3 1488 00844 6445

MW00583619

ComicLink
AUCTIONS AND EXCHANGE
SINCE 1996

The #1 Auction House and Original Online Comic Book Exchange

- It's our 27th Year Online
- We Have the Buyers You Want
- We Have an Expert Staff
- We Have a Solid Infrastructure
- We Give Upfront Cash Advances
- CGC/CBCS Screening Service
- CGC/CBCS Fee Advancement
- We Save You Time
- We Save You Money
- We Work for You

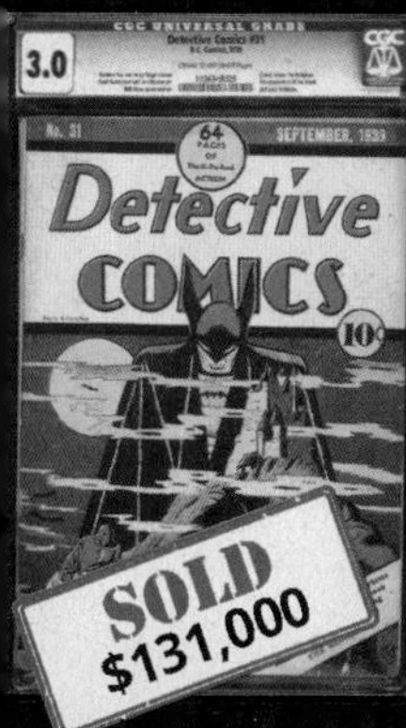

Visit us at
ComicLink.com

LET US MAXIMIZE YOUR NET RETURN!
ATTAINING RECORD SALES SINCE 1996!

Algonquin Area Public Library
2600 Harnish Dr.
Algonquin, IL 60102
www.aapld.org

ComicLink
AUCTIONS AND EXCHANGE
SINCE 1996

DOES SELLING YOUR COLLECTION STRESS YOU OUT?

Sold on ComicLink

Selling your comic book collection can be really hard work. Partnering with ComicLink's full team of professionals is the answer. For over a quarter of a century and hundreds of thousands of transactions, ComicLink has linked sellers with the best buyers in the world for their comic books, regularly setting sales records across eras.

Why ComicLink?

We do all of the heavy lifting, including:

- ✔ Evaluation and submission of your books for third-party grading (we even front the grading-costs)
- ✔ Scanning, listing and promoting your books to our aggressive base of global bidders
- ✔ Handling of all aspects of the promotion, fulfillment and customer service

Our service to you, the seller, is top-notch:

- ✔ We're available to speak to you any time during regular business hours
- ✔ More than a dozen team members work to provide you, the seller, with the best service possible, from start to finish

Interested?

Reach out to us. We will do the work, you will cash the check!

What could be easier than that?

LET US MAXIMIZE YOUR NET RETURN!
ATTAINING RECORD SALES SINCE 1996!

Visit us at
ComicLink.com
buysell@comiclink.com
(617) 517-0062
M-F 8:30am to 5:30pm ET

THE LARGEST DEALER OF VINTAGE COMIC BOOKS IN THE WORLD

METROPOLIS
COLLECTIBLES
www.metropoliscomics.com

YOUR COMICS

WE HAVE MILLIONS OF DOLLARS TO SPEND ON YOUR COLLECTION
GOLDEN TO MODERN AGE COMICS, COMIC ART, PULPS, VHS, & VIDEO GAMES
FREE APPRAISALS | IMMEDIATE PAYMENT | WE TRAVEL WORLWIDE

CALL TODAY TOLL FREE
1-800-229-6387

Stephen Fishler, CEO
Overstreet Advisor

OVER 100 YEARS COMBINED EXPERIENCE,
OUR KNOWLEDGE IS YOUR ADVANTAGE

SELL WITH THE BEST TO GET THE MOST
MONEY FOR YOUR COLLECTION

QES YOUR COM!

TALK TO OUR EXPERTS TODAY!

Vincent Zurzolo, President
Overstreet Advisor

P: 212.260.4147 | F: 212.260.4304 | 36 W 37TH ST, 6TH FL, NEW YORK, NY 10018
BUYING@METROPOLISCOMICS.COM | WWW.METROPOLISCOMICS.COM

CGC®

CGC UNIVERSAL GRADE
9.8
Batman Adventures #12
D.C. Comics, 9/93

CGC UNIVERSAL GRADE
9.8
Ultimate Fallout #4
Marvel Comics, 10/11

CGC UNIVERSAL GRADE
Saga #1
Image Comics, 4/12

CGCcomics.com

WHERE THE ACTION IS!

COMICCONNECT IS THE WORLD'S PREMIER ONLINE COMIC MARKETPLACE & AUCTIONEER

SOLD! $3,550,000

SOLD! $3,250,000

SOLD! $2,604,750

SOLD! $2,428,000

SOLD! $1,638,759

SOLD! $1,500,000

SOLD! $1,250,000

SOLD! $1,100,000

In 16 years, we've sold more record breaking books than anybody else!

ComicConnect was the first to sell a comic book for $1 MILLION!

ComicConnect brokered many of the most expensive comics ever sold!

ComicConnect has the BEST buyers and sellers! We are where the ACTION is!

IMMEDIATE CASH ADVANCES · SUPER FAST PAYMENT · FREE PRINT & ONLINE COLOR EVENT AUCTION CATALOG
TIME PAYMENTS AVAILABLE · PHONE & ABSENTEE BIDDING · SMALL COMMISSION · OPTIONAL BUYER'S PREMIUM

CONTACT US TODAY FOR A FREE CONSULTATION!

VINCENT ZURZOLO, *PRESIDENT*

36 W 37TH ST, FL. 6, NEW YORK, NEW YORK, 10018
P: 888.779.7377 | INT'L: 001.212.895.3999 | F: 212.260.4304
www.comicconnect.com | support@comicconnect.com

HERITAGE®

COMICS & COMIC ART AUCTIONS

HERITAGE HAS AUCTIONED $900 MILLION WORTH OF COMICS AND COMIC ART SINCE 2001, MORE THAN ALL OTHER COMIC AUCTIONEERS COMBINED!

BY FAR THE MOST WEBSITE VISITORS
No comics competitor comes remotely close — go to the independent tracking site SimilarWeb.com and see for yourself!

According to independent, third-party SimilarWeb.com: Heritage averages more Internet visits per month than our top two competitors' sites combined receive per year.

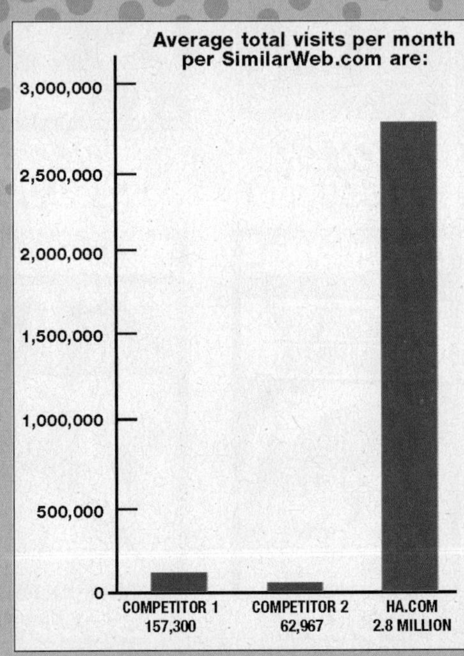

HERITAGE HAS BEEN CHOSEN AS AUCTIONEER BY:

Maggie Thompson | Stan Lee | Nicolas Cage
Joe Kubert| Steve Geppi | MAD Magazine
Random House | Playboy Magazine

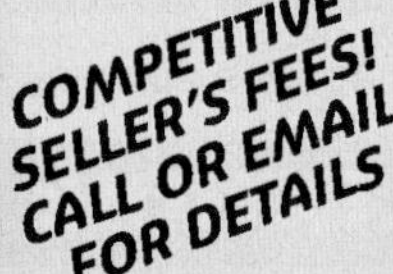

WE LOOK FORWARD TO HEARING FROM YOU.
877-HERITAGE (437-4824)

ED JASTER
Ext. 1288
EdJ@HA.com

LON ALLEN
Ext. 1261
LonA@HA.com

JOE MANNARINO
Ext. 1921
JoeM@HA.com

HERITAGE AUCTIONS
THE WORLD'S LARGEST COLLECTIBLES AUCTIONEER

HERITAGE®

COMICS & COMIC ART AUCTIONS

MORE EXPOSURE FOR SELLERS AT HERITAGE!

Our **Beautiful printed catalogs** entice bidders to bid higher.

Our **heavily advertised** Signature® auctions are among the biggest events in the comic book hobby. The live sessions bidders participate by phone, in person, and over the Internet.

Our **Auction archive** of Comics and Original Art includes every item we've ever auctioned with full descriptions, images and actual prices realized. We don't hide our past results (and we don't intermix retail sales with our auction records)!

Sold for:
$3.1 Million
January 2022

EXCLUSIVE AUCTIONEER OF THESE OUTSTANDING PERSONAL COLLECTIONS:

The Promise Collection
$24 million and Counting

The Doug Schmell Collection
$3.9 million 100% sold

The #1 Spider-Man Registry Set
$7.4 million 100% sold

Heritage's experts will guide you through the consignment process and help you get the most money for your treasured items. Immediate cash advances available!

DALLAS | NEW YORK | BEVERLY HILLS | CHICAGO | PALM BEACH
LONDON | PARIS | GENEVA | BRUSSELS | AMSTERDAM | HONG KONG

Always Accepting Quality Consignments in 50+ Categories
Immediate Cash Advances Available
1.5 Million+ Online Bidder-Members

HERITAGE AUCTIONS
THE WORLD'S LARGEST COLLECTIBLES AUCTIONEER

Paul R. Minshull #16591. BP 20%; see HA.com 71400

ComicLink
AUCTIONS AND EXCHANGE
SINCE 1996

LET'S TALK ABOUT THE ELEPHANT IN THE ROOM

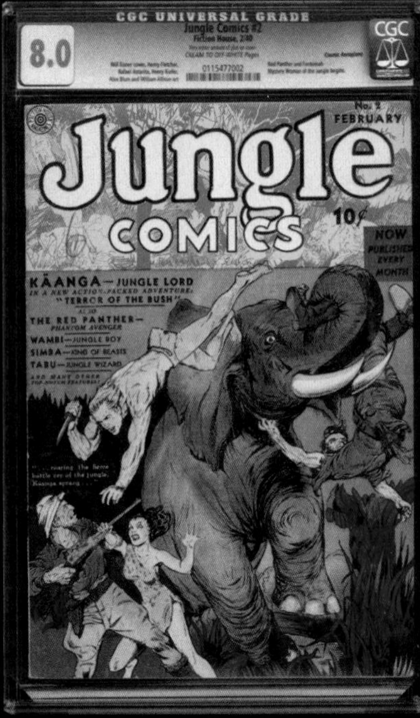
Sold on ComicLink

When selecting an auction house to partner with for the sale of your collection, it's easy to be drawn in by the glitzy corporate giant attempting to justify its high commissions with its bigness. You know the drill - guys in suits trying to sell you on cross-marketing your comic book collection to coin and dinosaur bone collectors who have never even purchased a comic book. The glitzy corporate giant also pushes their over-produced print catalog, which in reality doesn't impact bidding as today's buyers are all online–it's 2023 after all! Those glossy catalogs only exist to impress potential sellers like yourself, and make no mistake, the seller and buyer commission generated from your items is what pays for it! That does only one thing - it lowers your net return as a seller.

At ComicLink, we think differently. We pioneered the smartest, most cost-effective way to sell your comic book collection, and for over a quarter of a century, our sellers have reached the most aggressive bidders in the hobby. Comprised of a mid-sized team of more than a dozen full-time professionals with over 250 years of combined experience in the hobby and over half a billion in sales, our infrastructure is big enough–however, our objective for the seller is not to do things bigger but to do things better. Our longevity, expertise and reach combined with our low fee structure means the greatest net return for our sellers.

Come join our global consignor base and enjoy the best value proposition in the hobby!

Visit us at
ComicLink.com
buysell@comiclink.com
(617) 517-0062
M-F 8:30am to 5:30pm ET

LET US MAXIMIZE YOUR NET RETURN!
ATTAINING RECORD SALES SINCE 1996!

53RD EDITION

COMICS FROM THE 1500s–PRESENT INCLUDED
FULLY ILLUSTRATED CATALOGUE
& EVALUATION GUIDE

by ROBERT M. OVERSTREET
with YOLANDA RAMIREZ

GEMSTONE PUBLISHING

Stephen A. Geppi, Chief Executive Officer
J.C. Vaughn, President
Mark Huesman, Editor - Print
Amanda Sheriff, Editor - Digital
Yolanda Ramirez, Pricing Editor
Mike Wilbur, Warehouse Operations
Tom Garey, Kathy Weaver, Brett Canby, Angela Phillips-Mills, Accounting Services

SPECIAL CONTRIBUTORS TO THIS EDITION

Kevin N. Ammentorp • Julia Chiquete • Brendon & Brian Fraim • Dawn Guzzo • Mark L. Haynes
Mark Herr • Mark Huesman • Mindy Lopkin • Brian Miller • Gayle A. Olson, Ph.D.
Richard Olson, Ph.D. • Hans K. Pedersen • Troy A. Pierce, Ph.D. • Amanda Sheriff • J.C. Vaughn

SPECIAL ADVISORS TO THIS EDITION

Darren Adams • Grant Adey • Bill Alexander • David T. Alexander • Tyler Alexander • Lon Allen • Dave Anderson
David J. Anderson, DDS • L.E. Becker • Jim Berry • Peter Bilelis, Esq. • Mike Bollinger • Steve Borock
Scott Braden • Russ Bright • Richard M. Brown • Shawn Caffrey • Charles Cerrito • Jeff Cerrito
John Chruscinski • Paul Clairmont • Art Cloos • Gary Colabuono • Bill Cole • Ashley Cotter-Cairns
Jesse James Criscione • Brock Dickinson • Gary Dolgoff • John Dolmayan • Walter Durajlija • Ken Dyber
D'Arcy Farrell • Bill Fidyk • Paul M. Figura • Joseph Fiore • Stephen Fishler • Dan Fogel • Kevin Forbes
Eric Fournier • Dan Gallo • Stephen Gentner • Josh Geppi • Steve Geppi • Douglas Gillock • Sean Goodrich
Tom Gordon III • Jay Halstead • Terry Hoknes • Greg Holland • Steven Houston • Robert Isaac • Dr. Steven Kahn
Nick Katradis • Ivan Kocmarek • Timothy Kupin • Ben Labonog • Stephen Lipson • Paul Litch • Doug Mabry
Jim McCallum • Todd McDevitt • Steve Mortensen • Marc Nathan • Josh Nathanson • Tom Nelson
Jamie Newbold • Karen O'Brien • Terry O'Neill • Michael Pavlic • Bill Ponseti • Sean Prosje
Alex Reece • Austin Reece • Rob Reynolds • Stephen Ritter • Barry Sandoval • Buddy Saunders
Conan Saunders • Alika Seki • Todd Sheffer • Marc Sims • Lauren Sisselman
West Stephan • Al Stoltz • Doug Sulipa • Maggie Thompson • Michael Tierney • Ted VanLiew
John Verzyl II • Rose Verzyl • Lon Webb • Mike Wilbur • Harley Yee • Vincent Zurzolo, Jr.

See a full list of Overstreet Advisors on pages 1099-1103

NOTICE: Values for items listed or pictured in this book are based on author's experience, consultations with a network of advisors including collectors specializing in various categories, and actual prices realized for specific items sold through private sales and auctions. The values offered in this book are approximations influenced by many factors including condition, rarity and demand, and they should serve as only guidelines, presenting an average range of what one might expect to pay for the items. In the marketplace, knowledge and opinions held by both sellers and buyers determine prices asked and prices paid. This is not a price list of items for sale or items wanted by the author or publisher. The author and the publisher shall not be held responsible for losses that may occur in the purchase, sale or other transaction of property because of information contained herein. Efforts have been made to present accurate information, but the possibility of error exists. Readers who believe that have discovered an error are invited to mail corrective information to the author, Robert M. Overstreet, at Gemstone Publishing, 10150 York Rd., Suite 300, Hunt Valley, MD 21030. Verified corrections will be incorporated into future editions of this book.

THE OVERSTREET COMIC BOOK PRICE GUIDE. Copyright © 1992, 1993, 1994, 1995, 1996, 1997, 1998, 1999, 2000, 2001, 2002, 2002, 2003, 2004, 2005, 2006, 2007, 2008, 2009, 2010, 2011, 2012, 2013, 2014, 2015, 2016, 2017, 2018, 2019, 2020, 2021, 2022, 2023 by Gemstone Publishing, Inc. All rights reserved. Printed in the United States. No part of this book may be used or reproduced in any manner whatsoever without written permission except in the case of brief quotations embodied in critical articles and reviews. For information, write to: Gemstone Publishing, 10150 York Rd., Suite 300, Hunt Valley, MD 21030 or email feedback@gemstonepub.com

All rights reserved. **THE OVERSTREET COMIC BOOK PRICE GUIDE (53rd Edition)** is an original publication of Gemstone Publishing, Inc. This edition has never before appeared in book form.

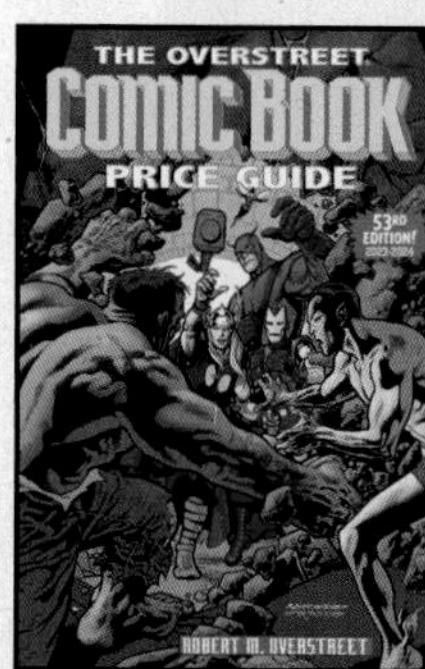

The Avengers: Art by Kevin Nowlan. The Avengers, Hulk and Sub-Mariner ©2023 MARVEL. All Rights Reserved.

Death Dealer: Art by Dan Lawlis. Death Dealer ©2023 Frazetta Girls LLC, under license to Incendium LLC

Hero Initiative: Art by John Tyler Christopher. Red Sonja ©2023 Red Sonja, LLC. All rights reserved.

Big, Big Edition: Blackout: Art by David Michael Beck.

The Avengers Hardcover Edition ISBN: 978-1-60360-619-6
The Avengers Soft Cover Edition ISBN: 978-1-60360-620-2

Death Dealer Hardcover Edition ISBN: 978-1-60360-621-9
Death Dealer Soft Cover Edition ISBN: 978-1-60360-622-6

Red Sonja - Hero Initiative Hardcover Edition ISBN: 978-1-60360-626-4

Blackout - Big, Big Edition ISBN: 978-1-60360-625-7

Printed in Canada.

10 9 8 7 6 5 4 3 2 1

Fifty-third Edition: July 2023

$2,428,000

$2,604,750

$3,550,000

$3,250,000

$1,638,75

$1,500,000

$1,050,00

$1,250,000

100,000 VINTAGE COMICS, ART, & VIDEO GAMES AVAILABLE

BEST BUYERS IN THE BUSINESS

IMMEDIATE CA$H ADVANCES

SUPER FAST PAYMENT

TIME PAYMENTS AVAILABLE*

*Time Payments are for certain lots only

PHONE & ABSENTEE BIDDING

GET YOUR COMICS QES CERTIFIED!

$1,000,00

$1,100,000

FREE PRINT & ONLINE COLOR EVENT AUCTION CATALOG

$815,000

WORLD'S PREMIER ONLINE COMIC MARKETPLACE & AUCTIONEER

LOW COMMISSIONS! MAXIMIZE YOUR PROFITS!

CALL TODAY TO CONSIGN FOR OUR NEXT EVENT AUCTION

Vincent Zurzolo, President

Rob Reynold
Dir. of Consignm

Visit our NEW website www.comicconnect.com or call us Toll Free at 888.779.7377

36 W 37TH ST, 6TH FL, NEW YORK, NY 10018 | P: 212.895.3[illegible] | F: 212.260.4304 | support@c[illegible]icconnect.com

ComicLink

AUCTIONS AND EXCHANGE

SINCE 1996

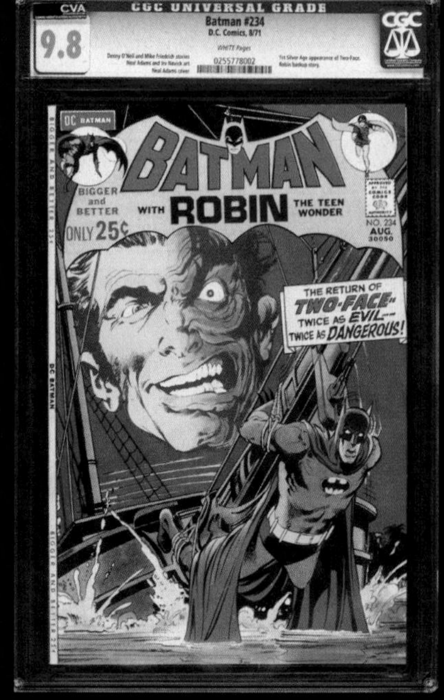

Sold on ComicLink

Ever Feel Like You're Being Trapped By This Guy?

Have you ever found yourself feeling trapped in a conversation with a disingenuous rep who acts like he's your best friend but is really just out for his own self-interest? You won't find any of that "two-faced, used car salesman" nonsense here at ComicLink. Like you, we are lifelong collectors and we understand how important selling your collection on your own terms is to you. We partner with every one of our clients to come up with customized solutions that work best for your benefit, not ours. With ComicLink you avoid the conflicts of interest that come with working with a consignment firm that is primarily a dealer or the limitations that come with working with a "ma and pa" operation being run out of someone's home. Neither situation provides you with the security or infrastructure you want in a consignment partner.

From the very inception of our firm over a quarter of a century ago, ComicLink has had a "win-win" mindset regarding collection owners, working for them, not against them. Believe it or not, this was a revolutionary approach then, and we are certainly the best at it now!

We have over a dozen full-time professionals working towards one goal – yours!

Give us a call and you'll see what we mean.

Visit us at
ComicLink.com
buysell@comiclink.com
(617) 517-0062
M-F 8:30am to 5:30pm ET

LET US MAXIMIZE YOUR NET RETURN!
ATTAINING RECORD SALES SINCE 1996!

TABLE OF CONTENTS

ACKNOWLEDGEMENTS

Kevin Nowlan returned to the *Guide* with his beautiful reinterpretation of Jack Kirby's cover for *The Avengers* #3. Dan Lawlis delivered a fiery take on Frank Frazetta's Death Dealer (with special thanks to Sara Frazetta and Frazetta Girls). John Tyler Christopher produced a stunning look at Red Sonja (special thanks to Nick Barrucci and Joe Rybandt at Dynamite) for the Hero Initiative edition, and David Michael Beck powerfully revived the almost-forgotten Golden Age character Blackout for the *Big, Big* edition.

Special thanks to Gemstone's own Yolanda Ramirez, Mark Huesman, J.C. Vaughn, and Amanda Sheriff, and a very fond retirement farewell to our Mike Wilbur.

Special Thanks to the Overstreet Advisors who contributed to this edition, including Darren Adams, Grant Adey, Bill Alexander, David T. Alexander, Tyler Alexander, Lon Allen, Dave Anderson, David J. Anderson, DDS, L.E. Becker, Jim Berry, Peter Bilelis, Esq., Steve Borock, Scott Braden, Russ Bright, Richard M. Brown, Shawn Caffrey, Charles Cerrito, Jeff Cerrito, John Chruscinski, Paul Clairmont, Art Cloos, Gary Colabuono, Bill Cole, Ashley Cotter-Cairns, Jesse James Criscione, Brock Dickinson, Gary Dolgoff, John Dolmayan, Walter Durajlija, Ken Dyber, Jon Engel, D'Arcy Farrell, Bill Fidyk, Paul M. Figura, Joseph Fiore, Stephen Fishler, Dan Fogel, Kevin Forbes, Eric Fournier, Brent Frankenhoff, Dan Gallo, Stephen Gentner, Josh Geppi, Steve Geppi, Douglas Gillock, Sean Goodrich, Tom Gordon III, Jim Halperin, Jay Halstead, Rick Hirsch, Terry Hoknes, Greg Holland, Steven Houston, Robert Isaac, Dr. Steven Kahn, Nick Katradis, Ivan Kocmarek, Robert Krause, Timothy Kupin, Ben Labonog, Stephen Lipson, Paul Litch, Doug Mabry, Jim McCallum, Todd McDevitt, Steve Mortensen, Marc Nathan, Josh Nathanson, Tom Nelson, Jamie Newbold, Karen O'Brien, Terry O'Neill, Michael Pavlic, Bill Ponseti, Sean Prosje, Alex Reece, Austin Reece, Rob Reynolds, Stephen & Sharon Ritter, Barry Sandoval, Buddy Saunders, Conan Saunders, Alika Seki, Todd Sheffer, Marc Sims, Lauren Sisselman, West Stephan, Al Stoltz, Doug Sulipa, Maggie Thompson, Michael Tierney, Anthony Tincani, Tom Tunnicliff, Ted VanLiew, John Verzyl II, Rose Verzyl, Lon Webb, Eddie Wendt, Mike Wilbur, Harley Yee, and Vincent Zurzolo, Jr., as well as to our additional contributors, including Stephen Baer, Dr. Jonathan Calure, Dawn Guzzo, and Kevin Poling. Without their active participation, this project would not have been possible.

Additionally, I would like to personally extend my thanks to all of those who encouraged and supported first the creation of and then subsequently the expansion of the *Guide* over the past five decades. While it's impossible in this brief space to individually acknowledge every individual, mention is certainly due to Lon Allen (Golden Age data), Mark Arnold (Harvey data), Larry Bigman (Frazetta-Williamson data), Bill Blackbeard (Platinum Age cover photos), Steve Borock and Mark Haspel (Grading), Glenn Bray (Kurtzman data), Gary M. Carter (DC data), J.B. Clifford Jr. (EC data), Gary Coddington (Superman data), Gary Colabuono (Golden Age ashcan data), Wilt Conine (Fawcett data), Chris Cormier (Miracleman data), Dr. S.M. Davidson (Cupples & Leon data), Al Dellinges (Kubert data), Stephen Fishler (10-Point Grading system), Chris Friesen (Glossary additions), David Gerstein (Walt Disney Comics data), Kevin Hancer (Tarzan data), Charles Heffelfinger and Jim Ivey (March of Comics listing), R.C. Holland and Ron Pussell (*Seduction* and *Parade of Pleasure* data), Grant Irwin (Quality data), Richard Kravitz (Kelly data), Phil Levine (giveaway data), Paul Litch (Copper & Modern Age data), Dan Malan & Charles Heffelfinger (Classic Comics data), Jon McClure (Whitman data), Fred Nardelli (Frazetta data), Marc Nathan (FCBD issues), Michelle Nolan (Love comics), Mike Nolan (MLJ, Timely, Nedor data), George Olshevsky (Timely data), Dr. Richard Olson (Grading and Yellow Kid info), Chris Pedrin (DC War data), Scott Pell ('50s data), Greg Robertson (National data), Don Rosa (Late 1940s to 1950s data), Matt Schiffman (Bronze Age data), Frank Scigliano (Little Lulu data), Gene Seger (Buck Rogers data), Rick Sloane (Archie data), David R. Smith, Archivist, Walt Disney Productions (Disney data), Bill Spicer and Zetta DeVoe (Western Publishing Co. data), Tony Starks (Silver and Bronze Age data), Al Stoltz (Golden Age & Promo data), Doug Sulipa (Bronze Age data), Don and Maggie Thompson (Four Color listing), Mike Tiefenbacher & Jerry Sinkovec (Atlas and National data), Raymond True & Philip J. Gaudino (Classic Comics data), Jim Vadeboncoeur Jr. (Williamson and Atlas data), Richard Samuel West (Victorian Age and Platinum Age data), Kim Weston (Disney and Barks data), Cat Yronwode (Spirit data), Andrew Zerbe and Gary Behymer (M. E. data).

A special thanks, as always, to my wife Caroline, for her encouragement and support on such a tremendous project, and to all who placed ads in this edition.

ComicLink

AUCTIONS AND EXCHANGE

SINCE 1996

WE'LL FIND THE HIDDEN GEMS IN YOUR COLLECTION!

›u likely know about the value of major keys like *Incredible Hulk* #181, *Amazing Spider-Man* #129 and *ant-size X-Men* #1, but did you know that books like *Fear* #11, *Sub-Mariner* #46 and *Avengers* #69 ›ve sold for over $5,000 at auction? "Keys" are just the tip of the iceberg when it comes to valuable mics from the late 60s, 70s and 80s. Many common books in high-grade can sell for hundreds or en thousands of dollars more than reflected in this guide. Let us identify the hidden nuggets in ›ur collection, advance your grading fees and maximize your return when selling! Check out these cent sales from our auctions to see what we mean:

$ 21,000
RESULT
Top Guide: $260

$14,250
RESULT
Top Guide: $600

$9,200
RESULT
Top Guide: $425

$8,300
RESULT
Top Guide: $35

$4,300
RESULT
Top Guide: $36

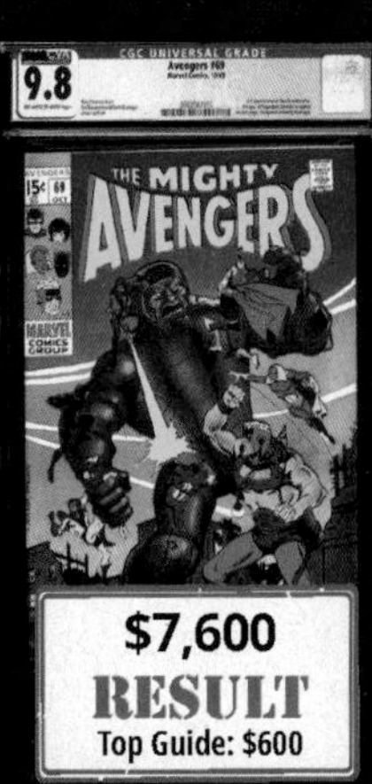

$7,600
RESULT
Top Guide: $600

$5,900
RESULT
Top Guide: $70

$5,285
RESULT
Top Guide: $18

›ide prices provided based on 2022-2023 ›erstreet Price Guide NM- price

Visit us at
ComicLink.com
buysell@comiclink.com
(617) 517-0062
M-F 8:30am to 5:30pm ET

›T US MAXIMIZE YOUR NET RETURN!
›TAINING RECORD SALES SINCE 1996!

Hit Parade®

REPACK PRODUCTS
FOR EVERY TYPE OF
COLLECTOR

CGC COMICS • AUTOGRAPHED CARDS • POP! VINYL
GRADED FIGURES • POP CULTURE • COINS/NOTES

Whether you carry them in your store or use them for online breaks,
Hit Parade offers a wide variety of repack product lines!

VOTED BEST REPACK BRAND OF THE YEAR
3 YEARS IN A ROW AT BECKETT'S INDUSTRY SUMMIT!

WWW.HITPARADECOLLECTION.COM

@hitparadecollection @hpcollect

Try Pedigree Comics' Awesome...

Raw to Riche$ CONSIGNMENT SERVICE!™

(P)edigree Comics will transport your ungraded comics and/or magazines directly to CGC headquarters for submission. After a consultation regarding what you plan on sending us, all you'll have to do is carefully pack and ship the books to our offices... and your work is done!!!

(P)edigree makes frequent trips to CGC's offices in Sarasota, Florida (usually once every 4 weeks). Your books will be safely and securely delivered for grading. Pedigree Comics, Inc. incurs all the risks involving the transport and delivery of your comics and magazines to and from CGC and is fully covered for any potential loss or damage to your books.

(P)edigree will submit your books in person under the Pedigree Comics, Inc. account in the appropriate grading service (tier) and fill out all necessary submission forms. You do not lay out any of the grading costs in advance. We will deduct the grading costs (at our 20% discounted rate) from the sale of your CGC graded books on our website. There are no hidden fees or costs!!

(P)edigree will pick up your graded books from CGC and safely transport them to our offices. This will save you from the potential hazards and expenses of having CGC ship the books back to you directly!

(P)edigree will inventory, scan and upload your CGC graded books onto the PedigreeComics.com website where they will be listed in the New Arrivals Section or an upcoming Grand Auction. The books will be listed under your personal account and you will receive email notification of every bid and purchase made.

(P)edigree does all the work while you can relax and watch your CGC graded books sell on our website. All of this for only 10% commission! You receive exactly 90% of the sale(s) price(s) of your book(s) after the deduction of the grading costs.

(P)edigree Pays Extremely Fast! Your consignment check(s) will be mailed out within two weeks of the respective sales!

Raw to Riche$ Consignment Service™ is a registered trademark of Pedigree Comics, Inc.

CGC Comics Guaranty, LLC Charter Member Dealer

Pedigree Comics, Inc. • 12541 Equine Lane • Wellington, FL 33414
PedigreeComics.com • email: DougSchmell@pedigreecomics.com
Office: (561) 422-1120 • Cell: (561) 596-9111 • Fax: (561) 422-1120

Sales Reporting Partner GPAnalysis

All Fantastic Four (the "Thing") Character(s) © Copyright of Disney / Marvel Comics

COMIC BOOK VAULTING WITH PWCC

FREE UP SPACE, KEEP YOUR COLLECTION SAFE

Let us take care of your comic book collection with our hassle-free, secure storage and insurance services.

With PWCC Vaulting you super power your collection with:

THE PWCC VAULT

- ✓ Secure vault storage
- ✓ Fully insured
- ✓ Portfolio management tools
- ✓ High-resolution digital assets
- ✓ Real-time valuations
- ✓ Expert appraisal pricing
- ✓ Asset-backed financing
- ✓ No-fee advances
- ✓ Concierge customer service
- ✓ Delivery on demand
- ✓ Buying or selling 24/7
- ✓ One-click selling
- ✓ Sales tax free purchasing

PWCCMARKETPLACE.COM

NEED A COMIC BOOK COLLECTION GRADED?

DO YOU WANT TO KNOW WHAT IT IS WORTH?

LOOK NO FURTHER THAN BILL COLE!

A Professional Comic Book Grader with over 50 Years of experience!

Senior Overstreet Price Guide Advisor since 1973!

Bill Cole

PROFESSIONAL COMIC BOOK GRADER

Bill Cole has been a paper preservation specialist since 1973 with executive industry experience, as well as a professional Comic Book Grader responsible for evaluating the condition and resale value of rare and collectible comic books. **Bill is an independent comic book grader and does not purchase books.**

JUST WHAT IS A "PROFESSIONAL" COMIC BOOK GRADER?

He or she is a skilled and knowledgeable expert responsible for evaluating and who accurately details/describes the exact condition and completeness of a comic book and determines its worth based upon a recognized grading process.

PLEASE CONTACT ME AT!

P.O. Box 87095
S. Dartmouth, MA 02748-0700
e-mail me at: bcole@bcemylar.com

CGC®

Superman #1 CGC 8.0
$5,300,000

Higher Prices Realized

Collectors and dealers trust the accuracy and integrity of CGC grading, which results in higher prices realized for CGC-certified collectibles.

In fact, CGC has graded the most valuable comic books in the world.

Highest Prices Realized in 2022

Amazing Fantasy #15 CGC 9.6
$3,600,000

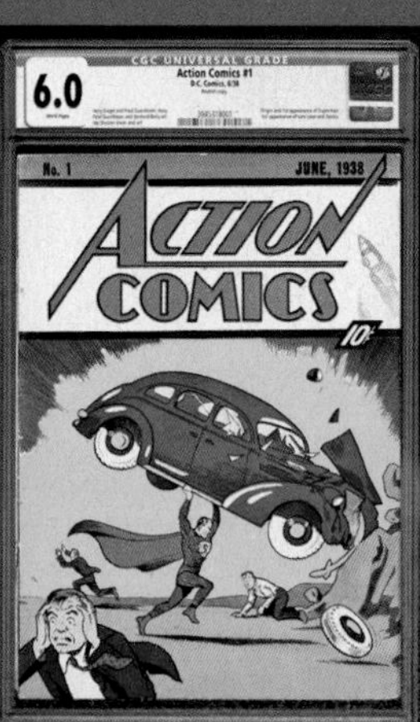

Action Comics #1 CGC 6.0
$3,400,000

Captain America Comics #1 CGC 9.4
$3,120,000

CGC Paid Memberships Are Loaded with Benefits

By joining as a paid CGC member, you can enjoy full submission privileges and other great benefits, such as 24/7 online tracking, free grader notes for your submissions and more.

Associate $25	Premium $149	Elite $299
Full Access to Online Resources	Full Access to Online Resources	Full Access to Online Resources
Full Submission Privileges	Full Submission Privileges	Full Submission Privileges
Free Grader Notes for Comics When Available	Free Grader Notes for Comics When Available	Free Grader Notes for Comics When Available
Free $15 Shipping Kit Voucher for New Members	Free $20 Shipping Kit Voucher for New Members	Free $20 Shipping Kit Voucher for New Members
10% Off at CCG Store	10% Off at CCG Store	10% Off at CCG Store
	$150 Credit with CGC	$150 Credit with CGC
		10% Off CGC Grading Tiers

Scan the QR Code to Join Today!

CGCcomics.com

MYCOMICSHOP MAKES SELLING EASY!!!

BOB MONTANA

Copyright © 2023 Archie Comics

We'll buy your entire collection, or consign it. Try us and you'll see why sellers entrusted us with the sale of over 112,000 consigned comics last year.

Visit mycomicshop.com/overstreet

MY COMIC SHOP

MY COMIC SHOP

SELL YOUR COMICS

Buying comic collections up to $2M+.
We pay top dollar for quality collections, 90-95% of current market retail for major Gold and Silver keys.

GET AN OFFER

Call or text 817-701-0704
Or email your list to
buying@mycomicshop.com

Selling comics since 1961

CONSIGN YOUR COMICS

112,000+ consigned comics sold in 2022
Industry's lowest commissions
Listings visible on MyComicShop & eBay
More customers = better prices, faster sales
Call or text 817-701-0702
Email consign@mycomicshop.com
mycomicshop.com/consign

Classic Collectible Services

Maximize Your Comic Book's Potential

CCS is the world's leading comic book pressing, restoration and restoration removal company.

CCS offers its services in conjunction with Certified Guaranty Company (CGC), the world's first and largest third-party comic book grading service, creating a streamlined process that saves submitters both time and money.

What Can CCS Do?

CCS specializes in the correction or removal of these defects and repairs to improve a comic's appearance or desirability.

- **Dirt**
- **Finger bends**
- **Writing**
- **Ripples**
- **Spine rolls**
- **Bends**
- **Stacking bends**
- **Corner Crunch**

To learn more, visit: CGCcomics.com/CCS-pressing

We Want Your Comics

We Buy it All!

- Golden-Age 1933-1955
- Silver-Age 1956-1969
- Bronze-Age 1970-1985
- Original Comic Artwork

No hassles and no excuses!

Just Cash, Baby!

- No Collection too Large or too Small
- Travel the Globe to Buy Books we Need
- 30 Years Experience

Senior Advisor Overstreet Price Guide

CGC Comics Guaranty, LLC CHARTER MEMBER DEALER

© Marvel

Call Today
800-731-1029
or
734-421-7921

Immediate Funds Available

Harley Yee
P.O. Box #51758
Livonia, MI 48151
734-421-7928 Fax

HarleyYeeComics.com eBay ID: harleycomics HarleyComx@aol.com

CAPTAIN AMERICA NO. 13
ALL OUT FOR AMERICA ISSUE!
10¢
YOU STARTED IT! NOW- WE'LL FINISH IT!

12¢ the AMAZING SPIDER-MAN 1 MAR.
2 GREAT FEATURE-LENGTH SPIDER-MAN THRILLERS!
THE FANTASTIC FOUR THINK I'M TRAPPED! BUT THEY DON'T SUSPECT MY REAL POWER!
EXTRA ADDED ATTRACTION: SPIDER-MAN MEETS THE FANTASTIC FOUR, AS "the CHAMELEON STRIKES!"

(972) 315-3664

2417 South Stemmons Fwy. #106
Lewisville, TX 75067
info@lewisvillecomics.com

Lewisvillecomics.com

We carry new and vintage Comic Books, Sport and Non-Sport Trading Cards (*Huge Pokemon Selection!*), Toys, Pops, Statues, Autographs, Posters, and More!

We are ALWAYS BUYING!
Stop by or call for a
FREE In-Store Appraisal!

Deepest selection of vintage comics and cards in the DFW Metroplex!

William Hughes
Senior Advisor
Overstreet
Price Guide

REECE'S RARE COMICS

Overstreet Advisor
10+ Years Experience
CGC Member Dealer

www.reececomics.com
Phone: 240-367-3662
Email: alex@reececomics.com
Frederick, MD

$2,000,000 CASH AVAILABLE FOR IMMEDIATE PAYMENT!

We travel anywhere!

Actual purchases from the last few years:

Toronto, CANADA $14,500
Chicago, IL $44,500
Cleveland, OH $6,500
Philadelphia, PA $50,000
Brooklyn, NY $135,000
Irving, TX $35,800
Columbus, OH $6,800
Bethesda, MD $113,000
Dutch Valley, TN $235,000
New Orleans, LA $55,000
Sterling, VA $85,000
Raleigh, NC $15,000
Fort Walton Beach, FL $5,000
Midlothian, VA $28,000
St Petersburg, FL $8,700
Blacksburg, VA $13,000

- No waiting for **YOUR Money**. Full payment made **on the spot!**
- **We buy it all**, no collection is too small or too large.
- No nonsense. We treat you **fairly.**
- References available.

A **PICTURE** IS WORTH A THOUSAND WORDS.

BIDS **STARTING**
AS LOW AS **$1.00**

DIG AUCTION.COM

DIGAuction.com

*Come "**DIG**" through our collection.*

MULTIPLE COMIC AUCTIONS EVERY WEEK! | **NO** BUYER'S PREMIUM

• SOLID GRADING, SOLID REPUTATION, COMPETITIVE PRICING •

CGC AND NON-CGC GOLDEN AGE, SILVER AGE AND BRONZE AGE. ALL GENRES

Have you been to large comic shows and only purchased 1 or 2 books?

Do you wish that all of a dealer's high grade selection could be in just one location?

Are you having difficulty in locating that hard-to-find issue?

Are you looking to upgrade from VF (8.0) to NM- (9.2) or NM (9.4)?

Large selection of CGC and non-CGC issues covering multiple genres.

All characters ©2009 respective copyright holders.

WELCOME TO THE WEB SITE DEDICATED TO THE BUYING AND SELLING OF CGC AND NON-CGC GOLDEN AGE, SILVER AGE AND BRONZE AGE COLLECTIBLES!

HighGradeComics.com

WILL BATTLE FOR YOUR BUSINESS!

I understand the emotional attachment involved when selling your collection. I pay very fairly and the most important thing will happen: the check will clear.

ROBERT C. STORMS
17 Bethany Drive, Commack, NY 11725
Tel # 631-543-1917 Fax # 631-864-1921
Email: BobStorms@Highgradecomics.com

Want lists accepted and actually looked at.

CGC AND NON-CGC GOLDEN AGE, SILVER AGE AND BRONZE AGE. ALL GENRES

• SOLID GRADING, SOLID REPUTATION, COMPETITIVE PRICING •

MILLER KUBERT MARANVILLE SILVESTRI
FOUR
ANCIENT ENEMIES
ENTER THE GEEK
DiDIO BEYRUTH
OF 6
RONIN BOOK II
MILLER • TAN • HENRIQUES
FRANK MILLER PRESENTS
FRANK MILLER'S
PANDORA
FIERCELY
INDEPENDENT

FMP

SEE OUR OTHER ADS IN THIS GUIDE FOR MORE INFORMATION

THAN RARE BOOKS & COMICS
WHEN THINKING OF SELLING YOUR COLLECTION!

WE BUY...

Golden, Silver and Bronze Age Comics, Big Little Books, Pulp Magazines and original art.

No collection is too large!

Immediate funds available for $500,000 or more...

WHAT WE DO FOR YOU

Pay exceptional prices for collections of interest.

We pay up to 110% of Guide for many desirable comics.

Travel to you to review your collection.

Provide a fair and honest value assessment.

Buy all grades and comic titles before 1975.

We will respect you and your collection. (No high pressure calls)

Offer generous finder fees that result in the purchase of a collection.

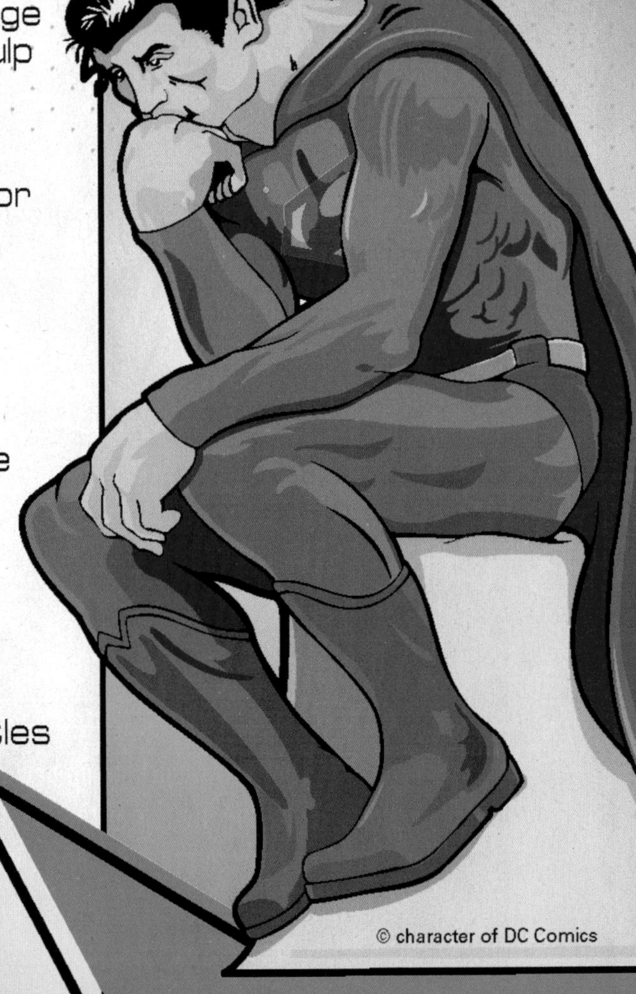

© character of DC Comics

CREDENTIALS
Special Advisor to the Overstreet Guide 1985–present
(see our other ads in this book for further credential information)

JAMES PAYETTE
RARE BOOKS & COMICS
P.O. Box 750 • Bethlehem, NH 03574
Tel (603) 869-2097 • Fax (603) 869-3475
jimpayette@msn.com
jamespayettecomics.com

COMING SEPTEMBER 2023

Ironjaw ©2023 Nemesis, Inc. Shi ©2023 William Tucci. Kent Menace ©2023 Scott Braden & Mike Malbrough. Overstreet® is a Registered Trademark of Gemstone Publishing. All rights reserved.

Whether you're picking up new comics off the shelves each week or bidding on the highest of the high-end back issues, there are things you need to know in order to collect effectively. This book introduces them.

- How do you collect comics?
- How do you care for them?
- How do you grade them?
- How do you sell them?
- Who have been the greatest comic creators?
- How do you turn your comics hobby into a job in the industry?

This brand new edition of *The Overstreet Guide To Collecting Comics* offers answers and insights into these questions and more facing new collectors and experienced enthusiasts alike.

GEMSTONE PUBLISHING

www.gemstonepub.com

AMERICA'S FIRST
COLLECTIBLES AUCTION HOUSE

HAKES.COM

CONSIGN YOUR
COMICS TODAY!

"WHEN I SOLD MY COLLECTION, HAKE'S WAS THE ONLY CHOICE."
- BOB OVERSTREET

PROVEN RESULTS SINCE 1967

- CONTACT US ABOUT OUR FAVORABLE RATES- WE MATCH OR BEAT OUR COMPETITION FOR THE RIGHT MATERIAL
- WE HELP YOU EVERY STEP OF THE WAY FROM THIRD PARTY GRADING TO SELLING
- WANT YOUR BOOK TO STAND OUT? ASK ABOUT OUR *NO DUPLICATE GRADE GUARANTEE* - THE ONLY SUCH ASSURANCE IN THE HOBBY WHY COMPETE AGAINST YOURSELF - MAXIMIZE YOUR INVESTMENT
- CASH ADVANCES FOR QUALITY CONSIGNMENTS

CBCS

AND WE SELL MORE THAN JUST COMIC BOOKS -

PROTOTYPE
SOLD $236,000

SOLD $79,178

SOLD $112,015

SOLD $234,171

HERO PROP
SOLD $259,570

SOLD $76,700

SOLD $24,806

THE WORLD'S #1 VINTAGE COMIC BOOK COMPANY!

www.QualityComix.com

TRANSPARENCY. PROFESSIONAL GRADING. SERVICE. INTEGRITY.

WE BUY VINTAGE COMICS PRODUCED BEFORE 1980!

SMALL & LARGE COLLECTIONS!

Our entire team understands that we have one goal, earn your business. We sell vintage comic books. You have them and we need them. It's as simple and transparent as that.

It's time for a change from the way the "Other" dealers do business. Come let our family take care of your family."

-Brent Moeshlin, OWNER

FREE CONSULTATION

FREE EVALUATION

PAYMENT UP FRONT

FASTEST RESPONSE TIME IN THE INDUSTRY

WE TRAVEL TO YOU FOR LARGE COLLECTIONS

REFER PEOPLE YOU KNOW AND GET PAID IF WE BUY

1-800-548-3314

CALL US OR EMAIL US TODAY!

BUY@QUALITYCOMIX.COM

500 EASTERN BOULEVARD SUITE 101 MONTGOMERY, AL 36117

You Tube
POP! XP
NETWORK!
THE NEW GOLDEN AGE OF CREATORS
CROWDFUNDING COMICS
THURSDAY NIGHT
LIVE!
With BILLY TUCCI
STEVE...AND CIMINO
SAYS
BOOM!!
SHOW!
SUBSCRIBE TO THE BEST CHANNEL ON YOUTUBE
FOR COMIC BOOK CREATOR INTERVIEWS, HOW TO STREAMS,
BOOK REVIEWS, AND INTERACTIVE LIVE STREAMS
WITH THE BIGGEST NAMES IN COMICS!
@POPXP

WE'VE ALL GONE WORLDWIDE!

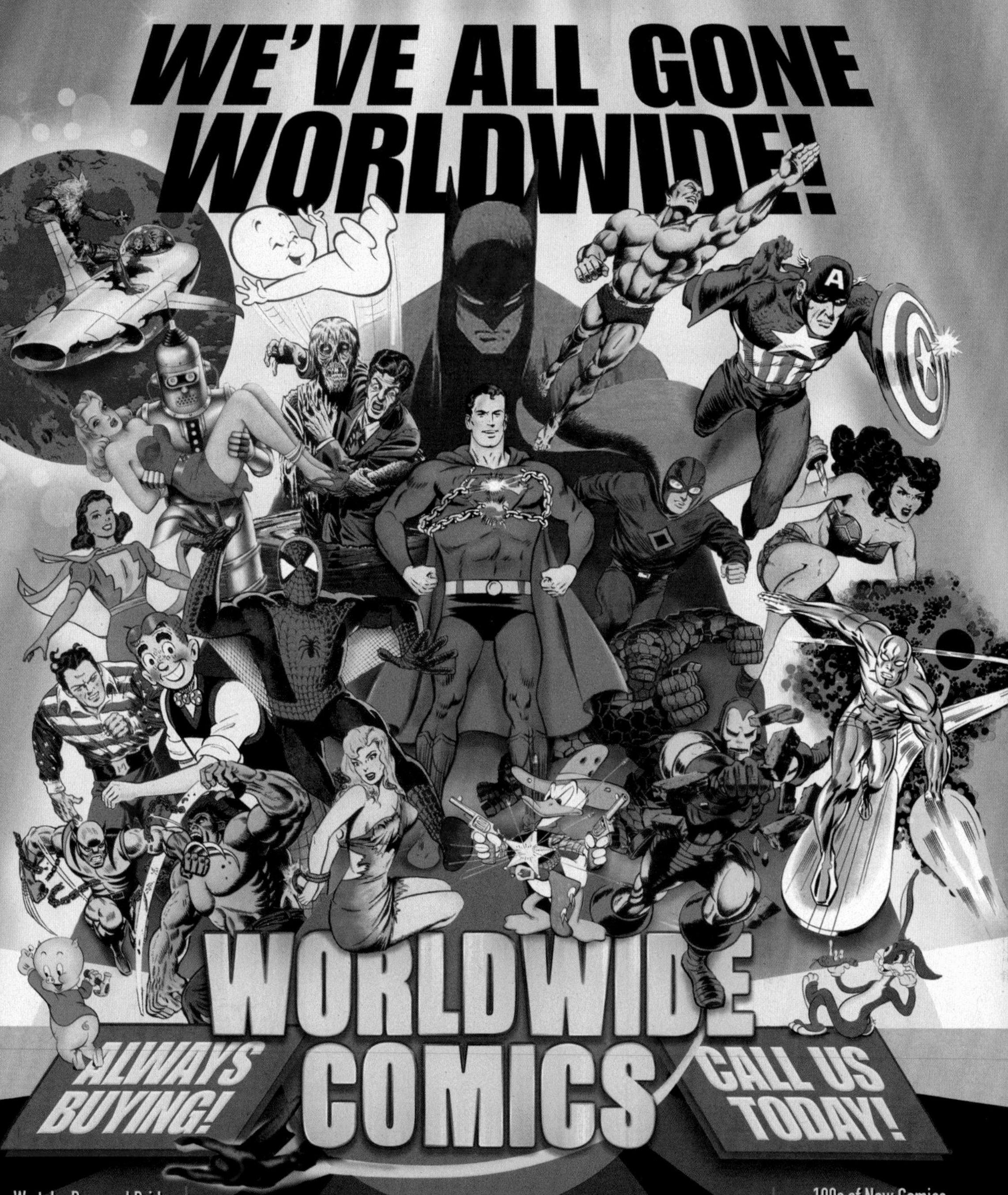

WORLDWIDE COMICS

ALWAYS BUYING!

CALL US TODAY!

We take Personal Pride in our Grading Accuracy!
...and we price all our books at current market value!
We buy and sell at major conventions!
SENIOR OVERSTREET ADVISOR

On-Line Web-Site with Huge Scans of Every Comic.
Selling and Buying 1930s to 1990 Comics.
One of the Largest Stocks of CGC Books anywhere!
The #1 Dealer in Comic Pedigrees!

100s of New Comics Listed Each Week, Low and High Grade, CGC and Raw, with Current CGC Census Data!
We offer FREE onsite Appraisals of your collection!

wwcomics.com

STEPHEN RITTER • stephen@wwcomics.com
Tel: (830) 368-4103 • 29369 Raintree Ridge, Fair Oaks Ranch, TX 78015 (San Antonio Area)

COMICS GUARANTY, LLC Charter Member Dealer

BUYING AND SELLING COMICS FOR 30 YEARS!

All characters © 2013 respective copyright holders.

HAVE YOU SEEN WHAT Archie IS DOING NOW?!

HORROR

MADAM SATAN

CHILLING ADVENTURES IN SORCERY

SCI-FI

WEIRDER MYSTERIES

JINX

THRILLERS

CAMP PICKENS

BETTY THE FINAL GIRL

NEW CHARACTERS

Archie COMICS DIGEST

50TH ANNIVERSARY

SUPERHEROES

AVAILABLE AT FINER COMIC SHOPS NEAR YOU

ArchieComics.com ArchieComicsOfficial  @ArchieComics

I USED TO BUY OLD COMICS
I STILL DO!
BUYING OLD COMIC BOOKS FOR OVER 50 YEARS!
ND US ONLINE!
OESONLINE.COM
@HEROESONLINE
#HEROESCON
#CLTMINICON
#UNDERTHEWATERTOWER
HEROES
Aren't Hard To Find
AMERICA'S COMIC SOURCE SINCE 1980
SINCE 1977
CHARLOTTE MINI-CON
OP BY,
LL OR EMAIL US:
OESARENTHARDTOFIND@GMAIL.COM
17 PECAN AVENUE · CHARLOTTE, NC 28204 · 704-375-7462
HOST OF AMERICA'S FAVORITE COMIC CONVENTION
HEROES CONVENTION
SINCE 1982
COMICS' GREATEST CREATORS & VENDORS!
FOR OVER 40 YEARS!

TED VANLIEW

LISA VANLIEW

Why Sell to Us?

HIGH PRICES PAID

CASH AVAILABLE IMMEDIATELY

WE TRAVEL TO YOU

35 YEARS IN BUSINESS

FAIR AND HONEST

WANT-LIST MATCHING

GREAT CUSTOMER SERVICE!

LIVE SHOWS

@SUPERWORLD_COMICS

@SHRINKYS

SUPERWORLD
COMICS
MAY No.1

You've spent years assembling your collection.
Sell it to someone you *trust.*

SUPERWORLDCOMICS.COM
TED@SUPERWORLDCOMICS.COM
508-829-2259

MAKE MINE
SILVERLINE
TRUMPS
TWILIGHT GRIMM
BEYOND THE STARS
They fight to save a universe!
KAYLESS
DIVINITY
silverlinecomics.com • indyplanet.com/silverline

WWW.NICKKATRADIS.COM

TITLE: ISSUE: PAGE: DATE:

BLEED

FULL PAGE

SAFE ZONE

DO YOU LOVE ORIGINAL COMIC ART? I DO!

Hello, my name is Nick Katradis. If you love comic art as much as I do, and you are considering selling any of your comic art, please contact me. I am a lifelong collector of comics and I am one of the most serious collectors of comic art, specifically from the Bronze Age."

I want to purchase your comic art from DC, Marvel and Charlton. I collect mostly Bronze Age art from 1968 to 1979. But I will purchase Silver Age and Golden Age art too. I also collect Bronze Age Romance art, from DC, Marvel, and Charlton, from 1964 to 1977.

I collect comic art by Sal Buscema, Jim Aparo, Gil Kane, Gene Colan, Nick Cardy, John Romita, Jack Kirby, John Buscema, Steve Ditko, Irv Novick, Rich Buckler, Curt Swan, Herb Trimpe, Dick Giordano, Dick Dillin, Don Heck, George Tuska, Mike Sekowsky, Jim Mooney, Ross Andru, Marie Severin, etc.

If you are interested in selling your comic art to a fellow collector, or if you would like to purchase any of my comic art on my website, please contact me and we can discuss a possible sale or trade.

www.NickKatradis.com
ndde@aol.com • (917) 815-0777

Overstreet Advisor
CGC Authorized Representative
Visit My Site!

ARTIST:

SCALES TO 6.6"X7.75" MANGA SIZE

SHIELDS UP

Everyone knows the days of keeping unbagged comic books lying around are long gone – bags and boards are a forgone conclusion in this modern world of collecting. But what about when a bag and board aren't enough? Do you want to lie awake all night worrying that your comic is developing irreversible stresses that will reduce its value a thousandfold? You need something a little tougher to keep that comic safe, and Ironguard Supplies has just the thing. In addition to a full range of bags and boards in all sizes, Ironguard now offers comic toploaders, rigid sleeves that will keep your comic protected from even the most unforgiving longbox. Sleep easy, my friend.

Get 20% off with code

OVERSTREET

See the full line at ironguardsupplies.com

f ◎ /ironguardsupplies

© 2022 Ironguard Supplies. All rights Vreserved.

YOUR FAVORITE CHARACTERS RARELY STAY...

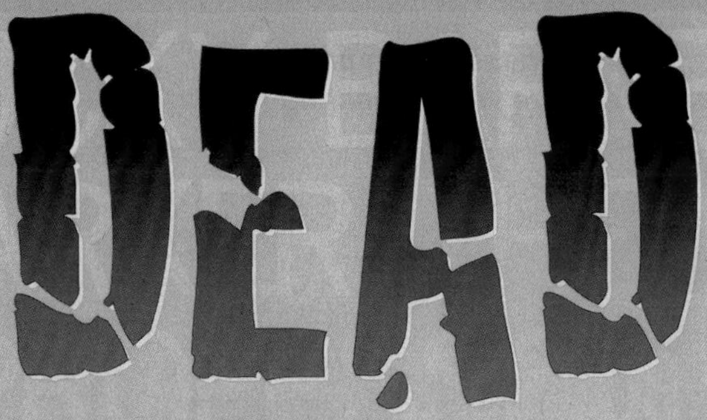

UNFORTUNATELY, THE SAME CANNOT BE SAID FOR YOUR COMICS.

The culprits are:

Air, UV Light, Heat, Humidity, Dirt, Fungi, Vermin, Insects, Acids, Chemicals and More.

Don't let your books turn yellow and brittle. Only our heat-sealed Mylar® sleeves can and will protect your books!

Want to know how to save them?

Then visit our website for 100s of high quality preservation and other comic book related items.

www.bcemylar.com

BCE

BILL COLE ENTERPRISES, INC.

Arklites™, Arklites 2™, Comic Gards™, Time-Loks™, Time-X-Tenders™, Life-X-Tenders™, Life-X-Tenders Plus™ and Thin-X-Tenders™ are trademarks of Bill Cole Enterprises, Inc. The Preservation Professionals is a service mark of Bill Cole Enterprises, Inc. Mylar® is a registered trademark of DuPont Teijin films. Their brands of archival quality polyester films are Mylar® type D and Melinex® 516 of which they are exclusive manufacturers.

Our faith-based team is always ready to serve your collecting needs.

BUYING ENTIRE COLLECTIONS REGULARLY

Bill

Our Friend and Associate Angelo

David

Rick

Ashton

Jason

Sharon

Jamie

Tina

Chad

Jordan

Richard

Chris

William Hughes' Vintage Collectibles

P.O. Box 270244 Flower Mound, TX 75027

Office: (972) 539-9190 Mobile: (973) 432-4070

Email: whughes199@yahoo.com

eBay User ID: **comic-warehouse**

www.VintageCollectables.net

Senior Advisor Overstreet Price Guide

ALWAYS SEEKING THE FOLLOWING

DC COMICS 1936-1993
MARVEL COMICS 1958-1991
TIMELY COMICS 1939-1947
ATLAS COMICS 1948-1957
PULPS/FANTASY MAGAZINES 1928-1981
OTHER MISC
GOLDEN AGE 1938-1955
ORIGINAL COMIC ART
POKÉMON CARDS
VINTAGE MOVIE POSTERS
SPORTSCARDS 1869-PRESENT

CALL NOW FOR IMMEDIATE PAYMENT!

DON'T WANT TO SELL WHOLESALE?

After 50 years in the hobby, I am extremely confident
hat I have the most consignor-friendly
onsignment program in the industry!

long with the better comics that come in each collection, I also andle the cheaper comics that most auction companies won't ke on consignment. Keep in mind that the only way to TRULY AXIMIZE the value of your collection is to sell every comic dividually. Don't let some other auction house bulk-lot your easured comics!

CALL NOW FOR DETAILS

Office (972) 539-9190
Mobile (973) 432-4070

William Hughes' Vintage Collectibles

MOVIE POSTERS • COMIC BOOKS • SPORTS MEMORABILIA

www.VintageCollectables.net
Email: whughes199@yahoo.com
eBay User: comic-warehouse

allas * New York * Los Angeles * Chicago

HIGHEST PRICES PAID REGULARLY!

ALL WINNERS COMICS No. 1

All Winners Comics #1
CGC NM+ 9.6
PAID
$93,500

Frankenstein Poster
PAID
$189,750

Babe Comes Home Poster
PAID
$138,000

Captain America Comics #1
CGC VF/NM 9.0
PAID
$96,686

Bill Hughes buys "Pay Copy" of Marvel Comics #1 for $350,000 from Steve Geppi

William Hughes' Vintage Collectibles

P.O. Box 270244 Flower Mound, TX 75027
Office (972) 539-9190 Mobile: (973) 432-4070
Email: whughes199@yahoo.com
Ebay User: comic-warehouse
www.VintageCollectables.net

Senior Advisor Overstreet Price Guide

CGC Comics Guaranty, LLC CHARTER MEMBER DEALER

Whether you are buying or selling any Fine Vintage Collectibles, I'd like to get acquainted with you to discuss your options. I'm Bill Hughes.

I have been instrumental in the buying and selling of many of the largest, most valuable and noteworthy collections and individual collectibles to ever surface in the comic book, trading card and movie poster marketplaces. From the finest certified copies of **Marvel Comics #1, Action Comics #1, Superman #1, Detective Comics #27** and **Batman #1** to the only known copy of the super-rare **Dracula Style A original one sheet movie poster**, to the **Original Artwork for the entire book of X-Men #1** to the first "Gem Mint 10" certified **Mickey Mantle rookie baseball card**. With over **50 Years of experience I have Seen and Done it ALL!**

Whether you are looking to Buy, Sell or Consign your collectibles, please give me a call. **With 30,000+ Active Buying Customers, I can Afford to Pay the Most because I Get the Most for Top Quality Items.** So Why Wait? If you want a **Few Dollars More**, give me a call right away to discuss what you have to offer, or, more importantly, what I have to offer you!

There is No One Quicker on the draw with Fast Cash! You will come away with a smile on your face and **A Fistful of Dollars**. I want all dealings to have a Win-Win outcome, so try me. You'll be happy you did!

Senior Advisor Overstreet Price Guide

CGC Comics Guaranty, LLC CHARTER MEMBER DEALER

ebay: comic-warehouse • whughes199@yahoo.com

This is a sampling of comics that have all been bought and sold by me, among so many other Mega-Keys!

Nobody is giving this stuff away! I have to pay huge prices to acquire these beauties, so why not take advantage of the hottest comic book market we've ever experienced and give me a call to discuss how I can enrich you by buying your treasures?

I am prepared to issue immediate payment in ANY FORM DESIRED!!

William Hughes' Vintage Collectibles

P.O. Box 270244 Flower Mound, TX 75027
Office: (972) 539-9190 Mobile: (973) 432-4070
Email: whughes199@yahoo.com
ebay: comic-warehouse

www.VintageCollectables.net

ALWAYS BUYING THE BIGGIES!

William Hughes' Vintage Collectibles

Senior Advisor Overstreet Price Guide

P.O. Box 270244 Flower Mound, TX 75027
Office: (972) 539-9190 Mobile: (973) 432-4070
Email: whughes199@yahoo.com
ebay: comic-warehouse
www.VintageCollectables.net

Grab yourself a refreshment!

• Marv Wolfman •
(Teen Titans)

• Larry Houston •
(X-Men animated)

• Rick Hoberg •
(Star Wars)

• Chris Ulm •
(Ultraverse/Rune)

• Shaun McLaughlin •
(Superman animated)

• Ed Catto •
(Captain Action)

• Kevin VanHook •
(Bloodshot)

Geekview Tavern
on YouTube

Host & bartender Dave Olbrich
(publisher Malibu Comics, Ultraverse, Bravura, Eternity)

All the geeky comic books, television, and movies you love!

www.youtube.com/@geekview

Record for this comic
in this grade
$1.7 M

Record for this comic
in this grade
$720,000

Record for this comic
in this grade
$510,000

Goldin

Sell Your Comics With Us

No upfront fees
Cash advances
Record-setting auctions

Record for this comic
in this grade
$450,000

Record for this comic
in this grade
$264,000

Record for this comic
in this grade
$210,000

There is only one Goldin.
goldin.co/comics
Quick Payouts | Cash Advances | Vetted Buyers
Email us at sell@goldin.co | Call us at 856.767.8550

Goldin

VISI 8

ENTERTAINMENT

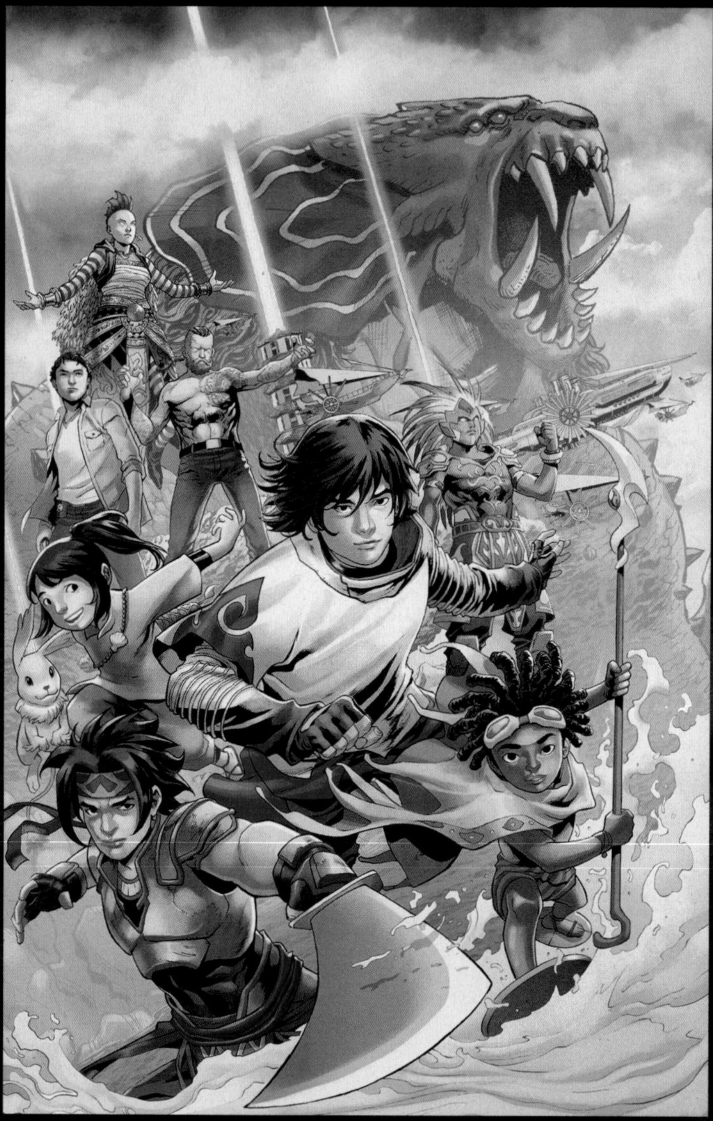

Changelings, Kara Guardian of The Realms, Galeo of the Seawalkers , The Seventh Tiger & Nusantara Falls © & TM 2023 PT VISI DELAPAN SEMESTA

This journey began several years ago when Mas (that roughly translates as Older Brother or Bro! in Indonesian) Raiyan Laksamana and Mas Farid Siddik were working together to tell stories through animation and by creating visual effects for film and television.

Along the way, they met comic book creator Kevin VanHook and after more than a year of looking at ways the three could collaborate, it was decided to tell many of their original stories with comics as well as in animated and even live-action form. Thus creating Visi8 Entertainment.

Visi8 Entertainment aims to develop stories into various media such as Animation, Augmented Reality (AR), Virtual Reality (VR), Extended Reality (XR). Using the latest technology combined with compelling stories, Visi8 aspires to present locally created content on to the International stage.

www.visi8.com | visi8.studio | visi8 entertainment

DISCOVER THE HERO WITHIN

a new source of family ENTERTAINMENT

Coming to the St. Louis area

2023

theherocomplex.stl

theherocomplex.stl

theherocomplex.com

info@theherocomplex.com

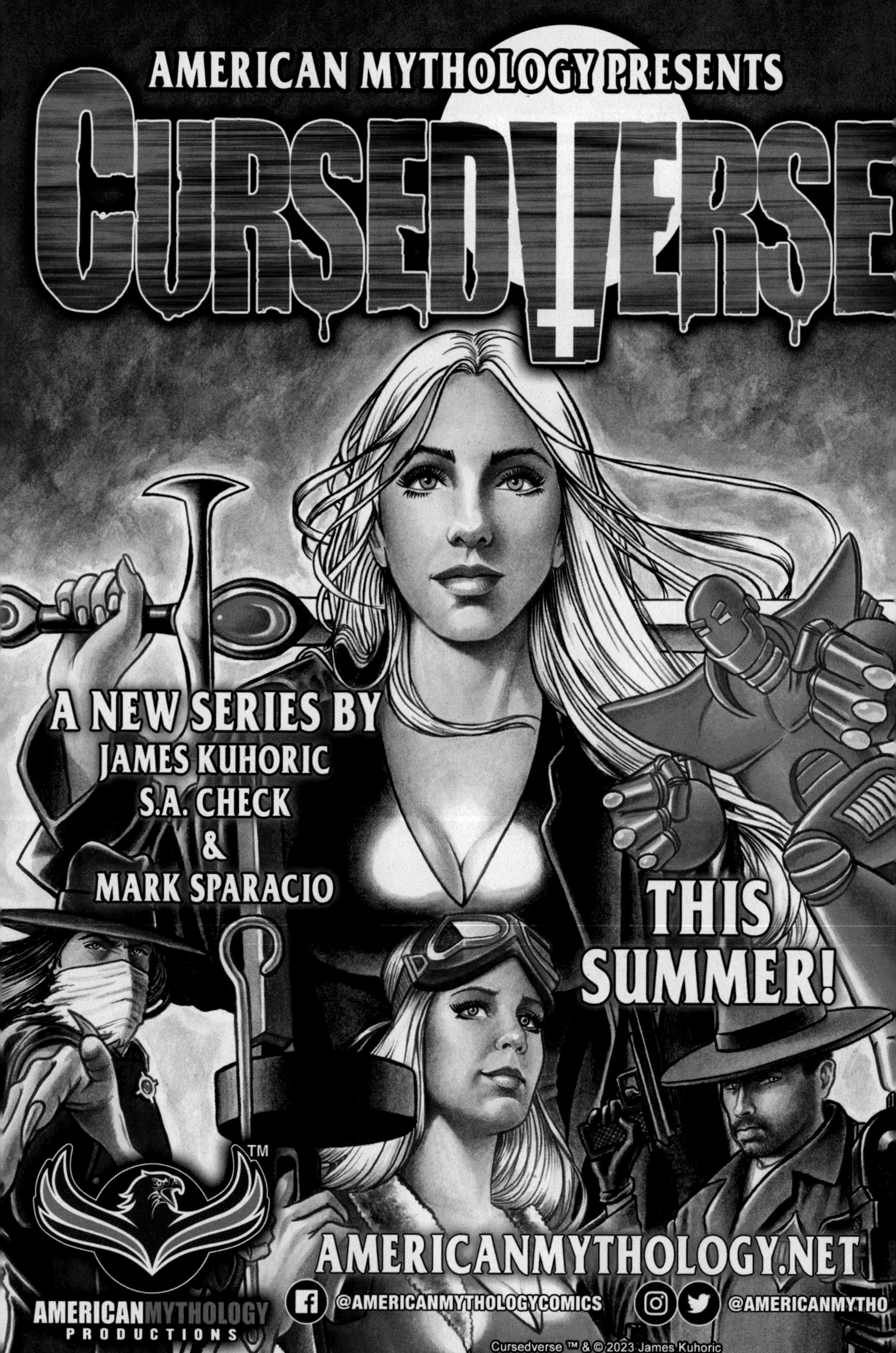
AMERICAN MYTHOLOGY PRESENTS
CURSEDVERSE
A NEW SERIES BY
JAMES KUHORIC
S.A. CHECK
&
MARK SPARACIO
THIS SUMMER!
AMERICANMYTHOLOGY.NET
@AMERICANMYTHOLOGYCOMICS
@AMERICANMYTHO
AMERICANMYTHOLOGY PRODUCTIONS
Cursedverse ™ & © 2023 James Kuhoric

WANTED
THE GREATEST COMICS OF ALL TIME!

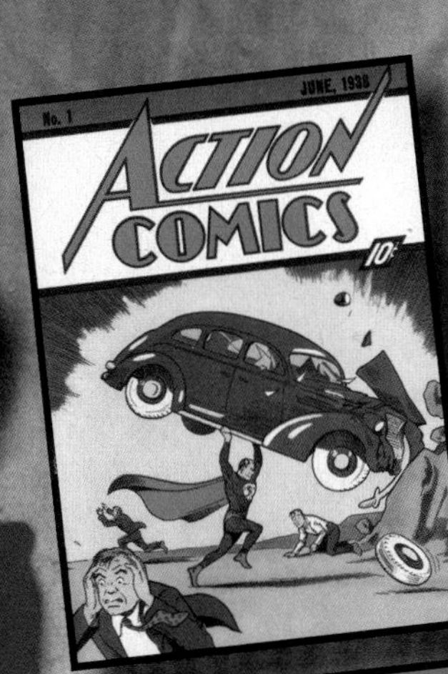

I WANT THESE BACK!

I'm looking for all those great comics you saw on the previous page, and for many others as well! Some people thought when I donated a major collection to the Library of Congress that I stopped collecting. Nothing could be further from the truth!

I'm buying all the time! Are you in the market to sell your Pre-1965 comics? Send me your list!

Steve

Steve Geppi
gsteve@diamondcomics.com

The Inside
COLLECTOR

July/
August 1991
Volume 2
Number 2
$3.95
Canada
$4.95

Scandal Rocks Toy World

Jewels by Jumeau

Fireworks!!

Claymation Art

Comics King Steve Geppi

10150 York Road, Suite 300
Hunt Valley, MD 21030

410.598.1773

BUYING BOUND VOLUMES

Looking for vintage bound volumes that were bound by the publisher and originally used for reference, but other types of bound volumes will be considered.

If you have bound volumes to sell, then you are "bound" to sell them to me because I have a higher respect and pay more for them than anyone!

Stephen A. Geppi

10150 York Road, Suite 300
Hunt Valley, MD 21030

410.598.1773

gsteve@diamondcomics.com

COLLECTOR

BUYING PRE-1965 COMIC BOOKS

AND RELATED COLLECTIBLES

I am the most serious collector you'll ever find...

I LOVE THIS STUFF!

All characters ©2022 respective copyright holders.

SEND YOUR SALE LIST !

Stephen A. Geppi

10150 York Road, Suite 300
Hunt Valley, MD 21030

410.598.1773

gsteve@diamondcomics.com

DIG DIAMOND INTERNATIONAL GALLERIES

IS BUYING!

WE'RE ACTIVELY SEEKING INDIVIDUAL TREASURES AND COMPLETE COLLECTIONS OF

COMIC BOOKS AND TOY PREMIUMS!

- Contact -

Kevin W. Poling • Vice President of Sales

pokevin@diamondgalleries.com

(443) 318-8441

ALSO INTERESTED IN

ORIGINAL COMIC ART • TIN LITHO TOYS • ACTION FIGURES • STATUES

BORDERLANDS

COMICS & GAMES

Upstate South Carolina's premier comic book and game shop, bringing the best in comics, graphic novels, collectibles and gaming to the region for more than THREE DECADES.

WE'RE ALWAYS BUYING!

WE PAY CASH FOR YOUR GEEKY STUFF!

We buy comics, toys, games, collectibles, RPGs, video games and more!

We **TRAVEL FOR COLLECTIONS**, and we pay a finder's fee for referrals!

PROUD ORGANIZER

SC COMICON
SCCOMICON.COM

October 29, 2023
April 6-7, 2024
SCCOMICON.COM

BORDERLANDS
READ · BUILD · PLAY

410 S. Pleasantburg Dr.
Greenville, SC 29607
864.235.3488

borderlands.us
borderlandscomics@gmail.com
/borderlandscomicsandgames
@borderlandscg

"SUPERB JUMPING-ON POINT!"
- Matt Meyer, Comic Watch

"POETIC SCRIPT AND OTHERWORLDLY ART."
- Sayantan Gayen, CBR

"IS THIS THE COOLEST THING THAT HAS BEEN PUBLISHED ALL YEAR??? HOT DAMN, THIS RULES."
- Spencer Perry, Comicbook.com

"DOWNRIGHT BIBLICAL!"
- Nathan Simmon AIPT!

FROM ACCLAIMED CREATORS
BECKY CLOONAN | MICHAEL W. CONRAD | LIAM SHARP

VALIANTENTERTAINMENT.COM | FACEBOOK.COM/VALIANTCOMICS | TWITTER.COM/VALIANTCOMICS

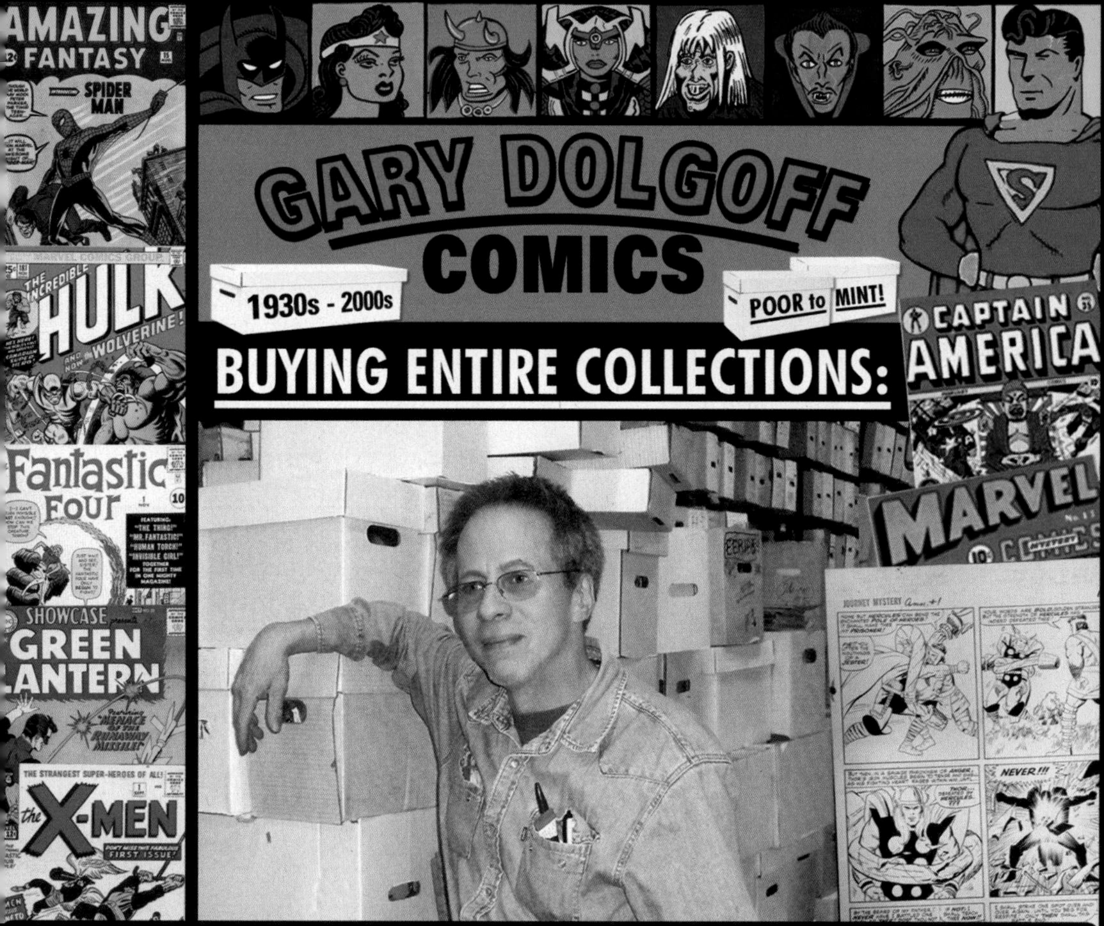

GARY DOLGOFF
COMICS

1930s - 2000s

POOR to MINT!

BUYING ENTIRE COLLECTIONS:

When I evaluate your collection, I can pay more, because I take everything into account ...

WANTED: 'One to 1-Million' Comics, Original Art pcs. & more!
NO COLLECTION is too BIG or too small ...we like 'em all!

COLLECTIONS, WAREHOUSES, STORE STOCK, INHERITANCE, ESTATES

COMIC BOOKS, ORIGINAL ART...
-ALL YEARS, GENRES, & CONDITIONS!
+TOYS, PUB.s, PULPs, CARDS, & more...

gary@gdcomics.com • gdcomics.com • #413-529-0326

GARY DOLGOFF COMICS • 116 PLEASANT ST. SUITE #213, EASTHAMPTON, MA 01027

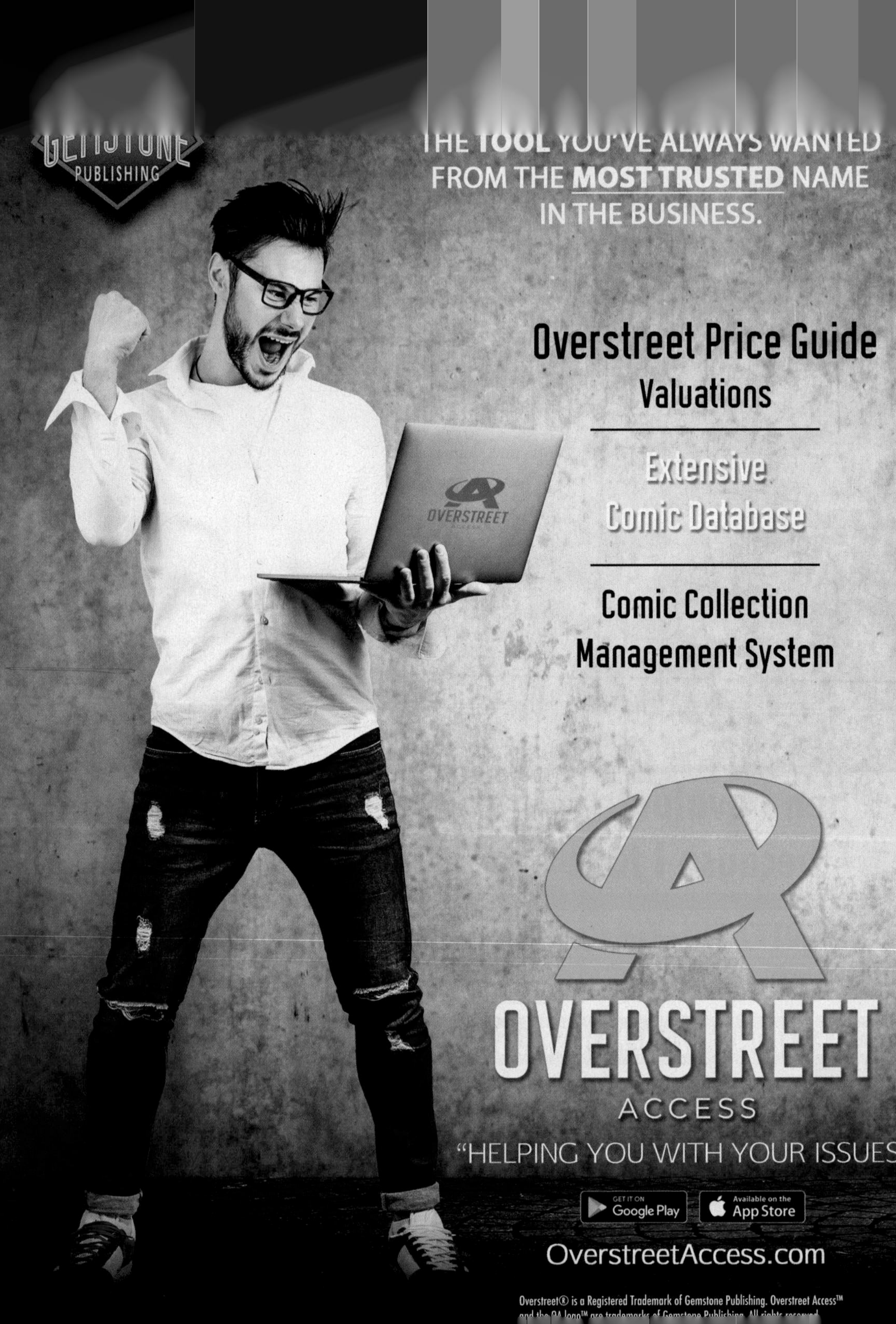

PUBLISHING
THE TOOL YOU'VE ALWAYS WANTED
FROM THE MOST TRUSTED NAME
IN THE BUSINESS.
OVERSTREET
Overstreet Price Guide
Valuations
Extensive
Comic Database
Comic Collection
Management System
OVERSTREET
ACCESS
"HELPING YOU WITH YOUR ISSUES.
GET IT ON
Google Play
Available on the
App Store
OverstreetAccess.com
Overstreet® is a Registered Trademark of Gemstone Publishing. Overstreet Access™
and the OA logo™ are trademarks of Gemstone Publishing. All rights reserved.

OVERSTREET
ACCESS

Want to get $30 off
Overstreet Access™?

OverstreetAccess.com

e's what you get with Overstreet Access:

Overstreet Prices!
Superior Collection Management Tools!
92,000 Variants just added!
mport/Export Tools just added!
Tracking Certified/Signed comics added!

Use this code to get a free Bronze Annual Membership or $30 off a Silver or Gold Annual membership with collection management capabilities!

OA531VN7PL9

OverstreetAccess.com

On Overstreet Access, you can...

- Create Collections!
- Create Boxes Within Collections!
- View and Organize Your Collections!
- Import and Export Collections!
- Want List!
- Gap List!
- Find Retailers!

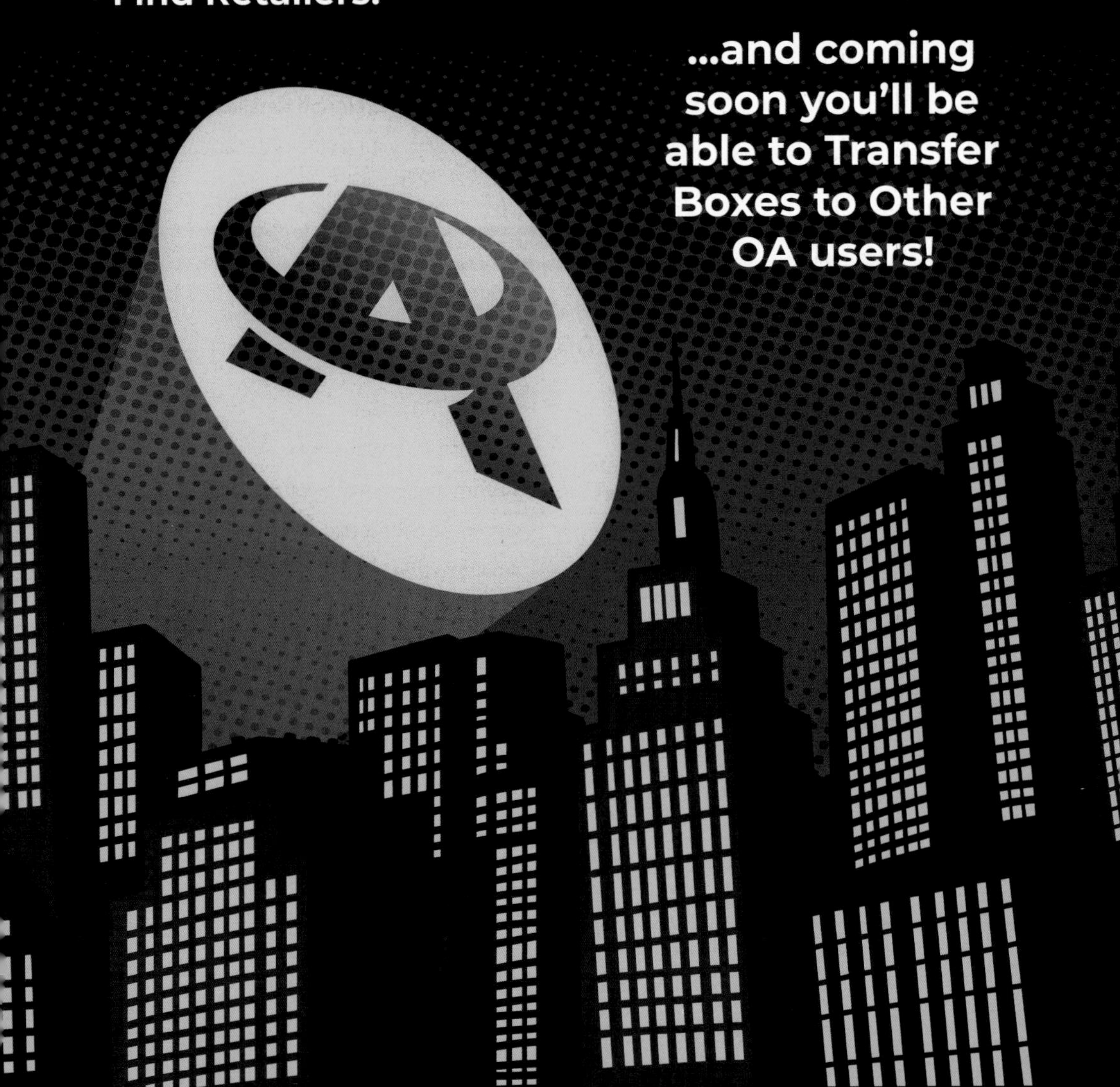

OverstreetAccess.com

Gold Membership

$9.00/month *or* $90.00/year (two months free!)

- Access to browse comic database and basic data, as well as meta data about publishers, titles, issues, story arcs, characters, and contributors
- View Overstreet Pricing information
- Access to special editorial content
- Access to collection management (4 Collections)
- Unlimited issues
- Add issues to Want List
- Automatically create your Gap List
- Access to the Mobile App
- Ability to add Preferred Retailers
- $30 off with your Guide purchase and your code

Silver Membership

$5.00/month *or* $50.00/year (two months free!)

- Access to browse comic database and basic data, as well as meta data about publishers, titles, issues, story arcs, characters, and contributors
- View Overstreet Pricing information
- Access to special editorial content
- Access to collection management (1 Collection)
- Up to 5000 issues
- Add issues to Want List
- Automatically create your Gap List
- Access to the Mobile App
- Ability to add Preferred Retailers
- $30 off with your Guide purchase and your code!

Bronze Membership

$3.00/month *or* $30.00/year (two months free!)

- Access to browse comic database and view basic data, as well as meta data about publishers, titles, issues, story arcs, characters, and contributors
- View Overstreet Pricing information
- Access to special editorial content
- Basically FREE with your Guide purchase and your code!

OverstreetAccess.com

BUYING & SELLING COMIC BOOKS, PULPS, ORIGINAL ARTWORK

SPECIALIZING IN: GOLDEN AGE - BRONZE AGE
HORROR | CRIME | TEEN | GGA | ROMANCE | SCI-FI

OWNER KEN DYBER
OVERSTREET ADVISOR SINCE 2008
CGC AUTHORIZED DEALER

I'VE REBRANDED!
MY NEW BUSINESS NAME IS:
TASTEECAT COMICS

SHOP ONLINE OR IN PERSON:

TASTEECATCOMICS.COM

@TASTEECATCOMICS | 503.236.8113

BRICK & MORTAR STORE OPEN 11 - 7 DAILY
2621 SE CLINTON ST. PORTLAND, OR

(Formerly Cloud 9 Comics of Portland, OR)

COMING MARCH 2024!

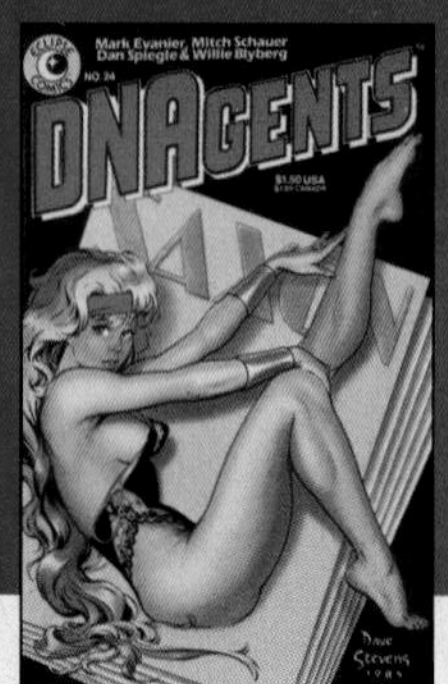

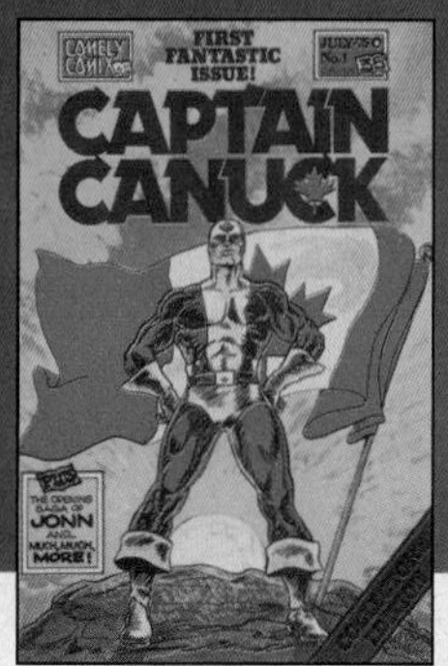

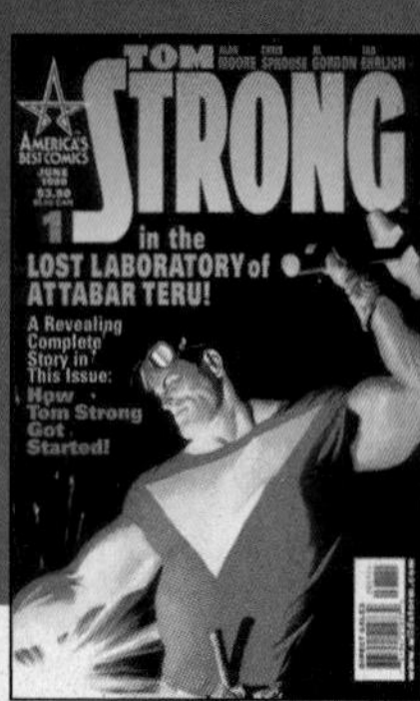

Featuring Fawcett's Marvel Family • Marvel 2099
America's Best Comics • BOOM!'s Stan Lee Universe • Captain Canuck
DNAgents • Scout • and MORE!

Timothy Truman's SCOUT 

From the pages of *Starslayer*, Grimjack and his graphic novel *Time Beavers* onward through his career, writer-artist Timothy Truman has offered readers hard-boiled action and no small amount of grit. It was at Eclipse that Truman created what is perhaps his signature title, *Scout*. And while Eclipse as a whole was clearly a non-universe, *Scout* and its spin-offs describe a single coherent reality.

"I'd always been interested in Native American culture when I was growing up. My great-grandmother on my father's side was a full-blooded Cherokee, and I'm sure that played a part in it. In college, the interest intensified, and I started reading a lot of scholarly studies and histories about various Native American tribes. Finally, my wife Beth purchased a big, thick book by a historian named Arthur Haley called *Apaches: A Culture and History Portrait* and gave it to me for my birthday. That book really set the scene for coming up with *Scout*. I became intensely interested in Apache culture. It was the Reagan era, so, as an unrepentant leftist, I saw things going on around me that concerned me quite a bit. So, I speculated about what might happen if these things were allowed to progress and eventually pictured this bleak future where America had basically become an impoverished third-world nation. It seemed to me that the only person who might have any sort of hope of existing in such a future would be someone with these old school traditional Apache cultural ideals that I was reading about. So, before I knew it, the whole scenario for the *Scout* series appeared, Truman said.

"The story takes place in the near future in a sort of ravaged, impoverished, dystopian United States. The country has split off into various smaller states or governments, the main one being centered in the American Southwest, called New America. The star of the series is an Apache named Emanuel Santana who is AWOL from a special Army training program. Scout learns, or at least thinks, that he is the reincarnation of the mythical Apache hero, Child of Water, and that it's his mission to destroy the Four Monsters of Apache legend. The monsters have taken the form of four businessmen and statesmen aligned with acting President, Jerry Grail - himself a former pro-wrestler. The reader never knows whether or not the Monsters are real or just a figment of Santana's imagination," he said.

FIRST PUBLICATION:
Scout #1
(September 1985)

LAST PUBLICATION:
Scout: War Shaman #16
(December 1989)

REVIVAL(S):
Scout: Marauder
graphic novel (TBD)

Scout #1 (September 1985) kicked off the original series, which ran 24 issues and concluded in October 1987. *Swords of Texas* #1 kicked off a four-issue mini-series that same month, and *New America* #1 launched another four-issue mini-series the following month. 1987 also saw the release of the *Scout Handbook*. *Scout: War Shaman* #1 (March 1988) launched a 16-issue run that concluded in December 1989.

"The second series, *Scout: War Shaman*, takes place about a decade or so after the first series, chronologically, during which time Scout married and had two small children, Tahzey and Victorio. After his wife dies, he and the boys set out on a trek across the southwest. Most people were really taken with the second series, the fact that you have this outlaw who has been branded a terrorist by the government, who is on the run and must worry about the welfare and safety of his two small children. In what was a pretty dramatic step for the time, at the end of the series, Scout dies. One boy, Tahzey, is adopted by one of Santana's allies, a militant missionary named Rev. Sanddog Yuma. However, the fate of the youngest boy, Victorio, is uncertain. When we last see him, he's very much alone, hiding in some rocks. Keeping his fate uncertain was a deliberate move on my part, as readers will hopefully discover in Scout: Marauder," Truman said.

Timothy Truman's original art for *Scout* #8 Page 2 (1986).
Image courtesy of Heritage Auctions.

2 **LOST UNIVERSES** **LOST UNIVERSES** 3

Full color! • Every comic listed is also pictured! • The latest prices!
Original art! • Interviews, feature articles and more!
Inside information on the birth, death, and revivals of Lost Universes!

THE OVERSTREET COMIC BOOK PRICE GUIDE TO
LOST UNIVERSES
2ND EDITION
ALL NEW!
Spider-Man 2099 cover by Butch Guice!
Plus a Scout cover by Timothy Truman!
BY ROBERT M. OVERSTREET & J.C. VAUGHN
DNAgents ©2023 Mark Evanier & Will Meugniot. Scout ©2023 Timothy Truman.
Overstreet® is a Registered Trademark of Gemstone Publishing. All rights reserved.
Interested in advertising?
Email feedback@gemstonepub.com!
GEMSTONE
WWW.GEMSTONEPUB.COM

CELEBRATING RED SONJA'S 50TH ANNIVERSARY IN COMICS ALL YEAR LONG WITH DYNAMITE ENTERTAINMENT!

COMICS AND GRAPHIC NOVELS
AVAILABLE AT YOUR FAVORITE COMIC SHOP

DYNAMITE® WWW.DYNAMITE.COM /dynamitecomics @dynamitecomics

RED SONJA ® and related logos, characters, names, and distinctive likenesses thereof are trademarks of Red Sonja, llc. unless otherwise noted. All Rights Reserved. "Dynamite" and "Dynamite Entertainment" are ®, and the "DE Logo" is ™ and ©, Dynamite Entertainment. All rights reserve

LIFE CAN CHANGE IN A FLASH.

When that happens for comic shop and bookstore employees and owners, Binc is a phone call away. Support your local indie comic shop and bookstore by supporting their safety net.

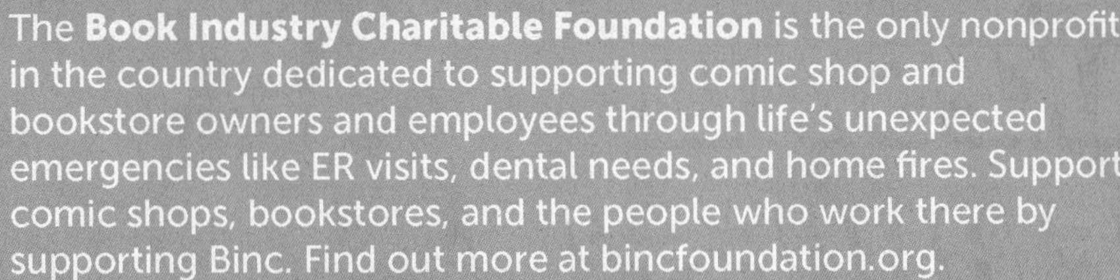

The **Book Industry Charitable Foundation** is the only nonprofit in the country dedicated to supporting comic shop and bookstore owners and employees through life's unexpected emergencies like ER visits, dental needs, and home fires. Support comic shops, bookstores, and the people who work there by supporting Binc. Find out more at bincfoundation.org.

GREATNONPROFITS 2022 TOP-RATED NONPROFIT

bincfoundation.org | 866.733.9064 | info@bincfoundation.org

"SHE WHO HAS ALL THE TOYS MAKES ALL THE RULES"

TUESDAYS

HERITAGE®

COMICS & COMIC ART AUCTIONS

QUESTIONS TO ASK YOUR **PROSPECTIVE AUCTIONEER**

- Are all of your previous results available online so I can judge your performance?
- Do you cross-market to other categories to drive interest in my consigned items?
- Do you have a world-class website that makes it easy for people to track and bid on my lots?
- Do you mail thousands of exquisite, printed catalogs to the top collectors throughout the world?
- Is in-person viewing open to the public, so my premium quality books won't sell for generic prices?
- Do you offer live public auctions for your top items, with proxy, real-time internet and telephone bidding?
- Do you offer extremely favorable terms on major consignments?

At Heritage Auctions, the answer to all of the above is **YES**.

Sold for:
$3,360,000
January 2022

Heritage has successfully auctioned more than 371,000 consignments, 94% from repeat consignors.

We invite you to call or email us right now to discuss your comic treasures and how Heritage can serve you.

WE LOOK FORWARD TO HEARING FROM YOU.
877-HERITAGE (437-4824)

ED JASTER
Ext. 1288
EdJ@HA.com

LON ALLEN
Ext. 1261
LonA@HA.com

JOE MANNARINO
Ext. 1921
JoeM@HA.com

HERITAGE
AUCTIONS
THE WORLD'S LARGEST
COLLECTIBLES AUCTIONEER

Comicpresser.com™

Comics, magazines & treasuries   Cleaning, pressing & conservation

"Incredible service! One of a kind company!! Hands down the best."

Golden Age before & after pressing

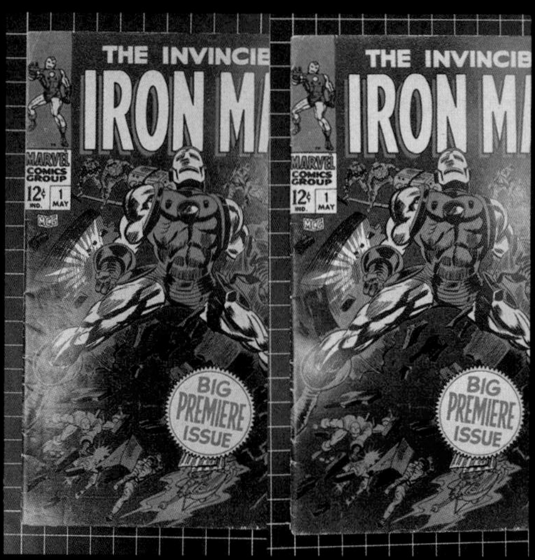

Silver Age before & after pressing

Bronze Age before & after pressing

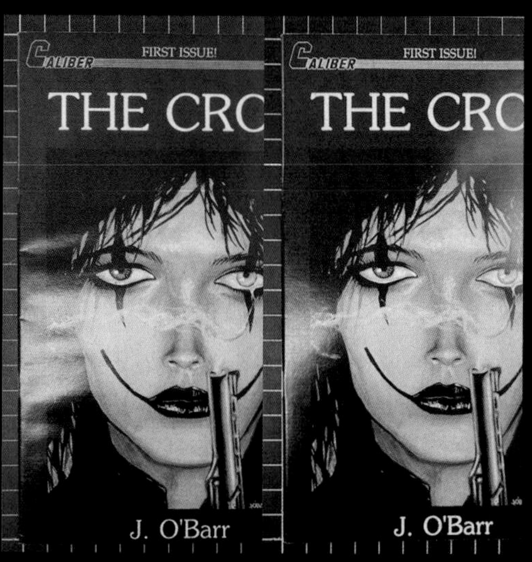

Modern Age before & after pressing

www.comicpresser.com   comic_presser

Reduce stains & defects
Raise grades & values

10% OFF CODE: OS-CPR-10
BULK DEALS TOO

"Great customer service, quick response, accurate turnaround. I recommend..."

Cover & page lightening

Foxing & tanning reduction

Tape & sticker removal

Mold & transfer stain treatment

Based in Atlanta, GA **info@comicpresser.com** +1 (507) 400-0661

MYCOMICSHOP MAKES SELLING EASY!!!

BOB MONTANA

Copyright © 2023 Archie Comics

We'll buy your entire collection, or consign it. Try us and you'll see why sellers entrusted us with the sale of over 112,000 consigned comics last year.

Visit mycomicshop.com/overstreet

MY COMIC SHOP

MY COMIC SHOP

SELL YOUR COMICS

Buying comic collections up to $2M+.
We pay top dollar for quality collections,
90-95% of current market retail for
major Gold and Silver keys.

GET AN OFFER

Call or text 817-701-0704
Or email your list to
buying@mycomicshop.com

Selling comics since 1961

CONSIGN YOUR COMICS

112,000+ consigned comics sold in 2022
Industry's lowest commissions
Listings visible on MyComicShop & eBay
More customers = better prices, faster sales
Call or text 817-701-0702
Email consign@mycomicshop.com
mycomicshop.com/consign

AMERICA'S FIRST COLLECTIBLES AUCTION HOUSE

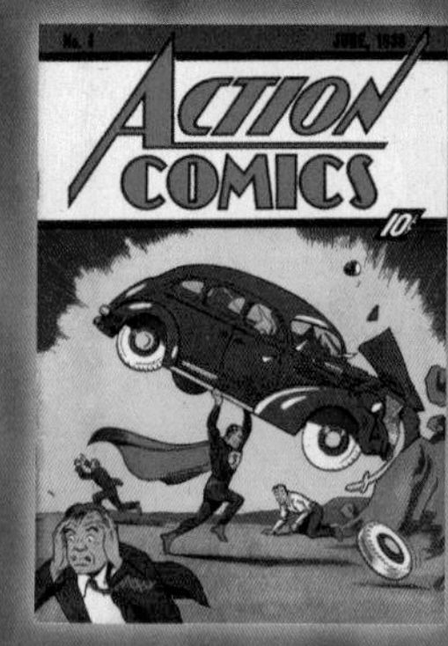

HAKES.COM

CONSIGN YOUR
COMICS TODAY!

PROVEN RESULTS SINCE 1967

- RECORD PRICES SET IN EVERY AUCTION
- NO AUCTION HOUSE HAS OFFERED COMIC BOOKS LONGER

- CONTACT US ABOUT OUR FAVORABLE RATES- WE MATCH OR BEAT OUR COMPETITION FOR THE RIGHT MATERIAL

CBCS

- WE HELP YOU EVERY STEP OF THE WAY FROM THIRD PARTY GRADING TO SELLING

- WANT YOUR BOOK TO STAND OUT? ASK ABOUT OUR *NO DUPLICATE GRADE GUARANTEE* - THE ONLY SUCH ASSURANCE IN THE HOBBY WHY COMPETE AGAINST YOURSELF - MAXIMIZE YOUR INVESTMENT

- CASH ADVANCES FOR QUALITY CONSIGNMENTS

KELLY McCLAIN TOM GORDON III

KELLY McCLAIN-SR. CONSIGNMENT MANAGER
(717) 434-1636 MKELLY@HAKES.COM

TOM GORDON III-COMIC BOOK SPECIALIST
(443) 776-1750 COMICART@HAKES.COM

"WHEN I SOLD MY COLLECTION, HAKE'S WAS THE ONLY CHOICE." - BOB OVERSTREET

"HAKE'S IS CHRISTIE'S AND SOTHEBY'S COMBINED FOR POP CULTURE ARTIFACTS. WHO DOESN'T LOOK FORWARD TO THEIR AUCTIONS?" - CHIP KIDD

AMERICA'S FIRST COLLECTIBLES AUCTION HOUSE

1.25"
SOLD $185,850

SOLD $234,171

THE CONSIGNOR'S BEST CHOICE
OVER 1 MILLION ITEMS SOLD

- OVER 200 CATALOGED AUCTIONS CONDUCTED SINCE 1967
- OUR EXPERTS USE THEIR COMBINED 400 YEARS OF KNOWLEDGE IN THE FIELD TO SHOWCASE YOUR ITEMS

SOLD $151,534

SOLD $7,475

SOLD $12,197

SOLD $24,035

HAKE'S AUCTIONS SELLS MORE THAN JUST COMIC BOOKS - WE HANDLE IT ALL - ORIGINAL ART, CCG/TCG & SPORTS CARDS, MOVIE & CONCERT POSTERS, PROPS, ACTION FIGURES, POLITICAL ITEMS, VIDEO GAMES AND MORE.

P.O. Box 12001
York, PA 17402
866-404-9800

CONSIGN ONE ITEM OR YOUR ENTIRE COLLECTION.

SOLD $34,462

SOLD $18,107

SOLD $18,497

SOLD $94,875

HAKES.COM

- CONTACT US ABOUT OUR FAVORABLE RATES- WE MATCH OR BEAT OUR COMPETITION FOR THE RIGHT MATERIAL

- CASH ADVANCES FOR QUALITY CONSIGNMENTS

CURT SWAN
ACTION COVER
ORIGINAL ART
$112,015

DAVE COCKRUM
X-MEN SPLASH
ORIGINAL ART
$75,673

ROB LIEFELD
NEW MUTANTS
ORIGINAL ART
$40,383

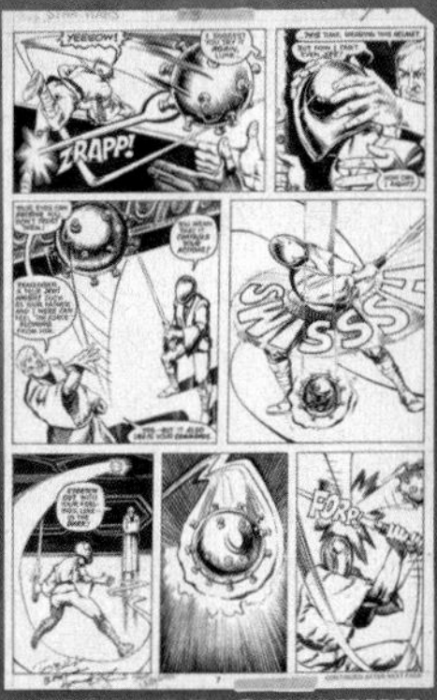

HOWARD CHAYKIN
STAR WARS
ORIGINAL ART
$33,748

WORLD RECORD PRICES SET IN EVERY AUCTION

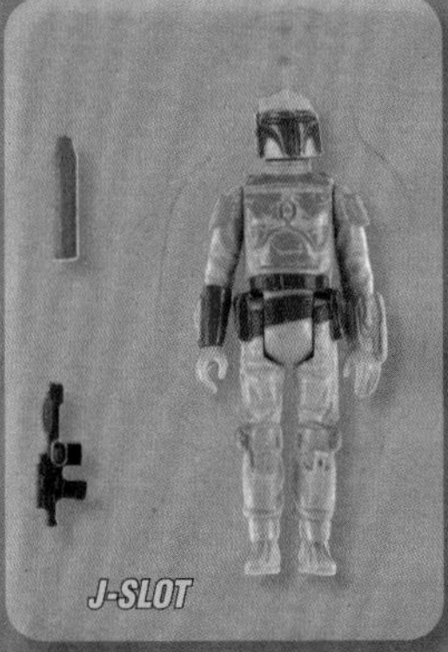

SOLD $204,435

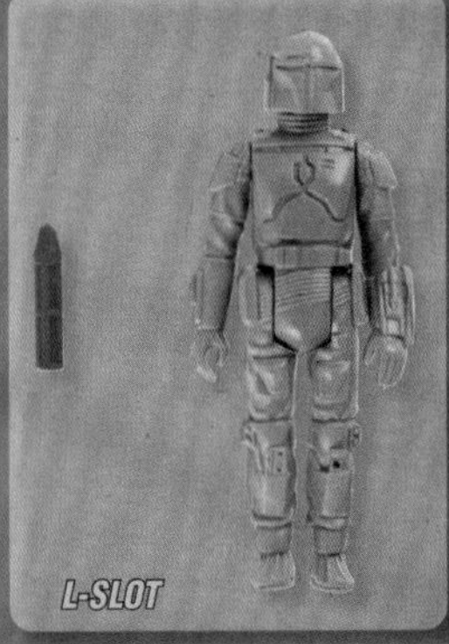

SOLD $236,000

HERO PROP
SOLD $259,570

SOLD $79,178

SOLD $64,900

SOLD $33,674

ComicLink

AUCTIONS AND EXCHANGE

SINCE 1996

THE SKY'S THE LIMIT!

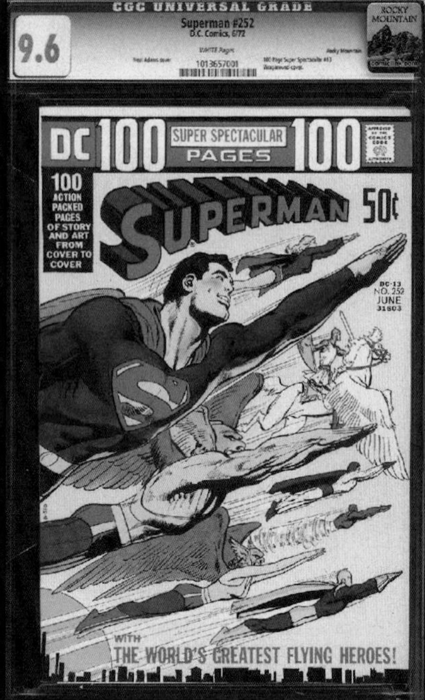

Sold on ComicLink

Vintage comic books are going for big money! If you are thinking about selling, do yourself a favor and reach out to us – you will be glad you did!

Here are some examples from the recent past showing what we've achieved in terms of results for our sellers. Note that most of these were record sales as of March of 2023 when this was written.

Golden Age (1933-1955)

***Detective Comics* #31 CGC 3.0 $131,000**
***Detective Comics* #1 CGC 3.0 $81,000**
***Mad* #1 CGC 9.2 $52,438**
***Action Comics* #7 CGC 1.0 $44,555**
***Detective Comics* #69 CGC 7.0 $36,999**
***Archie Comics* #1 CGC 3.5 $33,300**
***Thrilling Crime Cases* #49 CGC 9.4 $32,202**
***Adventure Comics* #40 CGC 3.5 $31,000**

Silver Age (1956-1969)

***Fantastic Four* #1 CGC 8.5 $350,000**
***Amazing Fantasy* #15 CGC 7.5 $270,052**
***Silver Surfer* #1 CGC 9.8 $222,000**
***Fantastic Four* #5 CGC 9.4 $210,000**
***Tales of Suspense* #39 CGC 9.0 $126,007**
***Incredible Hulk* #1 CGC 7.5 $126,000**
***Avengers* #1 CBCS 9.4 $100,000**
***Journey Into Mystery* #83 CGC 8.5 $92,000**

Bronze Age (1970-1979)

***Incredible Hulk* #181 CGC 9.8 $146,000**
***Marvel Spotlight* #5 CGC 9.6 $68,500**
***Giant-size X-Men* #1 CGC 9.8 $56,000**
***Amazing Spider-Man* #129 CGC 9.8 $39,000**
***Marvel Feature* #1 CGC 9.8 $15,250**
***Green Lantern* #87 CGC 9.8 $14,251**
***Amazing Spider-Man* #124 CGC 9.8 $14,250**
***Tomb of Dracula* #1 CGC 9.8 $10,250**

Modern Age (1980-Present)

***Amazing Spider-Man* #667 CGC 9.8 Variant $42,000**
***DC Comics Presents* #26 CGC 9.9 $40,005**
***Ultimate Fallout* #4 CGC 9.8 Variant $33,000**
***New Mutants* #87 CGC 9.9 $20,251**
***Gobbledygook* #1 CGC 7.5 $14,499**
***Daredevil* #168 CGC 9.8 Newsstand $13,916**
***Thorn: Tales From the Lantern* CGC 9.2 $13,138**
***The Crow* #1 CGC 9.8 $12,426**

Come join our global consignor base and enjoy the best value proposition in the hobby!

Visit us at
ComicLink.com
buysell@comiclink.com
(617) 517-0062
M-F 8:30am to 5:30pm ET

LET US MAXIMIZE YOUR NET RETURN!
ATTAINING RECORD SALES SINCE 1996!

"IN ONE FORM OR ANOTHER, COMIC BOOKS HAVE BEEN AROUND SINCE THE 1800S."
"WELL BEFORE THE BIRTH OF THE SUPERHEROES, THERE WERE COMIC BOOKS."

THESE DAYS, THERE ARE COMICS FOR JUST ABOUT EVERY TASTE...
AND IT'S ALWAYS A GOOD TIME TO DISCOVER THE CLASSICS!

THERE'S USUALLY A REASON THAT CERTAIN COMICS HAVE STOOD THE TEST OF TIME...
AND THE WHOLE REASON THAT THE OVERSTREET COMIC BOOK PRICE GUIDE EXISTS IS THAT MANY COMICS HAVE GONE UP IN VALUE SINCE THEY WERE PUBLISHED!

WHILE MANY COMICS ARE VERY AFFORDABLE TO EVEN THE NEWEST FANS, SEVERAL ISSUES HAVE SOLD FOR MORE THAN $1 MILLION!

BUT AN IMPORTANT COMPONENT OF COLLECTING WHAT YOU LOVE IS JUST THAT: COLLECTING WHAT YOU LOVE.
SUPERHEROES!
ANYTHING BUT SUPERHEROES!
MANGA!
ANYTHING BUT MANGA!

NOT WHAT SOMEONE ELSE SAYS YOU SHOULD LOVE!

GET INFORMED. SEE WHAT FITS YOUR TASTES. MAKE NEW DISCOVERIES. AND GO YOUR OWN WAY!

CAPTAIN ACTION & DR. EVIL ©2023 CAPTAIN ACTION ENTERPRISES.

COMICS ARE LISTED **ALPHABETICALLY** BY TITLE, **REGARDLESS** OF **PUBLISHER.** THE MAIN SECTION LISTS COMICS FROM **1934** TO THE **PRESENT.**

THIS BOOK ALSO INCLUDES...

BIG LITTLE BOOKS
PROMOTIONAL COMICS
PIONEER AGE COMICS
VICTORIAN AGE COMICS
PLATINUM AGE COMICS

9.2
9.0
8.5
8.0
7.5
7.0
6.5
6.0
5.5
5.0
4.5
4.0
3.5
3.0
2.5
2.0

PRICES ARE LISTED IN **SIX GRADES** FROM **2.0** TO **9.2** ON A 10.0 SCALE.

THERE ARE **MORE GRADES** THAN THE SIX LISTED, BUT THESE WILL GIVE YOU THE KEYS TO UNDERSTANDING THE MARKET.

WHILE PRICES **BELOW 9.2** ARE FAIRLY **STEADY,** IT'S IMPORTANT TO NOTE THAT PRICES **ABOVE 9.2** ARE FREQUENTLY CONSIDERED EXTREMELY **VOLATILE.**

SHI ©2023 WILLIAM TUCCI.

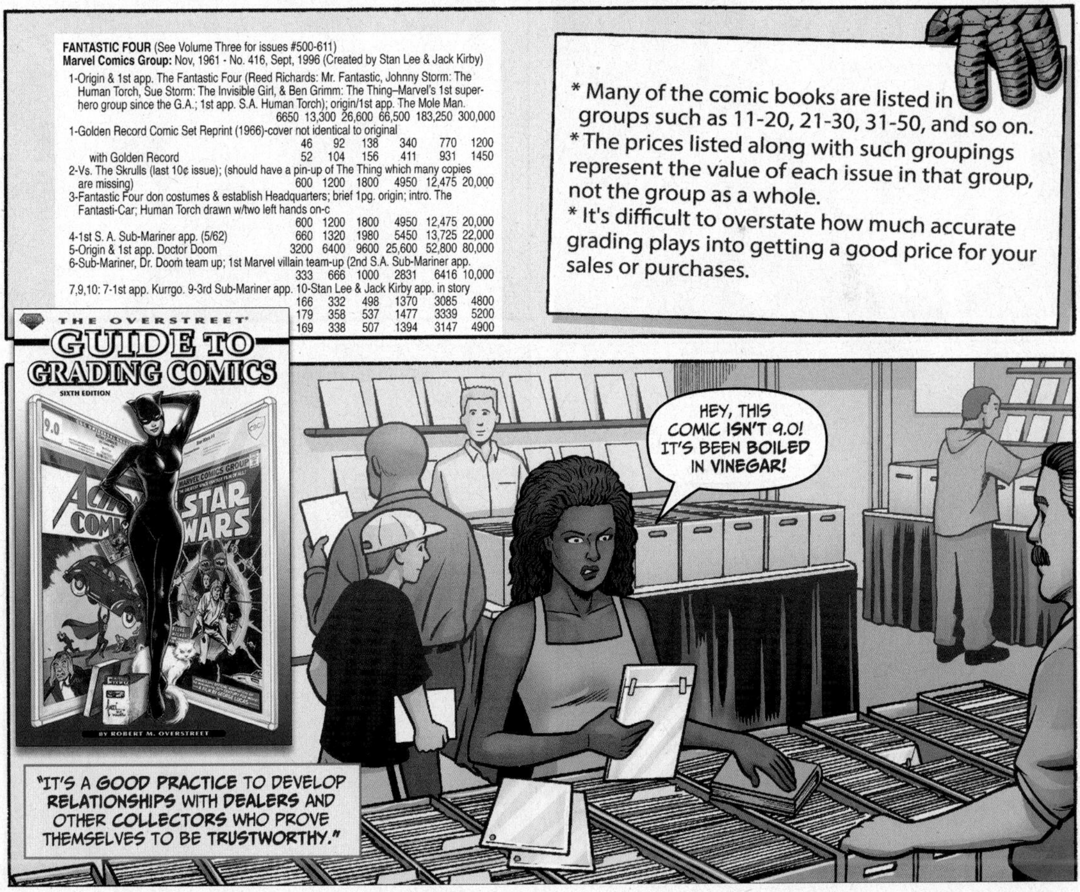

FANTASTIC FOUR (See Volume Three for issues #500-611)
Marvel Comics Group: Nov, 1961 - No. 416, Sept, 1996 (Created by Stan Lee & Jack Kirby)

1-Origin & 1st app. The Fantastic Four (Reed Richards: Mr. Fantastic, Johnny Storm: The Human Torch, Sue Storm: The Invisible Girl, & Ben Grimm: The Thing–Marvel's 1st super-hero group since the G.A.; 1st app. S.A. Human Torch); origin/1st app. The Mole Man. 6650 13,300 26,600 66,500 183,250 300,000
1-Golden Record Comic Set Reprint (1966)-cover not identical to original 46 92 138 340 770 1200
with Golden Record 52 104 156 411 931 1450
2-Vs. The Skrulls (last 10¢ issue); (should have a pin-up of The Thing which many copies are missing) 600 1200 1800 4950 12,475 20,000
3-Fantastic Four don costumes & establish Headquarters; brief 1pg. origin; intro. The Fantasti-Car; Human Torch drawn w/two left hands on-c 600 1200 1800 4950 12,475 20,000
4-1st S. A. Sub-Mariner app. (5/62) 660 1320 1980 5450 13,725 22,000
5-Origin & 1st app. Doctor Doom 3200 6400 9600 25,600 52,800 80,000
6-Sub-Mariner, Dr. Doom team up; 1st Marvel villain team-up (2nd S.A. Sub-Mariner app. 333 666 1000 2831 6416 10,000
7,9,10: 7-1st app. Kurrgo. 9-3rd Sub-Mariner app. 10-Stan Lee & Jack Kirby app. in story 166 332 498 1370 3085 4800
179 358 537 1477 3339 5200
169 338 507 1394 3147 4900

* Many of the comic books are listed in groups such as 11-20, 21-30, 31-50, and so on.
* The prices listed along with such groupings represent the value of each issue in that group, not the group as a whole.
* It's difficult to overstate how much accurate grading plays into getting a good price for your sales or purchases.

ISN'T THE BEST PART OF COLLECTING THAT THERE ARE SO MANY DIFFERENT WAYS TO COLLECT?

YOU BET! YOU CAN CHOOSE TO FOLLOW INDIVIDUAL WRITERS, ARTISTS, PUBLISHERS, OR CHARACTERS...

YOU CAN COLLECT SUPERHEROES, WAR COMICS, WESTERNS, ROMANCE COMICS, OR WHATEVER YOU LIKE!

YOU CAN CHOOSE #1 ISSUES, FIRST APPEARANCES, CROSSOVERS, OR MANY OTHER VARIATIONS.

SO YOU'RE SAYING IT'S TRULY ABOUT COLLECTING WHAT YOU LIKE AND NOT WHAT SOMEONE ELSE LIKES?

WHETHER IT'S SPIDER-MAN OR EVERY COMIC BOOK APPEARANCE OF JAMES BOND, MAKE YOUR OWN PLAN. THEN GO TO IT!

OVERSTREET
THE BEST WAY TO HAVE A GOOD PLAN IS TO GET INFORMED.
THE BEST WAY TO GET INFORMED IS TO GO TO THE EXPERTS.
LEARN THE INS AND OUTS OF COLLECTING, INCLUDING HOW TO TAKE CARE OF YOUR COLLECTION!
LEARN HOW TO GRADE YOUR COMICS AND WHY GRADES MAKE SUCH A DIFFERENCE!
LEARN WHAT TO EXPECT AT CONVENTIONS OR WHEN BUYING AND SELLING COMICS ELSEWHERE.
IT IS ALSO IMPORTANT TO REMEMBER THAT THIS BOOK IS A GUIDE, NOT A DEALER'S PRICE LIST. THE MARKET SETS THE PRICES.
GETTING THAT ISSUE YOU'VE BEEN AFTER IS A GREAT FEELING...
BUT DON'T BE IN SUCH A HURRY THAT YOU DON'T CHECK THINGS OUT THOROUGHLY.
AFTER DAVID MACK

THANKS TO OUR INCREDIBLE NETWORK OF **OVERSTREET ADVISORS**, WE **NEVER** STOP WORKING ON THIS STUFF!

AND AFTER MORE THAN 50 YEARS, WE'RE JUST GETTING **WARMED UP!**

Written by J.C. VAUGHN
Illustrated by BRENDON & BRIAN FRAIM
Colored by Hi-Fi's BRIAN MILLER
Lettered by MINDY LOPKIN
Edited by MARK HUESMAN

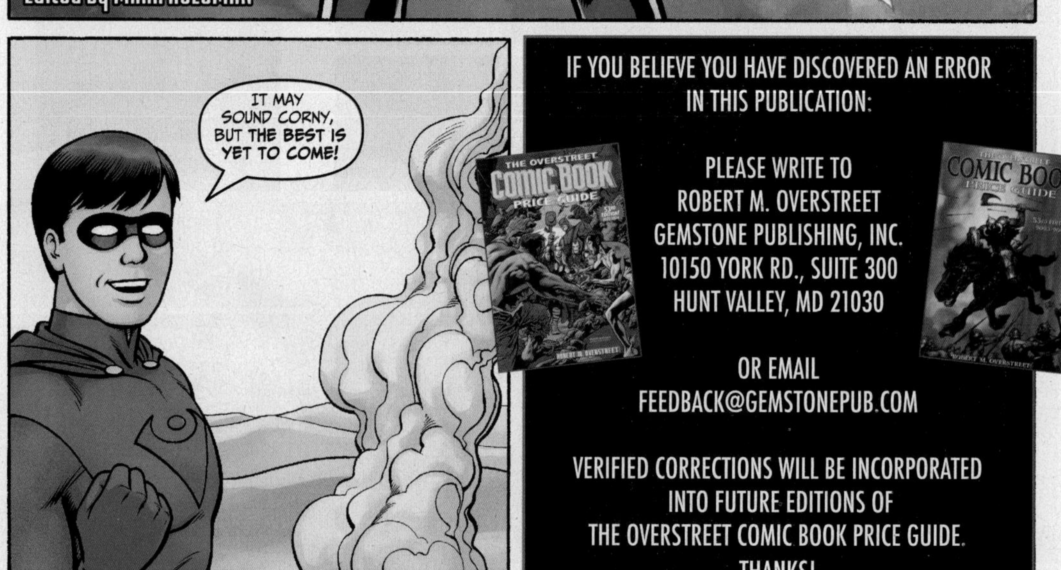

PRE-CODE HORROR REMAINED IN DEMAND WHILE OTHER PRICES VARIED WIDELY

MARKET REPORT 2023 • Robert M. Overstreet

I'd like to personally extend my thanks to everyone who has supported *The Overstreet Comic Book Price Guide* over the years.

As David Alexander reported, "2021 had rising prices and the trend continued into 2022, but early in the year we saw price support eroding. Key Marvel and DC issues lost their footing. An *X-Men* #1 (CGC 6.5) which sold for $60,000 last year failed to hit $30,000."

David Anderson agreed, "Although the comic book market remains very strong in 2022, there were some signs that it was slowing down."

Lauren Becker reported, "Golden Age has been a tremendous seller at shows and online. A copy of *Detective Comics* #36 graded 2.5 restored went for an amazing $19,200 through Heritage! I see more copies of *Action* #1 offered than I do *Punch Comics* #12 where a CGC 5.5 closed for $90,000 at Heritage."

Scott Braden reported, "Most of 2022 was a strong year for graded comics. Then in the 4th quarter, the sales of modern slabs began to slow down."

Jeff Cerrito pointed out, "Some shows were back to full capacity pre-pandemic and a few took steps forward and set record numbers for attendance. Mega-Con in Orlando would draw 100,000 people. This year, fans came out in droves with an attendance of 148,000. For San Diego, it was definitely what San Diego was pre-pandemic. The aisles were busy, the entire city was buzzing."

Paul Clairmont noted, "The pandemic began to wind down and with it came the slow down of record online sales from the past two years. The beginning of the year saw some of the strongest sales we've ever encountered in our ten years of business. The 2nd quarter of the year, people began to move back to regular activities. So began the decline of overinflated prices to a more normal level."

#1 $3.55 million

#8 $1.62 million

#12 $90,000

Gary Colabuano reported, "After 40 years of being an advisor to Bob Overstreet this will be my last market report. I've had a great run, discovering the Windy City pedigree collection and uncovering the original cache of authentic DC Golden Age ashcan editions." *Thanks for your decades of input Gary*.

Gary Dolgoff reported, "Comic collections and individual books continue to be bought and sold in a hearty and constant way."

Bill Fidyk noted, "There is a market correction that the hobby is currently undergoing."

Paul Figura reported, "For the past few years, comic coventions have been lacking in attendance due to the pandemic that has swept the world."

Joseph Fiore pointed out, "Markets have cooled substantially."

Kevin Forbes noted, "After the historic and meteoric rise in comic book prices across the board, we all expected a market correction at some point, but the substantial drop from late August to late November/December surprised most. To me it was Black Fall, the comic book version of the stock market crashing."

Dan Gallo reported, "The first half of 2022 was solid. The second half was a different story. We started to see prices decrease as demand waned."

Stephen Gentner noted, "The downturn in prices gives the collector an opportunity to get some nice deals now, as dealers accept lower offers to move their stock. The Pre-Code Horror segment is very hot and popular! The enthusiasm and competition for this material continues unabated."

Terry Hoknes reported, "Most of these prices crashed back to more or less where they had been before the big jump."

Doug Mabry stated, "The internet has really changed everything. First appearances, no matter how minor, are snatched up at quickly escalating prices while non-keys sit. So now, in the Golden Age market, prices have become extremely volatile. Keys are always at a premium."

Steve Mortensen wrote, "The demand for comics in general remains strong as buyers are still out there picking up deals."

Josh Nathanson at ComicLink reported, "We were the first online comic book and comic art consignment website. 2022 was another exceptional year for ComicLink. Thousands of new sales records were established in the hobby. The Golden Age market remained extremely healthy throughout 2022. Market growth is driven by first appearances an origin issues, early appearances of popular heroes and villains, Pre-Code Horror, Good Girl Art and classic covers by the likes of Schomburg, Baker, L.B. Cole and Frazetta."

Karen O'Brien pointed out, "As the pandemic ages into an endemic state, comic shops resumed regular business hours."

Terry O'Neill reported, "Sales at comic shows have been mixed, with a somewhat downward trend from the crazy highs of 2021. Catalog orders were significantly down in 2022."

Bill Ponseti reported, "Rapidly increasing prices across the board for Gold, Silver and Bronze comics. That trend continued into the first quarter of 2022, and then the regression in prices started and haven't really stabilized as of this writing."

Stephen & Sharon Ritter wrote, "Even though 2022 can be classified as a year most comics saw a decrease in value, it was not by any means a bad year for the comic market due to the tremendous surge of prices seen in 2021. 2022 can be better explained as the year prices stabilized to a more confident market for collectors and investors alike."

Conan & Buddy Saunders reported, "If the market peaked May-July of 2022, it's dropped relatively steadily through the end of 2022. As 2022 concludes and we move into 2023, it looks to me like price decreases have been flattening out, possibly hitting or nearing a bottom. Even with the pull-back, prices for major comic keys are still up significantly from where they were in early 2020 before Covid, even adjusting for inflation between then and now."

Todd Sheffer noted, "Early DC and Timely superhero titles have a continued following with film and TV features attracting new collectors. EC and other Pre-Code Horror have been running strong with that trend looking to continue."

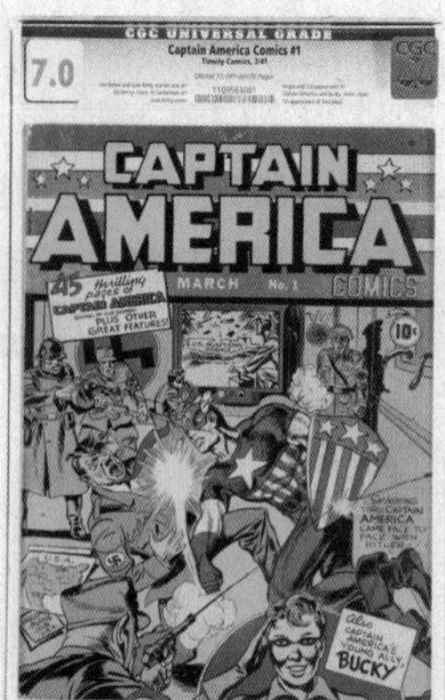

#1 $312,000

#27 $1.74 million

#1 $720,000

Marc Sims stated, "2022 truly was the year of the great market correction in comics. I would estimate prices on the majority of Copper/Bronze/Silver, and even most common Golden Age, are down an average of 40%."

West Stephan reported, "2022 has proven, once again, to be another crazy and unpredictable year for the hobby. The demand for graded books jumped to unparalleled heights."

Al Stoltz wrote, "November online sales have really slowed way down and regardless of what those on TV say, a recession is already here affecting sales heavily."

Michael Tierney reported, "Marvel Comics was back at full strength in 2022 and they dominated the new comics market with a superiority not seen since the heyday of editor Jim Shooter."

Ted VanLiew noted, "Overall, the overheated market we saw for a couple of years during the height of the pandemic has subsided. Prices have been adjusting to more where they should be."

Harley Yee noted, "The 2022 market can be described as a tale of two halves. The first half continued the hot 2021. The second half saw some price pressure on many books and titles."

Golden Age Sales:

Action Comics #1, CGC 6.0 $3,550,000
Adventure Comics #48 CGC 9.2 $168,000
All Flash #22 CGC 9.8 Promise Coll. $66,000
All Star Comics #8 CGC 9.4 $1,620,000, CGC 7.0 $168,000, CGC 6.0 $66,000
Batman #1 CGC 6.0 $552,000, CGC 1.8 $180,000, $126,000, CGC 3.5 $264,000, CGC 4.0 $264,000, CGC 6.0 Moderate $72,000, CGC 8.5 ext. rest. $69,000
Captain America Comics #1, CGC 7.0 $312,000, CGC 5.0 $180,000, CGC 5.0 Moderate $72,000, CGC 3.0 $144,000, CGC 4.5 $194,400,
Capt. America Comics #2 CGC 9.0 $78,000
Capt. America Comics #3 CGC 8.0 $90,000
Century of Comics nn CGC 5.5 $9,300
Chamber of Chills #19 CGC 9.2 $72,000
Cinderella Love #25, CGC 1.5 $6,000
Crime Does Not Pay #24 CGC 9.4 $102,000
Crime Does Not Pay #34 CGC 9.4 $2,640
Crime SuspenStories #22 CGC 9.0 $72,000,

Desert Dawn, nn CGC 6.5 $3720
Detective Comics #1 CGC 5.0 $108,000
Detective Comics #2, CGC 1.8 $8,700
Detective Comics #4, CGC 4.5 $560
Detective Comics #7 CGC 6.5 $5,600
Detective Comics #9 CGC 4.5 $9,000
Detective Comics #10 CGC 4.0 $10,200
Detective Comics #24 CGC 4.0 $3,600
Detective Comics #24 cover original art $84,000
Detective Comics #27 CGC 7.0 $1,500,000, CGC 4.5 $1,140,000, CGC 7.0 Slight $384,000, no cover $78,000
Detective Comics #28 CGC 6.0 $66,000
Detective Comics #29 CGC 8.5 $276,000
Detective Comics #31 CGC 2.0 $93,000, CGC 1.5 $66,000
Detective Comics #33 CGC 8.0 $192,000
Detective Comics #59 original art $180,000
Detective Comics #168 CGC 9.4 $324,000
Donald Duck Four Color #178 CGC 9.6 $90,000
Famous Funnies, A Carnival of Comics CGC 4.5 $2,880, CGC 7.0 $5,280
Famous Funnies #1, CGC 1.5 $6,000, CGC 4.0 $7,800, CGC 5.5 $19,200
Flash Comics #1 CGC 5.0 $192,000, CGC 1.8 $84,000
Frontline Combat #3 original cover art $78,000
Haunt of Fear #20 original cover art $114,000
Little Dot #1 CGC 9.6 $78,000
Marvel Comics #1, CGC 4.5 $360,000, #3 CGC 3.5 $312,000, CGC 3.0 $223,200
Marvel Family #1 CGC 9.0 $90,000
More Fun Comics #52 CGC 8.5 $264,000
More Fun Comics #55 CGC 9.0 $90,000
More Fun Comics #73 CGC 6.5 $192,000, $102,000, CGC 6.0 $90,000, CGC 2.0 $72,000
Punch Comics #12 CGC 5.5 $90,000
Sensation Comics #1 CGC 7.5 $96,000, CGC 6.5 $84,000
Superboy nn Ashcan CGC 6.5 $48,000
Superman #1 CGC 1.0 $69,000, CGC 1.5 $192,000, CGC 1.8 $288,000, CGC 5.0 $720,00, Nova Scotia copy $675,000, CGC 7.0 $96,000, CGC 0.5 $96,000
Superman nn Ashcan CGC 8.5 $288,000
Two-Fisted Tales #21 original cover art $72,000
Vault of Horror #16, 8-pg. story art by Craig $78,000
Whiz Comics #1 CGC 3.5 $120,000

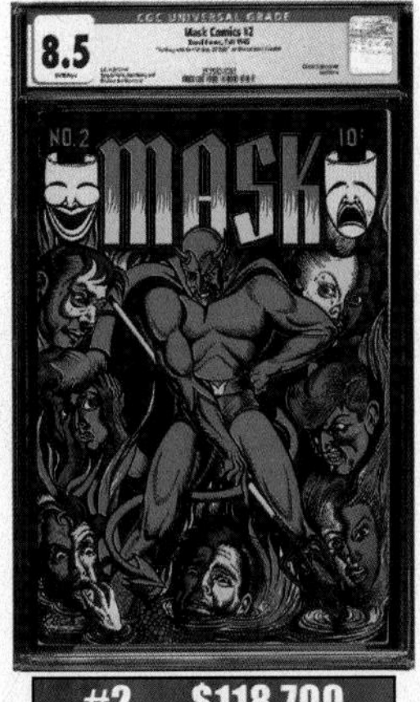

#2 $118,700

#52 $264,000

#15 $810,000

Silver Age: Dealers reported that the first half of 2022 sales were solid but the second half sales had slowed and prices dropped along with demand. Now may be a good time for collectors to pick up books on their want list before prices go up.

Dr. Steven Kahn pointed out, "Almost all graded Silver and Bronze keys are down from between 30 to 50 percent."

Jim McCallum reported, "*Daredevil* #1 when compared to the rest of the major keys still appears to be undervalued and the demand remains high. As soon as a copy comes in, it's usually sold within hours. Another 1960s book similar to this is *Iron Man* #1 as many collectors have resigned themselves to the fact that an *Iron Man* #1 is the closest they will ever get to his first appearance and even prefer it to an affordable copy of *Tales of Suspense* #40 (Iron Man's second appearance)."

Joe Engel reported, "2022 was a little crazy for comics. At the beginning we continued to see some of the mass buying of hotter books moving at a record pace. As the year went on, we saw this slow down and return to a 2019 pace."

Ben Labonog reported, "The market keys have cooled considerably, and are down as much as 50% on some books."

Steve Mortensen noted, "I suspect that 2023 will be like the second half of 2022 and that the true recovery in the collectible market will happen in 2024."

Josh Nathanson reported, "The Silver Age continues to be one of the most popular segments of the hobby, with the superhero genre dominating the activity within this category."

Tom Nelson stated, "Overall sales were very strong with the dollars flowing into the market this year. However the second half of the year there was a softening of prices on primarily Marvel keys from the Silver Age through the Modern Age."

Karen O'Brien reported, "Silver Age titles in all conditions remain desirable and continue to generate high prices."

Terry O'Neill noted, "Prices shot way up in 2021 but they have certainly settled back down this year."

Bill Ponseti wrote, "I have seen prices continue to drop, while others remain relatively stable after the initial few months of price drops."

Alex & Austin Reece reported, "2022

was also the return of a full year of conventions after some re-started in 2021."

Alika Seki, P.E. stated, "A period of cooling has set in. Prices are down across the board, less so obviously for the top books."

Silver Age through Modern Age Sales:
Amazing Fantasy #15, CGC 9.2 $810,000, CGC 8.5 $552,000, CGC 7.5 $300,000, CGC 7.5 $216,000, CGC 7.5 $198,000, CGC 7.0 $240,000, CGC 7.0 $222,000, CGC 7.0 $252,000, CGC 7.0 $168,000, CGC 6.5 $120,000, $96,000, CGC 5.5 $120,000, $117,000, $66,000, CGC 5.0 $84,000, $78,000, CGC 4.5 $72,000, $69,000, $66,000, CGC 4.0 $72,000
Amazing Spider-Man #1, CGC 9.6 $336,000, CGC 9.2 $168,000, CGC 9.0 $120,000, $72,000
Amazing Spider-Man #2 CGC 9.2 $69,000
Amazing Spider-Man #50 CGC 9.8 $99,000
Avengers #1 CGC 9.4 $120,000, CGC 8.0 $66,000, CGC 4.0 $72,000
Bone #1 CGC 9.8 $12,000
Captain America #117, CGC 9.8 $78,000
Daredevil #1 CGC 9.6 $111,000, $96,000, $90,000, CGC 9.4 $78,000, $72,000
Detective Comics #359 CGC 9.6 $78,000
Fantastic Four #1, CGC 9.2 $1,500,000, CGC 9.0 $420,000, CGC 9.0 $234,000, $288,000, CGC 8.5 $240,000, CGC 7.0 $81,000, CGC 7.5 $168,000, $84,000, CGC 6.5 $78,000
Fantastic Four #2 CGC 9.4 $ 84,000, $78,000
Fantastic Four #3 CGC 9.4 $102,000
Fantastic Four #49 CBCS 9.8 $192,000
Fantastic Four #5 CGC 9.2 $180,000, $150,150
Fantastic Four #5 CGC 9.4 $162,000
Hero for Hire #1 CGC 9.8 $102,000
Incredible Hulk #1 CGC 7.5 $78,000, CGC 7.0 $72,000, CGC 6.5 $75,000, $72,000
Incredible Hulk #181 CGC 9.8 $138,000, $102,000, $96.000, $90,000, CGC 6.5 $84,000, CGC 7.0 $84,000
Journey Into Mystery #83 CGC 9.4 $432,000, CGC 8.0 $66,000
Journey Into Mystery #85 CGC 9.4 $78,000
Marvel Spotlight #5 CGC 9.6 $90,000, $84,000
Showcase #22 CGC 8.5 $93,000
Strange Tales #110 CGC 9.4 $72,000, CGC

#1 $120,000

#1 $12,000

9.2 $72,000
Tales of Suspense #39 CGC 9.2 $168,000, CGC 9.2 $108,000, CGC 9.0 $78,000
Tales of Suspense #57 CGC 9.8 $102,000
Tales to Astonish #27 CGC 9.0 $66,000
Teenage Mutant Ninja Turtles #1 signed $192,000, CGC 9.8 $186,000, $156,000, CGC 9.6 $69,000
X-Men #1, CGC 9.6 $871,999.20, CGC 9.2 $276,000, $204,000, $186,000 CGC 9.0 $156,000, $114,000, $108,000, $102,000, CGC 8.5 $78,000, CGC 8.0 $102,000, $72,000, $66,000, CGC 7.5 $78,000, $66,000

Bronze Age: Gary Dolgoff reported, "Bronze Age Marvels are solid sellers, and there are a number of Bronze keys that sell for over *Guide*, such as *Amazing Spider-Man* #129 (1st Punisher), #194 (1st Black Cat), #258 (1st Hobgoblin), *Daredevil* #131 (1st Bullseye), #168 (1st Elektra), *Tomb of Dracula* #10 (1st Blade), *Werewolf By Night* #32 (1st Moon Knight) and others.

Ken Dyber reported, "Another period showing declines in value and in people collecting."

Kevin Forbes noted, "All the keys from this era have taken a substantial hit over the past few months, with only a few exceptions due to highest graded copy, or low numbers of copies IN grade."

Dan Gallo noted, "Marvels have been brutal. The super key issue books that we all thought were invincible proved otherwise. *Amazing Fantasy* #15 and *X-Men* #1, the two most popular books of the era had previously experienced massive increases so naturally when things got soft, they had the furthest to fall."

Dr. Steven Kahn stated, "Almost all graded Silver and Bronze keys are down from between 30 to 50 percent."

Josh Nathanson & Rick Hirsch reported, "Record prices were achieved for Bronze Age keys in pristine condition, many of which sold for sums unimaginable to those of us who remember plunking down 20 or 25 cents for some of these comics in our youth."

Karen O'Brien noted, "Bronze Age titles are killing it at auction houses, eBay, and social media live "Claim sales" are all netting solid results for these books."

Terry O'Neill reported, "While demand is high, it's been increasingly difficult to acquire collections of this material, especially Marvel comics. As always, *Amazing Spider-Man* and *X-Men* are the most collected."

Alika Seki, PE. noted, "After a huge pandemic/crypto fueled boom in the collectibles market, a period of cooling has set in."

Al Stolz stated, "Even big Marvel keys in lower grades that sold for nutty money now have tumbled back."

Ted VanLiew reported, "Bronze Age is an area where books were underappreciated for many years, then took off, then took off again."

Modern Age 1980-Present:

Lauren Becker reported, "During the pandemic, collectors were swarming the internet looking for the next big investment, and thanks to phone apps like Key Collector, they found it. Anything that was a first appearance related to a movie/ TV show or even a speculated scene that MIGHT appear, shot up fast. And then it died."

John Chruscinski pointed out, "It's been a solid year overall, even though the economy is not where it was a few years ago. The recovery continues and so does the passion for collecting and investing in comics and collectibles."

Paul Clairmont stated, "2022 was our most successful and interesting year in our ten years of business."

Art Cloos reported, "It's December 2022. We were asked to assess how Covid affected us in 2022. So as shows came back we debated over how many should we go to? In a normal year it can be as many as 40 shows, but that number has been drastically reduced since the beginning of the Covid outbreak to a relative handful in the last 3 years."

Brock Dickinson noted, "*Prices vary widely* could be the slogan for the 2022 market."

Walter Durajlija and Jay Halstead reported, "The second half of the year saw some major price drops, especially in the most heavily traded sectors of the key issue Silver, Bronze, Copper and Modern Ages."

Ken Dyber made a good point, "Late 2020 through early 2022 specifically showed the largest period of growth in not only comics, but all collectibles in history. So, as downward trending as 2022 has been, things are not all doom and gloom."

#4 $38,400

#1 $192,000

#1 $871,999

Bill Fidyk stated, "The end of 2022 saw prices for comics and magazines that soared in 2020-21 dip slightly and come back to reality. There is no bubble bursting, but there is a market price-correction."

Bill Ponseti reported, "We set up at two shows in 2022, Fan Fusion Phoenix and San Diego Comic-Con. Both shows were very strong for us in terms of sales."

Conan Saunders stated, "Comic retailers are running into more issues with newly published comics arriving with dings, bends, dents, and spine ticks. If you're a reader focused on reading the next issue, they still look great and you probably won't notice or care. But if you're a grade-sensitive collector looking for only Near Mint comics to add to your collection, many newly distributed books may not meet your standards."

Marc Sims noted, "2022 was the year of the great market correction in comics. Prices on all periods down an average of 40%."

Doug Sulipa reported, "All 1960s Marvel main-stream titles are selling in all grades, both raw and CGC graded."

Vincent Zurzolo and Rob Reynolds stated, "Some Silver and Bronze have decreased by 10-30%, Copper and Modern have dropped by 10-50%. The overall trajectory of books from this time period, due to how common they are, has been downward."

Rob Reynolds added, "Like the winds of March, the 2022 collectibles market raged in like a lion and left like a lamb. Prices that were easy to achieve at the start of the year got tougher to match as the year persisted."

The following market reports were submitted from some of our many advisors and are published here for your information. The opinions in these reports belong to each contributor and do not necessarily reflect the vews of the publisher or the staff of the Overstreet Comic Book Price Guide or Gemstone Publishing.

They will provide important insights into the thinking of many key players in the marketplace.

See you next year!

Bob

Robert M. Overstreet

THE JOHN VERZYL OVERSTREET® ADVISOR AWARD

The John Verzyl Overstreet Advisor Award, named in honor of our friend and longtime contributor John Verzyl, is presented annually to an Advisor or Advisors whose knowledge, contributions, ethics and reputation are held in the highest esteem by his or her peers.

Nominations may be made by any Overstreet Advisor in good standing by sending the nominee's name and description of why he or she represents the positive attributes that John embodied for our hobby. To make a nomination, email Gemstone Publishing's Mark Huesman at humark@gemstonepub.com. Nominations for our next edition must be received by March 15, 2024.

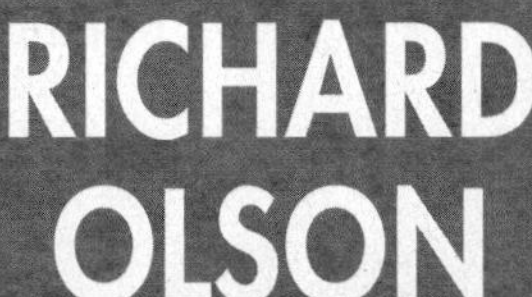

RICHARD OLSON

GARY GUZZO

RICHARD OLSON was a longtime Overstreet Advisor who actively supported the *Guide* and shared its goal of disseminating details of the rich history of our medium out to as many readers as possible. With a scholarly approach, he contributed information and frequently wrote articles, including his last one in this edition, about the Platinum Age. He passed away on April 30, 2023.

GARY GUZZO, with his outgoing passion for both the business and creative aspects of comics, a classic rock FM radio DJ voice, and a "can-do" problem-solving mentality, was known by many in the industry for his stint as Marvel Comics' Director of Publicity. During his tenure there, he virtually created the model for publishers to more actively reach out to the press, including the *Guide*, which he supported in myriad ways, frequently behind the scenes. He passed away on January 4, 2023.

Both consistently proved themselves willing to share their experience and expertise with collectors, dealers, historians, and others, including the readership of *The Overstreet Comic Book Price Guide*.

OVERSTREET COVER SUBJECTS
FIRST APPEARANCES

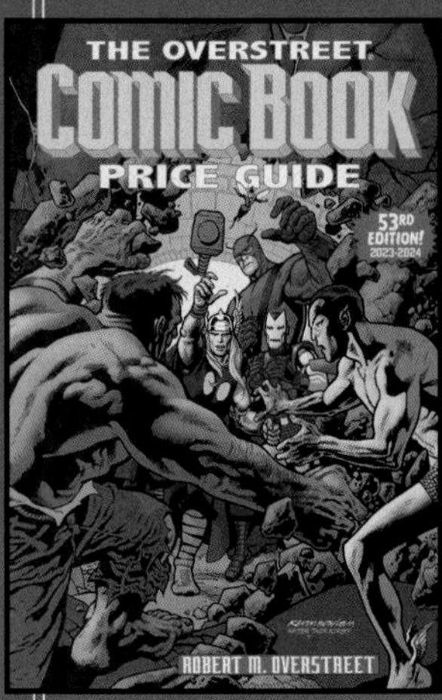

THE AVENGERS
The Avengers #1
September 1963
2023 NM- PRICE: $60,000

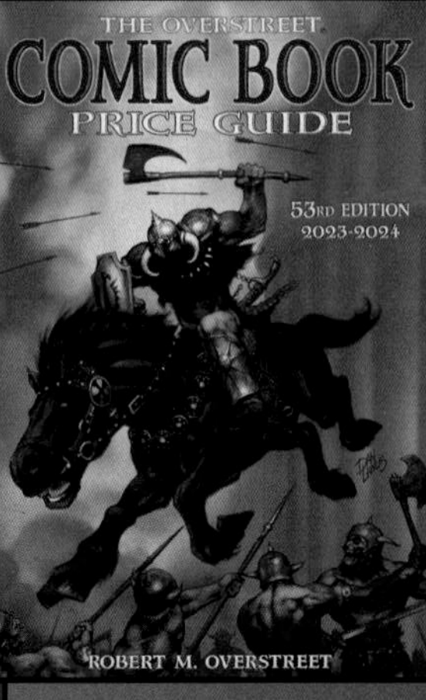

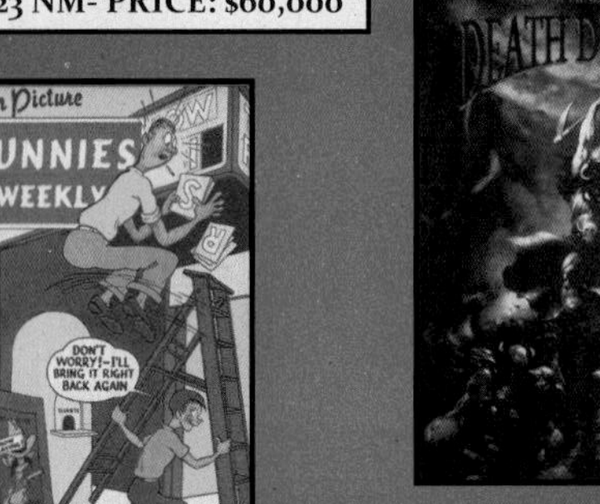

DEATH DEALER
(in comics)
Death Dealer #1
July 1995
2023 NM- PRICE: $30

SUB-MARINER
Motion Picture
Funnies Weekly #1
1939
2023 VF/NM PRICE: $65,000

BLACKOUT
Cat-Man Comics #10
May 1942
2023 NM- PRICE: $3,900

RED SONJA
Conan the Barbarian #23
February 1973
2023 NM- PRICE: $315

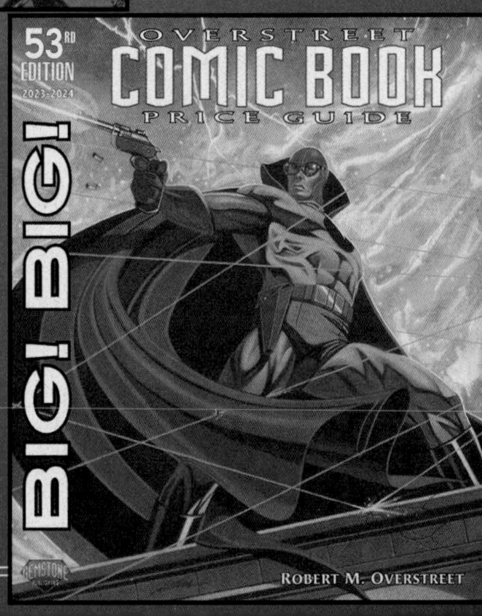

Large Finder Fee's Available!

Got Pokémon?™

We Buy!

Singles
Loose Boxes
Sealed Cases
Storage Units
Estates
Vintage & New

PRISTINECOMICS.COM
PRISTINE COMICS
CALL: (253) 941-1986

BUYING ALL POKEMON CARDS

SINGLES - SETS - BOXES - CASES - ENTIRE COLLECTIONS - ALL YEARS

WE ARE ALWAYS BUYING COMICS, SPORTSCARDS, MAGIC THE GATHERING & POKEMON
PRISTINE COMICS EST 1986
AND WEST COAST SPORTS CARDS
2008 SOUTH 314TH STREET. FEDERAL WAY, WA 98003
CALL: 253.941.1986 - WESTCOASTSPORTSCARDS.COM
I UNDERSTAND THE PAIN IN LETTING GO OF YOUR HIGHLY PRIZED COLLECTIBLES. I WILL TREAT YOUR ITEMS WITH GREAT RESPECT.
BUYING ALL COMIC BOOKS, ORIGINAL ART & VIDEO GAMES
Seattle
Tacoma
9.0
ALL STAR Comics
9.0
ACTION COMICS
100% Confidential
PRISTINECOMICS.COM
PRISTINE COMICS EST 1986
CALL: (253) 941-1986
BUYING COMICS 1930 TO PRESENT
SINGLE BOOKS - LARGE COLLECTIONS - ALL TITLES & GRADES

Grant Adey
Halo Certification Pty Ltd. - Australia

Some big surprises have unfolded this year, with an *Action Comics* #1 coming out of Darwin, Northern Territory. It was sold by 2nd generation to some businessmen from the Middle East, and just when I thought all the whales were gone. I graded the book as a GD/GD+. Page quality cream with tanning at edges. Maybe we're coming to a point in time where the high prices and aging collectors are ready to say goodbye to their treasures.

This leads me to an Australian icon, *The Phantom*. Eighteen years ago I had an educated guess that maybe twenty were in collections. Just this year, seven that I've never seen have come in for grading, so it appears there are a lot more than twenty. Grading in the 6.0 to 6.5 range, it's incredible for a 1948 comic with a newsprint cover. Auction prices were around $22,000. Highest graded were two comics in 6.5. Fifteen years ago, I graded two of my prime 1950's *Phantoms* with CGC, grading at 9.2. At the time, Eric Downton wrote to me and said that 8.5 was the best grade on a newsprint cover comic they had done.

Large private collections in for grading come from people who bought way back in the '70s. I sold off maybe half of the lower grade in the '90s/2000s.

Here's a common story: this week 3,000 books came in for grading, included was a bunch of Mile High 2 books. Yeah, *Incredible Hulk* #181 Mile High 2. From memory, Chuck got a full case of *Hulk* #181 at the time. Interesting to note, I'm not sure but did the last *Hulk* #181 in 9.8 sell at auction in the region of $180k? I think that's what I read in *Scoop*. My shop was buying and selling in the early 2000s books like *Strange Tales*, *Tales of Suspense*, *Tales To Astonish*, early ECs which were in plentiful supply. I could sell a run of Hulk, #2-6 tattered, #102 to #240 VG to VF, less #181 for $600, plus $200 for the #181. Replace them in a month. How those days are gone never to return.

Grading cards is very strong, I'm only taking pre '90s non-sports, focusing in on early Australian Scanlens or UK ABC cards. *Batman*, 1969 *Planet of the Apes* movie with Charlton Heston, early Rugby League football so on. The *Batman* 1966 series seem to be the favoured graded card.

Let's talk about fragments of comic books. A fragment isn't just a fragment. I've adapted a grading scale for fragments: 100 point scale. Goodbye to PG or NG. It is possible to grade a fragment or single page. For a few years I've collected for study Egyptian papyrus. Okay, hang on a minute, you can own a graded fragment of papyrus for as little as $100. So a splash page only of *Amazing Fantasy* #15 is $2,000 I guess. Why not grade it. We grade comics on 1 criteria, condition. Fragments take more into consideration. Fragments or single page will not be for everyone, but more for the collector who knows his Gerber scale. Watch the prices on Golden Age coverless or incomplete. Let's just focus on Alex Schomburg, Joe Simon, Jack Kirby, Joe Shuster, Walter Wood, Al Feldstein, and Bill Ward. To buy a *Batman* #1 is way out of reach for 99% of us. So the right page or panel clipped from a wreck can still bring joy. I've said enough on that.

Signing off from the furtherest outpost ... Grant.

Bill Alexander
Collector

This year I am starting my report with some disagreements as to what is accurate in the *Guide*, as well as providing a few amazing notable comic book sales of 2022 this year, some which were record high sales in the hobby.

The Guide states that *Amazing Spider-Man* #238 has no Canadian price variant edition copies that exist with the Tattoos inserts, but I myself have owned a Canadian price variant copy with the Tattoos insert in it, and CGC Label stated on it as well.

Marvel Age #87 has the first appearance of Danny Ketch as Ghost Rider. You only noted Danny Ketch as Ghost Rider which is known already and completely insignificant in my opinion. *Marvel Age* #2 (May 1983) predates *Alpha Flight* #1 August 1983 by 3 months, and features the 1st appearance of Alpha Flight team members Puck and Marrina on the cover and inside the book. CGC on its own has been labeling *Alpha Flight* #1 as the first appearance of Puck and Marrina for many years. I contacted CGC to correct them with no success sad to say. *(Editor's Note:* The Guide *considers the appearances of new characters in* Marvel Age *to be advance previews, not comic-story debuts, as apparently CGC agrees.)*

My reported noteworthy sales of 2022: Luke Cage *Hero For Hire* #1 CGC 9.8 $102,000 July 2022 on Heritage Auctions. *Amazing Spider-Man* #300 CGC 9.8 newsstand edition $13,600.00 on Heritage Auctions July 2022. *Marvel Age* #87 CGC 9.8 $1,200.00 (1st preview appearance of Danny Ketch) not noted in *OPG* as "1st appearance" of Danny Ketch. My personal purchase in 2022. *Marvel Two In One Annual* #7 CGC 9.9 $15,000 Apri 2022. A record high Canadian price variant sale in the hobby.

Greetings from sunny California! As all of you repeat *OPG* Market Report readers know, in addition to being an Overstreet Advisor I am a co-founder and advisor to the CPV Price Guide which aims to fill the void by valuing the newsstand-exclusive 1980's Type 1A US-published Canadian Price Variants that are still absent from within the pages of the *Overstreet Guide*. Newsstand comics from the 1980s with variant cover prices exist from Marvel (10/1982-8/1986), DC (10/1982-9/1988) and various other publishers as well.

Together with fellow Overstreet Advisors Paul Clairmont, Jay Halstead, Greg Holland, Jon McClure, Conan Saunders, and Doug Sulipa, and joined by Tim Bildhauser, Jayden Mitchell, Benjamin Nobel, and Angelo Virone, we have recently published the 2023 Edition of our CPV guide, available to read online without cost at www.cpvpriceguide.com. Below I am pleased to share our latest Top 25 CPV Comics Checklist [see our guide for Top Magazines].

Top Canadian Price Variant Checklist

#1 *G.I. Joe, a Real American Hero* #21 Marvel, 3/1984 $1000
#2 *Amazing Spider-Man* #238 Marvel, 3/1983 $750
#3 *Archie's Girls Betty and Veronica* #320 Archie, Oct-82 $680
#4 *Saga of the Swamp Thing* #37 DC, 6/1985 $600
#5 *Batman* #423 DC, 9/1988 $505
#6 *Blip* #1 Marvel, 2/1983 $500
#7 *Star Wars* #68 Marvel, 2/1983 $340
#8 *Amazing Spider-Man* #252 Marvel, 5/1984 $325
#9 *Marvel Super Heroes Secret Wars* #8 Marvel, 12/1984 $310
#10 *Transformers* #1 Marvel, 9/1984 $300
#11 *Batman* #357 DC, 3/1983 $298
#12 *Jughead* #325 Archie, Oct-82 $275
#13 *Amazing Spider-Man Annual* #16 Marvel, 12/1982 $230
#14 *Teenage Mutant Ninja Turtles Adventures* Mini Series #1 Archie, Aug-88 $222
#15 *ThunderCats* #1 Star, 12/1985 $200
#16 *Thor* #337 Marvel, 11/1983 $195
#17 *Teenage Mutant Ninja Turtles Adventures* #72 Archie, Oct-95 $190
#18 *Marvel Team-Up* #141 Marvel, 5/1984 $185
#19 *Batman* #386 DC, 8/1985 $181
#20 *Punisher* #1 Marvel, 1/1986 $180
#21 *Archie's Girls Betty and Veronica* #322 Archie, Feb-83 $175
#22 *Teenage Mutant Ninja Turtles Adventures* Mini Series #1DE Archie, Aug-88 $165
#23 *Archie's Girls Betty and Veronica* #321 Archie, Dec-82 $153
#24 *X-Factor* #6 Marvel, 7/1986 $150
#25 *Star Wars* #81 Marvel, 3/1984 $149

David T. Alexander, Tyler Alexander and Eddie Wendt DTAcollectibles.com CultureAndThrills.com

Where did all this info come from? I am about to begin my 55th year as a full time comic book salesman. My first comic con was the original San Diego Comic Con that took place at the U. S. Grant Hotel in downtown San Diego in 1970. I was co-founder of The American Comic Book Company, Southern California's most progressive comic book store chain, until I moved back to Florida in 1989. I have owned a dozen comic shops and helped open another 40 across the US. Years ago I lost count but I think I have participated in over 1000 comic cons and collectors shows. Maintaining a mail order operation was taxing during the years when I had so many stores but I think I produced in excess of 200 mail order catalogs before the internet took over. I hope the post office loves me because I have shipped over 200,000 mail orders and they only lost a few. I have sold many millions of dollars of comics and have been sorry to see each one of them go, but I had to keep moving them to get money to buy more.

The highlight of the past half century has been meeting and sharing the thrills of collecting with great people from all over the world. I would never have had the opportunity to meet so many exciting, interesting, unique and eccentric fans if we did not share the love of collecting.

We (I could not do this without some knowledgeable and dedicated help) currently maintain an inventory of around 750,000 items mostly consisting of comics from the 1800s thru 1989, pulp magazines, movie material and sports publications. We do not have a lot of comics from 1990 to date. To be sure there are many good issues, artists and writers from that time period but we are overwhelmed dealing with vintage material.

So, all of that gives you some insight into our thoughts about the developments during the last year. The theme for 2022 has been a combination of musical chairs and the laws of gravity. What goes up must come down and someone will be left holding the bag. 2021 ended on a positive note with enthusiastically rising prices and the trend continued the beginning of 2022 but early in the year we saw price support eroding. Key Marvel and DC issues lost their footing and collectors developed a wait and see attitude. When an *X-Men* #1 (CGC 6.5) which sold for over $60,000 last year failed to hit $30,000, it made many collectors hit the brake pedal.This is just one example of the trauma that has been prevalent in 2022.

A variety of reasons have led to price escalation in 2021 including the disruptions caused by Covid, many new collectors entering the market from the influence of the comic book movies, people being disenchanted with traditional investment opportunities, people looking for a new source of fun (which collecting certainly provides), an auction frenzy which has made some collectors think this is their last chance to obtain a key book, and various internet channels broadcasting ever-rising prices on key and presumed key books.

As many people have advised, "collect what you love", and I must admit I love it all. If you really love a book then hang on to it and let your love grow as you might have that book for many years.

When you are bidding and buying in an auction you are confident in your offer because there is someone willing to pay close to your bid and that drives the price up. That is the nature of the auction and unfortunately we usually do not know who the under bidder is. In the past there have been many prices manipulated by shill bidders, some working on behalf of the seller and some in the employ of the auction company. This practice has not been exposed recently but be careful when bidding.

Our buying this year has been extremely strong. We have picked up several large collections of Marvel and DC Silver Age super hero books. Although some people have been scared to buy or sell we have found many willing sellers and have boosted our inventory of 1960s 12 cent above pre-pandemic levels. We are always happy to get more of these although some dealers report many prices are declining.

We had a handful of impressive pulp collections arrive at our warehouse in the last 12 months. You might have noticed that several larger comic dealers are trying to get involved with pulp collecting this year. Maybe you should explore this area. Pulps are lots of fun to look for and the best ones are generally from the 1930s making many key issues around 90 years old.

The most significant collection that we received was the personal estate of famous pulp author Wyatt Blassingame. Using his own name and his pen name, William B. Rainey, he was very prolific in the weird menace and horror titles. We received many of the "Spicy" titles published by Trojan, plus *Horror Stories*, *Terror Tales*, *Dime Mystery*, *Ace G-Man*, *Scorpion*, *Black Mask*, *Captain Satan* and more. This collection showed up at the annual Florida Memorabilia Show which took place on the waterfront in historic Gulfport, Florida. You can be assured that we will attend that show next year.

As you might guess we are open to more buying as we are still trying to fill holes in our inventory.

In closing here is a short list of a few of the cool items that we parted with last year:

Amazing Spider-Man #129 CGC 9.4 : $8,269
Amazing Spider-Man #2 CGC 5.0 : $6,162
Detective Comics #225 CGC 4.5 : $6,000
Pictorial Romances #17 CGC 5.0 : $1,602
Daring Mystery #6 CBCS 6.5 : $3,895
Hit Comics #19 VF- : $2,970
Weird Mysteries #12 VG : $2,200
Journey Into Mystery #112 CGC 8.0 : $1,950
Crypt of Terror #19 CGC 5.5 : $1,766
Usagi Yojimbo #10 CGC 9.8 : $1,155
Strange Terrors #4 G+ : $910
Betty and Me #16 CGC 6.0 : $900

Dave Anderson, DDS
Collector

Although the comic book market remains very strong in 2022, there were some signs that it was slowing down. After the soaring prices seen over the last couple of years, we are seeing some cooling off, especially in Silver Age books, both key and non-key. Some good examples are books like *Amazing Fantasy* #15 and *Amazing Spider-Man* #1. Both books are still wildly popular and highly desirable, but because they both are relatively common, prices have come down. The same is true for most other Silver Age books as well. This trend generally applies to books in lower and mid grades only.

High grade Silver Age continues to sell for consistantly strong prices without the downturn seen for low and mid grade books. This cooling off was not seen in Golden Age books in any grades. Since Golden Age books are much less common than Silver Age, buyers will have fewer options when purchasing. There will always be another example of any Silver Age book available, but that's not always the case with Golden Age.

Lauren Becker
Comic*Pop Collectibles

The restrictions that Covid-19 affected have been unshackled. Society is starting to get back to (somewhat) normal. How has this affected the industry of comics and collectibles? Are we in a better place or have things gotten worse? Depends on who you ask and what you invested in.

Winners: Golden Age (especially esoteric issues) and original art. There were some record breaking numbers on many of the auction sites in 2022. A copy of *Detective Comics* #36 CGC graded 2.5 Restored went for an amazing $19,200.00 through Heritage! I personally had first hand knowledge of the book as it was a customer's of mine who I helped get everything graded for him. He had offered it to me first, but at a price that I thought was a little too high (but still less that 1/2 of what it went for). I guess, in hindsight, it was a pretty good deal.

For myself, personally, Golden Age has been a tremendous seller at shows and online. We had purchased a beautiful copy of *Hit Comics* #1 in about a FN+ condition, that lasted all of about 2 weeks before we sold it at Heroes Con in NC. The rarer the title, the faster it seems to sell. This doesn't go for everything, but it's amazing that titles that no one gave a second glance at even 5 years ago, are now some of the hottest commodities in the industry. I see more copies of *Action Comics* #1 offered than I do *Punch Comics* #12 (where a CGC 5.5 closed for $90,000 in November on Heritage). Granted, *Action* #1 is more significant, but *Punch* #12 is much rarer.

Then, there is original art. The prices have been so insane in the last 6-8 months, I have taken down many of my pieces for future auctions. The two biggest pieces that come to mind are *Marvel Super-Heroes Secret Wars* #8 (Pg. 25) by Mike Zeck that closed for $3.4 MILLION and the cover to *The Dark Knight Returns* #1 by Frank Miller for $2.4 MILLION! These are not the only large sales as many popular "modern age" pieces went for gargantuan prices. A page from Todd McFarlane's "adjective-less" Spider-Man run went for $20,000+. Doesn't sound like a lot, however, did I mention that the page was ALL STAT with NO original pencils/inks at all? Insane!

Losers: Modern Age (across the board) and Silver/Bronze/Copper Age Marvel. During the pandemic, collectors were swarming the internet looking for the next big investment, and thanks to phone apps like Key Collector, they found it. Anything that was a first appearance related to a movie/tv show or even a speculated scene that MIGHT appear, shot up fast.

And then it died.

A good example of this is *Action Comics* #9 (2nd Appearance/1st cover appearance of Calvin Ellis...Superman of Earth-23). Speculation of a movie spearheaded by Michael B. Jordan, and a comic that would languish in bulk boxes, becomes an instant $50-$75 comic, with CGC 9.8 copies as high as $650.00! Today, though? Barely over $100.00, with raw copies at barely at $20.

Key Marvel books from Silver-Bronze also lost some shine. Not saying that these are losers, but the insane prices that people were paying from 2020-2021 (and even at the beginning of 2022) has calmed down now as supply is shown to be much more plentiful than originally thought. *Amazing Spider-Man* #1 for example. A CGC 6.0 copy has dropped from a record high of $48,000 down to $18,528, all in the matter of 5 months.

Here are a listing of CGC comics we have sold this year. This is by no means EVERY one that we sold, but an example of how the market was for us.

Daredevil #1 CGC 7.0 $12,000
Moon Knight #1 (1980) CGC SS Sienkiewicz w/Moon Knight sketch 8.5 $400
Batman #234 CGC 7.0 $500.00
Police Comics #11 CBCS 3.0 verified Will Eisner signature $2000
Detective Comics #400 CGC 4.5 $290
Amazing Spider-Man #50 CGC SS qualified 6.0 (Stan Lee) $1000
Witchcraft #3 CGC 5.5 $650
Wanted Comics (1952) #52 CGC 3.5 $1250
Real Life Comics #39 (Mile High Pedigree) CGC 8.5 $600
Elektra: Assassin #1 CGC SS Sienkiewicz w/Elektra sketch 9.6 $500
New Mutants #26 CGC SS Sienkiewicz w/Professor X sketch 9.6 $380
Doctor Strange #169 CGC 7.5 $850
Doctor Strange #1 CGC 8.0 $230
Next Men #21 CGC 9.8 $500
Captain America Comics #78 CGC 1.8 $1500
Sgt. Fury and His Howling Commandos #1 CGC 2.5 $1200
Great Comics #1 CGC 9.2 $1500
Destroyer Duck #1 CBCS SS 9.2 (Evenier, Staton, Aragonés) $300
She-Hulk #1 (1980) CGC 9.8 $1250
She-Hulk #1 (1980) CGC 9.4 (newsstand) $450
Marvel Super-Heroes Secret Wars #8 (newsstand) CGC 8.5 $600
Uncanny X-Men #129 CGC 9.6 $1300
Tales of Suspense #57 CGC 6.5 $2400
Venus #6 CGC 5.0 $1000
Cat-Man Comics #29 CGC 3.5 $1500
Reform School Girls nn CGC 1.5 $3500
King Spawn #1 1:250 variant cover CGC ss (McFarlane) 9.8 $1200
Conan #1 CGC 8.5 $1000
Venom #3 CGC 9.8 $330
Fantastic Four #52 CGC 6.5 $3000
Chilling Tales #15 CGC 4.0 $4500
X-Men #2 CGC 4.0 $1425
Spirit #22 CGC 1.0 $1500
Savage Tales #1 CGC 8.5 $1800
Daredevil #131 CGC 9.0 $900
Shock SuspenStories #6 CGC 3.0 $1850
Batman #73 CGC 3.5 $1300
Ghost Rider #1 CGC 9.6 $5000
Doctor Solar Man of the Atom #1 CGC 6.5 $400
Firestorm #1 CGC 9.4 $150
Avengers Annual #10 newsstand variant CGC ss (Chris Claremont) 7.0 $300
X-Men #64 CGC 9.8 $10,000
Amazing Spider-Man #2 CGC 1.5 $1800
Amazing Spider-Man #9 CGC 5.0 $1900

Jim Berry
Collector

Greetings from Portland, Oregon. I'm a long time collector and dealer based in the Northwest with a small store I maintain on eBay as JB233 where I list mostly high-grade raw comics.

As a collector, I actively seek books from the 1940s-70s with a focus on pre-Code Horror, Science Fiction, and Crime featuring sex, drugs, bondage, exploding heads, injury to the eye, and monkey brains. - Everything your mother warned you about. I pair these interests with a love of the art from the many great masters from those decades – Fine, Schomburg, Baily, Ditko, Frazetta, Baker, L.B. Cole, Feldstein, Wood, Kirby, and so many more.

This past year we finally saw the inevitable rebound. After blasting through the stratosphere thanks to the massive influx of Covid relief money, prices crashed back to earth. There has been more volatility in the prices of comics, specifically Silver and Bronze age keys, than I have ever seen in forty yeas of collecting.

The same rebound, however, did not seem to affect top tier Golden Age, pre-Code Horror and Sci-Fi as well as early GA DC, Timely, etc. In fact, I've noticed that top Golden Age continues the steady climb that we've come to expect under normal circumstances. I chalk that up to supply and demand. As of this writing, there are over 500 listings for, "Hulk 181 CGC," while there are no copies of *Mister Mystery* #12 in any grade, raw or slabbed.

Still, with so many auction houses, eBay running 24-7, online sales everywhere, Facebook marketplace, there are endless possibilities online. So the good news is that there are still some incredible deals to be had out there in the corners of antique malls or regional auction houses. Even eBay yields some deals on occasion. You just have to keep digging - and that's half the fun (or so they say).

One bright spot for me this year is a new partnership formed with Shane Ahlvers who co-owns Sir Lonebuck's House of Comics and Geekery, in Woodinville, Washington, a small town about 30 miles NE of Seattle. Sir Lonebuck's is not your grandpa's comic shop. There are no dusty stacks, no tangy aroma of old paper – this is a clean, curated space with the modern vibe of a gallery. Shane specializes in new issues, graphic novels, toys, and there is a special section devoted to a selection of works of horror including some traditional novels. In addition to his handpicked inventory, Shane credits his devotion to the ideas of community and inclusion to his success.

When I noticed no old comics in the shop, I volunteered to be Shane's liaison should Gold, Silver or Bronze come walking through the door. Though the great majority of calls I've received have been curious collectors with modern books from the past ten years or so, we did close one deal for a small collection of Dell/Gold Key Ducks from the '50s - late '60s in nice grades and we're hopeful for 2023. Thanks, Shane!

Shout out to John Hill at Hill's Of Comics in Auburn, Washington. John's shop is absolutely huge, a hidden treasure not far from Seattle with selections of old, new and everything in between.

Two great reads from this past year: Fantagraphics produced two volumes featuring the works of Fletcher Hanks back in 2009. I found them this past year and was blown away by the 1st volume entitled, *You Shall Die By Your Own Evil Creation*. Hanks, deemed, "The Ed Wood," of comics wrote and illustrated for a few scant years in the early 1940s and he was a true iconoclast. His work is bizarre in the best way imaginable.

And then there's *Did You Hear What Eddie Gein Done?* by Harold Schechter and Eric Powell. This was the most affecting graphic novel I read all year. Though I'd follow Eric Powell through the gates of Hel, I wasn't all that excited by the idea of another piece of media about an infamous (maybe the most infamous) American serial killer. But the book was amazing, so well paced and heartbreaking. I dare you to read this book and not see Ed Gein as a lonely, misunderstood Frankenstein. Powell's art is remarkable, layered, textured, cinematic. It's his best work to date in my humble opinion.

Here's a list of raw books on eBay that I bid on but didn't win this year. In truth, I didn't come close on most of these as the prices sailed beyond my budget and any inkling of what I thought they were worth. Alas, the ones that got away:

Brenda Starr #14, GD, $2247
Haunted Thrills #17, FN+ $770
National #16, VG/FN $735
Blue Bolt #112, FN/VF $1686
Man O Mars #1, FN/VF $1075
Miss Fury #2, VF $4049
Foxhole #4, VG+ $1165
Menace #5, FN $2510
Captain America Comics #76, VG+, $1208

(Interestingly, I watched an Australian version of this book, called *Captain America* #1, reprinted with crazy garish colors, in similar raw condition, also published in 1954 and it went for $2030! Oi!)

Peter Bilelis, Esq.
Collector

It's December and the pandemic is now considered behind us. In the comic book hobby, it's been a bit of a rollercoaster year. The explosion of record high reported sale prices for vintage comics book in 2021 continued into early 2022. General perception was this record-setting seller's market would continue indefinitely, while many long-term hobbyists scratched their heads, wondering how so many books could be selling at such astronomical prices. The first half of 2022 saw multiple crypto-currency companies in financial difficulty. Consumer spending and continuing global supply chain issues contributed to growing inflation, causing the Fed to raise interest rates – but many experts showed concern that too much of an economic slow-down could result in a recession. By the second half of 2022, some companies announced layoffs, more jobs left U.S. borders, and, in November, some crypto exchanges filed for bankruptcy. Concurrent with these events, many vintage comic book segments began to experience a chill, which has persisted as of this writing. In contrast, many genres, titles, and individual books soared in interest.

Hobby Bedrock: Blue chips, true keys, and classic covers were king ("Demand Books"). This includes superhero books featuring first appearances and origins of key characters, such as *All Star Comics* #8, *Captain America Comics* #1, *Detective Comics* #33, #66, #140, #168, *Action Comics* #23, *More Fun Comics* #52-53, #55, #73, *Amazing Fantasy* #15, *Avengers* #4, *Hulk* #1, *Tales of Suspense* #39, and *Hulk* #181 to name a few. Classic covers were in extreme demand, regardless of genre, with many shattering previously reported record high sales prices, only to then shatter the new records. Books on this list include: *Crime SuspenStories* #22, *Startling Terror Tales* #11, *Crime Does Not Pay* #24, *True Crime Comics* #2, #3, *Daredevil Battles Hitler* #1, *Mask Comics* #1, #2, *Detective Comics* #71, #73, *Batman* #23, #37, #49, #52, *Young Allies* #1, #4, *Master Comics* #27, #29, and *Suspense* #3, #8.

Books sporting WWII covers continued to attract a ton of interest, especially Hitler covers. One key title book that astute hobbyists seek and can still buy at a relative discount due to it flying under the radar, is *More Fun Comics* #75. It features a sort of "hidden" Hitler cover (look closely at the framed picture falling from the wall) hidden in this WWII/Fifth Columnist cover. And two books that are revered as having transcended to almost legendary status are *All-American* #61 and *Master Comics* #27. The first Solomon Grundy appearance, with its stunning classic cover, rarely turns up in higher unrestored grade. It's a fan favorite and growing demand continues to drive its value to new heights. The Mac Raboy "V for Victory" cover, although not yet distinguished in the *Guide* as a "classic cover" book, is generally considered to be the most iconic WWII cover of the run and, pushing its demand even higher, is the fact that it's almost non-existent in the marketplace. This year, a strong CGC 8.0 sold for a staggering ~15X *Guide*. This book is so rare there's no established market for it. As such, the record sale price for the CGC 8.0 might ultimately prove to be a steal.

Hobby Marsh: In short, the softening part of the hobby is largely comprised of a vast array of speculation books, which includes books with no performance track record as well as good investment books (including pedigree copies) that attained unwarrantedly high prices.

Reported sale prices for many "C-list" character books kept rising. Generally, YouTube and the MCU helped drive this. In the past few years, there's been an explosion of YouTube personalities, some with thousands of followers. Many offer tremendous value via widespread hobby knowledge dispersion. Others, however, present themselves as more knowledgeable than they are, and most focus almost exclusively on the commodity aspect of the hobby, pushing books they deem "hot" based purely on value speculation. In 2020-2021, many YouTube personalities gained hordes of subscribers by pushing spec books – generally, books featuring some obscure character's first appearance based on announcements or rumor that the character might appear in an MCU production. The uptick in reported sale prices for many of these books was more serendipity than prophetic, as the aggressive spending trend of 2020-2021 in many hobbies and elsewhere was generally attributed to pandemic quarantine dynamics. In 2022, many of the books pushed by these YouTubers took backward steps in interest and value, as rumors turned out to be false or the character slated to appear in the MCU had notional popularity potential. On balance, many of these YouTube channels offer entertainment and value, but many foster commoditization of comic books and this can result in disillusionment (and upheaval/sell-off) that comes from buying very risky speculative material that underperforms.

Intertwined with this YouTube development, is the "MCU announcement/rumor factor," discussed above. At one point, MCU films were all blockbusters and any MCU film announcement had speculators smartly stocking up on the featured character's first comic book appearance. This mindset even extended to books like *Fantastic Four* #1, where MCU film announcements quickly turned *Fantastic Four* #1 into a very expensive "hot" book. The latest "phase" of MCU films, however, is considered by many hobbyists to be underwhelming. Adding to this, none of the prior *Fantastic Four* films were very successful. All this, coupled with the other dynamics discussed above, resulted in *Fantastic Four* #1 also experiencing the current chill, as many hobbyists don't necessarily see the upcoming film catapulting this book to new heights.

Some minor key books were also swept up in the "hot book" push, especially the "newsstand copy" version. Ironically, actual publishing statistics prove that up until approximately 1985, when newsstand and direct copies balanced in print runs, direct copies were far and away the much lower print run books. In any event, while books like *New Mutants* #98 and *Batman Adventures* #12 are great investments, many of these newer keys with bloated 2020-2021 values saw a downturn in 2022. Even pedigrees were not immune. The Promise pedigree collection, which included many impossibly high-grade copies, came to market during the pandemic. Many books from this collection sold for astronomical prices, in part due to the quarantine dynamic, but primarily because many rival the quality of the Edgar Church and Tom Reilly copies. In 2022, however, some Promise books were resold – only months after the initial sales – and, through a confluence of factors (e.g. economic dynamics, run books with too high initial sale prices, reselling too soon, not Demand Books), yielded fractions of initial respective reported sale prices. In essence, these books seeing lower resale prices wasn't a statement about the collection (which in fact has enormous importance). Instead, it was a statement about unreasonable expectations.

Despite the 2022 hobby chill and rollercoaster resulting in a buyer's market, it was clear that quality material remained solid and in-demand. The number of hobbyists is growing, and the wealth of quality material being brought to market isn't just getting absorbed, it's getting sucked up. And, books priced over their skis saw rationalization. All of these are indicators of a very healthy hobby. I can be contacted at pbilelis@yahoo.com. Good luck hunting in 2023.

Steve Borock
Senior Consignment Director
ComicLink

HAPPY 85TH BIRTHDAY TO BOB OVERSTREET!!!!!!

For over 50 years this great man has steered this ship and still attacks it like a true hobbyist to make our great hobby a safe and fun place to be in! We owe him so much! I know I do! Bob, you are the best!

I would like to take a moment not just to thank Bob, but also to thank all of the amazing people who help make this happen every year such as J.C. Vaughn, Mark Huesman and Amanda Sheriff, among others. I would also like to thank Steve Geppi for all the support he and his family have given, not just to me, but to this amazing guide and our hobby in general. THANK YOU ALL!

I am now the newest Senior Consignment Director for ComicLink! This is another amazing and fun road of the many roads I have taken in our great hobby! I started as a fanboy, have graded for Sotheby's and Christie's auction (before certification existed) and have been lucky enough to work for some of the giants in our industry all the while helping collectors with advice as well as helping them sell their precious comics and comic art, sometimes for a few million dollars! I love helping and talking with true hobbyists!

This is also very exciting for me as ComicLink Founder and President Josh Nathanson and I have been great friends for 25 years now, and IMHO, he has built an amazing and very safe place for buying and selling comic books and comic art, all the while setting record high sale prices for thousands and thousands of consignors and doing so with unparalleled ethics.

I would not have joined ComicLink if I did not truly believe this!

I have also helped create CGC as I was their 1st Primary grader and President as well as setting their grading standards (along with Mark Haspel) and ethics. What a trip it was trying to sell Certification to the collecting community! It was not easy, but it was fun and now CGC and CBCS (which I was also the Co-Founder of) graded comic books are everywhere!

What a lucky hobbyist I have been! The kid in me still is amazed!

Onto the Market: IT'S ALL OVER THE PLACE!!!!!! We are seeing record prices every day at ComicLink and more and more people are coming into our hobby every day as well. I am sure you will read all about these crazy high prices realized here in many of the other reports as many comic books are on fire and the downturn now on prices that went crazy the last 2 years on more common 1960s and 1970s non-key and non-high grade comic books. We are just now starting to see a large comeback. At the time, it was a buyer's market for sure!

As always, I want to give a shout out to our hobby's greatest charity: The Hero Initiative. Hero gives back to those in need who created or worked on the wonderful characters we all enjoy. They provide food, medical, housing and other help that is needed. Please check them out at www.heroinitiative.org. This marks the 14th year that there is a Hero Initiative limited edition of *The Overstreet Comic Book Price Guide* where the proceeds go directly to the charity. I hope this is the copy you are reading right now. I am proud to be on the board of directors!

I will end my market report the same way I do every year. This is for the newer collectors in our great hobby, as I would hope that the more seasoned collectors already know this information. Even though I really believe in this hobby, this market and its future, and have done so since I was a kid (I am 60 this year), there is no such thing as a free lunch. If you are going to invest in comic books, you had better love what you buy. If the economy ever goes really bad, just like stocks, precious metals, real estate, or anything else considered an investment, you will not be able to sell them for a really high price very quickly and you can certainly not use comic books to feed, house, or take care of your family.

The best advice I can give you is this: Buy what you like and can afford. It's really that simple. It has also been my war cry for so many years. Just enjoy collecting and reading comic books, enjoy the amazing friendships we make in this wonderful hobby, look around and enjoy all the cool stuff this hobby has to offer from original comic art and comic books, to the movies and TV shows based on the characters we all love so much, to comic memorabilia, going to the conventions and it will all seem worth it in the end.

I look forward to seeing and talking with many of you on the convention floor this year!

If you ever need help, not just selling, but need any advice, I am always happy to talk with other, especially newer, hobbyists.

Happy collecting!

Scott Braden
Collector

It's no secret that for most of 2022, it was a strong year for graded comics – commonly known among advanced collectors as "slabs." For the first three quarters of the year, this select comic book genre market – where comics were graded and encapsulated by the likes of CGC, CBCS, and others – showed strength across all comic book ages, usually selling at prices exponentially higher than *The Overstreet Comic Book Price Guide*.

Then, in the fourth quarter of 2022, the sales of modern slabs began to slow down. Collectors of graded comics, whether buying or selling, would find prices and demand discounted and reduced, respectively, both online and in brick-and-mortar shops.

Advanced collector Chris Haga of Westminster, Maryland, on the other hand, says the biggest disconnect in the current slab market right now is the difference in prices offered for graded comics by online and brick-and-mortar stores. Haga has experienced brick-and-mortar outlets selling books at 25 to 40 percent higher than what potential buyers see online.

In his mind, DC Comics' graded books are the "next big gold rush." Where Marvel Comics' *Moon Knight* #1 by writer Doug Moench and artist-extraordinaire Bill Sienkiewicz plateaued around 100 or 150 bucks – some collectors were even finding high grade copies at 90 to 100 dollars. This is even after the success of its Marvel Cinematic Universe adaptation that streamed earlier in the year on Disney+. All the while, similarly aged books like DC Comics' *DC Comics Presents* #26 is hitting the $200 to $250 mark without buyer hesitation. Haga added that other DC Comics' graded titles, like Silver and Bronze Age *World's Finest* issues, are also getting warm.

It appears that Superman is dominating the newly named DCU and that "The Man of Tomorrow" is living up to his nickname as related raw and graded comic titles are feeling the superstar property's positive reverberations in the comic book slab market -- which for the last several years, has followed in popularity with the success of its big and small screen adaptations.

"At the same time, if I was going to speculate," Haga said by telephone, "Vertigo titles, led by the strength of Neil Gaiman's *Sandman*, are poised to be the next successful boom."

Russ Bright
Mill Geek Comics

Looking back on the past year, it's difficult to sum up quickly. There has been an absolute rollercoaster of prices and demand. Sometimes we're seeing record highs swinging to record lows in a matter of a few months. This is a buyer's market which is fueled by nostalgia and speculation.

We had hoped that the post pandemic world would bring recovery to some of the facets of the industry that had been suffering. Conventions are back and mostly at capacity. New York Comic Con was incredibly crowded and most of the dealers I talked to had very successful shows. People are spending money when they have it. I'm constantly shocked at prices. On an almost weekly basis, we are seeing prices that are egregiously high or low, in every era of book.

The anticipation for new movies and TV shows is still driving the market, but the shelf life is much shorter. People are buying raw copies and getting them graded in the hopes that a book will spike when the movie releases. *Invincible Iron Man* #9 (1st Riri Williams as Ironheart) is a perfect example. Rumors started in 2020 that Ironheart would be in *Black Panther 2* and later we had confirmation of her own solo show. People started buying raw copies and getting them graded and by the middle of 2020, 9.8 graded copies had gone from around $150 to a $400 average. The *Black Panther 2* movie was delayed for a few reasons; the death of Chadwick Boseman, script rewrites and reshoots as well as schedule conflicts with the other actors. This delay caused a drastic downturn in demand and price. At one time commanding $800+ we saw prices in the $500-600 ranges by mid-2022. When the movie had released it was under $400 and at time of this writing, we're seeing 9.8 sales regularly below $300.

This is even happening with Silver Age keys. At the end of December 2021, Matt Murdock showed up in *Spider-Man: No Way Home* to be Peter's lawyer. It was a nice Easter egg that fueled rumors for the next 6 months until it was announced that there would be a new Daredevil TV series in 2024. There was already demand for *Daredevil* #1 and these announcements made it even higher. The strange thing is that prices slid all year. CGC 7.5 were selling in the $16k range after his 2021 movie appearance. Then 12 months later, we have seen two sales BELOW $10k. The CGC 7.0 has taken a similar turn, from $14k highs to $7k lows.

In the past, people had a longer time after the announcement before a spike, and prices didn't crash immediately after movie/TV release. We saw this same pattern with *Moon Knight* as well as *She-Hulk*. These were heavily anticipated shows with multiple comic books spiking before the release and fizzling immediately afterwards.

What does this mean?

Volatility is here to stay and fear of missing out (FOMO) drives the market. As a shop owner, I have people asking me what to buy or what to sell. Silver and Bronze keys can be found for below-market prices if you're patient and still have long term gains. There are new, perpetually relevant keys that should not be overlooked. If you're a collector of older books, make sure you're at least aware of the next generation of comic book superheroes. These young guns (Miles Morales, Young Avengers) can sometimes be purchased when some of the bigger keys get farther and farther out of reach. With more movies and TV coming, and some of the older actors aging out of their roles, we will be seeing more movement from the younger heroes in the coming years.

The bottom line is that we need to remember that comic books are supposed to be fun. They're meant to be enjoyed. The value should be secondary. As I try to impart to all collectors, young and old; Collect what you love, and you'll always love your collection.

As always, Geek Responsibly! (Many thanks from the Comic Sensei!)

Richard M. Brown
Collector

Journey Into Mystery #85 is fantastic! With the first Loki appearance, it exploded last year. Look for appearances of Loki, Joker, Harley Quinn and Doctor Strange to continue to climb. Iron Man, Hawkeye, Black Widow and the Hulk will always have fans.

Watch *Marvel Family* #1 and *Shazam!* #28, the first two appearances of Black Adam (amazingly 32 years apart), their popularity no doubt helped by the movie starring The Rock, Dwayne Johnson, who did double duty as the voice of Krypto in the *League of Super-Pets* movie. No word if that movie led to any increases in prices for the Super-Dog's debut in *Adventure Comics* #210.

Jeff and Charles Cerrito
Hotflips
Jeff Cerrito

Hey all, sorry I missed out on 2021. It was certainly a trying year personally, but the convention scene was to put it mildly, very underwhelming. But 2022?? Well let's just say conventions are back!!

The year started off slow with the Omnicron variant hanging around in the beginning of the year, but things started to pick up around May for sure. Some shows were back to full capacity pre-pandemic and a few took steps forward and set record numbers for attendance.

I'll start with Fan Expo's MegaCon in Orlando. Talk about a show that took a step forward!! Pre-pandemic this show would always draw 100,000 people and was always a good draw for fans. This year, fans came out in droves with an attendance of 148,000. Every aisle was jammed packed and with a stellar guest list and quality venders, this show has become a monster. If you ever thought about vending or attending this show, it is definitely a must do. I couldn't believe the crowds myself and I'm excited to see how much bigger this show will get. Plus, the show is moving dates closer to the winter, so who wouldn't want to go and visit Mickey the same time it's cold up in the north east (where I'm from).

Another show that looks like it took a step forward is a branded show, ReedPop's Star Wars Celebration. This is a show I geek out a little at because of my love for Star Wars. Imagine being with 100,000 people who all share the same passion? It's an amazing and well run show. The hardest part is figuring out what to spend your money on. This is one of the few conventions where you genuinely see attendees smile and having a good time. At the end of the day, that's what it's all about.

A convention that always hung in the middle tier is Fan Expo's Dallas Comic Con. This past year this show took a step forward, although not in terms of MegaCon, but it's on its way. It's always great to see my Texas friends while I'm there. I'll certainly be there again this coming year.

Then there was San Diego. Well, it was definitely what San Diego was pre-pandemic. The aisles were busy, the entire city was buzzing, and it's always a great show to catch up with my West Coast customers. It's always one of my favorite shows to do.

The one international show I'd like to mention is Fan Expo Toronto. This show has always been a busy show, but there was a jump in attendance due to the breadth of comics, toys, media guests and artists. A fun show for sure.

ReedPop's New York Comic Con came back with a bang for sure. Aisles were mobbed, people spending money, and dirty water dogs. What more do you need? A convention, like San Diego, where everyone in the industry is there. The Artist Alley, like all ReedPop shows is second to none. All the best of the best from a comic standpoint is here, artists, writers, colorists, etc. Any comic you are looking for from Golden Age to current can be had. If you walk out empty-handed at this show, you should probably find a new hobby.

Just a note: I compared all the conventions to 2019. It wouldn't be fair to compare 2020 and 2021 as all shows took a major hit as far as attendees and vendors. That all being said, the convention companies that know what they're doing are still around and obviously there is a reason for that. I can't wait for 2023 and see what all these conventions do for an encore. See you all at a convention near you.

Charles Cerrito

Hey everyone! For the last three years, since the pandemic started, everyone is still adjusting. Everyone was kept inside their homes and suddenly the entire collectible market went haywire. Comics, cards (sports & non-sports), and toys were spiking to levels that we have not seen before. Now that the world started to open up in late 2021, the collectible market started to correct itself slowly and the conventions were starting to reopen with precautions (mask and vaccination requirements). Then in 2022, we started to get back to a new normal, but now families are no longer getting that extra cash anymore.

The supply chain issue is still an issue, and it is slowly starting to get back to normal. When we order our supplies to be made, we were not getting them on schedule and this was a global problem. So the supplies that we carried were put on hold, The container ships that were carrying the emergency equipment was shipped out but the empty container was never shipped back (leading to a shortage on containers) which caused a spike on everything. To give an example, container ships would pick up containers three times a day, but now it was three times a week. Private companies saw an opportunity to make money and started to charge between $30K to $50K to deliver. These containers of goods were already made but delivery was put on hold to produce emergency equipment. So all the containers were all piling up at all the ports, which caused a huge massive overload in California and New York. The congestion of container ships made the oceans look like cities themselves.

Now that 2022 has come to a close, we were happy to see that all conventions, whether it was a four day convention or a small one day show, people were coming out in record numbers. A lot of these conventions are showing that there is a waiting list for vendors to get in. Looking forward to 2023 and we are finally going to run our own one day, hopefully monthly, show in Long Island.

On March 28, 2022, the market changed for us that day. A new collectors based app called Whatnot was introduced to us and it turned out to be a new avenue for us. We tried it not knowing what to expect. This became the alternative to eBay. This is a collectible app that you can easily download on your iPhone and it is a new auction site. We started with 30 auctions and listed it for 30 seconds. It is actually a live show with you being the host. There was a lot of learning in the beginning and now this is a priority for us for selling all kinds of collectibles. It is great that you do not have to wait days or a week until the auction is over. It took a while to get started but we got 25 followers on our first show, then in six months we reached 5,000 followers, and we are still growing. We want to thank everyone for their support of Hotflips.

As far as the comic book market goes, we have to thank Disney+ for making great shows and bringing characters to life whether it is Marvel or Star Wars. This brought a spike to a lot of first appearances like *Young Avengers* #1, *Darth Vader* #6, and *Darth Maul* #2, These comics were in the bargain boxes until the announcements were made. Now every dealer is holding onto the comics that are still in their bargain boxes until the next announcement is made. *Incredible Hulk* #449 was already up there, and now the announcement of a Thunderbolts movie brought it up more. For *Savage She-Hulk* #1 (1980), a CGC 9.8 used to sell for $250, now it's over $1,000. More exciting things are happening in the Marvel Universe and we're looking forward to 2023.

John Chruscinski
Tropic Comics

It's been another impressive year for comics and collectibles. We have all seen constant record prices for Golden Age keys to Modern keys in all grades. The news media has continued to follow these mega-sales and these have and will create new interest in the hobby. If it's a key book, then it continues to sell well and typically for strong prices. Lesser non-key issues having weaker demand continue to sell, but only when discounted.

While we primarily deal in comics and related comic and entertainment collectibles, we also sell many pop culture items and collectibles in other fields . It's been a solid year overall, even though the economy is not where it was a few years ago. The recovery continues and so does the passion for collecting and investing in comics and collectibles.

Our hobby has seen an even stronger than normal increase in first appearances, origin issues, and variant covers. As the TV shows and movies find more obscure characters, we see a constant demand for any new TV/movie appearance creating a fast influx of buyers for the related comics, especially in high grade. It seems like every week there is a new hot book to be pulled out of a dealers $1 box and sold for $20 and up. Characters that you never would have thought of in a million years can appear in a TV or Movie related tie-in, or even just the rumor of an upcoming appearance, can cause a book to skyrocket over night. Now they can also slow or even decrease in value almost as fast, ie, Moon Knight, Hawkeye, She-Hulk, etc.

Look for many more undiscovered treasures to become valuable for different reasons than was the norm 10 years ago. With many more entering our hobby on a daily basis, more books are going to be more sought after by the masses

Remember to collect what you like, and not what someone or website tells you should collect, and you will never lose in the true enjoyment of our wonderful hobby.

Paul Clairmont
PNJ Comics

2022 was our most successful and interesting year in our ten years of business. The pandemic began to wind down and with it came the slow down of record online sales from the past two years that will likely never be duplicated again.

My only regret was that I could not process inventory fast enough to take advantage of the overheated pandemic pricing. Books that were listed for $5.00 in NM- in the *Overstreet Guide* would routinely sell for $100.00 to $250.00 once it was graded and received a 9.8 grade. I was happy to repeat this process over and over as the margins were eye popping. It was like hitting a winner every time you scratched one of those Lotto scratch tickets. I'm not a gambler, but I would imagine that if you're buying a $5.00 scratch ticket and winning $50.00 to $200.00 every time you scratch, then I would think you are a very successful and lucky gambler.

We also knew that all good things eventually come to an end. We were cautious and insulated ourselves from taking on too much. As economic factors such as inflation and interest rates started rising throughout 2022, we understood a large portion of the buying demographic relied on credit to make a lot of their purchases and these economic changes would affect those buying decisions. The key was to know that everything is not going to continue to go up and not to then go and spend recklessly on inventory that people wanted us to buy from them. I'm not sure why so many people find it confusing that we're a business and as such we are not interested in paying for a collector to recoup everything they spent on their "emotional purchases." In essence, we're not an insurance policy for someone to get back everything they spent over the years.

If you want to maximize your profits by selling a comic collection then you must go the route of selling it yourself. This is not such an easy task. The seller needs to understand that if they want to liquidate quickly then there will be some give and take. Selling in volume means that you're not going to get the highest prices achievable as the effort to process, grade and find a buyer for everything is a slow venture and time is money.

The beginning of the year saw some of the strongest sales we've ever encountered in our ten years of business. As we entered the 2nd quarter of the year people began to move back to regular activities and disposable income was shifting to other entertainment as the weather became nicer and summer approached. It was as though people were beginning to awaken from their cocoons and venture back into the real world. So began the decline of overinflated prices to a more normal level of pricing for about 95% of the books in the hobby. There will always be exceptions as prices continued to skyrocket for some material but that would be more to do with blue chip keys and ultra rare or tough to find in high grade books. We're talking about material that cost the same as a modest house. Suffice to say, more than the 99.9% of comic collectors are not really the buyers of such material.

With the declining prices, "comic-chasers" looking for easy money or a sure thing started disappearing. Investors with the new money that came in spending and setting record prices on common books were also leaving. With the declining prices I'm sure regular collectors breathed a sigh of relief as they didn't have to compete with the new money buyers that had earlier entered the hobby to get books and fill holes in their collections

These unsavvy investors that were once dropping insane amounts of money on books such as *Eternals* #1 in CGC 9.8 for $3,500 USD began disappearing and likely licking their wounds. Let's face it… things got ridiculous. It defies logic, and a book like *Eternals* #1 should never be worth more then $10.00. This book, along with countless other examples, sat in dollar bins for over 40 years for a reason.

Another thing that emerged from the pandemic and got out of hand in this hobby was the term "influencer." Suddenly everyone was an expert. A fanboy that frequents comic stores, has an internet connection and buys a microphone at Best Buy shouldn't feel entitled to make videos on the internet about the comic industry. You could go on YouTube and see every person who ever held a comic thinking they were suddenly an expert, but it was the pandemic that was causing the collectible prices to climb as everyone was locked down spending free government money. The amount of disinformation and personal opinions to steer the public to buy common books and make them believe it's a solid investment exploded. If you could avoid all the noise and fluff being spewed, then you are probably a true collector still enjoying what you buy because you like it. Buyers should not be relying on these people to drive their purchasing decisions. Thankfully, as the money realized begins to correct and come back down to earth for these collectibles, you see more of these influencers disappear because they don't have a real sense of business.

I'll be honest, if I or one of my peers has some insight on what is good material to speculate on we are not running to the internet to share the information. We are buying the material up before our hunch becomes reality and prices rise. That is truly what speculating is, not following the herd once the news breaks and everyone starts to chase after the books as they are rising. It becomes comical to watch the "comic-chasers" fumble over each other for the next hot book. Inevitably, treating it like a hot potato by buying it during its price increase in hopes that the price continues to rise. Then they set up at some local comic show or flea market in hopes of selling it to the next mark at a higher price. The fatal error was that many of these "comic-chasers" didn't think prices would come down on these precious comics they were also attached to. I would imagine this practice would be incredibly tedious, yet this makes up a large percentage of the sellers trying to make it in the industry because the rising prices made everything look easy to do.

Now that the rush of overheated prices has come to pass there are many collections filled with common books sitting on the sidelines that investors overpaid for and are now afraid to sell as it would likely result in a big loss. The books will eventually make their way into the market again, but a cautionary lesson should be learned.

The comic market is certainly not going to crash but level heads in the community/hobby will always prevail over this new human nature that seems to be looking to "get-rich-quick" and ignore common rules of working hard to get ahead. Whether it's trying to be a comic dealer, investor or simply someone trying to leverage their own collection with a little buying and selling.

Art Cloos
Collector

It's December 2022, which means two things: the holidays are coming and once again it's time for the Overstreet Advisor reports to be handed in. We were asked to assess how Covid affected us in 2022 and that will be a big part of this report. As I have said before, my much better half and I are collectors, not dealers so how Covid affected us in 2022 is not from the perspective of a retailer but as a collector.

So as shows came back we debated, as many of our fellow collector friends did and I am sure as many of you out there did as well, over how many should we go to? In a normal year it can be as many as 40 shows, but that number has been drastically reduced since the beginning of the Covid outbreak to a relative handful in the last 3 years. In the end we decided that even though cons came back in a big way in 2022 with sometimes multiple shows on the same day or weekend, we would cut back in the number we go to by foregoing cons which required any extended traveling. However the number of requests for us to buy made up for our reduced show schedule though of course we very much missed the excitement of a live show. We live in the north east and most of the shows we go to are located in that part of the country, especially the tri state area, so that is the perspective here. We were fully vaccinated but we knew we could still catch it and we both did. Allie in the beginning of January and she was sick for almost the whole month suffering from post-Covid syndrome and I on the last day of the NYCC in October came down with it but thankfully that only lasted two weeks.

In terms of comics, it was a good year for us overall. My better half has her list of books she has been working on to add to her collection and she managed to acquire several in 2022. It was the same for me as I have a list of books I want too, and I managed to find several of them as well. In March, the spring Big Apple show led off the convention scene here and sales were brisk with a good turnout. Mike Carbo's shows are a must for us. Then the Garden State Comic con kicked off the summer featuring a very strong showing of Silver and Bronze Age books and was well attended by both sellers and buyers. The NYCC held every year in October is a highlight show for us, and it was an especially good show for Allie and I as we brought home some nice additions to the collections. The nice selection of books overall for sale at a major show like NYCC is to be expected. Ken Lawrence's November Collectorfest show in NJ had a nice mix of both

Gold, Silver and Bronze books and also was well attended. The Pug production monthly shows in New Jersey continued to be must-attend venues for collectors as well, as surprises show up at almost every show.

In 2022 the internet continued to be an important place for collectors to network and to find pieces for their collections, and while Allie and I prefer to see a book in person, we both used it to find books we needed. As for me I continued to get a lot of email requests to sell and buy in 2022 as I did in 2021, but I am not someone who sells, I (well we) only buy. In the first half of the year sales of Golden Age continued very strong in the auction houses and dealer's sell lists and walls, and prices kept rising for Silver and Bronze age Marvels, especially keys, that in particular were very hot. Then came the summer and with it things began to change somewhat. One dealer said it started literally on July 1st as prices began to level off and decline in some instances, especially for Silver and Bronze Age books with Marvel in particular reflecting the trend. This continued into the fall shows we attended. Dealers whose prices did not reflect this change had their books sit on their walls. On the other hand, sales of DC comics which had been depressed for years as compared to Marvels started to become more attractive to buyers even as prices were becoming stagnant overall, especially for Golden and Atomic age books. It is a good idea to look at them as a collecting alternative.

The Golden Age titles that Allie and I follow, such as *All-American*, *All Star*, *Sensation*, *Wonder Woman*, *Captain Marvel Adventures* (Fawcett), *Batman* and *Detective* mostly did continue to sell well, but prices on *All Stars* were very high in every grade and many sat unsold for a considerable amount of time. *All-American* is one title that is hot and does not show up much on dealer walls in this part of the world (though I scored 4 at NYCC.) They were being offered at way over *Guide* and GPA, but that did not stop them from selling. The Golden Age Wonder Woman and Batman titles continued to sell as well. But as I noted the same was not as true for Silver and Bronze DCs and Marvels. In 2021, it seemed that every month a different Bronze Age comic, especially Marvels, became hot all of a sudden based on the latest new movie or TV show, but in in late 2022 not so much.

So what does 2023 have in store for the hobby? Well in terms of Covid as the new year approaches we are facing a Covid, RSV, Flu trifecta here in NY (and in many parts of the country at large). Hospitals are filling up and the entire state is urged to wear masks indoors and there is talk of having NYS school kids once again wear masks. How this affects the convention scene and the hobby in general remains to be seen. I wish a good 2023 to everyone.

GARY COLABUONO
MOONDOGBUYSCOMICS.COM

After 40 years of being an advisor to Bob Overstreet and 35 years of monitoring the sales of authentic Golden Age ashcans, I've decided that this will be my last market report.

I've had a great run. Running the Moondog's chain of shops. Discovering the Windy City pedigree collection. Uncovering the original cache of authentic DC Golden Age ashcan editions that originated with Sol Harrison. Celebrating comics and their creators as the CEO of the Chicago Comicon (along with Larry Charet and the late Bob Weinberg). Bringing comics and pop culture to the masses as the host of the Moondog's Pop Culture Radio Hour. And meeting and becoming friends with Bob Overstreet, Steve Geppi and hundreds of other like-minded lovers of this original American art form.

In April I sold the remaining issues from my ashcan collection. This was the Superman family - the rarest and most important ashcans on the planet. The *Superman Comics* ashcan in CGC 8.5 sold for the highest price of any ashcan ever at $288,000 far surpassing the $204,000 figure that my *Action Comics* ashcan sold for in 2021. With only 2 copies of *Superman* known to exist it could be many years before another is available.

The *Superwoman* ashcan sold in CGC 7.0 for $43,200. Only 2 copies exist - this one and one in the DC vault. The *Superboy* ashcan in CGC 6.5 sold for $48,000. This is the only copy known to exist. The *Supergirl* ashcan, sold raw as a VF since the front cover overhang could damage the book if encapsulated, still sold for a whopping $28,800. This too is the only issue known to exist.

Other ashcan sales were just as strong during 2022 as this category keeps attracting more collectors who seek the rarest of the rare.

The DC *Flash Comics* ashcan in CGC 9.6 sold for $45,600 in June.

In the same auction Fawcett's *5 Cent Comics* in CGC 9.6 sold for a very strong $13,200 while its sister title *Nickel Comics* also in CGC 9.6 sold for $5,520.

During the past year I've been digitizing many videos, audio tapes and other memories from my archives and making them available on my website www.moondogbuyscomics.com. Stop by and let me know what you think.

Ashley Cotter-Cairns & Sean Goodrich Goldin

The biggest news of the year — for us, at least — was the acquisition of Sell My Comic Books by Goldin.

Our entire staff and operations are now run by Goldin, where Sean and I are tasked with growing the comics vertical. To say the process of being acquired was challenging would be an understatement. Neither of us has sold a business before! The deal closed in September, and we look forward to meeting you all in our new roles at various conventions this year.

No matter where you put your money during 2022, it seems to have been a bad call, as the stock markets, crypto currencies and collectibles have all struggled. Prices we routinely expected in Q1 of 2022 were in some cases halved or worse by the end of the year. Speculator special books, such as *What If?* #10 (What If Jane Foster was Thor?) have, to coin a phrase, been hammered. A double whammy in this case, as *Thor: Love and Thunder* was widely regarded as one of the worst misses the MCU has put out to date. At its peak, a CGC 9.8 would fetch in the $1,500-1,800 range, with a record sale of $2,150, but it's crashed back down to the $700 range.

Big Silver Age keys have also had the gloss taken off them. *X-Men* #1, a book which seemed rocket-powered for years, suddenly felt the inevitable pull of gravity, and we're seeing prices in upper grades close to early pandemic levels. What a wild ride! If you're the seller of a CGC 8.0 — a more than respectable grade for this tough issue — then you'd have been delighted with $102K in April, but not so thrilled with $43K in December.

Fortunately, some huge Golden Age sales have bucked the trend. Goldin sold the "rocket" copy of *Action Comics* #1 for $3.4 million in a private deal. This CGC 6.0 was at the time a record for any comic book. Goldin also sold a *Detective Comics* #27 CGC 6.5 for $1.74 million; a *Superman* #1 CGC 3.0 for $720K; and a *Batman* #1 CGC 5.0 for $510K, a CGC 4.0 for $336K and a CGC 2.0 for $174K.

Goldin sold an *Incredible Hulk* #1 CGC 8.0 for $210K and a *TMNT* #1 CGC 9.8 for $264K.

We also brought the cover art to *Showcase* #24 to market, which closed for $108K, along with some other Gil Kane pages from the same collection.

So what might we all expect from 2023? Economists are gloomily muttering into their eggnog about a probable recession, with a tight labor market potentially keeping inflation too high, which means more interest rate hikes in our futures.

If I were to peer into a crystal ball, then I'd expect less speculation on modern "keys", as the MCU effect seems to have run out of steam. We may look back on Q4 of 2022 as a time of opportunity, when big keys were available at prices we'd seldom dream of being able to afford again.

Incredible Hulk #1 is a book I've been banging on about for years. It did perk up along with the rest of the market during the boom times, but it does seem to be less affected by the drop-off, and it could be finding its deserved level at last.

Incredible Hulk #2 is not nearly as expensive, but very tough in higher grades, and the first green Hulk is more recognizable to fans, so perhaps that is one to add to your portfolio.

But there is one area of the hobby that is definitely growing. Foreign editions of Marvel and DC comics, especially overseas editions of recognized keys, have finally caught people's attention. There are many amusing foreign names for our favorite heroes, and collectors are trying to assemble all the available or known versions of big keys, like *Incredible Hulk* #181, *Batman* #181 and *Avengers* #4.

By far the most elusive and popular are the *El Sorpredente Hombre Arana* Spider-Man series produced after Gwen Stacy's death, where the Mexican publishers got permission to keep her alive and eventually marry Peter Parker in #128.

A mid-grade copy of *ESHA* #128 sold on eBay for $35K recently, and it's one for Spider-fans to lust after, with a truly iconic cover (also produced locally). As well as having a super-cool backstory worthy of any comic book.

But what of the UK editions of Marvel comics? Still these have failed to capture the imagination of US buyers — but you're going to be sorry if you don't invest in them soon.

Census numbers are crazy. These books were printed at the same time as the US editions, but with UK prices and no month in the box on the cover variants. Here are just a few examples of Universal CGC census numbers for US and UK editions:

Amazing Fantasy #15: 2396 US / 56 UK
Incredible Hulk #1: 1387 US / 38 UK
Journey into Mystery #83: 1714 US / 30 UK

The Bronze Age variants resemble the 30¢ test market variants in the US, with familiar flashes and circles, but with penny prices. These are affordable and super-cool to collect and not easy to come by in high grade.

Stay safe, and give us a call if you'd like us to get top dollar for your collection!

Jesse James Criscione Jesse James Comics

Wow, 2022 has been an amazing year for sales across the board. We saw a HUGE spike on our E-commerce pages. eBay got its second wind this year and really pushed our numbers to extemely higher than normal sales. We had our product on several static plaforms, and all of them out performed last year's numbers. Again, it was all about live streaming. Comic Book Shopping Network ended the year with almost a 300% increase in sales, and viewership hit a high at 150%. We didn't have a drop in the Big Item books either.

We did see a whole new customer base come to us this year. The prices points of $1, $2 and $3 books have been a huge increase in our overall business. The $3.00 books had a 500% increase in sales this year, outperfoming our new issue sales. We did see a small decline in new issues and graded book sales. The customers this year were looking for Price Points, minor Keys, lower shipping and service.

There seems to an abundance of live podcasts and platforms that are trying to price the market on a daily and weekly basis. This has created a HUGE increase in overvalued product. Within a 6 month period (after the price has been announced) a high number of these items have dropped more than half and leveled off to where they should have been to start. If I was to say there was a black mark on the industry, I would point to low informational spec shows and pages. In 2023, the industry needs to be part of this process more on a monthly level to even out this type of overpricing and misinforming the customers on what to buy. We need to see some industry-driven shows in the following years.

Crowdfunding continues to break record after record each year. Again we saw Coffin Comics (Brian Pulido) lead the way to sales that couldn't be imagined 10 years ago.

Overall, we see 2023 as our biggest year to come. We will see QR codes and apps take over as big part of the industry over the next 5 years. As A.I. comes in, we will also see a great amount of customers that are not tradtional floppy buyers, start hitting the stores and conventions soon.

Brock Dickinson
Collector

After the extreme highs and adrenaline rushes of the booming comic market in 2021, the 2022 market might best be described as an intense hangover. Where 2021 saw massive price rises and enormous quantities of new money flowing into the hobby – reflected by some aggressive price increases in the last *Overstreet Guide* – 2022 has been a year of fuzzy regrets and headaches. Beneath this gloomy assessment, though, lies some better news. While it's clear that many prices declined over the course of 2022, this decline was relative to the stellar growth observed in the 2020-2021 period. In other words, prices have retreated, but remain up substantially over what we saw just two years ago.

This year's downward trend was not unique to comics. Global stock markets declined by an average of 15% in 2022. Sotheby's reported that its art sales were down by 10%, and sports card collectors lamented the "crash" of their market. Even gold, a traditional place to invest when markets are uncertain, fell by 1.6% over the year. In this light, the slowdown in the comic market reflects a wider economic trend, rather than something specific to the hobby. And while the record prices for high end keys (especially more common Bronze and Copper keys) are now in the past, there are other elements of the market that are doing well. Many dealers have reported that sales of $1 books have increased dramatically, perhaps an indicator that comic collectors are still on the hunt, but preserving their funds until the market stabilizes.

Having said that, the 2022 market was often "uneven" with prices varying widely. In the old days, before the Internet, GPA and pricing apps allowed us to instantly know sales results from around the world, the *Overstreet Guide* used to include a notation on some listings suggesting "prices vary widely on this book". For me, this was an indicator of a book heating up, but one where some parts of the market hadn't yet caught on. "Prices vary widely" could be the slogan for the 2022 market, but by thinking of this as a kind of lens through which we can anticipate future market activity, I'd suggest five areas where the market seems to be poised for significant growth. As always, I'm sticking to the Bronze, Copper and Modern end of the market, where my expertise lies.

Company Crossovers: There was a time when Marvel and DC would periodically publish crossovers of their characters. Many of these books – perhaps led by the JLA Vs. Avengers series – began to rise in price this year. Although collectors think of these books as few and far between, there have been many published over the years, ranging from *Batman/Captain America* to *Incredible Hulk Vs. Superman* to *Darkseid Vs. Galactus*. As a group, these seem to be attracting increased interest, which is spilling over into other crossover properties linking multiple companies, such as *Batman/Spawn*, *Star Trek/X-Men* and *Aliens Vs. Predator Vs. Terminator*. Again, "prices vary widely" but the trend is clear. It's also worth noting that there are many reprints and collected editions of these titles that are not currently listed in the *Guide* that are selling for higher prices.

Marvel and DC Horror: Pre-Code Horror books have been hot for several years now, and this seems to be validating the collectability of horror titles in other eras. Bronze books in particular are heating up, including *House of Secrets* and *House of Mystery* from DC, or *Fear*, *Man-Thing* and *Werewolf by Night* from Marvel. In part, these books may have looked under-priced when compared to superhero titles, but there were other factors at play. For Marvel, the introduction of the characters Elsa Bloodstone, Werewolf by Night and Blade into their cinematic efforts sparked some market interest. For DC, the spark was the number of classic covers by highly regarded artists that can be found in the Horror runs. Which leads to the next trend…

Classic Covers by Classic Artists: The always-too-early deaths in 2022 of some giants of the comic art world, including Neal Adams and George Pérez, helped spur interest in the work of classic artists. Helped along by third-party grading companies like CGC, this portion of the market is accelerating again. Classic DC horror covers by Neal Adams, Bernie Wrightson and Michael Kaluta saw record prices being realized throughout the year in the most obvious display of this trend. However, there was also renewed interest in the work of Copper Age great Dave Stevens, and in the "classic" works of perennial fan favourites Todd McFarlane and Adam Hughes, for example.

Classic Stories: As the past years' binge on high-priced keys draws to a close, collectors are turning to different notions of value, which are not always focused on speculative potential. This has led to a modest return of "run collectors" but also a cadre that is seeking out classic storylines. These are the kinds of stories that are lauded by critics, fondly remembered by fans, and built on by succeeding generations of writers. Examples of books receiving increased attention include Batman: Year 1 in *Batman* #404-407, Batman: Hush in *Batman* #608-619, Kraven's Last Hunt spread across several Spider-Man titles, the Dark Phoenix storyline in *Uncanny X-Men*, *Batman: The Dark Knight Returns*, Barry Windsor-Smith's Weapon X in *Marvel Comics Presents* #72-84, and Alex Ross' *Kingdom Come*. While these books have typically been broken out from surrounding books in the *Guide*, price growth on these issues is accelerating

Magazines and Treasury Editions: Magazines have been an overlooked area of the hobby. The general scarcity (especially in high grade) and unnoticed range of key appearances in these books has reversed this trend. Marvel perhaps led this phenomenon, with popular characters such as Star-Lord (*Marvel Preview* #4), Rocket Raccoon (*Marvel Preview* #7), White Tiger (*Deadly Hands of Kung Fu* #19) and Man-Thing (*Savage Tales* #1) all debuting in magazines that were suddenly on the hobby's collective radar. This heat has since spilled over into the market for Warren Publishing titles (especially issues of *Vampirella*), where we continue to see record prices. While this is an area that still has room for growth, the market is increasingly focusing the same attention on treasury edition books. These titles – including *All-New Collector's Edition*, *Golden Picture Story Book*, *Limited Collector's Edition*, *Marvel Special Edition*, *Marvel Treasury Edition* – are increasingly sought after. Some books in this vein are well-known, such as Neal Adams' *Superman Vs. Muhammad Ali*, or the DC/Marvel collaborations on *Superman Vs. The Amazing Spider-Man*. At the same time, there are scarce books (like *Christmas with Archie*, *King Kong* and even two different versions of *The Jungle Book*) that could absolutely explode in price if this niche continues to catch on.

I've used the word "classic" a lot in this report, but in uncertain times, we retreat to safety. As I say, "prices vary widely" but this is my take on some of the silver linings in the currently cloudy marketplace. Thanks to Norm and Stephen at Mostly Comics in St. Catharines for keeping me supplied, thanks to Mark Huesman and the amazing team at the *Guide* for all the work they do, and thanks to each of you Market Report readers. I hope I've provided some insights of value for the upcoming year!

GARY DOLGOFF
GARY DOLGOFF COMICS

Still Shining Bright - The Comic Marketplace At A Glance: Comic books have been, and remain to be, a 'beacon of light' in our wacky yet ever-wondrous world. They have enjoyed years of enduring popularity - as we know that they have intrinsic value to accompany their collectibility. Folks still snap them up: comic collections and individual books continue to be bought and sold in a 'hearty and consistent' way. I continue to buy collections of comics, original comic art, magazines, hardcovers, TPBs, toys, cards & more with total confidence and at a steady clip. Collectors, well into their 70s are still buying treasured oldies, and are still enjoying them. While many of these folks will opt to sell their collections, or parts of them, for various reasons - their legacy has paved the way for countless collectors who are middle aged or younger. Collecting comics spans the ages of "man and woman-kind" now more than ever!

Market Breakdown - Certified, Slabbed Comics: Noteworthy enough, even when buying raw comics (those that haven't been encased or certified), I can value some of them at over *Guide*, and pay accordingly based on their potential. For example, if acquiring a given raw comic book, I can assess it at a premium provided that it would sell correspondingly if it were to be certified in the future.

Many comics get 'slabbed', and as a result, some sell for over *Guide*. Considering this, it may be tempting for some folks to have the majority of their collection certified. Nonetheless, people should be judicious about which they choose to send out to get processed. A number of comics are worth *Guide* or less 'slabbed'- while many others end up being worth less than the cost it was to have them certified.

Regarding the certification companies themselves, CGC and CBCS are still the two leading companies, but there are others - with CGC still maintaining the largest market share. Generally speaking, comics graded by CGC tend to sell for somewhat more money.

Market Breakdown - Golden Age (1930s thru 1954/ Pre-Code): In general, these are more solid sellers than ever, and many more of them are worth over *Guide* (by various amounts). Timely Comics (1940s Marvels) are tougher to get than ever. More of them are worth over *Guide*, as time goes on. I love those Timelys! One ol' friend of mine, Joey, says with wonder, that they even smell different, in a cool way. I myself have a nice collection of Timelys, led by over 40 Golden Age *Captain America Comics* (sorry, they are not for sale).They have been my Golden Age favorites since I was a teen-ager.

Golden Age DC comics are, in general, solid, steady sellers, and some sell for over *Guide*.My favorite Golden Age DC title, *Wonder Woman* is like that, as are *Detective Comics* up to #40 or #50, *Batman* #1, *Superman* #1, *Action Comics* #1 through 10; most *More Fun* issues with The Spectre, *All Star Comics* #8 (1st app. Wonder Woman!). I enjoy those late 1930s and early '40s DCs quite a bit, especially those early Batman and Superman appearances.

Other Golden Age (Quality, MLJ, Fawcett, Centaur, Dell, etc.)

Quality Comics: They had a lot of 'Quality' artists and interesting superheroes. Uncle Sam, drawn by Will Eisner, Lou Fine, etc. was a particularly notable character, well-drawn, and dynamic! In addition to their colorful superheroes (the well-known Plastic Man and The Spirit), the titles of the comics were often dynamic as well! *Crack*, *Smash*, *Hit* to name a few. Later 1940s Quality comics were okay, but they did not match the allure of the early issues. Most Quality comics sell for *Guide*, with some early '40s selling for *Guide* or more.

MLJ - The company that in the early 1940s launched Archie and the gang! They had primitive art for the most part, but interesting, with their own allure!

Centaur- A late 1930s/early '40s company- Mostly, Centaurs are worth well over *Guide*.

Fawcett - Captain Marvel/Jr., Mary Marvel- a number of Fawcett titles with those characters. They generally sell for *Guide*.

Dell - Donald Duck, Mickey Mouse, Uncle Scrooge, plus a whole lot of newspaper reprint characters - Dells sell for *Guide* or less.

Classics Comics/Illustrated - Slower sellers, often selling for less than Guide. (But they were great for homework projects back in the day!

Pre-Code Horror, and ECs - These are 'way cool books'. The Horror issues are mostly worth well over *Guide*, and I love to get them in. They sell like hotcakes. ECs had some of the best stories and art - ever! They sell quite well – best are the Horrors, then the Sci-Fi's, plus *Crime SuspenStories* and *Shock SuspenStories*.

Market Breakdown - Silver Age (1955 to 1971/ 10¢, 12¢, and 15¢ cover price)

Marvel Comics Silver Age: The "Foundation" of the comics industry. To me, I equate 1960s Marvels with the Silver Age rock group, The Beatles. Both have 50+ years of perennial staying power and are truly icons of that era. Many of us read them as youths, and that built up fond memories for us that last a lifetime and beyond. To me, and many others, they were so relatable. They had moods, ups and downs, human frailties, and yet had exciting superhero battles. Particularly relatable, was Spider-Man, who was bullied, but fought back against that bullying, sometimes. The characters still endure in the world, and probably always will.

The early 1960s #1s and 1st appearances have always sold for over Guide. Especially *Amazing Spider-Man* #1, *Avengers* #1, *Daredevil* #1, *Fantastic Four* #1, *Incredible Hulk* #1, *Journey Into Mystery* #83 (1st app. Thor), *Tales of Suspense* #39 (1st app. Iron Man), and *X-Men* #1. Other 1960s Marvels sell reliably, at *Guide* or more. When they're worth over-*Guide*, I pay accordingly.

DC Comics Silver Age: They are cool. They were also read, and treasured, by a number of us comics fans. However, they (for the most part), don't command the "over *Guide* respect" of some of their Marvel counterparts. *Batman*, *Brave and the Bold*, *Detective*, *Flash*, and *Wonder Woman* sell well enough.

Some Silver Age DC keys sell for over *Guide* such as *Batman* #121 (1st Mr Freeze), #181 (1st Poison Ivy), #227 (classic cover swipe from *Detective* #31), *Detective* #359 (1st Batgirl), *House of Secrets* #92 (1st app. Swamp Thing), *Showcase* #4 (1st app. S.A. Flash), #22 (1st app. S.A. Green Lantern), and some others.

Market Breakdown - Bronze Age (1972 thru early '80s): For a lot of folks growing up in the 1970s, the Bronze Age was the fun, funky, and sometimes quite imaginative era of comics.

Marvel - Bronze Age Marvels are solid sellers, and there are a number of Bronze Keys that sell for over *Guide*, such as *Amazing Spider-Man* #129 (1st Punisher), #194 (1st Black Cat), #238 (1st Hobgoblin); *Daredevil* #131 (1st Bullseye), #168 (1st Elektra); *Tomb of Dracula* #10 (1st Blade); *Werewolf By Night* #32 (1st Moon Knight); *Giant-Size X-Men* #1 (1st new X-Men); *X-Men* #101 (1st Phoenix), #129 (1st Kitty Pride); and the star of the show, *Incredible Hulk* #181 (1st Wolverine!) *Amazing Spider-Man* and *X-Men* are two of the best Bronze Age sellers in general.

DC Comics - Bronze Age DCs are pretty sold sellers, for the most part. *Batman* and *Detective* are two of the most solid titles, from this era. *Batman* #251 (classic Joker cover) is a spectacular one, quite popular, and a great seller. The funky '70s Kirby DCs are a fun read, and sell well, especially the Kirby Fourth World (*Forever People*, *Mister Miracle*, *New Gods*, and *Jimmy Olsen*.) In general, one can find buyers for Bronze Age DCs, who appreciate getting them for some entertaining reading.

Market Breakdown - Modern Era Comics (Mid/Later '80s Through The Present)

It's great that younger folks are enjoying these comics (they are "the future" after all).There are some great and interesting titles and storylines from these eras: anything from *Watchmen* and those terrific and gripping Alan Moore *Swamp Things*, to that Spider-Man series wherein Doc Ock takes over Peter Parker/Spider-Man's inner self, and starts socializing as such! And there are comics from this era that are worth multiples of *Guide*.

Market Breakdown - Original Comic Art: It has been dubbed the "Wild West" of the industry, price-wise, as some art has gone up to astronomical amounts. However, much art is still affordable, and these one-of-a-kind pieces are often a proud addition to most any collector's "repertoire of keepsies." I have the cover to *Howard The Duck* #19 (Howard the Human!), a 'take' on the cover of *Amazing Spider-Man* #50. I also own a few Alex Raymond pieces from the 1930s in my collection as well.

So, all told, it's been another great year in the biz. The market, although a bit variable at times, has held the bar.

Also, I'm still enjoying all types of comics as much as ever – everything from Horror to Hero and beyond... and all types of copies from faulty to flawless!

Thinking back, when I first discovered comics at age 11, my brother had beat-up boxes full of weathered comics (although they were only a few months to a couple of years old at the time.) I came to enjoy these comics, no matter how they presented themselves. As a result, I fashioned my comics business to enjoy and avidly deal with ALL comics, Poor to Mint, and I still do!

Over 50 years in the comics industry, and I'm still not even remotely tired of it. I have my wonderful crew at the ol' GD warehouse to "buoy things along", "Keep it goin', and keep it flowin'." All the best to you all!

Walter Durajlija and Jay Halstead Big B Comics/International Comic Exchange (ICE)

Walter Durajlija, Big B Comics, Hamilton Ontario and Niagara Falls Ontario

Congratulations to Bob, Jeff, Mark and the whole Overstreet crew on delivering another *Overstreet Price Guide* to the masses. The *Guide* is still the best resource out there for comics and this new one will take its place weighing down my briefcase as I retire last year's edition to my now quite large *Guide* archives.

It has been quite a tumultuous year, 2022 has. Prices for collectible comics started out at levels none of us veterans of the hobby could have ever imagined. The second half of the year though saw some major price drops, especially in the most heavily traded sectors of the key issue Silver, Bronze, Copper and Modern Ages. I've noticed many of these prices retreating back to 2020 and 2019 levels which in hindsight makes a lot of sense. Let's not forget that comic book values in the spring of 2020 were also at all time highs, the hobby had enjoyed the greatest decade it ever had in the 2010s. This period, thanks to the magic that was happening in the movie theatres, streaming services, amusement parks, video games and other media, saw comic book culture truly expand to every nook and cranny across the globe. Very few places in the world escaped the influence of comic book culture and this showed in the droves of new collectors and investors into the hobby.

The correction of 2022 was setting things back to the still lofty heights of 2020, if the values could stabilize there we would indeed be on very firm ground for future growth in the hobby.

Comics are a resilient commodity, even as the general trend in prices was heading downward there were strong pockets within the hobby still enjoying increases in values. Pre-Code Horror, Pre-Hero Golden Age (1933 to 1938), Classic Cover Golden Age, Scarce issues (especially in high grade) and a few other sectors remained strong throughout 2022 with some books enjoying strong value gains. This for me is a sign that the core of the hobby remained strong.

Our ICE Collectibles eBay auction (see Jay Halstead's report for more) produced great results throughout the year especially in the Golden Age sector and especially with our raw listings. Raw comics were in such demand in our auctions, they often sold for at or even above what graded versions would have sold for, this speaks well for the trust buyers were putting into our grading and delivery. Some highlight sales included a *Vampirella* #1 raw 6.0 - $1200, CGC 9.0 graded *Human Torch* #2 (Golden Age) - $9520, we had about 20 or so Golden Age *Batman* from #20 to #80 and they all sold raw at auction for prices very close to the values they were getting graded.

We can't ignore that a lot of books lost a lot of value, Modern Age keys were the hardest hit with many books losing well over half their market values over the course of 2022. Realistically though these books should not have been trading for the prices they were trading for in the early part of 2022. The whole pandemic bubble is something that I'm sure economists will be studying in the years to come. Sectors like real estate, stocks, digital currency, NFTs and collectibles all enjoyed levels that we all knew were too good to be true, the good news there is that we were all right.

I'm looking at the correction in a positive light, it was needed. The hobby is a strong, and as I said above, resilient one. Collectors can now rejoin the hobby with prices they can justify and investors and speculators can start buying again based on some well thought out research, inside tips and even hunches. Let's see what 2023 has in store for us.

I'd like to add a big thank you to the staff at Big B Comics and ICE Collectibles, these people do some amazing work for which I am eternally grateful.

Jay Halstead - icomicexchange.com

Hello gang, another year in the books, and as most of you realize reading this, this past year can be summed up by something Charles Dickens once said a long time ago! "It was the best of times, it was the worst of times!"

First, the good. Yes, slabs have slowed down for us, no denying that. So consciously, we've sent less and less to CGC. However, we have really ramped up our raw auctions and all I can say is WOW! I'd say there were a sizable amount of raw auctions where the consignor got more money than he would have had we graded them (and he or she had paid for grading--always remember that expense, it's funny how many tend to forget that when selling slabs). If you're going to get $150 for a raw 8.0, but $170 for a graded one, there is simply no use in grading it. Because we've stuck to our guns, we now have more followers and more active shoppers on ebay than we ever have, and our consignors are certainly enjoying the ride!

Now let's talk about the year overall. We'll start at the beginning of 2022. Things were humming along, essentially business as usual. Not nearly as crazy as the April through June/July of 2021 (we may never see that again frankly), but busy, lots of books changing hands, prices still going up on big Silver and Bronze keys, prices still hanging on on most of everything else. As the year moved forward, we started to see things change, slowly at first, but expected changes, like 9.6 Modern comics starting to drop significantly (there was just too much inventory available). Everyone at home, getting free money, just grading everything, was an expected mess a year later, and since mid-2022, that has certainly been the case.

Man, have things sure have changed since late 2021. With interest rates rising, and the incredible inflation we are feeling (esp. here in Canada), people just aren't spending like they were before. Again, a lot of this was expected, as it's impossible to ride that high forever, but I don't think many of us could forecast just how much things have changed. 9.8 Copper and Modern have cratered, literally. Unless it's a key, related to a movie or was simply scarce in the first place, this segment of the market is absolutely hemmoraging value. All the books I spoke about last year, the *Wolverine* #1 & #8, *War Journal* #6 & #7, *Amazing Spidey* in the #300s (let's not even talk about the blood bath that is *Spidey* #300), are falling off a cliff. Again, this was easy to see, I just thought it would take longer and the fall wouldn't be this sudden. The combination of availability, the lack of expendable income and the collector's who have simply abandoned ship, have caused this segment of the marketplace to free fall the hardest. However Silver and Bronze aren't fairing a heck of a lot better right now and 2023 doesn't look like it's going to offer any sort of let up.

I'm going to use just one book as an example of this, and then try to give my best advice going forward beyond 2023. *Incredible Hulk* #181, ahh yes, the book that actually isn't even a first appearance (don't get me started). Last year in my report I wrote about a 9.8 that came in to ICE (didn't have white pages), that sold immediately, which at the time, "we got a near record price for, however very soon afterwards, even that incredible price was surpassed." The book then took off like a rocket from then on. From $50k, to $80k, to $100k, then unbelievably, a few white pagers snagged $138k and $145k. That book with white pages today (near Christmas Day 2022), is between $90k and $100k, and who knows where it goes from here!

So here's my point. If a book comes up that you simply can't live without, but was available last week and will be available next week, in the same grade, you have to tread lightly. Can you afford to lose $30k? $40k? I know I can't. You want to believe when you buy something it will be yours forever, but sadly gang, that isn't the case most of the time, especially now when things get tight. So we're having guys drop stuff off and losing 20%-30%, from when they purchased! Those are guys that probably won't buy again, they are most likely gone from this hobby forever. The reason is they didn't use possibly the most important rule when buying high dollar books, which is the rule of scarcity. Keys are nice, Silver Age Marvels are too, but if you can buy the same book, in the same grade, over and over again, that book is susceptible to wild price variance, which you are seeing today. Comics are not cash, diversify, enjoy what you're doing, buy what you love (and can afford to lose), but most importantly, caveat emptor!

It's not all bad gang, comics are still fun, I've never added more comics to the personal collection than I have this past year (my high grade monster/Bronze DC and Canadian Price Variant collection continues to increase in size exponentially), and I will continue to buy. I'm still loving every second of it, and you should too!

Well thanks for reading, keep your stick on the ice, and keep collecting!

Ken Dyber
Tasteecat Comics

Hello comic friends, I own Tasteecat Comics, which has a brick & mortar store in Portland, OR that's been open for 8 years now. I've also been selling online and at conventions around the country for almost two decades.

Let's start off with the obvious/big news… I have rebranded, changing my business name from Cloud 9 Comics to Tasteecat Comics. I'm not going to get into the why, but just know, nothing about the business has changed other than the name. My brick and mortar store is in the same location (2621 SE Clinton St. Portland, OR) with the same hours (11 – 7 daily). I'm still the owner, employees are the same (shout out to Moises, Michael, Stephen & Duncan), website design, etc… all the same, just new business name, logo, URL & social names.

You can shop via my website: www.tasteecatcomics.com or check me out on Ebay & Social Media at: Tasteecatcomics). My website has several thousand comics for sale, a shopping cart, and a very useful Advanced Search, where one can shop by time period, genre, price and/or publisher.

Well, 2022… Let's start off with the vintage/collectible segment of the market. Corrections, corrections, and, yup, more market corrections. I am so thankful that I do not specialize in key Silver, Bronze & Copper Age superhero key books. Many have gone down 20-50% in less than one year. Don't get me wrong, I do sell them, but I'm not the dealer at cons with rows and rows of these key books. Now… perspective is paramount when looking inward at the market, as 2021 showed record gains from all time periods, so, as downward trending as 2022 has been, things are not all doom and gloom. If you're a press/flipper and over extended yourself in 2021, you may think differently, as in the short term, you have gotten crushed. X-Men #1's as an example in graded 2.0-6.0 have reduced by 50% this year, however, if you bought years before, and are simply holding as a long-term collector, you're going to be fine, so don't freak out. This is not inflation or supply chain stuff, simply, 2021 (end of 2020 – beginning of 2022 specifically) showed the largest period of growth in not only comics, but all collectibles in history from what I can tell. People at home unable to spend their money elsewhere due to Covid closures, coupled with stimulus money coming in, created the perfect spending frenzy. But, alas, reality has set in. Sure, inflation isn't helping, as it's causing people to spend less due to the value of their dollar not going as far, but this correction was going to happen regardless as the growth wasn't sustainable. The collapse of Crypto currencies hasn't helped the collectibles markets either, as the folks who did well there, were spending in collectibles, and they have all vanished along with their portfolios.

As for the reader based market (ie: trades/Manga, new comics), that is still moving along pretty consistently for me at least. Manga and trade sales are down very slightly from last year, but I was expecting this year to be down in some capacity as there was almost no way to match last year's growth. Percentage wise, my Manga sales are better than my general TPB/HC sales, but I have 3 bookshelves of Manga vs 12 bookshelves of U.S. comic TPB/HCs. If I had more room in the store, I would increase the size of my Manga selection.

New Comic sales have a really tough dynamic for me to explain as there are many factors that might make my shop's situation unique comparatively with the rest of the country. In general, I think I'm actually selling slightly less units or about the same as last year, but then there is the upward trend in cover prices to offset that. I have seen growth though with an increase in more Box (subscription) customers, especially the last 3 months or so. I don't order enough new books to really play the incentive variant game, but I do have to say, there are some pretty fantastic looking variant covers being created these days.

As a side note, my first comic as a creator should be coming out in 2023. I am the writer of *Stealing Action*, a five-issue 1 arc story about stealing the world's most valuable comic (no, this has nothing to do with what happened to Cage's copy, but does make for an interesting premise. I actually wrote this story years ago as a feature length screenplay not knowing anything about what had happened with Nic's book). Story is more about loss, redemption and love than the actual comic. I appreciate any/all of your help going to your local comic stores and requesting it/buying it (and store owners, please bring it in). Not sure who will publish it at present, but I am also excited in that it will also be the first published work by my artist, Aedan Baez, who is one of my shop's Box Customers, so it will be cool for us to "break into" the hobby together. OK, enough shameless PR and onto some more market specifics.

Conventions: This one is a bit harder to pinpoint than previous years, but in general, there seemed to be a spending regression from customers and dealers. Some conventions were outliers, like NYCC was good for back issue selling/buying, San Diego resuming back in July had many folks excited, but overall, there seemed to be less money exchanging hands this past year. I think there is less buyer confidence at present, and consumers and dealers don't seem to know where this downward market correction will end, so trying to determine what the bottom on a book or title is has proven to be a challenge. There has also been an increase/return to smaller size conventions that are more comic-book-centric like the new Collector's Summit. Portland's Frankenstein Comic Swap has returned, and Terry O'Neill's 1 day CA show is back in 2023. I fully believe that as large weekend cons continue to move more towards pop culture events, these comic-book-centric show will only increase over the next few years.

Golden Age: Interestingly enough, this seemed to be the one segment of the overall back issue market that wasn't too affected by the market correction. I didn't see as many record prices being realized as previous years, but there also wasn't the regression you saw in the superhero books from the Silver to Copper Age. Matt Baker and LB Cole books are still in demand, but have stabilized for the moment. Now is a great time to buy early Archie books. They have been flat for years now, and are quite hard to find in grade (think VG or better). I can't recall the last time I saw a *Pep* #22 at auction or in person. I sold quite a few War books this past year from the 1950s, all moving quite fast at prices way over *Guide*. Many of these have little to no copies graded. Pre-Code Horror is still selling quite well for the better covers, the average or uninteresting covers have slowed. I can only attribute the stabilization in this time period to the customer base being older, and most likely in better financial position to continue to buy.

Silver Age: Just getting crushed at present. All major keys are down, some considerably, and some, well, are actually a bit head scratching. *Fantastic Four* books shouldn't be going down as much as they are, as their debut MCU film is coming. Great time to get into *X-Men* #1, *Fantastic Four* #52, *Amazing Spider-Man* #50 and many others. What is interesting to me, is that I can't keep Silver Age *X-Men* in any condition in stock, where *Fantastic Four* are much slower for me to move. There is no X-Men movie announced, and even if there was tomorrow, it would be a year or two after the *Fantastic Four* movie at the earliest. I can only attribute this to the fact that the X-Men are the most popular super hero team, and not only so, but by a ton. I think this is a good thing, as we've become so accustomed to interest or gains on books/characters due to TV shows/movies, but we forget that so many of us cared about these characters well before the studios were producing all this stuff. Keep buying what you love here, and buy as much as you can afford right now, because just like in 2009 when the market bottomed out, it will come back, and I think this time, sooner than later.

Bronze Age: Another period showing declines in value and in people collecting. My back issues sales from $5-$20 books and more desirable books has really slowed here. Normally I'd put an *Amazing Spider-Man* #121 out for sale at a con or in my shop, and it would be gone. *Tomb of Dracula* #10 gone. *Werewolf By Night* #32 gone. Not so now... even priced at current market, not pre-bubble pricing, they are sitting with no interest, or needing to be discounted to create interest, which historically would be shocking. The declines here have not been as sharp as the Silver Age, but these books were also not as expensive to begin with so it's relative. Again, a good time to buy here, but not as great as the Silver Age, as the % gains in both might be the same in the next 5 years, but your dollar gains will be greater in the Silver Age.

Copper Age: Still tons of great deals to be had here with many new keys emerging from the $1-$10 price range, so lots of great affordable spec books here. Higher end books like *TMNT* #1 and *Albedo* #2 have cooled a bit, but don't expect this to continue for long. I still think *Albedo* #2 is really undervalued, especially in 9.2 or higher So... hear me out, I know the Turtles as a property are so much more popular than Usagi is, but think about these facts about both books which were published in 1984. *TMNT* #1: Print Run: 3000. CGC Census: 1153 (38%). In 9.8: 42 copies. Recent Graded 9.8 Sale: $156,000 (Nov 2022). *Albedo* #2: Print Run: 2000. CGC Census: 297 (15%). In 9.8: 20 copies. Recent Graded 9.8 Sale: $19,800 (July 2020). *Albedo* #2 is scarcer, with a lower overall % of the run graded. I feel given this info, *Albedo* #2 in 9.8 should be more like a $75,000-$100,000 book given this info. Time will tell I guess.

On a more specific note, and I can't believe I'm learning about this just now, as this is the time period I grew up with, but I just learned that *Marvel Super Heroes Secret Wars* #1 has a centerfold printing error of Galactus. Galactus is printed as blue & white in some copies in circulation instead of the normal purple coloring. You can find images of both versions online relatively easily. The blue error versions are currently selling at a bit of a premium (think about 25% or so more), but I think this margin may widen as more collectors begin to learn about this. If a store owner didn't know, then I'm guessing many of you don't as well. The *Guide* should make a note of this with a separate line listing, and I suggest a modest 25% increase is pricing for the initial listing and will see how the market changes over time with this.

Renaissance Age: To me this is the current comic book market, that began with *Walking Dead* #1, but the term hasn't caught on with everyone else yet so (spread the word!). Very hard these days to tell what the "next" book or series will be. Publishers are doing shorter and shorter print runs, with many titles just being one arc. It's interesting to me that *Saga* #1 (my store's best-selling series, and by a ton for that matter), sells for half of what *Something Is Killing The Children* #1 goes for raw or graded. Now is a good time to buy some *Saga* #1s!

Thanks to everyone who continues to support my small store (literally 680 feet of retail), and buying stuff online with me either via eBay, my website, Instagram or wherever. I look forward to meeting more of you in the coming years. Happy collecting!

D'Arcy Farrell
Pendragon Comics

We relocated to a bigger, better location within Cloverdale Mall in Toronto. With more foot traffic, and new comic fans, we had to expand. For the young and old, Dynamite's *Gargoyles* and *Darkwing Duck* is a welcome fresh addition to the shelves. There is still not enough content made for 4-8 year olds, and really nothing suitable for 9-12 (except maybe *Star Wars Adventures*). Many of this age group want mature content Marvel titles, and there just isn't any released consistently. DC has some, but it's not enough.

Movies have stagnated. After *Eternals*, *Black Adam* did so so, and even though the *Black Panther* sequel did great at the box office, it did not equate to more sales for us. I'd say the new *Batman* movie did amazing for sales for us, as I had many requests for items like the *Batman: Year One* TPB.

Vintage books sold not bad, but high values leveled off once conventions and comic stores could open freely with no Covid restrictions. I did sell way more mid-level valued items (under $100) than usual.

New DC of 2022: *Dark Crisis*, *Nubia*, *Black Adam*, *DC vs. Vampires* all sold under expectations. Chip Zdarsky on *Batman* starting at #125 was a big thing and it did sell well, but *Batman* is the top in comics, well over anything Marvel churns out. Most Batman titles are well written and supported with consistent decent art. I think the 2022 year had a bit too many Bat items on the shelves, but for the most, it's a good thing. The various *Batman: One Bad Day* one-shots are a good read as well.

Joker continues his slaughter on the shelves with consistent good sales with multiple titles and fans cannot get enough. It's about time DC took advantage of the best criminal/villain in all comics.

Batman/Spawn 1-shot is the biggest selling item in years. It's a shame McFarlane wrote it, but the many variant covers by great artists and interior by Capullo made this a top seller. Buy this only for the art.

New Marvel of 2022: The Punisher came back and was well received. I can't say the same for Ghost Rider's return as it flatlined after #1. Facsimile editions are a hit for sales, as these affordable classics give many fans a way to own and read a key comic.

Alex Ross covers definitely affect sales. *Black Panther* actually sells due to his cover art. His hardcover slipcase of *Fantastic Four: Full Circle* was a massive hit, as well as this beloved team's restart at #1 with Ross doing many great covers.

Fortnite X Zero War sold better than expected. A.X.E. sold so-so, but anything associated with Eternals I'd expect that at best. The failure of *The Eternals* (first in 1970s as a bad copy of Kirby's great DC work) has even affected confidence in the big movie churning machine known as Disney. It has hurt back issue sales and comic investors as they second guess what to buy as a wise investment that may be a big risk. The Disney 100th anniversary variants coming early 2023 will sell very well.

New Image of 2022: The best news of the year is the return of *Saga*!! The next best thing was the surprise hit *Eight Billion Genies* written by Charles Soule. By the time you read this, the 8-part mini series is over, and a trade or hardcover will be on sale, I highly suggest you purchase this, well worth it. *Bone Orchard* sequel written by Lemire is fabulous. *Creepshow* is a great new horror that appeals to any EC fan. *Art Brut* just arrived fresh and exciting to read. The covers are great as well.

New Boom! Studios of 2022: This company still rocks awesome horrors such as the best selling *Something Is Killing The Children*. Having a great cover artist David Mack definitely helps. *House of Slaughter* sales have not decreased either. The Killer, *Affairs of the State*, written by Matz, was a great sequel for 2022.

New Dynamite of 2022: Best for its many great covers, I'd wish for a more ongoing cohesive style for its flagship characters like Vampirella. This reminds me of the defunct company Chaos. This company sells more to cover collectors than readers and is missing out on greater sales. *The Boys* is a great TV hit, but it hasn't translated to many extra trade sales.*Gargoyles* and *Darkwing Duck* releases at end of 2022 was well done and sold well.

New IDW of 2022: Since the hit surprise *TMNT: The Last Ronin* ended in early 2022, sales have slid. I have seen increased interest in various Star Trek projects, and G.I. Joe. I think an ongoing Transformers title would be a good idea, it works for Power Rangers, both of their best selling properties after TMNT.

Bill Fidyk
Collector

2022 was another strong year for comics and comic magazine sales. However, the end of 2022 saw prices for comics and magazines that soared in 2020-21 dip slightly and come back to reality. I say dip because prices did not plummet. There is no bubble bursting, but there is a market price correction that the hobby is currently undergoing. As always, key blue chip books will always maintain the most value, but you will need to hold onto the book for a longer period of time as compared to last year or the year before if you are buying for investment. The days of grabbing a hot book for an instant flip with a sizeable profit seem to have past.

For comic magazines, the vintage market saw interest and prices remain strong for individual issues for certain titles.

Warren: While it is impossible to go through every title, I'll highlight the big four: With regard to *Famous Monsters*, it is issue #1 hands down. Nostalgia and interest continues to attract new collectors to this title and the first fifteen or so issues are very tough to find in high grade. These magazines were well loved by many kids of the 1950s/early '60s. Issue one in a grade of Very Fine or higher is nearly impossible to find. For *Creepy* and *Eerie*, any cover that has a Frazetta cover was sought after and commanded high prices. For *Vampirella*, issue one is still a high demand key. However, prices have stabilized with this magazine across all grades. It appears that the market correction the hobby is currently in has affected this book. As an honorable mention, *Blazing Combat* #1 is a key for Warren collectors with a tough black cover that is impossible to find in Very Fine/Near Mint condition.

Marvel: The Marvel horror titles are still wildly popular. All horror titles for Marvel/Curtis saw a slight rise in prices (especially high grade copies). *Vampire Tales* #2 (first Satana) and *Dracula Lives* #2 (first Marvel origin of Dracula) saw popularity and prices rise. For *Marvel Preview*, issues #4 and #7 have stabilized in price. However, issue #3 (early Blade appearance) is in demand and commands high prices. A high grade copy of this issue also rarely comes to market. The biggest surprise title that saw a bump in demand and price for several issues in its run is *Marvel Super Special*. This was mainly a title that was a melting pot of genres for Marvel that incorporated rock and roll (KISS and the Beatles) to sword and sorcery (Conan) to superheroes (Star-Lord). The title eventually found its identity with movie adaptations. Issue #1 featuring KISS is insane right now. The *Star Wars* issues have leveled off in demand and price, but the Indiana Jones issues have spiked in demand and price. Many dealers and collectors are citing issue #18 (the *Raiders of the Lost Ark* issue) as the first appearance of Indiana Jones in comics which seems to have caught the attention of speculators. Biggest magazine key for Marvel is still *Savage Tales* #1 (first appearance and origin of the Man-Thing).

Skywald/Eerie publications: Amazing books that are super scarce in high grade (very fine or above). Demand outstrips supply with high grade examples of any of these magazines which is why there are so many outliers regarding record prices when high grade copies do surface to market.

Paul Figura
CBCS - Modern and Vintage Grader

This year I went to fewer comic conventions, not by choice but to stay back and help sort through the formidable volume of books we have in the office.

So that everyone knows, we are making progress. The past few years, comic conventions have been lacking in attendance. Not because of lack of interest, but due to the pandemic that has swept the world. It was sad to see the drop in attendance and sales but it was understandable. This past year however, attendance was incredible. People flocked to the shows to once again support the hobby and see their favorite writers, artists and stars! Safety precautions were in place at many shows, and a majority of the sea of people seemed to follow them without any sort of a problem. As usual autographs were a top priority and the lines for artist and celebrities were massive. Signatures on comics once again seems to be leading the pack of "must do while there", as the never-ending lines for autographs grew with each day.

As the doors opened and the crowd spilled in, the retailers seemed eager to get back in the flow of the convention fun. Making those all-important sales after going through some slow years. Sadly though, at a few shows, the count on pure comic book retailers was low. There were more of the Pop Culture and cosplay vendors set up. Not that that is a bad thing. They all tie into the comic book experience!

Pricing on Gold and Silver Age books was at a new all time high at a few of the shows, and depending upon which titles you were looking at. In the Modern era of comics, some could be surprisingly high. As the year progressed, we did start to see some of the prices begin to drop. Over all it looked as though the vendors were doing well and that business was back to normal.

Last but not least were the writer, artist and celebrity signings! Most of the shows had a great line up of comic book professionals and celebrities. The fans turned out *en masse* to meet and greet their favorites, with fans getting pictures and selfies, and you could just feel the excitement in the convention hall. Others getting their comics signed by favorite artists and writers, meeting and chatting with them, watching the excitement in their faces as they scramble to another table in artist alley for another treasured signature.

All in all the convention experience is back in full swing and can only get better and bigger from here. Looking forward to the new convention experience in the coming year. Get out and join in the fun! As always, Happy Collecting!

Joseph Fiore
ComicWiz.com

The red ink stamp imprint on the cover of the "Rocket Copy" of *Action Comics* #1 and its sale in January 2022 appeared to really set the stage for a "red hot" year, and early in the year, it would seemingly symbolize an unrelenting upward trajectory of growth. As a mega-key that was slightly above mid-grade (CGC 6.0), it represented the kind of gains we continued to see with low to mid-grade keys across nearly every era. And the sale happening on Heritage evokes a memory of yesteryear where I was handling an estate with a good amount of Silver Age keys, and one of the consignment directors at the time told me low to mid-grade didn't sell. These changes we all began seeing, particularly as it pertained to these unprecedented value increases was astonishing. Many found themselves participating in the selling frenzy, and that's understandable. I was watching people paying the kind of prices on 1.5 - 2.5 CGC *Giant-Size X-Men* #1, *Amazing Spider-Man* #129 or *Hulk* #181 that I had been paying on 8.5 - 9.0 grades not more than 5-6 years ago.

In the over 30 years of buying and selling everything from trading cards, toys and comics, I don't ever remember finding myself holding back on selling anything, especially with the kind of demand we were seeing with anything that got suddenly hot. I began to quickly realize that buying back into the market on those hot books was going to cost me more the moment the book sold. This happened on several key issues I sold in February 2022, and the two I had the most trouble buying back were *Amazing Spider-Man* (ASM) *Annual* #1 and *ASM* #14. Then in the summer, I began seeing the market cooling and sometime in late August, a mid-grade copy of *ASM* #14 turned up and I couldn't believe the asking price was what a CGC 2.5 was commanding a few months prior. The Red Rocket that had once captured a can't miss growth trajectory began looking like it was making an emergency landing.

This pattern of low to mid-grade keys losing ground further reinforced my decision to not sell anything for the rest of the year. As appraisal work really began to pick up at a fever pitch in April, I began to notice a concerning trend, and it began with the process of vetting comparables from several of the major auction companies. Seeing items being relisted, that had formerly achieved record prices, only to see them sell at lower prices when they reappeared, was the beginning of the onset of resignation for the status quo in terms of selling venues lacking in transparency, particularly as it related to using outlier sales to bolster a can't miss narrative treating comics as a "new asset class."

The cascading moment was when I turned to an auction company asking for a value opinion - a value opinion they apparently offered "free" to anyone considering using them to auction their items.

That person gave me a value estimate which was so incredibly low, that I couldn't even use it to insure the item correctly if I had to ship it to them. I could have done the appraisal myself, but when I'm recommending a venue to someone looking to sell their inheritance, I need to know who I'm recommending before I find myself giving bad advice. During this time, I began to also become resigned with the fee structures, particularly the dreaded 'buyers' premiums. With values dipping, those fees felt like hands dipping into collectors pockets, because an auction managed approach wasn't guaranteeing you would get more than selling it yourself. It was during this time that I began immersing myself more in Facebook groups, particularly ones that did away with fees and outlier sale shenanigans. With markets fluctuating as they did in comics, the same began happening in other collecting categories. What started out as an accounting of incidents where people had received damaged items, were selling items that had degraded (either due to age, or in transit) and/or questions began to emerge on the authenticity of what they were listing for sale, became a moment of realization that there was a need for a service with the basic premises of determining authenticity and market value.

I launched ToyVerify.com and ComicVerify.com as two services where I could better streamline the appraisal process on individual items or large collections. Rather than a printed report, all appraisals/verifications being performed could be accessed online through PC or Smartphone by way of a digital badge with QR code or serial number. I'm happy to report that I've been able to help a number of collectors with requests ranging from making sure their collections are properly insured, to assisting them in circumstances where they need an appraisal update to ensure they have appropriate coverages. I also began seeing a number of circumstances I hadn't seen before, with several involving post-loss appraisal during shipping, and collectors wanting an impartial and accredited appraiser to direct the claimant on what they were entitled to regardless of the damage sustained during transit.

The more disconcerting assignments were people who were buying in peak markets, and finding out that a 30-50% correction in values occurred between April and September. In such situations, I try to remind people about Replacement Values (RV), and that they are not only useful in relation to insurance matters.

At the time of this writing, markets have cooled substantially, due in some part to global economic circumstances. In such instances, it isn't always the case that your ability to acquire items is guaranteed to be lower in a depressed market, and this relates to a phenomenon I call a "supply choke", where items acquired during peak markets are not going to be easy to buy or wriggle loose at the expense of someone taking a loss on it for someone else's benefit, unless it's a duress sale situation. In such instances, RV may also be a useful metric to quantify what you should expect your reacquisition costs to be if you need to go out and reacquire a piece you are considering selling. This concept is more abstractly understood in housing markets, particularly in instances where a hot market may allow you to do well on the resale of your home, however you need to consider the costs of buying or rebuilding in that same market. To those who bought in peak markets, or those awaiting some imminent "fire sale", consider RV as a metric to explain why a hasty sale may present challenges in reacquiring or upgrading an item in fluctuating markets.

2022 represents the year where I began to more seriously consider supporting platforms that were offering alternatives to the status quo, and during the summer months I began to learn about an app that was in development called TheCollectorAlliance.com. I was offered an opportunity to beta test the site, and was so impressed with its features and offerings that I joined. It operates on a low monthly membership cost and allows you to sell and list as much as you want with no fees. The website and app were developed by the same person who built the digital price guide Star Wars Tracker. More recently, I have been in discussions about partnering with the site to provide verifications via ToyVerify. All in all, this past year was about building on my collection and continuing to help collectors navigate areas of authentication and values, and I am hopeful we will start to see things picking back-up where they left off in terms of market growth in the year ahead. Happy collecting!

Dan Fogel
Hippy Comix

After two years of skipping live events due to the Covid pandemic, I retailed at four small-to-medium conventions in 2022. There was lots of business being done and plenty of dealers, creators, fans, collectors, and their families happy to be there! Although my current main gig is working on the next edition of *Fogel's Underground Comix Price Guide* while buying and selling mostly Underground, Alternative, Indy, and Adult Comix, I took advantage of being able to tempt my regular and new buyers in person!

2022 Golden Age Sales Highlights: Low grade books from this era have heated up and often sell for double *Guide* un-slabbed, since most collectors and many dealers can no longer afford even mid-grades, let alone high! Bowing to that wisdom I started selling some of my beloved Fawcetts that I had stuck away as investments. *Captain Marvel Adventures* #1 coverless, CGC NG, sold for $1,500, #17 in GD+ sold for $300, *Marvel Family* #1 missing the bottom third of the front cover sold for $1,000, and various lesser and lower grade GA Captain Marvel books sold for double *Overstreet*.

Bronze Age: Early *Cerebus the Aardvark* are definitely heating up! #2 FN-VF $300, #3 VF+ $300, #4 VF $250, #5 VF $125, #6 VF+ $125, #7 VF-NM $100, #8 VF+ $50, #9 FN-VF $30, #10 VF $40. *Love and Rockets* is even hotter, with a growing younger fanbase leading to record sales! #1 (1981 self-published) VF+ File Copy signed by Gilbert Hernandez $850, #1 (1982 Fantagraphics) in VF-NM $275, and various other early issues sold over *Guide*. I've seen increased demand since legendary artist Richard Corben's passing in December 2020, even though his comics, magazines and graphic novels have always been among my top sellers.

Copper to Modern Age: Still not my focus but I put out a box of inexpensive Marvels at a small show and made some younger buyers happy with *Deadpool* and *Doctor Strange*, although *Wolverine* had no takers.

Finally, congratulations are due to the fine folks at Overstreet and Gemstone Publishing for the beautiful new color and layout makeover and the launch of Overstreet Access. The Original is still the best and leading the way! Thanks to Bob Overstreet, Steve Geppi, J.C. Vaughn, Mark Huesman, Amanda Sheriff, Yolanda Ramirez, Mike Wilbur, and all the rest, for letting me be a small part of the fun since 1987!

Kevin Forbes
Comic Interlude

Greetings from Lexington, Kentucky! Many of you know me from shows and conventions all over the country the past 32 years. I've owned Comic Interlude almost 27 years now, and while retail isn't what it used to be, our customer base remains strong. As for 2022, the comic book market began just as strong as 2021, but heading into summer something seemed amiss. As the leaves began to fall, comic book prices followed suit. As of this writing, the carnage is mostly over, and a huge percentage of the price increases of the past few years have been wiped out by a market correction almost as swift and amazing as it all began. You're now seeing flagship titles *Amazing Spider-Man*, *Fantastic Four*, *Avengers*, *X-Men*, single issues as well as KEY issues, in the same grades and conditions, selling for 30-50% less in just the past few months. Sure you will still be seeing some record setting prices moving forward, since our hobby has always had truly rare books that can go toe to toe with any type of market conditions...but we might never again see the across the board increases we enjoyed these past few years.

It's not all doom and gloom though, as most of the comic book prices are back to near pre-pandemic levels, some doing better, some fairing worse, and of course some still to be determined, but hey, that's the comic book market for as long as I've known it. After the historic and meteoric rise in comic book prices across the board, we all expected a market correction at some point, but the substantial drop from late August to late November/December surprised most. To me it was Black Fall, the comic book version of the stock market crashing. If you've ever seen the movie *Margin Call*, you'll understand "the ground is shifting below our feet, and apparently, there's no other way out".

So what do we do now? As dealers, we do what we do best. We buy collections based on market prices, we go back to selling at market prices, whatever those might be, and we sell to whoever is buying them. As buyers and collectors, you go back to negotiating the best deal you can, based on where prices are now. Will there be holdouts? Oh yes, seeing many many already. Sellers not willing to adjust their prices down to compete with the current market, all the while thinking/hoping/praying prices go back up to where they were, and more power to them. We've all known (know lol) dealers that price how they price, regardless of past/current prices, so what's changed? If one dealer won't budge and has unrealistic prices, you do what you've always done...move on to the next one, and keep looking until you get the deal/price you want. I deal in return business, so I must have realistic prices and compete with anyone on anything daily. I'm constantly researching and adjusting prices, and most all my fellow dealers are exactly the same in that respect. As comic book dealers, we adapt to any market. We always have, and we always will.

Current/Modern Comics: Since I have a retail store, I can say demand for new product is constant. Definitely not as strong as past years, but rebounded nicely post pandemic. Having an online presence, and competing with other online businesses is essential these days. The demand for modern keys is strong, and it's nice to see so many of them holding their own pricewise. Most of the Dark Horse *Star Wars* books are down, but demand for them remains strong especially in CGC 9.6 to 9.8 grades. *Star Wars: The Clone Wars* #1 in CGC 9.8 is holding steady at $2,000....early in 2022 I sold one for $3,000 on eBay, and the lowest was in July for $2,200 at Fan Expo Chicago. *Star Wars: Heir to the Empire* #1 CGC 9.8s are way down to around $900-$1,100. Both books have long term potential. *New Mutants* #98 CGC 9.8 (1st Deadpool) seems to be steady at $1,400-$1700 and *Batman Adventures* #12 (1st Harley Quinn) has recent sales support around the $3,000 range, but I feel a drop to $2,500 is more likely than an increase to $3,500 in the near term. *Ultimate Fallout* #4 is consistently below $2,000 now. Recent sales have been as low as $1,700, and this was a book I was selling easily for $2,500-$2,800 in early to mid 2022. It's another great book with long term potential, since Miles Morales has yet to hit the live action screen. Some recent sales: *Star Wars: Thrawn* #1 CGC 9.8 $187, *Star Wars Jedi: Mace Windu* CGC 9.8 $308, *Spider-Man India* #1 CGC 9.8 $330, and *Spider-Man Noir* #1 CGC 9.8 $362.

Bronze Age Comics: My favorite era of comics, since I grew up in the '70s and starting buying comic books in 1975. Oh how the mighty have fallen. All the keys from this era have taken a substantial hit over the past few months, with only a few exceptions due to highest graded copy, or low numbers of copies IN grade. Most everything is down 10-30%, and as I mentioned earlier, most are back to pre-pandemic price levels. Lots of 2nd chances for many collectors here, since I see most all the key issues from this era slowly rebounding in price over the next 3-5 years. A great opportunity to pick up some investment books on the dip.

Some very recent sales: *Thor* #337 CGC 9.8 $717, *Iron Man* #54 CGC 8.5 $309, *Amazing Spider-Man* #100 CGC 6.5 $145, *X-Men* #120 CGC (Sig. Series) 8.5 $210, *X-Men* #130 CGC 9.6 $454, *Marvel Spotlight* #32 CGC 9.6 $513, *Iron Fist* #14 CGC 7.5 $450, *Thundercats* #1 CGC 9.8 $675, *Star Wars* #107 CGC 9.8 $938, *Star Wars* #1 CGC 9.6 $975, *Nova* #1 CGC 9.8 $1,400, and *Giant-Size Chillers* #1 CGC 9.6 $1,344.

Silver Age Comics: I sound like a broken record at this point, but prices are down across the board here as well, and there are some great opportunities here to buy on the cheap looking at long term appreciation. It's truly a solid era of comic books, and by far one of the most desired age of comic books among collectors and investors alike. The current down prices are a golden opportunity to get into some of the greatest comic books ever published. There are so many key 1st appearances in the Silver Age of comics, and I strongly feel these prices will stabilize and begin to move back up in the near term. While there's always been consistent demand for keys from this era from all age groups of collectors, the trend of much younger collectors buying these books is nice to see.

Here are some recent Silver Age sales: *Iron Man/Sub-Mariner* #1 CGC 8.5 $392, *Peacemaker* #1 CGC 8.5 $525, *Tales of Suspense* #40 CGC 4.0 $475, *Tales to Astonish* #93 CGC 8.5 $685, *Amazing Spider-Man* #15 CGC 4.5 $850,

Amazing Spider-Man #12 CGC 6.5 $756, and *Avengers* #8 CGC 9.0 $3,900.

Golden Age Comics: Not too much of a surprise that keys from this era are stable and even increasing, even with all the falling prices these past few months. Demand remains strong for books from this era, with Timely and Pre-Code Horror keys regularly selling for new highs each time they are offered for sale. A very desirable era among long time collectors, and one new investors are picking up on more and more. Lots of affordable books to be had, but in higher grade they will always command record prices in my opinion. I don't ever see supply outweighing demand, and the popular keys in this era in any grade constantly sell higher year to year.

Eric Fournier
Guardian Comics

If you were looking for excitement in the comic pricing world, well you certainly found it this year. Everyone knew that the absolute vertical prices couldn't continue forever. Just like the stock market of 2021 the comic market followed in line with the housing market. Once the powers started increasing rates, we saw asset prices across the board pull back to more normal numbers. What does this mean? It's made a lot of books more affordable (and rightly so), some books went nuclear the past few years like *Giant-Size X-Men* #1. Pre-Covid this book in mid grade was about $1,400, then Covid happened and pushed this book to a height of over $5,000, with it now trending back around the low $2k mark. The book is still up 50% from pre-Covid, wahooo! However, if you bought at the peak, ouch! No one was immune from this, as many books had similar trajectories and both dealers and collectors did not just stop buying so there will be some that are "underwater" on their books for a bit. However, like history has shown us, time will heal these wounds. With rates poised to stop increasing and many projecting decreasing late 2023, we could be in for another fun year of where do prices go from here.

We have yet to slow down both on the buying or selling side of the hustle. At the start of 2022 we purchased another 6-figure collection (we ended 2021 buying a similar collection). The seller was a huge Marvel fan and purchased almost every single issue from #1-100 (or #100-200 in the case of titles like *Captain America* and *Hulk*). It was complete with the big keys which were slabbed and the runs nicely organized with mylars and fullbacks. Is the trend changing? Is the price point causing "deals" in the raws? Are buyers going back to reading and feeling the books?. I'm not sure what it is but we've definitely seen a big shift at the shows and shop of buyers enjoying raws more than slabs. We have also noticed that speculation from MCU and DCU movies/TV has died down a significant amount (which we won't complain about in the least). It used to be that each time there was a hint of a character, it would explode and slowly drop until that character was confirmed and then explode again. Have their announcements slowed the roles? Or the rather lacklustre performances from the last few years have people gun shy? We always enjoy a balanced market. Everyone is happy on the sale and the buy, when the market is mixed someone feels like they got burnt. Our business has been ever growing. Last year I hinted that we'd be expanding in 2022, it was a bit tongue in cheek however we have added a staff member to our crew, mind you I don't think he'll be helpful for 7 or 8 years until he can actually help or it might take until he is 19 and driving haha. In regards to sales, we had some monster books pass through our hands like most years: a couple of *Amazing Fantasy* #15s, *Amazing Spider-Man* #1, *Showcase* #4, *Tales of Suspense* #39, *Journey Into Mystery* #83, *Fantastic Four* #5, *X-Men* #1, and *Strange Tales* #110. Honestly we had our best inventory so it isn't shocking we sold some of the best books in the hobby.

Conventions this year felt farther apart which is likely because our selling side was not as busy as there was some restructuring from promoters to reduce the number of shows they put on. We absolutely love doing shows as we finally get to interact with our web-based customers who we don't see in the shop. We didn't get to all the USA shows to do our regular route this year but hopefully 2023 allows us to. One of the highlights was that we were invited to attend a show and put on a grading seminar for attendees. We discussed everything from pressing, restoration, why grading matters and just about everything in between. It was an absolute blast. Conventions seemed to be less heavily packed in terms of numbers, however it seems like more comic people were out. By no means is that a complaint with only buyers showing up and not so much the lookers. We've seen however more and more 1 day shows trying to emerge and take force. Many have struggled their first few shows to get attendees out so it will be interesting to see if the trend continues. We could be set up at a show each weekend if we tried.

With just a week away from Christmas we are looking forward to what 2023 brings. I'm excited to see what the big shocker in the comic world will be of the year. Hopefully some stability will return to all lives not just in the hobby and allow everyone to continue loving life. Yet again I've got something big planned and the wheels are in motion. It really could become a game changer if you love the hobby as much as we do. Unfortunately another year meant more Greats passing which included the legendary Neal Adams and George Pérez. Their art and stories pulled in readers and they will be missed.

Until next time, keep Protecting Protectors!

Dan Gallo
Dealer

As I sit here writing this report Christmas is only a week away and a lot can happen between now and the time you read this. This time last year I wrote about how 2021 was the best year I ever had, a sentiment that was reflected by many in the hobby. Well, times have changed…

The first half of 2022 was solid. Although the frenzy had died down there was still demand and sales were brisk. The second half was a different story. Looking back, I can see that things started to slow down after Memorial Day and by the summer things had grown very quiet. We started to see prices decrease as demand waned, most notably for Marvel Silver and Bronze Age keys.

Over the last couple of months, the question I was most frequently asked was why? Why was this happening? Until now our hobby had been virtually bulletproof, unaffected by anything internal or external impacting us in a negative way but now for the first time we saw a downtick in areas where we never thought we would. Nevertheless, the comic book market is still a market and subject to ups and downs like any other asset class. Whether it be from a substandard economy, high inflation, a volatile stock market, a crypto drop, over inflated prices, way too many auctions, poor MCU offerings, bad luck or a little bit of everything.... here we are. It's not all doom and gloom. There are still segments that are strong and performing well. Let's break it down:

Golden Age: Although not affordable for most collectors, Big Gold, (most of the books on *Overstreet*'s top 25 G.A. list), are as strong as ever. More affordable, and what I have been buying as of late, are Timelys, specifically *Captain America*, *Marvel Mystery*, *All-Winners* and *All Select*. I buy clean, well presenting, blue label copies and because they are scarce, (most under 75 copies on the census), and don't trade as much they are less volatile than Silver Age and Bronze Age. I consider them safe.

Silver Age: Marvels have been brutal; no way to sugarcoat it. The super key issues, books that we all thought were invincible proved otherwise. *Amazing Fantasy* #15 and *X-Men* #1, the two most popular books of the era, had previously experienced massive increases so naturally when things got soft, they had the furthest to fall. The other big Marvel keys all took a hit as well. That being said, they are still great books and are now more affordable so anyone who was priced out or hadn't checked that box yet now may be the time. At some point dealers will back buying things up at these lower levels, (and you know what happens next)!

For the first time in ages, I am actively looking for DC keys. I had been down on DC S.A. for years, but I am now beginning to see an uptick in activity. Because prices had been so low for so long, the slowdown that hit Marvels had little if any effect on DCs. Also, DC Studios finally appears to have some direction, so hopefully we will start getting some better content in the upcoming years which can only help with demand.

Bronze Age & Copper Age: Bronze Age Marvel keys have had a rough going as of late for all the reasons previously stated plus the fact that they are common. In a soft market, common books find their way to market more than anything else. With more availability, pricing becomes more sensitive which can lead to a race to the bottom. Same is true for the Marvel Copper Age 9.8s. For now...

Original Art: This is a segment that keeps chugging along and I bought more original art in 2022 than ever before. Collecting OA is fun and its one-of-a-kind nature acts as a buffer to random market swings. It's a great feeling when you buy a piece of original art knowing that no one else has it but you. Just buy what you like, hang it on the wall, and enjoy!

MCU: What a disappointment. All of it.

Auctions: There are way too many auctions. It seems like there's something ending every single night and one auction will end and another one will begin. Tonight, as I sit here and write this report, there are three auctions ending plus we are in the middle of a stretch that will have auctions ending in 22 of 25 nights. It's total saturation. Hey auction houses, prices are going down and part of the reason is you!

Conclusion: 2022 was a mixed bag. There was some good and there was some not so good. At some point in 2023, or beyond, the negative factors I mentioned earlier will reverse themselves. Until then one can either wait it out or take advantage of the lower prices. If neither is appealing to you...buy original art!

Food for Thought: The sports card industry is running circles around us. They come off as young, hip, and fun while our hobby comes off as just the opposite; old, dated, and set in our ways. It does not mean that we love our hobby any less but how do we grow? How can we achieve higher levels of exposure? It seems like we have no major entity that is forward thinking; not the Overstreet, not the big auction houses, not the grading companies and not the publishers. I mean, where are our influencers?? If you have high profile buyers, shouldn't you be encouraging them to go to social media to show off and promote what they bought? Sometimes it's not about the high price realized but more about who made the purchase that could move the needle. Also, why not have a current cultural icon, whether it be a musician or an athlete, in a comic book? Have a variant cover, have them signed and graded and then let them put it out across all their social media platforms? It's how we grow and expand the hobby. Just food for thought...

Stephen Gentner
Golden Age Specialist

Greetings comic collectors! Another year has passed, and it has been very tumultuous! I wanted to say at the outset how wonderful it is to have our *Price Guide*! Each year I am so honored to share my impressions with you here! It is a high honor! *The Guide* is still a very useful tool. It provides title, price, and all sorts of great information at a glance without having to lug around a laptop and flog away on the Internet! The auction results of the year and great in-depth articles also grace its pages.

This year, the inflation-rate, recession, interest rates, and "you name it" have been thrown into a cocked hat for collectors, investors, and sellers in our comic hobby! I have noted a flattening and retreat of prices in general. There are those books which will always be relatively unfazed by the madness around us, but in general the breakneck pace of appreciation we have enjoyed has waned for now. That might not be a bad thing. The balloon was getting pretty big...and we certainly don't want it to POP! The downturn in prices gives the collector an opportunity to get some very nice deals now, as dealers accept lower offers to move their stock.

I don't collect the new books anymore and haven't for

some time. I lament the woke ideology that has forced its way into our hobby. It is corrosive. Men acting like women and women acting as men...what is that? Co-opting classic characters for social change is pathological. If the cause is so wonderful, create new characters to carry that banner. Don't put boobs on Batman and tell me to like it. The canon of our heroes has been built since before WWII. The stories and characters were painstakingly crafted with great art and great writing. Editorial direction and a consistent fidelity to who the characters were made the readers look forward to each month with anticipation. Now, you wonder who is coming out of the closet or going in.

I confess there are some books I do buy that are new. Good girl covers are the best in my lifetime now. The wonderful cast of great artists grace cover and variant covers with pulchritude I would have expired over in 1963! I collect and follow Golden Age and Silver Age predominantly. I have noted that the Pre-Code Horror (PCH) segment is very hot and popular! It was also coming on strong last year as well. I had no idea of the number and variety of skulls, blood, ghosts, monsters, and brains there were out there!! EC, Harvey, Avon, and a raft of other publishers' material gets posted on Instagram! A veritable sea of horror drifts by like the Lost Souls flying by with Marley's Ghost! The enthusiasm and competition for this material continues unabated.

The higher prices that characterized Timely, DC, Fiction House, Standard/Nedor, Quality, Fox, and others stabilized lower, with keys and icon covers less affected. It is an axiom that always works ...a motivated buyer and an aloof seller spell more money. The reverse pulls the opposite direction. The number of collectors after Golden Age material has grown. The supply cannot keep up with the demand, because in real terms the supply has always been low. Paper drives, angry mothers and grandmothers, attrition, neglect, offensive content(to some) and other factors had major effects towards a low survival rate. Especially in terms of the additional exposure and prices this material draws.

In Silver Age, the supply is much more approachable in size. Books were kept in their numbers by an entire generation of collectors. Here the supply is greater, but the enormous number of collectors in this Age still push certain books high, *Amazing Fantasy* #15 in particular. I continue to always preach that you should buy books that you love. If the winds of demand change, you always have a book you love to have. Investment-only books are a cold asset, perform or not...it's going anyway. My goal has always been heart first, and head second. If the two combine, love grows in both the joy of owning and an appreciated asset. I have picked up a few books this year. Here are one book each from Gold, Silver, and Modern. I bought a *Thun'da* #1 by Frank Frazetta, an *X-Men* #50 by Jim Steranko, and a delightful modern *Archie Comics* #645 by Tim Seeley! The *Thun'da* is a revelation, and the only comic book Frazetta did all the art for! Gardner Fox wrote the story inside. The first cover appearance of Polaris is just spectacular in execution by Steranko! Tim Seeley makes Betty as naughty as I ever saw her except for her tight white sweater cover on *Archie Comics* #50!

The biggest news by FAR in my collecting this year was managing to add a major Grail to my collection!! It is the Highest Graded Copy of *Betty and Veronica* #40! I have looked for a high-grade example for years, and this CGC 8.0 copy shares the honor with only one other copy in that grade. I had to step up to secure it financially, but I have absolutely NO regrets!

I hope we have reasoned leadership this coming year to keep us all safe! Good Hunting!

TERRY HOKNES
WWW.TERRYHOKNES.COM

2021 was a record breaking year for comics and collectibles sales as many key issues actually tripled in price in a single year. Late 2022 was a reality check as most of these prices crashed back to more or less where they had been before the big jump. Feeling like a roller coaster ride you made huge profits if you were selling early but for thousands who bought at the high prices they are now crying as the prices crashed right back down again. Almost no major key was untouched by this post-Covid crash. Just like the stock market the smart thing is to buy now while prices are low again and be patient and sit on the books you bought at top dollar.

In modern comics, the trends were still focused on ratio retailer comics such as 1:50, 1:100 etc due to small print runs and sometimes amazing cover art. But many collectors feel the new market is saturated with too many covers especially comic store exclusive variant covers that rarely hold their value.

I continue to index and teach comic book history from all eras covering all genres using the *Overstreet Guide* and prices as the main sources as the greatest reference tool ever. I have used the *Overstreet Guide* every year since 1980 (when I was 9 years old!)

There are 3 main comic book series that I teach every week on my YouTube video.

a) Platinum Age (1930's comics). Learn the history of the earliest comic books in the most in depth series ever on Platinum Age and early Golden Age comics.

b) Silver, Bronze, Copper and Modern Age comics history of Marvel and DC with tips on investing

c) New Release comics - speculation and investment picks for new releases every week

You can join my YouTube to learn more about comic book history and about investing by searching YouTube for Terry Hoknes Comic Books or going to this link:

https://www.youtube.com/c/TerryHoknesComicsInvestingCollecting

There is a dedicated group of comic book collectors who help the collecting community every single day with insightful articles about comics called CBSI. I joined the team a few years ago and help promote comic book collecting. Thousands of articles are posted every year at www.comicbookinvest.com . You can also join discussions with 17,000 collectors on the CBSI Facebook group. I also publish my own series of books on comic book history and investing at www.TerryHoknes.com. I have also published 10,000 articles on comic books at my website. You can also find me at Facebook at Terry Hoknes Comics.

Congrats to Overstreet for another great year of documenting comic history and collecting info!

GREG HOLLAND
SLABDATA.COM

The CGC Census increased from 6,875,047 in December 2021 to 8,771,445 in December 2022. This 27.5% increase in a single year is evidence of the significant increase in demand and fulfillment for CGC graded comic books, exceeding the 20% increase seen between December 2020 and December 2021. *Amazing Spider-Man* #300 is still the most-submitted comic book, now at 31,535 graded copies. *Amazing Spider-Man* #361 remained in 2nd place after being 5th three years ago. *Spawn* #1 moved up to 3rd this year, and *New Mutants* #98 is now 4th. It should be noted that all four of these most-submitted comic books to CGC are dated between 1988 and 1992, corresponding with the height of comic book popularity just prior to the overproduction of 1993 and the collapse that followed.

The most submitted comic from DC Comics, *Batman: The Killing Joke* is now in 27th place overall and also dated within the 1988 to 1992 timeframe. *Batman: The Killing Joke* was in 21st place last year. The only Top 100 book by a publisher other than Marvel, DC, and Image is *Rai* #0 from Valiant Comics, also from 1992. CGC has graded over 280,000 different titles and issues, but the Top 100 most-submitted books to CGC represent 11% of CGC graded comics. One in every nine CGC slabs comes from a short list of just 100 comics (see cgcdata.com for the full list). Approximately one in every three CGC slabs contains a comic book dated 2010 to present, demonstrating a continued demand for immediate CGC grading upon publication. Only a few comic books are in both the Top 100 submitted and printed since 2010 with *Ultimate Fallout* #4, *Amazing Spider-Man* #4 (2014), *Darth Vader* #3, *Edge of Spider-Verse* #2, *Venom* #3, and *Batman* #1 (2011) as the most prominent.

CGC Census Counts by Comic Decade (as of mid-December 2022):

1930s = 10,841 (0.12%)
1940s = 196,349 (2.2%)
1950s = 213,460 (2.4%)
1960s = 1,031,070 (11.8%)
1970s = 1,169,310 (13.3%)
1980s = 1,378,930 (15.7%)
1990s = 1,137,999 (13.0%)
2000s = 764,759 (8.7%)
2010s = 1,819,896 (20.7%)
2020s = 1,042,611 (11.9%)
Others = 6,220 (0.07%) – ("Others" includes undated books)
Total = 8,771,445.

CGC "Worthiness": There are now more CGC graded comic books printed between 2020 and 2022 than there are CGC graded comic books from 1960 to 1969. Is it accurate to say that more comics printed in the last three years are "CGC Worthy" than all of the comics printed at the height of the Silver Age in the whole decade of the 1960s? I doubt many would agree with this statement. The question of CGC "Worthiness" is more complex than the counts on the CGC Census. First of all, the fees associated with CGC grading are different for recent comics versus the 1960s (or any comic pre-1975). Secondly, there are hundreds of thousands of Signature Series comics for 2020 to 2022, but less than 50,000 for the whole decades of the 1960s. While the content of the comics may not be comparable, signed recent comics satisfy a market demand which is not possible for many popular creators of the 1960s who are no longer living. A third factor is the "newness" factor. Initial demand coincides with CGC grading for comic books printed today, while CGC did not exist until at least 30 years after the initial demand for 1960s comic books. Another factor is the survival of recent comics, which are mostly purchased for protected collections, compared to 1960s comics which have had more than fifty years of reduction in survival due to discarding and damage. There are many other factors which influence whether a comic is sent to CGC for grading, but the bottom line is that there are now more CGC slabbed comics from 2020 to 2022 than all of the 1960s comic books combined.

Accidental Demand: One aspect of the market that continually pops up in my research and analysis is the concept of "accidental demand". When we look at the origins of the comic book market, it really is "accidental demand" from the start. *Action Comics* #1 and *Detective Comics* #27 were successful, but disposable products, and the demand for copies of those issues years later could not be matched by remaining supplies.

While comic books were always intended to entertain, it was a complete accident that an entire industry and market for out-of-print comic books would be created. By the time of the Silver Age, the basic concept of comic book collecting was known, but the tales of carefully cultivated Silver Age collections being thrown away by parents or teenagers deciding they were unsuitable for "grown-ups" still populate message boards today.

The first few decades of the comic book market are almost entirely the result of the "accidental demand" many years later for products which were only intended to survive a few months. It's important to note that this "accidental demand" was always in opposition to the prevailing view of the day that there was no reason to hold onto those particular comic books. By the time the market was established in spite of the majority view, it was too late to save those comics which had been discarded decades earlier.

There have been particular instances of "accidental demand" in every decade since the Silver Age. One example is the 30-cent and 35-cent cover price test markets from Marvel in 1976 and 1977. Comic book prices were increased by five cents in select geographies to determine how the sales would be impacted by the price increase. Marvel did not intend to create a limited cover price variant for the back issue market. It was accidental demand which created the price variant market, many years after the original intention of the publisher, and in spite of many retailers and collectors who would have insisted for decades that there should be no market difference for otherwise identical books.

Canadian Price Variants and U.K. pence editions of comic books are other examples of "accidental demand" decades later. It would not take a majority of collectors to desire pence or Canadian variants for the market to shift from discounts to premiums. The supply of those issues is low enough that the interest of only a few collectors could shift the market from disdain to greater demand.

It is fascinating how much "accidental demand" has changed and shaped the comic book industry. We know the same is true in other popular collectible markets, whether it was old coins being melted down, sportscards in bicycle spokes, or action figures ripped from their packaging. "Accidental demand" seems like the best description looking back, and in each and every case, the majority of people (even the experts) would have argued against collecting, protecting, and securing those items for the future. As always, collect what you enjoy, and if some (experts) insist that your favorite collectible isn't anything special, see if they'll sell you all of theirs at a discount. Odds are, those frequent discouragers don't even have any of what you want, but they may have several variant comics from the past three years in CGC slabs as an alternative. Time will tell which collectibles would have been better choices.

STEVEN HOUSTON & JOHN DOLMAYAN TORPEDO COMICS

STEVEN HOUSTON

Greetings from Torpedo Comics in Las Vegas. Since the publication of last year's *Overstreet Guide,* the industry has witnessed a massive explosion of creative activity from Marvel Comics and the MCU, while DC Comics/Time Warner has struggled.

As if to finally announce to the world that the Covid pandemic was over, the entertainment industry unleashed project after project, be it from the *Star Wars* franchise, the world of super-heroes or even fantasy, via a return to the world of *The Lord of the Rings*. As for the aftereffects of the pandemic, shortly after the last year's *Guide*, the virus began to lose steam as new variants of Covid proved less deadly and the government and major corporations began to ease their Covid restrictions. However, the effects of Covid did not disappear overnight, in fact, as witnessed by the rather lackluster customer count at our store. We had some signings, but the customer count was way down as fear proved to be a powerful enemy to sales. After the lockdowns and major restrictions were removed, our customer count was down 75% from pre-pandemic levels. It has slowly increased, but if not for our aggressive online sales campaigns, we may have had to close the store. As of thiswriting, I have good news. We just did a signing with Jim Lee and the attendance level was much better and only a small minority wore masks. We may have turned the corner here in regards to Covid and the fear it caused.

As for comic book content, the industry has seen an unprecedented release of super-hero television and movie related material, with each show causing a knock-on effect of speculator driven sales. Shortly after the publication of the last *Guide* in 2021, the *What If?* animated series exploded across fandom, sending speculators off in search of the first appearance of The Watcher in *Fantastic Four* #13. Regarding the Fantastic Four, rumors ran rampant regarding both the Sub-Mariner and Doctor Doom as word spread that the *Fantastic Four* movie franchise was coming to the MCU. *Fantastic Four* #4 and #5 exploded in demand, especially in the lower to mid-grades. Word also spread that Namor could appear in the second *Black Panther* movie, driving up demand even further. As we moved into the fall of 2021, two Marvel movies were close to being released, both *Shang-Chi and the Legend of the Ten Rings* (September) and *Venom: Let There be Carnage* (October) caused reverberations thru fandom as the first appearance of Shang-Chi in *Special Marvel Edition* #15 peaked in 9.8 at $18,000!! Just for reference, the current going price of a 9.8 at time of writing is $7,500 – a lesson to be learned here for sure. As for the second *Venom* movie, sales of *Amazing Spider-Man* #361 peaked at $1,450 for a 9.8. Again, as of writing the price of a 9.8 has collapsed, with current prices being in the $350 range!!

Before continuing on with raw data and sales, I want to take a moment to discuss the current state of the collecting world. As you can see by the results of the aforementioned collapsing sales of Shang-Chi and Carnage, we are currently caught in a loop of rampant speculation leading to exploding and sometimes insane prices, followed by the inevitable crash and burn. This leads us to ask some pretty tough questions. Who are purchasing these issues? What percentage are pure flippers with no actual love for comics, opposed to fans who actually read the current product. Even more controversial, can it be that after nearly twenty years of the best super-hero exposure to the masses, readership of comics is actually down? Can it be that the market is filled with 'spec hunters' who follow the numerous online comic sites that scream about the next hot book? Contemporary comic readership has fallen by the wayside as the major two publishers seemingly follow a business plan to appeal to the smallest minority amongst us. Some of these questions are open to rabid debate to be sure, but what is not in doubt, is the fact that the big two, Marvel and DC seem to have forgotten their audiences and sneer at any suggestion they are moving in the wrong direction.

Let's talk about DC Comics for a moment. A tale of woe to be sure. The Arrowverse on the CW continued with *Arrow*, *Flash*, *Supergirl*, *Legends of Tomorrow*, *Black Lightning* and the controversial *Batwoman* culminating in the "Armageddon" crossover event of November 2021. As for any effect on DC Comics sales – ziltch – nothing! Even with *Stargirl*, *Doom Patrol*, *Swamp Thing*, *Lucifer* and *Titans* adding to the Warner Brothers DC character onslaught, we at Torpedo were unable to discern any effect on sales. That's including the addition of the Zack Snyder version of the Justice League. Silver Age DC sales are abysmal with only Batman selling at all, and only keys at that. Lower grade *Batman* and *Detective*s had to be discounted to get them to move. These dismal sales continued on into the Bronze Age, with only the super-keys moving such as Joker appearances and Neal Adams books. Even the Neal Adams' *Green Lantern*s died off, with only issue #76 garnering any attention. Update as of today, with the announcement that we are to get a John Stewart Green Lantern live action show, *Green Lantern* #87 has exploded! Same old story!!! In March of 2022, the long-awaited *Batman* movie featuring Robert Pattinson arrived to mixed reviews but first appearances for the Riddler and the Penguin, were not even asked for by customers. As for critical acclaim, *The Sandman* series, released in August of 2022 did have an impact on the Sandman's 1990s run, but nothing extraordinary. DC finished off the year with *Black Adam* (October 2022), The Rock's passion project finally seeing the light of day after years of development hell. The result? Mixed reviews and absolutely no interest in Black Adam's various comic appearances! There is much to say about DC's current editorial policy, but space does not permit that here. Rather, let it be known here, in all my years working in the comic book industry, I have never seen such fan apathy towards DC Comics product. If it's not Batman, it's dead.

As for Marvel and the MCU, it was time for Disney to take a gamble. *The Eternals* movie was released in November of 2021, a gamble indeed as there was no "civilian" knowledge of who or what these characters were. Marvel had to unleash a full advertising campaign so that people could get to know or at least be intrigued by these cosmic themed characters. The sales of *Eternals* issues from the 1970's had been strong for a year with 9.8 copies of issue #1 peaking at an astounding $2,300! Current prices for this book are at $600. In fact, once the movie was released and comic fans realized that the movie bore no relation to Jack Kirby's vision of the characters, sales across the board on *Eternals* died. The film did a reasonable $400 million at the box office, so when one takes into consideration the fact that this was an unknown franchise, Marvel dodged a bullet here. Marvel forged ahead into late 2021 with the massively successful *Spider-Man: No Way Home* movie, featuring a host of villains and all three versions of Peter Parker. With a box office of almost two billion dollars, this was the super-hero event of 2021, however to be fair, we at Torpedo saw no knock-on sales with the comics or trade paperbacks due to the movie. On a personal note, this was a very enjoyable movie, and showcased what can happen when good writers do not stray too far from the source material. Marvel finished out 2021 with the live action *Hawkeye* series on Disney Plus. Fan reaction was positive with the breakout star being Hawkeye's apprentice, Kate Bishop. Her first appearance in *Young Avengers* #1 (2005) peaked in 2021 at $900 for a 9.8, but even today, with the financial situation being a lot harsher, a 9.8 will still run you approximately $500.

As the industry forged into 2022, fandom was ablaze with 'specs', as the online community overflowed, hour by hour news of the hot books to look for. The hottest being *Werewolf by Night* #32 – the first appearance of Moon Knight. The *Moon Knight* series was slated for release in March and that book was flying, in any condition into collectors and flippers hands. I was very fortunate to film an episode with *Pawn Stars* where a young non-collector came to the show trying to sell as astonishing CGC 9.8 *Werewolf by Night* #32. I valued the book at the time at $50,000 but the book scared the Pawn Stars crew, the main problem being no 'name recognition' with Moon Knight! A 9.8 copy did indeed sell for $70,500 not long after the show, but as of today, the price has dropped to about $42,000. It was about this time that Marvel's entire monster and supernatural character library received intense collector activity, including fans hunting down any copy they could find of *Savage Tales* #1 – the first appearance of the Man-Thing. *Strange Tales* #169 – the first Brother Voodoo, *Marvel Premiere* #28 – the Legion of Monsters and of course, returning back into the fray, *Tomb of Dracula* #10, the first Blade. The new Blade movie had been announced and his first appearance exploded again, with a 9.8 copy selling for an incredible $40,000. In fact, sales have not dipped as we speak, with copies still at the $32,000 mark in 9.8. The other Marvel monster to get to some speculator activity was Morbius, the Living Vampire with the movie set to be released in April. However, his first appearance in *Amazing Spider-Man* #101 did not explode in value but in 9.8 this book has held its value, with a sale recently of $26,400. Lower grades have dropped off, but experienced collectors know just how tough this book is to find in a 9.8 condition. Interestingly, Morbius' other appearances in *Fear* #20-32 did see an increase in collector demand, however, all demand faded away when the movie was released to a disappointing $163 million box office. Perhaps the most surprising monster to get some collector activity was the

Robert E. Howard creation, Shuma-Gorath, originating from *Marvel Premiere* #10, a character that appeared in the previews for the second *Doctor Strange* movie, *In the Multiverse of Madness*, released in May. What is fascinating about this book is the fact that no 9.8 copies have been sold since 2020. A 9.6 copy recently sold for $2,000! While lower grades have dropped in value, it's information like this which reveals just how scarce super-high-grade comics can be.

With spec hunters unable to catch a proverbial breath, more comic tips begin to explode across social media, the strangest being perhaps the speculation that a on-set photo of Thor in a jacket was proof that he was going to appear as 'Thunderstrike' – a Thor type character from the early 1990s. Spec hunters could not resist and within hours, copies of *Thunderstrike* #1 were flying off eBay and out of stores! At the peak of the 'madness' a 9.8 copy sold for $175, but as time has progressed, cooler heads have proven that the spec hunters were way off, the current 9.8 price is about $40. The *Love and Thunder* Thor movie did have an effect on a few key modern books, with collectors and flippers hunting down the first appearance of Jane Foster as Thor from her issue #1 in 2014. This book was selling for over $500 at the height of the speculation on this book, but as with most other books in the current market, a 9.8 copy will cost you about $120 at this time. Spec hunters were also quick to jump on the first actual appearance of a female Thor from *What If* Vol.1 #10, with a 9.8 selling for the high of $2,150!! Incredible, for a book that was $10 in 9.2 for years. The main villain of the movie, Gorr, the God Butcher's first appearance from *Thor: God of Thunder* #2 was blazing hot since 2020, with a sale of $800, but as we moved into 2021 the price leveled off to about $600 and then after the movie, $120!!!!!! If there is any better example of the modern speculator filled comic world than this book, I've yet to see it.

The *Moon Knight* Disney Plus series debuted in May to critical acclaim and although the price of the book has cooled off, this book is an exception, being that it was always hard to find in high grade and as of writing is still one of the industry's hot books. The other live action television series to appear in August was *She-Hulk: Attorney at Law*. Spec hunters were grabbing as many 9.8 copies of *Savage She-Hulk* #1 from 1980, as possible. However, unlike *Werewolf by Night* #32, where copies were scarce, the She-Hulk issue was plentiful as seemingly, week after week dealers were finding, 10,20 or 30 copies at a time. Demand was so high at one point that a CGC 9.8 copy sold for $2,307 – the speculator market had gone insane and when more and more copies began to appear, 'out of the woodwork', the price began to drop. Then we got the first previews of the series and the book dropped again and finally after a fan backlash against the actual series, 9.8 copies dropped under $400. Instead of cooling the insatiable speculation desire, hunters simply moved on to new targets. Fandom was ablaze with the *Werewolf by Night* television special, keeping the prices of Man-Thing appearances high. *Savage Tales* #1 went from $4,000 in 9.8 in 2020, to an astonishing $37,200 in late 2021. Again, this is an example of a serious lack of high-grade copies being out there. Demand was high and remains high as of writing, leading to collectors seeking out other Man-Thing appearances such as *Astonishing Tales* #12 (his second appearance) which was listed at $100 in 9.2, but blew up to $1,795 in CGC 9.4. Interestingly enough, the last 9.8 sale was back in 2006! His third appearance in *Astonishing Tales* #13 also exploded, with a 9.8 copy selling for $1,960. *Fear* #10 (his 4th appearance and beginning of his solo series) saw a 9.8 selling for $3,120 in May 2022 and finally, *Man-Thing* #1 (1974) hit a stratospheric $3,840 in 2021 in CGC 9.8. The price on this issue has cooled, just as everything has cooled off in the last five months, but a 9.8 copy recently sold for $2,160. Pretty impressive, considering the *Overstreet* listed this book in 9.2 at $145. Perhaps the book with the biggest price increase per percentage was *Bloodstone* #1 from the 2001 four issue limited series. The first issue introduced Elsa Bloodstone, formally a book found in dollar bins at shows or stores suddenly became a spec hunter book, with rumors abound that she would be appearing in the MCU. Speculation hit its peak in early 2022, with a 9.8 copy selling for over $1,000! Yes, incredible as it may seem, a book that could be found in dollar bins was now $1,000 in high grade. Prices have calmed down, but this book will never be a dollar again, as Elsa did in fact appear in the *Werewolf by Night* television special. Current 9.8 prices are around the $400 range.

As of writing the *Wakanda Forever* movie has just been released and we finally got to see Namor on the big screen, however, Marvel decided to change the origin of the character, moving far away from the comic book origin. While 'civilians' who have no idea about Namor have been happy, comic fans less so. As for sales of key Namor appearances, the Golden Age first appearance was not affected at all, with the price already being out of the range of 99.9% of collectors. Even the first Silver Age appearance did not change much in the 9.2 or 9.4 ranges, however, the real heat on this book took place in the lower grades. Most collectors who were endeavoring to put together a full set of *Fantastic Four,* or at least a specific range, be it, #1-25, #1-50 or #1-100, usually had to deal with 2.0 or 3.0 grades for most of those early copies. Issue #4 with Namor was an easy $1,000 in raw good (2.0), $1,800 in 3.0 and $2,000 in 4.0, but when rumors of Namor's appearance in the MCU began to heat up, in came the speculators and those prices were left in the dust. Very quickly, a 4.0 CGC copy sold for $6,100, even a 2.0 hit $3,799! For some context, back in 2019, years before rumors of a big screen appearance an amazing 9.6 CGC copy sold for $81,000. Similar to the situation with Doctor Strange, when *Strange Tales* #110 was deemed out of reach by normal collectors, the heat fell on *Doctor Strange* #169. With Namor, the heat fell upon *Sub-Mariner* #1 from 1968. This was always an affordable key, with CGC 9.2 selling in 2020 for a maximum of $1,438, then in 2021 this book hit $3,050, however in December of 2022, as this report is being written, a 9.2 can be had for about $1,480. For some context, a 9.8 copy recently sold for $15,600, down from $19,950.

As one can see from the above information, speculators and flippers hold sway over the industry with prices exploding and crashing all year. But what of the immediate future? What's the next big thing? Well, as I write this report in December of 2022, the spec hunters have already been busy trying to get ahead of the curve, studying the upcoming slate of movies and television series that are planned not only for 2023, but also 2024. The MCU phase five and six are being scrutinized and online comic book 'influencers' are already pushing the next big thing. Disney Plus apparently has plans for a number of new series, including *What If?* season two, *Echo*, *Loki* season two, *Ironheart*, *X-Men '97*, *Agatha: Coven of Chaos*, *Daredevil: Born Again* and *Spider-Man: Freshman Year*. From the aforementioned series, the speculator heat was on the first Echo from *Daredevil* Vol. 2 #9 (1999) which peaked at an incredible $1,800 in CGC 9.8 back in 2021 and Ironheart from *Iron Man* (Vol. 3 #7, 2016) which peaked at $658 in 2021. Incredibly a 9.8 copy of the first Echo appearance just sold for $185! Obviously, market conditions are tough out there right now with inflation and other financial stress throughout the world, but how can one explain such a dramatic crash in price? As for the first Ironheart, the current going price ranges in the $100-150 range for a 9.8, while her first full appearance in *Iron Man* Vol. 4 #9 peaked at $1,000 in 2021 and is now down to $221 in 9.8. As for *Daredevil* Born Again, issues #227-233 are already moving on eBay. Issue #227 started 2022 with a bang as news first filtered out about the potential TV series. A 9.8 copy sold for $635, however as we get close to 2023, this issue has also crashed down to $175 for a 9.8. In conclusion, when taken in its entirety, one can see that the current speculation time period for issues, is a one-month window of maximizing your 'investments', as speculation heats up to boiling point and online 'collectors' make desperate purchases in the hope of not missing out. Then as time moves on and even if the character that has been invested in, is confirmed to have an upcoming MCU appearance, more and more copies get graded (for modern issues) everyone realizes that copies are plentiful and the price crashes.

To conclude this year's report, I feel I must clear the air. As a dealer who has been in the business since 1993, I've seen my fair share of ups and downs, but never before have I felt such trepidation regarding the industry's future. Our industry has NEVER received so much public advertising, with the world of super-heroes going through a proverbial Golden Age of exposure, ever since the first *Iron Man* movie. Massive movie after massive movie has shaken Hollywood to its core, as the MCU and to a lesser degree the DCU, have garnered billions upon billions of dollars for all concerned. However, it's my sad duty to report, as I write this report in December 2022, I can see no discernable increase in comic book readership. Print runs on 99.9% of all published (American) comics are embarrassingly low. Manga sales have been skyrocketing while the traditional American super-hero comic is dying on the vine. How can this be? How can classic American super-heroes that are seen on millions of people's televisions every day, be struggling to sell on new issue day? First, one has to look at the marketing departments of the big two, both companies guilty of rampant rebooting, with new issue #1s and its hundreds of variants being followed a few years later by another #1 issue, with the same greedy marketing ploy to drag any money out of collectors wallets with a new set of variants, be it 1/10, 1/50, 1/100 or even 1/5000!! Creative teams can't seem to stay on books anymore, so a brand-new issue #1 boasting a super-star creative team maybe has six issues in them, before they are done and a lackluster team takes over, causing sales to drop, which leads to a reboot and a whole new set of number #1 issues! Perhaps the most dangerous aspect of the modern super-hero world, is the hiring of a new generation of creators who actually do not like the subject matter they are working with. Some of these new 'star' creators openly state that they are not here to add to the wonderment of either the DC or Marvel Universes, but rather fix certain 'wrongs', to tear down characters with perceived biases and rebuild them for the new era. The result has been a falling away of any older readers, sending them off to trade paperback or omnibus land, to reread 'classic' stories of the past, while appealing to a minority of readers with heavy handed sermons. This is killing readership, leaving only speculators or to use the current term, 'flippers' left, with their incessant need to locate cheap books that will go up in price when an appearance in the MCU is announced. Manga comics have mostly been able to avoid all this self-administered judging, seeking to entertain and use comics as a pure escapist medium – thus huge sales in a supposedly dead market. And yet, with every new creator or editor breaking into the big two, the same self-recrimination and worst of all, the looking down on readers, especially the older readership, for apparently not reading the 'correct' comic stories all these years runs rampant. The only way either company is going to pull the money out of older readers' wallets these days is with reprint material, high-priced omnibus or deluxe hardcover editions of 'classic' material, that new creators seek to tear down in contemporary comics. It seems that editorial of both big two companies have decided that low sales are okay, as long as their pure message is being published. I'm 55-years old and I don't know any of my ilk who are reading anything from the big two, having moved onto reprints and the odd independent comic. We have the money to purchase almost every monthly book we want, we just can't find anything remotely similar to what we read in the 1990s or 1980s. Apparently, the people in charge have decided that they would rather sell one copy of a given title per month as long as it goes along with their beliefs and makes them sleep well at night. In the meantime, comic store owners are fighting for their lives out here.

This has been a rather dour report in many ways. I'm trying to think of positives, but facts don't care about feelings. Some hard decisions have to be made about the creative method of modern American super-hero comics, or we are going to lose an entire generation of readers during our supposed 'Golden Age' of super-hero exposure.

Robert Isaac
Red Hood Comics

Last year I had predicted that the market would continue to thrive. Even with the Marvel movies serving as catalysts to growing interest and investment in the hobby, I did NOT predict that the quality of the films based on our beloved characters would reduce so drastically to poor storytelling, pushed by woke agendas. We all knew the financial influx would eventually stabilize either back to what it was before the pandemic or plateau at a higher level than it used to be. I feel that both of these factors have caused many comic values to drop during the final months of the year, with drastic reductions from the high numbers they were commanding previously.

The Collector's Summit: Conventions have done well throughout most of the year, although we had less people in attendance at most shows. San Diego Comic-Con definitely had the highest sales over all other shows I exhibited. The Collector's Summit in Bellevue, WA and then again at the Heritage offices in Dallas, TX, I feel were the best two shows of the year for comic collectors and dealers. Strictly comic book shows, these two events showcased rooms packed full of high-dollar books and lots of rare Golden Age gems. These were the first shows put on by my friend Nathan Howerton, and he knocked it out of the park with the feedback from collectors, customers and dealers all the same. I know many are looking forward to the next in the series of Collector's Summit shows to come, and I know that I'll be at every one of them.

Shortboxed: There is a rising power in our hobby of comic book collecting and selling, and it's called Shortboxed – a company founded by my friends Gene Miguel and BJ Abordo. Their app, available for download for iOS & Android through the Apple and Google Play stores, allows users to shop THOUSANDS of books simply from their mobile device and make offers on any books available. For sellers, all you do is take a front and back picture of your graded book or upload existing images you may have previously scanned, etc. and the app will provide the information of the book on its own and just ask you for an asking price to list. It's such a smooth, seamless process that's been LONG overdue in the community when it comes to selling comics online. I've had several notable sales through their app, including a *Crow* (1989) #1 CGC 9.8 with White Pages for $20,000 and a *Detective Comics* #298 CGC 9.0 with White Pages for $7,000.

The Auction Houses: Auction house sales have been quite interesting throughout the year as well, I picked up a *Chamber of Chills* #19 in a 9.2 grade for $50,000 in January to see it re-sell ten months later in a November auction for $72,000. I picked up a *Tales from the Crypt* #46 File Copy graded at a 9.4 in San Diego, the same copy that sold earlier in the year on Heritage for $9,000 re-sell on ComicConnect for $21,000! Golden Age Pre-Code Horror seemed to be untouched by the dropping values in the market of most Silver Age, Bronze Age and Modern books the same, due to their scarcity in high grades and availability. My favorite book, the highest-graded copy of *Detective Comics* #168 featuring the origin of the Joker as the Red Hood, a 9.4 copy, sold on Heritage for $324,000. Unfortunately for me, I was out of the auction around the $250,000 mark. I did, however, pick up one of Jack Nicholson's suits from his iconic Joker performance in the 1989 *Batman* film for $125,000, a sale that made CNN and several other news stations, and then more recently I purchased one of Cesar Romero's Joker suits from the classic 1966 *Batman* television series for $87,000.

Dr. Steven Kahn
Inner Child Comics and Collectibles

What Happened?: Ladies and gentlemen and children of all ages, welcome to the New World where comics had sprouted wings, soared to new heights, and then lost them and crashed to earth. After rising to levels never seen before, harsh reality struck and we saw the end of the Covid era of "Comics on Steroids."

Before that, each week you needed only to visit your tracking site of choice or pick your favorite YouTube host to see or hear of records toppling, one after another. At Key Collector Comics, the requirement to break into the weekly top 10 listing was that there had to have been 3 record breaking prices achieved in at least 3 different grades and the list was bursting each week (hard to even remotely imagine that today). It seemed that the sky was the limit and that the smart collector could do no wrong.

Record breaking patterns extended deeply into sportscards, video games and coin markets as well. When Collector's Universe (now called Collectors) began grading the future Beanie Babies of our time, Funko Pops, their prices soared as well.

YouTube hosts bordered on maniacal as they trumpeted each shattered record. Forbes updated its article on Collectors, the aforementioned sportscard, coin and video game grading behemoth, and noted that the value of the company soared from just under one billion dollars to to over four billion in just a little over a year.

However, once you went beyond the hottest collectibles,

a different picture emerged. The record gains largely resided in specific sectors and sub-sectors and other collectibles languished. There were essentially no positive changes seen in the 'cold' collectible markets. With comics, all the action was focused on Key comics. The vast majority of comic titles and individual comics, which I have sorted out in detail in previous reports, remained on life support.

Why Did It Happen?: As a collector for nearly 7 decades, this felt unpleasantly familiar. I was taken back to the early 1990s, when over saturation of new product in almost all areas of Pop Culture collecting led to a global crash across the board. After nearly three decades, this has yet to fully recover.

How bad was that crash? In the comic book market, it led to the bankruptcy of many publishers and a shaking out of every aspect of comic collecting that still lingers today. For those who were not around at that time, I can cite just one example that tells it all.

Marvel had overproduced and mis-managed product and distribution in an attempt to take advantage of collector mania and monopolize the broader market. This ultimately drove them to self destruction. Marvel, which included everything that we now know of as The Marvel Universe, had been bought just 7 years earlier for a mere $82 million and yet in December, 1996, their mistakes forced them to declare bankruptcy. In addition to that, more than 4,000 brick and mortar comic book stores disappeared. Primarily caused by greed cut from a wide swath that included publishers, dealers and collectors, the resulting bloodbath caused both new and old collectors to leave their hobbies in droves.

Where Are We Now?: Now that we have some historical perspective, we can fast track to where we stand today. Before going into the weeds and to also provide background, monitoring sales of graded comics has never been easier due to the presence of services such as GoCollect and GPA. If you merely examine their charts for any book covering a variety of grades, trends easily come into focus. Any collector who subscribes to these services can now have the tools to make important collecting decisions with greater confidence.

If we look at books such as *Amazing Fantasy* #15, early Spider-Man keys and important key first appearances as well as *Giant-Size X-Men* #1 and *Hulk* #181s, we can see that they have all exhibited similar patterns. These books had sharp growth, starting with the Covid lockdown, followed by an unprecedented spike in the late Spring of 2021. This was followed by a drop that has yet to stop as I am submitting this report (12/2022).

The rare exceptions were a small number of the highest graded or super keys (see below), generally associated with extremely low population counts and high demand. Also included were iconic key covers such as Horror, Joker covers, etc., which shared this high demand and short supply.

Almost all graded Silver and Bronze keys are down from between 30 to 50 per cent as people finally realized that these books were not rare at all. The only books that proved to be bulletproof were the Crème de la Crème. It applied to the rarest of the rare, and always associated with unrelenting demand. *Amazing Fantasy* #15 in 9.0 and above did not suffer. Books like *Action* #1, *Batman* #1, *Superman* #1 or *Detective* #27 were immune as well. However, the formerly blue chip Bronze keys, like *Giant-Size X-Men* #1 in say 9.8, or even *Amazing Fantasy* #15 in grades 4.0 and below were off nearly 40 percent or more. Finally, the speculative market, based on characters being placed in upcoming TV series and movies, suffered even steeper declines.

How bad was the drop in the speculative market? Would you believe 80 percent and more! To cite just one example, *Eternals* #1 in 9.8 peaked at nearly $4000 when its movie was about to be released. Last week I saw a copy go for under $600. Examples such as that are evident everywhere.

As I have noted in previous Overstreet reports, I believe that certain auction houses' greed has contributed to this problem and resulted in high population key books being constantly available in virtually any grade almost all the time.

For example, if I had submitted a copy of *Hulk* #181 in 7.0 for auction, I might later visit the auction site only to find 6 or more copies listed next to me with grades between 5.0 and 8.5 and become very upset as I saw my book fall through the cracks. Please remember that when you submit books for auction, you generally lose any control as to how, where or when they will be listed.

It evokes memories of when eBay and internet selling originally began to gain steam, that people rushed towards collectibles like there was no tomorrow. When they ultimately discovered that most of it was always there, prices dropped dramatically.

What's Next?: So where do I think we will be when you are reading this in the Summer of 2023, when this report is 'hot off the presses'? I believe the market in the important keys will be moving sideways for the most part. Newer books will have fallen even more than they already have. Dealers will suddenly have more key books on their walls as the sell-off will continue. Bargains may still be hard to find unless you find people who are truly liquidating. However, I do not believe that prices will approach the pre-Covid levels. Even as many speculators will have left the hobby, the influx of new collectors over the last several years will still support prices.

In Closing: As always, I am eager to give advice or just share stories with any fellow collector virtually 365 days a year. Just call me at 847-971-1223 or email at Stevenkahn47@gmail.com. I will be delighted to help you in any way I can. Also, look for my profile on this season's METV's 'The Collectors Call', which may give you a better idea of the breadth of my collecting passion. My episode should be available by the time this report is in print.

I continue to search for an almost unlimited variety of Pop Culture collectibles to ultimately share with others and I am always buying to curate and save these great relics of our childhoods. I would love to hear from any of you in that regard as well.

In closing, my advice remains unchanged from every Overstreet report I have written. If you love collecting, you cannot lose if you continue to fill your passion. Prices may rise and fall, but it has never driven me. It has only limited me.

There is nothing more exciting than finding a treasured book or figure or toy in a little higher grade than you've ever had before. And finding a missing grail is exciting beyond description. I still come to my store every day with the hope that something new and exciting will fall into my hands. I want to add another brick to help build my museum. It is wonderful to dream and dreams can become manifestations and is one of the great joys of life. Finally, I hope to see or hear from you this year and share the blessing of good health and spirits. Inshallah!

Nick Katradis
Collector

As I sit in front of my computer a few days before Christmas 2022, I am once again stunned by the prices achieved by original comic art. In the January 2022 Heritage auction, the year started with a sale of a Mike Zeck *Secret Wars* #8 page of Spidey, which sold for an astounding $3,360,000. A panel page - let that sink in for a while!

Then in June 2022, Heritage sold the cover to *Batman: The Dark Knight* #1 for $2,400,000. What can I say, these absurd prices have now become commonplace in the movie-fueled world of comic art.

We all believed that after the world pandemic ended, that the market would settle down, especially as the Federal Reserve has now started tapering and is increasing interest rates at a furious pace to stave off double digit worldwide inflation. That has hardly been the case. As more and more people begin to go back to the workplace, after working from home for two years, the anticipated slowdown in price inflation of comic art has not materialized.

The once called "hobby" of comic art has now truly become an asset class to many, attracting speculators and "investors" into the once Geek-populated hobby. I personally know a few collectors that quit their jobs in the financial industry to devote their full time to buying and selling comic art, comics, and sports cards. Whether this signals a price plateau and a potential decline in prices, only time will tell. For true collectors, it is a dark time as most are priced out of buying the comic art they coveted for so many years.

A few more notable sales, were the Captain America *Tales of Suspense* #59 splash, which sold for an incredible $630,000 in April 2022. Most of these earth-shattering price results all occurred on Heritage featured auctions over the year. And being located in Texas, where "shill bidding" may not be illegal, who knows if there is any manipulation going on. I have noticed that some of this top tier art has been shopped privately at fraction of the prices realized at auction and many have gone unsold. Until they hit the auction route.

But I'm no conspiracy theorist and since I'm fully invested in this hobby as a top Bronze Age collector, I do want to believe that these prices are all legit. After all, as we all age and realize our own mortality, going forward we will all consider whether or when we sell some or most of our collections in our lifetimes.

There were a few trends that I have noticed this year. First, the past few years have been mostly "give me Marvel," as most of the highest comic art prices realized have been Marvel art. A few Top Tier DC comic art has achieved very high prices but in comparison to Marvel sales, they are inept at best.

Aside from the *Dark Knight* #1 sale, another notable DC top tier sale was the Jim Lee *Batman* #619 triple-gate cover, which sold for $504,000. And just a few weeks ago, the George Pérez *Justice League of America* #195 cover sold for a shocking $288,000. A cover from 1981 that many collectors felt would not even crack the six figure barrier.

Two more sales in 2022 that should be noted were: The *Amazing Spider-Man* #16 cover by Todd McFarlane sold in June 2022 for $408,000; and the cover to *Defenders* #1, by Sal Buscema, sold for $288,000 in January 2022. The *Defenders* #1 cover was especially dear to me as I am a huge Sal Buscema collector and I thought I would have a shot at landing it at $100-125K, which would have been 3-4 times the highest price I have ever bid for any other piece in my collection.

I watched it cross 100k early and I did not even bid on it. The sad reality is that most of us old time collectors can't even fathom bidding that high, even if we can afford to.

As I finish my market report, I venture to believe that the price escalation of comic art has not hit its zenith yet. I feel that a lot of new money has entered the hobby in the past few years. Many are speculators, but many are new collectors that branched out from collecting comics. It's a natural progression for many high-end collectors of comics to begin to purchase comic art. As the prices of graded comics have skyrocketed since 2019, many CGC collectors have sold part of their comics and used the "house money" to buy comic art. Since these new collectors don't have any price points for comic art, and there is no price guide for comic art, to them these prices might seem fair since they watched comics sell for seven figures for years.

To put this scenario in a more easily understood frame of reference, I will site an example with real estate in my neighborhood. A neighbor of mine in Tenafly, New Jersey bought an overpriced home nearby a few years ago. and even though I felt he over paid by $500k at the time, he felt otherwise. He sold a 2,000 sq. ft. co-op in Manhattan for $2.5m and bought a one acre 9,000 sq. ft. house for roughly the same price. He felt the exchange was awesome for him.

By the same comparison, a collector of CGC comics that sold his comics recently for seven figures, which were only worth $100K 4-5 years ago, might feel he is getting a bargain buying a few grail comic art covers for the same price. His frame of reference is different than a comic art collector that has witnessed fractional prices for that art. To a seasoned veteran comic art collector, an overpriced piece of art is overpriced strictly because he could have bought it for a fraction of that price only a few years prior. But when you remove that price reference, the new collector may feel he is getting a bargain.

In summary, to fellow collectors that always ask if this is the top, I say "prices will continue to go up, until they don't". And nobody can time the stock market, the real estate market, or the comic art market. Nuff, said!

Ivan Kocmarek
Collector

The huge Grodd Gorilla in the room, of course, is the massive price correction that most Silver Age and later books, especially slabbed copies, suffered this past year after soaring in the spring of 2021. Golden Age books, probably due to their relative scarcity when compared with post-1960 comics, seemed to suffer less so. Canadian 1940s books (WECA comics that appeared from 1941-46 and FECA or Canadian reprints of American comics that appeared from about 1948-53) are even scarcer in general than American Golden Age books (you are still hard pressed to find more than 10 copies of any WECA book in the CGC Census) seemed to hold solid worth points. This year, however, seemed to have the fewest WECA books come to market than any year I can remember—again, probably a function of their scarcity.

You'll see dozens of copies of *Hulk* #181 and multiple copies of just about any Marvel Key at most modern-day cons but try to find a Canadian war time book at one of them. Because of this, collectors of these old Canadian books tend to pick them up whenever they come across them because they're afraid that they might not see another copy for a long time, if ever. Scarcity seems to add a patina of recession proofness to comics and I think that's what we saw with recorded sales of Canadian comics from the forties.

As I said, there weren't many recorded sales of WECA books this past year, but those that happened showed that prices of these books certainly weren't in anyway on the decline. Here is a list of the top ten WECA books that I found were sold online in 2022.

Title	Grade	Sale Price
Better Comics Vol. 1 #1	5.5	$18,100
Super Comics nn (Citren)	5.5	$13,200
Three Ring Comics #3	3.0	$3,060
Wow Comics #16	6.5	$2,677
Captain Marvel Comics Vol 1 #2	7.0	$1,876
Triumph Comics #12	3.5	$1,525
Super Comics Vol. 2 #5	5.5	$1,302.77
Triumph Comics #17	3.0	$1,125
Joke Comics #12	5.0	$867
Wow Comics #10(#11)	6.5	$865

Better Comics Vol. 1 #1 (March 1941) is the first ever floppy style Canadian comic and this was the first time one of these (there are a half dozen known copies) has come to market. The price of $18,100 USD is the new highest price achieved by a Canadian war time comic book. The Citren *Super Comics* contains the first Archie story and reprints the Shield cover from *Pep Comics* #22 but alters his costume to depict the Union Jack rather than the Stars and Stripes. A 4.0 Qualified copy sold in 2021 for $1700. GPA doesn't track sales of Canadian comics from the 1940s and any sales are few and irregular so it's difficult to compare previous sales. The *Three Rings Comics* #3 has this same Shield cover but contains only funny animal American reprints so, in my estimation, overachieved in that final sale price. However, I can say that the prices for all of the comics on the above list reflect a healthy and even robust WECA comic market that can only see its sales prices continue to rise.

For me one of the big surprises of the past year has been the growth in values realized by FECA books (those books that appeared during the second ban on American comics from 1947 to the early 1950s) when, this time, the Canadian government allowed the reprinting of American comics from plates that were sent up from below the border. These Canadian editions often contained fewer pages than their American counterparts, sometimes they were right out mash ups of American books and they are all invariably scarcer than the American books they sourced.

Here is a list of the leading sales, this past year, of 20 books from this reprint period during the late 1940s and early 1950s.

Title	Grade	Sale Price
Super Duper Comics #3	9.2	$13,200.00
Sun Girl #1	8.0	$8,075.00
Manhunt #12	2.5	$5,280.00
Unusual Comics #6	6.5	$3,100.00
Three Ring Comics #3	3.0	$3,060.00
Red Seal Comics #30	6.0	$2,880.00
Weird Science #12 (#1)	7.5	$2,640.00
Vault of Horror #12 R (slight)	7.0	$2,640.00
Venus #1	8.0	$2,520.00
4-Most #22 BB cover	5.0	$1,800.00
Mad #1	4.0	$1,680.00
Tales from the Crypt #24	raw	$1,301.88
Vault of Horror #13	6.5	$960.00

Weird Fantasy #13 (#1)	6.0	$960.00
Colossal Comics #5	3.0	$910.00
Mad #5	VG+	$900.00
Two-Fisted Tales #18	7.0	$900.00
Fighting Yank #12	5.0	$898.00
Two-Gun Kid #1	8.5	$867.00

The high-grade *Super Duper Comics* #3 has the first Mr. Monster full story (this is the comic that went on to inspire Michael T. Gilbert to revive and recreate the character) and the last, and only, full-color Nelvana story. Copies of this are a little more abundant because it did receive some US distribution. Though it came out after the WECA period (May-June 1947), it contains all original Canadian stories and is often considered an honorary WECA book. I believe this is the highest price achieved by a post-1946 Canadian book. In fact, the listed value for a 9.2 of this book in last year's *Overstreet* is $1200 or less than a tenth of this sale.

The *Manhunt* #12 is a number in the title that never appeared in the US printings. It has a unique Ogden Whitney cover and first began to appear in auctions in 2020 when, in the feeding frenzy, a VG copy sold for $3351 (Jan. 2020), a 2.5 sold for $7200 (July 2020), a 5.5 sold for $10,500 (Nov. 2020) and dropped to $8400 when sold a year later (Nov. 2021). This book looks like it has had a bit of a correction but let's see if more copies are spit out of the wild in the next couple of years.

Unusual Comics #6 reprints the *All Winners* one shot from 1948 with the Blonde Phantom cover, and *Red Seal Comics* #30 has a unique cover whose source is unknown. What also stands out is that a buyer's tide seems to be lifting the prices of Canadian EC reprints.

Bottom line is that Canadian comics from the 1940s and early 1950s are still solid and growing in value in spite of what appears to be a current recession shark that's ripping huge bites out of Silver and Bronze and later keys. Let's see what next year holds.

(Thanks to Jim Finlay for keeping up and sharing sales data.)

Timothy Kupin
Koops Comics

For the fourth year in a row, I am honored to be given an opportunity to contribute to *The Overstreet Comic Book Price Guide*.

This has been a very busy year for me. I relocated from Tucson, Arizona to Lawton, Oklahoma. I still have a bunch of comics and stuff in Tucson but I should have the last of it moved here in February 2023. I made at least 10 round trips (Lawton to Tucson) between mid 2021 thru November 2022. I also drove back to the east coast in August to buy a van load of comics and again in October to buy the rest of a single owner Marvel collection.

I've done 14 shows in six states in 2023. Although I did pretty well at San Diego Comic Con, I have to say the show of the year was the Grand Forks Comic Con. Sales were not particularly good, but it was the 31st state in which I've setup at a comic con, thus my show of the year. The show was held in the University of North Dakota's football stadium. The old UND Fighting Hawks were fighting on the road that weekend. Like I said, sales were unremarkable but the buying was decent. I picked up a 1940 Superman coloring book, lots of trade paperbacks and hard covers and a few other goodies.

On the way up there we stopped to check out Comics Junction in Fargo, ND. Very cool old school comic store run by an old school dealer named Kip. We bought some cool comics for inventory and a few that I kept for the personal collection. Kip has numerous rooms of comics of all types. On the way back, we stopped in Omaha to see my old buddy Dean Phillips and his stupendous store, Krypton Comics. Dean had a few Italian *Batmans* for me and we had a nice visit. Krypton Comics has everything you might be looking for. It's huge and filled to the brim with comics, toys, pops, gaming product, magic cards, etc. If you find yourself in Fargo, do your self a favor and check out Comic Junction . If you happen to be in Omaha, make time to check out Krypton Comics. I highly recommend both stores.

And the big event of the year has to be Koops Comics now has a brick and mortar store in Lawton, Oklahoma. We are located at 1312 SW Lee Blvd., Lawton, OK 73501. I'm in my store now typing this year's report. As of this writing, the store is not yet open to the public but will be soon. I still need to get signage and a few more wooden magazine racks and shelving for the back rooms. We're getting close. In the meantime it serves as my office, my consolidated storage and show preparation area. My new home away from home!

Overall show sales weren't too bad. It did get worse towards the end of 2022. Very different than 2021, but still a solid year of sales for me.

Some notable sales from shows in 2022:

Journey into Mystery #84 CBCS 4.5 $2500
Strange Tales #101 CBCS 3.0 $400
Creatures on the Loose #32 CBCS 8.5 $150
Invincible #1 (Larry's Comics variant) CGC 9.8 $600
Giant-Size Defenders #3 CBCS 9.6 $1250
Sandman #1 CBCS 9.2 $250
Creepy #1 raw 9.0 $350
Fantastic Four #3 raw 2.5 $1200

2022 was solid but not spectacular. Looking forward to what 2023 will bring and to whatever comics that may just walk into my store.

Ben Labonog
Primetime Comics

It was great to finally see the Sub-Mariner on the big screen this past year. His trademark green shorts, pointed ears, and winged ankles were quite marvelous. Now we just need to see him team up with Dr. Doom, fight the Fantastic Four, and create the love triangle with Reed and Sue!

The market on keys has cooled considerably, and is down as much as 50% on some books. Now is the time to pick up an *Amazing Fantasy* #15 which is selling for roughly $8000 per point in low grades at the time of this report (Dec '22).

Timelys and key Golden Age books/covers, however, have not seen much price resistance at major auction houses or private exchanges. One would be fortunate to obtain any complete, early Timely for under $1000. This is no surprise, since Golden Age books like *Suspense Comics* #3 and *Marvel Mystery* #9 have the perfect storm of rarity and demand to keep prices from becoming relatively soft.

The "parts assembly" has taken on big operations, and is still in full force. Many collectors are cobbling books together from many sources in order to complete big keys, or early, scarce books at a more affordable price. The front cover and centerfold wrap are the most highly prized, sought after parts. Meanwhile, the back cover is probably the least important of the book that collectors can live the most without.

I would like to thank my fellow Timely collector, Lance Lee, for gifting me with many of his old *Comic Book Marketplace* issues a few years ago. I hadn't picked one up in years, and the information in them is precious and often long forgotten with the current collectors. The old timers will remember the *Comic Book Marketplace*, a fanzine publication that started in 1991 by Gary Carter. It had numerous articles about restoration, preservation of comics, pedigree collections, scarcity, pioneers in the hobby, and much more. Here are a few notable sales advertisements from those issues that are fun to look back upon: *Action Comics* #10 FR/GD $500 (Motor City, Mar '92), *Hulk* #181 VG $65 (Steven Ritter, Mar '92), *FF* #1 FR/GD signed Kirby $200 (21st Century, Apr '92), *Marvel Mystery* #4 VG/FN $800 (DTA Comics, Sept '92), *All Select* #1 Carson City NM $2700 (PCE, Nov '92), *Suspense* #3 GD/VG incomplete (trading hands 3x at a con for $500-$1500-$3000) (Mar, '95), *Adventure* #46 FN- $1100 (Jul '95), *All Select* #2 FN $500 (Stephen Gentner, Aug '95), *Captain America Comics* #3 GD+ $850 – *Marvel Mystery* #9 no back-c $400 (Now & Then, Jan '96), *Marvel Mystery* #5 GD $2000 – *All-American* #16 GD+ $10k (Feb '96), *Detective* #31 GD- $2920 (Nick Kronfeld, Jul '96), *USA* #7 FN/FN+ $2000 (Four Color Comics, Nov '96), *Sub-Mariner Comics* #1 GD $2200 (Jan '97), *Fantastic Four* #1 FR/GD $995-, *Detective* #31 FR $910 (Mar, '97), *Action* #7 GD $1200 (Oct '98), *Batman* #1 FR $4895 (Rob Hughes, Dec '99), and *Marvel Comics* #1 VG $22k (Apr '00).

Since it is the holiday season at the time of this publication (and I consider myself a historian of the hobby), I'd like to include some of the most notable, favored books that were released and distributed in the month of December. Any of these treasures could have ended up in a kid's stocking for Christmas – *Action Comics* #20 (12-1-39), *Whiz Comics* #2(#1) (12-1-39), *Donald Duck* Frozen Gold #62 (12-1-44), *Crime SuspenStories* #22 (12-1-53), *The Great Comic Book Heroes* (Jules Feiffer) (12-1-65), *Iron Man* #35 (12-1-70), *Batman* #121 (12-2-58), *Journey Into Mystery* #89 (12-3-62), *All Select Comics* #2 (12-5-43), *Sub-Mariner* #59 (12-5-72), *Detective Comics* #35 (12-7-39), *Amazing Spider-Man* #34 (12-9-65), *Fantastic Four* #48 (12-9-65), *Fantastic Comics* #3 (12-10-39), *Human Torch* #2 (12-10-40), *Amazing Spider-Man* #1, *Fantastic Four* #12, *Tales of Suspense* #39 (12-10-62), *New Mutants* #98 (12-11-90), *Adventure Comics* #46 (12-12-39), *Fantastic Four* #3 (12-12-61), *Daring Mystery* #2 (12-15-39), *Mystic Comics* #5 (12-15-40), *Marvel Mystery Comics* #4 (12-20-39), *Captain America Comics* #1 (12-20-40), *Detective Comics* #156 (12-21-49), *Marvel Team-Up* #1 (12-21-71), *Detective Comics* #168 (12-22-50), *Flash* #105 (12-23-58), *Adventure Comics* #34 (12-27-38), *Action Comics* #21 (12-27-39), *All Winners* #7 (12-27-42), *Mystic Comics* #8 (12-28-41), *Fighting Yank* #7 (12-28-43), *Detective Comics* #180 (12-28-51), *Brave and the Bold* #28 (12-29-59), *USA Comics* #7 (12-30-42), *All Winners* #11 (12-31-43), *Four Color* (Peanuts) #878 (12-31-57). For my money, December 1939 and December 1962 were absolutely the best December months to buy comics because they had the best selection on the newsstands for one to choose from.

Finally, I'll mention one book that I have been enjoying in my collection for several years now – *Adventure Comics* #46 (released December 12, 1939) published by DC Comics - one of seven early Creig Flessel Sandman covers in the run. It is possibly the toughest of the seven to come around, and has the lowest census count of the seven (CGC lists 25 total copies). The large logo and central Sandman image showing him hopping a fence to attack an armed thug is a Golden Age classic.

Stephen Lipson
Collector

In the year 2022, irrespective of the Covid-19 pandemic, the market continues to remain robust in the niche collecting arena of the Canadian Golden Age comics (AKA Canadian Whites due to their black and white interiors).

I was extremely fortunate to acquire a very large collection of 200 of these 1941-1946 books. A feat that is almost impossible in today's market, due to scarcity and limited availability of these vestiges of Canadian pop culture.

My area of collecting and focus is the Canadian Golden Age era. In 2022, I have sold several books this year to collectors and I see an upswing in prices realized:

Sampling of 2022 Personal Sales of Note:

Colossal Comics Bell Features Giant Uncertified $2000

Rocket Comics Vol 4 # 3 CGC 2.5 $1500

Wow Comics #14 Uncertified (Coupon cut out of front cover) $750

Joke Comics #17 Uncertified 4.0 $950

Joke Comics #6 Uncertified 3.0 $850

Wow Comics #19 Uncertified Missing Centerfold $650

Captain Marvel Comics Vol. 2 # 10 Uncertified 2.5 $1200

There still appears to be a dearth of availability of the Canadian Golden Age World War II era books from 1941-1946, due to low print runs, and the fact that comics were meant to be read and thrown away. The paper drives of the Second World War also had contributed to the scarcity as well.

Hopefully 2023 will yield more fruit, and an abundance of these rare books will come to market.

Doug Mabry
The Great Escape

It's been another volatile year in the comic collecting world. We've seen for the past few years how movies and TV shows have driven demand for first appearances. But truthfully, the internet itself has changed the way comics are valued. Twenty-five years ago the market was fairly stable. Comics values increased at a measured pace, people collected runs and average issues were sought after.

The internet has really changed everything. First appearances, no matter how minor, are snatched up at quickly escalating prices while non-keys sit. Runs of mainstream books can be had on eBay for pennies on the dollar. There is one place, however, where the internet has really turned things upside down: Golden Age comics.

Golden Age has always been scarce. That's a given. Many of us eagerly devoured the photo sections of *The Overstreet Price Guide* to see books that we'd never seen before. Many of those became "grails" for me as I wondered about the contents of the cool books I saw. And the way that it worked was that if your local shop got in an issue of *Prize* or *Zip* or *Speed*, it would be priced at *Guide* and you'd better snatch it up when you had the chance. But things began to change with the publishing of Gerber's *Photo-Journal*. Now people could see all the cool covers that they never knew existed and suddenly folks had MORE books on their want list, but still not an easy way to get them outside of conventions and mail order catalogs. Then came the internet and eBay. Now people could read public domain comics and actively bid on the books that they once never knew they wanted.

So now, in the Golden Age market, prices have become extremely volatile. Keys are always at a premium, but an especially cool cover can drive a book to 20 times *Guide*! Covers by Schomburg and L.B. Cole, Hitler covers, and many others can spike the price of a comic. And now interiors are starting to affect it. Particularly graphic or sexy interiors can also drive the prices up. This is especially true in the secondary publisher's books. I can't tell you how many times I've been outbid on a book on eBay that went for ten to fifteen times Guide price, or even more! Here are some recent sales from our store:

Golden Age: *Wonder Woman* #2, FN+ $1250, *Wonder Woman* #13, FN+, $2000, *All Flash* #19, FN, $800, *Fighting Yank* #19, FN $800, *Bulletman* #8, VF, $1200, *Sensation Comics* #53, FN, $900, *Smash* #15, VG, $900, *Exciting Comics* #4, GD/VG, $900, *All Flash* #23, CGC 7.5, $1200, *Exciting Comics* #46, FN, $700, *Green Hornet* #4, FN-, $900, *Hit Comics* #21, FN-, $900, *Wonder Woman* #48, GD+, $400, *All Star Comics* #31, VF, $1500.00, and *Clue Comics* #1, VG+, $900.

Silver Age: *Daredevil* #1, Poor, $1624.

Bronze Age: *X-Men* #133, VG+, $101 and *Daredevil* #131, FN+, $400.

Modern Age: *Incredible Hulk* #377 (3rd print), GD, $126.00 and *Amazing Spider-Man* (2014) #4 (1st Silk), VF/NM, $182.

Jim McCallum
Guardian Comics

How else can we describe 2022 other than a tale of two different halves? The first half of the year started exactly where the previous two years left off, with an absolutely booming back issue comic book market with no signs of letting up in sight. Then the interest rate hikes began, fast and furious and by the end of the convention season in early September 2022, the uncertainty of the comic book marketplace and collectibles in general started self correcting. Gone were the days of setting GPA highs with every sale, as the reality of a more disciplined marketplace took hold.

The true collectors are still firmly engrained in the hobby and attendance at your smaller one day shows, and the larger Fan Expo type conventions has never been stronger. Still jam packed, shoulder to shoulder with little room to manuever as people have been foaming at the mouth for the convention experience and in person sales for the last two years now, and came out in droves.

We have always tried to have the strongest inventory of CGC graded books in the Greater Toronto Area, if not the country with at least one copy of any possible key book you can think of, if not multiples in varying grades, but have noticed that raw books seem to be trending upward in desirability. As you can definitely see the swing from speculation and treating comic books like they are commodities back to collectability, collectors are less worried about what the new "hot book" is and going back to collecting what they enjoy and love. In June 2022 we brought the "Crown Collection" to market, which consisted of every mainstream Marvel title from #1-100 save a few issues. It consisted of 32 short boxes, all perfectly boarded and mylared and after our first show we sold half the collection. By the end of four shows we were down to half a short box and just mixed it into our regular inventory. People absolutely loved the thrill of buying single digit *Hulk*s raw again. Filling in their *Tales of Suspense* runs between #40 and #99 and feeling they got the most bang for their buck.

Don't get me wrong, slabs are still moving, but they need to be priced competitively and reflective of current market value. If they are priced at last March prices, then they will sit and sales will be non-existent. We just finished the process of repricing all our slabs in late November to fall in line with fair market value and I must say the entire process was a real eye opener. Of the close to a thousand slabs we have, on only three books did we need to raise the price. A couple stayed the same, but most had to be reduced to be competitive. Slashing thousands of dollars off the sticker price for a high-grade *Marvel Spotlight* #5 and *Tomb of Dracula* #10 were a bitter pill to swallow, but we all knew these continuously rising prices weren't going to last forever.

The books we are continually asked for and can't keep in stock are what I would call mid-tier keys, with the king being *Daredevil* #1. *Daredevil* #1 when compared to the rest of the major keys, like *Amazing Fantasy* #15, *Hulk* #1 and even *Avengers* and *X-Men* #1s still appears to be undervalued and the demand remains high. As soon as a copy comes in, it's usually sold within hours. Another 1960s book similar to this is *Iron Man* #1. Even with the lowest grades of a *Tales of Suspense* #39 approaching five figures, many collectors have resigned themselves to the fact that an *Iron Man* #1 is the closest they will ever get to his first appearance and actually even prefer it to an affordable copy of *Tales of Suspense* #40 (Iron Man's second appearance).

Another huge area of growth are 1980s Copper Age comics and we have seen an unprecedented run up in demand for a great many of the titles. Many of these books are what forty- and fifty-somethings grew up with, picking them up off the spinner racks at their favourite convenience stores and shelves of their local comic book stores in their youth. These are also the books that were tucked away in attics and basements and refound at the beginning of the pandemic. These are the books that are the reason many collectors are back because of the strong nostalgic ties to that era. The McFarlane run of *Amazing Spider-Man* and *Spider-Man*, the Jim Lee run on *X-Men* is continuously being asked for. As well as titles like *Iron Man*, *Excalibur*, *Marvel Comics Presents* and everything in between. Even the early Image books like *Spawn*, *Wildcats*, *Pitt* and *Savage Dragon* are being asked for, as collectors are trying to complete the runs where they left off with many collectors being flabbergasted when I tell them that *Spawn* is still being printed and has surpassed issue #300.

So as we say goodbye to the year of 2022, I think we are also saying goodbye to the casual speculator and investor. They came, they saw, they conquered and they've moved on to something else. What we are left with is a much stronger hobby. One with more sustainable and steady growth. A marketplace that doubles and triples in value overnight is not healthy to building long term growth. We need the collector that loves the books, more than their values not to be discouraged that they have been priced out of the market. This is the backbone of the hobby. It's their passion and love that keep this amazing hobby of ours going. It's also a passion that they will teach their children, who might take up the mantle someday to keep this hobby and love of the artform going for the next fifty years. That's my hope anyways!!!

Todd McDevitt
New Dimension Comics

Greetings from the Pittsburgh region of PA! And St. Clairsville, Ohio, too! I always think it's helpful for readers here to know from where these insights derive. We have five stores in the Pittsburgh region and one in Ohio. Two are in malls, two are on main streets, and two others are in shopping centers. I am happy to report that in 2023 I will celebrate my 37th year in business! I've seen lots of trends and industry changes that have threatened the comic business over those years, but the comic hobby is tenacious!

In addition to the six brick-and-mortar stores, I travel and attend conventions and also host one in Pittsburgh, the 3 Rivers Comicon, along with other cool events. We also sell online, primarily on eBay, as seller ID newdimensioncomics, and new in 2022, we added newdimensioncomics2. This wide variety of sources and personal experiences fuel the insights I am sharing with you.

The collectible comics side of things went a little bonkers last year. We are just starting to see a downturn in recent months. Not a giant nosedive, but the peak seems to have occurred and things are nudging a little less. This mostly applies to key issues. It's not a great surprise, as many collectors seem to have shaken loose things from their stash to cash in on them in while the economy was inflated with Covid stimulation money. It appears that many folks who wanted their "grail issues" used their extra money from the Covid stimulation to finally get them. This eventually created a bit of a market saturation, and it was a perfect storm - but that storm has passed.

Another consideration is that in the past ten or so years, many general investors have turned to comic books. They don't have a love for them specifically, it's just about the investment value, and they acknowledge that when it's time to cash out. To prove this point, I had an interesting conversation with a colleague from the sports card auction world. His company has turned to auctioning comic books in recent years because sports card folks have embraced the investment opportunity that key issue comic books present. It will be interesting to see where things land as these trends play out.

My next point is something I've watched evolve for many years. With certain books, I've seen a lot of gut instinct and subjectivity involved in pricing. Personally, I'm a big fan of researching what a growing market price should be, and usually hedging just a little less than that. My rationale behind that stems from the fact that I am in western Pennsylvania, and we have a lot of great comic collectors that have kept me in business for 37 years. However, it's certainly not a marketplace as vibrant as some other regions. (Sidenote, it's always fun to see our hobbies play out in the microcosm of a comic convention. If you've never been to one, it's an amazing pure comic book experience! That's where my two examples come from, specifically the Baltimore Comic-Con.)

In this meeting of "the best of the best," I brought some significant comic books along. I sold a *Marvel Mystery* #34 to a dealer for my full retail price of $1,000. Then he quickly sold it for $1,200 to another dealer. I must qualify that I thought that my $1000 price tag was aggressive. I'm sure it's no surprise for anyone to hear that these sorts of books never last long. That's why I keep scooting the prices up on them, and yet still two other dealers saw some opportunities in even a higher amount. After all this occurred, another dealer came into the picture and claimed he would've spent even more! The next example is a *Green Hornet* #1 from 1940, a rarity that my staff had purchased, and had suggested that the price should be put at $1,600. I thought differently and priced it at $2,000. Another dealer bought it from me and sold it promptly for $2,500. I suppose part to the point of all this is that while there are many resources to reference on going market prices, there are sales happening all the time that do not figure into those sort of statistics. And I really believe the only way this gets discerned is through the experience of veteran comic dealers. Personally, I'm certainly at a point that if I see a comic book that I've never seen in 37 years, I get excited and put a robust price on it. Many of my peers would agree - they know a true rarity when they see one. My favorite quote for something like that with a hefty price tag that raises complaints is "go buy the other one in the room!" There isn't one. So keep your eyes open for that true rarity, even if it's not the most popular item in the current market. It might just be worth more than you think!

As much as I'm sure you are enjoying reading my ramblings, I'd like to involve my awesome staff to share some better opinions from the front lines. I spend much of my time tucked away processing comic books, but these folks hear from customers every day. So, here's the snapshot of what they are witnessing.

Jon Engel, General Manager New Dimension Comics

2022 was a little crazy for comics. At the beginning we continued to see some of the mass buying of hotter books moving at a record pace. As the year went on, we saw this slow down and return to a 2019 era pace. As the world starts to get back more and more to "normal" we even saw the market cool off a bit. Newer items, like *Sandman*, *Moon Knight*, and Dark Horse *Star Wars* were some highlights.

When it comes to where and when books have been moving, I have seen comic cons, especially smaller ones, really move the needle on books. Those same books in our retail locations will sit longer than expected. Which I found especially weird as the prices marked did not change. My only real wish was that pricing was a little more uniform. Hopefully with the advent of Overstreet Access, this happens sooner than later.

I will also say that it is impressive how resilient the comic book industry is in these times. Publishers had to play catch up and released a lot of books this year, many that were delayed from 2021. Customers showed up for most of it and supported shops. A huge thank you to the collectors for helping all of us to keep the lights on.

Anthony Tincani, Manager at New Dimension Comics Butler, PA

As people are tightening their belts everywhere, the desire for comics seems to be running at an equal pace. While the demand for the key issues, hidden gems, and new hits is ever growing, long runs of comics from a few decades ago are also high on the hunt list. Especially with '90s nostalgia being in full force. It has been keeping us very busy trying to fill peoples' wish lists, but I can only see that as a good thing.

Tom Tunnicliff, Ellwood City, PA location

Investing vs. Collecting: "What's the most expensive book you have in the store?" What's going to be the next big thing?" Two questions we hear the most in our shop. The first one always gives me pause because I think, "Why, are you going to rob us?" Though I really know it's cause people usually want to tell me about the books their mom threw away.

The second question is a bit harder to respond to, 'cause if I knew the answer I wouldn't be working here. Investing in comics, in my opinion, is riskier than the stock market. We're not financial planners, but we can use some of the same advice. Stick with the blue chip: older books that have an established history of growth and avoid the "Hot Tip" books that the faceless speculators say is the next big thing.

We have a few regulars here that get hundreds of dollars a month in new books. Some read every issue, can't wait for the next issue of their latest favorite and just love the medium. Then a couple I will be ringing out their $400+ order and I comment that I was reading this run and have really enjoyed it or I'll ask if it is it any good because I was thinking about reading that series and I get, "I don't read them," or even "I've never read a comic book."

"Oh..." then I quietly continue to scan their books.

Most books are never going to be an investment of any kind beyond the joy or nostalgia that you get from them. 98% of new books will struggle to even maintain their cover price as value let alone be hot. This is why in our shop we have a couple of dozen long boxes of priced books and hundreds of boxes of dollar books.

The third question we get is, "I'm just getting into comics. What should I read?" After I get the smile on my face under control I reply, "Well what do you Like? Because if you don't enjoy it, it's not worth your money or time to collect."

That all said, one view isn't better than the other, they are just two parts of the industry we cater too.

Steve Mortensen
Miracle Comics

2022 was turbulent year for comics. Coming out of Covid, we saw some highs at the beginning of the year and then ended the year with lows. The comic market was divided in half in terms of value; only a handful of the high-end collectibles survived the cuts in prices. The value for high grade Golden Age, Silver Age and Bronze Age comics set new records, while 9.2 copies and below suffered a real carnage – in some cases dropping more than 80% from their highs. Despite the correction, the demand for comics in general remains strong as buyers are still out there picking up deals. *Amazing Fantasy* #15 in CGC 4.0 can be purchased for around $30,000 (as of this writing) while the high for the book in that grade was near $75,000 a year ago – almost a 60% drop.

The 2022 comic market correction mirrors that of the stock market, both of which were impacted by rising interest rates that affected overall spending. I believe this is the best buying opportunity in a decade for the comic book investor. Collectors with money can score tremendous deals on high grade Gold, Silver and Bronze collectibles. I think in years to come, people will look back at this time when the market experienced a pivot – a dip that few people had a chance to take advantage of due to the economic crisis.

At the beginning of 2022, *Ultimate Fallout* #4 in CGC 9.8 sold for as high as $4,500. In November 2022, the last sale at a major auction house was $1,560. How low can it go? I had planned to sell a few and hold onto a few. Selling it for $3,000 off its high seemed ridiculous; however, the all-time low for the book is $36 from when the book came out in 2011. There is speculation that dealers are still holding quantity of this book in bulk. The book had a high print run. So, there's still a lot of room left to drop. At the same time, the Miles Morales character has lots of room to grow, so I believe this book will be hot over the next 10 years. This may be an entry point for collectors looking to pick up a copy but remain cautious.

It was recently announced that Bob Iger returned to Disney as CEO for the second time. Bob was instrumental in the acquisitions of both the *Star Wars* franchise and the Marvel Universe. Some say that things at Marvel slipped a bit since Bob left, so I'm hoping that his new tenure lifts the MCU back to new heights, which will help the future of the comic book market. His influence has contributed to the expansion of the back issue market perhaps more than any other person in the past ten years.

I'm recommending three places to put collecting dollars in 2023: Golden Age Timelys, Pre-Code Horror and high-grade Bronze Age issues. Timely Comics from the '40s continue to command high dollars in all conditions and are holding strong during the recession. There are entry points for almost anyone willing to spend $1,000-$2,000+ on a copy. A Fair condition issue will cost you $1,000-$1,500, and it goes up from there. They are the prime pick of the Golden Age. Others include *Batman* and *Detective Comics* – especially ones with Joker stories and covers. Pre-Code Horror books are getting harder to find as collectors hold onto their copies. When they do come up for auction, most sell multiples of *Guide*.

Another great future investment that I see is high grade Bronze comics from the '70s. CGC 9.8s are priced at $600-$2,000 each for a common book – it really depends on the population report and how many 9.8s have been graded. I recently picked up a Bronze Age *Amazing Spider-Man* ungraded. I had it pressed and graded, and I was lucky to receive a 9.8. The population report was so low on the book that the 9.8 price was $3,750 as of the last copy sold. CGC 9.6s of some Bronze Age titles can sell for a fraction of 9.8 values. In this case, the CGC 9.6 sells for $300.

I suspect that 2023 will be like the second half of 2022 and that the true recovery in the collectible market will happen in 2024. It is an exciting time to be a buyer of comics, as there are many key books at attractive prices. The best way to make a deal is to do some research and check out the 3–5 year sales data before you buy.

Marc Nathan
Cards, Comics, and Collectibles/ Baltimore Comic-Con

Greetings from northwest Baltimore County Maryland. 2022 started very much like last year ended. Every good book, from any era, sold within days of us putting for sale. This seemed to last at least through the summer.

When school started, there was a natural slow down and that happens every year. This year, however, I noticed that some of the folks that bought the hot comic, slowed down. The first indicator that they were having trouble flipping it quickly. If this continues, sales may slow down some, but in the end, the person that wants them for their own collection will have a much better chance.

Right before our Baltimore Comic-Con this year, we were able to buy three substantial collections. Our booth was loaded with hundreds of vintage comics that we held for the convention. This helped to make it a record year in the booth.

As of this writing, it's a week before Christmas and we are trying to help shoppers with gift ideas. As you probably know, it's very hard to buy a gift for someone when you have no idea what they have or like. Fortunately, we have such a large store with a wide selection, that folks find something cool.

Lastly, new comics still sell well but we continue to worry about the escalating cover price. Spider-Man and Batman will always sell, but when they are $8 a month or so, other titles always get hurt.

Josh Nathanson & Rick Hirsch
ComicLink

For over a quarter of a century ComicLink.com has been a leading consignment and auction firm for comic books and related artwork. We were the first online comic book and comic art consignment website, serving buyers and sellers of comic books and comic/fantasy original artwork since 1996. We have facilitated the sale of just about every valuable comic book that exists in a multitude of conditions.

2022 was another exceptional year for ComicLink. Many thousands of certified comic books were sold through one of our online auctions or the ComicLink Exchange® and thousands of new sales records were established in the hobby. ComicLink has continued to generate many all-time record prices for our consignors each month including an October 2022 sale of an *Incredible Hulk* #181 in CGC 9.8 that closed at a record in grade of $146,000. Other notable sales on ComicLink this year include *Silver Surfer* #1 in CGC 9.8 for $222,000; *Fantastic Four* #1 in CGC 8.5 for $350,000; *Amazing Fantasy* #15 in CGC 7.5 for $270,021; *Incredible Hulk* #1 in CGC 8.5 for $270,000; *Giant-Size X-Men* #1 in CGC 9.8 for $67,500. A top Golden Age sale was *Suspense Comics* #3 in CGC 6.5 for $280,000, which is one of largest sales ever for a non-superhero comic. Top Modern Era sales include *Teenage Mutant Ninja Turtles* #1 9.6 $63,234 and *DC Comics Presents* #26 in CGC 9.9 for $40,005.

Comic and fantasy-related original artwork was strong in 2022. Some top ComicLink sales included Jack Kirby and Steve Ditko *Fantastic Four Annual* #1 page 1 Spider-Man title splash for $286,000; Jack Davis *Tales From the Crypt* #39 cover $181,000; Steve Ditko *Amazing Spider-Man* #34 page for $145,000; and Todd McFarlane *Marvel Tales* #239 cover for $130,000.

CertifiedLink.com, our partner firm in such categories as certified trading cards, coins, vintage video games, action figures, VHS and memorabilia, also had a solid year.

Here is a small sample of ComicLink comic book sales broken out by era that took place during 2022 on ComicLink.

Silver Age (1956-1969): The Silver Age continues to be one of the most popular segments of the hobby, with the superhero genre dominating the activity within this category. *Amazing Fantasy* #15 remains the leading "Holy Grail" of the era and ComicLink set record prices in 2022 for examples from all grade levels from CGC 7.5 on down. Led by *Amazing Spider-Man*, all mainline Marvel titles are popular, with DC coming in second. With the Fantastic Four and X-Men coming to the Marvel Cinematic Universe in a few years, high-grade examples of even some non-key issues from these titles are selling for thousands of dollars.

All comic book examples in this report are certified by CGC unless otherwise noted.

Some of the Golden Age sales that took place on ComicLink during 2022 included:

- *Amazing Fantasy* #15 7.5 $270,052, 6.5 $225,000, 5.5 $117,000, 4.0 $78,400, 3.5 $62,000, 3.0 $60,000 & 1.8 $43,000
- *Action Comics* #252 9.0 $40,000 & 8.0 $17,750
- *Amazing Spider-Man* #1 7.5 $60,000, 6.0 $33,111, 5.0 $23,751, #2 9.0 $50,775, #3 9.2 $37,250 & 9.0 $35,000, #4 9.0 $22,000, #10 9.8 $19,528, #11 9.6 $47,775, #13 9.4 $20,266, #14 9.4 $41,000 and 9.0 $21,751, #15 9.2 $22,250, #16 9.8 $44,000, #17 9.8 $27,000, #20 9.4 $23,252, #37 9.8 $31,001, #39 9.8 $44,000, #46 9.8 $24,694 and #50 9.2 $15,816
- *Avengers* #1 CBCS 9.4 $100,000 & 8.5 $35,900, #4 9.4 $30,138 & 9.0 $17,750 and #48 9.8 $26,250
- *Captain America* #100 9.8 $16,450
- *Daredevil* #1 9.2 $47,000
- *Doctor Strange* #169 9.8 $18,250
- *Fantastic Four* #1 8.5 $350,000, 7.5 $120,000, 6.5 $72,000, 5.0 $46,444 & 3.0 $29,250, #5 9.4 $210,000 & 9.0 $119,000, #6 9.4 $54,100, #25 9.6 $16,375, #45 9.8 $55,000, #48 9.2 $22,950, and *Annual* #2 9.6 $35,000
- *Incredible Hulk* #1 8.5 $270,000, 7.5 $126,000, 4.5 $43,044 & 2.5 SS $25,065
- *Journey Into Mystery* #83 8.5 $92,000, 7.5 $60,500, 7.0 $44,000, 6.5 $32,502, 5.5 $27,806 and *Annual* #1 9.6 $25,500
- *Showcase* #22 7.0 $20,265
- *Silver Surfer* #1 9.8 $222,000 and #4 9.6 $21,250
- *Star Trek* #1 9.4 $16,250
- *Strange Tales* #110 8.5 $24,012 & 7.5 $19,150
- *Tales of Suspense* #39 9.0 $126,007, 8.5, $88,910, 8.0 $78,088, 7.5 $60,888, 7.0 $44,100 & 4.5 $16,550 and #52 9.2 $16,566
- *X-Men* #1 8.5 $125,000, 5.5 $27,250, & 4.0 $16,111, #49 9.8 $18,700

Golden Age (1933-1955): The Golden Age market remained extremely healthy throughout 2022. Market growth is driven by first appearance and origin issues, early appearances of popular heroes and villains, Pre-Code Horror, Good Girl Art and classic covers by the likes of Schomburg (including his all-time classic *Suspense Comics* #3), Baker, L.B. Cole and Frazetta.

Some of the Golden Age sales that took place on ComicLink during 2022 included:

- *Suspense Comics* #3 6.5 $280,000
- *Action Comics* #2 4.0 $44,000, #7 1.0 $44,555 & #23 5.5 $26,250
- *All Star Comics* #8 3.5 $43,000 & 2.0 $23,250
- *All Winners Comics* #1 8.5 $25,000
- *Archie Comics* #1 2.5 $27,000
- *Astonishing* #30 9.2 $33,000
- *Batman* #2 6.0 $29,000, #20 9.0 $16,916 & #23 8.5 $16,250
- *Black Knight* #1 7.0 $21,150
- *Captain America Comics* #2 6.5 $31,000, #3 4.5 $47,000, #7 8.5 $16,305, #46 3.0 $20,250 & #74 7.0 $29,250

• *Cat-Man Comics* #28 6.0 $18,500
• *Champion Comics* #10 8.5 $22,750
• *Detective Comics* #1 3.0 $81,000, #29 4.5 $110,000 & 2.5 $76,100, #31 3.0 $131,000, #37 4.0 $20,050, #38 3.5 $43,250, #40 5.5 $20,805, #67 6.5 $16,249, #69 7.0 $36,999 & #140 5.5 $18,450
• *Great Comics* #3 6.0 $19,240
• *Human Torch* #1 6.0 $18,250
• *Mad* #1 9.2 $52,438
• *Marvel Mystery Comics* #4 7.5 $160,000 & #41 9.4 $27,555
• *Mask Comics* #1 8.0 $74,000 & #2 CGC 8.5 $118,700
• *More Fun Comics* #55 5.5 $45,000
• *Mystic Comics* #6 7.0 $32,000 & #10 6.5 $15,550
• *Pep Comics* #34 5.0 $21,555
• *Planet Comics* #1 7.0 $21,750
• *Startling Comics* #49 8.0 $25,750
• *Sub-Mariner Comics* #1 6.5 $40,950
• *Superman* #6 8.5 $20,350, #17 8.0 $16,450 & #76 9.4 $20,361
• *Suspense Comics* #1 8.5 $28,765
• *Thrilling Crime Cases* #49 9.4 $32,202
• *Tomb of Terror* #15 9.2 $38,795

Bronze Age (1970-1979): Record prices were achieved for Bronze Age keys in pristine condition, many of which sold for sums unimaginable to those of us who remember plunking down 20 or 25 cents for some of these comics in our youth. With the early Bronze Age comics now over 50 years old, the era has gained full recognition and major keys from the era in high grade are recognized as true blue chip collectibles with plenty of room for further growth. *Incredible Hulk* #181 remains the most popular Bronze Age book followed by *Giant-Size X-Men* #1. As mentioned above, ComicLink set record prices in grade for CGC 9.8 examples of these two highly desired mega-keys.

Some of the Bronze Age sales that took place on ComicLink during 2022 included:

• *Incredible Hulk* #181 9.8 $146,000 (Record price in CGC 9.8!)
• *Giant-Size X-Men* #1 9.8 $67,500 (and 9.6 for $18,027)
• *Amazing Spider-Man* #101 9.6 $16,387, #129 9.6 $10,252 & #194 9.9 $52,000
• *1st Issue Special* #8 (1st Warlord) 9.9 $11,250
• *House of Secrets* #92 9.4 $18,027
• *Incredible Hulk* #181 CBCS 9.4 $20,420
• *Marvel Spotlight* #5 9.6 $68,500
• *Tomb of Dracula* #10 9.8 $35,000 Higher than last sale but lower than 12-month average

Modern Age (1980-Present): With the Modern Age designation now covering a 40+ year period, there are numerous examples of high value comic books from the era and the list of new keys grows every week as new movie and streaming projects adapting comic book characters are announced. Collectors are also buying up books they believe have the potential to become keys. Highlights include:

• *Albedo* #2 9.4 $10,250
• *Amazing Spider-Man* #300 9.8 $12,000
• *DC Comics Presents* #26 9.9 $40,005
• *Edge of Spider-Verse* #2 CGC 9.8 SS Variant $13,750
• *G.I. Joe: A Real American Hero* #1 CGC 9.9 $27,256
• *Marvel Super Heroes: Secret Wars* #8 9.9 $11,749
• *New Mutants* #87 9.9 $20,251
• *New Teen Titans* #2 CGC 9.9 $27,572
• *Savage She-Hulk* #1 9.9 $27,250
• *Tales of the Teen Titans* #44 9.9 $10,850
• *Teenage Mutant Ninja Turtles* #1 9.6 $63,234 & 5.5 $13,805
• *The Crow* #1 9.8 $11,351
• *Thor* #337 9.9 $32,000
• *Thorn: Tales From the Lantern* #NN 9.2 $13,138
• *Ultimate Fallout* #4 9.6 Variant $11,111
• *Venom: Lethal Protector* #1 10.0 $12,250

Original Artwork: 2022 was a strong year for ComicLink in terms of sales of original artwork from the worlds of comics and fantasy. A small number of artwork highlights from the year includes:

• Jack Kirby and Steve Ditko *Fantastic Four Annual* #1 page 1 Spider-Man title splash $286,000
• Rob Prior *Iron Man Revealed!* An enormous painting from the Stan Lee Legacy Collection $285,000
• Jack Davis *Tales From the Crypt* #39 cover $181,000
• Steve Ditko *Amazing Spider-Man* #34 page $145,000
• Todd McFarlane *Marvel Tales* #239 cover $130,000; *Spider-Man* #11 splash page $84,311; *Amazing Spider-Man* #303 page $62,068
• Neal Adams *Justice League of America* #91 cover $102,000
• Barry Windsor-Smith *Conan the Barbarian* #6 cover $89,001 and page 1 title splash $58,000
• Gene Colan *Doctor Strange* #172 cover $86,009
• Marie Severin *Incredible Hulk* #102 page 1 title splash $75,000
• Jim Lee *Alpha Flight* #87 cover $72,000
• Boris Vallejo 1996 Marvel Masterpieces card art including Wolverine card art for $70,000 and Thanos card art for $69,000
• John Byrne *Marvel Fanfare* #45 wrap-around cover $68,000
• Frank Brunner *Marvel Premiere* #12 cover $64,666
• John Buscema *Silver Surfer* #14 page $59,200
• *Alex Ross Visions: X-Men* original art for lithograph $52,000
• Frank Frazetta Vampirella illustration $48,151
• Gil Kane *Marvel Team-up* #44 cover $45,200
• J. Scott Campbell *Amazing Spider-Man: Renew Your Vows* #1 incentive cover $44,800

If you have valuable comic books or related original artwork or other collectibles, we invite you to visit ComicLink.com, CertifiedLink.com and reach out to us if you have interest in selling. We'll work with you to optimize the value of your collection. We assist with everything including evaluating your collection for certification, processing, pricing, marketing and selling your material. We do all this work, and offer upfront cash advances, for a very minimal commission rate. All you have to do is ship us your comics or artwork or drop off the material at one of our offices or at our booth at one of the major conventions we take part in every year.

Tom Nelson
Top Notch Comics

Here I am at the end of December 2022 giving my annual comic market report. Overall sales were very strong with the dollars flowing into the market this year, however the second half of the year there was a softening of prices on primarily Marvel keys from the Silver Age through the Modern Age. The books that had the largest price increases in 2020 and 2021 were the books that saw the largest decreases in 2022. A lot of the DCs and Independents didn't see the huge run up in prices and therefore their prices are more stable this year. However it still comes down to supply and demand and when a book gets hot it can really go up in price quickly, but when the supply eventually works its way back into the marketplace those books do start to trend down.

I'd like to focus this year again on the top ten DC Silver Age books in very fine 8.0 condition, higher grades are very scarce and volatile with pricing:

Showcase #4	$100,000
Showcase #22	$50,000
Brave and the Bold #28	$22,000
Action Comics #242	$22,000
Our Army at War #83	$20,000
Adventure Comics #247	$18,000
Action Comics #252	$15,000
Batman #121	$12,500
Showcase #8	$12,000
Flash #105	$12,000

The top ten chart is dominated by Flash appearances, with the King being *Showcase* #4 which launched the rebirth of the Silver Age superheroes. Second is *Showcase* #22 the first appearance of Green Lantern, this book saw the largest dollar increase from the top ten charts from last year. Third is *Brave and the Bold* #28 the first Justice League of America. Fourth is *Action* #242 a deep purple cover with the first appearance of Brainiac. Then the biggest DC war book comes in fifth with *Our Army at War* #83, the first Sgt Rock. Sixth place is a highly demanded key featuring the first Legion of the Super Heroes in *Adventure* #247. We than get the first Supergirl in *Action* #252, the lone Bat book is *Batman* #121 with the first Mr. Freeze, then we round out the top ten with two more Flash books, *Showcase* #8 featuring the first Captain Cold and Flash #105 the first of his ongoing series.

My next top ten are Independents in Near Mint minus 9.2 from the Modern era that had standard comic shop distribution, excluding variants, mail aways and error editions.

Teenage Mutant Ninja Turtles #1 (1st print)	$30,000
Albedo #2	$10,000
Bone #1	$3,500
Teenage Mutant Ninja Turtles #1 (2nd print)	$3,500
Sentai #2	$1,500
Crow #1	$1,500
Walking Dead #1	$1,200
Primer #2	$1,000
Invincible #1	$1,000
Star Wars: The Clone Wars #1	$700

The biggest books in the Modern Age are full blown independents. They had a fraction of the print runs for a standard title. The first and fourth go to *Turtles* #1 first and second printings. Second is *Albedo* #2 first Usagi Yojimbo. Third is *Bone* #1 first printing, a cartoon series by Jeff Smith. Fifth is *Sentai* #2, first Power Rangers by Antarctic Press in 1994. We then have the all black cover of *Crow* #1 in sixth place. Seventh is *Walking Dead* #1 from 2003. *Primer* #2 is the first appearance of Grendel by Comico in 1982. *Invincible* #1 from Image comics breaks into this year's list at number nine. The final book is *Star Wars: The Clone Wars*, first Ahsoka Tano based on Cartoon Network from 2008.

My final group of books in high grade Near Mint minus 9.2 can be viewed as modern Independent comics featuring crossover Games and Video Games characters, primarily giveaways and promotional, yet a few had some comic shop distribution.

Nintendo Sneak Preview 1990 promotional *Comics Buyers Guide*	$800
Maximum Carnage #1 1994 promotional from game	$700
Blip #1 1983 first Donkey Kong and Mario in comics	$300
Super Mario Brothers #1 Valiant 1993	$300
Dragonball #1 1998 Viz	$300
Dragonball Z #1 1998 Viz	$300
Legends of Zelda #1 1990	$250
Sonic The Hedgehog #1 1991 promotional	$200
Mortal Kombat Midway #1 1992 mail away	$200
Pokemon: Electric Tale of Pikachu #1 1999 promotional	$200

The Modern collectible books with cover art by Todd McFarlane and Dave Stevens continue to sell well,and vintage artists like Baker, L.B. Cole, Lou Fine and Schomburg are all seeing price increases regardless of the book having any type of key issue story line. Low CGC census books from Gold, Silver, Bronze, Copper and Modern are still breaking records, and rare books still are commanding a premium despite the softening prices of popular keys. Modern newsstand editions in CGC 9.8 condition still command a premium over their regular cover edition, and there has been some similar sales from the 1980s and 1990s, with most of the exaggerated prices being from newsstands in the 2000s.

The back issue comic market is still very strong with similar dollars invested into CGC books in 2022 compared to 2021, as there was an increase in supply for many of the popular Silver to Modern keys causing a softening of sales. Once these books move to their second home and volume thins down, the prices should start to rebound again in the long term for the popular books.

We sold thousands of books this year, and here are a few notable sales: *Adam: Legend of Blue Marvel* #1 CGC 9.8 $979.99, *Amazing Spider-Man* #20 6.0 $1500, *Amazing Spider-Man* #238 9.8 $3,000, *Booster Gold* #1 CGC 9.8 $400, *Brave and the Bold* #25 CGC 3.0 $570, *Coyote* #11 CGC 9.8 $500, *Crow* #1 CGC 8.5 $965, *Daredevil* #4 7.0 $600, *Dragonball* #1 CGC 9.8 $1100, *Fantastic Four* #6 CGC 4.0 $1900, *Flash* #135 CGC 9.4 $3000, *Evil Ernie* #1 CGC 9.8 $4500, *Marvel Premiere* #28 CGC 9.4 $1000, *Romantic Marriage* #24 CGC 5.5 $1000, *Strange Tales* #101 7.5 $1500, *Suspense Comics* #8 1.0 $2,000, *X-Men* #50 CGC 9.2 $1200, and *Warlock* #1 CGC 9.2 $350.

Jamie Newbold with Matt Joaquin
Southern California Comics

Welcome to the summer of 2023 while it's the winter of 2022 as we write down our thoughts.

Covid temporarily robbed our store of walk-in customers after March of 2020. We filled the sales void with eBay, Instagram, Facebook, website, Twitter and phone call sales that helped topple previous annual earnings records. That was the tremendous upside. San Diego's Comic-Con International revved up our sales during the summer of 2022 and provided us with the second best show we've ever had. Considering I've been selling at the show since 1975, that was a welcome bounty after the dearth of shows during Covid.

The downside was the elevated prices that we all witnessed during the pandemic seemingly dropped overnight in the summer of 2022 and beyond. If I had to explain it I'd surmise that enough stay-at-home people marginalized government relief money for some internet fun and got caught up in the world of comic book collecting/speculation to impact worldwide sales trends. Once the boom ended and the relief dollars were spent, people needed to off-load all those key comics they thought would make them world-class comic dealers. Newer, pop-up sales sites such as Shortboxed and Whatnot became release points for collectors, investors and, pardon the pun, whatnot. Sales figures are all over the map, but the general consensus is there's a slump in the current inflationary market.

One reference site currently on the "hot list" of price comparisons is the on-line subscription home of Go-Collect. Their sales figures extend beyond GPA into the risky area of raw comics. Prices their crew have established at various websites work in real time, unlike *Overstreet*'s annual book-format, often with less-than-timely numbers. However, no documentarian can create their own fair market value prices unless the documenters sell comics on a daily basis and record their own numbers, much as we at So Cal Comics. We all have experienced the eBay seller with a VF comic book that arrives at the buyer's address in VG shape thanks to bad grading. Possession of the comic, as the story goes, is 9/10 ignorance. "I own it, therefore, I know it".

I believe that the wisest course of pricing for raw comics on wb sites is to post price ranges. For instance, a NM copy of *Silver Surfer* #5 would range in 2023 from $400 to $700 ($750 recorded slabbed on GPA. We extrapolated downward from that to $700 after roughly subtracting the cost of CGC grading. That pricing technique works very well for us for particular comics).

We believe in *OPG*'s general pricing for grades below the NMs in ungraded conditions. Trust in the book, but add other sources into the mix to be market fresh.

We watch collectors at our store and at shows attempt to discern purchase prices off various price sites on their phones. Their plans are to figure out if they can either get comics cheaper than ours, or sell their comics somewhere for more than they paid. We see more phones being whipped out to confer with e-sites than we hear questions being asked to gain knowledge. Lesson number one in this arena is to do the heavy-lifting and learn how to grade before trusting e-numbers. The prices on raw books are meaningless if the data was drawn from sales where it is unknown if the sellers knew how to grade.

I figured, based upon comments from some of those shoppers, that their attempts to capitalize on comic book back issue money back-fired when they couldn't figure out how to do what stores and dealers like us do to make real money. The fantasies about working from home to buy/sell comics while they were displaced from their normal places of work, or were shutdown, blew up in their faces. They were not practiced in the nuances of buying off the 'net, or anywhere else, and then selling for profit on the very same sites.

We've encountered quite a few people who chose that path temporarily and then came to us to unload stuff they bought but couldn't make a go of it. Some of the newbies ask for help and we provided. We gave them some ideas and perhaps game plans to at least get themselves out of a financial holes they dug to supplement incomes through comics.

I wrote the *Forensic Comicologist* as a teaching tool for comic book enthusiasts who want to learn to collect/trade/buy and sell, but avoid the pitfalls of inexperience and "bad actors" willing to take advantage of naive souls. Four years after the book's release I'm still getting royalties from sales. That's a nice surprise.

Covid's impact is a succession of reduced auction prices on many key comics. That's a disappointing display of red "down" arrows on GPA that indicate much of the good times from 2020-2021 have hit the skids. The market pulled that decrease to my business twice before. The first time was the second Gulf War. Deployed servicemen and women left town and took their business with them. The economy was in decline, evidenced by our 20%-25% drop in sales. Fortunately we recovered.

The second collapse came with the 2008-2009 mortgage collapse. San Diego properties rode a tidal wave of value increases thanks to sketchy home-lending practices and novice home-buyers easily taken to the cleaners by shady realtors and the banks they palled-up with. Our store dipped into red ink for most of those two years. That was partly our doing. Others in our hobby suffered and sacrificed their collections to us. We didn't lose as much money as it looked on paper. We just spent ourselves into the red buying up collections banking on better times ahead and with meaty inventories. We find ourselves back into a third downturn in business.

Covid could have, maybe should have put a headstone over our shop. Trump, Biden and our federal government helped save us with PPP forgivable loan money, twice. I used the government money to keep my employees paid if they took themselves off of unemployment.

All of that is behind us now, as we ride a momentum that rollercoastered downhill when we closed the store due to State 2020 mandates, and then re-opened to customers nervous about exposure. Most customers returned, with optional masks and we arrived at what seemed to be better than normal business days, only to be hit by high inflation returning us to decreases not seen since 2009. The inflation issue has affected our whole bottom line: store and website catalogue. Numbers on eBay for graded comics get about what they got pre-pandemic. Some are high and some are low and so on. Key comics are stressed. We see the drops in sales prices for comics we should be able to sell for more. Dealers are reluctant to give away the house on their best stuff while buyers feel it's their market, for now. I liked a comment I found on the internet somewhere: "There will be a $100 fee for anyone that shops with us and tells us they can get 'it' online for less." Ha!

So, we have to hunker down and see if the market on the most desired stuff returns to the numbers we had before the world got sick, or ally with the numbers of December 2021.

The modern and monthly comics game has more or less stayed the same over the past couple years for us. On the DC front, three out of every ten new Bat-related titles from DC make an impact, and the rest decrease in the amount ordered every month until they are cancelled or the mini-series runs to an end. The main *Batman* series still reigns over any and all DC titles, and Zdarsky is creating a very decent story. The inundation of a new character every week has thankfully seemed to have slowed at all publishing houses, with DC being the largest proprietor of that trend.

Marvel's ultimate blockbuster spanning the Avengers, X-Men and Eternals was received to little acclaim and the numbers showed. Uncertainties like the reception of *The Punisher* new storyline reads fine enough and has comparable orders to the last time it was published. *Amazing Spider-Man* still is the largest ordered title with its loyal, mostly unwavering readers. At our store, the movies hardly have any effect on sales now and rarely bring in a significant amount of new customers.

As far as independents go, Image still is on top, while BOOM! publishing is showing it can produce quality stories. The sales numbers are generally consistent from issue two until the end, as long as the books come with no surprise delays. As many as there are readers that are in it for the story and art, there are and always will be plenty of clueless speculators buying every first issue of anything coming out, hoping to strike gold.

Thievery, often the shoplifting variety, is stunning in its frequency and audacity. The store is forced to operate with at least one extra employee to watch the customers. Most of our best comics are locked up, off-site, out of reach, or under camera/person surveillance. Still, we can't get them all. One particular thief was caught after the fact. A shopper emptied bagged comics from their exterior, coded Mylars, ditched them and then concealed the comics. He pulled off this theft on surveillance camera, stuffing comics up his shirt. We discovered the Mylars and the guy one day after it happened. We posted the thief's picture on FB comic book groups and got a slew of responses from L.A. comic book stores. They all seemed to know him. Now, they put 2+2 together and realized the same thief was their problem, too. We had video and so did one of the L.A. stores. The thief pulled the same ploy and got busted at the scene. We posted both videos together and everyone saw him display his shoplifting technique.

The thief, a D-List actor, intrigued a lot of people. We gained 9,000 followers on Twitter. Eventually the story and videos found a grander audience when the tattle-tale web site, TMZ, outted the thief worldwide. Those damning videos left no room for alibi. Even the *National Enquirer* ran the story. Our local radio stations got in line and told their abbreviated versions of our theft. The actor pulled down all of his social networking presence, including his website and then just disappeared. He lives or lived in Long Beach, but our crime was reported to San Diego PD. As of November 17, the crime case is in the hands of the City Attorney's Office.

The thief earned his living through the internet promoting his acting skills for work. He royally screwed himself over with his criminal performance. His agent and his manager have the videos. I hoped that one of his contacts could induce him to give up, or return my comics. We had brief contact with him through his e-mail but he shut that down as soon as every other internet troll found it. He hurt a lot of stores who trusted his customer loyalty. Many of them are victims, but they didn't know it was my thief. The greater Los Angeles area stores talk to each other. The thief is done in that city and mine.

Karen O'Brien
Comics Journalist

As the pandemic ages into an endemic state, comic shops have resumed regular business hours and the "extra-curricular" activities that make each shop unique (welcome back, Free Comic Book Day). Rescheduled conventions and shows have enjoyed cautiously enthusiastic audiences (many early-year shows with local restrictions and precautions in place). And collectors have renewed their in-person comics hunting in local venues like estate sales and flea markets.

With the resumption of these more "normal" comics activities, it seems that some of our more positive pandemic-born practices may have become permanent routines.

Shop owners noted continued strong back issue sales, regular customers diligently emptying their pull bins, and a steady pace of in-shop visits on days without new comics releases. Requests for curbside pickups and comics-by-mail receded or are entirely gone. Shops that increased their social media presence during the lockdowns are seeing rewards for their efforts as collectors are still relying on Facebook, Instagram, and YouTube posts to receive comic shop news, event announcements, and new release information.

Key issues and the expanding definition of "key" remain hot topics. It's not just about the first appearance of a character anymore. Key hunters are also looking for "minor keys," including the first cover appearance, the first time a character guest starred in another character's book, costume changes (not *ASM* #252 because we'll all likely agree that's an actual key issue), the first use of a certain plot twist or super power—I'm not really sure where it ends. But this fervor has highlighted a very interesting collecting avenue to pursue—a creator's first published work. Just try to find a bargain bin-priced copy of *Astonishing Tales* #25 (Marvel, 1974) and you'll see what I mean. It's the first appearance of Deathok the Demolisher, but that's not the reason that a copy in NM condition can run you nearly $600. It's also the first published work of (future) comics legend George Pérez. (Rest in peace, Mr. Pérez—and thank you.)

And speaking of back issues, the impact of the Marvel cinematic universe (the films and the increasing number of limited series on Disney+) remains a strong short-term influence on associated comics titles—just follow the extreme pricing increases of *Black Knight* #1 (courtesy of *Eternals*) and the relative downturn of *Moon Knight* #1 (while values are still elevated, the book is returning to more historic levels). While these short-term effects are exciting for the moment and have increased the visibility of characters that hadn't received much popular attention, the long-term effects are a subject for debate. Will this focus on "smaller" characters inspire collectors to not only seek out first appearances and first issues because those are the "hot" titles of the day but to also pursue whole runs of these characters that would indicate a more long-term demand? That will be fun to watch. The good news is that the comic collecting realm has room for both short-term and long-term perspectives—and there are plenty of opportunities to enjoy both.

How are your pandemic projects coming along? The quest to organize my back issues continues, assisted by the increasing availability of comics-related supplies—bags, boards, and boxes were easier to find later in the year after familiar supply chain delays persisted through the first half of the year. I'm still slowly working on that Bronze Age run and even upgraded a few of its books along the way.

My observations on the comics marketplace for 2022: There is still a buzz around the Golden Age slabbed books from the Promise Collection—and with good reason, what a spectacular treasure trove!

Atomic Age space titles and early horror books are seeing prices on the rise for lesser conditions. Desire for the 1950s westerns was flat.

Silver Age titles in all conditions remain desirable and continue to generate high prices. Patience and homework are vital tools for collectors working on Silver Age runs, as books are available but opportunities for bargains are few, so verify condition on potential acquisitions. There's a perpetual interest in every era of *Amazing Spider-Man*, and Silver Age books continue to do well, but increasing demand for adjacent titles like *Spidey Super Stories* (1974), *The Spectacular Spider-Man* (1976), *Web of Spider-Man* (1985), and *Spider-Man* (1990) should keep collectors looking for runs within these titles busy this year.

Bronze Age titles are killing it at auction. Notable auction houses, eBay, and social media live "claim sales" are all netting solid results for these books. *Conan the Barbarian* is doing better this year, while most sword & sorcery books remain flat. The new *Ka-Zar* and *Lord of the Jungle* series may spark interest in their 1970s predecessors, *Ka-Zar* (1974) and *Tarzan Lord of the Jungle* (1977). Super hero titles are driving the bus on valuation and demand, however, so if you're working on runs, budget accordingly.

Increasing interest in key issues has seeped into the Copper Age books, which remain affordable and relatively easy to find. Frank Miller's masterpiece *The Dark Knight Returns* is a pillar of the era, but don't overlook Mike Grell's brilliant *Green Arrow: The Longbow Hunters*.

Modern Age demand is driven by popular characters, good genre books, some carryover interest from films and television series, slabbed book speculators, and variants. Batman has enjoyed a string of topnotch creative teams, but the flood of limited-run Bat titles is wearing budgets thin. Marvel and DC both released major event titles this year to a market already fatigued by mega events. I'm not sure if the re-published collections of CrossGen issues will generate any interest in the original issues this year, but it's on the radar because many of the CrossGen creators are still cranking out quality work.

Small publishers continue to release quality books that are drawing attention. And there has been a noticeable migration of big name creators from DC and Marvel to do creator-owned books. The well-done horror titles from BOOM! Studios are in demand. Image Comics' *Saga* and *Monstress* continue their success.

As I did with the last edition, I'll end this report with a call to encourage the next generation of collectors. Your knowledge of this hobby and approach to collecting can be a benefit to others, so reach out when you can. Opportunities exist to give talks or lead discussions at local libraries (donate this book to your local library immediately), Rotary, Kiwanis, Lion's Club, or scouting organization meetings

Collect what you enjoy and enjoy your collection!

Terry O'Neill
Terry's Comics/CalComicCon/ Nationwide Comics

This report focuses on convention and mail order aspects of vintage comic collecting. Sales at comic shows have been mixed, with a somewhat downward trend from the crazy highs of 2021. Catalog orders were significantly down in 2022 and we had to re-price many comics to remain competitive. Acquiring replacement inventory has been more difficult than in past years as many past customers are selling their own comics on the Internet through Facebook, chat boards, Instagram, Whatnot and so on. I don't mind paying a higher price for quality material, but when everyone is a dealer, it's more difficult to acquire large collections.

After many years of operating a warehouse, I moved to a new location in Washington State and have been liquidating approximately 1/4 million paper items. As a result, I no longer have access to just about every comic and magazine from the mid '70s and on. I'm now focused on acquiring an older, more high-end inventory My mail order business is also affected because my only full-time employee got married and moved back to California.

Golden Age (1938-1945): I consider Golden Age to be my specialty. I have a large diverse selection of all titles and genres in my inventory. Luckily for me, many of my older customers still call me to buy their comics. It sure helps to have been in this industry a long time. I bought back some DC comics such as *Action*, *Batman*, *Detective*, *Superman* and *Wonder Woman* from a customer who bought them from me back in the nineties. Most of these were in rather low grade, but that was what he could afford back then. Sales of note: *Amazing-Man Comics* #24 1.0 bound volume $2,400 *Action Comics* #148 6.0 $567, *Detective Comics* #107 4.0 restoration $210, *Whiz Comics* #17 1.0 bound volume $292, *Champ Comics* #19 2.0 $1350, *Archie Comics* #50 2.0 $630, *Blue Ribbon Comics* #13 3.0 $550, *Fight Comics* #1 CBCS 2.5 resto $570, #20 1.0 $500, *Mystery Men* #6 CBCS 2.5 $800, *Kid Comics* #1 CBCS 6.5 Restoration $1400, and *Fighting Yank* #6 0.5 Centerfold missing $400.

Atom Age (1946-1955): Although we have not purchased any large collections of this material, I have been able to acquire several small batches from other dealers and collectors. Some items of note were *Space Western*, *Weird Mystery*, *Weird Tales of the Future*, *Jetta*, *Fighting American*, *Stuntman* and several Avon One-Shots like *Out of this World*, *Robotmen of the Lost Planet*, and *Eerie*. We also picked up some Matt Baker Romance and War Comics such as *Teen-Age Temptations* and *Fightin' Marines* with *Canteen Kate*. Sales of note: *Out of this World* #nn 5.0 $800, *Sub-Mariner Comics* #42 2.5 $450, *True Love Pictorial* #2 3.5 $700, *Human Torch Comics* #37 3.0 $400, *Ghost Comics* #3 7.0 $1700, *Weird Tales of the Future* #7 4.0 $2000, *Starlet O'Hara* #3 5.0 $600, *Space Western* #44 4.0 $338, and *Authentic Police Case* #8 5.0 $550.

Silver Age (1956-1970): Wow, what a difference a year makes. Prices shot way up in 2021 but they have certainly settled back down this year. Marvel was especially out of control and DC also went up a bit before things began cooling down. After repricing in 2021 to the higher market, we're having to reprice them again. All this being what it is, we purchased no new collections of Silver Age in 2022, aside from the few small batches we bought at trade shows. Sales of note: *Amazing Spider-Man* #4 3.5 $1350, #31 4.0 $375, *Avengers* #1 3.0 color touch $1800, #19 7.5 $400, #25 7.0 $300, *Batman* #121 4.5 $2400, 1500, #123 5.0 $1000, *Tales of Suspense* #42 7,0 $575, #66 6.5 $222, *Green Lantern* #87 7.0 $675, *Tales to Astonish* #57 9.0 $600, *Thor* #168 CBCS 8.5 $406, *X-Men* #4 4.5 $400, #16 8.5 $500, and *Blue Beetle* (Charlton) #1 CGC 9.6 $1968.

Bronze Age (1971-1985): While demand is high, it's been increasingly difficult to acquire collections of this material, especially Marvel Comics. As always, *Amazing Spider-Man* and *X-Men* are the most collected titles from this era. Also in demand are those monster /mystery books like *Tomb of Dracula*, *Frankenstein*, *Ghost Rider*, *Moon Knight*, *Man-Thing*, *Witching Hour*, *Swamp Thing* and others with short one-shot stories. Sales of note: *Amazing Spider-Man* #122 7.0 $500, #129 4.0 $2000, *Mister Miracle* #1 8.5 $300, *House of Secrets* #92 CGC 4.5 $1100, *Incredible Hulk* #124 9.4 $360, *Tomb of Dracula* #1 6.5 $500, *Giant-Size Chillers* 35c #1 6.5 $200, *Conan the Barbarian* #11 9.2 $225, *Marvel Premiere* #28 9.0 $450, and *X-Men* #95 9.0 $400.

Magazines (All): Not much to report in this area as I wholesaled most of my Magazine inventory. That said, *Savage Tales* #1 in high grade is a definite sought-after magazine. Some sales of note: *Spectacular Spider-Man* #1 7.0 $40, and *Savage Sword of Conan* #1 2.0 $40.

Copper Age & Independents (1981-Now): I just realized that Copper Age comics are now over 40 years old. I remember when I was calling Silver Age Back-Issues, (Yes, I'm old)! *Amazing Spider-Man* #300 is in very high demand; however, Harley Quinn and *New Mutants* #98 has cooled. She-Hulk has done well along with anything with Carnage and Venom in them. *Watchmen* series is back in demand, as well as McFarland Batman. The *Marvel Super Heroes Secret Wars* entire series is in high demand. Sales of note: *Bone* #2 9.4 $100, *Batman Killing Joke* 1st #nn 9.4 $88, $357 9.4 #135, #428 7.0 $22, *Avengers* #257 9.8 $143, and *Amazing Spider-Man* #298 9.2 $200.

Graded Books: We mostly sell them at conventions and a few through auction houses such as Heritage, ComicLink, Comic Connect and Short Boxed. Some sales of note: *Amazing Spider-Man* #19 CGC 8.5 $681, #34 CGC 8.5 $333, *Batman* #232 CGC 7.5 $630, *Prize Comics* #2 CGC 6.0 $1,800, *True Comics* #55 CGC 9.4 $1,489, *War Victory Adventures* #2 CGC 3.0 restoration $630, *Lucky Comics* #2 CGC 7.5 $1,211, *Top Love Stories* #10 CGC 8.5 $900, and *Key Comics* #4 CGC 8.5 $436.

Internet Sales: The majority of our inventory is at www.terryscomics.com . We update our website about three or four times a year.

In summary, I am still excited while buying, selling and going through comic collections. I really enjoy this industry and the community of dealers, collectors and promoters I meet at the comic book conventions, such as the Little Giant Old School Show in New Hampshire, CalComicCon in California, Rocky Mountain Con in Denver and the Collectors Summit in Washington. Very often I get to meet long-time mail-order customers in person for the first time. I especially enjoy meeting and talking with all the new collectors excited about discovering new things related to Golden and Silver Age comics.

Michael Pavlic
Purple Gorilla Comics

This year the fine folks at Overstreet asked us advisors to comment on Covid and how it affected our businesses. Well, as of this writing (mid-December) I have recently experienced Covid for the first time and it forced me to close for four days. As my biz is only open Friday, Saturday and Sunday, that's a chunk of change that I may never get back. If I had Covid earlier, I could have applied for some government assistance but that now longer exists. That said, it could have been much worse and I'm grateful that I fully recovered.

The biggest change from pre-Covid to post-Covid (are we there yet?) is that seasonal buying has diminished, it seems to be spread out beyond the big months of June-August and November-December. These days, if I get a good collection of comics, I'm going to have a good month, if I don't get anything, it'll be a tough month. So I'm on "Feast or Famine" cycles. Fortunately, "Feast" does eventually happen, so much so that last year was the second best in terms of sales that Purple Gorilla Comics has had in 14 years. Now previous results do not necessarily reflect what will happen in the future, meaning I got to work hard to find comics that my people want or even more importantly, find comics my people didn't know they wanted until I show them!

That last sentence demonstrates how my biz works and why I don't do online or shipping. I guess I'm stuck in 1993 or something because of the way I run my shop. I like interacting with people, I use my knowledge to recommend comics that people don't know about that they might like. I feel this "value added" aspect makes it more appealing than just selling on eBay or whatever. So when Covid first hit and everyone was saying that "you HAVE to sell online!", I resisted. It's not my way. I'll be old school 'til I die! This inflationary situation we all find ourselves in may be more difficult to navigate than Covid. Time will tell.

While Covid destroyed many businesses, the comic market in Calgary remained resilient. Every shop that was around pre-Covid is still here. I suspect it's because each store has it's own "personality". Some stores only sell new comics, graphic novels and toys, others will do that plus some back issues. There's a store that handles high end and slabbed comics. Then there's me, just back issues and a few new comics for the kids (a big thumbs up to DC for the new *Batman/Scooby Doo* series, I sell 15 copies a month!). I don't do slabs and I don't overpay for "key books" just to say I have them. I deal with what I have and whatever happens to come in. I consider myself a "Turd Polisher", I take stock that others wouldn't touch or can't sell, give it some love with a new bag and board and present it to the world. My instincts seem to be pretty good, so far. Many stores have no calling for *Savage Sword of Conan* mags, *Heavy Metal*, kids comics, Undergrounds and Alternative press. All find a home with me.

That said, I could polish turds all day long and it wouldn't mean a thing without my regular, loyal customers. Without these folks no comic store could survive. Purple Gorilla has been around for 14 years because of these folks. It's my aim to keep them happy for another 14 years!

I need to thank these people because without them I doubt I'd be where I am today: Dave from Amazing Fantasy in Red Deer, Ben and Martin from Phoenix Comics in Calgary and Doyle, cos it will always be his fault!

Bill Ponseti
Fantastic Worlds Comics

Greetings comic lovers!

Last year we could hardly catch our breath while trying to keep up with the rapidly increasing prices across the board for Gold, Silver and Bronze comics. That trend continued into the first quarter of 2022, and then the regression in prices started and haven't really stabilized as of this writing.

The rapid decline should have been predicted as the prices for not particularly scarce comics had really gotten out of control. While many have been wailing, gnashing their teeth and once again predicting the eminent demise of the comic collecting hobby, my advice is to pump the brakes on that hysteria.

Price fluctuations up and down have been a part of this hobby across my entire 50 years of collecting and dealing comics. This downturn seems much more dramatic as prices have dropped on average 50% from their astronomical heights achieved in 2021. But that's okay, they are coming back down to the price range that more collectors can, and are, adding them to their collections.

Last year in our market report we used *X-Men* #1 in 4.5 as an example of the craziness that was 2021. That book went from $6000 to a high of over $30,000. That simply wasn't warranted or sustainable. Even after the huge drops in key comic prices this past year it's settled in around $13,000. Which is still a fine return on the investment for any copies bought before 2021.

I have seen some prices continue to drop, while others remain relatively stable after the initial few months of price drops. Certain issues are actually going back up somewhat in price, but at a much more common to the market rate of growth.

As far as categories of growth, not surprisingly Marvel was again king of the marketplace in 2022. But much like 2021 we sold many more DC Silver and Bronze Age comics in the shop than we have in any previous year. We've been considering moving some of our inventory to online platforms to broaden our reach and have made that a business priority for 2023. Although we still get lots of local and out of town collectors coming into our shop to fill in their collections or get that key they've always wanted.

One area that has been relatively immune to the price drops has been Golden Age. In fact, this area has continued to climb in prices as well as demand. We've enjoyed many more sales of Golden Age comics across the spectrum of genres. Not just superheroes sell in this era of comics. Our two biggest sales in 2022, by far, were big Golden Age keys. *Sub-Mariner* #1 CGC 8.5 Billy Wright Copy for $150,000 a record price for that grade, and *Superman* #1 CGC 0.5 for $130,000 also a record for that grade.

Original comic art sales didn't seem, from my perspective, to have any price drops. In fact, the opposite seems to be true. Finding a nice Silver Age superhero page for under $10,000 seems to be nearly impossible. Thus, I've seen an uptick in Bronze Age superhero page prices and demand.

We set up a two large shows in 2022, Fan Fusion in Phoenix and San Diego Comic Con. Both shows were very strong for us in terms of sales. Not as many buyers as in years past, but the overall sales were better by a good margin than the last time we set up at those shows. We continue to help promote our local Scottsdale show twice a year, and attendance has tripled since the 2021 show. This is a comic and comic art only show, so that is a great indicator of the collector's interest in shows like that.

Our new comic sales remained relatively flat year over year, but our ancillary product sales like apparel, toys, action figures and Pokémon cards has been a huge growth area for our shop.

As always, my advice is to keep the hobby fun, and it will amply reward you. Buy what you like, and you will never lose.

Sean Prosje
Comic Cave Canada

I have been collecting comic books for over 40 years. Over the past 10 years I began selling comics. I have quickly become the largest retail online seller in Canada. There has never been as much popularity or sales in comic books as in the past decade, and it is occurring right now. The following is my market overview report on what I have witnessed in the rapidly growing comic collecting community and my suggestions for the 53rd *Guide*.

Comic book character movies and television series are at an all-time high. They continue to produce more constantly. All comic book movies and television series weigh a heavy influence in the rising prices of characters' and comic issues relating to the media (television/cinematic movies). Some of the original issues, with the first appearances particularly, or 'key' issues, as the modern collectors call them, have risen exponentially in value. I believe this to be an important factor that we must recognize, but also be careful to give the value to only the comics that deserve this credibility and increase. There is a large misconception arising in society that any book with these characters' appearing in them, is valuable. Something has been lost in translation. If a comic book has a print run of 100 million copies available right now, and a 1960's first run book does not, then it is logical to say a new Spider-Man book should not be selling for more than the original 1960s book issues. Unfortunately this is not the case and it is happening daily. Collectors are overpaying for modern books and this is the direct result of uninformed new collectors, relying on current market trends, set by sellers on eBay. There are a lot of incorrect values placed on a lot of different and modern comics. We cannot control this. We can however, adjust society's perception to stay on top of the times and remain trustworthy and extremely reputable by our adjustments.

The older Golden and Silver Age books need price increases on the steady each season. This will ensure the valuable books stay where they should be and the modern mass-produced books where they belong. I believe it is our job to educate the comic book collectors, by significant changes in the evaluations of the older Gold and Silver comics. This will keep the eBay trends, and the high priced moderns at appropriate prices. In short, *Overstreet* must step up the values significantly to match and create a proper price guideline for true collectors. Some of the older books have begun to climb, but with the demand way up high with the population growth and the supply depleting more quickly on the 1940s-1970s books, we need to address the rarity (print run) and the availability of purchasing higher grade copies in these truly vintage older books. This is necessary to keep the industry growing correctly and the correct pricing in the *Overstreet Guide*. An infusion of greater values to the deserving Golden and Silver Age books will ensure the security of the future for investors, collectors and hobby readers alike.

Thank you for the opportunity and privilege, for including my facts, opinion and experiences into the 53rd *Overstreet Price Guide*.

Alex & Austin Reece
Reece's Rare Comics
Alex Reece

Hello to all! 2022 was another wild year in the world, and in the comic industry. The year began the same as 2021 ended, with an absolutely red-hot comic book market. Demand was insatiable for A-Level keys, but even B and C level keys (think *Darkhawk* #1) were shooting up at preposterous rates, sometimes doubling month over month. Just as we had said in 2021, Austin and I knew this rate of growth was unsustainable, and while we became worried about the potential for the bubble to pop, we continued running our business as we always had, namely buying collections and books that made sense. My philosophy was that we were going to keep buying on the way up, and all the way to the top. Obviously, this meant we would buy some material at the absolute peak of the market, but the opportunity on the way up had so much more upside that we kept the same strategy that we always had, and it worked out.

Different sections of the market found their peak at different times, but Bronze/Copper keys that had been on fire throughout 2021 started fading in the winter, while Silver Age that had seemed unassailable started lagging from May onwards. Gold has more or less held its own (more on that later). As I write this, most prices for Copper/Bronze have returned to pre-pandemic 2020 levels, while Silver Age has corrected quite a bit but in general is still a little over pre-pandemic 2020 levels. I think there are a few factors here that others will go over in more depth, but the comic correction is not an isolated market. Stocks are down, 0% interest money is gone, and geopolitical conflicts have rocked the world. Also, as much as we hate to admit it, the MCU is a factor. It is the machine that takes nothing books and turns them into keys overnight, and it reinforces the price points of even the most classic books and characters. Sadly, Phase 4 has been mostly a letdown from a story progression standpoint. While many of the movies were enjoyable as standalone pieces, few did anything to advance the MCU in a meaningful way, outside of the Multiverse concept. It seems as if Phase 4 was more of a holding pattern to regroup after the massive buildup to *Infinity War/Endgame*, but I have faith that the team has big plans for the next phase, which we all expect to include some familiar villains and superheroes. All of that said, if you look at almost any hobby (sports cards, comics, video games) they have all had massive corrections from their market peaks in the last two years. This tells me that it's not necessarily an issue with the comic market, but rather a global economic issue.

Now that we have that out of the way, let's focus on some of the positives! One of the best parts of our year was bringing to market a massive collection that we dubbed the Key City Collection. The collection was comprised of almost 3,000 CGC graded books, and included four *Amazing Fantasy* #15s, six *X-Men* #1s, a literal short box of *Incredible Hulk* #181s, and a multitude of other keys and high-grade books. We launched it on www.reececomics.com in March, and the response was incredible. In 6 months, we had sold through over two-thirds of the collection. The next best collection we sourced was a small group of about 75 Silver Age Marvel books that were incredible high grade. We named this group the Pacific Northwest Collection, as they were from an original owner who lived in that area. When I first saw these books raw, I couldn't believe how nice they were, both structurally and with their dripping wet inks. They were from a similar area as the famed Pacific Coast Pedigree, and almost looked like sister books to that pedigree, thanks to the advantageous climate. They were sent to CGC, and some of the highlights were: *Amazing Spider-Man* #13 CGC 9.6, *Amazing Spider-Man* #14 CGC 9.6, *Amazing Spider-Man* #31 CGC 9.6, *Fantastic Four* #67 CGC 9.6, *Incredible Hulk* #141 CGC 9.8, and many other high-grade examples from that era. Unfortunately, the owner had sold some books throughout the years, which is the only reason this collection would not have received a Pedigree. This collection was purchased in June, after the peak for Silver Age books, but as is almost always the case, I found that the best of the best continued to sell well. Most of these books were in the top 1-3% of copies graded on the census, and they were very desirable for the reasons I mentioned above, so we had no trouble moving them. As I alluded to earlier, this was also true of many Golden Age examples. These books are so much rarer than their Silver/Bronze counterparts, so while those were going down people began flocking to Golden Age as a safe haven, and so far, it seems to have worked. These have outperformed every other sector of the market, and if a given book had not traded during the pandemic years, you could pretty much blindly bet that it was going to explode in value, and we saw that time and time again at auction and through private sales. Obviously, nothing is completely foolproof, but Golden Age has had another renaissance and does not seem to be slowing down.

2022 was also the return of a full year of conventions after some restarted in 2021. It was nice to be back at our favorite shows, and without recapping them all I will just say that conventions are alive and well. While people were forced to shop online during the lockdown, they seemed very happy to be back on the show floor and shop in person. I have found that even in the midst of this market downturn, if you are priced at or near fair market value, then people are going to keep buying comics. In fact, this downturn is good in the fact that it is allowing true collectors to reenter the market on some specific keys that may have been out of reach during the pandemic. Collectors are the backbone of this hobby, so if they are the ones ending up with the keys they want, that is actually good for the long-term health of the hobby.

Overall, 2022 was an incredible year, and one I would not trade for anything. That said, I am looking forward to a hopefully more stable comic market in 2023 that does not have the wild swings in value that we have seen over the past two years. If we can find the market bottom in the next few months and get any kind of positive news on the "real world" side of things, I think 2023 can be a great year. Thank you as always to our customers, colleagues, and friends that have helped make this such a great year, we could not do what we do without you. I am looking forward to next year already!

Austin Reece

Hello to all! As my now-retired dad wrote his final Overstreet report last year, I figured it was time to pick up the mantle and begin contributing to the *Overstreet* in his stead. He left some big shoes to fill, but I have been lucky enough to have learned from the best. For those who don't know me, I am the brother of Alex and co-owner of Reece's Rare Comics. By the time you are reading this, I will be in my 8th year helping run our company, and am excited to offer a new perspective for the *Guide*!

Market Report: I'm not sure how it happened, but every year continues to feel busier than the last, and this one was no exception. While we were able to attend some shows in 2021, this year was the first year since pre-COVID that actually felt normal again. We were able to attend all of the major national shows and it felt like a big family reunion seeing dealers and customers that we haven't seen in several years. The highlights of these shows for us continue to be San Diego Comic-Con in July and New York Comic Con in October.

In particular, NYCC was one of the busiest shows we have ever attended, and though the market had started to slow down by that time, we had one of our best shows ever and found that if you were priced currently, that there were plenty of people spending. This was true for all of the shows we attended in the 2nd half of the year when the market had started to cool off. If you were priced at what books had been selling for in the last 90 days, rather than the previous 6 or 12 month averages, you would move product quickly. It also showed the power of in-person shopping. While some were quick to conclude that in-person conventions would be a thing of the past post-COVID, we found that people were extremely excited to get back to conventions to spend time with friends and buy books in person. Half of the fun of this job is the people, so I highly encourage you to attend a show with some friends and meet the wonderful people in this hobby.

While we had a great time getting to see everyone again, we definitely noticed a decrease in online sales. I believe this was a culmination of in-person shopping, the market cooling, and an uncertain economic outlook.

As far as the future of prices are concerned, my educated guess is that I think we are going to see prices continue on a downward trend until they get close to 2019 prices for most books excluding super key Golden Age books (*Superman* #1, *Action* #1, etc.) and extremely high-grade Silver Age keys (9.2+) before we see the market stabilize. Remember, we are writing these market reports in December, so it's always important to consider the context that we don't know what will happen in the months before you read this, or it may have happened already.

While prices did start to cool off in the 2nd half of 2022, I think there are always opportunities in this market, and a lot of times you just have to look where no one else is. The market started to see tremendous value in Golden Age DC and Pre-Code Horror as these had largely been overlooked during the Covid boom, and we saw many high-grade copies of these books scooped up during the last few months of auctions.

Speaking of DC books, we have always thought that Silver Age DC has been undervalued, and if they are able to create excitement with their revamped DCEU, the sky is the limit as these books are older and scarcer than their Marvel counterparts. I also think this next year could provide a great opportunity to get back into some Marvel Silver Age keys as those prices start to level off. The market has gotten extremely savvy over the last few years, so if you are going to make a large purchase, make sure you get a copy with nice eye appeal, limited or no Marvel chipping, and minimal or no writing. These copies have started to separate themselves from their similar graded counterparts, so you may have to pay up to get one, but I think it will serve you well down the road.

Key City Collection: We always like to say that buying is more fun than selling, and the biggest thrill of all is finding a new collection. In February, we launched the biggest CGC graded collection that we have ever had on our website. The collection consisted of nearly 3,000 CGC graded books, of which there were several copies of *Amazing Fantasy* #15, *Amazing Spider-Man* #1, *Avengers* #1, *Daredevil* #1, *X-Men* #1, and much more. We were extremely thrilled to bring this collection to market, and sold through nearly 60% of the books before the end of the Summer. As any big collection does, it provided the ultimate thrill in this business and gave us another reminder that you never know what's out there.

Conclusion: Every show we go to I get asked, "Austin, what should I buy?" and my answer remains the same as it always has: buy what you like and can afford. If you do those two things, you will have a good time in this hobby and potentially make some money down the road. We saw too many people the past few years looking to purchase books to make a quick flip. While I'm all for making a profit, I think it led to some serious price fluctuation and unsustainable spikes in prices and left a lot of people holding the bag with a bad taste in their mouth. Similar to the stock market, the best thing you can do is buy and hold books over an extended timeline.

By the time you have this in hand, we will have launched the newest version of our website, www.reececomics.com, and I think it is the best thing we have ever done. If you enjoy buying vintage comics and want to experience a website built just for you, I encourage you to give us a chance. As always, we are tremendously thankful for all of our customers who spend their time and hard-earned dollars with us. Thank you for allowing us to do what we do and see you all in 2023!

Stephen & Sharon Ritter
WorldWide Comics

What happens after the stunning year the comic market experienced in 2021? That was the question going into 2022 that was on the mind of comic dealers, collectors and investors. 2021 was a galactic year for the comic market with prices on all eras and all conditions of comics soaring to all time new heights. Was the quote "What goes up must come down?" to be expected, or was a stable market going to emerge from the ashes of the 2021 spike? In other words, were prices set during this surge going to be here to stay?

For those not familiar with us, we at WorldWide Comics are primarily an internet site selling vintage comics catering to both high and low end collectors. We offer comics from the Golden to the Copper Age with over 10,000 Third Party (CGC) graded comics on our website and about 50,000 non-Third party graded comics. We set up at a few major comic conventions each year and participate in all major auction houses around the country.

To begin analyzing 2022, we feel compelled to first review what we saw in 2021, a year that saw the COVID-19 in its second but first full year, where pandemic restrictions that were set in place caused world chaos in every market. Who would have guessed it would have been such a surge for the comic market, but most people were still shut in at home throughout most of the year giving collectors with a steady flow of income more time than ever to shop online.

September – December 2020: The surge for the market actually began at the end of 2020 when COVID restrictions were just put in place nationwide and comics began to heavily flow into the market at an increased pace not seen in a while. During the last quarter of 2020, we saw a 20%-30% rise in most Golden and Marvel Silver Age comics, especially keys.

January – December 2021: Through the first six months of 2021, prices on comics kept soaring, it was almost a race for buyers to purchase as quickly and as frequently as they could. Each month was more chaotic then the previous going well beyond just Golden Age and Marvel Silver Age. Our site was getting wiped out of most titles and we could not restock fast enough. By the end of June, auctions were seeing increases closer to three times last year's prices for most Marvel Silver Age and twice for Bronze Age comics. Our website sales were triple in numbers of previous years in the first half of 2021. The end of June though, the nation was almost fully back to work but beginning to experience economic difficulties which was bound to impact the comic market. In July, we felt we finally saw the peak of the year-long bubble. In August, we began to see prices dip slightly which continued throughout the remainder of the year. By December we recognized that about a 20% drop from the June peak was seen on key comics, but keep in mind, prices were still up over twice from the year before.

January – June 2022: The beginning of the new year saw a steadying of the market. There were slight drops on keys but mostly a plateau for all other comics. The surge of 2021 was definitely over, but prices for all comics were still selling at the higher prices seen at the top of the bubble. However, the state of the nation economy began to impact the comic market around March of 2022. At this point we started to see drops in most Silver to Modern keys. Based on our sales, we began to start seeing the buyer that is primarily an investor in comics make fewer and fewer purchases. Understandably, as each month continued to see a drop in price for all Silver Age and Bronze Age key type comics. Some issues saw as much as a 50% drop in prices from the beginning of the year. Only a few keys saw little drop (*Fantastic Four* #1 and *Incredible Hulk* #1 were two of the most stable). Our site sales still remained high at three times previous years in January but dipping to about twice normal by the end of June. We recognized our peak in sales during this elongated bubble was likely past.

July – December 2022: With the investors almost all but gone by August, key Marvel and even DC comics continued dipping almost every month. As a dealer, it was hard to buy these comics as they were no longer in high demand and would likely take a while to sell. And, if you held them longer than three months, they may not be worth what you paid. Now, here is the interesting trend we saw during this time frame. Most common comics (non-keys) were still holding steady from their original prices in January. These are the types of comics that collectors are buying and not the investor, so the investor's disappearance and the economical state of the country were not really impacting the general collector from still buying. Another area that was still selling strong were Golden Age comics, especially hot and scarce comics (WW II covers, skull covers, Hitler covers, violent covers, good-girl covers, etc.). These comics remained extremely healthy throughout the year and even increased in value during this time period.

By the end of 2022 and the beginning of 2023, it appeared the dip after the surge was ending. We began seeing sales from the investor type clients again and prices seen in auctions and online were becoming steadier and no longer dropping each month. We began to pursue Silver Age keys again ourselves, now that prices were more stable. Even though 2022 can be classified as a year most comics saw a decrease in value, it was not by any means a bad year for the comic market due to the tremendous surge of prices seen in 2021. 2022 can be better explained as the year prices stabilized to a more confident market for collectors and investors alike. Let's hope 2023 brings more confidence in all types of buyers which will only strengthen the comic market. Good hunting!!

Conan Saunders & Buddy Saunders
Lone Star Comics/MyComicShop.com

With the books closed on 2022, I would say we are now well and truly in the post-Covid comic market. 2020 was a year of initial uncertainty followed by rising sales and rising prices. 2021 saw the comic market reach another gear entirely, driven by a potent combination of low interest rates, stimulus payments, accumulated household savings due to reduced spending on services and travel, and a soaring stock market. Together these supercharged consumer confidence and sent demand for collectibles surging. In comics this effect was felt most strongly in the prices for key books from the Silver Age to the modern era.

We first observed the train slowing down June/July of 2022. Prices were still strong, but buyers were no longer snapping up big books at ever-increasing prices as quickly as they had in the previous year and a half. If the market peaked May-July of 2022, it's dropped relatively steadily through the end of 2022. As 2022 concludes and we move into 2023, it looks to me like price decreases have been flattening out, possibly hitting or nearing a bottom. Even with the pull-back, prices for major comic keys are still up significantly from where they were in early 2020 before Covid, even adjusting for inflation between then and now.

Here at MyComicShop, sales of our own collectible comic inventory at the end of 2022/early 2023 has been up 20%+ over the same period a year ago in late 2021/early 2022, which I think is a pretty impressive accomplishment given that we're comparing a weaker market now against a stronger market a year ago. But, sales of consignor-owned inventory have been down a bit.

I think part of the reason why sales of our inventory are up while consignor sales have been a little down is that we as a company can respond faster to changing markets. As the markets have moved down, we've been relatively quick to lower our prices to where the market's at, and as a result our sales are still strong. For some of our consignors, I think it's harder to adjust down as rapidly. In some cases collectors who bought into the market on the way up to the peak, or at the peak, are not in a big hurry to cut their losses and lower their prices.

Summarizing: prices are down from where they were at the beginning of 2022, but from where we sit it seems like the market is still quite active and there are plenty of buyers for comics all up and down the price spectrum, from Golden Age to Modern Age. Sellers just need to be realistic with their pricing and can't hold out for the prices they were seeing 6-12 months ago.

One other thing I'd like to cover: the condition of new comics.

This is a situation that seems to have originated with changes that happened during the Covid era. The past few years have seen major changes in comic distribution, with DC going with new distributor Lunar, and then Marvel going with mega book distributor Penguin Random House, and Diamond continuing to carry Marvels as a sub-distributor of PRH. In addition to the new faces and procedures in distribution, some publishers have also made changes to how they print comics, including what paper stock is used. In particular, the cover stock used for Marvel comics is now a flimsy lighter weight stock, the same paper stock as the comic interiors. Previously, covers used a heavier paper stock than interiors.

Comic retailers are running into more issues with newly published comics arriving with dings, bends, dents, and spine ticks. If you're a reader focused on reading the next issue, they still look great and you probably won't notice or care. But if you're a grade-sensitive collector looking for only Near Mint comics to add to your collection, many newly distributed books may not meet your standards.

We've recently been reviewing the comics we receive from the distributors and have found that overall about two thirds of the comics we receive are what we would consider NM, and one third would be VF or lower. This can create a difficult balancing act for retailers, trying to meet the needs of collectors wanting only NM copies when getting so many non-NM books in. Here at MyComicShop we haven't made any changes yet, but in the months ahead we may need to adjust how we handle new comics to better reflect the reality of what we receive from the publishers.

Hope 2023 is a good year for you and your family, and hope you continue to get massive enjoyment from the comics you read and collect!

Buddy Saunders

The comic book market continues to be an interesting one. Covid's impact on the market is well documented. Brick-and-mortar comic retailers, through no fault of their own, were the big loser. Government closures put them out of business for weeks and even months at a time. Internet retailers, by contrast, continue to operate and to pick up comic fans orphaned by government mandates. And in our case, and in the case of other comic Internet retailers, we benefited not just from our brick-and-mortar competition being shut down, but from the fact that other forms of entertainment and social activity shut down as well—such things as sports events, movies, dining out. We did a booming business in both new and back issue comics all through Covid.

But in terms of new comics sales for Internet retailers, that boom is over.

During Covid, MyComicShop saw a more-than-normal growth in sub-service preorders, and in orders from weekly new comic arrivals. Now, with the impact of Covid pretty much in the rearview mirror, brick-and-mortar is recovering lost customers. As a consequence, we are seeing short term negative growth in new comics sales, which is to be expected. Although new comic sales during Covid represent a single dramatic upward spike, the graph line to either side of that period points to continued growth in our new comic and graphic novel sales.

While new comics are an important part of our business, back issue sales are and always will be the backbone of our business. Even as our new comic sales ramped up dramatically during Covid, so too did our back issue sales. I was both surprised and pleased to see that the back issue comic sales boom has not let up and, if anything, is accelerating.

Inflation remains a big concern for us. It has to be affecting every retailer. When things cost more and more, the consumer buys less and less. But thus far, in terms of our own sales, I'm seeing little negative effects. We, all of us, retailers and fans alike, can only keep our fingers crossed, as we can do nothing about intemperate government spending.

On a brighter note, I'm pleased to be heading up our new Vintage Paper Department which has as its focus all sorts of collectible paper—pulps, the spicies, Big Little Books, men's interest magazines, general interest magazines, and pretty much anything I find interesting and that I think other collectors would likewise find interesting.

Pulp magazines are the core of our Vintage Paper Department. I am working with our software development team to polish our pulp listings to make them as comprehensive as are our comic listings. We are making tremendous progress. Pretty much every known pulp and spicy magazine already is in our database along with images of most covers, and we are constantly adding content data.

We see the market for such material as vibrant and growing as more collectors and readers discover these too often overlooked treasures of years past.

When it comes to pulp pricing, there's no sheriff in town. Everything is wide open. That's one of the reasons I find this category so challenging and correspondingly much fun. Pricing is whatever you make of it, whatever the market bears. No pulp price guide exists that reflects current market, and if there were, the market is changing so swiftly that any new price guide would soon be out of date. And for vintage paper in general, absolutely no price guides exist. It is like the days before the first *Overstreet* codified pricing.

Given that pulp and other vintage paper pricing is so fluid, initially we tend to price pretty optimistically, and if a newly listed item fails to sell at the initial price selected, from time to time our automated software will reduce the price until the item finds a buyer.

In addition to being one of the largest buyers of comic books in the nation, Lone Star Comics/MyComicShop is well on the way to being the largest pulp and vintage paper buyer in the country. For example, recently we purchased in excess of 3000 pulp magazines, an outstanding collection assembled by a collector over 40 years, ranging from publication dates as early as 1900 on up to the 1940s.

May we all--fans, collectors, dealers, creators, publishers, distributors, all alike--enjoy and prosper in this greatest of all hobbies.

Alika Seki, P.E.
Maui Comics & Collectibles

Aloha from Maui! When I write my annual report, I am tempted to talk about all the market impacts as I experience them. And then I remember that what I am experiencing as a small comic retailer is universal. Lunar and Penguin are stepping into the role of distributors, siphoning some business from Diamond. After a huge pandemic/crypto fueled boom in the collectibles market, a period of cooling has set in. Prices are down across the board, less so obviously for the top books. There is not much I could add to those discussions, aside from "I feel it too."

What has been exciting for our store is the rise of independent and local comic creators. With the means of production becoming more accessible, higher quality comics are appearing throughout Hawaii. We spent the most of this past year planning the Maui Comic Con, a free-to-the-public comic convention happening in December on Maui. This year's special guests included David Nakayama, Agnes Garbowska, Amy Mebberson, Geof Isherwood and of course the legendary Frank Cho. While those headliners do tend to draw the fans, most of the local hype is for the 30 local artists we hosted from across the islands. It was great to see the community and the creators both getting so much out of their interactions, and for the love of comics to be perpetuated.

Those who've been reading *The Guide* for a long time will remember my mentor Bruce Ellsworth (the third, but he hates that part) who was a senior advisor to *The Guide* on his passing in 2013. Bruce was an avid collector and lover of underground comix. At this past convention, an old, hippy man on a motorized scooter came and found me on the convention floor and asked me to come to his car to appraise 3 suitcases of comics. This old man reminded me of Bruce, but I could also see Bruce enjoying the collection he had me going through. One suitcase was almost entirely low-grade cartoon books from the '70s and '80s. The second suitcase was about 200 mid to high grade underground comix, each in individual mylars covering the entire range of what would be considered "head comix" by those who were there buying them from illicit sources when they originally came out. Unfortunately, while he did have early printings of books, the most important books were second printings or later, like *Zap* #1 and other Crumb hits. The third suitcase appeared at first glance to be low grade, low value Archie books, until the 10 cent covers started appearing. He had issues as early as the mid-50s and even had the infamous *Betty and Me* "Beat off" cover, which was the most valuable book in his entire collection. The old man appreciated the quick appraisal and set off on his way.

Over the course of this past year, I have been buying low grade silver age books, as they are a safe bet for quick turnover. Fantastic Four and Amazing Spider-Man lead demand and were our best sellers. Notable sales for our store include:

- 2 copies of *Amazing Spider-Man* #238, No Tattooz VF and NM for $700

- *Sentry* #1 (2000) CGC 9.8 White Pages for $385
- *Young Avengers* #1 (2005) CGC 9.2 White Pages for $300
- *Avengers* #5 (1964) CGC 6.0 Off-White Pages for $378

These notable sales just being our eBay sales, as in person sales have been difficult to recall. It used to be that any sale over $300 would register and be memorable, at this point they come and go so often that I barely recall what books have sold.

As discussed in previous reports, and witness by all, early *Teenage Mutant Ninja Turtles* had reached their peak values at the beginning of this year and slowly receded. Whereas this time last year a *TMNT* #1 first printing in CGC 9.2 condition was a sure $40,000 sale it is closer to $30,000 now. This is still a substantial amount more, and a much more reliable and consistent price, than prior to the pandemic. In previous years, when I first opened my store around 2015-2016 it was possible to find that book in CGC 9.2 for under $10,000. Most other Teenage Mutant Ninja Turtle books from all runs have earned respect on the market and tend to sell regularly at prices much higher than they had in the previous decade. Despite the downward trend in comics prices across the board, the progress in market valuation for these books is still on an upward trend overall.

Mahalo for checking out our report! If you plan on visiting our store let us know via social media on IG: @maui_comics, and FB: Maui Comics & Collectibles. If you are interested in attending the Maui Comic Con or even being a sponsor/vendor please visit MauiComicCon.com or contact us via social media on IG: @mauicomiccon, and FB: MAUI Comic Con. A hui hou!

Todd Sheffer
Hake's Auctions

Hake's Auctions enjoyed another great year of record results in 2022, with comics and collectibles continuing to be a strong investment. Sales and prices were still strong in all categories such as comics, comic art, action figures and collectibles.

Comic book sales show values keep rising for key books from the Golden, Silver and Bronze Age, while Modern Age comics and limited run variants are seeing amazing prices with the search for the next key high grade book. Interest in certified comics shows no slowing down as collectors try to build high grade runs of series. This looks to continue as third party grading companies have seen an onslaught of submissions over the past year, a trend that will continue into next year.

The comic art market keeps getting attention as record-breaking prices are paid at auction for covers and key pages from legends and hot new artists. Sadly, we lost several greats in the comic art industry in 2022, and as is often the case after these artists pass, interest in and demand for their art sees a corresponding increase. Look for interest in comic art to continue to build with every high dollar sale announcement, sending collectors scrambling to add to their collections.

Vintage *Star Wars* action figures continue to bring record-breaking prices. Hake's Auctions set a world record price with a Rocket-Firing Boba Fett prototype, fetching $236,000 (the most ever at auction for any *Star Wars* figure). Disney+ keeps airing new *Star Wars* series like *The Book Of Boba Fett*, *Obi-Wan Kenobi* and *Andor*, with more slated to hit the streaming service in 2023. The *Star Wars* collectibles market is as strong as ever and we look for this interest to continue as even more collections come to market thanks to these record prices.

Classic toys and collectibles from the 1980s and 1990s are seeing a steady increase in demand, with the generations that played with Masters of the Universe, G.I. Joe, ThunderCats and Teenage Mutant Ninja Turtles realizing the investment potential of their childhood toys. Growth continues in this sector as collectors look to reconnect to those childhood memories.

And just like certified comics, third party graded toys and action figures have seen another year of growth as well, with high grade examples of popular characters resulting in bidding wars that have frequently set new price benchmarks this year. These third party graders have seen sometimes overwhelming demand for their services, no doubt brought on in part from continued impressive prices for graded toys at auction.

Golden Age: Early DC and Timely superhero titles have a continued following with film and TV features attracting new collectors and driving already avid collectors to seek out the early appearances of key characters. EC and other pre-code horror have been running strong with that trend looking to continue. Pedigrees such as Larson, Mile High and others bring top dollar when they come to market. Uncertified issues also command high prices with scarce titles and issues getting scooped up by savvy collectors when they come up for sale.

Silver Age: Marvel continues to be the desired choice in Silver Age. *Amazing Fantasy* #15 shows no signs of slowing down, with increases in value across all grades this past year. Spider-Man leads the pack as the hottest character, with early issues being highly sought after by collectors, especially those with first appearances of key villains. First appearances of all major marvel characters continue to be in high demand as well. Look for more of this as Hollywood and various streaming platforms ramp up production for 2023.

Bronze/Copper/Modern Age: TV and movies continue to drive these newer issues forward as well with Disney+, Amazon Prime, Netflix and others pulling material from comics. Shows like *Moon Knight*, *Ms. Marvel*, *She-Hulk*, *Harley Quinn*, *Titans*, *Doom Patrol*, *Peacemaker*, *The Umbrella Academy*, *The Boys*, *Sandman* and much more are getting the attention of viewers hungry for more comic content, with big ratings for most. First appearances of characters such as Wolverine, Ghost Rider, Moon Knight and more modern characters like Harley Quinn, Deadpool, Cable,

Miles Morales and others keep increasing with each new film project announced. Variant covers for these newer books keep bringing record-breaking prices as well.

Notable 2022 Comic Sales at Hakes.com: *Amazing Fantasy* #15 CGC 2.5 $31,152, *Tales Of Suspense* #39 CGC 4.5 $14,992, *X-Men* #1 CGC 6.0 $24,645, *Incredible Hulk* #181 CGC 9.6 $23,883, *Journey Into Mystery* #83 CGC 5.5 $20,767, *Amazing Spider-Man* #1 CGC 4.5 $13,897, *Cat-Man* #20 CGC 3.5 $11,293, *Giant-Size X-Men* #1 CGC 9.6 $14,422, and *Marvel Family* #1 CGC 5.0 $17,134.

Notable 2022 Comic Art Sales at Hakes.com: *Famous Funnies* #217 cover art by Mike Roy $26,710, *Incredible Hulk* #283 cover art by Ed Hannigan $33,314, *Spectacular Spider-Man* #68 cover art by Ed Hannigan $17,387, *Justice League of America* #19 page art by Mike Sekowsky $14,278, *Amazing Spider-Man* #1 Marvel Masterworks color guides by Andy Yanchus $14,437, *Amazing Fantasy* #15 reprint from *Marvel Tales* color guides by Andy Yanchus $15,576, *Action Comics* #333 splash page art by Curt Swan $17,501, *Star Wars* daily strips #7-12 original art for a proposed series by Al Williamson with a combined price of $171,504, *Marvel Premiere* #15 page art by Gil Kane $20,350, *Star Wars* #3 page art by Howard Chaykin $23,559, and *Superman* #184 splash page art by Curt Swan $15,057.

Notable 2022 Pop Culture Collectible Sales at Hake's: *Star Wars* Boba Fett (Rocket-Firing L-Slot Prototype) AFA 80+ $236,000 (world record price), *Star Wars* Boba Fett (Rocket-Firing J-Slot Prototype) AFA 50 $204,435, *Star Wars* Vinyl Cape Jawa AFA 80 $40,887, *Star Wars* Double-Telescoping Obi-Wan Kenobi AFA 75 $79,178, *Star Wars: Return Of The Jedi* Princess Leia Pink Poncho Sample AFA 60 $42,834, Mego Green Goblin AFA 80+ $76,700 (world record price), G.I. Joe Snake Eyes AFA 80 $18,496, *Transformers* Optimus Prime Series 1 AFA 80 NM $9,735, and Nintendo 64 *Super Smash Bros.* game cartridge $11,800.

Marc Sims
Big B Comics - Barrie

Well, it had to happen eventually. After an absolutely insane 2021 where we saw record price after record price, 2022 truly was the year of the great market correction in comics. I would estimate prices on the majority of Copper/Bronze/Silver, and even most common Golden Age, are down an average of 40% from the crazy highs of 2021. That's a pretty harsh haircut if you bought at the peak, and the result I am seeing is a flood of people who jumped into the hobby at the start of the pandemic just as quickly jumping out. Turns out people really don't enjoy the feeling of what in hindsight looks like overpaying.

Of course this is about more than just comics. The broader economic trends are pretty terrible all around. Stocks in some of the most valuable companies in the world are down as much as 70% on the year. The housing market has crashed. Crypto went kaboom and people are going to go to jail for fraud. Household debt is at all time highs as interest rates have quadrupled and food prices keep going up every month. The scary part is, I don't think we've seen the worst of it yet. I am setting my budget for 2023 right now and my overall strategy is to be very cautious. I expect further price chops and weak sales results through at least the first two quarters of 2023.

All that being said, I remain bullish on comics and pop culture collectibles as a safe store of value for the future. The reality is prices last year went up too much and too quickly and needed to come down. Overall trends if you look at 2020 onwards are still really good on just about every book that remains in demand today. I like to look at bellwether books like *Incredible Hulk* #181, *Giant-Size X-Men* #1, *Amazing Fantasy* #15, and *Amazing Spider-Man* #129. These are 4 books that are constantly requested at my store and every other store in the world I'm sure. If you bought any of those books in 2021 or early 2022 you are probably not feeling great. But if you bought in 2020 or earlier, you are still up probably at least 50%. To me it still looks like a healthy market with strong fundamentals. Old comics are rare and fragile and the characters remain immensely popular and recognizable.

I believe so much in the comic industry in fact that this year I will have moved my store Big B Comics in Barrie, Ontario, Canada into a brand new storefront with twice the square footage, all of which will be devoted to more comics! I am immensely proud of our new comic book superstore at 45 Essa Road and look forward to buying and selling comics there for years to come. A big part of our strategy is doubling down on back issue comics and working hard to source new collections of quality material. It remains challenging of course, as even in a down market opportunities to buy good stuff are few and far between. We did however have good success this year and acquired some nice original owner Silver Age collections and brought them to market for the first time. A nearly complete run of *Amazing Spider-Man* bought fresh off the newsstands and kept in dresser drawers for 60 years was undoubtedly the highlight. Books from this collection sold quickly. A smaller original-owner collection of S.A. Marvels including *Daredevil* #1 and some early *Fantastic*

Fours also turned over almost immediately.

Each one of these books went to market just the way I like it – raw and in their fully natural, un-tinkered with glory. I am getting so tired of seeing perfectly good comics flattened like pancakes or the performative spectacle of showing off the coveted press/clean "Grade Bump". I'm going to lay down a marker here and say that the way amateur pressing and cleaning is almost completely ubiquitous today will in 10 or 15 years time be looked at as complete folly. You know how reinforcing the spine with glue on, say, a *More Fun* #52 was considered just preserving the book back in the day but now is like the mark of death? Attitudes change but permanent work can't be undone.

Lauren Sisselman
Comics Journalist

Manga Madness: Japanese comics, or manga as they're better known, might be the last thing you would expect to see in an Overstreet Report. But in the 1990s many popular manga titles were released in American comic shops in our standard floppy comic format. This was huge for me, as I consumed manga like it was air. Over the past few years, interest in single issues and complete sets has grown, with several titles commanding surprising amounts. While these books may never see *Action Comics* #1 money, they're still worth keeping an eye on. But there's a lot of manga out there. If you're not a fan, it can be daunting! As someone who grew up with anime and manga, I still have a keen eye for what's popular. Here are a few big hits you may have in your collection already.

Sailor Moon is one of the most well-known magical girl series in modern pop culture history. The series resurrected the at the time defunct magical-girl genre, was a gateway anime series for many Americans and is still popular 30 years later. When Mixxzine first translated Sailor Moon, fans were mainly mixed on it – some might say that translated version was a complete disaster. However, the Western-style issues have since become collector's items. *Sailor Moon* #1 currently has a fair market value of $700 for CGC blue label 9.8s – and this book can still be easily found in back issue bins. There are only 31 graded 9.8 copies on the census, but I'm willing to bet there are a ton of raw copies out there that could very well obtain a 9.8 grade. Sailor Moon fans aren't shy about spending money on this franchise! Be aware that Sailor Moon has been re-released several times in America – while the re-releases certainly are nice, the Mixxzine/ Tokyopop issues are where the money is.

Anyone who's been around pop culture and comic books have undoubtedly heard of *Akira*. The groundbreaking anime introduced an entire generation of Americans to what anime could truly be. The first translated printing of the manga, translated by Epic Comics (Marvel) in 1988 is a grail for many fans. The one-year average on *Akira* #1 blue label CGC 9.8s is $623, while the last issue – issue #38, has a one-year value of $1,100, also for blue label 9.8s. Raw copies of *Akira* #38 tend to sell for over $200 each time they appear on eBay. While interest in *Akira* has softened recently, the movie will be turning 40 in 2028. I expect interest in all things related will go up in value shortly before then.

Blending Spaghetti Western and Space Noir appeal, *Cowboy Bebop* became one of the most talked about series in the early 2000s. The series was a hit with fans and is still talked about today. Tokyopop's release of the *Cowboy Bebop* manga became a hot collector's item prior to Netflix's 2021 live-action series, but graded copies of the first issue are still in demand. Currently, the FMV for *Cowboy Bebop* #1 with a CGC blue label 9.8 is $750, though lower grades (under 9.4) sell for under $100. Interest on this title might have softened price-wise after the Netflix show aired, but this is still a series worth investing in. This is an essential comic and, much like *Sailor Moon* #1 can easily be found in back issue bins.

Giant robots are a staple in anime and manga. In 1985, *Robotech* began airing on US airwaves. *Robotech* is a mix of three shows - *The Super Dimension Fortress Macross*, *Super Dimension Cavalry Southern Cross*, and *Genesis Climber*. Before *Robotech* began airing, Comico released the English adaptation of the Macross manga. Issue one was the only comic to be released under this title. Eventually the comic would be reimagined with *Robotech* as the main series. The one-year average on a CGC blue label 9.8 copy is $1,367. There are only 64 9.8 copies on the census, though many more have been graded. Other popular giant robot shows that you may find some value in include *Gundam*, *Big O*, and *Neon Genesis Evangelion*.

Of course, we can't talk about manga without mentioning *Dragon Ball Z*. Akira Toriyama's shonen fighting manga is one of the most well-known series the world over – protagonist Son Goku even has a float in the Macy's Thanksgiving Day parade! The first issue of Viz's release of *Dragon Ball Z* is comic many people likely still have in their back issue bin. A CGC blue label 9.8 has a one-year average of $1,118, while lower grades such as an 8.0 have a one-year of $110. This is still a worthwhile book regardless of the grade and should be treated as such.

Dragon Ball Z's prequel series, *Dragon Ball*, is another comic to keep your eyes peeled for. Following Goku when he was younger, the series is just as fun and engrossing as the Z series. As always, higher grades mean more money, but you can't really go wrong with this book. A CGC blue-label 9.8 has a one-year average of $1,445, but even lower grades can still fetch a few hundred dollars. The first appearance of Dragon Ball, *Weekly Shonen Jump* issue 51 from 1984, is arguably the most valuable of all Dragon Ball comics. The Japanese magazine routinely sells for over $1,500 on eBay. This book is harder to find stateside, but if you're an avid Dragon Ball fan this is worth the hunt.

Manga graphic novels can also be a worthwhile find. Many series from the 1980s through the early 2000s are out of print, and collectors are always looking for them. Be advised that the first printing of most manga, as well as complete sets, is where you'll find value. Of course, not all manga is going to have any kind of monetary value, but there are some standout books. *GTO: The Early Years* was initially translated and published by Tokyopop in 2006. The series has not been translated since then. In October 2022, the entire 10-set collection sold for $1,500 on eBay.

Sometimes manga even gets the variant cover treatment. The popular shonen manga, *Naruto*, had a limited-edition holographic cover variant for the first volume. This one book can fetch over $1K on the secondary market. *Dragon Ball* volume one also had a holographic cover variant, which tends to fetch over $900 in auctions. *Sailor Moon* has a western-format style variant that was released during San Diego Comic-Con 2008. The all-over pink cover features a crescent moon in the center, and raw copies can fetch over $300 in an auction.

The world of manga and anime may seem overwhelming, but treat it as you would American comics. There are some incredible gems yet to be discovered, and sometimes it's fun to jump into something new! While the titles mentioned above are some of the more popular ones, there are countless others I urge you all to look into. Some titles you may already be familiar with, such as *Speed Racer*, *Pokémon*, and even *Astro Boy*. You may find some undiscovered gold, or you may find a new hobby! Either way, it's a win-win. Good luck and happy hunting!

West Stephan
Director of CBCS/Senior Grader

2022 has proven, once again, to be another crazy and unpredictable year for the hobby. The demand for graded books jumped to unparalleled heights, and as such, CBCS has hired many graders! We searched the entire country, literally hiring from coast to coast, to employ the best and most consistent graders out there. We introduced a new training academy to teach them how to stay consistent with our grading standards. I would like to take a minute to make a shoutout to all the graders here at CBCS: Daniel E, Scott M, Mark W, Joe A, Brian T, Joshua S, Jocelyn P, Angus I, Mark D, Donnell E, Mike V, Randi R, Andrew M, Wade S, Jacob H, Daniel F, Darren G, Michael (Moose) A, Kyle L and Matt H. These are all hard-working collectors who have a passion for the hobby!

The past year also proved to be more than our old building could handle! With the massive influx of items to be graded across the Beckett brand, we moved our location a few miles down the road. The new CBCS address is 2700 Summit Ave Suite #100, Plano, TX 75074. This building is about 6 times larger than the other! With huge quantities of packages arriving daily, let's hope she holds!

2022 was another phenomenal year for comics, the movies, cartoons and comic licensing in general. I saw a lot of really cool new comics come across my desk by an impressive array of artists! Speaking of artists, my good friend and fellow co-worker Steve Ricketts published his first comic book in December, called *Ripped!* It has several different covers including cover swipes of *Action Comics* #1 and *Mask Comics* #2. He did 99% of the work, writing, drawing, etc. I get .0001% credit for helping edit, give suggestions and ideas, but man, you should check it out! I can wait to see issue #2.

It was a sad year for all of us as we saw the passing of many greats in the hobby, including Neal Adams, George Pérez, Tim Sale, Alan Grant, Kazuki Takahashi, Ron Goulart, Vic Carrabotta, Tom Palmer and Lily Renée.

2022 definitely was a fun year for me, seeing many incredible vintage comics pass through. The Bethlehem copy of *Ghost Comics* #6 with its classic horror cover was incredible! One collector submitted 3 Marvel keys he bought in the mid '80s and kept this entire time! All 3 were fresh, high grade copies: *Incredible Hulk* #1, *Journey into Mystery* #83 and *Tales of Suspense* #39. Wow, what a treat!

2023, what will that bring? I can't wait to find out! Thank you to Bob Overstreet, Mark Huesman and J.C. Vaughn for all you do for the hobby!

Al Stoltz
Basement Comics / Basement Comics Pressing

"Free Cheap Money" poured out into the world and people finally stepping away from Covid lockdowns bought and sold comics, especially graded comics at record prices almost daily. The market was on fire for most of this year, and book prices were thought to never suffer an upset and have gravity yank them back down to earth...but it happened! In August, a hint of slowing and a slight downturn was just barely visible on the horizon, but it was peeking through just enough to get people to pay attention. By September it was evident that the bloom was off the roses as far as more modern books that were graded that reached nutty prices in the prior twelve months. November online sales have really slowed way down and regardless of what those on TV say, a recession is already here affecting sales heavily.

A book like *Thundercats* #1 in CGC 9.8 that was nothing, then almost $2K at one point, stands out in my mind showing a quick retreat in pricing. I was super happy with this phoenix of a book since I had over one hundred copies laying around the warehouse and figured no one would really even want them. We quickly pressed and sent them in for grading and sold them on the way up the "March to Madness" prices and then started selling just under GPA for the quick withdraw. People made money on this book and many more that exploded but those who bought in at the top end and figured they were building a future portfolio for early retirement got crushed. Even big Marvel keys in lower grades that sold for nutty money and now have tumbled back. As I'm writing this report in November, still have 10-20% more to drop before they level off. You want to treat this hobby like a stock market, then you have to be strapped in for the whole rollercoaster ride.

The good news for a seller like me that specializes in Golden Age and off title books and items like Mags, fanzines, really rare odd-ball items is that the market drifted to people buying those types of books and items now, Baltimore Comic-Con has just passed by and it was the only large show we set up at for 2022 and it was a huge show for us. We really put very little Bronze and Silver books on the walls and instead concentrated on books from a few collections that featured high grade Dells and Gold Keys books, Golden Age, Pre-Code Horror and lots of rare items we picked up with the almost two years we sat at home and did zero shows on the road. No big Marvel Keys or hot new books on the wall and we were mobbed all day long. Art, Animation cels from a large collection we bought sold in numbers. High Grade Dell and Gold Keys were gobbled up! My booth was so full of odd material that the great Steve Geppi himself seemed to like the books we offered that he hung out for a little while. However, I talked to many other dealers who were heavy sellers of the now slower material, and they said it was a tough battle to make sales at the show and with fast falling values of books they paid higher for just six to eight months prior when market was crazy hot. Will the Marvel and other Keys that went too high and too fast recover? Of course they will and probably in a year or two they will glide back up again.

Cons in 2022 for Basement Comics were very few and far between. We set up at all the comics shows for Clandestine Con, a local Maryland show that has been running for over thirty years by local legend Fred Edison, and I took a page from one of my show heroes Richie Mucheum and rolled in with one hand truck of goods and one display board for my one lone table. Easy in and easy out operation and brought new and exciting stuff that paid off each time I did a show. I was given a free pass to attend Heroes Convention in June by a gracious Shelton Drum since I could not set up at show this year because that weekend I was hosting a 100th Birthday for my Mother-in-Law and had to leave show by noon on Friday. Set up day madness was at usual pace at Heroes and at Earl Shaw's booth! It was mayhem after he let the mob start picking and it was like old time crazy comic buying like the good old days. Finally got to meet up with Buzzard Brothers Comics and they had a book on my Grail search, *Flash Gordon* Macy's giveaway, I was super jazzed to get it for only a few hundred bucks and add it to my eternal hoard pile. Having to leave on Friday by noon seriously cut into my search time, and I maybe really spent at six booths and could only wonder what treasures I was leaving behind. I heard later that show was great for the dealers I knew and as usual this Summer show is the BEST place to hunt comics from dealers you may only ever see here at this show.

Funny thing about the hobby I took note of was that long ago a dealer would never grade a comic that was not higher grade, especially not books that were now 1.8 or lower in grade. With demand or rarity of certain books, they are all getting graded and displayed prominently on the dealer show walls. We personally bought a *Detective* #38 graded 1.5 at Baltimore Comic-Con and were thrilled to be able to even buy it! We also have many Purple label books that are rare or great War covers that we readily buy now instead of passing them by. New buyers entering the market seem less put off by lower grades as well and just happy to be able to add that certain book to the keeper pile. I do realize that many of the early Golden Age books are slowly creeping up on one hundred years old and will not hold up perfect after that many years, so we will have to take what we can manage to find.

Basement Comics Pressing turned seven years old and the last two years of Covid poured so many books into our system it was almost maddening at times. That crazy cycle of press everything has given way to a more selective approach by our clients and work load has lessened a bit and turn around times have fallen back to 4-5 weeks at most. I think that pressing will remain a staple for those slabbing and looking for the bump in grade for a long while and I'm sure I will be busy in my pressing office for some time to come.

Where are we going in 2023? With the economy looking shaky at the moment I am sure many will pour money into tangible assets like comics and related items and hope for the best.

Doug Sulipa
Doug Sulipa's Comic World

The boom we saw during 2020-2021 through the Pandemic carried on to early 2022. Around March 2022, sales dropped off, but by June our sales were back to our normal levels of 2018 and 2019. With inflation everywhere and talk of a recession, it seems a natural state for sales to slow after a boom where prices went higher than expected on all the overly hot, over-hyped Key issues, especially on CGC graded comics. Some of the bigger price drops included *Eternals*, *G.I. Joe*, *Moon Knight*, *Morbius* and *She-Hulk* comics, but all still leveled off higher than the prices from the 2018 era. These were all blazing hot before their MCU releases, but all cooled after the Movies and TV shows debuted. Buyers quickly turned their attention to all the other "new" Key issues related to dozens of other upcoming movies and TV shows.

I have heard many fellow dealers complaint they got caught with too many copies of the over-hyped comics, and their sales have come to an abrupt halt. Since I have been selling comics since 1970, for me this was yet another five-year-cycle with many things changing, so I was expecting it and I was prepared. When things slowed, I saw it as an opportunity to list items on eBay and other sites at a rate of about 400% more than I did in 2020-2021. I went back to prioritizing the all-time most collected Silver and Bronze Age titles (*Amazing Spider-Man*, *Avengers*, *Batman*, *Daredevil*, *Fantastic Four*, *Hulk*, *Iron Man*, *JLA*, *Star Wars*, *Thor*, *Vampirella*, *Wonder Woman*, *X-Men* etc.). After a few months, sales climbed again, buyers were buying 2, 5 and 10 CGC at a time. We got busy enough that we did not have time for new listings for a few months.

Marvel comics dominate the back issue market, for many back-issue dealers they're up to 75% of their sales (even with my huge selection, it is still about 35% of my sales). Fueled by 14+ years of the Marvel Cinematic Universe, the demand for key issues is never ending, so even with big print runs, the prices continue to soar. There are over 16,400+ copies of *Incredible Hulk* #181 (1st Wolverine) graded by CGC as compared to around 220 copies of *Magnus Robot Fighter* #1(1963) with none in 9.8, yet #181 is much more valuable, showing that demand usually is more important that scarcity. There are 31,500+ *Amazing Spider-Man* #300 (1988) graded by CGC, yet most sellers find it near impossible to keep in stock in any grade. We sold nearly 1,000 copies of *Eternals* #1 in the last five years (over 650 were CGC graded.)

My all-time best-selling comic is *Captain Canuck* #1(1975), bought directly from Richard Comely the publisher. I have sold about 10,000 copies in total in the last 47+ years (about 6,000 copies from 1975-1980, plus 4,500 more from 1981-2015, and about 500 more from 2016-2022 (about 1-2 copies every week). I am down to my last 400 copies. Raw NM copies of #1 sell for around $30 with CGC 9.8 copies selling for around $200.

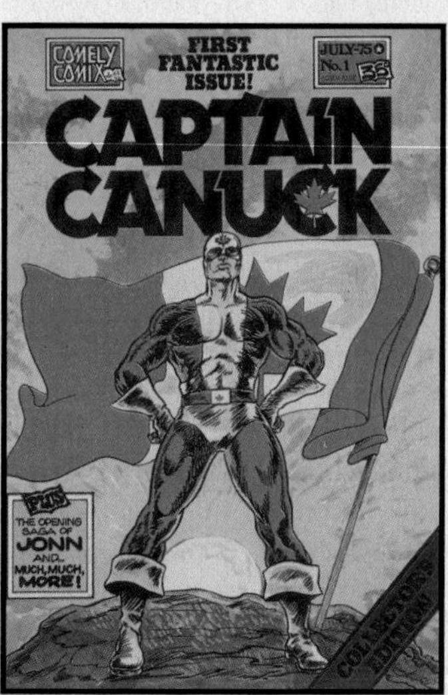

One of the trends that has happened is that all 1960s Marvel mainstream titles are selling in all grades, both Raw and CGC-Graded. Long-time collectors are scrambling to fill in the gaps in runs like *Amazing Spider-Man* #1-129, *Avengers* #1-100, *Batman* #171-251, *Daredevil* #1-18, *Fantastic Four* #1-100, *X-Men* #1-142. Even our Fair and Poor Silver Age issues are selling, as long as front cover and story are complete. Many with Pin-up or ad pages missing are now sold. Most S.A. Key issues and issues with top villains and characters (battle issues, Doctor Doom, Galactus, Joker, Juggernaut, Kang, Magneto, Mephisto, Riddler, Silver Surfer, Sinestro, Warlock, etc.) appearing, we are seeing GD to FN copies selling 200%, 400% and 600% of *Guide* prices for Raw copies, with CGC graded copies in 7.0 to 8.0 range bringing full 9.2 *Guide* prices or more.

This trend goes well beyond just Marvel and DC. The trend now also includes everything that was always in high demand with low supply. The *Overstreet Guide* being overly conservative, now has prices at wholesale or below wholesale on thousands of these high demand comics: Archie (Key issues, classic covers, swimsuits, suggestive/risque, monster/Sci-Fi), Archie Superheroes (*The Fly*, *Mighty Crusaders* etc., most later became DC heroes), most Atlas Marvel Comics of the 1950-1961 era, Charlton Super-Heroes (most became DC heroes in 1980s), Gold Key early and Key issues (*Dr. Solar*, *Magnus*, *Munsters*, *Phantom*, *Twilight Zone*), Pre-Code comics (Crime, Good Girl Art, Horror, parody/spoof, Science Fiction, Teen-Age, War), Hanna-Barbera comics (especially *Scooby Doo*), Comic Digests (1960s Gold Key, 1970s Charlton, 1990s Harvey), High Demand Top Artists (Neal Adams, Matt Baker, L.B. Cole, Corben, Dan DeCarlo, Ditko, EC artists, Frazetta, Russ Heath, Kirby, Mobius, Alex Schomburg, Todd McFarlane, Frank Miller, Steranko, Dave Stevens, Bill Ward, Wally Wood, Berni Wrightson, etc.), Comic Magazines (most 1950s-1960s, Eerie Pub., Marvel, Skywald, parody (*Cracked*, *Sick,* etc.), Top Comic Writers (Alan Moore, Stan Lee, etc.), Magazines and Fanzines with Preview First Appearances (McFarlane, black costume Spider-Man, *TMNT*, etc. in *Comics Journal*, *FOOM*, *Marvel Age*, *Comic Shop News* etc.), Underground, Eros and other Adult Comics, Low Print Self-Published Alternative Comics (*Cerebus*, *Jontar*, *Trial Run*, *Chakan*, early *TMNT* etc.)

The CPV (Canadian Price Variant - 1980's Newsstand Editions) market is strong and still growing, with many record-breaking prices. Do an internet search for "Canadian Price Variant Price Guide." CGC and CBCS now list Canadian Price Variant on the labels, and most Key issues sell for 50% to 300% more than the common Direct editions. The U.S. Newsstand editions of the 1980 through 2000 era are now commanding premium prices of 10% to 100% more than Direct Editions. In late 2022, CGC began listing Newsstand editions on their labels. In the 1980s most collectors bought their comics in comic stores, thus most have Direct editions. The survival rate of Newsstand editions (especially in High Grade) is much lower, as a large percentage sold to readers (mostly non-collectors). One of the reasons CPV higher values is that almost all are Newsstand editions. CGC will also now be listing "Multi-Pack" editions on their labels, more correctly termed Early Direct editions (non-polybag editions, were 100% distributed thru Seagate only, as far as I know). This pertains to Marvel comics from 2-12/1977, 1978 and 1979 (most with black diamond), which are often mistaken to be Whitman Marvel. In reality, only the plastic bag is Whitman. Once the comics are removed, they are identical to Marvel Direct editions. They are one and the same. There are approx. 400+ comics published thus in each of these years, with an estimated total of 1200-1300 existing in the period. The 1977 issues are usually scarcest, and typically command 50% over-*Guide* premiums, while 1978-1979 issues on average sell at about a 10-30% over-*Guide* premium. Since they are not broken out in the *Guide*, most collectors are not aware that they even exist. A few issues were not published as

Early Direct editions in the period (three entire months if I recall correctly). That was probably a publisher oversite error, and they seem likely to not exist. Knowledge and statistics are still hard to find on these, with no detailed research on scarcity. CGC Census will help in the future. Some issues seem quite rare, with a few collectors having searched to find in gaps in their collection for 5-10 years with little or no luck.

DC Early Direct editions started in December 1978 (see *Batman* #306 for example) through to December 1979. Many of the December 1978 DC comics were Whitman Logo Variants. Many might not exist as Early Direct editions. The Whitman Logo Variants of DC comics exist from March 1978 through to August 1980.

Once again, demand is up for most Licensed Character comics, with prices climbing on CGC graded Key issue copies, including: Horror (Universal Monsters, Godzilla, Freddy Krueger, *Friday the 13th*, Chucky, *Night of the Living Dead,* etc.), Video Games (*Blip*, *Legend of Zelda*, *Super Mario Brothers*), Movie and TV (*Aliens*, *Back to the Future*, *Beetlejuice*, *Blade Runner*, *Crow*, *Dune*, Elvira, John Wayne, *Jurassic Park*, *Munsters*, *Predator*, *Simpsons,* etc.), Animated and Toys (Disney Classics, Hanna-Barbera by all Publishers, G.I. Joe, Masters of the Universe, *TMNT*, *Transformers*), Manga (*Akira*, *Astro Boy*, *Battle of the Planets*, *Pokémon*, *Sailor Moon*), Role Playing (*Advanced Dungeon & Dragons*, *Magic the Gathering*, *Warhammer* etc.), Top Writers (Robert E. Howard, H.P. Lovecraft, George R.R. Martin, Edgar Allan Poe), 3-D and *How to Draw Comics.*

Maggie Thompson Collector

With Brent Frankenhoff

The back-issue market maintained a strong presence in 2022, building on its 2020 and 2021 pandemic-fueled expansion. Areas of speculation included previously undervalued first appearances, variant covers (as always), foreign reprints of key events, and the phenomenon of classifying character appearances in ordering catalogs and other promotional materials as "first appearances." (I might be encouraging that in a way, since my weekly column for Gemstone's *Scoop* newsletter has a focus on anniversaries of such events.)

Outside the field of that speculation, there's plenty of ongoing activity in back-issue sales, as collectors continue to fill holes in their collections. My colleague Brent Frankenhoff confirmed that his orders show that some of his sales provide inventory to other dealers.

New online streaming series showed little effect on back-issue prices, even though media appearances became more commonplace, doing deeper dives into publishers' character libraries. Underperforming big-screen releases have also been a drag on some back-issue prices.

Some online sellers also prepare random comics groupings to sell as separate lots. Sometimes, those lots don't have keys, and it's difficult to figure out what's driving prices. Some Facebook sales start with a set price at a certain hour, with the sale going to the first to buy at that price. These types of transactions are more difficult to track than simple one-on-one sales.

What appear to be warehouse purchases by such mass-market resellers as Half-Price Books has made a number of graphic novels available at steep discounts. Moreover, staffers sometimes let gems go unidentified. Savvy buyers can pick up bargains and fill their bookshelves inexpensively by being in the right place at the right time. For example, I found several plastic-wrapped $2 bundles of non-super-hero comics from the 1940s and 1950s at an area Half-Price Books a year or so ago. Whoever had done the sorting simply wrapped like with like, showing only the front cover of the issue on the top and the back cover of the issue on the bottom. I bought three or four in case they'd fill holes in my collection. When I unwrapped one, I found it included *Four Color* #48 in VG with an estimated value of a hundred times what I'd paid for the entire bundle.

Michael Tierney Collector's Edition & The Comic Book Store

Marvel Comics was back at full strength in 2022 and they dominated the new comics market with a superiority not seen since the heyday of editor Jim Shooter. DC dropped to a distant second place as the upheaval within that organization was intensified by the company changing ownership yet again. Huge turnover in their editorial ranks left the company seemingly rudderless while they waited for the latest restructure to be defined. Their output was not far off from what it was in the past, but it was primarily mini-series. What few ongoing series they did have in addition to their mainstays like *Batman* and *Detective Comics* did well, but the plethora of mini-series yielded no hits.

While Marvel's new comics sales were up, back issue sales went down with the economy. When the pandemic first hit in 2020, I saw my sales plummet from what was going to be one of my best years ever, collapsing 80% within a single month and staying at those levels not seen since the early-1980s. Customer traffic simply disappeared as the public was advised to stay home and not to venture outside. Then Diamond announced that they were shutting down their distribution network and it panicked all my employees into taking other jobs. Suddenly I was left with 5500 square feet of retail space in two cities to run single-handedly. That problem was compounded by the government paying people an extra bonus to stay unemployed, so no one showed for their interviews. Having just signed contracts to produce six fiction and non-fiction books over the next two years, I had other demands on my time and was left with no choice but to evolve from being a T-Rex of a retailer who dominated comic sales within my state, down to the size of a bird – as an online retailer. It was stunning how many of my customers made that transition with me. If I had tried to make a business model shift like this at any other time in the past, it would never have worked as effectively as it did.

My back issue sales also moved to online and, with the recession and spiraling inflation, soon took a downward spiral. When gas prices go up, I've always seen sales go down. When I was a brick-and-mortar retailer for nearly 40 years, operating in a largely rural state that meant most of my customers invested hours in making roundtrip drives to my stores, when gas prices went up something had to give – and it was always the comics hobby that was the first to go. Another recurring cyclical downturn to people's spending habits are the national elections. Some years people will freeze their spending while waiting to see the election results. That was never as prominent a factor for me as it was in 2022. But once the election was over, I did not see the expected bounce back start until the Thanksgiving Day weekend, which may have been more of a result of holiday shopping than renewed consumer confidence.

So my decision to evolve down in size and scope turned out to be the right one in every way. The hemorrhaging of expenses to keep two large retail locations going would have been digging me into a hole of debt that I might never have climbed out of. As it is, I've maintained profitability throughout all the recent upheavals in both the industry and the economy. It was fortunate that I'd built my retail stores with an emergency exit strategy by being my own landlord at one store. My North Little Rock location was in such a prime location, when I decided to explore that strategy, I received two offers by noon of the first day the property was listed, one for full price.

In the past I had thought about building a location for my Little Rock store and bought what I though was a nice, isolated parcel of land. The next month major retailers bought up the properties on either side and suddenly it was in a crowded location, so I sold it six months later for a multiple of the original purchase price. That deal and the purchase and sale of the North Little Rock property, which I operated for 30 years, were the most profitable business moves I've ever made—earning more money on those two transactions alone than the whole of my four decades as a retailer with multiple locations.

With my lease up at the other location at the same time that I sold my North Little Rock store, there was a keyhole-sized opportunity of exit that I hit squarely. Sold most of my excess inventory to another online retailer, who told me that if I had hesitated even a single month, the offer I received would have been halved because so many other retailers started failing at that time.

But I didn't sell all my back issues. I had already gathered a selection ear-marked for online sales, and continued to pursue that strategy, which did very well in 2020.

But, as mentioned earlier, back issue activity began slowing down in 2021 and that trend accelerated this year, but still included some key transactions, and another mylar horror story that has become an annual trend while liquidating a trinity of books that I once refused to sell, preferring to keep them on display. The previous two were platinum editions of *Superman* #75 and *Adventures of Superman* #500, featuring the death and rebirth of Superman, and both of which were still sealed in their black bags that had unfortunately adhered to their mylar cases.

When I went to sell my platinum *Spider-Man* #1, once again mylar damage was detected. Upon receipt, I immediately encased it in mylar and hung it in a frame with ultra-violet light protection. Expecting it to be in near 10 point condition when I opened it to list online, I discovered that at some point over the last thirty years some idiot employee decided to have a look for themselves, and damaged the back cover on the razor sharp mylar edge when they put it back in. The condition was downgraded from Mint to a Fine at best. Fortunately, I had also enclosed the original letter that Marvel sent with it, and this drew far more interest than the book itself. Apparently, few of those were saved, and I had numerous offers for the letter alone. Eventually I accepted $650 for the pair.

Another notable sale was *Wolverine* #88 in Near Mint for $75. The year before I had sold several high grade copies of this issue whose only significance was an appearance by Deadpool. That demand slowed this year to a single copy. The 1 copy per store variant of *Mighty Avengers* #1, which featured the first appearance of Monica Rambeau as Spectrum, sold in Near Mint for $100. *Secret Invasion* (2008) #1 sold in Near Mint for $50.

One area that has been growing steadily in recent years has been the demand for out-of-print graphic novels. Uncle Scrooge reprints from Fantagraphics sell very well, and in first print for a premium. My best graphic novel sale was the 2016 *Conan Omnibus: Birth of a Legend* from Dark Horse, in Near Mint for $75.

Ted VanLiew
Superworld Comics

Hi all. As always, it's been a fun year! Overall, the overheated market we saw for a couple years during the height of the pandemic has subsided. Prices have been adjusting to more where they should be, and the spastic speculation has calmed down for the time being.

Also, due to the interruption in folks' ability to go to the movie theater to see the latest releases, speculation on the latest movie and show announcements has lost some steam. It's still a factor, but things just aren't as crazy as they were for a while, and prices on modern books have generally gone down and stabilized.

We're still percolating along, and buying good quality books, and art never goes out of style! Golden, Silver, and Bronze Age books always are steady sellers. I've noticed that a lot of buyers are more excited by the scarcer older books than in the past. I think possibly because as great as the Silver and Bronze Age books are, we do see most of them quite frequently. Golden and Atomic Age books are genuinely scarce, so when we present them, collectors and investors get genuinely excited.

Another nice aspect of our hobby is that no matter what's happening in the overall economy or in the world, we're relatively unaffected. I've noticed that some other collectibles go through boom and bust cycles, but comics are always cool! Who'd have thought back in the day when we were the nerds who were in our own secret worlds, while the jocks and cool cats were getting the glory, that we'd wind up on top of the heap. It's quite gratifying!

Golden Age: Interest in Golden Age books has been increasing, and it's a bit surprising, as there's always concern that as the original collectors 'age out', interest might wane. I suspect that as collectors and investors educate themselves on the timelines of many of the characters and the overall history of comics, their increased awareness results in heightened desire to own some of these cool books. Also, many of the most well-known characters were featured in 1930s and '40s books prior to their '50s and '60s incarnations. Plus, the serialized nature of various series really helps in providing connective tissue between eras. It certainly doesn't hurt that there are some wonderful references, such as this very *Overstreet Guide*, and online, Grand Comics Database, which provides cover images and content info on nearly every comic ever published.

Timelys are tough to keep in stock, as they don't turn up as often as we'd like, and when they do, whoosh!... out the door, especially war era issues, scarcer ones, ones featuring really cool characters and classic covers.

DCs are quite a broad category. There are the more mainstream titles such as *Batman*, *Superman*, *Flash*, *Wonder Woman*, et al. and then there are the secondary titles, such as *Sensation Comics*, *All Flash*, *Leading*, *All-American* and a host of others. They are generally good sellers. As always, war covers are in demand, along with villain covers. Batman always has led the pack. Even though the All American hero Supes came first, Batman's more popular. Maybe it says something about us that we favor the nutcase who prowls the city at night over the All-American good guy.

There are a plethora of publishers from the Golden Age, some we've heard of, like Fox, Centaur, Fiction House, Fawcett, and many others, and then some that are less recognizable, like Hyper Publications, Ace Publications, and Novelty Pubs. All have some great titles, and some pretty good titles. Books that were published by these lesser known, small, or fly-by-night outfits are tough to locate and great to have.

An area that doesn't get the love it should is Platinum Age, which is basically anything pre-*Action* #1. Again, there are may wonderful books in this era. Most are 'funnies' or adventure stories. Definitely worth exploring if you feel ambitious.

Some sales from 2022: *Batman* #68 VF+ $3,800, *Captain Aero* #26 VG/F $3,600, *Captain America Comics* #47 VF $6,200, #57 VF $5,500, *Challenger Comics* NN CGC 5.0 $14,000, *Startling* #49 CGC 4.0 $15,000, *Spirit* #22 FN $4,700, *Superman* #8 $6,500, and *Thrilling* #44 CGC 5.0 $3,300.

Atomic Age (1950-1959 or so): Such a fertile area for searching for great, lesser known books! Almost anything published by EC, Avon, and Ziff-Davis is first rate. Besides the superhero books, which are always consistently interesting, there is the Pre-Code Horror and Crime genre, and an explosion of science fiction and fantasy books. This is the era that is most known for "cover collecting." There are many truly outrageous and grotesque covers amongst the Crime and Horror, and these move fast, and for rising prices. Competition for these books is also outrageous!

The 1950s was the era of B.E.M.s (bug-eyed monsters), and a lot of the sci-fi books reflected this. Some of the top artists in comics history were in their prime as well, such as Wally Wood, Bill Everett, LB Cole, George Saunders, and Bernard Baily, to name a few. Lots of classic covers to be found in this time period, as well as covers that are not 'classic', but are really cool nonetheless.

War and Western books are lesser sellers, but there is a plethora of really exceptional books in this group. Lots of great covers and stories by Heath, Kubert, Everett, Colan, Kirby, among others.

Some sales: *Astonishing* #30 VG/F $4,800, *Chilling Tales* #16 VG+ $3,300, *Crime Suspenstories* #22 FR/GD $1,800, *Eerie*(1947) #1 CGC 1.8 $3,500, *Underworld Crime* #7 VG $5,000, and *Weird Tales of the Future* #7 VG $2,400.

Silver Age: Possibly the most important era. This is when comics truly came into their own, and became a force to be reckoned with. DC kicked things off with some of their characters that they introduced or re-introduced, and not long after, Marvel followed suit and then steadily became a monster!

For Marvels, books published between late '61 and '63 are by far the most valuable, as Marvel was a small company at that point, and was proceeding to revolutionize the market. By 1964, they were really catching on, and their circulation was increasing, so more copies exist from each year they were growing. *Amazing Spider-Man* is certainly the king as always, but *Fantastic Four* has been creeping up on the web-slinger! Both titles, besides just being great, have a lot of key issues within their runs. This is in contrast to, say, *Daredevil*, who lacks the copious amount of key issues, and as a result, doesn't quite get the respect he deserves. All the # 1 issues and major first appearances are always in high demand, and we just can't turn up enough of them to take care of everyone who wants them. I always found it curious that a #1 is worth about 50 times more than a #2, considering they're only a month or two apart, but the market has spoken!

DCs aren't nearly as popular in general as the Marvels, which I think is unfortunate, as there are a ton of good to great DCs in the Silver Age. *Batman* pretty much leads the way as most consistently popular. *Detective*, *Flash*, *Brave & the Bold*, *Showcase*, *Wonder Woman* also are consistent sellers. Many titles, such as *Superman*, *Tales of the Unexpected*, *My Greatest Adventure*, *Atom*, *Metal Men*, *Aquaman*, and others don't sell as well as they should, with the exception of key issues (Jose'll kill me for including *Superman* in this group). Now that I think of it, the DC mystery titles, led by *House of Mystery* and *House of Secrets*, are consistently popular.

There are some really interesting books by other publishers as well. Gold Key published *Magnus, Robot Fighter*, *Doctor Solar*, *Space Family Robinson*, and tons of TV and movie tie-in titles with nice photo still covers. Charlton had a full slate of titles, some with Ditko covers and art, and others with early art by Aparo, Giordano, and others. Tower Comics are really exciting, but don't get the action they should. They were a company co-founded by Wally Wood to work outside of the tyranny of the 'Big Two', and they published *T.H.U.N.D.E.R. Agents*, *Dynamo*, *Noman*, *Undersea Agent*, and others, featuring art by Wood, Adkins, Sekowski, Ditko, Crandall, and other top artists.

Some Sales: *Amazing Spider-Man* #1 CGC 7.0 $48,000, #3 CGC 7.0 $8,500, #50 VF/NM $8,500, *Annual* #1 VF/VF- $7,000, *Avengers* #1 FN+ $12,000, #4 VF/VF+ $6,500, *Batman* #181 VF $4,800, *Daredevil* #1 CGC 8.5 $28,000, CGC 7.5 $16,000, *Fantastic Four* #1 GD+ $19,000, #3 VF $7,500, #5 CGC 7.5 $45,000, #48 VF $7,500, *Incredible Hulk* #1 CBCS 3.0 $26,500, #5 VF/NM $9,700, *Journey Into Mystery* #84 CGC 9.4 $40,000, #85 CGC 9.6 $85,000, *Justice League of America* #1 CGC 7.0 $6,500, *Silver Surfer* #4 CGC 9.4 $11,500, *X-Men* #1 CBCS 3.0 $18,000, and #4 VF/NM $16,000.

Bronze Age: This is an area where books were under-appreciated for many years, then took off, then leveled off, then took off again. There are zillions of worthy books in this time period, and lots of keys, including first appearances and special event issues. Again, Marvel leads by a mile, but DC has some goodies as well.

Any of the black 'picture frame' cover issues are very tough to find in superior grade, and picture frame covers are popular in general. Jack Kirby had left Marvel for DC, and launched his Fourth World opus, which lasted for about a year and a half. These books and the titles Kirby launched afterwards are gaining esteem in collectors' minds. In the mid-'70s, Kirby returned to Marvel, and created many new titles there as well.

By and large, books from the first half of the 1970s are far more sought after than the latter half books. The direct market was in its infancy, and speculation on certain books began in earnest, leading to a larger supply of certain issues, because they were saved with the express purpose of investment. They still have great collectibility though, because as a lot of time has elapsed, and some of the books have perished in flooding or fire, and have been disseminated into collections, they're tougher to locate than ever.

One of DC's strongest areas in the late '60s through the '70s was the mystery titles, led by *House of Mystery* and *House of Secrets*. Others soon followed, and these titles have stupendous covers and art by the likes of Adams, Wrightson, Wood, Nino, and many others. Marvel was inspired to launch several horror themed books as well, such as *Monster of Frankenstein*, *Tomb of Dracula*, *Werewolf by Night*, *Ghost Rider*, et al., which remain tremendously collectible.

Some Sales: *Amazing Spider-Man* #129 CGC 9.0 $4,200, *Batman* #251 CBCS 9.0 Signed Adams $2,500, *Giant-Size X-Men* #1 CGC 9.0 $8,000, *Incredible Hulk* #181 CGC 9.4 $20,000, and *Marvel Spotlight* #5 CGC 8.5 $6,300.

Copper and Modern Age: Gotta admit that I used to think that books from these eras wouldn't amount to much, but I have been proven wrong! As long as there are creative folks working in the industry, there are going to be hits. Good examples include the advent of Cable and Deadpool, co-created by Rob Liefeld, and *Teenage Mutant Ninja Turtles*, which captured lightning in a bottle for Eastman and Laird. There are many movie and TV show tie ins, and those tend to jump in demand and value. Lots of other interesting characters have been introduced in the years from 1981 or so to the present. I'm not expert in this era, but am gaining a greater appreciation for lots of the books.

Couple of Sales: *Albedo* #2 VF/NM $10,500 and *TMNT* #1 NM (2nd print) $4,200.

Well, hope this is all helpful, and not too long winded. May the Seven Rings of Raggador never close in on you! Best, Ted.

John Verzyl II & Rose Verzyl
Comic Heaven

Salutations, comic collectors! There is much to cover in this 2022-2023 Market Report as, at the time of writing this, there have been historic highs and the threat of looming lows.

Besides being a fantastic year for comic sales over the internet, it was also amazing for comic sales in person! Physical conventions are finally back to near capacity, unlike the half-filled aisleways of last year. In the previous two years, we have visited local comic book and trading card shows, wandering around for deals and fun, but this is the first year that Comic Heaven has set up as a vendor in a convention hall since the Covid-19 pandemic.

The first and largest convention we attended in 2022 was San Diego Comic-Con. It was bizarre and comforting wandering the convention hall, finally returning to a place I remember so vividly. Being able to catch up with friends and customers that I can only see in California was delightful, and, for a moment, it felt like Covid had never happened. This is reflected by the attendance being near what it was pre-Covid, as well as the smiles hidden underneath mandatory masks. Well, I'll take what I can get.

Further, sales at the show were terrific. At Comic Heaven, we do not disclose sales data on the grounds that some customers like to keep their collections private. With that being said, I can tell you that our numbers were quite good. The sales were lower than pre-Covid sales; however, we left certain items of Golden Age inventory home for security purposes, so I expected to sell less. What really shocked me was that some of the items I left home were requested! I am pleasantly surprised that in a market where Silver and Bronze have dominated, the Golden Age is finally getting its chance to shine. In that same vein, it was jarring having customers come to the booth and pay full sticker for books, no haggling required. An absolute godsend. I feel so blessed. To anyone reading this that attended SDCC 2022, I want to thank you for stopping by the booth, even if you didn't buy anything.

The final convention we attended this year was The Summit 2022. From what I have heard and have been told, this is a very new show, and it is a *faux pas* to bring Silver and Bronze. It was a very intimate affair held at the Heritage Auction's Headquarters in Dallas, Texas. Everyone in attendance was either another dealer or a collector in the Texas area that never leaves their house. The convention was packed to the gills with Golden Age goodies with some light Silver, Bronze, and Modern sprinkled in. The sales numbers were quite good but made even better when I found out the event was catered. Free miniature tacos with napkins are divine when you are busy at a convention and cannot get outside the booth. I look forward to going next year and am glad to see all the new and returning faces.

Well, that is enough sentimentality, time for some cold, hard numbers. This year was astounding for Golden Age sales. A ton of high-grade keys and collections have come out of the woodwork this year and done spectacularly. I'm sure everyone reading this has heard of the unprecedented $5.3-million-dollar sale of *Superman* #1 8.0 Mile High in April, but are you aware of the other record-shattering sales of *Captain America Comics* #1 and *Marvel Comics* #1?! A *Captain America Comics* #1 9.4 San Francisco copy sold for $3.12 million, a massive step up from its 2019 sale of $915,000. I repeat, the same book from three years ago sold for over three times its initial sale. Talk about a profit margin! Moreover, this increase can be seen in lower conditions as well. An 8.5 copy sold for $384,000 in January of 2021, and two 7.0 copies sold in May of this year for nearly the same amount ($312,000 and $339,761). Similarly, the *Marvel Comics* #1 9.2 Pay copy sold for $2,427,778 in March. A sizeable jump in price compared to the $1.26 million sale of the 9.4 Windy City copy at the tail end of 2019. These keys are in such demand that even No Grade/Coverless copies have gone up from a staggering $22,800 (September 2021) to $40,800 (January 2022)! And these extraordinary sales have a trickledown effect on all Golden Age books. Even if random Golden Age books go up $100 or so dollars over their usual rate of increase, they are selling much easier than they ever have.

However, for the first time in an extremely long time, it appears that the never-ending money train of Silver and Bronze keys may be coming to an end. With the lack of superpowered sales at the box office as well as fan apathy, comic book key speculation may no longer be as fruitful as years prior. For example, *Savage She-Hulk* #1 9.8, a book that was selling strong with anticipation for its Disney + miniseries, has slumped from average sales of $1,250 to a depressing average of $450 (the last five sales of December 2022 being $470, $425, $446, $460, and $475). To make matters even worse, this book has little to no chance to recover from this severe decrease seeing as the TV show is finished while also being received very negatively by fans and general audiences alike. For the movie side of things, let us look at *Fantastic Four* #4, the first Silver Age appearance of the Sub-Mariner. This book has been steadily increasing in the last few years with the imminent arrival of Subby to the silver screen. For instance, two 8.0 (VF) copies sold for $15,600 and $18,600 in 2021, while three copies in the same grade have sold for $19,800, $13,200, and $15,000 in 2022. On paper, that seems pretty good, especially considering that one sale was over last year's numbers. However, that $19,800 sale was in April, at the height of all the anticipation for the movie. With more details about the film being released, the sales were bound to plummet, a very different outcome compared to comics related to movies before Phase 4. As for after-movie impact, 4.0 has dropped from a rough average of $5,500 to around $3,250. This clearly indicates *Black Panther: Wakanda Forever*'s poor performance.

Well, not all is lost. The Fantastic Four is rumored to be hitting the silver screen soon, and their first appearance, *Fantastic Four* #1, is still selling at strong numbers above *Guide*. 8.5 copies of the book have jumped from $132,000 in 2021 to an average of about $260,000 (the three sales of 2022 are $350,000, $240,000, and $228,000). The only caveat may be that *Fantastic Four* #1 is a cornerstone of Silver Age comics, meaning the strong sales may be indicative of their collectable and historical value, not movie tie-in potential. Be warned collectors, while a lot of books may appear to be half price; they may only be worth the same amount they were in 2019-2020, which leaves little room for profit without an external modifier like a movie or TV special.

In closing, I would like to say that I am very proud to be a part of the comic-collecting community. Comics have survived the ever-changing landscape of investments gracefully, avoiding the lows of cryptocurrency, NFT scams, and negative stock yields. More importantly, I am thankful once again to meet collectors and investors in person and shake their hands. I hope all of you have a great year, and happy hunting!

Lon Webb
Dark Adventure Comics

I'm recovering from my third bout of Covid, complete with the essential brain fog, so I apologize if my writing is not as up to par or as astute as in my previous annual reports. That said, I think it is more than safe to state that 2021 was perhaps THE best year ever for significant sales in the history of the hobby, with 2022 batting a fine clean-up. Prices realized on many books actually doubled every couple of months and continued to do so well past year's end. It is also important to note that the rapid and steady increase was primarily seen on slabbed books (especially graded 9.6 and 9.8) and the shortage of those as key issues in the marketplace; after all, people were mainly buying instead of selling off at the time.

It is arguable that the shortage might very well have been fueled in part by the slow turnaround times from all third-party grading companies, dovetailing well into 2022. It is a known fact that the major percentage of books in queue for slabbing were modern comics, which also significantly added to the shortage of vintage items reaching the marketplace for ready sale in that given time due to the wait because of the modern glut. Plus, many of those desirable books that did hit the marketplace with detailed grader's notes were immediately snatched up by flippers in search of grading bumps by cracking, then cleaning/pressing and sending them for grading and then off to auction, further stalling final end-of-line sales to collectors for that period of time.

I note all of this as a partial explanation on the rapid price increases that were outside the increased buying and investor interest that was fired by the pandemic and lack of readily available product to buy from stores and conventions due to closures. When the main source of collector's crack or the highest graded copy around was to be found primarily at auction-only...well, expect end prices to soar, then settle a bit only when availability heightens.

Throughout this year, those slabbing queues shortened, inflation hit, venues fully opened back up, and product availability made a comeback-even though most high-end books were held and put into another queue for auction placement. Now, the high-end goodies continue to do very well at a slightly slowing price point, but the regular market items have dipped back into moderate to discounted sales as the availability of items increase and ready extra cash decrease among numerous collectors.

Many in the business reeled this year because just as rapidly as the prices and sales had increased across the board in the last years (seemingly with no end in sight), they suddenly began stalling and decreasing. Start-up open sourcing businesses that flourished during the pandemic years started falling like dominoes, eBay truly regressed to dollar store and flea market bargaining again with a startling immediacy, and the entire selling field seemed to revert to default settings. Normalcy and expedient business-as-usual was returning to the market and way too fast for many.

Seeing as how high-end keys and high-grade slabbed books remain (and probably will always remain) this hobby's largest cash source, the acknowledged impetus is, of course, on those books as the highest priority in the market. Added to this as an inescapable fact is that slabbed books increasingly are bringing ever larger money out of perceived added value while raw books continue to bring far less...even in comparable high grades or rarity or in key issues. That brings me to a series of important observations about the current and future of this market, third-party grading, and the growing counter-culture within the hobby that is focused in whole on grade manipulation.

In the past, we've all seen conservation and we've all seen restoration and we've delineated the difference to have a healthy hobby. I personally have no issue with either unless it is done poorly by amateurs or for no reason other than increasing the price-and neither do many buyers (in fact, some prefer the best visually appealing copy they can get at the lowest price) ...as long as any work done to a book is expressly noted when it changes hands and the buyer has that information.

I've been burned by this, and sadly, I've inadvertently burned others long ago due to lack of knowledge or disclosure about what I'll call "books that have been dicked-with" that I'd purchased, kept, or resold without being aware of the work or not being trained enough or had the tools or proper time to find and return them or note it in detail myself. That is true of almost every dealer if they are being honest, as everyone has made that unintentional dumbass mistake at some point because the more books you buy and the speed in which they are sold makes it more likely something gets right by you. And one suffers for it, yes, one does.

Thankfully, my mistakes were never intentional and it was a learning curve for a young man. Now, everyone has had access to the tools and knowledge for many years to spot an undisclosed, dicked-with book if they wish to know how to do so. If work is not disclosed...face it...it's a dicked-with book. Restoration spotting was the biggest reason I was a main supporter of third-party grading at its onset. I pushed for it, especially with the coming future that was online sales back in those early days of the internet, and especially because some work was incredibly tough to discern and overall comic values were rapidly increasing and trust was a must in sight-unseen transactions.

The big third-party graders have been around for over 20 years now and have mostly been exceptional in identifying dicked-with books, though sometimes erring on the side of caution. Today is a different story. Ever since pressing and cleaning a book was greenlit for a blue label to boost flagging slabbing revenues, the extremely small subculture of book-dicking began to explode. That culture is full of good people who do credible, non-invasive work, but is also overran with flippers and those fascinated with condition manipulation for fun and profit. It's the wild west out there now.

At first, it was about pushing the envelope of what was allowable by the exalted slabbing companies. Then, YouTube entered the picture and how to dick-with-books videos were posted, books on book-dicking were written, restoration techniques long known and created by professionals were dragged out into the light and touted as allowable new discoveries because some amateur tweaked something...and the list goes on.

The challenge most amateur restorers take and thrive on nowadays is how to get book-dicking past the graders to a blue label. They call it science-based, harmless to paper, a skill, and an art (which it can be); some do and don't understand that it is harmful and is restoration. Slab-cracking and re-submitting has been going on for years, but now it is a massive problem-so much so that grading company census numbers are a joke. That is a real issue for serious high-grade or census-based collectors and has been since cleaning/pressing was allowed.

I've been observing this sub-culture for some time in online forums, on video channels, in Facebook groups and literally everywhere. It is a shared and grass roots movement for book appearance manipulators that have blinded themselves to what they are actually doing. You'd be surprised how many of them fight for credit for having discovered the same old technique wheel over and over. The current thing is whitening, lightening, and stain-removal, mostly all done by chemical process, moisture, and LED lights...otherwise known as restoration because the paper itself is changed, added to in process, taken away from...dicked with...by processes far from new, just maybe tweaked.

There is comic conservation, which is cold-pressing, light cleaning, etc.-all laborious, time-consuming arts. Then, there is restoration-heat pressing, moisture, chemicals, staple cleaning/replacement, etc., all of which changes the originality and structure of the comic and affects the paper and shortens its life. Looks great now, but not so good in the future sealed in a slab with a front-end grade on a back-end hidden reality. They'll argue you the science of it like a specialist arguing evidence to the opposition's expert at a murder trial, and use paper reversion as an excuse for crossing a line, but any learned conservator will destroy those arguments in seconds with simple facts.

There are no longer hundreds of pressers out there... there are literally thousands, with hundreds of them practicing the arcane art of book-dicking as a hobby or for-profit profession. Hundreds of amateur restorers believing they are pros because of the visual results they achieve through practice. Actually, some of them have become pros of a sort, but it's a skillful con at the end of the day - both intentional and unintentional. It all seemed like a passing thing at first, like a trendy water challenge, but it is now a very dangerous movement within and for the hobby. It all used to generally be an under-the-table amateur thing you heard about - book surgeries in someone's downstairs lab, but now it's out in the open for everyone to see the step-by-step processes and results literally available for viewing anywhere...the grade bumps from cracked books...the Mile High that was 6.0 in 2000 that is now a 9.2 blue label. Suddenly, everyone is a book surgeon.

I would say conservatively that there are probably untold thousands of slabbed books out there (with hundreds more coming back as blue labels daily to weekly as we speak) that are dicked-with books, and I don't mean non-invasive and professionally conserved work, but restored by definition; undisclosed and in unknown quantities that are presently out there in the wild, in growing numbers. Restoration checks by the grading companies miss most of these because they are either done so well or they simply do not have the time or methodology to pick them all out or they are allowed for some reason. I wonder if any grader actually goes online and sees all of the pics of the returned grade-bumped and slabbed blue labels with identifying numbers on them that the proud practitioners post there to many congratulatory comments... and with a detailed commentary of exactly what they did and how they pulled it off...and the sheer numbers of them. The thought pattern is if you beat the graders, it's not restoration, if they catch it, then it is.

This concerns me enough that I devoted this report to the implications of this now-prevalent industry inside the hobby. Will this become as accepted a practice as cleaning and pressing has become? I pray not. Everything needs to tighten up. We are at a time similar to that of many years ago when rules and methodology concerning book-dicking had to be changed and almost regulated for the safety of the hobby to maintain trust in it by a sea-change in/of information and how it is managed and disseminated. Professionalism and disclosure won the day. The same needs to occur again, and quickly.

I do not wish to offend here as much as hopefully humorously inform and not waste space on dry scientific sides of all of this to anally prove what I'm stating in a general fashion due to space. I realize that there are myriad views on this subject out there, some of which differ greatly from mine. I just feel it is too important a subject not to address, considering the explosion in value perceived that Third-Party graded books are to the market as opposed to the continuing lessening of raw values, especially at a time when undisclosed restoration is at an all-time and ever-escalating high. Blessings to you all and have a great year and love and enjoy what you collect!

Sales of Note (Brokered, Consigned, or In-House): Group of Timely/Atlas Final Issues (All Raw) - *All Winners* #21 VG $2,200; *Sub-Mariner Comics* #42 VF $2,300; *Venus* #19 VF+ $16,000; *Human Torch* #38 VF/NM $2,800; and *Captain America Comics* #78 VF+ $3,800.

Also, *Space Western Comics* #44 VF/NM $3,000; *Doc Savage Comics* #1 6.0 $2,890; *Little Dot* #1 FN/VF $7,550; *Little Lotta* #1 NM- $4,000; *Cat-Man Comics* #30 VF $3,400; *Action Comics* #12 GD+ $7,200; *Four Color* #878 Peanuts VG+ $425; and *Mysterious Adventures* #13 FN $4,200.

Harley Yee
Harley Yee Comics

The 2022 market can be described as a tale of two halves. The first half continued the hot 2021. Fueled by multiple sources of money from crypto, cards and government money, comic book prices continued to increase across the board, from Golden Age to Modern Age.

The second half saw some price pressure on many books and titles. This happened mostly in the Silver Age and Bronze Age market, with Golden Age mostly holding steady.With many new ways of selling comics arriving almost monthly, adding to the old ways, it's causing the market to grow as seeing comic book characters displayed in everyday life has become commonplace.

As to the market, Golden Age continues to see inroads to a younger age group. Social media has made it popular for discussion groups with rarity, classic covers and classic artists driving that market. Pre-Code Horror, Good Girl art, and Matt Baker books are particularly strong. DC Golden Age continue being strong across the board with *Batman* and *Flash* leading the way. Timelys continue to be scarce and I cannot keep *Captain America Comics* in stock.

While the Silver Age Marvel market was steady, it was led by *Amazing Spider-Man*, *X-Men* and *Sub-Mariner*. Particularly strong demand was for *Fantastic Four* #4, #5, and #12, *X-Men* #4, *Avengers* #9 and *Daredevil* #7. The Silver Age DC market was led by the usual suspects in *Batman* and *Wonder Woman*.

The Bronze Age market was generally led by TV/movie characters such as Scooby-Doo, Moon Knight, Ghost Rider and Batman.

Overall, I see the market being steady in 2023 with Golden Age remaining strong. Silver Age and Bronze Age will be steady with TV/movie announcements and premieres creating hits.

Vincent Zurzolo & Rob Reynolds
Metropolis Collectibles
ComicConnect.com

Vincent Zurzolo - Metropolis Collectibles and ComicConnect.com

To paraphrase the novel *War & Peace*, "It was the best of times (it really was) and it was the worst of times (well, not really the worst). 2022 stormed in like a lion and left like a lion/lamb hybrid from a weird Sci-fi/fantasy movie. The Golden Age market, due to its rarity and overall demand, is doing very well with prices either plateauing or hitting new records. For the rest of the market, there have been a correction on many books. Some Silver and Bronze have decreased by 10-30%. Copper and Modern have dropped by 10-50%. That isn't to say that there aren't many books from these time periods that are still going strong and increasing. But the overall trajectory of books from this time period, due to how common they are, has been downward.

My advice to anybody out there who has been trying to figure out when to jump into the market, do it now. I believe the market will plateau, and similar to the Middle Ages Italian mathematician Fibonacci's Fibonacci Sequence, will eventually rise to heights greater than we saw over the last two years. When will this happen? I seem to have lost my crystal ball. I hope to find it before my next annual report.

The great thing about buying comics regardless of a bull or bear market, is you are buying something you love and enjoy as a nostalgic pop-culture collectible, and for the entertainment and escapist value it delivers. I know for me, whether a great comic book I own goes up or down in value, it doesn't change the smile it puts on my face when I look at it. I certainly hope that it is the same for you.

We've had many amazing prices this year. Here is a small sampling of some of the record sales (you can find everything sold in 2022 on comicconnect.com): *Action Comics* #1 CGC 6.0 Rocket Copy $3,550,000, *Batman* #1 CGC 8.0 $1,550,000, *Amazing Fantasy* #15 CGC 9.0 $1,100,000, *Action Comics* #1 CGC 9.4 restored $500,000, *Avengers* #1 CGC 9.4 $280,000, *Superman* #1 CGC 1.8 $240,000, *Incredible Hulk* #1 CGC 8.0 $200,000, *Captain America Comics* #1 CGC 7.0 restored $95,000, and *Werewolf by Night* #32 CGC 9.8 $63,000.

Original art is doing gangbusters and due to the unique nature of this collectible, it will continue to do so. Here are some of our biggest sales: *Avengers Classic* #1 cover by Art Adams $105,000, *Marvel Comics Presents* #100 page 18 by Sam Kieth $50,000, *X-Men* #100 page 4 by Dave Cockrum $36,750, *Paragon Pretty Girl Portfolio of the White Queen* by John Byrne $25,000, *X-Men* #110 page 23 by Tony Dezuniga $13,750, *Detective Comics* #534 cover by Gene Colan $17,000 and *Batman: Curse of the White Knight* #8 cover $25,000, and *Inferior Five* #9 cover by Win Mortimer $14,000.

The market for action figures continues to do very well.

We sold a Darth Vader AFA graded 85 12 back-A; DT Saber for $160,000, Luke Skywalker AFA 85 12 back-A; DT Saber $140,000 and an Obi-Wan Kenobi AFA 80 AFA 85 12 back-A; DT Saber $130,000.

One of the coolest items we sold in 2022 was Mark Zuckerberg's rookie baseball card. It is a card he and his mom made when he was 8 years old. He signed it for his favorite camp counselor who held onto it for 30 years. We sold it this year for $136,500.

In closing, thanks to all the buyers, sellers, consignors, bidders, friends and family who helped to make this year one to be remembered in a very positive way. As always, I wish you and yours all the best and hope to speak with you soon about the thing that brings us all together, comic books!

Rob Reynolds - ComicConnect.com

Like the winds of March, the 2022 collectibles market raged in like a lion and left like a lamb. Prices that were easy to achieve at the start of the year got tougher to match as the year persisted. While Golden Age keys and rarities maintained a higher percentage of value over the four major auctions with numerous records set by year's end, Silver Age books experienced more value adjustments. Several early sellers became late buyers as a few prices that were beyond reach in Spring eased into more budgets by Thanksgiving.

Still, ComicConnect produced results over 20% greater than 2021 for our best year ever, topping over $31 million in Event Auction sales. The other day a client called, pledged their ongoing loyalty, and said, "Til now, I've sold through every auction house, and I know the market is correcting some, but I don't lose money with ComicConnect like I do the other guys, I'm sending you all of my stuff going forward." Up against a market that has been tough for a few collectible categories, ComicConnect achieved record prices in grade throughout the year.

As ComicConnect expanded investment categories in 2021, we consolidated those efforts in 2022 to focus on comics, original comic art, pulps, and certified video tapes and games. Event #49 kicked off the auction season by offering a unique copy of *Marvel Comics* #1 9.2, Lloyd Jacquet's Pay Copy. Historically speaking, the Pay Copy is the most notable *Marvel* #1 in existence as it comes directly from the file of Lloyd Jacquet, founder of Funnies, Inc., who owned the rights at the time to 'The Human Torch' and 'Sub-Mariner.' Jacquet used the comic to record creator earnings, including Sub-Mariner artist Bill Everett and Human Torch creator Carl Burgos. The record-setting comic eclipsed $2.4 million at auction. Our second major pulp auction offered the first appearance of Buck Rogers in *Amazing Stories* (Aug. 1928) breaking $24,150, alongside over 850 high-grade sci-fi, classic hero, and horror pulps.

Event Auction 49 March 2022 Highlights:

- *Amazing Fantasy* #15 8.0 $520,000
- *Batman* #1 2.5 $270,000
- *Captain America Comics* #1 7.0 $339,761
- *Flash Comics* #1 1.5 $80,420
- *Incredible Hulk* #1 8.5 $245,000
- *Marvel Comics* #1 9.2 $2,427,778
- *Marvel Comics* #1 2.5 $363,528
- *Superman* #1 1.0 $141,45
- *Whiz Comics* #2 (#1) 4.0 $105,800
- *X-Men* #1 9.0 Stan Lee Signature $160,009
- *X-Men* #1 8.5 $132,000

By June, with inflation raging and the words 'turbulent' and 'stock market' matching more often than most medium-sized shareholders cared to manage, many turned to the haven of the collectibles market. Thousands of new clients joined and placed tens of thousands of bids in Event #50 that offered blue-chip Golden Age keys like *Action Comics* #1, *Batman* #1, and *Superman* #1 alongside nice copies of Silver Age investment books like *Amazing Fantasy* #15 8.0 and *Fantastic Four* #1 8.5. Pulps continue to become a larger part of every auction and 2023 will be filled with never-before-seen pulp rarities and foreign editions that have never been offered at auction. Bidders had a chance at another first appearance of Buck Rogers selling for $12,777.

Event Auction 50 June 2022 Highlights:

- *Action Comics* #1 9.4 R $575,500
- *Amazing Fantasy* #15 8.0 $448,500
- *Amazing Fantasy* #15 6.5 $180,000
- *Batman* #1 4.5 $345,000
- *Fantastic Four* #1 8.5 $350,000
- *Incredible Hulk* #1 7.5 $108,100
- *Punch Comics* #12 CGC 5.5 $71,300
- *Sensation Comics* #1 6.0 $86,250
- *Showcase* #4 7.5 $80,500
- *Superman* #1 4.0 $815,000
- *X-Men* #1 9.0 $94,000

In Event #51, a single consignor offered a collection that featured nearly every key from every comic age with *Action Comics* #1 and *Detective Comics* #27 ultimately tying at $350,750 as the seller reaped nearly $1.9 million in final sales. And a potentially once-in-a-lifetime opportunity was presented to investment Timely collectors with the entire, unbroken run of *Marvel Mystery Comics*, headed up by *Marvel Comics* #1 6.0 Kansas City copy that hit $729,000. The entire run ended at $1.3 million marking the first time the entire run was offered at auction in longer than anyone we spoke with could remember, if ever.

Event Auction 51 September 2022 Highlights:

- *Action Comics* #1 8.5 R $350,750
- *All-American Comics* #16 8.5 R $65,837
- *Amazing Fantasy* #15 6.0 $93,088
- *Amazing Man Comics* #22 7.5 $69,000
- *Amazing Spider-Man* #1 9.0 $196,138
- *Captain America Comics* #1 8.0 R $78,200
- *Daredevil* #1 9.6 $110,500
- *Detective Comics* #27 7.5 R $350,750
- *Fantastic Four* #1 7.5 $88,551
- *Flash Comics* #1 1.5 $85,000
- *Incredible Hulk* #1 7.5 $104,650
- *Marvel Comics* #1 CGC 6.0 $729,000
- *Superman* #1 6.5 R $92,000
- *X-Men* #1 9.6 $871,999

The final auction of the year closed out with blue-chip Golden Age keys, hundreds of original art lots, high-grade Silver and Bronze Age keys, more runs of rare Timelys, certified video tapes and games, pulps, and a TMNT collection filled with unique items and rarities from one of the creator's uncles, Quentin Eastman.

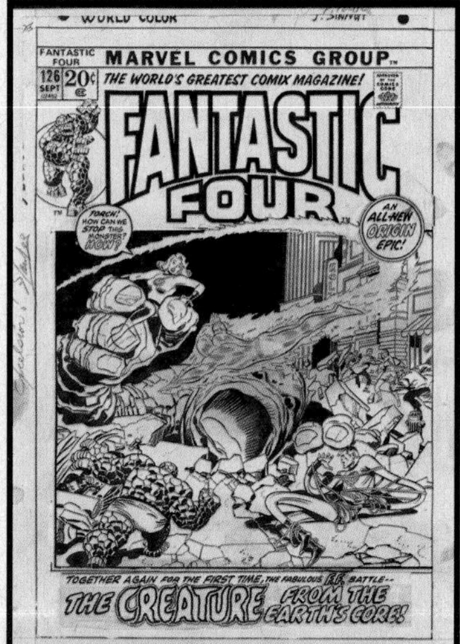

Eastman amassed his Turtles collection by first funding the start-up and eventually working for and with Kevin Eastman. Some of the top sales include a pair of signed *Gobbledygook* proof copies #1 for $37,055 and #2 at $14,055. Two original *TMNT* #1's sold, an Eastman Signature Series with sketch certified-9.4 hit $32,200 and a 9.0 (VF/NM) hammered at $23,115.

Leading the comic auction, the powerhouse trio *Superman* #1 4.5 at $517,500, *Marvel Comics* #1 2.5 at $293,250, and *Sensation Comics* #1 8.5 at $165,000. The rarity of Golden Age comics has allowed them to maintain their values where comics that have higher populations have not fared as well.

Event Auction 52 December 2022 Highlights:

- *All Star Comics* #8 4.5 $57,563
- *Amazing Fantasy* #15 6.5 $110,111
- *Amazing Fantasy* #15 5.0 $50,227
- *Detective Comics* #35 6.5 $79,988
- *Incredible Hulk* #1 7.5 $91,000
- *Marvel Comics* #1 2.5 $293,250
- *Sensation Comics* #1 8.5 $165,000
- *Showcase* #22 7.5 $50,728
- *Superman* #1 4.5 $517,500
- *Tales of Suspense* #39 8.0 $46,000

As we look forward to 2023, we are looking at foreign editions of U.S. comics to increase in value as collectors become aware of the scarcity of, and how incredibly difficult to nearly impossible it is to obtain many copies. Event Auction #52 offered Mexican Editions of *Amazing Spider-Man* #1 6.5 $6,100, *Famous Funnies* with Frazetta covers, and a *Witches Tales* #25. Event Auction #52 is the tip of the spear of the foreign edition market as 2023 auctions will assuredly bolster values each outing as investors continue to seek alternatives.

ComicConnect's Original Art auctions continue to thrive as consignors seek access to our extensive slate of exclusive bidders. A complete story from *Creepy* magazine by Richard Corben achieved $147,838 in Event #52 proving that, regardless of trends, quality art continues to be of great interest to collectors. The cover to *Fantastic Four* #126 by John Buscema and Joe Sinnott hit $115,000, and Rich Buckler's cover pencils with Sinnott's inks on the cover of *Avengers* #113 rounded out 2022's six-figure pieces at $109,250. The cover to *Captain America* #284 by Mike Zeck and John Beatty went for $87,400 while the cover to *Marvel Feature* #12 by Jim Starlin and John Romita finished at $81,000. To consign to one of our upcoming art auctions, email Micah Spivak (michas@metropoliscomics.com).

We also expect the pulp market to achieve never-before-seen prices in 2023 as more bidders catch on to the rarity and spectacle that are pulps. First issues, first appearances, high-grade copies, and iconic covers comprise the most desirable pulps. The market is continually attaining new value levels and if a collector is on the fence, it's time to get in the market before they're priced out. Highlights sales include the first issue of *Marvel Science Stories* (Aug. 1938) at $7,415 and the first appearance of Conan in *Weird Tales* (Dec. 1932) for $10,350.

We're looking to another strong 2023 as the current buyer's market shifts back to a seller's and the lion will roar again. If you have a collection for sale, we want to hear from you. We are looking to assist with comics, original comic art, certified video games and VHS tapes, pulps, and just about any collectible so please give us a try. To consign to an upcoming auction, email me, the Director of Consignments at robr@comicconnect.com. No fee cash advances are always available.

If you are looking to begin or add to your own investment portfolio, simply call us at 888-779-7377 to start your path to financial security with an investment collectibles portfolio. Please call us today and put over 100 years of experience to work for you.

That's A Wrap!

For the entirety of Gemstone Publishing's time with *The Overstreet Comic Book Price Guide*, Mike Wilbur has been the one to ship the books out to customers who ordered directly from Gemstone. He also led the team – often just him and our Mark Huesman – who took care of packing, shipping, and tracking the thousands of copies that have gone to our Overstreet Advisors and advertisers since Steve Geppi acquired the *Guide* in 1994. In more recent years, Mike and Mark also hand delivered the Advisor copies on the day of release at Comic-Con International: San Diego's Preview Night.

So, just as Steve has now owned the *Guide* for longer than Bob Overstreet did, Mike has been shipping the *Guide* longer than anyone before him. This one, though, marks his last one. In fact, while he'll be headed to our vast Olive Branch warehouse soon after these words are written and the book is sent to the printer, Mike actually retired on Friday, March 31, 2023.

We'll miss his skill, the stunningly small number of returns or damaged books over his tenure (despite the best efforts of the shipping services), and his approach to the job.

In addition to our friendship and our best wishes, Mike takes with him an incredible amount of industry and institutional knowledge (he made it almost a weekend before someone from the office called for his insight).

Thanks, Mike!

Steve Geppi (left) presents Mike Wilbur (right) with an award for his more than 30 years of service to Geppi Family Enterprises at his retirement dinner.

The result of a typical day of packing and shipping when it comes time for the annual release of *The Overstreet Comic Book Price Guide*.

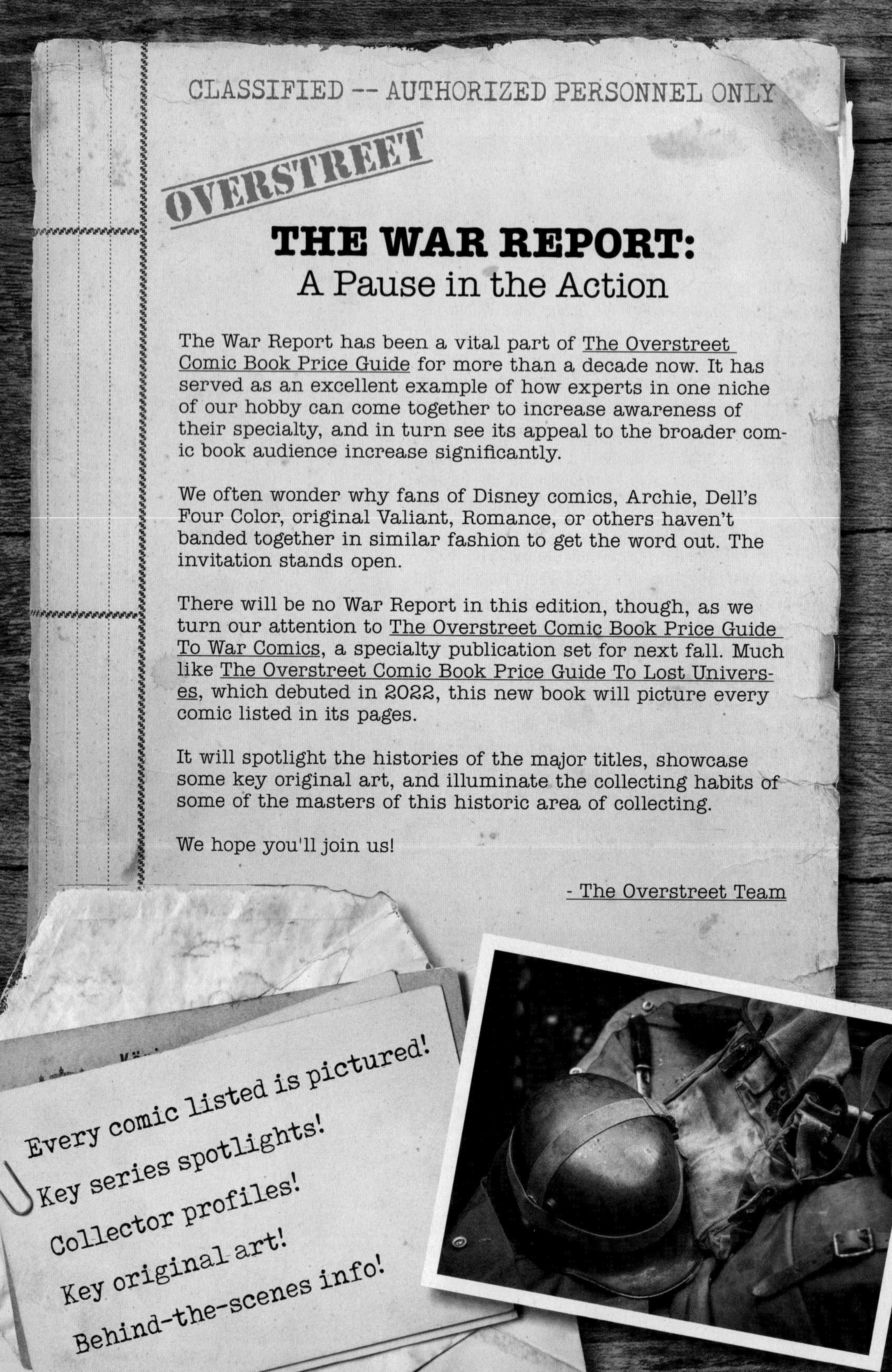

CLASSIFIED -- AUTHORIZED PERSONNEL ONLY

OVERSTREET

THE WAR REPORT:
A Pause in the Action

The War Report has been a vital part of The Overstreet Comic Book Price Guide for more than a decade now. It has served as an excellent example of how experts in one niche of our hobby can come together to increase awareness of their specialty, and in turn see its appeal to the broader comic book audience increase significantly.

We often wonder why fans of Disney comics, Archie, Dell's Four Color, original Valiant, Romance, or others haven't banded together in similar fashion to get the word out. The invitation stands open.

There will be no War Report in this edition, though, as we turn our attention to The Overstreet Comic Book Price Guide To War Comics, a specialty publication set for next fall. Much like The Overstreet Comic Book Price Guide To Lost Universes, which debuted in 2022, this new book will picture every comic listed in its pages.

It will spotlight the histories of the major titles, showcase some key original art, and illuminate the collecting habits of some of the masters of this historic area of collecting.

We hope you'll join us!

- The Overstreet Team

Every comic listed is pictured!
Key series spotlights!
Collector profiles!
Key original art!
Behind-the-scenes info!

THE OVERSTREET COMIC BOOK PRICE GUIDE TO

WAR COMICS

by Robert M. Overstreet

Russ Heath

Not Actual Cover Art

COMING FALL 2024!

Overstreet® is a Registered Trademark of Gemstone Publishing. Sgt. Rock ©2023 DC Comics. All rights reserved.

KEY SALES FROM 2022-2023

The following lists of sales were reported to Gemstone during the year and represent only a small portion of the total amount of important books that have sold. For other sales information, please see the Overstreet Market Report starting on page 89.

GOLDEN AGE SALES

Action Comics #33 CGC 1.5 $720
Air Ace V2 #3 VG/FN $252
All Top #8 CGC 8.0 $19,200
All Winners #13 CGC $7,300 (Penn Copy)
Batman #1 CGC 0.5 $9,500
(No Grade Back Cover Only)
Batman #2 CGC 8.0 $1,110,000
(Fantast Collection)
Batman #73 CGC 4.0 $1,440
Battle Action #9 C GC 9.0 $780
Battle Cry #2 CGC 8.0 $1,380
Battle Stories #3 CGC 9.0 $264
Blue Beetle #48 VG $630
Blue Bolt #113 CGC 7.0 $4,950
Captain Flight Comics #3 CGC 4.5 $1,080
Captain Jet #2 CGC 8.5 $2,160
Captain Marvel Adventures #1 $10,000
(Small Glue on Cover)
Chamber of Chills #19 VG $5,002
Combat Casey #12 CGC 7.0 $1,560
Comics Magazine, The #1 VG $11,600
Crime Must Stop Vol. 1 #1 CGC 3.5 $1,200
Crime Suspenstories #22 CGC 9.2 $72,000
(Gaines File Copy)
Crime Suspenstories #22 CGC 3.0 $5,500
Detective Comics #27 CGC 6.0 $1,740,000
(To My Friend Bob Crestohl- Bob Kane)
Detective Comics #122 CGC 4.5 $4,800
Exciting War #5 CGC 6.5 $660
Exciting War #6 CGC 5.0 $840
Fight Comics #21 CGC 7.0 $1,680
Fight Comics #32 CGC 5.0 $1,020
Fightin' Marines #5 CGC 8.5 $2,280
Giant Comics Edition #12 CGC 3.5 $19,200
G.I. Combat #14 CGC 8.5 $1,020
Indian Warriors #8 CGC 8.5 $1,320
Marvel Family #1 CGC 3.5 $7,500
More Fun #99 FN/VF $900
National Comics #26 VG/FN $1,320
Phantom Lady #23 CGC 8.5 $21,600
Planet Comics #12 CGC 8.0 $5,573
Raggedy Ann & Andy FC #306 CGC 9.4 $900
Rangers Comics #21 CGC 6.5 $4,080
Scamp Four Color #703 CGC 9.2 $384
Seven Seas Comics #4 CGC 9.2 $81,000
("D" Copy)
Silver Streak Comics #17 Good $396
Spirit, The #22 CGC 8.0 $14,400
Spirit Weekly Newspaper # 1-4-48 VF $456
Spirit Weekly Newspaper # 5-25-47 VF $504
Startling Comics #49 CGC 2.5 $7,999
Sunny #12 FN- $780
Superman #4 CGC 3.5 $13,300
Superman #57 VG $504
Teen-Age Romances #19 CGC 7.5 $10,800
Weird Mysteries #45 CGC 4.0 $9,000
Wonder Comics #15 CGC 4.5 $3,120
Wonder Woman #1 CGC 0.5 $17,000

SILVER AGE SALES

Action Comics #252 CGC 4.5 $2,640
Action Comics #276 CGC 4.0 $400
Air War Stories #7 CGC 9.6 $780 (File Copy)
Amazing Spider-Man #3 CGC 7.5 $7,877
Amazing Spider-Man #11 CGC 8.5 $6,605
Amazing Spider-Man #25 VG/FN $240
Batman #169 VG/FN $101
Batman #203 CGC 9.0 $432
Batman #251 CGC 9.8 $32,999
Brave and the Bold #57 CGC 9.2 $1,440

Combat #2 CGC 9.4 $780
Combat #11 CGC 9.0 $576 (File Copy)
Detective Comics #359 CGC 8.0 $3,360
Flash #105 CGC 5.5 $2,880
Flintstones #8 CGC 9.6 $1,140 (File Copy)
Flintstones #15 CGC 9.4 $720 (File Copy)
El Cid FC #1259 CGC 9.0 $660 (File Copy)
Ghost Stories #30 CGC 9.6 $504 (File Copy)
Giant Size X-Men #1 VF/NM $8500
Incredible Hulk #1 CGC 5.5 $33,600
Iron Man #1 CGC 5.0 $22,222 (Signed by the Legend Stan Lee)
Marvel Spotlight #5 NM $9300
Phantom Stranger #12 CGC 9.6 $360
Showcase #4 Good $14,889
Showcase #22 CGC 5.0 $6,689
Showcase #70 CGC $780
Silver Surfer #3 CGC 9.4 $5,400
Strange Tales #110 CGC 6.5 $5,760
Tales to Astonish #13 CGC 4.5 $3,120
Teen Titans #12 CGC 9.6 $8,400
Teen Titans #13 CGC 9.6 $6,000
X-Men #1 CGC 4.0 $12,600
X-Men #49 CGC 9.8 $19,200

BRONZE AGE SALES

Albedo #2 VF- $5,950
Archie Comics #271 VG+ $191
Cerebus the Aardvark #1 VG $3,500
Amazing Spider-Man #129 CGC 9.2 $4,900
Batman #227 NM- $1,799
Black Hole #4 CGC 9.6 $1,382 (Whitman)
Blip #1 CGC 9.8 $1,410
Bone #1 CGC 9.6 $7,100
Deadly Hands of Kung Fu #19 CGC 9.6 $1,500
Foom #10 CGC 9.0 $3,699
Green Lantern #87 CGC 9.4 $1,952
Iron Man #55 CGC 9.8 $8,999
Iron Man #128 CGC 9.6 $5,000 (Signed Robert Downey Jr.)
Marvel Premiere #28 CGC 9.8 $4,050
Scooby Doo #1 CGC 8.0 $3,494
Shanna The She-Devil #1 CGC 9.8 $3,383
Supergirl #1 CGC 9.2 $288
Superman #233 CGC 9.6 $3,403
Star Wars #1 CGC 9.4 $56,400 (35¢ Variant)
Star Wars #3 CBCS 9.0 $1,375
Star Wars #42 CGC 9.8 $7,500
Strange Tales #178 CGC 9.8 $7,000
Teen Age Mutant Ninja Turtles #1 CGC 6.0 $12,999
Tomb of Dracula #10 NM+ $6,889
Uncanny X-Men #266 CGC 9.8 $10,600
Werewolf by Night #32 CGC 5.5 $1,500

MODERN AGE SALES

Amazing Spider-Man #667 CGC 9.2 $10,600 (Dell'Otto Variant)
Alf #48 CGC 9.2 $298
Care Bears #7 FN- $124
Detective Comics #411 CGC 9.8 $56,400
G.I Joe Special #1 CGC 9.8 $870
Hulk #1 CGC 9.6 $165 (Red Hulk)
Infinite Crisis #5 CGC 9.6 $133
Labyrinth: The Movie #1 CGC 9.2 $105
Sandman #1 CGC 9.8 $960
She Hulk #6 CGC 9.8 $199
Spawn #185 CGC 9.0 $15,000 (Signature series, Sketch Cover, Signed by Todd McFarlane)
Star Wars: Heir to the Empire #1 CGC 9.8 $1,250
Star Wars: The Clone Wars #1 CGC 9.2 $1,550 (News Stand Edition)
Superman Adventures #21 NM $50
Ultimate Fallout #4 CGC 9.6 $8,150 (Ratio Variant)
Venom Lethal Protector #1 NM $10,663
Wolverine #145 CGC 8.5 $760 (Nabisco Variant Cover)
Wolverine #145 NM+ $150
Wolverine 2010 #1 CGC 9.8 $7,295 (Deadpool Variant Cover)
X-Man #120 CGC 9.8 $6,500

TOP COMICS

The following tables denote the rate of appreciation of the top Golden Age, Platinum Age, Silver Age and Bronze Age comics, as well as selected genres over the past year. The retail value for a Near Mint- copy of each comic (or VF where a Near Mint- copy is not known to exist) in 2023 is compared to its Near Mint- value in 2022. The rate of return for 2023 over 2022 is given. The place in rank is given for each comic by year, with its corresponding value in highest known grade. These tables can be very useful in forecasting trends in the market place. For instance, the investor might want to know which book is yielding the best dividend from one year to the next, or one might just be interested in seeing how the popularity of books changes from year to year. For instance, *More Fun Comics* #1 was in 18th place in 2022 and has increased to 16th place in 2023. Premium books are also included in these tables and are denoted with an asterisk(*).

The following tables are meant as a guide to the investor. However, it should be pointed out that trends may change at anytime and that some books can meet market resistance with a slowdown in price increases, while others can develop into real comers from a presently dormant state. In the long run, if the investor sticks to the books that are appreciating steadily each year, he shouldn't go very far wrong.

TOP 100 GOLDEN AGE COMICS

TITLE/ISSUE#	2023 RANK	2023 NM- PRICE	2022 RANK	2022 NM- PRICE	$ INCR.	% INCR.
Action Comics #1	1	$6,600,000	1	$6,000,000	$600,000	10%
Detective Comics #27	2	$4,500,000	2	$4,000,000	$500,000	13%
Superman #1	3	$2,700,000	3	$2,200,000	$500,000	23%
Marvel Comics #1	4	$1,200,000	4	$1,000,000	$200,000	20%
Batman #1	5	$1,100,000	4	$1,000,000	$100,000	10%
All-American Comics #16	6	$975,000	6	$950,000	$25,000	3%
Captain America Comics #1	7	$715,000	7	$650,000	$65,000	10%
Action Comics #7	8	$630,000	8	$600,000	$30,000	5%
Detective Comics #31	9	$490,000	9	$450,000	$40,000	9%
Whiz Comics #2 (#1)	10	$450,000	11	$420,000	$30,000	7%
Pep Comics #22	11	$440,000	10	$425,000	$15,000	4%
Action Comics #10	12	$415,000	12	$400,000	$15,000	4%
All Star Comics #8	13	$385,000	13	$380,000	$5,000	1%
Detective Comics #29	13	$385,000	14	$350,000	$35,000	10%
Flash Comics #1	15	$375,000	14	$350,000	$25,000	7%
More Fun Comics #52	16	$300,000	18	$250,000	$50,000	20%
Action Comics #2	17	$290,000	16	$260,000	$30,000	12%
Detective Comics #33	18	$275,000	16	$260,000	$15,000	6%
Wonder Woman #1	19	$250,000	19	$240,000	$10,000	4%
Sensation Comics #1	20	$240,000	22	$215,000	$25,000	12%
Detective Comics #35	21	$235,000	20	$230,000	$5,000	2%
Archie Comics #1	22	$232,000	21	$225,000	$7,000	3%
Action Comics #13	23	$225,000	23	$210,000	$15,000	7%
Detective Comics #38	24	$220,000	24	$200,000	$20,000	10%
Adventure Comics #40	25	$205,000	25	$195,000	$10,000	5%
More Fun Comics #73	26	$176,000	27	$160,000	$16,000	10%
Sub-Mariner Comics #1	27	$175,000	28	$150,000	$25,000	17%
Suspense Comics #3	27	$175,000	28	$150,000	$25,000	17%
Action Comics #3	29	$172,000	26	$165,000	$7,000	4%
All Star Comics #3	30	$150,000	30	$145,000	$5,000	3%
Detective Comics #1	30	VF $150,000	31	VF $140,000	$10,000	7%
Captain Marvel Adventures #1	33	$135,000	33	$120,000	$15,000	13%
Detective Comics #36	34	$125,000	33	$120,000	$5,000	4%
Marvel Mystery Comics #9	35	$119,000	35	$116,000	$3,000	3%
Fantastic Comics #3	36	$110,000	37	$100,000	$10,000	10%
Marvel Mystery Comics #2	36	$110,000	36	$107,000	$3,000	3%
Marvel Mystery Comics #5	38	$98,000	38	$94,000	$4,000	4%
Superman #2	39	$96,000	39	$92,000	$4,000	4%
Green Lantern #1	40	$95,000	41	$88,000	$7,000	8%

TITLE/ISSUE#	2023 RANK	2023 NM- PRICE	2022 RANK	2022 NM- PRICE	$ INCR.	% INCR.
More Fun Comics #53	41	$92,000	40	$90,000	$2,000	2%
Action Comics #23	42	$90,000	42	$86,000	$4,000	5%
Detective Comics #37	43	$85,000	43	$79,000	$6,000	8%
Captain America Comics #3	44	$82,000	45	$75,000	$7,000	9%
Marvel Mystery Comics #4	44	$82,000	44	$78,000	$4,000	5%
Human Torch #2 (#1)	46	$80,000	45	$75,000	$5,000	7%
Action Comics #6	47	$78,000	45	$75,000	$3,000	4%
Action Comics #4	48	$77,000	45	$75,000	$2,000	3%
Action Comics #5	48	$77,000	45	$75,000	$2,000	3%
Captain America Comics #2	50	$75,000	50	$72,000	$3,000	4%
Action Comics #12	51	$70,000	54	$65,000	$5,000	8%
Adventure Comics #48	51	$70,000	51	$68,000	$2,000	3%
All-American Comics #19	51	$70,000	51	$68,000	$2,000	3%
Marvel Mystery Comics #3	51	$70,000	51	$68,000	$2,000	3%
Batman #2	55	$68,000	54	$65,000	$3,000	5%
More Fun Comics #54	56	$65,000	66	$50,000	$15,000	30%
More Fun Comics #55	56	$65,000	66	$50,000	$15,000	30%
Motion Picture Funn. Wkly #1	56	$65,000	56	$62,000	$3,000	5%
Wonder Comics #1	56	$65,000	58	$60,000	$5,000	8%
Captain America Comics #74	60	$64,000	58	$60,000	$4,000	7%
Action Comics #15	61	$62,000	58	$60,000	$2,000	3%
New Fun Comics #1	61	VF $62,000	57	VF $61,000	$1,000	2%
Action Comics #8	63	$60,000	61	$57,000	$3,000	5%
Action Comics #9	63	$60,000	61	$57,000	$3,000	5%
All-American Comics #61	63	$60,000	66	$50,000	$10,000	20%
Amazing Man Comics #22	63	$60,000	66	$50,000	$10,000	20%
Daring Mystery Comics #1	63	$60,000	63	$56,000	$4,000	7%
Mask Comics #1	63	$60,000	66	$50,000	$10,000	20%
Punch Comics #12	63	$60,000	66	$50,000	$10,000	20%
Terrific Comics #5	63	$60,000	66	$50,000	$10,000	20%
Detective Comics #140	71	$58,000	66	$50,000	$8,000	16%
Silver Streak Comics #6	71	$58,000	65	$52,000	$6,000	12%
Phantom Lady #17	73	$56,000	66	$50,000	$6,000	12%
Walt Disney's Comics & Stories #1	73	$56,000	64	$54,000	$2,000	4%
All-Select Comics #1	75	$55,000	66	$50,000	$5,000	10%
Detective Comics #69	75	$55,000	66	$50,000	$5,000	10%
Detective Comics #168	75	$55,000	66	$50,000	$5,000	10%
Red Raven Comics #1	75	$55,000	66	$50,000	$5,000	10%
Four Color Ser. 1 (Donald Duck) #4	79	$52,000	66	$50,000	$2,000	4%
Detective Comics #40	80	$50,000	81	$45,000	$5,000	11%
Detective Comics #225	80	$50,000	80	$46,000	$4,000	9%
Marvel Mystery Comics 132 pg.	80	VF $50,000	79	VF $48,000	$2,000	4%
Marvel Mystery Comics #46	83	$48,000	90	$40,000	$8,000	20%
Superman #3	83	$48,000	81	$45,000	$3,000	7%
Detective Comics #30	85	$47,000	86	$43,000	$4,000	9%
Mystic Comics #1	85	$47,000	81	$45,000	$2,000	4%
Amazing Man Comics #5	87	$46,000	81	$45,000	$1,000	2%
Detective Comics #66	88	$45,000	90	$40,000	$5,000	13%
Famous Funnies-Series 1 #1	88	VF $45,000	85	VF $44,500	$500	1%
Marvel Mystery Comics #44	88	$45,000	90	$40,000	$5,000	13%
Detective Comics #2	91	VF $43,000	87	VF $42,500	$500	1%
Double Action Comics #2	91	$43,000	88	$42,000	$1,000	2%
Captain America Comics 132 pg.	93	VF $42,750	88	VF $42,000	$750	2%
Marvel Mystery Comics #8	94	$42,000	90	$40,000	$2,000	5%
All Winners Comics #1	95	$41,000	90	$40,000	$1,000	3%
Batman #11	96	$40,000	90	$38,000	$2,000	5%
Chamber of Chills #19	96	$40,000	90	$20,000	$20,000	100%
Mystery Men Comics #1	96	$40,000	93	$38,000	$2,000	5%
Planet Comics #1	96	$40,000	96	$35,000	$5,000	14%
Action Comics #17	100	$38,000	96	$35,000	$3,000	9%
Pep Comics #34	100	$38,000	96	$35,000	$3,000	9%

TOP 50 SILVER AGE COMICS

TITLE/ISSUE#	2023 RANK	2023 NM- PRICE	2022 RANK	2022 NM- PRICE	$ INCR.	% INCR.
Amazing Fantasy #15	1	$650,000	1	$550,000	$100,000	18%
Incredible Hulk #1	2	$400,000	2	$350,000	$50,000	14%
Fantastic Four #1	3	$300,000	3	$250,000	$50,000	20%
X-Men #1	4	$185,000	4	$180,000	$5,000	3%
Showcase #4	5	$182,000	4	$180,000	$2,000	1%
Amazing Spider-Man #1	6	$120,000	7	$100,000	$20,000	20%
Journey Into Mystery #83	6	$120,000	6	$110,000	$10,000	9%
Brave and the Bold #28	8	$94,000	8	$93,000	$1,000	1%
Tales of Suspense #39	9	$88,000	9	$80,000	$8,000	10%
Fantastic Four #5	10	$80,000	10	$75,000	$5,000	7%
Showcase #22	11	$65,000	11	$62,000	$3,000	5%
Avengers #1	12	$60,000	13	$55,000	$5,000	9%
Tales to Astonish #27	12	$60,000	12	$58,000	$2,000	3%
Adventure Comics #247	14	$40,000	14	$35,000	$5,000	14%
Flash #105	15	$37,000	14	$35,000	$2,000	6%
Action Comics #242	16	$35,000	16	$34,000	$1,000	3%
Action Comics #252	17	$34,000	17	$32,000	$2,000	6%
Justice League of America #1	18	$32,500	17	$32,000	$500	2%
Our Army at War #83	19	$31,000	19	$30,000	$1,000	3%
Sgt. Fury #1	19	$31,000	19	$30,000	$1,000	3%
Strange Tales #110	19	$31,000	19	$30,000	$1,000	3%
Daredevil (1964) #1	22	$29,000	22	$28,000	$1,000	4%
Amazing Spider-Man #2	23	$28,000	24	$25,000	$3,000	12%
Tales to Astonish #13	23	$28,000	23	$27,000	$1,000	4%
Amazing Spider-Man #3	25	$26,000	24	$25,000	$1,000	4%
Journey Into Mystery #85	25	$26,000	27	$24,000	$2,000	8%
Showcase #8	25	$26,000	24	$25,000	$1,000	4%
Fantastic Four #4	28	$22,000	28	$20,000	$2,000	10%
Incredible Hulk #2	28	$22,000	28	$20,000	$2,000	10%
Fantastic Four #2	30	$20,000	30	$19,000	$1,000	5%
Fantastic Four #3	30	$20,000	32	$17,500	$2,500	14%
Batman #121	32	$19,000	34	$16,000	$3,000	19%
Green Lantern #1	32	$19,000	31	$18,000	$1,000	6%
Amazing Spider-Man #4	34	$18,000	34	$16,000	$2,000	13%
Tales to Astonish #35	34	$18,000	34	$16,000	$2,000	13%
Showcase #17	36	$17,000	33	$16,500	$500	3%
Amazing Spider-Man #14	37	$16,000	39	$15,000	$1,000	7%
Fantastic Four #12	37	$16,000	37	$15,500	$500	3%
Superman's G.F. Lois Lane #1	37	$16,000	37	$15,500	$500	3%
Showcase #9	40	$15,000	39	$15,000	$0	0%
Showcase #6	41	$13,500	41	$12,500	$1,000	8%
Showcase #13	42	$13,000	42	$12,000	$1,000	8%
Showcase #14	42	$13,000	42	$12,000	$1,000	8%
Avengers #4	44	$12,200	42	$12,000	$200	2%
Fantastic Four #48	45	$12,000	42	$12,000	$0	0%
Journey Into Mystery #84	45	$12,000	48	$10,000	$2,000	20%
Richie Rich #1	45	$12,000	46	$11,000	$1,000	9%
Fantastic Four #52	48	$11,000	48	$10,000	$1,000	10%
Flash #106	49	$11,000	51	$9,900	$1,100	11%
Our Army at War #81	50	$11,000	47	$10,500	$500	5%

TOP 25 BRONZE AGE COMICS

TITLE/ISSUE#	2023 RANK	2023 NM- PRICE	2022 RANK	2022 NM- PRICE	$ INCR.	% INCR.
Star Wars #1 (35¢ price variant)	1	$15,000	1	$14,000	$1,000	7%
Incredible Hulk #181	2	$12,000	2	$12,000	$0	0%
Giant-Size X-Men #1	3	$10,000	3	$10,000	$0	0%
Marvel Spotlight #5	4	$9,000	4	$9,000	$0	0%
Cerebus #1	5	$7,000	7	$5,000	$2,000	40%
House of Secrets #92	6	$6,700	6	$6,500	$200	3%
Scooby Doo (1970) #1	7	$5,400	7	$5,000	$400	8%
Werewolf By Night #32	8	$5,000	5	$7,000	-$2,000	-29%
Iron Fist #14 (35¢ price variant)	9	$4,700	10	$4,700	$0	0%
Amazing Spider-Man #129	10	$4,000	11	$4,000	$0	0%
Tomb of Dracula #10	10	$4,000	7	$5,000	-$1,000	-20%
X-Men #94	12	$2,800	12	$3,000	-$200	-7%
Green Lantern #76	13	$2,700	14	$2,700	$0	0%
Incredible Hulk #180	14	$2,500	12	$3,000	-$500	-17%
Star Wars #2 (35¢ price variant)	15	$2,200	16	$2,200	$0	0%
Star Wars #3 (35¢ price variant)	16	$2,100	17	$2,000	$100	5%
Star Wars #4 (35¢ price variant)	16	$2,100	17	$2,000	$100	5%
Amazing Spider-Man #101	18	$2,000	15	$2,500	-$500	-20%
Hero For Hire #1	18	$2,000	17	$2,000	$0	0%
Iron Man #55	18	$2,000	17	$2,000	$0	0%
Batman #227	21	$1,900	21	$1,500	$400	27%
Batman #251	22	$1,650	21	$1,500	$150	10%
DC 100 Page Sup. Spec. #5	23	$1,450	23	$1,400	$50	4%
Batman #232	24	$1,300	24	$1,200	$100	8%
Tomb of Dracula #1	25	$1,100	30	$1,000	$100	10%

TOP 25 COPPER AGE COMICS

TITLE/ISSUE#	2023 RANK	2023 NM- PRICE	2022 RANK	2022 NM- PRICE	$ INCR.	% INCR.
Gobbledygook #1	1	$34,000	1	$30,000	$4,000	13%
Teenage Mutant Ninja Turtles #1	2	$22,000	2	$20,000	$2,000	10%
Gobbledygook #2	3	$10,000	3	$9,000	$1,000	11%
Albedo #2	4	$8,200	4	$8,000	$200	3%
Primer #2	5	$1,200	6	$1,200	$0	0%
Crow, The #1	6	$1,050	7	$1,000	$50	5%
Miracleman Gold #1	7	$1,000	5	$1,500	-$500	-33%
Miracleman Blue #1	8	$850	8	$850	$0	0%
Amazing Spider-Man #300	9	$650	8	$850	-$200	24%
Sandman #8	9	$650	10	$625	$25	4%
Teenage Mutant Ninja Turtles #2	11	$600	11	$600	$0	0%
Vampirella #113	12	$575	12	$575	$0	0%
Amazing Spider-Man #238	13	$500	13	$500	$0	0%
Caliber Presents #1	14	$425	14	$400	$25	6%
Swamp Thing #37	15	$400	14	$400	$0	0%
Spider-Man Platinum #1	16	$390	17	$360	$30	8%
Evil Ernie #1	17	$375	18	$350	$25	7%
New Mutants #98	17	$375	16	$375	$0	0%
Spider-Man #1 (Gold 2nd UPC)	19	$290	20	$270	$20	7%
Amazing Spider-Man #252	20	$275	19	$275	$0	0%
Grendel #1	21	$265	21	$250	$15	6%
Batman #423	22	$250	21	$250	$0	0%
Eightball #1	22	$250	23	$235	$15	6%
Cry For Dawn #1	24	$240	25	$200	$40	20%
Teenage Mutant Ninja Turtles #3	25	$225	24	$225	$0	0%

TOP 20 MODERN AGE COMICS

TITLE/ISSUE#	2023 RANK	2023 NM- PRICE	2022 RANK	2022 NM- PRICE	$ INCR.	% INCR.
Bone #1	1	$3,600	1	$3,500	$100	3%
Venom: Lethal Protector #1 (black-c)	2	$2,800	2	$2,500	$300	12%
Walking Dead #1	3	$1,250	3	$1,250	$0	0%
Hero Trade: A Brief Case #1	4	$1,000	4	$1,000	$0	0%
Invincible #1	4	$1,000	4	$1,000	$0	0%
Star Wars: The Clone Wars #1	6	$800	6	$800	$100	14%
Batman Adventures #12	7	$725	7	$700	$25	4%
Captain Marvel #17 (2012, 2nd printing)	8	$700	7	$700	$0	0%
Marvel Collectible Classics: Spider-Man #1	9	$650	9	$650	$0	0%
Spawn #1 (B&W edition)	10	$600	10	$600	$0	0%
Ultimate Fallout #4	11	$500	12	$500	$0	0%
The Goon #1	12	$475	13	$450	$25	6%
Adam: Legend of the Blue Marvel #1	13	$450	13	$450	$0	0%
Hero Trade #1	14	$400	15	$400	$0	0%
Ult. Spider-Man (3rd series) #1 var-c (city)	14	$400	15	$400	$0	0%
Ult. Spider-Man (3rd) #1 var-c (unmasked)	14	$400	15	$400	$0	0%
Walking Dead #2	17	$380	18	$380	$0	0%
Spawn #174	18	$365	11	$525	-$160	-30%
Incredible Hulk #377 (3rd printing)	19	$350	19	$350	$0	0%
Strangers in Paradise #1	20	$325	22	$300	$25	8%

TOP 10 PLATINUM AGE COMICS

TITLE/ISSUE#	2023 RANK	2023 PRICE	2022 RANK	2022 PRICE	$ INCR.	% INCR.
Yellow Kid in McFadden Flats	1	FN $18,000	1	FN $15,000	$3,000	00%
Little Sammy Sneeze	2	FN $8,700	2	FN $8,600	$100	1%
Mickey Mouse Book (1st printing)	3	VF $6,300	4	VF $6,200	$100	2%
Little Nemo 1906	4	FN $5,100	5	FN $5,100	$0	0%
Sam and His Laugh	5	VF $4,800	13	VF $3,000	$1,800	60%
Pore Li'l Mose	6	FN $4,500	6	FN $4,000	$500	13%
Yellow Kid #1	6	FN $4,500	6	FN $4,000	$500	13%
Little Nemo 1909	8	FN $4,000	6	FN $4,000	$0	0%
Dreams of the Rarebit Fiend	9	VF $3,600	15	VF $2,900	$700	24%
Happy Hooligan Book 1	9	VF $3,600	9	VF $3,500	$100	3%

TOP 10 CRIME COMICS

TITLE/ISSUE#	2023 RANK	2023 NM- PRICE	2022 RANK	2022 NM- PRICE	$ INCR.	% INCR.
Crime SuspenStories #22	1	$26,000	1	$20,000	$6,000	30%
Crime Does Not Pay #24	2	$25,000	1	$20,000	$5,000	25%
Crime Does Not Pay #22	3	$15,000	3	$14,500	$500	3%
Crime SuspenStories #20	4	$11,500	4	$10,000	$1,500	15%
Crime Does Not Pay #33	5	$8,000	5	$6,000	$2,000	33%
Crime Does Not Pay #23	6	$5,600	6	$5,600	$0	0%
Gangsters Can't Win #1	7	$5,400	7	$5,000	$400	8%
Crime Reporter #2	8	$5,000	9	$4,200	$800	19%
True Crime Comics #2	9	$4,700	8	$4,500	$200	4%
True Crime Comics #3	10	$4,000	10	$3,600	$400	11%

TOP 10 HORROR COMICS

TITLE/ISSUE#	2023 RANK	2023 NM- PRICE	2022 RANK	2022 NM- PRICE	$ INCR.	% INCR.
Chamber of Chills #19	1	$40,000	2	$20,000	$20,000	100%
Journey into Mystery #1	2	$24,000	1	$22,000	$2,000	9%
Eerie #1	3	$19,000	3	$17,000	$2,000	12%
Tales to Astonish #1	3	$19,000	3	$17,000	$2,000	12%
Tales of Terror Annual #1	5	VF $17,500	5	VF $16,000	$1,500	9%
Strange Tales #1	6	$17,000	6	$15,500	$1,500	10%
Vault of Horror #12	7	$16,500	7	$15,000	$1,500	10%
Chamber of Chills #23	8	$12,000	8	$10,000	$2,000	20%
Crime Patrol #15	8	$12,000	9	$8,000	$4,000	50%
Amazing Ghost Stories #14	10	$10,000	-	$5,000	$5,000	100%

TOP 10 ROMANCE COMICS

TITLE/ISSUE#	2023 RANK	2023 NM- PRICE	2022 RANK	2022 NM- PRICE	$ INCR.	% INCR.
Giant Comics Edition #12	1	$22,000	1	$18,000	$4,000	22%
Daring Love #1	2	$7,700	2	$7,500	$200	3%
Giant Comics Edition #15	3	$4,500	4	$3,800	$700	18%
Negro Romance #1	4	$4,100	3	$3,900	$200	5%
Negro Romances #4	5	$3,800	6	$3,300	$500	15%
Intimate Confessions #1	6	$3,600	5	$3,500	$100	3%
Giant Comics Edition #13	7	$3,400	9	$3,000	$400	13%
Moon, A Girl... Romance #12	7	$3,400	9	$3,000	$400	13%
Negro Romance #2	7	$3,400	6	$3,300	$100	3%
Negro Romance #3	7	$3,400	6	$3,300	$100	3%

TOP 10 SCI-FI COMICS

TITLE/ISSUE#	2023 RANK	2023 NM- PRICE	2022 RANK	2022 NM- PRICE	$ INCR.	% INCR.
Showcase #17 (Adam Strange)	1	$17,000	1	$16,500	$500	3%
Mystery In Space #1	2	$8,400	2	$8,200	$200	2%
Weird Science-Fantasy Annual 1952	3	$7,000	3	$6,000	$1,000	17%
Weird Science #12 (#1)	4	$5,800	4	$5,600	$200	4%
Strange Adventures #1	5	$5,300	5	$5,250	$50	1%
Showcase #15 (Space Ranger)	6	$5,200	6	$5,100	$100	2%
Journey Into Unknown Worlds #36	7	$4,800	7	$4,800	$0	0%
Mystery in Space #53	8	$4,600	8	$4,600	$0	1%
Weird Fantasy #13 (#1)	8	$4,600	9	$4,500	$100	2%
Fawcett Movie #15 (Man From Planet X)	10	$4,000	10	$4,000	$0	0%

TOP 10 WESTERN COMICS

TITLE/ISSUE#	2023 RANK	2023 NM- PRICE	2022 RANK	2022 NM- PRICE	$ INCR.	% INCR.
Gene Autry Comics #1	1	$6,000	1	$6,000	$0	0%
*Lone Ranger Ice Cream 1939 2nd	2	VF $4,700	2	VF $4,600	$100	2%
Roy Rogers Four Color #38	3	$4,500	3	$4,500	$0	0%
*Lone Ranger Ice Cream 1939	4	VF $4,200	4	VF $4,100	$100	2%
Western Picture Stories #1	4	$4,200	4	$4,100	$100	2%
John Wayne Adventure Comics #1	6	$4,100	4	$4,100	$0	0%
Red Ryder Comics #1	6	$4,100	4	$4,100	$0	0%
*Tom Mix Ralston #1	8	$3,500	8	$3,400	$100	3%
Hopalong Cassidy #1	9	$3,000	9	$3,000	$0	0%
*Red Ryder Victory Patrol '42	10	$1,500	10	$1,400	$100	7%

GRADING DEFINITIONS

When grading a comic book, common sense must be employed. The overall eye appeal and beauty of the comic book must be taken into account along with its technical flaws to arrive at the appropriate grade.

10.0 GEM MINT (GM): This is an exceptional example of a given book - the best ever seen. The slightest bindery defects and/or printing flaws may be seen only upon very close inspection. The overall look is "as if it has never been handled or released for purchase." Only the slightest bindery or printing defects are allowed, and these would be imperceptible on first viewing. No bindery tears. Cover is flat with no surface wear. Inks are bright with high reflectivity. Well centered and firmly secured to interior pages. Corners are cut square and sharp. No creases. No dates or stamped markings allowed. No soiling, staining or other discoloration. Spine is tight and flat. No spine roll or split allowed. Staples must be original, centered and clean with no rust. No staple tears or stress lines. Paper is white, supple and fresh. No hint of acidity in the odor of the newsprint. No interior autographs or owner signatures. Centerfold is firmly secure. No interior tears.

9.9 MINT (MT): Near perfect in every way. Only subtle bindery or printing defects are allowed. No bindery tears. Cover is flat with no surface wear. Inks are bright with high reflectivity. Generally well centered and firmly secured to interior pages. Corners are cut square and sharp. No creases. Small, inconspicuous, lightly penciled, stamped or inked arrival dates are acceptable as long as they are in an unobtrusive location. No soiling, staining or other discoloration. Spine is tight and flat. No spine roll or split allowed. Staples must be original, generally centered and clean with no rust. No staple tears or stress lines. Paper is white, supple and fresh. No hint of acidity in the odor of the newsprint. Centerfold is firmly secure. No interior tears.

9.8 NEAR MINT/MINT (NM/MT): Nearly perfect in every way with only minor imperfections that keep it from the next higher grade. Only subtle bindery or printing defects are allowed. No bindery tears. Cover is flat with no surface wear. Inks are bright with high reflectivity. Generally well centered and firmly secured to interior pages. Corners are cut square and sharp. No creases. Small, inconspicuous, lightly penciled, stamped or inked arrival dates are acceptable as long as they are in an unobtrusive location. No soiling, staining or other discoloration. Spine is tight and flat. No spine roll or split allowed. Staples must be original, generally centered and clean with no rust. No staple tears or stress lines. Paper is off-white to white, supple and fresh. No hint of acidity in the odor of the newsprint. Centerfold is firmly secure. Only the slightest interior tears are allowed.

9.6 NEAR MINT+ (NM+): Nearly perfect with a minor additional virtue or virtues that raise it from Near Mint. The overall look is "as if it was just purchased and read once or twice." Only subtle bindery or printing defects are allowed. No bindery tears are allowed, although on Golden Age books bindery tears of up to 1/8" have been noted. Cover is flat with no surface wear. Inks are bright with high reflectivity. Well centered and firmly secured to interior pages. One corner may be almost imperceptibly blunted, but still almost sharp and cut square. Almost imperceptible indentations are permissible, but no creases, bends, or color break. Small, inconspicuous, lightly penciled, stamped or inked arrival dates are acceptable as long as they are in an unobtrusive location. No soiling, staining or other discoloration. Spine is tight and flat. No spine roll or split allowed. Staples must be original, generally centered, with only the slightest discoloration. No staple tears, stress lines, or rust migration. Paper is off-white, supple and fresh. No hint of acidity in the odor of the newsprint. Centerfold is firmly secure. Only the slightest interior tears are allowed.

9.4 NEAR MINT (NM): Nearly perfect with only minor imperfections that keep it from the next higher grade. Minor feathering that does not distract from the overall beauty of an otherwise higher grade copy is acceptable for this grade. The overall look is "as if it was just purchased and read once or twice." Subtle bindery defects are allowed. Bindery tears must be less than 1/16" on Silver Age and later books, although on Golden Age books bindery tears of up to 1/4" have been noted. Cover is flat with no surface wear. Inks are bright with high reflectivity. Generally well centered and secured to interior pages. Corners are cut square and sharp with ever-so-slight blunting permitted. A 1/16" bend is permitted with no color break. No creases. Small, inconspicuous, lightly penciled, stamped or inked arrival dates are acceptable as long as they are in an unobtrusive location. No soiling, staining or other discoloration apart from slight foxing. Spine is tight and flat. No spine roll or split allowed. Staples are generally centered; may have slight discoloration. No staple tears are allowed; almost no stress lines. No rust migration. In rare cases, a comic was not stapled at the bindery and therefore has a missing staple; this is not considered a defect. Any staple can be replaced on books up to Fine, but only vintage staples can be used on books from Very Fine to Near Mint. Mint books must have original staples. Paper is cream to off-white, supple and fresh. No hint of acidity in the odor of the newsprint. Centerfold is secure. Slight interior tears are allowed.

9.2 NEAR MINT– (NM–): Nearly perfect with only

a minor additional defect or defects that keep it from Near Mint. A limited number of minor bindery defects are allowed. A light, barely noticeable water stain or minor foxing that does not distract from the beauty of the book is acceptable for this grade. Cover is flat with no surface wear. Inks are bright with only the slightest dimming of reflectivity. Generally well centered and secured to interior pages. Corners are cut square and sharp with ever-so-slight blunting permitted. A 1/16"-1/8" bend is permitted with no color break. No creases. Small, inconspicuous, lightly penciled, stamped or inked arrival dates are acceptable as long as they are in an unobtrusive location. No soiling, staining or other discoloration apart from slight foxing. Spine is tight and flat. No spine roll or split allowed. Staples may show some discoloration. No staple tears are allowed; almost no stress lines. No rust migration. In rare cases, a comic was not stapled at the bindery and therefore has a missing staple; this is not considered a defect. Any staple can be replaced on books up to Fine, but only vintage staples can be used on books from Very Fine to Near Mint. Mint books must have original staples. Paper is cream to off-white, supple and fresh. No hint of acidity in the odor of the newsprint. Centerfold is secure. Slight interior tears are allowed.

9.0 VERY FINE/NEAR MINT (VF/NM): Nearly perfect with outstanding eye appeal. A limited number of bindery defects are allowed. Almost flat cover with almost imperceptible wear. Inks are bright with slightly diminished reflectivity. An 1/8" bend is allowed if color is not broken. Corners are cut square and sharp with ever-so-slight blunting permitted but no creases. Several lightly penciled, stamped or inked arrival dates are acceptable. No obvious soiling, staining or other discoloration, except for very minor foxing. Spine is tight and flat. No spine roll or split allowed. Staples may show some discoloration. Only the slightest staple tears are allowed. A very minor accumulation of stress lines may be present if they are nearly imperceptible. No rust migration. In rare cases, a comic was not stapled at the bindery and therefore has a missing staple; this is not considered a defect. Any staple can be replaced on books up to Fine, but only vintage staples can be used on books from Very Fine to Near Mint. Mint books must have original staples. Paper is cream to off-white and supple. No hint of acidity in the odor of the newsprint. Centerfold is secure. Very minor interior tears may be present.

8.5 VERY FINE+ (VF+): Fits the criteria for Very Fine but with an additional virtue or small accumulation of virtues that improves the book's appearance by a perceptible amount.

8.0 VERY FINE (VF): An excellent copy with outstanding eye appeal. Sharp, bright and clean with supple pages. A comic book in this grade has the appearance of having been carefully handled. A limited accumulation of minor bindery defects is allowed. Cover is relatively flat with minimal surface wear beginning to show, possibly including some minute wear at corners. Inks are generally bright with moderate to high reflectivity. A 1/4" crease is acceptable if color is not broken. Stamped or inked arrival dates may be present. No obvious soiling, staining or other discoloration, except for minor foxing. Spine is almost flat with no roll. Possible minor color break allowed. Staples may show some discoloration. Very slight staple tears and a few almost very minor to minor stress lines may be present. No rust migration. In rare cases, a comic was not stapled at the bindery and therefore has a missing staple; this is not considered a defect. Any staple can be replaced on books up to Fine, but only vintage staples can be used on books from Very Fine to Near Mint. Mint books must have original staples. Paper is tan to cream and supple. No hint of acidity in the odor of the newsprint. Centerfold is mostly secure. Minor interior tears at the margin may be present.

7.5 VERY FINE– (VF–): Fits the criteria for Very Fine but with an additional defect or small accumulation of defects that detracts from the book's appearance by a perceptible amount.

7.0 FINE/VERY FINE (FN/VF): An above-average copy that shows minor wear but is still relatively flat and clean with outstanding eye appeal. A small accumulation of minor bindery defects is allowed. Minor cover wear beginning to show with interior yellowing or tanning allowed, possibly including minor creases. Corners may be blunted or abraded. Inks are generally bright with a moderate reduction in reflectivity. Stamped or inked arrival dates may be present. No obvious soiling, staining or other discoloration, except for minor foxing. The slightest spine roll may be present, as well as a possible moderate color break. Staples may show some discoloration. Slight staple tears and a slight accumulation of light stress lines may be present. Slight rust migration. In rare cases, a comic was not stapled at the bindery and therefore has a missing staple; this is not considered a defect. Any staple can be replaced on books up to Fine, but only vintage staples can be used on books from Very Fine to Near Mint. Mint books must have original staples. Paper is tan to cream, but not brown. No hint of acidity in the odor of the newsprint. Centerfold is mostly secure. Minor interior tears at the margin may be present.

6.5 FINE+ (FN+): Fits the criteria for Fine but with an additional virtue or small accumulation of virtues that improves the book's appearance by a perceptible amount.

6.0 FINE (FN): An above-average copy that shows minor wear but is still relatively flat and clean with no significant creasing or other serious defects. Eye appeal is somewhat reduced because of slight surface wear and the accumulation of small defects, especially on the spine and edges. A FINE condition comic book appears to have been read a few times and has been handled with moderate care. Some accumulation of minor bindery defects is allowed. Minor cover wear apparent, with minor to moderate creases. Inks show a major reduction in reflectivity. Blunted or abraded corners are more common, as is minor staining, soiling, discoloration, and/or foxing. Stamped or inked arrival dates may be present. A minor spine roll is allowed. There can also be a 1/4" spine split or severe color break. Staples show minor discoloration. Minor staple tears and an accumulation of stress lines may be present, as well as minor rust migration. In rare cases, a comic was not stapled at the bindery and therefore has a missing staple; this is not considered a defect. Any staple can be replaced on books up to Fine, but only vintage staples can be used on books from Very Fine to Near Mint. Mint books must have original staples. Paper is brown to tan and fairly supple with no signs of brittleness. No hint of acidity in the odor of the newsprint. Minor interior tears at the margin may be present. Centerfold may be loose but not detached.

5.5 FINE– (FN–): Fits the criteria for Fine but with an additional defect or small accumulation of defects that detracts from the book's appearance by a perceptible amount.

5.0 VERY GOOD/FINE (VG/FN): An above-average but well-used comic book. A comic in this grade shows some moderate wear; eye appeal is somewhat reduced because of the accumulation of defects. Still a desirable copy that has been handled with some care. An accumulation of bindery defects is allowed. Minor to moderate cover wear apparent, with minor to moderate creases and/or dimples. Inks have major to extreme reduction in reflectivity. Blunted or abraded corners are increasingly common, as is minor to moderate staining, discoloration, and/or foxing. Stamped or inked arrival dates may be present. A minor to moderate spine roll is allowed. A spine split of up to 1/2" may be present. Staples show minor discoloration. A slight accumulation of minor staple tears and an accumulation of minor stress lines may also be present, as well as minor rust migration. In rare cases, a comic was not stapled at the bindery and therefore has a missing staple; this is not considered a defect. Any staple can be replaced on books up to Fine, but only vintage staples can be used on books from Very Fine to Near Mint. Mint books must have original staples. Paper is brown to tan with no signs of brittleness. May have the faintest trace of an acidic odor. Centerfold may be loose but not detached. Minor tears may also be present.

4.5 VERY GOOD+ (VG+): Fits the criteria for Very Good but with an additional virtue or small accumulation of virtues that improves the book's appearance by a perceptible amount.

4.0 VERY GOOD (VG): The average used comic book. A comic in this grade shows some significant moderate wear, but still has not accumulated enough total defects to reduce eye appeal to the point that it is not a desirable copy. Cover shows moderate to significant wear, and may be loose but not completely detached. Moderate to extreme reduction in reflectivity. Can have an accumulation of creases or dimples. Corners may be blunted or abraded. Store stamps, name stamps, arrival dates, initials, etc. have no effect on this grade. Some discoloration, fading, foxing, and even minor soiling is allowed. As much as a 1/4" triangle can be missing out of the corner or edge; a missing 1/8" square is also acceptable. Only minor unobtrusive tape and other amateur repair allowed on otherwise high grade copies. Moderate spine roll may be present and/or a 1" spine split. Staples discolored. Minor to moderate staple tears and stress lines may be present, as well as some rust migration. Paper is brown but not brittle. A minor acidic odor can be detectable. Minor to moderate tears may be present. Centerfold may be loose or detached at one staple.

3.5 VERY GOOD– (VG–): Fits the criteria for Very Good but with an additional defect or small accumulation of defects that detracts from the book's appearance by a perceptible amount.

3.0 GOOD/VERY GOOD (GD/VG): A used comic book showing some substantial wear. Cover shows significant wear, and may be loose or even detached at one staple. Cover reflectivity is very low. Can have a book-length crease and/or dimples. Corners may be blunted or even rounded. Discoloration, fading, foxing, and even minor to moderate soiling is allowed. A triangle from 1/4" to 1/2" can be missing out of the corner or edge; a missing 1/8" to 1/4" square is also acceptable. Tape and other amateur repair may be present. Moderate spine roll likely. May have a spine split of anywhere from 1" to 1-1/2". Staples may be rusted or replaced. Minor to moderate staple tears and moderate stress lines may be present, as well as some rust migration. Paper is brown but not brittle. Centerfold may be loose or detached at one staple. Minor to moderate interior tears may be present.

2.5 GOOD+ (GD+): Fits the criteria for Good but with an additional virtue or small accumulation of virtues that improves the book's appearance by a perceptible amount.

2.0 GOOD (GD): Shows substantial wear; often considered a "reading copy." Cover shows significant wear and may even be detached. Cover reflectivity is low and in some cases completely absent. Book-length creases and dimples may be present. Rounded corners are more common. Moderate soiling, staining, discoloration and foxing may be present. The largest piece allowed missing from the front or back cover is usually a 1/2" triangle or a 1/4" square, although some Silver Age books such as 1960s Marvels have had the price corner box clipped from the top left front cover and may be considered Good if they would otherwise have graded higher. Tape and other forms of amateur repair are common in Silver Age and older books. Spine roll is likely. May have up to a 2" spine split. Staples may be degraded, replaced or missing. Moderate staple tears and stress lines may be present, as well as rust migration. Paper is brown but not brittle. Centerfold may be loose or detached. Moderate interior tears may be present.

1.8 GOOD– (GD–): Fits the criteria for Good but with an

additional defect or small accumulation of defects that detracts from the book's appearance by a perceptible amount.

1.5 FAIR/GOOD (FR/GD): A comic showing substantial to heavy wear. A copy in this grade still has all pages and covers, although there may be pieces missing up to and including missing coupons and/or Marvel Value Stamps that do not impact the story. Books in this grade are commonly creased, scuffed, abraded, soiled, and possibly unattractive, but still generally readable. Cover shows considerable wear and may be detached. Nearly no reflectivity to no reflectivity remaining. Store stamp, name stamp, arrival date and initials are permitted. Book-length creases, tears and folds may be present. Rounded corners are increasingly common. Soiling, staining, discoloration and foxing is generally present. Up to 1/10 of the back cover may be missing. Tape and other forms of amateur repair are increasingly common in Silver Age and older books. Spine roll is common. May have a spine split between 2" and 2/3 the length of the book. Staples may be degraded, replaced or missing. Staple tears and stress lines are common, as well as rust migration. Paper is brown and may show brittleness around the edges. Acidic odor may be present. Centerfold may be loose or detached. Interior tears are common.

1.0 FAIR (FR): A copy in this grade shows heavy wear. Some collectors consider this the lowest collectible grade because comic books in lesser condition are usually incomplete and/or brittle. Comics in this grade are usually soiled, faded, ragged and possibly unattractive. This is the last grade in which a comic remains generally readable. Cover may be detached, and inks have lost all reflectivity. Creases, tears and/or folds are prevalent. Corners are commonly rounded or absent. Soiling and staining is present. Books in this condition generally have all pages and most of the covers, although there may be up to 1/4 of the front cover missing or no back cover, but not both. Tape and other forms of amateur repair are more common. Spine roll is more common; spine split can extend up to 2/3 the length of the book. Staples may be missing or show rust and discoloration. An accumulation of staple tears and stress lines may be present, as well as rust migration. Paper is brown and may show brittleness around the edges but not in the central portion of the pages. Acidic odor may be present. Accumulation of interior tears. Chunks may be missing. The centerfold may be missing if readability is generally preserved (although there may be difficulty). Coupons may be cut.

0.5 POOR (PR): Most comic books in this grade have been sufficiently degraded to the point where there is little or no collector value; they are easily identified by a complete absence of eye appeal. Comics in this grade are brittle almost to the point of turning to dust with a touch, and are usually incomplete. Extreme cover fading may render the cover almost indiscernible. May have extremely severe stains, mildew or heavy cover abrasion to the point that some cover inks are indistinct/absent. Covers may be detached with large chunks missing. Can have extremely ragged edges and extensive creasing. Corners are rounded or virtually absent. Covers may have been defaced with paints, varnishes, glues, oil, indelible markers or dyes, and may have suffered heavy water damage. Can also have extensive amateur repairs such as laminated covers. Extreme spine roll present; can have extremely ragged spines or a complete, book-length split. Staples can be missing or show extreme rust and discoloration. Extensive staple tears and stress lines may be present, as well as extreme rust migration. Paper exhibits moderate to severe brittleness (where the comic book literally falls apart when examined). Extreme acidic odor may be present. Extensive interior tears. Multiple pages, including the centerfold, may be missing that affect readability. Coupons may be cut.

0.3 INCOMPLETE (INC): Books that are coverless, but are otherwise complete, or covers missing their interiors.

0.1 INCOMPLETE (INC): Coverless copies that have incomplete interiors, wraps or single pages will receive a grade of .1 as will just front covers or just back covers.

PUBLISHERS' CODES

The following abbreviations are used with cover reproductions throughout the book for copyright purposes:

ABC-America's Best Comics
AC-AC Comics
ACE-Ace Periodicals
ACG-American Comics Group
AJAX-Ajax-Farrell
ACP-Archie Comic Publications
BP-Better Publications
C & L-Cupples & Leon
CC-Charlton Comics
CEN-Centaur Publications
CCG-Columbia Comics Group
CG-Catechetical Guild
CHES-Harry 'A' Chesler
CM-Comics Magazine
CN-Cartoon Network
CPI-Conan Properties Inc.

DC-DC Comics, Inc.
DELL-Dell Publishing Co.
DH-Dark Horse
DIS-Disney Enterprises, Inc.
DMP-David McKay Publishing
DYN-Dynamite Entertainment
DS-D. S. Publishing Co.
EAS-Eastern Color Printing Co.
EC-E. C. Comics
ECL-Eclipse Comics
ENWIL-Enwil Associates
EP-Elliott Publications
ERB-Edgar Rice Burroughs
FAW-Fawcett Publications
FC-First Comics
FF-Famous Funnies

FH-Fiction House Magazines
FOX-Fox Feature Syndicate
GIL-Gilberton
GK-Gold Key
GP-Great Publications
HARV-Harvey Publications
H-B-Hanna-Barbera
HILL-Hillman Periodicals
HOKE-Holyoke Publishing Co.
IM-Image Comics
KING-King Features Syndicate
LEV-Lev Gleason Publications
MAL-Malibu Comics
MAR-Marvel Characters, Inc.
ME-Magazine Enterprises
MLJ-MLJ Magazines

MS-Mirage Studios
NOVP-Novelty Press
NYNS-New York News Syndicate
PG-Premier Group
PINE-Pines
PMI-Parents' Magazine Institute
PRIZE-Prize Publications
QUA-Quality Comics Group
REAL-Realistic Comics
RH-Rural Home
S & S-Street and Smith Publishers
SKY-Skywald Publications
STAR-Star Publications
STD-Standard Comics
STJ-St. John Publishing Co.
SUPR-Superior Comics

TC-Tower Comics
TM-Trojan Magazines
TMP-Todd McFarlane Prods.
TOBY-Toby Press
TOPS-Tops Comics
UFS-United Features Syndicate
VAL-Valiant
VITL-Vital Publications
WB-Warner Brothers.
WEST-Western Publishing Co.
WHIT-Whitman Publishing Co.
WHW-William H. Wise
WMG-William M. Gaines (E. C.)
WP-Warren Publishing Co.
YM-Youthful Magazines
Z-D-Ziff-Davis Publishing Co.

OVERSTREET ADVISORS

Even before the first edition of *The Overstreet Comic Book Price Guide* was printed, author Robert M. Overstreet solicited pricing data, historical notations, and general information from a variety of sources. What was initially an informal group offering input quickly became an organized field of comic book collectors, dealers and historians whose opinions are actively solicited in advance of each edition of this book. Some of these Overstreet Advisors are specialists who deal in particular niches within the comic book world, while others are generalists who are interested in commenting on the broader marketplace. Each advisor provides information from their respective areas of interest and expertise, spanning the history of American comics.

While some choose to offer pricing and historical information in the form of annotated sales catalogs, auction catalogs, or documented private sales, assistance from others comes in the form of the market reports such as those beginning on page 97 in this book. In addition to those who have served as Overstreet Advisors almost since *The Guide*'s inception, each year new contributors are sought.

With that in mind, we are pleased to present our newest Overstreet Advisors:

THE CLASS OF 2023

JAMES FAIR
Diamond Int. Galleries
Hunt Valley, MD

KEVIN FORBES
Comic Interlude
Lexington, KY

TERRENCE KEEGAN
Platinum Age Specialist
Phillipines

SEAN PROSJE
Comic Cave Canada
Dundas, ON, Canada

AUSTIN REECE
Reece's Rare Comics
Monrovia, MD

ROBERT YOUNG
Borderlands Comics and Games
Greenville, SC

METROPOLIS

www.metropoliscomics.com

THE LARGEST DEALER OF VINTAGE COMIC BOOKS IN THE WORLD

Bill Hughes
Paid You How Much?

CALL NOW FOR IMMEDIATE PAYMENT!!

ALWAYS SEEKING THE FOLLOWING:

Pre-1965 Disney Comics & Posters
Vintage Tarzan Books, Comics & Posters
Pre-1960 Western Comics & Posters
Early Popeye, Betty Boop & Krazy Kat
Vintage Our Gang, Marx Bros., 3-Stooges
Vintage Lone Ranger, Dick Tracy, Green Hornet
Charlie Chaplin, Buster Keaton, Harold Lloyd
Horror & Sci-Fi Poster and Stills
High-Grade Warren & Skywald Magazines
Pre-1937 Pulps & Fantasy Books

William Hughes' Vintage Collectables

P.O. Box 270244
Flower Mound, TX 75027

Office: 972-539-9190
Mobile: 973-432-4070

www.VintageCollectables.net
Email: whughes199@yahoo.com
eBay User Name: comic-warehouse

Senior Advisor Overstreet Price Guide

Bill Hughes
Paid You How Much?

ALWAYS SEEKING THE FOLLOWING:

Golden Age, Silver Age, & Bronze Age Comics
Vintage Original Comic & Collector Card Art
vintage Baseball Cards & Uncut Sheets
Movie Posters & Stills
Western, Sci-Fi, and Comedy Collectibles
Vintage Toys in Original Boxes
Vintage Disneyana & Other Animation
Original Comic Art

William Hughes' Vintage Collectables

P.O. Box 270244
Flower Mound, TX 75027
Office: 972-539-9190
Mobile: 973-432-4070

www.VintageCollectables.net
Email: whughes199@yahoo.com
eBay User Name: comic-warehouse

Senior Advisor Overstreet Price Guide

BUYING COMICS

METROPOLISCOMICS.COM 36 W 37TH ST, 6TH FL, NEW YORK, NY 10018

P: 212.260.4147 F: 212.260.4304 BUYING@METROPOLISCOMICS.COM

TOLL-FREE 1.800.229.METRO

$250,000
SILVER AGE COLLECTION

$597,000
GOLDEN AGE COLLECTION

$500,000
CHARLESTON COLLECTION

WE PAID $3.2 MILLION FOR ONE COMIC, IMAGINE WHAT WE CAN PAY FOR YOUR COLLECTION

$1 MILLION
AMAZING FANTASY #15

$1.2 MILLION
DETECTIVE COMICS #27

$657,250
AMAZING SPIDER-MAN #328

1-800-229-6387

CALL TOLL FREE TODAY FOR IMMEDIATE CA$H OFFER

CASH FOR COMICS, ORIGINAL ART, VIDEO GAMES, VHS, & PULPS

WE WILL TRAVEL THE WORLD TO BUY YOUR COLLECTION

WE SPEND MILLIONS EACH YEAR

TALK TO
UR EXPERTS
TODAY!

QES YOUR
COMICS!

Stephen Fishler
CEO,
Overstreet Advisor

METROPOLIS
COLLECTIBLES
www.metropoliscomics.com
VINTAGE COMIC BOOKS | ORIGINAL COMIC ART

Vincent Zurzolo
President,
Overstreet Advisor

METROPOLIS

RIDDLE ME THIS?

Is it still better to get more money for your comics than less?
Does the Earth still revolve around the Sun?
Are there still people out there who are not offering their books to Metropolis and losing money by selling to the wrong guy?

If anyone out there can shed some light on why this still happens in this day and age, could you please let us know?

The following is a true story...
At the biggest convention of the year, a dealer who traveled hundreds of miles to set up bought a high-grade Fantastic Four #1 for roughly 1/2 the price that we would have paid. After that comic passed through the hands of several dealers, Metropolis did in fact buy it. The fellow who initially sold it at the convention could easily have made *seven thousand dollars more* if he had sold it to Metropolis.

SHOULDN'T THESE GUYS KNOW BETTER? SHOULDN'T EVERYONE?

CONTACT US TODAY!
1.800.229.6387

CHECK OUT OUR WEBSITE! EASY TO MAKE OFFERS!
METROPOLISCOMICS.COM 36 W 37TH ST, 6TH FL, NEW YORK, NY 10018
P: 212.260.4147 F: 212.260.4304 BUYING@METROPOLISCOMICS.COM
TOLL-FREE 1.800.229.6387 INTERNATIONAL: 001.212.260.4147

METROPOLIS

COLLECTIBLES

www.metropoliscomics.com

We can afford to pay you more because we have the best customers. We travel to you. Metropolis is buying entire collections. We buy Golden, Silver, Bronze, and Modern Comics. No collection is too small. The prices below are for NM 9.4. **WE BUY ALL GRADES!** Email us your list or call today for a quote 1-800-229-METRO (6387)!

CA$H FOR COMICS

Action #1	**$4 MILLION**	Detective #38	**$250,000**	New Fun #6	**$55,000**
Action #7	**$500,000**	Detective #168	**$80,000**	Pep Comics #22	**$325,000**
Action #242	**$40,000**	Detective #225	**$80,000**	Phantom Lady #17	**$85,000**
Adventure #40	**$150,000**	Donald Duck #9	**$28,000**	Sensation Comics #1	**$325,000**
Adventure #48	**$80,000**	Fantastic Comics #3	**$150,000**	Showcase #4	**$825,000**
Adventure #210	**$50,000**	Fantastic Four #1	**$750,000**	Showcase #22	**$150,000**
All-American #16	**$600,000**	Fantastic Four #5	**$65,000**	Star Wars #1 (35c)	**$21,000**
All-American #19	**$70,000**	Flash Comics #1	**$1.3 MILLION**	Superboy #1	**$30,000**
All-Star #3	**$220,000**	Green Lantern #1 (GA)	**$60,000**	Superman #1	**$3 MILLION**
Amazing Fantasy #15	**$800,000**	Green Lantern #1 (SA)	**$28,000**	Superman #14	**$90,000**
Amazing Spider-Man #1	**$175,000**	House of Secrets #92	**$7,000**	Suspense Comics #3	**$150,000**
Amazing Spider-Man #129	**$4,500**	Human Torch #2(#1)	**$145,000**	Tales of Suspense #39	**$115,000**
Avengers #1	**$90,000**	Incredible Hulk #1	**$650,000**	Tales to Astonish #27	**$48,000**
Avengers #4	**$25,000**	Incredible Hulk #181	**$10,000**	Target Comics V1 #7	**$15,000**
Batman #1	**$1.3 MILLION**	Journey into Myst. #83	**$240,000**	Teenage Mutant Ninja Turtles #1	**$20,000**
Batman Adventures #12	**$700**	Justice League #1	**$90,000**	Walt Disney C&S #1	**$55,000**
Black Cat Mystery #50	**$60,000**	Marvel Comics #1	**$1.8 MILLION**	Whiz #2 (#1)	**$800,000**
Brave & the Bold #28	**$250,000**	Marvel Spotlight #5	**$6,000**	Wonder Woman #1	**$150,000**
Captain America #1	**$850,000**	More Fun #52	**$250,000**	X-Men #1	**$175,000**
Detective #1	**$350,000**	More Fun #54	**$60,000**	X-Men Giant-Size #1	**$5,000**
Detective #27	**$3.5 MILLION**	More Fun #55	**$55,000**	Young Allies #1	**$30,000**

Action Comics	#1-400	Classic Comics	#1-169	Jungle Comics	#1-163	Strange Tales	#1-145
Adventure Comics	#32-400	Comic Cavalcade	#1-63	Justice League	#1-110	Sub-Mariner	#1-42
Advs. Into Weird Worlds	#1-30	Daredevil Comics	#1-60	Mad	#1-50	Superboy	#1-110
All-American Comics	#1-102	Daring Mystery	#1-8	Marvel Mystery	#1-92	Superman	#1-250
All-Flash Quarterly	#1-32	Detective Comics	#1-450	Military Comics	#1-43	Suspense Comics	#1-11
All-Select	#1-11	Donald Duck 4-Colors	#4-up	More Fun Comics	#7-127	Tales From The Crypt	#20-46
All-Star Comics	#1-57	Exciting Comics	#1-69	Mystery in Space	#1-75	Tales of Suspense	#1-80
All-Winners	#1-21	Fantastic Four	#1-200	Mystic Comics	#1-up	Tales to Astonish	#1-80
Amazing Man	#5-26	Fight Comics	#1-86	National Comics	#1-75	Terrific Comics	#1-6
Amaz. Mystery Funnies	all	Flash	#105-150	New Adventure	#12-31	Thing	#1-17
Amazing Spider-Man	#1-328	Flash Comics	#1-104	New Comics	#1-11	USA Comics	#1-17
Avengers	#1-200	Funny Pages	#6-42	New Fun Comics	#1-6	Weird Comics	#1-20
Batman	#1-300	Green Lantern (GA)	#1-38	Our Army at War	#1-200	Weird Mysteries	#1-12
Blackhawk	#9-130	Green Lantern (SA)	#1-90	Our Fighting Forces	#1-180	Weird Tales From The Future	#1-8
Boy Commandos	#1-32	Hit Comics	#1-65	Planet Comics	#1-73	Whiz Comics	#1-155
Brave & the Bold	#1-100	Human Torch	#2 (#1)-38	Rangers Comics	#1-69	Wings Comics	#1-124
Captain America	#1-78	Incredible Hulk	#1-6	Reform School Girl	NN	Wonder Woman	#1-20
Captain Marvel Advs.	#1-150	Jimmy Olsen	#1-150	Sensation Comics	#1-116	Wonderworld	#3-33
Catman	#1-32	Journey into Mystery	#1-125	Showcase	#1-100	World's Finest	#1-200
Challengers	#1-25	Jumbo Comics	#1-167	Star-Spangled Comics	#1-130	X-Men	#1-30

CHECK OUT OUR WEBSITE! NEW COMICS ADDED DAILY!

METROPOLISCOMICS.COM 36 W 37TH ST, 6TH FL, NEW YORK, NY 10018

P: 212.260.4147 F: 212.260.4304 BUYING@METROPOLISCOMICS.COM

TOLL-FREE 1.800.229.6387 INTERNATIONAL: 001.212.260.4147

JUST THE FACTS

FACT 1: ABSOLUTELY NO OTHER COMIC DEALER BUYS MORE 1930'S - 1980'S COMICS THAN METROPOLIS.

Although the pages of the price guide are filled with other dealers offering to pay "top dollar," the simple truth is that Metropolis spends more money on more quality comic book collections year in and year out than any other dealers in the country. We have the funds and the expertise to back up our word. The fact is that we have spent nearly $8 million dollars on vintage comic books, comic art, video games, VHS, pulps, toys, memorabilia and movie posters over the last year. If you have comic books to sell, please call us at toll-free 1-800-229-6387. A generous finder's fee will be given if you know of any collections that we purchase. All calls will be strictly confidential.

FACT 2: ABSOLUTELY NO OTHER COMIC DEALER SELLS MORE 1930'S - 1980'S COMICS THAN METROPOLIS.

We simply have the best stock of Golden and Silver Age comic books in the world. Tens of thousands of collectors familiar with our strict grading standards and excellent service can attest to this. Chances are, if you want it, we have it!

CHECK OUT OUR WEBSITE! INTEREST FREE TIME PAYMENTS!

METROPOLISCOMICS.COM 36 W 37TH ST, 6TH FL, NEW YORK, NY 10018

P: 212.260.4147 F: 212.260.4304 BUYING@METROPOLISCOMICS.COM

TOLL-FREE 1 800 229 6387 INTERNATIONAL: 001 212 260 4147

ABSOLUTELY 100% FREE

APPRAISAL SERVICE

If you'd like to know the value of your comics, why not ask the guys who created the universal 10-point grading scale? Metropolis offers the following absolutely free!

1. **VALUE APPRAISAL** to determine your comics' retail value based on all parameters including condition, current desirability of the comic, relative scarcity, and historical significance.
2. **COMPLETE EXAMINATION** of comics for all types of restoration.
3. **DOUBLE GRADING SYSTEM** to ensure greatest accuracy.

1.800.229.METRO (6387)

Please limit the number of comics to 10. Comics should be from 1930-1990.

Our staff has over 100 years of comic evaluation and retail experience. There is not a more knowledgeable staff anywhere. Email us your list today!

SELLER TIP:

Sometimes having your comics sealed by a 3rd party grader increases the value. Other times it won't and you only lose money on grading fees. Our consultation determines when and when not to have a comic "slabbed" saving you money!

CHECK OUT OUR WEBSITE! IMMEDIATE CASH OFFERS!

METROPOLISCOMICS.COM 36 W 37TH ST, 6TH FL, NEW YORK, NY 10018

P: 212.260.4147 F: 212.260.4304 BUYING@METROPOLISCOMICS.COM

TOLL-FREE 1.800.229.6387 INTERNATIONAL: 001.212.260.4147

ISN'T IT BETTER TO GET **MORE MONEY** FOR YOUR COMICS?

COMIC CONNECT

WWW.COMICCONNECT.COM

WORLD'S PREMIER ONLINE COMIC MARKETPLACE & AUCTIONEER

For over 40 years, the experts at ComicConnect have been recognized and renowned for selling the most sought-after comic books and collections. Our services have been enlisted by individuals who are the most aggressive collectors in the market. ComicConnect will help you realize the best return when you are selling your comics.

In today's market, the decision of just how to sell your comics is critical. Making the right choice is like walking a tightrope without a net. Perhaps the most common pitfall novice sellers fall into is blindly consigning to the first auction house they come across. If you are considering parting with your collection, and think an auction house is the best way to go, we strongly advise you to consider the following:

Do The Math. How much is the auction house making on your consignment? Just add the seller's premium and the buyer's premium together and you will have your answer. We have seen buyer's premiums of 20% and even 25%. Seems a bit aggressive and greedy. Don't you think? And don't be fooled by auction houses that don't even put out a catalog. They save lots of money there, but you as the consignor pays for that in the end. ComicConnect has many options available to you to maximize your return on investment.

When you consign to ComicConnect, you have at your disposal the services of the most experienced comic book sellers in the world. More importantly, you benefit from the thousands upon thousands of long-term customer relationships we've developed over the past 40 years. We're in it for the long haul and will work with you to develop a strategy that will get you the highest return. We won't "square-peg" your collection into a formula that doesn't fit. We will pursue the avenue or avenues that work best for the comics you consign. Sometimes, that means selling your comics to the private individuals who pay the very best for being offered the very best. Oftentimes, we will arrange exclusive viewings at our showroom in Manhattan. We also maintain thousands of want lists of customers waiting in the wings for certain comic books to come to market - comic books that you may have in your collection.

If you're thinking about selling your comics, visit our website www.comicconnect.com!
For a free consultation, call us Toll Free at 888.779.7377 or email support@comicconnect.com

36 WEST 37TH STREET., 6TH FLOOR, NEW YORK, NY 10018 P: 212.895.3999 F: 212.260.4304 COMICCONNECT.COM

METROPOLIS

COLLECTIBLES

www.metropoliscomics.com

We understand how important your collection is to you.
We will treat you with the respect and professionalism you deserve.

Call us today to experience the Metropolis difference.

BIGGER AND BETTER 52 PAGES 25¢ COMICS INA FLASH! 52 PAGES 25¢

COMICS INA FLASH!

Giant-Size X-Men #1 © MCG

House of Secrets #92 © DC

We are the **KING** of Bronze Age books!

Detective Comics #225 © DC

Yes, we have plenty of **Silver Age** books too!

Showcase #4 © DC

BUY-SELL & TRADE COMICS 1956-1980

CONTACT US!! We'll send you our free photo packed catalogue which lists 1000's of comics with prices starting under $1.00!!

Tony Starks
COMICS INA FLASH®℠
PO Box 3611
Evansville, IN 47735-3611
Phone/Text 812-401-6127
Outside USA 812-401-6127

NOW OFFERING:
Fast, Affordable & Professional comic book pressing service.
See our website for full details.

www.comicsinaflash.com
email: comicflash@aol.com

Comics Ina Flash! is a registered service mark of Tony Starks

JHV ASSOCIATES
is
BUYING COMICS

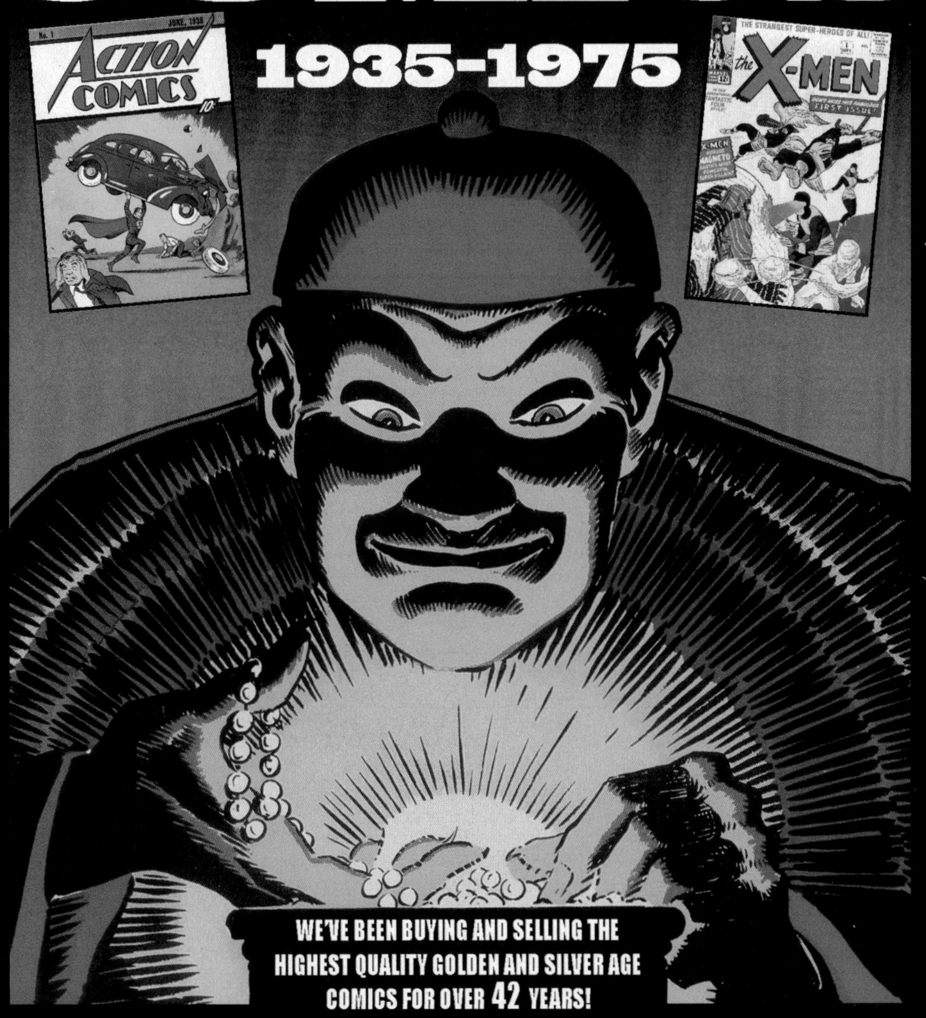

If you are thinking of selling your prized collection... call us!
We'll fly anywhere to meet with you and we guarantee we'll treat you right!

Ask around (Even our competitors)... Our reputation Can't Be Beat!

P.O. BOX 317, WOODBURY HEIGHTS, NEW JERSEY 08097 TEL: 856-845-4010

E-MAIL: JHVASSOC@HOTMAIL.COM

VISIT MY EBAY STORE JHV ASSOC

www.dougcomicworld.com

DOUG SULIPA'S

COMIC WORLD

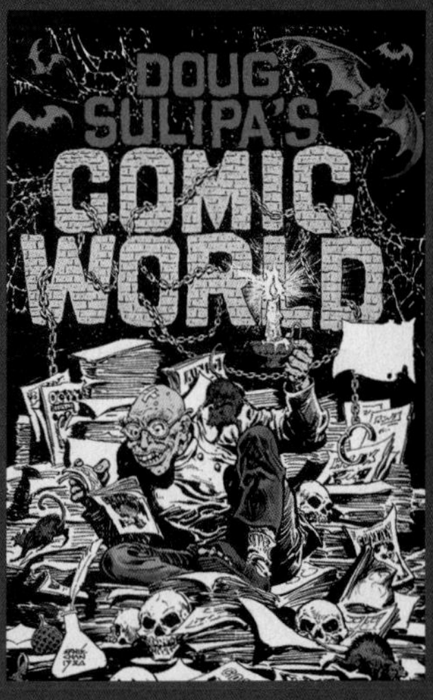

Box 21986
Steinbach, Manitoba
CANADA R5G 1B5
Ph: 1-204-346-3674 (8am-11pm)
Web site: www.dougcomicworld.com
Email:dsulipa@gmail.com Ebay Auction: "dwscw"
Mail order since 1971! Overstreet Advisor!
Specialist in EVERYTHING!

1,300,000 COMICS & RELATED ITEMS; Specializing in 1960-2010 = 95% of ALL comics by ALL companies in Stock; Likely THE World's BIGGEST selection with Approx 200,000 DIFFERENT Comics & Related items in stock; PLUS a Great Selection of 1940's-1950's & older too; (We especially like to carry everything valued at under $100); ** (200,000 Alternatives; 40,000 Archie; 35,000 Charlton; 3000 Classics; 6000 Comic/Cartoon Paperbacks; 15,000 Comic Digests; 70,000 Comic Magazines; 3000 Dennis the Menace; Fanzines & related; 350,000 DC; 20,000 DELL; 20,000 Disney; 3000 French & Foreign Language comics; 30,000 Gold Key; 5000 Hanna Barbera; 8000 Harvey; 450,000 Marvel; 12,000 Richie Rich; 2000 Treasure Chest; 1500 Undergrounds; 13,000 UK British Marvel; 6000 Warren); ** **PLUS a big selection of**; ACG, Adult Cartoon, Atlas/Seaboard, Atlas/Marvel, Bananas mags, BLB's, Capt Canuck,CARtoons, CGC graded, Coloring Books, Calendars, CBG, Christian/Religious, Comic Reader/Journal, Cracked, Dynamite, Eerie pub, Fanzines, Fawcett Westerns, Giveaways, Gladstone, Heavy Metal, Help, Horror, Humor/Parody, MAD, Misc Golden Age, National Lampoon, Platinum Age, Portfolios, RBCC, Romance, Sick, Skywald, Spire, Stanley, 3-D, Treasuries, Trib Comic, War, Tower, UK - British Annuals & Comics, Westerns & MORE; We have most of the hard to find Cartoon, Humor, Love,Teen, War & Western Comics & most mainstream Superhero & other popular titles too; Please ***SEND your*** SERIOUS ***WANT LIST*** of 50 or less "Most Wanted" items;
eBAY; See our many current auctions on eBay, for all the types of material we sell as " **dwscw** " (Our Feedback at over +12,000 = 100% Positive, at time of writing); ABE Books; See the BOOKS, Paperbacks,Pulps & other items we have listed on the internet at ABE books = "www.abebooks.com" & search sellers = " Comic World "; **POSTERS;** We have 10,000 Movie & Video store Posters (1960 up & some older), PLUS about another 10,000 Chain Store type posters; 3000 Comic & Comic Promo posters; Send your want lists!
100,000 Vinyl RECORDS; Most Standard issue records 1960-90 in stock & selection of 50's (most $5-25); 8000 Cassette tapes; VIDEO GAMES; Collectible Atari2600, Coleco, Intellivision, Nintendo, Sega,Vic-20 & some newer games; BOARD GAMES; Approx 1500 Vintage 1950's to 1980's Board Games; Character,TV,Comic & Misc; **16,000 VHS MOVIES;** Most Popular Theatre Movies in Stock; 1000's of Out-of-Print; Most are $5-$15 range; 3000 DVD's; Selection of; old NEWSPAPERS, Sunday Comic Pages (1960's-early1980's); 1000 AVON colectables; 1000 old SOFT DRINK bottles;
250,000 MAGAZINES; One of the World's biggest selection of ALL types of mags 1940's-2000+, some older; [70,000 Comic related; 10,000 Fantasy/SF/Horror; 10,000 SPORTS Illustrated; 5000 Misc Sports; 10,000 Music; 10,000 Car, Hot Rod, Motorcycle; 10,000 Playboy & Penthouse; 8000 Misc ADULT 1950's-2000+ (No XXX); 20,000 NEWS MAGS; Life, Time, Newsweek, McLeans, Look, Saturday Evening Post, Colliers,etc; 5000 TV/Movie/Personality; 15,000 Comic Digests; 5000 Misc DIGESTS; Readers,Coronet,Mystery,SF,Childrens,etc; 10,000 TV GUIDES 1950's-2000+; 3000 PULPS]; ** PLUS; Adventure, Aircraft, Argosy, Beckett, Bettie Page, Boxing, Childrens, Cosmopolitan, Crafts, Dime Novels (1885-1925), Ebony, Golf, High Times, Hobbies, Martial Arts, Model Airplane Cars Trains, Muscle mags, National Geographic, Omni, People Mag, Popular Mechanics, New Yorker, Price Guide mags, Punch, Railroad, RPG/Gaming, Rolling Stone, Scandal & Tabloid, Stephen King, Teen, Tennis, Traci Lords, True Detective, True Romance, UFO, US mag, Video Games,War/Military,Western, Womens Fashion, Wrestling; *** Please ***SEND your*** SERIOUS ***WANT LIST*** of 50 or less "Most Wanted" items.
MANITOBA Collection; (20,000+ Comics from this mainly 1971-1988 HIGH GRADE Pedigree Quality Collection from all Publishers);
250,000 Mass Market PAPERBACKS; ALL TYPES 1940-2000 from VINTAGE Rarities to Common Reading copies (40,000 F/SF/Horror; 60,000 Mystery; 10,000 Vintage Adult; 6000 Comic/Cartoon, 2000 Rare Canadian Collins White Circle; 3000 scarce Harlequin, #1-2000; 12,000 WAR/Military, 6000 TV; 4000 Biography; 15,000 Western; 10,000 Historical Fiction; Occult/UFO=4000; 10,000 NON-Fiction; 10,000 Romance; 50,000 Misc General Fiction; PLUS; Children/Juvenile, Sports, Music, Movie, Juvenile Delinquent, Drug, Estoteric, Good Girl Art, JFK, Star Trek, Character/Personality, Ace Doubles, ERB, REH, History, Literature, Religion & MORE; **60,000 HARDCOVERS**; A huge selection, of ALL types 1900-1990's+ including many lower cost Book Club & cheaper Reading copies; Most in the $5-$35 range; Some cheaper, some better.

** **We have 600,000 Pounds of Inventory:** Our Webite lists the equivalent of 6000 Typed Pages, in over 160 Catagories (& still growing) of what INVENTORY is IN STOCK & ready to sell. They are NOT catalogued by price & conditon; (1) REQUEST Condition, Price & confimation of availibility; (2) State preferred Condition; (3) List up to a MAXIMUM of 50 items that interest you; (4) We will respond ASAP;

** **NO COMPUTER ??** Send your want list, or Phone it in; We can make printouts & send by Mail = Phone for Cost of Printing Out & shipping; We will sell BULK Store & Dealer stock; SATISFACTION ALWAYS GUARANTEED; 99.9% Satisfaction Rate!! **Strict Grading;** FULL TIME Mail Order ONLY, from our WAREHOUSE; (NO Retail store); MAIL ORDER since 1971, with OVER 25,000 DIFFERENT Satisfied Customers, with over 250,000 completed Orders. VISA, MC, Amex, MO, PAYPAL.

www.dougcomicworld.com **If we don't have what you want, maybe no one does.**

GOLDEN AGE

WANT LIST COMICS

SILVER AGE

WE FILL WANT LISTS

We have a simple question to ask ... have you

E-MAILED

us your want list yet? Here is what it will cost you... 5 to 10 minutes of your time.
Here is what you could stand to gain . . . SOME OR ALL OF THE COMIC BOOKS (CGC OR RAW) THAT YOU HAVE BEEN SEARCHING FOR THE LAST FEW YEARS!!!

WHAT ARE YOU WAITING FOR?

"The **Batman #1** you sold me was in the **nicest, unrestored condition** I've ever seen!", **Bob Overstreet, author "The Official Overstreet Comic Book Price Guide."**

"I'm glad that you have a **great selection** of **Golden Age** and **Silver Age** comics in stock. You have been able to constantly find books to fill some very tough missing holes in my collection. I also appreciate your **consistent, tight** grading and **fair** prices!"

Dan Hampton, Las Cruces, NM

These are just two of the **many** satisfied customers that have bought books from us in the past. Over the years, we have developed a **very strong return customer base** because we **ACCURATELY** price, grade, and describe books (in detail) over the phone and through the mail/email. If CGC books are desired, we can definitely fill those needs as well !!! In the past few years, we have acquired nearly **EVERY** major **Golden Age** and **Silver Age** book **more than once** for our many want list clients. These include books like **Action 1, Detective 1, Detective 27, Marvel 1, Superman 1** and more recent gems like **AF 15, FF 1, Hulk 1, Flash 105** and **Showcase 4, 8, 22. OUR SPECIALTY IS GOLD, SILVER, BRONZE, AND COPPER AGE BOOKS (1933 - 1993)**. Please check out our **great selection** of old books! (CGC or Raw).

We don't claim that we can fill every list all the time, but if any company can accomplish this, it **would certainly** be us! We can say this with **much confidence** because our representatives travel to the **majority** of the 50 states and Canada plus attend many of the major comic book conventions (San Diego, Chicago, Detroit, New York, etc.) to uncover books **you would not** have the opportunity to find. When we are not on the road, we spend **MANY** hours on the phone locating books from our **long** list of past and present comic sources we've developed over the **25 years** we have been dealing in comic books. When sending your want list either **E-MAIL** us, or mail us and include a self-addressed stamped envelope (if possible), **your phone number,** and a good time to reach you. We **DON'T** send out catalogs, so **please** ask for **specific** books and **conditions** desired. We will contact you **when** we find the items you've requested. **Phone calls are also welcomed. WE WILL GLADLY SUGGEST AND PERSONALLY PUT TOGETHER COMIC BOOK INVESTMENT PORTFOLIOS FOR BIG AND SMALL INVESTORS. OUR ADVICE IS ALWAYS FREE!**

SAVE YOURSELF ALL THE HASSLE AND LET US DO THE LOOKING FOR YOU!
CALL, FAX, MAIL, OR EMAIL US YOUR WANT LIST!

YOU HAVE NOTHING TO LOSE AND EVERYTHING ON YOUR WANT LIST TO GAIN!

Competitive pricing always. Accurate grading. **MANY CGC BOOKS AVAILABLE.** Friendly, courteous service. **Interest free time payments/layaways possible.** Checks, Money Orders, Visa, Mastercard, Discover and American Express accepted for total payment **OR** down payment on books. 7 day money back guarantee before a sale is considered final on all non-CGC books. No collect calls please.

PayPal payments accepted

Our office/warehouse # is:
1-918-299-0440
Call us anytime between 1 pm and 8 pm, CST

WANT LIST COMICS
BOX 701932
TULSA, OK 74170-1932

Senior Advisor to the Overstreet Comic Price Guide
References gladly provided!

Please email your want list to our NEW address

wantlistcomics777@gmail.com

PENDRAGON COMICS

Canada's Premier Store for quality Silver, Golden, and Bronze Age comics!

WE BUY ALL COMICS!
WE TRADE AND HELP UPGRADE!
WE BUY ENTIRE COLLECTIONS!
NO COLLECTION TOO BIG OR SMALL
WE PAY CASH OR MONEY ORDER
WE CAN EVEN PAY BY PAYPAL!

pendragoncomicscanada@gmail.com

VINTAGE SPECIALISTS FOR OVER 3 DECADES, WE HAVE 200+ BINS OF GOLDEN AGE TO BRONZE AGE. WITH WALL TO WALL 50+ SHOWCASES OF TOP DEMAND KEY BOOKS NUMBERING OVER 1000+. OUR SELECTION IS VAST, WITH MANY COMPANIES REPRESENTED. ARCHIE, DELL, GOLD KEY, ATLAS, HARVEY AND OF COURSE DC AND MARVEL. COME ON IN, YOU WON'T BE DISAPPOINTED. WE SELL ONLINE AT OUR WEBSITE, AND WE CAN BE FOLLOWED ON FACEBOOK/TWITTER/INSTAGRAM AT PENDRAGONCOMICS.

SEE US AT TORONTO'S BEST COMIC CONVENTION HOSTED BY HOBBYSTAR IN AUGUST!

THE SHOW BOASTS OVER 100,000+ FANS FOR COMICS, TV/MOVIE, HORROR, SCI-FI AND ANIME. WE ARE THERE EVERY YEAR! (USUALLY LAST FRI, SAT & SUN IN AUGUST).

WE SPECIALIZE IN 1940-1970S COMICS
AN HONEST STORE FOR 30+ YEARS
AN OFFICIAL OVERSTREET ADVISOR
LAYAWAY POSSIBLE
GREAT RESERVING SYSTEM FOR NEW RELEASES!

PENDRAGON COMICS

CLOVERDALE MALL
ETOBICOKE, TORONTO

WWW.PENDRAGONCOMICS.COM

416-253-6974 • OPEN EVERY DAY

Collect Comics?

Get our free catalog!

We Do Platinum, Golden, Silver & Bronze Back Issue Mail Order Right!

Here's what a few of our many satisfied customers say!

"I was very impressed with the packaging and speed of delivery." - Jack Eastwood, Murrieta, CA

"I have never dealt with a better mail order service." -Garth Ferris, Chico, CA

"I can count on you,...Precise Grading." -Carsten Pedersen, Hvidovre, Denmark

"RTS is my first source to find older comics for reasonable prices. Easy to use catalog & great service!" -Lance Leber, Monument, CO

"Thank you so much for your prompt service. Ordering from you is a really delightful experience. Your grading is unusually strict - most items were better than I expected." -Schultz Riggs, Jackson, MS

RTS Unlimited Inc, P.O. Box 150412, Dept OS44, Lakewood, CO 80215-0412
(303) 403-1840, Fax: (303) 403-1837, RTSUnlimited@earthlink.net, www.RTSUnlimited.com

Contact us today to get our huge illustrated free catalog! Platinum, Golden, Silver & Bronze comics, CGC graded comics, supplies, and more!! Over 30 years in business! We have the Rocky Mountain Region's most diverse selection of collectible back issue comics and supplies.

Photo-Journals!

This awesome resource to comic book collecting contains thousands of full color cover pictures in each volume! A must have for every comic collector!!

We can't recommend these books enough!

Thousands of full color pictures! Includes publication dates, artist information, articles and much more! Vol 1 & 2 focus on the Golden Age and also have scarcity data! The Golden Age volumes are only $65.95 each or $119.95 for both. Vol 3 & 4 are dedicated to Marvel Comics and are $27.95 each or $53.95 for both.

Special: Get all four volumes for only $164.95!

Shipping and handling: Continental US: please add $9.00 for the first Vol and $4.00 for each additional one. All others: please call for rates.

Note: Some volumes may have some minor cosmetic damage (The clear plastic coating is delaminating). ALL volumes are NEW and UNREAD.

To order: Call, fax, or e-mail a credit card order or Send check or money order to:

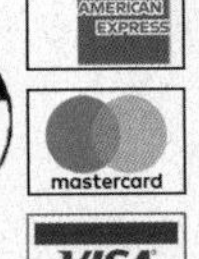

RTS Unlimited, Inc.
P.O. Box 150412
Lakewood, CO 80215
(303) 403-1840
Fax: (303) 403-1837
RTSUnlimited@earthlink.net
www.RTSUnlimited.com

RTS Unlimited, Inc.

Dedicated to Customer Satisfaction!

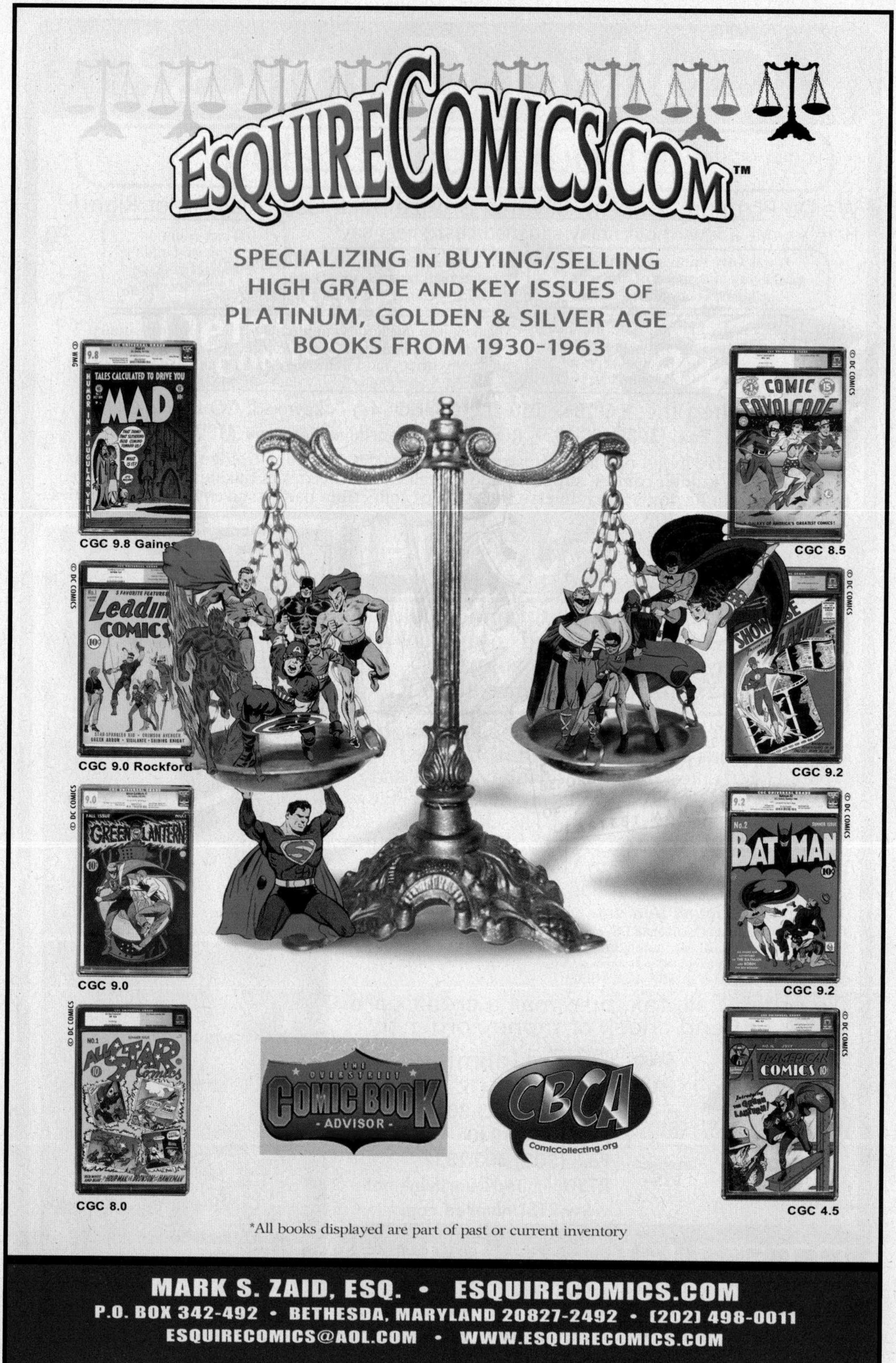

ESQUIRECOMICS.COM™

SPECIALIZING IN BUYING/SELLING HIGH GRADE AND KEY ISSUES OF PLATINUM, GOLDEN & SILVER AGE BOOKS FROM 1930-1963

CGC 9.8 Gaines

CGC 8.5

CGC 9.0 Rockford

CGC 9.2

CGC 9.0

CGC 9.2

CGC 8.0

CGC 4.5

*All books displayed are part of past or current inventory

MARK S. ZAID, ESQ. • ESQUIRECOMICS.COM

P.O. BOX 342-492 • BETHESDA, MARYLAND 20827-2492 • (202) 498-0011

ESQUIRECOMICS@AOL.COM • WWW.ESQUIRECOMICS.COM

David: **(813) 417-0510** Tyler: **(813) 417-7482**

DTACOLLECTIBLES.COM

PO BOX 273086, Tampa, FL 33618 • (813) 968-1805 • dtacollectibles@gmail.com

LONGEST RUNNING OVERSTREET PRICE GUIDE ADVERTISER • SINCE 1971

THE MOST TRUSTED NAME
IN COMIC BOOK GRADING
SIGNATURE VERIFICATION

Become Part of the CBCS
Preferred Partner Program to
Receive Special Pricing

cbcscomics.com

Nationwide Vintage Comic Dealers

Terry's Old School Comics
Terry O'Neill - owner
TerrysComics.com
Terry@TerrysComics.com
P.O. Box 2065, Orange, CA. 92859
P.O. Box 1186, Kelso, WA 98626
P: 714-288-8993 / C: 360-846-3714

Graham Crackers Comics
Jamie Graham - President/CEO/Co-owner
GrahamCrackers.com -
JamieGraham@AOL.Com
1271 Rickert Dr #135, Naperville, IL 60540

PHILADELPHIA COMIC-CON!
Derek Woywood - Promoter
Philadelphiacomic-con.com
dwoywood@yahoo.com
PO Box 313, Clementon, NJ 08021
PH: (856) 217-5737

CalComicCon
CalComicCon.com
Info@CalComicCon.com

PayPal VERIFIED

We buy and sell comics
Nationwide.

DISCOVER...

senior Advisor
Overstreet
Price Guide

MARVEL
MARCH
10¢
No. 5
MYSTERY COMICS
HUMAN TORCH
SUB-MARINER
ELECTRO The Robot
THE ANGEL
KA-ZAR The Great
Plus Other Features
like a flaming comet THE HUMAN TORCH streaked to the rescue!
NITRO CHLORIDE

NYOKA

12¢
the AMAZING SPIDER-MAN
APPROVED BY THE COMICS CODE AUTHORITY
1 MAR.
2 GREAT FEATURE-LENGTH SPIDER-MAN THRILLERS!
THE FANTASTIC FOUR THINK I'M TRAPPED! BUT THEY DON'T SUSPECT MY REAL POWER!
EXTRA ADDED ATTRACTION: SPIDER-MAN MEETS THE FANTASTIC FOUR, AS "the CHAMELEON STRIKES!"

...HARLEY'S TROVE OF TIMELESS TREASURES

Golden Age • Silver Age • Bronze Age

For over 25 years, we have been supplying our clientele with the ***Finest Quality and Selection of Vintage Comic Books.*** By traveling to more than 30 comic book conventions in the USA, Canada, England, Australia and New Zealand each year and diligently searching for those rare and desirable comics our clients demand, it provides us with golden opportunities to purchase and offer one of the most ***Vast Selections of Golden Age, Silver Age and Bronze Age comics*** in the marketplace today.

Our material is Very Special and quite Diverse -- An ideal reflection of our client base. We cater to various wish-lists worldwide; from the very rare and unique items to super high-grade investment comics to the lower to mid-grade collector copies... ***We Have it All!***

And so, whatever type of comics you may be looking for, CGC certified or non-certified, be sure to give us a call. Our 25 years of Experience, Customer Service and Reputation is ***Second-to-None!***

- Accurate and Consistent Grading • Great Selection
- Competitive Pricing • Prompt & Professional Service
- Want-Lists Always Welcome • Complete Customer Satisfaction

No collection is too large or small. We will travel anywhere to view your comics and ***Pay the Highest Prices with Immediate Cash*** on hand. ***Make sure to Call Us First!***

Always Buying
Immediate Cash

Harley Yee

eBay ID
harleycomics

P.O. Box #51758
Livonia, MI 48151-5758 • USA
(800) 731-1029 • (734) 421-7921
(734) 421-7928 Fax
HarleyComx@aol.com HarleyYeeComics.com

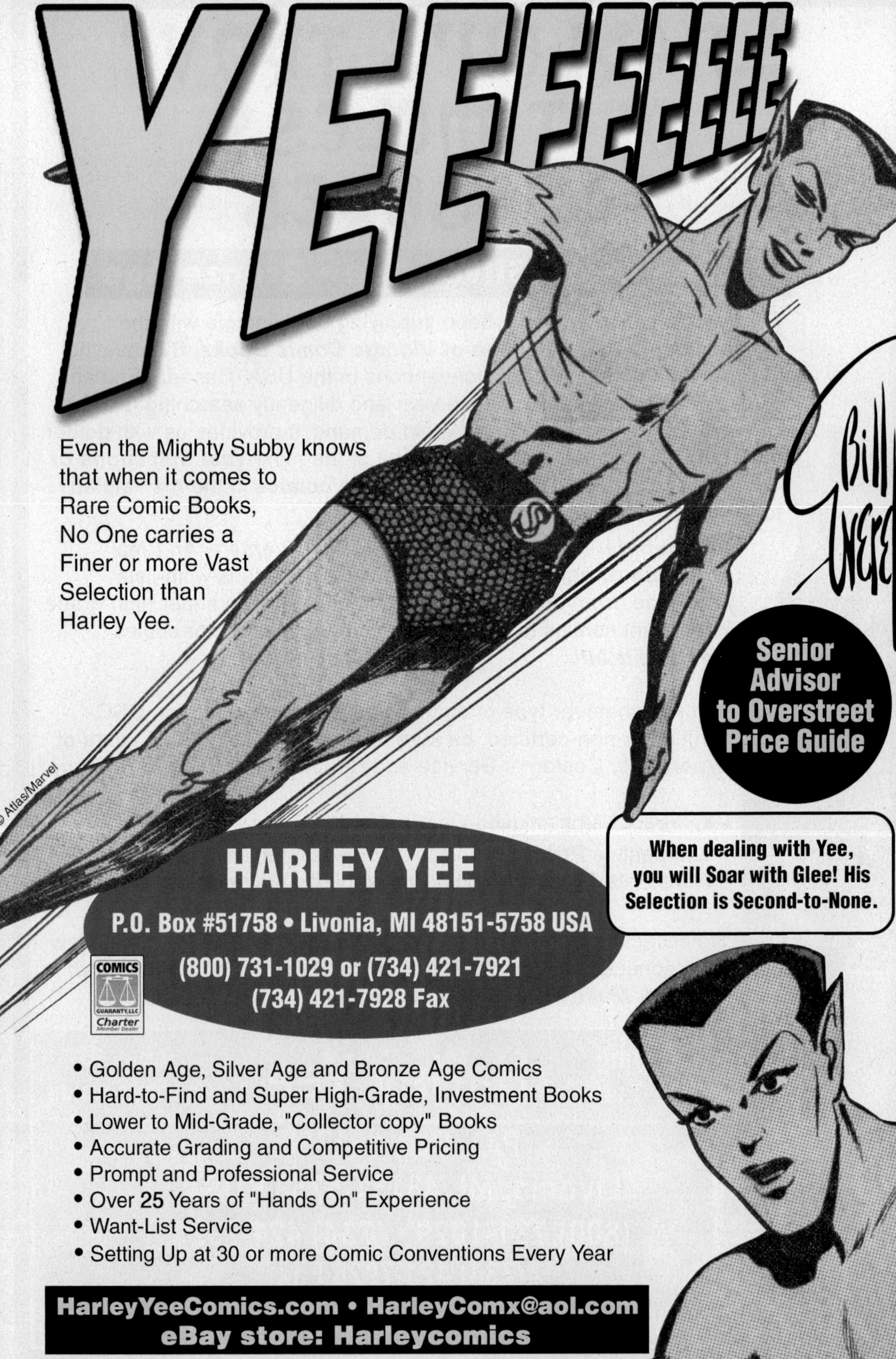
YEEEEEEEE
Even the Mighty Subby knows that when it comes to Rare Comic Books, No One carries a Finer or more Vast Selection than Harley Yee.
Bill Everett
Senior Advisor to Overstreet Price Guide
© Atlas/Marvel
When dealing with Yee, you will Soar with Glee! His Selection is Second-to-None.
HARLEY YEE
P.O. Box #51758 • Livonia, MI 48151-5758 USA
(800) 731-1029 or (734) 421-7921
(734) 421-7928 Fax
COMICS GUARANTY, LLC Charter Member Dealer
• Golden Age, Silver Age and Bronze Age Comics
• Hard-to-Find and Super High-Grade, Investment Books
• Lower to Mid-Grade, "Collector copy" Books
• Accurate Grading and Competitive Pricing
• Prompt and Professional Service
• Over 25 Years of "Hands On" Experience
• Want-List Service
• Setting Up at 30 or more Comic Conventions Every Year
HarleyYeeComics.com • HarleyComx@aol.com
eBay store: Harleycomics

COMIC COLLECTOR/DEALER

Paying up to 100% or more of Guide for many comics of interest

▼ POINTS TO CONSIDER ▼

TO SELL ON EBAY OR NOT TO SELL ON EBAY – THAT IS YOUR QUESTION?

- Consigning your comics to an eBay seller or an auction may not let you realize your collection's potential. eBay sellers and auctions charge 15% to 35% on every transaction regardless of if they sell for less than Guide. Many items sell for way below Guide and you still pay all related charges. Many dealers buy these items well below market value. After you consider all charges and the final selling price you will generally net much less than we would pay. Selling to us there will be no charges, no waiting for payment. It's easy, and you will be treated with honesty and fairness.
- We have over 25 years of experience in comic fandom. We have purchased many well known collections while competing against other interested parties. Give us the chance to show you your top price.
- Being a collector/dealer gives us the ability to buy your entire collection and pay you the most for it. You will maximize your collection's value.

You have everything to gain by contacting us. WHY miss out on your BEST OFFER? Call (603) 869-2097 today!

JAMES PAYETTE
Rare Books & Comics
P.O. Box 750 · Bethlehem, NH 03574
Tel (603) 869-2097 · Fax (603) 869-3475
www.jamespayettecomics.com
jimpayette@msn.com

COMICS
GUARANTY, LLC
Charter
Member Dealer

CREDENTIALS

Special Advisor to Overstreet *Guide*	1985-present
Member AACBC	1990-present
Sotheby's Authenticating, Certification, and Grading committee	1991-2002
Experience as a Dealer/Collector	since 1975
CBG Customer Service Award Winner for many years	

PLEASE SEE OUR OTHER ADS FOR FURTHER REFERENCE

We are paying 65% of Guide *for the following:*

Action 16-200
Adventure 32-100
All-American
All-Flash
All Top 8-18
Blonde Phantom
Blue Beetle 47-57
Brenda Starr 1-45
Crash
Daring Mystery
Fantastic
Flash (1st)
Hit 1-20
John Wayne
JO-JO 7-29
Kid Komics
Miss Fury
More Fun 52-107
Mysterious Adventure
Mystic (1st)
National 1-23
New Book of Comics
Pep 1-21
Phantom Lady
Phantom Stranger
Rangers 1-20
Rulah
Science (Fox)
Sensation
Silver Streak 1-17
Smash
Speed 1-20
Strange Tales 1-100
U.S.A. 1-5
Weird Comics
Zoot 7-16

We are paying 60% of Guide *for the following:*

Adventure 101-200
Adv. of Bob Hope 1-50
Adv. of Jerry Lewis 1-50
Adv. of Ozzie & Harriet
Air Fighters
All Star
Amazing Spider-Man 3-10
America's Greatest
Batman 2-100
Blue Ribbon 2-20
Brave & the Bold 1-20
Bulletman
Captain Marvel
Captain Marvel Jr.
Captain Midnight
Challengers 1-10
Comic Cavalcade 1-29
Daredevil 1st 1-20
Detective 28-100
Dollman
Fantastic Four 3-10
Fight 1-30
Frontier Fighters
Green Hornet 1-20
Green Lantern (1st)
House of Mystery 1-50
House of Secrets 1-25
Ibis
Journey Into Mystery 1-115
Jumbo 11-50
Jungle 1-50
Lash Larue 1-46
Leading 1-14
Legend of D. Boone
Marvel Family
Mary Marvel
Master
Military
Modern
Movie Comics (DC)
My Greatest Adv. 1-50
Mystery in Space 1-50
Nickel
Planet
Police 1-20
Red Ryder 1-100
Saint
Shadow (1st)
Showcase 1-3, 5-20
Shield Wizard
Spy Smasher
Star Spangled
Strange Adventure 1-120
Superboy 1-50
Superman 2-125
Superman's Pal Jimmy Olsen 2-30
Top-Notch
Walt Disney Comics & Stories 1-40
Whiz
World's Finest 1-110
Zip 1-39

We are also paying 50-100% of* Guide *for many other titles. Comics must be properly graded and complete. Please send your listing of comics for sale or a list of comics you wish to purchase. We are dealing in Marvels, DCs, Timelys, Nedors, Western, Funny Material and much more! Please check our website or send for our 100-page catalog. We will travel for large collections or, if you're passing through the area call for an appointment.

JAMES PAYETTE
Rare Books & Comics
P.O. Box 750 · Bethlehem, NH 03574
Tel (603) 869-2097 · Fax (603) 869-3475
www.jamespayettecomics.com
jimpayette@msn.com

COMICS GUARANTY, LLC Charter Member Dealer

CREDENTIALS

Special Advisor to Overstreet *Guide*	1985-present
Member AACBC	1990-present
Sotheby's Authenticating, Certification, and Grading committee	1991-2002
Experience as a Dealer/Collector	since 1975
CBG Customer Service Award Winner for many years	

PLEASE SEE OUR OTHER ADS FOR FURTHER REFERENCE

THE SELLER'S GUIDE

Yes, here are the pages you're looking for. These percentages will help you determine the sale value of your collection. If you do not find your title, call with any questions. We have purchased many of the major well known collections. We are serious about buying your comics and paying you the most for them.

If you have comics or related items for sale call or send your list for a quote. No collection is too large or small. Immediate funds available of 500K and beyond.

These are some of the high prices we will pay. Percentages stated will be paid for any grade unless otherwise noted. All percentages based on this Overstreet *Guide.*

–JAMES PAYETTE

We are paying 100% of Guide *for the following:*

All-Select 1-up
All Winners 6-up
America's Best 1-up
Black Terror 1-25
Captain Aero 3-25
Captain America 11-up
Cat-Man 1-up
Dynamic 2-15
Exciting 3-50
Human Torch 6-35
Marvel Mystery 11-up
Pep 22-45
Prize 2-50
Reform School Girl 1
Speed 10-30
Startling 2-up
Sub-Mariner 3-32
Thrilling 2-52
U.S.A. 6-up
Wonder (Nedor) 1-up

We are paying 75% of Guide *for the following:*

Action 1-15
Adventure 247
All New 2-13
All Winners 1-5
Amazing Man all
Amazing Mystery Funnies all
Amazing Spider-Man 1-2
Andy Devine
Arrow all
Captain America 1-10
Daredevil (2nd) 1
Detective 2-26
Detective Eye all
Detective Picture Stories all
Fantastic Four 1-2
Four Favorites 3-27
Funny Pages all
Funny Picture Stories all
Hangman all
Jumbo 1-10
Journey into Mystery 83
Keen Detective Funnies all
Marvel Mystery 1-10
Mystery Men all
Showcase 4
Superman 1
Superman's Pal 1
Tim McCoy all
Wonder (Fox)
Young Allies all

BUYING & SELLING GOLDEN & SILVER AGE COMICS SINCE 1975

YOUR BEST RESOURCE FOR GAMING NEWS

Each month Game Trade Magazine brings you EXCLUSIVE information about the Gaming Industry's most popular titles.

Find Us At Your Friendly Neighborhood Local Comic And Game Stores!

LOW COMMISSION RATES | MASSIVE CASH ADVANCES | SUPER FAST PAYMENT

OVER $5 MILLION IN ORIGINAL COMIC ART SOLD IN 2021.

GET MORE *FOR* YOUR ART, SO YOU CAN GET MORE ART!

WORLD'S PREMIER ONLINE COMIC ART MARKETPLACE & AUCTIONEER

Vincent Zurzolo
President

COMICCONNECT

WWW.COMICCONNECT.COM CALL TO CONSIGN 888-779-7377

Micah Spivak
Original Art
Coordinator & Buyer

36 W 37th ST, 6th FL, NEW YORK, NY 10018| P: 212.895.3999 | F: 212.260.4304| support@comicconnect.com

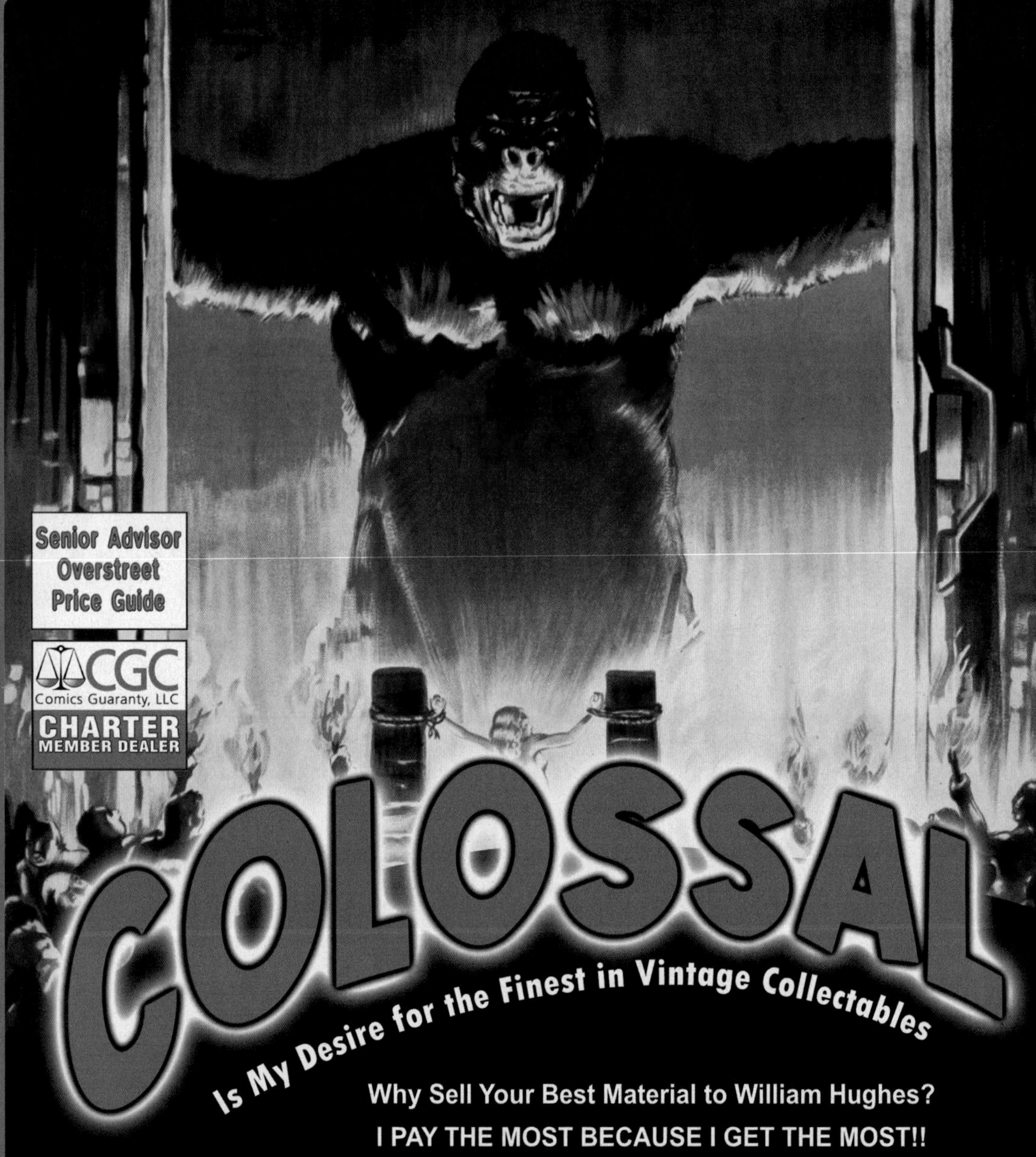

Why Sell Your Best Material to William Hughes?

I PAY THE MOST BECAUSE I GET THE MOST!!

Yes, you read correctly, I will usually pay the most for quality vintage COMIC BOOKS, MOVIE POSTERS or BASEBALL CARDS because I can usually get the most for these items through my vast network of associates and customer list of thousands of active buyers. I also sell many items "outside the hobby" to people that don't care what price guides say and who don't want to bid in auctions.

William Hughes'
Vintage Collectables
P.O. Box 270244
Flower Mound, TX 75027
Office: 972-539-9190
Mobile: 973-432-4070

I Am Up To The Challenge! I Will Do My Very Best To Pay Your Ultimate Desired Price, Just Try Me First

www.VintageCollectables.net • whughes199@yahoo.com

ALWAYS SEEKING THE FOLLOWING

Pre-1976 Baseball, Basketball, Football & Hockey Card Sets & Singles

Pre-1969 Non-Sports Card Sets & Singles

Vintage Advertising Signs

Hall-of-Famer Autographs

Superstar Game-Used Bats, Gloves & Uniforms

Pokémon Cards

Other Rare Memorabilia

Entire Collections My Specialty

CALL NOW FOR IMMEDIATE PAYMENT!

Why Sell Your Best Material to William Hughes?
I PAY THE MOST BECAUSE I GET THE MOST!!

Yes, you read correctly, I will usually pay the most for quality vintage COMIC BOOKS, MOVIE POSTERS or BASEBALL CARDS because I can usually get the most for these items through my vast network of associates and customer list of thousands of active buyers. I also sell many items "outside the hobby" to people that don't care what price guides say and who don't want to bid in auctions.

I Am Up To The Challenge! I Will Do My Very Best To Pay Your Ultimate Desired Price, Just Try Me First

William Hughes' Vintage Collectables

MOVIE POSTERS • COMIC BOOKS • SPORTS MEMORABILIA

P.O. Box 270244 Flower Mound, TX 75027
Office: 972-539-9190
Mobile: 973-432-4070 Fax: 972-691-8837

www.VintageCollectables.net
Email: whughes199@yahoo.com
eBay User: comic-warehouse

NOW AVAILABLE!

VISIT YOUR LOCAL COMIC BOOK RETAILER TODAY!

$25.00 SC SEP211561
$35.00 HC SEP211562

$24.95 SC JAN211364

$15.00 SC JUN201131

$30.00 SC SEP191814

$30.00 SC JUN201128

$20.00 SC JUN201130

$15.00 SC JUN201129

$15.00 SC JUN201133

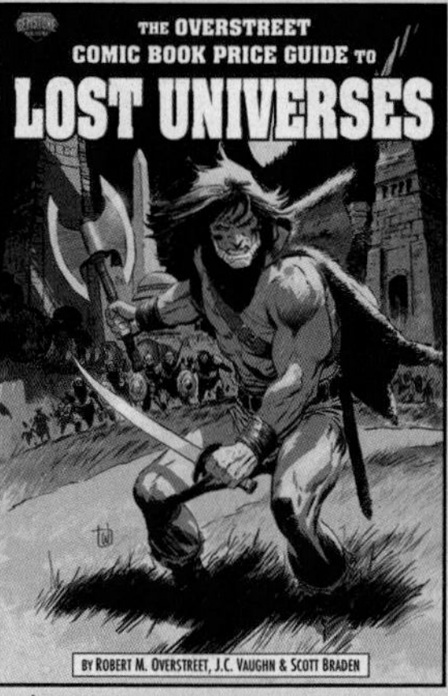

$25.00 SC SEP211559
$35.00 HC SEP211560

GEMSTONE PUBLISHING

www.gemstonepub.com

All characters ©2023 respective Copyright holders. Used by permission.
Overstreet® is a Registered Trademark of Gemstone Publishing. All rights reserved.

ACTIVELY BUYING

High prices paid. All genres wanted. One piece or lifetime collections. No collection too large or small.

ACTIVELY SELLING

Thousands of Pulps in stock.
We love servicing your want lists.
Items added to our website weekly.

www.FantasyIllustrated.net

DEALING SINCE 1969

Prompt professional service. Specializing in Pulp magazines and science fiction/fantasy/horror first editions. Vintage paperbacks and comic books.

Contact DAVE SMITH

(425) 750-4513 • (360) 652-0339
rocketbat@msn.com
P.O. Box 248 Silvana, WA 98287
www.FantasyIllustrated.net

MARVEL

1/7 SCALE BUSTS

AVAILABLE NOW:

SPIDER-MAN

Coming
Spring 2023

Diamond Select Toys and Collectibles is a trademark of Diamond Select Toys and Collectibles, LLC. © 2023 Diamond Select Toys and Collectibles. All Rights Reserved. Comic Shop Locator Service and CSLS logo © Diamond Comic Distributors Inc. All Rights Reserved. Final product may vary.

Collect Comics?

Get our free catalog!

We Do Platinum, Golden, Silver & Bronze Back Issue Mail Order Right!

Here's what a few of our many satisfied customers say!

"I was very impressed with the packaging and speed of delivery."
- Jack Eastwood, Murrieta, CA

"I have never dealt with a better mail order service."
-Garth Ferris, Chico, CA

"I can count on you,...Precise Grading."
-Carsten Pedersen, Hvidovre, Denmark

"RTS is my first source to find older comics for reasonable prices. Easy to use catalog & great service!"
-Lance Leber, Monument, CO

"Thank you so much for your prompt service. Ordering from you is a really delightful experience. Your grading is unusually strict - most items were better than I expected."
-Schultz Riggs, Jackson, MS

RTS Unlimited Inc, P.O. Box 150412, Dept OS44, Lakewood, CO 80215-0412
(303) 403-1840, Fax: (303) 403-1837, RTSUnlimited@earthlink.net, www.RTSUnlimited.com

Contact us today to get our huge illustrated free catalog! Platinum, Golden, Silver & Bronze comics, CGC graded comics, supplies, and more!! Over 30 years in business! We have the Rocky Mountain Region's most diverse selection of collectible back issue comics and supplies.

Photo-Journals!

This awesome resource to comic book collecting contains thousands of full color cover pictures in each volume!
A must have for every comic collector!!

We can't recommend these books enough!

Thousands of full color pictures! Includes publication dates, artist information, articles and much more! Vol 1 & 2 focus on the Golden Age and also have scarcity data! The Golden Age volumes are only $65.95 each or $119.95 for both. Vol 3 & 4 are dedicated to Marvel Comics and are $27.95 each or $53.95 for both.

Special: Get all four volumes for only $164.95!

Shipping and handling: Continental US: please add $9.00 for the first Vol and $4.00 for each additional one. All others: please call for rates.

Note: Some volumes may have some minor cosmetic damage (The clear plastic coating is delaminating). ALL volumes are NEW and UNREAD.

To order: Call, fax, or e-mail a credit card order or Send check or money order to:

RTS Unlimited, Inc.
P.O. Box 150412
Lakewood, CO 80215
(303) 403-1840
Fax: (303) 403-1837
RTSUnlimited@earthlink.net
www.RTSUnlimited.com

RTS Unlimited, Inc.

Dedicated to Customer Satisfaction!

FIND NEW WORLDS AND DISCOVER NEW STORYLINES AT YOUR LOCAL COMIC SHOP

BUYING: ALL COMICS POOR to MINT!

GARY DOLGOFF COMICS

GDCOMICS

SINCE 1969

- 40+ Years Experience (Buying Collections)
- Great Reputation for being Fair and Honest
- Longtime Overstreet Advisor
- Immediate Payment • Buying Worldwide
- Paying the Highest Prices Possible

gary@gdcomics.com • gdcomics.com • #413-529-0326

GARY DOLGOFF COMICS • 116 PLEASANT ST. SUITE #213, EASTHAMPTON, MA 01027

PX

EXCLUSIVE TO **PREVIEW**

YOURS TO COLLEC

READY TO POP

PREVIEWS Exclusive Funko Pop! vinyl figures featuring your favorite character

Packaged in a collector friendly window box, perfect for display.

Available to order now! ***PREVIEWS***world.com/Pullbox

THE COMIC CELLAR
WE'RE OPEN SEVEN DAYS A WEEK!
135 W. MAIN ST. ALHAMBRA, CA 91801
(626) 570-8743
WWW.COMICCELLAR.COM / COMICCELLAR@COMICCELLAR.COM

SAVE THE DATE

FREE COMIC BOOK DAY
May 4, 2024
freecomicbookday.com
™

SUBSCRIBE & FOLLOW

Our grading services just got

BIGGER

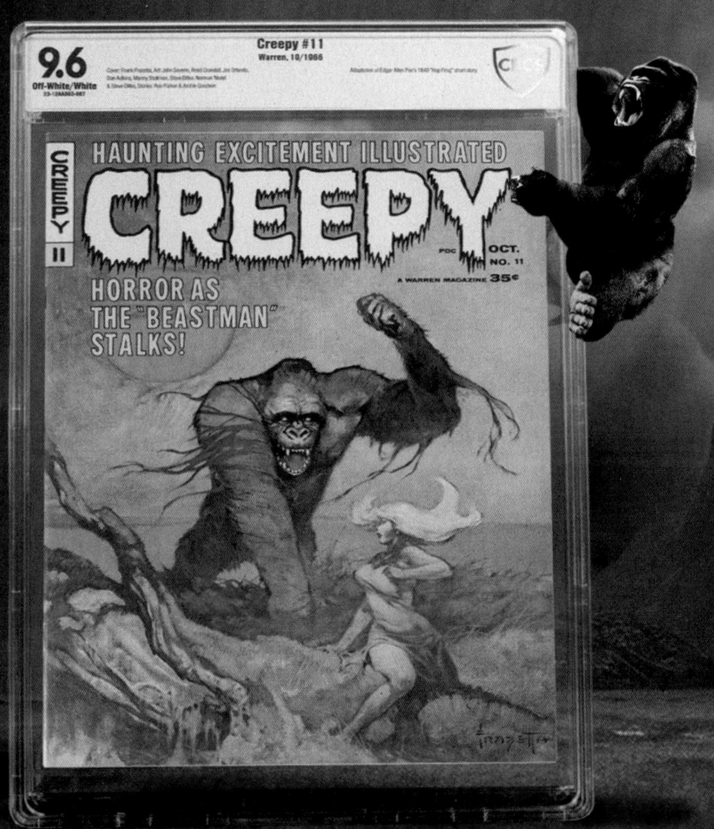

You can now submit your larger magazine-sized comics to CBCS for grading and encapsulation.

Special Introductory Pricing

$25 PER BOOK

cbcscomics.com/grading-pressing

BECKETT

Seasoned Collector • Pioneering Grading Expert • Original Art Expert
Veteran Overstreet Advisor • Respected Industry Figure

STEVE BOROCK HAS JOINED

Helped create CGC and launched CBCS
Honesty • Integrity • Experience

"Let me put my more than two decades of industry know-how to work for you!"

Steve Borock
sborock@comiclink.com
Call (617) 517-0062 ext. 107

COMIC HEAVEN

JOHN VERZYL II AND SISTER ROSE "HARD AT WORK"

In 1979, John Verzyl Sr., with his wife Nanette, opened "COMIC HEAVEN", a retail store devoted entirely to the buying and selling of rare comic books. John had started collecting comics in 1965, and within ten years, he had amassed thousands of Golden and Silver Age collectibles. Over the years, he had come to be recognized as an authority in the field of comic books, and served as a special advisor to *The Overstreet Comic Book Price Guide* for 30 years. Thousands of his "near mint" pedigree comics were photographed for Ernst Gerber's *Photo-Journal Guide to Comic Books*. The first annual **Comic Heaven Auction** was held in 1987 and ran continuously for 24 years.

Sadly, John Verzyl passed away in 2018. His untimely death was a shock and a great loss to everyone who knew him. But his children, John II and Rose, having had a love of the hobby instilled in them since childhood by their dad, will continue to operate the business. We will continue to set up our huge retail displays at the annual San Diego Comic-Con, the August Chicago Comic Con, and the New York City Comic Con in October, and will continue to wow our wonderful customers with super-rare collectibles. We will also be updating and using our website, **ComicHeaven.net**, in new and exciting ways, with periodic updates of newly acquired stock items and news about our upcoming convention appearances.

www.ComicHeaven.net

Comic Heaven LLC
John II, Rose & Nanette Verzyl
P.O. Box 900, Big Sandy, TX 75755
www.ComicHeaven.net
(903) 539-8875

COMIC

BUY

Sell us your Golden, Silver and Bronze Age comics

No collection is too large or too small.

We will travel anywhere in the USA to buy collections we want.
In previous years, we've traveled over 30,000 miles to buy comic books.

We are especially looking to buy:

- **Silver Age Marvels and DCs**
- **Golden Age Timelys and DCs**
- **Fox/ MLJ/ Nedor/ EC**
- **"Mile High" copies (Edgar Church Collection)**
- **Baseball cards, Movie posters and Original art**

HEAVEN

I N G

A TRADITION OF EXCELLENCE FOR OVER 40 YEARS!!

We Specialize In Purchasing Large Golden And Silver Age Collections

Comic Heaven
John II, Rose & Nanette Verzyl
P.O. Box 900
Big Sandy, TX 75755
www.ComicHeaven.net
(903) 539-8875

COMICHEAVEN.NET

OFFICIAL

- As a family-owned business, your questions and messages go directly to the source without any automated middleman.

- With our 40+ years of experience, we will work tirelessly to answer your questions.

- Send us your want lists. It's our goal to help complete them.

COMICHEAVEN.NET

ComicHeaven.net

WEBSITE

VISIT OUR STORE!

- **Featuring high-quality comics from the Golden Age, Silver Age, and Bronze Age.**
- **Orders are shipped Priority Mail with insurance and with a signature required. We want to make sure you get your precious books.**
- **Website is updated frequently.**

ComicHeaven.net

THESE DIDN'T HAPPEN WITHOUT YOUR HELP.

The Overstreet Comic Book Price Guide doesn't happen by magic. A network of advisors – made up of experienced dealers, collectors and comics historians – gives us input for every edition we publish. If you spot an error or omission in this edition or any of our publications, let us know!

Write to us at
Gemstone Publishing Inc.,
10150 York Rd., Suite 300,
Hunt Valley, MD 21030.
Or e-mail **feedback@gemstonepub.com**.

We want your help!

BIG LITTLE BOOKS

INTRODUCTION

In 1932, at the depths of the Great Depression, comic books were not selling despite their successes in the previous two decades. Desperate publishers had already reduced prices to 25¢, but this was still too much for many people to spend on entertainment.

Comic books quickly evolved into two newer formats, the comics magazine and the Big Little Book. Both types retailed for 10¢.

Big Little Books began by reprinting the art (and adapting the stories) from newspaper comics. As their success grew and publishers began commissioning original material, movie adaptations and other entertainment-derived stories became commonplace.

GRADING

Before a Big Little Book's value can be assessed, its condition or state of preservation must be determined. A book in **Near Mint** condition will bring many times the price of the same book in **Poor** condition. Many variables influence the grading of a Big Little Book and all must be considered in the final evaluation. Due to the way they are constructed, damage occurs with very little use - usually to the spine, book edges and binding. More important defects that affect grading are: Split spines, pages missing, page browning or brittleness, writing, crayoning, loose pages, color fading, chunks missing, and rolling or out of square. The following grading guide is given to aid the novice:

9.4 Near Mint: The overall look is as if it was just purchased and maybe opened once; only subtle defects are allowed; paper is cream to off-white, supple and fresh; cover is flat with no surface wear or creases; inks and colors are bright; small penciled or inked arrival dates are acceptable; very slight blunting of corners at top and bottom of spine are common; outside corners are cut square and sharp. Books in this grade could bring prices of guide and a half or more.

9.0 Very Fine/Near Mint: Limited number of defects; full cover gloss with only very slight wear on book corners and edges; very minor foxing; very minor tears allowed, binding still square and tight with no pages missing; paper quality still fresh from cream to off-white. Dates, stamps or initials allowed on cover or inside.

8.0 Very Fine: Most of the cover gloss retained with minor wear appearing at corners and around edges; spine tight with no pages missing; cream/tan paper allowed if still supple; up to 1/4" bend allowed on covers with no color break; cover relatively flat; minor tears allowed.

6.0 Fine: Slight wear beginning to show; cover gloss reduced but still clean, pages tan/brown but still supple (not brittle); up to 1/4" split or color break allowed; minor discoloration and/or foxing allowed.

4.0 Very Good: Obviously a read copy with original printing luster almost gone; some fading and discoloration, but not soiled; some signs of wear such as corner splits and spine rolling; paper can be brown but not brittle; a few pages can be loose but not missing; no chunks missing; blunted corners acceptable.

2.0 Good: An average used copy complete with only minor pieces missing from the spine, which may be partially split; slightly soiled or marked with spine rolling; color flaking and wear around edges, but perfectly sound and legible; could have minor tape repairs but otherwise complete.

1.0 Fair: Very heavily read and soiled with small chunks missing from cover; most or all of spine could be missing; multiple splits in spine and loose pages, but still sound and legible, bringing 50 to 70 percent of good price.

0.5 Poor: Damaged, heavily weathered, soiled or otherwise unsuited for collecting purposes.

IMPORTANT

Most BLBs on the market today will fall in the **Good** to **Fine** grade category. When **Very Fine** to **Near Mint** BLBs are offered for sale, they usually bring premium prices.

A WORD ON PRICING

The prices are given for **Good**, **Fine**, **Very Fine** and **Near Mint-** condition. A book in **Fair** would be 50-70% of the **Good** price. **Very Good** would be halfway between the **Good** and the **Fine** price. The prices listed were averaged from convention sales, dealers' lists, adzines, auctions, and by special contact with dealers and collectors from coast to coast. The prices and the spreads were determined from sales of copies in available condition or the highest grade known. Since most available copies are in the **Good** to **Fine** range, neither dealers nor collectors should let the **Very Fine** or **Near Mint-** column influence the prices they are willing to charge or pay for books in less than perfect condition.

The prices listed reflect spread ranges from 6 to 16 times, depending on the price level. We feel this spread accurately reflects the current market, especially when you condider the scarcity of books in **Very Fine** to **Near Mint-** condition. When one or both end sheets are missing, the book's value would drop about a half grade.

Books with movie scenes are of double importance due to the high crossover demand by movie collectors.

Abbreviations: a-art; c-cover; nn-no number; p-pages; r-reprint.

Publisher Codes: BRP-Blue Ribbon Press; **ERB**-Edgar Rice Burroughs; **EVW**-Engel van Wiseman; **FAW**-Fawcett Publishing Co.; **Gold**-Goldsmith Publishing Co.; **Lynn**-Lynn Publishing Co.; **McKay**-David McKay Co.; **Whit**-Whitman Publishing Co.; **World**-World Syndicate Publishing Co.

Terminology: *All Pictures Comics*-no text, all drawings; *Fast-Action*-A special series of Dell books highly collected; *Flip Pictures*-upper right corner of interior pages contain drawings that are put into motion when rifled; *Movie Scenes*-book illustrated with scenes from the movie. *Soft Cover*-A thin single sheet of cardboard used in binding most of the giveaway versions.

"Big Little Book" and "Better Little Book" are registered trademarks of Whitman Publishing Co. "Little Big Book" is a registered trademark of the Saalfield Publishing Co.

"Pop-Up" is a registered trademark of Blue Ribbon Press. "Little Big Book" is a registered trademark of the Saalfield Co.

Top 20 Big Little Books and related size books*

Issue#	Rank	Title	Price
731	1	Mickey Mouse the Mail Pilot (variant version of Mickey Mouse #717) (A VG copy sold at auction for $7,170)	
nn	2	Mickey Mouse and Minnie Mouse at Macy's	$5,000
nn	3	Mickey Mouse and Minnie March to Macy's	$4,200
717	4	Mickey Mouse (skinny Mickey on-c)	$3,800
725	5	Big Little Mother Goose HC	$2,600
W-707	6	Dick Tracy The Detective	$2,550
717	7	Mickey Mouse (reg. Mickey on-c)	$2,300
nn	8	Mickey Mouse Silly Symphonies	$2,000
nn	9	Mickey Mouse Mail Pilot (Great Big Midget Book)	$1,850
725	10	Big Little Mother Goose SC	$1,800
nn	10	Mickey Mouse and the Magic Carpet	$1,800
nn	10	Mickey Mouse (Great Big Midget Book)	$1,800
721	13	Big Little Paint Book (336 pg.)	$1,750
nn	14	Mickey Mouse Sails For Treasure Island (Great Big Midget Book)	$1,650
721	15	Big Little Paint Book (320 pg.)	$1,450
4063	16	Popeye Thimble Theater Starring... (2nd printing)	$1,300
1126	17	Laughing Dragon of Oz	$1,250
4063	18	Popeye Thimble Theater Starring... (1st printing)	$1,100
nn	19	Buck Rogers	$1,000
nn	19	Buck Rogers in the City of Floating Globes	$975

*Includes only the various sized BLBs; no premiums, giveaways or other divergent forms are included.

763 - Alley Oop and Dinny © WHIT

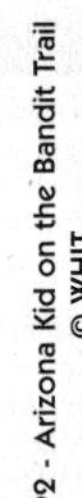

1192 - Arizona Kid on the Bandit Trail © WHIT

760 - Believe It or Not! © WHIT

	GD	FN	VF	VF/NM
1175-0- **Abbie an' Slats**, 1940, Saalfield, 400 pgs.	10	25	64	100
1182- **Abbie an' Slats-and Becky**, 1940, Saalfield, 400 pgs.	10	25	64	100
nn- **ABC's To Draw and Color, The**, 1930s, Whitman, 4" x 5 1/4" x 1 1/12" deep, cardboard box contains 320 double-sided sheets to color and a box of crayons	25	63	175	300
1177- **Ace Drummond**, 1935, Whitman, 432 pgs.	11	28	68	110
Admiral Byrd (See Paramount Newsreel ...)				
nn- **Adventures of Charlie McCarthy and Edgar Bergen, The**, 1938, Dell, 194 pgs., Fast-Action Story, soft-c	21	53	145	230
1422- **Adventures of Huckleberry Finn, The**, 1939, Whitman, 432 pgs., Henry E. Vallely-a	10	25	64	100
1648- **Adventures of Jim Bowie** (TV Series), 1958, Whitman, 280 pgs.	4	10	24	35
1056- **Adventures of Krazy Kat and Ignatz Mouse in Koko Land**, 1934, Saalfield, 160 pgs., oblong size, hard-c, Herriman-c/a	48	120	336	625
1306- **Adventures of Krazy Kat and Ignatz Mouse in Koko Land**, 1934, Saalfield, 164 pgs., oblong size, soft-c, Herriman-c/a	56	140	392	725
1082- **Adventures of Pete the Tramp, The**, 1935, Saalfield, hard-c, by C. D. Russell	10	25	60	95
1312- **Adventures of Pete the Tramp, The**, 1935, Saalfield, soft-c, by C. D. Russell	10	25	60	95
1053- **Adventures of Tim Tyler**, 1934, Saalfield, hard-c, oblong size, by Lyman Young	18	45	128	200
1303- **Adventures of Tim Tyler**, 1934, Saalfield, soft-c, oblong size, by Lyman Young	18	45	128	200
1058- **Adventures of Tom Sawyer, The**, 1934, Saalfield, 160 pgs., hard-c, Park Sumner-a	10	25	60	95
1308- **Adventures of Tom Sawyer, The**, 1934, Saalfield, 160 pgs., soft-c, Park Sumner-a	10	25	60	95
1448- **Air Fighters of America**, 1941, Whitman, 432 pgs., flip picture	11	28	68	110
Alexander Smart, ESQ. (See Top Line Comics)				
759- **Alice in Wonderland**, 1933, Whitman, 160 pgs., hard-c, photo-c, movie scenes	42	105	294	500
1481- **Allen Pike of the Parachute Squad U.S.A.**, 1941, Whitman, 432 pgs.	12	30	72	115
763- **Alley Oop and Dinny**, 1935, Whitman, 384 pgs., V. T. Hamlin-a	16	40	112	175
1473- **Alley Oop and Dinny in the Jungles of Moo**, 1938, Whitman, 432 pgs., V. T. Hamlin-a	16	40	112	175
nn- **Alley Oop and the Missing King of Moo**, 1938, Whitman, 36 pgs., 2 1/2" x 3 1/2", Penny Book	10	25	60	95
nn- **Alley Oop in the Kingdom of Foo**, 1938, Whitman, 68 pgs., 3 1/4" x 3 1/2", Pan-Am premium	18	45	128	200
nn- **Alley Oop Taming a Dinosaur**, 1938, Whitman, 68 pgs., 3 1/2" x 3 3/4", Pan-Am premium	18	45	128	200
nn- **"Alley Oop the Invasion of Moo,"** 1935, Whitman, 260 pgs., Cocomalt premium, soft-c; V. T. Hamlin-a	12	30	76	125
Andy Burnette (See Walt Disney's...)				
Andy Panda (Also see Walter Lantz ...)				
531- **Andy Panda**, 1943, Whitman, 3 3/4x8 3/4", Tall Comic Book, All Pictures Comics	16	42	119	185
1425- **Andy Panda and Tiny Tom**, 1944, Whitman, All Pictures Comics	12	30	76	125
1431- **Andy Panda and the Mad Dog Mystery**, 1947, Whitman, 288 pgs., by Walter Lantz	12	30	76	125
1441- **Andy Panda in the City of Ice**, 1948, Whitman, All Picture Comics, by Walter Lantz	12	30	76	125
1459- **Andy Panda and the Pirate Ghosts**, 1949, Whitman, 88 pgs., by Walter Lantz	12	30	76	125
1485- **Andy Panda's Vacation**, 1946, Whitman, All Pictures Comics, by Walter Lantz	12	30	76	125
15- **Andy Panda (The Adventures of)**, 1942, Dell, Fast-Action Story	16	41	119	185
707-10- **Andy Panda and Presto the Pup**, 1949, Whitman	12	30	76	125
1130- **Apple Mary and Dennie Foil the Swindlers**, 1936, Whitman, 432 pgs. (Forerunner to Mary Worth)	11	28	68	110

	GD	FN	VF	VF/NM
1403- **Apple Mary and Dennie's Lucky Apples**, 1939, Whitman, 432 pgs.	11	28	68	110
2017- **(#17)-Aquaman-Scourge of the Sea**, 1968, Whitman, 260 pgs., 39 cents, hard-c, color illos	3	8	22	32
1192- **Arizona Kid on the Bandit Trail, The**, 1936, Whitman, 432 pgs.	10	25	64	100
1469- **Bambi** (Walt Disney's), 1942, Whitman, 432 pgs.	21	53	145	230
1497- **Bambi's Children** (Disney), 1943, Whitman, 432 pgs., Disney Studios-a	21	53	145	230
1138- **Bandits at Bay**, 1938, Saalfield, 400 pgs.	9	23	56	90
1459- **Barney Baxter in the Air with the Eagle Squadron**, 1938, Whitman, 432 pgs.	9	23	54	95
1083- **Barney Google**, 1935, Saalfield, hard-c	14	35	100	160
1313- **Barney Google**, 1935, Saalfield, soft-c	14	35	100	160
2031-(#31)- **Batman and Robin in the Cheetah Caper**, 1969, Whitman, 258 pgs.	4	10	24	35
5771- **Batman and Robin in the Cheetah Caper**, 1974, Whitman, 258 pgs., 49 cents	1	3	10	14
5771-1- **Batman and Robin in the Cheetah Caper**, 1974, Whitman, 258 pgs., 69 cents	1	3	10	14
5771-2- **Batman and Robin in the Cheetah Caper**, 1975?, Whitman, 258 pgs.	1	3	10	14
nn- **Beauty and the Beast**, nd (1930s), np (Whitman), 36 pgs., 3" x 3 1/2" Penny Book	4	10	28	42
Beep Beep The Road Runner (See Road Runner)				
760- **Believe It or Not!**, 1933, Whitman, 160 pgs., by Ripley (c. 1931)	10	25	64	100
Betty Bear's Lesson (See Wee Little Books)				
1119- **Betty Boop in Snow White**, 1934, Whitman, 240 pgs., hard-c; adapted from Max Fleischer Paramount Talkartoon	48	120	336	625
1119- **Betty Boop in Snow White**, 1934, Whitman, 240 pgs., soft-c; same contents as hard-c (Rare)	62	155	434	800
1158- **Betty Boop in "Miss Gullivers Travels,"** 1935, Whitman, 288 pgs., hard-c (Scarce)	60	150	420	775
2070- **Big Big Paint Book**, 1936, Whitman, 432 pgs., 8 1/2" x 11 3/8", B&W pages to color	19	48	136	215
1432- **Big Chief Wahoo and the Lost Pioneers**, 1942, Whitman, 432 pgs., Elmer Woggon-a	12	30	72	115
1443- **Big Chief Wahoo and the Great Gusto**, 1938, Whitman, 432 pgs., Elmer Woggon-a	12	30	72	115
1483- **Big Chief Wahoo and the Magic Lamp**, 1940, Whitman, 432 pgs., flip pictures, Woggon-c/a	12	30	72	115
725- **Big Little Mother Goose, The**, 1934, Whitman, 580 pgs. (Rare) Hardcover	173	433	1384	2600
725- **Big Little Mother Goose, The**, 1934, Whitman, 580 pgs. (Rare) Softcover	123	308	925	1800
1005- **Big Little Nickel Book**, 1935, Whitman, 144 pgs., Blackie Bear stories and Donna the Donkey	9	23	54	85
1006- **Big Little Nickel Book**, 1935, Whitman, 144 pgs., Blackie Bear stories, folk tales in primer style	9	23	54	85
1007- **Big Little Nickel Book**, 1935, Whitman, 144 pgs., Peter Rabbit, etc.	9	23	54	85
1008- **Big Little Nickel Book**, 1935, Whitman, 144 pgs., Wee Wee Woman, etc.	9	23	54	85
721- **Big Little Paint Book,** The, 1933, Whitman, 320 pgs., 3 3/4" x 8 1/2", for crayoning; first printing has green page ends; second printing has purple page ends (both are rare)	104	250	700	1450
721- **Big Little Paint Book,** The, 1933, Whitman, 336 pgs., 3 3/4" x 8 1/2", for crayoning; first printing has green page ends; second printing has purple page ends (both are rare)	121	3030	900	1750
1178- **Billy of Bar-Zero**, 1940, Saalfield, 400 pgs.	10	25	64	100
773- **Billy the Kid**, 1935, Whitman, 432 pgs., Hal Arbo-a	11	28	68	110
1159- **Billy the Kid on Tall Butte**, 1939, Saalfield, 400 pgs.	10	25	64	100
1174- **Billy the Kid's Pledge**, 1940, Saalfield, 400 pgs.	10	25	64	100
nn- **Billy the Kid, Western Outlaw**, 1935, Whitman, 260 pgs., Cocomalt premium, Hal Arbo-a, soft-c	13	33	92	145
1057- **Black Beauty**, 1934, Saalfield, hard-c	8	20	50	80
1307- **Black Beauty**, 1934, Saalfield, soft-c	8	20	50	80

	GD	FN	VF	VF/NM
1414- **Black Silver and His Pirate Crew**, 1937, Whitman, 300 pgs.	11	28	68	110
1447- **Blaze Brandon with the Foreign Legion**, 1938, Whitman, 432 pgs.	11	28	68	110
1410- **Blondie and Dagwood in Hot Water**, 1946, Whitman, 352 pgs., by Chic Young	10	25	60	95
1415- **Blondie and Baby Dumpling**, 1937, Whitman, 432 pgs., by Chic Young	10	25	64	100
1419- **Oh, Blondie the Bumsteads Carry On**, 1941, Whitman, 432 pgs., flip pictures, by Chic Young	10	25	64	100
1423- **Blondie Who's Boss?**, 1942, Whitman, 432 pgs., flip pictures, by Chic Young	10	25	64	100
1429- **Blondie with Baby Dumpling and Daisy**, 1939, Whitman, 432 pgs., by Chic Young	10	25	64	100
1430- **Blondie Count Cookie in Too!**, 1947, Whitman, 288 pgs., by Chic Young	10	25	60	95
1438- **Blondie and Dagwood Everybody's Happy**, 1948, Whitman, 288 pgs., by Chic Young	10	25	60	95
1450- **Blondie No Dull Moments**, 1948, Whitman, 288 pgs., by Chic Young	10	25	60	95
1463- **Blondie Fun For All**, 1949, Whitman, 288 pgs., by Chic Young	10	25	60	95
1466- **Blondie or Life Among the Bumsteads**, 1944, Whitman, 352 pgs., by Chic Young	10	25	64	100
1476- **Blondie and Bouncing Baby Dumpling**, 1940, Whitman, 432 pgs., by Chic Young	10	25	64	100
1487- **Blondie Baby Dumpling and All!**, 1941, Whitman, 432 pgs. flip pictures, by Chic Young	10	25	64	100
1490- **Blondie Papa Knows Best**, 1945, Whitman, 352 pgs., by Chic Young	10	25	60	95
1491- **Blondie-Cookie and Daisy's Pups**, 1943, Whitman, 1st printing, 432 pgs.	10	25	64	100
1491- **Blondie-Cookie and Daisy's Pups**, 1943, Whitman, 2nd printing with different back-c & 352 pgs.	9	23	56	90
703-10- **Blondie and Dagwood Some Fun!**, 1949, Whitman, by Chic Young	8	20	48	75
21- **Blondie and Dagwood**, 1936, Lynn, by Chic Young	14	35	100	160
1108- **Bobby Benson on the H-Bar-O Ranch**, 1934, Whitman, 300 pgs., based on radio serial	12	30	72	115
Bobby Thatcher and the Samarang Emerald (See Top-Line Comics)				
1432- **Bob Stone the Young Detective**, 1937, Whitman, 240 pgs., movie scenes	12	30	74	120
2002- **(#2)-Bonanza-The Bubble Gum Kid**, 1967, Whitman, 260 pgs., 39 cents, hard-c, color illos	3	8	21	30
1139- **Border Eagle, The**, 1938, Saalfield, 400 pgs.	8	20	48	75
1153- **Boss of the Chisholm Trail**, 1939, Saalfield, 400 pgs.	8	20	48	75
1425- **Brad Turner in Transatlantic Flight**, 1939, Whitman, 432 pgs.	10	25	60	95
1058- **Brave Little Tailor, The** (Disney), 1939, Whitman, 5" x 5 1/2", 68 pgs., hard-c (Mickey Mouse)	12	30	76	125
1427- **Brenda Starr and the Masked Impostor**, 1943, Whitman, 352 pgs., Dale Messick-a	12	30	74	120
1426- **Brer Rabbit** (Walt Disney's ...), 1947, Whitman, All Picture Comics, from "Song Of The South" movie	20	50	143	225
704-10- **Brer Rabbit**, 1949, Whitman	16	40	119	185
1059- **Brick Bradford in the City Beneath the Sea**, 1934, Saalfield, hard-c, by William Ritt & Clarence Gray	15	38	105	165
1309- **Brick Bradford in the City Beneath the Sea**, 1934, Saalfield, soft-c, by Ritt & Gray	15	38	105	165
1468- **Brick Bradford with Brocco the Modern Buccaneer**, 1938, Whitman, 432 pgs., by Wm. Ritt & Clarence Gray	10	25	64	100
1133- **Bringing Up Father**, 1936, Whitman, 432 pgs., by George McManus	12	30	76	125
1100- **Broadway Bill**, 1935, Saalfield, photo-c, 4 1/2" x 5 1/4", movie scenes (Columbia Pictures, horse racing)	11	28	68	110
1580- **Broadway Bill**, 1935, Saalfield, soft-c, photo-c, movie scenes	11	28	68	110
1181- **Broncho Bill**, 1940, Saalfield, 400 pgs.	10	25	64	100
nn- **Broncho Bill**, 1935, Whitman, 148 pgs., 3 1/2" x 4", Tarzan Ice Cream cup lid premium	22	55	154	260
nn- **Broncho Bill in Suicide Canyon** (See Top-Line Comics)				
1417- **Bronc Peeler the Lone Cowboy**, 1937, Whitman, 432 pgs., by Fred Harman, forerunner of Red Ryder (also see Red Death on the Range)	10	25	60	95
nn- **Brownies' Merry Adventures, The**, 1993, Barefoot Books, 202 pgs., reprints from Palmer Cox's late 1800s books	3	8	20	28
1470- **Buccaneer, The**, 1938, Whitman, 240 pgs., photo-c, movie scenes	12	30	76	125
1646- **Buccaneers, The** (TV Series), 1958, Whitman, 4 1/2" x 5 1/4", 280 pgs., Russ Manning-a	3	8	21	30
1104- **Buck Jones in the Fighting Code**, 1934, Whitman, 160 pgs., hard-c, movie scenes	13	33	92	145
1116- **Buck Jones in Ride 'Em Cowboy** (Universal Presents), 1935, Whitman, 240 pgs., photo-c, movie scenes	13	33	92	145
1174- **Buck Jones in the Roaring West** (Universal Presents), 1935, Whitman, 240 pgs., movie scenes	13	33	92	145
1188- **Buck Jones in the Fighting Rangers** (Universal Presents), 1936, Whitman, 240 pgs., photo-c, movie scenes	13	33	85	135
1404- **Buck Jones and the Two-Gun Kid**, 1937, Whitman, 432 pgs.	10	25	60	95
1451- **Buck Jones and the Killers of Crooked Butte**, 1940, Whitman, 432 pgs.	10	25	60	95
1461- **Buck Jones and the Rock Creek Cattle War**, 1938, Whitman, 432 pgs.	10	25	60	95
1486- **Buck Jones and the Rough Riders in Forbidden Trails**, 1943, Whitman, flip pictures, based on movie; Tim McCoy app.	12	30	72	115
3- **Buck Jones in the Red Rider**, 1934, EVW, 160 pgs., movie scenes	21	53	145	230
8- **Buck Jones Cowboy Masquerade**, 1938, Whitman, 132 pgs., soft-c, 3 3/4" x 3 1/2", Buddy Book premium	22	55	154	260
15- **Buck Jones in Rocky Rhodes**, 1935, EVW, 160 pgs., photo-c, movie scenes	30	75	210	360
4069- **Buck Jones and the Night Riders**, 1937, Whitman, 7" x 9", 320 pgs., Big Big Book	33	83	235	400
nn- **Buck Jones on the Six-Gun Trail**, 1939, Whitman, 36 pgs., 2 1/2" x 3 1/2", Penny Book	10	25	60	95
nn- **Buck Jones Big Thrill Chewing Gum**, 1934, Whitman, 8 pgs., 2 1/2" x 3 1/2" (6 diff.) each...	13	33	95	150
742- **Buck Rogers in the 25th Century A.D.**, 1933, Whitman, 320 pgs., Dick Calkins-a	42	105	294	500
nn- **Buck Rogers in the 25th Century A.D.**, 1933, Whitman, 204 pgs.,Cocomalt premium, Calkins-a	28	70	196	340
765- **Buck Rogers in the City Below the Sea**, 1934, Whitman, 320 pgs., Dick Calkins-a	31	78	217	375
765- **Buck Rogers in the City Below the Sea**, 1934, Whitman, 324 pgs., soft-c, Dick Calkins-c/a (Rare)	52	130	364	675
1143- **Buck Rogers on the Moons of Saturn**, 1934, Whitman, 320 pgs., Dick Calkins-a	31	78	217	375
nn- **Buck Rogers on the Moons of Saturn**, 1934, Whitman, 324 pgs., premium w/no ads, soft 3-color-c, Dick Calkins-a	42	105	295	525
1169- **Buck Rogers and the Depth Men of Jupiter**, 1935, Whitman, 432 pgs., Calkins-a	31	78	217	375
1178- **Buck Rogers and the Doom Comet**, 1935, Whitman, 432 pgs., Calkins-a	31	78	217	375
1197- **Buck Rogers and the Planetoid Plot**, 1936, Whitman, 432 pgs., Calkins-a	31	78	217	375
1409- **Buck Rogers Vs. the Fiend of Space**, 1940, Whitman, 432 pgs., Calkins-a	33	83	235	400
1437- **Buck Rogers in the War with the Planet Venus**, 1938, Whitman, 432 pgs., Calkins-a	31	78	217	375
1474- **Buck Rogers and the Overturned World**, 1941, Whitman, 432 pgs., flip pictures, Calkins-a	31	78	217	375
1490- **Buck Rogers and the Super-Dwarf of Space**, 1943, Whitman, 11 Pictures Comics, Calkins-a	31	78	217	375
4057- **Buck Rogers, The Adventures of**, 1934, Whitman, 7" x 9 1/2", 320 pgs., Big Big Book, "The Story of Buck Rogers on the Planet Eros," Calkins-c/a	65	163	435	850
nn- **Buck Rogers**, 1935, Whitman, 4" x 3 1/2", Tarzan Ice Cream cup premium (Rare)	73	184	515	1000
nn- **Buck Rogers in the City of Floating Globes**, 1935, Whitman, 258 pgs., Cocomalt premium, soft-c, Dick Calkins-a	73	184	514	975
nn- **Buck Rogers Big Thrill Chewing Gum**, 1934, Whitman, 8 pgs., 2 1/2" x 3 " (6 diff.) each...	19	48	136	215
1135- **Buckskin and Bullets**, 1938, Saalfield, 400 pgs.	8	20	50	80
Buffalo Bill (See Wild West Adventures of ...)				
nn- **Buffalo Bill**, 1934, World Syndicate, All pictures, by J. Carroll Mansfield	10	25	60	95
713- **Buffalo Bill and the Pony Express**, 1934, Whitman, hard-c, 384 pgs., Hal Arbo-a	12	30	72	115
nn- **Buffalo Bill and the Pony Express**, 1934, Whitman, soft-c, 384 pgs., Hal Arbo-a; three-color premium (Rare)	37	93	260	450
1194- **Buffalo Bill Plays a Lone Hand**, 1936, Whitman, 432 pgs., Hal Arbo-a	10	25	60	95
530- **Bugs Bunny**, 1943, Whitman, All Pictures Comics, Tall Comic Book, 3 1/4" x 8 1/4", reprints/Looney Tunes 1 & 5	16	40	112	175
1403- **Bugs Bunny and the Pirate Loot**, 1947, Whitman, All Pictures Comics	11	28	66	105
1435- **Bugs Bunny**, 1944, Whitman, All Pictures Comics	11	28	68	110
1440- **Bugs Bunny in Risky Business**, 1948, Whitman, All Pictures & Comics	11	28	66	105
1455- **Bugs Bunny and Klondike Gold,** 1948, Whitman, 288 pgs.	11	28	66	105
1465- **Bugs Bunny The Masked Marvel**, 1949, Whitman, 288 pgs.	11	28	66	105
1496- **Bugs Bunny and His Pals,** 1945, Whitman, All Pictures Comics; r/Four Color Comics #33	11	28	66	105
13- **Bugs Bunny and the Secret of Storm Island**, 1942, Dell,194 pgs., Fast-Action Story	28	70	196	340

1181 - Broncho Bill © Saalfield

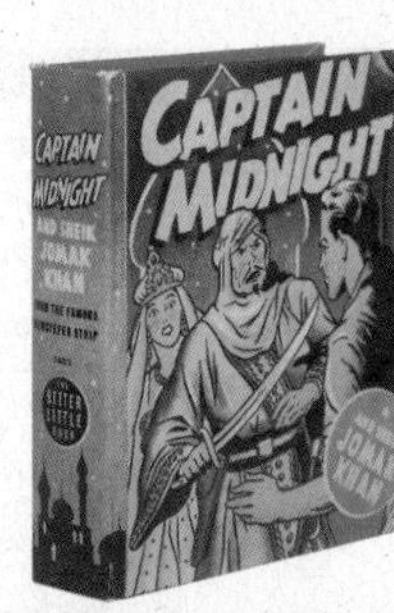

1402 - Captain Midnight and Sheik Jomak Khan © FAW

L14 - Chip Collins' Adventures on Bat Island © LYNN

	GD	FN	VF	VF/NM
706-10- **Bugs Bunny and the Giant Brothers**, 1949, Whitman	10	25	60	95
2007- **(#7)-Bugs Bunny-Double Trouble on Diamond Island**, 1967, Whitman, 260 pgs., 39 cents, hard-c, color illos	3	8	23	34
2029-(#29)- **Bugs Bunny, Accidental Adventure,** 1969, Whitman, 256 pgs., hard-c, color illos.	2	3	17	24
2952- **Bugs Bunny's Mistake**, 1949, Whitman, 3 1/4" x 4", 24 pgs., Tiny Tales, full color (5 cents) (1030-5 on back-c)	10	25	60	95
5757-2- **Bugs Bunny in Double Trouble on Diamond Island**,1967, (1980-reprints #2007), Whitman, 260 pgs., soft-c, 79 cents, B&W	1	3	10	14
5758- **Bugs Bunny, Accidental Adventure,** 1973, Whitman, 256 pgs., soft-c, B&W illos.	1	3	10	14
5758-1- **Bugs Bunny, Accidental Adventure,** 1973, Whitman, 256 pgs., soft-c, B&W illos.	1	3	10	14
5772- **Bugs Bunny the Last Crusader**, 1975, Whitman, 49 cents, flip-it book	1	3	10	14
5772-2- **Bugs Bunny the Last Crusader**, 1975, Whitman, $1.00, flip-it book	1	3	5	6
1169- **Bullet Benton**, 1939, Saalfield, 400 pgs.	10	25	64	100
nn- **Bulletman and the Return of Mr. Murder**, 1941, Fawcett, 196 pgs., Dime Action Book	42	105	294	500
1142- **Bullets Across the Border** (A Billy The Kid story), 1938, Saalfield, 400 pgs.	10	25	60	95
Bunky (See Top-Line Comics)				
837- **Bunty** (Punch and Judy), 1935, Whitman, 28 pgs., Magic-Action with 3 pop-ups	13	33	90	140
1091- **Burn 'Em Up Barnes**, 1935, Saalfield, hard-c, movie scenes	10	25	60	95
1321- **Burn 'Em Up Barnes**, 1935, Saalfield, soft-c, movie scenes	10	25	60	95
1415- **Buz Sawyer and Bomber 13**,1946, Whitman, 352 pgs., Roy Crane-a	10	25	60	95
1412- **Calling W-1-X-Y-Z, Jimmy Kean and the Radio Spies**, 1939, Whitman, 300 pgs.	11	28	66	105
Call of the Wild (See Jack London's...)				
1107- **Camels are Coming**, 1935, Saalfield, movie scenes	10	25	60	95
1587- **Camels are Coming**, 1935, Saalfield, movie scenes	10	25	60	95
nn- **Captain and the Kids, Boys Vill Be Boys, The**, 1938, 68 pgs., Pan-Am Oil premium, soft-c	12	30	76	125
1128- **Captain Easy Soldier of Fortune**, 1934, Whitman, 432 pgs., Roy Crane-a	12	30	76	125
nn- **Captain Easy Soldier of Fortune**, 1934, Whitman, 436 pgs., Premium, no ads, soft 3-color-c, Roy Crane-a	21	53	145	230
1474- **Captain Easy Behind Enemy Lines**, 1943, Whitman, 352 pgs., Roy Crane-a	11	28	68	110
nn- **Captain Easy and Wash Tubbs**, 1935, 260 pgs., Cocomalt premium, Roy Crane-a	11	28	68	110
1444- **Captain Frank Hawks Air Ace and the League of Twelve**, 1938, Whitman, 432 pgs.	11	28	68	110
nn- **Captain Marvel,** 1941, Fawcett, 196 pgs., Dime Action Book	52	130	364	675
1402- **Captain Midnight and Sheik Jomak Khan**, 1946, Whitman, 352 pgs.	17	43	123	190
1452- **Captain Midnight and the Moon Woman**, 1943, Whitman, 352 pgs.	20	50	143	225
1458- **Captain Midnight Vs. The Terror of the Orient**, 1942, Whitman, 432 pgs., flip pictures, Hess-a	20	50	143	225
1488- **Captain Midnight and the Secret Squadron**, 1941, Whitman, 432 pgs.	20	50	143	225
Captain Robb of.. (See Dirigible ZR90 ...)				
nn- **Cauliflower Catnip Pearls of Peril**, 1981, Teacup Tales, 290 pgs., Joe Wehrle Jr.-s/a; deliberately printed on aged-looking paper to look like an old BLB	3	8	20	28
20- **Ceiling Zero,** 1936, Lynn, 128 pgs., 7 1/2" x 5", hard-c, James Cagney, Pat O'Brien photos on-c, movie scenes, Warner Bros. Pictures	11	28	66	105
1093- **Chandu the Magician**, 1935, Saalfield, 5" x 5 1/4", 160 pgs., hard-c, Bela Lugosi photo-c, movie scenes	16	40	112	175
1323- **Chandu the Magician**, 1935, Saalfield, 5" x 5 1/4", 160 pgs., soft-c, Bela Lugosi photo-c	16	41	119	185
Charlie Chan (See Inspector ...)				
1459- **Charlie Chan Solves a New Mystery** (See Inspector..), 1940, Whitman, 432 pgs., Alfred Andriola-a	13	33	92	145
1478- **Charlie Chan of the Honolulu Police, Inspector**, 1939, Whitman, 432 pgs., Andriola-a	13	33	92	145
Charlie McCarthy (See Story Of ...)				
734- **Chester Gump at Silver Creek Ranch**, 1933, Whitman, 320 pgs., Sidney Smith-a	12	30	74	120
nn- **Chester Gump at Silver Creek Ranch**, 1933, Whitman, 204 pgs., Cocomalt premium, soft-c, Sidney Smith-a	13	33	85	135
nn- **Chester Gump at Silver Creek Ranch**, 1933, Whitman, 52 pgs., 4" x 5 1/2", premium-no ads, soft-c, Sidney Smith-a	16	41	117	185
766- **Chester Gump Finds the Hidden Treasure**, 1934, Whitman, 320 pgs., Sidney Smith-a	11	28	68	110
nn- **Chester Gump Finds the Hidden Treasure**, 1934, Whitman, 52 pgs., 3 1/2" x 5 3/4", premium-no ads, soft-c, Sidney Smith-a	16	41	119	185
nn- **Chester Gump Finds the Hidden Treasure**, 1934, Whitman, 52 pgs., 4" x 5 1/2", premium-no ads, Sidney Smith-a	16	41	119	185
1146- **Chester Gump in the City Of Gold**, 1935, Whitman, 432 pgs., Sidney Smith-a	12	30	72	115
nn- **Chester Gump in the City Of Gold**, 1935, Whitman, 436 pgs., premium-no ads, 3-color, soft-c, Sidney Smith-a	22	55	154	260
1402- **Chester Gump in the Pole to Pole Flight**, 1937, Whitman, 432 pgs.	11	28	68	110
5- **Chester Gump and His Friends,** 1934, Whitman, 132 pgs., 3 1/2" x 3 1/2", soft-c, Tarzan Ice Cream cup lid premium	22	55	154	260
nn- **Chester Gump at the North Pole**, 1938, Whitman, 68 pgs. soft-c, 3 3/4" x 3 1/2", Pan-Am giveaway	22	55	154	260
nn- **Chicken Greedy**, nd(1930s), np (Whitman), 36 pgs., 3" x 2 1/2", Penny Book	4	10	27	40
nn- **Chicken Licken**, nd (1930s), np (Whitman), 36 pgs., 3" x 2 1/2", Penny Book	4	10	27	40
1101- **Chief of the Rangers**, 1935, Saalfield, hard-c, Tom Mix photo-c, movie scenes from "The Miracle Rider"	13	33	90	140
1581- **Chief of the Rangers**, 1935, Saalfield, soft-c, Tom Mix photo-c, movie scenes	13	33	90	140
Child's Garden of Verses (See Wee Little Books)				
L14- **Chip Collins' Adventures on Bat Island**, 1935, Lynn, 192 pgs.	12	30	76	125
2025- **Chitty Chitty Bang Bang**, 1968, Whitman, movie photos	3	8	21	30
Chubby Little Books, 1935, Whitman, 3" x 2 1/2", 200 pgs.				
W803- **Golden Hours Story Book, The**	3	8	22	32
W803- **Story Hours Story Book, The**	3	8	22	32
W804- **Gay Book of Little Stories, The**	3	8	22	32
W804- **Glad Book of Little Stories, The**	3	8	22	32
W804- **Joy Book of Little Stories, The**	3	8	22	32
W804- **Sunny Book of Little Stories, The**	3	8	22	32
1453- **Chuck Malloy Railroad Detective on the Streamliner**,1938, Whitman, 300 pgs.	6	15	36	55
Cinderella (See Walt Disney's...)				
Clyde Beatty (See The Steel Arena)				
1410- **Clyde Beatty Daredevil Lion and Tiger Tamer**, 1939, Whitman, 300 pgs.	12	30	76	125
1480- **Coach Bernie Bierman's Brick Barton and the Winning Eleven**, 1938, 300 pgs.	10	25	60	95
1446- **Convoy Patrol** (A Thrilling U.S. Navy Story), 1942, Whitman, 432 pgs., flip pictures	10	25	60	95
1127- **Corley of the Wilderness Trail**, 1937, Saalfield, hard-c	10	25	60	95
1607- **Corley of the Wilderness Trail**, 1937, Saalfield, soft-c	10	25	60	95
1- **Count of Monte Cristo**, 1934, EVW, 160 pgs., (Five Star Library),				

GD FN VF VF/NM

movie scenes, hard-c (Rare) 19 48 136 215
1457- **Cowboy Lingo Boys' Book of Western Facts**, 1938,
Whitman, 300 pgs., Fred Harman-a 6 15 40 60
1171- **Cowboy Malloy**, 1940, Saalfield, 400 pgs. 5 12 30 45
1106- **Cowboy Millionaire**, 1935, Saalfield, movie scenes with
George O'Brien, photo-c, hard-c 12 30 72 115
1586- **Cowboy Millionaire**, 1935, Saalfield, movie scenes with
George O'Brien, photo-c, soft-c 12 30 72 115
724- **Cowboy Stories**, 1933, Whitman, 300 pgs., Hal Arbo-a
10 25 64 100
nn- **Cowboy Stories**, 1933, Whitman, 52 pgs., soft-c, premium-no ads,
4" x 5 1/2" Hal Arbo-a 12 30 72 115
1161- **Crimson Cloak, The**, 1939, Saalfield, 400 pgs.
10 25 60 95
L19- **Curley Harper at Lakespur**, 1935, Lynn, 192 pgs.
10 25 60 95
5785-2- **Daffy Duck in Twice the Trouble**, 1980, Whitman, 260 pgs.,
79 cents soft-c 1 3 5 6
2018-(#18)-**Daktari-Night of Terror**, 1968, Whitman, 260 pgs., 39 cents,
hard-c, color illos 3 8 20 28
1010- **Dan Dunn And The Gangsters' Frame-Up**, 1937, Whitman,
7 1/4" x 5 1/2", 64 pgs., Nickel Book 26 65 185 315
1116- **Dan Dunn "Crime Never Pays,"** 1934, Whitman, 320 pgs.,
by Norman Marsh 8 20 50 80
1125- **Dan Dunn on the Trail of the Counterfeiters**, 1936,
Whitman, 432 pgs., by Norman Marsh 8 20 50 80
1171- **Dan Dunn and the Crime Master**, 1937, Whitman, 432 pgs.,
by Norman Marsh 8 20 50 80
1417- **Dan Dunn and the Underworld Gorillas**, 1941, Whitman,
All Pictures Comics, flip pictures, by Norman Marsh 8 20 50 80
1454- **Dan Dunn on the Trail of Wu Fang**, 1938, Whitman, 432 pgs.,
by Norman Marsh 10 25 64 100
1481- **Dan Dunn and the Border Smugglers**, 1938, Whitman, 432 pgs.,
by Norman Marsh 6 15 40 60
1492- **Dan Dunn and the Dope Ring**, 1940, Whitman, 432 pgs.,
by Norman Marsh 6 15 40 60
nn- **Dan Dunn and the Bank Hold-Up**, 1938, Whitman, 36 pgs.,
2 1/2" x 3 1/2", Penny Book 9 23 54 85
nn- **Dan Dunn and the Zeppelin Of Doom**, 1938, Dell, 196 pgs.,
Fast-Action Story, soft-c 18 45 128 200
nn- **Dan Dunn Meets Chang Loo**, 1938, Whitman, 66 pgs., Pan-Am
premium, by Norman Marsh 23 58 165 280
nn- **Dan Dunn Plays a Lone Hand**, 1938, Whitman, 36 pgs.,
2 1/2" x 3 1/2", Penny Book 9 23 54 85
3 3/4" x 3 1/2", Buddy book 24 61 171 290
6- **Dan Dunn Secret Operative 48 and the Counterfeiter Ring**, 1938,
Whitman, 132 pgs., soft-c, 3 3/4" x 3 1/2", Buddy Book premium
24 61 171 290
9- **Dan Dunn's Mysterious Ruse**, 1936, Whitman, 132 pgs., soft-c,
3 1/2" x 3 1/2", Tarzan Ice Cream cup lid premium 24 61 171 290
1177- **Danger Trail North**, 1940, Saalfield, 400 pgs. 10 25 60 95
1151- **Danger Trails in Africa**, 1935, Whitman, 432 pgs. 10 30 80 130
nn- **Daniel Boone**, 1934, World Syndicate, High Lights of History Series,
hard-c, All in Pictures 10 25 60 95
1160- **Dan of the Lazy L**, 1939, Saalfield, 400 pgs. 10 25 60 95
1148- **David Copperfield**, 1934, Whitman, hard-c, 160 pgs., photo-c,
movie scenes (W. C. Fields) 13 33 90 140
nn- **David Copperfield**, 1934, Whitman, soft-c, 164 pgs., movie scenes
13 33 90 140
1151- **Death by Short Wave**, 1938, Saalfield 11 28 68 110
1156- **Denny the Ace Detective**, 1938, Saalfield, 400 pgs.
11 28 66 105
1431- **Desert Eagle and the Hidden Fortress, The**, 1941, Whitman,
432 pgs., flip pictures 11 28 68 110
1458- **Desert Eagle Rides Again, The**, 1939, Whitman, 300 pgs.
11 28 68 110
1136- **Desert Justice**, 1938, Saalfield, 400 pgs. 10 25 64 100
1484- **Detective Higgins of the Racket Squad**, 1938, Whitman,
432 pgs. 10 25 64 100
1124- **Dickie Moore in the Little Red School House**, 1936, Whitman,
240 pgs., photo-c, movie scenes (Chesterfield Motion Picts. Corp)
12 30 80 130
W-707- **Dick Tracy the Detective, The Adventures of**, 1933, Whitman,
320 pgs. (The 1st Big Little Book), by Chester Gould
(Scarce) 170 425 1360 2550
nn- **Dick Tracy Detective, The Adventures of**, 1933, Whitman,
52 pgs., 4" x 5 1/2", premium-no ads, soft-c, by Chester Gould
82 205 575 1150
nn- **Dick Tracy Detective, The Adventures of**, 1933, Whitman,
52 pgs., 4" x 5 1/2", inside back-c & back-c ads for Sundial Shoes,
soft-c, by Chester Gould 86 215 600 1200
710- **Dick Tracy and Dick Tracy, Jr.** (The Advs. of ...), 1933, Whitman,
320 pgs., by Chester Gould 60 150 420 775
nn- **Dick Tracy and Dick Tracy, Jr.** (The Advs. of ...), 1933, Whitman,
52 pgs., premium-no ads, soft-c, 4" x 5 1/2", by Chester Gould
60 150 420 775

GD FN VF VF/NM

nn- **Dick Tracy the Detective and Dick Tracy, Jr.**, 1933, Whitman,
52 pgs., premium-no ads, 3 1/2"x 5 1/4", soft-c, by Chester Gould
60 150 420 775
723- **Dick Tracy Out West**, 1933, Whitman, 300 pgs., by Chester Gould
37 93 260 450
749- **Dick Tracy from Colorado to Nova Scotia**, 1933, Whitman,
320 pgs., by Chester Gould 26 75 180 310
nn- **Dick Tracy from Colorado to Nova Scotia**, 1933, Whitman, 204 pgs.,
premium-no ads, soft-c, by Chester Gould 27 69 192 335
1105- **Dick Tracy and the Stolen Bonds**, 1934, Whitman, 320 pgs.,
by Chester Gould 16 41 119 185
1112- **Dick Tracy and the Racketeer Gang**, 1936, Whitman,
432 pgs., by Chester Gould 13 33 95 150
1137- **Dick Tracy Solves the Penfield Mystery**, 1934, Whitman,
320 pgs., by Chester Gould 16 40 116 180
nn- **Dick Tracy Solves the Penfield Mystery**, 1934, Whitman, 324 pgs.,
premium-no ads, 3-color, soft-c, by Chester Gould 41 103 287 490
1163- **Dick Tracy and the Boris Arson Gang**, 1935, Whitman,
432 pgs., by Chester Gould 15 38 108 170
1170- **Dick Tracy on the Trail of Larceny Lu**, 1935, Whitman,
432 pgs., by Chester Gould 14 35 100 160
1185- **Dick Tracy in Chains of Crime**, 1936, Whitman, 432 pgs.,
by Chester Gould 14 35 100 160
1412- **Dick Tracy and Yogee Yamma**, 1946, Whitman, 352 pgs.,
by Chester Gould 13 33 95 150
1420- **Dick Tracy and the Hotel Murders**, 1937, Whitman, 432 pgs.,
by Chester Gould 14 35 100 160
1434- **Dick Tracy and the Phantom Ship**, 1940, Whitman, 432 pgs.,
by Chester Gould 14 35 100 160
1436- **Dick Tracy and the Mad Killer**, 1947, Whitman, 288 pgs., by
Chester Gould 13 33 85 135
1439- **Dick Tracy and His G-Men**, 1941, Whitman, 432 pgs., flip pictures,
by Chester Gould 14 35 100 160
1445- **Dick Tracy and the Bicycle Gang**, 1948, Whitman, 288 pgs.,
by Chester Gould 13 33 85 135
1446- **Detective Dick Tracy and the Spider Gang**, 1937, Whitman, 240 pgs.,
scenes from "Adventures of Dick Tracy" serial 19 48 136 215
1449- **Dick Tracy Special F.B.I. Operative**, 1943, Whitman, 432 pgs.
by Chester Gould 14 35 100 160
1454- **Dick Tracy on the High Seas**, 1939, Whitman, 432 pgs.,
by Chester Gould 14 35 100 160
1460- **Dick Tracy and the Tiger Lilly Gang**, 1949, Whitman,
288 pgs., by Chester Gould 13 33 85 135
1478- **Dick Tracy on Voodoo Island**, 1944, Whitman, 352 pgs.,
by Chester Gould 13 33 85 135
1479- **Detective Dick Tracy Vs. Crooks in Disguise**, 1939, Whitman,
432 pgs., flip pictures, by Chester Gould 14 35 100 160
1482- **Dick Tracy and the Wreath Kidnapping Case**, 1945,
Whitman, 352 pgs. 13 33 95 150
1488- **Dick Tracy the Super-Detective**, 1939, Whitman, 432 pgs.,
by Chester Gould 14 35 100 160
1491- **Dick Tracy the Man with No Face**, 1938, Whitman, 432 pgs.
14 35 100 160
1495- **Dick Tracy Returns**, 1939, Whitman, 432 pgs., based on Republic
Motion Picture serial, Chester Gould-a 14 35 100 160
2001- (#1)-**Dick Tracy-Encounters Facey**, 1967, Whitman, 260 pgs.,
39 cents, hard-c, color illos 3 8 21 30
3912- **Dick Tracy Big Little Book Picture Puzzles**, 1938, Whitman,
7 1/2" x 10 1/4" box with 2 jigsaw puzzles 50 125 350 650
Variant set, same cover w/2 puzzles showing Dick Tracy & Jr. in crime
lab & Dick Tracy patting down a gangster 50 125 350 650
4055- **Dick Tracy, The Adventures of**, 1934, Whitman, 7" x 9 1/2", 320 pgs.,
Big Big Book, by Chester Gould 56 140 392 725
4071- **Dick Tracy and the Mystery of the Purple Cross**, 1938,
7" x 9 1/2", 320 pgs., Big Big Book, by Chester Gould
(Scarce) 52 130 364 675
nn- **Dick Tracy and the Invisible Man**, 1939, Whitman,
3 1/4" x 3 3/4", 132 pgs., stapled, soft-c, Quaker Oats premium;
NBC radio play script, Chester Gould-a 41 103 287 490
Vol. 2- **Dick Tracy's Ghost Ship**, 1939, Whitman, 3 1/2" x 3 1/2", 132 pgs.,
soft-c, stapled, Quaker Oats premium; NBC radio play script episode
from actual radio show; Gould-a 39 98 276 475
3- **Dick Tracy Meets a New Gang**, 1934, Whitman, 3" x 3 1/2", 132 pgs.,
soft-c, Tarzan Ice Cream cup lid premium 37 93 260 450
11- **Dick Tracy in Smashing the Famon Racket**, 1938, Whitman,
3 3/4" x 3 1/2", Buddy Book-ice cream premium, by Chester Gould
36 90 252 430
nn- **Dick Tracy Gets His Man**, 1938, Whitman, 36 pgs., 2 1/2" x 3 1/2",
Penny Book 8 20 50 80
nn- **Dick Tracy the Detective**, 1938, Whitman, 36 pgs., 2 1/2" x 3 1/2",
Penny Book 8 20 50 80
9- **Dick Tracy and the Frozen Bullet Murders**, 1941, Dell, 196 pgs.,
Fast-Action Story, soft-c, by Gould 37 93 260 450
6833- **Dick Tracy Detective and Federal Agent**, 1936, Dell, 244 pgs.,
Cartoon Story Books, hard-c, by Gould 40 101 283 485
nn- **Dick Tracy Detective and Federal Agent**, 1936, Dell, 244 pgs.,

1124 - Dickie Moore in the Little Red School House © WHIT

1411 - Donald Duck and Ghost Morgan's Treasure © DIS

10 - Dumbo the Flying Elephant © DIS

	GD	FN	VF	VF/NM
Fast-Action Story, soft-c, by Gould	34	85	238	410
nn- **Dick Tracy and the Blackmailers**, 1939, Dell, 196 pgs., Fast-Action Story, soft-c, by Gould	34	85	238	410
nn- **Dick Tracy and the Chain of Evidence, Detective**, 1938, Dell, 196 pgs., Fast-Action Story, soft-c, by Chester Gould	34	85	238	410
nn- **Dick Tracy and the Crook Without a Face**, 1938, Whitman, 68 pgs., 3 1/4" x 3 1/2", Pan-Am giveaway, Gould-c/a	29	73	203	350
nn- **Dick Tracy and the Maroon Mask Gang**, 1938, Dell, 196 pgs., Fast-Action Story, soft-c, by Gould	34	85	238	410
nn- **Dick Tracy Cross-Country Race**, 1934, Whitman, 8 pgs., 2 1/2" x 3", Big Thrill chewing gum premium (6 diff.)	13	33	85	135
nn- **Dick Whittington and his Cat**, nd(1930s), np(Whitman), 36 pgs., Penny Book	3	7	20	28
Dinglehoofer und His Dog Adolph (See Top-Line Comics)				
Dinky (See Jackie Cooper in ...)				
1464- **Dirigible ZR90 and the Disappearing Zeppelin** (Captain Robb of ...), 1941, Whitman, 300 pgs., Al Lewin-a	14	35	100	160
1167- **Dixie Dugan Among the Cowboys**, 1939, Saalfield, 400 pgs.	10	25	60	95
1188- **Dixie Dugan and Cuddles**, 1940, Saalfield, 400 pgs., by Striebel & McEvoy	10	25	60	95
Doctor Doom (See Foreign Spies... & International Spy...)				
Dog of Flanders, A (See Frankie Thomas in ...)				
1114- **Dog Stars of Hollywood**, 1936, Saalfield, photo-c, photo-illos	11	28	68	110
1594- **Dog Stars of Hollywood**, 1936, Saalfield, photo-c, soft-c, photo-illos	11	28	68	110
nn- **Dolls and Dresses Big Little Set**, 1930s, Whitman, box contains 20 dolls on paper, 128 sheets of clothing to color & cut out, includes crayons	37	93	260	450
Donald Duck (See Silly Symphony... & Walt Disney's ...)				
800- **Donald Duck in Bringing Up the Boys**, 1948, Whitman, hard-c, Story Hour series	10	25	60	95
1404- **Donald Duck (Says Such a Life)** (Disney), 1939, Whitman, 432 pgs., Taliaferro-a	19	48	136	215
1411- **Donald Duck and Ghost Morgan's Treasure** (Disney), 1946, Whitman, All Pictures Comics, Barks-a; reprints FC #9	24	60	168	285
1422- **Donald Duck Sees Stars** (Disney), 1941, Whitman, 432 pgs., flip pictures, Taliaferro-a	18	45	126	195
1424- **Donald Duck Says Such Luck** (Disney), 1941, Whitman, 432 pgs., flip pictures, Taliaferro-a	18	45	126	195
1430- **Donald Duck Headed For Trouble** (Disney), 1942, Whitman, 432 pgs., flip pictures, Taliaferro-a	18	45	126	195
1432- **Donald Duck and the Green Serpent** (Disney), 1947, Whitman, All Pictures Comics, Barks-a; reprints FC #108	20	50	140	220
1434- **Donald Duck Forgets To Duck** (Disney), 1939, Whitman, 432 pgs., Taliaferro-a	19	48	133	210
1438- **Donald Duck Off the Beam** (Disney), 1943, Whitman, 352 pgs., flip pictures, Taliaferro-a	18	45	126	195
1438- **Donald Duck Off the Beam** (Disney), 1943, Whitman, 432 pgs., flip pictures, Taliaferro-a	18	45	126	195
1449- **Donald Duck Lays Down the Law**, 1948, Whitman, 288 pgs., Barks-a	19	48	133	210
1457- **Donald Duck in Volcano Valley** (Disney), 1949, Whitman, 288 pgs., Barks-a	19	48	133	210
1462- **Donald Duck Gets Fed Up** (Disney), 1940, Whitman, 432 pgs.,Taliaferro-a	18	45	126	195
1478- **Donald Duck-Hunting For Trouble** (Disney), 1938, Whitman, 432 pgs., Taliaferro-a	19	48	133	210
1484- **Donald Duck is Here Again!**, 1944, Whitman, All Pictures Comics, Taliaferro-a	18	45	126	195
1486- **Donald Duck Up in the Air** (Disney), 1945, Whitman, 352 pgs., Barks-a	21	53	145	230
705-10- **Donald Duck and the Mystery of the Double X**, (Disney), 1949, Whitman, Barks-a	12	30	76	125
2033-(#33)- **Donald Duck, Luck of the Ducks**, 1969, Whitman, 256 pgs., hard-c, 39 cents, color illos.	3	8	19	26
2009-(#9)-**Donald Duck-The Fabulous Diamond Fountain**, (Walt Disney), 1967, Whitman, 260 pgs., 39 cents, hard-c, color illos	4	10	24	35
5756- **Donald Duck-The Fabulous Diamond Fountain**, (Walt Disney), 1973, Whitman, 260 pgs., 79 cents, soft-c, color illos	2	3	17	24
5756-1- **Donald Duck-The Fabulous Diamond Fountain**, (Walt Disney), 1973, Whitman, 260 pgs., 79 cents, soft-c, color illos	2	3	17	24
5756-2- **Donald Duck-The Fabulous Diamond Fountain**, (Walt Disney), 1973, Whitman, 260 pgs., 79 cents, soft-c, color illos	2	3	17	24
5760- **Donald Duck in Volcano Valley** (Disney), 1973, Whitman, 39 cents, flip-it book	2	3	17	24
5760-2- **Donald Duck in Volcano Valley** (Disney), 1973, Whitman, 79 cents, flip-it book	2	3	12	16
5764- **Donald Duck, Luck of the Ducks**, 1969, Whitman, 256 pgs., soft-c, 49 cents, color illos.	2	3	16	24
5773- **Donald Duck - The Lost Jungle City**, 1975, Whitman, 49 cents, flip-it book; 6 printings through 1980	2	3	12	16
nn- **Donald Duck and the Ducklings**, 1938, Dell, 194 pgs., Fast-Action Story, soft-c, Taliaferro-a	37	93	260	450
nn- **Donald Duck Out of Luck** (Disney), 1940, Dell, 196 pgs., Fast-Action Story, has Four Color #4 on back-c, Taliaferro-a	37	93	260	450
8- **Donald Duck Takes It on the Chin** (Disney), 1941, Dell, 196 pgs., Fast-Action Story, soft-c, Taliaferro-a	36	90	252	430
L13- **Donnie and the Pirates**, 1935, Lynn, 192 pgs.	10	25	60	95
1438- **Don O'Dare Finds War**, 1940, Whitman, 432 pgs.	10	25	60	95
1107- **Don Winslow, U.S.N.**, 1935, Whitman, 432 pgs.	13	33	95	150
nn- **Don Winslow, U.S.N.**, 1935, Whitman, 436 pgs., premium-no ads, 3-color, soft-c	16	40	116	180
1408- **Don Winslow and the Giant Girl Spy**, 1946, Whitman, 352 pgs.	10	25	64	100
1418- **Don Winslow Navy Intelligence Ace**, 1942, Whitman, 432 pgs., flip pictures	13	33	90	140
1419- **Don Winslow of the Navy Vs. the Scorpion Gang**, 1938, Whitman, 432 pgs.	13	33	90	140
1453- **Don Winslow of the Navy and the Secret Enemy Base**, 1943, Whitman, 352 pgs.	13	33	90	140
1489- **Don Winslow of the Navy and the Great War Plot**, 1940, Whitman, 432 pgs.	13	33	90	140
nn- **Don Winslow U.S. Navy and the Missing Admiral**, 1938, Whitman, 36 pgs., 2 1/2" x 3 1/2", Penny Book	6	15	36	55
1137- **Doomed To Die**, 1938, Saalfield, 400 pgs.	11	28	68	110
1140- **Down Cartridge Creek**, 1938, Saalfield, 400 pgs.	11	28	68	110
1416- **Draftie of the U.S. Army**, 1943, Whitman, All Pictures Comics	11	28	68	110
1100B- **Dreams** (Your dreams & what they mean), 1938, Whitman, 36 pgs., 2 1/2" x 3 1/2", Penny Book	4	10	24	35
24- **Dumb Dora and Bing Brown**, 1936, Lynn	12	30	72	115
1400- **Dumbo, of the Circus - Only His Ears Grew!** (Disney), 1941, Whitman, 432 pgs., based on Disney movie	20	50	143	225
10- **Dumbo the Flying Elephant** (Disney), 1944, Dell, 194 pgs., Fast-Action Story, soft-c	31	78	217	375
nn- **East O' the Sun and West O' the Moon**, nd (1930s), np (Whitman), 36 pgs., 3" x 2 1/2", Penny Book	3	8	21	30
774- **Eddie Cantor in An Hour with You**, 1934, Whitman, 154 pgs., 4 1/4" x 5 1/4", photo-c, movie scenes	12	30	80	130
nn- **Eddie Cantor in Laughland**, 1934, Goldsmith, 132 pgs., soft-c, photo-c, Vallely-a	12	30	80	130
1106- **Ella Cinders and the Mysterious House**, 1934, Whitman, 432 pgs.	13	33	85	135
nn- **Ella Cinders and the Mysterious House**, 1934, Whitman, 52 pgs., premium-no ads, soft-c, 3 1/2" x 5 3/4"	15	38	108	170
nn- **Ella Cinders and the Mysterious House**, 1934, Whitman, 52 pgs., Lemix Korlix desserts ad by Perkins Products Co. on back-c, soft-c, 3 1/2" x 5 3/4"	18	45	128	200
nn- **Ella Cinders**, 1935, Whitman, 148 pgs., 3 1/4" x 4", Tarzan Ice Cream cup lid premium	23	58	165	280
nn- **Ella Cinders Plays Duchess**, 1938, Whitman, 68 pgs., 3 3/4" x 3 1/2", Pan-Am Oil premium	16	41	119	185
nn- **Ella Cinders Solves a Mystery**, 1938, Whitman, 68 pgs., Pan-Am Oil				

	GD	FN	VF	VF/NM
premium, soft-c	16	41	119	185
11- **Ella Cinders' Exciting Experience**, 1934, Whitman, 3 1/2" x 3 1/2", 132 pgs., Tarzan Ice Cream cup lid giveaway	23	58	165	280
1406- **Ellery Queen the Adventure of the Last Man Club**, 1940, Whitman, 432 pgs.	12	30	80	130
1472- **Ellery Queen the Master Detective**, 1942, Whitman, 432 pgs., flip pictures	12	30	80	130
1081- **Elmer and his Dog Spot**, 1935, Saalfield, hard-c	8	20	50	80
1311- **Elmer and his Dog Spot**, 1935, Saalfield, soft-c	8	20	50	80
722- **Erik Noble and the Forty-Niners**, 1934, Whitman, 384 pgs.	8	20	50	80
nn- **Erik Noble and the Forty-Niners**, 1934, Whitman, 386 pgs., 3-color, soft-c (Rare)	33	83	235	400
684- **Famous Comics** (in open box), 1934, Whitman, 48 pgs., 3 3/4" x 8 1/2", (3 books in set): Book 1 - Katzenjammer Kids, Barney Google, & Little Jimmy; Book 2 - Polly and Her Pals, Little Jimmy, & Katzenjammer Kids; Book 3 - Little Annie Rooney, Katzenjammer Kids, & Polly and Her Pals; Complete set	48	120	336	625
2019-(#19)- **Fantastic Four in the House of Horrors,** 1968, Whitman, 256 pgs., hard-c, color illos.	3	8	21	30
5775- **Fantastic Four in the House of Horrors,** 1976, Whitman, 256 pgs., soft-c, B&W illos.	2	3	15	20
5775-1- **Fantastic Four in the House of Horrors,** 1976, Whitman, 256 pgs., soft-c, B&W illos.	2	3	15	20
1058- **Farmyard Symphony, The** (Disney), 1939, 5" X 5 1/2", 68 pgs., hard-c	12	30	72	115
1129- **Felix the Cat**, 1936, Whitman, 432 pgs., Messmer-a	24	60	168	285
1439- **Felix the Cat**, 1943, Whitman, All Pictures Comics, Messmer-a	21	53	149	250
1465- **Felix the Cat**, 1945, Whitman, All Pictures Comics, Messmer-a	16	40	112	175
nn- **Felix** (Flip book), 1967, World Retrospective of Animation Cinema, 188 pgs., 2 1/2" x 4" by Otto Messmer	3	8	21	30
nn- **Fighting Cowboy of Nugget Gulch, The**, 1939, Whitman, 2 1/2" x 3 1/2", Penny Book	3	8	21	30
1401- **Fighting Heroes Battle for Freedom**, 1943, Whitman, All Pictures Comics, from "Heroes of Democracy" strip, by Stookie Allen	8	20	50	80
6- **Fighting President, The**, 1934, EVW (Five Star Library), 160 pgs., photo-c, photo ill., F. D. Roosevelt	11	28	68	110
nn- **Fire Chief Ed Wynn and "His Old Fire Horse,"** 1934, Goldsmith, 132 pgs., H. Vallely-a, photo, soft-c	10	25	60	95
1464- **Flame Boy and the Indians' Secret**, 1938, Whitman, 300 pgs., Sekakuku-a (Hopi Indian)	8	20	50	80
22- **Flaming Guns**, 1935, EVW, with Tom Mix, movie scenes				
Hardcover	42	105	294	500
(Scarce) Softcover	44	110	308	550
1110- **Flash Gordon on the Planet Mongo**, 1934, Whitman, 320 pgs., by Alex Raymond	41	103	287	490
1166- **Flash Gordon and the Monsters of Mongo**, 1935, Whitman, 432 pgs., by Alex Raymond	39	98	273	470
nn- **Flash Gordon and the Monsters of Mongo**, 1935, Whitman, 436 pgs., premium-no ads, 3-color, soft-c, by Raymond	62	155	434	800
1171- **Flash Gordon and the Tournaments of Mongo**, 1935, Whitman, 432 pgs., by Alex Raymond	37	93	260	450
1190- **Flash Gordon and the Witch Queen of Mongo**, 1936, Whitman, 432 pgs., by Alex Raymond	37	93	260	450
1407- **Flash Gordon in the Water World of Mongo**, 1937, Whitman, 432 pgs., by Alex Raymond	31	80	226	385
1423- **Flash Gordon and the Perils of Mongo**, 1940, Whitman, 432 pgs., by Alex Raymond	29	73	203	350
1424- **Flash Gordon in the Jungles of Mongo**, 1947, Whitman, 352 pgs., by Alex Raymond	22	55	155	265
1443- **Flash Gordon in the Ice World of Mongo**, 1942, Whitman, 432 pgs., flip pictures, by Alex Raymond	30	75	210	360
1447- **Flash Gordon and the Fiery Desert of Mongo**, 1948, Whitman, 288 pgs., Raymond-a	22	55	154	260
1469- **Flash Gordon and the Power Men of Mongo**, 1943, Whitman, 352 pgs., by Alex Raymond	31	78	217	375
1479- **Flash Gordon and the Red Sword Invaders**, 1945, Whitman, 352 pgs., by Alex Raymond	29	73	203	350
1484- **Flash Gordon and the Tyrant of Mongo**, 1941, Whitman, 432 pgs., flip pictures, by Alex Raymond	31	78	217	375
1492- **Flash Gordon in the Forest Kingdom of Mongo**, 1938, Whitman, 432 pgs., by Alex Raymond	41	103	287	490
12- **Flash Gordon and the Ape Men of Mor**, 1942, Dell, 196 pgs., Fast-Action Story, by Alex Raymond	37	93	260	450
6833- **Flash Gordon Vs. the Emperor of Mongo**, 1936, Dell, 244 pgs., Cartoon Story Books, hard-c, Raymond-c/a	44	110	308	550
nn- **Flash Gordon Vs. the Emperor of Mongo**, 1936, Dell, 244 pgs., Fast-Action Story, soft-c, Alex Raymond-c/a	37	93	260	450
1467- **Flint Roper and the Six-Gun Showdown**, 1941, Whitman, 300 pgs.	10	25	60	95
2014-(#14)- **Flintstones-The Case of the Many Missing Things**, 1968, Whitman, 260 pgs., 39 cents, hard-c, color illos	3	8	20	28

	GD	FN	VF	VF/NM
nn- **Flintstones: A Friend From the Past**, 1977, Modern Promotions, 244 pgs., 49 cents, soft-c, flip pictures	1	3	8	12
nn- **Flintstones: It's About Time**, 1977, Modern Promotions, 244 pgs., 49 cents, soft-c, flip pictures	1	3	8	12
nn- **Flintstones: Pebbles & Bamm-Bamm Meet Santa Claus**, 1977, Modern Promotions, 244 pgs., 49 cents, soft-c, flip pictures	1	3	8	12
nn- **Flintstones: The Great Balloon Race**, 1977, Modern Promotions, 244 pgs., 49 cents, soft-c, flip pictures	1	3	8	12
nn- **Flintstones: The Mystery of the Many Missing Things**, 1977, Modern Promotions, 244 pgs., 49 cents, soft-c, flip pictures	1	3	8	12
2003-(#3)- **Flipper-Killer Whale Trouble**, 1967, Whitman, 260 pgs., hard-c, 39 cents, color illos	2	3	15	20
2032-(#32)- **Flipper, Deep-Sea Photographer,** 1969, Whitman, 256 pgs., hard-c, color illos.	2	3	15	20
1108- **Flying the Sky Clipper with Winsie Atkins**, 1936, Whitman, 432 pgs.	10	25	60	95
1460- **Foreign Spies Doctor Doom and the Ghost Submarine**, 1939, Whitman, 432 pgs., Al McWilliams-a	12	30	74	120
1100B- **Fortune Teller**, 1938, Whitman, 36 pgs., 2 1/2" x 3 1/2", Penny Book	2	3	16	22
1175- **Frank Buck Presents Ted Towers Animal Master**, 1935, Whitman, 432 pgs.	11	28	68	110
2015-(#15)-**Frankenstein, Jr. - The Menace of the Heartless Monster**, 1968, Whitman, 260 pgs., 39 cents, hard-c, color illos.	3	8	20	28
16- **Frankie Thomas in A Dog of Flanders**, 1935, EVW, movie scenes	11	28	68	110
1121- **Frank Merriwell at Yale**, 1935, 432 pgs.	10	25	60	95
Freckles and His Friends in the North Woods (See Top-Line Comics)				
nn- **Freckles and His Friends Stage a Play**, 1938, Whitman, 36 pgs., 2 1/2" x 3 1/2", Penny Book	10	25	60	95
1164- **Freckles and the Lost Diamond Mine**, 1937, Whitman, 432 pgs., Merrill Blosser-a	11	28	68	110
nn- **Freckles and the Mystery Ship**, 1935, Whitman, 66 pgs., Pan-Am premium	12	30	72	115
1100B- **Fun, Puzzles, Riddles**, 1938, Whitman, 36 pgs., 2 1/2" x 3 1/2", Penny Book	2	3	16	22
1433- **Gang Busters Step In**, 1939, Whitman, 432 pgs., Henry E. Vallely-a	11	28	68	110
1437- **Gang Busters Smash Through**, 1942, Whitman, 432 pgs.	11	28	68	110
1451- **Gang Busters in Action!**, 1938, Whitman, 432 pgs.	11	28	68	110
nn- **Gang Busters and Guns of the Law**, 1940, Dell, 4" x 5", 194 pgs., Fast-Action Story, soft-c	28	70	196	340
nn- **Gang Busters and the Radio Clues**, 1938, Whitman, 36 pgs., 2 1/2" x 3 1/2", Penny Book	8	20	48	75
1409- **Gene Autry and Raiders of the Range**, 1946, Whitman, 352 pgs.	12	30	76	125
1425- **Gene Autry and the Mystery of Paint Rock Canyon**, 1947, Whitman, 288 pgs.	12	30	76	125
1428- **Gene Autry Special Ranger**, 1941, Whitman, 432 pgs., Erwin Hess-a	15	38	105	165
1433- **Gene Autry in Public Cowboy No. 1**, 1938, Whitman, 240 pgs., photo-c, movie scenes (1st Autry BLB)	28	70	196	340
1434- **Gene Autry and the Gun-Smoke Reckoning**, 1943, Whitman, 352 pgs.	14	35	100	160
1439- **Gene Autry and the Land Grab Mystery**, 1948, Whitman, 290 pgs.	12	30	74	120
1456- **Gene Autry in Special Ranger Rule**, 1945, Whitman, 352 pgs., Henry E. Vallely-a	14	35	100	160
1461- **Gene Autry and the Red Bandit's Ghost**, 1949, Whitman, 288 pgs.	12	30	72	115
1483- **Gene Autry in Law of the Range**, 1939, Whitman, 432 pgs.	14	35	100	160
1493- **Gene Autry and the Hawk of the Hills**, 1942, Whitman, 428 pgs., flip pictures, Vallely-a	14	35	100	160
1494- **Gene Autry Cowboy Detective**, 1940, Whitman, 432 pgs., Erwin Hess-a	14	35	100	160
700-10- **Gene Autry and the Bandits of Silver Tip**, 1949, Whitman	12	30	72	115
714-10- **Gene Autry and the Range War**, 1950, Whitman	12	30	72	115
nn- **Gene Autry in Gun-Smoke**, 1938, Dell, 196 pgs., Fast-Action story, soft-c	27	68	189	325
2035-(#35)- **Gentle Ben, Mystery of the Everglades,** 1969, Whitman, 256 pgs., hard-c, color illos.	2	3	15	20
1176- **Gentleman Joe Palooka**, 1940, Saalfield, 400 pgs.	10	25	60	95
George O'Brien (See The Cowboy Millionaire)				
1101- **George O'Brien and the Arizona Badman**, 1936?, Whitman	10	25	60	95
1418- **George O'Brien in Gun Law**, 1938, Whitman, 240 pgs., photo-c, movie scenes, RKO Radio Pictures	10	25	60	95
1457- **George O'Brien and the Hooded Riders**, 1940, Whitman, 432 pgs., Erwin Hess-a	8	20	50	80

1129 - Felix the Cat © WHIT

700-10 - Gene Autry and the Bandits of Silver Tip © WHIT

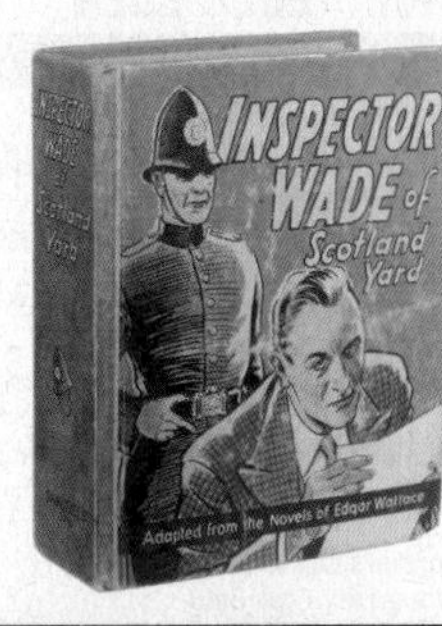

1186 - Inspector Wade of Scotland Yard © WHIT

GD FN VF VF/NM

nn- George O'Brien and the Arizona Bad Man, 1939, Whitman, 36 pgs., 2 1/2" x 3 1/2", Penny Book 8 20 50 80
1462- Ghost Avenger, 1943, Whitman, 432 pgs., flip pictures, Henry Vallely-a 10 25 60 95
nn- Ghost Gun Gang Meet Their Match, The, 1939. Whitman, 2 1/2" x 3 1/2", Penny Book 8 20 50 80
nn- Gingerbread Boy, The, nd(1930s), np(Whitman), 36 pgs., Penny Book 2 5 15 20
1118- G-Man on the Crime Trail, 1936, Whitman, 432 pgs. 12 30 74 120
1147- G-Man Vs. the Red X, 1936, Whitman, 432 pgs. 13 33 90 140
1162- G-Man Allen, 1939, Saalfield, 400 pgs. 12 30 74 120
1173- G-Man in Action, A, 1940, Saalfield, 400 pgs., J.R. White-a 12 30 74 120
1434- G-Man and the Radio Bank Robberies, 1937, Whitman, 432 pgs. 13 33 90 140
1469- G-Man and the Gun Runners, The, 1940, Whitman, 432 pgs. 13 33 90 140
1470- G-Man vs. the Fifth Column, 1941, Whitman, 432 pgs., flip pictures 13 33 90 140
1493- G-Man Breaking the Gambling Ring, 1938, Whitman, 432 pgs., James Gary-a 13 33 90 140
nn- G-Man on Lightning Island, 1936, Dell, 244 pgs., Fast-Action Story, soft-c, Henry E. Vallely-a 24 60 168 285
nn- G-Man, Underworld Chief, 1938, Whitman, Buddy Book premium, 27 68 189 325
6833- G-Man on Lightning Island, 1936, Dell, 244 pgs., Cartoon Story Book, hard-c, Henry E. Vallely-a 18 45 128 200
4- G-Men Foil the Kidnappers, 1936, Whitman, 132 pgs., 3 1/2" x 3 1/2", soft-c, Tarzan Ice Cream cup lid premium 23 58 165 280
1157- G-Men on the Trail, 1938, Saalfield, 400 pgs. 10 25 64 100
1168- G Men on the Job, 1935, Whitman, 432 pgs. 12 30 76 125
nn- G-Men on the Job Again, 1938, Whitman, 36 pgs., 2 1/2" x 3 1/2", Penny Book 10 25 64 100
nn- G-Men and Kidnap Justice, 1938, Whitman, 68 pgs., Pan-Am premium, soft-c 12 30 76 125
nn- G-Men and the Missing Clues, 1938, Whitman, 36 pgs., 2 1/2"x 3 1/2", Penny Book 10 25 64 100
1097- Go Into Your Dance, 1935, Saalfield, 160 pgs.. photo-c, movie scenes with Al Jolson & Ruby Keeler 12 30 80 130
1577- Go Into Your Dance, 1935, Saalfield, 160 pgs., photo-c, movie scenes, soft-c 12 30 80 130
2021- Goofy in Giant Trouble (Walt Disney's ...), 1968, Whitman, hard-c, 260 pgs., 39 cents, color illos. 2 3 15 20
5751- Goofy in Giant Trouble (Walt Disney's ...), 1968, Whitman, soft-c, 260 pgs., 39 cents, color illos. 2 3 15 20
5751-2- Goofy in Giant Trouble, 1968 (1980-reprint of '67 version), Whitman, soft-c, 260 pgs., 79 cents, B&W 1 3 6 10
8- Great Expectations, 1934, EVW, (Five Star Library), 160 pgs., photo-c, movie scenes 13 33 95 150
1453- Green Hornet Strikes!, The, 1940, Whitman, 432 pgs., Robert Weisman-a 35 88 248 425
1480- Green Hornet Cracks Down, The, 1942, Whitman, 432 pgs., flip pictures, Henry Vallely-a 33 83 235 400
1496- Green Hornet Returns, The, 1941, Whitman, 432 pgs., flip pictures 35 88 248 425
5778- Grimm's Ghost Stories, 1976, Whitman, 256 pgs., Laura French-s adapted from fairy tales; blue spine & back-c 2 3 10 14
5778-1- Grimm's Ghost Stories, 1976, Whitman, 256 pgs., reprint of #5778; yellow spine & back-c 2 3 10 14
1172- Gullivers' Travels, 1939, Saalfield, 320 pgs., adapted from Paramount Pict. Cartoons (Rare) Hardcover 25 63 175 300
(Scarce) Softcover 28 70 196 340
nn- Gumps In Radio Land, The (Andy Gump and the Chest of Gold), 1937, Lehn & Fink Prod. Corp., 100 pgs., 3 1/4" x 5 1/2", Pebeco Tooth Paste giveaway, by Gus Edson 20 50 140 220
nn- Gunmen of Rustlers' Gulch, The, 1939, Whitman, 36 pgs., 2 1/2" x 3 1/2", Penny Book 6 15 40 60
1426- Guns in the Roaring West, 1937, Whitman, 300 pgs. 6 15 40 60

GD FN VF VF/NM

1647- Gunsmoke (TV Series), 1958, Whitman, 280 pgs., 4 1/2" x 5 3/4" 4 10 27 40
1101- Hairbreath Harry in Department QT, 1935, Whitman, 384 pgs., by J. M. Alexander 9 23 56 90
1413- Hal Hardy in the Lost Land of Giants, 1938, Whitman, 300 pgs., "The World 1,000,000 Years Ago" 22 55 154 260
1159- Hall of Fame of the Air, 1936, Whitman, 432 pgs., by Capt. Eddie Rickenbacker 9 23 54 85
nn- Hansel and Grethel, The Story of, nd (1930s), no publ., 36 pgs., Penny Book 3 8 21 30
1145- Hap Lee's Selection of Movie Gags, 1935, Whitman, 160 pgs., photos of stars 12 30 80 130
Happy Prince, The (See Wee Little Books)
1111- Hard Rock Harrigan-A Story of Boulder Dam, 1935, Saalfield, hard-c, photo-c, photo illos. 10 25 64 100
1591- Hard Rock Harrigan-A Story of Boulder Dam, 1935, Saalfield, soft-c, photo-c, photo illos. 10 25 64 100
1418- Harold Teen Swinging at the Sugar Bowl, 1939, Whitman, 432 pgs., by Carl Ed 10 25 64 100
nn- Hercules - The Legendary Journeys, 1998, Chronicle Books, 310 pgs., based on TV series, 1-color (brown) illos 1 3 6 10
1100B- Hobbies, 1938, Whitman, 36 pgs., 2 1/2" x 3 1/2", Penny Book 3 8 18 25
1125- Hockey Spare, The, 1937, Saalfield, sports book 6 15 36 55
1605- Hockey Spare, The, 1937, Saalfield, soft-c 6 15 36 55
728- Homeless Homer, 1934, Whitman, by Dee Dobbin, for young kids 3 8 22 32
17- Hoosier Schoolmaster, The, 1935, EVW, movie scenes 12 30 80 130
715- Houdini's Big Little Book of Magic, 1927 (1933), 300 pgs. 16 41 119 185
nn- Houdini's Big Little Book of Magic, 1927 (1933), 196 pgs., American Oil Co. premium, soft-c 16 41 119 185
nn- Houdini's Big Little Book of Magic, 1927 (1933), 204 pgs., Cocomalt premium, soft-c 16 41 119 185
Huckleberry Finn (See The Adventures of...)
nn- Huckleberry Hound Newspaper Reporter, 1977, Modern Promotions, 244 pgs., 49 cents, soft-c, flip pictures 2 3 10 14
1644- Hugh O'Brian TV's Wyatt Earp (TV Series), 1958, Whitman, 280 pgs. 3 8 22 32
5782-2- Incredible Hulk Lost in Time, 1980, 260 pgs., 79¢-c, soft-c, B&W 1 3 8 12
1424- Inspector Charlie Chan Villainy on the High Seas, 1942, Whitman, 432 pgs., flip pictures 14 35 100 160
1186- Inspector Wade of Scotland Yard, 1940, Saalfield, 400 pgs. 10 25 60 95
1194- Inspector Wade and The Feathered Serpent, 1939, Saalfield, 400 pgs. 10 25 60 95
1448- Inspector Wade Solves the Mystery of the Red Aces, 1937, Whitman, 432 pgs. 10 25 60 95
1148- International Spy Doctor Doom Faces Death at Dawn, 1937, Whitman, 432 pgs., Arbo-a 12 30 74 120
1155- In the Name of the Law, 1937, Whitman, 432 pgs., Henry E. Vallely-a 10 25 60 95
2012-(#12)-Invaders, The-Alien Missile Threat (TV Series), 1967, Whitman, 260 pgs., hard-c, 39 cents, color illos. 3 8 20 28
1403- Invisible Scarlet O'Neil, 1942, Whitman, All Pictures Comics, flip pictures 13 33 90 140
1406- Invisible Scarlet O'Neil Versus the King of the Slums, 1946, Whitman, 352 pgs. 11 28 68 110
1098- It Happened One Night, 1935, Saalfield, 160 pgs., Little Big Book, Clark Gable, Claudette Colbert photo-c, movie scenes from Academy Award winner 14 35 100 160
1578- It Happened One Night, 1935, Saalfield, 160 pgs., soft-c 14 35 100 160
Jack and Jill (See Wee Little Books)
1432- Jack Armstrong and the Mystery of the Iron Key, 1939, Whitman, 432 pgs., Henry E. Vallely-a 13 33 90 140
1435- Jack Armstrong and the Ivory Treasure, 1937, Whitman, 432 pgs., Henry Vallely-a 13 33 90 140

Title	GD	FN	VF	VF/NM
Jackie Cooper (See Story Of..)				
1084- **Jackie Cooper in Peck's Bad Boy**, 1934, Saalfield, 160 pgs., hard, photo-c, movie scenes	14	35	100	160
1314- **Jackie Cooper in Peck's Bad Boy**, 1934, Saalfield, 160 pgs., soft, photo-c, movie scenes	14	35	100	160
1402- **Jackie Cooper in "Gangster's Boy,"** 1939, Whitman, 240 pgs., photo-c, movie scenes	14	35	100	160
13- **Jackie Cooper in Dinky**, 1935, EVW, 160 pgs., movie scenes	14	35	100	160
nn- **Jack King of the Secret Service and the Counterfeiters**, 1939, Whitman, 36 pgs., 2 1/2" x 3 1/2", Penny Book, by John G. Gray	10	25	64	100
L11- **Jack London's Call of the Wild**, 1935, Lynn, 20th Cent. Pic., movie scenes with Clark Gable	12	30	74	120
nn- **Jack Pearl as Detective Baron Munchausen**, 1934, Goldsmith, 132 pgs., soft-c	12	30	80	130
1102- **Jack Swift and His Rocket Ship**, 1934, Whitman, 320 pgs.	16	40	112	175
1498- **Jane Arden the Vanished Princess**, Whitman, 300 pgs.	10	25	60	95
1179- **Jane Withers in This is the Life** (20th Century-Fox Presents...), 1935, Whitman, 240 pgs., photo-c, movie scenes	12	30	80	130
1463- **Jane Withers in Keep Smiling**, 1938, Whitman, 240 pgs., photo-c, movie scenes	12	30	80	130
Jaragu of the Jungle (See Rex Beach's ...)				
1447- **Jerry Parker Police Reporter and the Candid Camera Clue**, 1941, Whitman, 300 pgs.	10	25	60	95
Jim Bowie (See Adventures of ...)				
nn- **Jim Brant of the Highway Patrol and the Mysterious Accident**, 1939, Whitman, 36 pgs., 2 1/2" x 3 1/2", Penny Book	9	23	54	85
1466- **Jim Craig State Trooper and the Kidnapped Governor**, 1938, Whitman, 432 pgs.	10	25	60	95
nn- **Jim Doyle Private Detective and the Train Hold-Up**, 1939, Whitman, 36 pgs., 2 1/2" x 3 1/2", Penny Book	10	25	64	100
1180- **Jim Hardy Ace Reporter**, 1940, Saalfield, 400 pgs., Dick Moores-a	10	25	64	100
1143- **Jimmy Allen in the Air Mail Robbery**, 1936, Whitman, 432 pgs.	10	25	64	100
27- **Jimmy Allen in The Sky Parade**, 1936, Lynn, 130 pgs., 5 x 7 1/2", Paramount Pictures, movie scenes	12	30	74	120
L15- **Jimmy and the Tiger**, 1935, Lynn, 192 pgs.	10	25	64	100
1428- **Jim Starr of the Border Patrol**, 1937, Whitman, 432 pgs.	10	25	64	100
Joan of Arc (See Wee Little Books)				
1105- **Joe Louis the Brown Bomber**, 1936, Whitman, 240 pgs., photo-c, photo-illos.	22	55	154	260
Joe Palooka (See Gentleman ...)				
1123- **Joe Palooka the Heavyweight Boxing Champ**, 1934, Whitman, 320 pgs., Ham Fisher-a	17	43	123	190
1168- **Joe Palooka's Great Adventure**, 1939, Saalfield	14	35	100	160
nn- **Joe Penner's Duck Farm**, 1935, Goldsmith, Henry Vallely-a	11	28	68	110
1402- **John Carter of Mars**, 1940, Whitman, 432 pgs., John Coleman Burroughs-a	52	130	364	675
nn- **John Carter of Mars**, 1940, Dell, 194 pgs., Fast-Action Story, soft-c	63	159	444	825
1164- **Johnny Forty Five**, 1938, Saalfield, 400 pgs.	10	25	64	90
John Wayne (See Westward Ho!)				
1100B- **Jokes** (A book of laughs galore), 1938, Whitman, 36 pgs., 2 1/2" x 3 1/2", Penny Book, laughing guy-c	2	3	15	20
1100B- **Jokes** (A book of side-splitting funny stories), 1938, Whitman, 36 pgs., 2 1/2" x 3 1/2", Penny Book, clowns on-c	2	3	15	20
2026-(#26)- **Journey to the Center of the Earth, The Fiery Foe**, 1968, Whitman	3	8	21	30
Jungle Jim (See Top-Line Comics)				
1138- **Jungle Jim**, 1936, Whitman, 432 pgs., Alex Raymond-a	22	55	154	260
1139- **Jungle Jim and the Vampire Woman**, 1937, Whitman, 432 pgs., Alex Raymond-a	22	55	154	260
1442- **Junior G-Men**, 1937, Whitman, 432 pgs., Henry E. Vallely-a	11	28	68	110
nn- **Junior G-Men Solve a Crime**, 1939, Whitman, 36 pgs., 2 1/2" x 3 1/2", Penny Book	11	28	68	110
1422- **Junior Nebb on the Diamond Bar Ranch**, 1938, Whitman, 300 pgs., by Sol Hess	11	28	68	110
1470- **Junior Nebb Joins the Circus**, 1939, Whitman, 300 pgs. by Sol Hess	11	28	68	110
nn- **Junior Nebb Elephant Trainer**, 1939, Whitman, 68 pgs., Pan-Am Oil premium, soft-c	13	33	85	135
1052- **"Just Kids"** (Adventures of ...), 1934, Saalfield, oblong size, by Ad Carter	17	43	123	190
1094- **Just Kids and the Mysterious Stranger**, 1935, Saalfield, 160 pgs., by Ad Carter	13	33	85	135
1184- **Just Kids and Deep-Sea Dan**, 1940, Saalfield, 400 pgs., by Ad Carter	12	30	72	115
1302- **Just Kids, The Adventures of**, 1934, Saalfield, oblong size, soft-c, by Ad Carter	18	45	128	200
1324- **Just Kids and the Mysterious Stranger**, 1935, Saalfield, 160 pgs., soft-c, by Ad Carter ,	13	33	85	135
1401- **Just Kids**, 1937, Whitman, 432 pgs., by Ad Carter	13	33	85	135
1055- **Katzenjammer Kids in the Mountains**, 1934, Saalfield, hard-c, oblong, H. H. Knerr-a	16	40	112	175
1305- **Katzenjammer Kids in the Mountains**, 1934, Saalfield, soft-c, oblong, H. H. Knerr-a	16	40	112	175
14- **Katzenjammer Kids, The**, 1942, Dell, 194 pgs., Fast-Action Story, H. H. Knerr-a	17	43	123	190
1411- **Kay Darcy and the Mystery Hideout**, 1937, Whitman, 300 pgs., Charles Mueller-a	12	30	80	130
1180- **Kayo in the Land of Sunshine** (With Moon Mullins), 1937, Whitman, 432 pgs., by Willard	13	33	90	140
1415- **Kayo and Moon Mullins and the One Man Gang**, 1939, Whitman, 432 pgs., by Frank Willard	11	28	68	110
7- **Kayo and Moon Mullins 'Way Down South**, 1938, Whitman, 132 pgs., 3 1/2" x 3 1/2", Buddy Book	20	50	140	220
1105- **Kazan in Revenge of the North** (James Oliver Curwood's...), 1937, Whitman, 432 pgs., Henry E. Vallely-a	10	25	60	95
1471- **Kazan, King of the Pack** (James Oliver Curwood's...), 1940, Whitman, 432 pgs.	9	23	54	85
1420- **Keep 'Em Flying! U.S.A. for America's Defense**, 1943, Whitman, 432 pgs., Henry E. Vallely-a, flip pictures	10	25	60	95
1133- **Kelly King at Yale Hall**, 1937, Saalfield	9	23	54	85
Ken Maynard (See Strawberry Roan & Western Frontier)				
5- **Ken Maynard in "Wheels of Destiny,"** 1934, EVW, 160 pgs., movie scenes (scarce)	18	45	128	200
776- **Ken Maynard in "Gun Justice,"** 1934, Whitman, 160 pgs., hard-c, movie scenes (Universal Pic.)	13	33	90	140
776- **Ken Maynard in "Gun Justice,"** 1934, Whitman, 160 pgs., soft-c, movie scenes (Universal Pic.)	13	33	90	140
1430- **Ken Maynard in Western Justice**, 1938, Whitman, 432 pgs., Irwin Myers-a	11	28	68	110
1442- **Ken Maynard and the Gun Wolves of the Gila**, 1939, Whitman, 432 pgs.	11	28	68	110
nn- **Ken Maynard in Six-Gun Law**, 1938, Whitman, 36 pgs., 2 1/2" x 3 1/2", Penny Book	9	23	54	85
1134- **King of Crime**, 1938, Saalfield, 400 pgs.	10	25	60	95
King of the Royal Mounted (See Zane Grey)				
nn- **Kit Carson**, 1933, World Syndicate, by J. Carroll Mansfield, High Lights Of History Series, hard-c	10	25	60	95
nn- **Kit Carson**, 1933, World Syndicate, same as hard-c above but with a black cloth-c	10	25	60	95
1105- **Kit Carson and the Mystery Riders**, 1935, Saalfield, hard-c, Johnny Mack Brown photo-c, movie scenes	13	33	85	135
1585- **Kit Carson and the Mystery Riders**, 1935, Saalfield, soft-c, Johnny Mack Brown photo-c, movie scenes	13	33	85	135
Krazy Kat (See Adventures of...)				
2004- (#4)-**Lassie-Adventure in Alaska** (TV Series), 1967, Whitman, hard-c, 260 pgs., 39 cents, color illos	3	8	20	28
5754- **Lassie-Adventure in Alaska** (TV Series), 1973, Whitman, soft-c, 260 pgs., 49 cents, color illos	2	3	12	16
2027- **Lassie and the Shabby Sheik** (TV Series), 1968, Whitman, hard-c, 260 pgs., 39 cents	3	8	19	26
5762- **Lassie and the Shabby Sheik** (TV Series), 1972, Whitman, soft-c, 260 pgs., 39 cents	2	3	12	16
5769- **Lassie, Old One-Eye** (TV Series), 1975, Whitman, soft-c, 260 pgs., 49 cents, three printings	2	3	10	15
1132- **Last Days of Pompeii, The**, 1935, Whitman, 5 1/4" x 6 1/4", 260 pgs., photo-c, movie scenes	13	33	95	150
1128- **Last Man Out** (Baseball), 1937, Saalfield, hard-c	10	25	64	100
L30- **Last of the Mohicans, The**, 1936, Lynn, 192 pgs., movie scenes with Randolph Scott, United Artists Pictures	13	33	90	140
1126- **Laughing Dragon of Oz, The**, 1934, Whitman 432 pgs., by Frank Baum (scarce)	89	224	625	1250
1086- **Laurel and Hardy**, 1934, Saalfield, 160 pgs., hard-c, photo-c, movie scenes	20	50	140	220
1316- **Laurel and Hardy**, 1934, Saalfield, 160 pgs. soft-c, photo-c, movie scenes	20	50	140	220
1092- **Law of the Wild, The**, 1935, Saalfield, 160 pgs., photo-c, movie scenes of Rex, The Wild Horse & Rin-Tin-Tin Jr.	11	28	68	110
1322- **Law of the Wild, The**, 1935, Saalfield, 160 pgs., photo-c, movie scenes, soft-c	11	28	68	110
1100B- **Learn to be a Ventriloquist**, 1938, Whitman, 36 pgs. 2 1/2" x 3 1/2", Penny Book	2	3	15	20
1149- **Lee Brady Range Detective**, 1938, Saalfield, 400 pgs.	10	25	60	95
L10- **Les Miserables** (Victor Hugo's ...), 1935, Lynn, 192 pgs., movie scenes	13	33	95	150
1441- **Lightning Jim U.S. Marshal Brings Law to the West**, 1940, Whitman, 432 pgs., based on radio program	10	25	64	100
nn- **Lightning Jim Whipple U.S. Marshal in Indian Territory**, 1939, Whitman, 36 pgs., 2 1/2" x 3 1/2", Penny Book	8	20	48	75
653- **Lions and Tigers** (With Clyde Beatty), 1934, Whitman, 160 pgs.,				

1447 - Jerry Parker Police Reporter
© WHIT

2004 - Lassie - Adventure in Alaska
© WHIT

716 - Little Orphan Annie and Sandy
© WHIT

GD FN VF VF/NM

photo-c movie scenes 12 30 80 130
1187- **Li'l Abner and the Ratfields**, 1940, Saalfield, 400 pgs., by Al Capp 13 33 95 150
1193- **Li'l Abner and Sadie Hawkins Day**, 1940, Saalfield, 400 pgs., by Al Capp 13 33 95 150
1198- **Li'l Abner in New York**, 1936, Whitman, 432 pgs., by Al Capp 14 35 100 160
1401- **Li'l Abner Among the Millionaires**, 1939, Whitman, 432 pgs., by Al Capp 14 35 100 160
1054- **Little Annie Rooney**, 1934, Saalfield, oblong - 4" x 8", All Pictures Comics, hard-c 14 35 98 155
1304- **Little Annie Rooney**, 1934, Saalfield, oblong - 4" x 8", All Pictures, soft-c 14 35 98 155
1117- **Little Annie Rooney and the Orphan House**, 1936, Whitman, 432 pgs. 11 289 68 110
1406- **Little Annie Rooney on the Highway to Adventure**, 1938, Whitman, 432 pgs. 11 289 68 110
1149- **Little Big Shot** (With Sybil Jason), 1935, Whitman, 240 pgs., photo-c, movie scenes 12 30 80 130
nn- **Little Black Sambo**, nd (1930s), np (Whitman), 36 pgs., 3" x 2 1/2", Penny Book 13 33 92 145
Little Bo-Peep (See Wee Little Books)
Little Colonel, The (See Shirley Temple)
1148- **Little Green Door, The**, 1938, Saalfield, 400 pgs. 9 23 56 90
1112- **Little Hollywood Stars**, 1935, Saalfield, movie scenes (Little Rascals, etc.), hard-c 12 30 80 130
1592- **Little Hollywood Stars**, 1935, Saalfield, movie scenes, soft-c 12 30 80 130
1087- **Little Jimmy's Gold Hunt**, 1935, Saalfield, 160 pgs., hard-c, Little Big Book, by Swinnerton 15 38 108 170
1317- **Little Jimmy's Gold Hunt**, 1935, Saalfield, 160 pgs., 4 1/4" x 5 3/4", soft-c, by Swinnerton 15 38 108 170
Little Joe and the City Gangsters (See Top-Line Comics)
Little Joe Otter's Slide (See Wee Little Books)
1118- **Little Lord Fauntleroy**, 1936, Saalfield, movie scenes, photo-c, 4 1/2" x 5 1/4", starring Mickey Rooney & Freddie Bartholomew, hard-c 10 25 60 95
1598- **Little Lord Fauntleroy**, 1936, Saalfield, photo-c, movie scenes, soft-c 10 25 60 95
1192- **Little Mary Mixup and the Grocery Robberies**, 1940, Saalfield 10 25 60 95
8- **Little Mary Mixup Wins A Prize**, 1936, Whitman, 132 pgs., 3 1/2" x 3 1/2", soft-c, Tarzan Ice Cream cup lid premium 23 58 163 275
1150- **Little Men**, 1934, Whitman, 4 3/4" x 5 1/4", movie scenes (Mascot Prod.), photo-c, hard-c 10 25 64 100
9- **Little Minister, The**,-Katharine Hepburn, 1935, 160 pgs., 4 1/4" x 5 1/2", EVW (Five Star Library), movie scenes (RKO) 14 35 98 155
1120- **Little Miss Muffet**, 1936, Whitman, 432 pgs., by Fanny Y. Cory 11 28 68 110
708- **Little Orphan Annie**, 1933, Whitman, 320 pgs., by Harold Gray, the 2nd Big Little Book 40 100 280 480
nn- **Little Orphan Annie**, 1928('33), Whitman, 52 pgs., 4" x 5 1/2", premium-no ads, soft-c, by Harold Gray 27 68 189 325
716- **Little Orphan Annie and Sandy**, 1933, Whitman, 320 pgs., by Harold Gray 23 58 163 275
716- **Little Orphan Annie and Sandy**, 1933, Whitman, 300 pgs., by Harold Gray 18 45 128 200
nn- **Little Orphan Annie and Sandy**, 1933, Whitman, 52 pgs., premium, no ads, 4" x 5 1/2", soft-c by Harold Gray 27 68 189 325
748- **Little Orphan Annie and Chizzler**, 1933, Whitman, 320 pgs., by Harold Gray 14 35 98 155
1010- **Little Orphan Annie and the Big Town Gunmen**, 1937, 7 1/4" x 5 1/2", 64 pgs., Nickel Book 12 30 80 130
nn- **Little Orphan Annie with the Circus**, 1934, Whitman, 320 pgs., same cover as L.O.A. 708 but with blue background, Ovaltine giveaway stamp inside front-c, by Harold Gray 31 78 217 375
1103- **Little Orphan Annie with the Circus**, 1934, Whitman, 320 pgs. 14 35 98 155
1140- **Little Orphan Annie and the Big Train Robbery**, 1934, Whitman, 300 pgs., by Gray 14 35 98 155
1140- **Little Orphan Annie and the Big Train Robbery**, 1934, Whitman, 300 pgs., premium-no ads, soft-c, by Harold Gray 21 53 149 250
1154- **Little Orphan Annie and the Ghost Gang**, 1935, Whitman, 432 pgs. by Harold Gray 14 35 98 155
nn- **Little Orphan Annie and the Ghost Gang**, 1935, Whitman, 436 pgs., premium-no ads, 3-color, soft-c, by Harold Gray 21 53 149 250
1162- **Little Orphan Annie and Punjab the Wizard**, 1935, Whitman, 432 pgs., by Harold Gray 14 35 98 155
1186- **Little Orphan Annie and the $1,000,000 Formula**, 1936, Whitman, 432 pgs., by Gray 13 33 90 140
1414- **Little Orphan Annie and the Ancient Treasure of Am**, 1939, Whitman, 432 pgs., by Gray 12 30 80 130
1416- **Little Orphan Annie in the Movies**, 1937, Whitman, 432 pgs., by Harold Gray 12 30 80 130
1417- **Little Orphan Annie and the Secret of the Well**, 1947, Whitman, 352 pgs., by Gray 11 28 68 110
1435- **Little Orphan Annie and the Gooneyville Mystery**, 1947, Whitman, 288 pgs., by Gray 12 30 72 115
1446- **Little Orphan Annie in the Thieves' Den**, 1949, Whitman, 288 pgs., by Harold Gray 12 30 72 115
1449- **Little Orphan Annie and the Mysterious Shoemaker**, 1938, Whitman, 432 pgs., by Harold Gray 12 30 80 130
1457- **Little Orphan Annie and Her Junior Commandos**, 1943, Whitman, 352 pgs., by H. Gray 10 25 60 95
1461- **Little Orphan Annie and the Underground Hide-Out**, 1945, Whitman, 352 pgs., by Gray 10 25 60 95
1468- **Little Orphan Annie and the Ancient Treasure of Am**, 1949 (Misdated 1939), 288 pgs., by Gray 10 25 60 95
1482- **Little Orphan Annie and the Haunted Mansion**, 1941, Whitman, 432 pgs., flip pictures, by Harold Gray 12 30 80 130
3048- **Little Orphan Annie and Her Big Little Kit**, 1937, Whitman, 384 pgs., 4 1/2" x 6 1/2" box, includes miniature box of 4 crayons-red, yellow, blue and green 62 155 434 800
4054- **Little Orphan Annie, The Story of**, 1934, Whitman, 7" x 9 1/2", 320 pgs., Big Big Book, Harold Gray-c/a 27 68 189 325
nn- **Little Orphan Annie Gets into Trouble**, 1938, Whitman, 36 pgs., 2 1/2" x 3 1/2", Penny Book 9 23 56 90
nn- **Little Orphan Annie in Hollywood**, 1937, Whitman, 3 1/2" x 3 1/4", Pan-Am premium, soft-c 21 53 149 250
nn- **Little Orphan Annie in Rags to Riches**, 1939, Dell, 194 pgs., Fast-Action Story, soft-c 21 53 149 250
nn- **Little Orphan Annie Saves Sandy**, 1938, Whitman, 36 pgs., 2 1/2" x 3 1/2", Penny Book 10 25 60 95
nn- **Little Orphan Annie Under the Big Top**, 1938, Dell, 194 pgs., Fast-Action Story, soft-c 21 53 149 250
nn- **Little Orphan Annie Wee Little Books** (In open box)
nn, 1934, Whitman, 44 pgs., by H. Gray
L.O.A. And Daddy Warbucks 9 23 54 85
L.O.A. And Her Dog Sandy 9 23 54 85
L.O.A. And The Lucky Knife 9 23 54 85
L.O.A. And The Pinch-Pennys 9 23 54 85
L.O.A. At Happy Home 9 23 54 85
L.O.A. Finds Mickey 9 23 54 85
Complete set with box 54 135 378 700
nn- **Little Polly Flinders, The Story of**, nd (1930s), no publ., 36 pgs., 2 1/2" x 3", Penny Book 2 3 15 20
nn- **Little Red Hen, The**, nd(1930s), np(Whitman), 36 pgs., Penny Book 2 3 15 20
nn- **Little Red Riding Hood**, nd(1930s), np(Whitman), 36 pgs., 3" x 2 1/2", Penny Book 2 3 15 20
nn- **Little Red Riding Hood and the Big Bad Wolf** (Disney), 1934, McKay, 36 pgs., stiff-c, Disney Studio-a
Sized (7 3/4" x 10") 23 58 160 270
Different version (6 1/4" x 8 1/2") blue spine 15 38 108 170
757- **Little Women**, 1934, Whitman, 4 3/4" x 5 1/4", 160 pgs., photo-c, movie scenes, starring Katharine Hepburn 14 35 100 160
Littlest Rebel, The (See Shirley Temple)
1181- **Lone Ranger and his Horse Silver**, 1935, Whitman, 432 pgs., Hal Arbo-a 18 45 128 200

	GD	FN	VF	VF/NM
1196- **Lone Ranger and the Vanishing Herd**, 1936, Whitman, 432 pgs.	14	35	100	160
1407- **Lone Ranger and Dead Men's Mine, The**, 1939, Whitman, 432 pgs.	13	33	90	140
1421- **Lone Ranger on the Barbary Coast, The**, 1944, Whitman, 352 pgs., Henry Vallely-a	12	30	74	120
1428- **Lone Ranger and the Secret Weapon, The**, 1943, Whitman,	12	30	74	120
1431- **Lone Ranger and the Secret Killer, The**, 1937, Whitman 432 pgs., H. Anderson-a	15	38	108	170
1450- **Lone Ranger and the Black Shirt Highwayman, The**, 1939, Whitman, 432 pgs.	13	33	90	140
1465- **Lone Ranger and the Menace of Murder Valley, The**, 1938, Whitman, 432 pgs., Robert Wiseman-a	12	30	80	130
1468- **Lone Ranger Follows Through, The**, 1941, Whitman, 432 pgs., H.E. Vallely-a	12	30	80	130
1477- **Lone Ranger and the Great Western Span, The**, 1942, Whitman, 424 pgs., H. E. Vallely-a	12	30	74	120
1489- **Lone Ranger and the Red Renegades, The**, 1939, Whitman, 432 pgs.	14	35	100	160
1498- **Lone Ranger and the Silver Bullets**, 1946, Whitman, 352 pgs., Henry E. Vallely-a	12	30	74	120
712-10- **Lone Ranger and the Secret of Somber Cavern, The**, 1950, Whitman	9	23	56	90
2013- **(#13)-Lone Ranger Outwits Crazy Cougar, The**, 1968, Whitman, 260 pgs., 39 cents, hard-c, color illos	3	8	20	28
5774- **Lone Ranger Outwits Crazy Cougar, The**, 1976, Whitman, 260 pgs., 49 cents, soft-c, color illos	2	3	16	22
5774-1- **Lone Ranger Outwits Crazy Cougar, The**, 1979, Whitman, 260 pgs., 69 cents, soft-c, color illos	2	3	16	22
nn- **Lone Ranger and the Lost Valley, The**, 1938, Dell, 196 pgs., Fast-Action Story, soft-c	23	58	165	280
1405- **Lone Star Martin of the Texas Rangers**, 1939, Whitman, 432 pgs.	12	30	80	130
19- **Lost City, The**, 1935, EVW, movie scenes	13	33	85	135
1103- **Lost Jungle, The** (With Clyde Beatty), 1936, Saalfield, movie scenes, hard-c	12	30	80	130
1583- **Lost Jungle, The** (With Clyde Beatty), 1936, Saalfield, movie scenes, soft -c	11	28	68	110
753- **Lost Patrol, The**, 1934, Whitman, 160 pgs., photo-c, movie scenes with Boris Karloff	12	34	74	120
nn- **Lost World, The - Jurassic Park 2**, 1997, Chronicle Books, 312 pgs., adapts movie, 1-color (green) illos	2	3	15	20
1189- **Mac of the Marines in Africa**, 1936, Whitman, 432 pgs.	10	25	64	100
1400- **Mac of the Marines in China**, 1938, Whitman, 432 pgs.	10	25	64	100
1100B- **Magic Tricks** (With explanations), 1938, Whitman, 36 pgs., 2 1/2" x 3 1/2", Penny Book, rabbit in hat-c	2	3	15	20
1100B- **Magic Tricks** (How to do them), 1938, Whitman, 36 pgs., 2 1/2" x 3 1/2", Penny Book, genie-c	2	3	15	20
Major Hoople (See Our Boarding House)				
2022-(#22)- **Major Matt Mason, Moon Mission,** 1968, Whitman, 256 pgs., hard-c, color illos.	3	8	20	28
1167- **Mandrake the Magician**, 1935, Whitman, 432 pgs., by Lee Falk & Phil Davis	16	40	116	180
1418- **Mandrake the Magician and the Flame Pearls**, 1946, Whitman, 352 pgs., by Lee Falk & Phil Davis	13	33	90	140
1431- **Mandrake the Magician and the Midnight Monster**, 1939, Whitman, 432 pgs., by Lee Falk & Phil Davis	14	35	100	160
1454- **Mandrake the Magician Mighty Solver of Mysteries**, 1941, Whitman, 432 pgs., by Lee Falk & Phil Davis, flip pictures	14	35	100	160
2011-(#11)-**Man From U.N.C.L.E., The**-The Calcutta Affair (TV Series), 1967, Whitman, 260 pgs., 39¢, hard-c, color illos	3	8	20	28
1429- **Marge's Little Lulu Alvin and Tubby**, 1947, Whitman, All Pictures Comics, Stanley-a	25	63	175	300
1438- **Mary Lee and the Mystery of the Indian Beads**, 1937, Whitman, 300 pgs.	10	25	60	95
1165- **Masked Man of the Mesa, The**, 1939, Saalfield, 400 pgs.	9	23	56	90
nn- **Mask of Zorro, The**, 1998, Chronicle Books, 312 pgs., adapts movie, 1-color (yellow-green) illos	1	3	6	10
1436- **Maximo the Amazing Superman**, 1940, Whitman, 432 pgs., Henry E. Vallely-a	13	33	92	145
1444- **Maximo the Amazing Superman and the Crystals of Doom**, 1941, Whitman,432 pgs., Henry E. Vallely-a	13	33	92	145
1445- **Maximo the Amazing Superman and the Supermachine**, 1941, Whitman, 432 pgs.	13	33	92	145
755- **Men of the Mounted**, 1934, Whitman, 320 pgs.	13	33	85	135
nn- **Men of the Mounted**, 1933, Whitman, 52 pgs., 3 1/2" x 5 3/4", premium-no ads; other versions with Poll Parrot & Perkins ad; soft-c	14	35	100	160
nn- **Men of the Mounted**, 1934, Whitman, Cocomalt premium, soft-c, by Ted McCall	10	25	60	95
1475- **Men With Wings,** 1938, Whitman, 240 pgs., photo-c, movie scenes (Paramount Pics.)	13	33	85	135

	GD	FN	VF	VF/NM
1170- **Mickey Finn**, 1940, Saalfield, 400 pgs., by Frank Leonard	13	33	95	150
717- **Mickey Mouse** (Disney), (1st printing) 1933, Whitman, 320 pgs., Gottfredson-a, skinny Mickey on cover	245	613	2083	3800
717- **Mickey Mouse** (Disney), (2nd printing)1933, Whitman, 320 pgs., Gottfredson-a, regular Mickey on cover	153	383	1224	2300
nn- **Mickey Mouse** (Disney), 1933, Dean & Son, Great Big Midget Book, 320 pgs.	123	308	925	1800
731- **Mickey Mouse the Mail Pilot** (Disney), 1933, Whitman, (This is the same book as the 1st Mickey Mouse BLB #717(2nd printing) but with "The Mail Pilot" printed on the front. Lower left of back cover has a small box printed over the existing "No. 717." "No. 731" is printed next to it.) (Sold at auction in 2014 in VG+ condition for $7170, and in FR/GD condition for $2,500)				
726- **Mickey Mouse in Blaggard Castle** (Disney), 1934, Whitman, 320 pgs., Gottfredson-a	31	78	217	375
731- **Mickey Mouse the Mail Pilot** (Disney), 1933, Whitman, 300 pgs., Gottfredson-a	33	83	235	400
731- **Mickey Mouse the Mail Pilot** (Disney), 1933, Whitman, 300 pgs., soft cover; Gottfredson-a (Rare)	72	180	504	950
nn- **Mickey Mouse the Mail Pilot** (Disney), 1933, Whitman, 292 pgs., American Oil Co. premium, soft-c, Gottfredson-a; another version 3 1/2" x 4 3/4"	33	83	235	400
nn- **Mickey Mouse the Mail Pilot** (Disney), 1933, Dean & Son, Great Big Midget Book (Rare)	125	313	1000	1850
750- **Mickey Mouse Sails for Treasure Island** (Disney), 1933, Whitman, 320 pgs., Gottfredson-a	33	83	235	400
nn- **Mickey Mouse Sails for Treasure Island** (Disney), 1935, Whitman, 196 pgs., premium-no ads, soft-c, Gottfredson-a (Scarce)	37	93	260	450
nn- **Mickey Mouse Sails for Treasure Island** (Disney), 1935, Whitman, 196 pgs., Kolynos Dental Cream premium (Scarce)	37	93	260	450
nn- **Mickey Mouse Sails for Treasure Island** (Disney), 1933, Dean & Son, Great Big Midget Book, 320 pgs.	118	295	826	1650
756- **Mickey Mouse Presents a Walt Disney Silly Symphony** (Disney), 1934, Whitman, 240 pgs., Bucky Bug app.	29	73	203	350
801- **Mickey Mouse's Summer Vacation**, 1948, Whitman, hard-c, Story Hour series	13	33	85	135
1058- **Mickey Mouse Box, The** (Disney), 1939, Whitman, 10" x 11 1/2" x 1", (set includes 6 books from the 1058 series, all 5" x 5 1/2", 68 pgs. Lid features Mickey & Minnie, Donald Duck, Goofy and Clarabelle Cow. The six books are: The Brave Little Tailor, Mother Pluto, The Ugly Ducklings, The Practical Pig, Timid Elmer, and The Farmyard Symphony (a VF set sold for $5175 in Nov, 2014)				
1111- **Mickey Mouse Presents Walt Disney's Silly Symphonies Stories,** 1936, Whitman, 432 pgs., Donald Duck app.	29	73	203	350
1128- **Mickey Mouse and Pluto the Racer** (Disney), 1936, Whitman, 432 pgs., Gottfredson-a	27	68	189	325
1139- **Mickey Mouse the Detective** (Disney), 1934, Whitman, 300 pgs., Gottfredson-a	30	76	212	365
1139- **Mickey Mouse the Detective** (Disney), 1934, Whitman, 304 pgs., premium-no ads, soft-c, Gottfredson-a (Scarce)	48	120	335	625
1153- **Mickey Mouse and the Bat Bandit** (Disney), 1935, Whitman, 432 pgs., Gottfredson-a	27	68	189	325
nn- **Mickey Mouse and the Bat Bandit** (Disney), 1935, Whitman, 436 pgs., premium-no ads, 3-color, soft-c, Gottfredson-a (Scarce)	48	120	335	625
1160- **Mickey Mouse and Bobo the Elephant** (Disney), 1935, Whitman, 432 pgs., Gottfredson-a	27	68	189	325
1187- **Mickey Mouse and the Sacred Jewel** (Disney), 1936, Whitman, 432 pgs., Gottfredson-a	27	68	189	325
1401- **Mickey Mouse in the Treasure Hunt** (Disney), 1941, Whitman, 430 pgs., flip pictures of Pluto, Gottfredson-a	23	58	165	280
1409- **Mickey Mouse Runs His Own Newspaper** (Disney), 1937, Whitman, 432 pgs., Gottfredson-a	24	61	170	290
1413- **Mickey Mouse and the 'Lectro Box** (Disney), 1946, Whitman, 352 pgs., Gottfredson-a	16	40	112	175
1417- **Mickey Mouse on Sky Island** (Disney), 1941, Whitman, 432 pgs., flip pictures, Gottfredson-a; considered by Gottfredson to be his best Mickey story	22	55	154	260
1428- **Mickey Mouse in the Foreign Legion** (Disney), 1940, Whitman, 432 pgs., Gottfredson-a	22	55	154	260
1429- **Mickey Mouse and the Magic Lamp** (Disney), 1942, Whitman, 432 pgs., flip pictures	22	55	154	260
1433- **Mickey Mouse and the Lazy Daisy Mystery** (Disney), 1947, Whitman, 288 pgs.	16	40	112	175
1444- **Mickey Mouse in the World of Tomorrow** (Disney), 1948, Whitman, 288 pgs., Gottfredson-a	24	60	168	285
1451- **Mickey Mouse and the Desert Palace** (Disney), 1948, Whitman, 288 pgs.	16	40	112	175
1463- **Mickey Mouse and the Pirate Submarine** (Disney), 1939, Whitman, 432 pgs., Gottfredson-a	23	58	163	275
1464- **Mickey Mouse and the Stolen Jewels** (Disney), 1949, Whitman, 288 pgs.	20	50	143	225
1471- **Mickey Mouse and the Dude Ranch Bandit** (Disney),				

The Mask of Zorro © ZPI

1409 - Mickey Mouse Runs His Own Newspaper © DIS

1116 - My Life and Times © Saalfield

	GD	FN	VF	VF/NM
1943, Whitman, 432 pgs., flip pictures	21	53	150	255
1475- **Mickey Mouse and the 7 Ghosts** (Disney), 1940, Whitman, 432 pgs., Gottfredson-a	23	58	163	275
1476- **Mickey Mouse in the Race for Riches** (Disney), 1938, Whitman, 432 pgs., Gottfredson-a	23	58	163	275
1483- **Mickey Mouse Bell Boy Detective** (Disney), 1945, Whitman, 352 pgs.	20	50	143	225
1499- **Mickey Mouse on the Cave-Man Island** (Disney), 1944, Whitman, 352 pgs.	20	50	143	225
2004- **Mickey Mouse With This Big Big Color Set, Here Comes** (Disney), 1936, Whitman, (Very Rare), 224 pgs., 12" x 8 1/4" box, with red, yellow and blue crayons, contains 224 loose pages to color, reprinted from early Mickey Mouse related movie and strip reprints. Attached to center of lid is a 5" tall separate die-cut cardboard Mickey Mouse figure (a VF/NM set sold for $1701 in July 2014)	239	598	2030	3700
2020-(#20)- **Mickey Mouse, Adventure in Outer Space,** 1968, Whitman, 256 pgs.,hard-c, color illos.	3	8	20	28
3059- **Mickey Mouse Big Little Set** (Disney), 1936, Whitman, 8 1/4" x 8 1/2", with crayons, box contains a 4" x 5 1/4" soft-c book with 160 pgs. of Mickey to color, reprinted from early Mickey Mouse BLBs, (Rare) (a copy in NM sold for $1897 in Nov, 2011, a VF copy sold for $1147 in 2013)				
5750- **Mickey Mouse, Adventure in Outer Space,** 1973, Whitman, 256 pgs.,soft-c, 39 cents, color illos.	2	3	11	15
3049- **Mickey Mouse and His Big Little Kit** (Disney), 1937, Whitman, 384 pgs., 4 1/2" x 6 1/2" box, includes miniature box of 4 crayons-red, yellow, blue and green (a copy in VF/NM sold for $335 in 2015)				
3061- **Mickey Mouse to Draw and Color** (The Big Little Set), nd (early 1930s), Whitman, with crayons; box contains 320 loose pages to color, reprinted from early Mickey Mouse BLBs	121	303	900	1750
4062- **Mickey Mouse, The Story Of,** 1935, Whitman, 7" x 9 1/2", 320 pgs., Big Big Book, Gottfredson-a	86	215	600	1200
4062- **Mickey Mouse and the Smugglers, The Story Of,** 1935, Whitman, (Scarce), 7" x 9 1/2", 320 pgs., Big Big Book, same contents as above version; Gottfredson-a	86	215	600	1200
708-10- **Mickey Mouse on the Haunted Island** (Disney), 1950, Whitman, Gottfredson-a	12	30	80	130
nn- **Mickey Mouse and Minnie at Macy's**, 1934 Whitman, 148 pgs., 3 1/4" x 3 1/2", soft-c, R. H. Macy & Co. Christmas giveaway (Rare, less than 20 known copies)	310	777	2800	5000
nn- **Mickey Mouse and Minnie March to Macy's**, 1935, Whitman, 148 pgs., 3 1/2" x 3 1/2", soft-c, R. H. Macy & Co. Christmas giveaway (scarce)	271	678	2300	4200
nn- **Mickey Mouse and the Magic Carpet**, 1935, Whitman, 148 pgs., 3 1/2"x 4", soft-c, giveaway, Gottfredson-a, Donald Duck app.	123	308	925	1800
nn- **Mickey Mouse Silly Symphonies**, 1934, Dean & Son, Ltd (England), 48 pgs., with 4 pop-ups, Babes In The Woods, King Neptune				
With dust jacket	133	333	1064	2000
Without dust jacket	93	233	650	1300
nn- **Mickey Mouse the Sheriff of Nugget Gulch** (Disney) 1938, Dell, 196 pgs., Fast-Action Story, soft-c, Gottfredson-a	35	88	248	425
nn- **Mickey Mouse Waddle Book**, 1934, BRP, 20 pgs., 7 1/2" x 10", forerunner of the Blue Ribbon Pop-Up books; with 4 removable articulated cardboard characters Book Only	75	188	525	1050
(A complete copy in VG/FN w/VF dustjacket sold for $5676 in 2010) (A complete copy in VF with dustjacket ramp & band sold for $573 in 2014)				
nn- **Mickey Mouse with Goofy and Mickey's Nephews**, 1938, Dell, Fast-Action Story, Gottfredson-a	37	93	260	450
16- **Mickey Mouse and Pluto** (Disney), 1942, Dell, 196 pgs., Fast-Action story	35	88	248	425
512- **Mickey Mouse Wee Little Books** (In open box), nn, 1934, Whitman, 44 pgs., small size, soft-c				
Mickey Mouse and Tanglefoot	13	33	90	140
Mickey Mouse at the Carnival	13	33	90	140
Mickey Mouse Will Not Quit!	13	33	90	140
Mickey Mouse Wins the Race!	13	33	90	140
Mickey Mouse's Misfortune	13	33	90	140
Mickey Mouse's Uphill Fight	13	33	90	140
Complete set with box	86	215	600	1200
1493- **Mickey Rooney and Judy Garland and How They Got into the Movies**, 1941, Whitman, 432 pgs., photo-c	13	33	85	135
1427- **Mickey Rooney Himself**, 1939, Whitman, 240 pgs., photo-c, movie scenes, life story	12	30	74	120
532- **Mickey's Dog Pluto** (Disney), 1943, Whitman, All Picture Comics, A Tall Comic Book , 3 3/4" x 8 3/4"	20	50	140	220
284- **Midget Jumbo Coloring Book**, 1935, Saalfield	42	105	294	500
2113- **Midget Jumbo Coloring Book**, 1935, Saalfield, 240 pgs.	42	105	294	500
21- **Midsummer Night's Dream**, 1935, EVW, movie scenes	13	33	92	145
nn- **Minute-Man** (Mystery of the Spy Ring), 1941, Fawcett, Dime Action Book	35	88	248	425
710- **Moby Dick the Great White Whale, The Story of,** 1934, Whitman, 160 pgs., photo-c, movie scenes from "The Sea Beast"	12	30	80	130
746- **Moon Mullins and Kayo** (Kayo and Moon Mullins-inside), 1933, Whitman, 320 pgs., Frank Willard-c/a	12	30	74	120
nn- **Moon Mullins and Kayo**, 1933, Whitman, Cocomalt premium, soft-c, by Willard	12	30	74	120
1134- **Moon Mullins and the Plushbottom Twins**, 1935, Whitman, 432 pgs., Willard-c/a	12	30	74	120
nn- **Moon Mullins and the Plushbottom Twins**, 1935, Whitman, 436 pgs., premium-no ads, 3-color, soft-c, by Willard	17	43	123	190
1058- **Mother Pluto** (Disney), 1939, Whitman, 68 pgs., hard-c	13	33	85	135
1100B- **Movie Jokes** (From the talkies), 1938, Whitman, 36 pgs., 2 1/2" x 3 1/2", Penny Book	2	3	14	16
1408- **Mr. District Attorney on the Job**, 1941, Whitman, 432 pgs., flip pictures	10	25	64	100
nn- **Musicians of Bremen, The**, nd (1930s), np (Whitman), 36 pgs., 3" x 2 1/2", Penny Book	2	3	12	16
1113- **Mutt and Jeff**, 1936, Whitman, 300 pgs., by Bud Fisher	25	63	175	300
1116- **My Life and Times** (By Shirley Temple), 1936, Saalfield, Little Big Book, hard-c, photo-c/illos	13	33	85	135
1596- **My Life and Times** (By Shirley Temple), 1936, Saalfield, Little Big Book, soft-c, photo-c/illos	13	33	85	135
1497- **Myra North Special Nurse and Foreign Spies**, 1938, Whitman, 432 pgs.	12	30	76	125
1400- **Nancy and Sluggo**, 1946, Whitman, All Pictures Comics, Ernie Bushmiller-a	12	30	74	120
1487- **Nancy Has Fun**, 1946, Whitman, All Pictures Comics	12	30	74	120
1150- **Napoleon and Uncle Elby**, 1938, Saalfield, 400 pgs., by Clifford McBride	11	28	68	110
1166- **Napoleon Uncle Elby And Little Mary**, 1939, Saalfield, 400 pgs., by Clifford McBride	11	28	68	110
1179- **Ned Brant Adventure Bound**, 1940, Saalfield, 400 pgs.	10	25	60	95
1146- **Nevada Rides The Danger Trail**, 1938, Saalfield, 400 pgs., J.R. White-a	10	25	60	95
1147- **Nevada Whalen, Avenger**, 1938, Saalfield, 400 pgs.	10	25	60	95
Nicodemus O'Malley (See Top-Line Comics)				
1115- **Og Son of Fire**, 1936, Whitman, 432 pgs.	13	33	85	135
1419- **Oh, Blondie the Bumsteads** (See Blondie)				
11- **Oliver Twist**, 1935, EVW (Five Star Library), movie scenes, starring Dickie Moore (Monogram Pictures)	12	30	80	130
718- **Once Upon a Time**, 1933, Whitman, 364 pgs., soft-c	12	30	80	130
712- **100 Fairy Tales for Children, The**, 1933, Whitman, 288 pgs., Circle Library	10	25	60	95
1099- **One Night of Love**, 1935, Saalfield, 160 pgs., hard-c, photo-c, movie scenes, Columbia Pictures, starring Grace Moore	13	33	95	150
1579- **One Night of Love**, 1935, Sat, 160 pgs., soft-c, photo-c, movie scenes, Columbia Pictures, starring Grace Moore	13	33	95	150
1155- **$1000 Reward**, 1938, Saalfield, 400 pgs.	10	25	60	95
Orphan Annie (See Little Orphan ...)				
L17- **O'Shaughnessy's Boy**, 1935, Lynn, 192 pgs., movie scenes,				

	GD	FN	VF	VF/NM
w/Wallace Beery & Jackie Cooper (Metro-Goldwyn-Mayer)	12	30	72	115
1109- **Oswald the Lucky Rabbit**, 1934, Whitman, 288 pgs.	16	40	112	175
1403- **Oswald Rabbit Plays G-Man**, 1937, Whitman, 240 pgs., movie scenes by Walter Lantz	18	45	128	200
1190- **Our Boarding House, Major Hoople and his Horse**, 1940, Saalfield, 400 pgs.	11	28	68	110
1085- **Our Gang**, 1934, Saalfield, 160 pgs., photo-c, movie scenes, hard-c	14	35	100	160
1315- **Our Gang**, 1934, Saalfield, 160 pgs., photo-c, movie scenes, soft-c	14	35	100	160
1451- **"Our Gang" on the March**, 1942, Whitman, 432 pgs., flip pictures, Vallely-a	14	35	100	160
1456- **Our Gang Adventures**, 1948, Whitman, 288 pgs.	12	30	80	130
nn- **Paramount Newsreel Men with Admiral Byrd in Little America**, 1934, Whitman, 96 pgs., 6 1/4" x 6 1/4", photo-c, photo ill.	14	35	98	155
nn- **Patch**, nd (1930s), np (Whitman), 36 pgs., 3" x 2 1/2", Penny Book	2	3	14	18
1445- **Pat Nelson Ace of Test Pilots**, 1937, Whitman, 432 pgs.	10	25	60	95
1411- **Peggy Brown and the Mystery Basket**, 1941, Whitman, 432 pgs., flip pictures, Henry E. Vallely-a	10	25	64	100
1423- **Peggy Brown and the Secret Treasure**, 1947, Whitman, 288 pgs., Henry E. Vallely-a	10	25	64	100
1427- **Peggy Brown and the Runaway Auto Trailer**, 1937, Whitman, 300 pgs., Henry E. Vallely-a	10	25	64	100
1463- **Peggy Brown and the Jewel of Fire**, 1943, Whitman, 352 pgs., Henry E. Vallely-a	10	25	64	100
1491- **Peggy Brown in the Big Haunted House**, 1940, Whitman, 432 pgs., Vallely-a	10	25	64	100
1143- **Peril Afloat**, 1938, Saalfield, 400 pgs.	10	25	64	100
1199- **Perry Winkle and the Rinkeydinks**, 1937, Whitman, 432 pgs., by Martin Branner	13	33	95	150
1487- **Perry Winkle and the Rinkeydinks get a Horse**, 1938, Whitman, 432 pgs., by Martin Branner	13	33	95	150
Peter Pan (See Wee Little Books)				
nn- **Peter Rabbit**, nd(1930s), np(Whitman), 36 pgs., Penny Book, 3" x 2 1/2"	5	12	30	45
Peter Rabbit's Carrots (See Wee Little Books)				
1100- **Phantom, The**, 1936, Whitman, 432 pgs., by Lee Falk & Ray Moore	31	78	217	375
1416- **Phantom and the Girl of Mystery, The**, 1947, Whitman, 352 pgs. by Falk & Moore	13	33	90	140
1421- **Phantom and Desert Justice, The**, 1941, Whitman, 432 pgs., flip pictures, by Falk & Moore	15	38	108	170
1468- **Phantom and the Sky Pirates, The**, 1945, Whitman, 352 pgs., by Falk & Moore	13	33	95	150
1474- **Phantom and the Sign of the Skull, The**, 1939, Whitman, 432 pgs., by Falk & Moore	16	41	119	185
1489- **Phantom, Return of the...**, 1942, Whitman, 432 pgs., flip pictures, by Falk & Moore	15	38	108	170
1130- **Phil Burton, Sleuth** (Scout Book), 1937, Saalfield, hard-c	5	12	30	45
Pied Piper of Hamlin (See Wee Little Books)				
1466- **Pilot Pete Dive Bomber**, 1941, Whitman, 432 pgs., flip pictures	10	25	60	95
5776- **Pink Panther Adventures in Z-Land, The**, 1976, Whitman, 260 pgs., soft-c, 49 cents, B&W	1	3	6	10
5776-2- **Pink Panther Adventures in Z-Land, The**, 1980, Whitman, 260 pgs., soft-c, 79 cents, B&W	1	3	6	10
5783-2- **Pink Panther at Castle Kreep, The**, 1980, Whitman, 260 pgs., soft-c, 79 cents, B&W	1	3	6	10
Pinocchio and Jiminy Cricket (See Walt Disney's ...)				
nn- **Pioneers of the Wild West** (Blue-c), 1933, World Syndicate, High Lights of History Series	5	12	34	50
With dustjacket	18	45	128	200
nn- **Pioneers of the Wild West** (Red-c), 1933, World Syndicate, High Lights of History Series	5	12	34	50
1123- **Plainsman, The**, 1936, Whitman, 240 pgs., photo-c, movie scenes with Gary Cooper (Paramount Pics.)	13	33	95	150
Pluto (See Mickey's Dog ... & Walt Disney's ...)				
2114- **Pocket Coloring Book**, 1935, Saalfield	25	63	175	300
1060- **Polly and Her Pals on the Farm**, 1934, Saalfield, 164 pgs., hard-c, by Cliff Sterrett	12	30	76	125
1310- **Polly and Her Pals on the Farm**, 1934, Saalfield, soft-c	12	30	76	125
1051- **Popeye, Adventures of...**, 1934, Saalfield, oblong-size, E.C. Segar-a, hard-c	42	105	295	525
1088- **Popeye in Puddleburg**, 1934, Saalfield, 160 pgs., hard-c, E. C. Segar-a	18	45	128	200
1113- **Popeye Starring in Choose Your Weppins**, 1936, Saalfield, 160 pgs., hard-c, Segar-a	35	88	248	425
1117- **Popeye's Ark**, 1936, Saalfield, 4 1/2" x 5 1/2", hard-c, Segar-a	18	45	128	200
1163- **Popeye Sees the Sea**, 1936, Whitman, 432 pgs., Segar-a	20	50	140	220
1301- **Popeye, Adventures of...**, 1934, Saalfield, oblong-size, Segar-a	42	105	295	525
1318- **Popeye in Puddleburg**, 1934, Saalfield, 160 pgs., soft-c, Segar-a	19	48	133	210
1405- **Popeye and the Jeep**, 1937, Whitman, 432 pgs., Segar-a	20	50	140	220
1406- **Popeye the Super-Fighter**, 1939, Whitman, All Pictures Comics, flip pictures, Segar-a	18	45	128	200
1422- **Popeye the Sailor Man**, 1947, Whitman, All Pictures Comics	12	30	80	130
1450- **Popeye in Quest of His Poopdeck Pappy**, 1937, Whitman, 432 pgs., Segar-c/a	14	35	100	160
1458- **Popeye and Queen Olive Oyl**, 1949, Whitman, 288 pgs., Sagendorf-a	13	33	85	135
1459- **Popeye and the Quest for the Rainbird**, 1943, Whitman, Winner & Zaboly-a	13	33	95	150
1480- **Popeye the Spinach Eater**, 1945, Whitman, All Pictures Comics	12	30	80	130
1485- **Popeye in a Sock for Susan's Sake**, 1940, Whitman, 432 pgs., flip pictures	13	33	95	150
1497- **Popeye and Caster Oyl the Detective**, 1941, Whitman, 432 pgs. flip pictures, Segar-a	16	40	112	175
1499- **Popeye and the Deep Sea Mystery**, 1939, Whitman, 432 pgs., Segar-c/a	16	40	116	180
1593- **Popeye Starring in Choose Your Weppins**, 1936, Saalfield, 160 pgs., soft-c, Segar-a	16	40	116	180
1597- **Popeye's Ark**, 1936, Saalfield, 4 1/2" x 5 1/2", soft-c, Segar-a	16	40	116	180
2008-(#8)- **Popeye-Ghost Ship to Treasure Island**, 1967, Whitman, 260 pgs., 39 cents, hard-c, color illos	3	8	20	28
5755- **Popeye-Ghost Ship to Treasure Island**, 1973, Whitman, 260 pgs., soft-c, color illos	2	3	11	15
2034-(#34)- **Popeye, Danger Ahoy!**, 1969, Whitman, 256 pgs., hard-c, color illos.	3	8	18	25
5768- **Popeye, Danger Ahoy!**, 1975, Whitman, 256 pgs., soft-c, color illos.	2	3	11	15
4063- **Popeye, Thimble Theatre Starring**, 1935, Whitman, 7" x 9 1/2", 320 pgs., Big Big Book, Segar-c/a; (Cactus cover w/yellow logo)	79	198	550	1100
4063- **Popeye, Thimble Theatre Starring**, 1935, Whitman, 7" x 9 1/2", 320 pgs., Big Big Book, Segar-c/a; (Big Balloon-c with red logo), (2nd printing w/same contents as above)	93	233	650	1300
5761- **Popeye and Queen Olive Oyl**, 1973, 260 pgs., B&W, soft-c	3	8	20	28
5761-2- **Popeye and Queen Olive Oyl**, 1973 (1980-reprint of 1973 version), 260 pgs., 79 cents, B&W, soft-c	2	3	11	15
103- **"Pop-Up" Buck Rogers in the Dangerous Mission** (with Pop-Up picture), 1934, BRP, 62 pgs., The Midget Pop-Up Book w/Pop-Up in center of book, Calkins-a	118	295	826	1650
206- **"Pop-Up" Buck Rogers - Strange Adventures in the Spider Ship, The**, 1935, BRP, 24 pgs., 8" x 9", 3 Pop-Ups, hard-c, by Dick Calkins	118	295	826	1650
nn- **"Pop-Up" Cinderella**, 1933, BRP, 7 1/2" x 9 3/4", 4 Pop-Ups, hard-c				
With dustjacket	63	159	438	825
Without dustjacket	56	140	392	725
207- **"Pop-Up" Dick Tracy-Capture of Boris Arson**, 1935, BRP, 24 pgs., 8" x 9", 3 Pop-Ups, hard-c, by Gould	63	159	438	825
210- **"Pop-Up" Flash Gordon Tournament of Death, The**, 1935, BRP, 24 pgs., 8" x 9", 3 Pop-Ups, hard-c, by Alex Raymond	119	298	850	1700
202- **"Pop-Up" Goldilocks and the Three Bears, The**, 1934, BRP, 24 pgs., 8" x 9", 3 Pop-Ups, hard-c	35	88	248	425
nn- **"Pop-Up" Jack and the Beanstalk**, 1933, BRP, hard-c (50 cents), 1 Pop-Up	35	88	248	425
nn- **"Pop-Up" Jack the Giant Killer**, 1933, BRP, hard-c (50 cents), 1 Pop-Up	35	88	248	425
nn- **"Pop-Up" Jack the Giant Killer**, 1933, BRP, 4 Pop-Ups, hard-c				
With dustjacket	62	155	434	800
Without dust jacket	54	135	378	700
105- **"Pop-Up" Little Black Sambo**, (with Pop-Up picture), 1934, BRP, 62 pgs., The Midget Pop-Up Book, one Pop-Up in center of book	50	125	350	650
208- **"Pop-Up" Little Orphan Annie and Jumbo the Circus Elephant**, 1935, BRP, 24 pgs., 8" x 9 1/2", 3 Pop-Ups, hard-c, by H. Gray	62	155	434	800
nn- **"Pop-Up" Little Red Ridinghood**, 1933, BRP, hard-c (50 cents), 1 Pop-Up	42	105	294	500
nn- **"Pop-Up" Mickey Mouse, The**, 1933, BRP, 34 pgs., 6 1/2" x 9", 3 Pop-Ups, hard-c, Gottfredson-a (75 cents)	52	130	364	675
nn- **"Pop-Up" Mickey Mouse in King Arthur's Court, The**, 1933, BRP, 56 pgs., 7 1/2" x 9 1/4", 4 Pop-Ups, hard-c, Gottfredson-a				
With dust jacket	128	320	973	1850
Without dustjacket	96	241	672	1350
101- **"Pop-Up" Mickey Mouse in "Ye Olden Days"** (with Pop-Up picture),				

1130 - Phil Burton, Sleuth © Saalfield

1408 - Porky Pig and Petunia © WB

1427 - Red Ryder and the Code of the West © WHIT

	GD	FN	VF	VF/NM
1934, 62 pgs., BRP, The Midget Pop-Up Book, one Pop-Up in center of book, Gottfredson-a	110	275	770	1550
nn- **"Pop-Up" Minnie Mouse, The**, 1933, BRP, 36 pgs., 6 1/2" x 9", 3 Pop-Ups, hard-c (75 cents), Gottfredson-a	52	130	364	675
203- **"Pop-Up" Mother Goose, The**, 1934, BRP, 24 pgs., 8" x 9 1/4", 3 Pop-Ups, hard-c	42	105	290	500
nn- **"Pop-Up" Mother Goose Rhymes, The**, 1933, BRP, 96 pgs., 7 1/2" x 9 1/4", 4 Pop-Ups, hard-c				
With dustjacket ($2)	46	115	322	600
Without dustjacket	42	105	290	500
209- **"Pop-Up" New Adventures of Tarzan**, 1935, BRP, 24 pgs., 8" x 9", 3 Pop-Ups, hard-c	107	268	749	1500
104- **"Pop-Up" Peter Rabbit, The** (with Pop-Up picture), 1934, BRP, 62 pgs., The Midget Pop-Up Book, one Pop-Up in center of book	50	125	350	650
nn- **"Pop-Up" Pinocchio**, 1933, BRP, 7 1/2" x 9 3/4", 4 Pop-Ups, hard-c				
With dustjacket	65	163	455	850
Without dust jacket	56	140	392	725
102- **"Pop-Up" Popeye among the White Savages** (with Pop-Up picture), 1934, BRP, 62 pgs., The Midget Pop-Up Book, one Pop-Up in center of book, E. C. Segar-a	62	155	434	800
205- **"Pop-Up" Popeye with the Hag of the Seven Seas, The**, 1935, BRP, 24 pgs., 8" x 9", 3 Pop-Ups, hard-c, Segar-a	68	170	476	875
201- **"Pop-Up" Puss In Boots, The**, 1934, BRP, 24 pgs., 3 Pop-Ups, hard-c	33	83	235	400
nn- **"Pop-Up" Silly Symphonies, The** (Mickey Mouse Presents His ...), 1933, BRP, 56 pgs., 9 3/4" x 7 1/2", 4 Pop-Ups, hard-c				
With dust jacket	100	250	700	1400
Without dust jacket	72	180	504	950
nn- **"Pop-Up" Sleeping Beauty**, 1933, BRP, hard-c, (50 cents), 1 Pop-up	42	105	295	525
212- **"Pop-Up" Terry and the Pirates in Shipwrecked, The**, 1935, BRP, 24 pgs., 8" x 9", 3 Pop-Ups, hard-c	72	180	504	950
211- **"Pop-Up" Tim Tyler in the Jungle, The**, 1935, BRP, 24 pgs., 8" x 9", 3 Pop-Ups, hard-c	42	105	294	500
1404- **Porky Pig and His Gang**, 1946, Whitman, All Pictures Comics, Barks-a, reprints Four Color #48	18	45	128	200
1408- **Porky Pig and Petunia**, 1942, Whitman, All Pictures Comics, flip pictures, reprints Four Color #16 & Famous Gang Book of Comics	12	30	80	130
1176- **Powder Smoke Range**, 1935, Whitman, 240 pgs., photo-c, movie scenes, Hoot Gibson, Harey Carey app. (RKO Radio Pict.)	11	28	68	110
1058- **Practical Pig!, The** (Disney), 1939, Whitman, 68 pgs., 5" x 5 1/2", hard-c	11	28	68	110
758- **Prairie Bill and the Covered Wagon**, 1934, Whitman, 384 pgs., Hal Arbo-a	10	25	60	95
nn- **Prairie Bill and the Covered Wagon**, 1934, Whitman, 390 pgs., premium-no ads, 3-color, soft-c, Hal Arbo-a	12	30	80	130
1440- **Punch Davis of the U.S. Aircraft Carrier**, 1945, Whitman, 352 pgs.	8	20	50	80
nn- **Puss in Boots**, nd(1930s), np(Whitman), 36 pgs., Penny Book	2	3	15	20
1100B- **Puzzle Book**, 1938, Whitman, 36 pgs., 2 1/2" x 3 1/2", Penny Book	2	3	16	22
1100B- **Puzzles**, 1938, Whitman, 36 pgs., 2 1/2" x 3 1/2", Penny Book	2	3	16	22
1100B- **Quiz Book, The**, 1938, Whitman, 36 pgs., 2 1/2" x 3 1/2", Penny Book	2	3	16	22
1142- **Radio Patrol**, 1935, Whitman, 432 pgs., by Eddie Sullivan & Charlie Schmidt (#1)	12	30	72	115
1173- **Radio Patrol Trailing the Safeblowers**, 1937, Whitman, 432 pgs.	9	23	56	90
1496- **Radio Patrol Outwitting the Gang Chief**, 1939, Whitman, 432 pgs.	9	23	56	90
1498- **Radio Patrol and Big Dan's Mobsters**, 1937, Whitman, 432 pgs.	9	23	56	90
nn- **Raiders of the Lost Ark**, 1998, Chronicle Books, 304 pgs., adapts movie, 1-color (green) illos	2	3	16	22
1441- **Range Busters, The**, 1942, Whitman, 432 pgs., Henry E. Vallely-a	10	25	60	95
1163- **Ranger and the Cowboy, The**, 1939, Saalfield, 400 pgs.	9	23	56	90
1154- **Rangers on the Rio Grande**, 1938, Saalfield, 400 pgs.	9	23	56	90
1447- **Ray Land of the Tank Corps, U.S.A.**, 1942, Whitman, 432 pgs., flip pictures, Hess-a	10	25	60	95
1157- **Red Barry Ace-Detective**, 1935, Whitman, 432 pgs., by Will Gould	12	30	80	130
1426- **Red Barry Undercover Man**, 1939, Whitman, 432 pgs., by Will Gould	12	30	72	115
20- **Red Davis**, 1935, EVW, 160 pgs.	11	28	68	110
1449- **Red Death on the Range, The**, 1940, Whitman, 432 pgs., Fred Harman-a (Bronc Peeler)	12	30	72	115
nn- **Red Falcon Adventures, The**, 1937, Seal Right Ice Cream, 8 pgs., set of 50 books, circular in shape				
Issue #1	39	98	276	475
Issue #2-5	27	68	189	325
Issue #6-10	23	58	163	275
Issue #11-50	16	40	112	175
nn- **Red Hen and the Fox, The**, nd(1930s), np(Whitman), 36 pgs., 3" x 2 1/2", Penny Book	2	3	15	20
1145- **Red-Hot Holsters**, 1938, Saalfield, 400 pgs.	9	23	56	90
1400- **Red Ryder and Little Beaver on Hoofs of Thunder**, 1939, Whitman, 432 pgs., Harman-c/a	13	33	85	135
1414- **Red Ryder and the Squaw-Tooth Rustlers**, 1946, Whitman, 352 pgs., Fred Harman-a	12	30	72	115
1427- **Red Ryder and the Code of the West**, 1941, Whitman, 432 pgs., flip pictures, by Harman	12	30	76	125
1440- **Red Ryder the Fighting Westerner**, 1940, Whitman, Harman-a	12	30	76	125
1443- **Red Ryder and the Rimrock Killer**, 1948, Whitman, 288 pgs., Harman-a	11	28	68	110
1450- **Red Ryder and Western Border Guns**, 1942, Whitman, 432 pgs., flip pictures, by Harman	12	30	76	125
1454- **Red Ryder and the Secret Canyon**, 1948, Whitman, 288 pgs., Harman-a	11	28	68	110
1466- **Red Ryder and Circus Luck**, 1947, Whitman, 288 pgs., by Fred Harman	11	28	68	110
1473- **Red Ryder in War on the Range**, 1945, Whitman, 352 pgs., by Fred Harman	12	30	72	115
1475- **Red Ryder and the Outlaw of Painted Valley**, 1943, Whitman, 352 pgs., by Harman	11	28	68	110
702-10- **Red Ryder Acting Sheriff**, 1949, Whitman, by Fred Hannan	10	25	64	100
nn- **Red Ryder Brings Law to Devil's Hole**, 1939, Dell, 196 pgs., Fast-Action Story, Harman-c/a	21	53	149	250
nn- **Red Ryder and the Highway Robbers**, 1938, Whitman, 36 pgs., 2 1/2" x 3 1/2", Penny Book	10	25	64	100
754- **Reg'lar Fellers**, 1933, Whitman, 320 pgs., by Gene Byrnes	11	28	68	110
nn- **Reg'lar Fellers**, 1933, Whitman, 202 pgs., Cocomalt premium, by Gene Byrnes	11	28	68	110
1424- **Rex Beach's Jaragu of the Jungle**, 1937, Whitman, 432 pgs.	8	20	50	80
12- **Rex, King of Wild Horses in "Stampede,"** 1935, EVW, 160 pgs., movie scenes, Columbia Pictures	9	23	56	90
1100B- **Riddles for Fun**, 1938, Whitman, 36 pgs., 2 1/2" x 3 1/2", Penny Book	3	8	18	25
1100B- **Riddles to Guess**, 1938, Whitman, 36 pgs., 2 1/2" x 3 1/2", Penny Book	3	8	18	25
1425- **Riders of Lone Trails**, 1937, Whitman, 300 pgs.	10	25	60	95
1141- **Rio Raiders** (A Billy The Kid Story), 1938, Saalfield, 400 pgs.	10	25	60	95
2023-(#23)- **The Road Runner, The Super Beep Catcher,** 1968, Whitman, 256 pgs., hard-c, color illos.	1	3	8	12
5759- **The Road Runner, The Super Beep Catcher,** 1973, Whitman, 256 pgs., soft-c, 39 cents, B&W illos., and flip pictures	1	3	8	12
5767-2- **Road Runner, The Lost Road Runner Mine, The,**				

	GD	FN	VF	VF/NM
1974 (1980), 260 pgs., 79 cents, B&W, soft-c	1	3	8	12
5784- **The Road Runner and the Unidentified Coyote,** 1974, Whitman, 260 pgs., soft-c, flip pictures	1	3	8	12
5784-2- **The Road Runner and the Unidentified Coyote,** 1980, Whitman, 260 pgs., soft-c, flip pictures	1	3	8	12
nn- **Road To Perdition**, 2002, Dreamworks, screenplay from movie, hard-c (Dreamworks and 20th Century Fox)	1	3	6	9
Robin Hood (See Wee Little Books)				
10- **Robin Hood**, 1935, EVW, 160 pgs., movie scenes w/Douglas Fairbanks (United Artists), hard-c	13	33	85	135
719- **Robinson Crusoe** (The Story of...), nd (1933), Whitman, 364 pgs., soft-c	11	28	68	110
1421- **Roy Rogers and the Dwarf-Cattle Ranch**, 1947, Whitman, 352 pgs., Henry E. Vallely-a	11	28	68	110
1437- **Roy Rogers and the Deadly Treasure**, 1947, Whitman, 288 pgs.	11	28	68	110
1448- **Roy Rogers and the Mystery of the Howling Mesa**, 1948, Whitman, 288 pgs.	11	28	68	110
1452- **Roy Rogers in Robbers' Roost**, 1948, Whitman, 288 pgs.	11	28	68	110
1460- **Roy Rogers Robinhood of the Range**, 1942, Whitman, 432 pgs., Hess-a (1st)	13	33	85	135
1462- **Roy Rogers and the Mystery of the Lazy M**, 1949, Whitman	10	25	60	95
1476- **Roy Rogers King of the Cowboys**, 1943, Whitman, 352 pgs., Irwin Myers-a, based on movie	15	38	105	165
1494- **Roy Rogers at Crossed Feathers Ranch**, 1945, Whitman, 320 pgs., Erwin Hess-a , 3 1/4" x 5 1/2"	11	28	68	110
701-10- **Roy Rogers and the Snowbound Outlaws**, 1949, 3 1/4" x 5 1/2"	9	23	56	90
715-10- **Roy Rogers Range Detective**, 1950, Whitman, 2 1/2" x 5"	9	23	56	90
nn- **Sandy Gregg Federal Agent on Special Assignment**, 1939, Whitman, 36 pgs., 2 1/2" x 3 1/2", Penny Book	9	23	54	85
Sappo (See Top-Line Comics)				
1122- **Scrappy**, 1934, Whitman, 288 pgs.	12	30	72	115
L12- **Scrappy** (The Adventures of...), 1935, Lynn, 192 pgs., movie scenes	12	30	72	115
1191- **Secret Agent K-7**,1940, Saalfield, 400 pgs., based on radio show	10	25	60	95
1144- **Secret Agent X-9**, 1936, Whitman, 432 pgs., Charles Flanders-a	15	38	108	170
1472- **Secret Agent X-9 and the Mad Assassin**, 1938, Whitman, 432 pgs., Charles Flanders-a	15	38	108	170
1161- **Sequoia**, 1935, Whitman, 160 pgs., photo-c, movie scenes	12	30	72	115
1430- **Shadow and the Living Death, The**, 1940, Whitman, 432 pgs., Erwin Hess-a	42	105	294	500
1443- **Shadow and the Master of Evil, The**, 1941, Whitman, 432 pgs., flip pictures, Hess-a	42	105	294	500
1495- **Shadow and the Ghost Makers, The**, 1942, Whitman, 432 pgs., John Coleman Burroughs-c	42	105	294	500
2024- **Shazzan, The Glass Princess**, 1968, Whitman, Hanna-Barbera	2	3	15	20
Shirley Temple (See My Life and Times & Story of..)				
1095- **Shirley Temple and Lionel Barrymore Starring In "The Little Colonel,"** 1935, Saalfield, photo hard-c, movie scenes	19	48	133	210
1115- **Shirley Temple in "The Littlest Rebel,"** 1935, Saalfield, photo-c, movie scenes, hard-c	19	48	133	210
1575- **Shirley Temple and Lionel Barrymore Starring In "The Little Colonel,"** 1935, Saalfield, photo soft-c, movie scenes	19	48	133	210
1595- **Shirley Temple in "The Littlest Rebel,"** 1935, Saalfield, photo-c, movie scenes, soft-c	19	48	133	210
1195- **Shooting Sheriffs of the Wild West**, 1936, Whitman, 432 pgs.	6	15	40	60
1169- **Silly Symphony Featuring Donald Duck** (Disney), 1937, Whitman, 432 pgs., Taliaferro-a	27	68	189	325
1441- **Silly Symphony Featuring Donald Duck and His (MIS) Adventures** (Disney), 1937, Whitman, 432 pgs., Taliaferro-a	27	68	189	325
1155- **Silver Streak, The**, 1935, Whitman, 160 pgs., photo-c, movie scenes (RKO Radio Pict.)	12	30	74	120
Simple Simon (See Wee Little Books)				
1649- **Sir Lancelot** (TV Series), 1958, Whitman, 280 pgs.	4	10	24	35
1112- **Skeezix in Africa**, 1934, Whitman, 300 pgs., Frank King-a	9	23	56	90
1408- **Skeezix at the Military Academy**, 1938, Whitman, 432 pgs., Frank King-a	9	23	54	85
1414- **Skeezix Goes to War**, 1944, Whitman, 352 pgs., Frank King-a	9	23	54	85
1419- **Skeezix on His Own in the Big City**, 1941, Whitman, All Pictures Comics, flip pictures, Frank King-a	8	20	48	75
761- **Skippy**, 1934, Whitman, 320 pgs., by Percy Crosby	8	20	48	75
4056- **Skippy, The Story of**, 1934, Whitman, 320 pgs., 7" x 9 1/2", Big Big Book, Percy Crosby-a	20	50	140	220

	GD	FN	VF	VF/NM
nn- **Skippy, The Story of**, 1934, Whitman, Phillips Dental Magnesia premium, soft-c, by Percy Crosby	8	20	48	75
1127- **Skyroads** (Hurricane Hawk's name not on cover), 1936, Whitman, 432 pgs., by Lt. Dick Calkins, Russell Keaton-a	10	25	64	100
1439- **Skyroads with Clipper Williams of the Flying Legion**, 1938, Whitman, 432 pgs., by Lt. Dick Calkins, Keaton-a	10	25	64	100
1127- **Skyroads with Hurricane Hawk**, 1936, Whitman, 432 pgs., by Lt. Dick Calkins, Russell Keaton-a	9	23	56	90
Smilin' Jack and his Flivver Plane (See Top-Line Comics)				
1152- **Smilin' Jack and the Stratosphere Ascent**, 1937, Whitman, 432 pgs., Zack Mosley-a	13	33	85	135
1412- **Smilin' Jack Flying High with "Downwind,"** 1942, Whitman, 432 pgs., Zack Mosley-a	12	30	80	130
1416- **Smilin' Jack in Wings over the Pacific**, 1939, Whitman, 432 pgs., Zack Mosley-a	12	30	80	130
1419- **Smilin' Jack and the Jungle Pipe Line**, 1947, Whitman, 352 pgs., Zack Mosley-a	12	30	74	120
1445- **Smilin' Jack and the Escape from Death Rock**, 1943, Whitman, 352 pgs., Mosley-a	12	30	74	120
1464- **Smilin' Jack and the Coral Princess**, 1945, Whitman, 352 pgs., Zack Mosley-a	12	30	74	120
1473- **Smilin' Jack Speed Pilot**, 1941, Whitman, 432 pgs., Zack Mosley-a	12	30	80	130
2- **Smilin' Jack and his Stratosphere Plane**, 1938, Whitman, 132 pgs., Buddy Book, soft-c, Zack Mosley-a	27	68	189	325
nn- **Smilin' Jack Grounded on a Tropical Shore**, 1938, Whitman, 36 pgs., 2 1/2" x 3 1/2", Penny Book	10	25	60	95
11- **Smilin' Jack and the Border Bandits**, 1941, Dell, 196 pgs., Fast-Action Story, soft-c, Zack Mosley-a	24	60	168	285
745- **Smitty Golden Gloves Tournament**, 1934, Whitman, 320 pgs., Walter Berndt-a	12	30	74	120
nn- **Smitty Golden Gloves Tournament**, 1934, Whitman, 204 pgs., Cocomalt premium, soft-c, Walter Berndt-a	13	33	85	135
1404- **Smitty and Herby Lost Among the Indians**, 1941, Whitman, All Pictures Comics	10	25	60	95
1477- **Smitty in Going Native**, 1938, Whitman, 300 pgs., Walter Berndt-a	11	28	68	110
2- **Smitty and Herby**, 1936, Whitman, 132 pgs., 3 1/2" x 3 1/2", soft-c, Tarzan Ice Cream cup lid premium	24	60	168	285
9- **Smitty's Brother Herby and the Police Horse**, 1938, Whitman, 132 pgs., 3 1/4" x 3 1/2", Buddy Book-ice cream premium, by Walter Berndt	24	60	168	285
1010- **Smokey Stover Firefighter of Foo**, 1937, Whitman, 7 1/4" x 5 1/2", 64 pgs., Nickel Book, Bill Holman-a	13	33	85	135
1413- **Smokey Stover**, 1942, Whitman, All Pictures Comics, flip pictures, Bill Holman-a	13	33	85	135
1421- **Smokey Stover the Foo Fighter**, 1938, Whitman, 432 pgs., Bill Holman-a	13	33	85	135
1481- **Smokey Stover the Foolish Foo Fighter**, 1942, Whitman, All Pictures Comics	13	33	85	135
1- **Smokey Stover the Fireman of Foo**, 1938, Whitman, 3 3/4" x 3 1/2", 132 pgs., Buddy Book-ice cream premium, by Bill Holman	21	53	149	250
1100A- **Smokey Stover**, 1938, Whitman, 36 pgs., 2 1/2" x 3 1/2", Penny Book	10	25	64	100
nn- **Smokey Stover and the Fire Chief of Foo**, 1938, Whitman, 36 pgs., 2 1/2" x 3 1/2", Penny Book, yellow shirt on-c	10	25	64	100
nn- **Smokey Stover and the Fire Chief of Foo**, 1938, Whitman, 36 pgs., Penny Book, green shirt on-c	10	25	64	100
1460- **Snow White and the Seven Dwarfs** (The Story of Walt Disney's ...), 1938, Whitman, 288 pgs.	19	48	136	215
1136- **Sombrero Pete**, 1936, Whitman, 432 pgs.	10	25	60	95
1152- **Son of Mystery**, 1939, Saalfield, 400 pgs.	10	25	60	95
1191- **SOS Coast Guard**, 1936, Whitman, 432 pgs., Henry E. Vallely-a	10	25	64	100
2016-(#16)-**Space Ghost-The Sorceress of Cyba-3** (TV Cartoon), 1968, Whitman, 260 pgs., 39¢-c, hard-c, color illos	10	25	60	95
1455- **Speed Douglas and the Mole Gang-The Great Sabotage Plot**, 1941, Whitman, 432 pgs., flip pictures	10	25	60	95
5779- **Spider-Man Zaps Mr. Zodiac**, 1976, 260 pgs., soft-c, B&W	2	3	11	15
5779-2- **Spider-Man Zaps Mr. Zodiac**, 1980, 260 pgs., 79¢-c, soft-c, B&W	1	3	6	8
1467- **Spike Kelly of the Commandos**, 1943, Whitman, 352 pgs.	10	25	60	95
1144- **Spook Riders on the Overland**, 1938, Saalfield, 400 pgs.	10	25	60	95
768- **Spy, The**, 1936, Whitman, 300 pgs.	10	30	80	130
nn- **Spy Smasher and the Red Death**, 1941, Fawcett, 4" x 5 1/2", Dime Action Book	44	110	308	550
1120- **Stan Kent Freshman Fullback**, 1936, Saalfield, 148 pgs., hard-c	6	15	36	55
1132- **Stan Kent, Captain**, 1937, Saalfield	6	15	36	55
1600- **Stan Kent Freshman Fullback**, 1936, Saalfield, 148 pgs., soft-c	6	15	36	55

1460 - Roy Rogers Robinhood of the Range © WHIT

1132 - Stan Kent, Captain © Saalfield

1183 - Tailspin Tommy Air Racer © Saalfield

	GD	FN	VF	VF/NM
1123- Stan Kent Varsity Man, 1936, Saalfield, 160 pgs., hard-c	6	15	36	55
1603- Stan Kent Varsity Man, 1936, Saalfield, 160 pgs., soft-c	6	15	36	55
nn- Star Wars - A New Hope, 1997, Chronicle Books, 320 pgs., adapts movie, 1-color (blue) illos	2	3	15	20
nn- Star Wars - Empire Strikes Back, The, 1997, Chronicle Books, 296 pgs., adapts movie, 1-color (blue) illos	2	3	15	20
nn- Star Wars - Episode 1 - The Phantom Menace, 1999, Chronicle Books, 344 pgs., adapts movie, 1-color (blue) illos	1	3	6	10
nn- Star Wars - Episode 2 - Attack of the Clones, 2002, Chronicle Books, 340 pgs., adapts movie, 1-color (blue) illos	1	3	6	10
nn- Star Wars - Return of the Jedi, 1997, Chronicle Books, 312 pgs., adapts movie, 1-color (blue) illos	2	3	15	20
1104- Steel Arena, The (With Clyde Beatty), 1936, Saalfield, hard-c, movie scenes adapted from "The Lost Jungle"	12	30	72	115
1584- Steel Arena, The (With Clyde Beatty), 1936, Saalfield, soft-c, movie scenes	12	30	72	115
1426- Steve Hunter of the U.S. Coast Guard Under Secret Orders, 1942, Whitman, 432 pgs.	10	25	60	95
1456- Story of Charlie McCarthy and Edgar Bergen, The, 1938, Whitman, 288 pgs.	10	25	60	95
Story of Daniel, The (See Wee Little Books)				
Story of David, The (See Wee Little Books)				
1110- Story of Freddie Bartholomew, The, 1935, Saalfield, 4 1/2" x 5 1/4", hard-c, movie scenes (MGM)	10	25	60	95
1590- Story of Freddie Bartholomew, The, 1935, Saalfield, 4 1/2" x 5 1/4", soft-c, movie scenes (MGM)	10	25	60	95
Story of Gideon, The (See Wee Little Books)				
W714- Story of Jackie Cooper, The, 1933, Whitman, 240 pgs., photo-c, movie scenes, "Skippy" & "Sooky" movie	12	30	74	120
Story of Joseph, The (See Wee Little Books)				
Story of Moses, The (See Wee Little Books)				
Story of Ruth and Naomi (See Wee Little Books)				
1089- Story of Shirley Temple, The, 1934, Saalfield, 160 pgs., hard-c, photo-c, movie scenes	12	30	72	115
1319- Story of Shirley Temple, The, 1934, Saalfield, 160 pgs., soft-c, photo-c, movie scenes	12	30	72	115
1090- Strawberry-Roan, 1934, Saalfield, 160 pgs., hard-c, Ken Maynard photo-c, movie scenes	12	30	72	115
1320- Strawberry-Roan, 1934, Saalfield, 160 pgs., soft-c, Ken Maynard photo-c, movie scenes	12	30	72	115
Streaky and the Football Signals (See Top-Line Comics)				
5780-2- Superman in the Phantom Zone Connection, 1980, 260 pgs., 79¢-c, soft-c, B&W	1	3	8	12
582- "Swap It" Book, The, 1949, Samuel Lowe Co., 260 pgs., 3 1/2" x 4 1/2"				
1. Little Tex in the Midst of Trouble	4	10	24	35
2. Little Tex's Escape	4	10	24	35
3. Little Tex Comes to the XY Ranch	4	10	24	35
4. Get Them Cowboy	4	10	24	35
5. The Mail Must Go Through! A Story of the Pony Express	4	10	24	35
6. Nevada Jones, Trouble Shooter	4	10	24	35
7. Danny Meets the Cowboys	4	10	24	35
8. Flint Adams and the Stage Coach	4	10	24	35
9. Bud Shinners and the Oregon Trail	4	10	24	35
10. The Outlaws' Last Ride	4	10	24	35
Sybil Jason (See Little Big Shot)				
747- Tailspin Tommy in the Famous Pay-Roll Mystery, 1933, Whitman, hard-c, 320 pgs., Hal Forrest-a (# 1)	12	30	74	120
747- Tailspin Tommy in the Famous Pay-Roll Mystery, 1933, Whitman, soft-c, 320 pgs., Hal Forrest-a (# 1)	12	30	74	120
nn- Tailspin Tommy the Pay-Roll Mystery, 1934, Whitman, 52 pgs., 3 1/2" x 5 1/4", premium-no ads, soft-c; another version with Perkins ad, Hal Forrest-a	16	40	112	175
1110- Tailspin Tommy and the Island in the Sky, 1936, Whitman, 432 pgs., Hal Forrest-a	11	28	68	110
1124- Tailspin Tommy the Dirigible Flight to the North Pole, 1934, Whitman, 432 pgs., H. Forrest-a	12	30	74	120

	GD	FN	VF	VF/NM
nn- Tailspin Tommy the Dirigible Flight to the North Pole, 1934, Whitman, 436 pgs., 3-color, soft-c, premium-no ads, Hal Forrest-a	20	50	140	220
1172- Tailspin Tommy Hunting for Pirate Gold, 1935, Whitman, 432 pgs., Hal Forrest-a	11	28	68	110
1183- Tailspin Tommy Air Racer, 1940, Saalfield, 400 pgs., hard-c	11	28	68	110
1184- Tailspin Tommy in the Great Air Mystery, 1936, Whitman, 240 pgs., photo-c, movie scenes	12	30	74	120
1410- Tailspin Tommy the Weasel and His "Skywaymen," 1941, Whitman, All Pictures Comics, flip pictures	10	25	64	100
1413- Tailspin Tommy and the Lost Transport, 1940, Whitman, 432 pgs., Hal Forrest-a	10	25	64	100
1423- Tailspin Tommy and the Hooded Flyer, 1937, Whitman, 432 pgs., Hal Forrest-a	11	28	68	110
1494- Tailspin Tommy and the Sky Bandits, 1938, Whitman 432 pgs., Hal Forrest-a	11	28	68	110
nn- Tailspin Tommy and the Airliner Mystery, 1938, Dell, 196 pgs., Fast-Action Story, soft-c, Hal Forrest-a	26	65	185	315
nn- Tailspin Tommy in Flying Aces, 1938, Dell, 196 pgs., Fast-Action Story, soft-c, Hal Forrest-a	26	65	185	315
nn- Tailspin Tommy in Wings Over the Arctic, 1934, Whitman, Cocomalt premium, Forrest-a	11	28	68	110
nn- Tailspin Tommy Big Thrill Chewing Gum, 1934, Whitman, 8 pgs., 2 1/2" x 3 " (6 diff.) each..	11	28	68	110
3- Tailspin Tommy on the Mountain of Human Sacrifice, 1938, Whitman, soft-c, Buddy Book	31	78	217	375
7- Tailspin Tommy's Perilous Adventure, 1934, Whitman, 132 pgs., 3 1/2" x 3 1/2" soft-c, Tarzan Ice Cream cup premium	21	53	149	250
nn- Tailspin Tommy, 1935, Whitman, 148 pgs., 3 1/2" x 4", Tarzan Ice Cream cup premium	23	58	163	275
L16- Tale of Two Cities, A, 1935, Lynn, movie scenes	12	30	74	120
744- Tarzan of the Apes, 1933, Whitman, 320 pgs., by Edgar Rice Burroughs (1st)	29	73	203	350
nn- Tarzan of the Apes, 1935, Whitman, 52 pgs., 3 1/2" x 5 1/4", soft-c, stapled, premium, no ad; another version with a Perkins ad; reprints panels from Hal Foster's newspaper adaptation	40	100	280	480
769- Tarzan the Fearless, 1934, Whitman, 240 pgs., Buster Crabbe photo-c, movie scenes, ERB	21	53	149	250
770- Tarzan Twins, The, 1934, Whitman, 432 pgs., ERB	50	125	350	650
770- Tarzan Twins, The, 1935, Whitman, 432 pgs., ERB	40	100	280	480
nn- Tarzan Twins, The, 1935, Whitman, 52 pgs., 3 1/2" x 5 3/4", premium-with & without ads, soft-c, ERB	42	105	290	500
nn- Tarzan Twins, The, 1935, Whitman, 436 pgs., 3-color, soft-c, premium-no ads, ERB	42	105	295	525
778- Tarzan of the Screen (The Story of Johnny Weissmuller), 1934, Whitman, 240 pgs., photo-c, movie scenes, ERB	21	53	149	250
1102- Tarzan, The Return of, 1936, Whitman, 432 pgs., Edgar Rice Burroughs	15	38	108	170
1180- Tarzan, The New Adventures of, 1935, Whitman, 160 pgs., Herman Brix photo-c, movie scenes, ERB	16	40	116	180
1182- Tarzan Escapes, 1936, Whitman, 240 pgs., Johnny Weissmuller photo-c, movie scenes, ERB	21	53	149	250
1407- Tarzan Lord of the Jungle, 1946, Whitman, 352 pgs., ERB	11	28	68	110
1410- Tarzan, The Beasts of, 1937, Whitman, 432 pgs., Edgar Rice Burroughs	14	35	100	160
1442- Tarzan and the Lost Empire, 1948, Whitman, 288 pgs., ERB	11	28	68	110
1444- Tarzan and the Ant Men, 1945, Whitman, 352 pgs., ERB	11	28	68	110
1448- Tarzan and the Golden Lion, 1943, Whitman, 432 pgs., ERB	13	33	95	150
1452- Tarzan the Untamed, 1941, Whitman, 432 pgs., flip pictures, ERB	13	33	95	150
1453- Tarzan the Terrible, 1942, Whitman, 432 pgs., flip pictures,				

	GD	FN	VF	VF/NM
ERB	13	33	95	150
1467- **Tarzan in the Land of the Giant Apes**, 1949, Whitman, ERB	11	28	68	110
1477- **Tarzan, The Son of**, 1939, Whitman, 432 pgs., ERB	13	33	95	150
1488- **Tarzan's Revenge**, 1938, Whitman, 432 pgs., ERB	13	33	95	150
1495- **Tarzan and the Jewels of Opar**, 1940, Whitman, 432 pgs.	13	33	95	150
4056- **Tarzan and the Tarzan Twins with Jad-Bal-Ja the Golden Lion**, 1936, Whitman, 7" x 9 1/2", 320 pgs., Big Big Book	42	105	290	500
709-10- **Tarzan and the Journey of Terror**, 1950, Whitman, 2 1/2" x 5", ERB, Marsh-a	7	18	45	70
2005- **(#5)-Tarzan: The Mark of the Red Hyena**, 1967, Whitman, 260 pgs., 39 cents, hard-c, color illos	3	8	20	28
nn- **Tarzan**, 1935, Whitman, 148 pgs., soft-c, 3 1/2" x 4", Tarzan Ice Cream cup premium, ERB (scarce)	52	130	364	675
nn- **Tarzan and a Daring Rescue**, 1938, Whitman, 68 pgs., Pan-Am premium, soft-c, ERB (blank back-c version also exists)	37	93	260	450
nn- **Tarzan and his Jungle Friends**, 1936, Whitman, 132 pgs., soft-c, 3 1/2" x 3 1/2", Tarzan Ice Cream cup premium, ERB (scarce)	52	130	364	675
nn- **Tarzan in the Golden City**, 1938, Whitman, 68 pgs., Pan-Am premium, soft-c, 3 1/2" x 3 3/4", ERB	37	93	260	450
nn- **Tarzan The Avenger**, 1939, Dell, 194 pgs., Fast-Action Story, ERB, soft-c	25	63	175	300
nn- **Tarzan with the Tarzan Twins in the Jungle**, 1938, Dell, 194 pgs., Fast-Action Story, ERB	25	63	175	300
1100B- **Tell Your Fortune**, 1938, Whitman, 36 pgs., 2 1/2" x 3 1/2", Penny Book	3	8	21	30
nn- **Terminator 2: Judgment Day**, 1998, Chronicle Books, 310 pgs., adapts movie, 1-color (blue-gray) illos	1	3	6	10
1156- **Terry and the Pirates**, 1935, Whitman, 432 pgs., Milton Caniff-a (#1)	13	33	95	150
nn- **Terry and the Pirates**, 1935, Whitman, 52 pgs., 3 1/2" x 5 1/4", soft-c, premium, Milton Caniff-a; 3 versions: No ad, Sears ad & Perkins ad	25	63	175	300
1412- **Terry and the Pirates Shipwrecked on a Desert Island**, 1938, Whitman, 432 pgs., Milton Caniff-a	12	30	72	115
1420- **Terry and War in the Jungle**, 1946, Whitman, 352 pgs., Milton Caniff-a	11	28	68	110
1436- **Terry and the Pirates The Plantation Mystery**, 1942, Whitman, 432 pgs., flip pictures, Milton Caniff-a	12	30	72	115
1446- **Terry and the Pirates and the Giant's Vengeance**, 1939, Whitman, 432 pgs., Caniff-a	12	30	72	115
1499- **Terry and the Pirates in the Mountain Stronghold**, 1941, Whitman, 432 pgs., Caniff-a	12	30	72	115
4073- **Terry and the Pirates, The Adventures of**, 1938, Whitman, 7" x 9 1/2", 320 pgs., Big Big Book, Milton Caniff-a	25	63	175	300
4- **Terry and the Pirates Ashore in Singapore**, 1938, Whitman, 132 pgs., 3 1/2" x 3 3/4", soft-c, Buddy Book premium	21	53	149	250
10- **Terry and the Pirates Meet Again**, 1936, Whitman, 132 pgs., 3 1/2" x 3 1/2", soft-c, Tarzan Ice Cream cup lid premium	25	63	175	300
nn- **Terry and the Pirates, Adventures of**, 1938, 36 pgs., 2 1/2" x 3 1/2", Penny Book, Caniff-a	7	18	45	70
nn- **Terry and the Pirates and the Island Rescue**, 1938, Whitman, 68 pgs., 3 1/4" x 3 1/2", Pan-Am premium	20	50	140	220
nn- **Terry and the Pirates on Their Travels**, 1938, 36 pgs., 2 1/2" x 3 1/2", Penny Book, Caniff-a	7	18	45	70
nn- **Terry and the Pirates and the Mystery Ship**, 1938, Dell, 194 pgs., Fast-Action Story, soft-c	25	63	175	300
1492- **Terry Lee Flight Officer U.S.A.**, 1944, Whitman, 352 pgs., Milton Caniff-a	12	30	72	115
7- **Texas Bad Man, The** (Tom Mix), 1934, EVW, 160 pgs., (Five Star Library), movie scenes	16	40	112	175
1429- **Texas Kid, The**, 1937, Whitman, 432 pgs.	6	15	40	60
1135- **Texas Ranger, The**, 1936, Whitman, 432 pgs., Hal Arbo-a	6	15	40	60
nn- **Texas Ranger, The**, 1935, Whitman, 260 pgs., Cocomalt premium, soft-c, Hal Arbo-a	12	30	72	115
nn- **Texas Ranger and the Rustler Gang, The**, 1936, Whitman, Pan-Am giveaway	21	53	145	230
nn- **Texas Ranger in the West, The**, 1938, Whitman, 36 pgs., 2 1/2" x 3 1/2", Penny Book	6	15	40	60
nn- **Texas Ranger to the Rescue, The**, 1938, Whitman, 36 pgs., 2 1/2" x 3 1/2", Penny Book	6	15	40	60
12- **Texas Ranger in Rustler Strategy, The**, 1936, Whitman, 132 pgs., 3 1/2" x 3 1/2", soft-c, Tarzan Ice Cream cup lid premium	21	53	145	230
Tex Thorne (See Zane Grey)				
Thimble Theatre (See Popeye)				
26- **13 Hours By Air**, 1936, Lynn, 128 pgs., 5" x 7 1/2", photo-c, movie scenes (Paramount Pictures)	12	30	74	120
nn- **Three Bears, The**, nd (1930s), np (Whitman), 36 pgs., 3" x 2 1/2", Penny Book	2	3	16	22
1129- **Three Finger Joe** (Baseball), 1937, Saalfield, Robert A. Graef-a	7	18	45	70
nn- **Three Little Pigs, The**, nd (1930s), np (Whitman), 36 pgs., 3" x 2 1/2", Penny Book	2	3	16	22
1131- **Three Musketeers**, 1935, Whitman, 182 pgs., 5 1/4" x 6 1/4", photo-c, movie scenes	13	33	90	140
1409- **Thumper and the Seven Dwarfs** (Disney), 1944, Whitman, All Pictures Comics	23	58	165	280
1108- **Tiger Lady, The** (The life of Mabel Stark, animal trainer), 1935, Saalfield, photo-c, movie scenes, hard-c	9	23	56	90
1588- **Tiger Lady, The**, 1935, Saalfield, photo-c, movie scenes, soft-c	9	23	56	90
1442- **Tillie the Toiler and the Wild Man of Desert Island**, 1941, Whitman, 432 pgs., Russ Westover-a	11	28	66	105
1058- **"Timid Elmer"** (Disney), 1939, Whitman, 5" x 5 1/2", 68 pgs., hard-c	11	28	66	105
1152- **Tim McCoy in the Prescott Kid**, 1935, Whitman, 160 pgs., hard-c, photo-c, movie scenes	16	40	116	180
1193- **Tim McCoy in the Westerner**, 1936, Whitman, 240 pgs., photo-c, movie scenes	12	30	76	125
1436- **Tim McCoy on the Tomahawk Trail**, 1937, Whitman, 432 pgs., Robert Weisman-a	11	28	68	110
1490- **Tim McCoy and the Sandy Gulch Stampede**, 1939, Whitman, 424 pgs.	10	25	60	95
2- **Tim McCoy in Beyond the Law**, 1934, EVW, Five Star Library, photo-c, movie scenes (Columbia Pict.) Hardcover	12	30	76	125
(Rare) Softcover	22	55	154	260
10- **Tim McCoy in Fighting the Redskins**, 1938, Whitman, 130 pgs., Buddy Book, soft-c	21	53	149	250
14- **Tim McCoy in Speedwings**, 1935, EVW, Five Star Library, 160 pgs., photo-c, movie scenes (Columbia Pictures)	13	33	95	150
nn- **Tim the Builder**, nd (1930s), np (Whitman), 36 pgs., 3" x 2 1/2", Penny Book	2	3	16	22
Tim Tyler (Also see Adventures of ...)				
1140- **Tim Tyler's Luck Adventures in the Ivory Patrol**, 1937, Whitman, 432 pgs., by Lyman Young	9	23	56	90
1479- **Tim Tyler's Luck and the Plot of the Exiled King**, 1939, Whitman, 432 pgs., by Lyman Young	9	23	56	90
767- **Tiny Tim, The Adventures of**, 1935, Whitman, 384 pgs., by Stanley Link	12	30	74	120
1172- **Tiny Tim and the Mechanical Men**, 1937, Whitman, 432 pgs., by Stanley Link	11	28	68	110
1472- **Tiny Tim in the Big, Big World**, 1945, Whitman, 352 pgs., by Stanley Link	11	28	68	110
2006- **(#6)-Tom and Jerry Meet Mr. Fingers**, 1967, Whitman, 39¢-c 260 pgs., hard-c, color illos.	3	8	20	28
5752- **Tom and Jerry Meet Mr. Fingers**, 1973, Whitman, 39¢-c 260 pgs., soft-c, color illos., 5 printings	2	3	11	15
2030-(#30)- **Tom and Jerry, The Astro-Nots,** 1969, Whitman, 256 pgs., hard-c, color illos.	2	3	15	20
5765- **Tom and Jerry, The Astro-Nots**, 1974, Whitman, 256 pgs., soft-c, color illos.	2	3	11	15
5787-2- **Tom and Jerry Under the Big Top**, 1980, Whitman, 79¢-c, 260 pgs., soft-c, B&W	2	3	11	15
723- **Tom Beatty Ace of the Service**, 1934, Whitman, 256 pgs., George Taylor-a	12	30	72	115
nn- **Tom Beatty Ace of the Service**, 1934, Whitman, 260 pgs., soft-c	12	30	72	115
1165- **Tom Beatty Ace of the Service Scores Again**, 1937, Whitman, 432 pgs., Weisman-a	11	28	66	105
1420- **Tom Beatty Ace of the Service and the Big Brain Gang**, 1939, Whitman, 432 pgs.	11	28	66	105
nn- **Tom Beatty Ace Detective and the Gorgon Gang**, 1938?, Whitman, 36 pgs., 2 1/2" x 3 1/2", Penny Book	10	25	60	95
nn- **Tom Beatty Ace of the Service and the Kidnapers**, 1938?, Whitman, 36 pgs., 2 1/2" x 3 1/2", Penny Book	10	25	60	95
1102- **Tom Mason on Top**, 1935, Saalfield, 160 pgs., Tom Mix photo-c, from Mascot serial "The Miracle Rider," movie scenes, hard-c	13	33	95	150
1582- **Tom Mason on Top**, 1935, Saalfield, 160 pgs., Tom Mix photo-c, movie scenes, soft-c	13	33	95	150
Tom Mix (See Chief of the Rangers, Flaming Guns & Texas Bad Man)				
762- **Tom Mix and Tony Jr. in "Terror Trail,"** 1934, Whitman, 160 pgs., movie scenes	13	33	95	150
1144- **Tom Mix in the Fighting Cowboy**, 1935, Whitman, 432 pgs., Hal Arbo-a	12	30	72	115
nn- **Tom Mix in the Fighting Cowboy**, 1935, Whitman, 436 pgs., premium-no ads, 3 color, soft-c, Hal Arbo-a	18	45	128	200
1166- **Tom Mix in the Range War**, 1937, Whitman, 432 pgs., Hal Arbo-a	10	25	60	95
1173- **Tom Mix Plays a Lone Hand**, 1935, Whitman, 288 pgs., hard-c, Hal Arbo-a	10	25	60	95

1129 - Three Finger Joe © Saalfield

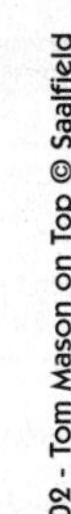

1102 - Tom Mason on Top © Saalfield

1411 - Union Pacific © WHIT

	GD	FN	VF	VF/NM
1183- Tom Mix and the Stranger from the South, 1936, Whitman, 432 pgs.	10	25	60	95
1462- Tom Mix and the Hoard of Montezuma, 1937, Whitman, H. E. Vallely-a	10	25	60	95
1482- Tom Mix and His Circus on the Barbary Coast, 1940, Whitman, 432 pgs., James Gary-a	10	25	60	95
3047- Tom Mix and His Big Little Kit, 1937, Whitman, 384 pgs., 4 1/2" x 6 1/2" box, includes miniature box of 4 crayons-red, yellow, blue and green	46	115	322	600
4068- Tom Mix and the Scourge of Paradise Valley, 1937, Whitman, 7" x 9 1/2", 320 pgs., Big Big Book, Vallely-a	21	53	145	230
6833- Tom Mix in the Riding Avenger, 1936, Dell, 244 pgs., Cartoon Story Book, hard-c	13	33	95	150
nn- Tom Mix Rides to the Rescue, 1939, 36 pgs., 2 1/2" x 3", Penny Book	7	18	42	65
nn- Tom Mix Avenges the Dry Gulched Range King, 1939, Dell, 196 pgs., Fast-Action Story, soft-c	14	35	100	160
nn- Tom Mix in the Riding Avenger, 1936, Dell, 244 pgs., Fast-Action Story	14	35	100	160
nn- Tom Mix the Trail of the Terrible 6, 1935, Ralston Purina Co., 84 pgs., 3" x 3 1/2", premium	13	33	90	140
4- Tom Mix and Tony in the Rider of Death Valley, 1934, EVW, Five Star Library, 160 pgs., movie scenes (Universal Pictures), hard-c	12	30	80	130
4- Tom Mix and Tony in the Rider of Death Valley, 1934, EVW, Five Star Library, 160 pgs., movie scenes (Universal Pictures), soft-c (Rare)	25	63	175	300
7- Tom Mix in the Texas Bad Man, 1934, EVW, Five Star Library, 160 pgs., movie scenes, hard-c	13	33	90	140
7- Tom Mix in the Texas Bad Man, 1934, EVW, Five Star Library, 160 pgs., movie scenes; soft-c (Rare)	25	63	175	300
10- Tom Mix in the Tepee Ranch Mystery, 1938, Whitman, 132 pgs., Buddy Book, soft-c	16	40	112	175
1126- Tommy of Troop Six (Scout Book), 1937, Saalfield, hard-c	7	18	42	65
1606- Tommy of Troop Six (Scout Book), 1937, Saalfield, soft-c	7	18	42	65
Tom Sawyer (See Adventures of ...)				
1437- Tom Swift and His Magnetic Silencer, 1941, Whitman, 432 pgs., flip pictures	21	53	149	250
1485- Tom Swift and His Giant Telescope, 1939, Whitman, 432 pgs., James Gary-a	16	40	116	180
540- Top-Line Comics (In Open Box), 1935, Whitman, 164 pgs., 3 1/2" x 3 1/2", 3 books in set, all soft-c:				
Bobby Thatcher and the Samarang Emerald	12	30	76	125
Broncho Bill in Suicide Canyon	12	30	76	125
Freckles and His Friends in the North Woods	12	30	76	125
Complete set with box	37	93	260	450
541- Top-Line Comics (In Open Box), 1935, Whitman, 164 pgs., 3 1/2" x 3 1/2", 3 books in set; all soft-c:				
Little Joe and the City Gangsters	12	30	76	125
Smilin' Jack and His Flivver Plane	12	30	76	125
Streaky and the Football Signals	12	30	76	125
Complete set with box	37	93	260	450
542- Top-Line Comics (In Open Box), 1935, Whitman, 164 pgs., 3 1/2" x 3 1/2", 3 books in set; all soft-c:				
Dinglehoofer Und His Dog Adolph by Knerr	12	30	76	125
Jungle Jim by Alex Raymond	13	33	95	150
Sappo by Segar	13	33	95	150
Complete set with box	42	105	290	500
543- Top-Line Comics (In Open Box), 1935, Whitman, 164 pgs., 3 1/2" x 3 1/2", 3 books in set; all soft-c:				
Alexander Smart, ESQ by Winner	12	30	76	125
Bunky by Billy de Beck	12	30	76	125
Nicodemus O'Malley by Carter	12	30	76	125
Complete set with box	37	93	260	450
1158- Tracked by a G-Man, 1939, Saalfield, 400 pgs.	8	20	48	75
25- Trail of the Lonesome Pine, The, 1936, Lynn, movie scenes	10	25	60	95
nn- Trail of the Terrible 6 (See Tom Mix ...)				
1185- Trail to Squaw Gulch, The, 1940, Saalfield, 400 pgs.	8	20	48	75
720- Treasure Island, 1933, Whitman, 362 pgs.	10	25	60	95
1141- Treasure Island, 1934, Whitman, 164 pgs., hard-c, 4 1/4" x 5 1/4", Jackie Cooper photo-c, movie scenes	10	25	60	95
1141- Treasure Island, 1934, Whitman, 164 pgs., soft-c, 4 1/4" x 5 1/4", Jackie Cooper photo-c, movie scenes	10	25	60	95
1018- Trick and Puzzle Book, 1939, Whitman, 100 pgs., soft-c	3	8	18	25
1100B- Tricks Easy to Do (Slight of hand & magic), 1938, Whitman, 36 pgs., 2 1/2" x 3 1/2", Penny Book	3	8	18	25
1100B- Tricks You Can Do, 1938, Whitman, 36 pgs., 2 1/2" x 3 1/2", Penny Book	3	8	18	25
5777- Tweety and Sylvester, The Magic Voice, 1976, Whitman, 260 pgs., soft-c, flip-it feature; 5 printings	1	3	8	12
1104- Two-Gun Montana, 1936, Whitman, 432 pgs., Henry E. Vallely-a	10	25	60	95
nn- Two-Gun Montana Shoots it Out, 1939, Whitman, 36 pgs., 2 1/2" x 3 1/2", Penny Book	10	25	60	95
1058- Ugly Duckling, The (Disney), 1939, Whitman, 68 pgs., 5" x 5 1/2", hard-c	12	30	74	120
nn- Ugly Duckling, The, nd (1930s), np (Whitman), 36 pgs., 3" x 2 1/2", Penny Book	2	3	17	24
Unc' Billy Gets Even (See Wee Little Books)				
1114- Uncle Don's Strange Adventures, 1935, Whitman, 300 pgs., radio star-Uncle Don Carney	10	25	64	100
722- Uncle Ray's Story of the United States, 1934, Whitman, 300 pgs.	10	25	64	100
1461- Uncle Sam's Sky Defenders, 1941, Whitman, 432 pgs., flip pictures	11	28	68	110
1405- Uncle Wiggily's Adventures, 1946, Whitman, All Pictures Comics	12	30	72	115
1411- Union Pacific, 1939, Whitman, 240 pgs., photo-c, movie scenes	11	28	66	105
With Union Pacific letter	22	55	154	260
1189- Up Dead Horse Canyon, 1940, Saalfield, 400 pgs.	7	18	42	65
1455- Vic Sands of the U.S. Flying Fortress Bomber Squadron, 1944, Whitman, 352 pgs.	11	28	66	105
nn- Visit to Santa Claus, 1938?, Whitman, Pan Am premium by Snow Plane; soft-c (Rare)	22	55	154	260
1645- Walt Disney's Andy Burnett on the Trail (TV Series), 1958, Whitman, 280 pgs.	3	8	20	28
803- Walt Disney's Bongo, 1948, Whitman, hard-c, Story Hour Series	9	23	56	90
711-10- Walt Disney's Cinderella and the Magic Wand, 1950, Whitman, 2 1/2" x 5", based on Disney movie	10	25	60	95
845- Walt Disney's Donald Duck and his Cat Troubles (Disney), 1948, Whitman, 100 pgs., 5" x 5 1/2", hard-c	12	30	72	115
845- Walt Disney's Donald Duck and the Boys, 1948, Whitman, 100 pgs., 5" x 5 1/2", hard-c, Barks-a	18	45	128	200
2952- Walt Disney's Donald Duck in the Great Kite Maker, 1949, Whitman, 24 pgs., 3 1/4" x 4", Tiny Tales, full color (5 cents)	10	25	60	95
804- Walt Disney's Mickey and the Beanstalk, 1948, Whitman, hard-c, Story Hour Series	12	30	72	115
845- Walt Disney's Mickey Mouse and the Boy Thursday, 194 pgs., Whitman, 5" x 5 1/2", 100 pgs.	12	30	72	115
845- Walt Disney's Mickey Mouse the Miracle Maker, 1948, Whitman, 5" x 5 1/2", 100 pgs.	12	30	72	115
2952- Walt Disney's Mickey Mouse and the Night Prowlers, Whitman, 1949, 24 pgs., 3 1/4" x 4", Tiny Tales, full color (5 ¢)	10	25	60	95
5770- Walt Disney's Mickey Mouse - Mystery at Disneyland, Whitman, 1975, 260 pgs., four printings	1	3	10	14
5781-2- Walt Disney's Mickey Mouse - Mystery at Dead Man's Cove, Whitman, 1980, 260 pgs., two printings	1	3	8	12
845- Walt Disney's Minnie Mouse and the Antique Chair, 1948, Whitman, 5" x 5 1/2", 100 pgs.	12	30	72	115
1435- Walt Disney's Pinocchio and Jiminy Cricket, 1940,				

	GD	FN	VF	VF/NM
Whitman, 432 pgs.	27	68	189	325
nn- **Walt Disney's Pinocchio and Jiminy Cricket**, Fast Action Story, 1940, Dell, 432 pgs.	35	88	248	425
845- **Walt Disney's Poor Pluto**, 1948, Whitman, 5" x 5 1/2", 100 pgs., hard-c	12	30	76	125
1467- **Walt Disney's Pluto the Pup** (Disney), 1938, Whitman, 432 pgs., Gottfredson-a	15	38	108	170
1066- **Walt Disney's Story of Clarabelle Cow** (Disney), 1938, Whitman, 100 pgs.	12	30	72	115
66- **Walt Disney's Story of Dippy the Goof** (Disney), 1938, Whitman, 100 pgs.	12	30	72	115
1066- **Walt Disney's Story of Donald Duck** (Disney), 1938, Whitman, 100 pgs., hard-c, Taliaferro-a	12	30	72	115
1066- **Walt Disney's Story of Goofy** (Disney), 1938, Whitman, 100 pgs., hard-c	12	30	76	125
1066- **Walt Disney's Story of Mickey Mouse** (Disney), 1938, Whitman, 100 pgs., hard-c, Gottfredson-a, Donald Duck app.	12	30	72	115
1066- **Walt Disney's Story of Minnie Mouse** (Disney), 1938, Whitman, 100 pgs., hard-c	12	30	72	115
1066- **Walt Disney's Story of Pluto the Pup**, (Disney), 1938, Whitman, 100 pgs., hard-c	12	30	76	125
2952- **Walter Lantz Presents Andy Panda's Rescue**, 1949, Whitman, Tiny Tales, full color (5 cents) (1030-5 on back-c)	11	28	66	105
751- **Wash Tubbs in Pandemonia**, 1934, Whitman, 320 pgs., Roy Crane-a	12	30	72	115
nn- **Wash Tubbs in Pandemonia**, 1934, Whitman, 52 pgs., 4" x 5 1/2", premium-no ads, soft-c, Roy Crane-a	18	45	128	200
1455- **Wash Tubbs and Captain Easy Hunting For Whales**, 1938, Whitman, 432 pgs., Roy Crane-a	12	30	76	125
6- **Wash Tubbs in Foreign Travel**, 1934, Whitman, soft-c, 3 1/2" x 3 1/2", Tarzan Ice Cream cup premium	21	53	149	250
513- **Wee Little Books** (In Open Box), 1934, Whitman, 44 pgs., small size, 6 books in set (children's classics) (Both Red box and Green box editions exist)				
Child's Garden of Verses	4	10	24	35
The Happy Prince (The Story of)	4	10	24	35
Joan of Arc (The Story of)	4	10	24	35
Peter Pan (The Story of)	4	10	24	35
Pied Piper Of Hamlin	4	10	24	35
Robin Hood (A Story of...)	4	10	24	35
Complete set with box	25	63	175	300
514- **Wee Little Books** (In Open Box), 1934, Whitman, 44 pgs., small size, 6 books in set				
Jack And Jill	4	10	24	35
Little Bo-Peep	4	10	24	35
Little Tommy Tucker	4	10	24	35
Mother Goose	4	10	24	35
Old King Cole	4	10	24	35
Simple Simon	4	10	24	35
Complete set with box	25	63	175	300
518- **Wee Little Books** (In Open Box), 1933, Whitman, 44 pgs., small size, 6 books in set, written by Thornton Burgess				
Betty Bear's Lesson-1930	4	10	24	35
Jimmy Skunk's Justice-1933	4	10	24	35
Little Joe Otter's Slide-1929	4	10	24	35
Peter Rabbit's Carrots-1933	4	10	24	35
Unc' Billy Gets Even-1930	4	10	24	35
Whitefoot's Secret-1933	4	10	24	35
Complete set with box	25	63	175	300
519- **Wee Little Books** (In Open Box) (Bible Stories), 1934, Whitman, 44 pgs., small size, 6 books in set, Helen Janes-a				
The Story of David	4	10	24	35
The Story of Gideon	4	10	24	35
The Story of Daniel	4	10	24	35
The Story of Joseph	4	10	24	35
The Story of Ruth and Naomi	4	10	24	35
The Story of Moses	4	10	24	35
Complete set with box	25	63	175	300
1471- **Wells Fargo**, 1938, Whitman, 240 pgs., photo-c, movie scenes	10	25	64	100
L18- **Western Frontier**, 1935, Lynn, 192 pgs., starring Ken Maynard, movie scenes	12	30	76	125
1121- **West Pointers on the Gridiron**, 1936, Saalfield, 148 pgs., hard-c, sports book	5	12	34	50
1601- **West Pointers on the Gridiron**, 1936, Saalfield, 148 pgs., soft-c, sports book	5	12	34	50
1124- **West Point Five, The**, 1937, Saalfield, 4 3/4" x 5 1/4", sports book, hard-c	5	12	34	50
1604- **West Point Five, The**, 1937, Saalfield, 4 1/4" x 5 1/4", sports book, soft-c	5	12	34	50
1164- **West Point of the Air**, 1935, Whitman, 160 pgs., photo-c, movie scenes	9	23	54	85
18- **Westward Ho!**, 1935, EVW, 160 pgs., movie scenes, star ring John Wayne (Scarce)	42	105	290	500

	GD	FN	VF	VF/NM
1109- **We Three**, 1935, Saalfield, 160 pgs., photo-c, movie scenes, by John Barrymore, hard-c	10	25	60	95
1589- **We Three**, 1935, Saalfield, 160 pgs., photo-c, movie scenes, by John Barrymore, soft-c	10	25	60	95
Whitefoot's Secret (See Wee Little Books)				
nn- **Who's Afraid of the Big Bad Wolf**, "Three Little Pigs" (Disney), 1933, McKay, 36 pgs., 6" x 8 1/2", stiff-c, Disney studio-a	21	53	149	250
nn- **Wild West Adventures of Buffalo Bill**, 1935, Whitman, 260 pgs., Cocomalt premium, soft-c, Hal Arbo-a	12	30	72	115
1096- **Will Rogers, The Story of**, 1935, Saalfield, photo-hard-c	7	18	45	70
1576- **Will Rogers, The Story of**, 1935, Saalfield, photo-soft-c	7	18	45	70
1458- **Wimpy the Hamburger Eater**, 1938, Whitman, 432 pgs., E.C. Segar-a	16	40	112	175
1433- **Windy Wayne and His Flying Wing**, 1942, Whitman, 432 pgs., flip pictures	10	25	60	95
1131- **Winged Four, The**, 1937, Saalfield, sports book, hard-c	10	25	60	95
1407- **Wings of the U.S.A.**, 1940, Whitman, 432 pgs., Thomas Hickey-a	10	25	60	95
nn- **Winning of the Old Northwest, The**, 1934, World Syndicate, High Lights of History Series, full color-c	10	25	60	95
nn- **Winning of the Old Northwest, The**, 1934, World Syndicate, High Lights of History Series; red & silver-c	10	25	60	95
1122- **Winning Point, The**, 1936, Saalfield, (Football), hard-c	5	12	30	45
1602- **Winning Point, The**, 1936, Saalfield, soft-c	5	12	30	45
nn- **Wizard of Oz Waddle Book**, 1934, BRP, 20 pgs., 7 1/2" x 10", forerunner of the Blue Ribbon Pop-Up books; with 6 removable articulated cardboard characters. Book only	42	105	290	500
Dust jacket only	46	115	322	600
Near Mint Complete - $12,500				
710-10- **Woody Woodpecker Big Game Hunter**, 1950, Whitman, by Walter Lantz	7	18	42	65
2010-(#10)- **Woody Woodpecker-The Meteor Menace**, 1967, Whitman, 260 pgs., 39¢-c, hard-c, color illos.	3	8	21	30
5753- **Woody Woodpecker-The Meteor Menace**, 1973, Whitman, 260 pgs., no price, soft-c, color illos.	1	3	6	8
2028- **Woody Woodpecker-The Sinister Signal**, 1969, Whitman	2	3	16	22
5763- **Woody Woodpecker-The Sinister Signal**, 1974, Whitman, 1st printing-no price; 2nd printing-39¢-c	1	3	5	6
23- **World of Monsters, The**, 1935, EVW, Five Star Library, movie scenes	14	35	100	160
779- **World War in Photographs, The**, 1934, Whitman, photo-c, photo illus.	10	25	60	95
Wyatt Earp (See Hugh O'Brian ...)				
nn- **Xena - Warrior Princess**, 1998, Chronicle Books, 310 pgs., based on TV series, 1-color (purple) illos	1	3	6	10
nn- **Yogi Bear Goes Country & Western**, 1977, Modern Promotions, 244 pgs., 49 cents, soft-c, flip pictures	1	3	10	14
nn- **Yogi Bear Saves Jellystone Park**, 1977, Modern Promotions, 244 pgs., 49 cents, soft-c, flip pictures	1	3	10	14
nn- **Zane Grey's Cowboys of the West**, 1935, Whitman, 148 pgs., 3 3/4" x 4", Tarzan Ice Cream Cup premium, soft-c, Arbo-a	21	53	149	250
Zane Grey's King of the Royal Mounted (See Men of the Mounted)				
1010- **Zane Grey's King of the Royal Mounted in Arctic Law**, 1937, Whitman, 7 1/4" x 5 1/2", 64 pgs., Nickel Book	10	25	64	100
1103- **Zane Grey's King of the Royal Mounted**, 1936, Whitman, 432 pgs.	10	25	60	95
nn- **Zane Grey's King of the Royal Mounted**, 1935, Whitman, 260 pgs., Cocomalt premium, soft-c	12	25	64	100
1179- **Zane Grey's King of the Royal Mounted and the Northern Treasure**, 1937, Whitman, 432 pgs.	10	25	60	95
1405- **Zane Grey's King of the Royal Mounted the Long Arm of the Law**, 1942, Whitman, All Pictures Comics	10	25	60	95
1452- **Zane Grey's King of the Royal Mounted Gets His Man**, 1938, Whitman, 432 pgs.	10	25	60	95
1486- **Zane Grey's King of the Royal Mounted and the Great Jewel Mystery**, 1939, Whitman, 432 pgs.	10	25	60	95
5- **Zane Grey's King of the Royal Mounted in the Far North**, 1938, Whitman, 132 pgs., Buddy Book, soft-c (Rare)	29	73	203	350
nn- **Zane Grey's King of the Royal Mounted in Law of the North**, 1939, Whitman, 36 pgs., 2 1/2" x 3 1/2", Penny Book	6	15	36	55
nn- **Zane Grey's King of the Royal Mounted Policing the Frozen North**, 1938, Dell, 196 pgs., Fast-Action Story, soft-c	13	33	95	150
1440- **Zane Grey's Tex Thorne Comes Out of the West**, 1937, Whitman, 432 pgs.	10	25	60	95
1465- **Zip Saunders King of the Speedway**, 1939, 432 pgs., Weisman-a	10	25	60	95

PROMOTIONAL COMICS

The Marketing of a Medium

By Carrie Wood

When it comes to four-letter words, most people probably rank "free" among some of their favorites. But of course, just because you didn't pay for something doesn't mean that there isn't a catch involved. Comic books have hardly been immune to this – a free comic usually meant that someone was trying to sell the reader something additional. And this practice of hiding a sales pitch behind some fun, colorful characters has been around in comics since the very beginning of the medium.

Even as early as the Platinum and Victorian Ages of comics, companies had realized the value of comic strips as promotional material. By the 1850s, free almanacs such as Hostetter's and Wright's were using comics as a way to help sell everything from shoe polish to patent medicine. These books are remarkably rare today, and it's difficult to compile an accurate or complete history (though you can read more about them in the Victorian Comics essay elsewhere in this book). By the end of the 1800s, the popularity of characters like the Yellow Kid and The Brownies heralded in a new age of comics-as-promos.

Some of the earliest characters that were used as successful tools in promotional comics were Palmer Cox's creation "The Brownies." The illustration shown here showcases them drinking and endorsing Seal Brand Coffee.

The very idea of funny pages within newspapers were, essentially, using comics as promotions to help sell more papers. The news publishers of the time started adding supplements to Sunday papers, and soon after, thanks to the key arrival of Buster Brown as a wildly popular character, comics were being nationally licensed for newspapers. And the sales-minded goal of using free comic strip pages to help driver readership? That worked remarkably well. The Yellow Kid, The Brownies, Buster Brown and others helped increase newspaper sales nationwide.

We can even attribute the debut of the comic book itself to promotions: in 1933, Harry Wildenberg managed to convince Procter & Gamble to sponsor the very first comic book, *Funnies on Parade*, as a premium item. *Funnies on Parade* was just a few pages long and contained reprints of various comic strips, and it was sent out for free to customers who mailed in coupons clipped from Procter & Gamble products. That book was such a success that it led to the creation of *Famous Funnies*, the first true "comic book" as we know it today.

A 1933 article in *Fortune* magazine recognized the incredible marketing power of the comic book, seemingly right away – but it wasn't such a fan of the idea, suggesting that businesses that engaged in such a thing were going against classic decorum and that using comics to sell products was somehow bringing those products "down to the level" of comics. In spite of that, it was clear from the get-go that businessfolk recognized what kind of promotional power comics held.

By the 1950s, promotional comics were being given away for more than just the sake of selling something inside; they were now being used to help educate children on a huge number of topics, from banking and mathematics to great moments in history. A few years later in the '70s, promotional comics were being included as a premium in just about everything, with major characters from DC and Marvel showing up to help save various company mascots in their time of need. By the '80s, comics were being included as premiums with action figures and video games – Atari especially took a liking to comics, leading to a regular newsstand comic series with the company's popular game characters.

In 2002, a whole holiday was created based around free promotional comics: Free Comic Book Day. Facilitated by Diamond Comic Distributors, the day (the first Saturday each May) features dozens of books given away at no charge to the customer, from some of the most popular publishers in the business. These books are often used to promote upcoming or current releases from these publishers, and by giving readers a taste of the story, they hope that the customer will then come back and spend their money on the rest of the series. For the comic shops that host it, these promo books serve the purpose of simply getting people in the door – at which point they'll hopefully find something to spend some money on, thanks to the typical big FCBD sales weekends that shop owners host to play up the event. It's comics-as-advertising in its purest form: giving free comics away for the sake of selling more comics.

*Every market and product has been on the promotional comic book bandwagon. Freihofer's Baking Company distributed a comic in the 1940s that featured reprinted pages from **All-American Comics**.*

*The promotional title **March of Comics** was a prolific comic that ran for 36 years and 488 issues featuring a variety of subjects and characters. (#20 shown)*

So much as a simple skim through this section will highlight the numerous purposes for which promotional comics have been created: from telling kids not to smoke (*Captain America Meets the Asthma Monster*), to trying to sway elections (*The Story of Harry Truman*), to showing the importance of environmentalism (*Our Spaceship Earth*), to explaining history (*Louisiana Purchase*), to recruiting for the armed forced (*Li'l Abner Joins the Navy*) and much more. There's also been the occasional oddball branded team-up that simply served to promote the brand, such as *The Craftsman Bolt-On System Saves the Justice League*, *The KFC Colonel Meets the DC Multiverse*, and *The X-Men at the Texas State Fair*.

Whether being used to educate, entertain or endorse, comics have proven themselves a powerful promotional tool. And as long as people still love the word "free," they'll keep picking them up – meaning that the industry will continue to produce promos.

Adventures of Big Boy #2 © MAR

Adventures of Quik Bunny #1 © MAR

Amazing Spider-Man #50 mini-comic © MAR

ACTION COMICS
DC Comics: 1947 - 1998 (Giveaway)

	GD 2.0	VG 4.0	FN 6.0	VF 8.0	VF/NM 9.0	NM- 9.2
1 (1976) paper cover w/10¢ price, 16 pgs. in color; reprints complete Superman story from #1 ('38)	5	10	15	30	50	70
1 (1976) Safeguard Giveaway; paper cover w/"free", 16 pgs. in color; reprints complete Superman story from #1 ('38)	5	10	15	30	50	70
1 (1983) paper cover w/10¢ price, 16 pgs. in color; reprints complete Superman story from #1 ('38)	3	6	9	15	22	28
1 (1987 Nestle Quik; 1988, 50¢)	2	4	6	8	10	12
1 (1992)-Came w/Reign of Superman packs						4.00
1 (1998 U.S. Postal Service, $7.95) Reprints entire issue; extra outer half-cover contains First Day Issuance of 32¢ Superman stamp with Sept. 10, 1998 Cleveland, OH postmark	1	2	3	5	6	8
Theater (1947, 32 pgs., 5" x 7", nn)-Vigilante story based on Columbia Vigilante serial; no Superman-c or story	77	154	231	493	847	1200

ACTION ZONE
CBS Television: 1994 (Promotes CBS Saturday morning cartoons)

	GD 2.0	VG 4.0	FN 6.0	VF 8.0	VF/NM 9.0	NM- 9.2
1-WildC.A.T.s, T.M.N.Turtles, Skeleton Warriors stories; Jim Lee-c						4.00

ADVENTURE COMICS
IGA: No date (early 1940s) (Paper-c, 32 pgs.)

	GD 2.0	VG 4.0	FN 6.0	VF 8.0	VF/NM 9.0	NM- 9.2
Two diff. issues; Super-Mystery V2 #3-r from 1941; Jim Mooney-c	24	48	72	142	234	325

ADVENTURE IN DISNEYLAND
Walt Disney Productions (Dist. by Richfield Oil): May, 1955 (Giveaway, soft-c., 16 pgs)

	GD 2.0	VG 4.0	FN 6.0	VF 8.0	VF/NM 9.0	NM- 9.2
nn	15	30	45	94	147	200

ADVENTURES @ EBAY
eBay: 2000 (6 3/4" x 4 1/2", 16 pgs.)

	GD 2.0	VG 4.0	FN 6.0	VF 8.0	VF/NM 9.0	NM- 9.2
1-Judd Winick-a/Rucka & Van Meter-s; intro to eBay comic buying						4.00

ADVENTURES IN JET POWER
General Electric: 1950

	GD 2.0	VG 4.0	FN 6.0	VF 8.0	VF/NM 9.0	NM- 9.2
nn	8	16	24	40	50	60

ADVENTURES OF BIG BOY (Also titled Adventures of the Big Boy)
Timely Comics/Webs Adv. Corp./Illus. Features: 1956 - Present
(Giveaway) (East & West editions of early issues)

	GD 2.0	VG 4.0	FN 6.0	VF 8.0	VF/NM 9.0	NM- 9.2
1-Everett-c/a	129	258	387	826	1413	2000
2-Everett-c/a	52	104	156	328	552	775
3-5: 4-Robot-c	21	42	63	126	206	285
6-10: 6-Sci/fic issue	10	20	30	67	141	215
11-20: 11,13-DeCarlo-a	6	12	18	41	76	110
21-30	4	8	12	27	44	60
31-50	3	6	9	17	26	35
51-100	2	4	6	9	13	16
101-150	2	4	6	8	10	12
151-240: 239-Wizard of Oz parody-c	1	2	3	5	7	9
241-265,267-269,271-300:						6.00
266-Superman x-over	3	6	9	17	26	35
270-TV's Buck Rogers-c/s	3	6	9	14	20	25
301-400						4.00
401-500						3.00
1-(2nd series - '76-'84,Paragon Prod.) (...Shoney's Big Boy)	1	3	4	6	8	10
2-20						5.00
21-76						3.00
Summer, 1959 issue, large size	7	14	21	46	86	125

ADVENTURES OF G. I. JOE
1969 (3-1/4x7") (20 & 16 pgs.)

First Series: 1-Danger of the Depths. 2-Perilous Rescue. 3-Secret Mission to Spy Island. 4-Mysterious Explosion. 5-Fantastic Free Fall. 6-Eight Ropes of Danger. 7-Mouth of Doom. 8-Hidden Missile Discovery. 9-Space Walk Mystery. 10-Fight for Survival. 11-The Shark's Surprise.
Second Series: 2-Flying Space Adventure. 4-White Tiger Hunt. 7-Capture of the Pygmy Gorilla. 12-Secret of the Mummy's Tomb.
Third Series: Reprinted surviving titles of First Series. Fourth Series: 13-Adventure Team Headquarters. 14-Search For the Stolen Idol.

	GD 2.0	VG 4.0	FN 6.0	VF 8.0	VF/NM 9.0	NM- 9.2
each....	3	6	9	17	26	35

ADVENTURES OF JELL-O MAN AND WOBBLY, THE
Welsh Publishing Group: 1991 ($1.25)

	GD 2.0	VG 4.0	FN 6.0	VF 8.0	VF/NM 9.0	NM- 9.2
1						4.00

ADVENTURES OF KOOL-AID MAN
Marvel Comics: 1983 - No. 3, 1985 (Mail order giveaway)
Archie Comics: No. 4, 1987 - No. 9, 1989

	GD 2.0	VG 4.0	FN 6.0	VF 8.0	VF/NM 9.0	NM- 9.2
1	2	4	6	11	16	20
2-9: 4-9-Dan DeCarlo-a/c	1	3	4	6	8	10

ADVENTURES OF MARGARET O'BRIEN, THE
Bambury Fashions (Clothes): 1947 (20 pgs. in color, slick-c, regular size) (Premium)

	GD 2.0	VG 4.0	FN 6.0	VF 8.0	VF/NM 9.0	NM- 9.2
In "The Big City" movie adaptation (scarce)	22	44	66	132	216	300

ADVENTURES OF QUIK BUNNY
Nestle's Quik: 1984 (Giveaway, 32 pgs.)

	GD 2.0	VG 4.0	FN 6.0	VF 8.0	VF/NM 9.0	NM- 9.2
nn-Spider-Man app.	2	4	6	10	14	18

ADVENTURES OF STUBBY, SANTA'S SMALLEST REINDEER, THE
W. T. Grant Co.: nd (early 1940s) (Giveaway, 12 pgs.)

	GD 2.0	VG 4.0	FN 6.0	VF 8.0	VF/NM 9.0	NM- 9.2
nn	10	20	30	56	76	95

ADVENTURES OF VOTEMAN, THE
Foundation For Citizen Education Inc.: 1968

	GD 2.0	VG 4.0	FN 6.0	VF 8.0	VF/NM 9.0	NM- 9.2
nn	4	8	12	27	44	60

ADVENTURES WITH SANTA CLAUS
Promotional Publ. Co. (Murphy's Store): No date (early 50's)
(9-3/4x 6-3/4", 24 pgs., giveaway, paper-c)

	GD 2.0	VG 4.0	FN 6.0	VF 8.0	VF/NM 9.0	NM- 9.2
nn-Contains 8 pgs. ads	8	16	24	42	54	65
16 pg. version	8	16	24	44	57	70

AIR POWER (CBS TV & the U.S. Air Force Presents)
Prudential Insurance Co.: 1956 (5-1/4x7-1/4", 32 pgs., giveaway, soft-c)

	GD 2.0	VG 4.0	FN 6.0	VF 8.0	VF/NM 9.0	NM- 9.2
nn-Toth-a? Based on 'You Are There' TV program by Walter Cronkite	11	22	33	62	86	110

ALASKA BUSH PILOT
Jan Enterprises: 1959 (Paper cover, 10¢)

1-Promotes Bush Pilot Club (A 9.0 copy sold for $77 in Sept. 2022)
NOTE: *A CGC certified 9.9 Mint sold for $632.50 in 2005.*

ALICE IN BLUNDERLAND
Industrial Services: 1952 (Paper cover, 16 pgs. in color)

	GD 2.0	VG 4.0	FN 6.0	VF 8.0	VF/NM 9.0	NM- 9.2
nn-Facts about government waste and inefficiency	17	34	51	105	165	225

ALICE IN WONDERLAND
Western Printing Company/Whitman Publ. Co.: 1965; 1969; 1982

	GD 2.0	VG 4.0	FN 6.0	VF 8.0	VF/NM 9.0	NM- 9.2
Meets Santa (1950s), nd, 16 pgs.	9	18	27	47	61	75
Rexall Giveaway(1965, 16 pgs., 5x7-1/4) Western Printing (TV, Hanna-Barbera)	3	6	9	21	33	45
Wonder Bakery Giveaway(1969, 16 pgs, color, nn, nd) (Continental Baking Company)	3	6	9	19	30	40

ALL ABOARD, MR. LINCOLN
Assoc. of American Railroads: Jan, 1959 (16 pgs.)

	GD 2.0	VG 4.0	FN 6.0	VF 8.0	VF/NM 9.0	NM- 9.2
nn-Abraham Lincoln and the Railroads	7	14	21	35	43	50

ALL NEW COMICS
Harvey Comics: Oct, 1993 (Giveaway, no cover price, 16 pgs.)(Hanna-Barbera)

	GD 2.0	VG 4.0	FN 6.0	VF 8.0	VF/NM 9.0	NM- 9.2
1-Flintstones, Scooby Doo, Jetsons, Yogi Bear & Wacky Races previews for upcoming Harvey's new Hanna-Barbera line-up	1	2	3	5	7	9

NOTE: *Material previewed in Harvey giveaway was eventually published by Archie.*

ALL STAR SUPERMAN SPECIAL EDITION (Sears promotion for the 2013 Man of Steel movie)
DC Comics: Jun, 2013 (Giveaway, no cover price, some copies bagged with Sears insert)

	GD 2.0	VG 4.0	FN 6.0	VF 8.0	VF/NM 9.0	NM- 9.2
1-Reprints 1st issue; regular Quitely cover and Sears exclusive cover by Camuncoli						7.00

AMAZING SPIDER-MAN, THE
Marvel Comics Group

	GD 2.0	VG 4.0	FN 6.0	VF 8.0	VF/NM 9.0	NM- 9.2
Acme & Dingo Children's Boots (1980)-Spider-Woman app.	3	6	9	17	26	35
Adventures in Reading Starring... (1990,1991) Bogdanove & Romita-c/a						5.00
Aim Toothpaste Giveaway (36 pgs., reg. size)-1 pg. origin recap; Green Goblin-c/story	3	6	9	15	22	28
Aim Toothpaste Giveaway (16 pgs., reg. size)-Dr. Octopus app.	3	6	9	14	19	24
All Detergent Giveaway (1979, 36 pgs.), nn-Origin-r	3	6	9	16	23	30
Amazing Fantasy #15 (8/02) reprint included in Spider-Man DVD Collector's Gift Set	1	3	4	6	8	10
Amazing Fantasy #15 (2006) News America Marketing newspaper giveaway						4.00
Amazing Spider-Man nn (1990, 6-1/8x9", 28 pgs.)-Shan-Lon giveaway; retells origin of Spider-Man; Bagley-a/Saviuk-c	2	4	6	8	10	12
Amazing Spider-Man nn (1990, 6-1/8x9", 28 pgs.)-Shan-Lon giveaway; reprints Amazing Spider-Man #303 w/McFarlane-c/a	2	4	6	9	12	15
Amazing Spider-Man #1 Reprint (1990, 4-1/4x6-1/4", 28 pgs.)-Packaged with the book "Start Collecting Comic Books" from Running Press						4.00
Amazing Spider-Man #3 Reprint (2004)-Best Buy/Sony giveaway						4.00
Amazing Spider-Man #50 (Sony Pictures Edition) (8/04)-mini-comic included in Spider-Man 2 movie DVD Collector's Gift Set; r/#50 & various ASM covers with Dr. Octopus						4.00
Amazing Spider-Man #129 (Lion Gate Films) (6/04)-promotional comic given away at movie theaters on opening night for The Punisher						4.00

...& Power Pack (1984, nn)(Nat'l Committee for Prevention of Child Abuse)

GD VG FN VF VF/NM NM-
2.0 4.0 6.0 8.0 9.0 9.2

(two versions, mail offer & store giveaway)-Mooney-a; Byrne-c
Mail offer 2 4 6 10 14 18
Store giveaway 1 3 4 6 8 10
...& The Hulk (Special Edition)(6/8/80; 20 pgs.)-Supplement to Chicago Tribune
3 6 9 14 20 26
...& The Incredible Hulk (1981, 1982; 36 pgs.)-Sanger Harris or May D&F supplement to Dallas Times, Dallas Herald, Denver Post, Kansas City Star, Tulsa World; Foley's supplement to Houston Chronicle (1982, 16 pgs.)- "Great Rodeo Robbery"; The Jones Store-giveaway (1983, 16 pgs.) 3 6 9 16 23 30
...and the New Mutants Featuring Skids nn (1990, National Committee for Prevention of Child Abuse/K-Mart giveaway)-Williams-c(i) 2 4 6 8 10 12
... Battles Ignorance (1992)(Sylvan Learning Systems) giveaway; Mad Thinker app. Kupperberg-a 2 4 6 8 10 12
...Captain America, The Incredible Hulk, & Spider-Woman (1981) (7-11 Stores giveaway; 36 pgs.) 3 6 9 14 19 24
...: Christmas in Dallas (1983) (Supplement to Dallas Times Herald) giveaway 3 6 9 14 19 24
...: Danger in Dallas (1983) (Supplement to Dallas Times Herald) giveaway 3 6 9 14 19 24
...: Danger in Denver (1983) (Supplement to Denver Post) giveaway for May D&F stores 3 6 9 14 19 24
..., Fire-Star, And Ice-Man at the Dallas Ballet Nutcracker (1983; supplement to Dallas Times Herald)-Mooney-p 3 6 9 14 19 24
Giveaway-Esquire Magazine (2/69)-Miniature-Still attached (scarce)
15 30 45 100 220 340
Giveaway-Eye Magazine (2/69)-Miniature-Still attached
10 20 30 67 141 215
...: Riot at Robotworld (1991; 16 pgs.)(National Action Council for Minorities in Engineering, Inc.) giveaway; Saviuk-c 1 2 3 5 6 8
..., Storm & Powerman (1982; 20 pgs.)(American Cancer Society) giveaway; also a 1991 2nd printing and a 1994 printing 2 4 6 8 10 12
...Vs. The Hulk (Special Edition; 1979, 20 pgs.)(Supplement to Columbus Dispatch)
3 6 9 16 23 30
...Vs. The Prodigy (Giveaway, 16 pgs. in color (1976, 5x6-1/2")-Sex education; (1 million printed; 35-50¢) 2 4 6 9 13 16
Spidey & The Mini-Marvels Halloween 2003 Ashcan (12/03, 8 1/2"x 5 1/2") Giarusso-s/a; Venom and Green Goblin app. 3.00

AMERICA MENACED!
Vital Publications: 1950 (Paper-c)
nn-Anti-communism 42 84 126 265 445 625

AMERICAN COMICS
Theatre Giveaways (Liberty Theatre, Grand Rapids, Mich. known): 1940's
Many possible combinations. "Golden Age" superhero comics with new cover added and given away at theaters. Following known: Superman #59, Capt. Marvel #20, 21, Capt. Marvel Jr. #5, Action #33, Classics Comics #8, Whiz #39. Value would vary with book and should be 70-80 percent of the original.

AMERICA UNDER SOCIALISM
National Research Bureau: 1950 (Paper-c)
nn-Anti-communism; 16 pages (a CGC 9.2 copy sold for $2520 in Nov. 2020)

ANDY HARDY COMICS
Western Printing Co.:
...& the New Automatic Gas Clothes Dryer (1952, 5x7-1/4", 16 pgs.) Bendix Giveaway (soft-c) 6 12 18 31 38 45

ANIMANIACS EMERGENCY WORLD
DC Comics: 1995
nn-American Red Cross 5.00

APACHE HUNTER
Creative Pictorials: 1954 (18 pgs. in color) (promo copy) (saddle stitched)
nn-Severin, Heath stories 15 30 45 88 137 185

AQUATEERS MEET THE SUPER FRIENDS
DC Comics: 1979
nn 2 4 6 11 16 20

ARCHIE AND HIS GANG (Zeta Beta Tau Presents...)
Archie Publications: Dec. 1950 (St. Louis National Convention giveaway)
nn-Contains new cover stapled over Archie Comics #47 (11-12/50) on inside; produced for Zeta Beta Tau 32 64 96 188 307 425

ARCHIE COMICS (Also see Sabrina)
Archie Publications
... And Friends and the Shield (10/02, 8 1/2"x 5 1/2") Diamond Comic Dist. 4.00
... And Friends - A Halloween Tale (10/98, 8 1/2"x 5 1/2") Diamond Comic Dist.; Sabrina and Sonic app.; Dan DeCarlo-a 4.00
... And Friends - A Timely Tale (10/01, 8 1/2"x 5 1/2") Diamond Comic Dist. 4.00
... And Friends Monster Bash 2003 (8 1/2"x 5 1/2") Diamond Comic Dist. Halloween 4.00
...And His Friends Help Raise Literacy Awareness In Mississippi nn (3/94)
1 2 3 5 6 8
...And His Friends Vs. The Household Toxic Wastes nn (1993, 16 pgs.) produced for the San Diego Regional Household Hazardous Materials Program
1 2 3 5 6 8
...And His Pals in the Peer Helping Program nn (2/91, 7"x4 1/2") produced by the FBI
1 2 3 5 6 8
...And the History of Electronics nn (5/90, 36 pgs.)-Radio Shack giveaway; Bender-c/a
1 2 3 5 6 8
Fairmont Potato Chips Giveaway-Mini comics 1970 (6 issues-nn's.,6 7/8" x 2 1/4", 8 pgs. each)
3 6 9 18 28 38
Fairmont Potato Chips Giveaway-Mini comics 1971 (4 issues-nn's.,6 7/8" x 5", 8 pgs. each)
3 6 9 18 28 38
Little Archie, The House That Wouldn't Move ('07, 8-1/2" x 5-3/8" Halloween mini-comic) 3.00
...'s Ham Radio Adventure (1997) Morse code instruction; Goldberg-a 6.00
...'s Weird Mysteries (9/99, 8 1/2"x 5 1/2") Diamond Comic Dist. Halloween giveaway 3.00
Tales From Riverdale (2006, 8 1/2"x 5 1/2") Diamond Comic Dist. Halloween giveaway 3.00
...: The Dawn of Time ('10, 8-1/2" x 5-3/8" Halloween mini-comic) 3.00
...: The Mystery of the Museum Sleep-In ('08, 8-1/2" x 5-3/8" Halloween mini-comic) 3.00
... Your Official Store Club Magazine nn (10/48, 9-1/2x6-1/2, 16 pgs.)- "Wolf Whistle" Archie on front-c; B. R. Baker Co. ad on back-c (a CGC 7.5 copy sold for $1912 in Feb. 2013)

ARCHIE SHOE-STORE GIVEAWAY
Archie Publications: 1944-50 (12-15 pgs. of games, puzzles, stories like Superman-Tim books, No nos. - came out monthly)
(1944-47)-issues 34 68 102 199 325 450
2/48-Peggy Lee photo-c 28 56 84 165 270 375
3/48-Marylee Robb photo-c 22 44 66 128 209 290
4/48-Gloria De Haven photo-c 28 56 84 165 270 375
5/48, 6/48, 7/48 22 44 66 128 209 290
8/48-Story on Shirley Temple 28 56 84 165 270 375
10/48-Wolf whistle-c 71 142 213 454 777 1100
5/49-Kathleen Hughes photo-c 21 42 63 124 202 280
6/49, 7/49, 9/49 20 40 60 114 182 250
8/49-Archie photo-c from radio show 34 68 102 199 325 450
10/49-Gloria Mann photo-c from radio show 24 48 72 142 234 325
11/49, 12/49, 2/50, 3/50 21 42 63 124 202 280

ARCHIE'S JOKE BOOK MAGAZINE (See Joke Book ...)
Archie Publications
Drug Store Giveaway (No. 39 w/new-c) 10 20 30 54 72 90

ARCHIE'S TEN ISSUE COLLECTOR'S SET (Title inside of cover only)
Archie Publications: June, 1997 - No. 10, June, 1997 ($1.50, 20 pgs.)
1-10: 1,7-Archie. 2,8-Betty & Veronica. 3,9-Veronica. 4-Betty. 5-World of Archie. 6-Jughead. 10-Archie and Friends each... 5.00

ASTRO COMICS
American Airlines (Harvey): 1968 - 1979 (Giveaway)(Reprints of Harvey comics)
1968-Richie Rich, Hot Stuff, Casper, Wendy on-c only; Spooky and Nightmare app. inside
4 8 12 23 37 50
1970-Casper, Spooky, Hot Stuff, Stumbo the Giant, Little Audrey, Little Lotta, & Richie Rich reprints. Five different versions 3 6 9 17 26 35
1973,1975,1976: 1973-Three different versions 2 4 6 11 16 20
1977-r/Richie Rich & Casper #20. 1978-r/Richie Rich & Casper #25. 1979-r/Richie Rich & Casper #30 (scarce) 2 4 6 9 13 16

ATARI FORCE (Given away with Atari games)
DC Comics: 1982 - No. 5, 1983
1-3 (1982, 5x7", 52 pgs.) 2 4 6 10 14 18
4,5 (1982-1983, 52 pgs.)(scarcer) 3 6 9 14 20 25

AURORA COMIC SCENES INSTRUCTION BOOKLET (Included with superhero model kits)
Aurora Plastics Co.: 1974 (6-1/4x9-3/4," 8 pgs., slick paper)
181-140-Tarzan; Neal Adams-a 3 6 9 18 27 38
182-140-Spider-Man. 4 8 12 23 37 50
183-140-Tonto(Gil Kane art). 184-140-Hulk. 185-140-Superman. 186-140-Superboy. 187-140-Batman. 188-140-The Lone Ranger(1974-by Gil Kane). 192-140-Captain America(1975). 193-140-Robin 3 6 9 16 23 30

BACK TO THE FUTURE
Harvey Comics
Special nn (1991, 20 pgs.)-Brunner-c; given away at Universal Studios in Florida
3 6 9 14 19 24

BALTIMORE COLTS
American Visuals Corp.: 1950 (Giveaway)
nn-Eisner-c 50 100 150 315 533 750

BAMBI (Disney)
K. K. Publications (Giveaways): 1941, 1942
1941-Horlick's Malted Milk & various toy stores; text & pictures; most copies mailed out with store stickers on-c 45 90 135 284 480 675
1942-Same as 4-Color #12, but no price (Same as '41 issue?) (Scarce)
100 200 300 640 1095 1550

BATMAN
DC Comics: 1966 - Present
Act II Popcorn mini-comic(1998) 1 2 3 5 6 8
Batman #121 Toys R Us edition (1997) r/1st Mr. Freeze
2 4 6 10 14 18
Batman #279 Mini-comic with Monogram Model kit (1995)
1 2 3 5 6 8
Batman #362 Mervyn's edition (1989) 6.00
Batman #608 New York Post edition (2002) 2 4 6 8 10 12
Batman Adventures #25 Best Western edition (1997) 5.00
Batman and Other DC Classics 1 (1989, giveaway)-DC Comics/Diamond Comic Distributors; Batman origin-r/Batman #47, Camelot 3000-r, Justice League-r('87), New Teen Titans-r 5.00
Batman and Robin movie preview (1997, 8 pgs.) Kellogg's Cereal promo 4.00
Batman Beyond Six Flags edition 1 2 3 5 6 8
Batman: Canadian Multiculturalism Custom (1992) 5.00
Batman Claritan edition (1999) 4.00
Kellogg's Poptarts comics (1966, Set of 6, 16 pgs.); All were folded and placed in Poptarts boxes. Infantino art on Catwoman and Joker issues.
"The Man in the Iron Mask", "The Penguin's Fowl Play", "The Joker's Happy Victims", "The Catwoman's Catnapping Caper", "The Mad Hatter's Hat Crimes", "The Case of the Batman II"
each.... 6 12 18 37 66 95
Mask of the Phantasm (1993) Mini-comic released w/video
2 4 6 8 10 12
Onstar - Auto Show Special Edition (OnStar Corp., 2001, 8 pgs.) Riddler app. 3.00
Pizza Hut giveaway (12/77)-exact-r of #122,123; Joker app.
2 4 6 13 18 22
Prell Shampoo giveaway (1966, 16 pgs.)- "The Joker's Practical Jokes" (6-7/8x3-3/8") 11 22 33 76 163 250
Revell in pack (1995) 4.00
...: The 10-Cent Adventure (3/02, 10¢) intro. to the "Bruce Wayne: Murderer" x-over; Rucka-s/ Burchett & Janson-a/Dave Johnson-c; these are alternate copies with special outer half-covers (at least 10 different) promoting comics, toys and games shops 3.00

Archie and Friends Monster Bash 2003 © ACP

Aurora Comic Scenes #184-140 Hulk © MAR

Blood is the Harvest #1 © CCG

	GD 2.0	VG 4.0	FN 6.0	VF 8.0	VF/NM 9.0	NM- 9.2
BATMAN RECORD COMIC						
National Periodical Publications: 1966 (one-shot)						
1-With record (still sealed)	14	28	42	96	211	325
Comic only	10	20	30	64	132	200
BEETLE BAILEY						
Charlton Comics: 1969-1970 (Giveaways)						
Armed Forces ('69)-same as regular issue (#68)	2	4	6	10	14	18
Armed Forces ('70)	2	4	6	10	14	18
Bold Detergent ('69)-same as regular issue (#67)	2	4	6	10	14	18
Cerebral Palsy Assn. V2#71('69) - V2#73(#1,1/70)						3.00
Red Cross (1969, 5x7", 16 pgs., paper-c)	2	4	6	10	14	18
BELLAIRE BICYCLE CO.						
Bellaire Bicycle Co.: 1940 (promotional comic)(64 pgs.)						
nn-Contains Wonderworld #12 w/new-c. Contents can vary w/diff. 1940's books	54	108	162	343	574	825
BEST WESTERN GIVEAWAY						
DC Comics: 1999						
nn-Best Western hotels						3.00
BETTER LIFE FOR YOU, A						
Harvey Publications Inc.: (16 pgs., paper cover)						
nn-Better living through higher productivity	3	6	9	15	22	28
BEWARE THE BOOBY TRAP						
Malcolm Alter: 1970 (5" x 7")						
nn-Deals with drug abuse	5	10	15	33	57	80
B-FORCE (Milwaukee Brewers and Wisconsin Dental Asso.)						
Dark Horse Comics: 2001 (School and stadium giveaway)						
nn-Brewers players combat the evils of smokeless tobacco						4.00
BIG BOY (see Adventures of...)						
BIG JIM'S P.A.C.K.						
Mattel, Inc. (Marvel Comics): No date (1975) (16 pgs.)						
nn-Giveaway with Big Jim doll; Buscema/Sinnott-c/a	4	8	12	27	44	60
"BILL AND TED'S EXCELLENT ADVENTURE" MOVIE ADAPTATION						
DC Comics: 1989 (No cover price)						
nn-Torres-a	1	2	3	5	6	8
BIONICLE (LEGO robot toys)						
DC Comics: Jun, 2001 - No. 27, Nov, 2005 ($2.25/$3.25, 16 pgs, available to LEGO club members)						
1	2	4	6	8	10	12
2-5						6.00
6-13						4.00
14-27						3.00
The Legend of Bionicle (McDonald's Mini-comic, 4-1/4 x 7")						4.00
Special Edition #0 (Six Heroes...One Destiny) '03 San Diego Comic Con; Ashley Wood-c	1	2	3	5	6	8
BLACK GOLD						
Esso Service Station (Giveaway): 1945? (8 pgs. in color)						
nn-Reprints from True Comics	7	14	21	35	43	50
BLADE SINS OF THE FATHER						
Marvel Comics: Aug, 1996 (24 pgs. with paper cover)						
1-Theatrical preview; possibly limited to 2000 copies (Value will be based on sale)						
BLAZING FOREST, THE (See Forest Fire and Smokey Bear)						
Western Printing: 1962 (20 pgs., 5x7", slick-c)						
nn-Smokey The Bear fire prevention	3	6	9	14	20	26
BLESSED PIUS X						
Catechetical Guild (Giveaway): No date (Text/comics, 32 pgs., paper-c)						
nn	12	24	36	69	97	125
BLIND JUSTICE (Also see Batman: Blind Justice)						
DC Comics/Diamond Comic Distributors: 1989 (Giveaway, squarebound)						
nn-Contains Detective #598-600 by Batman movie writer Sam Hamm, w/covers; published same time as originals?						6.00
BLONDIE COMICS						
Harvey Publications: 1950-1964						
1950 Giveaway	10	20	30	54	72	90
1962,1964 Giveaway	3	6	9	18	28	38
N. Y. State Dept. of Mental Hygiene Giveaway-(1950) Regular size; 16 pgs.; no #	5	10	15	31	53	75
N. Y. State Dept. of Mental Hygiene Giveaway-(1956) Regular size; 16 pgs.; no #	3	6	9	19	30	40
N. Y. State Dept. of Mental Hygiene Giveaway-(1961) Regular size; 16 pgs.; no #	3	6	9	16	24	32

	GD 2.0	VG 4.0	FN 6.0	VF 8.0	VF/NM 9.0	NM- 9.2
BLOOD IS THE HARVEST						
Catechetical Guild: 1950 (32 pgs., paper-c)						
(Scarce)-Anti-communism (35 known copies)	265	530	795	1694	2897	4100
Black & white version (5 known copies), saddle stitched	129	258	387	826	1413	2000
Untrimmed version (only one known copy); estimated value - $4500						
NOTE: *In 1979 nine copies of the color version surfaced from the old Guild's files plus the five black & white copies.*						
BLUE BIRD CHILDREN'S MAGAZINE, THE						
Graphic Information Service: V1#2, 1957 - No. 10 1958 (16 pgs., soft-c, regular size)						
V1#2-10: Pat, Pete & Blue Bird app.	2	4	6	10	14	18
BLUE BIRD COMICS						
Various Shoe Stores: 1947 - 1950 (Giveaway, 36 pgs.)						
Charlton Comics: 1959 - 1964 (Giveaway)						
nn-(1947-50, not Charlton)(36 pgs.)-Several issues; Human Torch, Sub-Mariner app. in some	21	42	63	126	206	285
1959-(Charlton) Lil Genius, Wild Bill Hickok, Black Fury, Masked Raider, Timmy The Timid Ghost, Freddy (All #1)	3	6	9	15	22	28
1959-(Charlton, same 6 titles; all #2-5) except (#5) Masked Raider #21	3	6	9	14	20	25
1959-(#5) Masked Raider #21	3	6	9	16	23	30
1960-(6 titles, all #6-9) Black Fury, Masked Raider, Freddy, Timmy the Timid Ghost, Li'l Genius, Six Gun Heroes	3	6	9	14	19	24
1961-(All #10's) Black Fury, Masked Raider, Freddy, Timmy the Timid Ghost, Li'l Genius, Six Gun Heroes (Charlton)	2	4	6	13	18	22
1961-(All #11-13) Lil Genius, Wyatt Earp, Black Fury, Timmy the Timid Ghost, Atomic Mouse, Freddy	2	4	6	13	18	22
1962-(All #14) Lil Genius, Wyatt Earp, Black Fury, Timmy the Timid Ghost, Atomic Mouse, Freddy	2	4	6	13	18	22
1962-(6 titles, all #15) Lil Genius, Six Gun Heroes, Black Fury, Timmy the Timid Ghost, Texas Rangers, Freddy	2	4	6	13	18	22
1962-(7 titles, all #16) Lil Genius, Six Gun Heroes, Black Fury, Timmy the Timid Ghost, Texas Rangers, Wyatt Earp, Atomic Mouse	2	4	6	13	18	22
1963-(All #17) My Little Margie, Lil Genius, Timmy the Timid Ghost, Texas Rangers (Charlton)	2	4	6	9	13	16
1964-(All #18) Mysteries of Unexplored Worlds, Teenage Hotrodders, War Heroes, Wyatt Earp (Charlton)	2	4	6	9	13	16
NOTE: *Reprints comics of regular issue, with Blue Bird shoe promo on back cover, with upper front cover imprint of various shoe retailers. Printed from 1959 to 1962, with issues 1 thru 16. The 8 different front cover imprints for issues 1 thru 16 are, 1) Blue Bird Shoes, 2) Schiff's Shoes, 3) Big Shoe Store, 4) E.D. Edwards Shoe Store, 5) R & S Shoe store, 6) Federal Shoe Store, 7) Kirby's Shoes, 8) Gallenkamps.*						
BOB & BETTY & SANTA'S WISHING WHISTLE (Also see A Christmas Carol, Merry Christmas From Sears Toyland, and Santa's Christmas Comic Variety Show)						
Sears Roebuck & Co.: 1941 (Christmas giveaway, 12 pgs., oblong)						
nn	26	52	78	154	252	350
BOBBY BENSON'S B-BAR-B RIDERS (Radio)						
Magazine Enterprises/AC Comics						
...in the Tunnel of Gold-(1936, 5-1/4x8"; 100 pgs.) Radio giveaway by Hecker-H.O. Company (H.O. Oats); contains 22 color pgs. of comics, rest in novel form	14	28	42	76	108	140
...And The Lost Herd-same as above	14	28	42	76	108	140
BOBBY GETS HEP						
Bell Telephone: 1946						
nn-Bell Telephone Systems giveaway	8	16	24	40	50	60
BOBBY SHELBY COMICS						
Shelby Cycle Co./Harvey Publications: 1949						
nn	6	12	18	31	36	45
BOY SCOUT ADVENTURE						
Boy Scouts of America: 1954 (16 pgs., paper cover)						
nn	5	10	15	24	30	35
BOYS' RANCH						
Harvey Publications: 1951						
Shoe Store Giveaway #5,6 (Identical to regular issues except Simon & Kirby centerfold replaced with ad)	14	28	42	76	108	140
BOZO THE CLOWN (TV)						
Dell Publishing Co.: 1961						
Giveaway-1961, 16 pgs., 3-1/2x7-1/4", Apsco Products	5	10	15	31	53	75
BRER RABBIT IN "ICE CREAM FOR THE PARTY"						
American Dairy Association: 1955 (5x7-1/4", 16 pgs., soft-c) (Walt Disney) (Premium)						
nn-(Scarce)	42	84	126	265	445	625
BUCK ROGERS (In the 25th Century)						
Kelloggs Corn Flakes Giveaway: 1933 (6x8", 36 pgs)						

GD 2.0 | VG 4.0 | FN 6.0 | VF 8.0 | VF/NM 9.0 | NM- 9.2

370A-By Phil Nowlan & Dick Calkins; 1st Buck Rogers radio premium & 1st app.
in comics (tells origin) (Reissued in 1995) 78 156 234 575 - -
with envelope 100 200 300 750 - -

BUGS BUNNY (Puffed Rice Giveaway)
Quaker Cereals: 1949 (32 pgs. each, 3-1/8x6-7/8")
A1-Traps the Counterfeiters, A2-Aboard Mystery Submarine, A3- Rocket to the Moon, A4-Lion Tamer, A5-Rescues the Beautiful Princess, B1-Buried Treasure, B2-Outwits the Smugglers, B3-Joins the Marines, B4-Meets the Dwarf Ghost, B5-Finds Aladdin's Lamp, C1-Lost in the Frozen North, C2-Secret Agent, C3-Captured by Cannibals, C4-Fights the Man from Mars, C5-And the Haunted Cave
each.... 8 16 24 40 50 60
Mailing Envelope (has illo of Bugs on front)(Each envelope designates what set it contains, A,B or C on front) 8 16 24 40 50 60

BUGS BUNNY (3-D)
Cheerios Giveaway: 1953 (Pocket size) (15 titles)
each.... 10 20 30 58 79 100
Mailing Envelope (has Bugs drawn on front) 10 20 30 58 79 100

BUGS BUNNY
DC Comics: May, 1997 ($4.95, 24 pgs., comic-sized)
1-Numbered ed. of 100,000; "1st Day of Issue" stamp cancellation on-c 6.00

BUGS BUNNY POSTAL COMIC
DC Comics: 1997 (64 pgs., 7.5" x 5")
nn -Mail Fan; Daffy Duck app. 4.50

BULLETMAN
Fawcett Publications
Well Known Comics (1942)-Paper-c, glued binding; printed in red (Bestmaid/Samuel Lowe giveaway) 17 34 51 100 158 215

BULLS-EYE (Cody of The Pony Express No. 8 on)
Charlton: 1955 (Great Scott Shoe Store giveaway)
Reprints #2 with new cover 20 40 60 114 182 250

BUSTER BROWN COMICS (Radio)(Also see My Dog Tige in Promotional sec.)
Brown Shoe Co.: 1945 - No. 43, 1959 (No. 5: paper-c)
nn, nd (#1,scarce)-Featuring Smilin' Ed McConnell & the Buster Brown gang "Midnight" the cat, "Squeaky" the mouse & "Froggy" the Gremlin; covers mention diff. shoe stores.
Contains adventure stories 68 136 204 435 743 1050
2 21 42 63 124 202 280
3,5-10 14 28 42 80 115 150
4 (Rare)-Low print run due to paper shortage 20 40 60 115 188 260
11-20 9 18 27 52 69 85
21-24,26-28 7 14 21 35 43 50
25,33-37,40,41-Crandall-a in all 10 20 30 58 79 100
29-32-"Interplanetary Police Vs. the Space Siren" by Crandall (pencils only #29) 11 22 33 62 86 110
38,39,42,43 7 14 21 35 43 50

BUSTER BROWN COMICS (Radio)
Brown Shoe Co: 1950s
...Goes to Mars (2/58-Western Printing), slick-c, 20 pgs., reg. size 15 30 45 83 124 165
...In "Buster Makes the Team!" (1959-Custom Comics) 9 18 27 47 61 75
...In The Jet Age ('50s), slick-c, 20 pgs., 5x7-1/4" 11 22 33 60 83 105
...Of the Safety Patrol ('60-Custom Comics) 3 6 9 19 30 40
...Out of This World ('59-Custom Comics) 7 14 21 37 46 55
...Safety Coloring Book ('58, 16 pgs.)-Slick paper 7 14 21 37 46 55

CALL FROM CHRIST
Catechetical Educational Society: 1952 (Giveaway, 36 pgs.)
nn 7 14 21 37 46 55

CANCELLED COMIC CAVALCADE
DC Comics, Inc.: Summer, 1978 - No. 2, Fall, 1978 (8-1/2x11", B&W)
(Xeroxed pgs. on one side only w/blue cover and taped spine)(Only 35 sets produced)
1-(412 pgs.) Contains xeroxed copies of art for: Black Lightning #12, cover to #13; Claw #13,14; The Deserter #1; Doorway to Nightmare #6; Firestorm #6; The Green Team #2,3.
2-(532 pgs.) Contains xeroxed copies of art for: Kamandi #60 (including Omac), #61; Prez #5; Shade #9 (including The Odd Man); Showcase #105 (Deadman), 106 (The Creeper); Secret Society of Super Villains #16 & 17; The Vixen #1; and covers to Army at War #2, Battle Classics #3, Demand Classics #1 & 2, Dynamic Classics #3, Mr. Miracle #26, Ragman #6, Weird Mystery #25 & 26, & Western Classics #1 & 2.
(A FN set of Number 1 & 2 was sold in 2005 for $3680; a VG set sold in 2007 for $2629)
NOTE: *In June, 1978, DC cancelled several of their titles. For copyright purposes, the unpublished original art for these titles was xeroxed, bound in the above books, published and distributed. Only 35 copies were made. Beware of bootleg copies.*

CAP'N CRUNCH COMICS (See Quaker Oats)
Quaker Oats Co.: 1963; 1965 (16 pgs.; miniature giveaways; 2-1/2x6-1/2")
(1963 titles)- "The Picture Pirates", "The Fountain of Youth", "I'm Dreaming of a Wide Isthmus". (1965 titles)- "Bewitched, Betwitched, & Betweaked", "Seadog Meets the Witch Doctor", "A Witch in Time" 5 10 15 33 57 80

CAPTAIN ACTION (Toy)
National Periodical Publications
...& Action Boy('67)-Ideal Toy Co. giveaway (1st app. Captain Action) 11 22 33 73 157 240

CAPTAIN AMERICA
Marvel Comics Group
...& The Campbell Kids (1980, 36pg. giveaway, Campbell's Soup/U.S. Dept. of Energy) 2 4 6 11 16 20
...Goes To War Against Drugs(1990, no #, giveaway)-Distributed to direct sales shops; 2nd printing exists 2 4 6 9 12 15
...Meets The Asthma Monster (1987, no #, giveaway, Your Physician and Glaxo, Inc.) 2 4 6 8 10 12
Return of The Asthma Monster Vol. 1 #2 (1992, giveaway, Your Physician & Allen & Hanbury's) 2 4 6 8 10 12
...Vs. Asthma Monster (1990, no #, giveaway, Your Physician & Allen & Hanbury's) 2 4 6 8 10 12

CAPTAIN AMERICA COMICS
Timely/Marvel Comics: 1954
Shoestore Giveaway #77 200 400 600 1280 2190 3100

CAPTAIN ATOM
Nationwide Publishers
...- Secret of the Columbian Jungle (16 pgs. in color, paper-c, 3-3/4x5-1/8")- Fireside Marshmallow giveaway 6 12 18 31 38 45

CAPTAIN BEN DIX
Bendix Aviation Corporation: 1943 (Small size)
nn 10 20 30 54 72 90

CAPTAIN BEN DIX IN ACTION WITH THE INVISIBLE CREW
Bendix Aviation Corp.: 1940s (nd), (20 pgs, 8-1/4"x11", heavy paper)
nn-WWII bomber-c; Japanese app. 9 18 27 47 61 75

CAPTAIN BEN DIX IN SECRETS OF THE INVISIBLE CREW
Bendix Aviation Corp.: 1940s (nd), (32 pgs, soft-c)
nn 9 18 27 47 61 75

CAPTAIN FORTUNE PRESENTS
Vital Publications: 1955 - 1959 (Giveaway, 3-1/4x6-7/8", 16 pgs.)
"Davy Crockett in Episodes of the Creek War", "Davy Crockett at the Alamo", "In Sherwood Forest Tells Strange Tales of Robin Hood" ('57), "Meets Bolivar the Liberator" ('59), "Tells How Buffalo Bill Fights the Dog Soldiers" ('57), "Young Davy Crockett" 4 8 12 17 21 24

CAPTAIN GALLANT (...of the Foreign Legion) (TV)
Charlton Comics
Heinz Foods Premium (#1?)(1955; regular size)-U.S. Pictorial; contains Buster Crabbe photos; Don Heck-a 1 3 4 6 8 10
Mailing Envelope 20.00

CAPTAIN JOLLY ADVENTURES
Johnston and Cushing: 1950's, nd (Post Corn Fetti cereal giveaway) (5-1/4" x 4-1/2")
1-3: 1-Captain Jolly Advs. 2-Captain Jolly and His Pirate Crew in Off To Treasure Island. 3-C.J. & His Pirate Crew in The Terror Of The Deep 3 6 8 12 14 16

CAPTAIN MARVEL ADVENTURES
Fawcett Publications
Bond Bread Giveaways-(24 pgs.; pocket size-7-1/4x3-1/2"; paper cover): "...& the Stolen City" ('48), "The Boy Who Never Heard of Capt. Marvel", "Meets the Weatherman" (1950) (reprint) each.... 26 52 78 154 252 350
...Well Known Comics (1944; 12 pgs.; 8-1/2x10-1/2")-printed in red & in blue; soft-c; glued binding - (Bestmaid/Samuel Lowe Co. giveaway) 19 38 57 112 179 245

CAPTAIN MARVEL ADVENTURES (Also see Flash and Funny Stuff)
Fawcett Publications (Wheaties Giveaway): 1945 (6x8", full color, paper-c)
nn- "Captain Marvel & the Threads of Life" plus 2 other stories (32 pgs.) 60 120 300 600 - -
NOTE: *All copies were taped at each corner to a box of Wheaties and are never found in Fine or Mint condition. Prices listed for each grade include tape. File copy stamped "June 21, 1947".*

CAPTAIN MARVEL AND THE LTS. OF SAFETY
Ebasco Services/Fawcett Publications: 1950 - 1951 (3 issues - no No.'s)
nn (#1) "Danger Flies a Kite" ('50, scarce), 40 80 120 246 441 575
nn (#2)"Danger Takes to Climbing" ('50), 28 56 84 165 270 375
nn (#3)"Danger Smashes Street Lights" ('51) 28 56 84 165 270 375

CAPTAIN MARVEL, JR.
Fawcett Publications: (1944; 12 pgs.; 8-1/2x10-1/2")
...Well Known Comics (Printed in blue; paper-c, glued binding)-Bestmaid/Samuel Lowe Co. giveaway 15 30 45 86 133 180

CARDINAL MINDSZENTY (The Truth Behind the Trial of...)
Catechetical Guild Education Society: 1949 (24 pgs., paper cover)
nn-Anti-communism 15 30 45 85 130 175
Press Proof-(Very Rare)-(Full color, 7-1/2x11-3/4", untrimmed) Only two known copies 460.00
Preview Copy (B&W, stapled), 18 pgs.; contains first 13 pgs. of Cardinal Mindszenty and was sent out as an advance promotion. Only one known copy 450.00 - 550.00
NOTE: *Regular edition also printed in French. There was also a movie released in 1949 called "Guilty of Treason" which is a fact-based account of the trial and imprisonment of Cardinal Mindszenty by the Communist regime in Hungary.*

CARNIVAL OF COMICS
Fleet-Air Shoes: 1954 (Giveaway)
nn-Contains a comic bound with new cover; several combinations possible; Charlton's Eh! known 6 12 18 28 34 40

CARTOON NETWORK
DC Comics: 1997 (Giveaway)
nn-reprints Cow and Chicken, Scooby-Doo, & Flintstones stories 6.00

CARVEL COMICS (Amazing Advs. of Capt. Carvel)
Carvel Corp. (Ice Cream): 1975 - No. 5, 1976 (25¢; #3-5: 35¢) (#4,5: 3-1/4x5")
1-3 1 2 3 5 6 8
4,5(1976)-Baseball theme 2 4 6 8 10 12

CASE OF THE WASTED WATER, THE
Rheem Water Heating: 1972? (Giveaway)
nn-Neal Adams-a 4 8 12 28 47 65

CASPER SPECIAL
Target Stores (Harvey): nd (Dec, 1990) (Giveaway with $1.00 cover)
Three issues-Given away with Casper video 6.00

CASPER, THE FRIENDLY GHOST (Paramount Picture Star...)(2nd Series)
Harvey Publications

Buster Brown Comics #25 © BBS

Carvel Comics #3 © Carvel

A Christmas Dream © PPC

	GD 2.0	VG 4.0	FN 6.0	VF 8.0	VF/NM 9.0	NM- 9.2

American Dental Association (Giveaways):
...'s Dental Health Activity Book-1977 2 4 6 8 11 14
...Presents Space Age Dentistry-1972 2 4 6 9 13 16
..., His Den, & Their Dentist Fight the Tooth Demons-1974
2 4 6 9 13 16
Casper Rides the School Bus (1960, 7x3.5", 16 pgs.) 2 4 6 9 13 16

CELEBRATE THE CENTURY SUPERHEROES STAMP ALBUM
DC Comics: 1998 - No. 5, 2000 (32 pgs.)
1-5: Historical stories hosted by DC heroes 4.00

CENTIPEDE
DC Comics: 1983
1-Based on Atari video game 2 4 6 13 18 22

CENTURY OF COMICS
Eastern Color Printing Co.: 1933 (100 pgs.)
Bought by Wheatena, Malt-O-Milk, John Wanamaker, Kinney Shoe Stores, & others to be used as premiums and radio giveaways. No publisher listed.
nn-Mutt & Jeff, Joe Palooka, etc. reprints 2050 4100 6150 15,500 - -

CHEERIOS PREMIUMS (Disney)
Walt Disney Productions: 1947 (16 titles, pocket size, 32 pgs.)
Mailing Envelope for each set "W,X,Y & Z" (has Mickey illo on front)(each envelope designates the set it contains on the front) 9 18 27 50 65 80
Set "W"
W1-Donald Duck & the Pirates 9 18 27 52 69 85
W2-Bucky Bug & the Cannibal King 6 12 18 27 33 38
W3-Pluto Joins the F.B.I. 6 12 18 27 33 38
W4-Mickey Mouse & the Haunted House 6 12 18 29 36 42
Set "X"
X1-Donald Duck, Counter Spy 9 18 27 50 65 80
X2-Goofy Lost in the Desert 6 12 18 27 33 38
X3-Br'er Rabbit Outwits Br'er Fox 6 12 18 27 33 38
X4-Mickey Mouse at the Rodeo 6 12 18 31 38 45
Set "Y"
Y1-Donald Duck's Atom Bomb by Carl Barks. Disney has banned reprinting this book
71 142 213 454 777 1100
Y2-Br'er Rabbit's Secret 6 12 18 27 33 38
Y3-Dumbo & the Circus Mystery 6 12 18 27 33 38
Y4-Mickey Mouse Meets the Wizard 6 12 18 33 41 48
Set "Z"
Z1-Donald Duck Pilots a Jet Plane (not by Barks) 9 18 27 47 61 75
Z2-Pluto Turns Sleuth Hound 5 10 15 25 31 36
Z3-The Seven Dwarfs & the Enchanted Mtn. 6 12 18 33 41 48
Z4-Mickey Mouse's Secret Room 6 12 18 33 41 48

CHEERIOS 3-D GIVEAWAYS (Disney)
Walt Disney Productions: 1954 (24 titles, pocket size) (Glasses came in envelopes)
Glasses only... 4 7 10 14 17 20
Mailing Envelope (no art on front) 6 12 18 27 33 38
(Set 1)
1-Donald Duck & Uncle Scrooge, the Firefighters 7 14 21 35 43 50
2-Mickey Mouse & Goofy, Pirate Plunder 7 14 21 35 43 50
3-Donald Duck's Nephews, the Fabulous Inventors 7 14 21 37 46 55
4-Mickey Mouse, Secret of the Ming Vase 6 12 18 29 36 42
5-Donald Duck with Huey, Dewey, & Louie; ...the Seafarers (title on 2nd page)
7 14 21 35 43 50
6-Mickey Mouse, Moaning Mountain 6 12 18 29 36 42
7-Donald Duck, Apache Gold 7 14 21 35 43 50
8-Mickey Mouse, Flight to Nowhere 6 12 18 29 36 42
(Set 2)
1-Donald Duck, Treasure of Timbuktu 7 14 21 35 43 50
2-Mickey Mouse & Pluto, Operation China 6 12 18 29 36 42
3-Donald Duck and the Magic Cows 7 14 21 35 43 50
4-Mickey Mouse & Goofy, Kid Kokonut 6 12 18 29 36 42
5-Donald Duck, Mystery Ship 7 14 21 35 43 50
6-Mickey Mouse, Phantom Sheriff 6 12 18 29 36 42
7-Donald Duck, Circus Adventures 7 14 21 35 43 50
8-Mickey Mouse, Arctic Explorers 6 12 18 29 36 42
(Set 3)
1-Donald Duck & Witch Hazel 7 14 21 35 43 50
2-Mickey Mouse in Darkest Africa 6 12 18 29 36 42
3-Donald Duck & Uncle Scrooge, Timber Trouble 7 14 21 35 43 50
4-Mickey Mouse, Rajah's Rescue 6 12 18 29 36 42
5-Donald Duck in Robot Reporter 7 14 21 35 43 50
6-Mickey Mouse, Slumbering Sleuth 6 12 18 29 36 42
7-Donald Duck in the Foreign Legion 7 14 21 35 43 50
8-Mickey Mouse, Airwalking Wonder 6 12 18 29 36 42

CHESTY AND COPTIE (Disney)
Los Angeles Community Chest: 1946 (Giveaway, 4pgs.)
nn-(One known copy) by Floyd Gottfredson (a GD copy sold for $371.65 on 2/12/17)

CHESTY AND HIS HELPERS (Disney)
Los Angeles War Chest: 1943 (Giveaway, 12 pgs., 5-1/2x7-1/4")
nn-Chesty & Coptie 53 106 159 334 567 800

CHOCOLATE THE FLAVOR OF FRIENDSHIP AROUND THE WORLD
The Nestle Company: 1955
nn 7 14 21 35 43 50

CHRISTMAS ADVENTURE, THE
S. Rose (H. L. Green Giveaway): 1963 (16 pgs.)
nn 2 4 6 11 16 20

CHRISTMAS ADVENTURES WITH ELMER THE ELF
1949 (paper-c)
nn 5 10 15 22 26 30

CHRISTMAS AT THE ROTUNDA (Titled Ford Rotunda Christmas Book 1957 on) (Regular size)
Ford Motor Co. (Western Printing): 1954 - 1961 (Given away every Christmas at one location)
1954-56 issues (nn's) 9 18 27 50 65 80
1957-61 issues (nn's) 8 16 24 44 57 70

CHRISTMAS CAROL, A
Sears Roebuck & Co.: No date (1942-43) (Giveaway, 32 pgs., 8-1/4x10-3/4", paper cover)
nn-Comics & coloring book 24 48 72 142 234 325

CHRISTMAS CAROL, A (Also see Bob & Santa's Wishing Whistle, Merry Christmas From Sears Toyland, and Santa's Christmas Comic Variety Show)
Sears Roebuck & Co.: 1940s? (Christmas giveaway, 20 pgs.)
nn-Comic book & animated coloring book 22 44 66 132 216 300

CHRISTMAS CAROLS
Hot Shoppes Giveaway: 1959? (16 pgs.)
nn 5 10 15 22 26 30

CHRISTMAS COLORING FUN
H. Burnside: 1964 (20 pgs., slick-c, B&W)
nn 2 4 6 11 16 20

CHRISTMAS DREAM, A
Promotional Publishing Co.: 1950 (Kinney Shoe Store Giveaway, 16 pgs.)
nn 6 12 18 28 34 40

CHRISTMAS DREAM, A
J. J. Newberry Co.: 1952? (Giveaway, paper cover, 16 pgs.)
nn 5 10 15 23 28 32

CHRISTMAS DREAM, A
Promotional Publ. Co.: 1952 (Giveaway, 16 pgs., paper cover)
nn 5 10 15 23 28 32

CHRISTMAS FUN AROUND THE WORLD
No publisher: No date (early 50's) (16 pgs., paper cover)
nn 5 10 15 25 31 36

CHRISTMAS FUN BOOK
G. C. Murphy Co.: 1950 (Giveaway, paper cover)
nn-Contains paper dolls 7 14 21 35 43 50

CHRISTMAS IS COMING!
No publisher: No date (early 50's?) (Store giveaway, 16 pgs.)
nn-Santa cover 6 12 18 32 39 46

CHRISTMAS JOURNEY THROUGH SPACE
Promotional Publishing Co.: 1960
nn-Reprints 1954 issue Jolly Christmas Book with new slick cover
3 6 9 16 23 30

CHRISTMAS ON THE MOON
W. T. Grant Co.: 1958 (Giveaway, 20 pgs., slick cover)
nn 10 20 30 54 72 90

CHRISTMAS PLAY BOOK
Gould-Stoner Co.: 1946 (Giveaway, 16 pgs., paper cover)
nn 11 22 33 62 86 110

CHRISTMAS ROUNDUP
Promotional Publishing Co.: 1960
nn-Marv Levy-c/a 2 4 6 9 13 16

CHRISTMAS STORY CUT-OUT BOOK, THE
Catechetical Guild: No. 393, 1951 (15¢, 36 pgs.)
393-Half text & half comics 9 18 27 47 61 75

CHRISTMAS USA (Through 300 Years) (Also see Uncle Sam's...)
Promotional Publ. Co.: 1956 (Giveaway)

	GD 2.0	VG 4.0	FN 6.0	VF 8.0	VF/NM 9.0	NM- 9.2
nn-Marv Levy-c/a	4	8	12	17	21	24

CHRISTMAS WITH SNOW WHITE AND THE SEVEN DWARFS
Kobackers Giftstore of Buffalo, N.Y.: 1953 (16 pgs., paper-c)

	GD 2.0	VG 4.0	FN 6.0	VF 8.0	VF/NM 9.0	NM- 9.2
nn	9	18	27	50	65	80

CHRISTOPHERS, THE
Catechetical Guild: 1951 (Giveaway, 36 pgs.) (Some copies have 15¢ sticker)

	GD 2.0	VG 4.0	FN 6.0	VF 8.0	VF/NM 9.0	NM- 9.2
nn-Stalin as Satan in Hell; Hitler & Lincoln app.	29	58	87	172	281	390

CHUCKY JACK'S A-COMIN'
Great Smoky Mountains Historical Assn., Gatlinburg, TN: 1956 (Reg. size)

	GD 2.0	VG 4.0	FN 6.0	VF 8.0	VF/NM 9.0	NM- 9.2
nn-Life of John Sevier, founder of Tennessee	8	16	24	42	54	65

CINDERELLA IN "FAIREST OF THE FAIR" (Walt Disney)
American Dairy Association (Premium): 1955 (5x7-1/4", 16 pgs., soft-c)

	GD 2.0	VG 4.0	FN 6.0	VF 8.0	VF/NM 9.0	NM- 9.2
nn	12	24	36	67	94	120

CINEMA COMICS HERALD
Paramount Pictures/Universal/RKO/20th Century Fox/Republic:
1941 - 1943 (4-pg. movie "trailers", paper-c, 7-1/2x10-1/2")(Giveaway)

	GD 2.0	VG 4.0	FN 6.0	VF 8.0	VF/NM 9.0	NM- 9.2
"Mr. Bug Goes to Town" (1941)	18	36	54	109	172	235
"Bedtime Story"	14	28	42	78	112	145
"Lady For A Night", John Wayne, Joan Blondell ('42)	21	42	63	126	206	285
"Reap The Wild Wind" (1942)	14	28	42	82	121	160
"Thunder Birds" (1942)	14	28	42	78	112	145
"They All Kissed the Bride"	14	28	42	81	118	155
"Arabian Nights" (nd)	14	28	42	82	121	160
"Bombardie" (1943)	14	28	42	78	112	145
"Crash Dive" (1943)-Tyrone Power	14	28	42	82	121	160

NOTE: *The 1941-42 issues contain line art with color photos. 1943 issues are line art.*

CLASSICS GIVEAWAYS (Classic Comics reprints)

	GD 2.0	VG 4.0	FN 6.0	VF 8.0	VF/NM 9.0	NM- 9.2
12/41–Walter Theatre Enterprises (Huntington, WV) giveaway containing #2 (orig.) w/new generic-c (only 1 known copy)	110	220	330	704	1202	1700
1942–Double Comics containing CC#1 (orig.) (diff. cover) (not actually a giveaway) (very rare) (also see Double Comics) (only one known copy)	181	362	543	1158	1979	2800
12/42–Saks 34th St. Giveaway containing CC#7 (orig.) (diff. cover) (very rare; only 6 known copies)	360	780	1080	2520	4410	6300
2/43–American Comics containing CC#8 (orig.) (Liberty Theatre giveaway) (different cover) (only one known copy) (see American Comics)	135	270	405	864	1482	2100
12/44–Robin Hood Flour Co. Giveaway - #7-CC(R) (diff. cover) (rare) (edition probably 5 [22])	271	542	813	1734	2967	4200

NOTE: How are above editions determined without CC covers? 1942 is dated 1942, and CC#1-first reprint did not come out until 5/43. 12/42 and 2/43 are determined by blue note at bottom of first text page only in original edition. 12/44 is estimated from page width each reprint edition had progressively slightly smaller page width.

	GD 2.0	VG 4.0	FN 6.0	VF 8.0	VF/NM 9.0	NM- 9.2
1951–Shelter Thru the Ages (C.I. Educational Series) (actually Giveaway by the Ruberoid Co.) (16 pgs.) (contains original artwork by H. C. Kiefer) (there are 5 diff. back cover ad variations: "Ranch" house ad, "Igloo" ad, "Doll House" ad, "Tree House" ad & blank) (scarce)	77	154	231	493	847	1200
1952–George Daynor Biography Giveaway (CC logo) (partly comic book/pictures/newspaper articles) (story of man who built Palace Depression out of junkyard swamp in NJ) (64 pgs.) (very rare; only 3 known copies, one missing back-c)	394	788	1182	2758	4829	6900
1953–Westinghouse/Dreams of a Man (C.I. Educational Series) (Westinghousebio./ Westinghouse Co. giveaway) (contains original artwork by H. C. Kiefer) (16 pgs.) (also French/Spanish/Italian versions) (scarce)	55	110	165	352	601	850

NOTE: Reproductions of 1951, 1952, and 1953 exist with color photocopy covers and black & white photocopy interior ("W.C.N. Reprint")

	GD 2.0	VG 4.0	FN 6.0	VF 8.0	VF/NM 9.0	NM- 9.2
(W.C.N. Reprint)	2	4	6	8	10	12
1951-53–Coward Shoe Giveaways (all editions very rare); 2 variations of back-c ad exist:						
With back-c photo ad: 5 (87), 12 (89), 22 (85), 32 (85), 49 (85), 69 (87), 72 (no HRN), 80 (0), 91 (0), 92 (0), 96 (0), 98 (0), 100 (0), 101 (0), 103-105 (all Os)	34	68	102	199	325	450
With back-c cartoon ad: 106-109 (all 0s), 110 (111), 112 (0)	34	68	102	204	332	460
1956–Ben Franklin 5-10 Store Giveaway (#65-PC with back cover ad) (scarce)	26	52	78	154	252	350
1956–Ben Franklin Insurance Co. Giveaway (#65-PC with diff. back cover ad) (very rare)	52	104	156	328	552	775
11/56–Sealtest Co. Edition - #4 (135) (identical to regular edition except for Sealtest logo printed, not stamped, on front cover) (only two copies known to exist)	32	64	96	188	307	425
1958–Get-Well Giveaway containing #15-CI (new cartoon-type cover) (Pressman Pharmacy) (only one copy known to exist)	32	64	96	188	307	425
1967-68–Twin Circle Giveaway Editions - all HRN 166, with back cover ad for National Catholic Press.						
2(R68), 4(R67), 10(R68), 13(R68)	3	6	9	21	33	45
48(R67), 128(R68), 535(576-R68)	4	8	12	23	37	50
16(R68), 68(R67)	5	10	15	30	50	70
12/69–Christmas Giveaway ("A Christmas Adventure") (reprints Picture Parade #4-1953, new cover) (4 ad variations)						
Stacey's Dept. Store	4	8	12	25	40	55
Anne & Hope Store	5	10	15	33	57	80
Gibson's Dept. Store (rare)	5	10	15	33	57	80
"Merry Christmas" & blank ad space	4	8	12	25	40	55

CLEAR THE TRACK!
Association of American Railroads: 1954 (paper-c, 16 pgs.)

	GD 2.0	VG 4.0	FN 6.0	VF 8.0	VF/NM 9.0	NM- 9.2
nn	6	12	18	31	38	45

CLIFF MERRITT SETS THE RECORD STRAIGHT
Brotherhood of Railroad Trainsmen: Giveaway (2 different issues)

	GD 2.0	VG 4.0	FN 6.0	VF 8.0	VF/NM 9.0	NM- 9.2
...and the Very Candid Candidate by Al Williamson	4	8	12	28	47	65
...Sets the Record Straight by Al Williamson (2 different-c: one by Williamson, the other by McWilliams)	4	8	12	28	47	65

CLYDE BEATTY COMICS (Also see Crackajack Funnies)
Commodore Productions & Artists, Inc.

	GD 2.0	VG 4.0	FN 6.0	VF 8.0	VF/NM 9.0	NM- 9.2
...African Jungle Book('56)-Richfield Oil Co. 16 pg. giveaway, soft-c	12	24	36	69	97	125

C-M-O COMICS
Chicago Mail Order Co.(Centaur): 1942 - No. 2, 1942 (68 pgs., full color)

	GD 2.0	VG 4.0	FN 6.0	VF 8.0	VF/NM 9.0	NM- 9.2
1-Invisible Terror, Super Ann, & Plymo the Rubber Man app. (all Centaur costume heroes)	174	348	522	1414	1907	2700
2-Invisible Terror, Super Ann app.	103	206	309	659	1130	1600

COCOMALT BIG BOOK OF COMICS
Harry 'A' Chesler (Cocomalt Premium): 1938 (Reg. size, full color, 52 pgs.)

	GD 2.0	VG 4.0	FN 6.0	VF 8.0	VF/NM 9.0	NM- 9.2
1-(Scarce)-Biro-c/a; Little Nemo by Winsor McCay Jr., Dan Hastings; Jack Cole, Guardineer, Gustavson, Bob Wood-a	232	464	696	1485	2543	3600

COLONEL OF TWO WORLDS, THE
DC Comics: 2015 (Kentucky Fried Chicken promotion, no price)

1-Flash, Green Lantern and Colonel Sanders vs. the evil Colonel of Earth-3; Derenick-a 3.00

COMIC BOOK (Also see Comics From Weatherbird)
American Juniors Shoe: 1954 (Giveaway)
Contains a comic rebound with new cover. Several combinations possible. Contents determine price.

COMIC BOOK CONFIDENTIAL
Sphinx Productions: 1988 (Giveaway, 16 pgs.)

	GD 2.0	VG 4.0	FN 6.0	VF 8.0	VF/NM 9.0	NM- 9.2
1-Tie-in to a documentary about comic creators; creator biographies; Chester Brown-c	1	2	3	5	6	8

COMIC BOOK MAGAZINE
Chicago Tribune & other newspapers: 1940 - 1943 (Similar to Spirit sections) (7-3/4x10-3/4"; full color; 16-24 pgs. ea.)

	GD 2.0	VG 4.0	FN 6.0	VF 8.0	VF/NM 9.0	NM- 9.2
1940 issues	9	18	27	47	61	75
1941, 1942 issues	8	16	24	40	50	60
1943 issues	7	14	21	37	46	55

NOTE: *Published weekly. Texas Slim, Kit Carson, Spooky, Josie, Nuts & Jolts, Lew Loyal, Brenda Starr, Daniel Boone, Captain Storm, Rocky, Smokey Stover, Tiny Tim, Little Joe, Fu Manchu appear among others. Early issues had photo stories with pictures from the movies; later issues had comic art.*

COMIC BOOKS (Series 1)
Metropolitan Printing Co. (Giveaway): 1950 (16 pgs.; 5-1/4x8-1/2"; full color; bound at top; paper cover)

	GD 2.0	VG 4.0	FN 6.0	VF 8.0	VF/NM 9.0	NM- 9.2
1-Boots and Saddles; intro The Masked Marshal	8	16	24	40	50	60
1-The Green Jet; Green Lama by Raboy	22	44	66	132	216	300
1-My Pal Dizzy (Teen-age)	6	12	18	28	34	40
1-New World; origin Atomaster (costumed hero)	11	22	33	62	86	110
1-Talullah (Teen-age)	6	12	18	28	34	40

COMIC CAVALCADE
All-American/National Periodical Publications

	GD 2.0	VG 4.0	FN 6.0	VF 8.0	VF/NM 9.0	NM- 9.2
Giveaway (1944, 8 pgs., paper-c, in color)-One Hundred Years of Co-operation-r/Comic Cavalcade #9	47	94	141	296	498	700
Giveaway (1945, 16 pgs., paper-c, in color)-Movie "Tomorrow The World" (Nazi theme); r/Comic Cavalcade #10	65	130	195	416	708	1000
Giveaway (c. 1944-45; 8 pgs, paper-c, in color)-The Twain Shall Meet-r/Comic Cavalcade #8	47	94	141	296	498	700

COMIC SELECTIONS (Shoe store giveaway)
Parents' Magazine Press: 1944-46 (Reprints from Calling All Girls, True Comics, True Aviation, & Real Heroes) (All contain WWII-c/s)

	GD 2.0	VG 4.0	FN 6.0	VF 8.0	VF/NM 9.0	NM- 9.2
1	6	12	18	31	38	45
2-6	5	10	15	23	28	32

COMICS FROM WEATHER BIRD (Also see Comic Book, Edward's Shoes, Free Comics to You & Weather Bird)
Weather Bird Shoes: 1954 - 1957 (Giveaway)
Contains a comic bound with new cover. Many combinations possible. Contents would determine price. Some issues do not contain complete comics, but only parts of comics. Value equals 40 to 60 percent of contents.

COMICS READING LIBRARIES (Educational Series)
King Features (Charlton Publ.): 1973, 1977, 1979 (36 pgs. in color) (Giveaways)

	GD 2.0	VG 4.0	FN 6.0	VF 8.0	VF/NM 9.0	NM- 9.2
R-01-Tiger, Quincy	2	4	6	9	13	16
R-02-Beetle Bailey, Blondie & Popeye	2	4	6	11	16	20
R-03-Blondie, Beetle Bailey	2	4	6	8	11	14
R-04-Tim Tyler's Luck, Felix the Cat	3	6	9	16	23	30
R-05-Quincy, Henry	2	4	6	8	11	14
R-06-The Phantom, Mandrake	3	6	9	18	27	36
1977 reprint(R-04)	2	4	6	9	13	16
R-07-Popeye, Little King	2	4	6	13	18	22
R-08-Prince Valiant (Foster), Flash Gordon	3	6	9	19	30	40
1977 reprint	2	4	6	11	16	20
R-09-Hagar the Horrible, Boner's Ark	2	4	6	10	14	18
R-10-Redeye, Tiger	2	4	6	8	11	14
R-11-Blondie, Hi & Lois	2	4	6	8	11	14
R-12-Popeye-Swee'pea, Brutus	2	4	6	13	18	22
R-13-Beetle Bailey, Little King	2	4	6	8	11	14
R-14-Quincy-Hamlet	2	4	6	8	11	14
R-15-The Phantom, The Genius	3	6	9	14	20	25
R-16-Flash Gordon, Mandrake	3	6	9	21	33	45
1977 reprint	2	4	6	10	14	18
Other 1977 editions....	2	4	6	8	10	12
1979 editions (68 pgs.)	2	4	6	8	10	12

NOTE: *Above giveaways available with purchase of $45.00 in merchandise. Used as a reading skills aid for small children.*

COMMANDMENTS OF GOD
Catechetical Guild: 1954, 1958

	GD 2.0	VG 4.0	FN 6.0	VF 8.0	VF/NM 9.0	NM- 9.2
300-Same contents in both editions; diff-c	5	10	15	24	29	34

COMPLIMENTARY COMICS
Sales Promotion Publ.: No date (1950's) (Giveaway)

	GD 2.0	VG 4.0	FN 6.0	VF 8.0	VF/NM 9.0	NM- 9.2
1-Strongman by Powell, 3 stories	8	16	24	42	54	65

COPPER - THE OLDEST AND NEWEST METAL
Commercial Comics: 1959

	GD 2.0	VG 4.0	FN 6.0	VF 8.0	VF/NM 9.0	NM- 9.2
nn	3	6	9	14	20	25

CRACKAJACK FUNNIES (Giveaway)

Cocomalt Big Book of Comics #1 © CHES

Detective Comics #38 Toy R Us Edition © DC

Doc Carter VD Comics © HPI

	GD 2.0	VG 4.0	FN 6.0	VF 8.0	VF/NM 9.0	NM- 9.2

Malto-Meal: 1937 (Full size, soft-c, full color, 32 pgs.)(Before No. 1?)
nn-Features Dan Dunn, G-Man, Speed Bolton, Buck Jones, The Nebbs, Clyde Beatty, Freckles, Major Hoople, Wash Tubbs 97 194 291 621 1061 1500

CRAFTSMAN BOLT-ON SYSTEMS SAVE THE JUSTICE LEAGUE
DC Comics: 2012 (Giveaway promo for Craftsman Bolt-On Tool System)
1-Christian Duce-a/c; New-52 Justice League, The Key and Royal Flush Gang app. 4.00

CRISIS AT THE CARSONS
Pictorial Media: 1958 (Reg. size)
nn 6 12 18 29 36 42

CROSLEY'S HOUSE OF FUN (Also see Tee and Vee Crosley...)
Crosley Div. AVCO Mfg. Corp.: 1950 (Giveaway, paper cover, 32 pgs.)
nn-Strips revolve around Crosley appliances 6 12 18 27 33 38

DAGWOOD SPLITS THE ATOM (Also see Topix V8#4)
King Features Syndicate: 1949 (Science comic with King Features characters) (Giveaway)
nn-Half comic, half text; Popeye, Olive Oyl, Henry, Mandrake, Little King, Katzenjammer Kids app. 8 16 24 42 54 65

DAISY COMICS (Daisy Air Rifles)
Eastern Color Printing Co.: Dec, 1936 (5-1/4x7-1/2")
nn-Joe Palooka, Buck Rogers (2 pgs. from Famous Funnies No. 18, 1st full cover app.), Napoleon Flying to Fame, Butty & Fally 40 80 120 246 411 575

DAISY LOW OF THE GIRL SCOUTS
Girl Scouts of America: 1954, 1965 (16 pgs., paper-c)
1954-Story of Juliette Gordon Low 5 10 15 24 30 35
1965 2 4 6 9 13 16

DAN CURTIS GIVEAWAYS
Western Publishing Co.:1974 (3x6", 24 pgs., reprints)
1-Dark Shadows 2 4 6 11 16 20
2,6-Star Trek 2 4 6 11 16 20
3,4,7-9: 3-The Twilight Zone. 4-Ripley's Believe It or Not! 7-The Occult Files of Dr. Spektor. 8-Dagar the Invincible. 9-Grimm's Ghost Stories 2 4 6 8 11 14
5-Turok, Son of Stone (partial-r/Turok #78) 2 4 6 10 14 18

DANNY AND THE DEMOXICYCLE
Virginia Highway Safety Division: 1970s (Reg. size, slick-c)
nn 3 6 9 19 30 40

DANNY KAYE'S BAND FUN BOOK
H & A Selmer: 1959 (Giveaway)
nn 7 14 21 35 43 50

DAREDEVIL
Marvel Comics Group: 1993
...Vs. Vapora 1 (Engineering Show Giveaway, 16 pg.) - Intro Vapora 6.00

DAVY CROCKETT (TV)
Dell Publishing Co.
...Christmas Book (no date, 16 pgs., paper-c)-Sears giveaway 6 12 18 31 38 45
...Safety Trails (1955, 16pgs, 3-1/4x7")-Cities Service giveaway 8 16 24 40 50 60

DAVY CROCKETT
Charlton Comics
Hunting With... nn ('55, 16 pgs.)-Ben Franklin Store giveaway (Publ.-S. Rose) 5 10 15 24 30 35

DAVY CROCKETT
Walt Disney Prod.: (1955, 16 pgs., 5x7-1/4", slick, photo-c)
...In the Raid at Piney Creek-American Motors giveaway 8 16 24 40 50 60

DC SAMPLER
DC Comics: nn (#1) 1983 - No. 3, 1984 (36 pgs.; 6 1/2" x 10", giveaway)
nn(#1) -3: nn-Wraparound-c, previews upcoming issues. 3-Kirby-a 1 2 3 4 5 7

DC SPOTLIGHT
DC Comics: 1985 (50th anniversary special) (giveaway)
1-Includes profiles on Batman: The Dark Knight & Watchmen 6.00

DENNIS THE MENACE
Hallden (Fawcett)
...& Dirt ('59)-Soil Conservation giveaway; r-# 36; Wiseman-c/a 3 6 9 16 23 30
...& Dirt ('68)-reprints '59 edition 2 4 6 10 14 18
...Away We Go('70)-Caladryl giveaway 2 4 6 9 12 15
...Coping with Family Stress-giveaway 2 4 6 9 12 15
...Takes a Poke at Poison('61)-Food & Drug Admin. giveaway; Wiseman-c/a 2 4 6 9 12 15
...Takes a Poke at Poison-Revised 1/66, 11/70 1 2 3 5 6 8
...Takes a Poke at Poison-Revised 1972, 1974, 1977, 1981 1 2 3 4 5 7

DESERT DAWN
E.C./American Museum of Natural History: 1935 (paper-c)
nn-Johnny Jackrabbit stars. Seven known copies: A CGC 2.5 copy (brittle) sold for $2034 in 2022. A CGC 6.5 copy sold for $3720 in Sept. 2022. Another CGC 6.5 sold for $1800 in Nov. 2022.

DETECTIVE COMICS (Also see other Batman titles)
National Periodical Publications/DC Comics
27 (1984)-Oreo Cookies giveaway (32 pgs., paper-c) r-/Det. #27,#38 & Batman #1 (1st Joker) 5 10 15 35 63 90
38 (1995) Blockbuster Video edition; reprints 1st Robin app. 2 4 5 7 8 10
38 (1997) Toys R Us edition 2 4 5 7 8 10
359 (1997) Toys R Us edition; reprints 1st Batgirl app. 2 4 5 7 8 10
373 (1997, 6 1/4" x 4") Warner Brothers Home Video 2 4 5 7 8 10

DICK TRACY GIVEAWAYS
1939 - 1958; 1990
Buster Brown Shoes Giveaway (1939, 36 pgs. in color); 1938-39-r by Gould 26 52 78 154 252 350
Gillmore Giveaway (See Superbook)
...Hatful of Fun (No date, 1950-52, 32pgs.; 8-1/2x10")-Dick Tracy hat promotion; Dick Tracy games, magic tricks. Miller Bros. premium 17 34 51 105 165 225
Motorola Giveaway (1953)-Reprints Harvey Comics Library #2; "The Case of the Sparkle Plenty TV Mystery" 7 14 21 37 46 55
Original Dick Tracy by Chester Gould, The (Aug, 1990, 16 pgs., 5-1/2x8-1/2")-Gladstone Publ.; Bread Giveaway 1 3 4 6 8 10
Popped Wheat Giveaway (1947, 16 pgs. in color)-1940-r; Sig Feuchtwanger Publ.; Gould-a 6 12 18 28 34 40
...Presents the Family Fun Book; Tip Top Bread Giveaway, no date or number (1940, Fawcett Publ., 16 pgs. in color)-Spy Smasher, Ibis, Lance O'Casey app. 34 68 102 199 325 450
Same as above but without app. of heroes & Dick Tracy on cover only 15 30 45 84 127 170
Service Station Giveaway (1958, 16 pgs. in color)(regular size, slick cover)-Harvey Info. Press 6 12 18 31 38 45
Shoe Store Giveaway (Weatherbird and Triangle Stores)(1939, 16 pgs.)-Gould-a 15 30 45 88 137 185

DICK TRACY SHEDS LIGHT ON THE MOLE
Western Printing Co.: 1949 (16 pgs.) (Ray-O-Vac Flashlights giveaway)
nn-Not by Gould 10 20 30 54 72 90

DICK WINGATE OF THE U.S. NAVY
Superior Publ./Toby Press: 1951; 1953 (no month)
nn-U.S. Navy giveaway 7 14 21 37 46 55
1(1953, Toby)-Reprints nn issue? (same-c) 6 12 18 29 36 42

DIG 'EM
Kellogg's Sugar Smacks Giveaway: 1973 (2-3/8x6", 16 pgs.)
nn-4 different issues 1 3 4 6 8 10

DISNEY MAGAZINE
Procter and Gamble giveaway: nn (#1), Sept, 1976 - nn (#4), Jan, 1977
nn-All have an original Mickey story in color, 12-13 pgs. ea. and info/articles on Disney movies, cartoons. All have partial photo covers of a movie star with 1-2 pg. story. Covers: 1-Bob Hope, 2-Debbie Reynolds, 3-Groucho Marx, 4-Rock Hudson. 2 4 6 10 14 18

DOC CARTER VD COMICS
Health Publications Institute, Raleigh, N. C. (Giveaway): 1949 (16 pgs. in color) (Paper-c)
nn 34 68 102 199 325 450

DONALD AND MICKEY MERRY CHRISTMAS (Formerly Famous Gang Book Of Comics)
K. K. Publ./Firestone Tire & Rubber Co.: 1943 - 1949 (Giveaway, 20 pgs.)
Put out each Christmas; 1943 issue titled "Firestone Presents Comics" (Disney)
1943-Donald Duck-r/WDC&S #32 by Carl Barks 95 190 285 608 1042 1475
1944-Donald Duck-r/WDC&S #35 by Barks 90 180 270 576 988 1400
1945- "Donald Duck's Best Christmas", 8 pgs. Carl Barks; intro. & 1st app. Grandma Duck in comic books 119 238 357 762 1306 1850
1946-Donald Duck in "Santa's Stormy Visit", 8 pgs. Carl Barks 74 148 222 470 810 1150
1947-Donald Duck in "Three Good Little Ducks", 8 pgs. Carl Barks 74 148 222 470 810 1150
1948-Donald Duck in "Toyland", 8 pgs. Carl Barks 74 148 222 470 810 1150
1949-Donald Duck in "New Toys", 8 pgs. Barks 68 136 204 435 743 1050

DONALD DUCK
K. K. Publications: 1944 (Christmas giveaway, paper-c, 16 pgs.)(2 versions)

	GD	VG	FN	VF	VF/NM	NM-
	2.0	4.0	6.0	8.0	9.0	9.2

nn-Kelly cover reprint 129 258 387 826 1413 2000

DONALD DUCK AND THE RED FEATHER
Red Feather Giveaway: 1948 (8-1/2x11", 4 pgs., B&W)
nn 22 44 66 132 216 300

DONALD DUCK IN "THE LITTERBUG"
Keep America Beautiful: 1963 (5x7-1/4", 16 pgs., soft-c) (Disney giveaway)
nn 5 10 15 33 57 80

DONALD DUCK "PLOTTING PICNICKERS" (See Frito-Lay Giveaway)

DONALD DUCK'S SURPRISE PARTY
Walt Disney Productions: 1948 (16 pgs.) (Giveaway for Icy Frost Twins Ice Cream Bars)
nn-(Rare)-Kelly-c/a 239 478 717 1530 2615 3700

DON FORTUNE MAGAZINE
Fawcett Publications: 1940s (Mini-comic)
1-3 (Rare) (A set of 3 in 9.0 sold for $116 in 2016)

DOT AND DASH AND THE LUCKY JINGLE PIGGIE
Sears Roebuck Co.: 1942 (Christmas giveaway, 12 pgs.)
nn-Contains a war stamp album and a punch out Jingle Piggie bank
14 28 42 76 108 140

DOUBLE TALK (Also see Two-Faces)
Feature Publications: No date (1961) (32 pgs., full color, slick-c)
Christian Anti-Communism Crusade (Giveaway)
nn-Sickle with blood-c 22 44 66 132 216 300

DRUMMER BOY AT GETTYSBURG
Eastern National Park & Monument Association: 1976
nn-Fred Ray-a 3 6 9 15 22 28

DUMBO (Walt Disney's..., The Flying Elephant)
Weatherbird Shoes/Ernest Kern Co.(Detroit)/ Wieboldt's (Chicago): 1941
(K.K. Publ. Giveaway)
nn-16 pgs., 9x10" (Rare) 48 96 144 302 514 725
nn-52 pgs., 5-1/2x8-1/2", slick cover in color; B&W interior; half text, half reprints 4-Color No. 17 (Dept. store) 26 52 78 150 245 340

DUMBO WEEKLY
Walt Disney Prod.: 1942 (Premium supplied by Diamond D-X Gas Stations)(4 pgs. each)
1 36 72 108 211 343 475
2-16 14 28 42 81 118 155
Binder only (linen-like stock) 180
NOTE: *A cover and binder came separate at gas stations. Came with membership card.*

EAT RIGHT TO WORK AND WIN
Swift & Company: 1942 (16 pgs.) (Giveaway)
Blondie, Henry, Flash Gordon by Alex Raymond, Toots & Casper, Thimble Theatre(Popeye), Tillie the Toiler, The Phantom, The Little King, & Bringing up Father - original strips just for this book -(in daily strip form which shows what foods we should eat and why)
32 64 96 188 307 425

EDWARD'S SHOES GIVEAWAY
Edward's Shoe Store: 1954 (Has clown on cover)
Contains comic with new cover. Many combinations possible. Contents determines price, 50-60 percent of original. (Similar to Comics From Weatherbird & Free Comics to You)

EE-YI-EE-YI-OH!
Consumer Power Co.: 1972 (Paper-c)
nn - A barnyard fable about ecology 1 3 4 6 8 10

ELSIE THE COW
D. S. Publishing Co.
Borden's cheese comic picture bk ("40, giveaway) 22 44 66 132 216 300
Borden Milk Giveaway-(16 pgs., nn) (3 ishs, "A Trip Through Space" and 2 others, 1957)
15 30 45 94 147 200
Elsie's Fun Book(1950; Borden Milk) 15 30 45 94 147 200
Everyday Birthday Fun With... (1957; 20 pgs.)(100th Anniversary); Kubert-a
15 30 45 94 147 200

ESCAPE FROM FEAR
Planned Parenthood of America: 1956, 1962, 1969 (Giveaway, 8 pgs., color) (On birth control)
1956 edition 14 28 42 78 112 145
1962 edition 5 10 15 30 50 70
1969 edition 3 6 9 21 33 45

EVEL KNIEVEL
Marvel Comics Group (Ideal Toy Corp.): 1974 (Giveaway, 20 pgs.)
nn-Contains photo on inside back-c 6 12 18 38 69 100

FAIR PLAY
Anti-Defamation League, NY: 1950s (soft-c, regular size)
nn-Anti-racism/anti-discrimination (A copy sold for $480 in Aug. 2018)

FAMOUS COMICS (Also see Favorite Comics)
Zain-Eppy/United Features Syndicate: No date; Mid 1930's (24 pgs., paper-c)
nn-Reprinted from 1933 & 1934 newspaper strips in color; Joe Palooka, Hairbreadth Harry, Napoleon, The Nebbs, etc. (Many different versions known)
94 188 282 597 1025 1450

FAMOUS FAIRY TALES
K. K. Publ. Co.: 1942; 1943 (32 pgs.); 1944 (16 pgs.) (Giveaway, soft-c)
1942-Kelly-a 41 82 123 256 428 600
1943-r-/Fairy Tale Parade No. 2,3; Kelly-a 28 56 84 165 270 375
1944-Kelly-a 26 52 78 154 252 350

FAMOUS FUNNIES - A CARNIVAL OF COMICS
Eastern Color: 1933
36 pgs., no date given, no publisher, no number; contains strip reprints of The Bungle Family, Dixie Dugan, Hairbreadth Harry, Joe Palooka, Keeping Up With the Jones, Mutt & Jeff, Reg'lar Fellers, S'Matter Pop, Strange As It Seems, and others. This book was sold by M. C. Gaines to Wheatena, Malt-O-Milk, John Wanamaker, Kinney Shoe Stores, & others to be given away as premiums and radio giveaways (1933). Originally came with a mailing envelope.
649 1298 1947 4738 8369 12,000

FAMOUS GANG BOOK OF COMICS (Becomes Donald & Mickey Merry Christmas 1943 on)
Firestone Tire & Rubber Co.: Dec, 1942 (Christmas giveaway, 32 pgs., paper-c)
nn-(Rare)-Porky Pig, Bugs Bunny, Mary Jane & Sniffles, Elmer Fudd; r/Looney Tunes
129 258 387 826 1413 2000

FANTASTIC FOUR
Marvel Comics
nn (1981, 32 pgs.) Young Model Builders Club 2 4 6 9 13 16
Vol. 3 #60 Baltimore Comic Book Show (10/02, newspaper supplement) 200,000 copies were distributed to Baltimore Sun home subscribers to promote Baltimore Comic Con 4.00

FATHER OF CHARITY
Catechetical Guild Giveaway: No date (32 pgs.; paper cover)
nn 6 12 18 27 33 38

FAVORITE COMICS (Also see Famous Comics)
Grocery Store Giveaway (Diff. Corp.) (detergent): 1934 (36 pgs.)
Book 1-The Nebbs, Strange As It Seems, Napoleon, Joe Palooka, Dixie Dugan, S'Matter Pop, Hairbreadth Harry, etc. reprints 344 688 1032 1550 – –
Book 2,3 228 456 684 1025 – –

FAWCETT MINIATURES (See Mighty Midget)
Fawcett Publications: 1946 (3-3/4x5", 12-24 pgs.) (Wheaties giveaways)
Captain Marvel "And the Horn of Plenty"; Bulletman story
14 28 42 76 108 140
Captain Marvel "& the Raiders From Space"; Golden Arrow story
14 28 42 76 108 140
Captain Marvel Jr. "The Case of the Poison Press!" Bulletman story
14 28 42 76 108 140
Delecta of the Planets; C. C. Beck art; B&W inside; 12 pgs.; 3 printing variations (coloring) exist 20 40 60 114 182 250

FEARLESS FOSDICK
Capp Enterprises Inc.: 1951
...& The Case of The Red Feather 7 14 21 37 46 55

FIFTY WHO MADE DC GREAT
DC Comics: 1985 (Reg. size, slick-c)
nn 1 3 4 6 8 10

FIGHT FOR FREEDOM
National Assoc. of Mfgrs./General Comics: 1949, 1951 (Giveaway, 16 pgs.)
nn-Dan Barry-c/a; used in **POP**, pg. 102 8 16 24 42 54 65

FIRE AND BLAST
National Fire Protection Assoc.: 1952 (Giveaway, 16 pgs., paper-c)
nn-Mart Baily A-Bomb-c; about fire prevention 19 38 57 111 176 240

FIRE CHIEF AND THE SAFE OL' FIREFLY, THE
National Board of Fire Underwriters: 1952 (16 pgs.) (Safety brochure given away at schools) (produced by American Visuals Corp.)(Eisner)
nn-(Rare) Eisner-c/a 43 86 129 271 461 650

FLASH, THE
DC Comics
nn-(1990) Brochure for CBS TV series 5.00
The Flash Comes to a Standstill (1981, General Foods giveaway, 8 pages, 3-1/2 x 6-3/4", oblong) 2 4 6 11 16 20

FLASH COMICS (Also see Captain Marvel and Funny Stuff)
National Periodical Publications: 1946 (6-1/2x8-1/4", 32 pgs.)(Wheaties Giveaway)
nn-Johnny Thunder, Ghost Patrol, The Flash & Kubert Hawkman app.; Irwin Hasen-c/a
100 200 700 1000 – –
NOTE: *All known copies were taped to Wheaties boxes and are never found in mint condition. Copies with light tape residue bring the listed prices in all grades*

FLASH GORDON
Dell Publishing Co.: 1943 (20 pgs.)
Macy's Giveaway-(Rare); not by Raymond 63 126 189 403 689 975

FLASH GORDON
Harvey Comics: 1951 (16 pgs. in color, regular size, paper-c) (Gordon Bread giveaway)
1,2: 1-r/strips 10/24/37 - 2/6/38. 2-r/strips 7/14/40 - 10/6/40; Reprints by Raymond each.... 3 6 9 16 24 32
NOTE: *Most copies have brittle edges.*

FLINTSTONES FUN BOOK, THE
Denny's giveaway: 1990
1-20 1 3 4 6 8 10

FLOOD RELIEF
Malibu Comics (Ultraverse): Jan, 1994 (36 pgs.)(Ordered thru mail w/$5.00 to Red Cross)
1-Hardcase, Prime & Prototype app. 6.00

FOREST FIRE (Also see The Blazing Forest and Smokey Bear)
American Forestry Assn.(Commerical Comics): 1949 (dated-1950) (16 pgs., paper-c)
nn-Intro/1st app. Smokey The Forest Fire Preventing Bear; created by Rudy Wendelein; Wendelein/Sparling-a; 'Carter Oil Co.' on back-c of original
21 42 63 126 206 285

FOREST RANGER HANDBOOK
Wrather Corp.: 1967 (5x7", 20 pgs., slick-c)
nn-WIth Corey Stuart & Lassie photo-c 2 4 6 13 18 22

FORGOTTEN STORY BEHIND NORTH BEACH, THE
Catechetical Guild: No date (8 pgs., paper-c)
nn 6 12 18 27 33 38

FORK IN THE ROAD
U.S. Army Recruiting Service: 1961 (16 pgs., paper-c)
nn 2 4 6 11 16 20

48 FAMOUS AMERICANS
J. C. Penney Co. (Cpr. Edwin H. Stroh): 1947 (Giveaway) (Half-size in color)

Escape From Fear 1956 © PPA

Fire and Blast © NFPA

Gulf Funny Weekly #56 © Gulf

	GD 2.0	VG 4.0	FN 6.0	VF 8.0	VF/NM 9.0	NM- 9.2
nn - Simon & Kirby-a; war cover	15	30	45	83	124	165
FOXHOLE ON YOUR LAWN **No Publisher:** No date						
nn-Charles Biro art	4	9	13	18	22	26
FRANKIE LUER'S SPACE ADVENTURES **Luer Packing Co.:** 1955 (5x7", 36 pgs., slick-c)						
nn - With Davey Rocket	5	10	14	20	24	28
FREDDY **Charlton Comics**						
Schiff's Shoes Presents... #1 (1959)-Giveaway	4	8	12	17	21	24
FREE COMIC BOOK DAY EDITIONS (Now listed in the regular section)						
FREE COMICS TO YOU FROM... (name of shoe store) (Has clown on cover & another with a rabbit) (Like comics from Weather Bird & Edward's Shoes) **Shoe Store Giveaway:** Circa 1956, 1960-61						
Contains a comic bound with new cover - several combinations possible; some Harvey titles known. Contents determine price.						
FREEDOM TRAIN **Street & Smith Publications:** 1948 (Giveaway)						
nn-Powell-c w/mailer; patriotic cover	20	40	60	114	182	250
FREIHOFER'S COMIC BOOK **All-American Comics:** 1940s (7 1/2 x 10 1/4")(Freihofer's Donuts promotional)						
2nd edition-(Scarce) Cover features All-American Comics characters Ultra-Man, Hop Harrigan, Red, White and Blue, Scribbly and others (A CGC 3.0 copy sold for $1200 in 2018)						
FRIENDLY GHOST, CASPER, THE **Harvey Publications:** 1967 (16 pgs.)						
American Dental Assoc. giveaway-Small size	3	6	9	17	25	32
FRITO-LAY GIVEAWAY **Frito-Lay:** 1962 (3-1/4x7", soft-c, 16 pgs.) (Disney)						
nn-Donald Duck "Plotting Picnickers"	5	10	15	30	50	70
nn-Ludwig Von Drake "Fish Stampede"	3	6	9	19	30	40
nn- Mickey Mouse & Goofy "Bicep Bungle"	3	6	9	21	33	45
FROM GOODWILL INDUSTRIES, A GOOD LIFE **Goodwill Industries:** 1950s (regular size)						
1	8	16	24	44	57	70
FRONTIER DAYS **Robin Hood Shoe Store (Brown Shoe):** 1956 (Giveaway)						
1	4	8	12	17	21	24
FRONTIERS OF FREEDOM **Institute of Life Insurance:** 1950 (Giveaway, paper cover)						
nn-Dan Barry-a	9	18	27	50	65	80
FUNNIES ON PARADE (Premium)(See Toy World Funnies) **Eastern Color Printing Co.:** 1933 (36 pgs., slick cover) No date or publisher listed						
nn-Contains Sunday page reprints of Mutt & Jeff, Joe Palooka, Hairbreadth Harry, Reg'lar Fellers, Skippy, & others (10,000 print run). This book was printed for Proctor & Gamble to be given away & came out before Famous Funnies or Century of Comics.	1275	2550	3825	9700	17,600	25,500
FUNNY PICTURE STORIES **Comics Magazine Co./Centaur Publications:** 1930s (Giveaway, 16-20 pgs., slick-c)						
Promotes diff. laundries; has box on cover where "your Laundry Name" is printed	58	116	174	371	636	900
FUNNY STUFF (Also see Captain Marvel & Flash Comics) **National Periodical Publications (Wheaties Giveaway):** 1946 (6-1/2x8-1/4")						
nn-(Scarce)-Dodo & the Frog, Three Mouseketeers, etc.; came taped to Wheaties box; never found in better than fine	48	96	144	480	-	-
FUTURE COP: L.A.P.D. (Electronic Arts video game) **DC Comics (WildStorm):** 1998						
nn-Ron Lim-a/Dave Johnson-c						4.00
GABBY HAYES WESTERN (Movie star) **Fawcett Publications**						
Quaker Oats Giveaway nn's(#1-5, 1951, 2-1/2x7") (Kagran Corp.)-...In Tracks of Guilt, ...In the Fence Post Mystery, ...In the Accidental Sherlock, ...In the Frame-Up, ...In the Double Cross Brand known	10	20	30	54	72	90
Mailing Envelope (has illo of Gabby on front)	10	20	30	54	72	90
GARY GIBSON COMICS (Donut club membership) **National Dunking Association:** 1950 (Included in donut box with pin and card)						
1-Western soft-c, 16 pgs.; folded into the box	6	12	18	31	38	45
GENE AUTRY COMICS						

	GD 2.0	VG 4.0	FN 6.0	VF 8.0	VF/NM 9.0	NM- 9.2
Dell Publishing Co.						
...Adventure Comics And Play-Fun Book ('47)-32 pgs., 8x6-1/2"; games, comics, magic (Pillsbury premium)	20	40	60	120	196	270
Quaker Oats Giveaway(1950)-2-1/2x6-3/4"; 5 different versions; "Death Card Gang", "Phantoms of the Cave", "Riddle of Laughing Mtn.", "Secret of Lost Valley", "Bond of the Broken Arrow" (came in wrapper) each...	10	20	30	58	79	100
Mailing Envelope (has illo. of Gene on front)	10	20	30	58	79	100
3-D Giveaway(1953)-Pocket-size; 5 different	10	20	30	58	79	100
Mailing Envelope (no art on front)	8	16	24	44	57	70
GENE AUTRY TIM (Formerly Tim) (Becomes Tim in Space) **Tim Stores:** 1950 (Half-size) (B&W Giveaway)						
nn-Several issues (All Scarce)	19	38	57	109	172	235
GENERAL FOODS SUPER-HEROES **DC Comics:** 1979, 1980						
1-4 (1979), 1-4 (1980) each...						12.00
G. I. COMICS (Also see Jeep & Overseas Comics) **Giveaways:** 1945 - No. 73?, 1946 (Distributed to U. S. Armed Forces)						
1-73-Contains Prince Valiant by Foster, Blondie, Smilin' Jack, Mickey Finn, Terry & the Pirates, Donald Duck, Alley Oop, Moon Mullins & Capt. Easy strip reprints (at least 73 issues known to exist)	9	18	27	47	61	75
GODZILLA VS. MEGALON **Cinema Shares Int.:** 1976 (4 pgs. on newsprint) (Movie theater giveaway)						
nn-1st. comic app. Godzilla in U.S.	7	14	21	46	86	125
GOLDEN ARROW **Fawcett Publications**						
...Well Known Comics (1944; 12 pgs.; 8-1/2x10-1/2"; paper-c; glued binding)- Bestmaid/Samuel Lowe giveaway; printed in green	12	24	36	67	94	120
GOLDILOCKS & THE THREE BEARS **K. K. Publications:** 1943 (Giveaway)						
nn	14	28	42	78	112	145
GREAT PEOPLE OF GENESIS, THE **David C. Cook Publ. Co.:** No date (Religious giveaway, 64 pgs.)						
nn-Reprint/Sunday Pix Weekly	5	10	15	23	28	32
GREAT SACRAMENT, THE **Catechetical Guild:** 1953 (Giveaway, 36 pgs.)						
nn	5	10	15	22	26	30
GREEN JET COMICS, THE (See Comic Books, Series 1)						
GRENADA **Commercial Comics Co.:** 1983 (Giveaway produced by the CIA)						
1-Air dropped over Grenada during 1983 invasion	5	10	15	30	50	70
GRIT (YOU'VE GOT TO HAVE...) **GRIT Publishing Co.:** 1959						
nn-GRIT newspaper sales recruitment comic; Schaffenberger-a. Later version has altered artwork	5	10	15	22	26	30
GROWING UP WITH JUDY 1952						
nn-General Electric giveaway	5	10	14	20	24	28
GULF FUNNY WEEKLY (Gulf Comic Weekly No. 1-4)(See Standard Oil Comics) **Gulf Oil Company (Giveaway):** 1933 - No. 422, 5/23/41 (in full color; 4 pgs.; tabloid size to 2/3/39; 2/10/39 on, regular comic book size)(early issues undated)						
1	84	168	252	538	919	1300
2-5	39	78	117	240	395	550
6-30	22	44	66	152	216	300
31-100	15	30	45	90	140	190
101-196	13	26	39	72	101	130
197-Wings Winfair begins(1/29/37); by Fred Meagher beginning in 1938	28	56	84	165	270	375
198-300 (Last tabloid size)	15	30	45	90	140	190
301-350 (Regular size)	10	20	30	56	76	95
351-422	8	16	24	44	57	70
GULLIVER'S TRAVELS **Macy's Department Store:** 1939, small size						
nn-Christmas giveaway	15	30	45	84	127	170
GUN THAT WON THE WEST, THE **Winchester-Western Division & Olin Mathieson Chemical Corp.:** 1956 (Giveaway, 24 pgs.)						
nn-Painted-c	7	14	21	35	43	50
HAPPINESS AND HEALING FOR YOU (Also see Oral Roberts'...) **Commercial Comics:** 1955 (36 pgs., slick cover) (Oral Roberts Giveaway)						
nn	12	24	36	67	94	120

	GD	VG	FN	VF	VF/NM	NM-
	2.0	4.0	6.0	8.0	9.0	9.2

NOTE: *The success of this book prompted Oral Roberts to go into the publishing business himself to produce his own material.*

HAPPI TIME FUN BOOK
Sears, Roebuck & Co.: 1940s - 1950s (32 pgs., soft-c)
nn-Comics, games, puzzles, & magic tricks cut -outs 5 10 15 24 30 35

HAPPY CHAMP, THE (The Story of Joker Osborn)
Western Publ.: 1965
nn-About water-skiing 3 6 9 19 30 40

HAPPY TOOTH
DC Comics: 1996
1 3.00

HARLEM YOUTH REPORT (Also see All-Negro Comics and Negro Romances)
Custom Comics, Inc.: 1964 (Giveaway)(No issues #1-4)
5-"Youth in the Ghetto" and "The Blueprint For Change"; distr. in Harlem only; has map of central Harlem on back-c; hypo-c (scarce) 66 132 198 528 1189 1850

HAVE MORE FUN BY PLAYING SAFE
Commercial Comics: 1965 (Sheriff's Youth Foundation, 16 pages, paper-c)
nn 3 6 9 19 30 40

HAWKMAN - THE SKY'S THE LIMIT
DC Comics: 1981 (General Foods giveaway, 8 pages, 3-1/2 x 6-3/4", oblong)
nn 2 4 6 10 14 18

HAWTHORN-MELODY FARMS DAIRY COMICS
Everybody's Publishing Co.: No date (1950's) (Giveaway)
nn-Cheerie Chick, Tuffy Turtle, Robin Koo Koo, Donald & Longhorn Legends 3 6 9 14 19 24

H-BOMB AND YOU
Commercial Comics: (? date) (small size, slick-c)
nn - H–Bomb explosion-c 41 82 123 256 428 600

HENRY ALDRICH COMICS (TV)
Dell Publishing Co.: 1951 (16 pgs., soft-c)
Giveaway - Capehart radio 4 8 12 27 44 60

HERE IS SANTA CLAUS
Goldsmith Publ. Co. (Kann's in Washington, D.C.): 1930s (16 pgs., 8 in color) (stiff paper covers)
nn 15 30 45 86 133 180

HERE'S HOW AMERICA'S CARTOONISTS HELP TO SELL U.S. SAVINGS BONDS
Harvey Comics: 1950? (16 pgs., giveaway, paper cover)
Contains: Joe Palooka, Donald Duck, Archie, Kerry Drake, Red Ryder, Blondie & Steve Canyon 22 44 66 128 209 290

HISTORY OF GAS
American Gas Assoc.: Mar, 1947 (Giveaway, 16 pgs., soft-c)
nn-Miss Flame narrates 10 20 30 58 79 100

HOME DEPOT, SAFETY HEROES
Marvel Comics.: Oct, 2005 (Giveaway)
nn-Spider-Man and the Fantastic Four on the cover; Olliffe-a/c; Roseman-s 4.00

HONEYBEE BIRDWHISTLE AND HER PET PEPI (Introducing...)
Newspaper Enterprise Assoc.: 1969 (Giveaway, 24 pgs., B&W, slick cover)
nn-Contains Freckles newspaper strips with a short biography of Henry Fornhals (artist) & Fred Fox (writer) of the strip 4 8 12 28 47 65

HOODS UP
Fram Corp.: 1953 (15¢, distributed to service station owners, 16 pgs.)
1-(Very Rare; only 2 known); Eisner-c/a in all (a CGC 9.0 copy sold for $1840 in 2006)
2-6-(Very Rare; only 1 known of #3, 2 known of #2,4) (a CGC 8.0 copy of #4 sold for $500 in 2012) 55 110 165 352 601 850
NOTE: *Convertible Connie gives tips for service stations, selling Fram oil filters.*

HOOKED (Anti-drug comic distributed at NYC methadone clinics)
U.S. Dept. of Health: 1966 (giveaway, oblong)
nn-Distributed between May and July, 1966 6 12 18 40 73 105

HOPALONG CASSIDY
Fawcett Publications
Grape Nuts Flakes giveaway (1950,9x6") 14 28 42 80 115 150
...& the Mad Barber (1951 Bond Bread giveaway)-7x5"; used in **SOTI**, pgs. 308,309 20 40 60 114 182 250
...Meets the Brend Brothers Bandits (1951 Bond Bread giveaway, color, paper-c, 16 pgs., 3-1/2x7")- Fawcett Publ. 9 18 27 50 65 80
...Strange Legacy (1951 Bond Bread giveaway) 9 18 27 50 65 80
White Tower Giveaway (1946, 16pgs., paper-c) 10 20 30 54 72 90

HOPPY THE MARVEL BUNNY (WELL KNOWN COMICS)
Fawcett Publications: 1944 (8-1/2x10-1/2", paper-c)
Bestmaid/Samuel Lowe (printed in red or blue) 14 28 42 76 108 140

HOT STUFF, THE LITTLE DEVIL
Harvey Publications (Illustrated Humor):1963
Shoestore Giveaway 3 6 9 21 33 45

HOW KIDS ENJOY NEW YORK
American Airlines: 1966 (Giveaway, 40 pgs., 4x9")
nn-Includes 8 color pages by Bob Kane featuring a tour of New York and his studio (a FN+ copy sold for $250 in 2004, and a VF copy sold for $800 in 2018)

HOW STALIN HOPES WE WILL DESTROY AMERICA
Joe Lowe Co. (Pictorial Media): 1951 (Giveaway, 16 pgs.)
nn 41 82 123 256 428 600

HURRICANE KIDS, THE (Also See Magic Morro, The Owl, Popular Comics #45)
R.S. Callender: 1941 (Giveaway, 7-1/2x5-1/4", soft-c)
nn-Will Ely-a. 9 18 27 52 69 85

IF THE DEVIL WOULD TALK
Roman Catholic Catechetical Guild/Impact Publ.: 1950; 1958 (32 pgs.; paper cover; in full color)
nn-(Scarce)-About secularism (20-30 copies known to exist); very low distribution 129 258 387 826 1413 2000
1958 Edition-(Impact Publ.); art & script changed to meet church criticism of earlier edition; 80 plus copies known to exist 36 72 108 211 343 475
Black & White version of nn edition; small size; only 4 known copies exist 39 78 117 240 395 550
NOTE: *The original edition of this book was printed and killed by the Guild's board of directors. It is believed that a very limited number of copies were distributed. The 1958 version was a complete bomb with very limited, if any, circulation. In 1979, 11 original, 4 1958 reprints, and 4 B&W's surfaced from the Guild's old files in St. Paul, Minnesota.*

IKE'S STORY
Sponsored Comics, Inc.: 1952 (soft-c)
nn-Dwight D. Eisenhower campaign (A 9.6 sold for $288 in 2018)

IN LOVE WITH JESUS
Catechetical Educational Society: 1952 (Giveaway, 36 pgs.)
nn 8 16 24 40 50 60

INTERSTATE THEATRES' FUN CLUB COMICS
Interstate Theatres: Mid 1940's (10¢ on cover) (B&W cover) (Premium)
Cover features MLJ characters looking at a copy of Top-Notch Comics, but contains an early Detective Comic on inside; many combinations 40 80 120 246 411 575

IN THE GOOD HANDS OF THE ROCKEFELLER TEAM
Country Art Studios: No date (paper cover, 8 pgs.)
nn-Joe Simon-a 9 18 27 52 69 85

IRON GIANT
DC Comics: 1999 (4 pages, theater giveaway)
1-Previews movie 1 2 3 5 6 8

IRON HORSE GOES TO WAR, THE
Association of American Railroads: 1960 (Giveaway, 16 pgs.)
nn-Civil War & railroads 3 6 9 19 30 40

IS THIS TOMORROW?
Catechetical Guild: 1947 (One Shot) (3 editions) (52 pgs.)
1-Theme of communists taking over the USA; (no price on cover) Used in **POP**, pg. 102 47 94 141 296 498 700
1-(10¢ on cover)(Red price on yellow circle) 47 94 141 296 498 700
1-(10¢ on cover)(Yellow price on red circle) 47 94 141 296 498 700
1-(10¢ on cover)(Yellow price on black circle) 47 94 141 296 498 700
1-Has blank circle with no price on cover 47 94 141 296 498 700
Black & White advance copy titled "Confidential" (52 pgs.)-Contains script and art edited out of the color edition, including one page of extreme violence showing mob nailing a Cardinal to a door; (only two known copies). A VF+ sold in 2/08 for $3346. A NM 9.2 sold in 11/16 for $2629.
NOTE: *The original color version first sold for 10 cents. Since sales were good, it was later printed as a giveaway. Approximately four million in total were printed. The two black and white copies listed plus two other versions as well as a full color untrimmed version surfaced in 1979 from the Guild's old files in St. Paul, Minnesota.*

IT'S FUN TO STAY ALIVE
National Automobile Dealers Association: 1948 (Giveaway, 16 pgs., heavy stock paper)
Featuring: Bugs Bunny, The Berrys, Dixie Dugan, Elmer, Henry, Tim Tyler, Bruce Gentry, Abbie & Slats, Joe Jinks, The Toodles, & Cokey; all art copyright 1946-48 drawn especially for this book 15 30 45 92 144 195

IT'S TIME FOR REASON - NOT TREASON
Liberty Lobby: 1967 (Reg. size, soft-c) (Anti-communist)
nn 8 16 24 51 96 140

JACK AND CHUCK LEARN THE HARD WAY
Commercia Comics/Wagner Electric Co.: 1950s (Reg. size, soft-c)
nn-Automotive giveaway 9 18 27 52 69 85

JACK & JILL VISIT TOYTOWN WITH ELMER THE ELF
Butler Brothers (Toytown Stores): 1949 (Giveaway, 16 pgs., paper cover)
nn 5 10 15 25 31 36

JACK ARMSTRONG (Radio)(See True Comics)
Parents' Institute: 1949
12-Premium version (distr. in Chicago only); Free printed on upper right-c; no price (Rare) 18 36 54 107 169 230

JACKIE JOYNER KERSEE IN HIGH HURDLES (Kellogg's Tony's Sports Comics)
DC Comics: 1992 (Sports Illustrated)
nn 5.00

JACKPOT OF FUN COMIC BOOK
DCA Food Ind.: 1957, giveaway (paper cover, regular size)
nn-Features Howdy Doody 13 26 39 72 101 130

JEDLICKA SHOES
DC Comics: 1961 (Funny animal-c)
nn-Contains Superman #142 9 18 27 60 120 180

JEEP COMICS
R. B. Leffingwell & Co.: 1945 - 1946 (16 pgs.)(King Features Syndicate)
1-(Giveaways)-Strip reprints in all issues; Tarzan, Flash Gordon, Blondie, The Nebbs, Little Iodine, Red Ryder, Don Winslow, The Phantom, Johnny Hazard, Katzenjammer Kids; distr. to U.S. Armed Forces from 1945-1946 20 40 60 118 192 265
2-5 15 30 45 88 137 185
6-46 7 14 21 35 43 50

JINGLE BELLS CHRISTMAS BOOK
Montgomery Ward (Giveaway): 1971 (20 pgs., B&W inside, slick-c)
nn 1 3 4 6 8 10

JOAN OF ARC
Catechetical Guild (Topix) (Giveaway): No date (28 pgs., blank back-c)
nn-Ingrid Bergman photo-c; Addison Burbank-a 14 28 42 80 115 150
NOTE: *Unpublished version exists which came from the Guild's files.*

Hooked © IMP

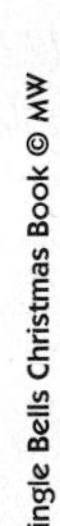
Jingle Bells Christmas Book © MW

Kite Fun Book 1968 - Bugs Bunny © WB

	GD 2.0	VG 4.0	FN 6.0	VF 8.0	VF/NM 9.0	NM- 9.2

JOE PALOOKA (2nd Series)
Harvey Publications

...Body Building Instruction Book (1958 B&M Sports Toy giveaway, 16 pgs., 5-1/4x7")-Origin	8	16	24	42	54	65
...Fights His Way Back (1945 Giveaway, 24 pgs.) Family Comics	12	24	36	67	94	120
...in Hi There! (1949 Red Cross giveaway, 12 pgs., 4-3/4x6")	8	16	24	40	50	60
...in It's All in the Family (1945 Red Cross giveaway, 16 pgs., regular size)	8	16	24	42	54	65

JOE THE GENIE OF STEEL (Also see "Return of...")
U.S. Steel Corp., Pittsburgh, PA: 1950 (16 pgs, reg size)

nn-Joe Magarac, the Paul Bunyan of steel 9 18 27 50 65 80

JOHNNY GETS THE WORD
Dept. of Health of New York City: 1963 (small size)

nn - Prevention of venereal diseases 5 10 15 35 63 90
NOTE: *A CGC 9.6 copy sold in 2016 for $263.*

JOHNNY JINGLE'S LUCKY DAY
American Dairy Assoc.: 1956 (16 pgs.; 7-1/4x5-1/8") (Giveaway) (Disney)

nn 5 10 15 24 30 35

JOHNSON MAKES THE TEAM
B.F. Goodrich: 1950 (Reg. size) (Football giveaway)

nn 6 12 18 31 38 45

JO-JOY (The Adventures of...)
W. T. Grant Dept. Stores: 1945 - 1953 (Christmas gift comic, 16 pgs., 7-1/16x10-1/4")

1945-53 issues 8 16 24 42 54 65

JOLLY CHRISTMAS BOOK (See Christmas Journey Through Space)
Promotional Publ. Co.: 1951; 1954; 1955 (36 pgs.; 24 pgs.)

1951-(Woolworth giveaway)-slightly oversized; no slick cover; Marv Levy-c/a	8	16	24	42	54	65
1954-(Hot Shoppes giveaway)-regular size-reprints 1951 issue; slick cover added; 24 pgs.; no ads	7	14	21	37	46	55
1955-(J. M. McDonald Co. giveaway)-reg. size	7	14	21	35	43	50

JOURNEY OF DISCOVERY WITH MARK STEEL (See Mark Steel)

JUMPING JACKS PRESENTS THE WHIZ KIDS
Jumping Jacks Stores giveaway: 1978 (In 3-D) with glasses (4 pgs.)

nn 1 3 4 6 8 10

JUNGLE BOOK FUN BOOK, THE (Disney)
Baskin Robbins: 1978

nn-Ice Cream giveaway 2 4 6 9 12 15

JUSTICE LEAGUE OF AMERICA
DC Comics: 1999 (included in Justice League of America Monopoly game)

nn - Reprints 1st app. in Brave and the Bold #28 4.00

KASCO KOMICS
Kasko Grainfeed (Giveaway): 1945; No. 2, 1949 (Regular size, paper-c)

1(1945)-Similar to Katy Keene; Bill Woggon-a; 28 pgs.; 6-7/8x9-7/8"	24	48	72	142	234	325
2(1949)-Woggon-c/a	15	30	45	94	147	200

KATY AND KEN VISIT SANTA WITH MISTER WISH
S. S. Kresge Co. : 1948 (Giveaway, 16 pgs., paper-c)

nn 7 14 21 37 46 55

KELLOGG'S CINNAMON MINI-BUNS SUPER-HEROES
DC Comics: 1993 (4 1/4" x 2 3/4")

4 editions: Flash, Justice League America, Superman, Wonder Woman and the Star Riders each..... 6.00

KERRY DRAKE DETECTIVE CASES
Publisher's Syndicate

...in the Case of the Sleeping City-(1951)-16 pg. giveaway for armed forces; paper cover 8 16 24 40 50 60

KEY COMICS
Key Clothing Co./Peterson Clothing: 1951 - 1956 (32 pgs.) (Giveaway)
Contains a comic from different publishers bound with new cover. Cover changed each year. Many combinations possible. Distributed in Nebraska, Iowa, & Kansas. Contents would determine price, 40-60 percent of original.

KING JAMES "THE KING OF BASKETBALL"
DC Comics: 2004 (Promo comic for LeBron James and Powerade Flava23 sports drink)

nn - Ten different covers by various artists; 4 covers for retail, 4 for mail-in, 1 for military commissaries, and 1 general market; Damion Scott-a/Gary Phillips-s 1 3 4 6 8 10

KIRBY'S SHOES COMICS
Kirby's Shoes: 1959 - 1961 (8 pgs., soft-c, several different editions)

nn-(1959) Features Kirby the Golden Bear	6	12	18	31	38	45
nn-(1960,1961) Features Kirby the Golden Bear	4	7	10	14	17	20

KITE FUN BOOK
Pacific, Gas & Electric/Sou. California Edison/Florida Power & Light/ Missouri Public Service Co.: 1952 - 1998 (16 pgs, 5x7-1/4", soft-c)

1952-Having Fun With Kites (P.G.&E.)	11	22	33	64	90	115
1953-Pinocchio Learns About Kites (Disney)	42	84	126	265	445	625
1954-Donald Duck Tells About Kites-Fla. Power, S.C.E. & version with label issues -Barks pencils-8 pgs.; inks-7 pgs. (Rare)	219	438	637	1402	2401	3400
1954-Donald Duck Tells About Kites-P.G.&E. issue -7th page redrawn changing middle 3 panels to show P.G.&E. in story line; (All Barks-a) Scarce	194	388	582	1242	2121	3000
1955-Brer Rabbit in "A Kite Tail" (Disney)	25	50	75	150	245	340
1956-Woody Woodpecker (Lantz)	12	24	36	67	94	120
1957-Ruff and Reddy (exist?)						
1958-Tom And Jerry (M.G.M.)	9	18	27	52	69	85
1959-Bugs Bunny (Warner Bros.)	4	8	12	27	44	60
1960-Porky Pig (Warner Bros.)	4	8	12	28	47	65
1960-Bugs Bunny (Warner Bros.)	4	8	12	28	47	65
1961-Huckleberry Hound (Hanna-Barbera)	5	10	15	31	53	75
1962-Yogi Bear (Hanna-Barbera)	4	8	12	25	40	55
1963-Rocky and Bullwinkle (TV)(Jay Ward)	5	10	15	35	63	90
1963-Top Cat (TV)(Hanna-Barbera)	3	6	9	19	30	40
1964-Magilla Gorilla (TV)(Hanna-Barbera)	3	6	9	17	26	35
1965-Jinks, Pixie and Dixie (TV)(Hanna-Barbera)	3	6	9	15	22	28
1965-Tweety and Sylvester (Warner); S.C.E. version with Reddy Kilowatt app.	2	4	6	9	13	16
1966-Secret Squirrel (Hanna-Barbera); S.C.E. version with Reddy Kilowatt app.	5	10	15	30	50	70
1967-Beep! Beep! The Road Runner (TV)(Warner)	2	4	6	11	16	20
1968-Bugs Bunny (Warner Bros.)	2	4	6	13	18	22
1969-Dastardly and Muttley (TV)(Hanna-Barbera)	3	6	9	19	30	40
1970-Rocky and Bullwinkle (TV)(Jay Ward)	4	8	12	27	44	60
1971-Beep! Beep! The Road Runner (TV)(Warner)	2	4	6	11	16	20
1972-The Pink Panther (TV)	2	4	6	10	14	18
1973-Lassie (TV)	3	6	9	15	22	28
1974-Underdog (TV)	2	4	6	11	16	20
1975-Ben Franklin	2	4	6	8	10	12
1976-The Brady Bunch (TV)	3	6	9	16	23	30
1977-Ben Franklin (exist?)	2	4	6	8	10	12
1977-Popeye	2	4	6	9	13	16
1978-Happy Days (TV)	2	4	6	11	16	20
1979-Eight is Enough (TV)	2	4	6	9	13	16
1980-The Waltons (TV, released in 1981)	2	4	6	9	13	16
1982-Tweety and Sylvester	2	4	6	8	11	14
1984-Smokey Bear	1	3	4	6	8	10
1986-Road Runner	1	2	3	5	6	8
1997-Thomas Edison						4.00
1998-Edison Field (Anaheim Stadium)						4.00

KNOWING'S NOT ENOUGH
Commercial Comics: 1956 (Reg. size, paper-c) (United States Steel safety giveaway)

nn 7 14 21 35 43 50

KNOW YOUR MASS
Catechetical Guild: No. 303, 1958 (35¢, 100 Pg. Giant) (Square binding)

303-In color 7 14 21 35 43 50

KOLYNOS PRESENTS THE WHITE GUARD
Whitehall Pharmacal Co.: 1949 (paper cover, 8 pgs.)

nn 6 12 18 31 38 45

KOLYNOS PRESENTS THE WICKED WITCH
Whitehall Pharmacal Co.: 1951 (paper cover, 8 pgs.)

nn-Anti-tooth decay 4 8 12 17 21 24

K. O. PUNCH, THE (Also see Lucky Fights It Through & Sidewalk Romance)
E. C. Comics: 1952 (VD Educational giveaway)

nn-Feldstein-splash; Kamen-a 432 864 1296 3154 5577 8000

KOREA MY HOME (Also see Yalta to Korea)
Johnstone and Cushing: nd (1950s, slick-c, regular size)

nn-Anti-communist; Korean War 30 60 90 177 289 400

KRIM-KO KOMICS
Krim-ko Chocolate Drink: 5/18/35 - No. 6, 6/22/35; 1936 - 1939 (weekly)

1-(16 pgs., soft-c, Dairy giveaways)-Tom, Mary & Sparky Advs. by Russell Keaton, Jim Hawkins by Dick Moores, Mystery Island! by Rick Yager begin	15	30	45	85	130	175
2-6 (6/22/35)	12	24	36	67	94	120

	GD	VG	FN	VF	VF/NM	NM-
	2.0	4.0	6.0	8.0	9.0	9.2

Lola, Secret Agent; 184 issues, 4 pg. giveaways - all original stories
each.... 9 18 27 47 61 75

LABOR IS A PARTNER
Catechetical Guild Educational Society: 1949 (32 pgs., paper-c)

nn-Anti-communism 47 94 141 296 498 750
Confidential Preview-(8-1/2x11", B&W, saddle stitched)-only one known copy; text varies from color version, advertises next book on secularism (If the Devil Would Talk)
(A VF- copy sold for $2629 in 11/2016 and a VG/FN copy sold for $454 in 1/2017)

LADIES - WOULDN'T IT BE BETTER TO KNOW
American Cancer Society: 1969 (Reg. size)

nn 4 8 12 22 35 48

LADY AND THE TRAMP IN "BUTTER LATE THAN NEVER"
American Dairy Assoc. (Premium): 1955 (16 pgs., 5x7-1/4", soft-c) (Disney)

nn 9 18 27 50 65 80

LASSIE (TV)
Dell Publ. Co

The Adventures of... nn-(Red Heart Dog Food giveaway, 1949)-16 pgs, soft-c;
1st app. Lassie in comics 40 80 120 246 411 575

LIFE OF THE BLESSED VIRGIN
Catechetical Guild (Giveaway): 1950 (68pgs.) (square binding)

nn-Contains "The Woman of the Promise" & "Mother of Us All" rebound
11 22 33 64 90 115

LIGHTNING RACERS
DC Comics: 1989

1 4.50

LI'L ABNER (Al Capp's) (Also see Natural Disasters!)
Harvey Publ./Toby Press

...& the Creatures from Drop-Outer Space-nn (Job Corps giveaway; 36 pgs., in color)
(entire book by Frank Frazetta) 22 44 66 128 209 290
...Joins the Navy (1950) (Toby Press Premium) 11 22 33 64 90 115
Al Capp by Li'l Abner (Circa 1946, nd, giveaway) Al Capp bio and his life as an amputee
11 22 33 64 90 115

LITTLE ALONZO
Macy's Dept. Store: 1938 (B&W, 5-1/2x8-1/2")(Christmas giveaway)

nn-By Ferdinand the Bull's Munro Leaf 10 20 30 58 79 100

LITTLE ARCHIE (See Archie Comics)

LITTLE DOT
Harvey Publications

Shoe store giveaway 2 4 8 12 28 47 65

LITTLE FIR TREE, THE
W. T. Grant Co. : nd (1942) (8-1/2x11") (12 pgs. with cover, color & B&W, heavy paper) (Christmas giveaway)

nn-Story by Hans Christian Anderson; 8 pg. Kelly-r/Santa Claus Funnies (not signed); X-Mas-c
97 194 291 621 1061 1500

LITTLE KLINKER
Little Klinker Ventures: Nov, 1960 (20 pgs.) (slick cover) (Montgomery Ward Giveaway)

nn - Christmas; Santa-c 3 6 9 14 20 25

LITTLE MISS SUNBEAM COMICS
Magazine Enterprises/Quality Bakers of America

Bread Giveaway 1-4(Quality Bakers, 1949-50)-14 pgs. each
8 16 24 42 54 65
Bread Giveaway (1957,61; 16pgs, reg. size) 6 12 18 31 38 45

LITTLE ORPHAN ANNIE
David McKay Publ./Dell Publishing Co.

Junior Commandos Giveaway (same-c as 4-Color #18, K.K. Publ.)(Big Shoe Store); same back cover as '47 Popped Wheat giveaway; 16 pgs; flag-c;
r/strips 9/7/42-10/10/42 26 52 78 154 252 350
Popped Wheat Giveaway ('47)-16 pgs. full color; reprints strips from 5/3/40 to 6/20/40
5 10 15 22 26 30
Quaker Sparkies Giveaway (1940) 18 36 54 103 162 220
Quaker Sparkies Giveaway (1941, full color, 20 pgs.); "LOA and the Rescue"; r/strips 4/13/39-6/21/39 & 7/6/39-7/17/39. "LOA and the Kidnappers";
r/strips 11/28/38-1/28/39 15 30 45 94 147 200
Quaker Sparkies Giveaway (1942, full color, 20 pgs.); "LOA and Mr. Gudge"; r/strips 2/13/38-3/21/38 & 4/18/37-5/30/37. "LOA and the Great Am"
15 30 45 88 137 185

LITTLE TREE THAT WASN'T WANTED, THE
W. T. Grant Co. (Giveaway): 1960, (Color, 28 pgs.)

nn-Christmas story, puzzles and games 4 8 12 23 37 50

LONE RANGER, THE
Dell Publishing Co.

Cheerios Giveaways (1954, 16 pgs., 2-1/2x7", soft-c) #1- "The Lone Ranger, His Mask & How He Met Tonto". #2- "The Lone Ranger & the Story of Silver"
each.... 12 24 36 69 97 125
Doll Giveaways (Gabriel Ind.)(1973, 3-1/4x5")- "The Story of The Lone Ranger," "The Carson City Bank Robbery" & "The Apache Buffalo Hunt"
2 4 6 12 16 20
How the Lone Ranger Captured Silver Book(1936)-Silvercup Bread giveaway
55 110 165 352 601 850
...In Milk for Big Mike (1955, Dairy Association giveaway), soft-c; 5x7-1/4",
16 pgs. 10 20 30 58 79 100
Legend of The Lone Ranger (1969, 16 pgs., giveaway)-Origin The Lone Ranger
4 8 12 21 33 45
Merita Bread giveaway (1954, 16 pgs., 5x7-1/4")- "How to Be a Lone Ranger
Health & Safety Scout" 14 28 42 80 115 150
Merita Bread giveaway (1955, 16 pgs., 5x7-1/4")- "Official Lone Ranger and Tonto
Coloring Book" 12 24 36 69 97 125
Merita Bread giveaway (1956, 16 pgs., 5x7-1/4")- "Tells the Story of Branding"
12 24 36 69 97 125

LONE RANGER COMICS, THE
Lone Ranger, Inc. : Book 1, 1939(inside) (shows 1938 on-c) (52 pgs. in color; regular size) (Ice cream mail order)

Book 1-(Scarce)-The first western comic devoted to a single character; not by
Vallely 600 1200 1800 4200 – –
2nd version w/large full color promo poster pasted over centerfold & a smaller poster pasted over back cover; includes new additional premiums not originally offered (Rare) (A CGC 7.0 copy sold in Nov. 2021 for $2,850)
670 1340 2010 4700 – –

LOONEY TUNES
DC Comics: 1991, 1998

Claritin promotional issue (1998); Colgate mini-comic (1998) 3.00
Tyson's 1-10 (1991) 4.00

LUCKY FIGHTS IT THROUGH (Also see The K. O. Punch & Sidewalk Romance)
Educational Comics: 1949 (Giveaway, 16 pgs. in color, paper-c)

nn-(Very Rare)-1st Kurtzman work for E.C.; V.D. prevention
187 374 561 1197 2049 2900
nn-Reprint in color (1977) 9.00
NOTE: *Subtitled "The Story of That Ignorant, Ignorant Cowboy". Prepared for Communications Materials Center, Columbia University.*

LUDWIG VON DRAKE (See Frito-Lay Giveaway)

MACO TOYS COMIC
Maco Toys/Charlton Comics: 1959 (Giveaway, 36 pgs.)

1-All military stories featuring Maco Toys 5 10 15 23 28 32

MAD MAGAZINE
DC Comics: 1997, 1999, 2008

Special Edition (1997, Tang giveaway) 6.00
Stocking Stuffer (1999) 6.00
San Diego Comic-Con Edition (2008) Watchmen parody with Fabry-a; Aragonés cartoons 3.00

MAGAZINELAND USA
DC Comics: 1977

nn-Kubert-c/a 3 6 9 21 33 45

MAGIC MORRO (Also see Super Comics #21, The Owl, & The Hurricane Kids)
K. K. Publications: 1941 (7-1/2 x 5-1/4", giveaway, soft-c)

nn-Ken Ernst-a. 10 20 30 58 79 100

MAGIC OF CHRISTMAS AT NEWBERRYS, THE
E. S. London: 1967 (Giveaway) (B&W, slick-c, 20 pgs.)

nn 1 3 4 6 8 10

MAGIC SHOE ADVENTURE BOOK
Western Publications: 1962 - No. 3, 1963 (Shoe store giveaway, Reg. size)

nn-(1962) 5 10 15 34 60 85
1 (1963)-And the Flaming Threat 4 8 12 28 47 65
2 (1963)-And the Winning Run 4 8 12 28 47 65
3 (1963)-And the Missing Masterpiece Mystery 4 8 12 28 47 65

MAJOR INAPAK THE SPACE ACE
Magazine Enterprises (Inapac Foods): 1951 (20 pgs.) (Giveaway)

1-Bob Powell-c/a 2 4 6 9 13 16
NOTE: *Many warehouse copies surfaced in 1973.*

MAMMY YOKUM & THE GREAT DOGPATCH MYSTERY
Toby Press: 1951 (Giveaway)

nn-Li'l Abner 17 34 51 103 162 220
nn-Reprint (1956) 5 10 15 24 30 35

MAN NAMED STEVENSON, A
Democratic National Committee: 1952 (20 pgs., 5 1/4 x 7")

nn 10 20 30 54 72 90

MAN OF PEACE, POPE PIUS XII
Catechetical Guild: 1950 (See Pope Pius XII... & To V2#8)

nn-All Powell-a 7 14 21 37 46 55

MAN OF STEEL BEST WESTERN
DC Comics: 1997 (Best Western hotels promo)

3-Reprints Superman's first post-Crisis meeting with Batman 4.00

MAN WHO RUNS INTERFERENCE
General Comics, Inc./Institute of Life Insurance: 1946 (Paper-c)

nn-Football premium 7 14 21 35 43 50

MAN WHO WOULDN'T QUIT, THE
Harvey Publications Inc.: 1952 (16 pgs., paper cover)

nn-The value of voting 5 10 15 23 28 32

MARCH OF COMICS (Boys' and Girls'...#3-353)
K. K. Publications/Western Publishing Co.: 1946 - No. 488, April, 1982 (#1-4 are not numbered) (K.K. Giveaway) (Founded by Sig Feuchtwanger)

Early issues were full size, 32 pages, and were printed with and without an extra cover of slick stock, just for the advertiser. The binding was stapled if the slick cover was added; otherwise, the pages were glued together at the spine. Most 1948 - 1951 issues were full size,24 pages, pulp covers. Starting in 1952 they were half-size (with a few exceptions) and 32 pages with slick covers.1959 and later issues had only 16 pages plus covers. 1952 -1959 issues read oblong; 1960 and later issues read upright. All have new stories except where noted.

nn (#1, 1946)-Goldilocks; Kelly back-c (16 pgs., stapled)
54 108 162 343 574 825
nn (#2, 1946)-How Santa Got His Red Suit; Kelly-a (11 pgs., r/4-Color #61
from 1944) (16pgs., stapled) 34 68 102 199 325 450
nn (#3, 1947)-Our Gang (Walt Kelly) 36 72 108 216 351 485
nn (#4)-Donald Duck by Carl Barks, "Maharajah Donald", 28 pgs.; Kelly-c?
(Disney) 811 1622 2433 5920 10,460 15,000
5-Andy Panda (Walter Lantz) 19 38 57 111 176 240
6-Popular Fairy Tales; Kelly-c; Noonan-a(2) 19 38 57 112 179 245

Lightning Racers #1 © DC

Magazineland USA © DC

March of Comics #51 © UFS

	GD 2.0	VG 4.0	FN 6.0	VF 8.0	VF/NM 9.0	NM- 9.2
7-Oswald the Rabbit	20	40	60	120	195	270
8-Mickey Mouse, 32 pgs. (Disney)	43	86	129	271	461	650
9(nn)-The Story of the Gloomy Bunny	13	26	39	74	105	135
10-Out of Santa's Bag	12	24	36	69	97	125
11-Fun With Santa Claus	11	22	33	62	86	110
12-Santa's Toys	11	22	33	62	86	110
13-Santa's Surprise	11	22	33	62	86	110
14-Santa's Candy Kitchen	11	22	33	62	86	110
15-Hip-It-Ty Hop & the Big Bass Viol	10	20	30	56	76	95
16-Woody Woodpecker (1947)(Walter Lantz)	14	28	42	78	112	145
17-Roy Rogers (1948)	20	40	60	120	195	270
18-Popular Fairy Tales	12	24	36	67	94	120
19-Uncle Wiggily	10	20	30	58	79	100
20-Donald Duck by Carl Barks, "Darkest Africa", 22 pgs.; Kelly-c (Disney)	271	542	813	1734	2967	4200
21-Tom and Jerry	11	22	33	62	86	110
22-Andy Panda (Lantz)	11	22	33	62	86	110
23-Raggedy Ann & Andy; Kerr-a	13	26	39	72	101	130
24-Felix the Cat, 1932 daily strip reprints by Otto Messmer	16	32	48	94	147	200
25-Gene Autry	17	34	51	100	158	215
26-Our Gang; Walt Kelly	16	32	48	96	151	205
27-Mickey Mouse; r/in M. M. #240 (Disney)	29	58	87	172	281	390
28-Gene Autry	17	34	51	98	154	210
29-Easter Bonnet Shop	9	18	27	47	61	75
30-Here Comes Santa	8	16	24	44	57	70
31-Santa's Busy Corner	8	16	24	44	57	70
32-No book produced						
33-A Christmas Carol (12/48)	9	18	27	47	61	75
34-Woody Woodpecker	11	22	33	62	86	110
35-Roy Rogers (1948)	19	38	57	112	179	245
36-Felix the Cat(1949); by Messmer; '34 strip-r	14	28	42	82	121	160
37-Popeye	14	28	42	78	112	145
38-Oswald the Rabbit	8	16	24	44	57	70
39-Gene Autry	16	32	48	94	147	200
40-Andy and Woody	8	16	24	44	57	70
41-Donald Duck by Carl Barks, "Race to the South Seas", 22 pgs.; Kelly-c	245	490	735	1568	2684	3800
42-Porky Pig	9	18	27	47	61	75
43-Henry	8	16	24	42	54	65
44-Bugs Bunny	9	18	27	52	69	85
45-Mickey Mouse (Disney)	22	44	66	128	209	290
46-Tom and Jerry	9	18	27	52	69	85
47-Roy Rogers	15	30	45	90	140	190
48-Greetings from Santa	6	12	18	31	38	45
49-Santa Is Here	6	12	18	31	38	45
50-Santa Claus' Workshop (1949)	6	12	18	31	38	45
51-Felix the Cat (1950) by Messmer	14	28	42	80	115	150
52-Popeye	11	22	33	62	86	110
53-Oswald the Rabbit	8	16	24	40	50	60
54-Gene Autry	15	30	45	84	127	170
55-Andy and Woody	8	16	24	40	50	60
56-Donald Duck; not by Barks; Barks art on back-c (Disney)	21	42	63	122	199	275
57-Porky Pig	8	16	24	40	50	60
58-Henry	7	14	21	35	43	50
59-Bugs Bunny	9	18	27	47	61	75
60-Mickey Mouse (Disney)	21	42	63	126	206	285
61-Tom and Jerry	8	16	24	40	50	60
62-Roy Rogers	15	30	45	90	140	190
63-Welcome Santa (1/2-size, oblong)	6	12	18	31	38	45
64(nn)-Santa's Helpers (1/2-size, oblong)	6	12	18	31	38	45
65(nn)-Jingle Bells (1950) (1/2-size, oblong)	6	12	18	31	38	45
66-Popeye (1951)	14	28	42	76	108	140
67-Oswald the Rabbit	7	14	21	35	43	50
68-Roy Rogers	14	28	42	80	115	150
69-Donald Duck; Barks-a on back-c (Disney)	21	42	63	122	199	275
70-Tom and Jerry	8	16	24	40	50	60
71-Porky Pig	8	16	24	42	54	65
72-Krazy Kat	9	18	27	47	61	75
73-Roy Rogers	14	28	42	82	121	160
74-Mickey Mouse (1951)(Disney)	20	40	60	115	190	250
75-Bugs Bunny	9	18	27	47	61	75
76-Andy and Woody	8	16	24	40	50	60
77-Roy Rogers	14	28	42	82	121	160
78-Gene Autry (1951); last regular size issue	14	28	42	80	115	150

Note: All pre #79 issues came with or without a slick protective wrap-around cover over the regular cover which advertised Poll Parrot Shoes, Sears, etc. This outer cover protects the inside pages making them in nicer condition.

Issues with the outer cover are worth 15-25% more

	GD 2.0	VG 4.0	FN 6.0	VF 8.0	VF/NM 9.0	NM- 9.2
79-Andy Panda (1952, 5x7" size)	7	14	21	35	43	50
80-Popeye	8	16	24	40	50	60
81-Oswald the Rabbit	6	12	18	29	36	42
82-Tarzan; Lex Barker photo-c	15	30	45	88	137	185
83-Bugs Bunny	7	14	21	37	46	55
84-Henry	6	12	18	29	36	42
85-Woody Woodpecker	6	12	18	29	36	42
86-Roy Rogers	11	22	33	62	86	110
87-Krazy Kat	8	16	24	44	57	70
88-Tom and Jerry	6	12	18	31	38	45
89-Porky Pig	6	12	18	29	36	42
90-Gene Autry	11	22	33	62	86	110
91-Roy Rogers & Santa	11	22	33	62	86	110
92-Christmas with Santa	5	10	15	24	30	35
93-Woody Woodpecker (1953)	5	10	15	23	28	32
94-Indian Chief	10	20	30	54	72	90
95-Oswald the Rabbit	5	10	15	23	28	32
96-Popeye	10	20	30	54	72	90
97-Bugs Bunny	7	14	21	35	43	50
98-Tarzan; Lex Barker photo-c	15	30	45	85	130	175
99-Porky Pig	5	10	15	23	28	32
100-Roy Rogers	10	20	30	58	79	100
101-Henry	5	10	15	22	26	30
102-Tom Corbett (TV)('53, early app).; painted-c	12	24	36	67	94	120
103-Tom and Jerry	5	10	15	23	28	32
104-Gene Autry	10	20	30	56	76	95
105-Roy Rogers	10	20	30	56	76	95
106-Santa's Helpers	5	10	15	24	30	35
107-Santa's Christmas Book - not published						
108-Fun with Santa (1953)	5	10	15	24	30	35
109-Woody Woodpecker (1954)	5	10	15	24	30	35
110-Indian Chief	6	12	18	31	38	45
111-Oswald the Rabbit	5	10	15	22	26	30
112-Henry	4	9	13	18	22	26
113-Porky Pig	5	10	15	22	26	30
114-Tarzan; Russ Manning-a	14	28	42	82	121	160
115-Bugs Bunny	6	12	18	27	33	38
116-Roy Rogers	10	20	30	56	76	95
117-Popeye	10	20	30	54	72	90
118-Flash Gordon; painted-c	12	24	36	69	97	125
119-Tom and Jerry	5	10	15	22	26	30
120-Gene Autry	10	20	30	58	76	95
121-Roy Rogers	10	20	30	58	76	95
122-Santa's Surprise (1954)	5	10	15	22	26	30
123-Santa's Christmas Book	5	10	15	22	26	30
124-Woody Woodpecker (1955)	4	9	13	18	22	26
125-Tarzan; Lex Barker photo-c	14	28	42	78	112	145
126-Oswald the Rabbit	4	9	13	18	22	26
127-Indian Chief	7	14	21	35	43	50
128-Tom and Jerry	4	9	13	18	22	26
129-Henry	4	8	12	17	21	24
130-Porky Pig	4	9	13	18	22	26
131-Roy Rogers	10	20	30	56	76	95
132-Bugs Bunny	5	10	15	23	28	32
133-Flash Gordon; painted-c	13	26	39	72	101	130
134-Popeye	8	16	24	42	54	65
135-Gene Autry	10	20	30	56	76	95
136-Roy Rogers	10	20	30	56	76	95
137-Gifts from Santa	4	7	10	14	17	20
138-Fun at Christmas (1955)	4	7	10	14	17	20
139-Woody Woodpecker (1956)	4	9	13	18	22	26
140-Indian Chief	7	14	21	35	43	50
141-Oswald the Rabbit	4	9	13	18	22	26
142-Flash Gordon	13	26	39	74	105	135
143-Porky Pig	4	9	13	18	22	26
144-Tarzan; Russ Manning-a; painted-c	13	26	39	72	101	130
145-Tom and Jerry	4	9	13	18	22	26
146-Roy Rogers; photo-c	10	20	30	56	76	95
147-Henry	4	8	11	16	19	22
148-Popeye	8	16	24	42	54	65
149-Bugs Bunny	5	10	15	22	26	30
150-Gene Autry	10	20	30	56	76	95
151-Roy Rogers	10	20	30	56	76	95
152-The Night Before Christmas	4	8	11	16	19	22
153-Merry Christmas (1956)	4	9	13	18	22	26
154-Tom and Jerry (1957)	4	9	13	18	22	26
155-Tarzan; photo-c	12	24	36	69	97	125
156-Oswald the Rabbit	4	9	13	18	22	26

	GD 2.0	VG 4.0	FN 6.0	VF 8.0	VF/NM 9.0	NM- 9.2
157-Popeye	7	14	21	35	43	50
158-Woody Woodpecker	4	9	13	18	22	26
159-Indian Chief	7	14	21	35	43	50
160-Bugs Bunny	5	10	15	22	26	30
161-Roy Rogers	9	18	27	52	69	85
162-Henry	4	8	11	16	19	22
163-Rin Tin Tin (TV)	8	16	24	42	54	65
164-Porky Pig	4	9	13	18	22	26
165-The Lone Ranger	9	18	27	50	65	80
166-Santa and His Reindeer	4	7	10	14	17	20
167-Roy Rogers and Santa	9	18	27	52	69	85
168-Santa Claus' Workshop (1957, full size)	4	8	11	16	19	22
169-Popeye (1958)	7	14	21	35	43	50
170-Indian Chief	7	14	21	35	43	50
171-Oswald the Rabbit	4	8	12	17	21	24
172-Tarzan	11	22	33	60	83	105
173-Tom and Jerry	4	8	12	17	21	24
174-The Lone Ranger	9	18	27	50	65	80
175-Porky Pig	4	8	12	17	21	24
176-Roy Rogers	9	18	27	47	61	75
177-Woody Woodpecker	4	8	12	17	21	24
178-Henry	4	8	11	16	19	22
179-Bugs Bunny	4	8	12	17	21	24
180-Rin Tin Tin (TV)	7	14	21	37	46	55
181-Happy Holiday	4	7	9	14	16	18
182-Happi Tim	4	8	11	16	19	22
183-Welcome Santa (1958, full size)	4	7	9	14	16	18
184-Woody Woodpecker (1959)	4	8	11	16	19	22
185-Tarzan; photo-c	10	20	30	58	79	100
186-Oswald the Rabbit	4	8	11	16	19	22
187-Indian Chief	6	12	18	28	34	40
188-Bugs Bunny	4	8	11	16	19	22
189-Henry	4	7	10	14	17	20
190-Tom and Jerry	4	8	11	16	19	22
191-Roy Rogers	8	16	24	44	57	70
192-Porky Pig	4	8	11	16	19	22
193-The Lone Ranger	9	18	27	47	61	75
194-Popeye	6	12	18	31	38	45
195-Rin Tin Tin (TV)	7	14	21	35	43	50
196-Sears Special - not published						
197-Santa Is Coming	4	7	10	14	17	20
198-Santa's Helpers (1959)	4	7	10	14	17	20
199-Huckleberry Hound (TV)(1960, early app.)	8	16	24	42	54	65
200-Fury (TV)	6	12	18	28	34	40
201-Bugs Bunny	4	8	11	16	19	22
202-Space Explorer	8	16	24	42	54	65
203-Woody Woodpecker	4	7	10	14	17	20
204-Tarzan	9	18	27	52	69	85
205-Mighty Mouse	6	12	18	33	41	48
206-Roy Rogers; photo-c	8	16	24	42	54	65
207-Tom and Jerry	4	7	10	14	17	20
208-The Lone Ranger; Clayton Moore photo-c	10	20	30	54	72	90
209-Porky Pig	4	7	10	14	17	20
210-Lassie (TV)	6	12	18	33	41	48
211-Sears Special - not published						
212-Christmas Eve	4	7	10	14	17	20
213-Here Comes Santa (1960)	4	7	10	14	17	20
214-Huckleberry Hound (TV)(1961)	7	14	21	35	43	50
215-Hi Yo Silver	8	16	24	40	50	60
216-Rocky & His Friends (TV)(1961); predates Rocky and His Fiendish Friends #1 (see Four Color #1128)	9	18	27	52	69	85
217-Lassie (TV)	6	12	18	31	38	45
218-Porky Pig	4	7	10	14	17	20
219-Journey to the Sun	5	10	15	24	30	35
220-Bugs Bunny	4	8	11	16	19	22
221-Roy and Dale; photo-c	8	16	24	42	54	65
222-Woody Woodpecker	4	7	10	14	17	20
223-Tarzan	9	18	27	50	65	80
224-Tom and Jerry	4	7	10	14	17	20
225-The Lone Ranger	8	16	24	40	50	60
226-Christmas Treasury (1961)	4	7	10	14	17	20
227-Letters to Santa (1961)	4	7	10	14	17	20
228-Sears Special - not published?						
229-The Flintstones (TV)(1962); early app.; predates 1st Flintstones Gold Key issue (#7)	10	20	30	58	79	100
230-Lassie (TV)	6	12	18	27	33	38
231-Bugs Bunny	4	8	11	16	19	22
232-The Three Stooges	10	20	30	54	72	90
233-Bullwinkle (TV) (1962, very early app.)	9	18	27	52	69	85
234-Smokey the Bear	5	10	15	23	28	32
235-Huckleberry Hound (TV)	7	14	21	35	43	50
236-Roy and Dale	7	14	21	35	43	50
237-Mighty Mouse	6	12	18	27	33	38
238-The Lone Ranger	8	16	24	40	50	60
239-Woody Woodpecker	4	7	10	14	17	20
240-Tarzan	8	16	24	44	57	70
241-Santa Claus Around the World	4	7	9	14	16	18
242-Santa's Toyland (1962)	4	7	9	14	16	18
243-The Flintstones (TV)(1963)	9	18	27	47	61	75
244-Mister Ed (TV); early app.; photo-c	7	14	21	35	43	50
245-Bugs Bunny	4	8	11	16	19	22
246-Popeye	6	12	18	27	33	38
247-Mighty Mouse	6	12	18	27	33	38
248-The Three Stooges	10	20	30	54	72	90
249-Woody Woodpecker	4	7	10	14	17	20
250-Roy and Dale	7	14	21	35	43	50
251-Little Lulu & Witch Hazel	11	22	33	60	83	105

	GD 2.0	VG 4.0	FN 6.0	VF 8.0	VF/NM 9.0	NM- 9.2
252-Tarzan; painted-c	8	16	24	42	54	65
253-Yogi Bear (TV)	8	16	24	40	50	60
254-Lassie (TV)	6	12	18	27	33	38
255-Santa's Christmas List	4	7	10	14	17	20
256-Christmas Party (1963)	4	7	10	14	17	20
257-Mighty Mouse	6	12	18	27	33	38
258-The Sword in the Stone (Disney)	8	16	24	42	54	65
259-Bugs Bunny	4	8	11	16	19	22
260-Mister Ed (TV)	6	12	18	31	38	45
261-Woody Woodpecker	4	7	10	14	17	20
262-Tarzan	8	16	24	40	50	60
263-Donald Duck; not by Barks (Disney)	9	18	27	52	69	85
264-Popeye	6	12	18	27	33	38
265-Yogi Bear (TV)	6	12	18	31	38	45
266-Lassie (TV)	5	10	15	23	28	32
267-Little Lulu; Irving Tripp-a	10	20	30	56	76	95
268-The Three Stooges	9	18	27	47	61	75
269-A Jolly Christmas	3	6	8	12	14	16
270-Santa's Little Helpers	3	6	8	12	14	16
271-The Flintstones (TV)(1965)	8	16	24	44	57	70
272-Tarzan	8	16	24	40	50	60
273-Bugs Bunny	4	8	11	16	19	22
274-Popeye	6	12	18	27	33	38
275-Little Lulu; Irving Tripp-a	9	18	27	50	65	80
276-The Jetsons (TV)	13	26	39	72	101	130
277-Daffy Duck	4	8	11	16	19	22
278-Lassie (TV)	5	10	15	23	28	32
279-Yogi Bear (TV)	6	12	18	31	38	45
280-The Three Stooges; photo-c	9	18	27	47	61	75
281-Tom and Jerry	4	7	9	14	16	18
282-Mister Ed (TV)	6	12	18	31	38	45
283-Santa's Visit	4	7	9	14	16	18
284-Christmas Parade (1965)	4	7	9	14	16	18
285-Astro Boy (TV); 2nd app. Astro Boy	36	72	108	211	343	475
286-Tarzan	7	14	21	37	46	55
287-Bugs Bunny	4	8	11	16	19	22
288-Daffy Duck	4	7	10	14	17	20
289-The Flintstones (TV)	8	16	24	44	57	70
290-Mister Ed (TV); photo-c	5	10	15	24	30	35
291-Yogi Bear (TV)	6	12	18	27	33	38
292-The Three Stooges; photo-c	9	18	27	47	61	75
293-Little Lulu; Irving Tripp-a	8	16	24	42	54	65
294-Popeye	5	10	15	24	30	35
295-Tom and Jerry	4	7	9	14	16	18
296-Lassie (TV); photo-c	5	10	15	22	26	30
297-Christmas Bells	3	6	8	12	14	16
298-Santa's Sleigh (1966)	3	6	8	12	14	16
299-The Flintstones (TV)(1967)	8	16	24	44	57	70
300-Tarzan	7	14	21	37	46	55
301-Bugs Bunny	4	7	10	14	17	20
302-Laurel and Hardy (TV); photo-c	6	12	18	28	34	40
303-Daffy Duck	3	6	8	12	14	16
304-The Three Stooges; photo-c	7	14	21	35	43	50
305-Tom and Jerry	3	6	8	12	14	16
306-Daniel Boone (TV); Fess Parker photo-c	7	14	21	35	43	50
307-Little Lulu; Irving Tripp-a	7	14	21	37	46	55
308-Lassie (TV); photo-c	5	10	15	22	26	30
309-Yogi Bear (TV)	5	10	15	24	30	35
310-The Lone Ranger; Clayton Moore photo-c	10	20	30	54	72	90
311-Santa's Show	4	7	9	14	16	18
312-Christmas Album (1967)	4	7	9	14	16	18
313-Daffy Duck (1968)	3	6	8	12	14	16
314-Laurel and Hardy (TV)	6	12	18	27	33	38
315-Bugs Bunny	4	7	10	14	17	20
316-The Three Stooges	8	16	24	40	50	60
317-The Flintstones (TV)	8	16	24	42	54	65
318-Tarzan	7	14	21	35	43	50
319-Yogi Bear (TV)	5	10	15	24	30	35
320-Space Family Robinson (TV); Spiegle-a	12	24	36	69	97	125
321-Tom and Jerry	3	6	8	12	14	16
322-The Lone Ranger	7	14	21	37	46	55
323-Little Lulu; not by Stanley	5	10	15	24	30	35
324-Lassie (TV); photo-c	5	10	15	22	26	30
325-Fun with Santa	4	7	9	14	16	18
326-Christmas Story (1968)	4	7	9	14	16	18
327-The Flintstones (TV)(1969)	8	16	24	42	54	65
328-Space Family Robinson (TV); Spiegle-a	12	24	36	69	97	125
329-Bugs Bunny	4	7	10	14	17	20
330-The Jetsons (TV)	10	20	30	56	76	95
331-Daffy Duck	3	6	8	12	14	16
332-Tarzan	6	12	18	28	34	40
333-Tom and Jerry	3	6	8	12	14	16
334-Lassie (TV)	4	9	13	18	22	26
335-Little Lulu	5	10	15	24	30	35
336-The Three Stooges	8	16	24	40	50	60
337-Yogi Bear (TV)	5	10	15	24	30	35
338-The Lone Ranger	7	14	21	37	46	55
339-(Was not published)						
340-Here Comes Santa (1969)	3	6	8	12	14	16
341-The Flintstones (TV)	8	16	24	42	54	65
342-Tarzan	3	6	9	19	30	40
343-Bugs Bunny	2	4	6	10	14	18
344-Yogi Bear (TV)	3	6	9	16	23	30
345-Tom and Jerry	2	4	6	9	13	16
346-Lassie (TV)	3	6	9	15	21	26
347-Daffy Duck	2	4	6	9	13	16
348-The Jetsons (TV)	6	12	18	37	66	95

March of Comics #222 © Walter Lantz

March of Comics #404 © WEST

Mark Steel Fights Pollution #1 © AISI

	GD	VG	FN	VF	VF/NM	NM-
	2.0	4.0	6.0	8.0	9.0	9.2
349-Little Lulu; not by Stanley	3	6	9	16	23	30
350-The Lone Ranger	3	6	9	17	26	35
351-Beep-Beep, the Road Runner (TV)	2	4	6	11	16	20
352-Space Family Robinson (TV); Spiegle-a	7	14	21	44	82	120
353-Beep-Beep, the Road Runner (1971) (TV)	2	4	6	11	16	20
354-Tarzan (1971)	3	6	9	17	26	35
355-Little Lulu; not by Stanley	3	6	9	16	23	30
356-Scooby Doo, Where Are You? (TV)	7	14	21	46	86	125
357-Daffy Duck & Porky Pig	2	4	6	8	11	14
358-Lassie (TV)	3	6	9	14	19	24
359-Baby Snoots	2	4	6	10	14	18
360-H. R. Pufnstuf (TV); photo-c	6	12	18	40	73	105
361-Tom and Jerry	2	4	6	8	11	14
362-Smokey Bear (TV)	2	4	6	8	11	14
363-Bugs Bunny & Yosemite Sam	2	4	6	9	13	16
364-The Banana Splits (TV); photo-c	5	10	15	33	57	80
365-Tom and Jerry (1972)	2	4	6	8	11	14
366-Tarzan	3	6	9	17	26	35
367-Bugs Bunny & Porky Pig	2	4	6	9	13	16
368-Scooby Doo (TV)(4/72)	6	12	18	37	66	95
369-Little Lulu; not by Stanley	3	6	9	14	19	24
370-Lassie (TV); photo-c	3	6	9	14	19	24
371-Baby Snoots	2	4	6	9	13	16
372-Smokey the Bear (TV)	2	4	6	8	11	14
373-The Three Stooges	4	8	12	23	37	50
374-Wacky Witch	2	4	6	8	11	14
375-Beep-Beep & Daffy Duck (TV)	2	4	6	8	11	14
376-The Pink Panther (1972) (TV)	2	4	6	10	14	18
377-Baby Snoots (1973)	2	4	6	9	13	16
378-Turok, Son of Stone; new-a	7	14	21	46	86	125
379-Heckle & Jeckle New Terrytoons (TV)	2	4	6	8	11	14
380-Bugs Bunny & Yosemite Sam	2	4	6	8	11	14
381-Lassie (TV)	2	4	6	11	16	20
382-Scooby Doo, Where Are You? (TV)	5	10	15	35	63	90
383-Smokey the Bear (TV)	2	4	6	8	11	14
384-Pink Panther (TV)	2	4	6	8	11	14
385-Little Lulu	2	4	6	13	18	22
386-Wacky Witch	2	4	6	8	11	14
387-Beep-Beep & Daffy Duck (TV)	2	4	6	8	11	14
388-Tom and Jerry (1973)	2	4	6	8	11	14
389-Little Lulu; not by Stanley	2	4	6	13	18	22
390-Pink Panther (TV)	2	4	6	8	11	14
391-Scooby Doo (TV)	4	8	12	28	47	65
392-Bugs Bunny & Yosemite Sam	2	4	6	8	10	12
393-New Terrytoons (Heckle & Jeckle) (TV)	2	4	6	8	10	12
394-Lassie (TV)	2	4	6	9	13	16
395-Woodsy Owl	2	4	6	8	10	12
396-Baby Snoots	2	4	6	8	11	14
397-Beep-Beep & Daffy Duck (TV)	2	4	6	8	10	12
398-Wacky Witch	2	4	6	8	10	12
399-Turok, Son of Stone; new-a	6	12	18	42	79	115
400-Tom and Jerry	2	4	6	8	10	12
401-Baby Snoots (1975) (r/#371)	2	4	6	8	11	14
402-Daffy Duck (r/#313)	1	3	4	6	8	10
403-Bugs Bunny (r/#343)	2	4	6	8	10	12
404-Space Family Robinson (TV)(r/#328)	6	12	18	37	66	95
405-Cracky	1	3	4	6	8	10
406-Little Lulu (r/#355)	2	4	6	10	14	18
407-Smokey the Bear (TV)(r/#362)	2	4	6	8	10	12
408-Turok, Son of Stone; c-r/Turok #20 w/changes; new-a						
	6	12	18	38	69	100
409-Pink Panther (TV)	1	3	4	6	8	10
410-Wacky Witch	1	2	3	5	6	8
411-Lassie (TV)(r/#324)	2	4	6	9	13	16
412-New Terrytoons (1975) (TV)	1	2	3	5	6	8
413-Daffy Duck (1976)(r/#331)	1	2	3	5	6	8
414-Space Family Robinson (r/#328)	5	10	15	35	63	90
415-Bugs Bunny (r/#329)	1	2	3	5	6	8
416-Beep-Beep, the Road Runner (r/#353)(TV)	1	2	3	5	6	8
417-Little Lulu (r/#323)	2	4	6	10	14	18
418-Pink Panther (r/#384) (TV)	1	2	3	5	6	8
419-Baby Snoots (r/#377)	1	3	4	6	8	10
420-Woody Woodpecker	1	2	3	5	6	8
421-Tweety & Sylvester	1	2	3	5	6	8
422-Wacky Witch (r/#386)	1	2	3	5	6	8
423-Little Monsters	1	3	4	6	8	10
424-Cracky (12/76)	1	2	3	5	6	8
425-Daffy Duck	1	2	3	5	6	8
426-Underdog (TV)	3	6	9	21	33	45
427-Little Lulu (r/#335)	2	4	6	8	11	14
428-Bugs Bunny	1	2	3	4	5	7
429-The Pink Panther (TV)	1	2	3	4	5	7
430-Beep-Beep, the Road Runner (TV)	1	2	3	4	5	7
431-Baby Snoots	1	2	3	5	6	8
432-Lassie (TV)	2	4	6	8	10	12
433-437: 433-Tweety & Sylvester. 434-Wacky Witch. 435-New Terrytoons (TV). 436-Wacky Advs. of Cracky. 437-Daffy Duck	1	2	3	4	5	7
438-Underdog (TV)	3	6	9	19	30	40
439-Little Lulu (r/#349)	2	4	6	8	11	14
440-442,444-446: 440-Bugs Bunny. 441-The Pink Panther (TV). 442-Beep-Beep, the Road Runner (TV). 444-Tom and Jerry. 445-Tweety and Sylvester. 446-Wacky Witch						
	1	2	3	5	6	8
443-Baby Snoots	1	2	3	5	6	8
447-Mighty Mouse	2	4	6	8	10	12
448-455,457,458: 448-Cracky. 449-Pink Panther (TV). 450-Baby Snoots. 451-Tom and Jerry. 452-Bugs Bunny. 453-Popeye. 454-Woody Woodpecker. 455-Beep-Beep, the Road Runner (TV). 457-Tweety & Sylvester. 458-Wacky Witch	1	2	3	5	6	8
456-Little Lulu (r/#369)	2	4	6	8	10	12
459-Mighty Mouse	2	4	6	8	10	12
460-466: 460-Daffy Duck. 461-The Pink Panther (TV). 462-Baby Snoots. 463-Tom and Jerry. 464-Bugs Bunny. 465-Popeye. 466-Woody Woodpecker						
	1	2	3	5	6	8
467-Underdog (TV)	3	6	9	17	26	35
468-Little Lulu (r/#385)	1	2	3	5	6	8
469-Tweety & Sylvester	1	2	3	5	6	8
470-Wacky Witch	1	2	3	5	6	8
471-Mighty Mouse	1	3	4	6	8	10
472-474,476-478: 472-Heckle & Jeckle(12/80). 473-Pink Panther(1/81)(TV). 474-Baby Snoots. 476-Bugs Bunny. 477-Popeye. 478-Woody Woodpecker						
	1	2	3	5	6	8
475-Little Lulu (r/#323)	1	3	4	6	8	10
479-Underdog (TV)	3	6	9	16	23	30
480-482: 480-Tom and Jerry. 481-Tweety and Sylvester. 482-Wacky Witch						
	1	2	3	4	5	8
483-Mighty Mouse	1	3	4	6	8	10
484-487: 484-Heckle & Jeckle. 485-Baby Snoots. 486-The Pink Panther (TV). 487-Bugs Bunny	1	2	3	4	5	8
488-Little Lulu (4/82) (r/#335) (Last issue)	2	4	6	10	14	18

MARCH TO MARKET, THE
Pictorial Media/Swift & Co.: 1948, 1950 (Giveaway)

	GD	VG	FN	VF	VF/NM	NM-
nn-The story of meat	5	10	14	20	24	28

MARGARET O'BRIEN (See The Adventures of...)

MARK STEEL
American Iron & Steel Institute: 1967, 1968, 1972 (Giveaway) (24 pgs.)

	GD	VG	FN	VF	VF/NM	NM-
1967,1968- "Journey of Discovery with..."; Neal Adams art	4	8	12	23	37	50
1972- "...Fights Pollution"; N. Adams-a	2	4	6	9	13	15

MARTIN LUTHER KING AND THE MONTGOMERY STORY
Fellowship Reconciliation: 1957 (Giveaway, 16 pgs.) (A Spanish edition also exists)

nn-In color with paper-c (a CGC 8.0 copy sold for $185 in 2017, a VF+ copy sold for $675 in 2019, a CGC 8.5 copy sold for $799 in May 2021, and a CGC 5.0 copy sold for $650 in April 2022)

MARTIN LUTHER KING AND THE MONTGOMERY STORY
Top Shelf/Fellowship Reconciliation: 2011, 2013 ($5.00, newsprint-c, 16 pgs.)

	NM-
nn-(2011) Reprint of the 1957 giveaway published by Fellowship Reconciliation; stapled	10.00
nn-(2013) Reprint has glued binding unlike the stapled 2011 version	10.00

MARVEL COLLECTOR'S EDITION: X-MEN
Marvel Comics: 1993 (3-3/4x6-1/2")

	NM-
1-4-Pizza Hut giveaways	6.00

MARVEL COMICS PRESENTS
Marvel Comics: 1987, 1988 (4 1/4 x 6 1/4, 20 pgs.)
...Mini Comic Giveaway

	GD	VG	FN	VF	VF/NM	NM-
nn-(1988) Alf	1	3	4	6	8	10
nn-(1987) Captain America r/ #250	1	3	4	6	8	10
nn-(1987) Care Bears (Star Comics...)	1	3	4	6	8	10
nn-(1988) Flintstone Kids	1	3	4	6	8	10
nn-(1987) Heathcliffe (Star Comics...)	1	3	4	6	8	10
nn-(1987) Spider-Man-r/Spect. Spider-Man #21	1	3	4	6	8	10
nn-(1988) Spider-Man-r/Amazing Spider-Man #1	1	3	4	6	8	10
nn-(1988) X-Men-reprints X-Men #53; B. Smith-a	1	3	4	6	8	10

MARVEL GUIDE TO COLLECTING COMICS, THE
Marvel Comics: 1982 (16 pgs., newsprint pages and cover)

	GD	VG	FN	VF	VF/NM	NM-
1-Simonson-c	2	4	6	8	10	12

MARVEL MINI-BOOKS

	GD 2.0	VG 4.0	FN 6.0	VF 8.0	VF/NM 9.0	NM- 9.2

Marvel Comics Group: 1966 (50 pgs., B&W; 5/8x7/8") (6 different issues) (Smallest comics ever published) (Marvel Mania Giveaways)

	GD	VG	FN	VF	VF/NM	NM-
Captain America, Millie the Model, Sgt. Fury, Hulk, Thor each...	3	6	9	21	33	45
Spider-Man	3	6	9	21	33	45

NOTE: Each came from gum machines in six different color covers, usually one color: Pink, yellow, green, etc.

MARVEL SUPER-HERO ISLAND ADVENTURES
Marvel Comics: 1999 (Sold at the park polybagged with Captain America V3 #19, one other comic, 5 trading cards and a cloisonn´e pin)

	GD	VG	FN	VF	VF/NM	NM-
1-Promotes Universal Studios Islands of Adventures theme park						5.00

MARY'S GREATEST APOSTLE (St. Louis Grignion de Montfort)
Catechetical Guild (Topix) (Giveaway): No date (16 pgs.; paper cover)

	GD	VG	FN	VF	VF/NM	NM-
nn	5	10	15	23	28	32

MASK (Made for Kenner Toys)
DC Comics: 1985

	GD	VG	FN	VF	VF/NM	NM-
1	4	8	12	23	37	50
2,3	2	4	6	8	10	12

MASKED PILOT, THE (See Popular Comics #43)
R.S. Callender: 1939 (7-1/2x5-1/4", 16 pgs., premium, non-slick-c)

	GD	VG	FN	VF	VF/NM	NM-
nn-Bob Jenney-a	10	20	30	56	76	95

MASTERS OF THE UNIVERSE (He-Man)
DC Comics: 1982 (giveaways with action figures, at least 35 different issues, unnumbered)

	GD	VG	FN	VF	VF/NM	NM-
nn	3	6	9	14	19	24

MATRIX, THE (1999 movie)
Warner Brothers: 1999 (Recalled by Warner Bros. over questionable content)

	GD	VG	FN	VF	VF/NM	NM-
nn-Paul Chadwick-s/a (16 pgs.); Geof Darrow-c	5	10	15	31	53	75

McCRORY'S CHRISTMAS BOOK
Western Printing Co: 1955 (36 pgs., slick-c) (McCrory Stores Corp. giveaway)

	GD	VG	FN	VF	VF/NM	NM-
nn-Painted-c	6	12	18	28	34	40

McCRORY'S TOYLAND BRINGS YOU SANTA'S PRIVATE EYES
Promotional Publ. Co.: 1956 (16 pgs.) (Giveaway)

	GD	VG	FN	VF	VF/NM	NM-
nn-Has 9 pg. story plus 7 pgs. toy ads	5	10	14	20	24	28

McCRORY'S WONDERFUL CHRISTMAS
Promotional Publ. Co.: 1954 (20 pgs., slick-c) (Giveaway)

	GD	VG	FN	VF	VF/NM	NM-
nn	6	12	18	28	34	40

McDONALDS COMMANDRONS
DC Comics: 1985

	GD	VG	FN	VF	VF/NM	NM-
nn-Four editions	1	2	3	5	6	8

MEDAL FOR BOWZER, A (Giveaway)
American Visuals Corp.: 1966 (8 pgs.)

	GD	VG	FN	VF	VF/NM	NM-
nn-Eisner-c/script; Bowzer (a dog) survives untried pneumonia cure and earns his medal; (medical experimentation on animals)	20	40	60	138	307	475

MEET HIYA A FRIEND OF SANTA CLAUS
Julian J. Proskauer/Sundial Shoe Stores, etc.: 1949 (18 pgs.?, paper-c)(Giveaway)

	GD	VG	FN	VF	VF/NM	NM-
nn	8	16	24	40	50	60

MEET THE NEW POST-GAZETTE SUNDAY FUNNIES
Pittsburgh Post Gazette: 3/12/49 (7-1/4x10-1/4", 16 pgs., paper-c)
Commercial Comics (insert in newspaper) (Rare)
Dick Tracy by Gould, Gasoline Alley, Terry & the Pirates, Brenda Starr, Buck Rogers by Yager, The Gumps, Peter Rabbit by Fago, Superman, Funnyman by Siegel & Shuster, The Saint, Archie, & others done especially for this book. A fine copy sold at auction in 1985 for $276.00.

	GD	VG	FN	VF	VF/NM	NM-
	260	520	780	1700	-	-

MEN OF COURAGE
Catechetical Guild: 1949

	GD	VG	FN	VF	VF/NM	NM-
Bound Topix comics-V7#2,4,6,8,10,16,18,20	7	14	21	37	46	55

MEN WHO MOVE THE NATION
Publisher unknown: (Giveaway) (B&W)

	GD	VG	FN	VF	VF/NM	NM-
nn-Neal Adams-a	7	14	21	35	43	50

MERRY CHRISTMAS, A
K. K. Publications (Child Life Shoes): 1948 (Giveaway)

	GD	VG	FN	VF	VF/NM	NM-
nn-Santa cover	9	18	27	47	61	75

MERRY CHRISTMAS
K. K. Publications (Blue Bird Shoes Giveaway): 1956 (7-1/4x5-1/4")

	GD	VG	FN	VF	VF/NM	NM-
nn-Santa cover	5	10	14	20	24	28

MERRY CHRISTMAS FROM MICKEY MOUSE
K. K. Publications: 1939 (16 pgs.) (Color & B&W) (Shoe store giveaway)

	GD	VG	FN	VF	VF/NM	NM-
nn-Donald Duck & Pluto app.; text with art (Rare); c-reprint/Mickey Mouse Mag. V3#3 (12/37)(Rare)	265	530	795	1694	2897	4100

MERRY CHRISTMAS FROM SEARS TOYLAND (See Santa's Christmas Comic, Bob & Betty & Santa's Wishing Whistle, and A Christmas Carol)
Sears Roebuck Giveaway: 1939 (16 pgs.) (Color)(Die-cut)

	GD	VG	FN	VF	VF/NM	NM-
nn-Dick Tracy, Little Orphan Annie, The Gumps, Terry & the Pirates	110	220	330	704	1202	1700

MICKEY MOUSE (Also see Frito-Lay Giveaway)
Dell Publ. Co

	GD	VG	FN	VF	VF/NM	NM-
...& Goofy Explore Business(1978)	2	4	6	8	10	12
...& Goofy Explore Energy(1976-1978, 36 pgs.); Exxon giveaway in color; regular size	2	4	6	8	10	12
...& Goofy Explore Energy Conservation(1976-1978)-Exxon	2	4	6	8	10	12
...& Goofy Explore The Universe of Energy(1985, 20 pgs.); Exxon giveaway in color; regular size	1	2	3	5	7	9
The Perils of Mickey nn (1993, 5-1/4x7-1/4", 16 pgs.)-Nabisco giveaway w/ games, Nabisco coupons & 6 pgs. of stories; Phantom Blot app.						6.00

MICKEY MOUSE MAGAZINE
Walt Disney Productions: V1#1, Jan, 1933 - V1#9, Sept, 1933 (5-1/4x7-1/4")
No. 1-3 published by Kamen-Blair (Kay Kamen, Inc.)
(Scarce)-Distributed by dairies and leading stores through their local theatres.
First few issues had 5¢ listed on cover, later ones had no price.

	GD	VG	FN	VF	VF/NM	NM-
V1#1	440	880	1760	5250	-	-
2	212	424	848	1700	-	-
3,4	165	330	660	1325	-	-
5-9	112	224	448	900	-	-

NOTE: A rare V1#1 Hardbound copy with a glassine dust jacket sold in July 2017 for $13,145.

MICKEY MOUSE MAGAZINE (Digest size)
Walt Disney Productions: V1#1, 11/33 - V2#12, 10/35 (Mills giveaways issued by different dairies)

	GD	VG	FN	VF	VF/NM	NM-
V1#1	168	336	504	1100	1850	-
2-12: 2-X-Mas issue	58	116	174	371	636	900
V2#1 (11/34) Donald Duck in sailor suit pg. 6 (cameo)	43	86	129	271	461	650
V2#2-4,6-12: 2-X-Mas issue. 4-St. Valentine-c	41	82	123	256	428	600
V2#5 (3/35) 1st app. Donald Duck in sailor outfit on-c	113	226	339	723	1237	1750

MICKEY MOUSE MAGAZINE
K.K. Publications: V4#1, Oct, 1938 (Giveaway)

	GD	VG	FN	VF	VF/NM	NM-
V4#1	47	94	141	296	498	700

MIGHTY ATOM, THE
Whitman

	GD	VG	FN	VF	VF/NM	NM-
Giveaway (1959, '63, Whitman)-Evans-a	3	6	9	16	23	30
Giveaway ('64r, '65r, '66r, '67r, '68r)-Evans-r?	2	4	6	10	14	18
Giveaway ('73r, '76r)	2	4	6	8	11	14

MILES THE MONSTER (Initially sold only at the Dover Speedway track)
Dover International Speedway, Inc.: 2006 ($3.00)

	GD	VG	FN	VF	VF/NM	NM-
1,2-Allan Gross & Mark Wheatley-s/Wheatley-a						3.00

MILITARY COURTESY
Harvey Publications: 1950 (16 pgs.)

	GD	VG	FN	VF	VF/NM	NM-
nn-Regulations and saluting instructions	5	10	15	24	30	35

MINUTE MAN
Sovereign Service Station giveaway: No date (16 pgs., B&W, paper-c blue & red)

	GD	VG	FN	VF	VF/NM	NM-
nn-American history	5	10	14	20	24	28

MINUTE MAN ANSWERS THE CALL, THE
By M. C. Gaines: 1942,1943,1944,1945 (4 pgs.) (Giveaway inserted in Jr. JSA Membership Kit)

	GD	VG	FN	VF	VF/NM	NM-
nn-Sheldon Moldoff-a	24	48	72	142	234	325

MIRACLE ON BROADWAY
Broadway Comics: Dec, 1995 (Giveaway)

	GD	VG	FN	VF	VF/NM	NM-
1-Ernie Colon-c/a; Jim Shooter & Co. story; 1st known digitally printed comic book; 1st app. Spire & Knights on Broadway (1150 print run)						20.00

NOTE: Miracle on Broadway was a limited edition comic given to 1100 VIPs in the entertainment industry for the 1995 Holiday Season.

MISS SUNBEAM (See Little Miss Sunbeam Comics)

MR. BUG GOES TO TOWN (See Cinema Comics Herald)
K.K. Publications: 1941 (Giveaway, 52 pgs.)

	GD	VG	FN	VF	VF/NM	NM-
nn-Cartoon movie (scarce)	71	142	213	454	777	1100

MR. PEANUT, THE PERSONAL STORY OF
Planters Nut & Chocolate Co.: 1956

	GD	VG	FN	VF	VF/NM	NM-
nn	4	8	12	23	37	50

MOTHER OF US ALL
Catechetical Guild Giveaway: 1950? (32 pgs.)

	GD	VG	FN	VF	VF/NM	NM-
nn	5	10	15	24	30	35

MOTION PICTURE FUNNIES WEEKLY (Amazing Man #5 on?)
First Funnies, Inc.: 1939 (Giveaway)(B&W, 36 pgs.) No month given; last panel in Sub-Mariner story dated 4/39 (Also see Colossus, Green Giant & Invaders No. 20)

	GD	VG	FN	VF	VF/NM	NM-
1-Origin & 1st printed app. Sub-Mariner by Bill Everett (8 pgs.); Fred Schwab-c; reprinted in Marvel Mystery #1 with color added over the craft tint which was used to shade the black & white version; Spy Ring, American Ace (reprinted in Marvel Mystery #3) app. (Rare)-only eight known copies, one near mint with white pages, the rest with brown pages.	9300	18,600	27,900	46,500	65,000	-
Covers only to #2-4 (set)						1000

NOTE: Eight copies (plus one coverless) were discovered in 1974 in the estate of the deceased publisher. Covers only to issues No. 2-4 were also found which evidently were printed in advance along with #1. #1 was to be distributed only through motion picture movie houses. However, it is believed that only advanced copies were sent out and the motion picture houses not going for the idea. Possible distribution at local theaters in Boston suspected. The "pay" copy (graded at 9.0) was discovered after 1974, bringing the total known to nine. The last panel of Sub-Mariner contains a rectangular box with "Continued Next Week" printed in it. When reprinted in Marvel Mystery, the box was left in with lettering omitted.

MY DOG TIGE (Buster Brown's Dog)
Buster Brown Shoes: 1957 (Giveaway)

	GD	VG	FN	VF	VF/NM	NM-
nn	5	10	15	24	30	35

MY GREATEST THRILLS IN BASEBALL
Mission of California: 1957 (16 pg. Giveaway)

	GD	VG	FN	VF	VF/NM	NM-
nn-By Mickey Mantle	59	118	165	352	601	850

MYSTERIOUS ADVENTURES WITH SANTA CLAUS
Lansburgh's: 1948 (paper cover)

	GD	VG	FN	VF	VF/NM	NM-
nn	15	30	45	84	127	170

NAKED FORCE!
Commercial Comics: 1958 (Small size)

	GD	VG	FN	VF	VF/NM	NM-
nn	4	8	11	16	19	22

NATURAL DISASTERS!
Graphic Information Service/ Civil Defense: 1956 (16 pgs., soft-c)

	GD	VG	FN	VF	VF/NM	NM-
nn-Al Capp Li'l Abner-c; Li'l Abner cameo (1 panel); narrated by Mr. Civil Defense	11	22	33	60	83	105

Motion Picture Funnies Weekly #1 © MAR

On the Air © NBC

Peter Wheat #20 © BA

NAVY: HISTORY & TRADITION
Stokes Walesby Co./Dept. of Navy: 1958 - 1961 (nn) (Giveaway)

	GD 2.0	VG 4.0	FN 6.0	VF 8.0	VF/NM 9.0	NM- 9.2
1772-1778, 1778-1782, 1782-1817, 1817-1865, 1865-1936, 1940-1945: 1772-1778-16 pg. in color	5	10	15	22	26	30
1861: Naval Actions of the Civil War: 1865-36 pg. in color; flag-c	5	10	15	22	26	30

NEW ADVENTURE OF WALT DISNEY'S SNOW WHITE AND THE SEVEN DWARFS, A
(See Snow White Bendix Giveaway)

NEW ADVENTURES OF PETER PAN (Disney)
Western Publishing Co.: 1953 (5x7-1/4", 36 pgs.) (Admiral giveaway)

	GD 2.0	VG 4.0	FN 6.0	VF 8.0	VF/NM 9.0	NM- 9.2
nn	14	28	42	80	115	150

NEW AVENGERS... (Giveaway for U.S Military personnel)
Marvel Comics: 2005 - Present (Distributed by Army & Air Force Exchange Service)

	GD 2.0	VG 4.0	FN 6.0	VF 8.0	VF/NM 9.0	NM- 9.2
... Guest Starring the Fantastic Four (4/05) Bendis-s/Jurgens-a/c						5.00
...: Pot of Gold (AAFES 110th Anniversary Issue) (10/05) Jenkins-s/Nolan-a/c						5.00
(#3) ...: Avengers & X-Men Time Trouble (4/06) Kirkman-s						5.00
(#4) ...: Letters Home (12/06) Capt. America, Punisher, Silver Surfer, Ghost Rider on-c						5.00
5-The Spirit of America (10/05) Captain America app.						5.00
6-Fireline (8/08) Spider-Man, Iron Man & Hulk app. Richards-a/Dave Ross-c						5.00
7-An Army of One (2009) Frank Cho pin-up on back-c						5.00
8-The Promise (12/09) Captain America (Bucky) app.						5.00

NEW FRONTIERS
Harvey Information Press (United States Steel Corp.) : 1958 (16 pgs., paper-c)

	GD 2.0	VG 4.0	FN 6.0	VF 8.0	VF/NM 9.0	NM- 9.2
nn-History of barbed wire	4	8	12	18	22	25

NEW TEEN TITANS, THE
DC Comics: Nov. 1983

	GD 2.0	VG 4.0	FN 6.0	VF 8.0	VF/NM 9.0	NM- 9.2
nn(11/83-Keebler Co. Giveaway)-In cooperation with "The President's Drug Awareness Campaign"; came in Presidential envelope w/letter from White House (Nancy Reagan)	1	2	3	5	6	8
nn-(re-issue of above on Mando paper for direct sales market); American Soft Drink Industry version; I.B.M. Corp. version						5.00

NEW USES FOR GOOD EARTH
Mined Land Conservation: 1960 (paper-c)

	GD 2.0	VG 4.0	FN 6.0	VF 8.0	VF/NM 9.0	NM- 9.2
nn	3	6	9	19	30	40

NOLAN RYAN IN THE WINNING PITCH (Kellogg's Tony's Sports Comics)
DC Comics: 1992 (Sports Illustrated)

	GD 2.0	VG 4.0	FN 6.0	VF 8.0	VF/NM 9.0	NM- 9.2
nn						5.00

OLD GLORY COMICS
Chesapeake & Ohio Railway: 1944 (Giveaway)

	GD 2.0	VG 4.0	FN 6.0	VF 8.0	VF/NM 9.0	NM- 9.2
nn-Capt. Fearless reprint	9	18	27	50	65	80

ON THE AIR
NBC Network Comic: 1947 (Giveaway, paper-c, regular size)

	GD 2.0	VG 4.0	FN 6.0	VF 8.0	VF/NM 9.0	NM- 9.2
nn-(Rare)	21	42	63	122	199	275

OPERATION SURVIVAL!
Graphic Information Service/ Civil Defense: 1957 (16 pgs., soft-c)

	GD 2.0	VG 4.0	FN 6.0	VF 8.0	VF/NM 9.0	NM- 9.2
nn-Al Capp Li'l Abner-c; Li'l Abner cameo (1 panel); narrated by Mr. Civil Defense	10	20	30	58	79	100

OUT OF THE PAST A CLUE TO THE FUTURE
E. C. Comics (Public Affairs Comm.): 1946? (16 pgs.) (paper cover)

	GD 2.0	VG 4.0	FN 6.0	VF 8.0	VF/NM 9.0	NM- 9.2
nn-Based on public affairs pamphlet "What Foreign Trade Means to You"	24	48	72	142	234	325

OUTSTANDING AMERICAN WAR HEROES
The Parents' Institute: 1944 (16 pgs., paper-c)

	GD 2.0	VG 4.0	FN 6.0	VF 8.0	VF/NM 9.0	NM- 9.2
nn-Reprints from True Comics	6	12	18	28	34	40

OVERSEAS COMICS (Also see G.I. Comics & Jeep Comics)
Giveaway (Distributed to U.S. Armed Forces): 1944 - No. 105?, 1946 (7-1/4x10-1/4"; 16 pgs. in color)

	GD 2.0	VG 4.0	FN 6.0	VF 8.0	VF/NM 9.0	NM- 9.2
23-105-Bringing Up Father (by McManus), Popeye, Joe Palooka, Dick Tracy, Superman, Gasoline Alley, Buz Sawyer, Li'l Abner, Blondie, Terry & the Pirates, Out Our Way	8	16	24	42	54	65

OWL, THE (See Crackajack Funnies #25 & Popular Comics #72)(Also see The Hurricane Kids & Magic Morro)
Western Pub. Co./R.S. Callender: 1940 (Giveaway)(7-1/2x5-1/4")(Soft-c, color)

	GD 2.0	VG 4.0	FN 6.0	VF 8.0	VF/NM 9.0	NM- 9.2
nn-Frank Thomas-a	17	34	51	100	158	215

OXYDOL-DREFT
Toby Press:1950 (Set of 6 pocket-size giveaways; distributed through the mail as a set) (Scarce)

	GD 2.0	VG 4.0	FN 6.0	VF 8.0	VF/NM 9.0	NM- 9.2
1-3: 1-Li'l Abner. 2-Daisy Mae. 3-Shmoo	9	18	27	50	65	80
4-John Wayne; Williamson/Frazetta-c from John Wayne #3	13	26	39	72	101	130
5-Archie	12	24	36	67	94	120
6-Terrytoons Mighty Mouse	9	18	27	52	69	85
Mailing Envelope (has All Capp's Shmoo on front)	9	18	27	52	69	85

OZZIE SMITH IN THE KID WHO COULD (Kellogg's Tony's Sports Comics)
DC Comics: 1992 (Sports Illustrated)

	GD 2.0	VG 4.0	FN 6.0	VF 8.0	VF/NM 9.0	NM- 9.2
nn-Ozzie Smith app.						5.00

PADRE OF THE POOR
Catechetical Guild: nd (Giveaway) (16 pgs., paper-c)

	GD 2.0	VG 4.0	FN 6.0	VF 8.0	VF/NM 9.0	NM- 9.2
nn	6	12	18	27	33	38

PAUL TERRY'S HOW TO DRAW FUNNY CARTOONS
Terrytoons, Inc. (Giveaway): 1940's (14 pgs.) (Black & White)

	GD 2.0	VG 4.0	FN 6.0	VF 8.0	VF/NM 9.0	NM- 9.2
nn-Heckle & Jeckle, Mighty Mouse, etc.	13	26	39	72	101	130

PERKY AND PAM
Kay Kamen: Late 1940's (soft-c)

nn-Christmas themes (a VF copy sold for $320 in 2019)

PETER PAN (See New Adventures of Peter Pan)

PETER PENNY AND HIS MAGIC DOLLAR
American Bankers Association, N. Y. (Giveaway): 1947 (16 pgs.; paper-c; regular size)

	GD 2.0	VG 4.0	FN 6.0	VF 8.0	VF/NM 9.0	NM- 9.2
nn-(Scarce)-Used in **SOTI**, pg. 310, 311	37	74	111	222	361	500
Diff. version (7-1/4x11")-redrawn, 16 pgs., paper-c	14	28	42	80	115	150

PETER WHEAT (The Adventures of...)
Bakers Associates Giveaway: 1948 - 1957? (16 pgs. in color) (paper covers)

	GD 2.0	VG 4.0	FN 6.0	VF 8.0	VF/NM 9.0	NM- 9.2
nn(No.1)-States on last page, end of 1st Adventure of...; Kelly-a	27	54	81	158	259	360
nn(4 issues)-Kelly-a	15	30	45	84	127	170
6-10-All Kelly-a	10	20	30	54	72	90
11-20-All Kelly-a	9	18	27	50	65	80
21-35-All Kelly-a	8	16	24	40	50	60
36-66	6	12	18	28	34	40
...Artist's Workbook ('54, digest size)	6	12	18	28	34	40
...Four-In-One Fun Pack (Vol. 2, '54), oblong, comics w/puzzles	7	14	21	35	43	50
...Fun Book ('52, 32 pgs., paper-c, B&W & color, 8-1/2x10-3/4")-Contains cut-outs, puzzles, games, magic & pages to color	8	16	24	44	57	70

NOTE: ***Al Hubbard** art #36 on; written by Del Connell.*

PETER WHEAT NEWS
Bakers Associates: 1948 - No. 63, 1953 (4 pgs. in color)

	GD 2.0	VG 4.0	FN 6.0	VF 8.0	VF/NM 9.0	NM- 9.2
Vol. 1-All have 2 pgs. Peter Wheat by Kelly	22	44	66	130	213	295
2-10	13	26	39	72	101	130
11-20	8	16	24	40	50	60
21-30	6	12	18	28	34	40
31-63	4	7	10	14	17	20

NOTE: *Early issues have no date & **Kelly** art.*

PINOCCHIO
Cocomalt/Montgomery Ward Co.: 1940 (10 pgs.; giveaway, linen-like paper)

	GD 2.0	VG 4.0	FN 6.0	VF 8.0	VF/NM 9.0	NM- 9.2
nn-Cocomalt edition	47	94	141	296	498	700
nn-store edition	39	78	117	240	395	550

PIUS XII MAN OF PEACE
Catechetical Guild: No date (12 pgs.; 5-1/2x8-1/2") (B&W)

	GD 2.0	VG 4.0	FN 6.0	VF 8.0	VF/NM 9.0	NM- 9.2
nn-Catechetical Guild Giveaway	6	12	18	33	41	48

PLOT TO STEAL THE WORLD, THE
Work & Unity Group: 1948, 16pgs., paper-c

	GD 2.0	VG 4.0	FN 6.0	VF 8.0	VF/NM 9.0	NM- 9.2
nn-Anti commumism	21	42	63	122	199	275

POCAHONTAS
Pocahontas Fuel Company (Coal): 1941 - No. 2, 1942

	GD 2.0	VG 4.0	FN 6.0	VF 8.0	VF/NM 9.0	NM- 9.2
nn(#1), 2-Feat. life story of Indian princess Pocahontas & facts about Pocahontas coal, Pocahontas, VA.	20	40	60	114	182	250

POLL PARROT
Poll Parrot Shoe Store/International Shoe
K. K. Publications (Giveaway): 1950 - No. 4, 1951; No. 2, 1959 - No. 16, 1962

	GD 2.0	VG 4.0	FN 6.0	VF 8.0	VF/NM 9.0	NM- 9.2
1 ('50)-Howdy Doody; small size	18	36	54	107	169	230
2-4('51)-Howdy Doody	15	30	45	88	137	185
2('59)-16('62): 2-The Secret of Crumbley Castle. 5-Bandit Busters. 6-Fortune Finders. 7-The Make-Believe Mummy. 8-Mixed Up Mission('60). 10-The Frightful Flight. 11-Showdown at Sunup. 12-Maniac at Mubu Island. 13-...and the Runaway Genie. 14-Bully for You. 15-Trapped In Tall Timber. 16-...& the Rajah's Ruby('62)	2	4	6	11	16	20

POPEYE
Whitman

	GD 2.0	VG 4.0	FN 6.0	VF 8.0	VF/NM 9.0	NM- 9.2
Bold Detergent giveaway (Same as regular issue #94)	2	4	6	9	13	16

Quaker Cereal premium (1989, 16pp, small size,4 diff.)(Popeye & the Time Machine,

GD VG FN VF VF/NM NM-
2.0 4.0 6.0 8.0 9.0 9.2

--On Safari, --& Big Foot, --vs. Bluto) 2 4 6 8 10 12

POPEYE
Charlton (King Features) (Giveaway): 1972 - 1974 (36 pgs. in color)

E-1 to E-15 (Educational comics) 2 4 6 9 13 16
nn-Popeye Gettin' Better Grades-4 pgs. used as intro. to above giveaways (in color) 2 4 6 9 13 16

POPSICLE PETE FUN BOOK (See All-American Comics #6)
Joe Lowe Corp.: 1947, 1948

nn-36 pgs. in color; Sammy 'n' Claras, The King Who Couldn't Sleep & Popsicle Pete stories, games, cut-outs 11 22 33 62 86 110
Adventure Book ('48)-Has Classics ad with checklist to HRN #343 (Great Expectations #43) 10 20 30 54 72 90

PORKY'S BOOK OF TRICKS
K. K. Publications (Giveaway): 1942 (8-1/2x5-1/2", 48 pgs.)

nn-7 pg. comic story, text stories, plus games & puzzles 55 110 165 352 601 850

POST GAZETTE (See Meet the New...)

PUNISHER: COUNTDOWN (Movie)
Marvel Comics: 2004 (7 1/4" X 4 3/4" mini-comic packaged with Punisher DVD)

nn-Prequel to 2004 movie; Ennis-s/Dillon-a/Bradstreet-c 3.00

PURE OIL COMICS (Also see Salerno Carnival of Comics, 24 Pages of Comics, & Vicks Comics)
Pure Oil Giveaway: Late 1930's (24 pgs., regular size, paper-c)

nn-Contains 1-2 pg. strips; i.e., Hairbreadth Harry, Skyroads, Buck Rogers by Calkins & Yager, Olly of the Movies, Napoleon, S'Matter Pop, etc. Also a 16 pg. 1938 giveaway with Buck Rogers 37 74 111 222 361 500

QUAKER OATS (Also see Cap'n Crunch)
Quaker Oats Co.: 1965 (Giveaway) (2-1/2x5-1/2") (16 pgs.)

"Plenty of Glutton", starring Quake & Quisp; 3 6 9 14 19 24
"Lava Come-Back", "Kite Tale" 1 3 4 6 8 10

RAILROADS DELIVER THE GOODS!
Assoc. of American Railroads: Dec, 1954; Sept, 1957 (16 pgs., paper-c)

nn-The story of railway freight 6 12 18 28 34 40

RAILS ACROSS AMERICA!
Assoc. of American Railroads: nd (16 pgs.)

nn 6 12 18 28 34 40

READY THEN, READY NOW
Western Publications: 1966 (National Guard military giveaway, regular size)

nn 5 10 15 34 60 85

REAL FUN OF DRIVING!!, THE
Chrysler Corp.: 1965, 1966, 1967 (Regular size, 16 pgs.)

nn-Schaffenberger-a (12 pgs.) 1 2 3 5 6 8

REAL HIT
Fox Feature Publications: 1944 (Savings Bond premium)

1-Blue Beetle-r; Blue Beetle on-c 20 40 60 115 190 260
NOTE: *Two versions exist, with and without covers. The coverless version has the title, No. 1 and price printed at top of splash page.*

RED BALL COMIC BOOK
Parents' Magazine Institute: 1947 (Red Ball Shoes giveaway)

nn-Reprints from True Comics 4 9 13 18 22 26

REDDY GOOSE
International Shoe Co. (Western Printing): No number, 1958?; No. 2, Jan, 1959 - No. 16, July, 1962 (Giveaway)

nn (#1) 4 8 12 23 37 50
2-16 3 6 9 14 20 25

REDDY KILOWATT (5¢) (Also see Story of Edison)
Educational Comics (E. C.): 1946 - No. 2, 1947; 1956 - 1965 (no month) (16 pgs., paper-c)

nn-A Visit With Reddy (1948-1954?) 10 20 30 56 76 95
nn-Reddy Made Magic (1946, 5¢) 14 28 42 78 112 145
nn-Reddy Made Magic (1958) 10 20 30 56 76 95
2-Edison, the Man Who Changed the World (3/4" smaller than #1) (1947, 5¢) 14 28 42 78 112 145
...Comic Book 2 (1954)- "Light's Diamond Jubilee" 11 22 33 60 83 105
...Comic Book 2 (1956, 16 pgs.)- "Wizard of Light" 10 20 30 56 76 95
...Comic Book 2 (1958, 16 pgs.)- "Wizard of Light" 9 18 27 52 69 85
...Comic Book 2 (1965, 16 pgs.)- "Wizard of Light" 4 8 12 28 47 65
...Comic Book 3 (1956, 8 pgs.)- "The Space Kite"; Orlando story; regular size 10 20 30 46 76 95
...Comic Book 3 (1960, 8 pgs.)- "The Space Kite"; Orlando story; regular size 5 10 15 33 57 80
NOTE: *Several copies surfaced in 1979.*

REDDY MADE MAGIC
Educational Comics (E. C.): 1956, 1958 (16 pgs., paper-c)

1-Reddy Kilowatt-r (splash panel changed) 11 22 33 64 90 115
1 (1958 edition) 7 14 21 35 43 50

RED ICEBERG, THE
Impact Publ. (Catechetical Guild): 1960 (10¢, 16 pgs., Communist propaganda)

nn-(Rare)- "We The People" back-c 38 76 114 281 628 975
2nd version- "Impact Press" back-c 30 60 90 216 483 750
3rd version- "Explains comic" back-c 30 60 90 216 483 750
4th version- "Impact Press w/World Wide Secret Heart Program ad" 30 60 90 216 483 750
5th version- "Chicago Inter-Student Catholic Action" back-c 30 60 90 216 483 750
NOTE: *This book was the Guild's last anti-communist propaganda book and had very limited circulation. 3 - 4 copies surfaced in 1979 from the defunct publisher's files. Other copies do turn up.*

RED RYDER COMICS

GD VG FN VF VF/NM NM-
2.0 4.0 6.0 8.0 9.0 9.2

Dell Publ. Co.

Buster Brown Shoes Giveaway (1941, color, soft-c, 32 pgs.) 22 44 66 128 209 290
Red Ryder Super Book of Comics (1944, paper-c, 32 pgs.; blank back-c) Magic Morro app. 22 44 66 128 209 290
Red Ryder Victory Patrol-nn(1942, 32 pgs.)(Langendorf bread; includes cut-out membership card and certificate, order blank and "Slide-Up" decoder, and a Super Book of Comics in color (same content as Super Book #4 w/diff. cover (Pan-Am)) (Rare) 97 194 291 621 1061 1500
Red Ryder Victory Patrol-nn(1943, 32 pgs.)(Langendorf bread; includes cut-out "Rodeomatic" radio decoder, order coupon for "Magic V-Badge", cut-out membership card and certificate and a full color Super Book of comics comic book) (Rare) 65 130 195 416 708 1000
Red Ryder Victory Patrol-nn(1944, 32 pgs.)-r-/#43,44; comic has a paper-c & is stapled inside a triple cardboard fold-out-c; contains membership card, decoder, map of R.R. home range, etc. Herky app. (Langendorf Bread giveaway; sub-titled 'Super Book of Comics') (Rare) 65 130 195 416 708 1000
Wells Lamont Corp. giveaway (1950)-16 pgs. in color; regular size; paper-c; 1941-r 15 30 45 83 124 165

RETURN OF JOE THE GENIE OF STEEL (Also see Joe The Genie of Steel)
U. S. Steel Corp., Pittsburgh, PA/Commercial Comics: 1951 (U. S. Steel Corp. giveaway)

nn-Joe Magarac, the Paul Bunyan of steel 5 10 15 33 57 80

REX MORGAN M.D. TALKS ABOUT YOUR UNBORN CHILD
(No publisher) Fetal Alcohol, Tobacco & Firearms giveaway, 1980 (Reg. size, paper-c)

nn 3 6 9 19 30 40

RICHIE RICH, CASPER & WENDY NATIONAL LEAGUE
Harvey Publications: June, 1976 (52 pgs.) (newsstand edition also exists)

1 (Released-3/76 with 6/76 date) 3 6 9 16 23 30
1 (6/76)-2nd version w/San Francisco Giants & KTVU 2 logos; has "Compliments of Giants and Straw Hat Pizza" on-c 3 6 9 16 23 30
1-Variants for other 11 NL teams, similar to Giants version but with different ad on inside front-c 3 6 9 16 23 30

RIDE THE HIGH IRON!
Assoc. of American Railroads: Jan, 1957 (16 pgs.)

nn-The Story of modern passenger trains 5 10 15 24 30 35

RIPLEY'S BELIEVE IT OR NOT!
Harvey Publications

J. C. Penney giveaway (1948) 10 20 30 56 76 95

ROBIN HOOD (New Adventures of...)
Walt Disney Productions: 1952 (Flour giveaways, 5x7-1/4", 36 pgs.)

"New Adventures of Robin Hood", "Ghosts of Waylea Castle", & "The Miller's Ransom" each.... 4 7 10 14 17 20

ROBIN HOOD'S FRONTIER DAYS (...Western Tales, Adventures of... #1)
Shoe Store Giveaway (Robin Hood Stores): 1956 (20 pgs., slick-c)(7 issues?)

nn 6 12 18 31 38 45
nn-Issues with Crandall-a 8 16 24 42 54 65

ROCKETS AND RANGE RIDERS
Richfield Oil Corp.: May, 1957 (Giveaway, 16 pgs., soft-c)

nn-Toth-a 22 44 66 128 209 290

ROMANCE OF MONEY, THE
Natamsa Publishing Co.: 1937,1947 (4-7/8" x 6-1/4")

1937 ed. -(Scarce) 24 pgs with blue logo and artwork; distributed by the National Savings Bank, Albany, NY. Art by H.T. Elmo, a pseudonym for Jacob Kurtzberg (Jack Kirby). Believed to be Kirby's first published comic book work 275 550 825 1650 - -
1947 ed. -(Scarce) 16 pgs with red logo and artwork 145 290 435 870 - -

ROUND THE WORLD GIFT
National War Fund (Giveaway): No date (mid 1940's) (4 pgs.)

nn 14 28 42 80 1151 150

ROY ROGERS COMICS
Dell Publishing Co.

...& the Man From Dodge City (Dodge giveaway, 16 pgs., 1954)-Frontier, Inc. (5x7-1/4") 12 24 36 69 97 125
Official Roy Rogers Riders Club Comics (1952; 16 pgs., reg. size, paper-c) 15 30 45 86 133 180

RUDOLPH, THE RED-NOSED REINDEER
Montgomery Ward: 1939 (2,400,000 copies printed); Dec, 1951 (Giveaway)

Paper cover-1st app. in print; written by Robert May; ill. by Denver Gillen 30 60 90 177 289 400
Hardcover version 22 44 66 132 216 300
1951 Edition (Has 1939 date)-36 pgs., slick-c printed in red & brown; pulp interior printed in four mixed-ink colors: red, green, blue & brown 14 28 42 76 108 140
1951 Edition with red-spiral promotional booklet printed on high quality stock, 8-1/2"x11", in red & brown, 25 pages composed of 4 fold outs, single sheets and the Rudolph comic book inserted (rare) 52 104 156 328 552 775

SABRINA THE TEENAGE WITCH AND HER BOOK OF MAGIC
Archie Comic Publications: 1970 (small size giveaway)

2 (A graded 9.4 copy sold for $121 in 2014 and a graded 7.5 copy sold for $31 in 2018)

SAD CASE OF WAITING ROOM WILLIE, THE
American Visuals Corp. (For Baltimore Medical Society): (nd, 1950?) (14 pgs. in color; paper covers; regular size)

nn-By Will Eisner (Rare) 53 106 159 334 567 800

SAD SACK COMICS
Harvey Publications: 1957-1962

Armed Forces Complimentary copies, HD #1 (1957) 5 10 15 34 60 85
2-40 (1957-1962) 3 6 9 16 24 32

SALERNO CARNIVAL OF COMICS (Also see Pure Oil Comics, 24 Pages of Comics, & Vicks

Reddy Goose #14 © ISC

Santa's Fun Book © PPC

Seeing Washington © CC

	GD 2.0	VG 4.0	FN 6.0	VF 8.0	VF/NM 9.0	NM- 9.2
Comics)						
Salerno Cookie Co.: Late 1930s (Giveaway, 16 pgs, paper-c)						
nn-Color reprints of Calkins' Buck Rogers & Skyroads, plus other strips from Famous Funnies	48	96	144	302	514	725
SALUTE TO THE BOY SCOUTS						
Association of American Railroads: 1960 (16 pgs., paper-c, regular size)						
nn-History of scouting and the railroad	3	6	9	16	23	30
SANTA AND POLLYANNA PLAY THE GLAD GAME						
Western Publ.: Aug, 1960 (16 pgs.) (Disney giveaway)						
nn	3	6	9	14	20	25
SANTA & THE BUCCANEERS						
Promotional Publ. Co.: 1959 (Giveaway, paper-c)						
nn-Reprints 1952 Santa & the Pirates	2	4	6	13	18	22
SANTA & THE CHRISTMAS CHICKADEE						
Murphy's: 1974 (Giveaway, 20 pgs.)						
nn	2	4	6	8	10	12
SANTA & THE PIRATES						
Promotional Publ. Co.: 1952 (Giveaway)						
nn-Marv Levy-c/a	5	10	15	22	26	30
SANTA CLAUS FUNNIES (Also see The Little Fir Tree)						
W. T. Grant Co./Whitman Publishing: nd; 1940 (Giveaway, 8x10"; 12 pgs., color & B&W, heavy paper)						
nn-(2 versions- no date and 1940)	47	94	141	296	498	700
SANTA IS HERE!						
Western Publ. (Giveaway): 1949 (oblong, slick-c)						
nn	7	14	21	35	43	50
SANTA ON THE JOLLY ROGER						
Promotional Publ. Co. (Giveaway): 1965						
nn-Marv Levy-c/a	2	4	6	8	10	12
SANTA! SANTA!						
R. Jackson: 1974 (20 pgs.) (Montgomery Ward giveaway)						
nn	1	3	4	6	8	10
SANTA'S BUNDLE OF FUN						
Gimbels: 1969 (Giveaway, B&W, 20 pgs.)						
nn-Coloring book & games	2	4	6	8	10	12
SANTA'S CHRISTMAS COMIC VARIETY SHOW (See Merry Christmas From Sears Toyland, Bob & Betty & Santa's Wishing Whistle, and A Christmas Carol)						
Sears Roebuck & Co.: 1943 (24 pgs.)						
Contains puzzles & new comics of Dick Tracy, Little Orphan Annie, Moon Mullins, Terry & the Pirates, etc.	55	110	165	352	601	850
SANTA'S CHRISTMAS TIME STORIES						
Premium Sales, Inc.: nd (Late 1940s) (16 pgs., paper-c) (Giveaway)						
nn	7	14	21	37	46	55
SANTA'S CIRCUS						
Promotional Publ. Co.: 1964 (Giveaway, half-size)						
nn-Marv Levy-c/a	2	4	6	9	12	15
SANTA'S FUN BOOK						
Promotional Publ. Co.: 1951, 1952 (Regular size, 16 pgs., paper-c) (Murphy's giveaway)						
nn	6	12	18	31	38	45
SANTA'S GIFT BOOK						
No Publisher: No date (16 pgs.)						
nn-Puzzles, games only	5	10	14	20	24	28
SANTA'S NEW STORY BOOK						
Wallace Hamilton Campbell: 1949 (16 pgs., paper-c) (Giveaway)						
nn	7	14	21	37	46	55
SANTA'S REAL STORY BOOK						
Wallace Hamilton Campbell/W. W. Orris: 1948, 1952 (Giveaway, 16 pgs.)						
nn	7	14	21	37	46	55
SANTA'S RIDE						
W. T. Grant Co.: 1959 (Giveaway)						
nn	4	9	13	18	22	26
SANTA'S RODEO						
Promotional Publ. Co.: 1964 (Giveaway, half-size)						
nn-Marv Levy-a	2	4	6	9	12	15
SANTA'S SECRET CAVE						
W.T. Grant Co.: 1960 (Giveaway, half-size)						

	GD 2.0	VG 4.0	FN 6.0	VF 8.0	VF/NM 9.0	NM- 9.2
nn	2	4	6	11	16	20
SANTA'S SECRETS						
Sam B. Anson Christmas giveaway: 1951, 1952? (16 pgs., paper-c)						
nn-Has games, stories & pictures to color	5	10	15	22	26	30
SANTA'S STORIES						
K. K. Publications (Klines Dept. Store): 1953 (Regular size, paper-c)						
nn-Kelly-a	16	32	48	98	154	210
nn-Another version (1953, glossy-c, half-size, 7-1/4x5-1/4")-Kelly-a	15	30	45	92	144	195
SANTA'S SURPRISE						
K. K. Publications: 1947 (Giveaway, 36 pgs., slick-c)						
nn	9	18	27	47	61	75
SANTA'S TOYTOWN FUN BOOK						
Promotional Publ. Co.: 1953 (Giveaway)						
nn-Marv Levy-c	4	9	13	18	22	26
SANTA TAKES A TRIP TO MARS						
Bradshaw-Diehl Co., Huntington, W.VA.: 1950s (nd) (Giveaway, 16 pgs.)						
nn	4	8	12	25	40	55
SCHWINN BIKE THRILLS						
Schwinn Bicycle Co.: 1959 (Reg. size)						
nn	8	16	24	44	57	70
SCIENCE FAIR STORY OF ELECTRONICS						
Radio Shack/Tandy Corp.: 1975 - 1987 (Giveaway)						
11 different issues (approx. 1 per year) each....						5.00
SECRETS BEHIND THE COMICS						
Famous Enterprises, Inc.: 1947 (Small size; advertised in Timely comics)						
nn - By Stan Lee; profile of Syd Shores (w/4 pgs. of his Blonde Phantom), Mike Sekowsky, Basil Wolverton, Al Jaffee & Martin Goodman; description of Captain America's creation with images	148	296	444	947	1624	2300
SEEING WASHINGTON						
Commercial Comics: 1957 (also sold at 25¢)(Slick-c, reg. size)						
nn	6	12	18	28	34	40
SERGEANT PRESTON OF THE YUKON						
Quaker Cereals: 1956 (4 comic booklets) (Soft-c, 16 pgs., 7x2-1/2" & 5x2-1/2") Giveaways						
"How He Found Yukon King", "The Case That Made Him A Sergeant", "How Yukon King Saved Him From The Wolves", "How He Became A Mountie" each...	9	18	27	50	65	80
SHAZAM! (Visits Portland Oregon in 1943)						
DC Comics: 1989 (69¢ cover)						
nn-Promotes Super-Heroes exhibit at Oregon Museum of Science and Industry; reprints Golden Age Captain Marvel story	3	6	9	16	23	30
SHERIFF OF COCHISE, THE (TV)						
Mobil: 1957 (16 pgs.) Giveaway						
nn-Schaffenberger-a	4	9	13	18	22	26
SIDEWALK ROMANCE (Also see The K. O. Punch & Lucky Fights It Through)						
Health Publications: 1950						
nn-VD educational giveaway	52	104	156	328	552	775
SILLY PUTTY MAN						
DC Comics: 1978						
1	2	4	6	11	16	20
SKATING SKILLS						
Custom Comics, Inc./Chicago Roller Skates: 1957 (36 & 12 pgs.; 5x7", two versions) (10¢)						
nn-Resembles old ACG cover plus interior art	4	7	10	14	17	20
SKIPPY'S OWN BOOK OF COMICS (See Popular Comics)						
No publisher listed: 1934 (Giveaway, 52 pgs., strip reprints)						
nn-(Scarce)-By Percy Crosby	354	708	1062	2478	4339	6200
Published by Max C. Gaines for Phillip's Dental Magnesia to be advertised on the Skippy Radio Show and given away with the purchase of a tube of Phillip's Tooth Paste. This is the first four-color comic book of reprints about one character.						
SKY KING "RUNAWAY TRAIN" (TV)						
National Biscuit Co.: 1964 (Regular size, 16 pgs.)						
nn	5	10	15	35	63	90
SLAM BANG COMICS						
Post Cereal Giveaway: No. 9, No date						
9-Dynamic Man, Echo, Mr. E, Yankee Boy app.	11	22	33	64	90	115
SMILIN' JACK						

	GD 2.0	VG 4.0	FN 6.0	VF 8.0	VF/NM 9.0	NM- 9.2

Dell Publishing Co.

Popped Wheat Giveaway (1947)-1938 strip reprints; 16 pgs. in full color	4	8	12	17	21	24
Shoe Store Giveaway-1938 strip reprints; 16 pgs.	6	12	18	28	34	40
Sparked Wheat Giveaway (1942)-16 pgs. in full color	6	12	18	28	34	40

SMOKEY BEAR (See Forest Fire for 1st app.)
Dell Publ. Co.: 1959,1960

True Story of..., The -U.S. Forest Service giveaway-Publ. by Western Printing Co.; reprints 1st 16 pgs. of Four Color #932. Inside front-c differs slightly in 1959 & 1960 editions	6	12	18	28	34	40
1964,1969 reprints	2	4	6	11	16	20

SMOKEY STOVER
Dell Publishing Co.

General Motors giveaway (1953)	9	18	27	50	65	80
National Fire Protection giveaway(1953 & 1954)-16 pgs., paper-c	9	18	27	50	65	80

SNOW FOR CHRISTMAS
W. T. Grant Co.: 1957 (16 pgs.) (Giveaway)

nn	5	10	14	20	24	28

SNOW WHITE AND THE SEVEN DWARFS
Bendix Washing Machines: 1952 (32 pgs., 5x7-1/4", soft-c) (Disney)

nn	14	28	42	80	115	150

SNOW WHITE AND THE SEVEN DWARFS
Promotional Publ. Co.: 1957 (Small size)

nn	7	14	21	37	46	55

SNOW WHITE AND THE SEVEN DWARFS
Western Printing Co.: 1958 (16 pgs, 5x7-1/4", soft-c) (Disney premium)

nn- "Mystery of the Missing Magic"	7	14	21	35	43	50

SNOW WHITE AND THE 7 DWARFS IN "MILKY WAY"
American Dairy Assoc.: 1955 (16 pgs., soft-c, 5x7-1/4") (Disney premium)

nn	8	16	24	40	50	60

SOLDIER OF GOD
Conventual Franciscans of Marytown: 1982 ($1.00)

nn-Story of Father Maximilian Kobe, priest in WWII Poland; Ray Chatton-a						6.00

SPACE GHOST COAST TO COAST
Cartoon Network: Apr, 1994 (giveaway to Turner Broadcasting employees)

1-(8 pgs.); origin of Space Ghost	2	4	6	8	10	12

SPACE PATROL (TV)
Ziff-Davis Publishing Co. (Approved Comics)

...'s Special Mission (8 pgs., B&W, Giveaway)	48	96	144	302	514	725

SPARKY
Fire Protection Association: 1961 (Reg. size, paper-c)

nn	3	6	9	16	24	32

SPECIAL AGENT
Assoc. of American Railroads: Oct, 1959 (16 pgs.)

nn-The Story of the railroad police	6	12	18	29	36	42

SPECIAL DELIVERY
Post Hall Synd.: 1951 (32 pgs.; B&W) (Giveaway)

nn-Origin of Pogo, Swamp, etc.; 2 pg. biog. on Walt Kelly (One copy sold in 1980 for $150.00)

SPECIAL EDITION (U. S. Navy Giveaways)
National Periodical Publs.: 1944 - 1945 (Reg. comic format with wording simplified, 52 pgs.)

1-Action (1944)-Reprints Action #80	90	180	270	576	988	1400
2-Action (1944)-Reprints Action #81	90	180	270	576	988	1400
3-Superman (1944)-Reprints Superman #33	90	180	270	576	988	1400
4-Detective (1944)-Reprints Detective #97	90	180	270	576	988	1400
5-Superman (1945)-Reprints Superman #34	90	180	270	576	988	1400
6-Action (1945)-Reprints Action #84	90	180	270	576	988	1400

NOTE: ***Wayne Boring** c-1, 2, 6. **Dick Sprang** c-4.*

SPIDER-MAN (See Amazing Spider-Man, The)

SPIRIT, THE (Weekly Comic Book)(Distributed through various newspapers & other sources)
Will Eisner: 6/2/40 - 10/5/52 (16 pgs.; 8 pgs.) (no cover) (in color)
NOTE: **Eisner** script, pencils/inks for the most part from 6/2/40-4/26/42; a few stories assisted by Jack Cole, Fine, Powell and Kotsky.

6/2/40(#1)-Origin/1st app. The Spirit; reprinted in Police #11; Lady Luck (Brenda Banks) (1st app.) by Chuck Mazoujian & Mr. Mystic (1st. app.) by S. R. (Bob) Powell begin (rare)	541	1082	1623	3950	6975	10,000
6/9/40(#2)	100	200	300	640	1095	1550
6/16/40(#3)-Black Queen app. in Spirit	47	94	141	295	498	700
6/23/40(#4)-Mr. Mystic receives magical necklace	36	72	108	211	343	475
6/30/40(#5)	36	72	108	211	343	475
7/7/40(#6)-1st app. Spirit carplane; Black Queen app. in Spirit	37	74	111	222	361	500
7/14/40(#7)-8/4/40(#10): 7/21/40-Spirit becomes fugitive wanted for murder	31	62	93	186	303	420
8/11/40-9/22/40: 9/15/40-Racist-c	29	58	87	172	281	390
9/29/40-Ellen drops engagement with Homer Creep	24	48	72	142	234	325
10/6/40-11/3/40	24	48	72	142	234	325
11/10/40-The Black Queen app.	24	48	72	142	234	325
11/17/40, 11/24/40	24	48	72	142	234	325
12/1/40-Ellen spanking by Spirit on cover & inside; Eisner-1st 3 pgs., J. Cole rest	39	78	117	240	395	550
12/8/40-3/9/41	17	34	51	103	162	220
3/16/41-Intro. & 1st app. Silk Satin	23	46	69	138	227	315
3/23/41-6/1/41: 5/11/41-Last Lady Luck by Mazoujian. 5/18/41-Lady Luck by Nick Viscardi begins, ends 2/22/42	17	34	51	103	162	220
6/8/41-2nd app. Satin; Spirit learns Satin is also a British agent	21	42	63	122	199	275
6/15/41-1st app. Twilight	19	38	57	112	179	245
6/22/41-Hitler app. in Spirit	18	36	54	107	169	230
6/29/41-1/25/42,2/8/42	15	30	45	84	127	170
2/1/42-1st app. Duchess	17	34	51	100	158	215
2/15/42-4/26/42-Lady Luck by Klaus Nordling begins 3/1/42	15	30	45	94	147	200
5/3/42-8/16/42-Eisner/Fine/Quality staff assists on Spirit	13	26	39	74	105	135
8/23/42-Satin cover splash; Spirit by Eisner/Fine although signed by Fine	19	38	57	111	176	240
8/30/42,9/27/42-10/11/42,10/25/42-11/8/42-Eisner/Fine/Quality staff assists on Spirit	13	26	39	72	101	130
9/6/42-9/20/42,10/18/42-Fine/Belfi art on Spirit; scripts by Manly Wade Wellman	9	18	27	52	69	85
11/15/42-12/6/42,12/20/42,12/27/42,1/17/43-4/18/43,5/9/43-8/8/43-Wellman/Woolfolk scripts, Fine pencils, Quality staff inks	9	18	27	52	69	85
12/13/42,1/3/43,1/10/43,4/25/43,5/2/43-Eisner scripts/layouts; Fine pencils, Quality staff inks	10	20	30	56	76	95
8/15/43-Eisner script/layout; pencils/inks by Quality staff; Jack Cole-a	9	18	27	47	61	75
8/22/43-12/12/43-Wellman/Woolfolk scripts, Fine pencils, Quality staff inks; Mr. Mystic by Guardineer-10/10/43-10/24/43	9	18	27	47	61	75
12/19/43-8/13/44-Wellman/Woolfolk/Jack Cole scripts; Cole, Fine & Robin King-a; Last Mr. Mystic-5/14/44	8	16	24	44	57	70
8/20/44-12/16/45-Wellman/Woolfolk scripts; Fine art with unknown staff assists	8	16	24	44	57	70

NOTE: *Scripts/layouts by Eisner, or Eisner/Nordling, Eisner/Mercer or Spranger/Eisner; inks by Eisner or Eisner/Spranger in issues 12/23/45-2/2/47.*

12/23/45-1/6/46: 12/23/45-Christmas-c	10	20	30	54	72	90
1/13/46-Origin Spirit retold	14	28	42	76	108	140
1/20/46-1st postwar Satin app.	12	24	36	69	97	125
1/27/46-3/10/46: 3/3/46-Last Lady Luck by Nordling	10	20	30	56	76	95
3/17/46-Intro. & 1st app. Nylon	12	24	36	69	97	125
3/24/46,3/31/46,4/14/46	10	20	30	54	72	90
4/7/46-2nd app. Nylon	10	20	30	58	79	100
4/21/46-Intro. & 1st app. Mr. Carrion & His Pet Buzzard Julia	14	28	42	76	108	140
4/28/46-5/12/46,5/26/46-6/30/46: Lady Luck by Fred Schwab in issues 5/5/46-11/3/46	10	20	30	54	72	90
5/19/46-2nd app. Mr. Carrion	10	20	30	58	79	100
7/7/46-Intro. & 1st app. Dulcet Tone & Skinny	12	24	36	69	97	125
7/14/46-9/29/46	10	20	30	54	72	90
10/6/46-Intro. & 1st app. P'Gell	14	28	42	78	112	145
10/13/46-11/3/46,11/16/46-11/24/46	10	20	30	54	72	90
11/10/46-2nd app. P'Gell	12	24	36	67	94	120
12/1/46-3rd app. P'Gell	10	20	30	56	76	95
12/8/46-2/2/47	9	18	27	52	69	85

NOTE: *Scripts, pencils/inks by Eisner except where noted in issues 2/9/47-12/19/48.*

2/9/47-7/6/47: 6/8/47-Eisner self satire	9	18	27	52	69	85
7/13/47- "Hansel & Gretel" fairy tales	12	24	36	69	97	125
7/20/47-Li'L Abner, Daddy Warbucks, Dick Tracy, Fearless Fosdick parody; A-Bomb blast-c	14	28	42	76	108	140
7/27/47-9/14/47	9	18	27	52	69	85
9/21/47-Pearl Harbor flashback	12	24	36	69	97	125
9/28/47-1st mention of Flying Saucers in comics - three months after 1st sighting in Idaho on 6/25/47	21	42	63	122	199	275
10/5/47- "Cinderella" fairy tales	12	24	36	69	97	125
10/12/47-11/30/47	9	18	27	52	69	85
12/7/47-Intro. & 1st app. Powder Pouf	14	28	42	80	115	150
12/14/47-12/28/47	9	18	27	52	69	85
1/4/48-2nd app. Powder Pouf	10	20	30	56	76	95
1/11/48-1st app. Sparrow Fallon; Powder Pouf app.	10	20	30	56	76	95
1/18/48-He-Man ad cover; satire issue	10	20	30	56	76	95
1/25/48-Intro. & 1st app. Castanet	14	28	42	76	108	140
2/1/48-2nd app. Castanet	10	20	30	54	72	90
2/8/48-3/7/48	9	18	27	52	69	85
3/14/48-Only app. Kretchma	10	20	30	54	72	90
3/21/48,3/28/48,4/11/48-4/25/48	9	18	27	52	69	85
4/4/48-Only app. Wild Rice	10	20	30	54	72	90
5/2/48-2nd app. Sparrow	9	18	27	52	69	85
5/9/48-6/27/48,7/11/48,7/18/48: 6/13/48-TV issue	9	18	27	52	69	85
7/4/48-Spirit by Andre Le Blanc	8	16	24	44	57	70
7/25/48-Ambrose Bierce's "The Thing" adaptation classic by Eisner/Grandenetti	17	34	51	103	162	220
8/1/48-8/15/48,8/29/48-9/12/48	9	18	27	52	69	85
8/22/48-Poe's "Fall of the House of Usher" classic by Eisner/Grandenetti	17	34	51	105	165	225
9/19/48-Only app. Lorelei	10	20	30	56	76	95
9/26/48-10/31/48	9	18	27	52	69	85
11/7/48-Only app. Plaster of Paris	12	24	36	69	97	125
11/14/48-12/19/48	9	18	27	52	69	85

NOTE: *Scripts by Eisner or Feiffer or Eisner/Feiffer or Nordling. Art by Eisner with backgrounds by Eisner, Grandenetti, Le Blanc, Stallman, Nordling, Dixon and/or others in issues 12/26/48-4/1/51 except where noted.*

12/26/48-Reprints some covers of 1948 with flashbacks	9	18	27	52	69	85
1/2/49-1/16/49	9	18	27	52	69	85
1/23/49,1/30/49-1st & 2nd app. Thorne	10	20	30	56	76	95
2/6/49-8/14/49	9	18	27	52	69	85
8/21/49,8/28/49-1st & 2nd app. Monica Veto	10	20	30	56	76	95
9/4/49,9/11/49	9	18	27	52	69	85
9/18/49-Love comic cover; has gag love comic ads on inside	10	20	30	56	76	95
9/25/49-Only app. Ice	10	20	30	54	72	90
10/2/49,10/9/49-Autumn News appears & dies in 10/9 issue	10	20	30	54	72	90
10/16/49-11/27/49,12/18/49,12/25/49	9	18	27	52	69	85
12/4/49,12/11/49-1st & 2nd app. Flaxen	10	20	30	54	72	90

1/1/50-Flashbacks to all of the Spirit girls-Thorne, Ellen, Satin, & Monica

Special Edition #4 © DC

The Spirit 8/25/40 © Will Eisner

The Story of Checks © FRB

	GD 2.0	VG 4.0	FN 6.0	VF 8.0	VF/NM 9.0	NM- 9.2
	15	30	45	83	124	165
1/8/50-Intro. & 1st app. Sand Saref	15	30	45	92	144	195
1/15/50-2nd app. Sand Saref	14	28	42	76	108	140
1/22/50-2/5/50	9	18	27	52	69	85
2/12/50-Roller Derby issue	10	20	30	56	76	95
2/19/50-Half Dead Mr. Lox - Classic horror	14	28	42	76	108	140
2/26/50-4/23/50,5/14/50,5/28/50,7/23/50-9/3/50	9	18	27	52	69	85
4/30/50-Script/art by Le Blanc with Eisner framing	8	16	24	42	54	65
5/7/50,6/4/50-7/16/50-Abe Kanegson-a	8	16	24	42	54	65
5/21/50-Script by Feiffer/Eisner, art by Blaisdell, Eisner framing	8	16	24	42	54	65
9/10/50-P'Gell returns	10	20	30	56	76	95
9/17/50-1/7/51	9	18	27	52	69	85
1/14/51-Life Magazine cover; brief biography of Comm. Dolan, Sand Saref, Silk Satin, P'Gell, Sammy & Willum, Darling O'Shea, & Mr. Carrion & His Pet Buzzard Julia, with pin-ups by Eisner	13	26	39	74	105	135
1/21/51,2/4/51-4/1/51	9	18	27	52	69	85
1/28/51- "The Meanest Man in the World" by Eisner	13	26	39	74	105	135
4/8/51-7/29/51,8/12/51-Last Eisner issue	9	18	27	52	69	85
8/5/51,8/19/51-7/20/52-Not Eisner	8	16	24	42	54	65
7/27/52-(Rare)-Denny Colt in Outer Space by Wally Wood; 7 pg. S/F story of E.C. vintage	58	116	174	371	636	900
8/3/52-(Rare)- "Mission...The Moon" by Wood	58	116	174	371	636	900
8/10/52-(Rare)- "A DP On The Moon" by Wood	58	116	174	371	636	900
8/17/52-(Rare)- "Heart" by Wood/Eisner	58	116	174	371	636	900
8/24/52-(Rare)- "Rescue" by Wood	58	116	174	371	636	900
8/31/52-(Rare)- "The Last Man" by Wood	58	116	174	371	636	900
9/7/52-(Rare)- "The Man in The Moon" by Wood	58	116	174	371	636	900
9/14/52-(Rare)-Eisner/Wenzel-a	39	78	117	240	395	550
9/21/52-(Rare)- "Denny Colt, Alias The Spirit/Space Report" by Eisner/Wenzel	39	78	117	240	395	550
9/28/52-(Rare)- "Return From The Moon" by Wood	53	106	159	334	567	800
10/5/52-(Rare)- "The Last Story" by Eisner	36	72	108	211	343	475

Large Tabloid pages from 1946 on (Eisner) - Price 200 percent over listed prices.
NOTE: *Spirit sections came out in both large and small format. Some newspapers went to the 8-pg. format months before others. Some printed the pages so they cannot be folded into a small comic book section; these are worth less. (Also see Three Comics & Spiritman).*

SPY SMASHER
Fawcett Publications

	GD	VG	FN	VF	VF/NM	NM-
Well Known Comics (1944, 12 pgs., 8-1/2x10-1/2"), paper-c, glued binding, printed in green; Bestmaid/Samuel Lowe giveaway	16	32	48	98	154	210

STANDARD OIL COMICS (Also see Gulf Funny Weekly)
Standard Oil Co.: 1932-1934 (Giveaway, tabloid size, 4 pgs. in color)

	GD	VG	FN	VF	VF/NM	NM-
nn (Dec. 1932)	68	136	204	435	743	1050
1-Series has original art	54	108	162	343	574	825
2-5	23	46	69	136	223	310
6-14: 14-Fred Opper strip, 1 pg.	15	30	45	88	137	185
1A (Jan 1933)	54	108	162	343	574	825
2A-14A (1933)	39	78	117	231	378	525
1B (1934)	42	84	126	265	445	625
2B-7B (1934)	39	78	117	231	318	525

NOTE: *Series A contains Frederick Opper's Si & Mirandi; Series B contains Goofus: He's From The Big City; McVittle by Walter O'Ehrle; interior strips include Pesty And His Pop & Smiling Slim by Sid Hicks.*

STARS AND STRIPES
Centaur Publications: Oct. 1942 (regular size)

5 - World's Greatest Parade of Comics and Fun Promotional Cover Edition (Atlas Theater) (A certified CGC 2.5 copy sold for $460 in 2019)

STAR TEAM
Marvel Comics Group: 1977 (6-1/2x5", 20 pgs.) (Ideal Toy Giveaway)

	GD	VG	FN	VF	VF/NM	NM-
nn	3	6	9	15	22	28

STEVE CANYON COMICS
Harvey Publications

	GD	VG	FN	VF	VF/NM	NM-
Dept. Store giveaway #3(6/48, 36pp)	10	20	30	56	76	95
...'s Secret Mission (1951, 16 pgs., Armed Forces giveaway); Caniff-a	9	18	27	50	65	80
Strictly for the Smart Birds (1951, 16 pgs.)-Information Comics Div. (Harvey) Premium	8	16	24	42	54	65

STORIES OF CHRISTMAS
K. K. Publications: 1942 (Giveaway, 32 pgs., paper cover)

	GD	VG	FN	VF	VF/NM	NM-
nn-Adaptation of "A Christmas Carol"; Kelly story "The Fir Tree"; Infinity-c	53	106	159	334	567	800

STORY HOUR SERIES (Disney)
Whitman Publ. Co.: 1948, 1949; 1951-1953 (36 pgs., paper-c) (4-3/4x6-1/2")
Given away with subscription to Walt Disney's Comics & Stories

	GD	VG	FN	VF	VF/NM	NM-
nn(1948)-Mickey Mouse and the Boy Thursday	12	24	36	67	94	120
nn(1948)-Mickey Mouse the Miracle Master	12	24	36	67	94	120
nn(1948)-Minnie Mouse and Antique Chair	12	24	36	67	94	120
nn(1949)-The Three Orphan Kittens(B&W & color)	9	18	27	47	61	75
nn(1949)-Danny-The Little Black Lamb	9	18	27	47	61	75
800(1948)-Donald Duck in "Bringing Up the Boys"	15	30	45	88	137	185
1953 edition	11	22	33	64	90	115
801(1948)-Mickey Mouse's Summer Vacation	10	20	30	56	76	95
1951, 1952 editions	7	14	21	35	43	50
802(1948)-Bugs Bunny's Adventures	9	18	27	50	65	80
803(1948)-Bongo	8	16	24	40	50	60
804(1948)-Mickey and the Beanstalk	9	18	27	47	61	75
805-15(1949)-Andy Panda and His Friends	8	16	24	40	50	60
806-15(1949)-Tom and Jerry	8	16	24	44	57	70
808-15(1949)-Johnny Appleseed	8	16	24	40	50	60

1948, 1949 Hard Cover Edition of each....30% - 40% more.

STOP AND GO, THE SAFETY TWINS
J.C. Penney: no date (giveaway)

	GD	VG	FN	VF	VF/NM	NM-
nn	5	10	15	24	30	35

STORY OF CHECKS THE
Federal Reserve Bank: 1979 (Reg. size)

	GD	VG	FN	VF	VF/NM	NM-
nn	1	3	4	6	8	10

STORY OF CHECKS AND ELECTRONIC PAYMENTS
Federal Reserve Bank: 1983 (Reg size)

	GD	VG	FN	VF	VF/NM	NM-
nn	1	2	3	5	6	8

STORY OF CONSUMER CREDIT
Federal Reserve Bank: 1980 (Reg. size)

	GD	VG	FN	VF	VF/NM	NM-
nn	1	2	3	5	6	8

STORY OF EDISON, THE
Educational Comics: 1956 (16 pgs.) (Reddy Killowatt)

	GD	VG	FN	VF	VF/NM	NM-
nn-Reprint of Reddy Kilowatt #2(1947)	8	16	24	40	50	60

STORY OF FOREIGN TRADE AND EXCHANGE
Federal Reserve Bank: 1985 (Reg. size)

	GD	VG	FN	VF	VF/NM	NM-
nn	1	2	3	5	6	8

STORY OF HARRY S. TRUMAN, THE
Democratic National Committee: 1948 (Giveaway, regular size, soft-c, 16 pg.)

	GD	VG	FN	VF	VF/NM	NM-
nn-Gives biography on career of Truman; used in **SOTI**, pg. 311	15	30	45	85	130	175

STORY OF INFLATION, THE
Federal Reserve Bank: 1980s (Reg size)

	GD	VG	FN	VF	VF/NM	NM-
nn	1	3	4	6	8	10

STORY OF MONEY
William C. Popper: 1962, 1965

	GD	VG	FN	VF	VF/NM	NM-
nn-Soft-c	3	6	9	16	23	30

STORY OF MONEY
Federal Reserve Bank: 1984 (Reg. size)

	GD	VG	FN	VF	VF/NM	NM-
nn	1	3	4	6	8	10

STORY OF THE BALLET, THE
Selva and Sons, Inc.: 1954 (16 pgs., paper cover)

	GD	VG	FN	VF	VF/NM	NM-
nn	5	10	14	20	24	28

STRANGE AS IT SEEMS
McNaught Syndicate: 1936 (B&W, 5" x 7", 24 pgs.)

	GD	VG	FN	VF	VF/NM	NM-
nn-Ex-Lax giveaway	10	20	30	58	79	100

STRIKES AND THE PUBLIC
Socialist Labor Party: no date

nn-Calling worker class to organize against capitalist class (a FN/VF copy sold for $216 in 2018)

SUGAR BEAR
Post Cereal Giveaway: No date, circa 1975? (2 1/2" x 4 1/2", 16 pgs.)

	GD	VG	FN	VF	VF/NM	NM-
"The Almost Take Over of the Post Office", "The Race Across the Atlantic", "The Zoo Goes Wild" each...	1	2	3	5	6	8

SUNDAY WORLD'S EASTER EGG FULL OF EASTER MEAT FOR LITTLE PEOPLE
Supplement to the New York World: 3/27/1898 (soft-c, 16pg, 4"x8" approx., opens at top, color & B&W)(Giveaway)(shaped like an Easter egg)

	GD	VG	FN	VF	VF/NM	NM-
nn-By R.F. Outcault	21	42	63	122	199	275

SUPER BOOK OF COMICS
Western Publ. Co.: nd (1942-1943?) (Soft-c, 32 pgs.) (Pan-Am/Gilmore Oil/Kelloggs premiums)

	GD	VG	FN	VF	VF/NM	NM-
nn-Dick Tracy (Gilmore)-Magic Morro app. (2 versions: Dick Tracy Jr. on cover and a filing cabinet cover)	40	80	120	246	411	575
1-Dick Tracy & The Smuggling Ring; Stratosphere Jim app. (Rare) (Pan-Am)	34	68	102	199	325	450
1-Smilin' Jack, Magic Morro (Pan-Am)	15	30	45	83	124	165
2-Smilin' Jack, Stratosphere Jim (Pan-Am)	15	30	45	83	124	165
2-Smitty, Magic Morro (Pan-Am)	15	30	45	83	124	165
3-Captain Midnight, Magic Morro (Pan-Am)	24	48	72	142	234	325

	GD 2.0	VG 4.0	FN 6.0	VF 8.0	VF/NM 9.0	NM- 9.2
3-Moon Mullins?	14	28	42	78	112	145
4-Red Ryder, Magic Morro (Pan-Am). Same content as Red Ryder Victory Patrol comic w/diff. cover	15	30	45	88	137	185
4-Smitty, Stratosphere Jim (Pan-Am)	14	28	42	78	112	145
5-Don Winslow, Magic Morro (Gilmore)	15	30	45	88	137	185
5-Don Winslow, Stratosphere Jim (Pan-Am)	15	30	45	88	137	185
5-Terry & the Pirates	17	34	51	103	162	220
6-Don Winslow, Stratosphere Jim (Pan-Am)-McWilliams-a	15	30	45	88	137	185
6-King of the Royal Mounted, Magic Morro (Pan-Am)	15	30	45	88	137	185
7-Dick Tracy, Magic Morro (Pan-Am)	20	40	60	115	185	255
7-Little Orphan Annie	12	24	36	67	94	120
8-Dick Tracy, Stratosphere Jim (Pan-Am)	17	34	51	100	158	215
8-Dan Dunn, Magic Morro (Pan-Am)	12	24	36	67	94	120
9-Terry & the Pirates, Magic Morro (Pan-Am)	17	34	51	100	158	215
10-Red Ryder, Magic Morro (Pan-Am)	15	30	45	86	133	180

SUPER-BOOK OF COMICS
Western Publishing Co.: (Omar Bread & Hancock Oil Co. giveaways) 1944 - No. 30, 1947 (Omar); 1947 - 1948 (Hancock) (16 pgs.)

NOTE: The Hancock issues are all exact reprints of the earlier Omar issues. The issue numbers were removed in some of the reprints.

	GD 2.0	VG 4.0	FN 6.0	VF 8.0	VF/NM 9.0	NM- 9.2
1-Dick Tracy (Omar, 1944)	17	34	51	98	154	210
1-Dick Tracy (Hancock, 1947)	14	28	42	78	112	145
2-Bugs Bunny (Omar, 1944)	8	16	24	40	50	60
2-Bugs Bunny (Hancock, 1947)	6	12	18	32	39	46
3-Terry & the Pirates (Omar, 1944)	11	22	33	60	83	105
3-Terry & the Pirates (Hancock, 1947)	10	20	30	54	72	90
4-Andy Panda (Omar, 1944)	8	16	24	40	50	60
4-Andy Panda (Hancock, 1947)	6	12	18	32	39	46
5-Smokey Stover (Omar, 1945)	6	12	18	32	39	46
5-Smokey Stover (Hancock, 1947)	5	10	15	24	30	35
6-Porky Pig (Omar, 1945)	8	16	24	40	50	60
6-Porky Pig (Hancock, 1947)	6	12	18	32	39	46
7-Smilin' Jack (Omar, 1945)	8	16	24	40	50	60
7-Smilin' Jack (Hancock, 1947)	6	12	18	32	39	46
8-Oswald the Rabbit (Omar, 1945)	6	12	18	32	39	46
8-Oswald the Rabbit (Hancock, 1947)	5	10	15	24	30	35
9-Alley Oop (Omar, 1945)	11	22	33	64	90	115
9-Alley Oop (Hancock, 1947)	11	22	33	60	83	105
10-Elmer Fudd (Omar, 1945)	6	12	18	32	39	46
10-Elmer Fudd (Hancock, 1947)	5	10	15	24	30	35
11-Little Orphan Annie (Omar, 1945)	8	16	24	42	53	64
11-Little Orphan Annie (Hancock, 1947)	7	14	21	36	45	54
12-Woody Woodpecker (Omar, 1945)	6	12	18	32	39	46
12-Woody Woodpecker (Hancock, 1947)	5	10	15	24	30	35
13-Dick Tracy (Omar, 1945)	11	22	33	64	90	115
13-Dick Tracy (Hancock, 1947)	11	22	33	60	83	105
14-Bugs Bunny (Omar, 1945)	6	12	18	32	39	46
14-Bugs Bunny (Hancock, 1947)	5	10	15	24	30	35
15-Andy Panda (Omar, 1945)	6	12	18	28	34	40
15-Andy Panda (Hancock, 1947)	5	10	15	24	30	35
16-Terry & the Pirates (Omar, 1945)	11	22	33	60	83	105
16-Terry & the Pirates (Hancock, 1947)	9	18	27	47	61	75
17-Smokey Stover (Omar, 1946)	6	12	18	32	39	46
17-Smokey Stover (Hancock, 1948?)	5	10	15	24	30	35
18-Porky Pig (Omar, 1946)	6	12	18	28	34	40
18-Porky Pig (Hancock, 1948?)	5	10	15	24	30	35
19-Smilin' Jack (Omar, 1946)	6	12	18	32	39	46
nn-Smilin' Jack (Hancock, 1948)	5	10	15	24	30	35
20-Oswald the Rabbit (Omar, 1946)	6	12	18	28	34	40
nn-Oswald the Rabbit (Hancock, 1948)	5	10	15	24	30	35
21-Gasoline Alley (Omar, 1946)	8	16	24	42	53	64
nn-Gasoline Alley (Hancock, 1948)	7	14	21	36	45	54
22-Elmer Fudd (Omar, 1946)	6	12	18	28	34	40
nn-Elmer Fudd (Hancock, 1948)	5	10	15	24	30	35
23-Little Orphan Annie (Omar, 1946)	8	16	24	40	50	60
nn-Little Orphan Annie (Hancock, 1948)	6	12	18	32	39	46
24-Woody Woodpecker (Omar, 1946)	6	12	18	28	34	40
nn-Woody Woodpecker (Hancock, 1948)	5	10	15	24	30	35
25-Dick Tracy (Omar, 1946)	11	22	33	60	83	105
nn-Dick Tracy (Hancock, 1948)	9	18	27	50	65	80
26-Bugs Bunny (Omar, 1946))	6	12	18	28	34	40
nn-Bugs Bunny (Hancock, 1948)	5	10	15	24	30	35
27-Andy Panda (Omar, 1946)	6	12	18	28	34	40
27-Andy Panda (Hancock, 1948)	5	10	15	24	30	35
28-Terry & the Pirates (Omar, 1946)	11	22	33	60	83	105
28-Terry & the Pirates (Hancock, 1948)	9	18	27	47	61	75
29-Smokey Stover (Omar, 1947)	6	12	18	28	34	40
29-Smokey Stover (Hancock, 1948)	5	10	15	24	30	35
30-Porky Pig (Omar, 1947)	6	12	18	28	34	40
30-Porky Pig (Hancock, 1948)	5	10	15	24	30	35
nn-Bugs Bunny (Hancock, 1948)-Does not match any Omar book	6	12	18	28	34	40

SUPER CIRCUS (TV)
Cross Publishing Co.

	GD 2.0	VG 4.0	FN 6.0	VF 8.0	VF/NM 9.0	NM- 9.2
1-(1951, Weather Bird Shoes giveaway)	9	18	27	50	65	80

SUPER FRIENDS
DC Comics: 1981 (Giveaway, no ads, no code or price)

	GD 2.0	VG 4.0	FN 6.0	VF 8.0	VF/NM 9.0	NM- 9.2
...Special 1 -r/Super Friends #19 & 36	3	6	9	14	20	25

SUPERGEAR COMICS
Jacobs Corp.: 1976 (Giveaway, 4 pgs. in color, slick paper)

	GD 2.0	VG 4.0	FN 6.0	VF 8.0	VF/NM 9.0	NM- 9.2
nn-(Rare)-Superman, Lois Lane; Steve Lombard app. (500 copies printed, over half destroyed?)	20	40	60	140	310	480

SUPERGIRL
DC Comics: 1984, 1986 (Giveaway, Baxter paper)

	GD 2.0	VG 4.0	FN 6.0	VF 8.0	VF/NM 9.0	NM- 9.2
nn-(American Honda/U.S. Dept. Transportation) Torres-c/a	2	4	6	10	14	18

SUPER HEROES PUZZLES AND GAMES
General Mills Giveaway (Marvel Comics Group): 1979 (32 pgs., regular size)

	GD 2.0	VG 4.0	FN 6.0	VF 8.0	VF/NM 9.0	NM- 9.2
nn-Four 2-pg. origin stories of Spider-Man, Captain America, The Hulk, & Spider-Woman	3	6	9	15	22	28

SUPERMAN
National Periodical Publ./DC Comics

	GD 2.0	VG 4.0	FN 6.0	VF 8.0	VF/NM 9.0	NM- 9.2
72-Giveaway(9-10/51)-(Rare)-Price blackened out; came with banner wrapped around book; without banner	84	168	252	538	919	1300
72-Giveaway with banner	129	258	387	826	1413	2000
Bradman birthday custom (1988)(extremely limited distribution) - a CGC 9.6 copy sold for $2600, a NM copy sold for $1125, and a FN/VF copy sold for $800 in 2011-2012, plus a CGC 9.0 sold for $421 in 12/12 and a CGC 9.6 copy sold for $1314 in 8/15						
... For the Animals (2000, Doris Day Animal Foundation, 30 pgs.) polybagged with Gotham Adventures #22, Hourman #12, Impulse #58, Looney Tunes #62, Stars and S.T.R.I.P.E. #8 and Superman Adventures #41						4.00
Kelloggs Giveaway-(2/3 normal size, 1954)-r-two stories/Superman #55	34	68	102	199	325	450
Kenner: Man of Steel (Doomsday is Coming) (1995, 16 pgs.) packaged with set of Superman and Doomsday action figures						5.00
...Meets the Quik Bunny (1987, Nestles Quik premium, 36 pgs.)	1	2	3	5	7	9
Pizza Hut Premiums (12/77)-Exact reprints of 1950s comics except for paid ads (set of 6 exist?); Vol. 1-r#97 (#113-r also known)	2	4	6	9	12	15
Radio Shack Giveaway-36 pgs. (7/80) "The Computers That Saved Metropolis", Starlin/ Giordano-a; advertising insert in Action #509, New Advs. of Superboy #7, Legion of Super-Heroes #265, & House of Mystery #282. (All comics were 68 pgs.) Cover of inserts printed on newsprint. Giveaway contains 4 extra pgs. of Radio Shack advertising that inserts do not have	1	2	3	5	7	9
Radio Shack Giveaway-(7/81) "Victory by Computer"	1	2	3	5	7	9
Radio Shack Giveaway-(7/82) "Computer Masters of Metropolis"	1	2	3	5	7	9

SUPERMAN ADVENTURES, THE (TV)
DC Comics: 1996 (Based on animated series)

	GD 2.0	VG 4.0	FN 6.0	VF 8.0	VF/NM 9.0	NM- 9.2
1-(1996) Preview issue distributed at Warner Bros. stores	1	2	3	5	6	8
Titus Game Edition (1998)						4.00

SUPERMAN AND THE GREAT CLEVELAND FIRE
National Periodical Publ.: 1948 (Giveaway, 4 pgs., no cover) (Hospital Fund)

	GD 2.0	VG 4.0	FN 6.0	VF 8.0	VF/NM 9.0	NM- 9.2
nn-In full color	90	180	270	576	988	1400

SUPERMAN AT THE GILBERT HALL OF SCIENCE
National Periodical Publ.: 1948 (Giveaway) (Gilbert Chemistry Sets / A.C. Gilbert Co.)

	GD 2.0	VG 4.0	FN 6.0	VF 8.0	VF/NM 9.0	NM- 9.2
nn-(8 1/2" x 5 1/2")	41	82	123	256	428	600

SUPERMAN (Miniature)
National Periodical Publ.: 1942; 1955 - 1956 (3 issues, no #'s, 32 pgs.)
The pages are numbered in the 1st issue: 1-32; 2nd: 1A-32A, and 3rd: 1B-32B

	GD 2.0	VG 4.0	FN 6.0	VF 8.0	VF/NM 9.0	NM- 9.2
No date-Py-Co-Pay Tooth Powder giveaway (8 pgs.; circa 1942)(The Adventures of...) Japanese air battle	40	80	120	246	411	575
1-The Superman Time Capsule (Kellogg's Sugar Smacks)(1955)	22	44	66	132	216	300
1A-Duel in Space (1955)	21	42	63	124	202	280
1B-The Super Show of Metropolis (also #1-32, no B)(1955)	21	42	63	124	202	280

NOTE: *Numbering variations exist. Each title could have any combination-#1, 1A, or 1B.*

SUPERMAN RECORD COMIC
National Periodical Publications: 1966 (Golden Records)

	GD 2.0	VG 4.0	FN 6.0	VF 8.0	VF/NM 9.0	NM- 9.2
(With record)-Record reads origin of Superman from comic; came with iron-on patch, decoder, membership card & button; comic-r/Superman #125,146	12	24	36	82	179	275
Comic only	6	12	18	38	69	100

SUPERMAN'S BUDDY (Costume Comic)
National Periodical Publs.: 1954 (4 pgs., slick paper-c; one-shot) (Came in box w/costume)

	GD 2.0	VG 4.0	FN 6.0	VF 8.0	VF/NM 9.0	NM- 9.2
1-With box & costume	142	284	426	909	1555	2200
Comic only	60	120	180	381	653	925
1-(1958 edition)-Printed in 2 colors	18	36	54	109	172	235

SUPERMAN'S CHRISTMAS ADVENTURE
National Periodical Publications: 1940, 1944 (Giveaway, 16 pgs.) Distributed by Nehi drinks, Bailey Store, Ivey-Keith Co., Kennedy's Boys Shop, Macy's Store, Boston Store

	GD 2.0	VG 4.0	FN 6.0	VF 8.0	VF/NM 9.0	NM- 9.2
1(1940)-Burnley-a; F. Ray-c/r from Superman #6 (Scarce)-Superman saves Santa Claus. Santa makes real Superman Toys offered in 1940. 1st merchandising story; versions with Royal Crown Cola ad on front-c & Boston Store ad on front-c; cover art on each has the same layout but different art	641	1282	1623	3950	6975	10,000
nn(1944) w/Santa Claus & X-mas tree-c	126	252	378	806	1378	1950
nn(1944) w/Candy cane & Superman-c	126	252	378	806	1378	1950
nn(1944) w/1940-c (Santa over chimney); Superman image (from Superman #6) on back-c	126	252	378	806	1378	1950

SUPERMAN-TIM (Becomes Tim)
Superman-Tim Stores/National Periodical Publ.: Aug, 1942 - May, 1950 (Half size) (B&W Giveaway w/2 color covers) (Publ. monthly 2/43 on)(All have Superman illos)

	GD 2.0	VG 4.0	FN 6.0	VF 8.0	VF/NM 9.0	NM- 9.2
8/42 (#1)- 2 pg. Superman story	158	316	474	1011	1731	2450
9/42 (#2) Superman/Uncle Sam flag-c	61	122	183	390	670	950
12/42-Christmas-c	50	100	150	315	533	750
1/43	48	96	144	302	514	725
2/43, 3/43-Classic flag-c	45	90	135	284	480	675
4/43, 5/43, 6/43, 8/43	39	78	117	240	395	550
7/43-Classic Superman bomb-c	43	86	129	271	461	650
9/43, 10/43, 11/43, 12/43	32	64	96	188	307	425
1/44-12/44	26	52	78	154	252	350

Super-Book of Comics #16 © KFS

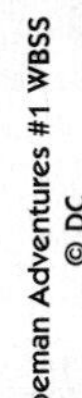
Supeman Adventures #1 WBSS © DC

Tom Mix #7 © R-P

	GD 2.0	VG 4.0	FN 6.0	VF 8.0	VF/NM 9.0	NM- 9.2
1/45-5/45, 8/45, 10-12/45 (X-mas-c), 1/46-8/46	24	48	72	140	230	320
6/45-Classic Superman-c	25	50	75	150	245	340
7/45-Classic Superman flag-c	26	52	78	154	252	350
9/45-1st stamp album issue	50	100	150	315	533	750
9/46-2nd stamp album issue	43	86	129	271	467	650
10/46-1st Superman story	31	62	93	182	296	410
11/46, 12/46, 1/47-8/47 issues-Superman story in each; 2/47-Infinity-c. All 36 pgs.	31	62	93	182	296	410
9/47-Stamp album issue & Superman story	41	82	123	256	428	600
10/47, 11/47, 12/47-Superman stories (24 pgs.)	29	58	87	174	285	395
1/48-7/48,10/48, 11/48, 12/48, 2/49, 4/49-11/49	24	48	72	142	234	325
8/48-Contains full page ad for Superman-Tim watch giveaway	24	48	72	142	234	325
9/48-Stamp album issue	32	64	96	192	314	435
1/49-Full page Superman bank cut-out	24	48	72	142	234	325
3/49-Full page Superman boxing game cut-out	24	48	72	142	234	325
12/49-3/50, 5/50-Superman stories	26	52	78	154	252	350
4/50-Superman story, baseball stories; photo-c without Superman	32	64	96	188	307	425

NOTE: *All issues have Superman illustrations throughout. The page count varies depending on whether a Superman-Tim comic story is inserted. If it is, the page count is either 36 or 24 pages. Otherwise all issues are 16 pages. Each issue has a special place for inserting a full color Superman stamp. The stamp album issues had spaces for the stamps given away the past year. The books were mailed as a subscription premium. The stamps were given away free (or when you made a purchase) only when you physically came into the store.*

	GD 2.0	VG 4.0	FN 6.0	VF 8.0	VF/NM 9.0	NM- 9.2
SUPER SEAMAN SLOPPY						
Allied Pristine Union Council, Buffalo, NY: 1940s, 8pg., reg. size (Soft-c)						
nn	30	60	90	177	289	400
SURVEY						
Marvel Comics Group: 1948 (Readership survey for advertisers, reg. size)						
nn-Harvey Kurtzman-c/a	110	220	330	704	1202	1700
SWAMP FOX, THE						
Walt Disney Productions: 1960 (14 pgs, small size) (Canada Dry Premiums)						
Titles: (A)-Tory Masquerade, (B)-Turnabout Tactics, (C)-Rindau Rampage; each came in paper sleeve, books 1,2 & 3; Set with sleeves	5	10	15	31	53	75
Comic only	2	4	6	13	18	22
SWORDQUEST						
DC Comics/Atari Pub.: 1982, 52pg., 5"x7" (Giveaway with video games)						
1,2-Roy Thomas & Gerry Conway-s; George Pérez & Dick Giordano-c/a in all	2	4	6	10	14	18
3-Low print	3	6	9	15	22	28
SYNDICATE FEATURES (Sci/fi)						
Harry A. Chesler Syndicate: V1#3, 11/15/37; V1#5, 12/15/37 (Tabloid size, 3 colors, 4 pgs.) (Editors premium) (Came folded)						
V1#3,5-Dan Hastings daily strips-Guardineer-a	168	336	504	1075	1838	2600
TAKING A CHANCE						
American Cancer Society: no date (giveaway)						
nn-Anti-smoking	3	6	9	14	19	24
TASTEE-FREEZ COMICS (Also see Harvey Hits and Richie Rich)						
Harvey Comics: 1957 (10¢, 36 pgs.)(6 different issues given away)						
1-Little Dot on cover; Richie Rich "Ride 'Em Cowboy" story published one year prior to being printed in Harvey Hits #9.	8	16	24	54	102	150
2,4,5: 2-Rags Rabbit. 4-Sad Sack. 5-Mazie	2	4	6	8	10	12
3-Casper	2	4	6	11	16	20
6-Dick Tracy	2	4	6	11	16	20
nn-Brings You Space Facts and Fun Book	1	2	3	5	6	8
TAYLOR'S CHRISTMAS TABLOID						
Dept. Store Giveaway: Mid 1930s, Cleveland, Ohio (Tabloid size; in color)						
nn-(Very Rare)-Among the earliest pro work of Siegel & Shuster; one full color page called "The Battle in the Stratosphere", with a pre-Superman look; Shuster art thoughout. (Only 1 known copy)						
TAZ'S 40TH BIRTHDAY BLOWOUT						
DC Comics: 1994 (K-Mart giveaway, 16 pgs.)						
nn-Six pg. story, games and puzzles						4.00
TEE AND VEE CROSLEY IN TELEVISION LAND COMICS (Also see Crosley's House of Fun)						
Crosley Division, Avco Mfg. Corp. : 1951 (52 pgs.; 8x11"; paper cover; in color) (Giveaway)						
Many stories, puzzles, cut-outs, games, etc.	8	16	24	44	57	70
TEEN-AGE BOOBY TRAP						
Commercial Comics: 1970 (Small size)						
nn	3	6	9	16	24	32
TENNESSEE JED (Radio)						
Fox Syndicate? (Wm. C. Popper & Co.): nd (1945) (16 pgs.; paper-c; reg. size; giveaway)						
nn	22	44	66	132	216	300
TENNIS (...For Speed, Stamina, Strength, Skill)						
Tennis Educational Foundation: 1956 (16 pgs.; soft cover; 10¢)						
Book 1-Endorsed by Gene Tunney, Ralph Kiner, etc. showing how tennis has helped them	6	12	18	28	34	40
TERRY AND THE PIRATES						
Dell Publishing Co.: 1939 - 1953 (By Milton Caniff)						
Buster Brown Shoes giveaway(1938)-32 pgs.; in color	21	42	63	124	202	280
Canada Dry Premiums-Books #1-3(1953, 36 pgs.; 2x5")-Harvey; #1-Hot Shot Charlie Flies Again; 2-In Forced Landing; 3-Dragon Lady in Distress)	14	28	42	82	121	160
Gambles Giveaway (1938, 16 pgs.)	10	20	30	56	76	95
Gillmore Giveaway (1938, 24 pgs.)	10	20	30	56	76	95
Popped Wheat Giveaway(1938)-Strip reprints in full color; Caniff-a	4	7	9	14	16	18
Shoe Store giveaway (Weatherbird & Poll-Parrot)(1938, 16 pgs., soft-c)(2-diff.)	10	20	30	58	79	100
Sparked Wheat Giveaway(1942, 16 pgs.)-In color	10	20	30	58	79	100
TERRY AND THE PIRATES						
Libby's Radio Premium: 1941 (16 pgs.; reg. size)(shipped folded in the mail)						
"Adventure of the Ruby of Genghis Khan" - Each pg. is a puzzle that must be completed to read the story	415	830	1245	2700	-	-
THAT THE WORLD MAY BELIEVE						
Catechetical Guild Giveaway: No date (16 pgs.) (Graymoor Friars distr.)						
nn	5	10	14	20	24	28
THREAT TO FREEDOM						
1965 (Small size)						
nn - Anti-communism pamphlet; hammer & sickle-c	10	20	30	64	132	200
3-D COLOR CLASSICS (Wendy's Kid's Club)						
Wendy's Int'l Inc.: 1995 (5 1/2" x 8", comes with 3-D glasses)						
The Elephant's Child, Gulliver's Travels, Peter Pan, The Time Machine, 20,000 Leagues Under the Sea: Neal Adams-a in all each....						5.00
350 YEARS OF AMERICAN DAIRY FOODS						
American Dairy Assoc.: 1957 (5x7", 16 pgs.)						
nn-History of milk	4	7	10	14	17	20
THUMPER (Disney)						
Grosset & Dunlap: 1942 (50¢, 32pgs., hardcover book, 7"x8-1/2" w/dust jacket)						
nn-Given away (along with a copy of Bambi) for a $2.00, 2-year subscription to WDC&S in 1942. (Xmas offer). Book only	19	38	57	111	176	240
Dust jacket only	12	24	36	67	94	120
TILLY AND TED-TINKERTOTLAND						
W. T. Grant Co.: 1945 (Giveaway, 20 pgs.)						
nn-Christmas comic	10	20	30	60	82	110
TIM (Formerly Superman-Tim; becomes Gene Autry-Tim)						
Tim Stores: June, 1950 - Oct, 1950 (B&W, half-size)						
4 issues; 6/50, 9/50, 10/50 known	17	34	51	105	165	225
TIM AND SALLY'S ADVENTURES AT MARINELAND						
Marineland Restaurant & Bar, Marineland, CA: 1957 (5x7", 16 pgs., soft-c)						
nn-copyright Oceanarium, Inc.	2	4	6	10	14	18
TIME OF DECISION						
Harvey Publications Inc.: Early 1950s (16 pgs., paper cover)						
nn-ROTC recruitment	6	12	18	28	34	40
TIM IN SPACE (Formerly Gene Autry Tim; becomes Tim Tomorrow)						
Tim Stores: 1950 (1/2 size giveaway) (B&W)						
nn	15	30	45	85	133	180
TIM TOMORROW (Formerly Tim In Space)						
Tim Stores: 8/51, 9/51, 10/51, Christmas, 1951 (5x7-3/4")						
nn-Prof. Fumble & Captain Kit Comet in all	15	30	45	85	133	180
TIM TYLER'S LUCK						
Standard Comics (King Feat. Syndicate): 1950s (Reg. size, slick-c)						
nn-Felix the Cat app.	5	10	15	23	28	32
TOM MIX (...Commandos Comics #10-12)						
Ralston-Purina Co.: Sept, 1940 - No. 12, Nov, 1942 (36 pgs.); 1983 (one-shot)						
Given away for two Ralston box-tops; 1983 came in cereal box						
1-Origin (life) Tom Mix; Fred Meagher-a	226	452	678	1448	2473	3500
2	50	100	150	315	533	750
3-9	39	78	117	240	395	550
10-12: 10-Origin Tom Mix Commando Unit; Speed O'Dare begins; Japanese sub-c. 12-Sci/fi-c	33	66	99	194	317	440
1983- "Taking of Grizzly Grebb", Toth-a; 16 pg. miniature	2	4	6	9	12	15

	GD 2.0	VG 4.0	FN 6.0	VF 8.0	VF/NM 9.0	NM- 9.2

TOM SAWYER COMICS
Giveaway: 1951? (Paper cover)
nn-Contains a coverless Hopalong Cassidy from 1951; other combinations known 5 10 15 24 29 34

TOO MUCH, TOO LITTLE
Federal Reserve Bank: 1989 (Reg. size)
9-13 1 3 4 6 8 10

TOP-NOTCH COMICS
MLJ Magazines/Rex Theater: 1940s (theater giveaway, sepia-c)
1-Black Hood-c; content & covers can vary 65 130 195 415 708 1000

TOWN THAT FORGOT SANTA, THE
W. T. Grant Co.: 1961 (Giveaway, 24 pgs.)
nn 3 6 9 16 23 30

TOY LAND FUNNIES (See Funnies On Parade)
Eastern Color Printing Co.: 1934 (32 pgs., Hecht Co. store giveaway)
nn-Reprints Buck Rogers Sunday pages #199-201 from Famous Funnies #5. A rare variation of Funnies On Parade; same format, similar contents, same cover except for large Santa placed in center (value will be based on sale)

TOY WORLD FUNNIES (See Funnies On Parade)
Eastern Color Printing Co.: 1933 (36 pgs., slick cover, Golden Eagle and Wanamaker giveaway)
nn-Contains contents from Funnies On Parade/Century Of Comics. A rare variation of Funnies On Parade; same format, similar contents, same cover except for large Santa placed in center. A GD/VG 3.0 copy sold for $5258 in May 2016.

TRAPPED
Harvey Publications (Columbia Univ. Press): 1951 (Giveaway, soft-c, 16 pgs)
nn-Drug education comic (30,000 printed?) distributed to schools.; mentioned in **SOTI**, pgs. 256,350 10 20 30 58 79 100
NOTE: *Many copies surfaced in 1979 causing a setback in price; beware of trimmed edges, because many copies have a brittle edge.*

TRIPLE-A BASEBALL HEROES
Marvel Comics: 2007 (Minor league baseball stadium giveaway)
1-Special John Watson painted-c for Memphis, Durham and Buffalo; generic cover with team logos for each of the other 27 teams; Spider-Man, Iron Man, FF app. 4.00

TRIP TO OUTER SPACE WITH SANTA
Sales Promotions, Inc/Peoria Dry Goods: 1950s (paper-c)
nn-Comics, games & puzzles 6 12 18 29 36 42

TRIP WITH SANTA ON CHRISTMAS EVE, A
Rockford Dry Goods Co.: No date (Early 1950s) (Giveaway, 16 pgs., paper-c)
nn 5 10 15 24 29 34

TRUTH BEHIND THE TRIAL OF CARDINAL MINDSZENTY, THE (See Cardinal Mindszenty)

TURNING WHEELS
Studebaker: 1954 (paper-c)
nn-The Studebaker story (A CGC 9.6 sold in 2018 for $1016 & a CGC 9.6 sold in 2019 for $156)

24 PAGES OF COMICS (No title) (Also see Pure Oil Comics, Salerno Carnival of Comics, & Vicks Comics)
Giveaway by various outlets including Sears: Late 1930s
nn-Contains strip reprints-Buck Rogers, Napoleon, Sky Roads, War on Crime 37 74 111 222 301 500

TWO FACES OF COMMUNISM (Also see Double Talk)
Christian Anti-Communism Crusade, Houston, Texas: 1961 (Giveaway, paper-c, 36 pgs.)
nn 34 68 102 199 325 450

2001, A SPACE ODYSSEY (Movie)
Marvel Comics Group
Howard Johnson giveaway (1968, 8pp); 6 pg. movie adaptation, 2 pg. games, puzzles; McWilliams-a 2 4 6 10 14 18

UNCLE SAM'S CHRISTMAS STORY
Promotional Publ. Co.: 1958 (Giveaway)
nn-Reprints 1956 Christmas USA 3 6 9 14 20 26

UNCLE WIGGILY COMICS
Herberger's Clothing Store: 1942 (32 pgs., paper cover)
nn-Comic panels with 6 pages of puzzles 15 30 45 88 137 185

UNKEPT PROMISE
Legion of Truth: 1949 (Giveaway, 24 pgs.)
nn-Anti-alcohol 12 24 36 69 97 125

UNTOLD LEGEND OF THE BATMAN, THE
DC Comics: 1989 (28 pgs., 6X9", limited series of cereal premiums)
1-1st & 2nd printings known; Byrne-a 2 4 6 9 13 16
2,3: 1st & 2nd printings known 1 3 4 6 8 10

UNTOUCHABLES, THE (TV)
Leaf Brands, Inc.
Topps Bubblegum premiums produced by Leaf Brands, Inc.-2-1/2x4-1/2", 8 pgs. (3 diff. issues) "The Organization, Jamaica Ginger, The Otto Frick Story (drug), 3000 Suspects, The Antidote, Mexican Stakeout, Little Egypt, Purple Gang, Bugs Moran Story, & Lily Dallas Story" 3 6 9 18 27 36

VICKS COMICS (See Pure Oil Comics, Salerno Carnival of Comics & 24 Pages of Comics)
Eastern Color Printing Co. (Vicks Chemical Co.): nd (circa 1938) (Giveaway, 68 pgs. in color)
nn-Famous Funnies-r (before #40); contains 5 pgs. Buck Rogers (4 pgs. from F.F. #15, & 1 pg. from #16) Joe Palooka, Napoleon, etc. app. 71 142 213 454 777 1100
nn-16 loose, untrimmed page giveaway; paper-c; r/Famous Funnies #14; Buck Rogers, Joe Palooka app. Has either "Vicks Comics" printed on cover or only a local store name as the logo. 28 56 84 165 270 375

WALT DISNEY'S COMICS & STORIES
K.K. Publications: 1942-1963 known (7-1/3"x10-1/4", 4 pgs. in color, slick paper) (folded horizontally once or twice as mailers) (Xmas subscription offer)
1942 mailer-r/Kelly cover to WDC&S 25; 2-year subscription + two Grosset & Dunlap hardcover books (32-pages each), of Bambi and of Thumper, offered for $2.00; came in an illustrated C&S envelope with an enclosed postage paid envelope (Rare) Mailer only 28 56 84 165 270 375
with envelopes 32 64 96 188 307 425
1947,1948 mailer 20 40 60 115 185 255
1949 mailer-A rare Barks item: Same WDC&S cover as 1942 mailer, but with art changed so that nephew is handing teacher Donald a comic book rather than an apple, as originally drawn by Kelly. The tiny, 7/8"x1-1/4" cover shown was a rejected cover by Barks that was intended for C&S 110, but was redrawn by Kelly for C&S 111. The original art has been lost and this is its only app. (Rare) 41 82 123 256 428 600
1950 mailer-P.1 r/Kelly cover to Dell Xmas Parade 1 (without title); p.2 r/Kelly cover to C&S 101 (w/o title), but with the art altered to show Donald reading C&S 122 (by Kelly); hardcover book, "Donald Duck in Bringing Up the Boys" given with a $1.00 one-year subscription; P.4 r/full Kelly Xmas cover to C&S 99 (Rare) 19 38 57 111 176 240
1952 mailer-P1 r/cover WDC&S #88 15 30 45 90 140 190
1953 mailer-P.1 r/cover Dell Xmas Parade 4 (w/o title); insides offer "Donald Duck Full Speed Ahead," a 28-page, color, 5-5/8"x6-5/8" book, not of the Story Hour series; P.4 r/full Barks C&S 148 cover (Rare) 15 30 45 90 140 190
1963 mailer-Pgs. 1,2 & 4 r/GK Xmas art; P.3 r/a 1963 C&S cover (Scarce) 7 14 21 44 82 120
NOTE: *It is assumed a different mailer was printed each Xmas for at least twenty years.*

WALT DISNEY'S COMICS & STORIES
Walt Disney Productions: 1943 (36 pgs.) (Dept. store Xmas giveaway)
nn-X-Mas-c with Donald & the Boys; Donald Duck by Jack Hannah; Thumper by Ken Hultgren 84 168 252 538 919 1300

WARLORD
DC Comics: (Remco Toy giveaway, 2-3/4x4")
nn 5.00

WATCH OUT FOR BIG TALK
General Comics: 1950
nn-Dan Barry-a; about crooked politicians 12 24 36 67 94 120

WEATHER-BIRD (See Comics From..., Dick Tracy, Free Comics to You..., Super Circus & Terry and the Pirates)
International Shoe Co./Western Printing Co.: 1958 - No. 16, July, 1962 (Shoe store giveaway)
1 4 8 12 24 38 52
2-16 3 6 9 14 19 24
NOTE: *The numbers are located in the lower bottom panel, pg. 1. All feature a character called Weather-Bird.*

WEATHER BIRD COMICS (See Comics From Weather Bird)
Weather Bird Shoes: 1955 - 1958 (Giveaway)
nn-Contains a comic bound with new cover. Several combinations possible; contents determine price (40 - 60 percent of contents).

WEEKLY COMIC MAGAZINE
Fox Publications: May 12, 1940 (16 pgs.) (Others exist w/o super-heroes)
(1st Version)-8 pg. Blue Beetle story, 7 pg. Patty O'Day story; two copies known to exist. (a VF copy sold in 5/07 for $1553)
(2nd Version)-7 two-pg. adventures of Blue Beetle, Patty O'Day, Yarko, Dr. Fung, Green Mask, Spark Stevens, & Rex Dexter (two known copies, a FN sold in 2007 for $1912, other is GD)
(3rd version)-Captain Valor (only one known copy, in VG+; it sold in 2005 for $480) -
Discovered with business papers, letters and exploitation material promoting **Weekly Comic Magazine** for use by newspapers in the same manner of **The Spirit** weeklies. Interesting note: these are dated three weeks before the first Spirit comic. Letters indicate that samples may have been sent to a few newspapers. These sections were actually 15-1/2x22" pages which will fold down to an approximate 8x10" comic booklet. Other various comic sections were found with the above, but were more like the Sunday comic sections in format.

WE HIT THE JACKPOT
General Comics, Inc./American Affairs: 1947 (Promotional comic)(Paper-c)
nn 8 16 24 40 50 60

WHAT DO YOU KNOW ABOUT THIS COMICS SEAL OF APPROVAL?
No publisher listed (DC Comics giveaway): nd (1955) (4 pgs., slick paper-c)
nn-(Rare) 258 516 774 1651 2826 4000

WHAT IF THEY CALL ME "CHICKEN"?
Kiwanis International: 1970 (giveaway)
nn-Educational anti-marijuana comic 4 8 12 27 44 60

WHAT'S BEHIND THESE HEADLINES
William C. Popper Co.: 1948 (16 pgs.)
nn-Comic insert "The Plot to Steal the World" 8 16 24 44 57 70

WHAT'S IN IT FOR YOU?
Harvey Publications Inc.: (16 pgs., paper cover)
nn-National Guard recruitment 4 8 11 16 19 22

WHEATIES (Premiums)
Walt Disney Productions: 1950 & 1951 (32 titles, pocket-size, 32 pgs.)
Mailing Envelope (no art on front)(Designates sets A,B,C or D on front) 7 14 21 37 46 55

(Set A-1 to A-8, 1950)
A-1-Mickey Mouse & the Disappearing Island, A-5-Mickey Mouse, Roving Reporter each... 6 12 18 31 38 45
A-2-Grandma Duck, Homespun Detective, A-6-Li'l Bad Wolf, Forest Ranger, A-7-Goofy, Tightrope Acrobat, A-8-Pluto & the Bogus Money each... 6 12 18 28 34 40
A-3-Donald Duck & the Haunted Jewels, A-4-Donald Duck & the Giant Ape each... 8 16 24 44 57 70

(Set B-1 to B-8, 1950)
B-1-Mickey Mouse & the Pharoah's Curse, B-4-Mickey Mouse & the Mystery Sea Monster each... 7 14 21 35 43 50
B-2-Pluto, Canine Cowpoke, B-5-Li'l Bad Wolf in the Hollow Tree Hideout, B-7-Goofy & the Gangsters each... 6 12 18 28 34 40
B-3-Donald Duck & the Buccaneers, B-6-Donald Duck,Trail Blazer, B-8 Donald Duck, Klondike Kid each... 8 16 24 44 57 70

Trapped © HARV

Weather-Bird #1 © ISC

Your Vote is Vital! © HARV

GD VG FN VF VF/NM NM-
2.0 4.0 6.0 8.0 9.0 9.2

(Set C-1 to C-8, 1951)
C-1-Donald Duck & the Inca Idol, C-5-Donald Duck in the Lost Lakes,
C-8-Donald Duck Deep-Sea Diver each... 8 16 24 44 57 70
C-2-Mickey Mouse & the Magic Mountain, C-6-Mickey Mouse & the Stagecoach Bandits
each... 7 14 21 35 45 50
C-3-Li'l Bad Wolf, Fire Fighter, C-4-Gus & Jaq Save the Ship, C-7-Goofy, Big Game Hunter
each... 6 12 18 28 34 40
(Set D-1 to D-8, 1951)
D-1-Donald Duck in Indian Country, D-5-Donald Duck, Mighty Mystic
each... 8 16 24 44 57 70
D-2-Mickey Mouse and the Abandoned Mine, D-6-Mickey Mouse & the Medicine Man
each... 7 14 21 35 43 50
D-3-Pluto & the Mysterious Package, D-4-Bre'r Rabbit's Sunken Treasure,
D-7-Li'l Bad Wolf and the Secret of the Woods, D-8-Minnie Mouse, Girl Explorer
each... 6 12 18 28 34 40
NOTE: *Some copies lack the Wheaties ad.*

WHEEL OF PROGRESS, THE
Assoc. of American Railroads: Oct, 1957 (16 pgs.)
nn-Bill Bunce 6 12 18 29 36 42

WHIZ COMICS (Formerly Flash Comics & Thrill Comics #1)
Fawcett Publications
Wheaties Giveaway(1946, Miniature, 6-1/2x8-1/4", 32 pgs.); all copies were taped at each corner to a box of Wheaties and are never found in very fine or mint condition; "Capt. Marvel & the Water Thieves", plus Golden Arrow, Ibis, Crime Smasher stories
83 166 415 - - -

WILD KINGDOM (TV) (Mutual of Omaha's...)
Western Printing Co.: 1965, 1966 (Giveaway, regular size, slick-c, 16 pgs.)
nn-Front & back-c are different on 1966 edition 2 4 6 9 12 15

WISCO/KLARER COMIC BOOK (Miniature)
Marvel Comics/Vital Publ./Fawcett Publ.: 1948 - 1964 (3-1/2x6-3/4", 24 pgs.)
Given away by Wisco "99" Service Stations, Carnation Malted Milk, Klarer Health Wieners, Fleers Dubble Bubble Gum, Rodeo All-Meat Wieners, Perfect Potato Chips, & others; see ad in Tom Mix #21
Blackstone & the Gold Medal Mystery (1948) 8 16 24 40 50 60
Blackstone "Solves the Sealed Vault Mystery" (1950) 8 16 24 40 50 60
Blaze Carson in "The Sheriff Shoots It Out" (1950) 8 16 24 40 50 60
Captain Marvel & Billy's Big Game (r/Capt. Marvel Adv. #76)
(Prices vary widely on this book) 26 52 78 154 252 350
China Boy in "A Trip to the Zoo" #10 (1948) 4 8 12 18 22 25
Indoors-Outdoors Game Book 3 6 9 11 13 15
Jim Solar Space Sheriff in "Battle for Mars", "Between Two Worlds", "Conquers Outer Space", "The Creatures on the Comet", "Defeats the Moon Missile Men", "Encounter Creatures on Comet", "Meet the Jupiter Jumpers", "Meets the Man From Mars", "On Traffic Duty", "Outlaws of the Spaceways", "Pirates of the Planet X", "Protects Space Lanes", "Raiders From the Sun", "Ring Around Saturn", "Robots of Rhea", "The Sky Ruby", "Spacetts of the Sky", "Spidermen of Venus", "Trouble on Mercury"
6 12 18 29 36 42
Johnny Starboard & the Underseas Pirates (1948) 4 8 12 18 22 25
Kid Colt in "He Lived by His Guns" (1950) 8 16 24 40 50 60
Little Aspirin as the "Crook Catcher" #2 (1950) 3 6 9 11 13 15
Little Aspirin in "Naughty But Nice" #6 (1950) 3 6 9 11 13 15
Return of the Black Phantom (not M.E. character)(Roy Dare)(1948)
6 12 18 27 33 38
Secrets of Magic 4 7 9 14 16 18
Slim Morgan "Brings Justice to Mesa City" #3 4 7 9 14 16 18
Super Rabbit(1950)-Cuts Red Tape, Stops Crime Wave!
8 16 24 44 57 70
Tex Farnum, Frontiersman (1948) 4 8 12 18 22 25
Tex Taylor in "Draw or Die, Cowpoke!" (1950) 6 12 18 28 34 40
Tex Taylor in "An Exciting Adventure at the Gold Mine" (1950)
6 12 18 27 33 38
Wacky Quacky in "All-Aboard" 3 5 7 10 12 14
When School Is Out 3 5 7 10 12 14
Willie in a "Comic-Comic Book Fall" #1 4 7 9 14 16 18
Wonder Duck "An Adventure at the Rodeo of the Fearless Quacker!" (1950)
8 16 24 44 57 70
Rare uncut version of three; includes Capt. Marvel, Tex Farnum, Black Phantom
(A VG copy sold in Sept. 2015 for $147)
Rare uncut version of three; includes China Boy, Blackstone, Johnny Starboard & the Underseas Pirates (A FN/VF copy sold in Sept. 2015 for $137)
Rare uncut version of three; all Jim Solar (A VG copy sold in Sept. 2015 for $79)
Rare uncut version of three; includes Willie in a "Comic-Comic Book Fall", Little Aspirin #2, Slim Morgan Brings Justice to Mesa City (a VF/FN copy sold for $54 in Nov. 2007)

WIZARD OF OZ
MGM: 1967 (small size)
"Dorothy and Friends Visit Oz", "Dorothy Meets the Wizard", "The Tin Woodsman Saves Dorothy" each... 2 4 6 11 16 20

WOLVERINE
Marvel Comics
145-(1999 Nabisco mail-in offer) Sienkiewicz-c 21 42 63 147 324 500
...Son of Canada (4/01, ed. of 65,000) Spider-Man & The Hulk app.; Lim-a
1 2 3 5 6 8

WOMAN OF THE PROMISE, THE
Catechetical Guild: 1950 (General Distr.) (Paper cover, 32 pgs.)
nn 6 12 18 28 34 40

WONDER BOOK OF RUBBER
B.F. Goodrich: 1947 (Promo giveaway
nn 5 10 15 24 30 35

WONDERFUL WORLD OF DUCKS (See Golden Picture Story Book)
Colgate Palmolive Co.: 1975
1-Mostly-r 1 3 4 6 8 10

WONDER WOMAN
DC Comics: 1977
Pizza Hut Giveaways (12/77)-Reprints #60,62 3 6 9 14 20 25
... - The Minotaur (1981, General Foods giveaway, 8 pages, 3-1/2 x 6-3/4", oblong) 3 6 9 14 20 26

WONDER WORKER OF PERU
Catechetical Guild: No date (5x7", 16 pgs., B&W, giveaway)
nn 6 12 18 28 34 40

WOODY WOODPECKER
Dell Publishing Co.
Clover Stamp-Newspaper Boy Contest('56)-9 pg. story-(Giveaway)
8 16 24 40 50 60
In Chevrolet Wonderland(1954-Giveaway)(Western Publ.)-20 pgs., full story line; Chilly Willy app. 18 36 54 105 165 225
...Meets Scotty MacTape(1953-Scotch Tape giveaway)-16 pgs., full size
18 36 54 105 165 225

WOOLWORTH'S CHRISTMAS STORY BOOK (See Jolly Christmas Book)
Promotional Publ. Co.(Western Printing Co.): 1952 - 1954 (16 pgs., paper-c)
nn: 1952 issue-Marv Levy c/a 8 16 24 44 57 70

WOOLWORTH'S HAPPY TIME CHRISTMAS BOOK
F. W. Woolworth Co. (Western Printing Co.): 1952 (Christmas giveaway)
nn-36 pgs. 8 16 24 42 54 65

WORLD'S FINEST COMICS
National Periodical Publ./DC Comics
Giveaway (c. 1944-45, 8 pgs., in color, paper-c)-Johnny Everyman-r/World's Finest
24 48 72 142 234 325
Giveaway (c. 1949, 8 pgs., in color, paper-c)- "Make Way For Youth" r/World's Finest; based on film of same name 21 42 63 122 199 275
#176, #179- Best Western reprint edition (1997) 5.00

WORLD'S GREATEST SUPER HEROES
DC Comics (Nutra Comics) (Child Vitamins, Inc.): 1977 (Giveaway, 3-3/4x3-3/4", 24 pgs.)
nn-Batman & Robin app.; health tips 2 4 6 13 18 22

WYOMING THE COWBOY STATE
1954 (Giveaway, slick-c)
nn 5 10 15 22 26 30

XMAS FUNNIES
Kinney Shoes: No date (Giveaway, paper cover, 36 pgs.?)
Contains 1933 color strip-r; Mutt & Jeff, etc. 34 68 102 199 325 450

X-MEN THE MOVIE
Marvel Comics/Toys R' Us: 2000
Special Movie Prequel Edition 2 4 6 8 10 12

X2 PRESENTS THE ULTIMATE X-MEN #2
Marvel Comics/New York Post: July, 2003
Reprint distributed inside issue of the New York Post 3.00

YALTA TO KOREA (Also see Korea My Home)
M. Phillip Corp. (Republican National Committee): 1952 (Giveaway, paper-c)
nn-(8 pgs.)-Anti-communist propaganda book 21 42 63 122 199 275

YOGI BEAR (TV)
Dell Publishing Co.
Giveaway ('84, '86)-City of Los Angeles, "Creative First Aid" & "Earthquake Preparedness for Children" 1 2 3 4 5 7

YOUR TRIP TO NEWSPAPERLAND
Philadelphia Evening Bulletin (Printed by Harvey Press): June, 1955 (14x11-1/2", 12 pgs.)
nn-Joe Palooka takes kids on newspaper tour 6 12 18 31 38 45

YOUR VOTE IS VITAL!
Harvey Publications Inc.: 1952 (5" x 7", 16 pgs., paper cover)
nn-The importance of voting 5 10 15 24 30 35

THE PIONEER AGE

The American Comic Book: 1500s-1828

For the last few years, we have featured a tremendous article by noted historian and collector Eric C. Caren on the foundations of what we now call "The Pioneer Age" of comics. We look forward to a new article on this significant topic in a future edition of *The Overstreet Comic Book Price Guide*. In the meantime, should you need it, Caren's article may be found in the 35th through 39th editions.

That said, even with the space constraints in this edition of the *Guide*, we could not possibly exclude reference to these incredible, formative works.

Why are these illustrations and sequences of illustrations important to the comic books of today?

German broadsheet, dated 1569.

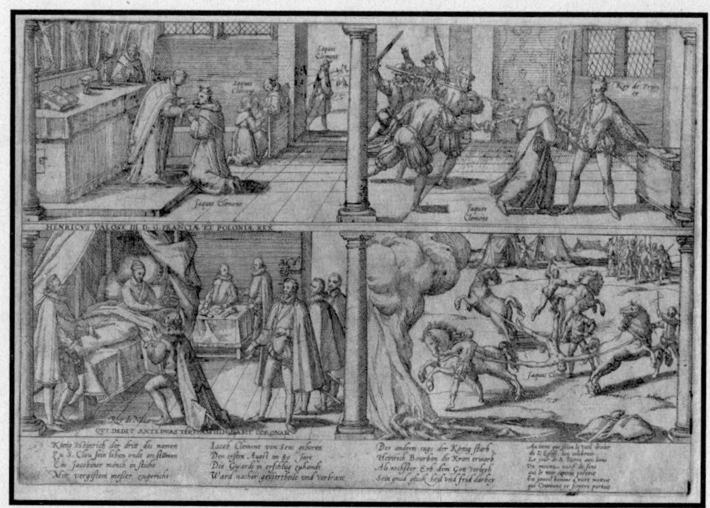

Quite frankly, because we can see in them the very building blocks of the comic art form.

The Murder of King Henry III (1589).

The shooting of the Italian Concini (1617).

Over the course of just a few hundred years, we the evolution of narration, word balloons, panel-to-panel progression of story, and so much more. If these stories aren't developed first, how would be every have reached the point that that *The Adventures of Mr. Obadiah Oldbuck* could have come along in 1842?

As the investigation of comic book history has blown away the notion that comic books were a 20 century invention, it hasn't been easy to convince some, even with the clear, linear progression of the artful melding of illustration and words.

"Want to avoid an argument in social discourse? Steer clear of politics and religion. In the latter category, the most controversial subject is human evolution. Collectors can become just as squeamish when you start messing with the evolution of a particular collectible," Eric Caren wrote in his article. "In most cases, the origin of a particular comic character will be universally agreed upon, but try tackling the origin of printed comics and you are asking for trouble."

"The Bubblers Medley" (1720).

"Join, or Die" from the **Pennsylvania Gazette**, *May 9, 1754.*

"Amusement for John Bull..." from **The European Magazine** *(1783).*

But the evidence is there for any who choose to look. Before the original comics of the Golden Age, there were comic strip reprints collected in comic book form. The practice dated back decades earlier, of course, but coalesced into the current form when the realities of the Great Depression spawned the modern incarnation of the comic book and its immediate cousin, the Big Little Book.

Everything that came later, though, did so because the acceptance of the visual language had already been worked out. Before Spider-Man and the Hulk, before Superman and Batman, before the Yellow Kid, Little Nemo, and the Brownies, cartoonists and editorial illustrators were working out how to tell a story or simply convey their ideas in this new artform.

Without this sort of work, without these pioneers, we simply wouldn't be where we are today.

CONNECTICUT MIRROR.

Cartoons satirizing Napoleon on the front page of the **Connecticut Mirror**, *dated January 7, 1811.*

Another Napoleon cartoon, this time dubbing him "The Corsican Munchausen," from the **London Strand**, *December 4, 1813.*

"A Consultation at the Medical Board" from **The Pasquin or General Satirist** *(1821).*

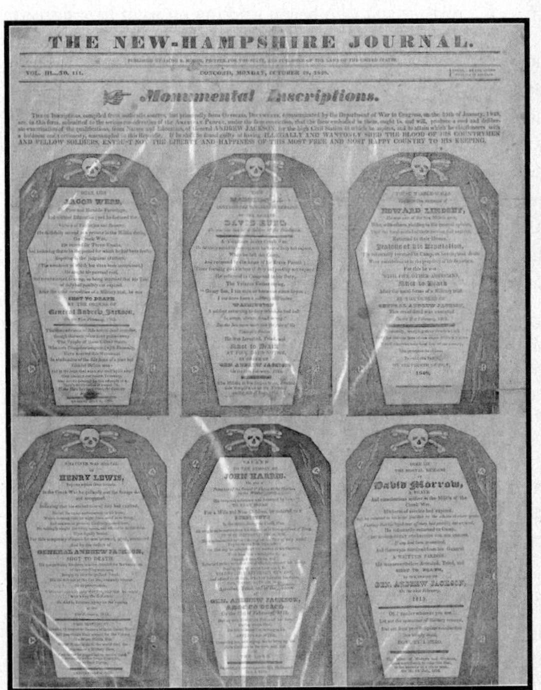

THE NEW-HAMPSHIRE JOURNAL.

CONCORD, MONDAY, OCTOBER 20, 1828.

Monumental Inscriptions.

JACOB WEBB,

EDWARD LINDSEY,

HENRY LEWIS,

JOHN HARRIS.

David Morrow,

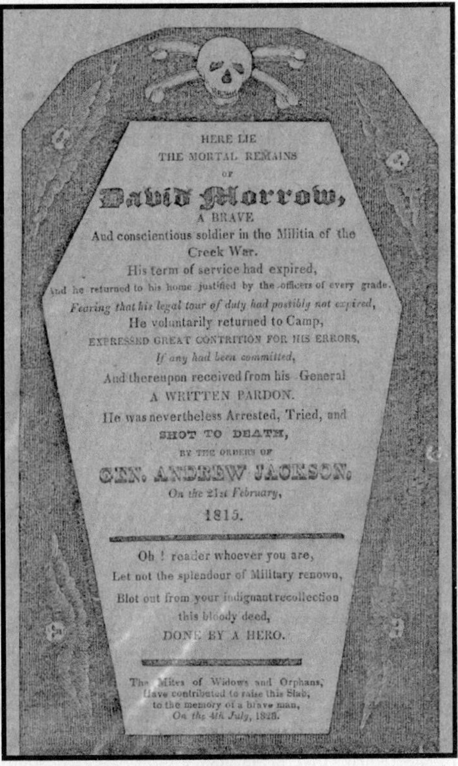

HERE LIE
THE MORTAL REMAINS
OF
David Morrow,
A BRAVE
And conscientious soldier in the Militia of the
Creek War.
His term of service had expired,
and he returned to his home justified by the officers of every grade.
Fearing that his legal tour of duty had possibly not expired,
He voluntarily returned to Camp,
EXPRESSED GREAT CONTRITION FOR HIS ERRORS,
If any had been committed,
And thereupon received from his General
A WRITTEN PARDON.
He was nevertheless Arrested, Tried, and
SHOT TO DEATH,
BY THE ORDERS OF
GEN. ANDREW JACKSON,
On the 21st February,
1815.

Oh! reader whoever you are,
Let not the splendour of Military renown,
Blot out from your indignant recollection
this bloody deed,
DONE BY A HERO.

The Mites of Widows and Orphans,
Have contributed to raise this Slab,
to the memory of a brave man,
On the 4th July, 1828.

Above left, the front page of **The New Hampshire Journal**, *dated October 20, 1828, with multiple tombstone "panels." To the right is a detail of the bottom right tombstone.*

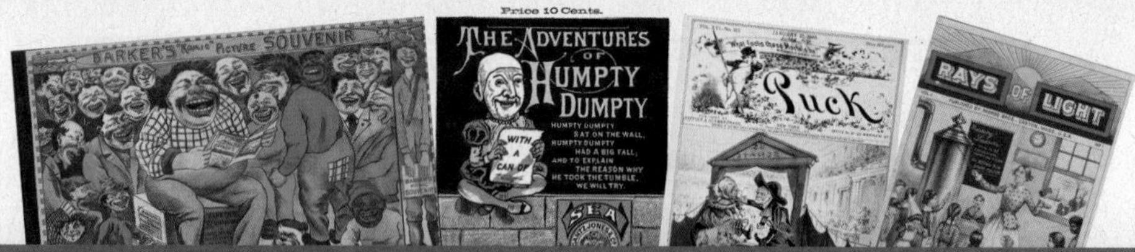

THE VICTORIAN AGE

Comic Strips and Books: 1646-1900

By Carrie Wood

Comics were appearing in publications long before caped heroes graced the newsstands around the country. The Victorian and Platinum Ages of comics pre-date the Golden Age arrival of superheroes by decades, though these eras are notable for far more than just the publication dates. We'll delve into the Platinum Age in the following section, and here we'll be focusing on Victorian comics, which began in the 1840s and ran through the end of the century, overlapping with the Platinum Age for a few years.

In terms of subject matter, the commonly-held attitudes and beliefs of 19th century America can be found throughout these cartoons – for better or for worse, by today's standards. And when it comes to the layout of the comics themselves, there's several things worth noting. For instance, word balloons in the Victorian Age were almost never used, and on the rare occasions they were found they were almost completely inconsequential. Typical comics of this time were single-panel illustrations, with narration or dialogue found beneath the panels rather than within the art itself.

There's a wealth of information to discuss about the Victorian Age, and especially with regards to pricing these historical comics, but we found it prudent to hit some of the most important events here before moving into this year's pricing section:

- The Victorian Age began in different countries at different times, depending entirely on when the first sequential comic art was published. Many European countries had a significant head start on the U.S. in this regard.
- America had non-sequential comic art in the years before the Victorian Age began, with woodcut prints occurring as early as the mid-1600s. The 1800s also introduced the States to memorable cartoon artwork, with one of the best-remembered being Benjamin Franklin's "Join or Die" piece, published in 1754; it represented the American Colonies at the time as severed snake parts. These early political cartoons helped introduce an initial baseline for comic art in publications around the country.
- In America, the Victorian Age began proper with the publication of *The Adventures of Mr. Obadiah Oldbuck* in 1842. This story was an unlicensed copy of the original work, *Histoire de M. Vieux Bois*, by Rodolphe Topffer, who had not granted permission of any sort to the periodical that published it (*Brother Jonathan Extra*).
- Topffer was a novelist, artist and teacher from Switzerland who began working on what he referred to

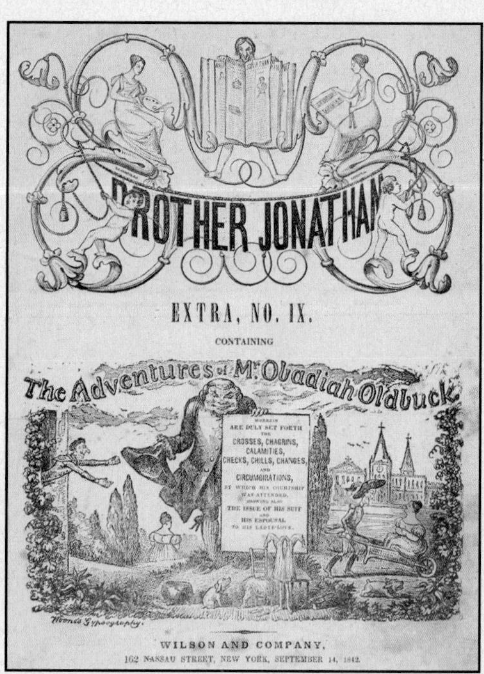
BROTHER JONATHAN

EXTRA, NO. IX.

CONTAINING

The Adventures of M. Obadiah Oldbuck

WHEREIN ARE DULY SET FORTH THE CROSSES, CHAGRINS, CALAMITIES, CHECKS, CHILLS, CHANGES, AND CIRCUMGYRATIONS, BY WHICH HIS COURTSHIP WAS ATTENDED, SHOWING ALSO THE ISSUE OF HIS SUIT AND HIS ESPOUSAL TO HIS LADYE-LOVE.

WILSON AND COMPANY,
162 NASSAU STREET, NEW YORK, SEPTEMBER 14, 1842.

The earliest-known sequential comic book published in America, ***The Adventures of Mr. Obadiah Oldbuck****, from September 1842.*

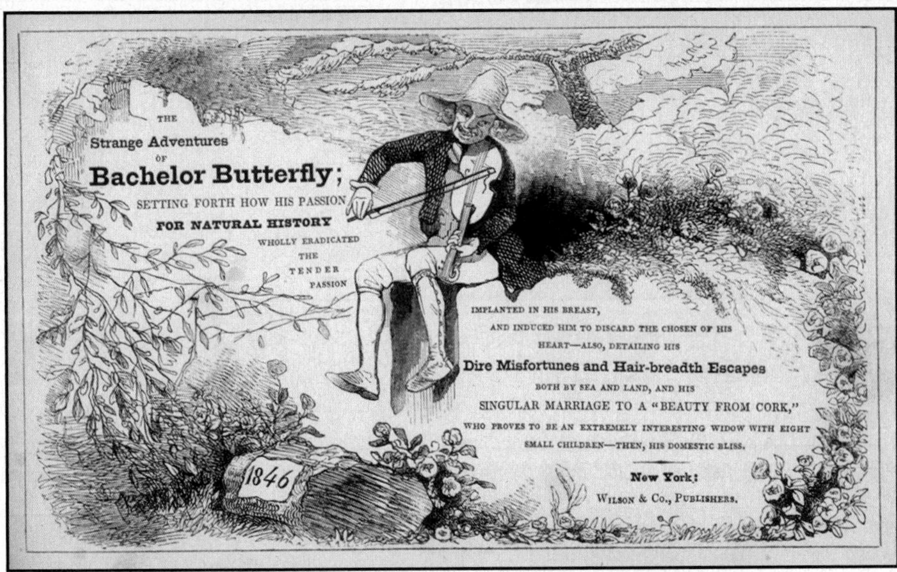

The Strange and Wonderful Adventures of Bachelor Butterfly
by Rodolphe Töpffer (New York, 1846), America's 3rd comic book.

as "picture novels" or "graphic literature" by the late 1820s. By the time his work found its way to Paris, they were a significant success. The demand for his work quickly outmatched the supply available, leading to the widespread piracy of his comics; in a world that didn't yet have any sort of international copyright law, this was perfectly legal at the time.

- *Brother Jonathan* began in 1839, with the newspaper being created to exploit a loophole in the postage rates, as magazines were held to a higher postage rate than newspapers. Despite being printed in newspaper format, it didn't contain any news, and instead focused on fictional stories, most of which were pirated from European works. Later that year, the publisher introduced *Brother Jonathan Extra*, a book-sized publication that reprinted novels. The publication of *Obadiah Oldbuck* in this format, which was reformatted from the European original, closely resembled a modern American comic book.
- George Cruikshank was another British cartoonist popular during this era. He was known for his caricature work during his early working years, and he later moved into providing illustrations for books such as *Grimms' Fairy Tales* and for his friend, novelist Charles Dickens. Cruikshank produced numerous cartoons over the course of his career, many of which saw international success.

George Cruikshank's ***The Bottle*** *from 1847, popular enough to be reprinted numerous times into the 20th century.*

- Thanks to the success of *Obadiah Oldbuck* in the U.S., it was followed up with printings of Cruikshank's *The Bachelor's Own Book*, which became the second known sequential comic book in the U.S.
- Cruikshank's *The Bottle* debuted in London in 1847 and told the story of a man with alcoholism and how it ruined his family and his life. It was reprinted in a British-American co-publication later that year. Both printings were in a large folio format. This was followed up with a smaller printing the following year, included in the volume *Temperance Tales; Or, Six Nights with the Washing-tonians*. *The Bottle* would see reprintings again and again by numerous publishers well into the 20th century.
- It was during this era that the humor magazine first made its debut, largely in part to the success of published comics in other periodicals. These included *Punch*, a British comic weekly which debuted in 1841. It was a huge success in both England and in the U.S., with thousands of copies being exported to the States with every issue.
- With the success of *Punch*, American businessmen quickly tried to seize upon the market for humorous content, founding the various short-lived publications of *Yankee Doodle, Judy, The John-Donkey* and *The Elephant* – none of which lasted more than a year, though all of which helped the comics market grow.

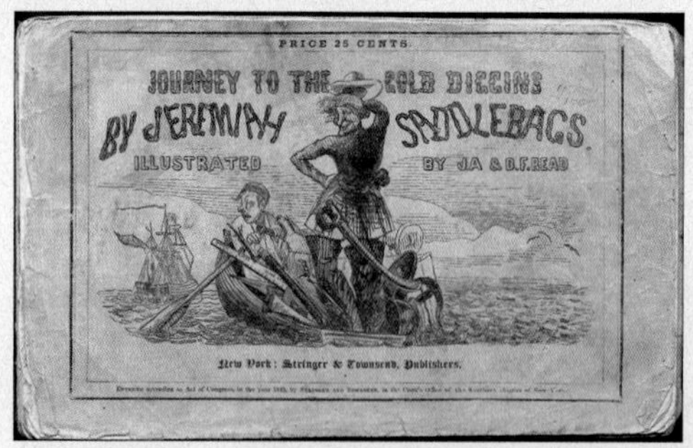

***Journey to the Gold Diggins By Jeremiah Saddlebags**, June 1849, so far the earliest known sequential comic book by American creators, J.A. and D.F. Read, shown with a pair of sample pages.*

- The earliest-known American-created comic book appeared in 1849: *Journey to the Gold Diggins by Jeremiah Saddlebags*, created by cartoonists James and Donald Read. The brothers had worked for *Yankee Doodle* before creating this work, which told of the California gold rush (a wildly popular subject matter for cartoonists of the era).
- Following the international success of *Punch* were collections that reprinted cartoons from the popular magazine, including *Merry Pictures by the Comic Hands* (1859) and others for decades to come. Newspapers would also reprint cartoons from *Punch*, which later would often be replaced by new original American cartoon work.
- *Harper's Monthly* began publishing comics shortly after it began publication in late 1850. The periodical began by reprinting *Punch* cartoons at the end of every issue, later moving into reprints from the British publication *Town Talk* before hiring Frank Bellew to create original comics.
- Bellew provided a huge number of sequential cartoon work during this era, and his work could be found in nearly every American comic or humor publication for decades. His work included contributions to *The Lantern, New York Picayune, The Comic Monthly, Wild Oats, Punchinello, Momus,* and plenty more. His work would go on to influence further generations of comic creators.
- Thomas Nast is another artist of note from this era, known more for his political cartoons than for his sequential comic artwork. Nast's work could be found in *Harper's Weekly*, where he worked from 1862-1886. His work helped to popularize the double-page folio-sized cartoon, a size which he practically invented on his own.
- The German humor magazine *Puck* launched first in 1871, founded by Joseph Keppler. An English-language version of the magazine launched the following year, though both were shut down by the end of 1872. Keppler relaunched *Puck* in 1876, this time to much greater success; it featured lithographed cartoons, and in color, and on top of that was being published on an ambitious weekly schedule. By 1880, *Puck* was a massive success, becoming the benchmark by which all other humor magazines were measured against.
- In 1881, *Judge* debuted, seeking to be the rival to *Puck*. This periodical was founded by former *Puck* artist James A. Wales, and it struggled financially for several years up until the point where politicians realized the power of these cartoons to influence the public. This led the Republican party at the time to help finance W.J. Arkell's purchase of the publication in 1886.
- *Life* arrived in 1883, becoming the third pillar of the comic scene during this era. Though it was priced the same as *Puck* and *Judge*, it was smaller in size and printed in black and white – though that didn't stop it from gaining a significant audience. Its earliest artists included Palmer Cox and Charles Dana Gibson. While *Puck* and *Judge* both altered their content as the world entered the 20th century, *Life* stayed almost exactly the same and maintained its audience better for it.
- On top of magazines, numerous almanacs and other publications rose around this time to start publishing comic art. We also started seeing promotional comics enter the scene during this era – you can learn more about those in our Promotional Comics section of this book.

***Puck** (January 27, 1885 shown) and **Judge** (June 7, 1890 shown) were the top two humor magazine titles of the late 19th century.*

The Strange and Wonderful Adventures
of Bachelor Butterfly by Rodolphe Töpffer
1870s © Dick & Fitzgerald, NYC

Barker's "Komic" Picture Souvenir, 3rd Edition
1894 © Barker, Moore & Klein Medicine Co.

FR1.0 GD2.0 FN6.0

COLLECTOR'S NOTE: Most of the books listed in this section were published well over a century before organized comics fandom began archiving and helping to preserve these fragile popular culture artifacts. With some of these comics now over 160 years old, they almost never surface in Fine+ or better shape. Be happy when you simply find a copy.

This year has seen price growth in quite a few comic books in this era. Since this section began growing almost a decade now, comic books from Wilson, Brother Jonathan, Huestis & Cozans, Garrett, Dick & Fitzgerald, Frank Leslie, Street & Smith and others continue to be recognized by the more savvy in this fine hobby as legitimate comic book collectors' items. We had been more concerned with simply establishing what is known to exist. For the most part, that work is now a *fait accompli* in this section compiled, revised, and expanded by Robert Beerbohm with special thanks this year to Terrance Keegan plus acknowledgment to Bill Blackbeard, Chris Brown, Alfredo Castelli, Darrell Coons, Leonardo De Sá, Scott Deschaine, Joe Evans, Ron Friggle, Tom Gordon III, Michel Kempeneers, Andy Konkykru, Don Kurtz, Richard Olson, Robert Quesinberry, Joseph Rainone, Steve Rowe, Randy Scott, John Snyder, Art Spiegelman, Steve Thompson, Richard Samuel West, Doug Wheeler and Richard Wright. Special kudos to long-time collector and scholar Gabriel Laderman.

The prices given for Fair, Good and Fine categories are for strictly graded editions. If you need help grading your item, we refer you to the grading section in this book or contact the authors of this essay. Items marked Scarce, Rare or Very Rare we are still trying to figure out how many copies might still be in existence. We welcome additions and corrections from any interested collectors and scholars at feedback@gemstonepub.com.

For ease ascertaining the contents of each item of this listing and the Platinum index list, we offer the following list of categories found immediately following most of the titles:

E - EUROPEAN ORIGINAL COMICS MATERIAL; Printed in Europe or reprinted in USA
G - GRAPHIC NOVEL (LONGER FORMAT COMIC TELLING A SINGLE STORY)
H - "HOW TO DRAW CARTOONS" BOOKS
I - ILLUSTRATED BOOKS NOTABLE FOR THE ARTIST, BUT NOT A COMIC.
M - MAGAZINE / PERIODICAL COMICS MATERIAL REPRINTS
N - NEWSPAPER COMICS MATERIAL REPRINTS
O - ORIGINAL COMIC MATERIAL NOT REPRINTED FROM ANOTHER SOURCE
P - PROMOTIONAL COMIC, EITHER GIVEN AWAY FOR FREE, OR A PREMIUM GIVEN IN CONJUNCTION WITH THE PURCHASE OF A PRODUCT.
S - SINGLE PANEL / NON-SEQUENTIAL CARTOONS

Measurements are in inches. The first dimension given is Height and the second is Width. Some original British editions are included in the section, so as to better explain and differentiate their American counterparts.

ACROBATIC ANIMALS
R.H. Russell: 1899 (9x11-7/8", 72 pgs, B&W, hard-c)

nn (Scarce) 125.00 250.00 750.00
NOTE: *Animal strips by Gustave Verbeck, presented 1 panel per page.*

ALMY'S SANTA CLAUS (P,E)
Edward C. Almy & Co., Providence, R.I.: nd (1880's) (5-3/4x4-5/8", 20 pgs, B&W, paper-c

nn - (Rare) 20.00 40.00 120.00
NOTE: *Department store Christmas giveaway containing an abbreviated 28-panel reprinting of George Cruikshank's **The Tooth-ache**. Santa Claus cover.*

AMERICAN COMIC ALMANAC, THE (OLD AMERICAN COMIC ALMANAC 1839-1846)
Charles Ellms: 1831-1846 (5x8, 52 pgs, B&W)

1-First American comic almanac ever prrinted 600.00 1200.00 3600.00
2-16 105.00 210.00 625.00
NOTE:#1 from 1831 is the First American Comic Almanac

AMERICAN PUNCH
American Punch Publishing Co: Jan 1879-March 1881, J.A. Cummings Engraving Co (last 3 issues) (Quarto Monthly)

Most issues 29.00 58.00 175.00

THE AMERICAN WIT
Richardson & Collins, NY: 1867-68 (18-1/2x13. 8 pgs, B&W)

2/3 Frank Bellew single panels 79.00 158.00 475.00

AMERICAN WIT AND HUMOR
Harper & Bros, NY: 1859 (

nn - numerous McLenan sequential comic strips 146.00 292.00 875.00

ATTWOOD'S PICTURES - AN ARTIST'S HISTORY OF THE LAST TEN YEARS OF THE NINETEENTH CENTURY (M,S)
Life Publishing Company, New York: 1900 (11-1/4x9-1/8", 156 pgs, B&W, gilted blue hard-c)

nn - By Attwood 37.00 74.00 220.00
NOTE: *Reprints monthly calendar cartoons which appeared in **LIFE**, for 1887 through 1899.*

BACHELOR BUTTERFLY, THE VERITABLE HISTORY OF MR. (E,G)
D. Bogue, London: 1845 (5-1/2x10-1/4", 74 pgs, B&W, gilted hardcover)

nn - By Rodolphe Töpffer (Scarce) 533.00 1066.00 3200.00
nn - Hand colored edition (Very Rare) (no known sales)
NOTE: *This is the British Edition, translated from the re-engraved by Cham serialization found in **L'Illustration** - a periodical from Paris publisher Dubochet. Predates the first French collected edition. Third Töpffer comic book published in English. The first story page is numbered Page 3. Page 17 shows Bachelor Butterfly being swallowed by a whale.*

BACHELOR BUTTERFLY, THE STRANGE ADVENTURES OF (E,G)
Wilson & Co., New York: 1846 (5-3/8x10-1/8", 68 pgs, B&W, soft-c)

nn - By Rodolphe Töpffer (Very Rare) 567.00 1134.00 3400.00
nn - At least one hand colored copy exists (Very Rare) (no known sales)
NOTE: *2nd Töpffer comic book printed in the U.S., 3rd earliest known sequential comic book in the USA. Reprinted from the British D. Bogue 1845 edition, itself from the earlier French language **Histoire de Mr. Cryptogame**. Released the same year as the French Dubochet edition. Two variations known, the earlier printing with Page number 17 placed on the inside (left) bottom corner in error, with slightly later printings corrected to place page number 17 on the outside (right) bottom corner of that page. Another first printing indicator is pages 17 and 20 are printed on the wrong side of the page. For both printings: the first story page is numbered 2. Page 17 shows Bachelor Butterfly already in the whale. In most panels with 3 lines of text, the third line is indented further than the second, which is in turn indented further than the first.*

BACHELOR BUTTERFLY, THE STRANGE ADVENTURES
Brother Jonathan Press, NY: 1854 (5-1/2x10-5/8", 68 pgs, paper-c, B&W) (Very Rare)

nn - By Rodolphe Töpffer 233.00 466.00 1400.00

BACHELOR BUTTERFLY,THE STRANGE & WONDERFUL ADVENTURES OF
Dick & Fitzgerald, New York: 1870s-1888 (various printings 30 Cent cover price, 68 pgs, B&W, paper cover) (all versions Rare) (E,G)

nn - Black print on blue cover (5-1/2x10-1/2"); string bound 104.00 208.00 625.00
nn - Black print on green cover (5-1/2x10-1/2"); string bound 83.00 166.00 500.00
NOTE: *Reprints the earlier Wilson & Co. edition. Page 2 is the first story page. Page 17 shows Bachelor Butterfly already in the whale. In most panels with 3 lines of text, the second and third lines are equally indented in from the first. Unknown which cover (blue or green) is earlier.*

BACHELOR'S OWN BOOK. BEING THE PROGRESS OF MR. LAMBKIN, (GENT.) IN THE PURSUIT OF PLEASURE AND AMUSEMENT (E,O,G)
(See also PROGRESS OF MR. LAMBKIN)
D. Bogue, London: August 1, 1844 (5x8-1/4", 28 pgs printed one side only, cardboard cover & interior) (all versions Rare)

nn - First printing hand colored 200.00 400.00 1200.00
nn - First printing black & white 183.00 366.00 1100.00
NOTE: *First printing has misspellings in the title. "PURSUIT" is spelled "PERSUIT", and "AMUSEMENT" is spelled "AMUSEMEMT".*
nn - Second printing hand colored 154.00 308.00 925.00
nn - Second printing black & white 150.00 300.00 900.00
NOTE: Second printing. The misspelling of "PURSUIT" has been corrected, but "AMUSEMEMT" error is still present.
nn - Third printing hand colored No misspellings 150.00 300.00 900.00
nn - Third printing black & white 150.00 300.00 900.00
NOTE: *By George Cruikshank. This is the British Edition. Issued both in black & white, and professionally hand-colored editions. Hand-colored editions have survived in higher quantities than uncolored. Originally made with thin paper sheets covering the plates.*

BACHELOR'S OWN BOOK; OR, THE PROGRESS OF MR. LAMBKIN, (GENT.), IN THE PURSUIT OF PLEASURE AND AMUSEMENT, AND ALSO IN SEARCH OF HEALTH AND HAPPINESS, THE (E,O,G)
David Bryce & Son: Glasgow: 1884 (one shilling; 7-5/8 x5-7/8", 62 pgs printed one side only, illustrated hardcover, page edges guilt

nn - Reprints the 1844 edition with altered title 25.00 50.00 150.00
nn - soft cover edition exists 12.00 24.00 75.00

BACHELOR'S OWN BOOK. BEIN-G TWENTY-FOUR PASSAGES IN THE LIFE OF MR. LAMBKIN, GENT. (E,G)
Burgess, Stringer & Co., New York on cover; Carey & Hart, Philadelphia on title page: 1845 (31-1/4 cents, 7-1/2x4-5/8", 52 pgs, B&W, paper cover)

nn - By George Cruikshank (Very Rare) (no known sales)
NOTE: *This is the second known sequential comic book story published in America. Reprints the earlier British edition. Pages printed on one side only. New cover art by an unknown artist.*

BAD BOY'S FIRST READER (O,S)
G.W. Carleton & Co.: 1881 (5-3/4 x 4-1/8", 44 pgs, B&W, paper cover)

nn - By Frank Bellew (Senior) 42.00 84.00 250.00
NOTE: *Parody of a children's ABC primer, one cartoon illustration plus text per page. Includes one panel of Boss Tweed. Frank Bellew is considered the "Father of the American Sequential Comics."*

BALL OF YARN OR, QUEER, QUIANT & QUIZZICAL STORIES, UNRAVELED WITH NEARLY 200 COMIC ENGRAVINGS OF FREAKS, FOLLIES & FOIBLES OF QUEER FOLKS BY THAT PRINCE OF COMICS, ELTON, THE (M)
Philip. J. Cozans, 116 Nassau St, NY: early 1850s (7-1/4x3-1/2", 76 pgs, yellow-wraps)

nn - sequential comic strips plus singles (no known sales)
NOTE: Mose Keyser-r, Jones, Smith & Robinson Goes To A Ball-r; The Adventures of Mr Goliah Starvemouse-r are all sequential comic strips printed in a number of sources

BARKER'S ILLUSTRATED ALMANAC (O,P,S)
Barker, Moore & Mein Medicine Co: 1878-1932+ (36 pgs, B&W, color paper-cr)

1878-1879 (Rare) 65.00 130.00 390.00
NOTE: *Not known yet what the cover art is.*
1880 Farmer Plowing Field-c 37.00 74.00 220.00
1881-1883 (Scarce,7-3/4x6-1/8") *4-mast ships & lighthouse-c* 27.00 54.00 160.00
1884-1889 (8x6-1/4") *Horse & Rider jumping picket fence-c* 27.00 54.00 160.00
1890-1897 (8-1/8x6-1/4") 27.00 54.00 160.00
1898-1899 (7-3/8x5-7/8") 27.00 54.00 160.00
1900+: see the Platinum Age Comics section (7x5-7/8")
NOTE: *Barker's Almanacs were actually issued in November of the year preceding the year which appears on the almanac. For example, the 1878 dated almanac was issued November 1877. They were given away to retailers of Barker's farm animal medicinal products, to in turn be given away to customers. Each Barker's Almanac contains 10 full page cartoons. These frequently included racist stereotypes of blacks. Each cartoon contained advertisements for Barker's products. It is unknown whether the cartoons appeared only in the almanacs, or if they also ran as newspaper ads or flyers. Originally issued with a metal hook attached in the upper left hand corner, which could be used to hang the almanac.*

BARKER'S "KOMIC" PICTURE SOUVENIR (P,S)
Barker, Moore & Mein Medicine Co: nd (1892-94) (color cardboard cover, B&W interior) (all unnumbered editions Very Rare)

nn - (1892) (1st edition, 6-7/8x10-1/2, 150 pgs) wraparound cover showing people headed towards Chicago for the 1893 World's Fair 200.00 400.00 1200.00
nn - (1893) (2nd edition, ??? pgs) same cover as 1st edition 167.00 334.00 1000.00

nn - (1894) (3rd edition, 180 pgs, 6-3/4x10-3/8") 167.00 334.00 1000.00
NOTE: *New cover art showing crowd of people laughing with a copy of Barker's Almanac. The crowd picture is flanked on both sides by picture of a tall thin person.*
nn - (1894) (4th edition, 124 pgs, 6-3/8x9-3/8") same-c as 3rd edition 133.00 266.00 800.00
NOTE: *Essentially same-c as 3rd edition, except flanking picture on left edge is now gone. The 2nd through 4th editions state their printing on the first interior page, in the paragraph beneath the picture of the Barker's Building. These have been confirmed as premium comic books, predating the Buster Brown premiums. They reprint advertising cartoons from Barker's Illustrated Almanac. For the 50 page booklets by this same name, numbered as "Part"s, see the PLATINUM AGE SECTION. All "Editions in Parts", without exception, were published after 1900.*

BEAU OGLEBY, THE COMICAL ADVENTURES OF (E,G)
Tilt & Bogue: nd (c1843) (5-7/8x9-1/8", 72 pgs, printed one side only, green gilted hard-c, B&W)
nn - By Rodolphe Töpffer (Rare) 333.00 666.00 2000.00
nn - Hand coloured edition (Very Rare) (no known sales)
NOTE: *British Edition; no known American Edition. 2nd Töpffer comic book published in English. Translated from Paris publisher Aubert's unauthorized redrawn 1839 bootleg edition of Töpffer's* ***Histoire de Mr. Jabot****. The back most interior page is an advertisement for* ***Obadiah Oldbuck****, showing its comic book cover*

BEE, THE
Bee Publishing Co: May 16 1898-Aug 2 1898 (Chromolithographic Weekly)
most issues 33.00 66.00 200.00
8 June Yellow Kid Hearst cover issue 138.00 276.00 825.00

BEFORE AND AFTER. A LOCOFOCO CHRISTMAS PRESENT. (O, C)
D.C. Johnston, Boston: 1837 (4-3/4x3", 1 page, hand colored cardboard)
nn - (Very Rare) by David Claypoole Johnston (sold at auction for $400 in GD)
NOTE: *Pull-tab cartoon envelope, parodying the 1836 New York City mayoral election, picturing the candidate of the Locofoco Party smiling "Before the N.York election", then, when the tab is pulled, picturing him with an angry sneer "After the N.York election".*

BILLY GOAT AND OTHER COMICALITIES, THE (M)
Charles Scribner's Sons: 1898 (6-3/4x8-1/2", 116 pgs., B&W, Hardcover)
nn - By E. W. Kemble 100.00 200.00 600.00

BLACKBERRIES, THE (N.S) (see Coontown's 400)
R. H. Russell: 1897 (9"x12", 76 pgs, hard-c, every other page in color, every other page in one color sepia tone)
nn - By E. W. Kemble 333.00 666.00 2000.00
NOTE: *Tastefully done comics about Black Americana during the USA's Jim Crow days.*

BOOK OF BUBBLES, YE (S)
Endicott & Co., New York: March 1864 (6-1/4 x 9-7/8",160 pgs, guilt-illus. hard-c, B&W
nn - By unknown 108.00 216.00 650.00
NOTE: *Subtitle: A contribution to the New York Fair in aid of the Sanitary Commission; 68 single-sided pages of B&W cartoons, each with an accompanying limerick. A few are sequential.*

BOOK OF DRAWINGS BY FRED RICHARDSON (N,S)
Lakeside Press, Chicago: 1899 (13-5/8x10-1/2", 116 pgs, B&W, hard-c)
nn - 58.00 116.00 350.00
NOTE: *Reprinted from the* ***Chicago Daily News****. Mostly single panel. Includes one* ***Yellow Kid*** *parody, some Spanish-American War cartoons.*

BOTTLE, THE (E,O) (see also THE DRUNKARD'S CHILDREN, and TEA GARDEN TO TEA POT, and TEMPERANCE TALES; OR, SIX NIGHTS WITH THE WASHINGTONIANS)
D. Bogue, London, with others in later editions: nd (1846) (16-1/2x11-1/2", 16 pgs, printed one side only, paper cover)
D. Bogue, London (nd; 1846): first edition:
nn - Black & white (Scarce) 200.00 400.00 1200.00
nn - Hand colored (Rare) (no known sales)
D. Bogue, London, and Wiley and Putnam, New York (nd; 1847) : second edition, misspells American publisher "Putnam" as "Putman":
nn - Black & white (Scarce) 125.00 250.00 750.00
nn - Hand colored (Rare) (no known sales)
D. Bogue, London, and Wiley and Putnam, New York (nd; 1847) : third edition has "Putnam" spelled correctly.
nn - Black & white (Scarce) 125.00 250.00 750.00
nn - Hand colored (Rare) (no known sales)
D. Bogue, London, Wiley and Putnam, New York, and J. Sands, Sydney, New South Wales: (nd; 1847) : fourth edition with no misspellings
nn - Black & white (Scarce) 125.00 250.00 750.00
nn - Hand colored (Rare) (no known sales)
NOTE: *By George Cruikshank. Temperance/anti-alcohol story. All editions are in precisely identical format. The only difference is to be found on the cover, where it lists who published it. Cover is text only - no cover art.*

BOTTLE, THE HISTORY OF THE
J.C. Becket, 22 Grea St James St, Montreal, Canada: 1851 (9-1/8x6", B&W)
nn - From Engravings by Cruikshank 129.00 258.00 775.00
NOTE: *As published in The Canada Temperance Advocate.*

BOTTLE, THE (E)
W. Tweedie, London: nd (1862) (11-1/2x17-1/3", 16 pgs, printed one side only, paper cover)
nn - Black & white; By George Cruikshank (Scarce) 67.00 134.00 400.00
nn - Hand colored (Scarce) (no known sales)

BOTTLE, THE (E)
Geo. Gebbie, Philadelphia: nd (c.1871) (11-3/8x17-1/8", 42 pgs, tinted interior, hard-c)
nn - By George Cruikshank 67.00 134.00 400.00
NOTE: *New cover art (cover not by Cruikshank).*

BOTTLE, THE (E)
National Temperance, London: nd (1881) (11-1/2x16-1/2", 16 pgs, printed one side only, paper-c, color)
nn - By George Cruikshank 67.00 134.00 400.00
NOTE: *See Platinum Age section for 1900s printings.*

BOTTLE, THE (E)
Marques, Pittsburgh, PA: 1884/85 (6x8", 8 plates, full color, illustrated envelope)
nn - art not by Cruickshank; New Art 42.00 84.00 250.00
NOTE: Says Presented by J.M. Gusky, Dealer in Boots and Shoes

BROAD GRINS OF THE LAUGHING PHILOSOPHER
Dick & Fitzgerald,NY: 1870s
nn - (4) panel sequential strip 27.00 54.00 160.00

BROTHER JONATHAN
Wilson & Co/Benj H Day, 48 Beekman, NYC: 1839-???
July 4 1846 - ads for Obadiah & Butterfly 46.00 92.00 275.00
July 4 1856 catalog list - front cover comic strip 67.00 134.00 400.00
Xmas/New Years 1856 50.00 100.00 300.00
average large size issues 19.00 38.00 115.00
NOTE: has full page advert for Fredinand Flipper comic book116

BULL CALF, THE (P,M)
Various: nd (c1890's) (3-7/8x4-1/8", 16 pgs, B&W, paper-c)
nn - By A.B. Frost Creme Oatmeal Toilet Soap 33.00 66.00 200.00
nn - By A.B. Frost Thompson & Taylor Spice Co, Chicago 33.00 66.00 200.00
NOTE: *Reprints the popular strip story by Frost, with the art modified to place a sign for Creme Oatmeal Soap within each panel. The back cover advertises the specific merchant who gave this booklet away - multiple variations exist.*

BULL CALF AND OTHER TALES, THE (M)
Charles Scribner's Sons: 1892 (120 pgs., 6-3/4x8-7/8", B&W, illus. hard cover)
nn - By Arthur Burdett Frost 50.00 100.00 300.00
NOTE: *Blue, grey, tan hard covers known to exist.*

BULL CALF, THE STORY OF THE MAN OF HUMANITY AND THE (P,M)
C.H. Fargo & Co.: 1890 (5-1/4x6-1/4", 24 pgs, B&W, color paper-c)
nn - By A.B. Frost 33.00 66.00 200.00
NOTE: *Fargo shoe company giveaway; pages alternate between shoe advertisements and the strip story.*

BUSHEL OF MERRY THOUGHTS, A (see Mischief Book, The) (E)
Sampson Low Son & Marsten: 1868 (68 pgs, handcolored hardcover, B&W)
nn - (6-1/4 x 9-7/8", 138 pgs) red binding, publisher's name on title page only; has hand colored interior by publisher 167.00 334.00 1000.00
nn - (6-1/2 x 10", 134 pgs) green binding, publisher's name on cover & title page; has hand colored interior by publisher 167.00 334.00 1000.00
NOTE: *Cover plus story title pages designed by Leighton Brothers, based on Busch art. Translated by Harry Rogers (who is credited instead of Busch). This is a British publication, notable as the earliest known English language anthology collection of Wilhelm Busch comic strips. Page 13 of second story missing from all editions (panel dropped). Unknown which of the two editions was published first. A modern reprint, by Dover in 1971.*

BUTTON BURSTER, THE (M) (says on cover "ten cents hard cash")
M.J. Ivers & Co., 86 Nassau St., New York: 1873 (11x8-1/8", soft paper, B&W)
By various cartoonists (Very Rare) 105.00 210.00 625.00
NOTE: *Reprints from various 1873 issues of Wild Oats; has (5) different sequential comic strips: (3) by Livingston Hopkins, (1) by Thomas Worth, other one creator presently unknown; Bellew, Sr. single panel cartoons.*

BUZZ A BUZZ OR THE BEES (E)
Griffith & Farran, London: September 1872 (8-1/2x5-1/2", 168 pgs, printed one side only, orange, black & white hardcover, B&W interior)
nn - By Wilhelm Busch (Scarce) 50.00 100.00 300.00
NOTE: *Reprint published by Phillipson & Golder, Chester; text written by English to accompany Busch art.*

BUZZ A BUZZ OR THE BEES (E)
Henry Holt & Company, New York: 1873 (9x6", 96 pgs, gilted hardcover, hand colored)
nn - By Wilhelm Busch (Scarce) 50.00 100.00 300.00
NOTE: *Completely different translation than the Griffith & Farran version. Also, contains 28 additional illustrations by Park Benjamin. The lower page count is because the Henry Holt edition prints on both sides of each page, and the Griffith & Farran edition is printed one side only.*

CALENDAR FOR THE MONTH; YE PICTORIAL LYSTE OF YE MATTERS OF INTEREST FOR SUMMER READING (P,M)
S.E. Bridgman & Company, Northampton, Mass: nd (c. late 1880's-1890's) (5-5/8x7-1/4", 64 pgs, paper-c, B&W)
nn - (Very Rare) T.S. Sullivant-c/a 83.00 166.00 500.00
NOTE: *Book seller's catalog, with every other page reprinting cartoons and strips (from Life??). Art by: Chips Bellew, Gibson, Howarth, Kemble, Sullivant, Townsend, Woolf.*

CARICATURE AND OTHER COMIC ART
Harper & Brothers, NY: 1877 (9-5/16x7-1/8", 360 pgs, B&W, green hard-c)
nn - By James Parton (over 200 illustrations) 54.00 108.00 325.00
NOTE: *This is the earliest known serious history of comics & related genre from around the world produced by an American. Parton was a cousin of Thomas Nast's wife Sarah. A large portion of this book was first serialized in* ***Harper's Monthly*** *in 1875.*

CARPET BAG, THE
Snow & Wilder, later Wilder & Pickard, Boston: March 21 1851-March 26 1853
Each average issue 17.00 34.00 100.00
Samuel "Mark Twain" Clemmons issues (first app in print) 583.00 1166.00 3500.00
NOTE: *Many issues contain cartoons by DC Johnston, Frank Bellew, others; literature includes Artemus Ward's Miss Partington who had a mischevious little Katzenjammer Kids-like brat. Carpet Bag was not considered derogatory pre-Civil War.*

CARROT-POMADE (O.G)
James G. Gregory, Publisher, New York: 1864 (9x6-7/8", 36 pgs, B&W)
nn - By Augustus Hoppin 50.00 100.00 300.00
NOTE; *The story of a quack remedy for baldness, sequentially told in the format parodying ABC primers. Has protective tissue pages (not part of page count).*

CARTOONS BY HOMER C. DAVENPORT (M,N,S)
De Witt Publishing House: 1898 (16-1/8x12", 102 pgs, hard-c, B&W)
nn 75.00 150.00 450.00
NOTE: *Reprinted from Harper's Weekly and the New York Journal. Includes cartoons about the Spanish-American War. Title page reads "Davenport's Cartoons".*

CARTOONS BY WILL E. CHAPIN (P,N,S)
The Times-Mirror Printing and Binding House, Los Angeles: 1899 (15-1/4x12", 98 pgs, hard-c, B&W)
nn - scarce 75.00 150.00 450.00
NOTE: *Premium item for subscribing to the Los-Angeles Times-Mirror newspaper, from which these cartoons were reprinted. Includes cartoons about the Spanish-American War.*

CARTOONS OF OUR WAR WITH SPAIN (N,S)
Frederick A. Stokes Company: 1898 (11-1/2x10", 72 pgs, hardcover, B&W)
nn - By Charles Nelan (r-New York Herald) 37.00 74.00 220.00
nn - 2nd printing noted on copy right page 22.00 44.00 130.00

CARTOONS OF THE WAR OF 1898 (E,M,N,S)
Belford, Middlebrook & Co., Chicago: 1898 (7x10-3/8",190 pgs, B&W, hard-c)
nn 30.00 66.00 200.00
NOTE: *Reprints single panel editorial cartoons on the Spanish-American War, from American, Spanish, Latino, and European newspapers and magazines, at rate of 2 to 6 cartoons per page. Art by Bart, Berryman, Bowman,*

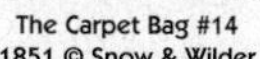

The Carpet Bag #14
1851 © Snow & Wilder

Centennial Fun (Keppler cover)
July 1876 © Frank Leslie

Comic Monthly v3 #11
April 1862 © J.C.Haney, NY

FR1.0 GD2.0 FN6.0

Bradley, Chapin, Gillam, Nelan, Tenniel, others.

CENTENNIAL FUN (O,S) (Rare)
Frank Leslie, Philadelphia: (July) 1876 (25¢, 11x8", 32 pgs, paper cover, B&W)
nn - By Joseph Keppler-c/a;Thomas Worth-a 125.00 250.00 750.00
NOTE: *Issued for the 1876 Centennial Exposition in Philadelphia. Exists with both black & white, and orange, black & white covers. One copy of the latter had an embossed newstand label from Partland, Maine, implying that the orange cover version, at least, was distributed and sold outside of Philadelphia.*

CHAMPAIGNE
Frank Leslie: June-Dec 1871
1-7 scarce 67.00 134.00 400.00

CHIC
Chic Publishing Co: 1880-81 (Chromolithographic Weekly)
1-38 Livingston Hopkins, Charles Kendrick, CW Weldon 54.00 108.00 325.00

CHILDREN'S CHRISTMAS BOOK, THE
The New York Sunday World: 1897 (10-1/4x8-3/4", 16 pgs, full color)
Dec 12, 1897 - By George Luks, G.H. Grant, Will Crawford, others) (Rare) 58.00 116.00 350.00

CHIP'S DOGS (M)
R.H. Russell and Son Publishers: 1895 hardcover, B&W)
nn - By Frank P. W. "Chip" Bellew 17.00 34.00 100.00
Early printing 80 pgs, 8-7/8x11-7/8"; dark green border of hardcover surrounds all four sides of pasted on cover image; pages arranged in error -- see NOTE below. (more scarce)
nn - By Frank P. W. "Chip" Bellew 8.00 16.00 50.00
Later printing 72 pgs, 8-7/8x11-3/4";green border only on the binding side (one side) of the cover image.
NOTE: *Both are strip reprints from* ***LIFE***. *The difference in page count is due to more blank pages in the first printing -- all printings have the same comics contents, but with the pages in the first printing arranged differently. This is noticeable particularly in the 2-page strip "Getting a Pointer", which appears on the 2nd & 3rd to last pages of the later printings, but in the early printing the first half of this strip is near the middle of the book, while the last half appears on the 2nd to last story page.*

CHIP'S OLD WOOD CUTS (M,S)
R.H. Russell & Son: 1895 (8-7/8x11-3/4", 72 pgs, hardcover, B&W)
nn - By Frank P. W. ("Chip") Bellew 25.00 50.00 150.00
nn - 1897 reprint 13.00 26.00 75.00

CHIP'S UN-NATURAL HISTORY (O,S)
Frederick A. Stokes & Brother: 1888 (7x5-1/4", 64 pgs, hardcover, B&W)
nn - By Frank P. W. ("Chip") Bellew 10.00 20.00 60.00
NOTE: *Title page lists publisher as "Successors to White, Stokes & Allen."*

CLOWN, OR THE BANQUET OF WIT, THE (E,M,O)
Fisher & Brother, Philadelphia, Baltimore, New York, Boston: nd (c.1851) (7-3/8x4-1/2", 88 pgs, paper cover, B&W)
nn - (Very Rare; 3 known copies) 483.00 966.00 2900.00
NOTE: *Earliest known multi-artist anthology of sequential comics; contains multiple sequential comics, plus numerous single panel cartoons. A mixture of reprinted and original material, involving both European and American artists. "Jones, Smith, and Robinson Goes to a Ball" by Richard Doyle (1st app. of Doyle's "Foreign Tour" in America, reprinted from PUNCH, August 24, 1850); "Moses Keyser The Bowery Bully's Trip to the Californian Gold Mines", by John H. Manning; "The Adventures of Mr. Gulp" (by the Read brothers?); more comics by artists unknown; cartoons by George Cruikshank, Grandville, Elton.*

COLD CUTS AND PICKLED EELS' FEET; DONE BROWN BY JOHN BROWN
P.J. Cozans, New York: nd (c1855-60) (B&W)
nn - (Very Rare) 63.00 126.00 375.00
NOTE: *Mostly a children's book. But, pages 87 to 110, and 111 to 122, contain narrative sequential stories.*

COLLEGE SCENES (O,G)
N. Hayward, Boston: 1850 (5x6-3/4", 72 pgs, printed one side only, B&W lithography)
nn - (Rare) by Nathan Hayward 129.00 258.00 775.00
NOTE: *This is the 2nd such production for an American University; the first issued at Yale circa 1845, decent funny art of story about life of a Harvard student from his entrance thru graduation entirely in caricature. Has art on back cover as well.*

COLLEGE CUTS Chosen From The Columbia Spectator 1880-81-82 (S)
White & Stokes, NY: 1882 (8x9-5/8", 92 pgs, B&W)
By F. Benedict Herzog, H. McVickar, W. Bard McVickar, others 21.00 42.00 125.00
nn - 2nd edition reprint (1888) (8-1/4x10-3/8) 8.00 16.00 50.00

COMICAL COONS (M)
R.H. Russell: 1898 (8-7/8 x 11-7/8", 68 pgs, hardcover, B&W)
nn - By E. W. Kemble 300.00 600.00 1800.00
NOTE: *Black Americana collection of 2-panel stories.*

COMICAL ALMANAC
Anton Bicker, Cincinnati, OH: 1885 (9x6, 260 pgs, B&W, illustrated-c)
nn - two (12) page sequential Busch comic strips 50.00 100.00 300.00

COMIC ALMANAC, THE
John Berger. Baltimore: 1854-? (7-1/2x6-1/4, 36 pgs, B&W)
nn - 50.00 100.00 300.00

COMIC ANNUAL, AMERICAN (O,I)
Richardson, Lord, & Holbrook, Boston: 1831 (6-7/8x4-3/8", 268 pgs, B&W, hard-c)
nn - (Scarce) 125.00 250.00 750.00
NOTE: *Mostly text; front & back cover illustrations, 13 full page, and scattered smaller illustrations by David Claypoole Johnston; edited by Henry J. Finn.*

COMIC HISTORY OF THE UNITED STATES, (I)
Carleton & Co., NY: 1876 (6-7/8x5-1/8", 336 pgs, hardcover, B&W)
nn - By Livingston Hopkins. 20.00 40.00 120.00
2nd printing: Cassell, Petter, Galpin & Co.: 1880 (6-7/8x5-1/8", 336 pgs, hardcover, B&W)
nn - By Livingston Hopkins. 17.00 34.00 100.00
NOTE: *Text with many B&W illustrations; some are multi-panel comics. Not to beconfused with* ***Bill Nye's Comic History Of The U.S.*** *which contains Frederick Opper illustrations.*

COMIC MONTHLY, THE
J.C. Haney, N.Y.: March 1859-1880 (16 x 11-1/2", 30 pgs average, B&W)
Certain average issues with sequential comics 40.00 80.00 240.00
11 (Jan 1860) Bellew-c 20.00 40.00 120.00
v2#2 (Apr 1860) Bellew-c 20.00 40.00 120.00
v2#3 (May 1860) Bellew-c 20.00 40.00 120.00
v2#4 (June 1860) Comic Strip Cover 40.00 80.00 240.00
v2#5 (July 1860) Bellew-c; (12) panel Explaining American Politics To An Intelligent Foreigner; (10) panel The Art of Stump Speaking; (15) panel Mr. Dibbs Goes to Pike's Peak and Comes Back Again 88.00 176.00 525.00
v2#7 (Sept 1860) Comic Strip Cover; (24) panel double page spread The Prince of Wales In America 40.00 80.00 240.00
v2#8 (18) panel The Three Young Friends Sillouette Strip 20.00 40.00 120.00
v2#9 (Nov 1860) (9) panel sequential 20.00 40.00 120.00
v2#10 11 not indexed 20.00 40.00 120.00
v2#12 (Jan 1861) (12) panel double page spread 20.00 40.00 120.00

COMIC TOKEN FOR 1836, A COMPANION TO THE COMIC ALMANAC, THE
Charles Ellms, Boston: 1836 (8x5', 48 pgs, B&W)
nn - 40.00 80.00 240.00

COMIC WEEKLY, THE
???, NYC: 1881-???
issues with comic strips (Chips, etc) 46.00 92.00 275.00

COMIC WORLD
???: 1876-1879 (Quarto Monthly)
issues with comic strips 46.00 92.00 275.00

COMICS FROM SCRIBNER'S MAGAZINE (M)
Scribner's: nd (1891) (10 cents, 9-1/2x6-5/8", 24 pgs, paper cover, side stapled, B&W)
nn - (Rare) F.M.Howarth C&A 120.00 240.00 725.00
NOTE: *Advertised in SCRIBNER'S MAGAZINE in the June 1891 issue, page 793, as available by mail order for 10 cents. Collects together comics material which ran in the back pages of Scribner's Magazine. Art by Attwood, "Chip" Bellew, Dōes, Frost, Gibson, Zim.*

COMUS OFFERING CONTAINING HUMOROUS SCRAPS OF DIVERTING COMICALITIES, THE (O, S)
B. Franklin Edmands, 25 Court St, Boston: c1830-31 (8-7/8x10-3/4", 16 pgs, thin brown paper-c, blank on backs,
nn - (William F Straton, Engraver, 15 Water St, Boston) (no known sales)
NOTE: All hand-colored single panel cartoons format definitely inspired by D.C. Johnston's Scraps with every panel character using well-defined word balloons. Might become a seminal step in the evolution of the American comic book. More research is needed.

CONTRASTS AND CONCEITS FOR CONTEMPLATION BY LUKE LIMNER (O)
Ackerman & Co, 96 Strand, London: c1848 (9-3/4x6-1/4, 48 pgs, B&W)
nn - By John Leighton 42.00 84.00 250.00

COONTOWN'S 400 (M) (see **Blackberries**) (M)
The Life (Magazine) Co.: 1899 (10-15/16x8-7/8, 68 pgs, cloth light-brown hard-c, B&W
nn - By E.W. Kemble (scarce) 350.00 700.00 2100.00
NOTE: *Tastefully drawn depictions of Black Americana over one hundred years ago during Jim Crow days.*

CROSSING THE ATLANTIC (O,G)
James R. Osgood & Co., Boston: 1872 (10-7/8x16", 68 pgs, hardcover, B&W);
Houghton, Osgood & Co., Boston: 1880
1st printing - by Augustus Hoppin 33.00 66.00 200.00
2nd printing (1880; 66 pgs; 8-1/8x11-1/8") 25.00 50.00 150.00

C.R. PITT'S COMIC ALMANAC
C.R. Pitt: 1880 (7-1/2x4-5/8", 28 pgs)
nn - contains (8) panel sequential 36.00 72.00 215.00

CRUIKSHANK'S OMNIBUS: A VEHICLE FOR FUN AND FROLIC (E,S)
E. Ferrett & Co., Philadelphia: 1845 (25 cents, 7-1/2" x 4-5/8", 96 pgs, B&W, paper-c)
nn - By George Cruikshank c/a (Very Rare) 142.00 284.00 850.00
NOTE: *Mostly prose, with 10 plates of cartoons printed on one-side (about half the plates with multiple cartoons), plus illustrated cover, all by George Cruikshank. First (perhaps only) American printing of Cruikshank's Omnibus, which was published first in Britain. It is only a partial reprinting.*

CYCLISTS' DICTIONARY (S)
Morgan & Wright, Chicago: 1894 (5 x3-3/4, 80 pgs, soft-c, B&W
nn - By Unknown 33.00 66.00 200.00

THE DAILY GRAPHIC
The Graphic Company, 39 Park Place, NY: 1873-Sept 23, 1889 (14x20-1/2, 8 pgs, B&W)
Average issues with comic strips 21.00 42.00 125.00
Average issues without comic strips 7.00 14.00 40.00

DAVY CROCKETT'S COMIC ALMANACK
???, Nashville, TN, then elsewhere: 1835-end (32 pages plus wraps)
1 450.00 900.00 2700.00
2-13 15 end 283.00 566.00 1700.00
14 contains (17) panel Crocket comic strip bio 1848 567.00 1134.00 3400.00

DAY'S DOINGS (was The Last Sensation) (Becomes New York Illustrated Times)
James Watts, NYC: #1 June 6 1868-early 1876 (11x16, 16 pgs, B&W)

average issue with comic strips 5.00 10.00 30.00
Paul Pry & Alley Sloper character issues 17.00 34.00 100.00
Aug 19 1871 - First Alley Sloper in America?? 33.00 66.00 200.00
NOTE: *James Watts was a shadow company for Frank Leslie; outright sold to Frank Leslie in 1873. There are a lot of issues with comic strips from 1868 up.*

DAY'S SPORT - OR, HUNTING ADVENTURES OF S. WINKS WATTLES, A SHOPKEEPER, THOMAS TITT, A "LEGAL GENT," AND MAJOR NICHOLAS NOGGIN, A JOLLY GOOD FELLOW GENERALLY, A (O)
Brother Jonathan, NY: c1850s (5-7/8x8-1/4, 44 pgs)

nn - By Henry L. Stephens, Philadelphia (Very Rare) (no known sales)

DEVIL'S COMICAL OLDMANICK WITH COMIC ENGRAVINGS OF THE PRINCIPAL EVENTS OF TEXAS, THE
Turner & Fisher, NY & Philadelphia: 1837 (7-7/8x5", 24 pgs)

nn - many single panel cartoons 96.00 192.00 575.00

DIE VEHME, ILLUSTRIRTES WOCHENBLATT FUR SCHERZ UND ERNEST (M,O)
Heinrich Binder, St. Louis: No.1 Aug 28, 1869 - No.?? Aug 20, 1870 (10 cents, 8 pgs, B&W, paper-c) (see also PUCK)

1-?? (Very Rare) by Joseph Keppler 71.00 142.00 425.00
NOTE: *Joseph Keppler's first attempt at a weekly American humor periodical. Entirely in German. The title translates into: **"The Star Chamber: An Illustrated Weekly Paper in Fun and Ernest"**.*

DOMESTIC MANNERS OF THE AMERICANS
The Imprint Society, Barre, Mass: 1969 (9-3/4 x 7-1/4", 390 pgs, hard-c in slipcase, B&W)

nn - 12.00 24.00 70.00
NOTE: *Reprints the 1832 edition of this book by Mrs. Trollope with an added insert. The 28-page insert is what is of primary interest to us -- it reproduces SCRAPS No. 4 (1833) by D.C. Johnston.*

DRUNKARD'S CHILDREN, THE (see also THE BOTTLE) (E,O)
David Bogue, London; John Wiley and G.P. Putnam, New York; J. Sands, Sydney, New South Wales: July 1, 1848 (16x11", 16 pgs, printed on one side only, paper-c)

nn - Black & white edition (Scarce) 217.00 434.00 1300.00
nn - Hand colored edition (Rare) (no known sales)
NOTE: *Sequel story to THE BOTTLE, by George Cruikshank. Temperance/anti-alcohol story. British-American-Australian co-publication. Cover is text only - no cover art.*

DRUNKARD'S PROGRESS, OR THE DIRECT ROAD TO POVERTY, WRETCHEDNESS & RUIN, THE
J. W. Barber, New Haven, Conn.: Sept 1826 (single sheet)

nn - By John Warner Barber (Very Rare) (no known sales)
NOTE: *Broadside designed and printed by barber contains four large wood engravings showing "The Morning Dram" which is "The Beginning of Sorrow"; "The Grog Shop" with its "Bad Company"; "The Confirmed Drunkard" in a state of "Beastly Intoxication"; and the "Concluding Scene" with the family being drive off to the alms house. It is an interesting set of cuts, faintly reminiscent of Hogarth. Many modern reprints exist.*

DUEL FOR LOVE, A (O,P)
E.C. DeWitt & Co., Chicago: nd (c1880's) (3-3/8" x 2-5/8", 12 pgs, B&W, paper-c)

nn - Art by F.M. Howarth (Rare) 25.00 50.00 150.00
NOTE: *Advertising giveaway for DeWitt's Little Early Risers, featuring an 8-panel strip story, spread out 1 panel per page.*

DURHAM WHIFFS (O, P)
Blackwells Durham Tobacco Co: Jan 8 1878 (9x6.5", 8 pgs, color-c, B&W)

v1 #1 w/Trade Card Insert 117.00 234.00 700.00
NOTE: Sold in 2008 CGC 9.4 $1250

DYNALENE LAFLETS (P)
The Dynalene Company: nd (3 x 3-1/2", 16 pgs, B&W, paper cover)

nn - Dynalene Dyes promo (9) panel comic strip 17.00 34.00 100.00

ELEPHANT, THE
William H Graham, Tribune Building, NYC: Jan 22 1848-Feb 19 1848 (11x8.5", B&W)

1-5 Rare - single panel cartoons 117.00 234.00 700.00

ELTON'S COMIC ALL-MY-NACK (E,O,S)
Elton, Publisher, 18 Division & 98 Nassau St, NY: 1833-1852 (7-1/2x4-1/2", 36pgs, B&W

1-5 99% single panel cartoons 79.00 158.00 475.00
6 (1839) 79.00 158.00 475.00
NOTE: Two different covers & different interiors exist for this title and number
7-15 - 99% single panel cartoons 71.00 142.00 425.00
16 - contains 6 panel "A Tales of A Tayl-or" 1848-49 117.00 234.00 700.00
17 - contains "Moses Keyser, The Bowery Bully's Trip To the California Gold Mines" 1850
By John H. Manning, early comics creator, told in 15 panels 117.00 234.00 700.00
18-19 presently unknown contents 75.00 150.00 450.00
NOTE: *Contains both original American, and pirated European, cartoons. All single panel material, except where noted. Almanacs are published near the end of the year prior to that for which they are printed -- like calendars today. Thus, the 1833 No. 1 issue was really published in the last months of 1832. #17 has Elton's Californian Comic-All-My-Nack on the cover.*

ELTON'S COMIC ALMANAC (Publsiher change)
GW Cottrell & Co, Publishers & C Cornhill, Boston, Mass: 1853 (7-7/8x4-5/8,36pgs,B&W
20 - (2) sequential comic strips (9) panel "Jones, Smith and Robinson Goes To A Ball; (21) panel "The Adventures of Mr. Gulp" Rare 250.00 500.00 1500.00
NOTE: *Both strips appear in* The Clown, Or The Banquet of Wit

ELTON'S FUNNY ALMANACK (title change to Almanac)
Elton Publisher and Engraver, New York: 1846 (8x6-1/2", 36 pgs)

1 54.00 108.00 325.00

ELTON'S FUNNY ALMANAC (#1 titled Almanack)
Elton & Co, New York: 1847-1853 (8x6-1/4, 36 pgs, B&W)
2 (1847) #3 (1848) 54.00 108.00 325.00
nn 1853 (8-1/8x4-7/8"; (5) panel comic strip "The Adventures of Mr. Goliah Starvemouse"

ELTON'S RIPSNORTER COMIC ALMANAC
Elton, 90 Nassau St, NY: 1850 (8x5, 24 pgs, B&W, paper-c)
nn - scarce 54.00 108.00 325.00

ENGLISH SOCIETY (S)
Harper & Brothers, Publishers, New York: 1897 (9-5/8x12-1/4", 206 pgs, B&W)

nn - by George Du Maurier 20.00 40.00 120.00

ENGLISH SOCIETY AT HOME (S)
James R. Osgood and Company: 1881 (10-7/8x8-5/8, 182 pgs, protective sheets on some pages - not included in pages count, hard-c, B&W)

nn - by George Du Maurier 20.00 40.00 120.00

ESQUIRE BROWN AND HIS MULE, STORY OF
A.C. Meyer, Baltimore, Maryland: 1880s (5x3/7/8", 28 pgs, B&W)

Booklet (9 panel story plus cough remedies catalog) 27.00 54.00 160.00
Fold-Out of Booklet (9 panel version) 27.00 54.00 160.00

"EVENTS OF THE WEEK" REPRINTED FROM THE CHICAGO TRIBUNE
Henry O. Shepard Co, Chicago: 1894 (5-3/8x15-7/8", 110 pg, B&W, hard-c)

First Series, Second Series - By HR Heaton 27.00 54.00 160.00

EVERYBODY'S COMICK ALMANACK
Turner & Fisher, NY & Philadelphia: 1837 (7-7/8x5", 36 pgs, B&W)

nn 42.00 84.00 250.00

EVOLUTION OF A DEMOCRAT - A DARWINIAN TALE, THE (O,G)
Paquet & Co., New York: 1888 (25 cents, 7-7/8x5-1/2", 100 pgs, printed one side only, orange paper cover, B&W) (Very Rare)

nn - Written by Henry Liddell, art by G. Roberty 267.00 534.00 1600.00
NOTE: *Political parody about the rise of an Irishman through Tammany Hall. Grover Cleveland appears as linked with Tammany. Ireland becomes the next state in the USA.*

FABLES FOR THE TIMES (S, I)
R.H. Russell & Son, New York: 1896 (9-1/8x12-1/8", 52 pgs, yellow hard-c)

nn - By H.W. Phillips and T.S. Sullivant Scarce 50.00 100.00 300.00

FERDINAND FLIPPER, ESQ., THE FORTUNES OF (O,G)
Brother Jonathan, Publisher, NY: nd (1851) (5-3/4 x 9-3/8", 84 pgs, B&W, printed both sides)

nn - By Various (Very Rare) 600.00 1200.00 3600.00
NOTE: *Extended title: "...Commencing With A Period of Four Months And Anterior To His Birth Going Thru The Various Stages of His Infancy, Childhood, Verdant Years, Manhood, Middle Life, and Green and Ripe Old Age, And Ending A Short Time Subsequent to His Sudden Decease With His Final Exit, Funeral And Burial." Extremely unique comic book, put together by gathering 145 independent single illustrations and cartoons, by various artists, and stringing them together into a sequential story. The majority of panels are by Grandville. Also included are at least 19 signed Charles Martin, reprinted from 1847 issues of Yankee Doodle, 5 panels from D.C. Johnston, plus other panels by F.O.C. Darley, T.H. Matheson, and others. The story also contains several panels of Gold Rush content . Printed by E.A. Alverds. The 1851 date is derived from an advertisement found in the Oct-Dec 1851 issue of the Brother Jonathan newspaper. It ispossible, however, that it actually came out even earlier.*

FERDINAND FLIPPER, ESQ., THE FORTUNES OF (G)
Dick & Fitzgerald, New York: nd (1870's to 1888) (30 Cents, 84 pgs, B&W, paper cover)

nn - (Very Rare reprint - several editions possible) 333.00 666.00 2000.00

FINN'S COMIC ALMANAC
Marsh, Capen, & Lyon; Boston: 1835-??? (4.5x7.5, 36 pgs, B&W)

nn 65.00 130.00 390.00

FINN'S COMIC SKETCHBOOK (S)
Peabody & Co., 223 Broadway, NY: 1831 (10-1/2x16", 12 pgs, B&W)

nn - By Henry J. Finn (Very Rare) (An incomplete copy sold for $1375 in Oct. 2014)
NOTE: *Designs on copper plates; etched by J. Harris, NY; should have tissue paper in front of each plate.*

50 GREAT CARTOONS (M,P,S)
Ram's Horn Press: 1895 (14x10-3/4, 112 pgs, hard-c)

nn - By Frank Beard 21.00 42.00 125.00
NOTE: *Premium in return for a subscription to **The Ram's Horn** magazine.*

FISHER'S COMIC ALMANAC
Ames Fisher and Brother, No 12 North Sixth St, Philadelphia , Charles Small in NYC, Also in Boston: 1841-1873 (4-1/2 x 7-1/4, 36 pgs, B&W)

1-7 (1841-1847) 80.00 160.00 475.00
12 reprints mermaid-c with word balloon (1868) 80.00 160.00 475.00

F**** A*** K*****, OUTLINES ILLUSTRATIVE OF THE JOURNAL OF** (O,S)
D.C. Johnston, Boston: 1835 (9-5/16 x 6", 12 pgs, printed one side only, blue paper cover, B&W interior) (see also **SCRAPS**)

nn - by David Claypoole Johnston (Scarce) 300.00 600.00 1800.00
NOTE: *This is a series of 8 plates parodying passages from the Journal of Fanny (Frances) A. Kemble, a British woman who wrote a highly negative book about American Culture after returning from the U.S. Though remembered now for her campaign against slavery, she was prejudiced against most everything American culture, thus inspiring Johnston's satire. Contains 4 protective sheets (not part of page count.)*

FLYING DUTCHMAN; OR, THE WRATH OF HERR VONSTOPPELNOZE, THE (E)
Carleton Publishing, New York: 1862 (7-5/8x5-1/4", 84 pgs, printed on one side only, gilted hardcover, B&W)

nn - By Wilhelm Busch (Scarce) 29.00 58.00 175.00
nn - 1975 Scarce 100 copy-r 74 pgs Visual Studies Workshop 3.00 6.00 20.00
NOTE: *This is the earliest known English language book publication of a Wilhelm Busch work. The story is plagiarized by American poet John G. Saxe, who is credited with the text, while the uncredited Busch cartoons are described merely as accompanying illustrations.*

FLYING LEAVES (E)
E.R. Herrick & Company, New York: nd (c1889/1890's) (8-1/4" x 11-1/2", 76 pgs, B&W interior, orange, b&w hard-c)

nn- (Scarce) 43.00 86.00 260.00
NOTE: *Reprints strips and single panel cartoons from 1888 Fliegende Blatter issues, translated into English. Various artists, including Bechstein, Adolf Hengeler, Lothar Meggendorfer, Emil Reinicke.*

FOOLS PARADISE WITH THE MANY ADVENTURES THERE AS SEEN IN THE STRANGE SURPRISING PEEP SHOW OF PROFESSOR WOLLEY COBBLE, THE (E)
(see also THE COMICAL PEEP SHOW)
John Camden Hotten, London: Nov 1871 (1 crown, 9-7/8x7-3/8", 172 pgs, printed one side only, gilted green hardcover, hand colored interior)

nn - By Wilhelm Busch (Rare) 350.00 700.00 2100.00
NOTE: *Title on cover is: **WALK IN! WALK IN!! JUST ABOUT TO BEGIN!!! the FOOLS PARADISE**; below the above title page. Anthology of Wilhelm Busch comics, translated into English.*

FOOLS PARADISE WITH THE MANY WONDERFUL SIGHTS AS SEEN IN THE STRANGE SURPRISING PEEP SHOW OF PROFESSOR WOLLEY COBBLE, FURTHER ADVENTURES IN (E)
Chatto & Windus, London: 1873 (10x7-3/8", 128 pgs, printed one side only, brown hardcover, hand colored interior)

nn - By Wilhelm Busch (Rare) 283.00 566.00 1700.00
NOTE: *Sequel to the 1871 **FOOLS PARADISE**, containing a completely different set of Busch stories, translated into English.*

The Daily Graphic #158
Sept. 4, 1873 © The Graphic Company, NY

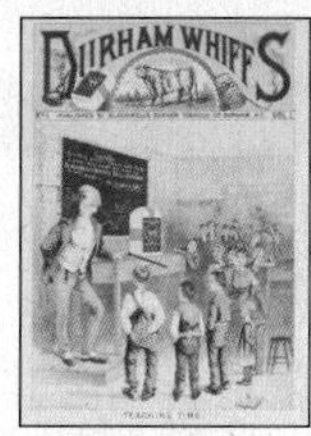

Durham Whiffs #1
1878 © Blackwells

Funny Folk by F.M. Howarth
1899© E.P. Dutton

FOOLS PARADISE MIRTH AND FUN FOR THE OLD & YOUNG (E)
Griffith & Farran, London: May 1883 (9-3/4x7-5/8", 78 pgs, color cover, color interior)
nn - By Wilhelm Busch (Rare) 92.00 184.00 550.00
NOTE: *Collection of selected stories reprinted from both the 1871 & 1873* ***FOOLS PARADISE.***

FOOLS PARADISE - MIRTH AND FUN FOR THE OLD & YOUNG (E)
E.P. Dutton and Co., NY: May 1883 (9-3/4x7-5/8", 78 pgs, color cover, color interior)
nn - By Wilhelm Busch (Rare) 83.00 166.00 500.00
NOTE: *Collection of selected stories reprinted from both the 1871 & 1873* ***FOOLS PARADISE.***

FOREIGN TOUR OF MESSRS. BROWN, JONES, AND ROBINSON, THE (see Messrs...,)

FRANK LESLIE'S BOYS AND GIRLS
Frank Leslie, NYC: Oct 13 1866-#905 Feb 9 1884
average issue with comic strip 11.00 22.00 65.00

FRANK LESLIE'S BUDGET OF FUN
Frank Leslie, Ross & Tousey, 121 Nassau St, NYC: Jan 1859-1878 (newspaper size)
1-5 no comic strips 50.00 100.00 300.00
6 June 1859 (9) panel "The Wonderful Hunting Tour of Mr Borridge After the Deer" 83.00 163.00 500.00
7-9 no comic strips 27.00 54.00 160.00
10 Sept 1859 sequential comic strip 48.00 96.00 290.00
11 (8) panel sequential "Apropos of the Great Eastern" 48.00 96.00 290.00
12-14 27.00 54.00 160.00
15 Feb 1860 (12) panel "The Ballet Girl" strip 48.00 96.00 290.00
16-18 27.00 54.00 160.00
19 June 1860 comic strip front cover 79.00 158.00 475.00
NOTE: Cover is (11) panel "The Very Latest Fashionable Amusement..."; Back cover comic strip "Mr Jogg's Reasons For Preferring to Board to Keeping House" (7) panels using word balloons. Plus centerfold double page (18) panel spread "The New York May, Moving in General, and Mrs. Grundy's In Particular."
20 24 25 no comic strips 27.00 54.00 160.00
21 (7/15/60) (8) panel Mr Septimus Verdilater Visits the Baltimore Convention" 48.00 96.00 290.00
22 (8/1/60) (3) panel 27.00 54.00 160.00
23 (8/15/60) (12) panel "Superb Scheme For Perfecting of Dramatic Entertainment" 48.00 96.00 290.00
25 (9/15/60 (9) panel sequential 27.00 54.00 160.00
27 AbrahamLincoln Word Balloon cover 48.00 96.00 290.00
28 Wilhelm Busch sequential strip-r begin 48.00 96.00 290.00
29, 31-51 27.00 54.00 160.00
30 (12/15/60) (3) panel sequential strip 27.00 54.00 160.00
31 (Jan 1861) (12) panel The Boarding School Miss 27.00 54.00 160.00
32 (Feb 1861) (10) panel Telegraphic Horrors; Or, Mr Buchanan Undergoing A Series of Electric Shocks 50.00 100.00 300.00
35 (4/1/61) Abraham Lincoln Word Balloon cover 50.00 100.00 300.00
43 44 no sequential comic strips 27.00 54.00 160.00
45 (Nov 1861) (6) panel sequential; (11) panel The Budget Army and Infantry Tactics; First Bellew here? - Many Bellew full pagers begin 48.00 96.00 290.00
48 (Feb 1862) Bellew-c; (2) panel Bellew strip plus singles 48.00 96.00 290.00
49 (Mar 1862) Bellew-c; (16) panel Wilhelm Busch "The Fly Or The Disturbed Dutchman A Story without Words" 48.00 96.00 290.00
50 (April 1862) Bellew-c "Succession Bath" plus singles 27.00 54.00 160.00
51 (May 1862) Bellew-c; (25) panel Busch The Toothache (6) panel Definitions of the Day 48.00 96.00 290.00
52 (June 1862) Bellew-c; (9) panel A Cock & A Bull Expedition; (6) panel Bellew The First Campaign of the Home Guard 48.00 96.00 290.00
NOTE: Johnny Bull & Louis Napoleon with Brother Jonathan
53-67 To Be Indexed in the Future 28.00 56.00 170.00
68 (11/18///63) (6) panel Bellew strip "Cuts On Cowards" 28.00 56.00 170.00
NOTE: contains (1) panel William Newman 1817-1870, mentor to Thomas Nast
71 (Feb 1864) Word Balloon Jefferson Davis-c 28.00 56.00 170.00
72 (Mar 1864) Word Balloon-c 28.00 56.00 170.00
73 (April 1864) Word Balloon-c in (6) panels 28.00 56.00 170.00
74 (May 1864) Newman Word Balloon-c 28.00 56.00 170.00
75 77 78 no sequentials 28.00 56.00 170.00
76 (July 1864) Newman Word Balloon-c 28.00 56.00 170.00
79 (Oct 1864) Word Balloon-c 28.00 56.00 170.00
80 (Nov 1864) Robt E Lee & Jeff Davis-c; no sequentials 28.00 56.00 170.00
81 (Dec 1864) Word Balloon "Abyss of War"-c 28.00 56.00 170.00
83 (2/18/65) Back-c (6) panel "Petroleum" 28.00 56.00 170.00
84 (Mar 1865) (6) panel sequential 28.00 56.00 170.00
85 (Apr 1865) Word Balloon-c 28.00 56.00 170.00
86 89 90 92 no sequentials 28.00 56.00 170.00
88 (7/6/65) (6) panel "Marriage" 28.00 56.00 170.00
91 (Oct 1865) (6) panel "Brief Confab At The Corner 28.00 56.00 170.00
93-98 yet to be indexed 28.00 56.00 170.00
99 (June 1866) (18) panel Mr Paul Peters Adventures While Trout-Fishing In The Adirondacks 48.00 96.00 290.00
100 (July 1866) (4) panel sequential comic strip 24.00 48.00 145.00
102 (Sept 1866) (6) panel sequential comic strip 24.00 48.00 145.00
103 (Oct 1866) (9) panel strip; (12) pane;l back cover Adventures of McTiffin At Long Branch 48.00 96.00 290.00
104 (Nov 1866) (4) panel; (23) panel "The Budget Rebuses; (2) panel Glut On Treason Market;back-c; (6) sequential strip 27.00 54.00 160.00
105 (12/18/66) Word Balloon-c; (20) panel sequential back-c 30.00 60.00 180.00
NOTE: Artists include William Newman (1863-1868), William Henry Shelton, Joseph Keppler (1873-1876), James A. Wales (1876-1878), Frederick Burr Opper (1878).

FRANK LESLIE'S LADY'S MAGAZINE
Frank Leslie, NYC: Feb 1863-Dec 1882 (8.5x12", typically 152 pgs)
issues with comic strips 12.00 24.00 70.00

FRANK LESLIE'S PICTORIAL WEEKLY
Frank Leslie, Ross & Tousey, 121 Nassau St, NYC:
average issue (Very Rare) 42.00 84.00 250.00

FRANK TOUSEY'S NEW YORK COMIC MONTHLY
Frank Tousey, NYC: (no known sales)

FREAKS
???, Philadelphia: Jan 8, 1881-April? 1881 (Chromolithographic Weekly)
(Very Rare) 100.00 200.00 600.00

FREELANCE, THE
A.M. Soteldo Jr, Edito, 292 Broadway, NYC: 1874-75 (Folio Weekly)
(Rare) 19.00 38.00 115.00

FREE MASONRY EXPOSED
Winchell & Small, 113 Fulton, NY: 1871 (7-5/8x10-1/2", 36pgs, blue paper-c, B&W)
nn- Thomas Worth Scarce 96.00 192.00 575.00
NOTE: Scathing satircal look at Free Masons thru many cartoons, their power waning by the 1870s

FREETHINKERS' PICTORIAL TEXT-BOOK, THE (S,O)
The Truth Seeker Company, New York: 1890, 1896, 1898 (9x12, hard-c, B&W)
1 (1890 edition) - Scarce 382 pgs By Watson Heston 192.00 384.00 1150.00
1 (1896 edition) - Scarce 378 pgs By Watson Heston (1890-r) 104.00 208.00 625.00
2 (1898 edition) - Scarce 408 pgs By Watson Heston 104.00 208.00 625.00
NOTE: *Sought after by collectors of Freethought/Atheism material. There is also 200 copy Modern Reprint.*

FRITZ SPINDLE-SHANKS, THE RAVEN BLACK
Cosack & C o, Buffalo, NY: 1870/80s (4-3/8x2-3/4", color)
(10) card comic strip set by Wilhelm Busch 18.00 36.00 110.00

FUN BY RALL
Unknown: circa 1865 (11x7-7/8", 68 pgs, soft-c, B&W)
nn - By presently unknown (Very Rare) 83.00 166.00 500.00
NOTE: *Wraparound soft cover like modern comic book; yellow paper cover with red & black ink.*

FUN FOR THE FAMILY IN PICTURES
D. Lothrop and Company: 1886 (4 x 7", 48 pgs, Silver & Red stiff-c; interior pages have various single color inks)
nn - By unknown hand 42.00 84.00 250.00
NOTE: *Single panel cartoons and sequential stories.*

FUN FROM LIFE
Frederick A Stokes & Brother, New York: 1889 (9 1/8 by 7 1/8, 72 pages, hard-c)
nn - Mostly by Frank "Chips" Bellew Jr 42.00 84.00 250.00
NOTE: *Contains both single panel and many sequential comics reprints from Life.*

FUNNYEST OF AWL AND THE FUNNIEST SORT OF PHUN, THE
AT Bellew Or W. Jennings Demorest, 121 Nassau St, NY : 1865-67 (30 issues, 16x11 tabloid 16 pgs B&W Monthly, 1-8 © American News; 9-on © A.T. Bellews)
1 (April 1864) Bellew-c 40.00 80.00 240.00
4 (1865) Bellew-c 38.00 76.00 225.00
5 (1865) Busch (20) panel comic srtip The Toothache 67.00 134.00 400.00
7 (1865) Bellew-c 38.00 76.00 225.00
8 (1865) Special Petroleum oil issue - much cartoon art 83.00 166.00 500.00
9 (July 1865) Bellew Bullfrog-c; centerfold double page spread hanging many Confederates; (6) panel strip hanging Jeff Davis 83.00 166.00 500.00
10 (Aug 1865) Bellew-c (13) panel Busch strip with two ducks, a frog and a butcher who gets the ducks in the end 83.00 166.00 500.00
11 (Sept 1865) Bellew Bull Frog Anti-French-c 38.00 76.00 225.00
13 14 15 (12/65-1/66) Bellew-c no sequential comic strips 38.00 76.00 225.00
16 (March 1866) address change to 39 Park Ave 38.00 76.00 225.00
22 (Sept 1866) 133 Nassau St 38.00 76.00 225.00
34 (Oct 1867) 133 Nassau St (7) panel Baseball comic strip; Last Known Issue - were there more? 83.00 166.00 500.00
NOTE: *Radical Republican politics distributed by Great American News Company; owned by Frank Bellew's wife as a front for her husband. When the Civil War ended, the brutal anti-Confederate comic strips and jokes switched to frogs and began attacking France. Funny thing, history says without France's help in the 1700s, there just might not have been a United States.*

FUNNY ALMANAC
Elton & Co., NY: 1853 (8-1/8x4-7/8, 36 pgs)
nn - sequential comic strip 38.00 76.00 230.00
NOTE: (5) panel strip "The Adventures of Mr. Goliah Starvemouse"

FUNNY FELLOWS OWN BOOK, A COMPANION FOR THE LOVERS OF FROLIC AND GLEE, THE (M,N)
Philip. J. Cozans, 116 Nassau ST, NY: 1852 (4-1/2x7-1/2", 196 pgs, burnt orange paper-c)
nn - contains many sequential comic strips (Very Rare) (no known sales)
NOTE: Collected from many different Comic Alamac(k)s including Mose Keyser (Calif Gold Rush); Jones, Smith and Robinson Goes To A Ball; Adventures of Mr. Gulp, Or the Effects of A Dinner Party; The Bowery Bully's Trip To The California Gold Mines plus lots more. This one is a sleeper so far.

FUNNY FOLK (M)
E. P. Dutton: 1899 (12x16-1/2", 90 pgs,14 strips in color-rest in b&w, hard-c)
nn - By Franklin Morris Howarth 333.00 666.00 2000.00
nn - London: J.M. Dent, 1899 embossed-c; same interior 208.00 416.00 1250.00

NOTE: *Reprints many sequential strips & single panel cartoons from* **Puck**. *This is considered by many to be yet another "missing link" between Victorian & Platinum Age comic books. Most comic books 1900-1917 reprinting Sunday newspaper comic strips follow this size format, except using cardboard-c rather than hard-c.*

FUNNY SKETCHES...Also Embracing Comic Illustrations
Frank Harrison, New York: 1881 (6-5/8x5", 68 pgs, B&W, Color-c)
nn - contains (3) sequential comic strips; one strip is (6) pages long; plus one (3) pages; one more (2) pager 58.00 116.00 350.00

GIBSON BOOK, THE (M,S)
Charles Scribner's Sons & R.H. Russell, New York: 1906 (11-3/8x17-5/8", gilted red hard-c, B&W)
Book I 33.00 66.00 200.00
NOTE: *Reprints in whole the books: Drawings, Pictures of People, London,Sketches and Cartoons, Education of Mr. Pipp, Americans. 414 pgs. 1907 2nd editions exist same value.*
Book II 33.00 66.00 200.00
NOTE: *Reprints in whole the books: A Widow and Her Friends, The Weaker Sex, Everyday People, Our Neighbors. 314 pgs 1907 second edition for both also exists. Same value.*

GIBSON'S PUBLISHED DRAWINGS, MR. (M,S) (see Plat index for later issues post 1900)
R.H. Russell, New York: No.1 1894 - No. 9 1904 (11x17-3/4", hard-c, B&W)
nn (No.1; 1894) Drawings 96 pgs 23.00 46.00 140.00
nn (No.2; 1896) Pictures of People 92 pgs 23.00 46.00 140.00
nn (No.3; 1898) Sketches and Cartoons 94 pgs 23.00 46.00 140.00
nn (No.4; 1899) The Education of Mr. Pipp 88 pgs 23.00 46.00 140.00
nn (No.5; 1900) Americans 23.00 46.00 140.00
NOTE: *By Charles Dana Gibson cartoons, reprinted from magazines, primarily* **LIFE**. *The Education of Mr. Pipp tells a story. Series continues how long after 1904? Each of these books originally came in a boxx and are worth more with the box.*

GIRL WHO WOULDN'T MIND GETTING MARRIED, THE (O)
Frederick Warne & Co., London & New York: nd (c1870's) (9-1/2x11-1/2", 28 pgs, printed 1 side, paper-c, B&W)
nn - By Harry Parkes 50.00 100.00 300.00
NOTE: *Published simultaneously with its companion volume,* ***The Man Who Would Like to Marry***.

GOBLIN SNOB, THE (O)
DeWitt & Davenport, New York: nd (c1853-56) (24 x 17 cm, 96 pgs, B&W, color hard-c)
nn - (Rare) by H.L. Stephens 200.00 400.00 1200.00

GOLDEN ARGOSY
Frank A. Munsey, 81 Warren St, NYC: 1880s (10-1/2x12, 16 pgs, B&W)
issues with full page comic strips by Chips and Bisbee 13.00 26.00 80.00

GOLDEN DAYS, THE
James Elverson, Publisher, NYC: March 6 1880-May 11 1907 weekly, 16 pgs
issues with comic strips 4.00 8.00 25.00
Horatio Alger issues 8.00 16.00 45.00
v10 #49-v11#1 1889 first Stratemeyer story 17.00 34.00 100.00

GOLDEN WEEKLY, THE
Frank Tousey, NYC: #1 Sept 25, 1889 - #145 Aug 18, 1892 (10-3/4x14-1/2, 16 pgs, B&W)
average issue with comic striips 12.00 24.00 70.00

GREAT LOCOFOCO JUGGERNAUT, THE (S)
publisher unknown: Fall/Winter 1837 (7-5/8x3-1/4, handbill single page)
nn - By David Claypoole Johnston (a GD copy sold for $1050 in 2018)
nn - **Imprint Society:** 1971 (reprint) 4.00 8.00 25.00

HALF A CENTURY OF ENGLISH HISTORY (S. M)
G.P. Putnam's Sons - The Knickerbocker Press, New York and London: 1884 (7-3/4 x 5-3/4", 316 pgs., illustrated hard-c)
nn - By Various 38.00 76.00 225.00
NOTE: *Subtitle: Pictorially Presented in a Series of Cartoons from the Collection of Mr. Punch. Comprising 150 plates by Doyle, Leech, Tenniel, and others, in which are portrayed the political careers of Peel, Palmerston, Russell, Cobden, Bright, Beaconsfield, Derby, Salisbury, Gladstone and other English statesmen.*

HAIL COLUMBIA! HISTORICAL, COMICAL, AND CENTENNIAL (O,S)
The Graphic Co., New York & Walter F. Brown, Providence, RI: 1876 (10x11-3/8", 60 pgs, red gilted hard-c, B&W)
nn - by Walter F. Brown (Scarce) 96.00 192.00 575.00

HANS HUCKEBEIN'S BATCH OF ODD STORIES ODDLY ILLUSTRATEDED
McLoughlin Bros., New York: 1880s (9-3/4x7-3/8, 36?? pg?
nn - By Wilhelm Busch (Rare) 54.00 108.00 325.00

HANS THE SWAPPER, THE STORY OF (O)
L. Pranc & Co., 159 Washington St, Boston: 1865 (33 inch long fold out in colors)
nn - Unique fold out comic book on one long piece of paper 57.00 114.00 340.00

HARPER'S NEW MONTHLY MAGAZINE
Harper & Brothers, Franklin Square, NY: 1850-1870s (6-3/4x10, 140 pgs, paper-c, B&W)
1850s issues with comic strips in back advert section 17.00 34.00 100.00

HEALTH GUYED (I)
Frederick A. Stokes Company: 1890 (5-3/8 x 8-3/8, 56 pgs, hardcover, B&W)
nn - By Frank P.W. ("Chip") Bellew (Junior) 33.00 66.00 200.00
NOTE: *Text & cartoon illustration parody of a health guide.*

HEATHEN CHINEE, THE (O)
Western News Co.: 1870 (5-1/32x7-1/4, B&W, paper)
nn - 10 sheets printed on one side came in envelope 71.00 142.00 425.00

HITS AT POLITICS (M,S)
R.H. Russell, New York: 1899 (15" x 12", 156 pgs, B&W, hard-c)
nn - W.A. Rogers c/a 58.00 116.00 350.00
NOTE: *Collection of W.A. Rogers cartoons, all reprinted from Harper's Weekly. Includes Spanish-American War cartoons.*

HOME CIRCLE, THE
Garrett & Co, NY: 1854-56 (26x19", 4 pgs, B&W)
1 (1/54) beautiful ad of Garrett Building 75.00 150.00 450.00
2/4 (4/66) Cover ad for Yale College Scraps 72.00 144.00 430.00
2/5 (5/55) First ad for Oscas Shanghai 50.00 100.00 300.00
2/6 (6/55) another ad forOscas Snanghai 50.00 100.00 300.00
2/8 (#20) (8/55) Oscar Shanghai comic book cover repro 183.00 366.00 1100.00
3/1 (#25) (1/56) 183.00 366.00 1100.00
NOTE: Garrett's 2nd comic book Courtship of Chavalier Slyfox-Wikoff
3/8 (#32) (8/56) 33.00 66.00 200.00
NOTE: First print ad for Foreign Tour of Messrs. Brown, Jones, and Robinson
35 (11/56) first official Garrett, Dick & Fitzgerald issue 33.00 66.00 200.00
37 (1/57) 75.00 150.00 450.00
NOTE: Front page comic strip repro ad for Messrs. Brown, Jones, and Robinson's Foreign Tour; Back cover full of short sequentials, singles panel

HOME MADE HAPPY. A ROMANCE FOR MARRIED MEN IN SEVEN CHAPTERS (O,P)
Genuine Durham Smoking Tobacco & The Graphic Co.: nd (c1870's) (5-1/4 tall x 3-3/8" wide folded, 27" wide unfolded, color cardboard)
nn - With all 8 panels attached (Scarce) 33.00 66.00 200.00
nn - Individual panels/cards 4.00 8.00 25.00
NOTE: *Consists of 8 attached cards, printed on one side, which unfold into a strip story of title card & 7 panels. Scrapbook hobbyists in the 19th Century tended to pull the panels apart to paste into their scrapbooks, making copies with all panels still attached scarce.*

HOME PICTURE BOOK FOR LITTLE CHILDREN (E,P)
Home Insurance Company, New York: July 1887 (8 x 6-1/8", 36 pgs, b&w, color paper-c)
nn (Scarce) 33.00 66.00 200.00
NOTE: *Contains an abbreviated 32-panel reprinting of "The Toothache" by George Cruikshank. Remainder of booklet does not contain comics. Some copies known to exist do not contain The Toothache - buyer beware!*

HOOD'S COMICALITIES. COMICAL PICTURES FROM HIS WORKS (E,S)
Porter & Coates: 1880 (8-1/2x10-3/8", 104 pgs, printed one side, hard-c, B&W)
nn 20.00 40.00 120.00
NOTE: *Reprints 4 cartoon illustrations per page from the British Hood's Comic Annuals, which were poetry books by Thomas Hood.*

HOOKEYBEAK THE RAVEN, AND OTHER TALES (see also JACK HUCKABACK, THE SCAPEGRACE RAVEN) (E)
George Routledge and Sons, London & New York: nd (1878) (7-1/4x5-5/8", 104 pgs, hardcover, B&W)
nn - By Wilhelm Busch (Rare) 83.00 166.00 500.00

HOW ADOLPHUS SLIM-JIM USED JACKSON'S BEST, AND WAS HAPPY. A LENGTHY TALE IN 7 ACTS. (O,P)
Jackson's Best Chewing Tobacco & Donaldson Brothers: nd(c1870's) (5-1/8 tall x 3-3/8" wide folded, 27" wide unfolded, color cardboard)
nn - With all 8 panels attached (Scarce) 36.00 72.00 215.00
nn - Individual panels/cards 4.00 8.00 25.00
NOTE: *Consists of 8 attached cards, printed on one side, which unfold into a strip story of title card & 7 panels. Scrapbook hobbyists in the 19th Century tended to pull the panels apart topaste into their scrapbooks, making copies with all panels still attached scarce.*

HOW DAYS' DURHAM STANDARD OF THE WORLD SMOKING TOBACCO MADE TWO PAIRS OF TWINS HAPPY (O,P)
J.R. Day & Bro. Standard Durham Smoking Tobacco, Durham, NC: nd (c late 1870's/ early 1880's) (3-5/8" x 5-1/2", folded, 21-3/4" tall unfolded, color cardboard)
nn- With all 6 panels attached (Scarce) 112.00 224.00 675.00
nn- Individual panels/cards 12.00 24.00 70.00
NOTE: *Highly sought by both Black Americana and Tobacciana collectors. Recurring mid-19th Century story about two African-American twin brothers who romance and marry a pair of African-American twin sisters. Although the text is racist at points, the art is not. Consists of 6 attached cards, printed on one side, which unfold downwards into a strip story of title card & 5 panels. Scrapbook hobbyists in the 19th Century tended to pull the panels apart and paste into their scrapbooks, making copies with all panels attached scarce. Note, there are numerous cartoon tellings of this same story, including several card series versions (with different art, and story variations, each time). But, the above is the only version which unfolds as a strip of attached cards. The cards from all the unattached versions are smaller sized, and thus distinguishable.*

HUGGINIANA; OR, HUGGINS' FANTASY, BEING A COLLECTION OF THE MOST ESTEEMED MODERN LITERARY PRODUCTIONS (I,S,P)
H.C. Southwick, New York: 1808 (296 pgs, printed one side, B&W, hard-c)
nn - (Very Rare)) (no known sales)
NOTE: *The earliest known surviving collected promotional cartoons in America. This is a booklet collecting 7 folded plus 1 full page flyer advertisements for barber John Richard Desborus Huggins, who hired American artists Elkanah Tisdale and William S. Leney to modify previously published illustrations into cartoons referring to his barber shop.*

HUMOROUS MASTERPIECES - PICTURES BY JOHN LEECH (E,M)
Frederick A. Stokes: nd (late 1900's - early 1910's) No.1-2 (5-5/8x3-7/8", 68 pgs, cardboard covers, B&W)
1- John Leech (single panel cartoon-r from **Punch**) 20.00 40.00 120.00
2- John Leech (single panel cartoon-r from **Punch**) 20.00 40.00 120.00

HUMOURIST, THE (E,I,S)
C.V. Nickerson and Lucas and Deaver, Baltimore: No.1 Jan 1829 - No.12 Dec 1829 (5-3/4x3-1/2", B&W text w/hand colored cartoon pg.)
Bound volume No.1-12 (Very Rare; copies in libraries 270 pgs) (no known sales)
NOTE: *Earliest known American published periodical to contain a cartoon every issue. Surviving individual issues currently unknown -- all information comes from 1 surviving bound volume. Each issue is mostly text, with one full page hand-colored cartoon. Bound volume contains an additional hand-colored cartoons at front of each six month set (total of 14 cartoons in volume). Cartoons appear to be of British origin, possibly by George Cruikshank.*

HUMPTY DUMPTY, ADVENTURES OF...(I,P)
1877 (Promotional 4x3-1/2", 12 page chapbook from Gantz, Jones & Co, 10¢-c.)
nn-Promotes Gantz Sea Foam Baking Powder; early app. of a costumed character, dressed as Humpty Dumpty 18.00 36.00 110.00

HUSBAND AND WIFE, OR THE STORY OF A HAIR. (O,P)
Garland Stoves and Ranges, Michigan Stove Co.: 1883 (4-3/16 tall x 2-11/16" wide folded, 16" wide unfolded, color cardboard)
nn - With all 6 panels attached (Scarce) 25.00 50.00 150.00
nn - Individual panels/cards 5.00 10.00 25.00
NOTE: *Consists of 6 attached cards, printed on one side, which unfold into a strip story of title card & 5 panels. Scrapbook hobbyists in the 19th Century tended to pull the panels apart topaste into their scrapbooks, making copies with all panels still attached scarce.*

ICHABOD ACADEMICUS, THE COLLEGE EXPERIENCES OF (O,G)
William T. Peters, New Haven, CT: 1850 (5-1/2x9-3/4",108 pgs, B&W)
nn - By William T. Peters (Rare) 733.00 1466.00 4400.00
NOTE: *Pages are not uniform in size. Also, a copy showed up on eBay with misspelled Academicus. Has "n" instead of "m" - not known yet which printing is earliest version.*

ICHABOD ACADEMICUS, THE COLLEGE EXPERIENCES OF (O,G)
Dick & Fitzgerald, New York: nd (1870s-1888) (paper-c, B&W)
nn - By William T. Peters (Very Rare) 200.00 400.00 1200.00
NOTE: *Pages are uniform in size.*

The Story of Han's The Swapper Cover & First Two Panels
1865 © L. Pranc & Co, Boston

Humpty Dumpty, The Adventures of...
© Gantz, Jones and Co.

Imagerie d'Epinal
1888 © Mumoristic Publishing Co.

FR1.0 GD2.0 FN6.0

ILLUSTRATED SCRAP-BOOK OF HUMOR AND INTELLIGENCE (M)
John J. Dyer & Co.: nd (c1859-1860)

	FR1.0	GD2.0	FN6.0
nn - Very Rare	183.00	366.00	1100.00

NOTE: *A "printed scrapbook" of images culled from some unidentified periodical. About half of it is illustrations that would have accompanied prose pieces. There are pages of single panel cartoons (multiple per page). And there are roughly 8 to 12 pages of sequential comics (all different stories, but appears to all be by the same presently unidentified artist).*

ILLUSTRATED WEEKLY, THE
Chars C Lucas & Co, 11 Dey St, NY: 1876 (15x18", 8pgs, 8¢ per issue)

	FR1.0	GD2.0	FN6.0
2/8 (2/19/76) back-c all sequential comic strips	70.00	140.00	425.00
2/12 (3/18/76) full page of British-r sequentials	70.00	140.00	425.00
2/14 (4/1/76) April Fool Issue - (6) panel center; plus more	70.00	140.00	425.00
2/15 (4/8/76) (6) panel sequential	70.00	140.00	425.00
issues without comic strips	21.00	42.00	125.00

ILLUSTRATIONS OF THE POETS: FROM PASSAGES IN THE LIFE OF LITTLE BILLY VIDKINS (See A Day's Sport...)
S. Robinson, Philadelphia: May 1849 (14.7 cm x 11.3 cm, 32 pgs, B&W)

nn - by Henry Stephens (very rare) (no known sales)
NOTE: *Predates Journey to the Gold Diggins By Jeremiah Saddlebags by a few months and is an original American proto-comic strip book. More research needs to be done. A later edition brought $800 in G/VG 2007*

IMAGERIE d'EPINAL (untrimmed individual sheets) (E)
Pellerin for Humoristic Publishing Co, Kansas City, Mo.: nd (1888) No.1-60 (15-7/8x11-3/4",single sheets, hand colored) (All are Rare)

	FR1.0	GD2.0	FN6.0
1-14, 21, 22, 25-46, 49-60 - in the Album d'Images	14.00	28.00	85.00
15-20, 23,24, 47, 48 - not in the Album d'Images	23.00	46.00	140.00

NOTE: *Printed and hand colored in France expressly for the Humoristic Publishing Company . Printed on one side only. These are single sheets, sold separately. Reprints and translates the sheets from their original French.*

IMAGERIE d'EPINAL ALBUM d'IMAGES (E)
Pellerin for Humoristic Publishing Co., Kansas City. Mo: nd (1888) (15-1/2x11-1/2",108 pgs plus full color hard-c, hand colored interior)

	FR1.0	GD2.0	FN6.0
nn - Various French artists (Rare)	333.00	666.00	2000.00

NOTE: *Printed and hand colored in France expressly for the Humoristic Publishing Company . Printed on one side only. This is supposedly a collection of sixty broadsheets, originally sold separately. All copies known only have fifty of the sixty known of these broadsheets (slightly bigger, before binding, trimming the margins in the process, down to 15-1/4x11-3/8".). Three slightly different covers known to exist, with or without the indication in French "Textes en Anglais" ("Texts in Englishi), with or without the general title "Contes de FEes" ("Fairy Tales"). All known copies were collected with sheets 15-20, 23,24, 47, and 48 missing.*

IN LAUGHLAND (M)
R.H. Russell, New York: 1899 (14-9/16x12", 72 pgs, hard-c)

	FR1.0	GD2.0	FN6.0
nn - By Henry "Hy" Mayer (scarce)	113.00	226.00	675.00

NOTE: *Mostly strips plus single panel cartoon-r from various magazines. The majority are reprinted from Life, with the rest from: Truth, Dramatic Mirror, Black and White, Figaro Illustre, Le Rire, and Fliegende Blatter.*

IN THE "400" AND OUT (M,S) (see also **THE TAILOR-MADE GIRL**)
Keppler & Schwarzmann, New York: 1888 (8-1/4x12", 64 pgs, hardc, B&W)

	FR1.0	GD2.0	FN6.0
nn - By C.J. Taylor	35.00	70.00	210.00

NOTE: *Cartoons reprinted from **Puck**. The "400" is a reference to New York City's aristocratic elite.*

IN VANITY FAIR (M,S)
R.H.Russell & Son, New York: 1896 (11-7/8x17-7/8", 80 pgs, hard-c, B&W)

	FR1.0	GD2.0	FN6.0
nn - By A.B.Wenzell, r-LIFE and HARPER'S	35.00	70.00	210.00

JACK HUCKABACK, THE SCAPEGRACE RAVEN (see also HOOKEYBEAK THE RAVEN) (E)
Stroefer & Kirchner, New York: nd (c1877) (9-3/8x6-3/8", 56 pgs, printed one side only, hand colored hardcover, B&W interior)

	FR1.0	GD2.0	FN6.0
nn - By Wilhelm Busch (Rare)	75.00	150.00	450.00

NOTE: *The 1877 date is derived from a gift signature on one known copy. The publication date might in truth be earlier. There are also professionally hand colored copies known to exist which would be worth more.*

JEFF PETTICOATS
American News Company, NY: July 1865 (23 inches folded out; 6-1/4x8 folded,, B&W)
nn - Very Rare Frank Bellew (6) panel sequential foldout (10¢) (no known sales)
NOTE: printed also in **FUNNYEST OF AWL AND THE FUNNIEST SORT OF PHUN** #9 (July 1865) (6) panel strip hanging Jeff Davis; This sold hundreds of thousand of copies in its day

JINGO (M,O)
Art Newspaper Co., Boston & New York: No.1 Sept 10, 1884 - No.11 Nov 19, 1884 (10 cents, 13-7/8" x 10-1/4",16 pgs, color front/back-c and center, remainder B&W, paper-c)

	FR1.0	GD2.0	FN6.0
1-11(Rare)	45.00	90.00	270.00

NOTE: *Satirical Republican propaganda magazine, modeled after **Puck** and **Judge**, which was published during the last couple months of the 1884 Presidential Election campaign. The Republicans lost, **Jingo** ceased publication, and Republican backers soon after purchased **Judge** magazine.*

JOHN-DONKEY, THE (O, S)
George Dexter, Burgess, Stringer & Co., NYC: 1848 (10x7.5",16 pgs,B&W, 6¢

	FR1.0	GD2.0	FN6.0
1 Jan 1 1848	71.00	142.00	425.00
2-end (last issue Aug 12 1848)	46.00	92.00	275.00

JOLLY JOKER
Frank Leslie, NY: 1862-1878 (B&W, 10¢)

	FR1.0	GD2.0	FN6.0
20/6 (July 1877) (Bellew Opper cover & single panels	108.00	216.00	650.00

JOLLY JOKER, OR LAUGH ALL-ROUND
Dick & Fitzgerald, NY: 1870s? (8-1/4x4-7/8", 148, B&W, illustrated green cover)

	FR1.0	GD2.0	FN6.0
nn - cartoons on every page	75.00	150.00	450.00

JONATHAN'S WHITTLINGS OF THE WAR (O, S)

FR1.0 GD2.0 FN6.0

T.W. Strong, 98 Nassau St, NYC: April 1854-July 8 1854 (11.5x8.5", 16 pgs, B&W)

	FR1.0	GD2.0	FN6.0
1 April 1854	70.00	140.00	420.00

NOTE: *Begins Frank Bellew's sequential comic strip "Mr. Hookemcumsnivey, A Russian Gentleman, Hears That His Country Is In A State of War"*

	FR1.0	GD2.0	FN6.0
2-12 (July 8 1854) Many Bellew & Hopkins	70.00	140.00	420.00

JOURNAL CARRIER'S GREETING
???, Minn, Minn: 1897-98? (giveaway promo, 10-1/8x8-1/4, 36, B&W, paper-c)

	FR1.0	GD2.0	FN6.0
nn - rare	32.00	64.00	190.00

JOURNEY TO THE GOLD DIGGINS BY JEREMIAH SADDLEBAGS (O,G)
Various publishers: 1849 (25 cents, 5-5/8 x 8-3/4", 68 pgs, green & black paper cover, B&W interior)

	FR1.0	GD2.0	FN6.0
nn -- New York edition, Stringer & Townsend, Publishers (Very Rare) By J.A. and D.F. Read.	2400.00	4800.00	14,400.00
nn -- Cincinnati, Ohio edition, published by U.P. James (Very Rare) By J.A. and D.F. Read.	2400.00	4800.00	14,400.00
nn -- 1950 reprint, with introduction, published by William P. Wreden, Burlingame, California: 1950 (5-7/8 x 9", 92 pgs, hardcover, color interior) (390 copies printed) By J.A. and D.F. Read.	10.00	20.00	60.00

NOTE: *Earliest known original sequential comic book by an American creator; directly inspired by Töpffer's **Obadiah Oldbuck** and **Bachelor Butterfly** The New York and Cincinnati editions were both published in 1849, one soon after the other. Antiquarian Book sources have traditionally cited that the Cincinnati edition preceded the New York, but without referencing their evidence. Conflicting with this, the Cincinnati edition lists the New York publishers' 1849 copyright, while the New York edition makes no reference to the Cincinnati publishers. Such would indicate that the New York edition was first. Both are very rare, and until resolved both will be regarded as published simultaneously. A New York copy with missing back cover, detached front cover, and G/VG interior sold for $2000 in 2000. Two copies sold at auction in 2006 for $11,500 and 12,000. (Prices vary widely.)*

JUDGE (M,O)
Judge Publishing, New York: No.1 Oct 29, 1881 - No. 950, Dec ??, 1899 (10 cents, color front/back c and centerspread, remainder B&W, paper-c)

	FR1.0	GD2.0	FN6.0
1 (Scarce)	(no known sales)		
2-26 (Volume 1; Scarce)	21.00	42.00	125.00
27-790,792-950	8.00	16.00	50.00
791 (12/12/1896; Vol.31) - classic satirical-c depicting Tammany Hall politicians as the Yellow Kid & Cox's Brownies	92.00	184.00	550.00
Bound Volumes (six month, 26 issue run each):			
Vol. 1 (Scarce)	(no known sales)		
Vol. 2-30,32-37	100.00	200.00	600.00
Vol. 31 - includes issue 791 **YK/Brownies** parody	150.00	300.00	700.00

NOTE: *Rival publication to Puck. Purchased by Republican Party backers, following their loss in the 1884 Presidential Election, to become a Republican propaganda satire magazine.*

JUDGE, GOOD THINGS FROM
Judge Publishing Co., NY: 1887 (13-3/4x10.5", 68 pgs, color paper-c)

	FR1.0	GD2.0	FN6.0
1 first printing	33.00	66.00	200.00

NOTE: Zimmerman, Hamilton, Victor, Woolf, Beard, Ehrhart, De Meza, Howarth, Smith, Alfred Mitchell

JUDGE'S LIBRARY (M)
Judge Publishing, New York: No.1, April 1890 - No. 141, Dec 1899 (10 cents, 11x8-1/8", 36 pgs, color paper-c, B&W)

	FR1.0	GD2.0	FN6.0
1	19.00	38.00	115.00
2-141	15.00	30.00	90.00

151-??? (post-1900 issues; see Platinum Age section)
NOTE: ***Judge's Library** was a monthly magazine reprinting cartoons & prose from **Judge**, with each issue's material organized around the same subject. The cover art was often original. All issues were kept in print for the duration of the series, so later issues are more scarce than earlier ones.*

JUDGE'S QUARTERLY (M)
Judge Publishing Company/Arkell Publishing Company, New York: No.1 April 1892 - 31 Oct 1899 (25¢, 13-3/4x10-1/4", 64 pgs, color paper-c, B&W)

	FR1.0	GD2.0	FN6.0
1-11 13-31 contents presently unknown to us	11.00	22.00	65.00
12 ZIM Sketches From Judge Jan 1895	75.00	150.00	450.00

NOTE: *Similar to **Judge's Library**, except larger in size, and issued quarterly. All reprint material, except for the cover art.*

JUDGE'S SERIALS (M,S)
Judge Publishing, New York: March 1888 (10x7.5", 36 pgs)

	FR1.0	GD2.0	FN6.0
#3 - Eugene Zimmerman	67.00	84.00	250.00

NOTE: *A bit of sequential comic strips; mostly single panel cartoons. This series runs to at least #8.*

JUDY
Burgess, Stringer & Co., 17 Ann St, NYC: Nov 28 1846-Feb 20 47 (11x8.5",12 pgs,B&W)

	FR1.0	GD2.0	FN6.0
1 Nov 28 1846	43.00	86.00	260.00
2-13	36.00	72.00	215.00

JUVENILE GEM, THE (see also THE ADVENTURES OF MR. TOM PLUMP, and OLD MOTHER MITTEN) (O,I)
Huestis & Cozans: nd (1850-1852) (6x3-7/8", 64 pgs, hand colored paper-c, B&W) (all versions Very Rare)

nn - First printing(s) publisher's address is 104 Nassau Street (1850-1851) (1 copy sold for $800.00 in Fair)
nn - 2nd printing(s) publisher's address is 116 Nassau Street (1851-1852) (no known sales)
nn - 3rd printing(s) publisher's address is 107 Nassau Street (1852+) (no known sales)
NOTE: *The JUVENILE GEM is a gathering of multiple booklets under a single, hand colored cover (none of the interior booklets have the covers which they were given when sold separately). The publisher appears to have gathered whichever printings of each booklet were available when copies of THE JUVENILE GEM was assembled, so that the booklets within, and the conglomerate cover, may be from a mixture of printings. Contains two sequential comic booklets: THE ADVENTURES OF MR. TOM PLUMP, and OLD MOTHER MITTEN AND HER FUNNY KITTEN, plus five heavily illustrated children's booklets - **The Pretty Primer, The***

Funny Book, The Picture Book, The Two Sisters, and Story Of The Little Drummer. Six of these -- including the two comic books -- were reprinted in the 1960's by Americana Review as a set of individual booklets, and included in a folder collectively titled "Six Children's Books of the 1850's".

LANTERN, THE
Stringer & Townsend: 1852-1853 (11x8-3/8", 12 pgs, soft paper, 6 ¢)

1 Jan 10, 1852	32.00	64.00	190.00
2	22.00	44.00	130.00
3-First Frank Bellew cartoons onwards each issue	31.00	62.00	185.00
4-Bellew 's Mr Blobb begins 1/31/52	42.00	84.00	250.00

NOTE: *Bellew serial sequential comic strip "Mr Blobb In Search Of A Physician" becomes 2nd earliest known recurring character in American comic strips plus full page single panel Bellew cartoon "The Modern Frankenstein" take-off on Shelly's story.*

5-Hunsdale 2-panel "The Horrors of Slavery"; Mr Blobb	38.00	76.00	230.00
6-DF Read 15 panel "A Volley of Valentines"; Mr Blobb	38.00	76.00	230.00
7-8,10-Bellew's Mr Blobb continues	21.00	42.00	125.00
9-Four panel "The Perils of Leap Year" MrBlobb	38.00	76.00	230.00
11-no Mr Blobb	19.00	38.00	115.00
12-Bellew's Mr Blobb continues 3/27/52	38.00	76.00	230.00
13-Bellew (10) panel sequential "Stump Speaking Studied"	38.00	76.00	230.00
14-no comic strips	18.00	36.00	110.00
15-Bellew's Mr Blobb ends (5) panel 4/17/52	38.00	76.00	230.00
16-Bellew begins new comic strip serial, "Mr. Bulbear, A Stockbroker, After having Supped at Delmonicos, Has A Dream", Part One, (6) panels	38.00	76.00	230.00
17-Bellew's Mr Bulbear continues	21.00	42.00	125.00
18-Bellew (8) panel "Trials of a Witness"	38.00	76.00	230.00
19-Bellew's Mr Bulbear's Dream continues	21.00	42.00	125.00
20-23-No comic strips	19.00	38.00	115.00
24 Bellew "Trials of a Publisher" (6) panel	38.00	76.00	230.00
25 comic strip "Travels of Jonathan Verdant"recurring character	21.00	42.00	125.00
26-49 contents still to be indexed			
50 (12/18/52) (2) panel Impertinent Smile	21.00	42.00	125.00
58 (2/12/53) (6) panel Trip to California	21.00	42.00	125.00
66 (4/9/53) (3) panel sequential strip	21.00	42.00	125.00

LAST SENSATION, THE (Becomes Day's Doings)
James Watts, NYC: Dec 27 1867-May 30 1868 (11x16 folio-size, 16 pgs, B&W)

Issues with comic strips	36.00	72.00	215.00

LAUGH AND GROW FAT COMIC ALMANAC
Fisher & Brother, Philadelphia, New York & Boston: 1860-? (36 pgs)

nn	48.00	96.00	275.00

LEGEND OF SAM'L OF POSEN (O)
M.B. Curtis Company: 1884-85 (8x3-3/8", 44 pgs, Color-c, B&W interior)

nn - By M.B. Curtis	36.00	72.00	215.00

NOTE: Cover blurb says: From Early Days in Fatherland to affluence And Success in the Land of His Adoption, America

LESLIE'S YOUNG AMERICA (O. S)
Leslie & Co, 98 Chamber St, NY: 1881-82 (11-1/2x8", 5¢, B&W)

1 (7/9/81) back cover (6) panel strip	108.00	216.00	650.00
2 (7/16/81) back cover (9) panel strip	43.00	86.00	260.00
3 (7/23/81) back cover (16) panel Busch strip	50.00	100.00	300.00
9 (9/3/81) sequentials; Hopkins singles	43.00	86.00	260.00
15 (10/15/81) Zim or Frost? (6) panel strip	43.00	86.00	260.00
19 (11/12/81) (9) panel back-c strip	43.00	86.00	260.00
24 (4) panel strip 25 (2) panel back-c strip	43.00	86.00	260.00
26 27 (6) panel back-c strip	43.00	86.00	260.00
29 31 (12) panel strip	43.00	86.00	260.00
32 (2/11/82) (8) panel strip	43.00	86.00	260.00
issues without comic strips or Jules Verne	21.00	42.00	125.00

NOTE: Jules Verne stories begin with #1 and run thru at least #42

LIFE (M,O) (continues with Vol.35 No. 894+ in the Platinum Age section)
J.A.Mitchell: Vol.1 No.1 Jan. 4, 1883 - Vol.1 No.26 June 29, 1883 (10-1/4x8", 16 pgs, B&W, paper cover); J.A. Mitchell: Vol. 2 No. 27, July 5, 1883 - Vol. 6 No.148, Oct 29, 1885 (10-1/4x8-1/4", 16 pgs., B&W, paper cover); Mitchell & Miller: Vol.6 No.149, Nov. 5, 1885 - Vol. 31, No. 796, March 17, 1898 (10-3/8x8-3/8", 16 pgs., B&W, paper cover); Life Publishing Company: Vol. 31 No. 797, March 24, 1898 - Vol. 34 No. 893, Dec 28, 1899 (10-3/8 x 8-1/2", 20 pgs., B&W, paper cover)

1-26 (Scarce) (no known individual sales, 1st 12-issues in a bound volume sold for $1554)			
27-799	5.00	10.00	30.00
800 (4/7/1898) parody Yellow Kid / Spanish-American War cover (not by Outcault)	54.00	108.00	325.00
801-893	4.00	8.00	25.00

NOTE: *All covers for issues 1 - 26 are identical, apart from issue number & date.*

Hard bound collected volumes:

V. 1 (No.1-26) (Scarce)	50.00	100.00	300.00
V. 2-34	30.00	60.00	180.00
V. 31 YK #800 parody-c not by RFO	54.00	108.00	325.00

NOTE: *Because the covers of all issues in Volume 1 are identical, it was common practice to remove the covers before binding the issues together. This is not true of later volumes, though, in all volumes it was common to drop the advertising pages which appeared at the rear of each issue. Information on many more individual issues will expand next Guide.*

LIFE AND ADVENTURES OF JEFF DAVIS (I)
J.C. Haney & Co., NY: 1865 (10 cents, 7-1/2" x 4", 36 pgs, B&W, paper-c)

nn - By McArone (Scarce)	146.00	292.00	875.00
nn - 1974 Reprint (350) copies 6-3/4x4-3/8	3.00	6.00	20.00
nn - 1997 Reprint (7th Fla. Sutler, Clearwater, 6-3/4x4-1/4")	–	–	5.00

NOTE: *Humorous telling of the capture of Confederate President Jeff Davis in women's clothing, from the publisher of Merryman's Monthly. It contains an ad page for that publication; the material is perhaps reprinted from it. J.C. Haney licensed it to local printers, and so various publishers are found -- all printings currently regarded as simultaneous. (The Geo. H. Hees printing, Oswego, NY, contains an ad for the upcoming October 1865 issue of Merryman's Monthly, thus placing that printing in September 1865). Modern facsimile editions have been produced.*

LIFE IN PHILADELPHIA
W. Simpson, 66 Chestnut, Philadelphia; Siltart, No. 65 South Third St, Philadelphia: 1830 (7-3/4x6-7/8", 15 loose plates, hand colored copies exist, maybe B&W also)

nn - By Edward Williams Clay (1799-1857) (Very Rare) (no known sales)

NOTE: *First 13 plates etched, with many word balloons; scenes of exaggerated Black Americana in Philadelphia viewed one by one as broadsides. Had several publishers over the years. Was also eventually collected into a book of same name but only with the first 13 plates used; the last two not used in book. Collected book not yet viewed to share info.*

LIFE'S BOOK OF ANIMALS (M.S)
Doubleday & McClure Co.: 1898 (7-1/4x10-1/8", 88 pgs, color hardcover, B&W)

nn	21.00	42.00	125.00

NOTE: *Reprints funny animal single panel and strip cartoons reprinted from LIFE. Art by Blaisdell, Chip Bellew, Kemble, Hy Mayer, Sullivant, Woolf.*

LIFE'S COMEDY (M,S)
Charles Scribner's Sons: Series 1 1897 - Series 3 1898 (12x9-3/8", hardcover, B&W)

1 (142 pgs). 2, 3 (138 pgs)	48.00	96.00	290.00

NOTE: *Gibson a-1-3; c-3. Hy Mayer a-1-3. Rose O'Neill a-2-3. Stanlaws a-2-3. Sullivant a-1-2. Verbeek a-2. Wenzell a-1-3; c(painted)-2.*

LIFE, THE GOOD THINGS OF (M,S)
White, Stokes, & Allen, NY: 1884 - No.3 1886 ; Frederick A. Stokes, NY: No.4 1887; Frederick Stokes & Brother, NY: No.5 1888 - No.6 1889; Frederick A. Stokes Company, NY: No. 7 1890 - No.10 1893 (8-3/8x10-1/2", 74 pgs, gilted hardcover, B&W)

nn - 1884 (most common issue)	27.00	54.00	160.00
2 - 1885	27.00	54.00	160.00
3 - 1886 (76 pgs)	27.00	54.00	160.00
4 - 1887 (76 pgs)	27.00	54.00	160.00
5 - 1888	27.00	54.00	160.00
6 - 1889	27.00	54.00	160.00
7 - 1890	27.00	54.00	160.00
8 - 1891 (scarce)	53.00	106.00	320.00
9 - 1892	27.00	54.00	160.00
10 - 1893	27.00	54.00	160.00

NOTE: *Contains mostly single panel, and some sequential, comics reprinted from LIFE. Attwood a-1-4,10. Roswell Bacon a-5. Chip Bellew a-4-6. Frank Bellew a-4,6. Palmer Cox a-1. H. E. Dey a-5. C. D. Gibson a-4-10. F.M. Howarth a-5-6. Kemble a-1-3. Klapp a-5. Walt McDougall a-1-2. H. McVickar a-5; J. A. Mitchell a-5. Peter Newell a-2-3. Gray Parker a-4-5,7. J. Smith a-5. Albert E. Steiner a-5; T. S. Sullivant a-7-9. Wenzell a-8-10. Wilder a-3. Woolf a-3-6.)*

LIFE, THE SPICE OF (E,M,)
White and Allen: NY & London: 1888 (8-3/8x10-1/2",76 pgs, hard-c, B&W)

nn	38.00	76.00	230.00

NOTE: *Resembles **THE GOOD THINGS OF LIFE** in layout and format, and appears to be an attempt to compete with their former partner Frederick A. Stokes. However, the material is not from **LIFE**, but rather is reprinted and translated German sequential and single panel comics.*

LIFE'S PICTURE GALLERY (becomes LIFE'S PRINTS) (M,S,P)
Life Publishing Company, New York: nd (1898-1899) (paper cover, B&W) (all are scarce)

nn - (nd; 1898, 100 pgs, 5-1/4x8-1/2") Gibson-c of a woman with closed umbrella; 1st interior page announcing that after January 1, 1899 Gibson will draw exclusively for LIFE; the word "SPECIMEN" is printed in red, diagonally, across every print; a-Gibson, Rose O'Neill, Sullivant	25.00	50.00	150.00
nn - (nd; 1899, 128 pgs, 4-7/8x7-3/8") Gibson-c of a woman golfer; 1st interior page announcing that Gibson & Hanna, Jr. draw exclusively for LIFE; the word "SPECIMEN" is printed in red, horizontally, across every print. Includes prints from Gibson's **THE EDUCATION OF MR. PIPP**; a-Gibson, Sullivant	25.00	50.00	150.00

NOTE: *Catalog of prints reprinted from **LIFE** covers & centerspreads. The first catalog was given away free to anyone requesting it, but after many people got the catalog without ordering anything, subsequent catalogs were sold at 10 cents.*

LIGHT AND SHADE
William Drey Doppel Soap: 1892 (3-3/4x5-3/8", 20 pgs, B&W, color cover)

nn - By J.C.	40.00	80.00	240.00

NOTE: Contains (8) panel comic strip of black boy whose skin turns white using this soap.

LITTLE SICK BEAR, THE
Edwin W. Joy Co, San Francisco, CA: 1897 (6-1/4x5", 20 pgs, B&W, Scarce)

nn - By James Swinnerton one long sequential comic strip	150.00	300.00	900.00

LONDON OUT OF TOWN, OR THE ADVENTURES OF THE BROWNS AT THE SEA SIDE BY LUKE LIMNER, ESQ. (O)
David Bogue, 86 Fleet St, London: c1847 (5-1/2x4-1/4, 32 pgs, yellow paper hard-c, B&W)

nn - By John Leighton	120.00	240.00	725.00

NOTE: one long sequential comic strip multiple-panel per page story; each page crammed with panels inspired by the Töpffer comic books Bogue began several years earlier.

LORGNETTE, THE (S)
George J Coombes, New York: 1886 (6-1/2x8-3/4, 38 pgs, hard-c, B&W

nn - By J.K. Bangs	33.00	66.00	200.00

LOVING BALLAD OF LORD BATEMAN, THE (E,I)
G.W. Carleton & Co., Publishers, Madison Square, NY: 1871 (9x5-7/8",16 pgs, soft-c, 6¢)

nn - By George Cruikshank	33.00	66.00	200.00

MADISON'S EXPOSITION OF THE AWFUL & TERRIFYING CEREMONIES OF THE ODD FELLOWS
T.E. Peterson & Brothers, 306 Chestnut St, Phila: 1870s? (5-3/4x9-1/4, 68 pgs, B&W)

nn - single panel cartoons	33.00	66.00	200.00

MANNERS AND CUSTOMS OF YE HARVARD STUDENTE (M,S)
Houghton Mifflin & Co., Boston & Moses King, Cambridge: 1877 (7-7/8x11", 72 pgs, printed one side, hardc, B&W)

nn - by F.G. Attwood	83.00	166.00	500.00

NOTE: *Collection of cartoons originally serialized in the **Harvard Lampoon**. Attwood later became a major cartoonist for **Life**.*

MAN WHO WOULD LIKE TO MARRY, THE (O)
Frederick Warne & Co., London & New York: nd (c 1880's) (9-1/2x11-1/2", 28 pgs, printed 1 side, paper-c, B&W)

nn - By Harry Parkes	54.00	108.00	325.00

NOTE: *Published simultaneously with its companion volume, **The Girl Who Wouldn't Mind Getting Married**.*

MAX AND MAURICE: A JUVENILE HISTORY IN SEVEN TRICKS (E)
(see also Teasing Tom and Naughty Ned)
Roberts Brothers, Boston: 1871 first edition (8-1/8 x 5-1/2", 76 pgs, hard & soft-c B&W)

nn - By Wilhelm Busch (green or brown cloth hardbound)	217.00	434.00	1300.00
nn - exactly the same, but soft paper cover	117.00	234.00	700.00

NOTE: *Page count includes 56 pgs of art, two blank endpapers at the front (one colored), 8 pgs of ads at the back, two blank endpapers at the end (one colored), and the covers. Green or brown illustrated hardcover. The name of the author is given on the title page as "William Busch." We assume this to be the 1st edition. Back side*

Merryman's Monthly v3#5 with Bellew strip
May 1865 © J. C. Haney & Co., New York

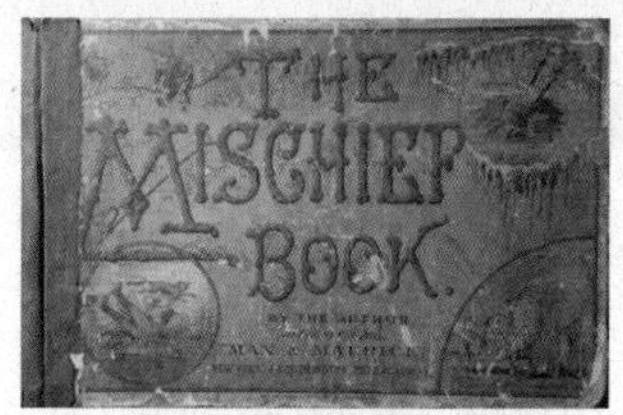
The Mischief Book by Wilhelm Busch
color cover art variation
1880 © R. Worthington, New York

FR1.0 GD2.0 FN6.0

of title page states: Entered according to Act of Congress, in the year 1870, by Roberts Brothers, In the office of the Librarian of Congress at Washington.

	FR1.0	GD2.0	FN6.0
nn - By Wilhelm Busch (1872 edition)	217.00	434.00	1300.00
nn - 1875 reprint	75.00	150.00	450.00
nn - 1882 reprint (76 pgs, hand colored- c/a, 75¢)	67.00	134.00	400.00
nn- 1889 reprint with new art on cover printed in full color	67.00	134.00	400.00

NOTE: *Each of the above contains 56 pages of art and text in a transitional format between a regular children's book and a comic book (the page count difference is ad pages in back). Seminal inspiration for William Randolph Hearst to acquire as a "new comic" (following the wild success of Outcault's Yellow Kid) to license M&M from Busch and hire Rudolph Dirks in late 1897 to create a New York American newspaper incarnation. In Hearst's English language newspapers it was called The Katzenjammer Kids and in his German language NYC newspaper it was titled Max & Moritz, Busch's original title. At least 50 other reprints versions are reputed to exist printed thru 1900. Translated from the 1865 German original. We are still sorting out the edition confusion.*

MAX AND MAURICE: A JUVENILE HISTORY IN SEVEN TRICKS (E)
(see also Teasing Tom and Naughty Ned)
Little, Brown, and Company, Boston: 1898-1902 (8-1/8 x 5-3/4", 72 pgs, hardcover, black ink on orange paper) (various early reprints)

nn - 1898 , 1899 By Wilhelm Busch	55.00	110.00	330.00
nn - 1902 (64 pages, B&W)	17.00	34.00	100.00

MERRY MAPLE LEAVES Or A Summer In The Country (S)
E.P. Dutton And Company, New York: 1872 (9-3/8x7-3/8", 90 and 86 pgs pgs, hard-c)

nn - By Abner Perk	28.00	56.00	170.00

NOTE: *Each drawing contained in a maple leaf motif by Livingston Hopkins and others.*

MERRYMAN'S MONTHLY A COMIC MAGAZINE FOR THE FAMILY (M,O,E)
J.C. Haney & Co, NY: 1863-1875 (10-7/8x7-13/16", 30 pgs average, B&W)

Certain issues with sequential comics	79.00	158.00	475.00

NOTE: *Sequential strips by Frank Bellew Sr, Wilhelm Busch found so far; others?*

MERRYTHOUGHT, OR LAUGHTER FROM YEAR TO YEAR, THE
Fisher & Brother, Phila, Baltimore: early 1850s (4-1/2x7", B&W)
nn - many singles, some sequential (Very Rare) (no known sales)
NOTE: *See Vict article for back cover pic which is earliest known use of the term Comic Book*

MESSRS BROWN JONES AND ROBINSON, THE AMERICAN TOUR OF (O,G)
D. Appleton & Co., New York: 1872 (11-5/8x9-1/2", 158 pgs, printed one side only, B&W, green gilted hard-c)

nn - By Toby	100.00	200.00	600.00

NOTE: *Original American graphic novel sequel to Richard Doyle's Foreign Tour of Brown, Jones, and Robinson, with the same characters visiting New York, Canada, and Cuba. Protective sheets between each page (not part of page count).*

MESSRS. BROWN, JONES, AND ROBINSON, THE FOREIGN TOUR OF
(see also **THE CLOWN, OR THE BANQUET OF WIT**) (E,M,O,G)
Bradbury & Evans, London: 1854 (11-5/8x9-1/2", 196 pgs, gilted hard-c, B&W)

nn - By Richard Doyle	45.00	90.00	270.00
nn - Bradbury & Evans 1900 reprint	17.00	34.00	100.00

NOTE: *Protective sheets between each page (not part of page count). Expanded and redrawn sequential comics story from the serialized episodes originally published in PUNCH. Also comes in a 174 pg 8-3/4x11" version.*

MESSRS. BROWN, JONES, AND ROBINSON, THE FOREIGN TOUR OF (E,M,G)
D. Appleton & Co., New York: 1860 & 1877 (11-5/8x9-1/2", 196 pgs, gilted hard-c, B&W)

nn - (1860 printing) by Richard Doyle	37.00	74.00	220.00
nn - (1871 printing) by Richard Doyle	25.00	50.00	150.00
nn - (1877 printing) by Richard Doyle	25.00	50.00	150.00

NOTE: *Protective sheets between each page (not part of page count). Reprints the Bradbury & Evans edition.*

MESSRS. BROWN, JONES, AND ROBINSON, THE LAUGHABLE ADVENTURES OF (E,M,G)
Garrett, Dick & Fitzgerald, NY: nd (1856 or 1857) (5-3/4x9-1/4", 100 pgs, printed one side only, paper-c, B&W)

nn - (Very Rare) by Richard Doyle c/a	242.00	434.00	1450.00

NOTE: *1st American reprinting of the "Foreign Tour"; reformatted into a small oblong format. Links the earlier Garrett & Co. to the later Dick & Fitzgerald. Back cover reprints full size the Garrett & Co. version cover for Oscar Shanghai. Interior front cover reprints full size the Garrett & Co. version cover for Slyfox-Wikof. Issued without a title page.*

MESSRS. BROWN, JONES, AND ROBINSON, THE LAUGHABLE ADVEN. OF (E,M,G)
Dick & Fitzgerald, NY: nd (late 1870's - 1888) (5-3/4x9-1/4", 100 pgs, printed one side only, green paper-c, B&W)

nn - (Scarce) by Richard Doyle	83.00	166.00	500.00

NOTE: *Reprints the Garrett, Dick & Fitzgerald printing, with the following changes: Takes what had been page 12 in the Garrett, D&F printing (art by M.H. Henry), and makes it a title page, which is numbered page 1. The first story page, "Go to the Races", is numbered 2 (whereas it is numbered 1 in the Garrett, Dick & Fitzgerald version). Numbering stays ahead of the G,D&F edition by 1 page up through page 12, after which the page numbering becomes identical.*

MINNEAPOLIS JOURNAL CARTOONS (N,S)
Minneapolis Journal: nn 1894 - No.2 1895 (7-3/4" x 10-7/8", 76 pgs, B&W, paper-c)

nn (1894) (Rare)	37.00	74.00	220.00
Second Series (1895) (Rare)	37.00	74.00	220.00
nn- "War Cartoons" Jan 1899 (9x8", 160 pgs, paperback, punched & string bound) (Scarce)	32.00	64.00	190.00

NOTE: *Reprints single panel cartoons from the prior year, by Charles "Bart" L. Bartholomew.*

MINNEAPOLIS TRIBUNE CARTOON BOOK FOR 1901
Roland C. Bowman: 1901
nn (a FR/GD copy sold in 2010 for $134)

MISCHIEF BOOK, THE (E)
R. Worthington, New York: 1880 (7-1/8 x 10-3/4", 176 pgs, hard-c, B&W)

nn - Green cloth binding; green on brown cover; cover art by R. Lewis based on Busch art by Wilhelm Busch	158.00	316.00	950.00
nn - Blue cloth binding; hand colored cover; completely different cover art based on Busch by Wilhelm Busch	158.00	316.00	950.00

NOTE: *Translated by Abby Langdon Alger. American published anthology collection of Wilhelm Busch comic strips. Includes two of the strips found in the British "Bushel of Merry-Thoughts" collection, translated better, and with the dropped panel restored. Unknown which cover version was first.*

MISSES BROWN, JONES AND ROBINSON, THE FOREIGN TOUR OF THE (E,O,G)
Bickers & Sons, London: nd (c1850's) (12-1/4" x 9-7/8", 108 pgs, printed on one side, B&W, hard-c)

nn- "by Miss Brown" (Rare)	73.00	146.00	440.00

NOTE: *A female take on Doyle's Foreign Tour, by an unknown woman artist, using the pseudonym "Miss Brown."*

MISS MILLY MILLEFLEUR'S CAREER (S)
Sheldon & Co., NY: 1869 (10-3/4x9-7/8", 74 pgs, purple hard-c)

nn - Artist unknown (Rare)	57.00	114.00	340.00

MR PODGER AT COUP'S GREATEST SHOW ON EARTH HIS HAPS AND MISHAPS, THE ADVENTURES OF (O,S)
W.C. Coup, New York: 1884 (5-5/8x4-1/4", 20 pgs, color-c, B&W)

nn - Circus Themes; Similar to Barker's Comic Almanacs	21.00	42.00	125.00

MR. TOODLES' GREAT ELEPHANT HUNT (See Peter Piper in Bengal)
Brother Jonathan, NYC: 1850s (4-1/4x7-7/8", page count presently unknown)
nn - catalog contains comic strip (Very Rare) (no known sales)

MR. TOODLES' TERRIFIC ELEPHANT HUNT
Dick & Fitzgerald, NYC: 1860s (5-3/4x9-1/4", 32 pgs, paper-c, B&W) (Very Rare)

nn - catalog reprint contains 28 panel comic strip	117.00	234.00	700.00

MRS GRUNDY
Mrs Grundy Publishing Co, NYC: July 8 1865-Sept 30 1865 (weekly)

1-13 Thomas Nast, Hoppin, Stephens,	37.00	74.00	220.00

MUSEUM OF WONDERS, A (O,I)
Routledge & Sons: 1894 (13x10", 64 pgs, color-c, color thru out)

nn - By Frederick Opper	92.00	184.00	550.00

MY FRIEND WRIGGLES, A (Laughter) Moving Panorama, of His Fortunes And Misfortunes, Illustrated With Over 200 Engravings, of Most Comic Catastrophes And Side-Splitting Merriment) (O,G)
Stearn & Co, 202 Williams St, NY: 1850s (5-7/8x9-3/4", 100 pgs, B&W)

nn - By S. P. Avery (also the engraver) (Very Rare)	192.00	384.00	1150.00

MY SKETCHBOOK (E,S)
Dana Estes & Charles E. Lauriat, Boston; J. Sabins & Sons, New York: circa 1880s (9-3/8x12", brown hard-c)

nn - By George Cruikshank	27.00	54.00	160.00

NOTE: *Reprints British editions 1834-36; extensive usage of word balloons.*

NASBY'S LIFE OF ANDY JONSON (O, M)
Jesse Haney Co., Publishers No. 119 Nassau St, NY: 1866 (4-1/2x7-1/2, 48 pgs, B&W)

nn - President Andrew Johnson satire	100.00	300.00	600.00

NOTE: Blurb further reads: With a True Pictorial History of His STumping Tour Out West By Petroleum V. Nasby, A Dimmicrat of Thirty Years Standing, And Who Allus Tuk His Licker Straight. Front of book has long sequential comic strip satire on President Andrew Johnson, misspelling his name on the cover on purpose.

NAST'S ILLUSTRATED ALMANAC
Harper & Brothers, Franklin Square, NYC: 1872-1874 (8x5.5", 80 pgs, B&W, 35¢)

nn	48.00	96.00	290.00

NAST'S WEEKLY (O,S)
???: 1892-93 (Quarto Weekly)

all issues scarce	33.00	66.00	200.00

NATIONAL COMIC ALMANAC
An Association of Gentlemen, Boston: 1836 (8.25x4.75", 34 pgs, B&W)

nn	50.00	100.00	300.00

NEW AMERICAN COMIC ALL-IMAKE (ELTON'S BASKET OF COMICAL SCRAPS), THE
Elton, Publisher, New York: 1839 (7-1/2x4-5/8, 24 pgs)

1	71.00	142.00	425.00

NEW BOOK OF NONSENSE, THE: A Contribution To The Great Central Fair In Aid of the Sanitary Commission (O,S)
Ashmead & Evans, No. 724 Chestnut St, Philadelphia: June 1864 (red hard-c)

nn - Artists unknown (Scarce)	58.00	116.00	350.00

NEW YORK ILLUSTRATED NEWS
Frank Leslie, NYC: 10/14/76-June 1884

average issues with comic strips	19.00	38.00	115.00

NEW YORK PICAYUNE (see PHUN FOTOCRAFT)
Woodward & Hutchings: 1850-1855 newspaper-size weekly; 1856-1857 Folio Monthly 16x10.5; 1857-1858 Quarto Weekly; 1858-1860 Quarto Weekly

Average Issue With Comic Strips	40.00	80.00	240.00
Issues with Full Front Page Comic Strip	71.00	142.00	425.00

NOTE: *Many issues contain Frank Bellew sequential comic strips & single panel cartoons. Later issues published by Woodward, Levison & Robert Gun (1853-1857) ; Levison & Thompson (1857-1860)*

NICK-NAX

Levison & Haney, NY: 1857-1858? (11x7-3/4", 32 pgs, B&W, paper-c)
v2 #10 Feb 1858 has many single panel cartoons 38.00 76.00 225.00

99 "WOOLFS" FROM TRUTH (see Sketches of Lowly Life in a Great City, Truth)
Truth Company, NY: 1896 (9x5-1/2", 72 pgs, varnished paper-like cloth hard-c, 25 cents)
nn - By Michael Angelo Woolf (Rare) 113.00 226.00 675.00
NOTE: *Woolf's cartoons are regarded as a primary influence on R.F. Outcault in the later development of The Yellow Kid newspaper strip. Copy sold in 2002 on eBay for $800.00.*

NONSENSE OR, THE TREASURE BOX OF UNCONSIDERED TRIFLES
Fisher & Brother, 12 North Sixth St, Phila, PA, 64 Baltimore St, Baltimore, MD: early 1850s (4-1/2x7", 128 pgs, B&W)
nn - much Davy Crocket sequential story-telling comic strips 242.00 484.00 1450.00

OBADIAH OLDBUCK, THE ADVENTURES OF MR. (E,G)
Tilt & Bogue, London: nd (1840-41) (5-15/16x9-3/16", 176 pgs,B&W, gilted hard-c)
nn - By Rodolphe Töpffer 567.00 1134.00 3400.00
nn - Hand coloured edition (Very Rare) (no known sales)
NOTE: *This is the British edition, translating the unauthorized redrawn 1839 edition from Parisian publisher Aubert, adapted from Töpffer's "Les Amours de Mr. Vieux Bois" (aka "Histoire de Mr. Vieux Bois"), originally published in French in Switzerland, in 1837 (2nd ed. 1839). Early 19th century books are often found rebound, with original cover and/or title page gone. To distinguish editions having no cover or title page: the British oblong editions (published by Tilt & Bogue) use Roman Numerals to number pages. American oblong shaped editions use Arabic Numerals. British are printed on one side only. This is the earliest known English language sequential comic book. Has a new title page with art by Robert Cruikshank.*

OBADIAH OLDBUCK, THE ADVENTURES OF MR. (E,G)
Wilson and Company, New York: September 14, 1842 (11-3/4x9", 44 pgs, B&W, yellow paper-c on bookstand editions, hemp paper interior)
Brother Jonathan Extra No. IX - Rare bookstand edition 2333.00 4666.00 14,000.00
Brother Jonathan Extra No. IX Very Rare subscriber/mailorder
2500.00 5000.00 15,000.00
NOTE: *By Rodolphe Töpffer. Earliest known sequential American comic book, reprinting the 1841 British edition. Pages are numbered via Roman numerals. States "BROTHER JONATHAN EXTRA - ADVENTURES OF MR. OBADIAH OLDBUCK." at the top of each page. Prints 2 to 3 tiers of panels on both sides of each page. Copies could be had for ten cents according to adverts in* ***Brother Jonathan****. By Rodolphe Töpffer with cover masthead design by David Claypool Johnston, and cover art beneath the masthead reprinting Robert Cruik-shank's title page art from the Tilt & Bogue edition. A special, additional cover was added for copies sold on stands (it was not issued with mail order or subscriber copies). Only 1 known copy possesses (partially) this very thin outer yellow cover. A decent (subscriber) copy sold on eBay in later October 2002 for over $3500.00.*
In 2005, a GD/VG for $20,000; and a VG for $20,000. An apparent GD copy sold in auction in 2007 for $9560. A FR/GD copy sold in 2008 for $4182.50. A bound edition sold in 2010 for $2270.50. A copy in GD (restored) sold in 2012 for $5377. A Poor condition copy sold in 2014 for $4780. A Fair condition copy sold for $3107 in 2018. (Prices vary widely.)

OBADIAH OLDBUCK, THE ADVENTURES OF MR. (E,G)
Wilson & Co, New York: nd (1849) (5-11/16x8-3/8", 84 pgs, B&W,paper-c)
nn - by Rodolphe Töpffer; title page by Robert Cruikshank (Very Rare)
750.00 1500.00 4500.00
NOTE: *2nd Wilson & Co printing, reformatted into a small oblong format, with nine panels edited out, and text modified to smooth out this removal. Results in four less printed tiers/strips. Pages are numbered via Arabic numerals. Every panel on Pages 11, 14, 19, 21, 24, 34, 35 has one line of text. Reformatted to conform with British first edition.*

OBADIAH OLDBUCK, THE ADVENTURES OF MR. (E,G)
Wilson & Co, 162 Nassau, NY: nd (early-1850s) (5-11/16x8-3/8", 84 pgs, B&W, yellow-c
nn - 3rd USA Printing by Rodolphe Töpffer; title page by Robert Cruikshank (Very Rare)
Says By Timothy Crayon, an obvious pseudonym 750.00 1500.00 4500.00
NOTE: *Front cover banner the giant is holding says "Done With Drawings By Timothy Crayon, Gypsographer, 188 Comic Etchings On Antimony" Title page changes address to No. 15 Spruce-Street. (Late 162 Nassau Street.)*

OBADIAH OLDBUCK, THE ADVENTURES OF MR..
Brother Jonathan Offices: ND (mid-1850s) (5-11/16x8-3/8", 84 pages, B&W, oblong)
nn - 4th printing; Originally by Rodolphe Töpffer (Very Rare) 750.00 1500.00 4500.00
NOTE: *Cover States: "New York: Published at the Brother Jonathan Office". Front cover banner the giant is holding says "Done With Drawings By Timothy Crayon, Gypsographer, 188 Comic Designs On Antimony."*

OBADIAH OLDBUCK, THE ADVENTURES OF MR. (E,G)
Dick & Fitzgerald, New York: nd (various printings; est. 1870s to 1888)
(Thirty Cents, 84 pgs, B&W, paper-c) (all versions scarce)
nn - Black print on green cover(5-11/16x8-15/16"); string bound 200.00 400.00 1200.00
nn - Black print on blue cover; same format as green-c 200.00 400.00 1200.00
nn - Black print on white cover(5-13/16x9-3/16"); staple bound beneath cover);
this is a later printing than the blue or green-c 200.00 400.00 1200.00
NOTE: *Reprints the abbreviated 1849 Wilson & Co. 2nd printing. Pages are numbered via Arabic numerals. Many of the panels on Pages 11, 14, 19, 21, 24, 34, 35 take two lines to print the same words found in the Wilson & Co version, which used only one text line for the same panels. Unknown whether the blue or green cover is earlier. White cover version has "thirty cents" line blackened out on the two copies known to exist. Robert Cruikshank's title page has been made the cover in the D&F editions.*

OLD FOGY'S COMIC ALMANAC
Philip J. Cozans, NY: 1858 (4-7/8x7-1/4, 48 pgs)
nn - sequential comic strip told one panel per page 46.00 92.00 275.00
NOTE: *Contains (12) panel "Fourth of July in New York" sequential*

OLD MOTHER MITTEN AND HER FUNNY KITTEN (see also **The Juvenile Gem**) (O)
Huestis & Cozans: nd(1850-1852) (6x3-7/8"12pgs, hand colored paper-c, B&W)
nn - first printing(s) publisher's address is 104 Nassau Street (1850-1851)
(Very Rare) (no known sales)
NOTE: *A hand colored outer cover is highly rare, with only 1 recorded copy possessing it. Front cover image and text is repeated precisely on page 3 (albeit b&w), and only interior pages are numbered, together leading owners of coverless copies to believe they have the cover. The true back cover has ads for the publisher. Cover was issued only with copies which were sold separately - books which were bound together as part of THE JUVENILE GEM never had such covers.*

OLD MOTHER MITTEN AND HER FUNNY KITTEN (see JUVENILE GEM) (O)
Philip J. Cozans: nd (1850-1852) (6x3-7/8",12 pgs, hand colored paper-c, B&W)
nn - Second printing(s) publisher's address is 116 Nassau Street (1851-1852)
(Very Rare) (no known sales)
nn - Third printing(s) publisher's address is 107 Nassau Street (1852+)
(Very Rare) (no known sales)

OLD MOTHER MITTEN AND HER FUNNY KITTEN
Americana Review, Scotia, NY: nd (1960's) (6-1/4x4-1/8", 8 pgs, side-stapled, cardboard, B&W)
nn - Modern reprint 4.00 8.00 25.00
NOTE: *Issued within a folder titled SIX CHILDREN'S BOOKS OF THE 1850'S. States "Reprinted by American Review" at bottom of front cover. Reprints the 104 Nassau Street address.*

ON THE NILE (O,G)
James R. Osgood & Co., Boston: 1874 ; **Houghton, Osgood & Co., Boston:** 1880 (112 pgs, gilted green hardcover, B&W)
1st printing (1874; 10-3/4x16") - by Augustus Hoppin 38.00 76.00 225.00
2nd printing (1880; smaller sized) 22.00 44.00 130.00

OSCAR SHANGHAI, THE EXTRAORDINARY AND MIRTH-PROVKING ADVENTURES BY SEA & LAND OF (O, G)
Garrett & Co., Publishers, No. 18 Ann Street, New York: May 1855 (5-3/4x9-1/4", 100 pgs, printed one side only, paper-c, 25¢, B&W)
nn - Samuel Avery-c; interior by ALC Very Rare) 700.00 1400.00 4200.00
NOTE: *Not much is known of this first edition as the data comes from a recently rediscovered* ***Brother Jonathan*** *catalog issued circa 1853-55. No original known yet to exist.*

OSCAR SHANGHAI, THE WONDERFUL AND AMUSING DOINGS BY SEA AND LAND OF (G)
Dick & Fitzgerald, 10 Ann St, NY: nd (1870s-1888) (25 ¢, 5-3/4x9-1/4", 100 pgs, printed one side only, green paper c, B&W)
nn - Cover by Samuel Avery; interior by ALC (Rare) 229.00 458.00 1375.00
NOTE: *Exact reprint of Garrett & Co original.*

OUR ARTIST IN CUBA (O)
Carleton, New York: 1865 (6-5/8x4-3/8", 120 pgs, printed one side only, gilted hard-c, B&W)
nn - By Geo. W. Carleton 38.00 76.00 225.00

OUR ARTIST IN CUBA, PERU, SPAIN, AND ALGIERS (O)
Carleton: 1877 (6-1/2x5-1/8", 156 pgs, hard-c, B&W)
nn - By Geo. W. Carleton 38.00 76.00 225.00
nn - By Geo. W. Carleton (wraps paper cover) (Rare) 38.00 76.00 225.00
NOTE: *Reprints OUR ARTIST IN CUBA and OUR ARTIST IN PERU, then adds new section on Spain and Algiers.*

OUR ARTIST IN PERU (O)
Carleton, New York: 1866 (7-3/4x5-7/8", 68 pgs, gilted hardcover, B&W)
nn- By Geo. W. Carleton 28.00 56.00 170.00
NOTE: *Contains advertisement for the upcoming books* ***OUR ARTIST IN ITALY*** *and* ***OUR ARTIST IN FRANCE****, but no such publications have been found to date.*

PARSON SOURBALL'S EUROPEAN TOUR (O)
Duff and Ashmead: 1867 (6x7-1/2", 76 pgs, blue embossed title hard-c)
nn - By Horace Cope 71.00 142.00 425.00
NOTE: *see* **REV. MR. SOURBALL'S EUROPEAN TOUR, THE** *for the soft paper cover version*

PEN AND INK SKETCHES OF YALE NOTABLES (O,S)
Soule, Thomas and Winsor, St. Louis: 1872 (12-1/4x9-3/4", B&W)
By Squills 22.00 44.00 130.00
NOTE: *Printed by Steamlith Press, The R.P. Studley Company, St Louis.*

PETER PIPER IN BENGAL
Bengamin H Day.Publisher, Brother Jonathan Cheap Book Establishment, 48 Beekman, NY: 1953-55 (6-5/8x4-1/4, 36 pgs, yellow paper-c, B&W, 3 cents - two dollars per hundred) (Very Rare)
nn - By John Tenniel - 32 panel comic strip Punch-r 416.00 832.00 2500.00
NOTE: *Actually also a catalog of inexpensive books, prints, maps and half a dozen comic books for sale on separate pages from publishers Day and Garrett - see full story of this brand new find in the Victorian Era essay. A complete copy with split spine sold in November 2002 for $750.00. Published date most likely 1855.*

THE PHILADELPHIA COMIC ALMANAC (S)
G. Strong, 44 Strawberry St, NYC: 1835 (8-1/2x5", 36 pgs)
nn - 104.00 208.00 625.00
NOTE: *77 engravings full of recurring cartoon characters but not sequential; early use of recurring characters.*

PHIL MAY'S SKETCH BOOK (E,S,M)
R.H. Russell, New York: 1899 (14-5/8x10", 64 pgs, brown hard-c, B&W)
nn - By Phil May 27.00 54.00 160.00
NOTE: *American reprint of the British edition.*

PHUNNY PHELLOW, THE
Oakie, Dayton & Jones: Oct 1859-1876; **Street & Smith** 1876: (Folio Monthly)
average issue with Thomas Nast 42.00 84.00 250.00

PHUN FOTOCRAFT, KEWREUS KONSEETS KOMICALLY ILLUSTRATED BY A KWEER FELLER (N) (see **NEW YORK PICAYUNE**)
The New York Picayune, NY: 1850s (104 pgs)
nn - Mostly Frank Bellew, some John Leach 250.00 500.00 1500.00
NOTE: *Many sequential comic strips as well as single cartoons all collected from The New York Picayune. Ross & Tousey, Agents, 121 Nassau St, NY. The Picayune ran many sequential comic strips in its decade.*

PICTORIAL HISTORY OF SENATOR SLIM'S VOYAGE TO EUROPE
Dr. Herrick & Brother, Chemists, Albany, NY: 1860 (3-1/4x4-3/4", 32 pgs, B&W)
nn - By John McLenan Very Rare 104.00 208.00 625.00

PICTURES OF ENGLISH SOCIETY (Parchment-Paper Series, No.4) (M,S,E)
D. Appleton & Co., New York: 1884 (5-5/8x4-3/8", 108 pgs, paper-c, B&W)
4 - By George du Maurier; Punch-r 23.00 46.00 135.00
NOTE: *Every other page is a full page cartoon, with the opposite page containing the cartoon's caption.*

PICTURES OF LIFE AND CHARACTER (M,S,E)
Bradbury and Evans, London: No.1 1855 - No.5 c1864 (12-1/2x18", 100 pgs, illustrated hard-c, B&W)
nn (No.1) (1855) 32.00 64.00 190.00
2 (1858), 3 (1860) 32.00 64.00 190.00
4 (nd; c1862) 5 (nd; c1864) 32.00 64.00 190.00
nn (nd (late 1860's) 28.00 56.00 170.00
NOTE: *2-1/2x18-1/4", 494 pgs, green gilted-c) reprints 1-5 in one book*
1-3 John Leech's... (nd; 12-3/8x10", ? pgs, red gilted-c). 20.00 40.00 120.00
NOTE: *Reprints John Leech cartoons from* ***Punch****. note that the Volume Number is mentioned only on the last page of these versions.*

PICTURES OF LIFE AND CHARACTER (E,M,S)
G.P. Putnam's Sons: 1880's (8-5/8x6-1/4", 218 pgs, hardcover, color-cr, B&W)
nn - John Leech (single panel **Punch** cartoon-r) 33.00 66.00 200.00
NOTE: *Leech reprints which extend back to the 1850s.*

PICTURES OF LIFE AND CHARACTER (Parchment-Paper Series) (E,M,S)
(see also Humerous Masterpieces)
D. Appleton & Co., NY: 1884 (30¢, 5-3/4 x 4-1/2", 104 pgs, paper-c, B&W)
nn - John Leech (single panel **Punch** cartoon-r) 28.00 56.00 170.00
NOTE: *An advertisment in the back refers to a cloth-bound edition for 50 cents.*

The Wonderful and Amusing Doings by Sea & Land of Oscar Shanghai
1870s © Dick & Fitzgerald, New York

The Adventures of Obadiah Oldbuck
© Brother Jonathan Offices, NY

FR1.0 GD2.0 FN6.0

PIPPIN AMONG THE WIDE-AWAKES (O,S)
Werill & Chapin, 113 Nassau St, NYC, NY): 1860 (6x4-1/2", 36 pgs, 6 cents)

nn - Artist unknown (Very Rare) 75.00 150.00 450.00

PLISH AND PLUM (E.G)
Roberts Brothers, Boston: 1883 (8-1/8x5-3/4", 80 pgs, hardcover, B&W)

nn - By Wilhelm Busch 38.00 76.00 230.00
nn - Reprint (Roberts Brothers, 1895) 33.00 66.00 200.00
nn - Reprint (Little, Brown & Co., 1899) 33.00 66.00 200.00
NOTE: *The adventures of two dogs.*

POUNDS OF FUN
Frank Tousey, 34 North Moore St, NY: 1881 (6-1/2x9-1/2", 68pgs, B&W)
nn - Bellew, Worth, Woolf, Chips 33.00 66.00 200.00

PRESIDENTS MESSAGE, THE
G.P. Putnam's Sons, NY: 1887 (5-3/4x7-5/8, 44 pgs)

nn - (19) Thomas Nast single panel full page cartoons 38.00 76.00 220.00

PROTECT THE U.S. FROM JOHN BULL - PROTECTION PICTURES FROM JUDGE
Judge Publishing, New York: 1888 ((10 cents, 6-7/8x10-3/8", 36 pgs, paper-c, B&W)

nn - (Scarce) 27.00 54.00 160.00
NOTE: *Reprints both cartoons and commentary from **Puck**, concerning the issue of tariffs which were then being debated in Congress. Art by Gillam, Hamilton, Victor.*

PUCK (German language edition, St. Louis) (M,O) (see also Die Vehme)
Publisher unknown, St. Louis: No.1, March 18, 1871 - No. ??, Aug. 24, 1872 (B&W, paper-c)

1-?? (Very Rare) by Joseph Keppler (no known sales)
NOTE: *Joseph Keppler's second attempt at a weekly humor periodical, following **Die Vehme** one year earlier. This was his first attempt to launch using the title **Puck**. This German language version ran for a full year before being joined by an English language version.*

PUCK (English language edition, St. Louis) (M,O)
Publisher unknown, St. Louis: No.1, March ?? 1872 - No. ??, Aug. 24, 1872 (B&W, paper c)

1-?? (Very Rare) by Joseph Keppler (no known sales)
NOTE: *Same material as in the German language edition, but in English.*

PUCK, ILLUSTRIRTES HUMORISTISCHES WOCHENBLATT (German language edition, NYC) (M,O)
Keppler & Schwarzmann, New York: No.1 Sept (27) 1876 - 1164 Dec ?? 1899 (10 cents, color front/back-c and centerspread, remainder B&W, paper-c)

1-26 (Volume 1; Rare) by Joseph Keppler - these issues precede the English language version, and contain cartoons not found in them. Includes cartoons on the controversial Tilden-Hayes 1876 Presidential Election debacle. (no known sales)
27-52 (Volume 2; Rare) by Joseph Keppler - contains some cartoon material not found in the English language editions. Particularly in the earlier issues. (no known sales)
53-1164 12.00 24.00 70.00
Bound Volumes (six month, 26 issue run each):
Vol. 1 (Rare) (no known sales)
Vol. 2-4 (Rare) (no known sales)
Vol. 5-47 52.00 104.00 310.00
NOTE: *Joseph Keppler's second, and successful, attempt to launch **Puck**. In German. The first six months precede the launch of the English language edition. Soon after (but not immediately after) the launch of the English edition, both editions began sharing the same cartoons, but, their prose material always remained different. The German language edition ceased publication at the end of 1899, while the English language edition continued into the early 20th Century. First American periodical to feature printed color every issue.*

PUCK (English language edition, NYC) (M,O)
Keppler & Schwarzmann, New York: No.1 March (14) 1877 - 1190 Dec ?? 1899 (10 cents, color front/back-c and centerspread, remainder B&W, paper-c)

1 (Rare) by Joseph Keppler (no known sales)
2-26 (Rare) by Joseph Keppler (no known sales)
27-1190 10.00 20.00 60.00
(see Platinum Age section for year 1900+ issues)
Bound volumes (six month, 26 issue run each):
Vol. 1 (Rare) (one set sold on eBay for $2300.00)
Vol. 2 (Scarce) (one set sold on eBay for $1500.00)
Vol. 3-6 (pre-1880 issues) 133.00 266.00 800.00
Vol. 7-46 100.00 200.00 600.00
NOTE: *The English language editions began six months after the German editions, and so the English edition numbering is always one volume number, and 26 issue numbers, behind its parallel German language edition. Pre-1880 & post-1900 issues are more scarce than 1880's & 1890's.*

PUCK (miniature) (M,P,I)
Keppler & Schwarzmann, New York: nd (c1895) (7x5-1/8", 12 pgs, color front & back paper-c, B&W interior)

nn - Scarce 20.00 40.00 120.00
NOTE: *C.J.Taylor-c; F.M.Howarth-a; F.Opper-a; giveaway item promoting **Puck's** various publications. Mostly text, with art reprinted from **Puck**.*

PUCK, CARTOONS FROM (M,S)
Keppler & Schwarzmann, New York: 1893 (14-1/4x11-1/2", 244 pgs, hard-c, mostly B&W)

nn - by Joseph Keppler (Signed and Numbered) 83.00 166.00 500.00
NOTE: *Reprints Keppler cartoons from 1877 to 1893, mostly in B&W, though a few in color, with a text opposite each cartoon explaining the situation then being satirized. Issued only in an edition of 300 numbered issues, signed by Keppler. Only 1/4 of the pages are cartoons.*

PUCK'S LIBRARY (M)
Keppler & Schwarzmann, New York: No.1, July, 1887 - No. 174, Dec, 1899 (10 cents, 11-1/2x8-1/4", 36 pgs, color paper-c, B&W)

1- "The National Game" (Baseball) 50.00 100.00 300.00

FR1.0 GD2.0 FN6.0

2-149 10.00 20.00 60.00
NOTE: ***Puck's Library** was a monthly magazine reprinting cartoons & prose from **Puck**, with each issue's material organized around the same subject. The cover art was often original. All issues were kept in print for the duration of the series, so later issues are more scarce than earlier ones.*

PUCK, PICKINGS FROM (M)
Keppler & Schwarzmann, New York: No.1, Sept, 1891 - No. 34, Dec, 1899 (25 cents, 13-1/4x10-1/4", 68 pgs, color paper-c, B&W)

1-34 Scarce 20.00 40.00 120.00
NOTE: *Similar to **Puck's Library**, except larger in size, and issued quarterly. All reprint material, except for the cover art. There also exist variations with "RAILROAD EDITION 30 CENTS" printed on the cover in place of the standard 25 cent price.*

PUCK PROOFS (M,P,S)
Keppler & Schwarzmann, New York: nd (1906-1909) (74 pgs, paper cover; B&W) (all are Scarce)

nn - (c.1906, no price, 4-1/8x5-1/4") B&W painted -c of couple kissing over a chess board; 1905 & 1906-r 21.00 42.00 125.00
nn- (c.1909, 10 cents, 4-3/8x5-3/8") plain green paper-c; 76 pgs 1905-1909-r 21.00 42.00 125.00
NOTE: *Catalog of prints available from **Puck**, reprinting mostly cover & centerspread art from **Puck**. There likely exist more as yet unreported **Puck Proofs** catalogs. Art by Rose O'Neill.*

PUCK'S OPPER BOOK (M)
Keppler & Schwarzmann, New York: 1888 (11-3/4x13-7/8", color paper-c, 68 pgs,interior B&W, 30¢)

nn - (Very Rare) by F. Opper 142.00 284.00 850.00
NOTE: *Puck's first book collecting work by a single artist.; mostly sequential comic strips.*

PUCK'S PRINTING BOOK FOR CHILDREN (S,O.I)
Keppler & Schwarzman, Pubs, NY: 1891 (10-3/8x7-7/8", 52 pgs, color-c, B&W and color)

nn - Frederick B Opper (Very Rare) (no known sales)

NOTE: *Left side printed in color; Right side B&W to be colored in.*

PUCK, THE TARIFF ?, CARTOONS AND COMMENTS FROM (M,S)
Keppler & Schwarzmann, New York: 1888 (10 cents, 6-7/8x10-3/8", 36 pgs, paper-c, B&W)

nn - (Scarce) 38.00 76.00 225.00
NOTE: *Reprints both cartoons and commentary from **Puck**, concerning the issue of tariffs which were then being debated in Congress. Art by Gillam, Keppler, Opper, Taylor.*

PUCK, WORLD'S FAIR
Keppler & Schwarzmann, PUCK BUILDING, World's Fair Grounds, Chicago: No.1 May 1, 1893 - No.26 Oct 30, 1893 (10 cents, 11-1/4x8-3/4, 14 pgs, paper-c, color front/back/center pages, rest B&W)(All issues Scarce to Rare)

1-26 27.00 54.00 160.00
1-26 bound volume: 417.00 834.00 2500.00
NOTE: *Art by Joseph Keppler, F. Opper, F.M. Howarth, C.J. Taylor, W.A. Rogers. This was a separate, parallel run of **Puck**, published during the 1893 Chicago World's Fair from within the fairgrounds, and containing all new and different material than the regular weekly **Puck**. Smaller sized and priced the same, this originally sold poorly, and had not as wide distribution as **Puck**, and so consequently issues are much more rare than regular **Puck** issues from the same period. Not to be confused with the larger sized regular **Puck** issues from 1893 which sometimes also contained World's Fair related material, and sometimes had the words "World's Fair" appear on the cover. Can also be distinguished by the fact that **Puck's** issue numbering was in the 800's in 1893, while these issue number 1 through 26.*

PUNCHINELLO
Punchinello Publishing Co, NYC: April 2-Dec 24 1870 (weekly)

1-39 Henry L. Stephens, Frank Bellew, Bowlend 19.00 38.00 115.00
NOTE: *Funded by the Tweed Ring, mild politics attacking Grant Admin & other NYC newspapers. Bound copies exist.*

QUIDDITIES OF AN ALASKAN TRIP (O,G)
G.A. Steel & Co., Portland, OR: 1873 (6-3/4x10-1/2", 80 pgs, gilted hard-c, Red-c and Blue-c exist, B&W) (A nice copy sold for $87 in 2018)

nn - By William H. Bell (Scarce) 300.00 600.00 1800.00
NOTE: *Highly sought Western Americana collectors. Parody of a trip from Washington DC to Alaska, by a member of the team which went to survey Alaska, purchase commonly known then as "Seward's Folly".*

"RAG TAGS" AND THEIR ADVENTURES, THE (N,S)
A. M. Robertson, San Francisco: 1899 (10-1/4x13-7/8, 84 pgs, color hard-c, B&W inside)

nn - By Arthur M. Lewis (SF Chronicle newspaper-r) (Scarce) 52.00 104.00 310.00

RAYS OF LIGHT (O,P)
Morse Bros., Canton, Mass.: No.1 1886 (7-1/8x5-1/8", 8 pgs, color paper-c, B&W)

1- (Rare) 33.00 66.00 200.00
NOTE: *Giveaway pamphlet in guise of an educational publication, consisting entirely of a sequential story in which a teacher instructs her classroom of young girls in the use of Rising Sun Stove Polish. Color front & back covers.*

RELIC OF THE ITALIAN REVOLUTION OF 1849, A
Gabici's Music Stores, New Orleans: 1849 (10-1/8x12-3/4", 144 pgs, hardcover)

nn - By G. Daelli (Scarce) 75.00 150.00 450.00
NOTE: *From the title page: "Album of fifty line engravings, executed on copper, by the most eminent artists at Rome in 1849; secreted from the papal police after the 'Restoration of Order,' And just imported into America."*

REMARKS ON THE JACOBINIAD (I,S)
E.W. Weld & W. Greenough, Boston: 1795-98 (8-1/4x5-1/8", 72 pgs, a number of B&W plates with text)

nn - Written by Rev. James Sylvester Gardner,artist unknown (Rare) (no known sales)
NOTE: *Early comics-type characters. Not sequential comics, but uses word balloons. Satire directed against "The Jacobin Club," supporters of the French Revolution and Radical Republicans. Gardner came to America from England in 1783, was minister of Trinity Church, Boston. There appears to be some reprints of this done as late as 1798.*

REV. MR. SOURBALL'S EUROPEAN TOUR, THE RECREATION OF A CITY, THE
Duffield Ashmead, Philadelphia: 1867 (7-5/8x6-1/4", 72 pgs, turquoise blue soft wrappers)
By Horace Cope (Rare) 38.00 75.00 225.00
NOTE: see **PARSON SOURBALL'S EUROPEAN TOUR** for the hard cover version.

RHYMES OF NONSENSE TRUTH & FICTION (S)
G.W. Carleton & Co, Publishers, NY: 1874 (10x7-3/4", 44 pgs, hard-c, B&W) (Very Rare)
nn - By Chaucer Jones and Michael Angelo Raphael Smith 92.00 184.00 550.00
NOTE: *Creator names obviously pseudonyms; looks like weak A.B. Frost.*

ROMANCE OF A HAMMOCK, THE - AS RECITED BY MR. GUS WILLIAMS IN "ONE OF THE FINEST" (O,P)
Unknown: 1880s (5-1/2x3-5/8" folded, 7 attached cardboard cards which fold out into a strip, color)
nn - By presently unknown Scarce 67.00 134.00 400.00
NOTE: *12-panel story, which one begins reading on one side of the folded-out strip, then flip to the other side to continue -- unlike the vast majority of folded strips, which are printed on only one side. This was a promotional handout, for a play titled "One of the Finest". The story pictured comes from a poem read in the play by then famous New York stage actor Gus Williams, who is pictured on the "cover"/title card."*

SAD TALE OF THE COURTSHIP OF CHEVALIER SLYFOX-WIKOF, SHOWING HIS HEART-RENDING ASTOUNDING & MOST WONDERFUL LOVE ADVENTURES WITH FANNY ELSSLER AND MISS GAMBOL, THE (O,G)
Garrett & Co., NY: Jan 1856 (25 ¢, 5-3/4x9-1/4", 100 pages, paper-c, B&W)
nn - By T.C. Bond ?? (Very Rare) 417.00 834.00 2500.00
NOTE: *No surviving copies yet reported -- known via ads in Home Circle published by Garrett. Cover art by John McLenan and Samuel Avery. Graphic novel parodying the real-life romance between European actress/ dancer Fanny Elssler and American aristocrat Henry Wikoff. The entire graphic novel is reprinted in the 1976 book "Fanny Elssler in America."*

SAD TALE OF THE COURTSHIP OF CHEVALIER SLYFOX-WIKOF, SHOWING HIS HEART-RENDING ASTOUNDING & MOST WONDERFUL LOVE ADVENTURES WITH FANNY ELSSLER AND MISS GUMBEL, THE (G) (25 cents printed on cover)
Dick And Fitzgerald, NY: 1870s-1888 (5-3/4x9-1/4", ??? pages, soft paper-c, B&W)
nn - By T.C. Bond ?? (Very Rare) 217.00 434.00 1300.00
NOTE: *Reprint of Garrett original printing before G,D&F partnership begins.*

SALT RIVER GUIDE FOR DISAPPOINTED POLITICIANS
Winchell, Small & Co., 113 Fulton St, NY: 1870s (16 pgs, 10¢)
nn - single panel cartoons from WIld Oats (Rare) 54.00 108.00 325.00

SAM SLICK'S COMIC ALMANAC
Philip J. Cozans, NYC: 1857 (7.5x4.5, 48 pgs, B&W) 73.00 146.00 440.00
NOTE: *Contains reprint of "Moses Keyser the Bowery Bully's Trip to the California Gold Mines" from Elton's Comic Almanac #17 1850.*

SCRAPS (O,S) (see also **F****** A*** K*******)
D.C. Johnston, Boston: 1828 - No.8 1840; New Series No.1 1849 (12 pgs, printed one side only, paper-c, B&W)
1 - 1828 (9-1/4 x 11-3/4") (Very Rare) (no known sales)
2 - 1830 (9-3/4 x 12-3/4") (Very Rare) (no known sales)
3 - 1832 (10-7/8 x 13-1/8") (Very Rare) (no known sales)
4 - 1833 (11 x 13-5/8") (Very Rare) (no known sales)
5- 1834 (10-3/8 x 13-3/8") (Very Rare) (no known sales)
6 - 1835 (10-3/8 x 13-1/4") red lettering in title SCRAPS (Very Rare)
217.00 434.00 1300.00
6 - 1835 (10-3/8 x 13-1/4") no red lettering in title (Rare)
183.00 366.00 1100.00
7 - 1837 (10-3/4 x 13-7/8") 1st Edition (Very Rare) 150.00 300.00 900.00
7 - 1837 (10-3/4 x 13-3/4") 2nd Edition (so stated) 63.00 125.00 375.00
NOTE: *20 pgs. of text (double-sided), 4 pgs. of art (single-sided), plus the covers. There are no protective sheets between the art pages.*
8 - 1840 (10-1/2 x 13-7/8") (Rare) 150.00 300.00 900.00
New Series 1- 1849 (10-7/8 x 13-3/4") 83.00 166.00 500.00
NOTE: *By David Claypoole Johnston. All issues consist of four one-sided sheets with 9 to 12 single panel cartoons per sheet. The other pages are blank or text. With #1-5 the size of the pages can vary up to an inch. Contains 4 protective sheets (not part of page count) Only 1 3 4 and the 1849 New Series Number 1 has cover art along with 4 art pgs. (single sided) with 4 protective sheets and no text pages.New Series Number 1, as well as #6 with bo red lettering and the second printing of issue 7, have survived in higher numbers due to a 1940s warehouse discovery.*

THE SETTLEMENT OF RHODE ISLAND (O)
The Graphic Co. Photo-Lith 39 & 41, Park Place, New York: 1874 (11-3/8x10, 40 pgs, gilted blue hard-c
nn - Charles T. Miller & Walter F. Brown 50.00 100.00 300.00
NOTE: *This is also the Same Walter F. Brown that did "Hail Columbia".*

SHAKESPEARE WOULD RIDE THE BICYCLE IF ALIVE TODAY. "THE REASON WHY" (O,P,S)
Cleveland Bicycles H.A. Lozier & Co., Toledo, OH: 1896 (5-1/2x4",16 pgs, paper-c, color)
nn - By F. Opper (Rare) 63.00 126.00 375.00
NOTE: *Original cartoons of Shakespearian characters riding bicycles; also popular amongst collectors of bicycle ephemera.*

SHAKINGS - ETCHINGS FROM THE NAVAL ACADEMY BY A MEMBER OF THE CLASS OF '67 (O,S)
Lee & Shepard, Boston: 1867 (7-7/8x10", 132 pages, blue hard-c)
By: Park Benjamin 29.00 58.00 175.00
NOTE: *Park Benjamin later became editor of Harper's Bazaar magazine.*

SHOO FLY PICTORIAL (S)
John Stetson, Chestnut sT Theatre, Phila, PA: June 1870 (15-1/2x11-1/2", 8 pgs, B&W)
1 50.00 100.00 300.00

SHYS AT SHAKSPEARE
J.P. and T.C.P., Philadelphia: 1869 (9-1/4x6", 52 pgs)
nn - Artist unknown 54.00 108.00 325.00

SKETCHES OF LOWLY LIFE IN A GREAT CITY (M,S) (See 99 "Woolfs" From Truth)
G. P. Puntam's Sons: 1899 (8-5/8x11-1/4", 200 pgs, hard-c, B&W)
(reprints from Life and Judge of Woolf's cartoons of NYC slum children)
nn - By Michael Angelo Woolf 71.00 142.00 425.00
NOTE: *Woolf's cartoons are regarded as a primary influence on R.F. Outcault in the later development of The Yellow Kid newspaper strip.*

SNAP (O,S)
Valentine & Townsend, Tribune Bldg, NYC: March 13,1885 (17x11, 8 pgs, B&W)
1-Contains a sequential comic strip 33.00 66.00 200.00

SOCIETY PICTURES (M,S,E)
Charles H. Sergel Company, Chicago: 1895 (5-1/4x7-3/4", 168 pgs, printed 1 side, paper-c, B&W)
nn - By George du Maurier; reprints from **Punch**. 21.00 42.00 125.00

SOLDIERS AND SAILORS HALF DIME TALES OF THE LATE REBELLION
Soldiers & Sailors Publishing Co: 1868 (5-1/4x7-7/8", 32 pgs)
v1#1-#16 v2#1-#10 10.00 20.00 60.00
v2 #11 contains (5) page comic strip 25.00 50.00 100.00
NOTE: *Changes to Soldiers & Sailors Half Dime Magazine with v2 #1.*

SOUVENIR CONTAINING CARTOONS ISSUED BY THE PRESS BUREAU OF THE OHIO STATE REPUBLICAN EXECUTIVE COMMITTEE, A (S)
Ohio State Republican Executive Committee, Columbus, OH: 1899 (10-3/8x13-1/2, 248 pgs, Hard-c, B&W
nn - By William L. Bloomer (Scarce) 79.00 158.00 475.00

SOUVENIR OF SOHMER CARTOONS FROM PUCK, JUDGE, AND FRANK LESLIE'S (M,S,P)
Sohmer Piano Co.: nd(c.1893) (6x4-3/4", 16 pgs, paper-c, B&W)
nn 17.00 34.00 100.00
NOTE: *Reprints painted "cartoon" Sohmer Piano advertisements which appeared in the above publications. Artists include Keppler, Gillam, others.*

SPORTING NEW YORKER, THE
Ornum & Co, Beekman ST, NYC: 1870s
issues with sequential comic strips (Rare) 33.00 66.00 200.00

STORY OF THE MAN OF HUMANITY AND THE BULL CALF, THE
(see Bull Calf, The Story of The Man Of Humanity And The)
NOTE: *Reprints of two of A. B. Frost's mostfamous sequential comic strips.*

STREET & SMITH'S LITERARY ALBUM
Street & Smith, NY: #1 Dec 23 1865-#225 Apr 9 1870 (11-3/4x16-3/4", 16 pgs, B&W)
1 (23 Dec 1865) 17.00 34.00 100.00
2-129 131-225 (issues with short sequential strips) 17.00 34.00 100.00
130 (Steam Man satire parody) 58.00 116.00 350.00

STUFF AND NONSENSE (Harper's Monthly strip-r) (M)
Charles Scribner's Sons: 1884 (10-1/4x7-3/4", 100 pgs, hardcover, B&W)
nn - By Arthur Burdett Frost 71.00 142.00 425.00
nn - By A.B. Frost (1888 reprint, 104 pgs) 36.00 72.00 215.00
NOTE: *Earliest known anthology devoted to collecting the comic strips of a single American artist. 1888 2nd printing has a different cover and is layed out somewhat differently inside with a new title page, 3 added pages of cartoons, and a couple more illustrations. For more Frost, the 2nd is worth checki ng out also.*

STUMPING IT (LAUGHING SERIES BRICKTOP STORIES #8) (O,S)
Collin & Small, NY: 1876 (6-5/8x9-1/4, 68 pgs, perfect bound, B&W)
nn - Thomas Worth art abounds (some sequentials) 71.00 142.00 425.00
NOTE: Mainly single panel cartoons w/text; however, some sequential comic strips inside worth picking up

SUMMER SCHOOL OF PHILOSOPHY AT MT. DESERT, THE
Henry Holt & Co.: 1881 (10-3/8x8-5/8", 60 pgs, illus. gilt hard-c, B&W)
nn - By J. A. Mitchell 44.00 88.00 265.00
NOTE: *J.A.Mitchell went on to found **LIFE** two years later in 1883. Also, the long-running mascot for **LIFE** was Cupid - which you see multitudes of Cupids flying around in this story.*

SURE WATER CURE, THE
Carey Grey & Hart, Phila, PA: c1841-43 (8-/2x5, 32 pgs, B&W
nn - proto-comic-strip Very Rare 142.00 284.00 850.00

TAILOR-MADE GIRL, HER FRIENDS, HER FASHIONS, AND HER FOLLIES, THE
(see also IN THE "400" AND OUT) (M)
Charles Scribner's Sons, New York: 1888 (8-3/8x10-1/2", 68 pgs, hard-c, B&W)
nn - Art by C.J. Taylor 22.00 44.00 130.00
NOTE: *Format is a full page cartoon on every other page, with a script style vignette, written by Philip H. Welch, on every page opposite the art.*

TALL STUDENT, THE
Roberts Brothers, Boston: 1873 (7x5", 48 pgs, printed one side only, gilted hard-c, B&W)
nn - By Wilhelm Busch (Scarce) 27.00 54.00 160.00

TARIFF ?, CARTOONS AND COMMENTS FROM PUCK, THE (see Puck, The Tariff...)

TEASING TOM AND NAUGHTY NED WITH A SPOOL OF CLARK'S COTTON, THE ADVENTURES OF (O,P)
Clark's O.N.T. Spool Cotton: 1879 (4-1/4x3", 12 pgs, B&W, paper-c)
nn 18.00 36.00 110.00
NOTE: *Knock-off of the "First Trick" in Wilhelm Busch's **Max and Maurice**, modified to involve Clark's Spool Cotton in the story, with similar but new art by an artist identified as "HB". The back cover advertises the specific merchant who gave this booklet away -- multiple variations of back cover suspected.*

TEMPERANCE TALES; OR, SIX NIGHTS WITH THE WASHINGTONIANS, VOL I & II
W.A. Leary & Co., Philadelphia: 1848 (50¢, 6-1/8x4", 328 pgs, B&W, hard-c)
nn 108.00 216.00 650.00
NOTE: *Mostly text. This edition gathers Volume I & II together. The first 8 pages reprints George Cruikshank's **THE BOTTLE**, re-drawn & re-engraved by Phil A. Pilliner. Later editions of this book do not include **THE BOTTLE** reprint and are therefore of little interest to comics collectors.*

TEXAS SIFTINGS
Texas Siftings Publishing Co, Austin, Texas (1881-1887), **NYC** (1887-1897): 1881-1885 newspaper-size weekly; 1886-1897 folio weekly (15x10-3/4", 16 pgs, B&W 10¢
1881-1885 issues 23.00 46.00 140.00
v6#1 (5/8/86) (8) panel strip Afterwhich He Emigrated;
(16) panel The Tenor's Triumph Veni Vidi Vici 17.00 34.00 100.00
v6#2 (5/16/86) (5) panel sewuential 17.00 34.00 100.00
v6#3 no sequentials 17.00 34.00 100.00
v6#4 (5/29/86) Worth-c (4) panel Worth strip; (2) panel 17.00 34.00 100.00
v6#5 no sequentials 17.00 34.00 100.00
v6#6 (6/12/86) Comic Strip Cover (11) panels The Rise of a Great Artist
(5) panel sequential 34.00 68.00 205.00
v6#7 (6/19/86) Worth-c (2) panel Wiorth;
(10) panel Ha! Ha! The Honest Youth & the Lordly Villain 18.00 36.00 110.00
v6#8 (6/26/86) Worth-c; (15) panel The Kangaroo Hunter 18.00 36.00 110.00
v6#9 (7/3/86) Worth-c; Bellew (2) panel How Wives Get What They Want
17.00 34.00 100.00
v6#10 ((7/10/86) Baseball-c; (3) panel;

Rays of Light
1886 © Morse Bros., Canton, Mass.

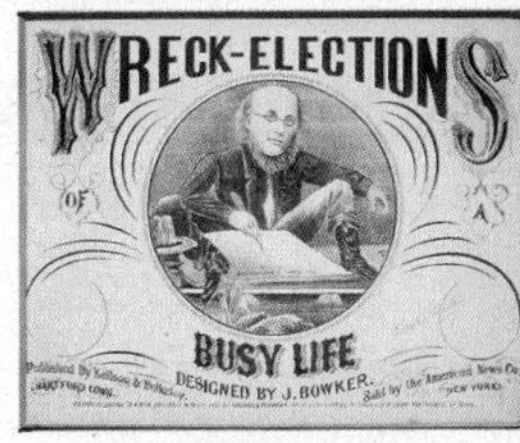

Wreck-Elections Of Busy Life
Kellogg & Buckeley © 1864?

Shakespeare Would Ride The Bicycle If Alive Today
1896 © Cleveland Bicycles, Toledo, OH.

FR1.0 GD2.0 FN6.0

(5) panel A Story Without Words from Fliegende Blätter 17.00 34.00 100.00
v6 #11 12 13 Worth-c no sequentials 17.00 34.00 100.00
v6#14 (8/7/86) Wiorth-c; (7) panel Mrs Cleveland Presents The President With A New Rocking Chair 17.00 34.00 100.00
v6#15 (8/14/86) Worth-c; (6) panel Worth strip 17.00 34.00 100.00
v6#16 (8/21/86) Worth-c Asleep At Post USA/Mexico Border (6) panel sequential 17.00 34.00 100.00
v6#17 no sequrntials 17.00 34.00 100.00
v6#18 (9/4/86) Worth-c; (3) panel from Fliegende 17.00 34.00 100.00
v6#19 (9/11/86) Worth Anarchist & Uncle Sam-c; (5) panel Duel of the Dudes 17.00 34.00 100.00
v6#20 (9/18/86) Worth-c (6) panel sequential 17.00 34.00 100.00
v6#21 (9/25/86) Worth-c; Verbeck single panel; (9) panel 17.00 34.00 100.00
v6#22 (10/2/86) Verbeck-c plus interiors 17.00 34.00 100.00
v6#23 (10/9/86) Worth-c Geronimo & Devil cover; Verbeck and Chips singles 17.00 34.00 100.00
v6#24 (10/16/86) Worth-c Verbeck strip "Evolution" 17.00 34.00 100.00
v6#25 no sequential strips 17.00 34.00 100.00
v6#26 (10/30/86) Worth-c; (6) panel Verbeck "A Warning To Smokers" 17.00 34.00 100.00
NOTE: *Many Thomas Worth sequential comic strips. Frank Bellew and Dan McCarthy appear. Wilhelm Busch-r from German Fligende Blaetter. Later issues in 1890s comics become sporadic*

THAT COMIC PRIMER (S)
G.W. Carleton & Co., Publishers: 1877 (6-5/8x5", 52 pgs, paper soft-c, B&W)
nn - By Frank Bellew 50.00 100.00 300.00
NOTE: *Premium for the United States Life Insurance Company, New York.*

TIGER, THE LEFTENANT AND THE BOSUN, THE
Prudential Insurance Home Office, 878 & 880 Broad St, Newark, NJ: 1889 (4.5x3.25", 12 pgs) (Scarce)
nn - 8 panel sequential story in color 40.00 80.00 240.00

TOM PLUMP, THE ADVENTURES OF MR. (see also The Juvenile Gem) (O)
Huestis & Cozans, New York: nd (c1850-1851) (6x3-7/8", 12 pgs, hand colored paper-c, B&W)
nn- First printing(s) publisher's address is 104 Nassau Street (1850-1851) (Very Rare) 567.00 1134.00 3400.00
NOTE: *California Gold Rush story. The hand colored outer cover is highly rare, with only 1 recorded copy possessing it. The front cover image and text is repeated precisely on page 3 (albeit b&w), and only interior pages are numbered, together leading owners of coverless copies to believe they have the cover. The true back cover contains ads for the publisher. The cover was issued only with copies which were sold separately - booklets which were bound together as part of* ***THE JUVENILE GEM*** *never had such covers.*

TOM PLUMP, THE ADVENTURES OF MR. (see also The Juvenile Gem) (O)
Philip J. Cozans: nd (1851-1852) (6x3-7/8", 12 pgs,hand colored paper-c, B&W)
nn- Second printing(s) publisher's address is 116 Nassau Street (1851-1852) (Very Rare) 300.00 600.00 1800.00
nn- Third printing(s) publisher's address is 107 Nassau Street (1852+) (Very Rare) 300.00 600.00 1800.00

TOM PLUMP, THE ADVENTURES OF MR.
Americana Review, Scotia, NY: nd(1960's) (6-1/4x4-1/8", 8 pgs, side-stapled, cardboard-c, B&W)
nn - Modern reprint 8.00 16.00 50.00
NOTE: *Issued within a folder titled SIX CHILDREN'S BOOKS OF THE 1850'S. States "Reprinted by American Review" at bottom of front cover. Reprints the 104 Nassau Street address.)*
nn - Modern rep. (Scarce 1980s) (5-1/2x4-1/4", 8 pgs,side-stapled) 3.00 6.00 20.00
NOTE: *Photocopy reprint by a comix zine publisher, from an Americana Review cop; vailable by mail order*

TOOTH-ACHE, THE (E,O)
D. Bogue, London: 1849 (5-1/4x3-3/4)
nn - By Cruikshank, B&W (Very Rare) 258.00 516.00 1550.00
nn - By Cruikshank, hand colored (Rare) (no known sales)
NOTE: *Scripted by Horace Mayhew, art by George Cruikshank. This is the British edition. Price 1/6 b&w, 3 hand colored. In British editions, the panels are not numbered. Publisher's name appears on cover. Booklet's "pages" unfold into a single, long, strip.*
J.L. Smith, Philadelphia, PA: nd (1849) (5-1/8"x 3-3/4" folded, 86-7/8" wide unfolded, 26 pgs, cardboard-c, color, 15¢)
nn - By Cruikshank, hand colored (Very Rare) 300.00 600.00 1800.00
NOTE: *Reprints the D. Bogue edition. In American editions, the panels are numbered (43 panels, not counting front & back cover). Publisher's name stamped on inside front cover, plus printed along left-hand side of first interior page. Page 1 is pasted to inside back cover, and unfolds from there. Front cover not attached to back cover by design. Booklet's "pages" unfold into a single, long, strip (made from four individual strips pasted together on the blank back side). There is a fairly common1974 British Arts Council reprint.*

TRAMP, THE: His Tricks, Tallies, and Tell-Tales, with His Signs, Countersigns, Grips, Passwords and Villainies Exposed (O,S)
Dick & Fitzgerald, New York: 1878 (11-3/8x8, 36 pgs, paper-c, B&W, 25¢) (Rare)
1 Frank Bellew 133.00 266.00 800.00
NOTE: *Edited by Frank Bellew, A Bee And A Chip (Bellew's daughter and son Frank).*

TRUTH (See Platinum Age section for 1900-1906 issues)
Truth Company, NY: 1886-1906? (13-11/16x10-5/16", 16 pgs, process color-c & centerfolds, rest B&W)
1886-1887 issues 18.00 36.00 110.00
1888-1895 issues non Outcault issues 19.00 28.00 85.00
Mar 10 1894 - precursor Yellow Kid RFO 79.00 158.00 475.00
#372 June 2 1894 - first app Yellow Kid RFO 217.00 434.00 1300.00
June 23 1894 - precursor Yellow Kid R. F. Outcault 75.00 150.00 450.00
July 14 1894 -2nd app Yellow Kid RFO 121.00 242.00 725.00

FR1.0 GD2.0 FN6.0

Sept 15 1894 - (2) 3rd app YK RFO plus YK precursor 121.00 242.00 725.00
Feb 9 1895 - 4th app Yellow Kid RFO 121.00 242.00 725.00
1896-1899 issues 10.00 20.00 60.00
NOTE: *This magazine contains the earliest known appearances of* ***The Yellow Kid*** *by Richard Felton Outcault. Feb 9 1895 issue's YK cartoon was reprinted one week later in the* ***New York World*** *Feb 17 1895 edition. We are still sorting out further Outcault appearances. Truth also contained full color sequential strips by Hy Mayer on the back plus Woolf, Verbeek, etc.*

TRUTH, SELECTIONS FROM
Truth Company, NY: 1894-Spr 1897 (13-11/16x10-1/4, color-c, quarterly)
1-4 17.00 34.00 100.00
5-Outcault's early Yellow Kid 83.00 166.00 500.00
6-13 13.00 26.00 80.00
NOTE: *#5 reprints all early Outcault Yellow Kid appearances*

TURNER'S COMIC ALMANAC
Charles Strong, 298 Pearl St, NYC: ???-1843 (7.25x4.5", 36 pgs, B&W)
nn 48.00 96.00 290.00

TURNER'S COMICK ALMA-NACK
Turner & Fisher, NYC: 1839-?? (7.25x4.5", 36 pgs, B&W)
nn 48.00 96.00 285.00

TWO HUNDRED SKETCHES, HUMOROUS AND GROTESQUE, BY GUSTAVE DORE (E)
Frederick Warne & Co, London: 1867 (13-3/4x11-3/8, 94 pgs, hard-c, B&W)
nn - (1867) by Gustave Dore 100.00 200.00 600.00
nn - (Second Edition; 1871)- by Gustave Dore 46.00 92.00 275.00
nn - (Third Edition; 1870's)- by Gustave Dore 43.00 86.00 260.00
nn - (Fourth Edition; 1870's- by Gustave Dore 43.00 86.00 260.00
NOTE: *Contains sequential comics stories, single panel cartoons, and sketches. Reprints and translates material which originally appeared in the French publications "Le Journal pour Rire", circa 1848-49. Although dated 1867, it was likely published & available for the 1866 Christmas Season, as has been confirmed for the American edition. Printed by Dalziel. The American & first British editions were printed simultaneously, the American edition is not a reprint of the British.*

TWO HUNDRED SKETCHES, HUMOROUS AND GROTESQUE, BY GUSTAVE DORE (E)
Roberts Brothers, Boston: 1867 (13-3/4x11-3/8", 96 pgs, hard-c, B&W)
nn - By Gustave Dore 113.00 226.00 675.00
NOTE: *Although dated 1867, it was published & available for the 1866 Christmas Season. Printed by Dalziel, in England, and imported to the USA expressly for a USA publisher.*

UNCLE JOSH'S TRUNK-FUL OF FUN
Dick & Fitzgerald, 18 Ann St, NY: 1870s (5-3/4x9", 68 pgs, B&W & Red-c, B&W inside)
nn - Rare 38.00 76.00 230.00
NOTE: *Many single panel cartoons; (2) pages of early boxing sequential strip*

UNCLE SAM'S COMIC ALMANAC
M.J. Meyers, NY: 1879 (11x8", 32 pgs)
nn - 36.00 72.00 215.00

UNDER THE GASLIGHT
Gaslight Publishing Co (Frank Tousey): Oct 13 1878-Apr 12 1879 (Folio, 16pgs)
1-27 33.00 66.00 200.00

UNITED STATES COMIC ALMANAC
King & Baird, Philadelphia: 1851-?? (7.5x4.5", 36 pgs, B&W)
nn 48.00 96.00 290.00

UPS AND DOWNS ON LAND AND WATER (O.G)
James R. Osgood & Co., Boston: 1871 ; **Houghton, Osgood & Co., Boston:** 1880 (108 pgs, gilted hard-c, B&W)
1st printing (1871; 10-3/4x16") - By Augustus Hoppin 36.00 72.00 215.00
2nd printing (1880; smaller sized) 22.00 44.00 130.00
NOTE: *Exists as blue or orange hard covers.*

VANITY FAIR
William A. Stephens (for Thompson & Camac): Dec 29 1859-July 4 1863 Quarto Weekly
Average issues with comic strips 20.00 40.00 120.00

VERDICT, THE
Verdict Publishing Co: Dec 19 1898-Nov 12 1900 (Chromolithographic Weekly)
Average Issues 45.00 90.00 270.00
NOTE: *Artists included George B. Luks, Horace Taylor, MIRS. Striking anti-Republican weekly full o fsome of the most savage political cartoons of the era. The last brilliant burst of energy for the political cartoon weekly*

VERY VERY FUNNY (M,S)
Dick & Fitzgerald, New York: nd(c1880's) (10¢, 7-1/2x5", 68 pgs, paper-c, B&W)
nn - (Rare) 63.00 125.00 375.00
NOTE: *Unauthorized reprints of prose and cartoons extracted from Puck, Texas Siftings, and other publications. Includes art by Chips Bellew, Bisbee, Graetz, Opper, Wales, Zim.*

VIM
H. Wimmel, NYC: June 22-Aug 24 1898 (Chromolithographic Weekly)
average issue 36.00 72.00 215.00
Yellow Kid by Leon Barritt issues 71.00 142.00 425.00

WAR IN THE MIDST OF AMERICA. FROM A NEW POINT OF VIEW. (E,O,G)
Ackermann & Co., London: 1864 (4-3/8" x 5-7/8", folded, 36 feet wide unfolded, 80 pgs, hard-c, B&W)
nn- by Charles Dryden (rare) 367.00 734.00 2200.00
NOTE: *British graphic novel about the American Civil War, with a pro-Confederate bent. Adventures of a British artist who decides to visually summarize the American Civil War for his countrymen, from newspaper accounts. Reaching current events, he finds he can not finish the story until the War ends, and so he travels to America, to*

end it. Book unfolds into a single long strip (binding was issued split, to enable the unfolding).

WASP, THE ILLUSTRATED SAN FRANCISCO
F. Korbel & Bros and Numerous Others: August 5 1876-April 25 1941 (Chromolithographic Weekly)

average 1800s issues with comic strips 35.00 70.00 210.00

WHAT I KNOW OF FARMING: Founded On The Experience of Horace Greeley (S)
The American News Company, New York: 1871 (7-1/4x4-1/2", paper-c, B&W)

nn - By Joseph Hull (Scarce) 32.00 64.00 190.00
NOTE: *Pay & Cox, Printers & Engravers, NY; political tract regarding Presidential elections.*

WILD FIRE
Wild Fire Co, NYC: Nov 30 1877-at least#16 Mar 1878 (Folio, 16 pgs)

1-16 21.00 42.00 125.00

WILD OATS, An Illustrated Weekly Journal of Fun, Satire, Burlesque, and Nits at Persons and Events of the Day (O)
Winchell & Small, 113 Fulton St /48 Ann St, NYC: Feb 1870-1881 (16-1/4x11", generally 16 pages, B&W, began as monthly, then bi-weekly, then weekly) All loose issues Very Rare (See *The Overstreet Price Guide* #35 2005 for a detailed index of single issue contents)

1-25 Very Rare - contents to be indexed in a future edition 50.00 100.00 300.00
26-28 30 32 35 36 39 40 41 43-46 1872 (sequential strips) 44.00 88.00 265.00
29 33 37 42 no sequential strips 30.00 60.00 180.00
31 34 38 47 Hopkins sequential comic strips 42.00 84.00 250.00
48 (1/16/73) Worth 13 panel sequential; first Woolf-c 42.00 84.00 250.00
49 51 53 54 60 62 61 64 65 66 67 69 1873 sequential strips 42.00 84.00 250.00
50 52 56 59 63 71 no sequential strips 30.00 60.00 180.00
51 (Worth 18 panel double page spread, Woolf 9 panel 42.00 84.00 250.00
55 Hopkins 22 panel double page spread; Bellew-c 54.00 108.00 325.00
57 Intense unknown 6 panel "Two Relics of Barbarism, or A Few Contrasted Pictures, Showing the origin of the North American Indian 42.00 84.00 250.00
58 (6/5/73) unknown 19 panel double pager "The Terrible Adventures of Messrs Buster & Stumps, About Exterminating the Indians" reads across both pages like Popeye #2095 (1933); Woolf-c 79.00 158.00 475.00
68 (10/16/73) unknown 9 panel "Adv of New jersey Mosquito" looks like Winsor McCay type style: early inspiration for McCay's animated cartoon? 42.00 84.00 250.00
70 unknown 6 panel; Hopkins 6 panel "Hopkins novel: A Tale of True Love, with all the variations"; Bellew-c 38.00 76.00 230.00
72 (12/11/73) Worth 11 panel; Wales President Grant war-c 38.00 76.00 230.00
73 74 75 Hopkins sequential comic strip 52.00 104.00 310.00
76 77 sequential strips 38.00 76.00 230.00
78 Bellew 5 panel double pager 38.00 76.00 230.00
79-105 (March 1874-Dec 1874) contents presently unknown 38.00 76.00 230.00
106 107 111 no sequentials;Bellew-c #106 110;Wales-c #107 38.00 76.00 230.00
108 (1/20/75) Wales 12 panel double pg spread; Bellew-c 38.00 76.00 230.00
109 (1/27/75) unknown 6 panel; Wales-c 38.00 76.00 230.00
111 Busch 13 panel "The Conundrum of the Day - Is Lager Beer Intoxicating?"; Bellew-c 38.00 76.00 230.00
112 116 sequential comic strips 38.00 76.00 230.00
113 114 115 no sequentials Worth-c #114 30.00 60.00 180.00
117 intense Wales 6 panel "One of the Oppresions of the Civil Rights Laws"' Bellew-c 58.00 116.00 350.00
118-137 (3/31/75-8/4/75) no sequential comic strips 30.00 60.00 180.00
138 (8/18/75) Bellew Sr & Bellew "Chips" Jr singles appear 38.00 76.00 225.00
139-143 145-147 154-157 159 no sequentials 30.00 60.00 180.00
144 (9/29/75) Hopkins 8 panel sequential; Wales-c 38.00 76.00 230.00
148 (10/27/75) Opper's first cover; many Opper singles 53.00 106.00 320.00
149 150 151 152 153 all Opper-c and much interior work 38.00 76.00 230.00
158 (1/5/76) Palmer Cox 1rst comic strip 24 panel double page spread "The Adv of Mr & Mrs Sprowl And Their Christmas Turkey - A Crashing Chasing Tearful Tragedy But Happily Ending Well"; Opper-c 75.00 150.00 450.00
159 160 162 165 167 169-173 no sequentials 30.00 60.00 180.00
161 163 164 166 168 179 182 Palmer Cox sequential strips 75.00 150.00 450.00
174 (4/26/76) Cox 24 panel double pager "The Tramp's Progress; A Story of the West And the Union Pacific Railroad" 75.00 150.00 450.00
175-178 183-189 no sequentials 30.00 60.00 180.00
180 (6/7/76) Beard & Opper jam; Woolf, Bellew singles 38.00 76.00 230.00
181 more Mann two panel jobs; Opper-c 38.00 76.00 230.00
190 Bellew 9 panel "Rodger's Patent Mosquito Armour" 53.00 106.00 320.00
191-end contents to be indexed in the near future 30.00 60.00 180.00
NOTE: *There are very few lknown oose issues. All loose issues are Very Rare. Prices vary widely on this magazine. Issues with sequential comic strips would be in higher demand than issues with no comic strips. We present this index from the Library of Congress and New York Historical Society bound sets. We would love to hear from any one who turns up loose copies. This scarce humor bi-weekly contains easily a couple hundred original first-time published sequential comic strips found in most issues plus innumerable single panel cartoons in every issue*

WOMAN IN SEARCH OF HER RIGHTS, THE ADVENTURES OF (G)
Lee & Shepard, Boston And New York: early 1870s (8-3/8x13", 40 pgs, hard-c)

By Florence Claxton (Very Rare) 383.00 766.00 2300.00
NOTE: *Earliest known original comic book sequential story by a woman; contains "nearly 100 original drawings by the author, which have been reproduced in fac-simile by the graphotype process of engraving." Tinted two color lithography; orange tint printed first, then printed 2nd time with black ink; early women's sufferage.*

WORLD OVER, THE (I)
G. W. Dillingham Company, New York: 1897 (192 pgs, hard-c)

nn - By Joe Kerr; 80 illustrations by R.F. Outcault (Rare) 225.00 450.00 1350.00
NOTE: soft cover editions also exist

WRECK-ELECTIONS OF BUSY LIFE (S)
Kellogg & Bulkeley: 1867 (9-1/4x11-3/4", ??? pages, soft-c)

nn - By J. Bowker (Rare) 75.00 150.00 450.00
NOTE: *Says "Sold by American News Company, New York" on cover.*

WYMAN'S COMIC ALMANAC FOR THE TIMES
T.W. Strong, NY: 1854 (8x5", 24 pgs)

nn - 37.00 74.00 220.00

YANKEE DOODLE
W.H. Graham, Tribune Building, NYC: Oct 10 1846-Oct 2 1847 (Quarto weekly)

average issue 45.00 90.00 270.00

YANKEE NOTIONS, OR WHITTLINGS OF JONATHAN'S JACK-KNIFE
T.W. Strong, 98 Nassau St, NYC: Jan. 1852-1875 (11x8, 32 pgs, paper-c, 12.5¢, monthly)

1 Brother Jonathan character single panel cartoons 46.00 92.00 275.00
NOTE: *Begins continuing character sequential comic strip, "The Adventures of Jeremiah Oldpot" in "A Bird in the Hand Is Worth Two in The Bush"*
2-4 23.00 46.00 140.00
5 British X-Over 23.00 46.00 140.00
NOTE: *Single panel of John Bull & Brother Jonathan exchanging civilities (issues of Punch & Yankee Notions)*
6 end of Jeremiah Oldpot continued strip 23.00 46.00 140.00
v2#1 begin "Hoosier Bragg" sequential strip - six issue serial 23.00 46.00 130.00
v2#2 Feb 1853 two pg 12 panel sequential "Mr Vanity's Exploits, Arising Out Of A Valentine" 33.00 66.00 200.00
v2#3-v2#5 continues Hoosier Bragg 23.00 46.00 130.00
v2#6 June 1853 Lion Eats Hoosier Bragg, end of story 23.00 46.00 130.00
v3#1 begins referring to its cartoons as "Comic Art" 33.00 66.00 200.00
v4#1-V4#6 v5#1-v5#2 no sequential comic strips 17.00 34.00 100.00
v5#3 two sequential comic strips 35.00 70.00 210.00
NOTE: *Mr Take-A-Drop And The Maine Law (5) panels and The First Segar (7) panels (about smoking tobacco)*
v5#4 April 1856 begin Billy Vidkins 35.00 70.00 210.00
NOTE: *Begins reprinting "From Passages in the Life of Little Billy Vidkins, first issued as a stand alone proto-comic book in 1849 Illustrations of the Poets*
v5#5 The McBargem Guards (9) panel sequential; Vidkins 22.00 44.00 130.00
v5#6 v5 #9 no comics 17.00 34.00 100.00
v5#7 Billy Vidkins continues 22.00 44.00 130.00
v5#8 end of Vidkins By HL Stephens, Esq. 22.00 44.00 130.00
v5#10 (6) panel "How We Learn To Ride"; Timber is hero 22.00 44.00 130.00
v5#11 (7) panel "How Mr. Green Sparrowgrass Voted-A Warning For the Benefit of Quiet Citizens About To Excercize the Elective Franchise" plus Pt Two "How We Learn to Ride" 33.00 66.00 200.00
v5#12 (6) panel "How Mr Pipp Got Struck"; "The Eclipse" featuring Mr Phips; Pt 3 "How We Learn to Ride" 22.00 44.00 130.00
v6#1 (Jan 1857) (12) panel "A Tale of An Umbrella; (4) panel begins a serial "The Man Who Bought The Elephant; (8) panel How Our Young New Yorkers Celebrate New Years Day 22.00 44.00 130.00
v6#2 (Feb 1857) Pt 2 (4) panels The Man Who Bought the Elephant; (7) panel A Game of All Fours 22.00 44.00 130.00
v6#3 (Mar 1857) Pt 3 (4) panels The Man Who Bought the Elephant ending; (4) panel Ye Great Crinoline Monopoly 22.00 44.00 130.00
v6#4 no comic strips 22.00 44.00 130.00
v6#5 (May 1850) (3) panel A Short Trip to Mr Bumps, And How It Ended; (2) panel How Mr Trembles Was Garrotted 22.00 44.00 130.00
v6#6 no comic strips 22.00 44.00 130.00
v6#7 (July 1857) (5) panel Alma Mater; (3) panel Three Tableaux In the Life of A Broadway Swell 22.00 44.00 130.00
v6 #8 9 no comic strips 22.00 44.00 130.00
v6#10 (Oct 1857) (3) panel Adv of Mr Near-Sight 22.00 44.00 130.00
v6#11 (Nov 1857) (11) panel Mrs Champignon's Dinner Party And the Way She Arranged Her Guests; (4) panel A Stroll in August 22.00 44.00 130.00
v6#12 (Dec 1857) (8) panel strip; (12) panel Young Fitz At A Blow Out in the Fifth Ave 22.00 44.00 130.00
v10#1 (Jan 1860) comic strip Bibbs at Central Park Skating Pond using word balloons 22.00 44.00 130.00

YE TRUE ACCOUNTE OF YE VISIT TO SPRINGFIELDE BY YE CONSTABEL HIS SPECIAL REPORTER
Frank Leslie: 1861 (5-1/8 x 5-1/4 or 93 inches when folded out, paper-c, B&W)

nn - Very Rare fold-out of 18 comic strip panels plus covers (a FN copy sold in 2010 for $101.85)
NOTE: *8 panels contain word balloons (Very Rare - only one copy known to exist.) First printed in Frank Leslie's Budget of Fun Jan 1 1861 issue. Abraham Lincoln Biography.*

YE VERACIOUS CHRONICLE OF GRUFF & POMPEY IN 7 TABLEAUX. (O,P)
Jackson's Best Chewing Tobacco & Donaldson Brothers: nd (c1870's) (5-1/8 tall x 3-3/8" wide folded, 27" wide unfolded, color cardboard)

nn - With all 8 panels attached (Scarce) 38.00 76.00 230.00
nn - Individual panels/cards 5.00 10.00 30.00
NOTE: *Black Americana interest. Consists of 8 attached cards, printed on one side, which unfold into a strip story of title card & 7 panels. Scrapbook hobbyists in the 19th Century tended to pull the panels apart and paste into their scrapbooks, making copies with all panels attached scarce.*

YOUNG AMERICA (continues as Yankee Doodle)
T.W. Strong, NYC: 1856

1-30 John McLennon 44.00 88.00 265.00

YOUNG AMERICA'S COMIC ALMANAC
T.W. Strong, NY: 1857 (7-1/2x5", 24 pgs)

nn 44.00 88.00 265.00

THE YOUNG MEN OF AMERICA (becomes Golden Weekly) (S)
Frank Tousey, NYC: 1887-88 (14x10-1/4", 16 pgs, B&W)

527 (10/13/87) Bellew strip "Story of A Black Eye" 19.00 38.00 115.00
530 (11/3/87) Thomas Worth (6) panel strip 21.00 42.00 125.00
531 (11/10/87) Thomas Worth(3) panel strip
537 (12/22/87) H.E. Patterson (3) panel strip
544 (2/9/88) Carans' Ache (6) panel strip-r 19.00 38.00 115.00
555 (4/26/88) Thomas Worth (3) panel strip
556 (5/3/88) Thomas Worth (6) panel strip; Kit Carson-c 60.00 120.00 360.00
569 (8/2/88) Frank Bellew (2) panel strip
570 (8/9/88) Kemble (2) panel strip
571 (8/16/88) Kemble (2) panel strip; first Davy Crockett 60.00 120.00 360.00
Issues with just single panel cartoons 8.00 16.00 50.00

ZIM'S QUARTERLY (M)
(13-13/16x10-1/4", 60 pgs, color-c; mostly B&W, some interior color)

1 - Eugene Zimmerman 88.00 176.00 525.00
NOTE: *Approx. half sequential comic strips, other half single panel cartoons.*

Any additions or corrections to this section are always welcome, very much encouraged and can be sent to **feedback@gemstonepub.com** to be processed for next year's Guide.

THE PLATINUM AGE

The American Comic Book: 1883-1938

The comic book ages tend to overlap a bit with one another – DC's Silver Age started with *Showcase* #4, but Marvel's didn't begin until *Fantastic Four* #1, for instance – so it's not surprising that the Platinum Age and Victorian Age tend to overlap a bit, with the Victorian Age in some ways running through the end of the 19th century. The Platinum Age of comics is marked by the introduction of several important elements, including three distinct and important features: the rise of licensed character merchandise, panel formats, and the evolution of the speech balloon.

The Platinum Age of Comics began with Palmer Cox's creation of *The Brownies* in 1883. Cox introduced a significant change to the medium with his work, and all at once rather than slowly and incrementally – he produced his art specifically with children in mind, and then merchandised his characters extensively. *The Brownies* became the first North American comic characters to be internationally merchandised. Their first standalone book, *The Brownies: Their Book*, debuted in 1887.

By the mid-1890s, newspaper publishers had caught on to the idea that comic characters could help sell more papers, having seen what they did to boost circulation of various magazines. The idea of a Sunday "comic supplement" was born at this time.

Throughout the Platinum Age, there are numerous important landmarks: James Swinnerton's *The Little Bears* (later *Little Bears & Tykes*), debuted in 1892, Richard F. Outcault's *Hogan's Alley* first appeared in 1894 in the *New York World* and The Yellow Kid first appeared in 1895 and had his first word balloon on October 25, 1896.

By the early 1900s, many other characters and strips were enjoying successful collections in volume format. Strips like *The Blackberries*, *Opper's Folks in Funnyville*, *Vaudevilles and Other Things*, *Mutt & Jeff*, *Bringing Up Father*, *The Katzenjammer Kids* and many others had circulations significantly higher than the early superheroes.

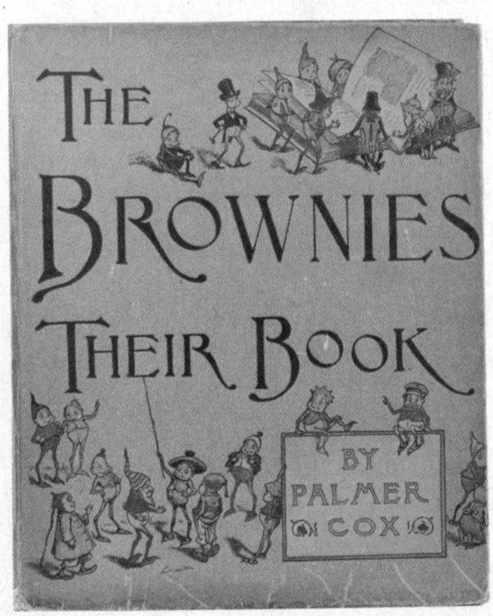

The Brownies' first book in 1887 set a precedent for the Platinum Age, collecting and reprinting previously published material.

R.F. OUTCAULT'S ADVERTISING COMICS

BY RICHARD D. OLSON, PH.D., GAYLE A. OLSON, PH.D., HANS K. PEDERSEN, KEVIN N. AMMENTORP AND TROY A. PIERCE, PH.D.

Merchants learned the value of advertising their wares and stores early and by the 19th Century, the use of trade cards and booklets became extremely popular means for increasing sales. When Palmer Cox introduced The Brownies in *St. Nicholas Magazine* in 1883, their popularity was so great that they became featured on trade cards and in booklets containing many of his Ivory Soap ads for children and adults.

The birth of newspaper comics in the 1890s quickly led to the most popular characters being used to promote merchandise. R. F. Outcault's Yellow Kid promoted everything from toys to whiskey. Not surprisingly, as the Yellow Kid only appeared in New York city papers, promotional material was limited to that area and is relatively scarce today.

However, in 1902 following the debut of his most famous character, Buster Brown, newspaper comics started to be distributed nationally, as were the ads for the products they promoted. This came to a head for Outcault in 1904. Legend has it that he opened a booth at the 1904 St. Louis World's Fair to market the use of his comic characters, emphasizing Buster Brown. The Brown Shoe Company was a large company with headquarters in St. Louis, and the rest was history, with Buster Brown becoming the symbol of the company.

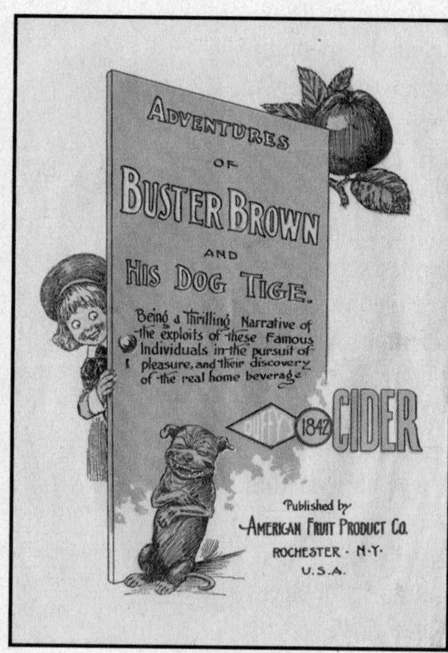

Figure 1. American Fruit Products Co., 1904, The Adventures of Buster Brown and his dog, Tige.

The company immediately had Outcault create a premium comic book for children visiting their stores which resulted in four distinct varieties of *Brown's Blue Ribbon Book of Jokes and Jingles* published in the first year. Variety 1 was published in red ink on light green paper. There is no record of its purpose and some people think it was a publisher's proof while others think it was a version for Canada. Its actual purpose may never be known but it is quite distinctive and appears to be the first publication of the 1904 book. Please note that the back cover shows Mary Jane, Buster Brown, Billie the Bear, and Pore Li'l Mose dancing along with some of the other animals from the newspaper comics.

Variety 2 is virtually the same comic but printed in four colors. The location, St. Louis, U.S.A. has been added to the bottom center of the front cover and some of the font sizes have been changed, most notably in the bottom right corner of the front page. The back cover is identical to Variety 1 except for the color.

Variety 3 has the same front cover but the German version of the Yellow Kid has replaced Pore Li'l Mose on the back cover. We can only speculate why this change occurred but St. Louis had a large German population in 1904 and the change may have been made to help them identify with the brand.

Variety 4 increased the emphasis on Buster Brown by adding his name in front of the Blue Ribbon Shoes motto at the bottom center of the front cover. The different varieties had very similar interiors but some of the pages, especially ads for the company, did vary throughout the year.

Figure 2. The Brown Shoe Company, 1904. Brown's Blue Ribbon Book of Jokes and Jingles. Variety 1.

Figure 3. The Brown Shoe Company, 1904. Brown's Blue Ribbon Book of Jokes and Jingles. Variety 2

Figure 4. The Brown Shoe Company, 1904, Brown's Blue Ribbon Book of Jokes and Jingles. Variety 3

Figure 5. The Brown Shoe Company, 1904, Brown's Blue Ribbon Book of Jokes and Jingles. Variety 4

The premium comic proved so popular that Outcault created a second book in 1905. This book was followed by two more in the series and then a separate **Buster Brown's Book of Travels**; however, none of which were created by Outcault. Examine the figures carefully for information on each comic and you will see that most of the other booklets were published in 1904 or the following decade. After that period, perhaps because of the production costs, the prospects of war, and the growing popularity of the calendar postcard which offered monthly contact with the customer, their popularity decreased. Please note that Figures 1-17 illustrate premium comic books featuring Buster Brown by Outcault as well as unlicensed issues by other artists. Further, Figures 18-23 illustrate scarce issues by Outcault not featuring any of his newspaper comic characters. These books are rarely seen and unknown to most collectors.

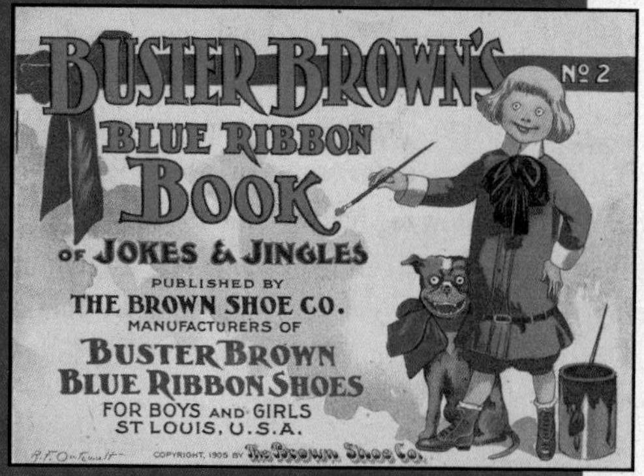

Figure 6, The Brown Shoe Co., 1905, Buster Brown's Blue Ribbon Book of Jokes and Jingles No. 2.

Figure 7. The Brown Shoe Co., 1909, Buster's Book of Jokes and Jingles No. 3.

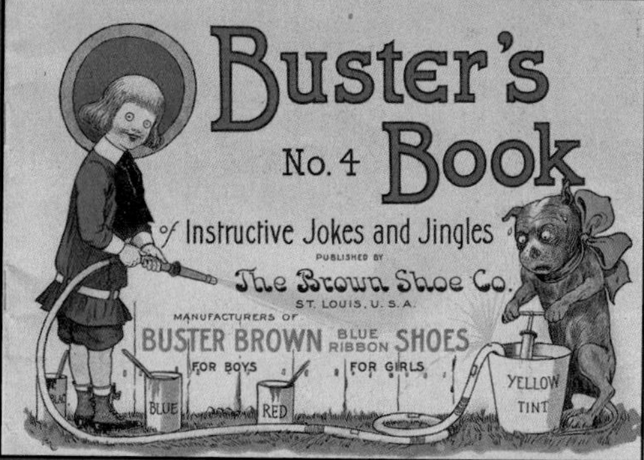

Figure 8. The Brown Shoe Co., 1910. Buster's Book of Instructive Jokes and Jingles No. 4.

Figure 9, The Brown Shoe Co., 1912. Buster Brown's Book of Travels.

Figure 10. Buster Brown Bread Co., 1904. The Buster Brown Bread Book of Rhymes.

Figure 11. C. Morton, no date, Merry Antics of Buster Brown, Buddy Tucker, and Tige.

Figure 12. Ivar Frank & Co., 1904. Buster Brown, Resolved.

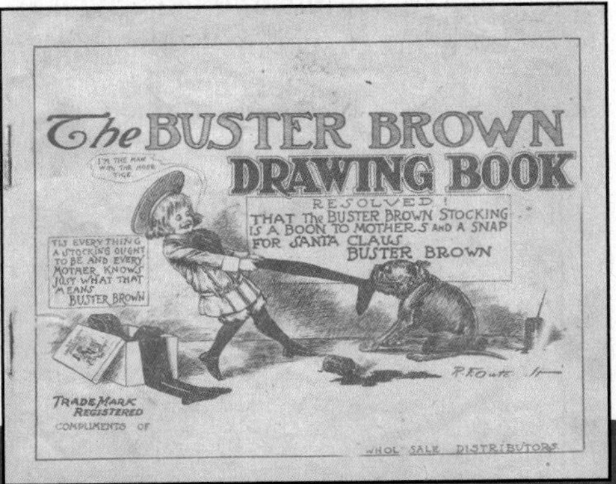

Figure 13. The Buster Brown Stocking Company, no date. The Buster Brown Drawing Book.

Figure 14. Pond's Extract, 1904. Buster Brown's Experiences with Pond's Extract.

Figure 15. Steinwender Stoffregen Coffee Co., 1905. Buster Brown Coffee.

Figure 16. Ringen Stove Company, no date. Quick Meal Steel Ranges.

Figure 17, Various Sponsors including Red Cross Coffee and Emerson Piano, 1906. The Drawing Book was very popular and had numerous versions.

Figure 18. The American National Bank, 1912. How Shall I Get Rich?

Figure 21. Tess and Ted School Shoes, early die cut undated. The Happy Days of Tess and Ted.

Figure 19. Hamilton Brown Shoe Company, Household Shoes Please Everybody Under The Roof.

Figure 22. Roberts, Johnson & Rand Shoe Co., undated. A Tess and Ted Shoe Story.

Figure 20. Keith Brothers & Co., no date. The Tiger Hat.

Figure 23. The Washington Shoe Manufacturir Co., undated. The Billy Buster Shoe Book.

Alphonse and Gaston and Their Friend Leon
1903 © Hearst's NY American & Journal

American-Journal-Examiner Joke Book Spec.
Supplement #2. 1911 © N.Y. American

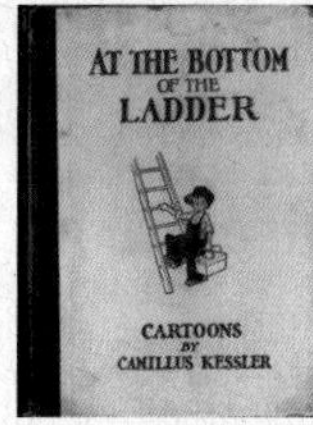

At The Bottom Of The Ladder
1926 © J.P. Lippincott Company

GD2.0 FN6.0 VF8.0

COLLECTOR'S NOTE: The books listed in this section were published many decades before organized comics fandom began archiving and helping to preserve these fragile popular culture artifacts. Consequently, copies of most all of these comics do not often surface in Fine+ or better shape. eBay has proven after more than a decade that many items once considered rare actually are not, though they almost always are in higher grades. For items marked scarce, we are trying to ascertain how many copies might still be in existence. Your input is always welcome.

Most Platinum Age comic books are in the Fair to VG range. If you want to collect these only in high grade, your collection will be extremely small. The prices given for Good, Fine and Very Fine categories are for strictly graded editions. If you need help grading your item, we refer you to the grading section in the front of this price guide or contact the authors of the Platinum essay. Most measurements are in inches. A few measurements are in centimeters. The first dimension given is Height and the second is Width.

For ease of ascertaining the contents of each item of this listing, there is a code letter or two following most titles we have been adding in over the years to aid you. A helpful list of categories pertaining to these codes can be found at the beginning of the Victorian Age pricing sections. This section created, revised, and expanded by Robert Beerbohm and Richard Olson with able assistance from Ray Agricola, Jon Berk, Bill Blackbeard, Roy Bonario, Ray Bottorff Jr., Chris Brown, Alfredo Castelli, Darrell Coons, Sol Davidson, Leonardo De Sá, Scott Deschaine, Mitchell Duval, Joe Evans, Tom Gordon III, Bruce Hamilton, Andy Konkykru, Don Kurtz, Gabriel Laderman, Bruce Mason, Donald Puff, Robert Quesinberry, Steve Rowe, Randy Scott, John Snyder, Art Spiegelman, Steve Thompson, Joan Crosby Tibbets, Richard Samuel West, Doug Wheeler, Richard Wright and Craig Yoe.

ADVENTURES OF EVA, PORA AND TED (M)
Evaporated Milk Association: 1932 (5x15", 16 pgs, B&W)
nn - By Steve 17.00 51.00 100.00
NOTE: *Appears to have had green, blue or white paper cover versions.*

ADVENTURES OF HAWKSHAW (N) (See Hawkshaw The Detective)
The Saalfield Publishing Co.: 1917 (9-3/4x13-1/2", 48 pgs., color & two-tone)
nn - By Gus Mager (only 24 pgs. of strips, reverse of each pg. is blank)
63.00 189.00 380.00
nn - 1927 Reprints 1917 issue 42.00 126.00 250.00
NOTE: *Started Feb 23, 1913-Sept 4, 1922, then begins again Dec 13, 1931-Feb 11, 1952.*

ADVENTURES OF SLIM AND SPUD, THE (M)
Prairie Farmer Publ. Co.: 1924 (3-3/4x 9-3/4", 104 pgs., B&W strip reprints)
nn 29.00 87.00 175.00
NOTE: *Illustrated mailing envelope exists postmarked out of Chicago, add 50%.*

ADVENTURES OF WILLIE WINTERS, THE (O,P)
Kelloggs Toasted Corn Flake Co.: 1912 (6-7/8x9-1/2", 20 pgs, full color)
nn - By Byron Williams & Dearborn Melvill 62.00 186.00 370.00

ADVENTURES OF WILLIE GREEN, THE (N) (see The Willie Green Comics)
Frank M. Acton Co.: 1915 (50¢, 52 pgs, 8-1/2X16", B&W, soft-c)
Book 1 - By Harris Brown; strip-r 62.00 186.00 370.00

A. E. F. IN CARTOONS BY WALLY, THE (N)
Don Sowers & Co.: 1933 (12x10-1/8", 88 pgs, hardcover B&W)
nn - By Wally Wallgren (WW One Stars & Stripes-r) 46.00 138.00 275.00

AFTER THE TOWN GOES DRY (I)
The Howell Publishing Co, Chicago: 1919 (48 pgs, 6-1/2x4", hardbound two color-c)
nn - By Henry C. Taylor; illus by Frank King 28.00 84.00 165.00

AIN'T IT A GRAND & GLORIOUS FEELING? (N) (Also see Mr. & Mrs.)
Whitman Publishing Co.: 1922 (9x9-3/4", 52 pgs., stiff cardboard-c)
nn - 1921 daily strip-r; B&W, color-c; Briggs-a 43.00 129.00 255.00
nn -(9x9-1/2", 28pgs., stiff cardboard-c)-Sunday strip-r in color (inside front-c says "More of the Married Life of Mr. & Mrs".) 43.00 129.00 255.00
NOTE: *Strip started in 1917; This is the 2nd Whitman comic book, after Brigg's MR. & MRS.*

ALL THE FUNNY FOLKS (I)
World Press Today, Inc.: 1926 (11-1/2x8-1/2", 112 pgs., color, hard-c)
nn-Barney Google, Spark Plug, Jiggs & Maggie, Tillie The Toiler, Happy Hooligan, Hans & Fritz, Toots & Casper, etc. 125.00 375.00 750.00
With Dust Jacket By Louis Biedermann 275.00 825.00 1650.00
NOTE: *Booklength race horse story masterfully enveloping all major King Features characters.*

ALPHONSE AND GASTON AND THEIR FRIEND LEON (N)
Hearst's New York American & Journal: 1902,1903 (10x15-1/4", Sunday strip reprints in color)
nn - (1902) - By Frederick Opper (scarce) 630.00 1890.00 2200.00
nn - (1903) - By Frederick Opper (scarce) (72 pages) 630.00 1890.00 –
NOTE: *Strip ran Sept 22, 1901 to at least July 17, 1904.*

ALWAYS BELITTLIN' (see Skippy; That Rookie From the 13th Squad; Between Shots)
Henry Holt & Co.: 1927 (6x8", hard-c with DJ,
nn -By Percy Crosby (text with cartoons) 53.00 159.00 320.00

ALWAYS BELITTLIN' (I) (see Skippy; That Rookie From the 13th Squad, Between Shots)
Percy Crosby, Publisher: 1933 (14 1/4 x 11", 72 pgs, hard-c, B&W)
nn - By Percy Crosby 53.00 159.00 315.00
NOTE: *Self-published; primarily political cartoons with text pages denouncing prohibition's gang warfare effects and cuts in the national defense budget as Crosby saw war looming in Europe and with Japan.*

AMERICAN-JOURNAL-EXAMINER JOKE BOOK SPECIAL SUPPLEMENT (O)
New York American: 1911-12 (12 x 9 3/4", 16 pgs) (known issues) (Very Rare)
1 Tom Powers Joke Book(12/10/11) 108.00 325.00 –
2 Mutt & Jeff Joke Book (Bud Fisher 12/17/11) 125.00 375.00 –
3 TAD's Joke Book (Thomas Dorgan 12/24/11) 103.00 310.00 –
4 F. Opper's Joke Book (Frederick Burr Opper 12/31/11) (contains Happy Hooligan) 104.00 375.00 –
5 not known to exist
6 Swinnerton's Joke Book (Jimmy Swinnerton 01/14/12) (contains Mr. Jack) 137.00 410.00 –
7 The Monkey's Joke Book (Gus Mager 01/21/12) (contains Sherlocko the Monk) 120.00 360.00 –
8 Joys And Glooms Joke Book (T. E. Powers 01/28/12) 103.00 310.00 –
9 The Dingbat Family's Joke Book (George Herriman 02/04/12) (contains early Krazy Kat & Ignatz) 275.00 825.00 –
10 Valentine Joke Book, A (Opper, Howarth, Mager, T. E. Powers 02/11/12) 105.00 315.00 –
11 Little Hatchet Joke Book (T. E. Powers 02/18/12) 105.00 315.00 –
12 Jungle Joke Book (Dirks, McCay 02/25/12) 137.00 410.00 –
13 The Hayseeds Joke Book (03/03/12) 103.00 310.00 –
14 Married Life Joke Book (T.E. Powers 03/10/12) 103.00 310.00 –
NOTE: *These were insert newspaper supplements similar to Eisner's later Spirit sections. A Valentine Joke Book recently surfaced from Hearst's Boston Sunday American proving that other cities besides New York City had these special supplements. Each issue also contains work by other cartoonists besides the cover featured creator and those already listed above such as Sidney Smith, Winsor McCay, Hy Mayer, Grace Weiderseim (later Drayton), others.*

AMERICA'S BLACK & WHITE BOOK 100 Pictured Reasons Why We Are At War (N,S)
Cupples & Leon: 1917 (10 3/4 x 8", 216 pgs)
nn - W. A. Rogers (New York Herald-r) 38.00 114.00 225.00

AMONG THE FOLKS IN HISTORY
Rand McNally Print Guild: 1928 (192 pgs, 8-1/2x9-1/2", hard-c, B&W)
nn - By Gaar Williams 25.00 75.00 150.00

AMONG THE FOLKS IN HISTORY
The Book and Print Guild: 1935 (200 pgs, 8-1/2x9-1/2:,
nn - By Gaar Williams 25.00 75.00 150.00
NOTE: *Both the above are evidently different editions and contain largely full-page, single panel cartoons similar to Briggs' work of that sort. 8 or 10 pages are broken into panels, usually with a "this is how it was in the old days, this is how it is today theme."*

ANGELIC ANGELINA (N)
Cupples & Leon Company: 1909 (11-1/2x17", 56 pgs., 2 colors)
nn - By Munson Paddock 69.00 207.00 415.00
NOTE: *Strip ran March 22, 1908-Feb 7, 1909.*

ANDY GUMP, HIS LIFE STORY (I)
The Reilly & Lee Co, Chicago: 1924 (192 pgs, hardbound)
nn - By Sidney Smith (over 100 illustrations) 41.00 123.00 245.00

ANIMAL CIRCUS, THE (from Puggery Wee)
Rand McNally + Company: 1908 (48 pgs, 11x8-1/2", color-c, 3-color insides)
nn - By unknown 27.00 81.00 160.00
NOTE: *Illustrated verse, many pages with multiple illustrations.*

ANIMAL SERIALS
T. Y. Crowell: 1906 (9x6-7/8", 214 pgs, hard-c, B&W)
nn - By E Warde Blaisdell 27.00 81.00 160.00
NOTE: *Multi-page comic strip stories. Reprints of Sunday strip "Bunny Bright He's All-Right".*

A NOBODY'S SCRAP BOOK
Frederik A. Stokes Co., New York: 1900 (11" x 8-5/8", hard-c, color)
nn- (Scarce) 71.00 213.00 425.00
NOTE: *Designed in England, printed in Holland, on English paper -- which likely explains the mispelling of Frederick Stokes' name. Highly fragile paper. Strips and cartoons, all by the same unidentified artist, "A Nobody", almost certainly reprinted from somewhere, as they are very professional.*

AT THE BOTTOM OF THE LADDER (M)
J.P. Lippincott Company: 1926 (11x8-1/4", 296 pgs, hardcover, B&W)
nn - By Camillus Kessler 47.00 141.00 280.00
NOTE: *Hilarious single panel cartoons showing first jobs of then important "captains of industry."*

AUTO FUN, PICTURES AND COMMENTS FROM "LIFE"
Thomas Y. Crowell & Co.: 1905 (152 pgs, 9x7", hard-c, B&W)
nn -By various 71.00 213.00 425.00
NOTE: *The cover just has "Auto Fun" but the title page also has the subheading listed here. This is similar to other reprint books of Life cartoons printed in the guide. Largely single panel cartoons but also several sequential. One or more cartoons by Kemble, Levering, Dirks, Flagg, Sullivant. Sequential cartoons by Kemble, Levering, Sullivant, and the highpoint, a 2 pg 6 panel piece by Winsor McCay.*

BANANA OIL (N) (see also HE DONE HER WRONG)
MS Publ. Co.: 1924 (9-7/8x10", 52 pgs., B&W)
nn - Milt Gross comic strips; not reprints 200.00 600.00 1200.00

BARKER'S ILLUSTRATED ALMANAC (O,P,S) (See Barkers in Victorian Era section)
Barker, Moore & Mein Medicine Co: 1900-1932+ (36 pgs, B&W, color paper-c)
1900-1932+ (7x5-7/8") 14.00 42.00 81.00

BARKER'S "KOMIC" PICTURE SOUVENIR (P,S) (see Barker's in Victorian)
Barker, Moore & Mein Medicine Co: nd (Parts 1-3, 1901-1903; Parts 1-4, 1906+) (color cardboard-c, B&W interior, 50 pages)
Parts 1-3 (Rare, earliest printing, nd (1901)) 167.00 500.00 1000.00

GD2.0 FN6.0 VF8.0

NOTE: *Same cover as 4th edition in Victorian Age Section, except has "Part 1", "Part 2", or "Part 3" printed in the blank space beneath the crate on which central figure is sitting. States "Edition in 3 Parts" on the first interior page, beneath the picture of the Barker's Building.*
Parts 1-3 (nd, c1901-1903) 125.00 375.00 750.00
NOTE: *New cover art on all Parts. States "Edition in 3 Parts" on the first interior page.*
Parts 1-4 (nd, c1906+) 100.00 300.00 600.00
NOTE: *States "Edition in 4 Parts" on the first interior page. Various printings known. These have been confirmed as premium comic books, predating the Buster Brown premiums. They reprint advertising cartoons from Barker's Illustrated Almanac. For the 50 page booklets by this same name, numbered as "Part"s, without exception, were published after 1900. Some editions are found to have 54 pages.*

BARNEY GOOGLE AND SPARK PLUG (N) (See **Comic Monthly**)
Cupples & Leon Co.: 1923 - No.6, 1928 (9-7/8x9-3/4"; 52 pgs., B&W, daily-r)
1 (nn)-By Billy DeBeck 108.00 325.00 650.00
2-4 (#5 & #6 do not exist) 55.00 165.00 330.00
NOTE: *Started June 17, 1919 as newspaper strip; Spark Plug introduced July 17, 1922; strip still running making it one of the oldest still in existence.*

BART'S CARTOONS FOR 1902 FROM THE MINNEAPOLIS JOURNAL (N,S)
Minneapolis Journal: 1903 (11x9", 102 pgs, paperback, B&W)
nn - By Charles L. Bartholomew 30.00 90.00 175.00

BELIEVE IT OR NOT! by Ripley (N,S)
Simon & Schuster: 1929 (8x 5-1/4", 68 pgs, red, B&W cover, B&W interior)
nn - By Robert Ripley (strip-r text & art) 46.00 138.00 275.00
NOTE: *1929 was the first printing of many reprintings. Strip began Dec 19, 1918 and is still running.*

BEN WEBSTER (N)
Standard Printing Company: 1928-1931 (13-3/4x4-7/16", 768 pgs, soft-c)
1 - "Bound to Win" 52.00 156.00 310.00
2 - "...in old Mexico 52.00 156.00 310.00
3 - "...At Wilderness Lake 52.00 156.00 310.00
4 - "...in the Oil Fields 52.00 156.00 310.00
NOTE: *Self Published by Edwin Alger, also contains fan's letter pages.*

BIG SMOKER
W.T. Blackwell & Co.: 1908 (16 pgs, 5-1/2x3-1/2", color-c & interior)
nn - By unknown 18.00 54.00 110.00
NOTE: *Stated reprint of 1878 version. no known copies yet of original printing.*

BILLY BOUNCE (I)
Donohue & Co.: 1906 (288 pgs, hardbound)
nn - By W.W. Denslow & Dudley Bragdon 217.00 651.00 1300.00
NOTE: *Billy Bounce was created in 1901 as a comic strip by W. W. Denslow (strip ran from 1901 NOV 11 to 1905 DEC 3), but the series is best remembered in the C. W. Kahles version (from 1902 SEP 28). Denslow resumed his character in the above illustrated book.*

BILLY HON'S FAMOUS CARTOON BOOK (H)
Wasley Publishing Co.: 1927 (7-1/2x10", 68 pgs, softbound wraparound)
nn - By Billy Hon 18.00 54.00 105.00

BILLY THE BOY ARTIST'S BOOK OF FUNNY PICTURES (N)
C.M.Clark Publishing Co.: 1910 (9x12", hardcover-c, Boston Globe strip-r)
nn - By Ed Payne 125.00 375.00 750.00
NOTE: *This long lived strip ran in **The Boston Globe** from Nov 5 1899-Jan 7 1955; one of the longer run strips.*

BILLY THE BOY ARTIST'S PAINTING BOOK OF FUNNY PICTURES
(known to exist; more data required) – – –

BIRD CENTER CARTOONS: A Chronicle of Social Happenings (N,S)
A. C. McClurg & Co.: 1904 (12-3/8x9-1/2", 216 pgs, hardcover, B&W, single panels)
nn - By John McCutcheon 42.00 126.00 250.00
NOTE: *Strip began in **The Chicago Tribune** in 1903. Satirical cartoons and text concerning a mythical town.*

BLASTS FROM THE RAM'S HORN
The Rams Horn Company: 1902 (330 pgs, 7x9", B&W)
nn - By various 27.00 81.00 160.00
NOTE: *Cartoons reprinted from what was, apparently, a religious newspaper. Many cartoons by Frank Beard. Mostly single panel but occasionally sequential. Allegorical cartoons similar to the Christian Cartoons book. This book mixes cartoons and text sort of like the Caricature books. One or more cartoons on every page.*

BOBBY THATCHER & TREASURE CAVE (N)
Altemus Co.: 1932 (9x7", 86 pgs., B&W, hard-c)
nn - Reprints; Storm-a 67.00 201.00 400.00

BOBBY THATCHER'S ROMANCE (N)
The Bell Syndicate/Henry Altemus Co.: 1931 (8-3/4x7", color cover, B&W)
nn - By Storm 67.00 201.00 400.00

BOOK OF CARTOONS, A (M,S)
Edward T. Miller: 1903 (12-1/4x9-1/4", 120 pgs, hardcover, B&W)
nn - By Harry J. Westerman (Ohio State Journal-r) 24.00 72.00 145.00

BOOK OF DRAWINGS BY A.B. FROST, A (M,S)
P.F. Collier & Son: 1904 (15-3/8 x 11", 96 pgs, B&W)
nn - A.B. Frost 51.00 153.00 305.00
NOTE: *Pages alternate verses by Wallace Irwin and full-page plated by A.B.Frost. 39 plates.*

BOTTLE, THE (E) (see Victorian Age section for earlier printings)
Gowans & Gray, London & Glasgow: June 1905 (3-3/4x6", 72 pgs, printed one side only, paper cover, B&W)
nn - 1st printing (June 1905) 27.00 81.00 160.00
nn - 2nd printing (March 1906) 20.00 60.00 120.00
nn - 3rd printing (January 1911) 20.00 60.00 120.00
NOTE: *By George Cruikshank. Reprints both THE BOTTLE and THE DRUNKARD'S CHILDREN. Cover is text only - no cover art.*

BOTTLE, THE (E)
Frederick A. Stokes: nd (c1906) (3-3/4x6", 72 pgs, printed one side only, paper-c, B&W)
nn- by George Cruikshank 20.00 60.00 120.00
NOTE: *Reprint of the Gowans & Gray edition. Reprints both THE BOTTLE and THE DRUNKARD'S CHILDREN. Cover is text only - no cover art.*

BOYS AND FOLKS (N).
George H. Dornan Company: 1917 (10-1/4 x 8-1/4", 232 pgs. (single-sided), B&W strip-r.
nn - By Webster 25.00 75.00 150.00
NOTE: *Four sections: Life's Darkest Moments, Mostly About Folks, The Thrill That Comes Once in a Lifetime, and Our Boyhood Ambitions. Most are single-panel cartoons, but there are some sequential comic strips.*

BOY'S & GIRLS' BIG PAINTING BOOK OF INTERESTING COMIC PICTURES (N)

GD2.0 FN6.0 VF8.0

M. A. Donohue & Co.: 1914-16 (9x15, 70 pgs)
nn - By Carl "Bunny" Schultze (Foxy Grandpa-r) 110.00 330.00 –
#2 (1914) 110.00 330.00 –
#337 (1914) (sez "Big Painting & Drawing Book") 110.00 330.00 –
nn - (1916) (sez "Big Painting Book")(9-1/4x15") 110.00 330.00 –
NOTE: *These are all **Foxy Grandpa** items.*

BRAIN LEAKS: Dialogues of Mutt & Flea (N)
O. K. Printing Co. (Rochester Evening Times): 1911 (76 pgs, 6-5/8x4-5/8, hard-c, B&W)
nn - By Leo Edward O'Melia; newspaper strip-r 35.00 105.00 210.00

BRAINY BOWERS AND DROWSY DUGGAN (N)
Star Publishing: 1905 (7-1/4 x 4-9/16", 98 pgs., blue, brown & white color cover, B&W interior, 25¢) (daily strip-r 1902-04 Chicago Daily News)
#74 - By R. W. Taylor (Scarce) 667.00 2000.00 –
NOTE: *Part of a series of Atlantic Library Heart Series. Strip begins in 1901 and runs thru 1915. Taylor also created Yen the Janitor for the **New York World.***

BRAIN BOWERS AND DROWSY DUGAN (N)
Max Stein Pub. House, Chicago: 1905 (6-3/16x4-3/8", 64 pgs, B&W)
nn - By R.W. Taylor (Scarce) 700.00 2100.00 –
NOTE: *A coverless copy of this surfaced on eBay in 2002 selling for $700.00.;*

BRAINY BOWERS AND DROWSY DUGGAN GETTING ON IN THE WORLD WITH NO VISIBLE MEANS OF SUPPORT (STORIES TOLD IN PICTURES TO MAKE THEIR TELLING SHORT) (N)
Max Stein/Star Publishing: 1905 (7-3/8x5 1/8", 164 pgs, slick black, red & tan color cover, interior newsprint) (daily strip-r 1902-04 Chicago Daily News)
nn - By R. W. Taylor (Scarce) 667.00 2000.00 –
nn - Possible hard cover edition also? – – –
NOTE: *These Brainy Bowers editions are the earliest known daily newspaper strip reprint books.*

BRINGING UP FATHER (N)
Star Co. (King Features): 1917 (5-1/2x16-1/2", 100 pgs., B&W, cardboard-c)
nn - (Scarcer)-Daily strip- by George McManus 200.00 600.00 1200.00

BRINGING UP FATHER (N)
Cupples & Leon Co.: 1919 - No. 26, 1934 (10x10", 52 pgs., B&W, stiff cardboard-c) (No. 22 is 9-1/4x9-1/2")
1-Daily strip-r by George McManus in all 68.00 204.00 410.00
2-10 51.00 153.00 305.00
11-20 68.00 204.00 410.00
21-26 (Scarcer) 102.00 306.00 610.00
The Big Book 1 (1926)-Thick book (hardcover, 142 pgs.) 183.00 549.00 1100.00
w/dust jacket (rare) 267.00 801.00 1600.00
The Big Book 2 (1929) 142.00 426.00 850.00
w/dust jacket (rare) 250.00 750.00 1500.00
NOTE: *The Big Books contain 3 regular issues rebound. Strip began Jan 2 1913-May 28 2000.*

BRINGING UP FATHER, THE TROUBLE OF (N)
Embee Publ. Co.: 1921 (9-3/4x15-3/4", 46 pgs, Sunday-r in color)
nn - (Rare) 121.00 363.00 725.00
NOTE: *Ties with Mutt & Jeff (EmBee) and Jimmie Dugan And The Reg'lar Fellers (C&L) as the last of the oblong size era. This was self published by George McManus.*

BRINGING UP FATHER (N) (see SAGARA'S ENGLISH CARTOONS
Publisher unknown (actually, unreadable), Tokyo: October 1924 (9-7/8" x 7-1/2", 90 pgs, color hard-c, B&W)
nn- (Scarce) by George McManus C&A (no known sales)
NOTE: *Published in Tokyo, Japan, with all strips in both English and Japanese, to facilitate learning English. Introduction by George McManus. Scarce in USA.*

BRONX BALLADS (I)
Simon & Schuster, NY: 1927 (9-1/2x7-1/4", hard-c with dust jacket, B&W)
nn - By Robert Simon and Harry Hershfield 54.00 162.00 325.00

BROWNIES, THE (not sequential comic strips)
The Century Co.: 1887 - 1914 (all came with dust jackets; add $100-150 to value if original dust jacket is included and intact)
Book 1 - The Brownies: Their Book (1887) 233.00 700.00 1400.00
Book 2 - Another Brownies Book (1890) 200.00 600.00 1200.00
Book 3 - The Brownies at Home (1893) 146.00 438.00 875.00
Book 4 - The Brownies Around the World (1894) 117.00 351.00 700.00
Book 5 - The Brownies Through the Union (1895) 117.00 351.00 700.00
Book 6 - The Brownies Abroad (1899) 117.00 351.00 700.00
Book 7 - The Brownies in the Philippines (1904) 117.00 351.00 700.00
Book 8 - The Brownies' Latest Adventures (1910) 117.00 351.00 700.00
Book 9 - The Brownies Many More Nights (1914) 117.00 351.00 700.00
...Raid on Kleinmaier Bros. (c. 1910, 16 pages) Kleinmaier Bros. Clothing, Marion, Ohio (no known sales)

BROWNIE CLOWN OF BROWNIE TOWN (N)
The Century Co.: 1908 (6-7/8 x 9-3/8", 112 pgs, color hardcover & interior)
nn - By Palmer Cox (rare; 1907 newspaper comic strip-r) 200.00 600.00 1200.00
NOTE: *The Brownies created 1883 in **St Nicholas Magazine.***

BUDDY TUCKER & HIS FRIENDS (N) (Also see **Buster Brown Nuggets**)
Cupples & Leon Co.: 1906 (11-5/8 x17", 58 pgs, color) (Scarce)
nn - 1905 Sunday strip-r by R. F. Outcault 517.00 1551.00 3100.00
NOTE: *Strip began Apr 30, 1905 thru at least Oct 1905.*

BUFFALO BILL'S PICTURE STORIES
Street & Smith Publications: 1909 (Soft cardboard cover)
nn - Very rare 79.00 237.00 475.00

BUGHOUSE FABLES (N) (see also **Comic Monthly**)
Embee Distributing Co. (King Features): 1921 (10¢, 4x4-1/2", 48 pgs.)
1-By Barney Google (Billy DeBeck) 71.00 213.00 425.00

BUG MOVIES (O) (Also see Clancy The Cop & Deadwood Gulch)
Dell Publishing Co.: 1931 (9-13/16x9-7/8", 52 pgs., B&W)
nn - Original material; Stookie Allen-a 105.00 315.00 630.00

BULL
Bull Publishing Company, New York: No.1, March, 1916 - No.12, Feb, 1917

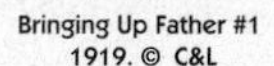
Bringing Up Father #1
1919. © C&L

Brownie Clown of Brownie Town
© The Century Co.

Buster Brown's Amusing Capers
1908 © Cupples & Leon

GD2.0 FN6.0 VF8.0

(10 cents, 10-3/4x8-3/4", 24 pgs, color paper-c, B&W)
1-12 (Very Rare) – – –
NOTE: *Pro-German, Anti-British cartoon/humor monthly, whose goal was to keep the U.S. neutral and out of World War I. We know of no copies which have sold in the past few years.*

BUNNY'S BLUE BOOK (see also Foxy Grandpa) (N)
Frederick A. Stokes Co.: 1911 (10x15, 60¢)
nn - By Carl "Bunny" Schultze strip-r 133.00 400.00 –

BUNNY'S RED BOOK (see also Foxy Grandpa) (N)
Frederick A. Stokes Co.: 1912 (10-1/4x15-3/4", 64 pgs.)
nn - By Carl "Bunny" Schultze strip-r 133.00 400.00 –

BUNNY'S GREEN BOOK (see also Foxy Grandpa) (N)
Frederick A. Stokes Co.: 1913 (10x15")
nn - By Carl "Bunny" Schultze 133.00 400.00 –

BUSTER BROWN (C) (Also see Brown's Blue Ribbon Book of Jokes and Jingles & Buddy Tucker & His Friends)
Frederick A. Stokes Co.: 1903 - 1916 (Daily strip-r in color)
1903...& His Resolutions (11-1/4x16", 66 pgs.) by R. F. Outcault (Rare)-1st nationally distributed comic. Distr. through Sears & Roebuck 1100.00 3300.00 –
1904...His Dog Tige & Their Troubles (11-1/4x16-1/4", 66 pgs.)(Rare) 567.00 1700.00 –
1905...Pranks (11-1/4x16-3/8", 66 pgs.) 483.00 1450.00 –
1906...Antics (11x16-3/8", 66 pgs.) 483.00 1450.00 –
1906...And Company (11x16-1/2", 66 pgs.) 333.00 1000.00 –
1906...Mary Jane & Tige (11-1/4x16, 66 pgs.) 333.00 1000.00 –
NOTE: ***Yellow Kid** pictured on two pages.*
1908 Collection of Buster Brown Comics 275.00 825.00 –
1909 Outcault's Real Buster and The Only Mary Jane (11x16, 66 pgs, Stokes) 275.00 825.00 –
1910...Up to Date (10-1/8x15-3/4", 66 pgs.) 167.00 501.00 1000.00
1911...Fun And Nonsense (10-1/8x15-3/4", 66 pgs.) 183.00 549.00 1100.00
1912...The Fun Maker (10-1/8x15-3/4", 66 pgs.) -Yellow Kid (4 pgs.) 183.00 549.00 1100.00
1913...At Home (10-1/8x15-3/4", 56 pgs.) 167.00 583.00 1000.00
1914...And Tige Here Again (10x16, 62 pgs, Stokes) 153.00 535.00 850.00
1915...And His Chum Tige (10x16, Stokes) 153.00 535.00 850.00
1916...The Little Rogue (10-1/8x15-3/4", 62 pgs.) 162.00 567.00 1000.00
1917...And the Cat (5-1/2x 6-1/2, 26 pgs, Stokes) 115.00 402.00 675.00
1917...Disturbs the Family (5-1/2x 6 1/2, 26 pgs, Stokes
NOTE: *Story featuring statue of "the Chinese Yellow Kid"* 115.00 402.00 675.00
1917...The Real Buster Brown (5-1/2x 6 -/2, 26 pgs, Stokes 115.00 402.00 675.00

Frederick A. Stokes Co. Hard Cover Series (I)
...Abroad (1904, 10-1/4x8", 86 pgs., B&W, hard-c)-R. F. Outcault-a (Rare) 180.00 600.00 850.00
...Abroad (1904, B&W, 67 pgs.)-R. F. Outcault-a 180.00 600.00 850.00
NOTE: *Buster Brown Abroad is not an actual comic book, but prose with illustrations.*
..."Tige" His Story 1905 (10x8", 63 pgs., B&W) (63 illos.)
nn-By RF Outcault 143.00 500.00 –
...My Resolutions 1906 (10x8", B&W, 68 pgs.)-R.F. Outcault-a (Rare) 233.00 817.00 1300.00
...Autobiography 1907 (10x8", B&W, 71 pgs.) (16 color plates & 36 B&W illos) 65.00 230.00 410.00
...And Mary Jane's Painting Book 1907 (10x13-1/4", 60 pgs, both card & hardcover versions exist
nn-RFO (first printing blank on top of cover) 67.00 233.00 430.00
First Series- this is a reprint if it says First Series 67.00 233.00 430.00
Volume Two - By RFO 67.00 233.00 430.00
... My Resolutions by Buster Brown (1907, 68 pgs, small size, cardboard covers) scarce 43.00 150.00 275.00
NOTE: *Not actual comic book per se, but a compilation of the Resolutions panels found at the end of Outcault's Buster Brown newspaper strips.*

BUSTER BROWN (N)
Cupples & Leon Co./N. Y. Herald Co.: 1906 - 1917 (11x17", color, strip-r)
NOTE: *Early issues by R. F. Outcault; most C&L editions are not by Outcault.*
1906...His Dog Tige And Their Jolly Times (11-3/8x16-5/8", 68 pgs.) 300.00 1100.00 2000.00
1906...His Dog Tige & Their Jolly Times (11x16, 46 pgs.) 163.00 600.00 1200.00
1907...Latest Frolics (11-3/8x16-5/8", 66 pgs., r/'05-06 strips) 163.00 600.00 1100.00
1908...Amusing Capers (58 pgs.) 129.00 475.00 760.00
1909...The Busy Body (11-3/8x16-5/8", 62 pgs.) 129.00 475.00 760.00
1910...On His Travels (11x16", 58 pgs.) 115.00 402.00 760.00
1911...Happy Days (11-3/8x16-5/8", 58 pgs.) 115.00 402.00 760.00
1912...In Foreign Lands (10x16", 58 pgs) 115.00 402.00 760.00
1913...And His Pets (11x16", 58 pgs.) STOKES???? 115.00 402.00 760.00
1913...And His Pets (26 pg partial reprint) – – –
1914...Funny Tricks (11-3/8x16-5/8", 58 pgs.) 115.00 402.00 760.00
1916...At Play (10x16, 58 pgs) 115.00 402.00 760.00

BUSTER BROWN NUGGETS (N)
Cupples & Leon Co./N.Y.Herald Co.: 1907 (1905, 7-1/2x6-1/2", 36 pgs., color, strip-r, hard-c)(By R. F. Outcault) (NOTE: books are all unnumbered)

GD2.0 FN6.0 VF8.0

Buster Brown Goes Fishing, Goes Swimming, Plays Indian, Goes Shooting, Plays Cowboy, On Uncle Jack's Farm, Tige And the Bull, And Uncle Buster 40.00 150.00 360.00
Buddy Tucker Meets Alice in Wonderland 75.00 225.00 450.00
Buddy Tucker Visits The House That Jack Built 40.00 150.00 360.00

BUSTER BROWN MUSLIN SERIES (N)
Saalfield: 1907 (also contain copyright Cupples & Leon)
...Goes Fishing, Plays Indian, And the Donkey (1907, 6-7/8x6-1/8", 24 pgs., color)-r/1905 Sunday comics page by Outcault (Rare) 75.00 175.00 350.00
...Plays Cowboy (1907, 6-3/4x6", 10 pgs., color)-r/1905 Sunday comics page by Outcault (Rare) 50.00 190.00 330.00
NOTE: *These are muslin versions of the C&L BB Nugget series. Muslin books are all cloth books, made to be washable so as not easily stained/destroyed by very young children. The Muslin books contain one strip each (the title strip), to the more common NUGGET's three strips.*

BUSTER BROWN PREMIUMS (Advertising premium booklets)
Various Publishers: 1904 - 1912 (3x5" to 5x7"; sizes vary)

American Fruit Product Company, Rochester, NY
Buster Brown Duffy's 1842 Cider (1904, 7x5". 12 pgs, C.E. Sherin Co, NYC)
nn - By R. F. Outcault (scarce) 100.00 350.00 650.00

The Brown Shoe Company, St. Louis, USA
Set of five books (5x7", 16 pgs., color)
Brown's Blue Ribbon Book of Jokes and Jingles Book 1 (nn, 1904)-By R. F. Outcault; Buster Brown & Tige, Little Tommy Tucker, Jack & Jill, Little Boy Blue, Dainty Jane; The Yellow Kid app. on back-c (1st BB comic book premium) 350.00 1100.00 2100.00
Buster Brown's Blue Ribbon Book of Jokes and Jingles Book 2 (1905)-
Original color art by Outcault 200.00 600.00 1250.00
Buster's Book of Jokes & Jingles Book 3 (1909)
not by R.F. Outcault 200.00 450.00 950.00
NOTE: *Reprinted from the Blue Ribbon post cards with advert jingles added.*
Buster's Book of Instructive Jokes and Jingles Book 4 (1910)-Original color art not by R.F. Outcault 150.00 585.00 1150.00
...Book of Travels nn (1912, 3x5")-Original color art not signed by Outcault 117.00 408.00 750.00
NOTE: *Estimated 5 or 6 known copies exist of books #1-4.*

The Buster Brown Bread Company
"Buster Brown" Bread Book of Rhymes, The (1904, 4x6", 12 pgs., half color, half B&W)- Original color art not signed by RFO 158.00 553.00 1200.00

Buster Brown's Hosiery Mills
"Buster Brown's Latest" nn (1909, 7x5-1/4". 20 pgs, color paper cover and color interior By R.F. Outcault (a GD+ copy sold for $150)
"How Buster Brown Got The Pie" nn (nd, 7x5-1/4". 16 pgs, color paper cover and color interior By R.F. Outcault 85.00 300.00 625.00
"The Autobiography of Buster Brown" nn (nd,9x6-1/8", 36 pgs, text story & art by R.F. Outcault 85.00 300.00 625.00
NOTE: *Similar to, but a distinctly different item than "Buster Brown's Autobiography."*

The Buster Brown Stocking Company
Buster Brown Drawing Book, The nn (nd, 5x6", 20 pgs.)-B&W reproductions of 1903 R.F. Outcault art to trace 65.00 165.00 450.00
NOTE: *Reprints a comic strip from Burr McIntosh Magazine, which includes Buster, Yellow Kid, and Pore Li'l Mose (only known story involving all three.)*
Buster Brown Stocking Magazine nn (Jan. 1906, 7-3/4x5-3/8", 36 pgs.) R.F. Outcault 50.00 100.00 300.00
NOTE: *This was actually a store bought item selling for 5 cents per copy.*

Collins Baking Company
Buster Brown Drawing Book nn (1904, 5x3", 12 pgs.)-Original B&W art to trace, not signed by R.F. Outcault 50.00 200.00 410.00

C. H. Morton, St. Albans, VT
Merry Antics of Buster Brown, Buddy Tucker & Tige nn (nd, 3-1/2x5-1/2", 16 pgs.) -Original B&W art by R.F. Outcault 83.00 292.00 550.00

Ivan Frank & Company
Buster Brown nn (1904, 3x5", 12 pgs.)-B&W repros of R. F. Outcault Sunday pages (First premium to actually reproduce Sunday comic pages – may be first premium comic strip-r book?) 150.00 475.00 1000.00
Buster Brown's Pranks (1904, 3-1/2x5-1/8", 12 pgs.)-reprints intro of Buddy Tucker into the BB newspaper strip before he was spun off into his own short lived newspaper strip 125.00 438.00 850.00

Kaufmann & Strauss
Buster Brown Drawing Book (1906, 28 pages, 5x3-1/2") Color Cover, B+W original story signed by Outcault, tracing paper inserted as alternate pages. Back cover imprinted for Nox' Em All Shoes 50.00 150.00 350.00

Pond's Extract
Buster Brown's Experiences With Pond's Extract nn (1904, 6-3/4x4-1/2", 28 pgs.) Original color art by R.F. Outcault (may be the first BB premium comic book with original art) 130.00 320.00 750.00

C. A. Cross & Co.
Red Cross Drawing Book nn (1906, 4-7/8x3-1/2", color paper -c, B&W interior, 12 pgs.) 75.00 175.00 340.00
NOTE: *This is for Red Cross coffee; not the health organization.*

Ringen Stove Company
Quick Meal Steel Ranges nn (nd, 5x3", 16 pgs.)-Original B&W art not signed by R.F. Outcault 100.00 240.00 450.00

Steinwender Stoffregen Coffee Co.
"Buster Brown Coffee" (1905, 4-7/8x3", color paper cover, B&W interior, 12 printed pages, plus 1 tracing paper page above each interior image (total of 8 sheets) (Very Rare)

105.00 310.00 650.00
NOTE: *Part of a BB drawing contest. If instructions had been followed, most copies would have ended up destroyed.*

U. S. Playing Card Company
Buster Brown - My Own Playing Cards (1906, 2-1/2x1-3/4", full color)
nn - By R. F. Outcault 42.00 147.00 275.00
NOTE: *Series of full color panels tell stories, average about 5 cards per story.*

Publisher Unknown
The Drawing Book nn (1906, 3-9/16x5", 8 pgs.)-Original B&W art to trace not by R.F. Outcault 75.00 175.00 350.00

BUTLER BOOK A Series of Clever Cartoons of Yale Undergraduate Life
Yale Record: June 16, 1913 (10-3/4 x 17", 34 pgs, paper cover B&W)
nn - By Alban Bernard Butler 25.00 75.00 160.00
NOTE: *Cartoons and strips reprinted from The Yale Record student newspaper.*

BUTTONS & FATTY IN THE FUNNIES
Whitman Publishing Co.: nd 1927 (10-1/4x15-1/2", 28pg., color)
W936 - Signed "M.E.B.", probably M.E. Brady; strips in color copyright The Brooklyn Daily Eagle; (very rare) 79.00 237.00 475.00

BY BRIGGS (M,N,P) (see also OLD GOLD THE SMOOTHER AND BETTER CIGARETTE)
Old Gold Cigarettes: nd (c1920's) (11" x 9-11/16", 44 pgs, cardboard-c, B&W)
nn- (Scarce) 55.00 110.00 225.00
NOTE: *Collection reprinting strip cartoons by Clare Briggs, advertising Old Gold Cigarettes. These strips originally appeared in various magazines, play program booklets, newspapers, etc. Some of the strips involve regular Briggs strip series. Contains all of the strips in the smaller, color "OLD GOLD" giveaways, plus more.*

CAMION CARTOONS
Marshall Jones Company: 1919 (7-1/2x5", 136 pgs, B&W)
nn - By Kirkland H. Day (W.W.One occupation) 20.00 70.00 135.00

CANYON COUNTRY KIDDIES (M)
Doubleday, Page & Co: 1923 (8x10-1/4", 88 pgs, hard-c, B&W)
nn - By James Swinnerton 39.00 137.00 250.00

CARLO (H)
Doubleday, Page & Co.: 1913 (8 x 9-5/8, 120 pgs, hardcover, B&W)
nn - By A.B. Frost 40.00 140.00 310.00
NOTE: *Original sequential strips about a dog. Became short lived newspaper comic strip in 1914. Originally published with a dust jacket which increases value 50%.*

CARTOON BOOK, THE
Bureau of Publicity, War Loan Organization, Treasury Department, Washington, D.C.: 1918 (6-1/2x4-7/8", 48 pgs, paper cover, B&W)
nn - By various artists 38.00 115.00 250.00
NOTE: *U.S. government issued booklet of WW I propaganda cartoons by 46 artists promoting the third sale of Liberty Loan bonds. The artists include: Berryman, Clare Briggs, Cesare, J. N. "Ding" Darling, Rube Goldberg, Kemble, McCutcheon, George McManus, F. Opper, T. E. Powers, Ripley, Satterfield, H. T. Webster, Gaar Williams.*

CARTOON CATALOGUE (S)
The Lockwood Art School, Kalamazoo, Mich.: 1919 (11-5/8x9, 52 pgs, B&W)
nn - Edited by Mr. Lockwood 20.00 60.00 140.00
NOTE: *Jammed with 100s of single panel cartoons and some sequential comics; Mr Lockwood began the very first cartoonist school back in 1892. Clare Briggs was one of his students.*

CARTOON COMICS
Lasco Publications, Detroit, Mich: #1, April 1930 - #2, May 1930 (8-3/6x5-1/5")
1, 2 - By Lu Harris 25.00 65.00 120.00
NOTE: *Contains recurring characters Hollywood Horace, Campus Charlie, Pair-A-Dice Alley and Jocko Monkey. Not much is presently known about the creator(s) or publisher.*

CARTOON HISTORY OF ROOSEVELT'S CAREER, A
The Review of Reviews Company: 1910 (276 pgs, 8-1/4x11",
nn - By various 105.00 210.00 415.00
NOTE: *Reprints editorial cartoons about Teddy Roosevelt from U.S. and international newspapers and cartoons from the humor magagines (Puck, Judge, etc.). A few cartoonists whose work is included are Dalrymple, Opper, McDougall, McCutcheon, Remington, Rogers, Kemble. Mostly single panel but 10 or so are sequential strips.*

CARTOON HUMOR
Collegian Press: 1938 (102 pgs, squarebound, B&W)
nn 20.00 70.00 130.00
NOTE: *Contains cartoons & strips by Otto Soglow, Syd Hoff, Peter Arno, Abner Dean, others.*

CARTOONIST'S PHILOSOPHY, A
Percy Crosby: 1931, HC, 252 pgs, 5-1/2x7-1/2", hard-c, celluloid dust wrapper
nn - By Percy Crosby (10 plates, 6 are of Skippy) 40.00 75.00 150.00
NOTE: *Crosby's partial autobiography regarding his return to France in 1929, and portrayals of Normandy, the "cliff dwellers" on Normandy cliffs (destroyed in WWII), his visit to London, comments on art, philosophy, several poems, and political dialogue. His description of his Cockney driver, "Harold" is amusing. Also describes his experience visiting Chicago to speak out against Capone, his concerns over the evils of Prohibition, and the economy prior to the 1929 crash. This book reveals he was aware of the dangers of his outspoken views, and is prophetic, re: his later years as political prisoner. Also reveals his religious beliefs.*

CARTOONS BY BRADLEY: CARTOONIST OF THE CHICAGO DAILY NEWS
Rand McNally & Company: 1917 (11-1/4x8-3/4", 112 pgs, hardcover, B&W)
nn - By Luther D. Bradley (editorial) 20.00 70.00 125.00

CARTOONS BY FONTAINE FOX (Toonerville Trolley) (S)
Harper & Brothers Publishers: nd early '20s (9x7-7/8",102 pgs., hard-c, B&W)
Second Book- By Fontaine Fox (Toonerville-r) 150.00 300.00 560.00

CARTOONS BY HALLADAY (N,S)
Providence Journal Co., Rhode Island: Dec 1914 (116 pgs, 10-1/2x 7-3/4", hard-c, B&W)
nn- (Scarce) 50.00 125.00 260.00
NOTE: *Cartoons on Rhode Island politics, plus some Teddy Roosevelt & WW I cartoons.*

CARTOONS BY McCUTCHEON (S)
A. C. McClurg & Co.: 1903 (12-3/8x9-3/4", 212 pgs., hardcover, B&W)
nn - By John McCutcheon 20.00 70.00 130.00

CARTOONS BY W. A. IRELAND (S)
The Columbus-Evening Dispatch: 1907 (13-3/4 x 10-1/2", 66 pgs, hardcover)
nn - By W. A. Ireland (strip-r) 30.00 75.00 140.00

CARTOONS MAGAZINE (I,N,S)
H. H. Windsor, Publisher: Jan 1912-June 1921; July 1921-1923; 1923-1924; 1924-1927 (1912-July 1913 issues 12x9-1/4", 68-76 pgs; 1913-1921 issues 10x7", average 112 to 188 pgs, color covers)
1912-Jan-Dec 30.00 75.00 165.00
1913-1917 30.00 75.00 165.00
1917-(Apr) "How Comickers Regard Their Characters" 30.00 105.00 175.00
1917-(June) "A Genius of the Comic Page" - long article on George Herriman, Krazy Kat, etc with lots of Herriman art; "Cartoonists and Their Cars" 150.00 300.00 775.00
1918-1919 30.00 75.00 160.00
1920-June 1921 30.00 75.00 160.00
July 1921-1923 titled Wayside Tales & Cartoons Magazine 30.00 75.00 160.00
1923-1924 becomes Cartoons Magazine again 30.00 75.00 160.00
1924-1927 becomes Cartoons & Movie Magazine 30.00 75.00 160.00
NOTE: *Many issues contain a wealth of historical background on then current cartoonists of the day with an international slant; each issue profusely illustrated with many cartoons. We are unsure if this magazine continued after 1927.*

CARTOONS BY J. N. DARLING (S,N - some sequential strips)
The Register & Tribune Co., Des Moines, Iowa: 1909?-1920 (12x8-7/8",B&W)
Book 1 20.00 55.00 160.00
Book 2 Education of Alonzo Applegate (1910) 18.00 52.00 125.00
2nd printing 18.00 52.00 125.00
Book 3 Cartoons From The Files (1911) 18.00 52.00 125.00
Book 4 18.00 52.00 125.00
Book 5 In Peace And War (1916) 18.00 52.00 125.00
Book 6 Aces & Kings War Cartoons (Dec 1, 1918) 18.00 52.00 125.00
Book 7 The Jazz Era (Dec 1920) 18.00 52.00 125.00
Book 8 Our Own Outlines of History (1922) 18.00 52.00 125.00
NOTE: *Some of the most inspired hard hitting cartoons ever printed. Are there more?*

CARTOONS THAT MADE PRINCE HENRY FAMOUS, THE (N,S)
The Chicago Record-Herald: Feb/March 1902 (12-1/8" x 9", 32 pgs, paper-c, B&W)
nn- (Scarce) by McCutcheon 25.00 55.00 110.00
NOTE: *Cartoons about the visit of the British Prince Henry to the U.S.*

CAVALRY CARTOONS (O)
R. Montalboddi: nd (c1918) (14-1/4" x 11", 30 pgs, printed on one side, olive & black construction paper-c, B&W interior)
nn - By R.Montalboddi 20.00 55.00 105.00
NOTE: *Comics about life in the U.S.Cavalry during World War I, by a soldier who was in the 1st Cavalry.*

CAWS AND EFFECT
L.D. Gallison Pub., NY: nd (7 two-sided panels, 4-5/8 x 3", B&W)
nn - By Edgar Ape O. (a GVG copy sold for $111.55 in 2010)

CHARLIE CHAPLIN (N)
Essanay/M. A. Donohue & Co.: 1917 (9x16", B&W, large size soft-c)
Series 1, #315-Comic Capers (9-3/4x15-3/4")-20 pgs. by Segar;
Series 1, #316-In the Movies 165.00 525.00 1300.00
#317-Up in the Air (20 pgs), #318-In the Army 165.00 525.00 1500.00
Funny Stunts-(12-1/2x16-3/8",16 color pgs) 165.00 525.00 1500.00
NOTE: *All contain pre-Thimble Theatre Segar art. The thin paper used makes high grade copies very scarce.*

CHASING THE BLUES
Doubleday Page: 1912 (7-1/2x10", 108 pgs., B&W, hard-c)
nn - By Rube Goldberg 200.00 600.00 1200.00
NOTE: *Contains a dozen Foolish Questions, baseball, a few Goldberg poems and lots of sequential strips.*

CHRISTIAN CARTOONS (N,S)
The Sunday School Times Company: 1922 (7-1/4 x 6-1/8,104 pgs, brown hard-c, B&W)
nn - E.J. Pace 19.00 57.00 115.00
NOTE: *Religious cartoons reprinted from The Sunday School Times.*

CLANCY THE COP (O)
Dell Publishing Co.: 1930 - No. 2, 1931 (10x10", 52 pgs., B&W, cardboard-c)
(Also see Bug Movies & Deadwood Gulch)
1, 2-By VEP Victor Pazimino (original material; not reprints) 120.00 280.00 580.00

CLIFFORD MCBRIDE'S IMMORTAL NAPOLEON & UNCLE ELBY (N)
The Castle Press: 1932 (12x17"; soft-c cartoon book)
nn - Intro. by Don Herod 36.00 144.00 240.00

COLLECTED DRAWINGS OF BRUCE BAIRNSFATHER, THE
W. Colston Leigh: 1931 (11-1/4x8-1/4 ", 168 pages, hardcover, B&W)
nn - By Bruce Bairnsfather 38.00 114.00 225.00

COMICAL PEEP SHOW
McLoughlin Bros: 1902 (36 pgs, B&W)
nn 32.00 96.00 190.00
NOTE: *Comic stories of Wilhelm Busch redrawn; two versions with green or gold front cover logos; back covers different.*

COMIC ANIMALS (I)
Charles E. Graham & Co.: 1903 (9-3/4x7-1/4", 90 pgs, color cover)
nn - By Walt McDougall (not comic strips) 90.00 180.00 295.00

COMIC CUTS (O)
H. L. Baker Co., Inc.: 5/19/34-7/28/34 (Tabloid size 10-1/2x15-1/2", 24 pgs., 5¢) (full color, not reprints; published weekly; created for news stand sales)
V1#1 - V1#7(6/30/34), V1#8(7/14/34), V1#9(7/28/34)-Idle Jack strips
200.00 600.00 1200.00
NOTE: *According to a 1958 Lloyd Jacquet interview, this short-lived comics mag was the direct inspiration for Major Malcolm Wheeler-Nicholson's **New Fun Comics**, not **Famous Funnies**.*

COMIC MONTHLY (N)
Embee Dist. Co.: Jan, 1922 - No. 12, Dec, 1922 (10¢, 8-1/2"x9", 28 pgs., 2-color covers) (1st monthly newsstand comic publication) (Reprints 1921 B&W dailies)
1-Polly & Her Pals by Cliff Sterrett 400.00 1200.00 2600.00
2-Mike & Ike by Rube Goldberg 150.00 500.00 1100.00
3-S'Matter, Pop? 150.00 500.00 1100.00
4-Barney Google by Billy DeBeck 150.00 500.00 1100.00
5-Tillie the Toiler by Russ Westover 150.00 500.00 1100.00
6-Indoor Sports by Tad Dorgan 150.00 500.00 1100.00
NOTE: *#6 contains more Judge Rummy than Indoor Sports.*
7-Little Jimmy by James Swinnerton 150.00 500.00 1100.00
8-Toots and Casper b y Jimmy Murphy 150.00 500.00 1100.00
9-New Bughouse Fables by Barney Google 150.00 500.00 1100.00

Charlie Chaplin in the Army by Segar
1917 © Essaney

Chasing the Blues
1912 © Rube Goldberg

How Dick Tracy and Dick Tracy, Jr.
Caught the Racketeers by Chester Gould
1933 © Cupples & Leon

GD2.0 FN6.0 VF8.0

10-Foolish Questions by Rube Goldberg 150.00 500.00 1100.00
11-Barney Google & Spark Plug by Billy DeBeck 150.00 500.00 1100.00
12-Polly & Her Pals by Cliff Sterrett 150.00 500.00 1100.00
NOTE: *This series was published by George McManus (Bringing Up Father) as Em & Rudolph Block, Jr., son of Hearst's cartoon editor for many years, as "Bee." One would have thought this series would have done very well considering the tremendous amount of talent assembled. All issues are extremely hard to find these days and rarely show up in any type of higher grade.*

COMIC PAINTING AND CRAYONING BOOK (H)
Saalfield Publ. Co.: 1917 (13-1/2x10", 32 pgs.) (No price on-c)
nn - Tidy Teddy by F. M. Follett, Clarence the Cop, Mr. & Mrs. Butt-In; regular comic stories to read or color 50.00 175.00 340.00

COMPLETE TRIBUNE PRIMER, THE (I)
Mutual Book Company: 1901 (7 1/4 x 5", 152 pgs, red hard-c)
nn - By Frederick Opper; has 75 Opper cartoons 35.00 80.00 160.00

COURTSHIP OF TAGS, THE (N)
McCormick Press: pre-1910 (9x4", 88 pgs, red & B&W-c, B&W interior)
nn - By O. E. Wertz (strip-r Wichita Daily Beacon) 35.00 80.00 160.00

DAFFYDILS (N)
Cupples & Leon Co.: 1911 (5-3/4x7-7/8", 52 pgs., B&W, hard-c)
nn - By "Tad" Dorgan 58.00 204.00 360.00
NOTE: *Also exists in self-published TAD edition: The T.A. Dorgan Company; unknown which is first printing.*

DAN DUNN SECRET OPERATIVE 48 (Also See Detective Dan) (N)
Whitman Publishing: 1937 ((5 1/2 x 7 1/4", 68pgs., color cardboard-c, B&W)
1010 And The Gangsters' Frame-Up 60.00 180.00 360.00
NOTE: *There are two versions of the book the later printing has a 5 cent cover price. Dick Tracy look-alike character by Norman Marsh.*

DANGERS OF DOLLY DIMPLE, THE (N)
Penn Tobacco Co.: nd (1930's) (9-3/8x7-7/8", 28 pgs, red cardboard-c, B&W)
nn - (Rare) by Walter Enright 29.00 87.00 175.00
NOTE: *Reprints newspaper comic strip advertisements, in which in every episode, Dolly Dimple's life is saved by Penn's Smoking Tobacco. - how very un-P.C. by today's standards.*

DEADWOOD GULCH (O) (See The Funnies 1929)(also see Bug Movies & Clancy The Cop)
Dell Publishing Co.: 1931 (10x10", 52 pgs., B&W, color covers, B&W interior)
nn - By Charles "Boody" Rogers (original material) 150.00 300.00 625.00

DESTINY A Novel In Pictures (O)
Farrar & Rinehart: 1930 (8x7", 424 pgs, B&W, hard-c with dust jacket)
nn - By Otto Nuckel (original graphic novel) 50.00 150.00 300.00

DICK TRACY & DICK TRACY JR. CAUGHT THE RACKETEERS, HOW
Cupples & Leon Co.: 1933 (8-1/2x7", 88 pgs., hard-c) (See Treasure Box of Famous Comics) (N)
2-(Numbered on pg. 84)-Continuation of Stooge Viller book (daily strip reprints from 8/3/33 thru 11/8/33)(Rarer than #1) 100.00 400.00 775.00
With dust jacket... 200.00 600.00 1200.00

DICK TRACY & DICK TRACY JR. AND HOW THEY CAPTURED "STOOGE" VILLER (N)
Cupples & Leon Co.: 1933 (8-1/2x7", 100 pgs., hard-c, one-shot)
Reprints 1932 & 1933 Dick Tracy daily strips
nn(No.1)-1st app. of "Stooge" Viller 100.00 400.00 750.00
With dust jacket... 183.00 549.00 1100.00

DIMPLES By Grace Drayton (N) (See Dolly Dimples)
Hearst's International Library Co.: 1915 (6 1/4 x 5 1/4, 12 pgs) (5 known)
nn-Puppy and Pussy; nn-She Goes For a Walk; nn-She Had A Sneeze; nn-She Has a Naughty Play Husband; nn-Wait Till Fido Comes Home 21.00 74.00 160.00

DOINGS OF THE DOO DADS, THE (N)
Detroit News (Universal Feat. & Specialty Co.): 1922 (50¢, 7-3/4x7-3/4", 34 pgs, B&W, red & white-c, square binding)
nn-Reprints 1921 newspaper strip "Text & Pictures" given away as prize in the Detroit News Doo Dads contest; by Arch Dale 43.00 173.00 340.00

DOING THE GRAND CANYON
Fred Harvey: 1922 (7 x 4-3/4", 24 pgs, B&W, paper cover)
nn - John McCutcheon 30.00 60.00 100.00
NOTE: *Text & 8 cartoons about visiting the Grand Canyon.*

DOINGS OF THE VAN-LOONS (N) (from same company as Mutt & Jeff #1-#5)
Ball Publications: 1912 (5-3/4X15-1/2", 68pg., B&W, hard-c)
nn - By Fred I. Leipziger (scarce) 72.00 252.00 600.00

DOLLY DIMPLES & BOBBY BOUNCE (See Dimples)
Cupples & Leon Co.: 1933 (8-3/4x7", color hardcover, B&W)
nn - Grace Drayton-a 27.00 81.00 160.00

DOO DADS, THE (Sleepy Sam and Tiny the Elephant)
Universal Feature * Specialty Co: 1922 (5-1/4x14", 36 pgs.,B&W, R&W-c,square binding)
nn - By Arch Dale 46.00 138.00 275.00

DRAWINGS BY HOWARD CHANDLER CHRISTIE (S, M)
Moffat, Yard & Company, NY: 1905 (11-7/8x16-1/2", 68 pgs, hard-c, B&W)
nn - Howard C. Christie 23.00 69.00 140.00
NOTE: *Reprints1898-1905 from Haprer & Bros, Ch. Scribners Sons, Leslie's, MacMillians, McLurg, Russell.*

GD2.0 FN6.0 VF8.0

DREAMS OF THE RAREBIT FIEND (N)
Frederick A. Stokes Co.:1905 (10-1/4x7-1/2", 68 pgs, thin paper cover all B&W) newspaper reprints from the New York Evening Telegram printed on yellow paper
nn-By Winsor "Silas" McCay (Very Rare) (Five copies known to exist)
Estimated value.... 1200.00 3600.00 –
NOTE: *A G/VG copy sold for $2,045 in May 2004. This item usually turns up with fragile paper.*

DRISCOLL'S BOOK OF PIRATES (O)
David McKay Publ.: 1934 (9x7", 124 pgs, B&W, hardcover)
nn - By Montford Amory ("Pieces of Eight strip-r) 29.00 87.00 175.00

DUCKY DADDLES
Frederick A. Stokes Co: July 1911 (15x10")
nn - By Grace Weiderseim (later Drayton) strip-r 58.00 174.00 350.00

DUMBUNNIES AND THEIR FRIENDS IN RABBITBORO, THE (O)
Albertine Randall Wheelan: 1931 (8-3/4x7-1/8", 82 pgs, color hardcover, B&W)
nn - By Albertine Randall Wheelan (self-pub) 40.00 120.00 240.00

EDISON - INSPIRATION TO YOUTH (N)(Also see Life of Thomas---)
Thomas A. Edison, Incorporated: 1939 (9-1/2 x 6-1/2, paper cover, B&W)
nn - Photo-c 50.00 150.00 310.00
NOTE: *Reprints strip material found in the 1928 Life of Thomas A. Edison in Word and Picture.*

'ERBIE AND 'IS PLAYMATES
Democratic National Committee: 1932 (8x9-1/2, 16 pgs, B&W)
nn - By Frederick Opper (Rare) 100.00 200.00 415.00
NOTE: *Anti-Hoover/Pro-Roosevelt political comics.*

EXPANSION BEING BART'S BEST CARTOONS FOR 1899
Minneapolis Journal: 1900 (10-1/4x8-1/4", 124 pgs, paperback, B&W)
v2#1 - By Charles L. Bartholomew 24.00 70.00 140.00

FAMOUS COMICS (N)
King Features Synd. (Whitman Pub. Co.): 1934 (100 pgs., daily newspaper-r) (3-1/2x8-1/2"; paper cover)(came in an illustrated box)
684 (#1) - Little Jimmy, Katz Kids & Barney Google 46.00 138.00 275.00
684 (#2) - Polly, Little Jimmy, Katzenjammer Kids 46.00 138.00 275.00
684 (#3) - Little Annie Rooney, Polly and Her Pals, Katzenjammer Kids 46.00 138.00 275.00
Box price... 75.00 225.00 450.00

FAMOUS COMICS CARTOON BOOKS (N)
Whitman Publishing Co.: 1934 (8x7-1/4", 72 pgs, B&W hard-c, daily strip-r)
1200-The Captain & the Kids; Dirks reprints credited to Bernard Dibble 38.00 114.00 225.00
1202-Captain Easy & Wash Tubbs by Roy Crane; 2 slightly different versions of cover exist 43.00 129.00 260.00
1203-Ella Cinders By Conselman & Plumb 38.00 114.00 225.00
1204-Freckles & His Friends 36.00 108.00 215.00
NOTE: *Called Famous Funnies Cartoon Books inside back area sales advertisement.*

FANTASIES IN HA-HA (M)
Meyer Bros & Co.: 1900 (14 x 11-7/8", 64 pgs, color cover hardcover, B&W)
nn - By Hy Mayer 54.00 162.00 325.00

FELIX (N)
Henry Altemus Company: 1931 (6-1/2"x8-1/4", 52 pgs., color, hard-c w/dust jacket)
1-3-Sunday strip reprints of Felix the Cat by Otto Messmer. Book No. 2 r/1931 Sunday panels mostly two to a page in a continuity format oddly arranged so each tier of panels reads across two pages, then drops to the next tier. (Books 1 & 3 have not been documented.)(Rare)
Each 275.00 550.00 1100.00
With dust jacket 300.00 800.00 1600.00

FELIX THE CAT BOOK (N)
McLoughlin Bros.: 1927 (8"x15-3/4", 52 pgs, half in color-half in B&W)
nn - Reprints 23 Sunday strips by Otto Messmer from 1926 & 1927, every other one in color, two pages per strip. (Rare) 333.00 1000.00 2000.00
260-Reissued (1931), reformatted to 9-1/2"x10-1/4" (same color plates, but one strip per every three pages), retitled ("Book" dropped from title) and abridged (only eight strips repeated from first issue, 28 pgs.).(Rare) 100.00 400.00 700.00

F. FOX'S FUNNY FOLK (see Toonerville Trolley; Cartoons by Fontaine Fox) (C)
George H. Doran Company: 1917 (10-1/4x8-1/4", 228 pgs, red, B&W cover, B&W interior, hardcover; dust jacket?)
nn - By Fontaine Fox (Toonerville Trolley strip-r) 150.00 450.00 775.00

52 CAREY CARTOONS (O,S)
Carey Cartoon Service, NY: 1915 (25 cents, 6-3/4" x 10-1/2", 118 pgs, printed on one side, color cardboard-c, B&W)
nn - (1915) War – – –
NOTE: *The Carey Cartoon Service supplied a weekly, hand-colored single panel cartoon broadsheet, on current news events, starting in 1906 or 1907, for window display in Carey Fountain Pen chain stores. These broadsheets were 22-1/2" x 33" in size. Starting circa 1915, Carey Fountain Pens began offering subscriptions for the broadsheets to other merchants, for window display in their stores as well. This collects, in B&W, the cartoons for 1915. An "Edition Deluxe" was also advertised, with all cartoons hand colored. It is currently unknown whether a reprint collection was only issued in 1915, or if other editions exist.*

52 LETTERS TO SALESMEN

GD2.0 FN6.0 VF8.0

Steven-Davis Company: 1926 - 1927

nn - (Rare) 25.00 100.00 140.00
NOTE: *52 motivational letters to salesmen, with page of comics for each week, bound into embossed leather binder.*

FOLKS IN FUNNYVILLE (S)
R.H. Russell: 1900 (12"x9-1/4", 48 pgs.)(cardboard-c)

nn - By Frederick Opper 367.00 1100.00 –
NOTE: *Reprinted from Hearst's NY Journal American Humorist supplements.*

FOOLISH QUESTIONS (S)
Small, Maynard & Co.: 1909 (6-7/8 x 5-1/2", 174 pgs, hardcover, B&W)

nn - By Rube Goldberg (first Goldberg item) 110.00 375.00 550.00
NOTE: *Comic strip began Oct 23, 1908 running thru 1941. Also drawn by George Frink in 1909.*

FOOLISH QUESTIONS THAT ARE ASKED BY ALL
Levi Strauss & Co./Small, Maynard & Co.: 1909 (5-1/2x5-3/4", 24 pgs, paper-c, B&W)

nn- (Rare) by Rube Goldberg 65.00 175.00 360.00

FOOLISH QUESTIONS (Boxed card set) (S)
Wallie Dorr Co., N.Y.: 1919 (5-1/4x3-3/4")(box & card backs are red)

nn - Boxed set w/52 B&W comics on cards; each a single panel gag complete set w/box 75.00 263.00 510.00
NOTE: *There are two diff sets put out simultaneously with the first set, by the same company. One set continues/picks up the numbering of the cards from the other set.*

FOOLISH QUESTIONS (S)
EmBee Distributing Co.: 1921 (10¢, 4x5 1/2; 52 pgs, 3 color covers; B&W)

1-By Rube Goldberg 46.00 160.00 305.00

FOXY GRANDPA
Foxy Grandpa Company, 33 Wall St, NY : 1900 (9x15", 84 pgs, full color, cardboard-c)

nn - By Carl Schultze (By Permission of New York Herald) 271.00 1300.00 –
NOTE: *This seminal comic strip began Jan 7, 1900 and was collected later that same year.*

FOXY GRANDPA (Also see The Funnies, 1st series) (N)
N. Y. Herald/Frederick A. Stokes Co./M. A. Donahue & Co./Bunny Publ. (L. R. Hammersly Co.): 1901 - 1916 (Strip-r in color, hard-c)

1901- 9x15" in color-N. Y. Herald 367.00 1100.00 –
1902- "Latest Larks of...", 32 pgs., 9-1/2x15-1/2" 197.00 590.00 –
1902- "The Many Advs. of...", 9x12", 148 pgs., Hammersly Co. 213.00 640.00 –
1903- "Latest Advs.", 9x15", 24 pgs., Hammersly Co. 197.00 590.00 –
1903- "...'s New Advs.", 11x15", 66 pgs., Stokes 197.00 590.00 –
1904- "Up to Date", 10x15", 66 pgs., Stokes 146.00 510.00 940.00
1904- "The Many Adventures of...", 9x15, 144pgs, Donohue 146.00 510.00 940.00
1905- "& Flip-Flaps", 9-1/2x15-1/2", 52 pgs. 146.00 510.00 940.00
1905- "The Latest Advs. of...", 9x15", 28, 52, & 68 pgs, M.A. Donohue Co.; re-issue of 1902 issue 104.00 365.00 720.00
1905- "Latest Larks of...", 9-1/2x15-1/2", 52 pgs., Donahue; re-issue of 1902 issue with more pages added 104.00 365.00 720.00
1905- "Latest Larks of...", 9-1/2x15-1/2", 24 pgs. edition, Donahue; re-issue of 1902 issue 104.00 365.00 720.00
1905- "Merry Pranks of...", 9-1/2x15-1/2", 28, 52 & 62 pgs., Donahue 104.00 365.00 720.00
1905-"...Surprises",10x15", color, 64 pg,Stokes, 60¢ 104.00 365.00 720.00
1906- "Frolics", 10x15", 30 pgs., Stokes 104.00 365.00 720.00
1907?-"...& His Boys",10x15", 64 color pgs, Stokes 104.00 365.00 720.00
1907- "Triumphs", 10x15", 62 pgs, Stokes 104.00 365.00 720.00
1908-"...Mother Goose", Stokes 104.00 365.00 720.00
1909- "...& Little Brother", 10x15, 58 pgs, Stokes 104.00 365.00 720.00
1911- "Latest Tricks", r-1910,1911 Sundays-Stokes Co. 104.00 365.00 720.00
1914-(9-1/2x15-1/2", 24 pgs.)-6 color cartoons/page, Bunny Publ. Co. 88.00 306.00 625.00
1915 - ...Always Jolly (10x16, Stokes) 88.00 306.00 625.00
1916- "Merry Book", (10x15", 64 pgs, Stokes) 88.00 306.00 625.00
1917-"...Adventures (5 1/2 x 6 1/2, 26 pgs, Stokes) 57.00 200.00 480.00
1917-"...Frolics (5 1/2 x 6 1/2, 26 pgs, Stokes) 57.00 200.00 480.00
1917-"...Triumphs (5 1/2 x 6 1/2, 26 pgs, Stokes) 57.00 200.00 480.00

FOXY GRANDPA, FUNNY TRICKS OF (The Stump Books)
M.A. Donahue Co, Chicago: approx 1903 (1-7/8x6-3/8", 44 pgs, blue hardcover)

nn - By Carl Schultze 63.00 189.00 375.00
NOTE: *One of a series of ten "stump" books; the only comics one.*

FOXY GRANDPA'S MOTHER GOOSE (I)
Stokes: October 1903 (10-11/16x8-1/2", 86 pgs, hard-c)

nn - By Carl Schultze (not comics - illustrated book) 63.00 189.00 375.00

FOXY GRANDPA SPARKLETS SERIES (N)
M. A. Donahue & Co.: 1908 (7-3/4x6-1/2"; 24 pgs., color)

"... Rides the Goat", "...& His Boys", "...Playing Ball", "...Fun on the Farm", "...Fancy Shooting", "...Show His Boys Up-To-Date Sports", "...Plays Santa Claus" each.... 88.00 306.00 600.00
900- "Playing Ball"; Bunny illos; 8 pgs., linen like pgs., no date 73.00 254.00 450.00

FOXY GRANDPA VISITS RICHMOND (O,P)
Dietz Printing Co., Richmond, VA / Hotel Rueger: nd (c1920's) (5-7/8" x 4-1/2", 16 pgs, paper-c, B&W)

nn - (Scarce) By Bunny 50.00 100.00 285.00
NOTE: *Promotional comic given away to its guests by the Hotel Rueger, about Foxy Grandpa visiting and enjoying the Hotel. Originally came in an envelope, with the words "Foxy Grandpa Visits Richmond -- and Rueger's" printed on it.*

FOXY GRANDPA VISITS WASHINGTON, D.C. (P)
Dietz Printing Co., Richmond, VA / Hamilton Hotel: nd (c1920's) (5-7/8" x 4-1/2", 16 pgs, paper-c, B&W)

nn - (Scarce) By Bunny 38.00 114.00 225.00
NOTE: *Mostly reprints "... Visits Richmond", changing all references to Hotel Rueger, to Hamilton Hotel instead. Also, changes depictions of a waiter and a cook from black to white, plus incompletely erases the cover art on a book Foxy Grandpa falls asleep with (the latter is how we know that the Richmond version was first).*

FRAGMENTS FROM FRANCE (S)
G. P. Putnam & Sons: 1917 (9x6-1/4", 168 pgs, hardcover, $1.75)

GD2.0 FN6.0 VF8.0

nn - By Bruce Bairnsfather 25.00 88.00 160.00
NOTE: *WW1 trench warfare cartoons; color dust jacket.*

FUNNIES, THE (H) (See Clancy the Cop, Deadwood Gulch, Bug Movies)
Dell Publishing Co.: 1929 - No. 36, 10/18/30 (10¢; 5¢ No. 22 on) (16 pgs.)
Full tabloid size in color; not reprints; published every Saturday

1-My Big Brudder, Jonathan, Jazzbo & Jim, Foxy Grandpa, Sniffy, Jimmy Jams & other strips begin; first four-color comic newsstand publication; also contains magic, puzzles & stories 300.00 900.00 1800.00
2-21 (1930, 10¢) 108.00 324.00 650.00
22(nn-7/12/30-5¢) 108.00 324.00 650.00
23(nn-7/19/30-5¢), 24(nn-7/26/30-5¢), 25(nn-8/2/30), 26(nn-8/9/30), 27(nn-8/16/30), 28(nn-8/23/30), 29(nn-8/30/30), 30(nn-9/6/30), 31(nn-9/13/30), 32(nn-9/20/30), 33(nn-9/27/30), 34(nn-10/4/30), 35(nn-10/11/30), 36(nn, no date-10/18/30) each.... 104.00 312.00 625.00

GASOLINE ALLEY (Also see Popular Comics & Super Comics) (N)
Reilly & Lee Publishers: 1929 (8-3/4x7", B&W daily strip-r, hard-c)

nn - By King (96 pgs.) 125.00 300.00 625.00
with scarce Dust Wrapper 250.00 500.00 1100.00
NOTE: *Of all the Frank King reprint books, this is the only one to reprint actual complete newspaper strips - all others are illustrated prose text stories.*

GIBSON'S PUBLISHED DRAWINGS, MR. (M,S) (see Victorian index for earlier issues)
R.H. Russell, New York: No.1 1894 - No. 9 1904 (11x17-3/4", hard-c, B&W)

nn (No.6; 1901) A Widow and her Friends (90 pgs.) 20.00 60.00 120.00
nn (No.7; 1902) The Social Ladder (88 pgs.) 20.00 60.00 120.00
8 - 1903 The Weaker Sex (88 pgs.) 20.00 60.00 120.00
9 - 1904 Everyday People (88 pgs.) 20.00 60.00 120.00
NOTE: *By Charles Dana Gibson cartoons, reprinted from magazines, primarily LIFE. The Education of Mr. Pipp tells a story. Series continues how long after 1904?*

GIGGLES
Pratt Food Co., Philadelphia, PA: 1908-09? (12x9", 8 pgs, color, 5 cents-c)

1-8: By Walt McDougall (#8 dated March 1909) 62.00 185.00 –
NOTE: *Appears to be monthly; almost tabloid size; yearly subscriptions was 25 cents.*

GOD'S MAN (H)
Jonathan Cape and Harrison Smith Inc.: 1929 (8-1/4x6", 298 pgs, B&W hardcover w/dust jacket) (original graphic novel in wood cuts)

nn - By Lynd Ward 58.00 174.00 350.00

GOLD DUST TWINS
N. K. Fairbank Co.: 1904 (4-5/8x6-3/4", 18 pgs, color and B&W)

nn - By E. W. Kemble (Rare) 46.00 138.00 275.00
NOTE: *Promo comic for Gold DustWashing Powder; includes page of watercolor paints.*

GOLF
Volland Co.: 1916 (9x12-3/4", 132 pgs, hard-c, B&W)

nn - By Clair Briggs 110.00 220.00 410.00

GUMPS, THE (N)
Landfield-Kupfer: No. 1, 1918 - No. 6, 1921; (B&W Daily strip-r)

Book No. 1 (1918)(scarce)-cardboard-c, 5-1/4x13-1/3", 64 pgs., daily strip-r by Sidney Smith 75.00 250.00 510.00
Book No. 2 (1918)-(scarce); 5-1/4x13-1/3"; paper cover; 36 pgs. daily strip reprints by Sidney Smith 75.00 250.00 510.00
Book No. 3 100.00 350.00 710.00
Book No. 4 (1918) 5-3/8x13-7/8", 20 pgs. Color card-c 100.00 350.00 710.00
Book No. 5 10-1/4x13-1/2", 20 pgs. Color paper-c 100.00 350.00 710.00
Book No. 6 (Rare, 20 pgs, 8x13-3/8, strip-r 1920-21) 121.00 423.00 760.00

GUMPS, ANDY AND MIN, THE (N)
Landfield-Kupfer Printing Co., Chicago/Morrison Hotel: nd (1920s) (Giveaway, 5-1/2"x14", 20 pgs., B&W, soft-c)

nn - Strip-r by Sidney Smith; art & logo embossed on cover w/hotel restaurant menu on back-c or a hotel promo ad; 4 different contents of issues known 50.00 175.00 310.00

GUMPS, THE (N)
Cupples & Leon: 1924-1930 (10x10, 52 pgs, B&W)

1 - By Sidney Smith 75.00 250.00 375.00
2-7 39.00 154.00 250.00

THE GUMPS (P)
Cupples & Leon Company: 1924 (9 x 7-1/2", 28 pgs, paper cover)

nn (1924) 50.00 175.00 260.00
NOTE: *Promotional comic for Sunshine Andy Gump Biscuits. Daily strip-r from 1922-24.*

GUMP'S CARTOON BOOK, THE (N)
The National Arts Company: 1931 (13-7/8x10", 36 pgs, color covers, B&W)

nn - By Sidney Smith 57.00 228.00 410.00

GUMPS PAINTING BOOK, THE (N)
The National Arts Company: 1931 (11 x 15 1/4", 20 pgs, half in full color)

nn - By Sidney Smith 57.00 228.00 410.00

HALT FRIENDS! (see also **HELLO BUDDY**)
???: 1918? (4-3/8x5-3/4", 36 pgs, color-c, B&W, no cover price listed)

nn - Unknown 20.00 60.00 120.00
NOTE: *Says on front cover: "Comics of War Facts of Service Sold on its merits by Unemployed or Disabled Ex-Service Men. Credentials Shown On Request. Price - Pay What You Please." These are very common; contents vary widely.*

HAMBONE'S MEDITATIONS
Jahl & Co.: 1917, no date (1920) (6-1/8 x 7-1/2, 108 pgs, paper cover, B&W)

nn - (1917, 68 pgs.) By J. P. Alley (a copy in GD sold in 2010 for $278)
nn - (nd, 108 pgs.) By J. P. Alley 55.00 175.00 350.00
NOTE: *Reprint of racist single panel newspaper series, 2 cartoons per page.*

HAN OLA OG PER (N)
Anundsen Publishing Co, Decorah, Iowa: 1927 (10-3/8 x 15-3/4", 54 pgs, paper-c, B&W)

nn - American origin Norwegian language strips-r 33.00 131.00 240.00
NOTE: *1940s and modern reprints exist.*

HANS UND FRITZ (N)

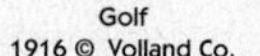
Golf
1916 © Volland Co.

The Gumps by Sidney Smith
1918 © Cupples & Leon

Happy Hooligan New Edition 1903
© Frederick A. Stokes

GD2.0 FN6.0 VF8.0

The Saalfield Publishing Co.: 1917, 1927-29 (10x13-1/2", 28 pgs., B&W)
nn - By R. Dirks (1917, r-1916 strips) 104.00 312.00 625.00
nn - By R. Dirks (1923 edition- reprint of 1917 edition) 54.00 162.00 325.00
nn - By R. Dirks (1926 edition- reprint of 1917 edition) 54.00 162.00 325.00
The Funny Larks Of... By R. Dirks (©1917 outside cover; ©1916 inside indicia) 104.00 312.00 625.00
The Funny Larks Of... (1927) reprints 1917 edition of 1916 strips Halloween-c 58.00 174.00 325.00
The Funny Larks Of... 2 (1929) 58.00 174.00 325.00
193 - By R. Dirks; contains 1916 Sunday strip reprints of Katzenjammer Kids & Hawkshaw the Detective - reprint of 1917 nn edition (1929) this edition is not rare 58.00 174.00 325.00

HAPPY DAYS (S)
Coward-McCann Inc.: 1929 (12-1/2x9-5/8", 110 pgs, hardcover B&W)
nn - By Alban Butler (WW 1 cartoons) 20.00 60.00 130.00

HAPPY HOOLIGAN (See Alphonse...) (N)
Hearst's New York American & Journal: 1902,1903
Book 1-(1902)-"And His Brother Gloomy Gus", By Fred Opper; has 1901-02-r; (yellow & black)(86 pgs.)(10x15-1/4") 600.00 1800.00 3600.00
New Edition, 1903 -10x15" 82 pgs. in color 500.00 1500.00 –
NOTE: *Strip ran March 26, 1900-Aug 14, 1932 and is widely recognized as setting the format standard for all newspaper comic strips which came after it. Opper (1857-1937) was going blind towards the end.*

HAPPY HOOLIGAN (N) (By Fredrick Opper)
Frederick A. Stokes Co.: 1906-08 (10-1/4x15-3/4", cardboard color-c)
1906 - :Travels of...), 68 pgs,10-1/4x15-3/4", 1905-r 317.00 950.00 –
1907 - "--Home Again", 68 pgs., 10x15-3/4", 60¢; full color-c 317.00 950.00 –
1908 - "Handy--", 68 pgs, color 317.00 950.00 –

HAPPY HOOLIGAN, THE STORY OF (G)
McLoughlin Bros.: No. 281, 1932 (12x9-1/2", 20 pgs., soft-c)
281-Three-color text, pictures on heavy paper 82.00 246.00 490.00
NOTE: *An homage to Opper's creation on its 30th Anniversary in 1932.*

HAROLD HARDHIKE'S REJUVENATION
O'Sullivan Rubber: 1917 (6-1/4x3-1/2, 16 pgs, B&W)
nn 38.00 114.00 225.00
NOTE: *Comic book to promote rubber shoe heels.*

HAROLD TEEN (N)
Cupples & Leon Co.: 1929 (9-7/8x9-7/8", 52 pgs, cardboard covers)
1 - By Carl Ed 88.00 264.00 530.00
nn - (1931, 8-11/16x6-7/8", 96 pgs, hardcover w/dj) 50.00 150.00 300.00
NOTE: *Title 2nd book: **HAROLD TEEN AND HIS OLD SIDE-KICK– POP JENKINS,** (Adv. of...). Precursor for Archie Andrews & crew; strip began May 4, 1919 running into 1959.*

HAROLD TEEN PAINT AND COLOR BOOK (N)
McLoughlin Bros Inc.: 1932 (13x9-3/4, 28 pgs, B&W and color)
#2054 36.00 108.00 215.00

HAWKSHAW THE DETECTIVE (See Advs. of..., Hans Und Fritz & Okay) (N)
The Saalfield Publishing Co.: 1917 (10-1/2x13-1/2", 24 pgs., B&W)
nn - By Gus Mager (Sunday strip-r) 60.00 180.00 360.00
nn - By Gus Mayer (1923 reprint of 1917 edition) 28.00 84.00 170.00
nn - By Gus Mager (1926 reprint of 1917 edition) 28.00 84.00 170.00
NOTE: *Runs Feb 23, 1913-Sept 4, 1922, starts again from Dec 13, 1931-Feb 11, 1952; Sherlock Holmes spoof.*

HEALTH IN PICTURES
American Public Health Association, NYC: 1930 (6-1/2" x 5-3/16", 76 pgs, green & black paper-c, B&W interior)
nn - By various 22.00 66.00 130.00
NOTE: *Collection of strips and cartoons put out by the Public Health Association, on topics ranging from boating and food safety, to small pox and typhoid prevention.*

HE DONE HER WRONG (O) (see also BANANA OIL)
Doubleday, Doran & Company: 1930 (8-1/4x 7-1/4", 276pgs, hard-c with dust jacket, B&W interiors)
nn - By Milt Gross 68.00 204.00 410.00
NOTE: *A seminal original-material wordless graphic novel, not reprints. Several modern reprints.*

HELLO BUDDY (see also **HALT FRIENDS**)
???: 1919? (4-3/8x5-3/4", 36 pgs, color-c, B&W, 15¢)
nn - Unknown 22.00 66.00 130.00
NOTE: *Says on front cover: "Comics of War Facts of Service Sold on its merits by Unemployed or Disabled Ex-Service Men." These are very common; contents vary widely.*

HENRY (N)
David McKay Co.: 1935 (25¢, soft-c with dust jacket)
Book 1 - By Carl Anderson 75.00 225.00 450.00
NOTE: *Strip began March 19 1932; this book ties with Popeye (David McKay) and Little Annie Rooney (David McKay) as the last of the 10x10" Platinum Age comic books.*

HENRY (M)
Greenberg Publishers Inc.: 1935 (11-1/4x 8-5/8", 72 pgs, red & blue color hard-c, dust jacket, B&W interiors) (strip-r from Saturday Evening Post)
nn - By Carl Anderson 71.00 213.00 425.00

HIGH KICKING KELLYS, THE (M)
Vaudeville News Corporation, NY: 1926 (5x11", B&W, two color soft-c)
nn - By Jack A. Ward (scarce) 52.00 156.00 310.00

HIGHLIGHTS OF HISTORY (N)
World Syndicate Publishing Co.: 1933-34 (4-1/2x4", 288 pgs)
nn - 5 different unnumbered issues; daily strip-r 18.00 54.00 110.00
NOTE: *Titles include Buffalo Bill, Daniel Boone, Kit Carson, Pioneers of the Old West, Winning of the Old Northwest. There are line drawing color covers and embossed hardcover versions. It is unknown which came out first.*

HOMER HOLCOMB AND MAY (N)
no publisher listed: 1920s (4 x 9-1/2", 40 pgs, paper cover, B&W)
nn - By Doc Bird Finch (strip-r) 13.00 39.00 80.00

HOME, SWEET HOME (N)
M.S. Publishing Co.: 1925 (10-1/4x10")
nn - By Tuthill 39.00 117.00 235.00

HOW THEY DRAW PROHIBITION (S)
Association Against Prohibition: 1930 (10x9", 100 pgs.)
nn - Single panel and multi-panel comics (rare) 108.00 324.00 650.00
NOTE: *Contains art by J.N. "Ding" Darling, James Flagg, Rollin Kirby, Winsor McCay, T.E. Powers, H.T. Webster, others. Also comes with a loose sheet listing all the newspapers where the cartoons originally appeared.*

HOW TO BE A CARTOONIST (H)
Saalfield Pub. Co: 1936 (10-3/8x12-1/2", 16 pgs, color-c, B&W)
nn - By Chas. H. Kuhn 20.00 60.00 120.00

HOW TO DRAW: A PRACTICAL BOOK OF INSTRUCTION (H)
Harper & Brothers: 1904 (9-1/4x12-3/8", 128 pgs, hardcover, B&W)
nn - Edited By Leon Barritt 67.00 201.00 400.00
NOTE: *Strips reprinted include: "Buster Brown" by Outcault, "Foxy Grandpa" by Bunny, "Happy Hooligan" by Opper, "Katzenjammer Kids" by Dirks, "Lady Bountiful" by Gene Carr, "Mr. Jack" by Swinnerton, "Panhandle Pete" by George McManus, "Mr E.Z. Mark" by F.M. Howarth others; non-character strips by Hy Mayer, Winsor McCay, T.E. Powers, others; single panel cartoons by Davenport, Frost, McDougall, Nast, W.A. Rogers, Sullivant, others.*

HOW TO DRAW CARTOONS (H)
Garden City Publishing Co.: 1926, 1937 (10 1/4 x 7 1/2, 150 pgs)
1926 first edition By Clare Briggs 30.00 90.00 180.00
1937 2nd edition By Clare Briggs 21.00 63.00 125.00
NOTE: *Seminal "how to" break into the comics syndicates with art by Briggs, Fisher, Goldberg, King, Webster, Opper, Tad, Hershfield, McCay, Ding, others. Came with Dust Jacket -add 50%.*

HOW TO DRAW FUNNY PICTURES: A Complete Course in Cartooning (H)
Frederick J. Drake & Co., Chicago: 1936 (10-3/8x6-7/8", 168 pgs, hardcover, B&W)
nn - By E.C. Matthews (200 illus by Eugene Zimmerman) 21.00 63.00 125.00

HY MAYER (M)
Puck Publishing: 1915 (13-1/2 x 20-3/4", 52 pgs, hardcover cover, color & B&W interiors)
nn - By Hy Mayer(strip reprints from Puck) 54.00 162.00 325.00

HYSTERICAL HISTORY OF THE CIVILIAN CONSERVATION CORPS
Peerless Engraving: 1934 (10-3/4x7-1/2", 104 pgs, soft-c, B&W)
nn - By various 28.00 84.00 165.00
NOTE: *Comics about CCC life, includes two color insert postcards in back.*

INDOOR SPORTS (N,S)
National Specials Co., New York: nd circa 1912 (25 cents, 6 x 9", 68 pgs, B&W)
nn - Tad 46.00 138.00 275.00
NOTE: *Cartoons reprinted from Hearst papers.*

IT HAPPENS IN THE BEST FAMILIES (N)
Powers Photo Engraving Co.: 1920 (52 pgs.)(9-1/2x10-3/4")
nn - By Briggs; B&W Sunday strips-r 40.00 120.00 240.00
Special Railroad Edition (30¢)-r/strips from 1914-1920 38.00 114.00 225.00

JIMMIE DUGAN AND THE REG'LAR FELLERS (N)
Cupples & Leon: 1921, 46 pgs. (11"x16")
nn - By Gene Byrne 88.00 264.00 525.00
NOTE: *Ties with EmBee's Mutt & Jeff and Trouble of Bringing Up Father as the last of this size.*

JIMMY (N) (see Little Jimmy Picture & Story Book)
N. Y. American & Journal: 1905 (10x15", 84 pgs., color)
nn - By Jimmy Swinnerton (scarce) 367.00 1100.00 2200.00
NOTE: *James Swinnerton was one of the original first pioneers of the American newspaper comic strip.*

JIMMY AND HIS SCRAPES (N)
Frederick A. Stokes: 1906, (10-1/4x15-1/4", 66 pgs, cardboard-c, color)
nn - By Jimmy Swinnerton (scarce) 317.00 951.00 1900.00

JOE PALOOKA (N)
Cupples & Leon Co.: 1933 (9-13/16x10", 52 pgs., B&W daily strip-r)
nn - By Ham Fisher (scarce) 192.00 576.00 1150.00

JOHN, JONATHAN AND MR. OPPER BY F. OPPER (S,I,N)
Grant, Richards, 48 Leicester Square, W.C.: 1903 (9-5/8x8-3/8", 108 pgs, hard-c B&W)
nn - Opper (Scarce) 73.00 219.00 440.00
NOTE: *British precursor-type companion to WIllie And His Poppa reprints from Hearst's NY American & Journal Opper cartoons interfacing Uncle Sam precursor Brother Jonathan, John Bull. Uses name Happy Hooligan in one cartoon, has John Bull smoking opium in another.*

GD2.0 FN6.0 VF8.0

JOLLY POLLY'S BOOK OF ENGLISH AND ETIQUETTE (S)
Jos. J. Frisch: 1931 (60 cents, 8 x 5-1/8, 88 pgs, paper-c, B&W)
nn - By Jos. J. Frisch 19.00 57.00 115.00
NOTE: *Reprint of single panel newspaper series, 4 per page, of English and etiquette lessons taught by a flapper.*

JOYS AND GLOOMS (N)
Reilly & Britton Co.: 1912 (11x8", 72 pgs, hard-c, B&W interior)
nn - By T. E. Powers (newspaper strip-r) 57.00 171.00 340.00

JUDGE - yet to be indexed

JUDGE'S LIBRARY - yet to be indexed

JUST KIDS COMICS FOR CRAYON COLORING
King Features. NYC: 1928 (11x8-1/2, 16 pgs, soft-c)
nn - By Ad Carter 38.00 114.00 225.00
NOTE: *Porous better grade paper; top pics printed in color; lower in b&w to color.*

JUST KIDS, THE STORY OF (I)
McLoughlin Bros.: 1932 (12x9-1/2", 20 pgs., paper-c)
283-Three-color text, pictures on heavy paper 47.00 141.00 280.00

KAPTIN KIDDO AND PUPPO (N)
Frederick A. Stokes Co.: 1910-1913 (11x16-1/2", 62 pgs)
1910-By Grace Wiederseim (later Drayton) 48.00 144.00 290.00
1910-Turr-ble Tales of... By Grace Wiederseim (Edward Stern & Co., 11x16-1/2", 64 pgs.) 42.00 126.00 250.00
1913- ...'Speriences By Grace Drayton 42.00 126.00 250.00
NOTE: *Strip ran approx. 1909-1912.*

KATZENJAMMER KIDS, THE (Also see Hans Und Fritz) (N)
New York American & Journal: 1902,1903 (10x15-1/4", 86 pgs., color)
(By Rudolph Dirks; strip first appeared in 1897) © W.R. Hearst
NOTE: *All KK books 1902-1905 all have the same exact title page with a 1902 copyright by W.R. Hearst; almost always look instead on the front cover.*
1902 (Rare) (red & black); has 1901-02 strips 967.00 2900.00 –
1903- **A New Edition** (Rare), 86 pgs 767.00 2300.00 –
1904- 10x15", 84 pgs 300.00 900.00 –
1905?-The Cruise of the, 10x15", 60¢, in color 300.00 900.00 –
1905-A Series of Comic Pictures, 10x15", 84 pgs. in color, possible reprint of 1904 edition 267.00 800.00 –
1905-Tricks of... (10x15", 66 pgs, Stokes) 267.00 800.00 –
1906-Stokes (10x16", 32 pgs. in color) 267.00 800.00 –
1907- The Cruise of the, 10x15", 62 pgs 1905-r? 267.00 800.00 –
1910-The Komical...(10x15) 133.00 400.00 800.00
1921-Embee Dist. Co., 10x16", 20 pgs. in color 133.00 400.00 800.00

KATZENJAMMER KIDS MAGIC DRAWING AND COLORING BOOK (N)
Sam L Gabriel Sons And Company: 1931 (8 1/2 x 12", 36 pages, stiff-c
838-By Knerr 63.00 189.00 380.00

KEEPING UP WITH THE JONESES (N)
Cupples & Leon Co.: 1920 - No. 2, 1921 (9-1/4x9-1/4",52 pgs.,B&W daily strip-r)
1,2-By Pop Momand 54.00 162.00 325.00

KID KARTOONS (N,S)
The Century Co.: 1922 (232 pgs, printed 1 side, 9-3/4 x 7-3/4", hard-c, B&W)
nn - By Gene Carr (Metropolitan Movies strip-r) 46.00 138.00 275.00

KING OF THE ROYAL MOUNTED (Also See Dan Dunn) (N)
Whitman Publishing: 1937 (5 1/2 x 7 1/4", 68 pgs., color cardboard-c, B&W)
1010 46.00 138.00 275.00

LADY BOUNTIFUL (N)
Saalfield Publ. Co./Press Publ. Co.: 1917 (13-3/8x10", 36 pgs, color cardboard-c, B&W interiors)
nn - By Gene Carr; 2 panels per page 52.00 156.00 310.00
1935 - 2nd printing (13-1/8x10",28 pgs color-c, B&W) 35.00 105.00 210.00

LAUGHS YOU MIGHT HAVE HAD From The Comic Pages of Six Week Day Issues of the Post-Dispatch (N)
St. Louis Post-Dispatch: 1921 (9 x 10 1/2", 28 pgs, B&W, red ink cover)
nn - Various comic strips 46.00 138.00 275.00

LIFE, DOGS FROM (M)
Doubleday, Page & Company: nn 1920 - No.2 1926 (130 pgs, 11-1/4 x 9", color painted-c, hard-c, B&W)
nn (No.1) 127.00 380.00 –
Second Litter 110.00 330.00 –
NOTE: *Reprints strips & cartoons featuring dogs, from Life Magazine. Editted by Thomas L. Masson. Highly sought by collectors of dog ephemera. Art in both books is mostly by Robert L. Dickey. Other art: Carl Anderson-1,2; Barbes-1; Chip Bellew-1; Lang Campbell-1,2; Percy Crosby-1,2; Edwina-2; Frueh-2; R.B. Fuller-1; Gibson-1,2; Don Herold-2; Gus Mager-2; Orr-1; J.R. Shaver-1,2; T.S. Sullivant-2; Russ Westover-1,2; Crawford Young-1.*

LIFE OF DAVY CROCKETT IN PICTURE AND STORY, THE
Cupples & Leon: 1935 (8-3/4x7", 64 pgs, B&W hard-c, dust jacket)
nn - By C. Richard Schaare 40.00 120.00 240.00

LIFE OF THOMAS A. EDISON IN WORD AND PICTURE, THE (N)(Also see Edison...)
Thomas A. Edison Industries: 1928 (10x8", 56 pgs, paper cover, B&W)
nn - Photo-c 67.00 201.00 400.00
NOTE: *Reprints newspaper strip which ran August to November 1927.*

LIFE'S LITTLE JOKES (S)
M.S. Publ. Co.: No date (1924)(10-1/16x10", 52 pgs., B&W)
nn - By Rube Goldberg 93.00 279.00 560.00

LIFE, MINIATURE (see also LIFE (miniature reprint of of issue No. 1)) (M,P,S)
Life Publishing Co.: No. 1 - No. 4 1913, 1916, 1919 (5-3/4x4-5/8", 20 pgs, color paper-c
1- 3 (1913) 4 (1916) 5 (1919) 33.00 100.00 200.00
NOTE: *Giveaway item from Life, to promote subscriptions. All reprint material. No.2: James Montgomery Flagg-c; a-Chip Bellew, Gus Dirks, Gibson, F.M.Howarth, Art Young.*

LIFE'S PRINTS (was **LIFE'S PICTURE GALLERY** - See Victorian Age section) (M,S,P)
Life Publishing Company, New York: nd (c1907) (7x4-1/2", 132 pgs, paper cover, B&W)
nn - (nd; c1907) unillustrated black construction paper cover; reprints art from 1895-1907; art by J.M.Flagg, A.B.Frost, Gibson (Scarce) – – –
nn - (nd; c1908) b&w cardboard painted cover by Gibson, showing angel raising a champagne glass; reprints art from 1901-1908; art by J.M.Flagg, A.B.Frost, Gibson, Walt Kuhn, Art Young (Scarce) – – –
NOTE: *Catalog of prints reprinted from LIFE covers & centerspreads. There are likely more as yet unreported catalogs.*

LIFE, THE COMEDY OF LIFE
Life Publishing Company: 1907 (130 pgs, 11-3/4x9-1/4",embossed printed cloth covered board-c, B+W
nn - By various 23.00 69.00 140.00
NOTE: *Single cartoons and some sequential cartoons). Artists include Charles Dana Gibson, Harrison Cady, E.W. Kemble, James Montgomery Flagg.*

LILY OF THE ALLEY IN THE FUNNIES
Whitman Publishing Co.: No date (1927) (10-1/4x15-1/2"; 28 pgs., color)
W936 - By T. Burke (Rare) 71.00 213.00 425.00

LITTLE ANNIE ROONEY (N)
David McKay Co.: 1935 (25¢, soft-c)
Book 1 60.00 180.00 360.00
NOTE: *Ties with Henry & Popeye (David McKay) as the last of the 10x10" size Plat comic books.*

LITTLE ANNIE ROONEY WISHING BOOK (G) (See Happy Hooligan, Story of #281)
McLoughlin Bros.: 1932 (12x9-1/2", 16 pgs., soft-c, 3-color text, heavier paper)
282 - By Darrell McClure 49.00 147.00 295.00

LITTLE BIRD TOLD ME, A (E)
Life Publishing Co.: 1905? (96 pgs, hardbound)
nn - By Walt Kuhn (Life-r) 49.00 147.00 295.00

LITTLE FOLKS PAINTING BOOK (N)
The National Arts Company: 1931 (10-7/8 x 15-1/4", 20 pgs, half in full color)
nn - By "Tack" Knight (strip-r) 49.00 147.00 295.00

LITTLE JIMMY PICTURE AND STORY BOOK (I) (see Jimmy)
McLaughlin Bros., Inc.: 1932 (13-1/4 x 9-3/4", 20 pgs, cardstock color cover)
284 Text by Marion Kincaird; illus by Swinnerton 79.00 237.00 475.00

LITTLE JOHNNY & THE TEDDY BEARS (Judge-r) (M) (see Teddy Bear Books)
Reilly & Britton Co.: 1907 (10x14".; 68 pgs, green, red, black interior color)
nn - By J. R. Bray-a/Robert D. Towne-s 79.00 237.00 475.00

LITTLE JOURNEY TO THE HOME OF BRIGGS THE SKY-ROCKET, THE
Lockhart Art School: 1917 (10-3/4x7-7/8", 20 pgs, B&W) (I)
nn - About Clare Briggs (bio & lots of early art) 48.00 144.00 285.00

LITTLE KING, THE (see New Yorker Cartoon Albums for 1st appearance) (M)
Farrar & Reinhart, Inc: 1933 (10-1/4 x 8-3/4, 80 pgs, hardcover w/dust jacket
nn - By Otto Soglow (strip-r The New Yorker) 93.00 279.00 560.00
NOTE: *Copies with dust jacket are worth 30% more. Also exists in a 12x8-3/4 edition.*

LITTLE LULU BY MARGE (M)
Rand McNally & Company, Chicago: 1936 (6-9/16x6", 68 pgs, yellow hard-c, B&W)
nn - By Marjorie Henderson Buell 52.00 156.00 310.00
NOTE: *Begins reprinting single panel Little Lulu cartoons which began with Saturday Evening Post Feb. 23, 1935. This book was reprinted several times as late as 1940.*

LITTLE NAPOLEON
No publisher listed: 1924 , 50 pages, 10" by 10"; Color cardstock-c, B&W
nn - By Bud Counihan (Cupples &Leon format) 43.00 129.00 260.00

LITTLE NEMO (...in Slumberland) (N) (see also Little Sammy Sneeze, Dreams...Rarebit F)
Doffield & Co.(1906)/Cupples & Leon Co.(1909): 1906, 1909 (Sunday strip-r in color, cardboard covers)
1906-11x16-1/2" by Winsor McCay; 30 pgs. (scarce) 1700.00 5100.00 –
1909-10x14" by Winsor McCay (scarce) 1333.00 4000.00 –

LITTLE ORPHAN ANNIE (See Treasure Box of Famous Comics) (N)
Cupples & Leon Co.: 1926 - 1934 (8-3/4x7", 100 pgs., B&W daily strip-r, hard-c)
1 (1926)-Little Orphan Annie (softback see Treasure Box) 68.00 204.00 410.00
2 (1927)-In the Circus (softback see Wonder Box...) 45.00 135.00 270.00
3 (1928)-The Haunted House (softback see Wonder Box...) 45.00 135.00 270.00
4 (1929)-Bucking the World 45.00 135.00 270.00
5 (1930)-Never Say Die 38.00 114.00 230.00
6 (1931)-Shipwrecked 38.00 114.00 230.00
7 (1932)-A Willing Helper 32.00 96.00 190.00
8 (1933)-In Cosmic City 32.00 96.00 190.00
9 (1934)-Uncle Dan (not rare) 32.00 96.00 190.00
NOTE: *Each book reprints dailies from the previous year. Each hardcover came with a dust jacket. Books with out dust jackets are worth 50% less. Many of copies of #9 Uncle Dan have been turning up on eBay recently.*

LITTLE ORPHAN ANNIE RUMMY CARDS (N)
Whitman Publishing Co., Racine: 1935 (box: 5 x 6 1/2" Cards: 3 1/2 x 2 1/4")
nn-Harold Gray 22.00 66.00 130.00
NOTE: *36 cards, including 1 instruction card, 5 character cards and 30 cards forming 5 sequential stories (6 cards each).*

LITTLE SAMMY SNEEZE (N) (see also Little Nemo, Dreams of A Rarebit Fiend)
New York Herald Co.: Dec 1905 (11x16-1/2", 72 pgs., color)
nn - By Winsor McCay (Very Rare) 2900.00 8700.00 –
NOTE: *Rarely found in fine to mint condition.*

LIVE AND LET LIVE
Travelers Insurance Co.: 1936 (5-3/4x7/3/4", 16 pgs. color and B&W)
nn - Bill Holman, Carl Anderson, etc 20.00 60.00 120.00

LULU AND LEANDER (N) (see also Funny Folk, 1899, in Victorian section)
New York American & Journal: 1904 (76 pgs); **William A Stokes & Co:** 1906
nn - By F.M. Howarth 300.00 900.00 1800.00
nn - The Trials of...(1906, 10x16", 68 pgs. in color) 300.00 900.00 1800.00
NOTE: *F. M. Howarth helped pioneer the American comic strip in the pages of PUCK magazine in the early 1890s before the Yellow Kid.*

MADMAN'S DRUM (O)
Jonathan Cape and Harrison Smith Inc.: 1930 (8-1/4x6", 274 pgs, B&W hardcover w/dust jacket) (original graphic novel in wood cuts)

The Katzenjammer Kids
1921 © NY American & Journal

Mickey Mouse Book
1930 © DIS

Mr. & Mrs.
1922 © WHIT

GD2.0 FN6.0 VF8.0

nn - By Lynd Ward 58.00 174.00 350.00

MAMA'S ANGEL CHILD IN TOYLAND (I)
Rand McNally, Chicago: 1915 (128 pgs, hardbound with dust jacket)
nn - By M.T. "Penny" Ross & Marie C, Sadler 42.00 126.00 250.00
NOTE: *Mamma's Angel Child published as a comic strip by the "Chicago Tribune" 1908 Mar 1 to 1920 Oct 17.This novel dedicated to Esther Starring Richartz, "the original Mamma's Angel Kid."*

MAUD (N) (see also **Happy Hooligan**)
Frederick A. Stokes Co.: 1906 - 1908? (10x15-1/2", cardboard-c)
1906-By Fred Opper (Scarce), 66 pgs. color 450.00 1400.00 -
1907-The Matchless, 10x15" 70 pgs in color 250.00 1100.00 -
1908-The Mirthful Mule, 10x15", 64 pgs in color 250.00 1100.00 -
NOTE: *First run of strip began July 24, 1904 to at least Oct 6, 1907, spun out of* ***Happy Hooligan.***

MEMORIAL EDITION The Drawings of Clare Briggs (S)
Wm H. Wise & Company: 1930 (7-1/2x8-3/4", 284 pgs, pebbled false black leather, B&W) (posthumous boxed set of 7 books by Clare Briggs)
nn - The Days of Real Sport; nn-Golf; nn-Real Folks at Home; nn-Ain't it a Grand and Glorious Feeling?; nn-That Guiltiest Feeling; nn-Somebody's Always Taking the Joy Out of Life; nn-When a Feller Needs a Friend
Each book... 25.00 75.00 150.00
NOTE: *Also exists in a whitish cream colored paper back edition; first edition unknown presently.*

MENACE CARTOONS (M, S)
Menace Publishing Company, Aurora, Missouri: 1914 (10-3/8x8", 80 pgs, cardboard-c, B&W)
nn - (Rare) 121.00 363.00 725.00
NOTE: *Reprints anti-Catholic cartoons from K.K.K. related publication* ***The Menace.***

MEN OF DARING (N)
Cupples & Leon Co.: 1933 (8-3/4x7", 100 pgs)
nn - By Stookie Allen, intro by Lowell Thomas 37.00 111.00 220.00

MICKEY MOUSE BOOK
Bibo & Lang: 1930-1931 (12x9", stapled-c, 20 pgs., 4 printings)
nn - First Disney licensed publication (a magazine, not a book–see first book, Adventures of Mickey Mouse). Contains story of how Mickey met Walt and got his name; games, cartoons & song "Mickey Mouse (You Cute Little Feller)," written by Irving Bibo; Minnie, Clarabelle Cow, Horace Horsecollar & caricature of Walt shaking hands with Mickey. The changes made with the 2nd printing have been verified by billing affidavits in the Walt Disney Archives and include:Two Win Smith Mickey strips from 4/15/30 and 4/17/30 added to page 8 & back-c; "Printed in U.S.A." added to front cover; Bobette Bibo's age of 11 years added to title page; faulty type on the word "tail" corrected top of page 3; the word "start" added to bottom of page 7, removing the words "start 1 2 3 4" from the top of page 7; music and lyrics were rewritten on pages 12-14. A green ink border was added beginning with 2nd printing and some covers have inking variations. Art by Albert Barbelle, drawn in an Ub Iwerks style. Total circulation : 97,938 copies varying from 21,000 to 26,000 per printing.
1st printing. Contains the song lyrics **censored** in later printings, "When little Minnie's pursued by a big bad villain we feel so bad then we're glad when you up and kill him." Attached to the Nov. 15, 1930 issue of the Official Bulletin of the Mickey Mouse Club notes: "Attached to this Bulletin is a new Mickey Mouse Book that has just been published." This is thought to be the reason why a slightly disproportionate larger number of copies of the first printing still exist 788.00 2364.00 6300.00
1st printing (variant) All white-c and has advertising on inside front & back-cvrs. All other examples have blank inside cvrs. Has word "kill" in the song. One of the ads is for a Mickey Mouse Club. A Fine copy sold on 12/24/17 for $2375.
2nd printing with a theater/advertising. Christmas greeting added to inside front cover (1 copy known with Dec. 27, 1930 date) - - -
2nd-4th printings 583.00 1750.00 3500.00
NOTE: *Theater/advertising copies do not qualify as separate printings. Most copies are missing pages 9 & 10 which had a puzzle to be cut out. Puzzle (pages 9 and 10) cut out or missing, subtract 60% to 75%.*

MICKEY MOUSE COLORING BOOK (S)
Saalfield Publishing Company:1931 (15-1/4x10-3/4", 32 pgs, color soft cover, half printed in full color interior, rest B&W
871 - By Ub Iwerks & Floyd Gottfredson (rare) 433.00 1300.00 2600.00
NOTE: *Contains reprints of first MM daily strip ever, including the "missing" speck the chicken is after found only on the original daily strip art by Iwerks plus other very early MM art. There were several other Saalfield Mickey Mouse coloring books manufactured around the same time.*

MICKEY MOUSE, THE ADVENTURES OF (I)
David McKay Co., Inc.: Book I, 1931 - Book II, 1932 (5-1/2"x8-1/2", 32 pgs.)
Book I-First Disney book, by strict definition (1st printing-50,000 copies)(see Mickey Mouse Book by Bibo & Lang). Illustrated text refers to Clarabelle Cow as "Carolyn" and Horace Horsecollar as "Henry". The name "Donald Duck" appears with a non-costumed generic duck on back cover & inside, not in the context of the character that later debuted in the Wise Little Hen.
Hardback w/characters on back-c 200.00 600.00 1200.00
Softcover w/characters on back-c 146.00 438.00 875.00
Version without characters on back-c 146.00 438.00 875.00
Book II-Less common than Book I. Character development brought into conformity with the Mickey Mouse cartoon shorts and syndicated strips. Captain Church Mouse, Tanglefoot, Peg-Leg Pete and Pluto appear with Mickey & Minnie 140.00 420.00 840.00

MICKEY MOUSE COMIC (N)
David McKay Co.: 1931 - No. 4, 1934 (10"x9-3/4", 52 pgs., card board-c)
(Later reprints exist)
1 (1931)-Reprints Floyd Gottfredson daily strips in black & white from 1930 & 1931, including the famous two week sequence in which Mickey tries to commit suicide 433.00 1299.00 2600.00
2 (1932)-1st app. of Pluto reprinted from 7/8/31 daily. All pgs. from 1931 233.00 699.00 1400.00
3 (1933)-Reprints 1932 & 1933 Sunday pages in color, one strip per page, including the "Lair of Wolf Barker" continuity pencilled by Gottfredson and inked by Al Taliaferro & Ted Thwaites. First app. Mickey's nephews, Morty & Ferdie, one identified by name of Mortimer Fieldmouse, not to be confused with Uncle Mortimer Mouse who is introduced in the Wolf Barker story 333.00 1000.00 2000.00
4 (1934)-1931 dailies, include the only known reprint of the infamous strip of 2/4/31 where the villainous Kat Nipp snips off the end of Mickey's tail with a pair of scissors 208.00 624.00 1250.00

MICKEY MOUSE (N)
Whitman Publishing Co.: 1933-34 (10x8-3/4", 34 pgs, cardboard-c)
948-1932 & 1933 Sunday strips in color, printed from the same plates as Mickey Mouse Book #3 by David McKay, but only pages 5-17 & 32-48 (including all of the "Wolf Barker" continuity) 250.00 750.00 1500.00
NOTE: *Some copies bound with back cover upside down. Variance doesn't affect value. Same art appears on front and back covers of all copies. Height of Whitman reissue trimmed 1/2 inch.*

MILITARY WILLIE
J. I. Austen Co.: 1907 (7x9-1/2", 12 pgs., every other page in color, stapled)
nn - By F. R. Morgan 63.00 189.00 380.00

MINNEAPOLIS TRIBUNE CARTOON BOOK (S)
Minneapolis Tribune: 1899-1903 (11-3/8x9-3/8", B&W, paper cover)
nn (#1) (1899) 50.00 110.00 225.00
nn (#2) (1900) 50.00 110.00 225.00
nn (#3) (1901) (published Jan 01, 1901) 50.00 110.00 225.00
nn (#4) (1902) (114 pgs) 50.00 110.00 225.00
nn (#5) (1903) (9x10-3/4",110 pgs, B&W; color-c) 50.00 110.00 225.00
NOTE: *All by Roland C. Bowman (editorial-r).*

MINUTE BIOGRAPHIES: INTIMATE GLIMPSES INTO THE LIVES OF 150 FAMOUS MEN AND WOMEN
Grossett & Dunlap: 1931, 1933 (10-1/4x7-3/4", 168 pgs, hardcover, B&W)
nn - By Nisenson (art) & Parker(text) 35.00 80.00 170.00
More.... (1933) 35.00 80.00 170.00

MISCHIEVOUS MONKS OF CROCODILE ISLE, THE (N)
J. I. Austen Co., Chicago: 1908 (8-1/2x11-1/2", 12 pgs., 4 pgs. in color)
nn - By F. R. Morgan; reads longwise 108.00 328.00 650.00

MR. & MRS. (Also see Ain't It A Grand and Glorious Feeling?) (N)
Whitman Publishing Co.: 1922 (9x9-1/2", 52 & 28 pgs., cardboard-c)
nn - By Briggs (B&W, 52 pgs.) 75.00 155.00 265.00
nn - 28 pgs.-(9x9-1/2")-Sunday strips-r in color 55.00 175.00 300.00
NOTE: *The earliest presently-known Whitman comic books*

MR. BLOCK (N)
Industrial Workers of the World (IWW): 1913, 1919
nn - By Ernest Riebe (C) 58.00 175.00 -
...And The Profiteers (original material) (H) 58.00 175.00 -
NOTE: *Mr Block was a daily strip published from 1912 NOV 7 to 1913 SEP ? by the socialist newspaper "Industrial Worker"; Mr Block was a "square" guy (his head was in fact a block) who enthusiastically supported the same system that exploited him. The noted Joe Hill wrote a song about him (Mr Block,1913, on the air of "It loooks me like a big time tonight") for the "Industrial Worker Songbook".*

MR. TWEE-DEEDLE (N)
Cupples & Leon: 1913, 1917 (11-3/8 x 16-3/4" color strips-r from NY Herald)
nn - By John B. Gruelle (later of Raggedy Ann fame) 367.00 1100.00 2200.00
nn - "Further Adventures of..." By Gruelle 367.00 1100.00 2200.00
NOTE: *Strip ran Feb 5, 1911-March 10, 1918.*

MONKEY SHINES OF MARSELEEN AND SOME OF HIS ADVENTURES (C)
McLaughlin Bros. New York: 1906 (10 x 12-3/8", 36 pgs, full color hardcover)
nn - By Norman E. Jennett strip-r NY Evening Telegram 92.00 276.00 550.00
NOTE: *Strip began in 1906 until at least March 13, 1910.*

MONKEY SHINES OF MARSELEEN (N)
Cupples & Leon Co.: 1909 (11-1/2 x 17", 58 pgs. in two colors)
nn - By Norman E. Jennett (strip-r New York Herald) 92.00 276.00 550.00

MOON MULLINS (N)
Cupples & Leon Co.: 1927 - 1933 (52 pgs., B&W daily strip-r)
Series 1 ('27)-By Willard 63.00 250.00 550.00
Series 2 ('28), Series 3 ('29), Series 4 ('30) 39.00 156.00 300.00
Series 5 ('31), 6 ('32), 7 ('33) 39.00 156.00 300.00
Big Book 1 ('30)-B&W (scarce) 100.00 400.00 725.00
w/dust jacket (rare) 175.00 700.00 1100.00

MOVING PICTURE FUNNIES
Saml Gabriel Sons & Company: 1918 (5-1/4 x 10-1/4", 52 pgs, B&W, illustrated hard-c)
nn 21.00 63.00 125.00
NOTE: *823 Comical illustrations that show a different scene when folded.*

MUTT & JEFF (...Cartoon, The) (N)
Ball Publications: 1911 - No. 5, 1916 (5-3/4 x 15-1/2", 72 pgs, B&W, hard-c)
1 (1910)(50¢) very common 85.00 300.00 575.00

GD2.0 FN6.0 VF8.0

2,3: 2 (1911)-Opium den panels; Jeff smokes opium (pipe dreams).
3 (1912) both very common 75.00 300.00 510.00
2-(1913) Reprint of 1911 edition with black ink cover 55.00 180.00 325.00
4 (1915) (50¢) (Scarce) 150.00 350.00 700.00
5 (1916) (Rare) -Photos of Fisher, 1st pg. (68 pages) 200.00 480.00 1050.00
5-Scarce 84 page reprint edition 150.00 450.00 875.00

NOTE: *Mutt & Jeff first appeared in newspapers in 1907. Cover variations exist showing Mutt & Jeff reading various newspapers; i.e., The Oregon Journal, The American, and The Detroit News. Reprinting of each issue began soon after publication. No. 4 and 5 may not have been reprinted. Values listed include the reprints. Mutt & Jeff was the first successful American daily newspaper comic strip and as such remains one of the seminal strips of all time.*

MUTT & JEFF (N)
Cupples & Leon Co.: No. 6, 1919 - No. 22, 1934? (9-1/2x9-1/2", 52 pgs., B&W dailies, stiff-c)
6, 7 - By Bud Fisher (very common) 32.00 128.00 210.00
8-10 46.00 186.00 315.00
11-18 (Somewhat Scarcer) (#19-#22 do not exist) 60.00 240.00 410.00
nn (1920) (Advs. of...) 11x16"; 44 pgs.; full color reprints of 1919 Sunday strips
93.00 372.00 650.00
Big Book nn (1926, 144 pgs., hardcovers) 114.00 456.00 750.00
w/dust jacket 193.00 772.00 1300.00
Big Book 1 (1928) - Thick book (hardcovers) 114.00 456.00 700.00
w/dust jacket (rare) 182.00 729.00 1250.00
Big Book 2 (1929) - Thick book (hardcovers) 114.00 456.00 750.00
w/dust jacket (rare) 182.00 729.00 1250.00

NOTE: *The Big Books contain three previous issues rebound.*

MUTT & JEFF (N)
Embee Publ. Co.: 1921 (9x15", color cardboard-c & interior)
nn - Sunday strips in color (Rare)- BY Bud Fisher 150.00 600.00 1100.00

NOTE: *Ties with The Trouble of Bringing Up Father (EmBee) and Jimmie Dugan & The Reg'lar Fellers (C&L) as the last of this size.*

MYSTERIOUS STRANGER AND OTHER CARTOONS, THE
McClure, Phillips & Co.: 1905 (12-3/8x9-3/4", 338 pgs, hardcover, B&W)
nn - By John McCutcheon 45.00 130.00 260.00

MY WAR - Szeged (Szuts)
Wm. Morrow Co.: 1932 (7x10-1/2", 210 pgs, hard-c, B&W)
nn - (All story panels, no words - powerful) 46.00 138.00 275.00

NAUGHTY ADVENTURES OF VIVACIOUS MR. JACK, THE
New York American & Journal: 1904 (15x10", color strips)
nn - By James Swinnerton; (Very Rare - 3 known copies) 450.00 1350.00 2700.00

NEBBS, THE (N)
Cupples & Leon Co.: 1928 (52 pgs., B&W daily strip-r)
nn - By Sol Hess; Carlson-a 60.00 180.00 300.00

NERVY NAT'S ADVENTURES (E)
Leslie-Judge Co.: 1911 (90 pgs, 85¢, 1903 strip reprints from **Judge**)
nn - By James Montgomery Flagg 75.00 263.00 460.00

THE NEWLYWEDS AND THEIR BABY (N)
Saalfield Publ. Co.: 1907 (13x10", 52 pgs., hardcover)
...& Their Baby' by McManus; daily strips 50% color 400.00 1200.00 –

NOTE: *Strip ran Apr 10, 1904 thru Jan 14, 1906 and then May 19, 1907-Dec 5, 1916; was a huge success with Baby Snookums long before McManus invented Bringing Up Father; Snookums brought back as a topper strip over BUF Nov 19, 1944-Dec 30, 1956.*

THE NEWLYWEDS AND THEIR BABY'S COMIC PICTURES FOR PAINTING AND CRAYONING (N)
Saalfield Publishign Company: 1916 (10-1/4x14-3/4", 52 pgs. Cardboard-c)
nn - 44 B&W pages, covers, and one color wrap glued to B&W title page.
Color wrap: color title pg. & 3 pgs of color strips 83.00 290.00 550.00
nn - (1917, 10x14", 20 pgs, oblong, cardboard-c) partial reprint of 1916 edition
31.00 124.00 280.00

THE NEWLYWEDS AND THEIR BABY (N)
Saalfield Publishing Company: 1917 (10-1/8x13-9/16 ", 52 pgs, full color cardstock-c, some pages full color, others two color (orange, blue))
nn 83.00 290.00 450.00

NEW YORKER CARTOON ALBUM, THE (M)
Doubleday, Doran & Company Inc.: (1928-1931); **Harper & Brothers.:** (1931-1933); **Random House** (1935-1937), 12x9", various pg counts, hardcovers w/dust jackets)
1928: nn-114 pgs Arno, Held, Soglow, Williams, etc 20.00 60.00 120.00
1928: SECOND-114 pgs Arno, Bairnsfather, Gross, Held, Soglow, Williams
10.00 30.00 75.00
1930: THIRD-172 pgs Arno, Bairnsfather, Held, Soglow, Art Young
10.00 30.00 75.00
1931: FOURTH-154 pgs Arno, Held, Soglow, Steig, Thurber, Williams, Art Young, "Little King" by Soglow begins 10.00 30.00 75.00
1932: FIFTH-156 pgs Arno, Bairnsfather, Held, Hoff, Soglow, Steig, Thurber, Williams 10.00 30.00 75.00
1933: SIXTH-156 pgs same as above 10.00 30.00 75.00
1935: SEVENTH-164 pgs 10.00 30.00 75.00
1937: 168 pgs; Charles Addams plus same as above but no Little King, two page "Gone With The Wind" parody strip 10.00 30.00 90.00

NOTE: *Some sequential strips but mostly single panel cartoons.*

NIPPY'S POP (N)
The Saalfield Publishing Co.: 1917 (10-1/2x13-1/2", 36 pgs., B&W, Sunday strip-r)
nn - Charles M Payne (better known as S'Matter Pop) 50.00 150.00 300.00

OH, MAN (A Bully Collection of Those Inimitable Humor Cartoons) (S)
P.F. Volland & Co.: 1919 (8-1/2x13"; 136 pgs.)
nn - By Briggs 50.00 160.00 290.00

NOTE: *Originally came in illustrated box with Briggs art (box is Rare - worth 50% more with box).*

OH SKIN-NAY! (S)
P.F. Volland & Co.: 1913 (8-1/2x13", 136 pgs.)
nn - The Days Of Real Sport by Briggs 50.00 165.00 275.00

NOTE: *Originally came in illustrated box with Briggs art (box is Rare - worth 50% more with box).*

OLD GOLD THE SMOOTHER AND BETTER CIGARETTE...NOT A COUGH IN A CARLOAD (M,N,P) (see also BY BRIGGS)
Old Gold Cigarettes: nd (c1920's) (16 pgs, paper-c, color) (both Scarce)
nn- (4-1/4" x 3-7/8") cover strip is "Oh, Man!"; also contains: "Real Folks at Home", "Ain't It a Grand and Glorious Feelin'?", "It Happens in the Best Regulated Families", and "Mr. and Mrs." (no known sales)
1440- (5-9/16" x 5-1/4") cover strip is "Frank and Ernest"; also contains: "That Guiltiest Feeling", "Real Folks at Home", "Oh, Man!", "When a Feller Needs a Friend". (no known sales)

NOTE: *Collection reprinting strip cartoons by Clare Briggs, advertising Old Gold Cigarettes. These strips originally appeared in various magazines, play program booklets, newspapers, etc. Some of the strips involve regular Briggs strip series. The two booklets contain a completely different set of comics.*

ON AND OFF MOUNT ARARAT (also see **Tigers**) (N)
Hearst's New York American & Journal: 1902, 86pgs. 10x15-1/4"
nn - Rare Noah's Ark satire by Jimmy Swinnerton (rare) 567.00 1700.00 –

ON THE LINKS (N)
Associated Feature Service: Dec, 1926 (9x10", 48 pgs.)
nn - Daily strip-r by Robert Hunter 43.00 129.00 260.00

ONE HUNDRED WAR CARTOONS (S)
Idaho Daily Statesman: 1918 (7-3/4x10", 102 pgs, paperback, B&W)
nn - By Villeneuve (WW I cartoons) 25.00 75.00 150.00

OUR ANTEDILUVIAN ANCESTORS (N,S)
New York Evening Journal, NY: 1903 (11-3/8x8-7/8", hardcover)
nn - By F Opper 75.00 200.00 460.00

NOTE: *There is a simultaneously published British edition, identical size and contents, from C. Arthur Pearson Ltd, London. A collection of single panel cartoons about cavemen. Similar to an earlier British cartoon book "Prehistoric Peeps from Punch", by E.T. Reed.*

OUTBURSTS OF EVERETT TRUE, THE (N)
Saalfield Publ. Co.(Werner Co.): 1907 (92 pgs, 9-7/16x5-1/4")
1907 (2-4 panel strips-r)-By Condo & Raper 125.00 375.00 750.00
1921-Full color-c; reprints 56 of 88 cartoons from 1907 ed. (10x10", 32 pgs B&W)
63.00 189.00 375.00

OVER THERE COMEDY FROM FRANCE
Observer House Printing: nd (WW 1 era) (6x14", 60 pgs, paper cover)
nn - Artist(s) unknown 22.00 66.00 130.00

OWN YOUR OWN HOME (I)
Bobbs-Merrill Company, Indianapolis: 1919 (7-7/16x5-1/4")
nn - By Fontaine Fox – – –

PECKS BAD BOY (N)
Charles C. Thompson Co, Chicago (by Walt McDougal): 1906-1908 (strip-r)
The Adventures of... (1906) 11-1/2x16-1/4", 68 pgs 142.00 426.00 850.00
...& His Country Cousin Cynthia (1907) 12x16-1/2," 34 pgs In color
142.00 429.00 850.00
Advs. of...And His Country Cousins (1907) 5-1/2x10-1/2", 18 pgs In color
67.00 200.00 400.00
Advs. of...And His Country Cousins (1907) 11-1/2x16-1/4", 36 pgs
67.00 200.00 400.00
...& Their Advs With The Teddy Bear (1907) 5-1/2x10-1/2", 18 pgs in color
67.00 200.00 400.00
...& Their Balloon Trip To the Country (1907) 5-1/2x 10-1/2, 18 pgs in color
67.00 200.00 400.00
...With the Teddy Bear Show (1907) 5-1/2x 10-1/2 67.00 200.00 400.00
...With The Billy Whiskers Goats (1907) 5-1/2 x 10-1/2, 18 pgs in color
67.00 200.00 400.00
...& His Chums (1908) - 11x16-3/8", 36 pgs. Stanton & Van Vliet Co
140.00 420.00 840.00
...& His Chums (1908)-Hardcover; full color;16 pgs. 117.00 350.00 700.00
Advs. of...in Pictures (1908) (11x17, 36 pgs)-In color; Stanton & Van V. Liet Co.
137.00 411.00 820.00

PERCY & FERDIE (N)
Cupples & Leon Co.: 1921 (10x10", 52 pgs., B&W dailies, cardboard-c)
nn - By H. A. MacGill (Rare) 87.00 261.00 520.00

PETER RABBIT (N)
John H. Eggers Co. The House of Little Books Publishers: 1922 - 1923
B1-B4-(Rare)-(Set of 4 books which came in a cardboard box)-Each book reprints half of a Sunday page per page and contains 8 B&W and 2 color pages; by Harrison Cady (9-1/4x6-1/4", paper-c) each.... 57.00 171.00 340.00
Box only 73.00 219.00 440.00

PHILATELIC CARTOONS (M)
Essex Publishing Company, Lynn, Mass.: 1916 (8-11/16" x 5-7/8", 40 pgs, light blue construction paper-c, B&W interior)
nn - By Leroy S. Bartlett 48.00 144.00 290.00

NOTE: *Comics reprinted from The New England Philatelist.*

PICTORIAL HISTORY OF THE DEPARTMENT OF COMMERCE UNDER HERBERT HOOVER (see Picture Life of a Great American) (O)
Hoover-Curtis Campaign Committee of New York State: no date, 1928 (3-1/4 x 5-1/4, 32 pgs, paper cover, B&W)
nn - By Satterfield (scarce) 48.00 144.00 290.00

NOTE: *1928 Presidential Campaign giveaway. Original material, contents completely different from Picture Life of a Great American.*

PICTURE LIFE OF A GREAT AMERICAN (see Pictorial History of the Department of Commerce under Herbert Hoover) (O)
Hoover-Curtis Campaign Committee of New York State: no date, 1928 (paper cover, B&W)
nn - (8-3/4 x 7, 20 pgs) Text cover, 2 page text introduction, 18 pgs of comics (scarcer first print) 46.00 138.00 275.00
nn - (9 x 6-3/4,24 pgs) Illustrated cover,5 page text introduction, 18 pgs of comics (scarce) 46.00 138.00 275.00

NOTE: *1928 Presidential Campaign giveaway. Unknown which above version was published first. Both contain the same original comics material by Satterfield.*

PINK LAFFIN (I)
Whitman Publishing Co.: 1922 (9x12")(Strip-r; some of these actually text joke books)
...the Lighter Side of Life, ...He Tells 'Em, ...and His Family, ...Knockouts;

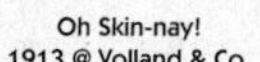
Oh Skin-nay!
1913 @ Volland & Co.

Secret Agent X-9 Book 2
1934 © David McKay

Winnie Winkle No. 2
1931 © Cupples & Leon

GD2.0 FN6.0 VF8.0

Ray Gleason-a (All rare) each... 29.00 87.00 175.00

POLLY (AND HER PALS) - (N)
Newspaper Feature Service: 1916 (3x2-1/2", color)

Altogether: Three Rahs and a Tiger! by Cliff Sterrett 28.00 84.00 170.00
There Is A Limit To Pa's Patience by Cliff Sterrett 28.00 84.00 170.00
Pa's Lil Book Has Some Uncut Pages by Sterrett 28.00 84.00 170.00
NOTE: *Single newsprint sheet printed in full color on both sides, unfolds to show 12 panel story.*

POPEYE PAINT BOOK (N)
McLaughlin Bros, Inc., Springfield, Mass.: 1932 (9-7/8x13", 28 pgs, color-c)

2052 - By E. C. Segar 113.00 339.00 675.00
NOTE: *Contains a full color panel above and the exact same art in below panel n B&W which one was to color in; strip-r panels.*

POPEYE CARTOON BOOK (N)
The Saalfield Co.: 1934 (8-1/2x13", 40 pgs, cardboard-c)

2095-(scarce)-1933 strip reprints in color by Segar. Each page contains a vertical half of a Sunday strip, so the continuity reads row by row completely across each double page spread. If each page is read by itself, the continuity makes no sense. Each double page spread reprints one complete Sunday page from 1933 300.00 900.00 2300.00
12 Page Version 133.00 400.00 1000.00

POPEYE (See **Thimble Theatre** for earlier Popeye-r from Sonnett) (N)
David McKay Publications: 1935 (25¢; 52 pgs, B&W) (By Segar)

1-Daily strip reprints- "The Gold Mine Thieves" 133.00 400.00 1000.00
2-Daily strip-r (scarce) 133.00 400.00 1000.00
NOTE: *Ties with Henry & Little Annie Rooney (David McKay) as the last of the 10x10" size books.*

PORE LI'L MOSE (N)
New York Herald Publ. by Grand Union Tea
Cupples & Leon Co.: 1902 (10-1/2x15", 78 pgs., color)

nn - By R. F. Outcault; Earliest known C&L comic book (scarce in high grade - very high demand) 1500.00 4500.00 –
NOTE: *Black Americana one page newspaper strips; falls in between Yellow Kid & Buster Brown. Complete copies have become scarce. Some have cut this book apart thinking that reselling individual pages will bring them more money.*

PRETTY PICTURES (M)
Farrar & Rinehart: 1931 (12 x 8-7/8", 104 pgs, color hardcover w/dust jacket, B&W; reprints from New Yorker, Judge, Life, Collier's Weekly)

nn - By Otto Soglow (contains "The Little King") 43.00 129.00 260.00

QUAINT OLD NEW ENGLAND (S)
Triton Syndicate: 1936 (5-1/4x6-1/4", 100 pgs, soft-c squarebound, B&W)

nn - By Jack Withycomb 40.00 120.00 240.00
NOTE: *Comics about weird doings in Old New England.*

RED CARTOONS (S)
Daily Worker Publishing Company: 1926 (12 x 9", 68 pgs,cardboard cover, B&W)

nn - By Various (scarce) 46.00 138.00 275.00
NOTE: *Reprint of American Communist Party editorial cartoons, from The Daily Worker, The Workers Monthly, and the Liberator. Art by Fred Ellis, William Gropper, Clive Weed, Art Young.*

REG'LAR FELLERS (See All-American Comics, Jimmie Dugan & The..., Popular Comics & Treasure Box of Famous Comics) (N)
Cupples & Leon Co./MS Publishing Co.: 1921-1929

1 (1921)-52 pgs. B&W dailies (Cupples & Leon, 10x10") 57.00 171.00 340.00
1925, 48 pgs. B&W dailies (MS Publ.) 50.00 150.00 300.00
Hardcover (1929, 8-3/4x7-1/2"; 96 pgs.)-B&W-r 71.00 213.00 425.00

REG'LAR FELLERS STORY PAINT BOOK
Whitman, Racine, Wisc.: 1932 (8-3/4x12-1/8", 132 pgs, red soft-c)

By Gene Byrnes 27.00 81.00 160.00

ROGER BEAN, R. G. (Regular Guy) (N)
The Indiana News Co, Distributers.: 1915 - No. 2, 1915 (5-3/8x17", 68 pgs., B&W, hardcovers); #3-#5 published by **Chas. B. Jackson:** 1916-1919
(No. 1 2 4 & 5 bound on side, No. 3 bound at top)

1-By Chas B. Jackson (68pgs.)(Scarce) 60.00 180.00 360.00
2- 5-5/8x17-1/8", 66 pgs (says 1913 inside - an obvious printing error) (red or green binding) 60.00 180.00 360.00
3-Along the Firing Line... (1916; 68 pgs, 6x17") 60.00 180.00 360.00
3-Along the Firing Line side-bound version 60.00 180.00 360.00
4-Into the Trenches and Out Again with... (1917, 68 pgs) 60.00 180.00 360.00
5 ...And The Reconstruction Period (1919, 5-3/8x15-1/2", 84 pgs) (Scarce) (has $1 printed on cover) 60.00 180.00 360.00
Baby Grand Editions 1-5 (10x10", cardboard-c) 60.00 180.00 360.00
NOTE: *No. 1 & 2 of the Twin Baby Grands (nd) 8-1/4x10-7/8", 52 pgs. #3 & #4 9x10-7/8" Cardboard cover. B&W strip reprints. Cover also says "Politics Pickles People Police."*
nn - 9x11, 68 pgs 60.00 180.00 360.00
NOTE: Has picture of Chic Jackson and a posthumous dedication from his three children. strip-r 1931-32

ROGER BEAN PHILOSOPHER
Schnull & Co: 1917 (5-1/2x17", 36 pgs., B&W, brown & black paper-c, square binding)

nn - By Chic Jackson (no known sales)

ROOKIE FROM THE 13TH SQUAD, THAT (N) (also Between Shots; Always Belittlin'; Skippy)
Harper & Brothers Publishers: Feb. 1918 (8x9-1/4", 72 pgs, hardcover, B&W)

nn - By Lieut. P(ercy) L. Crosby 63.00 189.00 380.00
NOTE: *Strip began in 1917 at an Army base during basic training.*

GD2.0 FN6.0 VF8.0

ROUND THE WORLD WITH THE DOO-DADS (see Doings of the Doo-Dads, Doo Dads)
Universal Feature And Specialty Co, Chicago: 1922 (12x10-1/2", 52 pgs, B&W, red & light blue-c, square binding)

nn - By Arch Dale newspaper strip-r 54.00 162.00 325.00
NOTE: *Intermixed single panel and sequential comic strips with scenes from Scotland, Ireland, England, Holland, Italy, Spain, Egypt, Africa, and Lions & Elephants along the Nile River, China, Australia & back home.*

RUBAIYKT OF THE EGG
The John C Winston Co, Philadelphia: 1905 (7x5/12", 64 pgs, purple-c, B&W)

nn - By Clare Victor Dwiggins 32.00 96.00 190.00
NOTE: *Book is printed & cut into the shape of an egg.*

RULING CLAWSS, THE (N,S)
The Daily Worker: 1935 (192 pgs, 10-1/4 x 7-3/8", hard-c, B&W)

nn - By Redfield 87.00 260.00 –
NOTE: *Reprints cartoons from the American Communist Party newspaper The Daily Worker.*

SAGARA'S ENGLISH CARTOONS AND CARTOON STORIES (N)
Bunkosha, Tokyo: nd (c1925) (6-5/8" x 4-1/4", 272 pgs, hard-c, B&W)

nn- (Scarce) – – –
NOTE: *Published in Tokyo, Japan, with all strips in both English and Japanese, to facilitate learning English. Majority of book is Bringing Up Father by George McManus. Also contains Japanese strip Father Takes it Easy, by T. Sagara, reprinted from the Kokusai News Agency.*

SAM AND HIS LAUGH (N)
Frederick A. Stokes: 1906 (10x15", cardboard-c, Sunday strip-r in color)

nn - By Jimmy Swinnerton (Extremely Rare) 800.00 2400.00 4800.00
NOTE: *Strip ran July 24, 1904-Dec 26 1906; its ethnic humor might be considered racist by today's standards.*

SCHOOL DAYS (N)
Harper & Bros.: 1919 (9x8", 104 pgs.)

nn - By Clare Victor Dwiggins 50.00 150.00 300.00

SEAMAN SI - A Book of Cartoons About the Funniest "Gob" in the Navy (N)
Pierce Publishing Co.: 1916 (4x8-1/2, 200 pgs, hardcover, B&W); 1918 (4-1/8x8-1/4, 104 pgs, hardcover, B&W)

nn - By Perce Pearce (1916) 50.00 150.00 305.00
nn - 1918 - (Reilly & Britton Co.) 35.00 105.00 210.00
NOTE: *There exists two different covers for the 1918 reprints. The earlier edition was self published by the artist. The newspaper strip is sometimes also known as "The American Sailor."*

SECRET AGENT X-9 (N)
David McKay Pbll.: 1934 (Book 1: 84 pgs; Book 2: 124 pgs.) (8x7-1/2")

Book 1-Contains reprints of the first 13 weeks of the strip by Dashiell Hammett & Alex Raymond, complete except for 2 dailies 108.00 324.00 650.00
Book 2-Contains reprints immediately following contents of Book 1, for 20 weeks by Dashiell Hammett & Alex Raymond; complete except for two dailies. Last 5 strips misdated from 6/34, continuity correct 108.00 324.00 650.00

SILK HAT HARRY'S DIVORCE SUIT (N)
M. A. Donoghue & Co.: 1912 (5-3/4x15-1/2", oblong, B&W)

nn - Newspaper-r by Tad (Thomas A. Dorgan) 71.00 213.00 425.00

SINBAD A DOG'S LIFE (M)
Coward - McCann, Inc.: 1930 (11x 8-3/4", 104 pgs., single-sided, illustrated hard-c, B&W

nn - By Edwina 23.00 69.00 135.00
Sinbad...Again (1932, 10-15/16x 8-9/16", 104 pgs.) 23.00 69.00 135.00
NOTE: *Wordless comic strips from LIFE.*

SIS HOPKINS OWN BOOK AND MAGAZINE OF FUN
Leslie-Judge Co.: 1899-July 1911 (36 pgs, color-c, B&W) (merged into Judge's Library, later titled Film Fun)

Any issue - By various 33.00 99.00 200.00
NOTE: *Zim, Flagg, Young, Newell, Adams, etc.*

SKEEZIX (Also see Gasoline Alley & Little Skeezix Books listed below) (I)
Reilly & Lee Co.: 1925 - 1928 (Strip-r, soft covers) (pictures & text)

...and Uncle Walt (1924)-Origin 38.00 114.00 225.00
...and Pal (1925), ...at the Circus (1926) 27.00 81.00 160.00
...& Uncle Walt (1927) (does this actually exist? reprint? never seen one yet)
...Out West (1928) 36.00 108.00 215.00
Hardback Editions... 42.00 126.00 250.00

SKEEZIX BOOKS, LITTLE (Also see Skeezix, Gasoline Alley) (G)
Reilly & Lee Co.: No date (1928, 1929) (Boxed set of three Skeezix books)

nn - Box with 3 issues of Skeezix. Skeezix & Pal, Skeezix at the Circus, Skeezix & Uncle Walt known. 1928 Set... 63.00 189.00 375.00
nn - Box with 4 issues of (3) above Skeezix plus "Out West" 92.00 276.00 550.00

SKEEZIX COLOR BOOK (N)
McLaughlin Bros. Inc, Springfield, Mass: 1929 (9-1/2x10-1/4", 28 pgs, one third in full color, rest in B&W)

2023 - By Frank King; strip-r to color 29.00 87.00 175.00

SKIPPY (see also Life Presents Skippy, Always Belittlin', That Rookie From 13th Squad)
No publisher listed: Circa 1920s (10x8", 16 pgs., color/B&W cartoons)

nn - By Percy Crosby 28.00 84.00 165.00

SKIPPY, LIFE PRESENTS (M)
Life Publishing Company & Henry Holt, NY: nd 1924 (134 pgs, 10-13/16x8-3/4", color hard-c, B&W

nn - By Percy L Crosby 96.00 288.00 575.00
NOTE: *Many sequential & single panel reprints from Skippy's earliest appearances in Life Magazine.*

SKIPPY
Greenberg, Publisher, Inc, NY: 1925. (11-14x8-5/8, 72 pgs, hard-c, B&W and color

nn - By Percy L. Crosby 48.00 144.00 285.00
NOTE: *Some but not all of these comics were also in Life Presents Skippy; issued with dust wrapper.*

SKIPPY AND OTHER HUMOR
Greenberg: Publisher, NY: 1929 (11-1/4x8-1/2",72 pgs,tan hard-c, B&W and color)

nn - By Percy L. Crosby 29.00 87.00 170.00
NOTE: *Came with a dust jacket.*

SKIPPY (I)
Grossett & Dunlap: 1929 (7-3/8x6, 370 pgs, hardcover text with some art)

nn - By Percy Crosby (issued with a dust jacket) 35.00 105.00 210.00
NOTE: *This is worth very little without the dust wrapper; very common without the dust jacket.*

SKIPPY
Greenberg Press: 1930 (soft cover, ca. 16 pp.,

nn - By Percy Crosby (scarce) 51.00 153.00 305.00
NOTE: *Reprints from LIFE cartoons, color, b/w. Crosby told Greenberg to withdraw from the market as it cheapened the hard cover prior editions. Greenberg then stopped publishing per agreement, and sent Crosby all the copper & zinc bookplates, which were in Crosby estate until 1996.*

SKIPPY CRAYON AND COLORING BOOK (N)
McLoughlin Bros, Inc., Springfield, MA: 1931 (13x9-3/4", 28 pgs, color-c, color & B&W)

2050 - By Percy Crosby 34.00 102.00 205.00
NOTE: *This item says on the front cover: "Licensed by Percy Crosby" because he owned his creation. About half the pages have one panel pre-printed in full color with same one b&w below for person to copy the colors.*

SKIPPY RAMBLES (I)
G.P. Putnam's Sons: 1932 (7 1/8 x 5 1/8, 202 pgs)

nn - By Percy Crosby 32.00 96.00 190.00
NOTE: *Issued with a dustjacket. Has Skippy plates by Crosby every 4 or 5 pages.*

SKUDDABUD STARRY STORY SERIES - FOLK FROM THE FUTURE (O,G)
no publisher listed: 1936 (9" x 11-7/8", 48 pgs, cardboard-c, B&W)

Book One (Rare) "Parachuting" (a VG/FN copy sold for $268 in 2010) 21.00 84.00 170.00
NOTE: *By Columba Krebs. Top half of each page is a continuing strip story, while bottom half are different stories, in prose, about the same characters -- a race of aliens who have migrated to Earth, from their dying world.*

S'MATTER POP? (N)
Saalfield Publ. Co.: 1917 (10x14", 44 pgs., B&W, cardboard-c,)

nn - By Charlie Payne; in full color; pages printed on one side 50.00 150.00 300.00

S'MATTER POP? (N) (25 ¢ cover price)
E.I. Company, New York: 1927 (8-15/16x7-1/8", 52 pgs, yellow soft-c perfect bound

nn - By C.M. Payne (scarce) 28.00 84.00 165.00
NOTE: *First comic book published by Hugo Gernsback, noted for inventing Amazing Stories among other memorable science fiction pulps. The World Science Fiction Convention Award, The Hugo, is named for him.*

SMITTY (See Treasure Box of Famous Comics) (N)
Cupples & Leon Co.: 1928 - 1933 (9x7", 96 pgs., B&W strip-r, hardcover)

1928-(96 pgs. 7x8-3/4") By Walter Berndt 58.00 174.00 350.00
1929-At the Ball Game (Babe Ruth on cover) 92.00 276.00 550.00
1930-The Flying Office Boy, 1931-The Jockey, 1932-In the North Woods
each... 51.00 153.00 305.00
1933-At Military School 51.00 153.00 305.00
NOTE: *Each hardbound was published with a dust jacket; worth 50% more with dust jacket. The 1929 edition is very popular with baseball collectors. Strip debuted Nov 27, 1922.*

SMOKEY STOVER (See Dan Dunn & King of the Royal Mounted) (N)
Whitman Publishing: 1937 (5 1/2 x 7 1/4", 68pgs., color cardboard-c, B&W)

1010 51.00 153.00 305.00

SOCIAL COMEDY (M)
Life Publishing Company: 1902 (11-3/4 x 9-1/2", 128 pgs, B&W, illustrated hardcover)

nn - Artists include C.D. Gibson & Kemble. 27.00 81.00 160.00
NOTE: *Reprints cartoons and a few sequential comics from LIFE. Came in unmarked slipcase.*

SOCIAL HELL, THE (O)
Rich Hill: 1902

nn - By Ryan Walker 27.00 81.00 160.00
NOTE: *"The conditions of workers and the corruption of a political system beholden to corporate interests have been a major focus of human rights concerns since the 19th century. This early graphic novel depicts the social evils of unreformed capitalism. Ryan Walker was a syndicate cartoonist for many mainstream newspapers as well as for the communist Daily Worker." This description comes from http://www.lib.uconn.edu/DoddCenter/ascexh3.html, where you can find also a reproduction of the cover. I add that Ryan Walker was the editor of "The Saint Louis Republic" comic section since its inception in 1897; the supplement published "Alma and Oliver", George McManus's first series.*

SPORT AND THE KID (see The Umbrella Man) (N)
Lowman & Hanford Co.: 1913 (6-1/4x6-5/8",114 pgs, hardcover, B&W&orange)

nn - By J.R. "Dok" Hager 26.00 78.00 155.00

STORY OF CONNECTICUT (N)
The Hartford Times: Vol.1 1935 - Vol.3 1936 (10-1/2" x 7-3/8",304 pgs,color hard-c, B&W)

Vol.1 - 3 27.00 81.00 160.00
NOTE: *Collects a newspaper strip on Connecticut State history, which ran in the Hartford Times. Strip is in a similar format to "Texas History Movies". Also published in a plain, blue hardcover.*

STORY OF JAPAN IN CHINA, THE (N,S)
Trans-Pacific News Service, NYC: Vol. 3, No.1 March 10, 1938 (9" x 6", 36 pgs, construction paper-c, B&W)

Vol.3 No.1 27.00 81.00 160.00
NOTE: *Part of the "China Reference Series" of booklets, detailing the Japanese occupation and brutalization of China. Consists entirely of cartoons. The other booklets in the series have no cartoons. Art by: Ding, Fitzpatrick, Herblock, Herman, Rollin Kirby, Knox, Low, Manning, Orr, Shoemaker, Talburt.*

STRANGE AS IT SEEMS (S)
Blue-Star Publishing Co.: 1932 (64 pgs., B&W, square binding)

1-Newspaper-r (*Published with & without No. 1 and price on cover.*) 38.00 114.00 225.00
Ex-Lax giveaway (1936, B&W, 24 pgs., 5x7") - McNaught Synd.
21.00 63.00 125.00

SULLIVANT'S ABC ZOO (I)
The Old Wine Press: 1946 (11-3/4x9-3/8", hardcover)

nn - By T.S. Sullivant (Rare) 58.00 174.00 350.00

NOTE: *Reprints Mitchell & Miller material 1895-1898 and Life Publishing 1898-1926.*

TAILSPIN TOMMY STORY & PICTURE BOOK (N)
McLoughlin Bros.: No. 266, 1931 (nd) (10x10-1/2", color strip-r)

266 - By Forrest 53.00 159.00 315.00

TAILSPIN TOMMY (Also see Famous Feature Stories & The Funnies)(N)
Cupples & Leon Co.: 1932 (100 pgs., hard-c) (B&W 1930 strip reprints)

nn - (Scarce)- by Hal Forrest & Glenn Chaffin 65.00 195.00 390.00

TALES OF DEMON DICK AND BUNKER BILL (O)
Whitman Publishing Co.: 1934 (5-1/4x10-1/2", 80 pgs, color hardcover, B&W)

793 - By Spencer 54.00 162.00 325.00

TARZAN BOOK (The Illustrated...) (N)
Grosset & Dunlap: 1929 (9x7", 80 pgs.)

1(Rare)-Contains 1st B&W Tarzan newspaper comics from 1929. By Hal Foster
Cloth reinforced spine & dust jacket (50¢); Foster-c
With dust jacket... 125.00 375.00 750.00
Without dust jacket... 63.00 189.00 375.00
2nd Printing(1934, 25¢, 76 pgs.)-4 Foster pgs. dropped; paper spine, circle in lower right cover with 25¢ price. The 25¢ is barely visible on some copies
46.00 138.00 275.00
1967-House of Greystoke reprint-7x10", using the complete 300 illustrations/text from the 1929 edition minus the original indicia, foreword, etc. Initial version bound in gold paper & sold for $5.00. Officially titled **Burroughs Bibliophile #2**. A very few additional copies were bound in heavier blue paper. Gold binding... 10.00 20.00 45.00
Blue binding... 10.00 20.00 45.00

TARZAN OF THE APES TO COLOR (N)
Saalfield Publishing Co.: No. 988, 1933 (15-1/4x10-3/4", 24 pgs) (Coloring book)

988-(Very Rare)-Contains 1929 daily reprints with some new art by Hal Foster. Two panels blown up large on each page with one at the top of opposing pages on every other double-page spread. Believed to be the only time these panels appeared in color. Most color panels are reproduced a second time in B&W to be colored
300.00 900.00 2400.00

TARZAN OF THE APES The Big Little Cartoon Book (N)
Whitman Publishing Company: 1933 (4-1/2x3 5/8", 320 pgs, color-c, B&W)

744 - By Hal Foster (comic strips on every page) 63.00 189.00 375.00

TECK HASKINS AT OHIO STATE (S)
Lea-Mar Press: 1908 (7-1/4x5-3/8", 84 pgs, B&W hardcover)

nn - By W.A. Ireland; football cartoons-r from Columbus Ohio Evening Dispatch
32.00 96.00 190.00
NOTE: *Small blue & white patch of cover art pasted atop a color cloth quilt patter; pasted patch can easily peel off some copies.*

TECK 1909 (S)
Lea-Mar Press: 1909 (8-5/8 x 8-1/8", 124 pgs., B&W hardcover, 25¢)

nn - By W.A. Ireland; Ohio State University baseball cartoons-r from Columbus Evening Dispatch 31.00 93.00 185.00

TEDDY BEAR BOOKS, THE (M) (see also LITTLE JOHNNY AND THE TEDDY BEARS)
Reilly & Britton Co., Chicago: 1907 (7-1/16" x 5-3/8", 24 pgs, hard-c, color

The Teddy Bears Come to Life, The Teddy Bears at the Circus, The Teddy Bears in a Smashup, The Teddy Bears on a Lark, The Teddy Bears on a Toboggan, The Teddy Bears at School, The Teddy Bears Go Fishing, The Teddy Bears in Hot Water
30.00 90.00 180.00
NOTE: *Books are all unnumbered. C & A by J.R. Bray; s-Robert D. Towne. Reprints "Little Johnny & the Teddy Bears" strips, from Judge Magazine. Similar in format to the Buster Brown Nuggets series. All eight books debuted simultaneously.*

TEDDY BEARS IN FUN AND FROLIC (M) (see LITTLE JOHNNY & THE TEDDY BEARS)
Reilly & Britton Co., Chicago: 1908 (8-3/4" x 8-3/4", 50 pgs, cardboard-c, color)

nn - (Rare) by J.R. Bray-a; Robert D. Towne-s 121.00 363.00 725.00
NOTE: *Reprints "Little Johnny & the Teddy Bears" strips, from Judge Magazine. Unknown if there were any other "Teddy Bear" titles published in this format.*

TEENIE WEENIES, THE
Reilly & Britton, Chicago: 1916 (16-3/8x10-1/2", 52 pgs, cardboard-c, full color)

nn - By Wm. Donahey (Chicago Tribune-r) 154.00 462.00 925.00

TERROR OF THE TINY TADS (see also UPSIDE DOWNS OF LITTLE LADY LOVEKINS AND OLD MAN MUFFAROO)
Cupples & Leon: 1909 (11x17, 26 Sunday strips in Black & Red, Stiff cardboard-c)

nn - By Gustave Verbeek (Very Rare) (no known sales)

TEXAS HISTORY MOVIES (N)
Various editions, 1928 to 1986 (B&W)

Book I -1928 Southwest Press (7-1/4 x 5-3/8, 56 pgs, cardboard cover)
for the Magnolia Petroleum Company 60.00 180.00 360.00
nn - 1928 Southwest Press (12-3/8 x 9-1/4, 232 pgs, HC) 79.00 237.00 475.00
nn - 1935 Magnolia Petroleum Company (6 x 9, 132 pgs, paper cover)
32.00 96.00 190.00
NOTE: *Exists with either Wagon Train or Texas Flag & Lafitte/pirate covers.*
nn - 1943 Magnolia Petroleum Company (132 pgs, paper-c) 23.00 69.00 140.00
nn - 1963 Graphic Ideas Inc (11 x 8-1/2, softcover) 14.00 42.00 85.00
NOTE: *Reprints daily newspaper strips from the Dallas News, on Texas history. 1935 editions onward distributed within the Texas Public School System. Prior to that they appear to be giveaway comic books for the Magnolia Petroleum Company. There are many more editions than the ones pointed out above.*

THAT ROOKIE FROM THE 13TH SQUAD
Harper & Brothers Publ.: 1918 (B&W)

1-By Lieut. Percy Crosby 27.00 81.00 160.00

THAT SON-IN-LAW OF PA'S! (N)
Newspaper Feature Service: 1914 (2-1/2 by 3", color)

nn - *Imprinted on back for THE LESTER SHOE STORE.* 13.00 39.00 80.00
NOTE: *Single sheet printed in full color on both sides, unfolds to show 12 panel story.*

THIMBLE THEATRE STARRING POPEYE (See also Popeye) (N)
Sonnet Publishing Co.: 1931 - No. 2, 1932 (25¢, B&W, 52 pgs.)(Rare)

1-Daily strip serial-r in both by Segar 200.00 600.00 1600.00
2 156.00 468.00 1250.00
NOTE: *The very first Popeye reprint book. The first Thimble Theatre Sunday page appeared Dec 19, 1919.*

Popeye first entered Thimble Theatre on Jan 17, 1929.

THREE FUN MAKERS, THE (N)
Stokes and Company: 1908 (10x15", 64 pgs., color) (1904-06 Sunday strip-r)
nn - Maud, Katzenjammer Kids, Happy Hooligan 767.00 2300.00 -
NOTE: *This is the first comic book to compile more than one newspaper strip together.*

TIGERS (Also see On and Off Mount Ararat) (N)
Hearst's New York American & Journal: 1902, 86 pgs. 10x15-1/4"
nn - Funny animal strip-r by Jimmy Swinnerton 600.00 1800.00 -
NOTE: *The strip began as The Journal Tigers in The New York Journal Dec 12, 1897-Sept 28 1903*

TILLIE THE TOILER (N)
Cupples & Leon Co.: 1925 - No. 8, 1933 (52 pgs., B&W, daily strip-r)
nn (#1) By Russ Westover 75.00 225.00 450.00
2-8 58.00 174.00 350.00
NOTE: *First newspaper strip appearance was in January, 1921.*

TILLIE THE TOILER MAGIC DRAWING AND COLORING BOOK
Sam L Gabriel Sons And Company: 1931 (8-1/2 x 12", 36 pages, stiff-c)
838-By Russ Westover 46.00 138.00 275.00

TIMID SOUL, THE (N)
Simon & Schuster: 1931 (12-1/4x9", 136 pgs, B&W hardcover, dust jacket?)
nn - By H. T. Webster (newspaper strip-r) 47.00 141.00 280.00

TIM McCOY, POLICE CAR 17 (O)
Whitman Publishing Co.: 1934 (14-3/4x11", 32 pgs, stiff color covers)
674-1933 original material 77.00 231.00 460.00
NOTE: *Historically important as first movie adaptation in comic books.*

TOAST BOOK
John C. Winston Co: 1905 (7-1/4 x 6,104 pgs, skull-shaped book, feltcover, B&W)
nn - By Clare Dwiggins 52.00 156.00 310.00
NOTE: *Cartoon illustrations accompanying toasts/poems, most involving alcohol.*

TOM SAWYER & HUCK FINN (N)
Stoll & Edwards Co.:1925 (10x10-3/4", 52 pgs, stiff covers)
nn - By "Dwig" Dwiggins; 1923, 1924-r color Sunday strips 60.00 180.00 360.00
NOTE: *By Permission of the Estate of Samuel L. Clemons and the Mark Twain Company.*

TOONERVILLE TROLLEY AND OTHER CARTOONS (N) (See Cartoons by Fontaine Fox)
Cupples & Leon Co.: 1921 (10 x10", 52 pgs., B&W, daily strip-r)
1 - By Fontaine Fox 104.00 312.00 625.00

TRAINING FOR THE TRENCHES (M)
Palmer Publishing Company: 1917 (5-3/8 x 7", 20 pgs., paper-c, 10¢)
nn - By Lieut. Alban B. Butler, Jr. 28.00 84.00 165.00
NOTE: *Subtitle: "A book of humorous cartoons on a serious subject." Single-panels about military training.*

TREASURE BOX OF FAMOUS COMICS (N) (see Wonder Chest of Famous Comics)
Cupples & Leon Co.: 1934 (8-1/2 x 6-7/8", 36 pgs, soft covers) (Boxed set of 5 books)
Little Orphan Annie (1926) 45.00 90.00 175.00
Reg'lar Fellers (1928) 19.00 76.00 155.00
Smitty (1928) 19.00 76.00 155.00
Harold Teen (1931) 19.00 76.00 155.00
How Dick Tracy & Dick Tracy Jr. Caught The Racketeers (1933)26.00 104.00 200.00
Softcover set of five books in box 267.00 800.00 1600.00
Box only 71.00 213.00 425.00
NOTE: *Dates shown are copyright dates; all books actually came out in 1934 or later. The softcovers are abbreviated versions of the hardcover editions listed under each character.*

T.R. IN CARTOONS (N)
A.C. McClurg & Co., Chicago: June 13, 1910 (10-5/8" x 8", 104? pgs, paper-c, B&W)
nn - By McCutcheon about Teddy Roosevelt - - -

TRUTH (See Victorian section for earlier issues including the first Yellow Kid appearances)
Truth Company, NY: 1886-1906? (13-11/16x10-5/16", 16 pgs, process color-c & centerfolds, rest B&W)
1900-1906 issues 20.00 60.00 120.00

TRUTH SAVE IT FROM ABUSE & OVERWORK BEING THE EPISODE OF THE HIRED HAND & MRS. STIX PLASTER, CONCERTIST (N)
Radio Truth Society of WBAP: no date, 1924 (6-3/8 x 4-7/8, 40 pgs, paper cover, B&W)
nn - By V.T. Hamlin (Very Rare) 125.00 375.00 750.00
NOTE: *Radio station WBAP giveaway reprints strips from the Ft. Worth Texas Star-Telegram set at local radio station. 1st collected work by V.T. Hamlin, pre-Alley Oop.*

TWENTY FIVE YEARS AGO (see At The Bottom Of The Ladder) (M,S)
Coward-McCann: 1931 (5-3/4x8-1/4, 328 pgs, hardcover, B&W)
nn - By Camillus Kessler 38.00 114.00 225.00
NOTE: *Multi-image panel cartoons showing historical events for dates during the year.*

UMBRELLA MAN, THE (N) (See Sport And The Kid)
Lowman & Hanford Co.: 1911 (8-7/8x5-7/8",112 pgs, hard-c, B&W & orange)
nn - By J.R. "Dok" Hager (Seattle Times-r) 23.00 69.00 140.00

UNCLE REMUS AND BRER RABBIT (N)
Frederick A. Stokes Co.: 1907 (64 pgs, hardbound, color)
nn - By Joel C Harris & J.M. Conde 63.00 189.00 375.00

UPSIDE DOWNS OF LITTLE LADY LOVEKINS AND OLD MAN MUFFAROO
New York Herald: 1905 (?) (N)
nn - By Gustav Verbeck; (Also see Terror Of The Tiny Tads) 142.00 426.00 850.00

VAUDEVILLES AND OTHER THINGS (N)
Isaac H. Blandiard Co.: 1900 (13x10-1/2", 22 pgs., color) plus two reprints
nn - By Bunny (Scarce) 317.00 950.00 -
nn - 2nd print "By the Creator of Foxy Grandpa" on-c but only has copyright info of 1900 (10-1/2x15 1/2, 28 pgs, color) 283.00 850.00 -
nn - 3rd print. "By the creator of Foxy Grandpa" on-c; has both 1900 and 1901 copyright info (11x13") 208.00 625.00 -

WALLY - HIS CARTOONS OF THE A.E.F. (N)
Stars & Stripes: 1917 (96 and 108 pgs, B&W)
nn - By Abian A "Wally" Wallgren (7x18; 96 pgs) 17.00 51.00 100.00
nn - another edition (108 pgs, 7x17-1/2) 17.00 51.00 100.00
NOTE: *World War One cartoons reprints from Stars & Stripes; sold to U.S. servicemen with profits to go to French War Orphans Fund. various editions from 1917-1920; there might be more than what we list here.*

WAR CARTOONS (S)
Dallas News: 1918 (11x9", 112 pgs, hardcover, B&W)
nn - By John Knott (WWOne cartoons) 26.00 78.00 155.00

WAR CARTOONS FROM THE CHICAGO DAILY NEWS (N,S)
Chicago Daily News: 1914 (10 cents, 7-3/4x10-3/4", 68 pgs, paper-c, B&W)
nn - By L.D. Bradley 25.00 75.00 150.00

WEBER & FIELD'S FUNNYISMS (S,M,O)
Arkell Comoany, NY: 1904 (10-7/8x8", 112 pgs, color-c, B&W)
1 - By various (only issue?) 27.00 81.00 160.00
NOTE: *Contains some sequential & many single panel strips by Outcault, George Luks, CA David, Houston, L Smith, Hy Mayer, Verbeck, Woolf, Sydney Adams, Frank "Chip" Bellew, Eugene "ZIM" Zimmerman, Phil May, FT Richards, Billy Marriner, Grosvenor and many others.*

WE'RE NOT HEROES (O,S)
E.C. Wells and J.W. Moss: 1933 (8-11/16" x 5-7/8", 52 pgs, B&W interior)
nn - By Eddie Wells; red & black paper-c 14.00 42.00 85.00
NOTE: *Amateurish cartoons about World War I vets in the Walter Reed Veteran's Hospital.*

WHEN A FELLER NEEDS A FRIEND (S)
P. F. Volland & Co.: 1914 (11-11/16x8-7/8)
nn - By Clare Briggs 33.00 100.00 200.00
NOTE: *Originally came in box with Briggs art (box is Rare); also numerous more modern reprints)*

WILD PILGRIMAGE (O)
Harrison Smith & Robert Haas: 1932 (9-7/8x7", 210 pgs, B&W hardcover w/dust jacket) (original wordless graphic novel in woodcuts)
nn - By Lynd Ward 50.00 150.00 300.00

WILLIE AND HIS PAPA AND THE REST OF THE FAMILY (I)
Grossett & Dunlap: 1901 (9-1/2x8", 200 pgs, hardcover from N.Y. Evening Journal by Permission of W. R. Hearst) (pictures & text)
nn - By Frederick Opper 71.00 213.00 425.00
NOTE: *Political satire series of single panel cartoons, involving whiny child Willie (President William McKinley), his rambunctious and uncontrollable cousin Teddy (Vice President Roosevelt), and Willie's Papa (trusts/ monopolies) and their Maid (Senator) Hanna.*

WILLIE GREEN COMICS, THE (N) (see Adventures of Willie Green)
Frank M. Acton Co./Harris Brown: 1915 (8x15, 36 pgs); 1921 (6x10-1/8", 52 pgs, color paper cover, B&W interior, 25¢)
Book No. 1 By Harris Brown 57.00 171.00 340.00
Book 2 (*#2 sold via mail order directly from the artist)(very rare)* 63.00 189.00 375.00
NOTE: *Book No. 1 possible reprint of Adv. of Willie Green; definitely two different editions.*

WILLIE WESTINGHOUSE EDISON SMITH THE BOY INVENTOR (N)
William A. Stokes Co.: 1906 (10x16", 36 pgs. in color)
nn - By Frank Crane (Scarce) 250.00 750.00 1500.00
NOTE: *Comic strip began May 27, 1900 and ran thru 1914. Parody of inventors Westinghouse and Edison.*

WINNIE WINKLE (N)*Strip began as a daily Sept 20, 1920.*
Cupples & Leon Co.: 1930 - No. 4, 1933 (52 pgs., B&W daily strip-r)
1 58.00 174.00 350.00
2-4 50.00 150.00 300.00

WISDOM OF CHING CHOW, THE (see also The Gumps)
R. J. Jefferson Printing Co.: 1928 (4x3", 100 pgs, red & B&W cardboard cover) (newspaper strip-r The Chicago Tribune)
nn - By Sidney Smith (scarce) 29.00 87.00 175.00

WONDER CHEST OF FAMOUS COMICS (N) see Treasure Chest of Famous Comics)
Cupples & Leon Co.: 1935? 8-1/2x(6-7/8", 36 pgs, soft covers) (Boxed set of 5 books)
Little Orphan Annie #2 (1927) (Haunted House) 26.00 78.00 155.00
Little Orphan Annie #3 (1928) (in the Circus) 26.00 78.00 155.00
Smitty #2 (1929) (Babe Ruth app.) 26.00 78.00 155.00
Dolly Dimples and Bobby Bounce (1933) by Grace Drayton 26.00 786.00 155.00
How Dick Tracy & Dick Tracy Jr. Caught The Racketeers (1933) 38.00 114.00 225.00
Softcover set of five books in box 163.00 489.00 1300.00
Box only 67.00 200.00 400.00
NOTE: *Dates shown are original copyright dates of the first printings; all actually came out in 1934 or later. Extremely abbreviated versions of the hardcover editions listed under each character. It is suspected this came out the Christmas season following Treasure Chest of Famous Comics. which contains earlier editions.*

WORLD OF TROUBLE, A (S)
Minneapolis Journal: 1901 (10x8-3/4", 100 pgs, 40 pgs full color)
v3#1 - By Charles L. Bartholomew (editorial-r) 30.00 100.00 190.00

WRIGLEY'S "MOTHER GOOSE"
Wm. Wrigley Jr. Company, Chicago: 1915 (6" x 4", 28 pgs, full color)
nn - *Promotional comics for Wrigley's gum. Intro Wrigley's "Spearmen* 25.00 80.00 160.00
Book No. 2 25.00 80.00 160.00

YELLOW KID, THE (Magazine)(I) (becomes **The Yellow Book** #10 on)
Howard, Ainslee & Co., N.Y.: Mar. 20, 1897 - #9, July 17, 1897 (5¢, B&W w/color covers, 52p., stapled) (not a comic book)
1-R.F. Outcault Yellow kid on-c only #1-6. The same Yellow Kid color ad app. on back-c #1-6 (advertising the New York Sunday Journal) 1500.00 4500.00 -
2-6 (#2 4/3/97, #5 5/22/97, #6, 6/5/97) 1067.00 3200.00 -
7-9 (Yellow Kid not on-c) 291.00 875.00 -
NOTE: *Richard Outcault's Yellow Kid from the Hearst New York American represents the very first successful newspaper comic strip in America. Listed here due to historical importance. A set of #1-9 sold in 2015 for $20,315.*

YELLOW KID IN MCFADDEN'S FLATS, THE (N)
G. W. Dillingham Co., New York: 1897 (50¢, 7-1/2x5-1/2", 196 pgs., B&W, squarebound)
nn - The first "comic" book featuring The Yellow Kid; E. W. Townsend narrative w/R. F. Outcault Sunday comic page art-r & some original drawings (Prices vary widely. Rare.) 7000.00 18,000.00 -
NOTE: *A Fair condition copy sold for $2,901 in August 2004.; restored app VF sold for $10,500 in 2005. A copy in Fine+ (spine intact) and loose back cover sold for $17,000 in 2006. An apparent FN+ copy sold for $6,572.50 in 2011. An apparent FN/VF copy sold for $4,182 in 2012.*

YESTERDAYS (S)
The Reilly & Lee Co.: 1930 (8-3/4 x 7-1/2", 128 pgs, illustrated hard-c with dust jacket
nn - Text and cartoons about Victorian times by Frank Wing 25.00 50.00 110.00

Image courtesy of Heritage Auctions

THERE IS A UNIVERSE THAT PREDATES OURS...

LET'S CALL THAT EARTH-2

By Mark Herr

Ever since *Flash* #123 (1961), with the introduction of the parallel universe dubbed Earth-2, the potential was there. Establishing that Golden Age heroes were still part of the DC Universe, it was only a matter of time before the groundbreaking Justice Society of America, the first superhero team in all of comics, was reintroduced. And the logical place to do it was in *Justice League of America*. It was such a smash hit, and quickly became an annual summer event that readers eagerly anticipated.

1963

In 1963, in *JLA* #21-22, the Justice Society of America were reintroduced into then-current continuity, with stories entitled "Crisis on Earth-1" and "Crisis on Earth-2," respectively. This set a titling theme that is still used by DC today (everything in DC is a crisis if you need a reason to get a bunch of heroes together). This JSA line-up included a nice mix of heroes with Earth-1 counterparts (Hawkman, Green Lantern, and the Atom) along with heroes unique to Earth-2 (Black Canary, Dr. Fate, and Hourman), joining forces with Batman, Superman, Wonder Woman, the Silver Age Green Lantern and Flash, and others from the JLA. The heroes join forces to defeat the evil Crime Champions. Much like the heroes they brought together, the villains are a mix of classic Golden Age villains (Fiddler, Icicle, and Wizard) and current Silver Age villains (Chronos, Felix Faust, and Dr. Alchemy).

The second team-up between the JLA and the JSA occurred in 1964's *JLA* #29-30. This crossover brought a slightly different line-up. Returning from their previous appearance was Hawkman, Dr. Fate, and Black Canary, joined by Starman and Dr. Mid-Nite. Oddly enough (or intentionally) these two newly resurrected heroes had joined the JSA together in *All Star Comics* #8, replacing Flash and Green Lantern. Similar to what they do here. Green Lantern, Flash, and Atom of Earth-2 have cameos in #29,

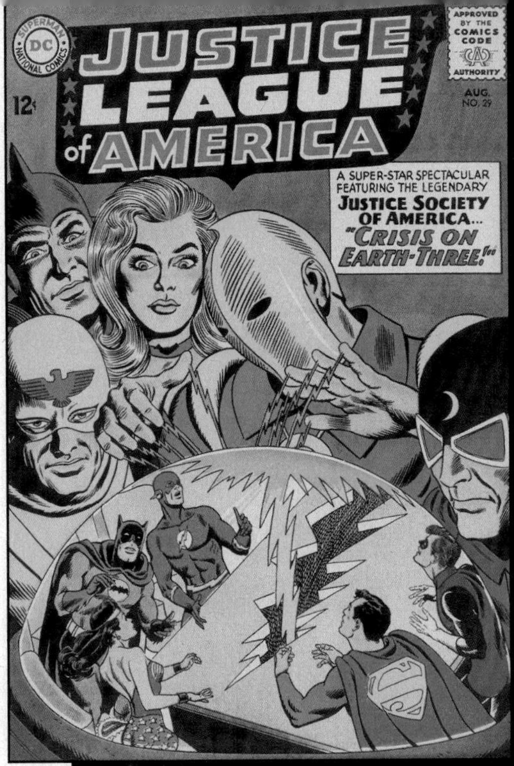

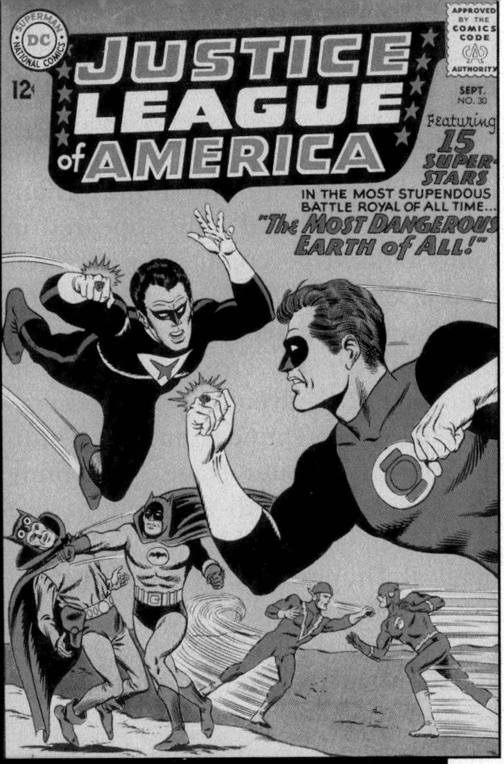

1964

but otherwise, are on the sidelines. The story introduced an entire new universe to the DC mythos, with Earth-3, a world where every historically significant hero was a villain and vice versa. So, logically, the heroes from our universe are reimagined as the world's greatest villains, the Crime Syndicate of America. The JLA's Superman, Green Lantern, Wonder Woman, Flash, and Batman initially defeated the Earth-3 villains, but it took the combined forces of both teams to stop a multiple universe conquest by the CSA.

Original art image courtesy of Heritage Auctions

JLA #37-38 saw the third team-up between the JLA and the JSA in the summer of 1965. The JSA line-up for this story included Hawkman, Green Lantern, Flash, Atom, Dr. Fate, and the reintroduced Mr. Terrific and Johnny Thunder. Mr. Terrific had only appeared in one Golden Age comic as a member of the JSA (*All Star Comics* #24), and so he appeared more frequently with the JSA in these crossovers than in the actual JSA adventures. The reintroduced Johnny Thunder and his Thunderbolt take center stage, as Johnny encounters his Earth-1 counterpart, a petty criminal who takes control of the magical Thunderbolt. When the Flash stops Earth-1 Johnny's crime spree, he uses Thunderbolt to go back in time and stop JLA members from becoming heroes. The evil Johnny then dubs this Earth-A, since they altered it to a significant degree. Only the JLA's allies from Earth-2 can help restore things to their proper settings.

Summer 1966 brought another team-up between the two legendary super-teams. *JLA* #46-47 saw Dr. Fate, Dr. Mid-Nite, and Black Canary fighting side by side with the Flash, Batman, and the Atom, as well as the reintroduced Sandman, Spectre, and Wildcat. Once again, with Wildcat, we have a hero who only appeared in two issues of *All Star Comics* (#24, along with Mr. Terrific, and #27). These annual crossover appearances help him to become a core fixture in the JSA's own title in the 1970s. This storyline features brute force villains (Solomon Grundy and Blockbuster) and introduces a villain on a cosmic level, the Anti-Matter Man. It's a good thing Spectre is on hand to help bring up the power level on both teams.

Using the *Batman* TV show's popularity, the 1967 crossover featured some Golden Age legends with the reintroduction of the Earth-2 Wonder Woman and the return of the original Robin, in a new hybrid costume of his and Batman's. At the start of this adventure, Robin finally joins the JSA. Of course, he won't appear in another crossover event for five years. *JLA* #55-56 also included the JLA's Superman, Green Arrow, Flash, and Green Arrow, and the JSA's Hawkman, Hourman, Wildcat, Mr. Terrific, and Johnny Thunder. This story involves black spheres from a dark matter universe creating supervillains that the heroes must defeat together.

Summer 1968 contained the reinvention of a Golden Age character, rather than a reintroduction. In the Golden Age, the Red Tornado was a comic relief character, a housewife who dressed up to fight crime. She even had a cameo in *All Star Comics* #3. But, the new Red Tornado is an android and the first major new Earth-2 character to be introduced since the universe was revealed. *JLA* #64-65 was a JSA-centric issue, featuring Hawkman, Green Lantern, Flash, Hourman, Starman, Sandman, Atom, Dr. Fate, Dr. Mid-Nite, Mr. Terrific, Black Canary, and of course, Red Tornado II. The villain of the story is Earth-1 villain T.O. Morrow, who escapes to Earth-2 and creates the robot, Red Tornado as part of a plot to destroy the JSA.

Dennis O'Neil penned his first JLA/JSA crossover in 1969, and it's an important one. *JLA* #73-74 not only give Golden Age Superman his first Silver Age appearance, but this storyline ends with Black Canary's husband Larry Lance dying. This leads into the following issue's storyline, in which Black Canary abandons Earth-2 for a new life on Earth-1 and the start of a long run with the Justice League. Sure, there's ret-con later, but that's a bunch of crossovers from now.

The 1970 summer crossover in *JLA* #82-83 featured many members of both teams and brought back Golden Age Batman for the first time. The story involves an alien being called the Creator2, who plans to merge Earth-1 and Earth-2 using Red Tornado as a pawn to do so. Ultimately, Dr. Fate and Thunderbolt must summon Spectre to save the day. And while Spectre apparently dies in the process, his death is short-lived.

JLA #91-92 in the summer of 1971 featured an alien boy, A-Rym, and his symbiotic pet, Teppy, who are separated into different universes, resulting in misunderstandings and mayhem. Solomon Grundy was also thrown into the mix (again). Robin of the JSA finally makes a return appearance, and for symmetry, Robin of Earth-1 also appears. The cover of the first part even has two columns of heroes featured in this story like Superman, Flash, Green Lantern, Hawkman, Atom, and Robin. While other heroes appear on the JLA side, it is the first time no one without an Earth-1 counterpart appears on the JSA side.

The JLA and JSA's tenth meeting was a major event. For the first time, it was a three-part story in #100-102. Written by Len Wein, this storyline brings back many JLA allies from the series, along with ten members of the JSA. In addition, this story reintroduces the Seven Solders of Victory back into continuity. This other super-team of the Golden Age comprised of Earth-2 heroes like Crimson Avenger, Green Arrow and Speedy, The Shining Knight, Star Spangled Kid and Stripesy, and the Vigilante. Apparently, the reason these heroes have been missing is the villainous Nebula Man, who flung them across time. The heroes must divide to find these stranded heroes, while also determining who is buried at the tomb

of the Unknown Soldier of Victory. This story culminates in the revelation of who is buried at the grave, and also the loss of a member of the JSA. (Don't worry, like the Spectre, he gets better, less than a year later).

Crisis on Earth-X is the focus of the JLA/JSA crossover from 1973. Told in *JLA* #107-108, this story introduces a new universe, one in which the Nazis won World War II, and it brings the old Quality characters into the DC Universe, under the team name, The Freedom Fighters. Uncle Sam, The Ray, Phantom Lady, Dollman, Black Condor, and the Human Bomb have been fighting Nazis for decades. And finally with some reinforcements, they can change the course of history on their Earth.

The 1974 *JLA* #113 crossover is a rarity, because it is one of two times that the annual team-up only lasted one issue "The Creature in the Velvet Cage." This story reveals the fate of Sandman's Golden Age boy sidekick Sandy, the Golden Boy. This smaller, quieter story also features a trimmed down cast on both teams, with only eight heroes in total, compared to the previous year's 13.

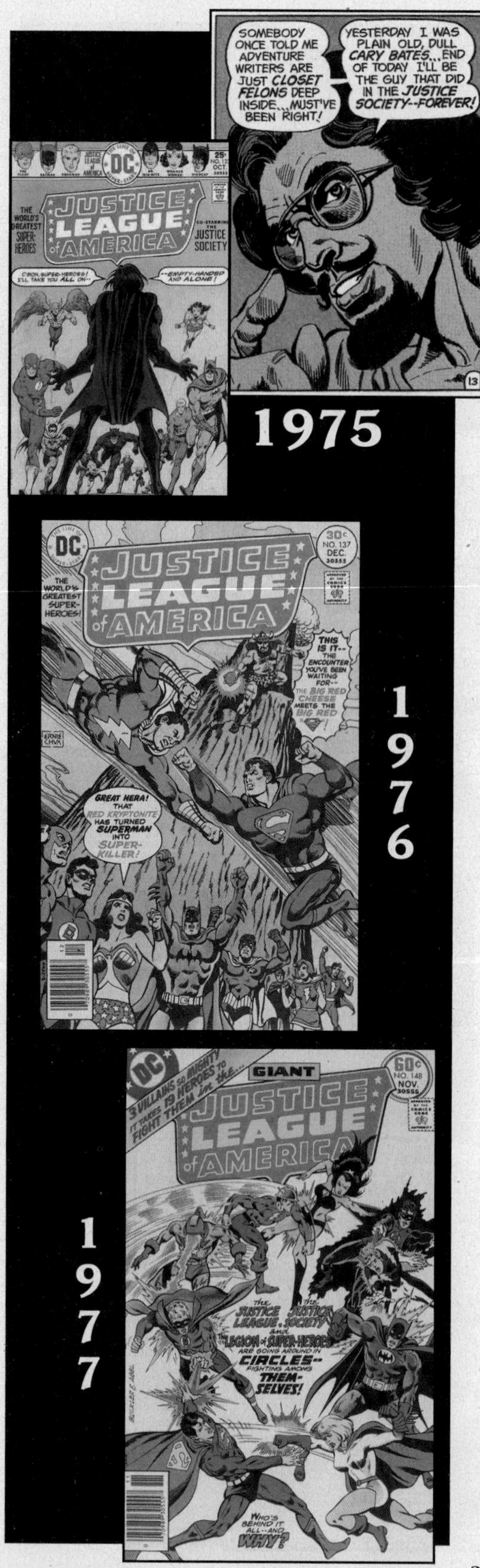

The '70s were a weird time, and a fine example was the 1975 crossover, *JLA* #123-124, written by Cary Bates and Elliot S. Maggin, where the main villain of the story is...Cary Bates. Using the Flash's cosmic treadmill, they travel to Earth-1 and Earth-2, where Bates becomes a supervillain and winds up tricking the JLA into killing the JSA, thinking that they are in fact the Injustice Society of America. This storyline also features the return of the Spectre, who, in the end, winds up helping the JSA become less dead.

It had been a few years since the JLA/JSA crossovers introduced a new universe and a new super-team. The 1976 three-parter in #135-137 featured the return of the Fawcett comic heroes. Bulletman, Bulletgirl, Ibid, Mr. Scarlet and Pinky, and Spy Smasher, along with the already reintroduced Marvel Family (Captain Marvel, Mary Marvel, and Captain Marvel Jr.). The JLA and JSA travel to Earth-S (for Shazam) in "Crisis In Eternity." The Fawcett heroes are called Shazam's Squadron of Justice, and our gathering of heroes face a multitude of villains from each of the three earths, under the leadership of Captain Marvel's old foe, King Kull. Before the story's end (thanks to Red Kryptonite), we get a fight between the powerhouses of Superman and Captain Marvel.

The significance of the 1977 crossover in *JLA* #147-148 revealed that the JSA line-up was connected to the current *All Star Comics* line-up, and the JSA finally had their own title again. Power Girl makes her first appearance in a JLA/JSA team-up, while Wildcat and Star Spangled Kid have cameos. In keeping with the more heroes than you can shake a stick at tradition, this one features our heroes joining forces to aid the Legion of Super-Heroes against Mordru, the Demons Three, and Psycho Pirate.

In 1978's *JLA* #159-160 "Crisis from Yesterday," the Time Lord pits our team against a random gathering of heroes from DC's past, including Jonah Hex, Black Pirate, Enemy Ace, Miss Liberty, and the Viking Prince. This crossover includes the newly introduced Huntress from the pages of *All Star Comics*, as well as the Wonder Woman of Earth-2, who was not an active member at the time.

By 1979, the adventures of the Justice Society had moved from *All Star Comics* over to *Adventure Comics*, and there was even a lead-in to that year's crossover in those pages when Mr. Terrific shows up to join the annual meet and greet, and was promptly killed. (He had last appeared in the 1972 crossover.) Now, there had been JSA members in the past who had died and gotten better. But, hot on the heels of the death of the Golden Age Batman, Mr. Terrific's death was permanent. Turns out he was murdered by his old enemy, the Spirit King, in possession of the Golden Age Flash's body. At the end, the villain escapes and the JSA vows to bring Terrific's killer to justice.

The following year, in another three-part adventure, the JLA and JSA meet the New Gods to face Darkseid and his minions. Sadly, longtime JLA artist Dick Dillin passed away after drawing the first part of this story in #183. He was succeeded by George Pérez, which started his significant run on this title with the second part of the story.

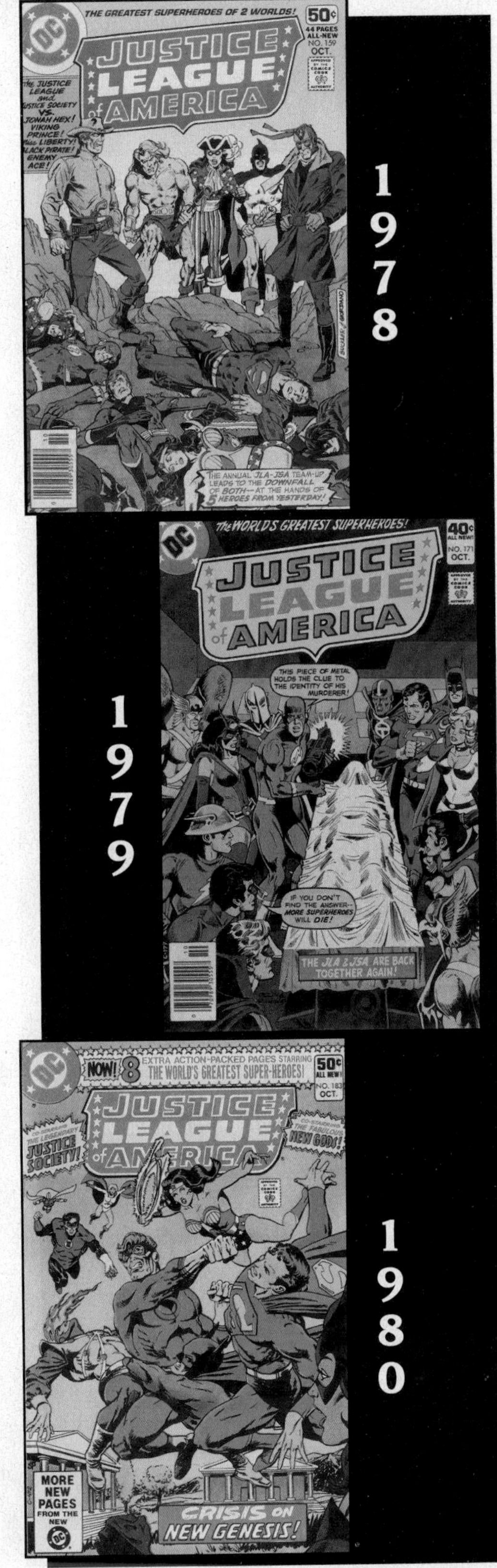

In 1981, the Ultra-Humanite built a new Secret Society of Super-Villains, with a group comprised of villains from Earth-1 and Earth-2. The genius gorilla has a plan to shift the cosmic balance by removing ten specific heroes and putting them in limbo. This three-part adventure takes place in *JLA* #195-197 with pencils by George Pérez.

By 1982, the new adventures on Earth-2 were stories from WWII found in the pages of *All Star Squadron*. So, it was only logical that the three-part crossover between the JLA and JSA also involves time travel back to the time of these great heroes of WWII. The Crime Syndicate of America, the evil versions of the JLA from Earth-3, along with time manipulator Per Degaton cause chaos across multiple universes.

The *JLA* #219-220 crossover in 1983, written by Roy Thomas and Gerry Conway, was a smaller scale story that revived the Crime Champions from the first JLA/JSA crossover, and the evil Johnny Thunder of Earth-1. More importantly, it reveals the true fate of the original Black Canary and the fact that the heroine who moved to Earth-1 was actually the daughter of the original, implanted with the memories of her mother by Johnny Thunder's Thunderbolt.

A two-part tale in *JLA* #231-232 featured another smaller grouping, as the two teams dealt with the evil Commander and the Crime Syndicate. It also introduces the Champion family, who are heavily linked to this story's battle. This story also features non-JLA heroine Supergirl.

The last JLA/JSA crossover, which is only the second crossover to be a single issue, came out in 1985. *JLA* #244 "The Final Crisis" also includes Infinity Inc, the Earth-2 successors to the JSA. But, most importantly, this is a "Crisis on Infinite Earths" tie-in, signaling the end of the multiverse (for a time). With the destruction of the parallel universe and the complete restructuring of DC's history, this series of summer stories came to an end.

1984

Overall, the JLA/JSA annual event was a reader favorite and something that was looked forward to by many. How would they top themselves this year? Which heroes would participate? And what evil would take the combined forces of these two great teams to defeat? Year after year, these stories answered the high expectations of the readers, and remain enduring favorites to this day.

1985

WHEN AUCTIONING YOUR COMICS, THERE'S ONLY ONE CHOICE.

COMICCONNECT

	TRADITIONAL AUCTIONS	INTERNET AUCTIONS	COMIC CONNECT
CBCS/CGC SELLER'S PREMIUMS	15%	10%	10%
BUYER'S PREMIUMS	20%	3%	OPTIONAL BUYER'S PREMIUM!
CONSIGNOR'S TOTAL COST	35%	13%	10%
PRINT CATALOG	YES	NO	YES
CA$H ADVANCES	1% INTEREST/MONTH	1% INTEREST/MONTH	INTEREST FREE!
TIME PAYMENTS	3% INTEREST/MONTH	1.5% INTEREST/MONTH	INQUIRE
MEDIA COVERAGE	SOME	BARELY	ALWAYS IN THE NEWS

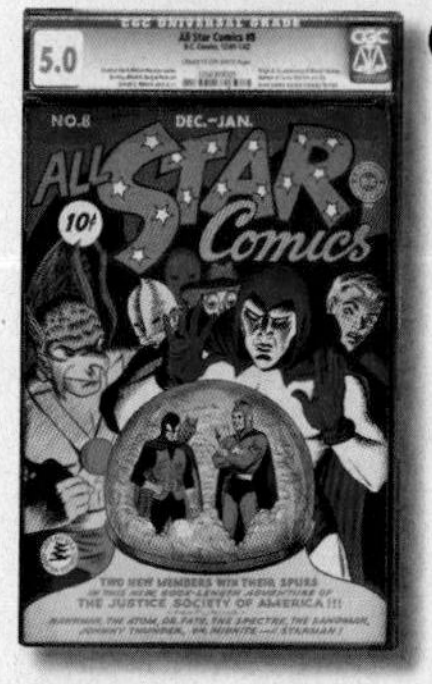

"After inheriting my grandfather's collection, I knew I'd only have one chance to make the right choice in selling it. I looked at all my options and ComicConnect was clearly the only way to go. The amazing prices they got for the comics for my family was a dream come true."

- Barbara R.

"They treated me like family. Their incredible efforts in promoting my collection put a lot more money in my pocket. I met with other auction houses before making my decision and I am so glad I went with ComicConnect."

- John W.

CONSIGN WITH US TODAY! QES YOUR COMICS!
36 WEST 37TH STREET, 6TH FLOOR, NEW YORK, NY 10018
P: 888.779.7377 | Int'l: 001.212.895.3999 | F: 212.260.4304
www.comicconnect.com | support@comicconnect.com

WHERE THE ACTION IS!

COMICCONNECT IS THE WORLD'S PREMIER ONLINE COMIC MARKETPLACE & AUCTIONEER

SOLD! $3,550,000

SOLD! $3,250,000

SOLD! $2,604,750

SOLD! $2,428,000

SOLD! $1,638,759

SOLD! $1,500,000

SOLD! $1,250,000

SOLD! $1,100,000

In 16 years, we've sold more record breaking books than anybody else!

ComicConnect was the first to sell a comic book for $1 MILLION!

ComicConnect brokered many of the most expensive comics ever sold!

ComicConnect has the BEST buyers and sellers! We are where the ACTION is!

IMMEDIATE CASH ADVANCES · SUPER FAST PAYMENT · FREE PRINT & ONLINE COLOR EVENT AUCTION CATALOG
TIME PAYMENTS AVAILABLE · PHONE & ABSENTEE BIDDING · SMALL COMMISSION · OPTIONAL BUYER'S PREMIUM

CONTACT US TODAY FOR A FREE CONSULTATION!

VINCENT ZURZOLO
PRESIDENT

COMIC CONNECT

36 W 37TH ST, FL. 6, NEW YORK, NEW YORK, 10018
P: 888.779.7377 | INT'L: 001.212.895.3999 | F: 212.260.4304
www.comicconnect.com | support@comicconnect.com

The correct title listing for each comic book can be determined by consulting the indicia (publication data) on the beginning interior pages of the comic. The official title is determined by those words of the title in capital letters only, and not by what is on the cover. Titles are listed in this book as if they were one word, ignoring spaces, hyphens, and apostrophes, to make finding titles easier. Exceptions are made in rare cases. Comic books listed should be assumed to be in color unless noted "B&W".

PRICING IN THIS GUIDE: Prices for **GD 2.0** (Good), **VG 4.0** (Very Good), **FN 6.0** (Fine), **VF 8.0** (Very Fine), **VF/NM 9.0** (Very Fine/Near Mint),and **NM– 9.2** (Near Mint–) are listed in whole U.S. dollars except for prices below $7 which show dollars and cents. **The minimum price listed is $3.00**, the cover price for current new comics. Many books listed at this price can be found in $1.00 boxes at conventions and dealers stores.

A-1 (See A-One)

A&A: THE ADVENTURES OF ARCHER & ARMSTRONG
Valiant Entertainment: Mar, 2016 - No. 12, Feb, 2017 ($3.99)

1-12: 1-Rafer Roberts-s/David Lafuente-a. 5-Faith app. 5-12-Norton-a 4.00
10-Cat cosplay photo variant-c 4.00

AARDVARK COMICS (Reprints from Cerebus in Hell)(Also see Batvark)
Aardvark-Vanaheim: Sept, 2017 ($4.00, B&W)

1-Cerebus figures placed over original Gustave Doré artwork of Hell; Action #1-c swipe 4.00

ABADAZAD
CrossGen (Code 6): Mar, 2004 - No. 3, May, 2004 ($2.95)

1-3-Ploog-a/c; DeMatteis-s 3.00
1-2nd printing with new cover 3.00

ABATTOIR
Radical Comics: Oct, 2010 - No. 6, Aug, 2011 ($3.99/$3.50, limited series)

1-($3.99) Cansino-a/Levin & Peteri-s 4.00
2-6-($3.50) 3.50

ABBIE AN' SLATS (...With Becky No. 1-4) (See Comics On Parade, Fight for Love, Giant Comics Edition 2, Giant Comics Editions #1, Sparkler Comics, Tip Topper, Treasury of Comics, & United Comics)
United Features Syndicate: 1940; March, 1948 - No. 4, Aug, 1948 (Reprints)

	GD 2.0	VG 4.0	FN 6.0	VF 8.0	VF/NM 9.0	NM- 9.2
Single Series 25 ('40)	43	86	129	271	461	650
Single Series 28	37	74	111	222	361	500
1 (1948)	20	40	60	114	182	250
2-4: 3-r/Sparkler #68-72	12	24	36	69	97	125

ABBOTT
BOOM! Studios: Jan, 2018 - No. 5, May, 2018 ($3.99, limited series)

	GD 2.0	VG 4.0	FN 6.0	VF 8.0	VF/NM 9.0	NM- 9.2
1-Saladin Ahmed-s/Sami Kivelä; red regular-c	3	6	9	14	20	25
1-Yellow-c by Micaela Dawn	2	4	6	11	16	20
1-Blue-c by Tula Lotay	3	6	9	14	20	25
1-Second printing with purple-c by Tag Tenfold	2	4	6	8	10	12
2	1	3	4	6	8	10
3-5						4.00

ABBOTT AND COSTELLO (...Comics)(See Giant Comics Editions #1 & Treasury of Comics)
St. John Publishing Co.: Feb, 1948 - No. 40, Sept, 1956 (Mort Drucker-a in most issues)

	GD 2.0	VG 4.0	FN 6.0	VF 8.0	VF/NM 9.0	NM- 9.2
1	97	194	291	621	1061	1500
2	58	116	174	371	638	900
3-9 (#8, 8/49; #9, 2/50)	37	74	111	218	354	490
10-Son of Sinbad story by Kubert (new)	41	82	123	250	418	585
11,13-20 (#11, 10/50; #13, 8/51; #15, 12/52)	25	50	75	147	241	335
12-Movie issue	28	56	78	154	252	350
21-30: 28-r/#8. 29,30-Painted-c	18	36	54	107	169	230
31-40: 33,36,38-Reprints	15	30	45	86	133	180
3-D #1 (11/53, 25¢)-Infinity-c	35	70	105	208	339	470

ABBOTT AND COSTELLO (TV)
Charlton Comics: Feb, 1968 - No. 22, Aug, 1971 (Hanna-Barbera)

	GD 2.0	VG 4.0	FN 6.0	VF 8.0	VF/NM 9.0	NM- 9.2
1	8	16	24	54	102	155
2	5	10	15	30	50	70
3-10	4	8	12	25	40	55
11-22	3	6	9	21	33	45

ABBOTT: 1973
BOOM! Studios: Jan, 2021 - No. 5, May, 2021 ($3.99, limited series)

1-5-Saladin Ahmed-s/Sami Kivelä 4.00

ABC (See America's Best TV Comics)

ABC: A-Z (one-shots)
America's Best Comics: Nov, 2005 - July, 2006 ($3.99, one-shots)

... Greyshirt and Cobweb (1/06) character bios; Veitch-s/a; Gebbie-a; Dodson-c 6.00
... Terra Obscura and Splash Brannigan (3/06) character bios; Barta-a; Dodson-c 6.00
... Tom Strong and Jack B. Quick (11/05) character bios; Sprouse-a; Nowlan-a; Dodson-c 4.00
... Top Ten and Teams (7/06) character bios; Ha & Cannon-a; Veitch-a; Dodson-c 4.00

ABE SAPIEN... (Hellboy character)
Dark Horse Comics: Apr, 2013 - No. 36, Aug, 2016 ($3.50/$3.99)

1-33: 1,2-Subtitled "Dark and Terrible"; Mignola & Allie-s/Fiumara-a/c. 8-Oeming-a. 23-Hellboy app.; Nowlan-a 3.50
34-36-($3.99) 4.00
...: Drums of the Dead (3/98, $2.95) 1-Thompson-a. Hellboy back-up; Mignola-s/a/c 4.00
...: The Abyssal Plain (6/10 - No. 2, 7/10, $3.50) 1,2-Mignola & Arcudi-s/Snejbjerg-a 3.50
...: The Devil Does Not Jest (9/11 - No. 2, 10/11, $3.50) Mignola & Arcudi-s. 1-Two covers by Johnson & Francavilla 3.50
...: The Drowning (2/08 - No. 5, 6/08, $2.99) 1-5-Mignola-s/c; Alexander-a 3.50
...: The Haunted Boy (10/09, $3.50) 1-Mignola & Arcudi-s/Reynolds-a/Johnson-c 3.50

ABIGAIL AND THE SNOWMAN
Boom Entertainment (KaBOOM!): Dec, 2014 - No. 4, Mar, 2015 ($3.99, limited series)

1-4-Roger Langridge-s/a. 1-Covers by Langridge & Liew 4.00

A. BIZARRO
DC Comics: Jul, 1999 - No. 4, Oct, 1999 ($2.50, limited series)

1-4-Gerber-s/Bright-a 4.00

ABOMINATIONS (See Hulk)
Marvel Comics: Dec, 1996 - No. 3, Feb, 1997 ($1.50, limited series)

1-3-Future Hulk storyline 4.00

ABRAHAM LINCOLN LIFE STORY (See Dell Giants)

ABRAHAM STONE
Marvel Comics (Epic): July, 1995 - No. 2, Aug, 1995 ($6.95, limited series)

1,2-Joe Kubert-s/a 7.00

ABSENT-MINDED PROFESSOR, THE (see Shaggy Dog & The... under Movie Comics)

ABSOLUTE CARNAGE
Marvel Comics: Oct, 2019 - No. 5, Jan, 2020 ($7.99/$4.99, limited series)

	GD 2.0	VG 4.0	FN 6.0	VF 8.0	VF/NM 9.0	NM- 9.2
1-($7.99) Donny Cates-s/Ryan Stegman-a; Venom, Carnage Spider-Man app.	2	4	6	9	12	15

2-5-($4.99) 2-Miles Morales & The Grendel Symbiote app. 3-Hulk app. 5-Knull freed 6.00
...: Avengers 1 (12/19, $4.99) Captain America, Hawkeye, The Thing, Wolverine app. 5.00
...: Captain Marvel 1 (1/20, $4.99) Carnage possesses the Flerkin Chewie 5.00
...: Immortal Hulk 1 (12/19, $4.99) Ewing-s/Andrade-a; Betty Ross & Venom app. 6.00
...: Separation Anxiety 1 (10/19, $4.99) The Life Foundation symbiotes app. 6.00
...: Symbiote of Vengeance 1 (11/19, $4.99) Ghost Rider vs. Carnage 5.00
...: Symbiote Spider-Man 1 (11/19, $4.99) Peter David-s; White Rabbit app. 5.00
...: Weapon Plus 1 (1/20, $4.99) Raffaele-a; Weapon Plus vs. Carnage 5.00

ABSOLUTE CARNAGE: LETHAL PROTECTORS
Marvel Comics: Oct, 2019 - No. 3, Dec, 2019 ($3.99, limited series)

1-Iron Fist, Misty Knight, Cloak & Dagger, Firestar & Morbius 6.00
2,3 4.00

ABSOLUTE CARNAGE: MILES MORALES
Marvel Comics: Oct, 2019 - No. 3, Dec, 2019 ($3.99, limited series)

1-Scorpion & Silver Sable app.; Ahmed-s/Vicentini-a 6.00
2,3 4.00

ABSOLUTE CARNAGE: SCREAM
Marvel Comics: Oct, 2019 - No. 3, Dec, 2019 ($3.99, limited series)

1-3-Bunn-s/Sandoval-a; Andi Benton app. 4.00

ABSOLUTE CARNAGE VS. DEADPOOL
Marvel Comics: Oct, 2019 - No. 3, Dec, 2019 ($3.99, limited series)

1-Tieri-s/Ferreira-a; Spider-Man app. 6.00
2,3 4.00

ABSOLUTE VERTIGO
DC Comics (Vertigo): Winter, 1995 (99¢, mature)

	GD 2.0	VG 4.0	FN 6.0	VF 8.0	VF/NM 9.0	NM- 9.2
nn-1st app. Preacher. Previews upcoming titles including Jonah Hex: Riders of the Worm, The Invisibles (King Mob), The Eaters, Ghostdancing & Preacher	2	4	6	10	14	18

ABSOLUTION
AWA Studios: Jul, 2022 - No. 5, Nov, 2022 ($3.99, limited series)

1-5-Peter Milligan-s/Mike Deodato Jr.-a. 1-Frank Cho-c 4.00

ABYSS, THE (Movie)
Dark Horse Comics: June, 1989 - No. 2, July, 1989 ($2.25, limited series)

1,2-Adaptation of film; Kaluta & Moebius-a 5.00

ACCELERATE
DC Comics (Vertigo): Aug, 2000 - No. 4, Nov, 2000 ($2.95, limited series)

1-4-Pander Bros.-a/Kadrey-s 3.00

ACCLAIM ADVENTURE ZONE
Acclaim Books: 1997 ($4.50, digest size)

	GD 2.0	VG 4.0	FN 6.0	VF 8.0	VF/NM 9.0	NM- 9.2
... Ninjak The Boss	3	6	9	19	30	40
... Turok Dinosaur Rodeo, ... Turok Extinction	1	3	4	6	8	10

ACCUSED, THE (Civil War II tie-in)
Marvel Comics: Oct, 2016 ($4.99, one-shot)

1-The trial of Hawkeye; Matt Murdock app.; Guggenheim-s/Bachs & Brown-a/Mack-c 5.00

ACE COMICS
David McKay Publications: Apr, 1937 - No. 151, Oct-Nov, 1949 (All contain some newspaper strip reprints)

	GD 2.0	VG 4.0	FN 6.0	VF 8.0	VF/NM 9.0	NM- 9.2
1-Jungle Jim by Alex Raymond, Blondie, Ripley's Believe It Or Not, Krazy Kat begin (1st app. of each)	383	766	1149	2681	4691	6700
2	118	236	348	742	1271	1800
3-5	73	146	219	467	798	1125
6-10	57	114	171	362	619	875
11-The Phantom begins (1st app., 2/38) (in brown costume)	541	1082	1623	3950	6975	10,000
12-20	43	86	129	271	461	650
21-25,27-30	39	78	117	240	395	550
26-Origin & 1st app. Prince Valiant (5/39); begins series?	206	412	618	1318	2259	3200
31-40: 37-Krazy Kat ends	24	48	72	142	234	325
41-60	15	30	45	92	144	195
61-64,66-76-(7/43; last 68 pgs.)	14	28	42	82	121	160
65-(8/42)-Flag-c	24	48	72	142	234	325
77-84 (3/44; all 60 pgs.)	13	26	39	72	101	130
85-99 (52 pgs.)	11	22	33	62	86	110
100 (7/45; last 52 pgs.)	13	26	39	72	101	130
101-134: 128-(11/47)-Brick Bradford begins. 134-Last Prince Valiant (all 36 pgs.)	10	20	30	58	79	100
135-151: 135-(6/48)-Lone Ranger begins	10	20	30	54	72	90

ACE KELLY (See Tops Comics & Tops In Humor)

ACE KING (See Adventures of Detective...)

ACES
Acme Press (Eclipse): Apr, 1988 - No. 5, Dec, 1988 ($2.95, B&W, magazine)

Abbott and Costello #1 © CC

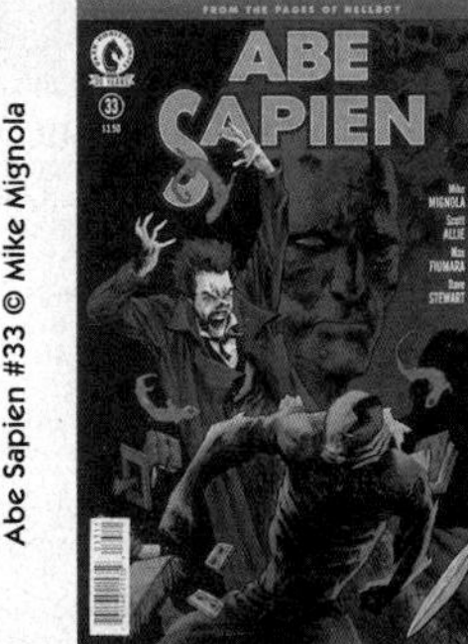

Abe Sapien #33 © Mike Mignola

Action Comics #7 © DC

	GD 2.0	VG 4.0	FN 6.0	VF 8.0	VF/NM 9.0	NM- 9.2

1,2 — 6.00
3-5 — 3.00

ACES HIGH
E.C. Comics: Mar-Apr, 1955 - No. 5, Nov-Dec, 1955

1-Not approved by code 41 82 123 256 428 600
2 23 46 69 138 227 315
3-5 21 42 63 124 202 280

NOTE: *All have stories by* ***Davis, Evans, Krigstein****, and* ***Wood. Evans*** *c-1-5.*

ACES HIGH
Gemstone Publishing: Apr, 1999 - No. 5, Aug, 1999 ($2.50)

1-Reprints E.C. issue 1 3 4 6 8 10
2-5-Reprints E.C. issues 6.00
Annual 1 ($13.50) r/#1-5 14.00

ACME NOVELTY LIBRARY, THE
Fantagraphics Books: Winter 1993-94 - Present (quarterly, various sizes)

1-Introduces Jimmy Corrigan; Chris Ware-s/a in all 3 6 9 17 26 35
1-2nd and later printings 1 3 4 6 8 10
2,3: 2-Quimby 2 4 6 10 14 18
4-Sparky's Best Comics & Stories 3 6 9 14 20 25
5-12: Jimmy Corrigan in all 2 4 6 9 12 15
13,15-($10.95-c) 2 4 6 11 16 20
14-($12.95-c) Concludes Jimmy Corrigan saga 22.00
16,19-($15.95, hardcover) Rusty Brown 22.00
17-($16.95, hardcover) Rusty Brown 22.00
18-($17.95, hardcover) 22.00
Jimmy Corrigan, The Smartest Kid on Earth (2000, Pantheon Books, Hardcover, $27.50, 380 pgs.) Collects Jimmy Corrigan stories; folded dust jacket 28.00
Jimmy Corrigan, The Smartest Kid on Earth (2003, Softcover, $17.95) 18.00

NOTE: *Multiple printings exist for most issues.*

ACROSS THE UNIVERSE: THE DC UNIVERSE STORIES OF ALAN MOORE (Also see DC Universe: The Stories of Alan Moore)
DC Comics: 2003 ($19.95, TPB)

nn-Reprints selected Moore stories from '85-'87; Superman, Batman, Swamp Thing app. 20.00

ACTION ADVENTURE (War) (Formerly Real Adventure)
Gillmor Magazines: V1#2, June, 1955 - No. 4, Oct, 1955

V1#2-4 9 18 27 50 65 80

ACTION COMICS (...Weekly #601-642) (Also see The Comics Magazine #1, More Fun #14-17 & Special Edition) (Also see Promotional Comics section)
National Periodical Publ./Detective Comics/DC Comics: 6/38 - No. 583, 9/86; No. 584, 1/87 - No. 904, Oct, 2011

1-Origin & 1st app. Superman by Siegel & Shuster, Marco Polo, Tex Thomson, Pep Morgan, Chuck Dawson & Scoop Scanlon; 1st app. Zatara & Lois Lane; Superman story missing 4 pgs. which were included when reprinted in Superman #1; Clark Kent works for Daily Star; story continued in #2 347,000 694,000 1,214,500 2,429,000 4,514,500 6,600,000
1-Reprint, Oversize 13-1/2x10". **WARNING:** for its size. DC published it in 1974 with a second cover titling it as a Famous First Edition. There have been many reported cases of the outer cover being removed and the interior sold as the original edition. The reprint with the new outer cover removed is practically worthless. See Famous First Edition for value.
2-O'Mealia non-Superman covers thru #6 15,600 31,200 46,800 117,000 203,500 290,000
3 (Scarce)-Superman apps. in costume in only one panel 9300 18,600 27,900 69,800 120,900 172,000
4,5 4150 8300 12,450 31,100 54,050 77,000
6-1st Jimmy Olsen (called office boy) 4200 8400 12,600 31,500 54,750 78,000
7-1st time the name Superman is printed on a comic cover; 2nd Superman cover 50,400 100,800 151,200 302,400 466,200 630,000
8,9 3250 6500 9750 24,400 42,200 60,000
10-3rd Superman cover by Shuster; splash panel used as cover art for Superman #1 33,200 66,400 99,600 199,200 307,100 415,000
11,14: 1st X-Ray Vision? 14-Clip Carson begins, ends #41; Zatara-c 1620 3240 4860 12,150 21,075 30,000
12-Has 1 panel Batman ad for Det. #27 (5/39); Zatara sci-fi cover 3800 7600 11,400 28,500 49,250 70,000
13-Shuster Superman-c; last Scoop Scanlon; centerspread has a 2-page ad for Superman #1 18,700 37,400 56,100 112,200 168,600 225,000
15-Guardineer Superman-c; has ad mentioning Detective Comics and Batman; full page ad for New York World's Fair 1939 with 25¢-c 3350 6700 10,050 25,000 43,500 62,000
16-Has full page ad and 1 panel ad for New York World's Fair 1939 25¢ cover edition 865 1730 2595 6500 11,250 16,000
17-Superman cover; last Marco Polo; full page ad for New York World's Fair 1939 with 15¢-c 2050 4100 6150 15,400 26,700 38,000
18-Origin 3 Aces; has a 1 panel ad for New York World's Fair 1939 at the end of the Superman story (ad also in #16,17,19) 865 1730 2595 6500 11,250 16,000
19-Superman covers begin 1950 3900 5850 14,600 25,300 36,000
20-The 'S' left off Superman's chest; Clark Kent works at 'Daily Star' 1900 3800 5700 14,250 24,625 35,000
21-Has 2 ads for More Fun #52 (1st Spectre) 1000 2000 3000 7400 13,200 19,000
22 811 1622 2433 5920 10,460 15,000
23-1st app. Luthor (w/red hair) & Black Pirate; Black Pirate by Moldoff; 1st mention of The Daily Planet (4/40)-Has 1 panel ad for Spectre in More Fun 5625 11,250 16,875 39,400 64,700 90,000
24,25: 24-Kent at Daily Planet. 25-Last app. Gargantua T. Potts, Tex Thomson's sidekick 541 1082 1623 3950 6975 10,000
26,28,30 481 962 1443 3511 6206 8900
27-(8/40) 1st Lois Lane-c 541 1082 1623 3950 6975 10,000
29-2nd Lois Lane-c 541 1082 1623 3950 6975 10,000
31,32: 32-Intro/1st app. Krypto Ray Gun in Superman story by Burnley 343 686 1029 2400 4200 6000
33-Origin Mr. America; Superman by Burnley; has half page ad for All Star Comics #3 371 742 1113 2600 4550 6500
34,35,38,39 314 628 951 2251 3976 5700
36,40: 36-Classic robot-c. 40-(9/41)-Intro/1st app. Star Spangled Kid & Stripesy; Jerry Siegel photo 389 778 1167 2723 4762 6800
37-Origin Congo Bill 331 662 993 2317 4059 5800
41,43-46,48-50: 44-Fat Man's i.d. revealed to Mr. America. 45-1st app. Stuff (Vigilante's Asian sidekick) 300 600 900 2010 3505 5000
42-1st app./origin Vigilante; Bob Daley becomes Fat Man; origin Mr. America's magic flying carpet; The Queen Bee & Luthor app; Black Pirate ends; not in #41 309 618 927 2163 3782 5400
47-1st Luthor cover in comics (4/42) 432 864 1296 3154 5577 8000
51-1st app. The Prankster 300 600 900 1980 3440 4900
52-Fat Man & Mr. America become the Ameri-commandos; origin Vigilante retold; classic Superman and back-ups-c 389 778 1167 2723 4762 6800
53-56,59: 56-Last Fat Man 271 542 813 1734 2967 4200
57-3rd Lois Lane-c in Action (2/43) 271 542 813 1734 2967 4200
58-"Slap a Jap"-c 514 1028 1542 3750 6625 9500
60-First app. Lois Lane as Super-woman 300 600 900 2010 3505 5000
61-Historic Atomic Radiation-c (6/43) 310 620 930 2170 3885 5600
62-Japan war-c 271 542 813 1734 2967 4200
63-Japan war-c; last 3 Aces 371 742 1113 2600 4550 6500
64-Intro Toyman 226 452 678 1446 2473 3500
65-70: 66-69-Kubert-i on Vigilante 183 366 549 1171 2011 2850
71-79: 74-Last Mr. America 145 290 435 928 1589 2250
80-2nd app. & 1st Mr. Mxyztplk-c (1/45) 181 362 543 1158 1979 2800
81-88,90: 83-Intro Hocus & Pocus 132 264 396 845 1448 2050
89-Classic rainbow cover 168 336 504 1075 1838 2600
91-99: 93-X-Mas-c. 99-1st small logo (8/46) 113 226 339 723 1237 1750
100 155 310 465 992 1696 2400
101-Nuclear explosion-c (10/46) 290 580 870 1856 3178 4500
102-Mxyztplk-c 113 226 339 723 1237 1750
103,104,106,107,109-116,118-120 106 212 318 682 1166 1650
105,117-Christmas covers 113 226 339 723 1237 1750
108-Classic molten metal-c 155 310 465 992 1696 2400
121,122,124-126,128-140: 135,136,138-Zatara by Kubert 100 200 300 640 1095 1550
123-(8/48) Superman flies (See Superman #30 for 1st time he flies, not leaps) 142 284 426 909 1555 2200
127-Vigilante by Kubert; Tommy Tomorrow begins (12/48, see Real Fact #6) 106 212 318 682 1166 1650
141-150,152-155,157,159-161: 161- Last 52 pgs. 94 188 282 597 1025 1450
151-Luthor/Mr. Mxyztplk/Prankster team-up 142 284 426 909 1555 2200
156-Lois as Super Woman 116 232 348 742 1271 1800
158-Origin Superman retold 155 310 465 992 1696 2400
162-180: 168,176-Used in **POP**, pg. 90. 173-Robot-c 90 180 270 576 988 1400
181-201: 191-Intro. Janu in Congo Bill. 198-Last Vigilante. 201-Last pre-code issue 84 168 252 538 919 1300
202-220,232: 212-(1/56)-Includes 1956 Superman calendar that is part of story. 232-1st Curt Swan-c in Action 68 136 204 435 743 1050
221-231,233-240: 221-1st S.A. issue. 224-1st Golden Gorilla story. 228-(5/57)-Kongorilla in Congo Bill story (Congorilla try-out) 57 114 171 362 619 875
241,243-251: 241-Batman x-over. 248-Origin/1st app. Congorilla; Congo Bill renamed Congorilla. 251-Last Tommy Tomorrow 48 96 144 302 514 725
242-Origin & 1st app. Brainiac (7/58); 1st mention of Shrunken City of Kandor 875 1750 3500 10,500 22,750 35,000
252-Origin & 1st app. Supergirl (5/59); 1st app. Metallo 850 1700 3400 10,200 22,100 34,000
253-2nd app. Supergirl 97 194 291 621 1061 1500

GD 2.0 | VG 4.0 | FN 6.0 | VF 8.0 | VF/NM 9.0 | NM- 9.2

254-1st meeting of Bizarro & Superman-c/story; 3rd app. Supergirl 90 180 270 576 988 1400
255-1st Bizarro Lois Lane-c/story & both Bizarros leave Earth to make Bizarro World; 4th app. Supergirl 63 126 189 403 689 975
256-260: 259-Red Kryptonite used 40 80 120 244 402 575
261-1st X-Kryptonite which gave Streaky his powers; last Congorilla in Action; origin & 1st app. Streaky The Super Cat 45 90 135 284 480 675
262,264-266,268-270 34 68 102 204 332 450
263-Origin Bizarro World (continues in #264) 43 86 129 271 461 650
267(8/60)-3rd Legion app; 1st app. Chameleon Boy, Colossal Boy, & Invisible Kid, 1st app. of Supergirl as Superwoman. 78 156 228 486 831 1175
271-275,277-282: 274-Lois Lane as Superwoman. 280-Brief origin of Superman & Supergirl retold; Brainiac-c. 282-Last 10¢ issue 28 56 84 165 270 375
276(5/61)-6th Legion app; 1st app. Brainiac 5, Phantom Girl, Triplicate Girl, Bouncing Boy, Sun Boy, & Shrinking Violet; Supergirl joins Legion 97 194 291 621 1061 1500
283(12/61)-Legion of Super-Villains app. 1st 12¢ 15 30 45 103 227 350
284(1/62)-Mon-El app. 15 30 45 105 233 360
285(2/62)-12th Legion app; Brainiac 5 cameo; Supergirl's existence revealed to world; JFK & Jackie, LBJ & Khrushchev cameos 35 70 105 252 564 875
286-287,289-292,294-299: 286(3/62)-Legion of Super Villains app. 287(4/62)-15th Legion app. (cameo). 289(6/62)-16th Legion app. (Adult); Lightning Man & Saturn Woman's marriage 1st revealed. 290(7/62)-Legion app. (cameo); Phantom Girl app. 1st Supergirl emergency squad. 291-1st meeting Supergirl & Mr. Mxyzptlk. 292-2nd app. Superhorse (see Adv.#293). 297-General Zod, Phantom Zone villains & Mon-El app. 298-General Zod app.; Legion cameo 12 24 36 82 179 275
288-Mon-El app.; r-origin Supergirl 12 24 36 82 179 275
293-Origin Comet (Superhorse) 16 32 48 108 239 370
300-(5/63) 15 30 45 103 227 350
301-303,305,307,308,310-312,315-320: 307-Saturn Girl app. 317-Death of Nor-Kan of Kandor. 319-Shrinking Violet app. 9 18 27 62 126 190
304,306,313: 304-Origin/1st app. Black Flame (9/63). 306-Brainiac 5, Mon-El app. 313-Batman app. 10 20 30 64 132 200
309-(2/64)-Legion app.; Batman & Robin-c & cameo; JFK app. (he died 11/22/63; on stands last week of Dec, 1963) 14 28 42 93 204 315
314-Retells origin Supergirl; J.L.A. x-over 10 20 30 65 135 205
321-333,335-339: 336-Origin Akvar (Flamebird) 8 16 24 54 102 150
334-Giant G-20; origin Supergirl, Streaky, Superhorse & Legion (all-r) 10 20 30 70 150 230
340-Origin, 1st app. of the Parasite; 2 pg. pin-up 25 50 75 175 388 600
341,344,350,358: 341-Batman app. in Supergirl back-up story. 344-Batman x-over. 350-Batman, Green Arrow & Green Lantern app. in Supergirl back-up story. 358-Superboy meets Supergirl 7 14 21 44 82 120
342,343,345,346,348,349,351-357,359: 342-UFO story. 345-Allen Funt/Candid Camera story. 6 12 18 42 79 115
347,360-Giant Supergirl G-33,G-45; 347-Origin Comet-r plus Bizarro story. 360-Legion app.-r; r/origin Supergirl 9 18 27 59 117 175
361-2nd app. Parasite 8 16 24 51 96 140
362-364,367-372,374-378: 362-366-Leper/Death story. 370-New facts about Superman's origin. 376-Last Supergirl in Action; last 12¢-c. 377-Legion begins (thru #392) 5 10 15 35 63 90
365,366: 365-JLA & Legion app. 366-JLA app. 6 12 18 38 69 100
373-Giant Supergirl G-57; Legion-r 8 16 24 56 108 160
379,380,382-399,401: 388-Sgt. Rock app. 392-Batman-c/app.; last Legion in Action; Saturn Girl gets new costume. 393-401-All Superman issues. 395-Bonus "Secrets of Superman's Fortress" 2-page spread 4 8 12 25 40 55
381-Superman as Dictator of Earth-c/s 7 14 21 46 86 125
400 5 10 15 33 57 80
402-Last 15¢ issue; Superman vs. Supergirl duel 4 8 12 25 40 55
403-413: All 52 pg. issues. 411-Origin Eclipso-(r). 413-Metamorpho begins, ends #418 4 8 12 23 37 50
414-418,420-424: 421-Intro Capt. Strong; Green Arrow begins. 422,423-Origin Human Target 2 4 6 11 16 20
419-Intro. Human Target 6 12 18 38 69 100
425-Neal Adams-a(p); The Atom begins 3 6 9 19 30 40
426-431,433-436,438,439 2 4 6 9 13 16
432-1st Bronze Age Toyman app. (2/74) 3 6 9 19 30 40
437,443-(100 pg. Giants) 5 10 15 35 63 90
440-1st Grell-a on Green Arrow 3 6 9 15 22 28
441,442,444-448: 441-Grell-a on Green Arrow continues 2 4 6 9 13 16
449-(68 pgs.) 3 6 9 14 20 25
450-465,467-470,474-483,486,489-499: 454-Last Atom. 456-Grell Jaws-c. 458-Last Green Arrow 1 3 4 6 8 10
466,487,488: 466-Batman, Flash app. 487,488-(44 pgs.). 487-Origin & 1st app. Microwave Man; origin Atom retold 2 4 6 8 10 12
471-(5/77) 1st app. Faora Hu-Ul 3 6 9 16 23 30
472,473-Faora app. 473-Faora, General Zod app. 3 6 9 14 19 24
481-483,486-492,495-499,501-505,507,508-Whitman variants (low print run; none show issue # on cover) 3 6 9 14 20 26
484-Earth II Superman & Lois Lane wed; 40th anniversary issue(6/78) 3 6 9 16 23 30
484-Variant includes 3-D Superman punchout doll in cello. pack; 4 different inserts; (Canadian promo?) 7 14 21 44 82 120
485-Classic Neal Adams Superman-c 3 6 9 14 20 25
485-Whitman variant 4 8 12 27 44 60
500-($1.00, 68 pgs.)-Infinity-c; Superman life story retold; shows Legion statues in museum 3 6 9 15 22 28
501-520,522-543,545,547-551: 511-514-Airwave II solo stories. 513-The Atom begins. 517-Aquaman begins; ends #541. 528-530-Three-part Brainiac storyline. 532,536-New Teen Titans cameo. 535,536-Omega Men app. 551-Starfire becomes Red-Star 1 3 4 6 8 10
521-1st app. The Vixen 5 10 15 34 60 85
544-(6/83, Mando paper, 68 pgs.)-45th Anniversary issue; origins new Luthor & Brainiac; Omega Men cameo; Shuster-a (pin-up); article by Siegel 3 6 9 14 20 25
546-J.L.A., New Teen Titans app. 2 4 6 8 11 14
552,553-Animal Man, Cave Carson, Congorilla, Sea Devils-c/app.; Dolphin, Immortal Man, Rip Hunter, Suicide Squad app (2/84 & 3/84) 1 3 4 6 8 10
554-582: 577-Intro. Caitiff, the First Vampire 1 2 3 5 6 8
583-(9/86) Alan Moore scripts; last Earth 1 Superman story (cont'd from Superman #423) 3 6 9 16 23 30
584-(1/87) Byrne-a begins; New Teen Titans app. 1 2 3 5 7 9
585-599: 586-Legends x-over. 595-1st app. Silver Banshee. 596-Millennium x-over; Spectre app. 598-1st Checkmate 6.00
600-($2.50, 84 pgs., 5/88) 2 4 6 8 10 12
601-608,610-642: (#601-642 are weekly issues) ($1.50, 52 pgs.) 601-Re-intro The Secret Six; death of Katma Tui. 611-614-Catwoman stories (new costume in #611). 613-618-Nightwing stories 1 2 3 5 6 8
609-Black Canary-c by Bolland 2 4 6 8 10 12
643-Superman & monthly issues begin again; Perez-c/a/scripts begin; swipes cover to Superman #1 1 3 4 6 8 10
644-649,651-661,663-666,668-673,675-682: 645-1st app. Maxima. 654-Part 3 of Batman storyline. 655-Free extra 8 pgs. 660-Death of Lex Luthor. 661-Begin $1.00-c. 675-Deathstroke cameo. 679-Last $1.00 issue 5.00
650,667: 650-($1.50, 52 pgs.)-Lobo cameo (last panel). 667-($1.75, 52 pgs.) 6.00
662-Clark Kent reveals i.d. to Lois Lane; story cont'd in Superman #53 6.00
674-Supergirl logo & c/story (reintro) 1 3 4 6 8 10
683-1st Jackal; Doomsday cameo 3 6 9 15 22 28
683-685-2nd & 3rd printings 3.00
684,685: 684-Doomsday battle issue. 685-Funeral for a Friend issue; Supergirl app. 2 4 6 11 16 20
686-Funeral for a Friend issue; Supergirl app. 5.00
687-($1.95)-Collector's Ed.w/die-cut-c 5.00
687-($1.50)-Newsstand Edition with mini-poster 4.00
688-699,701-703-($1.50): 688-Guy Gardner-c/story. 697-Bizarro-c/story. 703-(9/94)-Zero Hour 4.00
695-($2.50)-Collector's Edition w/embossed foil-c 6.00
700-($2.95, 68 pgs.)-Fall of Metropolis Pt 1, Guice-a; Pete Ross marries Lana Lang and Smallville flashbacks with Curt Swan art & Murphy Anderson inks 6.00
700-Platinum 20.00
700-Gold 25.00
704(11/94)-719,721-731: 710-Begin $1.95-c. 714-Joker app. 719-Batman-c/app. 721-Mr. Mxyzptlk app. 723-Dave Johnson-c. 727-Final Night x-over. 4.00
720-Lois breaks off engagement w/Clark 5.00
720-2nd print. 4.00
732-749,751-764,767,767: 732-New powers. 733-New costume, Ray app. 738-Immonen-s/a(p) begins. 741-Legion app. 744-Millennium Giants x-over. 745-747-70's-style Superman vs. Prankster. 753-JLA-c/app. 757-Hawkman-c. 760-1st Encantadora. 761-Wonder Woman app. 766-Batman-c/app. 4.00
750-($2.95) 5.00
765-Joker & Harley-c/app. 2 4 6 9 13 16
768,769,771-774: 768-Begin $2.25-c; Marvel Family-c/app. 771-Nightwing-c/app. 772,773-Ra's al Ghul app. 774-Martian Manhunter-c/app. 4.00
770-($3.50) Conclusion of Emperor Joker x-over 1 2 3 5 6 8
775-($3.75) Bradstreet-c; intro. The Elite 3 6 9 15 22 28
775-(2nd printing) 2 4 6 8 10 12
776-799: 776-Farewell to Krypton; Rivoche-c. 780-782-Our Worlds at War x-over. 781-Hippolyta and Major Lane killed. 782-War ends. 784-Joker: Last Laugh; Batman & Green Lantern app. 793-Return to Krypton. 795-The Elite app. 798-Van Fleet-c 4.00
800-(4/03, $3.95) Struzan painted-c; guest artists include Ross, Jim Lee, Jurgens, Sale 2 4 6 8 10 12
801-811: 801-Raney-a. 809-The Creeper app. 811-Mr. Majestic app. 3.00
812-Godfall part 1; Turner-c; Caldwell-a(p) 4.00
812-2nd printing; B&W sketch-c by Turner 3.00
813-Godfall pt. 4; Turner-c; Caldwell-a(p) 4.00
814-824,826-828,830-834,836: 814-Reis-a/Art Adams-c; Darkseid app.; begin $2.50-c. 815,816-Teen Titans-c/app. 820-Doomsday app. 826-Capt. Marvel app. 827-Byrne-c/a begin. 831-Villains United tie-in. 836-Infinite Crisis; revised origin 3.00
825-($2.99, 40 pgs.) Doomsday app. 4.00
829-Omac Project x-over Sacrifice pt. 2 5.00
829-(2nd printing) red tone cover 4.00
835-1st Livewire app. in regular DCU 3 6 9 14 19 24
837-843-One Year Later; powers return after Infinite Crisis; Johns & Busiek-s 3.00
844-Donner & Johns-s/Adam Kubert-a/c begin; brown-toned cover 4.00
844-Andy Kubert variant-c 6.00
844-2nd printing with red-toned Adam Kubert cover 3.00
845-849,851-857: 845-Bizarro-c/app.; re-intro. General Zod, Ursa & Non. 846-Jax-Ur app. 847-849-No Kubert-a. 851-Kubert-a/c. 855-857-Bizarro app.; Powell-a/c 3.00
850-($3.99) Supergirl and LSH app., origin re-told; Guedes-a/c 4.00
858-($3.50) Legion of Super-Heroes app.; 1st meeting re-told; Johns-s/Frank-a/c 4.00
858-Variant-c (Superman & giant Brainiac robot) by Frank 5.00
858-Second printing with regular cover with red background instead of yellow 3.00
858-Special Edition (7/10, $1.00) r/#858 with "What's Next?" cover logo 3.00
859-868,870-878: 859-863-Legion of Super-Heroes app.; var-c on each (859-Andy Kubert. 860-Lightle. 861-Grell. 862-Giffen. 863-Frank) 864-Batman and Lightning Lad app. 866-Brainiac returns. 870-Pa Kent dies. 871-New Krypton; Ross-c 3.00
869-Initial printing recalled because of beer bottles on cover 9 18 27 61 123 185
869-"Soda Pop" cover edition 6.00
879-896: 879-($3.99) Back-up Capt. Atom feature begins. 890-Luthor stories begin. 893-Comics debut of Chloe Sullivan (Smallville TV show) in regular DCU. 894-Death (from Sandman) app. 896-Secret Six app. 4.00
897-899, 901-903-($2.99) 897-Joker app. 898-Larfleeze app. 899-Brainiac app. 3.00
900 (6/11, $5.99, 96 pgs.) Conclusion of Luthor Black Ring saga; Doomsday app.; bonus short stories by various; Superman renounces U.S. citizenship 6.00
904-(10/11) Last issue of first volume; Doomsday app.; Rocafort-c 4.00
904-Variant-c by Ordway 1 2 3 5 6 8
#0-(10/94) Zero Hour tie-in; released between #703 & #704 3.00
#1,000,000 (11/98) Gene Ha-c; 853rd Century x-over 3.00
Annual 1 ('87, $2.95) Art Adams-c/a(p); Batman app. 1 3 4 6 8 10
Annual 2-6 ('89-'94, $2.95)-2-Pérez-c/a(i). 3-Armageddon 2001. 4-Eclipso vs. Shazam. 5-Bloodlines; 1st app. Loose Cannon. 6-Elseworlds story 5.00
Annual 7,9 ('95, '97, $3.95) 7-Year One story. 9-Pulp Heroes story 5.00

Action Comics #473 © DC

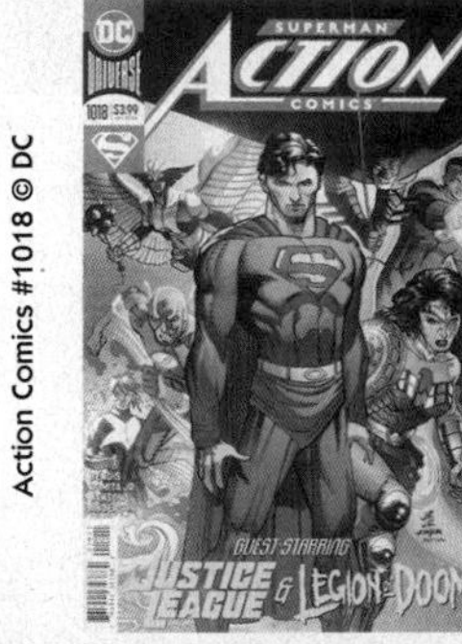

Action Comics #1018 © DC

Adam Strange Book 2 © DC

GD 2.0 | VG 4.0 | FN 6.0 | VF 8.0 | VF/NM 9.0 | NM- 9.2

Annual 8 (1996, $2.95) Legends of the Dead Earth story 5.00
Annual 10 ('07, $3.99) Short stories by Johns & Donner and various incl. A. Adams, J. Kubert, Wight, Morales; origin of Phantom Zone, Mon-El; Metallo app.; Adam & Joe Kubert-c 6.00
Annual 11 (7/08, $4.99) Conclusion to General Zod story continued from #851; Kubert-a 5.00
Annual 12 (8/09, $4.99) Origin of Nightwing and Flamebird 5.00
Annual 13 (2/11, $4.99) 1st meeting of Luthor and Darkseid; Ra's al Ghul app. 5.00

NOTE:***Supergirl's*** *origin in 262, 280, 285, 291, 305, 309.* ***N. Adams*** *c-356, 358, 359, 361-364, 366, 367, 370-374, 377-379i, 398-400, 402, 404,405, 419p, 466, 468, 469, 473i, 485.* ***Aparo*** *a-642.* ***Austin*** *c/a-682i.* ***Baily*** *a-24, 25.* ***Boring*** *a-164, 194, 211, 223, 233, 241, 250, 261, 266-268, 346, 348, 352, 356, 357.* ***Burnley*** *a-28-33; c-48?, 53-55, 58, 59?, 60-63, 65, 66p, 67p, 70p, 71p, 79p, 82p, 84-86p, 90-92p, 93p?, 94p, 107p, 108p.* ***Byrne*** *a-584-598p, 599i, 600p; c-584-591, 596-600.* ***Ditko*** *a-642.* ***Giffen*** *a-560, 563, 565, 577, 579; c-539, 560, 563, 565, 577, 579.* ***Grell*** *a-440-442, 444-446, 450-452, 456-458; c-456.* ***Guardineer*** *a-24, 25; c-8, 11, 12, 14-16, 18. 25.* ***Guice*** *a(p)-676-681, 683-698, 700; c-683, 685, 686, 687(direct), 688-693i, 694-696, 697i, 698-700.* ***Infantino*** *a-642.* ***Kaluta*** *c-613.* ***Bob Kane's*** *Clip Carson-14-41.* ***Gil Kane*** *a-443r, 493r, 539-541, 544-546, 551-554, 601-605, 642; c-535p, 540, 541, 544p, 545-549, 551-554, 580, 627.* ***Kirby*** *c-638.* ***Meskin*** *a-42-121(most).* ***Mignola*** *a-600, Annual 2; c-614.* ***Moldoff*** *a-23-25, 443r.* ***Mooney*** *a-667p.* ***Mortimer*** *c-153, 154, 159-172, 174, 178-181, 184, 186-189, 191-193, 196, 200, 206.* ***Orlando*** *a-617p; c-621.* ***Perez*** *a-600i, 643-652p, Annual 2p; c-529p, 602, 643-651, Annual 2p.* ***Quesada*** *c-Annual 4p.* ***Fred Ray*** *c-34, 36-46, 50-52.* ***Siegel & Shuster*** *a-1-27.* ***Paul Smith*** *c-608.* ***Starlin*** *a-509; c-631.* ***Leonard Starr*** *a-597i(part),* ***Staton*** *a-525p, 526p, 531p, 535p, 536p.* ***Swan/Moldoff*** *c-281, 286, 287, 293, 298, 334.* ***Thibert*** *c-676, 677p, 678-681, 684.* ***Toth*** *a-406, 407, 413, 431; c-616.* ***Tuska*** *a-486p, 550.* ***Williamson*** *a-568i.* ***Zeck*** *c-Annual 5*

ACTION COMICS (2nd series)(DC New 52)(Numbering reverts to original V1 #957 after #52)
DC Comics: Nov, 2011 - No. 52, Jul, 2016 ($3.99)

1-Grant Morrison-s/Rags Morales-a/c; re-introduces Superman
2 4 6 8 11 14
1-Variant-c by Jim Lee of Superman in new armor costume
2 4 6 11 16 20
1-(2nd - 5th printings) 4.00
2-12: 2-Morales & Brent Anderson-a; behind the scenes sketch art and commentary. 3-Gene Ha & Morales-a. 4-Re-intro. Steel. 5-Flashback to Krypton; Andy Kubert-a. 6-Legion of Super-Heroes app.; Andy Kubert-a. 7-Gets the new costume; intro. Steel 4.00
2-12-Variant covers. 2-Van Sciver. 3-Ha. 4-Choi. 5,6-Morales. 8-Frank 5.00
13-17,19-23: 13-Re-intro of Krypto. 14-Neil deGrasse Tyson app. 15-Legion app. 4.00
18-($4.99) Last Morrison-s; Mxyzptlk, The Legion and the Wanderers app. 5.00
23.1, 23.2, 23.3, 23.4 (11/13, $2.99, regular covers) 3.00
23.1 (11/13, $3.99, 3-D cover) "Cyborg Superman #1" on cover; Zor-El & Brainiac app. 5.00
23.2 (11/13, $3.99, 3-D cover) "Zod #1" on cover; origin of Zod on Krypton; Faora app. 5.00
23.3 (11/13, $3.99, 3-D cover) "Lex Luthor #1" on cover; Kuder-c 5.00
23.4 (11/13, $3.99, 3-D cover) "Metallo #1" on cover; Fisch-s/Pugh-a 5.00
24-49,51,52: 25-Zero Year. 30-Doomsday app. 31-35-Doomed x-over. 40-Bizarro app. 51-Supergirl app. 52-Wonder Woman, Batman and pre-Flashpoint Superman app. 4.00
50-($4.99) Vandal Savage and the Justice League app. 5.00
#0 (11/12, $3.99) Flashback to Lois' 1st Superman sighting; Oliver-a; 4.00
Annual 1 (12/12, $4.99) Superman vs. K-Man; Fisch-s/Hamner-a; Atomic Skull app. 5.00
Annual 2 (12/13, $4.99) Rocafort & Jurgens-a; H'El & Faora app.; back-up Mad sampler 5.00
Annual 3 (9/14, $4.99) Superman Doomed x-over; Brainiac app. 5.00
...: Futures End 1 (11/14, $2.99, regular-c) Five years later; Alixe-a 3.00
...: Futures End 1 (11/14, $3.99, 3-D cover) 4.00

ACTION COMICS (Numbering reverts to original V1 #957 after #52 from 2011-2016 series)
DC Comics: No. 957, Aug, 2016 - Present ($2.99/$3.99/$4.99)

957-974: 957-Jurgens-s/Zircher-a; the pre-52 Superman vs. Lex Luthor & Doomsday. 960-962-Wonder Woman app. 973-Superwoman & Steel app. 3.00
975-($3.99) Superman Reborn pt. 2; back-up with Mxyzptlk; Dini-s/Churchill-a 4.00
976-986,992-999: 976-Superman Reborn pt. 4. 977,978-Origin revised. 979-Cyborg Superman returns. 984-Intro Ursa and Lor-Zod. 992-998-Booster Gold app. 3.00
987-991-($2.99) The Oz Effect regular covers; Jor-El returns 3.00
987-991-($3.99) The Oz Effect lenticular covers 4.00
1000-(6/18, $7.99) Short stories and pin-ups by various incl. Jurgens, Swan, Coipel, Ordway, Gleason, García-López; intro. Rogol Zaar; Bendis-s/Jim Lee-a; 9 covers 8.00
1001-1028: 1001-Intro. Red Cloud; Gleason-a. 1004-1006-Sook-a. 1007-1011-Leviathan Rising; Epting-a. 1012-1016-Kudranski-a; Red Cloud and Thorn app. 1015-1016-Batman & Naomi app. 1017-1027-Romita, Jr.-a. 1017-1021-Legion of Doom app. 1020-1022-Young Justice app. 1028-Last Bendis-s 4.00
1029-1049-($4.99) P.K. Johnson-s begins. 1029-1034-Back-up with Midnighter; Cloonan-s. 1035-Superman & The Authority go to Warworld. 1037-1042-Martian Manhunter back-up 5.00
1050-(2/23, $5.99) Superman's secret ID restored; art by various 6.00
1051,1052-Metallo app.; back-up Power Girl story 5.00
2021 Annual 1 (9/21, $5.99) Tales of the House of El; Kara & future Supermen 6.00
2022 Annual 1 (7/22, $5.99) Mongul's secret origin; flashback to Clark's youth 6.00
... Special 1 (7/18, $4.99) Jurgens-s/Conrad-a; Russell-s/Thompson-a; Landis-s/Manapul-a 5.00

ACTION COMICS
DC Comics: (no date)

1-Ashcan comic, not distributed to newsstands, only for in-house use. Cover art is the rejected art to Detective Comics #2 and interior from Detective Comics #1.
A CGC certified 9.0 copy sold for $17,825 in 2002, $29,000 in 2008, and $50,000 in 2010.
A CGC certified 9.2 copy sold for $204,000 in April 2021.

GD 2.0 | VG 4.0 | FN 6.0 | VF 8.0 | VF/NM 9.0 | NM- 9.2

ACTION COMICS 1 (FACSIMILE EDITION)
DC Comics: 2022 ($6.99)

1-Reprints the entire 1938 Action Comics #1 with original ads 7.00

ACTION FORCE (Also see G.I. Joe European Missions)
Marvel Comics Ltd. (British): Mar, 1987 - No. 50, 1988 ($1.00, weekly, magazine)

	GD	VG	FN	VF	VF/NM	NM-
1,3: British G.I. Joe series. 3-w/poster insert	3	6	9	14	20	25
2,4	2	4	6	8	10	12
5-10	1	2	3	5	6	8
11-50						5.00
...Special 1 (7/87) Summer holiday special; Snake Eyes-c/app.	2	4	6	9	12	15
...Special 2 (10/87) Winter special						6.00

ACTION FUNNIES
DC Comics: 1937/1938

nn - Ashcan comic, not distributed to newsstands, only for in house use. Cover art is Action Comics #3 and interior from Detective Comics #10. The Mallette/Brown copy in VG+ condition sold for $15,000 in 2005. A VF+ copy sold for $10,157.50 in 2012.
A CGC certified 8.5 copy sold for $57,600 in April 2021.

ACTION GIRL
Slave Labor Graphics: Oct, 1994 - No. 19 ($2.50/$2.75/$2.95, B&W)

1-19: 4-Begin $2.75-c. 19-Begin $2.95-c 5.00
1-6 ($2.75, 2nd printings): All read 2nd Print in indicia. 1-(2/96). 2-(10/95). 3-(2/96). 4-(7/96). 5-(2/97). 6-(9/97) 3.00
1-4 ($2.75, 3rd printings): All read 3rd Print in indicia. 3.00

ACTION MAN (Based on the Hasbro G.I. Joe-type action figure)
IDW Publishing: Jun, 2016 - No. 4, Sept, 2016 ($3.99, limited series)

1-4-John Barber-s/Paolo Villanelli-a 4.00
...: Revolution (10/16, $3.99) Tie-in to Hasbro toy titles x-over; Barber-s/Villanelli-a 4.00

ACTION PHILOSOPHERS!
Dark Horse Comics: Oct, 2014 ($1.00, one-shot)

1-Van Lente-s/Dunlavey-a 3.00

ACTION PLANET COMICS
Action Planet: 1996 - No. 3, Sept, 1997 ($3.95, B&W, 44 pgs.)

1-3: 1-Intro Monster Man by Mike Manley & other stories 4.00
Giant Size Action Planet Halloween Special (1998, $5.95, oversized) 6.00

ACTUAL CONFESSIONS (Formerly Love Adventures)
Atlas Comics (MPI): No. 13, Oct, 1952 - No. 14, Dec, 1952

	GD	VG	FN	VF	VF/NM	NM-
13,14	14	28	42	82	121	160

ACTUAL ROMANCES (Becomes True Secrets #3 on?)
Marvel Comics (IPS): Oct, 1949 - No. 2, Jan, 1950 (52 pgs.)

	GD	VG	FN	VF	VF/NM	NM-
1-Photo-c	21	42	63	122	199	275
2-Photo-c	16	32	48	84	127	170

A.D.: AFTER DEATH
Image Comics: Book 1, Nov, 2016 - Book 3, May, 2017 ($5.99, limited series, square-bound 8"x11")

1-3-Scott Snyder-s/Jeff Lemire-a 6.00

ADAM AND EVE
Spire Christian Comics (Fleming H. Revell Co.): 1975,1978 (35¢/39¢/49¢)

	GD	VG	FN	VF	VF/NM	NM-
nn-By Al Hartley (1975 edition)	3	6	9	14	20	25
nn (1978 edition)	2	4	6	10	14	18

ADAM: LEGEND OF THE BLUE MARVEL
Marvel Comics: Jan, 2009 - No. 5, May, 2009 ($3.99, limited series)

	GD	VG	FN	VF	VF/NM	NM-
1-First app. Blue Marvel (Adam Brashear); Grevioux-s/Broome-a; Avengers app.	19	38	57	131	291	450
2	6	12	18	42	79	115
3,5	4	8	12	25	40	55
4-Namor app.	5	10	15	31	53	75

ADAM STRANGE (Also see Green Lantern #132, Mystery In Space #53 & Showcase #17)
DC Comics: 1990 - No. 3, 1990 ($3.95, 52 pgs, limited series, squarebound)

Book One - Three: Andy & Adam Kubert-c/a 5.00
...: The Man of Two Worlds (2003, $19.95, TPB) r/#1-3; sketch pages by Andy Kubert 20.00

ADAM STRANGE (Leads into the Rann/Thanagar War mini-series)
DC Comics: Nov, 2004 - No. 8, June, 2005 ($2.95, limited series)

1-8-Andy Diggle-s/Pascal Ferry-a/c. 1-Superman app. 3.00
...: Planet Heist TPB (2005, $19.99) r/series; sketch pages 20.00
... Special (11/08, $3.50) Takes place during Rann/Thanagar Holy War series; Starlin-s 4.00

ADAM STRANGE / FUTURE QUEST SPECIAL

GD 2.0 | VG 4.0 | FN 6.0 | VF 8.0 | VF/NM 9.0 | NM- 9.2

DC Comics: May, 2017 ($4.99, one-shot)

1-Adam Strange meets Jonny Quest and team; back-up Top Cat story; Batman app. 5.00

ADAM-12 (TV)
Gold Key: Dec, 1973 - No. 10, Feb, 1976 (Photo-c)

1 6 12 18 42 79 115
2-10 4 8 12 23 37 50

ADDAMS FAMILY (TV cartoon)
Gold Key: Oct, 1974 - No. 3, Apr, 1975 (Hanna-Barbera)

1 12 24 36 82 179 275
2,3 5 10 15 35 63 90

ADDAMS FAMILY
IDW Publishing: Oct, 2019 ($4.99, one-shot)

...: The Bodies Issue - Zöe Quinn-s/Philip Murphy-a 5.00

ADLAI STEVENSON
Dell Publishing Co.: Dec, 1966

12-007-612-Life story; photo-c 3 6 9 21 33 45

ADOLESCENT RADIOACTIVE BLACK BELT HAMSTERS (See Clint)
Comic Castle/Eclipse Comics: 1986 - No. 9, Jan, 1988 ($1.50, B&W)

1 2 4 6 8 11 14
1-In 3-D (7/86), 2-4 in 3-D ($2.50) 6.00
2-4 6.00
5-9 4.00
1-9 (Second printings) 4.00
Massacre The Japanese Invasion #1 (8/89, $2.00) 4.00

ADOLESCENT RADIOACTIVE BLACK BELT HAMSTERS
Dynamite Entertainment: 2008 - No. 4, 2008 ($3.50, limited series)

1-4-Tom Nguyen-a/Keith Champagne-s; 2 covers by Nguyen and Oeming 4.00

ADRENALYNN (See The Tenth)
Image Comics: Aug, 1999 - No. 4, Feb, 2000 ($2.50)

1-4-Tony Daniel-s/Marty Egeland-a; origin of Adrenalynn 3.00

ADULT TALES OF TERROR ILLUSTRATED (See Terror Illustrated)

ADVANCED DUNGEONS & DRAGONS (Also see TSR Worlds)
DC Comics: Dec, 1988 - No. 36, Dec, 1991 (Newsstand #1 is Holiday, 1988-89) ($1.25-$1.75)

1-Based on TSR role playing game 3 6 9 16 23 30
2 1 2 3 5 6 8
3-36: 25-$1.75-c begins 4.00
Annual 1 (1990, $3.95, 68 pgs.) 5.00

ADVENTURE BOUND
Dell Publishing Co.: Aug, 1949

Four Color 239 6 12 18 41 76 110

ADVENTURE COMICS (Formerly New Adventure)(...Presents Dial H For Hero #479-490)
National Periodical Publications/DC Comics: No. 32, 11/38 - No. 490, 2/82; No. 491, 9/82 - No. 503, 9/83

32-Anchors Aweigh (ends #52), Barry O'Neil (ends #60, not in #33), Captain Desmo (ends #47), Dale Daring (ends #47), Federal Men (ends #70), The Golden Dragon (ends #36), Rusty & His Pals (ends #52) by Bob Kane, Todd Hunter (ends #38) and Tom Brent (ends #39) begin 600 1200 1800 3250 4875 6500
33-35,38 415 830 1242 2240 3370 4500
36 (scarce) 740 1480 2220 4000 6000 8000
37-Cover used on Double Action #2 650 1300 1950 3500 5250 7000
39(6/39)- Jack Wood begins, ends #42; early mention of Marijuana in comics 555 1110 1665 3000 4500 6000
40-(Rare, 7/39, on stands 6/10/39)-The Sandman begins by Bert Christman (who died in WWII); believed to be 1st conceived story (see N.Y. World's Fair for 1st published app.); Socko Strong begins, ends #54 8400 16,800 25,200 62,200 133,600 205,000
41-O'Mealia shark-c 703 1406 2109 5132 9066 13,000
42,44-Sandman-c by Flessel. 44-Opium story 1000 2000 3000 7400 13,200 19,000
43,45: 45-Full page ad for Flash Comics #1 486 972 1458 3550 6275 9000
46-Sandman cover by Flessel 811 1622 2433 5920 10,460 15,000
47-Sandman cover by Flessel; Steve Conrad Adventurer begins, ends #76 732 1464 2196 5344 9422 13,500
48-1st app. The Hourman by Bernard Baily; Baily-c (Hourman c-48,50,52-59) 2950 5900 8850 22,000 46,000 70,000
49 314 628 942 2198 3849 5500
50-2nd Hourman-c; Cotton Carver by Jack Lehti begins, ends #64 334 668 1002 2338 4069 5800
51,60-Sandman-c: 51-Sandman-c by Flessel. 423 846 1269 3088 5444 7800
52-59: 53-1st app. Jimmy "Minuteman" Martin & the Minutemen of America in Hourman; ends #78. 58-Paul Kirk Manhunter begins (1st app.), ends #72 284 568 852 1818 3109 4400
61-1st app. Starman by Jack Burnley (4/41); Starman c-61-72; Starman by Burnley in #61-80 1667 3334 5000 12,500 24,250 36,000
62-65,67,68,70: 67-Origin & 1st app. The Mist; classic Burnley-c. 70-Last Federal Men 271 542 813 1734 2967 4200
66-Origin/1st app. Shining Knight (9/41) 300 600 900 2010 3505 5000
69-1st app. Sandy the Golden Boy (Sandman's sidekick) by Paul Norris (in a Bob Kane style); Sandman dons new costume 300 600 900 1950 3375 4800
71-Jimmy Martin becomes costumed aide to the Hourman; 1st app. Hourman's Miracle Ray machine 271 542 813 1734 2967 4200
72-1st Simon & Kirby Sandman (3/42, 1st DC work) 1000 2000 3000 7300 13,400 19,500
73-Origin Manhunter by Simon & Kirby; begin new series; Manhunter-c (scarce) 1275 2550 3825 9550 18,275 27,000
74-78,80: 74-Thorndyke replaces Jimmy, Hourman's assistant; new Sandman-c begin by S&K. 75-Thor app. by Kirby; 1st Kirby Thor (see Tales of the Unexpected #16). 77-Origin Genius Jones; Mist story. 80-Last S&K Manhunter & Burnley Starman 200 400 600 1280 2190 3100
79-Classic Manhunter-c 320 640 960 2240 3920 5600
81-90: 83-Last Hourman. 84-Mike Gibbs begins, ends #102 126 252 378 806 1378 1950
91-Last Simon & Kirby Sandman 129 258 387 826 1413 2000
92-99,101,102: 92-Last Manhunter. 101-Shining Knight origin retold. 102-Last Starman, Sandman, & Genius Jones; most-S&K-c (Genius Jones cont'd in More Fun #108) 100 200 300 640 1095 1550
100-S&K-c 135 270 405 864 1482 2100
103-Aquaman, Green Arrow, Johnny Quick & Superboy all move over from More Fun Comics #107; 8th app. Superboy; Superboy-c begin; 1st small logo (4/46) 314 628 942 2198 3849 5500
104-Needle in a haystack-c 129 258 387 826 1413 2000
105-110 90 180 270 576 988 1400
111,112,114-120 81 162 243 518 884 1250
113-X-Mas-c 135 270 405 864 1482 2100
121,122-126,128-130: 128-1st meeting Superboy & Lois Lane 74 148 222 470 810 1150
127-Brief origin Shining Knight retold 76 152 228 486 831 1175
131-141,143-149: 132-Shining Knight 1st return to King Arthur time; origin aide Sir Butch 65 130 195 416 708 1000
142-Origin Shining Knight & Johnny Quick retold 82 164 246 528 902 1275
150,151,153,155,157,159,161,163-All have 6 pg. Shining Knight stories by Frank Frazetta. 159-Origin Johnny Quick. 161-1st Lana Lang app. in this title 77 154 231 493 847 1200
152,154,156,158,160,162,164-169: 166-Last Shining Knight. 168-Last 52 pg. issue 57 114 171 362 619 875
170-180 54 108 162 343 574 825
181-199: 189-B&W and color illo in **POP** 53 106 159 334 567 800
200 (5/54) 65 130 195 416 708 1000
201-208: 207-Last Johnny Quick (not in 205) 50 100 150 315 533 750
209-Last pre-code issue; origin Speedy 54 108 162 343 574 825
210-1st app. Krypto (Superdog)-c/story (3/55) 850 1700 3400 7650 13,325 19,000
211-213,215-219 48 96 144 302 514 725
214-2nd app. Krypto 116 232 348 742 1271 1800
220-Krypto-c/sty 57 114 171 362 619 875
221-228,230-246: 237-1st Intergalactic Vigilante Squadron (6/57). 239-Krypto-c 39 78 117 240 395 550
229-1st S.A. issue; Green Arrow & Aquaman app. 77 154 231 493 847 1200
247(4/58)-1st Legion of Super Heroes app.; 1st app. Cosmic Boy, Saturn Girl & Lightning Boy (later Lightning Lad in #267) (origin) 1250 2500 5000 12,500 26,250 40,000
248-252,254,255-Green Arrow in all: 255-Intro. Red Kryptonite in Superboy (used in #252 but with no effect) 37 74 111 222 361 500
253-1st meeting of Superboy & Robin; Green Arrow by Kirby in #250-255 (also see World's Finest #96-99) 43 86 129 271 461 650
256-Origin Green Arrow by Kirby 75 150 225 490 1095 1700
257-259: 258-Green Arrow x-over in Superboy 30 60 90 177 289 400
260-1st Silver Age origin Aquaman (5/59) 125 250 375 1000 2000 3000
261-265,268,270: 262-Origin Speedy in Green Arrow. 270-Congorilla begins, ends #281,283 23 46 69 138 227 315
266-(11/59)-Origin & 1st app. Aquagirl (tryout, not same as later character) 37 74 111 222 361 500
267(12/59)-2nd Legion of Super Heroes; Lightning Boy now called Lightning Lad; new costumes for Legion 100 200 300 630 1815 3000
269-Intro. Aqualad (2/60); last Green Arrow (not in #206) 77 154 231 493 847 1200
271-Origin Luthor retold 55 110 165 352 601 850
272-274,277-280: 279-Intro White Kryptonite in Superboy. 280-1st meeting Superboy & Lori Lemaris 21 42 63 126 206 285
275-Origin Superman-Batman team retold (see World's Finest #94) 36 72 108 211 343 475
276-(9/60) Robinson Crusoe-like story 22 44 66 132 216 300
281,284,287-289: 281-Last Congorilla. 284-Last Aquaman in Adv.; Mooney-a. 287,288-Intro Dev-Em, the Knave from Krypton. 287-1st Bizarro Perry White & Jimmy Olsen. 288-Bizarro-c. 289-Legion cameo (statues) 20 40 60 117 189 260
282-(3/61) 5th Legion app; intro/origin Star Boy 45 90 135 284 480 675
283-Intro. The Phantom Zone; 1st app. of General Zod (cameo in 2 panels) 129 258 387 826 1413 2000
285-1st Tales of the Bizarro World-c/story (ends #299) in Adv. (see Action #255) 30 60 90 177 289 400
286-1st Bizarro Mxyzptlk; Bizarro-c 25 50 75 150 245 340
290(11/61)-9th Legion app; origin Sunboy in Legion (last 10¢ issue) 37 74 111 222 361 500
291,292,295-298: 291-1st 12¢ ish, (12/61). 292-1st Bizarro Lana Lang & Lucy Lane. 295-Bizarro-c; 1st Bizarro Titano 11 22 33 73 157 240
293(2/62)-13th Legion app; Mon-El app.; Legion of Super Pets 1st app./origin; 1st Superhorse; 2nd app. General Zod; 1st Bizarro Luthor & Kandor 48 96 144 302 514 725
294-1st Bizarro Marilyn Monroe, Pres. Kennedy 14 28 42 96 211 325
299-1st Gold Kryptonite (8/62) 11 22 33 76 163 250
300-Tales of the Legion of Super-Heroes series begins (9/62); Mon-El leaves Phantom Zone (temporarily), joins Legion 60 120 180 480 1215 1950
301-Origin Bouncing Boy 17 34 51 117 259 400
302-305: 303-1st app. Matter-Eater Lad. 304-Death of Lightning Lad in Legion 14 28 42 93 204 315
306-310: 306-Intro. Legion of Substitute Heroes. 307-1st app. Element Lad in Legion. 308-1st app. Lightning Lass in Legion. 309-1st app. Legion of Super-Monsters 12 24 36 83 182 280
311-320: 312-Lightning Lad back in Legion. 315-Last new Superboy story; Colossal Boy app. 316-Origins & powers of Legion given. 317-Intro. Dream Girl in Legion; Lightning Lass becomes Light Lass; Hall of Fame series begins. 320-Dev-Em 2nd app. 10 20 30 69 147 225
321-Intro. Time Trapper 10 20 30 66 138 210
322-330: 327-Intro/1st app. Lone Wolf in Legion. 329-Intro The Bizarro Legionnaires; intro. Legion flight rings 9 18 27 59 117 175
331-340: 337-Chlorophyll Kid & Night Girl app. 340-Intro Computo in Legion 8 16 24 56 108 160
341-Triplicate Girl becomes Duo Damsel 8 16 24 54 102 150
342-345,347-351: 345-Last Hall of Fame; returns in 356,371. 348-Origin Sunboy; intro Dr. Regulus in Legion. 349-Intro Universo & Rond Vidar. 351-1st app. White Witch 7 14 21 48 89 130

Adventure Comics #76 © DC

Adventure Comics #432 © DC

Adventureman #3 © Milkfed & Dodson

	GD 2.0	VG 4.0	FN 6.0	VF 8.0	VF/NM 9.0	NM- 9.2
346-1st app. Karate Kid, Princess Projectra, Ferro Lad, & Nemesis Kid.	27	54	81	189	420	650
352,354-360: 354,355-Superman meets the Adult Legion. 355-Insect Queen joins Legion (4/67)	7	14	21	44	82	120
353-Death of Ferro Lad in Legion	11	22	33	73	157	240
361-364,366,368-370: 369-Intro Mordru in Legion	6	12	18	41	76	110
365,367: 365-Intro Shadow Lass (memorial to Shadow Woman app. in #354's Adult Legion-s); lists origins & powers of L.S.H. 367-New Legion headquarters	8	16	24	54	102	150
371,372: 371-Intro. Chemical King (mentioned in #354's Adult Legion-s). 372-Timber Wolf & Chemical King join	8	16	24	51	96	140
373,374,376-380: 373-Intro. Tornado Twins (Barry Allen Flash descendants). 374-Article on comics fandom. 380-Last Legion in Adventure; last 12¢-c	6	12	18	37	66	95
375-Intro Quantum Queen & The Wanderers	6	12	18	41	76	110
381-Supergirl begins; 1st full length Supergirl story & her 1st solo book (6/69)	14	28	42	98	217	335
382-389	5	10	15	34	60	85
390-Giant Supergirl G-69	7	14	21	46	86	125
391-396,398	4	8	12	25	40	55
397-1st app. new Supergirl	5	10	15	35	63	90
399-Unpubbed G.A. Black Canary story	4	8	12	28	47	65
400-New costume for Supergirl (12/70)	6	12	18	38	69	100
401,402,404-408-(15¢-c)	3	6	9	18	28	38
403-68 pg. Giant G-81; Legion-r/#304,305,308,312	6	12	18	41	76	110
409-411,413-415,417-420-(52 pgs.): 413-Hawkman by Kubert r/B&B #44; G.A. Robotman-r/Det. #178; Zatanna by Morrow. 414-r-2nd Animal Man/Str. Advs. #184. 415-Animal Man-r/Str. Adv.#190 (origin recap). 417-Morrow Vigilante; Frazetta Shining Knight-r/Adv. #161; origin The Enchantress; no Zatanna. 418-Prev. unpub. Dr. Mid-Nite story from 1948; no Zatanna. 420-Animal Man-r/Str. Adv. #195	3	6	9	19	30	40
412-(52 pgs.) Reprints origin & 1st app. of Animal Man from Strange Adventures #180	3	6	9	21	33	45
416-Also listed as DC 100 Pg. Super Spectacular #10; Golden Age-r; r/1st app. Black Canary from Flash #86; no Zatanna	11	22	33	75	160	245
421-424: 424-Last Supergirl in Adventure	3	6	9	14	20	25
425-New look, content change to adventure; Kaluta-c; Toth-a, origin Capt. Fear	3	6	9	16	23	35
426,427: 426-1st Adventurers Club. 427-Last Vigilante	2	4	6	10	14	18
428-Origin/1st app. Black Orchid (c/story, 6-7/73)	11	22	33	76	163	250
429,430-Black Orchid-c/stories	4	8	12	25	40	55
431-Spectre by Aparo begins, ends #440.	6	12	18	38	69	100
432-439-Spectre app. 433-437-Cover title is Weird Adventure Comics. 436-Last 20¢ issue	3	6	9	21	33	45
440-New Spectre origin	4	8	12	25	40	55
441-458: 441-452-Aquaman app. 443-Fisherman app. 445-447-The Creeper app. 446-Flag-c. 449-451-Martian Manhunter app. 450-Weather Wizard app. in Aquaman story. 453-458-Superboy app. 453-Intro. Mighty Girl. 457,458-Eclipso app.	2	4	6	9	12	14
459,460 (68 pgs.): 459-New Gods/Darkseid storyline concludes from New Gods #19 (#459 is dated 9-10/78) without missing a month. 459-Flash (ends #466), Deadman (ends #466), Wonder Woman (ends #464), Green Lantern (ends #460). 460-Aquaman (ends #478)	3	6	9	16	24	32
461-($1.00, 68 pgs.) Justice Society begins; ends 466	4	8	12	27	44	60
462-($1.00, 68 pgs.) Death Earth II Batman	5	10	15	35	63	90
463-466 ($1.00 size, 68 pgs.)	2	4	6	11	16	20
467-Starman by Ditko & Plastic Man begins; 1st app. Prince Gavyn (Starman).	2	4	6	11	16	20
468-490: 470-Origin Starman. 479-Dial 'H' For Hero begins, ends #490. 478-Last Starman & Plastic Man. 480-490: Dial 'H' For Hero	2	4	6	8	10	12
491-503: 491-100pg. Digest size begins; r/Legion of Super Heroes/Adv. #247, 267; Spectre, Aquaman, Superboy, S&K Sandman, Black Canary-r & new Shazam by Newton begin. 492,495,496,499-S&K Sandman-r/Adventure in all. 493-Challengers of the Unknown begins by Tuska w/brief origin. 493-495,497-499-G.A. Captain Marvel-r. 494-499-Spectre-r/Spectre 1-3, 5-7. 496-Capt. Marvel Jr. new-s, Cockrum-a. 498-Mary Marvel new-s; Plastic Man-r begin; origin Bouncing Boy-r/ #301. 500-Legion-r (Digest size, 148 pgs.).						
501-503: G.A.-r	2	4	6	10	14	18
... 80 Page Giant (10/98, $4.95) Wonder Woman, Shazam, Superboy, Supergirl, Green Arrow, Legion, Bizarro World stories	2	4	6	8	10	12

NOTE: *Bizarro covers-285, 286, 288, 294, 295, 329. Vigilante app.-420, 426, 427.* **N. Adams** *a(r)-495i-498i; c-365-369, 371-373, 375-379, 381-383.* **Aparo** *a-431-433, 434i, 435, 436, 437i, 438i, 439-452, 503r; c-431-452.* **Austin** *a-449i 451i.* **Bernard Baily** *c-48, 50, 52-59.* **Bolland** *c-475.* **Burnley** *c-61-72, 116-120p.* **Chaykin** *a-438.* **Ditko** *a-467-478p; c-467p.* **Creig Flessel** *c-32, 33, 40, 42, 44, 46, 47, 51, 60.* **Giffen** *c-491p-494p, 500p.* **Grell** *a-435-437, 440.* **Guardineer** *c-34, 35, 45.* **Infantino** *a-416r.* **Kaluta** *c-425.* **Bob Kane** *a-38.* **G. Kane** *a-414r, 425; c-496-499, 537.* **Kirby** *a-250-256.* **Kubert** *a-413.* **Meskin** *a-81,125,127.* **Moldoff** *a-494i; c-49.* **Morrow** *a-413-415, 417, 422, 502r, 503r.* **Netzer/Nasser** *a-449-451.* **Newton** *a-459-461, 464-466, 491p, 492p.* **Paul Norris** *a-69.* **Orlando** *a-457p, 458p.* **Perez** *c-484-486, 490p.* **Simon/Kirby** *a-503r; c-73-97, 100-102.* **Starlin** *c-471.* **Staton** *a-445-447i, 456-458p, 459, 460, 461p-465p, 466,467p-478p, 502p(r); c-458, 461(back).* **Toth** *a-418, 419, 425, 431, 495p-497p.* **Tuska** *a-494p.*

ADVENTURE COMICS (Also see All Star Comics 1999 crossover titles)
DC Comics: May, 1999 ($1.99, one-shot)

1-Golden Age Starman and the Atom; Snejbjerg-a 4.00

ADVENTURE COMICS (See Final Crisis: Legion of Three Worlds)
DC Comics: No. 0, Apr, 2009 - No. 12, Aug, 2010; No. 516, Sept, 2010 - No. 529, Oct, 2011 ($1.00/$3.99)

0-($1.00) R/Adventure Comics #247; new Luthor & Brainiac back-up-s; Lopresti-c 3.00
1-7-($3.99) Superboy stories; Johns-s/Manapul-a; Legion back-up-s. 5-7-Blackest Night 4.00
1-12-Variant 7-panel covers by various numbered with original #504-#515 5.00
8-12: 8-11-New Krypton x-over. 11-Mon-El leaves 21st century. 12-Legion; Levitz-s 4.00
516-521: 516-(9/10, resumes original numbering) flashback to Legion formation; Atom back-ups. 521-Adult Legion resumes; Mon-El joins Green Lanterns 4.00
522-529-($2.99) Legion Academy. 523-527-Jimenez-a/c 3.00

ADVENTURE COMICS SPECIAL (See New Krypton issues in 2009 Superman titles)
DC Comics: Jan, 2009 ($2.99, one-shot)

... Featuring the Guardian - James Robinson-s/Pere Pérez-a; origin re-told; intro. Gwen 3.00

ADVENTURE INTO MYSTERY
Atlas Comics (BFP No. 1/OPI No. 2-8): May, 1956 - No. 8, July, 1957

	GD	VG	FN	VF	VF/NM	NM-
1-Powell s/f-a; Forte-a; Everett-c	90	180	270	576	988	1400
2-Flying Saucer story	40	80	120	246	411	575
3,6-Everett-c	37	74	111	222	361	500
4,5,7: 4-Williamson-a, 4 pgs; Powell-a. 5-Everett-c/a, Orlando-a. 7-Torres-a; Everett-c	39	78	117	231	378	525
8-Moreira, Sale, Torres, Woodbridge-a, Severin-c	39	78	117	231	378	525

ADVENTURE IS MY CAREER
U.S. Coast Guard Academy/Street & Smith: 1945 (44 pgs.)

	GD	VG	FN	VF	VF/NM	NM-
nn-Simon, Milt Gross-a	24	48	72	142	234	325

ADVENTUREMAN
Image Comics: Jun, 2020 - Present ($3.99, limited series)

1-9-Matt Fraction-s/Terry Dodson-a 4.00

ADVENTURERS, THE
Aircel Comics/Adventure Publ.: Aug, 1986 - No. 10, 1987 ($1.50, B&W)
V2#1, 1987 - V2#9, 1988; V3#1, Oct, 1989 - V3#6, 1990

	GD	VG	FN	VF	VF/NM	NM-
1-Peter Hsu-a	1	3	4	6	8	10
1-Cover variant, limited ed.	2	4	6	10	14	18
1-2nd print (1986); 1st app. Elf Warrior						3.00
2,3, 0 (#4, 12/86)-Origin, 5-10, Book II, reg. & Limited Ed. #1						4.00
Book II, #2,3,0,4-9						3.00
Book III, #1 (10/89, $2.25)-Reg. & limited-c, Book III, #2-6						3.00

ADVENTURES (No. 2 Spectacular... on cover)
St. John Publishing Co.: Nov, 1949 - No. 2, Feb, 1950 (No. 1 ...in Romance on cover) (Slightly larger size)

	GD	VG	FN	VF	VF/NM	NM-
1(Scarce); Bolle, Starr-a(2)	42	84	126	265	445	625
2(Scarce)-Slave Girl; China Bombshell app.; Bolle, L. Starr-a	53	106	159	334	567	800

ADVENTURES FOR BOYS
Bailey Enterprises: Dec, 1954

	GD	VG	FN	VF	VF/NM	NM-
nn-Comics, text, & photos	8	16	24	44	57	70

ADVENTURES IN PARADISE (TV)
Dell Publishing Co.: Feb-Apr, 1962

	GD	VG	FN	VF	VF/NM	NM-
Four Color 1301	6	12	18	37	66	95

ADVENTURES IN ROMANCE (See Adventures)

ADVENTURES IN SCIENCE (See Classics Illustrated Special Issue)

ADVENTURES IN THE DC UNIVERSE
DC Comics: Apr, 1997 - No. 19, Oct, 1998 ($1.75/$1.95/$1.99)

1-Animated style in all: JLA-c/app 5.00
2-11,13-17,19: 2-Flash app. 3-Wonder Woman. 4-Green Lantern. 6-Aquaman. 7-Shazam Family. 8-Blue Beetle & Booster Gold. 9-Flash. 10-Legion. 11-Green Lantern & Wonder Woman. 13-Impulse & Martian Manhunter. 14-Superboy/Flash race 3.50
12,18-JLA-c/app 3.50
Annual 1(1997, $3.95)-Dr. Fate, Impulse, Rose & Thorn, Superboy, Mister Miracle app. 4.50

ADVENTURES IN THE RIFLE BRIGADE
DC Comics (Vertigo): Oct, 2000 - No. 3, Dec, 2000 ($2.50, limited series)

1-3-Ennis-s/Ezquerra-a/Bolland-c 3.00
TPB (2004, $14.95) r/series and Operation Bollock series 15.00

ADVENTURES IN THE RIFLE BRIGADE: OPERATION BOLLOCK
DC Comics (Vertigo): Oct, 2001 - No. 3, Jan, 2002 ($2.50, limited series)

Issue	GD 2.0	VG 4.0	FN 6.0	VF 8.0	VF/NM 9.0	NM- 9.2
1-3-Ennis-s/Ezquerra-a/Fabry-c						3.00

ADVENTURES IN 3-D (With glasses)
Harvey Publications: Nov, 1953 - No. 2, Jan, 1954 (25¢)

Issue	GD 2.0	VG 4.0	FN 6.0	VF 8.0	VF/NM 9.0	NM- 9.2
1-Nostrand, Powell-a, 2-Powell-a	14	28	42	80	115	150

ADVENTURES INTO DARKNESS (See Seduction of the Innocent 3-D)
Better-Standard Publications/Visual Editions: No. 5, Aug, 1952- No. 14, 1954

Issue	GD 2.0	VG 4.0	FN 6.0	VF 8.0	VF/NM 9.0	NM- 9.2
5-Katz-c/a; Toth-a(p)	129	258	387	826	1413	2000
6-Tuska, Katz-a; skeleton cover	161	322	483	1030	1765	2500
7-Classic horror-c; Katz-c/a	226	452	678	1446	2473	3500
8,9-Toth-a(p)	97	194	291	621	1061	1500
10-Jack Katz-a; skeleton cover	65	130	195	416	708	1000
11,12-Classic horror-c: 11-Jack Katz-a. 12-Toth-a; lingerie panel	129	258	387	826	1413	2000
13-Toth-a(p); Cannibalism story cited by T. E. Murphy articles	142	284	426	909	1555	2200
14-Skeleton cover	129	258	387	826	1413	2000

NOTE: *Fawcette* a-13. *Moreira* a-5. *Sekowsky* a-10, 11, 13(2).

ADVENTURES INTO TERROR (Formerly Joker Comics)
Marvel/Atlas Comics (CDS): No. 43, Nov, 1950 - No. 31, May, 1954

Issue	GD 2.0	VG 4.0	FN 6.0	VF 8.0	VF/NM 9.0	NM- 9.2
43(#1)	116	232	348	742	1271	1800
44(#2, 2/51)-Sol Brodsky-c	106	212	318	673	1162	1650
3(4/51), 4	53	106	159	334	567	800
5-Wolverton-c panel/Mystic #6; Rico-c panel also; Atom Bomb story	58	116	174	371	636	900
6,8: 8-Wolverton text illo r-/Marvel Tales #104; prototype of Spider-Man villain The Lizard	50	100	150	315	533	750
7-Wolverton-a "Where Monsters Dwell", 6 pgs.; Tuska-c; Maneely-c panels	77	154	231	493	847	1200
9,10,12-Krigstein-a. 9-Decapitation panels	43	86	129	271	461	650
11,13-20	41	82	123	256	428	600
21-24,26-31	40	80	120	246	411	575
25-Matt Fox-a	43	86	129	271	461	650

NOTE: *Ayers* a-21. *Colan* a-3, 5, 14, 21, 24, 25, 28, 29; c-27. *Colletta* a-30. *Everett* c-13, 21, 25. *Fass* a-28, 29. *Forte* a-28. *Heath* a-43, 44, 4-6, 22, 24, 26; c-43, 9, 11. *Lazarus* a-7. *Maneely* a-7(3 pg.), 10, 11, 21., 22 c-15, 29. *Don Rico* a-4, 5(3 pg.). *Sekowsky* a-43, 3, 4. *Sinnott* a-8, 9, 11, 24, 28. *Tuska* a-14; c-7.

ADVENTURES INTO THE UNKNOWN
American Comics Group: Fall, 1948 - No. 174, Aug, 1967 (No. 1-33: 52 pgs.)
(1st continuous series Supernatural comic; see Eerie #1)

Issue	GD 2.0	VG 4.0	FN 6.0	VF 8.0	VF/NM 9.0	NM- 9.2
1-Guardineer-a; adapt. of 'Castle of Otranto' by Horace Walpole	568	1136	1704	4146	7323	10,500
2-Skull Island-c	271	542	813	1721	2961	4200
3-Feldstein-a (9 pgs)	135	270	405	864	1482	2100
4,5: 5- 'Spirit Of Frankenstein' series begins, ends #12 (except #11)	71	142	213	454	777	1100
6-10	40	80	120	246	411	575
11-14,16,18-20: 13-Starr-a	36	72	108	211	343	475
15-Hitler app.	39	78	117	240	395	550
17-Story similar to movie 'The Thing'	37	74	111	222	361	500
21-26,28-30	29	58	87	172	281	390
27-Williamson/Krenkel-a (8 pgs.)	53	106	159	334	567	800
31-37,39-50	22	44	66	132	216	300
38-Atom bomb panels; Devil-c	18	36	54	124	275	425
51-(1/54)-(3-D effect-c/story)-Only white cover	68	136	204	435	743	1050
52-58: (3-D effect-c/stories with black covers). 52-E.C. swipe/Haunt Of Fear #14	58	116	174	371	636	900
59-3-D effect story only; new logo	39	78	117	231	378	525
60-Wood*esque*-a by Landau	18	36	54	105	165	225
61-Last pre-code issue (1-2/55)	18	36	54	105	165	225
62-70	8	16	24	56	108	160
71-90: 80-Hydrogen bomb panel	7	14	21	44	82	120
91,96(#95 on inside),107,116-All have Williamson-a	7	14	21	48	89	130
92-95,97-99,101-106,108-115,117-128: 109-113,118-Whitney painted-c. 128-Williamson/Krenkel/Torres-a(r)/Forbidden Worlds #63; last 10¢ issue	6	12	18	37	66	95
100	6	12	18	41	78	110
129-153,157: 153,157-Magic Agent app.	4	8	12	28	47	65
154-Nemesis series begins (origin), ends #170	5	10	15	34	60	85
155,156,158-167,170-174: 174-Flying saucer-c	4	8	12	27	44	60
168-Ditko-a(p)	5	10	15	31	53	75
169-Nemesis battles Hitler	5	10	15	31	53	75
Nemesis Archives: Vol. One (Dark Horse Books, 9/08, $59.95) r/#154-170; creator bios						60.00

NOTE: *"Spirit of Frankenstein" series in 5, 6, 8-10, 12, 16.* *Buscema* a-100, 106, 108-110, 158r, 165r. *Cameron* a-34. *Craig* a-152, 160. *Goode* a-45, 47, 60. *Landau* a-51, 59-63. *Lazarus* a-34, 48, 51, 52, 56, 58, 79, 87; c-31-56, 58. *Reinman* a-102, 111, 112, 115-118, 124, 130, 137, 141, 145, 164. *Whitney* c-12-30, 57, 59-on (most.) *Torres/Williamson* a-116.

ADVENTURES INTO WEIRD WORLDS
Marvel/Atlas Comics (ACI): Jan, 1952 - No. 30, June, 1954

Issue	GD 2.0	VG 4.0	FN 6.0	VF 8.0	VF/NM 9.0	NM- 9.2
1-Atom bomb panels	145	290	435	928	1589	2250
2-Sci/fic stories (2); one by Maneely	55	110	165	352	601	850
3-10: 7-Tongue ripped out. 10-Krigstein, Everett-a	48	96	144	302	514	725
11-20	42	84	126	265	445	625
21-Hitler in Hell story	53	106	159	334	567	800
22-26: 24-Man holds hypo & splits in two-c	41	82	123	256	428	600
27-Matt Fox end of world story-a; severed head-c	71	142	213	454	777	1100
28-Atom bomb story; decapitation panels	47	94	141	296	498	700
29,30	41	82	123	256	428	600

NOTE: *Ayers* a-8, 26. *Everett* a-4, 5; c-6, 8, 10-13, 18, 19, 22, 24, 25; a-4, 25. *Fass* a-7. *Forte* a-21, 24. *Al Hartley* a-2. *Heath* a-1, 4, 17, 22; c-7, 9, 20. *Maneely* a-2, 3, 11, 20, 22, 23, 25; c-1, 3, 22, 25-27, 29. *Reinman* a-24, 28. *Rico* a-13. *Robinson* a-13. *Sinnott* a-25, 30. *Tuska* a-1, 2, 12, 15. *Whitney* a-7. *Wildey* a-28. Bondage c-22.

ADVENTURES IN WONDERLAND (Also see Uncle Charlies Fables)
Lev Gleason Publications: April, 1955 - No. 5, Feb, 1956 (Jr. Readers Guild)

Issue	GD 2.0	VG 4.0	FN 6.0	VF 8.0	VF/NM 9.0	NM- 9.2
1-Maurer-a	14	28	42	81	118	155
2-4	9	18	27	47	61	75
5-Christmas issue	9	18	27	50	65	80

ADVENTURES OF ALAN LADD, THE
National Periodical Publ.: Oct-Nov, 1949 - No. 9, Feb-Mar, 1951 (All 52 pgs.)

Issue	GD 2.0	VG 4.0	FN 6.0	VF 8.0	VF/NM 9.0	NM- 9.2
1-Photo-c	87	174	261	553	952	1350
2-Photo-c	41	82	123	256	428	600
3-6: Last photo-c	36	72	108	211	343	475
7-9	30	60	90	177	289	400

NOTE: *Dan Barry* a-1. *Moreira* a-3-7.

ADVENTURES OF ALICE (Also see Alice in Wonderland) (Becomes Alice at Monkey Island #3)
Civil Service Publ./Pentagon Publishing Co.: 1945

Issue	GD 2.0	VG 4.0	FN 6.0	VF 8.0	VF/NM 9.0	NM- 9.2
1	18	36	54	105	165	225
2-Through the Magic Looking Glass	14	28	42	81	118	155

ADVENTURES OF BARON MUNCHAUSEN, THE
Now Comics: July, 1989 - No. 4, Oct, 1989 ($1.75, limited series)

Issue	GD 2.0	VG 4.0	FN 6.0	VF 8.0	VF/NM 9.0	NM- 9.2
1-4: Movie adaptation						3.00

ADVENTURES OF BARRY WEEN, BOY GENIUS, THE
Image Comics: Mar, 1999 - No. 3, May, 1999 ($2.95, B&W, limited series)

Issue	GD 2.0	VG 4.0	FN 6.0	VF 8.0	VF/NM 9.0	NM- 9.2
1-3-Judd Winick-s/a						3.00
...: Secret Crisis Origin Files (Oni, 7/04, Free Comic Book Day giveaway) - Winick-s/a						3.00
TPB (Oni Press, 11/99, $8.95) r/#1-3						9.00

ADVENTURES OF BARRY WEEN, BOY GENIUS 2.0, THE
Oni Press: Feb, 2000 - No. 3, Apr, 2000 ($2.95, B&W, limited series)

Issue	GD 2.0	VG 4.0	FN 6.0	VF 8.0	VF/NM 9.0	NM- 9.2
1-3-Judd Winick-s/a						3.00
TPB (2000, $8.95)						9.00

ADVENTURES OF BARRY WEEN, BOY GENIUS 3, THE : MONKEY TALES
Oni Press: Feb, 2001 - No. 6, Feb, 2002 ($2.95, B&W, limited series)

Issue	GD 2.0	VG 4.0	FN 6.0	VF 8.0	VF/NM 9.0	NM- 9.2
1-6-Judd Winick-s/a						3.00
TPB (2001, $8.95) r/#1-3; intro. by Peter David						9.00
...4 TPB (5/02, $8.95) r/#4-6						9.00

ADVENTURES OF BAYOU BILLY, THE (Based on video game)
Archie Comics: Sept, 1989 - No. 5, June, 1990 ($1.00)

Issue	GD 2.0	VG 4.0	FN 6.0	VF 8.0	VF/NM 9.0	NM- 9.2
1-5: Esposito-c/a(i). 5-Kelley Jones-c						3.00

ADVENTURES OF BOB HOPE, THE (Also see True Comics #59)
National Per. Publ.: Feb-Mar, 1950 - No. 109, Feb-Mar, 1968 (#1-10: 52pgs.)

Issue	GD 2.0	VG 4.0	FN 6.0	VF 8.0	VF/NM 9.0	NM- 9.2
1-Photo-c	258	516	774	1651	2826	4000
2-Photo-c	92	184	276	584	1005	1425
3,4-Photo-c	57	114	171	362	619	875
5-10: 9-Horror-c	41	82	123	256	428	600
11-20	29	58	87	170	278	385
21-31 (2-3/55; last precode)	20	40	60	117	189	260
32-40	9	18	27	61	123	185
41-50	8	16	24	54	102	150
51-70	7	14	21	46	86	125
71-93	5	10	15	35	63	90
94-Aquaman cameo	6	12	18	42	79	115
95-1st app. Super-Hip & 1st monster issue (11/65)	9	18	27	60	120	180
96-105: Super-Hip and monster stories in all. 103-Batman, Robin, Ringo Starr cameos	6	12	18	38	69	100
106-109-All monster-c/stories by N. Adams-c/a	8	16	24	55	105	155

NOTE: *Buzzy in #34. Kitty Karr of Hollywood in #15, 17-20, 23, 28. Liz in #26, 109. Miss Beverly Hills of Hollywood in #7, 8, 10, 13, 14. Miss Melody Lane of Broadway in #15. Rusty in #23, 25. Tommy in #24. No 2nd feature in #2-4, 6, 8, 11, 12, 28-108.*

ADVENTURES OF CAPTAIN AMERICA
Marvel Comics: Sept, 1991 - No. 4, Jan, 1992 ($4.95, 52 pgs., squarebound, limited series)

Issue	GD 2.0	VG 4.0	FN 6.0	VF 8.0	VF/NM 9.0	NM- 9.2
1-4: 1-Origin in WW2; embossed-c; Nicieza scripts; Maguire-c/a(p) begins, ends #3. 2-4-Austin-c/a(i). 3,4-Red Skull app.						5.00

ADVENTURES OF CYCLOPS AND PHOENIX (Also See Askani'son & The Further Adventures of Cyclops And Phoenix)
Marvel Comics: May, 1994 - No. 4, Aug, 1994 ($2.95, limited series)

Issue	GD 2.0	VG 4.0	FN 6.0	VF 8.0	VF/NM 9.0	NM- 9.2
1-4-Characters from X-Men; origin of Cable						4.00
Trade paperback ($14.95)-reprints #1-4						15.00

ADVENTURES OF DEAN MARTIN AND JERRY LEWIS, THE
(The Adventures of Jerry Lewis #41 on) (See Movie Love #12)
National Periodical Publications: July-Aug, 1952 - No. 40, Oct, 1957

Issue	GD 2.0	VG 4.0	FN 6.0	VF 8.0	VF/NM 9.0	NM- 9.2
1	194	388	582	1242	2121	3000
2-Three pg. origin on how they became a team	60	120	180	381	653	925
3-10: 3- I Love Lucy text featurette	36	72	108	211	343	475
11-19: Last precode (2/55)	22	44	66	132	216	300
20-30	17	34	51	98	154	210
31-40	15	30	45	83	124	165

ADVENTURES OF DETECTIVE ACE KING, THE (Also see Bob Scully-- & Detective Dan)
Humor Publ. Corp.: No date (1933) (36 pgs., 9-1/2x12") (10¢, B&W, one-shot) (paper-c)

Issue	GD 2.0	VG 4.0	FN 6.0	VF 8.0	VF/NM 9.0	NM- 9.2
Book 1-Along with Bob Scully & Detective Dan, the first comic w/original art & the first of a single theme.; Not reprints; Ace King by Martin Nadle (The American Sherlock Holmes). A Dick Tracy look-alike	800	1600	2400	6400	-	-

ADVENTURES OF EVIL AND MALICE, THE
Image Comics: June, 1999 - No. 3, Nov, 1999 ($3.50/$3.95, limited series)

Issue	GD 2.0	VG 4.0	FN 6.0	VF 8.0	VF/NM 9.0	NM- 9.2
1-3-Jimmie Robinson-s/a. 3-($3.95-c)						4.00

ADVENTURES OF FELIX THE CAT, THE
Harvey Comics: May, 1992 ($1.25)

Issue	GD 2.0	VG 4.0	FN 6.0	VF 8.0	VF/NM 9.0	NM- 9.2
1-Messmer-r						5.00

ADVENTURES OF FORD FAIRLANE, THE
DC Comics: May, 1990 - No. 4, Aug, 1990 ($1.50, limited series, mature)

Issue	GD 2.0	VG 4.0	FN 6.0	VF 8.0	VF/NM 9.0	NM- 9.2
1-4: Andrew Dice Clay movie tie-in; Don Heck inks						4.00

ADVENTURES OF HOMER COBB, THE
Say/Bart Prod. : Sept, 1947 (Oversized) (Published in the U.S., but printed in Canada)

Adventures into Terror #13 © MAR

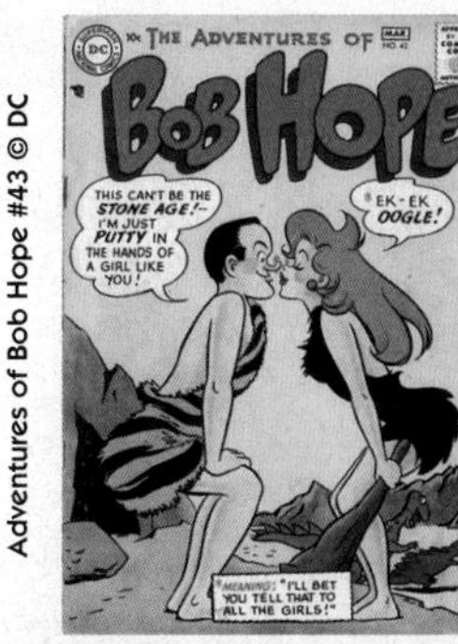

Adventures of Bob Hope #43 © DC

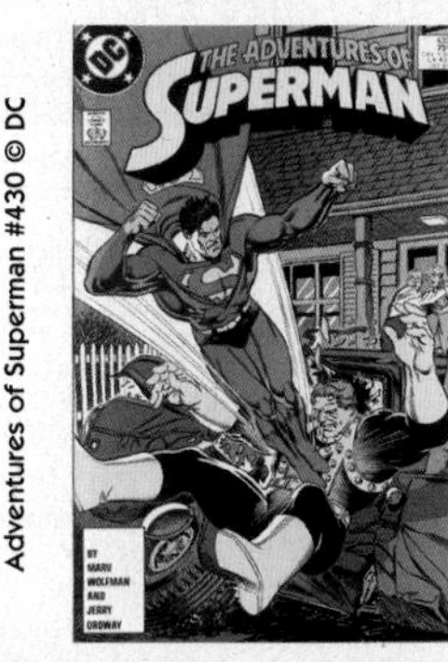

Adventures of Superman #430 © DC

	GD 2.0	VG 4.0	FN 6.0	VF 8.0	VF/NM 9.0	NM- 9.2
1-(Scarce)-Feldstein-c/a	53	106	159	334	567	800

ADVENTURES OF HOMER GHOST (See Homer The Happy Ghost)
Atlas Comics: June, 1957 - No. 2, Aug, 1957

	GD 2.0	VG 4.0	FN 6.0	VF 8.0	VF/NM 9.0	NM- 9.2
V1#1,2: 2-Robot-c	20	40	60	117	189	260

ADVENTURES OF JERRY LEWIS, THE (Adventures of Dean Martin & Jerry Lewis No. 1-40) (See Super DC Giant)
National Periodical Publ.: No. 41, Nov, 1957 - No. 124, May-June, 1971

	GD 2.0	VG 4.0	FN 6.0	VF 8.0	VF/NM 9.0	NM- 9.2
41	9	18	27	62	126	190
42-60	7	14	21	49	92	135
61-67,69-73,75-80	6	12	18	41	76	110
68,74-Photo-c (movie)	9	18	27	60	120	180
81,82,85-87,90,91,94,96,98,99	5	10	15	34	60	85
83,84,88: 83-1st Monsters-c/s. 84-Jerry as a Super-hero-c/s. 88-1st Witch, Miss Kraft	6	12	18	38	69	100
89-Bob Hope app.; Wizard of Oz & Alfred E. Neuman in MAD parody	8	16	24	51	96	140
92-Superman cameo	8	16	24	51	96	140
93-Beatles parody as babies	6	12	18	41	76	110
95-1st Uncle Hal Wack-A-Boy Camp-c/s	6	12	18	38	69	100
97-Batman/Robin/Joker-c/story; Riddler & Penguin app; Dick Sprang-c.	9	18	27	62	126	190
100	6	12	18	42	79	115
101,103,104-Neal Adams-c/a	8	16	24	54	102	150
102-Beatles app.; Neal Adams c/a	9	18	27	59	117	175
105-Superman x-over	6	12	18	41	76	110
106-111,113-116	4	8	12	28	47	65
112,117: 112-Flash x-over. 117-W. Woman x-over	6	12	18	41	76	110
118-124	4	8	12	27	44	60

NOTE: *Monster-c/s-90,93,96,98,101. Wack-A-Buy Camp-c/s-96,99,102,107,108.*

ADVENTURES OF JO-JOY, THE (See Jo-Joy)

ADVENTURES OF LASSIE, THE (See Lassie)

ADVENTURES OF LUTHER ARKWRIGHT, THE
Valkyrie Press/Dark Horse Comics: Oct, 1987 - No. 9, Jan, 1989 ($2.00, B&W) V2, #1, Mar, 1990 - V2#9, 1990 ($1.95, B&W)

	GD 2.0	VG 4.0	FN 6.0	VF 8.0	VF/NM 9.0	NM- 9.2
1-9: 1-Alan Moore intro., V2#1-9 (Dark Horse): r-1st series; new-c						4.00
TPB (1997, $14.95) r/#1-9 w/Michael Moorcock intro.						15.00

ADVENTURES OF MIGHTY MOUSE (Mighty Mouse Adventures No. 1)
St. John Publishing Co.: No. 2, Jan, 1952 - No. 18, May, 1955

	GD 2.0	VG 4.0	FN 6.0	VF 8.0	VF/NM 9.0	NM- 9.2
2	31	62	93	184	300	415
3-5	16	32	48	94	147	200
6-18	14	28	42	76	108	140

ADVENTURES OF MIGHTY MOUSE (2nd Series) (Becomes Mighty Mouse #161 on) (Two No. 144's; formerly Paul Terry's Comics; No. 129-137 have nn's)
St. John/Pines/Dell/Gold Key: No. 126, Aug, 1955 - No. 160, Oct, 1963

	GD 2.0	VG 4.0	FN 6.0	VF 8.0	VF/NM 9.0	NM- 9.2
126(8/55), 127(10/55), 128(11/55)-St. John	10	20	30	56	76	95
nn(129, 4/56)-144(8/59)-Pines	5	10	15	30	50	70
144(10-12/59)-155(7-9/62) Dell	4	8	12	27	44	60
156(10/62)-160(10/63) Gold Key	4	8	12	27	44	60

NOTE: *Early issues titled "Paul Terry's Adventures of ...."*

ADVENTURES OF MIGHTY MOUSE (Formerly Mighty Mouse)
Gold Key: No. 166, Mar, 1979 - No. 172, Jan, 1980

	GD 2.0	VG 4.0	FN 6.0	VF 8.0	VF/NM 9.0	NM- 9.2
166-172	1	3	4	6	8	10

ADVS. OF MR. FROG & MISS MOUSE (See Dell Junior Treasury No. 4)

ADVENTURES OF OZZIE & HARRIET, THE (See Ozzie & Harriet)

ADVENTURES OF PATORUZU
Green Publishing Co.: Aug, 1946 - Winter, 1946

	GD 2.0	VG 4.0	FN 6.0	VF 8.0	VF/NM 9.0	NM- 9.2
nn's-Contains Animal Crackers reprints	8	16	24	42	54	65

ADVENTURES OF PINKY LEE, THE (TV)
Atlas Comics: July, 1955 - No. 5, Dec, 1955

	GD 2.0	VG 4.0	FN 6.0	VF 8.0	VF/NM 9.0	NM- 9.2
1	30	60	90	177	289	400
2-5	19	38	57	111	176	240

ADVENTURES OF PIPSQUEAK, THE (Formerly Pat the Brat)
Archie Publications (Radio Comics): No. 34, Sept, 1959 - No. 39, July, 1960

	GD 2.0	VG 4.0	FN 6.0	VF 8.0	VF/NM 9.0	NM- 9.2
34	4	8	12	25	40	55
35-39	3	6	9	21	33	45

ADVENTURES OF QUAKE & QUISP, THE (See Quaker Oats "Plenty of Glutton")

ADVENTURES OF REX THE WONDER DOG, THE (Rex...No. 1)
National Periodical Publ.: Jan-Feb, 1952 - No. 45, May-June, 1959; No. 46, Nov-Dec, 1959

	GD 2.0	VG 4.0	FN 6.0	VF 8.0	VF/NM 9.0	NM- 9.2
1-(Scarce)-Toth-c/a	258	516	774	1651	2826	4000
2-(Scarce)-Toth-c/a	93	186	279	591	1021	1450
3-(Scarce)-Toth-a	68	136	204	435	743	1050
4,5	53	106	159	334	567	800
6-10	43	86	129	271	461	650
11-Atom bomb-c/story; dinosaur-c/sty	53	106	159	334	567	800
12-19: 19-Last precode (1-2/55)	34	68	102	199	325	450
20-46	24	48	72	142	234	325

NOTE: ***Infantino, Gil Kane** art in 5-19 (most)*

ADVENTURES OF ROBIN HOOD, THE (Formerly Robin Hood)
Magazine Enterprises (Sussex Publ. Co.): No. 6, Jun, 1957 - No. 8, Nov, 1957 (Based on Richard Greene TV Show)

	GD 2.0	VG 4.0	FN 6.0	VF 8.0	VF/NM 9.0	NM- 9.2
6-8-Richard Greene photo-c. 6,7-Powell-a	15	30	45	88	137	185

ADVENTURES OF ROBIN HOOD, THE
Gold Key: Mar, 1974 - No. 7, Jan, 1975 (Disney cartoon) (36 pgs.)

	GD 2.0	VG 4.0	FN 6.0	VF 8.0	VF/NM 9.0	NM- 9.2
1(90291-403)-Part-r of $1.50 editions	3	6	9	16	23	30
2-7: 1-7 are part-r	2	4	6	10	14	18

ADVENTURES OF SNAKE PLISSKEN
Marvel Comics: Jan, 1997 ($2.50, one-shot)

	GD 2.0	VG 4.0	FN 6.0	VF 8.0	VF/NM 9.0	NM- 9.2
1-Based on Escape From L.A. movie; Brereton-c	2	4	6	10	14	18

ADVENTURES OF SPAWN, THE
Image Comics (Todd McFarlane Prods.): Jan, 2007; Nov, 2008 ($5.99)

	GD 2.0	VG 4.0	FN 6.0	VF 8.0	VF/NM 9.0	NM- 9.2
1,2-Printed adaptation of the Spawn.com web comic; Khary Randolph-a	2	4	6	11	16	20

ADVENTURES OF SPIDER-MAN, THE (Based on animated TV series)
Marvel Comics: Apr, 1996 - No. 12, Mar, 1997 (99¢)

	GD 2.0	VG 4.0	FN 6.0	VF 8.0	VF/NM 9.0	NM- 9.2
1-Punisher app.	2	4	6	8	10	12
2-12: 2-Venom cameo. 3-X-Men. 6-Fantastic Four						4.00

ADVENTURES OF SUPERBOY, THE (See Superboy, 2nd Series)

ADVENTURES OF SUPERGIRL (Based on the TV series)
DC Comics: Early Jul, 2016 - No. 6, Sept, 2016 ($2.99)(Printing of stories first appearing online)

	GD 2.0	VG 4.0	FN 6.0	VF 8.0	VF/NM 9.0	NM- 9.2
1-Rampage app.; Bengal-a/Staggs-c	1	3	4	6	8	10
2-6						5.00

ADVENTURES OF SUPERMAN (Formerly Superman)
DC Comics: No. 424, Jan, 1987 - No. 499, Feb, 1993; No. 500, Early June, 1993 - No. 649, Apr, 2006 (This title's numbering continues with Superman #650, May, 2006)

	GD 2.0	VG 4.0	FN 6.0	VF 8.0	VF/NM 9.0	NM- 9.2
424-Ordway-c/a; Wolfman-s begin following Byrne's Superman revamp; 1st Cat Grant	2	4	6	8	10	12
425-435,437-462: 426-Legends x-over. 432-1st app. Jose Delgado who becomes Gangbuster in #434. 437-Millennium x-over. 438-New Brainiac app. 440-Batman app. 449-Invasion						4.00
436-Byrne scripts begin; Millennium x-over						5.00
463-Superman/Flash race; cover swipe/Superman #199	2	4	6	8	10	12
464-Lobo-c & app. (pre-dates Lobo #1)	1	3	4	6	8	10
465-1st app. Hank Henshaw (later becomes Cyborg Superman)	2	4	6	8	11	14
466-479,481-495: 467-Part 2 of Batman story. 473-Hal Jordan, Guy Gardner x-over. 477-Legion app. 491-Last $1.00-c. 495-Forever People-c/story; Darkseid app.						4.00
480,496,497: 480-($1.75, 52 pgs.). 496-Doomsday cameo. 497-Doomsday battle issue						4.00
496,497-2nd printings						4.00
498,499-Funeral for a Friend; Supergirl app.						5.00
498-2nd & 3rd printings						3.00
500-($2.95, 68 pgs.)-Collector's edition w/card	2	4	6	8	10	12
500-($2.50, 68 pgs.)-Regular edition w/different-c						6.00
500-Platinum edition						85.00
501-($1.95)-Collector's edition with die-cut-c						5.00
501-($1.50)-Regular edition w/mini-poster & diff.-c						4.00
502-516: 502-Supergirl-c/story. 508-Challengers of the Unknown app. 510-Bizarro-c/story. 516-(9/94)-Zero Hour tie-in (see #0 for next issue)						3.00
505-($2.50)-Holo-grafx foil-c edition						5.00
517-523: 517-(11/94)						3.00
524-549,551-580: 524-Begin $1.95-c. 527-Return of Alpha Centurion (Zero Hour). 533-Impulse-c/app. 535-Luthor-c/app. 536-Brainiac app. 537-Parasite app. 540-Final Night x-over. 541-Superboy-c/app.; Lois & Clark honeymoon. 545-New powers. 546-New costume. 555-Red & Blue Supermen battle. 557-Millennium Giants x-over. 558-560: Superman Silver Age-style story; Krypto app. 561-Begin $1.99-c. 565-JLA app.						3.00
550-($3.50)-Double sized						4.00
581-588: 581-Begin $2.25-c. 583-Emperor Joker. 588-Casey-s						3.00
589-595: 589-Return to Krypton; Rivoche-c. 591-Wolfman-s. 593-595-Our Worlds at War						

GD 2.0 | VG 4.0 | FN 6.0 | VF 8.0 | VF/NM 9.0 | NM- 9.2

x-over. 593-New Suicide Squad formed. 594-Doomsday-c/app. 3.00
596-Aftermath of "War" x-over has panel showing damaged World Trade Center buildings; issue went on sale the day after the Sept. 11 attack 6.00
597-599,601-624: 597-Joker: Last Laugh. 604,605-Ultraman, Owlman, Superwoman app. 606-Return to Krypton. 612-616,619-623-Nowlan-c. 624-Mr. Majestic app. 3.00
600-($3.95) Wieringo-a; painted-c by Adel; pin-ups by various 4.00
625,626-Godfall parts 2,5; Turner-c; Caldwell-a(p) 4.00
627-641,643-648: 627-Begin $2.50-c, Rucka-s/Clark-a/Ha-c begin. 628-Wagner-c. 631-Bagged with Sky Captain CD; Lois shot. 634-Mxyzptlk visits DC offices. 639-Capt. Marvel & Eclipso app. 641-OMAC app. 643-Sacrifice aftermath; Batman & Wonder Woman app. 3.00
642-OMAC Project x-over Sacrifice pt. 3; JLA app. 5.00
642-(2nd printing) red tone cover 3.00
649-Last issue; Infinite Crisis x-over, Superman vs. Earth-2 Superman 4.00
#0-(10/94) Zero Hour tie-in; released between #516 & #517 3.00
#1,000,000 (11/98) Gene Ha-c; 853rd Century x-over 5.00
Annual 1 (1987, $1.25, 52 pgs.)-Starlin-c & scripts 4.00
Annual 2,3 (1990, 1991, $2.00, 68 pgs.): 2-Byrne-c/a(i); Legion '90 (Lobo) app. 3-Armageddon 2001 x-over 4.00
Annual 4-6 ('92-'94, $2.50, 68 pgs.): 4-Guy Gardner/Lobo-c/story; Eclipso storyline; Quesada-c(p). 5-Bloodlines storyline. 6-Elseworlds sty. 4.00
Annual 7,9('95, '97, $3.95)-7-Year One story. 9-Pulp Heroes sty 4.00
Annual 8 (1996, $2.95)-Legends of the Dead Earth story 4.00
NOTE: *Erik Larsen a-431.*

ADVENTURES OF SUPERMAN
DC Comics: Jul, 2013 - No. 17, Nov, 2014 ($3.99)
1-17-Short story anthology by various. 1-Lemire-s/a. 4-Timm-c. 6-Mongul app. 14-Joker app.; Sugar & Spike app.; Hester-a 4.00

ADVENTURES OF SUPERMAN: JON KENT (Follows Superman: Son of Kal-El series)
DC Comics: May, 2023 - Present ($3.99)
1-Taylor-s/Henry-a; Val-Zod and Ultraman app. 4.00

ADVENTURES OF THE DOVER BOYS
Archie Comics (Close-up): September, 1950 - No. 2, 1950 (No month given)
1,2 12 24 36 69 97 125

ADVENTURES OF THE FLY (The Fly #1-6; Fly Man No. 32-39; See The Double Life of Private Strong, The Fly, Laugh Comics & Mighty Crusaders)
Archie Publications/Radio Comics: Aug, 1959 - No. 30, Oct, 1964; No. 31, May, 1965
1-Shield app.; origin The Fly; S&K-c/a 57 114 171 456 1028 1600
2-Williamson, S&K-a 29 58 87 209 467 725
3-Origin retold; Davis, Powell-a 27 54 81 189 420 650
4-Neal Adams-a(p)(1 panel); S&K-c; Powell-a; 2 pg. Shield story 38 76 114 285 641 1000
5,6,9,10: 10-Black Hood app. 12 24 36 82 179 275
7,8: 7-1st S.A. app. Black Hood (7/60). 8-1st S.A. app. Shield (9/60) 18 36 54 121 268 415
9-1st app. Cat Girl; Shield app. 14 28 42 96 211 325
11-13,15-20: 13-1st app. Fly Girl w/o costume. 16-Last 10¢ issue. 20-Origin Fly Girl retold 8 16 24 55 105 155
14-Origin & 1st app. Fly Girl in costume 9 18 27 60 120 180
21-30: 23-Jaguar cameo. 27-29-Black Hood 1 pg. strips. 30-Comet x-over (1st S.A. app.) in Fly Girl 7 14 21 44 82 120
31-Black Hood, Shield, Comet app. 7 14 21 46 86 125
Vol. 1 TPB ('04, $12.95) r/#1-4 & Double Life of Private Strong #1,2; foreward by Joe Simon 13.00
NOTE: *Simon c-2-4. Tuska a-1. Cover title to #31 is Flyman; Advs. of the Fly inside.*

ADVENTURES OF THE JAGUAR, THE (See Blue Ribbon Comics, Laugh Comics & Mighty Crusaders)
Archie Publications (Radio Comics): Sept, 1961 - No. 15, Nov, 1963
1-Origin Jaguar (1st app?) by J. Rosenberger 26 52 78 182 404 625
2,3: 3-Last 10¢ issue 11 22 33 77 166 255
4-6-Catgirl app. (#4's-c is same as splash pg.) 9 18 27 59 117 175
7-10: 10-Dinosaur-c 7 14 21 49 92 135
11-15: 13,14-Catgirl, Black Hood app. in both 6 12 18 42 79 115

ADVENTURES OF THE MASK (TV cartoon)
Dark Horse Comics: Jan, 1996 - No. 12, Dec, 1996 ($2.50)
1-Based on animated series 1 3 4 6 8 10
2-12 5.00

ADVENTURES OF THE NEW MEN (Formerly Newmen #1-21)
Maximum Press: No. 22, Nov, 1996; No. 23, March, 1997 ($2.50)
22,23-Sprouse-c/a 3.00

ADVENTURES OF THE OUTSIDERS, THE (Formerly Batman & The Outsiders; also see The Outsiders)
DC Comics: No. 33, May, 1986 - No. 46, June, 1987
33-46: 39-45-r/Outsiders #1-7 by Aparo 4.00

ADVENTURES OF THE SUPER MARIO BROTHERS (See Super Mario Bros.)
Valiant: Feb, 1991 - No. 9, Oct, 1991 ($1.50)
V2#1 9 18 27 59 117 175
2-9 3 6 9 14 19 24

ADVENTURES OF THE SUPER SONS (Jon Kent and Damian Wayne)
DC Comics: Oct, 2018 - No. 12, Sept, 2019 ($3.99)
1-12: 1-Intro Rex Luthor and Joker Jr.; Tomasi-s/Barberi-a. 6-Tommy Tomorrow app. 4.00

ADVENTURES OF THE THING, THE (Also see The Thing)
Marvel Comics: Apr, 1992 - No. 4, July, 1992, ($1.25, limited series)
1-4: 1-r/Marvel Two-In-One #50 by Byrne; Kieth-c. 2-4-r/Marvel Two-In-One #80,51 & 77; 2-Ghost Rider-c/story; Quesada-c. 3-Miller-r/Quesada-c; new Perez-a (4 pgs.) 4.00

ADVENTURES OF THE X-MEN, THE (Based on animated TV series)
Marvel Comics: Apr, 1996 - No. 12, Mar, 1997 (99¢)
1-Wolverine/Hulk battle 2 4 6 8 10 12
2-12: 3-Spider-Man-c. 5,6-Magneto-c/app. 4.00

ADVENTURES OF TINKER BELL (See Tinker Bell, 4-Color No. 896 & 982)

ADVENTURES OF TOM SAWYER (See Dell Junior Treasury No. 10)

ADVENTURES OF YOUNG DR. MASTERS, THE
Archie Comics (Radio Comics): Aug, 1964 - No. 2, Nov, 1964
1 4 8 12 25 40 55
2 3 6 9 16 23 30

ADVENTURES ON OTHER WORLDS (See Showcase #17 & 18)

ADVENTURES ON THE PLANET OF THE APES (Also see Planet of the Apes)
Marvel Comics Group: Oct, 1975 - No. 11, Dec, 1976
1-Planet of the Apes magazine-r in color; Starlin-c; adapts movie thru #6 6 12 18 38 69 100
2-5: 5-(25¢-c edition) 3 6 9 18 28 38
5-7-(30¢-c variants, limited distribution) 6 12 18 41 76 110
6-10: 6,7-(25¢-c edition). 7-Adapts 2nd movie (thru #11) 3 6 9 16 23 30
11-Last issue; concludes 2nd movie adaptation 3 6 9 21 33 45
NOTE: *Alcala a-6-11r. Buckler c-2p. Nasser c-7. Ploog a-1-9. Starlin c-6. Tuska a-1-5r.*

ADVENTURES WITH THE DC SUPER HEROES (Interior also inserted into some DC issues)
DC Comics/Geppi's Entertainment Museum: 2007 Free Comic Book Day giveaway
"The Batman and Cal Ripken, Jr. Hall of Fame Edition "A Rare Catch" " in indicia 1 3 4 6 8 10

ADVENTURE TIME (With Finn & Jake) (Based on the Cartoon Network animated series)
Boom Entertainment (KaBOOM!): Feb, 2012 - No. 75, Apr, 2018 ($3.99)
1-Cover A 32.00
1-Covers B & C; interlocking image 28.00
1-Cover D variant by Jeffrey Brown 35.00
1-Cover E wraparound 50.00
1-Second & third printings 5.00
2-Four covers 12.00
3-24,26-49,51-74-Multiple covers on all 4.00
25-($4.99) Art by Dustin Nguyen, Jess Fink, Jeffrey Brown & others; multiple covers 5.00
50-($4.99) Hastings-s/McGinty-a; multiple covers 5.00
75-($4.99) Last issue; multiple covers 5.00
2013 Annual #1 (5/13, $4.99) Three covers; s/a by Langridge, Nguyen & others 5.00
2013 Spoooktacular (10/13, $4.99) Halloween-themed; s/a by Fraser Irving & others 5.00
2013 Summer Special (7/13, $4.99) Multiple covers 5.00
2014 Annual #1 (4/14, $4.99) Three covers; stories printed sideways 5.00
2014 Winter Special (1/14, $4.99) Multiple covers 5.00
2015 Spoooktacular (10/15, $4.99) a Marceline story; s/a by Hanna K 5.00
2016 Spoooktacular (9/16, $4.99) Short stories by various; 2 covers by Bartel & McClaren 5.00
2017 Spoooktacular (10/17, $4.99) Short stories by various; 2 covers 5.00
... BMO Bonanza 1 (3/18, $7.99) Short stories by various 8.00
... Cover Showcase (12/12, $3.99) Gallery of variant covers for #1-9; Paul Pope-c 4.00
... Free Comic Book Day Edition (5/12) Giveaway flip book with Peanuts 4.00
... with Fionna and Cake 2018 Free Comic Book Day Special (5/18) Giveaway 3.00

ADVENTURE TIME: BANANA GUARD ACADEMY (Cartoon Network)
Boom Entertainment (KaBOOM!): Jul, 2014 - No. 6, Dec, 2014 ($3.99, limited series)
1-6-Multiple covers on all; Mad Rupert-a 4.00

ADVENTURE TIME: BEGINNING OF THE END (Cartoon Network)
Boom Entertainment (KaBOOM!): May, 2018 - No. 3, Jul, 2018 ($3.99, limited series)
1-3-Multiple covers on all; Ted Anderson-s/Marina Julia-a 4.00

ADVENTURE TIME: CANDY CAPERS (Cartoon Network)
Boom Entertainment (KaBOOM!): Jul, 2013 - No. 6, Dec, 2013 ($3.99, limited series)
1-6-Multiple covers on all; McGinty-a 4.00

ADVENTURE TIME COMICS (Cartoon Network)
Boom Entertainment (KaBOOM!): Jul, 2016 - No. 25, Jul, 2018 ($3.99)
1-24-Short stories by various. 1-Baltazar, Cook, Millionaire, Leyh-s/a 4.00
25-($4.99) Sonny Liew-s/a; Morgan Beem-s/a 5.00

ADVENTURE TIME: ICE KING (Cartoon Network)
Boom Entertainment (KaBOOM!): Jan, 2016 - No. 6, Jun, 2016 ($3.99, limited series)
1-6-Multiple covers on all; Naujokaitis-s/Andrewson-a 4.00

ADVENTURE TIME: MARCELINE AND THE SCREAM QUEENS (Cartoon Network)
Boom Entertainment (KaBOOM!): Jul, 2012 - No. 6, Dec, 2012 ($3.99, limited series)
1-6-Multiple covers on all 4.00

ADVENTURE TIME: MARCELINE GONE ADRIFT (Cartoon Network)
Boom Entertainment (KaBOOM!): Jan, 2015 - No. 6, Jun, 2015 ($3.99, limited series)
1-6-Multiple covers on all; Meredith Gran-s/Carey Pietsch-a 4.00

ADVENTURE TIME: MARCY & SIMON (Cartoon Network)
Boom Entertainment (KaBOOM!): Jan, 2019 - No. 6, Jun, 2019 ($3.99, limited series)
1-6-Multiple covers on all; Olivia Olson-s/Slimm Fabert; former Ice King apology tour 4.00

ADVENTURE TIME/ REGULAR SHOW (Cartoon Network)
Boom Entertainment (KaBOOM!): Aug, 2017 - No. 6, Jan, 2018 ($3.99, limited series)
1-6-McCreery-s/Di Meo-a; multiple covers on each 4.00

ADVENTURE TIME: SEASON 11 (Cartoon Network)
Boom Entertainment (KaBOOM!): Oct, 2018 - No. 6, Mar, 2019 ($3.99)
1-6-Follows the television finale; Ted Anderson-s/Marina Julia-a 4.00

ADVENTURE TIME: THE FLIP SIDE (Cartoon Network)
Boom Entertainment (KaBOOM!): Jan, 2014 - No. 6, Jun, 2014 ($3.99, limited series)
1-6-Multiple covers on all; Tobin & Coover-s; Wook Jin Clark-a 4.00

ADVENTURE TIME WITH FIONNA & CAKE (Cartoon Network)
Boom Entertainment (KaBOOM!): Jan, 2013 - No. 6, Jun, 2013 ($3.99, limited series)
1-6-Multiple covers on all 4.00

ADVENTURE TIME WITH FIONNA & CAKE CARD WARS (Cartoon Network)
Boom Entertainment (KaBOOM!): Jul, 2015 - No. 6, Dec, 2015 ($3.99, limited series)
1-6-Multiple covers on all; Jen Wang-s/Britt Wilson-a. 1-Polybagged with a game card 4.00

AEON FLUX (Based on the 2005 movie which was based on the MTV animated series)

Adventures of Superman: Jon Kent #1 © DC

Adventure Time Comics #13 © CN

Afterlife With Archie #5 © ACP

GD	VG	FN	VF	VF/NM	NM-
2.0	4.0	6.0	8.0	9.0	9.2

Dark Horse Comics: Oct, 2005 - No. 4, Jan, 2006 ($2.99, limited series)
1-Timothy Green II-a/Mike Kennedy-s 2 4 6 9 12 15
2-4 3.00
TPB (5/06, $12.95) r/series; cover gallery 13.00

AERO (See War of the Realms: New Agents of Atlas #4)
Marvel Comics: Sept, 2019 - No. 12, Dec, 2020 ($3.99)
1-Liefen-s/Kang-a; Shanghai-based heroine; origin back-up by Pak-s/Mhan-a 6.00
2-10 4.00

A-FORCE (Secret Wars tie-in)
Marvel Comics: Jul, 2015 - No. 5, Dec, 2015 ($3.99, limited series)
1-All-Female Avengers team; Bennett & Willow Wilson-s/Molina-a; intro. Singularity 2 4 6 9 12 15
2-5 4.00

A-FORCE (Follows Secret Wars)
Marvel Comics: Mar, 2016 - No. 10, Dec, 2016 ($3.99)
1-10: 1-Medusa, She-Hulk, Dazzler, Nico, Capt. Marvel, Singularity team; Wilson-s/Molina-a. 5-7-Thompson-s/Caldwell-a. 8-10-Civil War II tie-in 4.00

AFRICA
Magazine Enterprises: 1955
1(A-1 #137)-Cave Girl, Thun'da; Powell-c/a(4) 39 78 117 240 395 550

AFRICAN LION (Disney movie)
Dell Publishing Co.: Nov, 1955
Four Color 665 5 10 15 35 63 90

AFTER DARK
Sterling Comics: No. 6, May, 1955 - No. 8, Sept, 1955
6-8-Sekowsky-a in all 12 24 36 69 97 125

AFTER DARK (Co-created by Wesley Snipes)
Radical Comics: No. 0, Jun, 2010 - No. 3 ($1.00/$4.99, limited series)
0-($1.00) Milligan-s/Nentrup & Mattina-a 3.00
1-3-($4.99) Milligan-s/Manco-a 5.00

AFTERDARK
AfterShock Comics: Oct, 2021 ($6.99, oversized 8-1/2" x 10-7/8", one shot)
1-Horror anthology by various incl. Starlin, Bunn, Kudranski, Tieri, Pruett, Eisma 7.00

AFTERLIFE WITH ARCHIE
Archie Comic Publications: Sept, 2013 - Present ($2.99/$3.99)
1-Aguirre-Sacasa-s/Francavilla-a; zombies in Riverdale; Sabrina app.; 4 covers 28.00
1-Second printing; new cover by Francavilla 6.00
2-Covers by Francavilla & Seeley; back-up short story r/Chilling Advs. in Sorcery 14.00
3-6: 3,4-Covers by Francavilla & Seeley on each; back-up r/Chilling Advs. in Sorcery. 5,6-Pepoy variant-c. 6-Back-up preview of Chilling Advs. of Sabrina #1 8.00
7-10-($3.99) 7-Covers by Francavilla & Pepoy; back-up r/Chilling Advs. in Sorcery 6.00
... Halloween ComicFest Edition 1 (2014, giveaway) Grey-toned reprint of #1 4.00
... Halloween ComicFest Edition 1 (2016, giveaway) Grey-toned reprint of #7 4.00

AFTER REALM QUARTERLY, THE
Image Comics: Feb, 2020 - Present ($5.99, quarterly)
1-3-Michael Avon Oeming-s/a; intro/origin of Oona Lightfoot 6.00

AFTERSHOCK GENESIS
AfterShock Comics: May, 2016 ($1.00, one-shot)
1-Short stories by various and previews of upcoming AfterShock titles 3.00

AFTERSHOCK TRIPLE PLAY
AfterShock Comics: Dec, 2021 ($4.99, one-shot)
1-Stories from Animosity, Dark Ark & We Live; gatefold front-c 5.00

AFTER THE CAPE
Image Comics (Shadowline): Mar, 2007 - No. 3, May, 2007 ($2.99, B&W, limited series)
1-3-Jim Valentino-s/Marco Rudy-a 3.00
... Volume One TPB (9/07, $12.99) r/series; scripts, sketch pages, character profiles 13.00
...II (11/07 - No. 3, 1/08, $2.99) 1-3-Jim Valentino-s/Sergio Carrera-a 3.00

AGENCY, THE
Image Comics (Top Cow): August, 2001 - No. 6, Mar, 2002 ($2.50/$2.95/$4.95)
1-5: 1-Jenkins-s/Hotz-a; three covers by Hotz, Turner, Silvestri. 3-5-($2.95) 3.00
6-($4.95) Flip-c preview of Jeremiah TV series 5.00
Preview (2001, 16 pgs.) B&W pages, cover previews, sketch pages 3.00

AGENT CARTER: S.H.I.E.L.D. 50TH ANNIVERSARY
Marvel Comics: Nov, 2015 ($3.99, one-shot)
1-Kathryn Immonen-s/Rich Ellis-a; set in 1966; Sif, Dum Dum and Nick Fury app. 4.00

GD	VG	FN	VF	VF/NM	NM-
2.0	4.0	6.0	8.0	9.0	9.2

AGENT 47: BIRTH OF THE HITMAN (Based on the Io-Anteractive video game)
Dynamite Entertainment: 2017 - No. 6, 2018 ($3.99)
1-6: 1-Sebela-s/Lau-a; multiple covers on each 4.00

AGENT LIBERTY SPECIAL (See Superman, 2nd Series)
DC Comics: 1992 ($2.00, 52 pgs, one-shot)
1-1st solo adventure; Guice-c/a(i) 4.00

AGENTS, THE
Image Comics: Apr, 2003 - No. 6, Sept, 2003 ($2.95, B&W)
1-5-Ben Dunn-c/a in all 3.00
6-Five pg. preview of The Walking Dead #1 3 6 9 17 26 35

AGENTS OF ATLAS
Marvel Comics: Oct, 2006 - No. 6, Mar, 2007 ($2.99, limited series)
1-6: 1-Golden Age heroes Marvel Boy & Venus app.; Kirk-a 3.00
... MGC 1 (7/10, $1.00) r/#1 with "Marvel's Greatest Comics" logo on cover 3.00
HC (2007, $24.99, dustjacket) r/#1-6, What If? #9, agents' debuts in '40s-'50s Atlas comics, creator interviews, character design art 25.00

AGENTS OF ATLAS (Dark Reign)
Marvel Comics: Apr, 2009 - No. 11, Nov, 2009 ($3.99)
1-11: 1-Pagulayan-a; 2 covers by Art Adams and McGuinness; back-up with Wolverine app. 5-New Avengers app. 8-Hulk app. 4.00

AGENTS OF ATLAS (Continues in Atlantis Attacks #1)(Also see Future Fight Firsts)
Marvel Comics: Oct, 2019 - No. 5, Feb, 2020 ($4.99/$3.99)
1-($4.99) Team of Shang-Chi, Brawn, Silk, Jimmy Woo, Luna Snow, Aero & others 5.00
2-5-($3.99) Greg Pak-s/Nico Leon-a. 5-Namor app. 4.00

AGENTS OF LAW (Also see Comics' Greatest World)
Dark Horse Comics: Mar, 1995 - No. 6, Sept, 1995 ($2.50)
1-6: 5-Predator app. 6-Predator app.; death of Law 3.00

AGENTS OF S.H.I.E.L.D. (Characters from the TV series)
Marvel Comics: Mar, 2016 - No. 10, Dec, 2016 ($3.99)
1-10: 1-Guggenheim-s/Peralta-a; Tony Stark app. 3,4-Standoff tie-in. 5-Spider-Man app. 7-10-Civil War II tie-in. 9,10-Elektra app. 4.00

AGENT X (Continued from Deadpool)
Marvel Comics: Sept. 2002 - No. 15, Dec, 2003 ($2.99/$2.25)
1-($2.99) Simone-s/Udon Studios-a; Taskmaster app. 4.00
2-9-($2.25) 2-Punisher app. 3.00
10-15-($2.99) 10,11-Evan Dorkin-s. 12-Hotz-a 3.00

AGE OF APOCALYPSE (See Uncanny X-Force)
Marvel Comics: May, 2012 - No. 14, Jun, 2013 ($2.99)
1-14: 1-Lapham-s/De La Torre-a/Ramos-c. 13-Leads into X-Termination x-over 3.00

AGE OF APOCALYPSE (Secret Wars tie-in)
Marvel Comics: Sept, 2015 - No. 5, Dec, 2015 ($4.99/$3.99, limited series)
1-($4.99) Nicieza-s/Sandoval-a; alternate X-Men vs. Apocalypse 5.00
2-5-($3.99) Covers #1-5 form one image; Blink, Sabretooth & Magneto app. 4.00

AGE OF APOCALYPSE: THE CHOSEN
Marvel Comics: Apr, 1995 ($2.50, one-shot)
1-Wraparound-c 5.00

AGE OF BRONZE
Image Comics: Nov, 1998 - Present ($2.95/$3.50, B&W)
1-6-Eric Shanower-c/s/a 3.50
7-33-($3.50) 3.50
...Behind the Scenes (5/02, $3.50) background info and creative process 3.50
Image Firsts: Age of Bronze #1 (4/10, $1.00) r/#1 with "Image Firsts" cover logo 3.00
...Special (6/99, $2.95) Story of Agamemnon and Menelaus 3.50
A Thousand Ships (7/01, $19.95, TPB) r/#1-9 20.00
Sacrifice (9/04, $19.95, TPB) r/#10-19 20.00

AGE OF CONAN: BELIT
Marvel Comics: May, 2019 - No. 5, Sept, 2019 ($3.99, limited series)
1-5-Tini Howard-s/Kate Niemczyk-a/Sana Takeda-c; back-up serialized text story 4.00

AGE OF CONAN: VALERIA
Marvel Comics: Oct, 2019 - No. 5, Feb, 2020 ($3.99, limited series)
1-5-Meredith Finch-s/Aneke-a; origin from childhood; back-up serialized text story 4.00

AGE OF HEROES, THE
Halloween Comics/Image Comics #3 on: 1996 - No. 5, 1999 ($2.95, B&W)
1-5: James Hudnall scripts; John Ridgway-c/a 3.00
...Special ($4.95) r/#1,2 5.00

...Special 2 ($6.95) r/#3,4 7.00
...Wex 1 ('98, $2.95) Hudnall-s/Angel Fernandez-a 3.00

AGE OF HEROES (The Heroic Age)
Marvel Comics: Jul, 2010 - No. 4, Oct, 2010 ($3.99, limited series)

1-4-Short stories of Avengers members by various. 4-Jae Lee-c 4.00

AGE OF INNOCENCE: THE REBIRTH OF IRON MAN
Marvel Comics: Feb, 1996 ($2.50, one-shot)

1-New origin of Tony Stark 3.00

AGE OF REPTILES
Dark Horse Comics: Nov, 1993 - No. 4, Feb, 1994 ($2.50, limited series)

1-4: Delgado-c/a/scripts in all 4.00
... Ancient Egyptians 1-4 (6/15 - No. 4, 9/15, $3.99) Delgado-c/a/scripts; wraparound-c 4.00
... The Hunt 1-5 (5/96 - No. 5, 9/96, $2.95) Delgado-c/a/scripts in all; wraparound-c 4.00
... The Journey 1-4 (11/09 - No. 4, 7/10, $3.50) Delgado-c/a/scripts in all; wraparound-c 3.50

AGE OF THE SENTRY, THE
Marvel Comics: Nov, 2008 - No. 6, Mar, 2010 ($2.99, limited series)

1-6-Silver Age style stories. 1-Origin retold; Bullock-c. 3-Coover-a 3.00

AGE OF ULTRON
Marvel Comics: May, 2013 - No. 10, Aug, 2013 ($3.99, limited series)

1-Wraparound cardstock foil-c; Hitch-a/c 6.00
2-9: 2-5-Hitch-a/c. 6-Peterson & Pacheco-a, Hank Pym killed 4.00
10-Polybagged; Angela joins the Marvel Universe 1 3 4 6 8 10
10AU (8/13, $3.99) Waid-s/Aralijo-a/Pichelli-c; Hank Pym's origin re-told
2 4 6 9 12 15

AGE OF ULTRON VS. MARVEL ZOMBIES (Secret Wars tie-in)
Marvel Comics: Aug, 2015 - No. 4, Nov, 2015 ($3.99, limited series)

1-4-James Robinson-s/Steve Pugh-a; Vision, Wonder Man & Jim Hammond app. 4.00

AGE OF X (X-Men titles crossover)
Marvel Comics: ($3.99, limited series)

... Alpha 1 (3/11, $3.99) Short stories by various; covers by Bachalo & Coipel 6.00
...: Universe 1,2 (5/11 - No. 2, 6/11, $3.99) Pham-a; Bianchi-c; Avengers & Spider-Man app.
1 3 4 6 8 10

AGE OF X-MAN
Marvel Comics: Mar, 2019 - Sept, 2019 ($4.99/$3.99, limited series)

... Alpha 1 (3/19, $4.99) Rosanas-a; world where everyone is a mutant 5.00
...: Apocalypse and the X-Tracts 1-5 (5/19 - No. 5, 9/19 $3.99) Seeley-s/Espin-a 4.00
...: Nextgen 1-5 (4/19 - No. 5, 8/19, $3.99) 1-4-To-a; Bachalo-c. 5-Werneck-a 4.00
...: Omega 1 (9/19, $4.99) Conclusion; leads into House of X #1; Buonfantino-a 5.00
...: Prisoner X 1-5 (5/19 - No. 5, 9/19, $3.99) Peralta-a; Bishop, Polaris, Beast, Gabby app. 4.00
...: The Amazing Nightcrawler 1-5 (4/19 - No. 5, 8/19, $3.99) Frigeri-a 4.00
...: The Marvelous X-Men 1-5 (4/19 - No. 5, 8/19, $3.99) Failla-a/Noto-c; X-Man app. 4.00
...: X-Tremists 1-5 (4/19 - No. 5, 8/19, $3.99) Jeanty-a/Rahzzah-c 4.00

AGGIE MACK
Four Star Comics Corp./Superior Comics Ltd.: Jan, 1948 - No. 8, Aug, 1949

1-Feldstein-a, "Johnny Prep" 52 104 156 328 552 775
2,3-Kamen-c 31 62 93 184 300 415
4-Feldstein "Johnny Prep"; Kamen-c 39 78 117 231 378 525
5-8-Kamen-c/a. 7-Burt Lancaster app. on-c 32 64 96 192 314 435

AGGIE MACK
Dell Publishing Co.: Apr - Jun, 1962

Four Color 1335 6 12 18 37 66 95

AIR
DC Comics (Vertigo): Oct, 2008 - No. 24, Oct, 2010 ($2.99)

1-6,8-24-G. Willow Wilson-s/M.K. Perker-a 3.00
7-($1.00) Includes story re-cap 3.00
... A History of the Future TPB (2011, $14.99) r/#18-24 15.00
... Flying Machine TPB (2009, $12.99) r/#6-10; Wilson intro. 13.00
... Letters From Lost Countries TPB (2009, $9.99) r/#1-5; character sketch pages 10.00
... Pure Land TPB (2010, $14.99) r/#11-17 15.00

AIR ACE (Formerly Bill Barnes No. 1-12)
Street & Smith Publications: V2#1, Jan, 1944 - V3#8(No. 20), Feb-Mar, 1947

V2#1-Nazi concentration camp-c 103 206 309 659 1130 1600
V2#2-Classic Japanese WWII-c 300 600 900 2070 3635 5200
V2#3-WWII-c 34 68 102 199 325 450
V2#4-6,8-12 20 40 60 115 185 255
V2#7-Sci-fi-c; Powell-a 26 52 78 154 252 350
V3#1-Incinerated Japanese soldier on cover 24 48 72 142 234 325
V3#2-6: 2-Atomic explosion on-c 16 32 48 92 144 195
V3#7-Powell bondage-c/a; all atomic issue 58 116 174 371 636 900
V3#8 (V5#8 on-c)-Powell-c/a 17 34 51 100 158 215

AIRBOY (Also see Airmaidens, Skywolf, Target: Airboy & Valkyrie)
Eclipse Comics: July, 1986 - No. 50, Oct, 1989 (#1-8, 50¢, 20 pgs., bi-weekly; #9-on, 36 pgs.; #34-on monthly)

1 1 3 4 6 8 10
2-4: 2-1st Marisa; Skywolf gets new costume. 3-The Heap begins 5.00
5-Valkyrie returns; Dave Stevens-c 3 6 9 16 23 30
6-49: 9-Begin $1.25-c; Skywolf begins. 11-Origin of G.A. Airboy & his plane Birdie. 28-Mr. Monster vs. The Heap. 33-Begin $1.75-c. 38-40-The Heap by Infantino. 41-r/1st app. Valkyrie from Air Fighters. 42-Begin $1.95-c. 46,47-part-r/Air Fighters. 48-Black Angel-r/A.F
4.00
50 ($4.95, 52 pgs.)-Kubert-c 5.00
51-(It's Alive Press, Oct, 2019, $9.99) Chuck Dixon-s/Brent McKee-a; The Heap back-up 10.00
52-(It's Alive Press, Aug, 2022, $9.99) Chuck Dixon-s/Stipe Kalajzic-a; bonus pin-ups 10.00
NOTE: *Evans c-21. Gulacy c-7, 20. Spiegle a-34, 35, 37. Ken Steacy painted c-17, 33.*

AIRBOY
Image Comics: Jun, 2015 - No. 4, Nov, 2015 ($2.99, limited series, mature)

1-4: 1-Airboy meets writer James Robinson and artist Greg Hinkle. 3,4-Valkyrie app. 3.00

GD VG FN VF VF/NM NM-
2.0 4.0 6.0 8.0 9.0 9.2

AIRBOY COMICS (Air Fighters Comics No. 1-22)
Hillman Periodicals: V2#11, Dec, 1945 - V10#4, May, 1953 (No V3#3)

V2#11 68 136 204 435 743 1050
12-Valkyrie-c/app. 77 154 231 493 847 1200
V3#1,2(no #3) 43 86 129 271 461 650
4-The Heap app. in Skywolf 41 82 123 256 428 600
5,7,8,10,11 36 72 108 211 343 475
6-Valkyrie-c/app. 41 82 123 256 428 600
9-Origin The Heap 41 82 123 256 428 600
12-Skywolf & Airboy x-over; Valkyrie-c/app. 43 86 129 271 461 650
V4#1-Iron Lady app. 36 72 108 211 343 475
2,3,12: 2-Rackman begins 28 56 84 165 270 375
4-Simon & Kirby-c 34 68 102 199 325 450
5-7,9,11-All S&K-a 32 64 96 190 310 430
8-Classic bondage/torture-c; S&K-a 245 490 735 1568 2684 3800
10-Valkyrie-c/app. 40 80 120 246 411 575
V5#1-4,6-11: 4-Infantino Heap. 10-Origin The Heap 22 44 66 128 209 290
5-Skull-c. 30 60 90 177 289 400
12-Krigstein-a(p) 22 44 66 132 216 300
V6#1-3,5-12: 6,8-Origin The Heap 20 40 60 120 195 270
4-Origin retold 24 48 72 142 234 325
V7#1-12: 7,8,10-Origin The Heap. 12-(1/51) 20 40 60 118 192 265
V8#1-3,5-12: 5-UFO-c (6/51) 20 40 60 114 182 250
4-Krigstein-a 20 40 60 117 189 260
V9#1,3,4,6-12: 7-One pg. Frazetta ad 17 34 51 100 158 215
2-Valkyrie app. 19 38 57 109 172 235
5(#100) 18 36 54 105 165 225
V10#1-4 16 32 48 92 144 195
NOTE: *Barry a-V2#3, 7. Bolle a-V4#12. McWilliams a-V3#7, 9. Powell a-V7#2, 3, V8#1, 6. Starr a-V5#1, 12. Dick Wood a-V4#12. Bondage-c V5#8.*

AIRBOY MEETS THE PROWLER
Eclipse Comics: Aug, 1987 ($1.95, one-shot)

1-John Snyder, III-c/a 5.00

AIRBOY-MR. MONSTER SPECIAL
Eclipse Comics: Aug, 1987 ($1.75, one-shot)

1 5.00

AIRBOY VERSUS THE AIR MAIDENS
Eclipse Comics: July, 1988 ($1.95)

1 5.00

AIR FIGHTERS CLASSICS
Eclipse Comics: Nov, 1987 - No. 6, May, 1989 ($3.95, 68 pgs., B&W)

1-6: Reprints G.A. Air Fighters #2-7. 1-Origin Airboy 4.00

AIR FIGHTERS COMICS (Airboy Comics #23 (V2#11) on)
Hillman Periodicals: Nov, 1941; No. 2, Nov, 1942 - V2#10, Fall, 1945

V1#1-(Produced by Funnies, Inc.); No Airboy; Black Commander only app.
226 452 678 1446 2473 3500
2(11/42)-(Produced by Quality artists & Biro for Hillman); Origin & 1st app. Airboy & Iron Ace; Black Angel (1st app.), Flying Dutchman & Skywolf (1st app.) begin; Fuje-a; Biro-c/a 519 1038 1557 3789 6695 9600
3-Origin/1st app. The Heap; origin Skywolf; 2nd Airboy app./c
219 438 657 1402 2401 3400
4-Japan war-c 184 368 552 1168 2009 2850
5-Japanese octopus War-c 200 400 600 1280 2190 3100
6-Japanese soldiers as rats-c 232 464 696 1485 2543 3600
7-Classic Nazi swastika-c 219 438 657 1402 2401 3400
8-12: 8,10,11-War covers 93 186 279 591 1021 1450
V2#1-Classic Nazi War-c 110 220 330 704 1202 1700
2-Skywolf by Giunta; Flying Dutchman by Fuje; 1st meeting Valkyrie & Airboy (she worked for the Nazis in beginning); 1st app. Valkyrie (11/43); Valkyrie-c
271 542 813 1734 2967 4200
3,4,6,8,9 65 130 195 416 708 1000
5-Flag-c; Fuje-a 77 154 231 493 847 1200
7-Valkyrie app. 103 206 309 659 1130 1600
10-Origin The Heap & Skywolf 74 148 222 470 810 1150
NOTE: *Fuje a-V1#2, 5, 7, V2#2, 3, 5, 7-9. Giunta a-V2#2, 3, 7, 9.*

AIRFIGHTERS MEET SGT. STRIKE SPECIAL, THE
Eclipse Comics: Jan, 1988 ($1.95, one-shot, stiff-c)

1-Airboy, Valkyrie, Skywolf app. 4.00

AIR FORCES (See American Air Forces)

AIRMAIDENS SPECIAL
Eclipse Comics: August, 1987 ($1.75, one-shot, Baxter paper)

1-Marisa becomes La Lupina (origin) 5.00

AIR RAIDERS
Marvel Comics (Star Comics)/Marvel #3 on: Nov, 1987- No. 5, Mar, 1988 ($1.00)

1,5: Kelley Jones-a in all 4.00
2-4: 2-Thunderhammer app. 3.00

AIRTIGHT GARAGE, THE (Also see Elsewhere Prince)
Marvel Comics (Epic Comics): July, 1993 - No. 4, Oct, 1993 ($2.50, lim. series, Baxter paper)

1-Moebius-c/a/scripts in all 2 4 6 10 14 18
2,3 2 4 6 9 12 15
4 2 4 6 11 16 20

AIR WAR STORIES
Dell Publishing Co.: Sept-Nov, 1964 - No. 8, Aug, 1966

1-Painted-c; Glanzman-c/a begins 4 8 12 28 47 65
2-8: 2,3-Painted-c 3 6 9 19 30 40

A.K.A. GOLDFISH
Caliber Comics: 1994 - 1995 (B&W, $3.50/$3.95)

...:Ace; ...:Jack; ...:Queen; ...:Joker; ...:King -Brian Michael Bendis-s/a 4.00
TPB (1996, $17.95) 20.00
Goldfish: The Definitive Collection (Image, 2001, $19.95) r/series plus promo art and new

Air #9 © Wilson & Perker

Al Capone, Vampire #1 © Vaughn & Solof

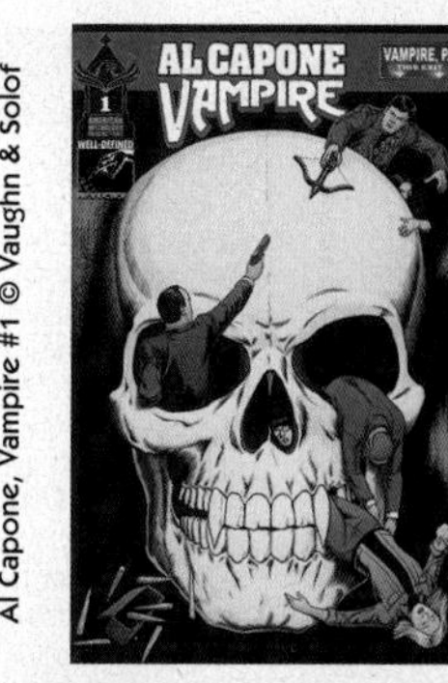

Alf #18 © MAR

	GD 2.0	VG 4.0	FN 6.0	VF 8.0	VF/NM 9.0	NM- 9.2
prose story; intro. by Matt Wagner						20.00
10th Anniversary HC (Image, 2002, $49.95)						50.00

AKIKO
Sirius: Mar, 1996 - No. 52, Feb, 2004 ($2.50/$2.95, B&W)

	GD 2.0	VG 4.0	FN 6.0	VF 8.0	VF/NM 9.0	NM- 9.2
1-Crilley-c/a/scripts in all						6.00
2						4.00
3-49,51,52: 25-($2.95, 32 pgs.)-w/Asala back-up pages. 40-Begin $2.95-c						3.00
50-($3.50)						3.50
Flights of Fancy TPB (5/02, $12.95) r/various features, pin-ups and gags						13.00
TPB Volume 1,4 ('97, 2/00, $14.95) 1-r/#1-7. 4-r/#19-25						15.00
TPB Volume 2,3 ('98, '99, $11.95) 2-r/#8-13. 3- r/#14-18						12.00
TPB Volume 5 (12/01, $12.95) r/#26-31						13.00
TPB Volume 6,7 (6/03, 4/04, $14.95) 6-r/#32-38. 7-r/#40-47						15.00

AKIKO ON THE PLANET SMOO
Sirius: Dec, 1995 ($3.95, B&W)

	GD 2.0	VG 4.0	FN 6.0	VF 8.0	VF/NM 9.0	NM- 9.2
V1#1-($3.95)-Crilley-c/a/scripts; gatefold-c						5.00
Ashcan ('95, mail offer)						3.00
Hardcover V1#1 (12/95, $19.95, B&W, 40 pgs.)						20.00
The Color Edition(2/00,$4.95)						5.00

AKIRA
Marvel Comics (Epic): Sept, 1988 - No. 38, Dec, 1995 ($3.50/$3.95/$6.95, deluxe, 68 pgs.)

	GD 2.0	VG 4.0	FN 6.0	VF 8.0	VF/NM 9.0	NM- 9.2
1-1st English translation of Katsuhiro Otomo's manga	4	8	12	25	40	55
1,2-2nd printings (1989, $3.95)						5.00
2	3	6	9	15	22	28
3-5	2	4	6	11	16	20
6-16	2	4	6	8	10	12
17-19: 17-$3.95-c begins	1	3	4	6	8	10
20-33 (Lower print run)	3	6	9	16	23	30
34,35: 34-(1994)-$6.95-c begins. 35-(1995)	3	6	9	19	30	40
36-Miyako's Last Stand	4	8	12	27	44	60
37-Texeira back-up, Gibbons, Williams pin-ups	6	12	18	41	76	110
38-Moebius, Allred, Pratt, Toth, Romita, Van Fleet, O'Neill, Madureira pin-ups; last Otomo issue	10	20	30	68	144	220

ALADDIN & HIS WONDERFUL LAMP (See Dell Jr Treasury #2)

ALAN LADD (See The Adventures of...)

ALAN MOORE'S AWESOME UNIVERSE HANDBOOK (Also see Across the Universe:...)
Awesome Entertainment: Apr, 1999 ($2.95, B&W)

	GD 2.0	VG 4.0	FN 6.0	VF 8.0	VF/NM 9.0	NM- 9.2
1-Alan Moore-text/ Alex Ross-sketch pages and 2 covers						5.00

ALAN MOORE...
DC Comics (WildStorm): TPB

	GD 2.0	VG 4.0	FN 6.0	VF 8.0	VF/NM 9.0	NM- 9.2
...'s Complete WildC.A.T.S. (2007, $29.99) r/#21-34,50; ...Homecoming & ...Gang War						30.00
...: Wild Worlds (2007, $24.99) r/various WildStorm one-shots and limited series						25.00

ALARMING ADVENTURES
Harvey Publications: Oct, 1962 - No. 3, Feb, 1963

	GD 2.0	VG 4.0	FN 6.0	VF 8.0	VF/NM 9.0	NM- 9.2
1-Crandall/Williamson-a	9	18	27	57	111	165
2-Williamson/Crandall-a	5	10	15	35	63	90
3-Torres-a	5	10	15	33	57	80

NOTE: ***Bailey*** *a-1, 3.* ***Crandall*** *a-1p, 2i.* ***Powell*** *a-2(2).* ***Severin*** *c-1-3.* ***Torres*** *a-2?* ***Tuska*** *a-1.* ***Williamson*** *a-1i, 2p.*

ALARMING TALES
Harvey Publications (Western Tales): Sept, 1957 - No. 6, Nov, 1958

	GD 2.0	VG 4.0	FN 6.0	VF 8.0	VF/NM 9.0	NM- 9.2
1-Kirby-c/a(4); Kamandi prototype story by Kirby	39	78	117	231	378	525
2-Kirby-a(4)	24	48	72	142	234	325
3,4-Kirby-a. 4-Powell, Wildey-a	19	38	57	111	176	240
5-Kirby/Williamson-a; Wildey-a; Severin-c	19	38	57	112	179	245
6-Williamson-a?; Severin-c	15	30	45	88	137	185

ALBATROSS EXPLODING FUNNYBOOKS
Albatross Funnybooks: 2022 - Present ($5.99)

	GD 2.0	VG 4.0	FN 6.0	VF 8.0	VF/NM 9.0	NM- 9.2
1-Anthology series with The Goon, La Diabla, Hillbilly, Lester and more; Eric Powell-s/a/c						6.00

ALBEDO
Thoughts And Images: Summer, 1983 - No. 14, Spring, 1989 (B&W)
Antarctic Press: (Vol. 2) Jun, 1991 - No. 10 ($2.50)

	GD 2.0	VG 4.0	FN 6.0	VF 8.0	VF/NM 9.0	NM- 9.2
0-Yellow cover; 50 copies	17	34	51	117	259	400
0-White cover, 450 copies	9	18	27	63	129	195
0-Blue, 1st printing, 500 copies	9	18	27	58	114	170
0-Blue, 2nd printing, 1000 copies	5	10	15	31	53	75
0-3rd & 4th printing	3	6	9	14	20	26
1-Dark red, 1st printing - low print run	27	54	81	189	420	650
1-Bright red, later printings - low print run	9	18	27	57	111	165
2-(11/84) 1st app. Usagi Yojimbo by Stan Sakai; 2000 copies - no 2nd printing	550	1100	1650	3850	6025	8200
3	10	20	30	67	144	215
4-Usagi Yojimbo-c	11	22	33	76	163	250
5-14	1	2	3	5	6	8
(Vol. 2) 1	2	4	6	8	10	12
2-10, Color Special	1	2	3	5	6	8

ALBEDO ANTHROPOMORPHICS
Antarctic Press: (Vol. 3) Spring, 1994 - No. 4, Jan, 1996 ($2.95, color);
(Vol. 4) Dec, 1999 - No. 2, Jan, 1999 ($2.95/$2.99, B&W)

	GD 2.0	VG 4.0	FN 6.0	VF 8.0	VF/NM 9.0	NM- 9.2
V3#1-Steve Gallacci-c/a	2	4	6	9	12	15
V3#2-4-Steve Gallacci-c/a. V4#1,2	1	3	4	6	8	10

ALBERTO (See The Crusaders)

ALBERT THE ALLIGATOR & POGO POSSUM (See Pogo Possum)

ALBION (Inspired by 1960s IPC British comics characters)
DC Comics (WildStorm): Aug, 2005 - No. 6, Nov, 2006 ($2.99, limited series)

	GD 2.0	VG 4.0	FN 6.0	VF 8.0	VF/NM 9.0	NM- 9.2
1-6-Alan Moore, Leah Moore & John Reppion-s/Shane Oakley-a; Dave Gibbons-c						3.00
TPB (2007, $19.99) r/series; intro by Neil Gaiman; reprints from 1960s British comics						20.00

ALBUM OF CRIME (See Fox Giants)

ALBUM OF LOVE (See Fox Giants)

AL CAPONE, VAMPIRE (Also see Vampire, PA)
American Myhtology Productions: Jul, 2022 - Present ($20.00)

	GD 2.0	VG 4.0	FN 6.0	VF 8.0	VF/NM 9.0	NM- 9.2
1-J.C. Vaughn-s/Brendon & Brian Fraim-a						20.00

AL CAPP'S DOGPATCH (Also see Mammy Yokum)
Toby Press: No. 71, June, 1949 - No. 4, Dec, 1949

	GD 2.0	VG 4.0	FN 6.0	VF 8.0	VF/NM 9.0	NM- 9.2
71(#1)-Reprints from Tip Top #112-114	18	36	54	105	165	225
2-4: 4-Reprints from Li'l Abner #73	14	28	42	80	115	150

AL CAPP'S SHMOO (Also see Oxydol-Dreft & Washable Jones & Shmoo)
Toby Press: July, 1949 - No. 5, Apr, 1950 (None by Al Capp)

	GD 2.0	VG 4.0	FN 6.0	VF 8.0	VF/NM 9.0	NM- 9.2
1-1st app. Super-Shmoo	31	62	93	182	296	410
2-5: 3-Sci-fi trip to moon. 4-X-Mas-c	20	40	60	120	195	270

AL CAPP'S WOLF GAL
Toby Press: 1951 - No. 2, 1952

	GD 2.0	VG 4.0	FN 6.0	VF 8.0	VF/NM 9.0	NM- 9.2
1-Edited-r from Li'l Abner #63	39	78	117	240	395	550
2-Edited-r from Li'l Abner #64	22	44	66	132	216	300

ALEISTER ARCANE
IDW Publishing: Apr, 2004 - No. 3, June, 2004 ($3.99, limited series)

	GD 2.0	VG 4.0	FN 6.0	VF 8.0	VF/NM 9.0	NM- 9.2
1-3-Steve Niles-s/Breehn Burns-a						4.00
TPB (10/04, $17.99) r/series; sketch pages						18.00

ALEXANDER THE GREAT (Movie)
Dell Publishing Co.: No. 688, May, 1956

	GD 2.0	VG 4.0	FN 6.0	VF 8.0	VF/NM 9.0	NM- 9.2
Four Color 688-Buscema-a; photo-c	7	14	21	46	86	125

ALEX + ADA
Image Comics: Nov, 2013 - No. 15, Jun, 2015 ($2.99/$3.99)

	GD 2.0	VG 4.0	FN 6.0	VF 8.0	VF/NM 9.0	NM- 9.2
1-14-Jonathan Luna-a/c; Sarah Vaughn & Luna-s						3.00
15-($3.99) Conclusion						4.00

ALF (TV) (See Star Comics Digest)
Marvel Comics: Mar, 1988 - No. 50, Feb, 1992 ($1.00)

	GD 2.0	VG 4.0	FN 6.0	VF 8.0	VF/NM 9.0	NM- 9.2
1-Photo-c	3	6	9	14	20	25
1-2nd printing						4.00
2-5	1	3	4	6	8	10
6-19: 6-Photo-c						6.00
20-22: 20-Conan parody. 21-Marx Brothers. 22-X-Men parody	1	2	3	5	6	8
23-30: 24-Rhonda-c/app. 29-3-D cover						4.00
31-43,46,47,49						4.00
44,45: 44-X-Men parody. 45-Wolverine, Punisher, Capt. America-c	1	3	4	6	8	10
48-(12/91) Risqué Alf with seal cover	10	20	30	64	132	200
50-($1.75, 52 pgs.)-Final issue; photo-c	1	3	4	6	8	10
Annual 1-3: 1-Rocky & Bullwinkle app. 2-Sienkiewicz-c. 3-TMNT parody						6.00
...Comics Digest 1,2: 1-(1988)-Reprints Alf #1,2	2	4	6	8	10	12
Holiday Special 1,2 ('88, Wint. '89, 68 pgs.): 2-X-Men parody-c						10.00
Spring Special 1 (Spr/89, $1.75, 68 pgs.) Invisible Man parody						10.00
TPB (1990, 68 pgs.) r/#1-3; photo-c						10.00

ALFRED HARVEY'S BLACK CAT
Lorne-Harvey Productions: 1995 ($3.50, B&W/color)

GD 2.0 | VG 4.0 | FN 6.0 | VF 8.0 | VF/NM 9.0 | NM- 9.2

1-Origin by Mark Evanier & Murphy Anderson; contains history of Alfred Harvey & Harvey Publications; 5 pg. B&W Sad Sack story; Hildebrandts-c 6.00

ALGIE (LITTLE...)
Timor Publ. Co.: Dec, 1953 - No. 3, 1954

1-Teenage 10 20 30 58 79 100
1-Algie #1 cover w/Secret Mysteries #19 inside 12 24 36 69 97 125
2 7 14 21 37 46 55
3-Good Girl-c 10 20 30 64 132 200
Accepted Reprint #2(nd) 4 7 10 14 17 20
Super Reprint #15 2 4 6 10 14 18

ALIAS:
Now Comics: July, 1990 - No. 5, Nov, 1990 ($1.75)

1-5: 1-Sienkiewicz-c 3.00

ALIAS (Also see Jessica Jones apps. in New Avengers and The Pulse)
Marvel Comics (MAX Comics): Nov, 2001 - No. 28, Jan, 2004 ($2.99)

1-Bendis-s/Gaydos-a/Mack-c; intro Jessica Jones; Luke Cage app. 7 14 21 46 86 125
2-4 1 2 3 5 6 8
5-23: 7,8-Sienkiewicz-a (2 pgs.) 16-21-Spider-Woman app. 22,23-Jessica's origin 5.00
24-Killgrave The Purple Man app.; Avengers app. 2 4 6 9 12 15
25-27-The Purple Man app.; Avengers app. 25,26-Flashback-a by Bagley. 26-Flashback-a by Rick Mays 1 3 4 6 8 10
28-Last issue; Purple Man app. 2 4 6 9 12 15
... MGC 1 (6/10, $1.00) r/#1 with "Marvel's Greatest Comics" logo on cover 3.00
HC (2002, $29.99) r/#1-9; intro. by Jeph Loeb 30.00
Omnibus (2006, $69.99, hardcover with dustjacket) r/#1-28 and What If Jessica Jones Had Joined the Avengers?; original pitch, script and sketch pages 70.00
Vol. 1: TPB (2003, $19.99) r/#1-9 20.00
Vol. 2: Come Home TPB (2003, $13.99) r/#11-15 14.00
Vol. 3: The Underneath TPB (2003, $16.99) r/#10,16-21 17.00

ALICE (New Adventures in Wonderland)
Ziff-Davis Publ. Co.: No. 10, 7-8/51 - No. 11(#2), 11-12/51

10-Painted-c; Berg-a 34 68 1025 199 325 450
11-(#2 on inside) Dave Berg-a 21 42 63 122 199 275

ALICE AT MONKEY ISLAND (Formerly The Adventures of Alice)
Pentagon Publ. Co. (Civil Service): No. 3, 1946

3 13 26 39 74 105 135

ALICE COOPER (Also see Last Temptation)
Dynamite Entertainment: 2014 - No. 6, 2015 ($3.99)

1-6: 1-5-Joe Harris-s/Eman Casallos-a/David Mack-c. 6-Jerwa-s/Tenorio-a 4.00

ALICE COOPER VS. CHAOS!
Dynamite Entertainment: 2015 - No. 6, 2016 ($3.99, limited series)

1-6-Chastity, Purgatori, Evil Ernie, Lady Demon & The Queen of Sorrows app. 4.00

ALICE EVER AFTER
BOOM! Studios: Apr, 2022 - No. 5, Aug, 2022 ($3.99, limited series)

1-5-Panosian-s/Spalletta & Panosian-a; adult Alice returning to Wonderland 4.00

ALICE IN WONDERLAND (Disney; see Advs. of Alice, Dell Jr. Treasury #1, The Dreamery, Movie Comics,Walt Disney Showcase #22, and World's Greatest Stories)
Dell Publishing Co.: No. 24, 1940; No. 331, 1951; No. 341, July, 1951

Single Series 24 (#1)(1940) 68 136 204 435 743 1050
Four Color 331, 341-"Unbirthday Party w/..." 18 36 54 124 275 425
1-(Whitman, 3/84, pre-pack only)-r/4-Color #331 4 8 12 25 40 55

ALIEN (Based on the creatures from the 1979 movie)
Marvel Comics: May, 2021 - No. 12, Jul, 2022 ($3.99)

1-12-P.K. Johnson-s/Salvador Larroca-a 4.00
Annual 1 (9/22, $4.99) P.K. Johnson-s/Salvador Larroca-a 5.00

ALIEN (Based on the creatures from the 1979 movie)
Marvel Comics: Nov, 2022 - Present ($3.99)

1-6-P.K. Johnson-s/Julius Ohta-a 4.00

ALIENATED
BOOM! Studios: Feb, 2020 - No. 6, Sept, 2020 ($3.99, limited series)

1-6-Spurrier-s/Wildgoose-a 4.00

ALIEN ENCOUNTERS (Replaces Alien Worlds)
Eclipse Comics: June, 1985 - No. 14, Aug, 1987 ($1.75, Baxter paper, mature)

1-10: Nudity, strong language in all. 9-Snyder-a 4.00
11-14-Low print run 5.00

ALIEN LEGION (See Epic & Marvel Graphic Novel #25)
Marvel Comics (Epic Comics): Apr, 1984 - No. 20, Sept, 1987

nn-With bound-in trading card; Austin-i 1 3 4 6 8 10
2-20: 2-$1.50-c. 7,8-Portacio-i 3.00

ALIEN LEGION (2nd Series)
Marvel Comics (Epic): Aug, 1987(indicia)(10/87 on-c) - No. 18, Aug, 1990

V2#1-18-Stroman-a in all. 7-18-Farmer-i 4.00
...: Force Nomad TPB (Checker Book Pub. Group, 2001, $24.95) r/#1-11 25.00
...: Piecemaker TPB (Checker Book Pub. Group, 2002, $19.95) r/#12-18 20.00

ALIEN LEGION: (Series of titles; all Marvel/Epic Comics)
--BINARY DEEP, 1993 ($3.50, one-shot, 52 pgs.), nn-With bound-in trading card 4.00
--JUGGER GRIMROD, 8/92 ($5.95, one-shot, 52 pgs.) Book 1 6.00
--ONE PLANET AT A TIME, 5/93 - Book 3, 7/93 ($4.95, squarebound, 52 pgs.) Book 1-3: Hoang Nguyen-a 5.00
--ON THE EDGE (The... #2 & 3), 11/90 - No. 3, 1/91 ($4.50, 52 pgs.) 1-3-Stroman & Farmer-a 4.50
--TENANTS OF HELL, '91 - No. 2, '91 ($4.50, squarebound, 52 pgs.) Book 1,2-Stroman-c/a(p) 4.50

ALIEN LEGION: UNCIVIL WAR
Titan Comics: Jul, 2014 - No. 4, Oct, 2014 ($3.99)

1-4-Dixon-s/Stroman-a 4.00

ALIEN LIFE (Cerebus in Hell)
Aardvark-Vanaheim: May, 2022 ($4.00, B&W)

1-Cerebus figures with Gustave Doré artwork of Hell; Alf #48-c swipe 4.00

ALIEN NATION (Movie)
DC Comics: Dec, 1988 ($2.50; 68 pgs.)

1-Adaptation of film; painted-c 4.00

ALIEN PIG FARM 3000
Image Comics (RAW Studios): Apr, 2007 - No. 4, July, 2007 ($2.99, limited series)

1-4-Steve Niles, Thomas Jane & Todd Farmer-s/Don Marquez-a 3.00

ALIEN RESURRECTION (Movie)
Dark Horse Comics: Oct, 1997 - No. 2, Nov, 1997 ($2.50; limited series)

1,2-Adaptation of film; Dave McKean-c 4.00

ALIENS, THE (Captain Johner and...)(Also see Magnus Robot Fighter...)
Gold Key: Sept-Dec, 1967; No. 2, May, 1982

1-Reprints from Magnus #1,3,4,6-10; Russ Manning-a in all 4 8 12 23 37 50
2-(Whitman) Same contents as #1 1 3 4 6 8 10

ALIENS (Movie) (See Alien: The Illustrated..., Dark Horse Comics & Dark Horse Presents #24)
Dark Horse Comics: May, 1988 - No. 6, July, 1989 ($1.95, B&W, limited series)

1-Based on movie sequel; 1st app. Aliens in comics 7 14 21 46 86 125
1-2nd printing 1 3 4 6 8 10
1-3rd - 6th printings; 4th w/new inside front-c 4.00
2 3 6 9 15 22 28
2-2nd & 3rd printing, 3-6-2nd printings 3.00
3 2 4 6 9 13 16
4,5 6.00
6-Last issue 1 3 4 6 8 10
Mini Comic #1 (2/89, 4x6")-Was included with Aliens Portfolio 5.00
Collection 1 ($10.95,)-r/#1-6 plus Dark Horse Presents #24 plus new-a 15.00
Collection 1-2nd printing (1991, $11.95)-On higher quality paper than 1st print; Dorman painted-c 12.00
Hardcover ('90, $24.95, B&W)-r/1-6, DHP #24 30.00
... Omnibus Vol. 1 (7/07, $24.95, 9x6") r/1st & 2nd series and Aliens: Earth War 50.00
... Omnibus Vol. 2 (12/07, $24.95, 9x6") r/Genocide, Harvest and Colonial Marines series 40.00
... Omnibus Vol. 3 (3/08, $24.95, 9x6") r/Rogue, Salvation and Sacrifice, Labyrinth series 40.00
... Omnibus Vol. 4 (8/08, $24.95, 9x6") r/Music of the Spears, Stronghold, Berserker, Mondo Pest and Mondo Heat series and one-shots 40.00
... Omnibus Vol. 5 (11/08, $24.95, 9x6") r/Alchemy, Survival, Havoc series and various 40.00
... Omnibus Vol. 6 (2/09, $24.95, 9x6") r/Apocalypse GN, Xenogenesis & one-shots 100.00
... Outbreak (3rd printing, 8/96, $17.95)-Bolton-c 18.00
Platinum Edition - (See Dark Horse Presents: Aliens Platinum Edition) -

ALIENS
Dark Horse Comics: V2#1, Aug, 1989 - No. 4, 1990 ($2.25, limited series)

V2#1-Painted art by Denis Beauvais 2 4 5 7 8 10
1-2nd printing (1990), 2-4 3.00
...: Nightmare Asylum TPB (12/96, $16.95) r/series; Bolton-c 17.00

ALIENS
Dark Horse Comics: May, 2009 - No. 4, Nov, 2009 ($3.50, limited series)

1-Howard-c 6.00
2-4-John Arcudi-s/Zach Howard-a. 2-Howard-c. 3,4-Swanland-c 4.00

ALIENS: (Series of titles, all Dark Horse)
--ALCHEMY, 10/97 - No. 3, 11/97 ($2.95),1-3-Corben-c/a, Arcudi-s 6.00
--APOCALYPSE - THE DESTROYING ANGELS, 1/99 - No. 4, 4/99 ($2.95) 1-4-Doug Wheatly-a/Schultz-s 5.00
--BERSERKERS, 1/95 - No. 4, 4/95 ($2.50) 1-4 6.00
--COLONIAL MARINES, 1/93 - No. 10, 7/94 ($2.50) 1-10 5.00
--DEAD ORBIT, 4/17 - No. 4, 12/17 ($3.99) 1-4-James Stokoe-s/a 6.00
--DEFIANCE, 4/16 - No. 12, 6/17 ($3.99) 1-Brian Wood-s/Tristan Jones-a 2 4 5 7 8 10
2-12: 2-Brian Wood-s/Tristan Jones-a 5.00
--DUST TO DUST, 4/18 - No. 4, 1/19 ($3.99) 1-4-Gabriel Hardman-s/a 5.00
--EARTH ANGEL, 8/94 ($2.95) 1-Byrne-a/story; wraparound-c 5.00
--EARTH WAR, 6/90 - No. 4, 10/90 ($2.50) 1-All have Sam Kieth-a & Bolton painted-c 6.00
1-2nd printing, 3,4 4.00
2 5.00
--GENOCIDE, 11/91 - No. 4, 2/92 ($2.50) 1-4-Suydam painted-c. 4-Wraparound-c, poster 4.00
--GLASS CORRIDOR, 6/98 ($2.95) 1-David Lloyd-s/a 10.00
--HARVEST (See Aliens: Hive)
--HAVOC, 6/97 - No. 2, 7/97 ($2.95) 1,2: Schultz-s, Kent Williams-c, 40 artists including Art Adams, Kelley Jones, Duncan Fegredo, Kevin Nowlan 6.00
--HIVE, 2/92 - No. 4,5/92 ($2.50) 1-4: Kelley Jones-c/a in all 4.00
...Harvest TPB ('98, $16.95) r/series; Bolton-c 17.00
--KIDNAPPED, 12/97 - No. 3, 2/98 ($2.50) 1-3 6.00
--LABYRINTH, 9/93 - No. 4, 1/94 ($2.50) 1-4: 1-Painted-c 5.00
--LIFE AND DEATH, 9/16 - No. 4, 12/16 ($3.99) 1-4-Abnett-s/Moritat-a 4.00
--LOVESICK, 12/96 ($2.95) 1 8.00
--MONDO HEAT, 2/96 ($2.50) nn-Sequel to Mondo Pest 8.00
--MONDO PEST, 4/95 ($2.95, 44 pgs.) nn-r/Dark Horse Comics #22-24 5.00
--MUSIC OF THE SPEARS, 1/94 - No. 4, 4/94 ($2.50) 1-4 4.00
--NEWT'S TALE, 6/92 - No. 2, 7/92 ($4.95) 1,2-Bolton-c 8.00
--PIG, 3/97 ($2.95)1 4.00

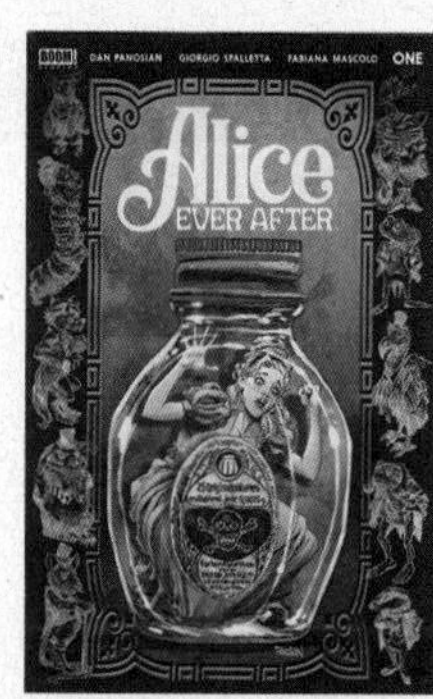

Alice Ever After #1 © Dan Panosian

Aliens: Defiance #6 © 20-FOX

All-American Comics #1 © DC

GD 2.0 | VG 4.0 | FN 6.0 | VF 8.0 | VF/NM 9.0 | NM- 9.2

--PREDATOR: THE DEADLIEST OF THE SPECIES, 7/93 - No. 12,8/95 ($2.50)
1-Bolton painted-c; Guice-a(p) 6.00
1-Embossed foil platinum edition 10.00
2-12: Bolton painted-c. 2,3-Guice-a(p) 4.00

--PURGE, 8/97 ($2.95) nn-Hester-a 8.00

--RESCUE, 7/19 - No. 4, 10/19 ($3.99) 1-4-Brian Wood-s/Kieran McKeown-a 5.00

--RESISTANCE, 1/19 - No. 4, 4/19 ($3.99) 1-4-Brian Wood-s/Robert Carey-a 6.00

--ROGUE, 4/93 - No. 4, 7/93 ($2.50) 1-4: Painted-c 4.00

--SACRIFICE, 5/93 ($4.95, 52 pgs.) nn-P. Milligan scripts; painted-c/a 6.00

--SALVATION, 11/93 ($4.95, 52 pgs.) nn-Mignola-c/a(p); Gibbons script 10.00

--SPECIAL, 6/97 ($2.50) 1 10.00

--STALKER, 6/98 ($2.50)1-David Wenzel-s/a 8.00

--STRONGHOLD, 5/94 - No. 4, 9/94 ($2.50) 1-4 5.00

--SURVIVAL, 2/98 - No. 3, 4/98 ($2.95) 1-3-Tony Harris-c 5.00

--TRIBES, 1992 ($24.95, hardcover graphic novel) Bissette text-s with Dorman painted-a 25.00
...softcover ($9.95) 10.00

ALIENS: AFTERMATH (Based on the creatures from the 1979 movie)
Marvel Comics: Sept, 2021 ($4.99, one-shot)
1-Benjamin Percy-s/Dave Wachter-a 4.00

ALIENS: FIRE AND STONE (Crossover with AvP, Predator, and Prometheus)
Dark Horse Comics: Sept, 2014 - No. 4, Dec, 2014 ($3.50, limited series)
1-4-Roberson-s/Reynolds-a 6.00

ALIENS/ VAMPIRELLA (See Vampirella/Aliens)

ALIENS VS. PARKER (Not based on the Alien movie series)
BOOM! Studios: Mar, 2013 - No. 4, May, 2013 ($3.99, limited series)
1-4: 1-Paul Scheer & Nick Giovannetti-s; Bracchi-a/Noto-c 4.00

ALIENS VS. PREDATOR (See Dark Horse Presents #36)
Dark Horse Comics: June, 1990 - No. 4, Dec, 1990 ($2.50, limited series)
1-Painted-c 2 4 6 11 16 20
1-2nd printing 4.00
0-(7/90, $1.95, B&W)-r/Dark Horse Pres. #34-36 2 4 6 11 16 20
2,3 6.00
4-Dave Dorman painted-c 5.00
Annual (7/99, $4.95) Jae Lee-c 5.00
... : Booty (1/96, $2.50) painted-c 4.00
... Omnibus Vol. 1 (5/07, $24.95, 9x6") r/#1-4 & Annual; ...: War; ...: Eternal 50.00
... Omnibus Vol. 2 (10/07, $24.95, 9x6") r/...: Xenogenesis #1-4; ...: Deadliest of the Species; ...: Booty and stories from ... Annual 40.00
...: One For One (8/10, $1.00) r/#1 with red cover frame 4.00
... : Thrill of the Hunt (9/04, $6.95, digest-size TPB) Based on 2004 movie 7.00
... Wraith 1 (7/98, $2.95) Jay Stephens-s 4.00

--VS. PREDATOR: DUEL, 3/95 - No. 2, 4/95 ($2.50) 1,2 4.00

--VS. PREDATOR: ETERNAL, 6/98 - No. 4, 9/98 ($2.50)1-4: Edginton-s/Maleev-a; Fabry-c 4.00

--VS. PREDATOR: THREE WORLD WAR, 1/10 - No. 6, 9/10 ($3.50) 1-6-Leonardi-a 5.00

--VS. PREDATOR VS. THE TERMINATOR, 4/00 - No. 4, 7/00 ($2.95) 1-4: Ripley app. 10.00

--VS. PREDATOR: WAR, No. 0, 5/95 - No. 4, 8/95 ($2.50) 0-4: Corben painted-c 4.00

--VS. PREDATOR: XENOGENESIS, 12/99 - No. 4, 3/00 ($2.95) 1-4: Watson-s/Mel Rubi-a 4.00

--XENOGENESIS, 8/99 - No. 4, 11/99 ($2.95) 1-4: T&M Bierbaum-s 4.00

ALIENS VS. ZOMBIES (Not based on the Alien movie series)
Zenescope Entertainment: Jul, 2015 - No. 5, Dec, 2015 ($3.99, limited series)
1-5: 1-Brusha-s/Riccardi-a; multiple covers on each 4.00

ALIEN TERROR (See 3-D Alien Terror)

ALIEN: THE ILLUSTRATED STORY (Also see Aliens)
Heavy Metal Books: 1980 ($3.95, soft-c, 8x11")
nn-Movie adaptation; Simonson-a 6 12 18 38 69 100

ALIEN: THE ORIGINAL SCREENPLAY
Dark Horse Comics: Aug, 2020 - Present ($3.99, limited series)
1-5-Adaptation of Dan O'Bannon's original 1976 screenplay; Seixas-s/Balbi-a 4.00

ALIEN ^{3} (Movie)
Dark Horse Comics: June, 1992 - No. 3, July, 1992 ($2.50, limited series)
1-3: Adapts 3rd movie; Suydam painted-c 5.00

ALIEN 3 (WILLIAM GIBSON'S...) (Movie)
Dark Horse Comics: Nov, 2018 - No. 5, Mar, 2019 ($3.99, limited series)
1-5-Adapts William Gibson's unproduced screenplay for Alien 3; Johnnie Christmas-s/a 4.00

ALIEN VS. PREDATOR: FIRE AND STONE (Crossover with Aliens, Predator, and Prometheus)
Dark Horse Comics: Oct, 2014 - No. 4, Jan, 2015 ($3.50, limited series)
1-4-Sebela-s/Olivetti-a 6.00

ALIEN VS. PREDATOR: LIFE AND DEATH (Crossover with Aliens, Predator, and Prometheus)
Dark Horse Comics: Dec, 2016 - No. 4, Mar, 2017 ($3.99, limited series)
1-4-Abnett-s/Theis-a 4.00

ALIEN VS. PREDATOR: THICKER THAN BLOOD
Dark Horse Comics: Dec, 2019 - No. 4 ($3.99, limited series)
1,2-Jeremy Barlow-s/Doug Wheatey-a 4.00

ALIEN WORLDS (Also see Eclipse Graphic Album #22)
Pacific Comics/Eclipse: Dec, 1982 - No. 9, Jan, 1985
1,2,4: 2,4-Dave Stevens-c/a 2 4 6 8 10 12
3,5-7 6.00
8,9 2 4 6 8 11 14
3-D No. 1-Art Adams 1st published art 2 4 6 8 11 14

ALISON DARE, LITTLE MISS ADVENTURES (Also see Return of ...)
Oni Press: Sept, 2000 ($4.50, B&W, one-shot)
1-J. Torres-s/J.Bone-c/a 4.50

ALISON DARE & THE HEART OF THE MAIDEN
Oni Press: Jan, 2002 - No. 2, Feb, 2002 ($2.95, B&W, limited series)
1,2-J. Torres-s/J.Bone-c/a 3.00

ALISTER THE SLAYER
Midnight Press: Oct, 1995 ($2.50)
1-Boris-c 3.00

ALL-AMERICAN COMICS (...Western #103-126, ...Men of War #127 on; also see The Big All-American Comic Book)
All-American/National Periodical Publ.: April, 1939 - No. 102, Oct, 1948
1-Hop Harrigan (1st app.), Scribbly by Mayer (1st DC app.), Toonerville Folks, Ben Webster, Spot Savage, Mutt & Jeff, Red White & Blue (1st app.), Adventures in the Unknown, Tippie, Reg'lar Fellers, Skippy, Bobby Thatcher, Mystery Men of Mars, Daiseybelle, Wiley of West Point begin 703 1406 2109 5132 9066 13,000
2-Ripley's Believe It or Not begins, ends #24 245 490 735 1568 2684 3800
3-5: 5-The American Way begins, ends #10 213 426 639 1363 2332 3300
6,7: 6-Last Spot Savage; Popsicle Pete begins, ends #26, 28. 7-Last Bobby Thatcher 161 322 483 1030 1765 2500
8-The Ultra Man begins & 1st-c app. 465 930 1395 3395 5998 8600
9,10: 10-X-Mas-c 155 310 465 992 1696 2400
11,15: 11-Ultra Man-c. 15-Last Tippie & Reg'lar Fellars; Ultra Man-c 219 438 657 1402 2401 3400
12-14: 12-Last Toonerville Folks 142 284 426 909 1555 2200
16-(Rare)-Origin/1st app. Green Lantern by Sheldon Moldoff (c/a)(7/40) & begin series; appears in costume on-c & only one panel inside; created by Martin Nodell. Inspired in 1940 by a switchman's green lantern that would give trains the go ahead to proceed. G.L. cover pose swiped from last panel of a Jan, 1939 Flash Gordon Sunday page. 29,900 59,800 89,700 221,200 598,100 975,000
17-2nd Green Lantern 1450 2900 4350 10,900 22,950 35,000
18-N.Y. World's Fair-c/story (scarce); The Atom app. in one panel announcing debut in next issue 1375 2750 4125 10,300 21,650 33,000
19-Origin/1st app. The Atom (10/40); last Ultra Man 3000 6000 9000 22,500 46,250 70,000
20-Atom dons costume; Ma Hunkle becomes Red Tornado (1st app.)(1st DC costumed heroine, before Wonder Woman, 11/40); Rescue on Mars begins, ends #25; 1 pg. origin Green Lantern 757 1514 2271 5526 9763 14,000
21-Last Wiley of West Point & Skippy; classic Moldoff-c 595 1190 1785 4350 7675 11,000
22,23: 23-Last Daiseybelle; 3 Idiots begin, end #82 377 754 1131 2639 4620 6600
24-Sisty & Dinky become the Cyclone Kids; Ben Webster ends; origin Dr. Mid-Nite & Sargon, The Sorcerer in text with app. 383 766 1149 2681 4691 6700
25-Origin & 1st story app. Dr. Mid-Nite by Stan Asch; Hop Harrigan becomes Guardian Angel; last Adventure in the Unknown (scarce) 1300 2600 3900 9750 20,375 31,000
26-Origin/1st story app. Sargon, the Sorcerer 411 822 1233 2877 5039 7200
27: #27-32 are misnumbered in indicia with correct No. appearing on-c. Intro. Doiby Dickles, Green Lantern's sidekick 400 800 1200 2800 4900 7000
28-Hop Harrigan gives up costumed i.d. 219 438 657 1402 2401 3400
29,30 213 426 639 1363 2332 3300
31-40: 35-Doiby learns Green Lantern's i.d. 181 362 543 1158 1979 2800
41-50: 50-Sargon ends 145 290 435 921 1586 2250
51-60: 59-Scribbly & the Red Tornado ends 123 246 369 757 1344 1900

	GD 2.0	VG 4.0	FN 6.0	VF 8.0	VF/NM 9.0	NM- 9.2
61-Origin/1st app. Solomon Grundy (11/44)	2825	5650	8475	21,200	40,600	60,000
62-70: 70-Kubert Sargon; intro Sargon's helper, Maximillian O'Leary	110	220	330	704	1202	1700
71-88: 71-Last Red White & Blue. 72-Black Pirate begins (not in #74-82); last Atom. 73-Winky, Blinky & Noddy begins, ends #82. 79,83-Mutt & Jeff-c. 85-1st Crusher Crock (becomes Sportsmaster); Hasen "Derby" cover	84	168	252	538	919	1300
89-Origin & 1st app. Harlequin (Molly Mayne)	443	886	1329	3234	5717	8200
90,92,96-99: 90-Origin/1st app. Icicle. 98-Sportsmaster-c. 99-Last Hop Harrigan	168	336	504	1075	1838	2600
91,93,94,95-Harlequin-c	226	452	678	1446	2473	3500
100-1st app. Johnny Thunder by Alex Toth (8/48); western theme begins (Scarce)	219	438	657	1402	2401	3400
101-Last Mutt & Jeff (Scarce)	148	296	444	947	1624	2300
102-Last Green Lantern, Black Pirate & Dr. Mid-Nite (Scarce)	271	542	813	1734	2967	4200

NOTE: *No Atom in 47, 62-69.* ***Kinstler*** *Black Pirate-89.* ***Stan Aschmeier*** *a (Dr. Mid-Nite) 25-84; c-7.* ***Mayer*** *c-1, 2(part), 6, 10.* ***Moldoff*** *c-16-23.* ***Nodell*** *c-31.* ***Paul Reinman*** *a (Green Lantern)-53-55p, 56-84, 87; (Black Pirate)-83-88, 90; c-52, 55-76, 78, 80, 81, 87.* ***Toth*** *a-88, 92, 96, 98-102; c(p)-92, 96-102. Scribbly by* ***Mayer*** *in #1-59. Ultra Man by* ***Mayer*** *in #8-19.*

ALL AMERICAN COMICS
DC Comics: April 1939

nn - Ashcan comic, not distributed to newsstands, only for in house use. Cover art is Adventure Comics #33 and interior from Detective Comics #23. A CGC 7.5 copy sold for $7466 in December 2014 and for $15,000 in July 2017.

ALL-AMERICAN COMICS (Also see All Star Comics 1999 crossover titles)
DC Comics: May, 1999 ($1.99, one-shot)

	GD 2.0	VG 4.0	FN 6.0	VF 8.0	VF/NM 9.0	NM- 9.2
1-Golden Age Green Lantern and Johnny Thunder; Barreto-a						4.00

ALL-AMERICAN MEN OF WAR (Previously All-American Western)
National Periodical Publ.: No. 127, Aug-Sept, 1952 - No. 117, Sept-Oct, 1966

	GD 2.0	VG 4.0	FN 6.0	VF 8.0	VF/NM 9.0	NM- 9.2
127 (#1, 1952)	141	282	423	1163	2632	4100
128 (1952)	61	122	183	488	1094	1700
2(12-1/'52-53)-5	54	108	162	432	966	1500
6-Devil Dog story; Ghost Squadron story	40	80	120	296	673	1050
7-10: 8-Sgt. Storm Cloud-s	40	80	120	296	673	1050
11-16,18: 18-Last precode; 1st Kubert-c (2/55)	36	72	108	259	580	900
17-1st Frogman-s in this title	38	76	114	281	628	975
19,20,22-27	28	56	84	202	451	700
21-Easy Co. prototype	34	68	102	245	548	850
28 (12/55)-1st Sgt. Rock prototype; Kubert-a	64	128	192	512	1156	1800
29,30,32-Wood-a	28	56	84	202	451	700
31,33,34,36-38,40: 34-Gunner prototype-s. 36-Little Sure Shot prototype-s. 38-1st S.A. issue	26	52	78	182	404	625
35-Greytone-c	34	68	102	245	548	850
39 (11/56)-2nd Sgt. Rock prototype; 1st Easy Co.?	44	88	132	326	738	1150
41,43-47,49,50: 46-Tankbusters-c/s	22	44	66	154	340	525
42-Pre-Sgt. Rock Easy Co.-c/s	28	56	84	202	451	700
48-Easy Co.-c/s; Nick app.; Kubert-a	28	56	84	202	451	700
51-56,58-62,65,66: 61-Gunner-c/s	18	36	54	124	275	425
57(5/58),63,64-Pre-Sgt. Rock Easy Co.-c/s	24	48	72	168	372	575
67-1st Gunner & Sarge by Andru & Esposito	57	114	171	456	1028	1600
68,69: 68-2nd app. Gunner & Sarge. 69-1st Tank Killer-c/s	22	44	66	154	340	525
70	15	30	45	103	227	350
71-80: 71,72,76-Tank Killer-c/s. 74-Minute Commandos-c/s	12	24	36	84	185	285
81-Greytone-c	13	26	39	86	188	290
82-Johnny Cloud begins(1st app.), ends #117	34	68	102	245	548	850
83-2nd Johnny Cloud	18	36	54	124	275	425
84-88: 88-Last 10¢ issue	11	22	33	72	154	235
89-100: 89-Battle Aces of 3 Wars begins, ends #98. 89,90-Panels from these issues used by artist Roy Lichtenstein for famous paintings	9	18	27	58	114	170
101-111,113-116: 110,11-Greytone-c. 111,114,115-Johnny Cloud	6	12	18	41	76	110
112-Balloon Buster series begins, ends #114,116	6	12	18	42	79	115
117-Johnny Cloud-c & 3-part story	6	12	18	42	79	115

NOTE: *Frogman stories in 17, 38, 44, 45, 50, 51, 53, 55-58, 63, 65, 66, 72, 76, 77.* ***Colan*** *a-112.* ***Drucker*** *a-47, 58, 61, 63, 65, 69, 71, 74, 77.* ***Grandenetti*** *c(p)-127, 128, 2-17(most).* ***Heath*** *a-14, 27, 32, 38, 41, 45, 47, 50, 51, 55-58, 62, 64, 71, 75, 76, 78, 95, 111-117; c-85, 91, 94-96, 100, 101, 110-112, others?* ***Infantino*** *a-8.* ***Kirby*** *a-29.* ***Krigstein*** *a-128('52), 2, 3, 5.* ***Kubert*** *a-22, 24, 28, 29, 33, 34, 36, 38, 39, 41-43, 47-50, 52, 53, 55, 56, 59, 60, 63-65, 69, 71-73, 76, 102, 103, 105, 106, 108, 114; c-41, 44, 52, 54, 55, 58, 64, 69, 76, 77, 79, 102-106, 108, 113-117, others? Tank Killer in 69, 71, 76 by* ***Kubert. P. Reinman*** *c-55, 57, 61, 62, 71, 72, 74-76, 80.* ***J. Severin*** *a-58.*

ALL AMERICAN MEN OF WAR
DC Comics: Aug/Sept. 1952

nn - Ashcan comic, not distributed to newsstands, only for in-house use. Cover art is All Star Western #58 and interior from Mr. District Attorney #21. A GD+ copy sold for $1195 in 2012.

ALL-AMERICAN SPORTS
Charlton Comics: Oct, 1967

	GD 2.0	VG 4.0	FN 6.0	VF 8.0	VF/NM 9.0	NM- 9.2
1	4	8	12	23	37	50

ALL-AMERICAN WESTERN (Formerly All-American Comics; Becomes All-American Men of War)
National Periodical Publ.: No. 103, Nov, 1948 - No. 126, June-July, 1952 (103-121: 52 pgs.)

	GD 2.0	VG 4.0	FN 6.0	VF 8.0	VF/NM 9.0	NM- 9.2
103-Johnny Thunder & his horse Black Lightning continues by Toth, ends #126; Foley of The Fighting 5th, Minstrel Maverick, & Overland Coach begin; Captain Tootsie by Beck; mentioned in Love and Death	63	126	189	403	689	975
104-Kubert-a	40	80	120	246	411	575
105,107-Kubert-a	36	72	108	211	343	475
106,108-110,112: 112-Kurtzman's "Pot-Shot Pete" (1 pg.)	29	58	87	170	278	385
111,114-116-Kubert-a	30	60	90	177	289	400
113-Intro. Swift Deer, J. Thunder's new sidekick (4-5/50); classic Toth-c; Kubert-a	34	68	102	199	325	450
117-126: 121-Kubert-a; bondage-c	21	42	63	126	206	285

NOTE: ***G. Kane*** *c(p)-112, 119, 120, 123.* ***Kubert*** *a-103-105, 107, 111, 112(1 pg.), 113-116, 121.* ***Toth*** *a-103-125; c(p)-103-111,113-116, 121, 122, 124-126. Some copies of #125 have #12 on-c.*

ALL COMICS
Chicago Nite Life News: 1945

	GD 2.0	VG 4.0	FN 6.0	VF 8.0	VF/NM 9.0	NM- 9.2
1	20	40	60	114	182	250

ALLEGRA
Image Comics (WildStorm): Aug, 1996 - No. 4, Dec, 1996 ($2.50)

	GD 2.0	VG 4.0	FN 6.0	VF 8.0	VF/NM 9.0	NM- 9.2
1-4						3.00

ALLEY CAT (Alley Baggett)
Image Comics: July, 1999 - No. 6, Mar, 2000 ($2.50/$2.95)

	GD 2.0	VG 4.0	FN 6.0	VF 8.0	VF/NM 9.0	NM- 9.2
Preview Edition						6.00
Prelude						5.00
Prelude w/variant-c						6.00
1-Photo-c						3.00
1-Painted-c by Dorian						4.00
1-Another Universe Edition, 1-Wizard World Edition						7.00
2-4: 4-Twin towers on-c						3.00
5,6-($2.95)						3.00
Lingerie Edition (10/99, $4.95) Photos, pin-ups, cover gallery						5.00
...Vs. Lady Pendragon ('99, $3.00) Stinsman-c						3.00

ALLEY OOP (See The Comics, The Funnies, Red Ryder and Super Book #9)
Dell Publishing Co.: No. 3, 1942

	GD 2.0	VG 4.0	FN 6.0	VF 8.0	VF/NM 9.0	NM- 9.2
Four Color 3 (#1)	54	108	162	432	966	1500

ALLEY OOP
Argo Publ.: Nov, 1955 - No. 3, Mar, 1956 (Newspaper reprints)

	GD 2.0	VG 4.0	FN 6.0	VF 8.0	VF/NM 9.0	NM- 9.2
1	20	40	60	117	189	260
2,3	14	28	42	80	115	150

ALLEY OOP
Dell Publishing Co.: 12-2/62-63 - No. 2, 9-11/63

	GD 2.0	VG 4.0	FN 6.0	VF 8.0	VF/NM 9.0	NM- 9.2
1	6	12	18	41	76	110
2	5	10	15	34	60	85

ALLEY OOP
Standard Comics: No. 10, Sept, 1947 - No. 18, Oct, 1949

	GD 2.0	VG 4.0	FN 6.0	VF 8.0	VF/NM 9.0	NM- 9.2
10	34	68	102	199	325	450
11-16	25	50	75	147	241	335
17,18-Schomburg-c	41	82	123	256	428	600

ALLEY OOP ADVENTURES
Antarctic Press: Aug, 1998 - No. 3, Dec, 1998 ($2.95)

	GD 2.0	VG 4.0	FN 6.0	VF 8.0	VF/NM 9.0	NM- 9.2
1-3-Jack Bender-s/a						3.00

ALLEY OOP ADVENTURES (Alley Oop Quarterly in indicia)
Antarctic Press: Sept, 1999 - No. 3, Mar, 2000 ($2.50/$2.99, B&W)

	GD 2.0	VG 4.0	FN 6.0	VF 8.0	VF/NM 9.0	NM- 9.2
1-3-Jack Bender-s/a						3.00

ALL-FAMOUS CRIME (2nd series - Formerly Law Against Crime #1-3; becomes All-Famous Police Cases #6 on)
Star Publications: No. 8, 5/51 - No. 10, 11/51; No. 4, 2/52 - No. 5, 5/52;

	GD 2.0	VG 4.0	FN 6.0	VF 8.0	VF/NM 9.0	NM- 9.2
8 (#1-1st series)	36	72	108	211	343	475
9 (#2)-Used in **SOTI**, illo- "The wish to hurt or kill couples in lovers' lanes is a not uncommon perversion;" L.B. Cole-c/a(r)/Law-Crime #3	50	100	150	315	533	750
10 (#3)	28	56	84	165	270	375
4 (#4-2nd series)-Formerly Law-Crime	28	56	84	165	270	375
5 (#5) Becomes All-Famous Police Cases #6	27	54	81	158	259	360

NOTE: *All have* ***L.B. Cole*** *covers.*

ALL FAMOUS CRIME STORIES (See Fox Giants)

ALL-FAMOUS POLICE CASES (Formerly All Famous Crime #5)
Star Publications: No. 6, Feb, 1952 - No. 16, Sept, 1954

	GD 2.0	VG 4.0	FN 6.0	VF 8.0	VF/NM 9.0	NM- 9.2
6	37	74	111	222	361	500
7-Matt Baker story	71	142	213	454	777	1100
8-Marijuana story	47	94	141	296	498	700
9-16	27	54	81	158	259	360

NOTE: ***L. B. Cole*** *c-all; a-15, 1pg.* ***Hollingsworth*** *a-15.*

ALL-FLASH (...Quarterly No. 1-5)
National Per. Publ./All-American: Summer, 1941 - No. 32, Dec-Jan, 1947-48

	GD 2.0	VG 4.0	FN 6.0	VF 8.0	VF/NM 9.0	NM- 9.2
1-Origin The Flash retold by E. E. Hibbard; Hibbard c-1-10,12-14,16,31p.	1425	2850	4275	9950	16,975	24,000
2-Origin recap	284	568	852	1818	3109	4400
3,4	168	336	504	1075	1838	2600
5-Winky, Blinky & Noddy begins (1st app.), ends #32	123	246	369	787	1344	1900
6-Has full page ad for Wonder Woman #1	116	232	348	742	1271	1800
7-10	113	226	339	723	1237	1750
11,13: 13-The King app.	100	200	300	635	1093	1550
12-Origin/1st The Thinker	123	246	369	787	1344	1900
14-Green Lantern cameo	113	226	339	723	1237	1750
15-20: 18-Mutt & Jeff begins, ends #22	87	174	261	553	952	1350
21-31	73	146	219	467	796	1125
32-Origin/1st app. The Fiddler; 1st Star Sapphire	300	600	900	2070	3635	5200
All-Flash Quarterly ashcan	(a CGC 7.0 copy sold for $8150 in 2012)					

NOTE: *Book length stories in 2-13, 16. Bondage c-31, 32.* ***Martin Nodell*** *c-15, 17-28.*

ALL FLASH (Leads into Flash [2nd series] #231)
DC Comics: Sept, 2007 ($2.99, one-shot)

	GD 2.0	VG 4.0	FN 6.0	VF 8.0	VF/NM 9.0	NM- 9.2
1-Wally West hunts down Bart's killers; Waid-s; two covers by Middleton & Sienkiewicz						3.00

ALL FOR LOVE (Young Love V3#5-on)
Prize Publications: Apr-May, 1957 - V3#4, Dec-Jan, 1959-60

	GD 2.0	VG 4.0	FN 6.0	VF 8.0	VF/NM 9.0	NM- 9.2
V1#1	11	22	33	76	163	250
2-6: 5-Orlando-c	6	12	18	42	79	115
V2#1-5(1/59), 5(3/59)	6	12	18	37	66	95
V3#1(5/59), 1(7/59)-4: 2-Powell-a	5	10	15	34	60	85

ALL FUNNY COMICS
Tilsam Publ./National Periodical Publications (Detective): Winter, 1943-44 - No. 23, May-June, 1948

1-Genius Jones (see Adventure #77 for debut), Buzzy (1st app., ends #4), Dover & Clover

All-American Men of War #82 © DC

All-Flash #8 © DC

All-New Captain America #1 © MAR

GD VG FN VF VF/NM NM-
2.0 4.0 6.0 8.0 9.0 9.2

GD VG FN VF VF/NM NM-
2.0 4.0 6.0 8.0 9.0 9.2

(see More Fun #93) begin; Bailey-a 59 118 177 375 650 925
2 25 50 75 150 245 340
3-10 16 32 48 92 144 195
11-13,15,18,19-Genius Jones app. 15 30 45 84 127 170
14,17,20-23 11 22 33 62 86 110
16-DC Super Heroes app. 36 72 108 211 343 475

ALL GOOD
St. John Publishing Co.: Oct, 1949 (50¢, 260 pgs.)

nn-(8 St. John comics bound together) 123 246 369 787 1344 1900
NOTE: *Also see Li'l Audrey Yearbook & Treasury of Comics.*

ALL GOOD COMICS (See Fox Giants)
Fox Feature Syndicate: No.1, Spring, 1946 (36 pgs.)

1-Joy Family, Dick Transom, Rick Evans, One Round Hogan
30 60 90 177 289 400

ALL GREAT
William H. Wise & Co.: nd (1945?) (132 pgs.)

nn-Capt. Jack Terry, Joan Mason, Girl Reporter, Baron Doomsday; Torture scenes
52 104 156 324 550 775

ALL GREAT COMICS (See Fox Giants)
Fox Feature Syndicate: 1946 (36 pgs.)

1-Crazy House, Bertie Benson Boy Detective, Gussie the Gob
29 58 87 172 281 390

ALL GREAT COMICS (Formerly Phantom Lady #13? Dagar, Desert Hawk No. 14 on)
Fox Feature Syndicate: No. 14, Oct, 1947 - No. 13, Dec, 1947 (Newspaper strip reprints)

14(#12)-Brenda Starr & Texas Slim-r (Scarce) 63 126 189 403 689 975
13-Origin Dagar, Desert Hawk; Brenda Starr (all-r); Kamen-c; Dagar covers
begin 129 258 387 826 1413 2000

ALL-GREAT CONFESSION MAGAZINE (See Fox Giants)

ALL-GREAT CONFESSIONS (See Fox Giants)

ALL GREAT CRIME STORIES (See Fox Giants)

ALL GREAT JUNGLE ADVENTURES (See Fox Giants)

ALL HALLOW'S EVE
Innovation Publishing: 1991 ($4.95, 52 pgs.)

1-Painted-c/a 1 3 4 6 8 10

ALL HERO COMICS
Fawcett Publications: Mar, 1943 (100 pgs., cardboard-c)

1-Capt. Marvel Jr., Capt. Midnight, Golden Arrow, Ibis the Invincible, Spy Smasher, Lance O'Casey; 1st Banshee O'Brien; Raboy-c 200 400 600 1280 2190 3100

ALL HUMOR COMICS
Quality Comics Group: Spring, 1946 - No. 17, December, 1949

1 26 52 78 154 252 350
2-Atomic Tot story; Gustavson-a 14 28 42 81 118 155
3-9: 3-Intro Kelly Poole who is cover feature #3 on. 5-1st app. Hickory? 8-Gustavson-a 10 20 30 54 72 90
10-17 9 18 27 50 65 80

ALL LOVE (...Romances No. 26)(Formerly Ernie Comics)
Ace Periodicals (Current Books): No. 26, May, 1949 - No. 32, May, 1950

26 (No. 1)-Ernie, Lily Belle app. 15 30 45 86 133 190
27-L. B. Cole-a 16 32 48 98 154 225
28-32 12 24 36 69 97 135

ALL-NEGRO COMICS
All-Negro Comics: June, 1947 (15¢)

1 (Rare) 2700 5400 8100 14,600 20,800 27,000
NOTE: *Seldom found in fine or mint condition; many copies have brown pages.*

ALL-NEW ALL-DIFFERENT AVENGERS (Follows Secret Wars event)
Marvel Comics: Jan, 2016 - No. 15, Dec, 2015 ($4.99/$3.99)

1-($4.99) Spider-Man (Miles), Ms. Marvel, Nova join; Waid-s/Adam Kubert & Asrar-a 5.00
2-15-($3.99) Main cover by Alex Ross. 2,3-Warbringer app.; Kubert-a. 4-6,9,10-Asrar-a. 7,8-Standoff tie-ins; Adam Kubert-a. 9-Intro. new Wasp (Nadia). 13-15-Civil War II tie-in 4.00
Annual 1(10/16, $4.99) Fan-fic short stories by various incl. Waid/Zdarsky & Allegri 5.00

ALL-NEW ALL-DIFFERENT MARVEL UNIVERSE
Marvel Comics: May, 2016 ($4.99, one-shot)

1-Handbook-style entries; profiles of major characters; Marquez-c 5.00

ALL-NEW ALL-DIFFERENT POINT ONE (Follows Secret Wars event)
Marvel Comics: Dec, 2015 ($5.99, one-shot)

1-Preludes to new titles: Carnage, Daredevil, All-New Inhumans, Agents of S.H.I.E.L.D., Rocket Raccoon & Groot, and Contest of Champions; Del Mundo-c 6.00

ALL-NEW ATOM, THE (See The Atom and DCU Brave New World)
DC Comics: Sept, 2006 - No. 25, Sept, 2008 ($2.99)

1-25: 1-18-Simone-s. 1-Intro Ryan Choi; Byrne-a thru #3. 4-11-Barrows-a. 12,13-Chronos app. 14,15-Countdown x-over. 17,18-Wonder Woman app. 3.00
...: Future/Past TPB (2007, $14.99) r/#7-11 15.00
...: My Life in Miniature TPB (2007, $14.99) r/#1-6 and app. in DCU Brave New World #1 15.00
...: Small Wonder TPB (2008, $17.99) r/#17,18,21-25 18.00
...: The Hunt For Ray Palmer TPB (2008, $14.99) r/#12-16 15.00

ALL-NEW BATMAN: BRAVE & THE BOLD (See Batman: The Brave and the Bold)

ALL-NEW CAPTAIN AMERICA (See Captain America #25 - 2014 series)
Marvel Comics: Jan, 2015 - No. 6, Jun, 2015 ($3.99)

1-Sam Wilson as Captain America, Ian as Nomad; Immonen-a
2 4 6 8 10 12
2-6 4.00
... Special 1 (7/15, $4.99) Loveness-s/Morgan-a; Inhumans & Spider-Man app. 5.00

ALL-NEW CAPTAIN AMERICA: FEAR HIM (Sam Wilson as Cap)
Marvel Comics: Jan, 2015 - No. 4, Apr, 2015 ($3.99, limited series)

1-4-Hopeless & Remender-s/Kudranski-a/Bianchi-c; The Scarecrow app. 4.00

ALL-NEW CLASSIC CAPTAIN CANUCK
Chapterhouse Comics: No. 0, Feb, 2016 - No. 4, Apr, 2017 ($4.99/$3.99)

0-($4.99) Short stories; Ed Brisson-s; art by various 5.00
1-4-($3.99) Brisson-s/Freeman-a; 2 covers on each 4.00

ALL-NEW COLLECTORS' EDITION (Formerly Limited Collectors' Edition: see for C-57, C-59)
DC Comics, Inc.: Jan, 1978 - Vol. 8, No. C-62, 1979 (No. 54-58: 76 pgs.)

C-53-Rudolph the Red-Nosed Reindeer 5 10 15 34 60 85
C-54-Superman Vs. Wonder Woman 5 10 15 35 63 90
C-55-Superboy & the Legion of Super-Heroes; Wedding of Lightning Lad & Saturn Girl; Grell-c/a 4 8 12 28 47 65
C-56-Superman Vs. Muhammad Ali: Wraparound Neal Adams-c/a; Adams & O'Neil-s (see "Superman Vs. Muhammad Ali" for reprint) 12 24 36 80 173 265
C-56-Superman Vs. Muhammad Ali (Whitman variant)-low print
14 28 42 94 207 320
C-57,C-59-(See Limited Collectors' Edition)
C-58-Superman Vs. Shazam; Buckler-c/a; Black Adam's 2nd Bronze Age app.
5 10 15 34 60 85
C-60-Rudolph's Summer Fun(8/78) 5 10 15 30 50 70
C-61-(See Famous First Edition-Superman #1)
C-62-Superman the Movie (68 pgs.; 1979)-Photo-c from movie plus photos inside (also see DC Special Series #25 for Superman II) 3 6 9 22 35 45

ALL-NEW COMICS (...Short Story Comics No. 1-3)
Family Comics (Harvey Publications): Jan, 1943 - No. 14, Nov, 1946; No. 15, Mar-Apr, 1947 (10 x 13-1/2")

1-Steve Case, Crime Rover, Johnny Rebel, Kayo Kane, The Echo, Night Hawk, Ray O'Light, Detective Shane begin (all 1st app.?); Red Blazer on cover only; Sultan-a; Nazi WWII-c
300 600 900 2070 3635 5200
2-Origin Scarlet Phantom by Kubert; Nazi WWII-c 161 322 483 1030 1765 2500
3-Nazi WWII-c 129 258 387 826 1413 2000
4-Sci-fi Nazi monsters bondage-c 290 580 870 1856 3178 4500
5-Classic Schomburg Japanese WWII-c showing Japanese using Human Suicide bombs falling on the Capitol building 258 516 774 1651 2826 4000
6-11: Schomburg-c on all. 9-11-Japanese WWII-c. 6-8 Nazi WWII-c. 6-The Boy Heroes & Red Blazer (text story) begin, end #12; Black Cat app.; intro. Sparky in Red Blazer. 7-Kubert, Powell-a; Black Cat & Zebra app. 8,9: 8-Shock Gibson app.; Kubert, Powell-a; Schomburg-c. 9-Black Cat app.; Kubert-a. 10-The Zebra app. (from Green Hornet Comics); Kubert-a(3). 11-Girl Commandos, Man In Black app.
181 362 543 1158 1979 2800
12-Kubert-a; Japanese WWII-c 90 180 270 576 988 1400
13-Stuntman by Simon & Kirby; Green Hornet, Joe Palooka, Flying Fool app.; Green Hornet-c 55 110 165 352 601 850
14-The Green Hornet & The Man in Black Called Fate by Powell, Joe Flying Fool app.; Flying Fool app.; J. Palooka-c by Ham Fisher 45 90 135 284 480 675
15-(Rare)-Small size (5-1/2x8-1/2"; B&W; 32 pgs.). Distributed to mail subscribers only. Black Cat and Joe Palooka app. 194 388 582 1242 2121 3000
NOTE: *Also see Boy Explorers No. 2, Flash Gordon No. 5, and Stuntman No. 3.* ***Powell*** *a-11.* ***Schomburg*** *c-5-11. Captain Red Blazer & Spark on c-5-11 (w/Boy Heroes #12).*

ALL-NEW DOOP (X-Men)
Marvel Comics: Jun, 2014 - No. 5, Nov, 2014 ($3.99, limited series)

1-5-Milligan-s/Lafuente-a; Kitty Pryde and X-Men app. 3-5-The Anarchist app. 4.00

ALL-NEW EXECUTIVE ASSISTANT: IRIS (Volume 4) (Also see Executive Assistant: Iris)

GD VG FN VF VF/NM NM- 2.0 4.0 6.0 8.0 9.0 9.2

Aspen MLT: Sept, 2013 - No. 5, Jun, 2014 ($1.00/$3.99)
1-($1.00) Buccellato-s/Qualano-a; multiple covers 3.00
2-5-($3.99) Multiple covers 4.00
...: Enemies Among Us 1 (12/16, $4.99) Wohl-s/Cafaro-a; Hernandéz-s/Green-a; multiple-c 5.00

ALL NEW FATHOM (See Fathom)

ALL-NEW FIREFLY (Also see Firefly)
BOOM! Studios: Feb, 2022 - No. 10, Nov, 2022 ($4.99)
1-10: 1-4-Booher-s/Pérez-a. 5-10-Federici-a 5.00
...: Big Damn Finale 1 (12/22, $8.99) Polybagged with cardboard to conceal cover image 9.00

ALL-NEW GHOST RIDER (Also see the 2017 Ghost Rider series)
Marvel Comics: May, 2014 - No. 12, May, 2015 ($3.99)
1-12: 1-Felipe Smith-s/Tradd Moore-a; origin of Robbie Reyes. 6-10-Damion Scott-a 4.00

ALL-NEW GUARDIANS OF THE GALAXY (Continues in Guardians of the Galaxy #146)
Marvel Comics: Jul, 2017 - No. 12, Dec, 2017 ($3.99)
1-12: 1-Grandmaster app.; Duggan-s/Kuder-a. 2,4-The Collector app. 3-Irving-a 4.00
Annual 1 (8/17, $4.99) Tie-in to Secret Empire; Beyruth-a; Yondu & Mantis app. 5.00

ALL-NEW HAWKEYE
Marvel Comics: May, 2015 - No. 5, Nov, 2015 ($3.99)
1-Jeff Lemire-s/Ramón Pérez-a/c; Kate Bishop app.; flashback to circus childhood 6.00
2-5 4.00

ALL-NEW HAWKEYE
Marvel Comics: Jan, 2016 - No. 6, Jun, 2016 ($3.99)
1-Lemire-s/Pérez-a/c; Kate Bishop app.; flashforward 30 years; Mandarin app. 6.00
2-6: 2,3-Flashforward 30 years; Mandarin app. 4.00

ALL-NEW INHUMANS
Marvel Comics: Feb, 2016 - No. 11, Nov, 2016 ($3.99)
1-($4.99)-Asmus & Soule-s/Caselli-a; Crystal & Gorgon app. 5.00
2-11-($3.99) 2-4-The Commissar app. 5,6-Spider-Man app. 4.00

ALL-NEW INVADERS
Marvel Comics: Mar, 2014 - No. 15, Apr, 2015 ($3.99)
1-15: 1-Capt. America, Bucky, Namor & Jim Hammond team; Robinson-s/Pugh-a. 6,7-Original Sin tie-in 4.00

ALL-NEW MARVEL NOW! POINT ONE
Marvel Comics: Mar, 2014 ($5.99, one-shot preview of upcoming series)
1-Previews of Loki, Silver Surfer, Black Widow, Ms. Marvel, Avengers, All-New Invaders 6.00

ALL NEW MICHAEL TURNER'S FATHOM (See Fathom)

ALL NEW MICHAEL TURNER'S SOULFIRE (See Soulfire)

ALL-NEW OFFICIAL HANDBOOK OF THE MARVEL UNIVERSE A TO Z
Marvel Comics: 2006 - No. 12, 2006 ($3.99, limited series)
1-12-Profile pages of Marvel characters not covered in 2004-2005 Official Handbooks 4.00
...: Update 1-4 (2007, $3.99) Profile pages 4.00

ALL-NEW ULTIMATES
Marvel Comics: Jun, 2014 - No. 12, Mar, 2015 ($3.99)
1-12: 1-Miles Morales Spider-Man, Spider-Woman, Cloak and Dagger, Kitty Pryde and Bombshell team. 5,6-Crossbones app. 4.00

ALL-NEW WOLVERINE (Laura Kinney X-23 as Wolverine)
Marvel Comics: Jan, 2016 - No. 35, Jul, 2018 ($4.99/$3.99)
1-($4.99) Tom Taylor-s/David Lopez-a; Angel app. 3 6 9 15 22 28
2-Intro. Gabby Kinney; Taskmaster app. 4 8 12 25 40 55
3-27,29-35-($3.99) 3-Taskmaster app. 4-Doctor Strange app. 5-Janet Van Dyne app. 7-Squirrel Girl app. 8,9-Fin Fang Foom app. 10-12-Civil War II tie-in. 16-18-Gambit app. 19-21-Ironheart app. 22-24-Guardians of the Galaxy app.; Yu-c. 25-30-Daken app. 31-Deadpool app. 33-"Old Woman Laura"; future against Doom 4.00
28-1st Honey Badger; Daken app. 6.00
Annual 1 (10/16, $4.99) Gwen Stacy app.; Tom Taylor-s/Marcio Takara-a 1 2 3 5 6 8

ALL-NEW X-FACTOR
Marvel Comics: Mar, 2014 - No. 20, Mar, 2015 ($3.99)
1-20: 1-12-David-s/DiGiandomenico-a; Gambit, Polaris, Quicksilver, Danger app. 13,14-Mhan-a. 14-Scarlet Witch app. 15-17-Axis tie-in 4.00

ALL-NEW X-MEN
Marvel Comics: Jan, 2013 - No. 41, Aug, 2015 ($3.99)
1-Bendis-s; Immonen-a and wraparound-c; original X-Men time travel to present 6.00
2-24: 6-8-Marquez-a; Mystique app. 8-Avengers app. 16,17-Battle of the Atom tie-ins. 18-New uniforms. 22-24-Trial of Jean Grey; Guardians of the Galaxy app. 4.00
25-($4.99) Art by Marquez with pages by Timm, Mack, Young, Campbell & many others 5.00
26-41: 30-Pichelli-a. 31-36-X-Men in Ultimate universe; Miles Morales app. 38,39-Black Vortex x-over; Ronan & Guardians of the Galaxy app.; Sorrentino-a. 40-Iceman revealed as gay 4.00
Annual 1 (2/15, $4.99) Sorrentino-a; Eva Bell and Morgana Le Fey in the past 5.00
Special #1 (12/13, $4.99) Superior Spider-Man and the Hulk app. 5.00

ALL-NEW X-MEN
Marvel Comics: Feb, 2016 - No. 19, May, 2017 ($3.99)
1-8-Hopeless-s/Bagley-a; original X-Men, Wolverine (X-23), Kid Apocalypse app. 4.00
9-($4.99) Apocalypse Wars x-over; Beast & Kid Apocalypse in ancient Egypt 5.00
10-19: 10,11-Apocalypse Wars; young Apocalypse app. 17,18-Inhumans app. 4.00
Annual 1 (1/17, $4.99) Spotlight on Idie; Sina Grace-s/Cory Smith-a 5.00
#1.MU (4/17, $4.99) Monsters Unleashed tie-in; Barberi & Lim-a; Gambit app. 5.00

ALL NIGHTER
Image Comics: Jun, 2011 - No. 5, Oct, 2011 ($2.99, B&W, limited series)
1-5-David Haun-s/a/c 3.00

ALL-OUT AVENGERS (Story continues in Avengers Beyond #1)
Marvel Comics: Nov, 2022 - No. 5, Mar, 2023 ($3.99)
1-5-Derek Landy-s/Greg Land-a; Avengers, Spider-Man and Blade app. 4.00

ALL-OUT WAR
DC Comics: Sept-Oct, 1979 - No. 6, Aug, 1980 ($1.00, 68 pgs.)
1-The Viking Commando (origin), Force Three(origin), & Black Eagle Squadron begin 2 4 6 13 18 22
2-6 2 4 6 8 10 12
NOTE: *Ayers a(p)-1-6. Elias r-2. Evans a-1-6. Kubert c-16.*

ALL PICTURE ADVENTURE MAGAZINE
St. John Publishing Co.: Oct, 1952 - No. 2, Nov, 1952 (100 pg. Giants, 25¢, squarebound)
1-War comics 58 116 174 371 636 900
2-Horror-crime comics 74 148 222 470 810 1150
NOTE: *Above books contain three St. John comics rebound; variations possible.* ***Baker*** *art known in both.*

ALL PICTURE ALL TRUE LOVE STORY
St. John Publishing Co.: Oct., 1952 - No. 2, Nov., 1952 (100 pgs., 25¢)
1-Canteen Kate by Matt Baker 194 388 582 1242 2121 3000
2-Baker-c/a 84 168 252 538 919 1300

ALL-PICTURE COMEDY CARNIVAL
St. John Publishing Co.: October, 1952 (100 pgs., 25¢)(Contains 4 rebound comics)
1-Contents can vary; Baker-a 54 108 162 343 574 825

ALL REAL CONFESSION MAGAZINE (See Fox Giants)

ALL ROMANCES (Mr. Risk No. 7 on)
A. A. Wyn (Ace Periodicals): Aug, 1949 - No. 6, June, 1950
1 22 44 66 132 216 300
2 14 28 42 80 115 150
3-6 12 24 36 69 97 125

ALL-SELECT COMICS (Blonde Phantom No. 12 on)
Timely Comics (Daring Comics): Fall, 1943 - No. 11, Fall, 1946
1-Capt. America (by Rico #1), Human Torch, Sub-Mariner begin; Black Widow story (4 pgs.); Classic Schomburg-c 2600 5200 7800 17,200 36,100 55,000
2-Red Skull app. 1000 2000 3000 7400 13,200 19,000
3-The Whizzer begins 486 972 1458 3550 6275 9000
4,5-Last Sub-Mariner 400 800 1200 2800 4900 7000
6-9: 6-The Destroyer app. 8-No Whizzer 300 600 900 2070 3635 5200
10-The Destroyer & Sub-Mariner app.; last Capt. America & Human Torch issue 308 616 924 2156 3778 5400
11-1st app. Blonde Phantom; Miss America app.; all Blonde Phantom-c by Shores 400 800 1200 2800 4900 7000
NOTE: ***Schomburg*** *c-1-10.* ***Sekowsky*** *a-7. #7 & 8 show 1944 in indicia, but should be 1945.*

ALL SELECT COMICS 70th ANNIVERARY SPECIAL
Marvel Comics: Sept, 2009 ($3.99, one-shot)
1-New stories of Blonde Phantom and Marvex the Super Robot; r/Marvex G.A. app. 6.00

ALL SPORTS COMICS (Formerly Real Sports Comics; becomes All Time Sports Comics No. 4 on)
Hillman Periodicals: No. 2, Dec-Jan, 1948-49; No. 3, Feb-Mar, 1949
2-Krigstein-a(p), Powell, Starr-a 39 78 117 240 395 550
3-Mort Lawrence-a 26 52 78 154 252 350

ALL STAR BATMAN
DC Comics: Oct, 2016 - No. 14, Dec, 2017 ($4.99)
1-Snyder-s/Romita Jr.-a; Two-Face app.; back-up with Shalvey-a 1 3 4 6 8 10
1-Director's Cut ($5.99) r/#1 with B&W art and original script; variant cover gallery 10.00
2-5-Snyder-s/Romita Jr.-a; Two-Face app.; back-up with Shalvey-a 5.00
6-9-Back-up w/Francavilla-a. 6-Jock-a; Mr. Freeze app. 7-Lotay-a; Poison Ivy app 5.00
10-14-Albuquerque-a; back-up with Fiumara-a 5.00

ALL STAR BATMAN & ROBIN, THE BOY WONDER
DC Comics: Sept, 2005 - No. 10, Aug, 2008 ($2.99)
1-Two covers; retelling of Robin's origin; Frank Miller-s/Jim Lee-a/c 1 3 4 6 8 10
1-Diamond Retailer Summit Edition (9/05) sketch-c 65.00
2-10: 2-7-Two covers by Lee and Miller. 3-Black Canary app. 4-Six pg. Batcave gatefold. 10-Edition without profanity 3.00
8-10: 8,9-Variant cover by Neal Adams. 10-Variant-c by Quitely 5.00
10-Recalled edition with insufficiently covered profanity inside; Jim Lee-c 24.00
10-Recalled edition with variant Quitely-c 45.00
... Special Edition (2/06, $3.99) r/#1 with Lee pencil pages and Miller script; new Miller-c 4.00
Vol. 1 HC (2008, $24.99, dustjacket) r/#1-9; cover gallery, sketch pages; Schreck intro. 25.00
Vol. 1 SC (2009, $19.99) r/#1-9; cover gallery, sketch pages; Schreck intro. 20.00

ALL STAR COMICS
DC Comics: Spring 1940
1-Ashcan comic, not distributed to newsstands, only for in-house use. Cover art is Flash Comics #1 and interior from Detective Comics #37. A CGC certified 7.0 copy sold for $15,600 in 2002 and for $21,000 in May 2014.

ALL STAR COMICS (All Star Western No. 58 on)
National Periodical Publ./All-American/DC Comics: Sum, 1940 - No. 57, Feb-Mar, 1951; No. 58, Jan-Feb, 1976 - No. 74, Sept-Oct, 1978
1-The Flash (#1 by E.E. Hibbard), Hawkman (by Shelly), Hourman (by Bernard Baily), The Sandman (by Creig Flessel), The Spectre (by Baily), Biff Bronson, Red White & Blue (ends #2) begin; Ultra Man's only app. (#1-3 are quarterly; #4 begins bi-monthly issues) 1450 2900 4350 10,900 20,450 30,000
2-Green Lantern (by Martin Nodell), Johnny Thunder begin; Green Lantern figure swipe from the cover of All-American Comics #16; Flash figure swipe from cover of Flash Comics #8; Moldoff/Bailey-c (cut & paste-c.) 649 1298 1947 4738 8369 12,000
3-Origin & 1st app. The Justice Society of America (Win/40); Dr. Fate & The Atom begin, Red Tornado cameo 6500 13,000 19,500 52,000 101,000 150,000
3-Reprint, Oversize 13-1/2x10". **WARNING:** This comic is an exact reprint of the original except for its size. DC published it in 1974 with a second cover titling it as a Famous First Edition. There have been many reported cases of the outer cover being removed and the interior sold as the original edition. The reprint with the new outer cover removed is practically worthless. See Famous First Edition for value.
4-1st adventure for J.S.A. 676 1352 2028 4935 8718 12,500
5-1st app. Shiera Sanders as Hawkgirl (1st costumed super-heroine, 6-7/41) 649 1298 1947 4738 8369 12,000
6-Johnny Thunder joins JSA 300 600 900 2010 3505 5000

All-New X-Men #22 © MAR

All Star Comics #3 © DC

All Star Superman #2 © DC

GD	VG	FN	VF	VF/NM	NM-
2.0	4.0	6.0	8.0	9.0	9.2

7-First time ever Superman and Batman appear in a story together; Superman, Batman and Flash become honorary members; last Hourman; Doiby Dickles app. 427 854 1281 3117 5509 7900

8-Origin & 1st app. Wonder Woman (12-1/41-42)(added as 9 pgs. book is 76 pgs.; origin cont'd in Sensation #1; see W.W. #1 for more detailed origin); Dr. Fate dons new helmet; Hop Harrigan text stories & Starman begin; Shiera app.; Hop Harrigan JSA guest; Starman & Dr. Mid-Nite become members 22,200 44,400 66,600 177,600 281,300 385,000

9-11: 9-JSA's girlfriends cameo; Shiera app.; J. Edgar Hoover of FBI made associate member of JSA. 10-Flash, Green Lantern cameo; Sandman new costume. 11-Wonder Woman begins; Spectre cameo; Shiera app.; Moldoff Hawkman-c 308 616 924 2156 3778 5400

12-Wonder Woman becomes JSA Secretary 303 606 909 2121 3711 5300

13,15: Sandman w/Sandy in #14 & 15. 13-Hitler app. in book-length sci-fi story. 15-Origin & 1st app. Brain Wave; Shiera app. 265 530 795 1694 2897 4100

14-(12/42) Junior JSA Club begins; w/membership offer & premiums 271 542 813 1734 2967 4200

16-20: 19-Sandman w/Sandy. 20-Dr. Fate & Sandman cameo 252 504 756 1613 2757 3900

21-23: 21-Spectre & Atom cameo; Dr. Fate by Kubert; Dr. Fate, Sandman end. 22-Last Hop Harrigan; Flag-c. 23-Origin/1st app. Psycho Pirate; last Spectre & Starman 194 388 582 1242 2121 3000

24-Flash & Green Lantern cameo; Mr. Terrific only app.; Wildcat, JSA guest; Kubert Hawkman begins; Hitler-c 200 400 600 1280 2190 3100

25-27: 25-Flash & Green Lantern start again. 26-Robot-c. 27-Wildcat, JSA guest (#24-26: only All-American imprint) 174 348 522 1114 1907 2700

28-32 161 322 483 1030 1765 2500

33-Solomon Grundy & Doiby Dickles app; classic Solomon Grundy cover 432 864 1296 3154 5377 8000

34,35-Johnny Thunder cameo in both 148 296 444 947 1624 2300

36-Batman & Superman JSA guests 400 800 1200 2800 4900 7000

37-Johnny Thunder cameo; origin & 1st app. Injustice Society; last Kubert Hawkman 290 580 870 1856 3178 4500

38-Black Canary begins; JSA Death issue 265 530 795 1694 2897 4100

39,40: 39-Last Johnny Thunder 168 336 504 1075 1838 2600

41-Black Canary joins JSA; Injustice Society app. (2nd app.?) 187 374 561 1197 2049 2900

42-Atom & the Hawkman don new costumes 206 412 618 1318 2259 3200

43-49,51-56: 43-New logo; Robot-c. 55-Sci/Fi story. 56-Robot-c 142 284 426 909 1555 2200

50-Frazetta art, 3 pgs. 148 296 444 947 1624 2300

57-Kubert-a, 6 pgs. (Scarce); last app. G.A. Green Lantern, Flash & Dr. Mid-Nite 219 438 657 1402 2401 3400

V12 #58-(1976) JSA (Flash, Hawkman, Dr. Mid-Nite, Wildcat, Dr. Fate, Green Lantern, Robin & Star Spangled Kid) app.; intro. Power Girl 11 22 33 73 157 240

V12 #59,60: 59-Estrada & Wood-a 3 6 9 21 33 45

V12 #61-68: 62-65-Superman app. 64,65-Wood-c/a; Vandal Savage app. 66-Injustice Society app. 68-Psycho Pirate app. 3 6 9 21 33 45

V12 #69-1st Earth-2 Huntress (Helena Wayne) 6 12 18 42 79 115

V12 #70-73: 70-Full intro. of Huntress. 72-Thorn on-c 3 6 9 21 33 45

V12 #74-(44 pgs.) Last issue, story continues in Adventure Comics #461 & 462 (death of Earth-2 Batman; Staton-c/a 5 10 15 30 50 70

(See Justice Society Vol. 1 TPB for reprints of V12 revival)

NOTE: *No Atom-27, 36; no Dr. Fate-13; no Flash-8, 9, 11-23; no Green Lantern-8, 9,11-23; Hawkman in 1-57 (only one to app. in all 57 issues); no Johnny Thunder-5, 36; no Wonder Woman-9, 10, 23. Book length stories in 4-9, 11-14, 18-22, 25, 26, 29, 30, 32-36, 40, 42, 43. Johnny Peril in #42-46, 48, 49, 51, 52,54-57.* ***Baily*** *a-1-10, 12, 13, 14i, 15-20.* ***Burnley*** *Starman-8-13; c-12, 13.* ***Grell*** *c-58.* ***E.E. Hibbard*** *c-3, 4, 6-10.* ***Infantino*** *c-40.* ***Kubert*** *Hawkman-24-30, 33-37.* ***Lampert/Baily/Flessel*** *c-1, 2.* ***Moldoff*** *Hawkman-3-23; c-11.* ***Mart Nodell*** *c-25i, 26i, 27-32.* ***Purcell*** *c-5.* ***Simon & Kirby*** *Sandman 14-17, 19.* ***Staton*** *a-66-74p. c-74p.* ***Toth*** *a-37(2), 38(2), 40, 41; c-38, 41.* ***Wood*** *a-58i-63i, 64, 65; c-63i, 64, 65. Issues 1-7, 9-16 are 68 pgs.; #8 is 76 pgs.; #17-19 are 60 pgs.; #20-57 are 52 pgs.*

ALL STAR COMICS (Also see crossover 1999 editions of Adventure, All-American, National, Sensation, Smash, Star Spangled and Thrilling Comics)
DC Comics: May, 1999 - No. 2, May, 1999 ($2.95, bookends for JSA x-over)

1,2-Justice Society in World War 2; Robinson-s/Johnson-c 5.00

1-RRP Edition 55.00

...80-Page Giant (9/99, $4.95) Phantom Lady app. 5.00

ALL STAR INDEX, THE
Independent Comics Group (Eclipse): Feb, 1987 ($2.00, Baxter paper)

1 1 3 4 6 8 10

ALL-STAR SECTION EIGHT (Also see Sixpack and Dogwelder: Hard Travelin' Heroz)
DC Comics: Aug, 2015 - No. 6, Feb, 2016 ($2.99, limited series)

1-6-Ennis-s/McCrea-a/Conner-c. 1-Batman app. 4-Wonder Woman app. 6-Superman 4.00

ALL-STAR SQUADRON (See Justice League of America #193)

GD	VG	FN	VF	VF/NM	NM-
2.0	4.0	6.0	8.0	9.0	9.2

DC Comics: Sept, 1981 - No. 67, Mar, 1987

1-Original Atom, Hawkman, Dr. Mid-Nite, Robotman (origin), Plastic Man, Johnny Quick, Liberty Belle, Shining Knight begin 2 4 6 10 14 18

2-10: 3-Solomon Grundy app. 4,7-Spectre app. 8-Re-intro Steel, the Indestructable Man 6.00

11-24,26-46,48,49: 12-Origin G.A. Hawkman retold. 15-JLA, JSA & Crime Syndicate app. 23-Origin/1st app. The Amazing Man. 24-Batman app. 26-Origin Infinity, Inc.(2nd app.); Robin app. 27-Dr. Fate vs. The Spectre. 30-35-Spectre app. 33-Origin Freedom Fighters of Earth-X. 36,37-Superman vs. Capt. Marvel; Ordway-c. 41-Origin Starman 5.00

25-1st app. Nuklon (Atom Smasher) & Infinity, Inc. (9/83) 3 6 9 19 30 40

47-Origin Dr. Fate; McFarlane-a (1st full story)/part-c (7/85) 3 6 9 21 33 45

50-Double size; Crisis x-over 2 4 6 8 10 12

51-66: 51-56-Crisis x-over. 61-Origin Liberty Belle. 62-Origin The Shining Knight. 63-Origin Robotman. 65-Origin Johnny Quick. 66-Origin Tarantula 6.00

67-Last issue; retells first case of the Justice Society 2 4 6 10 14 18

Annual 1-3: 1(11/82)-Retells origin of G.A. Atom, Guardian & Wildcat; Jerry Ordway's 1st pencils for DC. (1st work was inking Carmine Infantino in Mystery in Space #117). 2(11/83)-Infinity, Inc. app. 3(9/84) 6.00

NOTE: ***Buckler*** *a-1-5; c-1, 3-5, 51.* ***Kubert*** *c-2, 7-18. JLA app. in 14, 15. JSA app. in 4, 14, 15, 19, 27, 28.*

ALL-STAR STORY OF THE DODGERS, THE
Stadium Communications: Apr, 1979 ($1.00)

1 2 4 6 10 14 18

ALL-STAR SUPERMAN (Also see Sears Special Edition in the Promotional Comics section)
DC Comics: Jan, 2006 - No. 12, Oct, 2008 ($2.99)

1-Grant Morrison-s/Frank Quitely-a/c 1 3 4 6 8 10

1-Variant-c by Neal Adams 25.00

1-Special Edition (2009, $1.00) r/#1 with "After Watchmen" cover logo frame 3.00

2,4-12: 7,8-Bizarro app. 3.00

3-Lois gets super powers 1 2 3 5 6 8

Free Comic Book Day giveaway (6/08) reprints #1 4.00

Vol. 1 HC (2007, $19.99, dustjacket) r/#1-6; Bob Schreck intro. 20.00

Vol. 1 SC (2008, $12.99) r/#1-6; Schreck intro. 13.00

Vol. 2 HC (2009, $19.99, dustjacket) r/#7-12; Mark Waid intro. 20.00

Vol. 2 SC (2009, $12.99) r/#7-12; Mark Waid intro. 13.00

ALL STAR WESTERN (Formerly All Star Comics No. 1-57)
National Periodical Publ.: No. 58, Apr-May, 1951 - No. 119, June-July, 1961

58-Trigger Twins (ends #116), Strong Bow, The Roving Ranger & Don Caballero begin 56 110 165 352 601 850

59,60: Last 52 pgs. 32 64 96 190 310 430

61-66: 61-64-Toth-a 26 52 78 154 252 350

67-Johnny Thunder begins; Gil Kane-a 37 74 111 222 361 500

68-81: Last precode (2-3/55) 17 34 51 103 162 220

82-98: 97-1st S.A. issue 15 30 45 86 133 180

99-Frazetta-r/Jimmy Wakely #4 16 32 48 92 145 195

100 15 30 45 88 137 185

101-107,109-116,118,119: 103-Grey tone-c 14 28 42 82 121 160

108-Origin J. Thunder; J. Thunder logo begins 28 56 84 165 270 375

117-Origin Super Chief 20 40 60 118 192 265

NOTE: ***Gil Kane*** *c(p)-58, 59, 61, 63, 64, 68, 69, 70-95(most), 97-199(most).* ***Infantino*** *art in most issues. Madame .44 app.- #117-119.*

ALL-STAR WESTERN (Weird Western Tales No. 12 on)
National Periodical Publications: Aug-Sept, 1970 - No. 11, Apr-May, 1972

1-Pow-Wow Smith-r; Infantino-a 6 12 18 38 69 100

2-Outlaw begins; El Diablo by Morrow begins; has cameos by Williamson, Torres, Kane, Giordano & Phil Seuling 5 10 15 35 63 90

3-Origin El Diablo 5 10 15 31 53 75

4-6: 5-Last Outlaw issue. 6-Billy the Kid begins, ends #8 4 8 12 23 37 50

7-9-(52 pgs.) 9-Frazetta-a, 3pgs.(r) 4 8 12 25 40 55

10-(52 pgs.) Jonah Hex begins (1st app., 2-3/72) 38 76 114 285 641 1000

11-(52 pgs.) 2nd app. Jonah Hex; 1st cover 14 28 42 96 211 325

NOTE: ***Neal Adams*** *c-2-5;* ***Aparo*** *a-5.* ***G. Kane*** *a-3, 4, 6, 8.* ***Kubert*** *a-4r, 7-9r.* ***Morrow*** *a-2-4, 10, 11. No. 7-11 have 52 pgs.*

ALL STAR WESTERN (DC New 52)
DC Comics: Nov, 2011 - No. 34, Oct, 2014 ($3.99)

1-34: 1-Jonah Hex in 1880s Gotham City; Gray & Palmiotti-s/Moritat-a. 2,3-El Diablo back-up. 9-11-Court of Owls. 10-Bat Lash back-up; Garcia-López-a. 13-16-Tomahawk back-up. 19-21-Booster Gold app. 21-28-Hex in present day. 22-Batman app. 27-Superman app. 30,31-Madame .44 back-up; Garcia-López-a. 34-Darwyn Cooke-c/a 4.00

#0 (11/12, $3.99) Jonah Hex's full origin; Gray & Palmiotti-s/Moritat-a 4.00

ALL SURPRISE (Becomes Jeanie #13 on) (Funny animal)

	GD	VG	FN	VF	VF/NM	NM-
	2.0	4.0	6.0	8.0	9.0	9.2

Timely/Marvel (CPC): Fall, 1943 - No. 12, Winter, 1946-47

1-Super Rabbit, Gandy & Sourpuss begin 71 142 213 454 777 1100
2 29 58 87 172 281 390
3-10,12 22 44 66 128 209 290
11-Kurtzman "Pigtales" art 23 46 69 136 223 310

ALL TEEN (Formerly All Winners; All Winners & Teen Comics No. 21 on)
Marvel Comics (WFP): No. 20, January, 1947

20-Georgie, Mitzi, Patsy Walker, Willie app.; Syd Shores-c
45 90 135 284 480 675

ALL-TIME SPORTS COMICS (Formerly All Sports Comics)
Hillman Per.: V2, No. 4, Apr-May, 1949 - V2, No. 7, Oct-Nov, 1949 (All 52 pgs.)

V2#4 28 56 84 165 270 375
5-7: 5-(V1#5 inside)-Powell-a; Ty Cobb sty. 7-Krigstein-p; Walter Johnson & Knute Rockne sty 20 40 60 117 189 260

ALL TOP
William H. Wise Co.: 1944 (132 pgs.)

nn-Capt. V, Merciless the Sorceress, Red Robbins, One Round Hogan, Mike the M.P., Snooky, Pussy Katnip app. 65 130 195 416 708 1000

ALL TOP COMICS (My Experience No. 19 on)
Fox Feature Synd./Green Publ./Norlen Mag.: 1945; No. 2, Sum, 1946 - No. 18, Jul, 1949; 1957 - 1959

1-Cosmo Cat & Flash Rabbit begin (1st app.) 37 74 111 222 361 500
2 (#1-7 are funny animal) 19 38 57 111 176 240
3-7: 7-Two diff. issues (7/47 & 9/47) 15 30 45 86 133 180
8-Blue Beetle, Phantom Lady, & Rulah, Jungle Goddess begin (11/47); Kamen-c 303 606 909 2121 3711 5300
9-Kamen-c 174 348 522 1114 1907 2700
10-Classic Kamen bondage/torture/dwarf-c 213 426 639 1363 2332 3300
11-13,15,17: 11,12-Rulah-c. 15-No Blue Beetle 142 284 426 909 1555 2200
14-No Blue Beetle; used in **SOTI**, illo- "Corpses of colored people strung up by their wrists"
213 426 639 1363 2332 3300
16-Classic Good Girl octopus-c 459 918 1377 3350 5925 8500
18-Dagar, Jo-Jo app; no Phantom Lady or Blue Beetle
119 238 357 762 1306 1850
6(1957-Green Publ.)-Patoruzu the Indian; Cosmo Cat on cover only. 6(1958-Literary Ent.)-Muggy Doo; Cosmo Cat on cover only. 6(1959-Norlen)-Atomic Mouse; Cosmo Cat on-c only. 6(1959)-Little Eva. 6(Cornell)-Supermouse on-c 6 12 18 31 38 45
NOTE: *Jo-Jo by* ***Kamen****-12,18.*

ALL TRUE ALL PICTURE POLICE CASES
St. John Publishing Co.: Oct, 1952 - No. 2, Nov, 1952 (100 pgs.)

1-Three rebound St. John crime comics 63 126 183 403 689 975
2-Three comics rebound 48 96 144 302 514 725
NOTE: *Contents may vary.*

ALL-TRUE CRIME (...Cases No. 26-35; formerly Official True Crime Cases)
Marvel/Atlas Comics: No. 26, Feb, 1948 - No. 52, Sept, 1952
(OFI #26,27/CFI #28,29/LCC #30-46/LMC #47-52)

26(#1)-Syd Shores-c 48 96 144 302 514 725
27(4/48)-Electric chair-c 41 82 123 256 428 600
28-41,43-48,50-52: 35-37-Photo-c 19 38 57 111 176 240
42,49-Krigstein-a. 49-Used in **POP**, Pg 79 20 40 60 114 182 250
NOTE: ***Colan*** *a-46.* ***Keller*** *a-46.* ***Robinson*** *a-47, 50.* ***Sale*** *a-46.* ***Shores*** *c-26.* ***Tuska*** *a-48(3).*

ALL-TRUE DETECTIVE CASES (Kit Carson No. 5 on)
Avon Periodicals: #2, Apr-May, 1954 - No. 4, Aug-Sept, 1954

2(#1)-Wood-a 34 68 102 199 325 450
3-Kinstler-c 20 40 60 114 182 250
4-r/Gangsters And Gun Molls #2; Kamen-a 26 52 78 154 252 350
nn(100 pgs.)-7 pg. Kubert-a, Kinstler back-c 57 114 171 362 619 875

ALL TRUE ROMANCE (...Illustrated No. 3)
Artful Publ. #1-3/Harwell(Comic Media) #4-20?/Ajax-Farrell(Excellent Publ.) No. 22 on/Four Star Comic Corp.: 3/51 - No. 20, 12/54; No. 22, 3/55 - No. 30?, 7/57; No. 3(#31), 9/57;No. 4(#32), 11/57; No. 33, 2/58 - No. 34, 6/58

1 (3/51) 30 60 90 177 289 400
2 (10/51; 11/51 on-c) 17 34 51 100 158 215
3(12/51) - #5(5/52) 15 30 45 88 137 185
6-Wood-a, 9 pgs. (exceptional) 26 52 78 154 252 350
7-10 [two #7s: #7(11/52, 9/52 inside), #7(11/52, 11/52 inside)]. 10-Hollingsworth-c
15 30 45 85 130 175
11-13,16-19(9/54),20(12/54) (no #21): 11,13-Heck-a 14 28 42 80 115 150
14-Marijuana story 14 28 42 81 118 155
22- Last precode issue (1st Ajax, 3/55) 14 28 42 80 115 150
23-27,29,30(7/57): 29-Disbrow-a 13 26 39 72 101 130
28 (9/56)-L. B. Cole, Disbrow-a 15 30 45 90 140 190
3(#31, 9/57),4(#32, 11/57),33,34 (Farrell, '57- '58) 11 22 33 64 90 115

ALL WESTERN WINNERS (Formerly All Winners; becomes Western Winners with No. 5; see Two-Gun Kid No. 5)
Marvel Comics(CDS): No. 2, Winter, 1948-49 - No. 4, April, 1949

2-Black Rider (origin/1st app.) & his horse Satan, Kid Colt & his horse Steel, & Two-Gun Kid & his horse Cyclone begin; Shores c-2-4 97 194 291 621 1061 1500
3-Anti-Wertham editorial 45 90 135 284 480 675
4-Black Rider i.d. revealed; Heath, Shores-a 45 90 135 284 480 675

ALL WINNERS COMICS (All Teen #20) (Also see Timely Presents: ...)
USA No. 1-7/WFP No. 10-19/YAI No. 21: Summer, 1941 - No. 19, Fall, 1946; No. 21, Winter, 1946-47; (No #20) (No. 21 continued from Young Allies No. 20)

1-The Angel & Black Marvel only app.; Capt. America by Simon & Kirby, Human Torch & Sub-Mariner begin (#1 was advertised as All Aces); 1st app. All-Winners Squad in text story by Stan Lee 2050 4100 6150 14,500 27,750 41,000
2-The Destroyer & The Whizzer begin; Simon & Kirby Captain America
730 1460 2190 5329 9415 13,500
3 541 1082 1623 3950 6975 10,000
4-Classic War-c by Al Avison 919 1838 2757 6709 11,855 17,000
5 423 846 1269 3000 5250 7500
6-The Black Avenger only app.; no Whizzer story; Hitler, Hirohito & Mussolini-c
865 1730 2595 6315 11,158 16,000
7-10 411 822 1233 2877 5039 7200
11,13-15: 11-1st Atlas globe on-c (Winter, 1943-44; also see Human Torch #14). 14,15-No Human Torch 300 600 900 2070 3635 5200
12-Red Skull story; last Destroyer; no Whizzer story
541 1082 1623 3950 6975 10,000
16-18: 16-No Human Torch 271 542 813 1734 2967 4200
19-(Scarce)-1st story app. & origin All Winners Squad (Capt. America & Bucky, Human Torch & Toro, Sub-Mariner, Whizzer, & Miss America; r-in Fantasy Masterpieces #10
1030 2060 3090 7500 15,750 24,000
21-(Scarce)-All Winners Squad; bondage-c 730 1460 2190 5330 11,415 17,500
NOTE: ***Everett*** *Sub-Mariner-1, 3, 4;* ***Burgos*** *Torch-1, 3, 4.* ***Schomburg*** *c-1, 7-18.* ***Shores*** *c-19p, 21.*
(2nd Series - August, 1948, Marvel Comics (CDS))
(Becomes All Western Winners with No. 2)
1-The Blonde Phantom, Capt. America, Human Torch, & Sub-Mariner app.
337 674 1011 2359 4130 5900

ALL WINNERS COMICS 70th ANNIVERARY SPECIAL
Marvel Comics: Oct, 2009 ($3.99, one-shot)

1-New story of All Winners Squad; r/G.A. Capt America app. from All Winners #12 5.00

ALL-WINNERS SQUAD: BAND OF HEROES
Marvel Comics: Aug, 2011 - No. 5, Dec, 2011 ($2.99, unfinished limited series of 8 issues)

1-5-WWII story of the Young Avenger and Captain Flame; Jenkins-s/DiGiandomenico-a 3.00

ALL YOUR COMICS (See Fox Giants)
Fox Feature Syndicate (R. W. Voight): Spring, 1946 (36 pgs.)

1-Red Robbins, Merciless the Sorceress app. 34 68 102 199 325 450

ALMANAC OF CRIME (See Fox Giants)

ALMOST AMERICAN
AfterShock Comics: Sept, 2021 - No. 5, Feb, 2022 ($4.99/$3.99, limited series)

1-($4.99) Ron Marz-s/Marco Castiello-a; husband-and-wife Russian spies 5.00
2-5-($3.99) 4.00

AL OF FBI (See Little Al of the FBI)

ALOHA, HAWAIIAN DICK (Also see Hawaiian Dick)
Image Comics: Apr, 2016 - No. 5, Aug, 2016 ($3.99, limited series)

1-5-B. Clay Moore-s. 1-4-Jacob Wyatt-a. 5-Paul Reinwand-a 4.00

ALONE IN THE DARK (Based on video game)
Image Comics: Feb, 2003 ($4.95)

1-Matt Haley-c/a; Jean-Marc & Randy Lofficier-s 5.00

ALPHA AND OMEGA
Spire Christian Comics (Fleming H. Revell): 1978 (49¢)

nn 2 4 6 9 13 16

ALPHA: BIG TIME (See Amazing Spider-Man #692-694)
Marvel Comics: Apr, 2013 - No. 5, Aug, 2015 ($2.99)

1-5-Fialkov-s/Plati-a/Ramos-c. 1,3,5-Superior Peter Parker app. 4-Thor app. 3.00

ALPHA CENTURION (See Superman, 2nd Series & Zero Hour)
DC Comics: 1996 ($2.95, one-shot)

1 3.00

ALPHA FLIGHT (See X-Men #120,121 & X-Men/Alpha Flight)
Marvel Comics: Aug, 1983 - No. 130, Mar, 1994 (#52-on are direct sales only)

1-(52 pgs.) Byrne-a begins (thru #28) -Wolverine & Nightcrawler cameo
3 6 9 14 20 25
2-11,13-28: 2-Vindicator becomes Guardian; origin Marrina & Alpha Flight. 3-Concludes origin Alpha Flight. 6-Origin Shaman. 7-Origin Snowbird. 10,11-Origin Sasquatch. 13-Wolverine app. 16,17-Wolverine cameo. 17-X-Men x-over (mostly r-/X-Men #109). 19-Origin/1st app. Talisman. 20-New headquarters. 25-Return of Guardian. 28-Last Byrne issue 5.00
12-(52 pgs.)-Death of Guardian 6.00
29-32,35-49: 39-47,49-Portacio-a(i) 3.00
33-1st app. Lady Deathstrike; Wolverine app. 3 6 9 15 22 28
34-2nd app. Lady Deathstrike; origin Wolverine 6.00
50-Double size; Portacio-a(i) 4.00
51-Jim Lee's 1st work at Marvel (10/87); Wolverine cameo; 1st Lee Wolverine; Portacio-a(i)
2 4 6 13 18 22
52,53-Wolverine app.; Lee-a on Wolverine; Portacio-a(i); 53-Lee/Portacio-a 4.00
54-73,76-86,91-99,101-105: 54,63,64-No Jim Lee-a. 54-Portacio-a(i). 55-62-Jim Lee-a(p). 71-Intro The Sorcerer (villain). 91-Dr. Doom app. 94-F.F. x-over. 99-Galactus, Avengers app. 102-Intro Weapon Omega 3.00
74,75,87-90,100: 74-Wolverine, Spider-Man & The Avengers app. 75-Double size ($1.95, 52 pgs.). 87-90-Wolverine. 4 part story w/Jim Lee-c. 89-Original Guardian returns. 100-($2.00, 52 pgs.)-Avengers & Galactus app. 4.00
106-Northstar revealed to be gay 2 4 6 8 11 14
106-2nd printing (direct sale only) 3.00
107-109,112-119,121-129: 107-X-Factor x-over. 112-Infinity War x-overs. 115-1st Wyre 3.00
110,111: Infinity War x-overs, Wolverine app. (brief). 111-Thanos cameo 3.00
120-($2.25)-Polybagged w/Paranormal Registration Act poster 4.00
130-($2.25, 52 pgs.) 1 3 4 6 8 10
Annual 1,2 (9/86, 12/87) 4.00
...Classics Vol. 1 TPB (2007, $24.99) r/#1-8; character profile pages; Byrne interview 25.00
... No. 1 Facsimile Edition (7/19, $4.99) r/#1 with original 1983 ads and letter column 5.00
Special V2#1(6/92, $2.50, 52 pgs.)-Wolverine-c/story 4.00
NOTE: ***Austin*** *c-1i, 2i, 53i.* ***Byrne*** *c-81, 82.* ***Guice*** *c-85, 91-99.* ***Jim Lee*** *a(p)-51, 53, 55-62, 64; c-53, 87-90.* ***Mignola*** *a-29-31p.* ***Whilce Portacio*** *a(i)-39-47, 49-54.*

ALPHA FLIGHT (2nd Series)
Marvel Comics: Aug, 1997 - No. 20, Mar, 1999 ($2.99/$1.99)

1-($2.99)-Wraparound cover 6.00
2,3: 2-Variant-c 4.00
4-11: 8,9-Wolverine-c/app. 3.00
12-($2.99) Death of Sasquatch; wraparound-c 4.00

All True Romance #1 © Artful

Alpha Flight (2001) #1 © MAR

Amazing Adventures #8 © MAR

	GD 2.0	VG 4.0	FN 6.0	VF 8.0	VF/NM 9.0	NM- 9.2
13-15,18-20						3.00
16-1st app. cameo Honey Lemon (Big Hero 6)	1	2	3	5	6	8
17-1st app. Big Hero 6	2	4	6	10	14	18
.../Inhumans '98 Annual ($3.50) Raney-a						4.00

ALPHA FLIGHT (3rd Series)
Marvel Comics: May, 2004 - No. 12, April, 2005 ($2.99)

	GD 2.0	VG 4.0	FN 6.0	VF 8.0	VF/NM 9.0	NM- 9.2
1-12: 1-6-Lobdell-s/Henry-c/a						3.00
... Vol. 1: You Gotta Be Kiddin' Me (2004, $14.99) r/#1-6						15.00

ALPHA FLIGHT (4th Series)
Marvel Comics: No. 0.1, Jul, 2011 - No. 8, Mar, 2012 ($2.99)

	GD 2.0	VG 4.0	FN 6.0	VF 8.0	VF/NM 9.0	NM- 9.2
0.1-Pak & Van Lente-s/Oliver & Green-a; Kara Killgrave app.						3.00
1-(8/11, $3.99) Fear Itself tie-in; Eaglesham-a/Jimenez-c; bonus design sketch pages						4.00
2-8-($2.99) Fear Itself tie-ins. 2-Puck returns. 5-Taskmaster app. 7,8-Wolverine app.						3.00

ALPHA FLIGHT: IN THE BEGINNING
Marvel Comics: July, 1997 ($1.95, one-shot)

	GD 2.0	VG 4.0	FN 6.0	VF 8.0	VF/NM 9.0	NM- 9.2
(-1)-Flashback w/Wolverine						4.00

ALPHA FLIGHT SPECIAL
Marvel Comics: July, 1991 - No. 4, Oct, 1991 ($1.50, limited series)

	GD 2.0	VG 4.0	FN 6.0	VF 8.0	VF/NM 9.0	NM- 9.2
1-4: 1-3-r-A. Flight #97-99 w/covers. 4-r-A.Flight #100						4.00

ALPHA FLIGHT: TRUE NORTH
Marvel Comics: Nov, 2019 ($4.99, one-shot)

	GD 2.0	VG 4.0	FN 6.0	VF 8.0	VF/NM 9.0	NM- 9.2
1-Short stories by Canadian creators incl. Jim Zub, Dunbar, Brisson, MacKay, Hepburn						5.00

ALPHA KING (3 FLOYDS:...)
Image Comics: May, 2016 - No. 5, Nov, 2017 ($3.99)

	GD 2.0	VG 4.0	FN 6.0	VF 8.0	VF/NM 9.0	NM- 9.2
1-5-Azzarello & Floyd-s/Bisley-a/c						4.00

ALTERED IMAGE
Image Comics: Apr, 1998 - No. 3, Sept, 1998 ($2.50, limited series)

	GD 2.0	VG 4.0	FN 6.0	VF 8.0	VF/NM 9.0	NM- 9.2
1-3-Spawn, Witchblade, Savage Dragon; Valentino-s/a						4.00

ALTERED STATES
Dynamite Entertainment: 2015 ($3.99, series of one-shots)

	GD 2.0	VG 4.0	FN 6.0	VF 8.0	VF/NM 9.0	NM- 9.2
...: Doc Savage - Alternate reality Doc Savage in caveman past; Philip Tan-c						4.00
...: Red Sonja - Alternate reality Sonja in modern day New York City; Philip Tan-c						4.00
...: The Shadow - Alternate reality Shadow in sci-fi future; Philip Tan-c						4.00
...: Vampirella - Alternate reality Vampirella as a mortal on Drakulon; Collins-s						4.00

ALTER EGO
First Comics: May, 1986 - No. 4, Nov, 1986 (Mini-series)

	GD 2.0	VG 4.0	FN 6.0	VF 8.0	VF/NM 9.0	NM- 9.2
1-4						3.00

ALTER NATION
Image Comics: Feb, 2004 - No. 4, Jun, 2004 ($2.95, limited series)

	GD 2.0	VG 4.0	FN 6.0	VF 8.0	VF/NM 9.0	NM- 9.2
1-4: 1-Two covers by Art Adams and Barberi; Barberi-a						3.00

ALTERS
AfterShock Comics: Sept, 2016 - No. 10, Feb, 2018 ($3.99)

	GD 2.0	VG 4.0	FN 6.0	VF 8.0	VF/NM 9.0	NM- 9.2
1-10: 1-Paul Jenkins-s/Leila Leiz-a						4.00

ALVIN (TV) (See Four Color Comics No. 1042 or Three Chipmunks #1)
Dell Publishing Co.: Oct-Dec, 1962 - No. 28, Oct, 1973

	GD 2.0	VG 4.0	FN 6.0	VF 8.0	VF/NM 9.0	NM- 9.2
12-021-212 (#1)	9	18	27	62	126	190
2	5	10	15	33	57	80
3-10	4	8	12	28	47	65
11-"Chipmunks sing the Beatles' Hits"	5	10	15	33	57	80
12-28	4	8	12	23	37	50
Alvin For President (10/64)	5	10	15	30	50	70
...& His Pals in Merry Christmas with Clyde Crashcup & Leonardo 1 (25¢ Giant) (02-120-402)-(12-2/64)	7	14	21	46	86	125
Reprinted in 1966 (12-023-604)	4	8	12	23	37	50

ALVIN & THE CHIPMUNKS
Harvey Comics: July, 1992 - No. 5, May, 1994

	GD 2.0	VG 4.0	FN 6.0	VF 8.0	VF/NM 9.0	NM- 9.2
1-5: 1-Richie Rich app.						5.00

AMALGAM AGE OF COMICS, THE: THE DC COMICS COLLECTION
DC Comics: 1996 ($12.95, trade paperback)

	GD 2.0	VG 4.0	FN 6.0	VF 8.0	VF/NM 9.0	NM- 9.2
nn-r/Amazon, Assassins, Doctor Strangefate, JLX, Legends of the Dark Claw, & Super Soldier	4	8	12	23	37	50

AMANDA AND GUNN
Image Comics: Apr, 1997 - No. 4, Oct, 1997 ($2.95, B&W, limited series)

	GD 2.0	VG 4.0	FN 6.0	VF 8.0	VF/NM 9.0	NM- 9.2
1-4						3.00

AMAZING ADULT FANTASY (Formerly Amazing Adventures #1-6; becomes Amazing Fantasy #15) (See Amazing Fantasy for Omnibus HC reprint of #1-15)
Marvel Comics Group (AMI): No. 7, Dec, 1961 - No. 14, July, 1962

	GD 2.0	VG 4.0	FN 6.0	VF 8.0	VF/NM 9.0	NM- 9.2
7-Ditko-c/a begins, ends #14	62	124	186	500	1125	1750
8-Last 10¢ issue	54	108	162	432	966	1500
9-13: 12-1st app. Mailbag. 13-Anti-communist story	52	104	156	416	933	1450
13-2nd printing (1994)	2	4	6	9	12	15
14-Prototype issue (Professor X)	66	132	198	528	1189	1850

AMAZING ADVENTURE FUNNIES (Fantoman No. 2 on)
Centaur Publications: June, 1940 - No. 2, Sept. 1940

	GD 2.0	VG 4.0	FN 6.0	VF 8.0	VF/NM 9.0	NM- 9.2
1-The Fantom of the Fair by Gustavson (r/Amaz. Mystery Funnies V2#7,V2#8), The Arrow, Skyrocket Steele From the Year X by Everett (r/AMF #2); Burgos-a	290	580	870	1856	3178	4500
2-Reprints; Published after Fantoman #2	161	322	483	1030	1765	2500

NOTE: *Burgos a-1(2). Everett a-1(3). Gustavson a-1(5), 2(3). Pinajian a-2.*

AMAZING ADVENTURES (Also see Boy Cowboy & Science Comics)
Ziff-Davis Publ. Co.: 1950; No. 1, Nov, 1950 - No. 6, Fall, 1952 (Painted covers)

	GD 2.0	VG 4.0	FN 6.0	VF 8.0	VF/NM 9.0	NM- 9.2
1950 (no month given) (8-1/2x11) (8 pgs.) Has the front & back cover plus Schomburg story used in Amazing Advs. #1 (Sent to subscribers of Z-D s/f magazines & ordered through mail for 10¢. Used to test market)	100	200	300	640	1096	1550
1-Wood, Schomburg, Anderson, Whitney-a	116	232	348	742	1271	1800
2,3,5: 2-Schomburg-a. 2,5-Anderson-a. 3,5-Starr-a	55	110	165	352	601	850
4-Classic-c; Anderson-a	314	628	942	2198	3849	5500
6-Krigstein-a	53	106	159	334	567	800

AMAZING ADVENTURES (Becomes Amazing Adult Fantasy #7 on) (See Amazing Fantasy for Omnibus HC reprint of #1-15)
Atlas Comics (AMI)/Marvel Comics No. 3 on: June, 1961 - No. 6, Nov, 1961

	GD 2.0	VG 4.0	FN 6.0	VF 8.0	VF/NM 9.0	NM- 9.2
1-Origin Dr. Droom (1st Marvel-Age Superhero who later becomes Doctor Druid) by Kirby; Kirby/Ditko-a (5 pgs.) Ditko & Kirby-a in all; Kirby monster c-1-6	146	292	438	1209	2730	4250
2	57	114	171	456	1028	1600
3-6: 6-Last Dr. Droom	52	104	156	416	933	1450

AMAZING ADVENTURES
Marvel Comics Group: Aug, 1970 - No. 39, Nov, 1976

	GD 2.0	VG 4.0	FN 6.0	VF 8.0	VF/NM 9.0	NM- 9.2
1-Inhumans by Kirby(p) & Black Widow (1st app. in Tales of Suspense #52) double feature begins	9	18	27	57	111	165
2-4: 2-F.F. brief app. 4-Last Inhumans by Kirby	4	8	12	25	40	55
5-8: Adams-a(p); 8-Last Black Widow; last 15¢-c	5	10	15	31	53	75
9,10: Magneto app. 10-Last Inhumans (origin-r by Kirby)	5	10	15	31	53	75
11-New Beast begins(1st app. in mutated form; origin in flashback); X-Men cameo in flashback (#11-17 are X-Men tie-ins)	24	48	72	168	372	575
12-17: 12-Beast battles Iron Man. 13-Brotherhood of Evil Mutants x-over from X-Men. 15-X-Men app. 16-Rutland Vermont - Bald Mountain Halloween x-over; Juggernaut app. 17-Last Beast (origin); X-Men app.	8	16	24	51	96	140
18-War of the Worlds begins (5/73); 1st app. Killraven; Neal Adams-a(p)	5	10	15	35	63	90
19-35,38,39: 19-Chaykin-a. 25-Buckler-a. 35-Giffen's first published story (art), along with Deadly Hands of Kung-Fu #22 (3/76)	2	4	6	8	10	12
36,37-(Regular 25¢ edition)(7-8/76)	2	4	6	8	10	12
36,37-(30¢-c variants, limited distribution)	5	10	15	33	57	80

NOTE: *N. Adams c-6-8. Buscema a-1p, 2p. Colan a-3-5p, 26p. Ditko a-24r. Everett a(i)3-5, 7-9. Giffen a-35i, 38p. G. Kane c-11, 25p, 29p. Ploog a-12i. Russell a-27-32, 34-37, 39; c-28, 30-32, 33i, 34, 35, 37, 39i. Starliing a-17. Starlin c-15p, 16, 17, 27. Sutton a-11-15p.*

AMAZING ADVENTURES
Marvel Comics Group: Dec, 1979 - No. 14, Jan, 1981

	GD 2.0	VG 4.0	FN 6.0	VF 8.0	VF/NM 9.0	NM- 9.2
V2#1-Reprints story/X-Men #1 & 38 (origins)	3	6	9	19	30	40
2-14: 2-6-Early X-Men-r. 7,8-Origin Iceman	2	4	6	8	10	12

NOTE: *Byrne c-6p, 9p. Kirby a-1-14r; c-7, 9. Steranko a-12r. Tuska a-7-9.*

AMAZING ADVENTURES
Marvel Comics: July, 1988 ($4.95, squarebound, one-shot, 80 pgs.)

	GD 2.0	VG 4.0	FN 6.0	VF 8.0	VF/NM 9.0	NM- 9.2
1-Anthology; Austin, Golden-a						5.00

AMAZING ADVENTURES OF CAPTAIN CARVEL AND HIS CARVEL CRUSADERS, THE
(See Carvel Comics in the Promotional Comics section)

AMAZING BATVARK (Cerebus in Hell)
Aardvark-Vanaheim: Feb, 2021 ($4.00, B&W)

	GD 2.0	VG 4.0	FN 6.0	VF 8.0	VF/NM 9.0	NM- 9.2
1-Cerebus figures placed over Doré artwork of Hell; Amazing Spider-Man #50-c swipe						4.00

AMAZING CEREBUS (Reprints from Cerebus in Hell)(Also see Aardvark Comics)
Aardvark-Vanaheim: Feb, 2018 ($4.00, B&W)

	GD 2.0	VG 4.0	FN 6.0	VF 8.0	VF/NM 9.0	NM- 9.2
1-Cerebus figures placed over original Doré artwork; Amazing Spider-Man #300-c swipe						4.00

GD VG FN VF VF/NM NM-
2.0 4.0 6.0 8.0 9.0 9.2

AMAZING CHAN & THE CHAN CLAN, THE (TV)
Gold Key: May, 1973 - No. 4, Feb, 1974 (Hanna-Barbera)

1-Warren Tufts-a in all 4 8 12 27 44 60
2-4 3 6 9 17 26 35

AMAZING COMICS (Complete Comics No. 2)
Timely Comics (EPC): Fall, 1944

1-The Destroyer, The Whizzer, The Young Allies (by Sekowsky), Sergeant Dix;
Schomburg-c 300 600 900 1950 3375 4800

AMAZING DETECTIVE CASES (Formerly Suspense No. 2?)
Marvel/Atlas Comics (CCC): No. 3, Nov, 1950 - No. 14, Sept, 1952

3 37 74 111 222 361 500
4-6: 6-Jerry Robinson-a 22 44 66 128 209 290
7-10 20 40 60 115 185 255
11,12: 11-(3/52)-Horror format begins. 12-Krigstein-a 63 126 189 403 689 975
13-(Scarce)-Everett-a; electrocution-c/story 71 142 213 454 777 1100
14 57 114 171 362 619 875

NOTE: *Colan a-9. Maneely c-13. Sekowsky a-12. Sinnott a-13. Tuska a-10.*

AMAZING FANTASY (Formerly Amazing Adult Fantasy #7-14)
Atlas Magazines/Marvel: #15, Aug, 1962 (Sept, 1962 shown in indicia); #16, Dec, 1995 - #18, Feb, 1996

15-Origin/1st app. of Spider-Man by Steve Ditko (11 pgs.); 1st app. Aunt May & Uncle Ben;
Kirby/Ditko-c 13,850 27,700 55,400 159,300 404,650 650,000
16-18 ('95-'96, $3.95): Kurt Busiek scripts; painted-c/a by Paul Lee 5.00
Amazing Fantasy #15 Facsimile Edition (12/19, $3.99) r/#15 with original 1962 ads
3 6 9 16 23 30
Amazing Fantasy #15: Spider-Man! (8/12, $3.99) recolored rep. of #15 and ASM #1
2 4 6 11 16 20
Amazing Fantasy Omnibus HC ("Amazing Adult Fantasy" on-c) (2007, $75.00, dustjacket)
r/Amazing Adventures #1-6, Amazing Adult Fantasy #7-14 and Amazing Fantasy #15 with letter pages; foreword by Bissette; cover gallery from '70s reprint titles 200.00

AMAZING FANTASY (Continues from #6 in Araña: The Heart of the Spider)
Marvel Comics: Aug, 2004 - No. 20, June, 2006 ($2.99)

1-Intro. Anya Corazon; Avery-s/Brooks-c/a 3 6 9 21 33 45
2-6,8,9,11-14,16-20: 3,4-Roger Cruz-a. 13,14-Back-up Captain Universe stories.
16-20-Death's Head 3.00
7-Intro. new Scorpion; Kirk-a 3 6 9 19 30 40
10-Intro. Vampire By Night 6 12 18 38 69 100
15-($3.99, 1/06) Spider-Man app.; intro 6 new characters incl. Amadeus Cho/Mastermind Excello seen in World War Hulk series; s/a by various
9 18 27 60 120 180
Death's Head 3.0: Unnatural Selection TPB (2006, $13.99) r/#16-20 14.00
Scorpion: Poison Tomorrow (2005, $7.99, digest) r/#7-13 8.00

AMAZING FANTASY
Marvel Comics: Sept, 2021 - No. 5, Jan, 2022 ($4.99, limited series)

1-5-Kaare Andrews-s/a; WWII Capt. America, Teenage Spidey, & Black Widow app. 5.00

AMAZING FANTASY 1000
Marvel Comics: Oct, 2022 ($7.99, square-bound, one-shot)

1-Short Spider-Man stories by various incl. Busiek, Cheung, Coipel, Dodson, Gaiman, Hickman, Janson, McNiven, Nauck & Slott 8.00

AMAZING GHOST STORIES (Formerly Nightmare)
St. John Publishing Co.: No. 14, Oct, 1954 - No. 16, Feb, 1955

14-Pit & the Pendulum story by Kinstler; Baker-c 541 1082 1623 3950 6975 10,000
15-r/Weird Thrillers #5; Baker-c, Powell-a 110 220 330 704 1202 1700
16-Kubert reprints of Weird Thrillers #4; Baker-c; Roussos, Tuska-a;
Kinstler-a (1 pg.) 71 142 213 454 777 1100

AMAZING HIGH ADVENTURE
Marvel Comics: 8/84; No. 2, 10/85; No. 3, 10/86 - No. 5, 1986 ($2.00)

1-5: Painted-c on all. 3,4-Baxter paper. 4-Bolton-c/a. 5-Bolton-a 4.00

NOTE: *Bissette a-4. Severin a-1, 3. Sienkiewicz a-1,2. Paul Smith a-2. Williamson a-2i.*

AMAZING JOY BUZZARDS
Image Comics: 2005 - No. 4, 2005 ($2.95, B&W with pink spot color in #1)

1-4-Mark Andrew Smith-s/Dan Hipp-a. 1-Mahfood back-c. 2-Morse back-c 3.00
Vol. 1 TPB (2005, $11.95) r/#1-4; bonus art and character design sketches 12.00
TPB (2008, $19.99) r/#1-4 and Vol. 2 #1-5 20.00

AMAZING JOY BUZZARDS (Volume 2)
Image Comics: Oct, 2005 - No. 5, Aug, 2006 ($2.99, B&W)

1-5: 1-Mark Andrew Smith-s/Dan Hipp-a. 4-Mahfood-a; Crosland-a. 5-Holgate-a 3.00
Vol. 2 TPB (2006, $12.99) r/#1-4; bonus art, pin-ups and character sketches 13.00

AMAZING-MAN COMICS (Formerly Motion Picture Funnies Weekly?)
(Also see Stars And Stripes Comics, and Amazing Mystery Funnies nn)
Centaur Publications: No. 5, Sept, 1939 - No. 26, Jan, 1942

5(#1)(Rare)-Origin/1st app. A-Man the Amazing Man by Bill Everett; The Cat-Man by Tarpe Mills (also #8), Mighty Man by Filchock, Minimidget & sidekick Ritty, & The Iron Skull by Burgos begins 2240 4480 6720 17,900 31,950 46,000
6-Origin The Amazing Man retold; The Shark begins; Ivy Menace by Tarpe Mills app.
541 1082 1623 3950 6975 10,000
7-Magician From Mars begins; ends #11 354 708 1062 2478 4339 6200
8-Cat-Man dresses as woman 300 600 900 1920 3310 4700
9-Magician From Mars battles the 'Elemental Monster,' swiped into The Spectre in More Fun #54 & 55. Ties w/Marvel Mystery #4 for 1st Nazi War-c on a comic (2/40)
343 686 1029 2400 4200 6000
10,11: 11-Zardi, the Eternal Man begins; ends #16; Amazing Man dons costume;
last Everett issue 245 490 735 1568 2684 3800
12,13 226 452 678 1446 2473 3500
14-Reef Kinkaid, Rocke Wayburn (ends #20), & Dr. Hypno (ends #21) begin;
no Zardi or Chuck Hardy 200 400 600 1280 2190 3100
15,17-20: 15-Zardi returns; no Rocke Wayburn. 17-Dr. Hypno returns; no Zardi
168 336 504 1075 1838 2600
16-Mighty Man's powers of super strength & ability to shrink & grow explained; Rocke Wayburn returns; no Dr. Hypno; Al Avison (a character) begins, ends #18 (a tribute to the famed artist) 181 362 543 1158 1979 2800
21-Origin Dash Dartwell (drug-use story); origin & only app. T.N.T.
206 412 618 1318 2259 3200
22-Dash Dartwell, the Human Meteor & The Voice app; last Iron Skull & The Shark;
Silver Streak app. (classic Nazi monster-c) 3000 6000 9000 22,800 41,400 60,000
23-Two Amazing Man stories; intro/origin Tommy the Amazing Kid; The Marksman only app.
181 362 543 1158 1979 2800
24-King of Darkness, Nightshade, & Blue Lady begin; end #26; 1st app. Super-Ann
194 388 582 1242 2121 3000
25 (Scarce) Meteor Martin by Wolverton 919 1838 2757 6709 11,855 17,000
26 (Scarce) Meteor Martin by Wolverton; Electric Ray app.
1600 3200 4800 12,150 22,075 32,000

NOTE: *Everett a-5-11; c-5-11. Gilman a-14-20. Giunta/Mirando a-7-10. Sam Glanzman a-14-16, 18-21, 23. Louis Glanzman a-6, 9-11, 14-21; c-13-19, 21. Robert Golden a-9. Gustavson a-6; c-22, 23. Lubbers a-14-21. Simon a-10. Frank Thomas a-6, 9-11, 14, 15, 17-21.*

AMAZING MARY JANE (Mary Jane Watson)
Marvel Comics: Dec, 2019 - No. 6, May 2020 ($3.99)

1-6-Mary Jane & Mysterio filming a super-hero movie; Savage Six app.; Leah Williams-s
1 2 3 5 6 8

AMAZING MYSTERIES (Formerly Sub-Mariner Comics No. 31)
Marvel Comics (CCC): No. 32, May, 1949 - No. 35, Jan, 1950 (1st Marvel Horror Comic)

32-The Witness app. 194 388 582 1242 2121 3000
33-Horror format 77 154 231 493 847 1200
34,35: Changes to Crime. 34,35-Photo-c 31 62 93 184 300 415

AMAZING MYSTERY FUNNIES
Centaur Publications: Aug, 1938 - No. 24, Sept, 1940 (All 52 pgs.)

V1#1-Everett-c(1st); Dick Kent Adv. story; Skyrocket Steele in the Year X on cover only
865 1730 2595 6315 11,158 16,000
2-Everett 1st-a (Skyrocket Steele) 411 822 1233 2877 5039 7200
3 271 542 813 1734 2967 4200
3(#4, 12/38)-nn on cover, #3 on inside; bondage-c
300 600 900 1920 3310 4700
V2#1,3,4,6: 3-Air-Sub DX begins by Burgos. 4-Dan Hastings, Sand Hog begins (ends #5).
6-Last Skyrocket Steele 232 464 696 1485 2543 3600
2-Classic-c; drug use story 541 1082 1623 3950 6975 10,000
5-Classic Everett-c 975 1950 2919 7100 12,550 18,000
7 (Scarce)-Intro. The Fantom of the Fair & begins; Everett, Gustavson, Burgos-a
481 962 1443 3511 6206 8900
8-Origin & 1st app. Speed Centaur 239 478 717 1530 2615 3700
9-11: 11-Self portrait and biog. of Everett; Jon Linton begins; early Robot cover (11/39)
181 362 543 1158 1979 2800
12 (Scarce)-1st Space Patrol; Wolverton-a (12/39); new costume Phantom of the Fair
295 590 885 1888 3244 4600
V3#1(#17, 1/40)-Intro. Bullet; Tippy Taylor serial begins, ends #24
(continued in The Arrow #2) 155 310 465 992 1696 2400
18,20: 18-Fantom of the Fair by Gustavson 148 296 444 947 1624 2300
19,21-24: Space Patrol by Wolverton in all 174 348 522 1114 1907 2700

NOTE: *Burgos a-V2#3-9. Eisner a-V1#2, 3(2). Everett a-V1#2-4, V2#1, 3-6; c-V1#1-4,V2#3, 5, 18. Filchock a-V2#9. Flessel a-V2#6. Guardineer a-V1#4, V2#4-6; Gustavson a-V2#4, 5, 9-12, V3#1, 18, 19; c-V2#7, 9, 12, V3#1, 21, 22; McWilliams a-V2#9, 10. TarpeMills a-V2#2, 4-6, 9-12, V3#1. Leo Morey(Pulp artist) c-V2#10; text illo-V2#11. FrankThomas a-6-V2#11. Webster a-V2#4.*

AMAZING MYSTERY FUNNIES
Centaur Publications: 1942

nn (#23)-Cover from Amazing Man Comics #23 w/interior from Amazing Man Comics #25.
(2 known copies). A CGC 2.0 copy sold in March 2019 for $4,400.

AMAZING SAINTS
Logos International: 1974 (39¢)

nn-True story of Phil Saint 2 4 6 9 13 16

AMAZING SCARLET SPIDER
Marvel Comics: Nov, 1995 - No. 2, Dec, 1995 ($1.95, limited series)

1,2: Replaces "Amazing Spider-Man" for two issues. 1-Venom/Carnage cameos.
2-Green Goblin & Joystick-c/app. 3.00

AMAZING SCREW-ON HEAD, THE
Dark Horse Comics (Maverick): May, 2002 ($2.99, one-shot)

1-Mike Mignola-s/a/c 3.00

AMAZING SPIDER-GIRL (Also see Spider-Girl and What If...? (2nd series) #105)
Marvel Comics: No. 0, 2006; No. 1, Dec, 2006 - No. 30, May, 2009 ($2.99)

0-($1.99) Recap of the Spider-Girl series and character profiles; A.F. #15 cover swipe
2 4 6 9 12 15
1-Frenz & Buscema-a 1 3 4 6 8 10
2-14,16-24,26-($2.99) Frenz & Buscema-a. 9-Carnage returns. 19-Has #17 on cover 3.00
15,25,30-($3.99) 15-10th Anniversary issue. 25-Three covers 4.00
... Vol. 1: What Ever Happened to the Daughter of Spider-Man? TPB (2007, $14.99) r/#0-6 15.00
... Vol. 2: Comes the Carnage! TPB (2007, $13.99) r/#7-12 14.00
... Vol. 3: Mind Games TPB (2008, $13.99) r/#13-18 14.00

AMAZING SPIDER-MAN, THE (See All Detergent Comics, Amazing Fantasy, America's Best TV Comics, Aurora, Deadly Foes of..., Fireside Book Series, Friendly Neighborhood..., Giant-Size..., Giant Size Super-Heroes Featuring..., Marvel Age..., Marvel Collectors Item Classics, Marvel Fanfare, Marvel Graphic Novel, Marvel Knights..., Marvel Spec. Ed., Marvel Tales, Marvel Team-Up, Marvel Treasury Ed., New Avengers, Nothing Can Stop the Juggernaut, Official Marvel Index To..., Peter Parker..., Power Record Comics, Spectacular..., Spider-Man, Spider-Man Digest, Spider-Man Saga, Spider-Man 2099, Spider-Man Vs. Wolverine, Spidey Super Stories, Strange Tales Annual #2, Superior Spider-Man, Superman Vs. ..., Try-Out Winner Book, Ultimate Marvel Team-Up, Ultimate Spider-Man, Web of Spider- Man & Within Our Reach)

AMAZING SPIDER-MAN, THE
Marvel Comics Group: March, 1963 - No. 441, Nov, 1998

1-Retells origin by Steve Ditko; 1st Fantastic Four x-over (ties with F.F. #12 as first Marvel x-over); intro. John Jameson & The Chameleon; Spider-Man's 2nd app.; Kirby/Ditko-c;
Ditko-c/a #1-38 4800 9600 14,400 36,000 78,000 120,000
1-Reprint from the Golden Record Comic set 68 136 204 544 1222 1900
With record (1966) 64 128 192 512 1156 1800
2-1st app. the Vulture & the Terrible Tinkerer 1120 2240 3360 8000 18,000 28,000
3-1st app. Doc Octopus; 1st full-length story; Human Torch cameo;
Spider-Man pin-up by Ditko 1050 2100 3150 7550 16,775 26,000

Amazing Fantasy (2021) #1 © MAR

Amazing Spider-Girl #25 © MAR

Amazing Spider-Man #15 © MAR

	GD 2.0	VG 4.0	FN 6.0	VF 8.0	VF/NM 9.0	NM- 9.2
4-Origin & 1st app. The Sandman (see Strange Tales #115 for 2nd app.); 1st monthly issue; intro. Betty Brant & Liz Allen	720	1440	2160	5200	11,600	18,000
5-Dr. Doom app.	350	700	1050	2975	6737	10,500
6-1st app. Lizard	300	600	900	2550	5775	9000
7-Vs. The Vulture	190	380	570	1568	3534	5500
8-Fantastic Four app. in back-up story by Kirby & Ditko	132	264	396	1056	2378	3700
9-Origin & 1st app. Electro (2/64)	224	448	675	1848	4174	6500
10-1st app. Big Man & The Enforcers	111	222	333	888	1994	3100
11-1st app. Bennett Brant	172	344	516	1419	3210	5000
12-Doc Octopus unmasks Spider-Man-c/story	100	200	300	800	1800	2800
13-1st app. Mysterio	286	572	858	2402	5451	8500
14-(7/64)-1st app. The Green Goblin (c/story)(Norman Osborn); Hulk x-over	640	1280	1920	4600	10,300	16,000
15-1st app. Kraven the Hunter; 1st mention of Mary Jane Watson (not shown)	286	572	858	2402	5451	8500
16-Spider-Man battles Daredevil (1st x-over 9/64); still in old yellow costume	121	242	363	972	2186	3400
17-2nd app. Green Goblin (c/story); Human Torch x-over (also in #18 & #21)	89	178	267	712	1606	2500
18-1st app. Ned Leeds who later becomes Hobgoblin; Fantastic Four cameo; 3rd app. Sandman	59	118	177	472	1061	1650
19-Sandman app.	46	92	138	368	834	1300
20-Origin & 1st app. The Scorpion	145	290	435	1196	2698	4200
21-2nd app. The Beetle (see Strange Tales #123)	46	92	138	368	834	1300
22-1st app. Princess Python	46	92	138	340	770	1200
23-3rd app. The Green Goblin-c/story; Norman Osborn app.; Marvel Masterwork pin-up by Ditko; fan letter by Jim Shooter	52	104	156	416	933	1450
24	42	84	126	311	706	1100
25-(6/65)-1st brief app. Mary Jane Watson (face not shown); 1st app. Spencer Smythe; Norman Osborn app.	48	96	144	384	867	1350
26-4th app. The Green Goblin-c/story; 1st app. Crime Master; dies in #27; Norman Osborn app.	46	92	138	359	805	1250
27-5th app. The Green Goblin-c/story; Norman Osborn app.	44	88	132	326	738	1150
28-Origin & 1st app. Molten Man (9/65, scarcer in high grade)	166	332	498	1370	3085	4800
29-Vs. Scorpion	38	76	114	285	641	1000
30	34	68	102	245	548	850
31-(12/65)-1st app. Gwen Stacy, Prof. Warren, and Harry Osborn who later becomes 2nd Green Goblin	172	344	516	1419	3210	5000
32-38: 34-4th app. Kraven the Hunter. 36-1st app. Looter. 37-Intro. Norman Osborn. 38-(7/66)-2nd brief app. Mary Jane Watson (face not shown); last Ditko issue	25	50	75	175	388	600
39-The Green Goblin-c/story; Green Goblin's identity revealed as Norman Osborn; Osborn learns Spider-Man's secret identity; Romita-a begins (8/66; see Daredevil #16 for 1st Romita-a on Spider-Man)	75	150	225	600	1350	2100
40-1st told origin The Green Goblin-c/story	68	136	204	544	1222	1900
41-1st app. Rhino	100	200	300	800	1800	2800
42-(11/66)-3rd app. Mary Jane Watson (cameo in last 2 panels); 1st time face is shown	35	70	105	252	564	875
43-45,47-49: 43-Origin of the Rhino. 44,45-2nd & 3rd app. The Lizard. 47-M.J. Watson & Peter Parker 1st date. 47-Green Goblin cameo; Harry & Norman Osborn app. 47,49-5th & 6th app. Kraven the Hunter. 48-1st new Vulture (Blackie Drago)	20	40	60	138	307	475
46-Intro/origin The Shocker	50	100	150	400	900	1400
50-1st app. Kingpin (7/67)	300	600	900	2550	5775	9000
51-2nd app. Kingpin; Joe Robertson 1-panel cameo	50	100	150	400	900	1400
52-58,60: 52-1st app. Joe Robertson & 3rd app. Kingpin. 56-1st app. Capt. George Stacy. 57,58-Ka-Zar app.	15	30	45	103	227	350
59-1st app. Brainwasher (alias Kingpin); 1st-c app. M. J. Watson	18	36	54	124	275	425
61-74: 61-1st Gwen Stacy cover app. 67-1st app. Randy Robertson. 69-Kingpin-c. 69,70-Kingpin app. 70-1st app. Vanessa Fisk (Kingpin's wife)(only seen in shadow). 73-1st app. Silvermane. 74-Last 12¢ issue	12	24	36	79	170	260
75-77,79-83,87-89,91,92,95,99: 79-The Prowler app. 83-1st app. Schemer; Vanessa Fisk app. (only previously seen in shadow in #70)	10	20	30	69	147	225
78-1st app. The Prowler	23	46	69	161	356	550
84,85,93: 84,85-Kingpin-c/story. 93-1st app. Arthur Stacy	10	20	30	69	147	225
86-Re-intro & origin Black Widow in new costume	20	40	60	138	307	475
90-Death of Capt. Stacy	16	32	48	110	243	375
94-Origin retold	14	28	42	93	204	315
96-98-Green Goblin app. (97,98-Green Goblin-c); drug books not approved by CCA	13	26	39	89	195	300

	GD 2.0	VG 4.0	FN 6.0	VF 8.0	VF/NM 9.0	NM- 9.2
100-Anniversary issue (9/71); Green Goblin cameo (2 pgs.)	23	46	69	161	356	550
101-1st app. Morbius the Living Vampire; Lizard cameo; Stan Lee co-plots with Roy Thomas; last 15¢ issue (10/71)	71	142	213	568	1284	2000
101-Silver ink 2nd printing (9/92, $1.75)	5	10	15	33	57	80
101 Facsimile Edition 1 (4/21, $3.99) r/#101 with original 1971 ads and letter column						5.00
102-Origin & 2nd app. Morbius (25¢, 52 pgs.)	16	32	48	107	236	365
103-118: 103,104-Roy Thomas-s. 104,111-Kraven the Hunter-c/stories. 105-109-Stan Lee-s. 108-1st app. Sha-Shan. 109-Dr. Strange-c/story. 110-1st app. Gibbon; Conway-s begin. 113-1st app. Hammerhead. 116-118-Reprints story from Spectacular Spider-Man Mag. in color with some changes	8	16	24	51	96	140
119,120-Spider-Man vs. Hulk (4 & 5/73)	12	24	36	82	179	275
121-Death of Gwen Stacy (6/73) (killed by Green Goblin)(reprinted in Marvel Tales #98 & 192); Harry Osborn LSD overdose	38	76	114	281	628	975
122-Death of The Green Goblin-c/story (7/73) (reprinted in Marvel Tales #99 & 192)	28	56	84	202	451	700
123-Cage app.	9	18	27	62	126	190
124-1st app. Man-Wolf (9/73)	25	50	75	175	388	600
125-Man-Wolf origin	9	18	27	60	120	180
126-128: 126-1st mention of Harry Osborn becoming Green Goblin	6	12	18	42	79	115
129-1st app. The Punisher (2/74); 1st app. Jackal	400	800	1200	2000	3000	4000
130-133: 131-Last 20¢ issue	6	12	18	37	66	95
134-(7/74); 1st app. Tarantula; Harry Osborn discovers Spider-Man's ID; Punisher cameo	15	30	45	103	227	350
135-2nd full Punisher app. (8/74)	17	34	51	117	259	400
136-1st app. Harry Osborn in Green Goblin costume	10	20	30	67	141	215
137-Green Goblin-c/story (2nd Harry Osborn Goblin)	7	14	21	44	82	120
138-141: 139-1st Grizzly. 140-1st app. Glory Grant	4	8	12	28	47	65
142-Mysterio app.; Gwen Stacy clone cameo	5	10	15	35	63	90
143-Gwen Stacy clone cameo; 1st app. Cyclone	7	14	21	44	82	120
144-147: 144-Full app. of Gwen Stacy clone. 145,146-Gwen Stacy clone storyline continues. 147-Spider-Man learns Gwen Stacy is clone	4	8	12	28	47	65
148-Jackal revealed	7	14	21	49	92	135
149-Spider-Man clone story begins, clone dies (?); origin of Jackal	14	28	42	96	211	325
150-Spider-Man decides he is not the clone	6	12	18	38	69	100
151-Spider-Man disposes of clone body; Len Wein-s begins; thru #180	8	16	24	54	102	150
152-155,157-160-(Regular 25¢ editions). 152-vs. the Shocker. 154-vs. Sandman. 157-159-Doc Octopus & Hammerhead app. 159-Last 25¢ issue(8/76). 160-Spider-Mobile destroyed	4	8	12	25	40	55
155-159-(30¢-c variants, limited distribution)	9	18	27	63	129	195
156-1st Mirage	5	10	15	33	57	80
161-Nightcrawler app. from X-Men; Punisher cameo; Wolverine & Colossus app.	5	10	15	35	63	90
162-Punisher, Nightcrawler app.; 1st Jigsaw	6	12	18	42	79	115
163-168: 163-164-vs. the Kingpin. 165-vs. Stegron. 166-Stegron & the Lizard app. 167-1st app. Will O' The Wisp. 168-Will O' The Wisp app.	3	6	9	19	30	40
169-170,172-173: 169-Clone story recapped; Stan Lee Cameo. 170-Dr. Faustus app. 172-1st Rocket Racer. 173-vs Molten Man	3	6	9	19	30	40
171-Nova app. x-over w/Nova #12	4	8	12	23	37	50
169-173-(35¢-c variants, limited dist.)(6-10/77)	21	42	63	147	324	500
174,175-Punisher app.	4	8	12	25	40	55
176-180-Green Goblin (Barton Hamilton) app.; Harry Osborn Green Goblin in #180 only. 177-180-Silvermane app.	3	6	9	20	31	42
181-186: 181-Origin retold; gives life history of Spidey; Punisher cameo in flashback (1 panel). 182-(7/78)-Peter's first proposal to Mary Jane, but she declines (in #183). 183-Rocket Racer & the Big Wheel app. 184-vs. the second White Dragon. 185-Peter graduates college	3	6	9	16	23	30
187,188: 187-Captain America app. 188-vs. Jigsaw	3	6	9	21	33	45
189,190-Byrne-a; Man-Wolf app.	3	6	9	21	33	45
191-193,196-199: 191-vs. the Spider-Slayer. 192-Death of Spencer Smythe. 193-Peter & Mary Jane break up; the Fly app. 196-Faked death of Aunt May. 197-vs. the Kingpin. 198,199-Mysterio app.	3	6	9	14	20	25
NOTE: *Whitman 3-packs containing #192-194,196 exist.*						
194-1st app. Black Cat	22	44	66	154	340	525
195-2nd app. Black Cat & origin Black Cat	6	12	18	38	69	100
200-Giant origin issue (1/80); death of the burglar (from Amazing Fantasy #15)	4	8	12	28	47	65
201-Punisher app.; classic bullseye-c	5	10	15	33	57	80
202-Punisher app.	4	8	12	23	37	50
203-208,211,213-219: 203-3rd Dazzler (4/80). 204,205-Black Cat app. 204-Last Wolfman-s. 206-Byrne-a. 207-vs Mesmero. 211-Sub-Mariner app. 214,215-New Frightful Four app: Wizard, Trapster, Sandman & Llyra (Namor foe). 216-Madame Web app.						

GD 2.0 | VG 4.0 | FN 6.0 | VF 8.0 | VF/NM 9.0 | NM- 9.2

217-Sandman vs Hydro-Man. 219-Grey Gargoyle app.; Frank Miller-c
2 4 6 11 16 20
209-Kraven the Hunter app; 1st app. origin Calypso 3 6 9 17 26 35
210-1st app. Madame Web 10 20 30 64 132 200
212-1st app. & origin Hydro-Man 5 10 15 30 50 70
220-Moon Knight app. 4 8 12 23 37 50
221-225,228: 222-1st app. of the Whizzer as Speed Demon. 223-vs. The Red Ghost & the Super-Apes; Roger Stern-s begins. 224-Vulture app. 225-Foolkiller II-c/story
2 4 6 8 11 14
226,227-Black Cat returns 3 6 9 18 28 38
229,230: Classic 'Nothing can stop the Juggernaut' story
3 6 9 21 33 45
231-237: 231,232-Cobra & Mr Hyde app. 233-Tarantula app. 234-Free 16 pg. insert "Marvel Guide to Collecting Comics", Tarantula & Will O' The Wisp app. 235-Origin Will 'O The Wisp. 236-Tarantula dies. 237-Stilt-Man app. 2 4 6 8 11 14
238-(3/83)-1st app. Hobgoblin (Ned Leeds); came with skin "Tattooz" decal.
NOTE: The same decal appears in the more common Fantastic Four #252 which is being removed & placed in this issue as incentive to increase value. (No "Tattooz" were included in the Canadian edition)
(Value with tattooz) 21 42 63 147 324 500
(Value without tattooz) 6 12 18 38 69 100
238 Facsimile Edition 1 (5/22, $3.99) r/#238 with original 1983 ads and letter column 4.00
239-2nd app. Hobgoblin & 1st battle w/Spidey 5 10 15 33 57 80
240-243,246-248: 240,241-Vulture app. (origin in #241). 242-Mary Jane Watson cameo (last panel). 243-Reintro Mary Jane after 4 year absence. 248-Classic 'The Kid Who Collects Spider-Man' story; Spider-Man tells origin & reveals identity to young boy with leukemia
2 4 6 8 11 14
244-3rd app. Hobgoblin (cameo) 3 6 9 16 23 50
245-(10/83)-4th app. Hobgoblin (cameo); Lefty Donovan gains powers of Hobgoblin & battles Spider-Man 3 6 9 19 30 40
249-251: 3 part Hobgoblin/Spider-Man battle. 249-Retells origin & death of 1st Green Goblin. 251-Last old costume 3 6 9 14 19 24
252-Spider-Man dons new black costume (5/84); ties with Marvel Team-Up #141 & Spectacular Spider-Man #90 for 1st new costume in regular title (See Marvel Super-Heroes Secret Wars #8 (12/84) for acquisition of costume); last Roger Stern-s
12 24 36 82 179 275
252 Facsimile Edition 1 (6/19, $4.99) r/#252 with original 1984 ads and letter column 5.00
253-1st app. The Rose; Tom DeFalco-s begin 3 6 9 16 23 30
254,255: 254-Jack O' Lantern app. 255-1st app Black Fox
2 4 6 8 11 14
256,257: 256-1st app. Puma. 257-Hobgoblin cameo; 2nd app. Puma; M.J. Watson reveals she knows Spidey's i.d. 3 6 9 21 33 45
258-Spider-Man discovers black costume is an alien symbiote; Mister Fantastic, Human Torch, Hobgoblin app. 4 8 12 27 44 60
259-Full Hobgoblin app.; Spidey back to old costume; origin Mary Jane Watson
3 6 9 18 27 36
260,261-Hobgoblin app. 261-Painted-c by Vess 3 6 9 17 25 34
262-Spider-Man unmasked; photo-c 2 4 6 11 16 20
263,264,266-268: 266-Toad & Frogman app.; Peter David-s. 268-Secret Wars II x-over
2 4 6 8 10 12
265-1st app. Silver Sable (6/85) 5 10 15 33 57 80
265-Silver ink 2nd printing ($1.25) 2 4 6 11 16 20
269-274,277-280,282-283: 269-Spider-Man vs Firelord. 272-1st app. Slyde. 273-Secret Wars II x-over; Beyonder app. 274-Secret Wars II x-over; Zarathos app. (The Spirit of Vengeance). 277-Vess-c & back-up art. 278-Scourge app; death of the Wraith. 279-Jack O' Lantern-c/s. 280-1st Sinister Syndicate: Beetle, Boomerang, Hydro-Man, Rhino, Speed Demon. 282-X-Factor app. 2 4 6 8 10 12
270,276: 270-Avengers app. 276-Hobgoblin app. 2 4 6 10 14 18
275-($1.25, 52 pgs.)-Hobgoblin-c/story; origin-r by Ditko
3 6 9 17 26 35
281-Hobgoblin battles Jack O'Lantern 3 6 9 14 19 24
284,285: 284-Punisher cameo; Gang War Pt. 1; Hobgoblin-c/story. 285-Punisher app.; minor Hobgoblin app.; last Tom DeFalco-s; Gang War Pt. 2
2 4 6 8 11 14
286-288: Gang War Parts 3-5. 286-Hobgoblin-c & app. (minor). 287-Hobgoblin app. (minor). 288-Full Hobgoblin app.; Gang War ends 2 4 6 8 10 12
289-(6/87, $1.25, 52 pgs.)-Hobgoblin's i.d. revealed as Ned Leeds; death of Ned Leeds; Macendale (Jack O'Lantern) becomes new Hobgoblin (1st app.)
3 6 9 19 30 40
290-292,295-297: 290-Peter proposes to Mary Jane; 1st David Michelinie-s. 291,292-Spider-Slayer app. 292-She accepts; leads into wedding in Amazing Spider-Man Annual #21. 295-'Mad Dog Ward' Pt. 2; x-over w/Web of Spider-Man #33 & Spectacular Spider-Man #133. 296-297-Doc Octopus app. 1 3 4 6 8 10
293,294-Part 2 & 5 of Kraven story from Web of Spider-Man. 293-Continued from Web of Spider-Man #31; continues into Spectacular Spider-Man #131. 294-Death of Kraven; continued from Web of Spider-Man #32; continues in Spectacular Spider-Man #132
3 6 9 19 30 40
298-Todd McFarlane-c/a begins (3/88); 1st brief app. Eddie Brock who becomes Venom; (last pg.) 7 14 21 46 86 125
299-1st brief app. Venom with costume 7 14 21 46 86 125
300 ($1.50, 52 pgs.; 25th Anniversary)-1st full Venom app.; last black costume (5/88)
27 54 81 189 420 650
301-$1.00 issues begin. Classic McFarlane-c 6 12 18 42 79 115
302-305: 302-303-Silver Sable app. 304,305-Black Fox app. 304-1st bi-weekly issue
2 4 6 11 16 20
306-Swipes-c from Action #1 4 8 12 27 44 60
307-311,313,314: 307-Chameleon app. 308-Taskmaster app. 309-1st app. Styx & Stone. 310-Killer Shrike app. 311-Inferno x-over; Mysterio app. 313-Lizard app.; origin retold. 314-Christmas-c 2 4 6 10 14 18
312-Hobgoblin battles Green Goblin; Inferno x-over 3 6 9 18 27 36
315,317-Venom app. 4 8 12 23 37 50
316-Classic Venom-c 10 20 30 64 132 200
318-322: 318-Scorpion app. 319-Bi-weekly begins again; Scorpion, Rhino, Backlash app. 320-'Assassination Nation Plot' Pt.1 (ends in issue #325); Paladin & Silver Sable app. 321-Paladin & Silver Sable app. 322-Silver Sable app.; fan letters from Stan Lee and Charlie Novinskie 2 4 6 8 10 12
323,324: 323-Captain America app. 324-Sabretooth app.; McFarlane cover only
2 4 6 11 16 20
325-Captain America & Red Skull app. 3 6 9 16 23 30
326,327: 326-Acts of Vengeance x-over; vs Graviton. 327-Acts of Vengeance x-over; vs. Magneto; Cosmic storyline continues from Spectacular Spider-Man; Erik Larsen-a.
1 2 3 5 6 8
328-Acts of Vengeance x-over; vs. the Hulk; last McFarlane issue
3 6 9 17 26 35
329-Acts of Vengeance x-over; vs. the Tri-Sentinel; Sebastian Shaw app.; Erik Larsen-a (continuous through issue #344) 3 6 9 15 22 28
330-333: 330,331-Punisher app. 331-Minor Venom app. 332,333-Venom-c/story
3 6 9 14 20 25
334-336,338-343: 334-339-Return of the Sinister Six. 341-Tarantula app; Spider-Man loses his cosmic powers. 342,343-Black Cat app.
1 2 3 5 6 8
337-Hobgoblin app. 3 6 9 14 20 25
344-(2/91) 1st app. Cletus Kasady (Carnage) 4 8 12 28 47 65
345-1st full app. Cletus Kasady; Venom cameo on last pg.; 1st Mark Bagley-a on Spider-Man
3 6 9 19 30 40
346,347-Venom app. 3 6 9 19 30 40
347 Facsimile Edition (3/20, $3.99) r/#347 with original 1991 ads and letter column 4.00
348,349,351-359: 348-Avengers x-over. 351-Bagley-a begins. 351,352-Nova of New Warriors app. 353-Darkhawk app.; brief Punisher app. 354-Punisher cameo & Nova, Night Thrasher (New Warriors), Darkhawk & Moon Knight app. 357,358-Punisher, Darkhawk, Moon Knight, Night Thrasher, Nova x-over. 358-3 part gatefold-c; last $1.00-c 6.00
350-($1.50, 52pgs.)-Origin retold; Spidey vs. Dr. Doom; last Erik Larsen-a pin-ups; Uncle Ben app. 1 3 4 6 8 10
360-Carnage cameo 3 6 9 19 30 40
361-(4/92) Intro. Carnage (the Spawn of Venom); begin 3 part story; recap of how Spidey's alien costume became Venom 9 18 27 59 117 175
361-($1.25)-2nd printing; silver-c 5 10 15 33 57 80
362,363-Carnage & Venom-c/story 3 6 9 16 23 30
362-2nd printing 2 4 6 10 14 18
364,366-373,376,377,381-387: 364-The Shocker app. (old villain). 366-Peter's parents-c/story; Red Skull, Viper & Taskmaster app. 367-Red Skull, Viper & Taskmaster app. 368-Invasion of the Spider-Slayers Pt.1 (through Pt.6 in #373). 369-Harry Osborn back-up (Gr. Goblin II). Electro app. 370-Black Cat & Scorpion app. 373-Venom back-up. 376,377-Cardiac app. 381,382-Hulk app. 383-The Jury app. 383-385-vs The Jury. 384-Venom/Carnage app. 386-Vulture app. 387-Vulture is de-aged & gets new costume 4.00
365-(8/92, $3.95, 84 pgs.)-30th anniversary issue w/silver hologram on-c; Spidey/Venom/Carnage pull-out poster; contains 5 pg. preview of Spider-Man 2099 (intro., Spider-Man 2099 appears on a pull-out poster in Web of Spider-Man #90 one month earlier); Spidey's origin retold; Lizard app.; reintro Peter's parents in Stan Lee 3 pg. text w/illo (story continues thru #370)
4 8 12 23 37 50
374-Venom-c/story 2 4 6 11 16 20
375-(3/93, $3.95, 68 pgs.)-Holo-grafx foil-c; vs. Venom; ties into Venom: Lethal Protector #1; intro. Ann Weying; Pat Olliffe-a. 4 8 12 23 37 50
378-380: Parts 3,7 and 11 of Maximum Carnage. 378-Continued from Web of Spider-Man #101; Venom vs Carnage; continues in Spider-Man #35. 379-Continued from Web of Spider-Man #102; Deathlok, Firestar, Black Cat & Morbius app.; continued in Spider-Man #36. 380-Continued from Web of Spider-Man #103; Captain America & Cloak and Dagger app.; continued in Spider-Man #37 1 2 3 5 6 8
388-($2.25, 68 pgs.)-Newsstand edition; Venom back-up & Cardiac & chance back-up; last David Michelinie-s (6-year run) 6.00
388-($2.95, 68 pgs.)-Collector's edition w/foil-c 1 2 3 5 6 8
389-1st JM DeMatteis-s; Trading Card insert (3 cards) attached to the staples; harder to find in true high grade due to indents caused by the cards; Green Goblin app. 6.00
390-393,395,396: 390-393-vs. Shriek. 395-Puma app. 396-Daredevil & the Owl app. 4.00
390-($2.95)-Collector's edition polybagged w/16 pg. insert of new animated Spidey TV show plus animation cel 6.00
394-($2.95, 48 pgs.)-Deluxe edition; flip book w/Birth of a Spider-Man Pt. 2; silver foil both-c; Power & Responsibility Pt. 2; Judas Traveller, the Jackal and the Gwen Stacy Clone app. 1st app. Scrier 1 2 3 5 6 8
394-Newstand edition ($1.50-c) 1 2 3 5 6 8
397-($2.25)-Flip book w/Ultimate Spider-Man 6.00
398,399: 398-Web of Death Pt.3; continued from Spectacular Spider-Man #220; Doc Octopus & Kaine app.; continued in Spectacular Spider-Man #221. 399-Smoke and Mirrors Pt.2; continued from Web of Spider-Man #122; Jackal, Scarlet Spider, Gwen Stacy Clone app; continued in Spider-Man #56 6.00
400-($2.95)-Death of Aunt May; newsstand edition 3 6 9 19 30 40
400-($3.95)-Death of Aunt May; embossed grey overlay cover
3 6 9 15 22 28
400-Collector's Edition; white embossed-c; (10,000 print run)
5 10 15 34 60 85
401,402,405,406-409: 401-The Mark of Kaine Pt.2; continued from Web of Spider-Man #124; Scarlet Spider app; continues in Spider-Man #58. 402-Judas Traveller & Scrier app. 405-Exiled Pt.2; continued from Web of Spider-Man #128; Scarlet Spider app.; continues in Spider-Man #62. 406-1st full app. of the female Doc Octopus (Carolyn Trainer); continues in Spider-Man #63; Marvel Overpower card insert; harder to find in higher grades due to card indenting; last JM DeMatteis-s. 407-Human Torch, Sandman & Silver Sable app. Tom DeFalco-s (returns to Spider-Man; last-s in 1987). 408-Regular ed; Media Blizzard pt.2; Mysterio app; continued from Sensational Spider-Man #1; continues in Spider-Man #65. 409-The Return of Kaine Pt.3; continued from Spectacular Spider-Man #231; Kaine & Rhino app.; continues in Spider-Man #66 6.00
403-The Trial of Peter Parker Pt. 2; continued from Web of Spider-Man #126; Carnage app; continues in Spider-Man #60. 2 4 6 8 10 12
404-Maximum Clonage Pt.3; continued from Web of Spider-Man #127; Scarlet Spider, Jackal, Scrier & Kaine app; continued in Spider-Man #61 6.00
408-($2.95)-Polybagged version with TV theme song cassette; scarce in high grade due to damage caused by the cassette indenting the actual comic
9 18 27 60 120 180
408-Direct edition (without cassette & out of polybag) 4 8 12 23 37 50
408-Newstand edition; variant cover 5 10 15 31 53 75
410-Web of Carnage Pt.2; continued from Sensational Spider-Man #3; Carnage app; continues in Spider-Man #67 3 6 9 21 33 45
411,412,414,417-424: 411-Blood Brothers Pt.2; continued from Sensational Spider-Man #4; Gaunt app; continued in Spider-Man #68. 412-Blood Brothers Pt.6; continued from Sensational Spider-Man #5; vs Gaunt. 414-The Rose app. 417-Death of Scrier. 418-Revelations Pt.3; continued from Spectacular Spider-Man #240; Norman Osborn

Amazing Spider-Man #330 © MAR

Amazing Spider-Man Annual #8 © MAR

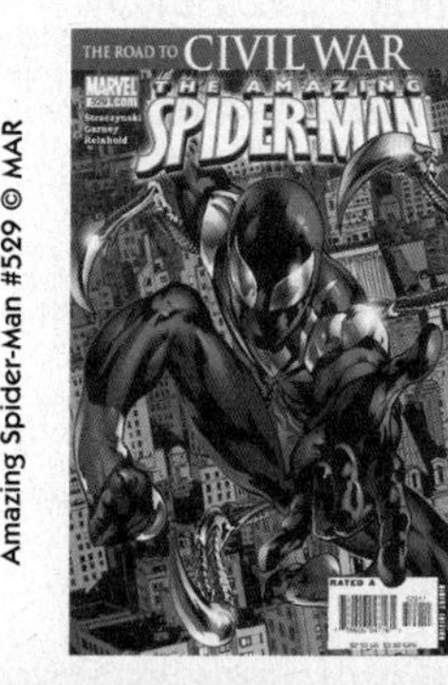

Amazing Spider-Man #529 © MAR

GD	VG	FN	VF	VF/NM	NM-
2.0	4.0	6.0	8.0	9.0	9.2

returns; 'death' of Peter and Mary Jane's baby (May Parker); continued in Spider-Man #75. 419-1st minor app. of The Black Tarantula. 420-X-Man app. 422,423-Electro app. 424-Elektra app. 6.00
413-Contains a free packet of Island Twists Kool-Aid and Spider-Man For Kids magazine subscriber card; harder to find in true high grade 1 3 4 6 8 10
415-Onslaught Impact 2; Green Goblin (Phil Urich) app. vs. Mark IV Sentinels; last Mark Bagley-a (5 year run) 1 2 3 5 6 8
416-Epilogue to Onslaught; harder to find in high grade due to Marvel Overpower card insert 2 4 6 9 13 16
425-($2.99)-48 pgs., wraparound-c; X-Man app 2 4 6 8 10 12
426,428,429,432,435-438,440: 426-Female Dr. Octopus app. 428-Dr. Octopus app. 429-Absorbing Man app. 432-Spider-Hunt Pt.2; continued from Sensational Spider-Man #25; Black Tarantula & Norman Osborn app. 433-Mr. Hyde app. 435-Identity Crisis; Black Tarantula & Kaine app. 436-Black Tarantula app. 437-Plantman app. 438-Daredevil app. 440-Gathering of Five Pt.2; continued from Sensational Spider-Man #32; John Byrne-s; Molten Man & Norman Osborn app; continued in Spider-Man #96 6.00
427-Return of Dr. Octopus; double-gatefold-c. 1 3 4 6 8 10
430-Carnage & Silver Surfer app. 4 8 12 23 37 50
431-Cosmic-Carnage vs Silver Surfer; Galactus cameo 4 8 12 28 47 65
432-Variant yellow-c 'Wanted Dead or Alive' 2 4 6 11 16 20
434-Identity Crisis; Black Tarantula app. 2 4 6 10 14 18
434-Variant 'Amazing Ricochet #1'-c 2 4 6 10 14 18
439-Alternate future story; Avengers app; last Tom DeFalco-s 2 4 6 8 11 14
441-The Final Chapter Pt.1; John Byrne-s; Norman Osborn app; last issue (Dec. 1998); story continues in Spider-Man #97 2 4 6 8 10 12
#500-up (See Amazing Spider-Man Vol. 2; series resumed original numbering after Vol. 2 #58)
#(-1) Flashback issue (7/97, $1.95-c) 5.00
Annual 1 (1964, 72 pgs.) Origin Spider-Man; 1st app. Sinister Six (Dr. Octopus, Electro, Kraven the Hunter, Mysterio, Sandman, Vulture) (new 41 pg. story); plus gallery of Spidey foes; early X-Men app. 333 666 1000 2831 6416 10,000
Annual #1 Facsimile Edition 1 (6/22, $7.99) rep. entire issue with original 1964 ads 8.00
Annual 2 (1965, 25¢, 72 pgs.) Reprints from #1,2,5 plus new Doctor Strange story 42 84 126 311 706 1100
Special 3 (11/66, 25¢, 72 pgs.) New Avengers story & Hulk x-over; Doctor Octopus-r from #11,12; Romita-a 22 44 66 154 340 525
Special 4 (11/67, 25¢, 68 pgs.) Spidey battles Human Torch (new 41 pg. story) 14 28 42 93 204 315
Special 5 (11/68, 25¢, 68 pgs.) New 40 pg. Red Skull story; 1st app. Peter Parker's parents; last annual with new-a 12 24 36 84 185 285
Special 5-2nd printing (1994) 2 4 6 9 13 16
Special 6 (11/69, 25¢, 68 pgs.) Reprints 41 pg. Sinister Six story from Annual #1 plus 2 Kirby/Ditko stories (r) 13 26 39 89 195 300
Special 7 (12/70, 25¢, 68 pgs.) All-r(#1,2) new Vulture-c 6 12 18 37 66 95
Special 8 (12/71) All-r 6 12 18 37 66 95
King Size 9 ('73) Reprints Spectacular Spider-Man (mag.) #2; 40 pg. Green Goblin-c/story (re-edited from 58 pgs.) 6 12 18 38 69 100
Annual 10 (1976) Origin Human Fly (vs. Spidey); new-a begins 4 8 12 27 44 60
Annual 11-13 ('77-'79): 12-Spidey vs. Hulk-r/#119,120. 13-New Byrne/Austin-a; Dr. Octopus x-over w/Spectacular S-M Ann. #1 3 6 9 15 22 28
Annual 14 (1980) Miller-c/a(p); Doctor Strange and Doctor Doom app. 3 6 9 16 24 32
Annual 15 (1981) Miller-c/a(p); Punisher and Doctor Octopus app.; 4 bonus pin-ups (Man-Wolf, The Jackal, Punisher and Tarantula) 3 6 9 19 30 40
Annual 16 (1982)-Origin/1st app. new Captain Marvel (female heroine Monica Rambeau) 8 16 24 54 102 150
Annual 17-20: 17 ('83)-Kingpin app. 18 ('84)-Scorpion app.; JJJ weds. 19 ('85). 20 ('86)-Origin Iron Man of 2020 2 4 6 8 11 14
Annual 21 (1987) Special wedding issue; newsstand & direct sale versions exist & are worth same 4 8 12 25 40 55
Annual 22 (1988, $1.75, 68 pgs.) 1st app. Speedball; Evolutionary War x-over; Daredevil app. 3 6 9 16 24 32
Annual 23 (1989, $2.00, 68 pgs.) Atlantis Attacks; origin Spider-Man retold; She-Hulk app.; Byrne-c; Liefeld-a(p), 23 pgs. 2 4 6 9 12 15
Annual 24 (1990, $2.00, 68 pgs.) -Ant-Man app. 1 2 3 5 6 8
Annual 25 (1991, $2.00, 68 pgs.) 3 pg. origin recap; Iron Man app.; 1st Venom solo story; Ditko-a (6 pgs.) 1 3 4 6 8 10
Annual 26 (1992, $2.25, 68 pgs.) New Warriors-c/story; Venom solo story cont'd in Spectacular Spider-Man Annual #12 2 4 6 9 13 16
Annual 27 ('93, $2.95, 68 pgs.) Bagged w/card; 1st app. Annex 6.00
Annual 28 ('94, $2.95, 68 pgs.) Carnage-c/story 2 4 6 8 11 14
'96 Special-($2.95, 64 pgs.)-"Blast From The Past" 6.00

GD	VG	FN	VF	VF/NM	NM-
2.0	4.0	6.0	8.0	9.0	9.2

'97 Special-($2.99)-Wraparound-c,Sundown app. 6.00
... : Carnage (6/93, $6.95)-r/ASM #344,345,359-363 2 4 6 8 11 14
Marvel Graphic Novel - Parallel Lives (3/89, $8.95) 2 4 6 8 11 14
...: Parallel Lives 1 (2012, $4.99) r/1989 GN 6.00
Marvel Graphic Novel - Spirits of the Earth (1990, $18.95, HC) 2 4 6 10 15 19
... No. 1 Facsimile Edition (12/22, $3.99) Reprints #1 with original 1963 ads 4.00
Super Special 1 (4/95, $3.95)-Flip Book 3 6 9 14 20 25
...: Skating on Thin Ice 1(1990, $1.25, Canadian)-McFarlane-c; anti-drug issue; Electro app. 2 4 6 8 10 12
...: Skating on Thin Ice 1 (2/93, $1.50, American) 6.00
...: Double Trouble 2 (1990, $1.25, Canadian) 1 2 3 5 6 8
...: Double Trouble 2 (2/93, $1.50, American) 1 3 4 6 8 10
...: Hit and Run 3 (1990, $1.25, Canadian)-Ghost Rider-c/story 1 2 3 5 7 9
...: Hit and Run 3 (2/93. $1.50, American) 5.00
...: Chaos in Calgary 4 (Canadian; part of 5 part series)-Turbine,Night Rider, Frightful app. 2 4 6 8 11 14
...: Chaos in Calgary 4 (2/93, $1.50, American) 5.00
...: Deadball 5 (1993, $1.60, Canadian)-Green Goblin-c/story; features Montreal Expos 2 4 6 10 14 18
Note: Prices listed above are for English Canadian editions. French editions are worth double.
...: Soul of the Hunter nn (8/92, $5.95, 52 pgs.)-Zeck-c/a(p) 1 2 3 5 6 8
...: Venom 3D No. 1 (10/19, $7.99) Reprints ASM #300 in 3D; bagged with glasses 25.00
Wizard #1 Ace Edition ($13.99) r/#1 w/ new Ramos acetate-c 18.00
Wizard #129 Ace Edition ($13.99) r/#129 w/ new Ramos acetate-c 25.00

NOTE: ***Austin*** *a(i)-248, 335, 337, Annual 13; c(i)-188, 241, 242, 248, 331, 334, 343, Annual 25.* ***J. Buscema*** *a(p)-72, 73, 76-81, 84, 85.* ***Byrne*** *a-189p, 190p, 206p, Annual 3r, 6r, 7r, 13p; c-189p, 268, 296, Annual 12.* ***Ditko*** *a-1-38, Annual 1, Special 3(r), 2, 24(2); c-1i, 2-38, Annual 1.* ***Guice*** *c/a-Annual 18i.* ***Gil Kane*** *a(p)-89-105, 120-124, 150, Annual 10, 12i, 24p; c-90p, 96, 98, 99, 101-105p, 129p, 131p, 132p, 137-140p, 143p, 148p, 149p, 151p, 153p, 160p, 161p, Annual 10p, 24.* ***Kirby*** *a-8.* ***Erik Larsen*** *a-324, 327, 329-350; c-327, 329-350, 354i, Annual 25.* ***McFarlane*** *a-298p, 299p, 300-303, 304-323p, 325p, 328; c-298-325, 328.* ***Miller*** *c-218, 219.* ***Mooney*** *a-65i, 67-82i, 84-88i, 173i, 178i, 189i, 190i, 192i, 193i, 196-202i, 207i, 211-219i, 221i, 222i, 226i, 227i, 229-233i, Annual 11i, 17i.* ***Nasser*** *c-228p.* ***Nebres*** *a-Annual 24i.* ***Russell*** *c-357i.* ***Simonson*** *c-222, 337i.* ***Starlin*** *a-113i, 114i, 187p.* ***Williamson*** *a-365i.*

AMAZING SPIDER-MAN (Volume 2) (Some issues reprinted in "Spider-Man, Best Of" hardcovers)
Marvel Comics: Jan, 1999 - No. 700, Feb, 2013 ($2.99/$1.99/$2.25)

1-($2.99)-Byrne-a; Avengers, Fantastic Four & Green Goblin app. 2 4 6 8 10 12
1-Sunburst variant-c 3 6 9 14 19 24
1-($6.95) Dynamic Forces variant-c by the Romitas 3 6 9 14 20 26
1-Marvel Matrix sketch variant-c 3 6 9 19 30 40
2-($1.99) Two covers -by Byrne & Andy Kubert 1 2 3 5 6 8
3,4,6-11: 4-Fantastic Four app. 4.00
5-1st Maddie Franklin as Spider-Woman 3 6 9 14 19 24
12-($2.99) Sinister Six return (cont. in Peter Parker #12) 5.00
13-17: 13-Mary Jane's plane explodes 4.00
18-Begin $2.25-c; Green Goblin app. 2 4 6 10 14 18
19,21-24,26-28: 19-Venom-c. 24-Maximum Security 4.00
20-($2.99, 100 pgs.) Spider-Slayer issue; new story and reprints 2 4 6 11 16 20
25-($2.99) Regular cover; Peter Parker becomes the Green Goblin 6.00
25-($3.99) Holo-foil enhanced cover 2 4 6 11 16 20
29-Peter is reunited with Mary Jane 5.00
30-Straczynski-s/Campbell-c begin; intro. Ezekiel 3 6 9 17 26 35
31-35: Battles Morlun 5.00
36-Black cover; aftermath of the Sept. 11 tragedy in New York 4 8 12 28 47 65
37-49: 39-'Nuff Said issue 42-Dr. Strange app. 43-45-Doctor Octopus app. 46-48-Cho-c 4.00
50-Peter and MJ reunite; Captain America & Dr. Doom app.; Campbell-c 1 3 4 6 8 10
51-58: 51,52-Campbell-c. 55,56-Avery scripts. 57,58-Avengers, FF, Cyclops app. 4.00
(After #58 [Nov, 2003] numbering reverts back to original Vol. 1 with #500, Dec, 2003)
500-($3.50) J. Scott Campbell-c; Romita Jr. & Sr.-a; Uncle Ben app. 2 4 6 11 16 20
501-524: 501-Harris-c. 503-504-Loki app. 506-508-Ezekiel app. 509-514-Sins Past; intro. Gabriel and Sarah Osborn; Deodato-a. 519-Moves into Avengers HQ. 521-Begin $2.50-c 524-Harris-c 4.00
525,526-Evolve or Die x-over. 525-David-s. 526-Hudlin-s; Spider-Man loses eye 5.00
525-528-2nd printings with variant-c. 525-Ben Reilly costume. 526-Six-Armed Spidey. 527-Spider-Man 2099. 528-Spider-Ham 6.00
527,528: Evolve or Die pt. 9,12 4.00
529-Debut of red and gold costume (Iron Spider); Garney-a 28.00
529-2nd printing 5.00
529-3rd printing with Wieringo-c 3.00
530,531-Titanium Man app.; Kirkham-a. 531-Begin $2.99-c 10.00

GD VG FN VF VF/NM NM-
2.0 4.0 6.0 8.0 9.0 9.2

532-538-Civil War tie-in. 538-Aunt May shot 6.00
539-543-Back in Black. 539-Peter wears the black costume 3.00
544-($3.99) "One More Day" pt. 1; Quesada-a/Straczynski-s 12.00
545-(12/08, $3.99) "One More Day" pt. 4; Quesada-a/Straczynski-s, Peter & MJ's marriage un-done; r/wedding from ASM Annual #21; 2 covers by Quesada and Djurdjevic 12.00
546-($3.99) Brand New Day begins; McNiven-a; Deodato, Winslade, Land, Romita Jr.-a; 1st app. Mr. Negative 50.00
546-Variant-c by Bryan Hitch 30.00
546-Second printing with new McNiven-c of Peter Parker 10.00
546-MGC (7/10, $1.00) r/#546 with "Marvel's Greatest Comics" logo on cover 3.00
547-549,551-564,566,567: 547,548-McNiven-a. 549-551-Larroca-a. 555-557-Bachalo-a. 559-Intro. Screwball. 560,561-MJ app. 566,567-Spidey in Daredevil costume 3.00
550-Intro. Menace (Lily Hollister) 12.00
565-Intro Ana Kravinoff 25.00
568-($3.99) Romita Jr.-a begins; two covers by Romita Jr. and Alex Ross 12.00
568-Variant-c by John Romita Sr. 28.00
568-2nd printing with Romita Jr. Anti-Venom costume cover 6.00
569-Debut of Anti-Venom; Norman Osborn and Thunderbolts app.; Romita Jr.-c 60.00
569-Variant Venom-c by Granov 50.00
569-2nd printing with Romita Jr.-c 165.00
570-572-Two covers on each 10.00
573-($3.99) New Ways to Die conclusion; Spidey meets Stephen Colbert back-up; Ollife-a; two covers by Romita Jr. and Maguire 6.00
573-Variant cover with Stephen Colbert; cover swipe of AF #15 by Quesada 25.00
574-582: 577-Punisher app. 3.00
583-($3.99) Spidey meets Obama back-up story; regular Romita Sr. "Cougars" cover 12.00
583-($3.99) Obama variant-c with Spidey on left; Spidey meets Obama back-up story 70.00
583-($3.99) Second printing Obama variant-c with Spidey on right and yellow bkgrd 8.00
583-($3.99) 3rd-5th printings Obama variant-c: 3rd-Blue bkgrd w/flag. 4th-White bkgrd w/flag. 5th-Lincoln Memorial bkgrd 5.00
584-587, 589-599: 585-Menace ID revealed. 590,591-Fantastic Four app. 594-Aunt May engaged. 595-599-American Son; Osborn Avengers app. app. 3.00
588-($3.99) Conclusion to "Character Assassination"; Romita Jr.-a 4.00
600-(9/09, $4.99) Aunt May's wedding; Romita Jr.-a; Doc Octopus, FF app.; Mary Jane cameo; back-up story by Stan Lee; back-up with Doran-a; 2 covers by Romita Jr. & Ross 18.00
600-Variant covers by Romita Sr. and Quesada 20.00
601-Mary Jane cover by Campbell; back-up w/Quesada-a 85.00
602-1st new Slyde 15.00
603,604,608-610,613-616,618-621,623-627: 612-The Gauntlet begins; Waid-s. 615,616-Sandman app. 621-Black Cat app. 624-Peter Parker fired. 626-Gaydos-a 3.00
605,612,617,622,628-($3.99): 605-Mayhew-c. 613-Rhino back-up story. 617-New Rhino. 622-Bianchi-c; Morbius app. 628-Captain Universe app. 4.00
606,607-Black Cat app.; Campbell-c 65.00
611-Deadpool-c/app. 25.00
629-633-($2.99)-Bachalo-a; Lizard app. 3.00
634-636,638-641-($3.99) 634-637-Grim Hunt; Kaine app. 635-Kraven returns. 638-641-"One Moment in Time" wedding flashback/retcon; Quesada-s 4.00
637-1st Araña(Anya Corazon) as Spider-Girl 50.00
638-641-Variant covers by Quesada 15.00
642-646-($2.99) Waid-s/Azaceta-a; interlocking covers by Djurdjevic 3.00
647-($4.99) Short stories by various; Djurdjevic-c; cover gallery of Brand New Day issues 5.00
648-650,652,653,655-691-($3.99) 648-Big Time begins; Ramos-a; Hobgoblin app. 655-Martin-a. 657-660-Fantastic Four app. 666-673-Spider Island. 667-672-Ramos-a; Avengers app. 677-X-over w/Daredevil #8. 682-687-Avengers app. 4.00
651-Hobgoblin & Black Cat app. 12.00
651-Tron variant-c by Mark Brooks 100.00
654-Flash Thompson becomes Venom; Marla Jameson killed 50.00
654.1-(4/11, $2.99) Flash Thompson as Venom; Ramos-a 20.00
679.1-(4/12, $2.99) Morbius the Living Vampire app. 10.00
692-($5.99) Debut of Alpha; Ramos-a; back-up short stories 10.00
693-697: 694-Cover swipe of Superman vs. Spider-Man 4.00
698, 699, 699.1: 698-Doctor Octopus brain switch revealed. 699.1-Morbius origin 4.00
700-($7.99) Collage cover; Leads into Superior Spider-Man #1; back-up short stories 36.00
700-Variant skyline-c by Marcos 55.00
700-Second printing cover with Doctor Octopus on an ASM #300 swipe 10.00
700.1 - 700.5 (2/14, weekly limited series, $3.99) 700.1-Janson-a/Ferry-c 5.00
1999, 2000 Annual ($2.99) (6/99, '00, $3.50) 1999-Buscema-a 4.00
2001 Annual ($2.99) Follows Peter Parker: S-M #29; last Mackie-s 4.00
Annual 1 (2008, $3.99) McKone-a; secret of Jackpot revealed; death of Jackpot 5.00
Annual 36 (9/09, $3.99) Debut of Raptor; Olliffe-a 4.00
Annual 37 (7/10, $3.99) Untold 1st meeting with Captain America; back-up w/Olliffe-a 4.00
Annual 38 (6/11, $3.99) Deadpool & Hulk app.; Garbett-a/McNiven-c 4.00
Annual 39 (7/12, $3.99) Avengers app.; Garbett-a/c 4.00
...: Big Time 1 (8/11, $5.99) r/#648-650 6.00
Collected Edition #30-32 ($3.95) reprints #30-32 w/cover #30 20.00
... 500 Covers HC (2004, $49.99) reprints covers for #1-500 & Annuals; yearly re-caps 50.00
...: Ends of the Earth (7/12, $3.99) Silas-a/Fiumara-c; Big Hero Six app. 4.00
...: Family Business HC (2014, $24.99) Kingpin app.; Waid & Robinson-s/Dell'Otto-a 25.00
Free Comic Book Day 2011 (Spider-Man) 1-Ramos-c/a; Spider-Woman & Shang-Chi app. 10.00
.../Ghost Rider: Motorstorm 1 ('11, $2.99) r/#558-560 8.00
...: Hooky 1 (2012, $4.99) r/Marvel Graphic Novel #22 (1986) with Wrightson-a 20.00
...: Infested 1 (11/11, $3.99) Spider Island tie-in; short stories by various; Ramos-c 6.00
... Omnibus HC (2007, $99.99, dustjacket) r/Amazing Fantasy #15, Amazing Spider-Man #1-38, Annual #1,2, Strange Tales Annual #2 & Fantastic Four Annual #1; letter pages, bonus art, intro. by Stan Lee; bios, essays, Marvel Tales cover gallery 200.00
Spider-Man: Brand New Day - Extra!! #1 (9/08, $3.99) short stories; Bachalo,Olliffe-a 4.00
Spider-Man: Brand New Day Yearbook #1 (2008, $4.99) plot synopses; profile pages 5.00
... Spidey Sunday Spectacuar (7/11, $3.99) collects back-ups from ASM #634-645 6.00
...: Swing Shift (2007 FCBD Edition) Jimenez-c/a; Slott-s 15.00
...: Swing Shift Director's Cut (2008, $3.99) story from 2007 FCBD; Brand New Day info 10.00
The Many Loves of the Amazing Spider-Man (7/10, $3.99) short stories of Black Cat, Gwen & Carlie, and Mary Jane; s/a by various 8.00
...: The Short Halloween (7/09, $3.99) Bill Hader & Seth Meyers-s/Maguire-a 7.00
...: You're Hired 1 (5/11, $3.99) r/story from New York Daily News insert 4.00
...Vol. 1: Coming Home (2001, $15.95) r/#30-35; J. Scott Campbell-c 16.00
...Vol. 2: Revelations (2002, $8.99) r/#36-39; Kaare Andrews-c 9.00
...Vol. 3: Until the Stars Turn Cold (2002, $12.99) r/#40-45; Romita Jr.-c 13.00
...Vol. 4: The Life and Death of Spiders (2003, $11.99) r/#46-50; Campbell-c 12.00
...Vol. 5: Unintended Consequences (2003, $12.99) r/#51-56; Dodson-c 13.00
...Vol. 6: Happy Birthday (2003, $12.99) r/#57,58,500-502 13.00
...Vol. 7: The Book of Ezekiel (2004, $12.99) r/#503-508; Romita Jr.-c 13.00
...Vol. 8: Sins Past (2005, $12.99) r/#509-514; cover sketch gallery 13.00
...Vol. 9: Skin Deep (2005, $9.99) r/#515-518 10.00
...Vol. 10: New Avengers (2005, $14.99) r/#519-524 15.00
Brand New Day #1-3 (11/08-1/09, $3.99) reprints #546-551 4.00
Civil War: Amazing Spider-Man TPB (2007, $17.99) r/#532-538; variant covers 18.00

AMAZING SPIDER-MAN (Follows Superior Spider-Man)(Also see Spider-Verse Team-Up)
Marvel Comics: Jun, 2014 - No. 20.1 , Oct, 2015 ($3.99)(there was no #19 or 20)

1-($5.99) 1st app. Cindy Moon (cameo, becomes Silk in #3); Slott-s/Ramos-a; bonus shorts with Electro, Black Cat, Spider-Man 2099, Kaine; bonus r/Inhuman #1; Ramos-c 12.00
1-Variant-c by J. Scott Campbell 15.00
2,3-Cindy Moon app.; Electro app. 2-Avengers app. 3-Black Cat app. 5.00
4-1st app. Silk (Cindy Moon); Original Sin tie-in 150.00
5-8: 5,6-Silk, Black Cat app. 7,8-Ms. Marvel app.; back-up Spider-Verse; Morlun app. 4.00
9-($4.99) Spider-Verse part 1; Variant Spider-Men & Spider-Gwen app.; Coipel-a 30.00
10-15-Spider-Verse; Superior Spider-Man returns. 13,14-Uncle Ben app.; Camuncoli-a 4.00
16-18-Ghost app.; Ramos-a; back-up with Black Cat 4.00
16.1, 17.1, 18.1, 19.1, 20.1-($3.99) Spiral parts 1-5; Conway-s/Barberi-a 4.00
Annual 1 (2/15, $4.99) Sean Ryan-s/Peterson-a/c; Nitz-s/Salas-a 5.00
Special 1 (5/15, $4.99) Crossover with Inhumans and All-New Captain America specials 5.00
#1.1-1.5 (Learning to Crawl) (7/14-11/14, $3.99) Re-tells early career; Alex Ross-c 4.00

AMAZING SPIDER-MAN (Follows Secret Wars)
Marvel Comics: Dec, 2015 - No. 32, Nov, 2017; No. 789, Dec, 2017 - No. 801, Aug, 2018 ($5.99/$3.99)

1-($5.99) Slott-s/Camuncoli-a; main-c by Alex Ross; back-up previews of Spider-titles 8.00
2-18-($3.99) 3,5-Human Torch app. 6-8-Cloak & Dagger app. 13-15-Iron Man app. 15-Mary Jane in the Iron Spider suit. 17-New female Electro 4.00
19-($4.99) Clone Conspiracy tie-in: Kingpin & Rhino app. 5.00
20-24: Clone Conspiracy tie-ins. 20-Doctor Octopus gets his body back. 21-Kaine returns 4.00
25-($9.99) Osborn Identity begins; Silver Sable returns; debut of The Superior Octopus 10.00
26-32: 26-28,32-Norman Osborn app.; Immonen-a. 29-31-Secret Empire tie-ins 4.00

[Title switches to legacy numbering after #32 (11/17)]

789-799,801: 789-791-"Fall of Parker"; Immonen-a. 792,793-Venom Inc. x-over. 795-Osborn merges with Carnage; Loki app. 4.00
800-(7/18, $9.99, 80 pages) Spider-Man vs. Red Goblin; death of Flash Thompson; art by Immonen, Ramos, Bradshaw, Camuncoli, Martin 12.00
#1.1-1.6 (Amazing Grace) (2/16-9/16, $3.99) The Santerians app.; Bianchi-a 4.00
Annual 1 (1/17, $4.99) Short stories by various incl. Wayne Brady, Ramos, Gage, Asmus 5.00
Annual 42 (4/18, $4.99) Dan Slott-s/Cory Smith-a 5.00

AMAZING SPIDER-MAN
Marvel Comics: Sept, 2018 - No. 93, May, 2022 ($5.99/$3.99)

1-($5.99) Spencer-s/Ottley-a; Mysterio app. 8.00
2-15-($3.99) 2-Taskmaster app. 6-10-Ramos-a. 8-10-Black Cat app. 14,15-Bachalo-a 4.00
16,17-($4.99) Kraven & Arcade app. 5.00
18-24: 18-23-Hunted. 18,20,22-Ramos-a. 22-Kraven dies. 23-Ottley-a. 24-Mysterio app. 4.00
16HU-($3.99) Hunted story arc; Coello-a; Black Cat, Taskmaster, Black Ant app. 4.00
18HU,19HU,20HU-($3.99) Hunted; 18-The Gibbon. 19-The Lizard; Bachalo-a. 20-Vulture 4.00
25-($7.99) Mysterio and Electro app.; art by Ottley, Ramos, Gleason, Walker 8.00
26-44,46-48: 30,31-Absolute Carnage tie-ins. 32-36-Spider-Man 2099. 41-Lethal Legion returns. 46-48-Sins Rising. 47,48-Norman Osborn app. 4.00
45-($4.99) Sins Rising begins; Spencer-s/Bagley-a; The Sin-Eater app. 5.00
49-($9.99) 850th issue celebration; Spidey vs. Green Goblin; back-up stories by various 10.00
50-($5.99) Last Remains; Dr. Strange app.; Kindred revealed as Harry Osborn 6.00
51-54,57-62,64-66: 51-54-Last Remains. 58,59-Mr. Negative app. 61-New costume 4.00
53.LR,54.LR-($3.99) Last Remains; Order of the Web vs. Kindred 4.00
55-Last Remains ends 24.00
56-($4.99) Last Remains Post Mortem; Norman Osborn, Kingpin app.; Bagley-a 5.00
63,67-($4.99) 63-King's Ransom pt. 1. 67-Chameleon Conspiracy pt. 1 5.00
68-73,76-92: 71-73-Sinister War. 77,78-Pichelli-a; Morbius app. 81-Miles app. 4.00
74-(11/21, $9.99) End of the Kindred saga; Mephisto app.; back-up with Ben Reilly 10.00
75-($5.99) Beyond pt. 1; Wells-s/Gleason-a; Ben Reilly back as Spider-Man 6.00
80.BEY-($4.99) Aunt May meets with Otto Octavius; Fiorelli-a 5.00
88.BEY-($4.99) The Slingers app.; Hobie Brown as The Hornet 5.00
92.BEY-($4.99) Morbius & Monica Rambeau app. 5.00
93-($5.99) Peter Parker vs. Ben Reilly 6.00
Annual 1 (11/18, $4.99) Flashback to early days with the black costume (Venom) 5.00
Annual 2 (9/21, $4.99) Infinite Destinies tie-in; Star app.; Pacheco-s/Carlini-a 5.00
...: Full Circle 1 (12/19, $9.99) Seven creative teams with successive chapters of 1 story; Hickman, Duggan, Zdarsky & others-s/Bachalo, Allred, Bagley & others-a 10.00
...: Going Big 1 (11/19, $4.99) Conway-s/Bagley-a; Macchio-s/Nauck-a; Larsen-s/a 5.00
...: Sins Rising Prelude 1 (9/20, $4.99) Spencer-s/Sanna-a; story of the Sin-Eater 5.00
...: The Sins of Norman Osborn 1 (11/20, $4.99) Spencer-s/Vicentini-a; leads into #49 5.00

AMAZING SPIDER-MAN
Marvel Comics: Jun, 2022 - Present ($5.99/$3.99)

1-($5.99) Zeb Wells-s/John Romita Jr.-a; Tombstone app. 6.00
2-5,7-13-($3.99) 5-Black Cat app. 7,8-Vulture app. 8-1st Spider-Glider. 9-Wolverine app. 4.00
6-($9.99) Legacy issue #900; The Sinister Seven app.; McGuinness-a 10.00
14-($4.99) Dark Web begins; Ben Reilly & Madelyne Pryor app. 5.00
15-20: 15-18-Dark Web; McGuinness-a. 19,20-Black Cat app.; Dodson-a 4.00

AMAZING SPIDER-MAN & SILK: THE SPIDER(FLY) EFFECT
Marvel Comics: May, 2016 - No. 4, Aug, 2016 ($4.99, limited series)

1-4: 1-Robbie Thompson-s/Todd Nauck-a; time-travelling Peter & Silk meet Ben Parker 1 2 3 5 6 8

AMAZING SPIDER-MAN EXTRA! (Continued from Spider-Man: Brand New Day - Extra!! #1)
Marvel Comics: No. 2, Mar, 2009 - No. 3, May, 2009 ($3.99)

2,3: 2-Anti-Venom app.; Bachalo-a. 3-Ana Kraven app.; Jimenez-a 4.00

AMAZING SPIDER-MAN FAMILY (Also see Spider-Man Family)
Marvel Comics: Oct, 2008 - No. 8, Sept, 2009 ($4.99, anthology)

1-8-New tales and reprints. 1-Includes r/ASM #300; Granov-c. 2-Deodato-c. 5-Spider-Girl

Amazing Spider-Man #700 © MAR

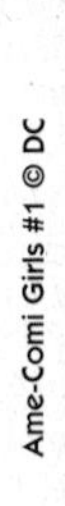

Ame-Comi Girls #1 © DC

America #10 © MAR

GD 2.0 VG 4.0 FN 6.0 VF 8.0 VF/NM 9.0 NM- 9.2

new story. 6-Origin of Jackpot 5.00

AMAZING SPIDER-MAN PRESENTS: AMERICAN SON
Marvel Comics: Jul, 2010 - No. 4, Oct, 2010 ($3.99, limited series)

1-4-Reed-s/Briones-a/Djurdjevic-c; Gabriel Stacy app. 4.00

AMAZING SPIDER-MAN PRESENTS: ANTI-VENOM - NEW WAYS TO LIVE
Marvel Comics: Nov, 2009 - No. 3, Feb, 2010 ($3.99, limited series)

1-3-Wells-s/Siqueira-a; Punisher app. 4.00

AMAZING SPIDER-MAN PRESENTS: JACKPOT
Marvel Comics: Mar, 2010 - No. 3, Jun, 2010 ($3.99, limited series)

1-3-Guggenheim-s/Melo-a; Boomerang and White Rabbit app. 4.00

AMAZING SPIDER-MAN: RENEW YOUR VOWS (Secret Wars tie-in)
Marvel Comics: Aug, 2015 - No. 5, Nov, 2015 ($3.99, limited series)

1-5-Adam Kubert-a; wife Mary Jane and daughter Annie app. 1-Venom app. 4.00

AMAZING SPIDER-MAN: RENEW YOUR VOWS (Series) (Leads into Spider-Girls #1)
Marvel Comics: Jan, 2017 - No. 23, Nov, 2018 ($4.99/$3.99)

1-($4.99) Conway-s/Stegman-a; Mole Man app.; back-up Holden-s/a; Leth-s/Sauvage-a 5.00
2-23-($3.99) 6,7-X-Men & Magneto app. 8,9-Venom app. 13-Jumps to 8 years later 4.00

AMAZING SPIDER-MAN: THE DAILY BUGLE
Marvel Comics: Mar, 2020 - No. 5 ($3.99, limited series)

1,2-Mat Johnson-s/Mack Chater-a 4.00

AMAZING SPIDER-MAN: THE MOVIE
Marvel Comics: Aug, 2012 - No. 2, Aug, 2012 ($3.99, limited series)

1,2-Partial adaptation of the 2012 movie; Neil Edwards-a; photo covers 4.00

AMAZING SPIDER-MAN: THE MOVIE ADAPTATION
Marvel Comics: Mar, 2014 - No. 2, Apr, 2014 ($2.99, limited series)

1,2-Adaptation of the 2012 movie; Wellington Alves-a; photo covers 3.00

AMAZING SPIDER-MAN: VENOM INC. (Crossover with ASM #792,793 & Venom #159,160)
Marvel Comics: 2018 ($4.99, bookends of crossover series)

... Alpha 1 (2/18, $4.99) Part 1 of x-over; Stegman-a; Eddie Brock & Anti-Venom app. 5.00
... Omega 1 (3/18, $4.99) Concluding Part 6 of x-over; Stegman-a 5.00

AMAZING SPIDER-MAN: WAKANDA FOREVER (Crossover with Wakanda Forever title)
Marvel Comics: Aug, 2018 ($4.99, one-shot)

1-Spider-Man teams with Dora Milaje; Nnedi Okorafor-s/Rafael Albuquerque-a 5.00

AMAZING WILLIE MAYS, THE
Famous Funnies Publ.: No date (Sept, 1954)

nn 87 174 261 553 952 1350

AMAZING WORLD OF DC COMICS
DC Comics: Jul, 1974 - No. 17, 1978 ($1.50, B&W, mail-order DC Pro-zine)

1-Kubert interview; unpublished Kirby-a; Infantino-c 7 14 21 46 86 125
2-4: 3-Julie Schwartz profile. 4-Batman; Robinson-c 5 10 15 33 57 80
5-Sheldon Mayer 5 10 15 30 50 70
6,8,13: 6-Joe Orlando; EC-r; Wrightson pin-up. 8-Infantino; Batman-r from Pop Tart giveaway. 13-Humor; Aragonés-c; Wood/Ditko-a; photos from serials of Superman, Batman, Captain Marvel 4 8 12 23 37 50
7,10-12: 7-Superman; r/1955 Pep comic giveaway. 10-Behind the scenes at DC; Showcase article. 11-Super-Villains; unpubl. Secret Society of S.V. story. 12-Legion; Grell-c/interview; 4 8 12 25 40 55
9-Legion of Super-Heroes; lengthy bios and history; Cockrum-c 7 14 21 46 86 125
14-Justice League 4 8 12 27 44 60
15-Wonder Woman; Nasser-c 5 10 15 31 53 75
16-Golden Age heroes 5 10 15 30 50 70
17-Shazam; G.A., '70s, TV and Fawcett heroes 4 8 12 27 44 60
Special 1 (Digest size) 3 6 9 21 33 45

AMAZING WORLD OF GUMBALL, THE (Based on the Cartoon Network series)
Boom Entertainment (kaBOOM!): Jun, 2014 - No. 8, Mar, 2015 ($3.99)

1-8-Multiple covers on each 4.00
... 2015 Grab Bag Special (9/15, $4.99) Short stories and pin-ups by various; 3 covers 5.00
... 2015 Special (1/15, $4.99) Short stories by various; 3 covers 5.00
... 2016 Grab Bag Special (8/16, $4.99) Short stories and pin-ups by various 5.00
... 2017 Grab Bag Special (8/17, $7.99) Short stories and pin-ups by various 8.00
... 2018 Grab Bag Special (8/18, $7.99) Short stories by various; Aguirre-c 8.00
... Spring Break Smash 1 (2/19, $7.99) Short stories by various 8.00

AMAZING WORLD OF SUPERMAN (See Superman)

AMAZING X-MEN
Marvel Comics: Mar, 1995 - No. 4, July, 1995 ($1.95, limited series)

1-Age of Apocalypse; Andy Kubert-c/a 6.00
2-4 4.00

AMAZING X-MEN
Marvel Comics: Jan, 2014 - No. 19, Jun, 2015 ($3.99)

1-19: 1-Nightcrawler returns; Aaron-s/McGuinness-a; wraparound-c. 7-Firestar, Iceman and Spider-Man app. 8-12-World War Wendigo. 19-Colossus vs. The Juggernaut 4.00
Annual 1 (8/14, $4.99) Larroca-a/c; back-up w/Juan Doe-a 5.00

AMAZON, THE
Comico: Mar, 1989 - No. 3, May, 1989 ($1.95, limited series)

1-3: Ecological theme; Steven Seagle-s/Tim Sale-a 5.00
1-3-(Dark Horse, 3/09 - No. 3, 5/09, $3.50) recolored reprint with creator interviews 3.50

AMAZON (Also see Marvel Versus DC #3 & DC Versus Marvel #4)
DC Comics (Amalgam): Apr, 1996 ($1.95, one-shot)

1-John Byrne-c/a/scripts 6.00

AMAZON ATTACK 3-D
The 3-D Zone: Sept, 1990 ($3.95, 28 pgs.)

1-Chaykin-a 6.00

AMAZONS ATTACK (See Wonder Woman #8 - 2006 series)
DC Comics: Jun, 2007 - No. 6, Late Oct, 2007 ($2.99, limited series)

1-6-Queen Hippolyta and Amazons attacks Wash., DC; Pfeifer-s/Woods-a 3.00

AMAZON WOMAN (1st Series)
FantaCo: Summer, 1994 - No. 2, Fall, 1994 ($2.95, B&W, limited series, mature)

1,2: Tom Simonton-c/a/scripts 3 6 9 14 19 24

AMAZON WOMAN (2nd Series)
FantaCo: Feb, 1996 - No. 4, May, 1996 ($2.95, B&W, limited series, mature)

1-4: Tom Simonton-a/scripts 2 4 6 11 16 20
...: Invaders of Terror ('96, $5.95) Simonton-a/s 2 4 6 8 12 15

AMBER BLAKE
IDW Publishing: Feb, 2019 - No. 4, May, 2019 ($3.99, oversized 8-3/8" x 11", limited series)

1-4:-Jade Lagardére-s/Butch Guice-a; 2 covers on each 3.00

AMBUSH BUG (Also see Son of...)
DC Comics: June, 1985 - No. 4, Sept, 1985 (75¢, limited series)

1-4: Giffen-c/a in all 5.00
Nothing Special 1 (9/92, $2.50, 68 pg.)-Giffen-c/a 5.00
Stocking Stuffer (2/86, $1.25)-Giffen-c/a 5.00

AMBUSH BUG: YEAR NONE
DC Comics: Sept, 2008 - No. 5, Jan, 2009; No. 7, Dec, 2009 ($2.99, limited series, no #6)

1-5,7-Giffen-s/a; Jonni DC app. 4-Conner-c. 7-Baltazar & Franco-a; Giffen-a 3.00

AME-COMI GIRLS (Based on the Anime-styled statue series)
DC Comics: Dec, 2012 - No. 5, Apr, 2013 ($3.99, printed version of digital-first series)

1-Wonder Woman; Conner-c/a 2 4 6 8 10 12
1-Variant-c by Dustin Nguyen 5 10 15 35 63 90
2-5: 2-Batgirl. 3-Duela Dent; Naifeh-a 4.00

AME-COMI GIRLS (Based on the Anime-styled statue series)
DC Comics: May, 2013 - No. 8, Dec, 2013 ($3.99)

1-8: 1-Palmiotti & Gray-s/Francisco-a; story continues from earlier series 4.00

AMERICA (From Young Avengers and The Ultimates)
Marvel Comics: May, 2017 - No. 12, Apr, 2018 ($3.99)

1-12: 1-Gabby Rivera-s/Joe Quinones-a; Captain Marvel & Spectrum app. 2-Moon Girl app. 3-Storm & the X-Men app. 4.00

AMERICA AT WAR - THE BEST OF DC WAR COMICS (See Fireside Book Series)

AMERICA CHAVEZ: MADE IN THE USA (From Young Avengers and The Ultimates)
Marvel Comics: May, 2021 - No. 5, Oct, 2021 ($3.99)

1-5-Kalinda Vasquez-s/Carlos Gómez-a. 1-Kate Bishop & Spider-Man app. 4.00

AMERICA IN ACTION
Dell (Imp. Publ. Co.)/ Mayflower House Publ.: 1942; Winter, 1945 (36 pgs.)

1942-Dell-(68 pgs.) 21 42 63 122 199 275
1-(1945)-Has 3 adaptations from American history; Kiefer, Schrotter & Webb-a 15 30 45 88 137 185

AMERICAN, THE
Dark Horse Comics: July, 1987 - No. 8, 1989 ($1.50/$1.75, B&W)

1-8: ($1.50) 3.00
Collection ($5.95, B&W)-Reprints 6.00
Special 1 (1990, $2.25, B&W) 3.00

GD 2.0 | VG 4.0 | FN 6.0 | VF 8.0 | VF/NM 9.0 | NM- 9.2

AMERICAN AIR FORCES, THE (See A-1 Comics)
William H. Wise(Flying Cadet Publ. Co./Hasan(No.1)/Life's Romances/ Magazine Ent. No. 5 on): Sept-Oct, 1944-No. 4, 1945; No. 5, 1951-No. 12, 1954
1-Article by Zack Mosley, creator of Smilin' Jack; German war-c 53 106 159 334 567 800
2-Classic-Japan war-c 161 322 483 1030 1765 2500
3-Japan war-c 30 60 90 177 289 400
4-Japan war-c 22 44 66 128 209 290
NOTE: *All part comic, part magazine. Art by* **Whitney, Chas. Quinlan, H. C. Kiefer**, *and* **Tony Dipreta**.
5(A-1 45)(Formerly Jet Powers), 6(A-1 54), 7(A-1 58), 8(A-1 65), 9(A-1 67), 10(A-1 74), 11(A-1 79), 12(A-1 91) 11 22 33 62 86 110
NOTE: **Powell** *c/a-5-12.*

AMERICAN CARNAGE
DC Comics (Vertigo): Jan, 2019 - No. 9, Sept, 2019 ($3.99)
1-9: 1-Bryan Hill-s/Leandro Fernandez-a 4.00

AMERICAN CENTURY
DC Comics (Vertigo): May, 2001 - No. 27, Oct, 2003 ($2.50/$2.75)
1-Chaykin-s/painted-c; Tischman-s; Laming-a 4.00
2-27: 5-New story arc begins. 10-16,22-27-Orbik-c. 17-21-Silke-c. 18-$2.75-c begins 3.00
Hollywood Babylon (2002, $12.95, TPB) r/#5-9; w/sketch-to-art pages 13.00
Scars & Stripes (2001, $8.95, TPB) r/#1-4; Tischman intro. 9.00

AMERICAN DREAM (From the M2 Avengers)
Marvel Comics: Jul, 2008 - No. 5, Sept, 2008 ($2.99, limited series)
1-5-DeFalco-s/Nauck-a 3.00

AMERICAN FLAGG! (See First Comics Graphic Novel 3,9,12,21 & Howard Chaykin's..)
First Comics: Oct, 1983 - No. 50, Mar, 1988
1,21-27: 1-Chaykin-c/a begins. 21-27-Alan Moore scripts 4.00
2-20,28-49: 31-Origin Bob Violence 3.00
50-Last issue 4.00
Special 1 (11/86)-Introduces Chaykin's Time2 4.00
...: Hard Times TPB (6/85, $11.95) r/#1-7; intro. by Michael Moorcock; bonus materials 12.00
...: Definitive Collection Volume 1 HC (2008, $49.99) r/#1-14 and material from the...: Hard Times TPB; intro by Michael Chabon; afterword by Jim Lee 50.00

AMERICAN FREAK: A TALE OF THE UN-MEN
DC Comics (Vertigo): Feb, 1994 - No. 5, Jun, 1994 ($1.95, mini-series, mature)
1-5 3.00

AMERICAN GODS (Based on the Neil Gaiman novel)
Dark Horse Comics: Mar, 2017 - No. 9, Nov, 2017 ($3.99)
1-9: 1-Gaiman & Russell-s/Scott Hampton-a. 3-Simonson-a (4 pgs). 4-Doran-a (9 pgs.) 4.00

AMERICAN GODS: MY AINSEL (Based on the Neil Gaiman novel)
Dark Horse Comics: Mar, 2018 - No. 9, Dec, 2018 ($3.99)
1-9: 1-Gaiman & Russell-s/Scott Hampton-a. 5-Buckingham-a 4.00

AMERICAN GODS: THE MOMENT OF THE STORM (Based on the Neil Gaiman novel)
Dark Horse Comics: Apr, 2019 - No. 9, Jan, 2020 ($3.99)
1-9-Gaiman & Russell-s/Scott Hampton-a 4.00

AMERICAN GRAPHICS
Henry Stewart: No. 1, 1954; No. 2, 1957 (25¢)
1-The Maid of the Mist, The Last of the Eries (Indian Legends of Niagara) (sold at Niagara Falls) 16 32 48 94 147 200
2-Victory at Niagara & Laura Secord (Heroine of the War of 1812) 9 18 27 50 65 80

AMERICAN INDIAN, THE (See Picture Progress)

AMERICAN JESUS: REVELATION (Also see Chosen)
Image Comics: Oct, 2022 - No. 3, Jan, 2023 ($3.99, limited series)
1-3-Mark Millar-s/Peter Gross-a 4.00

AMERICAN JESUS: THE NEW MESSIAH (Also see Chosen)
Image Comics: Dec, 2019 - No. 3, Feb, 2020 ($3.99, limited series)
1-3-Mark Millar-s/Peter Gross-a 4.00

AMERICAN LIBRARY
David McKay Publ.: 1943 - No. 6, 1944 (15¢, 68 pgs., B&W, text & pictures)
nn (#1)-Thirty Seconds Over Tokyo (movie) 48 96 144 302 514 725
nn (#2)-Guadalcanal Diary; painted-c (only 10¢) 36 72 108 211 343 475
3-6: 3-Look to the Mountain. 4-Case of the Crooked Candle (Perry Mason). 5-Duel in the Sun. 6-Wingate's Raiders 18 36 54 105 165 225

AMERICAN: LOST IN AMERICA, THE
Dark Horse Comics: July, 1992 - No. 4, Oct, 1992 ($2.50, limited series)
1-4: 1-Dorman painted-c. 2-Phillips painted-c. 3-Mignola-c. 4-Jim Lee-c 3.00

AMERICAN MONSTER
AfterShock Comics: Jan, 2016 - No. 6, May, 2017 ($3.99)
1-6-Brian Azzarello-s/Juan Doe-a 4.00

AMERICAN MYTHOLOGY ARCHIVES: LAUREL AND HARDY
American Mythology Prods.: 2020 ($3.99)
1-Reprints Laurel and Hardy #1 (1972) 4.00

AMERICAN MYTHOLOGY ARCHIVES PRESENTS ZORRO
American Mythology Prods.: 2019 ($3.99)
1-Reprints Four Color #882; art by Alex Toth 4.00

AMERICAN MYTHOLOGY DARK: WEREWOLVES VS DINOSAURS
American Mythology Prods.: 2016 - No. 2, 2017 ($3.99)
1,2-Chris Scalf & Eric Dobson-s/a; 3 covers 4.00

AMERICAN RONIN
AWA Inc.: Oct, 2020 - No. 5 ($3.99, limited series)
1-4-Peter Milligan-s/Aco-a 4.00

AMERICAN SPLENDOR: (Series of titles)
Dark Horse Comics: Aug, 1996 - Apr, 2001 (B&W, all one-shots)
--**COMIC-CON COMICS** (8/96) 1-H. Pekar script. --**MUSIC COMICS** (11/97) nn-H. Pekar-s/ Sacco-a; r/Village Voice jazz strips. --**ODDS AND ENDS** (12/97) 1-Pekar-s. --**ON THE JOB** (5/97) 1-Pekar-s. --**A STEP OUT OF THE NEST** (8/94) 1-Pekar-s. --**TERMINAL** (9/99) 1-Pekar-s. --**TRANSATLANTIC** (7/98) 1-"American Splendour" on cover; Pekar-s 3.00
--**A PORTRAIT OF THE AUTHOR IN HIS DECLINING YEARS** (4/01, $3.99) 1-Photo-c. --**BEDTIME STORIES** (6/00, $3.95) 4.00

AMERICAN SPLENDOR
DC Comics: Nov, 2006 - No. 4, Feb, 2007 ($2.99, B&W)
1-4-Pekar-s/art by Haspiel and various. 1-Fabry-c 3.00
...: Another Day TPB (2007, $14.99) r/#1-4 15.00

AMERICAN SPLENDOR (Volume 2)
DC Comics (Vertigo): Jun, 2008 - No. 4, Sept, 2008 ($2.99, B&W)
1-4-Pekar-s/art by Haspiel and various. 1-Bond-c. 3-Cooke-c 3.00
...: Another Dollar TPB (2009, $14.99) r/#1-4 15.00

AMERICAN SPLENDOR: UNSUNG HERO
Dark Horse Comics: Aug, 2002 - No. 3, Oct, 2002 ($3.99, B&W, limited series)
1-3-Pekar script/Collier-a; biography of Robert McNeill 4.00
TPB (8/03, $11.95) r/#1-3 12.00

AMERICAN SPLENDOR: WINDFALL
Dark Horse Comics: Sept, 1995 - No. 2, Oct,1995 ($3.95, B&W, limited series)
1,2-Pekar script 4.00

AMERICAN TAIL: FIEVEL GOES WEST, AN
Marvel Comics: Early Jan, 1992 - No. 3, Early Feb, 1992 ($1.00, limited series)
1-3-Adapts Universal animated movie; Wildman-a 4.00
1-($2.95-c, 69 pgs.) Deluxe squarebound edition 5.00

AMERICAN VAMPIRE
DC Comics (Vertigo): May, 2010 - No. 34, Feb, 2013 ($3.99/$2.99)
1-Snyder-s/Albuquerque-a; back-up story by Stephen King 2 4 6 10 14 18
1-5-Variant-c: 1-Jim Lee. 2-Berni Wrightson. 3-Andy Kubert. 5-Paul Pope 2 4 6 9 13 16
2-10: 2-9-Snyder-s/Albuquerque-a. 2-5-Back-up story by Stephen King continues 5.00
11-34-($2.99) 11-Santolouco-a. 12-Zezelj-a. 19-21-Bernet-a 3.00
... Anthology 1 (10/13, $7.99) Short stories by various; Albuquerque-c 8.00
...: The Long Road to Hell 1 (8/13, $6.99) Snyder-s/Albuquerque-a 7.00
HC (2010, $24.99, d.j.) r/#1-5; intro. by Stephen King; script pages and sketch art 25.00
...Volume Two HC (2011, $24.99, d.j.) r/#6-11; cover design art 25.00

AMERICAN VAMPIRE: LORD OF NIGHTMARES
DC Comics (Vertigo): Aug, 2012 - No. 5, Dec, 2012 ($2.99, limited series)
1-5-Set in 1954 England; Snyder-s/Nguyen-a/c. 2-Origin of Dracula 3.00

AMERICAN VAMPIRE: 1976
DC Comics (Vertigo): Dec, 2020 - No. 10, Oct, 2021 ($3.99/$4.99, limited series)
1-9-($3.99) Snyder-s/Albuquerque-a/c 4.00
10-($4.99) 5.00

AMERICAN VAMPIRE: SECOND CYCLE
DC Comics (Vertigo): May, 2014 - No. 11, Jan, 2016 ($3.99/$2.99, limited series)
1,8-10-($3.99) Snyder-s/Albuquerque-a/c 4.00
2-7-($2.99) 5-Bergara-a 3.00
11-($4.99) Snyder-s/Albuquerque-a/c 5.00

AMERICAN VAMPIRE: SURVIVAL OF THE FITTEST
DC Comics (Vertigo): Aug, 2011 - No. 5, Dec, 2011 ($2.99, limited series)
1-5-Set during WWII; Snyder-s/Murphy-a/c 3.00

AMERICAN VIRGIN
DC Comics (Vertigo): May, 2006 - No. 23, Mar, 2008 ($2.99)
1-23-Steven Seagle-s/Becky Cloonan-a in most. 1-3-Quitely-c. 4-14-Middleton-c 3.00
...: Head (2006, $9.99, TPB) r/#1-4; interviews with the creators and page development 10.00
...: Going Down (2007, $14.99, TPB) r/#5-9 15.00
...: Wet (2007, $12.99, TPB) r/#10-14 13.00
...: Around the World (Vol. 4) (2008, $17.99, TPB) r/#15-23 18.00

AMERICAN WAY, THE
DC Comics (WildStorm): Apr, 2006 - No. 8, Nov, 2006 ($2.99, limited series)
1-8-John Ridley-s/Georges Jeanty-a/c 3.00

AMERICAN WAY, THE: THOSE ABOVE AND THOSE BELOW
DC Comics (Vertigo): Sept, 2017 - No. 6, Apr, 2018 ($3.99, limited series)
1-6-John Ridley-s/Georges Jeanty-a/c; sequel set in 1972 4.00

AMERICA'S BEST COMICS
Nedor/Better/Standard Publications: Feb, 1942; No. 2, Sept, 1942 - No. 31, July, 1949 (New logo with #9)
1-The Woman in Red, Black Terror, Captain Future, Doc Strange, The Liberator, & Don Davis, Secret Ace begin 400 800 1200 2800 4900 7000
2-Origin The American Eagle; The Woman in Red ends 187 374 561 1197 2049 2900
3-Pyroman begins (11/42, 1st app.; also see Startling Comics #18, 12/42) 174 348 522 1114 1907 2700
4-6: 5-Last Capt. Future (not in #4); Lone Eagle app. 6-American Crusader app. 135 270 405 864 1482 2100
7-Hitler, Mussolini & Hirohito-c 389 778 1167 2723 4762 6800
8-Last Liberator 161 322 483 1030 1765 2500
9-The Fighting Yank begins; The Ghost app. 142 284 426 909 1555 2200
10-Flag-c 161 322 483 1030 1765 2500
11-Hirohito & Tojo-c. (10/44) 219 438 657 1402 2401 3400
12 118 236 348 742 1271 1800
13-Japanese WWII-c 135 270 405 864 1482 2100
14-17: 14-American Eagle ends; Doc Strange vs. Hitler story 84 168 252 538 919 1300
18-Classic-c 129 258 387 826 1413 2000
19-21: 21-Infinity-c 71 142 213 454 777 1100
22-Capt. Future app. 63 126 189 403 689 975

American Monster #1 © Brian Azzarello

America's Best Comics #35 © Nedor

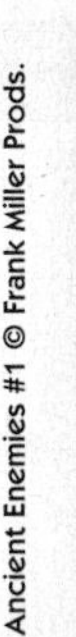

Ancient Enemies #1 © Frank Miller Prods.

	GD 2.0	VG 4.0	FN 6.0	VF 8.0	VF/NM 9.0	NM- 9.2

23-Miss Masque begins; last Doc Strange 116 232 348 742 1271 1800
24-Miss Masque bondage-c 110 220 330 704 1202 1700
25-Last Fighting Yank; Sea Eagle app. 74 148 222 470 810 1150
26-Miss Masque motorcycle-c; The Phantom Detective & The Silver Knight app.; Frazetta text illo & some panels in Miss Masque 123 246 369 787 1344 1900
27-31: 27,28-Commando Cubs. 27-Doc Strange. 28-Tuska Black Terror. 29-Last Pyroman 63 126 189 403 689 975

NOTE: *American Eagle not in 3, 8, 9, 13. Fighting Yank not in 10, 12. Liberator not in 2, 6, 7. Pyroman not in 9, 11, 14-16, 23, 25-27.* ***Schomburg (Xela)*** *c-5, 7-31. Bondage c-18, 24.*

AMERICA'S BEST COMICS
America's Best Comics: 1999 - 2008

... Preview (1999, Wizard magazine supplement) - Previews Tom Strong, Top Ten, Promethea, Tomorrow Stories 3.00
... Primer (2008, $4.99, TPB) r/Tom Strong #1, Tom Strong's Terrific Tales, Top Ten #1, Promethea #1, Tomorrow Stories #1,6 5.00
... Sketchbook (2002, $5.95, square-bound)-Design sketches by Sprouse, Ross, Adams, Nowlan, Ha and others 6.00
Special 1 (2/01, $6.95)-Short stories of Alan Moore's characters; art by various; Ross-c 7.00
TPB (2004, $17.95) Reprints short stories and sketch pages from ABC titles 18.00

AMERICA'S BEST TV COMICS (TV)
American Broadcasting Co. (Prod. by Marvel Comics): 1967 (25¢, 68 pgs.)

1-Spider-Man, Fantastic Four (by Kirby/Ayers), Casper, King Kong, George of the Jungle, Journey to the Center of the Earth stories (promotes new TV cartoon show) 10 20 30 69 147 225

AMERICA'S BIGGEST COMICS BOOK
William H. Wise: 1944 (196 pgs., one-shot)

1-The Grim Reaper, The Silver Knight, Zudo, the Jungle Boy, Commando Cubs, Thunderhoof app. 57 114 171 362 619 875

AMERICA'S FUNNIEST COMICS
William H. Wise: 1944 - No. 2, 1944 (15¢, 80 pgs.)

nn(#1), 2-Funny Animal 27 54 81 158 259 360

AMERICA'S GOT POWERS
Image Comics: Apr, 2012 - No. 7, Oct, 2013 ($2.99, limited series)

1-7-Jonathan Ross-s/Bryan Hitch-a/c. 1-Wraparound-c 3.00

AMERICA'S GREATEST COMICS
Fawcett Publications: May?, 1941 - No. 8, Summer, 1943 (15¢, 100 pgs., soft cardboard-c)

1-Bulletman, Spy Smasher, Capt. Marvel, Minute Man & Mr. Scarlet begin; Classic Mac Raboy-c. 1st time that Fawcett's major super-heroes appear together as a group on a cover. Fawcett's 1st squarebound comic 360 720 1080 2520 4410 6300
2 155 310 465 992 1696 2400
3 119 238 357 762 1306 1850
4,5: 4-Commando Yank begins; Golden Arrow, Ibis the Invincible & Spy Smasher cameo in Captain Marvel 81 162 243 518 884 1250
6,7: 7-Balbo the Boy Magician app.; Captain Marvel, Bulletman cameo in Mr. Scarlet 71 142 213 454 777 1100
8-Capt. Marvel Jr. & Golden Arrow app.; Spy Smasher x-over in Capt. Midnight; no Minute Man or Commando Yank 74 148 222 470 810 1150

AMERICA'S SWEETHEART SUNNY (See Sunny, ...)

AMERICA VS. THE JUSTICE SOCIETY
DC Comics: Jan, 1985 - No. 4, Apr, 1985 ($1.00, limited series)

1-Double size; Alcala-a(i) in all 2 4 6 8 10 12
2-4: 3,4-Spectre cameo 1 2 3 5 7 9

AMERICOMICS
Americomics: April, 1983 - No. 6, Mar, 1984 ($2.00, Baxter paper/slick paper)

1-Intro/origin The Shade; Intro. The Slayer, Captain Freedom and The Liberty Corps; Perez-c 5.00
1,2-2nd printings ($2.00) 3.00
2-6: 2-Messenger app. & 1st app. Tara on Jungle Island. 3-New & old Blue Beetle battle. 4-Origin Dragonfly & Shade. 5-Origin Commando D. 6-Origin the Scarlet Scorpion 3.00
Special 1 (8/83, $2.00)-Sentinels of Justice (Blue Beetle, Captain Atom, Nightshade & The Question) 5.00

AMETHYST
DC Comics: Jan, 1985 - No. 16, Aug, 1986 (75¢)

1-16: 8-Fire Jade's i.d. revealed 3.00
Special 1 (10/86, $1.25) 4.00
1-4 (11/87 - 2/88)(Limited series) 3.00

AMETHYST (Princess of Gemworld)(Also see Young Justice)
DC Comics (Wonder Comics): Apr, 2020 - No. 6, Feb, 2021 ($3.99)

1-6: 1-Amy Reeder-s/a; origin re-told in flashback 4.00

AMETHYST, PRINCESS OF GEMWORLD (See Legion of Super-Heroes #298)
DC Comics: May, 1983 - No. 12, Apr, 1984 (Maxi-series)

1-(60¢) 2 4 6 8 10 12
1,2-(35¢): tested in Austin & Kansas City 6 12 18 40 73 105
2-12, Annual 1(9/84): 5-11-Pérez-c(p) 4.00

NOTE: *Issues #1 & 2 also have Canadian variants with a 75¢ cover price.*

AMORY WARS (Based on the Coheed and Cambria album The Second Stage Turbine Blade)
Image Comics: Jun, 2007 - No. 5, Jan, 2008 ($2.99, limited series)

1-5: 1-Claudio Sanchez-s/Gus Vasquez-a 3.00

AMORY WARS II
Image Comics: Jun, 2008 - No. 5, Oct, 2008 ($2.99, limited series)

1-5-Claudio Sanchez-s/Gabriel Guzman-a 3.00

AMORY WARS: GOOD APOLLO, I'M BURNING STAR IV
BOOM! Studios: Apr, 2017 - No. 12, Oct, 2018 ($3.99)

1-12: 1-Claudio Sanchez & Chondra Echert-s/Rags Morales-a. 1-Four covers 4.00

AMORY WARS IN KEEPING SECRETS OF SILENT EARTH: 3
BOOM! Studios: May, 2010 - No. 12, Jun, 2011 ($3.99)

1-12: 1-Claudio Sanchez & Peter David-s/Chris Burnham-a. 1-Four covers 4.00

AMY RACECAR COLOR SPECIAL (See Stray Bullets)
El Capitán Books: July, 1997; Oct, 1999 ($2.95/$3.50)

1,2-David Lapham-a/scripts. 2-($3.50) 3.50

ANALOG
Image Comics: Apr, 2018 - No. 10, Mar, 2020 ($3.99)

1-10-Gerry Duggan-s/David O'Sullivan-a 4.00

ANARCHO DICTATOR OF DEATH (See Comics Novel)

ANARKY (See Batman titles)
DC Comics: May, 1997 - No. 4, Aug, 1997 ($2.50, limited series)

1 3.50
2-4 3.00

ANARKY (See Batman titles)
DC Comics: May, 1999 - No. 8, Dec, 1999 ($2.50)

1-8: 1-JLA app.; Grant-s/Breyfogle-a. 3-Green Lantern app. 7-Day of Judgment; Haunted Tank app. 8-Joker-c/app. 3.00

ANCHORS ANDREWS (The Saltwater Daffy)
St. John Publishing Co.: Jan, 1953 - No. 4, July, 1953 (Anchors the Saltwater... No. 4)

1-Canteen Kate by Matt Baker (9 pgs.) 36 72 108 211 343 475
2-4 14 28 42 80 115 150

ANCIENT ENEMIES
Frank Miller Presents: 2022 - No. 6 ($5.99, limited series)

1-($7.99) DiDio-s/Beyruth-a 8.00
2-($5.99) DiDio-s/Beyruth-a 6.00

ANDY & WOODY (See March of Comics No. 40, 55, 76)

ANDY BURNETT (TV, Disney)
Dell Publishing Co.: Dec, 1957

Four Color 865-Photo-c 9 18 27 57 111 165

ANDY COMICS (Formerly Scream Comics; becomes Ernie Comics)
Current Publications (Ace Magazines): No. 20, June, 1948-No. 21, Aug, 1948

20,21: Archie-type comic 18 36 54 105 165 225

ANDY DEVINE WESTERN
Fawcett Publications: Dec, 1950 - No. 2, 1951

1-Photo-c 47 94 141 296 498 700
2-Photo-c 32 64 96 192 314 435

ANDY GRIFFITH SHOW, THE (TV)(1st show aired 10/3/60)
Dell Publishing Co.: #1252, Jan-Mar, 1962; #1341, Apr-Jun, 1962

Four Color 1252(#1) 42 84 126 311 706 1100
Four Color 1341-Photo-c 36 72 108 266 596 925

ANDY HARDY COMICS (See Movie Comics #3 by Fiction House)
Dell Publishing Co.: April, 1952 - No. 6, Sept-Nov, 1954

Four Color 389(#1) 7 14 21 46 86 125
Four Color 447,480,515, #5,#6 5 10 15 30 50 70

ANDY PANDA (Also see Crackajack Funnies #39, The Funnies, New Funnies & Walter Lantz...)
Dell Publishing Co.: 1943 - No. 56, Nov-Jan, 1961-62 (Walter Lantz)

	GD	VG	FN	VF	VF/NM	NM-
	2.0	4.0	6.0	8.0	9.0	9.2
Four Color 25(#1, 1943)	50	100	150	390	870	1350
Four Color 54(1944)	25	50	75	175	388	600
Four Color 85(1945)	15	30	45	103	227	350
Four Color 130(1946),154,198	10	20	30	70	150	230
Four Color 216,240,258,280,297	8	16	24	55	105	155
Four Color 326,345,358	6	12	18	41	76	110
Four Color 383,409	5	10	15	35	63	90
16(11-1/52-53) - 30	4	8	12	28	47	65
31-56	4	8	12	23	37	50

(See March of Comics #5, 22, 79, & Super Book #4, 15, 27.)

A-NEXT (See Avengers)
Marvel Comics: Oct, 1998 - No. 12, Sept, 1999 ($1.99)

1-Next generation of Avengers; Frenz-a 1 3 4 6 8 10
2,3,5,6,8-11: 2-Two covers. 3-Defenders app. 3.00
4-1st app. American Dream 2 4 6 8 12 15
7-1st app. of Hope Pym 2 4 6 11 16 20
12-1st full app. of Hope Pym 1 3 4 6 8 10
Spider-Girl Presents Avengers Next Vol. 1: Second Coming (2006, $7.99, digest) r/#1-6 2 4 6 8 12 15

ANGEL
Dell Publishing Co.: Aug, 1954 - No. 16, Nov-Jan, 1958-59

Four Color 576(#1, 8/54) 5 10 15 34 60 85
2(5-7/55) - 16 3 6 9 17 26 35

ANGEL (TV) (Also see Buffy the Vampire Slayer)
Dark Horse Comics: Nov, 1999 - No. 17, Apr, 2001 ($2.95/$2.99)

1-17: 1-3,5-7,10-14-Zanier-a. 1-4,7,10-Matsuda & photo-c. 16-Buffy-c/app. 3.00
...: Earthly Possessions TPB (4/01, $9.95) r/#5-7, photo-c 10.00
...: Surrogates TPB (12/00, $9.95) r/#1-3; photo-c 10.00

ANGEL (Buffy the Vampire Slayer)
Dark Horse Comics: Sept, 2001 - No. 4, May, 2002 ($2.99, limited series)

1-4-Joss Whedon & Matthews-s/Rubi-a; photo-c and Rubi-c on each 3.00

ANGEL (Buffy the Vampire Slayer) (Previously titled Angel: After the Fall)
IDW Publishing: No. 18, Feb, 2009 - No. 44, Apr, 2011 ($3.99)

18-44: Multiple covers on all. 25-Juliet Landau-s 4.00

ANGEL (one-shots) (Buffy the Vampire Slayer)
IDW Publishing: ($3.99/$7.49)

...: Connor (8/06, $3.99) Jay Faerber-s/Bob Gill-a; 4 covers + 1 retailer cover 4.00
...: Doyle (7/06, $3.99) Jeff Mariotte-s/David Messina-a; 4 covers + 1 retailer cover 4.00
...: Gunn (5/06, $3.99) Dan Jolley-s/Mark Pennington-a; 4 covers + 2 retailer covers 4.00
...: Illyria (4/06, $3.99) Peter David-s/Nicola Scott-a; 4 covers + 2 retailer covers 4.00
...: Masks (10/06, $7.49) short stories of Angel, Illyria, Cordilia & Lindsay; puppet Angel app. 8.00
... 100-Page Spectacular (4/11, $7.99) reprints of 4 issues; Runge-c 8.00
... Special • Lorne (3/10, $7.99) John Byrne-s/a; The Groosalugg app. 8.00
Team Angel 100-Page Spectacular (4/11, $7.99) reprints; Runge-c 8.00
...: Vs. Frankenstein (10/09, $3.99) John Byrne-s/a/c 4.00
...: Vs. Frankenstein II (10/10, $3.99) John Byrne-s/a/c 4.00
...: Wesley (6/06, $3.99) Scott Tipton-s/Mike Norton-a; 4 covers + 1 retailer cover 4.00
Spotlight TPB (12/06, $19.99) r/Connor, Doyle, Gunn, Illyria & Wesley one-shots 20.00
... Yearbook (5/11, $7.99) short stories by various; 3 covers 8.00

ANGEL (Buffy the Vampire Slayer)(Title changes to Angel + Spike with #9)
BOOM! Studios: No. 0, Apr, 2019 - No. 8, Jan, 2020 ($3.99)

0-Bryan Edward Hill-s/Gleb Melnikov-a; Angel in Los Angeles; origin re-told 4.00
1-8: 1-(5/19). 3-Intro. Fred. 4-Intro. Gunn. 5-8-Hellmouth tie-ins with Buffy 4.00

ANGEL (Buffy the Vampire Slayer)
BOOM! Studios: Jan, 2022 - Present ($3.99)

1-8-Cantwell-s/Bayliss-a 4.00

ANGELA
Image Comics (Todd McFarlane Prod.): Dec, 1994 - No. 3, Feb, 1995 ($2.95, lim. series)

1-Gaiman scripts & Capullo-c/a in all; Spawn app. 2 4 6 9 12 15
2 6.00
3 5.00
Special Edition (1995)-Pirate Spawn-c 3 6 9 16 23 30
Special Edition (1995)-Angela-c 3 6 9 16 23 30
TPB ($9.95, 1995) reprints #1-3 & Special Ed. w/additional pin-ups 10.00

ANGELA: ASGARD'S ASSASSIN (The Image Comics character in the Marvel Universe)
Marvel Comics: Feb, 2015 - No. 6, Jul, 2015 ($3.99)

1-6: 1-Gillen-s/Jimenez-a; multiple covers. 4-6-Guardians of the Galaxy app. 4.00

ANGEL: AFTER THE FALL (Buffy the Vampire Slayer) (Follows the last TV episode)
IDW Publishing: Nov, 2007 - No. 17, Feb, 2009 ($3.99)(Continues as Angel with #18)

1-Whedon & Lynch-s; multiple covers 5.00
2-17: Multiple covers on all 4.00

ANGELA/GLORY: RAGE OF ANGELS (See Glory/Angela: Rage of Angels)
Image Comics (Todd McFarlane Productions): Mar, 1996 ($2.50, one-shot)

1-Liefeld-c/Cruz-a(p); Darkchylde preview flip book 4.00
1-Variant-c 4.00

ANGEL: A HOLE IN THE WORLD (Adaptation of the 2-part TV episode)
IDW Publishing: Dec, 2009 - No. 5, Apr, 2010 ($3.99, limited series)

1-5-Fred becomes Illyria; Casagrande-a/c 4.00

ANGEL & FAITH (Follows Buffy the Vampire Slayer Season Eight)
Dark Horse Comics: Aug, 2011 - No. 25, Aug, 2013 ($2.99)

1-Gage-s/Isaacs-a; two covers by Morris & Chen 3.00
2-25-Two covers by Morris & Isaacs. 5-Harmony & Clem app.; Noto-a. 7-Drusilla app. 11-14-Willow & Connor app. 20-Spike app.; Archie style-c 3.00

ANGEL & FAITH SEASON 10 (Buffy the Vampire Slayer)
Dark Horse Comics: Apr, 2014 - No. 25, Apr, 2016 ($3.50/$3.99)

1-15-Two covers on each. 1-Gischler-s/Conrad-a. 5-Santacruz-a. 6-10-Amy app. 10-Fred returns 3.50
16-25-($3.99) 17-Drusilla returns 4.00

ANGEL AND THE APE (Meet Angel No. 7) (See Limited Collector's Edition C-34 & Showcase #77)
National Periodical Publications: Nov-Dec, 1968 - No. 6, Sept-Oct, 1969

1-(11-12/68)-Not Wood-a 6 12 18 38 69 100
2-5-Wood inks in all. 4-Last 12¢ issue 4 8 12 25 40 55
6-Wood inks 4 8 12 28 47 65

ANGEL AND THE APE (2nd Series)
DC Comics: Mar, 1991 - No. 4, June, 1991 ($1.00, limited series)

1-4 5.00

ANGEL AND THE APE (3rd Series)
DC Comics (Vertigo): Oct, 2001 - No. 4, Jan 2002 ($2.95, limited series)

1-4-Chaykin & Tischman-s/Bond-a/Art Adams-c 3.00

ANGELA: QUEEN OF HEL (The Image Comics character in the Marvel Universe)
Marvel Comics: Dec, 2015 - No. 7, Jun, 2016 ($3.99)

1-5: 1-Bennett-s/Jacinto & Hans-a. 4,5-Hela app. 6,7-Thor (Jane) app. 4.00

ANGEL: AULD LANG SYNE (Buffy the Vampire Slayer)
IDW Publishing: Nov, 2006 - No. 5, Mar, 2007 ($3.99, limited series)

1-5: 1-Three covers plus photo-c; Tipton-s/Messina-a 4.00

ANGEL: BARBARY COAST (Buffy the Vampire Slayer)
IDW Publishing: Apr, 2010 - No. 3, Jun, 2010 ($3.99, limited series)

1-3-Angel in 1906 San Francisco; Tischman-s/Urru-a; 2 covers on each 4.00

ANGEL: BLOOD & TRENCHES (Buffy the Vampire Slayer)
IDW Publishing: Mar, 2009 - No. 4, June, 2009 ($3.99, B&W&Red, limited series)

1-4-Angel in World War II Europe; John Byrne-s/a/c 4.00

ANGEL: ILLYRIA: HAUNTED (Buffy the Vampire Slayer)
IDW Publishing: Nov, 2010 - No. 4, Feb, 2011 ($3.99, limited series)

1-4-Tipton & Huehner-s/Casagrande-a; 2 covers 4.00

ANGEL LOVE
DC Comics: Aug, 1986 - No. 8, Mar, 1987 (75¢, limited series)

1-8, Special 1 (1987, $1.25, 52 pgs.) 4.00

ANGEL: NOT FADE AWAY (Buffy the Vampire Slayer)
IDW Publishing: May, 2009 - No. 3, July, 2009 ($3.99, limited series)

1-3-Adaptation of TV show's final episodes; Mooney-a 4.00

ANGEL OF LIGHT, THE (See The Crusaders)

ANGEL: OLD FRIENDS (Buffy the Vampire Slayer)
IDW Publishing: Nov, 2005 - No. 5, Mar, 2006 ($3.99, limited series)

1-5: Four covers plus photo-c on each; Mariotte-s/Messina-a; Gunn, Spike and Illyria app. 4.00
... Cover Gallery (6/06, $3.99) gallery of variant covers for the series 4.00
... Cover Gallery (12/06, $3.99) gallery of variant covers; preview of Angel: Auld Lang Syne 4.00
TPB (2006, $19.99) r/series; gallery of Messina covers 20.00

ANGEL: ONLY HUMAN (Buffy the Vampire Slayer)
IDW Publishing: Aug, 2009 - No. 5, Dec, 2009 ($3.99, limited series)

1-5-Lobdell-s/Messina-a; covers by Messina and Dave Dorman 4.00

ANGEL + SPIKE (Buffy the Vampire Slayer)(Title changed from Angel after #8)
BOOM! Studios: No. 9, Feb, 2020 - No. 16, Nov, 2020 ($3.99)

9-16: 9-12-Hill-s/Melnikov-a. 13-Kowalski-a. 14-16-Sherman-a 4.00

ANGEL: REVELATIONS (X-Men character)
Marvel Comics: July, 2008 - No. 5, Nov, 2008 ($3.99, limited series)

1-5-Origin from childhood re-told; Adam Pollina-a/Aguirre-Sacasa-s 4.00

ANGEL SEASON 11 (Buffy the Vampire Slayer)
Dark Horse Comics: Jan, 2017 - No. 12, Dec, 2017 ($3.99)

1-12: 1-4-Bechko-s/Borges-a; Fred & Illyria app. 4.00

ANGEL: SMILE TIME (Buffy the Vampire Slayer)
IDW Publishing: Dec, 2008 - No. 3, Apr, 2009 ($3.99, limited series)

1-3-Adaptation of TV episode; Messina-a; Messina and photo covers for each 4.00

ANGEL: THE CURSE (Buffy the Vampire Slayer)
IDW Publishing: June, 2005 - No. 5, Oct, 2005 ($3.99, limited series)

1-5-Four covers on each; Mariotte-s/Messina-a 4.00
TPB (1/06, $19.99) r/#1-5; cover gallery of Messina covers 20.00

ANGELTOWN
DC Comics (Vertigo): Jan, 2005 - No. 5, May, 2005 ($2.95, limited series)

1-5-Gary Phillips-s/Shawn Martinbrough-a 3.00

ANGELUS
Image Comics (Top Cow): Dec, 2007; Dec, 2009 - Nov, 2010 ($2.99)

... Pilot Season 1-(12/07) Sejic-a/c; Edington-s; origin re-told 3.00
1-6-Marz-s/Sejic-a; multiple covers on each 3.00

ANGRY BIRDS COMICS (Based on the Rovio videogame)(Also see Super Angry Birds)
IDW Publishing: Jun, 2014 - No. 12, Jun, 2015 ($3.99)

1-12-Short stories by Jeff Parker, Paul Tobin and various; wraparound-c on most 4.00
Volume 2 (1/16 - 12/16, $3.99) 1-12-Wraparound-c on all 4.00
...: Holiday Special (12/14, $5.99) Terence in charge of the North Pole 6.00
... Quarterly: Furious Fowl (8/17, $5.99) Short stories by various 6.00
... Quarterly: Monsters and Mistletoe (12/17, $5.99) Short stories by various 6.00

ANGRY BIRDS: FLIGHT SCHOOL (Based on the Rovio videogame)
IDW Publishing: Feb, 2017 - No. 3, Jun, 2017 ($3.99)

1-3-Short stories by various 4.00

ANGRY BIRDS GAME PLAY (Based on the Rovio videogame)
IDW Publishing: Jan, 2017 - No. 3, May, 2017 ($3.99)

1-3-Short stories by various; wraparound-c 4.00

ANGRY BIRDS TRANSFORMERS (Based on the Rovio videogame)
IDW Publishing: Nov, 2014 - No. 4, Feb, 2015 ($3.99, limited series)

Angel & Faith #25 © 20-FOX

Angry Birds Comics #6 © Rovio

Animosity #7 © Marguerite Bennett

	GD	VG	FN	VF	VF/NM	NM-
	2.0	4.0	6.0	8.0	9.0	9.2

1-4-Barber-s; the Eggspark lands on Piggy Island 4.00

ANGRY CHRIST COMIX (See Cry For Dawn)

ANIMA
DC Comics: Mar, 1994 - No. 15, July, 1995 ($1.75/$1.95/$2.25)

1-7,0,8-15: 7-(9/94)-Begin $1.95-c; Zero Hour tie-in. 0-(10/94) released between #7 & #8 3.00

ANIMAL ADVENTURES
Timor Publications/Accepted Publ. (reprints): Dec, 1953 - No. 3, May?, 1954

1-Funny animal 11 22 33 62 86 110
2,3: 2-Featuring Soopermutt (2/54) 8 16 24 42 54 65
1-3 (reprints, nd) 4 7 9 14 16 18

ANIMAL ANTICS
DC Comics: Feb, 1946

nn - Ashcan comic, not distributed to newsstands, only for in-house use. Cover art is Star Spangled Comics #49 and interior is Boy Commandos #12; a NM cover sold for $1000 in 2012, and FN/VF copy sold for $1553.50 in 2012.

ANIMAL ANTICS (Movietown... No. 24 on)
National Periodical Publ: Mar-Apr, 1946 - No. 23, Nov-Dec, 1949 (All 52 pgs.?)

1-Raccoon Kids begins by Otto Feuer; many-c by Grossman; Seaman Sy Wheeler by Kelly in some issues; Grossman-a in most issues 58 116 174 371 636 900
2 26 52 78 154 252 350
3-10: 10-Post-c/a 18 36 54 103 162 220
11-23: 14,15,18,19-Post-a 14 28 42 76 108 140

ANIMAL COMICS
Dell Publishing Co.: Dec-Jan, 1941-42 - No. 30, Dec-Jan, 1947-48

1-1st Pogo app. by Walt Kelly (Dan Noonan art in most issues)
148 296 444 947 1624 2300
2-Uncle Wiggily begins 61 122 183 390 670 950
3,5 27 54 81 194 435 675
4,6,7-No Pogo 17 34 51 114 252 390
8-10 20 40 60 138 307 475
11-15 12 24 36 82 179 275
16-20 9 18 27 61 123 185
21-30: 24-30- "Jigger" by John Stanley 8 16 24 54 102 155
NOTE: *Dan Noonan a-18-30. Gollub art in most later issues; c-29, 30. Kelly c-7-26, part #27-30.*

ANIMAL CRACKERS (Also see Adventures of Patoruzu)
Green Publ. Co./Norlen/Fox Feat.(Hero Books): 1946; No. 31, July, 1950; No. 9, 1959

1-Super Cat begins (1st app.) 22 44 66 132 216 300
2 13 26 39 72 101 130
31(Fox)-Formerly My Love Secret 10 20 30 54 72 90
9(1959-Norlen)-Infinity-c 6 12 18 28 34 40
nn, nd ('50s), no publ.; infinity-c 6 12 18 28 34 40

ANIMAL FABLES
E. C. Comics (Fables Publ. Co.): July-Aug, 1946 - No. 7, Nov-Dec, 1947

1-Freddy Firefly (clone of Human Torch), Korky Kangaroo, Petey Pig, Danny Demon begin 76 152 228 486 831 1175
2-Aesop Fables begin 43 86 129 271 461 650
3-6 39 78 117 240 395 550
7-Origin Moon Girl 97 194 291 621 1061 1500

ANIMAL FAIR (Fawcett's...)
Fawcett Publications: Mar, 1946 - No. 11, Feb, 1947

1-Hoppy the Marvel Bunny-c 34 68 102 199 325 450
2 16 32 48 92 144 195
3-6 14 28 42 76 108 140
7-11 10 20 30 58 79 100

ANIMAL FUN
Premier Magazines: 1953 (25¢, came w/glasses)

1-(3-D)-Ziggy Pig, Silly Seal, Billy & Buggy Bear 43 86 129 271 461 650

ANIMAL MAN (See Action Comics #552, 553, DC Comics Presents #77, 78, Last Days of Animal Man, Secret Origins #39, Strange Adventures #180 & Wonder Woman #267, 268)
DC Comics (Vertigo imprint #57 on): Sept, 1988 - No. 89, Nov, 1995 ($1.25/$1.50/$1.75/$1.95/$2.25, mature)

1-Grant Morrison scripts begin, ends #26 2 4 6 10 14 18
2-4,6-10: 2-Superman cameo. 6-Invasion tie-in. 9-Manhunter-c/story. 10-Psycho Pirate app.
1 2 3 4 5 7
5-Crafty Coyote 2 4 6 9 13 16
11-49,51-55,57-89: 23,24-Psycho Pirate app. 24-Arkham Asylum story; Bizarro Superman app. 25-Inferior Five app. 26-Morrison apps. in story; part photo-c (of Morrison?) 4.00
50-($2.95, 52 pgs.)-Last issue w/Veitch scripts 5.00
56-($3.50, 68 pgs.) 5.00
Annual 1 (1993, $3.95, 68 pgs.)-Bolland-c; Children's Crusade Pt. 3 6.00
...: Deus Ex Machina TPB (2003, $19.95) r/#18-26; Morrison-s; new Bolland-c 20.00
...: Origin of the Species TPB (2002, $19.95) r/#10-17 & Secret Origins #39 20.00
NOTE: *Bolland c-1-63. 71-Sutton-a(i)*

ANIMAL MAN (DC New 52)
DC Comics: Nov, 2011 - No. 29, May, 2014 ($2.99)

1-Jeff Lemire-s/Travel Foreman-a/c; 1st printing with yellow cover background 8.00
1-Second printing (red cover background), Third printing (grey cover background) 3.00
2-29: 2-4 Foreman-a. 5-Huat-a. 10 Justice League Dark app. 13-17-Rotworld 3.00
#0 (11/12, $2.99) Lemire-s/Pugh-a/c; Buddy Baker's origin re-told 3.00
Annual 1 (7/12, $4.99) Swamp Thing app.; Lemire-s/Green-a 5.00
Annual 2 (9/13, $4.99) Lemire-s/Foreman-a 5.00

ANIMAL MYSTIC (See Dark One...)
Cry For Dawn/Sirius: 1993 - No. 4, 1995 ($2.95?/$3.50, B&W)

1 1 2 3 5 6 8
1-Alternate 2 4 6 10 14 18
1-2nd printing 4.00
2 4.00
2,3-2nd prints (Sirius) 3.50
3,4: 4-Color poster insert, Linsner-s 4.00
TPB ($14.95) r/series 15.00

ANIMAL MYSTIC WATER WARS
Sirius: 1996 - No. 6, Oct, 1998 ($2.95, limited series)

1-6-Dark One-c/a/scripts 4.00

ANIMAL WORLD, THE (Movie)
Dell Publishing Co.: No. 713, Aug, 1956

Four Color 713 5 10 15 34 60 85

ANIMANIACS (TV)
DC Comics: May, 1995 - No. 59, Apr, 2000 ($1.50/$1.75/$1.95/$1.99)

1 3 6 9 14 19 24
2-10 1 3 4 6 8 10
11-20: 13-Manga issue. 19-X-Files parody; Miran Kim-c; Adlard-a (4 pgs.) 6.00
21-59: 26-E.C. parody-c. 34-Xena parody. 43-Pinky & the Brain take over 4.00
A Christmas Special (12/94, $1.50, "1" on-c) 3 6 9 14 19 24

ANIMATED COMICS
E. C. Comics: No date given (Summer, 1947?)

1 (Rare) Funny Animal 116 232 348 742 1271 1800

ANIMATED FUNNY COMIC TUNES (See Funny Tunes)

ANIMATED MOVIE-TUNES (Movie Tunes No. 3)
Margood Publishing Corp. (Timely): Fall, 1945 - No. 2, Sum, 1946

1,2-Super Rabbit, Ziggy Pig & Silly Seal 45 90 135 284 480 675

ANIMAX
Marvel Comics (Star Comics): Dec, 1986 - No. 4, June, 1987

1-4: Based on toys; Simonson-a 3.00

ANIMOSITY (Also see World of Animosity one-shot)
AfterShock Comics: Aug, 2016 - Present ($3.99)

1-Marguerite Bennett-s/Rafael de Latorre-a; 2 covers 15.00
2 8.00
3-28: 17-Savarese-a. 19-28-Thomasi-a 4.00
... Tales 1 (5/19, Free Comic Book Day giveaway) Bennett-s/Thomasi-a 3.00

ANIMOSITY: EVOLUTION
AfterShock Comics: Oct, 2017 - No. 10, Jan, 2019 ($3.99, limited series)

1-10-Bennett-s/Gapstur-a; San Francisco one month after the awakening 4.00

ANIMOSITY: THE RISE
AfterShock Comics: Jan, 2017 - No. 3, Sept, 2017 ($3.99, limited series)

1-3-Bennett-s/Juan Doe-a; the early days after the animals awoke 4.00

ANITA BLAKE (Circus of the Damned - The Charmer on cover)
Marvel Comics: July, 2010 - No. 5, Dec, 2010 ($3.99, limited series)

1-5-Laurell K. Hamilton & Jess Ruffner-s/Ron Lim-a/ Brett Booth-c 4.00
... - The Ingenue 1-5 (3/11 - No. 5, 10/11, $3.99) Hamilton & Ruffner-s/Lim-a/Booth-c 4.00
... - The Scoundrel 1-4 (11/11 - No. 5, 5/12, $3.99) Hamilton & Ruffner-s/Lim-a/Booth-c 4.00

ANITA BLAKE: VAMPIRE HUNTER GUILTY PLEASURES
Marvel Comics (Dabel Brothers): Dec, 2006 - No. 12, Aug, 2008 ($2.99)

1-Laurell K. Hamilton-s/Brett Booth-a; blue cover 6.00
1-Variant-c by Greg Horn 20.00

1-Sketch cover 25.00
1-2nd printing with red cover 3.00
2-Two covers 5.00
3-12 3.00
...: Handbook (2007, $3.99) profile pages of characters; glossary 4.00
... Volume One HC (6/07, $19.99, dust jacket) r/#1-6; cover gallery 20.00

ANITA BLAKE: VAMPIRE HUNTER THE FIRST DEATH, (LAURELL K. HAMILTON'S...)
Marvel Comics (Dabel Brothers): July, 2007 - No. 2, Dec, 2007 ($3.99)

1,2-Laurell K. Hamilton & Jonathon Green-s/Wellington Alves-a. 2-Marvel Zombie var-c 4.00
... HC (2008, $19.99, dust jacket) r/#1,2 & Guilty Pleasures Handbook 20.00

ANITA BLAKE, VAMPIRE HUNTER: THE LAUGHING CORPSE
Marvel Comics: Dec, 2008 - No. 5, Apr, 2009 ($3.99)

... - Book One (12/08 - No. 5, 4/09) 1-5-Laurell K. Hamilton-s/Ron Lim-a/c 4.00
... - Necromancer 1-5 (6/09 - No. 5, 11/09, $3.99) Lim-a/c 4.00
Anita Blake (Executioner on-c) #11-15 (12/09 - No. 15, 5/10) numbering continued; Lim-a 4.00

ANNE RICE'S INTERVIEW WITH THE VAMPIRE
Innovation Books: 1991 - No. 12, Jan, 1994 ($2.50, limited series)

1-Adapts novel; Moeller-a 2 4 6 8 10 12
2-12-Continues adaptation 4.00

ANNE RICE'S THE MASTER OF RAMPLING GATE
Innovation Books: 1991 ($6.95, one-shot)

1-Bolton painted-c; Colleen Doran painted-a 7.00

ANNE RICE'S THE MUMMY OR RAMSES THE DAMNED
Millennium Publications: Oct, 1990 - No. 12, Feb, 1992 ($2.50, limited series)

1-Adapts novel; Mooney-p in all 1 3 4 6 8 10
2-12-Continues adaptation 4.00

ANNE RICE'S THE WITCHING HOUR
Millennium Publ./Comico: 1992 - No. 13, Jan, 1993 ($2.50, limited series)

1-13 3.00

ANNETTE (Disney, TV)
Dell Publishing Co.: No. 905, May, 1958; No. 1100, May, 1960
(Mickey Mouse Club)

Four Color 905-Annette Funicello photo-c 24 48 72 168 372 575
Four Color 1100-...'s Life Story (Movie); A. Funicello photo-c
18 36 54 125 276 430

ANNEX (See Amazing Spider-Man Annual #27 for 1st app.)
Marvel Comics: Aug, 1994 - No. 4, Nov, 1994 ($1.75)

1-4: 1,4-Spider-Man app. 3.00

ANNIE
Marvel Comics Group: Oct, 1982 - No. 2, Nov, 1982 (60¢)

1,2-Movie adaptation 5.00
Treasury Edition ($2.50, tabloid size) 3 6 9 17 26 35

ANNIE OAKLEY (See Tessie The Typist #19, Two-Gun Kid & Wild Western)
Marvel/Atlas Comics(MPI No. 1-4/CDS No. 5 on): Spring, 1948 - No. 4, 11/48; No. 5, 6/55 - No. 11, 6/56

1 (1st Series, 1948)-Hedy Devine app. 84 168 252 538 919 1300
2 (7/48, 52 pgs.)-Kurtzman-a, "Hey Look", 1 pg; Intro. Lana; Hedy Devine app; Captain Tootsie by Beck 41 82 123 256 428 600
3,4 36 72 108 211 343 475
5 (2nd Series, 1955)-Reinman-a; Maneely-c 25 50 75 150 245 340
6-9: 6,8-Woodbridge-a. 9-Williamson-a (4 pgs.) 19 38 57 112 179 240
10,11: 11-Severin-c 19 38 57 112 179 240

ANNIE OAKLEY AND TAGG (TV)
Dell Publishing Co./Gold Key: 1953 - No. 18, Jan-Mar, 1959; July, 1965 (Gail Davis photo-c #3 on)

Four Color 438 (#1) 13 26 39 89 195 300
Four Color 481,575 (#2,3) 9 18 27 59 117 175
4(7-9/55)-10 7 14 21 46 86 125
11-18(1-3/59) 6 12 18 38 69 100
1(7/65-Gold Key)-Photo-c (c-r/#6) 4 8 12 27 44 60
NOTE: *Manning a-13. Photo back c-4, 9, 11.*

ANNIHILATION
Marvel Comics: May, 2006 - No. 6, Mar, 2007 ($3.99/$2.99, limited x-over series)

Prologue (5/06, $3.99, one-shot) Nova, Thanos and Silver Surfer app. 4.00
1-6: 1-(10/06) Giffen-s/DiVito-a; Annihilus app. 3.00
...: Heralds of Galactus 1,2 (4/07-5/07, $3.99) 2-Silver Surfer app. 4.00
...: Nova 1-4 (6/06-9/06, $2.99) Abnett & Lanning-s/Walker-a/Dell'Otto-c. 2,3-Quasar app. 3.00
...: Ronan 1-4 (6/06-9/06, $2.99) Furman-s/Lucas-a/Dell'Otto-c 3.00
... Saga (2007, $1.99) re-cap of the series; DiVito-c 3.00
...: Silver Surfer 1-4 (6/06-9/06, $2.99) Giffen-s/Arlem-a/Dell'Otto-c 3.00
...: Super-Skrull 1-4 (6/06-9/06, $2.99) Grillo-Marxuach-s/Titus-a/Dell'Otto-c 3.00
...: The Nova Corps Files (2006, $3.99) profile pages of characters and alien races 4.00
Annihilation Book 1 HC (2007, $29.99, dustjacket) r/Drax the Destroyer #1-4, Annihilation Prologue and Annihilation: Nova #1-4; sketch and layout pages 30.00
Annihilation Book 1 SC (2007, $24.99) same content as HC 25.00
Annihilation Book 2 HC (2007, $29.99, dustjacket) r/Annihilation: Silver Surfer #1-4, ...: Super Skrull #1-4 and ...: Ronan #1-4; sketch and layout pages 30.00
Annihilation Book 2 SC (2007, $24.99) same content as HC 25.00
Annihilation Book 3 HC (2007, $29.99, dustjacket) r/Annihilation #1-6, Annihilation: Heralds of Galactus #1,2 and Annihilation: Nova Corps Files; sketch pages 30.00
Annihilation Book 3 SC (2007, $24.99) same content as HC 25.00

ANNIHILATION: CONQUEST (Also see Nova 2007 series)
Marvel Comics: Jan, 2008 - No. 6, Jun, 2008 ($3.99/$2.99, limited x-over series)

Prologue (8/07, $3.99, one-shot) the new Quasar, Moondragon app.; Perkins-a
2 4 6 10 14 18
1-5-Raney-a; Ultron app. 3-Moondragon dies 5.00
6-($3.99) Guardians of the Galaxy team forms 5 10 15 35 63 90
... - Quasar 1-4 (9/07-No. 4, 12/07, $2.99) Gage-s/Lilly-a. 1-Super-Adaptoid app. 3.00
... - Starlord 1-4 (9/07-No. 4, 12/07, $2.99) Giffen-s/Green-a 6.00
... - Wraith 1-4 (9/07-No. 4, 12/07, $2.99) Hotz-a/Grillo-Marxuach-s 3.00
Annihilation: Conquest Book 1 HC (2008, $29.99, dustjacket) r/Prologue; ...Quasar #1-4, ...Star-Lord #1-4; Annihilation Saga; design pages 30.00

ANNIHILATION – SCOURGE
Marvel Comics: Jan, 2020 - Feb, 2020 ($4.99, limited series)

Alpha (1/20, $4.99) Annihilus, Blastaar, Nova, and The Sentry app. 5.00
Omega 1 (2/20, $4.99) Conclusion of series; Lockjaw, Beta Ray Bill, Fantastic Four app. 5.00
...: Beta Ray Bill 1 (2/20, $4.99) Lockjaw and The Sentry app. 5.00
...: Fantastic Four 1 (2/20, $4.99) Gage-s/Olortegui-a 5.00
...: Nova 1 (2/20, $4.99) Rosenberg-s/Roberson-a; Richard Rider app. 5.00
...: Silver Surfer 1 (2/20, $4.99) Abnett-s/Davidson-a; Surfer merges with Bob Reynolds 5.00

ANNIHILATOR
Legendary Comics: Sept, 2014 - No. 6, Jun, 2015 ($3.99)

1-6-Grant Morrison-s/Frazer Irving-a/c 4.00

ANNIHILATORS
Marvel Comics: May, 2011 - No. 4, Aug, 2011 ($4.99, limited series)

1-4: Quasar, Silver Surfer, Beta-Ray Bill, Ronan, Gladiator app.; Huat-a 5.00

ANNIHILATORS: EARTHFALL
Marvel Comics: Nov, 2011 - No. 4, Feb, 2012 ($3.99, limited series)

1-4-Avengers app.; Abnett & Lanning-s/Huat-a/Christopher-c 4.00

ANNO DRACULA: 1895 SEVEN DAYS IN MAYHEM (Based on the Kim Newman novels)
Titan Comics: Apr, 2017 - No. 5, Sept, 2017 ($3.99, limited series)

1-5-Kim Newman-s/Paul McCaffrey-a; multiple covers on each 4.00

ANOTHER WORLD (See Strange Stories From...)

ANSWER!, THE
Dark Horse Comics: Jan, 2013 - No. 4 ($3.99, limited series)

1-3-Dennis Hopeless-s/Mike Norton-a 4.00

ANT
Image Comics: Aug, 2005 - No. 11, Feb, 2007; No. 12, Jun, 2021 ($2.99)

1-11: 1-Mario Gully-s/a. 2-Savage Dragon & Spawn app. 3-Spawn-c/app. 3.00
12-(6/21, $3.99) Series finished by Erik Larsen-s/a; covers by Larsen & Gully 4.00
Vol. 1: Reality Bites TPB (2006, $12.99) r/#1-4; sketch and concept art 13.00

ANT
Image Comics: Oct, 2021 - Present ($3.99)

1-6: 1-Erik Larsen-s/a/c; bonus sketch and concept art. 3,5,6-Spawn app. 4.00

ANTHEM (Based on the Electronic Arts videogame)
Dark Horse Comics: Feb, 2019 - No. 3, May, 2019 ($3.99, limited series)

1-3-Freed-s/Francisco-a 4.00

ANTHRO (See Showcase #74)
National Periodical Publications: July-Aug, 1968 - No. 6, July-Aug, 1969

1-(7-8/68)-Howie Post-a in all 5 10 15 33 57 80
2-5: 5-Last 12¢ issue 3 6 9 21 33 45
6-Wood-c/a (inks) 4 8 12 25 40 55

ANTI-HITLER COMICS
New England Comics Press: Summer, 1992 ($2.75, B&W, one-shot)

1-Reprints Hitler as Devil stories from wartime comics 1 2 3 5 6 8

ANT-MAN (See Irredeemable Ant-Man, The)

ANT-MAN (Also see Astonishing Ant-Man)
Marvel Comics: Mar, 2015 - No. 5, Jul, 2015 ($3.99)

1-($4.99) Scott Lang as Ant-Man; Spencer-s/Rosanas-a; main-c by Brooks 5.00
2-5-($3.99) 2,3-Taskmaster app. 4-Darren Cross returns 4.00
Annual 1 (9/15, $4.99) Giant-Man & Egghead app.; intro. Raz Malhotra 5.00
...: Larger Than Life 1 (8/15, $3.99) movie Hank Pym story; r/Tales to Astonish #27 & #35 4.00
...: Last Days 1 (10/15, $3.99) Secret Wars tie-in; Spencer-s; Miss Patriot app. 4.00

ANT-MAN
Marvel Comics: Apr, 2020 - No. 5, Oct, 2020 ($3.99, limited series)

1-5-Wells-s/Burnett-a; Scott Lang & Stinger (Cassie). 3-Spider-Man & Black Cat app. 4.00

ANT-MAN
Marvel Comics: Sept, 2022 - No. 4, Dec, 2022 ($3.99, limited series)

1-4-Al Ewing-s/Tom Reilly-a. 2-Eric O'Grady app. 3-Scott Lang & Cassie app. 4-Intro/origin Zayn Asghar, the future Ant-Man; Ultron app. 4.00

ANT-MAN & THE WASP
Marvel Comics: Aug, 2018 - No. 5, Nov, 2018 ($3.99, limited series)

1-5-Waid-s/Garrón-a; Scott Lang & Nadia Van Dyne 4.00
...: Living Legends 1 (8/18, $3.99) Macchio-s/Di Vito-a; Scott Lang & Janet Van Dyne 4.00

ANT-MAN & WASP
Marvel Comics: Jan, 2011 - No. 3, Mar, 2011 ($3.99, limited series)

1-3-Tim Seeley-s/a; Espin-c; Tigra app. 5.00

ANT-MAN'S BIG CHRISTMAS
Marvel Comics: Feb, 2000 ($5.95, square-bound, one-shot)

1-Bob Gale-s/Phil Winslade-a; Avengers app. 6.00

ANT-MAN: SEASON ONE
Marvel Comics: 2012 ($24.99, hardcover graphic novel)

HC - Origin story; DeFalco-s/Domingues-a/Tedesco painted-c 25.00

ANTONY AND CLEOPATRA (See Ideal, a Classical Comic)

ANYTHING GOES
Fantagraphics Books: Oct, 1986 - No. 6, 1987 ($2.00, #1-5 color & B&W/#6 B&W, lim. series)

1-6: 1-Flaming Carrot app. (1st in color?); G. Kane-c. 2-6: 2-Miller-c(p); Alan Moore scripts; Kirby-a; early Sam Kieth-a (2 pgs.). 3-Capt. Jack, Cerebus app.; Cerebus-c by N. Adams. 4-Perez-c. 5-3rd color Teenage Mutant Ninja Turtles app. 4.00

A-1
Marvel Comics (Epic Comics): 1992 - No. 4, 1993 ($5.95, limited series, mature)

Annie Oakley #9 © MAR

Ant-Man (2022) #1 © MAR

Apache Kid #17 © MAR

	GD 2.0	VG 4.0	FN 6.0	VF 8.0	VF/NM 9.0	NM- 9.2

1-4: 1-Fabry-c/a, Russell-a, S. Hampton-a. 3-Bisley-c; Kent Williams-a.
4-McKean-a; Dorman-s/a 1 2 3 4 5 7

A-1 COMICS (A-1 appears on covers No. 1-17 only)(See individual title listings for #11-139) (1st two issues not numbered.)
Life's Romances Publ.-No. 1/Compix/Magazine Ent.: 1944 - No. 139, Sept-Oct, 1955 (No #2)

nn-(1944) (See Kerry Drake Detective Cases)
1-Dotty Dripple (1 pg.), Mr. Ex, Bush Berry, Rocky, Lew Loyal (20 pgs.)
24 48 72 142 234 325
3-8,10: Texas Slim & Dirty Dalton, The Corsair, Teddy Rich, Dotty Dripple, Inca Dinca, Tommy Tinker, Little Mexico & Tugboat Tim, The Masquerader & others. 7-Corsair-c/s. 8-Intro Rodeo Ryan 14 28 42 80 115 150
9-All Texas Slim 14 28 42 81 118 155

(See Individual Alphabetical listings for prices)

11-Teena; Ogden Whitney-c
13-Guns of Fact & Fiction (1948). Used in **SOTI**, pg. 19; Ingels & Johnny Craig-a
17-Tim Holt #2; photo-c; last issue to carry A-1 on cover (9-10/48)
19-Tim Holt #3; photo-c
22-Dick Powell (1949)-Photo-c
23-Cowboys and Indians #6; Doc Holiday-c/story
25-Fibber McGee & Molly (1949) (Radio)
26-Trail Colt #2-Ingels-c
28-Christmas-(Koko & Kola #6) ("50)
30-Jet Powers #1-Powell-a
32-Jet Powers #2
33-Muggsy Mouse #1('51)
35-Jet Powers #3-Williamson/Evans-a
37-Ghost Rider #5-Frazetta-c (1951)
39-Muggsy Mouse #3
41-Cowboys 'N' Indians #7 (1951)
43-Dogface Dooley #2
45-American Air Forces #5-Powell-c/a
47-Thun'da, King of the Congo #1-Frazetta-c/a('52)
50-Danger Is Their Business #11 ('52)-Powell-a
53-Dogface Dooley #4
55-U.S. Marines #5-Powell-a
56-Thun'da #2-Powell-c/a
58-American Air Forces #7-Powell-a
60-The U.S. Marines #6-Powell-a
62-Starr Flagg, Undercover Girl #5 (#1) reprinted from A-1 #24
65-American Air Forces #8-Powell-a
67-American Air Forces #9-Powell-a
69-Ghost Rider #9(10/52)
71-Ghost Rider #10(12/52)-Vs. Frankenstein
74-American Air Forces #10-Powell-a
76-Best of the West #7
78-Thun'da #4-Powell-c/a
80-Ghost Rider #12(6/52)-One-eyed Devil-c
83-Thun'da #5-Powell-c/a
84-Ghost Rider #13(7-8/53)
86-Thun'da #6-Powell-c/a
88-Bobby Benson's B-Bar-B Riders #20
90-Red Hawk #11(1953)-Powell-c/a
91-American Air Forces #12-Powell-a
93-Great Western #8('54)-Origin The Ghost Rider; Powell-a
95-Muggsy Mouse #4
96-Cave Girl #12, with Thun'da; Powell-c/a
99-Muggsy Mouse #5
101-White Indian #12-Frazetta-a(r)
101-Dream Book of Romance #6 (4-6/54); Marlon Brando photo-c; Powell, Bolle, Guardineer-a
105-Great Western #9-Ghost Rider app.; Powell-a, 6 pgs.; Bolle-c
12,15-Teena
14-Tim Holt Western Adventures #1
16-Vacation Comics; The Pixies, Tom Tom, Flying Fredd, & Koko & Kola
18,20-Jimmy Durante; photo covers on both
21-Joan of Arc (1949)-Movie adaptation; Ingrid Bergman photo-covers & interior photos; Whitney-a
24-Trail Colt #1-Frazetta-r in-Manhunt #13; Ingels-c; L. B. Cole-a
27-Ghost Rider #1(1950)-Origin
29-Ghost Rider #2-Frazetta-c (1950)
31-Ghost Rider #3-Frazetta-c & origin ('51)
34-Ghost Rider #4-Frazetta-c (1951)
36-Muggsy Mouse #2; Racist-c
38-Jet Powers #4-Williamson/Wood-a
40-Dogface Dooley #1('51)
42-Best of the West #1-Powell-a
44-Ghost Rider #6
46-Best of the West #2
48-Cowboys 'N' Indians #8
49-Dogface Dooley #3
51-Ghost Rider #7 ('52)
52-Best of the West #3
54-American Air Forces #6(8/52)-Powell-a
57-Ghost Rider #8
59-Best of the West #4
61-Space Ace #5('53)-Guardineer-a
63-Manhunt #13-Frazetta
64-Dogface Dooley #5
66-Best of the West #5
68-U.S. Marines #7-Powell-a
70-Best of the West #6
72-U.S. Marines #8-Powell-a(3)
73-Thun'da #3-Powell-c/a
75-Ghost Rider #11(3/52)
77-Manhunt #14
79-American Air Forces #11-Powell-a
81-Best of the West #8
82-Cave Girl #11(1953)-Powell-c/a; origin (#1)
85-Best of the West #9
87-Best of the West #10(9-10/53)
89-Home Run #3-Powell-a; Stan Musial photo-c
92-Dream Book of Romance #5-Photo-c; Guardineer-a
94-White Indian #11-Frazetta-a(r); Powell-c
97-Best of the West #11
98-Undercover Girl #6-Powell-c
100-Badmen of the West #1-Meskin-a(?)
103-Best of the West #12-Powell-a
104-White Indian #13-Frazetta-a(r) ('54)
106-Dream Book of Love #1 (6-7/54) -Powell, Bolle-a; Montgomery Clift, Donna Reed photo-c
107-Hot Dog #1
108-Red Fox #15 (1954)-L.B. Cole-c/a; Powell-a
110-Dream Book of Romance #8 (10/54)-Movie photo-c
112-Ghost Rider #14 ('54)
114-Dream Book of Love #2- Guardineer, Bolle-a; Piper Laurie, Victor Mature photo-c
118-Undercover Girl #7-Powell-c
120-Badmen of the West #2
121-Mysteries of Scotland Yard #1; reprinted from Manhunt (5 stories)
124-Dream Book of Romance #8 (10-11/54)
126-I'm a Cop #2-Powell-a
128-I'm a Cop #3-Powell-a
130-Strongman #1-Powell-a (2-3/55)
132-Strongman #2
134-Strongman #3
136-Hot Dog #4
138-The Avenger #4-Powell-c/a
109-Dream Book of Romance #7 (7-8/54). Powell-a; movie photo-c
111-I'm a Cop #1 ('54); drug mention story; Powell-a
113-Great Western #10; Powell-a
115-Hot Dog #3
116-Cave Girl #13-Powell-c/a
117-White Indian #14
119-Straight Arrow's Fury #1 (origin); Fred Meagher-c/a
122-Black Phantom #1 (11/54)
123-Dream Book of Love #3 (10-11/54)-Movie photo-c
125-Cave Girl #14-Powell-c/a
127-Great Western #11('54)-Powell-a
129-The Avenger #1('55)-Powell-c
131-The Avenger #2('55)-Powell-c/a
133-The Avenger #3-Powell-c/a
135-White Indian #15
137-Africa #1-Powell-c/a(4)
139-Strongman #4-Powell-a

NOTE: *Bolle a-110. Photo-c-17-22, 89, 92, 101, 106, 109, 110, 114, 123, 124.*

APACHE
Fiction House Magazines: 1951

1 25 50 75 150 245 340
I.W. Reprint No. 1-r/#1 above 3 6 9 20 31 42

APACHE DELIVERY SERVICE
Dark Horse Comics: Jan, 2022 - No. 4, Apr, 2022 ($3.99, limited series)

1-4-Matt Kindt-s/Tyler Jenkins-a 4.00

APACHE KID (Formerly Reno Browne; Western Gunfighters #20 on)
(Also see Two-Gun Western & Wild Western)
Marvel/Atlas Comics(MPC No. 53-10/CPS No. 11 on): No. 53, 12/50 - No. 10, 1/52; No. 11, 12/54 - No. 19, 4/56

53(#1)-Apache Kid & his horse Nightwind (origin), Red Hawkins by Syd Shores begins
43 86 129 271 461 650
2(2/51) 20 40 60 117 189 265
3-5 15 30 45 86 133 180
6-10 (1951-52): 7-Russ Heath-a 14 28 42 80 115 150
11-19 (1954-56) 12 24 36 67 94 120

NOTE: ***Heath** a-7. c-11, 13. **Maneely** a-53; c-53(#1), 12, 14-16. **Powell** a-14. **Severin** c-17.*

APACHE MASSACRE (See Chief Victorio's...)

APACHE SKIES
Marvel Comics: Sept, 2002 - No. 4, Dec, 2002 ($2.99, limited series)

1-4-Apache Kid app.; Ostrander-s/Manco-c/a 3.00
TPB (2003, $12.99) r/#1-4 13.00

APACHE TRAIL
Steinway/America's Best: Sept, 1957 - No. 4, June, 1958

1 14 28 42 81 118 155
2-4: 2-Tuska-a 9 18 27 50 65 80

APE (Magazine)
Dell Publishing Co.: 1961 (52 pgs., B&W)

1-Comics and humor 5 10 15 31 53 75

APEX LEGENDS: OVERTIME (Based on the EA videogame)
Dark Horse Comics: Jun, 2021 - No. 4, Sept, 2022 ($3.99, limited series)

1-4-Jesse Stern-s/Neil Edwards-a 4.00

APHRODITE IX
Image Comics (Top Cow): Sept, 2000 - No. 4, Mar, 2002 ($2.50)

1-3: 1-Four covers by Finch, Turner, Silvestri, Benitez 4.00
1-Tower Record Ed.; Finch-c 3.00
1-DF Chrome ($14.99) 15.00
4-($4.95) Double-sized issue; Finch-c 5.00
Convention Preview 10.00
...: Time Out of Mind TPB (6/04, $14.99) r/#1-4, & #0; cover gallery 15.00
Wizard #0 (4/00, bagged w/Tomb Raider magazine) Preview & sketchbook 5.00
#0-(6/01, $2.95) r/Wizard #0 with cover gallery 3.00

APHRODITE IX (Volume 2)
Image Comics (Top Cow): May, 2013 - No. 11, Jun, 2014 ($2.99/$3.99)

1-Free Comic Book Day giveaway; Hawkins-s/Sejic-a 3.00

	GD 2.0	VG 4.0	FN 6.0	VF 8.0	VF/NM 9.0	NM- 9.2

2-10-($2.99) Hawkins-s/Sejic-a 3.00
11-($3.99) Leads into Aphrodite IX Cyber Force #1 4.00
...: Ares #1 (9/18, $3.99) Glaser-s/Knaepen-a; Marsh-s/Renna-a 4.00
... Cyber Force #1 (7/14, $5.99) Hawkins-s/Sejic-a; leads into IXth Generation #1 6.00
... Hidden Files 1 (1/14, $2.99) Character profiles; Sejic-a 3.00

APHRODITE V
Image Comics (Top Cow): Jul, 2018 - No. 4, Oct, 2018 ($3.99)
1-4-Bryan Hill-s/Jeff Spokes-a. 1-Origin re-told 4.00

A+X (Avengers Plus X-Men)
Marvel Comics: Dec, 2012 - No. 18, May, 2014 ($3.99)
1-18: 1-Hulk & Wolverine team-up; Keown-c. 2-Black Widow/Rogue; Bachalo-c/a. 14-Superior Spider-Man app. 4.00
1-Variant baby-c by Skottie Young 5.00

APOCALYPSE NERD
Dark Horse Comics: January, 2005 - No. 6, Oct, 2007 ($2.99, B&W)
1-6-Peter Bagge-s/a 3.00

APOLLO IX (See Aphrodite IX)
Image Comics (Top Cow): Aug, 2015 ($3.99, one-shot)
1-Ashley Robinson-s/Fernando Argosino-a; 2 covers 4.00

APPARITION
Caliber Comics: 1995 ($3.95, 52 pgs., B&W)
1 ($3.95) 4.00
V2#1-6 ($2.95) 3.00
Visitations 4.00

APPLESEED
Eclipse Comics: Sept, 1988 - Book 4, Vol. 4, Aug, 1991 ($2.50/$2.75/$3.50, 52/68 pgs, B&W)
Book One, Vol. 1-5: 5-(1/89), Book Two, Vol. 1(2/89) -5(7/89): Art Adams-c, Book Three, Vol. 1(8/89) -4 ($2.75), Book Three, Vol. 5 ($3.50), Book Four, Vol. 1 (1/91) - 4 (8/91) ($3.50, 68 pgs.) 1 3 4 6 8 10

APPLESEED DATABOOK
Dark Horse Comics: Apr, 1994 - No. 2, May, 1994 ($3.50, B&W, limited series)
1,2: 1-Flip book format 1 3 4 6 8 10

APPROVED COMICS (Also see Blue Ribbon Comics)
St. John Publishing Co. (Most have no c-price): March, 1954 - No. 12, Aug, 1954 (Painted-c on #1-5,7,8,10)

	GD	VG	FN	VF	VF/NM	NM-
1-The Hawk #5-r	14	28	42	76	108	140
2-Invisible Boy (3/54)-Origin; Saunders-c	20	40	60	114	182	250
3-Wild Boy of the Congo #11-r (4/54)	12	24	36	69	97	125
4,5: 4-Kid Cowboy-r. 5-Fly Boy-r	12	24	36	69	97	125
6-Daring Adv.-r (5/54); Krigstein-a(2); Baker-c	60	120	180	178	552	925
7-The Hawk #6-r	12	24	36	69	97	125
8-Crime on the Run (6/54); Powell-a; Saunders-c	12	24	36	69	97	125
9-Western Bandit Trails #3-r, with new-c; Baker-c/a	39	78	117	240	395	550
10-Dinky Duck (Terrytoons)	8	16	24	44	57	70
11-Fightin' Marines #3-r (8/54); Canteen Kate app; Baker-c/a	53	106	159	334	567	800
12-Northwest Mounties #4-r(8/54); new Baker-c	48	96	144	302	514	725

AQUAMAN (See Adventure Comics #260, Brave & the Bold, DC Comics Presents #5, DC Special #28, DC Special Series #1, DC Super Stars #7, Detective Comics, JLA, Justice League of America, More Fun #73, Showcase #30-33, Super DC Giant, Super Friends, and World's Finest Comics)

AQUAMAN (1st Series)
National Periodical Publications/DC Comics: Jan-Feb, 1962 - No. 56, Mar-Apr, 1971; No. 57, Aug-Sept, 1977 - No. 63, Aug-Sept, 1978

	GD	VG	FN	VF	VF/NM	NM-
1-(1-2/62)-Intro. Quisp	234	468	702	1931	4366	6800
2	38	76	114	281	628	975
3-5	22	44	66	154	340	525
6-10	15	30	45	100	220	340
11-1st app. Mera	111	222	333	888	1994	3100
12-17,19,20	12	24	36	79	170	260
18-Aquaman weds Mera; JLA cameo	18	36	54	122	271	420
21-28,30-32: 23-Birth of Aquababy. 26-Huntress app.(3-4/66). 30-Batman & Superman-c & cameo	8	16	24	55	105	155
29-1st app. Ocean Master, Aquaman's step-brother	44	88	132	326	738	1150
33-1st app. Aqua-Girl (see Adventure #266)	16	32	48	112	249	385
34,36-40: 40-Jim Aparo's 1st DC work (8/68)	7	14	21	46	86	125
35-1st app. Black Manta	71	142	213	568	1284	2000
41,43-46,47,49: 45-Last 12¢-c	6	12	18	38	69	100
42-Black Manta-c	13	26	39	91	201	310
48-Origin reprinted	7	14	21	46	86	125
50-52-Deadman by Neal Adams	8	16	24	56	108	160
53-56('71): 56-1st app. Crusader; last 15¢-c	4	8	12	23	37	50
57-('77) Black Manta-c	3	6	9	17	26	35
58-63: 58-Origin retold	2	4	6	10	14	18

...: Death of a Prince TPB (2011, $29.99) r/#58-63 and Adventure #435-437,441-455 30.00
NOTE: *Aparo a-40-45, 46p, 47-59; c-58-63.* ***Nick Cardy*** *c-1-40.* ***Newton*** *a-60-63.*

AQUAMAN (1st limited series)
DC Comics: Feb, 1986 - No. 4, May, 1986 (75¢, limited series)
1-New costume; 1st app. Nuada of Thierna Na Oge 2 4 6 9 12 15
2-4: 3-Retelling of Aquaman & Ocean Master's origins. 5.00
Special 1 (1988, $1.50, 52 pgs.) 5.00
NOTE: ***Craig Hamilton*** *c/a-1-4p.* ***Russell*** *c-2-4i.*

AQUAMAN (2nd limited series)
DC Comics: June, 1989 - No. 5, Oct, 1989 ($1.00, limited series)
1-Giffen plots/breakdowns; Swan-a(p) in all 6.00
2-5 4.00
Special 1 (Legend of..., $2.00, 1989, 52 pgs.)-Giffen plots/breakdowns; Swan-a(p) 4.00

AQUAMAN (2nd Series)
DC Comics: Dec, 1991 - No. 13, Dec, 1992 ($1.00/$1.25)
1 5.00
2-5 3.00
6-13: 6-Begin $1.25-c. 9-Sea Devils app. 3.00

AQUAMAN (3rd Series)(Also see Atlantis Chronicles)
DC Comics: Aug, 1994 - No. 75, Jan, 2001 ($1.50/$1.75/$1.95/$1.99/$2.50)
1-(8/94)-Peter David scripts begin; reintro Dolphin 6.00
2-(9/94)-Aquaman loses hand; continues in Aquaman #0 6.50
3-8: 3-(11/94)-Superboy-c/app. 4-Lobo app. 6-Deep Six app. 3.50
9-69: 9-Begin $1.75-c. 10-Green Lantern app. 11-Reintro Mera. 15-Re-intro Kordax. 16-vs. JLA. 18-Reintro Ocean Master & Atlan (Aquaman's father). 19-Reintro Garth (Aqualad). 23-1st app. Deep Blue (Neptune Perkins & Tsunami's daughter). 23,24-Neptune Perkins, Nuada, Tsunami, Arion, Power Girl, & The Sea Devils app. 26-Final Night. 28-Martian Manhunter-c/app. 29-Black Manta-c/app. 32-Swamp Thing-c/app. 37-Genesis x-over. 41-Maxima-c/app. 43-Millennium Giants x-over; Superman-c/app. 44-G.A. Flash & Sentinel app. 50-Larsen-s begins. 53-Superman app. 60-Tempest marries Dolphin; Teen Titans app. 63-Kaluta covers begin. 66-JLA app. 3.00
70-75: 70-Begin $2.50-c. 71-73-Warlord-c/app. 75-Final issue 3.00
#0-(10/94)-Aquaman replaces lost hand with hook; released between #2 & #3 6.50
#1,000,000 (11/98) 853rd Century x-over 3.00
Annual 1 (1995, $3.50)-Year One story 4.00
Annual 2 (1996, $2.95)-Legends of the Dead Earth story 4.00
Annual 3 (1997, $3.95)-Pulp Heroes story 4.00
Annual 4,5 ('98, '99, $2.95)-4-Ghosts; Wrightson-c. 5-JLApe 4.00
...Secret Files 1 (12/98, $4.95) Origin-s and pin-ups 5.00
NOTE: ***Art Adams****-c, Annual 5.* ***Mignola*** *c-6.* ***Simonson*** *c-15.*

AQUAMAN (4th Series)(Titled Aquaman: Sword of Atlantis #40-on) (Also see JLA #69-75)
DC Comics: Feb, 2003 - No. 57, Dec, 2007 ($2.50/$2.99)
1-Veitch-s/Guichet-a/Maleev-c 4.00
2-14: 2-Martian Manhunter app. 8-11-Black Manta app. 3.00
15-39: 15-San Diego flooded; Pfeifer-s/Davis-c begin. 23,24-Sea Devils app. 33-Mera returns. 39-Black Manta app. 3.00
40-Sword of Atlantis; One Year Later begins ($2.99-c) Guice-a ; two covers 4.00
41-49,51-57: 41-Two covers. 42-Sea Devils app. 44-Ocean Master app. 3.00
50-($3.99) Tempest app.; McManus-a 4.00
...Secret Files 2003 (5/03, $4.95) background on Aquaman's new powers; pin-ups 5.00
...: Once and Future TPB (2006, $12.99) r/#40-45 13.00
...: The Waterbearer TPB (2003, $12.95) r/#1-4, stories from Aquaman Secret Files and JLA/JSA Secret Files #1; JG Jones-c 13.00

AQUAMAN (DC New 52)
DC Comics: Nov, 2011 - No. 52, Jul, 2016 ($2.99/$3.99)
1-Geoff Johns-s/Ivan Reis-a/c 1 2 3 5 6 8
2-23,24,26-40: 7-13-Black Manta app. 14-17-Throne of Atlantis. 15,16-Justice League app. 24-Story of Atlan. 26-Pelletier-a. 31-Swamp Thing app. 37-Grodd app. 3.00
23.1, 23.2 (11/13, $2.99, regular covers) 3.00
23.1 (11/13, $3.99, 3-D cover) "Black Manta #1" on cover; Crime Syndicate app. 5.00
23.2 (11/13, $3.99, 3-D cover) "Ocean Master #1" on cover; Crime Syndicate app. 5.00
25-($3.99) "Death of a King" finale; last Johns-s 4.00
41-49,51,52: 41-($3.99-c begin) 4.00
50-($4.99) Booth-a 5.00
#0 (11/12, $2.99) Aquaman & Vulko's return to Atlantis; Johns-s/Reis-a/c 3.00
Annual 1 (12/13, $4.99) The Others app.; Pelletier-c/Ostrander-s 5.00
Annual 2 (9/14, $4.99) Wonder Woman app.; Parker-s/Guichet-a 5.00
...: Futures End 1 (11/14, $2.99, regular-c) Five years later; Jurgens-s 3.00
...: Futures End 1 (11/14, $3.99, 3-D cover) 4.00

AQUAMAN (DC Rebirth) (Also see Mera: Queen of Atlantis)
DC Comics: Aug, 2016 - No. 66, Feb, 2021 ($2.99/$3.99)
1-24: 1-Abnett-s/Walker-a; Black Manta app. 5,6-Superman app. 14,15-Black Manta app. 3.00
25-49-($3.99) 25-Sejic-a; leads into Justice League #24. 34-Kelley Jones-a. 39-X-over with Suicide Squad #45,46. 41,42-Drowned Earth. 43-DeConnick-s begin 4.00
50-($4.99) Black Manta returns; Wonder Woman app. 5.00
51-66: 51-54-Year of The Villain tie-ins; Black Manta app. 54-Acetate-c. 57-Princess Andy born. 57-61-Ocean Master app. 62,63-Black Manta app. 66-Endless Winter pt. 4 4.00
Annual 1 (1/18, $4.99) Fiumara-a; future Aquaman & Mera with son Tom 5.00
Annual 2 (12/19, $4.99) Year of the Villain tie-in; Aqualad app.; Ibáñez-a 5.00
.../ Jabberjaw Special 1 (7/18, $4.99) Abnett-s/Pelletier-a; back-up Capt. Caveman story 5.00
.../ Justice League: Drowned Earth Special 1 (1/19, $4.99) Leads into #43; Manapul-a 5.00
...: Rebirth (8/16, $2.99) Abnett-s/Eaton & Jiménez-a; Black Manta app. 3.00

AQUAMAN: ANDROMEDA
DC Comics (Black Label): Aug, 2022 - No. 3, Dec, 2022 ($6.99, oversized 8-1/2" x 10-3/4", limited series)
1-3-Ram V-s/Christian Ward-a; Black Manta app. 7.00

AQUAMAN & THE FLASH: VOIDSONG
DC Comics: Aug, 2022 - No. 3, Oct, 2022 ($6.99, squarebound, limited series)
1-3-Kelly & Lanzing-s/Georgiev-a 3.00

AQUAMAN AND THE OTHERS (DC New 52)
DC Comics: Jun, 2014 - No. 11, May, 2015 ($2.99)
1-11: 1-Jurgens-s/Medina-a 3.00
...: Futures End 1 (11/14, $2.99, regular-c) Five years later; Cont'd from Aquaman: FE #1 3.00
...: Futures End 1 (11/14, $3.99, 3-D cover) 4.00

AQUAMAN 80TH ANNIVERSARY 100-PAGE SUPER SPECTACULAR
DC Comics: Oct, 2021 ($9.99, squarebound, one-shot)
1-Short stories & pin-ups by various; Black Manta & Aqualad app.; multiple covers 10.00

AQUAMAN GIANT
DC Comics: 2019 - No. 4, 2020 ($4.99, 100 pgs., squarebound, Mass Market & Direct Market editions exist for each issue, with different covers)
1-4-Two new stories and reprints in each. 1-Black Manta app. 2-Sea Devils app. 5.00

AQUAMAN / GREEN ARROW - DEEP TARGET
DC Comics: Dec, 2021 - No. 7, Jun, 2022 ($3.99, limited series)
1-7-Thomas-s/Cliquet-a; Arthur Curry & Oliver Queen switch lives 4.00

AQUAMAN: THE BECOMING (Leads into Aquamen #1)
DC Comics: Nov, 2021 - No. 6, Apr, 2022 ($3.99, limited series)

Aquaman (2016) #6 © DC

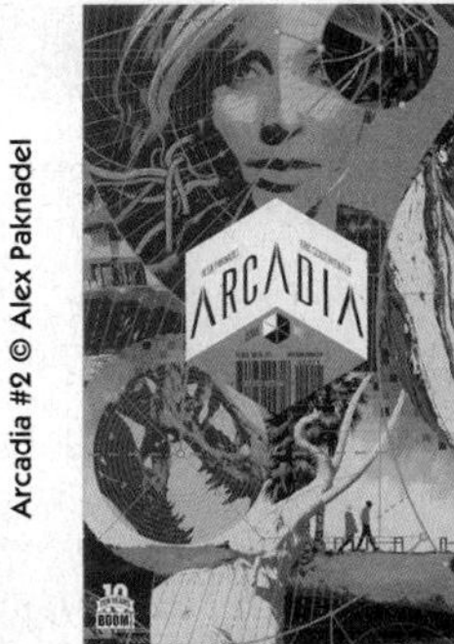

Arcadia #2 © Alex Paknadel

Archie (2015) #4 © ACP

GD VG FN VF VF/NM NM-
2.0 4.0 6.0 8.0 9.0 9.2

1-6-Spotlight on Aqualad Jackson Hyde. 3-Intro. Delilah 4.00

AQUAMAN: TIME & TIDE (3rd limited series) (Also see Atlantis Chronicles)
DC Comics: Dec, 1993 - No. 4, Mar, 1994 ($1.50, limited series)

1-4: Peter David scripts; origin retold. 3.00
Trade paperback ($9.95) 10.00

AQUAMEN (Follows Aquaman: The Becoming)
DC Comics: Feb, 2022 - No. 6, Sept, 2022 ($3.99, limited series)

1-6-Aquaman, Aqualad Jackson Hyde and Black Manta app. 3,4-Batwoman app. 4.00

AQUANAUTS (TV)
Dell Publishing Co.: May - July, 1961

Four Color 1197-Photo-c 8 16 24 51 96 140

ARABIAN NIGHTS (See Cinema Comics Herald)

ARACHNOPHOBIA (Movie)
Hollywood Comics (Disney Comics): 1990 ($5.95, 68 pg. graphic novel)

nn-Adaptation of film; Spiegle-a 6.00
Comic edition ($2.95, 68 pgs.) 4.00

ARAK/SON OF THUNDER (See Warlord #48)
DC Comics: Sept, 1981 - No. 50, Nov, 1985

1,24,50: 1-1st app. Angelica, Princess of White Cathay. 24,50-(52 pgs.) 4.00
2-23,25-49: 3-Intro Valda. 12-Origin Valda. 20-Origin Angelica 3.00
Annual 1(10/84) 4.00

ARAÑA THE HEART OF THE SPIDER (See Amazing Fantasy (2004) #1-6)
Marvel Comics: March, 2005 - No. 12, Feb, 2006 ($2.99)

1-12: 1-Avery-s/Cruz-a. 4-Spider-Man-c/app. 3.00
Vol. 1: Heart of the Spider (2005, $7.99, digest) r/Amazing Fantasy (2004) #1-6 8.00
Vol. 2: In the Beginning (2005, $7.99, digest) r/#1-6 8.00
Vol. 3: Night of the Hunter (2006, $7.99, digest) r/#7-12 8.00

ARCADIA
BOOM! Studios: May, 2015 - No. 8, Feb, 2016 ($3.99)

1-8-Paknadel-s/Pfeiffer-a 4.00

ARCANA (Also see Books of Magic limited & ongoing series and Mister E)
DC Comics (Vertigo): 1994 ($3.95, 68 pgs., annual)

1-Bolton painted-c; Children's Crusade/Tim Hunter story 4.00

ARCANUM
Image Comics (Top Cow Productions): Apr, 1997 - No. 8, Feb, 1998 ($2.50)

1/2 Gold Edition 12.00
1-Brandon Peterson-s/a(p), 1-Variant-c, 4-American Ent. Ed. 3.50
2-8 3.00
3-Variant-c 4.00
...: Millennium's End TPB (2005, $16.99) r/#1-8 & #1/2; cover gallery and sketch pages 17.00

ARCHANGEL (See Uncanny X-Men, X-Factor & X-Men)
Marvel Comics: Feb, 1996 ($2.50, B&W, one-shot)

1-Milligan story 3.00

ARCHANGEL 8
AWA Studios: Mar, 2020 - No. 5, Sept, 2020 ($3.99, limited series)

1-5-Michael Moreci-s/C.P. Smith-a 4.00

ARCHARD'S AGENTS (See Ruse)
CrossGeneration Comics: Jan, 2003; Nov, 2003; Apr, 2004 ($2.95)

1-Dixon-s/Perkins-a 3.00
...: The Case of the Puzzled Pugilist (11/03) Dixon-s/Perkins-a 3.00
Vol. 3 - Deadly Dare (4/04) Dixon-s/McNiven-a; preview of Lady Death: The Wild Hunt 3.00

ARCHENEMIES
Dark Horse Comics: Apr, 2006 - No. 4, July, 2006 ($2.99, limited series)

1-4-Melbourne-s/Guichet-a 3.00

ARCHER & ARMSTRONG
Valiant: July (June inside), 1992 - No. 26, Oct, 1994 ($2.50)

0-(7/92)-B. Smith-c/a; Reese-i assists 2 4 6 8 10 12
0-(with Gold Valiant Logo) 6 12 18 41 76 110
1,2: 1-(8/92)-Origin & 1st app. Archer; Miller-c; B. Smith/Layton-a. 2-2nd app. Turok (c/story); Smith/Layton-a; Simonson-c 5.00
3-7: 3,4-Smith-c&a(p) & scripts 4.00
8-($4.50, 52 pgs.)-Combined with Eternal Warrior #8; B. Smith-c/a & scripts; 1st app. Ivar the Time Walker 5.00
9-26: 10-2nd app. Ivar. 10,11-B. Smith-c. 21,22-Shadowman app. 22-w/bound-in trading card. 25-Eternal Warrior app. 26-Flip book w/Eternal Warrior #26 3.00

GD VG FN VF VF/NM NM-
2.0 4.0 6.0 8.0 9.0 9.2

...: First Impressions HC (2008, $24.95) recolored reprints #0-6; new "Formation of the Sect" story by Jim Shooter and Sal Velutto; Shooter commentary; new cover by Golden 25.00

ARCHER & ARMSTRONG
Valiant Entertainment: Aug, 2012 - No. 25, Oct, 2014 ($3.99)

1-24: 1-Van Lente-s/Henry-a; two covers; origin. 5-8-Eternal Warrior app. 4.00
1,4-8-Pullbox variants: 1-Clayton Henry. 4-Juan Doe. 7,8-Emanuela Lupacchino 4.00
1-Variant-c by David Aja 10.00
1-Variant-c by Neal Adams 28.00
25-($4.99) Van Lente-s/Henry-a; back-up short stories by various; cover gallery 5.00
#0-(5/13, $3.99) Van Lente-s/Henry-a 4.00
...Archer #0-(2/14, $3.99) Van Lente-s/Pere Pérez-a; childhood origin 4.00
...: The One Percent #1 (11/14, $3.99) Fawkes-s/Eisma-a/Juan Doe-c 4.00

ARCHER & ARMSTRONG FOREVER
Valiant Entertainment: May, 2022 - Present ($3.99)

1-4: 1-Steve Foxe-s/Marcio Fiorito-a 4.00

ARCHIE (See Archie Comics) (Also see Afterlife With..., Christmas & Archie, Everything's..., Explorers of the Unknown, Jackpot, Life With..., Little..., Oxydol-Dreft, Pep, Riverdale High, Teenage Mutant Ninja Turtles Adventures & To Riverdale and Back Again)

ARCHIE
Archie Comic Publs.: Sept, 2015 - No. 32, Sept, 2018; No. 699, Nov, 2018 - Present ($3.99)

1-32-Mark Waid-s; multiple covers on all; back-up classic reprints. 1-3-Fiona Staples-a. 4-Annie Wu-a. 5-10-Veronica Fish-a. 13-Re-intro. Cheryl Blossom; back-up r/1st app. from B&V #320. 13-17-Eisma-a. 18-22-Pete Woods-a. 23-32-Audrey Mok-a 4.00
699-(11/18, $1.00) Recaps of events from #1-32; preview of #700; Sauvage-c 3.00
700-713: 700-704-($3.99) Spencer-s/Sauvage-a; Sabrina app. 705-709-"Archie and Sabrina" on cover. 710-713-"Archie and Katy Keene" on cover 4.00
... Collector's Edition (2/16, $9.99) r/#1-3 with creator intros and variant cover gallery 10.00
FCBD Edition (2016, giveaway) r/#1; Staples-c; back-up Jughead story 3.00

ARCHIE ALL CANADIAN DIGEST
Archie Publications: Aug, 1996 ($1.75, 96 pgs.)

1 1 3 4 6 8 10

ARCHIE AMERICANA SERIES, BEST OF THE FORTIES
Archie Publications: 1991, 2002 ($10.95, trade paperback)

Vol. 1,2-r/early strips from 1940s 1-Intro. by Steven King. 2-Intro. by Paul Castiglia 12.00

ARCHIE AMERICANA SERIES, BEST OF THE FIFTIES
Archie Publications: 1991 ($8.95, trade paperback)

Vol. 2-r/strips from 1950's 12.00
2nd printing (1998, $9.95) 12.00
Book 2 (2003, $10.95) 12.00

ARCHIE AMERICANA SERIES, BEST OF THE SIXTIES
Archie Publications: 1995 ($9.95, trade paperback)

Vol. 3-r/strips from 1960s; intro. by Frankie Avalon 12.00

ARCHIE AMERICANA SERIES, BEST OF THE SEVENTIES
Archie Publications: 1997, 2008 ($9.95/$10.95, trade paperback)

Vol. 4 (1997, $9.95)-r/strips from 1970s 12.00
Vol. 8 Book 2 (2008, $10.95)-r/other strips from 1970s 12.00

ARCHIE AMERICANA SERIES, BEST OF THE EIGHTIES
Archie Publications: 2001 ($10.95, trade paperback)

Vol. 5-r/strips from 1980s; foreward by Steve Geppi 12.00

ARCHIE AMERICANA SERIES, BEST OF THE '90S
Archie Publications: 2008 ($11.95, trade paperback)

Vol. 9-r/strips from 1990s; new Lindsey cover 12.00

ARCHIE AND BIG ETHEL
Spire Christian Comics (Fleming H. Revell Co.): 1982 (69¢)

nn-(Low print run) 3 6 9 14 19 24

ARCHIE & FRIENDS
Archie Comics: Dec, 1992 - No. 159, Feb, 2012 ($1.25-$2.99)

1 5.00
2,4,10-14,17,18,20-Sabrina app. 20-Archie's Band-c 4.00
3,5-9,16 3.00
15-Babewatch-s with Sabrina app. 6.00
19-Josie and the Pussycats app.; E.T. parody-c/s 5.00
21-46 3.00
47-All Josie and the Pussycats issue; movie and actress profiles/photos 4.00
48-142: 48-56,58,60,96-Josie and the Pussycats-c/s. 79-Cheryl Blossom returns. 100-The Veronicas-c/app. 101-Katy Keene begins. 129-Begin $2.50. 130,131-Josie and the Pussycats. 137-Cosmo, Super Duck, Pat the Brat and other old characters app. 3.00

	GD 2.0	VG 4.0	FN 6.0	VF 8.0	VF/NM 9.0	NM- 9.2
143-159: 143-Begin $2.99-c. 145-Jersey Shore spoof. 146,147-Twilite. 154-Little Archie						3.00

ARCHIE & FRIENDS (Classic-style reprints with new lead story)
Archie Publications: Apr, 2019 - Present ($2.99, quarterly)

	GD 2.0	VG 4.0	FN 6.0	VF 8.0	VF/NM 9.0	NM- 9.2
...: Music #1; ...: Beach Party #1 (#2), ...: Back to School #1 (#3), ...: Travel #1 (#4), ...: Winter Wonderland #1 (#5), ...: Geeks and Games #1 (#6), ...: Endless Summer #1 (#7), ...: Fall Festival #1 (#8), ...: Guide to Dating #1 (#9), ...: Superheroes #1 (#10), ...: Summer Vacation #1 (#11), ...: Christmas Calamity #1 (#12), ...: Summer Lovin' #1 (#13), ...: Thrills and Chills #1 (#14)						3.00

ARCHIE & FRIENDS DOUBLE DIGEST MAGAZINE
Archie Comics: Feb, 2011 - No. 33, Jan, 2014 ($3.99, digest-size)

	GD 2.0	VG 4.0	FN 6.0	VF 8.0	VF/NM 9.0	NM- 9.2
1-32: 1-Staton-a. 7-13-SuperTeens app.						4.00
33-($5.99, 320 pages) Double Double Digest						6.00

ARCHIE AND ME (See Archie Giant Series Mag. #578, 591, 603, 616, 626)
Archie Publications: Oct, 1964; No. 2, Aug, 1965 - No. 161, Feb, 1987

	GD 2.0	VG 4.0	FN 6.0	VF 8.0	VF/NM 9.0	NM- 9.2
1	23	46	69	161	356	550
2-(8/65)	10	20	30	67	141	215
3-5: 3-(12/65)	6	12	18	41	76	110
6-10: 6-(8/66)	5	10	15	30	50	70
11-20: 11-(4/68)	3	6	9	21	33	45
21(6/68)-26,28-30: 21-UFO story. 26-X-Mas-c	3	6	9	16	24	32
27-Groovyman & Knowman superhero-s; UFO-sty	3	6	9	19	30	40
31-42: 37-Japan Expo '70-c/s	3	6	9	14	19	24
43-48,50-63-(All Giants): 43-(8/71) Mummy-s. 44-Mermaid-s. 62-Elvis cameo-c. 63-(2/74)	3	6	9	15	22	28
49-(Giant) Josie & the Pussycats-c/app.	4	8	12	22	35	48
64-66,68-99-(Regular size): 85-Bicentennial-s. 98-Collectors Comics	2	4	6	8	10	12
67-Sabrina app.(8/74)	2	4	6	10	14	18
100-(4/78)	2	4	6	8	11	14
101-120: 107-UFO-s	1	2	3	5	6	8
121(8/80)-159: 134-Riverdale 2001						6.00
160,161: 160-Origin Mr. Weatherbee; Caveman Archie gang story. 161-Last issue	1	2	3	5	6	8

ARCHIE & ME COMICS DIGEST
Archie Comics: Dec, 2017 - No. 23, Jan, 2020 ($6.99/$7.99, digest-size)

	GD 2.0	VG 4.0	FN 6.0	VF 8.0	VF/NM 9.0	NM- 9.2
1-20-Reprints include Archie Babies in early issues						7.00
21-23-($7.99)						8.00

ARCHIE AND MR. WEATHERBEE
Spire Christian Comics (Fleming H. Revell Co.): 1980 (59¢)

	GD 2.0	VG 4.0	FN 6.0	VF 8.0	VF/NM 9.0	NM- 9.2
nn - (Low print run)	3	6	9	14	19	24

ARCHIE...ARCHIE ANDREWS, WHERE ARE YOU? (...Comics Digest #9, 10; ...Comics Digest Mag. No. 11 on)
Archie Publications: Feb, 1977 - No. 114, May, 1998 (Digest size, 160-128 pgs., quarterly)

	GD 2.0	VG 4.0	FN 6.0	VF 8.0	VF/NM 9.0	NM- 9.2
1	3	6	9	19	30	40
2,3,5,7-9-N. Adams-a; 8-r-/origin The Fly by S&K. 9-Steel Sterling-r	2	4	6	10	14	18
4,6,10 ($1.00/$1.50)	2	4	6	8	11	14
11-20: 17-Katy Keene story	2	3	4	6	8	10
21-50,100	1	2	3	5	6	8
51-70						4.00
71-99,101-114: 113-Begin $1.95-c						3.00

ARCHIE AS PUREHEART THE POWERFUL (Also see Archie Giant Series #142, Jughead as Captain Hero, Life With Archie & Little Archie)
Archie Publications (Radio Comics): Sept, 1966 - No. 6, Nov, 1967

	GD 2.0	VG 4.0	FN 6.0	VF 8.0	VF/NM 9.0	NM- 9.2
1-Super hero parody	13	26	39	86	188	290
2	8	16	24	51	96	140
3-6	6	12	18	42	79	115

NOTE: *Evilheart cameos in all. Title: Archie As Pureheart the Powerful #1-3; ...As Capt. Pureheart-#4-6.*

ARCHIE AT RIVERDALE HIGH (See Archie Giant Series Magazine #573, 586, 604 & Riverdale High)
Archie Publications: Aug, 1972 - No. 113, Feb, 1987

	GD 2.0	VG 4.0	FN 6.0	VF 8.0	VF/NM 9.0	NM- 9.2
1	9	18	27	59	117	175
2	5	10	15	21	53	75
3-5	3	6	9	16	23	30
6-10	2	4	6	11	16	20
11-30	2	4	6	8	10	12
31(12/75)-46,48-50(12/77)	1	3	4	6	8	10
47-Archie in drag-s; Betty mud wrestling-s	2	4	6	11	16	20
51-80,100 (12/84)	1	2	3	5	6	8
81(8/81)-88, 91,93-95,98						6.00
89,90-Early Cheryl Blossom app. 90-Archies Band app.	3	6	9	15	22	28
92,96,97,99-Cheryl Blossom app. 96-Anti-smoking issue	2	4	6	13	18	22
101,102,104-109,111,112: 102-Ghost-c						6.00
103-Archie dates Cheryl Blossom-s	2	4	6	13	18	22
110,113: 110-Godzilla-s. 113-Last issue	1	2	3	5	6	8

ARCHIE CHRISTMAS SPECTACULAR
Archie Comics: Feb, 2018; Feb, 2019; Feb, 2020; Feb, 2021; Jan, 2022; Jan, 2023 ($2.99)

	GD 2.0	VG 4.0	FN 6.0	VF 8.0	VF/NM 9.0	NM- 9.2
1, nn (2019), nn (2020), nn (2021); 1 (2022), 1 (2023)-New story with reprints						3.00

ARCHIE COMICS (See Pep Comics #22 [12/41] for Archie's debut) (1st Teen-age comic; Radio show first aired 6/2/45 by NBC)
MLJ Magazines No. 1-19/Archie Publ. No. 20 on: Winter, 1942-43 - No. 19, 3-4/46; No. 20, 5-6/46 - No. 666, Jul, 2015

	GD 2.0	VG 4.0	FN 6.0	VF 8.0	VF/NM 9.0	NM- 9.2
1 (Scarce)-Jughead, Veronica app.; 1st app. Mrs. Andrews	15,000	30,000	52,500	105,000	168,500	232,000
2 (Scarce)	1950	3900	5850	14,600	24,300	34,000
3 (60 pgs.)(scarce)	1000	2000	3000	7400	13,200	19,000
4-Article about Archie radio series	568	1136	1704	4146	7323	10,500
5-Halloween-c	492	984	1476	3592	6346	9100
6-Christmas-c	371	742	1113	2600	4550	6500
7-1st definitive love triangle story	400	800	1200	2800	4900	7000
8-10: 9-1st Miss Grundy cover	320	640	960	2240	3920	5600
11-15: 15-Dotty & Ditto by Woggon	181	362	543	1158	1979	2800
16-20: 15,17,18-Dotty & Ditto by Woggon. 16,19-Woggon-a. 18-Halloween pumpkin-c.	155	310	465	992	1696	2400
21-30: 23-Betty & Veronica by Woggon. 25-Woggon-a. 30-Coach Piffle app., a Coach Kleats prototype. 34-Pre-Dilton try-out (named Dilbert)	97	194	291	621	1061	1500
31-40	58	116	174	371	636	900
41-49	47	94	141	296	498	700
50-Classic Montana Betty headlight-c (5-6/51)	503	1006	1509	3672	6486	9300
51-60	19	38	57	133	297	460
61-70 (1954): 65-70, Katy Keene app.	16	32	48	111	246	380
71-80: 72-74-Katy Keene app.	13	26	39	89	195	300
81-93,95-99	10	20	30	64	132	200
94-1st Coach Kleats in this title (see Pep #24)	12	24	36	83	182	280
100	15	30	45	105	233	360
101-Headlight-c	9	18	27	60	120	180
102-122,126,128-130 (1962)	7	14	21	44	82	120
123-125,127-Horror/SF covers. 123-UFO-c/s	11	22	33	76	163	250
131,132,134-157,159,160: 137-1st Caveman Archie gang story. 159-James Bond on cover	5	10	15	30	50	70
133 (12/62)-1st app. Cricket O'Dell	6	12	18	41	76	110
158-Archie in drag story	6	12	18	41	76	110
161(2/66)-184,186-188,190-195,197-199: 168-Superhero gag-c. 176,178-Twiggy-c 183-Caveman Archie gang story	3	6	9	19	30	40
185-1st "The Archies" Band story	4	8	12	28	47	65
189 (3/69)-Archie's band meets Don Kirshner who developed the Monkees	4	8	12	23	37	50
196 (12/69)-Early Cricket O'Dell app.	4	8	12	23	37	50
200 (6/70)	3	6	9	21	33	45
201-230(11/73): 213-Sabrina/Josie-c cameos. 229-Lost Child issue	3	6	9	14	19	24
231-260(3/77): 253-Tarzan parody	2	4	6	8	11	14
261-270,272-282, 284-299	1	3	4	6	8	10
271-Pearl necklace cover	14	28	42	96	211	325
283(8/79)-Cover/story plugs "International Children's Appeal" which was a fraudulent charity, according to TV's 20/20 news program broadcast July 20, 1979	2	4	6	8	10	12
300(1/81)-Anniversary issue	2	4	6	8	11	14
301-321,323-325,327-335,337-350: 323-Cheryl Blossom pin-up. 325-Cheryl Blossom app.						6.00
322-E.T. story	1	2	3	5	6	8
326-Early Cheryl Blossom story	2	4	6	11	16	20
336-Michael Jackson/Boy George parody	2	4	6	9	13	16
351-399: 356-Calgary Olympics Special. 393-Infinity-c; 1st comic book printed on recycled paper						5.00
400 (6/92)-Shows 1st meeting of Little Archie and Veronica						6.00
401-428						4.00
429-Love Showdown part 1						5.00
430-599: 467- "A Storm Over Uniforms" x-over parts 3,4. 538-Comic-Con issue						3.00
600-602: 600-(10/09) Archie proposes to Veronica. 601-Marries Veronica. 602-Twins born						4.00
603-605: 603-(1/10) Archie proposes to Betty. 604-Marries Betty. 605-Twins born						4.00
606-615,618-626: 609-Begin $2.99-c. 610-613-Man From RIVERDALE. 625-70th Anniversary. 626-Michael Strahan app.						3.00
616,617-Obama & Palin app.; two covers on each						4.00
627-630-Archie Meets KISS; 2 covers on each by Parent & Francavilla						4.00
631-658: 632-634-Archie marries Valerie from the Pussycats. 635-Jill Thompson var-c. 636-Gender swap. 641-644-Crossover with Glee; 2 covers. 648-Simonson var-c. 655-Cosmo the Merry Martian app. 656-Intro. Harper Lodge						3.00
650-Variant "Battle of the Bands" cover by Fiona Staples						5.00
659-665-($3.99) Two covers on each. 664-Game of Thrones parody. 665-Harper app.						4.00
666-Last issue; 6 interlocking covers with vintage title logos (Archie Comics, Blue Ribbon Comics, Top-Notch Comics, Pep Comics, Zip Comics, and Jackpot Comics)						4.00
Annual 1 ('50)-116 pgs. (Scarce)	320	640	960	2080	4340	6600
Annual 2 ('51)	124	248	372	790	1595	2400
Annual 3 ('52)	71	142	213	450	875	1300
Annual 4,5 (1953-54)	56	112	168	350	650	950
Annual 6-10 (1955-59): 8,9-(100 pgs.). 10-(84 pgs.) Elvis record on-c	19	38	57	131	291	450
Annual 11-15 (1960-65): 12,13-(84 pgs.) 14,15-(68 pgs.)	10	20	30	69	147	225
Annual 16-20 (1966-70)(all 68 pgs.): 20-Archie's band-c	6	12	18	42	79	115
Annual 21,22,24-26 (1971-75): 21,22-(68 pgs.). 22-Archie's band-s. 24-26-(52 pgs.). 25-Cavemen-s	4	8	12	25	40	55
Annual 23-Archie's band-c/s; Josie/Sabrina-c	5	10	15	31	53	75
Annual Digest 27 ('75)	4	8	12	25	40	55
...28-30	3	6	9	14	20	25
...31-34	2	4	6	9	13	16
...35-40 (...Magazine #35 on)	1	3	4	6	8	10
...41-65 ('94)						5.00
...66-69						3.00
...All-Star Specials (Winter '75, $1.25)-6 remaindered Archie comics rebound in each; titles: "The World of Giant Comics", "Giant Grab Bag of Comics", "Triple Giant Comics" & "Giant Spec. Comics	6	12	18	38	67	100

NOTE: *Archies Band-s-185, 188-192, 197, 198, 201, 204, 205, 208, 209, 215, 329, 330; Band-c-191, 330. Cavemen Archie Gang-s-183, 192, 197, 208, 210, 220, 223, 282, 333, 335, 338, 340.* ***Al Fagly*** *c-17-35.* ***Bob Montana*** *c-38, 41-50, 58, Annual 1-4.* ***Bill Woggon*** *c-53, 54.*

ARCHIE COMICS DIGEST (...Magazine No. 37-95)
Archie Publications: Aug, 1973 - No. 267, Nov, 2010 (Digest-size, 160-128 pgs.)

	GD 2.0	VG 4.0	FN 6.0	VF 8.0	VF/NM 9.0	NM- 9.2
1-1st Archie digest	10	20	30	70	150	230
2	5	10	15	34	60	85
3-5	4	8	12	23	37	50
6-10	3	6	9	16	23	30
11-33: 32,33-The Fly-r by S&K	2	4	6	10	14	18
34-60	1	3	4	6	8	10
61-80,100	1	2	3	5	6	8

Archie Comics #1 © ACP

Archie Comics #606 © ACP

Archie Giant Series #230 © ACP

GD VG FN VF VF/NM NM-
2.0 4.0 6.0 8.0 9.0 9.2

81-99 5.00
101-140: 36-Katy Keene story 4.00
141-165 3.00
166-235,237-267: 194-Begin $2.39-c. 225-Begin $2.49-c 3.00
236-65th Anniversary issue, r/1st app. in Pep #22 and entire Archie Comics #1 (1942) 5.00
NOTE: ***Neal Adams** a-1, 2, 4, 5, 19-21, 24, 25, 27, 29, 31, 33. X-mas c-88, 94, 100, 106.*

ARCHIE COMICS DIGEST (Continues from Archie's Double Digest #252)
Archie Publications: No. 253, Sept, 2014 - Present ($4.99-$9.99, digest-size)

253,254,257-259,261,262,264,267,269,270,272,273,275,277,279,281-($4.99) 5.00
255,260,266,274,276,282,283,285-300-($6.99) Titled Archie Jumbo Comics Digest 7.00
256,263,265,268,271,278,280,284-($5.99): 256,263,268,278-Titled Archie Comics Annual 6.00
302-325-($7.99) 8.00
326-336-($8.99) 9.00
337-339-($9.99) 10.00

ARCHIE COMICS (Free Comic Book Day editions) (Also see Pep Comics)
Archie Publications: 2003 - Present

... Free Comic Book Day Edition 1,2: 1-(7/03). 2-(9/04) 3.00
Little Archie "The Legend of the Lost Lagoon" FCBD Edition (5/07) Bolling-s/a 3.00
... Past, Present & Future Fun! (8/21) FCBD giveaway; 80th Anniversary celebration 3.00
... Presents the Mighty Archie Art Players ('09) Free Comic Book Day giveaway 3.00
...'s 65th Anniversary Bash ('06) Free Comic Book Day giveaway 3.00
...'s Summer Splash FCBD Edition (5/10) Parent-a; Cheryl Blossom app. 3.00

ARCHIE COMICS PRESENTS: THE LOVE SHOWDOWN COLLECTION
Archie Publications: 1994 ($4.95, squarebound)

nn-r/Archie #429, Betty #19, Betty & Veronica #82, & Veronica #39
1 3 4 6 8 10

ARCHIE COMICS SUPER SPECIAL
Archie Publications: Dec, 2012 - No. 7, Jan, 2017 ($9.99, squarebound magazine-sized, quarterly)

1-7: 1-Christmas themed. 2-Valentine's themed 10.00

ARCHIE DIGEST (Free Comic Book Day edition)
Archie Comic Publications: June/July 2014 (digest-size giveaway)

1-Reprints; Parent-c 3.00

ARCHIE DOUBLE DIGEST (See Archie's Double Digest Quarterly Magazine)

ARCHIE 80TH ANNIVERSARY: EVERYTHING'S ARCHIE
Archie Comic Publications: Aug, 2021 ($3.99, one-shot)

1-New story & reprints; includes r/Betty #46 (from 1997, Betty in 2021 AD with virtual school classes over video monitors) 4.00

ARCHIE 80TH ANNIVERSARY JUMBO COMICS DIGEST
Archie Comic Publications: Mar, 2021 - No. 5, Jan, 2022 ($7.99, digest-size)

1-5: 1-Reprints from all eras including Archie's debut in Pep Comics #22 8.00

ARCHIE GETS A JOB
Spire Christian Comics (Fleming H. Revell Co.): 1977

nn 3 6 9 14 20 26

ARCHIE GIANT SERIES MAGAZINE
Archie Publications: 1954 - No. 632, July, 1992 (No #36-135, no #252-451)
(#1 not code approved) (#1-233 are Giants; #12-184 are 68 pgs.,#185-194,197-233 are 52 pgs.; #195,196 are 84 pgs.; #234-up are 36 pgs.)

1-Archie's Christmas Stocking 194 388 582 1242 2121 3000
2-Archie's Christmas Stocking('55) 93 186 279 595 1023 1450
3-6-Archie's Christmas Stocking('56- '59) 58 116 174 371 636 900
7-10: 7-Katy Keene Holiday Fun(9/60); Bill Woggon-c. 8-Betty & Veronica Summer Fun (10/60); baseball story w/Babe Ruth & Lou Gehrig. 9-The World of Jughead (12/60); Neal Adams-a. 10-Archie's Christmas Stocking(1/61) 41 82 123 256 428 600
11,13,16,18: 11-Betty & Veronica Spectacular (6/61). 13-Betty & Veronica Summer Fun (10/61). 16-Betty & Veronica Spectacular (6/62). 18-Betty & Veronica Summer Fun (10/62)
28 56 84 165 270 375
12,14,15,17,19,20: 12-Katy Keene Holiday Fun (9/61). 14-The World of Jughead (12/61); Vampire-s. 15-Archie's Christmas Stocking (1/62). 17-Archie's Jokes (9/62); Katy Keene app. 19-The World of Jughead (12/62). 20-Archie's Christmas Stocking (1/63)
20 40 60 120 195 270
21,23,28: 21-Betty & Veronica Spectacular (6/63). 23-Betty & Veronica Summer Fun (10/63). 28-Betty & Veronica Summer Fun (9/64) 9 18 27 63 129 195
22,24,25,27,29,30: 22-Archie's Jokes (9/63). 24-The World of Jughead (12/63). 25-Archie's Christmas Stocking (1/64). 27-Archie's Jokes (8/64). 29-Around the World with Archie (10/64); Doris Day-s. 30-The World of Jughead (12/64) 8 16 24 56 108 160
26-Betty & Veronica Spectacular (6/64); all pin-ups; DeCarlo-c/a
10 20 30 67 141 215
31,33-35: 31-Archie's Christmas Stocking (1/65). 33-Archie's Jokes (8/65). 34-Betty & Veronica Summer Fun (9/65). 35-Around the World with Archie (10/65).
6 12 18 41 76 110
32-Betty & Veronica Spectacular (6/65); all pin-ups; DeCarlo-c/a
8 16 24 56 108 160
36-135-**Do not exist**
136-141: 136-The World of Jughead (12/65). 137-Archie's Christmas Stocking (1/66). 138-Betty & Veronica Spect. (6/66). 139-Archie's Jokes (6/66). 140-Betty & Veronica Summer Fun (8/66). 141-Around the World with Archie (9/66) 6 12 18 41 76 110
142-Archie's Super-Hero Special (10/66)-Origin Capt. Pureheart, Capt. Hero, and Evilheart
9 18 27 57 111 165
143-The World of Jughead (12/66); Capt. Hero-c/s; Man From R.I.V.E.R.D.A.L.E., Pureheart, Superteen app. 6 12 18 41 76 110
144-160: 144-Archie's Christmas Stocking (1/67). 145-Betty & Veronica Spectacular (6/67). 146-Archie's Jokes (6/67). 147-Betty & Veronica Summer Fun (8/67) 148-World of Archie (9/67). 149-World of Jughead (10/67). 150-Archie's Christmas Stocking (1/68). 151-World of Archie (2/68). 152-World of Jughead (2/68). 153-Betty & Veronica Spectacular (6/68). 154-Archie Jokes (6/68). 155-Betty & Veronica Summer Fun (8/68). 156-World of Archie (10/68). 157-World of Jughead (12/68). 158-Archie's Christmas Stocking (1/69). 159-Betty & Veronica Christmas Spectacular (1/69). 160-World of Archie (2/69); Frankenstein-s each... 4 8 12 25 40 55
161-World of Jughead (2/69); Super-Jughead-s; 11 pg. early Cricket O'Dell-s
4 8 12 27 44 60
162-183: 162-Betty & Veronica Spectacular (6/69). 163-Archie's Jokes(8/69). 164-Betty & Veronica Summer Fun (9/69). 165-World of Archie (9/69). 166-World of Jughead (9/69). 167-Archie's Christmas Stocking (1/70). 168-Betty & Veronica Christmas Spect. (1/70). 169-Archie's Christmas Love-In (1/70). 170-Jughead's Eat-Out Comic Book Mag. (12/69). 171-World of Archie (2/70). 172-World of Jughead (2/70). 173-Betty & Veronica Spectacular (6/70). 174-Archie's Jokes (8/70). 175-Betty & Veronica Summer Fun (9/70). 176-Li'l Jinx Giant Laugh-Out (8/70). 177-World of Archie (9/70). 178-World of Jughead (9/70). 179-Archie's Christmas Stocking(1/71). 180-Betty & Veronica Christmas Spect. (1/71). 181-Archie's Christmas Love-In (1/71). 182-World of Archie (2/71). 183-World of Jughead (2/71)-Last squarebound each... 3 6 9 19 30 40
184-189,193,194,197-199 (52 pgs.): 184-Betty & Veronica Spectacular (6/71). 185-Li'l Jinx Giant Laugh-Out (6/71). 186-Archie's Jokes (8/71). 187-Betty & Veronica Summer Fun (9/71). 188-World of Archie (9/71). 189-World of Jughead (9/71). 193-World of Archie (3/72).194-World of Jughead (4/72). 197-Betty & Veronica Spectacular (6/72). 198-Archie's Jokes (8/72). 199-Betty & Veronica Summer Fun (9/72)
each... 3 6 9 16 23 30
190-Archie's Christmas Stocking (12/71); Sabrina-c 5 10 15 31 53 75
191-Betty & Veronica Christmas Spect.(2/72); Sabrina app.
5 10 15 31 53 75
192-Archie's Christmas Love-In (1/72); Archie Band-c/s
3 6 9 21 33 45
195-(84 pgs.)-Li'l Jinx Christmas Bag (1/72). 4 8 12 23 37 50
196-(84 pgs.)-Sabrina's Christmas Magic (1/72) 6 12 18 41 76 110
200-(52 pgs.)-World of Archie (10/72) 3 6 9 21 33 45
201-206,208-219,221-230,232,233 (All 52 pgs.): 201-Betty & Veronica Spectacular (10/72). 202-World of Jughead (11/72). 203-Archie's Christmas Stocking (12/72). 204-Betty & Veronica Christmas Spectacular (2/73). 205-Archie's Christmas Love-In (1/73). 206-Li'l Jinx Christmas Bag (12/72). 208-World of Archie (3/73). 209-World of Jughead (4/73). 210-Betty & Veronica Spectacular (6/73). 211-Archie's Jokes (8/73). 212-Betty & Veronica Summer Fun (9/73). 213-World of Archie (10/73). 214-Betty & Veronica Spectacular (10/73). 215-World of Jughead (11/73). 216-Archie's Christmas Stocking (12/73). 217-Betty & Veronica Christmas Spectacular (2/74). 218-Archie's Christmas Love-In (1/74). 219-Li'l Jinx Christmas Bag (12/73). 221-Betty & Veronica Spectacular (Advertised as World of Archie) (6/74). 222-Archie's Jokes (advertised as World of Jughead) (8/74). 223-Li'l Jinx (8/74). 224-Betty & Veronica Summer Fun (9/74). 225-World of Archie (9/74). 226-Betty & Veronica Spectacular (10/74). 227-World of Jughead (10/74). 228-Archie's Christmas Stocking (12/74). 229-Betty & Veronica Christmas Spectacular (12/74). 230-Archie's Christmas Love-In (1/75). 232-World of Archie (3/75). 233-World of Jughead (4/75)
each... 3 6 9 14 19 24
207,220,231,243: Sabrina's Christmas Magic. 207-(12/72). 220-(12/73). 231-(1/75). 243-(1/76)
each... 3 6 9 18 27 36
234-242,244-251 (36 pgs.): 234-Betty & Veronica Spectacular (6/75). 235-Archie's Jokes (8/75). 236-Betty & Veronica Summer Fun (9/75). 237-World of Archie (9/75) 238-Betty & Veronica Spectacular (10/75). 239-World of Jughead (10/75). 240-Archie's Christmas Stocking (12/75). 241-Betty & Veronica Christmas Spectacular (12/75). 242-Archie's Christmas Love-In (1/76). 244-World of Archie (3/76). 245-World of Jughead (4/76). 246-Betty & Veronica Spectacular (6/76). 247-Archie's Jokes (8/76). 248-Betty & Veronica Summer Fun (9/76). 249-World of Archie (9/76). 250-Betty & Veronica Spectacular (10/76). 251-World of Jughead each.... 2 4 6 10 14 18
252-451-**Do not exist**
452-454,456-466,468-478, 480-490,492-499: 452-Archie's Christmas Stocking (12/76). 453-Betty & Veronica Christmas Spectacular (12/76). 454-Archie's Christmas Love-In (1/77). 456-World of Archie (3/77). 457-World of Jughead (4/77). 458-Betty & Veronica Spectacular

(6/77). 459-Archie's Jokes (8/77)-Shows 8/76 in error. 460-Betty & Veronica Summer Fun (9/77). 461-World of Archie (9/77). 462-Betty & Veronica Spectacular (10/77). 463-World of Jughead (10/77). 464-Archie's Christmas Stocking (12/77). 465-Betty & Veronica Christmas Spectacular (12/77). 466-Archie's Christmas Love-In (1/78). 468-World of Archie (2/78). 469-World of Jughead (2/78). 470-Betty & Veronica Spectacular(6/78). 471-Archie's Jokes (8/78). 472-Betty & Veronica Summer Fun (9/78). 473-World of Archie (9/78). 474-Betty & Veronica Spectacular (10/78). 475-World of Jughead (10/78). 476-Archie's Christmas Stocking (12/78). 477-Betty & Veronica Christmas Spectacular (12/78). 478-Archie's Christmas Love-In (1/79). 480-The World of Archie (3/79). 481-World of Jughead (4/79). 482-Betty & Veronica Spectacular (6/79). 483-Archie's Jokes (8/79). 484-Betty & Veronica Summer Fun(9/79). 485-The World of Archie (9/79). 486-Betty & Veronica Spectacular (10/79). 487-The World of Jughead (10/79). 488-Archie's Christmas Stocking (12/79). 489-Betty & Veronica Christmas Spectacular (1/80). 490-Archie's Christmas Love-in (1/80). 492-The World of Archie (2/80). 493-The World of Jughead (4/80). 494-Betty & Veronica Spectacular (6/80). 495-Archie's Jokes (8/80). 496-Betty & Veronica Summer Fun (9/80). 497-The World of Archie (9/80). 498-Betty & Veronica Spectacular (10/80). 499-The World of Jughead (10/80) each... 2 4 6 8 10 12

455,467,479,491,503-Sabrina's Christmas Magic: 455-(1/77). 467-(1/78). 479-(1/79) Dracula/Werewolf-s. 491-(1/80), 503(1/81) 2 4 6 13 18 22

500-Archie's Christmas Stocking (12/80) 2 4 6 8 11 14

501-514,516-527,529-532,534-539,541-543,545-550: 501-Betty & Veronica Christmas Spectacular (12/80). 502-Archie's Christmas Love-in (1/81). 504-The World of Archie (3/81). 505-The World of Jughead (4/81). 506-Betty & Veronica Spectacular (6/81). 507-Archie's Jokes (8/81). 508-Betty & Veronica Summer Fun (9/81). 509-The World of Archie (9/81). 510-Betty & Vernonica Spectacular (9/81). 511-The World of Jughead (10/81). 512-Archie's Christmas Stocking (12/81). 513-Betty & Veronica Christmas Spectacular (12/81). 514-Archie's Christmas Love-in (1/82). 516-The World of Archie(3/82). 517-The World of Jughead (4/82). 518-Betty & Veronica Spectacular (6/82). 519-Archie's Jokes (8/82). 520-Betty & Veronica Summer Fun (9/82). 521-The World of Archie (9/82). 522-Betty & Veronica Spectacular (10/82). 523-The World of Jughead (10/82).524-Archie's Christmas Stocking (1/83). 525-Betty and Veronica Christmas Spectacular (1/83). 526-Betty and Veronica Spectacular (5/83). 527-Little Archie (8/83). 529-Betty and Veronica Summer Fun (8/83). 530-Betty and Veronica Spectacular (9/83). 531-The World of Jughead (9/83). 532-The World of Archie (10/83). 534-Little Archie (1/84). 535-Archie's Christmas Stocking (1/84). 536-Betty and Veronica Christmas Spectacular (1/84). 537-Betty and Veronica Spectacular (6/84). 538-Little Archie (8/84). 539-Betty and Veronica Summer Fun (8/84). 541-Betty and Veronica Spectacular (9/84). 542-The World of Jughead (9/84). 543-The World of Archie (10/84). 545-Little Archie (12/84). 546-Archie's Christmas Stocking (12/84). 547-Betty and Veronica Christmas Spectacular (12/84). 548-Betty and Veronica Spectacular (6/85). 549-Little Archie. 550-Betty and Veronica Summer Fun each... 1 2 3 5 7 9

515,528,533,540,544: 515-Sabrina's Christmas Magic (1/82). 528-Josie and the Pussycats (8/83). 533-Sabrina; Space Pirates by Frank Bolling (10/83). 540-Josie and the Pussycats (8/84). 544-Sabrina the Teen-Age Witch (10/84). each... 2 4 6 11 16 20

551,562,571,584,597-Josie and the Pussycats 2 4 6 9 12 15

552-561,563-570,572-583,585-596,598-600: 552-Betty & Veronica Spectacular. 553-The World of Jughead. 554-The World of Archie. 555-Betty's Diary. 556-Little Archie (1/86). 557-Archie's Christmas Stocking (1/86). 558-Betty & Veronica Christmas Spectacular (1/86). 559-Betty & Veronica Spectacular. 560-Little Archie. 561-Betty & Veronica Summer Fun. 563-Betty & Veronica Spectacular. 564-World of Jughead. 565-World of Archie. 566-Little Archie. 567-Archie's Christmas Stocking. 568-Betty & Veronica Christmas Spectacular. 569-Betty & Veronica Spring Spectacular. 570-Little Archie. 571-Dracula-c/s. 572-Betty & Veronica Summer Fun. 573-Archie At Riverdale High. 574-World of Archie. 575-Betty & Veronica Spectacular. 576-Pep. 577-World of Jughead. 578-Archie And Me. 579-Archie's Christmas Stocking. 580-Betty and Veronica Christmas Spectacular. 581-Little Archie Christmas Special. 582-Betty & Veronica Spring Spectacular. 583-Little Archie. 585-Betty & Veronica Summer Fun. 586-Archie At Riverdale High. 587-The World of Archie (10/88); 1st app. Explorers of the Unknown. 588-Betty & Veronica Spectacular. 589-Pep (10/88). 590-The World of Jughead. 591-Archie & Me. 592-Archie's Christmas Stocking. 593-Betty & Veronica Christmas Spectacular. 594-Little Archie. 595-Betty & Veronica Spring Spectacular. 596-Little Archie. 598-Betty & Veronica Summer Fun. 599-The World of Archie (10/89); 2nd app. Explorers of the Unknown. 600-Betty and Veronica Spectacular each.... 6.00

601,602,604-609,611-629: 601-Pep. 602-The World of Jughead. 604-Archie at Riverdale High. 605-Archie's Christmas Stocking. 606-Betty and Veronica Christmas Spectacular. 607-Little Archie. 608-Betty and Veronica Spectacular. 609-Little Archie. 611-Betty and Veronica Summer Fun. 612-The World of Archie. 613-Betty and Veronica Spectacular. 614-Pep (10/90). 615-Veronica's Summer Special. 616-Archie and Me. 617-Archie's Christmas Stocking. 618-Betty & Veronica Christmas Spectacular. 619-Little Archie. 620-Betty and Veronica Spectacular. 621-Betty and Veronica Summer Fun. 622-Josie & the Pussycats; not published. 623-Betty and Veronica Spectacular. 624-Pep Comics. 625-Veronica's Summer Special. 626-Archie and Me. 627-World of Archie. 628-Archie's Pals 'n' Gals Holiday Special. 629-Betty & Veronica Christmas Spectacular. each.... 4.00

603-Archie and Me; Titanic app. 5.00

610-Josie and the Pussycats 1 3 4 6 8 10

630-631: 630-Archie's Christmas Stocking. 631-Archie's Pals 'n' Gals 4.00

632-Last issue; Betty & Veronica Spectacular 1 3 4 6 8 10

NOTE: *Archies Band-c-173,180,192; s-189,192. Archie Cavemen-165,225,232,244,249. Little Sabrina-527,534, 538,545,556,566. UFO-s-178,487,594.*

ARCHIE HALLOWEEN SPECTACULAR
Archie Comic Publs: Dec, 2017; Dec, 2018; Dec, 2019; Dec, 2020; Dec, 2021; Nov, 2022 ($2.99)

1-Halloween-themed reprints; Shultz-c 3.00
nn (12/18) Parent-c; nn (12/19) Parent-c; Sabrina app.; nn (12/20); nn (12/21); nn (11/22) 3.00

ARCHIE JUMBO COMICS DIGEST (See Archie Comic Digest)

ARCHIE – LOVE & HEARTBREAK SPECIAL
Archie Comic Publications: Apr, 2022 ($3.99, one-shot)

1-Short romantic stories by various incl. Pitilli, Grace, Cooke, Sterle, Zanfardino 4.00

ARCHIE MEETS BATMAN '66
Archie Comic Publications: Sept, 2018 - No. 6, Mar, 2019 ($3.99, limited series)

1-Parker & Moreci-s/Parent-a; multiple covers; Poison Ivy, Bookworm, Siren app. 1 3 4 6 8 10
2-6-Joker, Riddler, Penguin & Catwoman app. 6-Super Teens app. 5.00

ARCHIE MEETS RAMONES
Archie Comic Publications: 2016 ($4.99, one-shot)

1-Segura & Rosenberg-s/Lagacé-a; multiple covers; The Archies go to 1976; Sabrina app. 2 4 6 9 12 15

ARCHIE MEETS RIVERDALE
Archie Comic Publications: Jul, 2022 ($3.99, one-shot)

1-The Archie comics gang meet their TV counterparts; Kibblesmith-s 4.00

ARCHIE MEETS THE B-52s
Archie Comic Publications: Apr, 2020 ($3.99, one-shot)

1-Set in the '80s with the original line-up; Segura & Rosenberg-s/Parent-a; multiple covers 4.00

ARCHIE MEETS THE PUNISHER (Same contents as The Punisher Meets Archie)
Marvel Comics & Archie Comics Publ.: Aug, 1994 ($2.95, 52 pgs., one-shot)

1-Batton Lash story, John Buscema-a on Punisher, Stan Goldberg-a on Archie 3 6 9 14 19 24

ARCHIE MILESTONES JUMBO COMICS DIGEST
Archie Comics: Apr, 2019 - Present ($6.99/$7.99/$8.99, digest-size)

1-5-($6.99) 7.00
6-12-($7.99) 8.00
13-17-($8.99) 16-Best of the 2000s. 17-Best of the 1980s 9.00
18,19-($9.99) 18-Jughead Guide to Life 10.00

ARCHIE 1941
Archie Comic Publications: Nov, 2018 - No. 5, Mar, 2019 ($3.99, limited series)

1-5-Set in 1941 during WWII; Augustyn & Waid-s/Krause-a 4.00

ARCHIE 1955
Archie Comic Publications: Nov, 2019 - No. 5, Apr, 2020 ($3.99, limited series)

1-5-Set in 1955 at the dawn of Rock 'n' Roll; Augustyn & Waid-s/Grummett-a 4.00

ARCHIES, THE
Archie Comic Publications: Jul, 2017; Nov, 2017 - No. 7, Jul, 2018 ($4.99/$3.99)

1-7-($3.99) Segura & Rosenberg-s/Eisma-a. 3-Chvrches app. 4-The Monkees app. 6-Blondie app. 7-Josie and the Pussycats app. 4.00
... Anniversary Spectacular 1 (5/22, $2.99) New silent story; r/Life With Archie #80 3.00
..., One-Shot (7/17, $4.99) Segura & Rosenberg-s/Eisma-a; Archie forms the band 5.00

ARCHIE'S ACTIVITY COMICS DIGEST MAGAZINE
Archie Enterprises: 1985 - No. 4 (Annual, 128 pgs., digest size)

1 (Most copies are marked) 2 4 6 9 13 16
2-4 1 2 3 5 7 9

ARCHIE'S CAR
Spire Christian Comics (Fleming H. Revell co.): 1979 (49¢)

nn 3 6 9 14 19 24

ARCHIE'S CHRISTMAS LOVE-IN (See Archie Giant Series Mag. No. 169, 181,192, 205, 218, 230, 242, 454, 466, 478, 490, 502, 514)

ARCHIE'S CHRISTMAS STOCKING (See Archie Giant Series Mag. No. 1-6,10, 15, 20, 25, 31, 137, 144, 150, 158, 167, 179, 190, 203, 216, 228, 240, 452, 464, 476, 488, 500, 512, 524, 535, 546, 557, 567, 579, 592, 605, 617, 630)

ARCHIE'S CHRISTMAS STOCKING
Archie Comics: 1993 - No. 7, 1999 ($2.00-$2.29, 52 pgs.)(Bound-in calendar poster in all)

1-Dan DeCarlo-c/a 5.00
2-5 4.00
6,7: 6-(1998, $2.25). 7-(1999, $2.29) 4.00

ARCHIE'S CIRCUS
Barbour Christian Comics: 1990 (69¢)

nn 2 4 6 10 14 18

ARCHIE'S CLASSIC CHRISTMAS STORIES
Archie Comics: 2002 ($10.95, TPB)

Volume 1 - Reprints stories from 1955-1964 Archie's Christmas Stocking issues 12.00

ARCHIE'S CLEAN SLATE
Spire Christian Comics (Fleming H. Revell Co.): 1973 (35/49¢)

1-(35¢-c edition)(Some issues have nn) 3 6 9 14 19 24
1-(49¢-c edition) 2 4 6 10 14 18

ARCHIE'S DATE BOOK
Spire Christian comics (Fleming H. Revell Co.): 1981

nn-(Low print) 2 4 6 13 18 22

ARCHIE'S DOUBLE DIGEST QUARTERLY MAGAZINE
Archie Comics: 1981 - No. 252, Aug, 2014 ($1.95-$3.99, 256 pgs.) (Archie's Double Digest Magazine No. 10 on)(Title becomes Archie's Comics Digest #253 on)

1 3 6 9 16 23 30
2-10; 6-Katy Keene story. 2 4 6 10 14 18
11-30: 29-Pureheart story 2 4 6 8 10 12
31-50 1 2 3 4 5 7
51-70,100 5.00
71-99,101-237,239-251: 123-Begin $3.29-c. 170-Begin $3.69. 197-Begin $3.99-c 4.00
238-Titled Archie Double Double Digest (4/13, $5.99, 320 pages) 6.00
252-($4.99) Title changes to Archie's Comics Digest with #253 5.00

ARCHIE'S FAMILY ALBUM
Spire Christian Comics (Fleming H. Revell Co.): 1978 (39¢/49¢, 36 pgs.)

nn 2 4 6 13 18 22
nn (49¢-c edition) 2 4 6 9 13 16

ARCHIE'S FESTIVAL
Spire Christian Comics (Fleming H. Revell Co.): 1980 (49¢)

nn 2 4 6 13 18 22

ARCHIE'S FUNHOUSE DOUBLE DIGEST
Archie Comics: Feb, 2014 - No. 28, Nov, 2017 ($3.99-$7.99, digest-size)

1-5 4.00
6,19,21: 6,19-Titled Archie's Funhouse Double Double Digest ($5.99, 320 pgs.) 6.00
7-10,12-14,16,18,25,28-($4.99) Title becomes Archie's Funhouse Comics Digest 5.00
11-($7.99) Titled Archie's Funhouse Jumbo Comics Digest 8.00

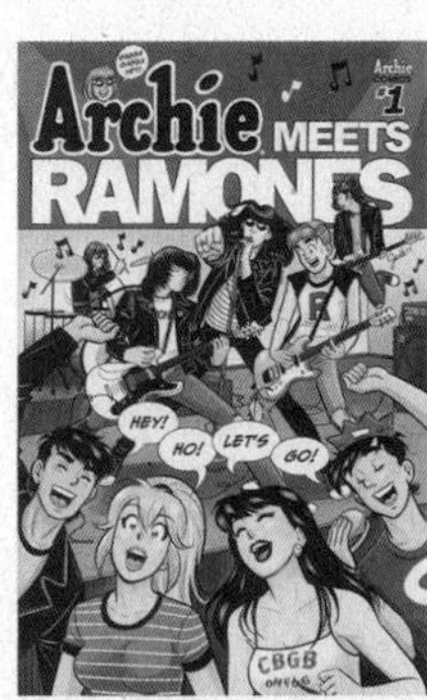

Archie Meets Ramones #1 © ACP

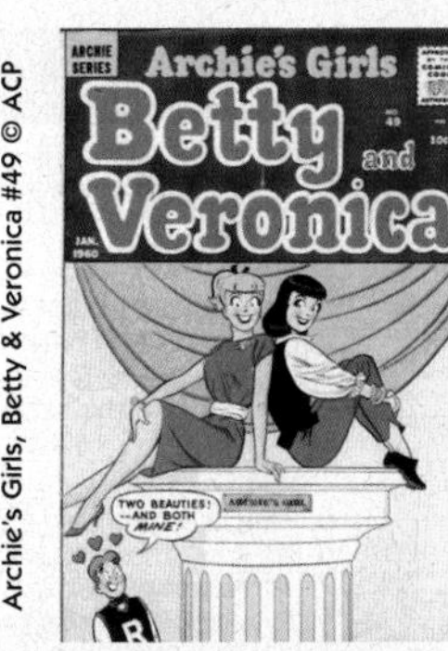

Archie's Girls, Betty & Veronica #49 © ACP

Archie's Mad House #23 © ACP

	GD 2.0	VG 4.0	FN 6.0	VF 8.0	VF/NM 9.0	NM- 9.2
15,17,20,22-($6.99) Archie's Funhouse Jumbo Comics Digest						7.00
23,24,26,27-($5.99) 23-Titled Archie's Funhouse Christmas Annual Double Digest						6.00

ARCHIE'S GIRLS, BETTY AND VERONICA (Becomes Betty & Veronica)(Also see Veronica)
Archie Publications (Close-Up): 1950 - No. 347, Apr, 1987

	GD 2.0	VG 4.0	FN 6.0	VF 8.0	VF/NM 9.0	NM- 9.2
1	360	720	1080	2520	4410	6300
2	155	310	465	992	1696	2400
3-5: 3-Betty's 1st ponytail. 4-Dan DeCarlo's 1st Archie work	97	194	291	621	1061	1500
6-10: 10-Katy Keene app. (2 pgs.)	65	130	195	416	708	1000
11-20: 11,13,14,17-19-Katy Keene app. 17-Last pre-code issue (3/55). 20-Debbie's Diary (2 pgs.)	47	94	141	296	498	700
21-30: 27,30-Katy Keene app. 29-Tarzan	37	74	111	222	361	500
31-43,45-50: 41-Marilyn Monroe and Brigitte Bardot mentioned. 45-Fabian 1 pg. photo & bio. 46-Bobby Darin 1 pg. photo & bio	21	42	63	126	206	285
44-Elvis Presley 1 pg. photo & bio	24	48	72	144	237	330
51-55,57-74: 67-Jackie Kennedy homage. 73-Sci-fi-c	9	18	27	57	111	165
56-Elvis and Bobby Darin records parody	10	20	30	66	138	210
75-Betty & Veronica sell souls to Devil	27	54	81	189	420	650
76-99: 82-Bobby Rydell 1 pg. illustrated bio; Elvis mentioned on-c. 83-Rick Nelson illo/text page. 84-Connie Francis 1 pg. illustrated bio	6	12	18	38	69	100
100	6	12	18	42	79	115
101-104, 106-117,120 (12/65): 113-Monsters-s	4	8	12	28	47	65
105-Beatles wig parody (5 pg. story)(9/64)	5	10	15	34	60	85
118-(10/65) 1st app./origin Superteen (also see Betty & Me #3)	6	12	18	42	79	115
119-2nd app./last Superteen story	5	10	15	33	57	80
121,122,124-126,128-140 (8/67): 135,140-Mod-c. 136-Slave Girl-s	3	6	9	19	30	40
123-"Jingo"-Ringo parody-c	4	8	12	23	37	50
127-Beatles Fan Club-s	5	10	15	31	53	75
141-156,158-163,165-180 (12/70)	3	6	9	15	22	28
157,164-Archies Band	3	6	9	18	28	38
181-193,195-199	2	4	6	11	16	20
194-Sabrina-c/s	4	8	12	23	37	50
200-(8/72)	3	6	9	14	19	24
201-205,207,209,211-215,217-240	2	4	6	8	10	12
206,208,210, 216: 206,208,216-Sabrina c/app. 206-Josie-c. 210-Sabrina app.	3	6	9	15	22	28
241 (1/76)-270 (6/78)	1	3	4	6	8	10
271-299: 281-UFO-s	1	2	3	5	7	9
300 (12/80)-Anniversary issue	2	4	6	8	10	12
301-309	1	2	3	4	5	7
310-John Travolta parody story	1	3	4	6	8	10
311-319						6.00
320 (10/82)-Intro. of Cheryl Blossom on cover and inside story (she also appears, but not on the cover, in Jughead #325 with same 10/82 publication date)	20	40	60	138	307	475
321-Cheryl Blossom app.	7	14	21	44	82	120
322-Cheryl Blossom app.; Cheryl meets Archie for the 1st time	7	14	21	49	92	135
323,326,329,330,331,333-338: 333-Monsters-s						6.00
324,325-Crickett O'Dell app.	2	4	6	9	12	15
327,328-Cheryl Blossom app.	3	6	9	20	31	42
332,339: 332-Superhero costume party. 339-(12/85) Betty dressed as Madonna.	2	4	6	10	14	18
340-346 Low print	1	3	4	6	8	10
347 (4/87) Last issue; low print	2	4	6	8	10	12
Annual 1 (1953)	148	296	444	947	1624	2300
Annual 2 (1954)	58	116	174	371	636	900
Annual 3-5 (1955-1957)	43	86	129	271	461	650
Annual 6-8 (1958-1960)	30	60	90	177	289	400

ARCHIE'S HOLIDAY FUN DIGEST
Archie Comics: Feb, 1997 - No. 12, Dec, 2007 ($1.75/$1.95/$1.99/$2.19/$2.39/$2.49, annual)

	GD 2.0	VG 4.0	FN 6.0	VF 8.0	VF/NM 9.0	NM- 9.2
1-12-Christmas stories						4.00

ARCHIE'S HOLIDAY MAGIC SPECIAL
Archie Comic Publications: Feb, 2022 ($3.99, one-shot)

	GD 2.0	VG 4.0	FN 6.0	VF 8.0	VF/NM 9.0	NM- 9.2
1-Short Christmas/Hanukkah stories by various incl. Ostow, Lusky, Schoening, Torres						4.00

ARCHIE SHOWCASE DIGEST
Archie Comics: Sept, 2020 - Present ($7.99/$8.99/$9.99, digest)

	GD 2.0	VG 4.0	FN 6.0	VF 8.0	VF/NM 9.0	NM- 9.2
1-6-Reprints from all eras. 2-Jughead spotlight. 3-Love Showdown						8.00
7-11-($8.99) 9,11-Christmas-c. 10-Sabrina						9.00
12-($9.99)						10.00

ARCHIE'S JOKEBOOK COMICS DIGEST ANNUAL (See Jokebook...)

ARCHIE'S JOKE BOOK MAGAZINE (See Joke Book ...)
Archie Publ: 1953 - No. 3, Sum, 1954; No. 15, Fall, 1954 - No. 288, 11/82 (subtitled...Laugh-In #127-140; ...Laugh-Out #141-194)

	GD 2.0	VG 4.0	FN 6.0	VF 8.0	VF/NM 9.0	NM- 9.2
1953-One Shot (#1)	164	328	492	1053	1802	2550
2	60	120	180	378	652	925
3 (no #4-14)	43	86	129	271	461	650
15-20: 15-Formerly Archie's Rival Reggie #14; last pre-code issue (Fall/54). 15-17-Katy Keene app.	27	54	81	162	266	370
21-30	16	32	48	98	154	210
31-43: 42-Bio of Ed "Kookie" Byrnes. 43-story about guitarist Duane Eddy	14	28	42	80	115	150
44-1st pro comic work by Neal Adams, 4 pgs.	36	72	108	214	347	480
45-47-N. Adams-a in all, 2-6 pgs.	21	42	63	122	199	275
48-Four pgs. N. Adams-a	21	42	63	122	199	275
49,50	6	12	18	57	66	95
51-56,60 (1962)	4	8	12	28	47	65
57-Elvis mentioned; Marilyn Monroe cameo	6	12	18	58	69	100
58,59-Horror/Sci-Fi-c	9	18	27	59	117	175
61-80 (8/64): 66-(12¢ cover). 76-Robot-c	3	6	9	19	30	40
66-(15¢ cover variant)	4	8	12	28	47	65
81-89,91,92,94-99	3	6	9	15	22	28
90,93: 90-Beatles gag. 93-Beatles cameo	3	6	9	17	26	35
100 (5/66)	3	6	9	16	24	32
101,103-117,119-123,127,129,131-140 (9/69): 105-Superhero gag-c. 108-110-Archies Archers Band-s. 116-Beatles/Monkees/Bob Dylan cameos (posters)	3	6	9	14	19	24
102 (7/66) Archie Band prototype-c; Elvis parody panel, Rolling Stones mention	3	6	9	18	28	38
118,124,125,126,128,130: 118-Archie Band-c; Veronica & Groovers band-s. 124-Archies Band-c/app. 125-Beatles cameo (poster). 126,130-Monkees cameo. 128-Veronica/Archies Band app.	3	6	9	16	24	32
141-173,175-181,183-199	2	4	6	9	13	16
174-Sabrina-c. 182-Sabrina cameo	2	4	6	10	14	18
200 (9/74)	2	4	6	10	14	18
201-230 (3/77)	1	3	4	6	8	10
231-239,241-287						6.00
240-Elvis record-c	2	4	6	8	10	12
288-Last issue	1	3	4	6	8	10

NOTE: *Archies Band-c-118,124,147,172; 1 pg.-s-127,128,138,140,143,147,167; 2 pg.-s-124,131, 155. Sabrina app.-247,248,252-259,261,262,264,266-270,274,277,284-286.*

ARCHIE'S JOKES (See Archie Giant Series Mag. No. 17, 22, 27, 33, 139, 146, 154, 163, 174, 186, 198, 211, 222, 235, 247, 459, 471, 483, 495, 519)

ARCHIE'S LOVE SCENE
Spire Christian Comics (Fleming H. Revell Co.): 1973 (35¢/39¢/49¢/no price)

	GD 2.0	VG 4.0	FN 6.0	VF 8.0	VF/NM 9.0	NM- 9.2
1-(35¢ Edition)	3	6	9	16	23	30
1-(39¢/49¢ Edition/no price) (Some copies have nn)	2	4	6	11	16	20

ARCHIE'S LOVE SHOWDOWN SPECIAL
Archie Publications: 1994 ($2.00, one-shot)

	GD 2.0	VG 4.0	FN 6.0	VF 8.0	VF/NM 9.0	NM- 9.2
1-Concludes x-over from Archie #429, Betty #19, B&V #82, Veronica #39	2	4	6	8	10	12

ARCHIE'S MADHOUSE (Madhouse Ma-ad No. 67 on)
Archie Publications: Sept, 1959 - No. 66, Feb, 1969

	GD 2.0	VG 4.0	FN 6.0	VF 8.0	VF/NM 9.0	NM- 9.2
1-Archie begins	46	92	138	368	834	1300
2	15	30	45	100	220	340
3-5	10	20	30	64	132	200
6-10	7	14	21	46	86	125
11-17 (Last w/regular characters)	6	12	18	35	63	90
18-21,23,29: 18-New format begins. 19-1st app. Witch Hilda. 23-No Sabrina. 29-Flying saucer-c	5	10	15	34	60	85
22-1st app. Sabrina, the Teen-age Witch and Salem the cat (10/62)	214	428	642	1766	3983	6200
24-2nd app. Sabrina and Salem; 1st app. Witch Hazel in a Sabrina story	24	48	72	168	372	575
25,26,28-Sabrina app. 25-1st app. Captain Sprocket (4/63); 3rd app. Sabrina; sci-fi/horror-c	14	28	42	93	204	315
27-Sabrina-c; no story	10	20	30	67	141	215
30-33,36,37-Sabrina app. 37-Witch Hilda now called Aunt Hilda	8	16	24	56	108	160
34,38-40: No Sabrina. 34-Bordered-c begin.	4	8	12	28	47	65
35-Beatles cameo. No Sabrina	5	10	15	31	53	75

41-44,46,47,51,54,56,57,60-62,64,66: No Sabrina. 43-Mighty Crusaders cameo. 44-Swipes Mad #4 (Super-Duperman) in "Bird Monsters From Outer Space".

	GD 2.0	VG 4.0	FN 6.0	VF 8.0	VF/NM 9.0	NM- 9.2
	4	8	12	23	37	50
45,48-50,52,53,55,58,59,63,65-Sabrina stories. 45-1st app. Rosalind. 65-1st app. Aunt Zelda	6	12	18	42	79	115
Annual 1 (1962-63) no Sabrina	12	24	36	82	179	275
Annual 2 (1964) no Sabrina	6	12	18	42	79	115
Annual 3 (1965)-r/1st app. Sabrina from #22	13	26	39	89	195	300
Annual 4,5('66-68)(Becomes Madhouse Ma-ad Annual #7 on); no Sabrina	5	10	15	31	53	75
Annual 6 (1969)-Sabrina the Teen-Age Witch-sty	8	16	24	52	99	145

NOTE: *Cover title to #61-65 is "Madhouse" and to #66 is "Madhouse Ma-ad Jokes". Sci-Fi/Horror covers 6, 8, 11, 13, 15-26, 29, 35, 36, 38, 42, 43, 48, 51, 58, 60.*

ARCHIE'S MECHANICS
Archie Publications: Sept, 1954 - No. 3, 1955

	GD	VG	FN	VF	VF/NM	NM-
1-(15¢; 52 pgs.)	116	232	348	742	1271	1800
2-(10¢)-Last pre-code issue	65	130	195	416	708	1000
3-(10¢)	55	110	165	352	601	850

ARCHIE'S MYSTERIES (Continued from Archie's Weird Mysteries)
Archie Comics: No. 25, Feb, 2003 - No. 34, June, 2004 ($2.19)

	GD	VG	FN	VF	VF/NM	NM-
25-34- Archie and gang as "Teen Scene Investigators"						4.00

ARCHIE'S ONE WAY
Spire Christian Comics (Fleming H. Revell Co.): 1972 (35¢/39¢/49¢, 36 pgs.)

	GD	VG	FN	VF	VF/NM	NM-
nn-(35¢ Edition)	3	6	9	16	23	30
nn-(39¢, 49¢, no price editions)	3	6	9	14	19	24

ARCHIE'S PAL, JUGHEAD (Jughead No. 126 on)
Archie Publications: 1949 - No. 125, Oct, 1965

	GD	VG	FN	VF	VF/NM	NM-
1 (1949)-1st app. Moose (see Pep #33)	300	600	900	2070	3635	5200
2 (1950)	116	232	348	742	1271	1800
3-5	61	122	183	390	670	950
6-10: 7-Suzie app.	41	82	123	256	428	600
11-20: 20-Jughead as Sherlock Holmes parody	28	56	84	165	270	375
21-30: 23-25,28-30-Katy Keene app. 23-Early Dilton-s. 28-Debbie's Diary app.	16	38	57	112	179	245
31-50: 49-Archies Rock 'N' Rollers band-c	8	16	24	54	102	150
51-57,59-70: 59- Bio of Will Hutchins of TV's Sugarfoot. 68-Early Archie Gang Cavemen-s	6	12	18	38	69	100
58-Neal Adams-a	7	14	21	44	82	120
71-76,83,89-99: 72-Jughead dates Betty & Veronica. 83 (4/62) 1st mention of Secret Society of Jughead Hating Girls. 95-2nd app. Cricket O'Dell	5	10	15	30	50	70
77,78,80-82,85,86,88-Horror/Sci-Fi-c. 86(7/62) 1st app. The Brain	9	18	27	57	111	165
79-Creature From the Black Lagoon-c; 1st app. Big Ethel	46	92	138	368	834	1300
84-2nd app. Big Ethel	11	22	33	73	157	240
87-3rd app. of Big Ethel; UGAJ (United Girls Against Jughead)-s	5	10	15	35	63	90
100	7	14	21	48	89	130
101-Return of Big Ethel	5	10	15	30	50	70
102-125	4	8	12	23	37	50
Annual 1 (1953, 25¢)	110	220	330	704	1202	1700
Annual 2 (1954, 25¢)-Last pre-code issue	57	114	171	362	619	875
Annual 3-5 (1955-57, 25¢)	37	74	111	218	354	490
Annual 6-8 (1958-60, 25¢)	23	46	69	138	227	315

ARCHIE'S PAL JUGHEAD COMICS (Formerly Jughead #1-45)
Archie Comic Publ.: No. 46, June, 1993 - No. 214, Sept, 2012 ($1.25-$2.99)

	GD	VG	FN	VF	VF/NM	NM-
46-214: 100-"A Storm Over Uniforms" x-over part 1,2. 166-Three Geeks cameo. 200-Tom Root-s; Sabrina cameo. 201-Begin $2.99-c						4.00

ARCHIE'S PALS 'N' GALS (Also see Archie Giant Series Magazine #628)
Archie Publ: 1952-53 - No. 6, 1957-58; No. 7, 1958 - No. 224, Sept, 1991
(...All News Stories on-c #49-59)

	GD	VG	FN	VF	VF/NM	NM-
1-(116 pgs., 25¢)	129	258	387	826	1413	2000
2(Annual)('54, 25¢)	54	108	162	343	574	825
3-5(Annual, '55-57, 25¢): 3-Last pre-code issue	39	78	117	240	395	550
6-10('58-'60)	25	50	75	150	245	340
11,13,14,16,17,20-(84 pgs.): 17-B&V paper dolls	14	28	42	82	121	160
12,15-(84 pgs.) Neal Adams-a. 12-Harry Belafonte 2 pg. photos & bio.	16	32	48	94	147	200
18-(84 pgs.) Horror/Sci-Fi-c	16	38	57	111	176	240
19-Marilyn Monroe app.	20	40	60	117	189	260
21,22,24-28,30 (68 pgs.)	7	14	21	44	82	120
23-(Wint./62) 6 pg. Josie-s with Pepper and Melody (1st app.) by DeCarlo; Betty in towel pin-up	71	142	213	568	1284	2000
29-Beatles satire (68 pgs.)	10	20	30	64	132	200
31(Wint. 64/65)-39 -(68 pgs.)	5	10	15	34	60	85
40-Early Superteen-s; with Pureheart	7	14	21	44	82	120
41(8/67)-43,45-50(2/69) (68 pgs.)	4	8	12	25	40	55
44-Archies Band-s; WEB cameo	4	8	12	28	47	65
51(4/69),52,55-64(6/71): 62-Last squarebound	3	6	9	18	28	38
53-Archies Band-c/s	3	6	9	21	33	45
54-Satan meets Veronica-s	5	10	15	34	60	85
65(8/70),67-70,73,74,76-81,83(6/74) (52 pgs.)	3	6	9	21	33	45
66,82-Sabrina-c	4	8	12	22	34	45
71,72-Two part drug story (8/72,9/72)	3	6	9	21	33	45
75-Archies Band-s	3	6	9	16	24	32
84-99	2	4	6	8	10	12
100 (12/75)	2	4	6	9	13	16
101-130(3/79): 125,126-Riverdale 2001-s	1	2	3	5	6	8
131-160,162-170 (7/84)						6.00
161 (11/82) 3rd app./1st solo Cheryl Blossom-s and pin-up; 2nd Jason Blossom	6	12	18	42	79	115
171-173,175,177-197,199: 197-G. Colan-a						5.00
174,176,198: 174-New Archies Band-s. 176-Cyndi Lauper-c. 198-Archie gang on strike at Archie Ent. offices						6.00
200(9/88)-Illiteracy-s						6.00
201,203-223: Later issues $1.00 cover						4.00
202-Explains end of Archie's jalopy; Dezerland-c/s; James Dean cameo						6.00
224-Last issue						6.00

NOTE: *Archies Band-c-45,47,49,53,56; s-44,53,75,174. UFO-s-50,63,209,220.*

ARCHIE'S PALS 'N' GALS DOUBLE DIGEST MAGAZINE
Archie Comic Publications: Nov, 1992 - No. 146, Dec, 2010 ($2.50-$3.99)

	GD	VG	FN	VF	VF/NM	NM-
1-Capt. Hero story; Pureheart app.	2	4	6	8	10	12
2-10: 2-Superduck story; Little Jinx in all. 4-Begin $2.75-c	1	2	3	4	5	7
11-29						4.00
30-146: 40-Begin $2.99-c. 48-Begin $3.19-c. 56-Begin $3.29-c. 72-Begin $3.59-c. 100-Story uses screen captures from classic animated series. 102-Begin $3.69-c 125-128-"New Look" art; Moose and Midge break up. 130-Begin $3.99-c. 133-Reggie spotlight, also reprints early apps.						4.00

ARCHIE'S PARABLES
Spire Christian Comics (Fleming H. Revell Co.): 1973,1975 (39/49¢, 36 pgs.)

	GD	VG	FN	VF	VF/NM	NM-
nn-By Al Hartley; 39¢ Edition	3	6	9	14	20	25
49¢, no price editions	2	4	6	10	14	18

ARCHIE'S R/C RACERS (Radio controlled cars)
Archie Comics: Sept, 1989 - No. 10, Mar, 1991 (95¢/$1)

	GD	VG	FN	VF	VF/NM	NM-
1						6.00
2,5-7,10: 5-Elvis parody. 7-Supervillain-c/s. 10-UFO-c/s						4.00
3,4,8,9						3.00

ARCHIE'S RIVAL REGGIE (Reggie & Archie's Joke Book #15 on)
Archie Publications: 1949 - No. 14, Aug, 1954

	GD	VG	FN	VF	VF/NM	NM-
1-Reggie 1st app. in Jackpot Comics #5	135	270	405	864	1482	2100
2	57	114	171	362	619	875
3-5	40	80	120	246	411	575
6-10	27	54	81	162	266	370
11-14: Katy Keene in No. 10-14, 1-2 pgs.	22	44	66	128	208	290

ARCHIE'S RIVERDALE HIGH (See Riverdale High)

ARCHIE'S ROLLER COASTER
Spire Christian Comics (Fleming H. Revell Co.): 1981 (69¢)

	GD	VG	FN	VF	VF/NM	NM-
nn-(Low print)	2	4	6	13	18	22

ARCHIE'S SOMETHING ELSE
Spire Christian Comics (Fleming H. Revell Co.): 1975 (39/49¢, 36 pgs.)

	GD	VG	FN	VF	VF/NM	NM-
nn-(39¢-c) Hell's Angels Biker on motorcycle-c	3	6	9	14	19	24
nn-(49¢-c)	2	4	6	10	14	18
Barbour Christian Comics Edition ('86, no price listed)	2	3	4	6	8	10

ARCHIE'S SONSHINE
Spire Christian Comics (Fleming H. Revell Co.): 1973, 1974 (39/49¢, 36 pgs.)

	GD	VG	FN	VF	VF/NM	NM-
39¢ Edition	3	6	9	14	19	24
49¢, no price editions	2	4	6	9	13	16

ARCHIE'S SPORTS SCENE
Spire Christian Comics (Fleming H. Revell Co.): 1983 (no cover price)

	GD	VG	FN	VF	VF/NM	NM-
nn-(Low print)	2	4	6	13	18	22

ARCHIE'S SPRING BREAK
Archie Comics: 1996 - No. 5, 2000 ($2.00/$2.49, 48 pgs., annual)

	GD	VG	FN	VF	VF/NM	NM-
1-5: 1,2-Dan DeCarlo-c						4.00

ARCHIE'S STORY & GAME COMICS DIGEST MAGAZINE
Archie Enterprises: Nov, 1986 - No. 39, Jan, 1998 ($1.25-$1.95, 128 pgs., digest-size)

	GD	VG	FN	VF	VF/NM	NM-
1: Marked-up copies are common	2	4	6	11	16	20
2-10	2	4	6	8	10	12
11-20	1	2	3	4	5	7
21-39: 39-($1.95)						4.00

ARCHIE'S SUPER HERO SPECIAL (See Archie Giant Series Mag. No. 142)

ARCHIE'S SUPER HERO SPECIAL (...Comics Digest Mag. 2)
Archie Publications (Red Circle): Jan, 1979 - No. 2, Aug, 1979 (95¢, 148 pgs.)

	GD	VG	FN	VF	VF/NM	NM-
1-Simon & Kirby r-/Double Life of Pvt. Strong #1,2; Black Hood, The Fly, Jaguar, The Web app.	3	6	9	16	23	30
2-Contains contents to the never published Black Hood #1; origin Black Hood; N. Adams, Wood, Channing, McWilliams, Morrow, S&K-a(r); N. Adams-c. The Shield, The Fly, Jaguar, Hangman, Steel Sterling, The Web, The Fox-r	3	6	9	15	22	28

ARCHIE'S SUPER TEENS
Archie Comic Publications, Inc.: 1994 - No. 4, 1996 ($2.00, 52 pgs.)

	GD	VG	FN	VF	VF/NM	NM-
1-Staton/Esposito-c/a; pull-out poster	2	4	6	8	10	12
2-4: 2-Fred Hembeck script; Bret Blevins/Terry Austin-a						4.00

ARCHIE'S SUPER TEENS VERSUS CRUSADERS
Archie Comic Publications: Aug, 2018 - No. 2, Sept, 2018 ($3.99, limited series)

	GD	VG	FN	VF	VF/NM	NM-
1,2-Black Hood, Steel Sterling, The Fox, The Web, The Comet, and The Shield app.						4.00

ARCHIE'S TV LAUGH-OUT ("...Starring Sabrina" on-c #1-50)
Archie Publications: Dec, 1969 - No. 105, Feb, 1986 (#1-7: 68 pgs.)

	GD	VG	FN	VF	VF/NM	NM-
1-Sabrina begins, thru #105. 1st app. Ambrose Spellman (Sabrina's cousin) and Harvey Kinkle (Sabrina's boyfriend). 1st app. of the Archie gang (Archie, Jughead, Reggie, Betty and Veronica) in a Sabrina story as Sabrina now attends Riverdale High	12	24	36	83	182	280
2 (68 pgs.)	6	12	18	42	79	115
3-6 (68 pgs.)	5	10	15	31	53	75
7-Josie begins, thru #105; Archie's & Josie's Bands cover logos begin	8	16	24	52	99	145
8-23 (52 pgs.): 10-1st Josie on-c. 12-1st Josie and Pussycats on-c. 14-Beatles cameo on poster	4	8	12	27	44	60
24-40: 37,39,40-Bicentennial-c	3	6	9	14	20	25
41,47,56: 41-Alexandra rejoins J&P band. 47-Fonz cameo; voodoo-s. 56-Fonz parody; B&V with Farrah hair-c	3	6	9	15	22	28
42-46,48-55,57-60	2	4	6	9	12	15

Archie's Pal Jughead Comics #172 © ACP

Archie's TV Laugh-Out #2 © ACP

Ares #1 © MAR

	GD 2.0	VG 4.0	FN 6.0	VF 8.0	VF/NM 9.0	NM- 9.2

61-68,70-80: 63-UFO-s. 79-Mummy-s 1 3 4 6 8 10
69-Sherlock Holmes parody 1 3 4 6 8 10
81-90,94,95,97-99: 84 Voodoo-s 1 2 3 5 6 8
91-Early Cheryl Blossom-s; Sabrina/Archies Band-c 3 6 9 21 33 45
92-A-Team parody 1 3 4 6 8 10
93-(2/84) Archie in drag-s; Hill Street Blues-s; Groucho Marx parody; cameo parody app. of Batman, Spider-Man, Wonder Woman and others 2 4 6 9 12 15
96-MASH parody-s; Jughead in drag; Archies Band-c 1 3 4 6 8 10
100-(4/85) Michael Jackson parody-c/s; J&P band and Archie band on-c 2 4 6 10 14 18
101-104-Lower print run. 104-Miami Vice parody-c 1 2 3 5 7 9
105-Wrestling/Hulk Hogan parody-c; J&P band-s 2 4 6 9 12 15

NOTE: ***Dan DeCarlo-a*** *78-up(most),* ***c****-89-up(most).* ***Archies Band-s*** *2,7,9-11,15,20,25,37,64,65,67,68,70,73,76,78,79,83,84,86,90,96,100,101;* ***Archies Band-c*** *2,17,20,91,94,96,99-103.* ***Josie-s*** *12,21,26,35,52,78,80,90.* ***Josie-c*** *10,91,94.* ***Josie and the Pussycats (as a band in costume)-s*** *7,9,10,37,38,41,42,66,84,99-101,105.* ***Josie w/Pussycats member Valerie &/or Melody-s*** *17,20,22,25,27-29,31,33,36,39,40,43-51,53-65,67-77,79,81-83,85-89,92-94,102-104.* ***Josie w/Pussycats band-c*** *12,14,17,18,22,24.* ***Sabrina-s*** *1-9,11-86,88-106.* ***Sabrina-c*** *1-18,21,23,27,49,91,94.*

ARCHIE'S VACATION SPECIAL
Archie Publications: Winter, 1994 - No. 8, 2000 ($2.00/$2.25/$2.29/$2.49, annual)

1 5.00
2-8: 8-(2000, $2.49) 4.00

ARCHIE'S VALENTINE'S SPECTACULAR
Archie Comic Publications: Mar, 2022; Mar, 2023 ($2.99, one-shot)

1-(2022) New romantic story by Rotante-s/Galvan-a; reprints by various incl. Parent 3.00
1-(2023) New story introducing Cassie Cloud 3.00

ARCHIE'S WEIRD MYSTERIES (Continues as Archie's Mysteries from #25 to #34)
Archie Comics: Feb, 2000 - No. 24, Dec, 2002 ($1.79/$1.99)

1 1 3 4 6 8 10
2-24: 3-Mighty Crusaders app. 14-Super Teens-c/app.; Mighty Crusaders app. 4.00

ARCHIE'S WORLD
Spire Christian Comics (Fleming H. Revell Co.): 1973, 1976 (39/49¢)

39¢ Edition 3 6 9 14 19 24
49¢ Edition, no price editions 2 4 6 9 13 16

ARCHIE: THE MARRIED LIFE – 10TH ANNIVERSARY
Archie Comics: Sept, 2019 - No. 6, Mar, 2020 ($3.99, limited series)

1-6-Sequel to future stories in Archie #600-605; Uslan-s/Parent-a; multiple covers 4.00

ARCHIE 3000
Archie Comics: May, 1989 - No. 16, July, 1991 (75¢/95¢/$1.00)

1,16: 16-Aliens-c/s 5.00
2-15: 6-Begin $1.00-c; X-Mas-c 4.00

ARCHIE VS. PREDATOR
Dark Horse Comics: Apr, 2015 - No. 4, Jul, 2015 ($3.99, limited series)

1-4-The Archie gang hunted by the Predator; de Campi-s/Ruiz-a; 3 covers on each 4.00

ARCHIE VS. PREDATOR II
Archie Comics: Sept, 2019 - No. 5, Mar, 2020 ($3.99, limited series)

1-5-Multiverse Archie gangs; de Campi-s/Hack-a; 3 covers on each 4.00

ARCHIE VS. SHARKNADO
Archie Comics: 2015 ($4.99, one-shot)

1-Based on the Sharknado movie series; Ferrante-s/Parent-a; 3 covers 5.00

ARCHIE VS. THE WORLD
Archie Comics: Mar, 2023 ($3.99, one-shot)

1-The Archie gang in a post-apocalyptic world; Sitterson-s/Dougherty-a 4.00

ARCOMICS PREMIERE
Arcomics: July, 1993 ($2.95)

1-1st lenticular-c on a comic (flicker-c) 4.00

AREA 52
Image Comics: Jan, 2001 - No. 4, June, 2001 ($2.95)

1-4-Haberlin-s/Henry-a 3.00

ARES
Marvel Comics: Mar, 2006 - No. 5, July, 2006 ($2.99, limited series)

1-5-Oeming-s/Foreman-a 3.00
...: God of War TPB (2006, $13.99) r/series 14.00

ARES IX: THE DARKNESS
Image Comics (Top Cow): Dec, 2018 ($3.99, one-shot)

1-Hodgdon-s/Valyogos-a; Crapo-s/Whitaker-a; The Darkness app. 4.00

ARE YOU AFRAID OF DARKSEID?
DC Comics: Dec, 2021 ($9.99, squarebound, one-shot)

1-Campfire-style ghost stories; Teen Titans, Darkseid, Harley Quinn, Batman app. 10.00

ARGUS (See Flash, 2nd Series) (Also see Showcase '95 #1,2)
DC Comics: Apr, 1995 - No. 6, Oct, 1995 ($1.50, limited series)

1-6: 4-Begin $1.75-c 3.00

ARIA
Image Comics (Avalon Studios): Jan, 1999 - No. 4, Nov, 1999 ($2.50)

Preview (11/98, $2.95) 5.00
1-Anacleto-c/a 1 2 3 5 6 8
1-Variant-c by Michael Turner 1 2 3 5 6 8
1-($10.00) Alternate-c by Turner 1 3 4 6 8 10
1,2-(Blanc & Noir) Black and white printing of pencil art 3.00
1-(Blanc & Noir) DF Edition 5.00
2-4: 2,4-Anacleto-c/a. 3-Martinez-a 3.00
4-($6.95) Glow in the Dark-c 1 3 4 6 8 10
Aria Angela 1 (2/00, $2.95) Anacleto-a; 4 covers by Anacleto, JG Jones, Portacio and Quesada 3.00
Aria Angela Blanc & Noir 1 (4/00, $2.95) Anacleto-c 3.00
Aria Angela European Ashcan 10.00
Aria Angela 2 (10/00, $2.95) Anacleto-a/c 3.00
...: A Midwinter's Dream 1 (1/02, $4.95, 7"x7") text-s w/Anacleto panels 5.00
...: Heavenly Creatures (2/21, $6.99) Reprints Aria Angela issues with Angela replaced 7.00
...: The Enchanted Collection (5/04, $16.95) r/Summer's Spell & The Uses of Enchantment 17.00

ARIA: SUMMER'S SPELL
Image Comics (Avalon Studios): Mar, 2002 - No. 2, Jun, 2002 ($2.95)

1,2-Anacleto-c/Holguin-s/Pajarillo & Medina-a 3.00

ARIA: THE SOUL MARKET
Image Comics (Avalon Studios): Mar, 2001 - No. 6, Dec, 2001 ($2.95)

1-6-Anacleto-c/Holguin-s 3.00
HC (2002, $26.95, 8.25" x 12.25") oversized r/#1-6 27.00
SC (2004, $16.95, 8.25" x 12.25") oversized r/#1-6 17.00

ARIA: THE USES OF ENCHANTMENT
Image Comics (Avalon Studios): Feb, 2003 - No. 4, Sept, 2003 ($2.95)

1-4-Anacleto-c/Holguin-s/Medina-a 3.00

ARIANE AND BLUEBEARD (See Night Music #8)

ARIEL & SEBASTIAN (See Cartoon Tales & The Little Mermaid)

ARION, LORD OF ATLANTIS (Also see Crisis on Infinite Earths & Warlord #55)
DC Comics: Nov, 1982 - No. 35, Sept, 1985

1-Story cont'd from Warlord #62 4.00
2-35 3.00
... Special #1 (11/85) 4.00

ARION THE IMMORTAL (Also see Arion, Lord of Atlantis & Showcase '95 #7)
DC Comics: July, 1992 - No. 6, Dec, 1992 ($1.50, limited series)

1-6: 4-Gustovich-a(i) 3.00

ARISTOCATS (See Movie Comics & Walt Disney Showcase No. 16)

ARISTOKITTENS, THE (...Meet Jiminy Cricket No. 1)(Disney)
Gold Key: Oct, 1971 - No. 9, Oct, 1975

1 3 6 9 19 30 40
2-5,7-9 3 6 9 14 19 24
6-(52 pgs.) 3 6 9 15 22 28

ARIZONA KID, THE (Also see The Comics & Wild Western)
Marvel/Atlas Comics(CSI): Mar, 1951 - No. 6, Jan, 1952

1 29 58 87 172 281 390
2-4: 2-Heath-a(3) 15 30 45 85 130 175
5,6 13 26 39 74 105 135

NOTE: ***Heath*** *a-1-3; c-1-3.* ***Maneely*** *c-4-6.* ***Morisi*** *a-4-6.* ***Sinnott*** *a-6.*

ARK, THE (See The Crusaders)

ARKAGA
Image Comics: Sept, 1997 ($2.95, one-shot)

1-Jorgensen-s/a 3.00

ARKANIUM
Dreamwave Productions: Sept, 2002 - No. 5 ($2.95)

1-5: 1-Gatefold wraparound-c 3.00

ARKHAM ASYLUM: LIVING HELL
DC Comics: July, 2003 - No. 6, Dec, 2003 ($2.50, limited series)

GD 2.0 | VG 4.0 | FN 6.0 | VF 8.0 | VF/NM 9.0 | NM- 9.2

1-6-Ryan Sook-a; Batman app. 3-Batgirl-c/app. 4.00

ARKHAM ASYLUM: MADNESS
DC Comics: 2010 ($19.99, HC graphic novel, dustjacket)
HC-Sam Kieth-s/a/c; Joker, Two-Face, Harley and Ivy app. 20.00
SC-(2011, $14.99) Sam Kieth-s/a/c; Joker, Two-Face, Harley and Ivy app. 15.00

ARKHAM CITY: THE ORDER OF THE WORLD
DC Comics: Dec, 2021 - No. 6, May, 2022 ($3.99, limited series)
1-6-Watters-s/Dani-a; Ten-Eyed Man, Mad Hatter, Ratcatcher & Azrael app. 4.00

ARKHAM MANOR (Follows events in Batman Eternal #30)
DC Comics: Dec, 2014 - No. 6, May, 2015 ($2.99)
1-6-Arkham Asylum re-opens in Wayne Manor; Duggan-s/Crystal-a 3.00
...: Endgame 1 (6/15, $2.99) Tieri-s/Albuquerque-c; tie-in with other Batman titles 3.00

ARKHAM REBORN
DC Comics: Dec, 2009 - No. 3, Feb, 2010 ($2.99, limited series)
1-3-David Hine-s/Jeremy Haun-a 3.00
Batman: Arkham Reborn TPB (2010, $12.99) r/#1-3, Detective Comics #864,865 and Batman: Battle For the Cowl: Arkham Asylum #1 16.00

ARMAGEDDON
Chaos! Comics: Oct, 1999 - No. 4, Jan, 2000 ($2.95, limited series)
Preview 5.00
1-4-Lady Death, Evil Ernie, Purgatori app. 3.00

ARMAGEDDON: ALIEN AGENDA
DC Comics: Nov, 1991 - No. 4, Feb, 1992 ($1.00, limited series)
1-4 3.00

ARMAGEDDON FACTOR, THE
AC Comics: 1987 - No. 2, 1987; No. 3, 1990 ($1.95)
1,2: Sentinels of Justice, Dragonfly, Femforce 3.00
3-($3.95, color)-Almost all AC characters app. 4.00

ARMAGEDDON: INFERNO
DC Comics: Apr, 1992 - No. 4, July, 1992 ($1.00, limited series)
1-4: Many DC heroes app. 3-A. Adams/Austin-a 3.00

ARMAGEDDON 2001
DC Comics: May, 1991 - No. 2, Oct, 1991 ($2.00, squarebound, 68 pgs.)
1-Features many DC heroes; intro Waverider 5.00
1-2nd & 3rd printings; 3rd has silver ink-c 4.00
2 4.00

ARMED & DANGEROUS
Acclaim Comics (Armada): Apr, 1996 - No.4, July, 1996 ($2.95, B&W)
1-4-Bob Hall-c/a & scripts 3.00
Special 1 (8/96, $2.95, B&W)-Hall-c/a & scripts. 3.00

ARMED & DANGEROUS HELL'S SLAUGHTERHOUSE
Acclaim Comics (Armada): Oct, 1996 - No. 4, Jan, 1997 ($2.95, B&W)
1-4: Hall-c/a/scripts. 3.00

ARMOR (AND THE SILVER STREAK) (Revengers Featuring... in indicia for #1-3)
Continuity Comics: Sept, 1985 - No.13, Apr, 1992 ($2.00)
1-Intro/origin Armor & the Silver Streak; Neal Adams-c/a (Newstand Ed.; red logo) 4.00
1-Direct Edition (silver logo) 5.00
2-12: 7-Origin Armor; Nebres-i 4.00
13-Direct Edition (green background) 5.00
13-Newstand Edition (purple background) 1 3 4 6 8 10

ARMORCLADS
Valiant Entertainment: Mar, 2022 - No. 5, Jul, 2022 ($3.99, limited series)
1-5-O'Connor & Buccellato-s/Garcia-a 4.00

ARMOR (DEATHWATCH 2000)
Continuity Comics: Apr, 1993 - No. 6, Nov, 1993 ($2.50)
1-6: 1-3-Deathwatch 2000 x-over 3.00

ARMOR HUNTERS
Valiant Entertainment: Jun, 2014 - No. 4, Sept, 2014 ($3.99)
1-4-Venditti-s/Braithwaite-a; X-O vs. the Hunters. 2-4-Bloodshot app. 4-Ninjak app. 4.00
...: Aftermath 1 (10/14, $3.99) Venditti-s/Cafu-a; leads into Unity #0 4.00

ARMOR HUNTERS: BLOODSHOT
Valiant Entertainment: Jul, 2014 - No. 3, Sept, 2014 ($3.99, limited series)
1-3-Joe Harris-s/Hairsine-a; Malgam app. 4.00

ARMOR HUNTERS: HARBINGER
Valiant Entertainment: Jul, 2014 - No. 3, Sept, 2014 ($3.99, limited series)
1-3-Dysart-s/Gill-a 4.00

ARMORINES (See X-O Manowar #25 for 16 pg. bound-in Armorines #0)
Valiant: June, 1994 - No. 12, June, 1995 ($2.25)
0-Stand-alone edition with cardstock-c 34.00
0-Gold 28.00
1 4.00
2-11: 7-Wraparound-c 3.00
12-Byrne-c/swipe (X-Men, 1st Series #138) 5.00

ARMORINES (Volume 2)
Acclaim Comics: Oct, 1999 - No. 4, Mar, 2000 ($3.95/$2.50, limited series)
1-($3.95) Calafiore & P. Palmiotti-a 6.00
2,3-($2.50) 4.00
4-Low print run 4 8 12 27 44 60

ARMOR WARS (Secret Wars tie-in)
Marvel Comics: Aug, 2015 - No. 5, Nov, 2015 ($3.99, limited series)
1-5-Tony Stark and other armor-clad citizens of Technopolis; Robinson-s/Takara-a 4.00

ARMOR X
Image Comics: March, 2005 - No. 4, June, 2005 ($2.95, limited series)
1-Keith Champagne-s/Andy Smith-a; flip covers on #2-4 3.00

ARMSTRONG AND THE VAULT OF SPIRITS (Archer and Armstrong)
Valiant Entertainment: Feb, 2018 ($3.99, one-shot)
1-Van Lente-s/Cafu & Robertson-a; Archer, Faith, Quantum & Woody, Ivar app. 4.00

ARMY AND NAVY COMICS (Supersnipe No. 6 on)
Street & Smith Publications: May, 1941 - No. 5, July, 1942

	GD 2.0	VG 4.0	FN 6.0	VF 8.0	VF/NM 9.0	NM- 9.2
1-Cap Fury & Nick Carter	71	142	213	454	777	1100
2-Cap Fury & Nick Carter	39	78	117	240	395	550
3,4: 4-Jack Farr-c/a	32	64	96	188	307	425
5-Supersnipe app.; see Shadow V2#3 for 1st app.; Story of Douglas MacArthur; George Marcoux-c/a	63	126	189	403	689	975

ARMY @ LOVE
DC Comics (Vertigo): May, 2007 - No. 12, Apr, 2008; V2 #1, Oct, 2008 - No. 6, Mar, 2009 ($2.99)
1-12-Rick Veitch-s/a(p); Gary Erskine-a(i) 3.00
(Vol. 2) 1-6-Veitch-s/a(p); Erskine-a(i) 3.00
...: Generation Pwned TPB (2008, $12.99) r/#6-12 13.00
...: The Hot Zone Club TPB (2007, $9.99) r/#1-5; intro. by Peter Kuper 10.00

ARMY ATTACK
Charlton Comics: July, 1964 - No. 4, Feb, 1965; V2#38, July, 1965 - No. 47, Feb, 1967

	GD 2.0	VG 4.0	FN 6.0	VF 8.0	VF/NM 9.0	NM- 9.2
V1#1	5	10	15	31	53	75
2-4(2/65)	3	6	9	21	33	45
V2#38(7/65)-47 (formerly U.S. Air Force #1-37)	3	6	9	16	24	32

NOTE: *Glanzman a-1-3. Montes/Bache a-44.*

ARMY AT WAR (Also see Our Army at War & Cancelled Comic Cavalcade)
DC Comics: Oct-Nov, 1978
1-Kubert-c; all new story and art 3 6 9 15 22 28

ARMY OF DARKNESS (Movie)
Dark Horse Comics: Nov, 1992 - No. 2, Dec, 1992; No. 3, Oct, 1993 ($2.50, limited series)

	GD 2.0	VG 4.0	FN 6.0	VF 8.0	VF/NM 9.0	NM- 9.2
1-Bolton painted-c/a in all	3	6	9	20	31	42
2,3	2	4	6	11	16	20

... Movie Adaptation TPB (2006, $14.99) r/#1-3; intro. by Busiek; Bruce Campbell interview 15.00

ARMY OF DARKNESS (Also see Marvel Zombies vs. Army of Darkness)
Dynamite Entertainment: 2005 - No. 13, 2007 ($2.99)
1-4 (Vs. Re-Animator):1,2-Four covers; Greene-a/Kuhoric-s. 3,4-Three covers 4.00
5-13: 5-7-Kuhoric-s/Sharpe-a; four covers. 8-11-Ash Vs. Dracula. 12,13-Death of Ash 4.00

ARMY OF DARKNESS: ... (Also see Death to the Army of Darkness)
Dynamite Entertainment: 2007 - No. 27, 2010 ($3.50/$3.99)
... From the Ashes 1-4-Kuhoric-s/Blanco-a; covers by Blanco & Suydam 4.00
5-8-(The Long Road Home); two covers on each 4.00
9-25: 9-12-(Home Sweet Hell), 13-King For a Day. 14-17-Hellbillies and Deadnecks 4.00
26,27-($3.99) Raicht-s/Cohn-a/c 4.00
#1992.1 (2014, $7.99, squarebound) Short stories by Kuhoric, Niles and others 8.00
...: Ash's Christmas Horror Special (2008, $4.99) Kuhoric-s/Simons-a; 2 covers 5.00
...: Convention Invasion (2014, $7.99, squarebound) Moreci-s/Peeples-a 8.00
... Election Special 1 (2016, $5.99) Serrano-s/Galindo-a 6.00
... Halloween Special One-Shot (2018, $4.99) art by Marron & Lofti; Blackbeard app. 5.00
.../ Reanimator One Shot (2013, $4.99) Rahner-s/Valiente-a 5.00

ARMY OF DARKNESS VOLUME 3
Dynamite Entertainment: 2012 - No. 13, 2013 ($3.99)
1-13: 1-Female Ash; Michaels-a 4.00

ARMY OF DARKNESS VOLUME 4
Dynamite Entertainment: 2014 - No. 5, 2015 ($3.99)
1-5-Ash in space; Bunn-s/Watts-a; multiple covers 4.00

ARMY OF DARKNESS: ASHES 2 ASHES (Movie)
Devil's Due Publ.: July, 2004 - No. 4, 2004 ($2.99, limited series)
1-4-Four covers for each; Nick Bradshaw-a 4.00
1-Director's Cut (12/04, $4.99) r/#1, cover gallery, script and sketch pages 5.00
TPB (2005, $14.99) r/series; cover gallery; Bradshaw interview and sketch pages 15.00

ARMY OF DARKNESS: ASH GETS HITCHED
Dynamite Entertainment: 2014 - No. 4, 2014 ($3.99, limited series)
1-4-Ash in medieval times; Niles-s/Tenorio-a; multiple covers 4.00

ARMY OF DARKNESS: ASH SAVES OBAMA
Dynamite Entertainment: 2009 - No. 4, 2009 ($3.50, limited series)
1-4-Serrano-s/Padilla-a; covers by Parrillo and Nauck. 4-Obama app. 6.00

ARMY OF DARKNESS/BUBBA HO-TEP
Dynamite Entertainment/IDW: 2019 - No. 4, 2019 ($3.99, limited series)
1-4-Ash meets Elvis; Duvall-s/Federici-a; multiple covers 4.00

ARMY OF DARKNESS FURIOUS ROAD
Dynamite Entertainment: 2016 - No. 6, 2016 ($3.99, limited series)
1-6-Nancy Collins-s/Kewber Baal-a. 1-Multiple covers 4.00

ARMY OF DARKNESS: 1979
Dynamite Entertainment: 2021 - No. 5, 2022 ($3.99, limited series)
1-5-Rodney Barnes-s/Tom Garcia & Ed Mennu-a; multiple covers on all; Ash in 1979 NY 4.00

ARMY OF DARKNESS: SHOP TILL YOU DROP DEAD (Movie)
Devil's Due Publ.: Jan, 2005 - No. 4, July, 2005 ($2.99, limited series)
1-4:1-Five covers; Bradshaw-a/Kuhoric-s. 2-4: Two covers. 3-Greene-a 4.00

ARMY OF DARKNESS VS. HACK/SLASH
Dynamite Entertainment: 2013 - No. 6, 2014 ($3.99, limited series)
1-6-Tim Seeley-s/Daniel Leister-a; multiple covers on each 4.00

ARMY OF DARKNESS VS. REANIMATOR: NECRONOMICON RISING
Dynamite Entertainment: 2022 - No. 5, 2022 ($3.99, limited series)
1-5-Burnham-s/Cassallos-a; multiple covers on each 4.00

ARMY OF DARKNESS / XENA

Arkham Asylum: Madness © DC

Armor Hunters #1 © VAL

Ascencia #12 © John Dolmayan

	GD	VG	FN	VF	VF/NM	NM-
	2.0	4.0	6.0	8.0	9.0	9.2

Dynamite Entertainment: 2008 - No. 4, 2008 ($3.50, limited series)
1-4-Layman-s/Montenegro-a; two covers on each 4.00

ARMY OF DARKNESS XENA: WARRIOR PRINCESS FOREVER... AND A DAY
Dynamite Entertainment: 2016 - No. 6, 2017 ($3.99, limited series)
1-6-Lobdell-s. 1-Multiple covers. 1,2-Fernandez-a. 3-6-Galindo-a 4.00

ARMY SURPLUS KOMIKZ FEATURING CUTEY BUNNY
Army Surplus Komikz/Eclipse Comics: 1982 - No. 5, 1985 ($1.50, B&W)
1-Cutey Bunny begins 2 4 6 10 14 18
2-5: 5-(Eclipse)-JLA/X-Men/Batman parody 5.00

ARMY WAR HEROES (Also see Iron Corporal)
Charlton Comics: Dec, 1963 - No. 38, June, 1970
1 8 16 24 51 96 140
2-10 4 8 12 25 40 55
11-21,23-30: 24-Intro. Archer & Corp. Jack series 3 6 9 16 23 30
22-Origin/1st app. Iron Corporal series by Glanzman 5 10 15 31 53 75
31-38 2 4 6 10 14 18
Modern Comics Reprint 36 ('78) 5.00
NOTE: ***Montes/Bache*** *a-1, 16, 17, 21, 23-25, 27-30.*

AROUND THE BLOCK WITH DUNC & LOO (See Dunc and Loo)

AROUND THE WORLD IN 80 DAYS (Movie) (See A Golden Picture Classic)
Dell Publishing Co.: Feb, 1957
Four Color 784-Photo-c 7 14 21 46 86 125

AROUND THE WORLD UNDER THE SEA (See Movie Classics)

AROUND THE WORLD WITH ARCHIE (See Archie Giant Series Mag. #29, 35, 141)

AROUND THE WORLD WITH HUCKLEBERRY & HIS FRIENDS (See Dell Giant No. 44)

ARRGH! (Satire)
Marvel Comics Group: Dec, 1974 - No. 5, Sept, 1975 (25¢)
1-Dracula story; Sekowsky-a(p) 3 6 9 20 31 42
2-5: 2-Frankenstein. 3-Mummy. 4-Nightstalker(TV); Dracula-c/app., Hunchback. 5-Invisible Man, Dracula 3 6 9 14 20 25
NOTE ***Alcala*** *a-2; c-3.* ***Everett*** *a-1r, 2r.* ***Grandenetti*** *a-4.* ***Maneely*** *a-4r.* ***Sutton*** *a-1-3.*

ARROW (See Protectors)
Malibu Comics: Oct, 1992 ($1.95, one-shot)
1-Moder-a(p) 4.00

ARROW (Based on the 2012 television series)
DC Comics: Jan, 2013 - No. 12, Dec, 2013 ($3.99, printings of digital-first stories)
1-Photo-c; origin retold; Grell-a 1 2 3 5 6 8
1-Special Edition (2012, giveaway) Grell-c; back-up preview of Green Arrow #0 3.00
2-12: 8-12-Photo-c 4.00

ARROW SEASON 2.5 (Follows the second season of the 2012 television series)
DC Comics: Dec, 2014 - No. 12, Nov, 2015 ($2.99, printings of digital-first stories)
1-12-Photo-c on most. 1-5-Brother Blood app. 5,6-Suicide Squad app. 3.00

ARROW, THE (See Funny Pages)
Centaur Publications: Oct, 1940 - No. 2, Nov, 1940; No. 3, Oct, 1941
1-The Arrow begins(r/Funny Pages) 423 846 1269 3088 5444 7800
2,3: 2-Tippy Taylor serial continues from Amazing Mystery Funnies #24. 3-Origin Dash Dartwell, the Human Meteor; origin The Rainbow-r; bondage-c
300 600 900 1950 3375 4800
NOTE: ***Gustavson*** *a-1, 2; c-3.*

ARROWHEAD (See Black Rider and Wild Western)
Atlas Comics (CPS): April, 1954 - No. 4, Nov, 1954
1-Arrowhead & his horse Eagle begin 26 52 78 154 252 350
2-4: 4-Forte-a 15 30 45 90 140 190
NOTE: ***Heath*** *c-3.* ***Jack Katz*** *a-3.* ***Maneely*** *c-2.* ***Pakula*** *a-2.* ***Sinnott*** *a-1-4; c-1.*

ARROWSMITH (Also see Astro City/Arrowsmith flip book)
DC Comics (Cliffhanger): Sept, 2003 - No. 6, May, 2004 ($2.95)
1-6-Pacheco-a/Busiek-s 3.00
...: So Smart in Their Fine Uniforms TPB (2004, $14.95) r/#1-6 15.00

ARROWSMITH: BEHIND ENEMY LINES
Image Comics: Jan, 2022 - No. 6, Jun, 2022 ($3.99)
1-6-Pacheco-a/Busiek-s 4.00

ARSENAL (Teen Titans' Speedy)
DC Comics: Oct, 1998 - No. 4, Jan, 1999 ($2.50, limited series)
1-4: Grayson-s. 1-Black Canary app. 2-Green Arrow app. 4.00

ARSENAL SPECIAL (See New Titans, Showcase '94 #7 & Showcase '95 #8)
DC Comics: 1996 ($2.95, one-shot)
1 4.00

ARTBABE
Fantagraphics Books: May, 1996 - Apr, 1999 ($2.50/$2.95/$3.50, B&W)
V1 #5, V2 #1-3 3.00
#4-($3.50) 3.50

ART BRUT
Image Comics: Dec, 2022 - Present ($3.99)
1-3-Prince-s/Morazzo-a 4.00

ARTEMIS & THE ASSASSIN
AfterShock Comics: Mar, 2020 - No. 5, Sept, 2020 ($4.99/$3.99)
1-($4.99) Stephanie Phillips-s/Meghan Hetrick & Francesca Fantini-a 5.00
2-5-($3.99) 3-5-Fantini-a 4.00

ARTEMIS IX (See Aphrodite IX)
Image Comics (Top Cow): Aug, 2015 ($3.99, one-shot)
1-Dan Wickline-s/Johnny Desjardins-a; 2 covers 4.00

ARTEMIS: REQUIEM (Also see Wonder Woman, 2nd Series #90)
DC Comics: June, 1996 - No. 6, Nov, 1996 ($1.75, limited series)
1-6: Messner-Loebs scripts & Benes-c/a in all. 1,2-Wonder Woman app. 3.00

ARTEMIS: WANTED (Wonder Woman)
DC Comics: Sept, 2022 ($5.99, one-shot)
1-Ayala-s/Patridge-a; Donna Troy and Cassie Sandsmark app. 6.00

ARTIFACT ONE
Aspen MLT: No. 0, Aug, 2018 - No. 4, Mar, 2019 ($3.99)
0-($1.50) Krul & Hernandez-s/Moranelli-a 3.00
1-4: 1-(10/18, $3.99) Krul & Hernandez-s/Moranelli-a; bonus Aspen Mascots story 4.00

ARTIFACTS
Image Comics (Top Cow): Jul, 2010 - No. 40, Nov, 2014 ($3.99, intended as a limited series)
0-(5/10, free) Free Comic Book Day edition; Sejic-a 3.00
1-39: 1-6-Marz-s/Broussard-a. 1-Multiple covers; back-up origin of Witchblade. 7,8-Portacio-a. 9-12-Haun-a. 10-Wraparound-c by Sejic. 13-Keown-a. 14-25-Sejic-a 4.00
40-($5.99) Steve Foxe-s/Adalor Alvarez-a/Sejic-c; back-up stories 6.00
... Lost Tales 1 (5/15, $3.99) Short stories by Talent Hunt runners-up 4.00
...Origins (1/12, $3.99) Two-page spread origins of the 13 artifacts; wraparound-c 4.00

ART OF HOMAGE STUDIOS, THE
Image Comics: Dec, 1993 ($4.95, one-shot)
1-Short stories and pin-ups by Jim Lee, Silvestri, Williams, Portacio & Chiodo 5.00

ART OF ZEN INTERGALACTIC NINJA, THE
Entity Comics: 1994 - No. 2, 1994 ($2.95)
1,2 3.00

ART OPS
DC Comics (Vertigo): Dec, 2015 - No. 12, Dec, 2016 ($3.99)
1-12: Shaun Simon-s/Mike Allred-c. 1-5,8,9,12-Mike Allred-a. 6,7-Eduardo Risso-a 4.00

ARZACH (See Moebius...)
Dark Horse Comics: 1996 ($6.95, one-shot)
nn-Moebius-c/a/scripts 6 12 18 38 69 100

ASCENCIA
Wake Entertainment: Jan, 2021 - Present ($3.99/$4.99)
1-11-John Dolmayan-s/Tony Parker-a 4.00
12-15 ($4.99) 13-Frank Cho-c 5.00

ASCENDER (Also see Descender)
Image Comics: Apr, 2019 - Aug, 2021 ($3.99)
1-18-Lemire-s/Nguyen-a/c in all. 4-Telsa app. 4.00

ASCENSION
Image Comics (Top Cow Productions): Oct, 1997 - No. 22, Mar, 2000 ($2.50)
Preview 6.00
Preview Gold Edition 1 3 4 6 8 10
Preview San Diego Edition 2 4 6 8 11 14
0 4.00
1/2 6.00
1-David Finch-s/a(p)/Batt-s/a(i) 4.00
1-Variant-c w/Image logo at lower right 6.00
2-22 3.00
... Collected Edition 1,2 (1998 - No. 2, $4.95, squarebound) 1-r/#1,2. 2-r/#3,4 5.00
Fan Club Edition 5.00

GD VG FN VF VF/NM NM- 2.0 4.0 6.0 8.0 9.0 9.2

ASGARDIANS OF THE GALAXY
Marvel Comics: Nov, 2018 - No. 10, Aug, 2019 ($3.99)

1-10-Angela, Valkyrie, Skurge, Thunderstrike, Throg (Thor Frog), The Destroyer team 4.00

ASH
Event Comics: Nov, 1994 - No. 6, Dec, 1995; No. 0, May, 1996 ($2.50/$3.00)

0-Present & Future (Both 5/96, $3.00, foil logo-c)-w/pin-ups 3.00
0-Blue Foil logo-c (Present and Future) (1000 each) 4.00
0-Silver Prism logo-c (Present and Future) (500 each) 10.00
0-Red Prism logo-c (Present and Future) (250 each) 20.00
0-Gold Hologram logo-c (Present and Future) (1000 each) 8.00
1-Quesada-p/story; Palmiotti-i/story: Barry Windsor-Smith pin-up 2 4 6 8 10 12
2-Mignola Hellboy pin-up 1 2 3 4 5 7
3,4: 3-Big Guy pin-up by Geoff Darrow. 4-Jim Lee pin-up 4.00
4-Fahrenheit Gold 7.00
4-6-Fahrenheit Red (5,6-1000) 8.00
4-6-Fahrenheit White 12.00
5, 6-Double-c w/Hildebrandt Bros.-a, Quesada & Palmiotti. 6-Texeira-c 3.00
5,6-Fahrenheit Gold (2000) 4.00
6-Fahrenheit White (500)-Texeira-c 12.00
Volume 1 (1996, $14.95, TPB)-r/#1-5, intro by James Robinson 15.00
Wizard Mini-Comic (1996, magazine supplement) 3.00
Wizard #1/2 (1997, mail order) 4.00

ASH AND THE ARMY OF DARKNESS (Leads into Army of Darkness: Ash Gets Hitched)
Dynamite Entertainment: 2013 - No. 8, 2014 ($3.99)

1-8: 1-5-Niles-s/Calero-a. 1-Three covers. 2-8-Two covers. 6-8-Tenorio-a 4.00

ASH & THORN
AHOY Comics: 2020 - No. 5, 2020 ($3.99)

1-5-Mariah McCourt-s/Soo Lee-a/ Jill Thompson-c 4.00

ASH: CINDER & SMOKE
Event Comics: May, 1997 - No. 6, Oct, 1997 ($2.95, limited series)

1-6: Ramos-a/Waid, Augustyn-s in all. 2-6-variant covers by Ramos and Quesada 3.00

ASH: FILES
Event Comics: Mar, 1997 ($2.95, one-shot)

1-Comics w/text 3.00

ASH: FIRE AND CROSSFIRE
Event Comics: Jan, 1999 - No. 5 ($2.95, limited series)

1,2-Robinson-s/Quesada & Palmiotti-c/a 3.00

ASH: FIRE WITHIN, THE
Event Comics: Sept, 1996 - No. 2, Jan, 1997 ($2.95, unfinished limited series)

1,2: Quesada & Palmiotti-c/s/a 3.00

ASH/ 22 BRIDES
Event Comics: Dec, 1996 - No. 2, Apr, 1997 ($2.95, limited series)

1,2: Nicieza-s/Ramos-c/a 3.00

ASH VS. THE ARMY OF DARKNESS
Dynamite Entertainment: No. 0, 2017 - No. 5, 2017 ($3.99)

0-5: 0-Sims & Bowers-s/Vargas-a; multiple covers on each 4.00

ASKANI'SON (See Adventures of Cyclops & Phoenix limited series)
Marvel Comics: Jan, 1996 - No. 4, May, 1996 ($2.95, limited series)

1-4: Story cont'd from Advs. of Cyclops & Phoenix; Lobdell/Loeb story; Gene Ha-c/a(p) 3.00
TPB (1997, $12.99) r/#1-4; Gene Ha painted-c 13.00

ASPEN (MICHAEL TURNER PRESENTS:...) (Also see Fathom)
Aspen MLT, Inc.: July, 2003 - No. 3, Aug, 2003 ($2.99)

1-Fathom story; Turner-a/Johns-s; interviews w/Turner & Johns; two covers by Turner 3.00
2,3:2-Fathom story; Turner-a/Johns-s; two covers by Turner; pin-ups and interviews 3.00
... Presents: The Adventures of the Aspen Universe (10/16, free) coloring book; Oum-a 3.00
... Seasons: Fall 2005 (12/05, $2.99) short stories by various; Turner-c 3.00
... Seasons: Spring 2005 (4/05, $2.99) short stories by various; Turner-c 3.00
... Seasons: Summer 2006 (10/06, $2.99) short stories by various; Turner-c 3.00
... Seasons: Winter 2009 (3/09, $2.99) short stories by various; Benitez-c 3.00
... Showcase: Aspen Matthews 1 (7/08, $2.99) Caldwell-a 3.00
... Showcase: Kiani 1 (10/09, $2.99) Scott Clark-a; covers by Clark and Caldwell 3.00
... Sketchbook 1 (2003, $2.99) sketch pages by Michael Turner and Talent Caldwell 3.00
... Splash: 2006 Swimsuit Spectacular 1 (3/06, $2.99) pin-up pages by various; Turner-c 3.00
... Splash: 2007 Swimsuit Spectacular 1 (8/07, $2.99) pin-up pages by various; Turner-c 3.00
... Splash: 2008 Swimsuit Spectacular 1 (7/08, $2.99) pin-up pages by various; Turner-c 3.00
... Splash: 2010 Swimsuit Spectacular 1 (8/10, $2.99) pin-up pages by various; 2 covers 3.00
... Splash: 2018 Swimsuit Spectacular 1 (7/18, $3.99) pin-up pages by various; 2 covers 4.00
...: The Year Ahead 2019 1 (2/19, 25¢) Previews, summaries of TPBs, creator profiles 3.00
... Universe Sourcebook 1 (7/16, $5.99) Character profiles for Fathom, Soulfire, Iris 6.00

ASPEN SHOWCASE
Aspen MLT: Oct, 2008 ($2.99)

...: Benoist 1 (10/08) - Krul-s/Gunnell-a; two covers by Gunnell & Manapul 3.00
...: Ember 1 (2/09) - Randy Green-a; two covers by Gunnell & Green 3.00

ASPEN UNIVERSE: DECIMATION
Aspen MLT: No. 0, May, 2017; No. 1, Oct, 2017 - No. 4, Jan, 2018 (free/$3.99)

0-(5/17, free) Prelude to Aspen crossover series; Hernandez-s/Renna & Bazaldua-a 3.00
1-4-($3.99) Hernandez-s/Renna-a 4.00

ASPEN UNIVERSE: REVELATIONS
Aspen MLT: Jul, 2016 - No. 5, Dec, 2016 ($3.99)

1-5-Fathom & Soulfire crossover; Fialkov & Krul-s/Gunderson-a; multiple covers 4.00

ASPEN VISIONS
Aspen MLT: Jan, 2019 - Mar, 2019 ($3.99)

...: Executive Assistant: Iris: The Midst of Chaos 1 (1/19) - Northcott-s/Tran-a; 4 covers 4.00
...: Fathom: Spinning Our Fate 1 (2/19) - Northcott-s/Sta Maria-a; 4 covers 4.00
...: Soulfire: The Heart of Eternity 1 (3/19) - Northcott-s/Cafaro-a; 4 covers 4.00

ASSASSINISTAS
IDW Publishing (Black Crown): Dec, 2017 - No. 6, May, 2018 ($3.99)

1-6-Tini Howard-s/Gilbert Hernandez-a 4.00

ASSASSIN NATION
Image Comics (Skybound): Mar, 2019 - No. 5, Jul, 2019 ($3.99, limited series)

1-5-Kyle Starks-s/Erica Henderson-a/c 4.00

ASSASSINS
DC Comics (Amalgam): Apr, 1996 ($1.95)

1 3.00

ASSASSIN'S APPRENTICE (Adaptation of Robin Hobb's fantasy novel)
Dark Horse Comics: Dec, 2022 - No. 6 ($3.99, limited series)

1-3-Robin Hobb & Jody Houser-s/Ryan Kelly-a 4.00

ASSASSIN'S CREED (Based on the Ubisoft Entertainment videogame)
Titan Comics: Nov, 2015 - No. 14, Feb, 2017 ($3.99/$4.99)

1-Trial By Fire; Del Col & McCreery-s/Edwards-a; multiple-c 6.00
2-12: 2-5-Trial By Fire. 6-11-Setting Sun 4.00
13,14-($4.99) Homecoming 5.00
... Free Comic Book Day (5/16, giveaway) Alves-a; Great Wall back-up w/Calero-a 3.00

ASSASSIN'S CREED: AWAKENING (Based on the Ubisoft Entertainment videogame)
Titan Comics: Dec, 2016 - No. 6, May, 2017 ($4.99, B&W manga style, reads right to left)

1-6-Takashi Yano-s/Kenji Oiwa-a 5.00

ASSASSIN'S CREED: CONSPIRACIES (Based on the Ubisoft Entertainment videogame)
Titan Comics: Sept, 2018 - No. 2, Oct, 2018 ($5.99, limited series)

1,2: 1-Dorison-s/Hostache-a. 2-Pion-a 6.00

ASSASSIN'S CREED: LOCUS (Based on the Ubisoft Entertainment videogame)
Titan Comics: Oct, 2016 - No. 4, Jan, 2017 ($3.99, limited series)

1-4-Edginton-s/Wijngaard-a 4.00

ASSASSIN'S CREED: ORIGINS (Based on the Ubisoft Entertainment videogame)
Titan Comics: Mar, 2018 - No. 4, Jul, 2018 ($3.99, limited series)

1-4-Del Col-s/Kaiowa-a. 1-Four covers. 2-4-Two covers 4.00

ASSASSIN'S CREED: REFLECTIONS (Based on the Ubisoft Entertainment videogame)
Titan Comics: Apr, 2017 - No. 4, Aug, 2017 ($3.99, limited series)

1-4-Edginton-s/Favoccia-a 4.00

ASSASSIN'S CREED: THE FALL (Based on the Ubisoft Entertainment videogame)
DC Comics: Jan, 2011 - No. 3, Mar, 2011 ($3.99, limited series)

1-3-Cam Stewart & Karl Kerschl-s/a 4.00

ASSASSIN'S CREED: UPRISING (Based on the Ubisoft Entertainment videogame)
Titan Comics: Feb, 2017 - No. 8, Nov, 2017 ($3.99)

1-Paknadel & Watters-s/Holder-a; multiple covers 1 2 3 5 6 8
2-8-Paknadel & Watters-s/Holder-a; multiple covers 5.00

ASSASSIN'S CREED VALHALLA: FORGOTTEN MYTHS (Ubisoft Entertainment videogame)
Dark Horse Comics: Mar, 2022 - No. 3, May, 2022 ($3.99)

1-3-Alexander Freed-s/Martín Túnica-a 4.00

ASSASSIN'S CREED VALHALLA: SONG OF GLORY (Ubisoft Entertainment videogame)
Dark Horse Comics: Oct, 2020 - No. 3, Dec, 2020 ($3.99)

1-3-Cavan Scott-s/Martín Túnica-a 4.00

ASSIGNMENT, THE (Adapts screenplay of 2017 movie The Assignment)
Titan Comics (Hard Case Crime): Feb, 2017 - No. 3, Apr, 2017 ($5.99)

1-3-Walter Hill & Denis Hamill-s/Jef-a; English version of French comic 6.00

ASSAULT ON NEW OLYMPUS PROLOGUE
Marvel Comics: Jan, 2010 ($3.99, one-shot)

1-Spider-Man, Hercules, Amadeus Cho app.; Granov-c; leads into Inc. Hercules #138 4.00

ASTONISHING (Formerly Marvel Boy No. 1, 2)
Marvel/Atlas Comics(20CC): No. 3, Apr, 1951 - No. 63, Aug, 1957

3-Marvel Boy continues; 3-5-Marvel Boy-c 219 438 657 1402 2401 3400
4-Classic skeletons-c; 4-Stan Lee app. 200 400 600 1280 2190 3100
5,6-Last Marvel Boy 142 284 426 909 1555 2200
7-10: 7-Maneely s/f story. 10-Sinnott s/f story 63 126 189 403 689 975
11,12,15,17,20 54 108 162 343 574 825
13,14,16,18,19-Krigstein-a. 18-Jack The Ripper sty 55 110 165 352 601 850
21,22,24 43 86 129 271 461 650
23-E.C. swipe "The Hole In The Wall" from Vault Of Horror #16 53 106 159 334 567 800
25,29: 25-Crandall-a. 29-Decapitation-c 43 86 129 271 461 650
26-28 41 82 123 256 428 600
30-Tentacled eyeball-c/story; classic-c 314 628 942 2198 3849 5500
31-Classic story: man develops atomic powers after exposure to A-bomb; four A-bomb panels 74 148 222 470 810 1150
32-37-Last pre-code issues 37 74 111 222 361 500
38-43,46,48-52,56,58,59,61 29 58 87 170 278 385
44,45,47,53-55,57,60: 44-Crandall swipe/Weird Fantasy #22. 45,47-Krigstein-a. 53-Ditko-a. 54-Torres-a, 55-Crandall, Torres-a. 57-Williamson/Krenkel-a (4 pgs.). 60-Williamson/Mayo-a (4 pgs.) 32 64 96 188 307 425
62,63: 62-Torres, Powell-a. 63-Woodbridge-a 32 64 96 188 307 425

NOTE: ***Ayers** a-16, 49. **Berg** a-36, 53, 56. **Cameron** a-50. **Gene Colan** a-12, 20, 29, 56. **Ditko** a-53. **Drucker** a-41, 62. **Everett** a-3-6(3), 6, 10, 12, 37, 47, 48, 58; c-3-5, 13,15, 16, 18, 29, 47, 49, 51, 53-55, 57, 59-63. **Fass** a-11, 34. **Forte** a-26, 48, 53, 58, 60. **Fuje** a-11. **Heath** a-8, 29; c-8, 9, 19, 22, 25, 26. **Kirby** a-56. **Lawrence** a-28, 37, 38, 42. **Maneely** a-7(2), 19; c-7, 31, 33, 34, 56. **Moldoff** a-33. **Morisi** a-10, 60. **Morrow** a-52, 61. **Orlando** a-47, 58, 61. **Pakula** a-10. **Powell** a-43, 44, 48. **Ravielli** a-26, 28. **Reinman** a-32, 34, 38. **Robinson** a-20. **J. Romita** a-7, 18, 24, 43, 57,61. **Roussos** a-55. **Sale** a-28, 38, 59; c-32. **Sekowsky** a-13. **Severin** c-46. **Shores** a-16, 60. **Sinnott** a-11, 30, 31. **Whitney** a-13. **Ed Win** a-20. Canadian reprints exist.*

ASTONISHING ANT-MAN (Scott Lang)
Marvel Comics: Dec, 2015 - No. 13, Dec, 2016 ($3.99)

1-12: 1-Spencer-s/Rosanas-a; Cassie Lang app. 2,3-Capt. America (Sam Wilson) app. 4.00
13-($4.99) Spencer-s/Schoonover & Rosanas-a; Yellowjacket app. 5.00

ASTONISHING SPIDER-MAN AND WOLVERINE

Aspen Universe: Revelations #2 © Aspen MLT

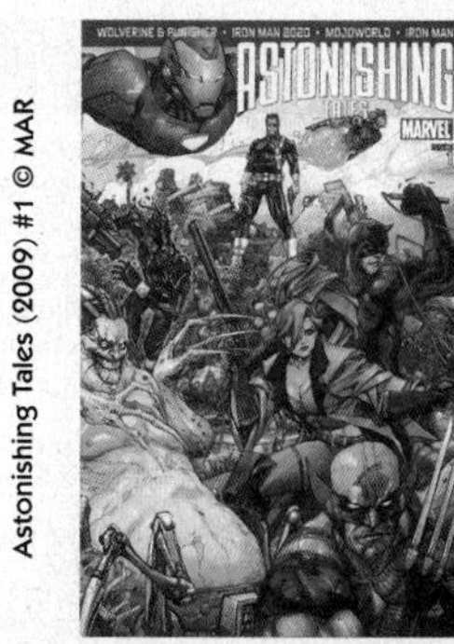

Astonishing Tales (2009) #1 © MAR

Astro City #23 © Juke Box

	GD	VG	FN	VF	VF/NM	NM-
	2.0	4.0	6.0	8.0	9.0	9.2

Marvel Comics: Jul, 2010 - No. 6, Jul. 2011 ($3.99, limited series)

1-6-Adam Kubert-a/Jason Aaron-s. 1-Bonus pin-up gallery; wraparound-c 4.00
1-Director's Cut (10/10, $4.99) r/#1 with full script & B&W art 5.00
...: Another Fine Mess (6/11, $4.99) r/#1-3; wraparound-c 5.00

ASTONISHING TALES (See Ka-Zar)
Marvel Comics Group: Aug, 1970 - No. 36, July, 1976 (#1-7: 15¢; #8: 25¢)

1-Ka-Zar (by Kirby(p) #1,2; by B. Smith #3-6) & Dr. Doom (by Wood #1-4; by Tuska #5,6; by Colan #7,8; 1st Marvel villain solo series) double feature begins; Kraven the Hunter-c/story; Nixon cameo 7 14 21 46 86 125
2-Kraven the Hunter-c/story; Kirby, Wood-a 4 8 12 25 40 55
3-5: B. Smith-p; Wood-a-#3,4. 5-Red Skull app. 4 8 12 27 44 60
6-1st app. Bobbi Morse (later becomes Mockingbird); Doctor Doom vs. Black Panther-c/sty; 15 30 45 103 227 350
7-Last 15¢ issue; Black Panther app. 3 6 9 18 28 38
8-(25¢, 52 pgs.)-Last Dr. Doom of series 4 8 12 27 44 60
9-All Ka-Zar issues begin; Lorna-r/Lorna #14 3 6 9 14 19 24
10-B. Smith/Sal Buscema-a. 3 6 9 15 22 28
11-Origin Ka-Zar & Zabu; death of Ka-Zar's father 3 6 9 15 22 28
12-2nd app.Man-Thing; by Neal Adams (see Savage Tales #1 for 1st app.) 10 20 30 69 147 225
13-3rd app.Man-Thing 7 14 21 46 86 125
14-20: 14-Jann of the Jungle-r (1950s); reprints censored Ka-Zar-s from Savage Tales #1. 17-S.H.I.E.L.D. begins. 19-Starlin-a(p). 20-Last Ka-Zar (continues into 1974 Ka-Zar series); Nick Fury & S.H.I.E.L.D. app. 2 4 6 8 10 12
21-(12/73)-It! the Living Colossus begins, ends #24 (see Supernatural Thrillers #1) 4 8 12 27 44 60
22 3 6 9 18 28 38
23,24-It! the Living Colossus vs. Fin Fang Foom 4 8 12 28 47 65
25-1st app. Deathlok the Demolisher; full length stories begin, end #36; Perez's 1st work, 2 pgs. (8/74) 24 48 72 168 372 575
26-Deathlok app. 4 8 12 25 40 55
27,28,30 3 6 9 15 22 28
29-Reprints origin/1st app. Guardians of the Galaxy from Marvel Super-Heroes #18 plus-c w/4 pgs. omitted; no Deathlok story 4 8 12 27 44 60
31,32,34: 31-Watcher-r/Silver Surfer #3 2 4 6 11 16 20
33-1st Hellinger 4 8 12 25 40 55
35,36-(Regular 25¢ edition)(5,7/76) 2 4 6 11 16 20
35,36-(30¢-c, low distribution) 8 16 24 31 96 140

NOTE: ***Buckler*** *a-13i, 16p, 25, 26p, 27p, 28, 29p-36p; c-13, 25p, 26-30, 32-35p, 36.* ***John Buscema*** *a-9, 12p-14p, 16p; c-4-6p, 12p.* ***Colan*** *a-7p, 8p.* ***Ditko*** *a-21r.* ***Everett*** *a-6i.* ***G. Kane*** *a-11p, 15p; c-9, 10p, 11p, 14, 15p, 21p.* ***McWilliams*** *a-30i.* ***Starlin*** *a-19p; c-16p.* ***Sutton & Trimpe*** *a-8.* ***Tuska*** *a-5p, 6p, 8p.* ***Wood*** *a-1-4.* ***Wrightson*** *c-31i.*

ASTONISHING TALES (Anthology)
Marvel Comics: Apr, 2009 - No. 6, Sept, 2009 ($3.99, limited series)

1-6-Wolverine, Punisher, Iron Man and Iron Man 2020 app. 1-Wraparound-c 4.00

ASTONISHING THOR
Marvel Comics: Jan, 2011 - No. 5, Sept, 2011 ($3.99, limited series)

1-5: 1-Robert Rodi-s/Mike Choi-a/Esad Ribic-c 4.00

ASTONISHING X-MEN
Marvel Comics: Mar, 1995 - No. 4, July, 1995 ($1.95, limited series)

1-Age of Apocalypse; Magneto-c 6.00
2-4 3.00

ASTONISHING X-MEN
Marvel Comics: Sept, 1999 - No. 3, Nov, 1999 ($2.50, limited series)

1-New team, Cable & X-Man app.; Peterson-a 6.00
2,3 3.00
TPB (11/00, $15.95) r/#1-3, X-Men #92 & #95, Uncanny X-Men #375 16.00

ASTONISHING X-MEN (See Giant-Size Astonishing X-Men for story folllowing #24)
Marvel Comics: July, 2004 - No. 68, Dec, 2013 ($2.99/$3.99)

1-Whedon-s/Cassaday-c/a; team of Cyclops, Beast, Wolverine, Emma Frost & Kitty Pryde 8.00
1-Director's Cut (2004, $3.99) different Cassaday partial sketch-c; cover gallery, sketch pages and script excerpt 6.00
1-Variant-c by Cassaday 12.00
1-Variant-c by Dell'Otto 10.00
2,5-X-Men battle Ord (in #2-6) 3.00
3-1st app. (cameo) Abigail Brand 3 6 9 14 19 24
4-Colossus returns 2 4 6 8 10 12
4-Variant Colossus cover by Cassaday 2 4 6 9 12 15
6-1st full app. Abigail Brand 3 6 9 16 24 32
7-24: 7-Fantastic Four app. 9,10-X-Men vs. the Danger Room 3.00
7,9,10-12,19-24-Second printing variant covers 3.00
25-35: 25-Ellis-s/Bianchi-a begins; Bianchi wraparound-c. 31-Jimenez-a begins 3.00
36-68-($3.99): 36-Pearson wraparound-c; Way-s/Pearson-a. 44-47-McKone-a. 51-Northstar wedding; wraparound-c. 60-X-Termination tie-in 4.00
Annual 1 (1/13, $4.99) Gage-s/Baldeon-a; bonus r/Alpha Flight #106 5.00
.../Amazing Spider-Man: The Gauntlet Sketchbook ('09, giveaway) flip book preview 3.00
...: Ghost Boxes 1,2 (12/08-1/09, $3.99) Ellis-s/Davis & Granov-a; full Ellis script 4.00
... Saga (2006, $3.99) reprints highlights from #1-12; sketch pages and cover gallery 4.00
... Sketchbook Special ('08, $2.99) Costume sketches & blueprints by Bianchi & Larroca 3.00
...Vol. 1 HC (2006, $29.99, dust jacket) r/#1-12; interviews, sketch pages and covers 30.00
...Vol. 1: Gifted (2004, $14.99) r/#1-6; variant cover gallery 15.00
...Vol. 2: Dangerous (2005, $14.99) r/#7-12; variant cover gallery 15.00
...Vol. 3: Torn (2007, $14.99) r/#13-18; variant & sketch cover gallery 15.00

ASTONISHING X-MEN
Marvel Comics: Sept, 2017 - No. 17, Jan, 2019 ($4.99/$3.99)

1-($4.99) Soule-s/Cheung-a; Old Man Logan, Rogue, Bishop, Gambit, Psylocke app. 5.00
2-17-($3.99) 2-Deodato-a; Mystique app. 3-McGuinness-a. 4-Pacheco-a. 7-Xavier returns; Noto-a. 13,14-Havok & Banshee return; Land-a 4.00
Annual 1 (10/18, $4.99) Rosenberg-s/Foreman-a; Xavier & Lucifer app. 5.00

ASTONISHING X-MEN: XENOGENESIS
Marvel Comics: July, 2010 - No. 5, Apr, 2011 ($3.99, limited series)

1-5-Warren Ellis-s/Kaare Andrews-a/c. 1-Wraparound-c; script 4.00
1-Director's Cut (10/10, $4.99) r/#1 with full script & B&W art; cover sketches 5.00

ASTOUNDING SPACE THRILLS: THE COMIC BOOK
Image Comics: Apr, 2000 - No. 4, Dec, 2000 ($2.95, limited series)

1-4-Steve Conley-s/a. 2,3-Flip book w/Crater Kid 3.00
Galaxy-Sized Astounding Space Thrills 1 (10/01, $4.95) 5.00

ASTOUNDING WOLF-MAN
Image Comics: Jun, 2007 - No. 25, Nov, 2010 ($2.99)

1-Free Comic Boy Day issue; Kirkman-s/Howard-a; origin story 3.00
2-24: 11-Invincible x-over from Invincble #57 3.00
25-($4.99) Wraparound-c; Wolfcorps app. 5.00
Vol. 1 TPB (2008, $14.99) r/#1-7; sketch pages; Kirkman intro. 15.00

ASTRA
CPM Manga: 2001 - No. 8 ($2.95, B&W, limited series)

1-8: Created by Jerry Robinson; Tanaka-a. 1-Balent variant-c 3.00
TPB (2002, $15.95) r/#1-8; JH Williams III-c from #3 16.00

ASTRO BOY (TV) (See March of Comics #285 & The Original...)
Gold Key: August, 1965 (12¢)

1(10151-508) 1st app. Astro Boy in comics 37 74 111 274 612 950

ASTRO BOY THE MOVIE (Based on the 2009 CGI movie)
IDW Publishing: 2009 ($3.99, limited series)

...Official Movie Adaptation 1-4 (8/09 - No. 4, 9/09, $3.99) EJ Su-a 4.00
...Official Movie Prequel 1-4 (5/09 - No. 4, 8/09) Jourdan-a/c; Ashley Wood var-c on each 4.00

ASTRO CITY (Also see Kurt Busiek's Astro City)
DC Comics (WildStorm Productions): Dec, 2004 - Dec, 2009 (one-shots)

...#1 Special Edition (8/10, $1.00) reprints first issue with "What's Next? cover logo 4.00
...: Astra Special 1,2 (11/09, 12/09, $3.99) Busiek-s/Anderson-a/Ross-c 4.00
... A Visitor's Guide (12/04, $5.95) short story, city guide and pin-ups by various; Ross-c 6.00
...: Beautie (4/08, $3.99) Busiek-s/Anderson-a/Ross-c; origin 4.00
...: Samaritan (9/06, $3.99) Busiek-s/Anderson-a/Ross-c; origin of Infidel 4.00
...: Shining Stars HC (2011, $24.99, d.j) r/...: Astra Special 1,2, ...: Beautie, ...: Samaritan, and ...: Silver Agent 1,2; bonus design art and Ross cover sketch art 25.00
...: Silver Agent 1,2 (8,9/10, $3.99) Busiek-s/Anderson-a/Ross-c 4.00

ASTRO CITY (Also see Kurt Busiek's Astro City)
DC Comics (Vertigo): Aug, 2013 - No. 52, Aug, 2018 ($3.99)

1-52-Busiek-s/Ross-c; Anderson-a in most. 12-Nolan-a. 17-Grummett-a. 22,25-Merino-a. 35,36-Ron Randall-a; Jack-In-The Box app. 39,40-Carnero-a. 47-Origin G-Dog 4.00

ASTRO CITY / ARROWSMITH (Flip book)
DC Comics (WildStorm Productions): Jun, 2004 ($2.95, one-shot flip book)

1-Intro. Black Badge; Ross-c; Arrowsmith a/c by Pacheco 5.00

ASTRO CITY: DARK AGE
DC Comics (WildStorm Productions): Aug, 2005 - No. 4, Dec, 2005 ($2.95, limited series)

Book One 1-4-Busiek-s/Anderson-a/Ross-c; Silver Agent and The Blue Knight app. 3.00
Book Two #1-4 (1/07-11/07, $2.99) Busiek-s/Anderson-a/Ross-c 3.00
Book Three #1-4 (7/09-10/09, $3.99) Busiek-s/Anderson-a/Ross-c 4.00
Book Four #1-4 (3/10-6/10, $3.99) Busiek-s/Anderson-a/Ross-c 4.00
... 1: Brothers and Other Strangers HC (2008, $29.99, d.j.) r/Book One #1-4, Book Two #1-4, and story from Astro City/Arrowsmith #1; Marc Guggenheim intro.; new Ross-c 30.00
... 1: Brothers and Other Strangers SC (2009, $19.99) same contents as HC 20.00

GD VG FN VF VF/NM NM-
2.0 4.0 6.0 8.0 9.0 9.2

... 2: Brothers in Arms HC ('10, $29.99, d.j.) r/Book Three #1-4, Book Four #1-4, Ross-c 30.00

ASTRO CITY: LOCAL HEROES
DC Comics (WildStorm Productions): Apr, 2003 - No. 5, Feb, 2004 ($2.95, limited series)
1-5-Busiek-s/Anderson-a/Ross-c 3.00
HC (2005, $24.95) r/series; Kurt Busiek's Astro City V2 #21,22; stories from Astro City/ Arrowsmith #1; and 9-11, The World's Finest... Vol. 2; Alex Ross sketch pages 25.00
SC (2005, $17.99) same contents as HC 18.00

ASTRO CITY: THAT WAS THEN... SPECIAL
Image Comics: Mar, 2022 ($3.99, one-shot)
1-Spotlight on the Jayhawks; Busiek-s/Anderson-a/Ross-c 4.00

ASTRO HUSTLE
Dark Horse Comics: Mar, 2019 - No. 2, Apr, 2019 ($3.99, unfinished limited series of 4 issues)
1,2-Jai Nitz-s/Tom Reilly-a 4.00

ASTRONAUTS IN TROUBLE
Image Comics: Jun, 2015 - No. 11 ($2.99, B&W, reprints of earlier Astronauts in Trouble)
1-11-Larry Young-s. 1-3-Reprints the Space: 1959 series; Charlie Adlard-a. 4-9-Reprints the Live From the Moon series. 4-6-Matt Smith-a. 7-11-Adlard-a 3.00

ASYLUM
Millennium Publications: 1993 ($2.50)
1-3: 1-Bolton-c/a; Russell 2-pg. illos 3.00

ASYLUM
Maximum Press: Dec, 1995 - No. 11, Jan, 1997 ($2.95/$2.99, anthology) (#1-6 are flip books)
1-11: 1-Warchild by Art Adams, Beanworld, Avengelyne, Battlestar Galactica. 2-Intro Mike Deodato's Deathkiss. 4-1st app.Christian; painted Battlestar Galactica story begins. 6-Intro Bionix (Six Million Dollar Man & the Bionic Woman). 7-Begin $2.99-c. 8-B&W-a. 9- Foot Soldiers & Kid Supreme. 10-Lady Supreme by Terry Moore-c/app. 4.00

ATARI FORCE (Also see Promotional comics section)
DC Comics: Jan, 1984 - No. 20, Aug, 1985 (Mando paper)
1-(1/84)-Intro Tempest, Packrat, Babe, Morphea, & Dart; García-López-a 1 3 4 6 8 10
2-20 5.00
Special 1 (4/86) 6.00
NOTE: *Byrne c-Special 1i. Giffen a-12p, 13i. Rogers a-18p, Special 1p.*

A-TEAM, THE (TV) (Also see Marvel Graphic Novel)
Marvel Comics Group: Mar, 1984 - No. 3, May, 1984 (limited series)
1-Marie Severin-a/John Romita-c 3 6 9 16 23 30
2,3: 2-Mooney-a. 3-Kupperberg-s/a 2 4 6 9 12 15
1,2-(Whitman bagged set) w/75¢-c 3 6 9 17 26 35
3-(Whitman, no bag) w/75¢-c 3 6 9 16 23 30

A-TEAM: SHOTGUN WEDDING (Based on the 2010 movie)
IDW Publishing: Mar, 2010 - No. 4, Apr, 2010 ($3.99, limited series)
1-4-Co-plotted by Joe Carnahan; Stephen Mooney-a; Snyder III-c 4.00

A-TEAM: WAR STORIES (Based on the 2010 movie)
IDW Publishing: Mar, 2010 - Apr, 2010 ($3.99, series of one-shots)
...: B.A. (3/10) Dixon & Burnham-s/Maloney-a/Gaydos & photo-c 4.00
...: Face (4/10) Dixon & Burnham-s/Muriel-a/Gaydos & photo-c 4.00
...: Hannibal (3/10) Dixon & Burnham-s/Petrus-a/Gaydos & photo-c 4.00
...: Murdock (4/10) Dixon & Burnham-s/Vilanova-a/Gaydos & photo-c 4.00

ATHENA INC. THE MANHUNTER PROJECT
Image Comics: Dec, 2001; Apr, 2002 - No. 6 ($2.95/$4.95/$5.95)
...The Beginning (12/01, $5.95) Anacleto-c/a; Haberlin-s 6.00
1-5: 1-(4/02, $2.95) two covers by Anacleto 3.00
6-($4.95) 5.00
...: Agents Roster #1 (11/02, $5.95, 8 1/2 x 11") bios and sketch pages by Anacleto 6.00
Vol. 1 TPB (4/03, $19.95) r/#1-6 & Agents Roster; cover gallery 20.00

ATHENA
Dynamite Entertainment: 2009 - No. 4, 2010 ($3.50)
1-4-Murray-s/Neves-a; multiple covers on each. 1-Obama flip cover 3.50

ATHENA IX (See Aphrodite IX)
Image Comics (Top Cow): Jul, 2015 ($3.99, one-shot)
1-Ryan Cady-s/Phillip Sevy; 3 covers 4.00

ATLANTIS ATTACKS (Continued from Agents of Atlas 2019-2020 series)
Marvel Comics: Mar, 2020 - No. 5, Feb, 2021 ($3.99, limited series)
1-5-Greg Pak-s/Ario Anindito-a; the current and the original Agents of Atlas app. 4.00

ATLANTIS CHRONICLES, THE (Also see Aquaman, 3rd Series & Aquaman: Time & Tide)
DC Comics: Mar, 1990 - No. 7, Sept, 1990 ($2.95, limited series, 52 pgs.)
1-7: 1-Peter David scripts. 7-True origin of Aquaman; nudity panels 4.00

ATLANTIS, THE LOST CONTINENT
Dell Publishing Co.: May, 1961
Four Color 1188-Movie, photo-c 9 18 27 62 126 190

ATLAS (See 1st Issue Special)

ATLAS
Dark Horse Comics: Feb, 1994 - No. 4, 1994 ($2.50, limited series)
1-4 3.00

ATLAS (Agents of Atlas)(The Heroic Age)
Marvel Comics: Jul, 2010 - No. 5, Nov, 2010 ($3.99/$2.99)
1-($3.99) Parker-s/Hardman-a/Dodson-c; 3-D Man app.; profile page 4.00
2-5-($2.99) 2,3,5-Pagulayan-c. 4-Jae Lee-c 3.00

ATLAS UNIFIED
Atlas Comics: No. 0, Oct, 2011 - No. 2, Feb, 2012 ($2.99, unfinished limited series)
0 Prelude: Midnight (10/11) Phoenix, Kromag, Sgt. Hawk app.; bonus sketch pages 3.00
1,2: 1-Three covers; Peyer-s/Salgado-a; x-over of Grim Ghost, Wulf, Phoenix & others 3.00

ATMOSPHERICS
Avatar Press: June, 2002 ($5.95, B&W, one-shot graphic novel)
1-Warren Ellis-s/Ken Meyer Jr.-painted-a/c 6.00

ATOM, THE (See Action #425, All-American #19, Brave & the Bold, D.C. Special Series #1, Detective Comics, Flash Comics #80, Hawkman, Identity Crisis, JLA, Power Of The Atom, Showcase #34 -36, Super Friends, Sword of The Atom, Teen Titans & World's Finest)

ATOM, THE (...& the Hawkman No. 39 on)
National Periodical Publ.: June-July, 1962 - No. 38, Aug-Sept, 1968
1-(6-7/62)-Intro Plant-Master; 1st app. Maya 114 228 342 912 2056 3200
2 31 62 93 223 499 775
3-1st Time Pool story; 1st app. Chronos (origin) 25 50 75 175 388 600
4,5: 4-Snapper Carr x-over 15 30 45 103 227 350
6,9,10 11 22 33 76 163 250
7-Hawkman x-over (6-7/63; 1st Atom & Hawkman team-up); 1st app. Hawkman since Brave & the Bold tryouts 23 46 69 161 356 550
8-Justice League, Dr. Light app. 13 26 39 91 201 310
11-15: 13-Chronos-c/story 9 18 27 60 120 180
16-18,20 7 14 21 46 86 125
19-Zatanna x-over; 2nd app. 19 36 54 124 275 425
21-28,30: 26-Two-page pin-up. 28-Chronos-c/story 6 12 18 41 76 110
29-1st solo Golden Age Atom x-over in S.A. 12 24 36 81 176 270
31-35,37,38: 31-Hawkman x-over. 37-Intro. Major Mynah; Hawkman cameo 5 10 15 35 63 90
36-G.A. Atom x-over 7 14 21 48 89 130
NOTE: *Anderson a-1-11i, 13i; c-inks-1-25, 31-35, 37. Sid Greene a-8i-37i. Gil Kane a-1p-37p; c-1p-28p, 29, 33p, 34; c-26i. George Roussos a-38i. Mike Sekowsky a-38p. Time Pool stories also in 6, 9,12, 17, 21, 27, 35.*

ATOM, THE (See All New Atom and Tangent Comics/ The Atom)

ATOM AGE (See Classics Illustrated Special Issue)

ATOM-AGE COMBAT
St. John Publishing Co.: June, 1952 - No. 5, Apr, 1953; Feb, 1958
1-Buck Vinson in all 63 126 189 403 689 975
2-Flying saucer story 39 78 117 240 395 550
3,5: 3-Mayo-a (6 pgs.). 5-Flying saucer-c/story 34 68 102 204 332 460
4 (Scarce) 39 78 117 240 395 550
1(2/58-St. John) 30 60 90 177 289 400

ATOM-AGE COMBAT
Fago Magazines: No. 2, Jan, 1959 - No. 3, Mar, 1959
2-A-Bomb explosion-c; 39 78 117 231 378 525
3 27 54 81 158 259 360

ATOMAN
Spark Publications: Feb, 1946 - No. 2, April, 1946
1-Origin & 1st app. Atoman; Robinson/Meskin-a; Kidcrusaders, Wild Bill Hickok, Marvin the Great app. 93 186 279 599 1025 1450
2-Robinson/Meskin-a; Robinson c-1,2 50 100 150 315 533 750

ATOM & HAWKMAN, THE (Formerly The Atom)
National Periodical Publ: No. 39, Oct-Nov, 1968 - No. 45, Oct-Nov, 1969; No. 46, Mar, 2010
39-43: 40-41-Kubert/Anderson-a. 43-(7/69)-Last 12¢ issue; 1st S.A. app. Gentleman Ghost 5 10 15 35 63 90
44,45: 44-(9/69)-1st 15¢-c; origin Gentleman Ghost 5 10 15 35 63 90
46-(3/10, $2.99) Blackest Night crossover one-shot; Geoff Johns-s/Ryan Sook-a/c 3.00
NOTE: *M. Anderson a-39, 40i, 41i, 43, 44. Sid Greene a-40i-45i. Kubert a-40p, 41p; c-39-45.*

ATOM ANT (TV) (See Golden Comics Digest #2) (Hanna-Barbera)
Gold Key: January, 1966 (12¢)
1(10170-601)-1st app. Atom Ant, Precious Pup, and Hillbilly Bears 16 32 48 110 243 375

ATOM ANT & SECRET SQUIRREL (See Hanna-Barbera Presents)

ATOMIC AGE
Marvel Comics (Epic Comics): Nov, 1990 - No. 4, Feb, 1991 ($4.50, limited series, squarebound, 52 pgs.)
1-4: Williamson-a(i); sci-fi story set in 1957 4.50

ATOMIC ATTACK (True War Stories; formerly Attack, first series)
Youthful Magazines: No. 5, Jan, 1953 - No. 8, Oct, 1953 (1st story is sci/fi in all issues)
5-Atomic bomb-c; science fiction stories in all 55 110 165 352 601 850
6-8 37 74 111 218 354 490

ATOMIC BOMB
Jay Burtis Publications: 1945 (36 pgs.)
1-Superheroes Airmale & Stampy (scarce) 84 168 252 538 919 1300

ATOMIC BUNNY (Formerly Atomic Rabbit)
Charlton Comics: No. 12, Aug, 1958 - No. 19, Dec, 1959
12 13 26 39 74 105 135
13-19 8 16 24 44 57 70

ATOMIC COMICS
Daniels Publications (Canadian): Jan, 1946 (Reprints, one-shot)
1-Rocketman, Yankee Boy, Master Key app. 52 104 156 323 549 775

ATOMIC COMICS
Green Publishing Co.: Jan, 1946 - No. 4, July-Aug, 1946 (#1-4 were printed w/o cover gloss)
1-Radio Squad by Siegel & Shuster; Barry O'Neal app.; Fang Gow cover-r/ Detective Comics (Classic-c) 97 194 291 621 1061 1500
2-Inspector Dayton; Kid Kane by Matt Baker; Lucky Wings, Congo King, Prop Powers (only app.) begin; atomic monster-c 68 136 204 435 743 1050
3,4: 3-Zero Ghost Detective app.; Baker-a(2) each; 4-Baker-c 48 96 144 302 514 725

ATOMIC KNIGHTS (See Strange Adventures #117)
DC Comics: 2010 ($39.99, HC with dustjacket)
HC-Reprints the original 1960-64 run from debut in Strange Adventures #117 to S.A. #160; new intro. by Murphy Anderson 40.00

ATOMIC MOUSE (TV, Movies) (See Blue Bird, Funny Animals, Giant Comics Edition & Wotalife Comics)

Atlas #1 © MAR

The Atom #36 © DC

Attack #57 © CC

Capitol Stories/Charlton Comics: 3/53 - No. 52, 2/63; No. 1, 12/84; V2#10, 9/85 - No. 12, 1/86

	GD 2.0	VG 4.0	FN 6.0	VF 8.0	VF/NM 9.0	NM- 9.2
1-Origin & 1st app.; Al Fago-c/a in most	41	82	123	256	428	600
2	15	30	45	90	140	190
3-10: 5-Timmy The Timid Ghost app.; see Zoo Funnies	10	20	30	58	79	100
11-13,16-25	8	16	24	40	50	60
14,15-Hoppy The Marvel Bunny app.	9	18	27	50	65	80
26-(68 pgs.)	12	24	36	67	94	120
27-40: 36,37-Atom The Cat app.	6	12	18	29	36	42
41-52	5	10	15	22	26	30
1 (1984)-Low print run; rep/#7-c w/diff. stories	2	4	6	8	10	12
V2#10 (9/85) -12(1/86)-Low print run	1	3	4	6	8	10

ATOMIC RABBIT (Atomic Bunny #12 on; see Giant Comics #3 & Wotalife)
Charlton Comics: Aug, 1955 - No. 11, Mar, 1958

	GD 2.0	VG 4.0	FN 6.0	VF 8.0	VF/NM 9.0	NM- 9.2
1-Origin & 1st app.; Al Fago-c/a in all?	37	74	111	218	354	490
2	15	30	45	84	127	170
3-10	10	20	30	58	79	100
11-(68 pgs.)	14	28	42	82	121	160

ATOMICS, THE
AAA Pop Comics: Jan, 2000 - No. 15, Nov, 2001 ($2.95)

	GD 2.0	VG 4.0	FN 6.0	VF 8.0	VF/NM 9.0	NM- 9.2
1-11-Mike Allred-s/a; 1-Madman-c/app.						3.00
12-15-($3.50): 13-15-Savage Dragon-c/app. 15-Afterword by Alex Ross; colored reprint of 1st Frank Einstein story						3.50
...King-Size Giant Spectacular: Jigsaw (2000, $10.00) r/#1-4						10.00
...King-Size Giant Spectacular: Lessons in Light, Lava, & Lasers (2000, $8.95) r/#5-8						9.00
...King-Size Giant Spectacular: Running With the Dragon ('02, $8.95) r/#13-15 and r/1st Frank Einstein app. in color						9.00
...King-Size Giant Spectacular: Worlds Within Worlds ('01, $8.95) r/#9-12						9.00
Madman and the Atomics, Vol. 1 TPB (2007, $24.99) r/#1-15, cover gallery, pin-ups, afterword by Alex Ross						25.00
...: Spaced Out & Grounded in Snap City TPB (10/03, $12.95) r/one-shots - It Girl, Mr. Gum, Spaceman and Crash Metro & the Star Squad; sketch pages						13.00

ATOMIC SPY CASES
Avon Periodicals: Mar-Apr, 1950 (Painted-c)

	GD 2.0	VG 4.0	FN 6.0	VF 8.0	VF/NM 9.0	NM- 9.2
1-No Wood-a; A-bomb blast panels; Fass-a	55	110	165	352	601	850

ATOMIC THUNDERBOLT, THE
Regor Company: Feb, 1946 (one-shot) (scarce)

	GD 2.0	VG 4.0	FN 6.0	VF 8.0	VF/NM 9.0	NM- 9.2
1-Intro. Atomic Thunderbolt & Mr. Murdo	97	194	291	621	1061	1500

ATOMIC TOYBOX
Image Comics: Dec, 1999 ($2.95)

	GD 2.0	VG 4.0	FN 6.0	VF 8.0	VF/NM 9.0	NM- 9.2
1- Aaron Lopresti-c/s/a						3.00

ATOMIC WAR!
Ace Periodicals (Junior Books): Nov, 1952 - No. 4, Apr, 1953

	GD 2.0	VG 4.0	FN 6.0	VF 8.0	VF/NM 9.0	NM- 9.2
1-Atomic bomb-c	200	400	600	1280	2190	3100
2,3: 3-Atomic bomb-c	77	154	231	493	847	1200
4-Used in **POP**, pg. 96 & illo.	90	180	270	576	988	1400

ATOMIKA
Speakeasy Comics/Mercury Comics: Mar, 2005 - No. 12, Jun, 2011 ($2.99)

	GD 2.0	VG 4.0	FN 6.0	VF 8.0	VF/NM 9.0	NM- 9.2
1-12: 1-Alex Ross-c/Sal Abbinanti-a/Dabb-s. 3-Fabry-c. 4-Four covers; Romita back-c						3.00
... God is Red TPB (5/06, $19.99) r/#1-6; cover gallery; Dabb foreword						20.00

ATOMIK ANGELS
Crusade Comics: May, 1996 - No. 4, Nov. 1996 ($2.50)

	GD 2.0	VG 4.0	FN 6.0	VF 8.0	VF/NM 9.0	NM- 9.2
1-4: 1-Freefall from Gen 13 app.						3.00
1-Variant-c						4.00
Intrep-Edition (2/96, B&W, giveaway at launch party)-Previews Atomik Angels #1; includes Billy Tucci interview.						4.00

ATOM SPECIAL (See Atom & Justice League of America)
DC Comics: 1993/1995 ($2.50/$2.95)(68pgs.)

	GD 2.0	VG 4.0	FN 6.0	VF 8.0	VF/NM 9.0	NM- 9.2
1,2: 1-Dillon-c/a. 2-McDonnell-a/Bolland-c/Peyer-s						4.00

ATOM THE CAT (Formerly Tom Cat; see Giant Comics #3)
Charlton Comics: No. 9, Oct, 1957 - No. 17, Aug, 1959

	GD 2.0	VG 4.0	FN 6.0	VF 8.0	VF/NM 9.0	NM- 9.2
9	10	20	30	56	76	95
10,13-17	7	14	21	37	46	55
11,12: 11(64 pgs)-Atomic Mouse app. 12(100 pgs.)	12	24	36	69	97	125

ATTACK
Youthful Mag./Trojan No. 5 on: May, 1952 - No. 4, Nov, 1952; No. 5, Jan, 1953 - No. 5, Sept, 1953

	GD 2.0	VG 4.0	FN 6.0	VF 8.0	VF/NM 9.0	NM- 9.2
1-(1st series)-Extreme violence	57	114	171	362	619	875
2,3-Both Harrison-c/a; bondage, whipping	32	64	96	188	307	425
4-Krenkel-a (7 pgs.); Harrison-a (becomes Atomic Attack #5 on)	32	64	96	188	307	425
5-(#1, Trojan, 2nd series)	20	40	60	117	189	260
6-8 (#2-4), 5	15	30	45	88	137	185

ATTACK
Charlton Comics: No. 54, 1958 - No. 60, Nov, 1959

	GD 2.0	VG 4.0	FN 6.0	VF 8.0	VF/NM 9.0	NM- 9.2
54 (25¢, 100 pgs.)	14	28	42	80	115	150
55-60	9	18	27	47	61	75

ATTACK!
Charlton Comics: 1962 - No. 15, 3/75; No. 16, 8/79 - No. 48, 10/84

	GD 2.0	VG 4.0	FN 6.0	VF 8.0	VF/NM 9.0	NM- 9.2
nn(#1)-('62) Special Edition	8	16	24	51	96	140
2('63), 3(Fall, '64)	4	8	12	27	44	60
V4#3(10/66), 4(10/67)-(Formerly Special War Series #2; becomes Attack At Sea V4#5): 3-Tokyo Rose story	3	6	9	21	33	45
1(9/71)-D-Day story	3	6	9	17	25	34
2-5: 2-Hitler app. 4-American Eagle app.	2	4	6	9	12	15
6-15(3/75): 8-Nixon app.	1	3	4	6	8	10
16(8/79) - 40						5.00
41-47 Low print run						7.00
48(10/84)-Wood-r; S&K-c (low print)	1	3	4	6	8	10
Modern Comics 13('78)-r						5.00

NOTE: *Sutton a-9,10,13.*

ATTACK!
Spire Christian Comics (Fleming H. Revell Co.): 1975 (39¢/49¢, 36 pgs.)

	GD 2.0	VG 4.0	FN 6.0	VF 8.0	VF/NM 9.0	NM- 9.2
nn	3	6	9	14	19	24

ATTACK AT SEA (Formerly Attack!, 1967)
Charlton Comics: V4#5, Oct, 1968 (one-shot)

	GD 2.0	VG 4.0	FN 6.0	VF 8.0	VF/NM 9.0	NM- 9.2
V4#5	3	6	9	21	33	45

ATTACK ON PLANET MARS (See Strange Worlds #18)
Avon Periodicals: 1951

	GD 2.0	VG 4.0	FN 6.0	VF 8.0	VF/NM 9.0	NM- 9.2
nn-Infantino, Fawcette, Kubert & Wood-a; adaptation of Tarrano the Conqueror by Ray Cummings	116	232	348	742	1271	1800

ATTRACTIVE COUSINS (Cerebus)
Aardvark-Vanaheim: Aug, 2020 ($4.00, B&W)

	GD 2.0	VG 4.0	FN 6.0	VF 8.0	VF/NM 9.0	NM- 9.2
1-Cerebus figures with original Gustave Doré artwork; Supergirl Action #252-c swipe						4.00

AUDREY & MELVIN (Formerly Little...)(See Little Audrey & Melvin)
Harvey Publications: No. 62, Sept, 1974

	GD 2.0	VG 4.0	FN 6.0	VF 8.0	VF/NM 9.0	NM- 9.2
62	2	4	6	10	14	18

AUGIE DOGGIE (TV) (See Hanna-Barbera Band Wagon, Quick-Draw McGraw, Spotlight #2, Top Cat & Whitman Comic Books)
Gold Key: October, 1963 (12¢)

	GD 2.0	VG 4.0	FN 6.0	VF 8.0	VF/NM 9.0	NM- 9.2
1-Hanna-Barbera character	16	32	48	107	236	365

AUNTIE AGATHA'S HOME FOR WAYWARD RABBITS
Image Comics: Nov, 2018 - No. 6, Apr, 2019 ($3.99, limited series)

	GD 2.0	VG 4.0	FN 6.0	VF 8.0	VF/NM 9.0	NM- 9.2
1-6-Keith Giffen-s/Benjamin Roman-a						4.00

AUTHENTIC POLICE CASES
St. John Publishing Co.: 2/48 - No. 6, 11/48; No. 7, 5/50 - No. 38, 3/55

	GD 2.0	VG 4.0	FN 6.0	VF 8.0	VF/NM 9.0	NM- 9.2
1-Hale the Magician by Tuska begins	74	148	222	470	810	1150
2-Lady Satan, Johnny Rebel app.	50	100	150	315	533	750
3-Veiled Avenger app.; blood drainage story plus 2 Lucky Coyne stories; used in **SOTI**, illo. from Red Seal #16	81	162	243	518	884	1250
4,5: 4-Masked Black Jack app. 5-Late 1930s Jack Cole-a(r); transvestism story	47	94	141	296	498	700
6-Matt Baker-c; used in **SOTI**, illo- "An invitation to learning", r-in Fugitives From Justice #3; Jack Cole-a; also used by the N.Y. Legis. Comm.	290	580	870	1856	3178	4500
7,8,10-14: 7-Jack Cole-a; Matt Baker-a begins #8, ends #?; Vic Flint in #10-14. 10-12-Baker-a(2 each)	61	122	183	390	670	950
9-No Vic Flint	55	110	165	352	601	850
15-Drug-c/story; Vic Flint app.; Baker-c	135	270	405	864	1482	2100
16,17,19,22-Baker-c	58	116	174	371	636	900
18,20,21,23: Baker-a(i)	43	86	129	271	461	650
24-28 (All 100 pgs.): 26-Transvestism	71	142	213	454	777	1100
29,31,32-Baker-c	53	106	159	334	567	800
30	34	68	102	199	325	450
33-38: 33-Baker-c. 34-Baker-c; drug story; r/#9. 35-Baker-c/a(2); r/#10. 36-r/#11; Vic Flint strip-r; Baker-c/a(2) unsigned. 37-Baker-c; r/#17. 38- Baker-c/a; r/#18	50	100	150	315	533	750

GD VG FN VF VF/NM NM-
2.0 4.0 6.0 8.0 9.0 9.2

NOTE: *Matt Baker c-6-16, 17, 19, 22, 27, 29, 31-38; a-13, 16. Bondage c-1, 3.*

AUTHORITY, THE (See Stormwatch and Jenny Sparks: The Secret History of...)
DC Comics (WildStorm): May, 1999 - No. 29, Jul, 2002 ($2.50)

1-Wraparound-c; Warren Ellis-s/Bryan Hitch and Paul Neary-a 1 3 4 6 8 10
1-Special Edition (7/10, $1.00) r/#1 with "What's Next?" logo on cover 3.00
2-4 5.00
5-12: 12-Death of Jenny Sparks; last Ellis-s 4.00
13-Mark Millar-s/Frank Quitely-c/a begins 6.00
14-16-Authority vs. Marvel-esque villains 4.00
17-29: 17,18-Weston-a. 19,20,22-Quitely-a. 21-McCrea-a. 23-26-Peyer-s/Nguyen-a; new Authority. 25,26-Jenny Sparks app. 27,28-Millar-s/Art Adams-a/c 3.00
Annual 2000 ($3.50) Devil's Night x-over; Hamner-a/Bermejo-c 4.00
Absolute Authority Slipcased Hardcover (2002, $49.95) oversized r/#1-12 plus script pages by Ellis and sketch pages by Hitch 50.00
...: Earth Inferno and Other Stories TPB (2002, $14.95) r/#17-20, Annual 2000, and Wildstorm Summer Special; new Quitely-c 15.00
...: Human on the Inside HC (2004, $24.95, dust jacket) Ridley-s/Oliver-a/c 25.00
...: Human on the Inside SC (2004, $17.99) Ridley-s/Oliver-a/c 18.00
...: Kev (10/02, $4.95) Ennis-s/Fabry-c/a 5.00
...: Relentless TPB (2000, $17.95) r/#1-8 18.00
...: Scorched Earth (2/03, $4.95) Robbie Morrison-s/Frazer Irving-a/Ashley Wood-c 5.00
...: Transfer of Power TPB (2002, $17.95) r/#22-29 18.00
...: Under New Management TPB (2000, $17.95) r/#9-16; new Quitely-c 18.00

AUTHORITY, THE (See previews in Sleeper, Stormwatch: Team Achilles and Wildcats Version 3.0)
DC Comics (WildStorm): Jul, 2003 - No. 14, Oct, 2004 ($2.95)

1-14: 1-Robbie Morrison-s/Dwayne Turner-a. 5-Huat-a. 14-Portacio-a 3.00
#0 (10/03, $2.95) r/preview back-up-s listed above; Turner sketch pages 3.00
...: Fractured Worlds TPB (2005, $17.95) r/#6-14; cover gallery 18.00
...: Harsh Realities TPB (2004, $14.95) r/#0-5; cover gallery 15.00
.../Lobo: Jingle Hell (2/04, $4.95) Bisley-c/a; Giffen & Grant-s 5.00
.../Lobo: Spring Break Massacre (8/05, $4.99) Bisley-c/a; Giffen & Grant-s 5.00

AUTHORITY, THE (Volume 4) (The Lost Year)
DC Comics (WildStorm): Dec, 2006 - No. 2, May 2007; No. 3, Jan, 2010 - No. 12, Oct, 2010 ($2.99)

1,2-Grant Morrison-s/Gene Ha-a/c 3.00
1-Variant cover by Art Adams 5.00
3-12: 3-(1/10) Morrison & Giffen-s/Robertson-a. 3-12-Ha-c. 12-Ordway-a 3.00
...Reader: The Lost Year (1/10, $2.99) r/#1,2 3.00
... Book One (2010, $17.99) r/#1-7; cover sketch art 18.00

AUTHORITY, THE (Volume 5) (World's End)
DC Comics (WildStorm): Oct, 2008 - No. 29, Jan, 2011 ($2.99)

1-29: 1-5-Simon Coleby-a/c; Lynch back-up story w/Hairsine-a/Gage-s. 21-Simonson-c 3.00
...: Rule Britannia TPB (2010, $19.99) r/#8-17 20.00
...: World's End TPB (2009, $17.99) r/#1-7 18.00

AUTHORITY, THE: MORE KEV
DC Comics (WildStorm): Jul, 2004 - No. 4, Dec, 2004 ($2.95, limited series)

1-4-Garth Ennis-s/Glenn Fabry-c/a 3.00
...: Kev TPB (2005, $14.99) r/Authority: Kev one-shot and Authority: More Kev series 15.00

AUTHORITY, THE: PRIME
DC Comics (WildStorm): Dec, 2007 - No. 6, May, 2008 ($2.99, limited series)

1-6-Gage-s/Robertson-c/a; Bendix app. 3.00
TPB (2008, $17.99) r/#1-6 18.00

AUTHORITY, THE: REVOLUTION
DC Comics (WildStorm): Dec, 2004 - No. 12, Dec, 2005 ($2.95/$2.99)

1-12-Brubaker-s/Nguyen-a. 5-Henry Bendix returns. 7-Jenny Sparks app. 3.00
...: Book One TPB (2005, $14.99) r/#1-6; cover gallery and Nguyen sketch pages 15.00
...: Book Two TPB (2006, $14.99) r/#7-12; cover gallery and Nguyen sketch pages 15.00

AUTHORITY, THE: THE MAGNIFICENT KEV
DC Comics (WildStorm): Nov, 2005 - No. 5, Feb, 2006 ($2.99, limited series)

1-5-Garth Ennis-s/Carlos Ezquerra-a/Glenn Fabry-c 3.00
TPB (2006, $14.99) r/#1-5 15.00

AUTOMATIC KAFKA
DC Comics (WildStorm): Sept, 2002 - No. 9, Jul, 2003 ($2.95)

1-9-Ashley Wood-c/a; Joe Casey-s 3.00

AUTUMN ADVENTURES (Walt Disney's...)
Disney Comics: Autumn, 1990; No. 2, Autumn, 1991 ($2.95, 68 pgs.)

1-Donald Duck-r(2) by Barks, Pluto-r, & new-a 4.00
2-D. Duck-r by Barks; new Super Goof story 4.00

AUTUMNLANDS: TOOTH & CLAW (Titled Tooth & Claw for issue #1, Autumnlands for #7-14)
Image Comics: Nov, 2014 - No. 14, Jan, 2017 ($2.99)

1-14: 1-Busiek-s/Dewey-a. 2-Variant-c by Alex Ross 3.00

AVANT-GUARDS, THE
BOOM! Studios (Boom! Box): Jan, 2019 - No. 8, Sept, 2019 ($3.99)

1-8-Carly Usdin-s/Noah Hayes-a 4.00

AVATAARS: COVENANT OF THE SHIELD
Marvel Comics: Sept, 2000 - No. 3, Nov, 2000 ($2.99, limited series)

1-3-Kaminski-s/Oscar Jimenez-a 3.00

AVATAR
DC Comics: Feb, 1991 - No. 3, Apr, 1991 ($5.95, limited series, 100 pgs.)

1-3: Based on TSR's Forgotten Realms 6.00

AVATAR: ADAPT OR DIE (Characters from the James Cameron movie)
Dark Horse Comics: May, 2022 - No. 6, Oct, 2022 ($3.99, limited series)

1-6-Corinna Bechko-s/Beni R. Lobel-a; Grace app. 4.00

AVATAR: THE NEXT SHADOW (Based on the James Cameron movie)
Dark Horse Comics: Jan, 2021 - No. 4, Apr, 2021 ($3.99, limited series)

1-4-Takes place 2 weeks after the movie; Jeremy Barlow-s/Josh Hood-a 4.00

AVATAR: TSU'TEY'S PATH (Based on the James Cameron movie)
Dark Horse Comics: Jan, 2019 - No. 6, Aug, 2019 ($3.99, limited series)

1-6-Sherri L. Smith-s/Jan Duursema-a 4.00

AVENGELYNE
Maximum Press: May, 1995 - No. 3, July, 1995 ($2.50/$3.50, limited series)

1/2 2 4 6 8 11 14
1/2 Platinum 18.00
1-Newstand ($2.50)-Photo-c; poster insert 6.00
1-Direct Market ($3.50)-Chromium-c; poster 1 2 3 5 6 8
1-Glossy edition 2 4 6 12 16 20
1-Gold 12.00
2-3: 2-Polybagged w/card 3.00
3-Variant-c; Deodato pin-up 5.00
...Bible (10/96, $3.50) 4.00
.../Glory (9/95, $3.95) 2 covers 4.00
.../Glory Swimsuit Special (6/96, $2.95) photo and illos. covers 3.00
.../Glory: The Godyssey (9/96, $2.99) 2 covers (1 photo) 3.00
...Revelation One (Avatar, 1/01, $3.50) 3 covers by Haley, Rio, Shaw; Shaw-a 3.50
.../Shi (Avatar, 11/01, $3.50) Eight covers; Waller-a 3.50
...Swimsuit (8/95, $2.95)-Pin-ups/photos. 3-Variant-c exist (2 photo, 1 Liefeld-a) 4.00
...Swimsuit (1/96, $3.50, 2nd printing)-photo-c 4.00
Trade paperback (12/95, $9.95) 10.00
.../Warrior Nun Areala 1 (11/96, $2.99) also see Warrior Nun/Avengelyne 3.00

AVENGELYNE
Maximum Press: V2#1, Apr, 1996 - No. 14, Apr, 1997 ($2.95/$2.50)

V2#1-Four covers exist (2 photo-c). 4.00
V2#2-Three covers exist (1 photo-c); flip book w/Darkchylde 5.00
V2#0, 3-14: 0-(10/96).3-Flip book w/Priest preview. 5-Flip book w/Blindside 3.00

AVENGELYNE (Volume 3)
Awesome Comics: Mar, 1999 ($2.50)

1-Fraga & Liefeld-a 3.00

AVENGELYNE (4th series)
Image Comics: Jul, 2011 - No. 8, May, 2012 ($2.99)

1-8-Liefeld & Poulson-s/Gieni-a. 1-Three covers by Liefeld, Gieni, and Benitez 3.00

AVENGELYNE: ARMAGEDDON
Maximum Press: Dec, 1996 - No. 3, Feb, 1997 ($2.99, limited series)

1-3-Scott Clark-a(p) 3.00

AVENGELYNE: DEADLY SINS
Maximum Press: Feb, 1996 - No. 2, Mar, 1996 ($2.95, limited series)

1,2: 1-Two-c exist (1 photo, 1 Liefeld-a). 2-Liefeld-c; Pop Mhan-a(p) 3.00

AVENGELYNE/POWER
Maximum Press: Nov, 1995 - No.3, Jan, 1996 ($2.95, limited series)

1-3: 1,2-Liefeld-c. 3-Three variant-c. exist (1 photo-c) 3.00

AVENGELYNE • PROPHET
Maximum Press: May, 1996; No. 2, Feb. 1997 ($2.95, unfinished lim. series)

1,2-Liefeld-c/a(p) 3.00

AVENGER, THE (See A-1 Comics)
Magazine Enterprises: Feb-Mar, 1955 - No. 4, Aug-Sept, 1955

1(A-1 #129)-Origin 61 122 183 390 670 950
2(A-1 #131), 3(A-1 #133) Robot-c, 4(A-1 #138) 58 116 174 371 636 900
IW Reprint #9('64)-Reprints #1 (new cover) 4 8 12 23 37 50
NOTE: *Powell a-2-4; c-1-4.*

AVENGER, THE (Pulp Hero from Justice Inc.)
Dynamite Entertainment: 2014 ($7.99)

... Special 2014: The Television Killers - Rahner-s/Menna-a/Hack-c 8.00

AVENGERS, THE (TV)(Also see Steed and Mrs. Peel)
Gold Key: Nov, 1968 ("John Steed & Emma Peel" cover title) (15¢)

1-Photo-c 10 20 30 67 141 215
1-(Variant with photo back-c) 17 34 51 117 259 400

AVENGERS, THE (See Essential..., Giant-Size..., JLA/..., Kree/Skrull War Starring..., Marvel Graphic Novel #27, Marvel Super Action, Marvel Super Heroes('66), Marvel Treasury Ed., Marvel Triple Action, New Avengers, Solo Avengers, Tales Of Suspense #49, West Coast Avengers & X-Men Vs....)

AVENGERS, THE (The Mighty Avengers on cover only #63-69)
Marvel Comics Group: Sept, 1963 - No. 402, Sept, 1996

1-Origin & 1st app. The Avengers (Thor, Iron Man, Hulk, Ant-Man, Wasp); Loki app. 1325 2650 5300 13,200 36,600 60,000
2-Hulk leaves Avengers 145 290 435 1196 2698 4200
3-2nd Sub-Mariner x-over outside the F.F. (see Strange Tales #107 for 1st); Sub-Mariner & Hulk team-up & battle Avengers; Spider-Man cameo (1/64) 114 228 342 912 2056 3200
4-Revival of Captain America who joins the Avengers; 1st Silver Age app. of Captain America & Bucky (3/64) 500 1000 1500 3500 7850 12,200
4-Reprint from the Golden Record Comic set 25 50 75 175 388 600
With Record (1966) 31 62 93 223 499 775
5-Hulk app. 61 122 183 488 1094 1700
6-1st app. original Zemo & his Masters of Evil 68 136 204 544 1222 1900
7-Rick Jones app. in Bucky costume 64 128 192 512 1156 1800
8-Intro Kang 172 344 516 1419 3210 5000
9-Intro Wonder Man who dies in same story 125 250 375 1000 2250 3500
10-Intro/1st app. Immortus; early Hercules app. (11/64) 50 100 150 400 900 1400
11-Spider-Man-c & x-over (12/64) 42 84 126 311 706 1100
12,13 47 94 141 296 498 700
14,15: 15-Death of original Zemo 37 74 111 222 361 500
16-New Avengers line-up (Hawkeye, Quicksilver, Scarlet Witch join; Thor, Iron Man, Giant-Man, Wasp leave) 50 100 150 400 900 1400
17,18: 17-Minor Hulk app. 15 30 45 103 227 350
19-1st app. Swordsman; origin Hawkeye (8/65) 32 64 96 230 515 800
20-22: Wood inks. 20-Intro. Power Man (Erik Josten) 12 24 36 80 173 265

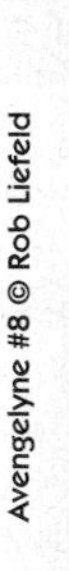
Avatar: Tsu'tey's Path #1 © 20-FOX

Avengelyne #8 © Rob Liefeld

Avengers #96 © MAR

	GD 2.0	VG 4.0	FN 6.0	VF 8.0	VF/NM 9.0	NM- 9.2
23-Romita Sr. inks (1st Silver Age Marvel work); Avengers vs. Kang; 1st app. Princess Ravonna	58	116	174	371	636	900
24,26,27,29,30: 24-Avengers vs. Kang	10	20	30	69	147	225
25-Dr. Doom-c/story	27	54	81	194	435	675
28-(5/66) First app. of The Collector; Giant-Man becomes Goliath	29	58	87	209	467	725
31-40: 32-1st Sons of the Serpent. 34-Last full Stan Lee plot/script. 35-1st Roy Thomas script w/Stan Lee plot. 38-40-Hercules app. 40-Sub-Mariner app.	9	18	27	59	117	175
41-46,50: 43-1st app. Red Guardian (dies in #44). 45-Hercules joins. 46-Ant-Man returns (re-intro, 11/67)	8	16	24	55	105	155
47-Magneto-c/story; 1st app. Dane Whitman who becomes the new Black Knight in #48	27	54	81	189	420	650
48-(1/68) Origin/1st app. new Black Knight (Dane Whitman)	71	142	213	568	1284	2000
49-Magneto-c/story	8	16	24	56	108	160
51-The Collector app.	8	16	24	56	108	160
52-Black Panther joins; 1st app. The Grim Reaper	16	32	48	107	236	365
53-X-Men app.	13	26	39	89	195	300
54-1st Ultron app. (1 panel); new Masters of Evil	12	24	36	84	185	285
55-1st full app. Ultron (8/68) (1 panel reveal in #54)	20	40	60	135	300	465
56-Zemo app; story explains how Capt. America became imprisoned in ice during WWII, only to be rescued in Avengers #4	10	20	30	69	147	225
57-1st app. S.A. Vision (10/68); death of Ultron-5	66	132	198	528	1189	1850
57 Facsimile Edition (1/21, $3.99) Reprints #57 with original ads and letter column						4.00
58-Origin The Vision	12	24	36	84	185	285
59-Intro. Yellowjacket	14	28	42	96	211	325
60,61,63-65: 60-Wasp & Yellowjacket wed. 61-Dr. Strange app. 63-Goliath becomes Yellowjacket; Hawkeye becomes the new Goliath. 65-Last 12¢ issue	8	16	24	54	102	150
62-1st Man-Ape	21	42	63	147	324	500
66-B. Smith-a; vs. Ultron-6; 1st mention of adamantium metal	10	20	30	64	132	200
67-Ultron-6 cvr/sty; B. Smith-a	10	20	30	68	144	220
68-Buscema-a	8	16	24	52	99	145
69-1st brief app. Squadron Sinister (Dr. Spectrum, Hyperion, Nighthawk)	27	54	81	189	420	650
70-1st full app. Nighthawk	17	34	51	117	259	400
71-1st app. The Invaders (12/69); Black Knight joins	22	44	66	154	340	525
72-79,81,82,84,86,90-91: 72-1st Zodiak; Captain Marvel & Nick Fury app. 73,74-Sons of the Serpent. 75-1st app. Arkon. 78-1st app. Lethal Legion (Man-Ape, Living Laser, Power Man, Grimm Reaper, Swordsman). 82-Daredevil app. 86-2nd Squadron Supreme app.	7	14	21	46	86	125
80-1st app. Red Wolf	12	24	36	84	185	285
83-Intro. The Liberators (Wasp, Valkyrie, Scarlet Witch, Medusa & the Black Widow)	21	42	63	147	324	500
85-1st app. Squadron Supreme (American Eagle, Dr. Spectrum, Hawkeye (Wyatt McDonald), Hyperion, Lady Lark, Nighthawk (Kyle Richmond), Tom Thumb, Whizzer)	23	46	69	161	356	550
87-Origin The Black Panther	15	30	45	100	220	340
88-Written by Harlan Ellison; Hulk app.	7	14	21	46	86	125
88-2nd printing (1994)	2	4	6	9	13	16
89-Classic Captain Marvel execution-c; beginning of Kree/Skrull War (runs through issue #97)	9	18	27	57	111	165
92-Last 15¢ issue; Neal Adams-c	9	18	27	59	117	175
93-(52 pgs.)-Neal Adams-c/a	18	36	54	124	275	425
94-96-Neal Adams-c/a	9	18	27	59	117	175
97-G.A. Capt. America, Sub-Mariner, Human Torch, Patriot, Vision, Blazing Skull, Fin, Angel, & new Capt. Marvel x-over	8	16	24	56	108	160
98,99: 98-Goliath becomes Hawkeye; Smith c/a(i). 99-Smith-c, Smith/Sutton-a	5	10	15	35	63	90
100-(6/72)-Smith-c/a; featuring everyone who was an Avenger	11	22	33	73	157	240
101-Harlan Ellison scripts	5	10	15	31	53	75
102-106,108,109	4	8	12	27	44	60
107-Starlin-a(p)	5	10	15	30	50	70
110,111-X-Men and Magneto app.	6	12	18	42	79	115
112-1st app. Mantis	13	26	39	89	195	300
113-115,119-124,126,128-130: 114-Swordsman returns; joins Avengers, first Mantis-c. 115-Prologue to Avengers/Defenders War. 119-Rutland, Vermont Halloween issue. 120-123-vs. Zodiac. 123,124-Mantis origin. 124-1st Star-Stalker. 126-Klaw & Solarr app. 129-Kang app; story continues in Giant-Size Avengers #2	4	8	12	23	37	50
116-118-Avengers/Defenders War; x-over w/Defenders #8-11. 116-Silver Surfer vs Vision. 117-Captain America vs. Sub-Mariner. 118-Avengers & Defenders vs. Loki & Dormammu	6	12	18	38	69	100
125-Thanos-c & brief app.; story continues in Captain Marvel #33	8	16	24	55	105	155
127-Ultron-7 app; story continues in Fantastic Four #150	4	8	12	27	44	60
131-133,136-140: 131,132-Vs. Kang. 131-1st Legion of the Unliving. 132-Continues in Giant-Size Avengers #3. 133-Origin of the Kree. 136-Ploog-r/Amazing Advs. #12. 137-Moondragon joins; Beast app; becomes provisional member; officially joins in #151; Wasp & Yellowjacket return	3	6	9	19	30	40
134,135-Origin of the Vision revised (also see Avengers Forever mini-series). 135-Continues in Giant-Size Avengers #4	4	8	12	28	47	65
141-143: 141-Squadron Supreme app; Pérez-a(p) begins. 142,143-Marvel Western heroes app. (Kid Colt, Rawhide Kid, Two-Gun Kid, Ringo Kid, Night Rider). 143-Vs. Kang (last 1970s app.)	3	6	9	17	25	34
144-Origin & 1st app. Hellcat (Patsy Walker)	8	16	24	55	105	155
145,146: Published out of sequence; Tony Isabella-s; originally intended to be in Giant-Size Avengers #5	3	6	9	15	22	28
146-149-(30¢-c variants, limited distribution)	7	14	21	48	89	130
147-149-(Reg. 25¢ editions)(5-7/76) Squadron Supreme app.	3	6	9	14	20	25
150-Kirby-a(r) pgs. 7-18 (from issue #16); pgs. 1-6 feature new-a by Pérez; new line-up: Capt. America, Iron Man, Scarlet Witch, Wasp, Yellowjacket, Vision & The Beast	3	6	9	20	31	42
150-(30¢-c variant, limited distribution)	7	14	21	48	89	130
151-Wonder Man returns w/new costume; Champions app.; The Collector app.	3	6	9	17	26	35
152-154,157,159,160,163: 152-1st app Black Talon. 154-vs. Attuma; continues in Super-Villain Team-up #9. 160-Grimm Reaper app. 163-Vs. The Champions	2	4	6	11	16	20
155,156-Dr. Doom app.	3	6	9	14	20	25
158-1st app. Graviton; Wonder Man vs. Vision; Jim Shooter plots begin	4	8	12	25	40	55
160-164-(35¢-c variants, limited dist.)(6-10/77)	10	20	30	66	138	210
161,162-Ultron-8 app; Henry Pym appears as Ant-Man. 162-1st app. Jocasta	3	6	9	17	26	35
164,165-Byrne-a; vs. Lethal Legion	3	6	9	14	20	25
166-Byrne-a; vs. Count Nefaria	3	6	9	16	23	30
167,168-Guardians of the Galaxy app.	3	6	9	15	21	27
169,172,178-180: 172-Hawkeye rejoins	2	4	6	9	12	15
170,171-Ultron & Jocasta app. 170-Minor Guardians of the Galaxy app.	3	6	9	15	22	28
173-177-Korvac Saga issues; 173-175-The Collector app. 173,177-Guardians of the Galaxy app. 174-Thanos cameo. 176-Starhawk app.	2	4	6	9	13	16
181-(3/79) Byrne-a/Pérez-c; new line-up: Capt. America, Scarlet Witch, Iron Man, Wasp, Vision, Beast & The Falcon; debut of Scott Lang who becomes Ant-Man in Marvel Premiere #47 (4/79)	6	12	18	38	69	100
182-184,187-191-Byrne-a: 183-Ms. Marvel joins. 184-vs. Absorbing Man. 187-vs. Morded the Mystic. 188-Intro. The Elements of Doom. 189-Deathbird app. 190,191-vs. Grey Gargoyle	2	4	6	9	13	16
185-Origin Quicksilver & Scarlet Witch	3	6	9	17	26	35
186-1st app. of Chthon in Avengers (1st app. was in Marvel Chillers #1 (1975))	5	10	15	34	60	85
192-194,197-199: 197-199-vs Red Ronin	2	4	6	8	10	12
195-1st Taskmaster cameo	4	8	12	27	44	60
196-1st full Taskmaster app.	9	18	27	59	117	175
200-(10/80, 52 pgs.)-Ms. Marvel leaves; 1st actual app. of Marcus Immortus	3	6	9	16	24	32
201,203-210,212: 204,205-vs. Yellow Claw	1	3	4	6	8	10
202-Ultron app.	3	6	9	15	22	28
211-New line-up: Capt. America, Iron Man, Tigra, Thor, Wasp & Yellowjacket; Angel, Beast, Dazzler app.	2	4	6	8	11	14
213,215,216,239,240,250: 213-Controversial Yellowjacket slapping Wasp issue; Yellowjacket leaves. 215,216-Silver Surfer app. 216-Tigra leaves. 239-(1/84) Avengers app. on David Letterman show. 240-Spider-Woman revived. 250-($1.00, 52 pgs; West Coast Avengers app. vs. Maelstrom	2	4	6	8	10	12
214-Ghost Rider app.	2	4	6	9	13	16
217-218,222,224-226,228-235,238: 217-Yellowjacket & Wasp return. 222-1st app. Egghead's Masters of Evil. 225,226-Black Knight app. 229-Death of Egghead. 230-Yellowjacket quits. 231-Iron Man leaves. 232-Starfox (Eros) joins. 233-Byrne-a. 234-Origin Quicksilver & Scarlet Witch. 238-Origin Blackout	1	3	4	6	8	10
219,220-Drax the Destroyer app. 220-Moondragon vs. Drax	2	4	6	8	11	14
221-Hawkeye & She-Hulk join; Spider-Man, Spider-Woman, Dazzler app.	3	6	9	21	33	45
223-Taskmaster app.	3	6	9	18	28	38

	GD	VG	FN	VF	VF/NM	NM-
	2.0	4.0	6.0	8.0	9.0	9.2

227-Captain Marvel (Monica Rambeau) joins; Roger Stern plots begin 3 6 9 14 20 25
236,237-Spider-Man tries to join the Avengers 2 4 6 9 12 15
241-249,251-256,258-262: 242-Dr. Strange app. 243-Vision becomes chairman. 244,245-vs. Dire Wraiths. 246-248-Eternals app. 249-x-over with Thor #350. 252-vs. the Blood Brothers. 253-Vision vs. Quasimodo. 254-West Coast Avengers app. 255-John Buscema & Tom Palmer return as artists; 1st app Nebula's pirate crew. 256-Terminus app. 258-x-over with Amazing Spider-Man #269-270; Spider-Man & Firelord app. 258-260-Nebula app. 260-261-Secret Wars II X-over; Beyonder app. 262-Hercules vs. Sub-Mariner 1 2 3 5 6 8
257-1st app. Nebula (from the Guardians of the Galaxy movie) 4 8 12 27 44 60
263-(1/86) Return of Jean Grey, leading into X-Factor #1(story continues in FF #286) 2 4 6 8 11 14
264-265,268,269: 264-1st new Yellowjacket (Rita Demara) 266-Secret Wars II x-over; vs. The Beyonder. 268,269-Kang app. 6.00
266-Secret Wars II epilogue; Silver Surfer & Molecule Man app. 1 2 3 5 6 8
267-Council of Kang 4 8 12 23 37 50
270-277-Baron Zemo and the new Masters of Evil app. 272-Alpha Flight app. 274-277-Siege of Avengers Mansion. 274-Hercules injured. 275-Jarvis severely beaten. 276-Thor returns. 277-Capt. America vs. Baron Zemo 1 2 3 5 6 8
278-283: 279-Capt. Marvel (Monica Rambeau) becomes Avengers leader; Dr. Druid joins. 280-Jarvis flashback issue. 281-283-Olympian Gods app. 282-Sub-Mariner rejoins 6.00
284,285-vs. the Olympian Gods. 285 Avengers vs. Zeus; Hercules recovers 1 2 3 5 6 8
286-299: 286-Fixer app. Awesome Android & Super Adaptoid app. 287-Mentallo app. 288-1st app. 'Heavy Metal' (TESS-One, Intergalactic Sentry #459, Machine Man, Super-Adaptoid). 290-West Coast Avengers app. 291-$1.00 issues begin. 292-1st app. the Leviathan (Marrina). 293-Death of Marrina. 294-Capt. Marvel (Monica Rambeau) leaves. 295-vs. the Cross-Time Kangs. 297-Dr. Druid leaves; Thor, Black Knight & She-Hulk resign. 298-Inferno x-over. 299-Inferno x-over; New Mutants app. 6.00
300-(2/89, $1.75, 68 pgs., squarebound) New line-up; the Captain (Steve Rogers), Thor, Invisible Woman, Mr. Fantastic & Gilgamesh (formerly the Forgotten one) Inferno x-over; Simonson-a 1 3 4 6 8 10
301-304,306-313,319-325,327,330-343: 301-Firelord app; 1st app. Super-Nova. 302-Re-intro Quasar; Firelord app. 303-vs. Super-Nova. Quasar, Firelord & West Coast Avengers app.; Mr. Fantastic & Invisible Woman leave. 308-310-Eternals app. 311-313-Acts of Vengeance x-over. 312-Freedom Force app. 320-324-Alpha Flight app. 327-2nd app. Rage. 332,333-Dr. Doom app. 334-Intro. Thane Ector & the Brethren; Inhumans & Quicksilver app. 335-339-vs. the Brethren. 335-1st Steve Epting art. 341,342-New Warriors & Sons of the Serpent app. 343-Intro. the Gatherers; Bob Harras scripts begin (end #395); last $1.00-c 5.00
305,314-318: 305-Byrne scripts begin; most current & non-active Avengers app. 314-318-Spider-Man x-over. 6.00
326-1st app. Rage (11/90) 2 4 6 8 10 12
328,329: 328-Origin Rage. 329-New line-up (Capt. America, Quasar, Sersi, She-Hulk, Thor, Vision, Black Widow) Spider-Man becomes a reserve member; Rage & Sandman become probationary members 6.00
344-346, 348-349,351-359: 344-1st app. Proctor, leader of the Gatherers. 345,346-Operation Galactic Storm x-overs. 345-Pt.5-Deathbird app. 346-Pt.12-Intro. Starforce (super-powered Kree warriors) 349-Thor vs. Hercules. 351-Starjammers app. 352-354-Grimm Reaper app. 5.00
347-Double-sized issue ($1.75, 39, pgs.) Operation Galactic Storm conclusion (Pt.19) end of the Kree/Shi'ar War; 'death' of the Supreme Intelligence 6.00
350-($2.50, 68 pgs.) Double gatefold-c showing-c to #1; r/#53 w/cover in flip book format; vs. The Starjammers 1 2 3 5 6 8
360-($2.95, 52 pgs.) Embossed all-foil-c; 30th ann. 2 4 6 8 10 12
361,362,364,365,367: 361-362-vs. the Gatherers. 364-365-vs. Galen-Kor of the Kree 5.00
363-($2.95, 52 pgs.)-All silver foil-c; vs. Proctor & the Gatherers; 1st cameo app. Deathcry (unnamed) 6.00
366-($3.95, 68 pgs.)-Embossed all gold foil-c; Deadpool app. in back-up story 6.00
368,376-378: 368-Bloodties pt.1; Avengers/X-Men x-over 5.00
369-($2.95)-Foil embossed-c; Bloodties pt.5; X-Men/Avengers vs. Exodus 6.00
370-373: 370-371-Ghaur the Deviant app. 372-373-vs. Proctor & the Gatherers 5.00
374-Bound-in trading card sheet; origin of Proctor as an alternate-Earth Black Knight revealed (scarcer in NM due to the card insert) 6.00
375-($2.00, 52 pgs.)-Regular ed.; Thunderstrike returns; leads into Malibu Comic's Black September; end of the Gatherers saga (since #343); death of Proctor; Black Knight & Sersi leave; last Epting-a 5.00
375-($2.50, 52 pgs.)-Collectors ed. 6.00
379-382-Regular editions: 379-Galen Kor & Kree Lunatic Legion app. 380-382-High Evolutionary app. 380-1st Mike Deodato-a. 381-Exodus app. 5.00
379-382-Marvel Double Feature editions ($2.50, 45 pgs.)-All have Giant-Man stories in a flip-book format 6.00
383-385: 383-Fantastic Force app. 384-Hercules stripped of immortality & banished from Olympus. 385-Red Skull app. 6.00
386-389, 398-399: 386-Red Skull app.; 'Taking of AIM' prelude; continues in Capt. America #440. 387-Taking of AIM Pt.2; Red Skull app.; re-intro Modok; continues in Capt. America #441. 388-Taking of AIM Pt.4; Red Skull & Modok app. 1 3 4 6 8 10
390-393: 390-'The Crossing' prelude; leads into Avengers: the Crossing #1. 391,392-The Crossing. 391-Overpower game card insert; scarcer in NM. 392-393-The Crossing 1 2 3 5 6 8
394,397: 394-The Crossing; 1st new Wasp; story cont. in Avengers Timeslide #1; 397-x-over w/Hulk #440-441 1 2 3 5 7 9
395-The Crossing/Timeslide; 'death' of Tony Stark; Bob Harras co-plot only, last work on Avengers 1 3 4 6 8 10
396-First Sign Pt.4; vs. the Zodiac 1 2 3 5 6 8
400-(Double-size, 32 pgs.)-Mark Waid scripts; Loki app. 1 2 3 5 7 9
401,402: 401-Onslaught Impact #1; Magneto app. 402-Onslaught Impact #2; vs. Onslaught & Holocaust; last issue; continues in X-Men #56 1 2 3 5 6 8
#500-503 (See Avengers Vol. 3; series resumed original numbering after Vol. 3 #84)
Special 1 (9/67, 25¢, 68 pgs.)-New-a; original & new Avengers team-up 13 26 39 91 201 310
Special 2 (9/68, 25¢, 68 pgs.)-New-a; original vs. new Avengers 14 28 42 96 207 325
Special 3 (9/69, 25¢, 68 pgs.)-r/Avengers #4 plus 3 Capt. America stories by Kirby (art); origin Red Skull 7 14 21 44 82 120
Special 4 (1/71, 25¢, 68 pgs.)-Kirby-r/Avengers #5,6 4 8 12 28 47 65
Special 5 (1/72, 52 pgs.)-All-reprint issue; Kirby-r Avengers #8/Heck-r w/Spider-Man from issue #11 5 10 15 31 53 75
Annual 6 (11/76) Pérez-a; Kirby-c; vs. Nuklo 3 6 9 17 26 35
Annual 7 (11/77)-Starlin-c/a; Warlock dies; Thanos app.; x-over w/Marvel Two-in-one Ann #2 7 14 21 46 86 125
Annual 8 (1978)-Dr. Strange, Ms. Marvel app. vs. Hyperion, Dr. Spectrum & Whizzer 2 4 6 11 16 20
Annual 9 (1979)-Newton-a(p); Intro. Arsenal 2 4 6 10 14 18
Annual 10 (1981)-Golden-a; X-Men cameo; 1st app. Rogue & Madelyne Pryor 8 16 24 54 102 150
Annual 11-13: 11 (1982)-Vs. The Defenders. 12 ('83)-Inhumans app. 13 ('84)-Ditko/Byrne-a 1 3 4 6 8 10
Annual 14-15,17-18: 14 ('85)-x-over w/Fantastic Four Ann. #19; vs. the Skrulls. 15 ('86)-vs. Freedom Force; x-over w/Avengers West Coast Ann. #1. 17('88)-Evolutionary War x-over. 18('89)-Atlantis Attacks 6.00
Annual 16 (1987)-x-over w/Avengers West Coast Ann. #2; Silver Surfer app. vs. the Grandmaster and Legion of the Unliving (including Drax, Captain Marvel & Green Goblin) 1 2 3 5 6 8
Annual 19-22: 19 ('90)-Terminus Factor Pt.5 (conclusion) continued from Avengers West Coast Ann. #5. 20 ('91)-Subterranean Saga Pt.1; cont. in Hulk Ann. #17. 21 ('92)-Citizen Kang pt.4; vs. Terminatrix. 22 ('93)-Bagged w/card; 1st app. Bloodwraith 5.00
Annual 23 (1994)-Buscema-a; Roy Thomas-s; vs. Loki & Pluto; x-over w/Thor Ann. #19 5.00
Avengers 1: The Coming of the Avengers! (2012, $3.99) recolored reprint/#1 1 2 3 4 5 7
...: Galactic Storm Vol. 1 ('06, $29.99, TPB) r/Kree-Shi'ar war from Avengers #345-346, Capt. America #398-399, Avengers West Coast #80-81, Quasar #32-33, Wonder Man #7-8, Iron Man #278 and Thor #445; new Epting-c 30.00
...: Galactic Storm Vol. 2 ('06, $29.99, TPB) r/Kree-Shi'ar war from Avengers #347, Capt. America #400-401, Avengers West Coast #82, Quasar #34-36, Wonder Man #9, Iron Man #279, Thor #446 and What If #55-56 30.00
...: Kang - Time and Time Again ('05, $19.99, TPB) r/Avengers #69-71 & 267-269, Thor #140 and Incredible Hulk #135 20.00
...Kree-Skrull War ('00, $24.95, TPB) new Neal Adams-c 25.00
...: Legends Vol. 3: George Perez ('03, $16.99)-r/#161,162,194-196,201, Ann. #6 & 8 17.00
Marvel Double Feature...Avengers/Giant-Man #379 ($2.50, 52 pgs.)-Same as Avengers #379 w/Giant-Man flip book 4.00
Marvel Graphic Novel - Deathtrap: The Vault (1991, $9.95) Venom-c/app. 2 4 6 11 16 20
The Korvac Saga TPB (2003, $19.95)-r/#167,168,170-177; Perez-c 20.00
The Serpent Crown TPB (2005, $15.99)-r/#141-144,147-149; Hellcat app. 16.00
The Yesterday Quest ($6.95)-r/#181,182,185-187 1 2 3 4 5 7
Under Siege ('98, $16.95, TPB) r/#270,271,273-277 17.00
...: Vision and the Scarlet Witch TPB (2005, $15.99) r/wedding from Giant-Size Avengers #4 and "Vision and the Scarlet Witch" mini-series #1-4 16.00
...: Visionaries ('99, $16.95)-r/early George Perez art 17.00
NOTE: ***Austin*** *c(i)-157, 167, 168, 170-177, 181, 183-188, 198-201, Annual 8.* ***John Buscema*** *a-41-44p, 46p, 47p, 49, 50, 51-62p, 74-77, 79-85, 87-91, 97, 105p, 121p, 124p,125p, 152, 153p, 255-279p, 281-302p; c-41-66, 68-71, 73-91, 97-99, 178, 256-259p, 261-279p, 281-302p.* ***Byrne*** *a-164-166p, 181-191p, 233p, Annual 13i, 14p; c-186-190p, 233p, 260, 305p; scripts-305-312.* ***Colan*** *a(p)-63-65, 111, 206-208, 210, 211; c(p)-65, 206-208, 210, 211.* ***Ditko*** *a-Annual 13.* ***Guice*** *a-Annual 12p.* ***Don Heck*** *a-9-15, 17-40, 157.* ***Kane*** *c-37p, 159p.* ***Kane/Everett*** *c-97.* ***Kirby*** *a-1-8p, Special 3r, 4r(p); c-1-30, 148, 151-158; layouts-14-16.* ***Ron Lim*** *c(p)-335-341.* ***Miller*** *c-193p.* ***Mooney*** *a-86i, 179p, 180p.* ***Nebres*** *a-178i; c-179i.* ***Newton*** *a-204p, Annual 9p.* ***Perez*** *a(p)-141, 143, 144, 148, 150, 154, 155, 160, 161, 162, 167,168, 170, 171, 194-196, 198-202, Annual 6, 8; c(p)-160-162, 164-166, 170-174, 181,183-185, 191, 192, 194-201, 379-382, Annual 8.* ***Starlin*** *c-121, 135.* ***Staton*** *a-127-134i.* ***Tuska*** *a-47i,48i, 51i, 53i, 54i, 106p, 107p, 135p, 137-140p, 163p. Guardians of the Galaxy app. in #167, 168, 170, 173, 175, 181.*

AVENGERS, THE (Volume Two)
Marvel Comics: V2#1, Nov, 1996 - No. 13, Nov, 1997 ($2.95/$1.95/$1.99) (Produced by Extreme Studios)

1-($2.95)-Heroes Reborn begins; intro new team (Captain America, Swordsman, Scarlet Witch, Vision, Thor, Hellcat & Hawkeye); 1st app. Avengers Island; Loki & Enchantress app.; Rob Liefeld-p & plot; Chap Yaep-p; Jim Valentino scripts; variant-c exists 1 2 3 4 5 7
1-($1.95)-Variant-c 6.00
2-13: 2,3-Jeph Loeb scripts begin, Kang app. 4-Hulk-c/app. 5-Thor/Hulk battle; 2 covers. 10,11,13-"World War 3"-pt. 2, x-over w/Image characters. 12-($2.99) "Heroes Reunited"-pt. 2 4.00
Heroes Reborn: Avengers (2006, $29.99, TPB) r/#1-12; pin-up and cover gallery 30.00

AVENGERS, THE (Volume Three)(See New Avengers for next series)
Marvel Comics: Feb, 1998 - No. 84, Aug, 2004; No. 500, Sept, 2004 - No. 503, Dec, 2004 ($2.99/$1.99/$2.25)

1-($2.99, 48 pgs.) Busiek-s/Pérez-a/wraparound-c; Avengers reassemble after Heroes Return; many Avengers app. vs. Morgan Le Fey 6.00
1-Variant Heroes Return sunburst cover 1 2 3 5 6 8
1-Dynamic Forces Ltd Edition (1500 copies); sunburst-c signed by Perez 4 8 12 25 40 55
1-Rough Cut-Features original script and pencil pages 4.00
2-($1.99) Pérez-c; vs. Morgan Le Fey, alternate painted-c by Lago 4.00
3,4: 3-Wonder Man-c/app. & "dies". 4-Final roster chosen; Captain America, Thor, Hawkeye, Iron Man, Scarlet Witch, Vision, Warbird (formally Ms. Marvel: Carol Danvers) 3.00
5-6,8-11; 5-6: Squadron Supreme-c/app.: Hyperion, Dr. Spectrum, Power Princess, Whizzer, Haywire, Lady Lark, Shape & Moonglow. 8-1st app; Triathlon & Silverclaw; vs. Moses Magnum. 9-1st mention of the Triune Understanding. 10-Grimm Reaper & Ultron app; return of the Legion of the Unliving: Captain Mar-Vell, Dr. Druid, Mockingbird, Swordsman, Wonder Man & Thunderstrike. 11-Legion of the Unliving app; Hellcat, Spider-Man, Daredevil & Fantastic Four guest app; Wonder Man returns to life 3.00
7-Live Kree or Die pt. 4; continued from Quicksilver #10; Warbird leaves; vs. Kree Lunatic Legion 4.00
12-($2.99, 38 pgs.) Thunderbolts app; Firebird and Justice (of the New Warriors) join the Avengers. 4.00
12-Alternate-c of Avengers w/white background; no logo 3 6 9 16 23 30
12-Dynamic Forces alternate-c; ltd. to 5000 copies 2 4 6 8 10 12
12-Dynamic Forces alternate-c; ltd. to 1500 copies; signed by Pérez, Vey and Smith 3 6 9 15 22 28

Avengers #255 © MAR

Avengers #674 © MAR

Avengers (2013) #1 © MAR

	GD 2.0	VG 4.0	FN 6.0	VF 8.0	VF/NM 9.0	NM- 9.2

13-18,23,26: 13-New Warriors app.; 1st app. Lord Templar; 1st (shadowed) app. Jonathan Tremont – leader of the Triune Understanding. 14-Beast app. vs. Lord Templar; 1st app. Pagan. 15-1st full app. of Jonathan Tremont; Pagan and Lord Templar, the Wrecking Crew and Ultron app. 16-18-Ordway-s/a; vs. the Doomsday Man in #17; vs. the Wrecking Crew in #18. 23-Vision & Scarlet Witch history retold. 26-Immonen-a; Lord Templar & Taskmaster app. 3.00
16-Variant-c w/purple background 5.00
19,20: Ultron Unlimited pt. 1-2; Black Panther app.; Giant-Man (Henry Pym app. in #20-22) 1 2 3 5 6 8
21,22-Ultron Unlimited pt. 3-4; vs. Ultron; Black Panther app. 6.00
24-Continued from Juggernaut: the Eighth Day #1; vs. the Exemplars 4.00
25-Vs. the Exemplars; Spider-Man, New Warriors, Juggernaut and Quicksilver app. 5.00
27-($2.99, 100 pgs. 'Monster') New line up - Justice, Firestar & Thor leave, Triathlon & She-Hulk join, Wonder Man becomes a reserve member; Ant-Man app.; reprints issues (all Vol.1) #101,150,151, Annual #19; Note: Due to the 100 pages, this issue often suffers from tears around the staples. 6.00
28-32: 28-30-vs. Kulan Gath. 31-Vision rejoins; vs. Grimm Reaper. 32-Life story & secret origin of Madame Masque revealed 3.00
33-Thunderbolts x-over w/Thunderbolts #44; Madame Masque & Count Nefaria app. 2 4 6 9 12 15
34-($2.99, 38 pgs.) Last Perez-a; continued from Thunderbolts #44; vs. Count Nefaria; Black Widow app 6.00
35-37: 35-Maximum Security x-over; Romita Jr.-a; 36-37; vs. Bloodwraith; Epting-a 4.00
38-Davis-a begins ($1.99-c); new line-up: Captain America, Goliath (Henry Pym), Thor, Quicksilver, Wasp, Iron Man, Vision, Scarlet Witch, Triathlon, Wonder Man & Warbird (Carol Danvers) 4.00
39,40: Hulk app. 5.00
41-47,49: 41-Vs. Scarlet Centurion; Kang app. 42-44-Kang, Scarlet Centurion & the Presence app. 43-Jack of Hearts joins; last Davis-a. 45-Origin of the Scarlet Centurion; Kang & the Master of the World (from Alpha Flight issues) app. 46-Vs. Kang and his army; Scarlet Centurion & the Master of the World app. 47-Origin of Scarlet Centurion continued with flashback to issue #200 w/Ms. Marvel (Carol Danvers); 1st full app of the Triple Evil (ancient cosmic menace). 49-'Nuff Said story; Kang attacks Washington DC 3.00
48-($3.50, 100 pgs); vs. Kang and his legions; Scarlet Centurion app; death of Master of the World; Triple Evil app.; r/#98-100 4.00
50-($3.50); vs. the Triple Evil (destroyed); Lord Pagan & Templar app. (both die); Jonathan Tremont & the Triune Understanding revealed as villains; 3-D Man app. 5.00
51,52: 51-Kang app. as ruler of the Earth; Wonder Man and Scarlet Witch app.; features 2 pg. tribute to the late John Buscema who passed away on January 10th 2002. 52-Avengers vs. Kang; Scarlet Centurion & the Presence app. 4.00
53-Avengers vs. Kang; death of Jonathan Tremont. 6.00
54-56: 54-Conclusion of the Kang war w/Kang defeated; death of Scarlet Centurion. 55-Kang war aftermath; Thor leaves. 56-Beast app; last Busiek issue 4.00
57-62,65-84: 57-Geoff Johns-s begins; 'World Trust' pt. 1; ends with pt. 4 in issue #60. 64-Solo Falcon story; vs Scarecrow. 65-70-Red Zone pt. 1-6; vs. the Red Skull. Wasp and Yellowjacket (Henry Pym) story; vs. Plantman and Whirlwind. 71-74; Search for She-Hulk pt. 1-4; Hulk app. in #73-74. 77-Last Johns issue. 78-81; Chuck Austen-s begin; Lionheart of Avalon pt. 1-5; special 50-¢t issue. 79-81; Captain Britain (Brian Braddock) app. 82-84-Once an Invader pt. 1-4; intro. New invaders team: Blazing Skull, Spitfire, US Agent & Union Jack; Namor app. in #83-84 4.00
63-Standoff pt. 3; continued from Thor (Vol. 2) #58; Thor vs. Iron Man; Dr. Doom app. 2 4 6 9 12 15

(After #84 [Aug, 2004], numbering reverted back to original Vol. 1 with #500, Sept, 2004)

500-($3.50) "Avengers Disassembled" begins; Bendis-s/Finch-a; Ant-Man (Scott Lang) and Jack of Hearts killed, Vision destroyed by the Scarlet Witch 1 2 3 5 6 8
500-Director's Cut ($4.99) Cassaday foil variant-c plus interviews and galleries 2 4 6 8 10 12
501, 502-($2.25): 501-Numerous Avengers and ex-team members app. 502-Hawkeye killed 5.00
503-($3.50) "Avengers Disassembled" ends; reprint pages from Avengers V1#16; Dr. Strange and Magneto app; story continues in Avengers Finale #1 4.00
#11/2 (12/99, $2.50) Timm-c/a; Stern-s; 1963-style issue 3.00
.../ Squadron Supreme '98 Annual ($2.99) 4.00
1999, 2000 Annual (7/99, '00, $3.50) 1999-Manco-a. 2000-Breyfogle-a 4.00
2001 Annual ($2.99) Reis-a; back-up-s art by Churchill 4.00
...: Above and Beyond TPB ('05, $24.99) r/#36-40,56, Annual 2001, & Avengers: The Ultron Imperative; Alan Davis-c 25.00
... Assemble HC ('04, $29.95, oversized) r/#1-11 & '98 Annual; Busiek intro.; Pérez pencil art and Busiek script from Avengers #1 30.00
... Assemble Vol. 2 HC ('05, $29.95, oversized) r/#12-22, #0 & Ann. 1999; Ordway intro. 30.00
... Assemble Vol. 3 HC ('06, $34.99, oversized) r/#23-34, #1 1/2 & Thunderbolts #42-44 35.00
... Assemble Vol. 4 HC ('07, $34.99, oversized) r/#35-40, Avengers 2000, Avengers 2001, Avengers: The Ultron Imperative, Maximum Security #1-3 & ...Dangerous Planet 35.00
... Assemble Vol. 5 HC ('07, $39.99, oversized) r/#41-56 and Avengers 2001 40.00
...: Clear and Present Dangers TPB ('01, $19.95) r/#8-15 20.00
...: Defenders War HC ('07, $19.99) r/#115-118 & Defenders #8-11; Englehart intro. 20.00
...: Disassembled HC ('06, $24.99) r/#500-503 & Avengers Finale; Director's Cut extras 25.00
...: Disassembled TPB ('05, $15.99) r/#500-503 & Avengers Finale; Director's Cut extras 16.00
...Finale 1 (1/05, $3.50) Epilogue to Avengers Disassembled; Neal Adams-c; art by various incl. Peréz, Maleev, Oeming, Powell, Mayhew, Mack, McNiven, Cheung, Frank 4.00
Free Comic Book Day (5/09, giveaway) New Avengers 1st battle vs. Dark Avengers 4.00
...: Living Legends TPB ('04, $19.99) r/#23-30; last Busiek/Pérez arc 20.00
...Supreme Justice TPB (4/01, $17.95) r/Squadron Supreme appearances in Avengers #5-7, '98 Annual, Iron Man #7, Capt. America #8, Quicksilver #10; Pérez-c 18.00
The Kang Dynasty TPB ('02, $29.99) r/#41-55 & 2001 Annual 30.00
The Morgan Conquest TPB ('00, $14.95) r/#1-4 15.00
.../Thunderbolts Vol. 1: The Nefaria Protocols (2004, $19.99) r/#31-34, 42-44 20.00
Ultron Unleashed TPB (8/99, $3.50) reprints early app. 4.00
Ultron Unlimited TPB (4/01, $14.95) r/#19-22 & #0 prelude 15.00
Wizard #0-Ultron Unlimited prelude 4.00
Vol. 1: World Trust TPB ('03, $14.99) r/#57-62 & Marvel Double-Shot #2 15.00
Vol. 2: Red Zone TPB ('04, $14.99) r/#64-70 15.00
Vol. 3: The Search For She-Hulk TPB ('04, $12.99) r/#71-76 13.00
Vol. 4: The Lionheart of Avalon TPB ('04, $11.99) r/#77-81 12.00
Vol. 5: Once an Invader TPB ('04, $14.99) r/#82-84, V1 #71; Invaders #0 & Ann #1 ('77) 15.00

AVENGERS (The Heroic Age)
Marvel Comics: July, 2010 - No. 34, Jan, 2013 ($3.99)

1-New team assembled; Bendis-s/Romita Jr.-a; Kang app.; back-up text Avengers history 6.00
1-Variant-c by Land 8.00
1-Variant covers by Djurdjevic and John Romita Sr. 12.00
1-3-Second printings 4.00
2,3: 2-Wonder Man app. 5.00
4-12: 4-6-Ultron app. 7-Red Hulk app. 12-Red Hulk joins 4.00
12.1 -(6/11, $2.99) Hitch & Neary-c/a; The Wizard & The Intelligencia app.; Ultron returns 3.00
13-24: 13-17-Fear Itself tie-ins. 13,15-Bachalo-a. 17-New Avengers app. 18-20-Acuña-a. 19-Vision returns, Storm joins 4.00
24.1 -(5/12, $2.99) Peterson-a; Magneto, She-Hulk app. 3.00
25-33: 25-30-Avengers vs. X-Men tie-in; Simonson-a. 31-34-Janet Van Dyne app. 4.00
34-($4.99) Art by Peterson, Mayhew & Dodson; Deodato, Simonson, Yu, Cheung, Coipel art pages; Bendis afterword 5.00
... Annual 1 (3/12, $4.99) Bendis-s/Dell'Otto-c/a; Wonder Man app. 5.00
... Assemble 1 (7/10, $3.99) Handbook-style profiles of Avengers, enemies, allies 4.00
...: Infinity Quest 1 (8/11, $4.99) r/#7-9 with variant covers 5.00
... Roll Call 1 (2012, $4.99) Updated handbook-style profiles of Avengers & enemies 5.00
... Spotlight (7/10, $3.99) Creator interviews, previews, history of the team; trivia 4.00

AVENGERS (Marvel NOW!)
Marvel Comics: Feb, 2013 - No. 44, Jun, 2015 ($3.99)

1-13: 1-Hickman-s/Opeña-a/Weaver-c. 4-6-Adam Kubert-a 4.00
14-23: 14-17-Prelude to Infinity. 18-23-Infinity tie-ins 4.00
24-($4.99) Rogue Planet; Ribic-a; Iron Man 3030 app. 5.00
25-28-Hickman-s/Larroca-a. 27-Includes reprint of All-New Invaders #1 4.00
29-($4.99) Original Sin tie-in; Yu-a/Cho-c 5.00
30-34-Original Sin tie-in; Hickman-s/Yu-a 4.00
34.1 (11/14), 34.2 (3/15), 35-($4.99) 34.1-Spotlight on Hyperion; Keown-a. 34.2-Spotlight on Starbrand; Bengal-a. 35-Cheung, Medina-a 5.00
36-39,41-43: 37,39,41-Deodato-a. 39-Leads into New Avengers #28 4.00
40-($4.99) Thanos-c/app.; Caselli-a 5.00
44-($4.99) Follows New Avengers #33; Thanos app.; leads into Secret Wars #1 5.00
Annual (2/14, $4.99) Christmas-themed; Lafuente-a 5.00
...: Endless Wartime HC (2013, $24.99, OGN) Ellis-s/McKone-a; intro by Clark Gregg 25.00
...: No More Bullying (3/15, $1.99) Short stories; Avengers, Spider-Man, GOTG app. 3.00
... Now! Handbook 1 (2/15, $4.99) Updated version with new characters from 2014 5.00
...: The Enemy Within (7/13, $2.99) DeConnick-s/Hepburn-a; Captain Marvel tie-in 3.00
...: Vs 1 (7/15, $5.99) Printing of 4 digital-first stories; Raney-c 6.00
100th Anniversary Special: Avengers 1 (9/14, $3.99) James Stokoe-s/a 4.00

AVENGERS (After Secret Wars)
Marvel Comics: No. 0, Dec, 2015 ($5.99)

0-Short story preludes for the various Avengers 2016 titles; Deadpool app. 6.00

AVENGERS (Follows events of Civil War II)
Marvel Comics: Jan, 2017 - No. 11, Nov, 2017; No. 672, Dec, 2017 - No. 690, Jun, 2018 ($4.99/$3.99)

1-($4.99) Spider-Man, Capt. America (Sam), Thor (Jane), Wasp, Vision, Hercules team 5.00
2-11-($3.99) 2-6-Kang app.; Waid-s/del Mundo-a. 7,8-Infamous Iron Man app.; Noto-a. 9,10-Secret Empire tie-ins 4.00

[Title switches to legacy numbering after #11 (11/17)]

672-674,676-683,685-688,690: 672-674-The Champions app. 676-690-No Surrender.

GD VG FN VF VF/NM NM-
2.0 4.0 6.0 8.0 9.0 9.2

681-Origin of Voyager. 682-Hulk returns 4.00
675-($4.99) No Surrender Part 1; "return" of Voyager; lenticular wraparound-c by Brooks 5.00
684-($4.99) No Surrender Part 10; re-cap of Hulk origin and many deaths 5.00
689-($4.99) No Surrender Part 15; Larraz-a 5.00
#1.MU (3/17, $4.99) Monsters Unleashed tie-in; Zub-s/Izaakse-a 5.00
...: Shards of Infinity 1 (6/18, $3.99) Macchio-s/Di Vito-a; Black Panther app. 4.00

AVENGERS
Marvel Comics: Jul, 2018 - Present ($4.99/$3.99)

1-($4.99) Aaron-s/McGuinness-a; Avengers re-form vs. the Celestials 5.00
2-9-($3.99) Loki app. 7-Origin of prehistoric Ghost Rider; Pichelli-a. 9-Namor app. 4.00
10-($5.99) 700th issue; Namor and The Winter Guard app.; McGuinness-a 6.00
11-30,32-49,51-65: 11-Phil Coulson app. 12-Blade joins. 15-17-Marquez-a. 16-Johnny Blaze app. 18-20-War of the Realms tie-ins; McGuinness-a. 18,21-Squadron Supreme app. 22,23-Hellstrom app. 23-25-Cosmic Ghost Rider app. 32-Mephisto & Dracula app. 39,41-44-Enter The Phoenix. 39-Keown-a. 40-Doom app. 46-49-World War She-Hulk. 60-AXE Judgment Day tie-in; Russell-s/Land-a 4.00
31-($4.99) "The Temptation of Anthony Stark"; Aaron-s; art by various 5.00
50-($9.99) 750th issue; Doctor Doom & Galactus app.; McGuinness, Pacheco, Kuder-a 10.00
Annual 1-(10/21, $4.99) MacKay-s/Foreman-a; Infinite Fury tie-in 5.00
... & Moon Girl 1 (10/22, $4.99) Shuri & Captain Marvel app. 5.00
... Assemble Alpha 1 (1/23, $5.99) Aaron-s/Hitch-a; leads into Avengers #63 (2023) and Avengers Forever #12 6.00
...: Curse of the Man-Thing 1 (5/21, $4.99) Orlando-s/Mobili-a (Also see Spider-Man: Curse of the Man-Thing and X-Men: Curse of the Man-Thing) 5.00
...: Edge of Infinity 1 (6/19, $3.99) Macchio-s/Di Vito-a; M.O.D.O.K. app. 4.00
...: End Times 1 (4/23, $7.99) Reprints Avengers (2010) #31-34; return of Janet Van Dyne 8.00
... Halloween Special 1 (12/18, $4.99) Short stories by various; Geoff Shaw-c 5.00
...: Loki Unleashed 1 (11/19, $4.99) Takes place after Avengers #277; Stern-s/Lim-a 5.00
...: Marvels Snapshots 1 (1/21, $4.99) Barbara Kesel-s/Staz Johnson-a 5.00
... 1,000,000 BC #1 (10/22, $4.99) Aaron-s/Walker-a; Phoenix Force app. 5.00

AVENGERS (Flashback to new team roster from Avengers #16 [1965])
Marvel Comics: No. 1.1, Jan, 2017 - No. 5.1, May, 2017 ($3.99)

1.1, 2.1, 3.1, 4.1, 5.1- Hawkeye, Quicksilver and Scarlet Witch join team; Waid-s/Kitson-a 4.00

AVENGERS (Marvel Action all ages)(Title changes to Marvel Action: Avengers with #6)
IDW Publishing: Dec, 2018 - No. 5, Apr, 2019 ($3.99)

1-5-Iron Man, Captain America, Thor, Hawkeye, Black Widow, Black Panther & Hulk app. 4.00

AVENGERS ACADEMY (The Heroic Age)(Also see Avengers Arena)
Marvel Comics: Aug, 2010 - No. 39, Jan, 2013 ($3.99/$2.99)

1-($3.99) Gage-s/McKone-a/c; Intro. team of Veil, Hazmat, Striker, Mettle, Finesse, Reptil 4.00
1-Variant-c by Djurdjevic 8.00
2-14,14.1 -($2.99) 3,4-Juggernaut app. 5-Molina-a. 7-Absorbing Man app.; Raney-a. 3.00
15-39: 15-20-Fear Itself tie-in. 22-Magneto app. 27,28-Runaways app. 29-33-Tie in to Avengers vs. X-Men event 3.00
... Giant Size 1 (7/11, $7.99) Young Allies and Arcade app.; Tobin-s/Baldeon-a 8.00

AVENGERS: AGE OF ULTRON POINT ONE (Free Comic Book Day)
Marvel Comics: 2012 (Free giveaway)

#0.1 - Reprints Avengers 12.1 (6/11); Bendis-s/Hitch & Neary-c/a 4.00

AVENGERS: A.I. (Follows Age of Ultron series)
Marvel Comics: Sept, 2013 - No. 12, Jun, 2014 ($2.99)

1-12: 1-Humphries-s/Araújo-a; Hank Pym, Vision app. 7-Daredevil app. 3.00

AVENGERS AND POWER PACK ASSEMBLE!
Marvel Comics: June, 2006 - No. 4, Sept, 2006 ($2.99, limited series)

1-4-GuriHiru-a/Sumerak-s. 1-Capt. America app. 2-Iron Man. 3-Spider-Man, Kang app. 3.00
TPB (2006, $6.99, digest-size) r/#1-4 7.00

AVENGERS AND THE INFINITY GAUNTLET
Marvel Comics: Oct, 2010 - No. 4, Jan, 2011 ($2.99, limited series)

1-4: 1-Clevinger-s/Churilla-a; Dr. Doom and Thanos app. 1-Ramos-c. 2-Lim-c 3.00

AVENGERS & X-MEN: AXIS
Marvel Comics: Dec, 2014 - No. 9, Feb, 2015 ($4.99/$3.99, limited series)

1-($4.99) Remender-s/Adam Kubert-a; Red Skull as Red Onslaught 5.00
2-8-($3.99): 2,7-Kubert-a. 3,4,8-Yu-a. 3-Adult Apocalypse app. 5,6-Dodson-a 4.00
9-($4.99) Cheung, Dodson, Yu & Kubert-a 5.00

AVENGERS ARENA
Marvel Comics: Feb, 2013 - No. 18, Jan, 2014 ($2.99)

1-18: 1-Avengers Academy members & Runaways in Arcade's Murder World; Walker-a 3.00

AVENGERS ASSEMBLE (Also see Marvel Universe Avengers Assemble)
Marvel Comics: May, 2012 - No. 25, May, 2014 ($3.99)

1-25: 1-Bendis-s/Bagley-a/c; movie roster in regular Marvel universe. 3-Thanos returns. 4-8-Guardians of the Galaxy app. 9-DeConnick-s begin. 13,14-Age of Ultron tie-in. 18-20-Infinity tie-in. 21-23-Inhumanity 4.00
Annual 1 (3/13, $4.99) Gage-s/Coker-a; spotlight on The Vision 5.00

AVENGERS: BACK TO BASICS
Marvel Comics: 2018 ($14.99, squarebound, printing of original digital comics)

nn-Peter David-s/Brian Level & Juanan Ramírez-a; Ms. Marvel & Kang app. 15.00

AVENGERS: CELESTIAL QUEST
Marvel Comics: Nov, 2001 - No. 8, June, 2002 ($2.50/$3.50, limited series)

1-7-Englehart-s/Santamaría-a; Thanos app. 3.00
8-($3.50) 4.00

AVENGERS: CLASSIC
Marvel Comics: Aug, 2007 - No. 12, Juy, 2008 ($3.99/$2.99)

1,12-($3.99) 1-Reprints Avengers #1 ('63) with new stories about that era; Art Adams-c 4.00
2-11-($2.99) R/#2-11 with back-up w/art by Oeming and others 3.00

AVENGERS COLLECTOR'S EDITION, THE
Marvel Comics: 1993 (Ordered through mail w/candy wrapper, 20 pgs.)

1-Contains 4 bound-in trading cards 5.00

AVENGERS: EARTH'S MIGHTIEST HEROES
Marvel Comics: Jan, 2005 - No. 8, Apr, 2005 ($3.50, limited series)

1-8-Retells origin; Casey-s/Kolins-a 4.00
HC (2005, $24.99, 7 1/2" x 11" with dustjacket) r/#1-8 25.00

AVENGERS: EARTH'S MIGHTIEST HEROES (Based on the Disney animated series)
Marvel Comics: Jan, 2011 - No. 4, Apr, 2011 ($3.99)

1-4-Yost-s/Wegener-a. 1-Hero profile pages. 2-Villain profile pages 4.00

AVENGERS EARTH'S MIGHTIEST HEROES (Titled Marvel Universe... for #1)
Marvel Comics: Jun, 2012 - No. 17, Oct, 2013 ($2.99)

1-17-All ages title. 13-FF & Dr. Doom app. 17-Ant-Man, Luke Cage & Iron Fist app. 4.00

AVENGERS: EARTH'S MIGHTIEST HEROES II
Marvel Comics: Jan, 2007 - No. 8, May, 2007 ($3.99, limited series)

1-8-Retells time when the Vision joined; Casey-s/Rosado-a. 6-Hank & Janet's wedding 4.00
HC (2007, $24.99, 7 1/2" x 11" with dustjacket) r/#1-8; cover sketches 25.00

AVENGERS FAIRY TALES
Marvel Comics: May, 2008 - No. 4, Dec, 2008 ($2.99, limited series)

1-4: 1-Peter Pan-style tale; Cebulski-a/Lemos-a. 2-The Vision. 3-Miyazawa-a 3.00

AVENGERS FOREVER
Marvel Comics: Dec, 1998 - No. 12, Feb, 2000 ($2.99)

1-Busiek-s/Pacheco-a in all 5.00
2-12: 4-Four covers. 6-Two covers. 8-Vision origin revised. 12-Rick Jones becomes Capt. Marvel 4.00
TPB (1/01, $24.95) r/#1-12; Busiek intro.; new Pacheco-c 25.00

AVENGERS FOREVER
Marvel Comics: Feb, 2022 - Present ($4.99/$3.99)

1-($4.99) Aaron-s/Kuder-a; Ant-Man Tony Stark and multiversal Avengers vs. Black Skull 5.00
2-14-($3.99) 2,3-Deathlok and Ghost Rider app. 9-Carol Corps 4.00

AVENGERS INFINITY
Marvel Comics: Sept, 2000 - No. 4, Dec, 2000 ($2.99, limited series)

1-4-Stern-s/Chen-a 4.00

AVENGERS/ INVADERS
Marvel Comics: Jul, 2008 - No. 12, Aug, 2009 ($2.99, limited series)

1-Invaders journey to the present; Alex Ross-c/Sadowski-a; Thunderbolts app. 3.00
2-12: 2-New Avengers app.; Perkins variant-c. 3-12-Variant-c on each 3.00
... Sketchbook (2008, giveaway) Ross and Sadowski sketch art; Krueger commentary 3.00

AVENGERS/ JLA (See JLA/Avengers for #1 & #3)
DC Comics: No, 2, 2003; No. 4, 2003 ($5.95, limited series)

2-Busiek-s/Pérez-a; wraparound-c; Krona, Galactus app. 3 6 9 14 20 25
4-Busiek-s/Pérez-a; wraparound-c 5 10 15 30 50 70

AVENGERS LOG, THE
Marvel Comics: Feb, 1994 ($1.95)

1-Gives history of all members; Pérez-c 6.00

AVENGERS MECH STRIKE
Marvel Comics: Apr, 2021 - No. 5, Sept, 2021 ($3.99, limited series)

1-5-Avengers with new giant robots vs. giant monsters; Jed MacKay-s/Carlos Magno-a 4.00

AVENGERS: MILLENNIUM
Marvel Comics: Jun, 2015 - No. 4, Jun, 2015 ($3.99, weekly limited series)

1-4-Di Giandomenico-a; Scarlet Witch & Quicksilver app. 1-Yu-c. 2-4-Deodato-c. 4.00

AVENGERS NEXT (See A-Next and Spider-Girl)
Marvel Comics: Jan, 2007 - No. 5, Mar, 2007 ($2.99, limited series)

1-5-Lim-a/Wieringo-c; Spider-Girl app. 1-Avengers vs. zombies. 2-Thena app. 3.00
...: Rebirth TPB (2007, $13.99) r/#1-5 14.00

AVENGERS 1959
Marvel Comics: Dec, 2011 - No. 5, Mar, 2012 ($2.99, limited series)

1-5-Chaykin-s/a/c; Nick Fury, Kraven, Namora, Sabretooth, Dominic Fortune app. 3.00

AVENGERS NO ROAD HOME
Marvel Comics: Apr, 2019 - No. 10, Jun, 2019 ($4.99/$3.99, weekly limited series)

1-($4.99) Waid, Ewing & Zub-s/Medina-a; intro Nyx; Rocket Raccoon & Hercules app. 5.00
2-5,7-9-($3.99) 2-Nightmare app. 4-Izaakse-a. 5-Conan cameo on last page. 7-9-Conan app. 7,9-Medina-a. 8-Barberi-a 4.00
6-($4.99) Conan the Barbarian and Scarlet Witch team-up; Izaakse-a 5.00
10-($4.99) Izaakse-a; Conan goes to the Savage Land 5.00

AVENGERS OF THE WASTELANDS
Marvel Comics: Mar, 2020 - No. 5, Nov, 2020 ($3.99, limited series)

1-5-Brisson-s/Scharf-a; set in the future during Old Man Logan & Dead Man Logan series 4.00

AVENGERS: OPERATION HYDRA
Marvel Comics: Jun, 2015 ($3.99, one-shot)

1-Movie team; Pilgrim-s/Di Vito-a; bonus reprint of Avengers #16 (1965) 4.00

AVENGERS ORIGINS (Series of one-shots)
Marvel Comics: Jan, 2012 ($3.99)

...: Ant-Man & The Wasp 1 (1/12) Aguirre-Sacasa-s/Hans-a/Djurdjevic-c; origin of both 4.00
...: Luke Cage 1 (1/12) Glass & Benson-s/Talajic-a/Djurdjevic-c; 4.00
...: Scarlet Witch & Quicksilver 1 (1/12) McKeever-s/Pierfederici-a/Djurdjevic-c 4.00
...: Thor 1 (1/12) K. Immonen-s/Barrionuevo-a/Djurdjevic-c 4.00
...: Vision 1 (1/12) Higgins & Siegel-s/Perger-a/Djurdjevic-c; Ultron-5 app. 4.00

AVENGERS PRIME (The Heroic Age)
Marvel Comics: Aug, 2010 - No. 5, Mar, 2011 ($3.99, limited series)

1-5-Thor, Iron Man & Steve Rogers; Bendis-s/Davis-a; Enchantress app. 4.00
1-Variant-c by Djurdjevic 8.00

AVENGERS: RAGE OF ULTRON
Marvel Comics: 2015 ($24.99, hardcover graphic novel)

HC - Remender-s/Opeña-a; intro by Busiek 25.00

AVENGERS: SEASON ONE
Marvel Comics: 2013 ($24.99, hardcover graphic novel)

Avengers Academy #18 © MAR

Avengers Prime #1 © MAR

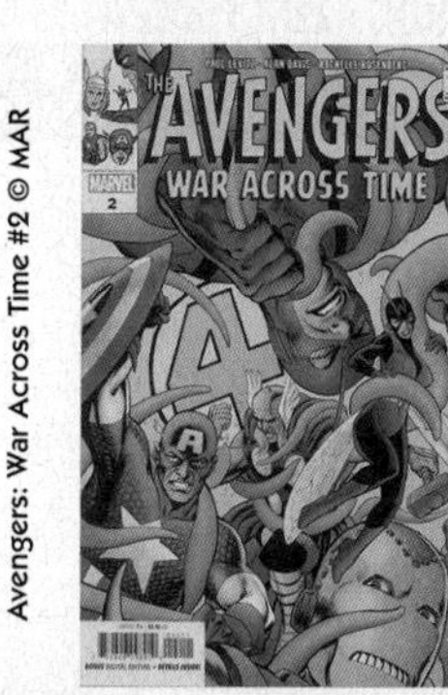

Avengers: War Across Time #2 © MAR

	GD	VG	FN	VF	VF/NM	NM-
	2.0	4.0	6.0	8.0	9.0	9.2

HC - Origin story; Peter David-a/Tedesco painted-c; bonus script outline 25.00

AVENGERS: SOLO
Marvel Comics: Dec, 2011 - No. 5, Apr, 2012 ($3.99, limited series)
1-5-Hawkeye; back-up Avengers Academy 4.00

AVENGERS SPOTLIGHT (Formerly Solo Avengers #1-20)
Marvel Comics: No. 21, Aug, 1989 - No. 40, Jan, 1991 (75¢/$1.00)
21-Byrne-c/a 5.00
22-40: 26-Acts of Vengeance story. 31-34-U.S. Agent series. 36-Heck-i. 37-Mortimer-i. 40-The Black Knight app. 4.00

AVENGERS STANDOFF (Crossover with Avengers titles and other Marvel titles)
Marvel Comics: Apr, 2016 - Jun, 2016 ($4.99)
...: Assault on Pleasant Hill Alpha 1 (5/16) Part 2 of crossover; Spencer-s/Saiz-a 5.00
...: Assault on Pleasant Hill Omega 1 (6/16) Part 3 of crossover; Spencer-s/Acuña-a; new Quasar debut; Red Skull app. 5.00
...: Welcome to Pleasant Hill 1 (4/16) Part 1 of crossover; Spencer-s/Bagley-a/Acuña-c 5.00

AVENGERS STRIKEFILE
Marvel Comics: Jan, 1994 ($1.75, one-shot)
1 4.00

AVENGERS: TECH-ON
Marvel Comics: Oct, 2021 - No. 6, Mar, 2022 ($3.99, limited series)
1-6-Power-drained Avengers & Spider-Man with mech-suits; Jim Zub-s/Jeffrey Cruz-a 4.00

AVENGERS: THE CHILDREN'S CRUSADE
Marvel Comics: Sept, 2010 - No. 9, May, 2012 ($3.99, limited series)
1-9-Young Avengers search for Scarlet Witch; Heinberg-s/Cheung-a. 6-9-X-Men app. 4.00
1-4-Variant-c. 1-Jelena Djurdjevic. 2-Travis Charest. 3,4-Art Adams 6.00
... - Young Avengers (5/11, $3.99) Takes place between #4&5; Alan Davis-a/c 4.00

AVENGERS: THE CROSSING
Marvel Comics: July, 1995 ($4.95, one-shot)
1-Deodato-c/a; 1st app. Thor's new costume 1 2 3 5 6 8

AVENGERS: THE INITIATIVE (See Civil War and related titles)
Marvel Comics: Jun, 2007 - No. 35, Jun, 2010 ($2.99)
1-Caselli-a/Slott-s/Cheung-c; War Machine app. 4.00
2-35: 4,5-World War Hulk. 6-Uy-a. 14-19-Secret Invasion; 3-D Man app. 16-Skrull Kill Krew returns. 20-Tigra pregnancy revealed, 21-25-Ramos-a. 32-35-Siege 3.00
Annual 1 (1/08, $3.99) Secret Invasion tie-in; Cheung-c 4.00
... Featuring Reptil (5/09, $3.99) Gage-s/Uy-a 4.00
... Special 1 (1/09, $3.99) Slott & Gage-s/Uy-a 4.00
...: Vol. 1 - Basic Training HC (2007, $19.99, d.j.) r/#1-6 20.00
...: Vol. 1 - Basic Training SC (2008, $14.99) r/#1-6 15.00

AVENGERS: THE ORIGIN
Marvel Comics: Jun, 2010 - No. 5, Oct, 2010 ($3.99, limited series)
1-5-Casey-s/Noto-a/c; team origin (pre-Capt. America) re-told; Loki app. 4.00

AVENGERS: THE TERMINATRIX OBJECTIVE
Marvel Comics: Sept, 1993 - No. 4, Dec, 1993 ($1.25, limited series)
1 ($2.50)-Holo-grafx foil-c 1 3 4 6 8 10
2-4-Old vs. current Avengers 4.00

AVENGERS: THE ULTRON IMPERATIVE
Marvel Comics: Nov, 2001 ($5.99, one-shot)
1-Follow-up to the Ultron Unlimited ending in Avengers #42; BWS-c 6.00

AVENGERS, THOR & CAPTAIN AMERICA: OFFICIAL INDEX TO THE MARVEL UNIVERSE
Marvel Comics: Jun, 2010 - No. 15, 2001 ($3.99)
1-15-Each issue has chronological synopsies, creator credits, character lists for 30-40 issues of Avengers, Captain America and Journey Into Mystery starting with debuts 4.00

AVENGERS/THUNDERBOLTS
Marvel Comics: May, 2004 - No. 6, Sept, 2004 ($2.99, limited series)
1-6: Busiek & Nicieza-s/Kitson-c. 1,2-Kitson-a. 3-6-Grummett-a 3.00
Vol. 2: Best Intentions (2004, $14.99) r/#1-6 15.00

AVENGERS: TIMESLIDE
Marvel Comics: Feb, 1996 ($4.95, one-shot)
1-Foil-c 5.00

AVENGERS TWO: WONDER MAN & BEAST
Marvel Comics: May, 2000 - No. 3, July, 2000 ($2.99, limited series)
1-3: Stern-s/Bagley-c/a 3.00
... - Marvel Tales 1 (3/23, $7.99) Reprints series; intro. by Ralph Macchio 8.00

AVENGERS/ULTRAFORCE (See Ultraforce/Avengers)
Marvel Comics: Oct, 1995 ($3.95, one-shot)
1-Wraparound foil-c by Pérez 4.00

AVENGERS: ULTRON FOREVER
Marvel Comics: Jun, 2015 ($4.99)(Continues in New Avengers: Ultron Forever)
1-Part 1 of 3-part crossover with New Avengers and Uncanny Avengers; Ewing-s/ Alan Davis-a; team-up of past, present and future Avengers vs. Ultron 5.00

AVENGERS UNDERCOVER (Follows Avengers Arena series)
Marvel Comics: May, 2014 - No. 10, Nov, 2014 ($2.99)
1-10: Hopeless-s in all; Masters of Evil app. 1,2,4,5,7,Kev Walker-a. 3,6,9-Green-a 3.00

AVENGERS UNITED THEY STAND
Marvel Comics: Nov, 1999 - No. 7, June, 2000 ($2.99/$1.99)
1-Based on the animated series 5.00
2-6-($1.99) 2-Avengers battle Hydra. 6-The Collector app. 4.00
7-($2.99) Devil Dinosaur-c/app.; The Collector app.; r/Avengers Action Figure Comic 5.00

AVENGERS UNIVERSE
Marvel Comics: Jun, 2000 - No. 3, Oct, 2000 ($3.99)
1-3-Reprints recent stories 4.00

AVENGERS UNPLUGGED
Marvel Comics: Oct, 1995 - No. 6, Aug, 1996 (99¢, bi-monthly)
1-4,6 4.00
5-Monica Rambeau becomes Photon 3 6 9 17 26 35

AVENGERS VS. ATLAS (Leads into Atlas #1)
Marvel Comics: Mar, 2010 - No. 4, Jun, 2010 ($3.99, limited series)
1-4-Hardman-a; Ramos-c. 1-Back-up w/Miyazawa-a. 2-4-Original Avengers app. 4.00

AVENGERS VS INFINITY
Marvel Comics: Jan, 2016 ($5.99, one-shot)
1-Short stories with The Wrecker, Doctor Doom, Bossman & Dracula; Alves & Lim-a 6.00

AVENGERS VS. PET AVENGERS
Marvel Comics: Dec, 2010 - No. 4, Mar, 2011 ($2.99, limited series)
1-4-Eliopoulos-s/Guara-a; Fin Fang Foom app. 3.00

AVENGERS VS. X-MEN (Also see AVX: VS and AVX: Consequences)
Marvel Comics: No. 0, May, 2012 - No. 12, Dec, 2012 ($3.99/$4.99, bi-weekly limited series)
0-Bendis & Aaron-s; Frank Cho-a/c; Scarlet Witch and Hope featured 4.00
1-11: 1-5-Romita Jr. -a. 6,7,11-Coipel-a. 8-10-Adam Kubert-a. 11-Hulk app. 4.00
12-($4.99) Adam Kubert-a; Cyclops as Dark Phoenix 5.00

AVENGERS: WAR ACROSS TIME
Marvel Comics: Mar, 2023 - No. 5 ($5.99/$3.99, limited series)
1-($5.99) Paul Levitz-s/Alan Davis-a; takes place after Avengers #11 (1964); Kang app. 6.00
2-($3.99) Sindri, forger of Mjolnir app. 4.00

AVENGERS WEST COAST (Formerly West Coast Avengers)
Marvel Comics: No. 48, Sept, 1989 - No. 102, Jan, 1994 ($1.00/$1.25)
48,49: 48-Byrne-c/a & scripts continue thru #57 4.00
50-Re-intro original Human Torch 5.00
51-69,71-74,76-83,85,86,89-99: 54-Cover swipe/F.F. #1. 78-Last $1.00-c. 79-Dr. Strange x-over. 93-95-Darkhawk app. 4.00
70,75,84,87,88: 70-Spider-Woman app. 75 (52 pgs.)-Fantastic Four x-over. 84-Origin Spider-Woman retold; Spider-Man app. (also in #85,86). 87,88-Wolverine-c/story 5.00
100-($3.95, 68 pgs.)-Embossed all red foil-c 5.00
101,102: 101-X-Men x-over 5.00
Annual 5-8 ('90- '93, 68 pgs.)-5,6-West Coast Avengers in indicia. 7-Darkhawk app. 8-Polybagged w/card 4.00
...: Darker Than Scarlet TPB (2008, $24.99) r/#51-57,60-62; Byrne-s/a 25.00
...: Vision Quest TPB (2005, $24.99) r/#42-50; Byrne-s/a 25.00

AVENGERS WORLD
Marvel Comics: Mar, 2014 - No. 21, Jul, 2015 ($3.99)
1-21: 1-Hickman & Spencer-s/Caselli-a. 6-Neal Adams-c. 15,16-Doctor Doom app. 16-Cassie Lang brought back to life. 21-Leads into Secret Wars #1 4.00

AVENGERS: X-SANCTION
Marvel Comics: Feb, 2012 - No. 4, May, 2012 ($3.99, limited series)
1-4-Loeb-s/McGuinness-a/c; Cable battles the Avengers. 3,4-Wolverine & Spidey app. 4.00

AVENGING SPIDER-MAN (Spider-Man and Avengers member team-ups)
Marvel Comics: Jan, 2012 - No. 22, Aug, 2013 ($3.99)
1-Madureira-a/Wells-s; Madureira-c; Red Hulk & Avengers app. 1 2 3 5 6 8
1-Variant-c by Ramos 2 4 6 8 10 12

	GD	VG	FN	VF	VF/NM	NM-
	2.0	4.0	6.0	8.0	9.0	9.2

1-Variant-c by J. Scott Campbell 2 4 6 8 10 12
2-8,10-15: 2,3-Madureira-a/Wells-s; Madureira-c. 2,3-Red Hulk & Avengers app. 4-Hawkeye. 5-Captain America app.; Yu-a. 11-Dillon-a. 12,13-Deadpool app. 14,15-Devil Dinosaur 4.00
9-(9/12) Carol Danvers (Ms. Marvel) takes the name Captain Marvel
6 12 18 37 66 95
15.1 (2/13, $2.99) Follows Amazing Spider-Man #700; 1st Superior Spider-Man 5.00
16-22-Superior Spider-Man. 16-Wolverine & X-Men app. 18-Thor app. 22-Punisher app. 4.00
Annual 1 (12/12, $4.99) Spider-Man (Peter Parker) and The Thing; Zircher-c 5.00

AVIATION ADVENTURES AND MODEL BUILDING (True Aviation Advs. ...No. 15)
Parents' Magazine Institute: No. 16, Dec, 1946 - No. 17, Feb, 1947
16,17-Half comics and half pictures 9 18 27 50 65 80

AVIATION CADETS
Street & Smith Publications: 1943
nn 21 42 63 122 199 275

A-V IN 3-D
Aardvark-Vanaheim: Dec, 1984 ($2.00, 28 pgs. w/glasses)
1-Cerebus, Flaming Carrot, Normalman & Ms. Tree 4.00

AVX: CONSEQUENCES (Aftermath of Avengers Vs. X-Men series)
Marvel Comics: Dec, 2012 - No. 5, Jan, 2013 ($3.99, weekly limited series)
1-5-Cyclops in prison; Gillen-s/art by various 4.00

AVX: VS (Tie-in to Avengers Vs. X-Men series)
Marvel Comics: Jun, 2012 - No. 6, Nov, 2012 ($3.99, limited series)
1-6-Spotlight on the individual fights from Avengers Vs. X-Men #2; art by various 4.00

AWAKEN SKIES
Aspen MLT: No. 0, Jun, 2018 ($1.50, one-shot)
0-($1.50) Mastromauro-s/Lorenzana-a; two covers 3.00

AWESOME ADVENTURES
Awesome Entertainment: Aug, 1999 ($2.50)
1-Alan Moore-s/ Steve Skroce-a; Youngblood story 3.00

AWESOME HOLIDAY SPECIAL
Awesome Entertainment: Dec, 1997 ($2.50, one-shot)
1-Flip book w/covers of Fighting American & Coven. Holiday stories also featuring Kaboom and Shaft by regular creators. 3.00
1-Gold Edition 5.00

AWFUL OSCAR (Formerly & becomes Oscar Comics with No. 13)
Marvel Comics: No. 11, June, 1949 - No. 12, Aug, 1949
11,12 18 36 54 105 165 225

AW YEAH COMICS: ACTION CAT & ADVENTURE BUG
Dark Horse Graphics: Mar, 2016 - No. 4, Jun, 2016 ($2.99, limited series)
1-4-Art Baltazar & Franco-s/a 3.00

AXA
Eclipse Comics: Apr, 1987 - No. 2, Aug, 1987 ($1.75)
1,2 6.00

AXCEND
Image Comics: Oct, 2015 - No. 5, Jul, 2016 ($3.50/$3.99)
1-3-Shane Davis-s/a 3.50
4,5-($3.99) 4.00

A.X.E.: AVENGERS (Tie-in to A.X.E.: Judgment Day)
Marvel Comics: Nov, 2022 ($3.99, one-shot)
1-Gillen-s/Vicentini-a; Iron Man, Wolverine, Jean Grey & Mr. Sinister app. 4.00

AXE COP: BAD GUY EARTH
Dark Horse Comics: Mar, 2011 - No. 3, May, 2011 ($3.50, limited series)
1-3-Malachai Nicolle-s/Ethan Nicolle-a 3.50

AXE COP: PRESIDENT OF THE WORLD
Dark Horse Comics: Jul, 2012 - No. 3, Sept, 2012 ($3.50, limited series)
1-3-Malachai Nicolle-s/Ethan Nicolle-a 3.50

AXE COP: THE AMERICAN CHOPPERS
Dark Horse Comics: May, 2014 - No. 3, Jul, 2014 ($3.99, limited series)
1-3-Malachai Nicolle-s/Ethan Nicolle-a. 3-Origin of Axe Cop 4.00

A.X.E.: DEATH TO THE MUTANTS (Tie-in to A.X.E.: Judgment Day)
Marvel Comics: Oct, 2022 - No. 3, Dec, 2022 ($3.99, limited series)
1-3-Gillen-s/Vilanova-a; Eternals' Druig vs. the Mutants 4.00

A.X.E.: ETERNALS (Tie-in to A.X.E.: Judgment Day)
Marvel Comics: Dec, 2022 ($3.99, one-shot)
1-Gillen-s/Ferry-a; Iron Man, Wolverine, Jean Grey & Mr. Sinister app. 4.00

A.X.E.: EVE OF JUDGMENT (Tie-in to A.X.E.: Judgment Day)
Marvel Comics: Sept, 2022 ($3.99, one-shot)
1-Gillen-s/Ferry-a; prelude to A.X.E.: Judgment Day series; Uranos app. 4.00

A.X.E.: IRON FIST (Tie-in to A.X.E.: Judgment Day)
Marvel Comics: Dec, 2022 ($3.99, one-shot)
1-Alyssa Wong-s/Michael Yg & Marika Cresta-a; Iron Fist (Lin Lie) & Loki app. 4.00

A.X.E.: JUDGMENT DAY (Avengers, X-Men, Eternals)
Marvel Comics: Sept, 2022 - No. 6, Dec, 2022 ($5.99/$4.99, limited series)
1,6-($5.99)-Gillen-s/Schiti-a; Eternals launch war on the mutants 6.00
2-5-($4.99)-Gillen-s/Schiti-a. 2-Intro. The Progenitor. 3,4-Starfox app. 5.00
...: Omega 1 (1/23, $4.99) Gillen-s/Vilanova-a; follows #6 5.00

AXEL PRESSBUTTON (Pressbutton No. 5; see Laser Eraser &...)
Eclipse Comics: Nov, 1984 - No. 6, July, 1985 ($1.50/$1.75, Baxter paper)
1-6: Reprints Warrior (British mag.). 1-Bolland-c; origin Laser Eraser & Pressbutton 4.00

A.X.E.: STARFOX (Tie-in to A.X.E.: Judgment Day)
Marvel Comics: Dec, 2022 ($3.99, one-shot)
1-Gillen-s/Di Nicuolo-a; Mentor, Sui-San & Zuras app. 4.00

A.X.E.: X-MEN (Tie-in to A.X.E.: Judgment Day)
Marvel Comics: Dec, 2022 ($3.99, one-shot)
1-Gillen-s/Mobili-a; Sersi, Iron Man, Wolverine, Jean Grey & Mr. Sinister app. 4.00

AXIS ALPHA
Axis Comics: Feb, 1994 ($2.50, one-shot)
V1-Previews Axis titles including, Tribe, Dethgrip, B.E.A.S.T.I.E.S. & more; Pitt app. in Tribe story. 4.00

AXIS: CARNAGE (Tie-in to Avengers & X-Men Axis series)
Marvel Comics: Dec, 2014 - No. 3, Feb, 2015 ($3.99, limited series)
1-3-Spears-s/Peralta-a; Carnage as a hero; Sin-Eater app. 4.00

AXIS: HOBGOBLIN (Tie-in to Avengers & X-Men Axis series)
Marvel Comics: Dec, 2014 - No. 3, Feb, 2015 ($3.99, limited series)
1-3-Shinick-s/Rodriguez-a; Hobgoblin as a hero; Goblin King app. 4.00

AXIS: RESOLUTIONS (Tie-in to Avengers & X-Men Axis series)
Marvel Comics: Dec, 2014 - No. 4, Feb, 2015 ($3.99, limited series)
1-4-Two stories per issue; s/a by various. 1-Lashley-a. 4-Chaykin-s/a 4.00

AZ
Comico: 1983 - No. 2, 1983 ($1.50, limited series)
1,2-Phil Lasorda-s/a 3.00

AZRAEL (...Agent of the Bat #47 on)(Also see Batman: Sword of Azrael)
DC Comics: Feb, 1995 - No. 100, May, 2003 ($1.95/$2.25/$2.50/$2.95)
1-Dennis O'Neil scripts begin 1 2 3 5 6 8
2,3 4.00
4-46,48-62: 5,6-Ras Al Ghul app. 13-Nightwing-c/app. 15-Contagion Pt. 5 (Pt. 4 on-c). 16-Contagion Pt. 10. 22-Batman-c/app. 23,27-Batman app. 27,28-Joker app. 35-Hitman app. 36-39-Batman, Bane app. 50-New costume. 53-Joker-c/app. 56,57,60-New Batgirl app. 3.00
47-($3.95) Flip book with Batman: Shadow of the Bat #80 4.00
63-74,76-92: 63-Huntress-c/app.; Azrael returns to old costume. 67-Begin $2.50-c. 70-79-Harris-c. 83-Joker x-over. 91-Bruce Wayne: Fugitive pt. 15 3.00
75-($3.95) New costume; Harris-c 4.00
93-100: 93-Begin $2.95-c. 95,96-Two-Face app. 100-Last issue; Zeck-c 3.00
#1,000,000 (11/98) Giarrano-a 3.00
Annual 1 (1995, $3.95)-Year One story 4.00
Annual 2 (1996, $2.95)-Legends of the Dead Earth story 4.00
Annual 3 (1997, $3.95)-Pulp Heroes story; Orbik-c 4.00
.../Ash (1997, $4.95) O'Neil-s/Quesada, Palmiotti-a 5.00
Plus (12/96, $2.95)-Question-c/app. 4.00

AZRAEL
DC Comics: Dec, 2009 - No. 18, May, 2011 ($2.99)
1-18: 1-9-Nicieza-s/Bachs-a. 1-Covers by Jock & Irving. 2,3-Jock-c. 5-Ragman app. 3.00
...: Angel in the Dark TPB (2010, $17.99) r/#1-6; cover gallery 18.00

AZRAEL: DEATH'S DARK KNIGHT
DC Comics: May, 2009 - No. 3, Jul, 2009 ($2.99, limited series)
1-Battle For the Cowl tie-in; Nicieza-s/Irving-a/March-c 3.00
TPB (2010, $14.99) r/#1-3, Batman Annual #27 and Detective Annual #11 15.00

AZTEC ACE
Eclipse Comics: Mar, 1984 - No. 15, Sept, 1985 ($2.25/$1.50/$1.75, Baxter paper)
1-$2.25-c (52 pgs.) 4.00
2-15: 2-Begin 36 pgs. 3.00
NOTE: *N. Redondo a-1i-8i, 10i. c-6-8i.*

AZTEK: THE ULTIMATE MAN
DC Comics: Aug, 1996 - No. 10, May 1997 ($1.75)
1-1st app. Aztek & Synth; Grant Morrison & Mark Millar scripts in all 6.00
2-9: 2-Green Lantern app. 3-1st app. Death-Doll. 4-Intro The Lizard King. 5-Origin. 6-Joker app.; Batman cameo. 7-Batman app. 8-Luthor app. 9-vs. Parasite-c/app. 4.00
10-Joins the JLA; JLA-c/app. 1 2 4 6 8 10
JLA Presents: Aztek the Ultimate Man TPB (2008, $19.99) r/#1-10 20.00
NOTE: ***Breyfogle** c-5p. **N. Steven Harris** a-1-5p. **Porter** c-1p. **Wieringo** c-2p.*

BABE (...Darling of the Hills, later issues)(See Big Shot and Sparky Watts)
Prize/Headline/Feature: June-July, 1948 - No. 11, Apr-May, 1950
1-Boody Rogers-a 65 130 195 416 708 1000
2-Boody Rogers-a 40 80 120 246 411 575
3-11-All by Boody Rogers 30 60 90 177 289 400

BABE
Dark Horse Comics (Legend): July, 1994 - No. 4, Jan, 1994 ($2.50, lim. series)
1-4: John Byrne-c/a/scripts; ProtoTykes back-up story 4.00

BABE RUTH SPORTS COMICS (Becomes Rags Rabbit #11 on?)
Harvey Publications: April, 1949 - No. 11, Feb, 1951
1-Powell-a 43 86 129 271 461 650
2-Powell-a 29 58 87 170 278 385
3-11: Powell-a in most 23 46 69 136 223 310
NOTE: *Baseball c-2-4, 9. Basketball c-1, 6. Football c-5. Yogi Berra c/story-8. Joe DiMaggio c/story-3. Bob Feller c/story-4. Stan Musial c-9.*

BABES IN TOYLAND (Disney, Movie) (See Golden Pix Story Book ST-3)
Dell Publishing Co.: No. 1282, Feb-Apr, 1962
Four Color 1282-Annette Funicello photo-c 13 26 39 86 188 290

BABES OF BROADWAY
Broadway Comics: May, 1996 ($2.95, one-shot)
1-Pin-ups of Broadway Comics' female characters; Alan Davis, Michael Kaluta, J.G. Jones, Alan Weiss, Guy Davis & others-a; Giordano-c. 5.00

BABE 2
Dark Horse Comics (Legend): Mar, 1995 - No. 2, May, 1995 ($2.50, lim. series)
1,2: John Byrne-c/a/scripts 3.00

BABY HUEY
Harvey Comics: No. 1, Oct, 1991 - No. 9, June, 1994 ($1.00/$1.25/$1.50, quarterly)

A.X.E.: Judgment Day #1 © MAR

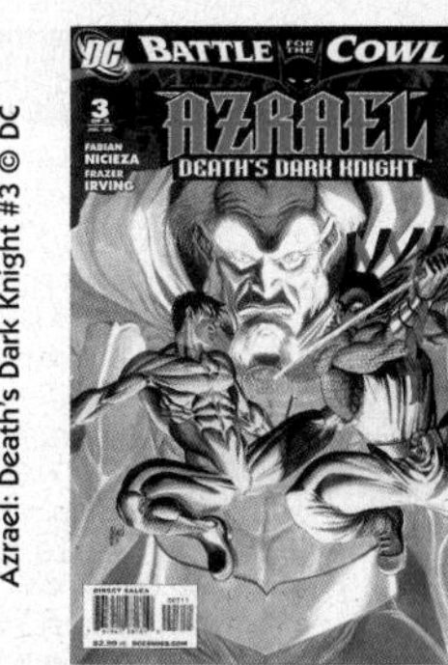
Azrael: Death's Dark Knight #3 © DC

Babyteeth #13 © Cates & Brown

	GD 2.0	VG 4.0	FN 6.0	VF 8.0	VF/NM 9.0	NM- 9.2
1 ($1.00): 1-Cover says "Big Baby Huey"						5.00
2-9 ($1.25-$1.50)						3.00

BABY HUEY AND PAPA (See Paramount Animated...)
Harvey Publications: May, 1962 - No. 33, Jan, 1968 (Also see Casper The Friendly Ghost)

	GD 2.0	VG 4.0	FN 6.0	VF 8.0	VF/NM 9.0	NM- 9.2
1	13	26	39	86	188	290
2	7	14	21	49	92	135
3-5	5	10	15	33	57	80
6-10	3	6	9	20	31	42
11-20	3	6	9	15	22	28
21-33	2	4	6	13	18	22

BABY HUEY DIGEST
Harvey Publications: June, 1992 (Digest-size, one-shot)

	GD 2.0	VG 4.0	FN 6.0	VF 8.0	VF/NM 9.0	NM- 9.2
1-Reprints	1	3	4	6	8	10

BABY HUEY DUCKLAND
Harvey Publications: Nov, 1962 - No. 15, Nov, 1966 (25¢ Giants, 68 pgs.)

	GD 2.0	VG 4.0	FN 6.0	VF 8.0	VF/NM 9.0	NM- 9.2
1	10	20	30	66	138	210
2-5	5	10	15	34	60	85
6-15	3	6	9	21	33	45

BABY HUEY, THE BABY GIANT (Also see Big Baby Huey, Casper, Harvey Hits #22, Harvey Comics Hits #60, & Paramount Animated Comics)
Harvey Publ: 9/56 - #97, 10/71; #98, 10/72; #99, 10/80; #100, 10/90; #101, 11/90

	GD 2.0	VG 4.0	FN 6.0	VF 8.0	VF/NM 9.0	NM- 9.2
1-Infinity-c	54	108	162	432	966	1500
2	21	42	63	147	324	500
3-Baby Huey takes anti-pep pills	13	26	39	89	195	300
4,5	9	18	27	61	123	185
6-10	6	12	18	40	73	105
11-20	5	10	15	31	53	75
21-40	4	8	12	23	37	50
41-60	3	6	9	16	23	30
61-79 (12/67)	2	4	6	13	18	22
80(12/68) - 95-All 68 pg. Giants	3	6	9	16	24	32
96,97-Both 52 pg. Giants	3	6	9	14	19	24
98-Regular size	2	4	6	9	12	15
99-Regular size	1	2	3	5	6	8
100,101 ($1.00)						4.00

BABYLON 5 (TV)
DC Comics: Jan, 1995 - No. 11, Dec, 1995 ($1.95/$2.50)

	GD 2.0	VG 4.0	FN 6.0	VF 8.0	VF/NM 9.0	NM- 9.2
1	2	4	6	9	13	16
2-5	1	2	3	5	7	9
6-11: 7-Begin $2.50-c	1	2	3	4	5	7
... The Price of Peace (1998, $9.95, TPB) r/#1-4,11						10.00

BABYLON 5: IN VALEN'S NAME
DC Comics: Mar, 1998 - No. 3, May, 1998 ($2.50, limited series)

	GD 2.0	VG 4.0	FN 6.0	VF 8.0	VF/NM 9.0	NM- 9.2
1-3						5.00

BABY SNOOTS (Also see March of Comics #359,371,396,401,419,431,443,450,462,474,485)
Gold Key: Aug, 1970 - No. 22, Nov, 1975

	GD 2.0	VG 4.0	FN 6.0	VF 8.0	VF/NM 9.0	NM- 9.2
1	3	6	9	19	30	50
2-11	2	4	6	11	16	20
12-22: 22-Titled Snoots, the Forgetful Elefink	2	4	6	8	10	12

BABYTEETH
AfterShock Comics: Jun, 2017 - No. 20, Sept, 2021 ($3.99)

	GD 2.0	VG 4.0	FN 6.0	VF 8.0	VF/NM 9.0	NM- 9.2
1-Donny Cates-s/Garry Brown-a	1	3	4	6	8	10
2-20						4.00
... #1: Halloween Edition (10/17, giveaway) r/#1 in B&W; Elizabeth Torque-c						3.00

BABY YODA CEREBUS
Aardvark-Vanaheim: May, 2021 ($4.00, B&W)

	GD 2.0	VG 4.0	FN 6.0	VF 8.0	VF/NM 9.0	NM- 9.2
1-Yoda-type character placed over original Gustave Doré background art						4.00

BACCHUS (Also see Eddie Campbell's ...)
Harrier Comics (New Wave): 1988 - No. 2, Aug, 1988 ($1.95, B&W)

	GD 2.0	VG 4.0	FN 6.0	VF 8.0	VF/NM 9.0	NM- 9.2
1,2: Eddie Campbell-c/a/scripts.						3.00

BACHELOR FATHER (TV)
Dell Publishing Co.: No. 1332, 4-6/62 - No. 2, Sept.-Nov., 1962

	GD 2.0	VG 4.0	FN 6.0	VF 8.0	VF/NM 9.0	NM- 9.2
Four Color 1332 (#1), 2-Written by Stanley	7	14	21	46	86	125

BACHELOR'S DIARY
Avon Periodicals: 1949 (15¢)

	GD 2.0	VG 4.0	FN 6.0	VF 8.0	VF/NM 9.0	NM- 9.2
1(Scarce)-King Features panel cartoons & text-r; pin-up, girl wrestling photos; similar to Sideshow	155	310	465	992	1696	2400

BACKLASH (Also see The Kindred)
Image Comics (WildStorm Prod.): Nov,1994 - No. 32, May, 1997 ($1.95/$2.50)

	GD 2.0	VG 4.0	FN 6.0	VF 8.0	VF/NM 9.0	NM- 9.2
1-Double-c; variant-double-c						4.00
2-24,26-32: 5-Intro Mindscape; 2 pinups. 8-Wildstorm Rising Pt 8 (newsstand & Direct Market versions. 19-Fire From Heaven Pt 2. 20-Fire From Heaven Pt 10. 31-WildC.A.T.S app.						3.00
25-($3.95)-Double-size						4.00
...& Taboo's African Holiday (9/99, $5.95) Booth-s/a(p)						6.00

BACKLASH/SPIDER-MAN
Image Comics (WildStorm Productions): Aug, 1996 - No. 2, Sept, 1996 ($2.50, lim. series)

	GD 2.0	VG 4.0	FN 6.0	VF 8.0	VF/NM 9.0	NM- 9.2
1,2: Pike (villain from WildC.A.T.S) & Venom app.	1	3	4	6	8	10

BACKPACK MARVELS (B&W backpack-sized reprint collections)
Marvel Comics: Nov, 2000 ($6.95, B&W, digest-size)

	GD 2.0	VG 4.0	FN 6.0	VF 8.0	VF/NM 9.0	NM- 9.2
Avengers 1 -r/Avengers #181-189; profile pages						7.00
Spider-Man 1-r/ASM #234-240						7.00
X-Men 1-r/Uncanny X-Men #167-173						7.00
X-Men 2-r/Uncanny X-Men #174-179; new painted-c by Greg Horn						7.00

BACKSTAGERS, THE
Boom Entertainment (BOOM! Box): Aug, 2016 - No. 8, Mar, 2017 ($3.99)

	GD 2.0	VG 4.0	FN 6.0	VF 8.0	VF/NM 9.0	NM- 9.2
1-8: 1-James Tynion IV-s/Rian Sygh-a/Veronica Fish-c						4.00
...: Halloween Intermission 1 (10/18, $7.99) Short stories by Tynion, Sygh and others						8.00
...: Valentine's Intermission 1 (2/18, $7.99) Short stories by Tynion, Sygh and others						8.00

BACK TO THE FUTURE (Movie, TV cartoon)
Harvey Comics: Nov, 1991 - No. 4, June, 1992 ($1.25)

	GD 2.0	VG 4.0	FN 6.0	VF 8.0	VF/NM 9.0	NM- 9.2
1-Gil Kane-c; based on animated cartoon	3	6	9	14	20	25
2-4: 2-Gil Kane-c						6.00

BACK TO THE FUTURE (Movie, TV cartoon)
IDW Publishing: Oct, 2015 - No. 25, Oct, 2017 ($3.99)

	GD 2.0	VG 4.0	FN 6.0	VF 8.0	VF/NM 9.0	NM- 9.2
1-Story by Bob Gale; multiple covers; Doc & Marty's first meeting	1	2	3	5	6	8
2-24-Multiple covers. 3-Archie variant-c						4.00
25-($4.99)						5.00

BACK TO THE FUTURE: BIFF TO THE FUTURE
IDW Publishing: Jan, 2017 - No. 6, Jun, 2017 ($3.99, limited series)

	GD 2.0	VG 4.0	FN 6.0	VF 8.0	VF/NM 9.0	NM- 9.2
1-5-Biff's rise to power with the sports almanac; Gale & Fridolfs-s/Alan Robinson-a						4.00

BACK TO THE FUTURE: CITIZEN BROWN (Based on the Telltale Games video game)
IDW Publishing: May, 2016 - No. 5, Sept, 2016 ($4.99, limited series)

	GD 2.0	VG 4.0	FN 6.0	VF 8.0	VF/NM 9.0	NM- 9.2
1-5-Erik Burnham-s/Alan Robinson-a; multiple covers on all						5.00

BACK TO THE FUTURE: FORWARD TO THE FUTURE
Harvey Comics: Oct, 1992 - No. 3, Feb, 1993 ($1.50, limited series)

	GD 2.0	VG 4.0	FN 6.0	VF 8.0	VF/NM 9.0	NM- 9.2
1	2	4	6	9	12	15
2,3						5.00

BACK TO THE FUTURE: TALES FROM THE TIME TRAIN
IDW Publishing: Dec, 2017 - No. 6, May, 2018 ($3.99, limited series)

	GD 2.0	VG 4.0	FN 6.0	VF 8.0	VF/NM 9.0	NM- 9.2
1-6-Doc Brown, Clara and their kids; Gale & Barber-s/Levens-a. 2-6-1939 World's Fair						4.00

BACKWAYS
AfterShock Comics: Dec, 2107 - No. 5, May, 2018 ($3.99)

	GD 2.0	VG 4.0	FN 6.0	VF 8.0	VF/NM 9.0	NM- 9.2
1-5-Justin Jordan-s/Eleonora Carlini-a						4.00

BAD ASS
Dynamite Entertainment: 2014 - No. 4. 2014 ($3.99)

	GD 2.0	VG 4.0	FN 6.0	VF 8.0	VF/NM 9.0	NM- 9.2
1-4-Hanna-s/Bessadi-a						4.00

BAD BLOOD
Dark Horse Comics: Jan, 2014 - No. 5, May, 2014 ($3.99, limited series)

	GD 2.0	VG 4.0	FN 6.0	VF 8.0	VF/NM 9.0	NM- 9.2
1-5-Vampire story; Jonathan Maberry-s/Tyler Crook-a						4.00

BAD BOY
Oni Press: Dec, 1997 ($4.95, one-shot)

	GD 2.0	VG 4.0	FN 6.0	VF 8.0	VF/NM 9.0	NM- 9.2
1-Frank Miller-s/Simon Bisley-a/painted-c						5.00

BAD COMPANY
Quality Comics/Fleetway Quality #15 on: Aug, 1988 - No. 19?, 1990 ($1.50/$1.75, high quality paper)

	GD 2.0	VG 4.0	FN 6.0	VF 8.0	VF/NM 9.0	NM- 9.2
1-19: 5,6-Guice-c						3.00

BADGE OF JUSTICE (Formerly Crime And Justice #21)
Charlton Comics: No. 22, Jan, 1955; No. 2, Apr, 1955 - No. 4, Oct, 1955

	GD 2.0	VG 4.0	FN 6.0	VF 8.0	VF/NM 9.0	NM- 9.2
22(#1)-Giordano-c	14	28	42	81	118	155
2-4	10	20	30	56	76	95

BADGER, THE

GD 2.0 | VG 4.0 | FN 6.0 | VF 8.0 | VF/NM 9.0 | NM- 9.2

Capital Comics(#1-4)/First Comics: Dec, 1983 - No. 70, Apr, 1991; V2#1, Spring, 1991
1 2 4 6 8 10 12
2-49,51-70: 52-54-Tim Vigil-c/a 3.00
50-($3.95, 52 pgs.) 4.00
V2#1 (Spring, 1991, $4.95) 5.00

BADGER, THE
Image Comics: V3#78, May, 1997 - V3#88 ($2.95, B&W)
78-Cover lists #1, Baron-s 3.00
79/#2, 80/#3, 81(indicia lists #80)/#4,82-88/#5-11 3.00

BADGER, THE
Devil's Due/1First Comics: 2016 - No. 5, 2016 ($3.99)
1-5: 1-Mike Baron-s/Jim Fern-a/Val Mayerik-c; origin story. 2-5-Putin app. 4.00

BADGER GOES BERSERK
First Comics: Sept, 1989 - No. 4, Dec, 1989 ($1.95, lim. series, Baxter paper)
1-4: 2-Paul Chadwick-c/a(2pgs.) 3.00

BADGER: SHATTERED MIRROR
Dark Horse Comics: July, 1994 - No. Oct, 1994 ($2.50, limited series)
1-4 3.00

BADGER: ZEN POP FUNNY-ANIMAL VERSION
Dark Horse Comics: July, 1994 - No. 2, Aug, 1994 ($2.50, limited series)
1,2 3.00

BAD GIRLS
DC Comics: Oct, 2003 - No. 5, Feb, 2004 ($2.50, limited series)
1-5-Steve Vance-s/Jennifer Graves-a/Darwyn Cooke-c 3.00
TPB (2009, $14.99) r/#1-5; Graves sketch pages 15.00

BAD IDEA CRASS PROMOTIONAL MODULE
Bad Idea: Jan, 2021 (giveaway)
1-Previews Eniac & Tankers series 5.00

BAD IDEAS
Image Comics: Apr, 2004 - No. 2, July, 2004 ($5.95, B&W, limited series)
1,2-Chinsang-s/Mahfood & Crosland-a 6.00
..., Vol. 1: Collected! (2005, $12.99) r/#1,2 13.00

BAD KITTY ONE SHOT (CHAOS!...)
Dynamite Entertainment: 2014 ($5.99)
1-Spence-s/Rafael-a/c; origin 6.00

BADLANDS
Vortex Comics: May, 1990 ($3.00, glossy stock, mature)
1-Chaykin-c 3.00

BADLANDS
Dark Horse Comics: July, 1991 - No. 6, Dec, 1991 ($2.25, B&W, limited series)
1-6: 1-John F. Kennedy-c; reprints Vortex Comics issue 3.00

BAD LUCK CHUCK
Dark Horse Comics: Mar, 2019 - No. 4, Jun, 2019 ($3.99, limited series)
1-4-Lela Gwenn-s/Matthew Dow Smith-a 4.00

BADMEN OF THE WEST
Avon Periodicals: 1951 (Giant) (132 pgs., painted-c)
1-Contains rebound copies of Jesse James, King of the Bad Men of Deadwood, Badmen of Tombstone; other combinations possible.
Issues with Kubert-a... 57 114 171 362 619 875

BADMEN OF THE WEST! (See A-1 Comics)
Magazine Enterprises: 1953 - No. 3, 1954
1 (A-1 100)-Meskin-a? 27 54 81 160 263 365
2 (A-1 120), 3: 2-Larsen-a 17 34 51 98 154 210

BADMEN OF TOMBSTONE
Avon Periodicals: 1950
nn 20 40 60 115 190 260

BAD MOTHER
AWA Studios: Aug, 2020 - No. 5, Dec, 2020 ($3.99, limited series)
1-5-Christa Faust-s/Mike Deodato Jr.-a 4.00

BAD PLANET
Image Comics (Raw Studios): Dec, 2005 - No. 6, Nov, 2008 ($2.99)
1-6: 1-Thomas Jane & Steve Niles-s/Larosa & Bradstreet-a/c. 2-Wrightson-c. 3-"3-D" pgs. 3.00

BAD RECEPTION
AfterShock Comics: Aug, 2019 - No. 5, Jul, 2020 ($3.99, limited series)
1-5-Juan Doe-s/a 4.00

BADROCK (Also see Youngblood)
Image Comics (Extreme Studios): Mar, 1995 - No. 2, Jan, 1996 ($1.75/$2.50)
1-Variant-c (3) 4.00
2-Liefeld-c/a & story; Savage Dragon app, flipbook w/Grifter/Badrock #2; variant-c exist 3.00
Annual 1(1995,$2.95)-Arthur Adams-c 4.00
Annual 1 Commemorative ($9.95)-3,000 printed 10.00
.../Wolverine (6/96, $4.95, squarebound)-Sauron app; pin-ups; variant-c exists 5.00
.../Wolverine (6/96)-Special Comicon Edition 5.00

BADROCK AND COMPANY (Also see Youngblood)
Image Comics (Extreme Studios): Sept, 1994 - No.6, Feb, 1995 ($2.50)
1-6 : 6-Indicia reads "October 1994"; story cont'd in Shadowhawk #17 3.00

BAFFLING MYSTERIES (Formerly Indian Braves No. 1-4; Heroes of the Wild Frontier No. 26-on)
Periodical House (Ace Magazines): No. 5, Nov, 1951 - No. 26, Oct, 1955
5 57 114 171 362 619 875
6,9-19,21-24: 10-E.C. Crypt Keeper swipe on-c. 24-Last pre-code issue
41 82 123 250 418 585
7,8-Classic-c: 8-Woodish-a by Cameron 129 258 387 826 1413 2000
20-Classic bondage-c 54 108 162 343 574 825

GD 2.0 | VG 4.0 | FN 6.0 | VF 8.0 | VF/NM 9.0 | NM- 9.2

25-Reprints; surrealistic-c 37 74 111 222 361 500
26-Reprints 30 60 90 177 289 400
NOTE: ***Cameron*** *a-8, 10, 16-18, 20-22.* ***Colan*** *a-5, 11, 25r/5.* ***Sekowsky*** *a-5, 6, 22. Bondage c-20, 23. Reprints in 18(1), 19(1), 24(3).*

BAKER STREET PECULIARS, THE
Boom Entertainment (kaboom!): Mar, 2016 - No. 4, Jun, 2016 ($3.99, limited series)
1-4-Roger Langridge-s/Andy Hirsch-a 4.00

BALBO (See Master Comics #33 & Mighty Midget Comics)

BALDER THE BRAVE (Character from Thor)
Marvel Comics Group: Nov, 1985 - No. 4, 1986 (Limited series)
1-4: Walt Simonson-c/s; Sal Buscema-a 4.00

BALLAD OF HALO JONES, THE
Quality Comics: Sept, 1987 - No. 12, Aug, 1988 ($1.25/$1.50)
1-12: Alan Moore scripts in all 3.00

BALL AND CHAIN
DC Comics (Homage): Nov, 1999 - No. 4, Feb, 2000 ($2.50, limited series)
1-4-Lobdell-s/Garza-a 5.00

BALLISTIC (Also See Cyberforce)
Image Comics (Top Cow Productions): Sept, 1995 - No. 3, Dec, 1995 ($2.50, limited series)
1-3: Wetworks app, Turner-c/a 3.00
... Action (5/96, $2.95) Pin-ups of Top Cow characters participating in outdoor sports 3.00
... Imagery (1/96, $2.50, anthology) Cyberforce app. 3.00
.../ Wolverine (2/97, $2.95) Devil's Reign pt. 4; Witchblade cameo (1 page) 4.00

BALOO & LITTLE BRITCHES (Disney)
Gold Key: Apr, 1968
1-From the Jungle Book 4 8 12 28 47 65

BALTIMORE: ... (One-shots)
Dark Horse Comics: ($3.50)
... The Inquisitor (6/13) Mignola & Golden-s; Stenbeck-a/c 3.50
... The Play (11/12) Mignola & Golden-s; Stenbeck-a/c 3.50
... The Widow and the Tank (2/13) Mignola & Golden-s; Stenbeck-a/c 3.50

BALTIMORE: CHAPEL OF BONES
Dark Horse Comics: Jan, 2014 - No. 2, Feb, 2014 ($3.50, limited series)
1,2-Mignola & Golden-s; Stenbeck-a/c 3.50

BALTIMORE: EMPTY GRAVES
Dark Horse Comics: Apr, 2016 - No. 5, Aug, 2016 ($3.99, limited series)
1-5-Mignola & Golden-s; Bergting-a; Stenbeck-c 4.00

BALTIMORE: DR. LESKOVAR'S REMEDY
Dark Horse Comics: Jun, 2012 - No. 2, Jul, 2012 ($3.50, limited series)
1,2-Mignola & Golden-s; Stenbeck-a/c 3.50

BALTIMORE: THE CULT OF THE RED KING
Dark Horse Comics: May, 2015 - No. 5, Sept, 2015 ($3.99, limited series)
1-5-Mignola & Golden-s; Bergting-a; Stenbeck-c 4.00

BALTIMORE: THE CURSE BELLS
Dark Horse Comics: Aug, 2011 - No. 5, Dec, 2011 ($3.50, limited series)
1-5-Mignola-s/c; Stenbeck-a. 1-Variant-c by Francavilla 3.50

BALTIMORE: THE INFERNAL TRAIN
Dark Horse Comics: Sept, 2013 - No. 3, Nov, 2013 ($3.50, limited series)
1-3-Mignola & Golden-s; Stenbeck-a/c 3.50

BALTIMORE: THE PLAGUE SHIPS
Dark Horse Comics: Aug, 2010 - No. 5, Dec, 2010 ($3.50, limited series)
1-5-Mignola-s/c; Stenbeck-a; Lord Baltimore hunting vampires in 1916 Europe 3.50

BALTIMORE: THE RED KINGDOM
Dark Horse Comics: Feb, 2017 - No. 5, Jun, 2017 ($3.99, limited series)
1-5-Mignola & Golden-s; Bergting-a; Stenbeck-c 4.00

BALTIMORE: THE WITCH OF HARJU
Dark Horse Comics: Jul, 2014 - No. 3, Sept, 2014 ($3.50, limited series)
1-3-Mignola & Golden-s; Bergting-a; Stenbeck-c 3.50

BALTIMORE: THE WOLF AND THE APOSTLE
Dark Horse Comics: Oct, 2014 - No. 2, Nov, 2014 ($3.50, limited series)
1,2-Mignola & Golden-s; Stenbeck-a/c 3.50

BAMBI (Disney) (See Movie Classics, Movie Comics, and Walt Disney Showcase No. 31)
Dell Publishing Co.: No. 12, 1942; No. 30, 1943; No. 186, Apr, 1948; 1984
Four Color 12-Walt Disney's... 50 100 150 400 900 1400
Four Color 30-Bambi's Children (1943) 44 88 132 326 738 1150
Four Color 186-Walt Disney's...; reprinted as Movie Classic Bambi #3 (1956)
16 32 48 110 243 375
1-(Whitman, 1984; 60¢)-r/Four Color #186 (3-pack) 2 4 6 11 16 20

BAMBI (Disney)
Grosset & Dunlap: 1942 (50¢, 7"x8-1/2", 32 pg, hard-c w/dust jacket)
nn-Given away w/a copy of Thumper for a $2.00, 2-yr. subscription to WDC&S in 1942 (Xmas offer). Book only 24 48 72 140 230 320
w/dust jacket 40 80 120 244 402 560

BAMM BAMM & PEBBLES FLINTSTONE (TV)
Gold Key: Oct, 1964 (Hanna-Barbera)
1 9 18 27 58 114 170

BANANA SPLITS, THE (TV) (See Golden Comics Digest & March of Comics No. 364)
Gold Key: June, 1969 - No. 8, Oct, 1971 (Hanna-Barbera)
1-Photo-c on all 10 20 30 67 141 215
2-8 5 10 15 35 63 90

B&V FRIENDS FOREVER (See Betty and Veronica Friends Forever)

BAND WAGON (See Hanna-Barbera Band Wagon)

Bad Mother #1 © AWA Inc.

Bang! #1 © Kindt & Torres

Barbie #3 © Mattel

	GD 2.0	VG 4.0	FN 6.0	VF 8.0	VF/NM 9.0	NM- 9.2

BANE: CONQUEST
DC Comics: Jul, 2017 - No. 12, Aug, 2018 ($3.99, limited series)
1-12: 1-Chuck Dixon-s/Graham Nolan-a; covers by Nolan and Kelley Jones. 4,5-Catwoman app. 6-12-Kobra app. 4.00

BANG!
Dark Horse Comics: Feb, 2020 - No. 5, Nov, 2020 ($3.99, limited series)
1-5-Matt Kindt-s/Wilfredo Torres-a 4.00

BANG! TANGO
DC Comics (Vertigo): Apr, 2009 - No. 6, Sept, 2009 ($2.99, limited series)
1-6-Kelly-s/Sibar-a/Chaykin-c 3.00

BANG-UP COMICS
Progressive Publishers: Dec, 1941 - No. 3, June, 1942

	GD	VG	FN	VF	VF/NM	NM-
1-Nazi WWII-c; Cosmo Mann & Lady Fairplay begin; Buzz Balmer by Rick Yager in all (origin #1)	135	270	405	864	1482	2100
2-Nazi zeppelin WWII-c	90	180	270	576	988	1400
3-Japanese WWII-c	74	148	222	470	810	1150

BANISHED KNIGHTS (See Warlands)
Image Comics: Dec, 2001 - No. 4, June, 2002 ($2.95)
1-4-Two covers (Alvin Lee, Pat Lee) 3.00

BANNER COMICS (Becomes Captain Courageous No. 6)
Ace Magazines: No. 3, Sept, 1941 - No. 5, Jan, 1942

	GD	VG	FN	VF	VF/NM	NM-
3-Captain Courageous (1st app.) & Lone Warrior & Sidekick Dicky begin; Nazi WWII-c by Jim Mooney	295	590	885	1888	3244	4600
4,5: 4-Flag-c	194	388	582	1242	2121	3000

BARACK OBAMA (See Presidential Material: Barack Obama, Amazing Spider-Man #583, Savage Dragon #137)

BARACK THE BARBARIAN
Devil's Due Publishing: Jun, 2009 - No. 4, Oct, 2009 ($3.50/$3.99, limited series)
...Quest For The Treasure of Stimuli 1-3-($3.50) Conan spoof with Barack Obama; Hama-s 3.50
...Quest For The Treasure of Stimuli 4-($3.99) 4.00
...: The Red of Red Sarah 1 ($5.99, B&W) Sarah Palin satire; Hama-s 6.00

BARBALIEN: RED PLANET (From Black Hammer)
Dark Horse Comics: Nov, 2020 - No. 5, Mar, 2021 ($3.99, limited series)
1-5-Lemire & Brombal-s/Walta-a 4.00

BARBARELLA (Volume 1)
Dynamite Entertainment: 2017 - No. 12, 2018 ($3.99)
1-12-Mike Carey-s/Kenan Yarar-a in most; multiple covers on each. 4-Fornés-a 4.00
... Holiday Special One Shot (2018, $5.99) Niklaus von Claus app.; J-M Lofficier-s 6.00

BARBARELLA (Volume 2)
Dynamite Entertainment: 2021 - No. 10, 2022 ($3.99)
1-10: 1-5-Sarah Hoyt-s/Madibek Musabekov-a; multiple covers on each 4.00

BARBARELLA / DEJAH THORIS
Dynamite Entertainment: 2019 - No. 4, 2019 ($3.99, limited series)
1-4-Leah Williams-s/Germán García-a; multiple covers on each 4.00

BARBARELLA: THE CENTER CANNOT HOLD
Dynamite Entertainment: 2023 - Present ($3.99)
1-Sarah Hoyt-s/Riccardo Bogani-a; multiple covers 4.00

BARBARIANS, THE
Atlas Comics/Seaboard Periodicals: June, 1975

	GD	VG	FN	VF	VF/NM	NM-
1-Origin, only app. Andrax; Iron Jaw app.; Marcos-a	3	6	9	16	24	32

BARBIE
Marvel Comics: Jan, 1991 - No. 63, Mar, 1996 ($1.00/$1.25/$1.50)

	GD	VG	FN	VF	VF/NM	NM-
1-Polybagged w/doorknob hanger; Romita-c	3	6	9	14	19	24
2-49,51-62	1	2	3	5	7	9
50,63: 50-(Giant). 63-Last issue	2	4	6	8	10	12
... And Baby Sister Kelly (1995, 99¢-c, part of a Marvel 4-pack) scarce	3	6	9	14	20	25

BARBIE & KEN
Dell Publishing Co.: May-July, 1962 - No. 5, Nov-Jan, 1963-64

	GD	VG	FN	VF	VF/NM	NM-
01-053-207(#1)-Based on Mattel toy dolls	40	80	120	296	673	1050
2-4	26	52	78	182	404	625
5 (Last issue)	27	54	81	189	420	650

BARBIE FASHION
Marvel Comics: Jan, 1991 - No. 53, May, 1995 ($1.00/$1.25/$1.50)

	GD	VG	FN	VF	VF/NM	NM-
1-Polybagged w/Barbie Pink Card	2	4	6	11	16	20
2-49,51,52: 4-Contains preview to Sweet XVI	1	2	3	5	7	9
50,53: 50-(Giant). 53-Last issue	2	4	6	8	10	12

BARB WIRE (See Comics' Greatest World)
Dark Horse Comics: Apr, 1994 - No. 9, Feb, 1995 ($2.00/$2.50)
1-9: 1-Foil logo 4.00
Trade paperback (1996, $8.95)-r/#2,3,5,6 w/Pamela Anderson bio 9.00

BARB WIRE (Volume 2)
Dark Horse Comics: Jul, 2015 - No. 8, Feb, 2016 ($3.99)
1-8-Adam Hughes-c on all. 1-Warner-s/Olliffe-a; two covers by Hughes 4.00

BARB WIRE: ACE OF SPADES
Dark Horse Comics: May, 1996 - No. 4, Sept, 1996 ($2.95, limited series)

	GD	VG	FN	VF	VF/NM	NM-
1-Chris Warner-c/a(p)/scripts; Tim Bradstreet-c/a(i) in all	1	3	4	6	8	10

2-4 4.00

BARB WIRE COMICS MAGAZINE SPECIAL
Dark Horse Comics: May, 1996 ($3.50, B&W, magazine, one-shot)

	GD	VG	FN	VF	VF/NM	NM-
nn-Adaptation of film; photo-c; poster insert.	1	3	4	6	8	10

BARB WIRE MOVIE SPECIAL
Dark Horse Comics: May, 1996 ($3.95, one-shot)

	GD	VG	FN	VF	VF/NM	NM-
nn-Adaptation of film; photo-c; 1st app. new look	2	4	6	9	12	15

BARKER, THE (Also see National Comics #42)
Quality Comics Group/Comic Magazine: Autumn, 1946 - No. 15, Dec, 1949

	GD	VG	FN	VF	VF/NM	NM-
1	32	64	96	188	307	425
2	17	34	51	100	158	215
3-10	13	26	39	72	101	130
11-14	10	20	30	54	72	90
15-Jack Cole-a(p)	11	22	33	60	83	105

NOTE: *Jack Cole art in some issues.*

BARNABY
Civil Service Publications Inc.: 1945 (25¢,102 pgs., digest size)

	GD	VG	FN	VF	VF/NM	NM-
V1#1-r/Crocket Johnson strips from 1942	7	14	21	35	43	50

BARNEY AND BETTY RUBBLE (TV) (Flintstones' Neighbors)
Charlton Comics: Jan, 1973 - No. 23, Dec, 1976 (Hanna-Barbera)

	GD	VG	FN	VF	VF/NM	NM-
1	5	10	15	30	50	70
2-11: 11(2/75)-1st Mike Zeck-a (illos)	3	6	9	14	20	25
12-23: 17-Columbo parody	2	4	6	10	14	18
Digest Annual (1972, B&W, 100 pgs.) (scarce)	4	8	12	27	44	60

BARNEY BAXTER (Also see Magic Comics)
David McKay/Dell Publishing Co./Argo: 1938 - No. 2, 1956

	GD	VG	FN	VF	VF/NM	NM-
Feature Books 15(McKay-1938)	48	96	144	302	514	725
Four Color 20(1942)	27	54	81	194	435	675
1,2 (1956-Argo)	9	18	27	52	69	85

BARNEY BEAR ...
Spire Christian Comics (Fleming H. Revell Co.): 1977-1982

	GD	VG	FN	VF	VF/NM	NM-
...Home Plate nn-(1979, 49¢), ...In Toyland nn-(1982, 49¢),...Lost and Found nn-(1979, 49¢), Out of The Woods nn-(1980, 49¢), Sunday School Picnic nn-(1981, 69¢), The Swamp Gang!-(1977, 39¢)	2	4	6	9	13	16

BARNEY GOOGLE & SNUFFY SMITH
Dell Publishing Co./Gold Key: 1942 - 1943; April, 1964

	GD	VG	FN	VF	VF/NM	NM-
Four Color 19(1942)	58	116	174	371	636	900
Four Color 40(1944)	20	40	60	140	310	480
Large Feature Comic 11(1943)	40	80	120	246	411	575
1(10113-404)-Gold Key (4/64)	4	8	12	25	40	55

BARNEY GOOGLE & SNUFFY SMITH
Toby Press: June, 1951 - No. 4, Feb, 1952 (Reprints)

	GD	VG	FN	VF	VF/NM	NM-
1	15	30	45	85	130	175
2,3	9	18	27	50	65	80
4-Kurtzman-a "Pot Shot Pete", 5 pgs.; reprints John Wayne #5	13	26	39	74	105	135

BARNEY GOOGLE AND SNUFFY SMITH
Charlton Comics: Mar, 1970 - No. 6, Jan, 1971

	GD	VG	FN	VF	VF/NM	NM-
1	3	6	9	18	27	36
2-6	2	4	6	11	16	20

BARNUM!
DC Comics (Vertigo): 2003; 2005 ($29.95, $19.95)
Hardcover (2003, $29.95, with dust jacket)-Chaykin & Tischman-s/Henrichon-a 30.00

Softcover (2005, $19.95)-Chaykin & Tischman-s/Henrichon-a 20.00

BARNYARD COMICS (Dizzy Duck No. 32 on)
Nedor/Polo Mag./Standard(Animated Cartoons): Jun, 1944 - No. 31, Sept, 1950; No. 10, 1957

	GD	VG	FN	VF	VF/NM	NM-
1 (nn, 52 pgs.)-Funny animal	28	56	84	165	270	375
2 (52 pgs.)	15	30	45	90	140	190
3-5	12	24	36	69	97	125
6-12,16	11	22	33	62	86	110
13-15,17,21,23,26,27,29-All contain Frazetta text illos	12	24	36	69	97	125
18-20,22,24,25-All contain Frazetta-a & text illos	14	28	42	82	121	160
28,30,31	10	20	30	54	72	90
10 (1957)(Exist?)	4	8	12	17	21	24

BARRIER
Image Comics: May, 2018 - No. 5, May, 2018 ($4.99/$3.99, limited series, printed sideways)

1,5-($4.99) Brian K. Vaughan-s/Marcos Martin-a 5.00
2-4-($3.99) 4.00

BARRY M. GOLDWATER
Dell Publishing Co.: Mar, 1965 (Complete life story)

12-055-503-Photo-c 4 8 12 28 47 65

BARRY WINDSOR-SMITH: STORYTELLER
Dark Horse Comics: Oct, 1996 - No. 9, July, 1997 ($4.95, oversize)

1-9: 1-Intro Young Gods, Paradox Man & the Freebooters; Barry Smith-c/a/scripts 5.00
Preview 4.00

BAR SINISTER (Also see Shaman's Tears)
Acclaim Comics (Windjammer): Jun, 1995 - No. 4, Sept, 1995 ($2.50, lim. series)

1-4: Mike Grell-c/a/scripts 3.00

BARTMAN (Also see Simpsons Comics & Radioactive Man)
Bongo Comics: 1993 - No. 6, 1994 ($1.95/$2.25)

1-($2.95)-Foil-c; bound-in jumbo Bartman poster 3 6 9 14 20 25
1-($1.95) Regular cover 2 4 6 8 10 12
2-6: 3-w/trading card 5.00
...: Spectacularly Super Secret Saga (2018, $7.99) Adult Bartman 20 years in the future 10.00

BART SIMPSON (See Simpsons Comics Presents Bart Simpson)

BASEBALL COMICS
Will Eisner Productions: Spring, 1949 (Reprinted later as a Spirit section)

1-Will Eisner-c/a 74 148 222 470 810 1150

BASEBALL COMICS
Kitchen Sink Press: 1991 ($3.95, coated stock)

1-r/1949 ish. by Eisner; contains trading cards 6.00

BASEBALL HEROES
Fawcett Publications: 1952 (one-shot)

nn (Scarce)-Babe Ruth photo-c; baseball's Hall of Fame biographies 90 180 270 576 988 1400

BASEBALL'S GREATEST HEROES
Magnum Comics: Dec, 1991 - No. 2, May, 1992 ($1.75)

1-Mickey Mantle #1; photo-c; Sinnott-a(p) 1 2 3 5 6 8
2-Brooks Robinson #1; photo-c; Sinnott-a(i) 6.00

BASEBALL THRILLS
Ziff-Davis Publ. Co.: No. 10, Sum, 1951 - No. 3, Sum, 1952 (Saunders painted-c No.1,2)

10(#1)-Bob Feller, Musial, Newcombe & Boudreau stories 45 90 135 284 480 675
2-Powell-a(2)(Late Sum, '51); Feller, Berra & Mathewson stories 32 64 96 188 307 425
3-Kinstler-c/a; Joe DiMaggio story 32 64 96 188 307 425

BASEBALL THRILLS 3-D
The 3-D Zone: May, 1990 ($2.95, w/glasses)

1-New L.B. Cole-c; life stories of Ty Cobb & Ted Williams 1 2 3 5 6 8

BASICALLY STRANGE (Magazine)
John C. Comics (Archie Comics Group): Dec, 1982 ($1.95, B&W)

1-(21,000 printed; all but 1,000 destroyed; pages out of sequence) 3 6 9 17 25 34
1-Wood, Toth-a; Corben-c; reprints & new art 2 4 6 13 18 22

BASIC HISTORY OF AMERICA ILLUSTRATED
Pendulum Press: 1976 (B&W) (Soft-c $1.50; Hard-c $4.50)

07-1999-America Becomes a World Power 1890-1920. 07-2251-The Industrial Era 1865-1915. 07-226x-Before the Civil War 1830-1860. 07-2278-Americans Move Westward 1800-1850. 07-2286-The Civil War 1850-1876; Redondo-a. 07-2294-The Fight for Freedom 1750-1783. 07-2308-The New World 1500-1750. 07-2316-Problems of the New Nation 1800-1830. 07-2324-Roaring Twenties and the Great Depression 1920-1940. 07-2332-The United States Emerges 1783-1800. 07-2340-America Today 1945-1976. 07-2359-World War II 1940-1945
Softcover editions each 1 2 3 4 5 7
Hardcover editions each 14.00

BASIL (...the Royal Cat)
St. John Publishing Co.: Jan, 1953 - No. 4, Sept, 1953

1-Funny animal 9 18 27 50 65 80
2-Hitler Mouse app. 10 20 30 54 72 90
3,4 6 12 18 31 38 45
I.W. Reprint 2 4 6 9 12 15

BASILISK
BOOM! Studios: Jun, 2021 - No. 12, Oct, 2022 ($3.99)

1-12-Cullen Bunn-s/Jonas Scharf-a 4.00

BASIL WOLVERTON'S FANTASTIC FABLES
Dark Horse Comics: Oct, 1993 - No. 2, Dec, 1993 ($2.50, B&W, limited series)

1-Wolverton-c/a(r) 1 3 4 6 8 10
2-Wolverton-c/a(r) 6.00

BASIL WOLVERTON'S GATEWAY TO HORROR
Dark Horse Comics: June, 1988 ($1.75, B&W, one-shot)

1-Wolverton-r 1 3 4 6 8 10

BASIL WOLVERTON'S PLANET OF TERROR
Dark Horse Comics: Oct, 1987 ($1.75, B&W, one-shot)

1-Wolverton-r; Alan Moore-c 1 2 3 5 6 8

BASKETFUL OF HEADS (Also see Refrigerator Full of Heads)
DC Comics (Hill House Comics): Dec, 2019 - No. 7, Jun, 2020 ($3.99, limited series)

1-7-Joe Hill-s/Leomacs-a; back-up serial Sea Dogs in each; Murakami-c 4.00
1-($4.99) Variant cardstock-c by Josh Middleton 5.00

BASTARD SAMURAI
Image Comics: Apr, 2002 - No. 3, Aug, 2002 ($2.95)

1-3-Oeming & Gunter-s; Shannon-a/Oeming-i 3.00
TPB (2003, $12.95) r/#1-3; plus sketch pages and pin-ups 13.00

BATGIRL (See Batman: No Man's Land stories)
DC Comics: Apr, 2000 - No. 73, Apr, 2006 ($2.50)

1-Scott & Campanella-a 2 4 6 9 12 15
1-(2nd printing) 3.00
2-10: 8-Lady Shiva app. 5.00
11-24: 12-"Officer Down" x-over. 15-Joker-c/app. 24-Bruce Wayne: Murderer pt. 2. 4.00
25-($3.25) Batgirl vs Lady Shiva 4.50
26-29: 27- Bruce Wayne: Fugitive pt. 5; Noto-a. 29-B.W.:F. pt. 13 4.00
30-49,51-73: 30-32-Connor Hawke app. 39-Intro. Black Wind. 41-Superboy-c/app. 53-Robin (Spoiler) app. 54-Bagged with Sky Captain CD. 55-57-War Games. 63,64-Deathstroke app. 67-Birds of Prey app. 70-1st app. Lazara (Nora Fries). 73-Lady Shiva origin; Sale-c 4.00
50-($3.25) Batgirl vs Batman 5.00
Annual 1 ('00, $3.50) Planet DC; intro. Aruna 5.00
...: A Knight Alone (2001, $12.95, TPB) r/#7-11,13,14 13.00
...: Death Wish (2003, $14.95, TPB) r/#17-20,22,23,25 & Secret Files and Origins #1 15.00
...: Destruction's Daughter (2006, $19.99, TPB) r/#65-73 20.00
...: Fists of Fury (2004, $14.95, TPB) r/#15,16,21,26-28 15.00
...: Kicking Assassins (2005, $14.99, TPB) r/#60-64 15.00
... Secret Files and Origins (8/02, $4.95) origin-s Noto-a; profile pages and pin-ups 5.00
...: Silent Running (2001, $12.95, TPB) r/#1-6 13.00

BATGIRL (Cassandra Cain)
DC Comics: Sept, 2008 - No. 6, Feb, 2009 ($2.99)

1-6-Beechen-s/Calafiore-a 4.00

BATGIRL (Spoiler/Stephanie Brown)(Batman: Reborn)
DC Comics: Oct, 2009 - No. 24, Oct, 2011 ($2.99)

1-Garbett-a/Noto-c 2 4 6 9 12 15
1-Variant-c by Hamner 3 6 9 14 20 25
2-24: 2-7-Garbett-a/Noto-c. 3-New costume. 8-Caldwell-a. 9-14-Lau-c. 14-Supergirl app. 4.00
...: Batgirl Rising TPB (2010, $17.99) r/#1-7 20.00
...: The Flood TPB (2011, $14.99) r/#9-14 30.00

BATGIRL (Barbara Gordon)(DC New 52)(See Secret Origins #10)
DC Comics: Nov, 2011 - No. 52, Jul, 2016 ($2.99)

1-Barbara Gordon back in costume; Simone-s/Syaf-a/Hughes-c 25.00
1-Second & Third printings 5.00
2-12: 2-6-Hughes-c. 3-Nightwing app. 7-12-Syaf-c. 9-Night of the Owls. 12-Batwoman app. 4.00
13-Die-cut cover; Death of the Family tie-in; Batwoman app. 10.00
13-24: 14-16-Death of the Family tie-in; Joker app. 20,21-Intro. The Ventriloquist 3.00
25-($3.99) Zero Year tie-in; Bennett-s/Pasarin-a 4.00
26-34: 27-Gothtopia tie-in. 28,29-Strix app. 31-34-Simone-s. 31-Ragdoll app. 3.00
35-49,51,52: 35-New costume; Tarr-a/Stewart-c. 37-Dagger Type app. 41,42-Batman (Gordon) & Livewire app. 45-Dick Grayson app. 48,49-Black Canary app. 3.00
50-($4.99) Black Canary, Spoiler & Bluebird app.; Tarr-a 5.00
#0 (11/12, $2.99) Batgirl origin updated; Simone-s/Benes-a 3.00
Annual 1 (12/12, $4.99) Catwoman and the Talons app.; Simone-s/Wijaya-a/Benes-c 5.00
Annual 2 (6/14, $4.99) Poison Ivy app.; Simone-s/Gill-a/Benes-c 5.00
Annual 3 (9/15, $4.99) Dick Grayson, Spoiler & Batwoman app. 5.00
...: Endgame 1 (5/15, $2.99) Tie-in with other Endgame stories in Batman titles 3.00
...: Futures End 1 (11/14, $2.99, regular-c) Five years later; Bane app.; Simone-s 3.00
...: Futures End 1 (11/14, $3.99, 3-D cover) 4.00

BATGIRL (DC Rebirth)
DC Comics: Sept, 2016 - No. 50, Dec, 2020 ($2.99/$3.99)

1-9: 1-Hope Larson-s/Rafael Albuquerque-a. 6-Poison Ivy app. 9-Penguin app. 3.00
10-24-($3.99): 10,11-Penguin app. 13-Catwoman app. 18-Harley Quinn app. 4.00
25-($4.99) Short stories by various; art by Derenick, Panosian, Pelletier, Lupacchino 5.00
26-49: 26-New costume. 30-34-Jason Bard app. 34-36-Terrible Trio app. 37-41-Year of the Villain tie-ins; new Oracle app. 41-Acetate-c. 47,48-Joker War tie-ins 4.00
50-($5.99) Intro. Ryan Wilder (1 pg.); Lupacchino-a; back-up w/Sauvage-a 6.00
Annual 1 (5/17, $4.99) Supergirl app. (story cont'd in Supergirl #9); Larson-s; Bengal-c 5.00
Annual 2 (10/18, $4.99) Casagrande-a; brother James Gordon app. 5.00

BATGIRL ADVENTURES (See Batman Adventures, The)
DC Comics: Feb, 1998 ($2.95, one-shot) (Based on animated series)

1-Harley Quinn and Poison Ivy app.; Timm-c 5 10 15 30 50 70

BATGIRL AND THE BIRDS OF PREY (DC Rebirth)
DC Comics: Aug, 2016 - No. 22, Jul, 2018 ($2.99/$3.99)

1-8: 1-Julie & Shawna Benson-s/Claire Roe-a. 3-6,8-Antonio-a. 8-Nightwing app. 3.00
9-22-($3.99) 10-Nightwing & Green Arrow app. 12-17-Catwoman & Poison Ivy app. 4.00
...: Rebirth 1 (9/16, $2.99) Batgirl, Black Canary & Huntress team up; Claire Roe-a 3.00

BATGIRLS (Stephanie Brown and Cassandra Cain)
DC Comics: Feb, 2022 - Present ($3.99)

1-16: 1-6-Cloonan & Conrad-s/Corona-a; vs. the Saints (Tarsus, Valentine & Assisi) 4.00
2022 Annual (1/23, $5.99) Rodriguez-a; Steph and Cass switch bodies; continues in #13 6.00

BATGIRL SPECIAL
DC Comics: 1988 ($1.50, one-shot, 52 pgs)

Basketful of Heads #1 © Joe Hill

Batgirls #1 © DC

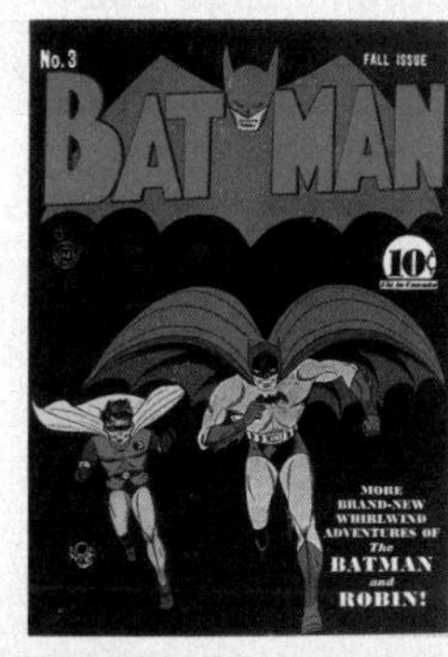

Batman #3 © DC

	GD 2.0	VG 4.0	FN 6.0	VF 8.0	VF/NM 9.0	NM- 9.2

1-Kitson-a/Mignola-c 2 4 6 11 16 20

BATGIRL: YEAR ONE
DC Comics: Feb, 2003 - No. 9, Oct, 2003 ($2.95, limited series)

1-Barbara Gordon becomes Batgirl; Killer Moth app.; Beatty & Dixon-s
2 4 6 8 10 12
2-9 4.00
TPB (2003, $17.95) r/#1-9 25.00

BAT LASH (See DC Special Series #16, Showcase #76, Weird Western Tales)
National Periodical Publications: Oct-Nov, 1968 - No. 7, Oct-Nov, 1969 (12¢/15¢)

1-(10-11/68, 12¢-c)-2nd app. Bat Lash; classic Nick Cardy-c/a in all
7 14 21 46 86 125
2-7: 6,7-(15¢-c) 4 8 12 27 44 60

BAT LASH
DC Comics: Feb, 2008 - No. 6, Jul, 2008 ($2.99, limited series)

1-6-Aragonés & Brandvold-s/John Severin-a. 1-Two covers by Severin and Simonson 3.00

BATMAN (See All Star Batman & Robin, Anarky, Aurora [in Promo. Comics section], Azrael, The Best of DC #2, Blind Justice, The Brave & the Bold, Cosmic Odyssey, DC 100-Page Super Spec. #14,20, DC Special, DC Special Series, Detective Comics, Dynamic Classics, 80-Page Giants, Gotham By Gaslight, Gotham Nights, Greatest Batman Stories Ever Told, Greatest Joker Stories Ever Told, Heroes Against Hunger, JLA, The Joker, Justice League of America, Justice League Int., Legends of the Dark Knight, Limited Coll. Ed., Man-Bat, Nightwing, Power Record Comics, Real Fact #5, Robin, Saga of Ra's al Ghul, Shadow of the..., Star Spangled, Super Friends, 3-D Batman, Untold Legend of..., Wanted... & World's Finest Comics)

BATMAN
National Per. Publ./Detective Comics/DC Comics: Spring, 1940 - No. 713, Oct, 2011 (#1-5 were quarterly)

1-Origin The Batman reprinted (2 pgs.) from Detective Comics #33 w/splash from #34 by Bob Kane; 1st app. Joker (2 stories intended for 2 separate issues of Detective which would have been 1st & 2nd app.); splash pg. to 2nd Joker story is similar to cover of Detective #40 (story intended for #40); 1st app. The Cat (Catwoman)(1st villainess in comics); has Batman story (w/Hugo Strange) without Robin originally planned for Detective #38; mentions location (Manhattan) where Batman lives (see Detective #31). This book was created entirely from the inventory of Detective Comics; 1st Batman/Robin pin-up on back-c; has text piece & photo of Bob Kane
73,300 146,600 219,900 498,000 799,000 1,100,000

1-Reprint, oversize 13-1/2x10". **WARNING**: This comic is an exact duplicate reprint of the original except for its size. DC published it in 1974 with a second cover titling it as a Famous First Edition. There have been many reported cases of the outer cover being removed and the interior sold as the original edition. The reprint with the new outer cover removed is practically worthless. See Famous First Edition for value.

2-2nd app. The Joker; 2nd app. Catwoman (out of costume) in Joker story; 1st time called Catwoman (NOTE: A 15¢-c for Canadian distr. exists.)
3450 6900 10,350 24,500 46,250 68,000
3-3rd app Catwoman (1st in costume & 1st costumed villainess); 1st Puppet Master app.; classic Kane & Robinson-c 1567 3134 4700 11,750 22,875 34,000
4-4th app. The Joker (see Det. #45 for 3rd); 1st mention of Gotham City in a Batman comic (on newspaper)(Win/40) 1567 3134 4700 11,750 22,875 34,000
5-1st app. the Batmobile with its bat-head front 1000 2000 3000 7300 12,900 18,500
6,7: 7-Bullseye-c; Joker app. 838 1676 2514 6117 10,809 15,500
8-Infinity-c by Fred Ray; Joker app. 784 1568 2352 5723 10,112 14,500
9-1st Batman Christmas story; Burnley-c 730 1460 2190 5329 9415 13,500
10-Catwoman story (gets new costume) 595 1190 1785 4344 7672 11,000
11-Classic Joker-c by Ray/Robinson (3rd Joker-c, 6-7/42); Joker & Penguin app.
2000 4000 6000 15,200 27,600 40,000
12,15: 12-Joker app. 15-New costume Catwoman 432 864 1296 3154 5577 8000
13-Jerry Siegel (Superman's co-creator) appears in a Batman story; Batman parachuting on black-c 443 886 1329 3234 5717 8200
14-2nd Penguin-c; Penguin app. (12-1/42-43) 428 856 1284 3124 5512 7900
16-Intro/origin Alfred (4-5/43); cover is a reverse of #9 cover by Burnley; 1st small logo
1250 2500 3750 9500 17,250 25,000
17-Classic war-c; Penguin app. 400 800 1200 2800 4900 7000
18-Hitler, Hirohito, Mussolini-c. 676 1352 2028 4935 8718 12,500
19-Joker app. 290 580 870 1856 3178 4500
20-1st Batmobile-c (12-1/43-44); Joker app. 486 972 1458 3550 6275 9000
21,24,26,28-30: 21-1st skinny Alfred in Batman (2-3/44). 21,30-Penguin app. 28-Joker story
219 438 657 1402 2401 3400
22-1st Alfred solo-c/story (Alfred solo stories in 22-32,36); Catwoman & The Cavalier app.
300 600 900 2010 3505 5000
23-Joker-c/story; classic black-c 865 1730 2595 6315 11,158 16,000
25-Only Joker/Penguin team-up; 1st team-up between two major villains
486 972 1458 3550 6275 9000
27-Classic Burnley Christmas-c; Penguin app. 274 548 822 1740 3020 4300
31,34-36,39: 35-Catwoman story (in new costume w/o cat head mask). 36-Penguin app.
161 322 483 1030 1765 2500
32-Origin Robin retold; Joker app. 213 426 639 1363 2332 3300
33-Christmas-c 194 388 582 1242 2121 3000
37-Joker spotlight on black-c 486 972 1458 3550 6275 9000
38-Penguin-c/story 314 628 942 2198 3849 5500
40-Joker-c/story 383 766 1149 2681 4591 6700
41-1st Sci-fi cover/story in Batman; Penguin app.(6-7/47)
168 336 504 1075 1838 2600
42-2nd Catwoman-c (1st in Batman)(8-9/47); Catwoman story also.
432 864 1296 3154 5577 8000
43-Penguin-c/story 258 516 774 1651 2826 4000
44-Classic Joker-c 811 1622 2433 5920 10,460 15,000
45-Christmas-c/story; Catwoman story 168 336 504 1075 1838 2600
46-Joker app. 290 580 870 1856 3178 4500
47-1st detailed origin The Batman (6-7/48); 1st Bat-signal-c this title (see Detective #108); Batman tracks down his parent's killer and reveals i.d. to him
1000 2000 3000 7600 13,800 20,000
48-1000 Secrets of the Batcave; r-in #203; Penguin story
343 686 1029 2400 4200 6000
49-Joker-c/story; 1st app. Mad Hatter; 1st app. Vicki Vale
541 1082 1623 3950 6975 10,000
50-Two-Face impostor app. 343 686 1029 2400 4200 6000
51-Pee-Wee, the Talking Penguin 194 388 582 1242 2121 3000
52-Joker-c/story 514 1028 1542 3750 6625 9500
53-Joker story 187 374 561 1197 2049 2900
54,56,57,60: 57-Centerfold is a 1950 calendar; Joker app.
135 270 405 864 1482 2100
55-Joker-c/stories 432 864 1296 3154 5577 8000
58,61: 58-Penguin-c. 61-Origin Batplane II 219 438 657 1402 2401 3400
59-1st app. Deadshot; Batman in the future-c/sty 519 1038 1557 3789 6695 9600
62-Origin Catwoman; Catwoman-c 432 864 1296 3154 5577 8000
63-1st app. Killer Moth; Joker story; flying saucer story(2-3/51)
343 686 1029 2400 4200 6000
64,70-72,74-77,79: 70-Robot-c. 72-Last 52 pg. issue. 74-Used in **POP**, Pg. 90. 75-Gorilla-c. 76-Penguin story. 79-Vicki Vale in "The Bride of Batman"
113 226 339 723 1237 1750
65,69-Catwoman-c/stories 371 742 1113 2600 4550 6500
66,73-Joker-c/stories. 66-Pre-2nd Batman & Robin team try-out. 73-Vicki Vale story
400 800 1200 2800 4900 7000
67-Joker story 148 296 444 947 1624 2300
68,81-Two-Face-c/stories 290 580 870 1856 3178 4500
78-(8-9/53)-Roh Kar, The Man Hunter from Mars story-the 1st lawman of Mars to come to Earth (green skinned) 271 542 813 1734 2967 4200
80-Joker stories 148 296 444 947 1624 2300
82,83,87-89: 89-Last pre-code issue 103 206 309 659 1130 1600
84-Catwoman-c/story; Two-Face app. 300 600 900 2070 3635 5200
85,86-Joker story. 86-Intro Batmarine (Batman's submarine)
113 226 339 723 1237 1750
90,91,93-96,98,99: 99-(4/56)-Last G.A. Penguin app.
90 180 270 576 988 1400
92-1st app. Bat-Hound-c/story 314 628 942 2198 3849 5500
97-2nd app. Bat-Hound-c/story; Joker story 219 458 657 1402 2401 3400
100-(6/56) 354 708 1062 2478 4339 6200
101-(8/56)-Clark Kent x-over who protects Batman's i.d. (3rd story)
94 188 282 597 1024 1450
102-104,106-109: 103-1st S.A. issue; 3rd Bat-Hound-c/story
81 162 243 518 884 1250
105-1st Batwoman in Batman (2nd anywhere) 168 336 504 1075 1838 2600
110-Joker story 87 174 261 553 952 1350
111-120: 112-1st app. Signalman (super villain). 113-1st app. Fatman; Batman meets his counterpart on Planet X w/a chest plate similar to S.A. Batman's design (yellow oval w/black design inside). 71 142 213 454 777 1100
121-Origin/1st app. of Mr. Zero (Mr. Freeze) 1000 2000 3000 7400 13,200 19,000
122,124-126,128,130: 122,126-Batwoman-c/story. 124-2nd app. Signal Man. 128-Batwoman cameo. 130-Lex Luthor app. 59 118 177 381 653 925
123,127: 123-Joker story; Bat-Hound-c/app. 127-(10/59)-Batman vs. Thor the Thunder God c/story; Joker story; Superman cameo 59 118 177 381 653 925
129-Origin Robin retold; bondage-c; Batwoman-c/story (reprinted in Batman Family #8)
77 154 231 493 847 1200
131-135,137,138,141-143: 131-Intro 2nd Batman & Robin series (see #66; also in #135,145, 154,159,163). 133-1st Bat-Mite in Batman (3rd app. anywhere). 134-Origin The Dummy (not Vigilante's villain). 141-2nd app. original Bat-Girl. 143-(10/61)-Last 10¢ issue
50 100 150 315 533 750
136-Joker-c/story 68 136 204 435 743 1050
139-Intro 1st original Bat-Girl; only app. Signalman as the Blue Bowman
206 412 618 1318 2259 3200
140-Joker story, Batwoman-c/s; Superman cameo 52 104 156 328 552 775

	GD 2.0	VG 4.0	FN 6.0	VF 8.0	VF/NM 9.0	NM- 9.2
144-(12/61)-1st 12¢ issue; Joker story	50	100	150	315	533	750
145,148-Joker-c/stories	74	148	222	470	810	1150
146,147,149,150	43	86	129	271	461	650
151-154,156-158,160-162,164-168,170: 152-Joker story. 156-Ant-Man/Robin team-up(6/63). 164-New Batmobile(6/64) new look & Mystery Analysts series begins	36	72	108	211	343	475
155-1st S.A. app. The Penguin (5/63)	258	516	774	1651	2826	4000
159,163-Joker-c/stories. 159-Bat-Girl app. 163-Last Bat-Girl app. until Teen Titans #50	50	100	150	315	533	750
169-2nd SA Penguin app.	45	90	135	284	480	675
171-1st Riddler app.(5/65) since Dec. 1948	213	426	639	1363	2332	3600
172-175,177,178,180,184	12	24	36	82	179	275
176-(80-Pg. Giant G-17); Joker-c/story; Penguin app. in strip-r; Catwoman reprint	16	32	48	110	243	375
179-2nd app. Silver Age Riddler	27	54	81	189	420	650
181-Intro. Poison Ivy; Batman & Robin poster insert	286	572	858	2402	5451	8500
181-(Facsimile Edition)(2019, $3.99) reprints issue with original ads and letter column						6.00
182,187-(80 Pg. Giants G-24, G-30); Joker-c/stories	12	24	36	84	185	285
183-2nd app. Poison Ivy	18	36	54	124	275	425
185-(80 Pg. Giant G-27)	12	24	36	84	185	285
186-Joker-c/story	17	34	51	117	259	400
188,191,192,194-196,199	10	20	30	64	132	200
189-1st S.A. app. Scarecrow; retells origin of G.A. Scarecrow from World's Finest #3 (1st app.)	61	122	183	488	1094	1700
190-Penguin-c/app.	17	34	51	117	259	400
193-(80-Pg. Giant G-37)	11	22	33	75	160	245
197-4th S.A. Catwoman app. cont'd from Det. #369; 1st new Batgirl app. in Batman (5th anywhere)	18	36	54	124	275	425
198-(80-Pg. Giant G-43); Joker-c/story-r/World's Finest #61; Catwoman-r/Det. #211; Penguin-r; origin-r/#47	12	24	36	80	173	265
200-(3/68)-Scarecrow app.; Joker, Penguin, Killer Moth cameos; retells origin of Batman & Robin; 1st Neal Adams work this title (cover only)	14	28	42	93	204	315
201-Joker story	8	16	24	56	108	160
202,204-207,209-212: 210-Catwoman-c/app. 212-Last 12¢ issue	8	16	24	51	96	140
203-(80 Pg. Giant G-49); r/#48, 61, & Det. 185; Batcave Blueprints	10	20	30	69	147	225
208-(80 Pg. Giant G-55); New origin Batman by Gil Kane plus 3 G.A. Batman reprints w/Catwoman, Vicki Vale & Batwoman	9	18	27	62	126	190
213-(80-Pg. Giant G-61); 30th anniversary issue (7-8/69); origin Alfred (r/Batman #16), Joker(r/Det. #168), Clayface; new origin Robin with new facts	9	18	27	63	129	195
214-217: 216-Alfred given a new last name- "Pennyworth" (see Detective #96)	7	14	21	44	82	120
218-(68 pg. Giant G-67)	9	18	27	63	129	195
219-Neal Adams-a	10	20	30	66	138	210
220,221,224-226,229-231	6	12	18	37	66	95
222-Beatles take-off; art lesson by Joe Kubert	20	40	60	140	310	480
223,228,233: 223,228-(68 pg. Giants G-73,G-79). 233-G-85-(68 pgs., "64 pgs." on-c)	7	14	21	48	89	130
227-Neal Adams cover swipe of Detective #31	68	136	204	544	1222	1900
232-(6/71) Adams-a. Intro/1st app. Ra's al Ghul; origin Batman & Robin retold; last 15¢ issue (see Detective #411 (5/71) for Talia's debut)	46	92	138	368	834	1300
232-(Facsimile Edition)(2019, $3.99) reprints issue with original ads and letter column						4.00
234-(9/71)-1st modern app. of Harvey Dent/Two-Face with origin re-told in brief; (see World's Finest #173 for Batman as Two-Face; only S.A. mention of character); N. Adams-a; 52 pg. issues begin, end #242	36	72	108	259	580	900
235,236,239-242: 239-XMas-c. 241-Reprint/#5	6	12	18	41	76	110
237-N. Adams-c/a. 1st Rutland Vermont - Bald Mountain Halloween x-over. 1st app. The Reaper; Holocaust reference; Wrightson/Ellison plots; G.A. Batman-r/Detective #37	20	40	60	138	307	475
238-Also listed as DC 100 Page Super Spectacular #8; Batman, Legion, Aquaman-r; G.A. Atom, Sargon (r/Sensation #57), Plastic Man (r/Police #14) stories; Doom Patrol origin-r; N. Adams wraparound-c	18	36	54	124	275	425
243,245-Neal Adams-a	11	22	33	73	157	240
244-Ra's al Ghul app.; Neal Adams-a	21	42	63	147	324	500
246-250,252,253: 246-Scarecrow app. 253-Shadow-c & app.	6	12	18	37	66	95
251-(9/73)-N. Adams-c/a; Joker-c/story	59	118	177	472	1061	1650
251-(Facsimile Edition)(2019, $3.99) reprints issue with original ads and letter column						20.00
254,256,257,259,261-All 100 pg. editions; part-r: 254-(2/74)-Man-Bat-c/app. 256-Catwoman app. 257-Joker & Penguin app. 259-Shadow-c/app.	7	14	21	49	92	135
255-(100 pgs.)-N. Adams-c/a; tells of Bruce Wayne's father who wore bat costume & fought crime (r/Det. #235); r/story Batman #22	9	18	27	59	117	175
258-First mention of Arkham (Hospital, renamed Arkham Asylum in #260)	10	20	30	66	138	210
260-(100 pgs.) Joker-c/story; 2nd Arkham Asylum (see #258 for 1st mention)	9	18	27	58	114	170
262 (68 pgs.)	6	12	18	40	73	105
263,264,266-285,287-290,292,293,295-299: 266-Catwoman back to old costume	3	6	9	17	26	35
265-Wrightson-a(i)	3	6	9	18	28	38
286,291,294: 294-Joker-c/stories	4	8	12	23	37	50
300-Double-size	5	10	15	31	53	75
301-(7/78)-306,308-310,312,314,315,317-320,325-331,333-352: 304-(44 pgs.). 306-3rd app. Black Spider. 308-Mr. Freeze app. 310-1st modern app. The Gentleman Ghost in Batman; Kubert-c. 312,314-Two-Face-c/stories. 318-Intro Firebug. 319-2nd modern age app. of The Gentleman Ghost; Kubert-c. 331-1st app./death original Electrocutioner. 344-Poison Ivy app. 345-1st app. new Dr. Death. 345,346,351-Catwoman back-ups. 346-Two-Face-c/app.	2	4	6	11	16	20
306-308,311-320,323,324,326-(Whitman variants; low print run; none show issue # on cover)	3	6	9	17	25	34
307-1st app. Lucius Fox (1/79)	4	8	12	25	40	55
311,316,322-324: 311-Batgirl-c/story; Batgirl reteams w/Batman. 316-Robin returns. 322-324-Catwoman (Selina Kyle) app. 322,323-Cat-Man cameos (1st in Batman, 1 panel each). 323-1st meeting Catwoman & Cat-Man. 324-1st full app. Cat-Man this title	3	6	9	14	20	25

	GD 2.0	VG 4.0	FN 6.0	VF 8.0	VF/NM 9.0	NM- 9.2
313-1st app. Timothy Fox (7/79)(see Future State: The Next Batman); Two-Face app.; 2nd app. Calendar Man	10	20	30	69	147	225
321-Joker-c/story	5	10	15	35	63	90
332-Catwoman's 1st solo	3	6	9	19	30	40
353-Joker-c/story; preview of Masters of the Universe	3	6	9	21	33	45
354-356,360,362-365,369,370: 362-Riddler-c/story with origin retold in brief	2	4	6	9	13	16
357-1st app. Jason Todd (3/83); see Det. #524; brief app. Croc (see Detective #523 (2/83) for earlier cameo)	9	18	27	58	114	170
357-(Facsimile Edition)(2023, $3.99) reprints issue with original ads and letter column						4.00
358-Early Croc app.	3	6	9	17	26	35
359-Joker-c/story	4	8	12	23	37	50
361-Debut of Harvey Bullock (7/83)(see Detective #441,('74) for a similar Lt. Bullock, no first name given, appeared in 3 panels)	3	6	9	17	26	35
366-Jason Todd 1st in Robin costume; Joker-c/story	4	8	12	28	47	65
367-Jason in red & green costume (not as Robin)	2	4	6	10	14	18
368-1st new Robin in costume (Jason Todd)	4	8	12	25	40	55
371,372,375-385,388-399,401-403: 371-Cat-Man-c/story; brief origin Cat-Man (cont'd in Det. #538). 390-391-Catwoman app. 398-Catwoman & Two-Face app. 401-2nd app. Magpie (see Man of Steel #3 for 1st). 403-Joker cameo	2	4	6	8	10	12
373-Scarecrow-c	3	6	9	14	19	24
374-Elongated Man app.	2	4	6	11	16	20

NOTE: *Issues 397-399, 401-403, 408-416, 421-425, 430-432 all have 2nd printings in 1989; some with up to 8 printings. Some are not identified as reprints but have newer ads copyrighted after cover dates. All reprints have different back-c ads. All reprints are scarcer than 1st prints and have same value to variant collectors.*

	GD 2.0	VG 4.0	FN 6.0	VF 8.0	VF/NM 9.0	NM- 9.2
386-Intro Black Mask (villain)	5	10	15	35	63	90
387-Intro Black Mask continues	2	4	6	13	18	22
400 ($1.50, 68pgs.)-Dark Knight special; intro by Stephen King; Art Adams/Austin-a	4	8	12	23	37	50
404-Miller scripts begin (end 407); Year 1; 1st modern app. Catwoman (2/87)	4	8	12	23	37	50
405-407: 407-Year 1 ends (See Detective Comics #575-578 for Year 2)	3	6	9	14	20	25
408-410: New Origin Jason Todd (Robin)	2	4	6	13	18	22
411-416,421,422,424,425: 411-Two-face app. 412-Origin/1st app. Mime. 414-Starlin scripts begin, end #429. 416-Nightwing-c/story	1	3	4	6	8	10
417-420: "Ten Nights of the Beast" storyline	2	4	6	8	11	14
423-McFarlane-c	11	22	33	76	163	250
426-($1.50, 52 pgs.)- "A Death In The Family" storyline begins, ends #429	4	8	12	22	35	48
427- "A Death In The Family" part 2. (Direct Sales version has inside back-c page for phone poll; newsstand version has an ad on inside back-c and UPC code on front-c)	3	6	9	19	30	40
428-Death of Robin (Jason Todd)	5	10	15	30	50	70
429-Joker-c/story; Superman app.	3	6	9	17	26	35
430-435: 433-435-Many Deaths of the Batman story by John Byrne-c/scripts	1	2	3	5	6	8
436-Year 3 begins (ends #439); origin original Robin retold by Nightwing (Dick Grayson); 1st app. Timothy Drake (8/89)	3	6	9	16	23	30
436-441: 436-2nd printing. 437-Origin Robin cont. 440,441: "A Lonely Place of Dying" Parts 1 & 3	1	2	3	5	6	8
442-1st app. Timothy Drake in Robin costume	2	4	6	11	16	20
443-456,458,459,462-464: 445-447-Batman goes to Russia. 448,449-The Penguin Affair Pts 1 & 3. 450-Origin Joker. 450,451-Joker-c/stories. 452-454-Dark Knight Dark City storyline; Riddler app. 455-Alan Grant scripts begin, ends #466, 470. 464-Last solo Batman story; free 16 pg. preview of Impact Comics line						6.00
457-Timothy Drake officially becomes Robin & dons new costume	3	6	9	16	23	30
457-Direct sale edition (has #000 in indicia)	3	6	9	17	26	35
460,461,465-487: 460,461-Two part Catwoman story. 465-Robin returns to action with Batman. 470-War of the Gods x-over. 475-1st app. Renee Montoya. 475,476-Return of Scarface. 476-Last $1.00-c. 477,478-Photo-c						6.00
488-Cont'd from Batman: Sword of Azrael #4; Azrael-c & app.	1	3	4	6	8	10
489-Bane-c/story; 1st app. Azrael in Bat-costume	2	4	6	10	14	18
490-Riddler-c/story; Azrael & Bane app.	2	4	6	8	10	12
491,492: 491-Knightfall lead-in; Joker-c/story; Azrael & Bane app.; Kelley Jones-c begin. 492-Knightfall part 1; Bane app.	1	3	4	6	8	10
492-Platinum edition (promo copy)	3	6	9	14	19	24
493-496: 493-Knightfall Pt. 3. 494-Knightfall Pt. 5; Joker-c & app. 495-Knightfall Pt. 7; brief Bane & Joker apps. 496-Knightfall Pt. 9, Joker-c/story; Bane cameo	1	2	3	5	6	8
497-(Late 7/93)-Knightfall Pt. 11; Bane breaks Batman's back; B&W outer-c; Aparo-a(p); Giordano-a(i)	3	6	9	14	19	24
497-499: 497-2nd printing. 497-Newsstand edition w/o outer cover. 498-Knightfall part 15; Bane & Catwoman-c & app. (see Showcase 93 #7 & 8) 499-Knightfall Pt. 17; Bane app.						6.00
500-($2.50, 68 pgs.)-Knightfall Pt. 19; Azrael in new Bat-costume; Bane-c/story	2	4	6	9	12	15
500-($3.95, 68 pgs.)-Collector's Edition w/die-cut double-c w/foil by Joe Quesada & 2 bound-in post cards	2	4	6	11	16	20
501-508,510,511: 501-Begin $1.50-c. 501-508-Knightquest. 503,504-Catwoman app. 507-Ballistic app.; Jim Balent-a(p). 510-KnightsEnd Pt. 7. 511-(9/94)-Zero Hour; Batgirl-c/story						5.00
509-($2.50, 52 pgs.)-KnightsEnd Pt. 1	1	2	3	5	6	8
512-514,516-518: 512-(11/94)-Dick Grayson assumes Batman role						5.00
515-Special Ed.($2.50)-Kelley Jones-a begins; all black embossed-c; Troika Pt. 1	1	3	4	6	8	10
515-Regular Edition						5.00
519-534,536-549: 519-Begin $1.95-c. 521-Return of Alfred, 522-Swamp Thing app. 525-Mr. Freeze app. 527,528-Two Face app. 529-Contagion Pt. 6. 530-532-Deadman app. 533-Legacy prelude. 534-Legacy Pt. 5. 536-Final Night x-over; Man-Bat-c/app. 540,541-Spectre-c-app. 544-546-Joker & The Demon. 548,549-Penguin-c/app.						5.00
530-532 ($2.50)-Enhanced edition; glow-in-the-dark-c.						6.00
535-(10/96, $2.95)-1st app. The Ogre						6.00
535-(10/96, $3.95)-1st app. The Ogre; variant, cardboard, foldout-c	1	2	3	5	6	8
550-($3.50)-Collector's Ed., includes 4 collector cards; intro. Chase, return of Clayface;						

Batman #291 © DC

Batman #655 © DC

Batman (2011) #39 © DC

	GD 2.0	VG 4.0	FN 6.0	VF 8.0	VF/NM 9.0	NM- 9.2
Kelley Jones-c	1	2	3	5	6	8
550-($2.95)-Standard Ed.; Williams & Gray-c						6.00
551-562: 551,552-Ragman c/app. 553-Cataclysm pt.3. 554-Cataclysm pt. 12.						5.00
563-No Man's Land; Joker-c by Campbell; Gale-s	2	4	6	8	11	14
564-566,568,569,571-574: 569-New Batgirl-c/app.						5.00
567-1st Cassandra Cain	5	10	15	30	50	70
570-Joker and Harley Quinn story	3	6	9	16	23	30
575-579: 575-New look Batman begins; McDaniel-a						5.00
580-599: 580-Begin $2.25-c. 587-Gordon shot. 591,592-Deadshot-c/app. 599-Bruce Wayne: Murderer pt. 7						5.00
600-($3.95) Bruce Wayne: Fugitive pt. 1; back-up homage stories in '50s, 60's, & 70s styles; by Aragonés, Gaudiano, Shanower and others	1	2	3	5	6	8
600-(2nd printing)						5.00
601-604, 606,607: 601,603-Bruce Wayne: Fugitive pt.3,13. 606,607-Deadshot-c/app.						5.00
605-($2.95) Conclusion to Bruce Wayne: Fugitive x-over; Noto-c						5.00
608-(12/02) Hush begins; Jim Lee-a/c & Jeph Loeb-s begin; Poison Ivy & Catwoman app.	3	6	9	14	20	25
608-2nd printing; has different cover with Batman standing on gargoyle						160.00
608-Special Edition; has different cover; 200 printed; used for promotional purposes (a CGC certified 9.2 copy sold for $700, and a CGC certified 9.8 copy sold for $2,100)						
608-Special Edition (9/09, $1.00) printing has new "After Watchmen" logo cover frame						8.00
609-Huntress app.	3	6	9	15	22	28
610,611: 610-Killer Croc-c/app.; Batman & Catwoman kiss	2	4	6	8	10	12
612-Batman vs. Superman; 1st printing with full color cover						26.00
612-2nd printing with B&W sketch cover						38.00
613-Harley Quinn & Joker-c/app.	2	4	6	10	14	18
614-Joker-c/app.	2	4	6	8	10	12
615-617: 615-Reveals ID to Catwoman. 616-Ra's al Ghul app. 617-Scarecrow app.						8.00
618-Batman vs. "Jason Todd"						6.00
619-Newsstand cover; Hush story concludes; Riddler app.						6.00
619-Two variant tri-fold covers; one Heroes group, one Villains group						6.00
619-2nd printing with Riddler chess cover						6.00
620-Broken City pt. 1; Azzarello-s/Risso-a/c begin; Killer Croc app.						6.00
621-633: 621-625-Azzarello-s/Risso-a/c. 626-630-Winick-s/Nguyen-a/Wagner-c; Penguin & Scarecrow app. 631-633-War Games. 633-Conclusion to War Games x-over						5.00
634,636,637-Winick-s/Nguyen-a/Wagner-c; Red Hood app. 637-Amazo app.						6.00
635-1st app. Red Hood (later revealed as Jason Todd in #638)	8	16	24	56	108	160
638-Red Hood unmasked as Jason Todd; Nguyen-a	2	4	6	10	14	18
639-650: 640-Superman app. 641-Begin $2.50-c. 643,644-War Crimes; Joker app. 650-Infinite Crisis; Joker and Jason Todd app.						5.00
651-654-One Year Later; Bianchi-c						6.00
655-Begin Grant Morrison-s/Andy Kubert-a; Kubert-c w/red background	4	8	12	23	37	50
655-Variant cover by Adam Kubert, brown-toned image	6	12	18	41	76	110
656-Intro. Damian, son of Talia and Batman (see Batman: Son of the Demon)	3	6	9	16	24	32
657-Damian in Robin costume	2	4	6	8	11	14
658-665: 659-662-Mandrake-a. 663-Van Fleet-a. 664-Bane app.						5.00
666-Future story of adult Damian; Andy Kubert-a	3	6	9	19	30	40
667-675: 667-669-Williams III-a. 670,671-Resurrection of Ra's al Ghul; Daniel-a. 671-2nd printing						5.00
676-Batman R.I.P. begins; Morrison-s/Daniel-a/Alex Ross-c						10.00
676-Variant-c by Tony Daniel						14.00
676-Second (red-tinted Daniel-c) & third (B&W Daniel-c) printings						4.00
677-685: Batman R.I.P.; Alex Ross-c. 678-Bat-Mite app. 681-($3.99) Batman R.I.P. conclusion. 682-685-Last Rites						5.00
677-Variant-c with Red Hood by Tony Daniel						14.00
677-Second printing with B&W&red-tinted Daniel-c						5.00
686-($3.99) Gaiman-s/Andy Kubert-a; continues in Detective #853; Kubert sketch pgs.; covers by Kubert and Ross; 2nd & 3rd printings exist						6.00
687-($3.99) Batman: Reborn begins; Dick Grayson becomes Batman; Winick-s/Benes-a						6.00
688-699: 688-691-Bagley-a. 692-697,699-Tony Daniel-s/a. 692-Catwoman app.						6.00
700-(8/10, $4.99) Morrison-s; art by Daniel, Quitely, Finch & Andy Kubert; Finch-c						16.00
700-Variant-c by Mignola						55.00
701-712: 701,702-Morrison-s; R.I.P story. 704-Batman Inc. begins; Daniel-s/a						5.00
713-(10/11) Last issue of first volume; Nicieza-s; Robin flashbacks						12.00
#0 (10/94)-Zero Hour issue released between #511 & #512; origin retold						5.00
#1,000,000 (11/98) 853rd Century x-over						5.00
Annual 1 (8-10/61)-Swan-c	61	122	183	488	1094	1700
Annual 2	27	54	81	194	435	675
Annual 3 (Summer, '62)-Joker-c/story	26	52	78	182	404	625
Annual 4,5	14	28	42	96	211	325
Annual 6 (80 pgs., 25¢)	12	24	36	84	185	285
Annual 7 (7/64, 25¢, 80 pgs.)	12	24	36	82	179	275
Annual V5#8 (1982)-Painted-c	2	4	6	8	11	14
Annual 9,10,12: 9(7/85). 10(1986). 12(1988, $1.50)	1	3	4	6	8	10
Annual 11 (1987, $1.25)-Penguin-c/story; Moore-s	2	4	6	8	11	14
Annual 13 (1989, $1.75, 68 pgs.)-Gives history of Bruce Wayne, Dick Grayson, Jason Todd, Alfred, Comm. Gordon, Barbara Gordon (Batgirl) & Vicki Vale; Morrow-i						6.00
Annual 14-17 ('90-'93, 68 pgs.)-14-Origin Two-Face. 15-Armageddon 2001 x-over; Joker app. 15 (2nd printing). 16-Joker-c/s; Kieth-c. 17 (1993, $2.50, 68 pgs.)-Azrael in Bat-costume; intro Ballistic						5.00
Annual 18 (1994, $2.95)						5.00
Annual 19 (1995, $3.95)-Year One story; retells Scarecrow's origin						5.00
Annual 20 (1996, $2.95)-Legends of the Dead Earth story; Giarrano-a						5.00
Annual 21 (1997, $3.95)-Pulp Heroes story						5.00
Annual 22,23 ('98, '99, $2.95)-22-Ghosts; Wrightson-c. 23-JLApe; Art Adams-c						5.00
Annual 24 ('00, $3.50) Planet DC; intro. The Boggart; Aparo-a						5.00
Annual 25 ('06, $4.99) Infinite Crisis-revised story of Jason Todd; unused Aparo page						12.00
Annual 26 ('07, $3.99) Origin of Ra's al Ghul; Damian app.						5.00
Annual 27 ('09, $4.99) Azrael app.; Calafiore-a; back-up story w/Kelley Jones-a						5.00
Annual 28 (2/11, $4.99) The Question, Nightrunner and Veil app.; Lau-c						5.00

NOTE: ***Art Adams*** *a-400p.* ***Neal Adams*** *c-200, 203, 210, 217, 219-222, 224-227, 229, 230, 232, 234, 236-241, 243-246, 251, 255, Annual 14.* ***Aparo*** *a-414-420, 426-435, 440-448, 450, 451, 480-483, 486-491, 494-500; c-414-416, 481, 482, 463i, 486, 487i.* ***Bolland*** *a-400; c-445-447.* ***Burnley*** *a-10, 12-18, 20, 22, 25, 27; c-9, 15, 16, 27, 28p, 40p, 42p.* ***Byrne*** *c-401, 433-435, 533-535, Annual 11.* ***Travis Charest*** *c-488-490p.* ***Colan*** *a-340p, 343-345p, 348-351p, 373p, 383p; c-343p, 345p, 350p.* ***J. Cole*** *a-238r.* ***Cowan*** *a-Annual 10p.* ***Golden*** *a-295p, 303p, 484, 485.* ***Alan Grant*** *scripts-455-466, 470, 474-476, 479, 480, Annual 16(part).* ***Grell*** *a-287, 288p, 289p, 290; c-287-290.* ***Infantino/Anderson*** *c-167, 173, 175, 181, 186, 191, 192, 194, 195, 198, 199.* ***Infantino/Giella*** *c-190.* ***Kelley Jones*** *a-513-519, 521-525, 527; c-491-499, 500(newsstand), 501-510, 513.* ***Kaluta*** *c-242, 248, 253, Annual 12.* ***G. Kane/Anderson*** *c-178-180.* ***Bob Kane*** *a-1, 2, 5; c-1-5, 7, 17.* ***G. Kane*** *a-(r)-254, 255, 259, 261, 353i.* ***Kubert*** *a-238r, 400; c-310, 319p, 327, 328, 344.* ***McFarlane*** *c-423.* ***Mignola*** *c-426-429, 452-454, Annual 18.* ***Moldoff*** *c-101-140.* ***Moldoff/Giella*** *a-164-175, 177-181, 183, 184, 186.* ***Moldoff/Greene*** *a-169, 172-174, 177-179, 181, 184.* ***Mooney*** *a-255r.* ***Morrow*** *a-Annual 13i.* ***Newton*** *a-305, 306, 328p, 331p, 332p, 337p, 338p, 346p, 352-357p, 360-372p, 374-378p; c-374p, 378p.* ***Nino*** *a-Annual 9.* ***Irv Novick*** *c-201, 202.* ***Perez*** *a-400; c-436-442.* ***Fred Ray*** *c-8, 10; w/* ***Robinson****-11.* ***Robinson/Roussos*** *a-12-17, 20, 22, 24, 25, 27, 28, 31, 33, 37.* ***Robinson*** *a-12, 14, 18, 22-32,34, 36, 37, 255r, 260r, 261r; c-6, 10, 12-14, 18, 21, 24, 26, 30, 37, 39.* ***Simonson*** *a-300p, 312p, 321p; c-300p, 312p, 366, 413i.* ***P. Smith*** *a-Annual 9.* ***Dick Sprang*** *c-19, 20, 22, 23, 25, 29, 31-36, 38, 51, 55, 66, 73, 76.* ***Starlin*** *c/a-402.* ***Staton*** *a-334.* ***Sutton*** *a-400.* ***Wrightson*** *a-265i, 400; c-320r. Bat-Hound app. in 92, 97, 103, 123, 125, 133, 156, 158. Bat-Mite app. in 133, 136, 144, 146, 158, 161. Batwoman app. in 105, 116, 122, 125, 128, 129, 131, 133, 139, 140, 141, 144, 145, 150, 151, 153, 154, 157, 159, 162, 163.* ***Zeck*** *c-417-420. Catwoman back-ups in 332, 345, 346, 348-351. Joker app. in 1, 2, 4, 5, 7-9, 11-13, 19, 20, 23, 25, 28, 32 & many more. Robin solo back-up stories in 337-339, 341-343.*

BATMAN (DC New 52)
DC Comics: Nov, 2011 - No. 52, Jul, 2016 ($2.99/$3.99)

	GD 2.0	VG 4.0	FN 6.0	VF 8.0	VF/NM 9.0	NM- 9.2
1-Snyder-s/Capullo-a/c	5	10	15	33	57	80
1-Variant-c by Van Sciver	5	10	15	30	50	70
1-2nd-5th printings	3	6	9	17	26	35
2-4	2	4	6	10	14	18
2-5-Variant covers. 2-Jim Lee. 3-Ivan Reis. 4-Mike Choi, 5-Burnham. 6-Gary Frank	2	4	6	11	16	20
5-7-Court of Owls. 7-Debut Harper Row	1	3	4	6	8	10
5-7 Combo Pack ($3.99) polybagged with digital download code	2	4	6	8	10	12
8-11: 8-Begin $3.99-c. 8,9-Night of the Owls. 11-Court of the Owls finale						6.00
12-Story of Harper Row; Cloonan-a						5.00
13-Death of the Family; Joker and Harley Quinn app.; die-cut-c	2	4	6	8	11	14
14-20: 14-17-Death of the Family. 17-Death of the Family conclusion. 18-Andy Kubert-a						5.00
21-23: 21-Zero Year begins; 1st app. Duke Thomas (unnamed)						5.00
23.1, 23.2, 23.3, 23.4 (11/13, $2.99, regular covers)						4.00
23.1 (11/13, $3.99, 3-D cover) "Joker #1" on cover; Andy Kubert-s/Andy Clarke-a						12.00
23.2 (11/13, $3.99, 3-D cover) "Riddler #1" on cover; Jeremy Haun-a						8.00
23.3 (11/13, $3.99, 3-D cover) "Penguin #1" on cover; Tieri-s/Duce-a/Fabok-c						8.00
23.4 (11/13, $3.99, 3-D cover) "Bane #1" on cover; Nolan-a/March-c						8.00
24-(12/13, $6.99) Batman vs. Red Hood at Ace Chemicals re-told; Dark City begins						10.00
24-New York Comic Con variant with Detective #27 cover swipe	3	6	9	15	22	28
25,29,33-($4.99) 25-All black cover; Doctor Death app. 33-Zero Year finale						6.00
26-28,30-32,34: 28-Nguyen-a; Harper Row as Bluebird; Stephanie Brown returns						4.00
35-($4.99) Endgame pt. 1; Justice League app.; back-up with Kelley Jones-a						5.00
36-39-Endgame; Joker app.; (back-up stories in each; 37-McCrea-a, 38-Kieth-a, 39-Nguyen) 39-Alfred attacked						4.00
40-($4.99) Endgame conclusion						5.00
41-43,45-49,51,52: 41-Gordon dons the robot suit. 49-Paquette-a. 52-Tynion-s						4.00
44-($4.99) Snyder & Azzarello-s/Jock-a						5.00
50-($5.99) Bruce Wayne back as Batman; new costume						6.00
#0 (11/12, $3.99) Flashbacks; Red Hood gang app.						5.00
Annual 1 (7/12, $4.99) Origin of Mr. Freeze; Snyder-s/Fabok-a	2	4	6	11	16	20

GD VG FN VF VF/NM NM-
2.0 4.0 6.0 8.0 9.0 9.2

Annual 2 (9/13, $4.99) Origin of the Anchoress; Jock-c 6.00
Annual 3 (2/15, $4.99) Joker app.; Tynion-s/Antonio-a/Albuquerque-c 5.00
Annual 4 (11/15, $4.99) Joker app.; Tynion-s/Antonio-a/Murphy-c 5.00
... Endgame 40 Director's Cut 1 (1/16, $5.99) Pencil art and original script for #40 6.00
...: Futures End 1 (11/14, $2.99, regular-c) Five years later; Fawkes-s; Bizarro app. 3.00
...: Futures End 1 (11/14, $3.99, 3-D cover) 4.00
... Zero Year Director's Cut (9/13, $5.99) Reprints Batman #21 original pencil art pages with word balloons; Scott Snyder's script 6.00

BATMAN (DC Rebirth)
DC Comics: Aug, 2016 - Present ($2.99/$3.99)
1-King-s/Finch-a/c; intro. Gotham and Gotham Girl 5.00
1-Director's Cut (1/17, $5.99) r/#1 in pencil-a; original script; variant cover gallery 6.00
2-20: 2-Hugo Strange app. 3-Psycho Pirate returns. 5-Justice League app. 7,8-Night of the Monster Men x-overs; Batwoman & Nightwing app. 9-13-I Am Suicide; Bane app. 3.00
21,22-The Button x-over with Flash #21,22; Eobard Thawne & Flashpoint Batman app. 3.00
23,24: 23-Swamp Thing app. 24-Batman proposes to Catwoman 3.00
25-($3.99) War of Jokes and Riddles part 1; Joker & Riddler app. 4.00
26-35,38-49: 26-32-War of Jokes and Riddles. 27-Kite Man app. 33-35,39,40,44-Joëlle Jones-a. 42-Justice League app. 45-47-Booster Gold app. 3.00
36,37-Superman & Lois app.; Clay Mann-a 3.00
50-(9/18, $4.99) The Wedding; art by Janin with pages by Adams, Miller, Kubert, Sale, Conner, Garcia-Lopez, Finch, Jim Lee, Capullo, Cloonan, Fabok and others 5.00
51-74: 51-53-Weeks-a; trial of Mr. Freeze. 54-Wagner-a. 55-Nightwing shot. 64,65-X-over with Flash #64,65; tie-in to Heroes in Crisis. 67-Weeks-a. 68-Conner-a 4.00
75-($4.99) City of Bane part 1; Gotham Girl app.; Daniel-a 5.00
76-84-City of Bane. 77-Alfred killed by Bane. 80,81-Romita Jr.-a. 82-Acetate-c 4.00
85-($4.99) City of Bane conclusion 5.00
86-88,90,91,93,94: 86-Tynion IV-s begin; Deathstroke & Cheshire app.; 1st app. the Nightclimber. 91,93-Harley Quinn app. 93,94-Joker and Punchline app. 4.00
89-1st app. Punchline in cameo; intro. The Designer 4 8 12 25 40 55
92-1st full app. Punchline in title; Joker & Harley app. 2 4 6 8 10 12
95-99-Joker War: 96-1st app. Clownhunter 4.00
100-(Early 12/20, $6.99) Conclusion to Joker War; intro. The Ghost-Maker 7.00
101-105: 101-Grifter app. 102-105-The Ghost-Maker & Clownhunter app. 4.00
106-124,126-133-($4.99) 106-Back-up Robin story. 107-109-Backup Ghost-Maker. 108-Debut of Miracle Molly. 112-117-Fear State. 118-Williamson-s begins 5.00
125-(9/22, $5.99) Zdarsky-s/Jimenez-a begins; intro Failsafe; back-up Catwoman story 6.00
Annual 1 (1/17, $4.99) Short stories by various incl. Adams, Dini, Snyder, Finch; Finch-c 5.00
Annual 2 (1/18, $4.99) King-s/Weeks & Lark-a; Batman & Catwoman's early encounters 5.00
Annual 3 (2/19, $4.99) Taylor-s/Schmidt-a; spotlight on Alfred 5.00
Annual 4 (2/20, $4.99) King-s/Fornes & Norton-a; Alfred's diary of Batman's exploits 5.00
Annual 5 (2/21, $4.99) Origin of Clownhunter; Tynion IV-s/Stokoe-a 5.00
2021 Annual 1 (1/22, $5.99) Ghost-Maker saga concludes; Tynion IV-s/Ortiz-a 6.00
2022 Annual 1 (7/22, $5.99) Ghost-Maker takes over Batman Inc.; Brisson-s/Timms-a 6.00
...: Rebirth 1 (8/16, $2.99) King & Snyder-s/Janín-a; Duke Thomas & Calendar Man app. 3.00

BATMAN (Hardcover books and trade paperbacks)
...: ABSOLUTION (2002, $24.95)-Hard-c.; DeMatteis-s/Ashmore painted-a 25.00
...: ABSOLUTION (2003, $17.95)-Soft-c.; DeMatteis-s/Ashmore painted-a 18.00
...: A LONELY PLACE OF DYING (1990, $3.95, 132 pgs.)-r/Batman #440-442 & New Titans #60,61; Perez-c 18.00
...: ANARKY TPB (1999, $12.95) r/early appearances 18.00
...AND DRACULA: RED RAIN nn (1991, $24.95)-Hard-c; Elseworlds storyline 35.00
...AND DRACULA: RED RAIN nn (1992, $9.95)-SC 16.00
...AND SON HC (2007, $24.99, dustjacket) r/Batman #655-658,663-666 25.00
...AND SON SC (2008, $14.99) r/Batman #655-658,663-666 15.00
...ANNUALS (See DC Comics Classics Library for reprints of early Annuals)
ARKHAM ASYLUM Hard-c; Morrison-s/McKean-a (1989, $24.95) 30.00
ARKHAM ASYLUM Soft-c ($14.95) 20.00
ARKHAM ASYLUM 15TH ANNIVERSARY EDITION Hard-c (2004, $29.95) reprint with Morrison's script and annotations, original page layouts; Karen Berger afterword 30.00
ARKHAM ASYLUM 15TH ANNIVERSARY EDITION Soft-c (2005, $17.99) 18.00
...: AS THE CROW FLIES-(2004, $12.95) r/#626-630; Nguyen sketch pages 13.00
BIRTH OF THE DEMON Hard-c (1992, $24.95)-Origin of Ra's al Ghul 40.00
BIRTH OF THE DEMON Soft-c (1993, $12.95) 20.00
BLIND JUSTICE nn (1992, $7.50)-r/Det. #598-600 12.00
BLOODSTORM (1994, $24.95,HC) Kelley Jones-c/a 28.00
BRIDE OF THE DEMON Hard-c (1990, $19.95) 25.00
BRIDE OF THE DEMON Soft-c ($12.95) 15.00
...: BROKEN CITY HC-(2004, $24.95) r/#620-625; new Johnson-c; intro by Schreck 25.00
...: BROKEN CITY SC-(2004, $14.99) r/#620-625; new Johnson-c; intro by Schreck 15.00
...: BRUCE WAYNE: FUGITIVE Vol. 1 ('02, $12.95)-r/ story arc 15.00
...: BRUCE WAYNE: FUGITIVE Vol. 2 ('03, $12.95)-r/ story arc 15.00
...: BRUCE WAYNE: FUGITIVE Vol. 3 ('03, $12.95)-r/ story arc 15.00
...: BRUCE WAYNE-MURDERER? ('02, $19.95)-r/ story arc 25.00
...: BRUCE WAYNE - THE ROAD HOME HC ('11, $24.99) r/Bruce Wayne: The Road Home one-shots 25.00
...: CATACLYSM ('99, $17.95)-r/ story arc 40.00
...: CHILD OF DREAMS (2003, $24.95, B&W, HC) Reprint of Japanese manga with Kia Asamiya-s/a/c; English adaptation by Max Allan Collins; Asamiya interview 25.00
...: CHILD OF DREAMS (2003, $19.95, B&W, SC) 20.00
...CHRONICLES VOL. 1 (2005, $14.99)-r/apps. in Detective Comics #27-38; Batman #1 15.00
...CHRONICLES VOL. 2 (2006, $14.99)-r/apps. in Detective Comics #39-45 and NY World's Fair 1940; Batman #2,3 15.00
...CHRONICLES VOL. 3 (2007, $14.99)-r/apps. in Detective Comics #46-50 and World's Best Comics #1; Batman #4,5 15.00
...CHRONICLES VOL. 4 (2007, $14.99)-r/apps. in Detective Comics #51-56 and World's Finest Comics #2,3; Batman #6,7 15.00
...CHRONICLES VOL. 5 (2008, $14.99)-r/apps. in Detective Comics #57-61 and World's Finest Comics #4; Batman #8,9 15.00
...CHRONICLES VOL. 6 (2008, $14.99)-r/apps. in Detective Comics #62-65 and World's Finest Comics #5,6; Batman #10,11 15.00
...CHRONICLES VOL. 7 (2009, $14.99)-r/apps. in Detective Comics #66-70 and World's Finest Comics #7; Batman #12,13 15.00
...CHRONICLES VOL. 8 (2009, $14.99)-r/apps. in Detective Comics #71-74 and World's Finest Comics #8,9; Batman #14,15 15.00
...CHRONICLES VOL. 9 (2010, $14.99)-r/apps. in Detective Comics #75-77 and World's Finest Comics #10; Batman #16,17 15.00
...CHRONICLES VOL. 10 (2010, $14.99)-r/apps. in Detective Comics #78-81 and World's Finest Comics #11; Batman #18,19 15.00
...: CITY OF CRIME (2006, $19.99) r/Detective Comics #800-808,811-814; Lapham-s 20.00
...: COLLECTED LEGENDS OF THE DARK KNIGHT nn (1994, $12.95)-r/Legends of the Dark Knight #32-34,38,42,43 18.00
...: CRIMSON MIST (1999, $24.95,HC)-Vampire Batman Elseworlds story Doug Moench-s/Kelley Jones-c/a 50.00
...: CRIMSON MIST (2001, $14.95,SC) 20.00
...: DARK JOKER-THE WILD (1993, $24.95,HC)-Elseworlds story; Moench-s/Jones-c/a 30.00
...: DARK JOKER-THE WILD (1993, $9.95,SC) 12.00
...DARK KNIGHT DYNASTY nn (1997, $24.95)-Hard-c.; 3 Elseworlds stories; Barr-s/ S. Hampton painted-a, Gary Frank, McDaniel-a(p) 28.00
...DARK KNIGHT DYNASTY Softcover (2000, $14.95) Hampton-c 15.00
...DEADMAN: DEATH AND GLORY nn (1996, $24.95)-Hard-c.; Robinson-s/ Estes-c/a 32.00
...DEADMAN: DEATH AND GLORY ($12.95)-SC 18.00
DEATH AND THE CITY (2007, $14.99, TPB)-r/Detective #827-834 15.00
DEATH BY DESIGN (2012, $24.99, HC)-Chip Kidd-s/Dave Taylor-s 25.00
DEATH IN THE FAMILY (1988, $3.95, trade paperback)-r/Batman #426-429 by Aparo 20.00
DEATH IN THE FAMILY: (2nd - 5th printings) 9.00
...: DETECTIVE (2007, $14.99, SC)-r/Detective Comics #821-826 15.00
...: DETECTIVE #27 HC (2003, $19.95)-Elseworlds; Uslan-s/Snejbjerg-a 20.00
...: DETECTIVE #27 SC (2004, $12.95)-Elseworlds; Uslan-s/Snejbjerg-a 13.00
DIGITAL JUSTICE nn (1990, $24.95, Hard-c.)-Computer generated art 25.00
... EARTH ONE HC (2012, $22.99)-Updated re-imagining of Batman's origin & debut; Geoff Johns-s/Gary Frank-a 23.00
... : EGO AND OTHER TALES HC (2007, $24.99)-r/Batman: Ego, Catwoman: Selina's Big Score, and stories from Batman Black and White and Solo; Darwyn Cooke-s/a 25.00
... : EGO AND OTHER TALES SC (2008, $17.99) same contents as HC 18.00
... :EVOLUTION (2001, $12.95, SC)-r/Detective Comics #743-750 13.00
... FACES (1995, $9.95, TPB) r/Legends of the Dark Knight #28-30 15.00
... FACES (2008, $12.99, TPB) Second printing 13.00
...: FACE THE FACE (2006, $14.99, TPB)-r/Batman #651-654, Detective #817-820 15.00
...: FALSE FACES HC (2008, $19.99)-r/Batman #588-590, Wonder Woman #160,161; Batman: Gotham City Secret Files #1 and Detective #787; Brian K. Vaughn intro. 20.00
...: FALSE FACES SC (2008, $14.99)-r/Batman #588-590, Wonder Woman #160,161; Batman: Gotham City Secret Files #1 and Detective #787; Brian K. Vaughn intro. 15.00
...: FORTUNATE SON HC (1999, $24.95) Gene Ha-a 25.00
...: FORTUNATE SON SC (2000, $14.95) Gene Ha-a 15.00
FOUR OF A KIND TPB (1998, $14.95)-r/1995 Year One Annuals featuring Poison Ivy, Riddler, Scarecrow, & Man-Bat 35.00
... GOING SANE (2008, $14.95, TPB) r/Legends of the Dark Knight #65-68,200 15.00
...: GOTHAM BY GASLIGHT (2006, $12.99, TPB) r/Gotham By Gaslight & Master of the Future one-shots; Elseworlds Batman vs. Jack the Ripper 13.00
...GOTHIC (1992, $12.95, TPB)-r/Legends of the Dark Knight #6-10 20.00
...GOTHIC (2007, $14.99, TPB)-r/Legends of the Dark Knight #6-10 15.00
...: HARVEST BREED-(2000, $24.95) George Pratt-s/painted-a 25.00
...: HARVEST BREED-(2003, $17.95) George Pratt-s/painted-a 18.00
...: HAUNTED KNIGHT-(1997, $12.95) r/ Halloween specials 18.00
...: HEART OF HUSH HC-(2009, $19.99) r/#Detective #846-850; pin-ups 20.00
...: HEART OF HUSH SC-(2010, $14.99) r/#Detective #846-850; pin-ups 15.00
...: HONG KONG HC (2003, $24.95, with dustjacket) Doug Moench-s/Tony Wong-a 25.00
...: HONG KONG SC (2004, $17.95) Doug Moench-s/Tony Wong-a 18.00
...: HUSH DOUBLE FEATURE-(2003, $3.95) r/#608,609(1st 2 Jim Lee-a issues) 6.00
...: HUSH SC-(2009, $24.99) r/#608-619; Wizard 0; variant cover gallery; Loeb intro 25.00
...: HUSH UNWRAPPED-(2011, $39.99, HC) r/#608-619's original Jim Lee pencil art 40.00
...: HUSH VOLUME 1 HC-(2003, $19.95) r/#608-612; & new 2 pg. origin w/Lee-a 20.00
...: HUSH VOLUME 1 SC-(2004, $12.95) r/#608-612; includes CD of DC GN art 13.00
...: HUSH VOLUME 2 HC-(2003, $19.95) r/#613-619; Lee intro & sketchpages 20.00
...: HUSH VOLUME 2 SC-(2004, $12.95) r/#613-619; Lee intro & sketchpages 13.00
...: ILLUSTRATED BY NEAL ADAMS VOLUME 1 HC-(2003, $49.95) r/Batman, Brave and the Bold, and Detective Comics stories and covers 50.00
...: ILLUSTRATED BY NEAL ADAMS VOLUME 2 HC-(2004, $49.95) r/Adams' Batman art from 1969-71; intro. by Dick Giordano 50.00
...: ILLUSTRATED BY NEAL ADAMS VOLUME 3 HC-(2006, $49.99) r/Adams' Batman art from 1971-74; covers, pin-ups and design art; intro. by Denny O'Neil 50.00
... IMPOSTERS TPB (2011, $14.99) r/Detective Comics #867-870 15.00
... INTERNATIONAL TPB (2010, $17.99) R/Batman: Scottish Connection, Batman in Barcelona: Dragon's Knight and Batman: Legends of the DK #52,53; Jim Lee-c 18.00
... IN THE FORTIES TPB ($19.95) Intro. by Bill Schelly 20.00
... IN THE FIFTIES TPB ($19.95) Intro. by Michael Uslan 20.00
... IN THE SIXTIES TPB ($19.95) Intro. by Adam West 20.00
... IN THE SEVENTIES TPB ($19.95) Intro. by Dennis O'Neil 20.00
... IN THE EIGHTIES TPB ($19.95) Intro. by John Wells 20.00
.../ JUDGE DREDD FILES (2004, $14.95) reprints cross-overs 15.00
... :KING TUT'S TOMB TPB (2010, $14.99) r/Batman Confidential #26-28, Batman #353 and Brave and the Bold #164,171 15.00
... LEGACY-(1996, $17.95) reprints Legacy 30.00
...: LIFE AFTER DEATH HC-(2010, $19.99, dustjacket) r/#Batman #692-699 20.00
...: LONG SHADOWS HC-(2010, $19.99, dustjacket) r/#Batman #687-691 20.00
...: LONG SHADOWS SC-(2011, $14.99) r/#Batman #687-691 15.00
...: LOVERS & MADMEN-(See Batman Confidential)
...: MAD LOVE AND OTHER STORIES HC (2009, $19.99) r/Batman Adventures: Mad Love, Batman Advs. Holiday Special and other Dini/Timm collaborations; commentary 20.00
...: THE MANY DEATHS OF THE BATMAN (1992, $3.95, 84 pgs.)-r/Batman #433-435 w/new Byrne-c 12.00
...: MONSTERS (2009, $19.99, TPB)-r/Legends of the Dark Knight #71-73,83,84,89,90 20.00
...: THE MOVIES (1997, $19.95)-r/movie adaptations of Batman, Batman Returns, Batman Forever, Batman and Robin 30.00
...: NINE LIVES HC (2002, $24.95, sideways format) Motter-s/Lark-a 25.00
...: NINE LIVES SC (2003, $17.95, sideways format) Motter-s/Lark-a 18.00
...: OFFICER DOWN (2001, $12.95)-r/Commissioner shot x-over; Talon-c 13.00
.../ PLANETARY DELUXE HC (2011, $22.99)-r/Planetary/Batman: Night on Earth; script 23.00
...: PREY (1992, $12.95)-Gulacy/Austin-a 24.00
...: PRIVATE CASEBOOK HC (2008, $19.99)-r/Detective Comics #840-845 and story from DC Infinite Halloween Special #1 20.00
...: PRODIGAL (1997, $14.95)-Gulacy/Austin-a 45.00

Batman (2016) #86 © DC

Batman: Ego and Other Tales HC © DC

Batman: Mitefall © DC

GD 2.0 VG 4.0 FN 6.0 VF 8.0 VF/NM 9.0 NM- 9.2

...: R.I.P.: THE DELUXE EDITION HC (2009, $24.99)-r/Batman #676-683 and story from DC Universe #0 25.00
...: R.I.P.: SC (2010, $14.99)-r/Batman #676-683 and story from DC Universe #0 15.00
... SCARECROW TALES (2005, $19.99, TPB) r/Scarecrow stories & pin-ups from World's Finest #3 to present 20.00
...: SECRETS OF THE BATCAVE (2007, $17.99, TPB) r/Batcave stories 18.00
SHAMAN (1993, $12.95)-r/Legends/D.K. #1-5 50.00
...: SNOW (2007, $14.99, TPB)-r/Legends of the Dark Knight #192-196; Fisher-a 15.00
...: SON OF THE DEMON Hard-c (9/87, $14.95) (see Batman #655-658) 35.00
...: SON OF THE DEMON limited signed & numbered Hard-c (1,700) 60.00
...: SON OF THE DEMON Soft-c w/new-c ($8.95) 20.00
...: SON OF THE DEMON Soft-c (1989, $9.95, 2nd printing - 5th printing) 10.00
... : STRANGE APPARITIONS ($12.95) r/'77-'78 Englehart/Rogers stories from Detective #469-479; also Simonson-a 25.00
...: TALES OF THE DEMON (1991, $17.95, 212 pgs.)-Intro by Sam Hamm; reprints by Neal Adams(3) & Golden; contains Saga of Ra's al Ghul #1 20.00
TALES OF THE MULTIVERSE: BATMAN - VAMPIRE (2007, $19.99) r/Batman & Dracula: Red Rain, Batman: Bloodstorm and Batman: Crimson Mist; Van Lustbader foreword 20.00
...: TEN NIGHTS OF THE BEAST (1994, $5.95)-r/Batman #417-420 18.00
...: TERROR (2003, $12.95, TPB)-r/Legends of the Dark Knight #137-141; Gulacy-c 13.00
...: THE BLACK GLOVE (2009, $17.99, TPB) r/Batman #667-669,672-675 18.00
...: THE CHALICE (HC, '99, $24.95) Van Fleet painted-a 25.00
...: THE CHALICE (SC, '00, $14.95) Van Fleet painted-a 15.00
...: THE GREATEST STORIES EVER TOLD (2005, $19.99, TPB) Les Daniels intro. 20.00
...: THE GREATEST STORIES EVER TOLD VOLUME TWO (2007, $19.99, TPB) 20.00
...: THE JOKER'S LAST LAUGH ('08, $17.99) r/Joker's Last Laugh series #1-6 18.00
...: THE LAST ANGEL (1994, $12.95, TPB) Lustbader-s 15.00
...: THE RESURRECTION OF RA'S AL GHUL (2008, $29.99, HC w/DJ) r/x-over 30.00
...: THE RESURRECTION OF RA'S AL GHUL (2009, $19.99, SC) r/x-over 20.00
...: THE RING, THE ARROW AND THE BAT (2003, $19.95, TPB) r/Legends of the DCU #7-9 & Batman: Legends of the Dark Knight #127-131; Green Lantern & Green Arrow app. 20.00
...: THE STRANGE DEATHS OF BATMAN ('09, $19.99) r/Batman #291-294, Det. #347, World's Finest #184,269, Brave & the Bold #115, Nightwing #52; Aparo-c 20.00
...: THE WORLD ('21, $24.99) New stories set around the world by non-American creators incl. Bermejo, Kowalski, Mauro, Valdés, Jaekwang Park, Qiu Kun 25.00
...: THE WRATH ('09, $17.99) r/Batman Special #1 and Batman Confidential #13-16 18.00
...: THRILLKILLER (1998, $12.95, TPB)-r/series & Thrillkiller '62 20.00
...: TIME AND THE BATMAN HC ('11, $19.99) r/Batman #700-703; cover gallery 20.00
...: TWO-FACE AND SCARECROW YEAR ONE (2009, $19.99, TPB)-r/Year One: Batman Scarecrow #1,2 and Two Face: Year One #1,2 20.00
...: UNDER THE COWL (2010, $17.99, TPB)-r/app. Dick Grayson, Tim Drake, Damian Wayne, Jean Paul Valley and Terry McGinnis as Batman 18.00
...: UNDER THE HOOD (2005, $9.99, TPB)-r/Batman #635-641 10.00
...: UNDER THE HOOD Vol. 2 (2006, $9.99, TPB)-r/Batman #645-650 & Annual #25 10.00
...: UNDER THE RED HOOD (2011, $29.99, TPB)-r/Batman #635-641,645-650, Ann. #25 30.00
...: VENOM (1993, $9.95, TPB)-r/Legends of the Dark Knight #16-20; embossed-c 25.00
... VS. TWO-FACE (2008, $19.99, TPB) r/initial (Det. #80) & classic battles; Bianchi-c 20.00
...: WAR CRIMES (2006, $12.99, TPB) r/x-over; James Jean-c 13.00
... WAR DRUMS (2004, $17.95) r/Detective #790-796 & Robin #126-128 18.00
...: WAR GAMES ACT 1,2,3 (2005, $14.95/$14.99, TPB) r/x-over; James Jean-c; each.. 15.00
...: WHATEVER HAPPENED TO THE CAPED CRUSADER? HC-(2009, $24.99, d.j.) r/Batman #686, Detective #853 and other Gaiman Batman stories; Gaiman intro.; Andy Kubert sketch pages; new Kubert cover 25.00
...: WHATEVER HAPPENED TO THE CAPED CRUSADER? SC-(2010, $14.99) 15.00
YEAR ONE Hard-c (1988, $12.95) r/Batman #404-407 25.00
YEAR ONE (1988, $9.95, TPB)-r/Batman #404-407 by Miller; intro by Miller 15.00
YEAR ONE (TPB, 2nd & 3rd printings) 10.00
YEAR ONE Deluxe HC (2005, $19.99, die-cut d.j.) new intro. by Miller and developmental material from Mazzucchelli; script pages and sketches 20.00
YEAR ONE (Deluxe) SC (2007, $14.99) r/story plus bonus material from 2005 HC 15.00
YEAR TWO (1990, $9.95, TPB)-r/Det. 575-578 by McFarlane; wraparound-c 15.00

BATMAN (one-shots)
... ABDUCTION, THE (1998, $5.95) 6.00
... ALLIES SECRET FILES AND ORIGINS 2005 (8/05, $4.99) stories/pin-ups by various 5.00
... & ROBIN (1997, $5.95)-Movie adaptation 8.00
...: ARKHAM ASYLUM - TALES OF MADNESS (5/98, $2.95) Cataclysm x-over pt. 16 8.00
... : BANE (1997, $4.95)-Dixon-s/Burchett-a; Stelfreeze-c; cover art interlocks w/Batman:(Batgirl, Mr. Freeze, Poison Ivy) 10.00
... : BATGIRL (1997, $4.95)-Puckett-s/Haley,Kesel-a; Stelfreeze-c; cover art interlocks w/Batman:(Bane, Mr. Freeze, Poison Ivy) 10.00
... : BATGIRL (6/98, $1.95)-Girlfrenzy; Balent-a 4.00
... : BLACKGATE (1/97, $3.95) Dixon-s 5.00
... : BLACKGATE - ISLE OF MEN (4/98, $2.95) Cataclysm x-over pt. 8; Moench-s/Aparo-a 4.00
... BOOK OF SHADOWS, THE (1999, $5.95) 6.00
BROTHERHOOD OF THE BAT (1995, $5.95)-Elseworlds-s 8.00

GD 2.0 VG 4.0 FN 6.0 VF 8.0 VF/NM 9.0 NM- 9.2

... BULLOCK'S LAW (8/99, $4.95) Dixon-s 5.00
.../CAPTAIN AMERICA (1996, $5.95, DC/Marvel) Elseworlds story; Byrne-c/s/a 12.00
...: CASTLE OF THE BAT (1994, $5.95)-Elseworlds story 6.00
... : CATWOMAN DEFIANT nn (1992, $4.95, prestige format)-Milligan scripts; cover art interlocks w/Batman: Penguin Triumphant; special foil logo 10.00
.../CATWOMAN: FOLLOW THE MONEY (1/11, $4.99) Chaykin-c/s/a 8.00
... /DANGER GIRL (2/05, $4.95)-Leinil Yu-a/c; Joker, Harley Quinn & Catwoman app. 8.00
... /DAREDEVIL (2000, $5.95)-Barreto-a 12.00
...: DARK ALLEGIANCES (1996, $5.95)-Elseworlds story, Chaykin-c/a 7.00
...: DARK KNIGHT GALLERY (1/96, $3.50)-Pin-ups by Pratt, Balent, & others 8.00
...:DAY OF JUDGMENT (11/99, $3.95) 5.00
... DAY SPECIAL EDITION 1 (10/17, giveaway) r/Batman #16 (2017) with Harley Quinn framing pages by Palmiotti & Conner-s/Blevins-a 3.00
...:DEAR DETECTIVE (2022, $7.99)-Lee Bermejo's Batman covers reprinted w/new story 8.00
...:DEATH OF INNOCENTS (12/96, $3.95)-O'Neil-s/ Staton-a(p) 8.00
.../DEMON (1996, $4.95)-Alan Grant scripts 8.00
.../DEMON: A TRAGEDY (2000, $5.95)-Grant-s/Murray painted-a 12.00
...:D.O.A. (1999, $6.95)-Bob Hall-s/a 7.00
...:/DOC SAVAGE SPECIAL (2010, $4.99)-Azzarello-s/Noto-a/covers by JG Jones & Morales; preview of First Wave line (Batman, Doc Savage, The Spirit, Blackhawks) 5.00
...:DREAMLAND (2000, $5.95)-Grant-s/Breyfogle-a 6.00
... : EGO (2000, $6.95)-Darwyn Cooke-s/a 7.00
... 80-PAGE GIANT (8/98, $4.95) Stelfreeze-c 6.00
... 80-PAGE GIANT 1 (2/10, $5.99) Andy Kubert-c; Catwoman, Poison Ivy app. 6.00
... 80-PAGE GIANT 2 (10/99, $4.95) Luck of the Draw 6.00
... 80-PAGE GIANT 3 (7/00, $5.95) Calendar Man 6.00
... 80-PAGE GIANT 2011 (2/11, $5.95) Nguyen-c; short stories of villains by various 6.00
... 80-PAGE GIANT 2011 (10/11, $5.99) Nguyen-c; art by Naifeh & others 6.00
... /ELMER FUDD SPECIAL 1 (8/17, $4.99) Tom King-s/Lee Weeks-a; cartoony back-up with Bugs Bunny; King-s/Vaughns-a 18.00
... /ELMER FUDD SPECIAL 1 (10/17, $4.99) 2nd printing; brighter red bkgd on cover 8.00
.../ FAZE CLAN 1 (5/22, $3.99) Trujillo-s/Eaton-a; real life gamer group app. 4.00
... FOREVER (1995, $5.95, direct market) 8.00
... FOREVER (1995, $3.95, newsstand) 6.00
FULL CIRCLE nn (1991, $5.95, 68 pgs.)-Sequel to Batman: Year Two 10.00
...GALLERY, The 1 (1992, $2.95)-Pin-ups by Miller, N. Adams & others 4.00
...GOLDEN STREETS OF GOTHAM (2003, $6.95) Elseworlds in early 1900s 14.00
...GOTHAM BY GASLIGHT (1989, $3.95) Elseworlds; Mignola-a/Augustyn-s 10.00
...GOTHAM CITY SECRET FILES 1 (4/00, $4.95) Batgirl app. 6.00
...: GOTHAM NOIR (2001, $6.95)-Elseworlds; Brubaker-s/Phillips-c/a 28.00
.../GREEN ARROW: THE POISON TOMORROW nn (1992, $5.95, square-bound, 68 pgs.) Netzer-c/a 8.00
... HALLOWEEN COMIC FEST SPECIAL EDITION 1 (11/17, giveaway) r/Batman #7 ('16) 3.00
...: HIDDEN TREASURES 1 (12/10, $4.99) unpubl. story Wrightson-a; r/Swamp Thing #7 5.00
HOLY TERROR nn (1991, $4.95, 52 pgs.)-Elseworlds story 6.00
.../HOUDINI: THE DEVIL'S WORKSHOP (1993, $5.95) 10.00
... :HUNTRESS/SPOILER - BLUNT TRAUMA (5/98, $2.95) Cataclysm pt. 13; Dixon-s/Barreto & Sienkiewicz-a 4.00
...: I, JOKER nn (1998, $4.95)-Elseworlds story; Bob Hall-s/a 8.00
...: IN BARCELONA: DRAGON'S KNIGHT 1 (7/09, $3.99) Waid-s/Olmos-a/Jim Lee-c 4.00
...: IN DARKEST KNIGHT nn (1994, $4.95, 52 pgs.)-Elseworlds story; Batman w/Green Lantern's ring. 10.00
...:JOKER'S APPRENTICE (5/99, $3.95) Von Eeden-a 5.00
...:JOKER'S DAUGHTER (4/14, $4.99) Bennett-s/Hetrick-a/Jeanty-c 5.00
.../ JOKER: SWITCH (2003, $6.95)-Bolton-a/Grayson-s 7.00
...:JUDGE DREDD: JUDGEMENT ON GOTHAM nn (1991, $5.95, 68 pgs.) Simon Bisley-c/a; Grant/Wagner scripts 8.00
...:JUDGE DREDD: JUDGEMENT ON GOTHAM nn (2nd printing) 6.00
...:JUDGE DREDD: THE ULTIMATE RIDDLE (1995, $4.95) 6.00
...:JUDGE DREDD: VENDETTA IN GOTHAM (1993, $5.95) 7.00
...: KNIGHTGALLERY (1995, $3.50)-Elseworlds sketchbook. 4.00
...– KNIGHTWATCH BATMAN DAY SPECIAL EDITION 1 (11/21, giveaway) Torres-s 3.00
...: LEGENDS OF GOTHAM (3/23, $5.99) Katana, Red Hood & Black Lightning app. 6.00
.../ LOBO (2000, $5.95)-Elseworlds; Joker app.; Bisley-a 6.00
...: MASK OF THE PHANTASM (1994, $2.95)-Movie adapt. 15.00
...: MASK OF THE PHANTASM (1994, $4.95)-Movie adapt. 20.00
...: MASQUE (1997, $6.95)-Elseworlds; Grell-c/s/a 7.00
...: MASTER OF THE FUTURE nn (1991, $5.95, 68 pgs.)-Elseworlds; sequel to Gotham By Gaslight; Barreto-a; embossed-c 6.00
...: MITEFALL (1995, $4.95)-Alan Grant script, Kevin O'Neill-a 6.00
... : MR. FREEZE (1997, $4.95)-Dini-s/Buckingham-a; Stelfreeze-c; cover art interlocks w/Batman:(Bane, Batgirl, Poison Ivy) 10.00
... /NIGHTWING: BLOODBORNE (2002, $5.95) Cypress-a; McKeever-c 6.00
...: NOEL (2011, $22.99, HC graphic novel with dustjacket) Lee Bermejo-s/a; Jim Lee intro.; Catwoman, Superman & The Joker app.; bonus sketch & layout art pages 23.00

GD 2.0 | VG 4.0 | FN 6.0 | VF 8.0 | VF/NM 9.0 | NM- 9.2

...: NOSFERATU (1999, $5.95) McKeever-a 15.00
...: OF ARKHAM (2000, $5.95)-Elseworlds; Grant-s/Alcatena-a 6.00
...: OUR WORLDS AT WAR (8/01, $2.95)-Jae Lee-c 3.00
...: PENGUIN TRIUMPHANT nn (1992, $4.95)-Staton-a(p); foil logo 8.00
...: PENNYWORTH R.I.P. 1 (4/20, $4.99) Short story reminiscences after Alfred's death 5.00
...•PHANTOM STRANGER nn (1997, $4.95) nn-Grant-s/Ransom-a 6.00
... : PLUS (2/97, $2.95) Arsenal-c/app. 4.00
... : POISON IVY (1997, $4.95)-J.F. Moore-s/Apthorp-a; Stelfreeze-c; cover art interlocks w/Batman:(Bane, Batgirl, Mr. Freeze) 6.00
.../POISON IVY: CAST SHADOWS (2004, $6.95) Van Fleet-c/a; Nocenti-s 7.00
.../PUNISHER: LAKE OF FIRE (1994, $4.95, DC/Marvel) 6.00
... :REIGN OF TERROR ('99, $4.95) Elseworlds 6.00
...RETURNS MOVIE SPECIAL (1992, $3.95) 4.00
...RETURNS MOVIE PRESTIGE (1992, $5.95, squarebound)-Dorman painted-c 6.00
...:RIDDLER-THE RIDDLE FACTORY (1995, $4.95)-Wagner script 6.00
...: ROOM FULL OF STRANGERS (2004, $5.95) Scott Morse-s/c/a 6.00
...: SCARECROW 3-D (12/98, $3.95) w/glasses 6.00
.../ SCARFACE: A PSYCHODRAMA (2001, $5.95)-Adlard-a/Sienkiewicz-c 6.00
...: SCAR OF THE BAT nn (1996, $4.95)-Elseworlds; Max Allan Collins script; Barreto-a 6.00
... :SCOTTISH CONNECTION (1998, $5.95) Quitely-a 6.00
... :SEDUCTION OF THE GUN nn (1992, $2.50, 68 pgs.) 5.00
.../SPAWN: WAR DEVIL nn (1994, $4.95, 52 pgs.) 1 3 4 6 8 10
... SPECIAL 1 (4/84)-Mike W. Barr story; Golden-c/a 2 4 6 11 16 20
... SPECIAL EDITION (FCBD) 1 (10/21)-Preview to Fear State storyline & I Am Batman #0 3.00
.../SPIDER-MAN (1997, $4.95) Dematteis-s/Nolan & Kesel-a 6.00
... : THE ABDUCTION ('98, $5.95) 6.00
...: THE AUDIO ADVENTURES SPECIAL (12/21, $9.99) Short stories by various; 3 covers 10.00
...: THE BLUE, THE GREY, & THE BAT (1992, $5.95)-Weiss/Lopez-a 7.00
... :THE HILL (5/00, $2.95)-Priest-s/Martinbrough-a 3.00
...: THE JOKER WAR ZONE (11/20, $5.99)-Short stories by various incl. Coipel, Stokoe 6.00
... :THE KILLING JOKE (1988, deluxe 52 pgs., mature readers)-Bolland-c/a; Alan Moore scripts; Joker cripples Barbara Gordon 5 10 15 34 60 85
...: THE KILLING JOKE (2nd thru 14th printings) 3 6 9 14 20 25
...: THE KILLING JOKE : THE DELUXE EDITION (2008, $17.99, HC) re-colored version along with Bolland-s/a from Batman Black and White #4; sketch pages; Tim Sale intro. 18.00
...: THE MAN WHO LAUGHS (2005, $6.95)-Retells 1st meeting with the Joker; Mahnke-a 7.00
...: THE OFFICIAL COMIC ADAPTATION OF THE WARNER BROS. MOTION PICTURE (1989, $2.50, regular format, 68 pgs.)-Ordway-c 2 4 6 9 12 15
...: THE OFFICIAL COMIC ADAPTATION OF THE WARNER BROS. MOTION PICTURE (1989, $4.95, prestige format, 68 pgs.)-same interiors but different-c 2 4 6 9 12 15
...: THE ORDER OF BEASTS (2004, $5.95)-Elseworlds; Eddie Campbell-a 6.00
...: THE SMILE KILLER (8/20, $5.99)-Epilogue to Joker: Killer Smile series; Sorrentino-a 6.00
...: THE SPIRIT (1/07, $4.99)-Loeb-s/Cooke-a; P'Gell & Commissioner Dolan app. 5.00
...: THE 10-CENT ADVENTURE (3/02, 10¢) intro. to the "Bruce Wayne: Murderer" x-over; Rucka-s/Burchett & Janson-a/Dave Johnson-c 3.00

NOTE: (Also see Promotional Comics section for alternate copies with special outer half-covers promoting local comic shops)

...: THE 12-CENT ADVENTURE (10/04, 12¢) intro. to the "War Games" x-over; Grayson-s/Bachs-a; Catwoman & Spoiler app. 3.00
...: THE WORLD BATMAN DAY SPECIAL EDITION 1 (11/21, giveaway) r/from GN 3.00
...: TWO-FACE-CRIME AND PUNISHMENT-(1995, $4.95)-McDaniel-a 6.00
... : TWO FACES (11/98, $4.95) Elseworlds 6.00
...Vs. THE INCREDIBLE HULK (1995, $3.95)-r/DC Special Series #27 20.00
...: VILLAINS SECRET FILES (10/98, $4.95) Origin-s 8.00
... VILLAINS SECRET FILES AND ORIGINS 2005 (7/05, $4.99) Clayface origin w/ Mignola-a; Black Mask story, pin-up of villains by various; Barrionuevo-c 6.00

BATMAN ADVENTURES, THE (Based on animated series)(See DC Classics for reprints)
DC Comics: Oct, 1992 - No. 36, Oct, 1995 ($1.25/$1.50)

1-Penguin-c/story 3 6 9 16 24 32
1 ($1.95, Silver Edition)-2nd printing 4.00
2,4-6,8-11,13-15,17-19: 2-Catwoman-c/story. 5-Scarecrow-c/story. 10-Riddler-c/story. 11-Man-Bat-c/story. 18-Batgirl-c/story. 19-Scarecrow-c/story 5.00
3-Joker-c/story 2 4 6 11 16 20
7-Special edition polybagged with Man-Bat trading card 1 3 4 6 8 10
12-(9/93) 1st Harley Quinn app. in comics; 1st animated-version Batgirl app. in title 75 150 225 340 533 725
16-Joker-c/story; begin $1.50-c 3 6 9 17 26 35
20-24,26,27,29-32: 26-Batgirl app. 5.00
25-($2.50, 52 pgs.)-Superman app. 2 4 6 9 13 16
28-Joker & Harley Quinn-c; 2nd app. Harley Quinn 3 6 9 17 26 35
33-36: 33-Begin $1.75-c 5.00
Annual 1 ('94) 3rd app. Harley Quinn 3 6 9 21 33 45
Annual 2 ('95) Demon-c/story; Ra's al Ghul app. 6.00
...: Dangerous Dames & Demons (2003, $14.95, TPB) r/Annual 1,2, Mad Love & Adventures in the DC Universe #3; Bruce Timm painted-c 30.00
Holiday Special 1 (1995, $2.95) Harley Quinn app. 5 10 15 34 60 85
The Collected Adventures Vol. 1,2 ('93, '95, $5.95) 15.00
TPB ('98, $7.95) r/#1-6; painted wraparound-c 10.00

BATMAN ADVENTURES (Based on animated series)
DC Comics: Jun, 2003 - No. 17, Oct, 2004 ($2.25)

1-Timm-c 3 6 9 14 19 24
1-Free Comic Book Day edition (6/03) Timm-c 4.00
1-Halloween Fest Special Edition (12/15) Timm-c 4.00
2,4-9,11-15,17: 4-Ra's al Ghul app. 6-8-Phantasm app. 14-Grey Ghost app. 4.00
3-Joker & Harley Quinn-c/app. 3 6 9 19 30 40
10-Catwoman-c/app. 3 6 9 16 24 32
16-Joker & Harley Quinn-c/app. 5 10 15 34 60 85
Batman/Scooby-Doo Halloween Fest 1 (12/12, giveaway flipbook with Scooby-Doo) r/#1 1 3 4 6 8 10
Vol. 1: Rogues Gallery (2004, $6.95, digest size) r/#1-4 & Batman: Gotham Advs. #50 7.00
Vol. 2: Shadows & Masks (2004, $6.95, digest size) r/#5-9 7.00

BATMAN ADVENTURES, THE: MAD LOVE
DC Comics: Feb, 1994 ($3.95/$4.95)

1-Origin of Harley Quinn; Dini-s/Timm-c/a 6 12 18 38 69 100
1-($4.95, Prestige format) new Timm painted-c 6 12 18 41 72 110

BATMAN ADVENTURES, THE: THE LOST YEARS (TV)
DC Comics: Jan, 1998 - No. 5, May, 1998 ($1.95) (Based on animated series)

1-Leads into Fall '97's new animated episodes 2 4 6 8 10 12
2-5: 4-Tim Drake becomes Robin. 5-Dick becomes Nightwing 1 2 3 5 6 8
TPB-(1999, $9.95) r/series 35.00

BATMAN/ALIENS
DC Comics/Dark Horse: Mar, 1997 - No. 2, Apr, 1997 ($4.95, limited series)

1,2: Wrightson-c/a. 1 3 4 6 8 10
TPB-(1997, $14.95) w/prequel from DHP #101,102 30.00

BATMAN/ALIENS II
DC Comics/Dark Horse: 2003 - No. 3, 2003 ($5.95, limited series)

1-3-Edginton-s/Staz Johnson-a 1 3 4 6 8 10
TPB-(2003, $14.95) r/#1-3 20.00

BATMAN AND... (See Batman and Robin [2011 series] #19-on)

BATMAN AND ROBIN (See Batman R.I.P. and Batman: Battle For The Cowl series)
DC Comics: Aug, 2009 - No. 26, Oct, 2011 ($2.99)

1-Grant Morrison-s/Frank Quitely-a/c; Dick Grayson & Damian Wayne team 8.00
1-Variant cover by J.G. Jones 20.00
1-Second thru Fourth printings - recolored Quitely covers 3.00
2-16-Quitely-c. 2-Three printings. 4-6-Tan-a. 7-9-Stewart-a; Batwoman & Squire app. 13-15-Joker app.; Irving-a. 16-Bruce Wayne returns; Batman Inc. announced 3.00
2-Variant-c by Adam Kubert 10.00
17-26: 17-McDaniel-a/March-c. 21,22-Gleason-a. 23-25-Red Hood app. 3.00
... #1 Special Edition (6/10, $1.00) r/#1 with "What's Next?" cover logo 3.00
...: Batman and Robin Must Die - The Deluxe Edition HC (2011, $24.99) r/#13-16; cover and costume design sketch art 25.00
...: Batman Reborn - The Deluxe Edition HC (2010, $24.99) r/#1-6; design sketch art 25.00
...: Batman Reborn SC (2011, $14.99) r/#1-6; cover and character design sketch art 15.00
...: Batman vs. Robin - The Deluxe Edition HC (2010, $24.99) r/#7-12; cover sketch art 25.00

BATMAN AND ROBIN (DC New 52)(Cover title changes each issue from #19-32)
DC Comics: Nov, 2011 - No. 40, May, 2015 ($2.99)

1-Bruce and Damian Wayne in costume; Tomasi-s/Gleason-a 4.00
2-14: 5,6-Ducard flashback. 9-Night of the Owls 3.00
15-Death of the Family tie-in; die-cut Joker cover 5.00
16-18: 16-Death of the Family tie-in. 18-Requiem 3.00
19-23: 19-Red Robin. 20-Red Hood. 21-Batgirl. 22-Catwoman. 23-Nightwing 3.00
23.1, 23.2, 23.3, 23.4 (11/13, $2.99, regular covers) 3.00
23.1 (11/13, $3.99, 3-D cover) "Two Face #1" on cover; March-a; Scarecrow app. 6.00
23.2 (11/13, $3.99, 3-D cover) "Court of Owls #1" on cover; history of the Owls 5.00
23.3 (11/13, $3.99, 3-D cover) "Ra's al Ghul #1" on cover; history of Ra's retold 5.00
23.4 (11/13, $3.99, 3-D cover) "Killer Croc #1" on cover; Croc's origin 5.00
24-40: 24-28-Two-Face. 25-Matches Malone app. 29-Aquaman. 30-Wonder Woman. 31-Frankenstein. 32-Ra's al Ghul. 33-38-Title back to Batman and Robin. 37-Darkseid app.; Damian returns; cont'd in Robin Rises: Alpha. 39,40-Justice League app. 3.00
#0 (11/12, $2.99) Damian's childhood training with Talia; Tomasi-s/Gleason-a 3.00
Annual 1 (3/13, $4.99) Damian in the Batman #666 costume; Andy Kubert-c 5.00
Annual 2 (3/14, $4.99) Mahnke-a; flashback to Dick Grayson's first week as Robin 5.00
Annual 3 (6/15, $4.99) Ryp-a/Syaf-c 5.00
...: Futures End 1 (11/14, $2.99, regular-c) Five years later; Nguyen-a; 1st app. Duke Thomas as future Robin 3.00
...: Futures End 1 (11/14, $3.99, 3-D cover) 4.00

BATMAN AND ROBIN ADVENTURES (TV)
DC Comics: Nov, 1995 - No. 25, Dec, 1997 ($1.75) (Based on animated series)

1-Dini-s 2 4 6 10 14 18
2-4,6,7,9-15,17,19,20,22,23: 2-4-Dini script. 4-Penguin-c/app. 9-Batgirl & Talia-c/app. 10-Ra's al Ghul-c/app. 11-Man-Bat app. 12-Bane-c/app. 13-Scarecrow-c/app. 15 Deadman-c/app. 5.00
5-Joker-c/story 1 3 4 6 8 10
8-Poison Ivy & Harley Quinn-c/app. 3 6 9 14 20 25
16,24: 16-Catwoman-c/app. 24-Poison Ivy app. 2 4 6 8 11 14
18-Joker-c/app. 3 6 9 15 22 28
21-Batgirl-c 3 6 9 21 33 45
25-($2.95, 48 pgs.) 1 2 3 5 6 8
Annual 1 (11/96) Phantasm-c/app. 3 6 9 19 30 40
Annual 2 (11/97) Zatara & Zatanna-c/app. 2 4 6 8 10 12
...: Sub-Zero(1998, $3.95) Adaptation of animated video 2 4 6 9 12 15

BATMAN & ROBIN ETERNAL (Sequel to Batman Eternal)
DC Comics: Dec, 2015 - No. 26, May, 2016 ($3.99/$2.99, weekly series)

1-($3.99) Tynion IV & Snyder-s/Daniel-a; Cassandra Cain app. 4.00
2-25-($2.99) Dick Grayson, Red Hood, Red Robin, Bluebird, Spoiler app. 6-1st app. Mother. 9,10,15,16,24,25-Azrael app. 23-25-Midnighter app. 3.00
26-($3.99) Conclusion; Tony Daniel-c 4.00

BATMAN & SCOOBY-DOO MYSTERIES, THE
DC Comics: Jun, 2021 - No. 12, May, 2022 ($2.99, limited series)

1-12: 4-Black Mask app. 8-Joker & Harley app. 10-The Question (Renee) app. 3.00

BATMAN & SCOOBY-DOO MYSTERIES, THE
DC Comics: Dec, 2022 - No. 12 ($2.99, limited series)

1-6: 1-Batmen of All Nations app. 2-Poison Ivy app. 5-Batwoman app. 3.00

BATMAN AND SUPERMAN ADVENTURES: WORLD'S FINEST
DC Comics: 1997 ($6.95, square-bound, one-shot) (Based on animated series)

1-Adaptation of animated crossover episode; Dini-s/Timm-c; Harley Quinn on cover 3 6 9 14 20 25

BATMAN AND SUPERMAN: WORLD'S FINEST
DC Comics: Apr, 1999 - No. 10, Jan, 2000 ($4.95/$1.99, limited series)

1-($4.95, squarebound) Taylor-a 1 3 4 6 8 10

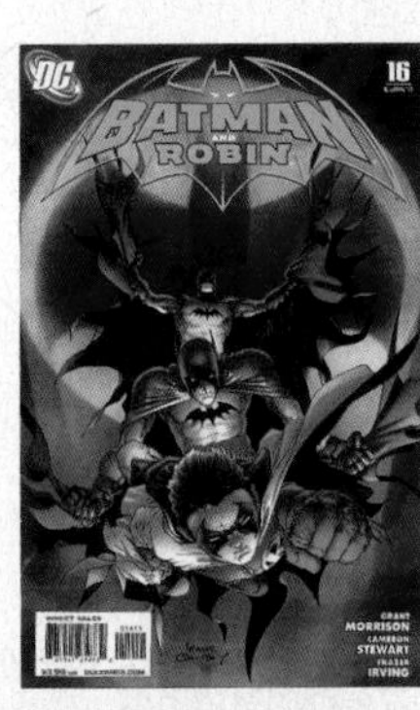

Batman and Robin #16 © DC

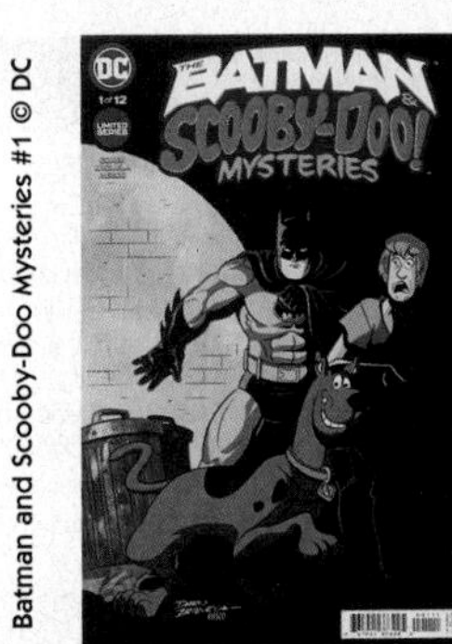

Batman and Scooby-Doo Mysteries #1 © DC

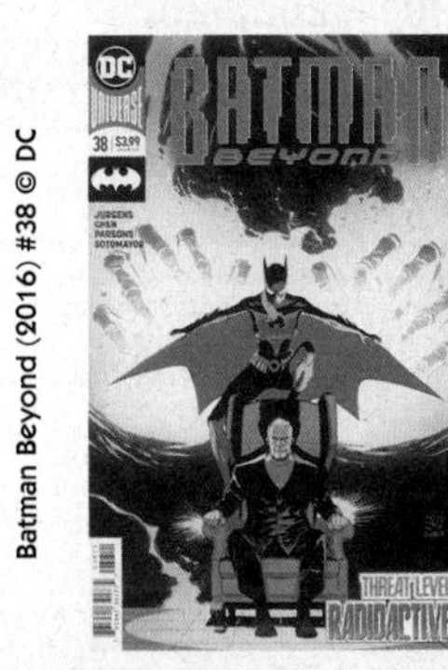

Batman Beyond (2016) #38 © DC

	GD 2.0	VG 4.0	FN 6.0	VF 8.0	VF/NM 9.0	NM- 9.2

2-9-($1.99) 5-Batgirl app. 8-Catwoman-c/app. 4.00
10-($4.95, squarebound) Taylor-a 6.00
TPB (2003, $19.95) r/#1-10 20.00

BATMAN & THE JOKER: THE DEADLY DUO
DC Comics: Jan, 2023 - Present ($4.99, limited series)

1-5-Marc Silvestri-s/a; Harley Quinn app. 5.00

BATMAN AND THE OUTSIDERS (The Adventures of the Outsiders #33 on)
(Also see Brave & The Bold #200 & The Outsiders) (Replaces The Brave and the Bold)
DC Comics: Aug, 1983 - No. 32, Apr, 1986 (Mando paper #5 on)

1-Batman, Halo, Geo-Force, Katana, Metamorpho & Black Lightning begin 3 6 9 14 19 24
2-32: 5-New Teen Titans x-over. 9-Halo begins. 11,12-Origin Katana. 18-More info on Metamorpho's origin. 28-31-Lookers origin. 32-Team disbands 4.00
Annual 1,2 (9/84, 9/85): 2-Metamorpho & Sapphire Stagg wed 5.00
NOTE: ***Aparo*** *a-1-9, 11-13p, 16-20; c-1-4, 5i, 6-21, Annual 1, 2.* ***B. Kane*** *a-3r.* ***Layton*** *a-19i, 20i.* ***Lopez*** *a-3p.* ***Miller*** *c-Annual 1.* ***Perez*** *c-5p.* ***B. Willingham*** *a-14p.*

BATMAN AND THE OUTSIDERS (Continues as The Outsiders for #15-39)
DC Comics: Dec, 2007 - No. 14, Feb, 2009; No. 40, Jul, 2011 ($2.99)

1-14: 1-Batman, Catwoman, Martian Manhunter, Katana, Metamorpho, Thunder & Grace begin. 4-Batgirl joins. 11-13-Batman R.I.P. 3.00
40 (7/11) Final issue; Didio-s/Tan-a; history of the team 3.00
... Special (3/09, $3.99) Alfred assembles a new team; Andy Kubert-a; two covers 4.00
...: The Chrysalis TPB (2008, $14.99) r/#1-5 15.00
...: The Snare TPB (2008, $14.99) r/#6-10 15.00

BATMAN & THE OUTSIDERS
DC Comics: Jul, 2019 - No. 17, Dec, 2020 ($3.99)

1-17: 1-Batman, Black Lightning, Katana, The Signal and Orphan team; Hill-s/Soy-a 4.00
Annual 1 (12/19, $4.99) Max Raynor-a; spotlight on Katana 5.00

BATMAN & THE SIGNAL
DC Comics: Mar, 2018 - No. 3, Jun, 2018 ($3.99)

1-3-Batman and Duke Thomas; Hamner-a 4.00

BATMAN: ARKHAM CITY (Prequel to the video game)
DC Comics: Early Jul, 2011 - No. 5, Oct, 2011 ($2.99, limited series)

1-5-Dini-s/D'Anda-a; Joker app. 3.00
...: End Game (1/13, $6.99) Story bridges Arkham City and Arkham Unhinged series 7.00

BATMAN: ARKHAM KNIGHT (Prequel to the Arkham video game trilogy finale)
DC Comics: May, 2015 - No. 12, Feb, 2016 ($3.99)

1-Tomasi-s/Bogdanovic-a/Panosian-c; 1st comic app. of Arkham Knight 6.00
2-12: 2-Harley Quinn cover 4.00
Annual 1 (11/15, $4.99) Tomasi-s/Segovia-a; Firefly app. 5.00
...: Robin 1 (1/16, $2.99) Tomasi-s/Rocha-a 3.00

BATMAN: ARKHAM KNIGHT: GENESIS
DC Comics: Oct, 2015 - No. 6 ($2.99, limited series)

1-4: 1-Tomasi-s/Borges-a/Sejic-c; Jason Todd's origin. 4-Harley Quinn cover 3.00

BATMAN: ARKHAM UNHINGED (Based on the Batman: Arkham City video game)
DC Comics: Jun, 2012 - No. 20, Jan, 2014 ($2.99)

1-20: 1-Wilkins-c; Catwoman, Two-Face & Hugo Strange app. 3.00

BATMAN: BANE OF THE DEMON
DC Comics: Mar, 1998 - No. 4, June, 1998 ($1.95, limited series)

1-4-Dixon-s/Nolan-a; prelude to Legacy x-over 5.00

BATMAN: BATTLE FOR THE COWL (Follows Batman R.I.P. storyline)
DC Comics: May, 2009 - No. 3, Jul, 2009 ($3.99, limited series)

1-3-Tony Daniel-s/a/c; 2 covers on each 4.00
...: Arkham Asylum (6/09, $2.99) Hine-s/Haun-a/Ladronn-c 3.00
...: Commissioner Gordon (5/09, $2.99) Mandrake-a/Ladronn-c; Mr. Freeze app. 3.00
...: Man-Bat (6/09, $2.99) Harris-s/Calafiore-a/Ladronn-c; Dr. Phosphorus app. 3.00
...: The Network (7/09, $2.99) Nicieza-s/Calafiore & Kramer-a/Ladronn-c 3.00
...: The Underground (6/09, $2.99) Yost-s/Raimondi-a/Ladronn-c; Harley Quinn app. 3.00
Companion SC (2009, $14.99) r/ five one-shots 15.00
HC (2009, $19.99) r/#1-3 & Gotham Gazette: Batman Dead & Gotham Gazette: Batman Alive; gallery of variant covers and sketch art 20.00
SC (2010, $14.99) same contents as HC 15.00

BATMAN BEYOND (Based on animated series)
DC Comics: Mar, 1999 - No. 6, Aug, 1999 ($1.99, limited series)

1-Adaptation of pilot episode, Timm-c 16 32 48 107 236 365
2-Adaptation of pilot episode cont., Timm-c 5 10 15 30 50 70
3 4 8 12 23 37 50
4,5: 4-Darwyn Cooke-c; The Demon app. 2 4 6 9 13 16
6-1st app. Inque 4 8 12 28 47 65
TPB (1999, $9.95) r/#1-6 15.00

BATMAN BEYOND (Based on animated series)(Continuing series)
DC Comics: Nov, 1999 - No. 24, Oct, 2001 ($1.99)

1-Rousseau-a; Batman vs. Batman 3 6 9 14 20 25
2 2 4 6 9 12 15
3,5-24: 14-Demon-c/app. 21,22-Justice League Unlimited-c/app. 6.00
4-1st app. Melanie Walker/Ten (Royal Flush Gang) 4 8 12 25 40 55
...: Return of the Joker (2/01, $2.95) adaptation of video release 4 8 12 25 40 55

BATMAN BEYOND (Animated series)(See Superman/Batman Annual #4)
DC Comics: Aug, 2010 - No. 6, Jan, 2011 ($2.99, limited series)

1-Benjamin-a; Nguyen-c; return of Hush 2 4 6 9 12 15
1-Variant-c by J.H. Williams III 2 4 6 11 16 20
2-6 4.00
...: Hush Beyond TPB (2011, $14.99) r/#1-6 15.00

BATMAN BEYOND
DC Comics: Mar, 2011 - No. 8, Oct, 2011 ($2.99)

1-8: 1-3-Justice League app.; Beechen-s/Benjamin-a/Nguyen-c. 8-Inque app. 4.00
1-Variant-c by Darwyn Cooke 5.00

BATMAN BEYOND (Tim Drake as Batman)
DC Comics: Aug, 2015 - No. 16, Nov. 2016 ($2.99)

1-16: 1-Jurgens-s/Chang-a. 2-Inque app. 5-New suit. 7,16-Stephen Thompson-a. 10-Tuftan app. 11-Superman's son app. 12-Tan-a. 16-Terry McGinnis back as Batman 3.00

BATMAN BEYOND (DC Rebirth)
DC Comics: Dec, 2016 - No. 50, Feb, 2021 ($2.99/$3.99)

1-6: 1-3,6-Dan Jurgens-s/Bernard Chang-a. 4,5-Pete Woods-a 3.00
7-24,26-50-($3.99) 8-11,44-47-Damian app. 22-24-New Scarecrow. 26-30-Joker app. 36-Flash app. 37-Intro. new Batwoman. 40-Batwoman ID revealed; Dick Grayson app. 48,49-Booster Gold app. 50-Wonder Woman & Inque app. 4.00
25-($4.99) Jurgens-s/Hamner-a; Joker app. 5.00
...: Rebirth 1 (11/16, $2.99) Terry McGinnis in the suit; Jurgens-s/Sook-a 3.00

BATMAN BEYOND: NEO-YEAR
DC Comics: Jun, 2022 - No. 6, Nov, 2022 ($3.99, limited series)

1-6-Kelly & Lanzing-s/Dunbar-a; The Sword of Gotham app. 4.00

BATMAN: BEYOND THE WHITE KNIGHT
DC Comics: May, 2022 - No. 8, Apr, 2023 ($4.99, limited series)

1-8-Sean Murphy-s/a; intro Terry McGinnis with the Batman Beyond suit 5.00
1-Second printing (7/22) Variant-c with Terry McGinnis in the Batman Beyond suit 5.00
... Showcase Edition (7/22, $5.99) Reprints #1 & 2 6.00

BATMAN BEYOND UNIVERSE
DC Comics: Oct, 2013 - No. 16, Jan, 2015 ($3.99)

1-12: 1-Superman & the JLB app.; Sean Murphy-c. 8-12-Wonder Woman app. 9-12-Justice Lords app. 13,14-Phantasm returns. 15-Royal Flush Gang app. 4.00

BATMAN BEYOND UNLIMITED
DC Comics: Apr, 2012 - No. 18, Sept, 2013 ($3.99)

1-18: 1-Beechen-s/Breyfogle-a; Superman & Justice League back-ups; Nguyen-c. 17-Metal Men return; Marvel Family app. 18-New Batgirl 4.00

BATMAN: BLACK & WHITE
DC Comics: June, 1996 - No. 4, Sept, 1996 ($2.95, B&W, limited series)

1-Stories by McKeever, Timm, Kubert, Chaykin, Goodwin; Jim Lee-c; Allred inside front-c; Moebius inside back-c 1 3 4 6 8 10
2-4: 2-Stories by Simonson, Corben, Bisley & Gaiman; Miller-c. 3-Stories by M. Wagner, Janson, Sienkiewicz, O'Neil & Kristiansen; B. Smith-c; Russell inside front-c; Silvestri inside back-c. 4-Stories by Bolland, Goodwin & Gianni, Strnad & Nowlan, O'Neil & Stelfreeze; Toth-c; pin-ups by Neal Adams & Alex Ross 4.00
Hardcover ('97, $39.95) r/series w/new art & cover plate 40.00
Softcover ('00, $19.95) r/series 20.00
Volume 2 HC ('02, $39.95, 7 3/4"x12") r/B&W back-up-s from Batman: Gotham Knights #1-16; stories and art by various incl. Ross, Buscema, Byrne, Ellison, Sale; Mignola-c 40.00
Volume 2 SC ('03, $19.95, 7 3/4"x12") same contents as HC 20.00
Volume 2 SC ('08, $19.99, reg. size) same contents as HC 20.00
Volume 3 HC ('07, $24.99, reg. size) r/B&W back-up-s from Batman: Gotham Knights #17-49; stories and art by various incl. Davis, DeCarlo, Morse, Schwartz, Thompson; Miller-c 25.00

BATMAN: BLACK & WHITE
DC Comics: Nov, 2013 - No. 6, Apr, 2014 ($4.99, B&W, limited series)

1-6-Short story anthology by various. 1-Silvestri-c; Neal Adams-a. 2-Steranko-c; Nino-a.

3-Bermejo-s/a. 4-Conner-c; Allred-s/a. 6-Mahnke-c; Hughes, Cloonan, Chiang-a 5.00

BATMAN: BLACK & WHITE

DC Comics: Jan, 2021 - No. 6, Jul, 2021 ($5.99, B&W, limited series)

1-6-Short story anthology by various. 1-Dini-s/Kubert-a; JH Williams III-s/a. 2-King-s/Gerads-a. 3-Future State Batman by Ridley-s/Coipel-a; Bengal-s/a. 6-Snyder-s/Romita Jr.-a 6.00

BATMAN: BOOK OF THE DEAD

DC Comics: Jun, 1999 - No. 2, July, 1999 ($4.95, limited series, prestige format)

1,2-Elseworlds; Kitson-a 8.00

BATMAN CACOPHONY

DC Comics: Jan, 2009 - No. 3, Mar, 2009 ($3.99, limited series)

1-3-Kevin Smith-s/Walt Flanagan-a; Joker and Onomatoapoeia app.; Adam Kubert-c 4.00

1-3-Variant-c by Sienkiewicz 15.00

HC (2009, $19.99, d.j.) r/#1-3; Kevin Smith intro.; script for #3, cover gallery 20.00

SC (2010, $14.99) r/#1-3; Kevin Smith intro.; script for #3, cover gallery 15.00

BATMAN / CATWOMAN

DC Comics (Black Label): Feb, 2021 - Present ($4.99)

1-12: 1-King-s/Mann-a; Andrea Beaumont and The Joker app. 3-Intro. Helena Wayne. 5-Harley Quinn app. 7-9-Liam Sharp-a 5.00

... Special 1 (3/22, $9.99) Tom King-s/John Paul Leon & others-a; tributes to J.P. Leon 10.00

BATMAN: CATWOMAN DEFIANT (See Batman one-shots)

BATMAN/ CATWOMAN: TRAIL OF THE GUN

DC Comics: 2004 - No. 2, 2004 ($5.95, limited series, prestige format)

1,2-Elseworlds; Van Sciver-a/Nocenti-s 8.00

BATMAN CHRONICLES, THE (See the Batman TPB listings for the Golden Age reprint series that shares this title)

DC Comics: Summer, 1995 - No. 23, Winter, 2001 ($2.95, quarterly)

1-3,5-19: 1-Dixon/Grant/Moench script. 3-Bolland-c. 5-Oracle Year One story, Richard Dragon app., Chaykin-c. 6-Kaluta-c; Ra's al Ghul story. 7-Superman-c/app.11-Paul Pope-s/a. 12-Cataclysm pt. 10. 18-No Man's Land 5.00

4-Hitman story by Ennis, Contagion tie-in; Balent-c 2 4 6 9 12 15

20,22,23: 20-Catwoman and Relative Heroes-c/app. 4.00

21-Brian Michael Bendis-s (1st for DC)/Gaydos-a; Giordano-a; Pander Bros.-a/c 6.00

...Gallery (3/97, $3.50) Pin-ups 4.00

...Gauntlet, The (1997, $4.95, one-shot) 6.00

BATMAN: CITY OF LIGHT

DC Comics: Dec, 2003 - No. 8, July, 2004 ($2.95, limited series)

1-8-Pander Brothers-a/s; Paniccia-s 3.00

BATMAN CONFIDENTIAL

DC Comics: Feb, 2007 - No. 54, May, 2011 ($2.99)

1-49,51-54: 1-6-Diggle-s/Portacio-a/c. 7-12-Cowan-a; Joker's origin. 13-16-Morales-a. 17-21-Batgirl vs. Catwoman; Maguire-a. 22-25-McDaniel-a; Joker app. 26-28-King Tut app.; Garcia-Lopez-a. 40-43-Kieth-s/a. 44-48-Mandrake-a/c 3.00

50-($4.99) Bingham-a; back-up Silver Age-style JLA story 5.00

...: Dead to Rights SC (2010, $14.99) r/#22-25,29,30 15.00

...: Lovers and Madmen HC (2008, $24.99, dustjacket) r/#7-12; Brad Meltzer intro. 25.00

...: Lovers and Madmen SC (2009, $14.99) r/#7-12; Brad Meltzer intro. 15.00

...: Rules of Engagement HC (2007, $24.99, dustjacket) r/#1-6 25.00

...: The Bat and the Beast SC (2010, $12.99) r/#31-35 13.00

...: The Cat and the Bat SC (2009, $12.99) r/#17-21 13.00

...: Vs. The Undead SC (2010, $14.99) r/#44-48 15.00

BATMAN: CREATURE OF THE NIGHT

DC Comics: Jan, 2018 - No. 4, Jan, 2020 ($5.99, squarebound, limited series)

1-4-Kurt Busiek-s/John Paul Leon-a; story of Bruce Wainwright 6.00

BATMAN: CURSE OF THE WHITE KNIGHT (Sequel to Batman: White Knight series)

DC Comics (Black Label): Sept, 2019 - No. 8, May, 2020 ($4.99, limited series)

1-8-Sean Murphy-s/a; flashbacks to 1685 Edmond Wayne in Gotham; Azrael returns 6.00

BATMAN: DAMNED

DC Comics (Black Label): Nov, 2018 - No. 3, Aug, 2019 ($6.99, squarebound, oversized, limited series)

1-Azzarello-s/Bermejo-a/c; Constantine & Deadman app.; nudity
3 6 9 19 30 40

1-Variant cover by Jim Lee 4 8 12 23 37 50

2,3-Harley Quinn, Constantine & Deadman app.; covers by Bermejo & Lee
1 3 4 6 8 10

BATMAN: DARK DETECTIVE

DC Comics: Early July, 2005 - No. 6, Late September, 2005 ($2.99, limited series)

1-Englehart-s/Rogers & Austin-a; Silver St. Cloud and The Joker app.; Joker-c
1 3 4 6 8 10

2-6 4.00

BATMAN: DARK KNIGHT OF THE ROUND TABLE

DC Comics: 1999 - No. 2, 1999 ($4.95, limited series, prestige format)

1,2-Elseworlds; Giordano-a 7.00

BATMAN: DARK VICTORY

DC Comics: 1999 - No. 13, 2000 ($4.95/$2.95, limited series)

Wizard #0 Preview 4.00

1-($4.95) Loeb-s/Sale-c/a 6.00

2-12-($2.95) 3.00

13-($4.95) 5.00

Hardcover (2001, $29.95) with dust jacket; r/#0,1-13 30.00

Softcover (2002, $19.95) r/#0,1-13 20.00

BATMAN: DEATH AND THE MAIDENS

DC Comics: Oct, 2003 - No. 9, Aug, 2004 ($2.95, limited series)

1-Ra's al Ghul app.; Rucka-s/Janson-a 4.00

2-9: 9-Ra's al Ghul dies 3.00

TPB (2004, $19.95) r/#1-9 & Detective #783 20.00

BATMAN/ DEATHBLOW: AFTER THE FIRE

DC Comics/WildStorm: 2002 - No. 3, 2002 ($5.95, limited series)

1-3-Azzarello-s/Bermejo & Bradstreet-a 6.00

TPB (2003, $12.95) r/#1-3; plus concept art 13.00

BATMAN: DEATH MASK

DC Comics/CMX: Jun, 2008 - No. 4, Sept, 2008 ($2.99, B&W, lim. series, right-to-left manga style)

1-4-Yoshinori Natsume-s/a 3.00

TPB (2008, $9.99, digest size) r/#1-4; interview with Yoshinori Natsume 10.00

BATMAN '89 (Based on the 1989 Michael Keaton movie)

DC Comics: Oct, 2021 - No. 6, Sept, 2022 ($3.99, limited series)

1-6-Hamm-s/Quinones-a; Harvey Dent app. 1-Intro. Drake Winston. 2-Selina Kyle app. 4.00

BATMAN ETERNAL (Also see Arkham Manor series)

DC Comics: Jun, 2014 - No. 52, Jun, 2015 ($2.99, weekly series)

1-Snyder-s/Fabok-a; Professor Pyg & Jason Bard app. 5.00

2-51: 2-Carmine Falcone returns. 3-Stephanie Brown app. 6,14-17,26,29,30,37-Joker's Daughter app. 20-Spoiler dons costume. 30-Arkham Asylum destroyed. 41-Bluebird in costume 3.00

52-($3.99) Jae Lee-c; art by various 4.00

BATMAN: EUROPA

DC Comics: Jan, 2016 - No. 4, Apr, 2016 ($4.99, limited series)

1-4: 1-Joker app.; Casali & Azzarello-a/Camuncoli & Jim Lee-a. 2-Camuncoli-a 5.00

... Director's Cut 1 (8/16, $5.99) r/#1 with Jim Lee's pencil art; bonus original script 6.00

BATMAN FAMILY, THE

National Periodical Pub./DC Comics: Sept-Oct, 1975 - No. 20, Oct-Nov, 1978 (#1-4, 17-on: 68 pgs.) (Combined with Detective Comics with No. 481)

1-Origin/2nd app. Batgirl-Robin team-up (The Dynamite Duo); reprints plus one new story begins; N. Adams-a(r); r/1st app. Man-Bat from Det. #400
5 10 15 33 57 80

2-5: 2-r/Det. #369. 3-Batgirl & Robin learn each's i.d.; r/Batwoman app. from Batman #105. 4-r/1st Fatman app. from Batman #113. 5-r/1st Bat-Hound app. from Batman #92
3 6 9 16 23 30

6-(7-8/76) Joker's daughter on cover (1st app.) 9 18 27 59 117 175

7,8,14-16: 8-r/Batwoman app.14-Batwoman app. 15-3rd app. Killer Moth. 16-Bat-Girl cameo (last app. in costume until New Teen Titans #47) 2 4 6 13 18 22

9-Joker's daughter-c/app. 6 12 18 37 66 95

10-1st revival Batwoman; Cavalier app.; Killer Moth app.
3 6 9 20 31 42

11-13,17-20: 11-13-Rogers-a(p): 11-New stories begin; Man-Bat begins. 13-Batwoman cameo. 17-($1.00 size)-Batman, Huntress begin; Batwoman & Catwoman 1st meet. 18-20: Huntress by Staton in all. 20-Origin Ragman retold
3 6 9 17 26 35

NOTE: ***Aparo*** *a-17; c-11-16.* ***Austin*** *a-12i.* ***Chaykin*** *a-14p.* ***Michael Golden*** *a-15-17,18-20p.* ***Grell*** *a-1; c-1.* ***Gil Kane*** *a-2r.* ***Kaluta*** *c-17, 19.* ***Newton*** *a-13.* ***Robinson*** *a-1r, 3i(r), 9r.* ***Russell*** *a-18i, 19i.* ***Starlin*** *a-17; c-18, 20.*

BATMAN: FAMILY

DC Comics: Dec, 2002 - No. 8, Feb, 2003 ($2.95/$2.25, weekly limited series)

1,8-($2.95): 1-John Francis Moore-s/Hoberg & Gaudiano-a 5.00

2-7-($2.25): 3-Orpheus & Black Canary app. 3.00

BATMAN: FEAR STATE

DC Comics: Alpha, Oct, 2021 - Omega, Jan, 2022 ($4.99, bookends of crossover event)

...: Alpha 1 - Tynion IV-s/Federici-a; Scarecrow app. 5.00

...: Omega 1 - Tynion IV-s/Federici, Duce, Benjamin, March & Hairsine-a 5.00

BATMAN / FORTNITE: FOUNDATION (Based on the videogame)

DC Comics: Dec, 2021 ($4.99, one-shot, bagged with a Fortnite code)

1-Batman, Justice League, Lex Luthor and The Batman Who Laughs app.; Hixson-a 5.00

BATMAN / FORTNITE: ZERO POINT (Based on the videogame)

DC Comics: Jun, 2021 - No. 6, Sept, 2021 ($4.99, limited series, bagged with a Fortnite code)

1-6: Batman and Catwoman in the land of Fortnite 5.00

... Batman Day Special Edition 1 (11/21, free giveaway, not bagged) r/#1 3.00

BATMAN: FORTRESS

DC Comics: Jul, 2022 - No. 8, Mar, 2023 ($3.99, limited series)

1-8-Gary Whitta-s/Darick Robertson-a 4.00

BATMAN: GATES OF GOTHAM

DC Comics: Jul, 2011 - No. 5, Late Oct, 2011 ($2.99, limited series)

1-5-Flashbacks to 1880s Gotham City; Snyder-s/Higgins-a 4.00

BATMAN: GCPD

DC Comics: Aug, 1996 - No. 4, Nov, 1996 ($2.25, limited series)

1-4: Features Jim Gordon; Aparo/Sienkiewicz-a 4.00

BATMAN GIANT (See reprint of new stories in Batman Universe)

DC Comics: 2018 - No. 14, 2019 ($4.99, 100 pgs., squarebound, Walmart exclusive)

1-New story Palmiotti-s/Zircher-a; reprints from Batman #608 (Hush), Nightwing ('11), and Harley Quinn ('14) in all 10.00

2,3,5-14: 2-Palmiotti-s/Zircher-a plus reprints. 3-Bendis-s/Derrington-a begins plus reprints. 8-Green Lantern & Jonah Hex app. in new story; Batgirl reprints replace Harley Quinn 5.00

4-Debut of Ginny Hex (Young Justice) in new story; Bendis-s/Derrington-a 8.00

BATMAN GIANT

DC Comics: 2019 - No. 5, 2020 ($4.99, 100 pgs., squarebound, Mass Market & Direct Market editions exist for each issue, with different covers)

1-5-Two new stories and reprints in each. 1-Batwoman vs. Lord Death Man 5.00

BATMAN: GORDON OF GOTHAM

DC Comics: June, 1998 - No. 4, Sept, 1998 ($1.95, limited series)

1-4: Gordon's early days in Chicago 4.00

BATMAN: GORDON'S LAW

DC Comics: Dec, 1996 - No. 4, Mar, 1997 ($1.95, limited series)

1-4: Dixon-s/Janson-c/a 4.00

BATMAN: GOTHAM ADVENTURES (Based on Kids WB Batman animated series)

DC Comics: June, 1998 - No. 60, May, 2003 ($2.95/$1.95/$1.99/$2.25)

1-($2.95) 3 6 9 14 19 24

Batman / Catwoman #3 © DC

Batman Eternal #50 © DC

Batman Incorporated (2012) #1 © DC

	GD 2.0	VG 4.0	FN 6.0	VF 8.0	VF/NM 9.0	NM- 9.2
2-($1.95) Two-Face-c/app.						5.00
3-($1.95) Grey Ghost app.	3	6	9	16	23	30
4-9,11-13,15-28: 4-Begin $1.99-c. 5-Deadman-c. 13-MAD #1 cover swipe						4.00
10,14-Harley Quinn c/app.	2	4	6	13	18	22
29,43-Harley Quinn c/app.	2	4	6	13	18	22
30,32-42,44,46-52,54-59: 50-Catwoman-c/app. 58-Creeper-c/app.						4.00
31-Joker-c/app.	1	2	3	5	6	8
45-Harley Quinn c/app.	3	6	9	16	24	35
53-Poison Ivy-c/app.; Harley Quinn cameo	2	4	6	9	12	15
60-Joker-c/app.	3	6	9	15	22	28
TPB (2000, $9.95) r/#1-6						24.00

BATMAN: GOTHAM AFTER MIDNIGHT
DC Comics: July, 2008 - No. 12, Jun, 2009 ($2.99, limited series)
1-12-Steve Niles-s/Kelley Jones-a/c. 1-Scarecrow app. 2-Man-Bat app. 5,6-Joker app. 4.00
TPB (2009, $19.99) r/#1-12; John Carpenter intro.; Jones sketch pages 20.00

BATMAN: GOTHAM COUNTY LINE
DC Comics: 2005 - No. 3, 2005 ($5.99, square-bound, limited series)
1-3-Steve Niles-s/Scott Hampton-a. 2,3-Deadman app. 6.00
TPB (2006, $17.99) r/#1-3 18.00

BATMAN: GOTHAM KNIGHTS
DC Comics: Mar, 2000 - No. 74, Apr, 2006 ($2.50/$2.75)
1-Grayson-s; B&W back-up by Warren Ellis & Jim Lee 6.00
2-10-Grayson-s; B&W back-ups by various. 6-Killing Joke flashback 3.00
11-($3.25) Bolland-c; Kyle Baker back-up story 4.00
12-24: 13-Officer Down x-over; Ellison back-up-s. 15-Colan back-up. 20-Superman-c/app. 3.00
25,26-Bruce Wayne: Murderer pt. 4,10 3.50
27-31: 28,30,31-Bruce Wayne: Fugitive pt. 7,14,17 3.00
32-49: 32-Begin $2.75-c; Kaluta-a back-up. 33,34-Bane-c/app. 35-Mahfood-a back-up. 38-Bolton-a back-up. 43-Jason Todd & Batgirl app. 44-Jason Todd flashback 3.00
50-54-Hush returns-Barrionuevo-a/Bermejo-c. 53,54-Green Arrow app. 4.00
55-($3.75) Batman vs. Hush; Joker & Riddler app. 5.00
56-74: 56-58-War Games; Jae Lee-c. 60-65-Hush app. 66-Villains United tie-in; Talia app. 3.00
Batman: Hush Returns TPB (2006, $12.99) r/#50-55,66; cover gallery 13.00

BATMAN: GOTHAM KNIGHTS – GILDED CITY (Based on the Gotham Knights videogame)
DC Comics: Dec, 2022 - No. 6 ($4.99, limited series)
1-5-Narcisse-s/Abel-a; prequel series to the video game: Gotham Knights 5.00

BATMAN: GOTHAM NIGHTS II (First series listed under Gotham Nights)
DC Comics: Mar, 1995 - No. 4, June, 1995 ($1.95, limited series)
1-4 4.00

BATMAN/GRENDEL (1st limited series)
DC Comics: 1993 - No. 2, 1993 ($4.95, limited series, squarebound; 52 pgs.)
1,2: Batman vs. Hunter Rose. 1-Devil's Riddle; Matt Wagner-c/a/scripts. 2-Devil's Masque; Matt Wagner-c/a/scripts 7.00

BATMAN/GRENDEL (2nd limited series)
DC Comics: June, 1996 - No. 2, July, 1996 ($4.95, limited series, squarebound)
1,2: Batman vs. Grendel Prime. 1-Devil's Bones. 2-Devil's Dance; Wagner-c/a/s 6.00

BATMAN: HARLEY & IVY
DC Comics: Jun, 2004 - No. 3, Aug, 2004 ($2.50, limited series)

	GD 2.0	VG 4.0	FN 6.0	VF 8.0	VF/NM 9.0	NM- 9.2
1-Paul Dini-s/Bruce Timm-c/a in all	3	6	9	20	31	42
2,3	3	6	9	14	20	26
TPB (2007, $14.99) r/series; newly colored story from Batman: Gotham Knights #14 and Harley and Ivy: Love on the Lam series						20.00

BATMAN: HARLEY QUINN
DC Comics: 1999 ($5.95, prestige format)

	GD 2.0	VG 4.0	FN 6.0	VF 8.0	VF/NM 9.0	NM- 9.2
1-Intro. of Harley Quinn into regular DC continuity; Dini-s/Alex Ross-c	8	16	24	56	108	160
1-(2nd printing)	5	10	15	30	50	70

BATMAN: HAUNTED GOTHAM
DC Comics: 2000 - No. 4, 2000 ($4.95, limited series, squarebound)
1-4-Doug Moench-s/Kelley Jones-c/a 6.00
TPB (2009, $19.99) r/#1-4 20.00

BATMAN/ HELLBOY/STARMAN
DC Comics/Dark Horse: Jan, 1999 - No. 2, Feb, 1999 ($2.50, limited series)
1,2: Robinson-s/Mignola-a. 2-Harris-c 6.00

BATMAN: HOLLYWOOD KNIGHT
DC Comics: Apr, 2001 - No. 3, Jun, 2001 ($2.50, limited series)
1-3-Elseworlds Batman as a 1940's movie star; Giordano-a/Layton-s 3.00

BATMAN/ HUNTRESS: CRY FOR BLOOD
DC Comics: Jun, 2000 - No. 6, Nov, 2000 ($2.50, limited series)
1-6: Rucka-s/Burchett-a; The Question app. 3.00
TPB (2002, $12.95) r/#1-6 13.00

BATMAN, INC.
DC Comics: Jan, 2011 - No. 8, Aug, 2011 ($3.99/$2.99)
1-3-Morrison-s/Paquette-a; covers by Paquette & Williams 4.00
4-8-($2.99) 4-Burnham-a, original Batwoman (Kathy Kane) app. 3.00
...: Leviathan Strikes (2/12, $6.99) Morrison-s/Burnham & Stewart-a; cover gallery 7.00

BATMAN INCORPORATED
DC Comics: Jul, 2012 - No. 13, Sept, 2013 ($2.99)
1-7-Morrison-s/Burnham-a/c. 2-Origin of Talia. 3-Matches Malone returns 3.00
1-Variant-c by Quitely 5.00
8-Death of Damian 5.00
9-13: 9,10,12,13-Morrison-s/Burnham-a/c 3.00
#0 (11/12, $2.99) Frazer Irving-a; the start of Batman Incorporated 3.00
... Special 1 (10/13, $4.99) Short stories about international Batmen; s/a by various 5.00

BATMAN INCORPORATED
DC Comics: Dec, 2022 - Present ($3.99)
1-6: 1-Brisson-s/Timms-a; Ghost-Maker leads the team. 6-Bandini-a 4.00

BATMAN: JEKYLL & HYDE
DC Comics: June, 2005 - No. 6, Nov, 2005 ($2.99, limited series)
1-6-Paul Jenkins-s; Two-Face app. 1-3-Jae Lee-a. 4-6-Sean Phillips-a 3.00
TPB (2008, $14.99) r/#1-6 15.00

BATMAN: JOKER TIME (...: It's Joker Time! on cover)
DC Comics: 2000 - No. 3 ($4.95, limited series, squarebound)
1-3-Bob Hall-s/a 6.00

BATMAN: JOURNEY INTO KNGHT
DC Comics: Oct, 2005 - No. 12, Nov, 2006 ($2.50/$2.99, limited series)
1-9-Andrew Helfer-s/Tan Eng Huat-a/Pat Lee-c 3.00
10-12-($2.99) Joker app. 3.00

BATMAN/ JUDGE DREDD "DIE LAUGHING"
DC Comics: 1998 - No. 2, 1999 ($4.95, limited series, squarebound)

	GD 2.0	VG 4.0	FN 6.0	VF 8.0	VF/NM 9.0	NM- 9.2
1,2: 1-Fabry-c/a. 2-Jim Murray-c/a	1	3	4	6	8	10

BATMAN: KILLING TIME
DC Comics: May, 2022 - No. 6, Oct, 2022 ($4.99, limited series)
1-6-Tom King-s/David Marquez-a. 1-Intro The Help 5.00

BATMAN: KINGS OF FEAR
DC Comics: Oct, 2018 - No. 6, Mar, 2019 ($3.99, limited series)
1-6-Scott Peterson-s/Kelley Jones-a; Scarecrow app. 4.00

BATMAN: KNIGHTGALLERY (See Batman one-shots)

BATMAN – KNIGHTWATCH
DC Comics: Nov, 2022 - No. 5, Mar, 2023 ($2.99, printing of the digital-first series)
1-5: 1-Clayface & Mr. Freeze app. 2-Penguin & Joker app. 3-Man-Bat & Firefly app. 3.00

BATMAN: LAST KNIGHT ON EARTH
DC Comics: Jul, 2019 - No. 3, Feb, 2020 ($5.99, limited series, squarebound)
1-3-Snyder-s/Capullo-a 6.00

BATMAN: LEAGUE OF BATMEN
DC Comics: 2001 - No. 2, 2001 ($5.95, limited series, squarebound)
1,2-Elseworlds; Moench-s/Bright & Tanghal-a/Van Fleet-c 6.00

BATMAN: LEGENDS OF THE DARK KNIGHT (Legends of the Dark...#1-36)
DC Comics: Nov, 1989 - No. 214, Mar, 2007 ($1.50/$1.75/$1.95/$1.99/$2.25/$2.50/$2.99)

	GD 2.0	VG 4.0	FN 6.0	VF 8.0	VF/NM 9.0	NM- 9.2
1- "Shaman" begins, ends #5; outer cover has four different color variations, all worth same; O'Neil-s/Hannigan-a	1	2	3	5	6	8
2-10: 6-10- "Gothic" by Grant Morrison (scripts)						4.00
11-15: 11-15-Gulacy/Austin-a. 13-Catwoman app.						4.00
16-Intro drug Bane uses; begin Venom story						6.00
17-20						5.00
21-49,51-63: 38-Bat-Mite-c/story. 46-49-Catwoman app. w/Heath-c/a. 51-Ragman app.; Joe Kubert-c. 59,60,61-Knightquest x-over. 62,63-KnightsEnd Pt. 4 & 10						3.00
50-($3.95, 68 pgs.)-Bolland embossed gold foil-c; Joker-c/story; pin-ups by Chaykin, Simonson, Williamson, Kaluta, Russell, others	2	4	6	13	18	22
64-99: 64-(9/94)-Begin $1.95-c. 71-73-James Robinson-s,Watkiss-c/a. 74,75-McKeever-c/a/s. 76-78-Scott Hampton-c/a/s. 81-Card insert. 83,84-Ellis-s. 85-Robinson-s. 91-93-Ennis-s. 94-Michael T. Gilbert-s/a.						3.00
100-($3.95) Alex Ross painted-c; gallery by various						5.00

GD VG FN VF VF/NM NM-
2.0 4.0 6.0 8.0 9.0 9.2

101-115: 101-Ezquerra-a. 102-104-Robinson-s 3.00
116-No Man's Land stories begin; Huntress-c 4.00
117-119,121-126: 122-Harris-c 3.00
120-ID of new Batgirl revealed 2 4 6 9 13 16
127-131: Return to Legends stories; Green Arrow app. 3.00
132-199, 201-204: 132-136 ($2.25-c) Archie Goodwin-s/Rogers-a. 137-141-Gulacy-a. 142-145-Joker and Ra's al Ghul app. 146-148-Kitson-a. 158-Begin $2.50-c 169-171-Tony Harris-c/a. 182-184-War Games. 182-Bagged with Sky Captain CD 3.00
200-($4.99) Joker-c/app. 1 2 3 5 6 8
205-214: 205-Begin $2.99-c. 207,208-Olivetti-a. 214-Deadshot app. 3.00
#0-(10/94)-Zero Hour; Quesada/Palmiotti-c; released between #64 & #65 3.00
Annual 1-7 ('91-'97, $3.50-$3.95, 68 pgs.): 1-Joker app. 2-Netzer-c/a. 3-New Batman (Azrael) app. 4-Elseworlds story. 5-Year One; Man-Bat app. 6-Legend of the Dead Earth story. 7-Pulp Heroes story 4.00
... Halloween Special 1 (12/93, $6.95, 84 pgs.)-Embossed & foil stamped-c 2 4 6 8 10 12
... Halloween Special Edition 1 (12/14, giveaway) Sale-a/c 3.00
Batman Madness-...Halloween Special (1994, $4.95) 6.00
Batman Ghosts-...Halloween Special (1995, $4.95) 6.00
NOTE: *Aparo a-Annual 1. Chaykin scripts-24-26. Giffen a-Annual 1. Golden a-Annual 1. Alan Grant scripts-38, 52, 53. Gil Kane c/a-24-26. Mignola a-54; c-54, 62. Morrow a-Annual 3i. Quesada a-Annual 1. James Robinson scripts- 71-73. Russell c/a-42, 43. Sears a-21, 23; c-21, 23. Zeck a-69, 70; c-69, 70.*

BATMAN-LEGENDS OF THE DARK KNIGHT: JAZZ
DC Comics: Apr, 1995 - No. 3, June, 1995 ($2.50, limited series)
1-3 3.00

BATMAN: LI'L GOTHAM
DC Comics: Jun, 2013 - No. 12, May, 2014 ($2.99, printings of stories that 1st appeared online)
1-12-Dustin Nguyen-a/c; Nguyen & Fridolfs-s; holiday themed short stories 3.00
Halloween Comic Fest 2013 (12/13, no cover price) Halloween giveaway; r/#1 3.00

BATMAN/LOBO
DC Comics: Oct, 2007 - No. 2, Nov, 2007 ($5.99, squarebound, limited series)
1,2-Sam Kieth-s/a 1 2 3 5 6 8

BATMAN: LOST (Tie-in to Dark Nights: Metal series)
DC Comics: Jan, 2018 ($4.99, one-shot)
1-Snyder, Tynion IV & Williamson-s/Mahnke, Paquette & Jimenez-a; Coipel foil-c 5.00

BATMAN: MANBAT
DC Comics: Oct, 1995 - No. 3, Dec, 1995 ($4.95, limited series)
1-3-Elseworlds-Delano-script; Bolton-a 6.00
TPB-(1997, $14.95) r/#1-3 15.00

BATMAN: MITEFALL (See Batman one-shots)

BATMAN MINIATURE (See Batman Kellogg's)

BATMAN: NEVERMORE
DC Comics: June, 2003 - No. 5, Oct, 2003 ($2.50, limited series)
1-5-Elseworlds Batman & Edgar Allan Poe; Wrightson-c/Guy Davis-a/Len Wein-s 4.00

BATMAN: NO MAN'S LAND (Also see 1999 Batman titles)
DC Comics: (one shots)
nn (3/99, $2.95) Alex Ross-c; Bob Gale-s; begins year-long story arc 4.00
Collector's Ed. (3/99, $3.95) Ross lenticular-c 6.00
#0 (: Ground Zero on cover) (12/99, $4.95) Orbik-c 6.00
...: Gallery (7/99, $3.95) Jim Lee-c 4.00
...: Secret Files (12/99, $4.95) Maleev-c 6.00
TPB ('99, $12.95) r/early No Man's Land stories; new Batgirl early app. 13.00
No Law and a New Order TPB(1999, $5.95) Ross-c 6.00
Volume 2 ('00, $12.95) r/later No Man's Land stories; Batgirl (Huntress) app.; Deodato-c 13.00
Volume 3-5 ('00,'01 $12.95) 3-Intro. new Batgirl. 4-('00). 5-('01) Land-c 13.00

BATMAN: ODYSSEY
DC Comics: Sept, 2010 - No. 6, Feb, 2011 ($3.99, limited series)
1-6-Neal Adams-s/a/c. 1-Man-Bat app.; bonus sketch pages. 5,6-Joker app. 4.00
1-6-Variant B&W-version cover 5.00
Vol. 2 (12/11 - No. 7, 6/12) 1-7-Neal Adams-s/a/c 4.00

BATMAN – ONE BAD DAY
DC Comics: Oct, 2022 - Present ($7.99, series of one-shots)
...: Bane 1 (3/23) Williamson-s/Porter-a 8.00
...: Catwoman 1 (2/23) G. Willow Wilson-s/Jamie McKelvie-a 8.00
...: Clayface 1 (4/23) Kelly & Lanzing-s/Xermánico-a 8.00
...: Mr. Freeze 1 (1/23) Duggan-s/Scalera-a 8.00
...: Penguin 1 (12/22) Ridley-s/Camuncoli-a; Penguin vs. The Umbrella Man 8.00
...: The Riddler 1 (10/22) Tom King-s/Mitch Gerads-a; childhood flashback 8.00
...: Two-Face 1 (11/22) Mariko Tamaki-s/Javier Fernandez-a 8.00

BATMAN: ONE DARK KNIGHT
DC Comics (Black Label): Feb, 2022 - No. 3, Sept, 2022 ($6.99, oversized 8-1/2" x 10-3/4", lim. series)
1-3-Jock-s/a/c 7.00

BATMAN: ORPHANS
DC Comics: Early Feb, 2011 - No. 2, Late Feb, 2011 ($3.99, limited series)
1,2-Berganza-s/Barberi-a/c 4.00

BATMAN: ORPHEUS RISING
DC Comics: Oct, 2001 - No. 5, Feb, 2002 ($2.50, limited series)
1-5-Intro. Orpheus; Simmons-s/Turner & Miki-a 3.00

BATMAN: OUTLAWS
DC Comics: 2000 - No. 3, 2000 ($4.95, limited series)
1-3-Moench-s/Gulacy-a 5.00

BATMAN: PENGUIN TRIUMPHANT (See Batman one-shots)

BATMAN/PREDATOR III: BLOOD TIES
DC Comics/Dark Horse Comics: Nov, 1997 - No. 4, Feb, 1998 ($1.95, lim. series)
1-4: Dixon-s/Damaggio-c/a 1 2 3 5 6 8
TPB-(1998, $7.95) r/#1-4 15.00

BATMAN: PRELUDE TO THE WEDDING
DC Comics: Jul, 2018 - Aug, 2018 ($3.99, series of one-shots)
...: Batgirl vs. Riddler 1 (8/18) Tim Seeley-s/Minkyu Jung-a 4.00
...: Harley Quinn vs. Joker 1 (8/18) Tim Seeley-s/Sami Basri-a; leads into Batman #48 4.00
...: Nightwing vs. Hush 1 (8/18) Tim Seeley-s/Travis Moore-a; Superman app. 4.00
...: Red Hood vs. Anarky 1 (8/18) Tim Seeley-s/Javier Fernandez-a; Joker app. 4.00
...: Robin vs. Ra's al Ghul 1 (7/18) Tim Seeley-s/Brad Walker-a; Selina Kyle app. 4.00

BATMAN/RA'S AL GHUL (See Year One:...)

BATMAN: REPTILIAN
DC Comics: Aug, 2021 - No. 6, Dec, 2021 ($4.99, limited series)
1-6-Garth Ennis-s/Liam Sharp-a; Killer Croc app. 5.00

BATMAN RETURNS MOVIE SPECIAL (See Batman one-shots)

BATMAN: RIDDLER-THE RIDDLE FACTORY (See Batman one-shots)

BATMAN: RUN, RIDDLER, RUN
DC Comics: 1992 - Book 3, 1992 ($4.95, limited series)
Book 1-3: Mark Badger-a & plot 6.00

BATMAN SCARECROW (See Year One:...)

BATMAN SCOOBY-DOO MYSTERIES, THE (See The Batman & Scooby-Doo Mysteries)

BATMAN: SECRET FILES
DC Comics: Oct, 1997; Dec, 2018; Sept, 2019; Jun, 2020; 2021 ($4.95/$4.99)
1-New origin-s and profiles 6.00
1-(12/18, $4.99) Short stories by various; Detective Chimp app. 5.00
2-(9/19, $4.99) Short stories by various; Joker, Riddler, Bane, Hugo Strange app. 5.00
3-(6/20, $4.99) Short stories; Deathstroke, Cheshire, Merlyn, Mr. Teeth & Gunsmith 5.00
...: Clownhunter 1 (10/21, $4.99) Punchline & Red Hood app.; Brisson-s/Kämpe-a 5.00
...: Huntress 1 (9/21, $4.99) Tamaki-s/Lapham-a 5.00
...: Miracle Molly 1 (11/21, $4.99) Tynion IV-s/Dani-a 5.00
...: Peacekeeper-01 1 (12/21, $4.99) "Fear State" tie-in; Tynion IV & Brisson-s/Hixson-a 5.00
...: The Gardener 1 (12/21, $4.99) "Fear State" tie-in; Poison Ivy app.; Ward-a 5.00
...: The Signal 1 (9/21, $4.99) Patrick-s/Duce-a 5.00

BATMAN: SECRETS
DC Comics: May, 2006 - No. 5, Sept, 2006 ($2.99, limited series)
1-5-Sam Kieth-s/a/c; Joker app. 3.00
TPB (2007, $12.99) r/series 13.00

BATMAN'S GRAVE, THE
DC Comics: Dec, 2019 - No. 12, Feb, 2021 ($3.99, limited series)
1-12-Warren Ellis-s/Bryan Hitch-a 4.00

BATMAN / SHADOW (Pulp hero)
DC Comics: June, 2017 - No. 6, Nov, 2017 ($3.99, limited series)
1-6: Snyder & Orlando-s/Rossmo-a; Lamont Cranston in current Gotham City 4.00

BATMAN: SHADOW OF THE BAT
DC Comics: June, 1992 - No. 94, Feb, 2000 ($1.50/$1.75/$1.95/$1.99)
1-The Last Arkham-c/story begins; 1st app. Victor Zsasz; Alan Grant scripts in all 2 4 6 10 14 18
1-($2.50)-Deluxe edition polybagged w/poster, pop-up & book mark 2 4 6 10 14 18
2-7: 4-The Last Arkham ends. 7-Last $1.50-c 4.00
8-28: 14,15-Staton-a(p). 16-18-Knightfall tie-ins. 19-28-Knightquest tie-ins w/Azrael as Batman. 25-Silver ink-c; anniversary issue 4.00
29-($2.95, 52 pgs.)-KnightsEnd Pt. 2 5.00
30-72: 30-KnightsEnd Pt. 8. 31-(9/94)-Begin $1.95-c; Zero Hour. 32-(11/94). 33-Robin-c. 35-Troika-Pt.2. 43,44-Cat-Man & Catwoman-c. 48-Contagion Pt. 1; card insert. 49-Contagion Pt.7. 56,57,58-Poison Ivy-c/app. 62-Two-Face app. 69,70-Fate app. 4.00
35-($2.95)-Variant embossed-c 5.00
73,74,76-78: Cataclysm x-over pts. 1,9. 76-78-Orbik-c 4.00
75-($2.95) Mr. Freeze & Clayface app.; Orbik-c 5.00
79,81,82: 79-Begin $1.99-c; Orbik-c 4.00
80-($3.95) Flip book with Azrael #47 5.00
83-No Man's Land; intro. new Batgirl (Huntress) 2 4 6 11 16 20
84,85-No Man's Land 5.00
86-92,94: 87-Deodato-a. 90-Harris-c. 92-Superman app. 94-No Man's Land ends 4.00
93-Joker and Harley app. 5.00
#0 (10/94) Zero Hour tie-in; released between #31 & #32 4.00
#1,000,000 (11/98) 853rd Century x-over; Orbik-c 4.00
Annual 1-5 ('93-'97 $2.95-$3.95, 68 pgs.): 3-Year One story; Poison Ivy app. 4-Legends of the Dead Earth story; Starman cameo. 5-Pulp Heroes story; Poison Ivy app. 5.00

BATMAN: SINS OF THE FATHER (Based on the Batman: The Telltale Series video game)
DC Comics: Apr, 2018 - No. 6, Sept, 2018 ($2.99, printing of digital first stories)
1-6-Gage-s/Ienco-a; Deadshot app. 3.00

BATMAN '66 (Characters and likenesses based on the 1966 television series)
DC Comics: Sept, 2013 - No. 30, Feb, 2016 ($3.99/$2.99, printings of stories that first appeared online)
1-Jeff Parker-s/Jonathan Case-a/Mike Allred-c; Riddler & Catwoman app. 2 4 6 8 10 12
1-Variant-c by Jonathan Case 2 4 6 8 11 14
1-San Diego Comic-Con variant action figure photo-c 3 6 9 17 26 35
2-12: 2-Penguin & Mr. Freeze app.; Templeton-a. 3,11,20-Joker app. 5,10,11-Batgirl app. 8-King Tut app. 4.00
13-24,26-30: 14-Selfie variant-c. 16,20-Egghead app. 18,21,27,29-Batgirl app. 21-Lord Death Man app. 22-Oeming-a. 26-Poison Ivy app. 27-Bane app. 30-Allred-a 3.00
25-1st app. The Harlequin; back-up Mad Men spoof with Batgirl 1 3 4 6 8 10
... Meets the Legion of Super-Heroes 1 (9/17, $3.99) Lee Allred-s/Mike Allred-a/c 4.00
... The Lost Episode 1 (1/15, $9.99) Harlan Ellison 1960s script adapted by Len Wein; García-López-a; Two-Face app.; covers by García-López & Ross; original pencil art 10.00

BATMAN '66 MEETS STEED AND MRS. PEEL (TV's The Avengers)
DC Comics: Sept, 2016 - No. 6, Feb, 2017 ($2.99, printings of stories that first appeared online)
1-6-Edginton-s/Dow Smith-a/Allred-c. 1,2-Catwoman app. 3-6-Mr. Freeze app. 3.00

Batman: Li'l Gotham #2 © DC

Batman '66 #3 © DC

Batman / Superman: World's Finest #8 © DC

	GD	VG	FN	VF	VF/NM	NM-
	2.0	4.0	6.0	8.0	9.0	9.2

BATMAN '66 MEETS THE GREEN HORNET
DC Comics: Aug, 2014 - No. 6, Jan, 2015 ($2.99, printings of stories that first appeared online)
1-6-Kevin Smith & Ralph Garman-s/Ty Templeton-a/Alex Ross-c 3.00

BATMAN '66 MEETS THE MAN FROM U.N.C.L.E.
DC Comics: Feb, 2016 - No. 6, Jul, 2016 ($2.99, limited series)
1-6-Jeff Parker-s/David Haun-a/Allred-c. 1-Olga and Penguin app. 3.00

BATMAN '66 MEETS WONDER WOMAN '77
DC Comics: Mar, 2017 - No. 6, Aug, 2017 ($3.99, limited series)
1-6-Parker & Andreyko-s/Haun-a; Ra's al Ghul & Talia app. 5,6-Robin as Nightwing 6.00

BATMAN: SON OF THE DEMON (Also see Batman #655-658 and Batman Hardcovers)
DC Comics: 2006 ($5.99, reprints the 1987 HC in comic book format)
nn-Talia has Batman's son; Mike W. Barr-s/Jerry Bingham-a; new Andy Kubert-c 6.00

BATMAN/SPAWN
DC Comics: Feb, 2023 ($6.99, squarebound one-shot)
1-McFarlane-s/Capullo-a; the Court of Owls and the Joker app. 7.00
... Unplugged 1 (4/23, $6.99) The story as B&W inked pages with no text 7.00

BATMAN-SPAWN: WAR DEVIL (See Batman one-shots)

BATMAN SPECTACULAR (See DC Special Series No. 15)

BATMAN: STREETS OF GOTHAM (Follows Batman: Battle For The Cowl series)
DC Comics: Aug, 2009 - No. 21, May, 2011 ($3.99$2.99)
1-18: 1-Dini-s/Nguyen-a; back-up Manhunter feature; Jeanty-a. 10,11-Zsasz app. 4.00
19-21-($2.99) 19-Joker app. 3.00
...- Hush Money HC (2010, $19.99) r/#1-4, Detective #852 and Batman #685 20.00
...- Hush Money SC (2011, $14.99) r/#1-4, Detective #852 and Batman #685 15.00
...- Leviathan HC (2010, $19.99) r/#5-11 20.00
...- The House of Hush HC (2011, $22.99) r/#12-14,16-21 23.00

BATMAN STRIKES!, THE (Based on the 2004 animated series)
DC Comics: Nov, 2004 - No. 50, Dec, 2008 ($2.25)
1-Penguin app. 1 2 3 5 6 8
1-Free Comic Book Day edition (6/05) Penguin app. 3.00
2,4-27,29-31,33,34,36-38,40,42,44,46,48-50: 2-Man-Bat app. 4-Bane app. 9-Joker app. 11-Penguin app. 18-Batgirl debut. 29-Robin debuts. 33-Cal Ripken 8-pg. insert. 44-Superman app. 3.00
3-($2.95) Joker-c/app.; Catwoman & Wonder Woman-r from Advs. in the DCU 4.00
28,32-Joker-c/app. 32-Cal Ripken 8-pg. insert. 5.00
35-Joker & Harley Quinn-c/app. 2 4 6 10 14 18
39,47-Black Mask-c/app. 6.00
41-Harley Quinn & Poison Ivy-c/app. 2 4 6 11 16 20
43-Harley Quinn-c/app. 2 4 6 10 14 18
45-Harley Quinn, Poison Ivy, Catwoman-c/app. 2 4 6 11 16 20
Jam Packed Action (2005, $7.99, digest) adaptations of two TV episodes 8.00
... Vol. 1: Crime Time (2005, $6.99, digest) r/#1-5 7.00
... Vol. 2: In Darkest Knight (2005, $6.99, digest) r/#6-10 7.00

BATMAN/ SUPERMAN
DC Comics: Aug, 2013 - No. 32, Jul, 2016 ($3.99)
1-4-Greg Pak-s/Jae Lee-a/c; Catwoman & Wonder Woman app. 4.00
3.1 (11/13, $2.99, regular cover) 3.00
3.1 (11/13, $3.99, 3-D cover) "Doomsday #1" on cover; Booth-a; Zod app. 6.00
5-7-Booth-a; reads sideways; Mongul app. 4.00
8,9-First Contact x-over with Worlds' Finest #20,21; Power Girl & Huntress app.; Lee-a 4.00
10-31: 11-Doomed tie-in. 13-Jae Lee-a. 13-15-Catwoman app. 17-Lobo app. 21-Batman (Gordon in robot suit). 23,24-Aquaman app. 25-27-Vandal Savage app. 4.00
32-The Great Ten app.; 1st app. Chinese Super-Man (Kong Kenan) 5.00
Annual 1 (5/14, $5.99) Supergirl, Krypto, Cyborg, Batgirl, Red Hood app.; Jae Lee-c 6.00
Annual 2 (5/15, $4.99) Killer Croc, Cheshire & Bane app.; Syaf-c 5.00
...: Futures End 1 (11/14, $2.99, regular-c) Five years later; Pak-s 3.00
...: Futures End 1 (11/14, $3.99, 3-D cover) 4.00

BATMAN/ SUPERMAN
DC Comics: Oct, 2019 - No. 22, Nov, 2021 ($3.99)
1-22: 1-5-The Batman Who Laughs app.; Williamson-s/Marquez-a. 4-Acetate-c. 7,8-General Zod & Ra's al Ghul app. 9-11-Ultra-Humanite app. 15-Solomon Grundy app. 4.00
Annual 1 (11/20, $4.99) Bat-Mite and Mr. Mxyzptlk app.; Eaglesham & Melnikov-a 5.00
2021 Annual 1 (10/21, $5.99) Yang-s/Francavilla & Pelletier-a 6.00
...: The Authority Special 1 (1/22, $5.99) P.K. Johnson-s/Hairsine, Beredo, Templesmith-a 6.00

BATMAN/ SUPERMAN/WONDER WOMAN: TRINITY
DC Comics: 2003 - No. 3, 2003 ($6.95, limited series, squarebound)
1-3-Matt Wagner-s/a/c. 1-Ra's al Ghul & Bizarro app. 7.00
HC (2004, $24.95, with dust-jacket) r/series; intro. by Brad Meltzer 30.00

	GD	VG	FN	VF	VF/NM	NM-
	2.0	4.0	6.0	8.0	9.0	9.2

SC (2004, $17.99) r/series; intro. by Brad Meltzer 18.00

BATMAN/ SUPERMAN: WORLD'S FINEST
DC Comics: May, 2022 - Present ($3.99)
1-12: 1-5-Waid-s/Mora-a; Doom Patrol app. 6-Travis Moore-a. 7-Intro Boy Thunder. 9-11-Joker and The Key app. 4.00

BATMAN: SWORD OF AZRAEL (Also see Azrael & Batman #488,489)
DC Comics: Oct, 1992 - No. 4, Jan, 1993 ($1.75, limited series)
1-Wraparound gatefold-c; Quesada-c/a(p) in all; 1st app. Azrael 3 6 9 14 19 24
2-4: 4-Cont'd in Batman #488 1 2 3 5 6 8
Silver Edition 1-4 (1993, $1.95)-Reprints #1-4 3.00
Trade Paperback (1993, $9.95)-Reprints #1-4 12.00
Trade Paperback Gold Edition 18.00

BATMAN/ TARZAN: CLAWS OF THE CAT-WOMAN
Dark Horse Comics/DC Comics: Sept, 1999 - No. 4, Dec, 1999 ($2.95, limited series)
1-4: Marz-s/Kordey-a 3.00

BATMAN/ TEENAGE MUTANT NINJA TURTLES
DC Comics: Feb, 2016 - No. 6, Jul, 2016 ($3.99, limited series)
1-6-Tynion IV-s/Williams II-a; Penguin, Croc & Shredder app. 5.00
... Director's Cut 1 (11/16, $5.99) r/#1 in B&W and pencil-a; original script 6.00

BATMAN/ TEENAGE MUTANT NINJA TURTLES II
DC Comics: Feb, 2018 - No. 6, Jun, 2018 ($3.99, limited series)
1-6-Tynion IV-s/Williams II-a; Bane app. 4.00

BATMAN/ TEENAGE MUTANT NINJA TURTLES III
DC Comics: Jul, 2019 - No. 6, Dec, 2019 ($3.99, limited series)
1-6-Tynion IV-s/Williams II-a; Crisis in a Half Shell; Anti-Monitor and Krang app. 4.00

BATMAN/ TEENAGE MUTANT NINJA TURTLES ADVENTURES
IDW Publishing: Nov, 2016 - No. 6, Apr, 2017 ($3.99, limited series)
1-6-Manning-s/Sommariva-a; Clayface, Joker and Harley Quinn app.; multiple covers 4.00
... Director's Cut 1 (2/17, $4.99) r/#1 in B&W and pencil-a; original script 5.00

BATMAN: TENSES
DC Comics: 2003 - No. 2, 2003 ($6.95, limited series)
1,2-Joe Casey-s/Cully Hamner-a; Bruce Wayne's first year back in Gotham 7.00

BATMAN: THE ADVENTURES CONTINUE (Set in Batman: The Animated Series continuity)
DC Comics: Jun, 2020 - No. 8, Mar, 2021 ($3.99, printing of digital first stories)
1-7-Dini & Burnett-s/Templeton-a. 2,3-Deathstroke app. 4-Azrael app. 5,6-Red Hood app.; Jason Todd origin as Robin. 6-Joker & Harley Quinn app. 4.00
8-($4.99) Harley Quinn, Poison Ivy, Scarface and Joker app. 5.00

BATMAN: THE ADVENTURES CONTINUE SEASON TWO (Batman: The Animated Series)
DC Comics: Aug, 2021 - No. 7, Feb, 2022 ($3.99, printing of digital first stories)
1-7: 1,2-Dini & Burnett-s/Templeton-a. 3,5-7-Burchett-a 4.00

BATMAN: THE ADVENTURES CONTINUE SEASON THREE (Batman: The Animated Series)
DC Comics: Mar, 2023 - Present ($3.99, printing of digital first stories)
1-3: 1-Dini & Burnett-s/Gibson-a. 2-Altieri-a. 3-Templeton-a; Task Force X app. 4.00

BATMAN: THE ANKH
DC Comics: 2002 - No. 2, 2002 ($5.95, limited series)
1,2-Dixon-s/Van Fleet-a 6.00

BATMAN: THE AUDIO ADVENTURES
DC Comics: Nov, 2022 - No. 7 ($3.99)
1-5: Killer Croc app. 4.00

BATMAN: THE BRAVE AND THE BOLD (Based on the 2008 animated series)
DC Comics: Mar, 2009 - No. 22, Dec, 2010 ($2.50/$2.99)
1-18: 1-Power Girl app. 4-Sugar & Spike cameo. 7-Doom Patrol app. 9-Catman app. 3.00
19-22-($2.99) Cyborg Superman and the Green Lantern Corps app. 22-Aquaman app. 3.00
TPB (2009, $12.99) r/#1-6 13.00
...: Emerald Knight TPB (2011, $12.99) r/#13,14,16,18,19,21 13.00
...: The Fearsome Fangs Strike Again TPB (2010, $12.99) r/#7-12 13.00

BATMAN: THE BRAVE AND THE BOLD (Titled "All New Batman: Brave & the Bold" for #1-13)
DC Comics: Jan, 2011 - No. 16, Apr, 2012 ($2.99)
1-16: 1-Superman. 4-Wonder Woman app. 8-Aquaman app. 9-Hawkman app. 3.00

BATMAN: THE CULT
DC Comics: 1988 - No. 4, Nov, 1988 ($3.50, deluxe limited series)
1-Wrightson-a/painted-c in all 1 3 4 6 8 10
2-4 6.00

GD 2.0 | VG 4.0 | FN 6.0 | VF 8.0 | VF/NM 9.0 | NM- 9.2

Trade Paperback (1991, $14.95)-New Wrightson-c; Starlin intro. 25.00
Trade Paperback (2009, $19.99) 20.00

BATMAN: THE DARK KNIGHT
DC Comics: Jan, 2011 - No. 5, Oct, 2011 ($3.99/$2.99)

1-David Finch-s/a; Penguin & Killer Croc app.; covers by Finch and Clarke 4.00
2-5-($2.99) Demon app. 3.00

BATMAN: THE DARK KNIGHT (DC New 52)
DC Comics: Nov, 2011 - No. 29, May, 2014 ($2.99)

1-29: 1-Jenkins & Finch-s/Finch-a/c; White Rabbit debut. 3-Flash app. 5,6-Superman app. 6,7-Bane app. 9-Night of the Owls. 22-25-Maleev-a. 28-Van Sciver-a/c 3.00
23.1, 23.2, 23.3, 23.4 (11/13, $2.99, regular covers) 3.00
23.1 (11/13, $3.99, 3-D cover) "Ventriloquist #1" on cover; Simone-s/Santacruz-a 6.00
23.2 (11/13, $3.99, 3-D cover) "Mr. Freeze #1" on cover; Gray & Palmiotti-s 5.00
23.3 (11/13, $3.99, 3-D cover) "Clayface#1" on cover; Richards-a 5.00
23.4 (11/13, $3.99, 3-D cover) "Joker's Daughter #1" on cover; origin story; Jeanty-a 12.00
#0 (11/12, $2.99) Hurwitz-s/Suayan & Ryp-a; flashback to aftermath of parents' murder 3.00
Annual 1 (7/13, $4.99) Hurwitz-s/Kudranski-a/Maleev-c; Scarecrow, Penguin Mad Hatter 5.00

BATMAN: THE DARK KNIGHT RETURNS (Also see Dark Knight Strikes Again)
DC Comics: Mar, 1986 - No. 4, 1986 ($2.95, squarebound, limited series)

	GD	VG	FN	VF	VF/NM	NM-
1-Miller story & c/a(p); set in the future	8	16	24	54	102	150
1,2-2nd & 3rd printings, 3-2nd printing	3	6	9	17	26	35
2-Carrie Kelley becomes 1st female Robin	5	10	15	30	50	70
3-Death of Joker; Superman app.	3	6	9	20	31	42
4-Death of Alfred; Superman app.	3	6	9	20	31	42
Hardcover, signed & numbered edition ($40.00)(4000 copies)						300.00
Hardcover, trade edition						70.00
Softcover, trade edition (1st printing only)	2	4	6	11	16	20
Softcover, trade edition (2nd thru 8th printings)	2	4	6	8	10	12

10th Anniv. Slipcase set ('96, $100.00): Signed & numbered hard-c edition (10,000 copies), sketchbook, copy of script for #1, 2 color prints 135.00
10th Anniv. Hardcover ('96, $45.00) 50.00
10th Anniv. Softcover ('97, $14.95) 18.00
Hardcover 2nd printing ('02, $24.95) with 3 1/4" tall partial dustjacket 25.00
NOTE: *The #2 second printings can be identified by matching the grey background colors on the inside front cover and facing page. The inside front cover of the second printing has a dark grey background which does not match the lighter grey of the facing page. On the true 1st printings, the backgrounds are both light grey. All other issues are clearly marked.*

BATMAN: THE DARK PRINCE CHARMING
DC Comics: Jan, 2018 - No. 2, Jun, 2018 ($12.99, HC, limited series)

1,2-Enrico Marini-s/a; Joker & Harley Quinn app. 13.00

BATMAN: THE DAWNBREAKER (Tie-in to Dark Nights: Metal series)
DC Comics: Dec, 2017 ($3.99, one-shot)

1-Humphries-s/Van Sciver-a; Fabok foil-c; Wayne as Dark Multiverse Green Lantern 4.00

BATMAN: THE DETECTIVE
DC Comics: Jun, 2021 - No. 6, Jan, 2022 ($3.99, limited series)

1-6-Tom Taylor-s/Andy Kubert-a; Knight and Squire app. 4.00

BATMAN: THE DOOM THAT CAME TO GOTHAM
DC Comics: 2000 - No. 3, 2001 ($4.95, limited series)

1-3-Elseworlds; Mignola-c/s; Nixey-a; Etrigan app. 6.00

BATMAN: THE DEVASTATOR (Tie-in to Dark Nights: Metal series)
DC Comics: Jan, 2018 ($3.99, one-shot)

1-Tieri-s/Daniel-a; Fabok foil-c; Bruce Wayne as Dark Multiverse Doomsday 4.00

BATMAN: THE DROWNED (Tie-in to Dark Nights: Metal series)
DC Comics: Dec, 2017 ($3.99, one-shot)

1-Abnett-s/Tan-a; Fabok foil-c; female Bryce Wayne as Dark Multiverse Aquawoman 4.00

BATMAN: THE IMPOSTER
DC Comics (Black Label): Dec, 2021 - No. 3, Feb, 2022 ($5.99, limited series)

1-3-Mattson Tomlin-s/Andrea Sorrentino-a 6.00

BATMAN: THE KILLING JOKE (See Batman one-shots)

BATMAN: THE KNIGHT
DC Comics: Mar, 2022 - No. 10, Dec, 2022 ($4.99, limited series)

1-10-Zdarsky-s/Di Giandomenico-a; flashbacks to his training days. 7-Zatanna app. 5.00
...: Compendium Edition 1 (7/22, $7.99) Reprints #1-3 8.00

BATMAN: THE LONG HALLOWEEN
DC Comics: Oct, 1996 - No. 13, Oct, 1997 ($2.95/$4.95, limited series)

	GD	VG	FN	VF	VF/NM	NM-
1-($4.95)-Loeb-s/Sale-c/a in all	4	8	12	28	47	65
2,4,5 ($2.95): 2-Solomon Grundy-c/app.	2	4	6	8	11	14
3-Joker-c/app., Catwoman, Poison Ivy app.	3	6	9	14	20	25
6,8-10: 6-Poison Ivy-c	1	2	3	5	6	8
7-Riddler-c/app.	2	4	6	11	16	20
11,12	1	2	3	5	6	8
13-($4.95, 48 pgs.)-Killer revelations	2	4	6	10	14	18

Special 1 (12/21, $7.99) Loeb-s/Sale-a; continuation of story; Calendar Man app. 8.00
Special Edition (Halloween Comic Fest 2013) (12/13, free giveaway) r/#1 5.00
Absolute Batman: The Long Halloween (2007, $75.00, oversized HC) r/series; interviews with the creators; Sale sketch pages; action figure line; unpubbed 4-page sequence 130.00
HC-($29.95) r/series 65.00
SC-($19.95) 20.00

BATMAN: THE MAD MONK ("Batman & the Mad Monk" on cover)
DC Comics: Oct, 2006 - No. 6, Mar, 2007 ($3.50, limited series)

1-6-Matt Wagner-s/a/c. 1-Catwoman app. 3.50
TPB (2007, $14.99) r/#1-6 15.00

BATMAN / THE MAXX: ARKHAM DREAMS
IDW Publishing/DC Comics: Sept, 2018 - No. 5 ($4.99, limited series)

1-3-Sam Kieth-s/a; 3 covers on each. 2-Joker app. 5.00
... The Lost Year Compendium (9/20, $7.99) Reprints #1-3; thumbnail previews of #4 8.00

BATMAN: THE MERCILESS (Tie-in to Dark Nights: Metal series)
DC Comics: Dec, 2017 ($3.99, one-shot)

1-Tomasi-s/Manapul-a; Fabok foil-c; Bruce Wayne as Dark Multiverse God of War 4.00

BATMAN: THE MONSTER MEN ("Batman & the Monster Men" on cover)
DC Comics: Jan, 2006 - No. 6, June, 2006 ($2.99, limited series)

1-6-Matt Wagner-s/a/c 3.00
TPB (2006, $14.99) r/#1-6 15.00

BATMAN: THE MURDER MACHINE (Tie-in to Dark Nights: Metal series)
DC Comics: Nov, 2017 ($3.99, one-shot)

1-Tieri-s/Federici-a; Fabok foil-c; Bruce Wayne as Dark Multiverse Cyborg 4.00

BATMAN: THE OFFICIAL COMIC ADAPTATION OF THE WARNER BROS. MOTION PICTURE (See Batman one-shots)

BATMAN: THE RED DEATH (Tie-in to Dark Nights: Metal series)
DC Comics: Nov, 2017 ($3.99, one-shot)

1-Williamson-s/Di Giandomenico-a; Fabok foil-c; Bruce Wayne as Dark Multiverse Flash 4.00

BATMAN: THE RETURN
DC Comics: Jan, 2011 ($4.99, one-shot)

1-Morrison-s/Finch-a; covers by Finch & Ha; costume design sketch art; script pages 5.00

BATMAN: THE RETURN OF BRUCE WAYNE (Follows Batman's "death" in Final Crisis #6)
DC Comics: Early Jul, 2010 - No. 6, Dec, 2010 ($3.99, limited series)

1-6-Bruce Wayne's time travels; Morrison-s/Andy Kubert-c. 1-Sprouse-a. 4-Jeanty-a 4.00
1-Second & third printings; 4.00
1-6-Variant covers: 1-Sprouse. 2-Irving. 3-Paquette. 4-Jeanty. 5-Sook. 6-Garbett 8.00
... - The Deluxe Edition HC (2011, $29.99) r/#1-6; sketch pages 30.00

BATMAN: THE ULTIMATE EVIL
DC Comics: 1995 ($5.95, limited series, prestige format)

1,2-Barrett, Jr. adaptation of Vachss novel. 6.00

BATMAN: THE WIDENING GYRE
DC Comics: Oct, 2009 - No. 6, Sept, 2010 ($3.99/$2.99/$4.99, limited series)

1-($3.99) Kevin Smith-s/Walt Flanagan-a; debut Baphomet; Demon app.; Sienkiewicz-c 4.00
1-5-Variant covers by Gene Ha 8.00
2-5-($2.99) 2-Silver St. Cloud returns. 5-Catwoman app. 3.00
6-($4.99) Joker, Deadshot & Catwoman app. 5.00
6-Variant cover by Gene Ha 10.00
HC (2010, $19.99, dj) r/#1-6; variant covers; afterword by Kevin Smith 20.00

BATMAN 3-D (Also see 3-D Batman)
DC Comics: 1990 ($9.95, w/glasses, 8-1/8x10-3/4")

	GD	VG	FN	VF	VF/NM	NM-
nn-Byrne-a/scripts; Riddler, Joker, Penguin & Two-Face app. plus r/1953 3-D Batman; pin-ups by many artists	2	4	6	9	13	16

BATMAN: THREE JOKERS
DC Comics (Black Label): Oct, 2020 - No. 3, Dec, 2020 ($6.99, limited series)

	GD	VG	FN	VF	VF/NM	NM-
1-3-Johns-s/Fabok-a. 1-Red Hood & Batgirl app. 2,3-Joe Chill app.	2	4	6	8	10	12

BATMAN: TOYMAN
DC Comics: Nov, 1998 - No. 4, Feb, 1999 ($2.25, limited series)

1-4-Hama-s 3.00

BATMAN: TURNING POINTS
DC Comics: Jan, 2001 - No. 5, Jan, 2001 ($2.50, weekly limited series)

1-5: 2-Giella-a. 3-Kubert-c/Giordano-a. 4-Chaykin-c/Brent Anderson-a. 5-Pope-c/a 3.00
TPB (2007, $14.99) r/#1-5 15.00

BATMAN: TWO-FACE-CRIME AND PUNISHMENT (See Batman one-shots)

BATMAN: TWO-FACE STRIKES TWICE
DC Comics: 1993 - No. 2, 1993 ($4.95, 52 pgs.)

1,2-Flip book format w/Staton-a (G.A. side) 6.00

BATMAN UNIVERSE (Reprints serialized story from Walmart exclusive Batman Giant)
DC Comics: Sept, 2019 - No. 6, Feb, 2020 ($4.99, limited series)

1-6: 1-Ginny Hex debut. 2-Green Arrow & Vandal Savage app. 3,4,6-Jonah Hex app. 5.00

BATMAN UNSEEN
DC Comics: Early Dec, 2009 - No. 5, Feb, 2010 ($2.99, limited series)

1-5-Doug Moench-s/Kelley Jones-a/c. Black Mask app. 3.00
SC (2010, $14.99) r/#1-5 15.00

BATMAN: URBAN LEGENDS
DC Comics: May, 2021 - No. 23, Mar, 2023 ($7.99, squarebound, anthology)

1-23: 1-Short stories with Red Hood, The Outsiders, Harley & Ivy, Grifter. 11-16-Ace the Bat-Hound; Russell-s 8.00

BATMAN: VENGEANCE OF BANE (Also see Batman #491)
DC Comics: Jan, 1993; 1995 ($2.50, 68 pgs.)

	GD	VG	FN	VF	VF/NM	NM-
... Special 1 - Origin & 1st app. Bane; Dixon-s/Nolan & Barreto-a/Fabry-c	6	12	18	41	76	110
... Special 1 (2nd printing)	3	6	9	16	23	30
.... II nn (1995, $3.95)-sequel; Dixon-s/Nolan & Barreto-a/Fabry-c	2	4	6	11	16	20

BATMAN VS. BIGBY! A WOLF IN GOTHAM
DC Comics (Black Label): Nov, 2021 - No. 6, Apr, 2022 ($3.99, limited series)

1-6-Willingham-s/Level-a; Batman hunts Bigby Wolf from Fables 4.00

BATMAN VERSUS PREDATOR
DC Comics/Dark Horse Comics: 1991 - No. 3, 1992 ($4.95/$1.95, limited series) (1st DC/Dark Horse x-over)

	GD	VG	FN	VF	VF/NM	NM-
1 (Prestige format, $4.95)-1 & 3 contain 8 Batman/Predator trading cards; Andy & Adam Kubert-a; Suydam painted-c	2	4	6	9	12	15
1-3 (Regular format, $1.95)-No trading cards						4.00
2,3-(Prestige)-2-Extra pin-ups inside; Suydam-c						6.00
TPB (1993, $5.95, 132 pgs.)-r/#1-3 w/new introductions & forward plus new wraparound-c by Dave Gibbons	2	4	6	11	16	20

BATMAN VERSUS PREDATOR II: BLOODMATCH
DC Comics: Late 1994 - No. 4, 1995 ($2.50, limited series)

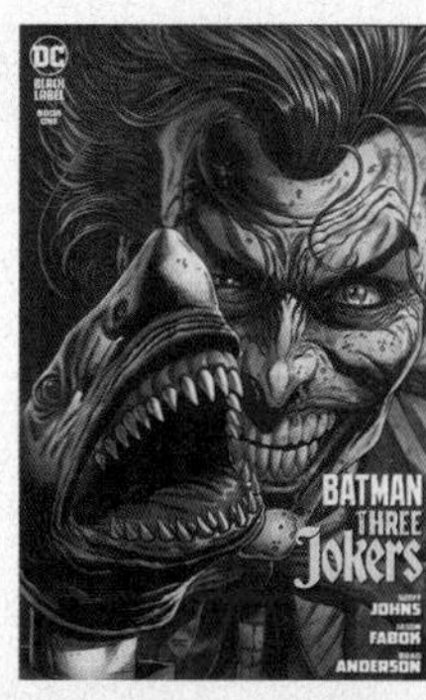

Batman: Three Jokers #1 © DC

Batman: White Knight #1 © DC

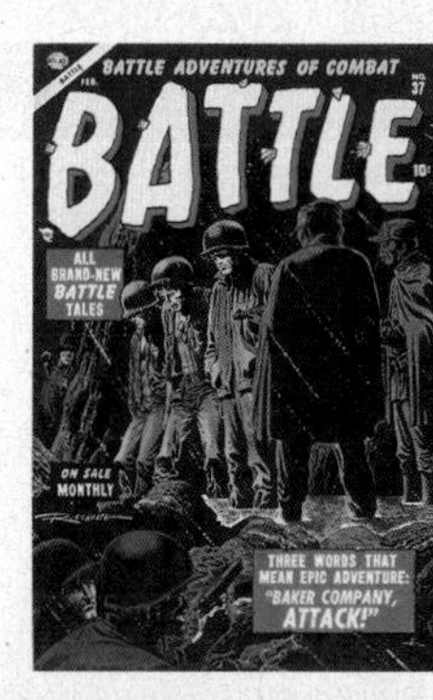

Battle #37 © MAR

	GD 2.0	VG 4.0	FN 6.0	VF 8.0	VF/NM 9.0	NM- 9.2
1-4-Huntress app.; Moench scripts; Gulacy-a						4.00
TPB (1995, $6.95)-r/#1-4	1	3	4	6	8	10

BATMAN VS. RA'S AL GHUL
DC Comics: Nov, 2019 - No. 6, Jun, 2021 ($3.99, limited series)

	GD	VG	FN	VF	VF/NM	NM-
1-6-Neal Adams-s/a; Deadman app.						4.00

BATMAN VS. ROBIN (Leads into Lazarus Planet mini-series)
DC Comics: Nov, 2022 - No. 5, Apr, 2023 ($5.99, limited series)

	GD	VG	FN	VF	VF/NM	NM-
1-5: 1-Waid-s/Asrar-a; Damian attacks; Alfred & Zatanna app. 5-Lazarus Planet epilogue						6.00

BATMAN VS. THE INCREDIBLE HULK (See DC Special Series No. 27)

BATMAN: WAR ON CRIME
DC Comics: Nov, 1999 ($9.95, treasury size, one-shot)

	GD	VG	FN	VF	VF/NM	NM-
nn-Painted art by Alex Ross; story by Alex Ross and Paul Dini						25.00

BATMAN: WHITE KNIGHT
DC Comics: Dec, 2017 - No. 8, Jul, 2018 ($3.99, limited series)

	GD	VG	FN	VF	VF/NM	NM-
1-7-Sean Murphy-s/a; Joker is cured. 2-7-Harley Quinn app.						4.00
8-($4.99) Murphy-s/a						5.00
... Presents Von Freeze (Black Label, 1/20, $5.99) Murphy-s/Janson-a; Fries flashback						6.00

BATMAN: WHITE KNIGHT PRESENTS HARLEY QUINN
DC Comics (Black Label): Dec, 2020 - No. 6, May, 2021 ($4.99, limited series)

	GD	VG	FN	VF	VF/NM	NM-
1-6-Katana Collins & Sean Murphy-s/Matteo Scalera-a						5.00

BATMAN: WHITE KNIGHT PRESENTS: RED HOOD
DC Comics (Black Label): Sept, 2022 - No. 6, ($4.99, limited series)

	GD	VG	FN	VF	VF/NM	NM-
1-2-Clay McCormack & Sean Murphy-s/Simone Di Meo-a						5.00

BATMAN WHO LAUGHS, THE (See Dark Nights: Metal)
DC Comics: Feb, 2019 - No. 7, Sept, 2019 ($4.99, limited series)

	GD	VG	FN	VF	VF/NM	NM-
1-7-Snyder-s/Jock-a; Joker and The Grim Knight app.						5.00
...: The Grim Knight 1 (5/19, $4.99) origin of the Grim Knight; Risso-a						5.00

BATMAN/ WILDCAT
DC Comics: Apr, 1997 - No. 3, June, 1997 ($2.25, mini-series)

	GD	VG	FN	VF	VF/NM	NM-
1-3: Dixon/Smith-s: 1-Killer Croc app.						4.00

BATMAN: YEAR 100
DC Comics: 2006 - No. 4, 2006 ($5.99, squarebound, limited series)

	GD	VG	FN	VF	VF/NM	NM-
1-4-Paul Pope-s/a/c						6.00
TPB (2007, $19.99) r/series						20.00

BAT MASTERSON (TV) (Also see Tim Holt #28)
Dell Publishing Co.: Aug-Oct, 1959; Feb-Apr, 1960 - No. 9, Nov-Jan, 1961-62

	GD	VG	FN	VF	VF/NM	NM-
Four Color 1013 (#1) (8-10/59)	11	22	33	72	154	235
2-9: Gene Barry photo-c on all. 2,3,6-Two different back-c exist; variants have a comic strip on the back-c	6	12	18	40	73	105

BAT-MITE
DC Comics: Aug, 2015 - No. 6, Jan, 2016 ($2.99, limited series)

	GD	VG	FN	VF	VF/NM	NM-
1-Jurgens-s/Howell-a; Batman app.						5.00
2-6: 4-Booster Gold app. 5-Inferior Five app.						3.00

BATS (See Tales Calculated to Drive You Bats)

BATS, CATS & CADILLACS
Now Comics: Oct, 1990 - No. 2, Nov, 1990 ($1.75)

	GD	VG	FN	VF	VF/NM	NM-
1,2: 1-Gustovich-a(i); Snyder-c						3.00

BAT-THING
DC Comics (Amalgam): June, 1997 ($1.95, one-shot)

	GD	VG	FN	VF	VF/NM	NM-
1-Hama-s/Damaggio & Sienkiewicz-a						5.00

BATTLE
Marvel/Atlas Comics(FPI #1-62/ Male #63 on): Mar, 1951 - No. 70, Jun, 1960

	GD	VG	FN	VF	VF/NM	NM-
1	81	162	243	518	884	1250
2	39	78	117	240	395	550
3-10: 4-1st Buck Pvt. O'Toole. 10-Pakula-a	32	64	96	188	307	425
11-20: 11-Check-a. 17-Classic Hitler story	27	54	81	158	259	360
21,23-Krigstein-a	28	56	84	165	270	375
22,24-36: 32-Tuska-a. 36-Everett-a	22	44	66	132	216	300
37-Kubert-a (Last precode, 2/55)	24	48	72	142	234	325
38-40,42-48	21	42	63	122	199	275
41,49: 41-Kubert/Moskowitz-a. 49-Davis-a	22	44	66	132	216	300
50-54,56-58: 56-Colan-a; Ayers-a	20	40	60	118	192	265
55-Williamson-a (5 pgs.)	22	44	66	132	216	300
59-Torres-a	21	42	63	124	202	275
60-62: 60,62-Combat Kelly app. 61-Combat Casey app.	22	44	66	132	216	300
63-Ditko-a	34	68	102	199	325	450
64-66-Kirby-a. 66-Davis-a; has story of Fidel Castro in pre-Communism days (an admiring profile)	32	64	96	188	307	425
67,68: 67-Williamson/Crandall-a (4 pgs.); Kirby, Davis-a. 68-Kirby/Williamson-a (4 pgs.); Kirby/Ditko-a	36	72	108	211	343	475
69,70: 69-Kirby-a. 70-Kirby/Ditko-a	32	64	96	188	307	425

NOTE: ***Andru** a-37. **Berg** a-8, 38, 14, 60-62. **Colan** a-19, 33, 43, 55. **Everett** a-36, 50, 70; c-56, 57. **Heath** a-6, 9, 13, 31, 69; c-6, 9, 12, 26, 35, 37. **Kirby** c-64-69. **Maneely** a-4-7, 31, 61; c-4, 22, 27, 33, 43, 48, 59, 61. **Orlando** a-47. **Powell** a-53, 55. **Reinman** a-4, 8-10, 14, 26, 32, 48. **Robinson** a-9, 39. **Romita** a-14, 26. **Severin** a-28, 32-34, 66-69; c-36, 50, 55. **Sinnott** a-33, 37, 63, 66. **Whitney** s-10.**Woodbridge** a-52, 55.*

BATTLE ACTION
Atlas Comics (NPI): Feb, 1952 - No. 12, 5/53; No. 13, 10/54 - No. 30, 8/57

	GD	VG	FN	VF	VF/NM	NM-
1-Pakula-a	55	110	165	352	601	850
2	30	60	90	177	289	400
3,4,6,7,9,10: 6-Robinson-c/a. 7-Partial nudity	20	40	60	117	189	260
5-Used in **POP**, pg. 93,94	21	42	63	122	199	275
8-Krigstein-a	22	44	66	132	216	300
11-15 (Last precode, 2/55)	20	40	60	114	182	250
16-30: 20-Romita-a. 22-Pakula-a. 27,30-Torres-a	18	36	54	107	169	230

NOTE: *Battle Brady app. 5-7, 10-12. **Berg** a-3. **Check** a-11. **Everett** a-7; c-13, 25. **Heath** a-3, 8, 18; c-3,15, 18, 21. **Maneely** a-1; c-5. **Reinman** a-1, 2, 20. **Robinson** a-6, 7; c-6. **Shores** a-7(2), 12, 20; c-11. **Sinnott** a-3, 27. **Woodbridge** a-28, 30.*

BATTLE ATTACK
Stanmor Publications: Oct, 1952 - No. 8, Dec, 1955

	GD	VG	FN	VF	VF/NM	NM-
1	19	38	57	111	176	240
2	12	24	36	67	94	120
3-8: 3-Hollingsworth-a	10	20	30	56	76	95

BATTLEAXES
DC Comics (Vertigo): May, 2000 - No. 4, Aug, 2000 ($2.50, limited series)

	GD	VG	FN	VF	VF/NM	NM-
1-4: Terry LaBan-s/Alex Horley-a						3.00

BATTLE BEASTS
Blackthorne Publishing: Feb, 1988 - No. 4, 1988 ($1.50/$1.75, B&W/color)

	GD	VG	FN	VF	VF/NM	NM-
1-4: 1-3- (B&W)-Based on Hasbro toys. 4-Color						3.00

BATTLE BEASTS
IDW Publishing: Jul, 2012 - No. 4, Oct, 2012 ($3.99, limited series)

	GD	VG	FN	VF	VF/NM	NM-
1-4-Curnow-s/Schiti-a; 2 covers on each						4.00

BATTLE BRADY (Formerly Men in Action No. 1-9; see 3-D Action)
Atlas Comics (IPC): No. 10, Jan, 1953 - No. 14, June, 1953

	GD	VG	FN	VF	VF/NM	NM-
10: 10-12-Syd Shores-c	37	74	111	222	361	500
11-Used in **POP**, pg. 95 plus B&W & color illos	24	48	72	142	234	325
12-14	20	40	60	114	182	250

BATTLE CHASERS
Image Comics (Cliffhanger): Apr, 1998 - No. 4, Dec, 1998; .
DC Comics (Cliffhanger): No. 5, May, 1999 - No. 8, May, 2001 ($2.50)
Image Comics: No. 9, Sept, 2001 ($3.50)

	GD	VG	FN	VF	VF/NM	NM-
Prelude (2/98)	2	4	6	8	10	12
Prelude Gold Ed.	3	6	9	14	19	24
1-Madureira & Sharrieff-s/Madureira-a(p)/Charest-c	2	4	6	10	14	18
1-American Ent. Ed. w/"racy" cover	2	4	6	8	10	12
1-Gold Edition	3	6	9	19	30	40
1-Chromium cover	4	8	12	23	37	50
1-2nd printing						4.00
2						5.00
2-Dynamic Forces BattleChrome cover	2	4	6	8	10	12
3-Red Monika cover by Madureira						4.00
4-8: 4-Four covers. 6-Back-up by Adam Warren-s/a. 7-Three covers (Madureira, Ramos, Campbell)						3.00
9-($3.50, Image) Flip cover/story by Adam Warren						4.00
...: A Gathering of Heroes HC ('99, $24.95) r/#1-5, Prelude, Frank Frazetta Fantasy Ill.; cover gallery						25.00
...: A Gathering of Heroes SC ('99, $14.95)						15.00
...Collected Edition 1,2 (11/98, 5/99, $5.95) 1-r/#1,2. 2-r/#3,4						6.00

BATTLE CLASSICS (See Cancelled Comic Cavalcade)
DC Comics: Sept-Oct, 1978 (44 pgs.)

	GD	VG	FN	VF	VF/NM	NM-
1-Kubert-r; new Kubert-c	2	4	6	8	10	12

BATTLE CRY
Stanmor Publications: 1952 (May) - No. 20, Sept, 1955

	GD	VG	FN	VF	VF/NM	NM-
1-Russian soldier flame broiled on cover	300	600	900	2070	3635	5200
2-(7/52)	15	30	45	88	137	185

	GD 2.0	VG 4.0	FN 6.0	VF 8.0	VF/NM 9.0	NM- 9.2
3,5-10: 8-Pvt. Ike begins, ends #13,17	14	28	42	78	112	145
4-Classic E.C. swipe	32	64	96	188	307	425
11-20	13	26	39	72	101	130

NOTE: *Hollingsworth a-9; c-20.*

BATTLEFIELD (War Adventures on the...)
Atlas Comics (ACI): April, 1952 - No. 11, May, 1953

	GD	VG	FN	VF	VF/NM	NM-
1-Pakula, Reinman-a	50	100	150	315	533	750
2-5: 2-Heath, Maneely, Pakula, Reinman-a	24	48	72	142	234	325
6-11	20	40	60	118	185	265

NOTE: *Colan a-11. Everett a-8. Heath a-1, 2, 5p,7; c-2, 8, 9, 11. Ravielli a-11.*

BATTLEFIELD ACTION (Formerly Foreign Intrigues)
Charlton Comics: No. 16, Nov, 1957 - No. 62, 2-3/66; No. 63, 7/80 - No. 89, 11/84

	GD	VG	FN	VF	VF/NM	NM-
V2#16	10	20	30	58	79	100
17,20-30: 29-D-Day story	7	14	21	35	43	50
18,19-Check-a (2 stories in #18)	4	8	12	25	40	55
31-34,36-62(1966): 40-Panel from this issue used by artist Roy Lichtenstein for famous painting. 55,61-Hitler app.	3	6	9	19	30	40
35-Hitler-c	5	10	15	31	53	75
63-80(1983-84)						5.00
81-83,85-89 (Low print run)	1	2	3	4	5	7
84-Kirby reprints; 3 stories	1	3	4	6	8	10

NOTE: *Montes/Bache a-43, 55, 62. Glanzman a-87r.*

BATTLEFIELDS
Dynamite Entertainment: 2008 - No. 9, 2010 ($3.50, limited series then numbered issues)

	NM-
...: Dear Billy 1-3 ('09 - No. 3, '09, $3.50) Ennis-s/Snejbjerg-a/Cassaday-c.1-Leach var-c	3.50
...: Happy Valley 1-3 ('09 - No. 3, '09, $3.50) Ennis-s/Holden-a/Leach-c	3.50
...: The Night Witches 1-3 ('08 - No. 3, '09, $3.50) Ennis-s/Braun-a/Cassaday-c; Russian female pilots in WW2. 1-Leach var-c	3.50
...: The Tankies 1-3 ('09 - No. 3, '09, $3.50) Ennis-s/Ezquerra-a/Cassaday-c. 1-Leach var-c	3.50
4-9: 4-6-Ezquerra-a/Leach-c. 7-9-Sequel to "The Night Witches"; Braun-a	3.50

BATTLEFIELDS (Volume 2)
Dynamite Entertainment: 2012 - No. 6, 2013 ($3.99, limited series)

	NM-
1-6: 1-3-Ennis-s/Ezquerra-a/Leach-c. 4-6-Braun-a	4.00

BATTLE FIRE
Aragon Magazine/Stanmor Publications: Apr, 1955 - No. 7, 1955

	GD	VG	FN	VF	VF/NM	NM-
1	19	38	57	111	176	240
2-(6/55)	12	24	36	69	97	125
3-7	11	22	33	62	86	110

BATTLE FOR A THREE DIMENSIONAL WORLD
3D Cosmic Publications: May, 1983 (20 pgs., slick paper w/stiff-c, $3.00)

	GD	VG	FN	VF	VF/NM	NM-
nn-Kirby c/a in 3-D; shows history of 3-D	2	4	6	8	11	14

BATTLEFORCE
Blackthorne Publishing: Nov, 1987 - No. 2, 1988 ($1.75, color/B&W)

	NM-
1,2: Based on game. 1-In color. 2-B&W	3.00

BATTLE FOR INDEPENDENTS, THE (Also See Cyblade/Shi & Shi/Cyblade: The Battle For Independents)
Image Comics (Top Cow Productions)/Crusade Comics: 1995 ($29.95)

	GD	VG	FN	VF	VF/NM	NM-
nn-Boxed set of all editions of Shi/Cyblade & Cyblade/Shi plus new variant	3	6	9	19	30	40

BATTLE FOR THE PLANET OF THE APES (See Power Record Comics)

BATTLEFRONT
Atlas Comics (PPI): June, 1952 - No. 48, Aug, 1957

	GD	VG	FN	VF	VF/NM	NM-
1-Heath-c	58	116	174	371	636	900
2-Robinson-a(4)	32	64	96	188	307	425
3-5-Robinson-a	26	52	78	154	252	350
6-10: Combat Kelly in No. 6-10. 6-Romita-a	22	44	66	128	209	290
11-22,24-28: 14,16-Battle Brady app. 22-Teddy Roosevelt & His Rough Riders story. 28-Last pre-code (2/55)	20	40	60	120	195	270
23,43-Check-a	21	42	63	122	199	275
29-39,41,44-47	20	40	60	114	182	250
40,42-Williamson-a	20	40	60	120	195	270
48-Crandall-a	20	40	60	117	189	260

NOTE: *Ayers a-18, 19, 25, 32, 35. Berg a-44. Colan a-21, 22, 24, 25, 32, 33-35, 38, 40, 42, 43, 45. Drucker a-28, 29. Everett a-44. Heath c-23, 26, 27, 29, 32. Maneely a-21-23, 26; c-2, 7, 13, 22, 24, 25, 34, 35, 41. Morisi a-42. Morrow a-41. Orlando a-47. Powell a-19, 21, 25, 29, 32, 40, 47. Robinson a-1-3, 4&5(4); c-4, 5. Robert Sale a-19, 24. Severin a-32; c-40, 42, 45. Sinnott a-26, 45, 48. Woodbridge a-45, 46.*

BATTLEFRONT
Standard Comics: No. 5, June, 1952

	GD	VG	FN	VF	VF/NM	NM-
5-Toth-a	20	40	60	118	192	265

BATTLE GODS: WARRIORS OF THE CHAAK
Dark Horse Comics: Apr, 2000 - No. 4, July, 2000 ($2.95)

	NM-
1-4-Francisco Ruiz Velasco-s/a	3.00

BATTLE GROUND
Atlas Comics (OMC): Sept, 1954 - No. 20, Sept, 1957

	GD	VG	FN	VF	VF/NM	NM-
1	43	86	129	271	461	650
2-Jack Katz-a (11/54)	24	48	72	142	234	325
3,4: 3-Jack Katz-a. 4-Last precode (3/55)	20	40	60	120	195	270
5-8,10 (3/56)	19	38	57	111	176	240
9,11,13,18: 9-Krigstein-a. 11,13,18-Williamson-a in each	20	40	60	117	189	260
12,15-17,19,20	18	36	54	105	165	225
14-Kirby-a	22	44	66	132	216	300

NOTE: *Ayers a-4, 6, 13, 16. Colan a-3, 11, 13. Drucker a-7, 12, 13, 20. Heath c-2, 3, 5, 7, 13. Maneely a-3, 14, 19; c-1, 6, 18, 19. Orlando a-17. Pakula a-6, 11. Reinman a-2. Severin a-4, 5, 12, 19. c-20. Sinnott a-7, 16. Tuska a-11.*

BATTLE HEROES
Stanley Publications: Sept, 1966 - No. 2, Nov, 1966 (25¢, squarebound giants)

	GD	VG	FN	VF	VF/NM	NM-
1	4	8	12	27	44	60
2	3	6	9	19	30	40

BATTLE HYMN
Image Comics: Jan, 2005 - No. 5, Oct, 2005 ($2.95/$2.99, limited series)

	NM-
1-5-WW2 super team; B. Clay Moore-s/Jeremy Haun-a; flip cover on #1-4	3.00

BATTLE OF THE BULGE (See Movie Classics)

BATTLE OF THE PLANETS (Based on syndicated cartoon by Sandy Frank)
Gold Key/Whitman No. 6 on: 6/79 - No. 10, 12/80

	GD	VG	FN	VF	VF/NM	NM-
1: Mortimer a-1-4,7-10	9	18	27	61	123	185
2-6,10	4	8	12	25	40	55
7-Low print run	8	16	24	51	96	140
8,9-Low print run: 8(11/80). 9-(3-pack only?)	6	12	18	38	69	100

BATTLE OF THE PLANETS (Also see Thundercats/...)
Image Comics (Top Cow): Aug, 2002 - No. 12, Sept, 2003 ($2.95/$2.99)

	NM-
1-($2.95) Alex Ross-c & art director; Tortosa-a(p); re-intro. G-Force	3.00
1-($5.95) Holofoil-c by Ross	6.00
2-11-($2.99) Ross-c on all	3.00
12-($4.99)	5.00
#1/2 (7/03, $2.99) Benitez-c; Alex Ross sketch pages	3.00
... Battle Book 1 (5/03, $4.99) background info on characters, equipment, stories	5.00
... : Jason 1 (7/03, $4.99) Ross-c; Erwin David-a; preview of Tomb Raider: Epiphany	5.00
... : Mark 1 (5/03, $4.99) Ross-c; Erwin David-a; preview of BotP: Jason	5.00
.../Thundercats 1 (Image/WildStorm, 5/03, $4.99) 2 covers by Ross & Campbell	5.00
.../Witchblade 1 (2/03, $5.95) Ross-c; Christina and Jo Chen-a	6.00
Vol. 1: Trial By Fire (2003, $7.99) r/#1-3	8.00
Vol. 2: Blood Red Sky (9/03, $16.95) r/#4-9	17.00
Vol. 3: Destroy All Monsters (11/03, $19.95) r/#10-12, ...: Jason, ...: Mark, .../Witchblade	20.00
Vol. 1: Digest (1/04, $9.99, 7-3/8x5", B&W) r/#1-9 & ...: Mark	10.00
Vol. 2: Digest (8/04, $9.99, B&W) r/#10-12, ...: Jason, ...: Manga #1-3, .../Witchblade	10.00

BATTLE OF THE PLANETS: MANGA
Image Comics (Top Cow): Nov, 2003 - No. 3, Jan, 2004 ($2.99, B&W)

	NM-
1-3-Edwin David-a/David Wohl-s; previews for Wanted & Tomb Raider #35	3.00

BATTLE OF THE PLANETS: PRINCESS
Image Comics (Top Cow): Nov, 2004 - No. 6, May, 2005 ($2.99, B&W, limited series)

	NM-
1-6-Tortosa-a/Wohl-s. 1-Ross-c. 2-Tortosa-c	3.00

BATTLE POPE
Image Comics: June, 2005 - No. 14, Apr, 2007 ($2.99/$3.50, reprints 2000 B&W series in color)

	NM-
1-5-Kirkman-s/Moore-a	3.50
6-10,12-14-($3.50) 14-Wedding	3.50
11-($4.99) Christmas issue	5.00
... Vol. 1: Genesis TPB (2006, $12.95) r/#1-4; sketch pages	13.00
... Vol. 2: Mayhem TPB (2006, $12.99) r/#5-8; sketch pages	13.00
... Vol. 3: Pillow Talk TPB (2007, $12.99) r/#9-11; sketch pages	13.00

BATTLEPUG
Image Comics: Sept, 2019 - No. 5, Jan, 2020 ($3.99)

	NM-
1-5-Mike Norton-s/a	4.00

BATTLER BRITTON (British comics character who debuted in 1956)
DC Comics (WildStorm): Sept, 2006 - No. 5, Jan, 2007 ($2.99, limited series)

	NM-
1-5-WWII fighter pilots; Garth Ennis-s/Colin Wilson-a	3.00
TPB (2007, $19.99) r/#1-5; background of the character's British origins in the 1950s	20.00

BATTLE REPORT
Ajax/Farrell Publications: Aug, 1952 - No. 6, June, 1953

	GD	VG	FN	VF	VF/NM	NM-
1	19	38	57	111	176	240
2-6	12	24	36	69	97	125

BATTLE SCARS
Marvel Comics: Jan, 2012 - No. 6, Jun, 2012 ($2.99, limited series)

	GD	VG	FN	VF	VF/NM	NM-
1-Intro. Marcus Johnson and Cheese (later ID'd as Phil Coulson in #6); Eaton-a/Pagulayan-c	2	4	6	8	10	12
2-5: 4-Deadpool app. 5-Nick Fury app.						4.00
6-Marcus Johnson becomes Nick Fury Jr.; resembles movie version; Cheese joins SHIELD and is ID'd as Agent Coulson	2	4	6	8	10	12

BATTLE SQUADRON
Stanmor Publications: April, 1955 - No. 5, Dec, 1955

	GD	VG	FN	VF	VF/NM	NM-
1	16	32	48	94	147	200
2-5: 3-Iwo Jima & flag-c	11	22	33	62	86	110

BATTLESTAR GALACTICA (TV) (Also see Marvel Comics Super Special #8)
Marvel Comics Group: Mar, 1979 - No. 23, Jan, 1981

	GD	VG	FN	VF	VF/NM	NM-
1: 1-5 adapt TV episodes	3	6	9	16	24	32
2-23: 1-3-Partial-r	2	4	6	8	10	12

NOTE: *Austin c-9i, 10i. Golden c-18. Simonson a(p)-4, 5, 11-13, 15-20, 22, 23; c(p)-4, 5,11-17, 19, 20, 22, 23.*

BATTLESTAR GALACTICA (TV) (Also see Asylum)
Maximum Press: July, 1995 - No. 4, Nov, 1995 ($2.50, limited series)

	NM-
1-4: Continuation of 1978 TV series	4.00
Trade paperback (12/95, $12.95)-reprints series	13.00

BATTLESTAR GALACTICA (1978 TV series)
Realm Press: Dec, 1997 - No. 5, July, 1998 ($2.99)

	NM-
1-5-Chris Scalf-s/painted-a/c	3.00
...Search For Sanctuary (9/98, $2.99) Scalf & Kuhoric-s	3.00
...Search For Sanctuary Special (4/00, $3.99) Kuhoric-s/Scalf & Scott-a	4.00

BATTLESTAR GALACTICA (2003-2009 TV series)
Dynamite Entertainment: No. 0, 2006 - No. 12, 2007 (25¢/$2.99)

	NM-
0-(25¢-c) Two covers; Pak-s/Raynor-a	3.00
1-($2.99) Covers by Turner, Tan, Raynor & photo-c; Pak-s/Raynor-a	3.00
2-12-Four covers on each	3.00
... Pegasus (2007, $4.99) story of Battlestar Pegasus & Admiral Cain; 2 covers	5.00
... Volume 1 HC (2007, $19.99) r/#0-4; cover gallery; Raynor sketch pages; commentary	20.00
... Volume 1 TPB (2007, $14.99) r/#0-4; cover gallery; Raynor sketch pages; commentary	15.00
... Volume 2 HC (2007, $19.99) r/#5-8; cover gallery; Raynor sketch pages	20.00
... Volume 2 TPB (2007, $14.99) r/#5-8; cover gallery; Raynor sketch pages	15.00

BATTLESTAR GALACTICA, (Classic...) (1978 TV series characters)

Battlefront #26 © MAR

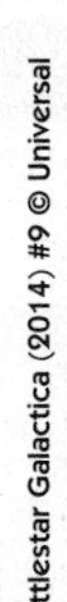
Battlestar Galactica (2014) #9 © Universal

Batwing #16 © DC

	GD	VG	FN	VF	VF/NM	NM-
	2.0	4.0	6.0	8.0	9.0	9.2

Dynamite Entertainment: 2006 - No. 5, 2006 ($2.99)

1-5: 1-Two covers by Dorman & Caldwell; Rafael-a. 2-Two covers 3.00

BATTLESTAR GALACTICA, (Classic...) (Volume 2) (1978 TV series characters)
Dynamite Entertainment: 2013 - No. 12, 2014 ($3.99)

1-12: 1-5-Two covers by Alex Ross & Chris Eliopoulos on each; Abnett & Lanning-s 4.00

BATTLESTAR GALACTICA, (Classic...) (Volume 3) (1978 TV series characters)
Dynamite Entertainment: 2016 - No. 5, 2016 ($3.99)

1-5: 1-Cullen Bunn-s/Alex Sanchez-a; multiple covers 4.00

BATTLESTAR GALACTICA, (Classic...) (Volume 4) (1978 TV series characters)
Dynamite Entertainment: No. 0, 2018 - No. 5, 2019 ($3.99)

0-(35¢, listed as #1 in indicia) John Jackson Miller-s/Daniel HDR-a; multiple covers 3.00
1-5-Multiple covers on each 4.00

BATTLESTAR GALACTICA: APOLLO'S JOURNEY (1978 TV series)
Maximum Press: Apr, 1996 - No. 3, June, 1996 ($2.95, limited series)

1-3: Richard Hatch scripts 4.00

BATTLESTAR GALACTICA: BSG VS. BSG (1978 characters meet 2003 characters)
Dynamite Entertainment: 2018 - No. 6, 2018 ($3.99, limited series)

1-6-Peter David-s; multiple covers. 1-3-Johnny DesJardins-a. 4-6-Edu Menna-a 4.00

BATTLESTAR GALACTICA: CYLON APOCALYPSE (1978 TV series characters)
Dynamite Entertainment: 2007 - No. 4, 2007 ($2.99, limited series)

1-4-Carlos Rafael-a; 4 covers on each 3.00
TPB (2007, $14.99) r/series with cover gallery 15.00

BATTLESTAR GALACTICA: CYLON WAR (2003-2009 TV series)
Dynamite Entertainment: 2009 - No. 4, 2010 ($3.99, limited series)

1-3-First cylon war 40 years before the Caprica attack; Raynor-a; 2 covers 4.00

BATTLESTAR GALACTICA 1880, STEAMPUNK... (1978 TV series characters)
(Title changes from "(Classic) Battlestar Galactica Vol. 2" after #1)
Dynamite Entertainment: 2014 - No. 4, 2014 ($3.99, limited series)

1-4-Tony Lee-s/Aneke-a; multiple covers 4.00

BATTLESTAR GALACTICA: GHOSTS (2003-2009 TV series)
Dynamite Entertainment: 2008 - No. 4, 2009 ($4.99, 40 pgs., limited series)

1-4-Intro. of the Ghost Squadron; Jerwa-s/Lau-a/Calero-c 5.00

BATTLESTAR GALACTICA: GODS AND MONSTERS (2003-2009 TV series)
Dynamite Entertainment: 2016 - No. 5, 2017 ($3.99, limited series)

1-5-Karl Kesel-s/Alec Morgan & Dan Schkade-a 4.00

BATTLESTAR GALACTICA: JOURNEY'S END (1978 TV series)
Maximum Press: Aug, 1996 - No. 4, Nov, 1996 ($2.99, limited series)

1-4-Continuation of the T.V. series 4.00

BATTLESTAR GALACTICA: ORIGINS (2003-2009 TV series)
Dynamite Entertainment: 2007 - No. 11, 2008 ($3.50)

1-11: 1-4-Baltar's origin; multiple covers. 5-8-Adama's origin. 9-11-Starbuck & Helo 3.50

BATTLESTAR GALACTICA: SEASON III
Realm Press: June/July, 1999 - No. 3, Sept, 1999 ($2.99)

1-3: 1-Kuhoric-s/Scalf & Scott-a; two covers by Scalf & Jae Lee. 2,3-Two covers 3.00
Gallery (4/00, $3.99) short story and pin-ups 4.00
1999 Tour Book (5/99, $2.99) 3.00
1999 Tour Book Convention Edition (6.99) 7.00
...Special: Centurion Prime (12/99, $3.99) Kuhoric-s 4.00

BATTLESTAR GALACTICA: SEASON ZERO (2003-2009 TV series)
Dynamite Entertainment: 2007 - No. 12, 2008 ($2.99)

1-12-Set 2 years before the Cylon attack; multiple covers 3.00
.../The Lone Ranger 2007 Free Comic Book Day Edition; flip book with Cassaday Lone Ranger-c 3.00

BATTLESTAR GALACTICA: SIX (2003-2009 TV series)
Dynamite Entertainment: No. 1, 2014 - No. 5, 2015 ($3.99, limited series)

1-5: 1-J.T. Krul-s/Igor Lima-a; multiple covers. 3-5-Rodolfo-a. 5-Baltar app. 4.00

BATTLESTAR GALACTICA: SPECIAL EDITION (TV)
Maximum Press: Jan, 1997 ($2.99, one-shot)

1-Fully painted; Scalf-c/s/a; r/Asylum 3.00

BATTLESTAR GALACTICA: STARBUCK (TV)
Maximum Press: Dec, 1995 - No. 3, Mar, 1996 ($2.50, limited series)

1-3 4.00

BATTLESTAR GALACTICA: STARBUCK, (Classic...) (1978 TV series characters)
Dynamite Entertainment: 2013 - No. 4, 2014 ($3.99, limited series)

1-4-Tony Lee-s/Eman Casallos-a. 1-Childhood flashback 4.00

BATTLESTAR GALACTICA: THE COMPENDIUM (TV)
Maximum Press: Feb, 1997 ($2.99, one-shot)

1 3.00

BATTLESTAR GALACTICA: THE DEATH OF APOLLO, (Classic...) (1978 TV series)
Dynamite Entertainment: 2014 - No. 6, 2015 ($3.99, limited series)

1-6-Dan Abnett-s/Dietrich Smith-a; multiple covers on each 4.00

BATTLESTAR GALACTICA: THE ENEMY WITHIN (TV)
Maximum Press: Nov, 1995 - No. 3, Feb, 1996 ($2.50, limited series)

1-3: 3-Indicia reads Feb, 1995 in error. 4.00

BATTLESTAR GALACTICA: THE FINAL FIVE (2003 series)
Dynamite Entertainment: 2009 - No. 4, 2009 ($3.99, limited series)

1-4-Raynor-a; 2 covers on each 4.00

BATTLESTAR GALACTICA: TWILIGHT COMMAND (2003 series)
Dynamite Entertainment: 2019 - No. 5, 2019 ($3.99, limited series)

1-5-Moreci-s/Tamura-a; 2 covers; takes place during season 3 of the 2003 series 4.00

BATTLESTAR GALACTICA ZAREK (2003 series)
Dynamite Entertainment: 2007 - No. 4, 2007 ($3.50, limited series)

1-4-Origin story of political activist Tom Zarek; 2 covers on each 3.50

BATTLE STORIES (See XMas Comics)
Fawcett Publications: Jan, 1952 - No. 11, Sept, 1953

	GD	VG	FN	VF	VF/NM	NM-
1-Evans-a (Korean War)	21	42	63	122	199	275
2	14	28	42	78	112	145
3-11	11	22	33	62	86	110

BATTLE STORIES
Super Comics: 1963 - 1964

	GD	VG	FN	VF	VF/NM	NM-
Reprints #10-13,15-18: 10-r/U.S Tank Commandos #? 11-r/? 11, 12,17-r/Monty Hall #?; 13-Kintsler-a (1pg).15-r/American Air Forces #7 by Powell; Bolle-r. 18-U.S. Fighting Air Force #?	2	4	6	10	14	18

BATTLETECH (See Blackthorne 3-D Series #41 for 3-D issue)
Blackthorne Publishing: Oct, 1987 - No. 6, 1988 ($1.75/$2.00)

1-6: Based on game. 1-Color. 2-Begin B&W 3.00
Annual 1 ($4.50, B&W) 5.00

BATTLETECH
Malibu Comics: Feb, 1995 ($2.95)

0 3.00

BATTLETECH FALLOUT
Malibu Comics: Dec, 1994 - No. 4, Mar, 1995 ($2.95)

1-4-Two edi. exist #1; normal logo 3.00
1-Gold version w/foil logo stamped "Gold Limited Edition 8.00
1-Full-c holographic limited edition 6.00

BATTLETIDE (Death's Head II & Killpower...)
Marvel Comics UK, Ltd.: Dec, 1992 - No. 4, Mar, 1993 ($1.75, mini-series)

1-4: Wolverine, Psylocke, Dark Angel app. 3.00

BATTLETIDE II (Death's Head II & Killpower...)
Marvel Comics UK, Ltd.: Aug, 1993 - No. 4, Nov, 1993 ($1.75, mini-series)

1-($2.95)-Foil embossed logo 4.00
2-4: 2-Hulk-c/story 3.00

BATVARK (Reprints from Cerebus in Hell)
Aardvark-Vanaheim: Aug, 2017 ($4.00, B&W)

1-Cerebus figures placed over original Gustave Doré artwork of Hell; Batman #1-c swipe 4.00
... A Poet in the Family (4/22, $4.00) Batman #428-c swipe 4.00
... Penis (9/20, $4.00) Homage to Batman: Damned; Michelangelo's David app. 4.00
... XXXXX (1/21, $4.00) 2nd printing 4.00

BATWING (DC New 52)
DC Comics: Nov, 2011 - No. 34, Oct, 2014 ($2.99)

1-24: 1-3,5-Judd Winick-s/Ben Oliver-a. 4-Origin; Chriscross-a. 9-Night of the Owls 3.00
25-($3.99) Zero Year tie-in; Luke Fox's first meeting with Batman; Conner-c 4.00
26-34: 26,27-Darwyn Cooke-c 3.00
#0 (11/12, $2.99) origin of David Zavimbe; Winick-s/To-a 3.00
...: Futures End 1 (11/14, $2.99, regular-c) Five years later; Panosian-c 3.00
...: Futures End 1 (11/14, $3.99, 3-D cover) 4.00

BATWOMAN (See 52 #9 & 11 for debut and Detective Comics #854-860)

DC Comics: No. 0, Jan, 2011; No. 1, Nov, 2011 - No. 40, May, 2015 ($2.99)

0-(1/11) Williams III-s; art by Williams III and Reeder; Williams III-c 3.00
0-(1/11)-Variant-c by Reeder 5.00
1-New DC 52; Williams III-a; Williams III & Blackman-s; Bette Kane app. 5.00
2-24: 2-Cameron Chase returns. 6-8-Reeder-a/c. 9-11,15,18-20,22,23-McCarthy-a. 12-17-Wonder Woman app. 21-Francavilla-a; Killer Croc app. 3.00
25-($3.99) Zero Year tie-in; Maggie Sawyer & Bruce Wayne app. 4.00
26-40: 26-31-Wolf Spider. 35-Etrigan, Clayface, Ragman & Alice app. 3.00
#0 (11/12, $2.99) Flashback to Kate's training; Williams III-a 3.00
Annual 1 (6/14, $4.99) Continued from #24; Batman app.; McCarthy & Moritat-a 5.00
Annual 2 (6/15, $4.99) Continued from #40; Jeanty-c/a 5.00
... Elegy The Deluxe Edition HC (2010, $24.99, d.j.) r/Detective #854-860; gallery of variant covers, sketch art and script pages; intro. by Rachel Maddow 25.00
... Elegy SC (2011, $17.99) same contents as Deluxe HC 18.00
...: Futures End 1 (11/14, $2.99, regular-c) Five years later; Red Alice app. 3.00
...: Futures End 1 (11/14, $3.99, 3-D cover) 4.00

BATWOMAN (DC Rebirth)
DC Comics: May, 2017 - No. 18, Oct, 2018 ($2.99/$3.99)

1-18: 1-($3.99) M. Bennett & Tynion IV-s/Epting-a; covers by Epting & JG Jones. 6-Arlem-a 8-10-Scarecrow app. 13-Alice returns 4.00
...: Rebirth 1 (4/17, $2.99) Bennett & Tynion-s/Epting-a; origin re-capped 3.00

BATWOMAN/SUPERGIRL: WORLD'S FINEST GIANT
DC Comics: 2019 - Present ($4.99, 100 pgs., squarebound, Mass Market & Direct Market editions exist for each issue, with different covers)

1-Three new stories plus reprints; Alice app.; Joëlle Jones-c 5.00

BAY CITY JIVE
DC Comics (WildStorm): Jul, 2001 - No. 3, Sept, 2001 ($2.95, limited series)

1-3: Intro Sugah Rollins in 1970s San Francisco; Layman-s/Johnson-a 3.00

BAYWATCH COMIC STORIES (TV) (Magazine)
Acclaim Comics (Armada): May, 1996 - No. 4, 1997 ($4.95) (Photo-c on all)

1-Photo comics based on TV show 3 6 9 14 20 25
2-4 2 4 6 8 10 12

BEACH BLANKET BINGO (See Movie Classics)

BEAGLE BOYS, THE (Walt Disney)(See The Phantom Blot)
Gold Key: 11/64; No. 2, 11/65; No. 3, 8/66 - No. 47, 2/79 (See WDC&S #134)

1 5 10 15 35 63 90
2-5 3 6 9 17 26 35
6-10 3 6 9 15 22 28
11-20: 11,14,19-r 2 4 6 11 16 20
21-30: 27-r 2 4 6 8 11 14
31-47 1 3 4 6 8 10

BEAGLE BOYS VERSUS UNCLE SCROOGE
Gold Key: Mar, 1979 - No. 12, Feb, 1980

1 2 4 6 9 13 16
2-12: 9-r 1 2 3 5 6 8

BEANBAGS
Ziff-Davis Publ. Co. (Approved Comics): Winter, 1951 - No. 2, Spring, 1952

1,2 17 34 51 78 154 210

BEANIE THE MEANIE
Fago Publications: No. 3, May, 1959

3 7 14 21 35 43 50

BEANY AND CECIL (TV) (Bob Clampett's...)
Dell Publishing Co.: Jan, 1952 - 1955; July-Sept, 1962 - No. 5, July-Sept, 1963

Four Color 368 25 50 75 175 388 600
Four Color 414,448,477,530,570,635(1/55) 14 28 42 96 211 325
01-057-209 (#1) 12 24 36 84 185 285
2-5 9 18 27 63 129 195

BEAR COUNTRY (Disney)
Dell Publishing Co.: No. 758, Dec, 1956

Four Color 758-Movie 5 10 15 34 60 85

BEAST (See X-Men)
Marvel Comics: May, 1997 - No. 3, 1997 ($2.50, mini-series)

1-3-Giffen-s/Nocon-a 4.00

BEAST BOY (See Titans)
DC Comics: Jan, 2000 - No. 4, Apr, 2000 ($2.95, mini-series)

1-4-Justiano-c/a; Raab & Johns-s 4.00

BEASTS OF BURDEN (See Dark Horse Book of Hauntings, ...Monsters, ...The Dead, ...Witchcraft)
Dark Horse Comics: Sept, 2009 - No. 4, Dec, 2009 ($2.99, limited series)

1-4-Evan Dorkin-s/Jill Thompson-a/c 3.00
...: Hunters & Gatherers (3/14, $3.50) Evan Dorkin-s/Jill Thompson-a/c 3.50
...: Neighborhood Watch (8/12, $3.50) Evan Dorkin-s/Jill Thompson-a/c 3.50
...: What the Cat Dragged In (5/16, $3.99) Evan Dorkin & Sarah Dyer-s/Jill Thompson-a/c 4.00
Volume 1: Animal Rites HC (6/10, $19.99) r/#1-4 & short stories from Dark Horse Books 20.00

BEASTS OF BURDEN: OCCUPIED TERRITORY
Dark Horse Comics: Apr, 2021 - No. 4, Jul, 2021 ($3.99, limited series)

1-4-Evan Dorkin & Sarah Dyer-s/Benjamin Dewey-a/c 4.00

BEASTS OF BURDEN: THE PRESENCE OF OTHERS
Dark Horse Comics: May, 2019 - No. 2, Jun, 2019 ($3.99, limited series)

1,2-Evan Dorkin-s/Jill Thompson-a/c 4.00

BEASTS OF BURDEN: WISE DOGS AND ELDRITCH MEN
Dark Horse Comics: Aug, 2018 - No. 4, Dec, 2018 ($3.99, limited series)

1-4-Evan Dorkin-s/Benjamin Dewey-a/c 4.00

BEATLES, THE (See Girls' Romances #109, Go-Go, Heart Throbs #101, Herbie #5, Howard the Duck Mag. #4, Laugh #166, Marvel Comics Super Special #4, My Little Margie #54, Not Brand Echh, Strange Tales #130, Summer Love, Superman's Pal Jimmy Olsen #79, Teen Confessions #37, Tippy's Friends & Tippy Teen)

BEATLES, THE (Life Story)
Dell Publishing Co.: Sept-Nov, 1964 (35¢)

1-(Scarce)-Stories with color photo pin-ups; Paul S. Newman-s/Joe Sinnott-a; photo-c 50 100 150 400 900 1400

BEATLES EXPERIENCE, THE
Revolutionary Comics: Mar, 1991 - No. 8, 1991 ($2.50, B&W, limited series)

1-8: 1-Gold logo 5.00

BEATLES YELLOW SUBMARINE (See Movie Comics under Yellow...)

BEAUTIFUL KILLER
Black Bull Comics: Sept., 2002 - No. 3, Jan, 2003 ($2.99, limited series)

...Limited Preview Edition (5/02, $5.00) preview pgs. & creator interviews 5.00
1-Noto-a/Palmiotti-s; Hughes-c; intro Brigit Cole 3.00
2,3: 2-Jusko-c. 3-Noto-c 3.00
TPB (5/03, $9.99) r/#1-3; cover gallery and Adam Hughes sketch pages 10.00

BEAUTIFUL PEOPLE
Slave Labor Graphics: Apr, 1994 ($4.95, 8-1/2x11", one-shot)

nn 5.00

BEAUTIFUL STORIES FOR UGLY CHILDREN
DC Comics (Piranha Press): 1989 - No. 30, 1991 ($2.00/$2.50, B&W, mature)

Vol. 1 2 4 6 11 16 20
2-8 1 2 3 5 6 8
9-20: 12-$2.50-c begins 5.00
21-25 5.00
26-29-(Lower print run) 1 3 4 6 8 10
30-(Lower print run) 2 4 6 10 14 18
A Cotton Candy Autopsy ($12.95, B&W)-Reprints 1st two volumes 20.00

BEAUTY, THE (Also see Pilot Season: The Beauty)
Image Comics: Aug, 2015 - Sept, 2021 ($3.50/$3.99)

1-6-Jeremy Haun & Jason Hurley-s/Haun-a. 1-Three covers; reprints Pilot Season issue 4.00
7-29-($3.99) 7-Huddleston-a. 8-10-Weldele-a. 12-Haun-a. 13-29-Nachlik-a 4.00
... All Good Things (9/21, $4.99) Conclusion of the series 5.00

BEAUTY AND THE BEAST, THE
Marvel Comics Group: Jan, 1985 - No. 4, Apr, 1985 (limited series)

1-4: Dazzler & the Beast from X-Men; Sienkiewicz-c on all 5.00

BEAUTY AND THE BEAST (Graphic novel)(Also see Cartoon Tales & Disney's New Adventures of...)
Disney Comics: 1992

nn-($4.95, prestige edition)-Adapts animated film 7.00
nn-($2.50, newsstand edition) 4.00

BEAUTY AND THE BEAST
Disney Comics: Sept., 1992 - No. 2, 1992 ($1.50, limited series)

1,2 4.00

BEAUTY AND THE BEAST: PORTRAIT OF LOVE (TV)
First Comics: May, 1989 - No. 2, Mar, 1990 ($5.95, 60 pgs., squarebound)

1,2: 1-Based on TV show, Wendy Pini-a/scripts. 2-...: Night of Beauty; by Wendy Pini 6.00

BEAVER VALLEY (Movie)(Disney)
Dell Publishing Co.: No. 625, Apr, 1955

Four Color 625 6 12 18 37 66 95

BEAVIS AND BUTTHEAD (MTV's...)(TV cartoon)
Marvel Comics: Mar, 1994 - No. 28, June, 1996 ($1.95)

1-Silver ink-c. 1, 2-Punisher & Devil Dinosaur app. 3 6 9 14 19 24
1-2nd printing 4.00
2,3: 2-Wolverine app. 3-Man-Thing, Spider-Man, Venom, Carnage, Mary Jane & Stan Lee cameos; John Romita, Sr. art (2 pgs.) 1 2 3 5 6 8
4-28: 5-War Machine, Thor, Loki, Hulk, Captain America & Rhino cameos. 6-Psylocke, Polaris, Daredevil & Bullseye app. 7-Ghost Rider & Sub-Mariner app. 8-Quasar & Eon app. 9-Prowler & Nightwatch app. 11-Black Widow app. 12-Thunderstrike & Bloodaxe app. 13-Night Thrasher app. 14-Spider-Man 2099 app. 15-Warlock app. 16-X-Factor app. 25-Juggernaut app. 5.00

BECK & CAUL INVESTIGATIONS
Gauntlet Comics (Caliber): Jan, 1994 - No. 5, 1995? ($2.95, B&W)

1-5 3.00
Special 1 ($4.95) 5.00

BEDKNOBS AND BROOMSTICKS (See Walt Disney Showcase No. 6 & 50)

BEDLAM!
Eclipse Comics: Sept, 1985 - No. 2, Sept, 1985 (B&W-r in color)

1,2: Bissette-a 4.00

BEDTIME STORIES FOR IMPRESSIONABLE CHILDREN
Moonstone Books/American Mythology: Nov, 2010; Feb, 2017 ($3.99, B&W)

1-(11/10) Short story anthology; Vaughn, Kuhoric & Tinnell-s; 3 covers 4.00
1-(2/17) Short story anthology; Vaughn, Shooter & Nelms-s; 4 covers 4.00

BEDTIME STORY (See Cinema Comics Herald)

BEE AND PUPPYCAT
Boom Entertainment (KaBOOM!): May, 2014 - No. 11, Apr, 2016 ($3.99)

1-11: Multiple covers on each. 1,2-Natasha Allegri-s/a 4.00

BEELZELVIS
Slave Labor Graphics: Feb, 1994 ($2.95, B&W, one-shot)

1 3.00

BEEP BEEP, THE ROAD RUNNER (TV) (See Dell Giant Comics Bugs Bunny Vacation Funnies #8 for 1st app.) (Also see Daffy & Kite Fun Book)
Dell Publishing Co./Gold Key No. 1-88/Whitman No. 89 on: July, 1958 - No. 14, Aug-Oct, 1962; Oct, 1966 - No. 105, 1984

Four Color 918 (#1, 7/58) 14 28 42 96 211 325
Four Color 1008,1046 (11-1/59-60) 8 16 24 54 102 150
4(2-4/60)-14(Dell) 7 14 21 46 86 125

Batwoman #17 © DC

Bee and Puppycat #6 © Frederator

Before Watchmen: Nite Owl #2 © DC

	GD 2.0	VG 4.0	FN 6.0	VF 8.0	VF/NM 9.0	NM- 9.2
1(10/66, Gold Key)	6	12	18	42	79	115
2-5	4	8	12	27	44	60
6-14	3	6	9	19	30	40
15-18,20-40	3	6	9	16	23	30
19-With pull-out poster	4	8	12	25	40	55
41-50	3	6	9	14	19	24
51-70	2	4	6	9	13	16
71-88	2	3	4	6	8	10
89,90,94-101: 100(3/82), 101(4/82)	2	4	6	8	10	12
91(8/80), 92(9/80), 93 (3-pack?) (low printing)	8	16	24	51	96	140
102-105 (All #90189 on-c; nd or date code; pre-pack) 102(6/83), 103(7/83), 104(5/84), 105(6/84)	3	6	9	19	30	40
#63-2970 (Now Age Books/Pendulum Pub. Comic Digest, 1971, 75¢, 100 pages, B&W) collection of one-page gags	4	8	12	27	44	60

NOTE: *See March of Comics #351, 353, 375, 387, 397, 416, 430, 442, 455. #5, 8-10, 35, 53, 59-62, 68-r; 96-102, 104 are 1/3-r.*

BEETLE BAILEY (See Giant Comic Album, Sarge Snorkel; also Comics Reading Libraries in the Promotional Comics section)
Dell Publishing Co./Gold Key #39-53/King #54-66/Charlton #67-119/Gold Key #120-131/ Whitman #132: #459, 5/53 - #38, 5-7/62; #39, 11/62 - #53, 5/66; #54, 8/66 - #65, 12/67;#67, 2/69 - #119, 11/76; #120, 4/78 - #132, 4/80

	GD 2.0	VG 4.0	FN 6.0	VF 8.0	VF/NM 9.0	NM- 9.2
Four Color 469 (#1)-By Mort Walker	13	26	39	89	195	300
Four Color 521,552,622	7	14	21	49	92	135
5(2-4/56)-10(5-7/57)	5	10	15	35	63	90
11-20(4-5/59)	4	8	12	28	47	65
21-38(5-7/62)	3	6	9	20	31	42
39-53(5/66)	3	6	9	17	26	35
54-65	3	6	9	16	23	30
66 (only exists as U.S. published complimentary copies given away overseas)	3	6	9	16	23	30
67-69: 69-Last 12¢ issue	3	6	9	14	20	25
70-99	2	4	6	9	13	16
100	2	4	6	11	16	20
101-111,114-119	1	3	4	6	8	10
112,113-Byrne illos. (4 each)	2	4	6	9	12	18
120-132	1	2	3	4	5	7

BEETLE BAILEY
Harvey Comics: V2#1, Sept, 1992 - V2#9, Aug, 1994 ($1.25/$1.50)

	GD 2.0	VG 4.0	FN 6.0	VF 8.0	VF/NM 9.0	NM- 9.2
V2#1						5.00
2-9-($1.50)						3.50
Big Book 1(11/92),2(5/93)(Both $1.95, 52 pgs.)						4.00
Giant Size V2#1(10/92),2(3/93)(Both $2.25,68 pgs.)						4.00

BEETLEJUICE (TV)
Harvey Comics: Oct, 1991 ($1.25)

	GD 2.0	VG 4.0	FN 6.0	VF 8.0	VF/NM 9.0	NM- 9.2
1	4	8	12	25	40	55

BEETLEJUICE CRIMEBUSTERS ON THE HAUNT
Harvey Comics: Sept, 1992 - No. 3, Jan, 1993 ($1.50, limited series)

	GD 2.0	VG 4.0	FN 6.0	VF 8.0	VF/NM 9.0	NM- 9.2
1-3	3	6	9	14	20	25

BEE 29, THE BOMBARDIER
Neal Publications: Feb, 1945

	GD 2.0	VG 4.0	FN 6.0	VF 8.0	VF/NM 9.0	NM- 9.2
1-(Funny animal)	40	80	120	246	411	575

BEFORE THE FANTASTIC FOUR: BEN GRIMM AND LOGAN
Marvel Comics: July, 2000 - No. 3, Sept, 2000 ($2.99, limited series)

1-3-The Thing and Wolverine app.; Hama-s — 3.00

BEFORE THE FANTASTIC FOUR: REED RICHARDS
Marvel Comics: Sept, 2000 - No. 3, Dec, 2000 ($2.99, limited series)

1-3-Peter David-s/Duncan Fegredo-c/a — 3.00

BEFORE THE FANTASTIC FOUR: THE STORMS
Marvel Comics: Dec, 2000 - No. 3, Feb, 2001 ($2.99, limited series)

1-3-Adlard-a — 3.00

BEFORE WATCHMEN: COMEDIAN (Prequel to 1986 Watchmen series)
DC Comics: Aug, 2012 - No. 6, Jun, 2013 ($3.99, limited series)

1-6-Brian Azzarello-s/J.G. Jones-a/c; The Comedian during the Vietnam War; back-up Crimson Corsair serial in #1-4; Higgins-a — 5.00
1-Variant-c by Jim Lee — 60.00
1-6-Variant covers. 1-Risso. 2-Bradstreet. 3-Leon. 4-Stelfreeze. 5-Frank. 6-Albuquerque — 10.00

BEFORE WATCHMEN: DOLLAR BILL (Prequel to 1986 Watchmen series)
DC Comics: Mar, 2013 ($3.99, one-shot)

1-Len Wein-s/Steve Rude-a/c; origin and demise of Dollar Bill — 5.00
1-Variant-c by Jim Lee — 60.00
1-Variant-c by Darwyn Cooke — 10.00

BEFORE WATCHMEN: DR. MANHATTAN (Prequel to 1986 Watchmen series)
DC Comics: Oct, 2012 - No. 4, Apr, 2013 ($3.99, limited series)

1-4-Straczynski-s/Hughes-a/c; back-up Crimson Corsair serial in #1-3; Higgins-a — 5.00
1-Variant-c by Jim Lee — 60.00
1-4-Variant covers. 1-Pope. 2-Russell. 3-Neal Adams. 4-Sienkiewicz — 10.00

BEFORE WATCHMEN: MINUTEMEN (Prequel to 1986 Watchmen series)
DC Comics: Aug, 2012 - No. 6, Mar, 2013 ($3.99, limited series)

1-6-Darwyn Cooke-a/c; The team flashback to 1939; back-up Crimson Corsair serial in #1-5; Higgins-a — 5.00
1-Variant-c by Jim Lee — 40.00
1-6-Variant covers. 1-Golden. 2-Garcia-Lopez-c. 3-Chiang. 4-Rude. 6-Cloonan — 10.00

BEFORE WATCHMEN: MOLOCH (Prequel to 1986 Watchmen series)
DC Comics: Jan, 2013 - No. 2, Feb, 2013 ($3.99, limited series)

1,2-Straczynski-s/Risso-a/c; origin; back-up Crimson Corsair serial in both; Higgins-a — 5.00
1-Variant-c by Jim Lee — 40.00
1,2-Variant covers. 1-Matt Wagner. 2-Olly Moss — 10.00

BEFORE WATCHMEN: NITE OWL (Prequel to 1986 Watchmen series)
DC Comics: Aug, 2012 - No. 4, Feb, 2013 ($3.99, limited series)

1-4-Straczynski-s/Andy Kubert-a/c; Joe Kubert-a(i) in #1-3; back-up Crimson Corsair serial in #1-3; Higgins-a — 5.00
1-Variant-c by Jim Lee — 50.00
1-4-Variant covers. 1-Nowlan. 2-Finch. 3-Samnee. 4-Van Sciver — 10.00

BEFORE WATCHMEN: OZYMANDIAS (Prequel to 1986 Watchmen series)
DC Comics: Sept, 2012 - No. 6, Apr, 2013 ($3.99, limited series)

1-6-Len Wein-s/Jae Lee-a/c; origin of master plan; back-up Crimson Corsair serial in #1-4; Higgins-a — 4.00
1-Variant-c by Jim Lee — 50.00
1-6-Variant covers. 1-Jimenez. 2-Noto. 3-Carnevale. 4-Kaluta. 5-Thompson. 6-Sook — 8.00

BEFORE WATCHMEN: RORSCHACH (Prequel to 1986 Watchmen series)
DC Comics: Oct, 2012 - No. 4, Apr, 2013 ($3.99, limited series)

1-4-Azzarello-s/Bermejo-a/c; back-up Crimson Corsair serial in #1-3; Higgins-a — 5.00
1-Variant-c by Jim Lee — 75.00
1-4-Variant covers. 1-Steranko. 2-Jock. 3-Kidd. 4-Reis — 10.00

BEFORE WATCHMEN: SILK SPECTRE (Prequel to 1986 Watchmen series)
DC Comics: Aug, 2012 - No. 4, Dec, 2013 ($3.99, limited series)

1-4-Cooke & Conner-s/Conner-a/c; back-up Crimson Corsair serial in all; Higgins-a — 5.00
1-Variant-c by Jim Lee — 60.00
1-4-Variant covers. 1-Dave Johnson. 2-Middleton. 3-Allred. 4-Timm — 10.00

BEHIND PRISON BARS
Realistic Comics (Avon): 1952

	GD 2.0	VG 4.0	FN 6.0	VF 8.0	VF/NM 9.0	NM- 9.2
1-Kinstler-c	53	106	159	334	567	800

BEHOLD THE HANDMAID
George Pflaum: 1954 (Religious) (25¢ with a 20¢ sticker price)

	GD 2.0	VG 4.0	FN 6.0	VF 8.0	VF/NM 9.0	NM- 9.2
nn	7	14	21	37	46	55

BELIEVE IT OR NOT (See Ripley's...)

BÊLIT & VALERIA: SWORDS VS. SORCERY (From The Cimmerian)
Ablaze Publishing: 2022 - No. 5, 2022 ($3.99)

1-5-Robert E. Howard characters; Bemis-s/Buchemi-a — 4.00

BEN AND ME (Disney)
Dell Publishing Co.: No. 539, Mar, 1954

	GD 2.0	VG 4.0	FN 6.0	VF 8.0	VF/NM 9.0	NM- 9.2
Four Color 539	5	10	15	33	57	80

BEN BOWIE AND HIS MOUNTAIN MEN
Dell Publishing Co.: 1952 - No. 17, Nov-Jan, 1958-59

	GD 2.0	VG 4.0	FN 6.0	VF 8.0	VF/NM 9.0	NM- 9.2
Four Color 443 (#1)	9	18	27	63	129	195
Four Color 513,557,599,626,657	5	10	15	34	60	85
7(5-7/56)-11: 11-Intro/origin Yellow Hair	4	8	12	25	40	55
12-17	4	8	12	23	37	50

BEN CASEY (TV)
Dell Publishing Co.: June-July, 1962 - No. 10, June-Aug, 1965 (Photo-c)

	GD 2.0	VG 4.0	FN 6.0	VF 8.0	VF/NM 9.0	NM- 9.2
12-063-207 (#1)	5	10	15	35	63	90
2(10/62),3,5-10	4	8	12	23	37	50
4-Marijuana & heroin use story	5	10	15	30	50	70

BEN CASEY FILM STORIES (TV)
Gold Key: Nov, 1962 (25¢) (Photo-c)

	GD	VG	FN	VF	VF/NM	NM-
	2.0	4.0	6.0	8.0	9.0	9.2

30009-211-All photos 6 12 18 38 69 100

BENEATH THE PLANET OF THE APES (See Movie Comics & Power Record Comics)

BEN FRANKLIN (See Kite Fun Book)

BEN HUR
Dell Publishing Co.: No. 1052, Nov, 1959

Four Color 1052-Movie, Manning-a 10 20 30 66 138 210

BEN ISRAEL
Logos International: 1974 (39¢)

nn-Christian religious 2 4 6 10 14 18

BEN REILLY: SCARLET SPIDER
Marvel Comics: Jun, 2017 - No. 25, Dec, 2018 ($3.99)

1-25: 1-Peter David-s/Mark Bagley-a. 6,7-Sliney-a. 7-Death app. 8-10-The Hornet app. 15-17-Damnation tie-in; Mephisto app. 23,25-Mephisto app. 4.00

BEN REILLY: SPIDER-MAN
Marvel Comics: Mar, 2022 - No. 5, Jul, 2022 ($3.99, limited series)

1-5-DeMatteis-s/Baldeón-a. 1,2,5-Scorpion app. 4.00

BEN 10 (Cartoon Network)
IDW Publishing: Nov, 2013 - No. 4, Feb, 2014 ($3.99, limited series)

1-4: Henderson-s/Purcell-a; multiple covers on each 4.00

BEOWULF (Also see First Comics Graphic Novel #1)
National Periodical Publications: Apr-May, 1975 - No. 6, Feb-Mar, 1976

1 2 4 6 11 16 20
2,3,5,6: 5-Flying saucer-c/story 1 2 3 5 6 8
4-Dracula-c/s 1 3 4 6 8 10

BEQUEST, THE
AfterShock Comics: Mar, 2021 - No. 4, Jun, 2021 ($4.99, limited series)

1-4-Tim Seeley-s/Freddie Williams II-a 5.00

BERMUDA
IDW Publishing: Jul, 2021 - No. 4, Oct, 2021 ($4.99, limited series)

1-4-John Layman-s/Nick Bradshaw-a; multiple covers on each 5.00

BERNI WRIGHTSON, MASTER OF THE MACABRE
Pacific Comics/Eclipse Comics No. 5: July, 1983 - No. 5, Nov, 1984 ($1.50, Baxter paper)

1-5: Wrightson-c/a(r). 4-Jeff Jones-r (11 pgs.) 6.00

BERRYS, THE (Also see Funny World)
Argo Publ.: May, 1956

1-Reprints daily & Sunday strips & daily Animal Antics by Ed Nofziger 7 14 21 37 46 55

BERZERKER (Milo Ventimiglia Presents...)
Image Comics (Top Cow): No. 0, Feb, 2009 - No. 6, Jun, 2010 ($2.99/$3.99)

0-3-Jeremy Haun-a/Rick Loverd-s/Dale Keown-c. 0-Creator interviews 3.00
4-6-($3.99) Covers by Haun & Keown 4.00

BERZERKERS (See Youngblood V1#2)
Image Comics (Extreme Studios): Aug, 1995 - No. 3, Oct, 1995 ($2.50, limited series)

1-3: Beau Smith scripts, Fraga-a 3.00

BERZERKER UNBOUND
Dark Horse Comics: Aug, 2019 - No. 4, Nov, 2019 ($3.99, limited series)

1-4-Jeff Lemire-s/Mike Deodato-a/c. 1-Mignola var-c. 2-Sorrentino var-c. 3-Nguyen var-c 4.00

BEST ARCHIE COMIC EVER!, THE
Archie Comic Publications: Aug, 2022 ($3.99, one-shot)

1-Three short stories by various; Pureheart the Powerful app. 4.00

BEST COMICS
Better Publications: Nov, 1939 - No. 4, Feb, 1940(10-11/16" wide x 8" tall, reads sideways)

1-(Scarce)-Red Mask begins (1st app., 1st African American superhero in comics) & c/s-all 459 918 1377 3350 5925 8500
2-4: 3-Racist-c. 4-Cannibalism story 258 516 774 1651 2826 4000

BEST FROM BOY'S LIFE, THE
Gilberton Company: Oct, 1957 - No. 5, Oct, 1958 (35¢)

1-Space Conquerors & Kam of the Ancient Ones begin, end #5; Bob Cousy photo/story 14 28 42 76 108 140
2,3,5 8 16 24 42 54 65
4-L.B. Cole-a 8 16 24 44 57 70

BEST LOVE (Formerly Sub-Mariner Comics No. 32)
Marvel Comics (MPI): No. 33, Aug, 1949 - No. 36, April, 1950 (Photo-c 33-36)

33-Kubert-a 20 40 60 117 189 260
34 (10/49) 14 28 42 81 118 155
35,36-Everett-a 15 30 45 84 127 170

BEST OF ARCHIE, THE
Perigee Books: 1980 ($7.95, softcover TPB)

nn-Intro by Michael Uslan & Jeffrey Mendel 5 10 15 35 63 90

BEST OF BUGS BUNNY, THE
Gold Key: Oct, 1966 - No. 2, Oct, 1968

1,2-Giants 4 8 12 27 44 60

BEST OF DC, THE (Blue Ribbon Digest) (See Limited Coll. Ed. C-52)
DC Comics: Sept-Oct, 1979 - No. 71, Apr, 1986 (100-148 pgs; mostly reprints)

1-Superman, w/"Death of Superman"-r 3 6 9 14 20 25
2,5-9: 2-Batman 40th Ann. Special. 5-Best of 1979. 6,8-Superman. 7-Superboy. 9-Batman, Creeper app. 2 4 6 8 10 12
3-Superfriends 2 4 6 9 12 15
4-Rudolph the Red Nosed Reindeer 2 4 6 9 13 16
10-Secret Origins of Super Villains; 1st ever Penguin origin-s 3 6 9 16 23 30
11-16,18-20: 11-The Year's Best Stories. 12-Superman Time and Space Stories.13-Best of DC Comics Presents. 14-New origin stories of Batman villains. 15-Superboy. 16-Superman Anniv. 18-Teen Titans new-s., Adams, Kane-a; Perez-c. 19-Superman. 20-World's Finest 1 2 3 5 7 9
17-Supergirl 2 4 6 8 10 12
21,22: 21-Justice Society. 22-Christmas; unpublished Sandman story w/Kirby-a 2 4 6 10 14 18
23-27: 23-(148 pgs.)-Best of 1981. 24 Legion, new story and 16 pgs. new costumes. 25-Superman. 26-Brave & Bold. 27-Superman vs. Luthor 2 4 6 9 12 15
28,29: 28-Binky, Sugar & Spike app. 29-Sugar & Spike, 3 new stories; new Stanley & his Monster story 2 4 6 9 13 16
30,32-36,38,40: 30-Detective Comics. 32-Superman. 33-Secret origins of Legion Heroes and Villains. 34-Metal Men; has #497 on-c from Adv. Comics. 35-The Year's Best Comics Stories (148 pgs.). 36-Superman vs. Kryptonite. 38-Superman. 40-World of Krypton 2 4 6 9 12 15
31-JLA 2 4 6 10 14 18
34-Corrected version with "#34" on cover 2 4 6 10 14 18
37,39: 37-"Funny Stuff", Mayer-a. 39-Binky 2 4 6 10 14 18
41,43,45,47,49,53,55,58,60,63,65,68,70: 41-Sugar & Spike new stories with Mayer-a. 43,49,55-Funny Stuff. 45,53,70-Binky. 47,65,68-Sugar & Spike. 58-Super Jrs. Holiday Special; Sugar & Spike. 60-Plop!; Wood-c(r) & Aragonés-r (5/85). 63-Plop!; Wrightson-a(r) 3 6 9 14 19 24
42,44,46,48,50-52,54,56,57,59,61,62,64,66,67,69,71: 42,56-Superman vs. Aliens. 44,57,67-Superboy & LSH. 46-Jimmy Olsen. 48-Superman Team-ups. 50-Year's best Superman. 51-Batman Family. 52 Best of 1984. 54,56,59-Superman. 61-(148 pgs.)Year's best. 62-Best of Batman 1985. 69-Year's best Team stories. 71-Year's best 2 4 6 10 14 18

NOTE: ***N. Adams** a-2r, 14r, 18r, 26, 51. **Aparo** a-9, 14, 26, 30; c-9, 14, 26. **Austin** a-51i. **Buckler** a-40p; c-16, 22. **Giffen** a-50, 52; c-33p. **Grell** a-33p. **Grossman** a-37. **Heath** a-26. **Infantino** a-10r, 18. **Kaluta** a-40. **G. Kane** a-10r, 18r; c-40, 44. **Kubert** a-10r, 21, 26. **Layton** a-21. **S. Mayer** c-29, 37, 41, 43, 47; a-28, 29, 37, 41, 43, 47, 58, 65, 68. **Moldoff** c-64p. **Morrow** a-40; c-40. **W. Mortimer** a-39p. **Newton** a-5, 51. **Perez** a-24, 50p; c-18, 21, 23. **Rogers** a-14, 51p. **Simonson** a-11r. **Spiegle** a-52. **Starlin** a-51. **Staton** a-5, 21. **Tuska** a-24. **Wolverton** a-60. **Wood** a-60, 63; c-60, 63. **Wrightson** a-60. New art in #14, 18, 24.*

BEST OF DENNIS THE MENACE, THE
Hallden/Fawcett Publications: Summer, 1959 - No. 5, Spring, 1961 (100 pgs.)

1-All reprints; Wiseman-a 6 12 18 42 79 115
2-5: 2-Christmas-c 5 10 15 34 50 65

BEST OF DONALD DUCK, THE
Gold Key: Nov, 1965 (12¢, 36 pgs.)(Lists 2nd printing in indicia)

1-Reprints Four Color #223 by Barks 7 14 21 49 92 135

BEST OF DONALD DUCK & UNCLE SCROOGE, THE
Gold Key: Nov, 1964 - No. 2, Sept, 1967 (25¢ Giants)

1(30022-411)('64)-Reprints 4-Color #189 & 408 by Carl Barks; cover of F.C. #189 redrawn by Barks 8 16 24 54 102 150
2(30022-709)('67)-Reprints 4-Color #256 & "Seven Cities of Cibola" & U.S. #8 by Barks 7 14 21 44 82 120

BEST OF HORROR AND SCIENCE FICTION COMICS
Bruce Webster: 1987 ($2.00)

1-Wolverton, Frazetta, Powell, Ditko-r 2 4 6 8 10 12

BEST OF JOSIE AND THE PUSSYCATS
Archie Comics: 2001 ($10.95, TPB)

1-Reprints 1st app. and noteworthy stories 12.00

BEST OF MARMADUKE, THE
Charlton Comics: 1960

1-Brad Anderson's strip reprints 3 6 9 21 33 45

BEST OF MS. TREE, THE
Pyramid Comics: 1987 - No. 4, 1988 ($2.00, B&W, limited series)

1-4 3.00

BEST OF THE BRAVE AND THE BOLD, THE (See Super DC Giant)
DC Comics: Oct, 1988 - No. 6, Jan, 1989 ($2.50, limited series)

1-6: Neal Adams-r, Kubert-r & Heath-r in all 4.00

BEST OF THE SPIRIT, THE
DC Comics: 2005 ($14.99, TPB)

nn-Reprints 1st app. and noteworthy stories; intro by Neil Gaiman; Eisner bio. 15.00

BEST OF THE WEST (See A-1 Comics)
Magazine Enterprises: 1951 - No. 12, April-June, 1954

1(A-1 42)-Ghost Rider, Durango Kid, Straight Arrow, Bobby Benson begin 50 100 150 315 533 750
2(A-1 46) 24 48 72 142 234 325
3(A-1 52), 4(A-1 59), 5(A-1 66) 20 40 60 114 182 250
6(A-1 70), 7(A-1 76), 8(A-1 81), 9(A-1 85), 10(A-1 87), 11(A-1 97), 12(A-1 103) 15 30 45 90 140 190

NOTE: ***Bolle** a-9. **Borth** a-12. **Guardineer** a-5, 12. **Powell** a-1, 12.*

BEST OF UNCLE SCROOGE & DONALD DUCK, THE
Gold Key: Nov, 1966 (25¢)

1(30030-611)-Reprints part 4-Color #159 & 456 & Uncle Scrooge #6,7 by Carl Barks 7 14 21 44 82 120

BEST OF WALT DISNEY COMICS, THE
Western Publishing Co.: 1974 ($1.50, 52 pgs.) (Walt Disney)
(8-1/2x11" cardboard covers; 32,000 printed of each)

96170-Reprints 1st two stories less 1 pg. each from 4-Color #62 6 12 18 37 66 95
96171-Reprints Mickey Mouse and the Bat Bandit of Inferno Gulch from 1934 (strips) by Gottfredson 6 12 18 37 66 95
96172-r/Uncle Scrooge #386 & two other stories 6 12 18 37 66 95
96173-Reprints "Ghost of the Grotto" (from 4-Color #159) & "Christmas on Bear Mountain" (from 4-Color #178) 6 12 18 37 66 95

BEST ROMANCE
Standard Comics (Visual Editions): No. 5, Feb-Mar, 1952 - No. 7, Aug, 1952

5-Toth-a; photo-c 20 40 60 117 189 260

Ben Reilly: Scarlet Spider #7 © MAR

Bettie Page V2 #1 © Bettie Page LLC

Betty and Veronica V4 #2 © ACP

	GD 2.0	VG 4.0	FN 6.0	VF 8.0	VF/NM 9.0	NM- 9.2
6,7-Photo-c	14	28	42	78	112	145

BEST SELLER COMICS (See Tailspin Tommy)

BEST WESTERN (Formerly Terry Toons? or Miss America Magazine
Marvel Comics (IPC): V7#24(#57)?; Western Outlaws & Sheriffs No. 60 on)
No. 58, June, 1949 - No. 59, Aug, 1949

	GD	VG	FN	VF	VF/NM	NM-
58,59-Black Rider, Kid Colt, Two-Gun Kid app.; both have Syd Shores-c	32	64	96	188	307	425

BETA RAY BILL (Thor)
Marvel Comics: May, 2021 - No. 5, Sept, 2021 ($4.99/$3.99, limited series)

1-($4.99)-Daniel Warren Johnson-s/a; Fin Fang Foom app.; Walt Simonson interview 5.00
2-5-($3.99) 2,3-Skurge & Pip app. 4,5-Surtur app. 4.00

BETA RAY BILL: GODHUNTER
Marvel Comics: Aug, 2009 - No. 3, Oct, 2009 ($3.99, limited series)

1-3-Kano-a; Thor and Galactus app.; reprints form Thor #337-339. 2,3-Silver Surfer app. 4.00

BETRAYAL OF THE PLANET OF THE APES (Set 20 years before the first movie)
BOOM! Studios: Nov, 2011 - No. 4, Feb, 2012 ($3.99, limited series)

1-4-Dr. Zaius app.; Bechko-s/Hardman-a. 1-Three covers. 2-Two covers 4.00

BETROTHED
AfterShock Comics: Mar, 2018 - No. 5, Jul, 2018 ($3.99, limited series)

1-5-Sean Lewis-s/Steve Uy-a 4.00

BETSY BRADDOCK: CAPTAIN BRITAIN
Marvel Comics: Apr, 2023 - Present ($3.99, limited series)

1-Morgan LeFay & Rachel Summers app.; Howard-s/Georgiev-a 4.00

BETTIE PAGE
Dynamite Entertainment: 2017 - No. 8, 2018 ($3.99)

	GD	VG	FN	VF	VF/NM	NM-
1-Bettie Page in 1951 Hollywood; Avallone-s/Worley-a; multiple covers	1	3	4	6	8	10
2-8-Multiple covers on each						6.00
... Halloween Special One-Shot (2018, $4.99) Avallone-s; art by Ohta & Ruiz						8.00
... Halloween Special One-Shot (2019, $4.99) Avallone-s; art by Martinez & Ruiz						8.00

BETTIE PAGE AND THE ALIEN AGENDA, VOLUME 6
Dynamite Entertainment: 2022 - No. 5, 2022 ($3.99)

1-5-Bettie Page alien-hunting in Egypt in 1950s; Ani-Mia-s; multiple covers on each 4.00

BETTIE PAGE AND THE CURSE OF THE BANSHEE, VOLUME 5
Dynamite Entertainment: 2021 - No. 5, 2021 ($3.99)

1-5-Bettie Page monster-hunting in Ireland in 1954; multiple covers on each 4.00

BETTIE PAGE COMICS
Dark Horse Comics: Mar, 1996 ($3.95)

	GD	VG	FN	VF	VF/NM	NM-
1-Dave Stevens-c; Blevins & Heath-a; Jaime Hernandez pin-up	3	6	9	16	23	30

BETTIE PAGE COMICS: QUEEN OF THE NILE
Dark Horse Comics: Dec, 1999 - No. 3, Apr, 2000 ($2.95, limited series)

	GD	VG	FN	VF	VF/NM	NM-
1-Silke-s/a; Stevens-c	3	6	9	14	20	25
2,3-Silke-s/a; Stevens-c	2	4	6	10	14	18

BETTIE PAGE COMICS: SPICY ADVENTURE
Dark Horse Comics: Jan, 1997 ($2.95, one-shot, mature)

	GD	VG	FN	VF	VF/NM	NM-
nn-Silke-c/s/a	2	4	6	8	10	12

BETTIE PAGE UNBOUND (Volume 3)
Dynamite Entertainment: 2019 - No. 10, 2020 ($3.99)

1-10-Multiple covers on each: 1-Bettie as Red Sonja. 2-Bettie as Vampirella 4.00

BETTIE PAGE: VOLUME 2
Dynamite Entertainment: 2018 - No. 5, 2019 ($3.99)

1-5-Bettie Page in 1952 England. 1-4-Avallone-s/Ohta-a; multiple covers on each 5.00

BETTIE PAGE: VOLUME 3
Dynamite Entertainment: 2020 - No. 5, 2020 ($3.99)

1-5-Bettie Page shooting a movie in the Caribbean; multiple covers on each 4.00

BETTY (See Pep Comics #22 for 1st app.)
Archie Comics: Sept, 1992 - No. 195, Jan, 2012 ($1.25-$2.99)

	GD	VG	FN	VF	VF/NM	NM-
1	2	4	6	8	10	12
2-7,9-18,20-24: 20-1st Super Sleuther-s						5.00
8-Risqué bikini-c	5	10	15	34	60	85
19-Love Showdown part 2						6.00
25-Pin-up page of Betty as Marilyn Monroe, Madonna, Lady Di						6.00
26-45,47-50						3.00
46-(2/97) "High School 2021 A.D." shows future with virtual classes over computer monitors						8.00
51-195: 57- "A Storm Over Uniforms" x-over part 5,6. 186-Begin $2.99-c						3.00

BETTY AND HER STEADY (Going Steady with Betty No. 1)
Avon Periodicals: No. 2, Mar-Apr, 1950

	GD	VG	FN	VF	VF/NM	NM-
2	15	30	45	86	133	180

BETTY AND ME
Archie Publications: Aug, 1965 - No. 200, Aug, 1992

	GD	VG	FN	VF	VF/NM	NM-
1	23	46	69	161	356	550
2,3: 3-Origin Superteen	8	16	24	56	108	160
4-8: Superteen in new costume #4-7; dons new helmet in #5, ends #8.	5	10	15	34	60	85
9,10: Girl from R.I.V.E.R.D.A.L.E. 9-UFO-s	4	8	12	27	44	60
11-15,17-20(4/69)	3	6	9	21	33	45
16-Classic cover; w/risqué cover dialogue	38	76	114	285	641	1000
21,24-35: 33-Paper doll page	3	6	9	16	23	30
22-Archies Band-s	3	6	9	16	24	32
23-I Dream of Jeannie parody	3	6	9	19	30	40
36(8/71),37,41-55 (52 pgs.): 42-Betty as vamp-s	3	6	9	16	23	30
38-Sabrina app.	4	8	12	23	37	50
39-Josie and Sabrina cover cameos	3	6	9	19	30	40
40-Archie & Betty share a cabin	3	6	9	17	26	35
56(4/71)-80(12/76): 79 Betty Cooper mysteries thru #86. 79-81-Drago the Vampire-s	2	4	6	9	13	16
81-99: 83-Harem-c. 84-Jekyll & Hyde-c/s	2	4	6	8	10	12
100(3/79)	2	4	6	9	12	15
101,118: 101-Elvis mentioned. 118-Tarzan mentioned	1	2	3	5	7	9
102-117,119-130(9/82): 103,104-Space-s. 124-DeCarlo-c begins						7.00
131-135,137,138,140,142-147,149-154,156-158: 135-Jason Blossom app. 137-Space-s. 138-Tarzan parody						5.00
136-Classic-c; Cheryl Blossom cameo	5	10	15	33	57	80
139,141,148: 139-Katy Keene collecting-s; Archie in drag-s. 141-Tarzan parody-s. 148-Cyndi Lauper parody-s						6.00
155,159,160(8/87): 155-Archie in drag-s. 159-Superhero gag-c. 160-Wheel of Fortune parody						6.00
161-169,171-199						4.00
170,200: 170-New Archie Superhero-s						6.00

BETTY AND VERONICA (Also see Archie's Girls...)
Archie Enterprises: June, 1987 - No. 278, Dec, 2015 (75¢-$3.99)

	GD	VG	FN	VF	VF/NM	NM-
1	3	6	9	16	23	30
2-10						6.00
11-30						4.00
31-81						3.00
82-Love Showdown part 3						5.00
83-271: 242-Begin $2.50-c. 247-Begin $2.99-c. 264-271-Two covers						3.00
267-Mermaid variant-c by Fiona Staples						10.00
272-274,276-278-($3.99): 272-274,276,277-Two covers. 278-Last issue; 6 covers						4.00
275-($4.99) Five covers by Adam Hughes, Ramona Fradon & others						5.00
... Free Comic Book Day Edition #1 (6/05) Katy Keene-c/app.; Cheryl Blossom app.						3.00

BETTY AND VERONICA (Volume 3)
Archie Comic Publications: Sept, 2016 - No. 3, Aug, 2017 ($3.99, limited series)

1-3-Adam Hughes-s/a; multiple covers on each; back-up classic pin-ups 4.00
... No. 1: FCBD Edition (5/17, giveaway) r/#1; bonus Riverdale TV show character guide 3.00

BETTY AND VERONICA (Volume 4)
Archie Comic Publications: Feb, 2019 - No. 5, Jul, 2019 ($3.99, limited series)

1-5-Rotante-s/Lanz-a; Senior year in high school 4.00

BETTY & VERONICA ANNUAL DIGEST (...Digest Magazine #1-4, 44 on; ...Comics Digest Mag. #5-43)(Continues as Betty & Veronica Friends Double Digest #209-on)
Archie Publications: Nov, 1980 - No. 208, Nov, 2010 ($1.00/-$2.69, digest size)

	GD	VG	FN	VF	VF/NM	NM-
1	3	6	9	16	23	30
2-10: 2(11/81-Katy Keene story), 3(8/82)	2	4	6	9	13	16
11-30	1	3	4	6	8	10
31-50	1	2	3	4	5	7
51-70						4.00
71-191: 110-Begin $2.19-c. 135-Begin $2.39-c. 165-Begin $2.49. 185-Includes reprint of Archie's Girls B&V #1 (1950) and new story where 1950 & 2008 B&V meet						3.00
192-208: 192-Begin $2.69-c						3.00

BETTY & VERONICA ANNUAL DIGEST MAGAZINE
Archie Comics: Sept, 1989 - No. 16, Aug, 1997 ($1.50/$1.75/$1.79, 128 pgs.)

	GD	VG	FN	VF	VF/NM	NM-
1	1	2	3	5	7	9
2-10: 9-Neon ink logo						5.00

	GD 2.0	VG 4.0	FN 6.0	VF 8.0	VF/NM 9.0	NM- 9.2
11-16: 16-Begin $1.79-c						3.00

BETTY & VERONICA CHRISTMAS SPECTACULAR (See Archie Giant Series Magazine #159, 168, 180, 191, 204, 217, 229, 241, 453, 465, 477, 489, 501, 513, 525, 536, 547, 558, 568, 580, 593, 606, 618)

BETTY & VERONICA DOUBLE DIGEST MAGAZINE
Archie Enterprises: 1987 - Present ($2.25-$9.99, digest size, 256 pgs.)(...Digest #12 on)

	GD 2.0	VG 4.0	FN 6.0	VF 8.0	VF/NM 9.0	NM- 9.2
1	2	4	6	8	10	12
2-10	1	2	3	4	5	7
11-25: 5,17-Xmas-c. 16-Capt. Hero story						5.00
26-50						4.00
51-150: 87-Begin $3.19-c. 95-Begin $3.29-c. 114-Begin $3.59-c. 142-Begin $3.69-c						4.00
151-211,213-222: 151-(7/07)-Realistic style Betty & Veronica debuts (thru #154). 160-Cheryl Blossom spotlight. 170-173-Realistic style						4.00
212,223,237,240-($5.99) Titled Betty & Veronica Double Double Digest (320 pages)						6.00
224-($5.99) Titled Betty & Veronica Comics Annual (192 pgs.)						6.00
225,228,238,242,247,250,255,257,260-275-($6.99) Titled Betty & Veronica Jumbo Comics Digest (320 pgs.)						7.00
226,227,229-232,234-236,239,241,243,245,246,249,251,254,256-($4.99) Titled Betty & Veronica Comics Digest or Comics Double Digest						5.00
244,248,252,253,258-($5.99) 244,253-Titled Betty & Veronica Summer Ann.						6.00
276-299-($7.99): 287-Halloween-c						8.00
300-309-($8.99)						9.00
310-313-($9.99)						10.00
Betty & Veronica: in Bad Boy Trouble Vol.1 TPB (2007, $7.49) r/new style from #151-154						8.00

BETTY & VERONICA FRIENDS DOUBLE DIGEST (Continues from B&V Digest Mag. #208)
Archie Publications: No. 209, Jan, 2011 - No. 286, Jan, 2021 ($3.99-$7.99, digest size)

	GD 2.0	VG 4.0	FN 6.0	VF 8.0	VF/NM 9.0	NM- 9.2
209-236,238: 209-Cheryl Blossom app.						4.00
237,246-Titled Betty & Veronica Friends Double Double Digest ($5.99, 320 pages)						6.00
239-($4.99) Double Digest						5.00
240,245,250,252,254,256,257-273-($6.99) 257-Winter Annual						7.00
241-244,248-($4.99) Titled Betty & Veronica Friends Comics Digest. 244-Pussycats app.						5.00
247,249,251,253,255-($5.99) 247-Easter Annual. 251-Halloween Annual						6.00
274-286-($7.99)						8.00

BETTY & VERONICA FRIENDS FOREVER
Archie Publications: Jun, 2018 - Present ($2.99, quarterly)

	GD 2.0	VG 4.0	FN 6.0	VF 8.0	VF/NM 9.0	NM- 9.2
1-Classic-style stories; Parent-a						3.00
1-(#2) Travel Tales on cover, 1-(#3) Storybook Tales, 1-(#4) Go To Work, 1-(#5) Pets, 1-(#6) Return to Storybook Land, 1-(#7) Supernatural Stories, 1-(#8) What If...?, 1(#9) It's All Relative. 1-(#10) Danger Zone. 1-(#11) Good Citizens. 1-(#12) Winterfest 1(#13) Spring Break. 1-(#14) Summer Fun. 1-(#15) Halloween Spooktacular 1(#16) Power-Ups. 1(#17) Summer Surf Party. 1(#18) Christmas Party						3.00

BETTY & VERONICA JUMBO COMICS DIGEST (See Betty & Veronica Double Digest Magazine)

BETTY & VERONICA SPECTACULAR (See Archie Giant Series Mag. #11, 16, 21, 26, 32, 138, 145, 153, 162, 173, 184, 197, 201, 210, 214, 221, 226, 234, 238, 246, 250, 458, 462, 470, 482, 486, 494, 498, 506, 510, 518, 522, 526, 530, 537, 552, 559, 563, 569, 575, 582, 588, 600, 608, 613, 620, 623, and Betty & Veronica)

BETTY AND VERONICA SPECTACULAR
Archie Comics: Oct, 1992 - No. 90, Sept, 2009 ($1.25/$1.50/$1.75/$1.99/$2.19/$2.25/$2.50)

	GD 2.0	VG 4.0	FN 6.0	VF 8.0	VF/NM 9.0	NM- 9.2
1-Dan DeCarlo-c/a						5.00
2-90: 48-Cheryl Blossom leaves Riverdale. 64-Cheryl Blossom returns						3.00

BETTY & VERONICA SPRING SPECTACULAR (See Archie Giant Series Magazine #569, 582, 595)

BETTY & VERONICA SUMMER FUN (See Archie Giant Series Mag. #8, 13, 18, 23, 28, 34, 140, 147, 155, 164, 175, 187, 199, 212, 224, 236, 248, 460, 484, 496, 508, 520, 529, 539, 550, 561, 572, 585, 598, 611, 621)
Archie Comics: 1994 - No. 6, 1999 ($2.00/$2.25/$2.29, annual)

	GD 2.0	VG 4.0	FN 6.0	VF 8.0	VF/NM 9.0	NM- 9.2
1-($2.00, 52 pgs. plus poster)						4.00
2-6: 5-($2.25-c). 6-($2.29-c)						3.00
Vol. 1 (2003, $10.95) reprints stories from Archie Giant Series editions						12.00

BETTY & VERONICA: VIXENS
Archie Comics Publications: Jan, 2018 - No. 10, Nov, 2018 ($3.99)

	GD 2.0	VG 4.0	FN 6.0	VF 8.0	VF/NM 9.0	NM- 9.2
1-10: 1-Betty & Veronica form a biker gang; Cabrera-a; South Side Serpents app.						4.00

BETTY BOOP (Volume 1)
Dynamite Entertainment: 2016 - No. 4, 2017 ($3.99)

	GD 2.0	VG 4.0	FN 6.0	VF 8.0	VF/NM 9.0	NM- 9.2
1-4-Langridge-s/Lagacé-a; Koko app.; multiple covers on each						4.00

BETTY BOOP'S BIG BREAK
First Publishing: 1990 ($5.95, 52 pgs.)

	GD 2.0	VG 4.0	FN 6.0	VF 8.0	VF/NM 9.0	NM- 9.2
nn-By Joshua Quagmire; 60th anniversary ish.						6.00

BETTY PAGE 3-D COMICS
The 3-D Zone: 1991 ($3.95, "7-1/2x10-1/4," 28 pgs., no glasses)

	GD 2.0	VG 4.0	FN 6.0	VF 8.0	VF/NM 9.0	NM- 9.2
1-Photo inside covers; back-c nudity	2	4	6	11	16	20

BETTY'S DIARY (See Archie Giant Series Magazine No. 555)
Archie Enterprises: April, 1986 - No. 40, Apr, 1991 (#1:65¢; 75¢/95¢)

	GD 2.0	VG 4.0	FN 6.0	VF 8.0	VF/NM 9.0	NM- 9.2
1	1	2	3	4	5	7
2-10						4.00
11-40						3.00

BETTY'S DIGEST
Archie Enterprises: Nov, 1996 - No. 2 ($1.75/$1.79)

	GD 2.0	VG 4.0	FN 6.0	VF 8.0	VF/NM 9.0	NM- 9.2
1,2						3.00

BEVERLY HILLBILLIES (TV)
Dell Publishing Co.: 4-6/63 - No. 18, 8/67; No. 19, 10/69; No. 20, 10/70; No. 21, Oct, 1971

	GD 2.0	VG 4.0	FN 6.0	VF 8.0	VF/NM 9.0	NM- 9.2
1-Photo-c	17	34	51	117	259	400
2-Photo-c	8	16	24	55	105	155
3-9: All have photo covers	6	12	18	40	73	105
10: No photo cover	5	10	15	30	50	70
11-21: All have photo covers. 18-Last 12¢ issue. 19-21-Reprint #1-3 (covers and insides)	5	10	15	33	57	80

NOTE: *#1-9, 11-21 are photo covers.*

BEWARE (Formerly Fantastic; Chilling Tales No. 13 on)
Youthful Magazines: No. 10, June, 1952 - No. 12, Oct, 1952

	GD 2.0	VG 4.0	FN 6.0	VF 8.0	VF/NM 9.0	NM- 9.2
10-E.A. Poe's Pit & the Pendulum adaptation by Wildey; Harrison/Bache-a; atom bomb and shrunken head-c	107	214	321	679	1165	1650
11-Harrison-a; Ambrose Bierce adapt.	71	142	213	454	777	1100
12-Used in SOTI, pg. 388; Harrison-a	71	142	213	454	777	1100

BEWARE
Trojan Magazines/Merit Publ. No. ?: No. 13, 1/53 - No. 16, 7/53; No. 5, 9/53 - No. 15, 5/55

	GD 2.0	VG 4.0	FN 6.0	VF 8.0	VF/NM 9.0	NM- 9.2
13(#1)-Harrison-a	103	206	309	659	1130	1600
14(#2, 3/53)-Krenkel/Harrison-c; dismemberment, severed head panels; Good Girl-c	181	362	543	1158	1979	2800
15,16(#3, 5/53; #4, 7/53)-Harrison-a	57	114	171	362	619	875
5,9,12,13(1/55)	54	108	162	343	574	825
6-Ill. in **SOTI**- "Children are first shocked and then desensitized by all this brutality." Corpse on cover swipe/V.O.H. #26; girl on cover swipe/Advs. Into Darkness #10	290	580	870	1856	3178	4500
7,8-Check-a	65	130	195	416	708	1000
10-Frazetta/Check-c; Disbrow, Check-a	423	846	1269	3000	5250	7500
11-Disbrow-a; heart torn out, blood drainage story	129	258	387	826	1413	2000
14,15: 14-Myron Fass-c. 15-Harrison-a	53	106	159	334	567	800

NOTE: ***Fass** a-5, 6, 8; c-6, 11, 14. **Forte** a-8. **Hollingsworth** a-15(#3), 16(#4), 9; c-16(#4), 8, 9. **Kiefer** a-16(#4), 5, 6, 10.*

BEWARE (Becomes Tomb of Darkness No. 9 on)
Marvel Comics Group: Mar, 1973 - No. 8, May, 1974 (All reprints)

	GD 2.0	VG 4.0	FN 6.0	VF 8.0	VF/NM 9.0	NM- 9.2
1-Everett-c; Kirby & Sinnott-r ('54)	6	12	18	37	66	95
2-8: 2-Forte, Colan-r. 6-Tuska-a. 7-Torres-r/Mystical Tales #7	4	8	12	23	37	50

NOTE: ***Infantino** a-4r. **Gil Kane** c-4. **Wildey** a-7r.*

BEWARE TERROR TALES
Fawcett Publications: May, 1952 - No. 8, July, 1953

	GD 2.0	VG 4.0	FN 6.0	VF 8.0	VF/NM 9.0	NM- 9.2
1-E.C. art swipe/Haunt of Fear #5 & Vault of Horror #26	84	168	252	538	919	1300
2	55	110	165	352	601	850
3-5,7	45	90	135	284	480	675
6-Classic skeleton-c	90	180	270	576	970	1400
8-Tothish-a; people being cooked-c	155	310	465	992	1696	2400

NOTE: ***Andru** a-2. **Bernard Bailey** a-1; c-1-5. **Powell** a-1, 2, 8. **Sekowsky** a-2.*

BEWARE THE BATMAN (Based on the Cartoon Network series)
DC Comics: Dec, 2013 - No. 6, May, 2014 ($2.99)

	GD 2.0	VG 4.0	FN 6.0	VF 8.0	VF/NM 9.0	NM- 9.2
1-6: 1-Anarky app. 4-Man-Bat app. 6-Killer Croc app.						3.00

BEWARE THE CREEPER (See Adventure, Best of the Brave & the Bold, Brave & the Bold, 1st Issue Special, Flash #318-323, Showcase #73, World's Finest Comics #249)
National Periodical Publications: May-June, 1968 - No. 6, Mar-Apr, 1969 (All 12¢ issues)

	GD 2.0	VG 4.0	FN 6.0	VF 8.0	VF/NM 9.0	NM- 9.2
1-(5-6/68)-Classic Ditko-c; Ditko-a in all	9	18	27	57	111	165
2-6: 2-5-Ditko-c. 2-Intro. Proteus. 6-Gil Kane-c	5	10	15	33	57	80

BEWARE THE CREEPER
DC Comics (Vertigo): Jun, 2003 - No. 5, Oct, 2003 ($2.95, limited series)

	GD 2.0	VG 4.0	FN 6.0	VF 8.0	VF/NM 9.0	NM- 9.2
1-5-Female vigilante in 1920s Paris; Jason Hall-s/Cliff Chiang-a						3.00

BEWARE THE EYE OF ODIN
Image Comics: Jun, 2022 - No. 4, Sept, 2022 ($4.99)

	GD 2.0	VG 4.0	FN 6.0	VF 8.0	VF/NM 9.0	NM- 9.2
1-4-Doug Wagner-s/Tim Odland-a						5.00

BEWITCHED (TV)
Dell Publishing Co.: 4-6/65 - No. 11, 10/67; No. 12, 10/68 - No. 13, 1/69; No. 14, 10/69

	GD 2.0	VG 4.0	FN 6.0	VF 8.0	VF/NM 9.0	NM- 9.2
1-Photo-c	16	32	48	110	243	375
2-No photo-c	8	16	24	54	102	150
3-13-All have photo-c. 12-Rep. #1. 13-Last 12¢-c	6	12	18	42	79	115
14-No photo-c; reprints #2	5	10	15	34	60	85

BEYOND!
Marvel Comics: Sept, 2006 - No. 6, Feb, 2007 ($2.99, limited series)

	GD 2.0	VG 4.0	FN 6.0	VF 8.0	VF/NM 9.0	NM- 9.2
1-6-McDuffie-s/Kolins-a; Spider-Man, Venom, Gravity, Wasp app. 6-Gravity dies						3.00

BEYOND, THE
Ace Magazines: Nov, 1950 - No. 30, Jan, 1955

	GD 2.0	VG 4.0	FN 6.0	VF 8.0	VF/NM 9.0	NM- 9.2
1-Bakerish-a(p)	129	258	387	826	1413	2000
2-Bakerish-a(p)	48	96	144	302	514	725
3-10: 10-Woodish-a by Cameron	39	78	117	240	395	550
11-20: 18-Used in **POP**, pgs. 81,82	34	68	102	204	332	450
21-26,28-30	30	60	90	177	289	400
27-Used in **SOTI**, pg. 111	129	258	387	826	1413	2000

NOTE: ***Cameron** a-10, 11p, 12p, 15, 16, 21-27, 30; c-20. **Colan** a-6, 13, 17. **Sekowsky** a-2, 3, 5, 7, 11, 14, 27r. No. 1 was to appear as Challenge of the Unknown No. 7.*

BEYONDERS
AfterShock Comics: Aug, 2018 - No. 5, Mar, 2019 ($3.99, limited series)

	GD 2.0	VG 4.0	FN 6.0	VF 8.0	VF/NM 9.0	NM- 9.2
1-5-Paul Jenkins-s/Wesley St. Claire-a						4.00

BEYOND THE BREACH
AfterShock Comics: Jul, 2021 - Present ($4.99/$3.99)

	GD 2.0	VG 4.0	FN 6.0	VF 8.0	VF/NM 9.0	NM- 9.2
1-($4.99) Ed Brisson-s/Damian Couceiro						5.00
2-5-($3.99)						4.00

BEYOND THE FRINGE (Based on the TV series Fringe)
DC Comics: May, 2012 ($3.99, one-shot)

	GD 2.0	VG 4.0	FN 6.0	VF 8.0	VF/NM 9.0	NM- 9.2
1-Joshua Jackson-s/Jorge Jimenez-a/Drew Johnson-c						4.00

BEYOND THE GRAVE
Charlton Comics: July, 1975 - No. 6, June, 1976; No. 7, Jan, 1983 - No. 17, Oct, 1984

	GD 2.0	VG 4.0	FN 6.0	VF 8.0	VF/NM 9.0	NM- 9.2
1-Ditko-a (6 pgs.); Sutton painted-c	5	10	15	30	50	70
2-6: 2-5-Ditko-a; Ditko c-2,3,6	3	6	9	17	26	35
7-17: ('83-'84) Reprints. 8,11,16-Ditko-a. 11-Staton-a. 13-Aparo-c(r). 15-Sutton-c (low print run). 16-Palais-a	1	2	3	6	8	10
Modern Comics Reprint 2('78)						6.00

NOTE: ***Howard** a-4. **Kim** a-1. **Larson** a-4, 6.*

BIBLE, THE: EDEN
IDW Publishing: 2003 ($21.99, hardcover graphic novel)

	GD 2.0	VG 4.0	FN 6.0	VF 8.0	VF/NM 9.0	NM- 9.2
HC-Scott Hampton painted-a; adaptation of Genesis by Dave Elliot and Keith Giffen						22.00

Beware the Batman #1 © DC

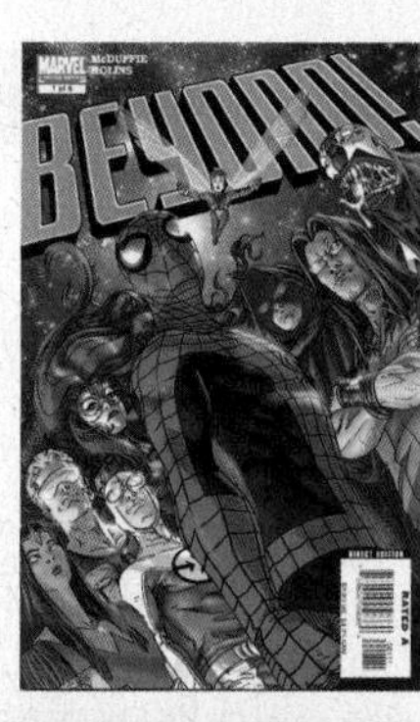

Beyond! #1 © MAR

Big Hero 6 #2 © MAR

	GD	VG	FN	VF	VF/NM	NM-
	2.0	4.0	6.0	8.0	9.0	9.2

BIBLE TALES FOR YOUNG FOLK (...Young People No. 3-5)
Atlas Comics (OMC): Aug, 1953 - No. 5, Mar, 1954

1 32 64 96 188 307 425
2-Everett, Krigstein, Maneely-a; Robinson-c 19 38 57 109 172 235
3-5: 4,5-Robinson-c 16 32 48 92 144 195

BIG (Movie)
Hit Comics (Dark Horse Comics): Mar, 1989 ($2.00)

1-Adaptation of film; Paul Chadwick-c 4.00

BIG ALL-AMERICAN COMIC BOOK, THE (See All-American Comics)
All-American/National Per. Publ.: 1944 (132 pgs., one-shot) (Early DC Annual)

1-Wonder Woman, Green Lantern, Flash, The Atom, Wildcat, Scribbly, The Whip, Ghost Patrol, Hawkman by Kubert (1st on Hawkman), Hop Harrigan, Johnny Thunder, Little Boy Blue, Mr. Terrific, Mutt & Jeff app.; Sargon on cover only; cover by Kubert/Hibbard/Mayer and others 700 1400 2100 5100 9550 14,000

BIG BABY HUEY (See Baby Huey)

BIG BANG COMICS (Becomes Big Bang #4)
Caliber Press: Spring, 1994 - No. 4, Feb, 1995; No. 0, May, 1995 ($1.95, lim. series)

1-4-($1.95-c) 4.00
0-(5/95, $2.95) Alex Ross-c; color and B&W pages 3.00
Your Big Book of Big Bang Comics TPB ('98, $11.00) r/#0-2 11.00

BIG BANG COMICS (Volume 2)
Image Comics (Highbrow Ent.): V2#1, May, 1996 - No. 35, Jan, 2001 ($1.95-$3.95)

1-23,26: 1-Mighty Man app. 2-4-S.A. Shadowhawk app. 5-Begin $2.95-c. 6-Curt Swan/Murphy Anderson-c. 7-Begin B&W. 12-Savage Dragon-c/app. 16,17,21-Shadow Lady 3.00
24,25,27-35-($3.95): 35-Big Bang vs. Alan Moore's "1963" characters 4.00
...Presents the Ultiman Family (2/05, $3.50) 3.50
...Round Table of America (2/04, $3.95) Don Thomas-a 4.00
...Summer Special (8/03, $4.95) World's Nastiest Nazis app. 5.00

BIG BANG PRESENTS (Volume 3)
Big Bang Comics: July, 2006 - No. 5 ($2.95/$3.95, B&W)

1,2: 1-Protoplasman (Plastic Man homage) 3.00
3-5-($3.95) 3-Origin of Protoplasman. 4-Flip book 4.00

BIG BANG UNIVERSE
AC Comics: 2015 ($9.95, B&W)

1-Four new stories; Ultiman, Knight Watchman, Galahad & Whiz Kids app. 10.00

BIG BLACK KISS
Vortex Comics: Sep, 1989 - No, 3, Nov, 1989 ($3.75, B&W, lim. series, mature)

1-3-Chaykin-s/a 5.00

BIG BLOWN BABY (Also see Dark Horse Presents)
Dark Horse Comics: Aug, 1996 - No. 4, Nov, 1996 ($2.95, lim. series, mature)

1-4: Bill Wray-c/a/scripts 3.00

BIG BOOK OF ..., THE
DC Comics (Paradox Press): 1994 - 1999 (B&W)($12.95 - $14.95)

nn-...**BAD,**1998 ($14.95),...**CONSPIRACIES,** 1995 ($12.95), ...**DEATH,**1994 ($12.95), ...**FREAKS,** 1996 ($14.95), ...**GRIMM,** 1999 ($14.95), ...**HOAXES,** 1996 ($14.95), ...**LITTLE CRIMINALS,** 1996 ($14.95), ...**LOSERS,**1997 ($14.95), **MARTYRS,** 1997 ($14.95), ...**SCANDAL,**1997 ($14.95), ...**THE WEIRD WILD WEST,**1998 ($14.95), ...**THUGS,** 1997 ($14.95), ...**UNEXPLAINED,** 1997 ($14.95), ...**URBAN LEGENDS,** 1994 ($12.95), ...**VICE,** 1999 ($14.95), ...**WEIRDOS,** 1995 ($12.95) cover price

BIG BOOK OF FUN COMICS (See New Book of Comics)
National Periodical Publications: Spring, 1936 (Large size, 52 pgs.)
(1st comic book annual & DC annual)

1 (Very rare)-r/New Fun #1-5 2500 5000 7500 16,500 - -

BIG BOOK ROMANCES
Fawcett Publications: Feb, 1950 (no date given) (148 pgs.)

1-Contains remaindered Fawcett romance comics - several combinations possible
93 186 279 591 1021 1450

BIG CHIEF WAHOO
Eastern Color Printing/George Dougherty (distr. by Fawcett): July, 1942 - No. 7, Wint., 1943/44?(no year given)(Quarterly)

1-Newspaper-r (on sale 6/15/42) 50 100 150 315 533 750
2-Steve Roper app. 24 48 72 144 237 330
3-5: 4-Chief is holding a Katy Keene comic in one panel
19 38 57 112 179 245
6-7 15 30 45 84 127 170

NOTE: *Kerry Drake in some issues.*

BIG CIRCUS, THE (Movie)
Dell Publishing Co.: No. 1036, Sept-Nov, 1959

Four Color 1036-Photo-c 6 12 18 40 73 105

BIG CON JOB, THE (PALMIOTTI & BRADY'S...)
BOOM! Studios: Mar, 2015 - No. 4, Jun, 2015 ($3.99, limited series)

1-4-Palmiotti & Brady-s/Stanton-a/Conner-c 4.00

BIG COUNTRY, THE (Movie)
Dell Publishing Co.: No. 946, Oct, 1958

Four Color 946-Photo-c 6 12 18 42 79 115

BIG DADDY DANGER
DC Comics: Oct, 2002 - No. 9, June, 2003 ($2.95, limited series)

1-9-Adam Pollina-s/a/c 3.00

BIG DADDY ROTH (Magazine)
Millar Publications: Oct-Nov, 1964 - No. 4, Apr-May, 1965 (35¢)

1-Toth-a; Batman & Robin parody 21 42 63 147 324 500
2-4-Toth-a 13 26 39 89 195 300

BIGFOOT
IDW Publishing: Feb, 2005 - No. 4, May, 2005 ($3.99, limited series)

1-4-Steve Niles & Rob Zombie-s/Richard Corben-a/c 4.00

BIG GIRLS
Image Comics: Aug, 2020 - No. 6, Jan, 2021 ($3.99)

1-6-Jason Howard-s/a 4.00

BIGG TIME
DC Comics (Vertigo): 2002 ($14.95, B&W, graphic novel)

nn-Ty Templeton-s/c/a 15.00

BIG GUY AND RUSTY THE BOY ROBOT, THE (Also See Madman Comics #6,7 & Martha Washington Stranded In Space)
Dark Horse (Legend): July, 1995 - No. 2, Aug, 1995 ($4.95, oversize, limited series)

1,2-Frank Miller scripts & Geoff Darrow-c/a 1 3 4 6 8 10

BIG HERO ADVENTURES (See Jigsaw)

BIG HERO 6 (Also see Sunfire & Big Hero Six)
Marvel Comics: Nov, 2008 - No. 5, Mar, 2009 ($3.99, limited series)

1-Claremont-s/Nakayama-a; 1-Character design pages & Handbook entries
3 6 9 21 33 45
2-5 1 3 4 6 8 10
...: Brave New Heroes 1 (11/12, $8.99) r/#1-5 2 4 6 8 11 14

BIG HERO 6: THE SERIES (Based on the Disney Channel animated series)
IDW Publishing: Nov, 2019 - Present ($3.99)

1-Blumenreich & Caramagna-s/Baldari-a; two covers 4.00

BIG JON & SPARKIE (Radio)(Formerly Sparkie, Radio Pixie)
Ziff-Davis Publ. Co.: No. 4, Sept-Oct, 1952 (Painted-c)

4-Based on children's radio program 21 42 63 122 199 275

BIG LAND, THE (Movie)
Dell Publishing Co.: No. 812, July, 1957

Four Color 812-Alan Ladd photo-c 8 16 24 52 99 145

BIG LIE, THE
Image Comics: Sept, 2011 ($3.99, one-shot)

1-Revisits the 9-11 attacks; Rick Veitch-s/a(p); Thomas Yeates-c 4.00

BIG MAN PLANS
Image Comics: Mar, 2015 - No. 4 ($3.50, limited series)

1-4-Eric Powell & Tim Wiesch-s/Powell-a/c 3.50

BIG MOOSE (Character from Archie Comics)
Archie Comics Publications: Jun, 2017 ($4.99, limited series)

..., One Shot - short stories by various; art by Cory Smith, Pitilli & Jampole 4.00

BIG RED (See Movie Comics)

BIG SHOT COMICS
Columbia Comics Group: May, 1940 - No. 104, Aug, 1949

1-Intro. Skyman; The Face (1st app.; Tony Trent), The Cloak (Spy Master), Marvelo, Monarch of Magicians, Joe Palooka, Charlie Chan, Tom Kerry, Dixie Dugan, Rocky Ryan begin; Charlie Chan moves over from Feature Comics #31 (4/40)
300 600 900 1950 3375 4800
2 103 206 309 659 1130 1600
3-The Cloak called Spy Chief; Skyman-c 97 194 291 621 1061 1500

	GD 2.0	VG 4.0	FN 6.0	VF 8.0	VF/NM 9.0	NM- 9.2
4,5	63	126	189	403	689	975
6-10: 8-Christmas-c	52	104	156	328	552	775
11-13	48	96	144	302	514	725
14-Origin & 1st app. Sparky Watts (6/41)	53	106	159	334	567	800
15-Origin The Cloak	61	122	183	390	670	950
16-20	40	80	120	246	411	575
21-23,27,30: 30-X-Mas-c, WWII-c	36	72	108	211	343	475
24-Classic Tojo-c.	142	284	426	909	1555	2200
25-Hitler-c	110	220	330	704	1202	1700
26,29-Japanese WWII-c. 29-Intro. Capt. Yank; Bo (a dog) newspaper strip-r by Frank Beck begin, ends #104.	45	90	135	284	480	675
28-Hitler, Tojo & Mussolini-c	148	296	444	947	1624	2300
31,33-40	26	52	78	152	249	340
32-Vic Jordan newspaper strip reprints begin, ends #52; Hitler, Tojo & Mussolini-c	123	246	369	787	1344	1900
41,42,44,45,47-50: 42-No Skyman. 50-Origin The Face retold	22	44	66	128	209	290
43-Hitler-c	119	238	357	762	1306	1850
46-Hitler, Tojo-c (6/44)	116	232	348	742	1271	1800
51-Tojo Japanese war-c	47	94	141	296	498	700
52-56,58-60:	19	38	57	111	176	240
57-Hitler, Tojo Halloween mask-c	48	96	144	302	514	725
61-70: 63 on-Tony Trent, the Face	15	30	45	85	130	175
71-80: 73-The Face cameo. 74-(2/47)-Mickey Finn begins. 74,80-The Face app. in Tony Trent. 78-Last Charlie Chan strip-r	14	28	42	80	115	150
81-90: 85-Tony Trent marries Babs Walsh. 86-Valentines-c	12	24	36	67	94	120
91-99,101-104: 69-94-Skyman in Outer Space. 96-Christmas-c	11	22	33	60	83	105
100	14	28	42	76	108	140

NOTE: ***Mart Bailey** art on "The Face" No. 1-104. **Guardineer** a-5. Sparky Watts by **Boody Rogers**-No. 14-42, 77-104, (by others No. 43-76). Others than Tony Trent wear "The Face" mask in No. 46-63, 93. Skyman by **Ogden Whitney**-No. 1, 2, 4, 12-37, 49, 70-101. Skyman covers-No. 1, 3, 7-12, 14, 16, 20, 27, 89, 95, 100.*

BIG SMASH BARGAIN COMICS
No publisher listed: 1950 - No. 6, 1951 (25¢, 160pgs., Canadian reprints)

	GD	VG	FN	VF	VF/NM	NM-
1-6: Contains 4 comics from various companies bundled with new cover (scarce)	48	96	144	302	514	725

BIG TEX
Toby Press: June, 1953

	GD	VG	FN	VF	VF/NM	NM-
1-Contains (3) John Wayne stories-r with name changed to Big Tex	15	30	45	84	127	170

BIG-3
Fox Feature Syndicate: Fall, 1940 - No. 7, Jan, 1942

	GD	VG	FN	VF	VF/NM	NM-
1-Blue Beetle, The Flame, & Samson begin	300	600	900	2010	3505	5000
2	126	252	378	806	1378	1950
3-5	97	194	291	621	1061	1500
6-Last Samson	74	148	222	470	810	1150
7-WWII Nazi-c; V-Man app.	97	194	291	621	1061	1500

BIG THUNDER MOUNTAIN RAILROAD (Disney Kingdoms)
Marvel Comics: May, 2015 - No. 5, Oct, 2015 ($3.99, limited series)

1-5: 1-Dennis Hopeless-s/Tigh Walker-a/Pasqual Ferry-c. 3-Ruiz-a 4.00

BIG TOP COMICS, THE (TV's Great Circus Show)
Toby Press: 1951 - No. 2, 1951 (No month)

	GD	VG	FN	VF	VF/NM	NM-
1	14	28	42	81	118	155
2	11	22	33	62	86	110

BIG TOWN (Radio/TV) (Also see Movie Comics, 1946)
National Periodical Publ: Jan, 1951 - No. 50, Mar-Apr, 1958 (No. 1-9: 52pgs.)

	GD	VG	FN	VF	VF/NM	NM-
1-Dan Barry-a begins	74	148	222	470	810	1150
2	39	78	117	231	378	525
3-10	24	48	72	142	234	325
11-20	19	38	57	111	176	240
21-31: Last pre-code (1-2/55)	14	28	42	80	115	150
32-50: 46-Grey tone cover	11	22	33	60	83	105

BIG TROUBLE IN LITTLE CHINA (Based on the 1986 Kurt Russell movie)
BOOM! Studios: Jun, 2014 - No. 25, Jun, 2016 ($3.99)

1-12-Continuing advs. of Jack Burton; John Carpenter & Eric Powell-s; Brian Churilla-a; multiple covers by Powell and others on each 4.00
13-24: 13-16-Van Lente-s/Eisma-a. 17-20-McDaid-a. 21-24-Santos-a 4.00
25-($4.99) Van Lente-s/Santos-a 5.00

BIG TROUBLE IN LITTLE CHINA / ESCAPE FROM NEW YORK (Based on the movies)
BOOM! Studios: Oct, 2016 - No. 6, Mar, 2017 ($3.99)

1-6-Jack Burton meets Snake Plisskin; Greg Pak-s/Daniel Bayliss-a 4.00

BIG TROUBLE IN LITTLE CHINA: OLD MAN JACK (Based on the movie)
BOOM! Studios: Sept, 2017 - No. 12, Aug, 2018 ($3.99)

1-12-Old Jack Burton battles Lo Pan; Carpenter & Burch-s/Corona-a; multiple covers 4.00

BIG VALLEY, THE (TV)
Dell Publishing Co.: June, 1966 - No. 5, Oct, 1967; No. 6, Oct, 1969

	GD	VG	FN	VF	VF/NM	NM-
1: Photo-c #1-5	5	10	15	33	57	80
2-6: 6-Reprints #1	3	6	9	21	33	45

BIKER MICE FROM MARS (TV)
Marvel Comics: Nov, 1993 - No. 3, Jan, 1994 ($1.50, limited series)

1-3: 1-Intro Vinnie, Modo & Throttle. 2-Origin 5.00

BILL & TED... (Movie)
OPUS: Sept, 2020 - No. 4, Dec, 2020 ($3.99, limited series)

...Present: Death (10/22, $6.66) Burnham-s/Manfredi-a; Beethoven app. 6.66
...'s Day of the Dead (11/22, $6.99) Montezuma, Freda Khalo, Death app. 7.00
...'s Excellent Holiday Special (12/22, $6.99) Christmas-themed 7.00

BILL & TED ARE DOOMED (Movie)
Dark Horse Comics: Sept, 2020 - No. 4, Dec, 2020 ($3.99, limited series)

1-4-Evan Dorkin-s/Roger Langridge-a; set in the year 2000 after the 2nd movie 4.00

BILL & TED GO TO HELL (Movie)
BOOM! Studios: Feb, 2016 - No. 4, May, 2016 ($3.99, limited series)

1-4-Joines-s/Bachan-a 4.00

BILL & TED ROLL THE DICE (Prequel to Bill & Ted's Bogus Journey)
OPUS: Jun, 2022 - No. 4, Sept, 2022 ($4.99, limited series)

1-4-Dungeons & Dragons themed adventure set before the 2nd movie 5.00

BILL & TED SAVE THE UNIVERSE (Movie)
BOOM! Studios: Jun, 2017 - No. 5, Oct, 2017 ($3.99, limited series)

1-5-Joines-s/Bachan-a 4.00

BILL & TED'S BOGUS JOURNEY
Marvel Comics: Sept, 1991 ($2.95, squarebound, 84 pgs.)

1-Adapts movie sequel 6.00

BILL & TED'S EXCELLENT COMIC BOOK (Movie)
Marvel Comics: Dec, 1991 - No. 12, 1992 ($1.00/$1.25)

1-12: 3-Begin $1.25-c 4.00

BILL & TED'S MOST TRIUMPHANT RETURN (Movie)
BOOM! Studios: Mar, 2015 - No. 6, Aug, 2015 ($3.99, limited series)

1-6: 1-Follows the end of the second movie; Lynch-s/Gaylord-a/Guillory-c 4.00

BILL BARNES COMICS (...America's Air Ace Comics No. 2 on) (Becomes Air Ace V2#1 on; also see Shadow Comics)
Street & Smith Publications: Oct, 1940(No. month given) - No. 12, Oct, 1943

	GD	VG	FN	VF	VF/NM	NM-
1-23 pgs.-comics; Rocket Rooney begins	119	238	357	762	1306	1850
2-Barnes as The Phantom Flyer app.; Tuska-a	61	122	183	390	670	950
3-5-War covers	48	96	144	302	514	725
6,8,10,12-War covers	42	84	126	265	445	625
7-(1942) Story about dropping atomic bomb on Japan	300	600	900	2070	3635	5200
9-Classic WWII cover	77	154	231	493	847	1200
11-Japanese WWII Gremlin cover	52	106	159	334	567	800

BILL BATTLE, THE ONE MAN ARMY (Also see Master Comics No. 133)
Fawcett Publications: Oct, 1952 - No. 4, Apr, 1953 (All photo-c)

	GD	VG	FN	VF	VF/NM	NM-
1	17	34	51	98	154	210
2	11	22	33	60	83	105
3,4	10	20	30	54	72	90

BILL BLACK'S FUN COMICS
Paragon #1-3/Americomics #4: Dec, 1982 - No. 4, Mar, 1983 ($1.75/$2.00, Baxter paper) (1st AC comic)

	GD	VG	FN	VF	VF/NM	NM-
1-(B&W fanzine; 7x8-1/2"; low print) Intro. Capt. Paragon, Phantom Lady & Commando D	3	6	9	16	23	30
2-4: 2,3-(B&W fanzines; 8-1/2x11"). 3-Kirby-c. 4-($2.00, color)-Origin Nightfall (formerly Phantom Lady); Nightveil app.; Kirby-a	2	4	6	8	11	14

BILL BOYD WESTERN (Movie star; see Hopalong Cassidy & Western Hero)
Fawcett Publ: Feb, 1950 - No. 23, June, 1952 (1-3,7,11,14-on: 36 pgs.)

	GD	VG	FN	VF	VF/NM	NM-
1-Bill Boyd & his horse Midnite begin; photo front/back-c	32	64	96	188	307	425
2-Painted-c	16	32	48	94	147	200
3-Photo-c begin, end #23; last photo back-c	14	28	42	80	115	150
4-6(52 pgs.)	12	24	36	69	97	125
7,11(36 pgs.)	10	20	30	56	76	95
8-10,12,13(52 pgs.)	10	20	30	58	79	100
14-22	9	18	27	52	69	85
23-Last issue	10	20	30	56	76	95

BILL BUMLIN (See Treasury of Comics No. 3)

BILL ELLIOTT (See Wild Bill Elliott)

BILLI 99
Dark Horse Comics: Sept, 1991 - No. 4, 1991 ($3.50, B&W, lim. series, 52 pgs.)

1-4: Tim Sale-c/a 4.00

BILLIONAIRE ISLAND
AHOY Comics: 2020 - No. 6, 2020 ($3.99, limited series)

1-6-Mark Russell-s/Steve Pugh-a 4.00

BILLIONAIRE ISLAND: CULT OF DOGS
AHOY Comics: 2022 - No. 6, 2023 ($3.99, limited series)

1-4-Mark Russell-s/Steve Pugh-a 4.00

BILL STERN'S SPORTS BOOK
Ziff-Davis Publ. Co.(Approved Comics): Spring-Sum, 1951 - V2#2, Win, 1952

	GD	VG	FN	VF	VF/NM	NM-
V1#10-(1951) Whitney painted-c	22	44	66	128	209	290
2-(Sum/52; reg. size)	17	34	51	100	158	215
V2#2-(1952, 96 pgs.)-Krigstein, Kinstler-a	22	44	66	132	216	300

BILL THE BULL: ONE SHOT, ONE BOURBON, ONE BEER
Boneyard Press: Dec, 1994 ($2.95, B&W, mature)

1 3.00

BILLY AND BUGGY BEAR (See Animal Fun)
I.W. Enterprises/Super: 1958; 1964

	GD	VG	FN	VF	VF/NM	NM-
I.W. Reprint #1, #7('58)-All Surprise Comics #?(Same issue-r for both)	2	4	6	13	18	22
Super Reprint #10(1964)	2	4	6	10	14	18

BILLY BATSON AND THE MAGIC OF SHAZAM! (Follows Shazam: The Monster Society of Evil mini-series)
DC Comics: Sept, 2008 - No. 21, Dec, 2010 ($2.25/$2.50, all ages title)

1-17: 1-4-Mike Kunkel-s/a/c; Theo (Black) Adam app. 5-DeStefano-a. 13-16-Black Adam 4.00
1-Variant B&W sketch cover 4.00
18-21 ($2.99) 21-Justice League cameo 4.00
TPB (2010, $12.99) r/#1-6; cover and haracter sketches 13.00
...: Mr. Mind Over Matter TPB (2011, $12.99) r/#7-12 13.00

Big Trouble in Little China #8 © 20-FOX

Bill Boyd Western #23 © FAW

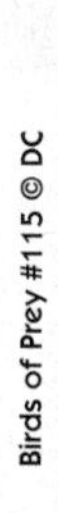
Birds of Prey #115 © DC

BILLY BUCKSKIN WESTERN (2-Gun Western No. 4)
Atlas Comics (IMC No. 1/MgPC No. 2,3): Nov, 1955 - No. 3, Mar, 1956

	GD 2.0	VG 4.0	FN 6.0	VF 8.0	VF/NM 9.0	NM- 9.2
1-Mort Drucker-a; Maneely-c/a	20	40	60	117	189	260
2-Mort Drucker-a	12	24	36	69	97	125
3-Williamson, Drucker-a	14	28	42	80	115	150

BILLY BUNNY (Black Cobra No. 6 on)
Excellent Publications: Feb-Mar, 1954 - No. 5, Oct-Nov, 1954

	GD 2.0	VG 4.0	FN 6.0	VF 8.0	VF/NM 9.0	NM- 9.2
1	11	22	33	64	90	115
2	8	16	24	40	50	60
3-5	6	12	18	31	38	45

BILLY BUNNY'S CHRISTMAS FROLICS
Farrell Publications: 1952 (25¢ Giant, 100 pgs.)

	GD 2.0	VG 4.0	FN 6.0	VF 8.0	VF/NM 9.0	NM- 9.2
1	24	48	72	142	234	325

BILLY MAKE BELIEVE
United Features Syndicate: No. 14, 1939

	GD 2.0	VG 4.0	FN 6.0	VF 8.0	VF/NM 9.0	NM- 9.2
Single Series 14	34	68	102	199	325	450

BILLY NGUYEN, PRIVATE EYE
Caliber Press: V2#1, 1990 ($2.50)

	GD 2.0	VG 4.0	FN 6.0	VF 8.0	VF/NM 9.0	NM- 9.2
V2#1						3.00

BILLY THE KID (Formerly The Masked Raider; also see Doc Savage Comics & Return of the Outlaw)
Charlton Publ. Co.: No. 9, Nov, 1957 - No. 121, Dec, 1976; No. 122, Sept, 1977 - No. 123, Oct, 1977; No. 124, Feb, 1978 - No. 153, Mar, 1983

	GD 2.0	VG 4.0	FN 6.0	VF 8.0	VF/NM 9.0	NM- 9.2
9	12	24	36	69	97	125
10,12,14,17-19: 12-2 pg Check-sty	8	16	24	42	54	65
11-(68 pgs.)-Origin & 1st app. The Ghost Train	9	18	27	52	69	85
13-Williamson/Torres-a	9	18	27	47	61	75
15-Origin; 2 pgs. Williamson-a	9	18	27	47	61	75
16-Williamson-a, 2 pgs.	8	16	24	44	57	70
20-26-Severin-a(3-4 each)	9	18	27	47	61	75
27-30: 30-Masked Rider app.	3	6	9	20	31	42
31-40	3	6	9	15	22	28
41-60	2	4	6	13	18	22
61-65	2	4	6	10	14	18
66-Bounty Hunter series begins.	3	6	9	14	20	25
67-80: Bounty Hunter series; not in #79,82,84-86	2	4	6	10	14	18
81-84,86-90: 87-Last Bounty Hunter. 88-1st app. Mr. Young of the Boothill Gazette	2	4	6	8	10	12
85-Early Kaluta-a (4 pgs.)	2	4	6	9	13	16
91-123: 110-Mr. Young of Boothill app. 111-Origin The Ghost Train. 117-Gunsmith & Co., The Cheyenne Kid app.	1	2	3	5	6	8
124(2/78)-153						6.00
Modern Comics 109 (1977 reprint)						5.00

NOTE: *Boyette a-88-110. Kim a-73. Morsi a-12,14. Sattler a-118-123. Severin a(r)-121-129, 134; c-23, 25. Sutton a-111.*

BILLY THE KID ADVENTURE MAGAZINE
Toby Press: Oct, 1950 - No. 29, 1955

	GD 2.0	VG 4.0	FN 6.0	VF 8.0	VF/NM 9.0	NM- 9.2
1-Williamson/Frazetta-a (2 pgs) r/from John Wayne Adventure Comics #2; photo-c	33	66	99	194	317	440
2-Photo-c	13	26	39	74	105	135
3-Williamson/Frazetta "The Claws of Death", 4 pgs. plus Williamson art	36	72	108	211	343	475
4,5,7,8,10: 4,7-Photo-c	9	18	27	52	69	85
6-Frazetta assist on "Nightmare"; photo-c	15	30	45	86	133	180
9-Kurtzman Pot-Shot Pete; photo-c	11	22	33	64	90	115
11,12,15-20: 11-Photo-c	8	16	24	42	54	65
13-Kurtzman-r/John Wayne #12 (Genius)	9	18	27	47	61	75
14-Williamson/Frazetta; r-of #1 (2 pgs.)	10	20	30	56	76	95
21,23-29	7	14	21	37	46	55
22-Williamson/Frazetta-r(1pg.)/#1; photo-c	8	16	24	42	54	65

BILLY THE KID AND OSCAR (Also see Fawcett's Funny Animals)
Fawcett Publications: Winter, 1945 - No. 3, Fall, 1946 (Funny animal)

	GD 2.0	VG 4.0	FN 6.0	VF 8.0	VF/NM 9.0	NM- 9.2
1	17	34	51	100	158	215
2,3	12	24	36	69	97	125

BILLY THE KID'S OLD TIMEY ODDITIES
Dark Horse Comics: Apr, 2005 - No. 4, July, 2005 ($2.99, limited series)

	GD 2.0	VG 4.0	FN 6.0	VF 8.0	VF/NM 9.0	NM- 9.2
1-4-Eric Powell-s/c; Kyle Hotz-a						4.00
TPB (2005, $13.95) r/series						14.00
... and the Ghostly Fiend of London (9/10 - No. 4, 12/10, $3.99) 1-4-Powell-s/c; Kyle Hotz-a; Goon back-up; Powell-s/a						4.00
... and the Orm of Loch Ness (10/12 - No. 4, 1/13, $3.50) 1-4-Powell-s/Hotz-a/c						4.00

BILLY WEST (Bill West No. 9,10)
Standard Comics (Visual Editions): 1949-No. 9, Feb, 1951; No. 10, Feb, 1952

	GD 2.0	VG 4.0	FN 6.0	VF 8.0	VF/NM 9.0	NM- 9.2
1	21	42	63	122	199	275
2	14	28	42	80	115	150
3-6,9,10	11	22	33	62	86	110
7,8-Schomburg-c	14	28	42	78	112	145

NOTE: *Celardo a-1-6, 9; c-1-3. Moreira a-3. Roussos a-2.*

BING CROSBY (See Feature Films)

BINGO (...Comics) (H. C. Blackerby)
Howard Publ.: 1945 (Reprints National material)

	GD 2.0	VG 4.0	FN 6.0	VF 8.0	VF/NM 9.0	NM- 9.2
1-L. B. Cole opium-c; blank back-c	45	90	135	284	480	675

BINGO, THE MONKEY DOODLE BOY
St. John Publishing Co.: Aug, 1951; Oct, 1953

	GD 2.0	VG 4.0	FN 6.0	VF 8.0	VF/NM 9.0	NM- 9.2
1(8/51)-By Eric Peters	13	26	39	74	105	135
1(10/53)	10	20	30	54	72	90

BINKY (Formerly Leave It to...)
National Periodical Publ./DC Comics: No. 72, 4-5/70 - No. 81, 10-11/71; No. 82, Summer/77

	GD 2.0	VG 4.0	FN 6.0	VF 8.0	VF/NM 9.0	NM- 9.2
72-76	5	10	15	30	50	70
77-79: (68 pgs.). 77-Bobby Sherman 1pg. story w/photo. 78-1 pg. sty on Barry Williams of Brady Bunch. 79-Osmonds 1pg. story	6	12	18	38	69	100
80,81 (52 pgs.)-Sweat Pain story	5	10	15	34	60	85
82 (1977, one-shot)	5	10	15	30	50	70

BINKY'S BUDDIES
National Periodical Publications: Jan-Feb, 1969 - No. 12, Nov-Dec, 1970

	GD 2.0	VG 4.0	FN 6.0	VF 8.0	VF/NM 9.0	NM- 9.2
1	9	18	27	58	114	170
2-12: 3-Last 12¢ issue	5	10	15	30	50	70

BIONIC MAN (TV)
Dynamite Entertainment: 2011 - No. 26, 2013 ($3.99)

	GD 2.0	VG 4.0	FN 6.0	VF 8.0	VF/NM 9.0	NM- 9.2
1-26: 1-Kevin Smith & Phil Hester-s; Lau-a; multiple covers. 12-15-Bigfoot app.						4.00
Annual 1 (2013, $4.99) The Venus Probe; Beatty-s/Mayhew-c						5.00

BIONIC MAN VS. THE BIONIC WOMAN (TV)
Dynamite Entertainment: 2013 - No. 5, 2013 ($3.99, limited series)

	GD 2.0	VG 4.0	FN 6.0	VF 8.0	VF/NM 9.0	NM- 9.2
1-5-Champagne-s/Luis-a; 3 covers on each						4.00

BIONIC WOMAN, THE (TV)
Charlton Publications: Oct, 1977 - No. 5, June, 1978

	GD 2.0	VG 4.0	FN 6.0	VF 8.0	VF/NM 9.0	NM- 9.2
1	6	12	18	38	69	100
2-5	4	8	12	23	37	50

BIONIC WOMAN, THE (TV)
Dynamite Entertainment: 2013 - No. 10, 2013 ($3.99)

	GD 2.0	VG 4.0	FN 6.0	VF 8.0	VF/NM 9.0	NM- 9.2
1-10: 1-Tobin-s/Renaud-c/Carvalho-a; origin re-told						4.00

BIONIC WOMAN, THE: SEASON FOUR (TV)
Dynamite Entertainment: 2014 - No. 4, 2014 ($3.99, limited series)

	GD 2.0	VG 4.0	FN 6.0	VF 8.0	VF/NM 9.0	NM- 9.2
1-4-Jerwa-s/Cabrera-a. 1-Reg & photo-c						4.00

BIRDS OF PREY (Also see Black Canary/Oracle: Birds of Prey)
DC Comics: Jan, 1999 - No. 127, Apr, 2009 ($1.99/$2.50/$2.99)

	GD 2.0	VG 4.0	FN 6.0	VF 8.0	VF/NM 9.0	NM- 9.2
1-Dixon-s/Land-c/a	2	4	6	10	14	18
2-4						6.00
5-7,9-15: 15-Guice-a begins.						4.00
8-Nightwing-c/app.; Barbara & Dick's circus date	4	8	12	27	44	60
16-38: 23-Grodd-c/app. 26-Bane app. 32-Noto-c begin						3.00
39,40-Bruce Wayne: Murderer pt. 5,12						3.50
41-Bruce Wayne: Fugitive pt. 2						4.00
42-46: 42-Fabry-a. 45-Deathstroke-c/app.						3.00
47-74,77-91: 47-49-Terry Moore-s/Conner & Palmiotti-a; Noto-c. 50-Gilbert Hernandez-s begin. 52,54-Metamorpho app. 56-Simone-s/Benes-a begin. 65,67,68,70-Land-c. 86-Timm-a (7 pgs.)						3.00
75-($2.95) Pearson-c; back-up story of Lady Blackhawk						4.00
76-Debut of Black Alice (from Day of Vengeance)	2	4	6	9	12	15
92-99,101-127: 92-One Year Later. 94-Begin $2.99-c; Prometheus app. 96,97-Black Alice app. 98,99-New Batgirl app. 99-Black Canary leaves the team. 104-107-Secret Six app.						3.00
100-($3.99) new team recruited; Black Canary origin re-told						4.00
TPB (1999, $17.95) r/ previous series and one-shots						18.00
...: Batgirl 1 (2/98, $2.95) Dixon-s/Frank-c						5.00
...: Batgirl/Catwoman 1 ('03, $5.95) Robertson-a; cont'd in BOP: Catwoman/Oracle 1						6.00
...: Between Dark & Dawn TPB (2006, $14.99) r/#69-75						15.00
...: Blood and Circuits TPB (2007, $17.99) r/#96-103						18.00
...: Catwoman/Oracle 1 ('03, $5.95) Cont'd from BOP: Batgirl/Catwoman 1; David Ross-a						6.00
...: Club Kids TPB (2008, $17.99) r/#109-112,118						18.00

...: Dead of Winter TPB (2008, $17.99) r/#104-108 18.00
...: Metropolis or Dust TPB (2008, $17.99) r/#113-117 18.00
...: Of Like Minds TPB (2004, $14.95) r/#55-61 15.00
...: Old Friends, New Enemies TPB (2003, $17.95) r/#1-6, ...: Batgirl, ...: Wolves 18.00
...: Perfect Pitch TPB (2007, $17.99) r/#86-90,92-95 18.00
...: Platinum Flats TPB (2009, $17.99) r/#119-124 18.00
...: Revolution 1 (1997, $2.95) Frank-c/Dixon-s 5.00
... Secret Files 2003 (8/03, $4.95) Short stories, pin-ups and profile pages; Noto-c 5.00
...: Sensei and Student TPB (2005, $17.95) r/#62-68 18.00
...: The Battle Within TPB (2006, $17.99) r/#76-85 18.00
...: The Ravens 1 (6/98, $1.95)-Dixon-s; Girlfrenzy issue 4.00
...: Wolves 1 (10/97, $2.95) Dixon-s/Giordano & Faucher-a 5.00

BIRDS OF PREY (Brightest Day)
DC Comics: Jul, 2010 - No. 15, Oct, 2011 ($2.99)

1-Simone-s/Benes-a/c; Hawk and Dove join team, Penguin app. 4.00
1-Variant cover by Chiang 6.00
2-15: 2-4-Penguin app. 7-10-"Death of Oracle". 11-Catman app. 14,15-Tucci-a 3.00
... End Run HC (2011, $22.99, d.j.) r/#1-6 23.00

BIRDS OF PREY (DC New 52)
DC Comics: Nov, 2011 - No. 34, Oct, 2014 ($2.99)

1-24: 1-Swierczynski-s/Saiz-a; intro. Starling. 2-Katana & Poison Ivy join. 4-Batgirl joins. 9-Night of the Owls. 16-Strix joins. 18-20-Mr. Freeze app. 3.00
25-($3.99) Zero Year tie-in; flashback to Dinah's childhood; John Lynch app. 4.00
26-34: 26-Birds vs. Basilisk. 28-Gothtopia tie-in; Ra's al Ghul app. 32-34-Suicide Squad 3.00
#0 (11/12, $2.99) Black Canary and Batgirl first meeting; Molenaar-a/Lau-c 3.00
...: Futures End 1 (11/14, $2.99, regular-c) Five years later; The Red League 3.00
...: Futures End 1 (11/14, $3.99, 3-D cover) 4.00

BIRDS OF PREY GIANT
DC Comics: 2019 - Present ($4.99, 100 pgs., squarebound, Mass Market & Direct Market editions exist for each issue, with different covers)

1-Three new stories plus reprints; Harley Quinn app.; Lupacchino-c 5.00

BIRDS OF PREY: MANHUNT
DC Comics: Sept, 1996 - No. 4, Dec, 1996 ($1.95, limited series)

1-Features Black Canary, Oracle, Huntress, & Catwoman; Chuck Dixon scripts; Gary Frank-c on all. 1-Catwoman cameo only 1 2 3 5 6 8
2-4 6.00
NOTE: *Gary Frank c-1-4. Matt Haley a-1-4p. Wade Von Grawbadger a-1i.*

BIRTH CAUL, THE
Eddie Campbell Comics: 1999 ($5.95, B&W, one-shot)

1-Alan Moore-s/Eddie Campbell-a 6.00

BIRTH OF THE DEFIANT UNIVERSE, THE
Defiant: May, 1993

nn-Contains promotional artwork & text; limited edition of 1000 copies signed & numbered by Jim Shooter 6 12 18 38 69 100
Regular unsigned issue 5 10 15 31 53 75

BIRTHRIGHT
Image Comics (Skybound): Oct, 2014 - No. 50, Jun, 2021 ($2.99/$3.99)

1-25-Joshua Williamson-s/Andrei Bressan-a 3.00
26-50-($3.99) 27-Regular & Walking Dead tribute covers. 45-Bonus preview of Stillwater 4.00

BISHOP (See Uncanny X-Men & X-Men)
Marvel Comics: Dec, 1994 - No.4, Mar, 1995 ($2.95, limited series)

1-4: Foil-c; Shard & Mountjoy in all. 1-Storm app. 4.00

BISHOP THE LAST X-MAN
Marvel Comics: Oct, 1999 - No. 16, Jan, 2001 ($2.99/$1.99/$2.25)

1-($2.99)-Jeanty-a 5.00
2-8-($1.99): 2-Two covers 4.00
9-11,13-16: 9-Begin $2.25-c. 15-Maximum Security x-over; Xavier app. 4.00
12-($2.99) 5.00

BISHOP: WAR COLLEGE
Marvel Comics: Apr, 2023 - Present ($4.99, limited series)

1-($4.99) Holtham-s/Hill-a; Armor & Surge app. 5.00

BISHOP: XAVIER SECURITY ENFORCER
Marvel Comics: Jan, 1998 - No.3, Mar, 1998 ($2.50, limited series)

1-3: Ostrander-s 4.00

BITCH PLANET
Image Comics: Dec, 2014 - No. 9, Apr, 2017 ($3.50/$3.99)

1-DeConnick-s/De Landro-a/c 5.00
2-9: 3-Origin of Penny Rolle. 5-Begin $3.99-c. 6-Meiko flashback 4.00

BITCH PLANET: TRIPLE FEATURE
Image Comics: Jun, 2017 - No. 5, Oct, 2017 ($3.99)

1-5-Short story anthology by various; De Landro-c. 5-Charretier-a 4.00

BITE CLUB
DC Comics (Vertigo): Jun, 2004 - No. 6, Nov, 2004 ($2.95, limited series)

1-6-Chaykin-s/Tischman-a/Quitely-c 3.00
TPB Digest (2005, $9.99) r/#1-6; cover gallery 10.00
The Complete Bite Club TPB (2007, $19.99) r/#1-6 and ...: Vampire Crime Unit #1-5 20.00

BITE CLUB: VAMPIRE CRIME UNIT
DC Comics (Vertigo): Jun, 2006 - No. 5, Oct, 2006 ($2.99, limited series)

1-5: 1-Chaykin & Tischman-s/Hahn-a/Quitely-c. 4-Chaykin-c 3.00

BITTER ROOT
Image Comics: Nov, 2018 - Present ($3.99)

1-15-David F. Walker & Chuck Brown-s/Sanford Greene-a 4.00
... Red Summer Special 1 (7/19, $5.99) Short stories by various; Greene-c 6.00

BIZARRE ADVENTURES (Formerly Marvel Preview)
Marvel Comics Group: No. 25, 3/81 - No. 34, 2/83 (#25-33: Magazine-$1.50)

25-Lethal Ladies 3 6 9 17 25 34
26-King Kull; Bolton-c/a 2 4 6 10 14 18
27,28: 27-Phoenix, Iceman & Nightcrawler app. 28-The Unlikely Heroes; Elektra by Miller; Neal Adams-a 2 4 6 13 18 22
29,30,32,33: 29-Stephen King's Lawnmower Man. 30-Tomorrow; 1st app. Silhouette. 32-Gods; Thor-c/s. 33-Horror; Dracula app.; photo-c. 2 3 4 6 8 10
31-After The Violence Stops; new Hangman story; Miller-a 2 4 6 8 12 15
34 ($2.00, Baxter paper, comic size)-Son of Santa; Christmas special; Howard the Duck by Paul Smith 2 4 6 9 13 16
No. 1 (12/19, $4.99) Short stories; Bloodstone, Shang-Chi, Dracula; Black Goliath app. 5.00
NOTE: *Alcala a-27i. Austin a-25i, 28i. Bolton a-26, 32. J. Buscema a-27p, 29, 30p; c-26. Byrne a-31 (2 pg.). Golden a-25p, 28p. Perez a-27p. Rogers a-25p. Simonson a-29; c-29. Paul Smith a-34.*

BIZARRO
DC Comics: Aug, 2015 - No. 6, Jan, 2016 ($2.99, limited series)

1-6-Corson-s/Duarte-a; Jimmy Olsen app. 4-Zatanna app. 6-Superman app. 3.00

BIZARRO COMICS!
DC Comics: 2001 ($29.95, hardcover, one-shot)

HC-Short stories of DC heroes by various alternative cartoonists including Dorkin, Pope, Haspiel, Kidd, Kochalka, Millionaire, Stephens, Wray; includes "Superman's Babysitter" by Kyle Baker from Elseworlds 80-Page Giant recalled by DC; Groening-c 30.00
Softcover (2003, $19.95) 20.00

BIZARRO WORLD
DC Comics: 2005 ($29.95, hardcover, one-shot)

HC-Short stories by various alternative cartoonists including Bagge, Baker, Dorkin, Dunn, Kupperman, Morse, Oswalt, Pekar, Simpson, Stewart; Jaime Hernandez-c 30.00
Softcover (2006, $19.99) 20.00

BLACK ADAM (See 52 and Countdown)
DC Comics: Oct, 2007 - No. 6, Mar, 2008 ($2.99, limited series)

1-Mahnke-a/c; Isis returns; Felix Faust app. 2 4 6 10 14 18
1-Variant-c by Alex Ross 6 12 18 38 69 100
2-6 5.00
....: Endless Winter Special (2/21, $3.99) Part 8 of crossover event; Frost King app. 4.00
...: The Dark Age TPB (2008, $17.99) r/#1-6; Alex Ross-c 18.00
...: Year of the Villain 1 (12/19, $4.99) Jenkins-s/Miranda-a; battles King Shazam 5.00

BLACK ADAM
DC Comics: Aug, 2022 - No. 12 ($3.99, limited series)

1-8: 1-5-Priest-s/Sandoval-a. 1-Intro. Malik White. 2-Debut of White Adam. 6-Batman app. 4.00

BLACK ADAM – THE JUSTICE SOCIETY FILES (From the 2022 movie)
DC Comics: Sept, 2022 - Dec, 2022 ($5.99, series of one-shots)

...: Atom Smasher 1 (11/22) Early adventures; Cavan Scott-s/Travis Mercer-a 6.00
...: Cyclone 1 (10/22) Maxine Hunkel's invite to the JSA; Hawkman app.; Scott-s/Sanapo-a 6.00
...: Dr. Fate 1 (12/22) Prelude to the movie; Scott-s/Merino-a 6.00
...: Hawkman 1 (9/22) Gentleman Ghost app.; Scott-s/Eaton-a 6.00

BLACK AND WHITE (See Large Feature Comic, Series I)

BLACK & WHITE (Also see Codename: Black & White)
Image Comics (Extreme): Oct, 1994 - No. 3, Jan, 1995 ($1.95, limited series)

1-3: Thibert-c/story 3.00

BLACK & WHITE MAGIC
Innovation Publishing: 1991 ($2.95, 98 pgs., B&W w/30 pgs. color, squarebound)

1-Contains rebound comics w/covers removed; contents may vary 4.00

BLACK AXE
Marvel Comics (UK): Apr, 1993 - No. 7, Oct, 1993 ($1.75)

1-4: 1-Romita Jr.-c. 2-Sunfire-c/s 3.00
5-7: 5-Janson-c; Black Panther app. 6,7-Black Panther-c/s 3.00

BLACK BADGE
BOOM! Studios: Aug, 2018 - No. 12, Jul, 2019 ($3.99)

1-12-Matt Kindt-s/Tyler Jenkins-a 4.00

BLACKBALL COMICS
Blackball Comics: Mar, 1994 ($3.00)

1-Trencher-c/story by Giffen; John Pain by O'Neill 3.00

BLACK BAT, THE
Dynamite Entertainment: 2013 - No. 12, 2014 ($3.99)

1-12-Buccellato-s/Cliquet-a; multiple covers on each 4.00

BLACKBEARD'S GHOST (See Movie Comics)

BLACK BEAUTY (See Son of Black Beauty)
Dell Publishing Co.: No. 440, Dec, 1952

Four Color 440 6 12 18 35 69 100

BLACK BEETLE, THE
Dark Horse Comics: Jan, 2013 - No. 4, Jun, 2013 ($3.99, limited series)

1-4-Francavilla-s/a/c 4.00

BLACKBIRD
Image Comics: Oct, 2018 - No. 6, Mar, 2019 ($3.99)

1-6-Sam Humphries-s/Jen Bartel-a 4.00

BLACK BOLT (The Inhumans)
Marvel Comics: Jul, 2017 - No. 12, Jun, 2018 ($3.99)

1-12: 1-6-Saladin Ahmed-s/Christian Ward-a; Absorbing Man app. 7-Irving-a 4.00

BLACK BOLT: SOMETHING INHUMAN THIS WAY COMES
Marvel Comics: Sept, 2013 ($7.99, one-shot)

1-Reprints Black Bolt app. in Amazing Adventures #5-10 & Avengers #95 8.00

BLACKBURNE COVENANT, THE
Dark Horse Comics: Apr, 2003 - No. 4, July, 2003 ($2.99, limited series)

1-4-Nicieza-s/Raffaele-a 3.00
TPB (2003, $12.95) r/#1-4 13.00

BLACK CANARY (See All Star Comics #38, Flash Comics #86, Justice League of America

Bitch Planet #4 © Milkfed Criminals

Black Cat Comics #45 © HARV

Black Cloud #1 © Againdemon

GD 2.0 | VG 4.0 | FN 6.0 | VF 8.0 | VF/NM 9.0 | NM- 9.2

#75 & World's Finest #244)
DC Comics: Nov, 1991 - No. 4, Feb, 1992 ($1.75, limited series)
1-4 3.00

BLACK CANARY
DC Comics: Jan, 1993 - No. 12, Dec, 1993 ($1.75)
1-Sarah Byam-s/Trevor Von Eeden-a/c 6.00
2-7 3.00
8-12: 8-The Ray-c/story. 9,10-Huntress-c/story 3.00

BLACK CANARY (Follows Oliver Queen's marriage proposal in Green Arrow #75)
DC Comics: Early Sept, 2007 - No. 4, Late Oct, 2007 ($2.99, bi-weekly limited series)
1-4-Bedard-s/Siqueira-a 3.00
... Wedding Planner 1 (11/07, $2.99) Roux-c/Ferguson & Norrie-a 3.00

BLACK CANARY
DC Comics: Aug, 2015 - No. 12, Aug, 2016 ($2.99)
1-12: 1-Fletcher-s/Annie Wu-a/c. 4,5-Guerra-a. 8-Vixen app. 9-Moritat-a. 10-Batgirl app. 3.00

BLACK CANARY AND ZATANNA; BLOODSPELL
DC Comics: 2014 ($22.99, hardcover graphic novel, dustjacket)
HC-Paul Dini-s/Joe Quinones-a; includes script and sketch art 23.00

BLACK CANARY/ORACLE: BIRDS OF PREY (Also see Showcase '96 #3)
DC Comics: 1996 ($3.95, one-shot)
1-Chuck Dixon scripts & Gary Frank-c/a. 2 4 6 13 18 22

BLACK CAT (From Spider-Man)
Marvel Comics: Aug, 2019 - No. 12, Oct, 2020 ($4.99/$3.99)
1-($4.99) MacKay-s/Foreman-a; back-up story with The Black Fox & Dracula 5.00
2-12-($3.99) 4,5-Johnny Storm app. 9,10-Wolverine app. 11,12-Iron Man app. 4.00
Annual 1 (1/20, $4.99) MacKay-s; "Wedding" of Spider-Man & Black Cat 5.00

BLACK CAT (From Spider-Man)(Story concludes in Giant-Size Black Cat: Infinity Score)
Marvel Comics: Feb, 2021 - No. 10, Nov, 2021 ($3.99)
1-10: 1-3-"King In Black" tie-ins; MacKay-s/Villa-a. 10-Nighthawk app. 4.00
Annual 1 (8/21, $4.99) MacKay-s/Vazquez-a; Infinite Destinies; The White Fox app. 5.00

BLACK CAT (AMAZING SPIDER-MAN PRESENTS...)
Marvel Comics: Aug, 2010 - No. 4, Dec, 2010 ($3.99, limited series)
1-4-Van Meter-s/Pulido-a/Conner-c; Spider-Man & Ana Kraven app. 5.00

BLACK CAT COMICS (...Western #16-19; ...Mystery #30 on)
(See All-New #7,9, The Original Black Cat, Pocket & Speed Comics)
Harvey Publications (Home Comics): June-July, 1946 - No. 29, June, 1951
1-Kubert-a; Joe Simon c-1,2 103 206 309 659 1130 1600
2-Kubert-a 48 96 144 302 514 725
3,4: 4-The Red Demons begin (The Demon #4 & 5)
39 78 117 240 395 550
5,6,7: 5,6-The Scarlet Arrow app. in ea. by Powell; S&K-a in both. 6-Origin Red Demon.
7-Vagabond Prince by S&K plus 1 more story 43 86 129 271 461 650
8-S&K-a; Kerry Drake begins, ends #13 47 94 141 296 498 700
9-Origin Stuntman (r/Stuntman #1) 43 86 129 271 461 650
10-20: 14,15,17-Mary Worth app. plus Invisible Scarlet O'Neil-#15,20,24
31 62 93 182 296 410
21-26 24 48 72 140 230 320
27,28: 27-Used in **SOTI**, pg. 193; X-Mas-c; 2 pg. John Wayne story. 28-Intro.
Kit, Black Cat's new sidekick 28 56 84 168 274 380
29-Black Cat bondage-c; Black Cat stories 31 62 93 182 296 410

BLACK CAT MYSTERY (Formerly Black Cat; ...Western Mystery #54; ...Western #55,56; ...Mystery #57; ...Mystic #58-62; Black Cat #63-65)
Harvey Publications: No. 30, Aug, 1951 - No. 65, Apr, 1963
30-Black Cat on cover and first page only 45 90 135 284 480 675
31,32,34,37,38,40 37 74 111 222 361 500
33-Used in **POP**, pg. 89; electrocution-c 61 122 183 390 670 950
35-Atomic disaster cover/story 50 100 150 315 533 750
36,39-Used in **SOTI**: #36-Pgs. 270,271; #39-Pgs. 386-388
65 130 195 416 708 1000
41-43 36 72 108 214 347 480
44-Eyes, ears, tongue cut out; Nostrand-a 65 130 195 416 708 1000
45-Classic "Colorama" by Powell; Nostrand-a 142 284 426 909 1555 2200
46-49,51-Nostrand-a in all. 51-Story has blank panel covering censored art (post-Code)
39 78 117 231 378 525
50-Check-a; classic Warren Kremer-c showing a man's face & hands burning away
1000 2000 3000 7600 13,800 20,000
52,53 (r/#34 & 35) 24 48 72 142 234 325
54-Two Black Cat stories (2/55, last pre-code) 26 54 78 154 252 350
55,56-Black Cat app. 22 44 66 132 216 300
57(7/56)-Kirby-c 24 48 72 142 234 325
58-60-Kirby-a(4). 58,59-Kirby-c. 60,61-Simon-c 28 56 84 165 270 375
61-Nostrand-a; "Colorama" r/#45 26 52 78 154 252 350
62 (3/58)-E.C. story swipe 22 44 66 132 216 300
63-65: Giants(10/62,1/63, 4/63); Reprints; Black Cat app. 63-origin Black Kitten.
65-1 pg. Powell-a 26 52 78 154 252 350
NOTE: ***Kremer** a-37, 39, 43; c-36, 37, 47. **Meskin** a-51. **Palais** a-30, 31(2), 32(2), 33-35, 37-40. **Powell** a-32-35, 36(2), 40, 41, 43-53, 57. **Simon** c-63-65. **Sparling** a-44. Bondage c-32, 34, 43.*

BLACK CLOUD
Image Comics: Apr, 2017 - No. 10, Jun, 2018 ($3.99)
1-10: 1-Latour & Brandon-s/Hinkle-a 4.00

BLACK COBRA (Bride's Diary No. 4 on) (See Captain Flight #8)
Ajax/Farrell Publications(Excellent Publ.): No. 1, 10-11/54; No. 6(No. 2), 12-1/54-55; No. 3, 2-3/55
1-Re-intro Black Cobra & The Cobra Kid (costumed heroes)
48 96 144 302 514 725
6(#2)-Formerly Billy Bunny 26 52 78 154 252 350
3-(Pre-code)-Torpedoman app. 25 50 75 150 245 340

BLACK CONDOR (Also see Crack Comics, Freedom Fighters & Showcase '94 #10,11)
DC Comics: June, 1992 - No. 12, May, 1993 ($1.25)
1-8-Heath-c 3.00
9-12: 9,10,12-Heath-c. 9,10-The Ray app. 12-Batman-c/app. 3.00

BLACK CROSS SPECIAL (See Dark Horse Presents)
Dark Horse Comics: Jan, 1988 ($1.75, B&W, one-shot)(Reprints & new-a)
1-1st printing 4.00
1-(2nd printing) has 2 pgs. new-a 3.00
...: Dirty Work 1 (4/97, $2.95) Chris Warner-c/s/a 3.00

BLACK CROWN QUARTERLY
IDW Publishing: Oct, 2017 - No. 3, Apr, 2018 ($6.99, quarterly)
1-3-Short story anthology with creator interviews and series previews 7.00

BLACK DIAMOND
Americomics: May, 1983 - No. 5, 1984 (no month)($2.00-$1.75, Baxter paper)
1-3-Movie adapt.; 1-Colt back-up begins 4.00
4,5 3.00
NOTE: ***Bill Black** a-1i; c-1. **Gulacy** c-2-5. Sybil Danning photo back-c-1.*

BLACK DIAMOND WESTERN (Formerly Desperado No. 1-8)
Lev Gleason Publ: No. 9, Mar, 1949 - No. 60, Feb, 1956 (No. 9-28: 52 pgs.)
9-Black Diamond & his horse Reliapon begin; origin & 1st app. Black Diamond
22 44 66 132 216 300
10 12 24 36 69 97 125
11-15 10 20 30 54 72 90
16-28(11/49-11/51)-Wolverton's Bingbang Buster 14 28 42 76 108 140
29-40: 31-One pg. Frazetta anti-drug ad 9 18 27 47 61 75
41-50,53-59 8 16 24 40 50 60
51-3-D effect-c/story 15 30 45 85 130 175
52-3-D effect story 14 28 42 81 118 155
60-Last issue 8 16 24 44 57 70
NOTE: ***Biro** c-9-35?. **Cooper** a-12. **Myron Foss** a-54-58, c-54-56, 58. **Guardineer** a-9, 12, 15, 18. **Jack Keller** a-12. **Kida** a-9. **Maurer** a-10. **Ed Moore** a-16. **Morisi** a-55. **William Overgard** a-9-23. **Tuska** a-10, 48. **Bill Walton** a-57.*

BLACK DRAGON, THE
Marvel Comics (Epic Comics): May, 1985 - No. 6, Oct, 1985 (Baxter paper, mature)
1-6: 1-Chris Claremont story & John Bolton painted-c/a in all 4.00
TPB (Dark Horse, 4/96, $17.95, B&W, trade paperback) r/#1-6; intro by Anne McCaffrey 18.00

BLACK DYNAMITE (Based on the Michael Jai White film)
IDW Publishing: Dec, 2013 - No. 4, Aug, 2014 ($3.99)
1-4: 1-Ash-s/Wimberly-a; multiple covers. 2,3-Ferreira-a 4.00

BLACKEST NIGHT (2009 Green Lantern & DC crossover) (Leads into Brightest Day series)
DC Comics: No. 0, Jun, 2009 - No. 8, May, 2010 ($3.99, limited series)
0-Free Comic Book Day edition; Johns-s/Reis-a; profile pages of different corps 3.00
1-8: 1-($3.99) Black Lantern Corps arises; Johns-s/Reis-c/a; Hawkman & Hawkgirl killed.
4-Nekron rises. 8-Dead heroes return 5.00
1-Variant cover by Van Sciver 10.00
1-3,5: 2nd-4th printings 4.00
2-8: 2-Cascioli variant-c. 3-Van Sciver variant-c. 4-7-Migliari variant-c. 8-Mahnke var-c 8.00
... Director's Cut (6/10, $5.99) Commentary with story panels; cover gallery, script pgs. 6.00
HC (2010, $29.99, d.j.) r/#0-8 & Blackest Night Director's Cut; variant cover gallery 30.00
SC (2011, $19.99) r/#0-8 & Blackest Night Director's Cut; variant cover gallery 20.00
...: Black Lantern Corps Vol. 1 HC (2010, $24.99, d.j.) r/BN: Batman, BN: Superman, and

BN: Titans series; cover gallery and character sketch designs 25.00
...: Black Lantern Corps Vol. 1 SC (2011, $19.99) same contents as HC edition 20.00
...: Black Lantern Corps Vol. 2 HC (2010, $24.99, d.j.) r/BN: The Flash, BN: JSA, and BN: Wonder Woman series; cover gallery and character sketch designs 25.00
...: Rise of the Black Lanterns HC (2010, $24.99) r/one-shots Atom and Hawkman #46, Catwoman #83, Phantom Stranger #42, Power of Shazam #48, The Question #37, Starman #81, Weird Western Tales #71, Green Arrow #30 & Adventure Comics #7; sketch art 25.00
...: Rise of the Black Lanterns SC (2011, $19.99) same contents as HC edition 20.00

BLACKEST NIGHT: BATMAN (2009 Green Lantern & DC crossover)
DC Comics: Oct, 2009 - No. 3, Dec, 2009 ($2.99, limited series)

1-3: 1-Bat-parents rise as Black Lanterns; Deadman app.; Syaf-a/Andy Kubert-c; 2 printings. 3-Flying Graysons return 3.00
1-3-Variant-c by Sienkiewicz 5.00

BLACKEST NIGHT: JSA (2009 Green Lantern & DC crossover)
DC Comics: Feb, 2010 - No. 3, Apr, 2010 ($2.99, limited series)

1-3-Original Sandman, Dr. Midnite and Mr. Terrific rise; Barrows-a/c 3.00
1-3-Variant-c by Gene Ha 5.00

BLACKEST NIGHT: SUPERMAN (2009 Green Lantern & DC crossover)
DC Comics: Oct, 2009 - No. 3, Dec, 2009 ($2.99, limited series)

1-3-Earth-2 Superman and Lois become Black Lanterns; Barrows-a/c; 2 printings 3.00
1-3-Variant-c by Shane Davis 5.00

BLACKEST NIGHT: TALES OF THE CORPS (2009 Green Lantern & DC crossover)
DC Comics: Sept, 2009 - No. 3, Sept, 2009 ($3.99, weekly limited series)

1-3-Short stories by various; interlocking cover images. 3-Commentary on B.N. #0 4.00
HC (2010, $24.99) r/#1-3 & Adventure Comics #4,5 & Green Lantern #49; sketch art 25.00
SC (2011, $19.99) r/#1-3 & Adventure Comics #4,5 & Green Lantern #49; sketch art 20.00

BLACKEST NIGHT: THE FLASH (2009 Green Lantern & DC crossover)
DC Comics: Feb, 2010 - No. 3, Apr, 2010 ($2.99, limited series)

1-3-Rogues vs. Dead Rogues; Johns-s/Kolins-a 3.00
1-3-Variant-c by Manapul 5.00

BLACKEST NIGHT: TITANS (2009 Green Lantern & DC crossover)
DC Comics: Oct, 2009 - No. 3, Dec, 2009 ($2.99, limited series)

1-3-Terra and the original Hawk return; Benes-a/c 3.00
1-3-Variant-c by Brian Haberlin 5.00

BLACKEST NIGHT: WONDER WOMAN (2009 Green Lantern & DC crossover)
DC Comics: Feb, 2010 - No. 3, Apr, 2010 ($2.99, limited series)

1-3-Maxwell Lord returns; Rucka-s/Scott-a/Horn-c. 2,3-Mera app.; Star Sapphire 3.00
1-3-Variant-c by Ryan Sook 5.00

BLACK-EYED KIDS
AfterShock Comics: Apr, 2016 - No. 15, Dec, 2017 ($3.99)

1-15: 1-($1.99) Joe Pruett-s/Szymon Kudranski-a/Francesco Francavilla-c. 2-15-($3.99) 4.00

BLACK FLAG (See Asylum #5)
Maximum Press: Jan, 1995 - No.4, 1995; No. 0, July, 1995 ($2.50, B&W) (No. 0 in color)

Preview Edition (6/94, $1.95, B&W)-Fraga/McFarlane-c. 3.00
0-4: 0-(7/95)-Liefeld/Fraga-c. 1-(1/95). 3.00
1-Variant cover 5.00
2,4-Variant covers 3.00

NOTE: ***Fraga** a-0-4, Preview Edition; c-1-4. **Liefeld/Fraga** c-0. **McFarlane/Fraga** c-Preview Edition.*

BLACK FURY (Becomes Wild West No. 58) (See Blue Bird)
Charlton Comics Group: May, 1955 - No. 57, Mar-Apr, 1966 (Horse stories)

	GD	VG	FN	VF	VF/NM	NM-
1	12	24	36	67	94	120
2	7	14	21	37	46	55
3-10	6	12	18	28	34	40
11-15,19,20	4	8	10	18	22	25
16-18-Ditko-a	12	24	36	67	94	120
21-30	4	7	10	14	17	20
31-57	3	6	8	12	14	16

BLACK GOLIATH (See Avengers #32-35,41,54 and Civil War #4)
Marvel Comics Group: Feb, 1976 - No. 5, Nov, 1976

	GD	VG	FN	VF	VF/NM	NM-
1-Tuska-a(p) thru #3	5	10	15	31	53	75
2-5: 2-4-(Regular 25¢ editions). 4-Kirby-c/Buckler-a	2	4	6	11	16	20
2-4-(30¢-c variants, limited distribution)(4,6,8/76)	6	12	18	37	66	95

BLACK HAMMER
Dark Horse Comics: Jul, 2016 - No. 13, Sept, 2017 ($3.99)

	GD	VG	FN	VF	VF/NM	NM-
1-Lemire-s/Ormston-a; covers by Ormston & Lemire	3	6	9	17	25	34
2	2	4	6	9	12	15
3-13: 3-8,10,11,13-Lemire-s/Ormston-a; covers by Ormston & Lemire. 9,12-Rubín-a						6.00
...: Cthu-Louise (12/18, $3.99) Lemire-s/Lenox-a; two covers by Lenox & Jill Thompson						4.00
... Director's Cut (1/19, $4.99) r/#1 in original B&W ink with original script	2	4	6	13	18	22
... Giant-Sized Annual (1/17, $5.99) Short stories by various incl. Nguyen, Allred, Kindt	2	4	6	8	10	12

BLACK HAMMER: AGE OF DOOM
Dark Horse Comics: Apr, 2018 - No. 12, Sept, 2019 ($3.99)

	GD	VG	FN	VF	VF/NM	NM-
1-Lemire-s/Ormston-a	1	2	3	5	6	8
2-12: 2-5,8-12-Lemire-s/Ormston-a. 6,7-Tammaso-a						4.00

BLACK HAMMER '45
Dark Horse Comics: Mar, 2019 - No. 4, Jun, 2019 ($3.99, limited series)

1-4-Fawkes-s/Kindt-a; flashbacks to the Black Hammer Squadron in WWII 4.00

BLACK HAMMER / JUSTICE LEAGUE: HAMMER OF JUSTICE!
Dark Horse Comics: Jul, 2019 - No. 5, Nov, 2019 ($3.99, limited series)

1-5-Lemire-s/Walsh-a; Justice League switches places with the Black Hammer crew 4.00

BLACK HAMMER REBORN
Dark Horse Comics: Jun, 2021 - No. 12, May, 2022 ($3.99, limited series)

1-12: 1-The daughter of the original Black Hammer. 3,4,7,8,12-Colonel Weird app. 4.00

BLACK HAMMER: VISIONS
Dark Horse Comics: Feb, 2021 - No. 8, Sept, 2021 ($3.99, limited series)

1-8: 1-Spotlight on Golden Gail; Patton Oswalt-s/Dean Kotz-a. 2-Johns-s. 3-Zdarsky-s 4.00

BLACKHAWK (Formerly Uncle Sam #1-8; see Military Comics & Modern Comics)
Comic Magazines(Quality)No. 9-107(12/56); National Periodical Publications No. 108 (1/57) -250; DC Comics No. 251 on: No. 9, Winter, 1944 - No. 243, 10-11/68; No. 244, 1-2/76 - No. 250, 1-2/77; No. 251, 10/82 - No. 273, 11/84

	GD	VG	FN	VF	VF/NM	NM-
9 (1944)	290	580	870	1856	3178	4500
10 (1946)	116	232	348	742	1271	1800
11-15: 14-Ward-a; 13,14-Fear app.	84	168	252	538	919	1300
16-19	68	136	204	435	743	1050
20-Classic Crandall bondage-c; Ward Blackhawk	129	258	387	806	1378	2000
21-30 (1950)	52	104	156	328	552	775
31-40: 31-Chop Chop by Jack Cole	41	82	123	250	418	585
41-49,51-60: 42-Robot-c	36	72	108	216	351	485
50-1st Killer Shark; origin in text	40	80	120	246	411	575
61,62: 61-Used in **POP**, pg. 91. 62-Used in **POP**, pg. 92 & color illo	36	72	108	211	343	475
63-70,72-80: 65-H-Bomb explosion panel. 66-B&W & color illos **POP**. 67-Hitler-s. 70-Return of Killer Shark; atomic explosion panel. 75-Intro. Blackie the Hawk	31	62	93	186	303	420
71-Origin retold; flying saucer-c; A-Bomb panels	37	74	111	222	361	500
81-86: Last precode (3/55)	27	54	81	162	266	370
87-92,94-99,101-107: 91-Robot-c. 105-1st S.A.	22	44	66	132	216	300
93-Origin in text	23	46	69	136	223	310
100	31	62	93	186	303	420
108-1st DC issue (1/57); re-intro. Blackie, the Hawk, their mascot; not in #115	44	88	132	326	738	1150
109-117: 117-(10/57)-Mr. Freeze app.	15	30	45	100	220	340
118-(11/57)-Frazetta-r/Jimmy Wakely #4 (3 pgs.)	16	32	48	110	243	375
119-130 (11/58): 120-Robot-c	12	24	36	79	170	260
131,132,134-140 (9/59)	10	20	30	66	138	210
133-Intro. Lady Blackhawk	148	296	444	947	1624	2300
141-Cat-Man returns-c/s	20	40	60	118	192	265
142-150,152-163,165,166: 143-Kurtzman-r/Jimmy Wakely #4. 150-(7/60)-King Condor returns. 166-Last 10¢ issue	8	16	24	54	102	150
151-Lady Blackhawk receives & loses super powers	17	34	51	100	158	215
164-Origin retold	9	18	27	60	120	180
167-180	6	12	18	37	66	95
181-190	5	10	15	31	53	75
191-196,199: 196-Combat Diary series begins	4	8	12	27	44	60
197,198,200: 197-New look for Blackhawks. 198-Origin retold	4	8	12	28	47	65
201,202,204-210	3	6	9	21	33	45
203-Origin Chop Chop (12/64)	4	8	12	27	44	60
211-227,229-243(1968): 230-Blackhawks become superheroes; JLA cameo 242-Return to old costumes	3	6	9	17	26	35
228-Batman, Green Lantern, Superman, The Flash cameos.	5	10	15	30	50	70
244 ('76) -250: 250-Chuck dies	1	2	3	5	6	8
251-273: 251-Origin retold; Black Knights return. 252-Intro Domino. 253-Part origin Hendrickson. 258-Blackhawk's Island destroyed. 259-Part origin Chop-Chop. 265-273 (75¢ cover price)						5.00

NOTE: ***Chaykin** a-260; c-257-260, 262. **Crandall** a-10, 11, 13, 16?, 18-20, 22-26, 30-33, 35p, 36(2), 37, 38?, 39-44, 46-50, 52-58, 60, 63, 64, 66, 67; c-14-20, 22-63(most except #28-33, 36, 37, 39). **Evans** a-244, 245,246i, 248-250i. **G. Kane** c-263, 264. **Kubert c**-244, 245. **Newton** a-266p. **Severin** a-257.**Spiegle** a-261-267, 269-273; c-265-272. **Toth** a-260p. **Ward** a-16-27(Chop Chop, 8pgs. ea.); pencilled stories-No. 17-63(approx.). **Wildey** a-268. Chop Chop solo stories in #10-95?*

BLACKHAWK
DC Comics: Mar, 1988 - No. 3, May, 1988 ($2.95, limited series, mature)

1-3: Chaykin painted-c/a/scripts 4.00

BLACKHAWK (Also see Action Comics #601)
DC Comics: Mar, 1989 - No. 16, Aug, 1990 ($1.50, mature)

1 4.00
2-6,8-16: 16-Crandall-c swipe 3.00
7-($2.50, 52 pgs.)-Story-r/Military #1 4.00
Annual 1 (1989, $2.95, 68 pgs.)-Recaps origin of Blackhawk, Lady Blackhawk, and others 4.00
Special 1 (1992, $3.50, 68 pgs.)-Mature readers 4.00

BLACKHAWK INDIAN TOMAHAWK WAR, THE
Avon Periodicals: 1951 (Also see Fighting Indians of the Wild West)

	GD	VG	FN	VF	VF/NM	NM-
nn-Kinstler-c; Kit West story	23	46	69	136	223	310

BLACKHAWKS (DC New 52)
DC Comics: Nov, 2011 - No. 8, Jun, 2012 ($2.99)

1-8: 1-Costa-s/Nolan & Lashley-a 3.00

BLACK HOLE (See Walt Disney Showcase #54) (Disney, movie)
Whitman Publishing Co.: Mar, 1980 - No. 4, Sept, 1980

	GD	VG	FN	VF	VF/NM	NM-
11295(#1) (1979, Golden, $1.50-c, 52 pgs., graphic novel; 8 1/2x11") Photo-c; Spiegle-a.	3	6	9	15	22	28
1-3: 1,2-Movie adaptation. 2,3-Spiegle-a. 3-McWilliams-a; photo-c. 3-New stories	2	4	6	10	14	18
4-Sold only in pre-packs; new story; Spiegle-a	33	66	99	238	532	825

BLACK HOOD, THE (See Blue Ribbon, Flyman & Mighty Comics)
Red Circle Comics (Archie): June, 1983 - No. 3, Oct, 1983 (Mandell paper)

	GD	VG	FN	VF	VF/NM	NM-
1-Morrow, McWilliams, Wildey-a; Toth-c	1	2	3	5	6	8
2,3: The Fox by Toth-c/a; Boyette-a. 3-Morrow-a; Toth wraparound-c						4.00

NOTE: *Also see Archie's Super-Hero Special Digest #2*

BLACK HOOD
DC Comics (Impact Comics): Dec, 1991 - No. 12, Dec, 1992 ($1.00)

1 4.00
2-12: 11-Intro The Fox. 12-Origin Black Hood 3.00
Annual 1 (1992, $2.50, 68 pgs.)-w/Trading card 4.00

BLACK HOOD, THE
Archie Comic Publications (Dark Circle Comics): Apr, 2015 - No. 11, Aug, 2016 ($3.99)

Black Hammer: Visions #1 © 171 Studios & Ormston

Blackhawks (2011) #1 © DC

Black Lightning: Year One #5 © DC

	GD 2.0	VG 4.0	FN 6.0	VF 8.0	VF/NM 9.0	NM- 9.2

1-11: 1-Origin retold; Swierczynski-s/Gaydos-a; five covers. 6-Chaykin-a. 8-Hack-a 4.00

BLACK HOOD, THE (Volume 2)
Archie Comic Publications (Dark Circle Comics): Dec, 2016 - No. 5, Aug, 2017 ($3.99)

1-5-Swierczynski-s/Greg Scott-a 4.00

BLACK HOOD COMICS (Formerly Hangman #2-8; Laugh Comics #20 on; also see Black Swan, Jackpot, Roly Poly & Top-Notch #9)
MLJ Magazines: No. 9, Wint., 1943-44 - No. 19, Sum., 1946 (on radio in 1943)

	GD	VG	FN	VF	VF/NM	NM-
9-The Hangman & The Boy Buddies cont'd	174	348	522	1114	1907	2700
10-Hangman & Dusty, the Boy Detective app.	116	232	348	742	1271	1800
11-Dusty app.; no Hangman	84	168	252	538	919	1300
12,13,15-18: 17-Hal Foster swipe from Prince Valiant; 1st issue with "An Archie Magazine" on-c	73	146	219	467	796	1125
14-Kinstler blood-c	135	270	405	864	1482	2100
19-I.D. exposed; last issue	93	186	279	591	1021	1450

NOTE: *Hangman by* ***Fuje*** *in 9, 10.* ***Kinstler*** *a-15, c-14-16.*

BLACK JACK (Rocky Lane's...; formerly Jim Bowie)
Charlton Comics: No. 20, Nov, 1957 - No. 30, Nov, 1959

	GD	VG	FN	VF	VF/NM	NM-
20	10	20	30	54	72	90
21,27,29,30	6	12	18	31	38	45
22,23: 22-(68 pgs.). 23-Williamson/Torres-a	8	16	24	42	54	65
24-26,28-Ditko-a	11	22	33	60	83	105

BLACK KNIGHT, THE
Toby Press: May, 1953; 1963

	GD	VG	FN	VF	VF/NM	NM-
1-Bondage-c	290	580	870	1856	3178	4500
Super Reprint No. 11 (1963)-Reprints 1953 issue	3	6	9	19	30	40

BLACK KNIGHT, THE
Atlas Comics (MgPC): May, 1955 - No. 5, April, 1956

	GD	VG	FN	VF	VF/NM	NM-
1-Origin Crusader; Maneely-c/a	811	1622	2433	5920	10,460	15,000
2-Maneely-c/a(4)	226	452	678	1446	2473	3500
3-5: 4-Maneely-c/a. 5-Maneely-c, Shores-a	213	426	618	1318	2259	3200
...No. 1 Facsimile Edition (4/21, $3.99) Reprints #1 with original ads						8.00

BLACK KNIGHT (See The Avengers #48, Marvel Super Heroes & Tales To Astonish #52)
Marvel Comics: June, 1990 - No. 4, Sept, 1990 ($1.50, limited series)

	GD	VG	FN	VF	VF/NM	NM-
1-Original Black Knight returns	4	8	12	23	37	50
2-4: 3,4-Dr. Strange app.						5.00
... (MDCU) 1 (01/10, $3.99) Origin re-told; Frenz-a; originally from Marvel Digital Comics						4.00

NOTE: ***Buckler*** *c-1-4p*

BLACK KNIGHT (See Weirdworld and Secret Wars 2015 series)
Marvel Comics: Jan, 2016 - No. 5, May, 2016 ($3.99)

	GD	VG	FN	VF	VF/NM	NM-
1-Tieri-s/Pizzari-a	1	3	4	6	8	10
2-5-Uncanny Avengers app.						4.00

BLACK KNIGHT: CURSE OF THE EBONY BLADE (Dane Whitman)
Marvel Comics: May, 2021 - No. 5, Sept, 2021 ($3.99, limited series)

1-5-Spurrier-s/Dávila-a. 1-Avengers app. 2-5-Mordred app. 4.00

BLACK KNIGHT: EXODUS
Marvel Comics: Dec, 1996 ($2.50, one-shot)

1-Raab-s; Apocalypse-c/app. 5.00

BLACK LAMB, THE
DC Comics (Helix): Nov, 1996 - No, 6, Apr, 1997 ($2.50, limited series)

1-6: Tim Truman-c/a/scripts 3.00

BLACK LAUGHTER
Black Laughter Publ.: Nov, 1972 (35¢)

V1#1-African American humor; James Dixon-s/a; 1st app. of Mr. Habeus Corpus
(a CGC 8.5 copy sold for $1400 in 6/2021, and a CGC 7.5 sold for $750 in 12/2021)

BLACKLIGHT (From ShadowHawk)
Image Comics: June, 2005 - No. 2, Jul, 2005 ($2.99)

1,2-Toledo & Deering-a/Wherle-s 3.00

BLACK LIGHTNING (See The Brave & The Bold, Cancelled Comic Cavalcade, DC Comics Presents #16, Detective Comics #490 and World's Finest #257)
National Periodical Publ./DC Comics: Apr, 1977 - No. 11, Sept-Oct, 1978

	GD	VG	FN	VF	VF/NM	NM-
1-Origin Black Lightning; 1st app. Tobias Whale	7	14	21	46	86	125
2,3,6-10: 2-Talia and Merlyn app.	2	4	6	9	13	16
4,5-Superman-c/s. 4-Intro Cyclotronic Man	2	4	6	13	18	22
11-The Ray new solo story	2	4	6	11	16	20

NOTE: ***Buckler*** *c-1-3p, 6-11p. #11 is 44 pgs.*

BLACK LIGHTNING (2nd Series)
DC Comics: Feb, 1995 - No. 13, Feb, 1996 ($1.95/$2.25)

	GD	VG	FN	VF	VF/NM	NM-
1-Tony Isabella scripts begin, ends #8	1	3	4	6	8	10
2-1st app. Painkiller	1	3	4	6	8	10
3-13: 6-Begin $2.25-c. 13-Batman-c/app.						3.00

BLACK LIGHTNING: COLD DEAD HANDS
DC Comics: Jan, 2018 - No. 6, Jun, 2018 ($3.99, limited series)

1-6-Tony Isabella-s/Clayton Henry-a; Tobias Whale app. 4.00

BLACK LIGHTNING / HONG KONG PHOOEY SPECIAL
DC Comics: Jul, 2018 ($3.99, one-shot)

1-Cowan & Sienkiewicz-a/Hill-s; takes place in 1976; Funky Phantom back-up story 4.00

BLACK LIGHTNING: YEAR ONE
DC Comics: Mar, 2009 - No. 6, May, 2009 ($2.99, bi-weekly limited series)

1-6-Van Meter-s/Hamner-a. 1-Two printings (white and yellow cover title logos) 3.00
TPB (2009, $17.99) r/#1-6 18.00

BLACK LIST, THE (Based on the TV show)
Titan Comics: Aug, 2015 - No. 10, Jul, 2016 ($3.99)

1-10-Art & photo-c for each: 1-Nicole Phillips-s/Beni Lobel-a. 4.00

BLACK MAGIC (...Magazine) (Becomes Cool Cat V8#6 on)
Crestwood Publ. V1#1-4,V6#1-V7#5/Headline V1#5-V5#3,V7#6-V8#5: 10-11/50 - V4#1, 6-7/53: V4#2, 9-10/53 - V5#3, 11-12/54; V6#1, 9-10/57 - V7#2, 11-12/58: V7#3, 7-8/60 - V8#5, 11-12/61 (V1#1-5, 52pgs.; V1#6-V3#3, 44pgs.)

	GD	VG	FN	VF	VF/NM	NM-
V1#1-S&K-a, 10 pgs.; Meskin-a(2)	181	362	543	1158	1979	2800
2-S&K-a, 17 pgs.; Meskin-a	77	154	231	493	847	1200
3-6(8-9/51)-S&K, Roussos, Meskin-a	65	130	195	416	708	1000
V2#1(10-11/51),4,5,7(#13),9(#15),12(#18)-S&K-a	43	86	129	271	461	650
2,3,6,8,10,11(#17)	37	74	111	218	354	490
V3#1(#19, 12/52) - 6(#24, 5/53)-S&K-a	37	74	111	222	361	500
V4#1(#25, 6-7/53), 2(#26, 9-10/53)-S&K-a(3-4)	39	78	117	231	378	525
3(#27, 11-12/53)-S&K-a; Ditko-a (2nd published-a); also see Captain 3-D, Daring Love #1, Strange Fantasy #9, & Fantastic Fears #5 (Fant. Fears was 1st drawn, but not 1st publ.)	74	148	222	470	810	1150
4(#28)-Eyes ripped out/story-S&K, Ditko-a	53	106	159	334	567	800
5(#29, 3-4/54)-S&K, Ditko-a	39	78	117	236	388	540
6(#30, 5-6/54)-S&K, Powell?-a	32	64	96	192	314	435
V5#1(#31, 7-8/54 - 3(#33, 11-12/54)-S&K-a	22	44	66	128	209	290
V6#1(#34, 9-10/57), 2(#35, 11-12/57)	14	28	42	78	112	145
3(1-2/58) - 6(7-8/58)	13	26	39	74	105	135
V7#1(9-10/58) - 3(7-8/60), 4(9-10/60)	11	22	33	60	83	105
5(11-12/60)-Hitler-c; Torres-a	24	48	72	142	234	325
6(1-2/61)-Powell-a(2)	11	22	33	60	83	105
V8#1(3-4/61)-Powell-c/a	11	22	33	60	83	105
2(5-6/61)-E.C. story swipe/W.F. #22; Ditko, Powell-a	12	24	36	67	94	120
3(7-8/61)-E.C. story swipe/W.F. #22; Powell-a(2)	12	24	36	67	94	120
4(9-10/61)-Powell-a(5)	11	22	33	60	83	105
5-E.C. story swipe/W.S.F. #28; Powell-a(3)	11	22	33	64	90	115

NOTE: ***Bernard Baily*** *a-V4#6?, V5#3(2).* ***Grandenetti*** *a-V2#3, 11.* ***Kirby*** *c-V1#1-6, V2#1-12, V3#1-6, V4#1, 2, 4-6, V5#1-3.* ***McWilliams*** *a-V3#2i.* ***Meskin*** *a-V1#1(2), 2, 3, 4(2), 5(2), 6, V2/1, 2, 3(2), 4(3), 5, 6(2), 7-9, 11; 12i, V3#1(2), 5, 6, V5#1(2), 2.* ***Orlando*** *a-V6#1, 4, V7#2; c-V6/1-6.* ***Powell*** *a-V5#1?.* ***Roussos*** *a-V1#3-5, 6(2), V2#3(2), 4, 5(2), 6, 8, 9, 10(2), 11, 12p, V3#1(2), 2i, 5, V5#2.* ***Simon*** *a-V2#12, V3#2, V7#5? c-V4#3?, V7#3?, 4, 5?, 6?, V8#1-5.* ***Simon & Kirby*** *a-V1#1, 2(2), 3-6, V2#1, 4, 5, 7, 9, 12, V3#1-6, V4#1(3), 2(4), 3(2), 4(2), 5, 6, V5#1-3; c-V2#1.* ***Leonard Starr*** *a-V1#1.* ***Tuska*** *a-V6#3, 4.* ***Woodbridge*** *a-V7#4.*

BLACK MAGIC
National Periodical Publications: Oct-Nov, 1973 - No. 9, Apr-May, 1975

	GD	VG	FN	VF	VF/NM	NM-
1-S&K reprints	3	6	9	19	30	40
2-8-S&K reprints	2	4	6	11	16	20
9-S&K reprints	3	6	9	14	19	24

BLACK MAGICK
Image Comics: Oct, 2015 - Present ($3.99)

1-16-Greg Rucka-s/Nicola Scott-a 4.00

BLACKMAIL TERROR (See Harvey Comics Library)

BLACK MANTA
DC Comics: Nov, 2021 - No. 6, Apr, 2022 ($3.99, limited series)

1-6: 1-Black Manta vs. Capt. Demo. 2,3-Gentleman Ghost app. 4.00

BLACK MARKET
BOOM! Studios: Jul, 2014 - No. 4, Oct, 2014 ($3.99, limited series)

1-4-Barbiere-s/Santos-a 4.00

BLACK MASK
DC Comics: 1993 - No. 3, 1994 ($4.95, limited series, 52 pgs.)

1-3 5.00

GD 2.0 | VG 4.0 | FN 6.0 | VF 8.0 | VF/NM 9.0 | NM- 9.2

BLACK MASK: YEAR OF THE VILLAIN
DC Comics: Oct, 2019 ($4.99, one-shot)
1-Tom Taylor-s/Cully Hamner-a; Apex Lex Luthor & Batwoman app. 5.00

BLACK MONDAY MURDERS, THE
Image Comics: Aug, 2016 - No. 8, Feb, 2018 ($4.99/$3.99, limited series)
1-4-Jonathan Hickman-s/Tomm Coker-a 5.00
5-8-($3.99) 4.00

BLACK OPS
Image Comics (WildStorm): Jan, 1996 - No. 5, May, 1996 ($2.50, lim. series)
1-5 3.00

BLACK ORCHID (See Adventure Comics #428 & Phantom Stranger)
DC Comics: Holiday, 1988-89 - No. 3, 1989 ($3.50, lim. series, prestige format)
Book 1,3: Gaiman scripts & McKean painted-a in all 6.00
Book 2-Arkham Asylum story; Batman app. 1 2 3 5 6 8
TPB (1991, $19.95) r/#1-3; new McKean-c 20.00

BLACK ORCHID
DC Comics: Sept, 1993 - No. 22, June, 1995 ($1.95/$2.25)
1-22: Dave McKean-c all issues 3.00
1-Platinum Edition 12.00
Annual 1 (1993, $3.95, 68 pgs.)-Children's Crusade 4.00

BLACK ORDER (The Warmasters of Thanos)
Marvel Comics: Jan, 2019 - No. 5, May, 2019 ($3.99, limited series)
1-5: 1-Landy-s/Tan-a. 3-5-Nova app. 5-Magno-a 4.00

BLACKOUT
Dark Horse Comics: Mar, 2014 - No. 4, Jul, 2014 ($2.99, limited series)
1-4-Barbiere-s/Lorimer-a; King Tiger back-up by Stradley-s/Doug Wheatley-a 3.00

BLACKOUTS (See Broadway Hollywood...)

BLACK PANTHER, THE (Also see Avengers #52, Fantastic Four #52, Jungle Action, Marvel Premiere #51-53 and Rise of the Black Panther)
Marvel Comics Group: Jan, 1977 - No. 15, May, 1979
1-Jack Kirby-s/a thru #12 9 18 27 62 126 190
2 4 8 12 27 44 60
3-5: 4,5-(Regular 30¢ editions). 3 6 9 21 33 45
4,5-(35¢-c variants, limited dist.)(7,9/77) 10 20 30 69 147 225
6-13: 8-Origin 3 6 9 19 30 40
14,15-Avengers x-over. 14-Origin 3 6 9 20 31 42
...By Jack Kirby Vol. 1 TPB (2005, $19.99) r/#1-7; unused covers and sketch pages 20.00
...By Jack Kirby Vol. 2 TPB (2006, $19.99) r/#8-12 by Kirby and #13 non-Kirby 20.00
NOTE: ***J. Buscema** c-15p. **Layton** c-13i.*

BLACK PANTHER
Marvel Comics Group: July, 1988 - No. 4, Oct, 1988 ($1.25)
1-Gillis-s/Cowan & Delarosa-a 2 4 6 11 16 20
2-4 1 2 3 5 6 8

BLACK PANTHER (Marvel Knights)
Marvel Comics: Nov, 1998 - No. 62, Sept, 2003 ($2.50)
1-Texeira-a/c; Priest-s 4 8 12 27 44 60
1-($6.95) DF edition w/Quesada & Palmiotti-c 3 6 9 19 30 40
2,3: 2-Two covers by Texeira and Timm. 3-Fantastic Four app. 1 2 3 5 6 8
4-1st White Wolf 3 6 9 15 22 28
5-22,24-35,37-40: 5-Evans-a. 6-8-Jusko-a. 8-Avengers-c/app. 15-Hulk app. 22-Moon Knight app. 25-Maximum Security x-over. 26-Storm-c/app. 28-Magneto & Sub-Mariner-c/app. 29-WWII flashback meeting w/Captain America. 35-Defenders-c/app. 37-Luke Cage and Falcon-c/app. 3.00
23-Deadpool & the Avengers app. 3 6 9 15 22 28
36-($3.50, 100 pgs.) 35th Anniversary issue incl. r/1st app. in FF #52 4.00
41-56: 41-44-Wolverine app. 47-Thor app. 48,49-Magneto app. 3.00
57-62: 57-Begin $2.99-c. 59-Falcon app. 3.00
...: The Client (6/01, $14.95, TPB) r/#1-5 15.00
... 2099 #1 (11/04, $2.99) Kirkman-s/Hotz-a/Pat Lee-c 3.00

BLACK PANTHER (Marvel Knights)
Marvel Comics: Apr, 2005 - No. 41, Nov, 2008 ($2.99)
1-Reginald Hudlin-s/John Romita Jr. & Klaus Janson-a; covers by Romita & Ribic 2 4 6 10 14 18
2-1st app. Shuri 8 16 24 51 96 140
3-7,9-15,17-20: 7-House of M; Hairsine-a. 10-14-Luke Cage app. 12,13-Blade app. 17-Linsner-c. 19-Doctor Doom app. 3.00
8-Cho-c; X-Men app. 5.00
8-2nd printing variant-c 3.00
16-($3.99) Wedding of T'Challa and Storm; wraparound Cho-c; Hudlin-s/Eaton-a 4.00
21-Civil War x-over; Namor app. 8.00
21-2nd printing with new cover and Civil War logo 3.00
22-25-Civil War: 23-25-Turner-c 4.00
26-41: 26-30-T'Challa and Storm join the Fantastic Four. 27-30-Marvel Zombies app. 28-30-Suydam-c. 39-41-Secret Invasion 3.00
Annual 1 (4/08, $3.99) Hudlin-s/Stroman & Lashley-a; alternate future; Uatu app. 4.00
...: Bad Mutha TPB (2006, $10.99) r/#10-13 11.00
...: Civil War TPB (2007, $17.99) r/#19-25 18.00
...: Four the Hard Way TPB (2007, $13.99) r/#26-30; page layouts and character designs 14.00
...: Little Green Men TPB (2008, $10.99) r/#31-34 11.00
...: The Bride TPB (2006, $14.99) r/#14-18; interview with the dress designer 15.00
...: Who Is The Black Panther HC (2005, $21.99) r/#1-6; Hudlin afterword; cover gallery 22.00
...: Who Is The Black Panther SC (2006, $14.99) r/#1-6; Hudlin afterword; cover gallery 15.00

BLACK PANTHER
Marvel Comics: Apr, 2009 - No. 12, Mar, 2010 ($3.99/$2.99)
1-($3.99) Hudlin-s/Lashley-a; covers by Campbell & Lashley; Dr. Doom & Shuri app. 7 14 21 44 82 120
2-12-($2.99) 2-6-Campbell-c. 6-Shuri becomes female Black Panther 4.00

BLACK PANTHER
Marvel Comics: Jun, 2016 - No. 18, Nov, 2017; No. 166, Dec, 2017 - No. 172, Jun, 2018 ($4.99/$3.99)
1-($4.99) Ta-Nehisi Coates-s/Brian Stelfreeze-a; bonus Stelfreeze interview & art 1 3 4 6 8 10
2,4-18-($3.99) 2,4,9,12-Stelfreeze-a. 5-8,10-12,16-18-Sprouse-a. 13-17-Ororo app. 4.00
3-1st Midnight Angels; Stelfreeze-a 1 3 4 6 8 10
[Title switches to legacy numbering after #18 (11/17)]
166-172: 166-Klaw app.; Coates-s/Kirk-a 4.00
Annual 1 (4/18, $4.99) Stories by Priest, Perkins, McGregor, Acuña, Hudlin & Lashley 5.00

BLACK PANTHER
Marvel Comics: Jul, 2018 - No. 25, Jul, 2021 ($4.99/$3.99)
1-($4.99) Ta-Nehisi Coates-s/Daniel Acuña-a; Intergalactic Empire of Wakanda 5.00
2-24-($3.99) 2-Intro Emperor N'Jadaka. 6,12-Jen Bartel-a. 7-11-Walker-a. 14-17-Acuña-a 4.00
25-($5.99) Coates-s/Acuña & Stelfreeze-a 6.00

BLACK PANTHER
Marvel Comics: Jan, 2022 - Present ($4.99/$3.99)
1-($4.99) John Ridley-s/Juann Cabal-a; Avengers app. 5.00
2,4-14-($3.99) Shuri app. 7,8-Ororo app. 9-14-Avengers app. 13,14-Namor app. 4.00
3-($5.99) Legacy 200th issue; X-Men app.; back up by Juni Ba-s/a; intro. Tosin Oduye 6.00
...: Unconquered 1 (1/23, $3.99) Bryan Hill-s/Alberto Foche-a 4.00

BLACK PANTHER (All ages title)
IDW Publishing (Marvel): Jan, 2019 - No. 6, Jun, 2019 ($3.99, limited series)
1-6: 1-3-Kyle Baker-s; Shuri app. 4-6-Vita Ayala-s 4.00

BLACK PANTHER AND THE AGENTS OF WAKANDA
Marvel Comics: Nov, 2019 - Present ($3.99)
1-8: 1-Team with Janet Van Dyne, Okoye, Gorilla-Man, and Broo. 5,6-Deadpool app. 4.00

BLACK PANTHER AND THE CREW
Marvel Comics: Jun, 2017 - No. 6, Oct, 2017 ($3.99)
1-6-Storm, Luke Cage, Misty Knight & Manifold app.; Ta-Nehisi Coates-s/Butch Guice-a 4.00

BLACK PANTHER/CAPTAIN AMERICA: FLAGS OF OUR FATHERS
Marvel Comics: Jun, 2010 - No. 4, Sept, 2010 ($3.99, limited series)
1-4-Hudlin-s/Cowan-a; WW2 story; Howling Commandos & Red Skull app. 4.00

BLACK PANTHER LEGENDS
Marvel Comics: Dec, 2021 - No. 4, Jun, 2022 ($3.99, limited series)
1-4-T'Challa-s childhood revisited; Onyebuchi-s/Fiadzigbey-a. 2-Ororo app. 4.00

BLACK PANTHER: PANTHER'S PREY
Marvel Comics: May, 1991 - No. 4, Oct, 1991 ($4.95, squarebound, lim. series, 52 pgs.)
1-4: McGregor-s/Turner-a 6.00

BLACK PANTHER: THE MAN WITHOUT FEAR (Continues from Daredevil #512)
Marvel Comics: No. 513, Feb, 2011 - No. 523, Nov, 2011 ($2.99)
513-523: 513-Shadowland aftermath; Liss-s/Francavilla-a/Bianchi-c. 521-523-Fear Itself 3.00
513-Variant-c by Francavilla 5.00

BLACK PANTHER: THE MOST DANGEROUS MAN ALIVE
Marvel Comics: No. 523.1, Nov, 2011 - No. 529, Apr, 2012 ($2.99)
523.1, 524-529: 523.1-Palo-a/Zircher-c. 524-Spider Island tie-in; Lady Bullseye app. 3.00

BLACK PANTHER: THE SOUND AND THE FURY
Marvel Comics: Apr, 2018 ($3.99, one-shot)
1-Klaw app.; Macchio-s/Di Vito-a; reprint of Fantastic Four #53 (origin/1st app. Klaw) 4.00

BLACK PANTHER VS. DEADPOOL
Marvel Comics: Dec, 2018 - No. 5, Apr, 2019 ($3.99, limited series)
1-5: 1-Kibblesmith-s/Ortiz-a; Willie Lumpkin app. 4.00

BLACK PANTHER: WORLD OF WAKANDA
Marvel Comics: Jan, 2017 - No. 6, Jun, 2017 ($4.99/$3.99, limited series)
1-($4.99) Roxanne Gay-s/Alitha E. Martinez-a; spotlight on The Dora Milaje 1 3 4 6 8 10
2-6-($3.99) 6-Rembert Browne-s/Joe Bennett-a; White Tiger app. 4.00

BLACK PEARL, THE
Dark Horse Comics: Sept, 1996 - No. 5, Jan, 1997 ($2.95, limited series)
1-Mark Hamill scripts in all 1 2 3 5 6 8
2-5 3.00

BLACK PHANTOM (See Tim Holt #25, 38)
Magazine Enterprises: Nov, 1954 (one-shot) (Female outlaw)
1 (A-1 #122)-The Ghost Rider story plus 3 Black Phantom stories; Headlight-c/a 77 154 231 493 847 1200

BLACK PHANTOM
AC Comics: 1989 - No. 3, 1990 ($2.50, B&W; #2 color)(Reprints & new-a)
1-3: 1-Ayers-r, Bolle-r/B.P. #1-3-Redmask-r 6.00

BLACK PHANTOM, RETURN OF THE (See Wisco)

BLACK RACER AND SHILO NORMAN SPECIAL, THE (Jack Kirby 100th Birthday tribute)
DC Comics: Oct, 2017 ($4.99, one-shot)
1-Black Racer origin; Hudlin-s/Cowan-a; reprint pages from New Gods #5,7,8 5.00

BLACK RIDER (Western Winners #1-7; Western Tales of Black Rider #28-31; Gunsmoke Western #32 on)(See All Western Winners, Best Western, Kid Colt, Outlaw Kid, Rex Hart, Two-Gun Kid, Two-Gun Western, Western Gunfighters, Western Winners, & Wild Western)
Marvel/Atlas Comics(CDS No. 8-17/CPS No. 19 on): No. 8, 3/50 - No. 18, 1/52; No. 19, 11/53 - No. 27, 3/55
8 (#1)-Black Rider & his horse Satan begin; 36 pgs; Stan Lee photo-c as Black Rider) 71 142 213 568 1284 2000
9-52 pgs. begin, end #14 32 64 96 188 307 425
10-Origin Black Rider 37 74 111 218 354 490
11-14: 14-Last 52pgs. 21 42 63 126 206 285
15-19: 19-Two-Gun Kid app. 19 38 57 112 179 245
20-Classic-c; Two-Gun Kid app. 22 44 66 132 216 300
21-27: 21-23-Two-Gun Kid app. 24,25-Arrowhead app. 26-Kid Colt app. 27-Last issue; last

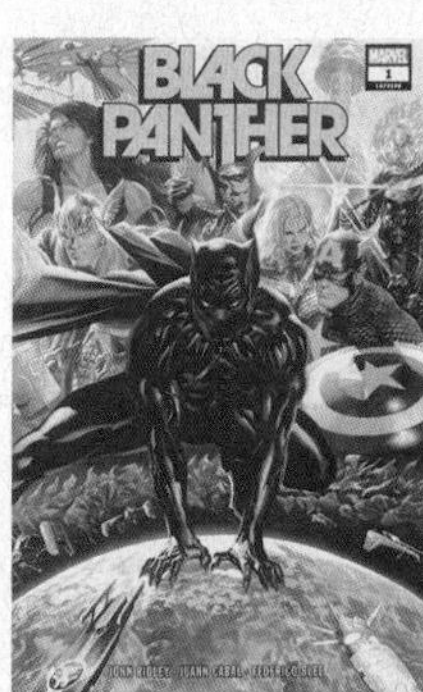
Black Panther (2022) #1 © MAR

Black Science #10 © Remender & Scalera

Black Terror V2 #1 © DYN

	GD 2.0	VG 4.0	FN 6.0	VF 8.0	VF/NM 9.0	NM- 9.2

precode. Kid Colt app. The Spider (a villain) burns to death 17 34 51 100 158 215

NOTE: *Ayers c-22. Jack Keller a-15, 26, 27. Maneely a-14; c-9, 16, 17, 24, 25, 27. Syd Shores a-19, 21, 22, 23(3), 24(3), 25-27; c-19, 21, 23. Sinnott a-24, 25. Tuska a-12, 19-21.*

BLACK RIDER RIDES AGAIN!, THE
Atlas Comics (CPS): Sept, 1957

1-Kirby-a(3); Powell-a; Severin-c 41 82 123 256 428 600

BLACK ROAD
Image Comics: Apr, 2016 - No. 10, May, 2017 ($3.99)

1-10-Brian Wood-s/Garry Brown-a 4.00

BLACK SCIENCE
Image Comics: Nov, 2013 - No. 43, Sept, 2019 ($3.50/$3.99)

1-Remender-s/Scalera-a; multiple covers 2 4 6 8 10 12
2 6.00
3-33: 11,16,21-33,35-43-$3.99-c 4.00
34-($4.99) 5.00

BLACK SEPTEMBER (Also see Avengers/Ultraforce, Ultraforce (1st series) #10 & Ultraforce/Avengers)
Malibu Comics (Ultraverse): 1995 ($1.50, one-shot)

Infinity-Intro to the new Ultraverse; variant-c exists. 3.00

BLACK'S MYTH
AHOY Comics: 2021 - No. 5, 2021 ($3.99, B&W, limited series)

1-5-Palicki-s/Cavalcanti-a 4.00

BLACKSTONE (See Super Magician Comics & Wisco Giveaways)

BLACKSTONE, MASTER MAGICIAN COMICS
Vital Publ./Street & Smith Publ.: Mar-Apr, 1946 - No. 3, July-Aug, 1946

1 42 84 126 265 445 625
2,3 26 52 78 154 252 350

BLACKSTONE, THE MAGICIAN (...Detective on cover only #3 & 4)
Marvel Comics (CnPC): No. 2, May, 1948 - No. 4, Sept, 1948 (No #1) (Cont'd from E.C. #1?)

2-The Blonde Phantom begins, ends #4 110 220 330 704 1202 1700
3,4: 3-Blonde Phantom by Sekowsky 61 122 183 390 670 950

BLACKSTONE, THE MAGICIAN DETECTIVE FIGHTS CRIME
E. C. Comics: Fall, 1947

1-1st app. Happy Houlihans 84 168 252 538 919 1300

BLACK SUN (X-Men Black Sun on cover)
Marvel Comics: Nov, 2000 - No. 5, Nov, 2000 ($2.99, weekly limited series)

1-(...: X-Men), 2-(...: Storm), 3-(...: Banshee and Sunfire), 4-(...: Colossus and Nightcrawler), 5-(...: Wolverine and Thunderbird); Claremont-s in all; Evans interlocking painted covers; Magik returns 4.00

BLACK SUN
DC Comics (WildStorm): Nov, 2002 - No. 6, Jun, 2003 ($2.95, limited series)

1-6-Andreyko-s/Scott-a 3.00

BLACK SWAN COMICS
MLJ Magazines (Pershing Square Publ. Co.): 1945

1-The Black Hood reprints from Black Hood No. 14; Bill Woggon-a; Suzie app. Caribbean Pirates-c 28 56 84 165 270 375

BLACK TAPE
Artists, Writers, & Artisans, Inc.: Feb, 2023 - No. 4 ($3.99, limited series)

1-Panosian-s/Talajic-a 4.00

BLACK TARANTULA (See Feature Presentations No. 5)

BLACK TERROR (See America's Best Comics & Exciting Comics)
Better Publications/Standard: Winter, 1942-43 - No. 27, June, 1949

1-Black Terror, Crime Crusader begin; Japanese WWII-c 432 864 1296 3154 5577 8000
2 232 464 696 1485 2543 3600
3-Nazi WWII-c 219 438 657 1402 2401 3400
4,5-Nazi & Japanese WWII-c 174 348 522 1114 1907 2700
6-8: 6,8-Classic Nazi WWII-c. 7-Classic Japanese WWII-c; The Ghost app. 206 412 618 1318 2259 3200
9,10-Nazi & Japanese WWII-c 155 310 465 992 1696 2400
11,13-19 77 154 231 493 847 1200
12-Japanese WWII-c 106 212 318 682 1166 1650
20-Classic-c; The Scarab app. 129 258 387 826 1413 2000
21-Miss Masque app. 97 194 291 621 1061 1500
22-Part Frazetta-a on one Black Terror story 103 206 309 659 1130 1600
23,25-27 65 130 195 416 708 1000
24-Frazetta-a (1/4 pg.) 110 220 330 704 1202 1700

NOTE: *Schomburg (Xela) c-2-27; bondage c-2, 17, 24. Meskin a-27. Moreira a-27. Robinson/Meskin a-23, 24(3), 25, 26. Roussos/Mayo a-24. Tuska a-26, 27.*

BLACK TERROR, THE (Also see Total Eclipse)
Eclipse Comics: Oct, 1989 - No. 3, June, 1990 ($4.95, 52 pgs., squarebound, limited series)

1-3: Beau Smith & Chuck Dixon scripts; Dan Brereton painted-c/a 5.00

BLACK TERROR (Also see Project Superpowers)
Dynamite Entertainment: 2008 - No. 14, 2011 ($3.50/$3.99)

1-14-Golden Age hero. 1-Alex Ross-c/Mike Lilly-a; various variant-c exist 4.00

BLACK TERROR VOLUME 2
Dynamite Entertainment: 2019 - No. 5, 2020 ($3.99, limited series)

1-5: 1-Set in 1974; Bemis-s/Gaudio-a. 2-5-Coleman-a; multiple covers for each 4.00

BLACKTHORNE 3-D SERIES
Blackthorne Publishing Co.: May, 1985 - No. 80, 1989 ($2.25/$2.50)

1-Sheena in 3-D #1. D. Stevens-c/retouched-a 2 4 6 8 11 14
2-10: 2-MerlinRealm in 3-D #1. 3-3-D Heroes #1. Goldyn in 3-D #1. 5-Bizarre 3-D Zone #1. 6-Salimba in 3-D #1. 7-Twisted Tales in 3-D #1. 8-Dick Tracy in 3-D #1. 9-Salimba in 3-D #2. 10-Gumby in 3-D #1 6.00
11-19: 11-Betty Boop in 3-D #1. 12-Hamster Vice in 3-D #1. 13-Little Nemo in 3-D #1. 14-Gumby in 3-D #2. 15-Hamster Vice #6 in 3-D. 16-Laffin' Gas #6 in 3-D. 17-Gumby in 3-D #3. 18-Bullwinkle and Rocky in 3-D #1. 19-The Flintstones in 3-D #1 6.00
20(#1),26(#2),35(#3),39(#4),52(#5),62,71(#6)-G.I. Joe in 3-D. 62-G.I. Joe Annual 2 4 6 8 11 14
21-24,27-28: 21-Gumby in 3-D #4. 22-The Flintstones in 3-D #2. 23-Laurel & Hardy in 3-D #1. 24-Bozo the Clown in 3-D #1. 27-Bravestarr in 3-D #1. 28- Gumby in 3-D #5 6.00
25,29,37-The Transformers in 3-D 2 4 6 11 16 20
30-Star Wars in 3-D #1 3 6 9 17 26 35
31-34,36,38,40: 31-The California Raisins in 3-D #1. 32-Richie Rich & Casper in 3-D #1. 33-Gumby in 3-D #6. 34-Laurel & Hardy in 3-D #2. 36-The Flintstones in 3-D #3. 38-Gumby in 3-D #7. 40-Bravestarr in 3-D #2 6.00
41-46,49,50: 41-Battletech in 3-D #1. 42-The Flintstones in 3-D #4. 43-Underdog in 3-D #1 44-The California Raisins in 3-D #2. 45-Red Heat in 3-D #1 (movie adapt.). 46-The California Raisins in 3-D #3. 49-Rambo in 3-D #1. 49-Sad Sack in 3-D #1. 50-Bullwinkle For President in 3-D #1 6.00
47,48-Star Wars in 3-D #2,3 3 6 9 14 19 24
51,53-60: 51-Kull in 3-D #1. 53-Red Sonja in 3-D #1. 54-Bozo in 3-D #2. 55-Waxwork in 3-D #1 (movie adapt.). 57-Casper in 3-D #1. 58-Baby Huey in 3-D #1. 59-Little Dot in 3-D #1. 60-Solomon Kane in 3-D #1 6.00
61,63-70,72-74,76-80: 61-Werewolf in 3-D #1. 63-The California Raisins in 3-D #4. 64-To Die For in 3-D #1. 65-Capt. Holo in 3-D #1. 66-Playful Little Audrey in 3-D #1. 67-Kull in 3-D #2. 69-The California Raisins in 3-D #5. 70-Wendy in 3-D #1. 72-Sports Hall of Shame #1. 74-The Noid in 3-D #1. 80-The Noid in 3-D #2 1 2 3 4 5 7
75-Moonwalker in 3-D #1 (Michael Jackson movie adapt.) 5 10 15 30 50 70

BLACK VORTEX (See Guardians of the Galaxy & X-Men: The Black Vortex)

BLACK WIDOW (Marvel Knights) (Also see Marvel Graphic Novel)
Marvel Comics: May, 1999 - No. 3, Aug, 1999 ($2.99, limited series)

1-(June on-c) Devin Grayson-s/J.G. Jones-c/a; intro. Yelena Belova; Daredevil app. 3 6 9 19 30 40
1-Variant-c by J.G. Jones 5 10 15 30 50 70
2,3 5.00
...Web of Intrigue (6/99, $3.50) r/origin & early appearances 1 2 3 5 6 7
TPB (7/01, $15.95) r/Vol. 1 & 2; Jones-c 16.00

BLACK WIDOW (Marvel Knights) (Volume 2)
Marvel Comics: Jan, 2001 - No. 3, May, 2001 ($2.99, limited series)

1-3-Grayson & Rucka-s/Scott Hampton-c/a; Daredevil app. 4.00

BLACK WIDOW (Marvel Knights)
Marvel Comics: Nov, 2004 - No. 6, Apr, 2005 ($2.99, limited series)

1-6-Sienkiewicz-a/Land-c 4.00

BLACK WIDOW (Continues in Widowmaker #1)
Marvel Comics: Jun, 2010 - No. 8, Jan, 2011 ($3.99/$2.99)

1-($3.99) Liu-s/Acuña-a; Wolverine app.; back-up history text 1 2 3 5 6 8
1-Variant photo-c of Scarlett Johansson from Iron Man 2 movie 9 18 27 59 117 175
2-8-($2.99) 2-5-Acuña-a. 2,3-Elektra app. 3.00

BLACK WIDOW (All-New Marvel Now!)

GD 2.0 | VG 4.0 | FN 6.0 | VF 8.0 | VF/NM 9.0 | NM- 9.2

Marvel Comics: Mar, 2014 - No. 20, Sept, 2015 ($3.99)

1-20: 1-Edmonson-s/Noto-a/c. 7-Daredevil app. 8-Winter Soldier app. 11-X-23 app. 4.00

BLACK WIDOW
Marvel Comics: May, 2016 - No. 12, May, 2017 ($3.99)

1-12: 1-Waid-s/Samnee-s&a. 6-Iron Man app. 9,10-Winter Soldier app. 4.00

BLACK WIDOW
Marvel Comics: Mar, 2019 - No. 5, Jul, 2019 ($3.99, limited series)

1-5: 1-Jen & Sylvia Soska-s/Flaviano-a; Captain America app. 2,3-Madame Masque app. 4.00

BLACK WIDOW
Marvel Comics: Jun, 2020 - No. 15, May, 2022 ($3.99)

1-15: 1-Kelly Thompson-s/Elena Casagrande; Yelena Belova & Arcade app. 4.00
...: Widow's Sting 1 (12/20, $3.99) Macchio-s/Buonfantino-a 4.00

BLACK WIDOW & THE MARVEL GIRLS
Marvel Comics: Feb, 2010 - No. 4, Apr, 2010 ($2.99, limited series)

1-4-Tobin-s. 1-Enchantress app. 2-Avengers app. 4-Storm app.; Miyazawa-a 4.00

BLACK WIDOW: DEADLY ORIGIN
Marvel Comics: Jan, 2010 - No. 4, Apr, 2010 ($3.99, limited series)

1-4-Granov-c; origin retold. 1-Wolverine and Bucky app. 3-Daredevil app. 4.00

BLACK WIDOW: PALE LITTLE SPIDER (Marvel Knights) (Volume 3)
Marvel Comics: Jun, 2002 - No. 3, Aug, 2002 ($2.99, limited series)

1-3-Rucka-s/Kordey-a/Horn-c 4.00

BLACK WIDOW 2 (THE THINGS THEY SAY ABOUT HER) (Marvel Knights)
Marvel Comics: Nov, 2005 - No. 6, Apr, 2006 ($2.99, limited series)

1-6-Phillips & Sienkiewicz-a/Morgan-s; Daredevil app. 4.00
TPB (2006, $15.99) r/#1-6 16.00

BLACKWOOD
Dark Horse Comics: May, 2018 - No. 4, Aug, 2018 ($3.99, limited series)

1-4-Evan Dorkin-s/Veronica Fish-a 4.00

BLACKWOOD: THE MOURNING AFTER
Dark Horse Comics: Feb, 2020 - No. 4, Sept, 2020 ($3.99, limited series)

1-4-Evan Dorkin-s/Veronica Fish-a 4.00

BLACKWULF
Marvel Comics: June, 1994 - No. 10, Mar, 1995 ($1.50)

1-($2.50)-Embossed-c; Angel Medina-a 4.00
2-10 3.00

BLADE (The Vampire Hunter)
Marvel Comics

1-(3/98, $3.50) Colan-a(p)/Christopher Golden-s 6.00
... Black & White TPB (2004, $15.99, B&W) reprints from magazines Vampire Tales #8,9; Marvel Preview #3,6; Crescent City Blues #1 and Marvel Shadow and Light #1 16.00
San Diego Con Promo (6/97) Wesley Snipes photo-c 3.00
...Sins of the Father (10/98, $5.99) Sears-a; movie adaption 6.00
Blade 2: Movie Adaptation (5/02, $5.95) Ponticelli-a/Bradstreet-c 6.00

BLADE (The Vampire Hunter)
Marvel Comics: Nov, 1998 - No. 3, Jan, 1999 ($3.50/$2.99)

1-($3.50) Contains Movie insider pages; McKean-a 6.00
2,3-($2.99): 2-Two covers 3.00

BLADE (Volume 2)
Marvel Comics (MAX): May, 2002 -No. 6, Oct, 2002 ($2.99)

1-6-Bradstreet-c/Hinz-s. 1-5-Pugh-a. 6-Homs-a 3.00

BLADE
Marvel Comics: Nov, 2006 - No. 12, Oct, 2007 ($2.99)

1-12: 1-Chaykin-a/Guggenheim-s; origin retold; Spider-Man app. 2-Dr. Doom-c/app. 5-Civil War tie-in; Wolverine app. 6-Blade loses a hand. 10-Spider-Man app. 3.00
...: Sins of the Father TPB (2007, $14.99) r/#7-12; afterword by Guggenheim 15.00
...: Undead Again TPB (2007, $14.99) r/#1-6; letters pages from #1&2 15.00

BLADE OF THE IMMORTAL (Manga)
Dark Horse Comics: June, 1996 - No. 131, Nov, 2007 ($2.95/$2.99/$3.95, B&W)

1-Hiroaki Samura-s/a in all 2 4 6 8 11 14
2-5: 2-#1 on cover in error 6.00
6-10 5.00
11,19,20,34-($3.95, 48 pgs.): 34-Food one-shot 4.00
12-18,21-33,35-41,43-105,107-131: 12-20-Dreamsong. 21-28-On Silent Wings. 29-33-Dark Shadow. 35-42-Heart of Darkness. 43-57-The Gathering 3.00
42-($3.50) Ends Heart of Darkness 3.50
106-($3.99) 4.00

BLADE RUNNER (Movie)
Marvel Comics Group: Oct, 1982 - No. 2, Nov, 1982

1-r/Marvel Super Special #22; Williamson-c/a 3 6 9 21 33 45
2-Williamson-a 3 6 9 15 22 28

BLADE RUNNER
Titan Comics: 2021 (Free giveaway)

... Free Comic Book Day Issue (2021) Previews the Blad Runner Origins and 2029 series 3.00

BLADE RUNNER: BLACK LOTUS
Titan Comics: Sept, 2022 - No. 4, Dec, 2022 ($3.99)

1-4-Nancy A. Collins-s/Enid Balam-a; multiple covers on each 4.00

BLADE RUNNER ORIGINS
Titan Comics: Mar, 2021 - No. 12, Jul, 2022 ($3.99)

1-12-Story of the first Blade Runner. 1-Dagnino-a; multiple covers 4.00

BLADE RUNNER 2019
Titan Comics: Aug, 2019 - No. 12, Dec, 2020 ($3.99)

1-12: 1-Green & Johnson-s/Guinaldo-a; multiple covers on each. 5-Jumps to 2026 4.00

BLADE RUNNER 2029
Titan Comics: Jan, 2021 - No. 12, Mar, 2022 ($3.99)

1-12: 1-Mike Johnson-s/Andres Guinaldo-a; multiple covers on each 4.00

BLADE RUNNER 2039
Titan Comics: Jan, 2023 - Present ($3.99)

1-3: 1-Mike Johnson & Mellow Brown-s/Andres Guinaldo-a; multiple covers on each 4.00

BLADE: THE VAMPIRE-HUNTER
Marvel Comics: July, 1994 - No. 10, Apr, 1995 ($1.95)

1-($2.95)-Foil-c; Dracula returns; Wheatley-c/a 4 8 12 25 40 55
2-Dracula-c/app. 2 4 6 8 10 12
3-10: 3,10-Dracula-c/app. 8-Morbius app. 5.00

BLADE: VAMPIRE-HUNTER
Marvel Comics: Dec, 1999 - No. 6, May, 2000 ($3.50/$2.50)

1-($3.50)-Bart Sears-s; Sears and Smith-a 3 6 9 14 20 25
2-6-($2.50): 2-Regular & Wesley Snipes photo-c 5.00

BLADE: VAMPIRE NATION
Marvel Comics: Jan, 2023 ($4.99, one-shot)

1-Russell-s/Wachter-a; Dracula app. 5.00

BLAIR WITCH CHRONICLES, THE
Oni Press: Mar, 2000 - No. 4, July, 2000 ($2.95, B&W, limited series)

1-4-Van Meter-s.1-Guy Davis-a. 2-Mireault-a 4.00
1-DF Alternate-c by John Estes 5.00
TPB (9/00, $15.95) r/#1-4 & Blair Witch Project one-shot 16.00

BLAIR WITCH: DARK TESTAMENTS
Image Comics: Oct, 2000 ($2.95, one-shot)

1-Edington-s/Adlard-a; story of murderer Rustin Parr 3.00

BLAIR WITCH PROJECT, THE (Movie companion, not adaptation)
Oni Press: July, 1999 ($2.95, B&W, one-shot)

1-(1st printing) History of the Blair Witch, art by Edwards, Mireault, and Davis; Van Meter-s; only the stick figure is red on the cover 2 4 6 9 12 15
1-(2nd printing) Stick figure and title lettering are red on cover 4.00
1-(3rd printing) Stick figure, title, and creator credits are red on cover 3.00
DF Glow in the Dark variant-c ($10.00) 10.00

BLAST (Satire Magazine)
G & D Publications: Feb, 1971 - No. 2, May, 1971

1-Wrightson & Kaluta-a/Everette-c 8 16 24 51 96 140
2-Kaluta-c/a 5 10 15 35 63 90

BLAST CORPS
Dark Horse Comics: Oct, 1998 ($2.50, one-shot, based on Nintendo game)

1-Reprints from Nintendo Power magazine; Mahn-a 4.00

BLASTERS SPECIAL
DC Comics: 1989 ($2.00, one-shot)

1-Peter David scripts; Invasion spin-off 4.00

BLAST-OFF (Three Rocketeers)
Harvey Publications (Fun Day Funnies): Oct, 1965 (12¢)

1-Kirby/Williamson-a(2); Williamson/Crandall-a; Williamson/Torres/Krenkel-a; Kirby/Simon-c 7 14 21 44 82 120

BLAZE
Marvel Comics: Aug, 1994 - No. 12, July, 1995 ($1.95)

1-($2.95)-Foil embossed-c 4.00
2-12: 2-Man-Thing-c/story. 11,12-Punisher app. 3.00

BLAZE CARSON (Rex Hart #6 on)(See Kid Colt, Tex Taylor, Wild Western, Wisco)
Marvel Comics (USA): Sept, 1948 - No. 5, June, 1949

1-Tex Taylor app.; Shores-c 36 72 108 214 347 480
2,4,5: 2-Tex Morgan app.; Shores-c. 4-Two-Gun Kid app. 5-Tex Taylor app. 23 46 69 136 223 310
3-Used by N.Y. State Legis. Comm. (injury to eye splash); Tex Morgan app. 24 48 72 142 234 325

BLAZE: LEGACY OF BLOOD (See Ghost Rider & Ghost Rider/Blaze)
Marvel Comics (Midnight Sons imprint): Dec, 1993 - No. 4, Mar, 1994 ($1.75, limited series)

1-4 3.00

BLAZE OF GLORY
Marvel Comics: Feb, 2000 - No. 4, Mar, 2000 ($2.99, limited series)

1-4-Ostrander-s/Manco-a; Two-Gun Kid, Rawhide Kid, Red Wolf and Ghost Rider app. 3.00
TPB (7/02, $9.99) r/#1-4 10.00

BLAZE THE WONDER COLLIE (Formerly Molly Manton's Romances #1?)
Marvel Comics(SePI): No. 2, Oct, 1949 - No. 3, Feb, 1950 (Both have photo-c)

2(#1), 3-(Scarce) 32 64 96 188 307 425

BLAZING BATTLE TALES
Seaboard Periodicals (Atlas): July, 1975

1-Intro. Sgt. Hawk & the Sky Demon; Severin, McWilliams, Sparling-a; Nazi-c by Thorne 3 6 9 16 23 30

BLAZING COMBAT (Magazine)
Warren Publishing Co.: Oct, 1965 - No. 4, July, 1966 (35¢, B&W)

1-Frazetta painted-c on all 46 92 138 368 834 1300
2 10 20 30 64 132 200
3,4: 4-Frazetta half pg. ad 9 18 27 58 114 170
nn-Anthology (reprints from No. 1-4) (low print) 9 18 27 58 114 170

NOTE: ***Adkins*** *a-4.* ***Colan*** *a-3,4,nn.* ***Crandall*** *a-all.* ***Evans*** *a-1,4.* ***Heath*** *a-4,nn.* ***Morrow*** *a-1-3,nn.* ***Orlando*** *a-1-3,nn.* ***J. Severin*** *a-all.* ***Torres*** *a-1-4.* ***Toth*** *a-all.* ***Williamson*** *a-2. and* ***Wood*** *a-3,4,nn.*

BLAZING COMBAT: WORLD WAR I AND WORLD WAR II
Apple Press: Mar, 1994 ($3.75, B&W)

1,2: 1-r/Colan, Toth, Goodwin, Severin, Wood-a. 2-r/Crandall, Evans, Severin, Torres, Williamson-a 6.00

BLAZING COMICS (Also see Blue Circle Comics and Red Circle Comics)

Black Widow (2020) #11 © MAR

Blade Runner 2019 #6 © Alcon

Blondie Comics #45 © HARV

Enwil Associates/Rural Home: 6/44 - #3, 9/44; #4, 2/45; #5, 3/45; #5(V2#2), 3/55 - #6(V2#3), 1955?

	GD 2.0	VG 4.0	FN 6.0	VF 8.0	VF/NM 9.0	NM- 9.2
1-The Green Turtle, Red Hawk, Black Buccaneer begin; origin Jun-Gal; classic Japanese WWII splash	84	168	252	538	919	1300
2-5: 2-Japanese WWII-c. 3-Briefer-a. 5-(V2#2 inside)	50	100	150	315	533	750
5(3/55, V2#2-inside)-Black Buccaneer-c, 6(V2#3-inside, 1955)-Indian/Japanese-c; cover is from Apr. 1945	30	60	90	177	289	400

NOTE: *No. 5 & 6 contain remaindered comics rebound and the contents can vary. Cloak & Daggar, Will Rogers, Superman 64, Star Spangled 130, Kaanga known. Value would be half of contents.*

BLAZING SIXGUNS
Avon Periodicals: Dec, 1952

	GD 2.0	VG 4.0	FN 6.0	VF 8.0	VF/NM 9.0	NM- 9.2
1-Kinstler-c/a; Larsen/Alascia-a(2), Tuska?-a; Jesse James, Kit Carson, Wild Bill Hickok app.	47	94	141	296	498	700

BLAZING SIXGUNS
I.W./Super Comics: 1964

	GD 2.0	VG 4.0	FN 6.0	VF 8.0	VF/NM 9.0	NM- 9.2
I.W. Reprint #1,8,9: 1-r/Wild Bill Hickok #26, Western True Crime #? & Blazing Sixguns #1 by Avon; Kinstler-c. 8-r/Blazing Western #?; Kinstler-c. 9-r/Blazing Western #1; Ditko-r; Kintsler-c reprinted from Dalton Boys #1	3	6	9	14	20	25
Super Reprint #10,11,15-17: 10,11-r/The Rider #2,1. 15-r/Silver Kid Western #?. 16-r/Buffalo Bill #?; Wildey-r; Severin-c. 17(1964)-r/Western True Crime #?	3	6	9	14	20	25
12-Reprints Bullseye #3; S&K-a	4	8	12	23	37	50
18-r/Straight Arrow #? by Powell; Severin-c	3	6	9	14	20	25

BLAZING SIX-GUNS (Also see Sundance Kid)
Skywald Comics: Feb, 1971 - No. 2, Apr, 1971 (52 pgs.)

	GD 2.0	VG 4.0	FN 6.0	VF 8.0	VF/NM 9.0	NM- 9.2
1-The Red Mask (3-D effect, not true 3-D), Sundance Kid begin (new-s), Avon's Geronimo reprint by Kinstler; Wyatt Earp app.	3	6	9	14	20	25
2-Wild Bill Hickok, Jesse James, Kit Carson-r plus M.E. Red Mask-r (3-D effect)	2	4	6	10	14	18

BLAZING WEST (The Hooded Horseman #21 on)(52 pgs.)
American Comics Group (B&I Publ./Michel Publ.): Fall, 1948 - No. 20, Nov-Dec, 1951

	GD 2.0	VG 4.0	FN 6.0	VF 8.0	VF/NM 9.0	NM- 9.2
1-Origin & 1st app. Injun Jones, Tenderfoot & Buffalo Belle; Texas Tim & Ranger begins, ends #13	27	54	81	158	259	360
2,3 (1-2/49)	14	28	42	82	121	160
4-Origin & 1st app. Little Lobo; Starr-a (3-4/49)	14	28	42	80	115	150
5-10: 5-Starr-a	11	22	33	60	83	105
11-13	10	20	30	54	72	90
14(11-12/50)-Origin/1st app. The Hooded Horseman	16	32	48	92	144	195
15-20: 15,16,18,19-Starr-a	10	20	30	58	79	100

BLAZING WESTERN
Timor Publications: Jan, 1954 - No. 5, Sept, 1954

	GD 2.0	VG 4.0	FN 6.0	VF 8.0	VF/NM 9.0	NM- 9.2
1-Ditko-a (1st Western-a?); text story by Bruce Hamilton	22	44	66	132	216	300
2-4	11	22	33	60	83	105
5-Disbrow-a; L.B. Cole-c	11	22	33	62	86	110

BLINDSIDE
Image Comics (Extreme Studios): Aug, 1996 ($2.50)

	GD 2.0	VG 4.0	FN 6.0	VF 8.0	VF/NM 9.0	NM- 9.2
1-Variant-c exists						3.00

BLINK (See X-Men Age of Apocalypse storyline)
Marvel Comics: March, 2001 - No. 4, June, 2001 ($2.99, limited series)

	GD 2.0	VG 4.0	FN 6.0	VF 8.0	VF/NM 9.0	NM- 9.2
1-4-Adam Kubert-c/Lobdell-s/Winick-script; leads into Exiles #1						3.00

BLIP
Marvel Comics Group: Feb, 1983 - 1983 (Video game mag. in comic format)

	GD 2.0	VG 4.0	FN 6.0	VF 8.0	VF/NM 9.0	NM- 9.2
1-1st app. Donkey Kong & Mario Bros. in comics, 6pgs. comics; photo-c	10	20	30	64	132	200
2-Spider-Man photo-c; 6pgs. Spider-Man comics w/Green Goblin	4	8	12	25	40	55
3,4,6	2	4	6	9	12	15
5-E.T., Indiana Jones; Rocky-c	3	6	9	14	20	25
7-6pgs. Hulk comics; Pac-Man & Donkey Kong Jr. Hints	2	4	6	11	16	20

BLISS
Image Comics: Jul, 2020 - No. 8, Jun, 2021 ($3.99)

	GD 2.0	VG 4.0	FN 6.0	VF 8.0	VF/NM 9.0	NM- 9.2
1-8-Sean Lewis-s/Caitlin Yarsky-a						4.00

BLISS ALLEY
Image Comics: July, 1997 - No. 2, Sept, 1997 ($2.95, B&W)

	GD 2.0	VG 4.0	FN 6.0	VF 8.0	VF/NM 9.0	NM- 9.2
1,2-Messner-Loebs-s/a						3.00

BLITZKRIEG
National Periodical Publications: Jan-Feb, 1976 - No. 5, Sept-Oct, 1976

	GD 2.0	VG 4.0	FN 6.0	VF 8.0	VF/NM 9.0	NM- 9.2
1-Kubert-c on all	5	10	15	33	57	80
2-5	3	6	9	17	25	34

BLOCKBUSTERS OF THE MARVEL UNIVERSE
Marvel Comics: March, 2011 ($4.99, one-shot)

	GD 2.0	VG 4.0	FN 6.0	VF 8.0	VF/NM 9.0	NM- 9.2
1-Handbook-style summaries of Marvel crossover events like Civil War & Heroes Reborn						5.00

BLONDE PHANTOM (Formerly All-Select #1-11; Lovers #23 on)(Also see Blackstone, Marvel Mystery, Millie The Model #2, Sub-Mariner Comics #25 & Sun Girl)
Marvel Comics (MPC): No. 12, Winter, 1946-47 - No. 22, Mar, 1949

	GD 2.0	VG 4.0	FN 6.0	VF 8.0	VF/NM 9.0	NM- 9.2
12-Miss America begins, ends #14	290	580	870	1856	3178	4500
13-Sub-Mariner begins (not in #16)	161	322	483	1030	1765	2500
14,15: 15-Kurtzman's "Hey Look"	155	310	465	992	1696	2400
16-Captain America with Bucky story by Rico(p), 6 pgs.; Kurtzman's "Hey Look" (1 pg.)	181	362	543	1158	1979	2800
17-22: 22-Anti Wertham editorial	129	258	387	826	1413	2000

NOTE: ***Shores** c-12-18.*

BLONDIE (See Ace Comics, Comics Reading Libraries (Promotional Comics section), Dagwood, Daisy & Her Pups, Eat Right to Work..., King & Magic Comics)
David McKay Publications: 1942 - 1946

	GD 2.0	VG 4.0	FN 6.0	VF 8.0	VF/NM 9.0	NM- 9.2
Feature Books 12 (Rare)	110	220	330	704	1202	1700
Feature Books 27-29,31,34(1940)	24	48	72	142	234	325
Feature Books 36,38,40,42,43,45,47	21	42	63	126	206	285
...1944 (Hard-c, 1938, B&W, 128 pgs.)-1944 daily strip-r	18	36	54	103	162	220

BLONDIE & DAGWOOD FAMILY
Harvey Publ. (King Features Synd.): Oct, 1963 - No. 4, Dec, 1965 (68 pgs.)

	GD 2.0	VG 4.0	FN 6.0	VF 8.0	VF/NM 9.0	NM- 9.2
1	5	10	15	30	50	70
2-4	3	6	9	19	30	40

BLONDIE COMICS (...Monthly No. 16-141)
David McKay #1-15/Harvey #16-163/King #164-175/Charlton #177 on:
Spring, 1947 - No. 163, Nov, 1965; No. 164, Aug, 1966 - No. 175, Dec, 1967; No. 177, Feb, 1969 - No. 222, Nov, 1976

	GD 2.0	VG 4.0	FN 6.0	VF 8.0	VF/NM 9.0	NM- 9.2
1	53	106	159	334	567	800
2	23	46	69	138	227	315
3-5	17	34	51	100	158	215
6-10	14	28	42	82	121	160
11-15	11	22	33	60	83	105
16-(3/50; 1st Harvey issue)	12	24	36	67	94	120
17-20: 20-(3/51)-Becomes Daisy & Her Pups #21 & Chamber of Chills #21	5	10	15	34	60	85
21-30	5	10	15	31	53	75
31-50	4	8	12	27	44	60
51-80	4	8	12	23	37	50
81-99	3	6	9	21	33	45
100	4	8	12	25	40	55
101-124,126-130	3	6	9	17	26	35
125 (80 pgs.)	4	8	12	27	44	60
131-136,138,139	3	6	9	16	24	32
137,140-(80 pgs.)	4	8	12	25	40	55
141-147,149-154,156,160,164-167	3	6	9	16	23	30
148,155,157-159,161-163 are 68 pgs.	3	6	9	21	33	45
168-175	2	4	6	11	16	20
177-199 (no #176)-Moon landing-c/s	2	4	6	9	13	16
200-Anniversary issue; highlights of the Bumsteads	2	4	6	10	14	18
201-210,213-222	2	4	6	8	10	12
211,212-1st & 2nd app. Super Dagwood	2	4	6	9	13	16
Blondie, Dagwood & Daisy by Chic Young #1(Harvey, 1953, 100 pg. squarebound giant) new stories; Popeye (1 pg.) and Felix (1pg.) app.	11	22	33	64	90	115

BLOOD
Marvel Comics (Epic Comics): Feb, 1988 - No. 4, Apr, 1988 ($3.25, mature)

	GD 2.0	VG 4.0	FN 6.0	VF 8.0	VF/NM 9.0	NM- 9.2
1-4: DeMatteis scripts & Kent Williams-c/a						5.00

BLOOD AND GLORY (Punisher & Captain America)
Marvel Comics: Oct, 1992 - No. 3, Dec, 1992 ($5.95, limited series)

	GD 2.0	VG 4.0	FN 6.0	VF 8.0	VF/NM 9.0	NM- 9.2
1-3: 1-Embossed wraparound-c by Janson; Chichester & Clarke-s						6.00

BLOOD & ROSES: FUTURE PAST TENSE (Bob Hickey's...)
Sky Comics: Dec, 1993 ($2.25)

	GD 2.0	VG 4.0	FN 6.0	VF 8.0	VF/NM 9.0	NM- 9.2
1-Silver ink logo						3.00

BLOOD & ROSES: SEARCH FOR THE TIME-STONE (Bob Hickey's...)

GD 2.0 | VG 4.0 | FN 6.0 | VF 8.0 | VF/NM 9.0 | NM- 9.2

Sky Comics: Apr, 1994 ($2.50)
1 3.00

BLOOD AND SHADOWS
DC Comics (Vertigo): 1996 - Book 4, 1996 ($5.95, squarebound, mature)
Books 1-4: Joe R. Lansdale scripts; Mark A. Nelson-c/a. 6.00

BLOOD AND WATER
DC Comics (Vertigo): May, 2003 - No. 5, Sept, 2003 ($2.95, limited series)
1-5-Judd Winick-s/Tomm Coker-a/Brian Bolland-c 3.00
TPB (2009, $14.99) r/#1-5 15.00

BLOOD: A TALE
DC Comics (Vertigo): Nov, 1996 - No. 4, Feb, 1997 ($2.95, limited series)
1-4: Reprints Epic series w/new-c; DeMatteis scripts; Kent Williams-c/a 3.00
TPB (2004, $19.95) r/#1-4 20.00

BLOODBATH
DC Comics: Early Dec, 1993 - No. 2, Late Dec, 1993 ($3.50, 68 pgs.)
1-Neon ink-c; Superman app.; new Batman-c /app. 4.00
2-Hitman 2nd app. 1 2 3 4 5 7

BLOOD BLISTER
AfterShock Comics: Jan, 2017 - No. 2, Apr, 2017 ($3.99)
1,2-Phil Hester-s/Tony Harris-a 4.00

BLOODBORNE (Based on the Sony computer game)
Titan Comics: Mar, 2018 - No. 16, Nov, 2019 ($3.99)
1-16-Ales Kot-s/Piotr Kowalski-a 4.00

BLOODHOUND
DC Comics: Sept, 2004 - No. 10, June, 2005 ($2.95)
1-10: 1-Jolley-s/Kirk-a/Johnson-c. 5-Firestorm app. (cont. from Firestorm #7) 3.00

BLOODHOUND: CROWBAR MEDICINE
Dark Horse Comics: Oct, 2013 - No. 5, Mar, 2014 ($3.99)
1-5-Jolley-s/Kirk-a/c 4.00

BLOOD LEGACY
Image Comics (Top Cow): May, 2000 - No. 4, Nov, 2000; Apr, 2003 ($2.50/$4.99)
...: The Story of Ryan 1-4-Kerri Hawkins-s. 1-Andy Park-a(p); 3 covers 3.00
...: The Young Ones 1 (4/03, $4.99, one-shot) Basaldua-c/a 5.00
Preview Special ('00, $4.95) B&W flip-book w/The Magdalena Preview 5.00

BLOODLINE: DAUGHTER OF BLADE
Marvel Comics: Apr, 2023 - Present ($3.99, limited series)
1-Danny Lore-s/Karen S. Darboe-a 4.00

BLOODLINES
DC Comics: Jun, 2016 - No. 6, Nov, 2016 ($2.99, limited series)
1-6: 1-Krul-s/Marion-a 3.00

BLOODLINES: A TALE FROM THE HEART OF AFRICA (See Tales From the Heart of Africa)
Marvel Comics (Epic Comics): 1992 ($5.95, 52 pgs.)
1-Story cont'd from Tales From... 6.00

BLOOD OF DRACULA
Apple Comics: Nov, 1987 - No. 20?, 1990 ($1.75/$1.95, B&W)($2.25 #14,16 on)
1-3,5-14,20: 1-10-Chadwick-c 4.00
4,16-19-Lost Frankenstein pgs. by Wrightson 1 2 3 4 5 7
15-Contains stereo flexidisc ($3.75) 5.00

BLOOD OF THE DEMON (Etrigan the Demon)
DC Comics: May, 2005 - No. 17, Sept, 2006 ($2.50/$2.99)
1-14-Byrne-a(p) & plot/Pfeifer-script. 3,4-Batman app. 13-One Year Later 3.00
15-17-($2.99) 3.00

BLOOD OF THE INNOCENT (See Warp Graphics Annual)
WaRP Graphics: 1/7/86 - No. 4, 1/28/86 (Weekly mini-series, mature)
1-4 3.00

BLOODPACK
DC Comics: Mar, 1995 - No. 4, June,1995 ($1.50, limited series)
1-4 3.00

BLOODPOOL
Image Comics (Extreme): Aug, 1995 - No. 4, Nov, 1995 ($2.50, limited series)
1-4: Jo Duffy scripts in all 3.00
Special (3/96, $2.50)-Jo Duffy scripts 3.00
Trade Paperback (1996, $12.95)-r/#1-4 13.00

BLOOD QUEEN, THE
Dynamite Entertainment: 2014 - No. 6, 2014 ($3.99, limited series)
1-6-Brownfield-s/Casas-a/Anacleto-c; variant covers on each 4.00
Annual 2014 ($7.99) Prequel stories to the series 8.00

BLOOD QUEEN VS. DRACULA
Dynamite Entertainment: 2015 - No. 4, 2015 ($3.99, limited series)
1-4-Brownfield-s/Baal-a/Anacleto-c; variant covers on each 4.00

BLOOD RED DRAGON (Stan Lee and Yoshiki's...)
Image Comics: No. 0, Aug, 2011 - No. 3, Nov, 2011 ($3.99)
0-3-Goff-s/Soriano-a 4.00

BLOODSCENT
Comico: Oct, 1988 ($2.00, one-shot, Baxter paper)
1-Colan-p 3.00

BLOODSEED
Marvel Comics (Frontier Comics): Oct, 1993 - No. 2, Nov, 1993 ($1.95)
1,2: Sharp/Cam Smith-a 3.00

BLOODSHOT (See Eternal Warrior #4 & Rai #0)
Valiant/Acclaim Comics (Valiant): Feb, 1993 - No. 51, Aug, 1996 ($2.25/$2.50)
0-(3/94, $3.50)-Wraparound chromium-c by Quesada(p); origin 5.00
0-Gold variant; no cover price 40.00
Note: There is a "Platinum variant" ; press run error of Gold ed. (25 copies exist)
(A CGC certified 9.4 copy sold for $1690 in 2017 and a 9.0 sold for $1200 in 2020)
1-($3.50)-Chromium embossed-c by B. Smith w/poster
2 4 6 8 10 12
2-5,8-14: 3-$2.25-c begins; cont'd in Hard Corps #5. 4-Eternal Warrior-c/story. 5-Rai & Eternal Warrior app. 14-(3/94)-Reese-c(i) 4.00
6,7: 6-1st app. Ninjak (out of costume). 7-Ninjak in costume
2 4 6 8 10 12
15(4/94)-50: 16-w/bound-in trading card 3.00
51-Bloodshot dies? 4 8 12 25 40 55
Yearbook 1 (1994, $3.95) 4.00
Special 1 (3/94, $5.95)-Zeck-c/a(p); Last Stand 2 4 6 8 10 12
...: Blood of the Machine HC (2012, $24.99) r/#1-8; new 8 pg. story; intro. by VanHook 25.00

BLOODSHOT (Volume Two)
Acclaim Comics (Valiant): July, 1997 - No. 16, Oct, 1998 ($2.50)
1,2,4-14: 1-Two covers. 5-Copycat-c. X-O Manowar-c/app. 3.00
3-1st Chainsaw 2 4 6 8 10 12
15,16 6.00

BLOODSHOT (Re-titled Bloodshot and H.A.R.D.Corps for #14-23)
Valiant Entertainment: July, 2012 - No. 25, Nov, 2014 ($3.99)
1-13: 1-Sweirczynski-s/Garcia & Lozzi-a. 10-13-Harbinger Wars tie-ins 4.00
1-9-Pullbox variants 4.00
1-Variant-c by David Aja 2 4 6 9 12 15
1-Variant-c by Esad Ribic 2 4 6 11 16 20
14-24: 14-23-Bloodshot and H.A.R.D.Corps 4.00
25-($4.99) Milligan-s/Larosa-a; back-up Chaykin-s/a; short features by various 5.00
#0 (8/13) Kindt-s/ChrisCross-a; covers by Lupacchino & Bullock 4.00
Bloodshot and H.A.R.D.Corps #0 (2/14, $3.99) History of Project Rising Spirit 4.00
Bloodshot's Day Off 1 (7/17, $3.99) Rahal-s/Evans-a; Viet Man app. 4.00

BLOODSHOT
Valiant Entertainment: Sept, 2019 - No. 12, Mar, 2021 ($3.99)
1-12: 1-Tim Seeley-s/Brett Booth-a; multiple covers on each 4.00
#0 (2/20, $3.99) Tim Seeley-s/Marc Laming-a; Bloodshot in Siberia; leads into issue #7 4.00

BLOODSHOT REBORN
Valiant Entertainment: Apr, 2015 - No. 18, Oct, 2016 ($3.99)
1-18: 1-4-Lemire-s/Suayan-a. 1-1st app. Bloodsquirt. 6-9-Guice-a. 10-13-Set 30 years later. 14-1st app. Deathmate 4.00
#0 (3/17, $3.99) Lemire-s/Guedes-a 4.00
Annual 2016 #1 (3/16, $5.99) Short stories by various incl. Kano, Lemire, Bennett 6.00
...: Bloodshot Island - Director's Cut 1 (6/16, $4.99) r/#1 in B&W; original script 5.00

BLOODSHOT RISING SPIRIT
Valiant Entertainment: Nov, 2018 - No. 8, Jun, 2019 ($3.99)
1-8: 1-Grevioux-s/Lashley-a; Bloodshot prototype; bonus Livewire #12 preview 4.00

BLOODSHOT SALVATION
Valiant Entertainment: Sept, 2017 - No. 12, Aug, 2018 ($3.99)
1-12: 1-Lemire-s/LaRosa-a; bonus Ninjak #1 preview 4.00

BLOODSHOT UNLEASHED
Valiant Entertainment: Sept, 2022 - No. 4, Dec, 2022 ($3.99, limited series)
1-4: 1-Deniz Camp-s/Jon Davis-Hunt-a. 4-Zawadzki-a 4.00

BLOODSHOT U.S.A.
Valiant Entertainment: Oct, 2016 - No. 4, Jan, 2017 ($3.99, limited series)
1-4-Lemire-s/Braithwaite-a; Ninjak and Deathmate app. 4.00

BLOOD STAINED TEETH
Marvel Comics: Apr, 2022 - Present ($3.99)
1-9-Christian Ward-s/Patric Reynolds-a 4.00

BLOODSTONE
Marvel Comics: Dec, 2001 - No. 4, Mar, 2002 ($2.99)
1-Intro. Elsa Bloodstone; Abnett & Lanning-s/Lopez-a
10 20 30 64 132 200
2-4 2 4 6 8 10 12

BLOODSTRIKE (See Supreme V2#3) (Issue #25 published between #10 & #11)
Image Comics (Extreme Studios): 1993 - No. 22, May, 1995; No. 25, May, 1994 ($1.95/$2.50)
1-22, 25: Liefeld layouts in early issues. 1-Blood Brothers prelude. 2-1st app. Lethal. 5-1st app. Noble. 9-Black and White part 6 by Art Thibert; Liefeld pin-up. 9,10-Have coupon #3 & 7 for Extreme Prejudice #0. 10-(4/94). 11-(7/94). 16:Platt-c; Prophet app. 17-19-polybagged w/card . 25-(5/94)-Liefeld/Fraga-c 3.00
#0-(6/18, $3.99) Brutalists part 1; origin of the team; Michel Fiffe-s/a 4.00
#23,24-(6/18, $3.99) Brutalists parts 2&3; retroactively fills story gap between #22&25 4.00
... #1 Remastered Edition (7/17, $3.99) Two covers by Fraga & Liefeld 4.00
NOTE: ***Giffen** story/layouts-4-6. **Jae Lee** c-7, 8. **Rob Liefeld** layouts-1-3. **Art Thibert** c-6i.*

BLOODSTRIKE
Image Comics: No. 26, Mar, 2012 - No. 33, Dec, 2012 ($2.99/$3.99)
26-29: 26-Two covers by Seeley & Liefeld; Seeley-s/Gaston-a 3.00
30-33-($3.99) 32,33-Suprema app. 4.00

BLOODSTRIKE (Volume 2)
Image Comics: Jul, 2015 - No. 2, Sept, 2015 ($2.99/$3.99)
1-($3.99) Liefeld-s/a 4.00
2-(9/15, $2.99) Liefeld-s/a 3.00

BLOODSTRIKE ASSASSIN
Image Comics (Extreme Studios): June, 1995 - No. 3, Aug, 1995; No. 0, Oct, 1995 ($2.50, limited series)
0-3: 3-(8/95)-Quesada-c. 0-(10/95)-Battlestone app. 3.00

BLOOD SWORD, THE
Jademan Comics: Aug, 1988 - No. 53, Dec, 1992 ($1.50/$1.95, 68 pgs.)
1-53-Kung Fu stories in all 4.00

The Blood Queen #1 © DYN

Bloodshot (2019) #9 © VAL

Blue Beetle (2011) #11 © DC

	GD 2.0	VG 4.0	FN 6.0	VF 8.0	VF/NM 9.0	NM- 9.2

BLOOD SWORD DYNASTY
Jademan Comics: 1989 - No. 41, Jan, 1993 ($1.25, 36 pgs.)

1-Ties into Blood Sword 4.00
2-41: Ties into Blood Sword 3.00

BLOOD SYNDICATE
DC Comics (Milestone): Apr, 1993 - No. 35, Feb, 1996 ($1.50-$3.50)

1-($2.95)-Collector's Edition; polybagged with poster, trading card, & acid-free backing board (direct sale only) 1 3 4 6 8 10
1-9,11-24,26,27,29,33: 8-Intro Kwai. 15-Byrne-c. 16-Worlds Collide Pt. 6; Superman-c/app. 17-Worlds Collide Pt. 13. 29-(99¢); Long Hot Summer x-over 4.00
10-Shadow War, Milestone's 1st x-over, continues from Xombi #0; Simonson-c 1 2 3 5 6 8
25-($2.95, 52 pgs.) 5.00
28,30-32: 30-Long Hot Summer x-over 4.00
34 3 6 9 16 23 30
35-Kwai disappears; last issue 4 8 12 27 44 60

BLOOD SYNDICATE: SEASON ONE
DC Comics (Milestone): Jul, 2022 - No. 6, Jan, 2023 ($3.99, limited series)

1-6: 1-4-Geoffrey Thorne-s/Chriscross-a 4.00

BLOODWULF
Image Comics (Extreme): Feb, 1995 - No. 4, May, 1995 ($2.50, limited series)

1-4: 1-Liefeld-c w/4 diferent captions & alternate-c. 3.00
Summer Special (8/95, $2.50)-Jeff Johnson-c/a; Supreme app; story takes place between Legend of Supreme #3 & Supreme #23. 3.00

BLOODY MARY
DC Comics (Helix): Oct, 1996 - No. 4, Jan, 1997 ($2.25, limited series)

1-4: Garth Ennis scripts; Ezquerra-c/a in all 3.50
TPB (2005, $19.99) r/#1-4 and Bloody Mary: Lady Liberty #1-4 20.00

BLOODY MARY: LADY LIBERTY
DC Comics (Helix): Sept, 1997 - No. 4, Dec, 1997 ($2.50, limited series)

1-4: Garth Ennis scripts; Ezquerra-c/a in all 3.00

BLOSSOMS: 666 (Archie Comics' Cheryl & Jason Blossom Satanic Horror)
Archie Comic Publications: Mar, 2019 - No. 5, Sept, 2019 ($3.99, limited series)

1-5-Cullen Bunn-s/Laura Braga-a; multiple covers. 2-Intro. Julian Blossom 4.00

BLUE
Image Comics (Action Toys): Aug, 1999 - No. 2, Apr, 2000 ($2.50)

1,2-Aronowitz-s/Struzan-c 3.00

BLUE & GOLD (Blue Beetle and Booster Gold)
DC Comics: Sept, 2021 - No. 8, Jun, 2022 ($3.99, limited series)

1-8: 1-Jurgens-s/Sook-a: 1,2-Justice League app. 4-Flashback pages with Maguire-a 4.00

BLUEBEARD
Slave Labor Graphics: Nov, 1993 - No. 3, Mar, 1994 ($2.95, B&W, lim. series)

1-3: James Robinson scripts. 2-(12/93) 3.00
Trade paperback (6/94, $9.95) 13.00
Trade paperback (2nd printing, 7/96, $12.95)-New-c 13.00

BLUE BEETLE, THE (Also see All Top, Big-3, Mystery Men & Weekly Comic Magazine)
Fox Publ. No. 1-11, 31-60; Holyoke No. 12-30: Winter, 1939-40 - No. 57, 7/48; No. 58, 4/50 - No. 60, 8/50

1-Reprints from Mystery Men #1-5; Blue Beetle origin; Yarko the Great-r/from Wonder Comics /Wonderworld #2-5 all by Eisner; Master Magician app.; (Blue Beetle in 4 different costumes) 975 1950 2919 7100 12,550 18,000
2-K-51-r by Powell/Wonderworld #8,9 300 600 900 1950 3375 4800
3-Simon-c 206 412 618 1318 2259 3200
4-Marijuana drug mention story 155 310 465 992 1696 2400
5-Zanzibar The Magician by Tuska 123 246 369 787 1344 1900
6-Dynamite Thor begins (1st); origin Blue Beetle 116 232 348 742 1271 1800
7,8-Dynamo app. in both. 8-Last Thor 113 226 339 718 1234 1750
9-12: 9,10-The Blackbird & The Gorilla app. 10-Bondage/hypo-c. 11(2/42)-Bondage-c; The Gladiator app. 12(6/42)-The Black Fury app. 100 200 300 635 1093 1550
13-V-Man begins (1st app.), ends #19; Kubert-a; centerfold spread 116 232 348 742 1271 1800
14,15-Kubert-a in both. 14-Intro. side-kick (c/text only), Sparky (called Spunky #17-19); BB vs. The Red Robe (Red Skull swipe) 93 186 279 591 1021 1450
16-18: 17-Brodsky-c 71 142 213 454 777 1100
19-Kubert-a 74 148 222 470 810 1150
20-Origin/1st app. Tiger Squadron; Arabian Nights begin 81 162 243 518 884 1250
21-26: 24-Intro. & only app. The Halo. 26-General Patton story & photo 58 116 174 371 636 900
27-Tamaa, Jungle Prince app. 53 106 159 334 567 800
28-30(2/44): 29-WWII Nazi bondage-c(1/44) 52 104 156 322 549 775
31(6/44), 33,34,36-40: 34-38-"The Threat from Saturn" serial. 40-Shows #20 in indicia 41 82 123 256 428 600
32-Hitler-c 148 296 444 947 1624 2300
35-Extreme violence 50 100 150 315 533 750
41-45 (#43 exist?) 40 80 120 246 411 575
46-The Puppeteer app. 50 100 150 315 533 750
47-Kamen & Baker-a begin 213 426 639 1363 2332 3300
48-50 148 296 444 947 1624 2300
51,53 129 258 387 826 1413 2000
52-Kamen bondage-c; true crime stories begin 226 452 678 1446 2473 3500
54-Used in **SOTI**. Illo, "Children call these 'headlights' comics"; classic-c 975 1950 2919 7100 12,550 18,000
55-57: 56-Used in **SOTI**, pg. 145. 57(7/48)-Last Kamen issue; becomes Western Killers? 123 246 369 762 1306 1900
58(4/50)-60-No Kamen-a 30 60 90 177 289 400
NOTE: ***Kamen** a-47-51, 53, 55-57; c-47, 49-52.* ***Powell** a-4(2). Bondage-c 9-12, 46, 52. Headlight-c 46, 48, 57.*

BLUE BEETLE (Formerly The Thing; becomes Mr. Muscles No. 22 on) (See Charlton Bullseye & Space Adventures)
Charlton Comics: No. 18, Feb, 1955 - No. 21, Aug, 1955

18,19-(Pre-1944-r). 18-Last pre-code issue. 19-Bouncer, Rocket Kelly-r 45 90 135 284 480 675
20-Joan Mason by Kamen 50 100 150 315 533 750
21-New material 39 78 117 231 378 525

BLUE BEETLE (Unusual Tales #1-49; Ghostly Tales #55 on)(See Captain Atom #83 & Charlton Bullseye)
Charlton Comics: V2#1, June, 1964 - V2#5, Mar-Apr, 1965; V3#50, July, 1965 - V3#54, Feb-Mar, 1966; #1, June, 1967 - #5, Nov, 1968

V2#1-Origin/1st S.A. app. Dan Garrett-Blue Beetle 29 58 87 209 467 725
2-5: 5-Weiss illo; 1st published-a? 8 16 24 51 96 140
V3#50-54-Formerly Unusual Tales 7 14 21 48 89 130
1(1967)-Question series begins by Ditko 29 58 87 209 467 725
2-Origin Ted Kord-Blue Beetle (see Capt. Atom #83 for 1st Ted Kord Blue Beetle); Dan Garrett x-over 10 20 30 64 132 200
3-5 (All Ditko-c/a in #1-5) 6 12 18 41 76 110
1 (Modern Comics-1977)-Reprints 3 6 9 19 30 40
3 (Modern Comics-1977)-Reprints 2 4 6 9 12 15
NOTE: *#6 only appeared in the fanzine 'The Charlton Portfolio.'*

BLUE BEETLE (Also see Americomics, Crisis On Infinite Earths, Justice League & Showcase '94 #2-4)
DC Comics: June, 1986 - No. 24, May, 1988

1-Origin retold; intro. Firefist 3 6 9 16 23 30
2-10,15-19,21-24: 2-Origin Firefist. 5-7-The Question app. 21-Millennium tie-in 4.00
11-14,20: 11-14-New Teen Titans x-over. 20-Justice League app.; Millennium tie-in 4.00

BLUE BEETLE (See Infinite Crisis, Teen Titans, and Booster Gold #21)
DC Comics: May, 2006 - No. 36, Apr, 2009 ($2.99)

1-Hamner-a/Giffen & Rogers-s; Guy Gardner app. 4.00
1-2nd & 3rd printings 3.00
2-36: 2-2nd printing exists. 2-4-Oracle app. 5-Phantom Stranger app. 16-Eclipso app. 18,33-Teen Titans app. 20-Sinestro Corps. 21-Spectre app. 26-Spanish issue 3.00
...: Black and Blue TPB (2010, $17.99) r/#27,28,35,36 & Booster Gold #21-25,28,29 18.00
...: Boundaries TPB (2009, $14.99) r/#29-34 15.00
...: End Game TPB (2008, $14.99) r/#20-26; English script for #26 15.00
...: Reach For the Stars TPB (2008, $14.99) r/#13-19 15.00
...: Road Trip TPB (2007, $12.99) r/#7-12 13.00
...: Shellshocked TPB (2006, $12.99) r/#1-6 13.00

BLUE BEETLE (DC New 52) (Also see Threshold)
DC Comics: Nov, 2011 - No. 16, Mar, 2013 ($2.99)

1-16: 1-Bedard-s/Ig Guara-a; new origin. 9-Green Lantern (Kyle) app. 11-Booster Gold 3.00
#0 (11/12, $2.99) Origin of the scarab 3.00

BLUE BEETLE (DC Rebirth)
DC Comics: Nov, 2016 - No. 18, Apr, 2018 ($2.99/$3.99)

1-7-Giffen-s/Kolins-a. 4-7-Doctor Fate app. 3.00
8-18-($3.99) 8-11-Doctor Fate, Arion and OMAC app. 12-Batman app. 4.00
...: Rebirth 1 (10/16, $2.99) Giffen-s/Kolins-a; Ted Kord & Doctor Fate app. 3.00

BLUE BEETLE: GRADUATION DAY (Jaime Reyes)
DC Comics: Jan, 2023 - No. 6 ($3.99)

1-4-Trujillo-s/Gutierrez-a; intro. Dynastes. 2-4-Ted Kord app. 3-Starfire app. 4.00

BLUEBERRY (See Lt. Blueberry & Marshal Blueberry)

Marvel Comics (Epic Comics): 1989 - No. 5, 1990 ($12.95/$14.95, graphic novel)

	GD 2.0	VG 4.0	FN 6.0	VF 8.0	VF/NM 9.0	NM- 9.2
1-($12.95) Moebius-a	5	10	15	31	53	75
2-5: 2-($14.95). 3,4,5-($12.95)-Moebius-a in all	3	6	9	19	30	40

BLUE BOLT
Funnies, Inc. No. 1/Novelty Press/Premium Group of Comics: June, 1940 - No. 101 (V10#2), Sept-Oct, 1949

	GD 2.0	VG 4.0	FN 6.0	VF 8.0	VF/NM 9.0	NM- 9.2
V1#1-Origin Blue Bolt by Joe Simon, Sub-Zero Man, White Rider & Super Horse, Dick Cole, Wonder Boy & Sgt. Spook (1st app. of each)	423	846	1269	3000	5250	7500
2-Simon & Kirby's 1st art & 1st super-hero (Blue Bolt)	300	600	900	1980	3440	4900
3-1 pg. Space Hawk by Wolverton; 2nd S&K-a on Blue Bolt (same cover date as Red Raven #1); Simon-c	274	548	822	1740	3020	4300
4-S&K-a; classic Everett shark-c	258	516	774	1651	2826	4000
5-S&K-a; Everett-a begins on Sub-Zero; 1st time S&K names app. in a comic	213	426	639	1363	2332	3300
6,8-10-S&K-a	181	362	543	1158	1979	2800
7-Classic S&K-c/a (scarce)	258	516	774	1651	2826	4000
11-Classic Everett Giant Robot-c (scarce)	226	452	678	1446	2473	3500
12-Nazi submarine-c	187	374	561	1197	2049	2900
V2#1-Origin Dick Cole & The Twister; Twister x-over in Dick Cole, Sub-Zero, & Blue Bolt; origin Simba Karno who battles Dick Cole thru V2#5 & becomes main supporting character V2#6 on; battle-c	58	116	174	371	636	900
2-Origin The Twister retold in text	45	90	135	284	480	675
3-5: 5-Intro. Freezum	39	78	117	231	378	525
6-Origin Sgt. Spook retold	36	72	108	211	343	475
7-12: 7-Lois Blake becomes Blue Bolt's costume aide; last Twister. 12-Text-sty by Mickey Spillaine	30	60	90	177	289	400
V3#1-3	24	48	72	142	234	325
4-12: 4-Blue Bolt abandons costume	21	42	63	122	199	275
V4#1-Hitler, Tojo, Mussolini-c	135	270	405	864	1482	2100
V4#2-Liberty Bell-c	20	40	60	118	192	265
V4#3-12: 3-Shows V4#3 on-c, V4#4 inside (9-10/43). 5-Infinity-c. 8-Last Sub-Zero	17	34	51	100	158	215
V5#1-8, V6#1-3,5-7,9,10, V7#1-12	15	30	45	86	133	180
V6#4-Racist cover	43	86	129	271	461	650
V6#8-Girl fight-c	20	40	60	114	182	250
V8#1-6,8-12, V9#1-4,7,8, V10#1(#100),V10#2(#101)-Last Dick Cole, Blue Bolt	14	28	42	78	112	145
V8#7,V9#6,9-L. B. Cole-c	26	52	78	154	252	350
V9#5-Classic fish in the face-c	39	78	117	231	378	525

NOTE: *Everett c-V1#4, 11, V2#1, 2. **Gustavson** a-V1#1-12, V2#1-7. **Kiefer** c-V3#1. **Rico** a-V6#10, V7#4. Blue Bolt not in V9#8.*

BLUE BOLT (Becomes Ghostly Weird Stories #120 on; continuation of Novelty Blue Bolt) (...Weird Tales of Terror #111,112,...Weird Tales #113-119)
Star Publications: No. 102, Nov-Dec, 1949 - No. 119, May-June, 1953

	GD 2.0	VG 4.0	FN 6.0	VF 8.0	VF/NM 9.0	NM- 9.2
102-The Chameleon, & Target app.	53	106	159	334	567	800
103,104-The Chameleon app. 104-Last Target	45	90	135	284	480	675
105-Origin Blue Bolt (from #1) retold by Simon; Chameleon & Target app.; opium den story	757	1514	2271	5526	9763	14,000
106-Blue Bolt by S&K begins; Spacehawk reprints from Target by Wolverton begin, ends #110; Sub-Zero begins; ends #109	226	452	678	1446	2473	3500
107-110: 108-Last S&K Blue Bolt reprint. 109-Wolverton-c(r)/inside Spacehawk splash. 110-Target app.	97	194	291	621	1061	1500
111,112: 111-Red Rocket & The Mask-r; last Blue Bolt; 1pg. L. B. Cole-a; classic-c 112-Last Torpedo Man app.	206	412	618	1318	2259	3200
113-Wolverton's Spacehawk-r/Target V3#7	194	388	582	1242	2121	3000
114,116: 116-Jungle Jo-r	161	322	483	1030	1765	2500
115-Classic-c; Sgt. Spook app.	400	800	1200	2800	4900	7000
117-Jo-Jo & Blue Bolt-r; Hollingsworth-a	168	336	504	1075	1838	2600
118-"White Spirit" by Wood	161	322	483	1030	1765	2500
119-Disbrow/Cole-c; Jungle Jo-r	174	348	522	1114	1907	2700
Accepted Reprint #103(1957?, nd)	16	32	48	94	147	200

NOTE: ***L. B. Cole** c-102-108, 110 on. **Disbrow** a-112(2), 113(3), 114(2), 115(2), 116-118. **Hollingsworth** a-117. **Palais** a-112r. Sci/Fi c-105-110. Horror c-111.*

BLUE BOOK
Dark Horse Comics: Feb, 2023 - Present ($4.99, B&W& blue)

	GD 2.0	VG 4.0	FN 6.0	VF 8.0	VF/NM 9.0	NM- 9.2
1-Tynion IV-s/Oeming-a; retells 1961 UFO encounter by Betty & Barney Hill						5.00

BLUE BULLETEER, THE (Also see Femforce Special)
AC Comics: 1989 ($2.25, B&W, one-shot)

	GD 2.0	VG 4.0	FN 6.0	VF 8.0	VF/NM 9.0	NM- 9.2
1-Origin by Bill Black; Bill Ward-a						4.00

BLUE BULLETEER (Also see Femforce Special)
AC Comics: 1996 ($5.95, B&W, one-shot)

	GD 2.0	VG 4.0	FN 6.0	VF 8.0	VF/NM 9.0	NM- 9.2
1-Photo-c						6.00

BLUE CIRCLE COMICS (Also see Red Circle Comics, Blazing Comics & Roly Poly Comic Book)
Enwil Associates/Rural Home: June, 1944 - No. 6, Apr, 1945

	GD 2.0	VG 4.0	FN 6.0	VF 8.0	VF/NM 9.0	NM- 9.2
1-The Blue Circle begins (1st app.); origin & 1st app. Steel Fist	47	94	141	296	498	700
2	27	54	81	160	263	365
3-Hitler parody-c	258	516	774	1651	2826	4000
4-6: 5-Last Steel Fist.	23	46	69	138	227	315
6-(Dated 4/45, Vol. 2#3 inside)-Leftover covers to #6 were later restapled over early 1950's coverless comics; variations of the coverless comics exist. Colossal Features known.	52	104	156	328	552	775

BLUE DEVIL (See Fury of Firestorm #24, Underworld Unleashed, Starman (2nd) #38, Infinite Crisis and Shadowpact)
DC Comics: June, 1984 - No. 31, Dec, 1986 (75¢/$1.25)

	GD 2.0	VG 4.0	FN 6.0	VF 8.0	VF/NM 9.0	NM- 9.2
1						4.00
2-16,19-31: 4-Origin Nebiros. 7-Gil Kane-a. 8-Giffen-a						3.00
17,18-Crisis x-over						3.50
Annual 1 (11/85)-Team-ups w/Black Orchid, Creeper, Demon, Madame Xanadu, Man-Bat & Phantom Stranger						4.00

BLUE MONDAY: ... (one-shots)
Oni Press: Feb, 2002 - Dec, 2008 (B&W, Chynna Clugston-Major-s/a/c in all)

	GD 2.0	VG 4.0	FN 6.0	VF 8.0	VF/NM 9.0	NM- 9.2
Dead Man's Party (10/02, $2.95) Dan Brereton painted back-c						3.00
Inbetween Days (9/03, $9.95, 8" x 5-1/2") r/Dead Man's Party, Lovecats, & Nobody's Fool						10.00
Lovecats (2/02, $2.95) Valentine's Day themed						3.00
Nobody's Fool (2/03, $2.95) April Fool's Day themed						3.00
Thieves Like Us (12/08, $3.50) Part 1 of an unfinished 5-part series						3.50

BLUE MONDAY: ABSOLUTE BEGINNERS
Oni Press: Feb, 2001 - No. 4, Sept, 2001 ($2.95, B&W, limited series)

	GD 2.0	VG 4.0	FN 6.0	VF 8.0	VF/NM 9.0	NM- 9.2
1-4-Chynna Clugston-Major-s/a/c						3.00
TPB (12/01, $11.95, 8" x 6") r/series						12.00

BLUE MONDAY: PAINTED MOON
Oni Press: Feb, 2004 - No. 4, Mar, 2005 ($2.99, B&W, limited series)

	GD 2.0	VG 4.0	FN 6.0	VF 8.0	VF/NM 9.0	NM- 9.2
1-4-Chynna Clugston-Major-s/a/c						3.00
TPB (4/05, $11.95, digest-sized) r/series; sketch pages						12.00

BLUE MONDAY: THE KIDS ARE ALRIGHT
Oni Press: Feb, 2000 - No. 3, May, 2000 ($2.95, B&W, limited series)

	GD 2.0	VG 4.0	FN 6.0	VF 8.0	VF/NM 9.0	NM- 9.2
1-3-Chynna Clugston-Major-s/a/c. 1-Variant-c by Warren. 2-Dorkin-c						3.00
3-Variant cover by J. Scott Campbell						4.00
TPB (12/00, $10.95, digest-sized) r/#1-3 & earlier short stories						11.00

BLUE PHANTOM, THE
Dell Publishing Co.: June-Aug, 1962

	GD 2.0	VG 4.0	FN 6.0	VF 8.0	VF/NM 9.0	NM- 9.2
1(01-066-208)-by Fred Fredericks	4	8	12	22	35	48

BLUE RIBBON COMICS (...Mystery Comics No. 9-18)
MLJ Magazines: Nov, 1939 - No. 22, Mar, 1942 (1st MLJ series)

	GD 2.0	VG 4.0	FN 6.0	VF 8.0	VF/NM 9.0	NM- 9.2
1-Dan Hastings, Richy the Amazing Boy, Rang-A-Tang the Wonder Dog begin (1st app. of each); Little Nemo app. (not by W. McCay); Jack Cole-a(3) (1st MLJ comic)	295	590	885	1873	3237	4600
2-Bob Phantom, Silver Fox (both in #3), Rang-A-Tang Club & Cpl. Collins begin (1st app. of each); Jack Cole-a	226	452	678	1446	2473	3500
3-J. Cole-a	103	206	309	659	1130	1600
4-Doc Strong, The Green Falcon, & Hercules begin (1st app. each); origin & 1st app. The Fox & Ty-Gor, Son of the Tiger	116	232	348	742	1271	1800
5-8: 8-Last Hercules; 6,7-Biro, Meskin-a. 7-Fox app. on-c	90	180	270	576	988	1400
9-(Scarce)-Origin & 1st app. Mr. Justice (2/41)	389	778	1167	2723	4762	6800
10-13: 12-Last Doc Strong. 13-Inferno, the Flame Breather begins, ends #19; Devil-c	168	336	504	1075	1838	2600
14,15,18: 15-Last Green Falcon	155	310	465	992	1696	2400
16-Origin & 1st app. Captain Flag (9/41)	219	438	657	1402	2401	3400
17-Bondage-c	194	388	582	1242	2121	3000
19,20,22: 20-Last Ty-Gor. 22-Origin Mr. Justice retold	129	258	387	826	1413	2000
21-Classic Black Hood-c	343	686	1029	2400	4200	6000

NOTE: ***Biro** c-3-5; a-2 (Cpl. Collins & Scoop Cody). **S. Cooper** c-9-17. 20-22 contain "Tales From the Witch's Cauldron" (same strip as "Stories of the Black Witch" in Zip Comics). Mr. Justice c-9-18. Captain Flag c-16-18 (w/ Mr. Justice), 19-22.*

BLUE RIBBON COMICS (Becomes Teen-Age Diary Secrets #4)
(Also see Approved Comics, Blue Ribbon Comics and Heckle & Jeckle)
Blue Ribbon (St. John): Feb, 1949 - No. 6, Aug, 1949

	GD 2.0	VG 4.0	FN 6.0	VF 8.0	VF/NM 9.0	NM- 9.2
1-Heckle & Jeckle (Terrytoons)	19	38	57	111	176	240
2(4/49)-Diary Secrets; Baker-c	77	154	231	493	847	1200
3-Heckle & Jeckle (Terrytoons)	13	26	39	74	105	135
4(6/49)-Diary Secrets; Baker c/a(2)	103	206	309	659	1130	1600
5(8/49)-Teen-Age Diary Secrets; Oversize; photo-c; Baker-a(2)- Continues as Teen-Age Diary Secrets	110	220	330	704	1202	1700
6-Dinky Duck(8/49)(Terrytoons)	9	18	27	47	61	75

BLUE RIBBON COMICS
Red Circle Prod./Archie Ent. No. 5 on: Nov, 1983 - No. 14, Dec, 1984

	GD 2.0	VG 4.0	FN 6.0	VF 8.0	VF/NM 9.0	NM- 9.2
1-S&K-r/Advs. of the Fly #1,2; Williamson/Torres-r/Fly #2; Ditko-c	1	3	4	6	8	10
2-7,9,10: 3-Origin Steel Sterling. 5-S&K Shield-r; new Kirby-c. 6,7-The Fox app.						6.00
8-Toth centerspread; Black Hood app.; Neal Adams-a(r)	1	2	3	4	5	7
11,13,14: 11-Black Hood. 13-Thunder Bunny. 14-Web & Jaguar						6.00
12-Thunder Agents; Noman new Ditko-a	1	2	3	5	6	8

NOTE: ***N. Adams** a(r)-8. **Buckler** a-4i. **Nino** a-2i. **McWilliams** a-8. **Morrow** a-8.*

BLUE STREAK (See Holyoke One-Shot No. 8)

BLUNTMAN AND CHRONIC TPB(Also see Jay and Silent Bob, Clerks, and Oni Double Feature)
Image Comics: Dec, 2001 ($14.95, TPB)

	GD 2.0	VG 4.0	FN 6.0	VF 8.0	VF/NM 9.0	NM- 9.2
nn-Tie-in for "Jay & Silent Bob Strike Back" movie; new Kevin Smith-s/Michael Oeming-a; r/app. from Oni Double Feature #12 in color; Ben Affleck & Jason Lee afterwords						15.00

BLYTHE (Marge's)
Dell Publishing Co.: No. 1072, Jan-Mar, 1960

	GD 2.0	VG 4.0	FN 6.0	VF 8.0	VF/NM 9.0	NM- 9.2
Four Color 1072	5	10	15	34	60	85

B-MAN (See Double-Dare Adventures)

BO (Tom Cat #4 on) (Also see Big Shot #29 & Dixie Dugan)
Charlton Comics Group: June, 1955 - No. 3, Oct, 1955 (A dog)

	GD 2.0	VG 4.0	FN 6.0	VF 8.0	VF/NM 9.0	NM- 9.2
1-3: Newspaper reprints by Frank Beck; Noodnik the Eskimo app.	8	16	24	40	50	60

BOATNIKS, THE (See Walt Disney Showcase No. 1)

BOB BURDEN'S ORIGINAL MYSTERYMEN PRESENTS
Dark Horse Comics: 1999 - No. 4 ($2.95/$3.50)

	GD 2.0	VG 4.0	FN 6.0	VF 8.0	VF/NM 9.0	NM- 9.2
1-3-Bob Burden-s/Sadowski-a(p)						3.50
4-($3.50) All Villain issue						3.50

BOBBY BENSON'S B-BAR-B RIDERS (Radio) (See Best of The West, The Lemonade Kid & Model Fun)
Magazine Enterprises/AC Comics: May-June, 1950 - No. 20, May-June, 1953

	GD 2.0	VG 4.0	FN 6.0	VF 8.0	VF/NM 9.0	NM- 9.2
1-The Lemonade Kid begins; Powell-a (Scarce)	45	90	135	284	480	675

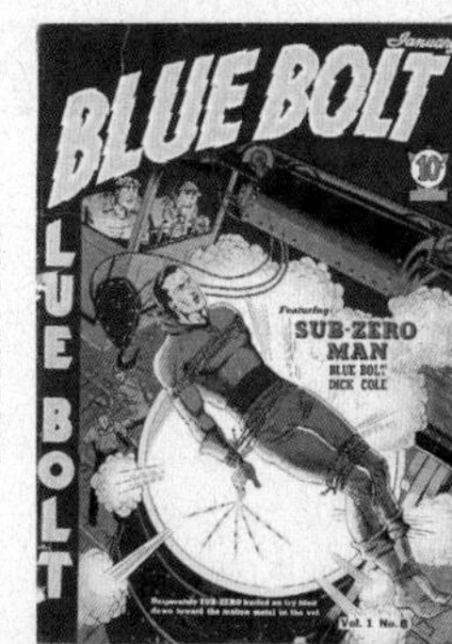

Blue Bolt #8 © NOV

Bob's Burgers #5 © Fox Ent.

Bolero #1 © Kennedy & Vecchio

	GD	VG	FN	VF	VF/NM	NM-
	2.0	4.0	6.0	8.0	9.0	9.2

2	18	36	54	103	162	220
3-5: 4,5-Lemonade Kid-c (#4-Spider-c)	14	28	42	78	112	145
6-8,10	13	26	39	74	105	135
9,11,13-Frazetta-c; Ghost Rider in #13-15 by Ayers-a. 13-Ghost Rider-c	42	84	126	265	445	625
12,17-20: 20-(A-1 #88)	12	24	36	67	94	120
14-Decapitation/Bondage-c & story; classic horror-c	50	100	150	315	533	750
15-Ghost Rider-c	26	52	78	152	249	350
16-Photo-c	14	28	42	81	118	155
1 (1990, $2.75, B&W)-Reprints; photo-c & inside covers						3.00

NOTE: *Ayers a-13-15, 20. **Powell** a-1-12(4 ea.), 13(3), 14-16(Red Hawk only); c-1-8,1 0, 12. Lemonade Kid in most 1-13.*

BOBBY COMICS
Universal Phoenix Features: May, 1946

1-By S. M. Iger	16	32	48	94	147	200

BOBBY SHERMAN (TV)
Charlton Comics: Feb, 1972 - No. 7, Oct, 1972

1-Based on TV show "Getting Together"	5	10	15	33	57	80
2-7: Photo-c on all. 7-Bobby Sherman for President	4	8	12	23	37	50

BOB COLT (See XMas Comics)
Fawcett Publications: Nov, 1950 - No. 10, May, 1952

1-Bob Colt, his horse Buckskin & sidekick Pablo begin; photo front/back-c begin	26	52	78	154	252	350
2	14	28	42	80	115	150
3-5	12	24	36	67	94	120
6-Flying Saucer story	10	20	30	58	79	100
7-10: 9-Last photo back-c	9	18	27	52	69	85

BOB HOPE (See Adventures of... & Calling All Boys #12)

BOB MARLEY, TALE OF THE TUFF GONG (Music star)
Marvel Comics: Aug, 1994 - No, 3, Nov, 1994 ($5.95, limited series)

1-3						6.00

BOB PHANTOM
Archie Comic Publications: Jan, 2023 ($3.99, one-shot)

1-Re-imagining of the 1939 hero; James III-s/Richard Ortiz & Juan Bobillo-a						4.00

BOB POWELL'S TIMELESS TALES
Eclipse Comics: March, 1989 ($2.00, B&W)

1-Powell-r/Black Cat #5 (Scarlet Arrow), 9 & Race for the Moon #1						3.00

BOB'S BURGERS (TV)
Dynamite Entertainment: 2014 - No. 5, 2014 ($3.99)

1-Short stories by various; multiple covers	3	6	9	15	22	28
2-5-Short stories by various						6.00

BOB'S BURGERS (Volume 2)(TV)
Dynamite Entertainment: 2015 - No. 16, 2016 ($3.99)

1-Short stories by various; multiple covers	2	4	6	8	10	12
2-16-Short stories by various; multiple covers on all						4.00
... Free Comic Book Day 2015 (giveaway) Reprints various short stories from Vol. 1						3.00
... Free Comic Book Day 2016 (giveaway) Reprints various short stories						3.00
... Free Comic Book Day 2018 (giveaway) Reprints various short stories						3.00
... Free Comic Book Day 2019 (giveaway) Reprints various short stories						3.00

BOB SCULLY, THE TWO-FISTED HICK DETECTIVE (Also see Advs. of Detective Ace King and Detective Dan)
Humor Publ. Co.: No date (1933) (36 pgs., 9-1/2x11", B&W, paper-c; 10¢-c)

nn-By Howard Dell; not reprints; along with Advs. of Detective Ace King and Detective Dan, the first comic w/original art & the first of a single theme; has a blue 2-tone cover	713	1426	2140	5700	--	--

BOB SON OF BATTLE
Dell Publishing Co.: No. 729, Nov, 1956

Four Color 729	5	10	15	30	50	70

BOB STEELE WESTERN (Movie star)
Fawcett Publications/AC Comics: Dec, 1950 - No. 10, June, 1952; 1990

1-Bob Steele & his horse Bullet begin; photo front/back-c begin	37	74	111	222	361	500
2	19	38	57	109	172	235
3-5: 4-Last photo back-c	14	28	42	82	121	160
6-10: 10-Last photo-c	13	26	39	72	101	130
1 (1990, $2.75, B&W)-Bob Steele & Rocky Lane reprints; photo-c & inside covers						3.00

BOB SWIFT (Boy Sportsman)
Fawcett Publications: May, 1951 - No. 5, Jan, 1952

1	11	22	33	62	86	110
2-5: Saunders painted-c #1-5	7	14	21	35	43	50

BOB, THE GALACTIC BUM
DC Comics: Feb, 1995 - No. 4, June, 1995 ($1.95, limited series)

1-4: 1-Lobo app.						3.00

BODIES
DC Comics (Vertigo): Sept, 2014 - No. 8, Apr, 2015 ($3.99, limited series)

1-8-Spencer-s; art by Hetrick, Ormston, Lotay & Winslade						4.00

BODY BAGS
Dark Horse Comics (Blanc Noir): Sept, 1996 - No. 4, Jan, 1997 ($2.95, mini-series, mature) (1st Blanc Noir series)

1,2-Jason Pearson-c/a/scripts in all. 1-Intro Clownface & Panda						5.00
3,4						4.00
Body Bags 1 (Image Comics, 7/05, $5.99) r/#1&2						6.00
Body Bags 2 (Image Comics, 8/05, $5.99) r/#3&4						6.00
...: 3 The Hard Way (Image, 2/06, $5.99) new story & r/Dark Horse Presents Annual 1997 and Dark Horse Maverick 2000; Pearson-c						6.00
...: One Shot (Image, 11/08, $5.99) wraparound-c; Pearson-c/a/s						6.00

BODYCOUNT (Also see Casey Jones & Raphael)
Image Comics (Highbrow Entertainment): Mar, 1996 - No. 4, July, 1996 ($2.50, lim. series)

1-4: Kevin Eastman-a(p)/scripts; Simon Bisley-c/a(i); Turtles app.	2	4	6	10	14	18
2-4	1	2	3	5	6	8

BODY DOUBLES (See Resurrection Man)
DC Comics: Oct, 1999 - No. 4, Jan, 2000 ($2.50, limited series)

1-4-Lanning & Abnett-s. 2-Black Canary app. 4-Wonder Woman app.						3.00
... (Villains) (2/98, $1.95, one-shot) 1-Pearson-c; Deadshot app.						3.00

BOFFO LAFFS
Paragraphics: 1986 - No. 5 ($2.50/$1.95)

1-($2.50) First comic cover with hologram						4.00
2-5						3.00

BOLD ADVENTURE
Pacific Comics: Nov, 1983 - No. 3, June, 1984 ($1.50)

1-Time Force, Anaconda, & The Weirdling begin						3.00
2,3: 2-Soldiers of Fortune begins. 3-Spitfire						3.00

NOTE: ***Kaluta** c-3. **Nebres** a-1-3. **Nino** a-2, 3. **Severin** a-3.*

BOLD STORIES (Also see Candid Tales & It Rhymes With Lust)
Kirby Publishing Co.: Mar, 1950 - July, 1950 (Digest size, 144 pgs.)

March issue (Very Rare) - Contains "The Ogre of Paris" by Wood	290	580	870	1856	3178	4500
May issue (Very Rare) - Contains "The Cobra's Kiss" by Graham Ingels (21 pgs.)	239	478	717	1530	2615	3700
July issue (Very Rare) - Contains "The Ogre of Paris" by Wood	239	478	717	1530	2615	3700

BOLERO
Image Comics: Jan, 2022 - No. 5, May, 2022 ($5.99, limited series, squarebound)

1-5-Wyatt Kennedy-s/Luana Vecchio-a						6.00

BOLT AND STAR FORCE SIX
Americomics: 1984 ($1.75)

1-Origin Bolt & Star Force Six						3.00
Special 1 (1984, $2.00, 52pgs., B&W)						4.00

BOMBARDIER (See Bee 29, the Bombardier & Cinema Comics Herald)

BOMBAST
Topps Comics: 1993 ($2.95, one-shot) (Created by Jack Kirby)

1-Polybagged w/Kirbychrome trading card; Savage Dragon app.; Kirby-c; has coupon for Amberchrome Secret City Saga #0						4.00

BOMBA THE JUNGLE BOY (TV)
National Periodical Publ.: Sept-Oct, 1967 - No. 7, Sept-Oct, 1968 (12¢)

1-Intro. Bomba; Infantino/Anderson-c	5	10	15	35	63	90
2-7	3	6	9	19	30	40

BOMBER COMICS
Elliot Publ. Co./Melverne Herald/Farrell/Sunrise Times: Mar, 1944 - No. 4, Winter, 1944-45

1-Wonder Boy, & Kismet, Man of Fate begin	113	226	339	723	1237	1750
2-Hitler-c and 8 pg. story	155	310	465	992	1696	2400
3: 2-4-Have Classics Comics ad to HRN 20	61	122	183	390	670	950

GD VG FN VF VF/NM NM-
2.0 4.0 6.0 8.0 9.0 9.2

4-Hitler, Tojo & Mussolini-c; Sensation Comics #13-c/swipe;
has Classics Comics ad to HRN 20. 168 336 504 1075 1838 2600

BOMB QUEEN
Image Comics (Shadowline): Feb, 2006 - No. 4, May, 2006 ($3.50, mature)
1-Jimmie Robinson-s/a in all 3 6 9 16 26 35
2-4 1 2 3 5 6 8
... Vs. Blacklight One Shot #1 (8/06, $3.50) Robinson-a; Shadowhawk app. 5.00
..., Vol. 1: WMD: Woman of Mass Destruction TPB (7/06, $12.99) r/#1-4; bonus art 13.00

BOMB QUEEN II
Image Comics (Shadowline): Oct, 2006 - No. 3, Dec, 2006 ($3.50, mature)
1-Jimmie Robinson-s/a; intro. The Four Queens 2 4 6 11 16 20
2,3 6.00
..., Vol. 2: Dirty Bomb - Queen of Hearts TPB (7/07, $14.99) r/#1-3 & Blacklight One Shot;
bonus art; Robinson interview 15.00

BOMB QUEEN III THE GOOD, THE BAD & THE LOVELY
Image Comics (Shadowline): Mar, 2007 - No. 4, Jun, 2007 ($3.50, mature)
1-4-Jimmie Robinson-a/Jim Valentino-s; Blacklight & Rebound app. 1-Linsner-c 4.00

BOMB QUEEN IV SUICIDE BOMBER
Image Comics (Shadowline): Aug, 2007 - No. 4, Dec, 2007 ($3.50, mature)
1-4-Jim Robinson-s/a. 3-She-Spawn app. 4.00

BOMB QUEEN (Volumes 5-8)
Image Comics (Shadowline): May, 2008 - Present ($3.50/$3.99, mature)
Vol. 5 #1-6 (5/08 - No. 6, 3/09) Jimmie Robinson-s/a 4.00
Vol. 6 #1-4 (9/09 - No. 4, 1/11, $3.50) Obama satire 3.50
Vol. 7 #1-4 (12/11 - No. 4, 5/12, $3.50) Bomb Queen returns in 2112 3.50
Vol. 8 #1-4 (8/20 - No. 4, 12/20, $3.99) Donald Trump satire 4.00
... Presents: All Girl Comics (5/09, $3.50) Dee Rail, Blacklight, Rebound, Tempest app. 3.50
... Presents: All Girl Special (7/11, $3.50) President Palin app. 3.50
... vs. Hack/Slash (2/11, $3.50) Cassie and Vlad app.; Robinson-s/a 3.50

BOMBSHELLS: UNITED (Continued from DC Comics: Bombshell series)
DC Comics: Nov, 2017 - No. 19, Early Aug, 2018 ($2.99)
1-19: 1-Bennett-s/Sauvage-a/Dodson-c; intro. Dawnstar & Clayface. 9,17-Siya Oum-a 3.00

BONANZA (TV)
Dell/Gold Key: June-Aug, 1960 - No. 37, Aug, 1970 (All Photo-c)
Four Color 1110 (6-8/60) 32 64 96 230 515 800
Four Color 1221,1283, & #01070-207, 01070-210 15 30 45 100 220 340
1(12/62-Gold Key) 16 32 48 110 243 375
2 9 18 27 58 114 170
3-10 7 14 21 44 82 120
11-20 5 10 15 34 60 85
21-37: 29-Reprints 5 10 15 30 50 70

BONE
Cartoon Books #1-20, 28 on/Image Comics #21-27: Jul, 1991 - No. 55, Jun, 2004 ($2.95, B&W)
1-Jeff Smith-c/a in all 129 258 387 1032 2316 3600
1-2nd printing 3 6 9 17 26 35
1-3rd thru 5th printings 5.00
2-1st printing 13 26 39 89 195 300
2-2nd & 3rd printings 1 2 3 5 6 8
3-1st printing 7 14 21 49 92 135
3-2nd thru 4th printings 4.00
4,5 5 10 15 35 63 90
6-10 3 6 9 14 20 25
11-20 1 2 3 5 6 8
13 1/2 (1/95, Wizard) 2 4 6 9 12 15
13 1/2 (Gold) 2 4 6 11 16 20
21-37: 21-1st Image issue 5.00
38-($4.95) Three covers by Miller, Ross, Smith 1 2 3 4 5 7
39-55-($2.95) 4.00
1-27-($2.95): 1-Image reprints begin w/new-c. 2-Allred pin-up. 3.00
nn (2008, 8-1/2" x 5-3/8" Halloween mini-comic giveaway) 3.00
... Holiday Special (1993, giveaway) 5.00
... Reader -($9.95) Behind the scenes info 10.00
... Sourcebook-San Diego Edition 4.00
...10th Anniversary Edition (8/01, $5.95) r/#1 in color; came with figure 6.00
Complete Bone Adventures Vol 1,2 ('93, '94, $12.95, r/#1-6 & #7-12) 15.00
...: One Volume Edition (2004, $39.95, 1300 pgs.) r/#1-54; extra material 40.00
...: One Volume Limited Edition HC (2004, signed by Jeff Smith, numbered edition of 2000)
21 42 63 147 324 500
Volume 1-($19.95, hard-c)-"Out From Boneville" 20.00
Volume 1-($12.95, soft-c) 13.00
Volume 2,5-($22.95, hard-c)-"The Great Cow Race" & "Rock Jaw" 23.00
Volume 2,5-($14.95, soft-c) 15.00
Volume 3,4-($24.95, hard-c)-"Eyes of the Storm" & "The Dragonslayer" 25.00
Volume 3,4,7-($16.95, soft-c) 17.00
Volume 6-($15.95, soft-c)-"Old Man's Cave" 16.00
Volume 7-($24.95, hard-c)-"Ghost Circles" 25.00
Volume 8-($23.95, hard-c)-"Treasure Hunters" 24.00
NOTE: *Printings not listed sell for cover price.*

BONE ORCHARD: TEN THOUSAND BLACK FEATHERS
Image Comics: Sept, 2022 - No. 5, Jan, 2023 ($3.99)
1-5-Lemire-s/Sorrentino-a 4.00

BONE ORCHARD: THE PASSAGEWAY
Image Comics: Jun, 2022 ($17.99, hardcover)
HC-Lemire-s/Sorrentino-a 18.00

BONE PARISH
BOOM! Studios: Jul, 2018 - No. 12, Aug, 2019 ($3.99)
1-12-Cullen Bunn-s/Jonas Scharf-a 4.00

BONGO (See Story Hour Series)

BONGO & LUMPJAW (Disney, see Walt Disney Showcase #3)
Dell Publishing Co.: No. 706, June, 1956; No. 886, Mar, 1958
Four Color 706 (#1) 6 12 18 41 76 110
Four Color 886 5 10 15 31 53 75

BONGO COMICS ...
Bongo Comics: 2005 - Present (Free Comic Book Day giveaways)
Gimme Gimme Giveaway! (2005) - Short stories from Simpsons Comics, Futurama Comics
and Radioactive Man 3.00
Free-For-All! (2006, 2007, 2008, 2009, 2010, 2011, 2013-2018) - Short stories 3.00
Free-For-All! 2012 - Flip book with SpongeBob Comics 3.00

BONGO COMICS PRESENTS RADIOACTIVE MAN (See Radioactive Man)

BON VOYAGE (See Movie Classics)

BOOF
Image Comics (Todd McFarlane Prod.): July, 1994 - No. 6, Dec, 1994 ($1.95)
1-6 3.00

BOOF AND THE BRUISE CREW
Image Comics (Todd McFarlane Prod.): July, 1994 - No. 6, Dec, 1994 ($1.95)
1-6 3.00

BOOK AND RECORD SET (See Power Record Comics)

BOOK OF ALL COMICS
William H. Wise: 1945 (196 pgs.)(Inside f/c has Green Publ. blacked out)
nn-Green Mask, Puppeteer & The Bouncer 77 154 231 493 847 1200

BOOK OF ANTS, THE
Artisan Entertainment: 1998 ($2.95, B&W)
1-Based on the movie Pi; Aronofsky-s 4.00

BOOK OF BALLADS AND SAGAS, THE
Green Man Press: Oct, 1995 - No. 4 ($2.95/$3.50/$3.25, B&W)
1-4: 1-Vess-c/a; Gaiman story. 3.50

BOOK OF COMICS, THE
William H. Wise: No date (1944) (25¢, 132 pgs.)
nn-Captain V app.; WWII-c 63 126 189 403 689 975

BOOK OF DEATH
Valiant Entertainment: Jul, 2015 - No. 4, Oct, 2015 ($3.99, limited series)
1-4-Venditti-s/Gill & Braithwaite-a; multiple covers on each. 4-Flip book with preview for
Wrath of the Eternal Warrior series 4.00
...: Fall of Bloodshot (7/15, $3.99) Lemire-s/Braithwaite-a; Armstrong app. 4.00
...: Fall of Harbinger (9/15, $3.99) Dysart-s/Kano-a; future deaths of the team 4.00
...: Fall of Ninjak (8/15, $3.99) Kindt-s/Hairsine-a 4.00
...: Fall of X-O Manowar (10/15, $3.99) Venditti-s/Henry-a; future death of Aric 4.00

BOOK OF FATE, THE (See Fate)
DC Comics: Feb, 1997 - No. 12, Jan, 1998 ($2.25/$2.50)
1-12: 4-Two-Face-c/app. 6-Convergence. 11-Sentinel app. 3.00

BOOK OF LOST SOULS, THE
Marvel Comics (Icon): Dec, 2005 - No. 6, June, 2006 ($2.99)
1-6-Colleen Doran-a/c; J. Michael Straczynski-s 3.00
... Vol. 1: Introductions All Around (2006, $16.99, TPB) r/series 17.00

BOOK OF LOVE (See Fox Giants)

BOOK OF NIGHT, THE
Dark Horse Comics: July, 1987 - No. 3, 1987 ($1.75, B&W)
1-3: Reprints from Epic Illustrated; Vess-a 3.00
TPB-r/#1-3 15.00
Hardcover-Black-c with red crest 120.00
Hardcover w/slipcase (1991) signed and numbered 60.00

BOOK OF SHADOWS
Valiant Entertainment: Jul, 2022 - No. 4, Feb, 2023 ($3.99)
1-4-Cullen Bunn-s/Vicente Cifuentes-a; Shadowman, Eternal Warrior, Punk Mambo app. 4.00

BOOK OF SLAUGHTER (From Something is Killing the Children and House of Slaughter)
BOOM! Studios: Dec, 2022 ($9.99, squarebound, one-shot)
1-Tynion IV-s/Dell'edera-a; bonus guidebook of the Order of St. George 10.00

BOOK OF THE DEAD
Marvel Comics: Dec, 1993 - No. 4, Mar, 1994 ($1.75, limited series, 52 pgs.)
1-Ploog Frankenstein & Morrow Man-Thing-r begin; Wrightson-r/Chamber of Darkness #7
2 4 6 9 12 15
2-4: 2-Morrow new painted-c; Chaykin/Morrow Man-Thing; Krigstein-r/Uncanny Tales #54;
r/Fear #10. 3-r/Astonishing Tales #10 & Starlin Man-Thing. 3,4-Painted-c
1 2 3 5 6 8

BOOKS OF DOOM (Dr. Doom from Fantastic Four)
Marvel Comics: Jan, 2006 - No. 6, June, 2006 ($2.99, limited series)
1-6-Life story/origin of Dr. Doom; Brubaker-s/Raimondi-a/Rivera-c 3.00
Fantastic Four: Books of Doom HC (2006, $19.99) r/#1-6 20.00
Fantastic Four: Books of Doom SC (2007, $14.99) r/#1-6 15.00

BOOKS OF FAERIE, THE
DC Comics (Vertigo): Mar, 1997 - No. 3, May, 1997 ($2.50, limited series)
1-3-Gross-a 4.00
TPB (1998, $14.95) r/#1-3 & Arcana Annual #1 15.00

BOOKS OF FAERIE, THE : AUBERON'S TALE
DC Comics (Vertigo): Aug, 1998 - No. 3, Oct, 1998 ($2.50, limited series)
1-3-Gross-a 4.00

BOOKS OF FAERIE, THE : MOLLY'S STORY
DC Comics (Vertigo): Sept, 1999 - No. 4, Dec, 1999 ($2.50, limited series)
1-4-Ney Rieber-s/Mejia-a 4.00

BOOKS OF MAGIC
DC Comics: 1990 - No. 4, 1991 ($3.95, 52 pgs., limited series, mature)

Bomb Queen III #2 © J. Robinson

Books of Magic (2018) #1 © DC

Booster Gold (2009) #21 © DC

	GD 2.0	VG 4.0	FN 6.0	VF 8.0	VF/NM 9.0	NM- 9.2

1-Bolton painted-c/a; Phantom Stranger app.; Gaiman scripts in all
2 4 6 9 12 15
2,3: 2-John Constantine, Dr. Fate, Spectre, Deadman app. 3-Dr. Occult app.; minor Sandman app. 1 2 3 4 5 7
4-Early Death-c/app. (early 1991) 1 2 3 5 6 8
Trade paperback-($19.95)-Reprints limited series 20.00

BOOKS OF MAGIC (Also see Hunter: The Age of Magic and Names of Magic)
DC Comics (Vertigo): May, 1994 - No. 75, Aug, 2000 ($1.95/$2.50, mature)

1-Charles Vess-c 2 4 6 9 12 15
1-Platinum 2 4 6 13 18 22
2-4: 4-Death app. 1 2 3 4 5 7
5-14: Charles Vess-c 4.00
15-75: 15-$2.50-c begins. 22-Kaluta-c. 25-Death-c/app; Bachalo-c. 51-Peter Gross-s/a begins. 55-Medley-a 3.00
Annual 1-3 (2/97, 2/98, '99, $3.95) 5.00
Bindings (1995, $12.95, TPB)-r/#1-4 13.00
Death After Death (2001, $19.95, TPB)-r/#42-50 20.00
Girl in the Box (1999, $14.95, TPB)-r/#26-32 15.00
Reckonings (1997, $12.95, TPB)-r/#14-20 13.00
Summonings (1996, $17.50, TPB)-r/#5-13, Vertigo Rave #1 17.50
The Burning Girl (2000, $17.95, TPB)-r/#33-41 18.00
Transformations (1998, $12.95, TPB)-r/#21-25 13.00

BOOKS OF MAGIC (The Sandman Universe)
DC Comics (Vertigo for #1-13, Black Label #14-on): Dec, 2018 - No. 23, Nov, 2020 ($3.99)

1-23: 1-Howard-s/Fowler-a; Tim Hunter's story continues from 1990 series; Dr. Rose app. 19-Barnett-s begins 4.00

BOOKS OF MAGICK, THE : LIFE DURING WARTIME (See Books of Magic)
DC Comics (Vertigo): Sept, 2004 - No. 15, Dec, 2005 ($2.50/$2.75)

1-15: 1-Spencer-s/Ormston-a/Quitely-c; Constantine app. 2-Bagged with Sky Captain CD 6-Fegredo-a. 7-Constantine & Zatanna-c 3.00
... Book One TPB (2005, $9.95) r/#1-5 10.00

BOOM! STUDIOS...
BOOM! Studios

... Free Comic Book Day 2019 No. 1 (5/19) Short stories of Buffy, Angel, Firefly 3.00
... Ten Year Celebration 2015 Free Comic Book Day Special (5/15, giveaway) short stories of Adventure Time, Peanuts, Garfield, Lumberjanes, Regular Show & others 3.00
... Summer Blast (5/16, FCBD giveaway) Mouse Guard, Labyrinth, Adventure Time 3.00
... 2017 Summer Blast (5/17) FCBD giveaway; Mouse Guard, Brave Chef Brianna 3.00

BOONDOCK SAINTS (Based on the movie)
12-Gauge Comics: May, 2010 - No. 2, Jun, 2010 ($3.99, limited series)

...: In Nomine Patris 1,2-Troy Duffy-s/Guus Floor-a 4.00
...: In Nomine Patris Vol. 2 (10/10 - No. 2, 11/10): 1,2-Duffy-s/Floor-a 4.00
...: In Nomine Patris Vol. 3 (3/11 - No. 2, 4/11): 1,2-Duffy-s/Floor-a 4.00

BOOSTER GOLD (See Justice League #4)
DC Comics: Feb, 1986 - No. 25, Feb, 1988 (75¢)

1-Dan Jurgens-s/a(p); 1st app. of Booster Gold 5 10 15 31 53 75
2-25: 4-Rose & Thorn app. 6-Origin. 6,7,23-Superman app. 8,9-LSH app. 22-JLI app. 24,25-Millennium tie-ins 5.00
NOTE: *Austin c-22i. Byrne c-23i.*

BOOSTER GOLD (See DC's weekly series 52)
DC Comics: Oct, 2007 - No. 47, Oct, 2011 ($3.50/$2.99/$3.99)

1-Geoff Johns-s/Dan Jurgens-a(p); covers by Jurgens and Art Adams; Rip Hunter app. 5.00
2-4,6-20: 3-Jonah Hex app. 4-Barry Allen app. 8-Superman app. 3.00
5-Joker and Batgirl app.; Killing Joke-style-c 6.00
21-29-($3.99) 21-Blue Beetle back-ups begin. 22-New Teen Titans app. 23-Photo-c. 26,27-Blackest Night; Ted Kord rises. 29-Cyborg Superman app. 4.00
30-47-($2.99): 32-34-Giffen & DeMatteis-s. 32-Emerald Empress app. 40-Origin retold. 43-Legion of S.H. app. 44-47-Flashpoint tie-in; Doomsday app. 3.00
#0-(4/08) Blue Beetle (Ted Cord) returns; takes place between #6&7 3.00
#1,000,000-(9/08) Michelle Carter returns; takes place between #10&11 3.00
...: Futures End 1 (11/14, $2.99, regular-c) Jurgens-s; Kamandi, LSH, Captain Atom app. 3.00
...: Futures End 1 (11/14, $3.99, 3-D cover) 4.00
.../ The Flintstones Special 1 (5/17, $4.99) Russell-s/Leonardi-a; Jetsons back-up 5.00

BOOTS AND HER BUDDIES
Standard Comics/Visual Editions/Argo (NEA Service):
No. 5, 9/48 - No. 9, 9/49; 12/55 - No. 3, 1956

5-Strip-r 39 78 117 240 395 550
6,8 15 30 45 88 137 185
7-(Scarce) 19 38 57 111 176 240
9-(Scarce)-Frazetta-a (2 pgs.) 53 106 159 334 567 800
1-3(Argo-1955-56)-Reprints 7 14 21 37 46 55

BOOTS & SADDLES (TV)
Dell Publ. Co.: No. 919, July, 1958; No. 1029, Sept, 1959; No. 1116, Aug, 1960

Four Color 919 (#1)-Photo-c 7 14 21 48 89 130
Four Color 1029, 1116-Photo-c 5 10 15 34 60 85

BORDERLANDS: ... (Based on the video game)
IDW Publishing: Jul, 2014 - No. 8, Feb, 2015 ($3.99)

1-8: 1-4-The Fall of Fyerstone. 5-8-Tannis and the Vault 4.00

BORDERLANDS: ORIGINS (Based on the video game)
IDW Publishing: Nov, 2012 - No. 4, Feb, 2013 ($3.99, limited series)

1-4: 1-Spotlight on Roland. 2-Lilith. 3-Mordecai. 4-Brick 4.00

BORDER PATROL
P. L. Publishing Co.: May-June, 1951 - No. 3, Sept-Oct, 1951

1 19 38 57 111 176 240
2,3 12 24 36 69 97 125

BORDER TOWN
DC Comics (Vertigo): Dec, 2018 - No. 4, Feb, 2019 ($3.99, unfinished series)

1-4-Esquivel-s/Villalobos-a 4.00

BORDER WORLDS (Also see Megaton Man)
Kitchen Sink Press: 7/86 - No. 7, 1987; V2#1, 1990 - No. 4, 1990 ($1.95-$2.00, B&W, mature)

1-7, V2#1-4: Donald Simpson-c/a/scripts 3.00

BORIS KARLOFF TALES OF MYSTERY (TV) (...Thriller No. 1,2)
Gold Key: No. 3, April, 1963 - No. 97, Feb, 1980

3-5-(Two #5's, 10/63,11/63): 5-(10/63)-11 pgs. Toth-a.
5 10 15 35 63 90
6-8,10: 10-Orlando-a 4 8 12 27 44 60
9-Wood-a 4 8 12 28 47 65
11-Williamson-a, 8 pgs.; Orlando-a, 5 pgs. 4 8 12 28 47 65
12-Torres, McWilliams-a; Orlando-a(2) 4 8 12 21 33 45
13,14,16-20 3 6 9 18 28 38
15-Crandall 3 6 9 19 30 40
21-Jeff Jones-a(3 pgs.) "The Screaming Skull" 3 6 9 19 30 40
22-Last 12¢ issue 3 6 9 16 23 30
23-30: 23-Reprint; photo-c 3 6 9 15 22 28
31-50: 36-Weiss-a 3 6 9 14 19 24
51-74: 74-Origin & 1st app. Taurus 2 4 6 10 14 18
75-79,87-97: 90-r/Torres, McWilliams-a/#12; Morrow-c2 2 4 6 9 12 15
80-86-(52 pgs.) 2 4 6 10 14 18
Story Digest 1(7/70-Gold Key)-All text/illos.; 148 pp. 5 10 15 31 53 75
(See Mystery Comics Digest No. 2, 5, 8, 11, 14, 17, 20, 23, 26)
NOTE: ***Bolle** a-51-54, 56, 58, 59. **McWilliams** a-12, 14, 18, 19, 72, 80, 81, 93. **Orlando** a-11-15, 21. Reprints: 78, 81-86, 88, 90, 92, 95, 97.*

BORIS KARLOFF THRILLER (TV) (Becomes Boris Karloff Tales...)
Gold Key: Oct, 1962 - No. 2, Jan, 1963 (84 pgs.)

1-Photo-c 11 22 33 77 166 255
2 6 12 18 42 79 115

BORIS THE BEAR
Dark Horse Comics/Nicotat Comics #13 on: Aug, 1986 - No. 34, 1990 ($1.50/$1.75/$1.95, B&W)

1, 8, Annual 1 (1988, $2.50): 8-(44 pgs.) 4.00
1 (2nd printing),2,3,4A,4B,5-12, 14-34 3.00
13-1st Nicotat Comics issue 3.00

BORIS THE BEAR INSTANT COLOR CLASSICS
Dark Horse Comics: July, 1987 - No. 3, 1987 ($1.75/$1.95)

1-3 3.00

BORN
Marvel Comics: 2003 - No. 4, 2003 ($3.50, limited series)

1-4-Frank Castle (the Punisher) in 1971 Vietnam; Ennis-s/Robertson-a 4.00
HC (2004, $17.99) oversized reprint of series; proposal, layout pages 18.00
Punisher: Born SC (2004, $13.99) r/series; proposal, layout pages 14.00

BORN AGAIN
Spire Christian Comics (Fleming H. Revell Co.): 1978 (39¢)

nn-Watergate, Nixon, etc. 3 6 9 19 30 40

BOUNCE, THE
Image Comics: May, 2013 - No. 12, May, 2014 ($2.99)

1-12-Casey-s/Messina-a 3.00

BOUNCER, THE (Formerly Green Mask #9)

GD VG FN VF VF/NM NM-
2.0 4.0 6.0 8.0 9.0 9.2

Fox Feature Syndicate: 1944 - No. 14, Jan, 1945

nn(1944, #10?) 39 78 117 231 378 525
11 (9/44)-Origin; Rocket Kelly, One Round Hogan app.
27 54 81 160 263 365
12-14: 14-Reprints no # issue 21 42 63 126 206 285

BOUNTY
Dark Horse Comics: Jul, 2016 - No. 5, Dec, 2016 ($3.99, limited series)

1-5-Kurtis Wiebe-s/Mindy Lee-a 4.00

BOUNTY GUNS (See Luke Short's..., Four Color 739)

BOX OFFICE POISON
Antarctic Press: 1996 - No. 21, Sept, 2000 ($2.95, B&W)

1-Alex Robinson-s/a in all 1 2 3 4 5 7
2-5 4.00
6-21, ...Kolor Karnival 1 (5/99, $2.99) 3.00
...Super Special 0 (5/97, $4.95) 5.00
Sherman's March: Collected BOP Vol. 1 (9/98, $14.95) r/#0-4 15.00
TPB (2002, $29.95, 608 pgs.) r/entire series 30.00

BOX OFFICE POISON COLOR COMICS
IDW Publishing: Jan, 2017 - No. 5, May, 2017 ($3.99)

1-5-Colored reprints of 1996 series; Alex Robinson-s/a in all; bonus commentary 4.00

BOY AND THE PIRATES, THE (Movie)
Dell Publishing Co.: No. 1117, Aug, 1960

Four Color 1117-Photo-c 6 12 18 37 66 95

BOY COMICS (Captain Battle No. 1 & 2; Boy Illustories No. 43-108) (Stories by Charles Biro) (Also see Squeeks)
Lev Gleason Publ. (Comic House): No. 3, Apr, 1942 - No. 119, Mar, 1956

3 (No.1)-1st app. & origin Crimebuster (ends #110), Bombshell (ends #8) Young Robin Hood (ends # 32), Yankee Longago (ends #28), Hero of the Month (ends #31), Case 1001-1005, 1006-1009 (ends #10); Swoop Storm begins (ends #32); Pepper Casey only app.; 1st app. Iron Jaw; Crimebuster's pet monkey Squeeks begins
343 686 1029 2400 4200 6000
4-Hitler, Tojo Mussolini-c; Iron Jaw app. Little Wise Guys (prototype of later version) begins, ends #5 300 600 900 2010 3505 5000
5-Japanese war-c 161 322 483 1030 1765 2500
6-Origin Iron Jaw; origin & death of Iron Jaw's son killed by his father; Hitler app.; Little Dynamite begins, ends #39; 1st Iron Jaw-c 337 674 1011 2359 4130 5900
7-Flag & Hitler, Tojo, Mussolini-c; Dickey Dean app. 258 516 774 1651 2826 4000
8-Death of Iron Jaw; Iron Jaw-c & spash pg. 113 226 339 735 1243 1750
9-Iron Jaw classic-c (does not appear in story) 314 628 942 2198 3849 5500
10-Return of Iron Jaw; classic Biro Iron Jaw/Nazi-c 343 686 1029 2400 4200 6000
11-Iron Jaw sty/classic-c 226 452 678 1446 2473 3500
12-Classic Japanese WWII bondage torture interrogation-c
142 284 426 909 1555 2200
13-Nazi firing squad-c 129 258 387 826 1413 2000
14-Iron Jaw-c 97 194 291 621 1061 1500
15-Death of Iron Jaw, killed by The Rodent 129 258 387 826 1413 2000
16,18,20 (2/45) 53 106 159 334 567 800
17-(8/44)-Flag-c; The Moth app. 61 122 183 390 670 950
19-One of the greatest all-time stories 57 114 171 362 619 875
21-24: 24-Concentration camp story 37 74 111 222 361 500
25-Devil-c; hanging story (52 pgs.) 41 82 123 256 428 600
26-Bondage, torture-c/story (68 pgs.) 48 96 144 302 514 725
27-29,31,32-(All 68 pgs.). 28-Yankee Longago ends. 32-Swoop Storm & Young Robin Hood end 36 72 108 211 343 475
30-(10/46, 68 pgs.)-Origin Crimebuster retold from #3 w/Iron Jaw; Nazi work camp story
42 84 126 265 445 625
33-40: 34-Crimebuster story (2); suicide-c/story 23 46 69 136 223 310
41-50-41-Daredevil illus. text story 19 38 57 111 176 240
51-59: 57(9/50)-Dilly Duncan begins, ends #71 16 32 48 94 147 200
60-(12/50)-Iron Jaw returns c/sty 19 38 57 111 175 240
61-Origin Crimebuster & Iron Jaw retold c/sty 20 40 60 114 182 250
62-(2/51)-Death of Iron Jaw explained w/Iron Jaw-c 19 38 57 111 176 240
63-67,69-72: 63-McWilliams-a 14 28 42 76 108 140
68,73-Iron Jaw c/sty; 73-Frazetta 1 pg. ad 14 28 42 80 115 150
74,78,81-Iron Jaw c/sty (2-3) 12 24 36 67 94 120
75-77,84 11 22 33 62 86 110
79,80-Iron Jaw sty: 80(8/52)-1st app. Rocky X of the Rocketeers; becomes "Rocky X" #101; Iron Jaw, Sniffer & the Deadly Dozen in #80-118 11 22 33 64 90 115
82-Iron Jaw-c (apps. in one panel) 11 22 33 62 86 110
83,85-88-Iron Jaw c/sty. 87-The Deadly Dozen begins; becomes Iron Jaw #88 (4/53)
11 22 33 64 90 115
89(5/53)-92-The Claw serial app. in Rocky X (also see Silver Streak & Daredevil); on-c. 89-"Iron Jaw" becomes "Sniffrer & Iron Jaw" (ends #118); Iron Jaw c/story in all
12 24 36 67 94 120
93-Claw cameo & last app.; Woodesque-a on Rocky X by Sid Check; Iron Jaw-c/sty
11 22 33 64 90 115
94-97-Iron Jaw-c/sty in all 11 22 33 60 83 105
98,100:(4/54): 98-Rocky X by Sid Check 11 22 33 62 86 110
99,101-107,109,111,119: 101-Rocky X becomes spy strip. 106-Robin Hood app. 111-Crimebuster becomes Chuck Chandler, ends #119
10 20 30 54 72 90
108-(2/55)-Kubert & Ditko-a (Crimebuster, 8 pgs.) 11 22 33 62 86 110
110,112-118-Kubert-a 10 20 30 58 79 100
(See Giant Boy Book of Comics)
NOTE: *Boy Movies in 3-5,40,41. Iron Jaw app. 3,4,6,8,10,11,13-15; returns-60,62, 68, 69, 72-79, 81-118; c-60-62, 73, 74, 78, 81-83, 85-97.* **Biro** *c-all.* **Jack Alderman** *a-26.* **Dan Barry** *a-31,32, 35-38.* **Al Borth** *a- 51.* **Dick Briefer** *a-3-28, 124.* **Sid Check** a-93, 98. **Ditko** a-108. **Bob Fujitani** (**Fuje**) *a-55, 18pgs.* **Jerry Gandenetti** *a-52.* **R. W. Hall** *a-19-22.* **Hubbell** *a-30, 106, 108, 110, 111.* **Joe Kubert** *a-108, 110, 112-118.* **Kenneth Landau** *a-92.* **George Mandel** *a-3-30.* **Norman Maurer** *a-4-9, 11-13, 31, 32, 35, 41, 43, 46, 51, 57, 61, 73, 74, 78-83.* **Bob Montana** *a-4, 16, 19.* **Pete Morisi** *a-111.* **William Overgard** *a-68, 71, 74, 86, 88.* **Palais** *a-14, 16, 17, 19, 20, 25, 26. among others.* **Tuska** *a-30.* **Bob Wood** *a-8-13.*

BOY COMMANDOS (See Detective #64 & World's Finest Comics #8)
National Periodical Publications: Winter, 1942-43 - No. 36, Nov-Dec, 1949

1-Origin Liberty Belle; The Sandman & The Newsboy Legion x-over in Boy Commandos; S&K-a, 48 pgs.; S&K cameo? (classic WWII-c) 400 800 1200 2800 4900 7000
2-Last Liberty Belle; Hitler-c; S&K-a, 46 pgs.; WWII-c
265 530 795 1694 2897 4100
3-S&K-a, 45 pgs.; WWII-c 135 270 405 864 1482 2100
4-6: All WWII-c. 6-S&K-a 87 174 261 553 952 1350
7-10: All WWII-c 55 110 165 352 601 850
11-13: All WWII-c. 11-Infinity-c 40 80 120 246 411 575
14,16,18-19-All have S&K-a. 18-2nd Crazy Quilt-c 34 68 102 204 332 460
15-1st app. Crazy Quilt, their arch nemesis 45 90 135 284 480 675
17,20-Sci/fi-c/stories 41 82 123 256 428 600
21,22,25: 22-3rd Crazy Quilt-c; Judy Canova x-over 27 54 81 162 266 370
23-S&K-c/a(all) 37 74 111 222 361 500
24-1st costumed superhero satire-c (11-12/47) 41 82 123 256 428 600
26-Flying Saucer story (3-4/48)-4th of this theme; see The Spirit 9/28/47(1st), Shadow Comics V7#10 (2nd, 1/48) & Captain Midnight #60 (3rd, 2/48)
36 72 108 211 343 475
27,28,30: 30-Cleveland Indians story 27 54 81 158 259 360
29-S&K story (1) 28 56 84 168 274 380
31-35: 32-Dale Evans app. on-c & in story. 33-Last Crazy Quilt-c. 34-Intro. Wolf, their mascot 24 48 72 140 230 320
36-Intro The Atomobile c/sci-fi story (Scarce) 45 90 135 284 480 675
The Boy Commandos by Joe Simon & Jack Kirby Volume One HC (2010, $49.99) reprints apps. in Detective #64-72, World's Finest #8,9 & Boy Commandos #1,2; Buhle intro. 50.00
NOTE: *Most issues signed by* **Simon & Kirby** *are not by them.* **S&K** *c-1-9, 13, 14, 17, 21, 23, 24, 30-32.* **Feller** *c-30.*

BOY COMMANDOS
National Per. Publ.: Sept-Oct, 1973 - No. 2, Nov-Dec, 1973 (G.A. S&K reprints)

1,2: 1-Reprints story from Boy Commandos #1 plus-c & Detective #66 by S&K. 2-Infantino/Orlando-c 2 4 6 10 14 18

BOY COMMANDOS COMICS
DC Comics: Sept/Oct. 1942

1-Ashcan comic, not distributed to newsstands, only for in-house use. Cover art is the splash page from the Boy Commandos story in Detective Comics #68 interior is from an unidentified issue of Detective Comics (A FN- copy sold for $1912 in 2012)
nn - (9-10/42) Ashcan comic, not distributed to newsstands, only for in-house use. Cover art is the splash page from the Boy Commandos story in Detective Comics #68 interior is from Detective Comics #68 (no known sales)

BOY COWBOY (Also see Amazing Adventures & Science Comics)
Ziff-Davis Publ. Co.: 1950 (8 pgs. in color)

nn-Sent to subscribers of Ziff-Davis mags. & ordered through mail for 10¢; used to test market for Kid Cowboy 39 78 117 231 378 525

BOY DETECTIVE
Avon Periodicals: May-June, 1951 - No. 4, May, 1952

1 28 56 84 165 270 375
2-4: 3,4-Kinstler-c 18 36 54 105 165 225

BOY EXPLORERS COMICS (Terry and The Pirates No. 3 on)
Family Comics (Harvey Publ.): May-June, 1946 - No. 2, Sept-Oct, 1946

1-Intro The Explorers, Duke of Broadway, Calamity Jane & Danny Dixon...Cadet; S&K-c/a, 24 pgs. 93 186 279 591 1021 1450
2-(Rare)-Small size (5-1/2x8-1/2"; B&W; 32 pgs.) Distributed to mail subscribers only; S&K-a 168 336 504 1075 1838 2600
(Also see All New No. 15, Flash Gordon No. 5, and Stuntman No. 3)

BOY ILLUSTORIES (See Boy Comics)

BOY LOVES GIRL (Boy Meets Girl No. 1-24)
Lev Gleason Publications: No. 25, July, 1952 - No. 57, June, 1956

25(#1) 18 36 54 105 165 225
26,27,29-33: 30-33-Serial, 'Loves of My Life 12 24 36 69 97 125
34-42: 39-Lingerie panels 12 24 36 67 94 120
28-Drug propaganda story 12 24 36 69 97 125
43-Toth-a 13 26 39 72 101 130
44-50: 47-Toth-a? 49-Roller Derby-c. 50-Last pre-code (2/55)
11 22 33 62 86 110
51-57: 57-Ann Brewster-a 10 20 30 56 76 95

BOY MEETS GIRL (Boy Loves Girl No. 25 on)
Lev Gleason Publications: Feb, 1950 - No. 24, June, 1952 (No. 1-17: 52 pgs.)

1-Guardineer-a 25 50 75 150 245 340
2 15 30 45 86 133 180
3-10 14 28 42 82 121 160
11-24 14 28 42 76 108 140
NOTE: **Briefer** *a-24.* **Fuje** *c-3,7. Painted-c 1-17. Photo-c 19-21, 23.*

BOYS, THE (Inspired the 2019 Amazon Prime TV series)
DC Comics (WildStorm)/Dynamite Ent. #7 on: Oct, 2006 - No. 72, 2012 ($2.99/$3.99)

1-Garth Ennis-s/Darick Robertson-a 6 12 18 42 79 115
2,3 3 6 9 21 33 45
4,5 3 6 9 14 20 25
6-20 1 3 4 6 8 10
21-50: 19-Origin of the Homelander. 23-Variant-c by Cassaday
1 2 3 5 6 8
51-64,66-71-($3.99) Russ Braun-a in most. 54,55-McCrea-a 5.00
65,72-($4.99): 65-End of the Homelander. 72-Last issue; bonus pin-ups; cover gallery
1 2 3 5 6 8
#1: Dynamite Edition (2009, $1.00) r/#1; flip book with Battlefields Night Witches 5.00
... Dynamite Edition 1-3 (2021 - Present, no price on-c) r/#1-3 4.00
... Volume 1: The Name of the Game TPB (2007, $14.99) r/#1-6; intro. by Simon Pegg 15.00
... Volume 2: Get Some TPB (2008, $19.99) r/#7-14 20.00
... Volume 3: Good For The Soul TPB (2008, $19.99) r/#15-22 20.00
... Volume 4: We Gotta Go Now TPB (2009, $19.99) r/#23-30; cover gallery 20.00
... Volume 5: Herogasm TPB (2009, $19.99) r/#Herogasm #1-6 20.00

BOYS, THE: BUTCHER, BAKER, CANDLESTICKMAKER
Dynamite Entertainment: 2011 - No. 6, 2011 ($3.99, mature)

1-6-Garth Ennis-s/Darick Robertson-a; Billy Butcher's early years 4.00

BOYS, THE: DEAR BECKY

Boy Comics #48 © LEV

The Boys #14 © Spitfire & Robertson

B.P.R.D.: Hell on Earth #120 © Mike Mignola

GD 2.0 VG 4.0 FN 6.0 VF 8.0 VF/NM 9.0 NM- 9.2

GD 2.0 VG 4.0 FN 6.0 VF 8.0 VF/NM 9.0 NM- 9.2

Dynamite Entertainment: 2020 - No. 8, 2020 ($3.99, mature)

1-8-Garth Ennis-s/Russ Braun-a/Darick Robertson-c; set 12 years later, plus flashbacks 4.00

BOYS, THE: HEROGASM
Dynamite Entertainment: 2009 - No. 6, 2009 ($2.99, mature)

	GD	VG	FN	VF	VF/NM	NM-
1-Garth Ennis-s/John McCrea-a	4	8	12	23	37	50
2-6						5.00

BOYS, THE: HIGHLAND LADDIE
Dynamite Entertainment: 2010 - No. 6, 2011 ($3.99, mature)

1-6-Garth Ennis-s/John McCrea-a 4.00

BOYS' AND GIRLS' MARCH OF COMICS (See March of Comics)

BOYS' RANCH (Also see Western Tales & Witches' Western Tales)
Harvey Publ.: Oct, 1950 - No. 6, Aug, 1951 (No.1-3, 52 pgs.; No. 4-6, 36 pgs.)

	GD	VG	FN	VF	VF/NM	NM-
1-S&K-c/a(3)	65	130	195	416	708	1000
2-S&K-c/a(3)	41	82	123	256	428	600
3-S&K-c/a(2); Meskin-a	40	80	120	244	402	560
4-S&K-c/a, 5 pgs.	36	72	108	211	343	475
5,6-S&K-c, splashes & centerspread only; Meskin-a	21	42	63	122	199	275

BOZO (Larry Harmon's Bozo, the World's Most Famous Clown)
Innovation Publishing: 1992 ($6.95, 68 pgs.)

	GD	VG	FN	VF	VF/NM	NM-
1-Reprints Four Color #285(#1)	1	2	3	4	5	7

BOZO THE CLOWN (TV) (Bozo No. 7 on)
Dell Publishing Co.: July, 1950 - No. 4, Oct-Dec, 1963

	GD	VG	FN	VF	VF/NM	NM-
Four Color 285(#1)	19	38	57	131	291	450
2(7-9/51)-7(10-12/52)	10	20	30	67	141	215
Four Color 464,508,551,594(10/54)	9	18	27	61	123	185
1(nn, 5-7/62)	7	14	21	46	86	125
2 - 4(1963)	6	12	18	38	69	95

BOZZ CHRONICLES, THE
Marvel Comics (Epic Comics): Dec, 1985 - No. 6, 1986 (Lim. series, mature)

1-6-Logan/Wolverine look alike in 19th century. 1,3,5-Blevins-a 3.00

B.P.R.D. (Bureau of Paranormal Research and Defense) (Also see Hellboy titles)
Dark Horse Comics: (one-shots)

... Dark Waters (7/03, $2.99) Guy Davis-c/a; Augustyn-s 3.00
... Night Train (9/03, $2.99) Johns & Kolins-s; Kolins & Stewart-a 3.00
... The Ectoplasmic Man (6/08, $2.99) Stenbeck-a/Mignola-c; origin of Johann Kraus 3.00
... There's Something Under My Bed (11/03, $2.99) Pollina-a/c 3.00
... The Soul of Venice (5/03, $2.99) Oeming-a/c; Gunter & Oeming-s 3.00
... The Soul of Venice and Other Stories TPB (8/04, $17.95) r/one-shots & new story by Mignola and Cam Stewart; sketch pages by various 18.00
... War on Frogs (6/08,12/08, 6/09, 12/09, $2.99) 1-Trimpe-a/Mignola-c; Abe Sapien app. 2-Severin-a. 3-Moline-a. 4-Snejbjerg 3.00

B.P.R.D.: GARDEN OF SOULS
Dark Horse Comics: Mar, 2007 - No. 5, July, 2007 ($2.99, limited series)

1-5-Mignola & Arcudi-s/Guy Davis-a/Mignola-c 3.00

B.P.R.D.: HELL ON EARTH
Dark Horse Comics: ($3.50, limited series)

... Exorcism (6/12 - No. 2, 7/12) 1,2-Mignola-s/Stewart-a/Kalvachev -c 3.50
... Gods (1/11 - No. 3, 3/11) 1-Mignola & Arcudi-s/Guy Davis-a; Ryan Sook-c 3.50
... Monsters (7/11 - No. 2, 8/11) 1,2-Mignola & Arcudi-s. 1-Sook & Francavilla covers 3.50
... New World (8/10 - No. 5, 12/10) 1-5-Mignola & Arcudi-s/Guy Davis-a/c 3.50
... Russia (9/11 - No. 5, 1/12) 1-5-Mignola & Arcudi-s/Crook-a 3.50
... The Devil's Engine (5/12 - No. 3, 7/12) 1-3-Mignola & Arcudi-s/Crook-a/Fegredo-c 3.50
... The Long Death (2/12 - No. 3, 4/12) 1-3-Mignola & Arcudi-s/Harren-a/Fegredo-c 3.50
... The Pickens County Horror (3/12 - No. 2, 4/12) 1,2-Mignola & Allie-s/Latour-a 3.50
... The Transformation of J.H. O'Donnell (5/12) 1-Mignola & Allie-s/Fiumara-a 3.50
... The Return of the Master (8/12 - No. 5, 12/12) 1-5-Mignola & Arcudi-s/Crook-a; 3-5-Also numbered as #100-102 on cover and indicia 3.50
103-141: 103-(1/13). 103,104-The Abyss of Time. 105,106-A Cold Day in Hell 3.50
142-147-($3.99) 4.00

B.P.R.D.: HOLLOW EARTH (Mike Mignola's...)
Dark Horse Comics: Jan, 2002 - No. 3, June, 2002 ($2.99, limited series)

1-3-Mignola, Golden & Sniegoski-s/Sook-a/Mignola-c; Hellboy and Abe Sapien app. 5.00
... and Other Stories TPB (1/03; 7/04, $17.95) r/#1-3, Hellboy: Box Full of Evil, Abe Sapien: Drums of the Dead, and Dark Horse Extra; plus sketch pages 18.00

B.P.R.D.: KILLING GROUND
Dark Horse Comics: Aug, 2007 - No. 5, Dec, 2007 ($2.99, limited series)

1-5-Mignola & Arcudi-s/Guy Davis-a/c 3.00

B.P.R.D.: KING OF FEAR
Dark Horse Comics: Jan, 2010 - No. 5, May, 2010 ($2.99, limited series)

1,2-Mignola & Arcudi-s/Guy Davis-a; Mignola-c 3.00

B.P.R.D.: 1946
Dark Horse Comics: Jan, 2008 - No. 5, May, 2008 ($2.99, limited series)

1-5-Mignola & Dysart-s/Azaceta-a; Mignola-c 3.00

B.P.R.D.: 1947
Dark Horse Comics: Jul, 2009 - No. 5, Nov, 2009 ($2.99, limited series)

1-5-Mignola & Dysart-s/Bá & Moon-a; Mignola-c 3.00

B.P.R.D.: 1948
Dark Horse Comics: Oct, 2012 - No. 5, Feb, 2013 ($3.50, limited series)

1-5-Mignola & Arcudi-s/Fiumara-a; Johnson-c 3.50

B.P.R.D.: PLAGUE OF FROGS
Dark Horse Comics: Mar, 2004 - No. 5, July, 2004 ($2.99, limited series)

1-5-Mignola-s/Guy Davis-c/a 3.00
TPB (1/05, $17.95) r/series; sketchbook pages & afterword by Davis & Mignola 18.00

B.P.R.D.: THE BLACK FLAME
Dark Horse Comics: Sept, 2005 - No. 6, Jan, 2006 ($2.99, limited series)

1-6-Mignola & Arcudi-s/Guy Davis-a/ Mignola-c 3.00
TPB (7/06, $17.95) r/series; sketchbook pages & afterword by Davis & Mignola 18.00

B.P.R.D.: THE BLACK GODDESS
Dark Horse Comics: Jan, 2009 - No. 5, May, 2009 ($2.99, limited series)

1-5-Mignola & Arcudi-s/Guy Davis-a/Nowlan-c 3.00

B.P.R.D.: THE DEAD
Dark Horse Comics: Nov, 2004 - No. 5, Mar, 2005 ($2.99, limited series)

1-5-Mignola-s/Guy Davis-c/a 3.00

B.P.R.D.: THE DEAD REMEMBERED
Dark Horse Comics: Apr, 2011 - No. 3, Jun, 2011 ($3.50, limited series)

1-3-Mignola-s; Moline-a; Jo Chen-c. 1-Variant-c by Moline 3.50

B.P.R.D.: THE DEVIL YOU KNOW
Dark Horse Comics: Jul, 2017 - No. 15, Apr, 2019 ($3.99, limited series)

1-15: 1-Mignola & Allie-s/Laurence Campbell-a/Fegredo-c. 6-8-Fiumara-a 4.00

B.P.R.D.: THE UNIVERSAL MACHINE
Dark Horse Comics: Apr, 2006 - No. 5, Aug, 2006 ($2.99, limited series)

1-5-Mignola & Arcudi-s/Guy Davis-a/Mignola-c. 5-Mignola-a (5 pgs.) 3.00
TPB (1/07, $17.95) r/series; sketchbook pages by Davis; Mignola afterword 18.00

B.P.R.D.: THE WARNING
Dark Horse Comics: July, 2008 - No. 5, Nov, 2008 ($2.99, limited series)

1-5-Mignola & Arcudi-s/Guy Davis-c/a 3.00

B.P.R.D.: VAMPIRE
Dark Horse Comics: Mar, 2013 - No. 5, Jul, 2013 ($3.50, limited series)

1-5-Mignola-s/Bá & Moon-a; Moon-c 3.50

BRADLEYS, THE (Also see Hate)
Fantagraphics Books: Apr, 1999 - No. 6, Jan, 2000 ($2.95, B&W, limited series)

1-6-Reprints Peter Bagge's-s/a 3.00

BRADY BUNCH, THE (TV)(See Kite Fun Book and Binky #78)
Dell Publishing Co.: Feb, 1970 - No. 2, May, 1970 (photo-c)

	GD	VG	FN	VF	VF/NM	NM-
1	13	26	39	89	195	300
2	10	20	30	64	132	200

BRAIN, THE
Sussex Publ. Co./Magazine Enterprises: Sept, 1956 - No. 7, 1958

	GD	VG	FN	VF	VF/NM	NM-
1-Dan DeCarlo-a in all including reprints	14	28	42	82	121	160
2,3	9	18	27	50	65	80
4-7	4	8	12	28	47	65
I.W. Reprints #1-4,8-10('63),14: 2-Reprints Sussex #2 with new cover added	2	4	6	9	13	16
Super Reprint #17,18(nd)	2	4	6	9	13	16

BRAINBANX
DC Comics (Helix): Mar, 1997 - No. 6, Aug, 1997 ($2.50, limited series)

1-6: Elaine Lee-s/Temujin-a 3.00

BRAIN BOY
Dell Publishing Co.: Apr-June, 1962 - No. 6, Sept-Nov, 1963 (Painted c-#1-6)

	GD	VG	FN	VF	VF/NM	NM-
	2.0	4.0	6.0	8.0	9.0	9.2

Four Color 1330(#1)-Gil Kane-a; origin 10 20 30 69 147 225
2(7-9/62),3-6: 4-Origin retold 6 12 18 41 76 110

BRAIN BOY
Dark Horse Comics: Sept, 2013 - No. 3, Nov, 2013 ($2.99, limited series)

1-3-Van Lente-s/Silva-a/Olivetti-c 3.00
#0-(12/13, $2.99) Reprints stories from Dark Horse Presents #23-25; Olivetti-c 3.00

BRAIN BOY: THE MEN FROM G.E.S.T.A.L.T.
Dark Horse Comics: May, 2014 - No. 4, Aug, 2014 ($2.99, limited series)

1-4-Van Lente-s/Freddie Williams II-a/c 3.00

BRAM STOKER'S DRACULA (Movie)(Also see Dracula: Vlad the Impaler)
Topps Comics: Oct, 1992 - No. 4, Jan, 1993 ($2.95, limited series, polybagged)

1-(1st & 2nd printing)-Adaptation of film begins; Mignola-c/a in all; 4 trading cards & poster; photo scenes of movie 5.00
1-Crimson foil edition (limited to 500) 20.00
2-4: 2-Bound-in poster & cards. 4 trading cards in both. 3-Contains coupon to win 1 of 500 crimson foil-c edition of #1. 4-Contains coupon to win 1 of 500 uncut sheets of all 16 trading cards 4.00

BRAND ECHH (See Not Brand Echh)

BRAND OF EMPIRE (See Luke Short's...Four Color 771)

BRASS
Image Comics (WildStorm Productions): Aug, 1996 - No. 3, May, 1997 ($2.50, lim. series)

1-($4.50) Folio Ed.; oversized 4.50
1-3: Wiesenfeld-s/Bennett-a. 3-Grunge & Roxy(Gen 13) cameo 3.00

BRASS
DC Comics (WildStorm): Aug, 2000 - No. 6, Jan, 2001 ($2.50, limited series)

1-6-Arcudi-s 3.00

BRATH
CrossGeneration Comics: Feb, 2003 - No. 14, June, 2004 ($2.95)

Prequel-Dixon-s/Di Vito-a 3.00
1-14: 1-(3/03)-Dixon-s/Di Vito-a 3.00
Vol. 1: Hammer of Vengeance (2003, $9.95) Digest-sized reprint of Prequel & #1-6 10.00

BRATS BIZARRE
Marvel Comics (Epic/Heavy Hitters): 1994 - No. 4, 1994 ($2.50, limited series)

1-4: All w/bound-in trading cards 3.00

BRAVADOS, THE (See Wild Western Action)
Skywald Publ. Corp.: Aug, 1971 (52 pgs., one-shot)

1-Red Mask, The Durango Kid, Billy Nevada-r; Bolle-a; 3-D effect story 3 6 9 16 23 30

BRAVE AND THE BOLD, THE (See Best Of... & Super DC Giant) (Replaced by Batman & The Outsiders)
National Periodical Publ./DC Comics: Aug-Sept, 1955 - No. 200, July, 1983

1-Viking Prince by Kubert, Silent Knight, Golden Gladiator begin; part Kubert-c 380 760 1140 3200 7350 11,500
2 141 282 423 1153 2602 4050
3,4 81 162 243 644 1447 2250
5-Robin Hood begins (4-5/56, 1st DC app.), ends #15; see Robin Hood Tales #7 84 168 252 700 1525 2350
6-10: 6-Robin Hood by Kubert; last Golden Gladiator app.; Silent Knight; no Viking Prince. 8-1st S.A. issue 54 108 162 432 966 1500
11-22,24: 12,14-Robin Hood-c. 18,21-23-Grey tone-c. 22-Last Silent Knight. 24-Last Viking Prince by Kubert (2nd solo book) 44 88 132 326 738 1150
23-Viking Prince origin by Kubert; 1st B&B single theme issue & 1st Viking Prince solo book 52 104 156 416 933 1450
25-1st app. Suicide Squad (8-9/59) 307 614 921 2610 5905 9200
26-Suicide Squad 48 96 144 374 862 1350
27-Suicide Squad 46 92 138 340 770 1200
28-(2-3/60)-Justice League 1st app.; battle Starro; origin/1st app. Snapper Carr 1435 2870 5740 18,400 56,200 94,000
28 (Facsimile Edition)(2020, $3.99) Reprints #28 with original ads and letter column 4.00
28 (Facsimile Edition)(2022, $3.99) Reprints #28 with original ads and letter column 4.00
29-Justice League (4-5/60)-2nd app. battle the Weapons Master; robot-c 255 510 765 2104 4752 7400
30-Justice League (6-7/60)-3rd app.; vs. Amazo 200 400 600 1650 3725 5800
31-1st app. Cave Carson (8-9/60); scarce in high grade; 1st try-out series 54 108 162 432 966 1500
32,33-Cave Carson 27 54 81 189 420 650
34-Origin/1st app. Silver-Age Hawkman, Hawkgirl & Byth (2-3/61); Gardner Fox story, Kubert-c/a ; 1st S.A. Hawkman tryout series; 2nd in #42-44; both series predate Hawkman #1 (4-5/64) 224 448 672 1848 4174 6500
35-Hawkman by Kubert (4-5/61)-2nd app. 42 84 126 311 706 1100
36-Hawkman by Kubert; origin & 1st app. Shadow Thief (6-7/61)-3rd app. 36 72 108 266 596 925
37-Suicide Squad (2nd tryout series) 30 60 90 216 483 750
38,39-Suicide Squad. 38-Last 10¢ issue 22 44 66 154 340 525
40,41-Cave Carson Inside Earth (2nd try-out series). 40-Kubert-a. 41-Meskin-a 14 28 42 96 211 325
42-Hawkman by Kubert (2nd tryout series); Hawkman earns helmet wings; Byth app. 22 44 66 154 340 525
43-Hawkman by Kubert; more detailed origin 24 48 72 168 372 575
44-Hawkman by Kubert; grey-tone-c 22 44 66 154 340 525
45-49-Strange Sports Stories by Infantino 9 18 27 61 123 185
50-The Green Arrow & Manhunter From Mars (10-11/63); 1st Manhunter x-over outside of Detective Comics (pre-dates House of Mystery #143); team-ups begin 21 42 63 147 324 500
51-Aquaman & Hawkman (12-1/63-64); pre-dates Hawkman #1 20 40 60 136 303 470
52-(2-3/64)-3 Battle Stars; Sgt. Rock, Haunted Tank, Johnny Cloud, & Mlle. Marie team-up for 1st time by Kubert (c/a) 25 50 75 175 388 600
53-Atom & The Flash by Toth 10 20 30 69 147 225
54-Kid Flash, Robin & Aqualad; 1st app./origin Teen Titans (6-7/64) 111 222 333 888 1994 3100
55-Metal Men & The Atom 9 18 27 61 123 185
56-The Flash & Manhunter From Mars 9 18 27 61 123 185
57-Origin & 1st app. Metamorpho (12-1/64-65) 26 52 78 182 404 625
58-2nd app. Metamorpho by Fradon 10 20 30 66 138 210
59-Batman & Green Lantern; 1st Batman team-up in Brave and the Bold 13 26 39 86 188 290
60-Teen Titans (2nd app.)-1st app. new Wonder Girl (Donna Troy), who joins Titans (6-7/65) 64 128 192 512 1158 1800
61-Origin Starman & Black Canary by Anderson 13 26 39 89 195 300
62-Origin Starman & Black Canary cont'd. 62-1st S.A. app. Wildcat (10-11/65); 1st S.A. app. of G.A. Huntress (W.W. villain) 11 22 33 75 160 245
63-Supergirl & Wonder Woman 10 20 30 64 132 200
64-Batman Versus Eclipso (see H.O.S. #61) 8 16 24 51 96 140
65-Flash & Doom Patrol (4-5/66) 7 14 21 44 82 120
66-Metamorpho & Metal Men (6-7/66) 7 14 21 44 82 120
67-Batman & The Flash by Infantino; Batman team-ups begin, end #200 (8-9/66) 8 16 24 55 105 155
68-Batman/Metamorpho/Joker/Riddler/Penguin-c/story; Batman as Bat-Hulk (Hulk parody) 8 16 24 54 102 150
69-Batman & Green Lantern 6 12 18 38 69 100
70-Batman & Hawkman; Craig-a(p) 6 12 18 38 69 100
71-Batman & Green Arrow 6 12 18 38 69 100
72-Spectre & Flash (6-7/67); 4th app. The Spectre; predates Spectre #1 7 14 21 46 86 125
73-Aquaman & The Atom 6 12 18 38 69 100
74-Batman & Metal Men 6 12 18 38 69 100
75-Batman & The Spectre (12-1/67-68); 6th app. Spectre; came out between Spectre #1 & #2 7 14 21 48 89 130
76-Batman & Plastic Man (2-3/68); came out between Plastic Man #8 & #9 6 12 18 40 73 105
77-Batman & The Atom 6 12 18 37 66 95
78-Batman, Wonder Woman & Batgirl 8 16 24 52 99 145
79-Batman & Deadman by Neal Adams (8-9/68); early Deadman app. 10 20 30 68 144 220
80-Batman & Creeper (10-11/68); N. Adams-a; early app. The Creeper; came out between Creeper #3 & #4 8 16 24 52 99 145
81-Batman & Flash; N. Adams-a 9 18 27 57 111 165
82-Batman & Aquaman; N. Adams-a; origin Ocean Master retold (2-3/69) 9 18 27 59 117 175
83-Batman & Teen Titans; N. Adams-a (4-5/69) 8 16 24 55 105 155
84-Batman (G.A., 1st S.A. app.) & Sgt. Rock; N. Adams-a; last 12¢ issue (6-7/69) 9 18 27 57 111 165
85-Batman & Green Arrow; 1st new costume for Green Arrow by Neal Adams (8-9/69) 15 30 45 105 233 360
86-Batman & Deadman (10-11/69); N. Adams-a; story concludes from Strange Adventures #216 (1-2/69) 9 18 27 59 117 175
87-Batman & Wonder Woman 5 10 15 33 57 80
88-Batman & Wildcat 4 8 12 27 44 60
89-Batman & Phantom Stranger (4-5/70); early Phantom Stranger app. (came out between Phantom Stranger #6 & 7 4 8 12 27 44 60
90-Batman & Adam Strange 4 8 12 27 44 60
91-Batman & Black Canary (8-9/70) 4 8 12 27 44 60
92-Batman; intro the Bat Squad 4 8 12 27 44 60
93-Batman-House of Mystery; N. Adams-a 10 20 30 64 132 200
94-Batman-Teen Titans 4 8 12 28 47 65
95-Batman & Plastic Man 3 6 9 21 33 45
96-Batman & Sgt. Rock; last 15¢ issue 3 6 9 21 33 45
97-Batman & Wildcat; 52 pg. issues begin, end #102; reprints origin & 1st app. Deadman from Strange Advs. #205 3 6 9 21 33 45
98-Batman & Phantom Stranger; 1st Jim Aparo Batman-a? 3 6 9 21 33 45
99-Batman & Flash 3 6 9 21 33 45
100-(2-3/72, 25¢, 52 pgs.)-Batman-Green Lantern-Green Arrow-Black Canary-Robin; Deadman-r by Adams/Str. Advs. #210 6 12 18 40 73 105
101-Batman & Metamorpho; Kubert Viking Prince 3 6 9 20 31 42
102-Batman-Teen Titans; N. Adams-a(p) 5 10 15 31 53 75
103-107,109,110: Batman team-ups: 103-Metal Men. 104-Deadman. 105-Wonder Woman. 106-Green Arrow. 107-Black Canary. 109-Demon. 110-Wildcat 3 6 9 16 23 30
108-Sgt. Rock 3 6 9 17 26 35
111-Batman/Joker-c/story 4 8 12 28 47 65
112-117: All 100 pgs.; Batman team-ups: 112-Mr. Miracle. 113-Metal Men; reprints origin/1st Hawkman from Brave and the Bold #34; r/origin Multi-Man/Challengers #14. 114-Aquaman. 115-Atom; r/origin Viking Prince from #23; r/Dr. Fate/Hourman/Solomon Grundy/Green Lantern from Showcase #55. 116-Spectre. 117-Sgt. Rock; last 100 pg. issue 5 10 15 30 50 70
118-Batman/Wildcat/Joker-c/story 3 6 9 21 33 45
119,121-123,125-128,132-140: Batman team-ups: 119-Man-Bat. 121-Metal Men. 122-Swamp Thing. 123-Plastic Man/Metamorpho. 125-Flash. 126-Aquaman. 127-Wildcat. 128-Mr. Miracle. 132-Kung-Fu Fighter. 133-Deadman. 134-Green Lantern. 135-Metal Men. 136-Metal Men/Green Arrow. 137-Demon. 138-Mr. Miracle. 139-Hawkman. 140-Wonder Woman 2 4 6 8 10 12
120-Kamandi (68 pgs.) 3 6 9 14 19 24
124-Sgt. Rock; Jim Aparo app. on cover & in story 2 4 6 10 14 18
129,130-Batman/Green Arrow/Atom parts 1 & 2; Joker & Two Face-c/stories 3 6 9 15 22 28
131-Batman & Wonder Woman vs. Catwoman-c/sty 3 6 9 14 20 25
141-Batman/Black Canary vs. Joker-c/story 3 6 9 15 22 28
142-160: Batman team-ups: 142-Aquaman. 143-Creeper; origin Human Target (44 pgs.). 144-Green Arrow; origin Human Target part 2 (44 pgs.). 145-Phantom Stranger. 146-G.A. Batman/Unknown Soldier. 147-Supergirl. 148-Plastic Man; X-Mas-c. 149-Teen Titans. 150-Anniversary issue; Superman. 151-Flash. 152-Atom. 153-Red Tornado. 154-Metamorpho. 155-Green Lantern. 156-Dr. Fate. 157-Batman vs. Kamandi (ties into Kamandi #59). 158-Wonder Woman. 159-Ra's Al Ghul. 160-Supergirl. 1 3 4 6 8 10
145(11/79)-147,150-159,165(8/80)-(Whitman variants; low print run;

Brave and the Bold #61 © DC

Brave and the Bold (2007) #5 © DC

Bravest Warriors #33 © Frederator

GD VG FN VF VF/NM NM-
2.0 4.0 6.0 8.0 9.0 9.2

none show issue # on cover) 2 4 6 11 16 20
161-181,183-190,192-195,198,199: Batman team-ups: 161-Adam Strange. 162-G.A. Batman/Sgt. Rock. 163-Black Lightning. 164-Hawkman. 165-Man-Bat. 166-Black Canary; Nemesis (intro) back-up story begins, ends #192; Penguin-c/story. 167-G.A. Batman/Blackhawk; origin Nemesis. 168-Green Arrow. 169-Zatanna. 170-Nemesis. 171-Scalphunter. 172-Firestorm. 173-Guardians of the Universe. 174-Green Lantern. 175-Lois Lane. 176-Swamp Thing. 177-Elongated Man. 178-Creeper. 179-Legion. 180-Spectre. 181-Hawk & Dove. 183-Riddler. 184-Huntress & Earth II Batman. 185-Green Arrow. 186-Hawkman. 187-Metal Men. 188,189-Rose & the Thorn. 190-Adam Strange. 192-Superboy vs. Mr. I.Q. 194-Flash. 195-I...Vampire. 198-Karate Kid. 199-Batman vs. The Spectre 6.00
182-G.A. Robin; G.A. Starman app.; 1st modern app. G.A. Batwoman 2 4 6 9 13 16
191-Batman/Joker-c/story; Nemesis app. 3 6 9 17 26 35
196-Ragman; origin Ragman retold. 1 2 3 5 6 8
197-Catwoman; Earth II Batman & Catwoman marry; 2nd modern app. of G.A. Batwoman; Scarecrow story in Golden Age style 3 6 9 16 24 32
200-Double-sized (64 pgs.); printed on Mando paper; Earth One & Earth Two Batman app. in separate stories; intro/1st app. Batman & The Outsiders; 1st app. Katana 4 8 12 23 37 50

NOTE: ***Neal Adams** a-79-86, 93, 100r, 102; c-75, 76, 79-86, 88-90, 93, 95, 99, 100r. **M. Anderson** a-115r; c-72i, 96i. **Andru/Esposito** c-25-27. **Aparo** a-98, 100-102, 104-125, 126i, 127-136, 138-145, 147, 148i, 149-152, 154, 155, 157-162, 168-170, 173-178, 180-182, 184, 186i-189i, 191i-193i, 195, 196, 200; c-105-109, 111-136, 137i, 138-175, 177, 180-184, 186-200. **Austin** a-166i. **Bernard Baily** c-32, 33, 58. **Buckler** a-185, 186p; c-137, 178p, 185p, 186p. **Giordano** a-143, 144. **Infantino** a-67p, 72p, 97r, 98r, 115r, 172p, 183p, 190p, 194p; c-45-49, 67p, 69p, 70p, 72p, 96p, 98r. **Kaluta** c-176. **Kane** a-115r; c-59, 64. **Kubert** &/or **Heath** a-1-24; reprints-101, 113, 115, 117. **Kubert** a-99r; c-22-24, 34-36, 40, 42-44, 52. **Mooney** a-114r. **Mortimer** a-64, 69. **Newton** a-153p, 156p, 165p. **Irv Novick** c-1(part), 2-21. **Fred Ray** a-78r. **Roussos** a-50, 76i, 114r. **Staton** 148p. 52 pgs.-97, 100; 68 pgs.-120; 100 pgs.-112-117.*

BRAVE AND THE BOLD, THE
DC Comics: Dec, 1991 - No. 6, June, 1992 ($1.75, limited series)

1-6: Green Arrow, The Butcher, The Question in all; Grell scripts in all 4.00
NOTE: ***Grell** c-3, 4-6.*

BRAVE AND THE BOLD, THE
DC Comics: Apr, 2007 - No. 35, Aug, 2010 ($2.99)

1-Batman & Green Lantern team-up; Roulette app.; Waid-s/Peréz-c/a; 2 covers 5.00
2-32,34,35: 2-GL & Supergirl. 3-Batman & Blue Beetle vs. Fatal Five; Lobo app. 4-6-LSH app. 12-Megistus conclusion; Ordway-a. 14-Kolins-a. 16-Superman & Catwoman. 28-Blackhawks app. 29-Batman/Brother Power the Geek. 31-Atom/Joker 3.00
33-Batgirl, Zatanna & W.W.; prelude to Killing Joke 3 6 9 17 26 35
...: Demons and Dragons HC (2009, $24.99, dustjacket) r/#13-16; Brave & the Bold V1 #181, Flash V3 #107 and Impulse #17; Mark Waid commentary 25.00
...: Demons and Dragons SC (2010, $17.99) same contents as HC 18.00
...: Milestone SC (2010, $17.99) r/#24-26 and Static #12, Hardware #16, Xombi #6 18.00
Team-ups of the Brave and the Bold HC (2010, $24.99) r/#27-33 25.00
...: The Book of Destiny HC (2008, $24.99, dustjacket) r/#7-12; Ordway sketch pages 25.00
...: The Book of Destiny SC (2009, $17.99) r/#7-12; Ordway sketch pages 18.00
...: The Lords of Luck HC (2007, $24.99, dustjacket) r/#1-6 with Waid intro & annotations 25.00
...: The Lords of Luck SC (2008, $17.99) r/#1-6 with Waid intro & annotations 18.00
...: Without Sin SC (2009, $17.99) r/#17-22 18.00

BRAVE AND THE BOLD ANNUAL NO. 1 1969 ISSUE, THE
DC Comics: 2001 ($5.95, one-shot)

1-Reprints Silver Age team-ups in 1960s-style 80 pg. Giant format 6.00

BRAVE AND THE BOLD: BATMAN AND WONDER WOMAN, THE
DC Comics: Apr, 2018 - No. 6, Sept, 2018 ($3.99, limited series)

1-6-Liam Sharp-s/a 4.00

BRAVE AND THE BOLD SPECIAL, THE (See DC Special Series No. 8)

BRAVE EAGLE (TV)
Dell Publishing Co.: No. 705, June, 1956 - No. 929, July, 1958

Four Color 705 (#1)-Photo-c 7 14 21 46 86 125
Four Color 770, 816, 879 (2/58), 929-All photo-c 5 10 15 33 57 80

BRAVE NEW WORLD (See DCU Brave New World)

BRAVE OLD WORLD (V2K)
DC Comics (Vertigo): Feb, 2000 - No. 4, May, 2000 ($2.50, mini-series)

1-4-Messner-Loeb-s/Guy Davis & Phil Hester-a 3.00

BRAVE ONE, THE (Movie)
Dell Publishing Co.: No. 773, Mar, 1957

Four Color 773-Photo-c 5 10 15 35 63 90

BRAVEST WARRIORS (Based on the animated web series)
BOOM! Entertainment (KaBOOM): Oct, 2012 - No. 36, Sept, 2015 ($3.99)

1-36-Multiple covers on each 4.00
2014 Annual (1/14, $4.99) Short stories featuring Catbug; multiple covers 5.00
2014 Impossibear Special 1 (6/14, $4.99) Short stories; multiple covers 5.00
... Paralyzed Horse Giant 1 (11/14, $4.99) Short stories; multiple covers 5.00
...: Tales From the Holo John 1 (5/15, $4.99) Short stories; multiple covers 5.00

BRAVURA
Malibu Comics (Bravura): 1995 (mail-in offer)

0-wraparound holographic-c; short stories and promo pin-ups of Chaykin's Power & Glory, Gil Kane's & Steven Grant's Edge, Starlin's Breed, & Simonson's Star Slammers 5.00
1 1/2 7.00

BREACH
DC Comics: Mar, 2005 - No. 11, Jan, 2006 ($2.95/$2.50)

1-11: 1-Marcos Martin-a/Bob Harras-s; origin. 4-JLA-c/app. 3.00

BREAKDOWN
Devil's Due Publ.: Oct, 2004 - No. 6, Apr, 2005 ($2.95)

1-6: 1-Two covers by Dave Ross and Leinil Yu; Dixon-s/Ross-a 3.00

BREAKFAST AFTER NOON
Oni Press: May, 2000 - No. 6, Jan, 2001 ($2.95, B&W, limited series)

1-6-Andi Watson-s/a 3.00
TPB (2001, $19.95) r/series 20.00

BREAKING INTO COMICS THE MARVEL WAY
Marvel Comics: May, 2010 - No. 2, May, 2010 ($3.99, limited series)

1,2-Short stories by various newcomer artists; artist profiles 4.00

BREAKNECK BLVD.
MotioN Comics/Slave Labor Graphics Vol. 2: No. 0, Feb, 1994 - No. 2, Nov, 1994; Vol. 2#1, Jul, 1995 - #6, Dec., 1996 ($2.50/$2.95, B&W)

0-2, V2#1-6: 0-Pérez/Giordano-c 3.00

BREAK-THRU (Also see Exiles V1#4)
Malibu Comics (Ultraverse): Dec, 1993 - No. 2, Jan, 1994 ($2.50, 44 pgs.)

1,2-Pérez-c/a(p); has x-overs in Ultraverse titles 4.00

BREATH OF BONES: A TALE OF THE GOLEM
Dark Horse Comics: Jun, 2013 - No. 3, Aug, 2013 ($3.99, B&W, limited series)

1-3-Niles-s/Wachter-a 4.00

BREATHTAKER
DC Comics: 1990 - No. 4, 1990 ($4.95, 52 pgs., prestige format, mature)

Book 1-4: Mark Wheatley-painted-c/a & scripts; Marc Hempel-a 5.00
TPB (1994, $14.95) r/#1-4; intro by Neil Gaiman 15.00

'BREED
Malibu Comics (Bravura): Jan, 1994 - No. 6, 1994 ($2.50, limited series)

1-(48 pgs.)-Origin/1st app. of 'Breed by Starlin; contains Bravura stamps; spot varnish-c 4.00
2-6: 2-5-contains Bravura stamps. 6-Death of Rachel 3.00
...:Book of Genesis (1994, $12.95)-reprints #1-6 13.00

'BREED II
Malibu Comics (Bravura): Nov, 1994 - No. 6, Apr, 1995 ($2.95, limited series)

1-6: Starlin-c/a/scripts in all. 1-Gold edition 3.00

'BREED III
Image Comics: May, 2011 - No. 7, Dec, 2011 ($2.99)

1-7: Starlin-c/a/scripts in all 3.00

BREEZE LAWSON, SKY SHERIFF (See Sky Sheriff)

BRENDA LEE'S LIFE STORY
Dell Publishing Co.: July-Sept., 1962

01-078-209 8 16 24 51 96 140

BRENDA STARR (Also see All Great)
Four Star Comics Corp./Superior Comics Ltd.: No. 13, 9/47; No. 14, 3/48; V2#3, 6/48 - V2#12, 12/49

V1#13-By Dale Messick 123 246 369 787 1344 1900
14-Classic Kamen bondage-c 975 1950 2919 7100 12,550 18,000
V2#3-Baker-a? 93 186 279 591 1021 1450
4-Used in **SOTI**, pg. 21; Kamen-c 142 284 426 909 1555 2200
5-10 81 162 243 518 884 1250
11,12 (Scarce) 84 168 252 538 919 1300
NOTE: *Newspaper reprints plus original material through #6. All original #7 on.*

BRENDA STARR (...Reporter)(Young Lovers No. 16 on?)
Charlton Comics: No. 13, June, 1955 - No. 15, Oct, 1955

13-15-Newspaper-r 36 72 108 211 343 475

BRENDA STARR REPORTER
Dell Publishing Co.: Oct, 1963

	GD 2.0	VG 4.0	FN 6.0	VF 8.0	VF/NM 9.0	NM- 9.2
1	11	22	33	75	160	245

BRER RABBIT (See Kite Fun Book, Walt Disney Showcase #28 and Wheaties)
Dell Publishing Co.: No. 129, 1946; No. 208, Jan, 1949; No. 693, 1956 (Disney)

	GD	VG	FN	VF	VF/NM	NM-
Four Color 129 (#1)-Adapted from Disney movie "Song of the South"	32	64	96	230	515	800
Four Color 208 (1/49)	12	24	36	82	179	275
Four Color 693-Part-r #129	10	20	30	64	132	200

BRIAN PULIDO'S LADY DEATH... (See Lady Death)

BRIAR
BOOM! Studios: Sept, 2022 - Present ($4.99/$3.99)

1-($4.99) A Sleeping Beauty pastiche; Cantwell-s/Garcia-a 5.00
2,3-($3.99) 4.00

BRICK BRADFORD (Also see Ace Comics & King Comics)
King Features Syndicate/Standard: No. 5, July, 1948 - No. 8, July, 1949 (Ritt & Grey reprints)

	GD	VG	FN	VF	VF/NM	NM-
5	23	46	69	138	227	315
6-Robot-c (by Schomburg?).	290	580	870	1856	3178	4500
7-Schomburg-c. 8-Says #7 inside, #8 on-c	19	38	57	112	179	245

BRICKLEBERRY (Based on the animated series)
Dynamite Entertainment: 2016 - No. 4, 2016 ($3.99, limited series)

1-4-Waco O'Guin & Roger Black-s 4.00

BRIDE'S DIARY (Formerly Black Cobra No. 3)
Ajax/Farrell Publ.: No. 4, May, 1955 - No. 10, Aug, 1956

	GD	VG	FN	VF	VF/NM	NM-
4 (#1)	14	28	42	82	121	160
5-8	11	22	33	60	83	105
9,10-Disbrow-a	12	24	36	69	97	125

BRIDES IN LOVE (Hollywood Romances & Summer Love No. 46 on)
Charlton Comics: Aug, 1956 - No. 45, Feb, 1965

	GD	VG	FN	VF	VF/NM	NM-
1	16	32	48	94	147	200
2	10	20	30	54	72	90
3-6,8-10	5	10	15	30	50	70
7-(68 pgs.)	5	10	15	34	60	85
11-20	4	8	12	23	37	50
21-45	3	6	9	16	24	32

BRIDES OF HELHEIM
Oni Press: Oct, 2014 - No. 6, May, 2015 ($3.99)

1-6-Cullen Bunn-s/Joëlle Jones-a 4.00

BRIDES ROMANCES
Quality Comics Group: Nov, 1953 - No. 23, Dec, 1956

	GD	VG	FN	VF	VF/NM	NM-
1	24	48	72	142	234	325
2	15	30	45	83	124	165
3-10: Last precode (3/55)	14	28	42	82	121	160
11-17,19-22: 15-Baker-a(p)?; Colan-a	14	28	42	76	108	140
18-Baker-a	15	30	45	90	140	190
23-Baker-c/a	28	56	84	165	270	375

BRIDE'S SECRETS
Ajax/Farrell(Excellent Publ.)/Four-Star: Apr-May, 1954 - No. 19, May, 1958

	GD	VG	FN	VF	VF/NM	NM-
1	20	40	60	118	192	265
2	14	28	42	81	118	155
3-6: Last precode (3/55)	12	24	36	69	97	125
7-11,13-19: 18-Hollingsworth-a	11	22	33	64	90	115
12-Disbrow-a	13	26	39	74	105	135

BRIDE-TO-BE ROMANCES (See True...)

BRIGADE
Image Comics (Extreme Studios): Aug, 1992 - No. 4, 1993 ($1.95, lim. series)

1-Liefeld part plots/scripts in all, Liefeld-c(p); contains 2 Brigade trading cards 4.00
1-Gold foil stamped logo edition 8.00
2-Contains coupon for Image Comics #0 & 2 trading cards 3.00
2-With coupon missing 2.00
3,4: 3-Contains 2 trading cards; 1st Birds of Prey. 4-Flip book featuring Youngblood #5 3.00

BRIGADE
Image Comics (Extreme): V2#1, May, 1993 - V2#22, July, 1995, V2#25, May, 1996 ($1.95/$2.50)

V2#1-22,25: 1-Gatefold-c; Liefeld co-plots; Blood Brothers part 1; Bloodstrike app. 2-(6/93, V2#1 on inside)-Foil merricote-c (newsstand ed. w/out foil-c exists). 3-Perez-c(i); Liefeld scripts. 8,9-Coupons #2 & 6 for Extreme Prejudice #0 bound-in. 11-(8/94, $2.50) WildC.A.T.S app. 16-Polybagged w/ trading card. 22-"Supreme Apocalypse" Pt. 4; w/ trading card 3.00
0-(9/93)-Liefeld scripts; 1st app. Warcry; Youngblood & Wildcats app.; 3.00
20-Variant-c. by Quesada & Palmiotti 3.00
Remastered Edition #1 (9/22, $3.99) #1's pages redrawn by modern artists; flipbook with Heirborne by Rob Liefeld-s/a 4.00
Sourcebook 1 (8/94, $2.95) 3.00
1-(Awesome Ent., 7/00, $2.99) Flip book w/Century preview 4.00
1-(6/10, $3.99) Liefeld-s/Mychaels-a; covers by Liefeld & Mychaels 4.00

BRIGAND, THE (See Fawcett Movie Comics No. 18)

BRIGGS LAND
Dark Horse Comics: Aug, 2016 - No. 6, Jan, 2017 ($3.99)

1-6-Brian Wood-s/Mack Chater-a/Tula Lotay-c 4.00

BRIGGS LAND: LONE WOLVES
Dark Horse Comics: Jun, 2017 - No. 6, Nov, 2017 ($3.99)

1-6: 1-Brian Wood-s/Mack Chater-a/Matthew Woodson-c. 4-Del Ray-a 4.00

BRIGHTEST DAY (Also see Blackest Night and Green Lantern)
DC Comics: No. 0, Jun, 2010 - No. 24, Late Jun, 2011 ($3.99/$2.99)

0-($3.99) Johns & Tomasi-s/Pasarin-a/Finch-c 4.00
0-Variant-c by Reis 8.00
1-23-($2.99) 1-Black Manta returns. 4-Intro. Jackson (new Aqualad) 16-Aqualad origin. 18-Hawkman & Hawkgirl killed. 20-Aquaman killed 3.00
1-23: Variant covers. 1-6,9-18,20-23-by Reis, 7,8 White Lantern by Sook. 19-by Frank 6.00
24-($4.99) Swamp Thing and John Constantine return to DC universe 5.00
24-($4.99) Variant cover by Reis 8.00
...: The Atom Special (9/10, $2.99) Lemire-s/Asrar-a/Frank-c 3.00
... Volume 1 HC (2010, $29.99) r/#0-7; cover gallery 30.00
... Volume 2 HC (2011, $29.99) r/#8-16; cover gallery 30.00

BRIGHTEST DAY AFTERMATH: THE SEARCH FOR SWAMP THING
DC Comics: Aug, 2011 - No. 3, Oct, 2011 ($2.99, limited series)

1-3-Vankin-s/Castiello-a; covers by Syaf & Jones; John Constantine & Zatanna app. 3.00

BRILLIANT
Marvel Comics (Icon): Jul, 2011 - No. 5, Mar, 2014 ($3.95, limited series)

1-5-Bendis-s/Bagley-a/c 4.00

BRILLIANT TRASH
AfterShock Comics: Nov, 2017 - No. 6, May, 2018 ($3.99)

1-6: 1-Tim Seeley-s/Priscilla Petraites-a. 6-Steve Kurth-a 4.00

BRING BACK THE BAD GUYS (Also see Fireside Book Series)
Marvel Comics: 1998 ($24.95, TPB)

1-Reprints stories of Marvel villains' secrets 25.00

BRINGING UP FATHER
Dell Publishing Co.: No. 9, 1942 - No. 37, 1944

	GD	VG	FN	VF	VF/NM	NM-
Large Feature Comic 9	39	78	117	240	395	550
Four Color 37	20	40	60	138	307	475

BRING ON THE BAD GUYS (See Fireside Book Series)

BRING THE THUNDER
Dynamite Entertainment: 2010 - No. 4, 2011 ($3.99)

1-4-Alex Ross-c/Ross & Nitz-s/Tortosa-a 4.00

BRITANNIA
Valiant Entertainment: Sept, 2016 - No. 4, Dec, 2016 ($3.99, limited series)

1-4-Milligan-a/Ryp-a; set in 60-66 A.D.; Emperor Nero app. 4.00
... One Dollar Debut #1 (5/19, $1.00) r/#1 3.00

BRITANNIA: LOST EAGLES OF ROME
Valiant Entertainment: Jul, 2018 - No. 4, Oct, 2018 ($3.99, limited series)

1-4-Milligan-a/Gill-a; Antonius Axia and Achillia in Egypt; multiple covers on each 4.00

BRITANNIA: WE WHO ARE ABOUT TO DIE
Valiant Entertainment: Apr, 2017 - No. 4, Jul, 2017 ($3.99, limited series)

1-4-Milligan-a/Ryp-a; further story of Antonius Axia; multiple covers on each 4.00

BRITISH PARANORMAL SOCIETY, THE : TIME OUT OF MIND (From Hellboy)
Dark Horse Comics: Apr, 2022 - No. 4, Oct, 2022 ($3.99, limited series)

1-4-Roberson-s/Mutti-a 4.00

BROADWAY HOLLYWOOD BLACKOUTS
Stanhall: Mar-Apr, 1954 - No. 3, July-Aug, 1954

	GD	VG	FN	VF	VF/NM	NM-
1	34	68	102	204	332	460
2,3	22	44	66	128	209	290

BROADWAY ROMANCES
Quality Comics Group: January, 1950 - No. 5, Sept, 1950

	GD	VG	FN	VF	VF/NM	NM-
1-Ward-c/a (9 pgs.); Gustavson-a	53	106	159	334	567	800
2-Ward-a (9 pgs.); photo-c	33	66	99	194	317	440
3-5: All-Photo-c	19	38	57	111	176	240

BROKEN ARROW (TV)
Dell Publishing Co.: No. 855, Oct, 1957 - No. 947, Nov, 1958

	GD	VG	FN	VF	VF/NM	NM-
Four Color 855 (#1)-Photo-c	7	14	21	44	82	120
Four Color 947-Photo-c	5	10	15	33	57	80

BROKEN CROSS, THE (See The Crusaders)

BROKEN MOON
American Gothic Press: Sept, 2015 - No. 4, Jan, 2016 ($3.99, limited series)

1-4-Steve Niles-s/Nat Jones-a; covers by Jones & Sanjulian 4.00

BROKEN PIECES
Aspen MLT: No. 0, Sept, 2011; Oct, 2011 - No. 5, Dec, 2012 ($2.50/$3.50, limited series)

0-($2.50)-Roslan-s/Kaneshiro-a; three covers 3.00
1-5: 1-($3.50)-Roslan-s/Kaneshiro-a; three covers 3.50

BROKEN TRINITY
Image Comics (Top Cow): July, 2008 - No. 3, Nov, 2008 ($2.99, limited series)

1-3-Witchblade, Darkness & Angelus app.; Marz-s/Sejic & Hester-a; two covers 3.00
...: Aftermath 1 (4/09, $2.99) Marz & Hill-s/Lucas & Kirkham-a 3.00
...: Angelus 1 (12/08, $2.99) Marz-s/Stelfreeze-a; two covers 3.00
...: Pandora's Box 1-6 (2/10 - No. 6, 4/11 $3.99) Tommy Lee Edwards-c 4.00
...: The Darkness 1 (8/08, $2.99) Hester-s/Lucas-a; two covers 3.00
...: Witchblade 1 (12/08, $2.99) Marz-s/Blake-a; two covers 3.00

BRONCHO BILL (See Comics On Parade, Sparkler & Tip Top Comics)
United Features Syndicate/Standard(Visual Editions) No. 5-on: 1939 - 1940; No. 5, 1?/48 - No. 16, 8?/50

	GD	VG	FN	VF	VF/NM	NM-
Single Series 2 ('39)	60	120	180	381	653	925
Single Series 19 ('40)(#2 on cvr)	47	94	141	296	498	700
5	17	34	51	100	158	215
6(4/48)-10(4/49)	12	24	36	67	94	120
11(6/49)-16	10	20	30	56	76	95

NOTE: *Schomburg c-6, 7, 9-13, 15, 16.*

BRONZE AGE BOOGIE
AHOY Comics: 2019 - No. 6, 2019 ($3.99, limited series)

1-6-Stuart Moore-s/Alberto Ponticelli-a 4.00

BROOKLYN ANIMAL CONTROL
IDW Publishing: Dec, 2015 ($7.99, square-bound, one-shot)

1-J.T. Petty-s/Stephen Thompson-a; werewolves in Brooklyn 8.00

BROOKS ROBINSON (See Baseball's Greatest Heroes #2)

Briggs Land #1 © Brian Wood

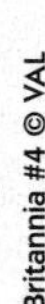
Britannia #4 © VAL

BRZRKR #8 © 74850 Inc.

GD 2.0 | VG 4.0 | FN 6.0 | VF 8.0 | VF/NM 9.0 | NM- 9.2

BROTHER BILLY THE PAIN FROM PLAINS
Marvel Comics Group: 1979 (68pgs.)

1-B&W comics, satire, Jimmy Carter-c & x-over w/Brother Billy peanut jokes. Joey Adams-a (scarce) 5 10 15 31 53 75

BROTHERHOOD, THE (Also see X-Men titles)
Marvel Comics: July, 2001 - No. 9, Mar, 2002 ($2.25)

1-Intro. Orwell & the Brotherhood; Ribic-a/X-s/Sienkiewicz-c 3.00
2-9: 2-Two covers (JG Jones & Sienkiewicz). 4-6-Fabry-c. 7-9-Phillips-c/a 3.00

BROTHER POWER, THE GEEK (See Saga of Swamp Thing Annual & Vertigo Visions)
National Periodical Publications: Sept-Oct, 1968 - No. 2, Nov-Dec, 1968

1-Origin; Simon-c(i?) 5 10 15 34 60 85
2 3 6 9 19 30 40

BROTHERS DRACUL
AfterShock Comics: Apr, 2018 - No. 5, Aug, 2018 ($3.99, limited series)

1-5-Cullen Bunn-s/Mirko Colak-a 4.00

BROTHERS, HANG IN THERE, THE
Spire Christian Comics (Fleming H. Revell Co.): 1979 (49¢)

nn 2 4 6 13 18 22

BROTHERS IN ARMS (Based on the World War II military video game)
Dynamite Entertainment: 2008 - No. 4, 2008 ($3.99/$3.50)

1-($3.99) Fabbri-a; two covers by Fabbri & Sejic 4.00
2-4-($3.50) Two covers by Fabbri & Sejic on each 3.50

BROTHERS OF THE SPEAR (Also see Tarzan)
Gold Key/Whitman No. 18: June, 1972 - No. 17, Feb, 1976; No. 18, May, 1982

1 5 10 15 31 53 75
2-Painted-c begin, end #17 3 6 9 18 28 38
3-10 3 6 9 15 22 28
11-18: 12-Line drawn-c. 13-17-Spiegle-a. 18(5/82)-r/#2; Leopard Girl-r 2 4 6 11 16 20

BROTHERS, THE CULT ESCAPE, THE
Spire Christian Comics (Fleming H. Revell Co.): 1980 (49¢)

nn 3 6 9 14 19 24

BROWNIES (See New Funnies)
Dell Publishing Co.: No. 192, July, 1948 - No. 605, Dec, 1954

Four Color 192(#1)-Kelly-a 14 28 42 96 211 325
Four Color 244(9/49), 293 (9/50)-Last Kelly c/a 10 20 30 68 144 220
Four Color 337(7-8/51), 365(12-1/51-52), 398(5/52) 6 12 18 38 69 100
Four Color 436(11/52), 482(7/53), 522(12/53), 605 5 10 15 35 63 90

BRUCE GENTRY
Better/Standard/Four Star Publ./Superior No. 3: Jan, 1948 - No. 8, Jul, 1949

1-Ray Bailey strip reprints begin, end #3; E.C. emblem appears as a monogram on stationery in story; negligee panels 84 168 252 538 919 1300
2,3: 2-Negligee panels 43 86 129 271 461 650
4-8 32 64 96 188 307 425
NOTE: *Kamenish a-2-7; c-1-8.*

BRUCE JONES' OUTER EDGE
Innovation: 1993 ($2.50, B&W, one-shot)

1-Bruce Jones-c/a/script 3.00

BRUCE LEE (Also see Deadly Hands of Kung Fu)
Malibu Comics: July, 1994 - No. 6, Dec, 1994 ($2.95, 36 pgs.)

1-6: 1-(44 pgs.)-Mortal Kombat prev., 1st app. in comics. 2,6-(36 pgs.) 6.00

BRUCE WAYNE: AGENT OF S.H.I.E.L.D. (Also see Marvel Vs. DC #3 & DC Vs. Marvel #4)
Marvel Comics (Amalgam): Apr, 1996 ($1.95, one-shot)

1-Chuck Dixon scripts & Cary Nord-c/a. 3.00

BRUCE WAYNE: THE ROAD HOME (See Batman: The Return of Bruce Wayne)
(See Batman: Bruce Wayne - The Road Home HC for reprints)
DC Comics: Dec, 2010 ($2.99, series of one-shots with interlocking covers)

...: Batgirl 1 - Bryan Miller-s/Pere Pérez-a 5.00
...: Batman and Robin 1 - Nicieza-s/Richards-a; Vicki Vale app. 5.00
...: Catwoman 1 - Fridolfs-s/Nguyen-a; Harley & Ivy app. 5.00
...: Commissioner Gordon 1 - Beechen-s/Kudranski-a; Penguin app. 5.00
...: Oracle 1 - Andreyko-s/Padilla-a; Man-Bat & Manhunter app. 5.00
...: Outsiders 1 - Barr-s/Saltares-a 5.00
...: Ra's al Ghul 1 - Nicieza-s/McDaniel-a 5.00
...: Red Robin 1 - Nicieza-s/Bachs-a; Ra's al Ghul app. 5.00

BRUTAL NATURE
IDW Publishing: May, 2016 - No. 4, Aug, 2016 ($3.99, limited series)

1-4-Ariel Olivetti-a/Luciano Saracino-s 4.00

BRUTAL NATURE: CONCRETE FURY
IDW Publishing: Mar, 2017 - No. 5, Jul, 2017 ($3.99, limited series)

1-5-Ariel Olivetti-a/Luciano Saracino-s 4.00

BRUTE, THE
Seaboard Publ. (Atlas): Feb, 1975 - No. 3, July, 1975

1-Origin & 1st app; Sekowsky-a(p) 3 6 9 17 26 35
2-Sekowsky-a(p); Fleisher-s 2 4 6 11 16 20
3-Brunner/Starlin/Weiss-a(p) 2 4 6 13 18 22

BRUTE & BABE
Ominous Press: July, 1994 - No. 2, Aug, 1994

1-($3.95, 8 tablets plus-c)-"...It Begins..."; tablet format 4.00
2-($2.50, 36 pgs.)-"Mael's Rage", 2-(40 pgs.)-Stiff additional variant-c 3.00

BRUTE FORCE
Marvel Comics: Aug, 1990 - No. 4, Nov, 1990 ($1.00, limited series)

1-4: Animal super-heroes; Delbo & DeCarlo-a 3.00

BRZRKR
BOOM! Studios: Feb, 2021 - No. 12 ($4.99/$3.99, limited series)

1-($4.99) Keanu Reeves & Matt Kindt-s/Ron Garney-a 1 3 4 6 8 10
2-($3.99) Origin story 1 3 4 6 8 10
3-11-($3.99) 3-Origin story continues 4.00

B-SIDES (The Craptacular...)
Marvel Comics: Nov, 2002 - No. 3, Jan, 2003 ($2.99, limited series)

1-3-Kieth-c/Weldele-a. 2-Dorkin-a (1 pg.) 2-FF cameo. 3-FF app. 3.00

BUBBA HO-TEP AND THE COSMIC BLOODSUCKERS
IDW Publications: Mar, 2018 - No. 5, Jul, 2018 ($3.99, limited series)

1-5-Jabcuga-s/Galusha-a; Elvis Presley vs. vampires and voodoo; Nixon app. 4.00

BUBBLEGUM CRISIS: GRAND MAL
Dark Horse Comics: Mar, 1994 - No. 4, June, 1994 ($2.50, limited series)

1-4-Japanese manga 4.00

BUBBLEGUN
Aspen MLT: Jun, 2013 - No. 5, Mar, 2014 ($1.00/$3.99)

1-($1.00) Roslan-s/Bowden-a; multiple covers 3.00
2-5-($3.99) Multiple covers on each 4.00

BUBBLEGUN (Volume 2)
Aspen MLT: May, 2017 - No. 5, Sept, 2017 ($3.99)

1-5-Roslan-s/Tovar-a; multiple covers 4.00

BUCCANEER
I. W. Enterprises: No date (1963)

I.W. Reprint #1(r-/Quality #20), #8(r-/#23): Crandall-a in each 3 6 9 17 26 35

BUCCANEERS (Formerly Kid Eternity)
Quality Comics: No. 19, Jan, 1950 - No. 27, May, 1951 (No. 24-27: 52 pgs.)

19-Captain Daring, Black Roger, Eric Falcon & Spanish Main begin; Crandall-a 52 104 156 328 552 775
20,23-Crandall-a 37 74 111 222 361 500
21-Crandall-c/a 40 80 120 246 411 575
22-Bondage-c 29 58 87 170 278 385
24-26: 24-Adam Peril, U.S.N. begins. 25-Origin & 1st app. Corsair Queen. 26-Last Spanish Main 24 48 72 142 234 325
27-Crandall-c/a 37 74 111 218 354 490
Super Reprint #12 (1964)-Crandall-r/#21 3 6 9 16 23 30

BUCCANEERS, THE (TV)
Dell Publishing Co.: No. 800, 1957

Four Color 800-Photo-c 6 12 18 42 79 115

BUCKAROO BANZAI (Movie)
Marvel Comics Group: Dec, 1984 - No. 2, Feb, 1985

1-Movie adaptation; r/Marvel Super Special #33; Texiera-c/a 1 3 4 6 8 10
2-Adaptation continues 6.00

BUCKAROO BANZAI: RETURN OF THE SCREW
Moonstone: 2006 - No. 3, 2006 ($3.50, limited series)

1-3: 1-Three covers by Haley, Stribling, Beck; Thompson-a 3.50
Preview (2006, 50¢) B&W preview; history of movie and spin-off projects 3.00

GD VG FN VF VF/NM NM-
2.0 4.0 6.0 8.0 9.0 9.2

BUCK DUCK
Atlas Comics (ANC): June, 1953 - No. 4, Dec, 1953
1-Funny animal stories in all 22 44 66 128 209 290
2-4: 2-Ed Win-a(5) 14 28 42 80 115 150

BUCK JONES (Also see Crackajack Funnies, Famous Feature Stories, Master Comics #7 & Wow Comics #1, 1936)
Dell Publishing Co.: No. 299, Oct, 1950 - No. 850, Oct, 1957 (All Painted-c)
Four Color 299(#1)-Buck Jones & his horse Silver-B begin; painted back-c begins, ends #5
14 28 42 93 204 315
2(4-6/51) 7 14 21 49 92 135
3-8(10-12/52) 6 12 18 38 69 100
Four Color 460,500,546,589 6 12 18 42 79 115
Four Color 652,733,850 5 10 15 35 63 90

BUCK ROGERS (Also see Famous Funnies, Pure Oil Comics, Salerno Carnival of Comics, 24 Pages of Comics, & Vicks Comics)
Famous Funnies: Winter, 1940-41 - No. 6, Sept, 1943
NOTE: Buck Rogers first appeared in the pulp magazine Amazing Stories Vol. 3 #5 in Aug, 1928.
1-Sunday strip reprints by Rick Yager; begins with strip #190; Calkins-c
365 730 1095 2555 4478 6400
2 (7/41)-Calkins-c 148 296 444 947 1624 2300
3 (12/41), 4 (7/42) 123 246 369 787 1344 1900
5,6: 5-Story continues with Famous Funnies No. 80; Buck Rogers, Sky Roads. 6-Reprints of 1939 dailies; contains B.R. story "Crater of Doom" (2 pgs.) by Calkins not-r from Famous Funnies 103 206 309 659 1130 1600

BUCK ROGERS
Toby Press: No. 100, Jan, 1951 - No. 9, May-June, 1951
100(#7)-All strip-r begin; Anderson, Chatton-a 36 72 108 211 343 475
101(#8), 9-All Anderson-a(1947-49-r/dailies) 24 54 81 160 263 365

BUCK ROGERS (...in the 25th Century No. 5 on) (TV)
Gold Key/Whitman No. 7 on: Oct, 1964; No. 2, July, 1979 - No. 16, May, 1982 (No #10; story was written but never released. #17 exists only as a press proof without covers and was never published)
1(10128-410, 12¢)-1st S.A. app. Buck Rogers & 1st new B. R. in comics since 1933 giveaway; painted-c; back-c pin-up 13 26 39 86 188 290
2(7/79)-6: 3,4,6-Movie adaptation; painted-c 2 4 6 11 16 20
7,11 (Whitman) 3 6 9 14 19 24
8,9 (prepack)(scarce) 5 10 15 34 60 85
12-16: 14(2/82), 15(3/82), 16(5/82) 2 4 6 8 10 12
Giant Movie Edition 11296(64pp, Whitman, $1.50), reprints GK #2-4 minus cover; tabloid size; photo-c (See Marvel Treasury) 3 6 9 17 26 35
Giant Movie Edition 02489(Western/Marvel, $1.50), reprints GK #2-4 minus cover
3 6 9 16 24 32
NOTE: *Bolle a-2p,3p, Movie Ed.(p). McWilliams a-2i,3i, 5-11, Movie Ed.(i). Painted c-1-9,11-13.*

BUCK ROGERS (Comics Module)
TSR, Inc.: 1990 - No. 10, 1991 ($2.95, 44 pgs.)
1-10 (1990): 1-Begin origin in 3 parts. 2-Indicia says #1. 2,3-Black Barney back-up story. 4-All Black Barney issue; B. B.-c. 5-Indicia says #6; Black Barney-c & lead story; Buck Rogers back-up story. 10-Flip book (72pgs.) 4.00

BUCK ROGERS
Dynamite Entertainment: No. 0, 2009 - No. 12, 2010 (25¢/$3.50)
0-(25¢) Beatty-s/Rafael-a/Cassaday-c 3.00
1-12: 1-($3.50) Three covers by Cassaday, Ross and Wagner; origin re-told 3.50
Annual 1 (2011, $4.99) Rafael-a; covers by Rafael & Sadowski 5.00

BUCK ROGERS
Hermes Press: 2013 - No. 4, 2013 ($3.99)
1-4-Howard Chaykin-s/a/c 4.00

BUCKSKIN (TV)
Dell Publishing Co.: No. 1011, July, 1959 - No. 1107, June-Aug, 1960
Four Color 1011 (#1)-Photo-c 7 14 21 44 82 120
Four Color 1107-Photo-c 6 12 18 40 73 105

BUCKY BARNES: THE WINTER SOLDIER (See Captain America titles)
Marvel Comics: Dec, 2014 - No. 11, Nov, 2015 ($3.99)
1-11: 1-Ales Kot-s/Marco Rudy-a; Daisy Johnson app. 2,8,9,10-Loki app. 4-7,9-Crossbones app. 7-Foss-a 4.00

BUCKY O'HARE (Funny Animal)
Continuity Comics: 1986 ($5.95, graphic novel)
1-Golden-c/a(r); r/serial-Echo of Futurepast #1-6 3 6 9 14 20 26
Deluxe Hardcover ($40.00, 52 pg., 8 x 11") 40.00

BUCKY O'HARE
Continuity Comics: Jan, 1991 - No. 5, 1991 ($2.00)
1-Michael Golden-c/a 3 6 9 14 19 24
2 1 2 3 5 6 8
3-6 4.00

BUDDIES IN THE U.S. ARMY
Avon Periodicals: Nov, 1952 - No. 2, 1953
1-Lawrence-c 43 86 129 271 461 650
2-Mort Lawrence-c/a 18 36 54 105 165 225

BUFFALO BEE (TV)
Dell Publishing Co.: No. 957, Nov, 1958 - No. 1061, Dec-Feb, 1959-60
Four Color 957 (#1) 9 18 27 59 117 175
Four Color 1002 (8-10/59), 1061 6 12 18 42 79 115

BUFFALO BILL (See Frontier Fighters, Super Western Comics & Western Action Thrillers)
Youthful Magazines: No. 2, Oct, 1950 - No. 9, Dec, 1951
2-Annie Oakley story 15 30 45 86 133 180
3-9: 2-4-Walter Johnson-c/a. 9-Wildey-a 11 22 33 62 86 110

BUFFALO BILL CODY (See Cody of the Pony Express)

BUFFALO BILL, JR. (TV) (See Western Roundup)
Dell/Gold Key: Jan, 1956 - No. 13, Aug-Oct, 1959; 1965 (All photo-c)
Four Color 673 (#1) 9 18 27 62 126 190
Four Color 742,766,798,828,856(11/57) 6 12 18 37 66 95
7(2-4/58)-13 5 10 15 31 53 75
1(6/65, Gold Key)-Photo-c(r/F.C. #798); photo-b/c 4 8 12 23 37 50

BUFFALO BILL PICTURE STORIES
Street & Smith Publications: June-July, 1949 - No. 2, Aug-Sept, 1949
1,2-Wildey, Powell-a in each 15 30 45 85 130 175

BUFFY '97
BOOM! Studios: Jun, 2022 ($7.99, one-shot)
1-Lambert-s/Ignazzi-a 8.00

BUFFY: THE HIGH SCHOOL YEARS (Based on the TV series)
Dark Horse Comics
... – Glutton For Punishment (10/16, $10.99, 6" x 9") McDonald-s/Li-a 11.00
... – Parental Parasite (6/17, $10.99, 6" x 9") McDonald-s/Li-a 11.00

BUFFY THE LAST VAMPIRE SLAYER
BOOM! Studios: Dec, 2021 - No. 4, Mar, 2022 ($4.99, limited series)
1-4-Set 50 years in the future; Gilly-s/Jaro-a 5.00
... Special 1 (3/23, $7.99) Thessaly & Spike app.; Gilly-s/Jaro-a 8.00

BUFFY THE VAMPIRE SLAYER (Based on the TV series)(Also see Angel and Faith, Spike, Tales of the Vampires and Willow)
Dark Horse Comics: 1998 - No. 63, Nov, 2003 ($2.95/$2.99)
1-Bennett-a/Watson-s; Art Adams-c 2 4 6 10 14 18
1-Variant photo-c 2 4 6 11 16 20
1-Gold foil logo Art Adams-c 18.00
1-Gold foil logo photo-c 20.00
2-4-Photo-c 1 3 4 6 8 10
5-15-Regular and photo-c. 4-7-Gomez-a. 5,8-Green-c 5.00
16-49: 29,30-Angel x-over. 43-45-Death of Buffy. 47-Lobdell-s begin. 48-Pike returns 3.00
50-($3.50) Scooby gang battles Adam; back-up story by Watson 4.00
51-63: 51-54-Viva Las Buffy; pre-Sunnydale Buffy & Pike in Vegas 3.00
Annual '99 ($4.95)-Two stories and pin-ups 1 2 3 4 5 7
...: A Stake to the Heart TPB (3/04, $12.95) r/#60-63 13.00
...: Chaos Bleeds (6/03, $2.99) Based on the video game; photo & Campbell-c 3.00
...: Creatures of Habit (3/02, $17.95) text with Horton & Paul Lee-a 18.00
...: Jonathan 1 (1/01, $2.99) two covers; Richards-a 3.00
...: Lost and Found 1 (3/02, $2.99) aftermath of Buffy's death; Richards-a 3.00
... Lovers Walk (2/01, $2.99) short stories by various; Richards & photo-c 3.00
...: Note From the Underground (3/03, $12.95) r/#47-50 13.00
...: Omnibus Vol. 1 (7/07, $24.95, 9x6") r/Spike & Dru #3, Origin #1-3 and Buffy #51-59 25.00
...: Omnibus Vol. 2 (9/07, $24.95, 9x6") r/Buffy #60-63 and various one-shots & specials 25.00
...: Omnibus Vol. 3 (1/08, $24.95, 9x6") r/Buffy #1-8,12,16, Annual '99 25.00
...: Omnibus Vol. 4 (5/08, $24.95, 9x6") r/Buffy #9-11,13-15,17-20,50 and various 25.00
...: Omnibus Vol. 5 (9/08, $24.95, 9x6") r/Buffy #21-28 and various one-shots & specials 25.00
...: Omnibus Vol. 6 (2/09, $24.95, 9x6") r/Buffy #29-38 and various one-shots & specials 25.00
...: One For One (9/10, $1.00) r/#1 with red cover frame 3.00
...: Reunion (6/02, $3.50) Buffy & Angel's; Espenson-s; art by various 3.50
...: Slayer Interrupted TPB (2003, $14.95) r/#56-59 15.00
...: Tales of the Slayers (10/02, $3.50) art by Matsuda and Colan; art & photo-c 3.50
...: The Death of Buffy TPB (8/02, $15.95) r/#43-46 16.00
...: Viva Las Buffy TPB (7/03, $12.95) r/#51-54 13.00
Wizard #1/2 1 2 3 6 8 9

BUFFY THE VAMPIRE SLAYER ("Season Eight" of the TV series)
Dark Horse Comics: Mar, 2007 - No. 40, Jan, 2011 ($2.99)
1-Joss Whedon-s/Georges Jeanty-a/Jo Chen-c 6.00
1-Variant cover by Jeanty 6.00
1-RRP with B&W Jeanty cover (edition of 1000) 85.00
1-4: 1-2nd thru 5th printings. 2-2nd-4th printings. 3,4-2nd & 3rd printings 3.00
2-5-Jeanty-a; covers by Chen & Jeanty 4.00
6-13,16-19-Two covers by Chen & Jeanty. 6-9-Faith app.; Vaughan-s. 10,11-Whedon-s. 12-15-Goddard-s; Dracula app. 16-19-Fray app.; Whedon-s/Moline-a 3.00
20-40: 20-28,31-40-Two covers by Chen and Jeanty. 20-Animation style flashback. 21,26-30-Espenson-s. 30-Hughes-c. 31-Whedon-s. 32-35-Meltzer-s. 36-40-Whedon-s 3.00
...: Riley (8/10, $3.50) Espensen-s/Moline-a; Riley Finn and Sam; Angel app. 3.50
... Tales of the Vampires (6/09, $2.99) Cloonan-s/Lolos-a; covers by Chen & Bá/Moon 3.00
...: Willow (12/09, $3.50) Whedon-s/Moline-a; Willow meets the Snake Guide 3.50

BUFFY THE VAMPIRE SLAYER ("Season Nine" of the TV series)
Dark Horse Comics: Sept, 2011 - No. 25, Sept, 2013 ($2.99)
1-25: 1-Whedon-s/Jeanty-a; covers by Morris & Chen. 2-5-Chambliss-s; two covers by Morris & Jeanty. 5-Moline-a; Nikki flashback. 6,7-Two covers by Jeanty & Noto. 8-10-Richards-a. 14-Espenson-s; intro. Billy. 16-19-Illyria app. 3.00
....: Buffyverse Sampler (1/13, $4.99) r/#1, Angel & Faith #1, Spike #1, Willow #1 5.00
FCBD (5/12, giveaway) Buffy vs. Alien; Jeanty-a; flip book with The Guild 3.00

BUFFY THE VAMPIRE SLAYER (SEASON TEN)
Dark Horse Comics: Mar, 2014 - No. 30, Aug, 2016 ($3.50/$3.99)
1-16: 1-Gage-s/Isaacs-a; covers by Morris & Isaacs. 2-5-Dracula app. 3-5,7,12,13-Nicholas Brendon & Gage-s. 8-Corben-a (3 pgs) 3.50
17-30-($3.99) 19-Nicholas Brendon & Gage-s. 25-Levens-a 4.00

BUFFY THE VAMPIRE SLAYER SEASON ELEVEN
Dark Horse Comics: Nov, 2016 - No. 12, Oct, 2017 ($3.99)
1-12: 1-Gage-s/Isaacs-a; covers by Morris & Isaacs. 5,9-Jeanty-a 4.00

BUFFY THE VAMPIRE SLAYER SEASON 12
Dark Horse Comics: Jun, 2018 - No. 4, Sept, 2018 ($3.99)
1-4-Gage & Whedon-s/Jeanty-a; Melaka Fray, Angel, Illyria app. 4.00

BUFFY THE VAMPIRE SLAYER
Dark Horse Comics: Jan, 2019 - No. 34, Feb, 2022 ($3.99)
1-24: 1-Rebooted Buffy first meets the Scooby gang in high school; Bellaire-s/Mora-a. 4-Xander attacked. 5-12-David López-a. 8-12-Hellmouth x-over with Angel #5-8. 10-Intro. Kendra. 11-Intro. Anya. 13-Valero-O'Connell-a. 19-Faith arrives 4.00

Buck Rogers (2013) #4 © Dille Family

Buffy the Vampire Slayer (2011) #17 © 20-FOX

Bugs Bunny #47 © WB

	GD 2.0	VG 4.0	FN 6.0	VF 8.0	VF/NM 9.0	NM- 9.2
25-($4.99) Scoobies travel to the 1998 TV series reality						5.00
26-34						4.00
...: Chosen Ones 1 (8/19, $7.99) Short stories of previous slayers						8.00
...: Every Generation 1 (4/20, $7.99) Short stories of previous slayers; Andolfo-c						8.00
...: Faith 1 (2/21, $7.99) Lambert-s/Carlini-a; flashbacks to childhood and recruitment						8.00
...: Tea Time 1 (6/21, $7.99) Mirka Andolfo-s/Siya Oum-a; "What If" Giles was a vampire						8.00

BUFFY THE VAMPIRE SLAYER: ANGEL
Dark Horse Comics: May, 1999 - No. 3, July, 1999 ($2.95, limited series)

1-Gomez-a; Matsuda-c & photo-c for each	1	2	3	5	6	8
2,3						4.00

BUFFY THE VAMPIRE SLAYER: GILES
Dark Horse Comics: Oct, 2000 ($2.95, one-shot)

1-Eric Powell-a; Powell & photo-c 4.00

BUFFY THE VAMPIRE SLAYER: HAUNTED
Dark Horse Comics: Dec, 2001 - No. 4, Mar, 2002 ($2.99, limited series)

1-4-Faith and the Mayor app.; Espenson-s/Richards-a 4.00
TPB (9/02, $12.95) r/series; photo-c 13.00

BUFFY THE VAMPIRE SLAYER: OZ
Dark Horse Comics: July, 2001 - No. 3, Sept, 2001 ($2.99, limited series)

1-3-Totleben & photo-c; Golden-s 4.00

BUFFY THE VAMPIRE SLAYER: SPIKE AND DRU
Dark Horse Comics: Apr, 1999; No. 2, Oct, 1999; No. 3, Dec, 2000 ($2.95)

1-Photo-c	1	2	3	5	6	8
2,3: 2-Photo-c. 3-Two covers (photo & Sook)						4.00

BUFFY THE VAMPIRE SLAYER: THE ORIGIN (Adapts movie screenplay)
Dark Horse Comics: Jan, 1999 - No. 3, Mar, 1999 ($2.95, limited series)

1-3-Brereton-s/Bennett-a; reg & photo-c for each 4.00

BUFFY THE VAMPIRE SLAYER 25th ANNIVERSARY SPECIAL
BOOM! Studios: Mar, 2022 ($9.99, one-shot)

1-Short stories by various; Frany-c 10.00

BUFFY THE VAMPIRE SLAYER: WILLOW
BOOM! Studios: Jul, 2020 - No. 5, Nov, 2020 ($3.99, limited series)

1-5-Mariko Tamaki-s/Natacha Bustos-a 4.00

BUFFY THE VAMPIRE SLAYER: WILLOW & TARA
Dark Horse Comics: Apr, 2001 ($2.99, one-shot)

1-Terry Moore-a/Chris Golden & Amber Benson-s; Moore-c & photo-c 4.00
TPB (4/03, $9.95) r/#1 & W&T - Wilderness; photo-c 10.00

BUFFY THE VAMPIRE SLAYER: WILLOW & TARA - WILDERNESS
Dark Horse Comics: Jul, 2002 - No. 2, Sept, 2002 ($2.99, limited series)

1,2-Chris Golden & Amber Benson-s; Jothikaumar-c & photo-c 4.00

BUG
Marvel Comics: Mar, 1997 ($2.99, one-shot)

1-Micronauts character	2	4	6	9	12	15

BUGALOOS (Sid & Marty Krofft TV show)
Charlton Comics: Sept, 1971 - No. 4, Feb, 1972

1	5	10	15	35	63	90
2-4	3	6	9	21	33	45

NOTE: *No. 3(1/72) went on sale late in 1972 (after No. 4) with the 1/73 issues.*

BUGHOUSE (Satire)
Ajax/Farrell (Excellent Publ.): Mar-Apr, 1954 - No. 4, Sept-Oct, 1954

V1#1	31	62	93	182	296	410
2-4	17	34	51	100	158	215

BUGS BUNNY (See The Best of..., Camp Comics, Comic Album #2, 6, 10, 14, Dell Giant #28, 32, 46, Dynabrite, Golden Comics Digest #1, 3, 5, 6, 8, 10, 14, 15, 17, 21, 26, 30, 34, 39, 42, 47, Kite Fun Book, Large Feature Comic #8, Looney Tunes and Merry Melodies, March of Comics #44, 59, 75, 83, 97, 115, 132, 149, 160, 179, 188, 201, 220, 231, 245, 259, 273, 287, 301, 315, 329, 343, 363, 367, 380, 392, 403, 415, 428, 440, 452, 464, 476, 487, Porky Pig, Puffed Wheat, Story Hour Series #802, Super Book #14, 26 and Whitman Comic Books)

BUGS BUNNY (See Dell Giants for annuals)
Dell Publishing Co./Gold Key No. 86-218/Whitman No. 219 on: 1942 - No. 245, April, 1984

Large Feature Comic 8(1942)-(Rarely found in fine-mint condition)	300	600	900	1950	3375	4800
Four Color 33 ('43) Bondage/torture-c	125	250	375	1000	2250	3500
Four Color 51	39	78	117	289	657	1025
Four Color 88-Sci-fi-c	25	50	75	175	388	600
Four Color 123('46),142,164	17	34	51	117	259	400
Four Color 187,200,217,233	12	24	36	84	185	285
Four Color 250-Used in **SOTI**, pg. 309	13	26	39	89	195	300
Four Color 266,274,281,289,298('50)	10	20	30	67	141	215
Four Color 307,317(#1),327(#2),338,347,355,366,376,393	9	18	27	59	117	175
Four Color 407,420,432(10/52)	8	16	24	54	102	150
Four Color 498(9/53),585(9/54),647(9/55)	6	12	18	41	76	110
Four Color 724(9/56),838(9/57),1064(12/59)	5	10	15	34	60	85
28(12-1/52-53)-30	5	10	15	34	60	85
31-50	4	8	12	28	47	65
51-85(7-9/62)	4	8	12	23	37	50
86(10/62)-88-Bugs Bunny's Showtime-(25¢, 80pgs.)	5	10	15	35	63	90
89-99	3	6	9	16	24	32
100	3	6	9	17	26	35
101-118: 108-1st Honey Bunny. 118-Last 12¢ issue	3	6	9	14	19	24
119-140	2	4	6	11	16	20
141-170	2	4	6	9	12	15
171-218: 218-Publ. by Whitman only?	2	4	6	8	10	12
219,220,225-237(5/82): 229-Swipe of Barks story/WDC&S #223. 233(2/82)	2	4	6	8	10	12
221(9/80),222(11/80)-Pre-pack? (Scarce)	4	8	12	28	47	65
223 (1/81, 50¢-c), 224 (3/81)-Low distr.	3	6	9	14	20	25
223 (1/81, 40¢-c) Cover price error variant	3	6	9	17	26	35
238-245 (#90070 on-c, nd, nd code; pre-pack): 238(5/83), 239(6/83), 240(7/83), 241(7/83), 242(8/83), 243(8/83), 244(3/84), 245(4/84)	3	6	9	15	22	28

NOTE: *Reprints-100,102-104,110,115,123,143,144,147,167,173,175-177,179-185,187,190.*

nn (Xerox Pub. Comic Digest, 1971, 100 pages, B&W) collection of one-page gags	4	8	12	23	37	50
...Comic-Go-Round 11196-(224 pgs.)($1.95)(Golden Press, 1979)	4	8	12	25	40	55
...Winter Fun 1(12/67-Gold Key)-Giant	5	10	15	30	50	70

BUGS BUNNY
DC Comics: June, 1990 - No. 3, Aug, 1990 ($1.00, limited series)

1-3: Daffy Duck, Elmer Fudd, others app. 5.00

BUGS BUNNY (...Monthly on-c)
DC Comics: 1993 - No. 3, 1994? ($1.95)

1-3-Bugs, Porky Pig, Daffy, Road Runner 3.50

BUGS BUNNY (Digest-size reprint from Looney Tunes)
DC Comics: 2005 ($6.99, digest)

Vol. 1: What's Up Doc? - Reprints from Looney Tunes #37,41,43-45,48,52,55,57-59,63 7.00

BUGS BUNNY & PORKY PIG
Gold Key: Sept, 1965 (Paper-c, giant, 100 pgs.)

1(30025-509)	6	12	18	38	69	100

BUGS BUNNY'S ALBUM (See Bugs Bunny, Four Color No. 498,585,647,724)

BUGS BUNNY LIFE STORY ALBUM (See Bugs Bunny, Four Color No. 838)

BUGS BUNNY MERRY CHRISTMAS (See Bugs Bunny, Four Color No. 1064)

BUG! THE ADVENTURES OF FORAGER (From New Gods)
DC Comics (Young Animal): Jul, 2017 - No. 6, Feb, 2018 ($3.99)

1-6-Lee Allred-s/Mike Allred-a/c. 1-Sandman, Brute & Glob app. 2-G.A. Sandman, Sandy, Blue Beetle and The Losers app. 3-Atlas app. 5-Omac app. 4.00

BUILDING, THE
Kitchen Sink Press: 1987; 2000 (8 1/2" x 11" sepia toned graphic novel)

nn-Will Eisner-s/c/a 15.00
nn-(DC Comics, 9/00, $9.95) reprints 1987 edition 10.00

BULLET CROW, FOWL OF FORTUNE
Eclipse Comics: Mar, 1987 - No. 2, Apr, 1987 ($2.00, B&W, limited series)

1,2-The Comic Reader-r & new-a 6.00

BULLETMAN (See Fawcett Miniatures, Master Comics, Mighty Midget Comics, Nickel Comics & XMas Comics)
Fawcett Publications: Sum, 1941 - #12, 2/12/43; #14, Spr, 1946 - #16, Fall, 1946 (No #13)

1-Silver metallic-c	411	822	1233	2877	5039	7200
2-Raboy-c	184	368	552	1178	2014	2850
3,5-Raboy-c each	145	290	435	921	1586	2250
4	100	200	300	635	1093	1550
6,8,9	87	174	261	553	952	1350
7-Ghost Stories told by night watchman of cemetery begins; Eisnerish-a; hidden message "Chic Stone is a jerk".	97	194	291	621	1061	1475
10-Intro. Bulletdog	95	190	285	603	1039	1475
11,12,14-16 (nn 13): 12-Robot-c	63	126	189	403	689	975

NOTE: ***Mac Raboy** c-1-3, 5, 6, 10. "Bulletman the Flying Detective" on cover #8 on.*

BULLET POINTS
Marvel Comics: Jan, 2007 - No. 5, May, 2007 ($2.99, limited series)

	GD 2.0	VG 4.0	FN 6.0	VF 8.0	VF/NM 9.0	NM- 9.2
1-5: 1-Steve Rogers becomes Iron Man; Straczynski-s/Edwards-a. 4,5-Galactus app.						3.00
TPB (2007, $13.99) r/#1-5; layout pages by Edwards						14.00

BULLETPROOF MONK (Inspired the 2003 film)
Image Comics (Flypaper Press): 1998 - No. 3, 1999 ($2.95, limited series)

	GD 2.0	VG 4.0	FN 6.0	VF 8.0	VF/NM 9.0	NM- 9.2
1-3-Oeming-a						3.00
...: Tales of the BPM (3/03, $2.95) Flip book; 2 covers by Sale; art by Sale, Oeming, Dave Johnson; Seann William Scott afterword						3.00
TPB (2002, $9.95) r/#1-3; foreword by John Woo						10.00

BULLETS AND BRACELETS (Also see Marvel Versus DC #3 & DC Versus Marvel #4)
Marvel Comics (Amalgam): Apr, 1996 ($1.95)

	GD 2.0	VG 4.0	FN 6.0	VF 8.0	VF/NM 9.0	NM- 9.2
1-John Ostrander script & Gary Frank-c/a						4.00

BULLSEYE (Daredevil villain)
Marvel Comics: Apr, 2017 - No. 5, Aug, 2017 ($4.99/$3.99, limited series)

	GD 2.0	VG 4.0	FN 6.0	VF 8.0	VF/NM 9.0	NM- 9.2
1-($4.99) Brisson-s/Sanna-a; back-up with Wolfman-s/Morgan-a						5.00
2-5-($3.99) Brisson-s/Sanna-a						4.00

BULLS-EYE (Cody of The Pony Express No. 8 on)
Mainline No. 1-5/Charlton No. 6,7: 7-8/54-No. 5, 3-4/55; No. 6, 6/55; No. 7, 8/55

	GD 2.0	VG 4.0	FN 6.0	VF 8.0	VF/NM 9.0	NM- 9.2
1-S&K-c, 2 pgs.-a	90	180	270	576	988	1400
2-S&K-c/a	65	130	195	416	708	1000
3-5-S&K-c/a(2 each). 4-Last pre-code issue (1-2/55). 5-Censored issue with tomahawks removed in battle scene	53	106	159	334	567	800
6-S&K-c/a	47	94	141	296	498	700
7-S&K-c/a(3)	53	106	159	334	567	800

BULLS-EYE COMICS (Formerly Komik Pages #10; becomes Kayo #12)
Harry 'A' Chesler: No. 11, 1944

	GD 2.0	VG 4.0	FN 6.0	VF 8.0	VF/NM 9.0	NM- 9.2
11-Origin K-9, Green Knight's sidekick, Lance; The Green Knight, Lady Satan, Yankee Doodle Jones app.	432	864	1296	3154	5577	8000

BULLSEYE: GREATEST HITS (Daredevil villain)
Marvel Comics: Nov, 2004 - No. 5, Mar, 2005 ($2.99, limted series)

	GD 2.0	VG 4.0	FN 6.0	VF 8.0	VF/NM 9.0	NM- 9.2
1-5-Origin of Bullseye; Steve Dillon-a/Deodato-c. 3-Punisher app.						3.00
TPB (2005, $13.99) r/#1-5						14.00

BULLSEYE: PERFECT GAME (Daredevil villain)
Marvel Comics: Jan, 2011 - No. 2, Feb, 2011 ($3.99, limited series)

	GD 2.0	VG 4.0	FN 6.0	VF 8.0	VF/NM 9.0	NM- 9.2
1,2-Huston-s/Martinbrough-a; Bullseye as baseball pitcher						4.00

BULLWHIP GRIFFIN (See Movie Comics)

BULLWINKLE (...and Rocky No. 22 on; See March of Comics #233 and Rocky & Bullwinkle) (TV) (Jay Ward)
Dell/Gold Key: 3-5/62 - #11, 4/74; #12, 6/76 - #19, 3/78; #20, 4/79 - #25, 2/80

	GD 2.0	VG 4.0	FN 6.0	VF 8.0	VF/NM 9.0	NM- 9.2
Four Color 1270 (3-5/62)	16	32	48	112	249	385
01-090-209 (Dell, 7-9/62)	13	26	39	89	195	300
1(11/62, Gold Key)	12	24	36	82	179	275
2(2/63)	8	16	24	54	102	150
3(4/72)-11(4/74-Gold Key)	5	10	15	31	53	75
12-14: 12(6/76)-Reprints. 13(9/76), 14-New stories	3	6	9	17	26	35
15-25	2	4	6	11	16	20
Mother Moose Nursery Pomes 01-530-207 (5-7/62, Dell)	16	32	48	107	236	365

NOTE: *Reprints: 6, 7, 20-24.*

BULLWINKLE AND ROCKY (TV)
Charlton Comics: July, 1970 - No. 7, July, 1971

	GD 2.0	VG 4.0	FN 6.0	VF 8.0	VF/NM 9.0	NM- 9.2
1-Has 1 pg. pin-up	6	12	18	42	79	115
2-7: 3-Snidely Whiplash app.	5	10	15	30	50	70

BULLWINKLE AND ROCKY
Star Comics/Marvel Comics No. 3 on: Nov, 1987 - No. 9, Mar, 1989

	GD 2.0	VG 4.0	FN 6.0	VF 8.0	VF/NM 9.0	NM- 9.2
1-9: Boris & Natasha in all. 3,5,8-Dudley Do-Right app. 4-Reagan-c						5.00
Marvel Moosterworks (1/92, $4.95)	2	4	6	8	10	12

BULLY WARS
Image Comics: Sept, 2018 - No. 5, Jan, 2019 ($3.99, limited series)

	GD 2.0	VG 4.0	FN 6.0	VF 8.0	VF/NM 9.0	NM- 9.2
1-5-Skottie Young-s/Aaron Conley-a						4.00

BUMMER
Fantagraphics Books: June, 1995 ($3.50, B&W, mature)

	GD 2.0	VG 4.0	FN 6.0	VF 8.0	VF/NM 9.0	NM- 9.2
1						3.50

BUNNY (Also see Harvey Pop Comics and Fruitman Special)
Harvey Publications: Dec, 1966 - No. 20, Dec, 1971; No. 21, Nov, 1976

	GD 2.0	VG 4.0	FN 6.0	VF 8.0	VF/NM 9.0	NM- 9.2
1-68 pg. Giants begin	7	14	21	49	92	135
2-10: 3-1st app. Fruitman. 6,8-10-Fruitman	4	8	12	28	47	65
11-18: 18-Last 68 pg. Giant	4	8	12	27	44	60
19-21-52 pg. Giants: 21-Fruitman app.	4	8	12	25	40	55

BUNNY MASK
AfterShock Comics: Jun, 2021 - No. 4, Sept, 2021 ($4.99, limited series)

	GD 2.0	VG 4.0	FN 6.0	VF 8.0	VF/NM 9.0	NM- 9.2
1-4-Paul Tobin-s/Andrea Mutti-a						5.00

BUNNY MASK VOL. 2 (... THE HOLLOW INSIDE on cover)
AfterShock Comics: May, 2022 - No. 4, Aug, 2022 ($4.99, limited series)

	GD 2.0	VG 4.0	FN 6.0	VF 8.0	VF/NM 9.0	NM- 9.2
1-4-Paul Tobin-s/Andrea Mutti-a						5.00

BURKE'S LAW (TV)
Dell Publ.: 1-3/64; No. 2, 5-7/64; No. 3, 3-5/65 (All have Gene Barry photo-c)

	GD 2.0	VG 4.0	FN 6.0	VF 8.0	VF/NM 9.0	NM- 9.2
1-Photo-c	5	10	15	31	53	75
2,3-Photo-c	4	8	12	23	37	50

BURNING FIELDS
BOOM! Studios: Jan, 2015 - No. 8, Sept, 2015 ($3.99, limited series)

	GD 2.0	VG 4.0	FN 6.0	VF 8.0	VF/NM 9.0	NM- 9.2
1-6-Moreci & Daniel-s/Lorimer-a						4.00

BURNING ROMANCES (See Fox Giants)

BURNOUTS
Image Comics: Sept, 2018 - No. 5, Jan, 2019 ($3.99)

	GD 2.0	VG 4.0	FN 6.0	VF 8.0	VF/NM 9.0	NM- 9.2
1-5-Dennis Culver-s/Geoffo-a						4.00

BUSTER BEAR
Quality Comics Group (Arnold Publ.): Dec, 1953 - No. 10, June, 1955

	GD 2.0	VG 4.0	FN 6.0	VF 8.0	VF/NM 9.0	NM- 9.2
1-Funny animal	14	28	42	80	115	150
2	8	16	24	40	50	60
3-10	6	12	18	31	38	45
I.W. Reprint #9,10 (Super on inside)	2	4	6	9	13	16

BUSTER BROWN COMICS (See Promotional Comics section)

BUSTER BUNNY
Standard Comics(Animated Cartoons)/Pines: Nov, 1949 - No. 16, Oct, 1953

	GD 2.0	VG 4.0	FN 6.0	VF 8.0	VF/NM 9.0	NM- 9.2
1-Frazetta 1 pg. text illo.	15	30	45	88	137	185
2	8	16	24	44	57	70
3-14,16	8	16	24	40	50	60
15-Racist-c	15	30	45	83	124	165

BUSTER CRABBE (TV)
Famous Funnies Publ.: Nov, 1951 - No. 12, 1953

	GD 2.0	VG 4.0	FN 6.0	VF 8.0	VF/NM 9.0	NM- 9.2
1-1st app.(?) Frazetta anti-drug ad; text story about Buster Crabbe & Billy the Kid	43	86	129	271	461	650
2-Williamson/Evans-c; text story about Wild Bill Hickok & Pecos Bill	39	78	117	240	395	550
3-Williamson/Evans-c/a	41	82	123	256	428	600
4-Frazetta-c/a, 1pg.; bondage-c	74	148	222	470	810	1150
5-Classic Frazetta sci-fi cover; Williamson/Krenkel/Orlando-a, 11pgs. (per Mr. Williamson)	194	388	582	1242	2121	3000
6,8	24	48	72	144	237	330
7-Frazetta one pg. ad	23	46	69	138	227	315
9-One pg. Frazetta Boy Scouts ad (1st?)	19	38	57	111	176	240
10-12	14	28	42	82	121	160

NOTE: Eastern Color sold 3 dozen each NM file copies of #s 9-12 a few years ago.

BUSTER CRABBE (The Amazing Adventures of...)(Movie star)
Lev Gleason Publications: Dec, 1953 - No. 4, June, 1954

	GD 2.0	VG 4.0	FN 6.0	VF 8.0	VF/NM 9.0	NM- 9.2
1,4: 1-Photo-c. 4-Flash Gordon-c	25	50	75	150	245	340
2,3-Toth-a	21	42	63	124	202	280

BUTCH CASSIDY
Skywald Comics: June, 1971 - No. 3, Oct, 1971 (52 pgs.)

	GD 2.0	VG 4.0	FN 6.0	VF 8.0	VF/NM 9.0	NM- 9.2
1-Pre-code reprints and new material; Red Mask reprint, retitled Maverick; Bolle-a; Sutton-a	3	6	9	15	22	28
2,3: 2-Whip Wilson-r. 3-Dead Canyon Days reprint/Crack Western No. 63; Sundance Kid app.; Crandall-a	2	4	6	10	14	18

BUTCH CASSIDY (...& the Wild Bunch)
Avon Periodicals: 1951

	GD 2.0	VG 4.0	FN 6.0	VF 8.0	VF/NM 9.0	NM- 9.2
1-Kinstler-c/a	27	54	81	160	263	365

NOTE: ***Reinman** story; Issue number on inside spine.*

BUTCH CASSIDY (See Fun-In No. 11 & Western Adventure Comics)

BUTCHER, THE (Also see Brave and the Bold, 2nd Series)
DC Comics: May, 1990 - No. 5, Sept, 1990 ($1.50, mature)

	GD 2.0	VG 4.0	FN 6.0	VF 8.0	VF/NM 9.0	NM- 9.2
1-5: 1-No indicia inside						3.00

BUTCHER KNIGHT
Image Comics (Top Cow): Jan, 2001 - No. 4, June, 2001 ($2.95, limited series)

	GD 2.0	VG 4.0	FN 6.0	VF 8.0	VF/NM 9.0	NM- 9.2
Preview (B&W, 16 pgs.) Dwayne Turner-c/a						3.00
1-4-Dwayne Turner-c/a						3.00

BUTCHER OF PARIS, THE
Dark Horse Comics: Dec, 2019 - No. 5, Apr, 2020 ($3.99, limited series)

	GD 2.0	VG 4.0	FN 6.0	VF 8.0	VF/NM 9.0	NM- 9.2
1-5-Serial killer in 1944 Paris; Stephanie Phillips-s/Dean Kotz-a						4.00

BUTTERFLY
Archaia: Sept, 2014 - No. 4, Dec, 2014 ($3.99, limited series)

	GD 2.0	VG 4.0	FN 6.0	VF 8.0	VF/NM 9.0	NM- 9.2
1-4: Phil Noto-c on all. 1-Marguerite Bennett-s/Antonio Fuso-a. 3,4-Simeone-a						4.00

BUZ SAWYER (Sweeney No. 4 on)
Standard Comics: June, 1948 - No. 3, 1949

	GD 2.0	VG 4.0	FN 6.0	VF 8.0	VF/NM 9.0	NM- 9.2
1-Roy Crane-a	30	60	90	177	289	400
2-Intro his pal Sweeney	17	34	51	98	154	210
3	13	26	39	72	101	130

BUZ SAWYER'S PAL, ROSCOE SWEENEY (See Sweeney)

BUZZ, THE (Also see Spider-Girl)
Marvel Comics: July, 2000 - No. 3, Sept, 2000 ($2.99, limited series)

	GD 2.0	VG 4.0	FN 6.0	VF 8.0	VF/NM 9.0	NM- 9.2
1-3-Buscema-a/DeFalco & Frenz-s						3.00

BUZZARD (See The Goon)
Dark Horse Comics: Jun, 2010 - No. 3, Aug, 2010 ($3.50, limited series)

	GD 2.0	VG 4.0	FN 6.0	VF 8.0	VF/NM 9.0	NM- 9.2
1-3-Eric Powell-c; Buzzard story w/Powell-s/a; Billy The Kid back-up; Powell-s/Hotz-a						3.50

BUZZ BUZZ COMICS MAGAZINE
Horse Press: May, 1996 ($4.95, B&W, over-sized magazine)

	GD 2.0	VG 4.0	FN 6.0	VF 8.0	VF/NM 9.0	NM- 9.2
1-Paul Pope-c/a/scripts; Moebius-a						5.00

BUZZY (See All Funny Comics)
National Periodical Publications/Detective Comics: Winter, 1944-45 - No. 75, 1-2/57; No. 76, 10/57; No. 77, 10/58

	GD 2.0	VG 4.0	FN 6.0	VF 8.0	VF/NM 9.0	NM- 9.2
1 (52 pgs. begin); "America's favorite teenster"	42	84	126	265	445	625
2 (Spr, 1945)	22	44	66	132	216	300
3-5	18	36	54	103	162	220
6-10	15	30	45	84	127	170
11-20	14	28	42	78	112	145
21-30	13	26	39	72	101	130
31,35-38	11	22	33	64	90	115
32-34,39-Last 52 pgs. Scribbly story by Mayer in each (these four stories were done for Scribbly #14 which was delayed for a year)	12	24	36	69	97	125

Bullseye (2017) #2 © MAR

By Night #2 © Allison & Larsen

Cable (2020) #7 © MAR

	GD 2.0	VG 4.0	FN 6.0	VF 8.0	VF/NM 9.0	NM- 9.2

40-77: 62-Last precode (2/55) 11 22 33 62 86 110

BUZZY THE CROW (See Harvey Comics Hits #60 & 62, Harvey Hits #18 & Paramount Animated Comics #1)

BY BIZARRE HANDS
Dark Horse Comics: Apr, 1994 - No. 3, June, 1994 ($2.50, B&W, mature)
1-3: Lansdale stories 3.00

BY NIGHT
Boom Entertainment (BOOM! Box): Jun, 2018 - No. 12, Jun, 2019 ($3.99)
1-12-John Allison-s/Christine Larsen-a 4.00

BYTE-SIZED
AWA, Inc.: Dec, 2020 - No. 4, Mar, 2021 ($3.99, limited series)
1-4-Cullen Bunn-s/Nelson Blake II-a 4.00

CABBOT: BLOODHUNTER (Also see Bloodstrike & Bloodstrike: Assassin)
Maximum Press: Jan, 1997 ($2.50, one-shot)
1-Rick Veitch-a/script; Platt-c; Thor, Chapel & Prophet cameos 3.00

CABLE (See Ghost Rider &..., & New Mutants #87) (Title becomes Soldier X)
Marvel Comics: May, 1993 - No. 107, Sept, 2002 ($3.50/$1.95/$1.50-$2.25)
1-($3.50, 52 pgs.)-Gold foil & embossed-c; Thibert a-1-4p; c-1-3
2 4 6 9 13 16
2,4-15: 4-Liefeld-a assist; last Thibert-a(p). 6-8-Reveals that Baby Nathan is Cable; gives background on Stryfe. 9-Omega Red-c/story. 11-Bound-in trading card sheet 4.00
3-1st Weasel; extra 16 pg. X-Men/Avengers ann. preview
1 2 3 5 6 8
16-Newsstand edition 3.00
16-Enhanced edition 5.00
17-20-($1.95)-Deluxe edition, 20-w/bound in '95 Fleer Ultra cards 4.00
17-20-($1.50)-Standard edition 3.00
21-24, 26-44, -1(7/97): 21-Begin $1.95-c; return from Age of Apocalyse. 24-Grizzly dies. 28-vs. Sugarman; Mr. Sinister app. 30-X-Man-c/app.; Exodus app. 31-vs. X-Man. 32-Post app. 33-Post-c/app; Mandarin app (flashback); includes "Onslaught Update". 34-Onslaught x-over; Hulk-c/app; Apocalypse app. (cont'd in Hulk #444). 35-Onslaught x-over; Apocalypse vs. Cable. 36-w/card insert. 38-Weapon X-c/app; Psycho Man & Micronauts app. 40-Scott Clark-a(p). 41-Bishop-c/app. 3.00
25 ($3.95)-Foil gatefold-c 5.00
45-49,51-74: 45-Operation Zero Tolerance. 51-1st Casey-s. 54-Black Panther. 55-Domino-c/app. 62-Nick Fury-c/app.63-Stryfe-c/app. 67,68-Avengers-c/app. 71,73-Liefeld-a 3.00
50-($2.99) Double sized w/wraparound-c 4.00
75-($2.99) Liefeld-c/a; Apocalypse: The Twelve x-over 4.00
76-79: 76-Apocalypse: The Twelve x-over 3.00
80-96: 80-Begin $2.25-c. 87-Mystique-c/app. 3.00
97-99,101-107: 97-Tischman-s/Kordey-a/c begin 3.00
100-($3.99) Dialogue-free 'Nuff Said back-up story 4.00
... Classic Vol. 1 TPB (2008, $29.99) r/#1-4, New Mutants #87, Cable: Blood & Metal #1,2 30.00
.../Machine Man '98 Annual ($2.99) Wraparound-c 4.00
.../X-Force '96 Annual ($2.95) Wraparound-c 4.00
...'99 Annual ($3.50) vs. Sinister; computer photo-c 4.00
...Second Genesis 1 (9/99, $3.99) r/New Mutants #99, 100 and X-Force #1; Liefeld-c 4.00
...: The End (2002, $14.99, TPB) r/#101-107 15.00

CABLE
Marvel Comics: May, 2008 - No. 25, Jun, 2010 ($2.99/$3.99)
1-23: 1-10-Olivetti-c/a. 1-Liefeld var-c. 2-Finch var-c. 3-Romita Jr. var-c. 4-Bishop app.; Djurdjevic var-c. 5-Silvestri var-c. 6-Liefeld var-c. 13-15-Messiah War x-over; Deadpool app. 16,17-Gulacy-a 3.00
24-($3.99) Bishop app. 4.00
25-($3.99) Deadpool app.; Medina-a 1 2 3 5 6 8

CABLE
Marvel Comics: Jul, 2017 - No. 5, Nov, 2017; No. 150, Dec, 2017 - No. 159, Sept, 2018 ($3.99)
1-5: 1-Robinson-s/Pacheco-a. 4,5-Cinar-a. 4-Rasputin app. 4.00
[Title switches to legacy numbering after #5 (11/17)]
150-159: 150-154-The Externals app. 4.00
... Deadpool Annual 1 (10/18, $4.99) David F. Walker-s; art by various 5.00

CABLE
Marvel Comics: May, 2020 - No. 12, Sept, 2021 ($4.99/$3.99)
1-($4.99) Duggan-s/Noto-a; young Cable on Krakoa; Wolverine app. 5.00
2-12-($3.99) 3-Space Knights and Deadpool app. 4-6-"X of Swords" tie-ins 4.00
... Reloaded 1 (10/21, $4.99) Ewing-s/Quinn-a; Rocket Raccoon app. 5.00

CABLE AND X-FORCE (Marvel NOW!)
Marvel Comics: Feb, 2013 - No. 19, Mar, 2014 ($3.99)
1-19: 1-Hopeless-s/Larroca-a; Cable, Colossus, Domino, Forge & Dr. Nemesis team 4.00

CABLE - BLOOD AND METAL (Also see New Mutants #87 & X-Force #8)
Marvel Comics: Oct, 1992 - No. 2, Nov, 1992 ($2.50, limited series, 52 pgs.)
1-Fabian Nicieza scripts; John Romita, Jr.-c/a in both; Cable vs. Stryfe; 2nd app. of The Wild Pack (becomes The Six Pack); wraparound-c 6.00
2-Prelude to X-Cutioner's Song 5.00

CABLE/DEADPOOL ("Cable & Deadpool" on cover)
Marvel Comics: May, 2004 - No. 50, Apr, 2008 ($2.99)
1-Nicieza-s/Liefeld-c 4 8 12 28 47 65
2,3 2 4 6 8 10 12
4-23,25-37: 7-9-X-Men app. 17-House of M. 21-Heroes For Hire app. 30,31-Civil War. 30-Great Lakes Avengers app. 33-Liefeld-c 5.00
24-Spider-Man app. 4 8 12 28 47 65
38-1st Bob, Agent of HYDRA 2 4 6 13 18 22
39-49: 43,44-Wolverine app. 4.00
50-($3.99) Final issue; Spider-Man and the Avengers app.; 1st Venompool
4 8 12 23 37 50
Cable & Deadpool MCG 1 (7/11, $1.00) r/#1 with "Marvel's Greatest Comics" cover logo 5.00
... Vol. 1: If Looks Could Kill TPB (2004, $14.99) r/#1-6 15.00
... Vol. 2: The Burnt Offering TPB (2005, $14.99) r/#7-12 15.00
... Vol. 3: The Human Race TPB (2005, $14.99) r/#13-18 15.00
... Vol. 4: Bosom Buddies TPB (2006, $14.99) r/#19-24 15.00
... Vol. 5: Living Legends TPB (2006, $13.99) r/#25-29 14.00
... Vol. 6: Paved With Good Intentions TPB (2007, $14.99) r/#30-35 15.00
... Vol. 7: Separation Anxiety TPB (2007, $17.99) r/#36-42; sketch pages 18.00
Deadpool Vs. The Marvel Universe TPB (2008, $24.99) r/#43-50 25.00

CADET GRAY OF WEST POINT (See Dell Giants)

CADILLACS & DINOSAURS (TV)
Marvel Comics (Epic Comics): Nov, 1990 - No. 6, Apr, 1991 ($2.50, limited series)
1-Reprints Xenozoic Tales in color w/new-c 1 3 4 6 8 10
2-6 5.00
...In 3-D #1 (7/92, $3.95, Kitchen Sink)-With glasses 1 3 4 6 8 10

CADILLACS AND DINOSAURS (TV)
Topps Comics: V2#1, Feb, 1994 - V2#9, 1995 ($2.50, limited series)
V2#1-($2.95)-Collector's edition w/Stout-c & bound-in poster; Buckler-a; foil stamped logo; Giordano-a in all 6.00
V2#1-9: 1-Newsstand edition w/Giordano-c. 2,3-Collector's editions w/Stout-c & posters. 2,3-Newsstand ed. w/Giordano-c; w/o posters. 4-6-Collectors & Newsstand editions; Kieth-c. 7-9-Linsner-c 3.00

CAGE (Also see Hero for Hire, Power Man & Punisher)
Marvel Comics: Apr, 1992 - No. 20, Nov, 1993 ($1.25)
1,3,10,12: 3-Punisher-c & minor app. 10-Rhino & Hulk-c/app. 12-(52 pgs.)-Iron Fist app. 4.00
2,4-9,11,13-20: 9-Rhino-c/story; Hulk cameo 3.00

CAGE (Volume 3)
Marvel Comics (MAX): Mar, 2002 - No. 5, Sept, 2002 ($2.99, mature)
1-5-Corben-c/a; Azzarello-s 3.00
HC (2002, $19.99, with dustjacket) r/#1-5; intro. by Darius James; sketch pages 20.00
SC (2003, $13.99) r/#1-5; intro. by Darius James 14.00

CAGE! (Luke Cage)
Marvel Comics: Dec, 2016 - No. 4, Mar, 2017 ($3.99, limited series)
1-4-Genndy Tartakovsky-s/a; set in 1977 4.00

CAGED HEAT 3000 (Movie)
Roger Corman's Cosmic Comics: Nov, 1995 - No. 3, Jan, 1996 ($2.50)
1-3: Adaptation of film 3.00

CAGE HERO
Dynamite Entertainment: 2015 - No. 4, 2016 ($3.99, limited series)
1-4-Kevin Eastman & Ian Parker-s/Renalto Rei-a 4.00

CAGES
Tundra Publ.: 1991 - No. 10, May, 1996 ($3.50/$3.95/$4.95, limited series)
1-Dave McKean-c/a in all 2 4 6 8 10 12
2-Misprint exists 1 2 3 5 6 8
3-9: 5-$3.95-c begins 4.00
10-($4.95) 5.00

CAIN'S HUNDRED (TV)
Dell Publishing Co.: May-July, 1962 - No. 2, Sept-Nov, 1962
nn (01-094-207) 3 6 9 21 33 45
2 3 6 9 15 22 28

CAIN/VAMPIRELLA FLIP BOOK

	GD 2.0	VG 4.0	FN 6.0	VF 8.0	VF/NM 9.0	NM- 9.2

Harris Comics: Oct, 1994 ($6.95, one-shot, squarebound)
nn-contains Cain #3 & #4; flip book is r/Vampirella story from 1993 Creepy Fearbook 1 3 4 6 8 10

CALAMITY KATE
Dark Horse Comics: Mar, 2019 - No. 4, Jun, 2019 ($3.99, limited series)
1-4-Magdalene Visaggio-s/Corin Howell-a 4.00

CALIBER PRESENTS
Caliber Press: Jan, 1989 - No. 24, 1991 ($1.95/$2.50, B&W, 52 pgs.)
1-Anthology; 1st app. The Crow; Tim Vigil-c/a 18 36 54 124 275 425
2-Deadworld story; Tim Vigil-a 2 4 6 11 16 20
3-24: 15-24 ($3.50, 68 pgs.) 4.00
...: Cinderella on Fire 1 (1994, $2.95, B&W, mature) 3.00

CALIBER SPOTLIGHT
Caliber Press: May, 1995 ($2.95, B&W)
1-Kabuki app. 4.00

CALIFORNIA GIRLS
Eclipse Comics: June, 1987 - No. 8, May, 1988 ($2.00, 40 pgs, B&W)
1-8: All contain color paper dolls 6.00

CALL, THE
Marvel Comics: June, 2003 - No. 4, Sept, 2003 ($2.25)
1-4-Austen-s/Olliffe-a 3.00

CALLING ALL BOYS (Tex Granger No. 18 on)
Parents' Magazine Institute: Jan, 1946 - No. 17, May, 1948 (Photo c-1-5,7,8)
1 22 44 66 132 216 300
2-Contains Roy Rogers article 14 28 42 76 108 140
3-7,9,11,14-17: 6-Painted-c. 11-Rin Tin Tin photo on-c; Tex Granger begins. 14-J. Edgar Hoover photo on-c. 15-Tex Granger-c begin 10 20 30 58 79 100
8-Milton Caniff story 14 28 42 76 108 140
10-Gary Cooper photo on-c 14 28 42 76 108 140
12-Bob Hope photo on-c 16 32 48 96 151 205
13-Bing Crosby photo on-c 15 30 45 86 133 180

CALLING ALL GIRLS
Parents' Magazine Institute: Sept, 1941 - No. 89, Sept, 1949 (Part magazine, part comic)
1-Photo-c 32 64 96 188 307 425
2-Photo-c 16 32 48 92 144 195
3-Shirley Temple photo-c 21 42 63 126 206 285
4-10: 4,5,7,9-Photo-c. 9-Flag-c 14 28 42 81 118 155
11-Tina Thayer photo-c; Mickey Rooney photo-b/c; B&W photo inside of Gary Cooper as Lou Gehrig in "Pride of Yankees" 15 30 45 86 133 180
12-20 12 24 36 67 94 120
21-39,41-43(10-11/45)-Last issue with comics 11 22 33 62 86 110
40-Liz Taylor photo-c 32 64 96 188 307 425
44-51(7/46)-Last comic book size issue 10 20 30 54 72 90
52-89 9 18 27 50 65 80
NOTE: *Jack Sparling art in many issues; becomes a girls' magazine "Senior Prom" with #90.*

CALLING ALL KIDS (Also see True Comics)
Parents' Magazine Institute: Dec-Jan, 1945-46 - No. 26, Aug, 1949
1-Funny animal 21 42 63 122 199 275
2 13 26 39 72 101 130
3-10 10 20 30 56 76 95
11-26 9 18 27 52 69 85

CALL OF DUTY: BLACK OPS III (Based on the Activision video game)
Dark Horse Comics: Nov, 2015 - No. 6, Oct, 2016 ($3.99, limited series)
1-Prequel to the game; Hama-s/Ferreira-a 1 2 3 5 6 8
2-6-Hama-s/Ferreira-a 4.00

CALL OF DUTY, THE : THE BROTHERHOOD
Marvel Comics: Aug, 2002 - No. 6, Jan, 2003 ($2.25)
1-Exploits of NYC Fire Dept.; Finch-c/a; Austen & Bruce Jones-s 4.00
2-6-Austen-s 3.00
...Vol 1: The Brotherhood & The Wagon TPB (2002, $14.99) r/#1-6 & ...The Wagon #1-4 15.00

CALL OF DUTY, THE : THE PRECINCT
Marvel Comics: Sept, 2002 - No. 5, Jan, 2003 ($2.25, limited series)
1-Exploits of NYC Police Dept.; Finch-c; Bruce Jones-s/Mandrake-a 3.00
2-4 3.00
...Vol 2: The Precinct TPB (2003, $9.99) r/#1-4 10.00

CALL OF DUTY, THE : THE WAGON
Marvel Comics: Oct, 2002 - No. 4, Jan, 2003 ($2.25, limited series)
1-4-Exploits of NYC EMS Dept.; Finch-c; Austen-s/Zelzej-a 3.00

CALL OF DUTY: ZOMBIES (Based on the Activision video game)
Dark Horse Comics: Oct, 2016 - No. 6, Aug, 2017 ($3.99, limited series)
1-Justin Jordan-s/Jonathan Wayshak-a/Bisley-c 3 6 9 16 23 30
2-6 1 3 4 6 8 10

CALL OF DUTY: ZOMBIES 2 (Based on the Activision video game)
Dark Horse Comics: Sept, 2018 - No. 3, Dec, 2018 ($3.99, limited series)
1-Justin Jordan-s/Andres Ponce-a/E.M. Gist-c 1 2 3 5 6 8
2,3 4.00

CALVIN (See Li'l Kids)

CALVIN & THE COLONEL (TV)
Dell Publishing Co.: No. 1354, Apr-June, 1962 - No. 2, July-Sept, 1962
Four Color 1354(#1) (The last Four Color issue) 9 18 27 60 120 180
2 5 10 15 35 63 90

CAMELOT 3000
DC Comics: Dec, 1982 - No. 11, July, 1984; No. 12, Apr, 1985 (Direct sales, maxi series, Mando paper)
1-12: 1-Mike Barr scripts & Brian Bolland-c/a in all. 5-Intro Knights of New Camelot 5.00
TPB (1988, $12.95) r/#1-12 15.00
...: The Deluxe Edition (2008, $34.99, HC) r/#1-12; oversized & recolored; Barr intro.; design and promotional art; original proposal page 40.00
NOTE: *Austin a-7i-12i. Bolland a-1-12p; c-1-12.*

CAMERA COMICS
U.S. Camera Publishing Corp./ME: July, 1944 - No. 9, Summer, 1946
nn (7/44) 43 86 129 271 461 650
nn (9/44) 33 66 99 194 317 440
1(10/44)-The Grey Comet (slightly smaller page size than subsequent issues); WWII-c 37 74 111 222 361 500
2-16 pgs. of photos with 32 pgs. of comics 23 46 69 138 227 315
3-Nazi WW II-c; photos 53 106 159 334 567 800
4-9: All 1/3 photos 20 40 60 118 192 265

CAMP CANDY (TV)
Marvel Comics: May, 1990 - No. 6, Oct, 1990 ($1.00, limited series)
1-Post-c/a(p); featuring John Candy 1 3 4 6 8 10
2-6 6.00

CAMP COMICS
Dell Publishing Co.: Feb, 1942 - No. 3, April, 1942 (All have photo-c)(All issues are scarce)
1- "Seaman Sy Wheeler" by Kelly, 7 pgs.; Bugs Bunny app.; Mark Twain adaptation 100 200 300 635 1093 1550
2-Kelly-a, 12 pgs.; Bugs Bunny app.; classic-c 97 194 291 621 1061 1500
3-(Scarce)-Dave Berg & Walt Kelly-a 68 136 204 435 743 1050

CAMP RUNAMUCK (TV)
Dell Publishing Co.: Apr, 1966
1-Photo-c 3 6 9 21 33 45

CAMPUS LOVES
Quality Comics Group (Comic Magazines): Dec, 1949 - No. 5, Aug, 1950
1-Ward-c/a (9 pgs.) 48 96 144 302 514 725
2-Ward-c/a 37 74 111 222 361 500
3-5 20 40 60 117 189 260
NOTE: *Gustavson a-1-5. Photo c-3-5.*

CAMPUS ROMANCE (...Romances on cover)
Avon Periodicals/Realistic: Sept-Oct, 1949 - No. 3, Feb-Mar, 1950
1-Walter Johnson-a; c-/Avon paperback #348 53 106 159 334 567 800
2-Grandenetti-a; c-/Avon paperback #151 37 74 111 222 361 500
3-c-/Avon paperback #201 37 74 111 222 361 500
Realistic reprint 20 40 60 114 182 250

CANADA DRY PREMIUMS (See Swamp Fox, The & Terry & The Pirates in the Promotional Comics section)

CANADIAN VARK! (Reprints from Cerebus in Hell)
Aardvark-Vanaheim: Dec, 2018 ($4.00, B&W)
1-Cerebus figures placed over original Doré artwork of Hell; American Flagg #1-c swipe 4.00

CANCELLED COMIC CAVALCADE (See the Promotional Comics section)

CANDID TALES (Also see Bold Stories & It Rhymes With Lust)
Kirby Publ. Co.: April, 1950; June, 1950 (Digest size) (144 pgs.) (Full color)
nn-(Scarce) Contains Wood female pirate story, 15 pgs., and 14 pgs. in June issue; Powell-a 300 600 900 2010 3505 5000
NOTE: *Another version exists with Dr. Kilmore by Wood; no female pirate story.*

CANDY (Teen-age)(Also see Police Comics #37)
Quality Comics Group (Comic Magazines): Autumn, 1947 - No. 64, Jul, 1956
1-Gustavson-a 32 64 96 188 307 425
2-Gustavson-a 19 38 57 111 176 240
3-10 14 28 42 78 112 145
11-30 11 22 33 62 86 110
31-64: 64-Ward-c(p)? 9 18 27 52 69 85
Super Reprint No. 2,10,12,16,17,18('63-'64):17-Candy #12 2 4 6 11 16 20
NOTE: *Jack Cole 1-2 pg. art in many issues.*

CANDY COMICS
William H. Wise & Co.: Fall, 1944 - No. 3, Spring, 1945
1-Two Scoop Scuttle stories by Wolverton 47 94 141 296 498 700
2,3-Scoop Scuttle by Wolverton, 2-4 pgs. 32 64 96 188 307 425

CANNON (See Heroes, Inc. Presents Cannon)

CANNIBAL
Image Comics: Oct, 2016 - No. 8, Oct, 2017 ($3.99)
1-8-Young & Buccellato-s/Bergara-a 4.00

CANNON: DAWN OF WAR (Michael Turner's...)
Aspen MLT, Inc.: Nov, 2004 ($2.99)
1-Turnbull-a; two covers by Turnbull and Turner 3.00

CANNONBALL COMICS
Rural Home Publishing Co.: Feb, 1945 - No. 2, Mar, 1945
1-The Crash Kid, Thunderbrand, The Captive Prince & Crime Crusader begin; skull-c 290 580 870 1856 3178 4500
2-Devil-c 226 452 678 1446 2473 3500

CANTEEN KATE (See All Picture All True Love Story & Fightin' Marines)
St. John Publishing Co.: June, 1952 - No. 3, Nov, 1952
1-Matt Baker-c/a 155 310 465 992 1696 2400
2-Matt Baker-c/a 71 142 213 454 777 1100
3-(Rare)-Used in **POP**, pg. 75; Baker-c/a 90 180 270 576 988 1400

CANTO
IDW Pubishing: Jun, 2019 - No. 6, Nov, 2019 ($3.99)
1-David M. Booher-s/Drew Zucker-a 5 10 15 33 57 80
2 2 4 6 9 12 15
3-6 6.00
... & The Clockwork Fairies (5/20, $3.99)-David M. Booher-s/Drew Zucker-a 1 2 3 5 6 8

CANTO & THE CITY OF GIANTS

Call of Duty: Zombies #5 © Activision

The Cape: Fallen #2 © Joe Hill

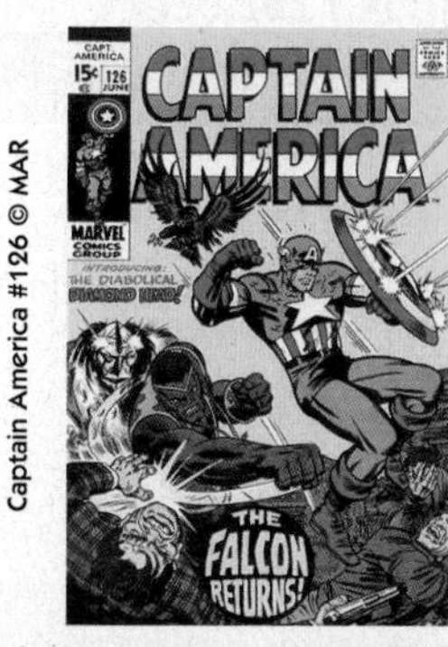

Captain America #126 © MAR

GD VG FN VF VF/NM NM-
2.0 4.0 6.0 8.0 9.0 9.2

IDW Pubishing: Apr, 2019 - No. 3, Jun, 2021 ($3.99)

1-3-David M. Booher-s/Sebastian Piriz-a 4.00

CANTO II: THE HOLLOW MEN
IDW Pubishing: Aug, 2020 - No. 5, Jan, 2021 ($3.99)

1-David M. Booher-s/Drew Zucker-a 2 4 6 9 12 15
2-5 4.00

CANTO III: LIONHEARTED
IDW Pubishing: Jul, 2021 - No. 6, Jan, 2022 ($3.99)

1-6-David M. Booher-s/Drew Zucker-a 4.00

CANTO: TALES OF THE UNNAMED WORLD
IDW Pubishing: Jun, 2022 - No. 2, Jul, 2022 ($3.99)

1,2-David M. Booher-s/Drew Zucker-a 4.00

CAPE, THE
IDW Publishing: Dec, 2010; Jul, 2011 - No. 4, Jan, 2012 ($3.99)

1-(12/10) Zach Howard-c/a; Jason Ciaramella-s 4.00
1-4: 1-(7/11) Story continues from 12/10 issue 4.00
...: Fallen (6/18 - No. 4, 12/18, $3.99) 1-4-Ciaramella-s; Zach Howard-a 4.00
...: Greatest Hits (6/18, $1.00) reprints #1 (12/10) and previews The Cape: Fallen series 3.00
...: Legacy Edition (6/11, $5.99) r/#1 (12/10) with Joe Hill's original short story 6.00
...: 1969 (7/12 - No. 4, 10/12, $3.99) 1-4-Ciaramella-s; origin in Vietnam 4.00

CAPER
DC Comics: Dec, 2003 - No. 12, Nov, 2004 ($2.95, limited series)

1-12: 1-4-Judd Winick-s/Farel Dalrymple-a. 5-8-John Severin-a. 9-12-Fowler-a 3.00

CAPES
Image Comics: Sept, 2003 - No. 3, Nov, 2003 ($3.50)

1-Robert Kirkman-s; 5 pg. preview of The Walking Dead #1
4 8 12 24 38 52
2,3-Robert Kirkman-s/Mark Englert-a/c 5.00

CAP'N QUICK & A FOOZLE (Also see Eclipse Mag. & Monthly)
Eclipse Comics: July, 1984 - No. 3, Nov, 1985 ($1.50, color, Baxter paper)

1-3-Rogers-c/a 3.00

CAPTAIN ACTION (Toy)
National Periodical Publications: Oct-Nov, 1968 - No. 5, June-July, 1969 (Based on Ideal toy)

1-Origin; Wally Wood-a; Superman-c app. 7 14 21 49 92 135
2,3,5-Gil Kane/Wally Wood-a 5 10 15 33 57 80
4- Gil Kane-c 4 8 12 28 47 65

CAPTAIN ACTION CAT: THE TIMESTREAM CATASTROPHE
Dynamite Entertainment: 2014 - No. 4, 2014 ($3.99, limited series)

1-4-Art Baltazar-s/a; Franco & Smits-s; all ages cat version of Capt. Action characters; Ghost, X, Captain Midnight, Skyman & The Occultist app. 4.00

CAPTAIN ACTION COMICS (Toy)
Moonstone: No. 0, 2008 - No. 5 (Based on the Ideal toy)

0-($1.99) Origin re-told; Sparacio-a; three covers; character history by Michael Eury 3.00
1-5: 1-($3.99) Sparacio-a; intro. by Jim Shooter 4.00
... Comics Special 1 (2010, $5.99) 3 covers by Barreto, Ordway & Spiegle 6.00
... Exclusive Special 1 (2011, no price) Gulacy-c; Barreto-a 4.00
...: First Mission, Last Day (2008, $3.99) origin story re-told; Nicieza-s/Procopio-a 4.00
... King Size Special 1 (2011, $6.99) 1-Covers by Byrne, Wheatley & M. Benes 7.00
... Season 2 (2010, $3.99) 1-3: 1-Covers by Allred & Texiera; Obama app. 4.00
... Winter Special (2011, $4.99) Green Hornet & Kato on-c & text story 5.00

CAPTAIN AERO COMICS (Samson No. 1-6; also see Veri Best Sure Fire & Veri Best Sure Shot Comics)
Holyoke Publishing Co.: V1#7(#1), Dec, 1941 - V2#4(#10), Jan, 1943; V3#9(#11), Sept, 1943 -V4#3(#17), Oct, 1944; #21, Dec, 1944 - #26, Aug, 1946 (No #18-20)

V1#7(#1)-Flag-Man & Solar, Master of Magic, Captain Aero, Cap Stone, Adventurer begin; Nazi WWII-c 232 464 696 1485 2543 3600
8,10: 8(#2)-Pals of Freedom app. 10(#4)-Origin The Gargoyle; Kubert-a
113 226 339 718 1234 1750
9(#3)-Hitler-sty; Catman back-c; Alias X begins; Pals of Freedom app.; Nazi WWII-c
142 284 426 909 1555 2200
11,12(#5,6)-Kubert-a; Miss Victory in #6 93 186 279 591 1021 1450
V2#1,2(#7,8): 8-Origin The Red Cross; Miss Victory app.; Brodsky-c(i)
74 148 222 470 810 1150
3(#9)-Miss Victory app. 129 258 387 826 1413 2000
4(#10)-Miss Victory app.; Japanese WWII-c 116 232 348 742 1271 1800
V3#9 - V3#12(#11-14): All Quinlan Japanese WWII-c. 9-Miss Victory app.
93 186 279 591 1021 1450

GD VG FN VF VF/NM NM-
2.0 4.0 6.0 8.0 9.0 9.2

V3#13(#15),V4#2(#16): Schomburg Japanese WWII-c. 13-Miss Victory app.
110 220 330 704 1202 1700
V4#3(#17)-Miss Victory app.; L.B. Cole Japanese WWII-c
84 168 252 538 919 1300
21-24-L.B. Cole Japanese WWII covers. 22-Intro/origin Mighty Mite
74 148 222 470 810 1150
25-L.B. Cole Sci-fi-c 103 206 309 659 1130 1600
26-L.B. Cole Sci-fi-c; Palais-a(2) (scarce) 400 800 1200 2800 4900 7000

NOTE: *L.B. Cole c-17, 21-26.* ***Hollingsworth*** *a-23.* ***Infantino*** *a-23, 26.* ***Schomburg*** *c-15, 16.*

CAPTAIN AMERICA (See Adventures of..., All-Select, All Winners, Aurora, Avengers #4, Blood and Glory, Captain Britain 16-20, Giant-Size..., The Invaders, Marvel Double Feature, Marvel Fanfare, Marvel Mystery, Marvel Super-Action, Marvel Super Heroes V2#3, Marvel Team-Up, Marvel Treasury Special, Power Record Comics, Ultimates, USA Comics, Young Allies & Young Men)

CAPTAIN AMERICA (Formerly Tales of Suspense #1-99) (Captain America and the Falcon #134-223 & Steve Rogers: Captain America #444-454 appears on cover only)
Marvel Comics Group: No. 100, Apr, 1968 - No. 454, Aug, 1996

100-Flashback on Cap's revival with Avengers & Sub-Mariner; story continued from Tales of Suspense #99; Kirby-c/a begins 100 200 300 700 1275 1850
101-The Sleeper-c/story; Red Skull app. 10 20 30 64 132 200
102-104: 102-Sleeper-c/s. 103,104-Red Skull-c/sty 8 16 24 54 102 150
105,106,108 7 14 21 44 82 120
107-Red Skull & Hitler-c 9 18 27 60 120 180
109-Origin Capt. America retold in detail 18 36 54 122 271 420
109-2nd printing (1994) 2 4 6 9 12 15
110-Rick Jones dons Bucky's costume & becomes Cap's partner; Hulk x-over; Steranko-a Classic Steranko-c 22 44 66 154 340 525
111-Classic Steranko-c/a; Death of Steve Rogers 15 30 45 100 220 340
112-S.A. recovery retold; last Kirby-c/a 8 16 24 54 102 150
113-Cap's funeral; Avengers app.; classic Steranko-c/a
12 24 36 81 176 270
114-116,119,120: 114-Red Skull Cosmic Cube story. 115,116-Red Skull app; last 12c issue. 119-Cap vs. Red Skull; Cosmic Cube "destroyed"; Falcon app.
5 10 15 34 60 85
117-1st app. The Falcon (9/69) 68 136 204 544 1222 1900
117 Facsimile Edition (3/21, $3.99) Reprints #117 with original ads and letter column
1 3 4 6 8 10
118-2nd app. The Falcon 14 28 42 94 207 320
121-136,139,140: 121-Retells origin; Avengers app. 122-Cap vs. Scorpion. 124-Modok app. 125-Mandarin app. 129-Red Skull app. 133-The Falcon becomes Cap's partner; origin Modok. 139,140-Grey Gargoyle app; origin in #140
4 8 12 28 47 65
137,138-Spider-Man x-over 5 10 15 34 60 85
141,142-Grey Gargoyle app. 141-Last Stan Lee issue. 142-Last 15¢ issue
4 8 12 27 44 60
143-(52 pgs) Cap vs. Red Skull 4 8 12 28 47 65
144-New costume Falcon 4 8 12 25 40 55
145-152: 145-147-Cap vs. the Supreme Hydra. 146-1st Sal Buscema-a on title. 147-Supreme Hydra revealed to be Kingpin's son. 148-Red Skull app. 150-The Stranger app. 151,152- Cap vs. Mr. Hyde & The Scorpion. 152-1st app. Boss Morgan
3 6 9 16 24 32
153-155: 153-1st brief app. Jack Monroe; return of 1950s Captain America. 154-1st full app. Jack Monroe (Nomad); 1950s Captain America and Avengers app. 155-Origin retold; origin Jack Monroe and the 1950s Captain America
5 10 15 30 50 70
156-Cap vs. the 1950s Captain America; Jack Monroe app; classic Cap vs Cap cover
3 6 9 21 33 45
157-162,165-167,177-179: 157-1st app. Viper. 159-Cap vs. Eel, Porcupine & Scarecrow. 160-1st app. Solarr. 161,162-Peggy Carter app. 164-1st Nightshade. 165-167-Cap vs. Yellow Claw. 177-Lucifer app. 178-1st time Peggy Carter meets Steve Rogers. 179-Hawkeye app. as the Golden Archer 3 6 9 14 19 24
163-1st Serpent Squad: Viper, Eel and Cobra 3 6 9 14 20 26
164-1st app. Nightshade, Queen of Werewolves 3 6 9 14 20 26
168-1st Helmut Zemo (as the Phoenix) 7 14 21 46 86 125
169-1st app. Quentin Harderman; Moonstone 1st app. (cameo)
3 6 9 15 22 28
170-New Falcon costume with wings for flying; Moonstone 1st full app. & origin
3 6 9 14 20 25
171-Black Panther & Iron Man app. 4 8 12 28 47 65
172-175: X-Men x-over. 174-1st app. Number 1 3 6 9 19 30 40
176-Steve Rogers quits being Cap.; Avengers app. 3 6 9 16 23 30
180-Intro/origin of Nomad (Steve Rogers) 9 18 27 62 126 190
181-Intro/origin new Cap. 3 6 9 19 30 40
182,184,185,187-191: 182,184,185-Red Skull app. 182-Frank Robbins-a. 189,190-Cap vs. Nightshade. 191-Iron Man app. 2 4 6 10 14 18
183-Death of new Cap; Steve Rogers drops Nomad I.D; returns to being Capt. America

GD VG FN VF VF/NM NM-
2.0 4.0 6.0 8.0 9.0 9.2

3 6 9 14 19 24
186-True origin The Falcon; Red Skull app. 3 6 9 16 23 30
192-1st app. Dr. Karla Sofen (later becomes Moonstone)
5 10 15 35 63 90
193-Kirby-c/a begins 5 10 15 31 53 75
194-199-(Regular 25¢ edition)(4-7/76) 3 6 9 14 19 24
196-199-(30¢-c variants, limited distribution) 7 14 21 44 82 120
200-(Regular 25¢ edition)(8/76) 3 6 9 15 22 28
200-(30¢-c variant, limited distribution) 8 16 24 52 99 145
201-214-Kirby-c/a. 208-1st Arnim Zola. 209,210- Arnim Zola app. 210-212 –vs Red Skull
2 4 6 10 14 18
210-214-(35¢-c variants, limited dist.)(6-10/77) 11 22 33 72 154 235
215,216,218-229: 215-Origin retold. 216-r/Strange Tales #114. 218-Sal Buscema-a resumes. 226,227-Red Skull app. 228-Cap vs. Constrictor. 229-Marvel Man app.
2 4 6 8 11 14
217-Intro. Marvel Boy (Wendell Vaughan); becomes Marvel Man in #218; later becomes Quasar (2/78) 8 16 24 54 102 150
230-Battles Hulk-c/story cont'd in Inc. Hulk #232 3 6 9 16 23 30
231-234,236-240,242-246: 233-"Death" of Sharon Carter. 234-Daredevil app. 244,245-Miller-c
1 3 4 6 8 10
235-(7/79) Daredevil x-over; Miller-a(p) 2 4 6 9 12 15
241-Punisher app.; Miller-c 6 12 18 37 66 95
241-2nd print 2 4 6 8 10 12
247-252-Byrne-a 2 4 6 8 10 12
253,255: 253-Byrne-a; Baron Blood app. 255-Origin retold; Miller-c
3 6 9 14 19 24
254-Byrne-a; death of Baron Blood; intro new Union Jack
3 6 9 16 23 30
256-262: 257-Hulk app. 258-Zeck-a begins. 259-Cap vs. Dr. Octopus. 261,262-Red Skull app.
1 2 3 5 6 8
263-266: 263-Red Skull-c/story. 264-Original X-Men app. 265,266-Spider-Man app.
1 3 4 6 8 10
267-280: 267-1st app. & origin Everyman. 268-Defenders app. 269-1st Team America. 272-1st Vermin. 273,274-Baron Strucker. 275-1st Baron Zemo (formally the Phoenix). 276-278-Cap vs. Baron Zemo. 279-(3/83)-Contains Tattooz skin decals. 280-Scarecrow app.
1 2 3 5 6 8
281-1950's Bucky returns. Spider-Woman and Viper app.
1 3 4 6 8 10
282-Bucky becomes new Nomad (Jack Monroe) 2 4 6 9 12 15
282-Silver ink 2nd print ($1.75) w/original date (6/83) 5.00
283-289,291-300: 283-Cap vs. Viper. 284-Patriot (Jack Mace) app. 285-Death of Patriot. 286-288-Deathlok app. 293,294-Nomad app. 293-299-Red Skull and Baron Zemo app. 298-Origin Red Skull. 300- "Death" of Red Skull 1 2 3 5 6 8
290-1st Mother Superior (Red Skull's daughter, later becomes Sin)
3 6 9 14 19 24
301-322,324-331: 301-Avengers app. 305,306-Captain Britain app. 307-1st Madcap; 1st Mark Gruenwald-s (begins 8-year run). 308-Secret Wars II x-over. 310-1st Serpent Society. 312-1st Flag Smasher. 313-Death of Modok. 314-Squadron Supreme x-over. 317-Hawkeye & Mockingbird app. 318-Scourge app; death of Blue Streak and Adder. 319-Scourge kills numerous villians. 320-"Death"of Scourge. 321-Cap vs. Flag Smasher; classic Zeck cover Cap with machine gun. 322-Cap vs. Flag Smasher. 325-Nomad app. 327-Cap vs Super-Patriot. 328,330-Demolition Man (D-Man) app.
1 2 3 5 6 8
323-1st app. new Super-Patriot (see Nick Fury) 4 8 12 27 44 60
332-Old Captain America resigns 3 6 9 14 20 26
333-Super Patriot becomes new Captain America 3 6 9 16 23 30
334-343,345-349: 334-Intro new Bucky; Freedom Force app. 337-Serpent Society app; Avengers #4 homage-c; Steve Rogers becomes 'the Captain'; becomes Captain America again in issue #350. 339-Fall of the Mutants tie-in. 341-Cap vs Iron Man; x-over with Iron Man #228. 342-Cap vs. Viper and the Serpent Squad
1 2 3 5 6 8
344-($1.50, 52 pgs.)-Ronald Reagan cameo as a snake man
1 3 4 6 8 10
350-($1.75, 68 pgs.)-Return of Steve Rogers (original Cap) to original costume
2 4 6 10 14 18
351,353,355-358,361-382,384-396: 351-Nick Fury app. 357-Bloodstone hunt Pt. 1 (of 6). 358-Baron Zemo app. 365,366-Acts of Vengeance x-overs. 367-Magneto vs Red Skull. 372-378-Streets of Poison. 374-Bullseye app. 375-Daredevil app. 376-Black Widow app. 377-Bullseye vs. Crossbones; Red Skull app. 379-Quasar app. 380-382-Serpent Society app. 386-U.S. Agent app. 387-392-Superia Stratagem. 387-389-Red Skull back-up stories. 394-Red Skull app. 395-Thor app. (Eric Masterson; also in #396-397); Red Skull app. 396-Red Skull and new (1st) Jack O Lantern app. 1 2 3 5 6 8
352-1st Supreme Soviet Soldiers 2 4 6 9 12 15
354-John Walker's 1st app. as U.S.Agent 5 10 15 31 53 75
354 Facsimile Edition (3/21, $3.99) Reprints #354 with original ads and letter column 4.00
359-Crossbones debut (cameo); Baron Zemo app. 2 4 6 8 11 14
360-1st app. Crossbones; Baron Zemo app. 3 6 9 19 30 40
383-($2.00, 68 pgs., squarebound)-50th anniversary issue; Red Skull story; Jim Lee-c(i)
2 4 6 9 12 15
397-399,401-424: 397-New Jack O Lantern app. 398,399-Operation Galactic Storm x-overs. 401-Operation Galactic storm epilogue. 402-Begin 6 part Man-Wolf story w/Wolverine in #403-407. 405-410-New Jack O Lantern app. in back-up story. 406-Cable & Shatterstar cameo. 407-Capwolf vs. Cable-c/story. 408-Infinity War x-over; Falcon back-up story. 409-Red Skull & Crossbones app. 410-Crossbones app. 414-Black Panther app. 419-Red Skull app; x-over with Silver Sable #15. 423- Cap vs. Namor-c/story 6.00
400-($2.25, 84 pgs.) Flip book format w/double gatefold-c; Operation Galactic Storm x-over; r/Avengers #4 plus-c contains cover pin-ups 1 3 4 6 8 10
425-($2.95, 52 pgs.)-Embossed Foil-c edition; Fighting Chance Pt. 1
2 4 6 8 10 12
425-($1.75, 52 pgs.)-non-embossed-c edition; Fighting Chance Pt. 1
2 4 6 8 10 12
426-439,442,443: 426-437-Fighting Chance Pt. 2-12. 427-Begins $1.50-c; bound-in trading card sheet. 428-1st Americop. 431-1st Free Spirit. 434-1st Jack Flag. 438-Fighting Chance epilogue. 443-Last Gruenwald issue 5.00
440,441,444,445: 440,441-Avengers x-overs; 'Taking A.I.M" story. 444-Mark Waid-s (1st on Cap) & Ron Garney-c/a(p) begins, ends #454; Avengers app. 445-Operation rebirth Pt.1; vs. Red Skull; Sharon Carter returns 6.00
446,447-Operation Rebirth; Red Skull app. 446-Hitler app.
1 2 3 5 6 8
448-($2.95, double-sized issue) Waid script & Garney-c/a; Red Skull "dies" 6.00
449-Thor app; story x-overs with Thor, Iron Man and Avengers titles 6.00
450- "Man Without a Country" begins; Steve Rogers-c 1 2 3 5 6 8
450-Captain America-c with white background 1 3 4 6 8 10
451-453: 451-1st app. Cap's new costume. 453-Cap gets old costume back; Bill Clinton app.
5.00
454-Last issue of the regular series (8/96) 6.00
#600-up (See Captain America 2005 series, resumed original numbering after #50)
Special 1(1/71)-All reprint issue from Tales Of Suspense #63,69,70,71,75
7 14 21 46 86 125
Special 2(1/72, 52 pgs.)-All reprint issue from Tales Of Suspense #72-74 and Not Brand Echh #5 5 10 15 30 50 70
Annual 3('76, 52 pgs.)-Kirby-c/a(new) 3 6 9 17 26 35
Annual 4('77, 34 pgs.)-Magneto-c/story 3 6 9 17 26 35
Annual 5-7: (52 pgs.)('81-'83) 1 2 3 5 6 8
Annual 8(9/86)-Wolverine-c/story;Zeck-c 4 8 12 28 47 65
Annual 9-13('90-'94, 68 pgs.)-9-Nomad back-up. 10-Origin retold (2 pgs.). 11-Falcon solo story. 12-Bagged w/card. 13-Red Skull-c/story 6.00
...Ashcan Edition ('95, 75¢) 4.00
... and the Falcon: Madbomb TPB (2004, $16.99) r/#193-200; Kirby-s/a 17.00
... and the Falcon: Nomad TPB (2006, $24.99) r/#177-186; Cap becomes Nomad 25.00
... and the Falcon: Secret Empire TPB (2005, $19.99) r/#169-176 20.00
... and the Falcon: The Swine TPB (2006, $29.99) r/#206-214 & Annual #3,4 30.00
... By Jack Kirby: Bicentennial Battles TPB (2005, $19.99) r/#201-205 & Marvel Treasury Special Featuring Captain America's Bicentennial Battles; Kirby-s/a 20.00
...: Deathlok Lives! nn(10/93, $4.95)-r/#286-288 6.00
...Drug War 1-(1994, $2.00, 52 pgs.)-New Warriors app. 4.00
...Man Without a Country(1998, $12.99, TPB)-r/#450-453 13.00
...Medusa Effect 1 (1994, $2.95, 68 pgs.)-Origin Baron Zemo 4.00
...Operation Rebirth (1996, $9.95)-r/#445-448 10.00
... 65th Anniversary Special (5/06, $3.99) WWII flashback with Bucky; Brubaker-s 5.00
...Streets of Poison ($15.95)-r/#372-378 16.00
...: The Movie Special nn (5/92, $3.50, 52 pgs.)-Adapts movie; printed on coated stock; The Red Skull app. 4.00

NOTE: ***Austin*** *c-225i, 239i, 246i.* ***Buscema*** *a-115p, 217p; c-136p, 217, 297.* ***Byrne*** *c-223(part), 238, 239, 247p-254p, 290, 291, 313p; a-247-254p, 255, 313p, 350.* ***Colan*** *a(p)-116-137, 256, Annual 5; c(p)-116-123, 126, 129.* ***Everett*** *a-136i, 137i; c-126i.* ***Garney*** *a(p)-444-454.* ***Gil Kane*** *a-145p; c-147p, 149p, 150p, 170p, 172-174, 180, 181p, 183-190p, 215, 216, 220, 221.* ***Kirby*** *a(p)-100-109, 112, 193-214, 216, Special 1, 2(layouts), Annual 3, 4; c-100-109, 112, 126p, 193-214.* ***Ron Lim*** *a(p)-366, 368-378, 380-386; c-366p, 368-378p, 379, 380-393p.* ***Miller*** *c-241p, 244p, 245p, 255p, Annual 5.* ***Mooney*** *a-149i.* ***Morrow*** *a-144.* ***Perez*** *c-243p, 246p.* ***Robbins*** *c(p)-183-187, 189-192, 225.* ***Roussos*** *a-140i, 168i.* ***Shores*** *a-102i, 107i, 109i.* ***Starlin/Sinnott*** *c-162.* ***Sutton*** *a-244i.* ***Tuska*** *a-112i, 215p, Special 2.* ***Waid*** *scripts-444-454.* ***Williamson*** *a-313i.* ***Wood*** *a-127i.* ***Zeck*** *a-263-289; c-300.*

CAPTAIN AMERICA (Volume Two)
Marvel Comics: V2#1, Nov, 1996 - No. 13, Nov, 1997($2.95/$1.95/$1.99)
(Produced by Extreme Studios)

1-($2.95)-Heroes Reborn begins; Liefeld-c/a; Loeb scripts; reintro Nick Fury
2 4 6 8 10 12
1-($2.95)-(Variant-c)-Liefeld-c/a 1 3 4 6 8 10
1-(7/96, $2.95)-(Exclusive Comicon Ed.)-Liefeld-c/a 2 4 6 8 11 14
2-4,6-11,13: 6-Cable-c/app. 13-"World War 3"-pt. 4, x-over w/Image 4.00
5-1st cover app. of Rikki Barnes; two covers 1 3 4 6 8 10
12-($2.99) "Heroes Reunited"-pt. 4 5.00
Heroes Reborn: Captain America (2006, $29.99, TPB) r/#1-12 & Heroes Reborn #1/2 30.00

CAPTAIN AMERICA (Vol. Three) (Also see Capt. America: Sentinel of Liberty)
Marvel Comics: Jan, 1998 - No. 50, Feb, 2002 ($2.99/$1.99/$2.25)

1-($2.99) Mark Waid-s/Ron Garney-a 4.00
1-Variant cover 6.00
2-($1.99): 2-Two covers 3.00
3-11: 3-Returns to old shield. 4-Hawkeye app. 5-Thor-c/app. 7-Andy Kubert-c/a begin. 9-New shield 3.00
12-($2.99) Battles Nightmare; Red Skull back-up story 4.00
13-17,19-Red Skull returns 3.00
18-($2.99) Cap vs. Korvac in the Future 4.00
20-24,26-29: 20,21-Sgt. Fury back-up story painted by Evans 3.00
25-($2.99) Cap & Falcon vs. Hatemonger 4.00
30-49: 30-Begin $2.25-c. 32-Ordway-a. 33-Jurgens-s/a begins; U.S. Agent app. 36-Maximum Security x-over. 41,46-Red Skull app. 3.00
50-($5.95) Stories by various incl. Jurgens, Quitely, Immonen; Ha-c 6.00
.../Citizen V '98 Annual ($3.50) Busiek & Kesel-s 4.00
1999 Annual ($3.50) Flag Smasher app. 4.00
2000 Annual ($3.50) Continued from #35 vs. Protocide; Jurgens-s 4.00
2001 Annual ($2.99) Golden Age flashback; Invaders app. 4.00
...: To Serve and Protect TPB (2/02, $17.95) r/Vol. 3 #1-7 18.00

CAPTAIN AMERICA (Volume 4)
Marvel Comics: Jun, 2002 - No. 32, Dec, 2004 ($3.99/$2.99)

1-Ney Rieber-s/Cassaday-c/a 4.00
2-9-($2.99) 3-Cap reveals Steve Rogers ID. 7-9-Hairsine-a 3.00
10-32: 10-16-Jae Lee-a. 17-20-Gibbons-s/Weeks-a. 21-26-Bachalo-a. 26-Bucky flashback. 27,28-Eddie Campbell-a. 29-32-Red Skull app. 3.00
...Vol. 1: The New Deal HC (2003, $22.99) r/#1-6; foreward by Max Allan Collins 23.00
...Vol. 2: The Extremists TPB (2003, $13.99) r/#7-11; Cassaday-c 14.00
...Vol. 3: Ice TPB (2003, $12.99) r/#12-16; Jae Lee-a; Cassaday-c 13.00
...Vol. 4: Cap Lives TPB (2004, $12.99) r/#17-22 & Tales of Suspense #66 13.00
Avengers Disassembled: Captain America TPB (2004, $17.99) r/#29-32 and Captain America and the Falcon #5-7 18.00

CAPTAIN AMERICA
Marvel Comics: Jan, 2005 - No. 50, Jul, 2009; No. 600, Aug, 2009 - No. 619, Aug, 2011 ($2.99/$3.99)

1-Brubaker-s/Epting-c/a; Red Skull app. 3 6 9 16 23 30
2-5 1 2 3 5 6 8
6-1st full app. of the Winter Soldier; swastika-c 6 12 18 38 69 100
6-Retailer variant cover 6 12 18 42 79 115
7-24: 10-House of M. 11-Origin of the Winter Soldier. 13-Iron Man app. 24-Civil War 5.00
8-Variant Red Skull cover 2 4 6 8 10 12

Captain America (2007) #25 © MAR

Captain America (2018) #25 © MAR

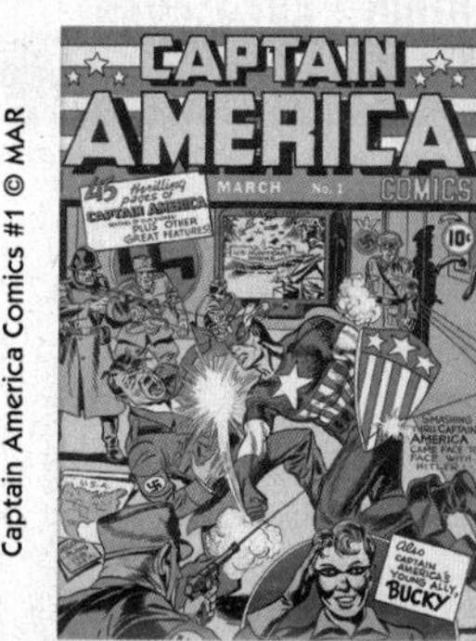

Captain America Comics #1 © MAR

GD VG FN VF VF/NM NM-
2.0 4.0 6.0 8.0 9.0 9.2

25-($3.99) Captain America shot dead; handcuffed red glove cover by Epting 14.00
25-($3.99) Variant edition with running Cap cover by McGuinness 10.00
25-($3.99) 2nd printing with "The Death of The Dream" cover by Epting 5.00
25-Director's Cut-($4.99) w/script with Brubaker commentary; pencil pages, variant and un-used covers gallery; article on media hype 8.00
26-33-Falcon & Winter Soldier app. 3.00
34-(3/08) Bucky becomes the new Captain America; Alex Ross-c 12.00
34-Variant-c by Steve Epting 8.00
34-($3.99) Director's Cut; includes script; pencil art, costume designs, cover gallery 5.00
34-DF Edition with Alex Ross portrait cover; signed by Ross 40.00
35-49-Bucky as Captain America. 43-45-Batroc app. 46,47-Sub-Mariner app. 3.00
50-(7/09, $3.99) Bucky's birthday flashbacks; Captain America's life synopsis; Martin-a 4.00
(After #50, numbering reverts to original with #600, Aug, 2009)
600-(8/09, $4.99) Covers by Ross and Epting; leads into Captain America: Reborn series; art by Guice, Chaykin, Ross, Eaglesham; commentary by Joe Simon; cover gallery 5.00
601-615,617-619-($3.99) 601-Gene Colan-a; 3 covers. 602-Nomad back-up feature begins. 606-Baron Zemo returns. 611-615-Trial of Captain America 4.00
615.1 (5/11, $2.99) Brubaker-s/Breitweiser-a/Acuña-c 3.00
616-(5/11, $4.99) 70th Anniversary Issue; short stories by Brubaker, Chaykin, Deodato, McGuinness, Grist and others, Charest-c 5.00
616-Variant-c by Epting 8.00
...: America's Avenger (8/11, $4.99) Handbook format profiles of friends and foes 5.00
... and Batroc (5/11, $3.99) Gillen-s/Arlem-a; Bucky vs. Batroc in Paris 4.00
... and Crossbones (5/11, $3.99) Harms-s/Shalvey-a/Tocchini-c 4.00
... and Falcon (5/11, $3.99) Williams-s/Isaacs-a/Tocchini-c 4.00
... and the First Thirteen (5/11, $3.99) Peggy Carter in WWII France 1943 4.00
... and the Secret Avengers (5/11, $3.99) DeConnick-s/Tocchini-a/c; Black Widow app. 4.00
... and Thor: Avengers 1 (9/11, $4.99) Movie version Cap; prequel to Thor movie; Lim-c 5.00
... By Ed Brubaker Omnibus Vol. 1 HC (2007, $74.99, dustjacket) r/#1-25; Capt. America 65th Anniv. Spec. and Winter Soldier: Winter Kills; Brubaker intro.; bonus material 75.00
Civil War: Captain America TPB (2007, $11.99) r/#22-24 & Winter Soldier: Winter Kills 12.00
...: Fighting Avenger (6/11, $4.99) 1st WWII mission; Gurihiru-a/c; Kitson var-c 5.00
...MGC #1 (5/10, $1.00) r/#1 with "Marvel's Greatest Comics" cover logo 3.00
...: Rebirth 1 (8/11, $4.99) r/origin & Red Skull apps. from Tales of Suspense #63,65-68 5.00
...: Red Menace Vol. 1 SC (2006, $11.99) r/#15-17 and 65th Anniversary Special 12.00
...: Red Menace Vol. 2 SC (2006, $10.99) r/#18-21; Brubaker interview 11.00
... Spotlight (7/11, $3.99) creator interviews; features on the movie and The Invaders 4.00
... Theater of War: America First! (2/09, $4.99) 1950s era tale; Chaykin-s/a; reprints 5.00
... Theater of War: America the Beautiful (3/09, $4.99) WW2 tale; Jenkins-s/Erskine-a 5.00
... Theater of War: Operation Zero-Point (12/08, $3.99) WW2 tale; Breitweiser-a 4.00
...: The Death of Captan America Vol. 1 HC (2007, $19.99) r/#25-30; variant covers 20.00
...: The Death of Captan America Vol. 2 HC (2008, $19.99) r/#31-36; variant covers 20.00
...Vol. 1: Winter Soldier HC (2005, $21.99) r/#1-7; concept sketches 22.00
...Vol. 1: Winter Soldier SC (2006, $16.99) r/#1-7; concept sketches 17.00
...: Who Won't Wield the Shield (6/10, $3.99) Deadpool & Forbush Man app. 4.00
...: Winter Soldier Vol. 2 HC (2006, $19.99) r/#8,9,11-14 20.00
...: Winter Soldier Vol. 2 SC (2006, $14.99) r/#8,9,11-14 15.00

CAPTAIN AMERICA
Marvel Comics: Sept, 2011 - No. 19, Dec, 2012 ($3.99)

1-19: 1-5-Brubaker-s/McNiven-c/a. 1-Nick Fury & Baron Zemo app. 6-10-Davis-a/c 4.00
1-Variant-c by John Romita Sr. 1 3 4 6 8 10
1-Movie photo variant-c of Chris Evans in costume 4 8 12 23 37 50

CAPTAIN AMERICA (Marvel NOW!)
Marvel Comics: Jan, 2013 - No. 25, Dec, 2014 ($3.99)

1-10-Remender-s/Romita Jr.-a/c; Cap in Dimension Z; Arnim Zola app.; 1st app. Jet Black. 10-Sharon Carter supposedly killed 4.00
11-24: 11,12,14,15-Pacheco-a; Nuke returns. 16-Red Skull app.; Alixe-a. 21-Steve Rogers rapidly aged. 22-24-Pacheco-a; Avengers app. 23-Sharon Carter returns 4.00
25-($4.99) Sam Wilson becomes the new Captain America; Pacheco-a
3 6 9 17 25 34
...: Homecoming 1 (5/14, $3.99) Van Lente-s/Grummett-a; bonus rep of Capt. Am. #117 4.00
...: Peggy Carter, Agent of S.H.I.E.L.D. (2014, $7.99) r/notable appearances 8.00

CAPTAIN AMERICA (Secret Empire tie-in)(Follows Captain America: Sam Wilson #24)
Marvel Comics: No. 25, Oct, 2017 ($4.99)

25-Leads into Secret Empire #8; Black Panther, Namor app.; Spencer-s/Saiz-a 5.00

CAPTAIN AMERICA (Marvel Legacy)
Marvel Comics: No. 695, Jan, 2018 - No. 704, Aug, 2018 ($3.99)

695-699: 695-Follows Secret Empire; Waid-s/Samnee-a. 697-Kraven app. 4.00
700-(6/18, $5.99) Waid-s/Samnee-a; back-up story by Waid using unpublished Kirby art 6.00
701-704-Romero-a. 701-Hughes-a (4 pgs). 702-Chaykin-a (5 pgs). 703-Davis-a (5 pgs) 4.00

CAPTAIN AMERICA
Marvel Comics: Sept, 2018 - No. 30, Sept, 2021 ($4.99/$3.99)

GD VG FN VF VF/NM NM-
2.0 4.0 6.0 8.0 9.0 9.2

1-($4.99) Ta-Nehisi Coates-s/Leinil Francis Yu-a; wraparound-c by Alex Ross 5.00
2-24,26-30-($3.99) 3-Black Panther app. 4,5-Taskmaster app. 7-12-Adam Kubert-a. 12-Daughters of Liberty regroup; back in Steve Rogers uniform. 14-Sin app. 16-John Walker app. 22,23-Shuri app. 23-Sharon Carter de-aged. 24-Red Skull app. 26-Red Hulk app. 4.00
25-($4.99) Red Skull, Falcon, Winter Soldier app.; back-up with Michael Cho-a 5.00
Annual 1 (11/18, $4.99) Howard-s/Sprouse & Lim-a; takes place in 1940; Bucky app. 5.00
Annual 1 (8/21, $4.99) Duggan-s/Castiello-a; "Infinite Destinies" tie-in; Black Widow app. 5.00
... & The Invaders: Bahamas Triangle 1 (9/19, $4.99) Roy Thomas-s/Jerry Ordway-a 5.00
... Anniversary Tribute 1 (5/21, $6.99) Captain America Comics #1 and Avengers #4 re-drawn by modern artists, one page each; McNiven-c swipe of Avengers #4 7.00
... The End 1 (4/20, $4.99) Erik Larsen-s/a; M.O.D.O.K. app. 5.00

CAPTAIN AMERICA (Leads into Captain America: Sentinel of Liberty #1 and Captain America: Symbol of Truth #1)
Marvel Comics: No. 0, Jun, 2022 ($4.99, one-shot)

0-De Iulis-a; Steve Rogers & Sam Wilson as Captain America; Arnim Zola app. 5.00

CAPTAIN AMERICA AND ... (Numbering continues from Captain America #619)
Marvel Comics: No. 620, Sept, 2011 - No. 640, Feb, 2013 ($2.99)

... Bucky 620-628: 620-624-Brubaker & Andreyko-s/Samnee-a/McGuinness-c. 620-Bucky's early WWII days. 625-628-Francavilla-c/a 3.00
... Hawkeye 629-632: 629-(6/12) Bunn-s/Vitti-aDell'Otto-c 3.00
... Iron Man 633-635: 635-(8/12) Bunn-s/Kitson-a/Andrasofszky-c; Batroc app. 3.00
... Namor 635.1 (10/12) World War II flashback; Will Conrad-a/Immonen-c 3.00
... Black Widow 636-640: 636-(11/12) Bunn-s/Francavilla-a/c 3.00

CAPTAIN AMERICA AND THE FALCON
Marvel Comics: May, 2004 - No. 14, June, 2005 ($2.99, limited series)

1-4-Priest-s/Sears-a 3.00
5-14: 5-8-Avengers Disassembled x-over. 6,7-Scarlet Witch app. 8-12-Modok app. 3.00
... Vol. 1: Two Americas (2005, $9.99) r/#1-4 10.00
... Vol. 2: Brothers and Keepers (2005, $17.99) r/#8-14 18.00

CAPTAIN AMERICA & THE KORVAC SAGA
Marvel Comics: Feb, 2011 - No. 4, May, 2011 ($2.99, limited series)

1-4-McCool-s/Rousseau-a/c. 4-Galactus app. 3.00

CAPTAIN AMERICA & THE MIGHTY AVENGERS (Sam Wilson as Captain America)
Marvel Comics: Jan, 2015 - No. 9, Aug, 2015 ($3.99)

1-9: 1-3-AXIS tie-ins; Luke Ross-a. 8,9-Secret Wars tie-in 4.00

CAPTAIN AMERICA & THE WINTER SOLDIER
Marvel Comics: Jan, 2023 ($4.99, one-shot)

1-Origin of the Outer Circle; story continues in Captain America: Sentinel of Liberty #7 5.00

CAPTAIN AMERICA/BLACK PANTHER (See Black Panther/Captain America: Flags of Our Fathers)

CAPTAIN AMERICA COMICS
Timely/Marvel Comics (TCI 1-20/CmPS 21-68/MjMC 69-75/Atlas Comics (PrPI 76-78):
Mar, 1941 - No. 75, Feb, 1950; No. 76, 5/54 - No. 78, 9/54
(No. 74 & 75 titled Capt. America's Weird Tales)

1-Origin & 1st app. Captain America & Bucky by Simon & Kirby; Hurricane, Tuk the Caveboy begin by S&K; 1st app. Red Skull; Hitler-c (by Simon?); intro of the "Capt. America Sentinels of Liberty Club" (advertised on inside front-c.); indicia reads Vol. 2, Number 1
37,600 75,200 112,800 250,800 413,600 715,000
2-S&K Hurricane; Tuk by Avison (Kirby splash); classic Hitler-c; 1st app. Cap's round shield
3125 6250 9375 23,400 49,200 75,000
3-Classic Red Skull-c & app; Stan Lee's 1st text (1st work for Marvel)
3550 7100 10,650 26,600 54,300 82,000
4-Early use of full pg. panel in comic; back-c pin-up of Captain America and Bucky
1530 3060 4590 11,500 21,750 32,000
5-Classic Kirby Nazi/torture Wheel of Death/Red Skull-c
1400 2800 4200 10,600 19,300 28,000
6-Origin Father Time; Tuk the Caveboy ends 1150 2300 3450 8700 15,850 23,000
7-Red Skull app.; classic-c 1300 2600 3900 9900 17,950 26,000
8-10-Last S&K issue, (S&K centerfold #6-10) 1000 2000 3000 7600 13,800 20,000
11-Last Hurricane, Headline Hunter; Al Avison Captain America begins, ends #20; Avison-c(p) 757 1514 2271 5526 9763 14,000
12-The Imp begins, ends #16; last Father Time 730 1460 2190 5329 9415 13,500
13-Origin The Secret Stamp; classic "Remember Pearl Harbor"-c
1350 2700 4050 10,250 18,625 27,000
14-"Remember Pearl Harbor" Japanese bondage/torture-c
975 1950 2919 7100 12,550 18,000
15 811 1622 2433 5920 10,460 15,000
16-Red Skull unmasks Cap; Red Skull-c 1100 2200 3300 8350 15,175 22,000
17-The Fighting Fool only app. 649 1298 1947 4738 8369 12,000
18-Classic-c 703 1406 2109 5132 9066 13,000
19-Human Torch begins #19 541 1082 1623 3950 6975 10,000

	GD 2.0	VG 4.0	FN 6.0	VF 8.0	VF/NM 9.0	NM- 9.2
20-Sub-Mariner app.; no Human Torch	514	1028	1542	3750	6625	9500
21-23,25: 25-Cap drinks liquid opium	497	994	1491	3628	6414	9200
24-Classic Japanese torture-c with boiling tar and fingernail removal	757	1514	2271	5526	9763	14,000
26-30: 27-Last Secret Stamp; Nazi WWII-c; last 68 pg. issue. 28-60 pg. issues begin.	497	994	1491	3628	6414	9200
31-35,38-40: 34-Centerfold poster of Cap. 38-Japanese bondage-c	459	918	1377	3350	5925	8500
36-Classic Hitler-c	1250	2500	3750	9500	17,250	25,000
37-Red Skull app.	1100	2200	3300	8350	15,175	22,000
41-Last Japan War-c	400	800	1200	2800	4900	7000
42-45	303	606	909	2121	3711	5300
46-German Holocaust-c; classic	3800	7600	11,400	25,300	44,650	64,000
47-Last German War-c	366	732	1098	2562	4481	6400
48-58,60	271	542	813	1734	2967	4200
59-Origin retold	411	822	1233	2877	5039	7200
61-Red Skull-c/story	459	918	1377	3350	5925	8500
62,64,65: 65-Kurtzman's "Hey Look"	300	600	900	1950	3375	4800
63-Intro/origin Asbestos Lady	300	600	900	2010	3505	5000
66-Bucky is shot; Golden Girl teams up with Captain America & learns his i.d; origin Golden Girl	411	822	1233	2877	5039	7200
67-69: 67-Captain America/Golden Girl team-up; Mxyztplk swipe; last Toro in Human Torch. 68-Sub-Mariner/Namora, and Captain America/Golden Girl team-up. 69-Human Torch/Sun Girl team-up.	371	742	1113	2600	4550	6500
70-73: 70-Sub-Mariner/Namora, and Captain America/Golden Girl team-up. 70-SciFi-c/story. 71-Anti Wertham editorial; The Witness, Bucky app.	423	846	1269	3000	5250	7500
74-(Scarce)(10/49)-Titled "Captain America's Weird Tales"; Red Skull-c & app.; classic-c	3800	7600	11,400	25,300	44,650	64,000
75(2/50)-Titled "C.A.'s Weird Tales"; no C.A. app.; horror cover/stories	423	846	1269	3000	5250	7500
76-78(1954): Human Torch/Toro stories; all have communist-c/stories	300	600	900	1950	3375	4800
132-Pg. Issue (B&W-1942)(Canadian)-Very rare. Has blank inside-c and back-c; contains Marvel Mystery #33 & Captain America #18 w/cover from Captain America #22; same contents as one version of the Marvel Mystery annuals	5700	11,400	17,100	42,750	--	--

NOTE: ***Crandall*** *a-2i, 3i, 9i, 10i.* ***Kirby*** *c-1, 2, 5-8p.* ***Rico*** *c-69-71.* ***Romita*** *c-77, 78.* ***Schomburg*** *c-3, 4, 26-29, 31, 33, 37-39, 41, 42, 45-54, 58.* ***Sekowsky*** *c-55, 56.* ***Shores*** *c-1i, 2i, 5-7i, 11i, 20-25, 30, 32, 34, 35, 40, 57, 59-67.* ***S&K*** *c-9, 10. Bondage c-3, 7, 15, 16, 34, 38.*

CAPTAIN AMERICA COMICS #1 70TH ANNIVERSARY EDITION
Marvel Comics: May, 2011 ($4.99, one-shot)

1-Recolored reprint of entire 1941 issue including Hurricane & Tuk stories; Ching-c 2 4 6 10 14 18

CAPTAIN AMERICA COMICS 70TH ANNIVERSARY SPECIAL
Marvel Comics: June, 2009 ($3.99, one-shot)

1-WWII flashback; Marcos Martin-a; Marcos-2 covers; r/Capt. America Comics #7 2 4 6 8 10 12

CAPTAIN AMERICA CORPS
Marvel Comics: Aug, 2011 - No. 5, Dec, 2011 ($2.99, limited series)

1-5-Stern-s/Briones-a/Jimenez-a; various versions of Captain America team-up 3.00

CAPTAIN AMERICA: DEAD MEN RUNNING
Marvel Comics: Mar, 2002 - No. 3, May, 2002 ($2.99, limited series)

1-3-Macan-s/Zezelj-a 3.00

CAPTAIN AMERICA: FIRST VENGEANCE (Based on the 2011 movie version)
Marvel Comics: Jul, 2011 - No. 4, Aug, 2011 ($2.99, limited series)

1-4-Van Lente-s; art by Luke Ross & others. 2-Movie photo-c 3.00

CAPTAIN AMERICA: FOREVER ALLIES
Marvel Comics: Oct, 2010 - No. 4, Jan, 2011 ($3.99, limited series)

1-4-Stern-s/Dragotta-a; Bucky in present & WW2 flashbacks; Young Allies app. 4.00

CAPTAIN AMERICA: HAIL HYDRA
Marvel Comics: Mar, 2011 - No. 5, Jul, 2011 ($2.99, limited series)

1-5-Cap vs. Hydra; Granov-c. 1-WWII flashback. 2-Kirby-style art by Scioli. 4-Hotz-a 3.00

CAPTAIN AMERICA / IRON MAN
Marvel Comics: Jan, 2022 - No. 5, May, 2022 ($3.99, limited series)

1-5-Landy-s/Unzueta-a; main covers by Alex Ross 4.00

CAPTAIN AMERICA: LIVING LEGEND
Marvel Comics: Dec, 2013 - No. 4, Feb, 2014 ($3.99, limited series)

1-4: 1-Diggle-s/Granov-a/c. 2-4-Alessio-a 4.00

CAPTAIN AMERICA: MAN OUT OF TIME
Marvel Comics: Jan, 2011 - No. 5, May, 2011 ($3.99, limited series)

1-5-Waid-s/Molina-a/Hitch-c; Cap's unfreezing in modern times re-told 4.00

CAPTAIN AMERICA/NICK FURY: BLOOD TRUCE
Marvel Comics: Feb, 1995 ($5.95, one-shot, squarebound)

nn-Chaykin story 6.00

CAPTAIN AMERICA/NICK FURY: THE OTHERWORLD WAR
Marvel Comics: Oct, 2001 ($6.95, one-shot, squarebound)

nn-Manco-a; Bucky and Red Skull app. 7.00

CAPTAIN AMERICA: PATRIOT
Marvel Comics: Nov, 2010 - No. 4, Feb, 2011 ($3.99, limited series)

1-4-Kesel-s/Breitweiser-a; 1-WW2 story; Patriot & the Liberty Legion app. 4.00

CAPTAIN AMERICA: REBORN (Titled Reborn in #1-3)
Marvel Comics: Sept, 2009 - No. 6, Mar, 2010 ($3.99, limited series)

1-6-Steve Rogers returns from the dead; Brubaker-s/Hitch & Guice-a. 1-Covers by Hitch, Ross & Quesada. 2-Origin re-told. 4-Joe Kubert var-c. 5-Cassaday var-c 4.00
1-4-Variant-c by Cassaday. 2-Variant-c by Sale. 5-Finch var-c 10.00
... MGC #1 (5/11, $1.00) r/#1 with "Marvel's Greatest Comics" logo on cover 3.00
...: Who Will Wield the Shield? (2/10, $3.99) Aftermath of series; Guice & Luke Ross-a 4.00

CAPTAIN AMERICA: RED, WHITE & BLUE
Marvel Comics: Sept, 2002 ($29.99, one-shot, hardcover with dustjacket)

nn-Reprints from Lee & Kirby, Steranko, Miller and others; and new short stories and pin-ups by various incl. Ross, Dini, Timm, Waid, Dorkin, Sienkiewicz, Miller, Bruce Jones, Collins, Piers-Rayner, Pope, Deodato, Quitely, Nino; Stelfreeze-c 30.00
TPB (2007, $19.99) 20.00

CAPTAIN AMERICA: ROAD TO WAR
Marvel Comics: Jun, 2016 ($4.99, one-shot)

1-Prelude to Captain America: Civil War movie; bonus r/Tales of Suspense #58 5.00

CAPTAIN AMERICA: SAM WILSON (Leads into Captain America #25 (Oct. 2017))
Marvel Comics: Dec, 2015 - No. 24, Sept, 2017 ($3.99)

1-6: 1-Spencer-s/Acuña-a; Misty Knight & D-Man app. 3-6-Sam as CapWolf 4.00
7-($5.99) 75th Anniversary issue; Steve Rogers regains his youth; Standoff tie-in; bonus short stories by Whedon & Cassaday, Tim Sale, and Rucka & Perkins 6.00
8-24: 8-Standoff tie-in; Baron Zemo app. 10-13-Civil War II tie-in. 11-13-U.S. Agent app. 22-24-Secret Empire tie-ins 4.00

CAPTAIN AMERICA, SENTINEL OF LIBERTY (See Fireside Book Series)

CAPTAIN AMERICA: SENTINEL OF LIBERTY
Marvel Comics: Sept, 1998 - No. 12, Aug, 1999 ($1.99)

1-Waid-s/Garney-a 5.00
1-Rough Cut ($2.99) Features original script and pencil pages 4.00
2-5: 2-Two-c; Invaders WW2 story 3.00
6-($2.99) Iron Man-c/app. 4.00
7-11: 8-Falcon-c/app. 9-Falcon poses as Cap 3.00
12-($2.99) Final issue; Bucky-c/app. 4.00

CAPTAIN AMERICA: SENTINEL OF LIBERTY (Steve Rogers as Captain America)
Marvel Comics: Aug, 2022 - Present ($4.99/$3.99)

1-($4.99) Lanzing & Kelly-s/Carnero-a; Bucky and The Destroyer app. 5.00
2-10-($3.99) 2-Peggy Carter returns 4.00

CAPTAIN AMERICA SPECIAL EDITION
Marvel Comics Group: Feb, 1984 - No. 2, Mar, 1984 ($2.00, Baxter paper)

	GD 2.0	VG 4.0	FN 6.0	VF 8.0	VF/NM 9.0	NM- 9.2
1-Steranko-c/a(r) in both; r/Capt. America #110,111	1	3	4	6	8	10
2-Reprints the scarce Our Love Story #5, and C.A. #113	1	3	4	6	8	10

CAPTAIN AMERICA: STEVE ROGERS (Also see Captain America: Sam Wilson)
Marvel Comics: Jul, 2016 - No. 19, Sept, 2017 ($4.99/$3.99)

1-Spencer-s/Saiz-a; childhood flashbacks to Hydra recruitment; Red Skull app. 5.00
2-19-($3.99) 2-Kobik app. 4-6-Civil War II tie-in. 14,15-Red Skull app. 16-19-Secret Empire tie-ins. 18-Namor app. 19-Leads into Captain America #25 (10/17) 4.00

CAPTAIN AMERICA: SYMBOL OF TRUTH (Sam Wilson as Captain America)
Marvel Comics: Aug, 2022 - Present ($4.99/$3.99)

1-($4.99) Onyebuchi-s/Silva-a; Misty Knight and Crossbones app. 5.00
2-10-($3.99) 2,3-Deadpool app. 3-Doctor Doom app. 4,5-Black Panther app. 4.00

CAPTAIN AMERICA THEATER OF WAR
Marvel Comics: 2009 - 2010 ($3.99, series of one-shots)

...: A Brother in Arms (6/09) Jenkins-s/McCrea-a; WWII story 4.00
...: Ghosts of My Country (12/09) Jenkins-s/Bonetti-a/Guice-c 4.00
...: Prisoners of Duty (2/10) Higgins & Siegel-s/Padilla-a; WWII story 4.00
...: To Soldier On (10/09) Jenkins-s/Blanco-a/Noto-c; Captain America in Iraq 4.00

CAPTAIN AMERICA: THE CHOSEN
Marvel Comics: Nov, 2007 - No. 6, Mar, 2008 ($3.99, limited series)

1-6-Breitweiser-a/Morrell-s 4.00

CAPTAIN AMERICA: THE CLASSIC YEARS
Marvel Comics: Jun, 1998 - No. 2 (trade paperbacks)

1-($19.95) Reprints Captain America Comics #1-5 25.00
2-($24.95) Reprints Captain America Comics #6-10 25.00

CAPTAIN AMERICA: THE FIRST AVENGER ADAPTATION (MARVEL'S...)
Marvel Comics: Jan, 2014 - No. 2, Feb, 2014 ($2.99, limited series)

1,2-Adaptation of the 2011 movie; Peter David-s/Wellinton Alves-a/photo-c 3.00

CAPTAIN AMERICA: THE LEGEND
Marvel Comics: Sept, 1996 ($3.95, one-shot)

1-Tribute issue; wraparound-c 5.00

CAPTAIN AMERICA: THE 1940S NEWSPAPER STRIP
Marvel Comics: Aug, 2010 - No. 3, Oct, 2010 ($3.99, limited series)

1-3-Karl Kesel-s/a; new stories set in WW2, formatted like 1940s newspaper comics 4.00

CAPTAIN AMERICA: WHAT PRICE GLORY
Marvel Comics: May, 2003 - No. 4, May, 2003 ($2.99, weekly limited series)

1-4-Bruce Jones-s/Steve Rude & Mike Royer-a 3.00

CAPTAIN AMERICA: WHITE
Marvel Comics: No. 0, Sept, 2008; No. 1, Nov, 2015 - No. 5, Feb, 2016 (limited series)

0-Bucky's origin retold; Loeb-s/Sale-a in all; interviews with creators; Sale sketch art 3.00
1-($4.99) Flashback to 1941; Sgt. Fury and the Howling Commandos app. 5.00
2-5-($3.99) 3-5-Red Skull app. 4.00

CAPTAIN AMERICA: WINTER SOLDIER DIRECTOR'S CUT
Marvel Comics: Jun, 2014 ($4.99, one-shot)

1-Reprints Captain America (2005) #1; bonus Brubaker script & series proposal 5.00

CAPTAIN AND THE KIDS, THE (See Famous Comics Cartoon Books)

CAPTAIN AND THE KIDS, THE (See Comics on Parade, Katzenjammer Kids, Okay Comics & Sparkler Comics)
United Features Syndicate/Dell Publ. Co.: 1938 -12/39; Sum, 1947 - No. 32, 1955; Four Color No. 881, Feb, 1958

	GD 2.0	VG 4.0	FN 6.0	VF 8.0	VF/NM 9.0	NM- 9.2
Single Series 1(1938)	126	252	378	806	1378	1950
Single Series 1(Reprint)(12/39- "Reprint" on-c)	50	100	150	315	533	750
1(Summer, 1947-UFS)-Katzenjammer Kids	20	40	60	115	185	255
2	11	22	33	62	86	110

Captain America: Sam Wilson #7 © MAR

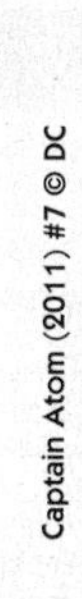
Captain Atom (2011) #7 © DC

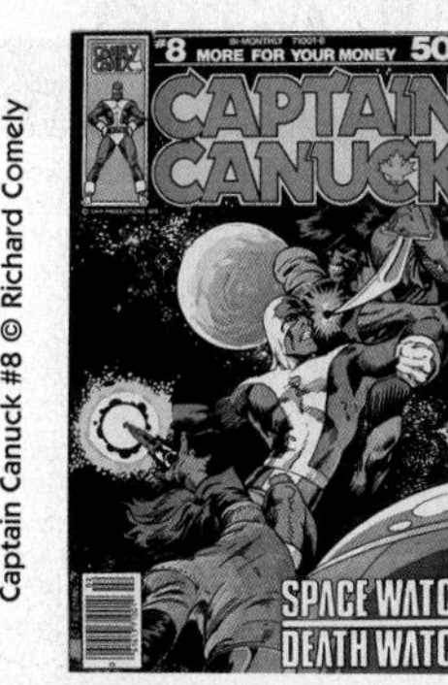
Captain Canuck #8 © Richard Comely

	GD 2.0	VG 4.0	FN 6.0	VF 8.0	VF/NM 9.0	NM- 9.2

3-10 10 20 30 54 72 90
11-20 8 16 24 44 57 70
21-32 (1955) 8 16 24 40 50 60
50th Anniversary issue-(1948)-Contains a 2 pg. history of the strip, including an account of the famous Supreme Court decision allowing both Pulitzer & Hearst to run the same strip under different names 19 38 57 111 176 240
Special Summer issue, Fall issue (1948) 12 24 36 69 97 125
Four Color 881 (Dell) 5 10 15 30 50 70

CAPTAIN ATOM
Nationwide Publishers: 1950 - No. 7, 1951 (5¢, 5x7-1/4", 52 pgs.)

1-Science fiction 43 86 129 271 461 650
2-7 27 54 81 158 259 360

CAPTAIN ATOM (Formerly Strange Suspense Stories #77)(Also see Space Adventures and Thunderbolt)
Charlton Comics: V2#78, Dec, 1965 - V2#89, Dec, 1967

V2#78-Origin retold; Bache-a (3 pgs.) 8 16 24 56 108 160
79-81: 79-1st app. Dr. Spectro; 3 pg. Ditko cut & paste /Space Adventures #24. 6 12 18 38 69 100
82-Intro. Nightshade (9/66) 12 24 36 82 179 275
83-(11/66)-1st app. Ted Kord/Blue Beetle 46 92 138 359 805 1250
84-86: Ted Kord Blue Beetle in all. 84-1st app. new Captain Atom. 85-1st app. Punch and Jewelee 5 10 15 35 63 90
87-89: Nightshade by Aparo in all 5 10 15 34 60 85
83-(Modern Comics-1977)-reprints 3 6 9 21 33 45
84,85-(Modern Comics-1977)-reprints 1 3 4 6 8 10
NOTE: *Aparo a-87-89.* ***Ditko*** *c/a(p) 78-89. #90 only published in fanzine 'The Charlton Bullseye' #1, 2.*

CAPTAIN ATOM (Also see Americomics & Crisis On Infinite Earths!)
DC Comics: Mar, 1987 - No. 57, Sept, 1991 (Direct sales only #35 on)

1-(44 pgs.)-Origin/1st app. with new costume 1 2 3 5 6 8
2-49: 5-Firestorm x-over. 6-Intro. new Dr. Spectro. 11-Millennium tie-in. 14-Nightshade app. 16-Justice League app. 17-$1.00-c begins; Swamp Thing app. 20-Blue Beetle x-over. 24,25-Invasion tie-in 4.00
50-($2.00, 52 pgs.) 5.00
51-57: 57-War of the Gods x-over 4.00
Annual 1,2 ('88, '89)-1-Intro Major Force 5.00

CAPTAIN ATOM (DC New 52)
DC Comics: Nov, 2011 - No. 12, Oct, 2012; No. 0, Nov, 2012 ($2.99)

1-12-J.T. Krul-s/Freddie Williams II-a. 3-Flash app. 3.00
#0 (11/12, $2.99) origin of Captain Atom re-told 3.00

CAPTAIN ATOM: ARMAGEDDON (Restarts the WildStorm Universe)
DC Comics (WildStorm): Dec, 2005 - No. 9, Aug, 2006 ($2.99, limited series)

1-9-Captain Atom appears in WildStorm Universe; Pfeifer-s/Camuncoli-a. 1-Lee-c 3.00
TPB (2007, $19.99) r/series 20.00

CAPTAIN BATTLE (Boy Comics #3 on) (See Silver Streak Comics)
New Friday Publ./Comic House: Summer, 1941 - No. 2, Fall, 1941

1-Origin Blackout by Rico; Captain Battle begins (1st appeared in Silver Streak #10, 5/41) classic hooded villain bondage/torture-c 232 464 696 1485 2543 3600
2-Origin Doctor Horror & only app.; classic story "House of Giants" 106 212 318 673 1162 1650

CAPTAIN BATTLE (2nd Series)
Magazine Press/Picture Scoop No. 5: No. 3, Wint, 1942-43; No. 5, Sum, 1943 (No #4)

3-Origin Silver Streak-r/SS#3; origin Lance Hale-r/SS #2; Cloud Curtis, Presto Martin 1st app.-r/SS #7; Simon-a(r) (52 pgs., nd) 116 232 348 742 1271 1800
5-Origin Blackout-r/#1 (68 pgs.); Japanese WWII-c 110 220 330 704 1202 1700

CAPTAIN BATTLE, JR.
Comic House (Lev Gleason): Fall, 1943 - No. 2, Winter, 1943-44

1-Nazi WWII-c by Rico. Hitler/Claw sty; The Claw vs. The Ghost 171 342 513 1086 1868 2650
2-Wolverton's Scoop Scuttle; Don Rico-c/a; The Green Claw story is reprinted from Silver Streak #6; Japanese WWII bondage/torture-c by Rico 106 212 318 673 1162 1650

CAPTAIN BEN DIX (See Promotional Comics section)

CAPTAIN BRITAIN (Also see Marvel Team-Up No. 65, 66)
Marvel Comics International: Oct. 13, 1976 - No. 39, July 6, 1977 (Weekly)

1-1st app & origin of Captain Britain (Brian Braddock); with Capt. Britain's face mask inside Claremont-s/Trimpe-a 27 54 81 189 420 650
2-Origin, part II; Capt. Britain's Boomerang inside 6 12 18 38 69 100
3-7: 3-Vs. Bank Robbers. 4-7-Vs. Hurricane 2 4 6 11 16 20
8-(12/76) 1st app. Betsy Braddock, the sister of Capt. Britain (Brian Braddock) who later becomes Psylocke (X-Men); 1st app. Dr. Synne 27 54 81 189 420 650
9-11-Battles Dr. Synne. 9,10-Betsy Braddock app. 2 4 6 11 16 20
12-23,25-27: (low print run)-12,13-Vs. Dr. Synne. 14,15-Vs. Mastermind. 16-23,25,26-With Captain America. 17-Misprinted & color section reprinted in #18. 27-Origin retold 3 6 9 17 25 34
24-With Capt. Britain's Jet Plane inside 5 10 15 34 60 85
28-32,36-39: 28-32-Vs. Lord Hawk. 30-32-Inhumans app. 35-Dr. Doom app. 37-39-Vs. Highwayman & Munipulator 2 4 6 8 10 12
33-35-More on origin 2 4 6 8 11 14
Annual (1978, Hardback, 64 pgs.)-Reprints #1-7 with pin-ups of Marvel characters 3 6 9 17 26 35
Summer Special (1980, 52 pgs.)-Reprints 2 4 6 8 10 12
NOTE: *No. 1, 2, & 24 are rarer in mint due to inserts. Distributed in Great Britain only. Nick Fury-r by* ***Steranko*** *in 1-20, 24-31, 35-37. Fantastic Four-r by* ***J. Buscema*** *in all. New* ***Buscema****-a in 24-30. Story from No. 39 continues in Super Spider-Man (British weekly) No. 231-247. Following cancellation of his series, new Captain Britain stories appeared in "Super Spider-Man" (British weekly) No. 231-247. Captain Britain stories which appear in Super-Spider-Man No 248-253 are reprints of Marvel Team-Up No. 65&66. Capt. Britain strips also appeared in Hulk Comic (weekly) 1, 3-30, 42-55, 57-60, in Marvel Superheroes (monthly) 377-388, in Daredevils (monthly) 1-11, Mighty World of Marvel (monthly) 7-16 & Captain Britain (monthly) 1-14. Issues 1-23 have B&W & color, paper-c, & are 32 pgs. Issues 24 on are all B&W w/glossy-c & are 36 pgs.*

CAPTAIN BRITAIN AND MI: 13 (Also see Secret Invasion x-over titles)
Marvel Comics: Jul, 2008 - No. 15, Sept, 2009 ($2.99)

1-Skrull invasion; Black Knight app.; Kirk-a 1 3 4 6 8 10
1-2nd printing with Kirk variant-c; 3rd printing with B&W cover 3.00
2-15: 5-Blade app. 9,10-Dracula app. 3.00
... Annual 1 (8/09, $3.99) Land-c; Meggan in Hell; Dr. Doom cameo; Collins-a 4.00

CAPTAIN BRITAIN AND THE MIGHTY DEFENDERS (Secret Wars tie-in)
Marvel Comics: Sept, 2015 - No. 2, Oct, 2015 ($3.99, limited series)

1,2-Ho Yinsen, Faiza Hussain, White Tiger, She-Hulk app.; Al Ewing-s/Alan Davis-a 4.00

CAPTAIN CANUCK
Comely Comix (Canada)(All distr. in U. S.): Jul,1975 - No. 4, Jul, 1977; No. 4, Jul-Aug, 1979 - No. 14, Mar-Apr, 1981

1-1st app. Captain Canuck, C.I.S.O. & Bluefox; Richard Comely-c/a 3 6 9 17 26 35
2,3(5-7/76): 2-1st app. Dr. Walker, Redcoat & Kebec. 3-1st app. Heather 1 3 4 6 8 10
4 (1st printing-2/77)-10x14-1/2"; (5.00); B&W; 300 copies serially numbered and signed with one certificate of authenticity 10 20 30 67 121 215
4 (2nd printing-7/77)-11x17", B&W; only 15 copies printed; signed by creator Richard Comely, serially #'d and two certificates of authenticity inserted; orange cardboard covers (Very Rare) 14 28 42 93 204 315
4-14: 4(7-8/79)-1st app. Tom Evans & Mr. Gold; origin The Catman. 5-Origin Capt. Canuck's powers; 1st app. Earth Patrol & Chaos Corps. 5-7-Three-part neo-Nazi story set in 1994. 8-Jonn 'The Final Chapter'; 1st app. Mike & Saskia. 9-1st World Beyond. 11-1st 'Chariots of Fire' story. 12-A-bomb explosion panel 1 2 3 5 6 8
15-(8/04, $15.00) Limited edition of unpublished issue from 1981; serially #'d edition of 150; signed by creator Richard Comely 8 16 24 51 96 140
... Legacy 1 (9-10/06) Comely-s/a 4.00
... Legacy Special Edition ($7.95, 52 pgs., limited ed. of 1000) Comely-s/a 2 4 6 8 10 12
Special Collectors Pack (#1 & #2 polybagged) 2 4 6 9 13 16
Summer Special 1(7-9/80, 95¢, 64 pgs.) George Freeman-c/a; pin-ups by Gene Day, Tom Grummett, Dave Sim and others 6.00
Summer Special / Canada Day Edition #1 (2014, no cover price) 2 new stories, background on animated web series; regular-c shows a parade; variants exist 5.00
NOTE: *30,000 copies of No. 2 were destroyed in Winnipeg.*

CAPTAIN CANUCK
Chapterhouse Comics: May, 2015 - No. 12, May, 2017 ($3.99)

1-Kalman Andrasofszky-s/a; 3 covers 1 3 4 6 8 10
2-12: 2-Andrasofszky-s/a. 3-12-Leonard Kirk-a 4.00
#0/FCBD Edition (5/15, giveaway) previews #1; origin re-told; character profiles 3.00
... Free Comic Book Day Issue 2019 (5/19) Intro. of a new Captain Canuck 3.00

CAPTAIN CANUCK (Season 5)
Chapterhouse Comics: Nov, 2020 - Present ($4.99)

1-Ho Che Anderson-s/Felipe Cunha-a 5.00

CAPTAIN CANUCK: UNHOLY WAR
Comely Comix: Oct, 2004 - No. 3, Jan, 2005; No. 4, Sept, 2007 ($2.50, limited series)

1-3-Riel Langlois-s/Drue Langlois-a: 1-1st app. David Semple (West Coast Capt. Canuck); Clair Sinclair as Bluefox 3.00
4-(Low print run) Black Mack the Lumberjack, Torchie, Splatter app. 6.00

CAPTAIN CANUCK YEAR ONE
Chapterhouse Comics: May, 2017; Nov, 2017 ($1.99)

GD VG FN VF VF/NM NM-
2.0 4.0 6.0 8.0 9.0 9.2

1-($1.99) Baruchel & Andrasofszky-s; Marcus To-a; back-up Die Kitty Die story 3.00
#1/FCBD Edition (5/17, giveaway) back-up Die Kitty Die story 3.00

CAPTAIN CARROT AND HIS AMAZING ZOO CREW (Also see New Teen Titans & Oz-Wonderland War)
DC Comics: Mar, 1982 - No. 20, Nov, 1983

1-Superman app. 2 4 6 8 10 12
2-20: 3-Re-intro Dodo & The Frog. 9-Re-intro Three Mouseketeers, the Terrific Whatzit. 10,11-Pig Iron reverts back to Peter Porkchops. 20-Changeling app. 5.00

CAPTAIN CARROT AND THE FINAL ARK (DC Countdown tie-in)
DC Comics: Dec, 2007 - No. 3, Feb, 2008 ($2.99, limited series)

1-3-Bill Morrison-s/Scott Shaw!-a. 3-Batman, Red Arrow, Hawkgirl & Zatanna app. 3.00
TPB (2008, $19.99) r/#1-3; Captain Carrot and His Amazing Zoo Crew #1,14,15; New Teen Titans #16 and stories from Teen Titans (2003 series) #30,31; cover gallery 20.00

CAPTAIN CARTER (Multiverse super soldier Peggy Carter)
Marvel Comics: May, 2022 - No. 5, Oct, 2022 ($3.99)

1-5-Adventures in modern times; McKelvie-s/Cresta-a. 4,5-Tony Stark app. 4.00

CAPTAIN CARVEL AND HIS CARVEL CRUSADERS (See Carvel Comics in the Promotional section)

CAPTAIN CONFEDERACY
Marvel Comics (Epic Comics): Nov, 1991 - No. 4, Feb, 1992 ($1.95)

1-All new stories 1 2 3 5 6 8
2-4-All new stories 4.00

CAPTAIN COURAGEOUS COMICS (Banner #3-5; see Four Favorites #5)
Periodical House (Ace Magazines): No. 6, March, 1942

6-Origin & 1st app. The Sword; Lone Warrior, Capt. Courageous app.; Capt. moves to Four Favorites #5 in May 142 284 426 909 1555 2200

CAPT'N CRUNCH COMICS (See Cap'n...)

CAPTAIN DAVY JONES
Dell Publishing Co.: No. 598, Nov, 1954

Four Color 598 6 12 18 38 69 100

CAPTAIN EASY (See The Funnies & Red Ryder #3-32)
Hawley/Dell Publ./Standard(Visual Editions)/Argo: 1939 - No. 17, Sept, 1949; April, 1956

nn-Hawley(1939)-Contains reprints from The Funnies & 1938 Sunday strips by Roy Crane 113 226 339 718 1234 1750
Four Color 24 (1942) 61 122 183 390 670 950
Four Color 111(6/46) 14 28 42 93 204 315
10(Standard-10/47) 16 32 48 94 147 200
11,12,14,15,17: 11-17 all contain 1930s & '40s strip-r 12 24 36 67 94 120
13,16: Schomburg-c 21 42 63 124 202 280
Argo 1(4/56)-Reprints 8 16 24 44 57 70

CAPTAIN EASY & WASH TUBBS (See Famous Comics Cartoon Books)

CAPTAIN ELECTRON
Brick Computer Science Institute: Aug, 1986 ($2.25)

1-Disbrow-a 3.00

CAPTAIN EO 3-D (Michael Jackson Disney theme parks movie)
Eclipse Comics: July, 1987 (Eclipse 3-D Special #18, $3.50, Baxter)

1-Adapts 3-D movie; Michael Jackson-c/app. 3 6 9 19 30 40
1-2-D limited edition 5 10 15 34 60 85
1-Large size (11x17", 8/87)-Sold only at Disney Theme parks ($6.95) 4 8 12 28 47 65

CAPTAIN FEARLESS COMICS (Also see Holyoke One-Shot #6, Old Glory Comics & Silver Streak #1)
Helnit Publishing Co. (Holyoke Publ. Co.): Aug, 1941 - No. 2, Sept, 1941

1-Origin Mr. Miracle, Alias X, Captain Fearless, Citizen Smith Son of the Unknown Soldier; Miss Victory (1st app.) begins (1st patriotic heroine? before Wonder Woman) 155 310 465 992 1696 2400
2-Grit Grady, Captain Stone app. 63 126 189 403 689 975

CAPTAIN FLAG (See Blue Ribbon Comics #16)

CAPTAIN FLASH
Sterling Comics: Nov, 1954 - No. 4, July, 1955

1-Origin; Sekowsky-a; Tomboy (female super hero) begins; only pre-code issue; atomic rocket-c 55 110 165 352 601 850
2-4: 4-Flying saucer invasion-c 36 72 108 211 343 475

CAPTAIN FLEET (Action Packed Tales of the Sea)
Ziff-Davis Publishing Co.: Fall, 1952

1-Painted-c 24 48 72 142 234 325

CAPTAIN FLIGHT COMICS
Four Star Publications: May, 1944 - No. 10, Dec, 1945; No. 11, Feb-Mar, 1947

nn-Captain Flight begins 87 174 261 553 952 1350
2-4: 4-Rock Raymond begins, ends #7 54 108 162 343 574 825
5-Bondage, classic torture-c; Red Rocket begins; the Grenade app. (scarce) 300 600 900 2010 3505 5000
6-L. B. Cole-a, 8 pgs. 61 122 183 390 670 950
7-10: 7-L. B. Cole covers begin, end #11. 7-9-Japanese WWII-c. 8-Yankee Girl begins; intro. Black Cobra & Cobra Kid & begins. 9-Torpedoman app.; last Yankee Girl; Kinstler-a. 10-Deep Sea Dawson, Zoom of the Jungle, Rock Raymond, Red Rocket, & Black Cobra app; bondage-c 132 264 396 838 1444 2050
11-Torpedoman, Blue Flame (Human Torch clone) app.; last Black Cobra, Red Rocket; classic L. B. Cole sci-fi robot-c (scarce) 622 1244 1866 4541 8021 11,500

CAPTAIN GALLANT (...of the Foreign Legion) (TV) (Texas Rangers in Action No. 5 on?)
Charlton Comics: 1955; No. 2, Jan, 1956 - No. 4, Sept, 1956

Non-Heinz version (#1)-Buster Crabbe photo on-c; full page Buster Crabbe photo inside front-c 9 18 27 47 61 75
(Heinz version is listed in the Promotional Comics section)
2-4: Buster Crabbe in all. 2-Crabbe photo back-c 7 14 21 35 43 50

CAPTAIN GINGER
AHOY Comics: 2018 - Present ($3.99)

1-4: Space-faring cats; Stuart Moore-s/June Brigman-a; back-up text stories by various 4.00
... Season Two (2020 - Present) 1,2-Moore-s/Brigman-a 4.00

CAPTAIN GLORY
Topps Comics: Apr, 1993 ($2.95) (Created by Jack Kirby)

1-Polybagged w/Kirbychrome trading card; Ditko-a & Kirby-c; has coupon for Amberchrome Secret City Saga #0 4.00

CAPTAIN HERO (See Jughead as...)

CAPTAIN HERO COMICS DIGEST MAGAZINE
Archie Publications: Sept, 1981

1-Reprints of Jughead as Super-Guy 2 4 6 10 14 18

CAPTAIN HOBBY COMICS
Export Publication Ent. Ltd. (Dist. in U.S. by Kable News Co.): Feb, 1948 (Canadian)

1 15 30 45 90 140 190

CAPT. HOLO IN 3-D (See Blackthorne 3-D Series #65)

CAPTAIN HOOK & PETER PAN (Movie)(Disney)
Dell Publishing Co.: No. 446, Jan, 1953

Four Color 446 10 20 30 66 138 210

CAPTAIN JET (Fantastic Fears No. 7 on)
Four Star Publ./Farrell/Comic Media: May, 1952 - No. 5, Jan, 1953

1-Bakerish-a 28 56 84 165 270 375
2 15 30 45 94 147 200
3-5,6(?) 14 28 42 78 112 145

CAPTAIN JOHNER & THE ALIENS
Valiant: May, 1995 - No. 2, May, 1995 ($2.95, shipped in same month)

1,2: Reprints Magnus Robot Fighter 4000 A.D. back-up stories; new Paul Smith-c 3.00

CAPTAIN JUSTICE (TV)
Marvel Comics: Mar, 1988 - No. 2, Apr, 1988 (limited series)

1,2-Based on the 1987 "Once a Hero" television series 3.00

CAPTAIN KANGAROO (TV)
Dell Publishing Co.: No. 721, Aug, 1956 - No. 872, Jan, 1958

Four Color 721 (#1)-Photo-c 13 26 39 91 201 310
Four Color 780, 872-Photo-c 12 24 36 79 170 260

CAPTAIN KID
AfterShock Comics: Jul, 2016 - No. 5, Mar, 2017 ($3.99)

1-5-Mark Waid & Tom Peyer-s/Wilfredo Torres-a 4.00

CAPTAIN KIDD (Formerly Dagar; My Secret Story #26 on)(Also see Comic Comics & Fantastic Comics)
Fox Feature Syndicate: No. 24, June, 1949 - No. 25, Aug, 1949

24,25: 24-Features Blackbeard the Pirate 19 38 57 111 176 240

CAPTAIN KRONOS - VAMPIRE HUNTER (Based on the 1974 Hammer film)
Titan Comics (Hammer Comics): Oct, 2017 - No. 4, Jan, 2018 ($3.99)

1-4-Abnett-s/Mandrake-a; multiple covers on each (art & photo) 4.00

CAPTAIN MARVEL (See All Hero, All-New Collectors' Ed., America's Greatest, Fawcett Miniature, Gift, JSA, Kingdom Come, Legends, Limited Collectors' Ed., Marvel Family, Master No. 21, Mighty Midget Comics, Power of Shazam!, Shazam, Special Edition Comics, Whiz, Wisco (in Promotional Comics section), World's Finest #253 and XMas Comics)

CAPTAIN MARVEL (Becomes ...Presents the Terrible 5 No. 5)
M. F. Enterprises: April, 1966 - No. 4, Nov, 1966 (25¢ Giants)

nn-(#1 on pg. 5)-Origin; created by Carl Burgos 7 14 21 49 92 135
2-4: 3-(#3 on pg. 4)-Fights the Bat 5 10 15 34 60 85

CAPTAIN MARVEL (Marvel's Space-Born Super-Hero! Captain Marvel #1-6; see Giant-Size..., Life Of..., Marvel Graphic Novel #1, Marvel Spotlight V2#1 & Marvel Super-Heroes #12)
Marvel Comics Group: May, 1968 - No. 19, Dec, 1969; No. 20, June, 1970 - No. 21, Aug, 1970; No. 22, Sept, 1972 - No. 62, May, 1979

1 23 46 69 161 356 550
2-Super Skrull-c/story 8 16 24 54 102 150
3-5: 4-Captain Marvel battles Sub-Mariner 6 12 18 38 69 100
6-11: 11-Capt. Marvel given great power by Zo the Ruler; Smith/Trimpe-c; Death of Una 4 8 12 25 40 55
12,13,15,19,20 3 6 9 17 26 35
14-Capt. Marvel vs. Iron Man; last 12¢ issue. 5 10 15 33 57 80
16-1st new Captain Marvel (cameo) 5 10 15 33 57 80
17-1st new Captain Marvel app. 11 22 33 73 157 240
18-Carol Danvers gets powers 11 22 33 75 160 245
21-Capt. Marvel battles Hulk; last 15¢ issue 6 12 18 40 73 105
22-24 3 6 9 17 26 35
25-Starlin-c/a begins; Starlin's 1st Thanos saga begins (3/73), ends #34; Thanos cameo (5 panels) 8 16 24 52 99 145
26-2nd app. Thanos (see Iron Man #55); 1st Thanos-c 10 20 30 67 141 215
27-2nd app. Eros (Starfox)(7/73); 3rd app. Thanos 12 24 36 83 182 280
28-Thanos-c/s (4th app.); Avengers app. 10 20 30 64 132 200
29,30-Thanos cameos. 29-C.M. gains more powers 5 10 15 34 60 85
31-Thanos app.; last 20¢ issue; Avengers app. 5 10 15 34 60 85
32-Thanos-c & app.; Avengers app. 5 10 15 35 63 90
33-Thanos-c & app.; Capt. Marvel battles Thanos; Thanos origin re-told 9 18 27 58 114 170
34-1st app. Nitro; C.M. contracts cancer which eventually kills him; last Starlin-c/a 5 10 15 31 53 75
35,37-40,42,46-48,50,53-56,59-62: 39-Origin Watcher. 42,59-62-Drax app. 2 4 6 8 10 12
36,41,43,49: 36-R-origin/1st app. Capt. Marvel from Marvel Super-Heroes #12. 41,43-Drax app.; Wrightson part inks; #43-c(i). 49-Starlin & Weiss-p assists 2 4 6 9 13 16
44,45-(Regular 25¢ editions)(5,7/76) 2 4 6 8 10 12
44,45-(30¢-c variants, limited distribution) 5 10 15 30 50 70
51,52-(Regular 30¢ editions)(7,9/77) 2 4 6 8 10 12
51,52-(35¢-c variants, limited distribution) 8 16 24 54 102 150

Captain Carter #1 © MAR

Captain Marvel (2019) #3 © MAR

Captain Marvel Adventures #47 © FAW

	GD 2.0	VG 4.0	FN 6.0	VF 8.0	VF/NM 9.0	NM- 9.2
57-Thanos appears in flashback	3	6	9	14	19	24
58-Thanos cameo; Drax app.	2	4	6	11	16	20

NOTE: ***Alcala*** *a-35.* ***Austin*** *a-46i, 49-53i; c-52i.* ***Buscema*** *a-18p-21p.* ***Colan*** *a(p)-1-4; c(p)-1-4, 8, 9.* ***Heck*** *a-5-10p, 16p.* ***Gil Kane*** *a-17-21p; c-17-24p, 37p, 53.* ***Starlin*** *a-36.* ***McWilliams*** *a-40i. #25-34 were reprinted in The Life of Captain Marvel.*

CAPTAIN MARVEL
Marvel Comics: Nov, 1989 ($1.50, one-shot, 52 pgs.)

	GD 2.0	VG 4.0	FN 6.0	VF 8.0	VF/NM 9.0	NM- 9.2
1-Monica Rambeau gains new powers; McDuffie-s	4	8	12	25	40	55

CAPTAIN MARVEL
Marvel Comics: Feb, 1994 ($1.75, 52 pgs.)

	GD 2.0	VG 4.0	FN 6.0	VF 8.0	VF/NM 9.0	NM- 9.2
1-(Indicia reads Vol 2 #2)-Minor Captain America app.	1	3	4	6	8	10

CAPTAIN MARVEL
Marvel Comics: Dec, 1995 - No. 6, May, 1996 ($2.95/$1.95)

	GD 2.0	VG 4.0	FN 6.0	VF 8.0	VF/NM 9.0	NM- 9.2
1 ($2.95)-Advs. of Mar-Vell's son begins; Fabian Nicieza scripts; foil-c	1	2	3	5	6	8
2-6: 2-Begin $1.95-c						4.00

CAPTAIN MARVEL (Vol. 3) (See Avengers Forever)
Marvel Comics: Jan, 2000 - No. 35, Oct, 2002 ($2.50)

	GD 2.0	VG 4.0	FN 6.0	VF 8.0	VF/NM 9.0	NM- 9.2
1-Peter David-s in all; two covers	1	2	3	5	6	8
2-10: 2-Two covers; Hulk app. 9-Silver Surfer app.						3.00
11-35: 12-Maximum Security x-over. 17,18-Starlin-a. 27-30-Spider-Man 2099 app.						3.00
Wizard #0-Preview and history of Rick Jones						4.00
...: First Contact (8/01, $16.95, TPB) r/#0,1-6						17.00

CAPTAIN MARVEL (Vol. 4) (See Avengers Forever)
Marvel Comics: Nov, 2002 - No. 25, Sept, 2004 ($2.25/$2.99)

	GD 2.0	VG 4.0	FN 6.0	VF 8.0	VF/NM 9.0	NM- 9.2
1-Peter David-s/Chriscross-a ; 3 covers by Ross, Jusko & Chriscross						5.00
2-7: 2,3-Punisher app. 3-Alex Ross-c; new costume debuts. 4-Noto-c. 7-Thor app.						3.00
3-Sketchbook Edition-($3.50) includes Ross' concept design pages for new costume						4.00
8-15,18-25: 8-Begin $2.99-c; Thor app. 10-Spider-Man-c/app. 15-Neal Adams-c						3.00
16-1st Phyla-Vell (cameo)	3	6	9	17	26	35
17-2nd Phyla-Vell (full app.)	5	10	15	30	50	70
Vol. 1: Nothing To Lose (2003, $14.99, TPB) r/#1-6						15.00
Vol. 2: Coven (2003, $14.99, TPB) r/#7-12						15.00
Vol. 3: Crazy Like a Fox (2004, $14.99, TPB) r/#13-18						15.00
Vol. 4: Odyssey (2004, $16.99, TPB) r/#19-25						17.00

CAPTAIN MARVEL (Vol. 5) (See Secret Invasion x-over titles)
Marvel Comics: Jan, 2008 - No. 5, Jun, 2008 ($2.99)

	GD 2.0	VG 4.0	FN 6.0	VF 8.0	VF/NM 9.0	NM- 9.2
1-5-Mar-Vell "from the past in the present"; McGuinness-c/Weeks-a						3.00
3,4-Skrull variant-c						4.00

CAPTAIN MARVEL
Marvel Comics: Sept, 2012 - No. 17, Jan, 2014 ($2.99)

	GD 2.0	VG 4.0	FN 6.0	VF 8.0	VF/NM 9.0	NM- 9.2
1-Carol Danvers as Captain Marvel; DeConnick-s/Soy-a	3	6	9	16	24	32
2-5						6.00
6-13,15,16: 13-The Enemy Within. 15,16-Infinity tie-in						5.00
14-1st cameo of Kamala Khan (new Ms. Marvel); Andrade-a; The Enemy Within cont'd	9	18	27	60	120	180
17-($3.99) Cameo of Kamala Khan (new Ms. Marvel); Andrade-a	3	6	9	21	33	45
17-($3.99, 2nd printing) Kamala Khan (new Ms. Marvel) in costume on cover	28	56	84	202	451	700

CAPTAIN MARVEL
Marvel Comics: May, 2014 - No. 15, Jul, 2015 ($3.99)

	GD 2.0	VG 4.0	FN 6.0	VF 8.0	VF/NM 9.0	NM- 9.2
1-Carol Danvers; DeConnick-s/Lopez-a	3	6	9	15	22	28
2,3-Guardians of the Galaxy app.						6.00
4-9,11-15: 7,8-Rocket Raccoon app. 14-Black Vortex x-over						4.00
10-($4.99) 100th issue; War Machine & Spider-Woman app.; Lopez & Takara-a						5.00

CAPTAIN MARVEL (Follows Secret Wars event)(Also see Mighty Captain Marvel)
Marvel Comics: Mar, 2016 - No. 10, Jan, 2017 ($3.99)

	GD 2.0	VG 4.0	FN 6.0	VF 8.0	VF/NM 9.0	NM- 9.2
1-5-Carol Danvers; Fazekas & Butters-s/Anka-a; Aurora, Sasquatch & Puck app.						4.00
6-9-Civil War II tie-ins						4.00
10-($4.99) Civil War II tie-in; Gage & Gage-s/Silas-a; Alpha Flight app.						5.00

CAPTAIN MARVEL (Follows Mighty Captain Marvel)
Marvel Comics: No. 125, Dec, 2017 - No. 129, Apr, 2018 ($3.99)

	GD 2.0	VG 4.0	FN 6.0	VF 8.0	VF/NM 9.0	NM- 9.2
125-129-Carol Danvers; Stohl-s/Bandini-a; Alpha Flight app.						4.00

CAPTAIN MARVEL (Carol Danvers)(Also see Star series)
Marvel Comics: Mar, 2019 - Present ($4.99/$3.99)

	GD 2.0	VG 4.0	FN 6.0	VF 8.0	VF/NM 9.0	NM- 9.2
1-($4.99) Thompson-s/Carnero-a; Spider-Woman, Hazmat, Nuclear Man app.						5.00
2-29,31-46-($3.99) 2,3-Echo & She-Hulk app. 3-5-Rogue app. 6,7-War of The Realms tie-in. 8-Debut of Star. 11-Star gets the Reality Stone. 12-16-The Last Avenger. 17-Wolverine app. 18-21-Empyre tie-in; Carol as The Accuser; intro. Lauri-ell. 31-Miyazawa-a						4.00
30-($4.99) Enchantress & Ove app.; back-up with McKelvie-s/a; Ms. Marvel app.						5.00
Annual 1 (6/22, $4.99) Starjammers app.; Gronbekk-s/Gomez-a						5.00
...: Braver & Mightier 1 (4/19, $3.99) Houser-s/Buonfantino-a						4.00
...: Marvels Snapshots 1 (4/21, $4.99) Mark Waid-s/Claire Roe-a; Kamala app.						5.00
...: The End 1 (3/20, $4.99) Carol's last adventure, set in 2051; Thompson-s/Carnero-a						5.00

CAPTAIN MARVEL ADVENTURES (See Special Edition Comics for pre #1)
Fawcett Publications: 1941 (March) - No. 150, Nov, 1953 (#1 on stands 1/16/41)

	GD 2.0	VG 4.0	FN 6.0	VF 8.0	VF/NM 9.0	NM- 9.2
nn(#1)-Captain Marvel & Sivana by Jack Kirby. The cover was printed on unstable paper stock and is rarely found in Fine or Mint condition; blank back inside-c	7500	15,000	30,000	60,000	97,500	135,000
2-(Advertised as #3, which was counting Special Edition Comics as the real #1); Tuska-a	486	972	1458	3550	6275	9000
3-Metallic silver-c	343	686	1029	2400	4200	6000
4-Three Lt. Marvels app.	245	490	735	1568	2684	3800
5-WWII-c	200	400	600	1280	2190	3100
6-10: 9-1st Otto Binder scripts on Capt. Marvel	142	284	426	909	1555	2200
11-15: 12-Capt. Marvel joins the Army. 13-Two pg. Capt. Marvel pin-up. 15-Comix Cards on back-c begin, end #26	113	226	339	718	1234	1750
16,17: 17-Painted-c	103	206	309	659	1130	1600
18-Origin & 1st app. Mary Marvel & Marvel Family (12/11/42); classic painted-c; Mary Marvel by Marcus Swayze	1000	2000	3000	7400	13,200	19,000
19-Mary Marvel x-over; classic Christmas-c	110	220	330	704	1202	1700
20,21,23-Attached to the cover, each has a miniature comic just like the Mighty Midget Comics #11, except that each has a full color promo ad on the back cover. Most copies were circulated without the miniature comic. These issues with miniatures attached are very rare, and should not be mistaken for copies with the similar Mighty Midget glued in its place. The Mighty Midgets had blank back covers except for a small victory stamp seal. Only the Capt. Marvel, Captain Marvel Jr. and Golden Arrow No. 11 miniatures have been positively documented as having been affixed to these covers. Each miniature was only partially glued by its back cover to the Captain Marvel comic making it easy to see if it's the genuine miniature rather than a Mighty Midget. with comic attached....	476	952	1428	3475	6138	8800
20,23-Without miniature	77	154	231	493	847	1200
21-Without miniature; Hitler-c	168	336	504	1075	1838	2600
22-Mr. Mind serial begins; Mr. Mind first heard	116	232	348	742	1271	1800
24,25	74	148	222	470	810	1150
26-28,30: 26-Flag-c; subtle Mr. Mind 2-panel cameo. 27-1st full Mr. Mind app. (his voice was only heard over the radio before now) (9/43)	60	120	180	381	653	925
29-1st Mr. Mind-c (11/43)	77	154	231	493	847	1200
31-35: 35-Origin Radar (5/44, see Master #50)	54	108	162	343	574	825
36-40: 37-Mary Marvel x-over	50	100	150	315	533	750
41-46: 42-Christmas-c. 43-Capt. Marvel 1st meets Uncle Marvel; Mary Batson cameo. 46-Mr. Mind serial ends	41	82	123	256	428	600
47-50	39	78	117	240	395	550
51-53,55-60: 51-63-Bi-weekly issues. 52-Origin & 1st app. Sivana Jr.; Capt. Marvel Jr. x-over	36	72	108	211	343	475
54-Special oversize 68 pg. issue	37	74	111	222	361	500
61-The Cult of the Curse serial begins	37	74	111	222	361	500
62-65-Serial cont.; Mary Marvel x-over in #65	34	68	102	204	332	460
66-Serial ends; Atomic War-c	42	84	126	265	445	625
67-77,79: 69-Billy Batson's Christmas; Uncle Marvel, Mary Marvel, Capt. Marvel Jr. x-over. 71-Three Lt. Marvels app. 72-Empire State Building photo-c. 79-Origin Mr. Tawny	31	62	93	186	303	420
78-Origin Mr. Atom	37	74	111	218	354	490
80-Origin Capt. Marvel retold; origin scene-c	97	194	291	621	1061	1500
81-84,86-90: 81,90-Mr. Atom app. 82-Infinity-c. 82,86,88,90-Mr. Tawny app.	31	62	93	186	305	420
85-Freedom Train issue	35	70	105	208	339	470
91-99: 92-Mr. Tawny app. 96-Gets 1st name "Tawky"	30	60	90	177	289	400
100-Origin retold; silver metallic-c	55	110	165	352	601	850
101-115,117-120	30	60	90	177	289	400
116-Flying Saucer issue (1/51)	35	70	105	208	339	470
121-Origin retold	39	78	117	240	395	550
122-137,139,140	30	60	90	177	289	400
138-Flying Saucer issue (11/52)	37	74	111	218	354	490
141-Pre-code horror story "The Hideous Head-Hunter"	39	78	117	231	378	525
142-149: 142-used in **POP**, pgs. 92,96	33	66	99	194	317	440
150-(Low distribution)	65	130	195	416	708	1000

NOTE: ***Swayze*** *a-12, 14, 15, 18, 19, 40; c-12, 15, 19.*

CAPTAIN MARVEL AND THE CAROL CORPS (Secret Wars tie-in)
Marvel Comics: Aug, 2015 - No. 4, Nov, 2015 ($3.99, limited series)

	GD 2.0	VG 4.0	FN 6.0	VF 8.0	VF/NM 9.0	NM- 9.2
1-4: 1-Carol Danvers' squad; DeConnick & Thompson-s/Lopez-a. 4-Braga-a						4.00

GD VG FN VF VF/NM NM-
2.0 4.0 6.0 8.0 9.0 9.2

CAPTAIN MARVEL AND THE GOOD HUMOR MAN (Movie)
Fawcett Publications: 1950
nn-Partial photo-c w/Jack Carson & the Captain Marvel Club Boys
58 116 174 371 636 900

CAPTAIN MARVEL COMIC STORY PAINT BOOK (See Comic Story...)

CAPTAIN MARVEL, JR. (See Fawcett Miniatures, Marvel Family, Master Comics, Mighty Midget Comics, Shazam & Whiz Comics)

CAPTAIN MARVEL, JR.
Fawcett Publications: Nov, 1942 - No. 119, June, 1953 (No #34)
1-Origin Capt. Marvel Jr. retold (Whiz #25); Capt. Nazi app. Classic Raboy-c
729 1458 2187 5322 9411 13,500
2-Vs. Capt. Nazi; origin Capt. Nippon 232 464 696 1485 2543 3600
3-Infinity Pied Piper-c 129 258 387 826 1413 2000
4-Classic Raboy-c 226 452 678 1446 2473 3500
5-Vs. Capt. Nazi 110 220 330 704 1202 1700
6-8: 8-Vs. Capt. Nazi 87 174 261 553 952 1350
9-Classic flag-c 110 220 330 704 1202 1700
10-Hitler-c 300 600 900 2010 3505 5000
11,12,15-Capt. Nazi app. 81 162 243 518 884 1250
13-Classic Hitler, Tojo and Mussolini football-c 300 600 900 2010 3505 5000
14,16-20: 14-Christmas-c. 16-Capt. Marvel & Sivana x-over. 17-Futuristic city-c; Raboy-c/a(3). 19-Capt. Nazi & Capt. Nippon app. 61 122 183 390 670 950
21-30: 25-Flag-c 48 96 144 302 514 725
31-33,36-40: 37-Infinity-c 35 70 105 208 339 470
35-#34 on inside; cover shows origin of Sivana Jr. which is not on inside. Evidently the cover to #35 was printed out of sequence and bound with contents to #34
36 72 108 214 347 480
41-70: 42-Robot-c. 53-Atomic Bomb-c/story 29 58 87 172 281 390
71-99,101-104: 87,93-Robot-c. 104-Used in **POP**, pg. 89
27 54 81 162 266 370
100 31 62 93 186 303 420
105-114,116-118: 116-Vampira, Queen of Terror app.
30 60 90 177 289 400
115-Classic injury to eye-c; Eyeball story w/injury-to-eye panels
194 388 582 1242 2121 3000
119-Electric chair-c (scarce) 90 180 270 576 988 1400
NOTE: ***Mac Raboy** c-1-28, 30-32, 57, 59 among others.*

CAPTAIN MARVEL PRESENTS THE TERRIBLE FIVE
M. F. Enterprises: Aug, 1966; V2#5, Sept, 1967 (No #2-4) (25¢)
1 6 12 18 41 76 110
V2#5-(Formerly Captain Marvel) 5 10 15 30 50 70

CAPTAIN MARVEL'S FUN BOOK
Samuel Lowe Co.: 1944 (1/2" thick) (cardboard covers)(25¢)
nn-Puzzles, games, magic, etc.; infinity-c 50 100 150 315 533 750

CAPTAIN MARVEL SPECIAL EDITION (See Special Edition)

CAPTAIN MARVEL STORY BOOK
Fawcett Publications: Summer, 1946 - No. 4, Summer?, 1948
1-Half text 65 130 195 416 708 1000
2-4 47 94 141 296 498 700

CAPTAIN MARVEL THRILL BOOK (Large-Size)
Fawcett Publications: 1941 (B&W w/color-c)
1-Reprints from Whiz #8,10, & Special Edition #1 (Rare)
480 960 1440 4800 -- --
NOTE: *Rarely found in Fine or Mint condition.*

CAPTAIN MIDNIGHT (TV, radio, films) (See The Funnies, Popular Comics & Super Book of Comics)(Becomes Sweethearts No. 68 on)
Fawcett Publications: Sept, 1942 - No. 67, Fall, 1948 (#1-14: 68 pgs.)
1-Origin Captain Midnight, star of radio and movies; Captain Marvel cameo on cover
343 686 1029 2400 4200 6000
2-Smashes the Jap Juggernaut 161 322 483 1030 1765 2500
3-Classic Nazi war-c 158 316 474 1003 1727 2450
4,5: 4-Grapples the Gremlins 119 238 357 762 1306 1850
6-8: 7-WWII-c 71 142 213 454 777 1100
9-Raboy-c 84 168 252 538 919 1300
10-Raboy Flag-c/WWII-c 81 162 243 518 884 1250
11-20: 11,17,18-Raboy-c. 16 (1/44) 50 100 150 315 533 750
21-Classic WWII-c 65 130 195 416 708 1000
22,25-30: 22-War savings stamp-c 40 80 120 246 411 575
23-WWII Concentration Camp-c 58 116 174 371 636 900
24-Japan flag sunburst-c 65 130 195 416 708 1000
31-40 32 64 96 188 307 425
41-59,61-67: 50-Sci/fi theme begins? 25 50 75 150 245 340
60-Flying Saucer issue (2/48)-3rd of this theme; see The Spirit 9/28/47 (1st), Shadow Comics V7#10 (2nd, 1/48) & Boy Commandos #26 (4th, 3-4/48)
40 80 120 246 411 575

CAPTAIN MIDNIGHT
Dark Horse Comics: No. 0, Jun, 2013 - No. 24, Jun, 2015 ($2.99)
0-24: 0-Williamson-s/Ibáñez-a; WWII hero appears in modern times. 4,5-Skyman app. 3.00
One For One: Captain Midnight #1 (1/14, $1.00) r/#1 3.00

CAPTAIN NICE (TV)
Gold Key: Nov, 1967 (one-shot)
1(10211-711)-Photo-c 6 12 18 38 69 100

CAPTAIN N: THE GAME MASTER (TV)
Valiant Comics: 1990 - No. 5, 1990 ($1.95, thick stock, coated-c)
1 5 10 15 31 53 75
2-4: 3-Quesada-a (1st pro work). 4-Layton-c 1 2 3 5 6 8
5-Last issue; Layton-c 3 6 9 19 30 40

CAPTAIN PARAGON (See Bill Black's Fun Comics)
Americomics: Dec, 1983 - No. 4, 1985
1-Intro/1st app. Ms. Victory 4.00
2-4 3.00

CAPTAIN PARAGON AND THE SENTINELS OF JUSTICE
AC Comics: April, 1985 - No. 6, 1986 ($1.75)
1-6: 1-Capt. Paragon, Commando D., Nightveil, Scarlet Scorpion, Stardust & Atoman 3.00

CAPTAIN PLANET AND THE PLANETEERS (TV cartoon)
Marvel Comics: Oct, 1991 - No. 12, Oct, 1992 ($1.00/$1.25)
1-N. Adams painted-c 2 4 6 11 16 20
2-12: 3-Romita-c 6.00

CAPTAIN POWER AND THE SOLDIERS OF THE FUTURE (TV)
Continuity Comics: Aug, 1988 - No. 2, 1988 ($2.00)
1,2: 1-Neal Adams-c/layouts/inks; variant-c exists. 4.00

CAPTAIN PUREHEART (See Archie as...)

CAPTAIN ROCKET
P. L. Publ. (Canada): Nov, 1951
1-Harry Harrison-a 65 130 195 416 708 1000

CAPT. SAVAGE AND HIS LEATHERNECK RAIDERS (...And His Battlefield Raiders #9 on)
Marvel Comics Group (Animated Timely Features): Jan, 1968 - No. 19, Mar, 1970 (See Sgt. Fury No. 10)
1-Sgt. Fury & Howlers cameo 7 14 21 46 86 125
2,7,11: 2-Origin Hydra. 7-Pre-"Thing" Ben Grimm story. 11-Sgt. Fury app.
3 6 9 17 26 35
3-6,8-10,12-14: 4-Origin Hydra. 14-Last 12¢ issue 3 6 9 16 23 30
15-19 3 6 9 14 19 24
NOTE: ***Ayres/Shores** a-1-8,11. **Ayres/Severin** a-9,10,17-19. **Heck/Shores** a-12-15.*

CAPTAIN SCIENCE (Fantastic No. 8 on)
Youthful Magazines: Nov, 1950; No. 2, Feb, 1951 - No. 7, Dec, 1951
1-Wood-a; origin; 2 pg. text w/ photos of George Pal's "Destination Moon."
123 246 369 787 1344 1900
2-Flying saucer-c swipes Weird Science #13(#2)-c 97 194 291 621 1061 1500
3,7; 3-Bondage c-swipes/Wings #94 65 130 195 416 708 1000
4,5-Wood/Orlando-c/a(2) each 110 220 330 704 1202 1700
6-Bondage c-swipes/Wings #91 155 310 465 992 1696 2400
NOTE: ***Fass** a-4. Bondage c-3, 6, 7.*

CAPTAIN SILVER'S LOG OF SEA HOUND (See Sea Hound)

CAPTAIN SINBAD (Movie Adaptation) (See Fantastic Voyages of... & Movie Comics)

CAPTAIN STERNN: RUNNING OUT OF TIME
Kitchen Sink Press: Sept, 1993 - No. 5, 1994 ($4.95, limited series, coated stock, 52 pgs.)
1-5: Berni Wrightson-c/a/scripts 6.00
1-Gold ink variant 10.00

CAPTAIN STEVE SAVAGE (...& His Jet Fighters, No. 2-13)
Avon Periodicals: 1950 - No. 8, 1/53; No. 5, 9-10/54 - No. 13, 5-6/56
nn(1st series)-Harrison/Wood art, 22 pgs. (titled "...Over Korea")
52 104 156 328 552 775
1(4/51)-Reprints nn issue (Canadian) 25 50 75 150 245 340
2-Kamen-a 20 40 60 117 189 260
3-11 (#6, 11-12/54, last precode) 16 32 48 92 144 195
12-Wood-a (6 pgs.) 20 40 60 117 189 260
13-Check, Lawrence-a 16 32 48 94 147 200
NOTE: ***Kinstler** c-2-5, 7-9, 11. **Lawrence** a-8. **Ravielli** a-5, 9.*
5(9-10/54-2nd series)(Formerly Sensational Police Cases)
13 26 39 74 105 135
6-Reprints nn issue; Harrison/Wood-a 14 28 42 76 108 140
7-13: 9,10-Kinstler-c. 10-r/cover #2 (1st series). 13-r/cover #8 (1st series)
11 22 33 62 86 110

CAPTAIN STONE (See Holyoke One-Shot No. 10)

CAPT. STORM (Also see G. I. Combat #138)
National Periodical Publications: May-June, 1964 - No. 18, Mar-Apr, 1967
1-Origin 10 20 30 69 147 225
2-7,9-18: 3,6,13-Kubert-a. 4-Colan-a. 12-Kubert-c 7 14 21 44 82 120
8-Grey-tone-c 8 16 24 54 102 150

CAPTAIN 3-D (Super hero)
Harvey Publications: December, 1953 (25¢, came with 2 pairs of glasses)
1-Kirby/Ditko-a (Ditko's 3rd published work tied with Strange Fantasy #9, see also Daring Love #1 & Black Magic V4 #3); shows cover in 3-D on inside; Kirby/Meskin-c 14 28 42 78 112 145
NOTE: *Half price without glasses*

CAPTAIN THUNDER AND BLUE BOLT
Hero Comics: Sept, 1987 - No. 10, 1988 ($1.95)
1-10: 1-Origin Blue Bolt. 3-Origin Capt. Thunder. 6-1st app. Wicket. 8-Champions x-over 3.00

CAPTAIN TOOTSIE & THE SECRET LEGION (Advs. of...)(Also see Monte Hale #30,39 & Real Western Hero)
Toby Press: Oct, 1950 - No. 2, Dec, 1950
1-Not Beck-a; both have sci/fi covers 41 82 123 256 428 600
2-The Rocketeer Patrol app.; not Beck-a 24 48 72 142 234 325

CAPTAIN TRIUMPH (See Crack Comics #27)

CAPTAIN UNIVERSE... (5-part x-over)
Marvel Comics: 2005; Jan, 2006
.../ Daredevil 1 (1/06, $2.99) Part 2; Faerber-s/Santacruz-a 3.00
.../ Hulk 1 (1/06, $2.99) Part 1; Faerber-s/Magno-a 3.00
.../ Invisible Woman 1 (1/06, $2.99) Part 4; Faerber-s/Raiz-a; Gladiator app. 3.00
.../ Silver Surfer 1 (1/06, $2.99) Part 5; Faerber-s/Magno-a 3.00
.../ X-23 1 (1/06, $2.99) Part 3; Faerber-s/Portella-a; Scorpion app. 3.00
...: Power Unimaginable TPB (2005, $19.99)-Reprints from Marvel Spotlight #9-11, Incredible Hulk Ann. #10, Marvel Fanfare #25, Web of Spider-Man Ann. #5&6, Marvel Comics Presents #148, Cosmic Power Unlimited #5 20.00
...: The Hero Who Could Be You 1 (7/13, $7.99) r/Marvel Spotlight #9-11 & early apps. 8.00

Captain Marvel Jr. #33 © FAW

Captain Science #2 © YF

Carnage (2010) #4 © MAR

	GD 2.0	VG 4.0	FN 6.0	VF 8.0	VF/NM 9.0	NM- 9.2

...: Universal Heroes TPB (2005, $13.99) reprints .../Hulk, .../Daredevil, ...X-23 and back-up stories from Amazing Fantasy (2005) #13,14 — 14.00

CAPTAIN VENTURE & THE LAND BENEATH THE SEA (See Space Family Robinson)
Gold Key: Oct, 1968 - No. 2, Oct, 1969

	GD	VG	FN	VF	VF/NM	NM-
1-r/Space Family Robinson serial; Spiegle-a	5	10	15	31	53	75
2-Spiegle-a	4	8	12	25	40	55

CAPTAIN VICTORY AND THE GALACTIC RANGERS (Also see Kirby: Genesis)
Pacific Comics: Nov, 1981 - No. 13, Jan, 1984 ($1.00, direct sales, 36-48 pgs.) (Created by Jack Kirby)

	GD	VG	FN	VF	VF/NM	NM-
1-1st app. Mr. Mind	1	2	3	5	6	8
2-13: 3-N. Adams-a						4.00
Special 1-(10/83)-Kirby c/a(p)						4.00

NOTE: **Conrad** a-10, 11. **Ditko** a-6. **Kirby** a-1-3p; c-1-13.

CAPTAIN VICTORY AND THE GALACTIC RANGERS
Jack Kirby Comics: July, 2000 - No. 2, Sept, 2000 ($2.95, B&W)

1,2-New Jeremy Kirby-s with reprinted Jack Kirby-a; Liefeld pin-up art — 3.00

CAPTAIN VICTORY AND THE GALACTIC RANGERS
Dynamite Entertainment: 2014 - No. 6, 2015 ($3.99)

1-6-Joe Casey-s; art by various. 3-Dalrymple & Mahfood-a — 4.00

CAPTAIN VIDEO (TV) (See XMas Comics)
Fawcett Publications: Feb, 1951 - No. 6, Dec, 1951 (No. 1,5,6-36 pgs.; 2-4, 52 pgs.)

	GD	VG	FN	VF	VF/NM	NM-
1-George Evans-a(2); 1st TV hero comic	106	212	318	678	1164	1650
2-Used in **SOTI**, pg. 382	74	148	222	470	810	1150
3-6-All Evans-a except #5 mostly Evans	58	116	174	371	636	900

NOTE: Minor **Williamson** assists on most issues. Photo c-1, 5, 6; painted c-2-4.

CAPTAIN WILLIE SCHULTZ (Also see Fightin' Army)
Charlton Comics: No. 76, Oct, 1985 - No. 77, Jan, 1986

	GD	VG	FN	VF	VF/NM	NM-
76,77-Low print run	1	2	3	5	6	8

CAPTAIN WIZARD COMICS (See Meteor, Red Band & Three Ring Comics)
Rural Home: 1946

	GD	VG	FN	VF	VF/NM	NM-
1-Capt. Wizard dons new costume; Impossible Man, Race Wilkins app.	52	104	156	328	552	775

CAPTAIN WONDER
Image Comics: Feb, 2011 ($4.99, 3-D comic with glasses)

1-Haberlin-s/Tan-a; sketch pages, crossword puzzle, paper dolls — 5.00

CAPTURE CREATURES
BOOM! Entertainment (kaboom!): Nov, 2014 - No. 4, May, 2015 ($3.99)

1-4-Frank Gibson-s/Becky Dreistadt-a; multiple covers on each — 4.00

CARBON GREY
Image Comics: Mar, 2011 - No. 3, May, 2011 ($2.99, limited series)

	NM-
1-3-Khari Evans, Kinsun Loh & Hoang Nguyen-a; Nguyen-c	3.00
... Origins 1,2 (11/11 - No. 2, 3/12, $3.99) 1-Pop Mhan-a	4.00
Vol. 2 (7/12 - No. 3, 2/13, $3.99) 1-3-Gardner-s/Evans & Nguyen-a	4.00
Vol. 3 (12/13 - No. 2, 1/14) 1,2-Gardner-s/Evans & Nguyen-a	4.00

CARE BEARS (TV, Movie)(See Star Comics Magazine)
Star Comics/Marvel Comics No. 15 on: Nov, 1985 - No. 20, Jan, 1989

	GD	VG	FN	VF	VF/NM	NM-
1-Post-a begins	3	6	9	21	33	45
2-20: 11-$1.00-c begins. 13-Madballs app.	2	4	6	8	10	12

CARE BEARS (TV, Movie)(Subtitled "Unlock the Magic" on cover)
IDW Publishing: Jul, 2019 - No. 3, Sept, 2019 ($3.99, limited series)

1-3-Garbowska-a — 4.00

CAREER GIRL ROMANCES (Formerly Three Nurses)
Charlton Comics: June, 1964 - No. 78, Dec, 1973

	GD	VG	FN	VF	VF/NM	NM-
V4#24-31	3	6	9	18	27	36
32-Elvis Presley, Herman's Hermits, Johnny Rivers line drawn-c	14	28	42	96	211	325
33-37,39-50: 39-Tiffany Sinn app.	3	6	9	16	23	30
38-(2/67) 1st app. Tiffany Sinn, C.I.A. Sweetheart, Undercover Agent (also see Secret Agent #10; Dominguel-a	3	6	9	19	30	40
51-78: 54-Jonnie Love anti-drup PSA. 67-Susan Dey pin-up. 70-David Cassidy pin-up	3	6	9	14	19	24

CAR 54, WHERE ARE YOU? (TV)
Dell Publishing Co.: Mar-May, 1962 - No. 7, Sept-Nov, 1963; 1964 - 1965 (All photo-c)

	GD	VG	FN	VF	VF/NM	NM-
Four Color 1257(#1, 3-5/62)	8	16	24	56	108	160
2(6-8/62)-7	5	10	15	30	50	70
2,3(10-12/64), 4(1-3/65)-Reprints #2,3,&4 of 1st series	3	6	9	19	30	40

CARL BARKS LIBRARY OF WALT DISNEY'S GYRO GEARLOOSE COMICS AND FILLERS IN COLOR, THE
Gladstone: 1993 ($7.95, 8-1/2x11", limited series, 52 pgs.)

	GD	VG	FN	VF	VF/NM	NM-
1-6: Carl Barks reprints	1	3	4	6	8	10

CARL BARKS LIBRARY OF WALT DISNEY'S COMICS AND STORIES IN COLOR, THE
Gladstone: Jan, 1992 - No. 51, Mar, 1996 ($8.95, 8-1/2x11", 60 pgs.)

	GD	VG	FN	VF	VF/NM	NM-
1,2,6,8-51: 1-Barks Donald Duck-r/WDC&S #31-35; 2-r/#36,38-41; 6-r/#57-61; 8-r/#67-71; 9-r/#72-76; 10-r/#77-81; 11-r/#82-86; 12-r/#87-91; 13-r/#92-96; 14-r/#97-101; 15-r/#102-106; 16-r/#107-111; 17-r/#112,114,117,124,125; 18-r/#126-130; 19-r/#131,132(2),133,134; 20-r/#135-139; 21-r/#140-144; 22-r/#145-149; 23-r/#150-154; 24-r/#155-159; 25-r/#160-164; 26-r/#165-169; 27-r/#170-174;28-r/#175-179; 29-r/#180-184; 30-r/#185-189; 31-r/#190-194; 32-r/#195-199;33-r/#200-204; 34-r/#205-209; 35-r/#210-214; 36-r/#215-219; 37-r/#220-224; 38-r/#225-229; 39-r/#230-234; 40-r/#235-239; 41-r/#240-244; 42r/#245-249; 43-r/#250-254; 44-50; All contain one Heroes & Villains trading card each	2	4	6	9	12	15
3,4,7: 3-r/#42-46. 4-r/#47-51. 7-r/#62-66.	2	4	6	11	16	20
5-r/#52-56	3	6	9	16	23	30

CARL BARKS LIBRARY OF WALT DISNEY'S DONALD DUCK ADVENTURES IN COLOR, THE
Gladstone: Jan, 1994 - No. 25, Jan, 1996 ($7.95-$9.95, 44-68 pgs., 8-1/2"x11") (all contain one Donald Duck trading card each)

	GD	VG	FN	VF	VF/NM	NM-
1-5,7-25-Carl Barks-r: 1-r/FC #9; 2-r/FC #29; 3-r/FC #62; 4-r/FC #108; 5-r/FC #147 & #79(Mickey Mouse); 7-r/FC #159. 8-r/FC #178 & 189. 9-r/FC #199 & 203; 10-r/FC 223 & 238; 11-r/Christmas Parade #1 & 2; 12-r/FC #296; 13-r/FC #263; 14-r/MOC #20 & 41; 15-r/FC 275 & 282; 16-r/FC #291&300; 17-r/FC #308 & 318; 18-r/Vac. Parade #1 & Summer Fun #2; 19-r/FC #328 & 367	2	4	6	9	12	15
6-r/MOC #4, Cheerios "Atom Bomb," D.D. Tells About Kites	3	6	9	14	20	25

CARL BARKS LIBRARY OF WALT DISNEY'S DONALD DUCK CHRISTMAS STORIES IN COLOR, THE
Gladstone: 1992 ($7.95, 44pgs., one-shot)

	GD	VG	FN	VF	VF/NM	NM-
nn-Reprints Firestone giveaways 1945-1949	2	4	6	10	14	18

CARL BARKS LIBRARY OF WALT DISNEY'S UNCLE SCROOGE COMICS ONE PAGERS IN COLOR, THE
Gladstone: 1992 - No. 2, 1993 ($8.95, limited series, 60 pgs., 8-1/2x11")

	GD	VG	FN	VF	VF/NM	NM-
1-Carl Barks one pg. reprints	3	6	9	16	23	30
2-Carl Barks one pg. reprints	2	4	6	10	14	18

CARNAGE
Marvel Comics: Dec, 2010 - No. 5, Aug, 2011 ($3.99, limited series)

	NM-
1-5-Spider-Man & Iron Man app.; Clayton Crain-a/c; Wells-s	4.00
...: It's a Wonderful Life (10/96, $1.95) David Quinn scripts	3.00
...: Mind Bomb (2/96, $2.95) Warren Ellis script; Kyle Hotz-a	4.00

CARNAGE
Marvel Comics: Jan, 2016 - No. 16, Mar, 2017 ($3.99)

1-16: 1-Conway-s/Perkins-a; Eddie Brock app. 3-Man-Wolf app. 4,5-Toxin app. — 4.00

CARNAGE
Marvel Comics: May, 2022 - Present ($3.99)

	NM-
1-($4.99) Ram V-s/Francesco Manna-a; Hydro-Man app.	5.00
2-10-($3.99) 3-The Spot app. 4-Spiderling app.	4.00
... Forever 1 (4/22, $4.99) Leads into Carnage #1; Johnson-s/Salazar-a; V-s/Larroca-a	5.00

CARNAGE: BLACK, WHITE & BLOOD
Marvel Comics: May, 2021 - No. 4, Sept, 2021 ($4.99, B&W&red, limited series)

1-4-Antholgy of short stories by various. 1-Spider-Man app. 2-Cates-s. 4-Bennett-a — 5.00

CARNAGE, U.S.A.
Marvel Comics: Feb, 2012 - No. 5, Jun, 2012 ($3.99, limited series)

1-4-Clayton Crain-a/c; Wells-s; Spider-Man & Avengers app. 3,4-Venom app. — 4.00

CARNATION MALTED MILK GIVEAWAYS (See Wisco/Klarer in the Promotional Comics section)

CARNEYS, THE
Archie Comics: Summer, 1994 ($2.00, 52 pgs)

1-Bound-in pull-out poster — 4.00

CARNIVAL COMICS (Formerly Kayo #12; becomes Red Seal Comics #14)
Harry 'A' Chesler/Pershing Square Publ. Co.: 1945

	GD	VG	FN	VF	VF/NM	NM-
nn (#13)-Guardineer-a	24	48	72	142	234	325

CAROLINE KENNEDY
Charlton Comics: 1961 (one-shot)

	GD	VG	FN	VF	VF/NM	NM-
nn-Interior photo covers of Kennedy family	11	22	33	77	166	255

GD VG FN VF VF/NM NM-
2.0 4.0 6.0 8.0 9.0 9.2

CAROUSEL COMICS
F. E. Howard, Toronto: V1#8, April, 1948
V1#8 15 30 45 85 130 175

CARS (Based on the 2006 Pixar movie)
Boom Entertainment: No. 0, Nov, 2009 - No. 7, Jun, 2010 ($2.99)
0-7: 0,1-Three covers on each. 2-7-Two covers on each 3.00
...: Adventures of Tow Mater 1-4 (7/10 - No. 4, 10/10, $2.99) 1-Two covers 3.00
...: Radiator Springs 1-4 (7/09 - No. 4, 10/09, $2.99) Two covers on each 3.00
...: The Rookie 1-4 (3/09 - No. 4, 6/09, $2.99) Origin of Lightning McQueen 3.00

CARS 2 (Based on the 2011 Pixar movie)
Marvel Worldwide (Disney Comics): Aug, 2011 - No. 2, Aug, 2011 ($3.99)
1,2-Movie adaptation; car profile pages 4.00

CARS, WORLD OF (Free Comic Book Day giveaway)
BOOM Kids!: May, 2009
1-Based on the Disney/Pixar movie 3.00

CARSON OF VENUS (Also see Edgar Rice Burroughs'...)
American Mythology Prods.: 2020 - 2020 ($3.99, limited series)
...: Realm of the Dead 1-3 - Wolfer-s/Mesarcia-a 4.00
...: The Eye of Amtor 1-3 - Wolfer-s/Carratu-a 4.00

CARTOON CARTOONS (Anthology)
DC Comics: Mar, 2001 - No. 33, Oct, 2004 ($1.99/$2.25)
1-33-Short stories of Cartoon Network characters. 3,6,10,13,15-Space Ghost. 13-Begin $2.25-c. 17-Dexter's Laboratory begins 3.00

CARTOON KIDS
Atlas Comics (CPS): 1957 (no month)
1-Maneely-c/a; Dexter The Demon, Willie The Wise-Guy, Little Zelda app. 19 38 57 111 176 240

CARTOON NETWORK ACTION PACK (Anthology)
DC Comics: July, 2006 - No. 67, May, 2012 ($2.25/$2.50/$2.99)
1-31-Short stories of Cartoon Network characters. 1,4,6-Rowdyruff Boys app. 3.00
32-67: 32-Begin $2.50-c. 50-Ben 10/Generator Rex team-up 3.00

CARTOON NETWORK BLOCK PARTY (Anthology)
DC Comics: Nov, 2004 - No. 59, Sept, 2009 ($2.25/$2.50)
1,2,4-51-Short stories of Cartoon Network characters 3.00
3-($2.95) Bonus pages 4.00
52-59: 52-Begin $2.50-c. 59-Last issue; Powerpuff Girls app. 3.00
Cartoon Network 2-in-1: Ben 10 Alien Force/The Secret Saturdays TPB (2010, $12.99) reprints stories from #26-42 13.00
Cartoon Network 2-in-1: Foster's Home For Imaginary Friends/Powerpuff Girls TPB (2010, $12.99) reprints stories from #19-21,23,25,26,28,30-32,34-38,41 13.00
... Vol. 1: Get Down! (2005, $6.99, digest) reprints from Dexter's Lab and Cartoon Cartoons 7.00
... Vol. 2: Read All About It! (2005, $6.99, digest) reprints 7.00
... Vol. 3: Can You Dig It?; ... Vol. 4: Blast Off! (2006, $6.99, digest) reprints 7.00

CARTOON NETWORK PRESENTS
DC Comics: Aug, 1997 - No. 24, Aug, 1999 ($1.75-$1.99, anthology)
1-Dexter's Lab 3 6 9 17 26 35
1-Platinum Edition 3 6 9 16 23 30
2-Space Ghost 1 3 4 6 8 10
3-10 4.00
11-24: 12-Bizarro World 3.00

CARTOON NETWORK PRESENTS SPACE GHOST
Archie Comics: Mar, 1997 ($1.50)
1-Scott Rosema-p 2 4 6 13 18 22

CARTOON NETWORK STARRING... (Anthology)
DC Comics: Sept, 1999 - No. 18, Feb, 2001 ($1.99)
1-Powerpuff Girls 4 8 12 28 47 65
2-18: 2,8,11,14,17-Johnny Bravo. 12,15,18-Space Ghost 4.00

CARTOON TALES (Disney's...)
W.D. Publications (Disney): nd, nn (1992) ($2.95, 6-5/8x9-1/2", 52 pgs.)
nn-Ariel & Sebastian-Serpent Teen; Beauty and the Beast; A Tale of Enchantment; Darkwing Duck - Just Us Justice Ducks; 101 Dalmatians - Canine Classics; Tale Spin - Surprise in the Skies; Uncle Scrooge - Blast to the Past 4.00

CARVERS
Image Comics (Flypaper Press): 1998 - No. 3, 1999 ($2.95)
1-3-Pander Bros.-a/Fleming-s 3.00

CAR WARRIORS
Marvel Comics (Epic): June, 1991 - No. 4, Sept, 1991 ($2.25, lim. series)
1-4: 1-Says April in indicia 3.00

CASANOVA
Image Comics: June, 2006 - No. 14, May, 2008 ($1.99, B&W & olive green or blue)
1-14: 1-7-Matt Fraction-s/Gabriel Bá-a/c. 8-14-Fabio Moon-a 3.00
...: Luxuria TPB (2008, $12.99) r/#1-7; sketch pages and cover gallery 13.00
1-4 (Marvel Comics, 10/10 - No. 4, 12/10, $3.99) Recolored reprints Image series #1-7 4.00
...: Acedia 1-8 (Image, 1/15 - No. 8, 3/17) Fraction-s/Moon-a; back-up by Chabon-s/Bá-a 4.00
...: Avaritia (III) 1-4 (Marvel, 11/11 - No. 4, 8/12, $4.99) new story; Fraction-s/Bá-a 5.00
...: Gula (Marvel, 1/11 - No. 4, 4/11) r/Image series #8-14. 4-New story pages 4.00

CASE FILES: SAM & TWITCH (Also see the Spawn titles)
Image Comics: May, 2003 - No. 25, July, 2006 ($2.50/$2.95, color #1-6/B&W #7-on)
1-25: 1-5-Scott Morse-a/Marc Andreyko-s. 7-13-Paul Lee-a. 13-Niles-s 3.00

CASE OF THE SHOPLIFTER'S SHOE (See Perry Mason, Feature Book No.50)

CASE OF THE WINKING BUDDHA, THE
St. John Publ. Co.: 1950 (132 pgs.; 25¢; B&W; 5-1/2x7-5-1/2x8")
nn-Charles Raab-a; reprinted in Authentic Police Cases No. 25 63 126 189 403 689 975

CASEY BLUE
DC Comics (WildStorm): Jul, 2008 - No. 6, Dec, 2008 ($2.99, limited series)
1-6-B. Clay Moore-s/Carlos Barberi-a 3.00
...: Beyond Tomorrow TPB (2009, $19.99) r/#1-6; Barberi sketch pages 20.00

CASEY-CRIME PHOTOGRAPHER (Two-Gun Western No. 5 on)(Radio)
Marvel Comics (BFP): Aug, 1949 - No. 4, Feb, 1950
1-Photo-c; 52 pgs. 39 78 117 240 395 550
2-4: Photo-c 25 50 75 150 245 340

CASEY JONES (TV)
Dell Publishing Co.: No. 915, July, 1958
Four Color 915-Alan Hale photo-c 6 12 18 40 73 105

CASEY JONES & RAPHAEL (See Bodycount)
Mirage Studios: Oct, 1994 ($2.75, unfinished limited series)
1-Bisley-c; Eastman story & pencils 3.00

CASEY JONES: NORTH BY DOWNEAST
Mirage Studios: May, 1994 - No. 2, July, 1994 ($2.75, limited series)
1,2-Rick Veitch script & pencils; Kevin Eastman story & inks 3.00

CASPER... (One-shots)
American Mythology Prods.: 2018 - 2019 ($3.99)
.. & Hot Stuff #1 (2018) Wolfer-s/Shanower-a and Shand-s/Scherer-a; r/Devil Kids #87 4.00
.. & Wendy #1 (2018) Check-s/Scherer-a and Shand-s/Sosa-a; r/Casper and Wendy #1 4.00
Casper's Classic Christmas #1 (2019, $3.99) Christmas-themed reprints; Hot Stuff app. 4.00
Casper's Haunted Halloween #1 (2019) Spooky, Nightmare and the Ghostly Trio reprints 4.00
... Spotlight: The Ghostly Trio #1 (2020) Reprints from 1971-1990 4.00
Casper's Spooksville #1 (2019) New stories by various 4.00

CASPER ADVENTURE DIGEST
Harvey Comics: V2#1, Oct, 1992 - V2#8, Apr, 1994 ($1.75/$1.95, digest-size)
V2#1: Casper, Richie Rich, Spooky, Wendy 5.00
2-8 3.50

CASPER AND...
Harvey Comics: Nov, 1987 - No. 12, June, 1990 (75¢/$1.00, all reprints)
1-Ghostly Trio 5.00
2-12: 2-Spooky; begin $1.00-c. 3-Wendy. 4-Nightmare. 5-Ghostly Trio. 6-Spooky. 7-Wendy. 8-Hot Stuff. 9-Baby Huey. 10-Wendy.11-Ghostly Trio. 12-Spooky 3.00

CASPER AND FRIENDS
Harvey Comics: Oct, 1991 - No. 5, July, 1992 ($1.00/$1.25)
1-Nightmare, Ghostly Trio, Wendy, Spooky 4.00
2-5 3.00

CASPER AND FRIENDS MAGAZINE: Mar, 1997 - No. 3, July, 1997 ($3.99)
1-3 4.00

CASPER AND NIGHTMARE (See Harvey Hits# 37, 45, 52, 56, 59, 62, 65, 68,71, 75)

CASPER AND NIGHTMARE (Nightmare & Casper No. 1-5)
Harvey Publications: No. 6, 11/64 - No. 44, 10/73; No. 45, 6/74 - No. 46, 8/74 (25¢)
6: 68 pg. Giants begin, ends #32 5 10 15 34 60 85
7-10 3 6 9 21 33 45
11-20 3 6 9 17 26 35
21-37: 33-37-(52 pg. Giants) 3 6 9 14 20 26
38-46 2 4 6 10 14 18
NOTE: *Many issues contain reprints.*

CASPER AND SPOOKY (See Harvey Hits No. 20)
Harvey Publications: Oct, 1972 - No. 7, Oct, 1973
1 3 6 9 21 33 45
2-7 2 4 6 10 14 18

CASPER AND THE GHOSTLY TRIO
Harvey Pub.: Nov, 1972 - No. 7, Nov, 1973; No. 8, Aug, 1990 - No. 10, Dec, 1990
1 3 6 9 21 33 45
2-7 2 4 6 10 14 18
8-10 6.00

CASPER AND WENDY
Harvey Publications: Sept, 1972 - No. 8, Nov, 1973
1: 52 pg. Giant 3 6 9 21 33 45
2-8 2 4 6 10 14 18

CASPER BIG BOOK
Harvey Comics: V2#1, Aug, 1992 - No. 3, May, 1993 ($1.95, 52 pgs.)
V2#1-Spooky app. 4.00
2,3 4.00

CASPER CAT (See Dopey Duck)
I. W. Enterprises/Super: 1958; 1963
1,7: 1-Wacky Duck #?.7-Reprint, Super No. 14('63) 2 4 6 11 16 20

CASPER DIGEST (...Magazine #?; ...Halloween Digest #8, 10)
Harvey Publications: Oct, 1986 - No. 18, Jan, 1991 ($1.25/$1.75, digest-size)
1 1 3 4 6 8 10
2-18: 11-Valentine-c. 18-Halloween-c 6.00

CASPER DIGEST (...Magazine #? on)
Harvey Comics: V2#1, Sept, 1991 - V2#14, Nov, 1994 ($1.75/$1.95, digest-size)
V2#1 5.00
2-14 3.50

CASPER DIGEST STORIES
Harvey Publications: Feb, 1980 - No. 4, Nov, 1980 (95¢, 132 pgs., digest size)
1 2 4 6 9 13 16
2-4 1 2 3 5 7 9

CASPER DIGEST WINNERS
Harvey Publications: Apr, 1980 - No. 3, Sept, 1980 (95¢, 132 pgs., digest size)
1 2 4 6 9 13 16
2,3 1 2 3 5 7 9

Cartoon Network Action Pack #49 © CN

Casper's Ghostland #24 © HARV

Castle: A Calm Before Storm #1 © ABC

GD VG FN VF VF/NM NM-
2.0 4.0 6.0 8.0 9.0 9.2

CASPER ENCHANTED TALES DIGEST
Harvey Comics: May, 1992 - No. 10, Oct, 1994 ($1.75, digest-size, 98 pgs.)
1-Casper, Spooky, Wendy stories 4 8 12 27 44 60
2-10 1 2 3 5 6 8

CASPER GHOSTLAND
Harvey Comics: May, 1992 ($1.25)
1 1 3 4 6 8 10

CASPER GIANT SIZE
Harvey Comics: Oct, 1992 - No. 4, Nov, 1993 ($2.25, 68 pgs.)
V2#1-Casper, Wendy, Spooky stories 5.00
2-4 4.00

CASPER HALLOWEEN TRICK OR TREAT
Harvey Publications: Jan, 1976 (52 pgs.)
1 3 6 9 17 26 35

CASPER IN SPACE (Formerly Casper Spaceship)
Harvey Publications: No. 6, June, 1973 - No. 8, Oct, 1973
6-8 2 4 6 11 16 20

CASPER'S CAPERS
American Mythology Prods.: 2018 - No. 6, 2019 ($3.99)
1-6-Classic reprints with digital recoloring. 1-Includes 1st apps. of Casper and Wendy4.00

CASPER'S GHOSTLAND
Harvey Publications: Winter, 1958-59 - No. 97, 12/77; No. 98, 12/79 (25¢)
1-84 pgs. begin, ends #10 20 40 60 138 307 475
2 9 18 27 61 123 185
3-10 7 14 21 44 82 120
11-20: 11-68 pgs. begin, ends #61. 13-X-Mas-c 5 10 15 35 63 90
21-40 4 8 12 28 47 65
41-61 3 6 9 16 24 32
62-77: 62-52 pgs. begin 2 4 6 9 13 16
78-98: 94-X-Mas-c 2 4 6 8 10 12
NOTE: *Most issues contain reprints w/new stories.*

CASPER'S GHOSTLAND
American Mythology Prods.: 2018 - No. 2, 2018 ($3.99)
1,2-New stories; art by Shanower & others; Wendy, Hot Stuff, Ghostly Trio app. 4.00

CASPER SPACESHIP (Casper in Space No. 6 on)
Harvey Publications: Aug, 1972 - No. 5, April, 1973
1: 52 pg. Giant 3 6 9 19 30 40
2-5 2 4 6 11 16 20

CASPER'S SCARE SCHOOL
Ape Entertainment: 2011 - No. 2 ($3.99, limited series)
1,2-New short stories and classic reprints 4.00

CASPER'S SPOOKSVILLE
American Mythology Prods.: 2020 - No. 4, 2020 ($3.99)
1-4-New stories & reprints; art by Shanower & others; Wendy, Hot Stuff, Spooky app. 4.00
... FCBD Edition 1 (2019, giveaway) New stories & reprints; art by Shanower 3.00

CASPER STRANGE GHOST STORIES
Harvey Publications: October, 1974 - No. 14, Jan, 1977 (All 52 pgs.)
1 3 6 9 18 28 38
2-14 2 4 6 11 16 20

CASPER, THE FRIENDLY GHOST (See America's Best TV Comics, Famous TV Funday Funnies, The Friendly Ghost..., Nightmare &..., Richie Rich and..., Tastee-Freez, Treasury of Comics, Wendy the Good Little Witch & Wendy Witch World)

CASPER, THE FRIENDLY GHOST (Becomes Harvey Comics Hits No. 61 (No. 6), and then continued with Harvey issue No. 7)(1st Series)
St. John Publishing Co.: Sept, 1949 - No. 5, Aug, 1951
1(1949)-Origin & 1st app. Baby Huey & Herman the Mouse (1st comic app. of Casper and the 1st time the name Casper app. in any media, even films)
784 1568 2352 5723 10,112 14,500
2,3 (2/50 & 8/50) 161 322 483 1030 1765 2500
4,5 (3/51 & 8/51) 106 212 318 673 1162 1650

CASPER, THE FRIENDLY GHOST (Paramount Picture Star...)(2nd Series)
Harvey Publications (Family Comics): No. 7, Dec, 1952 - No. 70, July, 1958
Note: No. 6 is Harvey Comics Hits No. 61 (10/52)
7-Baby Huey begins, ends #9 46 92 138 368 834 1300
8,9 24 48 72 168 372 575
10-Spooky begins (1st app., 6/53), ends #70? 44 88 132 326 738 1150
11,12: 2nd & 3rd app. Spooky 16 32 48 110 243 375
13-18: Alfred Harvey app. in story 13 26 39 87 191 295
19-1st app. Nightmare (4/54) 29 58 87 209 467 725
20-Wendy the Witch begins (1st app., 5/54) 62 124 186 496 1123 1750
21-30: 24-Infinity-c 10 20 30 66 138 210
31-40: 38-Early Wendy app. 39-1st app. Samson Honeybun. 40-1st app. Dr. Brainstorm
8 16 24 55 105 155
41-1st Wendy app. on-c 16 32 48 110 243 375
42-50: 43-2nd Wendy-c. 46-1st app. Spooky's girl Pearl.
7 14 21 44 82 120
51-70 (Continues as Friendly Ghost... 8/58) 58-Early app. Bat Balfrey. 63-2nd app. Something the Baby Ghost. 66-1st app. Wildcat Witch 5 10 15 35 63 90
Harvey Comics Classics Vol. 1 TPB (Dark Horse Books, 6/07, $19.95) Reprints Casper's earliest appearances in this title, Little Audrey, and The Friendly Ghost Casper, mostly B&W with some color stories; history, early concept drawings and animation art 20.00
NOTE: *Baby Huey app. 7-9, 11, 121, 14, 16, 20. Buzzy app. 14, 16, 20. Nightmare app. 19, 27, 36, 37, 42, 46, 51, 53, 56, 70. Spooky app. 10-70. Wendy app. 20, 29-31, 35, 37, 38, 41-49, 51, 52, 54-58, 61, 64, 68.*

CASPER THE FRIENDLY GHOST (Formerly The Friendly Ghost...)(3rd Series)
Harvey Comics: No. 254, July, 1990 - No. 260, Jan, 1991 ($1.00)
254-260 3.00

CASPER THE FRIENDLY GHOST (4th Series)
Harvey Comics: Mar, 1991 - No. 28, Nov, 1994 ($1.00/$1.25/$1.50)
1-Casper becomes Mighty Ghost; Spooky & Wendy app. 5.00
2-28: 7,8-Post-a. 11-28-($1.50) 3.00

CASPER THE FRIENDLY GHOST (5th Series)
American Mythology Prods.: 2017 - Present ($3.99)
1,2-New stories and reprints; Hot Stuff, Spooky & Wendy app. 4.00
... Presents Hot Stuff Sizzlers 1 (2020) Reprints Hot Stuff from 1958-62 4.00
... Presents Wendy & the Witch Widow 1 (2020) Reprints Casper from 1955-56 4.00

CASPER T.V. SHOWTIME
Harvey Comics: Jan, 1980 - No. 5, Oct, 1980
1 2 4 6 9 13 16
2-5 1 2 3 5 7 9

CASSETTE BOOKS (Classics Illustrated)
Cassette Book Co./I.P.S. Publ.: 1984 (48 pgs, b&w comic with cassette tape)
NOTE: *This series was illegal. The artwork was illegally obtained, and the Classics Illustrated copyright owner, Twin Circle Publ. sued to get an injunction to prevent the continued sale of this series. Many C.I. collectors obtained copies before the 1987 injunction, but now they are already scarce. Here again the market is just developing, but sealed mint copies of com ic and tape should be worth at least $25.*
1001 (CI#1-A2)New-PC 1002(CI#3-A2)CI-PC 1003(CI#13-A2)CI-PC
1004(CI#25)CI-LDC 1005(CI#10-A2)New-PC 1006(CI#64)CI-LDC

CASTILIAN (See Movie Classics)

CASTLE: A CALM BEFORE STORM (Based on the ABC TV series Castle)
Marvel Comics: Feb, 2013 - No. 5, Jul, 2013 ($3.99, limited series)
1-5-Peter David-s/Robert Atkins-a/Mico Suayan-c 4.00

CASTLE FULL OF BLACKBIRDS (From the world of Hellboy)
Dark Horse Comics: Sept, 2022 - No. 4, Mar, 2023 ($3.99, limited series)
1-4-Mignola & Slatter-s/Burzo-a 4.00

CASTLE: RICHARD CASTLE'S ... (Based on the ABC TV series Castle)
Marvel Comics: 2011, 2012 ($19.99, hardcover graphic novels with dustjacket)
Deadly Storm HC (2011) - An "adaptation" of the show's fictional Derrick Storm novel; Bendis & DeConnick-s 20.00
Storm Season HC (2012) - Bendis & DeConnick-s/Lupacchino-a 20.00

CASTLEVANIA: THE BELMONT LEGACY
IDW Publishing: March 2005 - No. 5, July, 2005 ($3.99, limited series)
1-5-Marc Andreyko-s/E.J. Su-a 4.00

CASTLE WAITING
Olio: 1997 - No. 7, 1999 ($2.95, B&W)
Cartoon Books: Vol. 2, Aug, 2000 - No. 16 ($2.95/$3.95, B&W)
Fantagraphics Books: Vol. 3, 2006 - No. 18, 2012 ($5.95/$3.95, B&W)
1-Linda Medley-s/a in all 1 2 3 5 6 8
2 4.00
3-7 3.00
The Lucky Road TPB r/#1-7 17.00
Hiatus Issue (1999) Crilley-c; short stories and previews 3.00
Vol. 2 #1-6,14-16 (#5&6 also have #12&13 on cover, for series numbering) 3.00
Vol. 3 #1 ($5.95) r/#15,16 and new story 6.00
Vol. 3 #2-18 ($3.95) 4.00

CASUAL FLING

GD VG FN VF VF/NM NM-
2.0 4.0 6.0 8.0 9.0 9.2

AWA Studios: Feb, 2021 - No. 4, May, 2021 ($3.99, limited series)
1-4-Jason Starr-s/Dalibor Talajic-a 4.00

CASUAL HEROES
Image Comics (Motown Machineworks): Apr, 1996 ($2.25, unfinished lim. series)
1-Steve Rude-c 3.00

CAT, T.H.E. (TV) (See T.H.E. Cat)

CAT, THE (See Movie Classics)

CAT, THE (Female hero)
Marvel Comics Group: Nov, 1972 - No. 4, June, 1973
1-Origin & 1st app. The Cat (who later becomes Tigra); Mooney-a(i); Wood-c(i)/a(i)
14 28 42 96 211 325
2,3: 2-Marie Severin/Mooney-a. 3-Everett inks 4 8 12 23 37 50
4-Starlin/Weiss-a(p) 4 8 12 25 40 55

CATACLYSM
Marvel Comics: No. 0.1, Dec, 2013 ($3.99)
0.1-Fialkov-s; Galactus threatens the Ultimate Universe 4.00

CATACLYSM: THE ULTIMATES LAST STAND (Leads into Survive #1)
Marvel Comics: Jan, 2014 - No. 5, Apr, 2014 ($3.99, limited series)
1-5-Galactus in the Ultimate Universe; Ultimates & Spider-Man app.; Bendis-s/Bagley-a 4.00

CATACLYSM: ULTIMATES
Marvel Comics: Jan, 2014 - No. 3, Mar, 2014 ($3.99, limited series)
1-3-Ultimates vs. Galactus; Fialkov-s/Giandomenico-a 4.00

CATACLYSM: ULTIMATE SPIDER-MAN
Marvel Comics: Jan, 2014 - No. 3, Mar, 2014 ($3.99, limited series)
1-3-Spider-Man vs. Galactus; Bendis-s/Marquez-a 4.00

CATACLYSM: ULTIMATE X-MEN
Marvel Comics: Jan, 2014 - No. 3, Mar, 2014 ($3.99, limited series)
1-3-Fialkov-s/Martinez-a; Captain Marvel app. 4.00

CATALYST: AGENTS OF CHANGE (Also see Comics' Greatest World)
Dark Horse Comics: Feb, 1994 - No. 7, Nov, 1994 ($2.00, limited series)
1-7: 1-Foil stamped logo 3.00

CATALYST COMIX (From Comics' Greatest World)
Dark Horse Comics: Jul, 2013 - No. 9, Mar, 2014 ($2.99)
1-9: Amazing Grace, Frank Wells, and Agents of Change app.; Casey-s/Grampá-c 3.00

CATECHISM IN PICTURES
Catechetical Guild: Jan, 1958
311-Addison Burbank-a 8 16 24 44 57 70

CAT FROM OUTER SPACE (See Walt Disney Showcase #46)

CATHOLIC COMICS (See Heroes All Catholic...)
Catholic Publications: June, 1946 - V3#10, July, 1949
1 34 68 102 199 325 450
2 19 38 57 111 176 240
3-13(7/47): 11-Hollingsworth-a 15 30 45 90 140 190
V2#1-10 13 26 39 72 101 130
V3#1-10: Reprints 10-part Treasure Island serial from Target V2#2-11 (see Key Comics #5)
13 26 39 74 105 135
NOTE: *Orlando c-V2#10, V3#5, 6, 8.*

CATHOLIC PICTORIAL
Catholic Guild: 1947
1-Toth-a(2) (Rare) 42 84 126 265 445 625

CAT-MAN AND KITTEN (From Project Superpowers)
Dynamite Entertainment: 2022 ($4.99, one-shot)
Volume 1 - Set in 1948; Jeff Parker-s/Joseph Cooper-a 4.00

CAT-MAN COMICS (Formerly Crash Comics No. 1-5)
Holyoke Publishing Co./Continental Magazines V2#12, 7/44 on:
5/41 - No. 17, 1/43; No. 18, 7/43 - No. 22, 12/43; No. 23, 3/44 - No. 26, 11/44; No. 27, 4/45 - No. 30, 12/45; No. 31, 6/46 - No. 32, 8/46
1(V1#6)-The Cat-Man new costume (see Crash Comics for 1st app.) by Charles Quinlan; Origin The Deacon & Sidekick Mickey, Dr. Diamond & Rag-Man; The Black Widow app. Blaze Baylor begins 811 1622 2433 5920 10,460 15,000
2(V1#7) 276 552 828 1753 3027 4300
3(V1#8)-The Pied Piper begins; classic Hitler, Stalin & Mussolini-c
508 1016 1524 3708 6554 9400
4(V1#9) 271 542 813 1734 2967 4200
5(V2#10, 12/41)-Origin/1st app. The Kitten, Cat-Man's sidekick; The Hood begins. (cover re-dated w/cat image printed over Nov. date). Most of The Kitten's cover image blocked with sidebar 300 600 900 1980 3440 4900
6(V2#11) Mad scientist-c 459 918 1377 3350 5925 8500
7(V2#12) 271 542 813 1734 2967 4200
8(V2#13,3/42)-Origin Little Leaders; Volton by Kubert begins (his 1st comic book work)
314 628 942 2198 3849 5500
9 (V2#14, 4/42)-Classic-c showing a laughing Kitten slaughtering Japanese soldiers with a machine gun 514 1028 1542 3750 6625 9500
10 (V2#15, 5/42)-Origin Blackout; Phantom Falcon begins
252 504 756 1613 2757 3900
11 (V3#1, 6/42)-Kubert-a 245 490 735 1568 2684 3800
12 (V3#2),15,17(1/43): 12-Volton by Brodsky, not Kubert
239 478 717 1530 2615 3700
13-(9/42)(scarce) Weed of Doom (marijuana) 975 1950 2919 7100 12,550 18,000
14-(10/42) World War II-c; Brodsky-a 295 590 885 1888 3244 4600
16 (V3#5, 12/42)-Hitler, Tojo, Mussolini, Goehring-c
850 1700 2550 4450 7725 11,000
18 (V3#8, 7/43)-(scarce) 360 720 1080 1890 2755 4700
19 (V2#6, 9/43)-Hitler, Tojo, Mussolini-c 880 1760 2640 4600 8050 11,500
20 (V2#7, 10/43)-Classic Hitler-c 1700 3400 5100 8900 15,450 22,000
21,22 (V2#8, V2#9) 226 452 678 1446 2473 3500
23 (V2#10, 3/44) World War II-c 245 490 735 1568 2684 3800
nn(V3#13, 5/44) Rico-a; Schomburg Japanese WWII bondage-c (Rare)
400 800 1200 2800 4900 7000
nn(V2#12, 7/44) L.B. Cole-a (4 pgs) 174 348 522 1114 1907 2700
nn(V3#1, 9/44)-Origin The Golden Archer; Leatherface app.
174 348 522 1114 1907 2700
nn(V3#2, 11/44)-L. B. Cole-c 206 412 618 1318 2259 3200
27-Origins Catman & Kitten retold; L. B. Cole Flag-c; Infantino-a
290 580 870 1856 3178 4500
28-Dr. Macabre app.; L. B. Cole-c/a 541 1082 1623 3950 6975 10,000
29-32-L. B. Cole-c; bondage-#30 290 580 870 1856 3178 4500
NOTE: ***Fuje** a-11, 27, 28(2), 29(3), 30. **Palais** a-11, 16, 27, 28, 29(2), 30(2), 32; c-25(7/44). **Rico** a-11(2), 23, 27, 28.*

CAT TALES (3-D)
Eternity Comics: Apr, 1989 ($2.95)
1-Felix the Cat-r in 3-D 5.00

CATWOMAN (Also see Action Comics Weekly #611, Batman #404-407, Detective Comics, & Superman's Girlfriend Lois Lane #70, 71)
DC Comics: Feb, 1989 - No. 4, May, 1989 ($1.50, limited series, mature)
1 2 4 6 10 14 18
2-4: 3-Batman cameo. 4-Batman app. 1 2 3 5 7 9
Her Sister's Keeper (1991, $9.95, trade paperback)-r/#1-4
2 4 6 11 16 20

CATWOMAN (Also see Showcase '93, Showcase '95 #4, & Batman #404-407)
DC Comics: Aug, 1993 - No. 94, Jul, 2001 ($1.50-$2.25)
1-($1.95)-Embossed-c; Bane app.; Balent c-1-10; a-1-10p
1 2 3 5 6 8
2-20: 3-Bane flashback cameo. 4-Brief Bane app. 6,7-Knightquest tie-ins; Batman (Azrael) app. 8-1st app. Zephyr. 12-KnightsEnd pt. 6. 13-new Knights End Aftermath. 14-(9/94)-Zero Hour 4.00
21-24, 26-30, 33-49: 21-$1.95-c begins. 28,29-Penguin cameo app. 36-Legacy pt. 2. 38-40-Year Two; Batman, Joker, Penguin & Two-Face app. 46-Two-Face app. 3.00
25,31,32: 25-($2.95)-Robin app. 31,32-Contagion pt. 4 (Reads pt. 5 on-c) & pt. 9. 4.00
50-($2.95, 48 pgs.)-New armored costume 4.00
50-($2.95, 48 pgs.)-Collector's Ed. w/metallic ink-c 5.00
51-77: 51-Huntress-c/app. 54-Grayson-s begins. 56-Cataclysm pt.6. 57-Poison Ivy-c/app. 63-65-Joker-c/app. 72-No Man's Land; Ostrander-s begins 3.00
78-82: 80-Catwoman goes to jail 3.00
83,84,89-Harley Quinn-c/app. 83-Begin $2.25-c 2 4 6 8 10 12
85-88,90-94 3.00
#0-(10/94)-Zero Hour tie-in; origin retold; released between #14 & #15 5.00
#1,000,000 (11/98) 853rd Century x-over 3.00
Annual 1 (1994, $2.95, 68 pgs.)-Elseworlds story; Batman app.; no Balent-a 4.00
Annual 2,4 ('95, '97, $3.95) 2-Year One story. 4-Pulp Heroes 4.00
Annual 3 (1996, $2.95)-Legends of the Dead Earth story 4.00
...Plus 1 (11/97, $2.95) Screamqueen (Scare Tactics) app. 4.00
TPB ($9.95) r/#15-19, Balent-c 12.00

CATWOMAN (Also see Detective Comics #759-762)
DC Comics: Jan, 2002 - No. 82, Oct, 2008; No. 83, Mar, 2010 ($2.50/$2.99)
1-Darwyn Cooke & Mike Allred-a; Ed Brubaker-s 2 4 6 9 13 16
2-4 1 3 4 6 8 10
5-43: 5-9-Rader-a/Paul Pope-c. 10-Morse-c. 16-JG Jones-c. 22-Batman-c/app. 34-36-War Games. 43-Killer Croc app. 5.00
44-Adam Hughes-c begin 2 4 6 8 10 12
45-Headlights-c; Hush & Clayface app. 4 8 12 23 37 50
46-Captain Cold app. 3 6 9 15 22 28
47,49,52-57,59-68,71,73,75-79: 52-Catwoman kills Black Mask. 53-One Year Later; Helena born. 55-Begin $2.99-c. 56-58-Wildcat app. 75-78-Salvation Run 5.00
48,69 1 2 3 5 6 8
50,58,72-Zatanna-c/app. 1 3 4 6 8 10
51-Classic Selina Kyle mugshot-c 7 14 21 44 82 120
70-Classic-c; "Amazons Attack" tie-in 4 8 12 27 44 60
74-Zatanna app. 4 8 12 27 44 60
80-82 1 3 4 6 8 10
83-(3/10, $2.99) Blackest Night one-shot; Harley Quinn & Black Mask app.; Adam Hughes-c
1 3 4 6 8 10
...: Catwoman Dies TPB (2008, $14.99) r/#66-72; Hughes cover gallery 15.00
...: Crime Pays TPB (2008, $14.99) r/#73-77 15.00
...: Crooked Little Town TPB (2003, $14.95) r/#5-10 & Secret Files; Oeming-c 15.00
...: It's Only a Movie TPB (2007, $19.99) r/#59-65 20.00
...: Relentless TPB (2005, $19.95) r/#12-19 & Secret Files 20.00
... Secret Files and Origins (10/02, $4.95) origin-s Oeming-a; profiles and pin-ups 5.00
...Selina's Big Score HC (2002, $24.95) Cooke-s/a; pin-ups by various 25.00
...Selina's Big Score SC (2003, $17.95) Cooke-s/a; pin-ups by various 18.00
...: The Dark End of the Street TPB (2002, $12.95) r/#1-4 & Slam Bradley back-up stories from Detective Comics #759-762 13.00
...: The Long Road Home TPB (2009, $17.99) r/#78-82 18.00
...: The Replacements TPB (2007, $14.99) r/#53-58 15.00
...: Wild Ride TPB (2005, $14.99) r/#20-24 & Secret Files #1 15.00

CATWOMAN (DC New 52)
DC Comics: Nov, 2011 - No. 52, Jul, 2016 ($2.99)
1-Winick-s/March-a; Batman app. 1 2 3 5 6 8
2-12: 2-6-March-a. 7,8-Melo-a. 9-Night of the Owls 3.00
13-(12/12) Death of the Family tie-in; die-cut Joker mask-c 12.00
13-Second printing with chessboard-c 5.00
14-22: 14-Death of the Family tie-in; Joker app 3.00
23,24: 23-(10/13) Debut of Joker's Daughter in final panel. 24-Joker's Daughter app. 5.00
25,26,28-49: 25-Zero Year. 26-Joker's Daughter app. 28-Gothtopia. 35-40-Jae Lee-c 3.00
27-($3.99) Gothtopia x-over with Detective Comics #27; Olliffe & Richards-a 4.00
50-($4.99) Harley Quinn, Poison Ivy app.; back-up origin of Black Mask's mask 5.00
51,52: Black Mask & the False Face Society app.; Middleton-c 3.00
#0 (11/12, $2.99) Origin re-told; Nocenti-s/Melo-a/March-c 3.00
Annual 1 (7/13, $4.99) Nocenti-s/Duce-a; Penguin app. 5.00
Annual 2 (2/15, $4.99) Olliffe & McCrea-a 5.00
...: Election Night 1 (1/17, $4.99) Meredith Finch-s/Shane Davis-a; Prez app. 5.00

Cat-Man Comics #21 © HOKE

Catwoman (2002) #74 © DC

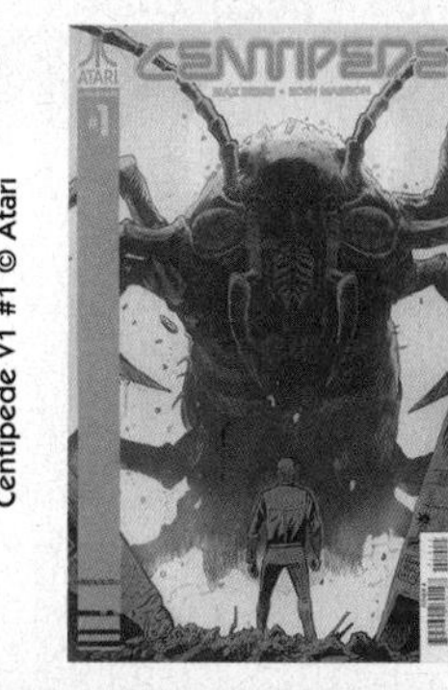

Centipede V1 #1 © Atari

GD 2.0 | VG 4.0 | FN 6.0 | VF 8.0 | VF/NM 9.0 | NM- 9.2

...: Futures End 1 (11/14, $2.99, regular-c) Five years later; Olliffe-a/Dodson-c 3.00
...: Futures End 1 (11/14, $3.99, 3-D cover) 4.00

CATWOMAN (Follows Batman #50 [2018])
DC Comics: Sept, 2018 - Present ($3.99)
1-12: 1-Joëlle Jones-s/a; new costume. 7,8-Casagrande-a; Penguin app. 9-Timms-a 4.00
13-24,26-49: 13-17-Year of the Villain tie-ins. 15-Andolfo-a. 17-Acetate-c. 18-Zatanna app. 23,24-Sean Murphy-c. 35-37-"Fear State" tie-ins. 36,37,43,44-Harley Quinn app. 4.00
13-($4.99) Year of the Villain cardstock-c by Artgerm 5.00
25-($5.99) Joker War tie-in; Riddler and Penguin app.; 2 back-up stories; J.P. Leon-a 6.00
50-($5.99) Punchline app. 6.00
51,52-Eiko Hasigawa as Catwoman 4.00
Annual 1 (7/19, $4.99) Casagrande & Petrus-a 5.00
2021 Annual 1 (8/21, $5.99) Ram V-s/Kyle Hotz-a; Azrael app. 6.00
.../Tweety & Sylvester 1 (10/18, $4.99) Simone-s/Miranda-a; Black Canary app. 5.00

CATWOMAN 80TH ANNIVERSARY 100-PAGE SUPER SPECTACULAR
DC Comics: Jun, 2020 ($9.99, squarebound, one-shot)
1-Short stories & pin-ups by various; birth of Helena by King-s/Janin-a; multiple covers 10.00

CATWOMAN/ GUARDIAN OF GOTHAM
DC Comics: 1999 - No. 2, 1999 ($5.95, limited series)
1,2-Elseworlds; Moench-s/Balent-a 2 4 6 8 10 12

CATWOMAN: LONELY CITY
DC Comics (Black Label): Dec, 2021 - No. 4, Dec, 2022 ($6.99, oversized 8-1/2" x 10-3/4", lim. series)
1-4-Cliff Chiang-s/a/c; world without Batman; Killer Croc, Poison Ivy, Etrigan app. 7.00

CATWOMAN: NINE LIVES OF A FELINE FATALE
DC Comics: 2004 ($14.95, TPB)
nn-Reprints notable stories from Batman #1 to the present; pin-ups by various; Bolland-c 15.00

CATWOMAN: THE MOVIE (2004 Halle Berry movie)
DC Comics: 2004 ($4.95/$9.95)
1-($4.95) Movie adaptation; Jim Lee-c and sketch pages; Derenick-a 1 2 3 5 6 8
... & Other Cat Tales TPB (2004, $9.95)-r/Movie adaptation; Jim Lee sketch pages, r/Catwoman #0, Catwoman (2nd series) #11 & 25; photo-c 10.00

CATWOMAN/VAMPIRELLA: THE FURIES
DC Comics/Harris Publ.: Feb, 1997 ($4.95, squarebound, 46 pgs.) (1st DC/Harris x-over)
nn-Reintro Pantha; Chuck Dixon scripts; Balent-c/a 2 4 6 10 14 18

CATWOMAN: WHEN IN ROME
DC Comics: Nov, 2004 - No. 6, Aug, 2005 ($3.50, limited series)
1-6-Jeph Loeb-s/Tim Sale-a/c; Riddler app. 3.50
HC (2005, $19.99, dustjacket) r/series; intro by Mark Chiarello; sketch pages 20.00
SC (2007, $12.99) r/series; intro by Mark Chiarello; sketch pages 13.00

CATWOMAN/WILDCAT
DC Comics: Aug, 1998 - No. 4, Nov, 1998 ($2.50, limited series)
1-4-Chuck Dixon & Beau Smith-s; Stelfreeze-c 4.00

CAUGHT
Atlas Comics (VPI): Aug, 1956 - No. 5, Apr, 1957
1 37 74 111 222 361 500
2-4: 3-Maneely, Pakula, Torres-a. 4-Maneely-a 19 38 57 111 176 240
5-Crandall, Krigstein-a 20 40 60 114 182 250
NOTE: *Drucker a-2. Heck a-4. Severin c-1, 2, 4, 5. Shores a-4.*

CAVALIER COMICS
A. W. Nugent Publ. Co.: 1945; 1952 (Early DC reprints)
2(1945)-Speed Saunders, Fang Gow 23 46 69 136 223 310
2(1952) 14 28 42 80 115 150

CAVALRY, THE : S.H.I.E.L.D. 50TH ANNIVERSARY
Marvel Comics: Nov, 2015 ($3.99, one-shot)
1-Agent Melinda May on a training mission; Luke Ross-a; Keown-c 4.00

CAVE CARSON HAS A CYBERNETIC EYE
DC Comics (Young Animal): Dec, 2016 - No. 12, Nov, 2017 ($3.99)
1-12-Jonathan Rivera & Gerald Way-s/Michael Avon Oeming-a; back-up Tom Scioli-s/a in #1-6. 7-Superman-c/app. 4.00
.../ Swamp Thing Special 1 (4/18, $4.99) Part 4 of Milk Wars crossover; Rivera-a/Foss-a 5.00

CAVE CARSON HAS AN INTERSTELLAR EYE
DC Comics (Young Animal): May, 2018 - No. 6, Oct, 2018 ($3.99)
1-6-Jonathan Rivera-s/Michael Avon Oeming-a; back-up with Maybury-a in #1-5 4.00

CAVE GIRL (Also see Africa)
Magazine Enterprises: No. 11, 1953 - No. 14, 1954
11(A-1 82)-Origin; all Cave Girl stories 65 130 195 416 708 1000
12(A-1 96), 13(A-1 116), 14(A-1 125)-Thunda by Powell in each 43 86 129 271 461 650
NOTE: *Powell c/a in all.*

CAVE GIRL
AC Comics: 1988 ($2.95, 44 pgs.) (16 pgs. of color, rest B&W)
1-Powell-r/Cave Girl #11; Nyoka photo back-c from movie; Powell/Bill Black-c; Special Limited Edition on-c 4.00

CAVE KIDS (TV) (See Comic Album #16)
Gold Key: Feb, 1963 - No. 16, Mar, 1967 (Hanna-Barbera)
1 6 12 18 38 69 100
2-5 4 8 12 23 37 50
6-16: 7,12-Pebbles & Bamm Bamm app. 16-1st Space Kidettes 3 6 9 19 30 40

CAVEWOMAN
Basement Comics: Jan, 1994 - No. 6, 1995 ($2.95)
1 9 18 27 62 126 190
2 4 8 12 25 40 55
3-6 2 4 6 10 14 18
...: Meets Explorers ('97, $2.95) 5.00
...: One-Shot Special (7/00, $2.95) Massey-s/a 5.00

CBLDF (Comic Book Legal Defense Fund) (See Liberty Comics)

CELESTINE (See Violator Vs. Badrock #1)
Image Comics (Extreme): May, 1996 - No. 2, June, 1996 ($2.50, limited series)
1,2: Warren Ellis scripts 3.00

CEMETERY BEACH
Image Comics: Sept, 2018 - No. 7, Mar, 2019 ($3.99)
1-7-Warren Ellis-s/Jason Howard-a 4.00

CENTIPEDE (Based on Atari videogame)
Dynamite Entertainment: 2017 - No. 5, 2017 ($3.99)
1-5: 1-Bemis-s/Marron-a; covers by Marron, Francavilla & Schkade 4.00

CENTURION OF ANCIENT ROME, THE
Zondervan Publishing House: 1958 (no month listed) (B&W, 36 pgs.)
(Rare) All by Jay Disbrow 113 226 339 718 1234 1750

CENTURIONS (TV)
DC Comics: June, 1987 - No. 4, Sept, 1987 (75¢, limited series)
1-4 4.00

CENTURY: DISTANT SONS
Marvel Comics: Feb, 1996 ($2.95, one-shot)
1-Wraparound-c 4.00

CENTURY OF COMICS (See Promotional Comics section)

CENTURY WEST
Image Comics: Sept, 2013 ($7.99, squarebound, graphic novel)
nn-Howard Chaykin-s/a/c 8.00

CEREBUS BI-WEEKLY
Aardvark-Vanaheim: Dec. 2, 1988 - No. 27, Nov. 24, 1989 ($1.25, B&W)
Reprints Cerebus The Aardvark #1-27
1-16, 18, 19, 21-27: 3.00
17-Hepcats app. 2 4 6 8 10 12
20-Milk & Cheese app. 2 4 6 10 12 15

CEREBUS: CHURCH & STATE
Aardvark-Vanaheim: Feb, 1991 - No. 30, Apr, 1992 ($2.00, B&W, bi-weekly)
1-30: r/Cerebus #51-80 3.00

CEREBUS: HIGH SOCIETY
Aardvark-Vanaheim: Feb, 1990 - No. 25, 1991 ($1.70, B&W)
1-25: r/Cerebus #26-50 3.00

CEREBUS IN HELL?
Aardvark-Vanaheim: No. 0, 2016; No. 1, Jan, 2017 - No. 4, Apr, 2017 ($4.00, B&W)
0-4-Sim & Atwal-s; Cerebus figures placed over original Gustave Doré artwork of Hell 4.00
Cerebus In Hell 1 (12/18, $4.00) new pages and reprints; cover swipe of Cerebus #1 4.00
Cerebus The Vark Knight Returns 1 (12/17, $4.00) new pages and reprints 4.00
...Presents #59: Defective Comics 1 (2/22, $8.00) Cover swipe of Detective Comics #27 8.00
The Death of Cerebus in Hell 1 (11/17, $4.00) new pages and reprints 4.00
... 2021 1 (1/21, $4.00) Cerebus figures with Doré art; calendar pages with parody covers 4.00

	GD	VG	FN	VF	VF/NM	NM-
	2.0	4.0	6.0	8.0	9.0	9.2

CEREBUS JAM
Aardvark-Vanaheim: Apr, 1985

1-Eisner, Austin, Dave Sim-a (Cerebus vs. Spirit) 6.00

CEREBUS THE AARDVARK (See A-V in 3-D, Nucleus, Power Comics)
Aardvark-Vanaheim: Dec, 1977 - No. 300, March, 2004 ($1.70/$2.00/$2.25, B&W)

0 5.00
0-Gold 20.00
1-1st app. Cerebus; 2000 print run; most copies poorly printed
241 482 723 1988 4494 7000

Note: *There is a counterfeit version known to exist. It can be distinguished from the original in the following ways: inside cover is glossy instead of flat, black background on the front cover is blotted or spotty. Reports show that a counterfeit #2 also exists.*

2-Dave Sim art in all 22 44 66 154 340 525
3-Origin Red Sophia 14 28 42 96 211 325
4-Origin Elrod the Albino 10 20 30 70 150 230
5,6 9 18 27 57 111 165
7-10 6 12 18 37 66 95
11,12: 11-Origin The Cockroach 5 10 15 31 53 75
13-15: 14-Origin Lord Julius 4 8 12 28 47 65
16-20 3 6 9 21 33 45
21-Barry Smith letter in letter column 5 10 15 33 57 80
22-Low distribution; no cover price 4 8 12 25 40 55
23-30: 23-Preview of Wandering Star by Teri S. Wood. 26-High Society begins, ends #50
3 6 9 16 23 30
31-Origin Moonroach 3 6 9 16 24 32
32-40, 53-Intro. Wolveroach (brief app.) 2 4 6 8 10 12
41-50,52: 48-1st app. Joshua "Wolverine" MacAlistaire in back-up. 52-Church & State begins, ends #111; Cutey Bunny app. 1 2 3 5 7 9
51,54: 51-Cutey Bunny app. 54-1st full Wolveroach story
2 4 6 8 11 14
55,56-Wolveroach app.; Normalman back-ups by Valentino
1 3 4 6 8 10
57-100: 61,62: Flaming Carrot app. 65-Gerhard begins 4.00
101-160: 104-Flaming Carrot app. 112/113-Double issue. 114-Jaka's Story begins, ends #136. 139-Melmoth begins, ends #150. 151-Mothers & Daughters begins, ends #200 3.00
161-Bone app. 1 3 4 6 8 10
162-231: 175-($2.25, 44 pgs). 186-Strangers in Paradise cameo. 201-Guys storyline begins; Eddie Campbell's Bacchus app. 220-231-Rick's Story 3.00
232-265-Going Home 3.00
266-288,291-299-Latter Days: 267-Five-Bar Gate. 276-Spore (Spawn spoof) 3.00
289&290 ($4.50) Two issues combined 5.00
300-Final issue 3.00
Free Cerebus (Giveaway, 1991-92?, 36 pgs.)-All-r 5.00

CEREBUS THE DUCK
Aardvark-Vanaheim: Apr, 2021 ($4.00, B&W, one-shot)

1-Cerebus figures placed over original Gustave Doré artwork; Howard the Duck #1 c-swipe 4.00

CEREBUS THE EMILY
Aardvark-Vanaheim: Mar, 2022 ($4.00, B&W, one-shot)

1-Cerebus figures placed over original Gustave Doré artwork; Emily the Strange #4 c-swipe 4.00

CEREBUS WOMAN
Aardvark-Vanaheim: May, 2019 ($4.00, B&W, one-shot)

1-Cerebus figures placed over original Gustave Doré artwork; Wonder Woman #1 c-swipe 4.00

CHAIN GANG WAR
DC Comics: July, 1993 - No. 12, June, 1994 ($1.75)

1-($2.50)-Embossed silver foil-c, Dave Johnson-c/a 4.00
2-4,6-12: 3-Deathstroke app. 4-Brief Deathstroke app. 6-New Batman (Azrael) cameo. 11-New Batman-c/story. 12-New Batman app. 3.00
5-($2.50)-Foil-c; Deathstroke app; new Batman cameo (1 panel) 4.00

CHAINS OF CHAOS
Harris Comics: Nov, 1994 - No. 3, Jan, 1995 ($2.95, limited series)

1-3-Re-Intro of The Rook w/ Vampirella 5.00

CHALLENGE OF THE SUPER SONS (Jon Kent and Damian Wayne)
DC Comics: Jun, 2021 - No. 7, Dec, 2021 ($3.99, limited series)

1-7-Tomasi-s/Raynor-a; Justice League, Felix Faust & Vandal Savage app. 4.00

CHALLENGE OF THE UNKNOWN (Formerly Love Experiences)
Ace Magazines: No. 6, Sept, 1950 (See Web Of Mystery No. 19)

6- "Villa of the Vampire" used in N.Y. Joint Legislative Comm. Publ; Sekowsky-a
65 130 195 416 708 1000

CHALLENGER, THE
Interfaith Publications/T.C. Comics: 1945 - No. 4, Oct-Dec, 1946

nn; nd; 32 pgs.; Origin the Challenger Club; Anti-Fascist with funny animal filler
541 1082 1623 3950 6975 10,000
2-Classic Pandora's Box demons-c; Kubert-a 110 220 330 704 1202 1700
3,4: Kubert-a; 4-Fuje-a 60 120 180 381 653 925

CHALLENGERS OF THE FANTASTIC
Marvel Comics (Amalgam): June 1997 ($1.95, one-shot)

1-Karl Kesel-s/Tom Grummett-a 4.00

CHALLENGERS OF THE UNKNOWN (See Showcase #6, 7, 11, 12, Super DC Giant, and Super Team Family) (See Showcase Presents for B&W reprints)
National Per. Publ./DC Comics: 4-5/58 - No. 77, 12-1/70-71; No. 78, 2/73 - No. 80, 6-7/73; No. 81, 6-7/77 - No. 87, 6-7/78

1-(4-5/58)-Kirby/Stein-a(2); Kirby-c 238 476 714 1964 4432 6900
2-Kirby/Stein-a(2) 71 142 213 568 1284 2000
3-Kirby/Stein-a(2); Rocky returns from space with powers similar to the Fantastic Four (9/58)
68 136 204 544 1222 1900
4-8-Kirby/Wood-a plus cover to #8 44 88 132 326 738 1150
9,10 27 54 81 189 420 650
11-Grey tone-c 36 72 108 259 580 900
12-15: 14-Origin/1st app. Multi-Man (villain) 18 36 54 126 281 435
16-22: 18-Intro. Cosmo, the Challengers Spacepet. 22-Last 10¢ issue
12 24 36 83 182 280
23-30 9 18 27 58 114 170
31-Retells origin of the Challengers 9 18 27 59 117 175
32-40 7 14 21 44 82 120
41-47,49,50,52-60: 43-New look begins. 47-1st Sponge-Man. 49-Intro. Challenger Corps. 55-Death of Red Ryan. 60-Red Ryan returns 5 10 15 33 57 80
48,51: 48-Doom Patrol app. 51-Sea Devils app. 5 10 15 34 60 85
61-68: 64,65-Kirby origin-r, parts 1 & 2. 66-New logo. 68-Last 12¢ issue.
4 8 12 25 40 55
69-73,75-80: 69-1st app. Corinna. 77-Last 15¢ issue 3 6 9 17 26 35
74-Deadman by Tuska/Adams; 1 pg. Wrightson-a 7 14 21 44 82 120
81,83-87: 81-(6-7/77). 83-87-Swamp Thing app. 84-87-Deadman app.
2 4 6 9 12 15
82-Swamp Thing begins (thru #87, c/s 2 4 6 11 16 20

NOTE: ***N. Adams** c-67, 68, 70, 72, 74i, 81i. **Buckler** c-83-86p. **Giffen** a-83-87p. **Kirby** a-75-80r; c-75, 77, 78. **Kubert** c-64, 66, 69, 76, 79. **Nasser** c/a-81p, 82p. **Tuska** a-73. **Wood** r-76.*

CHALLENGERS OF THE UNKNOWN
DC Comics: Mar, 1991 - No. 8, Oct, 1991 ($1.75, limited series)

1-Jeph Loeb scripts & Tim Sale-a in all (1st work together); Bolland-c 5.00
2-8: 2-Superman app. 3-Dr. Fate app. 6-G. Kane-c(p). 7-Steranko-c/swipe by Art Adams 4.00
... Must Die! (2004, $19.95, TPB) r/series; intro by Bendis; Sale sketch pages 20.00

NOTE: ***Art Adams** c-7. **Hempel** c-5. **Gil Kane** c-6p. **Sale** a-1-8; c-3, 8. **Wagner** c-4.*

CHALLENGERS OF THE UNKNOWN
DC Comics: Feb, 1997 - No. 18, July, 1998 ($2.25)

1-18: 1-Intro new team; Leon-c/a(p) begins. 4-Origin of new team. 11,12-Batman app. 15-Millennium Giants x-over; Superman-c/app. 4.00

CHALLENGERS OF THE UNKNOWN
DC Comics: Aug, 2004 - No. 6, Jan, 2005 ($2.95, limited series)

1-6-Intro. new team; Howard Chaykin-s/a 3.00

CHALLENGE TO THE WORLD
Catechetical Guild: 1951 (10¢, 36 pgs.)

nn 7 14 21 35 43 50

CHAMBER (See Generation X and Uncanny X-Men)
Marvel Comics: Oct, 2002 - No. 4, Jan, 2003 ($2.99, limited series)

1-4-Bachalo-c/Vaughan-s/Ferguson-a. 1-Cyclops app. 3.00

CHAMBER OF CHILLS (Formerly Blondie Comics #20; ...of Clues No. 27 on)
Harvey Publications/Witches Tales: No. 21, June, 1951 - No. 26, Dec, 1954

21 (#1) 168 336 504 1075 1838 2600
22,24 (#2,4) 55 110 165 352 601 850
23 (#3)-Excessive violence; eyes torn out 61 122 183 390 670 950
5(2/52)-Decapitation, acid in face scene 48 96 144 302 514 725
6-Woman melted alive 53 106 159 334 567 800
7-Used in **SOTI**, pg. 389; decapitation/severed head panels
55 110 165 352 601 850
8-10: 8-Decapitation panels 43 86 129 271 461 650
11,12 40 80 120 246 411 575
13,15-17,22,24-Nostrand-a in all. 13,21-Decapitation panels.
42 84 126 265 445 625
14-Spider-Man precursor (11/52) 53 106 159 334 567 800
18-Atom bomb panels 97 194 291 621 1061 1500
19-Classic-c; Nostrand-a 2000 4000 6000 15,200 27,600 40,000
20-Classic Nostrand-c 65 130 195 416 708 1000
21-Classic skull-c 129 258 387 826 1413 2000
23-Classic-c of corpse kissing woman; Nostrand-a 649 1298 1947 4738 8369 12,000
25,26 37 74 111 222 361 500

NOTE: *About half the issues contain bondage, torture, sadism, perversion, gore, cannibalism, eyes ripped out, acid in face, etc. **Elias** c-4-11, 14-19, 21-26. **Kremer** a-12, 17. **Palais** a-21(1), 23. **Nostrand/Powell** a-13, 15, 16. **Powell** a-21, 23, 24('51), 5-8, 11, 13, 18-21, 23-25. Bondage-c-21, 24('51), 7. 25-r/#5; 26-r/#9.*

CHAMBER OF CHILLS
Marvel Comics Group: Nov, 1972 - No. 25, Nov, 1976

1-Harlan Ellison adaptation 5 10 15 35 63 90
2-5: 2-1st app. John Jakes' Brak the Barbarian 3 6 9 17 26 35
6-25: 22,23-(Regular 25¢ editions) 3 6 9 16 23 30
22,23-(30¢-c variants, limited distribution)(5,7/76) 8 16 24 51 96 140

NOTE: ***Adkins** a-1i, 2i. **Brunner** a-2-4; c-4. **Chaykin** a-4. **Ditko** r-14, 16, 19, 23, 24. **Everett** a-3i, 11r,21r. **Heath** a-1r. **Gil Kane** c-2p. **Kirby** r-11, 18, 19, 22. **Powell** a-13r. **Russell** a-1p, 2p. **Shores** a-5 . **Williamson/Mayo** a-13r. **Robert E. Howard** horror story adaptation-2, 3.*

CHAMBER OF CLUES (Formerly Chamber of Chills)
Harvey Publications: No. 27, Feb, 1955 - No. 28, April, 1955

27-Kerry Drake-r/#19; Powell-a; last pre-code 8 16 24 42 54 65
28-Kerry Drake 7 14 21 35 43 50

CHAMBER OF DARKNESS (Monsters on the Prowl #9 on)
Marvel Comics Group: Oct, 1969 - No. 8, Dec, 1970

1-Buscema-a(p) 8 16 24 54 102 150
2,3: 2-Neal Adams scripts. 3-Smith, Buscema-a 4 8 12 28 47 65
4-A Conan-esque tryout by Smith (4/70); reprinted in Conan #16; Marie Severin/Everett-c 9 18 27 62 126 190
5,8: 5-H.P. Lovecraft adaptation. 8-Wrightson-c 4 8 12 25 40 55
6 3 6 9 21 33 45
7-Wrightson-c/a, 7pgs. (his 1st work at Marvel); Wrightson draws himself in 1st & last panels; Kirby/Ditko-r; last 15¢-c 6 12 18 38 69 100
1-(1/72; 25¢ Special, 52 pgs.) 4 8 12 25 40 55

NOTE: ***Adkins/Everett** a-8. **Buscema** a-Special 1r. **Craig** a-5. **Ditko** a-6-8r. **Heck** a-1, 2, 8, Special 1r. **Kirby** a(p)-4, 5, 7r. **Kirby/Everett** c-5. **Severin/Everett** c-6. **Shores** a-2, 3i, Special 1r. **Sutton** a-1, 2i, 4, 7, Special 1r. **Wrightson** c-7, 8.*

CHAMP COMICS (Formerly Champion No. 1-10)
Worth Publ. Co./Champ Publ./Family Comics(Harvey Publ.): No. 11, Oct, 1940 - No. 24, Dec, 1942; No. 25, April, 1943

11-Human Meteor cont'd. from Champion 158 316 474 1003 1727 2450
12-17,20: 14,15-Crandall-c. 20-The Green Ghost app.; Japanese WWII-c
132 264 396 846 1448 2050
18,19-Simon-c. 19-The Wasp app. 161 322 483 1030 1765 2500

Cerebus Woman #1 © A-V

Champions (2019) #1 © MAR

Chaos! #1 © DYN

	GD 2.0	VG 4.0	FN 6.0	VF 8.0	VF/NM 9.0	NM- 9.2
21-23,25: 22-The White Mask app. 23-Flag-c	103	206	309	659	1130	1600
24-Hitler, Tojo & Mussolini-c	295	590	885	1888	3244	4600

CHAMPION (See Gene Autry's...)

CHAMPION COMICS
Worth Publ. Co.: Oct, 1939 (ashcan)

nn-Ashcan comic, not distributed to newsstands, only for in house use. A FN/VF copy sold for $2,261.76 in 2010.

CHAMPION COMICS (Formerly Speed Comics #1?; Champ Comics No. 11 on)
Worth Publ. Co.(Harvey Publications): No. 2, Dec, 1939 - No. 10, Aug, 1940 (no No.1)

	GD 2.0	VG 4.0	FN 6.0	VF 8.0	VF/NM 9.0	NM- 9.2
2-The Champ, The Blazing Scarab, Neptina, Liberty Lads, Jungleman, Bill Handy, Swingtime Sweetie begin	148	296	444	947	1624	2300
3-Classic-c	129	258	387	826	1413	2000
4-7: 7-The Human Meteor begins?	100	200	300	635	1093	1550
8,10: 8-Simon-c. 10-Bondage-c by Kirby	300	600	900	2070	3635	5200
9-1st S&K-c (1st collaboration together)	364	728	1092	2548	4474	6400

CHAMPIONS, THE
Marvel Comics Group: Oct, 1975 - No. 17, Jan, 1978

	GD 2.0	VG 4.0	FN 6.0	VF 8.0	VF/NM 9.0	NM- 9.2
1-Origin & 1st app. The Champions (The Angel, Black Widow, Ghost Rider, Hercules, Iceman) Venus x-over	6	12	18	37	66	95
2-6,8-10: 2-3 vs. Pluto, Venus x-over. 5,6-(Regular 25¢ edition)(4-6/76). 5-1st Rampage. 6-Kirby-c. 8-Champions vs. Darkstar, Griffin & Titanium Man; 1st Yuri Petrovitch as new Crimson Dynamo. 10-Champions vs. Crimson Dynamo & Titanium Man	2	4	6	13	18	22
5,6-(30¢-c variants, limited distribution)	5	10	15	31	53	75
7-(Regular 25¢ edition)(8/76) 1st Darkstar, Griffin & Titanium Man app.	5	10	15	31	53	75
7-(30¢-c variant, limited distribution)	7	14	21	46	86	125
11-15: 11-Byrne-a begins; Black Goliath app; Darkstar joins. 12-Stilt-Man, Black Goliath & The Stranger app. 13-Black Goliath & The Stranger app. 14,15-(Regular 30¢ edition). 14-1st Swarm; Iceman dons new costume. 15-Origin Swarm	3	6	9	14	19	24
14,15-(35¢-c variant, limited distribution)	6	12	18	42	79	115
16-Continued from Super-Villain Team-Up #14; Magneto & Dr. Doom app; Hulk & Beast guest app.	2	4	6	13	18	25
17-Last issue; vs. The Brotherhood of Evil Mutants; Sentinels app.; Champions app. next in Spectacular Spider-Man #17	3	6	9	14	19	24

... Classic Vol. 1 TPB (2006, $19.99) r/#1-11; unused cover to #7 — 20.00
... Classic Vol. 2 TPB (2007, $19.99) r/#12-17, Iron Man Ann. #4, Avengers #163, Super-Villain Team-Up #14 and Peter Parker, The Spectacular Spider-Man #17-18 — 20.00
...: No Time For Losers (2016, $7.99) r/#1-3,14,15; art by Heck, Tuska & Byrne — 8.00

NOTE: ***Buckler/Adkins** c-3. **Byrne** a-11-15, 17. **Kane/Adkins** c-1. **Kane/Layton** c-11. **Tuska** a-3p, 4p, 6p, 7p. Ghost Rider c-1-4, 7, 8, 10, 14, 16, 17 (4, 10, 14 are more prominent).*

CHAMPIONS (Game)
Eclipse Comics: June, 1986 - No. 6, Feb, 1987 (limited series)

1-6: 1-Intro Flare; based on game. 5-Origin Flare — 4.00

CHAMPIONS (Also see The League of Champions)
Hero Comics: Sept, 1987 - No. 12, 1989 ($1.95)

1-12: 1-Intro The Marksman & The Rose. 4-Origin Malice — 4.00
Annual 1(1988, $2.75, 52 pgs.)-Origin of Giant — 5.00

CHAMPIONS
Marvel Comics: Dec, 2016 - No. 27, Feb, 2019 ($4.99/$3.99)

1-($4.99) Ms. Marvel, Spider-Man (Miles), Hulk (Amadeus), Nova, Viv Vision team — 5.00
2-24,26,27-($3.99) 3-Young Cyclops joins. 5-Gwenpool app. 9-Intro. Red Locust. 10,11-Secret Empire tie-ins. 13-15-Avengers app. 21-Zub-s/Izaakse-a begins. 22-New Ironheart armor. 23-Man-Thing app. 27-Champions in Weirdworld — 4.00
25-($4.99) Champions go to Weirdworld; Man-Thing app. — 5.00
#1.MU (4/17, $4.99) Monsters Unleashed tie-in; Whitely-s/Stein & Brandt-a — 5.00
Annual 1 (2/19, $4.99) Spotlight on Snowguard; Marcus To-a — 5.00

CHAMPIONS
Marvel Comics: Mar, 2019 - No. 10, Dec, 2019 ($3.99)

1-10: 1-Zub-s/Cummings-a; Mephisto app. 5,6-War of The Realms tie-in — 4.00

CHAMPIONS (Takes place after Outlawed #1)
Marvel Comics: Dec, 2020 - No. 10, Dec, 2021 ($3.99)

1-10: 1-Eve L. Ewing-s/Simone Di Meo-a; Ms. Marvel, Nova, Spider-Man (Miles) app. — 4.00

CHAMPION SPORTS
National Periodical Publications: Oct-Nov, 1973 - No. 3, Feb-Mar, 1974

	GD 2.0	VG 4.0	FN 6.0	VF 8.0	VF/NM 9.0	NM- 9.2
1	3	6	9	16	23	30
2,3	2	4	6	9	12	15

CHANNEL ZERO
Image Comics: Feb, 1998 - No. 5 ($2.95, B&W, limited series)

1-5, ...Dupe (1/99) -Brian Wood-s/a — 3.00

CHAOS (See The Crusaders)

CHAOS!
Dynamite Entertainment: 2014 - No. 6, 2014 ($3.99, limited series)

1-6-Seeley-s/Andolfo-a; multiple covers on each. Purgatori, Evil Ernie, Chastity app. — 4.00
... Holiday Special 2014 ($5.99) Short stories by various; Lupacchino-c — 6.00
...: Smiley The Psychotic Button 1 (2015, $4.99) origin re-told; Andolfo-c — 5.00

CHAOS! BIBLE
Chaos! Comics: Nov, 1995 ($3.30, one-shot)

1-Profiles of characters & creators — 3.50

CHAOS! CHRONICLES
Chaos! Comics: Feb, 2000 ($3.50, one-shot)

1-Profiles of characters, checklist of Chaos! comics and products — 3.50

CHAOS EFFECT, THE
Valiant: 1994

Alpha (Giveaway w/trading card checklist) — 4.00
Alpha-Red variant — 5.00
Omega (11/94, $2.25); Epilogue Pt. 1, 2 (12/94, 1/95; $2.95) — 4.00

	GD 2.0	VG 4.0	FN 6.0	VF 8.0	VF/NM 9.0	NM- 9.2
Omega-Gold variant	1	3	4	6	8	10

CHAOS! GALLERY
Chaos! Comics: Aug, 1997 ($2.95, one-shot)

1-Pin-ups of characters — 5.00

CHAOS! QUARTERLY
Chaos! Comics: Oct, 1995 -No. 3, May, 1996 ($4.95, quarterly)

1-3: 1-Anthology; Lady Death-c by Julie Bell. 2-Boris "Lady Demon"-c — 5.00
1-Premium Edition (7,500) — 25.00

CHAOS WAR
Marvel Comics: Dec, 2010 - No. 4, Mr, 2011 ($3.99, limited series)

1-5-Hercules, Thor and others vs. Chaos King; Pham-a. 3-5-Galactus app. — 4.00
...: Alpha Flight 1 (1/11, $3.99) McCann-s/Brown-a — 4.00
...: Ares 1 (2/11, $3.99) Oeming-s/Segovia-a — 4.00
...: Chaos King 1 (1/11, $3.99) Kaluta-a/c; Monclair-s — 4.00
...: Dead Avengers 1-3 (1/11 - No. 3, 3/11, $3.99) Grummett-a; Capt. Marvel app. — 4.00
...: God Squad 1 (2/11, $3.99) Sumerak-s/Panosian-a — 4.00
...: Thor 1,2 (1/11 - No. 2, 2/11, $3.99) DeMatteis-s/Ching-a — 4.00
...: X-Men 1,2 (2/11 - No. 2, 3/11, $3.99) Braithwaite-a; Thunderbird, Banshee app. — 4.00

CHAPEL (Also see Youngblood & Youngblood Strikefile #1-3)
Image Comics (Extreme Studios): No. 1 Feb, 1995 - No. 2, Mar, 1995 ($2.50, limited series)

1,2 — 4.00

CHAPEL (Also see Youngblood & Youngblood Strikefile #1-3)
Image Comics (Extreme Studios): V2 #1, Aug, 1995 - No. 7, Apr, 1996 ($2.50)

V2#1-7: 4-Babewatch x-over. 5-vs. Spawn. 7-Shadowhawk-c/app; Shadowhunt x-over — 4.00
#1-Quesada & Palmiotti variant-c — 4.00

CHAPEL (Also see Youngblood & Youngblood Strikefile #1-3)
Awesome Entertainment: Sept, 1997 ($2.99, one-shot)

1 (Reg. & alternate covers) — 4.00

CHARIOT
Artists, Writers & Artisans, Inc.: Mar, 2021 - No. 5, Jul, 2021 ($3.99, limited series)

1-5-Bryan Edward Hill-s/Priscilla Petraites-a — 4.00

CHARISMAGIC
Aspen MLT: No. 0, Mar, 2011 - No. 6, Jul, 2012 ($1.99/$2.99/$3.50)

0-($1.99) Khary Randolph-a/ Vince Hernandez-s; 3 covers — 3.00
1-4-($2.99) 1-4-Four covers on each — 3.00
5,6-($3.50) Multiple covers on each — 3.50
... Primer 1 (2/18, 25¢) Character profiles and story histories — 3.00
...: The Death Princess 1-3 (11/12 - No. 3, 7/13, $3.99) Hernandez-s/Emilio Lopez-a — 4.00

CHARISMAGIC (Volume 2)
Aspen MLT: May, 2013 - No. 6, Nov, 2013 ($1.00/$3.99)

1-($1.00) Vincenzo Cucca-a/ Vince Hernandez-s; multiple covers — 3.00
2-6-($3.99) Multiple covers on each — 4.00

CHARISMAGIC (Volume 3)
Aspen MLT: Feb, 2018 - No. 5, Jun, 2018 ($3.99)

1-5-Joey Vazquez-a/ Vince Hernandez-s; multiple covers — 4.00

CHARLEMAGNE (Also see War Dancer)

GD VG FN VF VF/NM NM-
2.0 4.0 6.0 8.0 9.0 9.2

Defiant: Mar, 1994 - No. 5, July, 1994 ($2.50)

1-(3/94, $3.50, 52 pgs.)-Adam Pollina-c/a. 4.00
2,3,5: Adam Pollina-c/a. 2-War Dancer app. 5-Pre-Schism issue. 3.00
4-($3.25, 52 pgs.) 4.00
#0 (Hero Illustrated giveaway)-Adam Pollina-c/a; 1st app. of Ngu 3.00

CHARLIE CHAN (See Big Shot Comics, Columbia Comics, Feature Comics & The New Advs. of...)

CHARLIE CHAN (The Adventures of...) (Zaza The Mystic No. 10 on) (TV)
Crestwood(Prize) No. 1-5; Charlton No. 6(6/55) on: 6-7/48 - No. 5, 2-3/49; No. 6, 6/55 - No. 9, 3/56

1-S&K-c, 2 pgs.; Infantino-a 103 206 309 659 1130 1600
2-5-S&K-c: 3-S&K-c/a 54 108 162 343 574 825
6 (6/55-Charlton)-S&K-c 39 78 117 240 395 550
7-9 22 44 66 132 216 300

CHARLIE CHAN
Dell Publishing Co.: Oct-Dec, 1965 - No. 2, Mar, 1966

1-Springer-a/c 5 10 15 31 53 75
2-Springer-a/c 3 6 9 21 33 45

CHARLIE McCARTHY (See Edgar Bergen Presents...)
Dell Publishing Co.: No. 171, Nov, 1947 - No. 571, July, 1954 (See True Comics #14)

Four Color 171 27 54 81 194 435 675
Four Color 196-Part photo-c; photo back-c 17 34 51 119 265 410
1(3-5/49)-Part photo-c; photo back-c 13 26 39 87 191 295
2-9(7/52; #5,6-52 pgs.) 8 16 24 51 96 140
Four Color 445,478,527,571 7 14 21 44 82 120

CHARLIE'S ANGELS (Based on the 1970s TV series)
Dynamite Entertainment: 2018 - No. 5, 2018 ($3.99)

1-5-John Layman-s/Joe Eisma-a; multiple covers on each; Jimmy Carter app. 4.00

CHARLIE'S ANGELS VS. THE BIONIC WOMAN (Based on the 1970s TV series)
Dynamite Entertainment: 2019 - No. 4, 2019 ($3.99)

1-4-Cameron DeOrdio-s/Soo Lee-a; multiple covers on each 4.00

CHARLTON ACTION: FEATURING "STATIC" (Also see Eclipse Monthly)
Charlton Comics: No, 11, Oct, 1985 - No. 12, Dec, 1985

11,12-Ditko-c/a; low print run 1 2 3 5 6 8

CHARLTON ARROW
Charlton Neo: 2017 ($7.99)

1-New E-Man and Nova by Cuti & Staton; Monster Hunter, Mr. Mixit 8.00

CHARLTON BULLSEYE
CPL/Gang Publications: 1975 - No. 5, 1976 ($1.50, B&W, bi-monthly, magazine format)

1: 1 & 2 are last Capt. Atom by Ditko/Byrne intended for the never published
Capt. Atom #90; Nightshade app.; Jeff Jones-a 5 10 15 31 53 75
2-Part 2 Capt. Atom story by Ditko/Byrne 3 6 9 21 33 45
3-Wrong Country by Sanho Kim 2 4 6 13 18 22
4-Doomsday + 1 by John Byrne 3 6 9 17 26 36
5-Doomsday + 1 by Byrne, The Question by Toth; Neal Adams back-c; Toth-c
5 10 15 33 57 80

CHARLTON BULLSEYE
Charlton Publications: June, 1981 - No. 10, Dec, 1982; Nov, 1986

1-1st Blue Beetle app. since '74, 1st app. The Question since '75; 1st app. Rocket Rabbit;
Neil The Horse shown on preview page 3 6 9 20 31 42
2-5: 2-Charlton debut of Neil The Horse; Rocket Rabbit app. 4-Vanguards 6.00
6-10: Low print run. 6-Origin & 1st app. Thunderbunny. 7-1st apps. of Captain Atom &
Nightshade since '75. 9-1st app. Bludd. 2 4 6 8 10 12
NOTE: *Material intended for issue #11-up was published in* ***Scary Tales*** *#37-up.*

CHARLTON CLASSICS
Charlton Comics: Apr, 1980 - No. 9, Aug, 1981

1-Hercules-r by Glanzman in all 6.00
2-9 5.00

CHARLTON CLASSICS LIBRARY (1776)
Charlton Comics: V10 No.1, Mar, 1973 (one-shot)

1776 (title) - Adaptation of the film musical "1776"; given away at movie theatres;
also a newsstand version 3 6 9 14 19 24

CHARLTON PREMIERE (Formerly Marine War Heroes)
Charlton Comics: V1#19, July, 1967; V2#1, Sept, 1967 - No. 4, May, 1968

V1#19, V2#1,2,4: V1#19-Marine War Heroes. V2#1-Trio; intro. Shape, Tyro Team &
Spookman. 2-Children of Doom; Boyette classic-a. 4-Unlikely Tales; Aparo, Ditko-a
3 6 9 16 24 32
V2#3-Sinistro Boy Fiend; Blue Beetle & Peacemaker x-over
3 6 9 19 30 40

CHARLTON SPORT LIBRARY - PROFESSIONAL FOOTBALL
Charlton Comics: Winter, 1969-70 (Jan. on cover) (68 pgs.)

1 3 6 9 21 33 45

CHARMED (TV)
Zenescope Entertainment: No. 0, Jun, 2010 - No. 24, Oct, 2012 ($3.50)

0-24-Multiple covers on most 3.50

CHARMED SEASON 10 (TV)
Zenescope Entertainment: Oct, 2014 - No. 17, Mar, 2016 ($3.99)

1-17: 1-Shand-s/Feliz-a/Seidman-c 4.00

CHARMED (Volume 1) (TV)
Dynamite Entertainment: 2017 - No. 5, 2017 ($3.99)

1-5-Schultz-s/Sanapo-a; multiple covers on all 4.00

CHASE (See Batman #550 for 1st app.)(Also see Batwoman)
DC Comics: Feb, 1998 - No. 9, Oct, 1998; #1,000,000 Nov, 1998 ($2.50)

1-9: Williams III & Gray-a. 1-Includes 4 Chase cards. 4-Teen Titans app. 7,8-Batman app.
9-GL Hal Jordan-c/app. 3.00
#1,000,000 (11/98) Final issue; 853rd Century x-over 3.00

CHASING DOGMA (See Jay and Silent Bob)

CHASSIS
Millenium Publications: 1996 - No. 3 ($2.95)

1-3: 1-Adam Hughes-c. 2-Conner var-c. 3.00

CHASSIS
Hurricane Entertainment: 1998 - No. 3 ($2.95)

0,1-3: 1-Adam Hughes-c. 0-Green var-c. 3.00

CHASSIS (Vol. 3)
Image Comics: Nov, 1999 - No. 4 ($2.95, limited series)

1-4: 1-Two covers by O'Neil and Green. 2-Busch var-c. 3.00
1-($6.95) DF Edition alternate-c by Wieringo 7.00

CHASTITY
Chaos! Comics: (one-shots)

#1/2 (1/01, $2.95) Batista-a 3.00
Heartbreaker (3/02, $2.99) Adrian-a/Molenaar-c 3.00
Love Bites (3/01, $2.99) Vale-a/Romano-c 3.00
Reign of Terror 1 (10/00, $2.95) Grant-s/Ross-a/Rio-c 3.00
Re-Imagined 1 (7/02, $2.99) Conner-c; Toledo-a 3.00

CHASTITY
Dynamite Entertainment: 2014 - No. 6, 2014 ($3.99, limited series)

1-6: 1-Andreyko-s/Acosta-a; origin retold. Multiple covers on each 4.00

CHASTITY (VOLUME 2)
Dynamite Entertainment: 2019 - No. 5, 2020 ($3.99, limited series)

1-5: 1-Leah Williams-s/Daniel Maine-a; multiple covers on each 4.00

CHASTITY: CRAZYTOWN
Chaos! Comics: Apr, 2002 - No. 3, June, 2002 ($2.99, limited series)

1-3-Nicieza-s/Batista-c/a 3.00

CHASTITY: LUST FOR LIFE
Chaos! Comics: May, 1999 - No. 3, July, 1999 ($2.95, limited series)

1-3-Nutman-s/Benes-c/a 3.00

CHASTITY: ROCKED
Chaos! Comics: Nov, 1998 - No. 4, Feb, 1999 ($2.95, limited series)

1-4-Nutman-s/Justiniano-c/a 3.00

CHASTITY: SHATTERED
Chaos! Comics: Jun, 2001 - No. 3, Sept, 2001 ($2.99, limited series)

1-3-Kaminski & Pulido-s/Batista-c/a 3.00

CHASTITY: THEATER OF PAIN
Chaos! Comics: Feb, 1997 - No. 3, June, 1997 ($2.95, limited series)

1-3-Pulido-s/Justiniano-c/a 3.00
TPB (1997, $9.95) r/#1-3 10.00

CHECKMATE (TV)
Gold Key: Oct, 1962 - No. 2, Dec, 1962

1-Photo-c on both 5 10 15 34 60 85
2 5 10 15 31 53 75

CHECKMATE! (See Action Comics #598 and The OMAC Project)
DC Comics: Apr, 1988 - No. 33, Jan, 1991 ($1.25)

1-33: 13: New format begins 3.00
NOTE: ***Gil Kane*** *c-2, 4, 7, 8, 10, 11, 15-19.*

CHECKMATE (See Infinite Crisis and The OMAC Project)
DC Comics: Jun, 2006 - No. 31, Dec, 2008 ($2.99)

1-Rucka-s/Saiz-a/Bermejo-c; Alan Scott, Mr. Terrific, Sasha Bordeaux app. 4.00
1-2nd printing with B&W cover 3.00
2-31: 2,3-Kobra, King Faraday, Amanda Waller, Fire app. 4-The Great Ten app.
13-15-Outsiders app. 26-Chimera origin 3.00
...: A King's GameTPB (2007, $14.99) r/#1-7 15.00
...: Chimera TPB (2009, $17.99) r/#26-31 18.00
...: Fall of the Wall TPB (2008, $14.99) r/#16-22 15.00
...: Pawn Breaks TPB (2007, $14.99) r/#8-12 15.00

CHECKMATE
DC Comics: Aug, 2021 - No. 6, Jan, 2022 ($3.99, limited series)

1-6-Bendis-s/Maleev-a; Checkmate vs. Leviathan; Damian & Talia app. 4.00

CHERISH
Dynamite Entertainment: 2022 - No. 5, 2023 ($3.99, limited series)

1-4-Katana Collins-s/Gabriel Caitano-a 4.00

CHERYL BLOSSOM (See Archie's Girls, Betty and Veronica #320 for 1st app.)
Archie Publications: Sept, 1995 - No. 3, Nov, 1995 ($1.50, limited series)

1 3 6 9 14 20 26
2,3 1 3 4 6 8 10
Special 1-4 ('95, '96, $2.00) 1 3 4 6 8 10

CHERYL BLOSSOM (Cheryl's Summer Job)
Archie Publications: July, 1996 - No. 3, Sept, 1996 ($1.50, limited series)

1-3 1 3 4 6 8 10

CHERYL BLOSSOM (...Goes Hollywood)
Archie Publications: Dec, 1996 - No. 3, Feb, 1997 ($1.50, limited series)

1-3 1 3 4 6 8 10

CHERYL BLOSSOM
Archie Publications: Apr, 1997 - No. 37, Mar, 2001 ($1.50/$1.75/$1.79/$1.99)

1-Dan DeCarlo-c/a 2 4 6 9 12 15
2-10: 2-7-Dan DeCarlo-c/a 1 2 3 5 6 8
11-37: 32-Begin $1.99-c. 34-Sabrina app. 5.00

CHESTY SANCHEZ
Antarctic Press: Nov, 1995 - No. 2, Mar, 1996 ($2.95, B&W)

1,2 1 2 3 5 6 8
...Super Special (2/99, $5.99) 1 2 3 5 6 8

Charlton Arrow V2 #1 © Staton & 1First

Chew #29 © John Layman

Children of the Atom #1 © MAR

CHEVAL NOIR
Dark Horse Comics: 1989 - No. 50, Jan, 1994 ($3.50, B&W, 68 pgs.)

	GD 2.0	VG 4.0	FN 6.0	VF 8.0	VF/NM 9.0	NM- 9.2
1 ($3.50) Dave Stevens-c	3	6	9	21	33	45
2-6,8,10 ($3.50): 6-Moebius poster insert	1	3	4	6	8	10
7-Dave Stevens-c	3	6	9	21	33	45
9,11,13,15,17,20,22 ($4.50, 84 pgs.)	1	3	4	6	8	10
12,18,19,21,23 ($3.95): 12-Geary-a; Mignola-c						6.00
14-($4.95, 76 pgs.)(7 pgs. color)	1	2	3	5	6	8
16-($3.75): 16-19-Contain trading cards						6.00
24-($3.75) Good girl art-c	2	4	6	9	12	15
25-($3.95)						6.00
26-($3.95) Moebius-a begins	2	4	6	9	12	15
27-48 ($2.95): 33-Snyder III-c						5.00
49,50-Low print run	2	4	6	11	16	20

NOTE: ***Bolland** a-2, 6, 7, 13, 14. **Bolton** a-2, 4, 45; c-4, 20, 49. **Chadwick** c-13. **Dorman** painted c-16. **Geary** a-13, 14. **Kelley Jones** c-27. **Kaluta** a-6; c-6, 18. **Moebius** c-5, 9, 26. **Dave Stevens** c-1, 7. **Sutton** painted c-36.*

CHEW (See Walking Dead #61 for preview)(Also see Chu)
Image Comics: Jun, 2009 - No. 60, Nov, 2016 ($2.99/$3.50/$3.99)

	GD 2.0	VG 4.0	FN 6.0	VF 8.0	VF/NM 9.0	NM- 9.2
1-Layman-s/Guillory-a	8	16	24	56	108	160
1-(2nd-4th printings)	2	4	6	9	12	15
2-1st printing	3	6	9	19	30	40
2-5-(2nd & 3rd printings)						6.00
3-1st printing	2	4	6	10	14	18
4,5-1st printings	2	4	6	8	10	12
6-10	1	3	4	6	8	10
11-15: 15-Gatefold wraparound-c	1	2	3	5	6	8
16-24: 19-Neon green cover ink						5.00
25-44,46-49: 27-(6/12) Second Helping Edition						3.00
27-(5/11) Future issue released between #18 & #19						5.00
45,50-55-($3.50) 49-Poyo cover. 53-Flintstones cover						3.50
56-59-($3.99)						4.00
60-($5.99) Final issue; double cover with gatefold; set in the future						6.00
...: Demon Chicken Poyo One-Shot (4/16, $3.99) Layman-s/Guillory-a; pin-up gallery						4.00
.../ Revival One Shot (5/14, $4.99) Flip book: Layman-s/Guillory-a & Selley-s/Norton-a						5.00
...: Warrior Chicken Poyo (7/14, $3.50) Layman-s/Guillory-a; bonus pin-up gallery						3.50
Image Firsts: Chew #1 (4/10, $1.00) r/#1 with "Image Firsts" cover logo						5.00

CHEWBACCA (Star Wars)
Marvel Comics: Dec, 2015 - No. 5, Feb, 2016 ($3.99, limited series)

	GD 2.0	VG 4.0	FN 6.0	VF 8.0	VF/NM 9.0	NM- 9.2
1-5-Duggan-s/Noto-a; takes place after Episode 4 Battle of Yavin						4.00

CHEYENNE (TV)
Dell Publishing Co.: No. 734, Oct, 1956 - No. 25, Dec-Jan, 1961-62

	GD 2.0	VG 4.0	FN 6.0	VF 8.0	VF/NM 9.0	NM- 9.2
Four Color 734(#1)-Clint Walker photo-c	13	26	39	89	195	300
Four Color 772,803: Clint Walker photo-c	8	16	24	54	102	150
4(8-10/57) - 20: 4-9,13-20-Clint Walker photo-c. 10-12-Ty Hardin photo-c	6	12	18	37	66	95
21-25-Clint Walker photo-c on all	6	12	18	38	69	100

CHEYENNE AUTUMN (See Movie Classics)

CHEYENNE KID (Formerly Wild Frontier No. 1-7)
Charlton Comics: No. 8, July, 1957 - No. 99, Nov, 1973

	GD 2.0	VG 4.0	FN 6.0	VF 8.0	VF/NM 9.0	NM- 9.2
8 (#1)	8	16	24	44	57	70
9,15-19	6	12	18	29	36	42
10-Williamson/Torres-a(3); Ditko-c	11	22	33	60	83	105
11-(68 pgs.)-Cheyenne Kid meets Geronimo	10	20	30	58	79	100
12-Williamson/Torres-a(2)	10	20	30	58	79	100
13-Williamson/Torres-a (5 pgs.)	8	16	24	44	57	70
14-Williamson-a (5 pgs.?)	8	16	24	42	54	65
20-22,24,25-Severin c/a(3) each	4	8	12	21	33	45
23,27-29	3	6	9	15	22	28
26,30-Severin-a	3	6	9	17	26	35
31-59	2	4	6	10	14	18
60-65	2	4	6	8	11	14
66-Wander by Aparo begins, ends #87	2	4	6	10	14	18
67-80	2	4	6	8	11	14
81-99: Apache Red begins #88, origin in #89	2	4	6	8	11	14
Modern Comics Reprint 87,89(1978)						5.00

CHIAROSCURO (THE PRIVATE LIVES OF LEONARDO DA VINCI)
DC Comics (Vertigo): July, 1995 - No. 10, Apr, 1996 ($2.50/$2.95, limited series, mature)

	GD 2.0	VG 4.0	FN 6.0	VF 8.0	VF/NM 9.0	NM- 9.2
1-9: McGreal and Rawson-s/Truog & Kayanan-a						3.00
10-($2.95)						3.00
TPB (2005, $24.99) r/series; intro. by Alisa Kwitney, afterword by Pat McGreal						25.00

CHICAGO MAIL ORDER (See C-M-O Comics in the Promotional Comics section)

CHICKEN DEVIL
AfterShock Comics: Oct, 2021 - No. 4, Jan, 2022 ($4.99, limited series)

	GD 2.0	VG 4.0	FN 6.0	VF 8.0	VF/NM 9.0	NM- 9.2
1-4-Brian Buccellato-s/Hayden Sherman-a						5.00
Vol. 2 (10/22 - Present) 1,2						5.00

CHIEF, THE (Indian Chief No. 3 on)
Dell Publishing Co.: No. 290, Aug, 1950 - No. 2, Apr-June, 1951

	GD 2.0	VG 4.0	FN 6.0	VF 8.0	VF/NM 9.0	NM- 9.2
Four Color 290(#1)	9	18	27	57	111	165
2	6	12	18	38	69	100

CHIEF CRAZY HORSE (See Wild Bill Hickok #21)
Avon Periodicals: 1950 (Also see Fighting Indians of the Wild West!)

	GD 2.0	VG 4.0	FN 6.0	VF 8.0	VF/NM 9.0	NM- 9.2
nn-Fawcette-c	28	56	84	165	270	375

CHIEF VICTORIO'S APACHE MASSACRE (See Fight Indians of/Wild West!)
Avon Periodicals: 1951

	GD 2.0	VG 4.0	FN 6.0	VF 8.0	VF/NM 9.0	NM- 9.2
nn-Williamson/Frazetta-a (7 pgs.); Larsen-a; Kinstler-c	69	138	207	442	750	1075

CHILD IS BORN, A
Apostle Arts: Nov, 2011 ($5.99, one-shot)

	GD 2.0	VG 4.0	FN 6.0	VF 8.0	VF/NM 9.0	NM- 9.2
nn-Story of the birth of Jesus; Billy Tucci-s/a; cover by Tucci & Sparacio						6.00
HC (7/12, $15.99) Includes bonus interview with Billy Tucci and sketch art						16.00

CHILDREN OF FIRE
Fantagor Press: Nov, 1987 - No. 3, 1988 ($2.00, limited series)

	GD 2.0	VG 4.0	FN 6.0	VF 8.0	VF/NM 9.0	NM- 9.2
1-3: by Richard Corben						4.00

CHILDREN OF THE ATOM (X-Men)
Marvel Comics: May, 2021 - No. 6, Oct, 2021 ($4.99/$3.99, limited series)

	GD 2.0	VG 4.0	FN 6.0	VF 8.0	VF/NM 9.0	NM- 9.2
1-($4.99)-New team of teen "mutants"; X-Men app.; Ayala-s/Chang-a						5.00
2-6-($3.99) 4,5-X-Men app.						4.00

CHILDREN OF THE PLAGUE
Dark Horse Comics: Sept, 2021 ($4.99, one-shot)

	GD 2.0	VG 4.0	FN 6.0	VF 8.0	VF/NM 9.0	NM- 9.2
1-Robert Love-s/a						5.00

CHILDREN OF THE VOYAGER (See Marvel Frontier Comics Unlimited)
Marvel Frontier Comics: Sept, 1993 - No. 4, Dec, 1993 ($1.95, limited series)

	GD 2.0	VG 4.0	FN 6.0	VF 8.0	VF/NM 9.0	NM- 9.2
1-($2.95)-Embossed glow-in-the-dark-c; Paul Johnson-c/a						4.00
2-4						3.00

CHILDREN'S BIG BOOK
Dorene Publ. Co.: 1945 (25¢, stiff-c, 68 pgs.)

	GD 2.0	VG 4.0	FN 6.0	VF 8.0	VF/NM 9.0	NM- 9.2
nn-Comics & fairy tales; David Icove-a	16	32	48	98	154	210

CHILDREN'S CRUSADE, THE
DC Comics (Vertigo): Dec, 1993 - No. 2, Jan, 1994 ($3.95, limited series)

	GD 2.0	VG 4.0	FN 6.0	VF 8.0	VF/NM 9.0	NM- 9.2
1,2-Gaiman scripts & Bachalo-a; framing issues for Children's Crusade x-over						4.00

CHILD'S PLAY: THE SERIES (Movie)
Innovation Publishing: May, 1991 - No. 5, Dec, 1991 ($2.50, 28pgs.)

	GD 2.0	VG 4.0	FN 6.0	VF 8.0	VF/NM 9.0	NM- 9.2
1	3	6	9	17	26	35
2,3	2	4	6	11	16	20
4,5-Low print run	2	4	6	9	12	15

CHILD'S PLAY 2 THE OFFICIAL MOVIE ADAPTATION (Movie)
Innovation Publishing: 1990 - No. 3, 1990 ($2.50, bi-weekly limited series)

	GD 2.0	VG 4.0	FN 6.0	VF 8.0	VF/NM 9.0	NM- 9.2
1-Adapts movie sequel	3	6	9	19	30	40
2,3	2	4	6	11	16	20

CHILI (Millie's Rival)
Marvel Comics Group: 5/69 - No. 17, 9/70; No. 18, 8/72 - No. 26, 12/73

	GD 2.0	VG 4.0	FN 6.0	VF 8.0	VF/NM 9.0	NM- 9.2
1	10	20	30	69	147	225
2,4,5	5	10	15	35	63	90
3-Millie & Chili visit Marvel and meet Stan Lee & Stan Goldberg (6 pgs.)	7	14	21	44	82	120
6-17	5	10	15	30	50	70
18-26	4	8	12	27	44	60
Special 1(12/71, 52 pgs.)	5	10	15	35	63	90

CHILLER
Marvel Comics (Epic): Nov, 1993 - No. 2, Dec, 1993 ($7.95, lim. series)

	GD 2.0	VG 4.0	FN 6.0	VF 8.0	VF/NM 9.0	NM- 9.2
1,2-(68 pgs.)	1	2	3	5	6	8

CHILLING ADVENTURES IN SORCERY (...as Told by Sabrina #1, 2)
(Red Circle Sorcery No. 6 on)
Archie Publications (Red Circle Prods.): 9/72 - No. 2, 10/72; No. 3, 10/73 - No. 5, 2/74

	GD 2.0	VG 4.0	FN 6.0	VF 8.0	VF/NM 9.0	NM- 9.2
1-Sabrina cameo as narrator	6	12	18	42	79	115
2-Sabrina cameo as narrator	4	8	12	22	35	48

GD VG FN VF VF/NM NM-
2.0 4.0 6.0 8.0 9.0 9.2

3-5: Morrow-c/a, all. 4,5-Alcazar-a 3 6 9 14 19 24

CHILLING ADVENTURES IN SORCERY (Also see Return of ...)
Archie Comic Publications: Dec, 2021 ($3.99)
1-Anthology of short horror stories hosted by Madam Satan; art by Federici, Charm 4.00

CHILLING ADVENTURES OF SABRINA (Inspired the 2018 Netflix series)(See Madam Satan)
Archie Comic Publications: Dec, 2014 - No. 8, Aug, 2017; No. 9, Dec, 2021 - Present ($3.99, mature content)
1-9: 1-Aguirre-Sacasa-s/Hack-a; two covers; origin re-told, set in the 1960s 4.00
1-(12/18, $1.00) r/#1 with Netflix art cover 3.00
... - Halloween ComicFest Edition 1 (2015, free) r/#1 in B&W 3.00
... - Halloween ComicFest Edition #1 2017 (free) r/#7 in B&W 3.00
... Monster-Sized One-Shot 1 (5/19, $7.99) r/#6-8; Hack-c 8.00

CHILLING ADVENTURES OF SALEM (From Sabrina the Teenage Witch)
Archie Comic Publications: Dec, 2022 ($3.99, one-shot)
1-Short horror stories with the Archie characters 4.00

CHILLING ADVENTURES PRESENTS...
Archie Comic Publications: Oct, 2022 ($3.99, series of one-shots)
... Betty The Final Girl 1 (4/23) Short horror stories; Josie and the Pussycats app. 4.00
...: Jinx Grim Fairy Tales 1 (10/22) Short horror stories 4.00
...: Weirder Mysteries 1 (11/22) Crashed UFO sci-fi story; Bingo Wilkin app. 4.00

CHILLING TALES (Formerly Beware)
Youthful Magazines: No. 13, Dec, 1952 - No. 17, Oct, 1953
13(No.1)-Harrison-a; Matt Fox-c/a 371 742 1113 2600 4550 6500
14-Harrison-a 142 284 426 909 1555 2200
15-Matt Fox-c; Harrison-a 371 742 1113 2600 4550 6500
16-Poe adapt.-'Metzengerstein'; Rudyard Kipling adapt.- 'Mark of the Beast,' by Kiefer; bondage-c 389 778 1167 2723 4762 6800
17-Matt Fox-c; Sir Walter Scott & Poe adapt. 194 388 582 1242 2121 3000

CHILLING TALES OF HORROR (Magazine)
Stanley Publications: V1#1, 6/69 - V1#7, 12/70; V2#2, 2/71 - V2#6, 10/71(50¢, B&W, 52 pgs.)
V1#1 10 20 30 67 141 215
2-4,(no #5),6,7: 7-Cameron-a 7 14 21 48 89 130
V2#2-6: 2-Two different #2 issues exist (2/71 & 4/71). 2-(2/71) Spirit of Frankenstein -r/Adventures into the Unknown #16. 4-(8/71) different from other V2#4(6/71) 6 12 18 41 76 110
V2#4-(6/71) r/9 pg. Feldstein-a from Adventures into the Unknown #3 7 14 21 44 82 120
NOTE: *Two issues of V2#2 exist, Feb, 1971 and April, 1971. Two issues of V2#4 exist, Jun, 1971 and Aug, 1971.*

CHILLY WILLY (Also see New Funnies #211)
Dell Publ. Co.: No. 740, Oct, 1956 - No. 1281, Apr-June, 1962 (Walter Lantz)
Four Color 740 (#1) 9 18 27 59 117 175
Four Color 852 (2/58),967 (2/59),1017 (9/59),1074 (2-4/60),1122 (8/60), 1177 (4-6/61),1212 (7-9/61),1281 6 12 18 37 66 95

CHIMERA
CrossGeneration Comics: Mar, 2003 - No. 4, July, 2003 ($2.95, limited series)
1-4-Marz-s/Peterson-c/a 3.00
Vol. 1 TPB (2003, $15.95) r/#1-4 plus sketch pages, 3-D models, how-to guides 16.00

CHIMICHANGA
Albatross Exploding Funny Books: 2010 ($3.00, B&W)
1-3-Eric Powell-s/a/c 5.00

CHIMICHANGA: THE SORROW OF THE WORLD'S WORST FACE
Dark Horse Comics: Oct, 2016 - No. 4, Dec, 2017 ($3.99, limited series)
1-4-Eric Powell-s/Stephanie Buscema-a 4.00

CHINA BOY (See Wisco in the Promotional Comics section)

CHIN MUSIC
Image Comics: May, 2013 - No. 2, Aug, 2013 ($2.99)
1,2-Steve Niles-s/Tony Harris-a/c 3.00

CHIP 'N' DALE (Walt Disney)(See Walt Disney's C&S #204)
Dell Publishing Co./Gold Key/Whitman No. 65 on: Nov, 1953 - No. 30, June-Aug, 1962; Sept, 1967 - No. 83, July, 1984
Four Color 517(#1) 12 24 36 79 170 260
Four Color 581,636 6 12 18 42 79 115
4(12/55-2/56)-10 5 10 15 33 57 80
11-30 4 8 12 28 47 65
1(Gold Key, 1967)-Reprints 3 6 9 19 30 40
2-10 2 4 6 13 18 22
11-20 2 4 6 9 12 15
21-40 2 4 6 8 10 12
41-64,70-77: 75(2/82), 76(2-3/82), 77(3/82) 1 2 3 5 7 9
65,66 (Whitman) 2 4 6 8 11 14
67-69 (3-pack? 1980): 67(8/80), 68(10/80) (scarce) 4 8 12 28 47 65
78-83 (All #90214; 3-pack, nd, nd code): 78(4/83), 79(5/83), 80(7/83), 81(8/83), 82(5/84), 83(7/84) 3 6 9 15 22 28
NOTE: *All Gold Key/Whitman issues have reprints except No. 32-35, 38-41, 45-47. No. 23-28, 30-42, 45-47, 49 have new covers.*

CHIP 'N DALE RESCUE RANGERS
Disney Comics: June, 1990 - No. 19, Dec, 1991 ($1.50)
1-New stories; origin begins 2 4 6 8 10 12
2-19: 2-Origin continued 4.00

CHIP 'N' DALE RESCUE RANGERS
BOOM! Studios: Dec, 2010 - No. 8, Jul, 2011 ($3.99)
1-8: 1-Brill-s/Castellani-a; 3 covers 4.00
... Free Comic Book Day Edition (5/11) Flip book with Darkwing Duck 5.00

CHITTY CHITTY BANG BANG (See Movie Comics)

C.H.I.X.
Image Comics (Studiosaurus): Jan, 1998 ($2.50)
1-Dodson, Haley, Lopresti, Randall, and Warren-s/c/a 3.00
1-($5.00) "X-Ray Variant" cover 5.00
C.H.I.X. That Time Forgot 1 (8/98, $2.95) 3.00

CHOICE COMICS
Great Publications: Dec, 1941 - No. 3, Feb, 1942
1-Origin Secret Circle; Atlas the Mighty app.; Zomba, Jungle Fight, Kangaroo Man, & Fire Eater begin 168 336 504 1075 1838 2600
2 135 270 405 864 1482 2100
3-Double feature; Features movie "The Lost City" (classic cover); continued from Great Comics #3 232 464 696 1485 2543 3600

CHOLLY AND FLYTRAP (Arthur Suydam's...)(Also see New Adventures of...)
Image Comics: Nov, 2004 - No. 4, June, 2005 ($4.95/$5.95, limited series)
1-($4.95) Arthur Suydam-s/a/c 6.00
2-4-($5.95) 6.00

CHOO CHOO CHARLIE
Gold Key: Dec, 1969
1-John Stanley-a 5 10 15 35 63 90

CHOSEN
Dark Horse Comics: Jan, 2004 - No. 3, Aug, 2004 ($2.99, limited series)
1-Story of the second coming; Mark Millar-s/Peter Gross-a 2 4 6 9 12 15
2,3 5.00

CHRIS CLAREMONT ANNIVERSARY SPECIAL
Marvel Comics: Mar, 2021 ($4.99, one-shot)
1-Claremont-s; art by Sienkiewicz, Chen, Olortegui, and Booth; Dani Moonstar app. 5.00

CHRISTIAN (See Asylum)
Maximum Press: Jan, 1996 ($2.99, one-shot)
1-Pop Mhan-a 3.00

CHRISTIAN HEROES OF TODAY
David C. Cook: 1964 (36 pgs.)
nn 3 6 9 17 26 35

CHRISTMAS (Also see A-1 Comics)
Magazine Enterprises: No. 28, 1950
A-1 28 13 26 39 72 101 130

CHRISTMAS ADVENTURE, A (See Classics Comics Giveaways, 12/69)

CHRISTMAS ALBUM (See March of Comics No. 312)

CHRISTMAS ANNUAL
Golden Special: 1975 ($1.95, 100 pgs., stiff-c)
nn-Reprints Mother Goose stories with Walt Kelly-a 3 6 9 21 33 45

CHRISTMAS & ARCHIE
Archie Comics: Jan, 1975 ($1.00, 68 pgs., 10-1/4x13-1/4" treasury-sized)
1-(scarce) 5 10 15 35 63 90

CHRISTMAS BELLS (See March of Comics No. 297)

CHRISTMAS CARNIVAL
Ziff-Davis Publ. Co./St. John Publ. Co. No. 2: 1952 (25¢, one-shot, 100 pgs.)
nn 40 80 120 246 411 575
2-Reprints Ziff-Davis issue plus-c 18 36 54 109 172 235

CHRISTMAS CAROL, A (See March of Comics No. 33)

CHRISTMAS EVE, A (See March of Comics No. 212)

CHRISTMAS IN DISNEYLAND (See Dell Giants)

CHRISTMAS PARADE (See Dell Giant No. 26, Dell Giants, March of Comics No. 284, Walt Disney Christmas Parade & Walt Disney's...)

CHRISTMAS PARADE (Walt Disney's)
Gold Key: 1962 (no month listed) - No. 9, Jan, 1972 (#1,5: 80 pgs.; #2-4,7-9: 36 pgs.)
1 (30018-301)-Giant 8 16 24 56 108 160
2-6: 2-r/F.C. #367 by Barks. 3-r/F.C. #178 by Barks. 4-r/F.C. #203 by Barks. 5-r/Christmas Parade #1 (Dell) by Barks; giant. 6-r/Christmas Parade #2 (Dell) by Barks (64 pgs.); giant 5 10 15 35 63 90
7-Pull-out poster (half price w/o poster) 5 10 15 30 50 70
8-r/F.C. #367 by Barks; pull-out poster 5 10 15 35 63 90
9 4 8 12 25 40 55

CHRISTMAS PARTY (See March of Comics No. 256)

CHRISTMAS STORIES (See Little People No. 959, 1062)

CHRISTMAS STORY (See March of Comics No. 326 in the Promotional Comics section)

CHRISTMAS STORY, THE
Catechetical Guild: 1955 (15¢)
393-Addison Burbank-a 8 16 24 44 57 70

CHRISTMAS STORY BOOK (See Woolworth's Christmas Story Book)

CHRISTMAS TREASURY, A (See Dell Giants & March of Comics No. 227)

CHRISTMAS WITH ARCHIE
Spire Christian Comics (Fleming H. Revell Co.): 1973, 1974 (49¢, 52 pgs.)
nn-Low print run 3 6 9 16 24 32

CHRISTMAS WITH MOTHER GOOSE
Dell Publishing Co.: No. 90, Nov, 1945 - No. 253, Nov, 1949
Four Color 90 (#1)-Kelly-a 15 30 45 104 230 365
Four Color 126 ('46), 172 (11/47)-By Walt Kelly 12 24 36 82 179 275
Four Color 201 (10/48), 253-By Walt Kelly 10 20 30 66 138 210

CHRISTMAS WITH SANTA (See March of Comics No. 92)

CHRISTMAS WITH THE SUPER-HEROES (See Limited Collectors' Edition)
DC Comics: 1988; No. 2, 1989 ($2.95)
1,2: 1-(100 pgs.)-All reprints; N. Adams-r, Byrne-c; Batman, Superman, JLA, LSH Christmas stories; r-Miller's 1st Batman/DC Special Series #21. 2-(68 pgs.)-Superman by Chadwick; Batman, Wonder Woman, Deadman, Green Lantern, Flash app.; Morrow-a; Enemy Ace

Chilling Adventures of Sabrina #4 © ACP

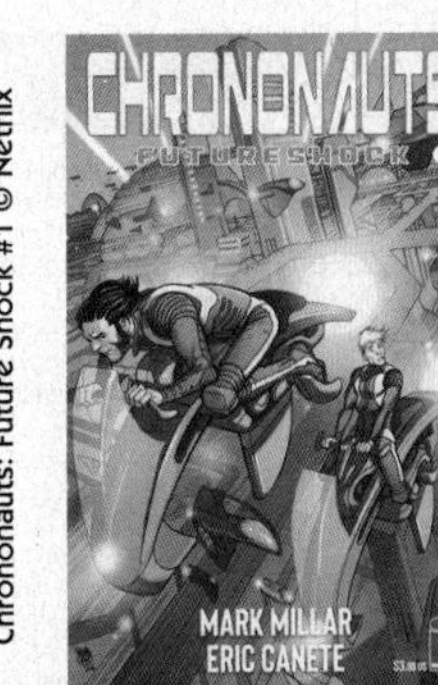

Chrononauts: Future Shock #1 © Netflix

Cinderella: Fables are Forever #4 © BW & DC

	GD 2.0	VG 4.0	FN 6.0	VF 8.0	VF/NM 9.0	NM- 9.2

by Byrne; all new-a 1 3 4 6 8 10

CHROMA-TICK, THE (...Special Edition, #1,2) (Also see The Tick)
New England Comics Press: Feb, 1992 - No. 8, Nov, 1993 ($3.95/$3.50, 44 pgs.)

1,2-Includes serially numbered trading card set 1 3 4 6 8 10
3-8 ($3.50, 36 pgs.): 6-Bound-in card 5.00

CHROME
Hot Comics: 1986 - No. 3, 1986 ($1.50, limited series)

1-3 3.00

CHROMIUM MAN, THE
Triumphant Comics: Aug, 1993 - No.10, May, 1994 ($2.50)

1-1st app. Mr. Death; all serially numbered 3.00
2-10: 2-1st app. Prince Vandal. 3-1st app. Candi, Breaker & Coil. 4,5-Triumphant Unleashed x-over. 8,9-(3/94). 10-(5/94) 3.00
0-(4/94)-Four color-c, 0-All pink-c & all blue-c; no cover price 3.00

CHROMIUM MAN: VIOLENT PAST, THE
Triumphant Comics: Jan, 1994 - No. 2, Jan, 1994 ($2.50, limited series)

1,2-Serially numbered to 22,000 each 3.00

CHRONICLES OF CONAN, THE (See Conan the Barbarian)

CHRONICLES OF CORUM, THE (Also see Corum...)
First Comics: Jan, 1987 - No. 12, Nov, 1988 ($1.75/$1.95, deluxe series)

1-12: Adapts Michael Moorcock's novel; Thomas-s; Mignola-a/c 3.00

CHRONONAUTS
Image Comics: Mar, 2015 - No. 4, Jun, 2015 ($3.50/$5.99)

1-3-Mark Millar-s/Sean Murphy-a 3.50
4-($5.99) 6.00

CHRONONAUTS: FUTURE SHOCK
Image Comics: Oct, 2019 - No. 4, Oct, 2019 ($3.99/$5.99, all 4 issues released the same day)

1-3-Mark Millar-s/Eric Canete-a/Pasqual Ferry-c 3.50
4-($5.99) 6.00

CHRONOS
DC Comics: Mar, 1998 - No. 11, Feb. 1999 ($2.50)

1-11-J.F. Moore-s/Guinan-a 3.00
#1,000,000 (11/98) 853rd Century x-over 3.00

CHU (Characters from Chew)
Image Comics: Jul, 2020 - Present ($3.99)

1-10-Layman-s/Boultwood-a; Tony Chu and Saffron Chu app. 4.00

CHUCK (Based on the NBC TV series)
DC Comics (WildStorm): Aug, 2008 - No. 6, Jan, 2009 ($2.99, limited series)

1-6-Jeremy Haun-a/Kristian Donaldson-c; Noto back-up-a 3.00
TPB (2009, $19.99) r/#1-6; photo-c 20.00

CHUCKLE, THE GIGGLY BOOK OF COMIC ANIMALS
R. B. Leffingwell Co.: 1945 (132 pgs., one-shot)

1-Funny animal 30 60 90 177 289 400

CHUCK NORRIS (TV)
Marvel Comics (Star Comics): Jan, 1987 - No. 4, July, 1987

1-Ditko-a 3 6 9 14 20 26
2,3: Ditko-a 1 3 4 6 8 10
4-No Ditko-a (low print run) 2 4 6 8 10 12

CHUCK WAGON (See Sheriff Bob Dixon's...)

CHUCKY (Based on the 1988 killer doll movie Child's Play)
Devil's Due Publishing: Apr, 2007 - No. 4, Nov, 2007 ($3.50/$5.50)

1-Pulido-s/Medors-a; art & photo covers 3 6 9 16 23 30
2,3 2 4 6 8 10 12
4-($5.50) 3 6 9 14 20 25
TPB (2007, $18.99) r/series; gallery of variant covers; 4 pages of script and sketch art 19.00

CHYNA (WWF Wrestling)
Chaos! Comics: Sept, 2000; July, 2001 ($2.95/$2.99, one-shots)

1-Grant-s/Barrows-a; photo-c 1 3 4 6 8 10
1-($9.95) Premium Edition; Cleavenger-c 2 4 6 9 12 15
II -(7/01, $2.99) Deodato-a; photo-c 4.00

CICERO'S CAT
Dell Publishing Co.: July-Aug, 1959 - No. 2, Sept-Oct, 1959

1-Cat from Mutt & Jeff 4 8 12 28 47 65
2 4 8 12 25 40 55

CIMARRON STRIP (TV)
Dell Publishing Co.: Jan, 1968

1-Stuart Whitman photo-c 4 8 12 23 37 50

CIMMERIAN: BEYOND THE BLACK RIVER
Ablaze Publishing: 2020 - No. 2, 2020 ($3.99)

1,2-Conan adaptation from 1935; Mathieu Gabella-s/Anthony Jean-a; text back-up 4.00

CIMMERIAN: HOUR OF THE DRAGON
Ablaze Publishing: 2022 - No. 4, 2022 ($3.99)

1-4-Conan adaptation from 1935,1936; Valentin Sécher-a; text back-up 4.00

CIMMERIAN: IRON SHADOWS IN THE MOON
Ablaze Publishing: 2020 - No. 3, 2020 ($3.99)

1-3-Conan adaptation from 1934; Virginie Augustin-s/a; text back-up 4.00

CIMMERIAN: QUEEN OF THE BLACK COAST
Ablaze Publishing: 2020 - No. 2, 2020 ($3.99)

1,2-Conan adaptation from Queen of the Black Coast; Morvan-s/Alary-a; text back-up 4.00

CIMMERIAN: THE MAN-EATERS OF ZAMBOULA
Ablaze Publishing: 2020 - No. 2, 2020 ($3.99)

1,2-Conan adaptation from 1935; Gess-s/a; text back-up 4.00

CIMMERIAN, THE: PEOPLE OF THE BLACK CIRCLE
Ablaze Publishing: 2020 - No. 3, 2020 ($3.99, limited series)

1-3-Conan adaptation; Yasmina app.; Runberg-s/Jae Kwang Park-a; text back-up 4.00

CIMMERIAN, THE: FROST-GIANT'S DAUGHTER
Ablaze Publishing: 2020 - No. 3, 2020 ($3.99, limited series)

1-3-Conan adaptation; Atali app.; Robin Recht-a; text back-up 4.00

CIMMERIAN, THE: RED NAILS
Ablaze Publishing: 2020 - No. 2, 2020 ($3.99)

1,2-Conan adaptation; Valeria app.; Hautiere-s/Vatine & Cassegrain-a; text back-up 4.00

CINDER AND ASHE
DC Comics: May, 1988 - No. 4, Aug, 1988 ($1.75, limited series)

1-4: Mature readers 3.00

CINDERELLA (Disney) (See Movie Comics)
Dell Publishing Co.: No. 272, Apr, 1950 - No. 786, Apr, 1957

Four Color 272 14 28 42 96 211 325
Four Color 786-Partial-r #272 8 16 24 54 102 150

CINDERELLA
Whitman Publishing Co.: Apr, 1982

nn-Reprints 4-Color #272 1 2 3 4 5 7

CINDERELLA: FABLES ARE FOREVER (See Fables)
DC Comics (Vertigo): Apr, 2011 - No. 6, Sept, 2011 ($2.99, limited series)

1-6-Roberson-s/McManus-a/Zullo-c; Dorothy Gale app. 3.00

CINDERELLA: FROM FABLETOWN WITH LOVE (See Fables)
DC Comics (Vertigo): Jan, 2010 - No. 6, Jun, 2010 ($2.99, limited series)

1-6: Roberson-s/McManus-a/Zullo-c 3.00
TPB (2010, $14.99) r/#1-6 15.00

CINDERELLA LOVE
Ziff-Davis/St. John Publ. Co. No. 12 on: No. 10, 1950; No. 11, 4-5/51; No. 12, 9/51; No. 4, 10-11/51 - No. 11, Fall, 1952; No. 12, 10/53 - No. 15, 8/54; No. 25, 12/54 - No. 29, 10/55 (No #16-24)

10(#1)(1st Series, 1950)-Painted-c 32 64 96 188 307 425
11(#2, 4-5/51)-Crandall-a; Saunders painted-c 21 42 63 124 202 280
12(#3, 9/51)-Photo-c 18 36 54 103 162 220
4-8: 4,6,7-Photo-c 16 32 48 94 147 200
9-Kinstler-a; photo-c 17 34 51 98 154 210
10,11(Fall/'52): 10,11-Photo-c 16 32 48 94 147 200
12(St. John-10/53)-#13: 13-Painted-c. 16 32 48 92 144 195
14-Matt Baker-a 41 82 123 256 428 600
15(8/54)-Matt Baker-c 110 220 330 704 1202 1700
25(2nd Series)(Formerly Romantic Marriage) Classic Matt Baker-c 343 686 1029 2400 4200 6000
26-Matt Baker-c; last precode (2/55) 161 322 483 1030 1765 2500
27-29: Matt Baker-c 116 232 348 742 1271 1800

CINDY COMICS (...Smith No. 39, 40; Crime Can't Win No. 41 on)(Formerly Krazy Komics) (See Junior Miss & Teen Comics)
Timely Comics: No. 27, Fall, 1947 - No. 40, July, 1950

27-Kurtzman-a, 3 pgs: Margie, Oscar begin 52 104 156 328 552 775

GD 2.0 | VG 4.0 | FN 6.0 | VF 8.0 | VF/NM 9.0 | NM- 9.2

28-31-Kurtzman-a 34 68 102 199 325 450
32-36,38-40: 33-Georgie story; anti-Wertham editorial. 39-Louise Altson painted-c
28 56 84 165 270 375
37-Classic greytone-c 370 740 1110 1850 2775 3700
NOTE: *Kurtzman's "Hey Look"-#27(3), 29(2), 30(2), 31; "Giggles 'n' Grins"-28.*

CINNAMON: EL CICLO
DC Comics: Oct, 2003 - No. 5, Feb, 2004 ($2.50, limited series)
1-5-Van Meter-s/Chaykin-c/Paronzini-a 3.00

CIRCUS (...the Comic Riot)
Globe Syndicate: June, 1938 - No. 3, Aug, 1938
1-(Scarce)-Spacehawks (2 pgs.), & Disk Eyes by Wolverton (2 pgs.), Pewee Throttle by Cole (2nd comic book work; see Star Comics V1#11), Beau Gus, Ken Craig & The Lords of Crillon, Jack Hinton by Eisner, Van Bragger by Kane
508 1016 1524 3708 6554 9400
2,3-(Scarce)-Eisner, Cole, Wolverton, Bob Kane-a in each
300 600 900 1980 3440 4900

CIRCUS BOY (TV) (See Movie Classics)
Dell Publishing Co.: No. 759, Dec, 1956 - No. 813, July, 1957
Four Color 759 (#1)-The Monkees' Mickey Dolenz photo-c
13 26 39 87 191 295
Four Color 785 (4/57), 813-Mickey Dolenz photo-c 10 20 30 64 132 200

CIRCUS COMICS
Farm Women's Pub. Co./D. S. Publ.: Apr, 1945 - No. 2, Jun, 1945; Wint., 1948-49
1-Funny animal 21 42 63 122 199 275
2 13 26 39 72 101 130
1(1948)-D.S. Publ.; 2 pgs. Frazetta 29 58 87 172 281 390

CIRCUS OF FUN COMICS
A. W. Nugent Publ. Co.: 1945 - No. 3, Dec, 1947 (A book of games & puzzles)
1 15 30 45 94 147 200
2,3 10 20 30 56 76 95

CISCO KID, THE (TV)
Dell Publishing Co.: July, 1950 - No. 41, Oct-Dec, 1958
Four Color 292(#1)-Cisco Kid, his horse Diablo, & sidekick Pancho & his horse Loco begin; line drawn cover 23 46 69 156 348 540
2(1/51) Painted-c begin 10 20 30 64 132 200
3-5 9 18 27 59 117 175
6-10 8 16 24 51 96 140
11-20 7 14 21 44 82 120
21-36-Last painted-c 6 12 18 37 66 95
37-41: All photo-c 7 14 21 46 86 125
NOTE: ***Buscema** a-40. **Ernest Nordli** painted c-5-16, 20, 35.*

CISCO KID COMICS
Bernard Bailey/Swappers Quarterly: Winter, 1944 (one-shot)
1-Illustrated Stories of the Operas: Faust; Funnyman by Giunta; Cisco Kid (1st app.) & Superbaby begin; Giunta-c 47 94 141 296 498 700

CITIZEN JACK
Image Comics: Nov, 2015 - No. 6, May, 2016 ($3.99, limited series)
1-6-Sam Humphries-s/Tommy Patterson-a 4.00

CITIZEN SMITH (See Holyoke One-Shot No. 9)

CITIZEN V AND THE V-BATTALION (See Thunderbolts)
Marvel Comics: June, 2001 - No. 3, Aug, 2001 ($2.99, limited series)
1-3-Nicieza-a; Michael Ryan-c/a 3.00
...: The Everlasting 1-4 (3/02 - No. 4, 7/02) Nicieza-s/LaRosa-a(p) 3.00

CITY OF HEROES (Online game)
Dark Horse Comics/Blue King Studios: Sept, 2002; May, 2004 - No. 7 ($2.95)
1-(no cover price) Dakan-s/Zombo-a 3.00
1-7-($2.95) 3.00

CITY OF HEROES (Online game)
Image Comics: June, 2005 - No. 20, Aug, 2007 ($2.99)
1-20: 1-Waid-s; Pérez-c. 6-Flip-c with City of Villains. 7-9-Jurgens-s 3.00

CITY OF OTHERS
Dark Horse Comics: Apr, 2007 - No. 4, Aug, 2007 ($2.99, limited series)
1-4-Bernie Wrightson-a/c; Steve Niles & Wrightson-s 3.00
TPB (2/08, $14.95) r/#1-4; Wrightson sketch pages 15.00

CITY OF SILENCE
Image Comics: May, 2000 - No. 3, July, 2000 ($2.50)
1-3-Ellis-s/Erskine-a 3.00
TPB (6/04, $9.95) r/#1-3; pin-up gallery 10.00

CITY OF THE LIVING DEAD (See Fantastic Tales No. 1)
Avon Periodicals: 1952
nn-Hollingsworth-c/a 126 252 378 806 1378 1950

CITY OF TOMORROW
DC Comics (WildStorm): June, 2005 - No. 6, Nov, 2005 ($2.99, limited series)
1-6-Howard Chaykin-s/a 3.00
TPB (2006, $19.99) r/#1-6 20.00

CITY PEOPLE NOTEBOOK
Kitchen Sink Press: 1989 ($9.95, B&W, magazine sized)
nn-Will Eisner-s/a 15.00
nn-(DC Comics, 2000) Reprint 10.00

CITY SURGEON (Blake Harper...)
Gold Key: August, 1963
1(10075-308)-Painted-c 4 8 12 23 37 50

CIVIL WAR (Also see Amazing Spider-Man for TPB)
Marvel Comics: July, 2006 - No. 7, Jan, 2007 ($3.99/$2.99, limited series)
1-($3.99) Millar-s/McNiven-a & wraparound-c 3 6 9 14 19 24
1-Variant cover by Michael Turner 4 8 12 23 37 50
1-Aspen Comics Variant cover by Turner 3 6 9 19 30 40
1-Sketch Variant cover 3 6 9 16 23 30
1-Director's Cut (2006, $4.99) r/#1 plus promo art, variant covers, sketches and script
2 4 6 11 16 20
2-($2.99) Spider-Man unmasks 2 4 6 8 10 12
2-Turner variant cover 2 4 6 11 16 20
2-B&W sketch variant cover 3 6 9 16 23 30
2-2nd printing 5.00
3-7: 3-Thor returns. 4-Goliath killed 1 2 3 5 6 8
3-7-Turner variant covers 1 2 3 6 8 10
3-7-B&W sketch variant covers 3 6 9 14 20 25
TPB (2007, $24.99) r/#1-7; gallery of variant covers 25.00
...: Battle Damage Report (2007, $3.99) Post-Civil War character profiles; McGuinness-c 4.00
...: Choosing Sides (2/07, $3.99) Colan-c; Howard the Duck app.; 2 covers by Yu & Colan 5.00
... Companion TPB (2007, $13.99) r/Civil War Files, ...:Battle Damage Report, Marvel Spotlight: Millar/McNiven, Marvel Spotlight: Civil War Aftermath and Daily Bugle CW 14.00
Daily Bugle Civil War Newspaper Special #1 (9/06, 50¢, newsprint) Daily Bugle "newspaper" overview of the crossover; Mayhew-a 3.00
...Files (2006, $3.99) profile pages of major Civil War characters; McNiven-c 4.00
...: Marvels Snapshots 1 (2/21, $4.99) Ahmed-s/Kelly-a; Alex Ross-c; Captain America app. 5.00
...: Marvel Universe TPB (2007, $11.99) r/Civil War: Choosing Sides, CW: The Return, She-Hulk #8, CW: The Initiative; She-Hulk sketch page; variant cover gallery 12.00
...: MGC #1 (6/10, $1.00) r/#1 with "Marvel's Greatest Comics" cover logo 3.00
...: The Confession (5/07, $2.99) Maleev-c/a; Bendis-s 3.00
...: The Initiative (4/07, $4.99) Silvestri-c/a; previews of post-Civil War series 5.00
...: The Return (3/07, $2.99) Captain Marvel returns; The Sentry app.; Raney-a 3.00
...: The Road to Civil War TPB (2007, $14.99) r/New Avengers: Illuminati, Fantastic Four #536 & 537, Amazing Spider-Man #529-531; Spider-Man costume sketches by Bachalo 15.00
... War Crimes (2/07, $3.99) Kingpin in prison; Tieri-s/Staz Johnson-a 4.00
... War Crimes TPB (2007, $17.99) r/Civil War: War Crimes one-shot and Underworld #1-5 18.00
... X-Men Universe TPB (2007, $13.99) r/Cable & Deadpool #30-32; X-Factor #8,9 14.00

CIVIL WAR (Secret Wars tie-in)
Marvel Comics: Sept, 2015 - No. 5, Dec, 2015 ($4.99/$3.99, limited series)
1-($4.99) Soule-s/Yu-a; Stark vs. Rogers on Battleworld 5.00
2-5-($3.99) 4.00

CIVIL WAR CHRONICLES (Reprints of Civil War and related Marvel issues)
Marvel Comics: Oct, 2007 - No. 12, Sept, 2008 ($4.99, limited series)
1-12: Reprints Civil War, Civil War: Frontline and x-over issues 5.00

CIVIL WAR: FRONTLINE (Tie-in to Civil War and related Marvel issues)
Marvel Comics: Aug, 2006 - No. 11, Apr, 2007 ($2.99, limited series)
1-Jenkins-s/Bachs-a/Watson-c; back-up stories by various 4.00
2-11: 3-Green Goblin app. 11-Aftermath of Civil War #7 3.00
... Book 1 TPB (2007, $14.99) r/#1-6 15.00
... Book 2 TPB (2007, $14.99) r/#7-11 15.00

CIVIL WAR: HOUSE OF M
Marvel Comics: Nov, 2008 - No. 5, Mar, 2009 ($2.99, limited series)
1-5-Gage-s/DiVito-a 3.00

CIVIL WAR MUSKET, THE (Kadets of America Handbook)
Custom Comics, Inc.: 1960 (25¢, half-size, 36 pgs.)
nn 3 6 9 15 22 28

CIVIL WAR II
Marvel Comics: No. 0, Jul, 2016 - No. 8, Feb, 2017 ($4.99/$5.99, limited series)
0-($4.99) Bendis-s/Coipel-a; intro. Ulysses 5.00
1-($5.99) Bendis-s/Marquez-a; Thanos kills War Machine 6.00
2-8-($4.99) 3-Banner killed. 4,5-Guardians of the Galaxy app. 7-Sorrentino-a (2 pgs.) 5.00
...: The Oath 1 (3/17, $4.99) Spencer-s; Capt. America named Director of SHIELD 5.00

CIVIL WAR II: AMAZING SPIDER-MAN
Marvel Comics: Aug, 2016 - No. 4, Nov, 2016 ($3.99, limited series)
1-4-Gage-s/Foreman-a; Ulysses app.; Clash returns 4.00

CIVIL WAR II: CHOOSING SIDES
Marvel Comics: Aug, 2016 - No. 6, Nov, 2016 ($4.99/$3.99, limited series)
1-($4.99) Short stories; Nick Fury, Night Thrasher & Damage Control app. 5.00
2-6-($3.99) Nick Fury story in all. 2-War Machine. 4-Punisher. 6-Jessica Jones 4.00

CIVIL WAR II: GODS OF WAR
Marvel Comics: Aug, 2016 - No. 4, Nov, 2016 ($3.99, limited series)
1-4-Abnett-s/Laiso-a/Anacleto-c. 1-Amadeus Cho app. 3-Avengers app. 4.00

CIVIL WAR II: KINGPIN
Marvel Comics: Sept, 2016 - No. 4, Dec, 2016 ($4.99/$3.99, limited series)
1-($4.99) Two stories; Rosenberg-s/Ortiz-a; Talajic-a; intro./origin Janus Jardeesh 5.00
2-4-($3.99) Rosenberg-s/Ortiz-a. 3-Punisher app. 4.00

CIVIL WAR II: ULYSSES
Marvel Comics: Oct, 2016 - No. 3, Dec, 2016 ($4.99, limited series)
1-3-Ewing-s/Kesel & Palo-a/Francavilla-c; Karnak and the Inhumans app. 4.00

CIVIL WAR II: X-MEN
Marvel Comics: Aug, 2016 - No. 4, Nov, 2016 ($3.99, limited series)
1-4-Bunn-s/Broccardo-a; Magneto app. 2-The Brood & Fantomex app. 4-Ulysses app. 4.00

CIVIL WAR: X-MEN (Tie-in to Civil War)
Marvel Comics: Sept, 2006 - No. 4, Dec, 2006 ($2.99, limited series)
1-4-Paquette-a/Hine-s; Bishop app. 3.00
1-Variant cover by Michael Turner 10.00
TPB (2007, $11.99) r/#1-4, profile pages of minor characters 12.00

CIVIL WAR: YOUNG AVENGERS & RUNAWAYS (Tie-in to Civil War)
Marvel Comics: Sept, 2006 - No. 4, Dec, 2006 ($2.99, limited series)
1-4-Caselli-a/Wells-s/Cheung-c 3.00
TPB (2007, $11.99) r/#1-4, profile pages of characters 12.00

CLAIRE VOYANT (Also see Keen Teens)

The Cisco Kid #14 © DELL

Civil War #3 © MAR

Clandestine (2008) #4 © MAR

	GD 2.0	VG 4.0	FN 6.0	VF 8.0	VF/NM 9.0	NM- 9.2
Leader Publ./Standard/Pentagon Publ.: 1946 - No. 4, 1947 (Sparling strip reprints)						
nn	103	206	309	659	1130	1600
2-Kamen-c	81	162	243	518	884	1250
3-Kamen bridal-c; contents mentioned in Love and Death, a book by Gershom Legman(1949) referenced by Dr. Wertham in **SOTI**	116	232	348	742	1271	1800
4-Kamen bondage-c	100	200	300	635	1093	1550

CLANDESTINE (Also see Marvel Comics Presents & X-Men: ClanDestine)
Marvel Comics: Oct, 1994 - No.12, Sept, 1995 ($2.95/$2.50)

1-($2.95)-Alan Davis-c/a(p)/scripts & Mark Farmer-c/a(i) begin, ends #8; Modok app.; Silver Surfer cameo; gold foil-c 4.00
2-12: 2-Wraparound-c. 2,3-Silver Surfer app. 5-Origin of ClanDestine. 6-Capt. America, Hulk, Spider-Man, Thing & Thor-c; Spider-Man cameo. 7-Spider-Man-c/app; Punisher cameo. 8-Invaders & Dr. Strange app. 10-Captain Britain-c/app. 11-Sub-Mariner app. 3.00
Preview (10/94, $1.50) 3.00
... Classic HC (2008, $29.99, DJ) r/#1-8, Marvel Comics Presents #158, X-Men and Clandestine #1&2, sketch pages and cover gallery; Alan Davis afterword 30.00

CLANDESTINE
Marvel Comics: Apr, 2008 - No. 5, Aug, 2008 ($2.99, limited series)

1-5: 1-Alan Davis-c/a(p)/scripts & Mark Farmer-c/a(i). 2-5-Excalibur app. 3.00

CLARENCE (Based on the Cartoon Network series)
BOOM! Studios (kaboom): Jun, 2015 - No. 4, Sept, 2015 ($3.99)

1-4-Short stories by various; multiple covers on each 4.00
...: Quest 1 (6/16, $4.99) Cron-DeVico-s; art by Smigiel & Omac 5.00
...: Rest Stops 1 (12/15, $4.99) Short stories by various; two covers 5.00

CLANKILLERS
AfterShock Comics: Jul, 2018 - No. 5, Dec, 2018 ($3.99, limited series)

1-5-Sean Lewis-s/Antonio Fuso-a 4.00

CLANS OF BELARI
AfterShock Comics: Jul, 2021 - No. 4, Oct, 2021 ($4.99, limited series)

1-4-Peter & Rob Blackie-s/Daniel Maine-a 5.00

CLASH
DC Comics: 1991 - No. 3, 1991 ($4.95, limited series, 52 pgs.)

Book One - Three: Adam Kubert-c/a 5.00

CLASSIC BATTLESTAR GALACTICA (See Battlestar Galactica, Classic...)

CLASSIC COMICS/ILLUSTRATED - INTRODUCTION
by Dan Malan

Since the first publication of this special introduction to the **Classics** section, a number of revisions have been made to further clarify the listings. **Classics** reprint editions prior to 1963 had either incorrect dates or no dates listed. Those reprint editions should be identified only by the highest number on the reorder list (HRN). Past *Guides* listed what were calculated to be approximately correct dates, but many people found it confusing for the *Guide* to list a date not listed in the comic itself.

We have also attempted to clear up confusion about edition variations, such as color, printer, etc. Such variations are identified by letters. Editions are determined by three categories. Original edition variations are designated as Edition 1A, 1B, etc. All reprint editions prior to 1963 are identified by HRN only. All reprint editions from 9/63 on are identified by the correct date listed in the comic.

Information is also included on four reprintings of **Classics**. From 1968-1976, Twin Circle, the Catholic newspaper, serialized over 100 **Classics** titles. That list can be found under non-series items at the end of this section. In 1972, twelve **Classics** were reissued as **Now Age Books Illustrated**. They are listed under **Pendulum Illustrated Classics**. In 1982, 20 **Classics** were reissued, adapted for teaching English as a second language. They are listed under **Regents Illustrated Classics**. Then in 1984, six **Classics** were reissued with cassette tapes. See the listing under **Cassette Books**.

UNDERSTANDING CLASSICS ILLUSTRATED
by Dan Malan

Since **Classics Illustrated** is the most complicated comic book series, with all its reprint editions and variations, changes in covers and artwork, a variety of means of identifying editions, and the most extensive worldwide distribution of any comic-book series, this introductory section is provided to assist you in gaining expertise about this series.

THE HISTORY OF CLASSICS

The **Classics** series was the brain child of Albert L. Kanter, who saw in the new comic-book medium a means of introducing children to the great classics of literature. In October of 1941 his Gilberton Co. began the **Classic Comics** series with **The Three Musketeers**, with 64 pages of storyline. In those early years, the struggling series saw irregular schedules and numerous printers, not to mention variable art quality and liberal story adaptations. With No.13 the page total was reduced to 56 (except for No. 33, originally scheduled to be No. 9), and with No. 15 the coming-next ad on the outside back cover moved inside. In 1945 the Jerry Iger Shop began producing all new CC titles, beginning with No. 23. In 1947 the search for a classier logo resulted in **Classics Illustrated**, beginning with No. 35, **Last Days of Pompeii**. With No. 45 the page total dropped again to 48, which was to become the standard.

Two new developments in 1951 had a profound effect upon the success of the series. One was the introduction of painted covers, instead of the old line drawn covers, beginning with No. 81, **The Odyssey**. The second was the switch to the major national distributor Curtis. They raised the cover price from 10 to 15 cents, making it the highest priced comic-book, but it did not slow the growth of the series, because they were marketed as books, not comics. Because of this higher quality image, **Classics** flourished during the fifties while other comic series were reeling from outside attacks. They diversified with their new **Juniors**, **Specials**, and **World Around Us** series.

Classics artwork can be divided into three distinct periods. The pre-Iger era (1941-44) was mentioned above for its variable art quality. The Iger era (1945-53) was a major improvement in art quality and adaptations. It came to be dominated by artists Henry Kiefer and Alex Blum, together accounting for some 50 titles. Their styles gave the first real personality to the series. The EC era (1954-62) resulted from the demise of the EC horror series, when many of their artists made the major switch to classical art.

But several factors brought the production of new CI titles to a complete halt in 1962. Gilberton lost its 2nd class mailing permit. External factors like television, cheap paperback books, and Cliff Notes were all eating away at their market. Production halted with No.167, **Faust**, even though many more titles were already in the works. Many of those found their way into foreign series, and are very desirable to collectors. In 1967, **Classics Illustrated** was sold to Patrick Frawley and his Catholic publication, Twin Circle. They issued two new titles in 1969 as part of an attempted revival, but succumbed to major distribution problems in 1971. In 1988, First Publishing acquired the rights to use the old CI series art, logo, and name from the Frawley Group, and released a short-lived series featuring contributions of modern creators. Acclaim Books and Twin Circles issued a series of **Classics** reprints from 1997-1998.

One of the unique aspects of the **Classics Illustrated** (CI) series was the proliferation of reprint variations. Some titles had as many as 25 editions. Reprinting began in 1943. Some **Classic Comics** (CC) reprints (r) had the logo format revised to a banner logo, and added a motto under the banner. In 1947 CC titles changed to the CI logo, but kept their line drawn covers (LDC). In 1948, Nos. 13, 18, 29 and 41 received second covers (LDC2), replacing covers considered too violent, and reprints of Nos. 13-44 had pages reduced to 48, except for No. 26, which had 48 pages to begin with.

Starting in the mid-1950s, 70 of the 80 LDC titles were reissued with new painted covers (PC). Thirty of them also received new interior artwork (A2). The new artwork was generally higher quality with larger art panels and more faithful but abbreviated storylines. Later on, there were 29 second painted covers (PC2), mostly by Twin Circle. Altogether there were 199 interior art variations (169 (O)s and 30 A2 editions) and 272 different covers (169 (O)s, four LDC2s, 70 new PCs of LDC (O)s, and 29 PC2s). It is mildly astounding to realize that there are nearly 1400 different editions in the U.S. CI series.

FOREIGN CLASSICS ILLUSTRATED

If U.S. Classics variations are mildly astounding, the veritable plethora of foreign CI variations will boggle your imagination. While we still anticipate additional discoveries, we presently know about series in 25 languages and 27 countries. There were 250 new CI titles in foreign series, and nearly 400 new foreign covers of U.S. titles. The 1400 U.S. CI editions pale in comparison to the 4000 plus foreign editions. The very nature of CI lent itself to flourishing as an international series. Worldwide, they published over one billion copies! The first foreign CI series consisted of six Canadian Classic Comic reprints in 1946.

The following chart shows when CI series first began in each country:
1946: Canada. 1947: Australia. 1948: Brazil/The Netherlands. 1950: Italy. 1951: Greece/ Japan/ Hong Kong(?)/England/Argentina/Mexico. 1952: West Germany. 1954: Norway. 1955: New Zealand/South Africa. 1956: Denmark/Sweden/Iceland. 1957: Finland/France. 1962: Singapore(?). 1964: India (8 languages). 1971: Ireland (Gaelic). 1973: Belgium(?) / Philippines(?) & Malaysia(?).

Significant among the early series were Brazil and Greece. In 1950, Brazil was the first country to begin doing its own new titles. They issued nearly 80 new CI titles by Brazilian authors. In Greece in 1951 they actually had debates in parliament about the effects of Classics Illustrated on Greek culture, leading to the inclusion of 88 new Greek History & Mythology titles in the CI series.

But by far the most important foreign CI development was the joint European series which began in 1956 in 10 countries simultaneously. By 1960, CI had the largest European distribution of any American publication, not just comics! So when all the problems came up with U.S. distribution, they literally moved the CI operation to Europe in 1962, and continued producing new titles in all four CI series. Many of them were adapted and drawn in the U.S., the most famous of which was the British CI #158A. Dr. No, drawn by Norman Nodel. Unfortunately, the British CI series ended in late 1963, which limited the European CI titles available in English to 15. Altogether there were 82 new CI art titles in the joint European series, which ran until 1976.

IDENTIFYING CLASSICS EDITIONS

HRN: This is the highest number on the reorder list. It should be listed in ( ) after the title number. It is crucial to understanding various CI editions.

ORIGINALS (O): This is the all-important First Edition. To determine (O)s,there is one primary rule and two secondary rules (with exceptions):

Rule No. 1: All (O)s and only (O)s have coming-next ads for the next number. **Exceptions**: No. 14(15) (reprint) has an ad on the last inside text page only. No. 14(0) also has a full-page outside back cover ad (also rule 2). Nos.55(75) and 57(75) have coming-next ads. (Rules 2 and 3 apply here). Nos. 168(0) and 169(0) do not have coming-next ads. No.168 was never reprinted; No. 169(0) has HRN (166). No. 169(169) is the only reprint.

Rule No. 2: On nos.1-80, all (O)s and only (O)s list 10c on the front cover. **Exceptions**: Reprint variations of Nos. 37(62), 39(71), and 46(62) list 10c on the front cover. (Rules 1 and 3 apply here.)

Rule No. 3: All (O)s have HRN close to that title No. **Exceptions**: Some reprints also have HRNs close to that title number: a few CC(r)s, 58(62), 60(62), 149(149), 152(149) 153(149), and title nos. in the 160's. (Rules 1 and 2 apply here.)

DATES: Many reprint editions list either an incorrect date or no date. Since Gilberton apparently kept track of CI editions by HRN, they often left the (O) date on reprints. Often, someone with a CI collection for sale will swear that all their copies are originals. That is why we are so detailed in pointing out how to identify original editions. Except for original editions, which should have a coming-next ad, etc., all CI dates prior to 1963 are incorrect! So you want to go by HRN only if it is (165) or below, and go by listed date if it is 1963 or later. There are a few (167) editions with incorrect dates. They could be listed either as (167) or (62/3), which is meant to indicate that they were issued sometime between late 1962 and early 1963.

COVERS: A change from CC to LDC indicates a logo change, not a cover change; while a change from LDC to LDC2, LDC to PC, or from PC to PC2 does indicate a new cover. New PCs can be identified by HRN, and PC2s can be identified by HRN and date. Several covers had color changes, particularly from purple to blue.

Notes: If you see 15 cents in Canada on a front cover, it does not necessarily indicate a Canadian edition. Editions with an HRN between 44 and 75, with 15 cents on the cover are Canadian. Check the publisher's address. An HRN listing two numbers with a / between them indicates that there are two different reorder lists in the front and back covers. Official Twin Circle editions have a full-page back cover ad for their TC magazine, with no CI reorder list. Any CI with just a Twin Circle sticker on the front is not an official TC edition.

TIPS ON LISTING CLASSICS FOR SALE

It may be easy to just list Edition 17, but Classics collectors keep track of CI editions in terms of HRN and/or date, (O) or (r), CC or LDC, PC or PC2, A1 or A2, soft or stiff cover, etc. Try to help them out. For originals, just list (0), unless there are variations such as color (Nos. 10 and 61), printer (Nos. 18-22), HRN (Nos. 95, 108, 160), etc. For reprints, just list HRN if it's (165) or below. Above that, list HRN and date. Also, please list type of logo/cover/art for the convenience of buyers. They will appreciate it.

CLASSIC COMICS (Also see Best from Boys Life, Cassette Books, Famous Stories, Fast Fiction, Golden Picture Classics, King Classics, Marvel Classics Comics, Pendulum Illustrated Classics, Picture Parade, Picture Progress, Regents Ill. Classics, Spitfire, Stories by Famous Authors, Superior Stories, and World Around Us.)

CLASSIC COMICS (Classics Illustrated No. 35 on)
Elliot Publishing #1-3 (1941-1942)/Gilberton Publications #4-167 (1942-1967) /Twin Circle Pub. (Frawley) #168-169 (1968-1971):
10/41 - No. 34, 2/47; No. 35, 3/47 - No. 169, Spring 1969
(Reprint Editions of almost all titles 5/43 - Spring 1971)
(Painted Covers (0)s No. 81 on, and (r)s of most Nos. 1-80)

Abbreviations:
A–Art; C or c–Cover; CC–Classic Comics; CI–Classics Ill.; Ed–Edition; LDC–Line Drawn Cover; PC–Painted Cover; r–Reprint

1. The Three Musketeers

Ed	HRN	Date	Details	A	C	GD 2.0	VG 4.0	FN 6.0	VF 8.0	VF/NM 9.0	NM- 9.2
1	–	10/41	Date listed-1941; Elliot Pub; 68 pgs.	1	1	516	1032	1548	3767	6659	9550
2	10	–	10¢ price removed on all (r)s; Elliot Pub; CC-r	1	1	39	78	117	231	378	525
3	15	–	Long Isl. Ind. Ed.; CC-r	1	1	26	52	78	154	252	350
4	18/20	–	Sunrise Times Ed.; CC-r	1	1	19	38	57	109	172	235
5	21	–	Richmond Courier Ed.; CC-r	1	1	17	34	51	98	154	210
6	28	1946	CC-r	1	1	14	28	42	80	115	150
7	36	–	LDC-r	1	1	8	16	24	42	54	65
8	60	–	LDC-r	1	1	6	12	18	27	33	38
9	64	–	LDC-r	1	1	5	10	15	22	26	30
10	78	–	C-price 15¢;LDC-r	1	1	4	9	13	18	22	26
11	93	–	LDC-r	1	1	4	9	13	18	22	26
12	114	–	Last LDC-r	1	1	4	8	11	16	19	22
13	134	–	New-c; old-a; 64 pg. PC-r	1	2	3	6	9	18	28	38
14	143	–	Old-a; PC-r; 64 pg.	1	2	2	4	6	11	16	20
15	150	–	New-a; PC-r; Evans/Crandall-a	2	2	3	6	9	16	24	32
16	149	–	PC-r	2	2	2	4	6	8	11	14
17	167	–	PC-r	2	2	2	4	6	8	11	14
18	167	4/64	PC-r	2	2	2	4	6	8	11	14
19	167	1/65	PC-r	2	2	2	4	6	8	11	14
20	167	3/66	PC-r	2	2	2	4	6	8	11	14
21	166	11/67	PC-r	2	2	2	4	6	8	11	14
22	166	Spr/69	C-price 25¢ ; stiff-c; PC-r	2	2	2	4	6	8	11	14
23	169	Spr/71	PC-r; stiff-c	2	2	2	4	6	8	11	14

2. Ivanhoe

Ed	HRN	Date	Details	A	C	GD 2.0	VG 4.0	FN 6.0	VF 8.0	VF/NM 9.0	NM- 9.2
1	(O)	12/41?	Date listed-1941; Elliot Pub; 68 pgs.	1	1	252	504	756	1613	2757	3900
2	10	–	Price & 'Presents' removed; Elliot Pub; CC-r	1	1	33	66	99	194	317	440
3	15	–	Long Isl. Ind. ed.; CC-r	1	1	21	42	63	124	202	280
4	18/20	–	Sunrise Times ed.; CC-r	1	1	18	36	54	103	162	225
5	21	–	Richmond Courier ed.; CC-r	1	1	16	32	48	94	147	200
6	28	1946	Last 'Comics'-r	1	1	15	30	45	83	124	165
7	36	–	1st LDC-r	1	1	9	18	27	47	61	75
8	60	–	LDC-r	1	1	6	12	18	27	33	38
9	64	–	LDC-r	1	1	5	10	15	22	26	30
10	78	–	C-price 15¢; LDC-r	1	1	4	9	13	18	22	26
11	89	–	LDC-r	1	1	4	8	12	17	21	24
12	106	–	LDC-r	1	1	4	7	10	14	17	20
13	121	–	Last LDC-r	1	1	4	7	10	14	17	20
14	136	–	New-c&a; PC-r	2	2	5	10	15	25	31	36
15	142	–	PC-r	2	2	2	4	6	9	13	16
16	153	–	PC-r	2	2	2	4	6	9	13	16
17	149	–	PC-r	2	2	2	4	6	9	13	16
18	167	–	PC-r	2	2	2	4	6	8	11	14
19	167	5/64	PC-r	2	2	2	4	6	8	11	14
20	167	1/65	PC-r	2	2	2	4	6	8	11	14
21	167	3/66	PC-r	2	2	2	4	6	8	11	14
22A	166	9/67	PC-r	2	2	2	4	6	8	11	14
22B	166	–	Center ad for Children's Digest & Young Miss; rare; PC-r	2	2	6	12	18	40	73	105
23	166	R/68	C-Price 25¢; PC-r	2	2	2	4	6	8	11	14
24	169	Win/69	Stiff-c	2	2	2	4	6	8	11	14
25	169	Win/71	PC-r; stiff-c	2	2	2	4	6	8	11	14

3. The Count of Monte Cristo

Ed	HRN	Date	Details	A	C	GD 2.0	VG 4.0	FN 6.0	VF 8.0	VF/NM 9.0	NM- 9.2
1	(O)	3/42	Elliot Pub; 68 pgs.	1	1	164	328	492	1041	1796	2550
2	10	–	Conray Prods; CC-r	1	1	30	60	90	177	289	400
3	15	–	Long Isl. Ind. ed.; CC-r	1	1	22	44	66	132	216	300
4	18/20	–	Sunrise Times ed.; CC-r	1	1	20	40	60	114	182	250
5	20	–	Sunrise Times ed.; CC-r	1	1	17	34	51	98	154	210
6	21	–	Richmond Courier ed.; CC-r	1	1	16	32	48	94	147	200
7	28	1946	CC-r; new Banner logo	1	1	14	28	42	80	115	150
8	36	–	1st LDC-r	1	1	9	18	27	47	61	75
9	60	–	LDC-r	1	1	6	12	18	27	33	38
10	62	–	LDC-r	1	1	6	12	18	29	36	42
11	71	–	LDC-r	1	1	5	10	14	20	24	28
12	87	–	C-price 15¢; LDC-r	1	1	4	9	13	18	22	26
13	113	–	LDC-r	1	1	4	7	10	14	17	20
14	135	–	New-c&a; PC-r; Cameron-a	2	2	3	6	9	17	26	35
15	143	–	PC-r	2	2	2	4	6	8	13	16
16	153	–	PC-r	2	2	2	4	6	8	13	16
17	161	–	PC-r	2	2	2	4	6	8	13	16
18	167	–	PC-r	2	2	2	4	6	8	11	14
19	167	7/64	PC-r	2	2	2	4	6	8	11	14
20	167	7/65	PC-r	2	2	2	4	6	8	11	14
21	167	7/66	PC-r	2	2	2	4	6	8	11	14
22	166	R/68	C-price 25¢; PC-r	2	2	2	4	6	8	11	14
23	169	–	Win/69 Stiff-c; PC-r	2	2	2	4	6	8	11	14

4. The Last of the Mohicans

Ed	HRN	Date	Details	A	C	GD 2.0	VG 4.0	FN 6.0	VF 8.0	VF/NM 9.0	NM- 9.2
1	(O)	8/42	Date listed-1942; Gilberton #4(0) on; 68 pgs.	1	1	145	290	435	921	1586	2250
2	12	–	Elliot Pub; CC-r	1	1	27	54	81	158	259	360
3	15	–	Long Isl. Ind. ed.; CC-r	1	1	20	40	60	120	195	270
4	20	–	Long Isl. Ind. ed.; CC-r; banner logo	1	1	18	36	54	105	165	225
5	21	–	Queens Home News ed.; CC-r	1	1	16	32	48	94	147	200
6	28	1946	Last CC-r; new	1	1	15	30	45	83	124	165
7	36	–	1st LDC-r	1	1	9	18	27	47	61	75
8	60	–	LDC-r	1	1	6	12	18	27	33	38
9	64	–	LDC-r	1	1	5	10	14	20	24	28
10	78	–	C-price 15¢; LDC-r	1	1	4	9	13	18	22	26
11	89	–	LDC-r	1	1	4	8	12	17	21	24
12	117	–	Last LDC-r	1	1	4	7	10	14	17	20
13	135	–	New-c; PC-r	1	2	5	10	15	24	30	35
14	141	–	PC-r	1	2	4	7	9	14	16	18
15	150	–	New-a; PC-r; Severin, L.B. Cole-a	2	2	6	12	18	27	33	38
16	161	–	PC-r	2	2	2	4	6	8	11	14
17	167	–	PC-r	2	2	2	4	6	8	11	14
18	167	6/64	PC-r	2	2	2	4	6	8	11	14
19	167	8/65	PC-r	2	2	2	4	6	8	11	14
20	167	8/66	PC-r	2	2	2	4	6	8	11	14
21	166	R/67	C-price 25¢; PC-r	2	2	2	4	6	8	11	14
22	169	Spr/69	Stiff-c; PC-r	2	2	2	4	6	8	11	14

5. Moby Dick

Ed	HRN	Date	Details	A	C	GD 2.0	VG 4.0	FN 6.0	VF 8.0	VF/NM 9.0	NM- 9.2
1A	(O)	9/42	Date listed-1942; Gilberton; 68 pgs.	1	1	177	354	531	1124	1937	2750
1B			inside-c, rare free promo			271	542	813	1734	2967	4200

Classic Comics #2 © GIL

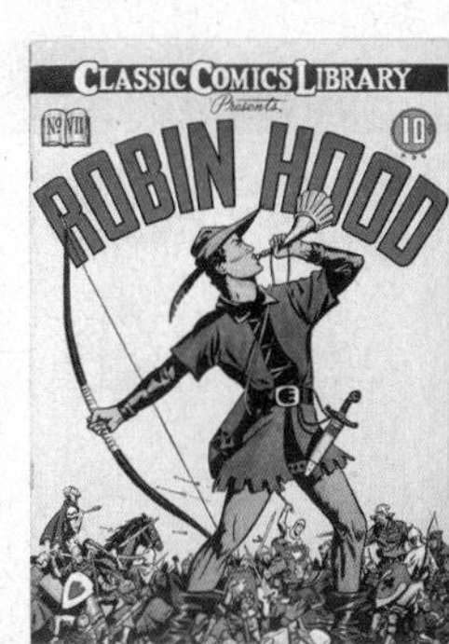

Classic Comics #7 © GIL

Classic Comics #9 © GIL

Ed	HRN	Date	Details	A	C	GD 2.0	VG 4.0	FN 6.0	VF 8.0	VF/NM 9.0	NM- 9.2
2	10	–	Conray Prods; Pg. 64 changed from 105 title list to letter from Editor; CC-r	1	1	30	60	90	177	289	400
3	15	–	Long Isl. Ind. ed.; Pg. 64 changed from Letter to the Editor to Ill. poem-Concord Hymn; CC-r	1	1	25	50	75	150	245	340
4	18/20	–	Sunrise Times ed.; CC-r	1	1	20	40	60	117	189	260
5	20	–	Sunrise Times ed.; CC-r	1	1	19	38	57	112	179	245
6	21	–	Sunrise Times ed.; CC-r	1	1	17	34	51	98	154	210
7	28	1946	CC-r; new banner logo	1	1	15	30	45	83	124	165
8	36	–	1st LDC-r	1	1	9	18	27	52	69	85
9	60	–	LDC-r	1	1	6	12	18	27	33	38
10	62	–	LDC-r	1	1	6	12	18	29	36	42
11	71	–	LDC-r	1	1	5	10	15	22	26	30
12	87	–	C-price 15¢; LDC-r	1	1	5	10	14	20	24	28
13	118	–	LDC-r	1	1	4	8	12	17	21	24
14	131	–	New c&a; PC-r	2	2	5	10	15	25	31	36
15	138	–	PC-r	2	2	2	4	6	9	12	16
16	148	–	PC-r	2	2	2	4	6	9	12	16
17	158	–	PC-r	2	2	2	4	6	9	12	16
18	167	–	PC-r	2	2	2	4	6	8	11	14
19	167	6/64	PC-r	2	2	2	4	6	8	11	14
20	167	7/65	PC-r	2	2	2	4	6	8	11	14
21	167	3/66	PC-r	2	2	2	4	6	8	11	14
22	166	9/67	PC-r	2	2	2	4	6	8	11	14
23	166	Win/69	New-c & c-price 25¢; Stiff-c; PC-r	2	3	3	6	9	16	23	30
24	169	Win/71	PC-r	2	3	3	6	9	14	19	24

6. A Tale of Two Cities

Ed	HRN	Date	Details	A	C	GD 2.0	VG 4.0	FN 6.0	VF 8.0	VF/NM 9.0	NM- 9.2
1	(O)	10/42	Date listed-1942; 68 pgs. Zeckerberg c/a	1	1	135	270	405	864	1482	2100
2	14	–	Elliot Pub; CC-r	1	1	25	50	75	150	245	340
3	18	–	Long Isl. Ind. ed.; CC-r	1	1	20	40	60	114	182	250
4	20	–	Sunrise Times ed.; CC-r	1	1	18	36	54	105	165	225
5	28	1946	Last CC-r; new banner logo	1	1	14	28	42	80	115	150
6	51	–	1st LDC-r	1	1	8	16	24	42	54	65
7	64	–	LDC-r	1	1	5	10	15	23	28	32
8	78	–	C-price 15¢; LDC-r	1	1	5	10	14	20	24	28
9	89	–	LDC-r	1	1	4	7	10	14	17	20
10	117	–	LDC-r	1	1	4	7	10	14	17	20
11	132	–	New-c&a; PC-r; Joe Orlando-a	2	2	5	10	15	25	31	36
12	140	–	PC-r	2	2	2	4	6	8	11	14
13	147	–	PC-r	2	2	2	4	6	8	11	14
14	152	–	PC-r; very rare	2	2	17	34	51	98	154	210
15	153	–	PC-r	2	2	2	4	6	9	13	16
16	149	–	PC-r	2	2	2	4	6	9	13	16
17	167	–	PC-r	2	2	2	4	6	8	11	14
18	167	6/64	PC-r	2	2	2	4	6	8	11	14
19	167	8/65	PC-r	2	2	2	4	6	8	11	14
20	166	5/67	PC-r	2	2	2	4	6	8	11	14
21	166	Fall/68	New-c & 25¢; PC-r	2	3	3	6	9	16	24	32
22	169	Sum/70	Stiff-c; PC-r	2	3	2	4	6	13	18	22

7. Robin Hood

Ed	HRN	Date	Details	A	C	GD 2.0	VG 4.0	FN 6.0	VF 8.0	VF/NM 9.0	NM- 9.2
1	(O)	12/42	Date listed-1942; first Gift Box ad-bc; 68 pgs.	1	1	103	206	309	659	1130	1600
2	12	–	Elliot Pub; CC-r	1	1	24	48	72	140	230	320
3	18	–	Long Isl. Ind. ed.; CC-r	1	1	19	38	57	111	176	240
4	20	–	Nassau Bulletin ed.; CC-r	1	1	18	36	54	103	162	220
5	22	–	Queens Cty. Times ed.; CC-r	1	1	16	32	48	94	147	200
6	28	–	CC-r	1	1	14	28	42	81	118	155
7	51	–	LDC-r	1	1	8	16	24	42	54	65
8	64	–	LDC-r	1	1	5	10	15	24	30	35
9	78	–	LDC-r	1	1	4	9	13	18	22	26
10	97	–	LDC-r	1	1	4	8	12	17	21	24
11	106	–	LDC-r	1	1	4	7	10	14	17	20
12	121	–	LDC-r	1	1	4	7	10	14	17	20
13	129	–	New-c; PC-r	1	2	5	10	15	25	31	36
14	136	–	New-a; PC-r	2	2	5	10	15	24	29	34
15	143	–	PC-r	2	2	2	4	6	9	13	16
16	153	–	PC-r	2	2	2	4	6	9	13	16
17	164	–	PC-r	2	2	2	4	6	8	11	14
18	167	–	PC-r	2	2	2	4	6	8	11	14
19	167	6/64	PC-r	2	2	2	4	6	8	11	14
20	167	5/65	PC-r	2	2	2	4	6	8	11	14
21	167	7/66	PC-r	2	2	2	4	6	8	11	14
22	166	12/67	PC-r	2	2	2	4	6	8	11	14
23	169	Sum/69	Stiff-c; c-price 25¢; PC-r	2	2	2	4	6	8	11	14

8. Arabian Nights

Ed	HRN	Date	Details	A	C	GD 2.0	VG 4.0	FN 6.0	VF 8.0	VF/NM 9.0	NM- 9.2
1	(O)	2/43	Original; 68 pgs. Lilian Chestney-c/a	1	1	152	304	456	965	1658	2350
2	17	–	Long Isl. ed.; pg. 64 changed from Gift Box ad to Letter from British Medical Worker; CC-r	1	1	52	104	156	323	549	775
3	20	–	Nassau Bulletin; Pg. 64 changed from letter to article-Three Men Named Smith; CC-r	1	1	42	84	126	265	445	625
4A	28	1946	CC-r; new banner logo, slick-c	1	1	31	62	93	182	296	410
4B	28	1946	Same, but w/stiff-c	1	1	31	62	93	182	296	410
5	51	–	LDC-r	1	1	22	44	66	128	209	290
6	64	–	LDC-r	1	1	19	38	57	111	176	240
7	78	–	LDC-r	1	1	18	36	54	105	165	225
8	164	–	New-c&a; PC-r	2	2	15	30	45	90	140	190

9. Les Miserables

Ed	HRN	Date	Details	A	C	GD 2.0	VG 4.0	FN 6.0	VF 8.0	VF/NM 9.0	NM- 9.2
1A	(O)	3/43	Original; slick paper cover; 68 pgs.	1	1	103	206	309	659	1130	1600
1B	(O)	3/43	Original; rough, pulp type-c; 68 pgs.	1	1	123	246	369	787	1344	1900
2	14	–	Elliot Pub; CC-r	1	1	26	52	78	154	252	350
3	18	3/44	Nassau Bul. Pg. 64 changed from Gift Box ad to Bill of Rights article; CC-r	1	1	22	44	66	128	209	290
4	20	–	Richmond Courier ed.; CC-r	1	1	19	38	57	111	176	240
5	28	1946	Gilberton; pgs. 60-64 rearranged/ illos added; CC-r	1	1	14	28	42	81	118	155
6	51	–	LDC-r	1	1	9	18	27	47	61	75
7	71	–	LDC-r	1	1	6	12	18	29	36	42
8	87	–	C-price 15¢; LDC-r	1	1	6	12	18	27	33	38
9	161	–	New-c&a; PC-r	2	2	7	14	21	37	46	55
10	167	9/63	PC-r	2	2	2	4	6	11	16	20
11	167	12/65	PC-r	2	2	2	4	6	11	16	20
12	166	R/1968	New-c & price 25¢; PC-r	2	3	3	6	9	17	26	35

10. Robinson Crusoe (Used in **SOTI**, pg. 142)

Ed	HRN	Date	Details	A	C	GD 2.0	VG 4.0	FN 6.0	VF 8.0	VF/NM 9.0	NM- 9.2
1A	(O)	4/43	Original; Violet-c; 68 pgs; Zuckerberg c/a	1	1	86	172	258	546	936	1325
1B	(O)	4/43	Original; blue-grey-c, 68 pgs.	1	1	94	188	282	597	1024	1450
2A	14	–	Elliot Pub; violet-c;	1	1	29	58	87	170	278	385

Ed	HRN	Date	Details	A	C	GD 2.0	VG 4.0	FN 6.0	VF 8.0	VF/NM 9.0	NM- 9.2
			68 pgs; CC-r								
2B	14	–	Elliot Pub; blue-grey-c; CC-r	1	1	25	50	75	147	241	335
3	18	–	Nassau Bul. Pg. 64 changed from Gift Box ad to Bill of Rights article; CC-r	1	1	19	38	57	111	176	240
4	20	–	Queens Home News ed.; CC-r	1	1	16	32	48	94	147	200
5	28	1946	Gilberton; pg. 64 changes from Bill of Rights to WWII article-One Leg Shot Away; last CC-r	1	1	14	28	42	80	115	150
6	51	–	LDC-r	1	1	8	16	24	42	54	65
7	64	–	LDC-r	1	1	6	12	18	27	33	38
8	78	–	C-price 15¢; LDC-r	1	1	5	10	14	20	24	28
9	97	–	LDC-r	1	1	4	9	13	18	22	26
10	114	–	LDC-r	1	1	4	7	10	14	17	20
11	130	–	New-c; PC-r	1	2	5	10	15	25	31	36
12	140	–	New-a; PC-r	2	2	5	10	15	24	29	34
13	153	–	PC-r	2	2	2	4	6	8	11	14
14	164	–	PC-r	2	2	2	4	6	8	11	14
15	167	–	PC-r	2	2	2	4	6	8	11	14
16	167	7/64	PC-r	2	2	2	4	6	10	14	18
17	167	5/65	PC-r	2	2	2	4	6	10	14	18
18	167	6/66	PC-r	2	2	2	4	6	8	11	14
19	166	Fall/68	C-price 25¢; PC-r	2	2	2	4	6	8	11	14
20	166	R/68	(No Twin Circle ad)	2	2	2	4	6	9	13	16
21	169	Sm/70	Stiff-c; PC-r	2	2	2	4	6	9	13	16

11. Don Quixote

Ed	HRN	Date	Details	A	C	GD 2.0	VG 4.0	FN 6.0	VF 8.0	VF/NM 9.0	NM- 9.2
1	10	5/43	First (O) with HRN list; 68 pgs.	1	1	89	178	267	565	970	1375
2	18	–	Nassau Bulletin ed.; CC-r	1	1	23	46	69	136	223	310
3	21	–	Queens Home News ed.; CC-r	1	1	19	38	57	111	176	240
4	28	–	CC-r	1	1	14	28	42	81	118	155
5	110	–	New-PC; PC-r	1	2	7	14	21	35	43	50
6	156	–	Pgs. reduced 68 to 52; PC-r	1	2	4	7	10	14	17	20
7	165	–	PC-r	1	2	2	4	6	9	13	16
8	167	1/64	PC-r	1	2	2	4	6	9	13	16
9	167	11/65	PC-r	1	2	2	4	6	9	13	16
10	166	R/1968	New-c & price 25¢; PC-r	1	3	3	6	9	18	27	36

12. Rip Van Winkle and the Headless Horseman

Ed	HRN	Date	Details	A	C	GD 2.0	VG 4.0	FN 6.0	VF 8.0	VF/NM 9.0	NM- 9.2
1	11	6/43	Original; 68 pgs.	1	1	92	184	276	584	1005	1425
2	15	–	Long Isl. Ind. ed.; CC-r	1	1	24	48	72	142	234	325
3	20	–	Long Isl. Ind. ed.;	1	1	20	40	60	114	182	250
4	22	–	Queens Cty. Times ed.; CC-r	1	1	16	32	48	94	147	200
5	28	–	CC-r	1	1	14	28	42	80	115	150
6	60	–	1st LDC-r	1	1	8	16	24	40	50	60
7	62	–	LDC-r	1	1	5	10	15	23	28	32
8	71	–	LDC-r	1	1	4	9	13	18	22	26
9	89	–	C-price 15¢; LDC-r	1	1	4	8	12	17	21	24
10	118	–	LDC-r	1	1	4	7	10	14	17	20
11	132	–	New-c; PC-r	1	2	5	10	15	25	31	36
12	150	–	New-a; PC-r	2	2	5	10	15	24	29	34
13	158	–	PC-r	2	2	2	4	6	9	13	16
14	167	–	PC-r	2	2	2	4	6	9	13	16
15	167	12/63	PC-r	2	2	2	4	6	8	11	14
16	167	4/65	PC-r	2	2	2	4	6	8	11	14
17	167	4/66	PC-r	2	2	2	4	6	8	11	14
18	166	R/1968	New-c&price 25¢; PC-r; stiff-c	2	3	3	6	9	14	20	26
19	169	Sm/70	PC-r; stiff-c	2	3	2	4	6	10	14	18

13. Dr. Jekyll and Mr. Hyde (Used in **SOTI**, pg. 143)(1st horror comic?)

Ed	HRN	Date	Details	A	C	GD 2.0	VG 4.0	FN 6.0	VF 8.0	VF/NM 9.0	NM- 9.2
1	12	8/43	Original 60 pgs.	1	1	148	296	444	947	1624	2300
2	15	–	Long Isl. Ind. ed.; CC-r	1	1	37	74	111	218	354	490
3	20	–	Long Isl. Ind. ed.; CC-r	1	1	25	50	75	150	245	340
4	28	–	No c-price; CC-r	1	1	19	38	57	112	179	245
5	60	–	New-c; Pgs. reduced from 60 to 52; H.C. Kiefer-c; LDC-r	1	2	9	18	27	50	65	80
6	62	–	LDC-r	1	2	6	12	18	28	34	40
7	71	–	LDC-r	1	2	5	10	15	23	28	32
8	87	–	Date returns (erroneous); LDC-r	1	2	5	10	15	22	26	30
9	112	–	New-c&a; PC-r; Cameron-a	2	3	7	14	21	35	43	50
10	153	–	PC-r	2	3	2	4	6	9	13	16
11	161	–	PC-r	2	3	2	4	6	9	13	16
12	167	–	PC-r	2	3	2	4	6	8	11	14
13	167	8/64	PC-r	2	3	2	4	6	8	11	14
14	167	11/65	PC-r	2	3	2	4	6	8	11	14
15	166	R/68	C-price 25¢; PC-r	2	3	2	4	6	8	11	14
16	169	Wn/69	PC-r; stiff-c	2	3	2	4	6	8	11	14

14. Westward Ho!

Ed	HRN	Date	Details	A	C	GD 2.0	VG 4.0	FN 6.0	VF 8.0	VF/NM 9.0	NM- 9.2
1	13	9/43	Original; last outside bc coming-next ad; 60 pgs.	1	1	194	388	582	1242	2121	3000
2	15	–	Long Isl. Ind. ed.; CC-r	1	1	58	116	174	371	636	900
3	21	–	Queens Home News; Pg. 56 changed from coming-next ad to Three Men Named Smith; CC-r	1	1	46	92	138	290	488	685
4	28	1946	Gilberton; Pg. 56 changed again to WWII article-Speaking for America; last CC-r	1	1	39	78	117	242	401	560
5	53	–	Pgs. reduced from 60 to 52; LDC-r	1	1	36	72	108	216	351	485

15. Uncle Tom's Cabin (Used in **SOTI**, pgs. 102, 103)

Ed	HRN	Date	Details	A	C	GD 2.0	VG 4.0	FN 6.0	VF 8.0	VF/NM 9.0	NM- 9.2
1	14	11/43	Original; Outside-bc ad: 2 Gift Boxes; 60 pgs.; color var. on-c; green tree trunk on left & brown trunk, root on left	1	1	87	174	261	553	952	1350
2	15	–	Long Isl. Ind. listed- bottom inside-fc; also Gilberton listed bottom-pg. 1; CC-r; no green tree trunk on cover	1	1	28	56	84	165	270	375
3	21	–	Nassau Bulletin ed.; CC-r has the normal fallen tree trunk & the green fallen tree trunk on cover	1	1	21	42	63	122	199	275
4	28	–	No c-price; CC-r	1	1	15	30	45	85	130	175
5	53	–	Pgs. reduced 60 to 52; LDC-r	1	1	8	16	24	44	57	70
6	71	–	LDC-r	1	1	6	12	18	29	38	42
7	89	–	C-price 15¢; LDC-r	1	1	6	12	18	27	33	38
8	117	–	New-c/lettering changes; PC-r	1	2	6	12	18	28	34	40
9	128	–	'Picture Progress' promo; PC-r	1	2	2	4	6	10	14	18
10	137	–	PC-r	1	2	2	4	6	9	13	16
11	146	–	PC-r	1	2	2	4	6	9	13	16
12	154	–	PC-r	1	2	2	4	6	9	13	16
13	161	–	PC-r	1	2	2	4	6	8	11	14
14	167	–	PC-r	1	2	2	4	6	8	11	14
15	167	6/64	PC-r	1	2	2	4	6	8	11	14
16	167	5/65	PC-r	1	2	2	4	6	8	11	14
17	166	5/67	PC-r	1	2	2	4	6	8	11	14
18	166	Wn/69	New-stiff-c; PC-r	1	3	3	6	9	15	22	28
19	169	Sm/70	PC-r; stiff-c	1	3	2	4	6	10	14	18

16. Gulliver's Travels

Ed	HRN	Date	Details	A	C	GD 2.0	VG 4.0	FN 6.0	VF 8.0	VF/NM 9.0	NM- 9.2
1	15	12/43	Original-Lilian Chestney c/a; 60 pgs.	1	1	81	162	243	518	884	1250
2	18/20	–	Price deleted; Queens Home News ed; CC-r	1	1	22	44	66	128	209	290
3	22	–	Queens Cty. Times ed.; CC-r	1	1	18	36	54	105	165	225
4	28	–	CC-r	1	1	14	28	42	80	115	150
5	60	–	Pgs. reduced to 48; LDC-r	1	1	6	12	18	31	38	45
6	62	–	LDC-r	1	1	5	10	15	23	28	32
7	78	–	C-price 15¢; LDC-r	1	1	5	10	14	20	24	28
8	89	–	LDC-r	1	1	4	8	12	17	21	24
9	155	–	New-c; PC-r	1	2	5	10	15	25	31	36
10	165	–	PC-r	1	2	2	4	6	8	11	14
11	167	5/64	PC-r	1	2	2	4	6	8	11	14
12	167	11/65	PC-r	1	2	2	4	6	8	11	14
13	166	R/1968	C-price 25¢; PC-r	1	2	2	4	6	8	11	14
14	169	Wn/69	PC-r; stiff-c	1	2	2	4	6	8	11	14

17. The Deerslayer

Ed	HRN	Date	Details	A	C	GD 2.0	VG 4.0	FN 6.0	VF 8.0	VF/NM 9.0	NM- 9.2
1	16	1/44	Original; Outside-bc ad: 3 Gift Boxes; 60 pgs.	1	1	68	136	204	435	743	1050
2A	18	–	Queens Cty Times (inside-fc); CC-r	1	1	24	48	72	140	230	320
2B	18	–	Gilberton (bottom-pg. 1); CC-r; Scarce	1	1	34	68	102	199	325	450
3	22	–	Queens Cty. Times ed.; CC-r	1	1	19	38	57	112	179	245
4	28	–	CC-r	1	1	14	28	42	81	118	155
5	60	–	Pgs.reduced to 52; LDC-r	1	1	7	14	21	37	46	55
6	64	–	LDC-r	1	1	5	10	15	22	26	30
7	85	–	C-price 15¢; LDC-r	1	1	4	8	12	17	21	24
8	118	–	LDC-r	1	1	4	7	10	14	17	20
9	132	–	LDC-r	1	1	4	7	10	14	17	20
10	167	11/66	Last LDC-r	1	1	2	4	6	11	16	20
11	166	R/1968	New-c & price 25¢;	1	2	3	6	9	17	26	35

Classic Comics #14 © GIL

Classic Comics #17 © GIL

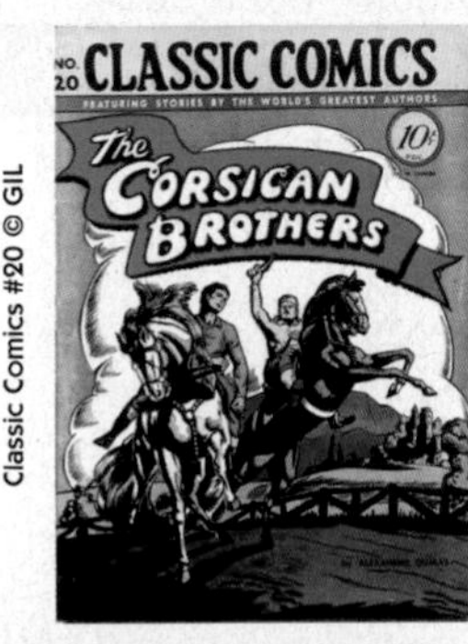

Classic Comics #20 © GIL

Ed	HRN	Date	Details	A	C	GD 2.0	VG 4.0	FN 6.0	VF 8.0	VF/NM 9.0	NM- 9.2
			PC-r								
12	169	Spr/71	Stiff-c; letters from parents & educators; PC-r	1	2	2	4	6	10	14	18

18. The Hunchback of Notre Dame

Ed	HRN	Date	Details	A	C	GD 2.0	VG 4.0	FN 6.0	VF 8.0	VF/NM 9.0	NM- 9.2
1A	17	3/44	Orig.; Gilberton ed; 60 pgs.	1	1	110	220	330	704	1202	1700
1B	17	3/44	Orig.; Island Pub. Ed.; 60 pgs.	1	1	93	186	279	591	1021	1450
2	18/20	–	Queens Home News ed.; CC-r	1	1	29	58	87	170	278	385
3	22	–	Queens Cty. Times ed.; CC-r	1	1	23	46	69	136	223	310
4	28	–	CC-r	1	1	21	42	63	122	199	275
5	60	–	New-c; 8pgs. deleted; Kiefer-c; LDC-r	1	2	9	18	27	50	65	80
6	62	–	LDC-r	1	2	5	10	15	22	26	30
7	78	–	C-price 15¢; LDC-r	1	2	5	10	14	20	24	28
8A	89	–	H.C.Kiefer on bottom right-fc; LDC-r	1	2	4	9	13	18	22	26
8B	89	–	Name omitted; LDC-r	1	2	5	10	15	24	30	35
9	118	–	LDC-r	1	2	4	8	12	17	21	24
10	140	–	New-c; PC-r	1	3	7	14	21	35	43	50
11	146	–	PC-r	1	3	4	9	13	18	22	26
12	158	–	New-c&a; PC-r; Evans/Crandall-a	2	4	5	10	15	25	31	36
13	165	–	PC-r	2	4	2	4	6	9	13	16
14	167	9/63	PC-r	2	4	2	4	6	9	13	16
15	167	10/64	PC-r	2	4	2	4	6	9	13	16
16	167	4/66	PC-r	2	4	2	4	6	8	11	14
17	166	R/1968	New price 25¢; PC-r	2	4	2	4	6	8	11	14
18	169	Sp/70	Stiff-c; PC-r	2	4	2	4	6	8	11	14

19. Huckleberry Finn

Ed	HRN	Date	Details	A	C	GD 2.0	VG 4.0	FN 6.0	VF 8.0	VF/NM 9.0	NM- 9.2
1A	18	4/44	Orig.; Gilberton ed.; 60 pgs.	1	1	57	114	171	362	619	875
1B	18	4/44	Orig.; Island Pub.; 60 pgs.	1	1	60	120	180	381	653	925
2	18	–	Nassau Bulletin ed.; fc-price 15¢-Canada; no coming-next ad; CC-r	1	1	24	48	72	140	230	320
3	22	–	Queens City Times ed.; CC-r	1	1	20	40	60	114	182	250
4	28	–	CC-r	1	1	14	28	42	82	121	160
5	60	–	Pgs. reduced to 48; LDC-r	1	1	6	12	18	31	38	45
6	62	–	LDC-r	1	1	5	10	15	23	28	32
7	78	–	LDC-r	1	1	4	9	13	18	22	26
8	89	–	LDC-r	1	1	4	8	12	17	21	24
9	117	–	LDC-r	1	1	4	7	10	14	17	20
10	131	–	New-c&a; PC-r	2	2	5	10	15	24	30	35
11	140	–	PC-r	2	2	2	4	6	9	13	16
12	150	–	PC-r	2	2	2	4	6	9	13	16
13	158	–	PC-r	2	2	2	4	6	9	13	16
14	165	–	PC-r (scarce)	2	2	3	6	9	14	19	24
15	167	–	PC-r	2	2	2	4	6	8	11	14
16	167	6/64	PC-r	2	2	2	4	6	8	11	14
17	167	6/65	PC-r	2	2	2	4	6	8	11	14
18	167	10/65	PC-r	2	2	2	4	6	8	11	14
19	166	9/67	PC-r	2	2	2	4	6	8	11	14
20	166	Win/69	C-price 25¢; PC-r; stiff-c	2	2	2	4	6	8	11	14
21	169	Sm/70	PC-r; stiff-c	2	2	2	4	6	8	11	14

20. The Corsican Brothers

Ed	HRN	Date	Details	A	C	GD 2.0	VG 4.0	FN 6.0	VF 8.0	VF/NM 9.0	NM- 9.2
1A	20	6/44	Orig.; Gilberton ed.; bc-ad: 4 Gift Boxes; 60 pgs.	1	1	51	102	153	321	546	770
1B	20	6/44	Orig.; Courier ed.; 60 pgs.	1	1	43	86	129	271	461	650
1C	20	6/44	Orig.; Long Island Ind. ed.; 60 pgs.	1	1	43	86	129	271	461	650
2	22	–	Queens Cty. Times ed.; white logo banner; CC-r	1	1	20	40	60	115	190	260
3	28	–	CC-r	1	1	19	38	57	109	172	235
4	60	–	CI logo; no price; 48 pgs.; LDC-r	1	1	15	30	45	90	140	190
5A	62	–	LDC-r; Classics Ill. logo at top of pgs.	1	1	15	30	45	83	124	165
5B	62	–	w/o logo at top of pg. (scarcer)	1	1	15	30	45	86	133	180
6	78	–	C-price 15¢; LDC-r	1	1	14	28	42	81	118	155
7	97	–	LDC-r	1	1	14	28	42	78	112	145

21. 3 Famous Mysteries ("The Sign of the 4", "The Murders in the Rue Morgue", "The Flayed Hand")

Ed	HRN	Date	Details	A	C	GD 2.0	VG 4.0	FN 6.0	VF 8.0	VF/NM 9.0	NM- 9.2
1A	21	7/44	Orig.; Gilberton ed.; 60 pgs.	1	1	106	212	318	673	1162	1650
1B	21	7/44	Orig. Island Pub. Co.; 60 pgs.	1	1	110	220	330	704	1202	1700
1C	21	7/44	Original; Courier Ed.; 60 pgs.	1	1	97	194	291	621	1061	1500
2	22	–	Nassau Bulletin ed.; CC-r	1	1	41	82	123	256	428	600
3	30	–	CC-r	1	1	30	60	90	177	289	400
4	62	–	LDC-r; 8 pgs. deleted; LDC-r	1	1	23	46	69	138	227	315
5	70	–	LDC-r	1	1	21	42	63	126	206	285
6	85	–	C-price 15¢; LDC-r	1	1	20	40	60	114	182	250
7	114	–	New-c; PC-r	1	2	20	40	60	114	182	250

22. The Pathfinder

Ed	HRN	Date	Details	A	C	GD 2.0	VG 4.0	FN 6.0	VF 8.0	VF/NM 9.0	NM- 9.2
1A	22	10/44	Orig.; No printer listed; ownership statement inside fc lists Gilberton & date; 60 pgs.	1	1	50	100	150	315	533	750
1B	22	10/44	Orig.; Island Pub. ed.; 60 pgs.	1	1	48	96	144	302	514	625
1C	22	10/44	Orig.; Queens Cty Times ed. 60 pgs.	1	1	48	96	144	302	514	625
2	30	–	C-price removed; CC-r	1	1	15	30	45	85	130	175
3	60	–	Pgs. reduced to 52; LDC-r	1	1	6	12	18	27	33	38
4	70	–	LDC-r	1	1	5	10	15	22	26	30
5	85	–	C-price 15¢; LDC-r	1	1	4	9	13	18	22	26
6	118	–	LDC-r	1	1	4	8	12	17	21	24
7	132	–	LDC-r	1	1	4	7	10	14	17	20
8	146	–	LDC-r	1	1	4	7	10	14	17	20
9	167	11/63	New-c; PC-r	1	2	4	8	12	23	37	50
10	167	12/65	PC-r	1	2	2	4	6	11	16	20
11	166	8/67	PC-r	1	2	2	4	6	11	16	20

23. Oliver Twist (1st Classic produced by the Iger Shop)

Ed	HRN	Date	Details	A	C	GD 2.0	VG 4.0	FN 6.0	VF 8.0	VF/NM 9.0	NM- 9.2
1	23	7/45	Original; 60 pgs.	1	1	52	104	156	328	552	775
2A	30	–	Printers Union logo on bottom left-fc same as 23(Orig.) (very rare); CC-r	1	1	31	62	93	184	300	415
2B	30	–	Union logo omitted; CC-r	1	1	15	30	45	84	127	170
3	60	–	Pgs. reduced to 48; LDC-r	1	1	6	12	18	29	36	42
4	62	–	LDC-r	1	1	5	10	15	23	28	32
5	71	–	LDC-r	1	1	5	10	14	20	24	28
6	85	–	C-price 15¢; LDC-r	1	1	4	9	13	18	22	26
7	94	–	LDC-r	1	1	4	7	10	14	17	20
8	118	–	LDC-r	1	1	4	7	10	14	17	20
9	136	–	New-PC, old-a; PC-r	1	2	5	10	15	24	30	35
10	150	–	Old-a; PC-r	1	2	4	7	10	14	17	20

(continued)

Ed	HRN	Date	Details	A	C	GD 2.0	VG 4.0	FN 6.0	VF 8.0	VF/NM 9.0	NM- 9.2
11	164	–	Old-a; PC-r	1	2	4	8	11	16	19	22
12	164	–	New-a; PC-r; Evans/Crandall-a	2	2	4	8	12	23	37	50
13	167	–	PC-r	2	2	2	4	6	11	16	20
14	167	8/64	PC-r	2	2	2	4	6	8	11	14
15	167	12/65	PC-r	2	2	2	4	6	8	11	14
16	166	R/1968	New 25¢; PC-r	2	2	2	4	6	8	11	14
17	169	Win/69	Stiff-c; PC-r	2	2	2	4	6	8	11	14

24. A Connecticut Yankee in King Arthur's Court

Ed	HRN	Date	Details	A	C	GD 2.0	VG 4.0	FN 6.0	VF 8.0	VF/NM 9.0	NM- 9.2
1	–	9/45	Original	1	1	47	94	141	296	498	700
2	30	–	No price circle; CC-r	1	1	15	30	45	90	140	190
3	60	–	8 pgs. deleted; LDC-r	1	1	6	12	18	27	33	38
4	62	–	LDC-r	1	1	5	10	15	23	28	32
5	71	–	LDC-r	1	1	5	10	15	22	26	30
6	87	–	C-price 15¢; LDC-r	1	1	4	9	13	18	22	26
7	121	–	LDC-r	1	1	4	8	12	17	21	24
8	140	–	New-c&a; PC-r	2	2	5	10	15	25	31	36
9	153	–	PC-r	2	2	2	4	6	9	13	16
10	164	–	PC-r	2	2	2	4	6	8	11	14
11	167	–	PC-r	2	2	2	4	6	8	11	14
12	167	7/64	PC-r	2	2	2	4	6	8	11	14
13	167	6/66	PC-r	2	2	2	4	6	8	11	14
14	166	R/1968	C-price 25¢; PC-r	2	2	2	4	6	8	11	14
15	169	Spr/71	PC-r; stiff-c	2	2	2	4	6	8	11	14

25. Two Years Before the Mast

Ed	HRN	Date	Details	A	C	GD 2.0	VG 4.0	FN 6.0	VF 8.0	VF/NM 9.0	NM- 9.2
1	–	10/45	Original; Webb/Heames-a&c	1	1	43	86	129	271	461	650
2	30	–	Price circle blank; CC-r	1	1	15	30	45	86	133	180
3	60	–	8 pgs. deleted; LDC-r	1	1	6	12	18	27	33	38
4	62	–	LDC-r	1	1	5	10	15	23	28	32
5	71	–	LDC-r	1	1	4	9	13	18	22	26
6	85	–	C-price 15¢; LDC-r	1	1	4	8	12	17	21	24
7	114	–	LDC-r	1	1	4	7	10	14	17	20
8	156	–	3 pgs. replaced by fillers; new-c; PC-r	1	2	5	10	15	25	31	36
9	167	12/63	PC-r	1	2	2	4	6	8	11	14
10	167	12/65	PC-r	1	2	2	4	6	8	11	14
11	166	9/67	PC-r	1	2	2	4	6	8	11	14
12	169	Win/69	C-price 25¢; stiff-c PC-r	1	2	2	4	6	8	11	14

26. Frankenstein (2nd horror comic?)

Ed	HRN	Date	Details	A	C	GD 2.0	VG 4.0	FN 6.0	VF 8.0	VF/NM 9.0	NM- 9.2
1	26	12/45	Orig.; Webb/Brewster a&c; 52 pgs.	1	1	135	270	405	864	1482	2100
2A	30	–	Price circle blank; no indicia; CC-r	1	1	37	74	111	222	361	500
2B	30	–	With indicia; scarce; CC-r	1	1	40	80	120	244	402	560
3	60	–	LDC-r	1	1	19	38	57	109	172	235
4	62	–	LDC-r	1	1	16	32	48	96	151	205
5	71	–	LDC-r	1	1	9	18	27	47	61	75
6A	82	–	C-price 15¢; soft-c LDC-r	1	1	8	16	24	42	54	65
6B	82	–	Stiff-c; LDC-r	1	1	9	18	27	47	61	75
7	117	–	LDC-r	1	1	5	10	15	22	26	30
8	146	–	New Saunders-c; PC-r	1	2	6	12	18	31	38	45
9	152	–	Scarce; PC-r	1	2	8	16	24	44	57	70
10	153	–	PC-r	1	2	2	4	6	10	14	18
11	160	–	PC-r	1	2	2	4	6	10	14	18
12	165	–	PC-r	1	2	2	4	6	9	13	16
13	167	–	PC-r	1	2	2	4	6	9	13	16
14	167	6/64	PC-r	1	2	2	4	6	9	13	16
15	167	6/65	PC-r	1	2	2	4	6	9	13	16
16	167	10/65	PC-r	1	2	2	4	6	9	13	16
17	166	9/67	PC-r	1	2	2	4	6	9	13	16
18	169	Fall/69	C-price 25¢; stiff-c PC-r	1	2	2	4	6	9	13	16
19	169	Spr/71	PC-r; stiff-c	1	2	2	4	6	9	13	16

27. The Adventures of Marco Polo

Ed	HRN	Date	Details	A	C	GD 2.0	VG 4.0	FN 6.0	VF 8.0	VF/NM 9.0	NM- 9.2
1	–	4/46	Original	1	1	45	90	135	284	480	675
2	30	–	Last 'Comics' reprint; CC-r	1	1	15	30	45	90	140	190
3	70	–	8 pgs. deleted; no c-price; LDC-r	1	1	5	10	15	24	30	35
4	87	–	C-price 15¢; LDC-r	1	1	4	9	13	18	22	26
5	117	–	LDC-r	1	1	4	7	10	14	17	20
6	154	–	New-c; PC-r	1	2	5	10	15	24	30	35
7	165	–	PC-r	1	2	2	4	6	8	11	14
8	167	4/64	PC-r	1	2	2	4	6	8	11	14
9	167	6/66	PC-r	1	2	2	4	6	8	11	14
10	169	Spr/69	New price 25¢; stiff-c; PC-r	1	2	2	4	6	8	11	14

28. Michael Strogoff

Ed	HRN	Date	Details	A	C	GD 2.0	VG 4.0	FN 6.0	VF 8.0	VF/NM 9.0	NM- 9.2
1	–	6/46	Original	1	1	42	84	126	265	445	625
2	51	–	8 pgs. cut; LDC-r	1	1	15	30	45	86	133	180
3	115	–	New-c; PC-r	1	2	6	12	18	31	38	45
4	155	–	PC-r	1	2	4	7	10	14	17	20
5	167	11/63	PC-r	1	2	2	4	6	9	13	16
6	167	7/66	PC-r	1	2	2	4	6	9	13	16
7	169	Sm/69	C-price 25¢; stiff-c PC-r	1	3	3	6	9	15	21	26

29. The Prince and the Pauper

Ed	HRN	Date	Details	A	C	GD 2.0	VG 4.0	FN 6.0	VF 8.0	VF/NM 9.0	NM- 9.2
1	–	7/46	Orig.; "Horror"-c	1	1	65	130	195	416	708	1000
2	60	–	8 pgs. cut; new-c by Kiefer; LDC-r	1	2	10	20	30	46	76	95
3	62	–	LDC-r	1	2	5	10	15	24	30	35
4	71	–	LDC-r	1	2	4	9	13	18	22	26
5	93	–	LDC-r	1	2	4	8	12	17	21	24
6	114	–	LDC-r	1	2	4	7	10	14	17	20
7	128	–	New-c; PC-r	1	3	5	10	15	24	30	35
8	138	–	PC-r	1	3	2	4	6	9	13	16
9	150	–	PC-r	1	3	2	4	6	9	13	16
10	164	–	PC-r	1	3	2	4	6	8	11	14
11	167	–	PC-r	1	3	2	4	6	8	11	14
12	167	7/64	PC-r	1	3	2	4	6	8	11	14
13	167	11/65	PC-r	1	3	2	4	6	8	11	14
14	166	R/68	C-price 25¢; PC-r	1	3	2	4	6	8	11	14
15	169	Sm/70	PC-r; stiff-c	1	3	2	4	6	8	11	14

30. The Moonstone

Ed	HRN	Date	Details	A	C	GD 2.0	VG 4.0	FN 6.0	VF 8.0	VF/NM 9.0	NM- 9.2
1	–	9/46	Original; Rico-c/a	1	1	42	84	126	265	445	625
2	60	–	LDC-r; 8pgs. cut	1	1	9	18	27	52	69	85
3	70	–	LDC-r	1	1	8	16	24	42	54	65
4	155	–	New L.B. Cole-c; PC-r	1	2	4	8	12	28	44	60
5	165	–	PC-r; L.B. Cole-c	1	2	3	6	9	16	23	30
6	167	1/64	PC-r; L.B. Cole-c	1	2	2	4	6	11	16	20
7	167	9/65	PC-r; L.B. Cole-c	1	2	2	4	6	10	14	18
8	166	R/1968	C-price 25¢; PC-r	1	2	2	4	6	9	13	16

31. The Black Arrow

Ed	HRN	Date	Details	A	C	GD 2.0	VG 4.0	FN 6.0	VF 8.0	VF/NM 9.0	NM- 9.2
1	30	10/46	Original	1	1	40	80	120	246	411	575
2	51	–	CI logo; LDC-r 8pgs. deleted	1	1	7	14	21	37	46	55
3	64	–	LDC-r	1	1	5	10	14	20	24	28
4	87	–	C-price 15¢; LDC-r	1	1	4	8	12	17	21	24
5	108	–	LDC-r	1	1	4	7	10	14	17	20
6	125	–	LDC-r	1	1	4	7	10	14	17	20
7	131	–	New-c; PC-r	1	2	6	12	18	28	34	40
8	140	–	PC-r	1	2	2	4	6	9	13	16
9	148	–	PC-r	1	2	2	4	6	9	13	16
10	161	–	PC-r	1	2	2	4	6	8	11	14
11	167	–	PC-r	1	2	2	4	6	8	11	14
12	167	7/64	PC-r	1	2	2	4	6	8	11	14
13	167	11/65	PC-r	1	2	2	4	6	8	11	14
14	166	R/1968	C-price 25¢; PC-r	1	2	2	4	6	8	11	14

32. Lorna Doone

Ed	HRN	Date	Details	A	C	GD 2.0	VG 4.0	FN 6.0	VF 8.0	VF/NM 9.0	NM- 9.2
1	–	12/46	Original; Matt Baker c&a	1	1	55	110	165	352	601	850
2	53/64	–	8 pgs. deleted; LDC-r	1	1	10	20	30	56	76	95
3	85	1951	C-price 15¢; LDC-r; Baker c&a	1	1	8	16	24	42	54	65
4	118	–	LDC-r	1	1	5	10	15	22	26	30
5	138	–	New-c; old-c becomes new title pg.; PC-r	1	2	6	12	18	31	38	45
6	150	–	PC-r	1	2	2	4	6	8	11	14
7	165	–	PC-r	1	2	2	4	6	8	11	14
8	167	1/64	PC-r	1	2	2	4	6	9	13	16
9	167	11/65	PC-r	1	2	2	4	6	9	13	16
10	166	R/1968	New-c; PC-r	1	3	3	6	9	16	24	32

33. The Adventures of Sherlock Holmes

Ed	HRN	Date	Details	A	C	GD 2.0	VG 4.0	FN 6.0	VF 8.0	VF/NM 9.0	NM- 9.2
1	33	1/47	Original; Kiefer-c; contains Study in Scarlet & Hound of the Baskervilles; 68 pgs.	1	1	139	278	417	883	1517	2150
2	53	–	"A Study in Scarlet" (17 pgs.) deleted; LDC-r	1	1	50	100	150	315	533	750
3	71	–	LDC-r	1	1	39	78	117	231	378	525
4A	89	–	C-price 15¢; LDC-r	1	1	30	60	90	117	289	400
4B	89	–	Kiefer's name omitted from-c	1	1	31	62	93	186	303	420

34. Mysterious Island (Last "Classic Comics" issue)

Ed	HRN	Date	Details	A	C	GD 2.0	VG 4.0	FN 6.0	VF 8.0	VF/NM 9.0	NM- 9.2
1	35	2/47	Original; Webb/Heames-c/a	1	1	41	82	123	256	428	600
2	60	–	8 pgs. deleted; LDC-r	1	1	7	14	21	37	46	55
3	62	–	LDC-r	1	1	5	10	15	23	28	32
4	71	–	LDC-r	1	1	6	12	18	31	38	45
5	78	–	C-price 15¢ in circle; LDC-r	1	1	5	10	14	20	24	28
6	92	–	LDC-r	1	1	4	9	13	18	22	26
7	117	–	LDC-r	1	1	4	7	10	14	17	20
8	140	–	New-c; PC-r	1	2	5	10	15	24	30	35

Classic Comics #26 © GIL

Classic Comics #33 © GIL

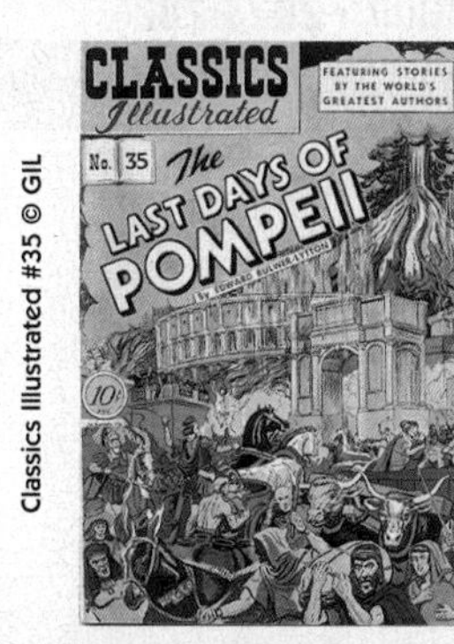

Classics Illustrated #35 © GIL

Ed	HRN	Date	Details	A	C	GD 2.0	VG 4.0	FN 6.0	VF 8.0	VF/NM 9.0	NM- 9.2
9	156	–	PC-r	1	2	2	4	6	9	13	16
10	167	10/63	PC-r	1	2	2	4	6	8	11	14
11	167	5/64	PC-r	1	2	2	4	6	8	11	14
12	167	6/66	PC-r	1	2	2	4	6	8	11	14
13	166	R/1968	C-price 25¢; PC-r	1	2	2	4	6	8	11	14

35. Last Days of Pompeii (First "Classics Illustrated")

Ed	HRN	Date	Details	A	C	GD 2.0	VG 4.0	FN 6.0	VF 8.0	VF/NM 9.0	NM- 9.2
1	35	3/47	Original; LDC; Kiefer-c/a	1	1	41	82	123	256	428	600
2	161	–	New c&a; 15¢; PC-r; Kirby/Ayers-a	2	2	5	10	15	31	53	75
3	167	1/64	PC-r	2	2	3	6	9	16	22	28
4	167	7/66	PC-r	2	2	3	6	9	16	22	28
5	169	Spr/70	New price 25¢; stiff-c; PC-r	2	2	3	6	9	16	22	28

36. Typee

Ed	HRN	Date	Details	A	C	GD 2.0	VG 4.0	FN 6.0	VF 8.0	VF/NM 9.0	NM- 9.2
1	36	4/47	Original	1	1	33	66	99	194	317	440
2	64	–	No c-price; 8 pg. ed.; LDC-r	1	1	8	16	24	42	54	65
3	155	–	New-c; PC-r	1	2	6	12	18	28	34	40
4	167	9/63	PC-r	1	2	2	4	6	9	13	16
5	167	7/65	PC-r	1	2	2	4	6	9	13	16
6	169	Sm/69	C-price 25¢; stiff-c PC-r	1	2	2	4	6	9	13	16

37. The Pioneers

Ed	HRN	Date	Details	A	C	GD 2.0	VG 4.0	FN 6.0	VF 8.0	VF/NM 9.0	NM- 9.2
1	37	5/47	Original; Palais-c/a	1	1	31	62	93	182	296	410
2A	62	–	8 pgs. cut; LDC-r; price circle blank	1	1	6	12	18	31	38	45
2B	62	–	10¢; LDC-r;	1	1	31	62	93	184	300	415
3	70	–	LDC-r	1	1	4	8	12	17	21	24
4	92	–	15¢; LDC-r	1	1	4	8	11	16	19	22
5	118	–	LDC-r	1	1	4	7	10	14	17	20
6	131	–	LDC-r	1	1	4	7	10	14	17	20
7	132	–	LDC-r	1	1	4	7	10	14	17	20
8	153	–	LDC-r	1	1	4	7	10	14	17	20
9	167	5/64	LDC-r	1	1	2	4	6	9	13	16
10	167	6/66	LDC-r	1	1	2	4	6	9	13	16
11	166	R/1968	New-c; 25¢; PC-r	1	2	3	6	9	18	27	36

38. Adventures of Cellini

Ed	HRN	Date	Details	A	C	GD 2.0	VG 4.0	FN 6.0	VF 8.0	VF/NM 9.0	NM- 9.2
1	–	6/47	Original; Froehlich c/a	1	1	32	64	96	192	314	435
2	164	–	New-c&a; PC-r	2	2	3	6	9	18	27	36
3	167	12/63	PC-r	2	2	2	4	6	10	14	18
4	167	7/66	PC-r	2	2	2	4	6	10	14	18
5	169	Spr/70	Stiff-c; new price 25¢; PC-r	2	2	2	4	6	11	16	20

39. Jane Eyre

Ed	HRN	Date	Details	A	C	GD 2.0	VG 4.0	FN 6.0	VF 8.0	VF/NM 9.0	NM- 9.2
1	–	7/47	Original	1	1	32	64	96	190	310	430
2	60	–	No c-price; 8 pgs. cut; LDC-r	1	1	7	14	21	35	43	50
3	62	–	LDC-r	1	1	5	10	15	24	30	35
4	71	–	LDC-r; c-price 10¢	1	1	5	10	15	22	26	30
5	92	–	C-price 15¢; LDC-r	1	1	4	9	13	18	22	26
6	118	–	LDC-r	1	1	4	8	12	17	21	24
7	142	–	New-c; old-a; PC-r	1	2	6	12	18	28	34	40
8	154	–	Old-a; PC-r	1	2	4	8	12	17	21	24
9	165	–	New-a; PC-r	2	2	3	6	9	17	26	35
10	167	12/63	PC-r	2	2	3	6	9	14	19	24
11	167	4/65	PC-r	2	2	2	4	6	13	18	22
12	167	8/66	PC-r	2	2	2	4	6	13	18	22
13	166	R/1968	New-c; PC-r	2	3	5	10	15	31	53	75

40. Mysteries ("The Pit and the Pendulum", "The Advs. of Hans Pfall" & "The Fall of the House of Usher")

Ed	HRN	Date	Details	A	C	GD 2.0	VG 4.0	FN 6.0	VF 8.0	VF/NM 9.0	NM- 9.2
1	40	8/47	Original; Kiefer-c/a, Froehlich, Griffiths-a	1	1	63	126	189	403	689	975
2	62	–	LDC-r; 8pgs. cut	1	1	26	52	78	154	252	350
3	75	–	LDC-r	1	1	20	40	60	115	185	255
4	92	–	C-price 15¢; LDC-r	1	1	17	34	51	100	158	215

41. Twenty Years After

Ed	HRN	Date	Details	A	C	GD 2.0	VG 4.0	FN 6.0	VF 8.0	VF/NM 9.0	NM- 9.2
1	–	9/47	Original; 'horror'-c	1	1	39	78	117	235	385	535
2	62	–	New-c; no c-price 8 pgs. cut; LDC-r; Kiefer-c	1	2	7	14	21	37	46	55
3	78	–	C-price 15¢; LDC-r	1	2	5	10	15	23	28	32
4	156	–	New-c; PC-r	1	3	5	10	15	24	30	35
5	167	12/63	PC-r	1	3	2	4	6	8	11	14
6	167	11/66	PC-r	1	3	2	4	6	8	11	14
7	169	Spr/70	New price 25¢; stiff-c; PC-r	1	3	2	4	6	8	11	14

42. Swiss Family Robinson

Ed	HRN	Date	Details	A	C	GD 2.0	VG 4.0	FN 6.0	VF 8.0	VF/NM 9.0	NM- 9.2
1	42	10/47	Orig.; Kiefer-c&a;	1	1	30	60	90	177	289	400
2A	62	–	8 pgs. cut; outside bc: Gift Box ad; LDC-r	1	1	7	14	21	37	46	55
2B	62	–	8 pgs. cut; outside-bc: Reorder list; scarce; LDC-r	1	1	14	28	42	82	121	160
3	75	–	LDC-r	1	1	5	10	14	20	24	28
4	93	–	LDC-r	1	1	5	10	14	20	24	28
5	117	–	LDC-r	1	1	3	6	9	14	19	24
6	131	–	New-c; old-a; PC-r	1	2	3	6	9	15	21	26
7	137	–	Old-a; PC-r	1	2	2	4	6	10	14	18
8	141	–	Old-a; PC-r	1	2	2	4	6	10	14	18
9	152	–	New-a; PC-r	2	2	3	6	9	16	23	30
10	158	–	PC-r	2	2	2	4	6	8	11	14
11	165	–	PC-r	2	2	3	6	9	16	24	32
12	167	12/63	PC-r	2	2	2	4	6	8	11	14
13	167	4/65	PC-r	2	2	2	4	6	8	11	14
14	167	5/66	PC-r	2	2	2	4	6	8	11	14
15	166	11/67	PC-r	2	2	2	4	6	8	11	14
16	169	Spr/69	PC-r; stiff-c	2	2	2	4	6	8	11	14

43. Great Expectations (Used in **SOTI**, pg. 311)

Ed	HRN	Date	Details	A	C	GD 2.0	VG 4.0	FN 6.0	VF 8.0	VF/NM 9.0	NM- 9.2
1	43	11/47	Original; Kiefer-a/c	1	1	94	188	282	597	1025	1450
2	62	–	No c-price; 8 pgs. cut; LDC-r	1	1	58	116	174	371	636	900

44. Mysteries of Paris (Used in **SOTI**, pg. 323)

Ed	HRN	Date	Details	A	C	GD 2.0	VG 4.0	FN 6.0	VF 8.0	VF/NM 9.0	NM- 9.2
1A	44	12/47	Original; 56 pgs.; Kiefer-c/a	1	1	68	136	204	435	743	1050
1B	44	12/47	Orig.; printed on white/heavier paper; (rare)	1	1	77	154	231	493	847	1200
2A	62	–	8 pgs. cut; outside-bc: Gift Box ad; LDC-r	1	1	30	60	90	177	289	400
2B	62	–	8 pgs. cut; outside-bc: reorder list; LDC-r	1	1	30	60	90	177	289	400
3	78	–	C-price 15¢; LDC-r	1	1	25	50	75	147	241	335

45. Tom Brown's School Days

Ed	HRN	Date	Details	A	C	GD 2.0	VG 4.0	FN 6.0	VF 8.0	VF/NM 9.0	NM- 9.2
1	44	1/48	Original; 1st 48pg. issue	1	1	21	42	63	122	199	275
2	64	–	No c-price; LDC-r	1	1	8	16	24	40	50	60
3	161	–	New-c&a; PC-r	2	2	3	6	9	17	26	35
4	167	2/64	PC-r	2	2	2	4	6	9	13	16
5	167	8/66	PC-r	2	2	2	4	6	9	13	16
6	166	R/1968	C-price 25¢; PC-r	2	2	2	4	6	9	13	16

46. Kidnapped

Ed	HRN	Date	Details	A	C	GD 2.0	VG 4.0	FN 6.0	VF 8.0	VF/NM 9.0	NM- 9.2
1	47	4/48	Original; Webb-c/a	1	1	22	44	66	132	216	300
2A	62	–	Price circle blank; LDC-r	1	1	8	16	24	40	50	60
2B	62	–	C-price 10¢; rare; LDC-r	1	1	33	66	99	194	317	440
3	78	–	C-price 15¢; LDC-r	1	1	5	10	14	20	24	28
4	87	–	LDC-r	1	1	4	9	13	18	22	26

Ed	HRN	Date	Details	A	C	GD 2.0	VG 4.0	FN 6.0	VF 8.0	VF/NM 9.0	NM- 9.2
5	118	–	LDC-r	1	1	4	7	10	14	17	20
6	131	–	New-c; PC-r	1	2	5	10	15	23	28	32
7	140	–	PC-r	1	2	2	4	6	9	13	16
8	150	–	PC-r	1	2	2	4	6	9	13	16
9	164	–	Reduced pg.width; PC-r	1	2	2	4	6	8	11	14
10	167	–	PC-r	1	2	2	4	6	8	11	14
11	167	3/64	PC-r	1	2	2	4	6	8	11	14
12	167	6/65	PC-r	1	2	2	4	6	8	11	14
13	167	12/65	PC-r	1	2	2	4	6	8	11	14
14	166	9/67	PC-r	1	2	2	4	6	8	11	14
15	166	Win/69	New price 25¢; PC-r; stiff-c	1	2	2	4	6	8	11	14
16	169	Sm/70	PC-r; stiff-c	1	2	2	4	6	8	11	14

47. Twenty Thousand Leagues Under the Sea

Ed	HRN	Date	Details	A	C	GD	VG	FN	VF	VF/NM	NM-
1	47	5/48	Orig.; Kiefer-a&c;	1	1	23	46	69	136	223	310
2	64	–	No c-price; LDC-r	1	1	6	12	18	31	38	45
3	78	–	C-price 15¢; LDC-r	1	1	4	9	13	18	22	26
4	94	–	LDC-r	1	1	4	8	12	17	21	24
5	118	–	LDC-r	1	1	4	7	10	14	17	20
6	128	–	New-c; PC-r	1	2	5	10	15	24	30	35
7	133	–	PC-r	1	2	2	4	6	10	14	18
8	140	–	PC-r	1	2	2	4	6	9	13	16
9	148	–	PC-r	1	2	2	4	6	9	13	16
10	156	–	PC-r	1	2	2	4	6	9	13	16
11	165	–	PC-r	1	2	2	4	6	9	13	16
12	167	–	PC-r	1	2	2	4	6	9	13	16
13	167	3/64	PC-r	1	2	2	4	6	9	13	16
14	167	8/65	PC-r	1	2	2	4	6	9	13	16
15	167	10/66	PC-r	1	2	2	4	6	9	13	16
16	166	R/1968	C-price 25¢; new-c PC-r	1	3	3	6	9	15	22	28
17	169	Spr/70	Stiff-c; PC-r	1	3	2	4	6	13	18	22

48. David Copperfield

Ed	HRN	Date	Details	A	C	GD	VG	FN	VF	VF/NM	NM-
1	47	6/48	Original; Kiefer-c/a	1	1	21	42	63	126	206	285
2	64	–	Price circle replaced by motif of boy reading; LDC-r	1	1	6	12	18	31	38	45
3	87	–	C-price 15¢; LDC-r	1	1	4	8	12	17	21	24
4	121	–	New-c; PC-r	1	2	5	10	15	22	26	30
5	130	–	PC-r	1	2	2	4	6	9	13	16
6	140	–	PC-r	1	2	2	4	6	9	13	16
7	148	–	PC-r	1	2	2	4	6	9	13	16
8	156	–	PC-r	1	2	2	4	6	9	13	16
9	167	–	PC-r	1	2	2	4	6	8	11	14
10	167	4/64	PC-r	1	2	2	4	6	8	11	14
11	167	6/65	PC-r	1	2	2	4	6	8	11	14
12	166	5/67	PC-r	1	2	2	4	6	8	11	14
13	166	R/67	PC-r; C-price 25¢	1	2	2	4	6	10	14	18
14	166	Spr/69	C-price 25¢; stiff-c PC-r	1	2	2	4	6	8	11	14
15	169	Win/69	Stiff-c; PC-r	1	2	2	4	6	8	11	14

49. Alice in Wonderland

Ed	HRN	Date	Details	A	C	GD	VG	FN	VF	VF/NM	NM-
1	47	7/48	Original; 1st Blum a & c	1	1	36	72	108	211	343	475
2	64	–	No c-price; LDC-r	1	1	9	18	27	47	61	75
3A	85	–	C-price 15¢; soft-c LDC-r	1	1	8	16	24	40	50	60
3B	85	–	Stiff-c; LDC-r	1	1	8	16	24	42	54	65
4	155	–	New PC, similar to orig.; PC-r	1	2	4	8	12	27	44	60
5	165	–	PC-r	1	2	3	6	9	18	28	38
6	167	3/64	PC-r	1	2	3	6	9	16	24	32
7	167	6/66	PC-r	1	2	4	8	12	28	47	65
8A	166	Fall/68	New-c; soft-c; 25¢ c-price; PC-r	1	3	4	8	12	27	44	60
8B	166	Fall/68	New-c; stiff-c; 25¢ c-price; PC-r	1	3	7	14	21	44	82	120

50. Adventures of Tom Sawyer (Used in **SOTI**, pg. 37)

Ed	HRN	Date	Details	A	C	GD	VG	FN	VF	VF/NM	NM-
1A	51	8/48	Orig.; Aldo Rubano a&c	1	1	21	42	63	122	199	275
1B	51	9/48	Orig.; Rubano c&a	1	1	21	42	63	122	199	275
1C	51	9/48	Orig.; outside-bc: blue & yellow only; rare	1	1	27	54	81	160	263	365
2	64	–	No c-price; LDC-r	1	1	5	10	15	23	28	32
3	78	–	C-price 15¢; LDC-r	1	1	4	8	12	17	21	24
4	94	–	LDC-r	1	1	4	7	10	14	17	20
5	117	–	LDC-r	1	1	2	4	6	10	14	18
6	132	–	LDC-r	1	1	2	4	6	10	14	18
7	140	–	New-c; PC-r	1	2	3	6	9	17	26	35
8	150	–	PC-r	1	2	2	4	6	9	13	16
9	164	–	New-a; PC-r	2	2	3	6	9	17	26	35
10	167	–	PC-r	2	2	2	4	6	9	13	16
11	167	1/65	PC-r	2	2	2	4	6	8	11	14
12	167	5/66	PC-r	2	2	2	4	6	8	11	14
13	166	12/67	PC-r	2	2	2	4	6	8	11	14
14	169	Fall/69	C-price 25¢; stiff-c; PC-r	2	2	2	4	6	8	11	14
15	169	Win/71	PC-r	2	2	2	4	6	8	11	14

51. The Spy

Ed	HRN	Date	Details	A	C	GD	VG	FN	VF	VF/NM	NM-
1A	51	9/48	Original; inside-bc illo: Christmas Carol	1	1	20	40	60	120	195	270
1B	51	9/48	Original; inside-bc illo: Man in Iron Mask	1	1	20	40	60	120	195	270
1C	51	8/48	Original; outside-bc: full color	1	1	20	40	60	120	195	270
1D	51	8/48	Original; outside-bc: blue & yellow only; scarce	1	1	22	44	66	128	209	290
2	89	–	C-price 15¢; LDC-r	1	1	5	10	14	20	24	28
3	121	–	LDC-r	1	1	4	8	12	17	21	24
4	139	–	New-c; PC-r	1	2	3	6	9	18	27	35
5	156	–	PC-r	1	2	2	4	6	9	13	16
6	167	11/63	PC-r	1	2	2	4	6	8	11	14
7	167	7/66	PC-r	1	2	2	4	6	8	11	14
8A	166	Win/69	C-price 25¢; soft-c; scarce; PC-r	1	2	3	6	9	15	21	26
8B	166	Win/69	C-price 25¢; stiff-c; PC-r	1	2	2	4	6	8	11	14

52. The House of the Seven Gables

Ed	HRN	Date	Details	A	C	GD	VG	FN	VF	VF/NM	NM-
1	53	10/48	Orig.; Griffiths a&c	1	1	22	44	66	132	216	300
2	89	–	C-price 15¢; LDC-r	1	1	6	12	18	28	34	40
3	121	–	LDC-r	1	1	4	8	12	17	21	24
4	142	–	New-c&a; PC-r; Woodbridge-a	2	2	5	10	15	25	31	36
5	156	–	PC-r	2	2	2	4	6	9	13	16
6	165	–	PC-r	2	2	2	4	6	8	11	14
7	167	5/64	PC-r	2	2	2	4	6	9	13	16
8	167	3/66	PC-r	2	2	2	4	6	8	11	14
9	166	R/1968	C-price 25¢; PC-r	2	2	2	4	6	8	11	14
10	169	Spr/70	Stiff-c; PC-r	2	2	2	4	6	8	11	14

53. A Christmas Carol

Ed	HRN	Date	Details	A	C	GD	VG	FN	VF	VF/NM	NM-
1	53	11/48	Original & only ed; Kiefer-c/a	1	1	32	64	96	188	307	425

54. Man in the Iron Mask

Ed	HRN	Date	Details	A	C	GD	VG	FN	VF	VF/NM	NM-
1	55	12/48	Original; Froehlich-a, Kiefer-c	1	1	21	42	63	122	199	275
2	93	–	C-price 15¢; LDC-r	1	1	5	10	15	23	28	32
3A	111	–	(O) logo lettering; scarce; LDC-r	1	1	6	12	18	31	38	45
3B	111	–	New logo as PC; LDC-r	1	1	5	10	15	23	28	32
4	142	–	New-c&a; PC-r	2	2	5	10	15	24	30	35
5	154	–	PC-r	2	2	2	4	6	9	13	16
6	165	–	PC-r	2	2	2	4	6	8	11	14
7	167	5/64	PC-r	2	2	2	4	6	8	11	14
8	167	4/66	PC-r	2	2	2	4	6	8	11	14
9A	166	Win/69	C-price 25¢; soft-c PC-r	2	2	3	6	9	15	21	26
9B	166	Win/69	Stiff-c	2	2	2	4	6	8	11	14

55. Silas Marner (Used in **SOTI**, pgs. 311, 312)

Ed	HRN	Date	Details	A	C	GD	VG	FN	VF	VF/NM	NM-
1	55	1/49	Original-Kiefer-c	1	1	20	40	60	117	189	260
2	75	–	Price circle blank; 'Coming Next' ad; LDC-r	1	1	6	12	18	28	34	40
3	97	–	LDC-r	1	1	3	6	9	14	19	24
4	121	–	New-c; PC-r	1	2	3	6	9	18	27	35
5	130	–	PC-r	1	2	2	4	6	9	13	16
6	140	–	PC-r	1	2	2	4	6	9	13	16
7	154	–	PC-r	1	2	2	4	6	9	13	16
8	165	–	PC-r	1	2	2	4	6	8	11	14
9	167	2/64	PC-r	1	2	2	4	6	8	11	14
10	167	6/65	PC-r	1	2	2	4	6	8	11	14
11	166	5/67	PC-r	1	2	2	4	6	8	11	14
12A	166	Win/69	C-price 25¢; soft-c PC-r	1	2	3	6	9	15	21	26
12B	166	Win/69	C-price 25¢; stiff-c PC-r	1	2	2	4	6	8	11	14

56. The Toilers of the Sea

Ed	HRN	Date	Details	A	C	GD	VG	FN	VF	VF/NM	NM-
1	55	2/49	Original; A.M. Froehlich-c/a	1	1	27	54	81	158	259	360
2	165	–	New-c&a; PC-r; Angelo Torres-a	2	2	8	16	24	44	57	70
3	167	3/64	PC-r	2	2	3	6	9	16	23	30
4	167	10/66	PC-r	2	2	3	6	9	16	23	30

57. The Song of Hiawatha

Ed	HRN	Date	Details	A	C	GD	VG	FN	VF	VF/NM	NM-
1	55	3/49	Original; Alex Blum-c/a	1	1	20	40	60	117	189	260
2	75	–	No c-price w/15¢ sticker; 'Coming Next' ad; LDC-r	1	1	6	12	18	28	34	40
3	94	–	C-price 15¢; LDC-r	1	1	5	10	14	20	24	28
4	118	–	LDC-r	1	1	3	6	9	14	19	24
5	134	–	New-c; PC-r	1	2	3	6	9	17	26	35
6	139	–	PC-r	1	2	2	4	6	9	13	16
7	154	–	PC-r	1	2	2	4	6	9	13	16

Classics Illustrated #49 © GIL

Classics Illustrated #60 © GIL

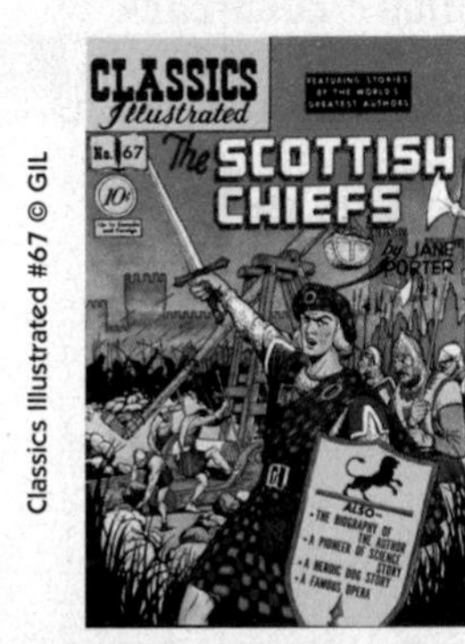

Classics Illustrated #67 © GIL

Ed	HRN	Date	Details	A	C	GD 2.0	VG 4.0	FN 6.0	VF 8.0	VF/NM 9.0	NM- 9.2
8	167	–	Has orig.date; PC-r	1	2	2	4	6	8	11	14
9	167	9/64	PC-r	1	2	2	4	6	8	11	14
10	167	10/65	PC-r	1	2	2	4	6	8	11	14
11	166	F/1968	C-price 25¢; PC-r	1	2	2	4	6	8	11	14
58. The Prairie											
1	60	4/49	Original; Palais c/a	1	1	18	36	54	107	169	230
2A	62	–	No c-price; no coming-next ad; LDC-r	1	1	9	18	27	47	61	75
2B	62		10¢ (rare)	1	1	20	40	60	115	185	255
3	78	–	C-price 15¢ in dbl. circle; LDC-r	1	1	5	10	15	22	26	30
4	114	–	LDC-r	1	1	4	8	12	17	21	24
5	131	–	LDC-r	1	1	4	7	10	14	17	20
6	132	–	LDC-r	1	1	4	7	10	14	17	20
7	146	–	New-c; PC-r	1	2	5	10	15	23	28	32
8	155	–	PC-r	1	2	2	4	6	9	13	16
9	167	5/64	PC-r	1	2	2	4	6	8	11	14
10	167	4/66	PC-r	1	2	2	4	6	8	11	14
11	169	Sm/69	New price 25¢; stiff-c; PC-r	1	2	2	4	6	8	11	14
59. Wuthering Heights											
1	60	5/49	Original; Kiefer-c/a	1	1	20	40	60	114	182	250
2	85	–	C-price 15¢; LDC-r	1	1	6	12	18	31	38	45
3	156	–	New-c; PC-r	1	2	5	10	15	25	31	36
4	167	1/64	PC-r	1	2	2	4	6	9	13	16
5	167	10/66	PC-r	1	2	2	4	6	9	13	16
6	169	Sm/69	C-price 25¢; stiff-c; PC-r	1	2	2	4	6	9	13	16
60. Black Beauty											
1	62	6/49	Original; Froehlich-c/a	1	1	18	36	54	103	162	220
2	62	–	No c-price; no coming-next ad; LDC-r (rare)	1	1	20	40	60	114	182	250
3	85	–	C-price 15¢; LDC-r	1	1	5	10	15	23	28	32
4	158	–	New L.B. Cole-c/a; PC-r	2	2	7	14	21	35	43	50
5	167	2/64	PC-r	2	2	2	4	6	11	16	20
6	167	3/66	PC-r	2	2	2	4	6	11	16	20
7	166	R/1968	New-c&price, 25¢; PC-r	2	3	5	10	15	30	50	70
61. The Woman in White											
1A	62	7/49	Original; Blum-c/a fc-purple; bc: top illos light blue	1	1	21	42	63	126	206	285
1B	62	7/49	Original; Blum-c/a fc-pink; bc: top illos light violet	1	1	21	42	63	126	206	285
2	156	–	New-c; PC-r	1	2	6	12	18	28	34	40
3	167	1/64	PC-r	1	2	2	4	6	11	16	20
4	166	R/1968	C-price 25¢; PC-r	1	2	2	4	6	11	16	20
62. Western Stories ("The Luck of Roaring Camp" and "The Outcasts of Poker Flat")											
1	62	8/49	Original; Kiefer-c/a	1	1	18	36	54	103	162	220
2	89	–	C-price 15¢; LDC-r	1	1	5	10	15	23	28	32
3	121	–	LDC-r	1	1	3	6	9	15	21	26
4	137	–	New-c; PC-r	1	2	3	6	9	17	26	35
5	152	–	PC-r	1	2	2	4	6	8	11	14
6	167	10/63	PC-r	1	2	2	4	6	8	11	14
7	167	6/64	PC-r	1	2	2	4	6	8	11	14
8	167	11/66	PC-r	1	2	2	4	6	8	11	14
9	166	R/1968	New-c&price 25¢; PC-r	1	3	3	6	9	16	24	32
63. The Man Without a Country											
1	62	9/49	Original; Kiefer-c/a	1	1	20	40	60	120	195	270
2	78	–	C-price 15¢ in double circle; LDC-r	1	1	5	10	15	23	28	32
3	156	–	New-c, old-a; PC-r	1	2	6	12	18	28	34	40
4	165	–	New-a & text pgs.; PC-r; A. Torres-a	2	2	5	10	15	23	28	32
5	167	3/64	PC-r	2	2	2	4	6	8	11	14
6	167	8/66	PC-r	2	2	2	4	6	8	11	14
7	169	Sm/69	New price 25¢; stiff-c; PC-r	2	2	2	4	6	8	11	14
64. Treasure Island											
1	62	10/49	Original; Blum-c/a	1	1	20	40	60	120	195	265
2A	82	–	C-price 15¢; soft-c LDC-r	1	1	5	10	15	22	26	30
2B	82	–	Stiff-c; LDC-r	1	1	5	10	15	23	28	32
3	117	–	LDC-r	1	1	3	6	9	15	21	26
4	131	–	New-c; PC-r	1	2	3	6	9	17	26	35
5	138	–	PC-r	1	2	2	4	6	9	13	16
6	146	–	PC-r	1	2	2	4	6	9	13	16
7	158	–	PC-r	1	2	2	4	6	9	13	16
8	165	–	PC-r	1	2	2	4	6	8	11	14
9	167	–	PC-r	1	2	2	4	6	8	11	14
10	167	6/64	PC-r	1	2	2	4	6	8	11	14
11	167	12/65	PC-r	1	2	2	4	6	8	11	14
12A	166	10/67	PC-r	1	2	2	4	6	8	11	14
12B	166	10/67	w/Grit ad stapled in book	1	2	10	20	30	66	138	210
13	169	Spr/69	New price 25¢; stiff-c; PC-r	1	2	2	4	6	9	13	16
14	–	1989	Long John Silver's Seafood Shoppes; $1.95, First/Berkley Publ.; Blum-r	1	2						5.00
65. Benjamin Franklin											
1	64	11/49	Original; Kiefer-c; Iger Shop-a	1	1	20	40	60	114	182	250
2	131	–	New-c; PC-r	1	2	6	12	18	28	34	40
3	154	–	PC-r	1	2	2	4	6	9	13	16
4	167	2/64	PC-r	1	2	2	4	6	9	13	16
5	167	4/66	PC-r	1	2	2	4	6	9	13	16
6	169	Fall/69	New price 25¢; stiff-c; PC-r	1	2	2	4	6	9	13	16
66. The Cloister and the Hearth											
1	67	12/49	Original & only ed; Kiefer-a & c	1	1	36	72	108	216	350	485
67. The Scottish Chiefs											
1	67	1/50	Original; Blum-a&c	1	1	15	30	45	94	147	200
2	85	–	C-price 15¢; LDC-r	1	1	5	10	15	23	28	32
3	118	–	LDC-r	1	1	3	6	9	15	21	26
4	136	–	New-c; PC-r	1	2	3	6	9	18	27	36
5	154	–	PC-r	1	2	2	4	6	9	13	16
6	167	11/63	PC-r	1	2	2	4	6	10	14	18
7	167	8/65	PC-r	1	2	2	4	6	9	13	16
68. Julius Caesar (Used in **SOTI**, pgs. 36, 37)											
1	70	2/50	Original; Kiefer-c/a	1	1	18	36	54	105	165	225
2	85	–	C-price 15¢; LDC-r	1	1	5	10	15	22	26	30
3	108	–	LDC-r	1	1	4	9	13	18	22	26
4	156	–	New L.B. Cole-c; PC-r	1	2	6	12	18	28	34	40
5	165	–	New-a by Evans, Crandall; PC-r	2	2	5	10	15	24	30	35
6	167	2/64	PC-r	2	2	2	4	6	8	11	14
7	167	10/65	Tarzan books inside cover; PC-r	2	2	2	4	6	8	11	14
8	166	R/1967	PC-r	2	2	2	4	6	8	11	14
9	169	Win/69	PC-r; stiff-c	2	2	2	4	6	8	11	14
69. Around the World in 80 Days											
1	70	3/50	Original; Kiefer-c/a	1	1	18	36	54	105	165	225

Ed	HRN	Date	Details	A	C	GD 2.0	VG 4.0	FN 6.0	VF 8.0	VF/NM 9.0	NM- 9.2
2	87	–	C-price 15¢; LDC-r	1	1	5	10	15	22	26	30
3	125	–	LDC-r	1	1	4	9	13	18	22	26
4	136	–	New-c; PC-r	1	2	5	10	15	25	31	36
5	146	–	PC-r	1	2	2	4	6	9	13	16
6	152	–	PC-r	1	2	2	4	6	9	13	16
7	164	–	PC-r	1	2	2	4	6	8	11	14
8	167	–	PC-r	1	2	2	4	6	8	11	14
9	167	7/64	PC-r	1	2	2	4	6	8	11	14
10	167	11/65	PC-r	1	2	2	4	6	8	11	14
11	166	7/67	PC-r	1	2	2	4	6	8	11	14
12	169	Spr/69	C-price 25¢; stiff-c; PC-r	1	2	2	4	6	8	11	14

70. The Pilot

Ed	HRN	Date	Details	A	C	GD 2.0	VG 4.0	FN 6.0	VF 8.0	VF/NM 9.0	NM- 9.2
1	71	4/50	Original; Blum-c/a	1	1	15	30	45	88	137	185
2	92	–	C-price 15¢; LDC-r	1	1	5	10	15	23	28	32
3	125	–	LDC-r	1	1	4	9	13	18	22	26
4	156	–	New-c; PC-r	1	2	6	12	18	28	34	40
5	167	2/64	PC-r	1	2	2	4	6	11	16	20
6	167	5/66	PC-r	1	2	2	4	6	9	13	16

71. The Man Who Laughs

Ed	HRN	Date	Details	A	C	GD 2.0	VG 4.0	FN 6.0	VF 8.0	VF/NM 9.0	NM- 9.2
1	71	5/50	Original; Blum-c/a	1	1	22	44	66	132	216	300
2	165	–	New-c&a; PC-r	2	2	15	30	45	85	130	175
3	167	4/64	PC-r	2	2	12	24	36	69	97	125

72. The Oregon Trail

Ed	HRN	Date	Details	A	C	GD 2.0	VG 4.0	FN 6.0	VF 8.0	VF/NM 9.0	NM- 9.2
1	73	6/50	Original; Kiefer-c/a	1	1	14	28	42	81	118	155
2	89	–	C-price 15¢; LDC-r	1	1	5	10	15	23	28	32
3	121	–	LDC-r	1	1	4	9	13	18	22	26
4	131	–	New-c; PC-r	1	2	5	10	15	25	31	36
5	140	–	PC-r	1	2	2	4	6	9	13	16
6	150	–	PC-r	1	2	2	4	6	9	13	16
7	164	–	PC-r	1	2	2	4	6	8	11	14
8	167	–	PC-r	1	2	2	4	6	8	11	14
9	167	8/64	PC-r	1	2	2	4	6	8	11	14
10	167	10/65	PC-r	1	2	2	4	6	8	11	14
11	166	R/1968	C-price 25¢; PC-r	1	2	2	4	6	8	11	14

73. The Black Tulip

Ed	HRN	Date	Details	A	C	GD 2.0	VG 4.0	FN 6.0	VF 8.0	VF/NM 9.0	NM- 9.2
1	75	7/50	1st & only ed.; Alex Blum-c/a	1	1	39	78	117	236	388	540

74. Mr. Midshipman Easy

Ed	HRN	Date	Details	A	C	GD 2.0	VG 4.0	FN 6.0	VF 8.0	VF/NM 9.0	NM- 9.2
1	75	8/50	1st & only edition	1	1	38	76	114	228	369	510

75. The Lady of the Lake

Ed	HRN	Date	Details	A	C	GD 2.0	VG 4.0	FN 6.0	VF 8.0	VF/NM 9.0	NM- 9.2
1	75	9/50	Original; Kiefer-c/a	1	1	15	30	45	88	137	185
2	85	–	C-price 15¢; LDC-r	1	1	5	10	15	24	30	35
3	118	–	LDC-r	1	1	5	10	14	20	24	28
4	139	–	New-c; PC-r	1	2	5	10	15	25	31	36
5	154	–	PC-r	1	2	2	4	6	9	13	16
6	165	–	PC-r	1	2	2	4	6	8	11	14
7	167	4/64	PC-r	1	2	2	4	6	8	11	14
8	167	5/66	PC-r	1	2	2	4	6	8	11	14
9	169	Spr/69	New price 25¢; stiff-c; PC-r	1	2	2	4	6	8	11	14

76. The Prisoner of Zenda

Ed	HRN	Date	Details	A	C	GD 2.0	VG 4.0	FN 6.0	VF 8.0	VF/NM 9.0	NM- 9.2
1	75	10/50	Original; Kiefer-c/a	1	1	15	30	45	88	137	185
2	85	–	C-price 15¢; LDC-r	1	1	5	10	15	23	28	32
3	111	–	LDC-r	1	1	3	6	9	16	21	26
4	128	–	New-c; PC-r	1	2	3	6	9	17	26	35
5	152	–	PC-r	1	2	2	4	6	9	13	16
6	165	–	PC-r	1	2	2	4	6	8	11	14
7	167	4/64	PC-r	1	2	2	4	6	8	11	14
8	167	9/66	PC-r	1	2	2	4	6	8	11	14
9	169	Fall/69	New price 25¢; stiff-c; PC-r	1	2	2	4	6	8	11	14

77. The Iliad

Ed	HRN	Date	Details	A	C	GD 2.0	VG 4.0	FN 6.0	VF 8.0	VF/NM 9.0	NM- 9.2
1	78	11/50	Original; Blum-c/a	1	1	15	30	45	88	137	185
2	87	–	C-price 15¢; LDC-r	1	1	6	12	18	28	34	40
3	121	–	LDC-r	1	1	3	6	9	15	21	26
4	139	–	New-c; PC-r	1	2	3	6	9	16	24	32
5	150	–	PC-r	1	2	2	4	6	9	13	16
6	165	–	PC-r	1	2	2	4	6	8	11	14
7	167	10/63	PC-r	1	2	2	4	6	8	11	14
8	167	7/64	PC-r	1	2	2	4	6	8	11	14
9	167	5/66	PC-r	1	2	2	4	6	8	11	14
10	166	R/1968	C-price 25¢; PC-r	1	2	2	4	6	8	11	14

78. Joan of Arc

Ed	HRN	Date	Details	A	C	GD 2.0	VG 4.0	FN 6.0	VF 8.0	VF/NM 9.0	NM- 9.2
1	78	12/50	Original; Kiefer-c/a	1	1	15	30	45	88	137	185
2	87	–	C-price 15¢; LDC-r	1	1	5	10	15	23	28	32
3	113	–	LDC-r	1	1	3	6	9	15	21	26
4	128	–	New-c; PC-r	1	2	3	6	9	17	26	35
5	140	–	PC-r	1	2	2	4	6	9	13	16
6	150	–	PC-r	1	2	2	4	6	9	13	16
7	159	–	PC-r	1	2	2	4	6	9	13	16
8	167	–	PC-r	1	2	2	4	6	8	11	14
9	167	12/63	PC-r	1	2	2	4	6	8	11	14
10	167	6/65	PC-r	1	2	2	4	6	8	11	14
11	166	6/67	PC-r	1	2	2	4	6	8	11	14
12	166	Win/69	New-c&price, 25¢; PC-r; stiff-c	1	3	3	6	9	16	24	32

79. Cyrano de Bergerac

Ed	HRN	Date	Details	A	C	GD 2.0	VG 4.0	FN 6.0	VF 8.0	VF/NM 9.0	NM- 9.2
1	78	1/51	Orig.; movie promo inside front-c; Blum-c/a	1	1	15	30	45	85	130	175
2	85	–	C-price 15¢; LDC-r	1	1	5	10	15	23	28	32
3	118	–	LDC-r	1	1	3	6	9	17	23	28
4	133	–	New-c; PC-r	1	2	3	6	9	16	24	32
5	156	–	PC-r	1	2	2	4	6	11	16	20
6	167	8/64	PC-r	1	2	2	4	6	11	16	20

80. White Fang (Last line drawn cover)

Ed	HRN	Date	Details	A	C	GD 2.0	VG 4.0	FN 6.0	VF 8.0	VF/NM 9.0	NM- 9.2
1	79	2/51	Orig.; Blum-c/a	1	1	15	30	45	83	124	165
2	87	–	C-price 15¢; LDC-r	1	1	5	10	15	24	30	35
3	125	–	LDC-r	1	1	3	6	9	15	21	26
4	132	–	New-c; PC-r	1	2	3	6	9	16	24	32
5	140	–	PC-r	1	2	2	4	6	9	13	16
6	153	–	PC-r	1	2	2	4	6	9	13	16
7	167	–	PC-r	1	2	2	4	6	8	11	14
8	167	9/64	PC-r	1	2	2	4	6	8	11	14
9	167	7/65	PC-r	1	2	2	4	6	8	11	14
10	166	6/67	PC-r	1	2	2	4	6	8	11	14
11	169	Fall/69	New price 25¢; PC-r; stiff-c	1	2	2	4	6	8	11	14

81. The Odyssey (1st painted cover)

Ed	HRN	Date	Details	A	C	GD 2.0	VG 4.0	FN 6.0	VF 8.0	VF/NM 9.0	NM- 9.2
1	82	3/51	First 15¢ Original; Blum-c	1	1	15	30	45	85	130	175
2	167	8/64	PC-r	1	1	2	4	6	11	16	20
3	167	10/66	PC-r	1	1	2	4	6	11	16	20
4	169	Spr/69	New, stiff-c; PC-r	1	2	3	6	9	18	27	36

82. The Master of Ballantrae

Ed	HRN	Date	Details	A	C	GD 2.0	VG 4.0	FN 6.0	VF 8.0	VF/NM 9.0	NM- 9.2
1	82	4/51	Original; Blum-c	1	1	14	28	42	76	108	140
2	167	8/64	PC-r	1	1	3	6	9	14	19	24
3	166	Fall/68	New, stiff-c; PC-r	1	2	3	6	9	18	27	36

83. The Jungle Book

Ed	HRN	Date	Details	A	C	GD 2.0	VG 4.0	FN 6.0	VF 8.0	VF/NM 9.0	NM- 9.2
1	85	5/51	Original; Blum-c Bossert/Blum-a	1	1	15	30	45	85	130	175
2	110	–	PC-r	1	1	2	4	6	10	14	18
3	125	–	PC-r	1	1	2	4	6	9	13	16
4	134	–	PC-r	1	1	2	4	6	9	13	16
5	142	–	PC-r	1	1	2	4	6	9	13	16
6	150	–	PC-r	1	1	2	4	6	9	13	16
7	159	–	PC-r	1	1	2	4	6	9	13	16
8	167	–	PC-r	1	1	2	4	6	8	11	14
9	167	3/65	PC-r	1	1	2	4	6	8	11	14
10	167	11/65	PC-r	1	1	2	4	6	8	11	14
11	167	5/66	PC-r	1	1	2	4	6	8	11	14
12	166	R/1968	New c&a; stiff-c; PC-r	2	2	3	6	9	18	28	38

84. The Gold Bug and Other Stories ("The Gold Bug", "The Tell-Tale Heart", "The Cask of Amontillado")

Ed	HRN	Date	Details	A	C	GD 2.0	VG 4.0	FN 6.0	VF 8.0	VF/NM 9.0	NM- 9.2
1	85	6/51	Original; Blum-c/a; Palais, Laverly-a	1	1	15	30	45	88	137	185
2	167	7/64	PC-r	1	1	11	22	33	64	90	115

85. The Sea Wolf

Ed	HRN	Date	Details	A	C	GD 2.0	VG 4.0	FN 6.0	VF 8.0	VF/NM 9.0	NM- 9.2
1	85	7/51	Original; Blum-c/a	1	1	13	26	39	72	101	130
2	121	–	PC-r	1	1	2	4	6	9	13	16
3	132	–	PC-r	1	1	2	4	6	9	13	16
4	141	–	PC-r	1	1	2	4	6	9	13	16
5	161	–	PC-r	1	1	2	4	6	8	11	14
6	167	2/64	PC-r	1	1	2	4	6	8	11	14
7	167	11/65	PC-r	1	1	2	4	6	8	11	14
8	169	Fall/69	New price 25¢; stiff-c; PC-r	1	1	2	4	6	8	11	14

86. Under Two Flags

Ed	HRN	Date	Details	A	C	GD 2.0	VG 4.0	FN 6.0	VF 8.0	VF/NM 9.0	NM- 9.2
1	87	8/51	Original; first delBourgo-a	1	1	13	26	39	74	105	135
2	117	–	PC-r	1	1	2	4	6	10	14	18
3	139	–	PC-r	1	1	2	4	6	9	13	16
4	158	–	PC-r	1	1	2	4	6	9	13	16
5	167	2/64	PC-r	1	1	2	4	6	8	11	14
6	167	8/66	PC-r	1	1	2	4	6	8	11	14
7	169	Sm/69	New price 25¢; stiff-c; PC-r	1	1	2	4	6	8	11	14

87. A Midsummer Nights Dream

Ed	HRN	Date	Details	A	C	GD 2.0	VG 4.0	FN 6.0	VF 8.0	VF/NM 9.0	NM- 9.2
1	87	9/51	Original; Blum c/a	1	1	13	26	39	74	105	135
2	161	–	PC-r	1	1	2	4	6	9	13	16
3	167	4/64	PC-r	1	1	2	4	6	8	11	14
4	167	5/66	PC-r	1	1	2	4	6	8	11	14
5	169	Sm/69	New price 25¢; stiff-c; PC-r	1	1	2	4	6	8	11	14

88. Men of Iron

Ed	HRN	Date	Details	A	C	GD 2.0	VG 4.0	FN 6.0	VF 8.0	VF/NM 9.0	NM- 9.2
1	89	10/51	Original	1	1	14	28	42	78	112	145
2	154	–	PC-r	1	1	2	4	6	9	13	16

Classics Illustrated #75 © GIL

Classics Illustrated #91 © GIL

Classics Illustrated #101 © GIL

Ed	HRN	Date	Details	A	C	GD 2.0	VG 4.0	FN 6.0	VF 8.0	VF/NM 9.0	NM- 9.2
3	167	1/64	PC-r	1	1	2	4	6	8	11	14
4	166	R/1968	C-price 25¢; PC-r	1	1	2	4	6	8	11	14

89. Crime and Punishment (Cover illo. in **POP**)

Ed	HRN	Date	Details	A	C	GD 2.0	VG 4.0	FN 6.0	VF 8.0	VF/NM 9.0	NM- 9.2
1	89	11/51	Original; Palais-a	1	1	15	30	45	83	124	165
2	152	–	PC-r	1	1	2	4	6	9	13	16
3	167	4/64	PC-r	1	1	2	4	6	8	11	14
4	167	5/66	PC-r	1	1	2	4	6	8	11	14
5	169	Fall/69	New price 25¢ stiff-c; PC-r	1	1	2	4	6	8	11	14

90. Green Mansions

Ed	HRN	Date	Details	A	C	GD 2.0	VG 4.0	FN 6.0	VF 8.0	VF/NM 9.0	NM- 9.2
1	89	12/51	Original; Blum-c/a	1	1	14	28	42	78	112	145
2	148	–	New L.B. Cole-c; PC-r	1	2	5	10	15	24	29	34
3	165	–	PC-r	1	2	2	4	6	8	11	14
4	167	4/64	PC-r	1	2	2	4	6	8	11	14
5	167	9/66	PC-r	1	2	2	4	6	8	11	14
6	169	Sm/69	New price 25¢; stiff-c; PC-r	1	2	2	4	6	8	11	14

91. The Call of the Wild

Ed	HRN	Date	Details	A	C	GD 2.0	VG 4.0	FN 6.0	VF 8.0	VF/NM 9.0	NM- 9.2
1	92	1/52	Orig.; delBourgo-a	1	1	14	28	42	80	115	150
2	112	–	PC-r	1	1	2	4	6	9	13	16
3	125	–	'Picture Progress' on back-c; PC-r	1	1	2	4	6	9	13	16
4	134	–	PC-r	1	1	2	4	6	9	13	16
5	143	–	PC-r	1	1	2	4	6	9	13	16
6	165	–	PC-r	1	1	2	4	6	9	13	16
7	167	–	PC-r	1	1	2	4	6	8	11	14
8	167	4/65	PC-r	1	1	2	4	6	8	11	14
9	167	3/66	PC-r	1	1	2	4	6	8	11	14
10	166	11/67	PC-r	1	1	2	4	6	8	11	14
11	169	Spr/70	New price 25¢; stiff-c; PC-r	1	1	2	4	6	8	11	14

92. The Courtship of Miles Standish

Ed	HRN	Date	Details	A	C	GD 2.0	VG 4.0	FN 6.0	VF 8.0	VF/NM 9.0	NM- 9.2
1	92	2/52	Original; Blum-c/a	1	1	14	28	42	78	112	145
2	165	–	PC-r	1	1	2	4	6	9	13	16
3	167	3/64	PC-r	1	1	2	4	6	9	13	16
4	166	5/67	PC-r	1	1	2	4	6	9	13	16
5	169	Win/69	New price 25¢ stiff-c; PC-r	1	1	2	4	6	9	13	16

93. Pudd'nhead Wilson

Ed	HRN	Date	Details	A	C	GD 2.0	VG 4.0	FN 6.0	VF 8.0	VF/NM 9.0	NM- 9.2
1	94	3/52	Orig.; Kiefer-c/a;	1	1	14	28	42	78	112	145
2	165	–	New-c; PC-r	1	2	2	4	6	11	16	25
3	167	3/64	PC-r	1	2	2	4	6	9	13	16
4	166	R/1968	New price 25¢; soft-c; PC-r	1	2	2	4	6	9	13	16

94. David Balfour

Ed	HRN	Date	Details	A	C	GD 2.0	VG 4.0	FN 6.0	VF 8.0	VF/NM 9.0	NM- 9.2
1	94	4/52	Original; Palais-a	1	1	12	24	36	69	97	125
2	167	5/64	PC-r	1	1	2	4	6	11	16	20
3	166	R/1968	C-price 25¢; PC-r	1	1	2	4	6	13	18	22

95. All Quiet on the Western Front

Ed	HRN	Date	Details	A	C	GD 2.0	VG 4.0	FN 6.0	VF 8.0	VF/NM 9.0	NM- 9.2
1A	96	5/52	Orig.; del Bourgo-a	1	1	15	30	45	90	140	190
1B	99	5/52	Orig.; del Bourgo-a	1	1	14	28	42	82	121	160
2	167	10/64	PC-r	1	1	3	6	9	15	22	28
3	167	11/66	PC-r	1	1	3	6	9	15	22	28

96. Daniel Boone

Ed	HRN	Date	Details	A	C	GD 2.0	VG 4.0	FN 6.0	VF 8.0	VF/NM 9.0	NM- 9.2
1	97	6/52	Original; Blum-a	1	1	12	24	36	67	94	120
2	117	–	PC-r	1	1	2	4	6	9	13	16
3	128	–	PC-r	1	1	2	4	6	9	13	16
4	132	–	PC-r	1	1	2	4	6	9	13	16
5	134	–	"Story of Jesus" on back-c; PC-r	1	1	2	4	6	9	13	16
6	158	–	PC-r	1	1	2	4	6	9	13	16
7	167	1/64	PC-r	1	1	2	4	6	8	11	14
8	167	5/65	PC-r	1	1	2	4	6	8	11	14
9	167	11/66	PC-r	1	1	2	4	6	8	11	14
10	166	Win/69	New-c; price 25¢; PC-r; stiff-c	1	2	3	6	9	15	22	28

97. King Solomon's Mines

Ed	HRN	Date	Details	A	C	GD 2.0	VG 4.0	FN 6.0	VF 8.0	VF/NM 9.0	NM- 9.2
1	96	7/52	Orig.; Kiefer-a	1	1	14	28	42	76	108	140
2	118	–	PC-r	1	1	2	4	6	9	13	16
3	131	–	PC-r	1	1	2	4	6	9	13	16
4	141	–	PC-r	1	1	2	4	6	9	13	16
5	158	–	PC-r	1	1	2	4	6	9	13	16
6	167	2/64	PC-r	1	1	2	4	6	8	11	14
7	167	9/65	PC-r	1	1	2	4	6	8	11	14
8	169	Sm/69	New price 25¢; stiff-c; PC-r	1	1	2	4	6	8	11	14

98. The Red Badge of Courage

Ed	HRN	Date	Details	A	C	GD 2.0	VG 4.0	FN 6.0	VF 8.0	VF/NM 9.0	NM- 9.2
1	98	8/52	Original	1	1	14	28	42	76	108	140
2	118	–	PC-r	1	1	2	4	6	9	13	16
3	132	–	PC-r	1	1	2	4	6	9	13	16
4	142	–	PC-r	1	1	2	4	6	9	13	16
5	152	–	PC-r	1	1	2	4	6	9	13	16
6	161	–	PC-r	1	1	2	4	6	9	13	16
7	167	–	Has orig.date; PC-r	1	1	2	4	6	9	13	16
8	167	9/64	PC-r	1	1	2	4	6	9	13	16
9	167	10/65	PC-r	1	1	2	4	6	9	13	16
10	166	R/1968	New-c&price 25¢; PC-r; stiff-c	1	2	3	6	9	16	23	30

99. Hamlet (Used in **POP**, pg. 102)

Ed	HRN	Date	Details	A	C	GD 2.0	VG 4.0	FN 6.0	VF 8.0	VF/NM 9.0	NM- 9.2
1	98	9/52	Original; Blum-a	1	1	12	24	36	69	97	125
2	121	–	PC-r	1	1	2	4	6	9	13	16
3	141	–	PC-r	1	1	2	4	6	9	13	16
4	158	–	PC-r	1	1	2	4	6	9	13	16
5	167	–	Has orig.date; PC-r	1	1	2	4	6	8	11	14
6	167	7/65	PC-r	1	1	2	4	6	8	11	14
7	166	4/67	PC-r	1	1	2	4	6	8	11	14
8	169	Spr/69	New-c&price 25¢; PC-r; stiff-c	1	2	3	6	9	16	23	30

100. Mutiny on the Bounty

Ed	HRN	Date	Details	A	C	GD 2.0	VG 4.0	FN 6.0	VF 8.0	VF/NM 9.0	NM- 9.2
1	100	10/52	Original	1	1	11	22	33	62	86	110
2	117	–	PC-r	1	1	2	4	6	9	13	16
3	132	–	PC-r	1	1	2	4	6	9	13	16
4	142	–	PC-r	1	1	2	4	6	9	13	16
5	155	–	PC-r	1	1	2	4	6	9	13	16
6	167	–	Has orig. date;PC-r	1	1	2	4	6	8	11	14
7	167	5/64	PC-r	1	1	2	4	6	8	11	14
8	167	3/66	PC-r	1	1	2	4	6	8	11	14
9	169	Spr/70	PC-r; stiff-c	1	1	2	4	6	8	11	14

101. William Tell

Ed	HRN	Date	Details	A	C	GD 2.0	VG 4.0	FN 6.0	VF 8.0	VF/NM 9.0	NM- 9.2
1	101	11/52	Original; Kiefer-c delBourgo-a	1	1	14	28	42	76	108	140
2	118	–	PC-r	1	1	2	4	6	9	13	16
3	141	–	PC-r	1	1	2	4	6	9	13	16
4	158	–	PC-r	1	1	2	4	6	9	13	16
5	167	–	Has orig.date; PC-r	1	1	2	4	6	8	11	14
6	167	11/64	PC-r	1	1	2	4	6	8	11	14
7	166	4/67	PC-r	1	1	2	4	6	8	11	14
8	169	Win/69	New price 25¢; stiff-c; PC-r	1	1	2	4	6	8	11	14

102. The White Company

Ed	HRN	Date	Details	A	C	GD 2.0	VG 4.0	FN 6.0	VF 8.0	VF/NM 9.0	NM- 9.2
1	101	12/52	Original; Blum-a	1	1	15	30	45	85	130	175
2	165	–	PC-r	1	1	3	6	9	16	23	30
3	167	4/64	PC-r	1	1	3	6	9	16	23	30

103. Men Against the Sea

Ed	HRN	Date	Details	A	C	GD 2.0	VG 4.0	FN 6.0	VF 8.0	VF/NM 9.0	NM- 9.2
1	104	1/53	Original; Kiefer-c; Palais-a	1	1	14	28	42	76	108	140
2	114	–	PC-r	1	1	4	8	11	16	19	22
3	131	–	New-c; PC-r	1	2	5	10	15	24	30	35
4	158	–	PC-r	1	2	4	7	10	14	17	20

Ed	HRN	Date	Details	A	C	GD 2.0	VG 4.0	FN 6.0	VF 8.0	VF/NM 9.0	NM- 9.2
5	149	–	White reorder list; came after HRN-158; PC-r	1	2	5	10	15	22	26	30
6	167	3/64	PC-r	1	2	2	4	6	9	13	16

104. Bring 'Em Back Alive

Ed	HRN	Date	Details	A	C	GD 2.0	VG 4.0	FN 6.0	VF 8.0	VF/NM 9.0	NM- 9.2
1	105	2/53	Original; Kiefer-c/a	1	1	13	26	39	72	101	130
2	118	–	PC-r	1	1	2	4	6	9	13	16
3	133	–	PC-r	1	1	2	4	6	9	13	16
4	150	–	PC-r	1	1	2	4	6	9	13	16
5	158	–	PC-r	1	1	2	4	6	9	13	16
6	167	10/63	PC-r	1	1	2	4	6	8	11	14
7	167	9/65	PC-r	1	1	2	4	6	8	11	14
8	169	Win/69	New price 25¢; stiff-c; PC-r	1	1	2	4	6	8	11	14

105. From the Earth to the Moon

Ed	HRN	Date	Details	A	C	GD 2.0	VG 4.0	FN 6.0	VF 8.0	VF/NM 9.0	NM- 9.2
1	106	3/53	Original; Blum-a	1	1	13	26	39	72	101	130
2	118	–	PC-r	1	1	2	4	6	9	13	16
3	132	–	PC-r	1	1	2	4	6	9	13	16
4	141	–	PC-r	1	1	2	4	6	9	13	16
5	146	–	PC-r	1	1	2	4	6	9	13	16
6	156	–	PC-r	1	1	2	4	6	9	13	16
7	167	–	Has orig. date; PC-r	1	1	2	4	6	8	11	14
8	167	5/64	PC-r	1	1	2	4	6	8	11	14
9	167	5/65	PC-r	1	1	2	4	6	8	11	14
10A	166	10/67	PC-r	1	1	2	4	6	8	11	14
10B	166	10/67	w/Grit ad stapled in book	1	1	9	18	27	59	117	175
11	169	Sm/69	New price 25¢; stiff-c; PC-r	1	1	2	4	6	8	11	14
12	169	Spr/71	PC-r	1	1	2	4	6	8	11	14

106. Buffalo Bill

Ed	HRN	Date	Details	A	C	GD 2.0	VG 4.0	FN 6.0	VF 8.0	VF/NM 9.0	NM- 9.2
1	107	4/53	Orig.; delBourgo-a	1	1	11	22	33	64	90	115
2	118	–	PC-r	1	1	2	4	6	9	13	16
3	132	–	PC-r	1	1	2	4	6	9	13	16
4	142	–	PC-r	1	1	2	4	6	9	13	16
5	161	–	PC-r	1	1	2	4	6	8	11	14
6	167	3/64	PC-r	1	1	2	4	6	8	11	14
7	166	7/67	PC-r	1	1	2	4	6	8	11	14
8	169	Fall/69	PC-r; stiff-c	1	1	2	4	6	8	11	14

107. King of the Khyber Rifles

Ed	HRN	Date	Details	A	C	GD 2.0	VG 4.0	FN 6.0	VF 8.0	VF/NM 9.0	NM- 9.2
1	108	5/53	Original; Ditko-a (earliest published; about 1/3 of book)	1	1	13	26	39	74	105	135
2	118	–	PC-r	1	1	2	4	6	9	13	16
3	146	–	PC-r	1	1	2	4	6	9	13	16
4	158	–	PC-r	1	1	2	4	6	9	13	16
5	167	–	Has orig.date; PC-r	1	1	2	4	6	8	11	14
6	167	10/66	PC-r	1	1	2	4	6	8	11	14

108. Knights of the Round Table

Ed	HRN	Date	Details	A	C	GD 2.0	VG 4.0	FN 6.0	VF 8.0	VF/NM 9.0	NM- 9.2
1A	108	6/53	Original; Blum-a	1	1	14	28	42	78	112	145
1B	109	6/53	Original; scarce	1	1	14	28	42	80	115	150
2	117	–	PC-r	1	1	2	4	6	9	13	16
3	165	–	PC-r	1	1	2	4	6	8	11	14
4	167	4/64	PC-r	1	1	2	4	6	8	11	14
5	166	4/67	PC-r	1	1	2	4	6	8	11	14
6	169	Sm/69	New price 25¢; stiff-c; PC-r	1	1	2	4	6	8	11	14

109. Pitcairn's Island

Ed	HRN	Date	Details	A	C	GD 2.0	VG 4.0	FN 6.0	VF 8.0	VF/NM 9.0	NM- 9.2
1	110	7/53	Original; Palais-a	1	1	13	26	39	74	105	135
2	165	–	PC-r	1	1	2	4	6	9	13	16
3	167	3/64	PC-r	1	1	2	4	6	9	13	16
4	166	6/67	PC-r	1	1	2	4	6	9	13	16

110. A Study in Scarlet

Ed	HRN	Date	Details	A	C	GD 2.0	VG 4.0	FN 6.0	VF 8.0	VF/NM 9.0	NM- 9.2
1	111	8/53	Original	1	1	15	30	45	86	133	180
2	165	–	PC-r	1	1	12	24	36	67	94	120

111. The Talisman

Ed	HRN	Date	Details	A	C	GD 2.0	VG 4.0	FN 6.0	VF 8.0	VF/NM 9.0	NM- 9.2
1	112	9/53	Original; last H.C. Kiefer-a	1	1	12	24	36	69	97	125
2	165	–	PC-r	1	1	2	4	6	9	13	16
3	167	5/64	PC-r	1	1	2	4	6	9	13	16
4	166	Fall/68	C-price 25¢; PC-r	1	1	2	4	6	9	13	16

112. Adventures of Kit Carson

Ed	HRN	Date	Details	A	C	GD 2.0	VG 4.0	FN 6.0	VF 8.0	VF/NM 9.0	NM- 9.2
1	113	10/53	Original; Palais-a	1	1	11	22	33	62	86	110
2	129	–	PC-r	1	1	2	4	6	9	13	16
3	141	–	PC-r	1	1	2	4	6	9	13	16
4	152	–	PC-r	1	1	2	4	6	9	13	16
5	161	–	PC-r	1	1	2	4	6	8	11	14
6	167	–	PC-r	1	1	2	4	6	8	11	14
7	167	2/65	PC-r	1	1	2	4	6	8	11	14
8	167	5/66	PC-r	1	1	2	4	6	8	11	14
9	166	Win/69	New-c&price 25¢; PC-r; stiff-c	1	2	3	6	9	14	20	25

113. The Forty-Five Guardsmen

Ed	HRN	Date	Details	A	C	GD 2.0	VG 4.0	FN 6.0	VF 8.0	VF/NM 9.0	NM- 9.2
1	114	11/53	Orig.; delBourgo-a	1	1	14	28	42	80	115	150
2	166	7/67	PC-r	1	1	4	8	12	25	40	55

114. The Red Rover

Ed	HRN	Date	Details	A	C	GD 2.0	VG 4.0	FN 6.0	VF 8.0	VF/NM 9.0	NM- 9.2
1	115	12/53	Original	1	1	14	28	42	80	115	150
2	166	7/67	PC-r	1	1	4	8	12	25	40	55

115. How I Found Livingstone

Ed	HRN	Date	Details	A	C	GD 2.0	VG 4.0	FN 6.0	VF 8.0	VF/NM 9.0	NM- 9.2
1	116	1/54	Original	1	1	14	28	42	82	121	160
2	167	1/67	PC-r	1	1	4	8	12	27	44	60

116. The Bottle Imp

Ed	HRN	Date	Details	A	C	GD 2.0	VG 4.0	FN 6.0	VF 8.0	VF/NM 9.0	NM- 9.2
1	117	2/54	Orig.; Cameron-a	1	1	14	28	42	82	121	160
2	167	1/67	PC-r	1	1	4	8	12	27	44	60

117. Captains Courageous

Ed	HRN	Date	Details	A	C	GD 2.0	VG 4.0	FN 6.0	VF 8.0	VF/NM 9.0	NM- 9.2
1	118	3/54	Orig.; Costanza-a	1	1	14	28	42	78	112	145
2	167	2/67	PC-r	1	1	3	6	9	14	20	26
3	169	Fall/69	New price 25¢; stiff-c; PC-r	1	1	3	6	9	14	20	26

118. Rob Roy

Ed	HRN	Date	Details	A	C	GD 2.0	VG 4.0	FN 6.0	VF 8.0	VF/NM 9.0	NM- 9.2
1	119	4/54	Original; Rudy & Walter Palais-a	1	1	14	28	42	82	121	160
2	167	2/67	PC-r	1	1	4	8	12	27	44	60

119. Soldiers of Fortune

Ed	HRN	Date	Details	A	C	GD 2.0	VG 4.0	FN 6.0	VF 8.0	VF/NM 9.0	NM- 9.2
1	120	5/54	Schaffenberger-a	1	1	14	28	42	76	108	140
2	166	3/67	PC-r	1	1	3	6	9	14	20	26
3	169	Spr/70	New price 25¢; stiff-c; PC-r	1	1	3	6	9	14	20	26

120. The Hurricane

Ed	HRN	Date	Details	A	C	GD 2.0	VG 4.0	FN 6.0	VF 8.0	VF/NM 9.0	NM- 9.2
1	121	6/54	Orig.; Cameron-a	1	1	14	28	42	80	115	150
2	166	3/67	PC-r	1	1	4	8	12	22	34	50

121. Wild Bill Hickok

Ed	HRN	Date	Details	A	C	GD 2.0	VG 4.0	FN 6.0	VF 8.0	VF/NM 9.0	NM- 9.2
1	122	7/54	Original	1	1	11	22	33	62	86	110
2	132	–	PC-r	1	1	2	4	6	9	13	16
3	141	–	PC-r	1	1	2	4	6	9	13	16
4	154	–	PC-r	1	1	2	4	6	9	13	16
5	167	–	PC-r	1	1	2	4	6	8	11	14
6	167	8/64	PC-r	1	1	2	4	6	8	11	14
7	166	4/67	PC-r	1	1	2	4	6	8	11	14
8	169	Win/69	PC-r; stiff-c	1	1	2	4	6	8	11	14

122. The Mutineers

Ed	HRN	Date	Details	A	C	GD 2.0	VG 4.0	FN 6.0	VF 8.0	VF/NM 9.0	NM- 9.2
1	123	9/54	Original	1	1	12	24	36	69	97	125
2	136	–	PC-r	1	1	2	4	6	9	13	16
3	146	–	PC-r	1	1	2	4	6	9	13	16
4	158	–	PC-r	1	1	2	4	6	9	13	16
5	167	11/63	PC-r	1	1	2	4	6	8	11	14
6	167	3/65	PC-r	1	1	2	4	6	8	11	14
7	166	8/67	PC-r	1	1	2	4	6	8	11	14

123. Fang and Claw

Ed	HRN	Date	Details	A	C	GD 2.0	VG 4.0	FN 6.0	VF 8.0	VF/NM 9.0	NM- 9.2
1	124	11/54	Original	1	1	12	24	36	69	97	125
2	133	–	PC-r	1	1	2	4	6	9	13	16
3	143	–	PC-r	1	1	2	4	6	9	13	16
4	154	–	PC-r	1	1	2	4	6	9	13	16
5	167	–	Has orig.date; PC-r	1	1	2	4	6	8	11	14
6	167	9/65	PC-r	1	1	2	4	6	8	11	14

124. The War of the Worlds

Ed	HRN	Date	Details	A	C	GD 2.0	VG 4.0	FN 6.0	VF 8.0	VF/NM 9.0	NM- 9.2
1	125	1/55	Original; Cameron-c/a	1	1	15	30	45	86	133	180
2	131	–	PC-r	1	1	2	4	6	10	14	18
3	141	–	PC-r	1	1	2	4	6	10	14	18
4	148	–	PC-r	1	1	2	4	6	10	14	18
5	156	–	PC-r	1	1	2	4	6	10	14	18
6	165	–	PC-r	1	1	2	4	6	13	18	22
7	167	–	PC-r	1	1	2	4	6	9	13	16
8	167	11/64	PC-r	1	1	2	4	6	10	14	18
9	167	11/65	PC-r	1	1	2	4	6	9	13	16
10	166	R/1968	C-price 25¢; PC-r	1	1	2	4	6	9	13	16
11	169	Sm/70	PC-r; stiff-c	1	1	2	4	6	9	13	16

125. The Ox Bow Incident

Ed	HRN	Date	Details	A	C	GD 2.0	VG 4.0	FN 6.0	VF 8.0	VF/NM 9.0	NM- 9.2
1	–	3/55	Original; Picture Progress replaces reorder list	1	1	11	22	33	64	90	115
2	143	–	PC-r	1	1	2	4	6	9	13	16
3	152	–	PC-r	1	1	2	4	6	9	13	16
4	149	–	PC-r	1	1	2	4	6	9	13	16
5	167	–	PC-r	1	1	2	4	6	8	11	14
6	167	11/64	PC-r	1	1	2	4	6	8	11	14
7	166	4/67	PC-r	1	1	2	4	6	8	11	14
8	169	Win/69	New price 25¢; stiff-c; PC-r	1	1	2	4	6	8	11	14

126. The Downfall

Ed	HRN	Date	Details	A	C	GD 2.0	VG 4.0	FN 6.0	VF 8.0	VF/NM 9.0	NM- 9.2
1	–	5/55	Orig.; 'Picture Pro-	1	1	12	24	36	69	97	125

Classics Illustrated #110 © GIL

Classics Illustrated #128 © GIL

Classics Illustrated #139 © GIL

Ed	HRN	Date	Details	A	C	GD 2.0	VG 4.0	FN 6.0	VF 8.0	VF/NM 9.0	NM- 9.2
			gress' replaces reorder list; Cameron-c/a								
2	167	8/64	PC-r	1	1	2	4	6	13	18	22
3	166	R/1968	C-price 25¢; PC-r	1	1	2	4	6	13	18	22

127. The King of the Mountains

Ed	HRN	Date	Details	A	C	GD 2.0	VG 4.0	FN 6.0	VF 8.0	VF/NM 9.0	NM- 9.2
1	128	7/55	Original	1	1	12	24	36	69	97	125
2	167	6/64	PC-r	1	1	2	4	6	11	16	20
3	166	F/1968	C-price 25¢; PC-r	1	1	2	4	6	11	16	20

128. Macbeth (Used in **POP**, pg. 102)

Ed	HRN	Date	Details	A	C	GD 2.0	VG 4.0	FN 6.0	VF 8.0	VF/NM 9.0	NM- 9.2
1	128	9/55	Orig.; last Blum-a	1	1	12	24	36	69	97	125
2	143	–	PC-r	1	1	2	4	6	9	13	16
3	158	–	PC-r	1	1	2	4	6	9	13	16
4	167	–	PC-r	1	1	2	4	6	8	11	14
5	167	6/64	PC-r	1	1	2	4	6	8	11	14
6	166	4/67	PC-r	1	1	2	4	6	8	11	14
7	166	R/1968	C-Price 25¢; PC-r	1	1	2	4	6	8	11	14
8	169	Spr/70	Stiff-c; PC-r	1	1	2	4	6	8	11	14

129. Davy Crockett

Ed	HRN	Date	Details	A	C	GD 2.0	VG 4.0	FN 6.0	VF 8.0	VF/NM 9.0	NM- 9.2
1	129	11/55	Orig.; Cameron-a	1	1	14	28	42	82	121	160
2	167	9/66	PC-r	1	1	11	22	33	62	86	110

130. Caesar's Conquests

Ed	HRN	Date	Details	A	C	GD 2.0	VG 4.0	FN 6.0	VF 8.0	VF/NM 9.0	NM- 9.2
1	130	1/56	Original; Orlando-a	1	1	12	24	36	69	97	125
2	142	–	PC-r	1	1	2	4	6	9	13	16
3	152	–	PC-r	1	1	2	4	6	9	13	16
4	149	–	PC-r	1	1	2	4	6	9	13	16
5	167	–	PC-r	1	1	2	4	6	8	11	14
6	167	10/64	PC-r	1	1	2	4	6	8	11	14
7	167	4/66	PC-r	1	1	2	4	6	8	11	14

131. The Covered Wagon

Ed	HRN	Date	Details	A	C	GD 2.0	VG 4.0	FN 6.0	VF 8.0	VF/NM 9.0	NM- 9.2
1	131	3/56	Original	1	1	6	12	18	40	73	105
2	143	–	PC-r	1	1	2	4	6	9	13	16
3	152	–	PC-r	1	1	2	4	6	9	13	16
4	158	–	PC-r	1	1	2	4	6	9	13	16
5	167	–	PC-r	1	1	2	4	6	8	11	14
6	167	11/64	PC-r	1	1	2	4	6	8	11	14
7	167	4/66	PC-r	1	1	2	4	6	8	11	14
8	169	Win/69	New price 25¢; stiff-c; PC-r	1	1	2	4	6	8	11	14

132. The Dark Frigate

Ed	HRN	Date	Details	A	C	GD 2.0	VG 4.0	FN 6.0	VF 8.0	VF/NM 9.0	NM- 9.2
1	132	5/56	Original	1	1	12	24	36	69	97	125
2	150	–	PC-r	1	1	2	4	6	9	13	16
3	167	1/64	PC-r	1	1	2	4	6	9	13	16
4	166	5/67	PC-r	1	1	2	4	6	9	13	16

133. The Time Machine

Ed	HRN	Date	Details	A	C	GD 2.0	VG 4.0	FN 6.0	VF 8.0	VF/NM 9.0	NM- 9.2
1	132	7/56	Orig.; Cameron-a	1	1	7	14	21	49	92	135
2	142	–	PC-r	1	1	2	4	6	11	16	20
3	152	–	PC-r	1	1	2	4	6	11	16	20
4	158	–	PC-r	1	1	2	4	6	10	14	18
5	167	–	PC-r	1	1	2	4	6	10	14	18
6	167	6/64	PC-r	1	1	2	4	6	11	16	20
7	167	3/66	PC-r	1	1	2	4	6	10	13	18
8	166	12/67	PC-r	1	1	2	4	6	10	13	18
9	169	Win/71	New price 25¢; stiff-c; PC-r	1	1	2	4	6	10	13	18

134. Romeo and Juliet

Ed	HRN	Date	Details	A	C	GD 2.0	VG 4.0	FN 6.0	VF 8.0	VF/NM 9.0	NM- 9.2
1	134	9/56	Original; Evans-a	1	1	7	14	21	46	86	125
2	161	–	PC-r	1	1	2	4	6	9	13	16
3	167	9/63	PC-r	1	1	2	4	6	8	11	14
4	167	5/65	PC-r	1	1	2	4	6	8	11	14
5	166	6/67	PC-r	1	1	2	4	6	8	11	14
6	166	Win/69	New c&price 25¢; stiff-c; PC-r	1	2	3	6	9	18	27	36

135. Waterloo

Ed	HRN	Date	Details	A	C	GD 2.0	VG 4.0	FN 6.0	VF 8.0	VF/NM 9.0	NM- 9.2
1	135	11/56	Orig.; G. Ingels-a	1	1	6	12	18	42	79	115
2	153	–	PC-r	1	1	2	4	6	9	13	16
3	167	–	PC-r	1	1	2	4	6	8	11	14
4	167	9/64	PC-r	1	1	2	4	6	8	11	14
5	166	R/1968	C-price 25¢; PC-r	1	1	2	4	6	8	11	14

136. Lord Jim

Ed	HRN	Date	Details	A	C	GD 2.0	VG 4.0	FN 6.0	VF 8.0	VF/NM 9.0	NM- 9.2
1	136	1/57	Original; Evans-a	1	1	6	12	18	42	79	115
2	165	–	PC-r	1	1	2	4	6	8	11	14
3	167	3/64	PC-r	1	1	2	4	6	8	11	14
4	167	9/66	PC-r	1	1	2	4	6	8	11	14
5	169	Sm/69	New price 25 ¢; stiff-c; PC-r	1	1	2	4	6	8	11	14

137. The Little Savage

Ed	HRN	Date	Details	A	C	GD 2.0	VG 4.0	FN 6.0	VF 8.0	VF/NM 9.0	NM- 9.2
1	136	3/57	Original; Evans-a	1	1	6	12	18	42	79	115
2	148	–	PC-r	1	1	2	4	6	9	13	16
3	156	–	PC-r	1	1	2	4	6	9	13	16
4	167	–	PC-r	1	1	2	4	6	8	11	14
5	167	10/64	PC-r	1	1	2	4	6	8	11	14
6	166	8/67	PC-r	1	1	2	4	6	8	11	14
7	169	Spr/70	New price 25¢; stiff-c; PC-r	1	1	2	4	6	8	11	14

138. A Journey to the Center of the Earth

Ed	HRN	Date	Details	A	C	GD 2.0	VG 4.0	FN 6.0	VF 8.0	VF/NM 9.0	NM- 9.2
1	136	5/57	Original	1	1	8	16	24	54	102	150
2	146	–	PC-r	1	1	2	4	6	11	16	20
3	156	–	PC-r	1	1	2	4	6	11	16	20
4	158	–	PC-r	1	1	2	4	6	9	13	16
5	167	–	PC-r	1	1	2	4	6	8	11	14
6	167	6/64	PC-r	1	1	2	4	6	13	18	22
7	167	4/66	PC-r	1	1	2	4	6	13	18	22
8	166	R/68	C-price 25¢; PC-r	1	1	2	4	6	10	14	18

139. In the Reign of Terror

Ed	HRN	Date	Details	A	C	GD 2.0	VG 4.0	FN 6.0	VF 8.0	VF/NM 9.0	NM- 9.2
1	139	7/57	Original; Evans-a	1	1	6	12	18	42	79	115
2	154	–	PC-r	1	1	2	4	6	9	13	16
3	167	–	Has orig.date; PC-r	1	1	2	4	6	8	11	14
4	167	7/64	PC-r	1	1	2	4	6	8	11	14
5	166	R/1968	C-price 25¢; PC-r	1	1	2	4	6	8	11	14

140. On Jungle Trails

Ed	HRN	Date	Details	A	C	GD 2.0	VG 4.0	FN 6.0	VF 8.0	VF/NM 9.0	NM- 9.2
1	140	9/57	Original	1	1	6	12	18	40	73	105
2	150	–	PC-r	1	1	2	4	6	9	13	16
3	160	–	PC-r	1	1	2	4	6	9	13	16
4	167	9/63	PC-r	1	1	2	4	6	8	11	14
5	167	9/65	PC-r	1	1	2	4	6	8	11	14

141. Castle Dangerous

Ed	HRN	Date	Details	A	C	GD 2.0	VG 4.0	FN 6.0	VF 8.0	VF/NM 9.0	NM- 9.2
1	141	11/57	Original	1	1	7	14	21	44	82	120
2	152	–	PC-r	1	1	2	4	6	9	13	16
3	167	–	PC-r	1	1	2	4	6	9	13	16
4	166	7/67	PC-r	1	1	2	4	6	9	13	16

142. Abraham Lincoln

Ed	HRN	Date	Details	A	C	GD 2.0	VG 4.0	FN 6.0	VF 8.0	VF/NM 9.0	NM- 9.2
1	142	1/58	Original	1	1	6	12	18	42	79	115
2	154	–	PC-r	1	1	2	4	6	9	13	16
3	158	–	PC-r	1	1	2	4	6	9	13	16
4	167	10/63	PC-r	1	1	2	4	6	8	11	14
5	167	7/65	PC-r	1	1	2	4	6	8	11	14
6	166	11/67	PC-r	1	1	2	4	6	8	11	14
7	169	Fall/69	New price 25¢; stiff-c; PC-r	1	1	2	4	6	8	11	14

143. Kim

Ed	HRN	Date	Details	A	C	GD 2.0	VG 4.0	FN 6.0	VF 8.0	VF/NM 9.0	NM- 9.2
1	143	3/58	Original; Orlando-a	1	1	6	12	18	40	73	105
2	165	–	PC-r	1	1	2	4	6	8	11	14
3	167	11/63	PC-r	1	1	2	4	6	8	11	14
4	167	8/65	PC-r	1	1	2	4	6	8	11	14
5	169	Win/69	New price 25¢; stiff-c; PC-r	1	1	2	4	6	8	11	14

144. The First Men in the Moon

Ed	HRN	Date	Details	A	C	GD 2.0	VG 4.0	FN 6.0	VF 8.0	VF/NM 9.0	NM- 9.2
1	143	5/58	Original; Woodbridge/Williamson/Torres-a	1	1	8	16	24	55	105	155
2	152	–	(Rare)-PC-r	1	1	9	18	27	58	114	170
3	153	–	PC-r	1	1	2	4	6	9	13	16
4	161	–	PC-r	1	1	2	4	6	8	11	14
5	167	–	PC-r	1	1	2	4	6	8	11	14
6	167	12/65	PC-r	1	1	2	4	6	8	11	14
7	166	Fall/68	New-c&price 25¢; PC-r; stiff-c	1	2	3	6	9	16	23	30
8	169	Win/69	Stiff-c; PC-r	1	2	2	4	6	10	16	20

145. The Crisis

Ed	HRN	Date	Details	A	C	GD 2.0	VG 4.0	FN 6.0	VF 8.0	VF/NM 9.0	NM- 9.2
1	143	7/58	Original; Evans-a	1	1	7	14	21	46	86	125
2	156	–	PC-r	1	1	2	4	6	9	13	16
3	167	10/63	PC-r	1	1	2	4	6	8	11	14
4	167	3/65	PC-r	1	1	2	4	6	8	11	14
5	166	R/68	C-price 25¢; PC-r	1	1	2	4	6	8	11	14

146. With Fire and Sword

Ed	HRN	Date	Details	A	C	GD 2.0	VG 4.0	FN 6.0	VF 8.0	VF/NM 9.0	NM- 9.2
1	143	9/58	Original; Woodbridge-a	1	1	7	14	21	46	86	125
2	156	–	PC-r	1	1	2	4	6	10	14	18
3	167	11/63	PC-r	1	1	2	4	6	9	13	16
4	167	3/65	PC-r	1	1	2	4	6	9	13	16

147. Ben-Hur

Ed	HRN	Date	Details	A	C	GD 2.0	VG 4.0	FN 6.0	VF 8.0	VF/NM 9.0	NM- 9.2
1	147	11/58	Original; Orlando-a	1	1	8	16	24	51	96	140
2	152	–	Scarce; PC-r	1	1	7	14	21	49	92	135
3	153	–	PC-r	1	1	2	4	6	9	13	16
4	158	–	PC-r	1	1	2	4	6	9	13	16
5	167	–	Orig.date; but PC-r	1	1	2	4	6	8	11	14
6	167	2/65	PC-r	1	1	2	4	6	8	11	14
7	167	9/66	PC-r	1	1	2	4	6	8	11	14
8A	166	Fall/68	New-c&price 25¢; PC-r; soft-c	1	2	3	6	9	16	24	32
8B	166	Fall/68	New-c&price 25¢; PC-r; stiff-c; scarce	1	2	4	8	12	23	37	50

148. The Buccaneer

Ed	HRN	Date	Details	A	C	GD 2.0	VG 4.0	FN 6.0	VF 8.0	VF/NM 9.0	NM- 9.2
1	148	1/59	Orig.; Evans/Jenny-a; Saunders-c	1	1	6	12	18	42	79	115
2	568	–	Juniors list only PC-r	1	1	2	4	6	9	13	16
3	167	–	PC-r	1	1	2	4	6	8	11	14
4	167	9/65	PC-r	1	1	2	4	6	8	11	14
5	169	Sm/69	New price 25¢; PC-r; stiff-c	1	1	2	4	6	8	11	14

149. Off on a Comet

Ed	HRN	Date	Details	A	C	GD 2.0	VG 4.0	FN 6.0	VF 8.0	VF/NM 9.0	NM- 9.2
1	149	3/59	Orig.;G.McCann-a; blue reorder list	1	1	7	14	21	46	86	125
2	155	–	PC-r	1	1	2	4	6	9	13	16
3	149	–	PC-r; white reorder list; no coming-next ad	1	1	2	4	6	9	13	16
4	167	12/63	PC-r	1	1	2	4	6	8	11	14
5	167	2/65	PC-r	1	1	2	4	6	8	11	14
6	167	10/66	PC-r	1	1	2	4	6	8	11	14
7	166	Fall/68	New-c & price 25¢; PC-r	1	2	3	6	9	17	26	35

150. The Virginian

Ed	HRN	Date	Details	A	C	GD 2.0	VG 4.0	FN 6.0	VF 8.0	VF/NM 9.0	NM- 9.2
1	150	5/59	Original	1	1	7	14	21	44	82	120
2	164	–	PC-r	1	1	2	4	6	11	16	20
3	167	10/63	PC-r	1	1	3	6	9	15	21	26
4	167	12/65	PC-r	1	1	2	4	6	11	16	20

151. Won By the Sword

Ed	HRN	Date	Details	A	C	GD 2.0	VG 4.0	FN 6.0	VF 8.0	VF/NM 9.0	NM- 9.2
1	150	7/59	Original	1	1	6	12	18	42	79	115
2	164	–	PC-r	1	1	2	4	6	10	14	18
3	167	10/63	PC-r	1	1	2	4	6	10	14	18
4	166	7/67	PC-r	1	1	2	4	6	10	14	18

152. Wild Animals I Have Known

Ed	HRN	Date	Details	A	C	GD 2.0	VG 4.0	FN 6.0	VF 8.0	VF/NM 9.0	NM- 9.2
1	152	9/59	Orig.; L.B. Cole c/a	1	1	7	14	21	46	86	125
2A	149	–	PC-r; white reorder list; no coming-next ad; IBC: Jr. list #572	1	1	2	4	6	9	13	16
2B	149	–	PC-r; inside-bc: Jr. list to #555	1	1	2	4	6	9	13	16
2C	149	–	PC-r; inside-bc: has World Around Us ad; scarce	1	1	3	6	9	15	21	26
3	167	9/63	PC-r	1	1	2	4	6	8	11	14
4	167	8/65	PC-r	1	1	2	4	6	8	11	14
5	169	Fall/69	New price 25¢; stiff-c; PC-r	1	1	2	4	6	8	11	14

153. The Invisible Man

Ed	HRN	Date	Details	A	C	GD 2.0	VG 4.0	FN 6.0	VF 8.0	VF/NM 9.0	NM- 9.2
1	153	11/59	Original	1	1	9	18	27	59	117	175
2A	149	–	PC-r; white reorder list; no coming-next ad; inside-bc: Jr. list to #572	1	1	3	6	9	15	22	28
2B	149	–	PC-r; inside-bc: Jr. list to #555	1	1	3	6	9	16	23	30
3	167	–	PC-r	1	1	2	4	6	9	13	16
4	167	2/65	PC-r	1	1	2	4	6	9	13	16
5	167	9/66	PC-r	1	1	2	4	6	9	13	16
6	166	Win/69	New price 25¢; PC-r; stiff-c	1	1	2	4	6	9	13	16
7	169	Spr/71	Stiff-c; letters spelling 'Invisible Man' are 'solid' not 'invisible;' PC-r	1	1	2	4	6	9	13	16

154. The Conspiracy of Pontiac

Ed	HRN	Date	Details	A	C	GD 2.0	VG 4.0	FN 6.0	VF 8.0	VF/NM 9.0	NM- 9.2
1	154	1/60	Original	1	1	7	14	21	41	82	120
2	167	11/63	PC-r	1	1	2	4	6	13	18	22
3	167	7/64	PC-r	1	1	2	4	6	13	18	22
4	166	12/67	PC-r	1	1	2	4	6	13	18	22

155. The Lion of the North

Ed	HRN	Date	Details	A	C	GD 2.0	VG 4.0	FN 6.0	VF 8.0	VF/NM 9.0	NM- 9.2
1	154	3/60	Original	1	1	6	12	18	42	79	115
2	167	1/64	PC-r	1	1	2	4	6	11	16	20
3	166	R/1967	C-price 25¢; PC-r	1	1	2	4	6	10	14	18

156. The Conquest of Mexico

Ed	HRN	Date	Details	A	C	GD 2.0	VG 4.0	FN 6.0	VF 8.0	VF/NM 9.0	NM- 9.2
1	156	5/60	Orig.; Bruno Premiani-c/a	1	1	6	12	18	42	79	115
2	167	1/64	PC-r	1	1	2	4	6	10	14	18
3	166	8/67	PC-r	1	1	2	4	6	10	14	18
4	169	Spr/70	New price 25¢; stiff-c; PC-r	1	1	2	4	6	9	13	16

157. Lives of the Hunted

Ed	HRN	Date	Details	A	C	GD 2.0	VG 4.0	FN 6.0	VF 8.0	VF/NM 9.0	NM- 9.2
1	156	7/60	Orig.; L.B. Cole-c	1	1	7	14	21	44	82	120
2	167	2/64	PC-r	1	1	2	4	6	13	18	22
3	166	10/67	PC-r	1	1	2	4	6	13	18	22

158. The Conspirators

Ed	HRN	Date	Details	A	C	GD 2.0	VG 4.0	FN 6.0	VF 8.0	VF/NM 9.0	NM- 9.2
1	156	9/60	Original	1	1	7	14	21	44	82	120
2	167	7/64	PC-r	1	1	2	4	6	13	18	22
3	166	10/67	PC-r	1	1	2	4	6	13	18	22

159. The Octopus

Ed	HRN	Date	Details	A	C	GD 2.0	VG 4.0	FN 6.0	VF 8.0	VF/NM 9.0	NM- 9.2
1	159	11/60	Orig.; Gray Morrow-a; L.B. Cole-c	1	1	8	16	24	54	102	150
2	167	2/64	PC-r	1	1	2	4	6	13	18	22
3	166	R/1967	C-price 25¢; PC-r	1	1	2	4	6	13	18	22

160. The Food of the Gods

Ed	HRN	Date	Details	A	C	GD 2.0	VG 4.0	FN 6.0	VF 8.0	VF/NM 9.0	NM- 9.2
1A	159	1/61	Original	1	1	8	16	24	55	105	155
1B	160	1/61	Original; same, except for HRN	1	1	8	16	24	52	99	145
2	167	1/64	PC-r	1	1	2	4	6	13	18	22
3	166	6/67	PC-r	1	1	2	4	6	13	18	22

161. Cleopatra

Ed	HRN	Date	Details	A	C	GD 2.0	VG 4.0	FN 6.0	VF 8.0	VF/NM 9.0	NM- 9.2
1	161	3/61	Original	1	1	8	16	24	54	102	150
2	167	1/64	PC-r	1	1	3	6	9	14	19	24
3	166	8/67	PC-r	1	1	3	6	9	14	19	24

162. Robur the Conqueror

Ed	HRN	Date	Details	A	C	GD 2.0	VG 4.0	FN 6.0	VF 8.0	VF/NM 9.0	NM- 9.2
1	162	5/61	Original	1	1	8	16	24	54	102	130
2	167	7/64	PC-r	1	1	3	6	9	14	19	24
3	166	8/67	PC-r	1	1	3	6	9	14	19	24

163. Master of the World

Ed	HRN	Date	Details	A	C	GD 2.0	VG 4.0	FN 6.0	VF 8.0	VF/NM 9.0	NM- 9.2
1	163	7/61	Original; Gray Morrow-a	1	1	7	14	21	44	82	120
2	167	1/65	PC-r	1	1	2	4	6	13	18	22
3	166	R/1968	C-price 25¢; PC-r	1	1	2	4	6	13	18	22

164. The Cossack Chief

Ed	HRN	Date	Details	A	C	GD 2.0	VG 4.0	FN 6.0	VF 8.0	VF/NM 9.0	NM- 9.2
1	164	(1961)	Orig.; nd(10/61?)	1	1	6	12	18	41	76	110
2	167	4/65	PC-r	1	1	2	4	6	13	18	22
3	166	Fall/68	C-price 25¢; PC-r	1	1	2	4	6	13	18	22

165. The Queen's Necklace

Ed	HRN	Date	Details	A	C	GD 2.0	VG 4.0	FN 6.0	VF 8.0	VF/NM 9.0	NM- 9.2
1	164	1/62	Original; Morrow-a	1	1	7	14	21	48	89	130
2	167	4/65	PC-r	1	1	2	4	6	13	18	22
3	166	Fall/68	C-price 25¢; PC-r	1	1	2	4	6	13	18	22

166. Tigers and Traitors

Ed	HRN	Date	Details	A	C	GD 2.0	VG 4.0	FN 6.0	VF 8.0	VF/NM 9.0	NM- 9.2
1	165	5/62	Original	1	1	9	18	27	57	111	165
2	167	2/64	PC-r	1	1	3	6	9	21	33	45
3	167	11/66	PC-r	1	1	3	6	9	21	33	45

167. Faust

Ed	HRN	Date	Details	A	C	GD 2.0	VG 4.0	FN 6.0	VF 8.0	VF/NM 9.0	NM- 9.2
1	165	8/62	Original	1	1	12	24	36	82	179	275
2	167	2/64	PC-r	1	1	5	10	15	35	63	90
3	166	6/67	PC-r	1	1	5	10	15	35	63	90

Classics Illustrated #152 © GIL

Classics Illustrated #161 © GIL

Classics Illustrated Junior #542 © GIL

	GD 2.0	VG 4.0	FN 6.0	VF 8.0	VF/NM 9.0	NM- 9.2

168. In Freedom's Cause

Ed	HRN	Date	Details	A	C	GD	VG	FN	VF	VF/NM	NM-
1	169	Win/69	Original; Evans/ Crandall-a; stiff-c; 25¢; no coming-next ad;	1	1	13	26	39	89	195	300

169. Negro Americans The Early Years

Ed	HRN	Date	Details	A	C	GD	VG	FN	VF	VF/NM	NM-
1	166	Spr/69	Orig. & last issue; 25¢; Stiff-c; no coming-next ad; other sources indicate publication date of 5/69	1	1	13	26	39	89	195	300
2	169	Spr/69	Stiff-c	1	1	8	16	24	55	105	155

NOTE: *Many other titles were prepared or planned but were only issued in British/European series.*

CLASSIC POPEYE (See Popeye, Classic)

CLASSIC PUNISHER (Also see Punisher)
Marvel Comics: Dec, 1989 ($4.95, B&W, deluxe format, 68 pgs.)

	GD	VG	FN	VF	VF/NM	NM-
1-Reprints Marvel Super Action #1 & Marvel Preview #2 plus new story	1	3	4	6	8	10

CLASSIC RED SONJA
Dynamite Entertainment: 2010 - No. 4, 2010 ($3.99)

1-4-Newly colored reprints of stories from Savage Sword of Conan magazine 4.00

CLASSICS ILLUSTRATED
First Publishing/Berkley Publishing: Feb, 1990 - No. 27, July, 1991 ($3.75/$3.95, 52 pgs.)

1-27: 1-Gahan Wilson-c/a. 4-Sienkiewicz painted-c/a. 6-Russell scripts/layouts. 7-Spiegle-a. 9-Ploog-c/a. 16-Staton-a. 18-Gahan Wilson-c/a; 20-Geary-a. 26-Aesop's Fables (6/91). 26,27-Direct sale only 5.00

CLASSICS ILLUSTRATED
Acclaim Books/Twin Circle PublishingCo.: Feb, 1997 - Jan, 1998 ($4.99, digest-size) (Each book contains study notes)

A Christmas Carol-(12/97), A Connecticut Yankee in King Arthur's Court-(5/97), All Quiet on the Western Front-(1/98), A Midsummer's Night Dream-(4/97) Around the World in 80 Days-(1/98), A Tale of Two Cities-(2/97)Joe Orlando-r, Captains Courageous-(11/97), Crime and Punishment-(3/97), Dr. Jekyll and Mr. Hyde-(10/97), Don Quixote-(12/97), Frankenstein-(10/97), Great Expectations-(4/97), Hamlet-(3/97), Huckleberry Finn-(3/97), Jane Eyre-(2/97), Kidnapped-(1/98), Les Miserables-(5/97), Lord Jim-(9/97), Macbeth-(5/97), Moby Dick-(4/97), Oliver Twist-(5/97), Robinson Crusoe-(9/97), Romeo & Juliet-(2/97), Silas Marner-(11/97), The Call of the Wild-(9/97), The Count of Monte Cristo-(1/98), The House of the Seven Gables-(9/97), The Iliad-(12/97), The Invisible Man-(10/97), The Last of the Mohicans-(12/97), The Master of Ballantrae-(11/97), The Odyssey-(3/97), The Prince and the Pauper-(4/97), The Red Badge Of Courage-(9/97), Tom Sawyer-(2/97) Wuthering Heights-(11/97) 5.00

NOTE: *Stories reprinted from the original Gilberton Classic Comics and Classics Illustrated.*

CLASSICS ILLUSTRATED GIANTS
Gilberton Publications: Oct, 1949 (One-Shots - "OS")
These Giant Editions, all with new front and back covers, were advertised from 10/49 to 2/52. They were 50¢ on the newsstand and 60¢ by mail. They are actually four Classics in one volume. All the stories are reprints of the Classics Illustrated Series.
NOTE: There were also British hardback Adventure & Indian Giants in 1952, with the same covers but different contents: Adventure - 2, 7, 10; Indian - 17, 22, 37, 58. They are also rare.

	GD	VG	FN	VF	VF/NM	NM-
"An Illustrated Library of Great Adventure Stories" - reprints of No. 6,7,8,10 (Rare); Kiefer-c	165	330	495	1048	1799	2550
"An Illustrated Library of Exciting Mystery Stories" - reprints of No. 30,21,40, 13 (Rare); Blum-c	177	354	531	1124	1937	2750
"An Illustrated Library of Great Indian Stories" - reprints of No. 4,17,22,37 (Rare); Blum-c	168	336	504	1075	1838	2600

INTRODUCTION TO CLASSICS ILLUSTRATED JUNIOR

Collectors of Juniors can be put into one of two categories: those who want any copy of each title, and those who want all the originals. Those seeking every original and reprint edition are a limited group, primarily because Juniors have no changes in art or covers to spark interest, and because reprints are so low in value it is difficult to get dealers to look for specific reprint editions.

In recent years it has become apparent that most serious Classics collectors seek Junior originals. Those seeking reprints seek them for low cost. This has made the previous note about the comparative market value of reprints inadequate. Three particular reprint editions are worth even more. For the 535-Twin Circle edition, see Giveaways. There are also reprint editions of 501 and 503 which have a full-page bc ad for the very rare Junior record. Those may sell as high as $10-$15 in mint. Original editions of 557 and 558 also have that ad.

There are no reprint editions of 577. The only edition, from 1969, is a 25 cent stiff-cover edition with no ad for the next issue. All other original editions have coming-next ad. But 577, like C.I. #168, was prepared in 1962 but not issued. Copies of 577 can be found in 1963 British/European series, which then continued with dozens of additional new Junior titles.

PRICES LISTED BELOW ARE FOR ORIGINAL EDITIONS, WHICH HAVE AN AD FOR THE NEXT ISSUE.

NOTE: *Non HRN 576 copies- many are written on or colored . Reprints with 576 HRN are worth about 1/3 original prices. All other HRN #'s are 1/2 original price*

CLASSICS ILLUSTRATED JUNIOR
Famous Authors Ltd. (Gilberton Publications): Oct, 1953 - Spring, 1971

	GD	VG	FN	VF	VF/NM	NM-
501-Snow White & the Seven Dwarfs; Alex Blum-a	12	24	36	69	97	125
502-The Ugly Duckling	9	18	27	47	61	75
503-Cinderella	8	16	24	40	50	60
504-512: 504-The Pied Piper. 505-The Sleeping Beauty. 506-The Three Little Pigs. 507-Jack & the Beanstalk. 508-Goldilocks & the Three Bears. 509-Beauty and the Beast. 510-Little Red Riding Hood. 511-Puss-N Boots. 512-Rumpelstiltskin	6	12	18	27	33	38
513-Pinocchio	7	14	21	37	46	55
514-The Steadfast Tin Soldier	8	16	24	44	57	70
515-Johnny Appleseed	6	12	18	27	33	38
516-Aladdin and His Lamp	6	12	18	29	36	42
517-519: 517-The Emperor's New Clothes. 518-The Golden Goose. 519-Paul Bunyan	6	12	18	27	33	38
520-Thumbelina	6	12	18	29	36	42
521-King of the Golden River	6	12	18	27	33	38
522,523,530: 522-The Nightingale. 523-The Gallant Tailor. 530-The Golden Bird	5	10	15	24	30	35
524-The Wild Swans	6	12	18	29	36	42
525,526: 525-The Little Mermaid. 526-The Frog Prince	6	12	18	29	36	42
527-The Golden-Haired Giant	6	12	18	27	33	38
528-The Penny Prince	6	12	18	27	33	38
529-The Magic Servants	6	12	18	27	33	38
531-Rapunzel	6	12	18	27	33	38
532-534: 532-The Dancing Princesses. 533-The Magic Fountain. 534-The Golden Touch	5	10	15	23	28	32
535-The Wizard of Oz	8	16	24	44	57	70
536-The Chimney Sweep	6	12	18	27	33	38
537-The Three Fairies	6	12	18	28	34	40
538-Silly Hans	5	10	15	23	28	32
539-The Enchanted Fish	6	12	18	31	38	45
540-The Tinder-Box	6	12	18	31	38	45
541-Snow White & Rose Red	5	10	15	24	30	35
542-The Donkey's Tale	5	10	15	24	30	35
543-The House in the Woods	6	12	18	27	33	38
544-The Golden Fleece	6	12	18	31	38	45
545-The Glass Mountain	5	10	15	24	30	35
546-The Elves & the Shoemaker	5	10	15	24	30	35
547-The Wishing Table	6	12	18	27	33	38
548-551: 548-The Magic Pitcher. 549-Simple Kate. 550-The Singing Donkey. 551-The Queen Bee	5	10	15	23	28	32
552-The Three Little Dwarfs	6	12	18	27	33	38
553,556: 553-King Thrushbeard. 556-The Elf Mound	5	10	15	23	28	32
554-The Enchanted Deer	6	12	18	29	36	42
555-The Three Golden Apples	5	10	15	24	30	35
557-Silly Willy	6	12	18	28	34	40
558-The Magic Dish; L.B. Cole-c; soft and stiff-c exist on original	7	14	21	35	43	50
559-The Japanese Lantern; 1 pg. Ingels-a; L.B. Cole-c	7	14	21	35	43	50
560-The Doll Princess; L.B. Cole-c	7	14	21	35	43	50
561-Hans Humdrum; L.B. Cole-c	6	12	18	29	36	42
562-The Enchanted Pony; L.B. Cole-c	7	14	21	35	43	50
563,565-568,570: 563-The Wishing Well; L.B. Cole-c. 565-The Silly Princess; L.B. Cole-c. 566-Clumsy Hans; L.B. Cole-c. 567-The Bearskin Soldier; L.B. Cole-c. 570-The Pearl Princess	6	12	18	27	33	38
564-The Salt Mountain; L.B.Cole-c. 568-The Happy Hedgehog; L.B. Cole-c.	6	12	18	28	34	40
569,573: 569-The Three Giants.573-The Crystal Ball	5	10	15	23	28	32
571,572: 571-How Fire Came to the Indians. 572-The Drummer Boy	6	12	18	29	36	42
574-Brightboots	5	10	15	24	30	35
575-The Fearless Prince	6	12	18	28	34	40
576-The Princess Who Saw Everything	7	14	21	35	43	50
577-The Runaway Dumpling	8	16	24	44	57	70

NOTE: *Prices are for original editions. Last reprint - Spring, 1971.* ***Costanza** & **Schaffenberger** art in many issues.*

CLASSICS ILLUSTRATED SPECIAL ISSUE

GD VG FN VF VF/NM NM-
2.0 4.0 6.0 8.0 9.0 9.2

Gilberton Co.: (Came out semi-annually) Dec, 1955 - Jul, 1962 (35¢, 100 pgs.)
129-The Story of Jesus (titled ...Special Edition) "Jesus on Mountain" cover
18 36 54 105 165 225
"Three Camels" cover (12/58) 19 38 57 109 172 235
"Mountain" cover (no date)-Has checklist on inside b/c to HRN #161 & different testimonial on back-c 14 28 42 76 108 140
"Mountain" cover (1968 re-issue; has white 50¢ circle) 10 20 30 56 76 95
132A-The Story of America (6/56); Cameron-a 12 24 36 67 94 120
135A-The Ten Commandments(12/56) 11 22 33 64 90 115
138A-Adventures in Science(6/57); HRN to 137 11 22 33 60 83 105
138A-(6/57)-2nd version w/HRN to 149 7 14 21 35 43 50
138A-(12/61)-3rd version w/HRN to 149 7 14 21 35 43 50
141A-The Rough Rider (Teddy Roosevelt)(12/57); Evans-a
11 22 33 62 86 110
144A-Blazing the Trails West(6/58)- 73 pgs. of Crandall/Evans plus Severin-a 11 22 33 64 90 115
147A-Crossing the Rockies(12/58)-Crandall/Evans-a 11 22 33 62 86 110
150A-Royal Canadian Police(6/59)-Ingels, Sid Check-a
11 22 33 62 86 110
153A-Men, Guns & Cattle(12/59)-Evans-a (26 pgs.); Kinstler-a
11 22 33 62 86 110
156A-The Atomic Age(6/60)-Crandall/Evans, Torres-a
11 22 33 62 86 110
159A-Rockets, Jets and Missiles(12/60)-Evans, Morrow-a
11 22 33 62 86 110
162A-War Between the States(6/61)-Kirby & Crandall/Evans-a; Ingels-a
17 34 51 100 158 215
165A-To the Stars(12/61)-Torres, Crandall/Evans, Kirby-a
14 28 42 76 108 140
166A-World War II('62)-Torres, Crandall/Evans, Kirby-a
15 30 45 85 130 175
167A-Prehistoric World(7/62)-Torres & Crandall/Evans-a; two versions exist (HRN to 165 & HRN to 167) 14 28 42 81 118 155
nn Special Issue-The United Nations (1964; 50¢; scarce); this is actually part of the European Special Series, which cont'd on after the U.S. series stopped issuing new titles in 1962. This English edition was prepared specifically for sale at the U.N. It was printed in Norway
50 100 150 315 533 750
NOTE: *There was another U.S. Special Issue prepared in 1962 with artwork by* ***Torres*** *entitled World War I. Unfortunately, it was never issued in any English-language edition. It was issued in 1964 in West Germany, The Netherlands, and some Scandanavian countries, with another edition in 1974 with a new cover.*

CLASSICS LIBRARY (See King Classics)

CLASSIC STAR WARS (Also see Star Wars)
Dark Horse Comics: Aug, 1992 - No. 20, June, 1994 ($2.50)
1-Begin Star Wars strip-r by Williamson; Williamson redrew portions of the panels to fit comic book format 1 2 3 5 6 8
2-10: 8-Polybagged w/Star Wars Galaxy trading card. 8-M. Schultz-c 4.00
11-19: 13-Yeates-c. 17-M. Schultz-c. 19-Evans-c 3.00
20-($3.50, 52 pgs.)-Polybagged w/trading card 4.00
Escape To Hoth TPB ($16.95) r/#15-20 17.00
The Rebel Storm TPB - r/#8-14 17.00
Trade paperback ($29.95, slip-cased)-Reprints all movie adaptations 30.00
NOTE: *Williamson c-1-5,7,9,10,14,15,20.*

CLASSIC STAR WARS: (Title series). **Dark Horse Comics**
--A NEW HOPE, 6/94 - No. 2, 7/94 ($3.95)
1,2: 1-r/Star Wars #1-3, 7-9 publ; 2-r/Star Wars #4-6, 10-12 publ. by Marvel Comics
1 2 3 5 6 8
--DEVILWORLDS, 8/96 - No. 2, 9/96 ($2.50) 1,2: r/Alan Moore-s
1 2 3 5 6 8
--HAN SOLO AT STARS' END, 3/97 - No. 3, 5/97 ($2.95)
1-3: r/strips by Alfredo Alcala 4.00
--RETURN OF THE JEDI, 10/94 - No. 2, 11/94 ($3.50)
1-r/1983-84 Marvel series; polybagged with w/trading card
2 4 6 11 16 20
2 1 2 3 5 6 8
--THE EARLY ADVENTURES, 8/94 - No. 9, 4/95 ($2.50) 1-8 4.00
9-Boba Fett-c 2 4 6 9 12 15
--THE EMPIRE STRIKES BACK, 8/94 - No. 2, 9/94 ($3.95)
1-r/Star Wars #39-44 published by Marvel Comics 6.00

CLASSIC X-MEN (Becomes X-Men Classic #46 on)
Marvel Comics Group: Sept, 1986 - No. 45, Mar, 1990
1-Begins-r of New X-Men 3 6 9 17 26 35
2-10: 10-Sabretooth app. 6.00
11-42,44,45: 11-1st origin of Magneto in back-up story. 17-Wolverine-c. 27-r/X-Men #121. 26-r/X-Men #120; Wolverine-c/app. 35-r/X-Men #129. 39-New Jim Lee back-up story (2nd-a on X-Men) 4.00
43-Byrne-c/a(r); ($1.75, double-size) 5.00
NOTE: ***Art Adams*** *c(p)-1-10, 12-16, 18-23.* ***Austin*** *c-10,15-21,24-28i.* ***Bolton*** *back up stories in 1-28,30-35.* ***Williamson*** *c-12-14i.*

CLAW (See Capt. Battle, Jr., Daredevil Comics & Silver Streak Comics)

CLAWS (See Wolverine & Black Cat: Claws 2 for sequel)
Marvel Comics: Oct, 2006 - No. 3, Dec, 2006 ($3.99, limited series)
1-3-Wolverine and Black Cat team-up; Linsner-a/c 4.00
Wolverine & Black Cat: Claws HC (2007, $17.99, dustjacket) r/#1-3 & bonus Linsner art 18.00

CLAW THE UNCONQUERED (See Cancelled Comic Cavalcade)
National Periodical Publications/DC Comics: 5-6/75 - No. 9, 9-10/76; No. 10, 4-5/78 - No. 12, 8-9/78
1-1st app. Claw 2 4 6 10 14 18
2-12: 3-Nudity panel. 9-Origin 1 2 3 4 5 7
NOTE: ***Giffen*** *a-8-12p.* ***Kubert*** *c-10-12.* ***Layton*** *a-9i, 12i.*

CLAW THE UNCONQUERED (See Red Sonja/Claw: The Devil's Hands)
DC Comics: Aug, 2006 - No. 6, Jan, 2007 ($2.99)
1-6: 1,2-Chuck Dixon-s/Andy Smith; two covers by Smith & Van Sciver 3.00
TPB (2007, $17.99) r/#1-6; cover gallery 18.00

CLAY CODY, GUNSLINGER
Pines Comics: Fall, 1957
1-Painted-c 7 14 21 35 43 50

CLEAN FUN, STARRING "SHOOGAFOOTS JONES"
Specialty Book Co.: 1944 (10¢, B&W, oversized covers, 24 pgs.)
nn-Humorous situations involving Negroes in the Deep South
White cover issue... 36 72 108 211 343 475
Dark grey cover issue... 34 68 102 199 325 450

CLEAN ROOM
DC Comics (Vertigo): Dec, 2015 - No. 18, Jun, 2017 ($3.99)
1-18: 1-Gail Simone-s/Jon Davis-Hunt-a/Jenny Frison-c 4.00

CLEMENTINA THE FLYING PIG (See Dell Jr. Treasury)

CLEOPATRA (See Ideal, a Classical Comic No. 1)

CLERKS: THE COMIC BOOK (Also see Tales From the Clerks and Oni Double Feature #1)
Oni Press: Feb, 1998 ($2.95, B&W, one-shot)
1-Kevin Smith-s 3 6 9 14 19 24
1-Second printing 6.00
...Holiday Special (12/98, $2.95) Smith-s 1 2 3 5 6 8
...The Lost Scene (12/99, $2.95) Smith-s/Hester-a 1 3 4 6 8 10

CLIFFHANGER (See Battle Chasers, Crimson, and Danger Girl)
WildStorm Prod./Wizard Press: 1997 (Wizard supplement)
0-Sketchbook preview of Cliffhanger titles 6.00

CLIMAX! (Mystery)
Gillmor Magazines: July, 1955 - No. 2, Sept, 1955
1 20 40 60 118 192 265
2 15 30 45 86 133 180

CLINT (Also see Adolescent Radioactive Black Belt Hamsters)
Eclipse Comics: Sept, 1986 - No. 2, Jan, 1987 ($1.50, B&W)
1,2 4.00

CLINT & MAC (TV, Disney)
Dell Publishing Co.: No. 889, Mar, 1958
Four Color 889-Alex Toth-a, photo-c 10 20 30 67 141 215

CLIVE BARKER'S BOOK OF THE DAMNED: A HELLRAISER COMPANION
Marvel Comics (Epic): Oct, 1991 - No. 3, Nov, 1992 ($4.95, semi-annual, 52 pgs.)
1-Simon Bisley-c 2 4 6 9 12 15
2,3: 2-(4/92). 3-(11/92)-McKean-a (1 pg.) 1 3 4 6 8 10

CLIVE BARKER'S HELLRAISER (Also see Epic, Hellraiser Nightbreed –Jihad, Revelations, Son of Celluloid, Tapping the Vein & Weaveworld)
Marvel Comics (Epic Comics): 1989 - No. 20, 1993 ($4.50-6.95, mature, quarterly, 68 pgs.)
Book 1: Based on Hellraiser & Hellbound movies 2 4 6 11 16 20
Book 2-4,10-16,18,19: Based on Hellraiser & Hellbound movies; Bolton-c/a; Spiegle & Wrightson-a (graphic album). 10-Foil-c. 12-Sam Kieth-a 1 3 4 6 8 10
Book 5-9 ($5.95): 7-Bolton-a. 8-Morrow-a 1 2 3 5 6 8
Book 17-Alex Ross-a, 34 pgs. 2 4 6 8 10 12
Book 20-By Gaiman/McKean 2 4 6 11 16 20
...Collected Best (Checker Books, '02, $21.95)-r/by various incl. Ross, Gaiman, Mignola 22.00
...Collected Best II ('03, $19.95)-r/by various incl. Bolton, L. Wachowski, Dorman 20.00
...Collected Best III ('04, $26.95)-r/by various incl. Bolton, L. Wachowski, Wrightson 27.00
...Dark Holiday Special ('92, $4.95)-Conrad-a 1 3 4 6 8 10
...Spring Slaughter 1 ('94, $6.95, 52 pgs.)-Painted-c 2 4 6 11 16 20
...Summer Special 1 ('92, $5.95, 68 pgs.) 1 3 4 6 8 10

CLIVE BARKER'S HELLRAISER
BOOM! Studios: Mar, 2011 - No. 20, Nov, 2012 ($3.99)
1-20: 1-Barker & Monfette-s/Manco-a; preview of Hellraiser Masterpieces; 3 covers 4.00
Annual 1 (3/12, $4.99) Hervás-a; three covers 5.00
2013 Annual (10/13, $4.99) Seifert-s/Hervás-a; Barker & Meares-s/Ordon-a 5.00
...: Bestiary 1-6 (8/14 - No. 6, 1/15, $3.99) short stories by various; multiple covers 4.00
... Masterpieces 1-12 (11/11 - No. 12, 4/12, $3.99) reps from Marvel series. 1-Wrightson-a 4.00
...: The Dark Watch 1-12 (2/13 - No. 12, 1/14, $3.99) Tom Garcia-a; multiple covers 4.00
...: The Road Below 1-4 (10/12 - No. 4, 1/13, $3.99) Haemi Jang-a; multiple covers 4.00

CLIVE BARKER'S NEXT TESTAMENT
BOOM! Studios: May, 2013 - No. 12, Aug, 2014 ($3.99)
1-12: 1-Clive Barker & Mark Miller-s/Haemi Jang-a. 1-Four covers 4.00

CLIVE BARKER'S NIGHTBREED (Also see Epic)
Marvel Comics (Epic Comics): Apr, 1990 - No. 25, Mar, 1993 ($1.95/$2.25/$2.50, mature)
1-Adapts the horror movie 1 3 4 6 8 10
2-25: 2-4-Adapt horror movie. 5-New stories; Guice-a(p) 3.00

CLIVE BARKER'S NIGHTBREED
BOOM! Studios: May, 2014 - No. 12, Apr, 2015 ($3.99)
1-12: 1-8-Andreyko-s/Kowalski-a. 9-11-Javier & Pramanik-a 4.00

CLIVE BARKER'S THE HARROWERS
Marvel Comics (Epic Comics): Dec, 1993 - No. 6, May, 1994 ($2.50)
1-($2.95)-Glow-in-the-dark-c; Colan-c/a in all 4.00
2-6 3.00
NOTE: ***Colan*** *a(p)-1-6; c-1-3, 4p, 5p.* ***Williamson*** *a(i)-2, 4, 5(part).*

CLOAK AND DAGGER
Ziff-Davis Publishing Co.: Fall, 1952
1-Saunders painted-c 42 84 126 265 445 625

CLOAK AND DAGGER (Also see Marvel Fanfare and Spectacular Spider-Man #64)
Marvel Comics Group: Oct, 1983 - No. 4, Jan, 1984 (Mini-series)
1-Mantlo-s/Leonardi-a/Austin-a(i) in all 1 2 3 5 6 8
2-4: 4-Origin 5.00

CLOAK AND DAGGER (2nd Series)(Also see Marvel Graphic Novel #34 & Strange Tales)

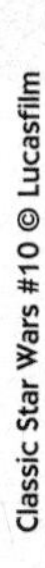
Classic Star Wars #10 © Lucasfilm

Clean Room #7 © Gail Simone

Cobra #18 © Hasbro

	GD 2.0	VG 4.0	FN 6.0	VF 8.0	VF/NM 9.0	NM- 9.2

Marvel Comics Group: July, 1985 - No. 11, Jan, 1987
1-Mantlo-s/Leonardi-a/Austin-a(i) 1 2 3 5 6 8
2-11: 7,8-Mignola-c. 9-Art Adams-p 4.00
...And Power Pack (1990, $7.95, 68 pgs.) 8.00

CLOAK AND DAGGER (3rd Series listed as Mutant Misadventures Of...)

CLOAK AND DAGGER
Marvel Comics: May, 2010 ($3.99, one-shot)
1-Stuart Moore-s/Mark Brooks-a; X-Men app. 6.00

CLOAK AND DAGGER: NEGATIVE EXPOSURE
Marvel Comics: 2019 ($19.99, squarebound TPB, printing of digital-first story)
nn-Hopeless-s/Manna & Coleman-a; Mister Negative app.; bonus inked art pages 20.00

CLOAK AND DAGGER: SHADES OF GREY
Marvel Comics: 2018 ($19.99, squarebound TPB, printing of digital-first story)
nn-Hopeless-s/Messina-a; bonus inked art pages 20.00

CLOAKED
Dark Horse Comics: Dec, 2021 - No. 4, Mar, 2022 ($3.99, limited series)
1-4-Mike Richardson-s/Jordi Armengol-a 4.00

CLOAKS
BOOM! Studios: Sept, 2014 - No. 4, Dec, 2014 ($3.99, limited series)
1-4-Monroe-s/Navarro-a 4.00

CLOBBERIN' TIME
Marvel Comics: Sept, 1995 ($1.95) (Based on card game)
nn-Overpower game guide; Ben Grimm story 3.00

CLOCK, THE
Image Comics: Jan, 2020 - No. 2, Feb, 2020 ($3.99)
1,2-Matt Hawkins-s/Colleen Doran-a 4.00

CLOCK MAKER, THE
Image Comics: Jan, 2003 - No. 4, May, 2003 ($2.50, comic unfolds to 10"x13" pages)
1-4-Krueger-s 3.00
... Act Two (4/04, $4.95, standard format) Krueger-s/Matt Smith-c 5.00

CLOCKWORK ANGELS (Based on Neil Peart's story and lyrics from Rush's album)
BOOM! Studios: Mar, 2014 - No. 6, Nov, 2014 ($3.99, limited series)
1-6-Kevin J. Anderson-s/Nick Robles-a; two covers on each 4.00

CLONE CONSPIRACY, THE (Also see Amazing Spider-Man [2017] #18)
Marvel Comics: Dec, 2016 - No. 5, Apr, 2017 ($4.99/$3.99)
1-($4.99) Slott-s/Cheung-a; Miles Warren, Gwen Stacy, Doc Ock & Rhino app. 5.00
2-5-($3.99) Kaine app. 3-Ben Reilly returns 4.00
...: Omega 1 (5/17, $4.99) Three short stories by various; aftermath of series 5.00

CLONEZONE SPECIAL
Dark Horse Comics/First Comics: 1989 ($2.00, B&W)
1-Back-up series from Badger & Nexus 3.00

CLOSE ENCOUNTERS (See Marvel Comics Super Special & Marvel Special Edition)

CLOSE SHAVES OF PAULINE PERIL, THE (TV cartoon)
Gold Key: June, 1970 - No. 4, March, 1971
1 4 8 12 27 44 60
2-4 3 6 9 17 26 35

CLOSET, THE
Image Comics: Jun, 2022 - No. 3, Aug, 2022 ($3.99, limited series)
1-3-James Tynion IV-s/Gavin Fullerton-a 4.00

CLOUDBURST
Image Comics: June, 2004 ($7.95, squarebound)
1-Gray & Palmiotti-s/Shy & Gouveia-a 8.00

CLOUDFALL
Image Comics: Nov, 2003 ($4.95, B&W, squarebound)
1-Kirkman-s/Su-a/c 5.00

CLOWN COMICS (No. 1 titled Clown Comic Book)
Clown Comics/Home Comics/Harvey Publ.: 1945 - No. 3, Win, 1946
nn (#1) 17 34 51 98 154 210
2,3 11 22 33 62 86 110

CLOWNS, THE (I Pagliacci)
Dark Horse Comics: 1998 ($2.95, B&W, one-shot)
1-Adaption of the opera; P. Craig Russell-script 3.00

CLUBHOUSE RASCALS (#1 titled ...Presents?) (Also see Three Rascals)
Sussex Publ. Co. (Magazine Enterprises): June, 1956 - No. 2, Oct, 1956
1-The Brain app. in both; DeCarlo-a 9 18 27 50 65 80
2 7 14 21 37 46 55

CLUB "16"
Famous Funnies: June, 1948 - No. 4, Dec, 1948
1-Teen-age humor 27 54 81 158 259 360
2-4 15 30 45 90 140 190

CLUE (Based on the boardgame)
IDW Publishing: Jun, 2017 - No. 6, Nov, 2017 ($3.99)
1-6-Paul Allor-s/Nelson Daniel-a; multiple covers on each 4.00

CLUE: CANDLESTICK (Based on the boardgame)
IDW Publishing: May, 2019 - No. 3, Jul, 2019 ($4.99, limited series)
1-3-Dash Shaw-s/a; multiple covers on each 5.00

CLUE COMICS (Real Clue Crime V2#4 on)
Hillman Periodicals: Jan, 1943 - No. 15(V2#3), May, 1947
1-Origin The Boy King, Nightmare, Micro-Face, Twilight, & Zippo
194 388 582 1242 2121 3000
2 (scarce) 97 194 291 621 1061 1500
3-5 (9/43) 50 100 150 315 533 750
6,8,9: 8-Palais-c/a(2) 39 78 117 231 378 525
7-Classic concentration camp torture-c (3/44) 135 270 405 864 1482 2100
10-Origin/1st app. The Gun Master & begin series; content changes to crime
(10/46) 40 80 120 246 411 575
11 (12/46) 30 60 90 177 289 400
12-Origin Rackman; McWilliams-a, Guardineer-a(2) 40 80 120 246 411 575
V2#1-Nightmare new origin; Iron Lady app.; Simon & Kirby-a (3/47)
84 168 252 538 919 1300
V2#2-S&K-a(2)-Bondage/torture-c; man attacks & kills people with electric iron.
Infantino-a 400 800 1200 2800 4900 7000
V2#3-S&K-a(3) 65 130 195 416 708 1000

CLUELESS: SENIOR YEAR (Movie)
Boom Entertainment (BOOM Box): Aug, 2017 ($14.99, SC, graphic novel)
nn-Sarah Kuhn & Amber Benson-s/Siobhan Keenan-a; sequel to the movie; bonus art 15.00

CLUELESS SPRING SPECIAL (TV)
Marvel Comics: May, 1997 ($3.99, magazine sized, one-shot)
1-Photo-c from TV show 4.00

CLUSTER
BOOM! Studios: Feb, 2015 - No. 8, Oct, 2015 ($3.99, limited series)
1-8-Ed Brisson-s/Damian Couceiro-a 4.00

CLUTCHING HAND, THE
American Comics Group: July-Aug, 1954
1-Gustavson, Moldoff-a 68 136 204 435 743 1050

CLYDE BEATTY COMICS (Also see Crackajack Funnies)
Commodore Productions & Artists, Inc.: October, 1953 (84 pgs.)
1-Photo front/back-c; movie scenes and comics 26 52 78 154 252 350

CLYDE CRASHCUP (TV)
Dell Publishing Co.: Aug-Oct, 1963 - No. 5, Sept-Nov, 1964
1-All written by John Stanley 6 12 18 41 76 110
2-5 4 8 12 27 44 60

COBB
IDW Publishing: May, 2006 - No. 3, July, 2007 ($3.99, B&W)
1-3-Beau Smith-s/Eduardo Barreto-a/c; regular and retailer incentive covers 4.00

COBRA (G.I. Joe)
IDW Publishing: No. 10, Feb, 2012 - No. 21, Jan, 2013 ($3.99)
10-21 4.00
... Annual 2012: The Origin of Cobra Commander (1/12, $7.99) Dixon-s 8.00

COBRA KAI: THE KARATE KID SAGA CONTINUES (Based on the Karate Kid movie)
IDW Publishing: Oct, 2019 - Present ($3.99)
1-3-Johnny Lawrence's story before & during the movie; Kagan McLeod-a 4.00

CODENAME: ACTION
Dynamite Entertainment: 2013 - No. 5, 2014 ($3.99, limited series)
1-5-Captain Action; Chris Roberson-s/Jonathan Lau-a; multiple covers on each 4.00

CODE NAME: ASSASSIN (See 1st Issue Special)

CODENAME: BABOUSHKA

	GD 2.0	VG 4.0	FN 6.0	VF 8.0	VF/NM 9.0	NM- 9.2

Image Comics: Oct, 2015 - No. 5, Mar, 2016 ($3.99, limited series)
1-5: 1-Antony Johnston-s/Shari Chankhamma-a 4.00

CODENAME: DANGER
Lodestone Publishing: Aug, 1985 - No. 4, May, 1986 ($1.50)
1-4 3.00

CODENAME: FIREARM (Also see Firearm)
Malibu Comics (Ultraverse): June, 1995 - No. 5, Sept, 1995 ($2.95, bimonthly limited series)
0-5: 0-2-Alec Swan back-up story by James Robinson. 0-Pérez-c 3.00

CODENAME: GENETIX
Marvel Comics UK: Jan, 1993 - No. 4, May, 1993 ($1.75, limited series)
1-4: Wolverine in all 3.00

CODENAME: KNOCKOUT
DC Comics (Vertigo): No. 0, Jun, 2001 - No. 23, June, 2003 ($2.50/$2.75)
0-15: Rodi-s in all. 0-5-Small Jr. -a. 1-Two covers by Chiodo & Cho. 7,8,10,11,12-Paquette-a. 6,9,13,14-Conner-a 3.00
16-23: 16-Begin $2.75-c. 23-Last issue; JG Jones-c 3.00

CODENAME SPITFIRE (Formerly Spitfire And The Troubleshooters)
Marvel Comics Group: No. 10, July, 1987 - No. 13, Oct, 1987
10-13: 10-Rogers-c/a (low printing) 3.50

CODENAME: STRYKE FORCE (Also See Cyberforce V1#4 & Cyberforce/Stryke Force: Opposing Forces
Image Comics (Top Cow Productions): Jan, 1994 - No. 14, Sept, 1995 ($1.95-$2.25)
0,1-14: 1-12-Silvestri stories, Peterson-a. 4-Stormwatch app. 14-Story continues in Cyberforce/Stryke Force: Opposing Forces; Turner-a 3.00
1-Gold, 1-Blue 4.00

CODE OF HONOR
Marvel Comics: Feb, 1997 - No. 4, May, 1997 ($5.95, limited series)
1-4-Fully painted by various; Dixon-s 6.00

CODY OF THE PONY EXPRESS (See Colossal Features Magazine)
Fox Feature Syndicate: Sept, 1950 (See Women Outlaws)(One shot)

	GD	VG	FN	VF	VF/NM	NM-
1-Painted-c	15	30	45	90	140	190

CODY OF THE PONY EXPRESS (Buffalo Bill...) (Outlaws of the West #11 on; Formerly Bullseye)
Charlton Comics: No. 8, Oct, 1955; No. 9, Jan, 1956; No. 10, June, 1956

	GD	VG	FN	VF	VF/NM	NM-
8-Bullseye on splash pg; not S&K-a	8	16	24	44	57	70
9,10: Buffalo Bill app. in all	6	12	18	29	36	42

CODY STARBUCK (1st app. in Star Reach #1)
Star Reach Productions: July, 1978

	GD	VG	FN	VF	VF/NM	NM-
nn-Howard Chaykin-c/a	3	6	9	14	20	25
2nd printing	2	4	6	8	10	12

NOTE: *Both printings say First Printing. True first printing is on lower-grade paper, somewhat off-register, and snow in snow sequence has green tint.*

CO-ED ROMANCES
P. L. Publishing Co.: November, 1951

	GD	VG	FN	VF	VF/NM	NM-
1	15	30	45	85	130	175

COFFEE WORLD
World Comics: Oct, 1995 ($1.50, B&W, anthology)
1-Shannon Wheeler's Too Much Coffee Man story 4.00

COFFIN, THE
Oni Press: Sept, 2000 - No. 4, May, 2001 ($2.95, B&W, limited series)
1-4-Hester-s/Huddleston-a 3.00

COFFIN BOUND
Image Comics: Aug, 2019 - No. 8, Nov, 2020 ($3.99/$4.99, limited series)
1-3,5,6,8-($3.99) Dan Watters-s/Dani-a 4.00
4,7-($4.99) 4-Bonus preview of Protector #1 5.00

COFFIN HILL
DC Comics (Vertigo): Dec, 2013 - No. 20, Sept, 2015 ($2.99/$3.99)
1-18: 1-Caitlin Kittredge-s/Inaki Miranda-a; covers by Dave Johnson & Gene Ha 3.00
19,20-($3.99) Johnson-c 4.00

COJACARU THE SKINNER
Dark Horse Comics: Apr, 2021 - No. 2, May, 2021 ($3.99, limited series)
1,2-Mignola & Golden-s/Bergting-a 4.00

COLDER
Dark Horse Comics: Nov, 2012 - No. 5, Mar, 2013 ($3.99, limited series)
1-5-Tobin-s/Ferreyra-a/c 4.00

COLDER: THE BAD SEED
Dark Horse Comics: Oct, 2014 - No. 5, Feb, 2015 ($3.99, limited series)
1-5-Tobin-s/Ferreyra-a/c 4.00

COLDER: TOSS THE BONES
Dark Horse Comics: Sept, 2015 - No. 5, Jan, 2016 ($3.99, limited series)
1-5-Tobin-s/Ferreyra-a/c 4.00

COLD WAR
IDW Publishing: Oct, 2011 - No. 4, Jan, 2012 ($3.99, limited series)
1-4-John Byrne-s/a/c; two covers on each 4.00

COLD WAR
AfterShock Comics: Feb, 2018 - No. 5, Jun, 2018 ($3.99, limited series)
1-5-Sebela-a/Sherman-a 4.00

COLLAPSER
DC Comics (Young Animal): Sept, 2019 - No. 6, Feb, 2020 ($3.99, limited series)
1-6-Mikey Way & Shaun Simon-s/Ilias Kyriazis-a. 5-Superman #1 cover swipe 4.00

COLLECTORS DRACULA, THE
Millennium Publications: 1994 - No. 2, 1994 ($3.95, color/B&W, 52 pgs., limited series)
1,2-Bolton-a (7 pgs.) 4.00

COLLECTORS ITEM CLASSICS (See Marvel Collectors Item Classics)

COLLECTOR, THE : UNIT 731
Dark Horse Comics: Apr, 2022 - No. 4, Jul, 2022 ($3.99, limited series)
1-4-Will Conrad & Rod Monteiro-s/Conrad-a; set in a WWII Japanese POW camp 4.00

COLLIDER (See FBP: Federal Bureau Of Physics; title changed after issue #1)

COLONEL WEIRD: COSMAGOG (From Black Hammer)
Dark Horse Comics: Oct, 2020 - No. 4, Jan, 2021 ($3.99, limited series)
1-4-Jeff Lemire-s/Tyler Crook-a 4.00

COLONIZED, THE
IDW Publishing: Apr, 2013 - No. 4, Jul, 2013 ($3.99, limited series)
1-4-Aliens vs. Zombies; Dave Sim-c/Chris Ryall-s/Drew Moss-a 4.00

COLORS IN BLACK
Dark Horse Comics: Mar, 1995 - No. 4, June, 1995 ($2.95, limited series)
1-4 3.00

COLOSSAL FEATURES MAGAZINE (Formerly I Loved) (See Cody of the Pony Express)
Fox Feature Syndicate: No. 33, 5/50 - No. 34, 7/50; No. 3, 9/50 (Based on Columbia serial)

	GD	VG	FN	VF	VF/NM	NM-
33,34: Cody of the Pony Express begins. 33-Painted-c. 34-Photo-c	20	40	60	118	192	265
3-Authentic criminal cases	68	136	204	435	743	1050

COLOSSAL SHOW, THE (TV cartoon)
Gold Key: Oct, 1969

	GD	VG	FN	VF	VF/NM	NM-
1	5	10	15	30	50	70

COLOSSUS (See X-Men)
Marvel Comics: Oct, 1997 ($2.99, 48 pgs., one-shot)
1-Raab-s/Hitch & Neary-a, wraparound-c 5.00

COLOSSUS COMICS (See Green Giant & Motion Picture Funnies Weekly)
Sun Publications (Funnies, Inc.?): March, 1940

	GD	VG	FN	VF	VF/NM	NM-
1-(Scarce)-Tulpa of Tsang(hero); Colossus app.	1050	2100	3150	8000	14,500	21,000

NOTE: *Cover by artist that drew Colossus in Green Giant Comics.*

COLOUR OF MAGIC, THE (Terry Pratchett's...)
Innovation Publishing: 1991 - No. 4, 1991 ($2.50, limited series)
1-4: Adapts 1st novel of the Discworld series 3.00

COLOUR YOUR OWN CEREBUS IN HELL?
Aardvark-Vanaheim: Oct, 2019 ($4.00, B&W)
1-Cerebus figures placed over original Gustave Doré artwork of Hell 4.00

COLT .45 (TV)
Dell Publishing Co.: No. 924, 8/58 - No. 1058, 11-1/59-60; No. 4, 2-4/60 - No. 9, 5-7/61

	GD	VG	FN	VF	VF/NM	NM-
Four Color 924(#1)-Wayde Preston photo-c on all	9	18	27	62	126	190
Four Color 1004,1058: 1004-Photo-b/c	7	14	21	48	89	130
4,5,7-9	7	14	21	48	89	130
6-Toth-a	8	16	24	51	96	140

COLUMBIA COMICS
William H. Wise Co.: 1943

	GD	VG	FN	VF	VF/NM	NM-
1-Joe Palooka, Charlie Chan, Capt. Yank, Sparky Watts, Dixie Dugan app.	36	72	108	211	343	475

COMANCHE
Dell Publishing Co.: No. 1350, Apr-Jun, 1962

	GD	VG	FN	VF	VF/NM	NM-
Four Color 1350-Disney movie; reprints FC #966 with title change from "Tonka" to "Comanche"; Sal Mineo photo-c	5	10	15	35	63	90

COMANCHEROS, THE
Dell Publishing Co.: No. 1300, Mar-May, 1962

	GD	VG	FN	VF	VF/NM	NM-
Four Color 1300-Movie, John Wayne photo-c	15	30	45	100	220	340

COMBAT
Atlas Comics (ANC): June, 1952 - No. 11, April, 1953

	GD	VG	FN	VF	VF/NM	NM-
1	53	106	159	334	567	800
2-Heath-c/a	29	58	87	172	281	390
3,5-9,11: 3-Romita-a. 6-Robinson-c; Romita-a	21	42	63	124	202	280
4-Krigstein-a	21	42	63	122	199	275
10-B&W and color illos. in **POP**; Sale-a, Forte-a	34	68	102	199	325	450

NOTE: *Combat Casey in 7-11.* **Heath** *a-2, 3; c-1, 2, 5, 9.* **Maneely** *a-1; c-3, 10.* **Pakula** *a-1.* **Reinman** *a-1.*

COMBAT
Dell Publishing Co.: Oct-Nov, 1961 - No. 40, Oct, 1973 (No #9)

	GD	VG	FN	VF	VF/NM	NM-
1-Painted-c (thru #17)	9	18	27	57	111	165
2,3,5	5	10	15	34	60	85
4-John F. Kennedy c/story (P.T. 109)	7	14	21	46	86	125
6,7,8(4-6/63), 8(7-9/63)	5	10	15	30	50	70
10-26: 26-Last 12¢ issue	4	8	12	25	40	55
27-40(reprints #1-14). 30-r/#4	3	6	9	16	24	32

COMBAT CASEY (Formerly War Combat)
Atlas Comics (SAI): No. 6, Jan, 1953 - No. 34, July, 1957

	GD	VG	FN	VF	VF/NM	NM-
6 (Indicia shows 1/52 in error)	39	78	117	231	378	525
7-R.Q. Sale-a	22	44	66	132	216	300
8-Used in **POP**, pg. 94	20	40	60	120	195	270
9,10,13-19-Violent art by R.Q. Sale; Battle Brady x-over #10	26	52	78	154	252	350
11,12,20-Last Precode (2/55)	18	36	54	103	162	220
21-34: 22,25-R.Q. Sale-a	17	34	51	98	154	210

NOTE: **Everett** *a-6.* **Heath** *c-10, 17, 19, 23, 30.* **Maneely** *c-6, 8, 15.* **Powell** *a-29(5), 30(5), 34.* **Severin** *c-26, 33, 34.*

COMBAT KELLY
Atlas Comics (SPI): Nov, 1951 - No. 44, Aug, 1957

	GD	VG	FN	VF	VF/NM	NM-
1-1st app. Combat Kelly; Heath-a	53	106	159	334	567	800
2	28	56	84	165	270	375
3-10	21	42	63	122	199	275

Coffin Bound #1 © Dan Watters & Dani

Combat #1 © MAR

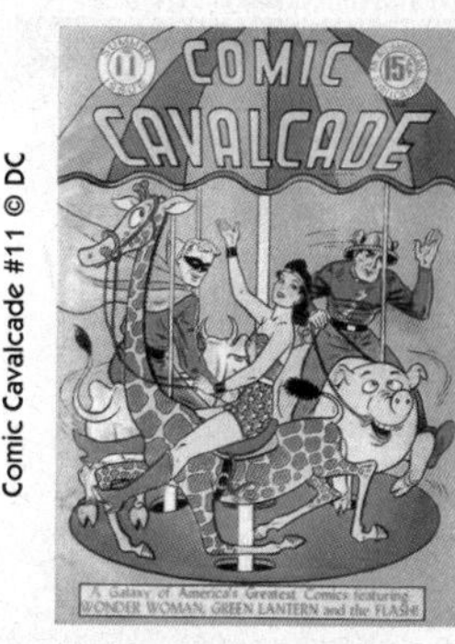

Comic Cavalcade #11 © DC

	GD 2.0	VG 4.0	FN 6.0	VF 8.0	VF/NM 9.0	NM- 9.2

11-Used in **POP**, pgs. 94,95 plus color illo. 22 44 66 132 216 300
12-Color illo. in **POP** 20 40 60 115 185 255
13-16 18 36 54 107 169 230
17-Violent art by R. Q. Sale; Combat Casey app. 23 46 69 138 227 315
18-20,22-28: 18-Battle Brady app. 28-Last precode (1/55)
18 36 54 103 162 220
21-Transvestism-c 21 42 63 122 199 275
29-44: 38-Green Berets story (8/56) 16 32 48 96 151 205
NOTE: ***Berg** a-8, 12-14, 15-17, 19-23, 25, 26, 28, 31-37, 39, 41-44; c-2. **Colan** a-42. **Heath** a-4, 18; c-31. **Lawrence** a-23. **Maneely** a-3-5(2), 6, 7(3), 8, 9(2), 11; c-4, 5, 7, 8, 10, 11, 25, 29, 39. **R.Q. Sale** a-17, 25. **Severin** c-41, 42. **Whitney** a-5.*

COMBAT KELLY (...and the Deadly Dozen)
Marvel Comics Group: June, 1972 - No. 9, Oct, 1973
1-Intro & origin new Combat Kelly; Ayers/Mooney-a; Severin-c (20¢)
5 10 15 34 60 85
2,5-8 3 6 9 14 20 25
3,4: 3-Origin. 4-Sgt. Fury-c/s 3 6 9 16 24 32
9-Death of the Deadly Dozen 4 8 12 25 40 55

COMBAT ZONE: TRUE TALES OF GIS IN IRAQ
Marvel Comics: 2005 ($19.99, squarebound)
Vol. 1-Karl Zinsmeister scripts adapted from his non-fiction books; Dan Jurgens-a 20.00

COMBINED OPERATIONS (See The Story of the Commandos)

COMEBACK (See Zane Grey 4-Color 357)

COMEDY CARNIVAL
St. John Publishing Co.: no date (1950's) (100 pgs.)
nn-Contains rebound St. John comics 40 80 120 246 411 575

COMEDY COMICS (1st Series) (Daring Mystery #1-8) (Becomes Margie Comics #35 on)
Timely Comics (TCI 9,10): No. 9, April, 1942 - No. 34, Fall, 1946
9-(Scarce)-The Fin by Everett, Capt. Dash, Citizen V, & The Silver Scorpion app.; Wolverton-a; 1st app. Comedy Kid; satire on Hitler & Stalin; The Fin, Citizen V & Silver Scorpion cont. from Daring Mystery 308 616 924 2156 3778 5400
10-(Scarce)-Origin The Fourth Musketeer, Victory Boys; Monstro, the Mighty app.
245 490 735 1568 2684 3800
11-Vagabond, Stuporman app. 74 148 222 470 810 1150
12,13 34 68 102 199 325 450
14-Origin/1st app. Super Rabbit (3/43) plus-c 110 220 330 704 1202 1700
15-19 30 60 90 177 289 400
20-Hitler parody-c 84 168 252 538 919 1300
21-Tojo-c 65 130 195 416 708 1000
22-Hitler parody-c 123 246 369 787 1344 1900
23-32 22 44 66 132 216 300
33-Kurtzman-a (5 pgs.) 23 46 69 136 223 310
34-Intro Margie; Wolverton-a (5 pgs.) 45 90 135 284 480 675

COMEDY COMICS (2nd Series)
Marvel Comics (ACI): May, 1948 - No. 10, Jan, 1950
1-Hedy, Tessie, Millie begin; Kurtzman's "Hey Look" (he draws himself)
93 186 279 591 1021 1450
2 60 120 180 381 653 925
3,4-Kurtzman's "Hey Look": 3-(1 pg). 4-(3 pgs) 77 154 231 493 847 1200
5-10 33 66 99 194 317 440

COMET, THE (See The Mighty Crusaders & Pep Comics #1)
Red Circle Comics (Archie): Oct, 1983 - No. 2, Dec, 1983
1-Re-intro & origin The Comet; The American Shield begins. Nino & Infantino art in both. Hangman in both 6.00
2-Origin continues. 5.00

COMET, THE
DC Comics (Impact Comics): July, 1991 - No. 18, Dec, 1992 ($1.00/$1.25)
1 4.00
2-18: 4-Black Hood app. 6-Re-intro Hangman. 8-Web x-over. 10-Contains Crusaders trading card. 4-Origin. Netzer (Nasser) c(p)-11,14-17 3.00
Annual 1 (1992, $2.50, 68 pgs.)-Contains Impact trading card; Shield back-up story 4.00

COMET MAN, THE (Movie)
Marvel Comics Group: Feb, 1987 - No. 6, July, 1987 (limited series)
1-6: 3-Hulk app. 4-She-Hulk shower scene-c/s. Fantastic 4 app. 5-Fantastic 4 app. 3.00
NOTE: ***Kelley Jones** a-1-6p.*

COMIC ALBUM (Also see Disney Comic Album)
Dell Publishing Co.: Mar-May, 1958 - No. 18, June-Aug, 1962
1-Donald Duck 9 18 27 62 126 190
2-Bugs Bunny 5 10 15 31 53 75
3-Donald Duck 6 12 18 41 76 110
4-6,8-10: 4-Tom & Jerry. 5-Woody Woodpecker. 6,10-Bugs Bunny. 8-Tom & Jerry. 9-Woody Woodpecker 4 8 12 27 44 60
7,11,15: Popeye. 11-(9-11/60) 4 8 12 28 47 65
12-14: 12-Tom & Jerry. 13-Woody Woodpecker. 14-Bugs Bunny
4 8 12 27 44 60
16-Flintstones (12-2/61-62)-3rd app. Early Cave Kids app.
7 14 21 46 86 125
17-Space Mouse (3rd app.) 5 10 15 30 50 70
18-Three Stooges; photo-c 7 14 21 46 86 125

COMIC BOOK
Marvel Comics-#1/Dark Horse Comics-#2: 1995 ($5.95, oversize)
1-Spumco characters by John K. 1 2 3 4 5 7
2-(Dark Horse) 6.00

COMIC BOOK GUY: THE COMIC BOOK (BONGO COMICS PRESENTS...) (Simpsons)
Bongo Comics: 2010 - No. 5, 2010 ($3.99/$2.99, limited series)
1-($3.99) Four-layer cover w/classic swipes incl. FF#1; intro Graphic Novel Kid
3 6 9 16 23 30
2-5-($2.99) 2-Stan Lee cameo. 3-Includes Little Lulu spoof. 4-Comic Book Guy origin
1 2 3 5 6 8

COMIC CAPERS
Red Circle Mag./Marvel Comics: Fall, 1944 - No. 6, Fall, 1946
1-Super Rabbit, The Creeper, Silly Seal, Ziggy Pig, Sharpy Fox begin
50 100 150 315 533 750
2 27 54 81 158 259 360
3-6: 4-(Summer 1945) 23 46 69 136 223 310

COMIC CAVALCADE
All-American/National Periodical Publications: Winter, 1942-43 - No. 63, June-July, 1954
(Contents change with No. 30, Dec-Jan, 1948-49 on)
1-The Flash, Green Lantern, Wonder Woman, Wildcat, The Black Pirate by Moldoff (also #2), Ghost Patrol, and Red White & Blue begin; Scribbly app.; Minute Movie
1025 2050 3075 7800 14,150 20,500
2-Mutt & Jeff begin; last Ghost Patrol & Black Pirate; Minute Movies
290 580 870 1856 3178 4500
3-Hop Harrigan & Sargon, the Sorcerer begin; The King app.
187 374 561 1197 2049 2900
4,5: 4-The Gay Ghost, The King, Scribbly, & Red Tornado app. 5-Christmas-c. 5-Prints ad for Jr. JSA membership kit that includes "The Minute Man Answers The Call"
181 362 543 1158 1979 2800
6-10: 7-Red Tornado & Black Pirate app.; last Scribbly. 9-Fat & Slat app.; X-Mas-c
155 310 465 992 1696 2400
11-Wonder Woman vs. The Cheetah 135 270 405 864 1482 2100
12,14: 12-Last Red White & Blue 119 238 357 762 1306 1850
13-Solomon Grundy app.; X-Mas-c 229 458 687 1454 2502 3550
15-Just a Story begins 116 232 348 742 1271 1800
16-20: 19-Christmas-c 110 220 330 704 1202 1700
21-23: 22-Johnny Peril begins. 23-Harry Lampert-c (Toth swipes)
100 200 300 635 1093 1550
24-Solomon Grundy x-over in Green Lantern 135 270 405 864 1482 2100
25-28: 25-Black Canary app.; X-Mas-c. 26-28-Johnny Peril app. 28-Last Mutt & Jeff
93 186 279 591 1021 1450
29-(10-11/48)-Last Flash, Wonder Woman, Green Lantern & Johnny Peril; Wonder Woman invents "Thinking Machine"; 2nd computer in comics (after Flash Comics #52); Leave It to Binky story (early app.) 132 264 396 838 1444 2050
30-(12-1/48-49)-The Fox & the Crow, Dodo & the Frog & Nutsy Squirrel begin
47 94 141 296 498 700
31-35 24 48 72 142 234 325
36-49: 41-Last squarebound issue 18 36 54 105 165 225
50-62(Scarce) 21 42 63 126 206 285
63(Rare) 40 80 120 246 411 575
NOTE: ***Grossman** a-30-63. **E.E. Hibbard** c-(Flash only)-1-4, 7-14, 16-19, 21. **Sheldon Mayer** a(2-3)-40-63. **Moulson** c(G.L.)-7, 15. **Nodell** c(G.L.)-9. **H.G. Peter** c(W. Woman only)-1, 3-21, 24. **Post** a-31, 36. **Purcell** c(G.L.)-2-5, 10. **Reinman** a(Green Lantern)-4-6, 8, 9, 13, 15-21; c(Gr. Lantern)-6, 8, 19. **Toth** a(Green Lantern)-26-28; c-27. Atom app.-22, 23.*

COMIC COMICS
Fawcett Publications: Apr, 1946 - No. 10, Feb, 1947
1-Captain Kid; Nutty Comics #1 in indicia 20 40 60 115 185 255
2-10-Wolverton-a, 4 pgs. each. 5-Captain Kidd app. Mystic Moot by Wolverton in #2-10? 17 34 51 100 158 215

COMIC LAND
Fact and Fiction Publ.: March, 1946
1-Sandusky & the Senator, Sam Stupor, Sleuth, Marvin the Great, Sir Passer, Phineas Gruff

	GD 2.0	VG 4.0	FN 6.0	VF 8.0	VF/NM 9.0	NM- 9.2
app.; Irv Tirman & Perry Williams art	19	38	57	111	176	240

COMICO CHRISTMAS SPECIAL
Comico: Dec, 1988 ($2.50, 44 pgs.)

	GD	VG	FN	VF	VF/NM	NM-
1-Rude/Williamson-a; Dave Stevens-c	2	4	6	10	14	18

COMICO COLLECTION (Also see Grendel)
Comico: 1987 ($9.95, slipcased collection)

nn-Contains exclusive Grendel: Devil's Vagary, 9 random Comico comics, a poster and newsletter in black slipcase w/silver ink 25.00

COMICO PRIMER (See Primer)

COMIC PAGES (Formerly Funny Picture Stories)
Centaur Publications: V3#4, July, 1939 - V3#6, Dec, 1939

	GD	VG	FN	VF	VF/NM	NM-
V3#4-Bob Wood-a	142	284	426	909	1555	2200
5,6: 6-Schwab-c	129	258	387	826	1413	2000

COMICS (See All Good)

COMICS, THE
Dell Publ. Co.: Mar, 1937 - No. 11, Nov, 1938 (Newspaper strip-r; bi-monthly)

	GD	VG	FN	VF	VF/NM	NM-
1-1st app. Tom Mix in comics; Wash Tubbs, Tom Beatty, Myra North, Arizona Kid, Erik Noble & International Spy w/Doctor Doom begin	194	388	582	1242	2121	3000
2	90	180	270	576	988	1400
3-11: 3-Alley Oop begins	74	148	222	470	810	1150

COMICS AND STORIES (See Walt Disney's Comics and Stories)

COMICS & STORIES (Also see Wolf & Red)
Dark Horse Comics: Apr, 1996 - No. 4, July, 1996 ($2.95, lim. series) (Created by Tex Avery)

1-4: Wolf & Red app; reads Comics and Stories on-c. 1-Terry Moore-a. 2-Reed Waller-a 3.00

COMICS CALENDAR, THE (The 1946...)
True Comics Press (ordered through the mail): 1946 (25¢, 116 pgs.) (Stapled at top)

	GD	VG	FN	VF	VF/NM	NM-
nn-(Rare) Has a "strip" story for every day of the year in color	52	104	156	328	552	775

COMICS DIGEST (Pocket size)
Parents' Magazine Institute: Winter, 1942-43 (B&W, 100 pgs)

	GD	VG	FN	VF	VF/NM	NM-
1-Reprints from True Comics (non-fiction World War II stories)	14	28	42	81	118	155

COMICS EXPRESS
Eclipse Comics: Nov, 1989 - No. 2, Jan, 1990 ($2.95, B&W, 68pgs.)

1,2: Collection of strip-r; 2(12/89-c, 1/90 inside) 4.00

COMICS FOR KIDS
London Publ. Co./Timely: 1945 (no month); No. 2, Sum, 1945 (Funny animal)

	GD	VG	FN	VF	VF/NM	NM-
1-Puffy Pig, Sharpy Fox	39	78	117	231	378	525
2-Puffy Pig, Sharpy Fox	26	52	78	154	252	350

COMICS' GREATEST WORLD
Dark Horse Comics: Jun, 1993 - V4#4, Sept, 1993 ($1.00, weekly, lim. series)

	GD	VG	FN	VF	VF/NM	NM-
Arcadia (Wk 1): V1#1,2,4: 1-X: Frank Miller-c. 2-Pit Bulls. 4-Monster.						3.00
1-B&W Press Proof Edition (1500 copies)	1	3	4	6	8	10
1-Silver-c; distr. retailer bonus w/print & cards	1	2	3	5	6	8
3-Ghost, Dorman-c; Hughes-a						4.00
Retailer's Prem. Emb. Silver Foil Logo-r/V1#1-4	1	3	4	6	8	10
Golden City (Wk 2: V2#1-4: 1-Rebel; Ordway-c. 2-Mecha; Dave Johnson-c.						
3-Titan; Walt Simonson-c. 4-Catalyst; Perez-c.						3.00
1-Gold-c; distr. retailer bonus w/print & cards.						6.00
Retailer's Prem. Embos. Gold Foil Logo-r/V2#1-4	1	2	3	5	6	8
Steel Harbor (Week 3): V3#1-Barb Wire; Dorman-c; Gulacy-a(p)						4.00
2-4: 2-The Machine. 3-Wolfgang. 4-Motorhead						3.00
1-Silver-c; distr. retailer bonus w/print & cards	1	2	3	5	6	8
Retailer's Prem. Emb. Red Foil Logo-r/V3#1-4.	1	3	4	6	8	10
Vortex (Week 4): V4#1-4: 1-Division 13; Dorman-c. 2-Hero Zero; Art Adams-c.						
3-King Tiger; Chadwick-a(p); Darrow-c. 4-Vortex; Miller-c.						3.00
1-Gold-c; distr. retailer bonus w/print & cards.						6.00
Retailer's Prem. Emb. Blue Foil Logo-r/V4#1-4.	1	2	3	5	6	8

COMICS' GREATEST WORLD: OUT OF THE VORTEX (See Out of The Vortex)

COMICS HITS (See Harvey Comics Hits)

COMICS MAGAZINE, THE (...Funny Pages #3)(Funny Pages #6 on)
Comics Magazine Co. (1st Comics Mag./Centaur Publ.): May, 1936 - No. 5, Sept, 1936 (Paper covers)

	GD	VG	FN	VF	VF/NM	NM-
1-1st app. Dr. Mystic (a.k.a. Dr. Occult) by Siegel & Shuster (the 1st app. of a Superman prototype in comics). Dr. Mystic is not in costume but later appears in costume as a more pronounced prototype in More Fun #14-17. (1st episode of "The Koth and the Seven"; continues in More Fun #14; originally scheduled for publication at DC). 1 pg. Kelly-a; Sheldon Mayer-a	4250	8500	12,750	25,500	--	--
2-Federal Agent (a.k.a. Federal Men) by Siegel & Shuster; 1 pg. Kelly-a	460	920	1380	2760	3680	4600
3-5	400	800	1200	2400	3200	4000

COMICS NOVEL (Anarcho, Dictator of Death)
Fawcett Publications: 1947

	GD	VG	FN	VF	VF/NM	NM-
1-All Radar; 51 pg anti-fascism story	45	90	135	284	480	675

COMICS ON PARADE (No. 30 on are a continuation of Single Series)
United Features Syndicate: Apr, 1938 - No. 104, Feb, 1955

	GD	VG	FN	VF	VF/NM	NM-
1-Tarzan by Foster; Captain & the Kids, Little Mary Mixup, Abbie & Slats, Ella Cinders, Broncho Bill, Li'l Abner begin	400	800	1200	2800	4900	7000
2 (Tarzan & others app. on-c of #1-3,17)	148	296	444	947	1624	2300
3	116	232	348	742	1271	1800
4,5	82	164	246	528	902	1275
6-10	55	110	165	352	601	850
11-16,18-20	42	84	126	267	451	635
17-Tarzan-c	55	110	165	352	601	850
21-29: 22-Son of Tarzan begins. 22,24,28-Tailspin Tommy-c. 29-Last Tarzan issue	36	72	108	216	351	485
30-Li'l Abner	20	40	60	114	182	250
31-The Captain & the Kids	15	30	45	85	130	175
32-Nancy & Fritzi Ritz	14	28	42	78	112	145
33,36,39,42-Li'l Abner	16	32	48	94	147	200
34,37,40-The Captain & the Kids (10/41,6/42,3/43)	15	30	45	83	124	165
35,38-Nancy & Fritzi Ritz. 38-Infinity-c	14	28	42	76	108	140
41-Nancy & Fritzi Ritz	12	24	36	67	94	120
43-The Captain & the Kids	15	30	45	83	124	165
44 (3/44),47,50: Nancy & Fritzi Ritz	12	24	36	67	94	120
45-Li'l Abner	15	30	45	84	127	170
46,49-The Captain & the Kids	13	26	39	74	105	135
48-Li'l Abner (3/45)	15	30	45	84	127	170
51,54-Li'l Abner	14	28	42	76	108	140
52-The Captain & the Kids (3/46)	12	24	36	69	97	125
53,55,57-Nancy & Fritzi Ritz	11	22	33	62	86	110
56-The Captain & the Kids (r/Sparkler)	11	22	33	62	86	110
58-Li'l Abner; continues as Li'l Abner #61?	14	28	42	76	108	140
59-The Captain & the Kids	10	20	30	54	72	90
60-70-Nancy & Fritzi Ritz	9	18	27	47	61	75
71-99,101-104-Nancy & Sluggo: 71-76-Nancy only	8	16	24	42	54	65
100-Nancy & Sluggo	14	28	42	76	108	140
Special Issue, 7/46; Summer, 1948 - The Captain & the Kids app.	14	28	42	76	108	140

NOTE: Bound Volume (Very Rare) includes No. 1-12; bound by publisher in pictorial comic boards & distributed at the 1939 World's Fair and through mail order from ads in comic books (also see Tip Top) 300 600 900 2010 3505 5000

NOTE: *Li'l Abner reprinted from Tip Top.*

COMICS READING LIBRARIES (See the Promotional Comics section)

COMICS REVUE
St. John Publ. Co. (United Features Synd.): June, 1947 - No. 5, Jan, 1948

	GD	VG	FN	VF	VF/NM	NM-
1-Ella Cinders & Blackie	15	30	45	88	137	185
2,4: 2-Hap Hopper (7/47). 4-Ella Cinders (9/47)	10	20	30	56	76	95
3,5: 3-Iron Vic (8/47). 5-Gordo No. 1 (1/48)	10	20	30	54	72	90

COMIC STORY PAINT BOOK
Samuel Lowe Co.: 1943 (Large size, 68 pgs.)

	GD	VG	FN	VF	VF/NM	NM-
1055-Captain Marvel & a Captain Marvel Jr. story to read & color; 3 panels in color per pg. (reprints)	87	174	261	553	952	1350

COMING OF RAGE
Liquid Comics: 2015 - No. 5, 2016 ($3.99, limited series)

1-5-Wes Craven & Steve Niles-s/Francesco Biagini-a. 1-Afterword by Wes Craven 4.00

COMIX BOOK
Marvel Comics Group/Krupp Comics Works No. 4,5: 1974 - No. 5, 1976 ($1.00, B&W, magazine) (#1-3 newsstand; #4,5 were direct distribution only)

	GD	VG	FN	VF	VF/NM	NM-
1-Underground comic artists; 2 pgs. Wolverton-a	3	6	9	15	22	28
2,3: 2-Wolverton-a (1 pg.)	3	6	9	14	19	24
4(2/76), 4(5/76), 5 (Low distribution)	3	6	9	16	23	30

NOTE: *Print run No. 1-3: 200,000-250,000; No. 4&5: 10,000 each.*

COMIX INTERNATIONAL
Warren Magazines: Jul, 1974 - No. 5, Spring, 1977 (Full color, stiff-c, mail only)

	GD	VG	FN	VF	VF/NM	NM-
1-Low distribution; all Corben story remainders from Warren; Corben-c on all	9	18	27	62	126	190
2,4: 2-Two Dracula stories; Wood, Wrightson-r; Crandall-a; Maroto-a. 4-Printing w/ 3 Corben sty	6	12	18	37	66	95
3-5: 3-Dax story. 4-(printing without Corben story). 4-Crandall-a. 4,5-Vampirella stories. 5-Spirit story; Eisner-a	5	10	15	33	57	80

NOTE: *No. 4 had two printings with extra **Corben** story in one. No. 3 may also have a variation. No. 3 has two Jeff Jones reprints from Vampirella.*

COMMANDER BATTLE AND THE ATOMIC SUB
Amer. Comics Group (Titan Publ. Co.): Jul-Aug, 1954 - No. 7, Aug-Sep, 1955

	GD	VG	FN	VF	VF/NM	NM-
1 (3-D effect)-Moldoff flying saucer-c	77	154	231	493	847	1200
2,4-7: 2-Moldoff-c. 4-(1-2/55)-Last pre-code; Landau-a. 5-3-D effect story (2 pgs.). 6,7-Landau-a. 7-Flying saucer-c	43	86	129	271	461	650
3-H-Bomb-c; Atomic Sub becomes Atomic Spaceship	50	100	150	315	533	750

COMMANDERS IN CRISIS
Image Comics: Oct, 2020 - No. 12, Sept, 2021 ($3.99)

1-12-Steve Orlando-s/Davide Tinto-a 4.00

COMMANDO ADVENTURES
Atlas Comics (MMC): June, 1957 - No. 2, Aug, 1957

	GD	VG	FN	VF	VF/NM	NM-
1-Severin-c	20	40	60	117	189	260
2-Severin-c; Reinman & Romita-a; Drucker-a?	14	28	42	82	121	160

COMMANDOS
DC Comics: Oct. 1942

1-Ashcan comic, not distributed to newsstands, only for in-house use. Cover art is Boy Commandos #1 with interior being a Boy Commandos story from an unidentified issue of Detective Comics (a VF copy sold for $2629 in 2018)

COMMANDO YANK (See The Mighty Midget Comics & Wow Comics)

COMMON GROUNDS
Image Comics (Top Cow): Feb, 2004 - No. 6, July, 2004 ($2.99)

1-6: 1-Two covers; art by Jurgens and Oeming. 3-Bachalo, Jurgens-a. 4-Peréz-a 3.00
...: Baker's Dozen TPB (12/04, $14.99) r/#1-6; cover gallery; Holey Crullers pages 15.00

COMPASS
Image Comics: Jun, 2021 - No. 5, Oct, 2021 ($3.99)

1-5-MacKenzie & Walker-s/Greenwood-a 4.00

COMPLETE ALICE IN WONDERLAND (Adaptation of Carroll's original story)
Dynamite Entertainment: 2009 - No. 4 ($4.99, limited series)

1-4-Leah Moore & John Reppion-s/Erica Awano-a/John Cassaday-c 5.00

COMPLETE BOOK OF COMICS AND FUNNIES

Comics on Parade #38 © UFS

Compass #1 © M, W, & G

Conan Red Sonja #4 © CPI & RS LLC

	GD	VG	FN	VF	VF/NM	NM-
	2.0	4.0	6.0	8.0	9.0	9.2

William H. Wise & Co.: 1944 (25¢, one-shot, 196 pgs.)

1-Origin Brad Spencer, Wonderman; The Magnet, The Silver Knight by Kinstler, & Zudo the Jungle Boy app. 77 154 231 493 847 1200

COMPLETE BOOK OF TRUE CRIME COMICS
William H. Wise & Co.: No date (Mid 1940's) (25¢, 132 pgs.)

nn-Contains Crime Does Not Pay rebound (includes #22) 200 400 600 1280 2190 3100

COMPLETE COMICS (Formerly Amazing Comics No. 1)
Timely Comics (EPC): No. 2, Winter, 1944-45

2-The Destroyer, The Whizzer, The Young Allies & Sergeant Dix; Schomburg-c 200 400 600 1280 2190 3100

COMPLETE DRACULA (Adaptation of Stoker's original story)
Dynamite Entertainment: 2009 - No. 5, 2009 ($4.99, limited series)

1-5-Leah Moore & John Reppion-s/Colton Worley-a/John Cassaday-c 5.00

COMPLETE FRANK MILLER BATMAN, THE
Longmeadow Press: 1989 ($29.95, hardcover, silver gilded pages)

HC-Reprints Batman: Year One, Wanted: Santa Claus--Dead or Alive, and The Dark Knight Returns 50.00

COMPLETE GUIDE TO THE DEADLY ARTS OF KUNG FU AND KARATE
Marvel Comics: 1974 (68 pgs., B&W magazine)

V1#1-Bruce Lee-c and 5 pg. story (scarce) 7 14 21 49 92 135

COMPLETE LOVE MAGAZINE (Formerly a pulp with same title)
Ace Periodicals (Periodical House): V26#2, May-June, 1951 - V32#4(#191), Sept, 1956

	GD	VG	FN	VF	VF/NM	NM-
V26#2-Painted-c (52 pgs.)	19	38	57	112	179	245
V26#3-6(2/52), V27#1(4/52)-6(1/53)	14	28	42	81	118	155
V28#1(3/53), V28#2(5/53), V29#3(7/53)-6(12/53)	13	26	39	74	105	135
V30#1(2/54), V30#1(#176, 4/54),2,4-6(#181, 1/55)	13	26	39	74	105	135
V30#3(#178)-Rock Hudson photo-c	14	28	42	80	115	150
V31#1(#182, 3/55)-Last precode	13	26	39	72	101	130
V31#2(5/55)-6(#187, 1/56)	12	24	36	69	97	125
V32#1(#188, 3/56)-4(#191, 9/56)	12	24	36	69	97	125

NOTE: *(34 total issues). Photo-c V27#5-on. Painted-c V26#3.*

COMPLETE MYSTERY (True Complete Mystery No. 5 on)
Marvel Comics (PrPl): Aug, 1948 - No. 4, Feb, 1949 (Full length stories)

1-Seven Dead Men 65 130 195 416 708 1000
2-4: 2-Jigsaw of Doom!; Shores-a. 3-Fear in the Night; Burgos-c/a (28 pgs.). 4-A Squealer Dies Fast 50 100 150 315 533 750

COMPLETE ROMANCE
Avon Periodicals: 1949

1-(Scarce)-Reprinted as Women to Love 65 130 195 416 708 1000

CONAN (See Chamber of Darkness #4, Giant-Size..., Handbook of..., King Conan, Marvel Graphic Novel #19, 28, Marvel Treasury Ed., Power Record Comics, Robert E. Howard's.., Savage Sword of Conan, and Savage Tales)

CONAN
Dark Horse Comics: Feb, 2004 - No. 50, May, 2008 ($2.99)

0-(11/03, 25¢-c) Busiek-s/Nord-a 3.00
1-($2.99) Linsner-c/Busiek-s/Nord-a 1 2 3 5 6 8
1-(2nd printing) J. Scott Campell-c 3.00
1-(3rd printing) Nord-c 3.00
2-49: 18-Severin & Timm-a. 22-Kaluta-a (6 pgs.) 24-Harris-c. 29-31-Mignola-s 3.00
24-Variant-c with nude woman (also see Conan and the Demons of Khitai #3 for ad) 150.00
50-($4.99) Harris-c; new story and reprint from Conan the Barbarian #30 1 2 3 5 6 8
... and the Daughters of Midora (10/04, $4.99) Texiera-a/c 5.00
...: Born on the Battlefield TPB (6/08, $17.95) r/#0,8,15,23,32,45,46; Ruth sketch pages 18.00
...: FCBD 2006 Special (5/06) Paul Lee-a; flip book with Star Wars FCBD 2006 Special 3.00
...: One For One (8/10, $1.00) r/#1 with red cover frame 3.00
...: The Blood-Stained Crown and Other Stories TPB (1/08, $14.95) r/#18,26-28,39 15.00
...: The Weight of the Crown (1/10, $3.50) Darick Robertson-s/a; 2 covers by Robertson 3.50
HC Vol. 1: The Frost Giant's Daughter and Other Stories (2005, $24.95) r/#1-6, partial #7; signed by Busiek; Nord sketch pages 25.00
Vol. 1: The Frost Giant's Daughter and Other Stories (2005, $15.95) r/#1-6, partial #7 16.00
Vol. 2: The God in the Bowl and Other Stories HC (2005, $24.95) r/#9-14 25.00
Vol. 2: The God in the Bowl and Other Stories SC (2006, $15.95) r/#9-14 16.00
Vol. 3: The Tower of the Elephant and Other Stories HC (5/06, $24.95) r/#0,16,17,19-22 25.00
Vol. 3: The Tower of the Elephant and Other Stories SC (6/06, $15.95) r/#0,16,17,19-22 16.00
Vol. 4: The Hall of the Dead and Other Stories HC (5/07, $24.95) r/#0,24,25,29-31,33,34 25.00
Vol. 4: The Hall of the Dead and Other Stories SC (6/07, $17.95) r/#0,24,25,29-31,33,34 18.00
Vol. 5: Rogues in the House and Other Stories SC (3/08, $17.95) r/#0,37,38,41-44 18.00
Vol. 6: The Hand of Nergal HC (10/08, $24.95) r/#0,47-50; sketch pages 25.00

GD	VG	FN	VF	VF/NM	NM-
2.0	4.0	6.0	8.0	9.0	9.2

CONAN AND THE DEMONS OF KHITAI
Dark Horse Comics: Oct, 2005 - No. 4, Jan, 2006 ($2.99, limited series)

1,2,4-Paul Lee-a/Akira Yoshida-s/Pat Lee-c 4.00
3-1st printing with red cover logo; letters page has image of Conan #24 nude variant-c 6.00
3-2nd printing with black cover logo; letters page has image of Conan #24 regular-c 3.00
TPB (7/06, $12.95) r/series 13.00

CONAN AND THE JEWELS OF GWAHLUR
Dark Horse Comics: Apr, 2005 - No. 3, June, 2005 ($2.99, limited series)

1-3-P. Craig Russell-s/a/c 3.00
HC (12/05, $13.95) r/series; P. Craig Russell interview and sketch pages 14.00

CONAN AND THE MIDNIGHT GOD
Dark Horse Comics: Dec, 2006 - No. 5, May, 2007 ($2.99, limited series)

1-5-Dysart-s/Conrad-a/Alexander-c 3.00
TPB (10/07, $14.95) r/#1-5 and Age of Conan: Hyborian Adventures one-shot 15.00

CONAN AND THE PEOPLE OF THE BLACK CIRCLE
Dark Horse Comics: Oct, 2013 - No. 4, Jan, 2014 ($3.50, limited series)

1-4-Van Lente-s/Olivetti-a/c 3.50

CONAN AND THE SONGS OF THE DEAD
Dark Horse Comics: July, 2006 - No. 5, Nov, 2006 ($2.99, limited series)

1-5-Timothy Truman-a/c; Joe Lansdale-s 3.00
TPB (4/07, $14.95) r/series; Truman sketch pages 15.00

CONAN: (Title Series): Marvel Comics

CONAN, 8/95 - No. 11, 6/96 ($2.95), 1-11: 4-Malibu Comic's Rune app. 5.00
...CLASSIC, 6/94 - No. 11, 4/95 ($1.50), 1-11: 1-r/Conan #1 by B. Smith, r/covers w/changes. 2-11-r/Conan #2-11 by Smith. 2-Bound w/cover to Conan The Adventurer #2 by mistake 5.00
...DEATH COVERED IN GOLD, 9/99 - No. 3, 11/99 ($2.99), 1-3-Roy Thomas-s/ John Buscema-a 5.00
...FLAME AND THE FIEND, 8/00 - No. 3, 10/00 ($2.99), 1-3-Thomas-s 5.00
...RETURN OF STYRM, 9/98 - No. 3, 11/98 ($2.99), 1-3-Parente & Soresina-a; painted-c 5.00
...RIVER OF BLOOD, 6/98 - No. 3, 8/98 ($2.50), 1-3 5.00
...SCARLET SWORD, 12/98 - No. 3, 2/99 ($2.99), 1-3-Thomas-s/Raffaele-a 5.00

CONAN: BATTLE FOR THE SERPENT CROWN
Marvel Comics: Apr, 2020 - No. 5, Nov, 2020 ($3.99, limited series)

1-5-Saladin Ahmed-s/Luke Ross-a; set in the present; Black Cat & Mephisto app. 3-Black Panther app. 4-Namor app. 4.00

CONAN: ISLAND OF NO RETURN
Dark Horse Comics: Jun, 2011 - No. 2, Jul, 2011 ($3.50, limited series)

1,2-Marz-s/Sears-a 4.00

CONAN RED SONJA
Dark Horse Comics: Jan, 2015 - No. 4, Apr, 2015 ($3.99, limited series)

1-4-Gail Simone & Jim Zub-s/Dan Panosian-a/c 6.00

CONAN: ROAD OF KINGS
Dark Horse Comics: Dec, 2010 - No. 12, Jan, 2012 ($3.50)

1-12: 1-Roy Thomas-s/Mike Hawthorne-a; covers by Wheatley & Keown 4.00

CONAN SAGA, THE
Marvel Comics: June, 1987 - No. 97, Apr, 1995 ($2.00/$2.25, B&W, magazine)

1-Barry Smith-r; new Smith-c 2 4 6 9 13 16
2-27: 2-9,11-new Barry Smith-c. 13,15-Boris-c. 17-Adams-r.18,25-Chaykin-r. 22-r/Giant-Size Conan 1,2 4.00
28-90: 28-Begin $2.25-c. 31-Red Sonja-r by N. Adams/SSOC #1; 1 pg. Jeff Jones-r. 32-Newspaper strip-r begin by Buscema. 33-Smith/Conrad-a. 39-r/Kull #1('71) by Andru & Wood. 44-Swipes-c/Savage Tales #1. 57-Brunner-r/SSOC #30. 66-r/Conan Annual #2 by Buscema. 79-r/Conan #43-45 w/Red Sonja. 85-Based on Conan #57-63 3.00
91-96 5.00
97-Last issue 1 2 3 5 6 8

NOTE: ***J. Buscema** r-32-on; c-86. **Chaykin** r-34. **Chiodo** painted c-63, 65, 66, 82. **G. Colan** a-47p. **Jusko** painted c-64, 83. **Kaluta** c-84. **Nino** a-37. **Ploog** a-50. **N. Redondo** painted c-48, 50, 51, 53, 57, 62. **Simonson** r-50-54, 56. **B. Smith** r-51. **Starlin** c-34. **Williamson** r-50i.*

CONAN: SERPENT WAR
Marvel Comics: Feb, 2020 - No. 4, Mar, 2020 ($4.99/$3.99, limited series)

1-($4.99) Jim Zub-s/Scot Eaton-a; Moon Knight, Solomon Kane and Dark Agnes app.; back-up Solomon Kane text serial 5.00
2-4-($3.99) Solomon Kane text serial in each. 2-Segovia-a. 3-Pizzari-a. 4-Guara-a 4.00

CONAN THE ADVENTURER
Marvel Comics: June, 1994 - No. 14, July, 1995 ($1.50)

	GD 2.0	VG 4.0	FN 6.0	VF 8.0	VF/NM 9.0	NM- 9.2
1-($2.50)-Embossed foil-c; Kayaran-a						4.00
2-14						3.00
2-Contents are Conan Classics #2 by mistake						3.00

CONAN THE AVENGER
Dark Horse Comics: Apr, 2014 - No. 25, Apr, 2016 ($3.99/$3.50)

	GD 2.0	VG 4.0	FN 6.0	VF 8.0	VF/NM 9.0	NM- 9.2
1-25: 1-Van Lente-s/Ching-a. 4-Staples-c. 13-15-Powell-c. 25-Bisley-c						4.00

CONAN THE BARBARIAN
Marvel Comics: Oct, 1970 - No. 275, Dec, 1993

	GD 2.0	VG 4.0	FN 6.0	VF 8.0	VF/NM 9.0	NM- 9.2
1-Origin/1st app. Conan (in comics) by Barry Smith; 1st brief app. Kull; #1-9 are 15¢ issues	38	76	114	285	641	1000
2	10	20	30	69	147	225
3-(Low distribution in some areas)	13	26	39	89	195	300
4,5	8	16	24	52	99	145
6-9: 8-Hidden panel message, pg. 14. 9-Last 15¢-c	6	12	18	38	69	100
10,11 (25¢ 52 pg. giants): 10-Black Knight-r; Kull story by Severin	7	14	21	48	89	130
12,13: 12-Wrightson-c(i)	5	10	15	35	63	90
14,15-Elric app.	6	12	18	42	79	115
16,19,20: 16-Conan-r/Savage Tales #1	5	10	15	34	60	85
17,18-No Barry Smith-a	4	8	12	28	47	65
21,22: 22-Has reprint from #1	5	10	15	30	50	70
23-1st app. Red Sonja (2/73)	14	28	42	93	204	315
24-1st full Red Sonja story; last Smith-a	15	30	45	103	227	350
25-John Buscema-c/a begins	3	6	9	19	30	40
26-30: 28-Centerfold ad by Mark Jewelers	3	6	9	14	19	24
31-36,38-40	2	4	6	10	14	18
37-Neal Adams-c/a; last 20¢ issue; contains pull-out subscription form	3	6	9	21	33	45
41-43,46-50: 48-Origin retold	2	4	6	8	11	14
44,45-N. Adams-i(Crusty Bunkers). 45-Adams-c	2	4	6	9	13	16
51-57,59,60: 59-Origin Belit	1	3	4	6	8	10
58-2nd Belit app. (see Giant-Size Conan #1)	2	4	6	11	16	20
61-65-(Regular 25¢ editions)(4-8/76)	1	3	4	6	8	10
61-65-(30¢-c variants, limited distribution)	6	12	18	38	69	100
66-99: 68-Red Sonja story cont'd from Marvel Feature #7. 75-79-(Reg. 30¢-c). 84-Intro. Zula. 85-Origin Zula. 87-r/Savage Sword of Conan #3 in color	1	2	3	5	6	8
75-79-(35¢-c variants, limited distribution)	8	16	24	54	102	150
100-(52 pg. Giant)-Death of Belit	2	4	6	9	13	16
101-114						6.00
115-Double size	1	2	3	5	6	8
116-199,201-231,233-249: 116-r/Power Record Comic PR31. 244-Zula returns						6.00
200,232: 200-(52 pgs.). 232-Young Conan storyline begins; Conan is born						6.00
250-(60 pgs.)	1	2	3	5	6	8
251-270: 262-Adapted from R.E. Howard story						6.00
271-274	1	3	4	6	8	10
275-($2.50, 68 pgs.)-Final issue; painted-c (low print)	4	8	12	28	47	65
King Size 1(1973, 35¢)-Smith-r/#2,4; Smith-c	6	12	18	41	76	110
Annual 2(1976, 50¢)-New full length story	3	6	9	15	22	28
Annual 3,4: 3('78)-Chaykin/N. Adams-r/SSOC #2. 4('78)-New full length story	2	4	6	8	11	14
Annual 5,6: 5(1979)-New full length Buscema story & part-c, 6(1981)-Kane-c/a	1	2	3	5	6	8
Annual 7-12: 7('82)-Based on novel "Conan of the Isles" (new-a). 8(1984). 9(1984). 10(1986). 11(1986). 12(1987)						5.00
No. 1 Facsimile Edition (2/22, $3.99) Reprints #1 with original ads and Bullpen pages						4.00
Special Edition 1 (Red Nails)						5.00
The Chronicles of Conan Vol. 1: Tower of the Elephant and Other Stories (Dark Horse, 2003, $15.95) r/#1-8; afterword by Roy Thomas						16.00
The Chronicles of Conan Vol. 2: Rogues in the House and Other Stories (Dark Horse, 2003, $15.95) r/#9-13,16; afterword by Roy Thomas						16.00
The Chronicles of Conan Vol. 3: The Monster of the Monoliths and Other Stories (Dark Horse, 2003, $15.95) r/#14,15,17-21; afterword by Roy Thomas						16.00
The Chronicles of Conan Vol. 4: The Song of Red Sonja and Other Stories (Dark Horse, 2004, $15.95) r/#23-26 & "Red Nails" from Savage Tales; afterword by Roy Thomas						16.00
The Chronicles of Conan Vol. 5: The Shadow in the Tomb and Other Stories (Dark Horse, 2004, $15.95) r/#27-34; afterword by Roy Thomas						16.00
The Chronicles of Conan Vol. 6: The Curse of the Skull and Other Stories (Dark Horse, 2004, $15.95) r/#35-42; afterword by Roy Thomas						16.00
The Chronicles of Conan Vol. 7: The Dweller in the Pool and Other Stories (Dark Horse, 2005, $15.95) r/#43-51; afterword by Roy Thomas						16.00
The Chronicles of Conan Vol. 8: Brothers of the Blade and Other Stories (Dark Horse, 2005, $16.95) r/#52-59; afterword by Roy Thomas						17.00
The Chronicles of Conan Vol. 9: Riders of the River-Dragons and Other Stories (Dark Horse, 11/05, $16.95) r/#60-63,65,69-71; afterword by Roy Thomas						17.00
The Chronicles of Conan Vol. 10: When Giants Walk the Earth and Other Stories (Dark Horse, 3/06, $16.95) r/#72-77,79-82; afterword by Roy Thomas						17.00
The Chronicles of Conan Vol. 11: The Dance of the Skull and Other Stories (Dark Horse, 2/07, $16.95) r/#82-86,88-90; afterword by Roy Thomas						17.00
The Chronicles of Conan Vol. 12: The King Beast of Abombi and Other Stories (Dark Horse, 7/07, $16.95) r/#91,93-100; afterword by Roy Thomas						17.00
The Chronicles of Conan Vol. 13: Whispering Shadows and Other Stories (Dark Horse, 12/07, $16.95) r/#92,100-107; afterword by Roy Thomas						17.00
The Chronicles of Conan Vol. 14: Shadow of the Beast and Other Stories (Dark Horse, 3/08, $16.95) r/#92,108-115; afterword by Roy Thomas						17.00
The Chronicles of Conan Vol. 15: The Corridor of Mullah-Kajar and Other Stories (Dark Horse, 7/08, $16.95) r/#116-121 & Annual #2; afterword by Roy Thomas						17.00

NOTE: ***Arthur Adams*** *c-248, 249.* ***Neal Adams*** *a-116r(i); c-49i.* ***Austin*** *a-125, 126; c-125i, 126i.* ***Brunner*** *c-17i. c-40.* ***Buscema*** *a-25-36p, 38, 39, 41-56p, 58-63p, 65-67p, 68, 70-78p, 84-86p, 88-91p, 93-126p, 136p, 140, 141-144p, 146-158p, 159, 161, 162, 163p, 165-185p, 187-190p, Annual 2(3pgs.). 3-5p, 7p; c(p)-26, 36, 44, 46, 52, 56, 58, 59, 64, 65, 72, 78-80, 83-91, 93-103, 105-126, 136-151, 155-159, 161, 162, 168, 169, 171, 172, 174, 175, 178-185, 188, 189, Annual 4, 5, 7.* ***Chaykin*** *a-79-83.* ***Golden*** *c-152.* ***Kaluta*** *c-167.* ***Gil Kane*** *a-12p, 17p, 18p, 127-130, 131-134p; c-12p, 17p, 18p, 23, 25, 27-32, 34, 35, 38, 39, 41-43, 45-51, 53-55, 57, 60-63, 65-71, 73p, 76p, 127-134.* ***Jim Lee*** *c-242.* ***McFarlane*** *c-241p.* ***Ploog*** *a-57.* ***Russell*** *a-21; c-251i.* ***Simonson*** *c-135.* ***B. Smith*** *a-1-11p, 12, 13-15p, 16, 19-21, 23, 24; c-1-11, 13-16, 19-24p.* ***Starlin*** *a-64.* ***Wood*** *a-47r. Issue Nos. 3-5, 7-9, 11, 16-18, 21, 23, 25, 27-30, 35, 37, 38, 42, 45, 52, 57, 58, 65, 69-71, 73, 79-83, 99, 100, 104, 114, Annual 2 have original Robert E. Howard stories adapted. Issues #32-34 adapted from Norvell Page's novel* ***Flame Winds****.*

CONAN THE BARBARIAN (Volume 2)
Marvel Comics: July, 1997 - No. 3, Oct, 1997 ($2.50, limited series)

	GD 2.0	VG 4.0	FN 6.0	VF 8.0	VF/NM 9.0	NM- 9.2
1-3-Castellini-a						5.00

CONAN THE BARBARIAN
Dark Horse Comics: Feb, 2012 - No. 25, Feb, 2014 ($3.50)

	GD 2.0	VG 4.0	FN 6.0	VF 8.0	VF/NM 9.0	NM- 9.2
1-Brian Wood-s/Becky Cloonan-a; two covers by Carnevale & Cloonan	1	2	3	5	6	8
2-25: 2,3-Brian Wood-s/Becky Cloonan-a						4.00
One for One: Conan the Barbarian #1 (1/14, $1.00) r/#1						4.00

CONAN THE BARBARIAN
Marvel Comics: Mar, 2019 - Present ($4.99/$3.99)

	GD 2.0	VG 4.0	FN 6.0	VF 8.0	VF/NM 9.0	NM- 9.2
1-($4.99) Jason Aaron-s/Mahmud Asrar-a; part 1 of a bonus text novella						5.00
2-24-($3.99)-Bonus text novella continues: 2,3,5-7,9-12-Asrar-a. 4,8-Zaffino-a						4.00
25-($4.99) 300th legacy issue; Belit app.; stories by Zub, Hama, Slott, Owsley						5.00
...: Exodus 1 (10/19, $3.99) Esad Ribic-s/a; bonus thumbnails of layout sketches						4.00

CONAN THE BARBARIAN MOVIE SPECIAL (Movie)
Marvel Comics Group: Oct, 1982 - No. 2, Nov, 1982

	GD 2.0	VG 4.0	FN 6.0	VF 8.0	VF/NM 9.0	NM- 9.2
1,2-Movie adaptation; Buscema-a	1	2	3	5	6	8

CONAN THE BARBARIAN: THE MASK OF ACHERON (Based on the 2011 movie)
Dark Horse Comics: Jul, 2011 ($6.99, one-shot)

	GD 2.0	VG 4.0	FN 6.0	VF 8.0	VF/NM 9.0	NM- 9.2
1-Stuart Moore-s/Gabriel Guzman-a/c						7.00

CONAN THE BARBARIAN: THE USURPER
Marvel Comics: Dec, 1997 - No. 3, Feb, 1998 ($2.50, limited series)

	GD 2.0	VG 4.0	FN 6.0	VF 8.0	VF/NM 9.0	NM- 9.2
1-3-Dixon-s						4.00

CONAN: THE BOOK OF THOTH
Dark Horse Comics: Mar, 2006 - No. 4, June, 2006 ($4.99, limited series)

	GD 2.0	VG 4.0	FN 6.0	VF 8.0	VF/NM 9.0	NM- 9.2
1-4-Origin of Thoth-amon; Len Wein & Kurt Busiek-s/Kelley Jones-a/c						5.00
TPB (12/06, $17.95) r/#1-4						18.00

CONAN THE CIMMERIAN
Dark Horse Comics: No. 0, Jun, 2008 - No. 25, Nov, 2010 (99¢/$2.99)

	GD 2.0	VG 4.0	FN 6.0	VF 8.0	VF/NM 9.0	NM- 9.2
0-Follows Conan #50; Truman-s/Giorello-a/c						4.00
1-(7/08, $2.99) Two covers by Joe Kubert and Cho; Giorello & Corben-a						4.00
2-25: 2-7-Cho-c; Giorello & Corben-a. 8-18-Linsner-c. 14-Joe Kubert-a (7 pgs.)						4.00

CONAN THE DESTROYER (Movie)
Marvel Comics Group: Jan, 1985 - No. 2, Mar, 1985

	GD 2.0	VG 4.0	FN 6.0	VF 8.0	VF/NM 9.0	NM- 9.2
1,2-r/Marvel Super Special						6.00

CONAN THE FRAZETTA COVER SERIES
Dark Horse Comics: Dec, 2007 - No. 8 ($3.50/$5.99/$6.99)

	GD 2.0	VG 4.0	FN 6.0	VF 8.0	VF/NM 9.0	NM- 9.2
1-($3.50) Reprints from Dark Horse series with Frazetta covers	2	4	6	9	12	15
2,3-($5.99)	1	3	4	6	8	10
4-8-($6.99)	2	4	6	8	10	12

CONAN THE KING (Formerly King Conan)
Marvel Comics Group: No. 20, Jan, 1984 - No. 55, Nov, 1989

	GD 2.0	VG 4.0	FN 6.0	VF 8.0	VF/NM 9.0	NM- 9.2
20-49						5.00
50-54						6.00
55-Last issue	2	4	6	9	12	15

NOTE: ***Kaluta*** *c-20-23, 24i, 26, 27, 30, 50, 52.* ***Williamson*** *a-37i; c-37i, 38i.*

CONAN: THE LEGEND (See Conan 2004 series)

CONAN: THE LORD OF THE SPIDERS
Marvel Comics: Mar, 1998 - No. 3, May, 1998 ($2.50, limited series)

	GD 2.0	VG 4.0	FN 6.0	VF 8.0	VF/NM 9.0	NM- 9.2
1-3-Roy Thomas-s/Raffaele-a						5.00

CONAN THE SAVAGE
Marvel Comics: Aug, 1995 - No. 10, May, 1996 ($2.95, B&W, Magazine)

	GD 2.0	VG 4.0	FN 6.0	VF 8.0	VF/NM 9.0	NM- 9.2
1-10: 1-Bisley-c. 4-vs. Malibu Comics' Rune. 5,10-Brereton-c						5.00

CONAN THE SLAYER
Dark Horse Comics: Jul, 2016 - No. 12, Aug, 2017 ($3.99)

	GD 2.0	VG 4.0	FN 6.0	VF 8.0	VF/NM 9.0	NM- 9.2
1-12: 1-Bunn-s/Dávila-a/Bermejo-c. 11-Verma-a						4.00

CONAN 2099
Marvel Comics: Jan, 2020 ($4.99, one-shot)

	GD 2.0	VG 4.0	FN 6.0	VF 8.0	VF/NM 9.0	NM- 9.2
1-Duggan-s/Antonio-a; Morgan Le Fay app.						5.00

CONAN VS. RUNE (Also See Conan #4)
Marvel Comics: Nov, 1995 ($2.95, one-shot)

	GD 2.0	VG 4.0	FN 6.0	VF 8.0	VF/NM 9.0	NM- 9.2
1-Barry Smith-c/a/scripts	1	3	4	6	8	10

CONCRETE (Also see Dark Horse Presents & Within Our Reach)
Dark Horse Comics: March, 1987 - No. 10, Nov, 1988 ($1.50, B&W)

	GD 2.0	VG 4.0	FN 6.0	VF 8.0	VF/NM 9.0	NM- 9.2
1-Paul Chadwick-c/a in all	2	4	6	9	13	16
1-2nd print						3.00
2						6.00
3-Origin						5.00
4-10						4.00
A New Life 1 (1989, $2.95, B&W)-r/#3,4 plus new-a (11 pgs.)						4.00
Celebrates Earth Day 1990 ($3.50, 52 pgs.)						6.00
Color Special 1 (2/89, $2.95, 44 pgs.)-r/1st two Concrete apps. from Dark Horse Presents #1,2 plus new-a						6.00
Depths TPB (7/05, $12.95)-r/#1-5, stories from DHP #1,8,10,150; other short stories						13.00
Land And Sea 1 (2/89, $2.95, B&W)-r/#1,2						6.00
Odd Jobs 1 (7/90, $3.50)-r/5,6 plus new-a						4.00
...Vol. 1: Depths ('05, $12.95, 9"x6") r/#1-5 & short stories						13.00
...Vol. 2: Heights ('05, $12.95, 9"x6") r/#6-10 & short stories						13.00
...Vol. 3: Fragile Creatures (1/06, $12.95, 9"x6") r/mini-series & short stories from DHP						13.00
...Vol. 4: Killer Smile (3/06, $12.95, 9"x6") r/mini-series & short stories from various						13.00
...Vol. 5: Think Like a Mountain (5/06, $12.95, 9"x6") r/mini-series & short stories						13.00
...Vol. 6: Strange Armor (7/06, $12.95, 9"x6") r/mini-series & short stories						13.00
...Vol. 7: The Human Dilemma (4/06, $12.95, 9"x6") r/mini-series						13.00

Conan the Barbarian #44 © CPI

Constantine #1 © DC

Contact Comics #1 © Aviation

	GD 2.0	VG 4.0	FN 6.0	VF 8.0	VF/NM 9.0	NM- 9.2
CONCRETE: (Title series), **Dark Horse Comics**						
--ECLECTICA, 4/93 - No. 2, 5/93 ($2.95) 1,2						4.00
--FRAGILE CREATURE, 6/91 - No. 4, 2/92 ($2.50) 1-4						4.00
--KILLER SMILE, (Legend), 7/94 - No. 4, 10/94 ($2.95) 1-4						4.00
--STRANGE ARMOR, 12/97 - No. 5, 5/98 ($2.95, color) 1-5-Chadwick-s/c/a; retells origin						4.00
--THE HUMAN DILEMMA, 12/04 - No. 6, 5/05 ($3.50)						
1-6: Chadwick-a/c & scripts; Concrete has a child						3.50
--THINK LIKE A MOUNTAIN, (Legend), 3/96 - No. 6, 8/96 ($2.95)						
1-6: Chadwick-a/scripts & Darrow-c in all						4.00
CONDORMAN (Walt Disney)						
Whitman Publishing: Oct, 1981 - No. 3, Jan, 1982						
1-3: 1,2-Movie adaptation; photo-c	1	3	4	6	8	10
CONEHEADS						
Marvel Comics: June, 1994 - No. 4, 1994 ($1.75, limited series)						
1	1	3	4	6	8	10
2-4						5.00
CONFESSIONS ILLUSTRATED (Magazine)						
E. C. Comics: Jan-Feb, 1956 - No. 2, Spring, 1956						
1-Craig, Kamen, Wood, Orlando-a	36	72	108	211	343	475
2-Craig, Crandall, Kamen, Orlando-a	26	52	78	154	252	350
CONFESSIONS OF LOVE						
Artful Publ.: Apr, 1950 - No. 2, July, 1950 (25¢, 7-1/4x5-1/4", 132 pgs.)						
1-Bakerish-a	90	180	270	576	988	1400
2-Art & text; Bakerish-a	55	110	165	352	601	850
CONFESSIONS OF LOVE (Formerly Startling Terror Tales #10; becomes Confessions of Romance No. 7 on)						
Star Publications: No. 11, 7/52 - No. 14, 1/53; No. 4, 3/53- No. 6, 8/53						
11-13: 12,13-Disbrow-a	43	86	129	271	461	650
14,5,6	36	72	108	211	343	475
4-Disbrow-a	39	78	117	231	378	525
NOTE: *All have **L. B. Cole** covers.*						
CONFESSIONS OF ROMANCE (Formerly Confessions of Love)						
Star Publications: No. 7, Nov, 1953 - No. 11, Nov, 1954						
7	28	56	84	165	270	375
8	21	42	63	122	199	275
9-Wood-a	22	44	66	128	209	290
10,11-Disbrow-a	21	42	63	122	199	275
NOTE: *All have **L. B. Cole** covers.*						
CONFESSIONS OF THE LOVELORN (Formerly Lovelorn)						
American Comics Group (Regis Publ./Best Synd. Features): No. 52, Aug, 1954 - No. 114, June-July, 1960						
52 (3-D effect)	65	130	195	416	708	1000
53,55	21	42	63	122	199	275
54 (3-D effect)	42	86	129	271	461	650
56-Anti-communist propaganda story, 10 pgs; last pre-code (2/55)	21	42	63	122	199	275
57-90,100	14	28	42	78	112	145
91-Williamson-a	15	30	45	83	124	165
92-99,101-114	11	22	33	62	86	110
NOTE: ***Whitney** a-most issues; c-52, 53. Painted c-106, 107.*						
CONFIDENTIAL DIARY (Formerly High School Confidential Diary; Three Nurses #18 on)						
Charlton Comics: No. 12, May, 1962 - No. 17, Mar, 1963						
12-17	3	6	9	17	26	35
CONGO BILL (See Action Comics & More Fun Comics #56)						
National Periodical Publication: Aug-Sept, 1954 - No. 7, Aug-Sept, 1955						
1	215	430	645	1700	--	--
2,7	131	262	393	1050	--	--
3-6: 4-Last pre-Code issue	106	212	318	850	--	--
NOTE: *(Rarely found in fine to mint condition.)* ***Nick Cardy** c-1-7.*						
CONGO BILL						
DC Comics (Vertigo): Oct, 1999 - No. 4, Jan, 2000 ($2.95, limited series)						
1-4-Corben-c						3.00
CONGORILLA (Also see Action Comics #224)						
DC Comics: Nov, 1992 - No. 4, Feb, 1993 ($1.75, limited series)						
1-4: 1,2-Brian Bolland-c						4.00
CONJURORS						

	GD 2.0	VG 4.0	FN 6.0	VF 8.0	VF/NM 9.0	NM- 9.2
DC Comics: Apr, 1999 - No. 3, Jun, 1999 ($2.95, limited series)						
1-3-Elseworlds; Phantom Stranger app.; Barreto-c/a						3.00
CONNECTICUT YANKEE, A (See King Classics)						
CONNOR HAWKE: DRAGON'S BLOOD (Also see Green Arrow titles)						
DC Comics: Jan, 2007 - No. 6, Jun, 2007 ($2.99, limited series)						
1-6-Chuck Dixon-s/Derec Donovan-a/c						3.00
SC (2008, $19.99) r/#1-6						20.00
CONQUEROR, THE						
Dell Publishing Co.: No., 690, Mar, 1956						
Four Color 690-Movie, John Wayne photo-c	15	30	45	103	227	350
CONQUEROR COMICS						
Albrecht Publishing Co.: Winter, 1945						
nn	25	50	75	150	245	340
CONQUEROR OF THE BARREN EARTH (See The Warlord #63)						
DC Comics: Feb, 1985 - No. 4, May, 1985 (Limited series)						
1-4: Back-up series from Warlord						3.00
CONQUEST						
Store Comics: 1953 (6¢)						
1-Richard the Lion Hearted, Beowulf, Swamp Fox	14	28	42	76	108	140
CONQUEST						
Famous Funnies: Spring, 1955						
1-Crandall-a, 1 pg.; contains contents of 1953 ish.	16	32	48	94	147	200
CONSPIRACY						
Marvel Comics: Feb, 1998 - No. 2, Mar, 1998 ($2.99, limited series)						
1,2-Painted art by Korday/Abnett-s						3.00
CONSTANTINE (Also see Hellblazer)						
DC Comics (Vertigo): 2005 (Based on the 2005 Keanu Reeves movie)						
...: The Hellblazer Collection (2005, $14.95) Movie adaptation and r/#1, 27, 41; photo-c						15.00
...: The Official Movie Adaptation (2005, $6.95) Seagle-s/Randall-a/photo-c						7.00
CONSTANTINE (Also see Justice League Dark)						
DC Comics: May, 2013 - No. 23, May, 2015 ($2.99)						
1-Lemire & Fawkes-s/Guedes-a; two covers by Reis & Guedes						4.00
2-20: 2-The Spectre app. 5-Trinity War tie-in; Shazam app. 9-Forever Evil tie-in. 20-23-Constantine on Earth 2. 23-Darkseid app.						3.00
...: Futures End 1 (11/14, $2.99, regular-c) Five years later; Ferreyra-a/c						3.00
...: Futures End 1 (11/14, $3.99, 3-D cover)						4.00
.../Hellblazer Special Edition 1 (12/14, $1.00) Flipbook r/#1 and Hellblazer #1						3.00
CONSTANTINE: THE HELLBLAZER						
DC Comics: Aug, 2015 - No. 13, Aug, 2016 ($2.99)						
1-13: 1-Doyle & Tynion IV-s/Rossmo-a, covers by Rossmo & Doyle. 3,4-Doyle-a. 7-Swamp Thing app. 8-12-Neron app. 10,11-Foreman-a						3.00
CONSUMED						
Platinum Studios: July, 2007 - No. 4, Oct, 2007 ($2.99, limited series)						
1-4-Linsner-c/Budd-a/Shumskas-Tait-s						3.00
CONTACT COMICS						
Aviation Press: July, 1944 - No. 12, May, 1946						
nn-Black Venus, Flamingo, Golden Eagle, Tommy Tomahawk begin	97	194	291	621	1061	1500
2-Classic sci-fi-c	90	180	270	576	988	1400
3-5: 3-Last Flamingo. 3,4-Black Venus by L. B. Cole. 5-The Phantom Flyer app.	60	120	180	381	653	925
6,11-Kurtzman's Black Venus; 11-Last Golden Eagle, last Tommy Tomahawk; Feldstein-a	77	154	231	493	847	1200
7-10	53	106	159	334	567	800
12-Sky Rangers, Air Kids, Ace Diamond app.; L.B. Cole sci-fi cover	649	1298	1947	4738	8369	12,000
NOTE: ***L. B. Cole** a-3, 9; c-1-12. **Giunta** a-3. **Hollingsworth** a-5, 7, 10. **Palais** a-11, 12.*						
CONTAGION						
Marvel Comics: Dec, 2019 - No. 5, Dec, 2019 ($3.99, weekly limited series)						
1-5-Brisson-s; Fantastic Four, Iron Fist, Luke Cage, Avengers app.						4.00
CONTEMPORARY MOTIVATORS						
Pendelum Press: 1977 - 1978 ($1.45, 5-3/8x8", 31 pgs., B&W)						
14-3002 The Caine Mutiny; 14-3010 Banner in the Sky; 14-3029 God Is My Co-Pilot; 14-3037 Guadalcanal Diary; 14-3045 Hiroshima; 14-3053 Hot Rod; 14-3061 Just Dial a Number; 14-3088 The Diary of Anne Frank; 14-3096 Lost Horizon						

2 4 6 8 10 12

NOTE: *Also see Pendulum Illustrated Classics. Above may have been distributed the same.*

CONTEST OF CHAMPIONS (See Marvel Super-Hero...)

CONTEST OF CHAMPIONS
Marvel Comics: Dec, 2015 - No. 10, Sept, 2016 ($4.99/$3.99, limited series)

1-($4.99) The Collector, Venom, Mr. Fixit, Iron Man, Gamora & Maestro app.; Medina-a 5.00
2-9-($3.99) 2-Ares and Punisher 2099 app. 3-5-The Sentry app. 7,8-Ultimates app. 9-Revisits Civil War 4.00
10-($4.99) Finale; Ewing-s/Marcellius-a 5.00

CONTEST OF CHAMPIONS II
Marvel Comics: Sept, 1999 - No. 5, Nov, 1999 ($2.50, limited series)

1-5-Claremont-s/Jimenez-a 3.00

CONTRACT WITH GOD, A
Baronet Publishing Co./Kitchen Sink Press: 1978 ($4.95/$7.95, B&W, graphic novel)

nn-Will Eisner-s/a 3 6 9 17 26 35
Reprint (DC Comics, 2000, $12.95) 13.00

CONVERGENCE
DC Comics: No. 0, Jun, 2015 - No. 8, July, 2015 ($4.99/$3.99, weekly limited series)

0-Superman & multiple Brainiacs app.; intro Telos; Van Sciver-a/Jurgens & King-s 5.00
1-($4.99) Earth-2 heroes vs. Telos; Pagulayan-a; wraparound-c by Reis 5.00
2-7-($3.99) 2-Intro. Deimos; Pagulayan-a. 4,5-Warlord app. 5-Andy Kubert-a 4.00
8-($4.99) Conclusion; art by Segovia, Pagulayan, Pansica & Van Sciver 5.00

CONVERGENCE
DC Comics: June, 2015 - July, 2015 ($3.99, 2-part tie-in miniseries, each issue has a variant cover designed by Chip Kidd)

... Action Comics 1,2 - Pre-Crisis Earth Two Superman & Power Girl; Red Son Superman, Wonder Woman & Lex Luthor app.; Conner-c. 2-Bonus preview of Sinestro #12 4.00
... Adventures of Superman 1,2 - Pre-Crisis Earth One Superman & Supergirl app.; Wolfman-s. 2-Kamandi app.; bonus preview of Martian Manhunter #1 4.00
... Aquaman 1,2 - Harpoon-hand Aquaman & Deathblow app.; Cloonan-c; Richards-a. 2-Bonus preview of Doctor Fate #1 4.00
... Atom 1,2 - Pre-Flashpoint Ray Palmer & Deathstroke app.; Dillon-c/Yeowell-a. 2-Ryan Choi app.; bonus preview of Green Lantern #41 4.00
... Batgirl 1,2 - Stephanie Brown, Cassadra Cain, Tim Drake & Catman app; Leonardi-a. 2-Grodd app.; bonus preview of Prez #1 4.00
... Batman and Robin 1,2 - Pre-Flashpoint Batman, Damian & Red Hood app.; Cowan & Janson-a. 2-Superman app.; bonus preview of Omega Men #1 4.00
... Batman and The Outsiders 1,2 - Pre-Crisis Outsiders and Omac app.; Andy Kubert-c. 2-Bonus preview of Batman Beyond #1 4.00
... Batman: Shadow of the Bat 1,2 - Pre-Zero Hour Batman & Azrael app. 1-Philip Tan-a/c. 2-Leonardi-a; bonus preview of Deathstroke #7 5.00
... Blue Beetle 1,2 - Charlton Blue Beetle, Captain Atom & The Question app.; Blevins-c. 2-Legion of Super-Heroes app.; bonus preview of Black Canary #1 4.00
... Booster Gold 1,2 - Rip Hunter & the Legion of Super-Heroes app.; Jurgens-c. 2-Blue Beetle app.; bonus preview of Earth-2: Society #1 4.00
... Catwoman 1,2 - Pre-Zero Hour purple suit Catwoman & Kingdom Come Batman app.; Ron Randall-a. Bonus preview of Gotham By Midnight #6 4.00
... Crime Syndicate 1,2 - Earth-Three villains & 853rd Century JLA app.; Winslade-a. 2-Bonus preview of Cyborg #1 4.00
... Detective Comics 1,2 - Earth-Two pre-Crisis Robin & Huntress vs. Red Son Superman; Cowan & Sienkiewicz-a. 2-Red Son Batman app.; bonus preview of Flash #41 4.00
... Flash 1,2 - Earth-One pre-Crisis Barry Allen vs. Tangent Superman; Abnett-s/Dallocchio-a; 2-Bonus preview of New Suicide Squad #9 4.00
... Green Arrow 1,2 - Pre-Zero Hour Oliver Queen & Connor Hawke vs. Kingdom Come Black Canary & Dinah Lance; Morales-a; 2-Bonus preview of G.L.C. Lost Army #14.00
... Green Lantern Corps 1,2 - Earth-One pre-Crisis Guy Gardner, John Stewart & Hal Jordan; Hercules from Durvale app. 2-Bonus preview of Gotham Academy #7 4.00
... Green Lantern/Parallax 1,2 - Pre-Zero Hour Hal Jordan & Kyle Rayner; Ron Wagner-a. Princess Fern of Electropolis app. 2-Bonus preview of Lobo #7 4.00
... Harley Quinn 1,2 - Pre-Flashpoint Harley, Poison Ivy & Catwoman; Winslade-a. 2-Harley battles Captain Carrot. 2-Bonus preview of Section Eight #1 4.00
... Hawkman 1,2 - Earth-One pre-Crisis Katar Hol & Shayera; Parker-s/Truman-a. 2-Bonus preview of Grayson #9 4.00
... Infinity Inc. 1,2 - Earth-Two pre-Crisis Infinity Inc. vs. Future Jonah Hex & The Dogs of War; Ordway-s, 1-Ben Caldwell-a. 2-Bonus preview of Batgirl #41 4.00
... Justice League 1,2 - Pre-Flashpoint female Justice League vs. Flashpoint Aquaman; Buckingham-c. 2-Bonus preview of Detective Comics #41 4.00
... Justice League International 1,2 - Pre-Zero Hour JLI vs. Kingdom Come; Manley-a. 2-Bonus preview of Justice League 3001 #1 4.00
... Justice League of America 1,2 - Earth-One pre-Crisis Detroit JLA vs. Tangent Secret Six; ChrisCross-a. 2-Bonus preview of Batman/Superman #21 4.00
... Justice Society of America 1,2 - Earth-Two pre-Crisis JSA vs. Weaponers of Qward; Derenick-a. 2-Bonus preview of Superman/Wonder Woman #18 4.00
... New Teen Titans 1,2 - Earth-One pre-Crisis Teen Titans vs. Tangent Doom Patrol; Nicola Scott-a. 2-Bonus preview of Robin: Son of Batman #1 4.00
... Nightwing and Oracle 1,2 - Pre-Flashpoint version vs. Flashpoint Hawkman; Duursema-a/Thompson-c. 2-Bonus preview of Midnighter #1 4.00
... Plastic Man and the Freedom Fighters 1,2 - Earth-X team vs. Futures End cyborgs; Silver Ghost app.; McCrea-a/Barta-c. 2-Bonus preview of Harley Quinn #17 4.00
... The Question 1,2 - Pre-Flashpoint Question (Renee Montoya); Huntress, Batwoman & Two-Face app.; Rucka-s/Hamner-a. 2-Bonus preview of Starfire #1 4.00
... Shazam! 1,2 - Earth-S Marvel Family vs. Gotham By Gaslight Batman; Shaner-a Sivana, Ibac, Mr. Atom app. 2-Bonus preview of Constantine The Hellblazer #1 4.00
... Speed Force 1,2 - Pre-Flashpoint Flash (Wally West) vs. Flashpoint Wonder Woman Grummett-a; Fastback (Zoo Crew) app. 2-Bonus preview of Green Arrow #41 4.00
... Suicide Squad 1,2 - Pre-Zero Hour vs. Kingdom Come Green Lantern Mandrake-a; Lex Luthor app. 2-Bonus preview of Aquaman #41 4.00
... Superboy 1,2 - Pre-Zero Hour Kon-El vs. Kingdom Come Superman, Flash & Red Robin; Moline-a/Tarr-c. 2-Bonus preview of Action Comics #41 4.00
... Superboy and the Legion of Super-Heroes 1,2 - Pre-Crisis Legion vs. The Atomic Knights; Storms-a/Guerra-c. 2-Bonus preview of Teen Titans #9 4.00
... Supergirl: Matrix 1,2 - Pre-Zero Hour Supergirl vs. Lady Quark (Electropolis); Ambush Bug app.; Giffen-s/Green II-a/Porter-c. 2-Bonus preview of Bat-Mite #1 4.00
... Superman 1 - Pre-Flashpoint Superman & Lois vs. Flashpoint heroes; Jurgens-s/Weeks-a 4.00
2-Birth of Jonathan Kent (Superman: Son of Kal-El); bonus preview of Doomed #1 (See Superman: Lois & Clark series) 3 6 9 21 33 45
... Superman: Man of Steel 1,2 - Pre-Zero Hour Steel vs. Gen-13; Parasite app.; Louise Simonson-s/June Brigman-a/Walt Simonson-c. 2-Bonus preview of Bizarro #1 4.00
... Swamp Thing 1,2 - Earth-One pre-Crisis Swamp Thing vs. Red Rain vampire Batman; Len Wein-s/Kelley Jones-a. 2-Bonus preview of Catwoman #41 4.00
... Titans 1,2 - Pre-Flashpoint Titans vs. The Extremists; Nicieza-s/Wagner-a; 2-Bonus preview of Red Hood & Arsenal #1 4.00
... Wonder Woman 1,2 - Earth-One pre-Crisis Wonder Woman vs. Red Rain vampire Joker, Catwoman & Poison Ivy. 1-Middleton-a/c. 2-Lopresti-a; bonus preview of Secret Six 6.00
... World's Finest 1,2 - Earth-Two pre-Crisis Seven Soldiers of Victory vs. Weaponers of Qward; Scribbly Jibbet app.; Levitz-s. 2-Bonus preview of We Are Robin #1 4.00

CONVOCATIONS: A MAGIC THE GATHERING GALLERY
Acclaim Comics (Armada): Jan, 1996 ($2.50, one-shot)

1-pin-ups by various artists including Kaluta, Vess, and Dringenberg 4.00

COO COO COMICS (...the Bird Brain No. 57 on)
Nedor Publ. Co./Standard (Animated Cartoons): Oct, 1942 - No. 62, Apr, 1952

1-Origin/1st app. Super Mouse & begin series (cloned from Superman); the first funny animal super hero series (see Looney Tunes #5 for 1st funny animal super hero) 65 130 195 416 708 1000
2 24 48 72 142 234 325
3-10: 10-(3/44) 16 32 48 98 154 210
11-33: 33-1 pg. Ingels-a 14 28 42 82 121 160
34-40,43-46,48-50Text illos by Frazetta in all. 36-Super Mouse covers begin 17 34 51 100 158 215
41-Frazetta-a (6-pg. story & 3 text illos) 32 64 96 188 307 425
42,47-Frazetta-a & text illos. 22 44 66 128 209 290
51-62: 56-58,61-Super Mouse app. 14 28 42 76 108 140

"COOKIE" (Also see Topsy-Turvy)
Michel Publ./American Comics Group(Regis Publ.): Apr, 1946 - No. 55, Aug-Sept, 1955

1-Teen-age humor 36 72 108 211 343 475
2-1st app. Tee-Pee Tim who takes over Ha Ha Comics later 19 38 57 111 176 240
3-10: 8-Bing Crosby app. 15 30 45 85 130 175
11-20: 12-Hedy Lamarr app. 13-Jackie Robinson mentioned. 15-Gregory Peck cover app. 16-Ub Iwerks (a creator of Mickey Mouse) name used. 18-Jane Russell-type Jane Bustle. 19-Cookie takes a dog to see Lassie movie 14 28 42 78 112 145
21-23,26,28-30: 26-Milt Gross & Starlett O'Hara stories. 28,30-Starlett O'Hara stories 12 24 36 67 94 120
24,25,27-Starlett O'Hara stories 12 24 36 69 97 125
31-34,37-48,52-55 10 20 30 56 76 95
35,36-Starlett O'Hara stories 11 22 33 62 86 110
49-51: 49-(6-7/54)-3-D effect-c/s. 50-3-D effect. 51-(10-11/54) 8pg. TrueVision 3-D effect story 16 32 48 94 147 200

COOL CAT (What's Cookin' With...) (Formerly Black Magic)
Prize Publications: V8#6, Mar-Apr, 1962 - V9#2, July-Aug, 1962

V8#6, nn(V9#1, 5-6/62), V9#2 3 6 9 21 33 45

COOL WORLD (Movie by Ralph Bakshi)
DC Comics: Apr, 1992 - No. 4, Sept, 1992 ($1.75, limited series)

1-4: Prequel to animated/live action movie. 1-Bakshi-c. Bill Wray inks in all 1 3 4 6 8 10
Movie Adaptation nn ('92, $3.50, 68pg.)-Bakshi-c 2 4 6 8 10 12

COPPER CANYON (See Fawcett Movie Comics)

COPPERHEAD
Image Comics: Sept, 2014 - No. 19, Jun, 2018 ($3.50/$3.99)

1-19: 1-Faerber-s/Godlewski-a; multiple covers. 11-$3.99-c begins. 11-18-Moss-a 4.00

COPS (TV)
DC Comics: Aug, 1988 - No. 15, Aug, 1989 ($1.00)

1 ($1.50, 52 pgs.)-Based on Hasbro Toys 4.00
2-15: 14-Orlando-c(p) 3.00

COPS: THE JOB
Marvel Comics: June, 1992 - No. 4, Sept, 1992 ($1.25, limited series)

1-4: All have Jusko scripts & Golden-c 3.00

CORBEN SPECIAL, A
Pacific Comics: May, 1984 (one-shot)

1-Corben-c/a; E.A. Poe adaptation 6.00

CORE, THE
Image Comics: July, 2008 ($3.99)

Pilot Season - Hickman-s/Rocafort-a 4.00

CORKY & WHITE SHADOW (Disney, TV)
Dell Publishing Co.: No. 707, May, 1956 (Mickey Mouse Club)

Four Color 707-Photo-c 7 14 21 46 86 125

CORLISS ARCHER (See Meet Corliss Archer)

CORMAC MAC ART (Robert E. Howard's...)
Dark Horse Comics: 1990 - No. 4, 1990 ($1.95, B&W, mini-series)

1-4: All have Bolton painted-c; Howard adapts. 3.00

CORONAVIRUS BOOK (Cerebus in Hell)
Aardvark-Vanaheim: Dec, 2021 ($8.00, B&W)

1-Cerebus figures placed over original Gustave Doré artwork of Hell 8.00

CORPORAL RUSTY DUGAN (See Holyoke One-Shot #2)

CORPSES OF DR. SACOTTI, THE (See Ideal a Classical Comic)

CORSAIR, THE (See A-1 Comics No. 5, 7, 10 under Texas Slim)

CORUM: THE BULL AND THE SPEAR (See Chronicles Of Corum)
First Comics: Jan, 1989 - No. 4, July, 1989 ($1.95)

Convergence Flash #1 © DC

Cosmo the Mighty Martian #1 © ACP

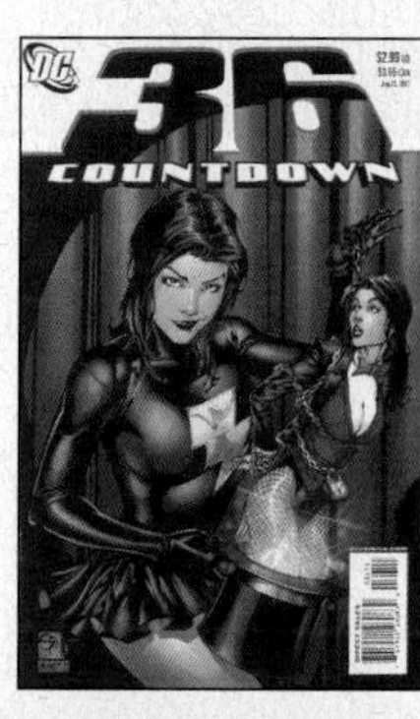

Countdown #36 © DC

	GD 2.0	VG 4.0	FN 6.0	VF 8.0	VF/NM 9.0	NM- 9.2
1-4: Adapts Michael Moorcock's novel						3.00

COSMIC BOOK, THE
Ace Comics: Dec, 1986 ($1.95)

	GD	VG	FN	VF	VF/NM	NM-
1-(44pgs.)-Wood, Toth-a	1	3	4	6	8	10

COSMIC BOY (Also see The Legion of Super-Heroes)
DC Comics: Dec, 1986 - No. 4, Mar, 1987 (limited series)

1-4: Legends tie-ins all issues 4.00

COSMIC GHOST RIDER (See Thanos 2017 series #13 for debut)
Marvel Comics: Sept, 2018 - No. 5, Jan, 2019 ($3.99)

1-Cates-s/Burnett-a; Frank Castle as Ghost Rider; Odin and baby Thanos app. 4.00
2-5: 2,3-Galactus app. 5-Leads into Guardians of the Galaxy 2019 series 4.00

COSMIC GHOST RIDER
Marvel Comics: May, 2023 - Present ($4.99)

1-($4.99) Stephanie Phillips-s/Juann Cabal-a 5.00

COSMIC GHOST RIDER DESTROYS MARVEL HISTORY
Marvel Comics: May, 2019 - No. 6, Oct, 2019 ($3.99, limited series)

1-6: 1-Scheer & Giovannetti-s/Sandoval-a: Uato the Watcher app. 2,4,6-Nauck-a 4.00

COSMIC GUARD
Devil's Due Publ.: Aug, 2004 - No. 6, Dec, 2005 ($2.99)

1-6-Jim Starlin-s/a 3.00

COSMIC HEROES
Eternity/Malibu Graphics: Oct, 1988 - No. 11, Dec, 1989 ($1.95, B&W)

1-11: Reprints 1934-1936's Buck Rogers newspaper strips #1-728 3.00

COSMIC ODYSSEY
DC Comics: 1988 - No. 4, 1988 ($3.50, limited series, squarebound)

1-4: Reintro. New Gods into DC continuity; Superman, Batman, Green Lantern (John Stewart) app; Starlin scripts, Mignola-c/a in all. 2-Darkseid merges Demon & Jason Blood (separated in Demon limited series #4) 5.00
TPB (1992,2009, $19.99) r/#1-4; Robert Greenberger intro. 20.00

COSMIC POWERS
Marvel Comics: Mar, 1994 - No. 6, Aug, 1994 ($2.50, limited series)

1,2-Thanos app. 1-Ron Lim-c/a(p). 2-Terrax 5.00
3-6: 3-Ganymede & Jack of Hearts app. 4.00

COSMIC POWERS UNLIMITED
Marvel Comics: May, 1995 - No. 5, May, 1996 ($3.95, quarterly)

1-5 4.00

COSMIC SLAM
Ultimate Sports Entertainment: 1999 ($3.95, one-shot)

1-McGwire, Sosa, Bagwell, Justice battle aliens; Sienkiewicz-c 4.00

COSMO (The Merry Martian)
Archie Comic Publications: Feb, 2018 - No. 5, Jul, 2018 ($2.99, limited series)

1-5-Cosmo, Astra, and Orbi app.; Ian Flynn-s/Tracy Yardley-a; multiple covers 3.00

COSMO CAT (Becomes Sunny #11 on; also see All Top & Wotalife Comics)
Fox Publications/Green Publ. Co./Norlen Mag.: July-Aug, 1946 - No. 10, Oct, 1947; 1957; 1959

	GD	VG	FN	VF	VF/NM	NM-
1	34	68	102	204	332	460
2	16	32	48	94	147	200
3-Origin (11-12/46)	20	40	60	115	185	255
4-Robot-c	16	32	48	92	144	195
5-10	11	22	33	62	86	110
2-4(1957-Green Publ. Co.)	6	12	18	27	33	38
2-4(1959-Norlen Mag.)	5	10	15	23	28	32
I.W. Reprint #1	2	4	6	11	16	20

COSMO THE MERRY MARTIAN
Archie Publications (Radio Comics): Sept, 1958 - No. 6, Oct, 1959

	GD	VG	FN	VF	VF/NM	NM-
1-Bob White-a in all	20	40	60	118	192	265
2-6	13	26	39	74	105	135

COSMO THE MIGHTY MARTIAN
Archie Comic Publications: Jan, 2020 - No. 5, Jun, 2020 ($3.99, limited series)

1-5-Ian Flynn-s/Tracy Yardley-a; multiple covers 4.00

COTTON WOODS (All-American athlete)
Dell Publishing Co.: No. 837, Sept, 1957

	GD	VG	FN	VF	VF/NM	NM-
Four Color 837	5	10	15	30	50	70

COUGAR, THE (Cougar No. 2)
Seaboard Periodicals (Atlas): April, 1975 - No. 2, July, 1975

	GD	VG	FN	VF	VF/NM	NM-
1,2: 1-Vampire; Adkins-a(p). 2-Cougar origin; werewolf-s; Buckler-c(p)	2	4	6	11	16	20

COUNT CROWLEY: AMATEUR MIDNIGHT MONSTER HUNTER
Dark Horse Comics: Mar, 2022 - No. 4, Nov, 2022 ($3.99, limited series)

1-4-David Dastmalchian-s/Lukas Ketner-a. 3-EC-style cover 4.00

COUNT CROWLEY: RELUCTANT MIDNIGHT MONSTER HUNTER
Dark Horse Comics: Oct, 2019 - No. 4, Jan, 2020 ($3.99, limited series)

1-4-David Dastmalchian-s/Lukas Ketner-a 4.00

COUNTDOWN (See Movie Classics)

COUNTDOWN
DC Comics (WildStorm): June, 2000 - No. 8, Jan, 2001 ($2.95)

1-8-Mariotte-s/Lopresti-a 3.00

COUNTDOWN (Continued from 52 weekly series)
DC Comics: No. 51, July, 2007 - No. 1, June, 2008 ($2.99, weekly, limited series) (issue #s go in reverse)

51-Gatefold wraparound-c by Andy Kubert; Duela Dent killed; the Monitors app. 3.00
50-1: 50-Joker-c. 48-Lightray dies. 47-Mary Marvel gains Black Adam's powers. 46-Intro. Forerunner. 43-Funeral for Bart Allen. 39-Karate Kid-c 3.00
Countdown to Final Crisis Vol. 1 TPB (2008, $19.99) r/#51-39 20.00
Countdown to Final Crisis Vol. 2 TPB (2008, $19.99) r/#38-26 20.00
Countdown to Final Crisis Vol. 3 TPB (2008, $19.99) r/#25-13 20.00
Countdown to Final Crisis Vol. 4 TPB (2008, $19.99) r/#12-1 20.00

COUNTDOWN: ARENA (Takes place during Countdown #21-18)
DC Comics: Feb, 2008 - No. 4, Feb, 2008 ($3.99, weekly, limited series)

1-4-Battles between alternate Earth heroes; McDaniel-a; Andy Kubert variant-c on each 4.00
TPB (2008, $17.99) r/#1-4; variant covers 18.00

COUNTDOWN PRESENTS: LORD HAVOK & THE EXTREMISTS
DC Comics: Dec, 2007 - No. 8 ($2.99, limited series)

1-6: 1-Tieri-s/Sharp-a/c; Challengers From Beyond app. 3.00
TPB (2008, $17.99) r/#1-6 18.00

COUNTDOWN PRESENTS THE SEARCH FOR RAY PALMER (Leads into Countdown #18)
DC Comics: Nov, 2007 - Feb, 2008 ($2.99, series of one-shots)

...: Wildstorm (11/07) Part 1; The Authority app.; Art Adams-c/Unzueta-a 3.00
...: Crime Society (12/07) Earth-3 Owlman & Jokester app.; Igle-a 3.00
...: Red Rain (1/08) Vampire Batman app.; Kelley Jones-c; Jones, Battle & Unzueta-a 3.00
...: Gotham By Gaslight (1/08) Victorian Batman app.; Tocchini-a/Nguyen-c 3.00
...: Red Son (2/08) Soviet Superman app.; Foreman-a 3.00
...: Superwoman/Batwoman (2/08) Conclusion; gender-reversed heroes; Sook-c 3.00
TPB (2008, $17.99) r/one-shots 18.00

COUNTDOWN SPECIAL
DC Comics: Dec, 2007 - Jun, 2008 ($4.99, collection of reprints related to Countdown)

...: Eclipso (5/08) r/Eclipso #10 & Spectre #17,18 (1994); Sook-c 5.00
...: Jimmy Olsen (1/08) r/Superman's Pal, Jimmy Olsen #136,147,148; Kirby-s/a; Sook-c 5.00
...: Kamandi (6/08) r/Kamandi: The Last Boy on Earth #1,10,29; Kirby-s/a; Sook-c 5.00
...: New Gods (3/08) r/Forever People #1, Mr. Miracle #1, New Gods #7; Kirby-s/a; Sook-c 5.00
...: Omac (4/08) r/Omac (1974) #1, Warlord #37-39, DC Comics Presents #61; Sook-c 5.00
...: The Atom 1,2 (2/08) r/stories from Super-Team Family #11-14; Sook-c on both 5.00
...: The Flash (12/07) r/Rogues Gallery in Flash (1st series) #106,113,155,174; Sook-c 5.00

COUNTDOWN TO ADVENTURE
DC Comics: Oct, 2007 - No. 8, May, 2008 ($3.99, limited series)

1-8: 1-Adam Strange, Animal Man and Starfire app.; origin of Forerunner 4.00
TPB (2008, $17.99) r/#1-8 18.00

COUNTDOWN TO INFINITE CRISIS (See DC Countdown)

COUNTDOWN TO MYSTERY (See Eclipso: The Music of the Spheres TPB for reprint)
DC Comics: Nov, 2007 - No. 8, Jun, 2008 ($3.99, limited series)

1-8: 1-Doctor Fate, Eclipso, The Spectre and Plastic Man app. 4.00
TPB (2008, $17.99) r/#1-8 18.00

COUNT DUCKULA (TV)
Marvel Comics: Nov, 1988 - No. 15, Jan, 1991 ($1.00)

1,8: 1-Dangermouse back-up. 8-Geraldo Rivera photo-c/& app.; Sienkiewicz-a(i) 7.00
2-7,9-15: Dangermouse back-ups in all 4.00

COUNT OF MONTE CRISTO, THE
Dell Publishing Co.: No. 794, May, 1957

	GD	VG	FN	VF	VF/NM	NM-
Four Color 794-Movie, Buscema-a	8	16	24	51	96	140

COUP D'ETAT (Oneshots)
DC Comics (WildStorm): April, 2004 ($2.95, weekly limited series)

	GD 2.0	VG 4.0	FN 6.0	VF 8.0	VF/NM 9.0	NM- 9.2
...: Sleeper 1 (part 1 of 4) Jim Lee-a; 2 covers by Lee and Bermejo						3.00
...: Stormwatch 1 (part 2 of 4) D'Anda-a; 2 covers by D'Anda and Bermejo						3.00
...: Wildcats Version 3.0 1 (part 3 of 4) Garza-a; 2 covers by Garza and Bermejo						3.00
...: The Authority 1 (part 4 of 4) Portacio-a; 2 covers by Portacio and Bermejo						3.00
...: Afterword 1 (5/04) Profile pages and prelude stories for Sleeper & Wetworks						3.00
TPB (2004, $12.95) r/series and profile pages from Afterword						13.00

COURAGE COMICS
J. Edward Slavin: 1945

	GD	VG	FN	VF	VF/NM	NM-
1,2,77	19	38	57	111	176	240

COURTNEY CRUMRIN
Oni Press: Apr, 2012 - No. 10, Feb, 2013 ($3.99)

	GD	VG	FN	VF	VF/NM	NM-
1-10-Ted Naifeh-s/a						4.00
#1 (5/14, Free Comic Book Day giveaway) r/#1						3.00

COURTNEY CRUMRIN...
Oni Press: July, 2005; July 2007; Dec, 2008 ($5.95, B&W, series of one-shots)

	GD	VG	FN	VF	VF/NM	NM-
... And The Fire Thief's Tale (7/07) Naifeh-s/a						6.00
... And The Prince of Nowhere (12/08) Naifeh-s/a						6.00
... Tales (5/11) sequel to Tales Portrait of the Warlock...; Naifeh-s/a						6.00
... Tales Portrait of the Warlock as a Young Man (7/05) origin Uncle Aloysius; Naifeh-s/a						6.00

COURTNEY CRUMRIN & THE COVEN OF MYSTICS
Oni Press: Dec, 2002 - No. 4, March, 2003 ($2.95, B&W, limited series)

	GD	VG	FN	VF	VF/NM	NM-
1-4-Ted Naifeh-s/a						3.00
TPB (9/03, $11.95, 8" x 5-1/2") r/#1-4						12.00

COURTNEY CRUMRIN & THE NIGHT THINGS
Oni Press: Mar, 2002 - No. 4, June, 2002 ($2.95, B&W, limited series)

	GD	VG	FN	VF	VF/NM	NM-
1-4-Ted Naifeh-s/a						3.00
Free Comic Book Day Edition (5/03) Naifeh-s/a						3.00
TPB (12/02, $11.95) r/#1-4						12.00

COURTNEY CRUMRIN IN THE TWILIGHT KINGDOM
Oni Press: Dec, 2003 - No. 4, May, 2004 ($2.99, B&W, limited series)

	GD	VG	FN	VF	VF/NM	NM-
1-4-Ted Naifeh-s/a						3.00
TPB (9/04, $11.95, digest-size) r/#1-4						12.00

COURTSHIP OF EDDIE'S FATHER (TV)
Dell Publishing Co.: Jan, 1970 - No. 2, May, 1970

	GD	VG	FN	VF	VF/NM	NM-
1-Bill Bixby photo-c on both	5	10	15	34	60	85
2	4	8	12	23	37	50

COVEN
Awesome Entertainment: Aug, 1997 - No. 5, Mar, 1998 ($2.50)

	GD	VG	FN	VF	VF/NM	NM-
Preview	1	2	3	5	6	8
1-Loeb-s/Churchill-a; three covers by Churchill, Liefeld, Pollina	1	2	3	5	6	8
1-Fan Appreciation Ed.(3/98); new Churchill-c						3.00
1+ :Includes B&W art from Kaboom	1	3	4	6	8	10
2-Regular-c w/leaping Fantom						6.00
2-Variant-c w/circle of candles	1	2	3	5	6	8
3-6-Contains flip book preview of ReGex						3.00
3-White variant-c	1	2	3	4	5	7
3,4: 3-Halloween wraparound-c. 4-Purple variant-c						3.00
...Black & White (9/98) Short stories						3.00
...Fantom Special (2/98) w/sketch pages						5.00

COVEN
Awesome Entertainment: Jan, 1999 - No. 3, June, 1999 ($2.50)

	GD	VG	FN	VF	VF/NM	NM-
1-3: 1-Loeb-s/Churchill-a; 6 covers by various. 2-Supreme-c/app. 3-Flip book w/Kaboom preview						3.00
... Dark Origins (7/99, 2.50) w/Lionheart gallery						3.00

COVENANT, THE
Image Comics (Top Cow): 2005 ($9.99, squarebound, one-shot)

	GD	VG	FN	VF	VF/NM	NM-
nn-Tone Rodriguez-a/Aron Coleite-s						10.00

COVENANT, THE
Image Comics: Jun, 2015 - No. 5, Dec, 2015 ($3.99)

	GD	VG	FN	VF	VF/NM	NM-
1-5-Rob Liefeld-s/c; Matt Horak-a; story of the Ark of the Covenant						4.00

COVER
DC Comics (Jinxworld): Nov, 2018 - No. 6, May, 2019 ($3.99)

	GD	VG	FN	VF	VF/NM	NM-
1-6-Brian Michael Bendis-s/David Mack-a/c; comic creator as spy						4.00

COVERED WAGONS, HO (Disney, TV)
Dell Publishing Co.: No. 814, June, 1957 (Donald Duck)

	GD	VG	FN	VF	VF/NM	NM-
Four Color 814-Mickey Mouse app.	7	14	21	46	86	125

COWBOY ACTION (Formerly Western Thrillers No. 1-4; Becomes Quick-Trigger Western No. 12 on)
Atlas Comics (ACI): No. 5, March, 1955 - No. 11, March, 1956

	GD	VG	FN	VF	VF/NM	NM-
5	15	30	45	90	140	190
6-10: 6-8-Heath-c	12	24	36	67	94	120
11-Williamson-a (4 pgs.); Baker-a	14	28	42	76	108	140

NOTE: *Ayers a-8. Drucker a-6.* ***Maneely*** *c/a-5, 6.* ***Severin*** *c-10.* ***Shores*** *a-7.*

COWBOY BEBOP (Based on the Netflix adaptation of the animated series)
Titan Comics: Feb, 2022 - No. 4, Jul, 2022 ($3.99, limited series)

	GD	VG	FN	VF	VF/NM	NM-
1-4-Dan Watters-s/Lamar Mathurin-a						4.00

COWBOY COMICS (Star Ranger #12, Stories #14)(Star Ranger Funnies #15)
Centaur Publishing Co.: No. 13, July, 1938 - No. 14, Aug, 1938

	GD	VG	FN	VF	VF/NM	NM-
13-(Rare)-Ace and Deuce, Lyin Lou, Air Patrol, Aces High, Lee Trent, Trouble Hunters begin	300	600	900	2010	3505	5000
14-(Rare)-Filchock-c	245	490	735	1568	2684	3800

NOTE: ***Guardineer*** *a-13, 14.* ***Gustavson*** *a-13, 14.*

COWBOY IN AFRICA (TV)
Gold Key: Mar, 1968

	GD	VG	FN	VF	VF/NM	NM-
1(10219-803)-Chuck Connors photo-c	4	8	12	25	40	55

COWBOY LOVE (Becomes Range Busters?)
Fawcett Publications/Charlton Comics No. 28 on: 7/49 - V2#10, 6/50; No. 11, 1951; No. 28, 2/55 - No. 31, 8/55

	GD	VG	FN	VF	VF/NM	NM-
V1#1-Rocky Lane photo back-c	20	40	60	117	189	260
2	9	18	27	52	69	85
V1#3,4,6 (12/49)	8	16	24	44	57	70
5-Bill Boyd photo back-c (11/49)	9	18	27	52	69	85
V2#7-Williamson/Evans-a	10	20	30	58	79	100
V2#8-11	8	16	24	40	50	60
V1#28 (Charlton)-Last precode (2/55) (Formerly Romantic Story?)	7	14	21	37	46	55
V1#29-31 (Charlton; becomes Sweetheart Diary #32 on)	7	14	21	35	43	50

NOTE: ***Powell*** *a-10.* ***Marcus Swayze*** *a-2, 3. Photo c-1-11. No. 1-3, 5-7, 9, 10 are 52 pgs.*

COWBOY ROMANCES (Young Men No. 4 on)
Marvel Comics (IPC): Oct, 1949 - No. 3, Mar, 1950 (All photo-c & 52 pgs.)

	GD	VG	FN	VF	VF/NM	NM-
1-Photo-c	29	58	87	172	281	390
2-William Holden, Mona Freeman "Streets of Laredo" photo-c	20	40	60	117	189	260
3-Photo-c	17	34	51	98	154	210

COWBOYS 'N' INJUNS (...and Indians No. 6 on)
Compix No. 1-5/Magazine Enterprises No. 6 on: 1946 - No. 5, 1947; No. 6, 1949 - No. 8, 1952

	GD	VG	FN	VF	VF/NM	NM-
1-Funny animal western	16	32	48	98	154	210
2-5-All funny animal western	10	20	30	58	79	100
6(A-1 23)-Half violent, half funny; Ayers-a	15	30	45	88	137	185
7(A-1 41, 1950), 8(A-1 48)-All funny	10	20	30	54	72	90
I.W. Reprint No. 1,7,10 (Reprinted in Canada by Superior, No. 7), 10('63)	3	6	9	14	19	24

COWBOY WESTERN COMICS (TV)(Formerly Jack In The Box; Becomes Space Western No. 40-45 & Wild Bill Hickok & Jingles No. 68 on; title: Cowboy Western Heroes No. 47 & 48; Cowboy Western No. 49 on)
Charlton (Capitol Stories): No. 17, 7/48 - No. 39, 8/52; No. 46, 10/53; No. 47, 12/53; No. 48, Spr, '54; No. 49, 5-6/54 - No. 67, 3/58 (nn 40-45)

	GD	VG	FN	VF	VF/NM	NM-
17-Jesse James, Annie Oakley, Wild Bill Hickok begin; Texas Rangers app.	20	40	60	114	182	250
18,19-Orlando-c/a. 18-Paul Bunyan begins. 19-Wyatt Earp story	10	20	30	58	79	100
20-25: 21-Buffalo Bill story. 22-Texas Rangers-c/story. 24-Joel McCrea photo-c & adaptation from movie "Three Faces West". 25-James Craig photo-c & adaptation from movie "Northwest Stampede"	9	18	27	52	69	85
26-George Montgomery photo-c and adaptation from movie "Indian Scout"; 1 pg. bio on Will Rogers	10	20	30	58	79	100
27-Sunset Carson photo-c & adapts movie "Sunset Carson Rides Again" plus 1 other Sunset Carson story	39	78	117	240	395	550
28-Sunset Carson line drawn-c; adapts movies "Battling Marshal" & "Fighting Mustangs" starring Sunset Carson	20	40	60	114	182	250
29-Sunset Carson line drawn-c; adapts movies "Rio Grande" with Sunset Carson & "Winchester '73" w/James Stewart plus 5 pg. life history of Sunset Carson featuring Tom Mix	20	40	60	114	182	250
30-Sunset Carson photo-c; adapts movie "Deadline" starring Sunset Carson plus 1 other Sunset Carson story	39	78	117	240	395	550
31-34,38,39,47-50 (no #40-45): 50-Golden Arrow, Rocky Lane & Blackjack (r?) stories	9	18	27	47	61	75
35,36-Sunset Carson-c/stories (2 in each). 35-Inside front-c photo of Sunset Carson plus photo on-c	20	40	60	120	195	270
37-Sunset Carson stories (2)	15	30	45	94	147	200
46-(Formerly Space Western)-Space western story	15	30	45	94	147	200
51-57,59-66: 51-Golden Arrow(r?) & Monte Hale-r renamed Rusty Hall. 53,54-Tom Mix-r. 55-Monte Hale story(r?). 66-Young Eagle story. 67-Wild Bill Hickok and Jingles-c/story	7	14	21	35	43	50
58-(1/56)-Wild Bill Hickok, Annie Oakley & Jesse James stories; Forgione-a	8	16	24	44	57	70
67-(15¢, 68 pgs.)-Williamson/Torres-a, 5 pgs.	9	18	27	50	65	80

NOTE: *Many issues trimmed 1" shorter.* ***Maneely*** *a-67(5). Inside front/back photo c-29.*

COWGIRL ROMANCES
Marvel Comics (CCC): No. 28, Jan, 1950 (52 pgs.)

	GD	VG	FN	VF	VF/NM	NM-
28(#1)-Photo-c	24	48	72	142	234	325

COWGIRL ROMANCES
Fiction House Magazines: 1950 - No. 12, Winter, 1952-53 (No. 1-3: 52 pgs.)

	GD	VG	FN	VF	VF/NM	NM-
1-Kamen-a	61	122	183	390	670	950
2	36	72	108	211	343	475
3-5: 5-12-Whitman-c (most)	28	56	84	168	274	380
6-9,11,12	26	52	78	156	256	355
10-Frazetta?/Williamson?-a; Kamen?/Baker-a; r/Mitzi story from Movie Comics #4 w/all new dialogue	55	110	165	352	601	850

C.O.W.L.
Image Comics: May, 2014 - No. 11, Jul, 2015 ($3.50)

	GD	VG	FN	VF	VF/NM	NM-
1-11: 1-Higgins & Siegel-s/Reis-a. 6-Origin of Grey Raven; Charretier-a						3.50

COW PUNCHER (...Comics)
Avon Periodicals: Jan, 1947; No. 2, Sept, 1947 - No. 7, 1949

	GD	VG	FN	VF	VF/NM	NM-
1-Clint Cortland, Texas Ranger, Kit West, Pioneer Queen begin; Kubert-a; Alabam stories begin	77	154	231	493	847	1200
2-Kubert, Kamen/Feldstein-a; Kamen-c	90	180	270	576	988	1400
3-5,7: 3-Kiefer story	41	82	123	256	428	600
6-Opium drug mention story; bondage, headlight-c; Reinman-a	65	130	195	416	708	1000

COWPUNCHER
Realistic Publications: 1953 (nn) (Reprints Avon's No. 2)

	GD	VG	FN	VF	VF/NM	NM-
nn-Kubert-a	17	34	51	100	158	215

COWSILLS, THE (See Harvey Pop Comics)

Cowboy Bebop #1 © Netflix

Crackajack Funnies #1 © DELL

Cracked #23 © MP

	GD 2.0	VG 4.0	FN 6.0	VF 8.0	VF/NM 9.0	NM- 9.2

COW SPECIAL, THE
Image Comics (Top Cow): Spring-Summer 2000; 2001 ($2.95)

Issue	GD	VG	FN	VF	VF/NM	NM-
1-Previews upcoming Top Cow projects; Yancy Butler photo-c						3.00
Vol. 2 #1-Witchblade-c; previews and interviews						3.00

COYOTE
Marvel Comics (Epic Comics): June, 1983 - No. 16, Mar, 1986

Issue	GD	VG	FN	VF	VF/NM	NM-
1-10,15: 7-10-Ditko-a						4.00
11-1st McFarlane-a.	5	10	15	31	53	75
12-14,16: 12-14-McFarlane-a. 14-Badger x-over. 16-Reagan c/app.						6.00
Coyote Collection Vol. 1 (2005, $14.99) reprints from Coyote #1-7 & Scorpio Rose #1,2 plus Rogers layout pages for unpublished #3; Englehart intro.						15.00
Coyote Collection Vol. 2 (2005, $12.99) reprints from Coyote #1-4						13.00
Coyote Collection Vol. 3 (2006, $12.99) reprints from Coyote #5-8						13.00
Coyote Collection Vol. 4 (2007, $14.99) reprints from Coyote #9-12						15.00
Coyote Collection Vol. 5 (2007, $12.99) reprints from Coyote #13-16						13.00

COYOTES
Image Comics: Nov, 2017 - No. 8, Nov, 2018 ($3.99, limited series)

Issue	GD	VG	FN	VF	VF/NM	NM-
1-8-Sean Lewis-s/Caitlin Yarsky-a						4.00

CRACKAJACK FUNNIES (Also see The Owl)
Dell Publishing Co.: June, 1938 - No. 43, Jan, 1942

Issue	GD	VG	FN	VF	VF/NM	NM-
1-Dan Dunn, Freckles, Myra North, Wash Tubbs, Apple Mary, The Nebbs, Don Winslow, Tom Mix, Buck Jones, Major Hoople, Clyde Beatty, Boots begin	200	400	600	1280	2190	3100
2	81	162	243	518	884	1250
3	60	120	180	381	653	925
4	48	96	144	302	514	725
5-Nude woman on cover (10/38)	61	122	183	390	670	950
6-8,10: 8-Speed Bolton begins (1st app.)	42	84	126	265	445	625
9-(3/39)-Red Ryder strip-r begin by Harman; 1st app. in comics & 1st cover app.	184	368	552	1168	2009	2850
11-14	36	72	108	216	351	485
15-Tarzan text feature begins by Burroughs (9/39); not in #26,35	39	78	117	240	395	550
16-24: 18-Stratosphere Jim begins (1st app., 12/39). 23-Ellery Queen begins plus-c (1st comic book app., 5/40)	32	64	96	188	307	425
25-The Owl begins (1st app., 7/40); in new costume #26 by Frank Thomas (also see Popular Comics #72)	97	194	291	621	1061	1500
26,27,29,30	52	104	156	328	552	775
28-Part Owl-c	65	130	195	416	708	1000
31-Owl covers begin, end #42	71	142	213	454	777	1100
32-Origin Owl Girl	77	154	231	493	847	1200
33-37: 36-Last Tarzan issue. 37-Cyclone & Midge begin (1st app.)	57	114	171	362	619	875
38-(scarce) Classic giant gorilla vs. Owl-c	93	186	279	591	1021	1450
39-Andy Panda begins (intro/1st app., 9/41)	87	174	261	553	952	1350
40-42: 42-Last Owl-c.	54	108	162	343	574	825
43-Terry & the Pirates-r	26	52	78	154	252	350

NOTE: ***McWilliams** art in most issues.*

CRACK COMICS (Crack Western No. 63 on)
Quality Comics Group: May, 1940 - No. 62, Sept, 1949

Issue	GD	VG	FN	VF	VF/NM	NM-
1-Origin & 1st app. The Black Condor by Lou Fine, Madame Fatal, Red Torpedo, Rock Bradden & The Space Legion; The Clock, Alias the Spider (by Gustavson), Wizard Wells, & Ned Brant begin; Powell-a; Note: Madame Fatal is a man dressed as a woman	470	940	1410	3431	6066	8700
2	232	464	696	1485	2543	3600
3	174	348	522	1114	1907	2700
4	138	276	414	876	1513	2150
5-10: 5-Molly The Model begins. 10-Tor, the Magic Master begins	116	232	348	742	1271	1800
11-20: 13-1 pg. J. Cole-a. 15-1st app. Spitfire	97	194	291	621	1061	1500
21-24: 23-Pen Miller begins; continued from National Comics #22. 24-Last Fine Black Condor	74	148	222	470	810	1150
25	60	120	180	381	653	925
26-Flag-c	74	148	222	470	810	1150
27-(1/43)-Intro & origin Captain Triumph by Alfred Andriola (Kerry Drake artist) & begin series	119	238	357	762	1306	1850
28-30	45	90	135	284	480	675
31-39: 31-Last Black Condor	25	50	75	150	245	340
40-46	18	36	54	107	169	230
47-57,59,60-Capt. Triumph by Crandall	19	38	57	112	179	245
58,61,62-Last Captain Triumph	15	30	45	88	137	185

NOTE: *Black Condor by **Fine**: No. 1, 2, 5, 6, 8, 10-24; by **Sultan**: No. 3, 7; by **Fugitani**: No. 9. **Cole** a-34. **Crandall** a-61(unsigned); c-48, 49, 51-61. **Guardineer** a-17. **Gustavson** a-1, 2, 4, 7, 13, 17, 23. **McWilliams** a-15-27. Black Condor c-2, 4, 6, 8, 10, 12, 14, 16, 18, 20-26. Capt. Triumph c-27-62. The Clock c-1, 3, 5, 7, 9, 11, 13, 15, 17, 19.*

CRACK COMICS (Next Issue Project)
Image Comics: No. 63, Oct, 2011 ($4.99, one-shot)

Issue	GD	VG	FN	VF	VF/NM	NM-
63-Mimics style & format of a 1949 issue; Weiss-c; s/a by various; Capt. Triumph app.						5.00

CRACK COMICS
Quality Comics: May 1940

1-Ashcan comic, not distributed to newsstands, only for in-house use. Cover art is the same as published version of Crack Comics #1with exception of text panel on bottom left of cover. A CGC certified 4.0 copy sold for $1,495 in 2005.

CRACKDOWN (Based on the videogame)
Dynamite Entertainment: 2018 - No. 4, 2018 ($3.99)

Issue	GD	VG	FN	VF	VF/NM	NM-
1-4-Jonathan Goff-s/Ricardo Jaime-a						4.00

CRACKED (Magazine) (Satire) (Also see The 3-D Zone #19)
Major Magazines(#1-212)/Globe Communications(#213-346/American Media #347 on): Feb-Mar, 1958 - No. 365, Nov, 2004

Issue	GD	VG	FN	VF	VF/NM	NM-
1-One pg. Williamson-a; Everett-c; Gunsmoke-s	40	80	120	296	673	1050
2-1st Shut-Ups & Bonus Cut-Outs; Superman parody-c by Severin (his 1st cover on the title) Frankenstein-s	19	38	57	131	291	450
3-5	13	26	39	86	188	290
6-10: 7-Reprints 1st 6 covers on-c. 8-Frankenstein-c. 10-Wolverton-a	10	20	30	66	138	210
11-12, 13(nn,3/60),	8	16	24	51	96	140
14-Kirby-a	8	16	24	56	108	160
15-17, 18(nn,2/61), 19,20	6	12	18	42	79	115
21-27(11/62), 27(No.28, 2/63; mis-#d), 29(5/63)	5	10	15	35	63	90
30-40(11/64): 37-Beatles and Superman cameos	4	8	12	27	44	60
41-45,47-56,59,60: 47,49,52-Munsters. 51-Beatles inside-c. 59-Laurel and Hardy photos	4	8	12	23	37	50
46,57,58: 46,58-Man From U.N.C.L.E. 46-Beatles. 57-Rolling Stones	4	8	12	25	40	55
61-80: 62-Beatles cameo. 69-Batman, Superman app. 70-(8/68) Elvis cameo. 71-Garrison's Gorillas; W.C. Fields photos	3	6	9	16	23	30
81-99: 99-Alfred E. Neuman on-c	3	6	9	14	20	25
100	3	6	9	17	26	35
101-119: 104-Godfather-c/s. 108-Archie Bunker-s. 112,119-Kung Fu (TV). 113-Tarzan-s. 115-MASH. 117-Cannon. 118-The Sting-c/s	2	4	6	10	14	18
120(12/74) Six Million Dollar Man-c/s; Ward-a	2	4	6	13	18	22
121,122,124-126,128-133,136-140: 121-American Graffiti. 122-Korak-c/s. 124,131-Godfather-c/s. 128-Capone-c. 129,131-Jaws. 132-Baretta-c/s. 133-Space 1999. 136-Laverne and Shirley/Fonz-c. 137-Travolta/Kotter-c/s. 138-Travolta/Laverne and Shirley/ Fonz-c. 139-Barney Miller-c/s. 140-King Kong-c/s; Fonz-s	2	4	6	10	14	18
123-Planet of the Apes-c/s; Six Million Dollar Man	3	6	9	15	22	28
127,134,135: 127-Star Trek-c/s; Ward-a. 134-Fonz-c/s; Starsky and Hutch. 135-Bionic Woman-c/s; Ward-a	3	6	9	14	20	25
141,151-Charlie's Angels-c/s. 151-Frankenstein	3	6	9	14	20	25
142,143,150,152-155,157: 142-MASH-c/s. 143-Rocky-c/s; King Kong-s. 150-(5/78) Close Encounters-c/s. 152-Close Enc./Star Wars-c/s. 153-Close Enc./Fonz-c/s. 154-Jaws II-c/s; Star Wars-s. 155-Star Wars/Fonz-c	2	4	6	9	13	16
144,149,156,158-160: 144-Fonz/Happy Days-c. 149-Star Wars/Six Mil.$ Man-c/s. 156-Grease/Travolta-c. 158-Mork & Mindy. 159-Battlestar Galactica-c/s; MASH-s. 160-Superman-c/s	2	4	6	11	16	20
145,147-Both have insert postcards: 145-Fonz/Rocky/L&S-c/s. 147-Star Wars-s; Farrah photo page (missing postcards-1/2 price)	3	6	9	15	22	28
146,148: 46-Star Wars-c/s with stickers insert (missing stickers-1/2 price). 148-Star Wars-c/s with inside-c color poster	3	6	9	18	28	38
161,170-Ward-a: 161-Mork & Mindy-c/s. 170-Dukes of Hazzard-c/s	2	4	6	8	11	14
162,165-168,171,172,175-178,180-Ward-a: 162-Sherlock Holmes-s. 165-Dracula-c/s. 167-Mork-c/s. 168,175-MASH-c/s. 168-Mork-s. 172-Dukes of Hazzard/CHiPs-c/s. 176-Barney Miller-c/s	2	4	6	8	10	12
163,179:163-Postcard insert; Mork & Mindy-c/s. 179-Insult cards insert; Popeye, Dukes of Hazzard-c/s	3	6	9	14	19	24
164,169: 164-Alien movie-c/s; Mork & Mindy-s. 169-Star Trek	2	4	6	9	13	16
173,174-Star Wars-Empire Strikes Back. 173-SW poster	3	6	9	14	20	25
181,182,185-191,193,194,196-198-most Ward-a: 182-MASH-c/s. 185-Dukes of Hazzard-c/s; Jefferson-s. 187-Love Boat. 188-Fall Guy-s. 189-Fonz/Happy Days-c. 190,194-MASH-c/s. 191-Magnum P.I./Rocky-c; Magnum-s. 193-Knight Rider-s. 196-Dukes of Hazzard/Knight Rider-c/s. 198-Jaws III-c/s; Fall Guy-s	1	2	3	5	7	9

183,184,192,195,199,200-Ward-a in all: 183-Superman-c/s. 184-Star Trek-c/s. 192-E.T.-c/s; Rocky-s. 195-E.T.-c/s. 199-Jabba-c; Star Wars-s. 200-(12/83)

GD VG FN VF VF/NM NM-
2.0 4.0 6.0 8.0 9.0 9.2

1 3 4 6 8 10
201,203,210-A-Team-c/s 6.00
202,204-206,211-224,226,227,230-233: 202-Knight Rider-s. 204-Magnum P.I.; A-Team-s. 206-Michael Jackson/Mr. T-c/s. 212-Prince-s; Cosby-s. 213-Monsters issue-c/s. 215-Hulk Hogan/Mr. T-c/s. 216-Miami Vice-s; James Bond-s. 217-Rambo-s; Cosby-s; A-Team-s. 218-Rocky-c/s. 219-Arnold/Commando-c/s; Rocky-s; Godzilla. 220-Rocky-c/s. 221-Stephen King app. 223-Miami Vice-s. 224-Cosby-s. 226-29th Anniv.; Tarzan-s; Aliens-s; Family Ties-s. 227-Cosby, Family Ties, Miami Vice-s. 230-Monkees-c/s; Elvis on-c; 232-Alf, Cheers, StarTrek-s. 233-Superman/James Bond-c/s; Robocop, Predator-s 5.00
207-209,225,234: 207-Michael Jackson-c/s. 208-Indiana Jones-c/s. 209-MichaelJackson/Gremlins-c/s; Star Trek III-s. 225-Schwarzenegger/Stallone/G.I. Joe-c/s. 234-Don Martin-a begins; Batman/Robocop/Clint Eastwood-c/s 6.00
228,229: 228-Star Trek-c/s; Alf, Pee Wee Herman-s. 229-Monsters issue-c/s; centerfold with many superheroes 6.00
235,239,243,249: 235-1st Martin-c; Star Trek:TNG-s; Alf-s. 239-Beetlejuice-c/s; Mike Tyson-s. 243-X-Men and other heroes app. 249-Batman/Indiana Jones/Ghostbusters-c/s 6.00
236,244,245,248: 236-Madonna/Stallone-c/s; Twilight Zone-s. 244-Elvis-c/s; Martin-c. 245-Roger Rabbit-c/s. 248-Batman issue 6.00
237,238,240-242,246,247,250: 237-Robocop-s. 238-Rambo-c/s; Star Trek-s. 242-Dirty Harry-s, Ward-a. 246-Alf-s; Star Trek-s., Ward-a. 247-Star Trek-s. 250-Batman/Ghostbusters-s 4.00
251-253,255,256,259,261-265,275-278,281,284,286-297,299: 252-Star Trek-s. 253-Back to the Future-c/s. 255-TMNT-c/s. 256-TMNT-c/s; Batman, Bart Simpson on-c. 259-Die Hard II, Robocop-s. 261-TMNT, Twin Peaks-s. 262-Rocky-c/s; Rocky Horror-s. 265-TMNT-s. 276-Aliens III, Batman-s. 277-Clinton-c. 284-Bart Simpson-c; 90210-s. 297-Van Damme-s/photo-c. 299-Dumb & Dumber-c/s 4.00
254,257,266,267,272,280,282,285,298,300: 254-Back to the Future, Punisher-s; Wolverton-a, Batman-s, Ward-a. 257-Batman, Simpsons-s; Spider-Man and other heroes app. 266-Terminator-c/s. 267-Toons-c/s. 272-Star Trek VI-s. 280-Swimsuit issue. 282-Cheers-c/s. 285-Jurassic Park-c/s. 298-Swimsuit issue; Martin-c. 300-(8/95) Brady Bunch-c/s 5.00
258,260,274,279,283: 258-Simpsons-c/s; Back to the Future-s. 260-Spider-Man-c/s; Simpsons-s. 274-Batman-c/s. 279-Madonna-c/s. 283-Jurassic Park-c/s; Wolverine app. inside back-c 5.00
301-305,307-365: 365-Freas-c 3.00
306-Toy Story-c/s 4.00
Biggest... (Winter, 1977) 2 4 6 13 18 22
Biggest, Greatest... nn('65) 5 10 15 30 50 70
Biggest, Greatest... 2('66/67) - #5('69/70) 3 6 9 19 30 40
Biggest, Greatest... 6('70) - #12(Wint. '77) 3 6 9 14 19 24
Biggest, Greatest...13(Fall '78) - #21(Fall/Wint. '86) 2 4 6 8 11 14
...Blockbuster 1(Sum '87), 2('88), 3(Sum. '89) 1 3 4 6 8 10
...Blockbuster 4 - 6(Sum. '92) 6.00
...Collectors' Edition 4 ('73; formerly ...Special) 2 4 6 13 18 22
5-9,10(10/75) 2 4 6 11 16 20
11-19,20(11/17) 2 4 6 8 11 14
21,22,23(5/78): 23-Ward-a 2 4 6 8 11 14
(#24-62,64 not numbered)
1978 (nn; July, Sept, Nov, Dec) (#24-27) 2 4 6 8 11 14
1979 (nn; May, July, Sept, Nov, Dec) (#28-33) 2 4 6 8 11 14
1980 (nn; Feb, May, July, Sept, Nov, Dec) (#34-39)1 3 4 6 8 10
1981 (nn; Feb, May, July, Sept, Nov, Dec) (#40-45)1 3 4 6 8 10
1982 (nn; Feb, May, July, Sept, Nov, Dec) (#46-51)1 3 4 6 8 10
1983 (nn; Feb, May, Sept, Nov, Dec) (#52-56) 1 3 4 6 8 10
1984 (nn; Feb, May, July, Nov) (#57-60) 1 2 3 4 5 7
1985 (nn; Feb) (#61) 1 2 3 4 5 7
62(9/85), nn(#63,11/85), 64(12/85), 65-69, 70(4/87) 1 2 3 4 5 7
71,72,73(100 pgs., 1/88), 74-79, 80(9/89) 5.00
81-96, 97(two diff. issues), 98-115: 83-Elvis, Batman parodies 5.00
116('98)-Last issue? 6.00
...Digest 1(Fall, '86, 148 pgs.), 2(1/87) 1 2 3 6 8 10
...Digest 3-5 1 2 3 4 5 7
...Party Pack 1,2('88) - 4('90) 4.00
...Shut-Ups 1(2/72) 3 6 9 17 26 35
...Shut-Ups 2('72) becomes Cracked Spec. #3 3 6 9 14 19 24
...Special 3('73; formerly Cracked Shut-Ups; ...Collectors' Edition#4 on) 2 4 6 13 18 22
... Summer Special 1(Sum. '91), 2(Sum. '92)-Don Martin-a 4.00
... Summer Special 3(Sum. '93) - 8(Sum. '98) 3.00
... Super (Vol. 2, formerly Super Cracked) 5(Wint. '91/92) - 14(Wint.'97/98) 3.00
Extra Special... 1(Spr. '76) 2 4 6 11 16 20
Extra Special... 2(Spr./Sum. '77) 2 4 6 10 14 18
Extra Special... 3(Wint. '79) - 9(Wint. '86) 1 2 3 4 5 7
Giant... nn('65) 5 10 15 33 57 80
Giant... 2('66) - 5('69) 3 6 9 21 33 45
Giant...6('70) - 12('76) 3 6 9 16 24 32
Giant...nn(9/77, #13), nn(1/78, #14), nn(3/78, #15), nn(5/78, #16), nn(7/78, #17), nn(11/78, #18), nn(3/79, #19), nn(7/79, #20), nn(10/79, #21), nn(12/79, #22), nn(3/80, #23), nn(7/80, #24) 2 4 6 11 16 20
Giant...nn(10/80, #25), nn(12/80, #26), nn(3/81, #27), nn(7/81, #28), nn(10/81, #29), nn(12/81, #30), nn(7/82, #31), nn(10/82, #32), nn(12/82, #33), nn(7/83, #34), 2 4 6 8 11 14
Giant...nn(10/83, #35), nn(12/83, #36), nn(3/84, #37), nn(7/84, #38), nn(10/84, #39), nn(3/85, #40), nn(7/85, #41), nn(10/85, #42) 1 2 3 5 7 9
Giant...43(3/86) - 46(1/87), 47(Wint. '88), 48(Wint. '89) 1 2 3 4 5 7
King Sized... 1('67) 4 8 12 25 40 55
King Sized... 2('68) - 5('71) 3 6 9 17 26 35
King Sized... 6('72) - 11('77) 3 6 9 14 20 26
King Sized... 12(Fall '78) - 17(Sum. '83) 2 4 6 8 11 14
King Sized... 18-20 (Sum/'86) (#21,22 exist?) 1 3 4 6 8 10
Spaced Out... 1-4 ('93 - '94) 5.00
Super... 1('68) 4 8 12 25 40 55
Super... 2('69) - 6('73) 3 6 9 19 30 40
Super... 7('74), 8(Spr. '75) - 10(Spr. '77) 3 6 9 15 22 28
Super... 11(Sum. '78) - 16(Fall '81) 2 4 6 11 16 20
Super... 17(Spr. '82) - 22(Fall '83) 2 4 6 8 11 14
Super... 23(Sum. '84, mis-numbered as #24) 2 4 6 8 11 14
Super... 24(Fall '84, correctly numbered) 2 4 6 8 11 14
Super... 25(Wint. '85) - 32(Fall '86) 2 4 6 8 10 12

GD VG FN VF VF/NM NM-
2.0 4.0 6.0 8.0 9.0 9.2

Super... (Vol. 2) 1('87, 100 pgs.)-Severin & Elder-a 1 3 4 6 8 10
Super... (Vol. 2) 2(Sum. '88), 3(Wint. '89), 4(exist?)(Becomes Cracked Super) 6.00
NOTE: ***Burgos** a-1-10. **Colan** a-257. **Davis** a-5, 11-17, 24, 40, 80; c-12-14, 16. **Elder** a-5, 6, 10-13; c-10. **Everett** a-1-10, 23-25, 61; c-1. **Heath** a-1-3, 6, 13, 14, 17, 110; c-6. **Jaffee** a-5, 6. **Don Martin** c-235, 244, 247, 259, 261, 264. **Morrow** a-8-10. **Reinman** a-1-4. **Severin** c/a-in most all issues. **Shores** a-3-7. **Torres** a-7-10. **Ward** a-22-24, 27, 35, 40, 120-193, 195, 197-205, 242, 244, 246, 247, 250, 252-257. **Williamson** a-1 (1 pg.). **Wolverton** a-10 (2 pgs.), Giant nn('65). **Wood** a-27, 35, 40. Alfred E. Neuman c-177, 200, 202. Batman c-234, 248, 249, 256, 274. Captain America c-256. Christmas c-234, 243. Spider-Man c-260. Star Trek c-127, 169, 207, 228. Star Wars c-145, 146, 148, 149, 152, 155, 173, 174, 199. Superman c-183, 233. #144, 146 have free full-color pre-glued stickers. #145, 147, 155, 163 have free full-color postcards. #123, 137, 154, 157 have free iron-ons.*

CRACKED MONSTER PARTY
Globe Communications: July, 1988 - No. 27, Wint. 1999/2000
1 3 6 9 14 20 25
2-4: 2-Wolfman, Frankenstein, Dracula, Nosferatu, The Mummy, Invisible Man & Mole Man-c. 3-Darth Vader/Chewbacca-c. 4-Elvira vs. Nanny 2 4 6 10 14 18
5-10 2 4 6 8 10 12
11-26 1 2 3 4 5 7
27-Interview with a Vampire-c/s 2 4 6 8 10 12

CRACKED'S FOR MONSTERS ONLY
Major Magazines: Sept, 1969 - No. 9, Sept, 1969; June, 1972
1 5 10 15 30 50 70
2-9, nn(6/72) 3 6 9 21 33 45

CRACK WESTERN (Formerly Crack Comics; Jonesy No. 85 on)
Quality Comics Group: No. 63, Nov, 1949 - No. 84, May, 1953 (36 pgs., 63-68,74-on)
63(#1)-Ward-c; Two-Gun Lil (origin & 1st app.)(ends #84), Arizona Ames, his horse Thunder (with sidekick Spurs & his horse Calico), Frontier Marshal (ends #70), & Dead Canyon Days (ends #69) begin; Crandall-a 19 38 57 112 179 245
64,65: 64-Ward-c. Crandall-a in both. 15 30 45 83 124 165
66,68-Photo-c. 66-Arizona Ames becomes A. Raines (ends #84) 13 26 39 72 101 130
67-Randolph Scott photo-c; Crandall-a 14 28 42 82 121 160
69(52pgs.)-Crandall-a 13 26 39 72 101 130
70(52pgs.)-The Whip (origin & 1st app.) & his horse Diablo begin (ends #84); Crandall-a 13 26 39 72 101 130
71(52pgs.)-Frontier Marshal becomes Bob Allen F. Marshal (ends #84); Crandall-c/a 14 28 42 80 115 150
72(52pgs.)-Tim Holt photo-c 12 24 36 67 94 120
73(52pgs.)-Photo-c 10 20 30 58 79 100
74-76,78,79,81,83-Crandall-c. 83-Crandall-a(p) 11 22 33 62 86 110
77,80,82 8 16 24 44 57 70
84-Crandall-c/a 12 24 36 67 94 120
NOTE: ***Crandall** c-71p, 74-81, 83p(w/**Cuidera**-i).*

CRASH COMICS (Cat-Man Comics No. 6 on)
Tem Publishing Co.: May, 1940 - No. 5, Nov, 1940
1-The Blue Streak, Strongman (origin), The Perfect Human, Shangra begin (1st app. of each); Kirby-a 389 778 1167 2723 4762 6800
2-Simon & Kirby-a 232 464 696 1485 2543 3600
3-Simon & Kirby-a 206 412 618 1318 2259 3200
4-Origin & 1st app. The Cat-Man; S&K-a 497 994 1491 3628 6414 9200
5-1st Cat-Man-c & 2nd app.; Simon & Kirby-a 284 568 852 1818 3109 4400
NOTE: *Solar Legion by **Kirby** No. 1-5 (5 pgs. each). Strongman c-1-4. Catman c-5.*

CRASH DIVE (See Cinema Comics Herald)

CRASH METRO AND THE STAR SQUAD
Oni Press: May, 1999 ($2.95, B&W, one-shot)
1-Allred-s/Ontiveros-a 3.00

CRASH RYAN (Also see Dark Horse Presents #44)
Marvel Comics (Epic): Oct, 1984 - No. 4, Jan, 1985 (Baxter paper, lim. series)
1-4 3.00

CRAZY (Also see This Magazine is Crazy)
Atlas Comics (CSI): Dec, 1953 - No. 7, July, 1954
1-Everett-c/a 84 168 252 538 919 1300
2 40 80 120 246 411 575
3-7: 4-I Love Lucy satire. 5-Satire on censorship 37 74 111 222 361 500
NOTE: ***Ayers** a-5. **Berg** a-1, 2. **Burgos** c-5, 6. **Drucker** a-6. **Everett** a-1-4. **Al Hartley** a-4. **Heath** a-3, 7; c-7. **Maneely** a-1-7, c-3, 4. **Post** a-3-6. Funny monster c-1-4.*

CRAZY (Satire)
Marvel Comics Group: Feb, 1973 - No. 3, June, 1973
1-Not Brand Echh-r; Beatles cameo (r) 3 6 9 18 28 38
2,3-Not Brand Echh-r; Kirby-a 2 4 6 13 18 22

CRAZY MAGAZINE (Satire)
Oct, 1973 - No. 94, Apr, 1983 (40-90¢, B&W magazine)
Marvel Comics: (#1, 44 pgs; #2-90, reg. issues, 52 pgs; #92-95, 68 pgs)'
1-Wolverton(1 pg.), Bode-a; 3 pg. photo story of Neal Adams & Dick Giordano; Harlan Ellison story; TV Kung Fu sty. 5 10 15 32 57 80
2-"Live & Let Die" c/s; 8pgs; Adams/Buscema-a; McCloud w5 pgs. Adams-a; Kurtzman's "Hey Look" 2 pg.-r 3 6 9 19 30 40
3-5: 3-"High Plains Drifter" w/Clint Eastwood c/s; Waltons app; Drucker, Reese-a. 4-Shaft-c/s; Ploog-a; Nixon 3 pg. app; Freas-a. 5-Michael Crichton's "Westworld" c/s; Nixon app. 3 6 9 16 24 32
6,7,18: 6-Exorcist c/s; Nixon app. 7-TV's Kung Fu c/s; Nixon app.; Ploog & Freas-a. 18-Six Million Dollar Man/Bionic Woman c/s; Welcome Back Kotter story 3 6 9 15 22 28
8-10: 8-Serpico c/s; Casper parody; TV's Police Story. 9-Joker cameo; Chinatown story; Eisner s/a begins; Has 1st 8 covers on-c. 10-Playboy Bunny-c; M. Severin-a; Lee Marrs-a begins; "Deathwish" story 3 6 9 14 20 26
11-17,19: 11-Towering Inferno. 12-Rhoda. 13-"Tommy" the Who Rock Opera. 14-Mandingo. 15-Jaws story. 16-Santa/Xmas-c; "Good Times" TV story; Jaws. 17-Bicentennial issue; Baretta; Woody Allen. 19-King Kong c/s; Reagan, J. Carter, Howard the Duck cameos, "Laverne & Shirley" 2 4 6 11 16 20
20,24,27: 20-Bicentennial-c; Space 1999 sty; Superheroes song sheet, 4pgs. 24-Charlie's Angels. 27-Charlie's Angels/Travolta/Fonz-c; Bionic Woman sty 3 6 9 14 19 24
21-23,25,26,28-30: 21-Starsky & Hutch. 22-Mount Rushmore/J. Carter-c; TV's Barney Miller;

Crack Western #74 © QUA

Crazy Magazine #35 © MAR

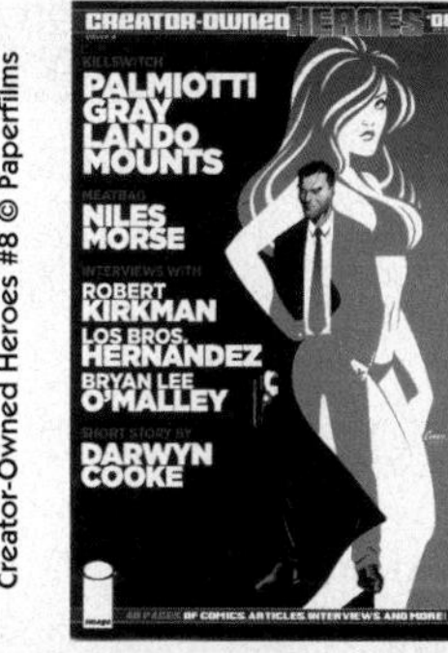

Creator-Owned Heroes #8 © Paperfilms

GD VG FN VF VF/NM NM-
2.0 4.0 6.0 8.0 9.0 9.2

Superheroes spoof. 23-Santa/Xmas-c; "Happy Days" sty; "Omen" sty. 25-J. Carter-c/s; Grandenetti-a begins; TV's Alice; Logan's Run. 26-TV Stars-c; Mary Hartman, King Kong. 28-Donny & Marie Osmond-c/s; Marathon Man. 29-Travolta/Kotter-c; "One Day at a Time", Gong Show. 30-1977, 84 pgs. w/bonus; Jaws, Baretta, King Kong, Happy Days 2 4 6 9 12 15

31,33-35,38,40: 31-"Rocky"-c/s; TV game shows. 33-Peter Benchley's "Deep". 34-J. Carter-c; TV's "Fish". 35-Xmas-c with Fonz/Six Million Dollar Man/Wonder Woman/Darth Vader/ Travolta, TV's "Mash" & "Family Matters". 38-Close Encounters of the Third Kind-c/s. 40-"Three's Company-c/s 1 3 4 6 8 11

32-Star Wars/Darth Vader-c/s; "Black Sunday" 3 6 9 15 22 28

36,42,47,49: 36-Farrah Fawcett/Six Million Dollar Man-c; TV's Nancy Drew & Hardy Boys; 1st app. Howard The Duck in Crazy, 2 pgs. 42-84 pgs. w/bonus; TV Hulk/Spider-Man-c; Mash, Gong Show, One Day at a Time, Disco, Alice. 47-Battlestar Galactica xmas-c; movie "Foul Play". 49-1979, 84 pgs. w/bonus; Mork & Mindy-c; Jaws, Saturday Night Fever, Three's Company 2 4 6 9 12 15

37-1978, 84 pgs. w/bonus. Darth Vader-c; Barney Miller, Laverne & Shirley, Good Times, Rocky, Donny & Marie Osmond, Bionic Woman 2 4 6 13 18 22

39,44: 39-Saturday Night Fever-c/s. 44-"Grease"-c w/Travolta/O. Newton-John 2 4 6 11 16 20

41-Kiss-c & 1pg. photos; Disaster movies, TV's "Family", Annie Hall 5 10 15 31 53 75

43,45,46,48,51: 43-Jaws-c; Saturday Night Fever. 43-E.C. swipe from Mad #131. 45-Travolta/O. Newton-John/J. Carter-c; Eight is Enough. 46-TV Hulk-c/s; Punk Rock. 48-"Wiz"-c, Battlestar Galactica-s. 51-Grease/Mork & Mindy/D&M Osmond-c, Mork & Mindy-sty. "Boys from Brazil" 1 3 4 6 8 11

50,58: 50-Superman movie-c/sty, Playboy Mag., TV Hulk, Fonz; Howard the Duck, 1 pg. 58-1980, 84 pgs. w/32 pg. color comic bonus insert-Full reprint of Crazy Comic #1, Battlestar Galactica, Charlie's Angels, Starsky & Hutch 2 4 6 11 16 20

52,59,60,64: 52-1979, 84 pgs. w/bonus. Marlon Brando-c; TV Hulk, Grease. Kiss, 1 pg. photos. 59-Santa Ptd-c by Larkin; "Alien", "Moonraker", Rocky-2, Howard the Duck, 1 pg. 60-Star Trek w/Muppets-c; Star Trek sty; 1st app/origin Teen Hulk; Severin-a. 64-84 pgs. w/bonus Monopoly game satire. "Empire Strikes Back", 8 pgs., One Day at a Time 2 4 6 11 16 20

53,54,65,67-70: 53-"Animal House"-c/sty; TV's "Vegas", Howard the Duck, 1 pg. 54-Love at First Bite-c/sty, Fantasy Island sty, Howard the Duck 1 pg. 65-(Has #66 on-c, Aug/'80). "Black Hole" w/Janson-a; Kirby,Wood/Severin-a(r), 5 pgs. Howard the Duck, 3 pgs.; Broderick-a; Buck Rogers, Mr. Rogers. 67-84 pgs. w/bonus; TV's Kung Fu, Exorcist; Ploog-a(r). 68-American Gigolo, Dukes of Hazzard, Teen Hulk; Howard the Duck, 3 pgs. Broderick-a; Monster sty/5 pg. Ditko-a(r). 69-Obnoxio the Clown-c/sty; Stephen King's "Shining", Teen Hulk, Richie Rich, Howard the Duck, 3pgs; Broderick-a. 70-84 pgs. Towering Inferno, Daytime TV; Trina Robbins-a 1 3 4 6 8 10

55-57,61,63: 55-84 pgs. w/bonus; Love Boat, Mork & Mindy, Fonz, TV Hulk. 56-Mork/Rocky/ J. Carter-c; China Syndrome. 57-TV Hulk with Miss Piggy-c, Dracula, Taxi, Muppets. 61-1980, 84 pgs. Adams-a(r), McCloud, Pro wrestling, Casper, TV's Police Story. 63-Apocalypse Now-Coppola's cult movie; 3rd app. Teen Hulk, Howard the Duck, 3 pgs. 2 4 6 8 11 14

62-Kiss-c & 2 pg. app; Quincy, 2nd app. Teen Hulk 4 8 12 28 47 65

66-Sept/'80, Empire Strikes Back-c/sty; Teen Hulk by Severin, Howard the Duck, 3pgs. by Broderick 3 6 9 14 20 25

71,72,75-77,79: 71-Blues Brothers parody, Teen Hulk, Superheroes parody, WKRP in Cincinnati, Howard the Duck, 3pgs. by Broderick. 72-Jackie Gleason/Smokey & the Bandit II-c/sty, Shogun, Teen Hulk. Howard the Duck, 3pgs. by Broderick. 75-Flash Gordon movie c/sty; Teen Hulk, Cat in the Hat, Howard the Duck 3pgs. by Broderick. 76-84 pgs. w/bonus; Monster-sty w/ Crandall-a(r), Monster-stys(2) w/Kirby-a(r), 5pgs. ea; Mash, TV Hulk, Chinatown. 77-Popeye movie/R. Williams-c/sty; Teen Hulk, Love Boat, Howard the Duck 3 pgs. 79-84 pgs. w/bonus color stickers; has new material; "9 to 5" w/Dolly Parton, Teen Hulk, Magnum P.I., Monster-sty w/5pgs, Ditko-a(r), "Rat" w/Sutton-a(r), Everett-a, 4 pgs.(r) 1 3 4 6 8 10

73,74,78,80: 73-84 pgs. w/bonus Hulk/Spiderman Finger Puppets-c & bonus; "Live & Let Die, Jaws, Fantasy Island. 74-Dallas/"Who Shot J.R."-c/sty; Elephant Man, Howard the Duck 3pgs. by Broderick. 78-Clint Eastwood-c/sty; Teen Hulk, Superheroes parody, Lou Grant. 80-Star Wars, 2 pg. app; "Howling", TV's "Greatest American Hero" 2 4 6 8 11 14

81,84,86,87,89: 81-.Superman Movie II-c/sty; Wolverine cameo, Mash, Teen Hulk. 84-American Werewolf in London, Johnny Carson app; Teen Hulk. 86-Time Bandits-c/sty; Private Benjamin. 87-Rubix Cube-c; Hill Street Blues, "Ragtime", Origin Obnoxio the Clown; Teen Hulk. 89-Burt Reynolds "Sharkey's Machine", Teen Hulk 1 3 4 6 8 10

82-X-Men-c w/new Byrne-a, 84 pgs. w/new material; Fantasy Island, Teen Hulk, "For Your Eyes Only", Spiderman/Human Torch-r by Kirby/Ditko; Sutton-a(r); Rogers-a; Hunchback of Notre Dame, 5 pgs. 3 6 9 14 19 24

83-Raiders of the Lost Ark-c/sty; Hart to Hart; Reese-a; Teen Hulk 2 4 6 9 13 20

85,88: 85-84 pgs; Escape from New York, Teen Hulk; Kirby-a(r), 5 pgs, Poseidon Adventure, Flintstones, Sesame Street. 88-84 pgs. w/bonus Dr. Strange Game; some new material; Jeffersons, X-Men/Wolverine, 10 pgs.; Byrne-a; Apocalypse Now, Teen Hulk 1 3 4 6 8 11

90-94: 90-Conan-c/sty; M. Severin-a; Teen Hulk. 91-84 pgs, some new material; Bladerunner-c/sty, "Deathwish-II, Teen Hulk, Black Knight, 10 pgs.-'50s-r w/Maneely-a. 92-Wrath of Khan Star Trek-c/sty; Joanie & Chachi, Teen Hulk. 93-"E.T."-c/sty, Teen Hulk, Archie Bunkers Place, Dr. Doom Game. 94-Poltergeist, Smurfs, Teen Hulk, Casper, Avengers parody-8pgs. Adams-a 2 4 6 10 14 18

Crazy Summer Special #1 (Sum, '75, 100 pgs.)-Nixon, TV Kung Fu, Babe Ruth, Joe Namath, Waltons, McCloud, Chariots of the Gods 3 6 9 14 20 26

NOTE: ***N. Adams*** *a-2, 61r, 94p.* ***Austin*** *a-82i.* ***Buscema*** *a-2, 82.* ***Byrne*** *c-82p.* ***Nick Cardy*** *c-7, 8, 10, 12-16, Super Special 1.* ***Crandall*** *a-76r.* ***Ditko*** *a-68r, 79r, 82r.* ***Drucker*** *a-3.* ***Eisner*** *a-9-16.* ***Kelly Freas*** *c-1-6, 9, 11; a-7.* ***Kirby/ Wood*** *a-66r.* ***Ploog*** *a-1, 4, 7, 67r, 73r.* ***Rogers*** *a-82.* ***Sparling*** *a-92.* ***Wood*** *a-65r. Howard the Duck in 36, 50, 51, 53, 54, 59, 63, 65, 66, 68, 69, 71, 72, 74, 75, 77. Hulk in 46, c-42, 46, 57, 73. Star Wars in 32, 66; c-37.*

CRAZY (Homage to the humor magazine)
Marvel Comics: Dec, 2019 ($4.99, one-shot)

1-Short stories by various incl. Duggan, Macchio, Koblish, Simpson, Bill Morrison 5.00

CRAZYMAN
Continuity Comics: Apr, 1992 - No. 3, 1992 ($2.50, high quality paper)

1-($3.95, 52 pgs.)-Embossed-c; N. Adams part-i 4.00
2,3 ($2.50): 2-N. Adams/Bolland-c 3.00

CRAZYMAN
Continuity Comics: V2#1, 5/93 - No. 4, 1/94 ($2.50, high quality paper)

V2#1-4: 1-Entire book is die-cut. 2-(12/93)-Adams-c(p) & part scripts. 3-(12/93). 4-Indicia says #3, Jan. 1993 3.00

CRAZY, MAN, CRAZY (Magazine) (Becomes This Magazine is...?)
(Formerly From Here to Insanity)
Humor Magazines (Charlton): V2#1, Dec, 1955 - V2#2, June, 1956

V2#1,V2#2-Satire; Wolverton-a, 3 pgs. 21 42 63 122 199 275

CREATOR-OWNED HEROES
Image Comics: Jun, 2012 - No. 8, Jan, 2013 ($3.99)

1-8-Anthology of short stories by various and creator interviews 4.00

CREATURE, THE (See Movie Classics)

CREATURE COMMANDOS (See Weird War Tales #93 for 1st app.)
DC Comics: May, 2000 - No. 8, Dec, 2000 ($2.50, limited series)

1-8: Truman-s/Eaton-a 3.00

CREATURES OF THE ID
Caliber Press: 1990 ($2.95, B&W)

1-Frank Einstein (Madman) app.; Allred-a 10 20 30 64 132 200

CREATURES OF THE NIGHT
Dark Horse Books: Nov, 2004 ($12.95, hardcover graphic novel)

HC-Neil Gaiman-s/Michael Zulli-a/c 13.00

CREATURES ON THE LOOSE (Formerly Tower of Shadows No. 1-9)(See Kull)
Marvel Comics: No. 10, March, 1971 - No. 37, Sept, 1975 (New-a & reprints)

10-(15¢)-1st full app. King Kull; see Kull the Conqueror; Wrightson-a 8 16 24 56 108 160
11-Classic story about an underground comic artist going to Hell 4 8 12 27 44 60
12-15: 13-Last 15¢ issue 4 8 12 23 37 50
16-Origin Warrior of Mars (begins, ends #21) 3 6 9 15 22 28
17-20 2 4 6 9 13 16
21-Steranko-c 3 6 9 17 26 35
22-Steranko-c; Thongor stories begin 3 6 9 18 28 38
23-29-Thongor-c/stories 1 3 4 6 8 10
30-Manwolf begins 3 6 9 21 33 45
31-33 2 4 6 9 13 16
34-37 2 4 6 8 10 12

NOTE: *Crandall a-13.* ***Ditko*** *r-15, 17, 18, 20, 22, 24, 27, 28.* ***Everett*** *a-16i(new).* ***Matt Fox*** *r-21i.* ***Howard*** *a-26i.* ***Gil Kane*** *a-16p, 17p, 19i; c-16, 17, 19, 20, 25, 29, 33p, 35p, 36p.* ***Kirby*** *a-10-15r, 16(2)r, 17r, 19r.* ***Morrow*** *a-20, 21.* ***Perez*** *a-33-37; c-34p.* ***Shores*** *a-11.* ***Innott*** *r-21.* ***Sutton*** *c-10.* ***Tuska*** *a-30-32p.*

CREECH, THE
Image Comics: Oct, 1997 - No. 3, Dec, 1997 ($1.95/$2.50, limited series)

1-3: 1-Capullo-s/c/a(p) 3.00
TPB (1999, $9.95) r/#1-3, McFarlane intro. 10.00
Out for Blood 1-3 (7/01 - No. 3, 11/01; $4.95) Capullo-s/c/a 5.00

CREED
Hall of Heroes Comics: Dec, 1994 - No. 2, Jan, 1995 ($2.50, B&W)

1-Trent Kaniuga-s/a 4 8 12 23 37 50
2 2 4 6 11 16 20

GD VG FN VF VF/NM NM-
2.0 4.0 6.0 8.0 9.0 9.2

CREED
Lightning Comics: June, 1995 - No. 3 ($2.75/$3.00, B&W/color)
1-($2.75) 4.00
1-($3.00, color) 5.00
1-($9.95)-Commemorative Edition 10.00
1-TwinVariant Edition (1250? print run) 10.00
1-Special Edition; polybagged w/certificate 4.00
1 Gold Collectors Edition; polybagged w/certificate 10.00
2,3-($3.00, color)-Butt Naked Edition & regular-c 3.00
3-($9.95)-Commemorative Edition; polybagged w/certificate & card 10.00

CREED: CRANIAL DISORDER
Lightning Comics: Oct, 1996 ($3.00, limited series)
1-3-Two covers 3.00
1-($5.95)-Platinum Edition 6.00
2,3-($9.95) Ltd. Edition 10.00

CREED/TEENAGE MUTANT NINJA TURTLES
Lightning Comics: May, 1996 ($3.00, one-shot)
1-Kaniuga-a(p)/scripts; Laird-c; variant-c exists 6.00
1-($9.95)-Platinum Edition 12.00
1-Special Edition; polybagged w/certificate 6.00

CREEP, THE
Dark Horse Books: No. 0, Aug, 2012 - No. 4, Dec, 2012 ($2.99/$3.50)
0-Frank Miller-c; Arcudi-s/Case-a 4.00
1-4-($3.50): 1-Mignola-c. 2-Sook-c 4.00

CREEPER BY STEVE DITKO, THE
DC Comics: 2010 ($39.99, hardcover with dustjacket)
HC-Reprints Showcase #73, Beware the Creeper #1-6, First Issue Special #7 and apps. in World's Finest #249-255 and Cancelled Comic Cavalcade #2; intro. by Steve Niles 40.00

CREEPER, THE (See Beware... , Showcase #73 & 1st Issue Special #7)
DC Comics: Dec, 1997 - No. 11; #1,000,000 Nov, 1998 ($2.50)
1-11-Kaminski-s/Martinbrough-a(p). 7,8-Joker-c/app. 4.00
#1,000,000 (11/98) 853rd Century x-over 4.00

CREEPER, THE (See DCU Brave New World)
DC Comics: Oct, 2006 - No. 6, Mar, 2007 ($2.99, limited series)
1-6-Niles-s/Justiniano-a/c; Jack Ryder becomes the Creeper. 2-6-Batman app. 3.00
... - Welcome to Creepsville TPB ('07, $19.99) r/#1-6 & story from DCU Brave New World 20.00

CREEPS
Image Comics: Oct, 2001 - No. 4, May, 2002 ($2.95)
1-4-Mandrake-a/Mishkin-s 3.00

CREEPSHOW
Plume/New American Library Pub.: July, 1982 (softcover graphic novel)
1st edition-nn-(68 pgs.) Kamen-c/Wrightson-a; screenplay by Stephen King for the George Romero movie 9 18 27 62 126 190
2nd-7th printings 3 6 9 17 26 35

CREEPSHOW
Image Comics (Skybound): Sept, 2022 - Present ($3.99)
1-5-Horror anthology. 2-Lapham-s/a. 3-Francavilla-a 4.00

CREEPY (See Warren Presents)
Warren Publishing Co./Harris Publ. #146: 1964 - No. 145, Feb, 1983; No. 146, 1985 (B&W, magazine)
1-Frazetta-a (his last story in comics?); Jack Davis-c; 1st Warren all comics magazine; 1st app. Uncle Creepy 18 36 54 128 284 440
2-Frazetta-c & 1 pg. strip 14 28 42 96 211 325
3-8,11-13,15-17: 3-7,9-11,15-17-Frazetta-c. 7-Frazetta 1 pg. strip. 15,16-Adams-a. 16-Jeff Jones-a 6 12 18 38 69 100
9-Creepy fan club sketch by Wrightson (1st published-a); has 1/2 pg. anti-smoking strip by Frazetta; Frazetta-c; 1st Wood and Ditko art on this title; Toth-a (low print) 9 18 27 58 114 170
10-Brunner fan club sketch (1st published work) 7 14 21 48 89 130
14-Neal Adams 1st Warren work 8 16 24 51 96 140
18-28,30,31: 27-Frazetta-c 5 10 15 30 50 70
29,34: 29-Jones-a 5 10 15 31 53 75
32-(scarce) Frazetta-c; Harlan Ellison sty 9 18 27 61 123 185
33,35,37,39,40,42-47,49: 35-Hitler/Nazi-s. 39-1st Uncle Creepy solo-s, Cousin Eerie app.; early Brunner-a. 42-1st San Julian-c. 44-1st Ploog-a. 46-Corben-a 4 8 12 25 40 55
36-(11/70)1st Corben art at Warren 5 10 15 31 53 75
38,41-(scarce): 38-1st Kelly-c. 41-Corben-a 5 10 15 34 60 85
48,55,65-(1972, 1973, 1974 Annuals) #55 & 65 contain an 8 pg. slick comic insert. 48-(84 pgs.). 55-Color poster bonus (1/2 price if missing). 65-(100 pgs.) Summer Giant 5 10 15 31 53 75
50-Vampirella/Eerie/Creepy-c 6 12 18 40 73 105
51,54,56-61,64: All contain an 8 pg. slick comic insert in middle. 59-Xmas horror. 54,64-Chaykin-a 4 8 12 28 47 65
52,53,66,71,72,75,76,78-80: 71-All Bermejo-a; Space & Time issue. 72-Gual-a. 78-Fantasy issue. 79,80-Monsters issue 3 6 9 21 33 45
62,63-1st & 2nd full Wrightson story art; Corben-a; 8 pg. color comic insert 4 8 12 28 47 65
67,73 4 8 12 23 37 50
68-"Twas the Night Before Christmas" 5 10 15 31 53 75
69,70-Edgar Allan Poe issues; Corben-a 4 8 12 25 40 55
74,77: 74-All Crandell-a. 77-Xmas Horror issue; Corben-a,Wrightson-a 4 8 12 25 40 55
81,84,85,88-90,92-94,96-99,102,104-112,114-118,120,122-130: 84,93-Sports issue. 85,97,102-Monster issue. 89-All war issue; Nino-a. 94-Weird Children issue. 96,109-Aliens issue. 99-Disasters. 103-Corben-a. 104-Robots issue. 106-Sword & Sorcery.107-Sci-fi. 116-End of Man. 125-Xmas Horror 2 4 6 11 16 20
82,100,101: 82-All Maroto issue. 100-(8/78) Anniversary. 101-Corben-a 3 6 9 16 23 30
83,95-Wrightson-a. 83-Corben-a. 95-Gorilla/Apes. 3 6 9 14 20 25
86,87,91,103-Wrightson-a. 86-Xmas Horror 3 6 9 14 20 25
113-All Wrightson-r issue 3 6 9 19 30 40
119,121: 119-All Nino issue.121-All Severin-r issue 3 6 9 14 20 25
131,133-136,138,140: 135-Xmas issue 3 6 9 14 20 25
132,137,139: 132-Corben. 137-All Williamson-r issue. 139-All Toth-r issue 3 6 9 16 23 30
141,143,144 (low dist.): 144-Giant, $2.25; Frazetta-c 3 6 9 18 28 38
142,145 (low dist.): 142-(10/82, 100 pgs.) All Torres issue. 145-(2/83) last Warren issue 3 6 9 21 33 45
146 ($2.95)-1st from Harris; resurrection issue 7 14 21 48 89 130
Year Book '68-'70: '70-Neal Adams, Ditko-a(r) 5 10 15 34 60 85
Annual 1971,1972 5 10 15 33 57 80
1993 Fearbook ($3.95)-Harris Publ.; Brereton-c; Vampirella by Busiek-s/Art Adams-a; David-s; Paquette-a 3 6 9 17 26 35
...:The Classic Years TPB (Harris/Dark Horse, '91, $12.95) Kaluta-c; art by Frazetta,Torres, Crandall, Ditko, Morrow, Williamson, Wrightson 25.00
NOTE: *All issues contain many good artists works:* ***Neal Adams, Brunner, Corben, Craig (Taycee), Crandall, Ditko, Evans, Frazetta, Heath, Jeff Jones, Krenkel, McWilliams, Morrow, Nino, Orlando, Ploog, Severin, Torres, Toth, Williamson, Wood, & Wrightson;*** *covers by* ***Crandall, Davis, Frazetta, Morrow, San Julian, Todd/Bode;*** *Otto Binder's "Adam Link" stories in No. 2, 4, 6, 8, 9, 12, 13, 15 with* ***Orlando*** *art.* ***Frazetta*** *c-2-7, 9-11, 15-17, 27, 32, 83r, 89r, 91r.* ***E.A. Poe*** *adaptations in 66, 69, 70.*

CREEPY (Mini-series)
Harris Comics/Dark Horse: 1992 - Book 4, 1992 (48 pgs, B&W, squarebound)
Book 1-4: Brereton painted-c on all. Stories and art by various incl. David (all), Busiek(2), Infantino(2), Guice(3), Colan(1) 2 4 6 8 10 12

CREEPY
Dark Horse Comics: July, 2009 - No. 24, Jun, 2016 ($4.99/$3.99, 48 pgs, B&W, quarterly)
1-13: 1-Powell-c; art by Wrightson, Toth, Alexander. 8,12-Corben-c. 5.00
14-24-($3.99) 18-Nguyen-c. 20,23,24-Corben-a 4.00

CREEPY THINGS
Charlton Comics: July, 1975 - No. 6, June, 1976
1-Sutton-c/a 3 6 9 16 24 32
2-6: Ditko-a in 3,5. Sutton c-3,4. 6-Zeck-c 2 4 6 9 12 15
Modern Comics Reprint 2-6(1977) 5.00
NOTE: ***Larson*** *a-2,6.* ***Sutton*** *a-1,2,4,6.* ***Zeck*** *a-2.*

CREW, THE
Marvel Comics: July, 2003 - No. 7, Jan, 2004 ($2.50)
1-7-Priest-s/Bennett-a; James Rhodes (War Machine) app. 3.00

CRIME AND JUSTICE (Badge Of Justice #22 on; Rookie Cop? No. 27 on)
Capitol Stories/Charlton Comics: March, 1951 - No. 21, Nov, 1954; No. 23, Mar, 1955 - No. 26, Sept, 1955 (No #22)
1 50 100 150 315 533 750
2 25 50 75 150 245 340
3-8,10-13: 6-Negligee panels 21 42 63 126 206 285
9-Classic story "Comics Vs. Crime" 40 80 120 246 411 575
14-Color illos in **POP**; story of murderer who beheads women 36 72 108 211 343 475
15-17,19-21,23,24: 15-Negligee panels. 23-Rookie Cop (1st app.) 15 30 45 86 133 180
18-Ditko-a 37 74 111 222 361 500
25,26: (scarce) 23 46 69 136 223 310
NOTE: ***Alascia*** *c-20.* ***Ayers*** *a-17.* ***Shuster*** *a-19-21; c-19. Bondage c-11, 12.*

CRIME AND PUNISHMENT (Title inspired by 1935 film)
Lev Gleason Publications: April, 1948 - No. 74, Aug, 1955
1-Mr. Crime app. on-c 50 100 150 315 533 750
2-Narrator, Officer Common Sense (a ghost) begins, ends #27? (see Crime Does Not Pay #41) 25 50 75 150 245 340
3-(6/48)-Used in **SOTI**, pg. 112; contains Biro & Gleason self censorship code of 12 listed restrictions 27 54 81 162 266 370
4,5 19 38 57 109 172 235
6-10 15 30 45 85 130 175
11-20 14 28 42 80 115 150
21-30 12 24 36 69 97 125
31-38,40-44,46: 46-One pg. Frazetta-a 11 22 33 62 86 110
39-Drug mention story "The Five Dopes" 19 38 57 111 176 240
45- "Hophead Killer" drug story 19 38 57 111 176 240
47-53,55,57,60-65,70-74: 10 20 30 58 79 100
54-Electric Chair-c 13 26 39 72 101 130
56-Classic dagger/torture-c 39 78 117 231 378 525
58-Used in **POP**, pg. 79 14 28 42 80 115 150
59-Used in **SOTI**, illo "What comic-book America stands for" 40 80 120 246 411 575
66-Toth-c/a(4); 3-D effect issue (3/54); 1st "Deep Dimension" process 45 90 135 284 480 675
67- "Monkey on His Back" heroin story; 3-D effect issue 40 80 120 246 411 575
68-3-D effect issue; Toth-c (7/54) 37 74 111 222 361 500
69- "The Hot Rod Gang" dope crazy kids 18 36 54 105 165 225
NOTE: ***Belfi*** *a- 2, 3, 5.* ***Biro*** *c-most.* ***Al Borth*** *a-9, 35.* ***Cooper*** *a-9.* ***Joe Certa*** *a-8.* ***Tony Dipreta*** *a-3, 5, 15, 34.* ***Everett*** *a-31.* ***Bob Fujitani (Fuje)*** *a-2-20, 26, 27.* ***Joseph Gaguardi*** *a-15, 18, 20.* ***Fred Guardineer*** *a-2-5, 10-12, 14, 15, 17, 18, 20, 26-28, 32, 34, 35, 38-44, 51, 54.* ***Jack Keller*** *a-18.* ***Kinstler*** *c-69.* ***Martinott*** *a-13.* ***Al McWilliams*** *a-36, 41, 48, 49.* ***William Overgard*** *a-36.* ***Dick Rockwell*** *a-35, 51.* ***Robert Q. Sale*** *a-43.* ***George Tuska*** *a-28, 30, 51, 64, 70. Painted-c-31.*

CRIME AND PUNISHMENT: MARSHALL LAW TAKES MANHATTAN
Marvel Comics (Epic Comics): 1989 ($4.95, 52 pgs., direct sales only, mature)
nn-Graphic album featuring Marshall Law 5.00

CRIME BIBLE: THE FIVE LESSONS (Aftermath of DC's 52 series)
DC Comics: Dec, 2007 - No. 5, Apr, 2008 ($2.99, limited series)
1-5-Rucka-s; The Question (Renee Montoya) app. 3-Batwoman app. 3.00
The Question: The Five Books of Blood HC (2008, $19.99) r/#1-5 20.00
The Question: The Five Books of Blood SC (2009, $14.99) r/#1-5 15.00

CRIME CAN'T WIN (Formerly Cindy Smith)
Marvel/Atlas Comics (TCI 41/CCC 42,43,4-12): No. 41, 9/50 - No. 43, 2/51;

The Creeper (2006) #5 © DC

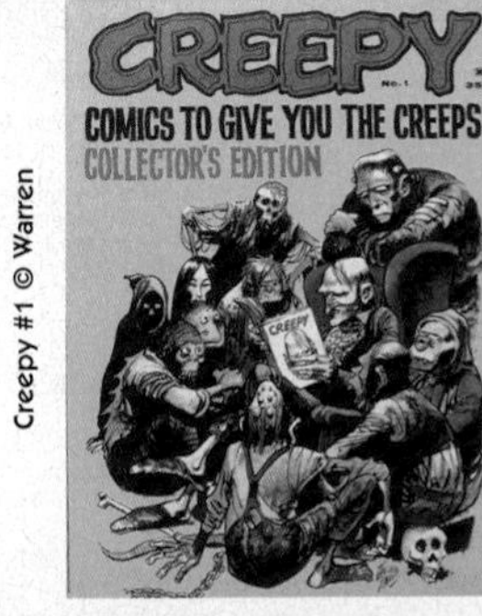

Creepy #1 © Warren

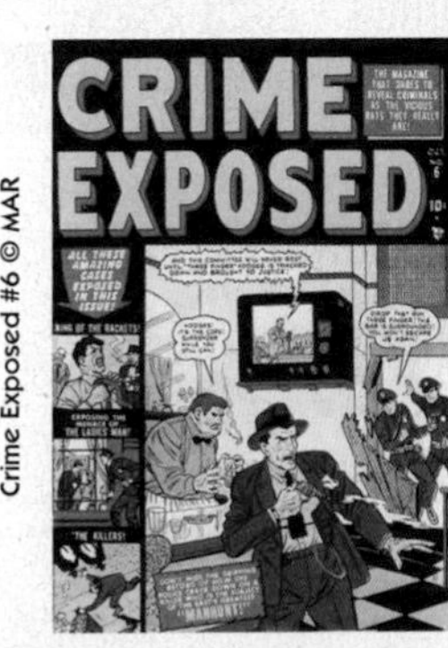

Crime Exposed #6 © MAR

	GD 2.0	VG 4.0	FN 6.0	VF 8.0	VF/NM 9.0	NM- 9.2
No. 4, 4/51 - No. 12, 9/53						
41(#1)-"The Girl Who Planned Her Own Murder"	37	74	111	222	361	500
42(#2)	22	44	66	128	209	290
43(#3)-Horror story	32	64	96	188	307	425
4(4/51),5-12: 10-Possible use in **SOTI**, pg. 161	18	36	54	103	162	220

NOTE: ***Robinson** a-9-11. **Tuska** a-43.*

CRIME CASES COMICS (Formerly Willie Comics)
Marvel/Atlas Comics(CnPC No.24-8/MJMC No.9-12): No. 24, 8/50 - No. 27, 3/51; No. 5, 5/51 - No. 12, 7/52

	GD 2.0	VG 4.0	FN 6.0	VF 8.0	VF/NM 9.0	NM- 9.2
24 (#1, 52 pgs.)-True police cases	28	56	84	165	270	375
25-27(#2-4): 27-Maneely & Morisi-a	22	44	66	128	209	290
5-12: 11-Robinson-a. 12-Tuska-a	19	38	57	109	172	235

CRIME CLINIC
Ziff-Davis Publishing Co.: No. 10, July-Aug, 1951 - No. 5, Summer, 1952

	GD 2.0	VG 4.0	FN 6.0	VF 8.0	VF/NM 9.0	NM- 9.2
10(#1)-Painted-c; origin Dr. Tom Rogers	45	90	135	284	480	675
11(#2),4,5: 4,5-Painted-c	34	68	102	204	332	460
3-Used in **SOTI**, pg. 18	39	78	117	231	378	525

NOTE: *All have painted covers by **Saunders**. **Starr** a-10.*

CRIME CLINIC
Slave Labor Graphics: May, 1995 - No. 2, Oct, 1995 ($2.95, B&W, limited series)

	GD 2.0	VG 4.0	FN 6.0	VF 8.0	VF/NM 9.0	NM- 9.2
1,2						4.00

CRIME DETECTIVE COMICS
Hillman Periodicals: Mar-Apr, 1948 - V3#8, May-June, 1953

	GD 2.0	VG 4.0	FN 6.0	VF 8.0	VF/NM 9.0	NM- 9.2
V1#1-The Invisible 6, costumed villains app; Fuje-c/a, 15 pgs.	50	100	150	315	533	750
2,5: 5-Krigstein-a	22	44	66	132	216	300
3,4,6,7,10-12: 6-McWilliams-a	20	40	60	114	182	250
8-Kirbyish-a by McCann	20	40	60	114	182	250
9-Used in **SOTI**, pg. 16 & "Caricature of the author in a position comic book publishers wish he were in permanently" illo.	54	108	162	343	574	825
V2#1,4,7-Krigstein-a: 1-Tuska-a	17	34	51	100	158	215
2,3,5,6,8-12 (1-2/52)	16	32	48	92	144	195
V3#1-Drug use-c	17	34	51	98	154	210
2-8	15	30	45	83	124	165

NOTE: ***Briefer** a-11, V3#1. **Kinstlerish**-a by **McCann**-V2#7, V3#2. **Powell** a-10, 11. **Starr** a-10.*

CRIME DETECTOR
Timor Publications: Jan, 1954 - No. 5, Sept, 1954

	GD 2.0	VG 4.0	FN 6.0	VF 8.0	VF/NM 9.0	NM- 9.2
1	36	72	108	211	343	475
2-Headlights-c	53	106	159	334	567	800
3,4	17	34	51	98	154	210
5-Disbrow-a (classic)	32	64	96	188	307	425

CRIME DOES NOT PAY (Formerly Silver Streak Comics No. 1-21)
Comic House/Lev Gleason/Golfing: No. 22, June, 1942 - No. 147, July, 1955
(1st crime comic)(Title inspired by film)

	GD 2.0	VG 4.0	FN 6.0	VF 8.0	VF/NM 9.0	NM- 9.2
22 (23 on cover, 22 on indicia)-Origin The War Eagle & only app.; Chip Gardner begins; #22 was rebound in Complete Book of True Crime (Scarce)	811	1622	2433	5920	10,460	15,000
23-(9/42) (Scarce)	320	640	960	2240	3920	5600
24-(11/42) Intro. & 1st app. Mr. Crime; classic Biro-c showing woman's head on fire being pushed onto hot stovetop burner	2000	4000	6000	10,000	17,500	25,000
25-(1/43) 2nd app. Mr. Crime; classic '40s crime-c	158	316	474	1003	1727	2450
26-(3/43) 3rd app. Mr. Crime	129	258	387	826	1413	2000
27-Classic Biro-c pushing man into hot oven	158	316	474	1003	1727	2450
28-30: 30-Wood and Biro app.	90	180	270	576	988	1400
31,32,34-40	52	104	156	328	552	775
33-(5/44) Classic Biro hanging & hatchet-c	432	864	1296	3154	5577	8000
41-(9/45) Origin & 1st app. Officer Common Sense	48	96	144	302	514	725
42-(11/45) Classic electrocution-c	116	232	348	742	1271	1800
43-46,48-50: 44-50 are 68 pg. issues. 44-"Legs" Diamond story. 50-(3/47)-1st issue to advertise 5 million readers on front-c. 58-(12/47)-shows 6 million readers (these ads believed to have influenced the crime comic wave of 1948)	34	68	102	199	325	450
47-(9/46)-Electric chair-c	61	122	183	390	670	950
51-70: 58(12/47)-Thomas Dun, killer of thousands (1565) story. 63,64-Possible use in **SOTI**, pg. 306. 63-Contains Biro & Gleason self censorship code of 12 listed restrictions (5/48)	25	50	75	150	245	340
71-99: 87-Chip Gardner begins, ends #100. 87-99-Painted-c	20	40	60	114	182	250
100-Painted-c	20	40	60	118	192	265
101-104,107-110: 101,102-Painted-c. 102-Chip Gardner app.	15	30	45	88	137	185
105-Used in **POP**, pg. 84	18	36	54	103	162	220
106,114-Frazetta-a, 1 pg.	16	32	48	94	147	200
111-Used in **POP**, pgs. 80 & 81; injury-to-eye sty illo	20	40	60	114	182	250
112,113,115-130	14	28	42	78	112	145
131-140	13	26	39	72	101	130
141,142-Last pre-code issue; Kubert-a(1)	14	28	42	80	115	150
143-Kubert-a in one story	14	28	42	80	115	150
144-146	13	26	39	72	101	130
147-Last issue (scarce); Kubert-a	19	38	57	112	179	245
1(Golfing-1945)	12	24	36	67	94	120
The Best of...(1944, 128 pgs.)-Series contains 4 rebound issues	142	284	426	909	1555	2200
...1945 issue	90	180	270	576	988	1400
...1946-48 issues	65	130	195	416	708	1000
...1949-50 issues	54	108	162	343	574	825
...1951-53 issues (25¢)	48	96	144	302	514	725

NOTE: *Many issues contain violent covers and stories. Who Dunit by **Guardineer**-39-42, 44-105, 108-110; Chip Gardner by **Bob Fujitani (Fuge)**-88-103. **Alderman** a-29, 41-44, 49. **Dan Barry** a-67, 75. **Charles Biro** c-1-76, 122, 142. **Dick Briefer** a-29(2), 30, 31, 33, 37, 39. **G. Colan** a-105. **Tony Dipreta** a-79, 90, 92. **Fuje** c-88, 89, 91-94, 96, 98, 99, 102, 103. **Fred Guardineer** a-51, 57, 58(2), 66-68, 71, 74, 79, 81, 90, 92. **Joe Kubert** c-143. **Landau** a-118. **Al Mandell** a-37. **Norman Maurer** a-29, 39, 41, 42. **McWilliams** a-91, 93, 95, 100-103. **Rudy Palais** a-30, 33, **Bob Powell** a-146, 147. **George Tuska** a-48-50(2ea.), 51, 52 56, 57(2), 58, 60-64, 66-68, 71, 74, 81. Painted c-87-103. Bondage c-43, 62, 98.*

CRIME EXPOSED
Marvel Comics (PPI)/Marvel Atlas Comics (PrPI): June, 1948; Dec, 1950 - No. 14, June, 1952

	GD 2.0	VG 4.0	FN 6.0	VF 8.0	VF/NM 9.0	NM- 9.2
1(6/48)	48	96	144	302	514	725
1(12/50)	31	62	93	182	296	410
2	20	40	60	114	182	250
3-9,11,14	17	34	51	98	154	210
10-Used in **POP**, pg. 81	20	40	60	117	189	260
12-Krigstein & Robinson-a	19	38	57	111	176	240
13-Used in **POP**, pg. 81; Krigstein-a	20	40	60	117	189	260

NOTE: ***Keller** a-8, 10. **Maneely** c-8. **Robinson** a-11, 12. **Sale** a-4. **Tuska** a-3, 4.*

CRIMEFIGHTERS
Marvel Comics (CmPS 1-3/CCC 4-10): Apr, 1948 - No. 10, Nov, 1949

	GD 2.0	VG 4.0	FN 6.0	VF 8.0	VF/NM 9.0	NM- 9.2
1-Some copies are undated & could be reprints	39	78	117	231	378	525
2,3: 3-Morphine addict story	20	40	60	118	192	265
4-10: 4-Early John Buscema-a. 6-Anti-Wertham editorial. 9,10-Photo-c	17	34	51	100	158	215

CRIME FIGHTERS (...Always Win)
Atlas Comics (CnPC): No. 11, Sept, 1954 - No. 13, Jan, 1955

	GD 2.0	VG 4.0	FN 6.0	VF 8.0	VF/NM 9.0	NM- 9.2
11-13: 11-Maneely-a,13-Pakula, Reinman, Severin-a	17	34	51	100	158	215

CRIME-FIGHTING DETECTIVE (Shock Detective Cases No. 20 on; formerly Criminals on the Run)
Star Publications: No. 11, Apr-May, 1950 - No. 19, June, 1952 (Based on true crime cases)

	GD 2.0	VG 4.0	FN 6.0	VF 8.0	VF/NM 9.0	NM- 9.2
11-L. B. Cole-c/a (2 pgs.); L. B. Cole-c on all	37	74	111	222	361	500
12,13,15-19: 17-Young King Cole & Dr. Doom app.	21	42	63	124	202	280
14-L. B. Cole-c/a, r/Law-Crime #2	22	44	66	132	216	300

CRIME FILES
Standard Comics: No. 5, Sept, 1952 - No. 6, Nov, 1952

	GD 2.0	VG 4.0	FN 6.0	VF 8.0	VF/NM 9.0	NM- 9.2
5-1pg. Alex Toth-a; used in **SOTI**, pg. 4 (text)	37	74	111	222	361	500
6-Sekowsky-a	18	36	54	105	165	225

CRIME ILLUSTRATED (Magazine)
E. C. Comics: Nov-Dec, 1955 - No. 2, Spring, 1956 (25¢, Adult Suspense Stories on-c)

	GD 2.0	VG 4.0	FN 6.0	VF 8.0	VF/NM 9.0	NM- 9.2
1-Ingels & Crandall-a	34	68	102	199	325	450
2-Ingels & Crandall-a	20	40	60	114	182	250

NOTE: ***Craig** a-2. **Crandall** a-1, 2; c-2. **Evans** a-1. **Davis** a-2. **Ingels** a-1, 2. **Krigstein/Crandall** a-1. **Orlando** a-1, 2; c-1.*

CRIME INCORPORATED (Formerly Crimes Incorporated)
Fox Feature Syndicate: No. 2, Aug, 1950; No. 3, Aug, 1951

	GD 2.0	VG 4.0	FN 6.0	VF 8.0	VF/NM 9.0	NM- 9.2
2	36	72	108	211	343	475
3(1951)-Hollingsworth-a	23	46	69	136	223	310

CRIME MACHINE (Magazine reprints pre-code crime and gangster comics)
Skywald Publications: Feb, 1971 - No. 2, May, 1971 (B&W, 68 pgs., roundbound)

	GD 2.0	VG 4.0	FN 6.0	VF 8.0	VF/NM 9.0	NM- 9.2
1-Kubert-a(2)(r)(Avon); bikini girl in cake-c	6	12	18	42	79	115
2-Torres, Wildey-a; violent-c/a	4	8	12	28	47	65

CRIME MUST LOSE! (Formerly Sports Action?)
Sports Action (Atlas Comics): No. 4, Oct, 1950 - No. 12, April, 1952

	GD 2.0	VG 4.0	FN 6.0	VF 8.0	VF/NM 9.0	NM- 9.2
4-Ann Brewster-a in all; c-used in N.Y. Legis. Comm. documents	30	60	90	177	289	400

	GD	VG	FN	VF	VF/NM	NM-
	2.0	4.0	6.0	8.0	9.0	9.2

5-10,12: 9-Robinson-a 20 40 60 114 182 250
11-Used in **POP**, pg. 89 20 40 60 117 189 260

CRIME MUST PAY THE PENALTY (Formerly Four Favorites; Penalty #47, 48)
Ace Magazines (Current Books): No. 33, Feb, 1948; No. 2, Jun, 1948 - No. 48, Jan, 1956

33(#1, 2/48)-Becomes Four Teeners #34? 63 126 189 403 689 975
2(6/48)-Extreme violence; Palais-a? 43 86 129 271 461 650
3,4,8: 3- "Frisco Mary" story used in Senate Investigation report, pg. 7. 4,8-Transvestism stories 26 52 78 154 252 350
5-7,9,10 20 40 60 115 185 255
11-19 19 38 57 109 172 235
20-Drug story "Dealers in White Death" 30 60 90 177 289 400
21-32,34-40,42-48: 44-Last pre-code 15 30 45 86 133 180
33(7/53)- "Dell Fabry-Junk King" drug story; mentioned in Love and Death 22 44 66 132 216 300
41-reprints "Dealers in White Death" 15 30 45 90 140 190

NOTE: ***Cameron** a-29-31, 34, 35, 39-41. **Colan** a-20, 31. **Kremer** a-3, 37r. **Larsen** a-32. **Palais** a-5?,37.*

CRIME MUST STOP
Hillman Periodicals: October, 1952 (52 pgs.)

V1#1(Scarce)-Similar to Monster Crime; Mort Lawrence, Krigstein-a 148 296 444 947 1624 2300

CRIME MYSTERIES (Secret Mysteries #16 on; combined with Crime Smashers #7 on)
Ribage Publ. Corp. (Trojan Magazines): May, 1952 - No. 15, Sept, 1954

1-Transvestism story; crime & terror stories begin 271 542 813 1734 2967 4200
2-Marijuana story (7/52) 194 388 582 1242 2121 3000
3-One pg. Frazetta-a 90 180 270 576 988 1400
4-Cover shows girl in bondage having her blood drained; 1 pg. Frazetta-a 420 840 1260 2940 5170 7400
5-10 54 108 162 343 574 825
11,12,14 50 100 150 315 533 750
13-(5/54)-Angelo Torres 1st comic work (inks over Check's pencils); Check-a 142 284 426 909 1555 2200
15-Acid in face-c 148 296 444 947 1624 2300

NOTE: ***Fass** a-13; c-4, 6, 10. **Hollingsworth** a-10-13, 15; c-2, 12, 13, 15. **Kiefer** a-4. **Woodbridge** a-13? Bondage-c-1, 8, 12.*

CRIME ON THE RUN (See Approved Comics #8)

CRIME ON THE WATERFRONT (Formerly Famous Gangsters)
Realistic Publications: No. 4, May, 1952 (Painted cover)

4 40 80 120 296 411 575

CRIME PATROL (Formerly International #1-5; International Crime Patrol #6; becomes Crypt of Terror #17 on)
E. C. Comics: No. 7, Summer, 1948 - No. 16, Feb-Mar, 1950

7-Intro. Captain Crime 116 232 348 742 1271 1800
8-14: 12-Ingels-a 90 180 270 576 988 1400
15-Intro. of Crypt Keeper (inspired by Witches Tales radio show) & Crypt of Terror (see Tales From the Crypt #33 for origin); used by N.Y. Legis. Comm.; last pg. Feldstein-a 649 1298 1947 4738 8369 12,000
16-2nd Crypt Keeper app.; Roussos-a 314 628 942 2198 3849 5500

NOTE: ***Craig** c/a in most issues. **Feldstein** a-9-16. **Kiefer** a-8, 10, 11. **Moldoff** a-7.*

CRIME PATROL
Gemstone Publishing: Apr, 2000 - No. 10, Jan, 2001 ($2.50)

1-10: E.C. reprints 4.00
Volume 1,2 (2000, $13.50) 1-r/#1-5. 2-r/#6-10 14.00

CRIME PHOTOGRAPHER (See Casey...)

CRIME REPORTER
St. John Publ. Co.: Aug, 1948 - No. 3, Dec, 1948 (Indicia shows Oct.)

1-Drug club story 106 212 318 673 1162 1650
2-Used in **SOTI**: illo- "Children told me what the man was going to do with the red-hot poker;" r/Dynamic #17 with editing; Baker-c; Tuska-a 300 600 900 2010 3505 5000
3-Baker-c; Tuska-a 116 232 348 742 1271 1800

CRIMES BY WOMEN
Fox Feature Syndicate: June, 1948 - No. 15, Aug, 1951; 1954 (True crime cases)

1-True story of Bonnie Parker 148 296 444 947 1624 2300
2 90 180 270 576 988 1400
3-Used in **SOTI**, pg. 234 142 284 426 909 1555 2200
4,5,7-9,11-15: 8-Used in **POP**. 14-Bondage-c 77 154 231 493 847 1200
6-Classic girl fight-c; acid-in-face panel 174 348 522 1114 1907 2700
10-Used in **SOTI**, pg. 72; girl fight-c 110 220 330 704 1202 1700
54(M.S. Publ.-'54)-Reprint; (formerly My Love Secret) 47 94 141 296 498 700

CRIMES INCORPORATED (Formerly My Past)
Fox Feature Syndicate: No. 12, June, 1950 (Crime Incorporated No. 2 on)

12 36 72 108 211 343 475

CRIMES INCORPORATED (See Fox Giants)

CRIME SMASHER (See Whiz #76)
Fawcett Publications: Summer, 1948 (one-shot)

1-Formerly Spy Smasher 48 96 144 302 514 725

CRIME SMASHERS (Becomes Secret Mysteries No. 16 on)
Ribage Publishing Corp.(Trojan Magazines): Oct, 1950 - No. 15, Mar, 1953

1-Used in **SOTI**, pg. 19,20, & illo "A girl raped and murdered;" Sally the Sleuth begins 110 220 330 704 1202 1700
2-Kubert-c 55 110 165 352 601 850
3,4 45 90 135 284 480 675
5-Wood-a 55 110 165 352 601 850
6,8-11: 8-Lingerie panel 37 74 111 222 361 500
7-Female heroin junkie story 40 80 120 246 411 575
12-Injury to eye panel; 1 pg. Frazetta-a 40 80 120 246 411 575
13-Used in **POP**, pgs. 79,80; 1 pg. Frazetta-a 40 80 120 246 411 575
14,15 32 64 96 188 307 425

NOTE: ***Hollingsworth** a-14. **Kiefer** a-15. Bondage c-7, 9.*

CRIME SUSPENSTORIES (Formerly Vault of Horror No. 12-14)
E. C. Comics: No. 15, Oct-Nov, 1950 - No. 27, Feb-Mar, 1955

15-Identical to #1 in content; #1 printed on outside front cover. #15 (formerly "The Vault of Horror") printed and blackened out on inside front cover with Vol. 1, No. 1 printed over it. Evidently, several of No. 15 were printed before a decision was made not to drop the Vault of Horror and Haunt of Fear series. The print run was stopped on No. 15 and continued on No. 1. All of the No. 15 issues were changed as described above. 229 458 687 1832 2916 4000
1 183 366 549 1464 2332 3200
2 91 182 273 728 1164 1600
3-5: 3-Poe adaptation. 3-Old Witch stories begin 66 132 198 528 839 1150
6-10: 9-Craig bio. 56 112 168 448 712 975
11,12,14,15: 15-The Old Witch guest stars 44 88 132 352 564 775
13,16-Williamson-a 59 118 177 472 749 1025
17-Classic "bullet in the head" cover; Williamson/Frazetta-a (6 pgs.); Williamson bio. 114 228 342 912 1456 2000
18,19: 19-Used in **SOTI**, pg. 235 47 94 141 376 601 825
20-Classic hanging cover used in **SOTI**, illo "Cover of a children's comic book"; issue was on display at the 1954 Senate hearing 657 1314 1971 5256 8378 11,500
21,24-26: 24- "Food For Thought" similar to "Cave In" in Amazing Detective Cases #13 (1952) 34 68 102 272 436 600
22-Classic ax decapitation-c; likely the single most notorious cover of the pre-Code era; exhibited in the 1954 Senate Investigation on juvenile delinquency trial; decapitation story 1486 2972 4458 11,888 18,944 26,000

NOTE: *Senator Kefauver questioning Bill Gaines: "Here is your May issue. This seems to be a man with a bloody ax holding a woman's head up which has been severed from her body. Do you think that's in good taste?" Gaines: "Yes I do - for the cover of a horror comic. A cover in bad taste, for example, might be defined as holding her head a little higher so that blood could be seen dripping from it and moving the body over a little further so that the neck of the body could be seen to be bloody." It was actually drawn this way first and Gaines had Craig change it to the published version.*

23-Used in Senate investigation on juvenile delinquency 66 132 198 528 839 1150
27-Last issue (Low distribution) 57 114 171 456 728 1000

NOTE: ***Craig** a-1-21; c-1-18, 20-22. **Crandall** a-18-26. **Davis** a-4, 5, 7, 9-12, 20. **Elder** a-17,18. **Evans** a-15, 19, 21, 23, 25, 27; c-23, 24. **Feldstein** c-19. **Ingels** a-1-12, 14, 15, 27. **Kamen** a-2, 4-18, 20-27; c-25-27. **Krigstein** a-22, 24, 25, 27. **Kurtzman** a-1, 3. **Orlando** a-16, 22, 24, 26. **Wood** a-1, 3. Issues No. 1-3 were printed in Canada as "Weird Suspenstories." Issues No. 11-15 have E. C. "quickie" stories. No. 25 contains the famous "Are You a Red Dupe?" editorial. Ray Bradbury adaptations-15, 17.*

CRIME SUSPENSTORIES
Russ Cochran/Gemstone Publ.: Nov, 1992 - No. 27, May, 1999 ($1.50/$2.00/$2.50)

1-27: Reprints Crime SuspenStories series 4.00

CRIME SYNDICATE (Legion of Justice cover logo on #5)
DC Comics: May, 2021 - No. 6, Oct, 2021 ($3.99, limited series)

1-6-Earth-3 villains vs. Starro; Schmidt-s/McKeown-a; back-up origins; Hitch-a 4.00

CRIMINAL (Also see Criminal: The Sinners)
Marvel Comics (Icon): Oct, 2006 - No. 10, Oct, 2007 ($2.99)
Volume 2: Feb, 2008 - No. 7, Nov, 2008 ($3.50)

1-10-Ed Brubaker-s/Sean Phillips-a/c 3.00
Volume 2: 1-7-Brubaker-s/Phillips-a 3.50
...: Tenth Anniversary Special Edition (Image Comics, 4/16, $5.99) Brubaker-s/Phillips-a; 1970s Kung Fu magazine pastishe within story; intro. Fang the Kung Fu Werewolf 6.00
...: The Special Edition (Image Comics, 2/15, $4.99) Brubaker-s/Phillips-a; 1970s Conan B&W magazine pastishe within story 5.00
... Vol. 1: Coward TPB (2007, $14.99) r/#1-5; intro. by Tom Fontana 15.00
... Vol. 2: Lawless TPB (2007, $14.99) r/#6-10; intro. by Frank Miller 15.00
... Vol. 3: The Dead and the Dying TPB (2008, $11.99) r/V2#1-4; intro. by John Singleton 12.00

CRIMINAL
Image Comics: Jan, 2019 - No. 12, Jan, 2020 ($3.99)

1-12-Ed Brubaker-s/Sean Phillips-a/c 4.00

CRIMINAL MACABRE: (limited series and one-shots)
Dark Horse Comics: ($2.99/$3.99)

...: Cellblock 666 (9/08 - No. 4, 5/09)(#25-28 in series) 1-4-Niles-s/Stakal-a/Bradstreet-c 3.00
.../ Count Crowley: From the Pit They Came (10/22, $3.99) Ketner-a 4.00
...: Die, Die, My Darling (4/12, $3.50) reprints serial from DHP #4-6; Staples-c 3.50
...: Feat of Clay (6/06, $2.99) Niles-s/Hotz-a/c 3.00
Free Comic Book Day: Criminal Macabre - Call Me Monster (5/11) flip book w/Baltimore 3.00
...: My Demon Baby (9/07 - No. 4, 4/08)(#21-24 in the series) 1-4-Niles-s/Stakal-a 3.00
...: No Peace For Dead Men (9/11, $3.99) Niles-s/Mitten-a/Staples-c 4.00
...: The Big Bleed Out (12/19 - No. 4, 3/20 $3.99) 1-4-Niles-s/Németh-a 4.00
...: The Eyes of Frankenstein (9/13 - No. 4, 12/13 $3.99) 1-4-Niles-s/Mitten-a 4.00
...: The Goon (7/11, $3.99) Niles-s/Mitten-a; covers by Powell & Staples 4.00
...: They Fight By Night (11/12, $3.99) reprints serial from DHP #10-13; Staples-c 4.00
...: Two Red Eyes (12/06 - No. 4, 3/07) 1-4-Niles-s/Hotz-a/Bradstreet-c 3.00

CRIMINAL MACABRE: A CAL MCDONALD MYSTERY (Also see Last Train to Deadsville)
Dark Horse Comics: May, 2003 - No. 5, Sept, 2003 ($2.99)

1-5-Niles-s/Templesmith-a 3.00

CRIMINAL MACABRE: FINAL NIGHT - THE 30 DAYS OF NIGHT CROSSOVER
Dark Horse Comics: Dec, 2012 - No. 4, Mar, 2013 ($3.99, limited series)

1-4-Niles-s/Mitten-a/Erickson-c 4.00

CRIMINAL MACABRE:THE THIRD CHILD
Dark Horse Comics: Sept, 2014 - No. 4, Dec, 2014 ($3.99, limited series)

1-4-Niles-s/Mitten-a/Erickson-c 4.00

CRIMINALS ON THE RUN (Formerly Young King Cole) (Crime Fighting Detective No. 11 on)
Premium Group (Novelty Press): V4#1, Aug-Sep, 1948-#10, Dec-Jan, 1949-50

V4#1-Young King Cole continues 41 82 123 258 428 600
2-6: 6-Dr. Doom app. 31 62 93 182 296 410
7-Classic "Fish in the Face" c by L. B. Cole 206 412 618 1318 2259 3200
V5#1,2 (#8,9),10: 9,10-L. B. Cole-c 27 54 81 158 259 360

NOTE: *Most issues have **L. B. Cole** covers. **McWilliams** a-V4#6, 7, V5#2, 10; c-V4#5.*

CRIMINAL: THE LAST OF THE INNOCENT
Marvel Comics (Icon): Jun, 2011 - No. 4, Sept, 2011 ($3.50)

1-4-Ed Brubaker-s/Sean Phillips-a/c 3.50

CRIMINAL: THE SINNERS

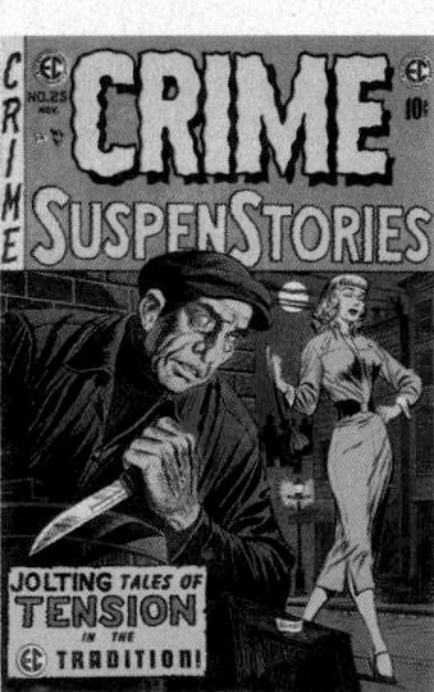

Crime SuspenStories #25 © WMG

Criminal V2 #1 © Brubaker & Phillips

Crisis on Infinite Earths Giant #1 © DC

GD VG FN VF VF/NM NM-
2.0 4.0 6.0 8.0 9.0 9.2

Marvel Comics (Icon): Sept, 2009 - No. 5, Mar, 2010 ($3.50)
1-5-Ed Brubaker-s/Sean Phillips-a/c 3.50

CRIMSON (Also see Cliffhanger #0)
Image Comics (Cliffhanger Productions): May, 1998 - No. 7, Dec, 1998;
DC Comics (Cliffhanger Prod.): No. 8, Mar, 1999 - No. 24, Apr, 2001 ($2.50)
1-Humberto Ramos-a/Augustyn-s 5.00
1-Variant-c by Warren 8.00
1-Chromium-c 15.00
2-Ramos-c with street crowd, 2-Variant-c by Art Adams 4.00
2-Dynamic Forces CrimsonChrome cover 15.00
3-7: 3-Ramos Moon background-c. 7-Three covers by Ramos, Madureira, & Campbell 3.50
8-23: 8-First DC issue 3.00
24-($3.50) Final issue; wraparound-c 4.00
DF Premiere Ed. 1998 ($6.95) covers by Ramos and Jae Lee 7.00
Crimson: Scarlet X Blood on the Moon (10/99, $3.95) 4.00
Crimson Sourcebook (11/99, $2.95) Pin-ups and info 3.00
Earth Angel TPB (2001, $14.95) r/#13-18 15.00
Heaven and Earth TPB (1/00, $14.95) r/#7-12 15.00
Loyalty and Loss TPB ('99, $12.95) r/#1-6 15.00
Redemption TPB ('01, $14.95) r/#19-24 15.00

CRIMSON AVENGER, THE (See Detective Comics #20 for 1st app.)(Also see Leading Comics #1 & World's Best/Finest Comics)
DC Comics: June, 1988 - No. 4, Sept, 1988 ($1.00, limited series)
1-4 4.00

CRIMSON CAGE, THE
Artists Writers & Artisans: Dec, 2021 - No. 5, Apr, 2022 ($3.99, limited series)
1-5-Horror tale told with professional wrestling; John Lees-s/Alex Cormack-a 4.00

CRIMSON DYNAMO
Marvel Comics (Epic): Oct, 2003 - No. 6, Apr, 2004 ($2.50/$2.99)
1-4,6: 1-John Jackson Miller-s/Steve Ellis-a/c 3.00
5-($2.99) Iron Man-c/app. 4.00

CRIMSON LOTUS
Dark Horse Comics: Nov, 2018 - No. 5, Mar, 2019 ($3.99, limited series)
1-5-John Arcudi-s/Mindy Lee-a/Tonci Zonjic-c 4.00

CRIMSON PLAGUE
Event Comics: June, 1997 ($2.95, unfinished mini-series)
1-George Perez-a 3.00

CRIMSON PLAGUE (George Pérez's...)
Image Comics (Gorilla): June, 2000 - No. 2, Aug, 2000 ($2.95, mini-series)
1-George Pérez-a; reprints 6/97 issue with 16 new pages 3.00
2-($2.50) 3.00

CRISIS AFTERMATH: THE BATTLE FOR BLUDHAVEN (Also see Infinite Crisis)
DC Comics: Jun, 2006 - No. 6, Sept, 2006 ($2.99, limited series)
1-Atomic Knights return; Teen Titans app.; Jurgens-a/Acuna-c 4.00
1-2nd printing with pencil cover 3.00
2-6: 2-Intro S.H.A.D.E. (new Freedom Fighters) 3.00
TPB (2007, $12.99) r/#1-6 13.00

CRISIS AFTERMATH: THE SPECTRE (Also see Infinite Crisis, Gotham Central and Tales of the Unexpected)
DC Comics: Jul, 2006 - No. 3, Sept, 2006 ($2.99, limited series)
1-3-Crispus Allen becomes the Spectre; Pfeifer-s/Chiang-a/c 3.00
TPB (2007, $12.99) r/#1-3 and Tales of the Unexpected #1-3 13.00

CRISIS IN INFINITE QUARANTINE (Cerebus in Hell)
Aardvark-Vanaheim: Aug, 2021 ($4.00, B&W)
1-Cerebus figures placed over original Gustave Doré artwork of Hell 4.00

CRISIS OF INFINITE CEREBI (Cerebus figures placed over original Gustave Doré artwork)
Aardvark-Vanaheim: Sept, 2018 ($4.00, B&W, one-shot)
1-Crisis on Infinite Earths #7-c swipe 4.00

CRISIS ON INFINITE EARTHS (Also see Official... Index and Legends of the DC Universe)
DC Comics: Apr, 1985 - No. 12, Mar, 1986 (maxi-series)
1-1st DC app. Blue Beetle & Detective Karp from Charlton; Pérez-c on all
3 6 9 17 26 35
2 2 4 6 11 16 20
3-6: 6-Intro Charlton's Capt. Atom, Nightshade, Question, Judomaster, Peacemaker & Thunderbolt into DC Universe 2 4 6 9 13 16
7-Double size; death of Supergirl 3 6 9 19 30 40
8-Death of the Flash (Barry Allen) 3 6 9 18 28 38

GD VG FN VF VF/NM NM-
2.0 4.0 6.0 8.0 9.0 9.2

8-Facsimile Edition (2019, $3.99) Reprints issue with original ads and letter column 4.00
9-11: 9-Intro. Charlton's Ghost into DC Universe. 10-Intro. Charlton's Banshee, Dr. Spectro, Image, Punch & Jewelee into DC Universe; Starman (Prince Gavyn) dies
2 4 6 8 10 12
12-(52 pgs.)-Deaths of Dove, Kole, Lori Lemaris, Sunburst, G.A. Robin & Huntress; Kid Flash becomes new Flash; 3rd & final DC app. of the 3 Lt. Marvels; Green Fury gets new look (becomes Green Flame in Infinity, Inc. #32) 2 4 6 9 13 16
Slipcased Hardcover (1998, $99.95) Wraparound dust-jacket cover pencilled by Pérez and painted by Alex Ross; sketch pages by Pérez; Wolfman intro.; afterword by Giordano 125.00
TPB (2000, $29.95) Wraparound-c by Pérez and Ross 30.00
NOTE: *Crossover issues: All Star Squadron 50-56,60; Amethyst 13; Blue Devil 17,18; DC Comics Presents 78,86-88,95; Detective Comics 558; Fury of Firestorm 41,42; G.I. Combat 274; Green Lantern 194-196,198; Infinity, Inc. 18-25 & Annual 1, Justice League of America 244,245 & Annual 3; Legion of Super-Heroes 16,18; Losers Special 1; New Teen Titans 13,14; Omega Men 31,33; Superman 413-415; Swamp Thing 44,46; Wonder Woman 327-329.*

CRISIS ON INFINITE EARTHS GIANT
DC Comics: 2019 - No. 2, 2020 ($4.99, 100 pgs., squarebound, Mass Market & Direct Market editions exist for each issue, with different covers)
1,2: 1-Two new stories tied to TV event plus reprints #1,7. 2-Include reprints #8,11 5.00

CRISIS ON MULTIPLE EARTHS
DC Comics: 2002 - 2010 ($14.95, trade paperbacks)
TPB-(2003) Reprints 1st 4 Silver Age JLA/JSA crossovers from J.L.ofA. #21,22; 29,30; 37,38; 46,47; new painted-c by Alex Ross; intro. by Mark Waid 15.00
Volume 2 (2003, $14.95) r/J.L.ofA. #55,56; 64,65; 73,74; 82,83; new Ordway-c 15.00
Volume 3 (2004, $14.95) r/J.L.ofA. #91,92; 100-102; 107,108; 113; Wein intro., Ross-c 15.00
Volume 4 (2006, $14.99) r/J.L.ofA. #123-124 (Earth-Prime),135-137 (Fawcett's Shazam characters), 147-148 (Legion of Super-Heroes); Ross-c 15.00
Volume 5 (2010, $19.99) r/J.L.ofA. #159-160 (Jonah Hex, Enemy Ace), #171-172 (Murder of Mr. Terrific), 1#83-185 (New Gods & Darkseid); Pérez-c 20.00
... The Team-Ups Volume 1 (2005, $14.99) r/Flash #123,129,137,151; Showcase #55,56; Green Lantern #40, Brave and the Bold #61 and Spectre #7; new Ordway-c 15.00

CRITICAL MASS (See A Shadowline Saga: Critical Mass)

CRITICAL ROLE: THE TALES OF EXANDRIA: THE BRIGHT QUEEN (Based on characters from the D&D web series)
Dark Horse Comics: Oct, 2021 - No. 4, Mar, 2022 ($3.99, limited series)
1-4-Poelgeest-s/CoupleofKooks-a 4.00

CRITICAL ROLE VOX MACHINA ORIGINS (Based on characters from the D&D web series)
Dark Horse Comics: Jul, 2019 - No. 6, Apr, 2020 ($3.99, limited series)
1-6-Matthew Mercer & Jody Houser-s/Olivia Samson-a 4.00
(Series) III 1-6-(2/21 - No. 6, 5/22, $3.99) Mercer & Houser-s/Samson-a 4.00

CRITTER
Big Dog Press: Jul, 2011 - No. 4, 2011; Jun, 2012 - No. 20, Apr, 2014 ($3.50)
1-4-Multiple covers on all 3.50
Vol. 2 1-20-Multiple covers on all 3.50

CRITTER
Aspen MLT: Jul, 2015 - No. 4, Oct, 2015 ($3.99)
1-4-Reprints the 2011 series; multiple covers on all 4.00

CRITTERS (Also see Usagi Yojimbo Summer Special)
Fantagraphics Books: 1986 - No. 50, 1990 ($1.70/$2.00, B&W)
1-Cutey Bunny, Usagi Yojimbo app. 4 8 12 23 37 50
2,4,5,8,9 1 2 3 5 6 8
3,6,7,10-Usagi Yojimbo app. 2 4 6 9 12 15
11,14-Usagi Yojimbo app. 11-Christmas Special (68 pgs.) 6.00
12,13,15-22,24-37,39,40: 22-Watchmen parody; two diff. covers exist 3.00
23-With Alan Moore Flexi-disc ($3.95) 5.00
38-($2.75-c) Usagi Yojimbo app. 5.00
41-49 4.00
50 ($4.95, 84 pgs.)-Neil the Horse, Capt. Jack, Sam & Max & Usagi Yojimbo app.; Quagmire, Shaw-a 2 4 6 8 10 12
Special 1 (1/88, $2.00) 4.00

CRONE
Dark Horse Comics: Nov, 2019 - No. 5, Mar, 2020 ($3.99, limited series)
1-5-Dennis Culver-s/Justin Greenwood-a 4.00

CROSS
Dark Horse Comics: No. 0, Oct, 1995 - No. 6, Apr, 1995 ($2.95, limited series, mature)
0-6: Darrow-c & Vachss scripts in all 3.00

CROSS AND THE SWITCHBLADE, THE
Spire Christian Comics (Fleming H. Revell Co.): 1972 (35-49¢)
1-Some issues have nn 3 6 9 21 33 45

	GD 2.0	VG 4.0	FN 6.0	VF 8.0	VF/NM 9.0	NM- 9.2

CROSS BRONX, THE
Image Comics: Sept, 2006 - No. 4, Dec, 2006 ($2.99, limited series)
1-4: 1-Oeming-a/c; Oeming & Brandon-s; Ribic var-c. 2-Johnson var-c. 4-Mack var-c 3.00

CROSSFIRE
Spire Christian Comics (Fleming H. Revell Co.): 1973 (39/49¢)
nn 2 4 6 13 18 22

CROSSFIRE (Also see DNAgents)
Eclipse Comics: 5/84 - No. 17, 3/86; No. 18, 1/87 - No. 26, 2/88 ($1.50, Baxter paper) (#18-26 are B&W)
1-11,14-26: 1-DNAgents x-over; Spiegle-c/a begins 4.00
12-Death of Marilyn Monroe; Dave Stevens-c 3 6 9 19 30 40
13-Death of Marilyn Monroe 1 3 4 6 8 10

CROSSFIRE AND RAINBOW (Also see DNAgents)
Eclipse Comics: June, 1986 - No. 4, Sept, 1986 ($1.25, deluxe format)
1-3: Spiegle-a 4.00
4-Elvis cover by Dave Stevens 6.00

CROSSGEN...
CrossGeneration Comics
CrossGenesis (1/00) Previews CrossGen universe; cover gallery 3.00
...Primer (1/00) Wizard supplement; intro. to the CrossGen universe 3.00
...Sampler (2/00) Retailer preview book 3.00

CROSSGEN CHRONICLES
CrossGeneration Comics: June, 2000 - No. 8, Jul, 2002 ($3.95)
1-Intro. to CrossGen characters & company 4.00
1-(no cover price) same contents, customer preview 4.00
2-8: 2-(3/01) George Pérez-c/a. 3-5-Pérez-a/Waid-s. 6,8-Maroto-c/a. 7-Nebres-c/a 4.00

CROSSGEN TALES
Marvel Comics: Jan, 2023 ($8.99, squarebound, one-shot)
1-Reprints Ruse #1, Mystic #1, Sigil #1, Sojourn #1; intro. by Ron Marz 9.00

CROSSING MIDNIGHT
DC Comics (Vertigo): Jan, 2007 - No. 19, Jul, 2008 ($2.99)
1-19: 1-Carey-s/Fern-a/Williams III-c. 10-12-Nguyen-a 3.00
...: Cut Here TPB (2007, $9.99) r/#1-5 10.00
...: A Map of Midnight TPB (2008, $14.99) r/#6-12; afterword by Carey 15.00
...: The Sword in the Soul TPB (2008, $14.99) r/#13-19 15.00

CROSSING THE ROCKIES (See Classics Illustrated Special Issue)

CROSSOVER
Image Comics: Nov, 2020 - Present ($3.99)
1-13: 1-Donny Cates-s/Geoff Shaw-a. 3-5-Madman app. 7-Zdarsky-s/Hester-a. 8-10-Walker & Pilgrim from Powers app. 10-13-Donny Cates app. 11-13-Negan app. 4.00
... #1 3-D Special (8/22, $8.99) Reprints #1 with 3-D effects; bagged with glasses 9.00

CROSSOVERS, THE
CrossGeneration Comics: Feb, 2003 - No. 9, Dec, 2003 ($2.95)
1-9-Robert Rodi-s. 1-6-Mauricet & Ernie Colon-a. 7-Staton-a begins 3.00
Vol. 1: Cross Currents (2003, $9.95) digest-sized reprints #1-6 10.00

CROSS TO BEAR
AfterShock Comics: Oct, 2021 - No. 4 ($4.99, limited series)
1-3-Stojanovic-s/Banovic-a 5.00

CROSSWIND
Image Comics: Jun, 2017 - No. 6, Jan, 2018 ($3.99)
1-6-Gail Simone-s/Cat Staggs-a 4.00

CROW, THE (Also see Caliber Presents)
Caliber Press: Feb, 1989 - No. 4, 1989 ($1.95, B&W, limited series)
1-James O'Barr-c/a/scripts 40 80 120 296 673 1050
1-2nd printing 17 34 51 117 259 400
2 10 20 30 69 147 225
2,3-2nd printing 3 6 9 19 30 40
2-3rd printing 3 6 9 14 20 25
3,4 8 16 24 54 102 150

CROW, THE
Tundra Publishing, Ltd.: Jan, 1992 - No. 3, 1992 ($4.95, B&W, 68 pgs.)
1-r/#1,2 of Caliber series 3 6 9 19 30 40
2,3: 2-r/#3 of Caliber series w/new material. 3-All new material 2 4 6 13 18 22

CROW, THE
Kitchen Sink Press: 1/96 - No. 3, 3/96 ($2.95, B&W)
1-James O'Barr-c/scripts in all 2 4 6 8 11 14
2,3 1 2 3 5 6 8
#0-A Cycle of Shattered Lives (12/98, $3.50) new story by O'Barr 1 3 4 6 8 10

CROW, THE
Image Comics (Todd McFarlane Prod.): Feb, 1999 - No. 10, Nov, 1999 ($2.50)
1-Two covers by McFarlane and Kent Williams; Muth-s in all 1 3 4 6 8 10
2-10: 2-6,10-Paul Lee-a 4.00
Book 1 - Vengeance (2000, $10.95, TPB) r/#1-3,5,6 15.00
Book 2 - Evil Beyond Reach (2000, $10.95, TPB) r/#4,7-10 15.00
Todd McFarlane Presents The Crow Magazine 1 (3/00, $4.95) 1 2 3 5 6 8

CROW, THE: CITY OF ANGELS (Movie)
Kitchen Sink Press: July, 1996 - No. 3, Sept, 1996 ($2.95, limited series)
1-Adaptation of film; two-c (photo & illos.); Vincent Perez interview 1 3 4 6 8 10
2,3-Adaptation continues 5.00

CROW, THE: CURARE
IDW Publishing: Jun, 2013 - No. 3, Aug, 2013 ($3.99, limited series)
1-3-James O'Barr-s/Antoine Dodé-a; multiple covers on each 4.00

CROW, THE: DEATH AND REBIRTH
IDW Publishing: Jul, 2012 - No. 5, Nov, 2012 ($3.99, limited series)
1-5-Shirley-s/Colden-a; multiple covers on each 4.00

CROW, THE: FLESH AND BLOOD
Kitchen Sink Press: May, 1996 - No. 3, July, 1996 ($2.95, limited series)
1-James O'Barr-c on all 1 3 4 6 8 10
2,3 4.00

CROW: HACK / SLASH
IDW Publishing: Jun, 2019 - No. 4, Sept, 2019 ($3.99, limited series)
1-4-Tim Seeley-s/Jim Terry-a; multiple covers on each 4.00

CROW: HARK THE HERALD
IDW Publishing: Nov, 2019 ($4.99, one-shot)
1-Tim Seeley-s/Meredith Laxton-a; four covers 5.00

CROW: LETHE
IDW Publishing: Feb, 2020 - Present ($3.99, limited series)
1-Tim Seeley-s/Ilias Kyriazis-a; four covers 4.00

CROW, THE: MEMENTO MORI
IDW Publishing: Mar, 2018 - No. 4, Jun, 2018 ($3.99, limited series)
1-4-Recchioni-s/Dell'edera-a in all; back-up short stories in each by various 4.00

CROW, THE: PESTILENCE
IDW Publishing: Mar, 2014 - No. 4, Jun, 2014 ($3.99, limited series)
1-4-Frank Bill-s/Drew Moss-a; two covers 4.00

CROW, THE: RAZOR - KILL THE PAIN
London Night Studios: Apr, 1998 - No. 3, July, 1998 ($2.95, B&W, lim. series)
1-Hartsoe-s/O'Barr-painted-c 1 2 3 5 6 8
2,3-Hartsoe-s/O'Barr-painted-c 4.00
0(10/98) Dorien painted-c, Finale (2/99) 4.00
The Lost Chapter (2/99, $4.95), Tour Book-(12/97) pin-ups; 4 diff.-c 1 2 3 5 6 8

CROW, THE: SKINNING THE WOLVES
IDW Publishing: Dec, 2012 - No. 3, Feb, 2013 ($3.99, limited series)
1-3-James O'Barr-s/Jim Terry-s/a; multiple covers on each 4.00

CROW, THE: WAKING NIGHTMARES
Kitchen Sink Press: Jan, 1997 - No. 4, 1998 ($2.95, B&W, limited series)
1-Miran Kim-c on all 1 3 4 6 8 10
2-4 5.00

CROW, THE: WILD JUSTICE
Kitchen Sink Press: Oct, 1996 - No. 3, Dec, 1996 ($2.95, B&W, limited series)
1-Prosser-s/Adlard-a in all 1 3 4 6 8 10
2,3 5.00

CROWN COMICS (Also see Vooda)
Golfing/McCombs Publ.: Wint, 1944-45; No. 2, Sum, 1945 - No. 19, July, 1949
1- "The Oblong Box" E.A. Poe adaptation 65 130 195 416 708 1000
2-Baker-a 39 78 117 231 378 525
3-Baker-a; Voodah by Baker; racist-c 54 108 162 343 574 825
4-6-Baker-c/a; Voodah app. #4,5 45 90 135 284 480 675
7-Feldstein, Baker, Kamen-a; Baker-c 142 284 426 909 1555 2200
8-Baker-a; Voodah app. 39 78 117 231 378 525
9-11,13-19: Voodah in #10-19. 13-New logo 22 44 66 132 216 300
12-Master Marvin by Feldstein, Starr-a; Voodah-c 23 46 69 136 223 310
NOTE: *Bolle a-11, 13-16, 18, 19; c-11p, 15. **Powell** a-19. **Starr** a-11-13; c-11i.*

CRUCIBLE
DC Comics (Impact): Feb, 1993 - No. 6, July, 1993 ($1.25, limited series)
1-6: 1-(99¢)-Neon ink-c. 1,2-Quesada-c(p). 1-4-Quesada layouts 3.00

CRUDE
Image Comics (Skybound): Apr, 2018 - No. 6, Sept, 2018 ($3.99, limited series)
1-6-Steve Orlando-s/Garry Brown-a 4.00

CRUEL AND UNUSUAL
DC Comics (Vertigo): June, 1999 - No. 4, Sept, 1999 ($2.95, limited series)
1-4-Delano & Peyer-s/McCrea-c/a 3.00

CRUSADER FROM MARS (See Tops in Adventure)
Ziff-Davis Publ. Co.: Jan-Mar, 1952 - No. 2, Fall, 1952 (Painted-c)
1-Cover is dated Spring 93 186 279 591 1021 1450
2-Bondage-c 65 130 195 416 708 1000

CRUSADER RABBIT (TV)
Dell Publishing Co.: No. 735, Oct, 1956 - No. 805, May, 1957
Four Color 735 (#1) 23 46 69 161 356 550
Four Color 805 17 34 51 119 265 410

CRUSADERS, THE (Religious)
Chick Publications: 1974 - Vol. 17, 1988 (39/69¢, 36 pgs.)
Vol.1-Operation Bucharest ('74). Vol.2-The Broken Cross ('74). Vol.3-Scarface ('74). Vol.4-Exorcists ('75). Vol.5-Chaos ('75) 3 6 9 16 23 30
Vol.6-Primal Man? ('76)-(Disputes evolution theory). Vol.7-The Ark-(claims proof of existence, destroyed by Bolsheviks). Vol.8-The Gift-(Life story of Christ). Vol.9-Angel of Light-(Story of the Devil). Vol.10-Spellbound?-(Tells how rock music is Satanic & produced by witches). 11-Sabotage?. 12-Alberto. 13-Double Cross. 14-The Godfathers. (No. 6-14 low in distribution; loaded with religious propaganda.). 15-The Force. 16-The Four Horsemen 3 6 9 16 23 30
Vol. 17-The Prophet (low print run) 3 6 9 17 26 35

CRUSADERS (Southern Knights No. 2 on)
Guild Publications: 1982 (B&W, magazine size)
1-1st app. Southern Knights 2 4 6 11 16 20

Crossfire #12 © ECL

The Crow: Memento Mori #1 © James O'Barr

CSI: Dying in the Gutters #1 © CBS

	GD 2.0	VG 4.0	FN 6.0	VF 8.0	VF/NM 9.0	NM- 9.2

CRUSADERS, THE (Also see Black Hood, The Jaguar, The Comet, The Fly, Legend of the Shield, The Mighty... & The Web)
DC Comics (Impact): May, 1992 - No. 8, Dec, 1992 ($1.00/$1.25)

1-8-Contains 3 Impact trading cards 4.00

CRUSADES, THE
DC Comics (Vertigo): 2001 - No. 20, Dec, 2002 ($3.95/$2.50)

...: Urban Decree ('01, $3.95) Intro. the Knight; Seagle-s/Kelley Jones-c/a 4.00
1-(5/01, $2.50) Sienkiewicz-c 3.00
2-20: 2-Moeller-c. 18-Begin $2.95-c 3.00

CRUSH
Dark Horse Comics: Oct, 2003 - No. 4, Jan, 2004 ($2.99, limited series)

1-4-Jason Hall-s/Sean Murphy-a 3.00

CRUSH, THE
Image Comics (Motown Machineworks): Jan, 1996 - No. 5, July, 1996 ($2.25, limited series)

1-5: Baron scripts 3.00

CRUSH & LOBO
DC Comics: Aug, 2021 - No. 8, Mar, 2022 ($3.99, limited series)

1-8-Lobo & his daughter from Teen Titans; Tamaki-s/Nahuelpan-a 4.00

CRUX
CrossGeneration Comics: May, 2001 - No. 33, Feb, 2004 ($2.95)

1-33: 1-Waid-s/Epting & Magyar-a/c. 6-Pelletier-a. 13-Dixon-s begin. 25-Cover has fake creases and other aging 3.00
Atlantis Rising Vol. 1 TPB (2002, $15.95) r/#1-6 16.00
Test of Time Vol. 2 TPB (12/02, $15.95) r/#7-12 16.00
Vol. 3: Strangers in Atlantis (2003, $15.95) r/#13-18 16.00
Vol. 4: Chaos Reborn (2003, $15.95) r/#19-24 16.00

CRY FOR DAWN
Cry For Dawn Pub.: 1989 - No. 9 ($2.25, B&W, mature)

	GD	VG	FN	VF	VF/NM	NM-
1	11	22	33	73	157	240
1-2nd printing	4	8	12	28	47	65
1-3rd printing	3	6	9	16	23	30
2	4	8	12	23	37	50
2-2nd printing	2	4	6	11	16	20
3	3	6	9	16	23	30
3a-HorrorCon Edition (1990, less than 400 printed, signed inside-c)						200.00
4-6	2	4	6	11	16	20
5-2nd printing	1	2	3	5	6	8
7-9	2	4	6	9	12	15
4-9-Signed & numbered editions	3	6	9	14	20	25

Angry Christ Comix HC (4/03, $29.99) reprints various stories; and 30 pgs. new material 30.00
...Calendar (1993) 35.00

CRY HAVOC
Image Comics: Jan, 2016 - No. 6, Jun, 2016 ($3.99)

1-6-Simon Spurrier-s/Ryan Kelly-a; 2 covers on each 4.00

CRYIN' LION COMICS
William H. Wise Co.: Fall, 1944 - No. 3, Spring, 1945

	GD	VG	FN	VF	VF/NM	NM-
1-Funny animal	18	36	54	107	169	230
2-Hitler and Tojo app.	15	30	45	84	127	170
3	11	22	33	62	86	110

CRYPT
Image Comics (Extreme): Aug, 1995 - No. 2, Oct. 1995 ($2.50, limited series)

1,2-Prophet app. 3.00

CRYPTIC WRITINGS OF MEGADETH
Chaos! Comics: Sept, 1997 - No. 4, Jun, 1998 ($2.95, quarterly)

1-4-Stories based on song lyrics by Dave Mustaine 3.00

CRYPTOCRACY
Dark Horse Comics: Jun, 2016 - No. 6, Nov, 2016 ($3.99)

1-6: 1-Van Jensen-s/Pete Woods-a 4.00

CRYPT OF DAWN (see Dawn)
Sirius: 1996 ($2.95, B&W, limited series)

	GD	VG	FN	VF	VF/NM	NM-
1-Linsner-c/s; anthology	1	3	4	6	8	10
2, 3 (2/98)						5.00
4,5: 4- (6/98), 5-(11/98)						4.00
Ltd. Edition						20.00

CRYPT OF SHADOWS
Marvel Comics Group: Jan, 1973 - No. 21, Nov, 1975 (#1-9 are 20¢)

	GD	VG	FN	VF	VF/NM	NM-
1-Wolverton-r/Advs. Into Terror #7	5	10	15	35	63	90
2-10: 2-Starlin/Everett-c	3	6	9	18	27	36
11-21: 18,20-Kirby-a	3	6	9	16	23	30

NOTE: ***Briefer** a-2r. **Ditko** a-13r, 18-20r. **Everett** a-6, 14r; c-2i. **Heath** a-1r. **Gil Kane** c-1, 6. **Mort Lawrence** a-1r, 8r. **Maneely** a-2r. **Moldoff** a-8. **Powell** a-12r, 14r. **Tuska** a-2r.*

CRYPT OF SHADOWS (Marvel 80th Anniversary salute to horror comics)
Marvel Comics: Mar, 2019 ($3.99, one-shot)

1-Al Ewing-s; art by Garry Brown, Stephen Green, Djibril Morissett-Phan; Kyle Hotz-c 4.00

CRYPT OF SHADOWS
Marvel Comics: Dec, 2022 ($5.99, one-shot)

1-Short stories featuring Moon Knight, Man-Thing, Werewolf By Night, Morbius & others 6.00

CRYPT OF TERROR (Formerly Crime Patrol; Tales From the Crypt No. 20 on)
(Also see EC Archives • Tales From the Crypt)
E. C. Comics: No. 17, Apr-May, 1950 - No. 19, Aug-Sept, 1950

	GD	VG	FN	VF	VF/NM	NM-
17-1st New Trend to hit stands	469	938	1407	3752	5976	8200
18,19	223	446	669	1784	2842	3900

NOTE: ***Craig** c/a-17-19. **Feldstein** a-17-19. **Ingels** a-19. **Kurtzman** a-18. **Wood** a-18. Canadian reprints known; see Table of Contents.*

CRYPTOZOIC MAN (Comic Book Men)
Dynamite Entertainment: 2013 - No. 4, 2014 ($3.99, limited series)

	GD	VG	FN	VF	VF/NM	NM-
1-Bryan Johnson-s/Walt Flanagan-a/c	2	4	6	11	16	20
2-4	2	4	6	8	10	12

CRYSIS (Based on the EA videogame)
IDW Publishing: Jun, 2011 - No. 6, Oct, 2011 ($3.99, limited series)

1-6: 1-Richard K. Moran-s/Peter Bergting-a; two covers 4.00

CSI: CRIME SCENE INVESTIGATION (Based on TV series)
IDW Publishing: Jan, 2003 - No. 5, May, 2003 ($3.99, limited series)

1-Two covers (photo & Ashley Wood); Max Allan Collins-s 4.00
2-5 4.00
Free Comic Book Day edition (7/04) Previews CSI: Bad Rap; The Shield: Spotlight; 24: One Shot; and 30 Days of Night 3.00
...: Case Files Vol. 1 TPB (8/06, $19.99) B&W rep/Serial TPB, CSI - Bad Rap and CSI - Demon House limited series 20.00
...: Serial TPB (2003, $19.99) r/#1-5; bonus short story by Collins/Wood 20.00
...: Thicker Than Blood (7/03, $6.99) Mariotte-s/Rodriguez-a 7.00

CSI: CRIME SCENE INVESTIGATION - BAD RAP
IDW Publishing: Aug, 2003 - No. 5, Dec, 2003 ($3.99, limited series)

1-5-Two photo covers; Max Allan Collins-s/Rodriguez-a 4.00
TPB (3/04, $19.99) r/#1-5 20.00

CSI: CRIME SCENE INVESTIGATION - DEMON HOUSE
IDW Publishing: Feb, 2004 - No. 5, Jun, 2004 ($3.99, limited series)

1-5-Photo covers on all; Max Allan Collins-s/Rodriguez-a 4.00
TPB (10/04, $19.99) r/#1-5 20.00

CSI: CRIME SCENE INVESTIGATION - DOMINOS
IDW Publishing: Aug, 2004 - No. 5, Dec, 2004 ($3.99, limited series)

1-5-Photo covers on all; Oprisko-s/Rodriguez-a 4.00

CSI: CRIME SCENE INVESTIGATION - DYING IN THE GUTTERS
IDW Publishing: Aug, 2006 - No. 5, Dec, 2006 ($3.99, limited series)

1-5-"Rich Johnston" murdered; comic creators (Quesada, Rucka, David, Brubaker, Silvestri and others) appear as suspects; Stephen Mooney-a; photo-c 4.00

CSI: CRIME SCENE INVESTIGATION - SECRET IDENTITY
IDW Publishing: Feb, 2005 - No. 5, Jun, 2005 ($3.99, limited series)

1-5-Photo covers on all; Steven Grant-s/Gabriel Rodriguez-a 4.00

CSI: MIAMI
IDW Publishing: Oct, 2003; Apr, 2004 ($6.99, one-shots)

... - Blood Money (9/04)-Oprisko-s/Guedes & Perkins-a 7.00
... - Smoking Gun (10/03)-Mariotte-s/Avilés & Wood-a 7.00
... - Thou Shalt Not... (4/04)-Oprisko-s/Guedes & Wood-a 7.00
TPB (2/05, $19.99) reprints one-shots 20.00

CSI: NY - BLOODY MURDER
IDW Publishing: July, 2005 - No. 5, Nov, 2005 ($3.99, limited series)

1-5-Photo covers on all; Collins-s/Woodward-a 4.00

C•23 (Jim Lee's...) (Based on Wizards of the Coast card game)
Image Comics: Apr, 1998 - No. 8, Nov, 1998 ($2.50)

1-8: 1,2-Choi & Mariotte-s/ Charest-c. 2-Variant-c by Jim Lee. 4-Ryan Benjamin-c. 5,8-Corben var-c. 6-Flip book with Planetary preview; Corben-c 3.00

GD VG FN VF VF/NM NM-
2.0 4.0 6.0 8.0 9.0 9.2

CUD
Fantagraphics Books: 8/92 - No. 8, 12/94 ($2.25-$2.75, B&W, mature)
1-8: Terry LaBan scripts & art in all. 6-1st Eno & Plum 3.00

CUD COMICS
Dark Horse Comics: Jan, 1995 - No. 8, Sept, 1997 ($2.95, B&W)
1-8: Terry LaBan-c/a/scripts. 5-Nudity; marijuana story 3.00
Eno and Plum TPB (1997, $12.95) r/#1-4, DHP #93-95 13.00

CUPID
Marvel Comics (U.S.A.): Dec, 1949 - No. 2, Mar, 1950
1-Photo-c 28 56 84 165 270 375
2-Bettie Page ('50s pin-up queen) photo-c; Powell-a (see My Love #4)
86 172 258 546 936 1325

CURB STOMP
BOOM! Studios: Feb, 2015 - No. 4, May, 2015 ($3.99, limited series)
1-4-Ryan Ferrier-s/Devaki Neogi-a 4.00

CURIO
Harry 'A' Chesler: 1930's(?) (Tabloid size, 16-20 pgs.)
nn 24 48 72 144 237 330

CURLY KAYOE COMICS (Boxing)
United Features Syndicate/Dell Publ. Co.: 1946 - No. 8, 1950; Jan, 1958
1 (1946)-Strip-r (Fritzi Ritz); biography of Sam Leff, Kayoe's artist
27 54 81 160 263 365
2 17 34 51 103 162 220
3-8 14 28 42 82 121 160
United Presents...(Fall, 1948) 14 28 42 82 121 160
Four Color 871 (Dell, 1/58) 5 10 15 33 57 80

CURSED
Image Comics (Top Cow): Oct, 2003 - No. 4, Feb, 2004 ($2.99)
1-4-Avery & Blevins-s/Molenaar-a 3.00

CURSED COMICS CAVALCADE
DC Comics: Dec, 2018 ($9.99, square-bound one-shot)
1-Short stories of DC heroes facing ghosts and monsters by various; Mahnke-c 10.00

CURSE OF BRIMSTONE, THE
DC Comics: Jun, 2018 - No. 12, May, 2019 ($2.99)
1-12: 1-3-Justin Jordan-s/Philip Tan-a. 6,11,12-Cowan-a. 9-Dr. Fate app. 3.00
Annual 1 (3/19, $4.99) Swamp Thing & Constantine app.; Perkins-a 5.00

CURSE OF DRACULA, THE
Dark Horse Comics: July, 1998 - No. 3, Sept, 1998 ($2.95, limited series)
1-3-Marv Wolfman-s/Gene Colan-a 4.00
TPB (2005, $9.95) r/series; intro. by Marv Wolfman 10.00

CURSE OF RUNE (Becomes Rune, 2nd Series)
Malibu Comics (Ultraverse): May, 1995 - No. 4, Aug, 1995 ($2.50, lim. series)
1-4: 1-Two covers form one image 3.00

CURSE OF THE SPAWN
Image Comics (Todd McFarlane Prod.): Sept, 1996 - No. 29, Mar, 1999 ($1.95)
1-Dwayne Turner-a(p) 2 4 6 10 14 18
1-B&W Edition 4 8 12 23 37 50
2-3 1 2 3 5 6 8
4-29: 12-Movie photo-c of Melinda Clarke (Priest) 4.00
Blood and Sutures ('99, $9.95, TPB) r/#5-8 10.00
Lost Values ('00, $10.95, TPB) r/#12-14,22; Ashley Wood-c 11.00
Sacrifice of the Soul ('99, $9.95, TPB) r/#1-4 10.00
Shades of Gray ('00, $9.95, TPB) r/#9-11,29 10.00
The Best of the Curse of the Spawn (6/06, $16.99, TPB) B&W r/#1-8,12-16,20-29 17.00

CURSE OF THE WEIRD
Marvel Comics: Dec, 1993 - No. 4, Mar, 1994 ($1.25, limited series)
(Pre-code horror-r)
1-4: 1,3,4-Wolverton-r(1-Eye of Doom; 3-Where Monsters Dwell; 4-The End of the World).
2-Orlando-r. 4-Zombie-r by Everett; painted-c 1 2 3 5 6 8
NOTE: *Briefer r-2. Davis a-4r. Ditko a-1r, 2r, 4r; c-1r. Everett r-1. Heath r-1-3. Kubert r-3. Wolverton a-1r, 3r, 4r.*

CURSE WORDS
Image Comics: Jan, 2017 - Present ($3.99)
1-25-Charles Soule-s/Ryan Browne-a 4.00
Holiday Special (12/17, $3.99) Mike Norton-a 4.00
... Spring Special (4/19, $3.99) Norton-a; takes place after #20; Ascender #1 preview 4.00
... Summer Swimsuit Special (8/18, $3.99) Joe Quinones-a; takes place after #15 4.00

CUSTER'S LAST FIGHT
Avon Periodicals: 1950
nn-Partial reprint of Cowpuncher #1 22 44 66 132 216 300

CUTEY BUNNY (See Army Surplus Komikz Featuring...)

CUTIE PIE
Junior Reader's Guild (Lev Gleason): May, 1955 - No. 3, Dec, 1955; No. 4, Feb, 1956; No. 5, Aug, 1956
1 11 22 33 64 90 115
2-5: 4-Misdated 2/55 8 16 24 40 50 60

CUTTING EDGE
Marvel Comics: Dec, 1995 ($2.95)
1-Hulk-c/story; Messner-Loebs scripts 3.00

CVO: COVERT VAMPIRIC OPERATIONS
IDW Publishing: June, 2003 ($5.99, one-shot)
1-Alex Garner-s/Mindy Lee-a(p) 6.00
... - Human Touch 1 (8/04, $3.99, one-shot) Hernandez & Garner-a 4.00
... - 100-Page Spectacular (4/11, $7.99) r/#1, African Blood #2 Rogue State #5 8.00
TPB (9/04, $19.99) r/#1 and ... - Artifact #1-3; intro. by Garner 20.00

CVO: COVERT VAMPIRIC OPERATIONS - AFRICAN BLOOD
IDW Publishing: Sept, 2006 - No. 4, May, 2007 ($3.99, limited series)
1-4-El Torres-s/Luis Czerniawski-a 4.00

CVO: COVERT VAMPIRIC OPERATIONS - ARTIFACT
IDW Publishing: Oct, 2003 - No. 3, Dec, 2003 ($3.99, limited series)
1-3-Jeff Mariotte-s/Gabriel Hernandez-a/Alex Garner-c 4.00

CVO: COVERT VAMPIRIC OPERATIONS - ROGUE STATE
IDW Publishing: Nov, 2004 - No. 5, Mar, 2005 ($3.99, limited series)
1-5-Jeff Mariotte-s/Vazquez-a 4.00
TPB (7/05, $19.99) r/#1-5; cover gallery 20.00

CYBERELLA
DC Comics (Helix): Sept, 1996 - No. 12, Aug, 1997 ($2.25/$2.50)(1st Helix series)
1-12: 1-5-Chaykin & Cameron-a. 1,2-Chaykin-c. 3-5-Cameron-c 3.00

CYBERFORCE
Image Comics (Top Cow Productions): Oct, 1992 - No. 4, 1993; No. 0, Sept, 1993 ($1.95, limited series)
1-Silvestri-c/a in all; coupon for Image Comics #0; 1st Top Cow Productions title 6.00
1-With coupon missing 2.00
2-4,0: 2-(3/93). 3-Pitt-c/story. 4-Codename: Stryke Force back-up (1st app.); foil-c.
0-(9/93)-Walt Simonson-c/a/scripts 3.00
...#1 30th Anniversary Edition (6/22, $4.99) R/#1 with creator interviews; cover gallery 5.00

CYBERFORCE
Image Comics (Top Cow Productions)/Top Cow Comics No. 28 on:
V2#1, Nov, 1993 - No. 35, Sept. 1997 ($1.95)
V2#1-24: 1-7-Marc Silvestri/Keith Williams-c/a. 8-McFarlane-c/a. 10-Painted variant-c exists.
18-Variant-c exists. 23-Velocity-c. 3.00
1-3: 1-Gold Logo-c. 2-Silver embossed-c. 3-Gold embossed-c 10.00
1-(99¢, 3/96, 2nd printing) 3.00
25-($3.95)-Wraparound, foil-c 4.00
26-35: 28-(11/96)-1st Top Cow Comics iss. Quesada & Palmiotti's Gabriel app.
27-Quesada & Palmiotti's Ash app. 3.00
Annual 1,2 (3/95, 8/96, $2.50, $2.95) 4.00
NOTE: *Annuals read Volume One in the indica.*

CYBERFORCE (Volume 3)
Image Comics (Top Cow): Apr, 2006 - No. 6, Nov, 2006 ($2.99)
1-6: 1-Pat Lee-a/Ron Marz-s; three covers by Pat Lee, Marc Silvestri and Dave Finch 3.00
#0-(6/06, $2.99) reprints origin story from Image Comics Hardcover Vol. 1 3.00
.../X-Men 1 (1/07, $3.99) Pat Lee-a/Ron Marz-s; 2 covers by Lee and Silvestri 4.00
Vol. 1 TPB (12/06, $14.99) r/#1-6, #0 & story from The Cow Quarterly; cover gallery 15.00

CYBER FORCE (Volume 4)
Image Comics (Top Cow): Dec, 2012 - No. 11 (no cover price/$2.99)
1-11: 1-Silvestri & Hawkins-s/Pham-a; multiple covers on each 3.00
...: Artifacts #0 (12/16, $3.99) Short stories by various; Khoi Pham-c 4.00

CYBER FORCE (Volume 5) (See Aphrodite IX and Ninth Generation)
Image Comics (Top Cow): Mar, 2018 - Present ($3.99)
1-11: 1-Matt Hawkins & Bryan Hill-s/Atilio Rojo-a; two covers; origin story 4.00

CYBERFORCE/HUNTER-KILLER
Image Comics (Top Cow Productions): July, 2009 - No. 5, Mar, 2010 ($2.99)
1-5-Waid-s/Rocafort-a; multiple covers on each 3.00

CYBERFORCE ORIGINS
Image Comics (Top Cow Productions): Jan, 1995 - No. 3, Nov, 1995 ($2.50)
1-Cyblade (1/95) 5.00
1-Cyblade (3/96, 99¢, 2nd printing) 3.00
1A-Exclusive Ed.; Tucci-c 4.00
2,3: 2-Stryker (2/95)-1st Mike Turner-a. 3-Impact 3.00
(#4) Misery (12/95, $2.95) 3.00

CYBERFORCE/STRYKEFORCE: OPPOSING FORCES (See Codename: Stryke Force #15)
Image Comics (Top Cow Productions): Sept, 1995 - No. 2, Oct, 1995 ($2.50, limited series)
1,2: 2-Stryker disbands Strykeforce. 3.00

CYBERFORCE UNIVERSE SOURCEBOOK
Image Comics (Top Cow Productions): Aug, 1994/Feb, 1995 ($2.50)
1,2-Silvestri-c 3.00

CYBERFROG
Hall of Heroes: June, 1994 - No. 2, Dec, 1994 ($2.50, B&W, limited series)
1-Ethan Van Sciver-c/a/scripts 9 18 27 62 126 190
2 5 10 15 35 63 90

CYBERFROG
Harris Comics: Feb, 1996 - No. 3, Apr, 1996 ($2.95)
0-3: Van Sciver-c/a/scripts. 2-Variant-c exists 2 4 6 8 11 14

CYBERFROG: (Title series), **Harris Comics**
--RESERVOIR FROG, 9/96 - No. 2, 10/96 ($2.95) 1,2: Van Sciver-c/a/scripts;
wraparound-c 2 4 6 9 12 15
--3RD ANNIVERSARY SPECIAL, 1/97 - #2, ($2.50, B&W) 1,2
2 4 6 8 10 12
--VS. CREED, 7/97 ($2.95, B&W)1 2 4 6 11 16 20

CYBERNARY (See Deathblow #1)
Image Comics (WildStorm Productions): Nov, 1995 - No.5, Mar, 1996 ($2.50)
1-5 3.00

CYBERNARY 2.0
DC Comics (WildStorm): Sept, 2001 - No. 6, Apr, 2002 ($2.95, limited series)
1-6: Joe Harris-s/Eric Canete-a. 6-The Authority app. 3.00

CYBERPUNK
Innovation Publishing: Sept, 1989 - No. 2, Oct, 1989 ($1.95, 28 pgs.) Book 2, #1, May, 1990 - No. 2, 1990 ($2.25, 28 pgs.)
1-Ken Steacy painted-cover (Adults) 2 4 6 9 12 15

The Curse of Brimstone #1 © DC

Cyborg (2016) #6 © DC

Daffy Duck #49 © WB

	GD	VG	FN	VF	VF/NM	NM-
	2.0	4.0	6.0	8.0	9.0	9.2

2, Book 2 #1,2: 2-Ken Steacy painted-covers (Adults) 6.00

CYBERPUNK: THE SERAPHIM FILES
Innovation Publishing: Nov, 1990 - No. 2, Dec, 1990 ($2.50, 28 pgs., mature)

1,2: 1-Painted-c; story cont'd from Seraphim 5.00

CYBERPUNK 2077: BLACKOUT (Based on the video game Cyberpunk 2077)
Dark Horse Comics: Jun, 2022 - No. 4, Sept, 2022 ($3.99, limited series)

1-3-Bartosz Sytybor-s/Roberto Ricci-a 4.00

CYBERPUNK 2077: TRAUMA TEAM (Based on the video game Cyberpunk 2077)
Dark Horse Comics: Sept, 2020 - No. 4, Dec, 2020 ($3.99, limited series)

1-4-Cullen Bunn-s/Miguel Valderrama-a 4.00

CYBERPUNK 2077: YOU HAVE MY WORD (Based on the video game Cyberpunk 2077)
Dark Horse Comics: Apr, 2021 - No. 4, Nov, 2022 ($3.99, limited series)

1-4-Bartosz Sztybor-s/Jesús Hervás-a 4.00

CYBERRAD
Continuity Comics: 1991 - No. 7, 1992 ($2.00)(Direct sale & newsstand-c variations) V2#1, 1993 ($2.50)

1-7: 5-Glow-in-the-dark-c by N. Adams (direct sale only). 6-Contains 4 pg. fold-out poster; N. Adams layouts 4.00
V2#1-($2.95, direct sale ed.)-Die-cut-c w/B&W hologram on-c; Neal Adams sketches 4.00
V2#1-($2.50, newsstand ed.)-Without sketches 3.00

CYBERRAD DEATHWATCH 2000 (Becomes CyberRad w/#2, 7/93)
Continuity Comics: Apr, 1993 - No. 2, 1993 ($2.50)

1,2: 1-Bagged w/2 cards; Adams-c & layouts & plots. 2-Bagged w/card; Adams scripts 4.00

CYBER 7
Eclipse Comics: Mar, 1989 - #7, Sept, 1989; V2#1, Oct, 1989 - #10, 1990 ($2.00, B&W)

1-7, Book 2 #1-10: Stories translated from Japanese 3.00

CYBLADE
Image Comics (Top Cow Productions): Oct, 2008 - No. 4, Mar, 2009 ($2.99)

1-4: 1,2-Mays-a/Fialkov-s. 1-Two covers. 3,4-Ferguson-a 3.00
.../ Ghost Rider 1 (Marvel/Top Cow, 1/97, $2.95) Devil's Reign pt. 2 4.00
...: Pilot Season 1 (9/07, $2.99) Rick Mays-a 3.00

CYBLADE/SHI (Also see Battle For The Independents & Shi/Cyblade: The Battle For The Independents)
Image Comics (Top Cow Productions): 1995 ($2.95, one-shot)

San Diego Preview 2 4 6 13 18 22
1-($2.95)-1st app. Witchblade 2 4 6 9 13 16
1-($2.95)-variant-c; Tucci-a 6.00

CYBORG (From Justice League)
DC Comics: Sept, 2015 - No. 12, Aug, 2016 ($2.99)

1-12: 1-Walker-s/Reis-a. 3-6-Metal Men app. 9,10-Shazam app. 3.00

CYBORG (DC Rebirth)
DC Comics: Nov, 2016 - No. 23, Aug, 2018 ($2.99/$3.99)

1-10: 1-Semper Jr.-s/Pelletier-a; Kilg%re app. 6-Intro. Variant 3.00
11-23: 11-Begin $3.99-c. 15-Metal Men app. 15-17-Beast Boy app. 4.00
...: Rebirth 1 (11/16, $2.99) Semper Jr.-s/Pelletier-a; origin retold 3.00

CYBRID
Maximum Press: July, 1995; No. 0, Jan, 1997 ($2.95/$3.50)

1-(7/95) 3.50
0-(1/97)-Liefeld-a/script; story cont'd in Avengelyne #4 3.50

CYCLONE COMICS (Also see Whirlwind Comics)
Bilbara Publishing Co.: June, 1940 - No. 5, Nov, 1940

1-Origin Tornado Tom; Volton (the human generator), Tornado Tom, Kingdom of the Moon, Mister Q begin (1st app. of each) 97 194 291 621 1061 1500
2 74 148 222 470 810 1150
3-Classic-c (scarce) 142 284 426 909 1555 2200
4-(9/40) 77 154 231 493 847 1200
5-(Scarce) 110 220 330 704 1202 1700
Ashcan - (5/40) Not distributed to newsstands, only for in house use. Cover produced on green stock paper. A CGC certified FN (6.0) copy sold for $2,000 in 2006.

CYCLOPS (X-Men)
Marvel Comics: Oct, 2001 - No. 4, Jan, 2002 ($2.50, limited series)

1-4-Texeira-c/a. 1,2-Black Tom and Juggernaut app. 4.00
1-(5/11, $2.99, one-shot) Haspiel-a; Batroc and the Circus of Crime app. 4.00

CYCLOPS (All-New X-Men)
Marvel Comics: Jul, 2014 - No. 12, Jun, 2015 ($3.99)

	GD	VG	FN	VF	VF/NM	NM-
	2.0	4.0	6.0	8.0	9.0	9.2

1-10: 1-Rucka-s/Dauterman-a; Corsair app. 6-12-Layman-s. 12-Black Vortex x-over 4.00

CYCLOPS: RETRIBUTION
Marvel Comics: 1994 ($5.95, trade paperback)

nn-r/Marvel Comics Presents #17-24 1 3 4 6 8 10

CY-GOR (See Spawn #38 for 1st app.)
Image Comics (Todd McFarlane Prod.): July, 1999 - No. 6, Dec, 1999 ($2.50)

1-6-Veitch-s 3.00

CYNTHIA DOYLE, NURSE IN LOVE (Formerly Sweetheart Diary)
Charlton Publications: No. 66, Oct, 1962 - No. 74, Feb, 1964

66-74 3 6 9 16 23 30

DAFFODIL
Marvel Comics (Soleil): 2010 - No. 3, 2010 ($5.99, limited series)

1-3-English version of French comic; Brrémaud-s/Rigano-a 6.00

DAFFY (Daffy Duck No. 18 on)(See Looney Tunes)
Dell Publishing Co./Gold Key No. 31-127/Whitman No. 128 on: #457, 3/53 - #30, 7-9/62; #31, 10-12/62 - #145, 6/84 (No #132,133)

Four Color 457(#1)-Elmer Fudd x-overs begin 12 24 36 83 182 280
Four Color 536,615('55) 8 16 24 52 99 145
4(1-3/56)-11('57) 5 10 15 33 57 80
12-19(1958-59) 4 8 12 28 47 65
20-40(1960-64) 3 6 9 20 31 42
41-60(1964-68) 3 6 9 16 23 30
61-90(1969-74)-Road Runner in most. 76-82-"Daffy Duck and the Road Runner" on-c 2 4 6 11 16 20
90-Whitman variant 3 6 9 14 19 24
91-110 2 4 6 8 11 14
111-127 1 3 4 6 8 10
128,134-141: 139(2/82), 140(2-3/82), 141(4/82) 2 4 6 8 10 12
129(8/80),130,131 (pre-pack?) (scarce). 129-Sherlock Holmes parody-s 4 8 12 28 47 65
142-145(#90029 on-c; nd, nd code, pre-pack): 142(6/83), 143(8/83), 144(3/84), 145(6/84) 3 6 9 17 26 35
Mini-Comic 1 (1976; 3-1/4x6-1/2") 1 3 4 6 8 10
NOTE: *Reprint issues-No.41-46, 48, 50, 53-55, 58, 59, 65, 67, 69, 73, 81, 96, 103-108; 136-142, 144, 145(1/3-2/3-r). (See March of Comics No. 277, 288, 303, 313, 331, 347, 357,375, 387, 397, 402, 413, 425, 437, 460).*

DAFFY DUCK (Digest-size reprints from Looney Tunes)
DC Comics: 2005 ($6.99, digest)

Vol. 1: You're Despicable! - Reprints from Looney Tunes #38,43,45,47,51,53,54,58,61,62,66,70 7.00

DAFFY TUNES COMICS
Four-Star Publications: June, 1947; No. 12, Aug, 1947

nn 13 26 39 74 105 135
12-Al Fago-c/a; funny animal 11 22 33 62 86 110

DAGAR, DESERT HAWK (Captain Kidd No. 24 on; formerly All Great)
Fox Feature Syndicate: No. 14, Feb, 1948 - No. 23, Apr, 1949 (No #17,18)

14-Tangi & Safari Cary begin; Good bondage-c/a 135 270 405 864 1482 2100
15,16-E. Good-a; 15-Headlight-c 68 136 204 435 743 1050
19,20,22: 19-Used in **SOTI**, pg. 180 (Tangi) 65 130 195 416 708 1000
21,23: 21-Bondage-c; "Bombs & Bums Away" panel in "Flood of Death" story used in **SOTI.** 23-Bondage-c 77 154 231 493 847 1200
NOTE: *Tangi by **Kamen**-14-16, 19, 20; c-20, 21.*

DAGAR THE INVINCIBLE (Tales of Sword & Sorcery...) (Also see Dan Curtis Giveaways & Gold Key Spotlight)
Gold Key: Oct, 1972 - No. 18, Dec, 1976; No. 19, Apr, 1982

1-Origin; intro. Villains Olstellon & Scor 4 8 12 23 37 50
2-5: 3-Intro. Graylin, Dagar's woman; Jarn x-over 3 6 9 14 19 24
6-1st Dark Gods story 2 4 6 9 13 16
7-10: 9-Intro. Torgus. 10-1st Three Witches story 2 4 6 9 13 16
11-18: 13-Durak & Torgus x-over; story continues in Dr. Spektor #15. 14-Dagar's origin retold. 18-Origin retold 2 4 6 8 10 12
19(4/82)-Origin-r/#18 6.00
NOTE: *Durak app. in 7, 12, 13. Tragg app. in 5, 11.*

DAGWOOD (Chic Young's) (Also see Blondie Comics)
Harvey Publications: Sept, 1950 - No. 140, Nov, 1965

1 20 40 60 138 307 475
2 10 20 30 64 132 200
3-10 7 14 21 44 82 120
11-20 5 10 15 35 63 90
21-30 5 10 15 31 53 75
31-50: 33-Sci-Fi-c 4 8 12 28 47 65

	GD 2.0	VG 4.0	FN 6.0	VF 8.0	VF/NM 9.0	NM- 9.2
51-70	3	6	9	21	33	45
71-100	3	6	9	17	26	35
101-121,123-128,130,135	3	6	9	16	23	30
122,129,131-134,136-140-All are 68-pg. issues	3	6	9	21	33	45

NOTE: *Popeye and other one page strips appeared in early issues.*

DAI KAMIKAZE!
Now Comics: June, 1987 - No. 12, Aug, 1988 ($1.75)

	GD	VG	FN	VF	VF/NM	NM-
1-1st app. Speed Racer	2	4	6	8	10	12
1-Second printing						4.00
2-12						3.00

DAILY BUGLE (See Spider-Man)
Marvel Comics: Dec, 1996 - No. 3, Feb, 1997 ($2.50, B&W, limited series)

1-3-Paul Grist-s 4.00

DAISY
Dark Horse Comics: Dec, 2021 - No. 5, Apr, 2022 ($3.99, limited series)

1-5-Colin Lorimer-s/a 4.00

DAISY AND DONALD (See Walt Disney Showcase No. 8)
Gold Key/Whitman No. 42 on: May, 1973 - No. 59, July, 1984 (no No. 48)

	GD	VG	FN	VF	VF/NM	NM-
1-Barks-r/WDC&S #280,308	4	8	12	27	44	60
2-5: 4-Barks-r/WDC&S #224	2	4	6	11	16	20
6-10	2	4	6	9	12	15
11-20	1	3	4	6	8	10
21-41: 32-r/WDC&S #308	1	2	3	5	6	8
36,42-44 (Whitman)	2	4	6	8	11	14
45 (8/80),46-(pre-pack?)(scarce)	4	8	12	27	44	60
47-(12/80)-Only distr. in Whitman 3-pack (scarce)	5	10	15	35	63	90
48(3/81)-50(8/81): 50-r/#3	2	4	6	10	14	18
51-54: 51-Barks-r/4-Color #1150. 52-r/#2. 53(2/82), 54(4/82)	2	4	6	9	13	16
55-59-(all #90284 on-c, nd, nd code, pre-pack): 55(5/83), 56(7/83), 57(8/83), 58(8/83), 59(7/84)	3	6	9	19	30	40

DAISY & HER PUPS (Dagwood & Blondie's Dogs)(Formerly Blondie Comics #20)
Harvey Publications: No. 21, 7/51 - No. 27, 7/52; No. 8, 9/52 - No. 18, 5/54

	GD	VG	FN	VF	VF/NM	NM-
21 (#1)-Blondie's dog Daisy and her 5 pups led by Elmer begin. Rags Rabbit app.	5	10	15	35	63	90
22-27 (#2-7): 26 has No. 6 on cover but No. 26 on inside. 23,25-The Little King app. 24-Bringing Up Father by McManus app. 25-27-Rags Rabbit app.	4	8	12	27	44	60
8-18: 8,9-Rags Rabbit app. 8,17-The Little King app. 11-The Flop Family Swan begins. 22-Cookie app. 11-Felix The Cat app. by 17,18-Popeye app.	4	8	12	25	40	55

DAISY DUCK & UNCLE SCROOGE PICNIC TIME (See Dell Giant #33)

DAISY DUCK & UNCLE SCROOGE SHOW BOAT (See Dell Giant #55)

DAISY DUCK'S DIARY (See Dynabrite Comics, & Walt Disney's C&S #298)
Dell Publishing Co.: No. 600, Nov, 1954 - No. 1247, Dec-Fef, 1961-62 (Disney)

	GD	VG	FN	VF	VF/NM	NM-
Four Color 600 (#1)	8	16	24	55	105	155
Four Color 659, 743 (11/56)	6	12	18	40	73	105
Four Color 858 (11/57), 948 (11/58), 1247 (12-2/61-62)	5	10	15	35	63	90
Four Color 1055 (11-1/59-60), 1150 (12-1/60-61)-By Carl Barks)	8	16	24	56	108	160

DAISY HANDBOOK
Daisy Manufacturing Co.: 1946; No. 2, 1948 (10¢, pocket-size, 132 pgs.)

	GD	VG	FN	VF	VF/NM	NM-
1-Buck Rogers, Red Ryder; Wolverton-a (2 pgs.)	27	54	81	158	259	360
2-Captain Marvel & Ibis the Invincible, Red Ryder, Boy Commandos & Robotman; Wolverton-a (2 pgs.); contains 8 pg. color catalog	27	54	81	158	259	360

DAISY MAE (See Oxydol-Dreft)

DAISY'S RED RYDER GUN BOOK
Daisy Manufacturing Co.: 1955 (25¢, pocket-size, 132 pgs.)

	GD	VG	FN	VF	VF/NM	NM-
nn-Boy Commandos, Red Ryder; 1pg. Wolverton-a	17	34	51	100	158	215

DAKEN: DARK WOLVERINE
Marvel Comics: Nov, 2010 - No. 23, May, 2012 ($3.99/$2.99)

1-Camuncoli-a/c; Way & Liu-s; back-up history of the character 5.00
2-9, 9.1, 10-23-($2.99) 3,4-Fantastic Four app. 7-9-Crossover with X-23 #8,9; Gambit app. 9.1-Avengers app. 13-16-Moon Knight app. 17-19-Runaways app. 3.00

DAKKON BLACKBLADE ON THE WORLD OF MAGIC: THE GATHERING
Acclaim Comics (Armada): June, 1996 ($5.95, one-shot)

1-Jerry Prosser scripts; Rags Morales-c/a. 6.00

DAKOTA LIL (See Fawcett Movie Comics)

DAKTARI (Ivan Tors) (TV)
Dell Publishing Co.: July, 1967 - No. 3, Oct, 1968; No. 4, Oct, 1969

	GD	VG	FN	VF	VF/NM	NM-
1-Marshall Thompson photo-c on all	4	8	12	25	40	55
2-4	3	6	9	18	28	38

DALE EVANS COMICS (Also see Queen of the West...)(See Boy Commandos #32)
National Periodical Publications: Sept-Oct, 1948 - No. 24, Jul-Aug, 1952 (No. 1-19: 52 pgs.)

	GD	VG	FN	VF	VF/NM	NM-
1-Dale Evans & her horse Buttermilk begin; Sierra Smith begins by Alex Toth	61	122	183	390	670	950
2-Alex Toth-a	31	62	93	186	303	420
3-11-Alex Toth-a	20	40	60	114	182	250
12-20: 12-Target-c	14	28	42	80	115	150
21-24	14	28	42	82	121	160

NOTE: *Photo-c-1, 2, 4-14.*

DALGODA
Fantagraphics Books: Aug, 1984 - No. 8, Feb, 1986 (High quality paper)

1,8: 1- Fujitake-c/a in all. 8-Alan Moore story 5.00
2-7: 2,3-Debut Grimwood's Daughter. 3.00

DALTON BOYS, THE
Avon Periodicals: 1951

	GD	VG	FN	VF	VF/NM	NM-
1-(Number on spine)-Kinstler-c	24	48	72	142	234	325

DAMAGE
DC Comics: Apr, 1994 - No. 20, Jan, 1996 ($1.75/$1.95/$2.25)

1-20: 6-(9/94)-Zero Hour. 0-(10/94). 7-(11/94). 14-Ray app. 3.00

DAMAGE
DC Comics: Mar, 2018 - No. 16, Jun, 2019 ($2.99/$3.99)

1-12: 1-Venditti-s/Daniel-a; intro. Ethan Avery. 2-Suicide Squad app. 2,3-Wonder Woman app. 4,5-Poison Ivy app. 4-Nord-a. 8,9-Unknown Soldier app. 10-12-Justice League app. 3.00
13-16-($3.99) 13-Batman app. 14-16-Congo Bill app. 4.00
Annual 1 (10/18, $4.99) Takes place between #8&9; Lopresti-a 5.00

DAMAGE CONTROL (See Marvel Comics Presents #19)
Marvel Comics: 5/89 - No. 4, 8/89; V2#1, 12/89 - No. 4, 2/90 ($1.00)
V3#1, 6/91 - No. 4, 9/91 ($1.25, all are limited series)

V1#1-4,V2#1-4,V3#1-4: V1#4-Wolverine app. V2#2,4-Punisher app. 1-Spider-Man app. 2-New Warriors app. 3,4-Silver Surfer app. 4-Infinity Gauntlet parody 3.00

DAMAGE CONTROL
Marvel Comics: Oct, 2022 - No. 5, Feb, 2023 ($4.99/$3.99)

1-($4.99) Adam Goldberg & Hans Rodionoff-s/Will Robson-a 5.00
2-5-($3.99) 4-Wrecking Crew app. 5-Sentinels app. 4.00

DAMAGED
Radical Comics: Jul, 2011 - No. 6 ($3.99/$3.50, limited series)

1-($3.99) Lapham-s/Manco-a; covers by Maleev & Manco 4.00
2-4-($3.50) Maleev-c 3.50

DAMIAN: SON OF BATMAN
DC Comics: Dec, 2013 - No. 4, Mar, 2014 ($3.99, limited series)

1-4-Andy Kubert-s/c/a; near-future Damian; Ra's al Ghul & Talia app. 4.00
1-Variant-c by Tony Daniel 8.00

DAMNATION: JOHNNY BLAZE - GHOST RIDER
Marvel Comics: May, 2018 ($3.99, one-shot)

1-Part of x-over with Doctor Strange: Damnation; Sebela-s/Noto-a/Crain-c 4.00

DAMNED
Image Comics (Homage Comics): June, 1997 - No. 4, Sept, 1997 ($2.50, limited series)

1-4-Steven Grant-s/Mike Zeck-c/a in all 3.00

DAMN NATION
Dark Horse Comics: Feb, 2005 - No. 3, Apr, 2005 ($2.99, limited series)

1-3-J. Alexander-a/Andrew Cosby-s 3.00

DAMN THEM ALL
BOOM! Studios: Oct, 2022 - Present ($3.99)

1-5-Spurrier-s/Adlard-a 4.00

DAMSELS
Dynamite Entertainment: 2012 - No. 13, 2014 ($3.99)

1-13: 1-Leah Moore & John Reppion-s/Aneke-a. 1-Campbell-c. 2-8-Linsner-c 4.00
... Giant Killer One Shot (2013, $4.99) Leah Moore & John Reppion-s/Dietrich Smith-a 5.00

DAMSELS IN EXCESS
Aspen MLT: Jul, 2014 - No. 5, May, 2015 ($3.99, limited series)

1-5-Vince Hernandez-s/Mirka Andolfo-a; multiple covers on each 4.00

DAMSELS: MERMAIDS
Dynamite Entertainment: No. 0, 2013 - No. 5, 2013 ($3.99)

0-Free Comic Book Day giveaway; Sturges-s/Deshong-a/Hans-c 3.00
1-5-($3.99) Sturges-s/Deshong-a. 1-Two covers by Anacleto & Renaud. 2-5-Renaud-c 4.00

DANCES WITH DEMONS (See Marvel Frontier Comics Unlimited)
Marvel Frontier Comics: Sept, 1993 - No. 4, Dec, 1993 ($1.95, limited series)

1-($2.95)-Foil embossed-c; Charlie Adlard & Rod Ramos-a 4.00
2-4 3.00

DAN DARE
Virgin Comics: Nov, 2007 - No. 7, July, 2008 ($2.99/$5.99)

1-6-Ennis-s/Erskine-a. 1-Two covers by Talbot and Horn. 2-6-Two covers on each 3.00
7-($5.99) Double sized finale with wraparound Erskine-c; Gibbons variant-c 6.00

DAN DARE
Titan Comics: Nov, 2017 - No. 4, Jan, 2018 ($3.99)

1-4-Milligan-s/Foche-a; multiple covers on each 4.00

DANDEE: Four Star Publications: 1947 (Advertised, not published)

DAN DUNN (See Crackajack Funnies, Detective Dan, Famous Feature Stories & Red Ryder)

DANDY COMICS (Also see Happy Jack Howard)
E. C. Comics: Spring, 1947 - No. 7, Spring, 1948

	GD	VG	FN	VF	VF/NM	NM-
1-Funny animal; Vince Fago-a in all; Dandy in all	55	110	165	252	601	850
2	37	74	111	222	361	500
3-7: 3-Intro Handy Andy who is c-feature #3 on	32	64	96	188	307	425

DANGER
Comic Media/Allen Hardy Assoc.: Jan, 1953 - No. 11, Aug, 1954

	GD	VG	FN	VF	VF/NM	NM-
1-Heck-c/a	39	78	117	231	378	525
2,3,5,7,9-11:	21	42	63	122	199	275
4-Marijuana cover/story	24	48	72	142	234	325
6- "Narcotics" story; begin spy theme	22	44	66	130	213	295
8-Bondage/torture/headlights panels	30	60	90	177	289	400

NOTE: *Morisi a-2, 5, 6(3), 10; c-2. Contains some reprints from Danger & Dynamite.*

DANGER (Formerly Comic Media title)
Charlton Comics Group: No. 12, June, 1955 - No. 14, Oct, 1955

	GD	VG	FN	VF	VF/NM	NM-
12(#1)	16	32	48	94	147	200
13,14: 14-r/#12	14	28	42	76	108	140

DANGER
Super Comics: 1964

Daisy #3 © Colin Lorimer

Damian: Son of Batman #1 © DC

Danger Street #1 © DC

	GD 2.0	VG 4.0	FN 6.0	VF 8.0	VF/NM 9.0	NM- 9.2
Super Reprint #10-12 (Black Dwarf; #10-r/Great Comics #1 by Novack. #11-r/Johnny Danger #1. #12-r/Red Seal #14), #15-r/Spy Cases #26. #16-Unpublished Chesler material (Yankee Girl), #17-r/Scoop #8 (Capt. Courage & Enchanted Dagger), #18(nd)-r/Guns Against Gangsters #5 (Gun-Master, Annie Oakley, The Chameleon; L.B. Cole-r)	2	4	6	13	18	22

DANGER AND ADVENTURE (Formerly This Magazine Is Haunted; Robin Hood and His Merry Men No. 28 on)
Charlton Comics: No. 22, Feb, 1955 - No. 27, Feb, 1956

	GD	VG	FN	VF	VF/NM	NM-
22-Ibis the Invincible-c/story (last G.A. app.); Nyoka app.; last pre-code issue	14	28	42	80	115	150
23-Lance O'Casey-c/sty; Nyoka app.; Ditko-a thru #27	15	30	45	84	127	170
24-27: 24-Mike Danger & Johnny Adventure begin	11	22	33	62	85	110

DANGER GIRL (Also see Cliffhanger #0)
Image Comics (Cliffhanger Productions): Mar, 1998 - No. 4, Dec, 1998;
DC Comics (Cliffhanger Prod.): No. 5, July, 1999 - No. 7, Feb, 2001

	GD	VG	FN	VF	VF/NM	NM-
Preview-Bagged in DV8 #14 Voyager Pack	2	4	6	11	16	20
Preview Gold Edition	4	8	12	22	35	50
1-($2.95) Hartnell & Campbell-s/Campbell/Garner-a	2	4	6	9	12	15
1-($4.95) Chromium cover	5	10	15	30	50	70
1-American Entertainment Ed.	1	3	4	6	8	10
1-American Entertainment Gold Ed., 1-Tourbook Ed.	2	4	6	11	16	20
1-"Danger-sized" ed.; over-sized format	3	6	9	16	24	32
2-($2.50)	1	2	3	5	6	8
2-Smoking Gun variant cover	6	12	18	41	76	110
2-Platinum Ed.	9	18	27	57	111	165
2-Dynamic Forces Omnichrome variant-c	3	6	9	16	23	30
2-Gold foil cover	3	6	9	14	20	25
2-Ruby red foil cover	14	28	42	96	211	325
3,4: 3-c by Campbell, Charest and Adam Hughes. 4-Big knife variant-c						4.00
3,5: 3-Gold foil cover. 5-DF Bikini variant-c						6.00
4-6						4.00
7-($5.95) Wraparound gatefold-c; Last issue						6.00
...: Dangerous Visions 3-D (IDW, 2/19, $6.99) r/#1 & Preview; bagged with glasses						7.00
...: Danger-Sized Treasury Edition #1 (IDW, 1/12, $9.99, 13" x 8-1/2") r/#1,2 & Preview						10.00
...: Hawaiian Punch (5/03, $4.95) Campbell-c; Phil Noto-a						5.00
...: Odd Jobs TPB (2004, $14.95) r/one-shots Hawaiian Punch, Viva Las Danger & Special; Campbell-c						15.00
San Diego Preview (8/98, B&W) flip book w/Wildcats preview						5.00
Sketchbook (2001, $6.95) Campbell-a; sketches for comics, toys, games						7.00
...Special (2/00, $3.50) art by Campbell, Chiodo, and Art Adams						3.50
... 3-D #1 (4/03, $4.95, bagged with 3-D glasses) r/ Preview & #1 in 3-D						5.00
...: Viva Las Danger (1/04, $4.95) Noto-a/Campbell-c						5.00
... :The Dangerous Collection nn (8/98; r-#1)						6.00
... :The Dangerous Collection 2,3: 2-(11/98, $5.95) r/#2,3. 3-('99) r/#4,5						6.00
... :The Dangerous Collection nn, 2-($10.00) Gold foil logo						10.00
... :The Ultimate Collection HC ($29.95) r/#1-7; intro by Bruce Campbell						30.00
... :The Ultimate Collection SC ($19.95) r/#1-7; intro by Bruce Campbell						20.00

DANGER GIRL AND THE ARMY OF DARKNESS
Dynamite Entertainment/ IDW Publ.: 2011 - No. 6, 2012 ($3.99, limited series)

	GD	VG	FN	VF	VF/NM	NM-
1-6-Hartnell-s/Bolson-a. 1,2 Covers by Campbell, Bradshaw & Renaud						4.00

DANGER GIRL: BACK IN BLACK
DC Comics (Cliffhanger): Jan, 2006 - No. 4, Apr, 2006 ($2.99, limited series)

	GD	VG	FN	VF	VF/NM	NM-
1-Hartnell-s/Bradshaw-a; Campbell-c	1	3	4	6	8	10
2-4-Hartnell-s/Bradshaw-a						3.00
TPB (2007, $12.99) r/series & covers						13.00

DANGER GIRL: BODY SHOTS
DC Comics (WildStorm): Jun, 2007 - No. 4, Sept, 2007 ($2.99, limited series)

	GD	VG	FN	VF	VF/NM	NM-
1-4-Hartnell-s/Bradshaw-a						5.00
TPB (2007, $12.99) r/series & covers						13.00

DANGER GIRL/ G.I. JOE
IDW Publishing: Jul, 2012 - No. 5, Nov, 2012 ($3.99, limited series)

	GD	VG	FN	VF	VF/NM	NM-
1-Hartnell-s/Royle-a; 2 covers by Campbell on each	1	3	4	6	8	10
2-5-Hartnell-s/Royle-a						6.00

DANGER GIRL KAMIKAZE
DC Comics (Cliffhanger): Nov, 2001 - No. 2, Dec., 2001 ($2.95, lim. series)

	GD	VG	FN	VF	VF/NM	NM-
1,2-Tommy Yune-s/a						3.00

DANGER GIRL: MAYDAY
IDW Publishing: Apr, 2014 - No. 4, Aug, 2014 ($3.99, limited series)

	GD	VG	FN	VF	VF/NM	NM-
1-4-Hartnell-s/Royle-a; 2 covers by Royle on each						4.00

DANGER GIRL: RENEGADE
IDW Publishing: Sept, 2015 - No. 4, Jan, 2016 ($3.99, limited series)

	GD	VG	FN	VF	VF/NM	NM-
1-4-Hartnell-s/Molnar-a/Campbell-c						4.00

DANGER GIRL: REVOLVER
IDW Publishing: Jan, 2012 - No. 4, Apr, 2012 ($3.99, limited series)

	GD	VG	FN	VF	VF/NM	NM-
1-4-Hartnell-s/Madden-a; covers by Campbell & Madden						5.00

DANGER GIRL: THE CHASE
IDW Publishing: Sept, 2013 - No. 4, Dec, 2013 ($3.99, limited series)

	GD	VG	FN	VF	VF/NM	NM-
1-4-Hartnell-s/Tolibao-a. 1-Three covers (Panosian, Wallace & photo)						5.00

DANGER GIRL: TRINITY
IDW Publishing: Apr, 2013 - No. 4, Jul, 2013 ($3.99, limited series)

	GD	VG	FN	VF	VF/NM	NM-
1-Hartnell-s/Campbell-c; art by Royle, Tolibao, & Molnar; variant-c by Garner	2	4	6	10	14	18
2-4	1	3	4	6	8	10

DANGER IS OUR BUSINESS!
Toby Press: 1953(Dec.) - No. 10, June, 1955

	GD	VG	FN	VF	VF/NM	NM-
1-Captain Comet by Williamson/Frazetta-a, 6 pgs. (science fiction)	68	136	204	435	743	1050
2	19	38	57	111	176	240
3-10	15	30	45	88	137	185
I.W. Reprint #9('64)-Williamson/Frazetta-r/#1; Kinstler-c	8	16	24	54	102	150

DANGER IS THEIR BUSINESS (Also see A-1 Comic)
Magazine Enterprises: No. 50, 1952

	GD	VG	FN	VF	VF/NM	NM-
A-1 50-Powell-a	19	38	57	111	176	240

DANGER MAN (TV)
Dell Publishing Co.: No. 1231, Sept-Nov, 1961

	GD	VG	FN	VF	VF/NM	NM-
Four Color 1231-Patrick McGoohan photo-c	11	22	33	77	166	255

DANGER STREET (Characters from 1st Issue Special series '74-'75)
DC Comics (Black Label): Feb, 2023 - No. 12 ($4.99, limited series)

	GD	VG	FN	VF	VF/NM	NM-
1-4-King-s/Fornés-a; Lady Cop, Creeper, Starman, Warlord, Metamorpho, Atlas app.						5.00

DANGER TRAIL (Also see Showcase #50, 51)
National Periodical Publ.: July-Aug, 1950 - No. 5, Mar-Apr, 1951 (52 pgs.)

	GD	VG	FN	VF	VF/NM	NM-
1-King Faraday begins, ends #4; Toth-a in all	161	322	483	1030	1765	2500
2	113	226	339	718	1234	1750
3-(Rare) one of the rarest early '50s DCs	174	348	522	1114	1907	2700
4,5: 5-Johnny Peril-c/story (moves to Sensation Comics #107); new logo (also see Comic Cavalcade #15-29)	81	162	243	518	884	1250

DANGER TRAIL
DC Comics: Apr, 1993 - No. 4, July, 1993 ($1.50, limited series)

	GD	VG	FN	VF	VF/NM	NM-
1-4: Gulacy-c on all						3.00

DANGER UNLIMITED (See San Diego Comic Con Comics #2 & Torch of Liberty Special)
Dark Horse (Legend): Feb, 1994 - No. 4, May, 1994 ($2.00, limited series)

	GD	VG	FN	VF	VF/NM	NM-
1-4: Byrne-c/a/scripts in all; origin stories of both original team (Doc Danger, Thermal, Miss Mirage, & Hunk) & future team (Thermal, Belebet, & Caucus). 1-Intro Torch of Liberty & Golgotha (cameo) in back-up story. 4-Hellboy & Torch of Liberty cameo in lead story						3.00
TPB (1995, $14.95)-r/#1-4; includes last pg. originally cut from #4						15.00

DAN HASTINGS (See Syndicate Features)

DANIEL BOONE (See The Exploits of..., Fighting... Frontier Scout...,The Legends of... & March of Comics No. 306)
Dell Publishing Co.: No. 1163, Mar-May, 1961

	GD	VG	FN	VF	VF/NM	NM-
Four Color 1163-Marsh-a	5	10	15	35	63	90

DANIEL BOONE (TV) (See March of Comics No. 306)
Gold Key: Jan, 1965 - No. 15, Apr, 1969 (All have Fess Parker photo-c)

	GD	VG	FN	VF	VF/NM	NM-
1-Back-c and last eight pages fold in half to form "Official Handbook Fess Parker as Daniel Boone Trail Blazers Club"	8	16	24	54	102	150
2-Back-c pin-up	5	10	15	30	50	70
3-5-Back-c pin-ups	4	8	12	25	40	55
6-15: 7,8-Back-c pin-up	3	6	9	19	30	40

DAN'L BOONE
Sussex Publ. Co.: Sept, 1955 - No. 8, Sept, 1957

	GD	VG	FN	VF	VF/NM	NM-
1	15	30	45	86	133	180
2	10	20	30	54	72	90
3-8	8	16	24	40	50	60

GD VG FN VF VF/NM NM-
2.0 4.0 6.0 8.0 9.0 9.2

DANNY BLAZE (...Firefighter) (Nature Boy No. 3 on)
Charlton Comics: Aug, 1955 - No. 2, Oct, 1955

1-Authentic stories of fire fighting 15 30 45 90 140 190
2 12 24 36 67 94 120

DANNY DINGLE (See Sparkler Comics)
United Features Syndicate: No. 17, 1940

Single Series 17 32 64 96 188 307 425

DANNY THOMAS SHOW, THE (TV)
Dell Publishing Co.: No. 1180, Apr-June, 1961 - No. 1249, Dec-Feb, 1961-62

Four Color 1180-Toth-a, photo-c 16 32 48 107 236 365
Four Color 1249-Manning-a, photo-c 12 24 36 80 173 265

DANTE'S INFERNO (Based on the video game)
DC Comics (WildStorm): Feb, 2010 - No. 6, Jul, 2010 ($3.99, limited series)

1-6-Christos Gage-s/Diego Latorre-a 4.00
TPB (2010, $19.99) r/#1-6 20.00

DAOMU (Based on a novel series from China)
Image Comics: Feb, 2011 - No. 8, Dec, 2011 ($2.99)

1-8-Kennedy Xu-s/Ken Chou-a 3.00

DAPHNE BYRNE
DC Comics (Hill House Comics): Mar, 2020 - No. 6, Sept, 2020 ($3.99)

1-6-Laura Marks-s/Kelley Jones-a; back-up Sea Dogs serial 4.00

DARBY O'GILL & THE LITTLE PEOPLE (Movie)(See Movie Comics)
Dell Publishing Co.: 1959 (Disney)

Four Color 1024-Toth-a; photo-c. 9 18 27 59 117 175

DAREDEVIL ("Daredevil Comics" on cover of #2) (See Silver Streak Comics)
Lev Gleason Publications (Funnies, Inc. No. 1): July, 1941 - No. 134, Sept, 1956
(52 pgs. #52-80; 64 pgs. #35-41)(Charles Biro stories)

1-No. 1 titled "Daredevil Battles Hitler," Classic battle issue as Daredevil teams up in each strip - The Silver Streak, Lance Hale, Cloud Curtis, Dickey Dean & Pirate Prince to battle Hitler; The Claw unites with Hitler and Japanese and battles Daredevil; Origin of Hitler feature story "The Man of Hate." Classic Hitler photo app. on-c
1600 3200 4800 11,900 20,950 30,000
2-London (by Jerry Robinson), Pat Patriot (by Reed Crandall), Nightro, Real American No. 1 (by Briefer #2-11), Dash Dillon, Whirlwind begin; Dickie Dean, Pirate Prince end; intro. & only app. Pioneer, Champion of America & Times Square. The Claw continues #2-4 411 822 1233 2877 5039 7200
3-Intro./origin of 13. Newspaper editor has name "Roussos." Daredevil battles the Claw ill. text story 277 554 831 1759 3030 4300
4-The Claw captured and taken to New York Central Park Zoo. Whirlwind, the Blond Bomber begins, ends #6 242 484 726 1537 2644 3750
5-Ghost vs. Claw begins by Bob Wood, ends #20; 13 & Jinx begin; origin 13 retold in text; intro./origin Jinx, 13's sidekick; intro. Sniffer in Daredevil
219 438 657 1402 2401 3400
6-(12/41)-Classic horror-c; Daredevil battles wolf with human brain; Dash Dillon ends
206 412 618 1318 2259 3200
7,9: 7-(2/42), shows #6 on cover; delayed one month due to Pearl Harbor attack. 9-Daredevil vs. Daredevil-c; Sniffer strip begins, ends #69
135 270 405 864 1482 2100
8-Nazi WWII war-c. Nightro ends. Sniffer/Daredevil fight Nazi insurgents;
161 322 483 1030 1765 2500
10-(5-42), "Remember Pearl Harbor" Japanese WWII-c; classic splash page w/American flag. Daredevil joins Air Corps. to fight Japanese. Ghost Battles Claw & Japanese. Last Whirlwind 300 600 900 2010 3505 5000
11-Classic Quasimodo (hunchback of Notre Dame) bondage/torture-c/sty. London, Pat Patriot, Real America #1 end 876 1752 2628 5606 8803 12,000
12-Origin of The Claw; Scoop Scuttle by Wolverton begins (2-4 pgs.), ends #22, not in #21. Charles Biro biography. Dickey Dean, Pirate Prince return (both end #32)
155 310 465 992 1696 2400
13-Intro of Little Wise Guys (10/42)(also see Boy #4); Daredevil fights Nazi hooded cult; Ghost battles Claw, Hitler & Nazis in Britain; Bob Wood biography
116 232 348 742 1271 1800
14-Classic Daredevil facial portrait-c; Hitler app.; "Slap the Jap" game included
106 212 318 673 1162 1650
15-Death of Meatball 119 238 357 762 1306 1850
16-WWII-c w/freighter hit by German torpedo. Meatball is buried & Curly joins Little Wise Guys team 93 186 279 591 1021 1450
17-Little Wise Guys hanging and beating Japanese soldiers on cover
239 478 717 1530 2615 3700
18-New origin of Daredevil (not same as Silver Streak #6). Hitler, Mussolini Tojo and Mickey Mouse app. on-c at carnival 155 310 465 992 1696 2400
19,20: Last Ghost vs. Claw 71 142 213 454 777 1100
21-Reprints cover of Silver Streak #6 (on inside) plus intro. of The Claw from Silver Streak #1. The Claw strip begins by Bob Q. Siege, ends #31 100 200 300 635 1093 1550
22,23: 22-Daredevil fights the Tramp. 23-Dickie Dean by Bob Montana
48 96 144 302 514 725
24-Bloody puppet show-c; classic Claw splash pg. 58 116 174 371 636 900
25-1st Little Wise Guys-c without Daredevil 39 78 117 231 378 525
26,28-30 42 84 126 265 445 625
27-Bondage/torture-c 116 232 348 742 1271 1800
31-Death of The Claw 93 186 279 591 1021 1450
32-34: 32,33-Egbert app. 33-Roger Wilco begins, ends #35
36 72 108 211 343 475
35-37,39-41: 35-Two Daredevil stories begin, end #68; Chauncey app. 37-39-Go Along Gallagher app. (#35-41 are 64 pgs.); 41-Dickie Dean ends
37 74 111 222 361 500
38-Origin Daredevil retold from #18 50 100 150 315 533 750
42-Intro. Kilroy in Daredevil who unveils Daredevil's I.D.-c/sty
32 64 96 188 307 425
43-45,47,48-All Daredevil-c. 43-Daredevil in costume on-c & 1 panel only inside; 44-DD back in costume; i.d. revealed on-c. 30 60 90 177 289 400
46,50: DD not on-c 25 50 75 150 245 340
49-Wise Guys fight secret hooded group c/sty. DD not on-c
30 60 90 177 289 400
51,52,56-60,63-66,68,69-Last Daredevil & Sniffer (12/50). 56-Wise Guys start their own circus. DD not on-c 20 40 60 118 192 265
53-Daredevil/Wise Guys find lost palace of Zanzarah, an underground Egyptian tomb w/mummy & treasure; classic c/story. DD-c 22 44 66 132 216 300
54,55-Daredevil-c 22 44 66 128 209 290
61-Daredevil & Wise Guys in haunted house classic c/story. Daredevil/Wise Guys fly rocket into stratosphere. DD not on-c 22 44 66 132 216 300
62-Wise Guys in medieval times, a dream by Peewee locked in a medieval museum; classic c/story. DD not on-c 22 44 66 132 216 300
67-Last Daredevil-c 22 44 66 128 209 290
70-Little Wise Guys take over book without Daredevil. Daredevil removed from-c & logo; Air Devils w/Hot Rock Flanagan begins, ends #80 14 28 42 82 121 160
71-78,81: 81-Dilly Duncan begins, ends #134 11 22 33 64 90 115
79,80: 79-(10/51)-Daredevil returns; Wise Guys go to Africa. 80-Daredevil & Wise Guys blast into space & land on Mars; last Daredevil app. in title
13 26 39 74 105 135
82,90: One pg. Frazetta ad in both 11 22 33 64 90 115
83-89,91-99,101-134 10 20 30 58 79 100
100-(7/53) 13 26 39 74 105 135

NOTE: *Biro a-1-22, 38; c-1-134; script-1-134.* ***Dan Barry*** *a(Daredevil) 40-48;* ***Roy Belft****-a (Daredevil) 49-55.* ***Bolle*** *a-125.* ***Al Borth****-a(Daredevil) #57-59.* ***Briefer*** *a-1-11 (Real American #1); Pirate Prince-#1, 2, 12-31.* ***Tony Dipreta****-a(Wise Guys) #108-110, 112-134.* ***R.W. Hall*** *a-22.* ***Carl Hubbell*** *a-9-21, 23-26, 27(Daredevil), 28-32.* ***Al Mandel*** *a-13.* ***Hy Mankin****-a(Wise Guys)-#80, 81.* ***Maurer****-a(Daredevil)-23, 31, 37, 38, 41, 43-51, 53-67, 69; (Little Wise Guys)-70-89.* ***McWilliams*** *a-70, 73-80.* ***Bob Montana*** *a-12, 23, 27, 28, 31-33.* ***Wm. Overgard****-a(Daredevil) #67, (Wise Guys) 74-79, 83-85, 87.* ***Jerry Robinson*** *a(London) #2-8.* ***Roussos*** *a(Nightro)-2-8.* ***Bob Q. Siege****-a(Claw) 27-31; (Daredevil)-#35.* ***Wolverton*** *a-12-22.* ***Bob Wood****-a(The Claw)-1-20; (The Ghost)-5-20.* ***Dick Wood*** *sty-2-10, 13-22, 27-32.* ***Daredevil*** *not on-c #46,49-52,56-66,68-134.*

DAREDEVIL (...& the Black Widow #92-107 on-c only; see Giant-Size...;Marvel Advs., Marvel Graphic Novel #24, Marvel Super Heroes, '66 & Spider-Man &...)
Marvel Comics Group: Apr, 1964 - No. 380, Oct, 1998

1-Origin/1st app. Daredevil; intro Foggy Nelson & Karen Page; death of Battling Murdock; Bill Everett-c/a; reprinted in Marvel Super Heroes #1 (1966)
1550 3100 4650 10,800 19,900 29,000
2-Fantastic Four cameo; 2nd app. Electro (Spidey villain); Thing guest star
114 228 342 912 2056 3200
3-Origin & 1st app. The Owl (villain) 52 108 162 432 966 1500
4-Origin & 1st app. The Purple Man 48 96 144 374 862 1350
5-Minor costume change; Wally Wood-a begins 36 72 108 266 596 925
6-Mr. Fear app. 38 76 114 285 641 1000
7-Daredevil battles Sub-Mariner & dons red costume for 1st time (4/65); Marvel Masterwork pin-up by Wood 121 242 363 968 2184 3400
8-10: 8-Origin/1st app. Stilt Man. 10-1st app. Cat Man, Bird Man, Ape Man & Frog Man
18 36 54 124 275 425
11,13-15: 11-Last Wally Wood. 13-Facts about Ka-Zar's origin; vs. the Plunderer; Kirby/Romita-a. 14-Romita-a begins; Ka-Zar & the Plunderer app. 15-1st app. the Ox
12 24 36 80 173 265
12-1st app. Plunderer; Ka-Zar app. Kirby/Romita-a begins
18 36 54 124 275 425
16-1st Romita-a on Spider-Man (5/66) 64 128 192 512 1156 1800
17-Spider-Man x-over continues 23 46 69 156 348 540
18-Origin & 1st app. Gladiator 18 36 54 124 275 425
19-DD vs. the Gladiator 9 18 27 63 129 195
20-DD vs. the Owl; 1st Gene Colan-a 12 24 36 81 176 270
21-DD vs. the Owl 9 18 27 58 114 170
22-26,28-30: 22-DD vs. the Owl, Gladiator & and Masked Marauder; 1st app the Tri-Man. 23-Owl, Gladiator, Masked Marauder & Tri-Man app. 24-Ka-Zar app. 25-1st app. Leap-Frog; 1st app. 'Mike Murdock' Daredevil's fake twin brother. 26-Stilt-Man app. 30-Thor app. vs. Cobra and Mr. Hyde 8 16 24 54 102 150
27-Spider-Man x-over; Stilt-Man & the Masked Marauder app.
9 18 27 60 120 180
31-36,39,40: 31,32-DD vs. Cobra & Mr. Hyde. 33,34-DD vs. the Beetle. 35-DD vs. the Trapster. 36-DD vs. the Trapster; Dr. Doom cameo. 39-1st app. Exterminator (later becomes Death-Stalker); Ape Man, Cat Man & Bird Man app. as the Unholy Three. 40-DD vs. the Unholy Three 6 12 18 42 79 115
37,38: 37-Daredevil vs. Dr. Doom. 38-Dr. Doom app; Fantastic Four x-over; continued in Fantastic Four #73 11 22 33 77 166 255
41,42-44-49: 41- 'Death' of Mike Murdock; Daredevil drops the fake twin persona; DD vs. the Exterminator and the Unholy Three. 42-1st app. Jester. 44-46-DD vs. the Jester. 48-DD vs. Stilt-Man. 49-1st app. Star Saxon & the Plastoid
6 12 18 40 73 105
43-Daredevil vs. Captain America; origin partially retold; Kirby-c
11 22 33 75 160 245
50-51,53: 50-Barry Smith-a; last Stan Lee-s; vs. Star Saxon & the Plastoid. 51-1st Roy Thomas-s; Barry Smith-a; vs. Star Saxon & the Plastoid. 53-Gene Colan-a returns; origin retold 6 12 18 42 79 115
52-Barry Smith-a; Black Panther app.; learns Daredevil's secret identity
8 16 24 54 102 150
54-56,58-60: 54-Spider-Man cameo; vs. Mr. Fear. 55-DD vs. Mr. Fear. 56-1st app. Death's Head (Star Saxon) (9/69); story continued in #57. 58-1st app. Stunt-Master. 59-1st app. Torpedo (dies this issue) 5 10 15 30 50 70
57-Reveals i.d. to Karen Page; Death's Head app. 7 14 21 44 82 120
61,63-68,70-72,74-76,78-80: 61-DD vs. the Jester, Cobra & Mr. Hyde. 63-vs. Gladiator. 64-Stunt-Master app. 67-Stilt-Man app. 71-Last Roy Thomas-s. 72-1st app Tagak 'Lord of Leopards'; 1st Gerry Conway-s. 75-1st app. El Condor. 76-Death El Condor. 78-1st app. Man-Bull. 79-DD vs. Man-Bull. 80-vs the Owl 4 8 12 27 44 60
62,69,73: 62-Origin of Nighthawk (Kyle Richmond). 69-Black Panther app. 73-Continued from Iron Man #35; Nick Fury app. vs. the Zodiac; concluded in Iron Man #36.
5 10 15 31 53 75
77-Spider-Man & Sub-Mariner app.; story continues in Sub-Mariner #40
6 12 18 41 76 110
81-(52 pgs.)-Black Widow becomes regular guest star (11/71); receives co-billing w/issue #92 through issue #107; vs. Mr. Kline and the Owl 8 16 24 56 108 160
82,84-87,89-98: 82-DD vs. Mr. Kline. 84-Conclusion of the Mr. Kline story; see Iron Man #41-45 & Sub-Mariner #42. 85-DD vs. Gladiator. 86-Death of the Ox. 87-Daredevil & the Black Widow relocate to San Francisco; Electro app. 89-Purple Man & Electro app. 90-Mr. Fear app. 91-Death of Mr. Fear. 92-Black Widow gets co-billing as of this issue. 93,94-DD vs. the Indestructible Man. 95,96-DD vs. the Man-Bull.

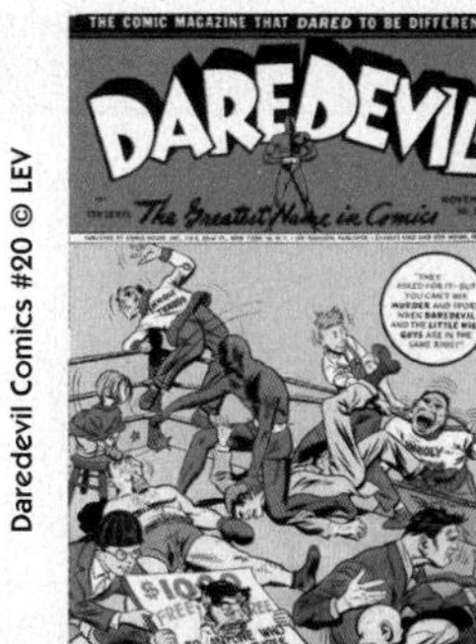

Daredevil Comics #20 © LEV

Daredevil #1 © MAR

Daredevil #104 © MAR

	GD 2.0	VG 4.0	FN 6.0	VF 8.0	VF/NM 9.0	NM- 9.2
97-99-DD vs. the Dark Messiah; Steve Gerber co-script; 98-Last Conway-s	4	8	12	23	37	50
83,99: 83-Barry Smith layouts/Weiss-p. 99-Hawkeye app; Steve Gerber-s begin; plot continues in Avengers #111	4	8	12	25	40	55
88-Purple Man app; early life of Black Widow revealed	5	10	15	31	53	75
100-1st app. Angar the Screamer; origin retold; Jann Wenner, editor of Rolling Stone app.	6	12	18	41	76	110
101,102,104,106,108-110: 101-vs Angar the Screamer. 102-vs. Stilt Man. 104-Kraven the Hunter app. 106-Moondragon app; vs. Terrex. 108-Title returns to 'Daredevil'. Moondragon app.; 1st app. Black Spectre; Beetle app; Daredevil and Black Widow break-up. 109-Shanna the She-Devil app.; vs. Nekra & Black Spectre; story continues in Marvel Two-in-One #3. 110-Continued from Marvel Two-in-One #3; vs. the Mandrill, Nekra & Black Spectre; brief Thing app.	3	6	9	19	30	40
103-1st app. & origin of Ramrod; Spider-Man app.	5	10	15	30	50	70
105-Origin of Moondragon by Starlin (12/73) Thanos cameo in flashback (early app.)	9	18	27	59	117	175
107-Starlin-c; Thanos cameo; Moondragon & Captain Marvel app; death of Terrex	4	8	12	25	40	55
111-1st app. Silver Samurai; Shanna the She-Devil, Mandrill, Nekra & Black Spectre app.	10	20	30	64	132	200
112-114,116-120: 112-Conclusion of the Black Spectre story; Mandrill & Nekra app. 113-1st brief app. Death-Stalker; Gladiator app. 114-1st full Death-Stalker app; Man-Thing & Gladiator app. 116,117-DD vs. the Owl; 117-Last Gerber-s. 118-1st app. Blackwing; vs. the Circus of Crime. 119-Tony Isabella-s begin. 120-1st app. El Jaguar Agent of HYDRA	3	6	9	17	26	35
115-Death-Stalker app.; advertisement for Wolverine in Incredible Hulk #181 (on pg. 19)	9	18	27	59	117	175
121-123,125-130,137: 121-vs. HYDRA; El Jaguar and the Dreadnaught app; Nick Fury app. 122-Return of Silvermane as the new Supreme HYDRA. 123-Silvermane, El Jaguar, Dreadnaught, Mentallo & HYDRA app; Nick Fury and SHIELD app; last Isabella-s. 125-Death of Copperhead; Wolfman-s begin. 126-1st app. the second and third Torpedos; 1st app. Heather Glenn. 127-vs. the third Torpedo (Brock Jones). 128-Death-Stalker app. 129-vs the Man-Bull	3	6	9	16	23	30
124-1st app. Copperhead; Black Widow leaves; Len Wein & Marv Wolfman co-plot	4	8	12	25	40	55
131-Origin/1st app. Bullseye (see Nick Fury #15)	25	50	75	175	388	600
132-2nd Bullseye app. new Bullseye (regular 25c edition)	6	12	18	41	76	110
132-(30¢-c variant, limited distribution)(4/76)	10	20	30	70	150	230
133-136: 133-Uri Geller & the Jester app. 134-Torpedo app. vs. the Chameleon. 135,136-vs. the Jester	3	6	9	15	22	28
133-136-(30¢-c variants, limited distribution)(5-8/76)	5	10	15	31	53	75
138-Ghost Rider-c/story; Death's Head is reincarnated; Byrne-a	3	6	9	20	31	42
139,140,142-145,147-154: 140-vs the Beetle & Gladiator. 142-vs. Cobra & Hyde; Nova cameo. 143-Cobra & Hyde app; last Wolfman-s. 144-vs the Man-Bull & Owl. 145-vs the Owl. 147-Purple Man app. 148-Death-Stalker app. 149-1st app. the third Smasher. 150-1st app. Paladin. 151-Reveals i.d. to Heather Glenn. 152-vs Death-Stalker; Roger McKenzie-s begin. 153-vs Cobra & Hyde. 154-vs Purple Man, Cobra & Hyde & Jester	3	6	9	14	19	24
141,146-Bullseye app.	4	8	12	27	44	60
146-(35¢-c variant, limited distribution)	12	24	36	80	173	265
147,148-(35¢-c variants, limited distribution)	9	18	27	57	111	165
155-157-DD vs. Death-Stalker; Black Widow, Hercules, Captain America & the Beast app.	3	6	9	15	22	28
158-Frank Miller-a begins (5/79) origin/death of Death-Stalker (see Captain America #235 & Spectacular Spider-Man #27)	9	18	27	59	117	175
159-Brief Bullseye app.	5	10	15	31	53	75
160,161-Bullseye and Black Widow app.	4	8	12	27	44	60
162-Ditko-a; no Miller-a; origin retold	3	6	9	15	22	28
163-Daredevil vs. the Hulk	6	12	18	38	69	100
164-Origin retold and expanded	3	6	9	21	33	45
165-167,170: 165-1st Miller co-plot w/McKenzie; Dr. Octopus app. 166-vs. Gladiator. 167-Last McKenzie co-plot; 1st app. Mauler. 170-Kingpin app.	3	6	9	17	25	34
168-(1/81) Origin/1st app. Elektra; 1st Miller scripts	19	38	57	131	291	450
169-2nd Elektra app; Bullseye app.	5	10	15	30	50	70
171-173: 171,172-vs. the Kingpin	3	6	9	18	28	38
174-1st app. the Hand (Ninjas who trained Elektra)	4	8	12	23	37	50
175-Elektra & Daredevil vs. the Hand	3	6	9	20	31	42
176-1st app. Stick (Daredevil's mentor)	4	8	12	27	44	60
177-180-Elektra app: 177-Kingpin & the Hand app. 178-Kingpin & Power Man & Iron Fist app. 179-Anti-smoking issue mentioned in the Congressional Record	3	6	9	17	26	35

	GD 2.0	VG 4.0	FN 6.0	VF 8.0	VF/NM 9.0	NM- 9.2
181-(4/82, 52-pgs)-Death of Elektra; Punisher cameo out of costume	4	8	12	28	47	65
182-184: 182-Bullseye app. 183,184 -'Angel Dust' drug story; Punisher app.	3	6	9	16	24	32
185-191: 186-Stilt-Man app. 187-New Black Widow vs. the Hand. 188-Black Widow app. 189-Death of Stick; Black Widow app. 190-Elektra returns, part origin; 2 pin-ups. 191-Classic 'Russian Roulette' story with Bullseye; last Miller Daredevil	2	4	6	8	11	14
192-195,198,199: 192-Alan Brennert story; Klaus Janson (p)&(i) begin. 193-Larry Hama-s. 194-Denny O'Neil-s begin. 198-Bullseye receives Adamantium bones. 199-Bullseye app; death of Dark Wind	1	2	3	5	6	8
196-Wolverine-c/app; 1st app. Dark Wind. Bullseye app.	3	6	9	17	26	35
197-Bullseye-c/app; 1st app. Yuriko Oyama (becomes Lady Deathstrike in Alpha Flight #33)	3	6	9	16	23	30
200-Bulleye vs. Daredevil; Byrne-c	2	4	6	8	11	14
201-207,209-218: 201-Black Widow solo story. 202-1st app. Micah Synn. 203-1st app. the Trump; Byrne-c. 204-1st app. Crossbow (Green Arrow homage?) 205-1st app. Gael (Irish Republican Army hitman). 206-DD vs. Micah Synn; 1st Mazzucchelli-p on DD. Kingpin app. 207-HYDRA & Black Widow app. 209-Harlan Ellison plot. 210-Crossbow & Kingpin app. 211,212-DD & Kingpin team-up vs. Micah Synn. 215-Two-Gun Kid flashback. 216-Gael app. 217-Gael app; 1st app. the Cossack; Barry-Windsor-Smith-c. 218-DD appears as the Jester						6.00
208,219: 208-Harlan Ellison and Arthur Byron Cover scripts borrowed from Avengers TV episode 'House that Jack Built'. 219-Miller-c/script						7.00
220-226,234-237: 220-Death of Heather Glenn. 222-Black Widow app. 223-Secret Wars II crossover; Beyonder gives DD his sight back; DD rejects the gift. 225-Vulture app. 226-Gladiator app.; last Denny O'Neil-s. 234-Madcap app. 235-DD vs. Mr. Hyde. 237-DD vs. Klaw; Black Widow app.						6.00
227-(2/86, 36 pgs.)-Miller scripts begin; classic 'Born Again' Pt.1 story begins; Kingpin learns DD's secret identity.	1	2	3	5	6	8
228-233: 'Born Again'; Kingpin ruins Matt Murdock's life. 232-1st app Nuke. 233-Last Miller script; Captain America app.; death of Nuke						5.00
238-Mutant massacre; Sabretooth app; 1st Ann Nocenti-s						6.00
239,240,242-247: 239-1st app. Rotgut. 243-1st app. Nameless One. 245-Black Panther app. 246-1st app. Chance. 247-Black Widow app.						4.00
241-Todd McFarlane-a(p)						5.00
248-Wolverine cameo; 1st app. Bushwacker. 249-DD vs. Wolverine; Bushwacker app.						6.00
250,251,253,258: 250-1st app. Bullet; Romita Jr-a begins. 251-vs. Bullet. 253-Kingpin app. 258-1st app. Bengal						4.00
252-(52 pgs)-Fall of the Mutants tie-in; 1st app. Ammo. 260-(52 pgs)-Bushwacker, Bullet, Ammo & Typhoid Mary vs. DD						5.00
254-Origin & 1st app. Typhoid Mary (5/88)	4	8	12	27	44	60
255,256: 2nd&3rd app. Typhoid Mary. 259-Typhoid Mary app.						5.00
257-Punisher app. (x-over w/Punisher #10)	2	4	6	10	14	18
261-269,271-281: 261-Typhoid Mary & Human Torch app. 262-Inferno tie-in. 263-Inferno tie-in; 1st new look 'monstrous' Mephisto. 264-vs the Owl. 265-Inferno tie-in; Mephisto app. 266-Mephisto app. 267-Bullet app. 269-Blob & Pyro (from Freedom Force) app. 272-1st app. Shotgun; Inhumans app. 273-DD vs. Shotgun; Inhumans app. 274-Black Bolt & the Inhumans app. 275,276-'Acts of Vengeance' x-over; Ultron app. 278-Mephisto & Blackheart app. 279-Mephisto app. 280-DD in Hell; Mephisto app. 281-Silver Surfer cameo; Mephisto & Blackheart app.						4.00
270-1st app. Blackheart (the son of Mephisto); Spider-Man app.	4	8	12	25	40	55
282-DD escapes Hell; Silver Surfer, Mephisto & Blackheart app.						5.00
283-287,289, 291-299: 283-Captain America app. 284-287,289-Bullseye impersonates DD; 284-1st Lee Weeks-a. 291-vs. Bullet; last Nocenti-s. 292,293-Punisher app. 295-Ghost Rider app. 297-'Last Rights' Pt.1; Typhoid Mary app. 298-Pt.2; Nick Fury & SHIELD app. 299-Pt. 3; Baron Strucker & Hydra vs. the Kingpin						4.00
288-Bullseye-c/s; Kingpin app; Elektra dream sequence						5.00
290-Bullseye vs. Daredevil	1	3	4	6	8	10
300-(52 pgs.)-'Last Rights' Pt.4; Kingpin loses criminal empire; last Weeks-a						5.00
301-318: 301-303-vs. the Owl. 305-306-Spider-Man app. 307-'Dead Man's Hand' Pt. 1; Nomad & Tombstone app.; continued in Nomad #4. 308-'Dead Man's Hand' Pt. 5; continued from Punisher War Journal #45; Punisher app; continues in Punisher War Journal #46. 309-'Dead Man's Hand' Pt. 7; continued from Nomad #5; continued in Punisher War Journal #47. 310-Infinity War tie-in; Calypso vs. DD doppelganger. 311-Calypso & Brother Voodoo app. 314,315-Shock & Mr. Fear app. 317,318-Taskmaster, Stilt-Man & Tatterdemalion app.						4.00
319-Prologue to Fall From Grace Pt. 1; Elektra returns; Silver Sable app.						6.00
319-2nd printing w/black-c						4.00
320-(9/93) Fall From Grace Pt. 1; Silver Sable app.						5.00
321-Fall From Grace regular ed; Pt. 2 new armored costume; Venom app.						4.00
321-($2.00)-Wraparound Glow-in-the-dark-c						5.00
322-325: 322-Fall From Grace Pt. 3; Eddie Brock app. 323,324: Fall From Grace Pts. 4,5.						

323-vs. Venom-c/story. 324-Morbius-c/story. 325-($2.50, 52 pgs.) Fall From Grace ends; contains bound-in poster; Elektra app. 5.00
326-338: 326-New logo; Captain America app. 327-Captain America-c/story. 328-Captain America & Baron Strucker app. 329-Iron Fist app. 330-Gambit app. 331,332-vs. Baron Strucker. 334-336-Bushwacker app. 338-Kingpin app. 4.00
339-343: 339-342-Kingpin app. 5.00
344-(9/95)-Title becomes part of the 'Marvel Edge' imprint; story continued from Double Edge: Alpha; Punisher & Nick Fury app.; continued in Ghost Rider #65 5.00
345-Original red costume returns; Marvel Overpower card insert 6.00
346-350: 348-1st Cary Nord-a in DD (1/96) 'Dec' on-c. 350-($2.95)-Double-Sized 4.00
350-($3.50)-Variant gold ink-c 5.00
351-353,355-360,362-364: 351-Last 'Marvel Edge' imprint issue. 353-Karl Kessel scripts; Nord-c/a begins. 354-Bullseye (illusion)-c. 355-Pyro app. 357-Enforcers app. 358-Mysterio app. 360-Absorbing Man app. 363-Colan-c/a. 364-Mr. Fear app. 4.00
354-Spider-Man app.; $1.50-c begins 1 3 4 6 8 10
361,365-367: 361-Black Widow & DD vs. Grey Gargoyle. 365-367: 365-Molten Man & Mr. Fear app. 366-Mr. Fear app.; Colan-c/a. 367-Colan-c/a; Mr. Fear & Gladiator app. 5.00
368-Omega Red & Black Widow app. 1 3 4 6 8 10
369-Black Widow app. 6.00
370-374: 370-Darkstar, Vanguard & Ursa Major app; last Colan-a. 371-Black Widow app. 372-Ghost Rider (Daniel Ketch) app. 373,374-Mr. Fear app. 5.00
375-($2.99)-Wraparound-c; Mr. Fear-c/app. 5.00
376-379: "Flying Blind", DD goes undercover for SHIELD 4.00
380-($2.99) Final issue; flashback story; Kingpin, Bullseye & Bushwacker app. 2 4 6 11 16 20
#(-1) Flashback issue (7/97, $1.95); Gene Colan-c/a 4.00
No. 181 Facsimile Edition (11/19, $4.99) r/#181 with original 1982 ads and letter column 5.00
Special 1 (9/67, 25¢, 68-pgs)-New art/story by Lee/Colan; DD vs. the 'Emissaries of Evil' (Electro, Leapfrog, Stilt-Man, Matador & Gladiator) 11 22 33 73 157 240
Special 2,3: 2 (2/71, 25¢, 52 pgs.) Reprints issues #10-11 by Wood. 3-(1/72, 25¢, 52 pgs.) Reprints issues #16-17 4 8 12 28 47 65
Annual 4 (10/76, squarebound) Sub-Mariner & Black Panther app. 4 8 12 27 44 60
Annual 4 (#5, 1989) Atlantis Attacks; continued from Spectacular Spider-Man Annual #9; Spider-Man app.; continued in Avengers Annual #18 6.00
Annual 6-9: 6-('90) Lifeform Pt. 2; continued from Punisher Annual #3; continues in Silver Surfer Annual #3. 7-('91) The Von Strucker Gambit Pt. 1; continued in Punisher Annual #4. Guice-a (7 pgs.). 8-('92) System Bites Pt. 2; Deathlok & Bushwacker app; continued in Wonder Man Annual #1. 9-('93) Polybagged w/card; 1st app. Devourer 6.00
Annual 10-('94) Elektra, Nick Fury, Shang-Chi (Master of Kung-Fu) vs. Ghostmaker 1 2 3 5 6 8
...: Born Again TPB ($17.95)-r/#227-233; Miller-s/Mazzucchelli-a & new-c 20.00
... By Frank Miller and Klaus Janson Omnibus HC (2007, $99.99, dustjacket) r/#158-161, 163-191 and What If...? #28; intros by Miller and Janson; interviews, bonus art 100.00
... By Frank Miller and Klaus Janson Omnibus Companion HC (2007, $59.99, die-cut d.j.) r/#219,226-233, Daredevil: The Man Without Fear #1-5, Daredevil: Love and War, and Peter Parker, the Spect. Spider-Man #27-28; bonus materials 60.00
.../Deadpool (Annual '97, $2.99)-Wraparound-c 6.00
...: Fall From Grace TPB ($19.95)-r/#319-325 20.00
...: Gang War TPB ($15.95)-r/#169-172,180; Miller-s/a(p) 16.00
...Legends: (Vol. 4) Typhoid Mary TPB (2003, $19.95) r/#254-257,259-263 20.00
... :Love's Labors Lost TPB ($19.99)-r/#215-217,219-222,225,226; Mazzucchelli-c 20.00
.../Punisher TPB (1988, $4.95)-r/D.D. #182-184 (all printings) 6.00
...Visionaries: Frank Miller Vol. 1 TPB ($17.95) r/#158-161,163-167 18.00
...Visionaries: Frank Miller Vol. 2 TPB ($24.95) r/#168-182; new Miller-c 25.00
...Visionaries: Frank Miller Vol. 3 TPB ($24.95) r/#183-191, What If? #28,35 & Bizarre Adventures #28; new Miller-c 25.00
... Vs. Bullseye Vol. 1 TPB (2004, $15.99) r/#131-132,146,169,181,191 16.00
Wizard Ace Edition: Daredevil (Vol. 1) #1 (4/03, $13.99) Acetate Campbell-c 14.00
NOTE: ***Art Adams*** *c-238p, 239.* ***Austin*** *a-191i; c-151i, 200i.* ***John Buscema*** *a-136, 137p, 234p, 235p; c-86p, 136i, 137p, 142, 219.* ***Byrne*** *c-200p, 201, 203, 223.* ***Capullo*** *a-286p.* ***Colan*** *a(p)-20-49, 53-82, 84-98, 100, 110, 112, 124, 153, 154, 156, 157, 363, 366-370, Spec. 1p; c(p)-20-42, 44-49, 53-60, 71, 92, 98, 138, 153, 154, 156, 157, Annual 1.* ***Craig*** *a-50i, 52i.* ***Ditko*** *a-162, 234p, 235p, 264p; c-162.* ***Everett*** *c/a-1; inks-21, 83.* ***Garney*** *c/a-304.* ***Gil Kane*** *a-141p, 146-148p, 151p; c(p)-85, 90, 91, 93, 94, 115, 116, 119, 120, 125-128, 133, 139, 147, 152.* ***Kirby*** *c-2-4, 12p, 13p, 43.* ***Layton*** *c-202.* ***Miller*** *scripts-168-182, 183(part), 184-191, 219, 227-233; a-158-161p, 163-184p, 191p; c-158-161p, 163-184p, 185-189, 190p, 191.* ***Orlando*** *a-2-4p.* ***Powell*** *a-9p, 11p, Special 1r, 2r.* ***Simonson*** *c-199, 236p.* ***B. Smith*** *a-236p; c-51p, 52p, 217.* ***Starlin*** *a-105p.* ***Steranko*** *c-44i.* ***Tuska*** *a-39i, 145p.* ***Williamson*** *a(i)-237, 239, 240, 243, 248-257, 259-282, 283(part), 284, 285, 287, 288(part), 289(part), 293-300; c(i)-237, 243, 244, 248-257, 259-263, 265-278, 280-289, Annual 8.* ***Wood*** *a-5-8, 9i, 10, 11i, Spec. 2i; c-5-11, 164i.*

DAREDEVIL (Volume 2)(Marvel Knights)(Becomes Black Panther: The Man Without Fear #513)
Marvel Comics: Nov, 1998 - No. 512, Feb, 2011 ($2.50/$2.99)

1-Kevin Smith-s/Quesada & Palmiotti-a 2 4 6 10 14 18
1-($6.95) DF Edition w/Quesada & Palmiotti var-c 2 4 6 11 16 20
1-($6.00) DF Sketch Ed. w/B&W-c 12.00
2-Two covers by Campbell and Quesada/Palmiotti 12.00
3-8: 4,5-Bullseye app. 5-Variant-c exists. 8-Spider-Man-c/app.; last Smith-s 6.00
9-15: 9-11-David Mack-s; intro Echo. 12-Begin $2.99-c; Haynes-a. 13,14-Quesada-a 4.00
16-19-Direct editions; Bendis-s/Mack-c/painted-a 4.00
18,19,21,22-Newsstand editions with variant cover logo "Marvel Unlimited Featuring... 4.00
20-($3.50) Gale-s/Winslade-a; back-up by Stan Lee-s/Colan-a; Mack-c 5.00
21-40: 21-25-Gale-s. 26-38-Bendis-s/Maleev-a. 32-Daredevil's ID revealed. 35-Spider-Man-c/app. 38-Iron Fist & Luke Cage app. 40-Dodson-a 3.50
41-(25¢-c) Begins "Lowlife" arc; Maleev-a; intro Milla Donovan 3.00
41-(Newsstand edition with 2.99¢-c) 3.00
42-45-"Lowlife" arc; Maleev-a 3.00
46-50-($2.99). 46-Typhoid Mary returns. 49-Bullseye app. 50-Art panels by various incl. Romita, Colan, Mack, Janson, Oeming, Quesada 3.00
51-64,66-74,76-81: 51-55-Mack-s/a; Echo app. 54-Wolverine-c/app. 61-64-Black Widow app. 71-Decalogue begins. 76-81-The Murdock Papers. 81-Last Bendis-s/Maleev-a 3.00
65-($3.99) 40th Anniversary issue; Land-c; art by Maleev, Horn, Bachalo and others 4.00
75-($3.99) Decalogue ends; Jester app. 4.00
82-99,101-119: 82-Brubaker-s/Lark-a begin; Foggy "killed". 84-86-Punisher app. 87-Other Daredevil ID revealed. 94-Romita-c. 111-Lady Bullseye debut 3.00
82-Variant-c by McNiven 4.00
100-($3.99) Three covers (Djurdjevic, Bermejo and Turner); art by Romita Sr., Colan, Lark, Sienkiewicz, Maleev, Bermejo & Djurdjevic; sketch art gallery; r/Daredevil #90 (1972) 4.00
(After Vol. 2 #119, Aug, 2009, numbering reverts to original Vol. 1 with #500)
500-(10/09, $4.99) Kingpin, Lady Bullseye app.; back-up stories, pin-up & cover galleries; r/#191; five covers by Djurdjevic, Darrow, Dell'Otto, Ross and Zircher 5.00
501-512: 501-Daredevil takes over The Hand; Diggle-s begins; Ribic-c. 508-Shadowland begins. 512-Black Panther app. 3.00
Annual #1 (12/07, $3.99) Brubaker-s/Fernandez-a/Djurdjevic-c; Black Tarantula app. 4.00
... & Captain America: Dead on Arrival (2008, $4.99) English version of Italian story 5.00
... Black & White 1 (10/10, $3.99) B&W short stories by various; Aja-c 4.00
... Blood of the Tarantula (6/08, $3.99) Parks & Brubaker-s/Samnee-a/Djurdjevic-c 4.00
... By Brian Michael Bendis Omnibus Vol. 1 HC (2008, $99.99) oversized r/#16-19,26-50, and 56-60 100.00
... By Ed Brubaker Saga (2008, giveaway) synopsis of issues #82-110, preview of #111 3.00
... Cage Match 1 (7/10, $2.99) flashback early Luke Cage team-up; Chen-a 3.00
... MGC #26 (8/10, $1.00) r/#26 with "Marvel's Greatest Comics" logo on cover 3.00
...2099 #1 (11/04, $2.99) Kirkman-s/Moline-a 3.00
TPB ($9.95) r/#1-3 10.00
...Vol. 1 HC (2001, $29.99, with dustjacket) r/#1-11,13-15 30.00
...Vol. 1 HC (2003, $29.99, with dustjacket) r/#1-11,13-15; larger page size 30.00
...Vol. 2 HC (2002, $29.99, with dustjacket) r/#26-37; afterword by Bendis 30.00
...Vol. 3 HC (2004, $29.99, with dustjacket) r/#38-50; Maleev sketch pages 30.00
...Vol. 4 HC (2005, $29.99, with dustjacket) r/#56-65; Vol. 1 #81 (1971) Black Widow 30.00
...Vol. 5 HC (2006, $29.99, with dustjacket) r/#66-75 30.00
...Vol. 6 HC (2006, $34.99, with dustjacket) r/#76-81 & What If Karen Page Had Lived? 35.00
(Vol. 1) Visionaries TPB ($19.95) r/#1-8; Ben Affleck intro. 20.00
(Vol. 2) Parts of a Hole TPB (1/02, $17.95) r/#9-15; David Mack intro. 18.00
(Vol. 3) Wake Up TPB (7/02, $9.99) r/#16-19 10.00
...Vol. 4: Underboss TPB (8/02, $14.99) r/#26-31 15.00
...Vol. 5: Out TPB (2003, $19.99) r/#32-40 20.00
...Vol. 6: Lowlife TPB (2003, $13.99) r/#41-45 14.00
...Vol. 7: Hardcore TPB (2003, $13.99) r/#46-50 14.00
...Vol. 8: Echo - Vision Quest TPB (2004, $13.99) r/#51-55; David Mack-s/a 14.00
...Vol. 9: King of Hell's Kitchen TPB (2004, $13.99) r/#56-60 14.00
...Vol. 10: The Widow TPB (2004, $16.99) r/#61-65 & Vol. 1 #81 17.00
...Vol. 11: Golden Age TPB (2005, $13.99) r/#66-70 14.00
...Vol. 12: Decalogue TPB (2005, $14.99) r/#71-75 15.00
...Vol. 13: The Murdock Papers TPB (2006, $14.99) r/#76-81 15.00
...: The Devil Inside and Out Vol. 1 (2006, $14.99) r/#82-87; Brubaker & Lark interview 15.00
...: The Devil Inside and Out Vol. 2 (2007, $14.99) r/#88-93; Bermejo cover sketches 15.00
...: Hell To Pay Vol. 1 TPB (2007, $14.99) r/#94-99; Djurdjevic cover sketches 15.00
...: Hell To Pay Vol. 2 TPB (2008, $15.99) r/#100-105 16.00

DAREDEVIL (Volume 3)
Marvel Comics: Sept, 2011 - No. 36, Apr, 2014 ($3.99/$2.99)

1-($3.99) Mark Waid-s/Paolo Rivera-a; back-up tale with Marcos Martin-a 4.00
1-Variant-c by Marcos Martin 8.00
1-Variant-c by Neal Adams 10.00
2-10,10.1,11-20,23,24,25,27-36-($2.99) 2-Capt. America app. 3-Klaw returns. 4-6-Marcos Martin-a. 8-X-over w/Amazing Spider-Man #677; Spider-Man and Black Cat app. 11-Spider-Man app. 17-Allred-a. 30-Silver Surfer app. 32,33-Satana & monsters app. 3.00
21,22: 21-1st Superior Spider-Man app. (cameo). 22-Superior Spider-Man app. 5.00
26-($3.99) Bullseye and Lady Bullseye app.; back-up "Fighting Cancer" story 4.00
Annual 1 (10/12, $4.99) Alan Davis-s/a/c; Dr. Strange & ClanDestine app. 5.00

DAREDEVIL (Volume 4)
Marvel Comics: May, 2014 - No. 18, Nov, 2015 ($3.99)

1-18-($3.99) Mark Waid-s/Chris Samnee-a; Murdock moves to San Francisco. 6,7-Original Sin tie-in. 8-10-Purple Man app. 14-Owl's daughter app. 15-18-Kingpin app. 4.00
#0.1-(9/14, $4.99) Waid-s/Krause-a/Samnee-c 5.00
#1.50-($4.99) 50th Anniversary issue; Murdock at 50; back-up Bendis-s/Maleev-a 5.00
#15.1-(7/15, $4.99) Waid-s/Samnee-a; Guggenheim-s/Krause-a 5.00

DAREDEVIL (Follows Secret Wars)
Marvel Comics: Feb, 2016 - No. 28, Dec, 2017; No. 595, Jan, 2018 - No. 612, Jan, 2019 ($3.99)

1-28: 1-Soule-s/Garney-a; Blindspot app. 2,3-The Hand app. 4-Steve Rogers app. 6,7-Elektra app.; Sienkiewicz-c. 9-Spider-Man app. 16-Bullseye app. 18,19-Purple Man app. 23-She-Hulk app. 28-Kingpin becomes mayor of New York 4.00
[Title switches to legacy numbering after #28 (12/17)]
595-599,601-611: 595-(1/18) Soule-s/Landini-a. 603,609-Elektra app. 4.00
600-(5/18, $5.99) Soule-s/Garney-a; Spider-Man and The Defenders app. 6.00
612-($4.99) Soule-s/Noto-a; leads into Man Without Fear 2019 series 5.00
Annual 1 (10/16, $4.99) Echo returns; Vanesa Del Ray-a 5.00
Annual 1 (10/18, $4.99) Schultz-s/Takara-a; flashback to 1st meeting with Misty Knight 5.00

DAREDEVIL (Follows Man Without Fear)
Marvel Comics: Apr, 2019 - No. 36, Jan, 2022 ($4.99/$3.99)

1-($4.99) Zdarsky-s/Checchetto-a; Kingpin app.; intro Det. Cole North 5.00
2-24,26-35 ($3.99) 3,4-Punisher app. 10-16-Elektra app. 19,20-Bullseye, Crossbones, Rhino app. 20,22,24,26-Typhoid Mary app. 23-Spider-Man app. 26-King in Black tie-in 4.00
25-Daredevil goes to jail; Elektra dons Daredevil costume 5.00
36-(4.99) Murdock leaves jail; leads into Devil's Reign #1 5.00
Annual 1 (10/20, $4.99) Zdarsky-s/Garcia-a; spotlight on Mike Murdock; The Hood app. 5.00

DAREDEVIL
Marvel Comics: Sept, 2022 - Present ($4.99/$3.99)

1-($4.99) Zdarsky-s/Checchetto-a; Spider-Man app. 5.00
2-($5.99) Legacy issue #650; back-up stories and bonus cover gallery 6.00
3-8-($3.99) 3-De Latorre-a; Luke Cage app. 6-Iron Man app. 7,8-Punisher app. 4.00

DAREDEVIL/ BATMAN (Also see Batman/Daredevil)
Marvel Comics/ DC Comics: 1997 ($5.99, one-shot)

nn-McDaniel-c/a 2 4 6 8 11 14

DAREDEVIL BATTLES HITLER (See Daredevil #1 [1941 series])

DAREDEVIL: BATTLIN' JACK MURDOCK
Marvel Comics: Aug, 2007 - No. 4, Nov, 2007 ($3.99, limited series)

1-4-Wells-s/DiGiandomenico-a; flashback to the fixed fight 4.00
TPB (2007, $12.99) r/#1-4; page layouts and cover inks 13.00

DAREDEVIL COMICS (Golden Age title) (See Daredevil)

DAREDEVIL: DARK NIGHTS

Daredevil V2 #106 © MAR

Daredevil: Woman Without Fear #2 © MAR

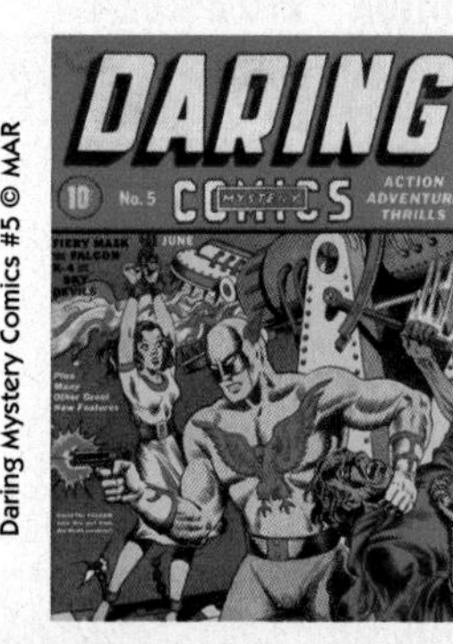

Daring Mystery Comics #5 © MAR

GD VG FN VF VF/NM NM-
2.0 4.0 6.0 8.0 9.0 9.2

Marvel Comics: Aug, 2013 - No. 8, Mar, 2014 ($3.99, limited series)

1-8: 1-3-Lee Weeks-s/a. 4,5-David Lapham-s/a; The Shocker app. 6-8-Conner-c 4.00

DAREDEVIL/ ELEKTRA: LOVE AND WAR
Marvel Comics: 2003 ($29.99, hardcover with dust jacket)

HC-Larger-size reprints of Daredevil: Love and War (Marvel Graphic Novel #24) & Elektra: Assassin; Frank Miller-s; Bill Sienkiewicz-a 30.00

DAREDEVIL: END OF DAYS
Marvel Comics: Dec, 2012 - No. 8, Aug, 2013 ($3.99, limited series)

1-8-Bendis & Mack-s/Janson & Sienkiewicz-a; death of Daredevil in the future 4.00

DAREDEVIL: FATHER
Marvel Comics: June, 2004 - No. 6, Feb, 2007 ($3.50/$2.99, limited series)

1-Quesada-s/a; Isanove-painted color 3.50
1-Director's Cut ($2.99) cover and page development art; partial sketch-c 3.00
2-6: 2-($2.99,10/05). 3-Santerians app. 3.00
HC (2006, $24.99) r/series; Lindelof intro.; sketch pages, cover pencils and bonus art 25.00

DAREDEVIL: NINJA
Marvel Comics: Dec, 2000 - No. 3, Feb, 2001 ($2.99, limited series)

1-3: Bendis-s/Haynes-a 3.00
1-Dynamic Forces foil-c 10.00
TPB (7/01, $12.95) r/#1-3 with cover and sketch gallery 13.00

DAREDEVIL NOIR
Marvel Comics: June, 2009 - No. 4, Sept, 2009 ($3.99, limited series)

1-4-Irvine-s/Coker-a; covers by Coker and Calero 4.00

DAREDEVIL / PUNISHER: SEVENTH CIRCLE
Marvel Comics: Jul, 2016 - No. 4, Oct, 2016 ($4.99, limited series)

1-4-Soule-s/Kudranski-a; Blindspot app. 3,4-Crimson Dynamo app. 5.00

DAREDEVIL: REBORN (Follows Shadowland x-over)
Marvel Comics: Mar, 2011 - No. 4, Jul, 2011 ($3.99, limited series)

1-4-Diggle-s/Gianfelice-a 4.00

DAREDEVIL: REDEMPTION
Marvel Comics: Apr, 2005 - No. 6, Aug, 2005 ($2.99, limited series)

1-6-Hine-s/Gaydos-a/Sienkiewicz-c 3.00
TPB (2005, $14.99) r/#1-6 15.00

DAREDEVIL: SEASON ONE
Marvel Comics: 2012 ($24.99, hardcover graphic novel)

HC - Story of early career, yellow costume; Johnston-s/Alves-a/Tedesco painted-c 25.00

DAREDEVIL/ SHI (See Shi/ Daredevil)
Marvel Comics/ Crusade Comics: Feb,1997 ($2.95, one-shot)

1 3.00

DAREDEVIL/ SPIDER-MAN
Marvel Comics: Jan, 2001 - No. 4, Apr, 2001 ($2.99, limited series)

1-4-Jenkins-s/Winslade-a/Alex Ross-c; Stilt Man app. 3.00
TPB (8/01, $12.95) r/#1-4; Ross-c 13.00

DAREDEVIL THE MAN WITHOUT FEAR
Marvel Comics: Oct, 1993 - No. 5, Feb, 1994 ($2.95, limited series) (foil embossed covers)

1-Miller scripts; Romita, Jr./Williamson-c/a 6.00
2-5 5.00
Hardcover 100.00
Trade paperback 20.00

DAREDEVIL: THE MOVIE (2003 movie adaptation)
Marvel Comics: March, 2003 ($3.50/$12.95, one-shot)

1-Photo-c of Ben Affleck; Bruce Jones-s/Manuel Garcia-a 3.50
TPB ($12.95) r/movie adaptation; Daredevil #32; Ultimate Daredevil & Elektra #1 and Spider-Man's Tangled Web #4; photo-c of Ben Affleck 13.00

DAREDEVIL: THE TARGET (Daredevil Bullseye on cover)
Marvel Comics: Jan, 2003 ($3.50, unfinished limited series)

1-Kevin Smith-s/Glenn Fabry-c/a 3.50

DAREDEVIL VS. PUNISHER
Marvel Comics: Sept, 2005 - No. 6, Jan, 2006 ($2.99, limited series)

1-5-David Lapham-s/a 3.00
TPB (2005, $15.99) r/#1-6 16.00

DAREDEVIL: WOMAN WITHOUT FEAR (Takes place during Devil's Reign series)
Marvel Comics: Mar, 2022 - No. 3, May, 2022 ($4.99/$3.99, limited series)

1-($4.99) Elektra continues as Daredevil; Zdarsky-s/De Latorre-a 5.00
2,3-($3.99) Kraven app.; prelude to Punisher #1 4.00

DAREDEVIL: YELLOW
Marvel Comics: Aug, 2001 - No. 6, Jan, 2002 ($3.50, limited series)

1-6-Jeph Loeb-s/Tim Sale-a/c; origin & yellow costume days retold 3.50
HC (5/02, $29.95) r/#1-6 with dustjacket; intro by Stan Lee; sketch pages 30.00
Daredevil Legends Vol. 1: Daredevil Yellow (2002, $14.99, TPB) r/#1-6 15.00

DARING ADVENTURES (Also see Approved Comics)
St. John Publishing Co.: Nov, 1953 (25¢, 3-D, came w/glasses)

1 (3-D)-Reprints lead story from Son of Sinbad #1 by Kubert 29 58 87 172 281 390

DARING ADVENTURES
I.W. Enterprises/Super Comics: 1963 - 1964

I. W. Reprint #8-r/Fight Comics #53; Matt Baker-a 5 10 15 34 60 85
I.W. Reprint #9-r/Blue Bolt #115; Disbrow-a(3) 5 10 15 35 63 90
Super Reprint #10,11('63)-r/Dynamic #24,16; 11-Marijuana story; Yankee Boy app.; Mac Raboy-a 4 8 12 23 37 50
Super Reprint #12('64)-Phantom Lady from Fox (r/#14 only? w/splash pg. omitted); Matt Baker-a 10 20 30 64 132 200
Super Reprint #15('64)-r/Hooded Menace #1 6 12 18 41 76 110
Super Reprint #16('64)-r/Dynamic #12 3 6 9 21 33 45
Super Reprint #17('64)-r/Green Lama #3 by Raboy 4 8 12 27 44 60
Super Reprint #18-Origin Atlas from unpublished Atlas Comics #1 4 8 12 25 40 55

DARING COMICS (Formerly Daring Mystery) (Jeanie Comics No. 13 on)
Timely Comics (HPC): No. 9, Fall, 1944 - No. 12, Fall, 1945

9-Human Torch, Toro & Sub-Mariner begin 343 686 1029 2400 4200 6000
10-12: 10-The Angel only app. 11,12-The Destroyer app. 245 490 735 1568 2684 3800

NOTE: ***Schomburg** c-9-11. **Sekowsky** c-12? Human Torch, Toro & Sub-Mariner c-9-12.*

DARING CONFESSIONS (Formerly Youthful Hearts)
Youthful Magazines: No. 4, 11/52 - No. 7, 5/53; No. 8, 10/53

4-Doug Wildey-a; Tony Curtis story 25 50 75 150 245 340
5-8: 5-Ray Anthony photo on-c. 6,8-Wildey-a 19 38 57 109 172 235

DARING ESCAPES
Image Comics: Sept, 1998 - No. 4, Mar, 1999 ($2.95/$2.50, mini-series)

1-Houdini; following app. in Spawn #19,20 3.00
2-4-($2.50) 3.00

DARING LOVE (Radiant Love No. 2 on)
Gilmor Magazines: Sept-Oct, 1953

1–Steve Ditko's 1st published work (1st drawn was Fantastic Fears #5)(Also see Black Magic #27)(scarce) 423 846 1269 3067 5384 7700

DARING LOVE (Formerly Youthful Romances)
Ribage/Pix: No. 15, 12/52; No. 16, 2/53-c, 4/53-Indicia; No. 17-4/53-c & indicia

15 19 38 57 112 179 245
16,17: 17-Photo-c 16 32 48 96 151 205

NOTE: ***Colletta** a-15. **Wildey** a-17.*

DARING LOVE STORIES (See Fox Giants)

DARING MYSTERY COMICS (Comedy Comics No. 9 on; title changed to Daring Comics with No. 9)
Timely Comics (TPI 1-6/TCI 7,8): 1/40 - No. 5, 6/40; No. 6, 9/40; No. 7, 4/41 - No. 8, 1/42

1-Origin The Fiery Mask (1st app.) by Joe Simon; Monako, Prince of Magic (1st app.), John Steele, Soldier of Fortune (1st app.), Doc Denton (1st app.) begin; Flash Foster & Barney Mullen, Sea Rover only app; bondage-c 2540 5080 7620 19,700 39,850 60,000
2-(Rare)-Origin The Phantom Bullet (1st & only app.); The Laughing Mask & Mr. E only app.; Trojak the Tiger Man begins, ends #6; Zephyr Jones & K-4 & His Sky Devils app., also #4 1380 2760 4140 10,400 20,200 30,000
3-The Phantom Reporter, Dale of FBI, Captain Strong only app.; Breeze Barton, Marvex the Super-Robot, The Purple Mask begin 757 1514 2271 5526 9763 14,000
4,5: 4-Last Purple Mask; Whirlwind Carter begins; Dan Gorman, G-Man app. 5-The Falcon begins (1st app.); The Fiery Mask, Little Hercules app. by Sagendorf in the Segar style; bondage-c 486 972 1458 3550 6275 9000
6-Origin & only app. Marvel Boy by S&K; Flying Flame, Dynaman, & Stuporman only app.; The Fiery Mask by S&K; S&K-c 541 1082 1623 3950 6975 10,000
7-Origin and 1st app. The Blue Diamond, Captain Daring by S&K, The Fin by Everett, The Challenger, The Silver Scorpion & The Thunderer by Burgos; Mr. Millions app 432 864 1296 3154 5577 8000
8-Origin Citizen V; Last Fin, Silver Scorpion, Capt. Daring by Borth, Blue Diamond & The Thunderer; Kirby & part solo Simon-c; Rudy the Robot only app.; Citizen V, Fin &

	GD	VG	FN	VF	VF/NM	NM-
	2.0	4.0	6.0	8.0	9.0	9.2

Silver Scorpion continue in Comedy #9 400 800 1200 2800 4900 7000
NOTE: *Schomburg c-1-4, 7. Simon a-2, 3, 5. Cover features: 1-Fiery Mask; 2-Phantom Bullet; 3-Purple Mask; 4-G-Man; 5-The Falcon; 6-Marvel Boy; 7, 8-Multiple characters.*

DARING MYSTERY COMICS 70th ANNIVERARY SPECIAL
Marvel Comics: Nov, 2009 ($3.99, one-shot)
1-New story of The Phantom Reporter; r/app. in Daring Mystery #3 (1940); 2 covers 5.00

DARING NEW ADVENTURES OF SUPERGIRL, THE
DC Comics: Nov, 1982 - No. 13, Nov, 1983 (Supergirl No. 14 on)
1-Origin retold; Lois Lane back-ups in #2-12 3 6 9 16 23 30
2-13: 8,9-Doom Patrol app. 13-New costume; flag-c 5.00
NOTE: *Buckler c-1p, 2p. Giffen c-3p, 4p. Gil Kane c-6,8, 9, 11-13.*

DARK, THE
Continum Comics: Nov, 1990 - No. 4, Feb, 1993; V2#1, May, 1993 - V2#7, Apr?, 1994 ($1.95)
1-4: 1-Bright-p; Panosian, Hanna-i; Stroman-c. 2-(1/92)-Stroman-c/a(p). 4-Perez-c & part-i 3.00
V2#1,V2#2-6: V2#1-Red foil Bart Sears-c. V2#1-Red non-foil variant-c. V2#1-2nd printing w/blue foil Bart Sears-c. V2#2-Stroman/Bryant-a. 3-Perez-c(i). 3-6-Foil-c. 4-Perez-c & part-i; bound-in trading cards. 5,6-(2,3/94)-Perez-c(i). 7-(B&W)-Perez-c(i) 3.00
Convention Book 1 ,2(Fall/94, 10/94)-Perez-c 3.00

DARK AGES
Dark Horse Comics: Aug, 2014 - No. 4, Nov, 2014 ($3.99, limited series)
1-4-Abnett-s/Culbard-a/c 4.00

DARK AGES
Marvel Comics: Mar, 2022 - No. 6, May, 2022 ($4.99/$3.99, limited series)
1-($4.99) Taylor-s/Coello-a; Marvel heroes in a world without electricity 5.00
2-6 ($3.99) Apocalypse & The Purple Man app. 4-Fin Fang Foom app. 4.00

DARK AGNES (Robert E. Howard character)
Marvel Comics: Apr, 2020 - No. 5 ($3.99, limited series)
1,2-Becky Cloonan-s/Luca Pizzari-a; set in 1521 France 4.00

DARK AND BLOODY, THE
DC Comics (Vertigo): Apr, 2016 - No. 6, Sept, 2016 ($3.99, limited series)
1-6-Aldridge-s/Godlewski-a 4.00

DARK ANGEL (Formerly Hell's Angel)
Marvel Comics UK, Ltd.: No. 6, Dec, 1992 - No. 16, Dec, 1993 ($1.75)
6-8,13-16: 6-Excalibur-c/story. 8-Psylocke app. 3.00
9-12-Wolverine/X-Men app. 3.50

DARK ANGEL: PHOENIX RESURRECTION (Kia Asamiya's...)
Image Comics: May, 2000 - No. 4, Oct, 2001 ($2.95)
1-4-Kia Asamiya-s/a. 3-Van Fleet variant-c 3.00

DARK ARK
AfterShock Comics: Sept, 2017 - No. 15, Mar, 2019 ($3.99)
1-15-Cullen Bunn-s/Juan Doe-a 4.00

DARK ARK: AFTER THE FLOOD
AfterShock Comics: Oct, 2019 - No. 5, Jul, 2020 ($3.99, limited series)
1-5: 1-Cullen Bunn-s/Juan Doe-a. 3-5-Jesus Hervas-a 4.00

DARK AVENGERS (See Secret Invasion and Dark Reign titles)
Marvel Comics: Mar, 2009 - No. 16, Jul, 2010 ($3.99)
1-Norman Osborn assembles his Avengers; Bendis-s/Deodato-a/c 3 6 9 16 23 30
1-Variant Iron Patriot armor cover by Djurdjevic 7 14 21 46 86 125
2-16: 2-6-Bendis-s/Deodato-a/c. 2-4 Dr. Doom app. 7,8-Utopia x-over; X-Men app. 9-Nick Fury app. 11,12-Deodato & Horn-a. 13-16-Siege. 13-Sentry origin 4.00
Annual 1 (2/10, $4.99) Bendis-s/Bachalo-a; Marvel Boy new costume; Siege preview 5.00
,,,/ Uncanny X-Men: Exodus (11/09, $3.99) Conclusion of x-over; Deodato & Dodson-a 4.00
,,,/ Uncanny X-Men: Utopia (8/09, $3.99) Part 1 of x-over w/Uncanny X-Men #513,514 4.00

DARK AVENGERS (Title continues from Thunderbolts #174)
Marvel Comics: No. 175, Aug, 2012 - No. 190, Jul, 2013 ($2.99)
175-190: 175-New team assembles; Parker-s/Shalvey-a/Deodato-c 3.00

DARK AVENGERS: ARES
Marvel Comics: Dec, 2009 - No. 3, Feb, 2010 ($3.99, limited series)
1-Garcia-a/Gillen-s/Nord-c 3 6 9 17 26 35
2,3: 2-Tan-c. 3-McGuinness-c 4.00

DARK BLOOD
BOOM! Studios: Jul, 2021 - No. 6, Jan, 2022 ($3.99, limited series)
1-6-Latoya Morgan-s. 1,2-Walt Barna-a. 3-6-Moisés Hidalgo-a 4.00

DARKCHYLDE (Also see Dreams of the Darkchylde)
Maximum Press #1-3/ Image Comics #4 on: June, 1996 - No. 5, Sept, 1997 ($2.95/ $2.50)
1-Randy Queen-c/a/scripts; "Roses" cover 1 3 4 6 8 10
1-American Entertainment Edition-wraparound-c 1 3 4 6 8 10
1-"Fashion magazine-style" variant-c 1 3 4 6 8 10
1-Special Comicon Edition (contents of #1) Winged devil variant-c 2 4 6 9 12 15
1-($2.50)-Remastered Ed.-wraparound-c 5.00
2(Reg-c),2-Spiderweb and Moon variant-c 1 3 4 6 8 10
3(Reg-c),3-"Kalvin Clein" variant-c by Drew 4.00
4,5(Reg-c), 4-Variant-c 4.00
5-B&W Edition, 5-Dynamic Forces Gold Ed. 8.00
0-(3/98, $2.50) 6.00
0-Remastered (1/01, $2.95) includes Darkchylde: Redemption preview 6.00
1/2-WIzard offer 1 2 3 5 6 8
1/2 Variant-c 1 3 4 6 8 10
... The Descent TPB ('98, $19.95) r/#1-5; bagged with Darkchylde The Legacy Preview Special 1998; listed price is for TPB only 20.00

DARKCHYLDE LAST ISSUE SPECIAL
Darkchylde Entertainment: June, 2002 ($3.95)
1-Wraparound-c; cover gallery 5.00

DARKCHYLDE REDEMPTION
Darkchylde Entertainment: Feb, 2001 - No. 2, Dec, 2001 ($2.95)
1,2: 1-Wraparound-c 3.00
1-Dynamic Forces alternate-c 6.00
1-Dynamic Forces chrome-c 16.00

DARKCHYLDE SKETCH BOOK
Image Comics (Dynamic Forces): 1998
1-Regular-c 8.00
1-DarkChrome cover 16.00

DARKCHYLDE SUMMER SWIMSUIT SPECTACULAR
DC Comics (WildStorm): Aug, 1999 ($3.95, one-shot)
1-Pin-up art by various 5.00

DARKCHYLDE SWIMSUIT ILLUSTRATED
Image Comics: 1998 ($2.50, one-shot)
1-Pin-up art by various 1 2 3 5 6 8
1-(6.95) Variant cover 1 3 4 6 8 10
1-Chromium cover 15.00

DARKCHYLDE THE DIARY
Image Comics: June, 1997 ($2.50, one-shot)
1-Queen-c/s/ art by various 3.00
1-Variant-c 5.00
1-Holochrome variant-c 8.00

DARKCHYLDE THE LEGACY
Image Comics/DC (WildStorm) #3 on: Aug, 1998 - No. 3, June, 1999 ($2.50)
1-3: 1-Queen-c. 2-Two covers by Queen and Art Adams 3.00

DARK CLAW ADVENTURES
DC Comics (Amalgam): June, 1997 ($1.95, one-shot)
1-Templeton-c/s/a & Burchett-a 3.00

DARK CRISIS (Title changes to Dark Crisis on Infinite Earths for #4-7)(See Justice League #75 from 2022)
DC Comics: No. 0, Jun, 2022 - No. 7, Feb, 2023 ($5.99/$4.99)
0 FCBD Special Edition 2022 (6/22, giveaway) Cheung-a; preview of Dark Crisis #1 3.00
1-(8/22, $5.99) Williamson-s/Sampere-a; Jon Kent forms a new Justice League 6.00
2-6 ($4.99) 2-Deathstroke vs. Nightwing. 4-Legion of Doom app. 6-Justice League returns 5.00
7 ($5.99) Conclusion; s/a by various 6.00
...: Big Bang 1 (2/23, $3.99) Waid-s/Jurgens-a; Flash vs. Anti-Monitor across Multiverse 4.00
...: The Dark Army 1 (1/23, $5.99) Damian Wayne vs. The Darkness 6.00
...: The Deadly Green 1 (12/22, $5.99) Jon Kent with Swamp Thing, Constantine, Raven 6.00
...: War Zone 1 (2/23, $5.99) Short battle stories with Wally West, various Green Lanterns 6.00
...: Worlds Without a Justice League - Batman 1 (1/23, $4.99) Back-up with Zatanna 5.00
...: Worlds Without a Justice League - Green Arrow 1 (12/22, $4.99) Black Canary app. 5.00
...: Worlds Without a Justice League - Green Lantern 1 (10/22, $4.99) Back-up w/Hawkgirl 5.00
...: Worlds Without a Justice League - Superman 1 (9/22, $4.99) Back-up with Aquaman 5.00
...: Worlds Without a Justice League - Wonder Woman 1 (11/22, $4.99) Martian Manhunter 5.00

DARK CRISIS: YOUNG JUSTICE
DC Comics: Aug, 2022 - No. 6, Jan, 2023 ($3.99, liimted series)
1-6-Fitzmartin-s/Braga-a. 4-6-Mickey Mxyzptlk app. 4.00

DARK CROSSINGS: DARK CLOUDS RISING
Image Comics (Top Cow): June, 2000; Oct, 2000 ($5.95, limited series)
1-Witchblade, Darkness, Tomb Raider crossover; Dwayne Turner-a 6.00
1-(Dark Clouds Overhead) 6.00

DARK CRYSTAL, THE (Movie)
Marvel Comics Group: April, 1983 - No. 2, May, 1983
1,2-Adaptation of film 2 4 6 11 16 20

DARK DAYS (See 30 Days of Night)
IDW Publishing: June, 2003 - No. 6, Dec, 2003 ($3.99, limited series)
1-6-Sequel to 30 Days of Night; Niles-s/Templesmith-a 4.00
1-Retailer variant (Diamond/Alliance Fort Wayne 5/03 summit) 15.00
TPB (2004, $19.99) r/#1-6; cover gallery; intro. by Eric Red 20.00

DARK DAYS (Tie-ins to Dark Nights: Metal series)
DC Comics: Aug, 2017 - Sept, 2017 ($4.99, one-shots)
...: The Casting 1 (9/17, $4.99) Snyder & Tynion IV-s; Jim Lee, Andy Kubert & Romita Jr.-a; Joker, Green Lantern & Hawkman app. 5.00
...: The Forge (8/17, $4.99) Lee, Kubert & Romita Jr.-a; Mister Miracle, Mr. Terrific app. 5.00
...: The Forge/The Casting Director's Cut (1/18, $7.99) reprints 2 issues with B&W pencil-a; original script for The Forge 8.00

DARKDEVIL (See Spider-Girl)
Marvel Comics: Nov, 2000 - No. 3, Jan, 2001 ($2.99, limited series)
1-3: 1-Origin of Darkdevil; Kingpin-c/app. 3.00

DARK DOMINION
Defiant: Oct, 1993 - No. 10, July, 1994 ($2.50)
1-10-Len Wein scripts begin. 1-Intro Chasm. 4-Free extra 16 pgs. 7-9-J.G. Jones-c/a (his 1st pro work). 10-Pre-Schism issue; Shooter/Wein script; John Ridgway-a 3.00

DARKER IMAGE (Also see Deathblow, The Maxx, & Bloodwulf)
Image Comics: Mar, 1993 ($1.95, one-shot)
1-The Maxx by Sam Kieth begins; Bloodwulf by Rob Liefeld & Deathblow by Jim Lee begin (both 1st app.); polybagged w/1 of 3 cards by Kieth, Lee or Liefeld 3.00
1-B&W interior pgs. w/silver foil logo 6.00

DARK FANG
Image Comics: Nov, 2017 - No. 5, Mar, 2018 ($3.99)
1-5-Gunter-s/Shannon-a 4.00

DARK FANTASIES
Dark Fantasy: 1994 - No. 8, 1995 ($2.95)
1-Test print Run (3,000)-Linsner-c 1 2 3 5 6 8
1-Linsner-c 5.00

Dark Ark #12 © Cullen Bunn

Dark Crisis: Young Justice #1 © DC

Dark Horse Present #3 © DH

	GD 2.0	VG 4.0	FN 6.0	VF 8.0	VF/NM 9.0	NM- 9.2

2-8: 2-4 (Deluxe), 2-4 (Regular), 5-8 (Deluxe; $3.95) 4.00
5-8 (Regular; $3.50) 3.50

DARK GUARD
Marvel Comics UK: Oct, 1993 - No. 4, Jan, 1994 ($1.75)

1-($2.95)-Foil stamped-c 4.00
2-4 3.00

DARKHAWK (See Marvel Age #97 {Feb. 1991} for debut, and War of Kings)
Marvel Comics: Mar, 1991 - No. 50, Apr, 1995 ($1.00/$1.25/$1.50)

1-Origin of Darkhawk; Hobgoblin cameo 3 6 9 17 26 35
2,3,13,14: 2-Spider-Man & Hobgoblin app. 3-Spider-Man & Hobgoblin app. 13,14-Venom-c/story 5.00
4-12,15-24,26-49: 6-Capt. America & Daredevil x-over. 9-Punisher app. 11,12-Tombstone app. 19-Spider-Man & Brotherhood of Evil Mutants-c/story. 20-Spider-Man app. 22-Ghost Rider-c/story. 23-Origin begins, ends #25. 27-New Warriors-c/story. 35-Begin 3 part Venom story. 39-Bound-in trading card sheet 4.00
25,50: (52 pgs.)-Red holo-grafx foil-c w/double gatefold poster; origin of Darkhawk armor 5.00
Annual 1,2 ('92, '93, 68 pgs.): 1-Vs. Iron Man. 2 -Polybagged w/card 5.00
Annual 3 ('94, 68 pgs.) Low print run 3 6 9 14 20 25

DARKHAWK (Marvel Legacy)
Marvel Comics: No. 51, Jan, 2018 ($3.99, one-shot)

51-Bowers & Sims-s/Kev Walker-a/Nakayama-c 6.00

DARKHAWK
Marvel Comics: Oct, 2021 - No. 5, Mar, 2022 ($4.99/$3.99, limited series)

1-($4.99) Higgins-s/Ramirez-a; intro. Connor Young as the new Darkhawk 5.00
2-5-($3.99) 3-5-Spider-Man (Miles) app. 4-Captain America app. 4.00
...: Heart of the Hawk (6/21, $4.99) Three short stories of the original Darkhawk 5.00

DARKHOLD, THE
Marvel Comics: Nov, 2021 - Mar, 2022 ($4.99/$3.99, series of one-shots)

... Alpha 1 (11/21, $4.99) 1st part; Orlando-s/Tormey-a; Scarlet Witch & Doom app. 5.00
... Black Bolt 1 (1/22, $3.99) Russell-s/Cutler-a; Maximus app. 4.00
... Blade 1 (12/21, $3.99) Kibblesmith-s/Sabbatini-a; vampire Amadeus Cho app. 4.00
... Iron Man 1 (12/21, $3.99) North-s/Sanna-a; alternate past with grey armor shown 4.00
... Omega 1 (3/22, $4.99) Conclusion; Orlando-s/Tormey-a; Chthon arrives 5.00
... Spider-Man 1 (2/22, $3.99) Paknadel-s/Neves-a; alternate past shown 4.00
... Wasp 1 (1/22, $3.99) Bellaire-s/Roe-a; alternate past with shown; Tigra app. 4.00

DARKHOLD: PAGES FROM THE BOOK OF SINS (See Midnight Sons Unlimited)
Marvel Comics (Midnight Sons imprint #15 on): Oct, 1992 - No. 16, Jan, 1994

1-($2.75, 52 pgs.)-Polybagged w/poster by Andy & Adam Kubert; part 4 of Rise of the Midnight Sons storyline 1 2 3 5 6 8
2-10,12-16: 3-Reintro Modred the Mystic (see Marvel Chillers #1). 4-Sabertooth-c/sty. 5-Punisher & Ghost Rider app. 15-Spot varnish-c. 15,16-Siege of Darkness pt. 4&12 3.00
11-($2.25)-Outer-c is a Darkhold envelope made of black parchment w/gold ink 4.00

DARK HORSE BOOK OF..., THE
Dark Horse Comics: Aug, 2003 - Nov, 2006 ($14.95/$15.95, HC, 9 1/4" x 6 1/4")

... Hauntings (8/03, $14.95)-Short stories by various incl. Mignola (Hellboy), Thompson, Dorkin, Russell; Gianni-c 15.00
... Monsters (11/06, $15.95)-Short-s by Mignola, Thompson, Dorkin, Giffen, Busiek; Gianni-c 16.00
... The Dead (6/05, $14.95)-Short-s by Mignola, Thompson, Dorkin, Powell; Gianni-c 15.00
... Witchcraft (6/04, $14.95)-Short-s by Mignola, Thompson, Dorkin, Millionaire; Gianni-c 15.00

DARK HORSE CLASSICS (Title series), **Dark Horse Comics**

1992 ($3.95, B&W, 52 pgs. nn's): The Last of the Mohicans. 20,000 Leagues Under the Sea 4.00

DARK HORSE CLASSICS
Dark Horse Comics: May, 1996 ($2.95, limited series)

1-Reprints Predator: Jungle Tales 1 2 3 5 6 8

DARK HORSE CLASSICS: ALIENS VERSUS PREDATOR
Dark Horse Comics: Feb, 1997 - No. 6, Jul, 1997 ($2.95, limited series)

1-Reprints Aliens Versus Predator series 1 3 4 6 8 10
2-6: R/Aliens Versus Predator 5.00

DARK HORSE CLASSICS: GODZILLA: KING OF THE MONSTERS
Dark Horse Comics: Apr, 1998 - No. 6, Sept, 1998 ($2.95, limited series)

1-Reprints Godzilla: Color Special; Art Adams-a 2 4 6 11 16 20
2-6 5.00

DARK HORSE CLASSICS: GODZILLA: TERROR OF GODZILLA
Dark Horse Comics: Aug, 1998 - No. 6, Jan, 1999 ($2.95, limited series)

1-Reprints manga Godzilla in color; Art Adams-c 2 4 6 11 16 20
2-6 1 2 3 5 6 8

DARK HORSE CLASSICS – STAR WARS: DARK EMPIRE
Dark Horse Comics: Mar, 1997 - No. 6, Aug, 1997 ($2.95, limited series)

1,3-Reprints Star Wars: Dark Empire 2 4 6 8 11 14
2,4-6: R/Star Wars: Dark Empire 5.00

DARK HORSE COMICS
Dark Horse Comics: Aug, 1992 - No. 25, Sept, 1994 ($2.50)

1-Dorman double gategold painted-c; Predator, Robocop, Timecop (3-part) & Renegade stories begin 1 2 3 5 6 8
2-6,11-25: 2-Mignola-c. 3-Begin 3-part Aliens story; Aliens-c. 4-Predator-c. 6-Begin 4 part Robocop story. 12-Begin 2-part Aliens & 3-part Predator stories. 13-Thing From Another World begins w/Nino-a(i). 15-Begin 2-part Aliens: Cargo story. 16-Begin 3-part Predator story. 17-Begin 3-part Star Wars: Droids story & 3-part Aliens: Alien story; Droids-c. 19-Begin 2-part X story; X cover 4.00
7-Begin Star Wars: Tales of the Jedi 3-part story 2 4 6 8 10 12
8-1st app. X and begins; begin 4-part James Bond 1 2 3 5 6 8
9,10: 9-Star Wars ends. 10-X ends; Begin 3-part Predator & Godzilla stories 5.00
NOTE: *Art Adams c-11.*

DARK HORSE DAY SAMPLER 2016
Dark Horse Comics: Jun, 2016 (no price, promotional one-shot)

nn-New Buffy the Vampire Slayer story; reprint stories of Sin City, AvP, Umbrella Academy 3.00

DARK HORSE DOWN UNDER
Dark Horse Comics: Jun, 1994 - No. 3, Oct, 1994 ($2.50, B&W, limited series)

1-3 3.00

DARK HORSE MAVERICK
Dark Horse Comics: July, 2000; July, 2001; Sept, 2002 (B&W, annual)

2000-($3.95) Short stories by Miller, Chadwick, Sakai, Pearson 4.00
2001-($4.99) Short stories by Sakai, Wagner and others; Miller-c 5.00
...: Happy Endings (9/02, $9.95) Short stories by Bendis, Oeming, Mahfood, Mignola, Miller, Kieth and others; Miller-c 10.00

DARK HORSE MONSTERS
Dark Horse Comics: Feb, 1997 ($2.95, one-shot)

1-Reprints 3.00

DARK HORSE PRESENTS
Dark Horse Comics: July, 1986 - No. 157, Sept, 2000 ($1.50-$2.95, B&W)

1-1st app. Concrete by Paul Chadwick 3 6 9 17 25 34
1-2nd printing (1988, $1.50) 4.00
1-Silver ink 3rd printing (1992, $2.25)-Says 2nd printing inside 4.00
2-9: 2-6,9-Concrete app. 6.00
10-1st app. The Mask; Concrete app. 4 8 12 25 40 55
11-19,21-23: 11-19,21-Mask stories. 12,14,16,18,22-Concrete app. 15(2/88). 17-All Roachmill issue 6.00
20-(68 pgs.)-Concrete, Flaming Carrot, Mask 2 4 6 8 10 12
24-Origin Aliens-c/story (11/88); Mr. Monster app. 3 6 9 17 26 35
25-27,29-31,37-39,41,44,45,47-49: 38-Concrete. 44-Crash Ryan. 48,49-Contain 2 trading cards 3.00
28,33,40: 28-(52 pgs.)-Concrete app.; Mr. Monster story (homage to Graham Ingels). 33-(44 pgs.). 40-(52 pgs.)-1st Argosy story 4.00
32,34,35: 32-(68 pgs.)-Annual; Concrete, American. 34-Aliens-c/story. 35-Predator-c/app. 5.00
36-1st Aliens Vs. Predator story; painted-c 3 6 9 15 22 28
36-Variant line drawn-c 3 6 9 19 30 40
42,43,46: 42,43-Aliens-c/stories. 46-Prequel to new Predator II mini-series 3.00
50-S/F story by Perez; contains 2 trading cards 4.00
51-53-Sin City by Frank Miller, parts 2-4; 51,53-Miller-c (see D.H.P. Fifth Anniversary Special for pt. 1) 1 3 4 6 8 10
54-61: 54-(9/91) The Next Men begins (1st app.) by Byrne; Miller-a/Morrow-c. Homocide by Morrow (also in #55). 55-2nd app. The Next Men; parts 5 & 6 of Sin City by Miller; Miller-c. 56-(68 pg. annual)-part 7 of Sin City by Miller; part prologue to Aliens: Genocide; Next Men by Byrne. 57-(52 pgs.)-Part 8 of Sin City by Miller; Next Men by Byrne; Byrne & Miller-c; Alien Fire story; swipes cover to Daredevil #1. 58,59-Alien Fire stories. 58-61- Part 9-12 Sin City by Miller 5.00
62-Last Sin City (entire book by Miller, c/a; 52 pgs.) 2 4 6 9 13 16
63-66,68-79,81-84-($2.25): 64-Dr. Giggles begins (1st app.), ends #66; Boris the Bear story. 66-New Concrete-c/story by Chadwick. 71-Begin 3 part Dominque story by Jim Balent; Balent-c. 72-(3/93)-Begin 3-part Eudaemon (1st app.) story by Nelson 3.00
67-($3.95, 68 pgs.)-Begin 3-part prelude to Predator: Race War mini-series; Oscar Wilde adapt. by Russell 4.00
80-Art Adams-c/a (Monkeyman & O'Brien) 4.00
85-87,92-99: 85-Begin $2.50-c. 92, 93, 95-Too Much Coffee Man 3.00
88-Hellboy by Mignola. 2 4 6 9 13 16
89-91-Hellboy by Mignola. 1 2 3 5 6 8
NOTE: *There are 5 different Dark Horse Presents #100 issues*

100-1-Intro Lance Blastoff by Miller; Milk & Cheese by Evan Dorkin 5.00
100-2-Hellboy-c by Wrightson; Hellboy story by Mignola; includes Roberta Gregory & Paul Pope stories 1 2 3 5 6 8
100-3-100-5: 100-3-Darrow-c, Concrete by Chadwick; Pekar story. 100-4-Gibbons-c: Miller story, Geary story/a. 100-5-Allred-c, Adams, Dorkin, Pope 3.00
101-125: 101-Aliens c/a by Wrightson, story by Pope. 103-Kirby gatefold-c. 106-Big Blown Baby by Bill Wray. 107-Mignola-c/a. 109-Begin $2.95-c; Paul Pope-c. 110-Ed Brubaker-a/s. 114-Flip books begin; Lance Blastoff by Miller; Star Slammers by Simonson. 115-Miller-c. 117-Aliens-c/app. 118-Evan Dorkin-c/a. 119-Monkeyman & O'Brien. 124-Predator. 125-Nocturnals 3.00
126-($3.95, 48 pgs.)-Flip book: Nocturnals, Starship Troopers 4.00
127-134,136-140: 127-Nocturnals. 129-The Hammer. 132-134-Warren-a 3.00
135-($3.50) The Mark 3.50
141-All Buffy the Vampire Slayer issue 4.00
142-149: 142-Mignola-c. 143-Tarzan. 146,147-Aliens vs. Predator. 148-Xena 3.00
150-($4.50) Buffy-c by Green; Buffy, Concrete, Fish Police app. 4.50
151-157: 151-Hellboy-c/app. 153-155-Angel flip-c. 156,157-Witch's Son 3.00
Annual 1997 ($4.95, 64 pgs.)-Flip book; Body Bags, Aliens. Pearson-c; stories by Allred & Stephens, Pope, Smith & Morrow 1 2 3 5 6 8
Annual 1998 ($4.95, 64 pgs.) 1st Buffy the Vampire Slayer comic app.; Hellboy story and cover by Mignola 4 8 12 25 40 55
Annual 1999 (7/99, $4.95) Stories of Xena, Hellboy, Ghost, Luke Skywalker, Groo, Concrete, the Mask and Usagi Yojimbo in their youth. 1 2 3 5 6 8
Annual 2000 ($4.95) Girl sidekicks; Chiodo-c and flip photo Buffy-c 1 3 4 6 8 10
...Aliens Platinum Edition (1992)-r/DHP #24,43,43,56 & Special 2 4 6 9 12 15
...Fifth Anniversary Special nn (4/91, $9.95)-Part 1 of Sin City by Frank Miller (c/a); Aliens, Aliens vs. Predator, Concrete, Roachmill, Give Me Liberty & The American stories 40.00
The One Trick Rip-off (1997, $12.95, TPB)-r/stories from #101-112 13.00
NOTE: ***Geary** a-59, 60. **Miller** a-Special, 51-53, 55-62; c-59-62, 100-1; c-51, 53, 55, 59-62, 100-1. **Moebius** a-63; c-63, 70. **Vess** a-78; c-75, 78.*

DARK HORSE PRESENTS
Dark Horse Comics: Apr, 2011 - No. 36, May, 2014 ($7.99, anthology)
1-36: 1-Frank Miller-c & Xerxes preview; Neal Adams-s/a. 1-3-Concrete by Chadwick. 1-8-Chaykin-s/a. 2,3,9-Corben-a. 3-Steranko interview. 7-Hellboy app. 10-Milk & Cheese. 12-17-Aliens; Kieth-a. 14-Flipbook. 18-Capt. Midnight. 23-26,29-34-Nexus. 25,26-Buffy. 28,29-Neal Adams-s/a. 31,32-Hellboy; McMahon-a 8.00

DARK HORSE PRESENTS (Volume 3)
Dark Horse Comics: Aug, 2014 - No. 33, Apr, 2017 ($4.99, anthology)
1-6: 1-Two covers. 1,2-Rusty & Big Guy by Darrow-s/a. 2-Aliens. 5-Alex Ross-c 5.00
7-(2/15) 200th Issue; Hellboy by Mignola & Bá, Groo, Mind Mgmt; Gibbons, Darrow-a5.00
8-15,17-33: 8-10-Tarzan by Grell. 14,15-The Rook; Gulacy-a. 17,18-Levitz-s 5.00
16-($5.99) Flip book with Hellboy by Mignola; art by Calero, Ordway, McCarthy 6.00

DARK HORSE TWENTY YEARS
Dark Horse Comics: 2006 (25¢, one-shot)
nn-Pin-ups by Dark Horse artists of other artists' Dark Horse characters; Mignola-c 3.00

DARK IVORY
Image Comics: Mar, 2008 - No. 4, Jan, 2009 ($2.99, limited series)
1-4-Eva Hopkins & Joseph Michael Linsner-s/Linsner-a/c 3.00

DARK KNIGHT (See Batman: The Dark Knight Returns & Legends of the...)

DARK KNIGHT RETURNS: THE GOLDEN CHILD
DC Comics (Black Label): Feb, 2020 ($5.99, squarebound, one-shot)
1-Frank Miller-s/Rafael Grampá-a; Lara & Carrie from DK III vs. Joker & Darkseid 6.00
1-Retailer incentive-c by Miller (limited 1 for 100) 40.00

DARK KNIGHT RETURNS, THE: THE LAST CRUSADE
DC Comics: Aug, 2016 ($6.99, squarebound, one-shot)
1-Miller & Azzarello-s/Romita Jr.-a; Jason Todd Robin vs. The Joker; Poison Ivy app. 7.00

DARK KNIGHTS OF STEEL
DC Comics: Jan, 2022 - No. 12 ($3.99, limited series)
1-9: 1-The El family's rocket lands in Medieval times; Taylor-s/Putri-a. 4-Bengal-a 4.00
...: Tales From the Three Kingdoms 1 (11/22, $5.99) Short stories; origin of the Robins 6.00
...: The Gathering Storm 1 (2022, $6.99) Reprints #1-3 7.00

DARK KNIGHTS RISING: THE WILD HUNT (See Dark Nights: Metal series and other tie-ins)
DC Comics: Apr, 2018 ($4.99, one-shot)
1-Snyder & Morrison-s/Porter & Mahnke-a; Detective Chimp app.; foil-c 5.00

DARK KNIGHT STRIKES AGAIN, THE (Also see Batman: The Dark Knight Returns)
DC Comics: 2001 - No. 3, 2002 ($7.95, prestige format, limited series)
1-Frank Miller-s/a/c; sequel set 3 years after Dark Knight Returns; 2 covers 10.00
2,3 10.00
HC (2002, $29.95) intro. by Miller; sketch pages and exclusive artwork; cover has 3 1/4" tall partial dustjacket 30.00
SC (2002, $19.95) intro. by Miller; sketch pages 20.00

DARK KNIGHT III: THE MASTER RACE (Also see Batman: The Dark Knight Returns)
DC Comics: Jan, 2016 - No. 9, Jul, 2017 ($5.99, cardstock cover, limited series)
1-9: 1-Miller & Azzarello-s/Andy Kubert-a; Dark Knight Universe Presents: The Atom mini-comic attached at centerfold, Miller-a. 2-Wonder Woman mini-comic. 3-Superman returns; Green Lantern mini-comic. 4-Batgirl mini-comic. 5-Lara mini-comic. 6-World's Finest mini-comic. 7-Strange Adventures mini-comic. 8-Detective mini. 9-Action mini 6.00
1-8-Deluxe Edition ($12.99, HC) reprints story plus mini-comic at full size; cover gallery 13.00
9-Deluxe Edition ($12.99, HC) Sold with slipcase fitting all 9 Deluxe Edition HCs 13.00
... Book One - Director's Cut (11/16, $7.99) r/ #1 in B&W art; script, variant cover gallery 8.00

DARKLON THE MYSTIC (Also see Eerie Magazine #79,80)
Pacific Comics: Oct, 1983 (one-shot)
1-Starlin-c/a(r) 4.00

DARKMAN (Movie)
Marvel Comics: Sept, 1990; Oct, 1990 - No. 3, Dec, 1990 ($1.50)
1 (9/90, $2.25, B&W mag., 68 pgs.)-Adaptation of film 4.00
1-3: Reprints B&W magazine 3.00

DARKMAN
Marvel Comics: V2#1, Apr, 1993 -No. 6, Sept, 1993 ($2.95, limited series)
V2#1 ($3.95, 52 pgs.) 4.00
2-6 3.00

DARK MANSION OF FORBIDDEN LOVE, THE (Becomes Forbidden Tales of Dark Mansion No. 5 on)
National Periodical Publ.: Sept-Oct, 1971 - No. 4, Mar-Apr, 1972 (52 pgs.)
1-Greytone-c on all 17 34 51 119 265 410
2-4: 2-Adams-c. 3-Jeff Jones-c 9 18 27 60 120 180

DARKMAN VS. THE ARMY OF DARKNESS (Movie crossover)
Dynamite Entertainment: 2006 - No. 4, 2007 ($3.50)
1-4: 1-Busiek & Stern-s/Fry-a; photo-c and Perez and Bradshaw covers 3.50

DARK MATTER (Inspired 2015 TV series on SyFy channel)
Dark Horse Comics.: Jan, 2012 - No. 4, Apr, 2012 ($3.50, limited series)
1-4-Joseph Mallozzi & Paul Mullie-s/Garry Brown-a 4.00

DARKMINDS
Image Comics (Dreamwave Prod.): July, 1998 - No. 8, Apr, 1999 ($2.50)
1-Manga; Pat Lee-s/a; 2 covers 1 3 4 6 8 10
1-2nd printing 3.00
2, 0-(1/99, $5.00) Story and sketch pages 5.00
3-8, 1/2-(5/99, $2.50) Story and sketch pages 3.00
... Collected 1,2 (1/99,3/99; $7.95) 1-r/#1-3. 2-r/#4-6 8.00
... Collected 3 (5/99; $5.95) r/#7,8 6.00

DARKMINDS (Volume 2)
Image Comics (Dreamwave Prod.): Feb, 2000 - No. 10, Apr, 2001 ($2.50)
1-10-Pat Lee-c 3.00
0-(7/00) Origin of Mai Murasaki; sketchbook 3.00

DARKMINDS: MACROPOLIS
Image Comics (Dreamwave Prod.): Jan, 2002 - No. 4, Dec, 2002 ($2.95)
Preview (8/01) Flip book w/Banished Knights preview 3.00
1-4-Jo Chen-a 3.00

DARKMINDS: MACROPOLIS (Volume 2)
Dreamwave Prod.: Sept, 2003 - No. 4, Jul, 2004 ($2.95)
1-4-Chris Sarracini-s/Kwang Mook Lim-a 3.00

DARKMINDS / WITCHBLADE (Also see Witchblade/Dark Minds)
Image Comics (Top Cow/Dreamwave Prod.): Aug, 2000 ($5.95, one-shot)
1-Wohl-s/Pat Lee-a; two covers by Silvestri and Lee 6.00

DARK MYSTERIES (Thrilling Tales of Horror & Suspense)
"Master" - "Merit" Publications: June-July, 1951 - No. 24, July, 1955
1-Wood-c/a (8 pgs.) 168 336 504 1075 1838 2600
2-Classic skull-c; Wood/Harrison-c/a (8 pgs.) 258 516 774 1651 2826 4000
3-9: 7-Dismemberment, hypo blood drainage stys 81 162 243 518 884 1250
10-Cannibalism story; witch burning-c 486 972 1458 3550 6275 9000
11-13,15-17: 11-Severed head panels. 13-Dismemberment-c/story. 17-The Old Gravedigger host 68 136 204 435 743 1050
14-Several E.C. Craig swipes 81 162 243 518 884 1250
18-Bondage, skeletons-c 116 232 348 742 1271 1800
19-Injury-to-eye panel; E.C. swipe; torture-c 432 864 1296 3154 5577 8000
20-Female bondage, blood drainage story 87 174 261 553 952 1350
21,22: 21-Devil-c. 22-Last pre-code issue, misdated 3/54 instead of 3/55 54 108 162 343 574 825
23,24 42 84 126 265 445 625
NOTE: ***Cameron** a-1, 2. **Myron Fass** c/a-21. **Harrison** a-3, 7; c-3. **Hollingsworth** a-7-17, 20, 21, 23. **Wildey** a-5. Woodish art by **Fleishman**-9; c-10, 14-17. Bondage c-10, 18, 19.*

DARK NEMESIS (VILLAINS) (See Teen Titans)
DC Comics: Feb, 1998 ($1.95, one-shot)
1-Jurgens-s/Pearson-c 4.00

DARKNESS, THE (See Witchblade #10)
Image Comics (Top Cow Productions): Dec, 1996 - No. 40, Aug, 2001 ($2.50)
Special Preview Edition-(7/96, B&W)-Ennis script; Silvestri-a(p) 2 4 6 9 13 16
0 2 4 6 8 10 12
0-Gold Edition 16.00
1/2 1 3 4 6 8 10
1/2-Christmas-c 3 6 9 14 19 24
1/2-(3/01, $2.95) r/#1/2 w/new 6 pg. story & Silvestri-c 3.00
1-Ennis-s/Silvestri-a, 1-Black variant-c 2 4 6 9 12 15
1-Platinum variant-c 20.00
1-DF Green variant-c 12.00
1-25th Anniversary Commemorative Edition (11/20, $4.99) r/#1 with creator interviews 5.00
1,2: 1-Fan Club Ed. 1 3 4 6 8 10
3-5 6.00
6-10: 9,10-Witchblade "Family Ties" x-over pt. 2,3 4.00
7-Variant-c w/concubine 1 2 3 5 7 9
8-American Entertainment 6.00
8-10-American Entertainment Gold Ed. 7.00
11-Regular Ed.; Ennis-s/Silverstri & D-Tron-c 3.00
11-Nine (non-chromium) variant-c (Benitez, Cabrera, the Hildebrandts, Finch, Keown, Peterson, Portacio, Tan, Turner 4.50
11-Chromium-c by Silvestri & Batt 20.00
12-19: 13-Begin Benitez-a(p) 3.00
20-24,26-40: 34-Ripclaw app. 3.00
25-($3.99) Two covers (Benitez, Silvestri) 4.00
25-Chromium-c variant by Silvestri 8.00
.../ Batman (8/99, $5.95) Silvestri, Finch, Lansing-a(p) 6.00
...Collected Editions #1-4 ($4.95,TPB) 1-r/#1,2. 2-r/#3,4. 3- r/#5,6. 4- r/#7,8 6.00
...Collected Editions #5,6 ($5.95, TPB)5- r/#11,12. 6-r/#13,14 6.00
Deluxe Collected Editions #1 (12/98, $14.95, TPB) r/#1-6 & Preview 15.00
...: Heart of Darkness (2001, $14.95, TPB) r/ #7,8, 11-14 15.00

Dark Knights of Steel #1 © DC

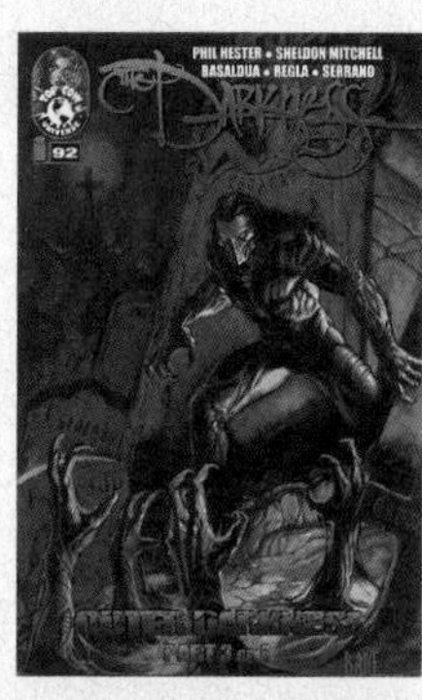

Darkness #92 © TCOW

Dark Reign: Elektra #5 © MAR

GD VG FN VF VF/NM NM-
2.0 4.0 6.0 8.0 9.0 9.2

Holiday Pin-up-American Entertainment 5.00
Holiday Pin-up Gold Ed.-American Entertainment 7.00
Image Firsts: Darkness #1 (9/10, $1.00) r/#1 with "Image Firsts" logo on cover 3.00
Infinity #1 (8/99, $3.50) Lobdell-s 3.50
Prelude-American Entertainment 4.00
Prelude Gold Ed.-American Entertainment 9.00
Volume 1 Compendium (2006, $59.99) r/#1-40, V2 #1, Tales of the Darkness #1-4; #1/2, Darkness/Witchblade #1/2, Darkness: Wanted Dead; cover and sketch gallery 60.00
...: Wanted Dead 1 (8/03, $2.99) Texiera-a/Tieri-s 3.00
Wizard ACE Ed.- Reprints #1 2 4 6 8 10 12

DARKNESS (Volume 2)
Image Comics (Top Cow Productions): Dec, 2002 - No. 24, Oct, 2004 ($2.99)

1-24: 1-6-Jenkins-s/Keown-a. 17-20-Lapham-s. 23,24-Magdalena app. 3.00
... Black Sails (3/05, $2.99) Marz-s/Cha-a; Hunter-Killer preview 3.00
... and Tomb Raider (4/05, $2.99) r/Darkness Prelude & Tomb Raider/Darkness Special 3.00
...: Resurrection TPB (2/04, $16.99) r/#1-6 & Vol. 1 #40 17.00
.../ The Incredible Hulk (7/04, $2.99) Keown-a/Jenkins-s 3.00
.../ Vampirella (7/05, $2.99) Terry Moore-s; two covers by Basaldua and Moore 3.00
... Vol. 5 TPB (2006, $19.99) r/#7-16 & The Darkness: Wanted Dead #1; cover gallery 20.00
... vs. Mr Hyde Monster War 2005 (9/05, $2.99) x-over w/Witchblade, Tomb Raider and Magdalena; two covers 3.00
.../ Wolverine (2006, $2.99) Kirkham-a/Tieri-s 3.00

DARKNESS (Volume 3) (Numbering jumps from #10 to #75)
Image Comics (Top Cow Productions): Dec, 2007 - No. 116, Dec, 2013 ($2.99)

1-10: 1-Hester-s/Broussard-a. 1-Three covers. 7-9-Lucas-a. 8-Aphrodite IV app. 3.00
75 (2/09, $4.99) Four covers; Hester-s/art by various 5.00
76-99,101-113,115-($2.99) 76-99,101-Multiple covers on each 3.00
100 (2/12, $4.99) Four covers; Hester-s/art by various; cover gallery; series timeline 5.00
114-($4.99) The Age of Reason Part 1; Hine-s/Haun-a; bonus Darkness timeline 5.00
116-($3.99) The Age of Reason Part 3; Hine-s/Haun-a 4.00
... : Butcher (4/08, $3.99) Story of Butcher Joyce; Levin-s/Broussard-a/c 4.00
... : Close Your Eyes (6/14, $3.99) Story of Adelmo Estacado in 1912; Kot-s/Oleksicki-a/c 4.00
...: Confession (5/11) Free Comic Boy Day giveaway; Broussard & Molnar-a 3.00
... / Darkchylde: Kingdom Pain 1 (5/10, $4.99) Randy Queen-s/a 5.00
... First Look (11/07, 99¢) Previews series; sketch pages 3.00
... : Hope (4/16, $3.99) Harmon-s/Dwyer-a/Linda Sejic-c 4.00
... : Lodbrok's Hand (12/08, $2.99) Hester-s/Oeming-a/c; variant-c by Carnevale 3.00
... : Shadows and Flame 1 (1/10, $2.99) Lucas-c/a 3.00
... : Vicious Traditions 1 (3/14, $3.99) Ales Kot-s/Dean Ormston-a/Dale Keown-c 4.00

DARKNESS: FOUR HORSEMEN
Image Comics (Top Cow): Aug, 2010 - No. 4, May, 2011 ($3.99, limited series)

1-4-Hine-s/Wamester-a 4.00

DARKNESS: LEVEL...
Image Comics (Top Cow): No. 0, Dec, 2006 - No. 5, Aug, 2007 ($2.99, limited series)

0-5: 0-Origin of The Darkness in WW1; Jenkins-s. 1-Jackie's origin retold; Sejic-a 3.00

DARKNESS/ PITT
Image Comics (Top Cow): Dec, 2006; Aug, 2009 - No. 3, Nov, 2009 ($2.99)

...: First Look (12/06) Jenkins script pages with Keown B&W and color art 3.00
1-3: 1-(8/09) Jenkins-s/Keown-a; covers by Keown and Sejic. 2,3-Two covers 3.00

DARKNESS/ SUPERMAN
Image Comics (Top Cow Productions): Jan, 2005 - No. 2, Feb, 2005 ($2.99, limited series)

1,2-Marz-s/Kirkham & Banning-a/Silvestri-c 3.00

DARKNESS VISIBLE
IDW Publishing: Feb, 2017 - No. 6, 2017 ($3.99)

1-6: 1-Mike Carey & Arvind David-s/Brendan Cahill-a. 3,6-Ramondelli-a 4.00

DARKNESS VS. EVA: DAUGHTER OF DRACULA
Dynamite Entertainment: 2008 - No. 4, 2008 ($3.50, limited series)

1-4-Leah Moore & John Reppion-s/Salazar-a; three covers on each 3.50

DARK NIGHT: A TRUE BATMAN STORY
DC Comics: 2016 ($22.99, HC Graphic Novel)

HC - Paul Dini-s/Eduardo Risso-a 23.00

DARK NIGHTS: DEATH METAL
DC Comics: Jul, 2020 - No. 7, Mar, 2021 ($4.99/$5.99, limited series)

1-6-Snyder-s/Capullo-a; sequel to Dark Nights: Metal; Batman Who Laughs app. 5.00
7-($5.99) Multiverse restored; leads into Future State titles 2 4 6 9 12 15
... - Guidebook 1 (10/20, $5.99) short s/a by various; Harley Quinn app. 6.00
... Infinite Hour Exxxtreme 1 (1/21, $5.99) Extremely violent stories hosted by Lobo 6.00
... Legends of the Dark Knights 1 (10/20, $5.99) Origin Robin King & other Batmen 6.00
... Multiverse's End 1 (11/20, $5.99) Capt. Carrot, Owlman. Pres. Superman & others 6.00
... Rise of the New God 1 (11/20, $5.99) Perpetua vs. The Batman Who Laughs 6.00
... Robin King 1 (11/20, $5.99) Robin King vs. the Robins; Rossmo & Sampere-a 6.00
... Speed Metal 1 (11/20, $5.99) Barrows-s; Wally West and other Flashes app. 6.00
... The Last 52: War of the Multiverses 1 (2/21, $8.99) Short stories by various 9.00
... The Last Stories of the DC Universe 1 (2/21, $8.99) Short stories by various 9.00
... The Multiverse That Laughs 1 (1/21, $5.99) Twisted humor short stories by various 6.00
... The Secret Origin 1 (2/21, $5.99) Origin/spotlight on Superboy-Prime 6.00
... Trinity Crisis 1 (11/20, $5.99) Snyder-s/Manapul-a; Batman, Superman, Wonder Woman 6.00

DARK NIGHTS: METAL (Also see Dark Days prelude one-shots)
DC Comics: Nov, 2017 - No. 6, May, 2018 ($4.99/$3.99)

1-($4.99) Snyder-s/Capullo-a; Justice League & Dream of the Endless app.; foil logo-c 1 3 4 6 8 10
1-Second printing; red title logo on cover 5.00
2-5-($3.99) 2-Barbatos app. 6.00
6-($4.99) Finale; leads into Justice League: No Justice series 1 2 3 5 6 8
Director's Cut 1 (2/18, $6.99) r/#1 pencil art; gallery of variant covers 1 3 4 6 8 10

DARK NIGHTS: THE BATMAN WHO LAUGHS (Dark Nights: Metal) (Also see Teen Titans #12 [11/17])
DC Comics: Jan, 2018 ($3.99, one-shot)

1-Tynion IV-s/Rossmo-a; Fabok foil-c; Bruce Wayne as Dark Multiverse Joker 3 6 9 14 20 25

DARK RED
AfterShock Comics: Mar, 2019 - No. 10, Jul, 2020 ($3.99)

1-10-Vampire Nazis in North Dakota; Tim Seeley-s/Corin Howell-a 4.00
1-Special Edition; r/#1 with bonus creator interviews and sketch art 4.00
...: Where Roads Lead 1 (1/22, $6.99, oversized 8-1/2" x 10-7/8") Seeley-s/Howell-a 7.00

DARK REIGN (Follows Secret Invasion crossover)
Marvel Comics: 2009 ($3.99/$4.99, one-shots)

...: Files 1 (2009, $4.99) profile pages of villains tied in to Dark Reign x-over 5.00
...: Made Men 1 (11/09, $3.99) short stories by various incl. Pham, Leon, Oliver 4.00
...: New Nation 1 (2/09, $3.99) previews of various series tied in to Dark Reign x-over 4.00
...: The Cabal 1 (6/09, $3.99) Cabal members stories by various incl. Granov, Acuña 4.00
...: The Goblin Legacy 1 (2009, $3.99) r/ASM #39,40; Osborn history; Mayhew-a 4.00

DARK REIGN: ELEKTRA
Marvel Comics: May, 2009 - No. 5, Oct, 2009 ($3.99, limited series)

1-5-Mann-a/Bermejo-c; Elektra after the Skrull replacement. 2,3-Bullseye app. 4.00

DARK REIGN: FANTASTIC FOUR
Marvel Comics: May, 2009 - No. 5, Sept, 2009 ($2.99, limited series)

1-5-Chen-a 3.00

DARK REIGN: HAWKEYE
Marvel Comics: June, 2009 - No. 5, Mar, 2010 ($3.99, limited series)

1-5-Bullseye in the Dark Avengers; Raney-a/Langley-c. 5-Guinaldo-a 4.00

DARK REIGN: LETHAL LEGION
Marvel Comics: Aug, 2009 - No. 3, Nov, 2009 ($3.99, limited series)

1-3-Santolouco-a/Edwards-c; Grim Reaper and Wonder Man app. 4.00

DARK REIGN: MR. NEGATIVE (Also see Amazing Spider-Man #546)
Marvel Comics: Aug, 2009 - No. 3, Oct, 2009 ($3.99, limited series)

1-3-Jae Lee-c/Gugliotta-a; Spider-Man app. 4.00

DARK REIGN: SINISTER SPIDER-MAN
Marvel Comics: Aug, 2009 - No. 4, Nov, 2009 ($3.99, limited series)

1-4-Bachalo-c/a; Venom/Scorpion as Dark Avenger Spider-Man 4.00

DARK REIGN: THE HOOD
Marvel Comics: Jul, 2009 - No. 5, Nov, 2009 ($3.99, limited series)

1-5-Hotz-a/Djurdjevic-c 4.00

DARK REIGN: THE LIST
Marvel Comics: 2009 - 2010 ($3.99, one-shots)

... - Amazing Spider-Man (1/10, $3.99) Adam Kubert-c/a; back-up r/Pulse #5 4.00
... - Avengers (11/09, $3.99) Bendis-s/Djurdjevic-c/a; Ronin (Hawkeye) app. 4.00
... - Daredevil (11/09, $3.99) Diggle-s/Tan-c/a; Bullseye app.; leads into Daredevil #501 4.00
... - Hulk (12/09, $3.99) Pak-s/Oliver-a; Skaar app.; back-up r/Amaz. Spider-Man #14 4.00
... - Punisher (12/09, $3.99) Romita Jr.-a/c; Castle killed by Daken; preview of Franken-Castle in Punisher #11 6.00
... - Secret Warriors (12/09, $3.99) McGuinness-a/c; Nick Fury; back-up r/Steranko-a 4.00

GD 2.0 | VG 4.0 | FN 6.0 | VF 8.0 | VF/NM 9.0 | NM- 9.2

... - Wolverine (12/09, $3.99) Ribic-a/c; Marvel Boy and Fantomex app. 4.00
... - X-Men (11/09, $3.99) Alan Davis-a/c; Namor app.; back-up r/Kieth-a 4.00

DARK REIGN: YOUNG AVENGERS
Marvel Comics: Jul, 2009 - No. 5, Dec, 2009 ($3.99, limited series)
1-Brooks-a; Osborn's Young Avengers vs. original Young Avengers 2 4 6 9 12 15
2-5 4.00

DARK REIGN: ZODIAC
Marvel Comics: Aug, 2009 - No. 3, Nov, 2009 ($3.99, limited series)
1-3-Casey-s/Fox-a. 1-Human Torch app. 4.00

DARK RIDE
Image Comics (Skybound): Oct, 2022 - Present ($3.99)
1-4-Williamson-s/Bressan-a 4.00

DARK ROOM, THE
Image Comics: Jun, 2022 ($19.99, HC graphic novel)
HC-Duggan-s/Buoncristiano-a 20.00

DARKSEID SPECIAL (Jack Kirby 100th Birthday tribute)
DC Comics: Oct, 2017 ($4.99, one-shot)
1-Evanier-s/Kolins-a; Omac story with Levitz-s/Hester-a; r/Forever People #6 (4 pgs) 5.00

DARKSEID (VILLAINS) (See Jack Kirby's New Gods and New Gods)
DC Comics: Feb, 1998 ($1.95, one-shot)
1-Byrne-s/Pearson-c 5.00

DARKSEID VS. GALACTUS: THE HUNGER
DC Comics: 1995 ($4.95, one-shot) (1st DC/Marvel x-over by John Byrne)
nn-John Byrne-c/a/script 2 4 6 9 13 16

DARK SHADOWS
Steinway Comic Publ. (Ajax)(America's Best): Oct, 1957 - No. 3, May, 1958

	GD	VG	FN	VF	VF/NM	NM-
1	36	72	108	211	343	475
2,3	23	46	69	136	223	310

DARK SHADOWS (TV) (See Dan Curtis Giveaways)
Gold Key: Mar, 1969 - No. 35, Feb, 1976 (Photo-c: 1-7)

	GD	VG	FN	VF	VF/NM	NM-
1(30039-903)-With pull-out poster (25¢)	24	48	72	168	372	575
1-With poster missing	7	14	21	48	89	130
2	8	16	24	54	102	150
3-With pull-out poster	9	18	27	62	126	190
3-With poster missing	5	10	15	35	63	90
4-7: 7-Last photo-c	6	12	18	38	69	100
8-10	5	10	15	30	50	70
11-20	4	8	12	27	44	60
21-35: 30-Last painted-c	4	8	12	23	37	50
Story Digest 1 (6/70, 148pp.)-Photo-c (low print)	7	14	21	46	86	125

DARK SHADOWS (TV) (See Nightmare on Elm Street)
Innovation Publishing: June, 1992 - No. 4, Spring, 1993 ($2.50, limited series, coated stock)
1-Based on 1991 NBC TV mini-series; painted-c 5.00
2-4 4.00

DARK SHADOWS: BOOK TWO
Innovation Publishing: 1993 - No. 4, July, 1993 ($2.50, limited series)
1-4-Painted-c. 4-Maggie Thompson scripts 4.00

DARK SHADOWS: BOOK THREE
Innovation Publishing: Nov, 1993 ($2.50)
1-(Whole #9) 4.00

DARK SHADOWS/VAMPIRELLA
Dynamite Entertainment: 2012 - No. 5, 2012 ($3.99, limited series)
1-5-Andreyko-s/Berkenkotter-a/Neves-c 5.00

DARK SHADOWS, VOLUME 1
Dynamite Entertainment: 2011 - No. 23, 2013 ($3.99)
1-23-Set in 1971. 1-Aaron Campbell-a; covers by Campbell & Francavilla 4.00

DARK SHADOWS: YEAR ONE
Dynamite Entertainment: 2013 - No. 6, 2013 ($3.99, limited series)
1-6-Origin of Barnabas Collins; Andreyko-s/Vilanova-a 4.00

DARK SOULS: LEGENDS OF THE FLAME (Based on the Bandai Namco video game)
Titan Comics: Sept, 2016 - No. 2, Nov, 2016 ($3.99, limited series)
1,2-Short stories by various; multiple covers on each 4.00

DARK SOULS: THE AGE OF FIRE (Based on the Bandai Namco video game)
Titan Comics: May, 2018 - No. 4, Oct, 2018 ($3.99, limited series)
1-4-O'Sullivan-s/Kokarev-a; multiple covers on each 4.00

DARK SOULS: THE BREATH OF ANDOLUS (Based on the Bandai Namco video game)
Titan Comics: May, 2016 - No. 4, Sept, 2016 ($3.99, limited series)
1-4-George Mann-s/Alan Quah-a; multiple covers on each 4.00

DARK SOULS: WINTER'S SPITE (Based on the Bandai Namco video game)
Titan Comics: Dec, 2016 - No. 4, Apr, 2017 ($3.99, limited series)
1-4-George Mann-s/Alan Quah-a; multiple covers on each 4.00

DARK SPACES: WILDFIRE
IDW Publishing: Jul, 2022 - No. 5, Nov, 2022 ($3.99, limited series)
1-5-Scott Snyder-s/Hayden Sherman-a 4.00

DARKSTAR AND THE WINTER GUARD
Marvel Comics: Aug, 2010 - No. 3, Oct, 2010 ($3.99, limited series)
1-3-Gallaher-s/Ellis-a/Henry-c; back-up reprint from X-Men Unlimited #28 4.00

DARKSTARS, THE
DC Comics: Oct, 1992 - No. 38, Jan, 1996 ($1.75/$1.95)
1-1st app. The Darkstars 4.00
2-24,25-38: 5-Hawkman & Hawkwoman app. 18-20-Flash app. 24-(9/94)-Zero Hour. 25-(11/94). 30-Green Lantern app. 31-...vs. Darkseid. 32-Green Lantern app. 3.00
#0-(10/94) Zero Hour issue released between #24 and #25 3.00
NOTE: *Travis Charest a(p)-4-7; c(p)-2-5; c-6-11. Stroman a-1-3; c-1.*

DARK TALES FROM THE VOKESVERSE
American Mythology: 2016 ($4.99, B&W)
1-Short horror stories by Neil Vokes and various; 2 covers 5.00

DARK TOWER: THE BATTLE OF JERICHO HILL (Based on Stephen King's Dark Tower)
Marvel Comics: Feb, 2010 - No. 5, Jun, 2010 ($3.99, limited series)
1-5-Peter David & Robin Furth-s/Jae Lee & Richard Isanove-a/c; variant-c for each 4.00

DARK TOWER: THE DRAWING OF THE THREE - BITTER MEDICINE (Stephen King)
Marvel Comics: Jun, 2016 - No. 5, Oct, 2016 ($3.99, limited series)
1-5-Peter David & Robin Furth-s/Jonathan Marks-a/Nimit Malavia-c 4.00

DARK TOWER: THE DRAWING OF THE THREE - HOUSE OF CARDS (Stephen King)
Marvel Comics: May, 2015 - No. 5, Sept, 2015 ($3.99, limited series)
1-5-Peter David & Robin Furth-s/Piotr Kowalski-a/J.T. Tedesco-c 4.00

DARK TOWER: THE DRAWING OF THE THREE - LADY OF SHADOWS (Stephen King)
Marvel Comics: Nov, 2015 - No. 5, Mar, 2016 ($3.99, limited series)
1-5-Peter David & Robin Furth-s/Jonathan Marks-a/Nimit Malavia-c 4.00

DARK TOWER: THE DRAWING OF THE THREE - THE PRISONER (Stephen King)
Marvel Comics: Nov, 2014 - No. 5, Feb, 2015 ($3.99, limited series)
1-5-Peter David & Robin Furth-s/Piotr Kowalski-a/J.T. Tedesco-c 4.00

DARK TOWER: THE DRAWING OF THE THREE - THE SAILOR (Stephen King)
Marvel Comics: Dec, 2016 - No. 5, Apr, 2017 ($3.99, limited series)
1-5-Peter David & Robin Furth-s/Ramirez-a/Anacleto-c 4.00

DARK TOWER: THE FALL OF GILEAD (Based on Stephen King's Dark Tower)
Marvel Comics: July, 2009 - No. 6, Jan, 2010 ($3.99, limited series)
1-6-Peter David & Robin Furth-s/Richard Isanove-a/Jae Lee-c; variant-c for each 4.00
Dark Tower: Guide to Gilead (2009, $3.99) profile pages of people and places 4.00

DARK TOWER: THE GUNSLINGER BORN (Based on Stephen King's Dark Tower series)
Marvel Comics: Apr, 2007 - No. 7, Oct, 2007 ($3.99, limited series)
1-Peter David & Robin Furth-s/Jae Lee & Richard Isanove-a; boyhood of Roland Deschain; afterword by Ralph Macchio; map of New Canaan 6.00
1-Variant cover by Quesada 10.00
1-Second printing with variant-c by Quesada 5.00
1-Sketch cover variant by Jae Lee 30.00
2-6-Jae Lee-c 4.00
2-Second printing with variant-c by Immonen 4.00
2-7-Variant covers. 2-Finch-c. 3-Yu-c. 4-McNiven-c. 5-Land-c. 6-Campbell. 7-Coipel 6.00
2-7-B&W sketch-c by Jae Lee 20.00
... MGC #1 (5/11, $1.00) r/#1 with "Marvel's Greatest Comics" logo on cover 3.00
... Sketchbook (2006, no cover price) pencil art and designs by Lee; coloring process 5.00
Dark Tower: Gunslinger's Guidebook (2007, $3.99) profile pages with Jae Lee-a 4.00
HC (2007, $24.99) r/#1-7; variant covers and sketch pages; Macchio intro. 25.00

DARK TOWER: THE GUNSLINGER - EVIL GROUND (Stephen King's Dark Tower)
Marvel Comics: Jun, 2013 - No. 2, Aug, 2013 ($3.99, limited series)
1,2-Robin Furth & Peter David-s/Richard Isanove-a/c 4.00

DARK TOWER: THE GUNSLINGER - SHEEMIE'S TALE (Stephen King's Dark Tower)
Marvel Comics: Mar, 2013 - No. 2, Apr, 2013 ($3.99, limited series)
1,2-Robin Furth-s/Richard Isanove-a/c 4.00

DARK TOWER: THE GUNSLINGER - SO FELL LORD PERTH (Stephen King's Dark Tower)
Marvel Comics: Sept, 2013 ($3.99, one-shot)
1-Robin Furth & Peter David-s/Richard Isanove-a/c 4.00

DARK TOWER: THE GUNSLINGER - THE BATTLE OF TULL (Stephen King's Dark Tower)
Marvel Comics: Aug, 2011 - No. 5, Dec, 2011 ($3.99, limited series)
1-5-Peter David & Robin Furth-s/Michael Lark-a/c 4.00

DARK TOWER: THE GUNSLINGER - THE JOURNEY BEGINS (Stephen King's Dark Tower)
Marvel Comics: Jul, 2010 - No. 5, Nov, 2010 ($3.99, limited series)
1-5-Peter David & Robin Furth-s/Sean Phillips-a/c 4.00
1-Variant cover by Jae Lee 5.00

DARK TOWER: THE GUNSLINGER - THE LITTLE SISTERS OF ELURIA (Stephen King)
Marvel Comics: Feb, 2011 - No. 5, Jun, 2011 ($3.99, limited series)
1-5: 1-Peter David & Robin Furth-s/Luke Ross-a/c 4.00

DARK TOWER: THE GUNSLINGER - THE MAN IN BLACK (Stephen King)
Marvel Comics: Aug, 2012 - No. 5, Dec, 2012 ($3.99, limited series)
1-5-Peter David & Robin Furth-s/Maleev-a/c 4.00

DARK TOWER: THE GUNSLINGER - THE WAY STATION (Stephen King)
Marvel Comics: Feb, 2012 - No. 5, Jun, 2012 ($3.99, limited series)
1-5-Peter David & Robin Furth-s/Laurence Campbell-a/c 4.00

DARK TOWER: THE LONG ROAD HOME (Based on Stephen King's Dark Tower series)
Marvel Comics: May, 2008 - No. 5, Sept, 2008 ($3.99, limited series)
1-Peter David & Robin Furth-s/Jae Lee & Richard Isanove-a 4.00
1-Variant cover by Deodato 6.00
1-Sketch cover variant by Jae Lee 30.00
2-5-Jae Lee-c 4.00
2-5: 2-Variant-c by Quesada. 3-Djurdjevic var-c. 4-Garney var-c. 5-Bermejo var-c 6.00
2-5-B&W sketch-c by Jae Lee 20.00
2-Second printing with variant-c by Lee 4.00
Dark Tower: End-World Almanac (2008, $3.99) guide to locations and inhabitants 4.00

DARK TOWER: THE SORCEROR (Based on Stephen King's Dark Tower)
Marvel Comics: June, 2009 ($3.99, one-shot)
1-Robin Furth-s/Richard Isanove-a/c; the story of Marten Broadcloak 4.00

DARK TOWER: TREACHERY (Based on Stephen King's Dark Tower series)
Marvel Comics: Nov, 2008 - No. 6, Apr, 2009 ($3.99, limited series)
1-6-Peter David & Robin Furth-s/Jae Lee & Richard Isanove-a 4.00

Dark Shadows (2013) #18 © Curtis Holdings

Darkwing Duck (2010) #1 © DIS

Darth Vader (2015) #13 © Lucasfilm

	GD	VG	FN	VF	VF/NM	NM-
	2.0	4.0	6.0	8.0	9.0	9.2

1-Variant cover by Dell'otto 10.00

DARK WEB (Spider-Man x-over event)
Marvel Comics: Feb, 2023 - Apr, 2023 ($4.99)

1-(2/23) Zeb Wells-s/Adam Kubert-a; Ben Reilly, Madelyne Pryor & Venom app. 5.00
...: Finale-(4/23) Wells-s/Adam Kubert-a; X-Men & Ms. Marvel app. 5.00

DARK WEB: MS. MARVEL
Marvel Comics: Feb, 2023 - No. 2, Mar, 2023 ($3.99, limited series)

1,2-Pirzada-s/Mortarino-a. 2-Miles Morales app. 4.00

DARK WEB: X-MEN
Marvel Comics: Feb, 2023 - No. 3, Mar, 2023 ($3.99, limited series)

1-3-Duggan-s. 1,2-Rod Reis-a. 2,3-Phil Noto-a 4.00

DARKWING DUCK (TV cartoon) (Also see Cartoon Tales)
Disney Comics: Nov, 1991 - No. 4, Feb, 1992 ($1.50, limited series)

1-Adapts hour-long premiere TV episode 5 10 15 31 53 75
2-4: Adaptation continues 2 4 6 8 10 12
...Facsimile Edition, Issue 1 (Dynamite Ent., 2023, $3.99) Reprints #1 without original ads 4.00

DARKWING DUCK (TV cartoon)
BOOM! Studios (KABOOM!): Jun, 2010 - No. 18, Nov, 2011 ($3.99)

1-Silvani-a; Launchpad McQuack app.; 3 covers 2 4 6 11 16 20
2 1 3 4 6 8 10
3-18-Multiple covers on all. 7-Batman #1 cover swipe. 8-Detective #31 cover swipe 6.00
Annual 1 (3/11, $4.99) 3 covers; Quackerjack app. 3 6 9 16 23 30
... Free Comic Book Day Edition (5/11) Flip book with Chip 'N' Dale Rescue Rangers
1 2 3 5 6 8

DARKWING DUCK (TV cartoon)
Dynamite Entertainment: 2023 - Present ($3.99)

1,2-Deibert-s/Lauro-a; multiple covers on each 4.00

DARK WOLVERINE (See Wolverine 2003 series)

DARK X-MEN (See Dark Avengers and the Dark Reign mini-series)
Marvel Comics: Jan, 2010 - No. 5, May, 2010 ($3.99, limited series)

1-5-Cornell-s/Kirk-a. 1-3-Bianchi-c. 1-Nate Grey returns 4.00
...: The Confession (11/09, $3.99) Cansino-a; Paquette-c 4.00

DARK X-MEN: THE BEGINNING (See Dark Avengers and the Dark Reign mini-series)
Marvel Comics: Sept, 2009 - No. 3, Oct, 2009 ($3.99, limited series)

1-3: 1-Cornell-s/Kirk-a; Jae Lee-c on all. 2-Daken app. 3-Mystique app.; Jock-a 4.00

DARLING LOVE
Close Up/Archie Publ. (A Darling Magazine): Oct-Nov, 1949 - No. 11, 1952 (no month) (52 pgs.)(Most photo-c)

1-Photo-c 31 62 93 182 296 410
2-Photo-c 17 34 51 100 158 215
3-8,10,11: 3-6-photo-c 15 30 45 83 124 165
9-Krigstein-a 15 30 45 85 130 175

DARLING ROMANCE
Close Up (MLJ Publications): Sept-Oct, 1949 - No. 7, 1951 (All photo-c)

1-(52 pgs.)-Photo-c 36 72 108 211 343 475
2 17 34 51 100 158 215
3-7 15 30 45 86 133 180

DARQUE PASSAGES (See Master Darque)
Acclaim (Valiant): April, 1998 - No. 4, Mar, 1998 ($2.50)

1-4-Christina Z.-s/Manco-c/a 3.00

DART (Also see Freak Force & Savage Dragon)
Image Comics (Highbrow Entertainment): Feb, 1996 - No. 3, May, 1996 ($2.50, lim. series)

1-3 3.00

DARTH MAUL (See Star Wars: Darth Maul)

DARTH VADER (Follows after the end of Star Wars Episode IV)
Marvel Comics: Apr, 2015 - No. 25, Dec, 2016 ($4.99/$3.99)

1-($4.99) Gillen-s/Larroca-a/Granov-c; intro. Wookiee bounty hunter Black Krrsantan;
Jabba the Hut & Boba Fett app. 3 6 9 21 33 45
2 2 4 6 11 16 20
3-Intro. Doctor Aphra and Triple Zero 8 16 24 54 102 150
3-Second printing 6 12 18 38 69 100
4-12-($3.99) 6-Boba Fett app. 1 2 3 5 6 8
13-19,21-24: 13-15-Vader Down x-over pts. 2,4,6. 24-Flashbacks to Episode III 6.00
20-($4.99) The Emperor app.; back-up Triple-Zero & Beetee story w/Norton-a
1 3 4 6 8 10
25-($5.99) Gillen-s/Larroca-a; back-up story with Fiumara-a; bonus cover gallery 6.00
Annual 1 (2/16, $4.99) Gillen-s/Yu-a/c 1 2 3 5 6 8
...: Doctor Aphra No. 1 Halloween Comic Fest 2016 (12/16, giveaway) r/#3
1 3 4 6 8 10

DARTH VADER (Follows after the end of Star Wars Episode III)
Marvel Comics: Aug, 2017 - No. 25, Feb, 2019 ($4.99/$3.99)

1,2: 1-($4.99) Soule-s/Camuncoli-a/Cheung-c; back-up by Eliopoulos-s/a. 2-($3.99)
1 3 4 6 8 10
3-5,7-18,20-24-($3.99) Soule-s/Camuncoli-a. 5-Vader acquires the red light saber 5.00
6-1st app. Grand Inquisitor 6 12 18 41 76 110
19-1st app. Trilla Suduri (Second Sister) 3 6 9 16 23 30
25-($4.99) Camuncoli-a/c; recap of Vader's life 1 3 4 6 8 10
Annual 2 (9/18, $4.99) Wendig-s/Kirk-a/Deodato-c; Commander Krennic app. 5.00

DASTARDLY & MUTTLEY (See Fun-In No. 1-4, 6 and Kite Fun Book)
DC Comics: Nov, 2017 - No. 6, Apr, 2018 ($3.99, limited series)

1-6: 1-New origin for the pair; Ennis-s/Mauricet-a 4.00

DATE WITH DANGER
Standard Comics: No. 5, Dec, 1952 - No. 6, Feb, 1953

5-Secret agent stories in both 71 142 213 454 777 1100
6-Atom bomb story 37 74 111 222 361 500

DATE WITH DEBBI (Also see Debbi's Dates)
National Periodical Publ.: Jan-Feb, 1969 - No. 17, Sept-Oct, 1971; No. 18, Oct-Nov, 1972

1-Teenage 10 20 30 64 132 200
2-5,17-(52 pgs) James Taylor sty. 5 10 15 31 53 75
6-12,18-Last issue 4 8 12 27 44 60
13-16-(68 pgs.): 14-1 pg. story on Jack Wild. 15-Marlo Thomas/"That Girl" story
5 10 15 30 50 70

DATE WITH JUDY, A (Radio/TV, and 1948 movie)
National Periodical Publications: Oct-Nov, 1947 - No. 79, Oct-Nov, 1960 (No. 1-25: 52 pgs.)

1-Teenage 47 94 141 296 498 700
2 21 42 63 122 199 275
3-10 16 32 48 92 144 195
11-20 14 28 42 78 112 145
21-40 13 26 39 74 105 135
41-45: 45-Last pre-code (2-3/55) 12 24 36 67 94 120
46-79: 79-Drucker-c/a 11 22 33 62 86 110

DATE WITH MILLIE, A (Life With Millie No. 8 on)(Teenage)
Atlas/Marvel Comics (MPC): Oct, 1956 - No. 7, Aug, 1957; Oct, 1959 - No. 7, Oct, 1960

1(10/56)-(1st Series)-Dan DeCarlo-a in #1-7 129 258 387 826 1413 2000
2 52 104 156 328 552 775
3-7 32 64 96 188 307 425
1(10/59)-(2nd Series) 60 120 180 381 653 925
2-7 19 38 57 111 176 240

DATE WITH PATSY, A (Also see Patsy Walker)
Atlas Comics: Sept, 1957 (One-shot)

1-Starring Patsy Walker 32 64 96 188 307 425

DAUGHTERS OF THE DRAGON (See Heroes For Hire)
Marvel Comics: 2005; Mar, 2006 - No. 6, Aug, 2006 ($2.99, limited series)

1-6-Palmiotti & Gray-s/Evans-a. 1-Rhino app. 5,6-Iron Fist app. 3.00
... Deadly Hands Special (2005, $3.99) reprints app. from Deadly Hands of Kung Fu #32,33 &
Bizarre Adventures #25; Claremont-s/Rogers-a; new Rogers-c & interview 4.00
...: Deep Cuts MPGN (2018, $19.99, SC) printing of digital-first story; MacKay-s 20.00
...: Samurai Bullets TPB (2006, $15.99) r/#1-6 16.00

DAVID AND GOLIATH (Movie)
Dell Publishing Co.: No. 1205, July, 1961

Four Color 1205-Photo-c 7 14 21 48 89 130

DAVID BORING (See Eightball)
Pantheon Books: 2000 ($24.95, hardcover w/dust jacket)

Hardcover - reprints David Boring stories from Eightball; Clowes-s/a 25.00

DAVID CASSIDY (TV)(See Partridge Family, Swing With Scooter #33 & Time For Love #30)
Charlton Comics: Feb, 1972 - No. 14, Sept, 1973

1-Most have photo covers 7 14 21 44 82 120
2-5 4 8 12 27 44 60
6-14 4 8 12 23 37 50

DAVID LADD'S LIFE STORY (See Movie Classics)

DAVY CROCKETT (See Dell Giants, Fightin..., Frontier Fighters, It's Game Time, Power Record Comics, Western Tales & Wild Frontier)

DAVY CROCKETT (Frontier Fighter...)

	GD	VG	FN	VF	VF/NM	NM-
	2.0	4.0	6.0	8.0	9.0	9.2

Avon Periodicals: 1951
nn-Tuska?, Reinman-a; Fawcette-c 26 52 78 154 252 350

DAVY CROCKETT (...King of the Wild Frontier No. 1,2)(TV)
Dell Publishing Co./Gold Key: 5/55 - No. 671, 12/55; No. 1, 12/63; No. 2, 11/69 (Walt Disney)
Four Color 631(#1)-Fess Parker photo-c 15 30 45 103 227 350
Four Color 639-Photo-c 12 24 36 82 179 275
Four Color 664,671(Marsh-a)-Photo-c 11 22 33 75 160 245
1(12/63-Gold Key)-Fess Parker photo-c; reprints 7 14 21 46 86 125
2(11/69)-Fess Parker photo-c; reprints 4 8 12 28 44 60

DAVY CROCKETT (...Frontier Fighter #1,2; Kid Montana #9 on)
Charlton Comics: Aug, 1955 - No. 8, Jan, 1957
1 12 24 36 67 94 120
2 7 14 21 37 46 55
3-8 6 12 18 28 34 40

DAWN
Sirius Entertainment/Image Comics: June, 1995 - No. 6, 1996 ($2.95)
1/2-w/certificate 1 2 3 5 6 8
1/2-Variant-c 2 4 6 10 14 18
1-Linsner-c/a 1 3 4 6 8 10
1-Black Light Edition 2 4 6 10 14 18
1-White Trash Edition 3 6 9 17 25 34
1-Look Sharp Edition 3 6 9 19 30 40
2-4: Linsner-c/a 4.50
2-Variant-c, 3-Limited Edition 2 4 6 13 18 22
4-6-Vibrato-c 3.50
4, 5-Limited Edition 2 4 6 8 10 12
6-Limited Edition 2 4 6 8 10 12
...Convention Sketchbook (Image Comics, 2002, $2.95) pin-ups 6.00
...2003 Convention Sketchbook (Image Comics, 3/03, $2.95) pin-ups 4.00
...2004 Convention Sketchbook (Image Comics, 4/04, $2.95) pin-ups 4.00
...2005 Convention Sketchbook (Image Comics, 5/05, $2.95) pin-ups 4.00
Genesis Edition ('99, Wizard supplement) previews Return of the Goddess 4.00
Lucifer's Halo TPB (11/97, $19.95) r/Drama, Dawn #1-6 plus 12 pages of new artwork 20.00
...: Not to Touch The Earth (9/10, $5.99) Linsner-s/c/a; pin-ups by various incl. Turner 6.00
...: Tenth Anniversary Special (9/99, $2.95) Interviews 3.00
The Portable Dawn ($9.95, 5"x4", 64 pgs.) Pocket-sized cover gallery 10.00
...: The Swordmaster's Daughter & Other Stories (2013, $3.99) Linsner-s/c/a 4.00

DAWN OF THE DEAD (George A. Romaro's...)
IDW Publishing: Apr, 2004 - No. 3, Jun, 2004 ($3.99, limited series)
1-3-Adaptation of the 2004 movie; Niles-s 2 4 6 8 10 12
TPB (9/04, $17.99) r/#1-3; intro. by George A. Romero 24.00

DAWN OF THE PLANET OF THE APES
BOOM! Studios: Nov, 2014 - No. 6, Apr, 2015 ($3.99, limited series)
1-6: 1-Takes place between the 2011 and 2014 movies; Moreci-s/McDaid-a 4.00

DAWN: THE RETURN OF THE GODDESS
Sirius Entertainment: Apr, 1999 - No. 4, July, 2000 ($2.95, limited series)
1-4-Linsner-s/a 4.00
TPB (4/02, $12.95) r/#1-4; intro. by Linsner 13.00

DAWN: THREE TIERS
Image Comics: Jun, 2003 - No. 6, Aug, 2005 ($2.95, limited series)
1-6-Linsner-s/a. 2-Preview of Vampire's Christmas 4.00

DAWN / VAMPIRELLA
Dynamite Entertainment: 2014 - No. 5, 2015 ($3.99, limited series)
1-5-Linsner-s/a/c. 3-Vampirella origin re-told 5.00

DAYDREAMERS (See Generation X)
Marvel Comics: Aug, 1997 - No. 3, Oct, 1997 ($2.50, limited series)
1-3-Franklin Richards, Howard the Duck, Man-Thing app. 4.00

DAY MEN
BOOM! Studios: Jul, 2013 - No. 8, Oct, 2015 ($3.99)
1-Stelfreeze-a/c; Gagnon & Nelson-s 5.00
2-8: 2-Covers by Stelfreeze & Pérez 4.00
...: Pen & Ink No. 1 (12/13, $9.99, 11"x17") Pen and ink art for #1&2 with commentary 10.00

DAY OF JUDGMENT
DC Comics: Nov, 1999 - No. 5, Nov, 1999 ($2.95/$2.50, limited series)
1-($2.95) Spectre possessed; Matt Smith-a 3.00
2-5: Parallax returns. 5-Hal Jordan becomes the Spectre 3.00
...Secret Files 1 (11/99, $4.95) Harris-c 5.00

DAY OF VENGEANCE (Prelude to Infinite Crisis)(Also see Birds of Prey #76 for 1st app. of Black Alice)
DC Comics: June, 2005 - No. 6, Nov, 2005 ($2.50, limited series)
1-6: 1-Jean Loring becomes Eclipso; Spectre, Ragman, Enchantress, Detective Chimp, Shazam app.; Justiniano-a. 2,3-Capt. Marvel app. 4-6-Black Alice app. 3.00
...: Infinite Crisis Special 1 (3/06, $4.99) Justiniano-a/Simonson-c 5.00
TPB (2005, $12.99) r/series & Action #826, Advs. of Superman #639, Superman #216 13.00

DAYS OF HATE
Image Comics: Jan, 2018 - No. 12, Jan, 2019 ($3.99)
1-12-Ales Kot-s/Danijel Zezelj-a 4.00

DAYS OF THE DEFENDERS (See Defenders, The)
Marvel Comics: Mar, 2001 ($3.50, one-shot)
1-Reprints early team-ups of members, incl. Marvel Feature #1; Larsen-c 3.50

DAYS OF THE MOB (See In the Days of the Mob)

DAYTRIPPER
DC Comics (Vertigo): Feb, 2010 - No. 10, Nov, 2010 ($2.99, limited series)
1-10-Gabriel Bá & Fábio Moon-s/a 3.00
TPB (2010, $19.99) r/#1-10; sketch art pages 20.00

DAZEY'S DIARY
Dell Publishing Co.: June-Aug, 1962
01-174-208: Bill Woggon-c/a 5 10 15 30 50 70

DAZZLER, THE (Also see Marvel Graphic Novel & X-Men #130)
Marvel Comics Group: Mar, 1981 - No. 42, Mar, 1986
1-X-Men app.; DeFalco-s/Romita Jr.-a 3 6 9 16 23 30
2-20,23,25,26,29-32,34-37,39-41: 2-X-Men app. 10,11-Galactus app. 23-Rogue/Mystique 1 pg. app. 26-Jusko-c. 40-Secret Wars II 4.00
21,22,24,27,28,38,42: 21-Double size; photo-c. 22 (12/82)-vs. Rogue Battle-c/sty. 24-Full app. Rogue w/Powerman (Iron Fist). 27-Rogue app. 28-Full app. Rogue; Mystique app. 38-Wolverine-c/app.; X-Men app. 42-Beast-c/app. 5.00
33-Michael Jackson "Thriller" swipe-c/sty 3 6 9 16 23 30
... No. 1 Facsimile Edition (4/19, $3.99) reprints #1 with original ads 4.00
One-shot (7/10, $3.99) Andrasofszky-a/c; Arcade app. 4.00
...: X-Song 1 (8/18, $3.99) Visaggio-s/Braga-a
NOTE: *No. 1 distributed only through comic shops.* ***Alcala*** *a-1i, 2i.* ***Chadwick*** *a-38-42p; c(p)-39, 41, 42.* ***Guice*** *a-38i, 42i; c-38, 40.*

DC CHALLENGE (Most DC superheroes appear)
DC Comics: Nov, 1985 - No. 12, Oct, 1986 ($1.25/$2.00, maxi-series)
1-11: 1-Colan-a. 2,8-Batman-c/app. 4-Gil Kane-c/a 4.00
12-($2.00-c) Giant; low print 5.00
NOTE: *Batman app. in 1-4, 6-12. Joker app. in 7.* ***Infantino*** *a-3.* ***Ordway*** *c-12.* ***Swan/Austin*** *c-10.*

DC CLASSICS: THE BATMAN ADVENTURES
DC Comics: Aug, 2020 - No. 7, Feb, 2021 ($1.99)
1-7-Reprints The Batman Adventures series. 2-Catwoman app. 3-Joker app. 3.00

DC COMICS: BOMBSHELLS (Continues in Bombshelss: United)
DC Comics: Oct, 2015 - No. 33, Oct, 2017 ($3.99, printings of digital-first stories)
1-Bennett-s/Sauvage-a/Lucia-a; set in 1940 WWII 2 4 6 8 10 12
2-13: 4-Harley Quinn-c/app. 1 2 3 5 6 8
14-Harley Quinn/Joker's Daughter-c 3 6 9 14 19 24
15-24: 15-18-Harley Quinn-c/app. 5.00
25-($4.99) Suicide Squad app.; intro. Faora Hu-Ul; Aneke-a 1 2 3 5 6 8
26-33: 27,32,33-Harley Quinn/Poison Ivy-c. 29-Superman app. 5.00
Annual 1 (10/16, $4.99) Bennett-s/Charretier-a; origin of vampire Batgirl 8.00

DC COMICS CLASSICS LIBRARY (Hardcover collections of classic DC stories)
DC Comics: 2009 - 2010 ($39.99, hardcover with dustjacket)
Batman: A Death in the Family ('09)- r/Batman #426-429, 440-442, New Titans #60,61 40.00
Batman Annuals ('09)- r/Batman Annual #1-3; afterword by Richard Bruning 40.00
Batman Annuals Volume 2 ('10)- r/Batman Annual #4-7; intro. by Michael Uslan 40.00
Flash of Two Worlds ('09)- r/Flash #123,129,137,151,170&173 team-ups with G.A. Flash 40.00
Justice League of America by George Pérez ('09) r/J.L.of A. #184-186, 192-194 40.00
Justice League of America by George Pérez Vol. 2 ('10) r/J.L.of A. #195-197,200 40.00
Legion of Super-Heroes: The Life and Death of Ferro Lad ('09) - r/Adventure Comics # 346, 347,352-355,357; intro. by Paul Levitz; afterword by Jim Shooter 40.00
Roots of the Swamp Thing ('09)- r/House of Secrets #92 & Swamp Thing #1-13; Wein intro. 40.00
Superman: Kryptonite Nevermore ('09)- r/Superman #233-238,240-242; afterword by Denny O'Neil 40.00

DC COMICS ESSENTIALS
DC Comics: ($1.00, flipbooks with DC Graphic Novel catalog of recommended titles)
...: Action Comics #1 (2/14, $1.00) Reprints Action #1 (2011) with flipbook of DC GNs 3.00
...: Batman #1 (12/13, $1.00) Reprints Batman #1 (2011) with flipbook of DC GNs 3.00
...: Batman and Robin #1 (4/16, $1.00) Reprints Batman and Robin #1 (2011) with flipbook 3.00
...: Batman and Son Special Ed. ('14, $1.00) Reprints Batman #655 with flipbook 3.00
...: Batman: Death of the Family (6/16, $1.00) Reprints Batman #13 (2011) with flipbook 3.00
...: Batman: Hush Spec. Ed. ('14, $1.00) Reprints Batman #608 with flipbook of DC GNs 3.00
...: Batman: The Black Mirror Special Ed. ('14, $1.00) Reprints Detective #871 w/flipbook 3.00
...: Batman: The Dark Knight Returns #1 (5/16, $1.00) Reprints #1 with flipbook 3.00
...: Batman: The Dark Knight Returns Special Ed. ('14, $1.00) Reprints #1 with flipbook 3.00
...: Batman: Year One #1 ('14, $1.00) Reprints Batman #404 with flipbook of DC GNs 3.00
...: DC: The New Frontier #1 (3/16, $1.00) Reprints first issue with flipbook 3.00
...: Green Lantern #1 (1/14, $1.00) Reprints Green Lantern #1 (2011) with flipbook 3.00
...: JLA #1 (6/16, $1.00) Reprints JLA #1 with flipbook of DC GNs 3.00
...: Justice League #1 (1/14, $1.00) Reprints Justice League #1 (2011) with flipbook 3.00
...: Superman Unchained #1 (5/16, $1.00) Reprints Superman Unchained #1 with flipbook 3.00
...: Watchmen #1 (2/14, $1.00) Reprints Watchmen #1 (1986) with flipbook 3.00
...: Wonder Woman #1 (12/13, $1.00) Reprints Wonder Woman #1 (2011) with flipbook 3.00

DC COMICS MEGA SAMPLER
DC Comics: 2009; Jul, 2010 (6-1/4" x 9-1/2", FCBD giveaways)
1, 2010- Short stories of kid-friendly titles; Tiny Titans, Billy Batson, Super Friends app. 3.00

DC COMICS PRESENTS
DC Comics: July-Aug, 1978 - No. 97, Sept, 1986 (Superman team-ups in all)
1-4th Superman/Flash race 4 8 12 28 47 65
1-(Whitman variant) 5 10 15 35 63 90
2-Part 2 of Superman/Flash race 3 6 9 15 22 28
2-(Whitman variant) 3 6 9 17 26 35
3,4,9-12,14-16,19,21,22-(Whitman variants, low print run, none have issue # on cover) 3 6 9 14 20 25
3-10: 3-Adam Strange. 4-Metal Men. 5-Aquaman. 6-Green Lantern. 7-Red Tornado. 8-Swamp Thing. 9-Wonder Woman. 10-Sgt. Rock 2 4 6 8 10 12
11-25,28-40: 12-Mister Miracle. 13-Legion of Super-Heroes. 19-Batgirl. 21-Elongated Man. 23-Dr. Fate. 24-Deadman. 30-Black Canary. 31-Robin. 34-Marvel Family. 35-Man-Bat. 36-Starman. 37-Hawkgirl. 38-The Flash 6.00
26-(10/80)-Green Lantern; intro Cyborg, Starfire, Raven (1st app. New Teen Titans in 16 pg. preview); Starlin-c/a; Sargon the Sorcerer back-up 11 22 33 76 163 250
27-1st app. Mongul 5 10 15 33 57 80
41-Superman/Joker-c/story; 1st app. New Wonder Woman in 16 pg. preview; Colan-a 2 4 6 9 13 16
42-46,48,50,52-71,73-76,79-83: 42-Sandman. 43,80-Legion of Super-Heroes. 52-Doom Patrol; 1st app. Ambush Bug. 58-Robin. 64-Kamandi. 82-Adam Strange. 83-Batman & Outsiders 4.00
47-(7/82) He-Man-c/s (1st app. in comics) 13 26 39 89 195 300
49-Black Adam & Captain Marvel app. 6 12 18 41 76 110

Dawn / Vampirella #5 © JML & DYN

DC Comics: Bombshells #27 © DC

DCeased #3 © DC

	GD 2.0	VG 4.0	FN 6.0	VF 8.0	VF/NM 9.0	NM- 9.2
51-Preview insert (16 pgs.) of He-Man (2nd app.)	2	4	6	10	14	18
72,77,78,97: 72-Joker/Phantom Stranger-c/story. 77,78-Animal Man app. (77-c also). 97-Phantom Zone						6.00
84-Challengers of the Unknown; Kirby-c/s.						6.00
85-Swamp Thing; Alan Moore scripts						6.00
86,88-96: 86-88-Crisis x-over. 88-Creeper						4.00
87-Origin/1st app. Superboy of Earth Prime	3	6	9	19	30	40
Annual 1(9/82)-G.A. Superman; 1st app. Alexander Luthor	2	4	6	8	10	12
Annual 2,3: 2(7/83)-Intro/origin Superwoman. 3(9/84)-Shazam						4.00
Annual 4(10/85)-Superwoman						4.00

NOTE: ***Adkins*** *a-2, 54; c-2.* ***Buckler*** *a-33, 34; c-30, 33, 34.* ***Giffen*** *a-39; c-59.* ***Gil Kane*** *a-28, 35, Annual 3; c-48p, 56, 58, 60, 62, 64, 68, Annual 2, 3.* ***Kirby*** *c/a-84.* ***Kubert*** *c/a-66.* ***Morrow*** *c/a-65.* ***Newton*** *c/a-54p.* ***Orlando*** *c-53i.* ***Perez*** *a-26p, 61p; c-38, 61, 94.* ***Starlin*** *a-26-29p, 36p, 37p; c-26-29, 36, 37, 93.* ***Toth*** *a-84.* ***Williamson*** *i-79, 85, 87.*

DC COMICS PRESENTS: ...(Julie Schwartz tribute series of one-shots based on classic covers)
DC Comics: Sept, 2004 - Oct, 2004 ($2.50)

The Atom -(Based on cover of Atom #10) Gibbons-s/Oliffe-a; Waid-s/Jurgens-a; Bolland-c 3.00
Batman -(Batman #183) Johns-s/Infantino-a; Wein-s/Kuhn-a; Hughes-c 3.00
The Flash -(Flash #163) Loeb-s/McGuinness-a; O'Neil-s/Mahnke-a; Ross-c 3.00
Green Lantern -(Green Lantern #31) Azzarello-s/Breyfogle-a; Pasko-s/McDaniel-a; Bolland-c 3.00
Hawkman -(Hawkman #6) Bates-s/Byrne-a; Busiek-s/Simonson-a; Garcia-Lopez-c 3.00
Justice League of America -(J.L. of A. #53) Ellison & David-s/Giella-a; Wolfman-s/Nguyen-a; Garcia-Lopez-c 3.00
Mystery in Space -(M.I.S. #82) Maggin-s/Williams-a; Morrison-s/Ordway-a; Ross-c 3.00
Superman -(Superman #264) Stan Lee-s/Cooke-a; Levitz-s/Giffen-a; Hughes-c 3.00

DC COMICS PRESENTS: ...
DC Comics: Dec, 2010 - Feb, 2016 ($7.99/$9.99, squarebound, one-shot reprints)

The Atom 1 (3/11) r/Legends of the DC Universe #28,29,40,41; Gil Kane-a 8.00
Batman 1 (12/10) r/Batman #582-585,600 8.00
Batman 2 (1/11) r/Batman #591-594 8.00
Batman 3 (2/11) r/Batman #595-598 8.00
Batman Adventures 1 (9/14) reprints; Burchett, Parobeck, Templeton, Timm-a 8.00
Batman: Arkham 1 (6/11) r/Batman Chronicles #6, Batman; Arkham Asylum - Tales of Madness #1, Batman Villains Secret Files #1 & Justice Leagues: J.L. of Arkham #1 8.00
Batman - Bad 1 (1/12) r/Batman: Legends of the D.K. #146-148 8.00
Batman Beyond 1 (2/11) r/Batman Beyond #13,14,21,22 8.00
Batman: Blaze of Glory 1 (2/12) r/Batman: Legends of the D.K. #197-199,212 8.00
Batman - Blink 1 (12/11) r/Batman: Legends of the D.K. #156-158 8.00
Batman/Catwoman 1 (12/10) r/Batman and Catwoman: Trail of the Gun 8.00
Batman - Conspiracy 1 (4/11) r/Batman: Legends of the D.K. #86-88; Detective #821 8.00
Batman - Dark Knight, Dark City 1 (7/11) r/Batman #452-454; Detective #633 8.00
Batman - Don't Blink 1 (1/12) r/Batman: Legends of the D.K. #164-167 8.00
Batman: Gotham Noir 1 (9/11) r/Batman: Gotham Noir #1 & Batman #604 8.00
Batman - Irresistible 1 (5/11) r/Batman: Legends of the D.K. #169-171; Hourman #22 8.00
Batman - The Demon Laughs 1 (12/11) r/Batman: Legends of the D.K. #142-145; Aparo-a 8.00
Batman: The Secret City 1 (2/12) r/Batman: Legends of the D.K. #180,181,190,191 8.00
Batman: Urban Legends 1 (2/12) r/Batman: Legends of the D.K. #168,177-179 8.00
Brightest Day 1 (12/10) r/Strange Advs. #205, Hawkman #27,34,36, Solo #8, DC Hol. '09 8.00
Brightest Day 2 (1/11) r/Firestorm #11-13 & Martian Manhunter #11,24 8.00
Brightest Day 3 (2/11) r/Legends of the DC Univ. #25-27 & Teen Titans #27,28 8.00
Captain Atom 1 (2/12) r/back-up stories from Action Comics #879-889 8.00
Catwoman - Guardian of Gotham 1 (12/11) r/Catwoman: Guardian of Gotham #1,2 8.00
Chase 1 (1/11) r/Chase #1,6-8 8.00
Darkseid War 1 (2/16, $7.99) r/New Gods #1,7, Mister Miracle #1 & Forever People #1 8.00
Demon Driven Out, The 1 (7/14, $9.99) r/The Demon: Driven Out #1-6 10.00
Elseworlds 80-Page Giant 1 (1/12) r/Elseworlds 80-Page Giant (pulled from distribution) 8.00
Flash 1 (7/11) r/Showcase #4,14 and Flash #125,130,139 8.00
Flash/Green Lantern: Faster Friends (1/11) r/G.L./Flash: Faster Friends & Flash/G.L.: FF 8.00
Green Lantern 1 (12/10) r/Green Lantern #137-140 (2001) 8.00
Green Lantern - Fear Itself 1 (4/11) r/Green Lantern: Fear Itself GN 8.00
Green Lantern - Willworld 1 (7/11) r/Green Lantern: Willworld GN 8.00
Harley Quinn 1 (4/14) r/Batman: Harley Quinn #1, Joker's Asylum II: HQ #1 and others 8.00
Impulse 1 (8/11) r/Impulse #50-53 8.00
Jack Kirby Omnibus Sampler 1 (12/11) r/Kirby art stories from 1957,1958 8.00
JLA 1 (2/11) r/JLA #90-93 8.00
JLA - Age of Wonder 1 (12/11) r/JLA: Age of Wonder 8.00
JLA: Black Baptism 1 (8/11) r/JLA: Black Baptism #1-4 8.00
JLA Heaven's Ladder 1 (10/11) comic-sized reprint; and r/Green Lantern #1,000,000 8.00
Legion of Super-Heroes 1 (6/11) r/Legion of Super-Heroes #122,123 & Legionnaires 79,80 8.00
Legion of Super-Heroes 2 (2/12) r/Adv. #247 and recent Legion short stories 8.00
Lobo 1 (3/11) r/Lobo #63,64 & DC First: Superman/Lobo #1 8.00
Metal Men 1 (4/11) r/Doom Patrol ('09) #1-7 and Silver Age: The Brave and the Bold #1 8.00
Night Force 1 (4/11) r/Night Force #1-4; Gene Colan-a 8.00
Ninja Boy 1 (6/11) r/Ninja Boy #1-4 8.00
Robin War 100-Page Super Spectacular 1 (2/16) Ryan Sook-c 8.00
Shazam! 1,2 (9/11,10/11) 1-r/Power of Shazam #38-41. 2-r/ #42-46 8.00
Son of Superman 1 (7/11) r/Son of Superman GN 8.00
Superboy's Legion 1 (12/11) r/Superboy's Legion #1,2 (Elseworlds) 8.00
Superman 1 (12/10) r/Superman: The Man of Steel #121 & Superman #179,180,185 8.00
Superman 2 (1/11) r/Action #798, Superman: The Man of Steel #133, Superman #189 & Advs. of Superman #611 8.00
Superman 3 (2/11) r/Superman #177,178,181,182 8.00
Superman 4 (9/11) r/Action #768,771-773 8.00
Superman Adventures 1 (8/12) r/Superman Adventures #16,19,22,23 8.00
Superman/Doomsday 1 (5/11) r/Doomsday Annual #1 & Superman #175 8.00
Superman - Infestation 1 (8/11) r/Action #778, Advs. of Superman #591, Superman #169 and Superman: The Man of Steel #113 8.00
Superman: Lois and Clark 100-Page S.S. 1 (1/16) r/Superman: The Wedding Album 8.00
Superman - Secret Identity 1 (12/11) r/Superman: Secret Identity #1,2 8.00
Superman - Secret Identity 2 (1/12) r/Superman: Secret Identity #3,4 8.00
Superman - Sole Survivor 1 (3/11) r/Legends of the DC Universe #1-3,39 8.00
Superman - The Kents 1,2 (1/12, 2/12) 1-r/The Kents #1-4. 2-The Kents #5-8 8.00
Teen Titans 1 (10/11) Teen Titans Lost Annual #1 and Solo #7; Allred-a 8.00
Titans Hunt 100-Page Super Spectacular 1 (1/16) r/Teen Titans early apps.; Sook-c 8.00
The Life Story of the Flash 1 (1/12) r/The Life Story of the Flash GN 8.00
T.H.U.N.D.E.R. Agents 1 (2/11) r/T.H.U.N.D.E.R. Agents #1,2,7 (1966) 8.00
Wonder Woman 1 (4/11) r/Wonder Woman #139-142 (1998) 8.00
Wonder Woman Adventures 1 (9/12) r/Advs. in the DC Universe #1,3,11,19 8.00
Young Justice 1 (12/10) r/JLA World Without Grownups #1,2 8.00
Young Justice 2 (1/11) r/Y.J: The Secret, Y.J. Secret Files #1, Y.J. In No Man's Land 8.00
Young Justice 3 (2/11) r/Young Justice #7 & Y.J Secret Origins 80-Page Giant #1 8.00

DC COMICS - THE NEW 52 FCBD SPECIAL EDITION
DC Comics: Jun, 2012 (giveaway one-shot)

1-Origin of The Trinity of Sin (Pandora, The Question, Phantom Stranger); Justice League app.; Jim Lee, Reis, Ha, Rocafort-a; previews Earth 2, G.I. Combat, Ravagers 3.00

DC COMICS THE NEW 52 PRESENTS: ...
DC Comics: Mar, 2012 ($7.99, squarebound, one-shot reprints)

The Dark 1 (3/12) r/Animal Man #1, Swamp Thing #1, I, Vampire #1, and J.L. Dark #1 8.00

DC COUNTDOWN (To Infinite Crisis)
DC Comics: May, 2005 ($1.00, 80 pages, one-shot)

1-Death of Blue Beetle; prelude to OMAC Project, Day of Vengeance, Rann/Thanagar War and Villains United mini-series; s/a by various; Jim Lee/Alex Ross-c 4.00

DCEASED
DC Comics: Jul, 2019 - No. 6, Dec, 2019 ($3.99, limited series)

1-5-Zombie apocalypse in DC universe; Taylor-s/Hairsine-a. 1-Darkseid app. 4.00
3,5-($4.99) 3-Variant zombie Wonder Woman-c by Mattina. 5-Zombie Harley Quinn-c 5.00
6-($4.99) Continues in DCeased: A Good Day to Die 5.00
6-($5.99) Variant Darkseid-c by Mattina 6.00
...: A Good Die to Die (11/19, $4.99) Taylor-s/Braga-a; Mr Miracle, Barda, Mr. Terrific app. 5.00
...: Hope at World's End SC (2022, $17.99) Collects Chapters #1-15 of digital series 18.00

DCEASED: DEAD PLANET
DC Comics: Sept, 2020 - No. 7, Mar, 2021 ($4.99/$3.99, limited series)

1-($4.99)-Zombie apocalypse; Damian Wayne, Jon Kent, Cassie Sandsmark app. 5.00
2-6-($3.99) John Constantine, Swamp Thing, Zatanna app. 4.00
7-($4.99)-Justice League vs. Amazo army; Constantine & Zatanna vs. Trigon 5.00

DCEASED: UNKILLABLES
DC Comics: Apr, 2020 - No. 3, Jul, 2020 ($4.99, limited series)

1-3-Zombie apocalypse continues; Deathstroke with a team of villains; Red Hood app. 5.00

DCEASED: WAR OF THE UNDEAD GODS
DC Comics: Oct, 2022 - No. 8 ($3.99, limited series)

1-6: 1-Intro. Supergirl & Brainiac; Superman cured. 3-Lobo app. 4.00

DC FESTIVAL OF HEROES: THE ASIAN SUPERHERO CELEBRATION
DC Comics: 2021 ($9.99, square-bound, one-shot)

1-Short stories of Asian characters incl. Batgirl, Katana, The Atom; intro Monkey Prince 10.00

DC FIRST: ...(series of one-shots)
DC Comics: July, 2002 ($3.50)

Batgirl/Joker 1-Sienkiewicz & Terry Moore-a; Nowlan-c 5.00
Green Lantern/Green Lantern 1-Alan Scott & Hal Jordan vs. Krona 3.50
Flash/Superman 1-Superman races Jay Garrick; Abra Kadabra app. 3.50
Superman/Lobo 1-Giffen-s; Nowlan-c 3.50

DC GOES APE
DC Comics: 2008 ($19.99, trade paperback)

	GD	VG	FN	VF	VF/NM	NM-
	2.0	4.0	6.0	8.0	9.0	9.2

Vol. 1 - Reprints app. of Grodd, Beppo, Titano and other monkey tales; Art Adams-c 20.00

DC GRAPHIC NOVEL (Also see DC Science Fiction...)
DC Comics: Nov, 1983 - No. 7, 1986 ($5.95, 68 pgs.)

1-3,5,7: 1-Star Raiders; García-López-c/a; prequel to Atari Force #1. 2-Warlords; not from regular Warlord series. 3-The Medusa Chain; Ernie Colon story/a. 5-Me and Joe Priest; Chaykin-c. 7-Space Clusters; Nino-c/a 2 4 6 9 12 15
4-The Hunger Dogs by Kirby; Darkseid kills Himon from Mister Miracle & destroys New Genesis 5 10 15 33 57 80
6-Metalzoic; Sienkiewicz-c ($6.95) 2 4 6 9 12 15

DC HOLIDAY SPECIAL
DC Comics: Feb, 2010 ($5.99/$9.99, one-shots)

... '09 (2/10, $5.99) 1-Christmas short stories by various incl. Tucci, Chaykin; Nguyen-c 6.00
... 2017 (2/18, $9.99) 1-Story/art by various incl. Rucka, King, Francavilla; Andy Kubert-c 10.00

DC HORROR PRESENTS: SGT. ROCK VS. THE ARMY OF THE DEAD
DC Comics: Nov, 2022 - No. 6, Apr, 2023 ($3.99, limited series)

1-6-Easy Company vs. zombies; Bruce Campbell-s/Eduardo Risso-a/Gary Frank-c 4.00

DC HORROR PRESENTS: SOUL PLUMMER
DC Comics: Jan, 2022 - No. 6, May, 2022 ($3.99, limited series)

1-6: 1-Parks & Zebrowski-s/McCrea-a 4.00

DC HORROR PRESENTS: THE CONJURING: THE LOVER
DC Comics: Aug, 2021 - No. 5, Dec, 2021 ($3.99, limited series)

1-5-Johnson-McGoldrick & Ogle-s/Garry Brown-a 4.00

DC HOUSE OF HORROR
DC Comics: Dec, 2017 ($9.99, square-bound one-shot)

1-Horror short stories by various incl. Giffen, Porter, Baker, Raney, Chaykin; Kaluta-c 10.00

DC INFINITE HALLOWEEN SPECIAL
DC Comics: Dec, 2007 ($5.99, one-shot)

1-Halloween short stories by various incl. Dini, Waid, Hairsine, Kelley Jones; Gene Ha-c 6.00

DC LEAGUE OF SUPER-PETS FCBD SPECIAL EDITION 2022
DC Comics: Jun, 2022 (Free Comic Book Day giveaway, one-shot)

1-Characters from the 2022 movie; preview of the graphic novel; preview of Primer 3.00

DC LOVE IS A BATTLEFIELD
DC Comics: Apr, 2021 ($9.99, squarebound, 80 pgs., one-shot)

1-Romance short stories by various; Harley Quinn, Poison Ivy, Batman, Catwoman app. 10.00

DC/MARVEL: ALL ACCESS (Also see DC Versus Marvel & Marvel Versus DC)
DC Comics: 1996 - No. 4, 1997 ($2.95, limited series)

1-4: 1-Superman & Spider-Man app. 2-Robin & Jubilee app. 3-Dr. Strange & Batman-c/app., X-Men, JLA app. 4-X-Men vs. JLA-c/app. rebirth of Amalgam 3.00

DC/MARVEL: CROSSOVER CLASSICS
DC Comics: 1998; 2003 ($14.95, TPB)

Vol. II-Reprints Batman/Punisher: Lake of Fire, Punisher/Batman: Deadly Knights, Silver Surfer/Superman, Batman & Capt. America 15.00
Vol. 4 (2003, $14.95) Reprints Green Lantern/Silver Surfer: Unholy Alliances, Darkseid/Galactus: The Hunger, Batman & Spider-Man, and Superman/Fantastic Four 15.00

DC: MECH
DC Comics: Sept, 2022 - No. 6, Feb, 2023 ($3.99, limited series)

1-6-Kenny Porter-s/Baldemar Rivas-a Justice League of giant robots vs. Darkseid 4.00

DC NATION
DC Comics: Jul, 2018 (25¢, one-shot)

0-Short stories; Joker by King-s/Mann-a; Superman by Bendis-s/García-López-a; prelude to Justice League: No Justice series; Jimenez-a 3.00

DC NATION FCBD SUPER SAMPLER
DC Comics: (Giveaway)

.../ Superman Adventures Flip Book (6/12) stories from Superman Family Adventures, Young Justice, Green Lantern: The Animated Series 3.00
... (7/13) Stories from Beware the Batman and Teen Titans Go! 3.00

DC NUCLEAR WINTER SPECIAL
DC Comics: Jan, 2019 ($9.99, square-bound, one-shot)

1-Wasteland short stories by various incl. Russell, Duce, Ordway, Hester; Paquette-c 10.00

DC 100 PAGE SUPER SPECTACULAR
(Title is 100 Page... No. 14 on)(Square bound) (Reprints, 50¢)
National Periodical Publications: No. 4, Summer, 1971 - No. 13, 6/72; No. 14, 2/73 - No. 22, 11/73 (No #1-3)

4-Weird Mystery Tales; Johnny Peril & Phantom Stranger; cover & splashes by Wrightson; origin Jungle Boy of Jupiter 27 54 81 194 435 675
5-Love Stories; Wood inks (7 pgs.)(scarcer) 52 104 156 406 928 1450
6- "World's Greatest Super-Heroes"; JLA, JSA, Spectre, Johnny Quick, Vigilante & Hawkman; contains unpublished Wildcat story; N. Adams wrap-around-c; r/JLA #21,22 18 36 54 128 284 440
6-Replica Edition (2004, $6.95) complete reprint w/wraparound-c 7.00
7-(Also listed as Superman #245) Air Wave, Kid Eternity, Hawkman-r; Atom-r/Atom #3 10 20 30 68 144 220
8-(Also listed as Batman #238) Batman, Legion, Aquaman-r; G.A. Atom, Sargon (r/Sensation #57), Plastic Man (r/Police #14) stories; Doom Patrol origin-r; Neal Adams wraparound-c 18 36 54 124 275 425
9-(Also listed as Our Army at War #242) Kubert-c 9 18 27 62 126 190
10-(Also listed as Adventure Comics #416) Golden Age-reprints; r/1st app. Black Canary from Flash #86; no Zatanna 11 22 33 75 160 245
11-(Also listed as Flash #214) origin Metal Men-r/Showcase #37; never before published G.A. Flash story. 9 18 27 58 114 170
12-(Also listed as Superboy #185) Legion-c/story; Teen Titans, Kid Eternity (r/Hit #46), Star Spangled Kid-r(S.S. #55) 8 16 24 56 108 160
13-(Also listed as Superman #252) Ray(r/Smash #17), Black Condor, (r/Crack #18), Hawkman(r/Flash #24); Starman-r/Adv. #67; Dr. Fate & Spectre-r/More Fun #57; Neal Adams-c 10 20 30 70 150 230
14-Batman-r/Detective #31,32,156; Atom-r/Showcase #34 8 16 24 54 102 150
15,16,18,19,21,22: 15-r/2nd Boy Commandos/Det. #64. 16-Sgt. Rock; r/Capt. Storm #1, 1st Johnny Cloud/All-American Men of War #82. 18-Superman. 21-Superboy; r/Brave & the Bold #54. 22-r/All-Flash #13 6 12 18 40 73 105
17,20: 17-JSA-r/All Star #37 (10-11/47, 38 pgs.), Sandman-r/Adv. #65 (8/41), JLA #23 (11/63) & JLA #43 (3/66). 20-Batman-r/Det. #66,68, Spectre; origin Two-Face 6 12 18 41 76 110
... : Love Stories Replica Edition (2000, $6.95) reprints #5 7.00

NOTE: ***Anderson*** *r-11, 14, 18i, 22.* ***B. Baily*** *r-18, 20.* ***Burnley*** *r-18, 20.* ***Crandall*** *r-14p, 20.* ***Drucker*** *r-4.* ***Grandenetti*** *a-22(2)r.* ***Heath*** *a-22r.* ***Infantino*** *r-17, 20, 22.* ***G. Kane*** *r-18.* ***Kirby*** *r-15.* ***Kubert*** *r-6, 7, 16, 17; c-16, 19.* ***Manning*** *a-19r.* ***Meskin*** *r-4, 22.* ***Mooney*** *r-15, 21.* ***Toth*** *r-17, 20.*

DC ONE MILLION (Also see crossover #1,000,000 issues and JLA One Million TPB)
DC Comics: Nov, 1998 - No. 4, Nov, 1998 ($2.95/$1.99, weekly lim. series)

1-($2.95) JLA travels to the 853rd century; Morrison-s 4.00
2-4-($1.99) 3.00
... Eighty-Page Giant (8/99, $4.95) 5.00
TPB ('99, $14.95) r/#1-4 and several x-over stories 15.00

DC POWER: A CELEBRATION
DC Comics: Mar, 2023 ($9.99, squarebound, one-shot)

1-Spotlight on DC's black heroes; short stories by various; Cyborg, John Stewart, Aqualad, Kid Flash, Batwing, Vixen, Amazing-Man and more app.; John Ridley intro. 10.00

DC PRIDE
DC Comics: Aug, 2021 ($9.99, squarebound, one-shot)

1-Spotlight on DC's LGBQT characters; short stories by various; Aqualad, Batwoman, Green Lantern Alan Scott, Renee Montoya, Midnighter & Apollo app. 10.00
... 2022 1-(8/22) Short stories by various incl. "Finding Batman" by Kevin Conroy-s 10.00
...: Tim Drake Special 1 (8/22, $5.99) R/stories from Batman: Urban Legends #4-6 & 10 6.00

DC REBIRTH HOLIDAY SPECIAL
DC Comics: Feb, 2017 ($9.99, one-shot)

1-Short stories by various; framing pages of Harley Quinn by Dini-s/Charretier-a 2 4 6 8 11 14

DC RETROACTIVE (New stories done in old style plus reprint from decade)
DC Comics: Sept, 2011 - Oct, 2011 ($4.99, series of one-shots)

...: Batman - The '70s (9/11, $4.99) Len Wein-s/Tom Mandrake-a; r/Batman #307 5.00
...: Batman - The '80s (10/11, $4.99) Mike Barr-s/Jerry Bingham-a; The Reaper app. 5.00
...: Batman - The '90s (10/11, $4.99) Grant-s/Breyfogle-a; Scarface & Ventriloquist app. 5.00
...: Flash - The '70s (9/11, $4.99) Bates-s/Gallego-a; r/DC Comics Presents #2 5.00
...: Flash - The '80s (10/11, $4.99) Messner-Loebs-s/LaRocque-a; r/Flash v2 #18 5.00
...: Flash - The '90s (10/11, $4.99) Augustyn-s/Bowden-a; r/Flash v2 #142 5.00
...: Green Lantern - The '70s (9/11, $4.99) O'Neil-s/Grell-a; r/Green Lantern #76 5.00
...: Green Lantern - The '80s (10/11, $4.99) Wein-s/Staton-a; r/Green Lantern #172 5.00
...: Green Lantern - The '90s (10/11, $4.99) Marz-s/Banks-a; r/Green Lantern v3 #78 5.00
...: JLA - The '70s (9/11, $4.99) Bates-s; Adam Strange app.; r/J.L. of A. #123 5.00
...: JLA - The '80s (10/11, $4.99) Conway-s/Randall-a; Felix Faust app.; r/J.L.of A. #239 5.00
...: JLA - The '90s (10/11, $4.99) Giffen & DeMatteis-s/Maguire-a; r/J.L.A. #6 5.00
...: Superman - The '70s (9/11, $4.99) Pasko-s/Barreto-a; r/Action Comics #484 5.00
...: Superman - The '80s (10/11, $4.99) Wolfman-s/Cariello-a; r/Superman #352 5.00
...: Superman - The '90s (10/11, $4.99) L. Simonson-s/Bogdanove-a; Guardian app. 5.00
...: Wonder Woman - The '70s (9/11, $4.99) O'Neil-s/J. Bone-a; r/Wonder Woman #201 5.00
...: Wonder Woman - The '80s (10/11, $4.99) Thomas-s/Buckler-a; r/W.W. #288 5.00
...: Wonder Woman - The '90s (10/11, $4.99) Messner-Loebs-s/Moder-a; r/W.W. v2 #66 5.00

DC/RWBY (Based on the online series from Rooster Teeth)
DC Comics: Apr, 2023 - Present ($3.99)

1-Marguerite Bennett/Meghan Hetrick-a; Batman app. 4.00

DC'S BEACH BLANKET BAD GUYS SUMMER SPECIAL
DC Comics: Sept, 2018 ($9.99, 80 pgs, square-bound, one-shot)

1-Summer short stories by various; Conner-c; Joker, Mr. Freeze, Black Manta app. 10.00

DC SCIENCE FICTION GRAPHIC NOVEL
DC Comics: 1985 - No. 7, 1987 ($5.95)

SF1-SF7: SF1-Hell on Earth by Robert Bloch; Giffen-p. SF2-Nightwings by Robert Silverberg; G. Colan-p. SF3-Frost & Fire by Bradbury. SF4-Merchants of Venus. SF5-Demon With A Glass Hand by Ellison; M. Rogers-a. SF6-The Magic Goes Away by Niven. SF7-Sandkings by George R.R. Martin 2 4 6 8 11 14

DC'S CRIMES OF PASSION
DC Comics: Apr, 2020 ($9.99, 80 pgs, square-bound, one-shot)

1-Romance-themed short stories by various; Yasmine Putri-c 10.00

DC'S GRIFTER GOT RUN OVER BY A REINDEER
DC Comics: Jan, 2023 ($9.99, 80 pgs, square-bound, one-shot)

1-Winter & Christmas-themed short stories by various; D'Anda-c; Harley Quinn app. 10.00

DC'S HARLEY QUINN ROMANCES
DC Comics: Mar, 2023 ($9.99, square-bound, one-shot)

1-Romance-themed short stories by various; Amanda Conner-c 10.00

DC SILVER AGE CLASSICS
DC Comics: 1992 ($1.00, all reprints)

...Action Comics #252-r/1st Supergirl. Adventure Comics #247-r/1st Legion of Super-Heroes. The Brave and the Bold #28-r/1st JLA. Detective Comics #225-r/1st Martian Manhunter. Detective Comics #327-r/1st new look Batman. Green Lantern #76-r/1st Green Lantern/Green Arrow. House of Secrets #92-r/1st Swamp Thing. Showcase #4-r/1st S.A. Flash. Showcase #22-r/1st S.A. Green Lantern 4.00
...Sugar and Spike #99; includes 2 unpublished stories 5.00

DC SPECIAL (Also see Super DC Giant)
National Per. Publ.: 10-12/68 - No. 15, 11-12/71; No. 16, Spr/75 - No. 29, 8-9/77

1-All Infantino issue; Flash, Batman, Adam Strange-r; begin 68 pg. issues, end #21 8 16 24 54 102 150
2-Teen humor; Binky, Buzzy, Harvey app. 9 18 27 62 126 190
3-All-Girl issue; unpubl. GA Wonder Woman story 9 18 27 60 120 180
4,11: 4-Horror (1st Abel, brief). 11-Monsters 5 10 15 35 63 90
5-10,12-15: 5-All Kubert issue; Viking Prince, Sgt. Rock-r. 6-Western. 7,9,13-Strangest Sports. 12-Viking Prince; Kubert-c/a (r/B&B almost entirely). 15-G.A. Plastic Man origin-r/

DC Love is a Battlefield #1 © DC

DC Pride 2022 #1 © DC

DC Super-Stars #15 © DC

GD 2.0 | VG 4.0 | FN 6.0 | VF 8.0 | VF/NM 9.0 | NM- 9.2

Police #1; origin Woozy by Cole; 14,15-(52 pgs.) 4 8 12 28 47 65
16-27: 16-Super Heroes Battle Super Gorillas. 17-Early S.A. Green Lantern-r. 22-Origin Robin Hood. 26-Enemy Ace. 27-Captain Comet story 3 6 9 16 23 30
28-Earth Shattering Disaster Stories; Legion of Super-Heroes story 3 6 9 17 25 34
29-New "The Untold Origin of the Justice Society"; Staton-a/Neal Adams-c; Hitler app. in story and on cover 5 10 15 34 60 85

NOTE: ***N. Adams*** *c-3, 4, 6, 11, 29.* ***Grell*** *a-20; c-17, 20.* ***Heath*** *a-12r.* ***G. Kane*** *a-6p, 13r, 17r, 19-21r.* ***Kirby*** *a-4,11.* ***Kubert*** *a-6r, 12r, 22.* ***Meskin*** *a-10.* ***Moreira*** *a-10.* ***Staton*** *a-29p.* ***Toth*** *a-13, 20r. #1-15: 25¢; 16-27: 50¢; 28, 29: 60¢. #1-13, 16-21: 68 pgs.; 14, 15: 52 pgs.; 25-27: oversized.*

DC SPECIAL BLUE RIBBON DIGEST
DC Comics: Mar-Apr, 1980 - No. 24, Aug, 1982

1,2,4: 1-Legion reprints. 2-Flash. 4-Green Lantern 2 4 6 9 13 16
3-Justice Society reprints; new Dr. Fate story 2 4 6 11 16 20
5-Secret Origins; new Zatara and Zatanna 3 6 9 14 20 25
6,8-10: 6-Ghosts. 8-Legion. 9-Secret Origins. 10-Warlord-"The Deimos Saga"-Grell-s/c/a 2 4 6 9 13 16
7-Sgt. Rock's Prize Battle Tales 3 6 9 14 19 24
11,16: 11-Justice League. 16-Green Lantern/Green Arrow-r; all Adams-a 2 4 6 13 18 22
12-Haunted Tank; reprints 1st app. 3 6 9 14 19 24
13-15,17-19: 13-Strange Sports Stories. 14-UFO Invaders; Adam Strange app. 15-Secret Origins of Super Villains; JLA app. 17-Ghosts. 18-Sgt. Rock; Kubert front & back-c. 19-Doom Patrol; new Perez-c 2 4 6 10 14 18
20-Dark Mansion of Forbidden Love (scarce) 5 10 15 30 50 70
21-Our Army at War 3 6 9 16 23 30
22-24: 22-Secret Origins. 23-Green Arrow, w/new 7 pg. story (Spiegle-a). 24-House of Mystery; new Kubert wraparound-c 3 6 9 14 19 24

NOTE: ***N. Adams*** *a-16(6)r, 17r, 23r; c-16.* ***Aparo*** *a-6r, 24r; c-23.* ***Grell*** *a-8, 10; c-10.* ***Heath*** *a-14.* ***Infantino*** *a-15r.* ***Kaluta*** *a-17r.* ***Gil Kane*** *a-15r, 22r.* ***Kirby*** *a-5, 9, 23r.* ***Kubert*** *a-3, 18r, 21r; c-7, 12, 14, 17, 18, 21, 24.* ***Morrow*** *a-24r.* ***Orlando*** *a-17r, 22r; c-1, 20.* ***Toth*** *a-21r, 24r.* ***Wood*** *a-3, 17r, 24r.* ***Wrightson*** *a-16r, 17r, 24r.*

DC SPECIAL: CYBORG (From Teen Titans) (See Teen Titans 2003 series for TPB collection)
DC Comics: Jul, 2008 - No. 6, Dec, 2008 ($2.99, limited series)

1-6: 1-Sable-s/Lashley-a; origin re-told. 3-6-Magno-a 3.00

DC SPECIAL: RAVEN (From Teen Titans) (See Teen Titans 2003 series for TPB collection)
DC Comics: May, 2008 - No. 5, Sept, 2008 ($2.99, limited series)

1-5-Marv Wolfman-s/Damion Scott-a 3.00

DC SPECIAL SERIES
National Periodical Publications/DC Comics: 9/77 - No. 16, Fall, 1978; No. 17, 8/79 - No. 27, Fall, 1981 (No. 18, 19, 23, 24 - digest size, 100 pgs.; No. 25-27 - Treasury sized)

1-"5-Star Super-Hero Spectacular 1977"; Batman, Atom, Flash, Green Lantern, Aquaman, in solo stories, Kobra app.; 1st app. Patty Spivot in Flash story; N. Adams-c 5 10 15 35 63 90
2(#1)-"The Original Swamp Thing Saga 1977"-r/Swamp Thing #1&2 by Wrightson; new Wrightson wraparound-c. 3 6 9 15 22 28
3,4,6-8: 3-Sgt Rock. 4-Unexpected. 6-Secret Society of Super Villains, Jones-a. 7-Ghosts Special. 8-Brave and Bold w/ new Batman, Deadman & Sgt Rock team-up 3 6 9 14 20 25
5-"Superman Spectacular 1977"-(84 pg, $1.00)-Superman vs. Brainiac & Lex Luthor, new 63 pg. story 3 6 9 17 26 35
9-Wonder Woman; Ditko-a (11 pgs.); Hitler-c 4 8 12 23 37 50
10-"Secret Origins of Superheroes Special 1978"-(52 pgs.)-Dr. Fate, Lightray & Black Canary on-c/new origin stories; Staton, Newton-a 3 6 9 16 23 30
11-"Flash Spectacular 1978"-(84 pgs.) Flash, Kid Flash, GA Flash & Johnny Quick vs. Grodd; Wood-i on Kid Flash chapter 2 4 6 13 18 22
12-"Secrets of Haunted House Special Spring 1978" 2 4 6 13 18 22
13-"Sgt. Rock Special Spring 1978", 50 pg new story 3 6 9 14 19 24
14,17,20-"Original Swamp Thing Saga", Wrightson-a: 14-Sum '78, r/#3,4. 17-Sum '79 r/#5-7. 20-Jan/Feb '80, r/#8-10 2 4 6 13 16
15-"Batman Spectacular Summer 1978", Ra's Al Ghul-app.; Golden-a. Rogers-a/front & back-c 4 8 12 27 44 60
16-"Jonah Hex Spectacular Fall 1978"; death of Jonah Hex, Heath-a; Bat Lash and Scalphunter stories 6 12 18 41 76 110
18,19-Digest size: 18-"Sgt. Rock's Prize Battle Tales Fall 1979". 19-"Secret Origins of Super-Heroes Fall 1979"; origins Wonder Woman (new-a),r/Robin, Batman-Superman team, Aquaman, Hawkman and others 2 4 6 13 18 22
21-"Super-Star Holiday Special Spring 1980", Frank Miller-a in "Batman--Wanted Dead or Alive" (1st Batman story); Jonah Hex, Sgt. Rock, Superboy & LSH and House of Mystery/ Witching Hour-c/stories 5 10 15 33 57 80
22-"G.I. Combat Sept. 1980", Kubert-c. Haunted Tank-s 3 6 9 14 19 24
23,24-Digest size: 23-World's Finest-r. 24-Flash 2 4 6 11 16 20
V5#25-($2.95)-"Superman II, the Adventure Continues Summer 1981"; photos from movie & photo-c (see All-New Coll. Ed. C-62 for first Superman movie) 3 6 9 17 26 35
26-($2.50)-"Superman and His Incredible Fortress of Solitude Summer 1981" 3 6 9 16 23 30
27-($2.50)-"Batman vs. The Incredible Hulk Fall 1981" 9 18 27 57 111 165

NOTE: ***Aparo*** *c-8.* ***Heath*** *a-12i, 16.* ***Infantino*** *a-19r.* ***Kirby*** *a-23, 19r.* ***Kubert*** *c-13, 19r.* ***Nasser/Netzer*** *a-1, 10i, 15.* ***Newton*** *a-10.* ***Nino*** *a-4, 7.* ***Starlin*** *c-12.* ***Staton*** *a-1.* ***Tuska*** *a-19r. #25 & 26. were advertised as All-New Collectors' Edition C-63, C-64. #26 was originally planned as All-New Collectors' Ed. C-30?; has C-630 & A.N.C.E. on cover.*

DC SPECIAL: THE RETURN OF DONNA TROY
DC Comics: Aug, 2005 - No. 4, Late Oct, 2005 ($2.99, limited series)

1-4-Jimenez-s/Garcia-Lopez-a(p)/Pérez-i 3.00

DC'S SAVED BY THE BELLE REVE
DC Comics: Oct, 2022 ($9.99, 80 pgs, square-bound, one-shot)

1-School-themed short stories by various; Juni Ba-c; Super Sons & Tiny Titans app. 10.00

DC'S TERROR THROUGH TIME
DC Comics: Dec, 2022 ($9.99, 80 pgs, square-bound, one-shot)

1-Tales of traumatizing time travel; short stories by various; John McCrea-c 10.00

DC SUPERHERO GIRLS
DC Comics: May, 2016; May, 2017; May 2018 (All-ages FCBD giveaway)

1 FCBD 2017 Special Edition (5/17); teenage girl heroes; Fontana-s/Labat-a 3.00
1 FCBD 2018 Special Edition (5/18); Date With Disaster; Fontana-s/Labat-a 3.00
1 Special Edition (5/16); teenage girl heroes at Super Hero High; Fontana-s/Labat-a 3.00
... 2017 Halloween Comic Fest Special Edition (11/17) Labat & Garbowska-a 3.00
... Halloween Fest Special Edition (12/16); teenage girl heroes at Super Hero High 3.00

DC SUPERHERO GIRLS GIANT
DC Comics: 2019 - No. 2, 2020 ($4.99, 100 pgs., squarebound, Mass Market & Direct Market editions exist for each issue, with different covers)

1,2-Direct Market Edition - New stories and reprints from graphic novels 5.00

DC SUPER-STARS
National Periodical Publ./DC Comics: March, 1976 - No. 18, Winter, 1978 (No. 3-18: 52 pgs.)

1-(68 pgs.)-Re-intro Teen Titans (predates T. T. #44 (11/76); tryout iss.) plus r/Teen Titans; W.W. as girl was original Wonder Girl 3 6 9 19 30 40
2-6,9,12,16: 2,4,6,8-Adam Strange; 2-(68 pgs.)-r/1st Adam Strange/Hawkman team-up from Mystery in Space #90 plus Atomic Knights origin-r. 3-Legion issue. 4-r/Tales/Unexpected #45. 2 4 6 8 11 14
7-Aquaman spotlight; Aqualad, Aquagirl, Ocean Master & Black Manta app.; Aparo-c 3 6 9 21 33 45
8-r/1st Space Ranger from Showcase #15, Adam Strange-r/Mystery in Space #89 & Star Rovers-r/M.I.S. #80 2 4 6 9 13 16
10-Strange Sports Stories; Batman/Joker-c/story 2 4 6 13 18 22
11-Magic; Zatanna-c/reprint from Adv. #413-415 with Morrow-a; Morrow-c; Flash vs. Abra Kadabra (r/Flash #128) 10 20 30 69 147 225
13-Sergio Aragonés Special 3 6 9 15 22 28
14,15,18: 15-Sgt. Rock 2 4 6 9 13 16
17-Secret Origins of Super-Heroes (origin of The Huntress); origin Green Arrow by Grell; Legion app.; Earth II Batman & Catwoman marry (1st revealed; also see B&B #197 & Superman Family #211) 9 18 27 62 126 190
#17 (Facsimile Edition) (2020, $4.99) Reprints #17 with original ads 5.00

NOTE: ***M. Anderson*** *r-2, 4, 6.* ***Aparo*** *c-7, 14, 18.* ***Austin*** *a-11i.* ***Buckler*** *a-14p; c-10.* ***Grell*** *a-17.* ***G. Kane*** *a-1r, 10r.* ***Kubert*** *c-15.* ***Layton*** *c/a-16i, 17i.* ***Mooney*** *a-4r, 6r.* ***Morrow*** *c/a-11r.* ***Nasser*** *a-11.* ***Newton*** *c/a-16p.* ***Staton*** *a-17; c-17. No. 10, 12-18 contain all new material; the rest are reprints. #1 contains new and reprint material.*

DC'S VERY MERRY MULTIVERSE
DC Comics: Feb, 2021 ($9.99, one-shot)

1-Short Holiday stories; Batman, Harley Quinn, Capt. Carrot, Lobo and others app. 10.00

DC'S YEAR OF THE VILLAIN SPECIAL
DC Comics: Jul, 2019 (25¢, one-shot)

1-Short preludes; Legion of Doom, Leviathan, Batman Who Laughs app.; Capullo-c 3.00

DC: THE DOOMED AND THE DAMNED
DC Comics: Dec, 2020 ($9.99, one-shot)

1-Short horror stories; Batman, Madame Xanadu, Man-Bat, Etrigan, Green Lantern app. 10.00

DC: THE NEW FRONTIER (Also see Justice League: The New Frontier Special)
DC Comics: Mar, 2004 - No. 6, Nov, 2004 ($6.95, limited series)

1-6-DCU in the 1940s-60s; Darwyn Cooke-c/s/a in all. 1-Hal Jordan and The Losers app. 2-Origin Martian Manhunter; Barry Allen app. 3-Challengers of the Unknown 7.00
...Volume One (2004, $19.95, TPB) r/#1-3; cover gallery & intro. by Paul Levitz 20.00
...Volume Two (2005, $19.99, TPB) r/#4-6; cover gallery & afterword by Cooke 20.00

DC TOP COW CROSSOVERS
DC Comics/Top Cow Productions: 2007 ($14.99, TPB)

SC-r/The Darkness/Batman; JLA/Witchblade; The Darkness/Superman; JLA/Cyberforce 15.00

DC 2000
DC Comics: 2000 - No. 2, 2000 ($6.95, limited series)

1,2-JLA visit 1941 JSA; Semeiks-a 7.00

DCU BRAVE NEW WORLD (See Infinite Crisis and tie-ins)
DC Comics: Aug, 2006 ($1.00, 80 pgs., one-shot)

1-Previews 2006 series Martian Manhunter, OMAC, The Creeper, The All-New Atom, The Trials of Shazam, and Uncle Sam and the Freedom Fighters; the Monitor app. 4.00

DCU (Halloween and Christmas one-shot anthologies)
DC Comics

... Halloween Special '09 (12/09, $5.99) Ha-c; art from Bagley, Tucci, K. Jones, Nguyen 6.00
... Halloween Special 2010 (12/10, $4.99) Ha-c; art from Tucci, Garbett; I...Vampire app. 5.00
... Holiday Special (2/09, $5.99) Christmas by various incl. Dini, Maguire, Reis; Quitely-c 6.00
... Holiday Special 2010 (2/11, $4.99) Jonah Hex, Spectre, Legion of S.H., Anthro app. 5.00
... Infinite Halloween Special (12/08, $5.99) Ralph & Sue Dibny app.; Gene Ha-c 6.00
... Infinite Holiday Special (2/07, $4.99) by various; Batwoman app.; Porter-c 5.00

DCU HEROES SECRET FILES
DC Comics: Feb, 1999 ($4.95, one-shot)

1-Origin-s and pin-ups; new Star Spangled Kid app. 5.00

DCU: LEGACIES
DC Comics: Jul, 2010 - No. 10, Apr, 2011 ($3.99, limited series)

1-10: 1,2-Andy Kubert-c; JSA app.; two covers on each. 3-JLA app.; Garcia-Lopez-a. 4-Sgt. Rock back-up; Joe Kubert-a. 5-Pérez-a. 8-Back-up Quitely-a 4.00

DC UNIVERSE CHRISTMAS, A
DC Comics: 2000 ($19.95)

TPB-Reprints DC Christmas stories by various 20.00

DC UNIVERSE: DECISIONS
DC Comics: Early Nov, 2008 - No. 4, Late Dec, 2008 ($2.99, limited series)

1-4-Assassination plot in the Presidential election; Winick & Willingham-s/Porter-a 3.00

DC UNIVERSE HOLIDAY BASH
DC Comics: 1997- 1999 ($3.95)

I,II-(X-mas '96,'97) Christmas stories by various 5.00
III (1999, for Christmas '98, $4.95) 5.00

DC UNIVERSE ILLUSTRATED BY NEAL ADAMS (Also see Batman Illustrated by Neal Adams HC Vol. 1-3)
DC Comics: 2008 ($39.99, hardcover with dustjacket)

Vol. 1 - Reprints Adams' non-Batman/non-Green Lantern work from 1967-1972; incl. Teen Titans, DC war, Enemy Ace, Superman and PSAs; promo art; Levitz foreword 40.00

DC UNIVERSE: LAST WILL AND TESTAMENT
DC Comics: Oct, 2008 ($3.99, one-shot)

1-Geo-Force vs. Deathstroke; DC heroes prepare for Final Crisis; Brad Meltzer-s; Adam Kubert & Joe Kubert-a; two covers 4.00

DC UNIVERSE ONLINE LEGENDS (Based on the online game)
DC Comics: Early Apr. 2011 - Late May, 2012 ($2.99)

1-26: 1-Wolfman & Bedard-s/Porter-a; DC heroes & Luthor vs. Brainiac. 1-Wraparound-c 3.00

DC UNIVERSE: ORIGINS
DC Comics: 2009 ($14.99, TPB)

nn-Reprints 2-page origins of DC characters from back-ups in 52, Countdown and Justice League: Cry For Justice #1-3; s/a by various; Alex Ross-c 15.00

DC UNIVERSE PRESENTS (DC New 52)
DC Comics: Nov, 2011 - No. 19, Jun, 2013 ($2.99)

1-5-Deadman. 1-Deadman origin re-told; Jenkins-s/Chang-a/Sook-c 3.00
6-8-Challengers of the Unknown; DiDio-s/Ordway-a/Sook-c 3.00
9-19: 9-11-Savage; Chang-a. 12-Kid Flash. 13-16-Black Lightning & Blue Devil 3.00
#0 (11/12, $5.99) O.M.A.C., Mr. Terrific, Hawk & Dove, Blackhawks, Deadman origins 6.00

DC UNIVERSE: REBIRTH
DC Comics: Jul, 2016 ($2.99, one-shot)

1-($2.99) Wally West returns; Johns-s; art by Frank, Van Sciver, Reis & Jimenez; wraparound-c by Gary Frank 3.00
1-2nd printing ($5.99, squarebound) same wraparound-c by Gary Frank 6.00
1-3rd printing ($5.99, squarebound) variant Kid Flash cover by Gary Frank 6.00

DC UNIVERSE SPECIAL
DC Comics: July, 2008 - Aug, 2008 ($4.99, collection of reprints related to Final Crisis)

...: Justice League of America (7/08) r/J.L. of A. #111,166-168 & Detective #274; Sook-c 5.00
...: Reign in Hell (8/08) r/Blaze/Satanus War x-over; Sook-c 5.00
...: Superman (7/08) r/Mongul app. in Superman #32, Showcase '95 #7,8, Flash #102 5.00

DC UNIVERSE: THE STORIES OF ALAN MOORE (Also see Across the Universe:...)
DC Comics: 2006 ($19.99)

TPB-Reprints Batman: The Killing Joke, "Whatever Happened to the Man of Tomorrow", "For The Man Who Has Everything, and other classic Moore DC stories; Bolland-c 20.00

DC UNIVERSE: TRINITY
DC Comics: Aug, 1993 - No. 2, Sept, 1993 ($2.95, 52 pgs, limited series)

1,2-Foil-c; Green Lantern, Darkstars, Legion app. 4.00

DC UNIVERSE VS. MASTERS OF THE UNIVERSE
DC Comics: Oct, 2013 - No. 6, May, 2014 ($2.99, limited series)

1-6: 1-3-Giffen-s/Soy-a/Benes-c; Constantine app. 4-6-Mhan-a 3.00

DCU VILLAINS SECRET FILES
DC Comics: Apr, 1999 ($4.95, one-shot)

1-Origin-s and profile pages 5.00

DC VERSUS MARVEL (See Marvel Versus DC) (Also see Amazon, Assassins, Bruce Wayne: Agent of S.H.I.E.L.D., Bullets & Bracelets, Doctor Strangefate, JLX, Legend of the Dark Claw, Magneto & The Magnetic Men, Speed Demon, Spider-Boy, Super Soldier, X-Patrol)
DC Comics: No. 1, 1996, No. 4, 1996 ($3.95, limited series)

1,4: 1-Marz script, Jurgens-a(p); 1st app. of Access. 5.00

.../Marvel Versus DC ($12.95, trade paperback) r/1-4 13.00

DC VS. VAMPIRES
DC Comics: Dec, 2021 - No. 12, Feb, 2023 ($3.99, limited series)

1-12-Tynion IV & Rosenberg-s/Schmidt-a. 1-I, Vampire (Andrew Bennett) app. 4.00
... Coffin Edition 1 (9/22, $5.99) Reprints #1-3; cover homage to Lost Boys movie poster 6.00
... Crypt Edition 1 (9/22, $5.99) Reprints #4-6; cover homage to Breakfast Club poster 6.00
... - Hunters 1 (7/22, $3.99) Damian in Gotham City; Googe-a 4.00
... - Killers 1 (8/22, $3.99) Harley Quinn & Catwoman app.; Bowden-a 4.00

DC VS. VAMPIRES: ALL-OUT WAR
DC Comics: Sept, 2022 - No. 6, Feb, 2023 ($3.99, B&W&red, limited series)

1-6-Rosenberg-s/Paknadel-a; John Constantine, Deathstroke, and Mary Marvel app. 4.00

DC/WILDSTORM DREAMWAR
DC Comics: Jun, 2008 - No. 6, Nov, 2008 ($2.99, limited series)

1-6-Giffen-s; Silver Age JLA, Teen Titans, JSA, Legion app. on WildStorm Earth 3.00
1-Variant-c of Superman & Midnighter by Garbett 6.00
TPB (2009, $19.99) r/series 20.00

DC: WORLD WAR III (See 52/WWIII)

D-DAY (Also see Special War Series)
Charlton Comics (no No. 3): Sum/63; No. 2, Fall/64; No. 4, 9/66; No. 5, 10/67; No. 6, 11/68

	GD 2.0	VG 4.0	FN 6.0	VF 8.0	VF/NM 9.0	NM- 9.2
1,2: 1(1963)-Montes/Bache-c. 2(Fall '64)-Wood-a(4)	4	8	12	27	44	60
4-6('66-'68)-Montes/Bache-a #5	3	6	9	14	20	25

DEAD AIR
Slave Labor Graphics: July, 1989 ($5.95, graphic novel)

	GD 2.0	VG 4.0	FN 6.0	VF 8.0	VF/NM 9.0	NM- 9.2
nn-Mike Allred's 1st published work	1	2	3	5	6	8

DEAD BODY ROAD: BAD BLOOD
Image Comics (Skybound): Jun, 2020 - No. 6, Dec, 2020 ($3.99)

1-6-Justin Jordan-s/Benjamin Tiesma-a/Matthew Scalera-c 4.00

DEADBOX
Vault Comics: Sept, 2021 - Present ($3.99, limited series)

1-3-Russell-s/Tiesma-a 4.00

DEAD BOY DETECTIVES
DC Comics (Vertigo): Feb, 2014 - No. 12, Feb, 2015 ($2.99, limited series)

1-12-Litt-s/Buckingham-a. 1-Covers by Buckingham & Chiang 3.00

DEAD CORPSE
DC Comics (Helix): Sept, 1998 - No. 4, Dec, 1998 ($2.50, limited series)

1-4-Pugh-a/Hinz-s 3.00

DEAD DAY
AfterShock Comics: May, 2020 - No. 5, Nov, 2020 ($3.99)

1-5-Ryan Parrott-s/Evgeniy Bornyakov-a 4.00

DEAD DOG'S BITE
Dark Horse Comics: Mar, 2021 - No. 4, Jun, 2021 ($4.99, limited series)

1-4-Tyler Boss-s/a 5.00

DEAD DROP
Valiant Entertainment: May, 2015 - No. 4, Aug, 2015 ($3.99, limited series)

1-4-Ales Kot-s/Adam Gorham-a; X-O Manowar app. 2-Archer app. 4.00

DEAD END CRIME STORIES
Kirby Publishing Co.: April, 1949 (52 pgs.)

	GD 2.0	VG 4.0	FN 6.0	VF 8.0	VF/NM 9.0	NM- 9.2
nn-(Scarce)-Powell, Roussos-a; painted-c	74	148	222	470	810	1150

DEAD ENDERS
DC Comics (Vertigo): Mar, 2000 - No. 16, June, 2001 ($2.50)

1-16-Brubaker-s/Pleece & Case-a 3.00
Stealing the Sun (2000, $9.95, TPB) r/#1-4, Vertigo Winter's Edge #3 10.00

DEAD EYES (Copies recalled due to trademark dispute, cancelled after #2)(See Dead Rabbit)
Image Comics: Oct, 2019 ($3.99)

1-Duggan-s/McCrea-a 6.00

DEAD-EYE WESTERN COMICS
Hillman Periodicals: Nov-Dec, 1948 - V3#1, Apr-May, 1953

	GD 2.0	VG 4.0	FN 6.0	VF 8.0	VF/NM 9.0	NM- 9.2
V1#1-(52 pgs.)-Krigstein, Roussos-a	27	54	81	158	259	360
V1#2,3-(52 pgs.)	15	30	45	85	130	175
V1#4-12-(52 pgs.)	12	24	36	67	94	120
V2#1,2,5-8,10-12: 1-7-(52 pgs.)	9	18	27	50	65	80
3,4-Krigstein-a	10	20	30	54	72	90
9-One pg. Frazetta ad	9	18	27	50	65	80
V3#1	9	18	27	50	65	80

NOTE: *Briefer a-V1#8. Kinstleresque stories by* ***McCann****-12, V2#1, 2, V3#1.* ***McWilliams*** *a-V1#5.* ***Ed Moore*** *a-V1#4.*

DEADFACE: DOING THE ISLANDS WITH BACCHUS
Dark Horse Comics: July, 1991 - No. 3, Sept, 1991 ($2.95, B&W, lim. series)

1-3: By Eddie Campbell 3.00

DEADFACE: EARTH, WATER, AIR, AND FIRE
Dark Horse Comics: July, 1992 - No. 4, Oct, 1992 ($2.50, B&W, limited series; British-r)

1-4: By Eddie Campbell 3.00

DEAD HAND, THE
Image Comics: Apr, 2018 - No. 6, Sept, 2018 ($3.99)

1-6-Kyle Higgins-s/Stephen Mooney-a 4.00

DEAD INSIDE
Dark Horse Comics: Dec, 2016 - No. 5, May, 2017 ($3.99)

1-5-Arcudi-s/Fejzula-a/Dave Johnson-c 4.00

DEAD IN THE WEST
Dark Horse Comics: Oct, 1993 - No. 2, Mar, 1994 ($3.95, B&W, 52 pgs.)

1,2-Timothy Truman-c 4.00

DEAD IRONS
Dynamite Entertainment: 2009 - No. 4, 2009 ($3.99)

DC vs. Vampires #1 © DC

Dead Boy Detectives #1 © DC

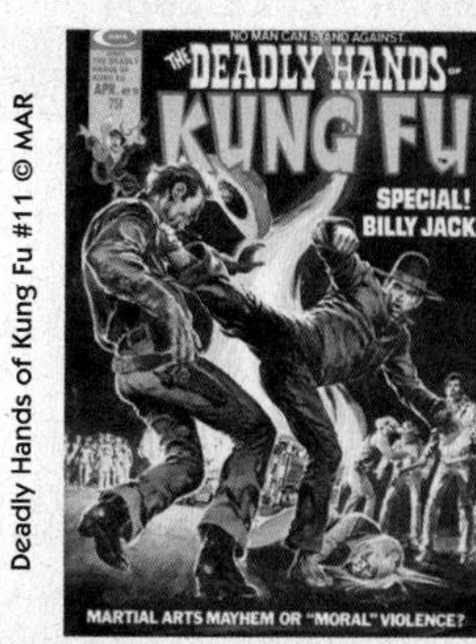

Deadly Hands of Kung Fu #11 © MAR

GD VG FN VF VF/NM NM-
2.0 4.0 6.0 8.0 9.0 9.2

1-4-Kuhoric-s/Alexander-a/Jae Lee-c 4.00

DEAD KINGS
AfterShock Comics: Oct, 2018 - No. 5, May, 2019 ($3.99)

1-5-Steve Orlando-s/Matthew Dow Smith-a 4.00

DEADLANDER (Becomes Dead Rider for #2)
Dark Horse Comics: Oct, 2007 - No. 4, ($2.99, limited series)

1-2-Kevin Ferrara-s/a 3.00

DEADLANDS (Old West role playing game)
Image Comics: Jul, 2011; Aug, 2011; Jan, 2012 ($2.99, one-shots)

...: Black Water (1/12) Mariotte-s/Brook Turner-a 3.00
...: Death Was Silent (8/11) Marz-s/Sears-a/c 3.00
...: Massacre at Red Wing (7/11) Palmiotti & Gray-s/Moder-a/c 3.00

DEADLIEST BOUQUET, THE
Image Comics: Aug, 2022 - No. 5, Dec, 2022 ($3.99)

1-5-Erica Schultz-s/Carola Borelli-a 4.00

DEADLIEST HEROES OF KUNG FU (Magazine)
Marvel Comics Group: Summer, 1975 (B&W)(76 pgs.)

1-Bruce Lee vs. Carradine painted-c; TV Kung Fu, 4pgs. photos/article; Enter the Dragon, 24 pgs. photos/article w/ Bruce Lee; Bruce Lee photo pinup 5 10 15 35 63 90

DEADLINE
Marvel Comics: June, 2002 - No. 4, Sept, 2002 ($2.99, limited series)

1-4: 1-Intro. Kat Farrell; Bill Rosemann-s/Guy Davis-a; Horn painted-c 3.00
TPB (2002. $9.99) r/#1-4 10.00

DEAD LUCKY, THE
Image Comics: Aug, 2022 - Present ($3.99)

1-6-Flores-s/Carlomagno-a 4.00

DEADLY CLASS (Inspired the 2018 SYFY Channel TV show)
Image Comics: Jan, 2014 - No. 56, Oct, 2022 ($3.99)

1-Remender-s/Craig-a 2 4 6 11 16 20
2-6 6.00
7-56: 40-44-Bone Machine 4.00
...: Killer Set, FCBD Special (5/19, giveaway) New story by Remender-s/Craig-a 3.00

DEADLY DUO, THE
Image Comics (Highbrow Entertainment): Nov, 1994 - No. 3, Jan, 1995 ($2.50, lim. series)

1-3: 1-1st app. of Kill Cat 4.00

DEADLY DUO, THE
Image Comics (Highbrow Entertainment): June, 1995 - No. 4, Oct, 1995 ($2.50, lim. series)

1-4: 1-Spawn app. 2-Savage Dragon app. 3-Gen 13 app. 4.00

DEADLY FOES OF SPIDER-MAN (See Lethal Foes of...)
Marvel Comics: May, 1991 - No. 4, Aug, 1991 ($1.00, limited series)

1-4: 1-Punisher, Kingpin, Rhino app. 4.00

DEADLY HANDS OF KUNG FU, THE (See Master of Kung Fu)
Marvel Comics Group: April, 1974 - No. 33, Feb, 1977 (75¢) (B&W, magazine)

1(V1#4 listed in error)-Origin Sons of the Tiger; Shang-Chi, Master of Kung Fu begins (ties w/Master of Kung Fu #17 as 3rd app. Shang-Chi); Bruce Lee painted-c by Neal Adams; 2pg. memorial photo pinup w/8 pgs. photos/articles; TV Kung Fu, 9 pgs. photos/articles; 15 pgs. Starlin-a 8 16 24 56 108 160
2-Adams painted-c; 1st time origin of Shang-Chi, 34 pgs. by Starlin. TV Kung Fu, 6 pgs. photos & article w/2 pg. pinup. Bruce Lee, 11 pgs. ph/a 6 12 18 37 66 95
3,4,7,10: 3-Adams painted-c; Gulacy-a. Enter the Dragon, photos/articles, 8 pgs. 4-TV Kung Fu painted-c by Neal Adams; TV Kung Fu 7 pg. article/art; Fu Manchu; Enter the Dragon, 10 pg. photos/article w/Bruce Lee. 7-Bruce Lee painted-c & 9 pgs. photos/articles-Return of Dragon plus 1 pg. photo pinup. 10-(3/75)-Iron Fist painted-c & 34 pg. sty-Early app. 4 8 12 27 44 60
5,6: 5-1st app. Manchurian, 6 pgs. Gulacy-a. TV Kung Fu, 4 pg. article; reprints books w/Barry Smith-a. Capt. America-sty, 10 pgs. Kirby-a(r). 6-Bruce Lee photos/article, 6 pgs.; 15 pgs. early Perez-a 4 8 12 23 37 50
8,9,11: 9-Iron Fist, 2 pg. Preview pinup; Nebres-a. 11-Billy Jack painted-c by Adams; 17 pgs. photos/article 3 6 9 19 30 40
12,13: 12-James Bond painted-c by Adams; 14 pg. photos/article. 13-16 pgs. early Perez-a; Piers Anthony, 7 pgs. photos/article 3 6 9 17 26 35
14-Classic Bruce Lee painted-c by Adams. Lee pinup by Chaykin. Lee 16 pg. photos/article w/2 pgs. Green Hornet TV 8 16 24 54 102 150
15-Sum, '75 Giant Annual #1; 20pgs. Starlin-a. Bruce Lee photo pinup & 3 pg. photos/ article re book; Man-Thing app. Iron Fist-c/sty; Gulacy-a 18pgs. 4 8 12 23 37 50

GD VG FN VF VF/NM NM-
2.0 4.0 6.0 8.0 9.0 9.2

16,18,20: 16-1st app. Corpse Rider, a Samurai w/Sanho Kim-a. 20-Chuck Norris painted-c & 16 pgs. interview w/photos/article; Bruce Lee vs. C. Norris pinup by Ken Barr. Origin The White Tiger, Perez-a 3 6 9 16 24 32
17-Bruce Lee painted-c by Adams; interview w/R. Clouse, director Enter Dragon 7 pgs. w/B. Lee app. 1st Giffen-a (1pg. 11/75) 5 10 15 34 60 85
19-Iron Fist painted-c & series begins; 1st White Tiger 25 50 75 175 388 600
21-Bruce Lee 1pg. photos/article 3 6 9 19 30 40
22-1st brief app. Jack of Hearts. 1st Giffen sty-a (along w/Amazing Adv. #35, 3/76) 6 12 18 41 76 110
23-1st full app. Jack of Hearts 5 10 15 34 60 85
24-26,29: 24-Iron Fist-c & centerfold pinup. early Zeck-a; Shang Chi pinup; 6 pgs. Piers Anthony text sty w/Pérez/Austin-a; Jack of Hearts app. early Giffen-a. 25-1st app. Shimuru, "Samurai", 20 pgs. Mantlo-sty/Broderick-a; "Swordquest"-c & begins 17 pg. sty by Sanho Kim; 11 pg. photos/article; partly Bruce Lee. 26-Bruce Lee painted-c & pinup; 16 pgs. interviews w/Kwon & Clouse; talk about Bruce Lee re-filming of Lee legend. 29-Ironfist vs. Shang Chi battle-c/sty; Jack of Hearts app. 3 6 9 18 28 38
27 3 6 9 15 22 28
28-All Bruce Lee Special Issue; (1st time in comics). Bruce Lee painted-c by Ken Barr & pinup. 36 pgs. comics chronicaling Bruce Lee's life; 15 pgs. B. Lee photos/article (Rare in high grade) 9 18 27 59 117 175
30-32: 30-Swordquest-c/sty & conclusion; Jack of Hearts app. 31-Jack of Hearts app; Staton-a. 32-1st Daughters of the Dragon-c/sty, 21 pgs. M. Rogers-a/Claremont-sty; Iron Fist pinup 3 6 9 16 23 30
33-Shang Chi-c/sty; Classic Daughters of the Dragon, 21 pgs. M. Rogers-a/Claremont-story with nudity; Bob Wall interview, photos/article, 14 pgs. 4 8 12 28 47 65
...Special Album Edition 1(Summer, '74)-Iron Fist-c/story (early app., 3rd?); 10 pgs. Adams-i; Shang Chi/Fu Manchu, 10 pgs.; Sons of Tiger, 11 pgs.; TV Kung Fu, 6 pgs. photos/article 5 10 15 33 57 80

NOTE: ***Bruce Lee:*** *1-7, 14, 15, 17, 25, 26, 28.* ***Kung Fu (TV):*** *1, 2, 4.* ***Jack of Hearts****: 22, 23, 29-33.* ***Shang Chi Master of Kung Fu****: 1-9, 11-18, 29, 31, 33.* ***Sons of Tiger:*** *1, 3, 4, 6-14, 16-19.* ***Swordquest:*** *25-27, 29-33.* ***White Tiger:*** *19-24, 26, 27, 29-33.* ***N. Adams*** *a-1i(part), 27i; c-1, 2-4, 11, 12, 14, 17.* ***Giffen*** *a-22p, 24p.* ***G. Kane*** *a-23p.* ***Kirby*** *a-5r.* ***Nasser*** *a-27p, 28.* ***Perez*** *a(p)-6-14, 16, 17, 19, 21.* ***Rogers*** *a-26, 32, 33.* ***Starlin*** *a-1, 2r, 15r.* ***Staton*** *a-28p, 31, 32.*

DEADLY HANDS OF KUNG FU
Marvel Comics: Jul, 2014 - No. 4, Oct, 2014 ($3.99, limited series)

1-4-Benson-s/Huat-a/Johnson-c. 2-4-Misty Knight & Colleen Wing app. 4.00

DEADLY NEIGHBORHOOD SPIDER-MAN
Marvel Comics: Dec, 2022 - No. 5, Apr, 2023 ($4.99/$3.99, limited series)

1-($4.99) B. Earl & Taboo-s/Juan Ferreyra-a 5.00
2-5-($3.99) 4.00

DEAD MALL
Dark Horse Comics: Oct, 2022 - No. 4, Feb, 2023 ($3.99, limited series)

1-4-Adam Cesare-s/David Stoll-a

DEADMAN (See The Brave and the Bold & Phantom Stranger #39)
DC Comics: May, 1985 - No. 7, Nov, 1985 ($1.75, Baxter paper)

1-7: 1-Deadman-r by Infantino, N. Adams in all. 5-Batman-c/story-r/Strange Adventures. 7-Batman-r 6.00
... Book One TPB (2011, $19.99) r/apps. in Strange Adventures #205-213 20.00

DEADMAN
DC Comics: Mar, 1986 - No. 4, June, 1986 (75¢, limited series)

1-4: Lopez-c/a. 4-Byrne-c(p) 5.00

DEADMAN
DC Comics: Feb, 2002 - No. 9, Oct, 2002 ($2.50)

1-9: 1-4-Vance-s/Beroy-a. 3,4-Mignola-c. 5,6-Garcia-Lopez-a 4.00

DEADMAN
DC Comics (Vertigo): Oct, 2006 - No. 13, Oct, 2007 ($2.99)

1-13: 1-Bruce Jones-s/John Watkiss-a/c; intro Brandon Cayce 3.00
...: Deadman Walking TPB (2007, $9.99) r/#1-5 10.00

DEADMAN
DC Comics: Jan, 2018 - No. 6, Jun, 2018 ($3.99, limited series)

1-6-Neal Adams-s/a; Zatanna, The Spectre, Hook and Commissioner Gordon app. 4.00

DEADMAN: DARK MANSION OF FORBIDDEN LOVE
DC Comics: Dec, 2016 - No. 3, Apr, 2017 ($5.99, limited series, squarebound)

1-3-Sarah Vaughn-s/Lan Medina-a/Stephanie Hans-c 6.00

DEADMAN: DEAD AGAIN (Leads into 2002 series)
DC Comics: Oct, 2001 - No. 5, Oct, 2001 ($2.50, weekly limited series)

GD 2.0 | VG 4.0 | FN 6.0 | VF 8.0 | VF/NM 9.0 | NM- 9.2

1-5: Deadman at the deaths of the Flash, Robin, Superman, Hal Jordan 3.00

DEADMAN: EXORCISM
DC Comics: 1992 - No. 2, 1992 ($4.95, limited series, 52 pgs.)
1,2: Kelley Jones-c/a in both 6.00

DEAD MAN LOGAN (Follows Old Man Logan series)
Marvel Comics: Jan, 2019 - No. 12, Dec, 2019 ($4.99/$3.99, limited series)
1-Ed Brisson-s/Mike Henderson-a; Mysterio, Miss Sinister & Hawkeye app. 5.00
2-10-($3.99) 2,3-Avengers app. 5-Mysterio app. 4.00
11,12: 11-1st Dani Cage. 12-Dani Cage becomes Thor 2 4 6 8 10 12

DEADMAN: LOVE AFTER DEATH
DC Comics: 1989 - No. 2, 1990 ($3.95, 52 pgs., limited series, mature)
Book One, Two: Kelley Jones-c/a in both. 1-Contains nudity 5.00

DEAD MAN'S RUN
Aspen MLT: No. 0, Dec, 2011 - No. 6, Jul, 2013 ($2.50/$3.50)
0-($2.50) Greg Pak-s/Tony Parker-a; 3 covers; bonus design sketch art 3.00
1-6: 1-(2/12, $3.50) Greg Pak-s/Tony Parker-a; 2 covers 3.50

DEAD OF NIGHT
Marvel Comics Group: Dec, 1973 - No. 11, Aug, 1975
1-Horror reprints 6 12 18 42 79 115
2-10: 10-Kirby-a. 6-Jack the Ripper-c/s 3 6 9 19 30 40
11-Intro Scarecrow; Kane/Wrightson-c 6 12 18 41 76 110
NOTE: *Ditko r-7, 10. Everett c-2. Sinnott r-1.*

DEAD OF NIGHT FEATURING DEVIL-SLAYER
Marvel Comics (MAX): Nov, 2008 - No. 4, Feb, 2009 ($3.99, limited series)
1-4-Keene-s/Samnee-a/Andrews-c 4.00

DEAD OF NIGHT FEATURING MAN-THING
Marvel Comics (MAX): Apr, 2008 - No. 4, July, 2008 ($3.99, limited series)
1-4: 1-Man-Thing origin re-told; Kano-a. 2-4-Jennifer Kale app. 4.00

DEAD OF NIGHT FEATURING WEREWOLF BY NIGHT
Marvel Comics (MAX): Mar, 2009 - No. 4, Jun, 2009 ($3.99, limited series)
1-4: 1-Werewolf By Night origin re-told; Swierczynski-s/Suayan-a 4.00

DEADPOOL (See New Mutants #98 for 1st app.)
Marvel Comics: Aug, 1994 - No. 4, Nov, 1994 ($2.50, limited series)
1-Mark Waid's 1st Marvel work; Ian Churchill-c/a 3 6 9 15 23 30
2-4 1 3 4 6 8 10

DEADPOOL (... : Agent of Weapon X on cover #57-60) (title becomes Agent X)
Marvel Comics: Jan, 1997 - No. 69, Sept, 2002 ($2.95/$1.95/$1.99)
1-($2.95)-Wraparound-c; Kelly-s/McGuinness-a 6 12 18 38 69 100
2-Begin-$1.95-c. 2 4 6 10 14 18
3,5-10,12,13,15-22,24: 12-Variant-c. 22-Cable app. 6.00
4-Hulk-c/app. 3 6 9 16 24 32
11-($3.99)-Deadpool replaces Spider-Man from Amazing Spider-Man #47; Kraven, Gwen Stacy app. 3 6 9 21 33 45
14-1st Ajax; begin McDaniel-a 3 6 9 14 20 25
23,25-($2.99); 23-Dead Reckoning pt. 1; wraparound-c 1 2 3 4 5 7
26-40: 27-Wolverine-c/app. 37-Thor app. 5.00
41,43-49,51-53,56-60: 41-Begin $2.25-c. 44-Black Panther-c/app. 46-49-Chadwick-a 51-Cover swipe of Detective #38. 57-60-BWS-c 4.00
42-G.I. Joe #21 cover swipe; silent issue 3 6 9 15 22 28
50-1st Kid Deadpool 2 4 6 11 16 20
54,55-Punisher-c/app. 54-Dillon-c. 55-Bradstreet-c 3 6 9 14 20 25
61-64,66-68: 61-64-Funeral For a Freak on cover. 66-69-Udon Studios-a. 67-Dazzler-c/app. 1 3 4 6 8 10
65-Girl in bunny suit-c; Udon Studios-a 4 8 12 27 44 60
69-Udon Studios-a 2 4 6 10 14 18
#(-1) Flashback (7/97) Lopresti-a; Wade Wilson's early days 2 4 6 10 14 18
.../Death '98 Annual ($2.99) Kelly-s 3 6 9 16 23 30
... Team-Up (12/98, $2.99) Widdle Wade-c/app. 2 4 6 9 12 15
Baby's First Deadpool Book (12/98, $2.99) 3 6 9 16 23 30
Encyclopædia Deadpoolica (12/98, $2.99) Synopses 3 6 9 15 22 28
.../GLI - Summer Fun Spectacular #1 (9/07, $3.99) short stories; Pelletier-c 2 4 6 8 10 12
... Classic Vol. 1 TPB (2008, $29.99) r/#1, New Mutants #98, Deadpool: The Circle Chase #1-4 and Deadpool (1994 series) #1-4 30.00
Mission Improbable TPB (9/98, $14.95) r/#1-5 20.00
Wizard #0 ('98, bagged with Wizard #87) 6.00

DEADPOOL
Marvel Comics: Nov, 2008 - No. 63, Dec, 2012 ($3.99/$2.99)
1-($3.99) Medina-a; Secret Invasion x-over; Crain-c 3 6 9 16 24 32
1-Variant cover by Liefeld 4 8 12 27 44 60
2 1 3 4 6 8 10
3-10: 4-10-Pearson-c. 8,9-Thunderbolts x-over. 10-Dark Reign 6.00
11-24,26-33, 33.1, 34-44,46-49-($2.99): 11-20-Pearson-c. 16-18-X-Men app. 19-21-Spider-Man & Hit-Monkey app. 26-Ghost Rider app. 27-29-Secret Avengers app. 30,31-Curse of the Mutants. 37-39-Hulk app. 4.00
25-($3.99) 3-D cover, fake 3-D glasses on back-c; back-up story w/Bond-a 5.00
45-1st full app. of Evil Deadpool 2 4 6 11 16 20
49.1, 51-63 ($2.99) 49-McCrea-a. 51-Garza-a. 61-Hit-Monkey app. 4.00
50-($3.99) Uncanny X-Force & Kingpin app.; Barberi-a 1 2 3 5 6 8
900-(12/09, $4.99) Stories by various incl. Liefeld, Baker; wraparound-c by Johnson 6.00
1000-(10/10, $4.99) Stories by various; gallery of variant covers; Johnson-c 6.00
Annual 1 (7/11, $3.99) "Identity Wars" crossover; Spider-Man & Hulk app. 5.00
... & Cable #26 (4/11, $3.99) Swierczynski-s/Fernandez-a 4.00
... Family 1 (6/11, $3.99) short stories by various; Pearson-c 4.00
...: Games of Death 1 (5/09, $3.99) Benson-s/Crystal-a/Land-c 4.00
... MCG (7/10, $1.00) r/#1 with "Marvel's Greatest Comics" logo on cover 3.00

DEADPOOL
Marvel Comics: Jan, 2013 - No. 45, Jun, 2015 ($2.99)
1-Posehn & Duggan-s/Tony Moore-a/Darrow-c; Deadpool vs. Zombie ex-Presidents 2 4 6 9 13 16
2-5 6.00
6-26: 7-Iron Man app.; spoof in 1980s style; Koblish-a/Maguire-c. 10-Spider-Man app. 13-Spoof in 1970s style; Heroes For Hire app. 15-19-Wolverine & Capt. America app. 4.00
27-($9.99) Wedding of Deadpool & Shiklah; wraparound-c with 236 characters 15.00
28-33,35-44-($3.99): 30-32-Dazzler app. 36-39-AXIS tie-in. 40-Gracking issue 4.00
34-($4.99) Original Sin tie-in; flashback in 1990s style; Sabretooth & Alpha Flight app. 1 2 3 5 6 8
45-(#250 on cover, 5/15, $9.99) Death of Deadpool; back-up short stories by various 10.00
Annual 1 (1/14, $4.99) Madcap and Avengers app.; Acker & Blacker-s/Shaner-a 5.00
Annual 2 (7/14, $4.99) Spider-Man and The Chameleon app.; Camagni-a/Nakayama-c 5.00
Bi-Annual 1 (11/14, $4.99) Scheer & Giovannetti-s/Espin-a; Brute Force app. 5.00
...: The Gauntlet (3/14, giveaway) printing of Marvel digital comics content; Cho-c 3.00

DEADPOOL (Continues in Despicable Deadpool #287)
Marvel Comics: Jan, 2016 - No. 36, Nov, 2017 ($4.99/$3.99)
1-($4.99) Duggan-s/Hawthorne-a; Deadpool starts a Heroes For Hire 1 2 3 5 6 8
2-6,8-12-($3.99) 3,4-Steve Rogers app. 6-Intro. Deadpool 2099; Koblish-a. 8-11-Sabretooth app. 12-Deadpool 2099 app. 4.00
7-($9.99) 25th Anniversary issue; back-up short stories about the Mercs For Money 10.00
13-($9.99) Crossover with Daredevil & Power Man and Iron Fist 10.00
14-20,22-24,26-29: 14-17-Civil War II tie-ins. 14-Ulysses app. 15-Black Panther app. 4.00
21-($9.99) Duggan-s/Lolli-a; Shakespeare-style story by Doescher-s/Oliveira-a 10.00
25-($5.99) Duggan-s/Koblish-a; Deadpool 2099 story 6.00
30-($9.99) Duggan-s/Hawthorne-a; Deadpool in space; Agent Adsit & Rocket app. 10.00
31-36: 31-35-Secret Empire tie-ins 4.00
#3.1-(2/16, $3.99) All-Spanish issue about the Mexican Deadpool Masacre; Koblish-a 4.00
Annual 1 (11/16, $4.99) Spoof of Spider-Man and His Amazing Friends cartoon; Koblish-a 5.00
...: Last Days of Magic 1 (7/16, $4.99) Koblish-a/Ramos-c; Doctor Strange app. 5.00
...: Masacre 1 (7/16, $3.99) Reprints #3.1 in English 4.00

DEADPOOL
Marvel Comics: Aug, 2018 - No. 15, Sept, 2019 ($4.99/$3.99)
1-($4.99) Skottie Young-s/Nic Klein-a; Scott Hepburn-a; Guardians of the Galaxy app. 5.00
2-14-($3.99) 2-Avengers and Champions app. 13,14-War of The Realms tie-in 4.00
15-($4.99) Mephisto app.; Young-s/Klein & Hepburn-a 5.00
Annual 1 (10/19, $4.99) "Acts of Evil" tie-in; Nightmare & Dr. Strange app. 5.00

DEADPOOL
Marvel Comics: Jan, 2020 - No. 10, Mar, 2021 ($4.99/$3.99)
1-($4.99) Kelly Thompson-s/Chris Bachalo-a; Elsa Bloodstone app. 5.00
2-10-($3.99) 2-4-Kraven The Hunter app. 2-Captain America app. 10-King in Black tie-in 4.00
...: Nerdy 30 #1 (5/21, $5.99) 30th Anniversary short stories by various 6.00
...: The End 1 (3/20, $4.99) Various "endings" to Deadpool; Kelly-s/Hawthorne-a 5.00

DEADPOOL
Marvel Comics: Jan, 2023 - Present ($4.99/$3.99)
1-($4.99) Wong-s/Coccolo-a; Doctor Octopus & Carnage app. 5.00
2-4-($3.99) Lady Deathstrike app. 4.00

DEADPOOL & CABLE: SPLIT SECOND
Marvel Comics: Feb, 2016 - No. 3, Apr, 2016 ($3.99, limited series)
1-3-Nicieza-s/Reilly Brown-a 4.00

DEADPOOL & THE MERCS FOR MONEY
Marvel Comics: Apr, 2016 - No. 5, Aug, 2016 ($3.99)
1-5: 1-Bunn-s/Espin-a; bonus reprint of Spidey #1 4.00

DEADPOOL & THE MERCS FOR MONEY
Marvel Comics: Sept, 2016 - No. 10, Jun, 2017 ($3.99)
1-10: 1-Bunn-s/Coello-a; Negasonic Teenage Warhead app. 10-Dracula app. 4.00

DEADPOOL: ASSASSIN
Marvel Comics: Aug, 2018 - No. 6, Oct, 2018 ($3.99)
1-($4.99) Bunn-s/Bagley-a; Weasel app. 5.00
2-6-($3.99) 4.00

DEADPOOL: BACK IN BLACK (Deadpool with the Venom symbiote right before ASM #300)
Marvel Comics: Dec, 2016 - No. 5, Feb, 2017 ($3.99, limited series)
1-5: 2-Power Pack app. 5-Spider-Man in black costume app.; Eddie Brock app. 4.00

DEADPOOL: BAD BLOOD
Marvel Comics: 2017 ($24.99, HC, original graphic novel)
1-Rob Liefeld-s/a/c; Cable, Domino and X-Force app. 25.00

DEADPOOL: BAD BLOOD (Reprints original 2017 HC graphic novel)
Marvel Comics: Jun, 2022 - No. 4, Oct, 2022 ($3.99, limited series)
1-4-Rob Liefeld-s/a/c; Cable, Domino and X-Force app. 4.00

DEADPOOL: BLACK, WHITE & BLOOD
Marvel Comics: Oct, 2021 - No. 4, Jan, 2022 ($4.99, B&W&red anthology)
1-4: 1-Noto, Stokoe, Portacio-a. 3-Baruchel-s/Medina-a; Sakai-s/a. 4-Allred-s/a 5.00

DEADPOOL: DRACULA'S GAUNTLET (Printing of Marvel digital comic mini-series)
Marvel Comics: Sept, 2014 - No. 7, Oct, 2014 ($3.99, weekly limited series)
1-7-Duggan & Posehn-s; Deadpool meets Shiklah. 2,3,6-Blade app. 4-Frightful Four app. 4.00

DEADPOOL CORPS (Continues from Prelude to Deadpool Corps series)
Marvel Comics: Jun, 2010 - No. 12, May, 2011 ($3.99/$2.99)
1-($3.99) Liefeld-a/c; Gischler-s; 2 covers by Liefeld 1 2 3 5 6 8
2-12-($2.99) 2-5,7,9-Liefeld-a. 6-Mychaels-a 3.00
...: Rank and Foul 1 (5/10, $3.99) Handbook-style profile pages of allies and enemies 4.00

DEADPOOL KILLS DEADPOOL
Marvel Comics: Sept, 2013 - No. 4, Dec, 2013 ($2.99, limited series)
1-Bunn-s/Espin-a; Deadpool Corps app. 1 2 3 5 6 8
2-4 3.00

Deadpool (2010) #33 © MAR

Deadpool the Duck #1 © MAR

Deadworld #17 © CAL

	GD	VG	FN	VF	VF/NM	NM-
	2.0	4.0	6.0	8.0	9.0	9.2

DEADPOOL KILLS THE MARVEL UNIVERSE
Marvel Comics: Oct, 2012 - No. 4, Oct, 2012 ($2.99, weekly limited series)

1-Bunn-s/Talajic-a/Andrews-c	3	6	9	18	28	38
2-4	2	4	6	8	10	12

DEADPOOL KILLS THE MARVEL UNIVERSE AGAIN
Marvel Comics: Sept, 2017 - No. 5, Nov, 2017 ($3.99, limited series)

1-5-Bunn-s/Talajic-a/Johnson-c. 3-Gwenpool app. 1,5-Red Skull app. 4.00

DEADPOOL KILLUSTRATED
Marvel Comics: Mar, 2013 - No. 4, Jun, 2013 ($2.99, limited series)

1-Bunn-s/Lolli-a/Del Mundo-c; stories/covers styled like Classics Illustrated	1	2	3	5	6	8
2-4						4.00

DEADPOOL MAX
Marvel Comics (MAX): Dec, 2010 - No. 12, Nov, 2011 ($3.99)

1-12: 1-8,10-12-David Lapham-s/Kyle Baker-a/c. 6,7-Domino app. 9-Crystal-a 4.00
... X-Mas Special 1 (2/12, $4.99) Lapham-s; art by Lapham, Baker & Crystal; Baker-c 5.00

DEADPOOL MAX 2
Marvel Comics (MAX): Dec, 2011 - No. 6, May, 2012 ($3.99)

1-6: 1,2-David Lapham-s/Kyle Baker-a/c. 3-Crystal-a 4.00

DEADPOOL: MERC WITH A MOUTH
Marvel Comics: Sept, 2009 - No. 13, Sept, 2010 ($3.99/$2.99)

1-($3.99) Suydam-c/Dazo-a; Zombie-head Deadpool & Ka-Zar app.; r/Deadpool #4 ('97)	2	4	6	10	14	18
2-6,8-12-($2.99) Suydam-c on all. 8-Deadpool goes to Zombie dimension						4.00
7-($3.99) Covers by Suydam & Liefeld; art by Liefeld, Baker, Pastoras, Dazo; 1st app. Lady Deadpool	4	8	12	27	44	60
13-($3.99) Silence of the Lambs-c	2	4	6	11	16	20

DEADPOOL PULP
Marvel Comics: Nov, 2010 - No. 4, Feb, 2011 ($3.99, limited series)

1-4-Alternate Deadpool in 1955; Glass & Benson-s/Laurence Campbell-a/Jae Lee-c 4.00

DEADPOOL'S ART OF WAR
Marvel Comics: Dec, 2014 - No. 4, Mar, 2015 ($3.99, limited series)

1-4-David-s/Koblish-a; Loki and Thor app. 4.00

DEADPOOL'S SECRET SECRET WARS (Secret Wars tie-in)
Marvel Comics: Jul, 2015 - No. 4, Oct, 2015 ($4.99/$3.99, limited series)

1-($4.99) Deadpool inserts himself into the 1984 Secret Wars series; Bunn-s/Harris-c 5.00
2-4-($3.99) Spider-Man, Avengers & X-Men app. 3-Black costume created 4.00
2-Gwenpool variant-c by Bachalo; 1st app. of Gwenpool 20.00

DEADPOOL: SUICIDE KINGS
Marvel Comics: Jun, 2009 - No. 5, Oct, 2009 ($3.99, limited series)

1-Barberi-a; Punisher, Daredevil, & Spider-Man app.	2	4	6	8	10	12
2-5						5.00

DEADPOOL TEAM-UP
Marvel Comics: No. 899, Jan, 2010 - No. 883, May, 2011 ($2.99, numbering runs in reverse)

899-883: 899-Hercules app.; Ramos-c. 897-Ghost Rider app. 894-Franken-Castle app. 887-Thor app. 883-Galactus & Silver Surfer app. 3.00

DEADPOOL: THE CIRCLE CHASE (See New Mutants #98)
Marvel Comics: Aug, 1993 - No. 4, Nov, 1993 ($2.00, limited series)

1-($2.50)-Embossed-c	3	6	9	16	24	32
2-4	1	3	4	6	8	10

DEADPOOL: THE DUCK
Marvel Comics: Mar, 2017 - No. 5, May, 2017 ($3.99, limited series)

1-5-Deadpool & Howard the Duck merge; Rocket Raccoon app.; Camagni-a 4.00

DEADPOOL: TOO SOON
Marvel Comics: Dec, 2016 - No. 4, Mar, 2017 ($4.99, limited series)

1-4-Corin-s/Nauck-a; Squirrel Girl, Howard the Duck, Punisher, Forbush Man app. 5.00

DEADPOOL V GAMBIT
Marvel Comics: Aug, 2016 - No. 5, Nov, 2016 ($3.99, limited series)

1-5-Acker & Blacker-s/Beyruth-s. 1-Spider-Man & Daredevil app. 4.00

DEADPOOL VS. CARNAGE
Marvel Comics: Jun, 2014 - No. 4, Aug, 2014 ($3.99, limited series)

1-Bunn-s/Espin-a/Fabry-c	2	4	6	8	10	12
2-4						6.00

DEADPOOL VS. OLD MAN LOGAN
Marvel Comics: Dec, 2017 - No. 5, Apr, 2018 ($3.99, limited series)

1-5-Declan Shalvey-s/Mike Henderson-a 4.00

DEADPOOL VS. THANOS
Marvel Comics: Nov, 2015 - No. 4, Dec, 2015 ($3.99, limited series)

1-4-Seeley-s/Bondoc-a; Death app. 2-Guardians of the Galaxy app. 4.00

DEADPOOL VS. THE PUNISHER
Marvel Comics: Jun, 2017 - No. 5, Aug, 2017 ($3.99, limited series)

1-5-Van Lente-s/Pere Pérez-a/Shalvey-c 4.00

DEADPOOL VS. X-FORCE
Marvel Comics: Sept, 2014 - No. 4, Nov, 2014 ($3.99, limited series)

1-4-Swierczynski-s/Larraz-a/Shane Davis-c 4.00

DEADPOOL: WADE WILSON'S WAR
Marvel Comics: Aug, 2010 - No. 4, Nov, 2010 ($3.99, limited series)

1-4-Swierczynski-s/Pearson-a/c; Bullseye, Domino & Silver Sable app. 4.00

DEAD RABBIT (Issues recalled due to trademark dispute, cancelled after #2)(See Dead Eyes)
Image Comics: Oct, 2018 - No. 2, Nov, 2018 ($3.99)

1-Duggan-s/McCrea-a 6.00
2-Bonus preview of Self/Made #1 4.00

DEAD RIDER (See Deadlander)

DEAD ROMEO
DC Comics: June, 2009 - No. 6, Nov, 2009 ($2.99, limited series)

1-6-Ryan Benjamin-a/Jesse Snider-s 3.00
TPB (2010, $19.99) r/#1-6; cover gallery 20.00

DEAD, SHE SAID
IDW Publishing: May, 2008 - No. 3, Sept, 2008 ($3.99, limited series)

1-3-Bernie Wrightson-a/Steve Niles-s 4.00

DEADSHOT (See Batman #59, Detective Comics #474, & Showcase '93 #8)
DC Comics: Nov, 1988 - No. 4, Feb, 1989 ($1.00, limited series)

1-Ostrander & Yale-s/Luke McDonnell-a	1	2	3	5	6	8
2-4						5.00

DEADSHOT
DC Comics: Feb, 2005 - No. 5, June 2005 ($2.95, limited series)

1-5-Zeck-c/Gage-s/Cummings-a. 3-Green Arrow app. 4.00

DEAD SPACE (Based on the Electronics Arts videogame)
Image Comics: Mar, 2008 - No. 6, Sept, 2008 ($2.99, limited series)

1-6-Templesmith-a/Johnston-s 3.00
... Extraction (9/09, $3.50) Templesmith-a/Johnston-s 3.50

DEAD VENGEANCE
Dark Horse Comics: Oct, 2015 - No. 4, Jan, 2016 ($3.99, limited series)

1-4-Bill Morrison-s. 1-Morrison-a. 2-4-Tone Rodriguez-a 4.00

DEAD WHO WALK, THE (See Strange Mysteries-Super Reprint #15,16 (1963-64))
Realistic Comics: 1952 (one-shot)

nn	155	310	465	992	1696	2400

DEADWORLD (Also see The Realm)
Arrow Comics/Caliber Comics: Dec, 1986 - No. 26 ($1.50/$1.95/#15-28: $2.50, B&W)

1-4 4.00
5-26-Graphic cover version 4.00
5-26-Tame cover version 3.00
...Archives 1-3 (1992, $2.50) 3.00

DEAN KOONTZ'S FRANKENSTEIN: STORM SURGE
Dynamite Entertainment: 2015 - No. 6, 2016 ($3.99)

1-6-Chuck Dixon-s/Andres Ponce-a 4.00

DEAN MARTIN & JERRY LEWIS (See Adventures of...)

DEAR BEATRICE FAIRFAX
Best/Standard Comics (King Features): No. 5, Nov, 1950 - No. 9, Sept, 1951 (Vern Greene art)

5-All have Schomburg air brush-c	21	42	63	122	199	275
6-9	15	30	45	85	130	175

DEAR HEART (Formerly Lonely Heart)
Ajax: No. 15, July, 1956 - No. 16, Sept, 1956

15,16	12	24	36	67	94	120

DEAR LONELY HEART (...Illustrated No. 1-6)
Artful Publications: Mar, 1951; No. 2, Oct, 1951 - No. 8, Oct, 1952

GD 2.0 | VG 4.0 | FN 6.0 | VF 8.0 | VF/NM 9.0 | NM- 9.2

1 24 48 72 142 234 325
2 15 30 45 83 124 165
3-Matt Baker Jungle Girl story 32 64 96 188 307 425
4-8 14 28 42 76 108 140

DEAR LONELY HEARTS (Lonely Heart #9 on)
Harwell Publ./Mystery Publ. Co. (Comic Media): Aug, 1953 -No. 8, Oct, 1954
1 19 38 57 111 176 240
2-8 14 28 42 81 118 155

DEARLY BELOVED
Ziff-Davis Publishing Co.: Fall, 1952
1-Photo-c 22 44 66 132 216 300

DEAR NANCY PARKER
Gold Key: June, 1963 - No. 2, Sept, 1963
1-Painted-c on both 4 8 12 25 40 55
2 3 6 9 17 26 35

DEATH, THE ABSOLUTE... (From Neil Gaiman's Sandman titles)
DC Comics (Vertigo): 2009 ($99.99, oversized hardcover in slipcase)
nn-Reprints 1st app. in Sandman #8, Sandman #20, Death: The High Cost of Living #1-3, Death: the Time of Your Life #1-3, Death Talks About Life; short stories and pin-ups; merchandise pics; script and sketch art for Sandman #8; Gaiman afterword 100.00

DEATH: AT DEATH'S DOOR (See Sandman: The Season of Mists)
DC Comics (Vertigo): 2003 ($9.95, graphic novel one-shot, B&W, 7-1/2" x 5")
1-Jill Thompson-s/a/c; manga-style; Morpheus and the Endless app. 10.00

DEATHBED
DC Comics (Vertigo): Apr, 2018 - No. 6, Sept, 2018 ($3.99)
1-6-Joshua Williamson-s/Riley Rossmo-a 4.00

DEATH BE DAMNED
BOOM! Studios: Feb, 2017 - No. 4, May, 2017 ($3.99, limited series)
1-4-Ben Acker, Ben Blacker & Andrew Miller-s/Hannah Christenson-a 4.00

DEATHBLOW (Also see Batman/Deathblow and Darker Image)
Image Comics (WildStorm Productions): May (Apr. inside), 1993 - No. 29, Aug, 1996 ($1.75/$1.95/$2.50)
0-(8/96, $2.95, 32 pgs.)-r/Darker Image w/new story & art; Jim Lee & Trevor Scott-a; new Jim Lee-c 4.00
1-($2.50)-Red foil stamped logo on black varnish-c; Jim Lee-c/a; flip-book side has Cybernary -c/story (#2 also) 4.00
1-($1.95)-Newsstand version w/o foil-c & varnish 3.00
2-29: 2-(8/93)-Lee-a; with bound-in poster. 2-($1.75)-Newsstand version w/o poster. 4-Jim Lee-c/Tim Sale-a begin. 13-W/pinup poster by Tim Sale & Jim Lee. 16-($1.95 Newsstand & $2.50 Direct Market editions)-Wildstorm Rising Pt. 6. 17-Variant "Chicago Comicon" edition exists. 20,21-Gen 13 app. 23-Backlash-c/app. 24,25-Grifter-c/app; Gen 13 & Dane from Wetworks app. 28-Deathblow dies. 29-Memorial issue 3.00
5-Alternate Portacio-c (Forms larger picture when combined with alternate-c for Gen 13 #5, Kindred #3, Stormwatch #10, Team 7 #1, Union #0, Wetworks #2 & WildC.A.T.S #11) 6.00
...:Sinners and Saints TPB ('99, $19.95) r/#1-12; Sale-c 20.00

DEATHBLOW (Volume 2)
DC Comics (WildStorm): Dec, 2006 - No. 9, Apr, 2008 ($2.99)
1-9: 1-Azzarello-s/D'Anda-a; two covers by D'Anda & Platt 3.00
...: And Then You Live! TPB (2008, $19.99) r/#1-9 20.00

DEATHBLOW BY BLOWS
DC Comics (WildStorm): Nov, 1999 - No. 3, Jan, 2000 ($2.95, limited series)
1-3-Alan Moore-s/Jim Baikie-a 3.00

DEATHBLOW/WOLVERINE
Image Comics (WildStorm Productions)/ Marvel Comics: Sept, 1996 - No. 2, Feb, 1997 ($2.50, limited series)
1,2: Wiesenfeld-s/Bennett-a 3.00
TPB (1997, $8.95) r/#1,2 9.00

DEATH DEALER (Also see Frank Frazetta's...)
Verotik: July, 1995 - No. 4, July, 1997 ($5.95)
1-Frazetta-c; Bisley-a 3 6 9 16 23 30
1-2nd print, 2-4-($6.95)-Frazetta-c; embossed logo 1 2 3 4 5 7

DEATH-DEFYING 'DEVIL, THE (Also see Project Superpowers)
Dynamite Entertainment: 2008 - No. 4, 2009 ($3.50, limited series)
1-4-Casey & Ross-s/Salazar-a; multiple covers; the Dragon app. 3.50

DEATH-DEFYING 'DEVIL (Volume 2)
Dynamite Entertainment: 2019 - No. 5, 2020 ($3.99, limited series)
1-5-Gail Simone-s/Walter Giovani-a; multiple covers 4.00

DEATH-DEFYING DOCTOR MIRAGE, THE
Valiant Entertainment: Sept, 2014 - No. 5, Jan, 2015 ($3.99, limited series)
1-5-Van Meter-s/de la Torre-a. 1-3-Foreman-c. 4,5-Wada-c 4.00

DEATH-DEFYING DOCTOR MIRAGE, THE: SECOND LIVES
Valiant Entertainment: Dec, 2015 - No. 4, Mar, 2016 ($3.99, limited series)
1-4-Van Meter-s/de La Torre-a 4.00

DEATH HEAD
Dark Horse Comics: Jul, 2015 - No. 6, Feb, 2016 ($3.99, limited series)
1-6-Zach & Nick Keller-s/Joanna Estep-a 4.00

DEATH, JR.
Image Comics: Apr, 2005 - No. 3, Aug, 2005 ($4.99, squarebound, limited series)
1-3-Gary Whitta-s/Ted Naifeh-a 5.00
Vol. 1 TPB (2005, $14.99) r/series; concept and promotional art 15.00

DEATH, JR. (Volume 2)
Image Comics: Jul, 2006 - No. 3, May, 2007 ($4.99, squarebound, limited series)
1-3-Gary Whitta-s/Ted Naifeh-a. 1-Dan Brereton-c 5.00

... Halloween Special (10/06, 8-1/2"x 5-1/2", Halloween giveaway) Guy Davis-a 3.00
Vol. 2 TPB (2007, $14.99) r/series; Halloween story w/Guy Davis-a; promotional art 15.00

DEATHLOK (Also see Astonishing Tales #25)
Marvel Comics: July, 1990 - No. 4, Oct, 1990 ($3.95, limited series, 52 pgs.)
1-4: 1,2-Guice-a(p). 3,4-Denys Cowan-a, c-4 5.00

DEATHLOK
Marvel Comics: July, 1991 - No. 34, Apr, 1994 ($1.75)
1-Silver ink cover; Denys Cowan-c/a(p) begins 1 3 4 6 8 10
2-18,20-24,26-34: 2-Forge (X-Men) app. 3-Vs. Dr. Doom. 5-X-Men & F.F. x-over. 6,7-Punisher x-over. 9,10-Ghost Rider-c/story. 16-Infinity War x-over. 17-Jae Lee-c. 22-Black Panther app. 27-Siege app. 3.00
19-($2.25)-Foil-c 4.00
25-($2.95, 52 pgs.)-Holo-grafx foil-c 4.00
Annual 1 (1992, $2.25, 68 pgs.)-Guice-p; Quesada-c(p) 5.00
Annual 2 (1993, $2.95, 68 pgs.)-Bagged w/card; intro Tracer 4.00
NOTE: *Denys Cowan a(p)-9-13, 15, Annual 1; c-9-12, 13p, 14.* ***Guice/Cowan*** *c-8.*

DEATHLOK
Marvel Comics: Sept, 1999 - No. 11, June, 2000 ($1.99)
1-11: 1-Casey-s/Manco-a. 2-Two covers. 4-Canete-a 3.00

DEATHLOK (... The Demolisher on cover)
Marvel Comics: Jan, 2010 - No. 7, Jul, 2010 ($3.99, limited series)
1-7-Huston-s/Medina-a/Peterson-c 4.00

DEATHLOK
Marvel Comics: Dec, 2014 - No. 10, Sept, 2015 ($3.99)
1-10: 1-Edmonson-s/Perkins-a; intro. Henry Hayes. 2-5,8-10-Domino app. 4.00

DEATHLOK SPECIAL
Marvel Comics: May, 1991 - No. 4, June, 1991 ($2.00, bi-weekly lim. series)
1-4: r/1-4(1990) w/new Guice-c #1,2; Cowan c-3,4 3.00
1-2nd printing w/white-c 3.00

DEATHMASK
Future Comics: Mar, 2003 - No. 3, June, 2003 ($2.99)
1-3-Giordano-a(p)/Michelinie & Layton-s 3.00

DEATHMATCH
BOOM! Studios: Dec, 2012 - No. 12, Nov, 2013 ($2.99)
1-($1.00) Jenkins-s/Magno-a; multiple covers 3.00
2-12 ($3.99) Multiple covers on each 4.00

DEATHMATE
Valiant (Prologue/Yellow/Blue)/Image Comics (Black/Red/Epilogue): Sept, 1993 - Epilogue (#6), Feb, 1994 ($2.95/$4.95, limited series)
Preview-(Advance Comics ed., 7/93, 8 pgs.) 1 3 4 6 8 10
Preview-(Comic Defense System ed., 7/93, 8 pgs.) 1 3 4 6 8 10
Preview-(Previews orange ed., 8/93, 8 pgs.) 4 8 12 23 37 50
Preview-(Previews pink ed., 8/93, 8 pgs.) 2 4 6 9 12 15
Prologue (#1)–Silver foil; Jim Lee/Layton-c; B. Smith/Lee-a; Liefeld-a(p) 3.00
Prologue–Special gold foil ed. of silver ed. 1 2 3 5 6 8
Black (#2)-(9/93, $4.95, 52 pgs.)-Silvestri/Jim Lee-c; pencils by Peterson/Silvestri/Capullo/ Jim Lee/Portacio; 1st story app. Gen 13 telling their rebellion against the Troika (see WildC.A.T.S. Trilogy) 1 2 3 5 6 8
Black-Special gold foil edition 2 4 6 9 12 15
Yellow (#3)-(10/93, $4.95, 52 pgs)-Yellow foil-c; Indicia says Prologue Sept 1993 by mistake; 3rd app. Ninjak; Thibert-c(i) 5.00
Yellow-Special gold foil edition 1 2 3 5 6 8
Blue (#4)-(10/93, $4.95, 52 pgs.)-Thibert blue foil-c(i); Reese-a(i) 5.00
Blue-Special gold foil edition 6.00
Red (#5), Epilogue (#6)-(2/94, $2.95)-Silver foil Quesada/Silvestri-c; Silvestri-a(p) 3.00

DEATH METAL
Marvel Comics UK: Jan, 1994 - No. 4, Apr, 1994 ($1.95, limited series)
1-4: 1-Silver ink-c. Alpha Flight app. 3.00

DEATH METAL VS. GENETIX
Marvel Comics UK: Dec, 1993 - No. 2, Jan, 1994 (Limited series)
1-($2.95)-Polybagged w/2 trading cards 3.00
2-($2.50)-Polybagged w/2 trading cards 3.00

DEATH OF CAPTAIN MARVEL (See Marvel Graphic Novel #1)

DEATH OF DOCTOR STRANGE
Marvel Comics: Nov, 2021 - No. 5, Mar, 2022 ($4.99/$3.99, limited series)
1-($4.99) MacKay-s/Garbett-a; Strange murdered; replaced with temporal remnant 5.00
2-5-($3.99) 2-Clea & the Avengers app.; intro The Three Mothers 4.00
...: Avengers 1 (12/21, $4.99) Paknadel-s/Bodenheim-a 5.00
...: Blade 1 (2/22, $4.99) Lore-s/Burnett-a; Dracula app. 5.00
...: Bloodstone 1 (3/22, $4.99) Howard-s/Guara-a 5.00
...: Spider-Man 1 (1/22, $4.99) MacKay-s/Ferreira-a; Ben Reilly Spidey & Black Cat app. 5.00
...: White Fox 1 (1/22, $4.99) Alyssa Wong-s/Andie Tong & Luciano Vecchio-a 5.00
...: X-Men / Black Knight 1 (3/22, $4.99) Spurrier-s/Quinn-a; Rogue, Jean Grey, Synch app. 5.00

DEATH OF DRACULA
Marvel Comics: Aug, 2010 ($3.99, one shot)
1-Gischler-s/Camuncoli-a/c 4.00

DEATH OF HAWKMAN, THE
DC Comics: Dec, 2016 - No. 6, May, 2017 ($3.99, limited series)
1-6-Andreyko-s/Lopresti-a; Adam Strange app. 2-6-Despero app. 4.00

DEATH OF MR. MONSTER, THE (See Mr. Monster #8)

DEATH OF SUPERMAN (See Superman, 2nd Series)

DEATH OF SUPERMAN 30TH ANNIVERSARY SPECIAL, THE
DC Comics: Oct, 2022 ($10.99, square-bound, one-shot)
1-Four new stories by the creators of the original event; Doomsday app. 11.00

DEATH OF THE INHUMANS
Marvel Comics: Sept, 2018 - No. 5, Jan, 2019($4.99/$3.99, limited series)

Deathblow (2008) #8 © DC

Death of Wolverine #4 © MAR

Deathstroke (2016) #38 © DC

GD VG FN VF VF/NM NM-
2.0 4.0 6.0 8.0 9.0 9.2

1-($4.99) Cates-s/Olivetti-a; Vox app. 5.00
2-5-($3.99) Karnak app. 4-Beta Ray Bill app. 4.00

DEATH OF THE NEW GODS (Tie-in to the Countdown series)
DC Comics: Early Dec, 2007 - No. 8, Jun, 2008 ($3.50, limited series)
1-8-Jim Starlin-s/a/c. 1-Barda killed. 6-Orion dies. 7-Scott Free and Metron die 3.50
TPB (2009, $19.99) r/#1-8; Starlin intro.; cover gallery 20.00

DEATH OF WOLVERINE
Marvel Comics: Nov, 2014 - No. 4, Dec, 2014 ($4.99, limited series)
1-4-Soule-s/McNiven-a; multiple covers on each; bonus art & commentary in each 5.00
...: Deadpool & Captain America (12/14, $4.99) Duggan-s/Kolins-a 5.00
...: Life After Logan (1/15, $4.99) Short stories by various; Cyclops, Nightcrawler app. 5.00

DEATH OF WOLVERINE: THE LOGAN LEGACY (Continues in Wolverines #1)
Marvel Comics: Dec, 2014 - No. 7, Feb, 2015 ($3.99, bi-weekly limited series)
1-7: 1-Soule-s; X-23, Daken, Deathstrike, Mystique & Sabretooth app. 4.00

DEATH OF WOLVERINE: THE WEAPON X PROGRAM
Marvel Comics: Jan, 2015 - No. 5, Mar, 2015 ($3.99, bi-weekly limited series)
1-5-Soule-s. 1-3-Larroca-a. 3-Sabretooth app. 4.00

DEATH OF X (Leads into X-Men vs. Inhumans)
Marvel Comics: Dec, 2016 - No. 4, Jan, 2017 ($4.99/$3.99, limited series)
1-($4.99) Soule & Lemire-s; Kuder-a; X-Men, Inhumans & Hydra app. 5.00
2-4-($3.99) 2-Kuder-a. 3,4-Kuder & Garrón-a. 4-Death of Cyclops 4.00

DEATH ORB
Dark Horse Comics: Oct, 2018 - No. 5, Feb, 2019 ($3.99, limited series)
1-5-Ryan Ferrier-s/Alejandro Aragon-a 4.00

DEATH OR GLORY
Image Comics: May, 2018 - No. 11, Jul, 2020 ($4.99/$3.99)
1-Remender-s/Bengal-a; three covers by Bengal, Fegredo & Harren 5.00
2-11-($3.99) 2-Three covers. 3-11-Two covers 4.00

DEATH RACE 2020
Roger Corman's Cosmic Comics: Apr, 1995 - No. 8, Nov, 1995 ($2.50)
1-8: Sequel to the Movie 3.00

DEATH RATTLE (Formerly an Underground)
Kitchen Sink Press: V2#1, 10/85 - No. 18, 1988, 1994 ($1.95, Baxter paper, mature); V3#1, 11/95 - No. 5, 6/96 ($2.95, B&W)
V2#1-7,9-18: 1-Corben-c. 2-Unpubbed Spirit story by Eisner. 5-Robot Woman-r by Wolverton. 6-B&W issues begin. 10-Savage World-r by by Williamson/Torres/Krenkel/Frazetta from Witzend #1. 16-Wolverton Spacehawk-r 5.00
8-(12/86)-1st app. Mark Schultz's Xenozoic Tales/Cadillacs & Dinosaurs 4 8 12 25 40 55
8-(1994)-r plus interview w/Mark Schultz 3.50
V3#1-5 ($2.95-c): 1-Mark Schultz-c 3.50

DEATH SENTENCE
Titan Comics: Nov, 2003 - No. 6, Apr, 2014 ($3.99)
1-6-Montynero-s/c; Dowling-a 4.00

DEATH SENTENCE LONDON
Titan Comics: Jun, 2015 - No. 6, Jan, 2016 ($3.99)
1-6-Montynero-s/c; Simmonds-a 4.00

DEATH'S HEAD (See Daredevil #56, Dragon's Claws #5 & Incomplete...)(See Amazing Fantasy (2004) for Death's Head 3.0)
Marvel Comics: Dec, 1988 - No. 10, Sept, 1989 ($1.75)
1-Dragon's Claws spin-off 3.00
2-Fantastic Four app.; Dragon's Claws x-over 3.00
3-10: 8-Dr. Who app. 9-F. F. x-over; Simonson-c(p) 3.00

DEATH'S HEAD
Marvel Comics: Sept, 2019 - No. 4, Dec, 2019 ($3.99, limited series)
1-4-Tini Howard-s/Kei Zama-a; Wiccan, Hulkling & Hawkeye (Kate) app. 4.00

DEATH'S HEAD II (Also see Battletide)
Marvel Comics UK, Ltd.: Mar, 1992 - No. 4, June (May inside), 1992 ($1.75, color, lim. series)
1-4: 2-Fantastic Four app. 4-Punisher, Spider-Man, Daredevil, Dr. Strange, Capt. America & Wolverine in the year 2020 4.00
1,2-Silver ink 2nd printiings 4.00

DEATH'S HEAD II (Also see Battletide)
Marvel Comics UK, Ltd.: Dec, 1992 - No. 16, Mar, 1994 ($1.75/$1.95)
V2#1-13,15,16: 1-Gatefold-c. 1-4-X-Men app. 15-Capt. America & Wolverine app. 4.00
V2# 14-($2.95)-Foil flip-c w/Death's Head II Gold #0 4.00

GD VG FN VF VF/NM NM-
2.0 4.0 6.0 8.0 9.0 9.2

...Gold 1 (1/94, $3.95, 68 pgs.)-Gold foil-c 4.00

DEATH'S HEAD II & THE ORIGIN OF DIE CUT
Marvel Comics UK, Ltd.: Aug, 1993 - No. 2, Sept, 1993 (limited series)
1-($2.95)-Embossed-c 5.00
2 ($1.75) 4.00

DEATHSTROKE (DC New 52)
DC Comics: Nov, 2011 - No. 20, Jul, 2013 ($2.99)
1-Higgins-s/Bennett-a/Bisley-c 6.00
2-20: 4-Blackhawks app. 9-12-Liefeld-s/a/c; Lobo app. 3.00
#0 (11/12, $2.99) Origin story, Team 7 app.; Liefeld-s/a/c 3.00

DEATHSTROKE (DC New 52)
DC Comics: Dec, 2014 - No. 20, Sept, 2016 ($2.99)
1-20: 1-Tony Daniel-s/a; I Ching app. 3-6-Harley Quinn app. 7-10-Wonder Woman app. 11-13-Harley Quinn & Suicide Squad app. 3.00
Annual 1 (9/15, $4.99) Takes place between #8 & 9; Wonder Woman app.; Kirkham-a 5.00
Annual 1 (8/16, $4.99) Hester-s/Colak & Viacava-a 5.00

DEATHSTROKE (DC Rebirth)
DC Comics: Oct, 2016 - No. 50, Feb, 2020 ($2.99/$3.99)
1-19: 1-Priest-s/Pagulayan-a; Clock King app. 4,5-Batman & Robin (Damian) app. 8-Superman app. 11-The Creeper app.; Cowan & Sienkiewicz-a. 19-Lazarus Contract tie-in with Teen Titans and Titans 3.00
20-49-($3.99) 21-The Defiance team forms; Terra app. 22-Dr. Light app. 32-35-Vs. Batman. 37-40-Two-Face app. 42,43-Crossover with Teen Titans #28-30. 44-Funeral 4.00
50-($4.99) Pagulayan & Pasarin-a; Raven app. 5.00
Annual 1 (3/18, $4.99) Priest-s/Cowan & Sienkiewicz-a; Power Girl app. 5.00
... Rebirth 1 (10/16, $2.99) Priest-s/Pagulayan-a; Clock King app. 3.00
.../ Yogi Bear Special 1 (12/18, $4.99) Texeira-a; Kirkham-c; Secret Squirrel back-up 5.00

DEATHSTROKE INC.
DC Comics: Nov, 2021 - Present ($3.99)
1-15: 1-Black Canary app.; Williamson-s/Porter-a. 10-Year One begins 4.00

DEATHSTROKE: THE TERMINATOR (Deathstroke: The Hunted #0-47; Deathstroke #48-60) (Also see Marvel & DC Present, New Teen Titans #2, New Titans, Showcase '93 #7,9 & Tales of the Teen Titans #42-44)
DC Comics: Aug, 1991 - No. 60, June, 1996 ($1.75-$2.25)
1-New Titans spin-off; Mike Zeck c-1-28 3 6 9 16 23 30
1-Gold ink 2nd printing ($1.75) 2 4 6 9 12 15
2 5.00
3-49,51-60: 6,8-Batman cameo. 7,9-Batman-c/story. 9-1st brief app. new Vigilante (female). 10-1st full app. new Vigilante; Perez-i. 13-Vs. Justice League; Team Titans cameo on last pg. 14-Total Chaos, part 1; story cont'd in New Titans #90. 15-1st app. Rose Wilson 3.00
50 ($3.50) 4.00
#0-(10/94) Zero Hour; begin Deathstroke, The Hunted; released between #40&41 3.00
Annual 1-4 ('92-'95, 68 pgs.): 1-Nightwing & Vigilante app.; minor Eclipso app. 2-Bloodlines Deathstorm; 1st app. Gunfire. 3-Elseworlds story. 4-Year One story 5.00
NOTE: ***Golden** a-12. **Perez** a-11i. **Zeck** c-Annual 1, 2.*

DEATH: THE HIGH COST OF LIVING (See Sandman #8) (Also see the Books of Magic limited & ongoing series)
DC Comics (Vertigo): Mar, 1993 - No. 3, May, 1993 ($1.95, limited series)
1-Bachalo/Buckingham-a; Dave McKean-c; Neil Gaiman scripts in all 1 2 3 5 6 8
1-Platinum edition 4 8 12 27 44 60
2 3.50
3-Pgs. 19 & 20 had wrong placement 3.00
3-Corrected version w/pgs. 19 & 20 facing each other 4.00
Death Talks About Life-giveaway about AIDS prevention 5.00
Hardcover (1994, $19.95)-r/#1-3 & Death Talks About Life; intro. by Tori Amos 20.00
Trade paperback (6/94, $12.95, Titan Books)-r/#1-3 & Death Talks About Life; prism-c 13.00

DEATH: THE TIME OF YOUR LIFE (See Sandman #8)
DC Comics (Vertigo): Apr, 1996 - No. 3, July, 1996 ($2.95, limited series)
1-3: Neil Gaiman story & Bachalo/Buckingham-a; Dave McKean-c. 2-(5/96) 3.00
Hardcover (1997, $19.95)-r/#1-3 w/3 new pages & gallery art by various 20.00
TPB (1997, $12.95)-r/#1-3 & Visions of Death gallery; Intro. by Claire Danes 13.00

DEATH 3
Marvel Comics UK: Sept, 1993 - No. 4, Dec, 1993 ($1.75, limited series)
1-($2.95)-Embossed-c 4.00
2-4 3.00

DEATH TO THE ARMY OF DARKNESS
Dynamite Entertainment: 2020 - No. 5, 2020 ($3.99, limited series)
1-5-Ryan Parrott-s/Jacob Edgar-a; intro. Lady Ash, dog Ash, skeleton Ash, mini Ash 4.00

DEATH VALLEY (Cowboys and Indians)
Comic Media: Oct, 1953 - No. 6, Aug, 1954

Issue	GD 2.0	VG 4.0	FN 6.0	VF 8.0	VF/NM 9.0	NM- 9.2
1-Billy the Kid; Morisi-a; Andru/Esposito-c/a	28	56	84	165	270	375
2-Don Heck-c	18	36	54	105	165	225
3-6: 3,5-Morisi-a. 5-Discount-a	15	30	45	88	137	185

DEATH VALLEY (Becomes Frontier Scout, Daniel Boone No.10-13)
Charlton Comics: No. 7, 6/55 - No. 9, 10/55 (Cont'd from Comic Media series)

Issue	GD 2.0	VG 4.0	FN 6.0	VF 8.0	VF/NM 9.0	NM- 9.2
7-9: 8-Wolverton-a (half pg.)	14	28	42	76	108	140

DEATH VIGIL
Image Comics (Top Cow): Jul, 2014 - No. 8, Sept, 2015 ($3.99)

Issue	GD 2.0	VG 4.0	FN 6.0	VF 8.0	VF/NM 9.0	NM- 9.2
1-8-Stjepan Sejic-s/a/c						4.00

DEATHWISH
DC Comics (Milestone Media): Dec, 1994 - No. 4, Mar, 1995 ($2.50, lim. series)

Issue	GD 2.0	VG 4.0	FN 6.0	VF 8.0	VF/NM 9.0	NM- 9.2
1-4						3.00

DEATH WRECK
Marvel Comics UK: Jan, 1994 - No. 4, Apr, 1994 ($1.95, limited series)

Issue	GD 2.0	VG 4.0	FN 6.0	VF 8.0	VF/NM 9.0	NM- 9.2
1-4: 1-Metallic ink logo; Death's Head II app.						3.00

DEBBIE DEAN, CAREER GIRL
Civil Service Publ.: April, 1945 - No. 2, July, 1945

Issue	GD 2.0	VG 4.0	FN 6.0	VF 8.0	VF/NM 9.0	NM- 9.2
1,2-Newspaper reprints by Bert Whitman	22	44	66	132	216	300

DEBBI'S DATES (Also see Date With Debbi)
National Periodical Publications: Apr-May, 1969 - No. 11, Dec-Jan, 1970-71

Issue	GD 2.0	VG 4.0	FN 6.0	VF 8.0	VF/NM 9.0	NM- 9.2
1	8	16	24	56	108	160
2,3,5,7-11: 2-Last 12¢ issue	5	10	15	30	50	70
4-Neal Adams text illo	5	10	15	33	57	80
6-Superman cameo	6	12	18	41	76	110

DECADE OF DARK HORSE, A
Dark Horse Comics: Jul, 1996 - No. 4, Oct, 1996 ($2.95, B&W/color, lim. series)

Issue	GD 2.0	VG 4.0	FN 6.0	VF 8.0	VF/NM 9.0	NM- 9.2
1-4: 1-Sin City-c/story by Miller; Grendel by Wagner; Predator. 2-Star Wars wraparound-c. 3-Aliens-c/story; Nexus, Mask stories						6.00

DECAPITATOR (Randy Bowen's...)
Dark Horse Comics: Jun, 1998 - No. 4, ($2.95)

Issue	GD 2.0	VG 4.0	FN 6.0	VF 8.0	VF/NM 9.0	NM- 9.2
1-4-Bowen-s/art by various. 1-Mahnke-c. 3-Jones-c						4.00

DECEPTION, THE
Image Comics (Flypaper Press): 1999 - No. 3, 1999 ($2.95, B&W, mini-series)

Issue	GD 2.0	VG 4.0	FN 6.0	VF 8.0	VF/NM 9.0	NM- 9.2
1-3-Horley painted-c						3.00

DECIMATION: THE HOUSE OF M
Marvel Comics: Jan, 2006 ($3.99)

Issue	GD 2.0	VG 4.0	FN 6.0	VF 8.0	VF/NM 9.0	NM- 9.2
... - The Day After (one-shot) Claremont-s/Green-a						4.00

DECISION 2012 (Biographies of the main 2012 presidential candidates)
BOOM! Studios: Nov, 2011 ($3.99, series of one-shots)

Issue	GD 2.0	VG 4.0	FN 6.0	VF 8.0	VF/NM 9.0	NM- 9.2
...: Barack Obama 1 (11/11, $3.99) biography; Damian Couceiro-a; 2 covers	1	2	3	5	6	8
...: Michelle Bachman 1 (11/11) biography; Aaron McConnell-a; 2 covers						4.00
...: Ron Paul 1 (11/11) biography; Dean Kotz-a; 2 covers						4.00
...: Sarah Palin 1 (11/11) biography; Damian Couceiro-a; 2 covers						4.00

DECORUM
Image Comics: Mar, 2020 - No. 8, Nov, 2021 ($4.99/$3.99)

Issue	GD 2.0	VG 4.0	FN 6.0	VF 8.0	VF/NM 9.0	NM- 9.2
1,5,8-($4.99): 1-Hickman-s/Huddleston-a. 8-Squarebound w/wraparoiund-c						5.00
2-4,6,7-($3.99)						4.00

DEEP, THE (Movie)
Marvel Comics Group: Nov, 1977 (Giant)

Issue	GD 2.0	VG 4.0	FN 6.0	VF 8.0	VF/NM 9.0	NM- 9.2
1-Infantino-c/a	2	4	6	8	10	12

DEEP BEYOND
Image Comics: Feb, 2021 - No. 12, Feb, 2022 ($3.99, limited series)

Issue	GD 2.0	VG 4.0	FN 6.0	VF 8.0	VF/NM 9.0	NM- 9.2
1-12-Andolfo & Goy-s/Broccardo-a						4.00

DEEP GRAVITY
Dark Horse Comics: Jul, 2014 - No. 4, Oct, 2014 ($3.99, limited series)

Issue	GD 2.0	VG 4.0	FN 6.0	VF 8.0	VF/NM 9.0	NM- 9.2
1-4-Hardman & Bechko-s/Baldó-a/Hardman-c						4.00

DEEP SLEEPER
Oni Press/Image Comics: Feb, 2004 - No. 4, Sept, 2004 ($3.50/$2.95, B&W, limited series)

Issue	GD 2.0	VG 4.0	FN 6.0	VF 8.0	VF/NM 9.0	NM- 9.2
1,2-(Oni Press, $3.50)-Hester-s/Huddleston-a						3.50
3,4-(Image Comics, $2.95)						3.00
... Omnibus (Image, 8/04, $5.95) r/#1,2						6.00
... Vol. 1 TPB (2005, $12.95) r/#1-4; cover gallery						13.00

DEEP STATE
BOOM! Studios: Nov, 2014 - No. 8, Jul, 2015 ($3.99)

Issue	GD 2.0	VG 4.0	FN 6.0	VF 8.0	VF/NM 9.0	NM- 9.2
1-8-Justin Jordan-s/Ariela Kristantina-a						4.00

DEFCON 4
Image Comics (WildStorm Productions): Feb, 1996 - No. 4, Sept, 1996 ($2.50, lim. series)

Issue	GD 2.0	VG 4.0	FN 6.0	VF 8.0	VF/NM 9.0	NM- 9.2
1/2	1	2	3	5	7	9
1/2 Gold-(1000 printed)						14.00
1-Main Cover by Mat Broome & Edwin Rosell						3.00
1-Hordes of Cymulants variant-c by Michael Golden						5.00
1-Backs to the Wall variant-c by Humberto Ramos & Alex Garner						5.00
1-Defcon 4-Way variant-c by Jim Lee	1	2	3	4	5	7
2-4						3.00

DEFEND COMICS (The CBLDF Presents...)
Comic Book Legal Defense Fund: May, 2015 - Present (giveaway)

Issue	GD 2.0	VG 4.0	FN 6.0	VF 8.0	VF/NM 9.0	NM- 9.2
FCBD Edition - (5/15) Short stories incl. Kevin Keller, Beanworld; art by Liew, Parent						3.00
...: FCBD 2016 Edition - Short stories by various incl. James Kochalka; Craig Thompson-c						3.00
...: FCBD 2017 Edition - Short stories by various incl. Ryan North; Jeffrey Brown-c						3.00
...: FCBD 2018 Edition - Reading Without Walls						3.00
...: FCBD 2019 Edition - Short stories by various incl. Bill Griffith; Derek Charm-c						3.00

DEFENDERS, THE (TV)
Dell Publishing Co.: Sept-Nov, 1962 - No. 2, Feb-Apr, 1963

Issue	GD 2.0	VG 4.0	FN 6.0	VF 8.0	VF/NM 9.0	NM- 9.2
12-176-211(#1)	4	8	12	25	40	55
12-176-304(#2)	3	6	9	20	31	42

DEFENDERS, THE (Also see Giant-Size..., Marvel Feature, Marvel Treasury Edition, Secret Defenders & Sub-Mariner #34, 35; The New...#140-on)
Marvel Comics Group: Aug, 1972 - No. 152, Feb, 1986

Issue	GD 2.0	VG 4.0	FN 6.0	VF 8.0	VF/NM 9.0	NM- 9.2
1-Englehart-s/Sal Buscema-a begins; The Hulk, Doctor Strange, Sub-Mariner app.; last app. as Defenders in Marvel Feature #3; 1st Necrodamus; plot continued from Incredible Hulk #126; minor Omegatron app.	17	34	51	117	259	400
2-Silver Surfer x-over; 1st Calizuma (a wizard in the service of the Nameless Ones)	9	18	27	62	126	190
3,5: 3-Silver Surfer x-over; vs. The Nameless Ones; Barbara Norris app. from Incredible Hulk #126. 5-vs. The Omegatron (destroyed)	5	10	15	34	60	85
4-Barbara Norris becomes the third incarnation of the Valkyrie (previously seen in Avengers #83 & Incredible Hulk #142; Enchantress, the Executioner & The Black Knight app (turned to stone); Valkyrie joins the Defenders	16	32	48	110	243	375
6,7: 6-Silver Surfer x-over. 7-Silver Surfer, Hawkeye app. vs. Red Ghost & Attuma	4	8	12	23	37	50
8,9: 8-Silver Surfer & Hawkeye app. vs. Red Ghost & Attuma; 4-pg story begins "Avengers/Defenders War"; Dormammu & Loki team-up; story continues in Avengers #116. 9-Continued from Avengers #116; Iron Man vs. Hawkeye, Dr. Strange vs. Mantis; continued in Avengers #117.	5	10	15	30	50	70
10-Hulk vs. Thor; continued in Avengers #118	10	20	30	64	132	200
11-"Avengers/Defenders War" concludes; Silver Surfer, Black Knight & King Richard app.; last Englehart-s	5	10	15	31	53	75
12-Last 20¢ issue; Wein-s begin; brief origin Valkyrie retold; vs. Xemnu the Titan; Defenders app. next in Giant-Size Defenders #1	3	6	9	15	22	28
13,14: 13-Nighthawk app. vs. The Squadron Sinister (Hyperion, Dr. Spectrum & the Whizzer; 1st app. Nebulon the Celestial Man. 14-vs. The Squadron Sinister & Nebulon; Sub-Mariner leaves; Nighthawk joins	3	6	9	17	26	35
15,16: 15-Magneto & Brotherhood of Evil Mutants app.; first Alpha the Ultimate Mutant; Professor X app. 16-Magneto & the Brotherhood of Evil mutants turned into children; Defenders app. next in Giant-Size Defenders #2	3	6	9	19	30	40
17-Power Man x-over (11/74); 1st app. of the Wrecking Crew (Thunderball, Bulldozer & Piledriver); Valkyrie leaves	11	22	33	76	163	250
18-1st full app. of the Wrecking Crew	10	20	30	64	132	200
19-20: 19-vs. the Wrecking Crew. 20-Continued from Marvel Two-in-one #7; Valkyrie returns (origin retold) 1st Gerber-s	2	4	6	10	14	18
21-25: 21-1st Headmen (Chondu the Mystic, Dr. Arthur Nagan, Jerold Morgan); Valkyrie origin continued from last issue; Hulk returns; story continued in Giant-Size Defenders #4. 22-25-vs. Sons of the Serpent. 23-Yellowjacket app. 24-25-Son of Satan, Daredevil, Yellowjacket & Power Man app; story continues in Giant-Size Defenders #5; 25-1st app. "Elf with a gun"	2	4	6	8	10	12
26-Continued from Giant-Size Defenders #5; Guardians of the Galaxy app. (pre-dates Marvel Presents #3); origin of Vance Astro; Killraven & Badoon x-over	3	6	9	19	30	40
27-1st brief app. Starhawk (unnamed); Guardians of the Galaxy & Defenders vs. the Badoon	4	8	12	27	44	60
28-1st full app. Starhawk; Guardians of the Galaxy & Badoon app.	7	14	21	44	82	120
29-Starhawk joins the Guardians of the Galaxy; 1st app. Aleta (Starhawks wife); Guardians story continues in Marvel Presents #3	2	4	6	11	16	20
30-Mantlo-s (fill-in issue)	2	4	6	8	10	12
31-40: 31-Headman app. 32-Origin of Nighthawk; Headmen & Son of Satan app; 1st app. Ruby Thursday; 2nd app. "Elf with a gun". 33-Origin Nighthawk continued; return of Nebulon. 34-38-(Regular 25¢ editions). 34-vs. Nebulon. 35-1st new Red Guardian (Dr. Tania Belinsky); Headmen & Nebulon app. 36-Red Guardian & Plant Man app. 37-Power Man guest app.; vs. Plant Man, Eel & Porcupine; Nebulon app. 38-Power Man app.; vs. Eel & Porcupine; "Elf with a gun" app. 39-Power Man app. 40-1st new Valkyrie (gold) costume; "Elf with a gun" app.; story continued in Defenders Annual #1	1	3	4	6	8	10
34-38 (30¢-c variants, limited distribution 4-8/76)	5	10	15	30	50	70
41-46: 41-Last Gerber-s/Sal Buscema-a. 42,43-Egg Head, Rhino, Solarr & Cobalt Man app.; Giffen-a; 43-1st Red Rajah; Power Man app. 44-Power Man & Hellcat app. 45-Power Man & Hellcat app. 46-Dr. Strange & Red Guardian leave; "Elf with a gun" app; vs. Scorpio	1	2	3	5	6	8
47-50-Moon Knight guest app. 47,48-Wonder Man app. 47-49-vs. Scorpio (Jacob Fury). 48-50-(Regular 30¢ editions). 50-Death Scorpio; SHIELD app.	1	2	3	5	6	8
48-52-(35c-c variants, limited distribution)(6-10/77)	8	16	24	57	96	140
51-60: 51,52-(Regular 30¢ editions). 51-Nighthawk vs. The Ringer. 52-Hulk vs. Sub-Mariner. 53-1st brief app. Lunatik (Lobo lookalike) created by Roger Slifer & Keith Giffen, six years before they create Lobo in Omega Men #3; 1st app. Sergie Krylov (The Presence). 54,55-vs. the Presence. 54-last Giffen-a. 55-Origin Red Guardian; Lunatik cameo. 56-Red Guardian leaves; Valkyrie vs. Lunatik. 57-Ms. Marvel (Carol Danvers) app. 58-60-Devil Slayer app.	1	2	3	5	6	8
61-vs. Lunatik; Spider-Man app.	1	2	3	5	6	8
62-"Defender for a day" issue; Jack of Hearts, Ms. Marvel (Carol Danvers), Hercules, Iron Man, White Tiger, Nova, Marvel Man (later Quasar), Son of Satan, Havok, Prowler, Paladin, Falcon, Torpedo, Black Goliath, Stingray, Polaris, Captain Ultra, Iron Fist, Captain Marvel (Mar-Vell), Tagak app. (all try to join Defenders)	1	2	3	5	6	8
63-93,97-99: 63-Various villains form their own Defenders team. 64-Villains defeated; the various new Defenders leave. 66-68-Defenders in Asgard. 66-Hulk returns. 68-Hela app. 69-Omegatron app. 70-vs. Lunatik. 71-Origin Lunatik; Dr. Strange returns. 72,73-Lunatik app. 73-Foolkiller app. 74-Nighthawk resigns as leader; Foolkiller app. 75-vs. Foolkiller. 76-Wasp, Omega the Unknown & Ruby Thursday app. 77-Origin Omega the Unknown; Moondragon & Wasp app. 78-Original Defenders return (Hulk, Dr. Strange & Namor; continue thru #101); Wasp, Yellowjacket & Moondragon app. 79,80-Mandrill app; Wasp & Yellowjacket app. 84-Atlantis vs. Wakanda; Namor vs. Black Panther. 85,86-Black Panther app. 87-Origin Hellcat retold. 90,91-vs. Mandrill; Daredevil app. 97,98-Devil Slayer & Man-Thing app. 98-Nighthawk leaves; Avengers app. 99-Mephisto app.						5.00
94-1st Gargoyle (Isaac Christians)	2	4	6	11	16	20
95,96: Ghost Rider app. 95-Dracula app.						6.00
100-(52-pgs.)-Hellcat (Patsy Walker) revealed as Satan's daughter; Silver Surfer app.	2	4	6	9	12	15

Deep Gravity #4 © DH

Defenders (2021) #4 © MAR

Dejah Thoris (2016) #1 © DYN

	GD	VG	FN	VF	VF/NM	NM-
	2.0	4.0	6.0	8.0	9.0	9.2

101-Silver Surfer app. 6.00
102-111,115-119-124: 104-Beast joins. 105-Son of Satan joins; Mr. Fantastic app. 106-Captain America app.; death of Nighthawk. 107-Daredevil & Captain America app. 109-Spider-Man app; Defenders app. next in Avengers Annual #11. 111-Overmind cameo. 120-122-Son of Satan-c/stories. 122-"Elf with a gun" returns; Silver Surfer & Iceman app. 123-"Elf with a Gun" app.; Moondragon cameo; 1st app. Cloud; Vision & Scarlet Witch app. 124-Origin of the "Elf with a gun" 5.00
112-114-Overmind & Squadron Supreme app. 5.00
125-(52 pgs)-Intro new Defenders (Angel, Beast, Iceman, Valkyrie, Gargoyle & Moondragon); Hulk, Dr. Strange, Namor & Silver Surfer resign; "Elf with a Gun" mystery resolved 6.00
126-149,151: 126-130-Secret Empire story. 129-New Mutants cameo (3/84, early x-over). 134-1st full app. Manslaughter. 139-Odin app. 140-New Moondragon costume. 145-Johnny Blaze (Ghost Rider) app. 147-1st app. Interloper; Sgt. Fury app. 151-Manslaughter app. 4.00
150-(52 pgs.)-Origin Cloud 5.00
152-(52 pgs.)-Continued from Secret Wars II #7; Beyonder app.; vs. The Dragon of the Moon; leads into X-Factor #1 6.00
Annual 1 (1976, 52 pgs-) Continued from Defenders #40; Power Man app.; vs. Nebulon, the Bozos and the Headmen 3 6 9 22 35 45
...: Marvel Feature No. 1 Facsimile Edition (7/19, $4.99) r/Marvel Feature #1 w/orig. ads 5.00

NOTE: ***Art Adams** c-142p. **Austin** a-53i; c-65i, 119i, 145i. **Frank Bolle** a-7i, 10i, 11i. **Buckler** c(p)-34, 38, 76, 77, 79-86, 90, 91. **J. Buscema** c-66. **Giffen** a-42-49p, 50, 51-54p. **Golden** a-53p, 54p; c-94, 96. **Guice** c-129. **G. Kane** c(p)-13, 16, 18, 19, 21-26, 31-33, 35-37, 40, 41, 52, 55. **Kirby** c-42-45. **Mooney** a-3i, 31-34i, 62i, 63i, 85i. **Nasser** c-88p. **Perez** c(p)-51, 53, 54. **Rogers** c-98. **Starlin** c-110. **Tuska** a-57p. Silver Surfer in No. 2, 3, 6, 8-11, 92, 98-101, 107, 112-115, 122-125.*

DEFENDERS, THE (Volume 2) (Continues in The Order)
Marvel Comics: Mar, 2001 - No. 12, Feb, 2002 ($2.99/$2.25)
1-Busiek & Larsen-s/Larsen & Janson-a/c 3.00
2-11: 2-Two covers by Larsen & Art Adams; Valkyrie app. 4-Frenz-a 3.00
12-($3.50) 'Nuff Said issue; back-up-s Reis-a 4.00
...: From the Vault (9/11, $2.99) Previously unpublished story; Bagley-a 3.00

DEFENDERS, THE
Marvel Comics: Sept, 2005 - No. 5, Jan, 2006 ($2.99, limited series)
1-5-Giffen & DeMatteis-s/Maguire-a. 2-Dormammu app. 3.00
...: Indefensible HC (2006, $19.99, dust jacket) r/#1-5; Giffen & Maguire sketch page 20.00
...: Indefensible SC (2007, $13.99) r/#1-5; Giffen & Maguire sketch page 14.00

DEFENDERS, THE
Marvel Comics: Feb, 2012 - No. 12, Jan, 2013 ($3.99)
1-12: 1-Dr. Strange, Namor, Silver Surfer, Red She-Hulk, Iron Fist team; Dodson-a 4.00
...: Strange Heroes 1 (2/12, $4.99) Handbook-style profiles of team members and foes 5.00
...: The Coming of the Defenders 1 (2/12, $5.99) r/Marvel Feature #1-3; recolored-c of #1 6.00
...: Tournament of Heroes 1 (3/12, $5.99) r/Defenders #62-65 (1978); recolored-c of #62 6.00

DEFENDERS
Marvel Comics: Aug, 2017 - No. 10, Apr, 2018 ($4.99/$3.99)
1-($4.99) Luke Cage, Jessica Jones, Daredevil, Iron Fist team; Bendis-s/Marquez-a 5.00
2-10-($3.99) 3-Punisher app. 6-8-Deadpool app. 4.00

DEFENDERS
Marvel Comics: Oct, 2021 - No. 5, March, 2022 ($3.99)
1-5-Masked Raider, Dr. Strange, Silver Surfer, Harpy & Cloud team vs. Omnimax 4.00

DEFENDERS: BEYOND
Marvel Comics: Sept, 2022 - No. 5, Jan, 2023 ($3.99, limited series)
1-5-Loki, Blue Marvel, America Chavez, Tigra, Taaia team; Ewing-s/Rodriguez-a 4.00

DEFENDERS OF DYNATRON CITY
Marvel Comics: Feb, 1992 - No. 6, July, 1992 ($1.25, limited series)
1-6-Lucasarts characters. 2-Origin 3.00

DEFENDERS OF THE EARTH (TV)
Marvel Comics (Star Comics): Jan, 1987 - No. 4, July, 1987
1-4: The Phantom, Mandrake The Magician, Flash Gordon begin. 3-Origin Phantom. 4-Origin Mandrake 4.00

DEFENDERS: THE BEST DEFENSE
Marvel Comics: Feb, 2019 ($4.99)
1-Doctor Strange, Immortal Hulk, Silver Surfer, Namor app.; Ewing-s/Bennett-a 5.00

DEFEX
Devil's Due Publ.: Oct, 2004 - No. 6, Apr, 2005 ($2.95)
1-6: 1-Wolfman-s/Caselli-a. 6-Pérez-c 3.00

DEFIANCE
Image Comics: Feb, 2002 - No. 8, Jun, 2003 ($2.95)
Preview Edition (12/01) 3.00
1-8-Barré-s/Kang & Suh-a 3.00

	GD	VG	FN	VF	VF/NM	NM-
	2.0	4.0	6.0	8.0	9.0	9.2

DEFINITIVE DIRECTORY OF THE DC UNIVERSE, THE (See Who's Who...)

DEJAH OF MARS (Warlord of Mars)
Dynamite Entertainment: 2014 - No. 4, 2014 ($3.99)
1-4-Rahner-s/Morales-a; multiple covers on each 4.00

DEJAH THORIS (Warlord of Mars)
Dynamite Entertainment: 2016 - No. 6, 2016 ($3.99)
1-6-Barbarie-s/Manna-a; multiple covers 4.00

DEJAH THORIS AND THE GREEN MEN OF MARS (Warlord of Mars)
Dynamite Entertainment: 2013 - No. 12, 2014 ($3.99)
1-12: 1-8-Rahner-s/Antonio-a; multiple covers on each. 9-12-Morales-a 4.00

DEJAH THORIS AND THE WHITE APES OF MARS (Warlord of Mars)
Dynamite Entertainment: 2012 - No. 3, 2012 ($3.99)
1-3-Rahner-s/Antonio-a; 2 covers by Peterson & Garza 4.00

DEJAH THORIS VERSUS JOHN CARTER
Dynamite Entertainment: 2021 - No. 6, 2021 ($3.99, limited series)
1-6-Abnett-s/Miracolo-a; multple covers on each 4.00

DEJAH THORIS, VOLUME 2
Dynamite Entertainment: No. 0, 2018 - No. 10, 2018 ($3.99)
0-(25¢-c) Amy Chu-s/Pasquale Qualano-a; multiple covers 3.00
1-10-($3.99) Chu-s/Qualano-a; multiple covers 4.00

DEJAH THORIS, VOLUME 3 (Leads into Dejah Thoris Versus John Carter)
Dynamite Entertainment: 2019 - No. 12, 2021 ($3.99)
1-12: 1-6-Dan Abnett-s/Vasco Georgiev-a; multiple covers on each. 7-10-Piriz-a 4.00
...: Fairy Tales 1 (2022, $4.99) Ron Marz-s/Andres Labrada-a; Snow White homage 5.00
...: Winter's End 1 (2021, $4.99) Short stories of Dejah Thoris and John Carter 5.00

DELECTA OF THE PLANETS (See Don Fortune & Fawcett Miniatures)

DELETE
1First Comics: 2016 - No. 4, 2016 ($4.99, limited series)
1-4-Palmiotti & Gray-s/Timms-a/Conner-c 5.00

DELICATE CREATURES
Image Comics (Top Cow): 2001 ($16.95, hardcover with dust jacket)
nn-Fairy tale storybook; J. Michael Straczynski-s; Michael Zulli-a 17.00

DELINQUENTS
Valiant Entertainment: Aug, 2014 - No. 4, Nov, 2014 ($3.99, limited series)
1-4-Quantum & Woody meet Archer & Armstrong; Asmus & Van Lente-s/Kano-a 4.00

DELIRIUM'S PARTY: A LITTLE ENDLESS STORYBOOK (Characters from The Sandman titles and The Little Endless Storybook)
DC Comics: 2011 ($14.99, hardcover, one-shot)
HC-Jill Thompson-s/painted-a/c; Little Delirium throws a party; watercolor page process 15.00

DELLA VISION (...The Television Queen) (Patty Powers #4 on)
Atlas Comics: April, 1955 - No. 3, Aug, 1955
1-Al Hartley-c 81 162 243 518 884 1250
2,3 42 84 126 265 445 625

DELLEC
Aspen MLT.: Aug, 2009 - No. 6, Oct, 2011 ($2.50)
1-6-Gunnell-a/c 3.00

DELLEC VOLUME 2
Aspen MLT.: Sept, 2018 - No. 4, Jan, 2019 ($3.99)
1-4-Frank Mastromauro & Vince Hernandez-s 4.00
... 2018 Primer 1 (9/18, 25¢) New short story and recap of Volume 1 3.00

DELL GIANT COMICS
Dell Publishing began to release square bound comics in 1949 with a 132-page issue called Christmas Parade #1. The covers were of a heavier stock to accommodate the increased number of pages. The books proved profitable at 25 cents, but the average number of pages was quickly reduced to 100. Ten years later they were converted to a numbering system similar to the Four Color Comics, for greater ease in distribution and the page counts cut back to mostly 84 pages. The label "Dell Giant" began to appear on the covers in 1954. Because of the size of the books and the heavier, less pliant cover stock, they are rarely found in high grade condition, and with the exception of a small quantity of copies released from Western Publishing's warehouse–are almost never found in near mint.

Abraham Lincoln Life Story 1(3/58) 9 18 27 72 129 185
Bugs Bunny Christmas Funnies 1(11/50, 116pp) 23 46 69 184 322 460
...Christmas Funnies 2(11/51, 116pp) 13 26 39 104 180 225
...Christmas Funnies 3-5(11/52-11/54,)-Becomes Christmas Party #6 10 20 30 80 140 200

	GD 2.0	VG 4.0	FN 6.0	VF 8.0	VF/NM 9.0	NM- 9.2
...Christmas Funnies 7-9(12/56-12/58)	9	18	27	72	124	175
...Christmas Party 6(11/55)-Formerly Bugs Bunny Christmas Funnies	9	18	27	72	124	175
...County Fair 1(9/57)	11	22	33	88	149	210
...Halloween Parade 1(10/53)	14	28	42	112	191	270
...Halloween Parade 2(10/54)-Trick 'N' Treat Halloween Fun #3 on	10	20	30	80	140	200
...Trick 'N' Treat Halloween Fun 3,4(10/55-10/56)-Formerly Halloween Parade #2	10	20	30	80	138	195
...Vacation Funnies 1(7/51, 112pp)	20	40	60	160	280	400
...Vacation Funnies 2('52)	13	26	39	104	180	255
...Vacation Funnies 3-5('53-'55)	10	20	30	80	138	195
...Vacation Funnies 6,7,9('56-'59)	9	18	27	72	124	175
...Vacation Funnies 8('58) 1st app. Beep Beep the Road Runner, Wile E. Coyote (1st meeting), Mathilda (Mrs. Beep Beep) and their 3 children who hatch from eggs; one month before Four Color #918	11	22	33	88	157	225
Cadet Gray of West Point 1(4/58)-Williamson-a, 10pgs.; Buscema-a; photo-c	8	16	24	64	107	150
Christmas In Disneyland 1(12/57)-Barks-a, 18 pgs.	25	50	75	200	350	500
Christmas Parade 1(11/49)(132 pgs.)(1st Dell Giant)-Donald Duck (25 pgs. by Barks, r-in G.K. Christmas Parade #5); Mickey Mouse & other film oriented stories; Cinderella (prior to movie), 7 Dwarfs, Bambi & Thumper, So Dear To My Heart, Flying Mouse, Dumbo, Cookieland & others	70	140	210	560	980	1400
Christmas Parade 2('50)-Donald Duck (132 pgs.)(25 pgs. by Barks, r-in Gold Key's Christmas Parade #6). Mickey, Pluto, Chip & Dale, etc. Contents shift to a holiday expansion of W.D. C&S type format	44	88	132	352	614	875
Christmas Parade 3-7('51-'55, #3-116pgs; #4-7, 100 pgs.)	14	28	42	112	196	280
Christmas Parade 8(12/56)-Barks-a, 8 pgs.	22	44	66	176	306	435
Christmas Parade 9(12/58)-Barks-a, 20 pgs.	25	50	75	200	350	500
Christmas Treasury, A 1(11/54)	10	20	30	80	135	190
Davy Crockett, King Of The Wild Frontier 1(9/55)-Fess Parker photo-c; Marsh-a	19	38	57	152	269	385
Disneyland Birthday Party 1(10/58)-Barks-a, 16 pgs. r-by Gladstone	25	50	75	200	350	500
Donald and Mickey In Disneyland 1(5/58)	12	24	36	96	166	235
Donald Duck Beach Party 1(7/54)-Has an Uncle Scrooge story (not by Barks) that prefigures the later rivalry with Flintheart Glomgold and tells of Scrooge's wild rivalry with another millionaire	18	36	54	144	252	360
...Beach Party 2(1955)-Lady & Tramp	12	24	36	96	168	240
...Beach Party 3-5(1956-58)	11	22	33	88	152	215
...Beach Party 6(8/59, 84pp)-Stapled	8	16	24	64	115	165
Donald Duck Fun Book 1,2 (1953 & 10/54)-Games, puzzles, comics & cut-outs (very rare in unused condition)(most copies commonly have defaced interior pgs.)	63	126	189	504	877	1250
Donald Duck In Disneyland 1(9/55)-1st Disneyland Dell Giant	16	32	48	128	227	325
Golden West Rodeo Treasury 1(10/57)	10	20	30	80	135	190
Huey, Dewey and Louie Back To School 1(9/58)	9	18	27	72	126	180
Lady and The Tramp 1(6/55)	19	38	57	152	261	370
Life Stories of American Presidents 1(11/57)-Buscema-a	8	16	24	64	112	160
Lone Ranger Golden West 3(8/55)-Formerly Lone Ranger Western Treasury	18	36	54	144	255	365
Lone Ranger Movie Story nn(3/56)-Origin Lone Ranger in text; Clayton Moore photo-c	36	72	108	288	507	725
...Western Treasury 1(9/53)-Origin Lone Ranger, Silver, & Tonto; painted cover	23	46	69	184	325	465
...Western Treasury 2(8/54)-Becomes Lone Ranger Golden West #3	18	36	54	144	255	365
Marge's Little Lulu & Alvin Story Telling Time 1(3/59)-r/#2,5,3,11,30,10,21,17,8, 14,16; Stanley-a	14	28	42	112	196	280
...& Her Friends 4(3/56)-Tripp-a	14	28	42	112	191	270
...& Her Special Friends 3(3/55)-Tripp-a	16	32	48	128	219	310
...& Tubby At Summer Camp 5,2: 5(10/57)-Tripp-a. 2(10/58)-Tripp-a	13	26	39	104	182	260
...& Tubby Halloween Fun 6,2: 6(10/57)-Tripp-a. 2(10/58)-Tripp-a	14	28	42	112	191	270
...& Tubby In Alaska 1(7/59)-Tripp-a	13	26	39	104	182	260
...On Vacation 1(7/54)-r/4C-110,14,4C-146,5,4C-97,4,4C-158,3,1;Stanley-a	25	50	75	200	350	500
...& Tubby Annual 1(3/53)-r/4C-165,4C-74,4C-146,4C-97,4C-158, 4C-139, 4C-131; Stanley-a (1st Lulu Dell Giant)	30	60	90	240	420	600
...& Tubby Annual 2('54)-r/4C-139,6,4C-115,4C-74,5,4C-97,3,4C-146,18; Stanley-a	25	50	75	200	350	500
Marge's Tubby & His Clubhouse Pals 1(10/56)-1st app. Gran'pa Feeb;1st app. Janie; written by Stanley; Tripp-a	15	30	45	120	210	300
Mickey Mouse Almanac 1(12/57)-Barks-a, 8pgs.	27	54	81	216	378	540
...Birthday Party 1(9/53)-r/entire 48pgs. of Gottfredson's "Mickey Mouse in Love Trouble" from WDC&S 36-39. Quality equal to original. Also reprints one story each from Four Color 27, 79, & 181 plus 6 panels of highlights in the career of Mickey Mouse	31	62	93	248	434	620
...Club Parade 1(12/55)-r/4-Color 16 with some death trap scenes redrawn by Paul Murry & recolored with night turned into day; quality less than original	22	44	66	176	308	440
...In Fantasy Land 1(5/57)	13	26	39	104	180	255
...In Frontier Land 1(5/56)-Mickey Mouse Club iss.	13	26	39	104	180	255
...Summer Fun 1(8/58)-Mobile cut-outs on back-c; becomes Summer Fun with #2; Canadian version exists with 30¢-c price	13	26	39	104	180	255
Moses & The Ten Commandments 1(8/57)-Not based on movie; Dell's adaptation; Sekowsky-a; variant version has "Gods of Egypt" comic back-c	8	16	24	64	107	150
Nancy & Sluggo Travel Time 1(9/58)	8	16	24	64	115	165
Peter Pan Treasure Chest 1(1/53, 212pp)-Disney; contains 54-page movie adaptation & other Peter Pan stories; plus Donald & Mickey stories w/P. Pan; a 32-page retelling of "D. Duck Finds Pirate Gold" with yellow beak, called "Capt. Hook & the Buried Treasure"	145	290	435	1160	2030	2900
Picnic Party 6,7(7/55-6/56)(Formerly Vacation Parade)-Uncle Scrooge, Mickey & Donald	12	24	36	96	166	235
Picnic Party 8(7/57)-Barks-a, 6pgs	21	42	63	168	289	410
Pogo Parade 1(9/53)-Kelly-a(r-/Pogo from Animal Comics in this order: #11,13,21,14,27,16,23,9,18,15,17)	25	50	75	200	350	500
Raggedy Ann & Andy 1(2/55)	17	34	51	136	238	340
Santa Claus Funnies 1(11/52)-Dan Noonan -A Christmas Carol adaptation	11	22	33	88	157	225
Silly Symphonies 1(9/52)-Redrawing of Gotfredson's Mickey Mouse strip of "The Brave Little Tailor;" 2 Good Housekeeping pages (from 1943); Lady and the Two Siamese Cats, three years before "Lady & the Tramp;" a retelling of Donald Duck's first app. in "The Wise Little Hen" & other stories based on 1930's Silly Symphony cartoons	35	70	105	280	490	700
Silly Symphonies 2(9/53)-M. Mouse in "The Sorcerer's Apprentice", 2 Good Housekeeping pages (from 1944); The Pelican & the Snipe, Elmer Elephant, Peculiar Penguins, Little Hiawatha, & others	24	48	72	192	339	485
Silly Symphonies 3(2/54)-r/Mickey & The Beanstalk (4-Color #157, 39pgs.), Little Minnehaha, Pablo, The Flying Gauchito, Pluto, & Bongo, & 2 Good Housekeeping pages (1944)	20	40	60	160	275	390
Silly Symphonies 4(8/54)-r/Dumbo (4-Color 234), Morris The Midget Moose, The Country Cousin, Bongo, & Clara Cluck	20	40	60	160	275	390
Silly Symphonies 5-8: 5(2/55)-r/Cinderella (4-Color 272), Bucky Bug, Pluto, Little Hiawatha, The 7 Dwarfs & Dumbo, Pinocchio. 6(8/55)-r/Pinocchio (WDC&S 63), The 7 Dwarfs & Thumper (WDC&S 45), M. Mouse "Adventures With Robin Hood" (40 pgs.), Johnny Appleseed, Pluto & Peter Pan, & Bucky Bug; Cut-out on back-c. 7(2/57)-r/Reluctant Dragon, Ugly Duckling, M. Mouse & Peter Pan, Jiminy Cricket, Peter & The Wolf, Brer Rabbit, Bucky Bug; Cut-out on back-c. 8(2/58)-r/Thumper Meets The 7 Dwarfs (4-Color #19), Jiminy Cricket, Niok, Brer Rabbit; Cut-out on back-c	16	32	48	128	224	320
Silly Symphonies 9(2/59)-r/Paul Bunyan, Humphrey Bear, Jiminy Cricket, The Social Lion, Goliath II; cut-out on back-c	15	30	45	120	210	300
Sleeping Beauty 1(4/59)	28	56	84	224	387	550
Summer Fun 2(8/59, 84pp, stapled binding)(Formerly Mickey Mouse...)-Barks-a(2), 24 pgs.	24	48	72	192	336	480
Tarzan's Jungle Annual 1(8/52)-Lex Barker photo on-c of #1,2	16	32	48	128	227	325
...Annual 2(8/53)	11	22	33	88	152	215
...Annual 3-7('54-9/58)(two No. 5s)-Manning-a-No. 3,5-7; Marsh-a in No. 1-7 plus painted-c 1-7	9	18	27	72	124	175
Tom And Jerry Back To School 1(9/56) 2 different back-c, variant has "Apple for the Teacher" cut-out	12	24	36	96	168	240
...Picnic Time 1(7/58)	10	20	30	80	135	190
...Summer Fun 1(7/54)-Droopy written by Barks	15	30	45	120	205	290
...Summer Fun 2-4(7/55-7/57)	8	16	24	64	107	150
...Toy Fair 1(6/58)	9	18	27	72	126	180
...Winter Carnival 1(12/52)-Droopy written by Barks	21	42	63	168	297	425
...Winter Carnival 2(12/53)-Droopy written by Barks	16	32	48	128	224	320
...Winter Fun 3(12/54)	8	16	24	64	115	165
...Winter Fun 4-7(12/55-11/58)	7	14	21	56	101	145
Treasury of Dogs, A 1(10/56)	8	16	24	64	107	150
Treasury of Horses, A (9/55)	8	16	24	64	107	150
Uncle Scrooge Goes To Disneyland 1(8/57p)-Barks-a, 20 pgs. r-by Gladstone; 2 different back-c; variant shows 6 snapshots of Scrooge	28	56	84	224	387	550
Vacation In Disneyland 1(8/58)	11	22	33	88	157	225
Vacation Parade 1(7/50, 132pp)-Donald Duck & Mickey Mouse; Barks-a, 55 pgs.	100	200	300	800	1400	2000
Vacation Parade 2(7/51,116pp)	26	52	78	208	367	525
Vacation Parade 3-5(7/52-7/54)-Becomes Picnic Party No. 6 on. #4-Robin Hood Advs.	14	28	42	112	194	275
Western Roundup 1(6/52)-Photo-c; Gene Autry, Roy Rogers, Johnny Mack Brown, Rex Allen, & Bill Elliott begin; photo back-c begin, end No. 14,16,18	25	50	75	200	350	500
Western Roundup 2(2/53)-Photo-c	14	28	42	112	196	280
Western Roundup 3-5(7-9/53 - 1-3/54)-Photo-c	11	22	33	88	157	225
Western Roundup 6-10(4-6/54 - 4-6/55)-Photo-c	11	22	33	88	149	210
Western Roundup 11-17,25: 11-17-Photo-c; 11-13,16,17-Manning-a. 11-Flying A's Range Rider, Dale Evans begin	9	18	27	72	129	185
Western Roundup 18-Toth-a; last photo-c; Gene Autry ends	11	22	33	88	149	210
Western Roundup 19-24-Manning-a. 19-Buffalo Bill Jr. begins (7-9/57; early app.). 19,20,22-Toth-a. 21-Rex Allen, Johnny Mack Brown end. 22-Jace Pearson's Texas Rangers, Rin Tin Tin, Tales of Wells Fargo (2nd app., 4-6/58) & Wagon Train (2nd app.) begin	9	18	27	72	129	185
Woody Woodpecker Back To School 1(10/52)	10	20	30	80	140	200
...Back To School 2-4,6('53-10/57)-County Fair No. 5	8	16	24	64	112	160
...County Fair 5(9/56)-Formerly Back To School	8	16	24	64	112	160
...County Fair 2(11/58)	7	14	21	56	101	145

DELL GIANTS (Consecutive numbering)
Dell Publishing Co.: No. 21, Sept, 1959 - No. 55, Sept, 1961 (Most 84 pgs., 25¢)

	GD 2.0	VG 4.0	FN 6.0	VF 8.0	VF/NM 9.0	NM- 9.2
21-(#1)-M.G.M.'s Tom & Jerry Picnic Time (84pp, stapled binding)-Painted-c	11	22	33	88	157	225
22-Huey, Dewey & Louie Back to School (Disney; 10/59, 84pp, square binding begins)	9	18	27	72	129	185
23-Marge's Little Lulu & Tubby Halloween Fun (10/59)-Tripp-a	12	24	36	96	168	240
24-Woody Woodpecker's Family Fun (11/59)(Walter Lantz)	8	16	24	64	112	160
25-Tarzan's Jungle World(11/59)-Marsh-a; painted-c	11	22	33	88	152	215
26-Christmas Parade(Disney; 12/59)-Barks-a, 16pgs.; Barks draws himself on wanted poster on pg. 13	21	42	63	168	289	410
27-Walt Disney's Man in Space (10/59) r-/4-Color 716,866, & 954 (100 pgs., 35¢)(TV)	9	18	27	72	129	185
28-Bugs Bunny's Winter Fun (2/60)	9	18	27	72	126	180
29-Marge's Little Lulu & Tubby in Hawaii (4/60)-Tripp-a	12	24	36	96	166	235
30-Disneyland USA(Disney; 6/60)	9	18	27	72	124	175
31-Huckleberry Hound Summer Fun (7/60)(TV)(HannaBarbera)-Yogi Bear & Pixie & Dixie						

Dell Giant #35 © DIS

The Demon: Hell is Earth #1 © DC

Dennis the Menace #41 © FAW

	GD 2.0	VG 4.0	FN 6.0	VF 8.0	VF/NM 9.0	NM- 9.2
app.	12	24	36	96	173	250
32-Bugs Bunny Beach Party	7	14	21	56	101	145
33-Daisy Duck & Uncle Scrooge Picnic Time (Disney; 9/60)	9	18	27	72	124	175
34-Nancy & Sluggo Summer Camp (8/60)	7	14	21	56	101	145
35-Huey, Dewey & Louie Back to School (Disney; 10/60)-1st app. Daisy Duck's Nieces, April, May & June	12	24	36	96	163	230
36-Marge's Little Lulu & Witch Hazel Halloween Fun (10/60)-Tripp-a	11	22	33	88	157	225
37-Tarzan, King of the Jungle (11/60)-Marsh-a; painted-c	9	18	27	72	129	185
38-Uncle Donald & His Nephews Family Fun (Disney; 11/60)-Cover painting based on a pencil sketch by Barks	12	24	36	96	173	250
39-Walt Disney's Merry Christmas (Disney; 12/60)-Cover painting based on a pencil sketch by Barks	12	24	36	96	173	250
40-Woody Woodpecker Christmas Parade (12/60)(Walter Lantz)	6	12	18	48	87	125
41-Yogi Bear's Winter Sports (12/60)(TV)(Hanna-Barbera)-Huckleberry Hound, Pixie & Dixie, Augie Doggie app.	12	24	36	96	173	250
42-Marge's Little Lulu & Tubby in Australia (4/61)	12	24	36	96	171	245
43-Mighty Mouse in Outer Space (5/61)	20	40	60	160	275	390
44-Around the World with Huckleberry and His Friends (7/61)(TV)(Hanna-Barbera)-Yogi Bear, Pixie & Dixie, Quick Draw McGraw, Augie Doggie app.; 1st app. Yakky Doodle	13	26	39	104	182	260
45-Nancy & Sluggo Summer Camp (8/61)	7	14	21	56	96	135
46-Bugs Bunny Beach Party (8/61)	7	14	21	56	96	135
47-Mickey & Donald in Vacationland (Disney; 8/61)	8	16	24	64	115	165
48-The Flintstones (No. 1)(Bedrock Bedlam)(7/61)(TV)(Hanna-Barbera) 1st app. in comics	30	60	90	240	420	600
49-Huey, Dewey & Louie Back to School (Disney; 9/61)	9	18	27	72	124	175
50-Marge's Little Lulu & Witch Hazel Trick 'N' Treat (10/61)	11	22	33	88	157	225
51-Tarzan, King of the Jungle by Jesse Marsh (11/61)-Painted-c	8	16	24	64	110	155
52-Uncle Donald & His Nephews Dude Ranch (Disney; 11/61)	8	16	24	64	115	165
53-Donald Duck Merry Christmas (Disney; 12/61)	8	16	24	64	112	160
54-Woody Woodpecker's Christmas Party (12/61)-Issued after No. 55	7	14	21	56	98	140
55-Daisy Duck & Uncle Scrooge Showboat (Disney; 9/61)	8	16	24	64	117	170

NOTE: All issues printed with & without ad on back cover.

DELL JUNIOR TREASURY
Dell Publishing Co.: June, 1955 - No. 10, Oct, 1957 (15¢) (All painted-c)

	GD 2.0	VG 4.0	FN 6.0	VF 8.0	VF/NM 9.0	NM- 9.2
1-Alice in Wonderland; r/4-Color #331 (52 pgs.)	8	16	24	56	108	160
2-Aladdin & the Wonderful Lamp	6	12	18	41	76	110
3-Gulliver's Travels (1/56)	6	12	18	37	66	95
4-Adventures of Mr. Frog & Miss Mouse	6	12	18	38	69	100
5-The Wizard of Oz (7/56)	6	12	18	41	76	110
6-10: 6-Heidi (10/56). 7-Santa and the Angel. 8-Raggedy Ann and the Camel with the Wrinkled Knees. 9-Clementina the Flying Pig. 10-Adventures of Tom Sawyer	6	12	18	37	66	95

DELTA 13
IDW Publishing: May, 2018 - No. 4, Aug, 2018 ($3.99, limited series)

1-4-Steve Niles-s/Nat Jones-a — 4.00

DEMOLITION MAN
DC Comics: Nov, 1993 - No. 4, Feb, 1994 ($1.75, limited series)

1-4-Movie adaptation — 4.00

DEMON, THE (See Detective Comics No. 482-485)
National Periodical Publications: Aug-Sept, 1972 - V3#16, Jan, 1974

	GD 2.0	VG 4.0	FN 6.0	VF 8.0	VF/NM 9.0	NM- 9.2
1-Origin; Kirby-s/c/a in all; 1st Morgaine Le Fey	19	38	57	131	291	450
2-5	4	8	12	28	47	65
6-16: 7-1st app. Klarion the Witch Boy	3	6	9	21	33	45

DEMON, THE (1st limited series)(Also see Cosmic Odyssey #2)
DC Comics: Nov, 1986 - No. 4, Feb, 1987 (75¢, limited series)(#2 has #4 of 4 on-c)

1-4: Matt Wagner-a(p) & scripts in all. 4-Demon & Jason Blood become separate entities — 4.00

DEMON, THE (2nd Series)
DC Comics: July, 1990 - No. 58, May, 1995 ($1.50/$1.75/$1.95)

	GD 2.0	VG 4.0	FN 6.0	VF 8.0	VF/NM 9.0	NM- 9.2
1-Grant scripts begin, ends #39: 1-4-Painted-c						5.00
2-18,20-27,29-39,41,42: 3,8-Batman app. (cameo #4). 12-Bisley painted-c. 12-15,21-Lobo app. (1 pg. cameo #11). 23-Robin app. 29-Superman app. 31,33-39-Lobo app.						3.00
19-($2.50, 44 pgs.)-Lobo poster stapled inside						5.00
28,40: 28-Superman-c/story; begin $1.75-c. 40-Garth Ennis scripts begin						4.00
43-45-Hitman app.	1	2	3	5	7	10
46-48 Return of The Haunted Tank-c/s. 48-Begin $1.95-c.						5.00
49,51,55-58: 51-(9/94) Followed by Demon #0 issue						3.00
50 ($2.95, 52 pgs.)						4.00
52-54-Hitman-s						5.00
#0-(10/94) Zero Hour issue released between #51&52						3.00
Annual 1 (1992, $3.00, 68 pgs.)-Eclipso-c/story						5.00
Annual 2 (1993, $3.50, 68 pgs.)-1st app. of Hitman	3	6	9	18	27	36

NOTE: ***Alan Grant*** *scripts in #1-16, 20, 21, 23-25, 30-39, Annual 1.* ***Wagner*** *a/scripts-22.*

DEMON DAYS (Reimagined Marvel characters set in Japanese folklore)
Marvel Comics: May, 2021 - May, 2022 ($4.99)

	NM- 9.2
...: Blood Feud 1 (5/22) Part 4 of The Yashida Saga; Peach Momoko-s/a; Hulk app.	5.00
...: Cursed Web 1 (11/21) Part 2 of The Yashida Saga; Peach Momoko-s/a; Mystique app.	5.00
...: Mariko 1 (8/21) Part 1 of The Yashida Saga; Peach Momoko-s/a; Black Widow app.	5.00
...: Rising Storm 1 (2/22) Part 3 of The Yashida Saga; Momoko-s/a; Thor & Storm app.	5.00
...: X-Men 1 (5/22) Momoko-s/a; Psylocke & Venom app.	5.00
...: X-Men Creator Cut 1 (2/22, $5.99) Shows B&W inked story with character & sketch art	6.00

DEMON DREAMS
Pacific Comics: Feb, 1984 - No. 2, May, 1984

1,2-Mostly r-/Heavy Metal — 3.00

DEMON: DRIVEN OUT
DC Comics: Nov, 2003 - No. 6, Apr, 2004 ($2.50, limited series)

1-6-Dysart-s/Mhan-a — 3.00

DEMON, THE: HELL IS EARTH (Etrigan)
DC Comics: Jan, 2018 - No. 6, Jun, 2018 ($2.99, limited series)

1-6-Andrew Constant-s/Brad Walker-a; Xanadu app. — 3.00

DEMON-HUNTER (See Marvel Spotlight #33)
Seaboard Periodicals (Atlas): Sept, 1975

	GD 2.0	VG 4.0	FN 6.0	VF 8.0	VF/NM 9.0	NM- 9.2
1-Origin/1st app. Demon-Hunter; Buckler-c/a	3	6	9	14	20	25

DEMON KNIGHT: A GRIMJACK GRAPHIC NOVEL
First Publishing: 1990 ($8.95, 52 pgs.)

nn-Flint Henry-a — 9.00

DEMON KNIGHTS (New DC 52) (Set in the Dark Ages)
DC Comics: Nov, 2011 - No. 23, Oct, 2013 ($2.99)

1-23: 1-Cornell-s/Neves-a/Daniel-c; Etrigan, Madame Xanadu & The Shining Knight app. — 3.00
#0 (11/12, $2.99) Origin of Etrigan The Demon; Merlin app.; Cornell-s/Chang-a — 3.00

DEMON WARS (Reimagined Marvel characters set in Japanese folklore)
Marvel Comics: Oct, 2022 - Present ($4.99)

	NM- 9.2
...: Down in Flames 1 (4/23) Into the Spirit World pt. 3; Peach Momoko-s/a	5.00
...: Shield of Justice 1 (1/23) Into the Spirit World pt. 2; Peach Momoko-s/a	5.00
...: The Iron Samurai 1 (10/22) Into the Spirit World pt. 1; Peach Momoko-s/a	5.00

DENNIS THE MENACE (TV with 1959 issues) (Becomes ...Fun Fest Series; See The Best of... & The Very Best of...)(...Fun Fest on-c only to #156-166)
Standard Comics/Pines No.15-31/Hallden (Fawcett) No.32 on: 8/53 - #14, 1/56; #15, 3/56 - #31, 11/58; #32, 1/59 - #166, 11/79

	GD 2.0	VG 4.0	FN 6.0	VF 8.0	VF/NM 9.0	NM- 9.2
1-1st app. Dennis, Mr. & Mrs. Wilson, Ruff & Dennis' mom & dad; Wiseman-a, written by Fred Toole-most issues	284	568	852	1818	3109	4400
2	74	148	222	470	810	1150
3-5	41	82	123	256	428	600
6-10: 8-Last pre-code issue	34	68	102	206	336	465
11-20	22	44	66	132	216	300
21,23-30	14	28	42	82	121	160
22-1st app. Margaret w/blonde hair	18	36	54	103	162	220
31-1st app. Joey	19	38	57	112	179	245
32-38,40(1/60): 37-A-Bomb blast panel	10	20	30	56	76	95
39-1st app. Gina (11/59)	14	28	42	76	108	140
41-60(7/62)	4	8	12	25	40	55
61-80(9/65),100(1/69)	3	6	9	16	23	30
81-99	2	4	6	11	16	20
101-117: 102-Last 12¢ issue	2	4	6	9	12	15
118(1/72)-131 (All 52 pages)	2	4	6	10	14	18
132(1/74)-142,144-160	1	2	3	5	7	9
143(3/76) Olympic-c/s; low print	2	4	6	10	14	18
161-166	1	3	4	6	8	10

NOTE: ***Wiseman*** *c/a-1-46, 53, 68, 69.*

DENNIS THE MENACE (Giants) (No. 1 titled Giant Vacation Special; becomes Dennis the Menace Bonus Magazine No. 76 on)
(#1-8,18,23,25,30,38: 100 pgs.; rest to #41: 84 pgs.; #42-75: 68 pgs.)
Standard/Pines/Hallden(Fawcett): Summer, 1955 - No. 75, Dec, 1969

	GD 2.0	VG 4.0	FN 6.0	VF 8.0	VF/NM 9.0	NM- 9.2
nn-Giant Vacation Special(Summ/55-Standard)	20	40	60	117	189	260
nn-Christmas issue (Winter '55)	18	36	54	103	162	220
2-Giant Vacation Special (Summer '56-Pines)	15	30	45	84	127	170
3-Giant Christmas issue (Winter '56-Pines)	14	28	42	78	112	145
4-Giant Vacation Special (Summer '57-Pines)	13	26	39	74	105	135
5-Giant Christmas issue (Winter '57-Pines)	13	26	39	74	105	135
6-In Hawaii (Giant Vacation Special)(Summer '58-Pines)	12	24	36	69	97	125
6-In Hawaii (Summer '59-Hallden)-2nd printing; says 3rd large printing on-c 6-In Hawaii (Summer '60)-3rd printing; says 4th large printing on-c 6-In Hawaii (Summer '62)-4th printing; says 5th large printing on-c each....	9	18	27	47	61	75
6-Giant Christmas issue (Winter '58)	12	24	36	69	97	125
7-In Hollywood (Winter '59-Hallden)	5	10	15	33	57	80
7-In Hollywood (Summer '61)-2nd printing	3	6	9	21	33	45
8-In Mexico (Winter '60, 100 pgs.-Hallden/Fawcett)	5	10	15	33	57	80
8-In Mexico (Summer '62, 2nd printing)	3	6	9	21	33	45
9-Goes to Camp (Summer '61, 84 pgs.)-1st CCA approved issue	5	10	15	31	53	75
9-Goes to Camp (Summer '62)-2nd printing	3	6	9	21	33	45
10-12: 10-X-Mas issue (Winter '61), 11-Giant Christmas issue (Winter '62), 12-Triple Feature (Winter '62)	5	10	15	34	60	85
13-17: 13-Best of Dennis the Menace (Spring '63)-Reprints, 14-And His Dog Ruff (Summer '63), 15-In Washington, D.C. (Summer '63), 16-Goes to Camp (Summer '63)-Reprints No. 9, 17-& His Pal Joey (Winter '63)	4	8	12	25	40	55
18-In Hawaii (Reprints No. 6)	3	6	9	21	33	45
19-Giant Christmas issue (Winter '63)	4	8	12	25	40	55
20-Spring Special (Spring '64)	4	8	12	25	40	55
21-40 (Summer '66): 30-r/#6. #35-Xmas spec.Wint,'65	3	6	9	19	30	40
41-60 (Fall '68)	3	6	9	15	22	28
61-75 (12/69): 68-Partial-r/#6	3	6	9	14	19	24

NOTE: ***Wiseman*** *c/a-1-8, 12, 14, 15, 17, 20, 22, 27, 28, 31, 35, 36, 41, 49.*

DENNIS THE MENACE
Marvel Comics Group: Nov, 1981 - No. 13, Nov, 1982

	GD 2.0	VG 4.0	FN 6.0	VF 8.0	VF/NM 9.0	NM- 9.2
1-New-a	2	4	6	10	14	18
2-13: 2-New art. 3-Part-r. 4,5-r. 5-X-Mas-c & issue, 7-Spider Kid-c/sty	1	2	3	4	5	7

NOTE: ***Hank Ketcham*** *c-most; a-3, 12.* ***Wiseman*** *a-4, 5.*

DENNIS THE MENACE AND HIS DOG RUFF
Hallden/Fawcett: Summer, 1961

	GD 2.0	VG 4.0	FN 6.0	VF 8.0	VF/NM 9.0	NM- 9.2
1-Wiseman-c/a	6	12	18	42	79	115

DENNIS THE MENACE AND HIS FRIENDS
Fawcett Publ.: 1969; No. 5, Jan, 1970 - No. 46, April, 1980 (All reprints)

	GD 2.0	VG 4.0	FN 6.0	VF 8.0	VF/NM 9.0	NM- 9.2
Dennis the Menace & Joey No. 2 (7/69)	2	4	6	13	18	22
Dennis the Menace & Ruff No. 2 (9/69)	2	4	6	13	18	22
Dennis the Menace & Mr. Wilson No. 1 (10/69)	3	6	9	15	22	28
Dennis & Margaret No. 1 (Winter '69)	3	6	9	15	22	28
5-12: 5-Dennis the Menace & Margaret. 6-...& Joey. 7-...& Ruff. 8-...& Mr. Wilson	2	4	6	8	11	14
13-21-(52 pg Giants): 13-(1/72). 21-(1/74)	2	4	6	10	14	18
22-37	1	3	4	6	8	10
38-46 (Digest size, 148 pgs., 4/78, 95¢)	2	4	6	8	11	14

NOTE: *Titles rotate every four issues, beginning with No. 5. Joey issues: #2(7/69),6,10,14,18,22,26,30,34. Ruff issues: #2(9/69), 7,11,15,19,23,27,31,35. Mr. Wilson issues: #1(10/69),8,12,16,20,24,28,32,36. Margaret issues: #1 (Wint./69),5,9,13,17,21,25,29,33,37.*

DENNIS THE MENACE AND HIS PAL JOEY
Fawcett Publ.: Summer, 1961 (10¢) (See Dennis the Menace Giants No. 45)

	GD 2.0	VG 4.0	FN 6.0	VF 8.0	VF/NM 9.0	NM- 9.2
1-Wiseman-c/a	6	12	18	42	79	115

DENNIS THE MENACE AND THE BIBLE KIDS
Word Books: 1977 (36 pgs.)

	GD 2.0	VG 4.0	FN 6.0	VF 8.0	VF/NM 9.0	NM- 9.2
1-6: 1-Jesus. 2-Joseph. 3-David. 4-The Bible Girls. 5-Moses. 6-More About Jesus	2	4	6	10	14	18
7-9-Low print run: 7-The Lord's Prayer. 8-Stories Jesus told. 9-Paul, God's Traveller	3	6	9	20	31	42
10-Low print run; In the Beginning	5	10	15	34	60	85

NOTE: ***Ketcham*** *c/a in all.*

DENNIS THE MENACE BIG BONUS SERIES
Fawcett Publications: No. 10, Feb, 1980 - No. 11, Apr, 1980

	GD 2.0	VG 4.0	FN 6.0	VF 8.0	VF/NM 9.0	NM- 9.2
10,11	1	2	3	5	6	8

DENNIS THE MENACE BONUS MAGAZINE (Formerly Dennis the Menace Giants Nos. 1-75)
(...Big Bonus Series on-c for #174-194)
Fawcett Publications: No. 76, 1/70 - No. 95, 7/71; No. 95, 7/71; No. 97, '71; No. 194, 10/79;
(No. 76-124: 68 pgs.; No. 125-163: 52 pgs.; No. 164 on: 36 pgs.)

	GD 2.0	VG 4.0	FN 6.0	VF 8.0	VF/NM 9.0	NM- 9.2
76-90(3/71)	2	4	6	10	14	18
91-95, 97-110(10/72): Two #95's with same date(7/71) A-Summer Games, and B-That's Our Boy. No #96	2	4	6	9	13	16
111-124	2	4	6	8	10	12
125-163-(52 pgs.)	2	4	6	8	10	12
164-194: 166-Indicia printed backwards	1	2	3	4	5	7

DENNIS THE MENACE COMICS DIGEST
Marvel Comics Group: April, 1982 - No. 3, Aug, 1982 ($1.25, digest-size)

	GD 2.0	VG 4.0	FN 6.0	VF 8.0	VF/NM 9.0	NM- 9.2
1-3-Reprints	1	3	4	6	8	10
1-Mistakenly printed with DC emblem on cover	2	4	6	10	12	15

NOTE: ***Ketcham*** *c-all.* ***Wiseman*** *a-all. A few thousand #1's were published with a DC emblem on cover.*

DENNIS THE MENACE FUN BOOK
Fawcett Publications/Standard Comics: 1960 (100 pgs.)

	GD 2.0	VG 4.0	FN 6.0	VF 8.0	VF/NM 9.0	NM- 9.2
1-Part Wiseman-a	6	12	18	42	79	115

DENNIS THE MENACE FUN FEST SERIES (Formerly Dennis the Menace #166)
Hallden (Fawcett): No. 16, Jan, 1980 - No. 17, Mar, 1980 (40¢)

	GD 2.0	VG 4.0	FN 6.0	VF 8.0	VF/NM 9.0	NM- 9.2
16,17-By Hank Ketcham	1	2	3	4	5	7

DENNIS THE MENACE POCKET FULL OF FUN!
Fawcett Publications (Hallden): Spring, 1969 - No. 50, March, 1980 (196 pgs.) (Digest size)

	GD 2.0	VG 4.0	FN 6.0	VF 8.0	VF/NM 9.0	NM- 9.2
1-Reprints in all issues	5	10	15	34	60	85
2-10	4	8	12	23	37	50
11-20	3	6	9	15	22	28
21-28	2	4	6	11	16	20
29-50: 35,40,46-Sunday strip-r	2	4	6	8	11	14

NOTE: *No. 1-28 are 196 pgs.; No. 29-36: 164 pgs.; No. 37: 148 pgs.; No. 38 on: 132 pgs. No. 8, 11, 15, 21, 25, 29 all contain strip reprints.*

DENNIS THE MENACE TELEVISION SPECIAL
Fawcett Publ. (Hallden Div.): Summer, 1961 - No. 2, Spring, 1962 (Giant)

	GD 2.0	VG 4.0	FN 6.0	VF 8.0	VF/NM 9.0	NM- 9.2
1	6	12	18	42	79	115
2	3	6	9	21	33	45

DENNIS THE MENACE TRIPLE FEATURE
Fawcett Publications: Winter, 1961 (Giant)

	GD 2.0	VG 4.0	FN 6.0	VF 8.0	VF/NM 9.0	NM- 9.2
1-Wiseman-c/a	6	12	18	42	79	115

DEPT. H
Dark Horse Comics: Apr, 2016 - No. 24, Mar, 2018 ($3.99)

	GD 2.0	VG 4.0	FN 6.0	VF 8.0	VF/NM 9.0	NM- 9.2
1-24-Matt Kindt-s/a. 1-Two covers						4.00

DEPARTMENT OF TRUTH
Image Comics: Sept, 2020 - Present ($3.99)

	GD 2.0	VG 4.0	FN 6.0	VF 8.0	VF/NM 9.0	NM- 9.2
1-James Tynion IV-s/Martin Simmonds-a	3	6	9	14	20	25
2-4-Tynion IV-s/Simmonds-a	1	3	4	6	8	10
5-22: 6-Elsa Charretier-a						4.00

DEPUTY, THE (TV)
Dell Publishing Co.: No. 1077, Feb-Apr, 1960 - No. 1225, Oct-Dec, 1961
(all-Henry Fonda photo-c)

	GD 2.0	VG 4.0	FN 6.0	VF 8.0	VF/NM 9.0	NM- 9.2
Four Color 1077 (#1)-Buscema-a	10	20	30	64	132	200
Four Color 1130 (9-11/60)-Buscema-a,1225	8	16	24	54	102	150

DEPUTY DAWG (TV) (Also see New Terrytoons)
Dell Publishing Co./Gold Key: Oct-Dec, 1961 - No. 1299, 1962; No. 1, Aug, 1965

	GD 2.0	VG 4.0	FN 6.0	VF 8.0	VF/NM 9.0	NM- 9.2
Four Color 1238,1299	9	18	27	63	129	195
1(10164-508)(8/65)-Gold Key	9	18	27	63	129	195

DEPUTY DAWG PRESENTS DINKY DUCK AND HASHIMOTO-SAN (TV)
Gold Key: August, 1965

	GD 2.0	VG 4.0	FN 6.0	VF 8.0	VF/NM 9.0	NM- 9.2
1(10159-508)	9	18	27	57	111	165

DESCENDENT, THE
AfterShock Comics: May, 2019 - No. 5, Sept, 2019 ($3.99)

	GD 2.0	VG 4.0	FN 6.0	VF 8.0	VF/NM 9.0	NM- 9.2
1-5-Stephanie Phillips-s/Evgeniv Bornyakov-a						4.00

DESCENDER (Also see Ascender)
Image Comics: Mar, 2015 - No. 32, Jul, 2018 ($2.99/$3.99)

	GD 2.0	VG 4.0	FN 6.0	VF 8.0	VF/NM 9.0	NM- 9.2
1-Lemire-s/Nguyen-a/c in all; bonus concept-a						5.00
1-Variant-c by Lemire						6.00
2-18-Lemire-s/Nguyen-a/c						3.00
19-32-($3.99)						4.00

DESERT GOLD (See Zane Grey 4-Color 467)

DESIGN FOR SURVIVAL (Gen. Thomas S. Power's...)
American Security Council Press: 1968 (36 pgs. in color) (25¢)

	GD 2.0	VG 4.0	FN 6.0	VF 8.0	VF/NM 9.0	NM- 9.2
nn-Propaganda against the Threat of Communism-Aircraft cover; H-Bomb panel	3	6	9	20	31	42
Twin Circle Edition-Cover shows panels from inside	3	6	9	15	22	28

DESOLATION JONES
DC Comics (WildStorm): July, 2005 - No. 8, Feb, 2007 ($2.95/$2.99)

	GD 2.0	VG 4.0	FN 6.0	VF 8.0	VF/NM 9.0	NM- 9.2
1-8: 1-6-Warren Ellis-s/J.H. Williams-a. 7,8-Zezelj-a						3.00

DESPERADO (Becomes Black Diamond Western No. 9 on)
Lev Gleason Publications: June, 1948 - No. 8, Feb, 1949 (All 52 pgs.)

	GD 2.0	VG 4.0	FN 6.0	VF 8.0	VF/NM 9.0	NM- 9.2
1-Biro-c on all; contains inside photo-c of Charles Biro, Lev Gleason & Bob Wood	20	40	60	117	189	260
2	12	24	36	67	94	120
3-Story with over 20 killings	12	24	36	69	97	125
4-8	9	18	27	50	65	80

NOTE: ***Barry*** *a-2.* ***Fuje*** *a-4, 8.* ***Guardineer*** *a-5-7.* ***Kida*** *a-3-7.* ***Ed Moore*** *a-4, 6.*

DESPERADO PRIMER
Image Comics (Desperado): Apr, 2005 ($1.99, one-shot)

	GD 2.0	VG 4.0	FN 6.0	VF 8.0	VF/NM 9.0	NM- 9.2
1-Previews of Roundeye, World Traveler, A Mirror To The Soul; Bolland-c						3.00

DESPERADOES
Image Comics (Homage): Sept, 1997 - No. 5, June, 1998 ($2.50/$2.95)

	GD 2.0	VG 4.0	FN 6.0	VF 8.0	VF/NM 9.0	NM- 9.2
1-5-Mariotte-s/Cassaday-c/a: 1-($2.50-c). 2-5-($2.95)						3.00
...: A Moment's Sunlight TPB ('98, $16.95) r/#1-5						17.00
...: Epidemic! (11/99, $5.95) Mariotte-s						6.00

DESPERADOES: BANNERS OF GOLD
IDW Publishing: Dec, 2004 - No. 5, Apr, 2005 ($3.99, limited series)

	GD 2.0	VG 4.0	FN 6.0	VF 8.0	VF/NM 9.0	NM- 9.2
1-5: Mariotte-s/Haun-a. 1-Cassaday-c						4.00

DESPERADOES: BUFFALO DREAMS
IDW Publishing: Jan, 2007 - No. 4, Apr, 2007 ($3.99, limited series)

	GD 2.0	VG 4.0	FN 6.0	VF 8.0	VF/NM 9.0	NM- 9.2
1-4: Mariotte-s/Dose-a/c						4.00

DESPERADOES: QUIET OF THE GRAVE
DC Comics (Homage): Jul, 2001 - No. 5, Nov, 2001 ($2.95)

	GD 2.0	VG 4.0	FN 6.0	VF 8.0	VF/NM 9.0	NM- 9.2
1-5-Jeff Mariotte-s/John Severin-c/a						3.00
TPB (2002, $14.95) r/#1-5; intro. by Brian Keene						15.00

DESPERATE TIMES (See Savage Dragon)

Descender #10 © 171 Studios & D. Nguyen

Desperado #1 © LEV

Detective Comics #38 © DC

	GD 2.0	VG 4.0	FN 6.0	VF 8.0	VF/NM 9.0	NM- 9.2

Image Comics: Jun, 1998 - No. 4, Dec, 1998; Nov, 2000 - No. 4, July, 2001 ($2.95, B&W)
1-Chris Eliopoulos-s/a in all 1 2 3 5 6 8
2-4 5.00
(Vol. 2) 1-4 3.00
(Vol. 3) 0-(1/04, $3.50) Pages read sideways 3.50
(Vol. 3) 1-Pages read sideways 3.00

DESPICABLE DEADPOOL (Marvel Legacy)
Marvel Comics: No. 287, Dec, 2017 - No. 300, Jul, 2018 ($3.99)
287-299: 287-Duggan-s/Koblish-a; Cable app. 293-Rogue app. 296-Capt. America app. 4.00
300-($5.99) Avengers and Champions app. 6.00

DESTINATION MOON (See Fawcett Movie Comics, Space Adventures #20, 23, & Strange Adventures #1)

DESTINY: A CHRONICLE OF DEATHS FORETOLD (See Sandman)
DC Comics (Vertigo): 1997 - No. 3, 1998 ($5.95, limited series)
1-3-Alisa Kwitney-s in all: 1-Kent Williams & Michael Zulli-a, Williams painted-c. 2-Williams & Scott Hampton-painted-c/a. 3-Williams & Guay-a 6.00
TPB (2000, $14.95) r/series 2 4 6 11 16 20

DESTROY!!
Eclipse Comics: 1986 ($4.95, B&W, magazine-size, one-shot)
1-Scott McCloud-s/a 4 8 12 23 37 50
3-D Special 1-r-/#1 ($2.50) 2 4 6 9 12 15

DESTROY ALL MONSTERS: A RECKLESS BOOK
Image Comics: Oct, 2021 ($24.99, HC graphic novel)
HC - Ed Brubaker-s/Sean Phillips-a; 3rd book in the Reckless series 25.00

DESTROYER
Marvel Comics: June, 2009 - No. 5, Oct, 2009 ($3.99, limited series)
1-5-Kirkman-s/Walker-a/Pearson-c 4.00

DESTROYER, THE
Marvel Comics (MAX): Nov, 1989 - No. 9, Jun, 1990 ($2.25, B&W, magazine, 52 pgs.)
1-Based on Remo Williams movie, paperbacks 6.00
2-9: 2-Williamson part inks. 4-Ditko-a 4.00

DESTROYER, THE
Marvel Comics: V2#1, March, 1991 ($1.95, 52 pgs.)
V3#1, Dec, 1991 - No. 4, Mar, 1992 ($1.95, mini-series)
V2#1,V3#1-4: Based on Remo Williams paperbacks. V3#1-4-Simonson-c. 3-Morrow-a 4.00

DESTROYER, THE (Also see Solar, Man of the Atom)
Valiant: Apr, 1995 ($2.50/$2.95, color, one-shot)
0-($2.50-c) Indicia indicates #1 4.00
0-($2.95-c) Indicia indicates #1 2 4 6 9 12 15

DESTROYER (VICTOR LAVALLE'S...)
BOOM! Studios: May, 2017 - No. 6, Oct, 2017 ($3.99, limited series)
1-6-LaValle-s/Dietrich Smith-a; Frankenstein's monster app. 4.00

DESTROYER DUCK
Eclipse Comics: Feb, 1982 - No. 7, May, 1984 (#2-7: Baxter paper) ($1.50)
1-Origin Destroyer Duck; 1st app. Groo; Kirby-c/a(p) 6 12 18 38 69 100
2-5: 2-Starling back-up begins; Kirby-c/a(p) thru #5 6.00
6,7 5.00
NOTE: ***Neal Adams** c-1i. **Kirby** c/a-1-5p. **Miller** c-7.*

DESTRUCTOR, THE
Atlas/Seaboard: February, 1975 - No. 4, Aug, 1975
1-Origin/1st app.; Ditko/Wood-a; Wood-c(i) 3 6 9 14 20 26
2-4: 2-Ditko/Wood-a. 3,4-Ditko-a(p) 2 4 6 9 13 16

DETECTIVE COMICS (Also see other Batman titles)
National Periodical Publications/DC Comics: Mar, 1937 - No. 881, Oct, 2011
1-(Scarce)-Slam Bradley & Spy by Siegel & Shuster, Speed Saunders by Stoner and Flessel, Cosmo, the Phantom of Disguise, Buck Marshall, Bruce Nelson begin; Chin Lung in 'Claws of the Red Dragon' serial begins; Vincent Sullivan-c
20,300 40,600 60,900 150,000 -- --
2 (Rare)-Creig Flessel-c begin; new logo 6600 13,200 19,800 43,000 -- --
3 (Rare) 4500 9000 13,500 34,000 -- --
4 3000 6000 9000 16,500 23,250 30,000
5-Larry Steele begins 2200 4400 6600 12,000 17,000 22,000
6,7,9,10 1750 3500 5250 9600 13,550 17,500
8-Mister Chang-c; classic-c 2850 5700 8550 15,700 22,100 28,500
11-14,17,19: 17-1st app. Fu Manchu in Detective 1500 3000 4500 8250 11,625 15,000
15,16-Have interior ad for Action Comics #1 1750 3500 5250 9600 13,550 17,500
18-Classic Fu Manchu-c; last Flessel-c 2400 4800 7200 13,200 18,600 24,000
20-The Crimson Avenger begins (1st app.) 1750 3500 5250 9600 13,550 17,500
21,23-25 1250 2500 3750 6900 9700 12,500
22-1st Crimson Avenger-c by Chambers (12/38) 1550 3100 4650 8500 12,000 15,500
26 1600 3200 4800 8800 12,400 16,000
27-The Bat-Man & Commissioner Gordon begin (1st app.), created by Bill Finger & Bob Kane (5/39); Batman-c (1st)(by Kane). Bat-Man's secret identity revealed as Bruce Wayne in six pg. story. Signed Rob't Kane (also see Det. Picture Stories #5 & Funny Pages V3#1)
307,000 614,000 921,000 2,048,000 3,274,000 4,500,000
27-Reprint, Oversize 13-1/2x10". WARNING: This comic is an exact duplicate reprint of the original except for its size. DC published it in 1974 with a second cover titling it as Famous First Edition. There have been many reported cases of the outer cover being removed and the interior sold as the original edition. The reprint with the new outer cover removed is practically worthless; see Famous First Edition for value.
28-2nd app. The Batman (6 pg. story); non-Bat-Man-c; signed Rob't Kane
11,200 22,400 33,600 61,600 100,800 140,000
29-1st app. Doctor Death-c/story, Batman's 1st name villain. 1st 2 part story (10 pgs.). 2nd Batman-c by Kane 28,000 56,000 84,000 154,000 269,500 385,000
30-Dr. Death app. Story concludes from issue #29. Classic Batman splash panel by Kane.
2900 5800 8700 20,300 33,650 47,000
31-Classic Batman over castle cover; 1st app. The Monk & 1st Julie Madison (Bruce Wayne's 1st love interest); 1st Batplane (Bat-Gyro) and Batarang; 2nd 2-part Batman adventure. Gardner Fox takes over script from Bill Finger. 1st mention of locale (New York City) where Batman lives 45,500 91,000 136,500 254,800 372,400 490,000
32-Batman story concludes from issue #31. 1st app. Dala (Monk's assistant). Batman uses gun for 1st time to slay The Monk and Dala. This was the 1st time a costumed hero used a gun in comic books. 1st Batman head logo on cover
2100 4200 6300 14,500 25,750 37,000
33-Origin The Batman (2 pgs.)(1st told origin); Batman gun holster-c; Batman w/smoking gun panel at end of story. Batman story now 12 pgs. Classic Batman-c
17,200 34,400 51,600 107,500 191,250 275,000
34-2nd Crimson Avenger-c by Creig Flessel and last non Batman-c. Story from issue #32 x-over as Bruce Wayne sees Julie Madison off to America from Paris. Classic Batman splash panel used later in Batman #1 for origin story. Steve Malone begins
2100 4200 6300 15,100 25,550 36,000
35-Classic Batman hypodermic needle-c that reflects story in issue #34. Classic Batman with smoking .45 automatic splash panel. Batman-c begin
19,400 38,800 58,200 124,200 179,600 235,000
36-Batman-c that reflects adventure in issue #35. Origin/1st app. of Dr. Hugo Strange (1st major villain, 2/40). 1st finned-gloves worn by Batman
8600 17,200 25,800 62,400 93,700 125,000
37-Last solo Golden-Age Batman adventure in Detective Comics. Panel at end of story reflects solo Batman adventure in Batman #1 that was originally planned for Detective #38. Cliff Crosby begins 5500 11,000 16,500 39,000 62,000 85,000
38-Origin/1st app. Robin the Boy Wonder (4/40); Batman and Robin-c begin; cover by Kane
16,300 32,600 48,900 114,000 167,000 220,000
39-Opium story; Clayface app. in 1 panel ad at the end of the Batman story
1400 2800 4200 10,600 19,300 28,000
40-Origin & 1st app. Clayface (Basil Karlo); 1st Joker cover app. (6/40); Joker story intended for this issue was used in Batman #1 instead; cover is similar to splash page in 2nd Joker story in Batman #1 3000 6000 9000 20,000 35,000 50,000
41-Robin's 1st solo 519 1038 1557 3789 6698 9600
42-44: 44-Crimson Avenger-new costume 423 846 1269 3046 5323 7600
45-1st Joker story in Det. (3rd book app. & 4th story app. over all, 11/40)
811 1622 2433 5920 10,460 15,000
46-50: 46-Death of Hugo Strange. 48-1st time car called Batmobile (2/41); Gotham City 1st mention in Detective (1st mentioned in Wow #1; also see Batman #4).
49-Last Clayface 389 778 1167 2723 4762 6800
51-53,55-57 300 600 900 2070 3635 5200
54-Cover mimics Detective #33 cover 314 628 942 2198 3849 5500
58-1st Penguin app. (12/41); last Speed Saunders; Fred Ray-c
2650 5300 7950 19,900 29,950 40,000
59-Last Steve Malone; 2nd Penguin; Wing becomes Crimson Avenger's aide.
300 600 900 1980 3440 4900
60-Intro. Air Wave; Joker app. (2nd in Det.) 343 686 1029 2400 4200 6000
61,63: 63-Last Cliff Crosby; 1st app. Mr. Baffle 290 580 870 1856 3178 4500
62-Joker-c/story (2nd Joker-c, 4/42) 1300 2600 3900 9900 17,950 26,000
64-Origin & 1st app. Boy Commandos by Simon & Kirby (6/42); Joker app.
519 1038 1557 3789 6695 9600
65-1st Boy Commandos-c (S&K-a on Boy Commandos & Ray/Robinson-a on Batman & Robin on-c; 4 artists on one-c) 349 698 1047 2548 4824 6100
66-Origin & 1st app. Two-Face (originally named Harvey Kent)
2900 5800 8700 20,600 32,800 45,000
67-1st Penguin-c (9/42) 1000 2000 3000 7600 13,800 20,000
68-Two-Face-c/story; 1st Two-Face-c 865 1730 2595 6315 11,158 16,000
69-Classic Joker with 2 guns in his hands-c 3550 7100 10,650 25,200 40,100 55,000
70 320 640 960 2240 3920 5600
71-Classic Joker black background calendar-c 1575 3150 4725 10,500 18,750 27,000

	GD 2.0	VG 4.0	FN 6.0	VF 8.0	VF/NM 9.0	NM- 9.2
72,74,75: 74-1st Tweedledum & Tweedledee plus-c; S&K-a	245	490	735	1568	2684	3800
73-Scarecrow-c/story (1st Scarecrow-c)	2000	4000	6000	13,300	23,650	34,000
76-Newsboy Legion & The Sandman x-over in Boy Commandos; S&K-a; Joker-c/story	465	930	1395	3395	5998	8600
77-79: All S&K-a	206	412	618	1318	2259	3200
80-Two-Face-c/sty; S&K-a	300	600	900	1950	3575	4800
81,82,84,86-90: 81-1st Cavalier-c & app. 87-Penguin app. 89-Last Crimson Avenger; 2nd Cavalier-c & app.	171	342	513	1086	1868	2650
83-1st "skinny" Alfred (1/44)(see Batman #21; last S&K Boy Commandos (also #92,128); most issues #84-on signed S&K are not by them	194	388	582	1242	2121	3000
85-Joker-c/story; last Spy; Kirby/Klech Boy Commandos	459	918	1377	3350	5925	8500
91-Joker-c/story	343	686	1029	2400	4200	6000
92-98: 96-Alfred's last name 'Beagle' revealed, later changed to 'Pennyworth' in #214	135	270	405	864	1482	2100
99-Penguin-c/story	206	412	618	1318	2259	3200
100 (6/45)	171	342	513	1095	1873	2650
101,103-107,110-113,115-117,119	119	238	357	762	1306	1850
102-Joker-c/story	300	600	900	2010	3505	5000
108-1st Bat-signal-c (2/46)	459	918	1377	3350	5925	8500
109-Joker-c/story	337	674	1011	2359	4130	5900
114,118-Joker-c/stories. 114-1st small logo (8/46)	300	600	900	2070	3635	5200
120-Penguin-c/story	232	464	696	1485	2543	3600
121,123,125,127,129,130	119	238	357	762	1306	1850
122-1st Catwoman-c (4/47)	1000	2000	3000	7400	13,200	19,000
124,128-Joker-c/stories	290	580	870	1856	3178	4500
126-Penguin-c	187	374	561	1197	2049	2900
131-134,136,139	113	226	339	718	1234	1750
135-Frankenstein-c/story	171	342	513	1086	1868	2650
137-Joker-c/story; last Air Wave	300	600	900	2010	3505	5000
138-Origin Robotman (see Star Spangled #7 for 1st app.); series ends #202	174	348	522	1114	1907	2700
140-The Riddler-c/story (1st app., 10/48)	3625	7250	10,875	24,200	41,100	58,000
141,143-148,150: 150-Last Boy Commandos	113	226	339	718	1234	1750
142-2nd Riddler-c/story	649	1298	1947	4738	8369	12,000
149-Joker-c/story	245	490	735	1568	2684	3800
151-Origin & 1st app. Pow Wow Smith, Indian lawman (9/49) & begins series	129	258	387	826	1413	2000
152,154,155,157-160: 152-Last Slam Bradley	113	226	339	718	1234	1750
153-1st app. Roy Raymond TV Detective (11/49); origin The Human Fly	126	252	378	806	1378	1950
156(2/50)-The new classic Batmobile	383	766	1149	2681	4691	6700
161-167,169,170,172-176: Last 52 pg. issue	110	220	330	704	1202	1700
168-Origin the Joker	4075	8150	12,225	25,400	40,200	55,000
171-Penguin-c	181	362	543	1158	1979	2800
177-179,181-186,188,189,191,192,194-199,201,202,204,206-210,212,214-216: 184-1st app. Fire Fly. 185-Secret of Batman's utility belt. 202-Last Robotman & Pow Wow Smith. 215-1st app. of Batmen of all Nations. 216-Last precode (2/55)	106	212	318	673	1162	1650
180,193-Joker-c/story	239	478	717	1530	2615	3700
187-Two-Face-c/story	354	708	1062	2478	4339	6200
190-Origin Batman retold	142	284	426	909	1555	2200
200(10/53), 205: 205-Origin Batcave	123	246	369	787	1344	1900
203,211-Catwoman-c/stories	161	322	483	1030	1765	2500
213-Origin & 1st app. Mirror Man	142	284	426	909	1555	2200
217-224: 218-Batman Jr. & Robin Sr. app.	90	180	270	576	988	1400
225-(11/55)-1st app. Martian Manhunter (J'onn J'onzz); origin begins; also see Batman #78	1775	3550	5325	13,100	31,550	50,000
226-Origin Martian Manhunter cont'd (2nd app.)	219	438	657	1402	2401	3400
227-229: Martian Manhunter stories in all	100	200	300	635	1093	1550
230-1st app. Mad Hatter (imposter, not the one from Batman #49, this one's appearance inspired the 1966 TV version); brief recap origin of Martian Manhunter	423	846	1269	3046	5323	7600
231-Brief origin recap Martian Manhunter	77	154	231	493	847	1200
232,234,237,238,240	68	136	204	435	743	1050
233-Origin & 1st app. Batwoman (7/56)	865	1730	2595	6315	11,158	16,000
235-Origin Batman & his costume; tells how Bruce Wayne's father (Thomas Wayne) wore Bat costume & fought crime (reprinted in Batman #255)	135	270	405	864	1482	2100
236-1st S.A. issue; J'onn J'onzz talks to parents and Mars-1st since being stranded on Earth; 1st app. Bat-Tank?	81	162	243	518	884	1250
239-Early DC grey tone-c	106	212	318	673	1162	1650
241-Rainbow Batman cover and story	174	348	522	1114	1907	2700
242-260: 246-Intro. Diane Meade, John Jones' girl. 249-Batwoman-c/app. 253-1st app. The Terrible Trio. 254-Bat-Hound-c/story. 257-Intro. & 1st app. Whirly Bats. 259-1st app. The Calendar Man	54	108	162	343	574	825
261-264,266,268-271: 261-J. Jones tie-in to sci/fi movie "Incredible Shrinking Man"; 1st app. Dr. Double X. 262-Origin Jackal. 268,271-Manhunter origin recap	42	84	126	265	445	625
265-Batman's origin retold with new facts	61	122	183	390	670	950
267-Origin & 1st app. Bat-Mite (5/59)	271	542	813	1734	2967	4200
272,274,275,277-280	37	74	111	218	354	490
273-J'onn J'onzz i.d. revealed for 1st time	39	78	117	240	395	550
276-2nd app. Bat-Mite	57	114	171	362	619	875
281-292, 294-297: 286,292-Batwoman-c/app. 287-Origin J'onn J'onzz retold. 289-Bat-Mite-c/story. 292-Last Roy Raymond. 297-Last 10¢ issue (11/61)	29	58	87	172	281	390
293-(7/61)-Aquaman begins (pre #1); ends #300	36	72	108	211	343	475
298-(12/61)-1st modern Clayface (Matt Hagen)	194	388	582	1242	2121	3000
299	29	58	87	172	281	390
300-(2/62)-1st Polka-Dot Man; Aquaman ends	103	206	309	659	1130	1600
301-(3/62)-J'onn J'onzz returns to Mars (1st time since stranded on Earth six years before)	15	30	45	105	233	360
302-Batwoman-c/app.	18	36	54	124	275	425
303-306,308-310,312-317,319-321,323,324,326,329,330: 321-2nd Terrible Trio. 326-Last J'onn J'onzz, story cont'd in House of Mystery #143; intro. Idol-Head of Diabolu	11	22	33	73	157	240
307-Batwoman-c/app.	12	24	36	82	179	275
311-1st app. Cat-Man; intro. Zook in John Jones	28	56	84	202	451	700
318-Cat-Man-c/story (2nd app.); also 1st app. Batwoman as the Cat-Woman	25	50	75	175	388	600
322,325: 322-Bat-Girl's 1st/only app. in Det. (6th in all); Batman cameo in J'onn J'onzz (only hero to app. in series). 325-Cat-Man-c/story (3rd app.); also 2nd app. Batwoman as the Cat-Woman	14	28	42	96	211	325
327-(5/64)-Elongated Man begins, ends #383; 1st new look Batman with new costume; Infantino/Giella new look-a begins; Batman with gun	18	36	54	124	275	425
328-Death of Alfred; Bob Kane biog, 2 pgs.	14	28	42	96	211	325
331,333-340: 334-1st app. The Outsider	9	18	27	61	123	185
332,341,365-Joker-c/stories	12	24	36	82	179	275
342-358,360,361,366-368: 345-Intro Block Buster. 347-"What If" theme story (1/66). 350-Elongated Man new costume. 355-Zatanna x-over in Elongated Man. 356-Alfred brought back in Batman, early SA app.	9	18	27	59	117	175
359-Intro/origin Batgirl (Barbara Gordon)-c/story (1/67); 1st Silver Age app. Killer Moth; classic Batgirl-c	197	394	591	1625	3663	5700
359-Facsimile Edition (2020, $3.99) Reprints issue with original ads and letter column	2	4	6	9	12	15
362,364-S.A. Riddler app. (early)	9	18	27	63	129	195
363-2nd app. new Batgirl	26	52	78	182	404	625
369(11/67)-N. Adams-a (Elongated Man); 3rd app. S.A. Catwoman (cameo; leads into Batman #197); 4th app. new Batgirl	20	40	60	138	307	475
370-1st Neal Adams-a on Batman (cover only, 12/67)	11	22	33	76	163	250
371-(1/68) 1st new Batmobile from TV show; classic Batgirl-c	16	32	48	111	246	380
372-376,378-386,389,390: 375-New Batmobile-c	7	14	21	48	89	130
377-S.A. Riddler-c/sty	8	16	24	55	105	155
387-r/1st Batman story from #27 (30th anniversary, 5/69); Joker-c; last 12¢ issue	12	24	36	79	170	260
388-Joker-c/story	12	24	36	82	179	275
391-394,396,398,399,401,403,406,409: 392-1st app. Jason Bard. 401-2nd Batgirl/Robin team-up	7	14	21	46	86	125
395-1st Neal Adams art on Detective	20	40	60	138	307	475
397,402,404,407,408,410-Neal Adams-a. 402-Man-Bat-c/app. (2nd app.). 404-Tribute to Enemy Ace	12	24	36	80	173	265
400-(6/70)-Origin & 1st app. Man-Bat; 1st Batgirl/Robin team-up (cont'd in #401); Neal Adams-a	40	80	120	296	673	1050
405-Debut League of Assassins	30	60	90	216	483	750
411-(5/71) Intro. Talia, daughter of Ra's al Ghul (Ra's mentioned, but doesn't appear until Batman #232 (6/71); Bob Brown-a	40	80	120	296	673	1050
412-413: 413-Last 15¢ issue	7	14	21	46	86	125
414-424: All-25¢, 52 pgs. 418-Creeper x-over. 424-Last Batgirl.	7	14	21	48	89	130
425-436: 426,430,436-Elongated Man app. 428,434-Hawkman begins, ends #467	5	10	15	34	60	85
437-New Manhunter begins (10-11/73, 1st app.) by Simonson, ends #443	6	12	18	38	69	100
438-440,442-445 (All 100 Page Super Spectaculars): 438-Kubert Hawkman-r. 439-Origin Manhunter. 440-G.A. Manhunter(Adv. #79) by S&K, Hawkman, Dollman, Green Lantern; Toth-a. 442-G.A. Newsboy Legion, Black Canary, Elongated Man, Dr. Fate-r. 443-Origin The Creeper-r; death of Manhunter; G.A. Green Lantern, Spectre-r; Batman-r/Batman #18. 444-G.A. Kid Eternity-r. 445-G.A. Dr. Midnite-r	7	14	21	44	82	120
441-(6,7/74)(100 Page S.S.) 1st app. Lt. (Harvey) Bullock, first name not given, appears in only 3 panels; G.A. Plastic Man, Batman, Ibis-r	8	16	24	51	96	140
446-456,458-460	3	6	9	19	30	40
457-Classic origin-c; origin retold & updated; 1st app. Leslie Thompkins	10	20	30	69	147	225
461,462,464,465,470,480: 480-(44 pgs.). 470-Intro. Silver St. Cloud	3	6	9	17	26	35
463-1st app. Black Spider	5	10	15	30	50	70
466-468,471-473,478,479-Rogers-a in all: 466-1st app. Signalman since Batman #139. 470,471-1st modern app. Hugo Strange. 478-1st app. 3rd Clayface (Preston Payne). 479-(44 pgs.)	4	8	12	27	44	60
469-Intro/origin Dr. Phosphorous; Simonson-a	5	10	15	31	53	75
474-1st app. new Deadshot	7	14	21	48	89	130
475-Joker-c/story; Rogers-a	9	18	27	62	126	190
475-Facsimile Edition (2020, $3.99) Reprints issue with original ads and letter column	1	3	4	6	8	10
476-Joker-c/story; Rogers-a	6	12	18	42	79	115
477-Neal Adams-a(r); Rogers-a (3 pgs.)	4	8	12	25	40	55
481-(Combined with Batman Family, 12-1/78-79, begin $1.00, 68 pg. issues, ends #495); 481-495-Batgirl, Robin solo stories	4	8	12	25	40	55
482,483: 482-Starlin/Russell, Golden-a; The Demon begins (origin-r), ends #485 (by Ditko #483-485). 483-40th Anniversary issue; origin retold in brief; Newton Batman begins; Human Target with Chaykin-a; Batman Family pin-up on back-c	3	6	9	16	23	30
484-495 (68 pgs): 484-Origin Robin. 485-Death of Batwoman. 486-Killer Moth app. 487-The Odd Man by Ditko. 489-Robin/Batgirl team-up. 490-Black Lightning begins. 491-(#492 on inside). 493-Intro. The Swashbuckler	2	4	6	10	14	18
496-499: 496-Clayface app.	2	4	6	8	11	14
500-($1.50, 52 pgs.)-Batman/Deadman team-up with Infantino-a; new Hawkman story by Joe Kubert; incorrectly says 500th Anniv. of Det.	3	6	9	18	28	38
501-503,505-522: 509-Catman-c. 510-Mad Hatter-c. 512-2nd app. new Dr. Death. 513-Two-Face app. 519-Last Batgirl. 521-Green Arrow series begins	2	4	6	8	10	12
504-Joker-c/story	3	6	9	14	19	24
523-1st Killer Croc (cameo); Solomon Grundy app.	4	8	12	28	47	65
524-2nd app. Jason Todd (cameo)(3/83)	4	8	12	28	47	65
525-3rd app. Jason Todd (See Batman #357)	3	6	9	19	30	40
526-Batman's 500th app. in Detective Comics ($1.50, 68 pgs.); Death of Jason Todd's parents, Joker-c/story (55 pgs.); Bob Kane pin-up	3	6	9	18	28	38
527-531,533,534,536-553,555-568,571,573: 538-Cat-Man-c/story cont'd from Batman #371. 542-Jason Todd quits as Robin (becomes Robin again #547). 549,550-Alan Moore scripts						

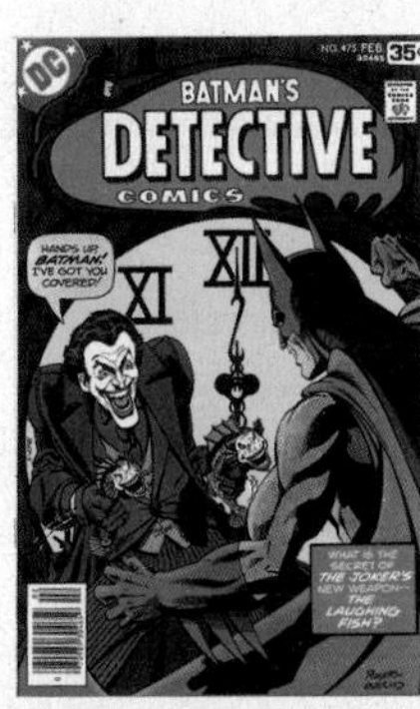

Detective Comics #475 © DC

Detective Comics #820 © DC

Detective Comics (2011) #9 © DC

GD 2.0 | VG 4.0 | FN 6.0 | VF 8.0 | VF/NM 9.0 | NM- 9.2

(Green Arrow). 566-Batman villains profiled. 567-Harlan Ellison scripts 1 3 4 6 8 10

532,569,570-Joker-c/stories 3 6 9 15 22 28

535-Intro new Robin (Jason Todd)-1st appeared in Batman 2 4 6 9 12 15

554-1st new Black Canary (9/85) 2 4 6 10 14 18

572-(3/87, $1.25, 60 pgs.)-50th Anniv. of Det. Comics 2 4 6 8 10 12

574-Origin Batman & Jason Todd retold 2 4 6 10 14 18

575-578: Year 2; McFarlane-c/a; The Reaper app. 3 6 9 19 30 40

579-584,586-597,599,601-607,609,610: 579-New bat wing logo. 583-1st app. villains Scarface & Ventriloquist. 589,595-(52 pgs.)-Each contain free 16 pg. Batman stories. 604-607-Mudpack storyline; 604,607-Contain Batman mini-posters. 610-Faked death of Penguin; artists names app. on tombstone on-c 1 2 3 5 6 8

585-The Ratcatcher debut (4/88) 2 4 6 8 10 12

598-($2.95, 84 pgs.)- "Blind Justice" storyline begins by Batman movie writer Sam Hamm, ends #600 2 4 6 8 10 12

600-(5/89, $2.95, 84 pgs.)-50th Anniv. of Batman in Det.; 1 pg. Neal Adams pin-up, among other artists 2 4 6 9 12 15

608-1st app. Anarky 3 6 9 14 19 24

611-626,628-646,649-658: 612-1st new look Cat-Man; Catwoman app. 615- "The Penguin Affair" part 2 (See Batman #448,449). 617-Joker-c/story. 624-1st new Catwoman (w/death) & 1st new Batwoman. 626-Batman's 600th app. in Detective. 642-Return of Scarface, part 2. 644-Last $1.00-c. 644-646-The (2nd) Electrocutioner (Lester Buchinsky) app. 652,653-Huntress-c/story w/new costume plus Charest-c on both 1 2 3 5 6 8

627-($2.95, 84 pgs.)-Batman's 601st app. in Det.; reprints 1st story/#27 plus 3 versions (2 new) of same story 2 4 6 8 10 12

647-1st app. Stephanie Brown 3 6 9 17 26 35

648-1st full app. Spoiler (Stephanie Brown) 2 4 6 8 11 14

659-664: 659-Knightfall part 2; Kelley Jones-c. 660-Knightfall part 4; Bane-c by Sam Kieth. 661-Knightfall part 6; brief Joker & Riddler app. 662-Knightfall part 8; Riddler app.; Sam Kieth-c. 663-Knightfall part 10; Kelley Jones-c. 664-Knightfall part 12; Bane-c/story; Joker app.; continued in Showcase 93 #7 & 8; Jones-c 1 3 4 6 8 10

665-675: 665,666-Knightfall parts 16 & 18; 666-Bane-c/story. 667-Knightquest: The Crusade & new Batman begins (1st app. in Batman #500). 669-Begin $1.50-c; Knightquest, cont'd in Robin #1. 671,673-Joker app. 6.00

675-($2.95)-Collectors edition w/foil-c 1 2 3 5 6 8

676-($2.50, 52 pgs.)-KnightsEnd pt. 3 1 2 3 5 6 8

677,678: 677-KnightsEnd pt. 9. 678-(9/94)-Zero Hour tie-in. 6.00

679-685: 679-(11/94). 682-Troika pt. 3 5.00

682-($2.50) Embossed-c Troika pt. 3 6.00

686-699,701-719: 686-Begin $1.95-c. 693,694-Poison Ivy-c/app. 695-Contagion pt. 2; Catwoman, Penguin app. 696-Contagion pt. 8. 698-Two-Face-c/app. 701-Legacy pt. 6; Batman vs. Bane-c/app. 702-Legacy Epilogue. 703-Final Night x-over. 705-707-Riddler-app. 714,715-Martian Manhunter-app. 5.00

700-($4.95, Collectors Edition)-Legacy pt. 1; Ra's Al Ghul-c/app; Talia & Bane app; book displayed at shops in envelope 2 4 6 8 11 14

700-($2.95, Regular Edition)-Different-c 1 3 4 6 8 10

720-736,738,739: 720,721-Cataclysm pts. 5,14. 723-Green Arrow app. 730-740-No Man's Land stories. 735-1st app. Mercy Graves in regular DCU 5.00

737-Harley Quinn-c/app. (1st app. in Detective); No Man's Land 3 6 9 16 23 30

740-Joker, Bane-c/app.; Harley Quinn app.; No Man's Land 2 4 6 8 11 14

741-($2.50) Endgame; Joker-c/app.; Harley Quinn app. 1 3 4 6 8 10

742-749,751-765: 742-New look Batman begins; 1st app. Crispus Allen (who later becomes the Spectre). 751,752-Poison Ivy app. 756-Superman-c/app. 759-762-Catwoman back-up 4.00

750-($4.95, 64 pgs.) Ra's al Ghul-c 1 2 3 4 5 7

766-772: 766,767-Bruce Wayne: Murderer pt. 1,8. 769-772-Bruce Wayne: Fugitive pts. 4,8,12,16 4.00

773,774,776-782,784-799: 773-Begin $2.75-c; Sienkiewicz-c. 777-784-Sale-c. 784-786-Alan Scott app. 787-Mad Hatter app. 797-799-War Games 4.00

775-($3.50) Sienkiewicz-c 5.00

783-1st Nyssa 1 3 4 6 8 10

800-($3.50) Jock-c; aftermath of War Games; back-up by Lapham 5.00

801-830,832-836,838-849,851,852: 801-814-Lapham-s. 804-Mr. Freeze app. 809-War Crimes. 817-820: One Year Later 8-part x-over with Batman #651-654; Robinson-s/Bianchi-c. 819-Begin $2.99-c. 820-Dini-s/Williams III-a. 821-Harley Quinn app. 825-Dr. Phosphorus app. 827-Debut of new Scarface. 833,834-Zatanna & Joker app. 838,839-Resurrection of Ra's al Ghul x-over. 846-847-Batman R.I.P. x-over 4.00

817,818,838,839-2nd printings. 817-Combo-c of #817̳ cover images. 818-Combo-c of #818 and Batman #653 cover images. 838-Andy Kubert variant-c. 839-Red bkgd-c 4.00

831,837-Harley Quinn-c/app. 831-Dini-s 1 3 4 6 8 10

850-($3.99) Batman vs. Hush; Dini-s/Nguyen-a 6.00

853-($3.99) Gaiman-s/Andy Kubert-a; continued from Batman #686; Kubert sketch pgs. 4.00

GD 2.0 | VG 4.0 | FN 6.0 | VF 8.0 | VF/NM 9.0 | NM- 9.2

853-Variant-c with red background by Andy Kubert 3 6 9 14 20 25

854-872-($3.99) 854-Batwoman features begin; Rucka-a/J.H. Williams-a/c; The Question back-ups begin. 858-860-Batwoman origin. 871-1st Scott Snyder Batman-s 5.00

854,858,859,860-Variant-c: 854-JG Jones. 858-Hughes. 859-Jock. 860-Alex Ross 6.00

854-Special Edition (8/10, $1.00) reprints issue with "What's Next?" logo on cover 3.00

873-879-($2.99) 874,875,879-Francavilla-a 4.00

880-Joker-c/app.; Jock-c/a 10 20 30 64 132 200

881-(10/11) Last issue of first volume; Snyder-s/Jock & Francavilla-a 2 4 6 11 16 20

#0-(10/94) Zero Hour tie-in, released between #678 & 679 4.00

#27-Facsimile Edition (2022, $6.99) Reprints entire issue with original ads 7.00

#38-Facsimile Edition (2020, $3.99) Reprints issue with original ads and letter column 4.00

#38-Facsimile Edition (2022, $6.99) Reprints issue with original ads and letter column 7.00

#1,000,000 (11/98) 853rd Century x-over 5.00

Annual 1 (1988, $1.50) 1 3 4 6 8 10

Annual 2-7,9 ('89-'94, '96, 68 pgs.)-4-Painted-c. 5-Joker-c/story (54 pgs.) continued in Robin Annual #1; Sam Kieth-c; Eclipso app. 6-Azrael as Batman in new costume; intro Geist the Twilight Man; Bloodlines storyline. 7-Elseworlds story. 9-Legends of the Dead Earth story 1 2 3 4 5 7

Annual 8 (1995, $3.95, 68 pgs.)-Year One story 5.00

Annual 10 (1997, $3.95)-Pulp Heroes story 5.00

Annual 11 (12/09, $4.99)-Azrael & The Question app.; continued from Batman Ann. #27 5.00

Annual 12 (2/11, $4.99)-Nightrunner & The Question app.; continued in Batman Ann. #28 5.00

NOTE: **Neal Adams** *c-370, 372, 385, 389, 391, 392, 394-422, 439.* **Aparo** *a-437, 438, 444-446, 500, 625-632p, 638-643p; c-430, 437, 440-446, 448, 468-470, 480, 484(back), 492-502,508, 509, 515, 518-522, 641, 716, 719, 722, 724.* **Austin** *a(i)-450, 451, 463-468, 471-476; c(i)-474-476, 478.* **Baily** *a-443r.* **Buckler** *a-434, 446p, 479p; c(p)-467, 482, 505-507, 511, 513-516, 518.* **Burnley** *a(Batman)-65, 75, 78, 83, 100, 103, 125; c-62i, 63i, 64, 73i, 78, 83p, 96p, 103p, 105p, 106, 108, 121p, 123p, 125p.* **Chaykin** *a-441.* **Colan** *a(p)-510, 512, 517, 523, 528-538, 540-546, 555-567; c(p)-510, 512, 528, 530-535, 537, 538, 540, 541, 543-545, 556-558, 560-564.* **J. Craig** *a-488.* **Ditko** *a-443r, 483-485, 487.* **Golden** *a-482p; c-625, 626, 628-631, 633, 644-646.* **Alan Grant** *scripts-584-597, 601-621, 641, 642, Annual 5.* **Grell** *a-445, 455, 463p, 464p; c-455.* **Guardineer** *c-23, 24, 26, 28, 30, 32.* **Gustavson** *a-441r.* **Infantino** *a-354, 442(2)r, 500, 572.* **Infantino/Anderson** *c-333, 337-340, 343, 344, 347, 351, 352, 359, 361-368, 371.* **Kelley Jones** *c-651, 657i, 658i, 659, 661, 663-675.* **Kaluta** *c-423, 424, 426-428, 431, 434, 438, 484, 486, 572.* **Bob Kane** *a-Most early issues #27 on, 297r, 356r, 438-440r, 442r, 443r.* **Kane/Robinson** *c-33.* **Gil Kane** *a(p)-368, 370-374, 384, 385, 388-407, 438r, 439r, 520.* **Kane/Anderson** *c-369.* **Sam Kieth** *c-654-656 (657, 658 w/***Kelley Jones***), 660, 662, Annual #5.* **Kubert** *a-438r, 439r, 500; c-348-350.* **McFarlane** *c/a(p)-576-578.* **Meskin** *a-420r.* **Mignola** *c-583.* **Moldoff** *c-233-354, 259, 266, 267, 275, 287, 289, 290, 297, 300.* **Moldoff/Giella** *a-328, 330, 332, 334, 336, 338, 340, 342, 344, 346, 348, 350, 352, 354, 356.* **Mooney** *a-444r.* **Moreira** *a-153-300, 419r, 444r, 445r.* **Nasser/Netzer** *a-654, 655, 657, 658.* **Newton** *a(p)-480, 481, 483-499, 501-509, 511, 513-516, 518-520, 524, 526, 539; c-526p.* **Irv Novick** *c-375-377, 383.* **Robbins** *a-426p, 429p.* **Robinson** *a-part: 66, 68, 71-73; all: 74-76, 79, 80; c-62, 64, 66, 68-74, 76, 79, 82, 86, 88, 442r, 443r.* **Rogers** *a-466-468, 471-479p, 481p; c-471p, 472p, 473, 474-479p.* **Roussos** *Airwave-76-105(most); c(i)-71, 72, 74-76, 79, 107.* **Russell** *a-481i, 482i.* **Simon/Kirby** *a-440r, 442r.* **Simonson** *a-437-443, 450, 469, 470, 500.* **Dick Sprang** *c-77, 82, 84, 85, 87, 89-93, 95-100, 102, 103i, 104i, 106, 108, 114, 117, 118, 122, 123, 128, 129, 131, 133, 135, 141, 148, 149, 168, 622-624.* **Starlin** *a-481p, 482p; c-503, 504, 567p.* **Starr** *a-444r.* **Toth** *a-442; r-414, 416, 418, 424, 440-441, 443, 444.* **Tuska** *a-486p, 490p.* **Matt Wagner** *c-647-649.* **Wrightson** *c-425.*

DETECTIVE COMICS (DC New 52)(Numbering reverts to original series #934 after #52)
DC Comics: Nov, 2011 - No. 52, Jul, 2016 ($2.99/$3.99)

1-Joker app.; Tony Daniel-s/a/c 3 6 9 16 23 30

2-7: 2-Intro of The Dollmaker. 5-7-Penguin app. 5.00

8,10-14,16-18: 8-($3.99) Catwoman & Scarecrow app.; back-up Two-Face story begins 4.00

9-Night of the Owls 5.00

15-Die-cut Joker cover; Death of the Family tie-in 8.00

19-(6/13, $7.99) 900th issue of Detective; bonus back-up stories and pin-up art 8.00

20-24,26: 21-23-Man-Bat back-up story. 26-Man-Bat app. 4.00

23.1, 23.2, 23.3, 23.4 (11/13, $2.99, regular covers) 1 2 3 5 6 8

23.1 (11/13, $3.99, 3-D cover) "Poison Ivy #1" on cover; Fridolfs-s/Pina-a 2 4 6 9 12 15

23.2 (11/13, $3.99, 3-D cover) "Harley Quinn #1" on cover; Googe-a/Kindt-s; origin 2 4 6 13 18 22

23.3 (11/13, $3.99, 3-D cover) "Scarecrow #1" on cover; Kudranski-a 15.00

23.4 (11/13, $3.99, 3-D cover) "Man-Bat #1" on cover; Tieri-s/Eaton-a 15.00

25-($3.99) Zero Year focus on Lt. Gordon; Fabok-a/c; Man-Bat back-up 4.00

27-($7.99) Start of Gothtopia; short stories by Meltzer, Hitch, Neal Adams, Francavilla, Murphy 8.00

28-49,51,52: 28,29-Gothtopia. 30-34,37-40-Manupul-a. 37-40-Anarky app. 43,44-Joker's Daughter. 45,46-Justice League app. 47-"Robin War" tie-in 4.00

50-($4.99) Bonus pin-up swipes of classic Detective covers by various 5.00

#0 (11/12, $3.99) Flashback to training and return to Alfred 4.00

Annual 1 (10/12, $4.99) Black Mask app.; Daniel-s/c; Molenaar-a 5.00

Annual 2 (9/13, $4.99) The Wrath app.; Eaton-a/Clarke-c 5.00

Annual 3 (9/14, $4.99) March-c 5.00

...: Endgame 1 (5/15, $2.99) Tie-in to Endgame story in Batman #35-40; Anarky app. 3.00

...: Futures End 1 (11/14, $2.99, regular-c) Five years later; Riddler app. 3.00

...: Futures End 1 (11/14, $3.99, 3-D cover) 4.00

DETECTIVE COMICS (Numbering reverts to original V1 #934 after #52 from 2011-2016 series)
DC Comics: No. 934, Aug, 2016 - Present ($2.99/$3.99)

934-Tynion IV-s/Barrows-a; Batwoman, Spoiler, Red Robin, Clayface app.

	GD 2.0	VG 4.0	FN 6.0	VF 8.0	VF/NM 9.0	NM- 9.2

1 2 3 5 6 8
935-949,951-974: 936-938-Alvaro Martinez-a. 937-Intro. Ulysses Armstrong. 940-Apparent death of Tim Drake. 941,942-Night of the Monster Men x-over. 944-Batwing returns. 948,949-Batwoman begins. 951-956-"League of Shadows." 958-961-Zatanna app. 965-Tim Drake vs. Mr. Oz. 965-967-Future Batman (Tim Drake) app. 3.00
950-($3.99) Prologue to "League of Shadows"; Takara-a; Shiva & Azrael app. 4.00
975-($3.99) Trial of Batwoman; Tynion IV-s/Martinez-a 4.00
976-987: 976-Batmen Eternal begins. 983-987-Black Lightning app. 3.00
988-999-($3.99) 989-993-Two-Face app. 994-999-Mahnke-a 4.00
1000-(5/19, $9.99) Short stories and pin-ups by various incl. Snyder/Capullo, Kevin Smith/Jim Lee, Dini/Nguyen, Ellis/Cloonan, O'Neil/Epting, Priest/Adams, Bendis/Maleev; Johns/Kelley Jones, Tynion IV/Martinez-Bueno, Daniel/Joëlle Jones; Slam Bradley app.; intro. The Arkham Knight by Tomasi-s/Mahnke-a; 10 regular covers 15.00
1001-1023: 1001-1005-Arkham Knight app. 1004-Arkham Knight origin. 1006,1007-Spectre app.; Kyle Hotz-a 1008-Joker app. 1008-1016-Mr. Freeze app. 1009-1011-Deadshot app. 1013-Nora Fries revived. 1023-Joker War tie-in
1024-1026-Joker War tie-ins. 1026-Killer Croc app. 2 4 6 8 10 12
1027-(11/20, $9.99) Short stories by various incl. Bendis-s/Marquez-a, Fraction-s/Zdarsky-a, Rucka-s/Risso-a, King-s/Simonson-a, Snyder-s/Reis-a; Jurgens-s/a with 1930s Batman meets Kamandi (leads into Generations Shattered #1); bonus pin-ups; multiple covers 12.00
1028-1033: 1029-Debut The Mirror. 1131-1133-Hush app. 4.00
1034-1049, 1051-1069-($4.99): 1044-1046-"Fear State" tie-ins. 1047-1049-Reis-a 5.00
1050-($5.99)-Shadows of the Bat; Psycho Pirate app.; bonus preview of World's Finest #1 6.00
Annual 1 (3/18, $4.99) Tynion IV-s/Barrows-a; Clayface origin re-told 5.00
Annual 2 (7/19, $4.99) Tomasi-s/Travis Moore-a; The Reaper app. 5.00
Annual 3 (Late March/20, $4.99) Spotlight on Alfred; back-up with Risso-a; Rude-c 5.00
2021 Annual 1 (1/22, $5.99) Prelude to Shadows of the Bat; Lapham-a 6.00
2022 Annual 1 (1/22, $5.99) Flashback to the Gathome Settlement in 1776; Mitten-a 6.00

DETECTIVE COMICS: BATMAN 80TH ANNIVERSARY GIANT
DC Comics: 2019 ($4.99, 100 pgs., squarebound, Walmart exclusive)

1-New story Venditti-s/Segovia-a; Two-Face app.; reprints 1st apps. of Batman, Robin, Batgirl, Leslie Thompkins, plus stories from Detective #500 and Batman Black and White #4 8 16 24 56 108 160

DETECTIVE DAN, SECRET OP. 48 (Also see Adventures of Detective Ace King and Bob Scully, The Two-Fisted Hick Detective)
Humor Publ. Co. (Norman Marsh): 1933 (10¢, 10x13", 36 pgs., B&W, one-shot) (3 color, cardboard-c)

nn-By Norman Marsh, 1st comic w/ original-a; 1st newsstand-c; Dick Tracy look-alike; forerunner of Dan Dunn. (Title and Wu Fang character inspired Detective Comics #1 four years later.) (1st comic of a single theme) 2160 4320 6480 13,000 -- --

DETECTIVE EYE (See Keen Detective Funnies)
Centaur Publications: Nov, 1940 - No. 2, Dec, 1940

1-Air Man (see Keen Detective) & The Eye Sees begins; The Masked Marvel & Dean Denton app. 300 600 900 1980 3440 4900
2-Origin Don Rance and the Mysticape; Binder-a; Frank Thomas-c 245 490 735 1568 2684 3800

DETECTIVE PICTURE STORIES (Keen Detective Funnies No. 8 on?)
Comics Magazine Company: Dec, 1936 - No. 5, Apr, 1937

1 (All issues are very scarce) 700 1400 2100 4000 6500 9000
2-The Clock app. (1/37, early app.) 360 720 1080 2050 3375 4700
3,4: 4-Eisner-a 300 600 900 1700 2800 3900
5-The Clock-c/story (4/37); "The Case of the Missing Heir" 1st detective/adventure art by Bob Kane; Bruce Wayne prototype app. (story reprinted in Funny Pages V3 #1) 500 1000 1500 2850 4725 6600

DETECTIVES, THE (TV)
Dell Publishing Co.: No. 1168, Mar-May, 1961 - No. 1240, Oct-Dec, 1961

Four Color 1168 (#1)-Robert Taylor photo-c 10 20 30 66 138 210
Four Color 1219-Robert Taylor, Adam West photo-c 10 20 30 66 138 210
Four Color 1240-Tufts-a; Robert Taylor photo-c; 2 different back-c 8 16 24 51 96 140

DETECTIVES, INC. (See Eclipse Graphic Album Series)
Eclipse Comics: Apr, 1985 - No. 2, Apr, 1985 ($1.75, both w/April dates)

1,2: 2-Nudity 4.00

DETECTIVES, INC.: A TERROR OF DYING DREAMS
Eclipse Comics: Jun, 1987 - No. 3, Dec, 1987 ($1.75, B&W& sepia)

1-3: Colan-a 4.00
TPB ('99, $19.95) r/series 20.00

DETENTION COMICS
DC Comics: Oct, 1996 ($3.50, 56 pgs., one-shot)

1-Robin story by Dennis O'Neil & Norm Breyfogle; Superboy story by Ron Marz & Ron Lim; Warrior story by Ruben Diaz & Joe Phillips; Phillips-c 5.00

DETHKLOK (Based on the animated series Metalocalypse)
Dark Horse Comics: Oct, 2010 - No. 3, Feb, 2011 ($3.99, limited series)

1-3-Small & Schnepp-s; covers by Schnepp & Eric Powell 4.00
...: Versus the Goon 1-(7/09, $3.50) Powell-s/a/c; Dethklok visits the Goon universe 2 4 6 8 10 12
...: Versus the Goon 1-Variant cover by Jon Schnepp 2 4 6 9 12 15
HC (7/11, $19.99) r/#1-3 & Dethklok: Versus the Goon 20.00

DETONATOR (Mike Baron's...)
Image Comics: Nov, 2004 - No. 4 ($2.50/$2.95)

1-4-Mike Baron-s/Mel Rubi-a 3.00

DEUS EX (Based on the Square Enix videogame)
DC Comics: Apr, 2011 - No. 6, Sept, 2011 ($2.99, limited series)

1-6-Robbie Morrison-s/Trevor Hairsine-a 3.00

DEUS EX: CHILDREN'S CRUSADE (Based on the Square Enix videogame)
Titan Comics: Mar, 2016 - No. 5, Jul, 2016 ($3.99, limited series)

1-5-Alex Irvine-s/John Aggs-a; 3 covers on each 4.00

DEVASTATOR
Image Comics/Halloween: 1998 - No. 3 ($2.95, B&W, limited series)

1,2-Hudnall-s/Horn-c/a 3.00

DEVI (Shekhar Kapur's...)
Virgin Comics: July, 2006 - No. 20, Jun, 2008 ($2.99)

1-20: 1-Mukesh Singh-a/Siddharth Kotian-s. 2-Greg Horn-c 3.00
.../Witchblade (4/08, $2.99) Singh-a/Land-c; continued from Witchblade/Devi 3.00
... Vol. 1 TPB (5/07, $14.99) r/#1-5 and Story from Virgin Comics Preview #0 15.00
... Vol. 2 TPB (9/07, $14.99) r/#6-10; character and cover sketches 15.00

DEVIL CHEF
Dark Horse Comics: July, 1994 ($2.50, B&W, one-shot)

nn 3.00

DEVIL DINOSAUR
Marvel Comics Group: Apr, 1978 - No. 9, Dec, 1978

1-Kirby/Royer-a in all; all have Kirby-c 5 10 15 30 50 70
2-9: 4-7-UFO/sci. fic. 8-Dinoriders-c/sty 2 4 6 11 16 20
... By Jack Kirby Omnibus HC (2007, $29.99, dustjacket) r/#1-9; intro. by Brevoort 70.00

DEVIL DINOSAUR SPRING FLING
Marvel Comics: June, 1997 ($2.99. one-shot)

1-(48 pgs.) Moon-Boy-c/app. 4.00

DEVIL-DOG DUGAN (Tales of the Marines No. 4 on)
Atlas Comics (OPI): July, 1956 - No. 3, Nov, 1956

1-Severin-c 26 52 78 154 252 350
2-Iron Mike McGraw x-over; Severin-c 15 30 45 83 124 165
3 14 28 42 81 118 155

DEVIL DOGS
Street & Smith Publishers: 1942

1-Boy Rangers, U.S. Marines; WWII Japanese slaughter-c 68 136 204 435 743 1050

DEVILERS
Dynamite Entertainment: 2014 - No. 7, 2015 ($2.99)

1-7-Fialkov-s/Triano-a/Jock-c 3.00

DEVILINA (Magazine)
Atlas/Seaboard: Feb, 1975 - No. 2, May, 1975 (B&W)

1-Art by Reese, Marcos; "The Tempest" adapt. 5 10 15 31 53 75
2 (Low printing) 5 10 15 33 57 80

DEVIL KIDS STARRING HOT STUFF
Harvey Publications (Illustrated Humor): July, 1962 - No. 107, Oct, 1981 (Giant-Size #41-55)

	GD	VG	FN	VF	VF/NM	NM-
1 (12¢ cover price #1-#41-9/69)	32	64	96	230	515	800
2	10	20	30	69	147	225
3-10 (1/64)	8	16	24	51	96	140
11-20	5	10	15	33	57	80
21-30	4	8	12	25	40	55
31-40: 40-(6/69)	3	6	9	19	30	40
41-50: All 68 pg. Giants	3	6	9	21	33	45
51-55: All 52 pg. Giants	3	6	9	19	30	40
56-70	2	4	6	11	16	20
71-90	2	4	6	8	11	14
91-107	1	2	3	5	6	8

DEVIL'S DUE FREE COMIC BOOK DAY
Devil's Due Publ.: May, 2005 (Free Comic Book Day giveaway)

nn-Short stories of G.I. Joe, Defex and Darkstalkers; Darkstalkers flip cover 3.00

DEVIL'S FOOTPRINTS, THE
Dark Horse Comics: March, 2003 - No. 4, June, 2003 ($2.99, limited series)

1-4-Paul Lee-c/a; Scott Allie-s 3.00

DEVIL'S HIGHWAY
AWA Studios: Jul, 2020 - No. 5, Nov, 2020 ($3.99, limited series)

1-5-Benjamin Percy-s/Brent Schoonover-a 4.00
Vol. 2 (5/22 - No. 5, 9/22) 1-5-Percy-s/Schoonover-a 4.00

DEVIL'S REIGN
Marvel Comics: Feb, 2022 - No. 6, Jun, 2022 ($5.99/$4.99, limited series)

1-($5.99) Zdarsky-s/Checchetto-a; Wilson Fisk outlaws heroes in New York City 6.00
2-5-($4.99) 2-Spider-Man vs. Taskmaster. 3-Superior Four app. 5.00
6-($5.99) Daredevil vs. Kingpin; Avengers vs. The Purple Man 6.00
...: Moon Knight 1 (5/22, $4.99) MacKay-s/Sabbatini-a 5.00
...: Omega 1 (7/22, $4.99) Coda to the series; leads into Daredevil #1 (2022) 5.00
...: Spider-Man 1 (4/22, $4.99) Ben Reilly Spidey; Anthony Piper-s/Zé Carlos-a 5.00
...: Winter Soldier 1 (3/22, $4.99) Nico Leon-a; leads into Captain America #0 (2022) 5.00
...: X-Men 1 (3/22, $4.99) Duggan-s/Noto-a; Emma Frost & Thunderbolts app. 5.00

DEVIL'S REIGN: SUPERIOR FOUR
Marvel Comics: Mar, 2022 - No. 3, May, 2022 ($3.99, limited series)

1-3-Doc Ock with multiverse Octaviuses as Wolverine, Hulk and Ghost Rider 4.00

DEVIL'S REIGN: VILLAINS FOR HIRE
Marvel Comics: Mar, 2022 - No. 3, May, 2022 ($3.99, limited series)

1-3-New Thunderbolts team; U.S.Agent app.; Chapman-s/Garcia-a 4.00

DEVIL'S REIGN: X-MEN
Marvel Comics: Mar, 2022 - No. 3, May, 2022 ($4.99/$3.99, limited series)

1-Duggan-s/Noto-a; Emma Frost & Thunderbolts app. 5.00
2,3-($3.99) 2-Spider-Man app. 3-Union Jack app. 4.00

DEVI / WITCHBLADE
Graphic India Pte, Ltd.: Jan, 2016 ($4.99, one-shot)

1-Ron Marz & Samit Basu-s/Eric & Rick Basuldua & Mukesh Singh-a; multiple covers 5.00

DEVOLUTION
Dynamite Entertainment: 2016 - No. 5, 2016 ($3.99)

1-5-Remender-s/Wayshak-a/Jae Lee-c 4.00

DEXTER (Character from the novels and Showtime series)
Marvel Comics: Sept, 2013 - No. 5, Jan, 2014 ($3.99, limited series)

Detective Comics #1043 © DC

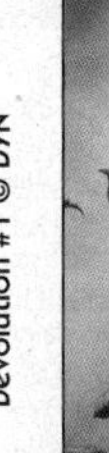
Devolution #1 © DYN

Dial H for Hero #4 © DC

	GD 2.0	VG 4.0	FN 6.0	VF 8.0	VF/NM 9.0	NM- 9.2
1-Linsday-s/Talajic-a/Mike Del Mundo-c in all	3	6	9	14	12	25
2-5						6.00

DEXTER COMICS
Dearfield Publ.: Summer, 1948 - No. 5, July, 1949

1-Teen-age humor	28	56	84	165	270	375
2-Junie Prom app.	18	36	54	105	165	225
3-5	15	30	45	83	124	165

DEXTER DOWN UNDER (Character from the novels and Showtime series)
Marvel Comics: Apr, 2014 - No. 5, Aug, 2014 ($3.99, limited series)

1-5-Jeff Lindsay-s/Dalibor Talajic-a/Mike Del Mundo-c 4.00

DEXTER'S LABORATORY (Cartoon Network)
DC Comics: Sept, 1999 - No. 34, Apr, 2003 ($1.99/$2.25)

1	3	6	9	15	22	28
2-10: 2-McCracken-s						6.00
11-24, 26-34: 31-Begin $2.25-c. 32-34-Wray-c						4.00
25-(50¢-c) Tartakovsky-s/a; Action Hank-c/app.						4.00

DEXTER'S LABORATORY (Cartoon Network)
IDW Publishing: Apr, 2014 - No. 4, Jul, 2014 ($3.99)

1-4-Fridolfs-s/Jampole-a; three covers on each 4.00

DEXTER THE DEMON (Formerly Melvin The Monster)(See Cartoon Kids & Peter the Little Pest)
Atlas Comics (HPC): No. 7, Sept, 1957

7	15	30	45	83	124	165

DHAMPIRE: STILLBORN
DC Comics (Vertigo): 1996 ($5.95, one-shot, mature)

1-Nancy Collins script; Paul Lee-c/a 6.00

DIABLO
DC Comics: Jan, 2012 - No. 5, Oct, 2012 ($2.99, limited series)

1-5-Aaron Williams-s/Joseph Lacroix-a/c 3.00

DIABLO HOUSE
IDW Publishing: Jul, 2017 - No. 4, Dec, 2017 ($3.99)

1-4-Horror anthology; Ted Adams-s/Santipérez-a 4.00

DIAL H (Dial H for HERO)(Also see Justice League #23.3)
DC Comics: Jul, 2012 - No. 15, Oct, 2013 ($2.99/$4.99)

1-14: 1-6-China Miéville-s/Mateus Santolouco-a/Brian Bolland-c. 1-Variant-c by Finch 3.00
15-($4.99) Mieville-s/Ponticelli-a/Bolland-c 5.00
#0 (11/12, $2.99) Origin of the dial; Miéville-s/Burchielli-a/Bolland-c 3.00

DIAL H FOR HERO
DC Comics: May, 2019 - No. 12, Apr, 2020 ($3.99)

1-12: 1-Intro. Miguel Montez; Humphries-s/Quinones-a. 3-Robby Reed returns 4.00

DIARY CONFESSIONS (Formerly Ideal Romance)
Stanmor/Key Publ.(Medal Comics): No. 9, May, 1955 - No. 14, Apr, 1955

9	15	30	45	85	130	175
10-14	12	24	36	67	94	120

DIARY LOVES (Formerly Love Diary #1; G. I. Sweethearts #32 on)
Quality Comics Group: No. 2, Nov, 1949 - No. 31, April, 1953

2-Ward-c/a, 9 pgs.	28	56	84	165	270	375
3 (1/50)-Photo-c begin, end #27?	15	30	45	85	130	175
4-Crandall-a	15	30	45	88	137	185
5-7,10	14	28	42	78	112	145
8,9-Ward-a 6,8 pgs. 8-Gustavson-a; Esther Williams photo-c	17	34	51	100	158	215
11,13,14,17-20	14	28	42	76	108	140
12,15,16-Ward-a 9,7,8 pgs.	16	32	48	94	147	200
21-Ward-a, 7 pgs.	15	30	45	86	133	180
22-31: 31-Whitney-a	13	26	39	74	105	135

NOTE: *Photo c-3-10, 12-28.*

DIARY OF HORROR
Avon Periodicals: December, 1952

1-Hollingsworth-c/a; bondage-c	290	580	870	1856	3178	4500

DIARY SECRETS (Formerly Teen-Age Diary Secrets)(See Giant Comics Ed.)
St. John Publishing Co.: No. 10, Feb, 1952 - No. 30, Sept, 1955

10-Baker-c/a most issues	142	284	426	909	1555	2200
11-16,18,19: 12,13,15-Baker-c	77	154	231	493	847	1200
17,20: Kubert-r/Hollywood Confessions #1. 17-r/Teen Age Romances #9	97	194	291	621	1061	1500
21-30: 22,27-Signed stories by Estrada. 28-Last precode (3/55)	71	142	213	454	777	1100
nn-(25¢ giant, nd (1950?)-Baker-c & rebound St. John comics	181	362	543	1158	1979	2800

DICK COLE (Sport Thrills No. 11 on)(See Blue Bolt & Four Most #1)
Curtis Publ./Star Publications: Dec-Jan, 1948-49 - No. 10, June-July, 1950

1-Sgt. Spook; L. B. Cole-c; McWilliams-a; Curt Swan's 1st work	40	80	120	246	411	575
2,5	18	36	54	105	165	225
3,4,6-10: All-L.B. Cole-c. 10-Joe Louis story	24	48	72	142	234	325
Accepted Reprint #7(V1#6 on-c)(1950's)-Reprints #7; L.B. Cole-c	9	18	27	50	65	80
Accepted Reprint #9(nd)-(Reprints #9 & #8-c)	9	18	27	50	65	80

NOTE: ***L. B. Cole** c-1, 3, 4, 6-10. **Al McWilliams** a-6. Dick Cole in 1-9. Baseball c-10. Basketball c-9. Football c-8.*

DICKIE DARE
Eastern Color Printing Co.: 1941 - No. 4, 1942 (#3 on sale 6/15/42)

1-Caniff-a, bondage-c by Everett	68	136	204	435	743	1050
2	32	64	96	188	307	425
3,4-Half Scorchy Smith by Noel Sickles who was very influential in Milton Caniff's development	34	68	102	199	325	450

DICK POWELL (Also see A-1 Comics)
Magazine Enterprises: No. 22, 1949 (one shot)

A-1 22-Photo-c	22	44	66	132	216	300

DICK QUICK, ACE REPORTER (See Picture News #10)

DICKS
Caliber Comics: 1997 - No. 4, 1998 ($2.95, B&W)

1-4-Ennis-s/McCrea-c/a; r/Fleetway 4.00
TPB ('98, $12.95) r/series 13.00

DICK'S ADVENTURES
Dell Publishing Co.: No. 245, Sept, 1949

Four Color 245	6	12	18	41	76	110

DICK TRACY (See Famous Feature Stories, Harvey Comics Library, Limited Collectors' Ed., Mammoth Comics, Merry Christmas, The Original..., Popular Comics, Super Book No. 1, 7, 13, 25, Super Comics & Tastee-Freez)

DICK TRACY
David McKay Publications: May, 1937 - Jan, 1938

Feature Books nn - 100 pgs., partially reprinted as 4-Color No. 1 (appeared before Large Feature Comics, 1st Dick Tracy comic book) (Very Rare-five known copies; two incomplete)	1750	3500	5250	13,100	24,050	35,000
Feature Books 4 - Reprints nn issue w/new-c	161	322	483	1022	1761	2500
Feature Books 6,9	110	220	330	704	1202	1700

DICK TRACY (...Monthly #1-24)
Dell Publishing Co.: 1939 - No. 24, Dec, 1949

Large Feature Comic 1 (1939) -Dick Tracy Meets The Blank	245	490	735	1568	2684	3800
Large Feature Comic 4,8	123	246	369	787	1344	1900
Large Feature Comic 11,13,15	106	212	318	673	1162	1650
Four Color 1(1939)('35-r)	1150	2300	3450	8750	16,625	24,500
Four Color 6(1940)('37-r)-(Scarce)	284	568	852	1818	3109	4400
Four Color 8(1940)('38-'39-r)	155	310	465	992	1696	2400
Large Feature Comic 3(1941, Series II)	113	226	339	718	1234	1750
Four Color 21('42)('38-r)	100	200	300	635	1093	1550
Four Color 34('44)('39-'40-r)	42	84	126	311	706	1100
Four Color 56('44)('40-r)	34	68	102	247	554	860
Four Color 96('46)('40-r)	23	46	69	161	356	550
Four Color 133('47)('40-'41-r)	18	36	54	124	275	425
Four Color 163('47)('41-r)	16	32	48	110	243	375
1(1/48)('34-r)	50	100	150	400	900	1400
2,3	24	48	72	168	377	585
4-10	19	38	57	133	297	460
11-18: 13-Bondage-c	14	28	42	97	214	330
19-1st app. Sparkle Plenty, B.O. Plenty & Gravel Gertie in a 3-pg. strip not by Gould	16	32	48	107	236	365
20-1st app. Sam Catchem; c/a not by Gould	13	26	39	91	201	310
21-24-Only 2 pg. Gould-a in each	13	26	39	89	195	300

NOTE: *No. 19-24 have a 2 pg. biography of a famous villain illustrated by **Gould**: 19-Little Face; 20-Flattop; 21-Breathless Mahoney; 22-Measles; 23-Itchy; 24-The Brow.*

DICK TRACY (Continued from Dell series)(...Comics Monthly #25-140)
Harvey Publications: No. 25, Mar, 1950 - No. 145, April, 1961

25-Flat Top-c/story (also #26,27)	11	22	33	76	163	250
26-28,30: 28-Bondage-c. 28,29-The Brow-c/stories	9	18	27	61	123	185
29-1st app. Gravel Gertie in a Gould-r	10	20	30	69	147	225

GD VG FN VF VF/NM NM-
2.0 4.0 6.0 8.0 9.0 9.2

31,32,34,35,37-40: 40-Intro/origin 2-way wrist radio (6/51)
8 16 24 52 99 145
33- "Measles the Teen-Age Dope Pusher" 9 18 27 61 123 185
36-1st app. B.O. Plenty in a Gould-r 9 18 27 61 123 185
41-50 7 14 21 46 86 125
51-56,58-80: 51-2pgs Powell-a 6 12 18 40 73 105
57-1st app. Sam Catchem in a Gould-r 7 14 21 46 86 125
81-99,101-140: 99-109-Painted-c 6 12 18 37 66 95
100, 141-145 (25¢)(titled "Dick Tracy") 6 12 18 40 73 105
NOTE: *Powell a(1-2pgs.)-43, 44, 104, 108, 109, 145. No. 110-120, 141-145 are all reprints from earlier issues.*

DICK TRACY ("Reuben Award" series)
Blackthorne Publishing: 12/84 - No. 24, 6/89 (1-12: $5.95; 13-24: $6.95, B&W, 76 pgs.)
1-8-1st printings; hard-c ed. ($14.95) 20.00
1-3-2nd printings, 1986; hard-c ed. 20.00
1-12-1st & 2nd printings; squarebound, thick-c 12.00
13-24 ($6.95): 21,22-Regular-c & stapled 14.00
NOTE: *Gould daily & Sunday strip-r in all. 1-12 r-12/31/45-4/5/49; 13-24 r-7/13/41-2/20/44.*

DICK TRACY (Disney)
WD Publications: 1990 - No. 3, 1990 (color) (Book 3 adapts 1990 movie)
Book One ($3.95, 52pgs.)-Kyle Baker-c/a 6.00
Book Two, Three ($5.95, 68pgs.)-Direct sale 6.00
Book Two, Three ($2.95, 68pgs.)-Newsstand 4.00

DICK TRACY ADVENTURES
Gladstone Publishing: May, 1991 ($4.95, 76 pgs.)
1-Reprints strips 2/1/42-4/18/42 5.00

DICK TRACY: DEAD OR ALIVE
IDW Publishing: Sept, 2018 - No. 4, Dec, 2018 ($3.99, limited series)
1-4-Lee & Michael Allred-s/Rich Tommaso-a 4.00

DICK TRACY, EXPLOITS OF
Rosdon Books, Inc.: 1946 ($1.00, hard-c strip reprints)
1-Reprints the near complete case of "The Brow" from 6/12/44 to 9/24/44
(story starts a few weeks late) 25 50 75 147 241 335
with dust jacket... 39 78 117 240 395 550

DICK TRACY FOREVER
IDW Publishing: Apr, 2019 - No. 4, Jul, 2019 ($3.99, limited series)
1-4-Michael A. Oeming-s/a. 1-Set in 1931. 2-Set in 1951. 3-Set in 2021. 4-Set in 2031 4.00

DICK TRACY MONTHLY/WEEKLY
Blackthorne Publishing: May, 1986 - No. 99, 1989 ($2.00, B&W)
(Becomes Weekly #26 on)
1-60: Gould-r. 30,31-Mr. Crime app. 4.00
61-90 4.00
91-95 6.00
96-99-Low print 1 2 3 5 7 9
NOTE: *#1-10 reprint strips 3/10/40-7/13/41; #10(pg.8)-51 reprint strips 4/6/49-12/31/55; #52-99 reprint strips 12/26/56-4/26/64.*

DICK TRACY SPECIAL
Blackthorne Publ.: Jan, 1988 - No. 3, Aug. (no month), 1989 ($2.95, B&W)
1-3: 1-Origin D. Tracy; 4/strips 10/12/31-3/30/32 4.00

DICK TRACY: THE EARLY YEARS
Blackthorne Publishing: Aug, 1987 - No. 4, Aug (no month) 1989 ($6.95, B&W, 76 pgs.)
1-3: 1-4-r/strips 10/12/31(1st daily)-8/31/32 & Sunday strips 6/12/32-8/28/32;
Big Boy apps. in #1-3 1 2 3 4 5 7
4 ($2.95, 52pgs.) 4.00

DICK TRACY UNPRINTED STORIES
Blackthorne Publishing: Sept, 1987 - No. 4, June, 1988 ($2.95, B&W)
1-4: Reprints strips 1/1/56-12/25/56 4.00

DICK TURPIN (See Legend of Young...)

DIE (Singular of dice)
Image Comics: Dec, 2018 - No. 20, Sept, 2021 ($3.99)
1-20-Kieron Gillen-s/Stephanie Hans-a; Dungeons & Dragons-themed story 4.00

DIE-CUT
Marvel Comics UK, Ltd: Nov, 1993 - No. 4, Feb, 1994 ($1.75, limited series)
1-4: 1-Die-cut-c; The Beast app. 3.00

DIE-CUT VS. G-FORCE
Marvel Comics UK, Ltd: Nov, 1993 - No. 2, Dec, 1993 ($2.75, limited series)
1,2-($2.75)-Gold foil-c on both 4.00

DIE!DIE!DIE!
Image Comics (Skybound): Jul, 2018 - Present ($3.99)
1-14: 1-Robert Kirkman-s/Chris Burnham-a. 14-Obama cover; Superman vs. Ali homage 4.00

DIE HARD: YEAR ONE (Based on the John McClane character)
BOOM! Studios: Aug, 2009 - No. 8, Mar, 2010 ($3.99, limited series)
1-8-Chaykin-s; Officer McClane in 1976 NYC; multiple covers on each 4.00

DIE KITTY DIE!
Chapterhouse Comics: Oct, 2016 - 2017 ($3.99/$4.99)
1,3,4-($3.99) Fernando Ruiz-s/Dan Parent-a; Harvey-style spoof 5.00
2-($4.99) Bonus faux 1969 reprint; Li'l Satan app. 6.00
... Christmas Special 1 (12/07, $4.99) Christmas stories 1 2 3 5 6 8
... Summer Vacation 1 (7/17, $3.99) Parent, Ruiz & Lagace-a 6.00

DIE KITTY DIE! HEAVEN & HELL
Chapterhouse Comics: No. 0, May, 2018 - No. 4, Jan, 2019 ($3.99/$4.99)
0-4-($3.99) Fernando Ruiz-s/Dan Parent-a 4.00
...: 2018 Halloween Special (10/18, $3.99) Art by Parent, Lagace, Bone, Pepoy 4.00

DIE KITTY DIE! HOLLYWOOD OR BUST
Chapterhouse Comics: Jul, 2017 - No. 4, Sept, 2017 ($3.99/$4.99)
1,2-($3.99) Fernando Ruiz-s/Dan Parent-a 4.00
3,4-($4.99) 5.00

DIE, MONSTER, DIE (See Movie Classics)

DIE!NAMITE
Dynamite Entertainment: 2020 - No. 5, 2021 ($3.99, limited series)
1-5-Vampirella, Red Sonja, Dejah Thoris, Peter Cannon Thunderbolt vs. zombies 4.00
... Valentine's Special, Our Bloody Valentine (2021, $4.99) short stories by various 5.00

DIE!NAMITE LIVES!
Dynamite Entertainment: 2021 - No. 5, 2021 ($3.99, limited series)
1-5-Ash (Evil Dead), Vampirella, Jennifer Blood, Project: Superpowers team vs. zombies 4.00

DIE!NAMITE NEVER DIES!
Dynamite Entertainment: 2022 - No. 5, 2022 ($3.99, limited series)
1-5-Tarzan, Vampirella, Evil Sonja, Pantha team vs. zombie John Carter & Dejah Thoris 4.00

DIESEL (TYSON HESSE'S...)
Boom Entertainment (BOOM! Box): Sept, 2015 - No. 4, Dec, 2015 ($3.99, limited series)
1-4-Tyson Hesse-s/a in all. 1-Three covers 4.00

DIGIMON DIGITAL MONSTERS (TV)
Dark Horse Comics: May, 2000 - No. 12, Nov, 2000 ($2.95/$2.99)
1 3 6 9 14 19 24
2-12 4.00
Sealed 4-pack ($9.99) 3 6 9 19 30 40

DIGITEK
Marvel UK, Ltd: Dec, 1992 - No. 4, Mar, 1993 ($1.95/$2.25, mini-series)
1-4: 3-Deathlock-c/story 3.00

DILLY (Dilly Duncan from Daredevil Comics; see Boy Comics #57)
Lev Gleason Publications: May, 1953 - No. 3, Sept, 1953
1-Teenage; Biro-c 12 24 36 67 94 120
2,3-Biro-c 8 16 24 42 54 65

DILTON'S STRANGE SCIENCE (See Pep Comics #78)
Archie Comics: May, 1989 - No. 5, May, 1990 (75¢/$1.00)
1-5 4.00

DIME COMICS
Newsbook Publ. Corp.: 1945; 1951
1-(32 pgs.) Silver Streak/Green Dragon-c/sty; Japanese WWII-c by L. B. Cole (Rare)
365 730 1095 2555 4478 6400
1(1951) 25 50 75 150 245 340

DINGBATS (See 1st Issue Special)

DING DONG
Compix/Magazine Enterprises: Summer?, 1946 - No. 5, 1947 (52 pgs.)
1-Funny animal 41 82 123 256 428 600
2 (9/46) 20 40 60 117 189 260
3 (Wint '46-'47) - 5 16 32 48 92 144 195

DINKY DUCK (Paul Terry's...) (See Approved Comics, Blue Ribbon, Giant Comics Edition #5A & New Terrytoons)
St. John Publishing Co./Pines No. 16 on: Nov, 1951 - No. 16, Sept, 1955; No. 16, Fall, 1956; No. 17, May, 1957 - No. 19, Summer, 1958
1-Funny animal 16 32 48 94 147 200
2 9 18 27 52 69 85
3-10 6 12 18 31 38 45
11-16(9/55) 6 12 18 28 34 40
16 (Fall, '56) - 19 5 10 15 23 28 32

DINKY DUCK & HASHIMOTO-SAN (See Deputy Dawg Presents...)

DINO (TV)(The Flintstones)
Charlton Publications: Aug, 1973 - No. 20, Jan, 1977 (Hanna-Barbera)
1 4 8 12 23 37 50
2-10 2 4 6 10 14 18
11-20 2 4 6 8 10 12
Digest nn (w/Xerox Pub., 1974) (low print run) 2 4 6 11 16 20

DINO ISLAND
Mirage Studios: Feb, 1994 - No. 2, Mar, 1994 ($2.75, limited series)
1,2-By Jim Lawson 4.00

DINO RIDERS
Marvel Comics: Feb, 1989 - No. 3, 1989 ($1.00)
1-3: Based on toys 4.00

DINOSAUR REX
Upshot Graphics (Fantagraphics): 1986 - No. 3, 1986 ($2.00, limited series)
1-3 4.00

DINOSAURS, A CELEBRATION
Marvel Comics (Epic): Oct, 1992 - No. 4, Oct, 1992 ($4.95, lim. series, 52 pgs.)
1-4: 2-Bolton painted-c 5.00

DINOSAURS ATTACK! (Based on Topps trading card set)
IDW Publishing: Jul, 2013 - No. 5, Nov, 2013 ($3.99, limited series)
1-5: 1,2-Remastered version of 1991 graphic novel. 3-5-New continuation of story 4.00

DINOSAURS ATTACK! THE GRAPHIC NOVEL
Eclipse Comics: 1991 ($3.95, coated stock, stiff-c)
Book One- Based on Topps trading cards 5.00

DINOSAURS FOR HIRE
Malibu Comics: Feb, 1993 - No. 12, Feb, 1994 ($1.95/$2.50)
1-12: 1,10-Flip bk. 8-Bagged w/Skycap; Staton-c. 10-Flip book 3.00

DINOSAURS GRAPHIC NOVEL (TV)
Disney Comics: 1992 - No. 2, 1993 ($2.95, 52 pgs.)
1,2-Staton-a; based on Dinosaurs TV show 4.00

DINOSAURUS

Dick Tracy Forever #3 © Tribune CA

Die Hard: Year One #8 © 20-FOX

Disney Comics and Stories #4 © DIS

	GD 2.0	VG 4.0	FN 6.0	VF 8.0	VF/NM 9.0	NM- 9.2

Dell Publishing Co.: No. 1120, Aug, 1960

Four Color 1120-Movie, painted-c	8	16	24	51	96	140

DIPPY DUCK
Atlas Comics (OPI): October, 1957

1-Maneely-a; code approved	16	32	48	94	147	200

DIRECTORY TO A NONEXISTENT UNIVERSE
Eclipse Comics: Dec, 1987 ($2.00, B&W)

1 — 3.00

DIRK GENTLY'S HOLISTIC DETECTIVE AGENCY
IDW Publishing: May, 2015 - No. 5, Oct, 2015 ($3.99, limited series)

1-5: 1-Ryall-s/Kyriazis-a; multiple covers on each — 4.00
...: A Spoon Too Short 1-5 (2/16 - No. 5, 6/16, $3.99) A.E. David-s/Kyriazis-a — 4.00
...: The Salmon of Doubt 1-9 (10/16 - No. 9, 6/17, $3.99) A.E. David-s/Kyriazis-a — 4.00

DIRTY DOZEN (See Movie Classics)

DIRTY PAIR (Manga)
Eclipse Comics: Dec, 1988 - No. 4, Apr, 1989 ($2.00, B&W, limited series)

1-4: Japanese manga with original stories — 5.00
...: Start the Violence (Dark Horse, 9/99, $2.95) r/B&W stories in color from Dark Horse Presents #132-134; covers by Warren & Pearson — 3.00

DIRTY PAIR: FATAL BUT NOT SERIOUS (Manga)
Dark Horse Comics: July, 1995 - No. 5, Nov, 1995 ($2.95, limited series)

1-5 — 4.00

DIRTY PAIR: RUN FROM THE FUTURE (Manga)
Dark Horse Comics: Jan, 2000 - No. 4, Mar, 2000 ($2.95, limited series)

1-Warren-s/c/a	3	6	9	19	30	40
1-Variant cover by Adam Hughes	8	16	24	54	102	150
2-4-Warren-s/c/a	1	3	4	6	8	10
2-4-Variant-c by Stelfreeze(2), Timm(3), Ramos(4)	2	4	6	11	16	20

DIRTY PAIR: SIM HELL (Manga)
Dark Horse Comics: May, 1993 - No. 4, Aug, 1993 ($2.50, B&W, limited series)

1-4 — 4.00
...Remastered #1-4 (5/01 - 8/01) reprints in color, with pin-up gallery — 3.00

DIRTY PAIR II (Manga)
Eclipse Comics: June, 1989 - No. 5, Mar, 1990 ($2.00, B&W, limited series)

1-5: 3-Cover is misnumbered as #1 — 4.00

DIRTY PAIR III, THE (A Plague of Angels) (Manga)
Eclipse Comics: Aug, 1990 - No. 5, Aug, 1991 ($2.00/$2.25, B&W, lim. series)

1-5 — 4.00

DISASTER INC.
AfterShock Comics: Apr, 2020 - No. 5, Dec, 2020 ($4.99/$3.99)

1-($4.99)-Joe Harris-s/Sebastian Piriz-a — 5.00
2-5-($3.99) — 4.00

DISCIPLINE
Image Comics: Mar, 2016 - No. 6, Aug, 2016 ($2.99)

1-6-Peter Milligan-s/Leandro Fernández-a — 3.00

DISNEY AFTERNOON, THE (TV)
Marvel Comics: Nov, 1994 - No. 10?, Aug, 1995 ($1.50)

1-10: 3-w/bound-in Power Ranger Barcode Card — 6.00

DISNEY AFTERNOON GIANT
IDW Publishing: Oct, 2018 - No. 8, Dec, 2019 ($5.99)

1-8: 1-4-DuckTales and Chip 'n' Dale stories. 5-Darkwing Duck and Chip 'n' Dale — 6.00

DISNEY COMIC ALBUM
Disney Comics: 1990(no month, year) - No. 8, 1991 ($6.95/$7.95)

1,2 ($6.95): 1-Donald Duck and Gyro Gearloose by Barks(r). 2-Uncle Scrooge by Barks(r); Jr. Woodchucks app. — 9.00
3-8: 3-Donald Duck-r/F.C. 308 by Barks; begin $7.95-c. 4-Mickey Mouse Meets the Phantom Blot; r/M.M Club Parade (censored 1956 version of story). 5-Chip 'n' Dale Rescue Rangers; new-a. 6-Uncle Scrooge. 7-Donald Duck in Too Many Pets; Barks-r(4) including F.C. #29. 8-Super Goof; r/S.G. #1, D.D. #102 — 9.00

DISNEY COMIC HITS
Marvel Comics: Oct, 1995 - No. 16, Jan, 1997 ($1.50/$2.50)

1-16: 4-Toy Story. 6-Aladdin. 7-Pocahontas. 10-The Hunchback of Notre Dame (Same story in Disney's The Hunchback of Notre Dame). 13-Aladdin and the Forty Thieves — 4.00

DISNEY COMICS
Disney Comics: June, 1990

Boxed set of #1 issues includes Donald Duck Advs., Ducktales, Chip 'n Dale Rescue Rangers, Roger Rabbit, Mickey Mouse Advs. & Goofy Advs.; limited to 10,000 sets	2	4	6	11	16	20

DISNEY COMICS AND STORIES
IDW Publishing: Sept, 2018 - No. 13, May, 2020 ($5.99)

1-13-Reprints of Danish and Italian stories — 6.00

DISNEY GIANT HALLOWEEN HEX
IDW Publishing: Oct, 2016 ($6.99)

1-Halloween-themed reprints of U.S., Dutch and Italian stories; three covers — 7.00

DISNEY KINGDOMS: FIGMENT 2 (Sequel to Figment series)
Marvel Comics: Nov, 2015 - No. 5, Mar, 2016 ($3.99)

1-5: 1-Jim Zub-s/Ramon Bachs-a/J. T. Christopher-c — 4.00

DISNEY KINGDOMS: SEEKERS OF THE WEIRD
Marvel Comics: Mar, 2014 - No. 5, Jul, 2014 ($3.99)

1-5: 1-Seifert-s/Moline-a/Del Mundo-c. 3-Andrade-a — 4.00

DISNEYLAND BIRTHDAY PARTY (Also see Dell Giants)
Gladstone Publishing Co.: Aug, 1985 ($2.50)

1-Reprints Dell Giant with new-photo-c	2	4	6	8	10	12
...Comics Digest #1-(Digest)	2	4	6	8	11	14

DISNEYLAND MAGAZINE
Fawcett Publications: Feb. 15, 1972 - ? (10-1/4"x12-5/8", 20 pgs, weekly)

1-One or two page painted art features on Dumbo, Snow White, Lady & the Tramp, the Aristocats, Brer Rabbit, Peter Pan, Cinderella, Jungle Book, Alice & Pinocchio. Most standard characters app.	3	6	9	17	25	34

DISNEYLAND, USA (See Dell Giant No. 30)

DISNEY MAGIC KINGDOM COMICS
IDW Publishing: May, 2016 - No. 2, Aug, 2016 ($6.99, squarebound, quarterly)

1,2-Reprints inspired by the theme parks; Barks-a — 7.00

DISNEY MOVIE BOOK
Walt Disney Productions (Gladstone): 1990 ($7.95, 8-1/2"x11", 52 pgs.) (w/pull-out poster)

1-Roger Rabbit in Tummy Trouble; from the cartoon film strips adapted to the comic format. Ron Dias-c	2	4	6	8	10	12

DISNEY'S ACTION CLUB
Acclaim Books: 1997 - No. 4 ($4.50, digest size)

1-4: 1-Hercules. 4-Mighty Ducks — 4.50

DISNEY'S ALADDIN (Movie)
Marvel Comics: no date (Oct, 1994) - No. 11, 1995 ($1.50)

1	1	3	4	6	8	10
2-11						4.00

DISNEY'S BEAUTY AND THE BEAST (Movie)
Marvel Comics: Sept, 1994 - No. 13, 1995 ($1.50)

1-13 — 4.00

DISNEY'S BEAUTY AND THE BEAST HOLIDAY SPECIAL
Acclaim Books: 1997 ($4.50, digest size, one-shot)

1-Based on The Enchanted Christmas video — 6.00

DISNEY'S COLOSSAL COMICS COLLECTION
Disney Comics: 1991 - No. 10, 1993 ($1.95, digest-size, 96/132 pgs.)

1,4,6,9: 4,6,9-Darkwing Duck-c. 4-r/Darkwing Duck #1-4. 6-Goofy begins	1	3	4	6	8	10
2,3,5,7,8,10: Ducktales, Talespin, Chip 'n Dale's Rescue Rangers. 8-Little Mermaid						5.00

DISNEY'S COMICS IN 3-D
Disney Comics: 1992 ($2.95, w/glasses, polybagged)

1-Infinity-c; Barks, Rosa, Gottfredson-r — 5.00

DISNEY'S ENCHANTING STORIES
Acclaim Books: 1997 - No. 5 ($4.50, digest size)

1-5: 1-Hercules. 2-Pocahontas — 4.50

DISNEY'S HERO SQUAD
BOOM! Studios: Jan, 2010 - No. 8, Aug, 2010 ($2.99)

1-8: 1-3-Phantom Blot app. 1-Back-up reprint of Super Goof #1 — 3.00

DISNEY'S NEW ADVENTURES OF BEAUTY AND THE BEAST (Also see Beauty and the Beast & Disney's Beauty and the Beast)
Disney Comics: 1992 - No. 2, 1992 ($1.50, limited series)

	GD 2.0	VG 4.0	FN 6.0	VF 8.0	VF/NM 9.0	NM- 9.2

1,2-New stories based on movie 5.00

DISNEY'S POCAHONTAS (Movie)
Marvel Comics: 1995 ($4.95, one-shot)

1-Movie adaptation 1 3 4 6 8 10

DISNEY'S TALESPIN LIMITED SERIES: "TAKE OFF" (TV) (See Talespin)
W. D. Publications (Disney Comics): Jan, 1991 - No. 4, Apr, 1991 ($1.50, lim. series, 52 pgs.)

1-4: Based on animated series; 4 part origin 5.00

DISNEY'S TARZAN (Movie)
Dark Horse Comics: June, 1999 - No. 2, July, 1999 ($2.95, limited series)

1,2: Movie adaptation 4.00

DISNEY'S THE LION KING (Movie)
Marvel Comics: July, 1994 - No. 2, July, 1994 ($1.50, limited series)

1,2: 2-part movie adaptation 1 2 3 5 6 8
1-($2.50, 52 pgs.)-Complete story 1 3 4 6 8 10

DISNEY'S THE LITTLE MERMAID (Movie)
Marvel Comics: Sept, 1994 - No. 12, 1995 ($1.50)

1 2 4 6 8 10 12
2-12 5.00

DISNEY'S THE LITTLE MERMAID LIMITED SERIES (Movie)
Disney Comics: Feb, 1992 - No. 4, May, 1992 ($1.50, limited series)

1-4: Peter David scripts; takes place before the movie 1 2 3 5 6 8
Set of #1-4 in unopened 4-issue Collector's Pack 65.00

DISNEY'S THE LITTLE MERMAID: UNDERWATER ENGAGEMENTS
Acclaim Books: 1997 ($4.50, digest size)

1-Flip book 1 3 4 6 8 10

DISNEY'S THE HUNCHBACK OF NOTRE DAME (Movie)(See Disney's Comic Hits #10)
Marvel Comics: July, 1996 ($4.95, squarebound, one-shot)

1-Movie adaptation. 1 2 3 4 5 9
NOTE: A different edition of this series was sold at Wal-Mart stores with new covers depicting scenes from the 1989 feature film. Inside contents and price were identical.

DISNEY'S THE PRINCE AND THE PAUPER
W. D. Publications: no date ($5.95, 68 pgs., squarebound)

nn-Movie adaptation 1 2 3 5 6 8

DISNEY'S THE THREE MUSKETEERS (Movie)
Marvel Comics: Jan, 1994 - No. 2, Feb, 1994 ($1.50, limited series)

1,2-Morrow-c; Spiegle-a; Movie adaptation 3.00

DISNEY'S TOY STORY (Movie)
Marvel Comics: Dec, 1995 ($4.95, one-shot)

nn-Adaptation of film 2 4 6 11 16 20

DISNEY TSUM TSUM KINGDOM ONE-SHOT (Based on the Japanese collectible stuffed toys)
IDW Publishing: Sept, 2018 ($7.99, squarebound, one-shot)

1-Short stories by various; Baldari-c 8.00

DISSENSION: WAR ETERNAL
Aspen MLT: Jul, 2018 - No. 5, Jan, 2019 ($3.99)

1-5-Fielder-s/Gunderson-a; Aspen Mascots bonus back-up story in each 4.00

DISTANT SOIL, A (1st Series)
WaRP Graphics: Dec, 1983 - No. 9, Mar 1986 ($1.50, B&W)

1-Magazine size 6.00
2-9: 2-4 are magazine size 4.00
NOTE: Second printings exist of #1, 2, 3 & 6.

DISTANT SOIL, A
Donning (Star Blaze): Mar, 1989 ($12.95, trade paperback)

nn-new material 13.00

DISTANT SOIL, A (2nd Series)
Aria Press/Image Comics (Highbrow Entertainment) #15 on:
June, 1991 - No. 42, Oct, 2013 ($1.75/$2.50/$2.95/$3.50/$3.95, B&W)

1-27: 13-$2.95-c begins. 14-Sketchbook. 15-(8/96)-1st Image issue 4.00
29-33,35,37-($3.95) 4.00
34-($4.95, 64 pages) includes sketchbook pages 5.00
36,38-($4.50) 36-Back-up story by Darnall & Doran. 38-Includes sketch pages 4.50
39-42-($3.50) 3.50
The Aria ('01, $16.95,TPB) r/#26-31 17.00
The Ascendant ('98, $18.95,TPB) r/#13-25 19.00
The Gathering ('97, $18.95,TPB) r/#1-13; intro. Neil Gaiman 19.00
Vol. 4: Coda (2005, $17.99, TPB) r/#32-38 18.00
NOTE: Four separate printings exist for #1 and are clearly marked. Second printings exist of #2-4 and are also clearly marked.

DISTANT SOIL, A: IMMIGRANT SONG
Donning (Star Blaze): Aug, 1987 ($6.95, trade paperback)

nn-new material 7.00

DISTRICT X (Also see X-Men titles) (Also see Mutopia X)
Marvel Comics: July, 2004 - No. 14, Aug, 2005 ($2.99)

1-14: 1-3-Bishop app.; Yardin-a/Hine-s 3.00
...Vol. 1: Mr. M (2005, $14.99) r/#1-6; sketch page by Yardin 15.00
...Vol. 2: Underground (2005, $19.99) r/#7-14; prologue from X-Men Unlimited #2 20.00

DIVER DAN (TV)
Dell Publishing Co.: Feb-Apr, 1962 - No. 2, June-Aug, 1962

Four Color 1254(#1), 2 10 20 30 69 147 225

DIVERGENCE FCBD SPECIAL EDITION
DC Comics: Jun, 2015 (Free Comic Book Day giveaway)

1-Previews Batman #41, Superman #41, Justice League Darkseid War 1 3 4 6 8 10

DIVIDED STATES OF HYSTERIA
Image Comics: Jun, 2017 - No. 6, Nov, 2017 ($3.99)

1-6-Howard Chaykin-s/a 4.00

DIVINE RIGHT
Image Comics (WildStorm Prod.): Sept, 1997 - No. 12, Nov, 1999 ($2.50)

Preview 5.00
1,2: 1-Jim Lee-s/a(p)/c, 1-Variant-c by Charest 4.00
1-($3.50)-Voyager Pack w/Stormwatch preview 4.00
1-American Entertainment Ed. 6.00
2-Variant-c of Exotica & Blaze 5.00
3-Chromium-c by Jim Lee 5.00
3-12: 3-5-Fairchild & Lynch app. 4-American Entertainment Ed. 8-Two covers. 9-1st DC issue. 11,12-Divine Intervention pt. 1,4 3.00
5-Pacific Comicon Ed. 6.00
6-Glow in the dark variant-c, European Tour Edition 20.00
...Book One TPB (2002, $17.95) r/#1-7 18.00
...Book Two TPB (2002, $17.95) r/#8-12 & Divine Intervention Gen13, ...Wildcats 18.00
...Collected Edition #1-3 ($5.95, TPB) 1-r/#1,2. 2-r/#3,4. 3-r/#5,6 6.00
Divine Intervention/Gen 13 (11/99, $2.50) Part 3; D'Anda-a 3.00
Divine Intervention/Wildcats (11/99, $2.50) Part 2; D'Anda-a 3.00

DIVINITY
Valiant Entertainment: Feb, 2015 - No. 4, May, 2015 ($3.99, limited series)

1-4-Kindt-s/Hairsine-a 4.00
#0 (8/17, $3.99) Kindt-s/Guedes-a; bonus preview of Eternity #1 4.00

DIVINITY II
Valiant Entertainment: Apr, 2016 - No. 4, Jul, 2016 ($3.99, limited series)

1-4-Kindt-s/Hairsine-a; 1-Origin of Myshka 4.00

DIVINITY III: STALINVERSE
Valiant Entertainment: Dec, 2016 - No. 4, Mar, 2017 ($3.99, limited series)

1-4-Kindt-s/Hairsine-a 4.00
Divinity III: Aric, Son of the Revolution 1 (1/17, $3.99) Joe Harris-s/Cafu-a 4.00
Divinity III: Escape From Gulag 396 1 (3/17, $3.99) Eliot Rahal-s/Francis Portela-a 4.00
Divinity III: Komandar Bloodshot 1 (12/16, $3.99) Jeff Lemire-s/Clayton Crain-a 4.00
Divinity III: Shadowman and the Battle for New Stalingrad 1 (2/17, $3.99) Robert Gill-a 4.00

DIVISION 13 (See Comic's Greatest World)
Dark Horse Comics: Sept, 1994 - Jan, 1995 ($2.50, color)

1-4: Giffen story in all. 1-Art Adams-c 4.00

DIXIE DUGAN (See Big Shot, Columbia Comics & Feature Funnies)
McNaught Syndicate/Columbia/Publication Ent.: July, 1942 - No. 13, 1949
(Strip reprints in all)

1-Joe Palooka x-over by Ham Fisher 36 72 108 211 343 475
2 20 40 60 114 182 250
3(1943) 15 30 45 83 124 165
4,5(1945-46)-Bo strip-r 12 24 36 67 94 120
6-13(1/47-49): 6-Paperdoll cut-outs 10 20 30 58 79 100

DIXIE DUGAN
Prize Publications (Headline): V3#1, Nov, 1951 - V4#4, Feb, 1954

V3#1 14 28 42 78 112 145
2-4 8 16 24 44 57 70
V4#1-4(#5-8) 8 16 24 40 50 60

DIZZY DAMES
American Comics Group (B&M Distr. Co.): Sept-Oct, 1952 - No. 6, Jul-Aug, 1953

1-Whitney-c 87 174 281 553 952 1350
2 47 94 141 296 498 700
3-6 28 56 84 165 270 375

DIZZY DON COMICS
F. E. Howard Publications/Dizzy Don Ent. Ltd (Canada): 1942 - No. 22, Oct, 1946; No. 3, Apr, 1947 - No. 4, Sept./Oct., 1947 (Most B&W)

1 (B&W) 60 120 180 381 653 925
2 (B&W) 39 78 117 231 378 525
4-21 (B&W) 34 68 102 199 325 450
22-Full color, 52 pgs. 37 74 111 222 361 500
3 (4/47), 4 (9-10/47)-Full color, 52 pgs. 37 74 111 222 361 500

DIZZY DUCK (Formerly Barnyard Comics)
Standard Comics: No. 32, Nov, 1950 - No. 39, Mar, 1952

32-Funny animal 13 26 39 72 101 130
33-39 8 16 24 44 57 70

DJANGO UNCHAINED (Adaptation of the 2012 movie)
DC Comics (Vertigo): Feb, 2013 - No. 7, Oct, 2013 ($3.99, limited series)

1-Adaptation of Quentin Tarantino's script; Guéra-a; Tarantino foreword; sketch pages 2 4 6 11 16 20
1-Variant-c by Jim Lee 5 10 15 33 57 80
2-Cowan-c; bonus concept art and cover sketch art 1 2 3 5 6 8
2-Variant-c by Mark Chiarello 3 6 9 17 26 35
3-7: 5-Quitely-c. 7-Alex Ross-c 5.00

DJANGO / ZORRO (Django from the 2012 Taratino movie)
Dynamite Entertainment: 2014 - No. 7, 2015 ($3.99/$5.99, limited series)

1-6-Tarantino & Matt Wagner-s/Esteve Polls-a; multiple covers on each 4.00
7-($5.99) Covers by Jae Lee & Francesco Francavilla 6.00

DMZ
DC Comics (Vertigo): Jan, 2006 - No. 72, Feb, 2012 ($2.99)

1-Brian Wood-s/Riccardo Burchielli-a 4.00
1-(2008, no cover price) Convention Exclusive promotional edition 3.00
2-49,51-72: 2-10-Brian Wood-s/Riccardo Burchielli-a. 11-Donaldson-a. 12-Wood-s/a 3.00
50-($3.99) Short stories by various incl. Risso, Moon, Gibbons, Bermejo, Jim Lee 4.00
...: Blood in the Game TPB (2009, $12.99) r/#29-34; intro. by Greg Palast 13.00
...: Body of a Journalist TPB (2007, $12.99) r/#6-12; intro. by D. Randall Blythe 13.00
...: Collective Punishment TPB (2011, $14.99) r/#55-59 15.00
...: Friendly Fire TPB (2008, $12.99) r/#18-22; intro. by Sgt. John G. Ford 13.00
...: Hearts and Minds TPB (2010, $16.99) r/#42-49; intro. by Morgan Spurlock 17.00

Divided States of Hysteria #4 © H. Chaykin

Doc Savage (2014) #8 © Conde Nast

Doctor Aphra #1 © Lucasfilm

GD VG FN VF VF/NM NM-
2.0 4.0 6.0 8.0 9.0 9.2

...: M.I.A. TPB (2011, $14.99) r/#50-54 15.00
...: On the Ground TPB (2006, $9.99) r/#1-5; intro. by Brian Azzarello 10.00
...: Public Works TPB (2007, $12.99) r/#13-17; intro. by Cory Doctorow 13.00
...: The Hidden War TPB (2008, $12.99) r/#23-28 13.00
...: War Powers TPB (2009, $14.99) r/#35-41 15.00

DNAGENTS (The New DNAgents V2/1 on)(Also see Surge)
Eclipse Comics: March, 1983 - No. 24, July, 1985 ($1.50, Baxter paper)

1-Origin. 5.00
2-23: 4-Amber app. 8-Infinity-c 4.00
24-Dave Stevens-c 4 8 12 25 40 55
... Industrial Strength Edition TPB (Image, 2008, $24.99) B&W r/#1-14; Evanier intro. 25.00

DOBERMAN (See Sgt. Bilko's Private...)

DOBERMAN
IDW Publishing (Darby Pop): Jul, 2014 - No. 5, Jan, 2015 ($3.99)

1-5-Marder, Rosell, & Lambert-s/McKinney-a 4.00

DOBIE GILLIS (See The Many Loves of...)

DOC FRANKENSTEIN
Burlyman Entertainment: Nov, 2004 - No. 6 ($3.50)

1-6-Wachowski brothers-s/Skroce-a 3.50

DOCK WALLOPER (Ed Burns' ...)
Virgin Comics: Nov, 2007 - No. 5, Jun, 2008 ($2.99)

1-5-Burns & Palmiotti-s/Siju Thomas-a; Prohibition time 3.00

DOC MACABRE
IDW Publishing: Dec, 2010 - No. 3, Feb, 2011 ($3.99)

1-3-Steve Niles-s/Bernie Wrightson-a/c 4.00

DOC SAMSON (Also see Incredible Hulk)
Marvel Comics: Jan, 1996 - No. 4, Apr, 1996 ($1.95, limited series)

1-4: 1-Hulk c/app. 2-She-Hulk-c/app. 3-Punisher-c/app. 4-Polaris-c/app. 3.00

DOC SAMSON (Incredible Hulk)
Marvel Comics: Mar, 2006 - No. 5, July, 2006 ($2.99, limited series)

1-5: 1-DiFilippo-s/Fiorentino-a. 3-Conner-c 3.00

DOC SAVAGE
Gold Key: Nov, 1966

1-Adaptation of the Thousand-Headed Man; James Bama c-r/1964 Doc Savage paperback
14 28 42 93 204 315

DOC SAVAGE (Also see Giant-Size...)
Marvel Comics Group: Oct, 1972 - No. 8, Jan, 1974

1 5 10 15 31 53 75
2,3-Steranko-c 3 6 9 21 33 45
4-8 2 4 6 10 14 18
...: The Man of Bronze TPB (DC Comics, 2010, $17.99) r/#1-8 18.00

NOTE: ***Gil Kane** c-5, 6. **Mooney** a-1i. No. 1, 2 adapts pulp story "The Man of Bronze"; No. 3, 4 adapts "Death in Silver"; No. 5, 6 adapts "The Monsters"; No. 7, 8 adapts "The Brand of The Werewolf".*

DOC SAVAGE (Magazine) (See Showcase Presents for reprint)
Marvel Comics Group: Aug, 1975 - No. 8, Spring, 1977 ($1.00, B&W)

1-Cover from movie poster; Ron Ely photo-c 3 6 9 21 33 45
2-5: 3-Buscema-a. 5-Adams-a(1 pg.), Rogers-a(1 pg) 2 4 6 9 13 16
6-8 2 4 6 10 14 18

DOC SAVAGE
DC Comics: Nov, 1987 - No. 4, Feb, 1988 ($1.75, limited series)

1-4: Dennis O'Neil-s/Adam & Andy Kubert-a/c in all 4.00
...: The Silver Pyramid TPB (2009, $19.99) r/#1-4 20.00

DOC SAVAGE
DC Comics: Nov, 1988 - No. 24, Oct, 1990 ($1.75/$2.00: #13-24)

1-16,19-24 4.00
17,18-Shadow x-over 5.00
Annual 1 (1989, $3.50, 68 pgs.) 5.00

DOC SAVAGE (First Wave)
DC Comics: Jun, 2010 - No. 18, Nov, 2011 ($3.99/$2.99)

1-9: 1-4-Malmont-s/Porter-a/J.G. Jones-c. Justice Inc. back-up; S. Hampton-a 4.00
1-6-Variant covers by Cassaday 5.00
10-17-($2.99) 10,16,17-Winslade-a 3.00

DOC SAVAGE
Dynamite Entertainment: 2013 - No. 8, 2014 ($3.99)

1-8: 1-Roberson-s/Evely-a; covers by Ross & Cassaday 4.00

GD VG FN VF VF/NM NM-
2.0 4.0 6.0 8.0 9.0 9.2

Annual 2014 ($5.99) Denton-s/Castro-a 6.00
Special 2014: Woman of Bronze ($7.99, squarebound) Walker-s/Baal-a; Patricia Savage 8.00

DOC SAVAGE COMICS (Also see Shadow Comics)
Street & Smith Publ.: May, 1940 - No. 20, Oct, 1943 (1st app. in Doc Savage pulp, 3/33)

1-Doc Savage, Cap Fury, Danny Garrett, Mark Mallory, The Whisperer, Captain Death, Billy the Kid, Sheriff Pete & Treasure Island begin; Norgil, the Magician app.
703 1406 2109 5132 9066 13,000
2-Origin & 1st app. Ajax, the Sun Man; Danny Garrett, The Whisperer end; classic sci-fi cover 265 530 795 1694 2897 4100
3 181 362 543 1158 1979 2800
4-Treasure Island ends; Tuska-a 142 284 426 909 1555 2200
5-Origin & 1st app. Astron, the Crocodile Queen, not in #9 & 11; Norgi the Magician app.; classic-c 126 252 378 806 1378 1950
6-10: 6-Cap Fury ends; origin & only app. Red Falcon in Astron story. 8-Mark Mallory ends; Charlie McCarthy app. on-c plus true life story. 9-Supersnipe app. 10-Origin & only app. The Thunderbolt 77 154 231 493 847 1200
11,12 61 122 183 390 670 950
V2#1-6,8(#13-18,20): 15-Origin of Ajax the Sun Man; Jack Benny on-c; Hitler app. 16-The Pulp Hero, The Avenger app.; Fanny Brice story. 17-Sun Man ends; Nick Carter begins; Duffy's Tavern part photo-c & story. 18-Huckleberry Finn part-c/story. 19-Henny Youngman part photo-c & life story. 20-Only all funny-c w/Huckleberry Finn
58 116 174 371 636 900
V2#7-Classic Devil-c 68 136 204 435 743 1050

DOC SAVAGE: CURSE OF THE FIRE GOD
Dark Horse Comics: Sept, 1995 - No, 4, Dec, 1995 ($2.95, limited series)

1-4 4.00

DOC SAVAGE: THE MAN OF BRONZE
Skylark Pub: Mar, 1979, 68pgs. (B&W comic digest, 5-1/4x7-5/8")(low print)

15406-0: Whitman-a, 60 pgs., new comics 4 8 12 23 37 50

DOC SAVAGE: THE MAN OF BRONZE
Millennium Publications: 1991 - No. 4, 1991 ($2.50, limited series)

1-4: 1-Bronze logo 4.00
...: The Manual of Bronze 1 ($2.50, B&W, color, one-shot)-Unpublished proposed Doc Savage strip in color, B&W strip-r 4.00

DOC SAVAGE: THE MAN OF BRONZE, DOOM DYNASTY
Millennium Publ.: 1992 (Says 1991) - No. 2, 1992 ($2.50, limited series)

1,2 4.00

DOC SAVAGE: THE MAN OF BRONZE - REPEL
Innovation Publishing: 1992 ($2.50)

1-Dave Dorman painted-c 4.00

DOC SAVAGE: THE MAN OF BRONZE THE DEVIL'S THOUGHTS
Millennium Publ.: 1992 (Says 1991) - No. 3, 1992 ($2.50, limited series)

1-3 4.00

DOC SAVAGE: THE RING OF FIRE
Dynamite Entertainment: 2017 - No. 4, 2017 ($3.99, limited series)

1-4-Avallone-s/Acosta-a; multiple covers on each 4.00

DOC SAVAGE: THE SPIDER'S WEB
Dynamite Entertainment: 2015 - No. 5, 2016 ($3.99, limited series)

1-5-Roberson-s/Razek-a. 1-Multiple covers 4.00

DOC STEARN...MR. MONSTER (See Mr. Monster)

DR. ANTHONY KING, HOLLYWOOD LOVE DOCTOR
Minoan Publishing Corp./Harvey Publications No. 4: 1952(Jan) - No. 3, May, 1953; No. 4, May, 1954

1 22 44 66 128 209 290
2-4: 4-Powell-a 14 28 42 80 115 150

DR. ANTHONY'S LOVE CLINIC (See Mr. Anthony's...)

DOCTOR APHRA (Star Wars)(Title changes to Star Wars: Doctor Aphra with #7)
(See Darth Vader #3 for debut)
Marvel Comics: Feb, 2017 - No. 6, Jun, 2017 ($4.99/$3.99)

1-Gillen-s/Walker-a; back-up with Larroca-a; BT-1, Triple-Zero and Black Krrsantan app.
3 6 9 14 20 25
2-6-($3.99) Walker-a 4.00

DOCTOR APHRA (Star Wars)(2nd series)(Listed under Star Wars: Doctor Aphra)

DR. BOBBS
Dell Publishing Co.: No. 212, Jan, 1949

Four Color 212 7 14 21 49 92 135

DOCTOR DOOM
Marvel Comics: Dec, 2019 - No. 10, Feb, 2021 ($4.99/$3.99)
1-($4.99) Cantwell-s/Larroca-a; Kang the Conqueror app. 5.00
2-10-($3.99) Blue Marvel, Morgan Le Fay, Mephisto app. 4.00

DOCTOR DOOM AND THE MASTERS OF EVIL (All ages title)
Marvel Comics: Mar, 2009 - No. 4, Jun, 2009 ($2.99)
1-4: 1-Sinister Six app. 4-Magneto app. 3.00

DR. DOOM'S REVENGE
Marvel Comics: 1989 (Came w/computer game from Paragon Software)
V1#1-Spider-Man & Captain America fight Dr. Doom 4 8 12 27 44 60

DR. FATE (See 1st Issue Special, The Immortal..., Justice League, More Fun #55, & Showcase)

DOCTOR FATE
DC Comics: July, 1987 - No. 4, Oct, 1987 ($1.50, limited series, Baxter paper)
1-Giffen-c/a in all 1 3 4 6 8 10
2-4 6.00

DOCTOR FATE
DC Comics: Winter, 1988-'89 - No. 41, June, 1992 ($1.25/$1.50 #5 on)
1,15: 15-Justice League app. 5.00
2-14,16-41: 25-1st new Dr. Fate. 36-Original Dr. Fate returns 4.00
Annual 1(1989, $2.95, 68 pgs.)-Sutton-a 5.00

DOCTOR FATE
DC Comics: Oct, 2003 - No. 5, Feb, 2004 ($2.50, limited series)
1-5-Golden-s/Kramer-a 4.00

DOCTOR FATE
DC Comics: Aug, 2015 - No. 18, Jan, 2017 ($2.99)
1-18: 1-Levitz-s/Liew-a; Khalid Nassour chosen as new Doctor. 12-15-Kent Nelson app. 3.00

DR. FU MANCHU (See The Mask of...)
I.W. Enterprises: 1964
1-r/Avon's "Mask of Dr. Fu Manchu"; Wood-a 8 16 24 55 105 155

DR. GIGGLES (See Dark Horse Presents #64-66)
Dark Horse Comics: Oct, 1992 - No. 2, Oct, 1992 ($2.50, limited series)
1,2-Based on movie 1 3 4 6 8 10

DOCTOR GRAVES (Formerly The Many Ghosts of...)
Charlton Comics: No. 73, Sept, 1985 - No. 75, Jan, 1986
73-75-Low print run. 73,74-Ditko-a 2 4 6 8 10 12
... Magic Book nn (Charlton Press/Xerox Education, 1977, 68 pgs., digest) Ditko-c/a; Staton-a
4 8 12 23 37 50

DR. HORRIBLE (Based on Joss Whedon's internet feature)
Dark Horse Comics: Nov, 2009 ($3.50, one-shot)
1-Zack Whedon-s/Joëlle Jones-a; Captain Hammer pin-up by Gene Ha; 3 covers 3.50
... and other Horrible Stories TPB (9/10, $9.99) r/#1 and 3 stories from MySpace DHP 10.00
...: Best Friends Forever one-shot (11/18, $3.99) Whedon-s/Beroy & Soler-a/Fabio Moon-c 4.00

DR. JEKYLL AND MR. HYDE (See A Star Presentation & Supernatural Thrillers #4)

DR. KILDARE (TV)
Dell Publishing Co.: No. 1337, 4-6/62 - No. 9, 4-6/65 (All Richard Chamberlain photo-c)
Four Color 1337(#1, 1962) 10 20 30 64 132 200
2-9 6 12 18 41 76 110

DR. MASTERS (See The Adventures of Young...)

DOCTOR MID-NITE (Also see All-American #25)
DC Comics: 1999 - No. 3, 1999 ($5.95, square-bound, limited series)
1-3-Matt Wagner-s/John K. Snyder III-painted art 6.00
TPB (2000, $19.95) r/series 20.00

DOCTOR MIRAGE (Also see Death-Defying Doctor Mirage)
Valiant Entertainment: Aug, 2019 - No. 5, Dec, 2019 ($3.99, limited series)
1-5-Visaggio-s/Robles-a 4.00

DOCTOR OCTOPUS: NEGATIVE EXPOSURE
Marvel Comics: Dec, 2003 - No. 5, Apr, 2004 ($2.99, limited series)
1-5-Vaughan-s/Staz Johnson-a; Spider-Man app. 3.00
Spider-Man/Doctor Octopus: Negative Exposure TPB (2004, $13.99) r/series 14.00

DR. ROBOT SPECIAL
Dark Horse Comics: Apr, 2000 ($2.95, one-shot)
1-Bernie Mireault-s/a; some reprints from Madman Comics #12-15 3.00

DOCTOR SOLAR, MAN OF THE ATOM (See The Occult Files of Dr. Spektor #14 & Solar)
Gold Key/Whitman No. 28 on: 10/62 - No. 27, 4/69; No. 28, 4/81 - No. 31, 3/82 (1-27 have painted-c)
1-(#10000-210)-Origin/1st app. Dr. Solar (1st original Gold Key character)
64 128 192 512 1156 1800
2-Prof. Harbinger begins 14 28 42 96 211 325
3,4 9 18 27 56 108 165
5-Intro. Man of the Atom in costume 10 20 30 70 150 230
6-10 6 12 18 38 69 100
11-14,16-20 5 10 15 31 53 75
15-Origin retold 5 10 15 35 63 90
21-23: 23-Last 12¢ issue 4 8 12 28 47 65
24-27 4 8 12 25 40 55
28-31: 29-Magnus Robot Fighter begins. 31-(3/82)The Sentinel app.
3 6 9 17 25 34
Hardcover Vol. One (Dark Horse Books, 2004, $49.95) r/#1-7; creator bios 50.00
Hardcover Vol. Two (Dark Horse Books, 6/05, $49.95) r/#8-14; Jim Shooter foreword 50.00
Hardcover Vol. Three (Dark Horse Books, 9/05, $49.95) r/#15-22; Mike Baron foreword 50.00
Hardcover Vol. Four (Dark Horse Books, 11/07, $49.95) r/#23-31 and The Occult Files of Dr. Spektor #14; Batton Lash foreword 50.00
NOTE: ***Frank Bolle*** *a-6-19, 29-31; c-29i, 30i.* ***Bob Fujitani*** *a-1-5.* ***Spiegle*** *a-29-31.* ***Al McWilliams*** *a-20-23.*

DOCTOR SOLAR, MAN OF THE ATOM
Valiant Comics: 1990 - No. 2, 1991 ($7.95, card stock-c, high quality, 96 pgs.)
1,2: Reprints Gold Key series 1 3 4 6 8 10

DOCTOR SOLAR, MAN OF THE ATOM
Dark Horse Comics: Jul, 2010 - No. 8, Sept, 2011 ($3.50)
1-(48 pgs.) Shooter-s/Calero-a; back-up reprint of origin/1st app. in D.S. #1 (1962) 4.00
2-8: 2-7-Roger Robinson-a 3.50
Free Comic Book Day Doctor Solar, Man of the Atom & Magnus, Robot Fighter (5/10, free) short story re-intros of Solar & Magnus; Shooter-s/Swanland-c; Calero & Reinhold-a 3.00

DOCTOR SPECTRUM (See Supreme Power)
Marvel Comics: Oct, 2004 - No. 6, Mar, 2005 ($2.99, limited series)
1-6-Origin; Sara Barnes-s/Travel Foreman-a 3.00
TPB (2005, $16.99) r/#1-6 17.00

DOCTOR SPEKTOR (See The Occult Files of..., & Spine-Tingling Tales)

DOCTOR SPEKTOR: MASTER OF THE OCCULT
Dynamite Entertainment: 2014 - No. 4, 2014 ($3.99)
1-4-Mark Waid-s; multiple covers on each 4.00

DOCTOR STAR AND THE KINGDOM OF LOST TOMORROW (Also see Black Hammer)
Dark Horse Comics: Mar, 2018 - No. 4, Jun, 2018 ($3.99, limited series)
1-4-Lemire-s/Fiumara-a 4.00

DOCTOR STRANGE (Formerly Strange Tales #1-168) (Also see The Defenders, Giant-Size..., Marvel Fanfare, Marvel Graphic Novel, Marvel Premiere, Marvel Treasury Edition, Strange & Strange Tales, 2nd Series)
Marvel Comics Group: No. 169, Jun, 1968 - No. 183, Nov, 1969
169(#1)-Origin retold; continued from Strange Tales #167; Roy Thomas-s/Dan Adkins-a; panel swipe/M.D. #1-c 50 100 150 400 900 1400
170-vs. Nightmare 10 20 30 69 147 225
171-176: 171-173-vs. Dormammu. 172-1st Colan-a. 174-1st Sons of Satannish
8 16 24 56 108 160
177-New masked costume 10 20 30 69 147 225
178-181: 178-Black Knight app.; continues in Avengers #61. 179-r/Spider-Man & Dr. Strange story from Amazing Spider-Man Annual #2. 180-Nightmare & Eternity app.; photo montage-c. 181-Brunner-c(part-i), last 12¢ issue 6 12 18 38 69 100
182-Juggernaut app. 8 16 24 54 102 150
183-Intro. The Undying Ones; cont'd in Sub-Mariner #22; concludes in Incredible Hulk #126; Dr. Strange returns in Marvel Feature #1 (second story)
8 16 24 54 102 150

DOCTOR STRANGE (2nd series)(Follows from Marvel Premiere #14)
Marvel Comics Group: Jun, 1974 - No. 81, Feb, 1987
1-Englehart-s/Brunner-c/a; 1st Silver Dagger 11 22 33 75 160 245
2-Silver Dagger app.; Defenders-c 6 12 18 41 76 110
3-5: 3-Mostly reprints; r-Strange Tales #126-127; 1 pg. original art. 4-5-Silver Dagger app. 5-Last Brunner-a 3 6 9 19 30 40
6-10: 6-Dormammu app; Colan-a begins. 7-Dormammu app.; story x-over with Giant-Size Avengers #4. 8-Dormammu app.; continued from Giant-Size Avengers #4. 9-Dormammu app.; Umar revealed as Clea's mother. 10-Baron Mordo & Eternity app.
2 4 6 13 18 22
11,12,15-20: 13,15-17-(Regular 25¢ editions). 15,16-Strange vs. Satan. 17-1st Stygyro. 18-vs. Stygyro; last Englehart-s. 19-Wolfman-s begin; 1st Xander & the Creators. 20-vs. Xander & the Creators; slight x-over w/Annual #1 2 4 6 8 10 12
13-Nightmare app; slight x-over with Tomb of Dracula #44
6 12 18 41 76 110
13,15-17-(30¢-c variants, limited distribution) 5 10 15 33 57 80
14-(5/76) (Regular 25¢ edition) Dracula app.; story continues from Tomb of Dracula #44 and leads into Tomb of Dracula #45 2 4 6 11 16 20
14-(30¢-c variant, limited distribution) 6 12 18 37 66 95
21,22: 21-Reprints origin from Dr. Strange #169. 22-1st Apalla, Queen of the Sun
2 4 6 9 12 15
23-25,30,32-40: 23-25-(Regular 30¢ editions). 23-Starlin layouts; last Wolfman-s. 24-Starlin-s. 25-Starlin-c/s. 30-1st full app. Dweller in Darkness. 32-vs. Dweller in Darkness; 1st Dream Weaver. 33-Dweller in Darkness & Dream Weaver app. 34-vs. Cyrus Black & Nightmare. 35-Captain America & Iron Man app; Black Knight statue app. 36-Ningal app. (from Chamber of Chills #3). 37-Ningal, Dweller in Darkness & D'Spayre app. 38-Claremont-s begin. 40-Baron Mordo app.; continues in Man-Thing Vol. 2 #4
1 3 4 6 8 10
23-25-(35¢-c variants, limited distribution)(6,8,10/77) 9 18 27 58 114 170
26-29,31: 26-Starlin-a (p); Ancient One & In-Betweener app. 27-vs. Stygyro; Roger Stern-s begin; Ancient One & In-Betweener app. 28-vs. In-Betweener; Brunner-c/a. 29-vs. Deathstalker; Nighthawk app; Brunner-c/a. 31-Sub-Mariner app.
1 3 4 6 8 10
41-57,63-77,79-81: 41-Continued from Man-Thing Vol. 2 #4; Man-Thing & Baron Mordo app. 46-Miller-c/p. 48,49-Brother Voodoo app; 48-Marshall Rogers-p begin. 49-Baron Mordo app. 50-vs. Baron Mordo. 51-Dormammu app. 52-Nightmare. 53-Fantastic Four & Rama-Tut app.; takes place during FF #19. 55-D'Spayre app; Golden-c/a. 56-Paul Smith-a; origin retold. 67-Hannibal King, Blade & Frank Drake app. 68,69-Black Knight app. 71-73 vs. Umar. 74-Secret Wars II x-over; Beyonder app. 75-Mignola-c; continued from FF #277; vs. Mephisto; last Stern-s. 79-1st Urthona. 80-1st Rintrah. 81-Last issue; Rintrah app; story continued in Strange Tales Vol. 2 #1 5.00
58-62: 58-Re-intro Hannibal King (cameo). 59-Hannibal King full app. 59-62-Dracula app. (Darkhold storyline). 61,62-Doctor Strange, Blade, Hannibal King & Frank Drake team-up to battle. Dracula. 62-Death of Dracula & Lilith 1 2 3 5 6 8
78-New costume; Cloak (from Cloak & Dagger) app. 1 3 4 6 8 10
Annual 1 (1976, 52 pgs.)-New Russell-a (35 pgs.) 4 8 12 22 35 48
...: From the Marvel Vault (4/11, $2.99) Stern-s/Vokes-a 3.00
.../Silver Dagger Special Edition 1 (3/83, $2.50)-r/#1,2,4,5; Wrightson-c 5.00
... Vs. Dracula TPB (2006, $19.99) r/#14,58-62 and Tomb of Dracula #44 20.00
...What Is It That Disturbs You, Stephen? #1 (10/97, $5.99, 48 pgs.) Russell-a/Andreyko & Russell-s, retelling of Annual #1 story 6.00
NOTE: ***Adkins*** *a-169, 170, 171i; c-169-171, 172i, 173.* ***Adams*** *a-4i.* ***Austin*** *a(i)-48-60, 66, 68, 70, 73; c(i)-38, 47-53, 55, 58-60, 70.* ***Brunner*** *a-1-5p; c-1-6, 22, 28-30, 33.* ***Colan*** *a(p)-172-178, 180-183, 6-18, 36-45, 47; c(p)-172, 174-183, 11-21, 23, 27, 35, 36, 47.* ***Ditko*** *a-179r, 3r.* ***Everett*** *c-183i.* ***Golden*** *a-46p, 55p; c-42-44, 46, 55p.* ***G. Kane*** *c(p)-8-10.* ***Miller*** *c-46p.* ***Nebres*** *a-20, 22, 23, 24i, 26i, 32i; c-32i, 34.* ***Rogers*** *a-48-53p; c-47p-53p.* ***Russell*** *a-34i, 46i, Annual 1.* ***B. Smith*** *c-179.* ***Paul Smith*** *a-54p, 56p, 65, 66p, 68p, 69, 71-73; c-56, 65, 66, 68, 71.* ***Starlin*** *a-23p, 26; c-25, 26.* ***Sutton*** *a-27-29p, 31i, 33, 34p. Painted c-62, 63.*

DOCTOR STRANGE (Volume 2)

Doctor Fate (2015) #13 © DC

Doctor Strange (2016) #11 © MAR

Doctor Tomorrow (2020) #3 © VAL

	GD 2.0	VG 4.0	FN 6.0	VF 8.0	VF/NM 9.0	NM- 9.2

Marvel Comics: Feb, 1999 - No. 4, May, 1999 ($2.99, limited series)

1-4: 1,2-Tony Harris-a/painted cover. 3,4-Chadwick-a 4.00

DOCTOR STRANGE (Follows Secret Wars event)
Marvel Comics: Dec, 2015 - No. 26, Dec, 2017; No. 381, Jan, 2018 - No. 390, Jul, 2018 ($4.99/$3.99)

1-($4.99) Aaron-s/Bachalo-a; back-up with Nowlan-a 5.00
2-5,7-19-($3.99) Aaron-s/Bachalo-a. 7-10-The Last Days of Magic 4.00
6-($4.99) The Last Days of Magic 5.00
20-($4.99) Doctor Strange in Weirdworld; art by Bachalo & Nowlan; last Aaron-s 5.00
21-24,26: 21-24-Secret Empire tie-ins; Kingpin & Baron Mordo app.; Henrichon-a 4.00
25-($4.99) Barber-s/Nowlan-a/c 5.00
[Title switches to legacy numbering after #26 (12/17)]
381-390: 381-385-Walta-a; Loki as Sorceror Supreme. 383-385-The Sentry app. 386-Mephisto app.; Henrichon-a. 387-389-Damnation tie-ins. 390-Irving-a 4.00
#1.MU (4/17, $4.99) Monsters Unleashed tie-in; Chip Zdarsky-s/Julian Lopez-a 5.00
Annual 1 (12/19, $4.99) Scarlet Witch, Talisman & Agatha Harkness app. 5.00
Annual 1 (11/16, $4.99) K. Immonen-s/Romero-a; Clea app. 5.00
...: Last Days of Magic 1 (6/16, $5.99) Story between #6 & 7; Doctor Voodoo & The Wu 6.00
...: Mystic Apprentice 1 (12/16, $3.99) New story w/Di Vito-a; r/Strange Tales #115, 110 4.00

DOCTOR STRANGE
Marvel Comics: Aug, 2018 - No. 20, Dec, 2019 ($3.99)

1-9,11-20: 1-Waid-s/Saiz-a; Strange goes to space. 2-Intro. Kanna. 3-Super-Skrull app. 11-17-Galactus app. 19-Strange's hands healed 4.00
10-($5.99) 400th issue; The Ancient One app.; bonus flashback with Nowlan-a 6.00
Annual 1 (12/19, $4.99) Scarlet Witch, Talisman & Agatha Harkness app. 5.00
...: Nexus of Nightmares 1 (6/22, $3.99) Baron Mordo app.; Macchio-s/Moustafa-a 4.00
...: The Best Defense 1 (2/19, $4.99) Duggan-s/Smallwood-a; x-over with other Defenders 5.00
...: The End 1 (3/20, $4.99) Leah Williams-s/Filipe Andrade-a; Illyana Rasputin app. 5.00

DR. STRANGE (... Surgeon Supreme on cover)
Marvel Comics: Feb, 2020 - No. 6, Oct, 2020 ($3.99)

1-6: 1-Waid-s/Walker-a; The Wrecker app. 2-6-Dr. Druid app. 5,6-Madame Masque app. 4.00

DOCTOR STRANGE AND THE SORCERERS SUPREME (Prelude in Doctor Strange Annual #1)
Marvel Comics: Dec, 2016 - No. 12, Nov, 2017 ($3.99)

1-12: 1-9-Thompson-s/Rodriguez-a; The Ancient One, Wiccan & Merlin app. 5.00

DOCTOR STRANGE CLASSICS
Marvel Comics Group: Mar, 1984 - No. 4, June, 1984 ($1.50, Baxter paper)

1-4: Ditko-r; Byrne-c. 4-New Golden pin-up 5.00
NOTE: ***Byrne*** *c-1i, 2-4.*

DOCTOR STRANGE: DAMNATION
Marvel Comics: Apr, 2018 - No. 4, Jun, 2018 ($3.99, limited series)

1-4-Spencer & Cates-s; Las Vegas is restored; Mephisto app. 1,2,4-Rod Reis-a 4.00

DOCTOR STRANGE: FALL SUNRISE
Marvel Comics: Jan, 2023 - No. 4, April 2023 ($4.99, limited series)

1-4-Tradd Moore-s/a 5.00

DOCTOR STRANGEFATE (See Marvel Versus DC #3 & DC Versus Marvel #4)
DC Comics (Amalgam): Apr, 1996 ($1.95)

1-Ron Marz script w/José Garcia-Lopez-(p) & Kevin Nowlan-(i). Access & Charles Xavier app. 6.00

DOCTOR STRANGE MASTER OF THE MYSTIC ARTS (See Fireside Book Series)

DOCTOR STRANGE/PUNISHER: MAGIC BULLETS
Marvel Comics: Feb, 2017 - No. 4, May, 2017 ($4.99, limited series)

1-4-Barber-s/Broccardo-a 5.00

DOCTOR STRANGE, SORCERER SUPREME
Marvel Comics (Midnight Sons imprint #60 on): Nov, 1988 - No. 90, June, 1996 ($1.25/$1.50/$1.75/$1.95, direct sales only, Mando paper)

1-Continued from Strange Tales Vol. 2 #19; Fantastic Four, Avengers, Spider-Man, Silver Surfer, Hulk, Daredevil app. (cameos); Dormammu app. 2 4 6 10 14 18
2-5,7-9: 2-Dormammu app. 3-New Defenders app. (Valkyrie, Andromeda, Interloper & Manslaughter.) 4-New Defenders becomes Dragoncircle; vs. Dragon of the Moon. 5-Roy & Dan Thomas-s & Guice-p begin; Rintrah app; vs. Baron Mordo. 7-Agamotto, Satannish, Mephisto app.; origin of Baron Mordo Pt. 2 (in back-up). 8-Mephisto vs. Satannish; origin of Baron Mordo Pt. 3 (in back-up). 9-History of Dr. Strange 1 2 3 5 6 8
6-1st Mephista (daughter of Mephisto); Satannish & Mephisto app; Rintrah appears as Howard the Duck this issue; origin of Baron Mordo Pt. 1 (in back-up) 3 6 9 15 22 28
10-45,48,49: 10-Re-intro Morbius w/new costume (11/89). 14-Origin Morbius. 15-Unauthorized Amy Grant photo-c. 16-vs. Baron Blood; Brother Voodoo app. also in back-up story (origin). 17-Morbius & Brother Voodoo app.; origin of Zombies in back-up. 19-Origin of the 1st Brother Voodoo in back-up. 20-Dormammu app. 21-24: Dormammu & Baron Mordo app.; last Guice-a. 26-Werewolf by Night app. 28-Ghost Rider story continued from Ghost Rider #12; published at the same time as Dr. Strange/Ghost Rider Special #1 (4/91). 31-Infinity Gauntlet x-over; continued from Infinity Gauntlet #1; Silver Surfer app. 33-Thanos app. 34-36-Infinity Gauntlet x-overs. 34-Dr. Doom app. 35-Scarlet Witch & Thor app. 41-Wolverine app. 42-47-Infinity War x-overs. 42-Galactus app.; continues in Silver Surfer #67. 43-Continued from Infinity War #2; Galactus vs. Agamotto. 44-Galactus, Silver Surfer & Juggernaut app. 45-Galactus, Silver Surfer & Death app. 1 2 3 5 6 8
46-1st app. Necromancer; Dr. Druid, Scarlet Witch & Agatha Harkness app. 3 6 9 16 23 30
47-1st cover app. Necromancer 3 6 9 14 20 25
50-($2.95, 52 pgs.)-Holo-grafx foil-c; Hulk, Ghost Rider & Silver Surfer app.; leads into new Secret Defenders series 2 4 6 9 13 16
51-74: 52,53-Nightmare & Morbius app. 54-56: Infinity Crusade x-overs. 61-Siege of Darkness Pt. 15; new Dr. Strange begins (cameo, 1st app. 'Strange'; continued from Marvel Comics Presents #146; continued in Ghost Rider/Blaze Spirits of Vengeance #18. 62-Dr. Doom vs. Strange. 64,65-Sub-Mariner app. 65-Begin $1.95-c; bound-in card sheet. 66-Midnight Sons app.; continued in Dr. Strange Annual #4. 67-Clea returns; continued from Dr. Strange Annual #4. 69-Polaris & Forge app.; story takes place between X-Factor #105,106. 70,71-Hulk app. 72-Silver ink-c; Last Rites Pt. 1. 73-Last Rites Pt. 2.; Salom app. 74-Last Rites Pt. 3; Salom app. 6.00
75-($3.50) Foil-c; Last Rites Pt. 4; death of 'Strange' 1 3 4 6 8 10
75-($2.50) Reg-c 5.00
76-89: 76-New look Dr. Strange. 80-Warren Ellis-s begin; another new look for Dr. Strange. 81-Begins "Over the Edge" branding. 82-Last Ellis-s. 84-DeMatteis-s begin; Baron Mordo app. 85-Baron Mordo revealed to have cancer. 86-Baron Mordo app. 87-'Death' of Baron Mordo 5.00
90-Last issue; Chthon app. 2 4 6 11 16 20
Annual 1 (See Doctor Strange 2nd series)
Annual 2 ('92, $2.25, 68 pgs.) Return of the Defenders Pt. 4; continued from Silver Surfer Annual #5; Hulk, Sub-Mariner, Silver Surfer app.; vs. Wild One 6.00
Annual 3 ('93, $2.95, 68 pgs.) Polybagged w/card; 1st Kyllian 6.00
Annual 4 ('94, $2.95, 68 pgs.) Story occurs between Doctor Strange #66-67 6.00
Ashcan (1995, 75¢) 4.00
.../Ghost Rider Special 1 (4/91, $1.50)-Same book as Doctor Strange, Sorceror Supreme #28 1 3 4 6 8 10
...Vs. Dracula 1 (3/94, $1.75, 52 pgs.)-r/Tomb of Dracula #44 & Dr. Strange #14 1 3 4 6 8 10
NOTE: ***Colan*** *c/a-19.* ***Golden*** *c-28.* ***Guice*** *a-5-16, 18, 20-24; c-5-12, 20-24.*

DOCTOR STRANGE: THE OATH
Marvel Comics: Dec, 2006 - No. 5, Apr, 2007 ($2.99, limited series)

1-5-Vaughan-s/Martin-a; Night Nurse app. 1-Origin re-told 4.00
1-Halloween Comic Fest 2015 (12/15, giveaway) r/#1 with logo on cover 4.00
TPB (2007, $13.99) r/#1-5; sketch pages and promotional art 14.00

DR. TOM BRENT, YOUNG INTERN
Charlton Publications: Feb, 1963 - No. 5, Oct, 1963

1 3 6 9 18 28 38
2-5 3 6 9 14 19 24

DR. TOMORROW
Acclaim Comics (Valiant): Sept, 1997 - No. 12, Aug, 1998 ($2.50)

1-12: 1-Mignola-c 4.00

DOCTOR TOMORROW
Valiant Entertainment: Feb, 2020 - No. 5, Aug, 2020 ($3.99, limited series)

1-5-Arbona-s/Towe-a; intro. new Doctor Tomorrow 4.00

DR. VOLTZ (See Mighty Midget Comics)

DOCTOR VOODOO: AVENGER OF THE SUPERNATURAL
Marvel Comics: Dec, 2009 - No. 5, Apr, 2010 ($2.99, limited series)

1-5-Dr. Doom, Son of Satan & Ghost Rider app.; Palo-a 3.00
Doctor Voodoo: The Origin of Jericho Drumm (1/10, $4.99) r/Strange Tales #169,170 5.00

DR. WEIRD
Big Bang Comics: Oct, 1994 - No. 2, May, 1995 ($2.95, B&W)

1,2: 1-Frank Brunner-c 4.00
... Special (2/94, $3.95, B&W, 68 pgs.) Origin-r by Starlin; Starlin-c 4.00

DOCTOR WHO (Also see Marvel Premiere #57-60)
Marvel Comics Group: Oct, 1984 - No. 23, Aug, 1986 ($1.50, direct sales, Baxter paper)

1-British-r 2 4 6 10 14 18
2-15-British-r 5.00
16-23 6.00

	GD	VG	FN	VF	VF/NM	NM-
	2.0	4.0	6.0	8.0	9.0	9.2

Graphic Novel Voyager (1985, $8.95) color reprints of B&W comic pages from Doctor Who Magazine #88-99; Colin Baker afterword 15.00

DOCTOR WHO (Based on the 2005 TV series with David Tennant)
IDW Publishing: Jan, 2008 - No. 6, Jun, 2008 ($3.99)

1-6: 1-Nick Roche-a/Gary Russell-s; two covers 4.00

DOCTOR WHO (Based on the 2005 TV series with David Tennant)
IDW Publishing: Jul, 2009 - No. 16, Oct, 2010 ($3.99)

1-16-Grist-c on all. 3-5,13-16-Art by Matt Smith (not the actor) 4.00
... Annual 2010 (7/10, $7.99) short stories by various; Yates-c; cameo by 11th Doctor 8.00
...: Autopia (6/09, $3.99) Ostrander-s; Yates-a/c; variant photo-c 4.00
...: Black Death White Life (9/09, $3.99) Mandrake-a; Guy Davis- c; variant photo-c 4.00
...: Cold-Blooded War (8/09, $3.99) Salmon-a/c; variant photo-c 4.00
...: Room With a Déjà View (6/09, $3.99) Eric J-a; Mandrake-c; variant photo-c 4.00
...: The Whispering Gallery (2/09, $3.99) Moore & Reppion-s; Templesmith-a/2 covers 4.00
...: Time Machination (5/09, $3.99) Paul Grist-a/c; variant photo-c 4.00

DOCTOR WHO (Based on the 2010 TV series with Matt Smith)
IDW Publishing: Jan, 2011 - No. 12, Apr, 2012 ($3.99)

1-16: 1-Edwards & photo-c; Currie-a. 5-Buckingham-a. 12-Grist-a 4.00
Annual 2011 (8/11, $7.99) short stories by Fialkov, Shedd, Smith, McDaid and others 8.00
... Convention Special (7/11, no cover price, BBC America Shop Exclusive) The Doctor, Amy, and Rory at the San Diego Comic-Con; Matthew Dow Smith-s/Domingues-a 15.00
... 100 Page Spectacular 1 (7/12, $7.99) Short story reprints from various eras 8.00

DOCTOR WHO (Volume 3)(Based on the 2010 TV series with Matt Smith)
IDW Publishing: Sept, 2012 - No. 16, Dec, 2013 ($3.99)

1-16-Regular & photo-c on each: 1,2-Diggle-s/Buckingham-a. 3,4-Bond-a 4.00
...: 2016 Convention Exclusive (7/16, $10.00) Short stories of the various doctors 10.00
... Special 2012 (8/12, $7.99) Short stories by various incl. Wein, Diggle; Buckingham-c 8.00
... Special 2013 (12/13, $7.99) Cornell-s/Broxton-a; The Doctor visits the real world 8.00

DOCTOR WHO (Based on the TV series with Jodie Whittaker)
Titan Comics: Dec, 2020 - No. 4, Mar, 2021 ($3.99)

1-4-The 13th and 10th Doctors team up; Rose app. 4.00

DOCTOR WHO: A FAIRYTALE LIFE (Based on the 2010 TV series with Matt Smith)
IDW Publishing: Apr, 2011 - No. 4, Jul, 2011 ($3.99, limited series)

1-4: 1-Sturges-s/Yeates-a; covers by Buckingham & Mebberson. 3-Shearer-a 4.00

DR. WHO & THE DALEKS (See Movie Classics)

DOCTOR WHO CLASSICS
IDW Publishing: Nov, 2005 - Oct, 2013 ($3.99)

1-10: Reprints from Doctor Who Weekly (1979); art by Gibbons, Neary and others 4.00
Series 2 (12/08 - No. 12, 11/09, $3.99) 1-12 4.00
Series 3 (3/10 - No. 6, 8/10, $3.99) 1-6 4.00
Series 4 (2/12 - No. 6, 7/12, $3.99) 1-6: Colin Baker era 4.00
Series 5 (3/13 - No. 5, 10/13 $3.99) 1-5: Sylvester McCoy era 4.00
...: The Seventh Doctor (2/11, $3.99) 1-5: 1-Furman-s/Ridgway-a; Sylvester McCoy-era 4.00

DOCTOR WHO: EMPIRE OF THE WOLF
Titan Comics: Dec, 2021 - No. 4, Mar, 2022 ($3.99, limited series)

1-4-Houser-s/Ingranata-a; 8th & 11th Doctors and Rose Tyler app. 4.00

DOCTOR WHO EVENT 2015: FOUR DOCTORS
Titan Comics: Sept, 2015 - No. 5, Oct, 2015 ($3.99, weekly limited series)

1-5-Paul Cornell-s/Neil Edwards-a; 10th, 11th, 12th and War Doctor app. 4.00

DOCTOR WHO EVENT 2016: SUPREMACY OF THE CYBERMEN
Titan Comics: Aug, 2016 - No. 5, Dec, 2016 ($3.99, limited series)

1-5-Mann & Scott-s; 9th, 10th, 11th, 12th Doctors app.; multiple covers on each 4.00

DOCTOR WHO: FREE COMIC BOOK DAY
Titan Comics: Jun, 2015; Jun, 2016; Jun, 2017, 2019 (giveaways)

1-Short stories with the 10th, 11th & 12th Doctors; Paul Cornell interview 3.00
2016 - (6/16) Short stories with the 9th, 10th, 11th & 12th Doctors 3.00
2017 - (6/17) 12th Doctor and Bill; flashbacks with the 9th, 10th, 11th Doctors 3.00
2018 - (2018) 7th, 10th, 11th, 12th and 13th Doctors app.; photo-c 3.00
2019 - (2019) 13th Doctor and companions; Houser-s/Angiolini-c 3.00

DOCTOR WHO: GHOST STORIES (Sequel to the 2016 Christmas episode with The Ghost)
IDW Publishing: May, 2017 - No. 4, Aug, 2017 ($3.99, limited series)

1-4-George Mann-s; Grant and Lucy app.; multiple covers on each. 3-Calero-a 4.00

DOCTOR WHO: MISSY
Titan Comics: May, 2021 - No. 4, Aug, 2021 ($3.99, limited series)

1-4-Houser-s/Ingranata-a; Missy teams with the original Master 4.00

DOCTOR WHO: ORIGINS (Based on the Jo Martin version)
Titan Comics: Jul, 2022 - No. 4, Oct, 2022 ($3.99, limited series)

1-4-Houser-s/Ingranata-a; features the Fugitive Doctor; multiple covers 4.00

DOCTOR WHO: PRISONERS OF TIME
IDW Publishing: Feb, 2013 - No. 12, Nov, 2013 ($3.99, limited series)

1-50th Anniversary series with each issue spotlighting one Doctor; Francavilla-c 6.00
1-12-Photo covers 5.00
2-12: Francavilla-c on all. 5-12-Dave Sim variant-c. 8-Langridge-a 4.00

DOCTOR WHO: SPECIAL (Also see Doctor Who: The Lost Dimension)
IDW Publishing: Nov, 2017 - No. 2, Nov, 2017 ($4.99)

1,2-The Lost Dimension x-over parts 5 & 7; River Song and the 4th Doctor app. 5.00

DOCTOR WHO: THE EIGHTH DOCTOR (Based on the Paul McGann version)
Titan Comics: Nov, 2015 - No. 5, Apr, 2016 ($3.99, limited series)

1-5: 1-Intro. Josephine; Vieceli-a; multiple covers on each 4.00

DOCTOR WHO: THE ELEVENTH DOCTOR (Based on the Matt Smith version)
Titan Comics: Aug, 2014 - No. 15, Sept, 2015 ($3.99)

1-15: 1-Intro. Alice; Fraser-a; multiple covers on each 4.00

DOCTOR WHO: THE ELEVENTH DOCTOR YEAR TWO (Matt Smith version)
Titan Comics: Oct, 2015 - No. 15, Dec, 2016 ($3.99)

1-15: 1-War Doctor & Abslom Daak app.; multiple covers on each 4.00

DOCTOR WHO: THE ELEVENTH DOCTOR YEAR THREE (Matt Smith version)
Titan Comics: Feb, 2017 - No. 13, Feb, 2018 ($3.99)

1-13: 1-The Doctor and Alice; Rob Williams-s; multiple covers on each. 10-Lost Dimension x-over part 4 4.00

DOCTOR WHO: THE FORGOTTEN (Based on the 2005 TV series with David Tennant)
IDW Publishing: Aug, 2008 - No. 6, Jan, 2009 ($3.99)

1-6: 1,2-Pia Guerra-a/Tony Lee-s; two covers 4.00

DOCTOR WHO: THE FOURTH DOCTOR (Based on the Tom Baker version)
Titan Comics: Apr, 2016 - No. 5, Oct, 2016 ($3.99)

1-5: Sarah Jane app.; Brian Williamson-a; multiple covers on each 4.00

DOCTOR WHO: THE LOST DIMENSION (Eight part x-over with 2017 Doctor Who titles)
Titan Comics: Sept, 2017 - Nov, 2017 ($3.99)

... Alpha (9/17, $3.99) Part one; multiple doctors and Capt. Jack app.; Stott-a 4.00
... Omega (11/17, $3.99) Concluding Part eight; multiple doctors and Jenny app. 4.00

DOCTOR WHO: THE NINTH DOCTOR (Based on the Christopher Eccleston version)
Titan Comics: Apr, 2015 - No. 5, Dec, 2015 ($3.99)

1-5: 1-Rose & Capt. Jack app.; Cavan Scott-s; multiple covers on each 4.00

DOCTOR WHO: THE NINTH DOCTOR ONGOING (Christopher Eccleston version)
Titan Comics: May, 2016 - No. 15, Sept, 2017 ($3.99)

1-15: 1-Rose & Capt. Jack app.; Cavan Scott-s; multiple covers on each 4.00
Doctor Who: The Ninth Special (Lost Dimension Part 2) (10/17, $3.99) Vastra app. 4.00

DOCTOR WHO: THE ROAD TO THE THIRTEEN DOCTOR
Titan Comics: Aug, 2018 - No. 3, Oct, 2018 ($3.99, limited series)

1-3: 1-The Tenth Doctor & companions; Peaty-s/Zanfardino-a. 2-Eleventh. 3-Twelfth 4.00

DOCTOR WHO: THE SEVENTH DOCTOR: OPERATION VOLCANO (Sylvester McCoy)
Titan Comics: Jul, 2018 - No. 3, Sept, 2018 ($5.99/$3.99)

1-($5.99) Ace & Gilmore app.; Andrew Cartmel-s/Christopher Jones-a 6.00
2,3-($3.99) 4.00

DOCTOR WHO: THE TENTH DOCTOR (Based on the David Tennant version)
Titan Comics: Aug, 2014 - No. 15, Sept, 2015 ($3.99)

1-15: 1-5-Casagrande-a; multiple covers on each. 1-Intro. Gabby. 6,7-Weeping Angels 4.00

DOCTOR WHO: THE TENTH DOCTOR YEAR TWO (David Tennant version)
Titan Comics: Oct, 2015 - No. 17, Jan, 2017 ($3.99)

1-17: 1-Abadzis-s/Carlini-a; multiple covers on each. 3-Captain Jack app. 4.00

DOCTOR WHO: THE TENTH DOCTOR YEAR THREE (David Tennant version)
Titan Comics: Feb, 2017 - No. 14, Mar, 2018 ($3.99)

1-14: 1-The Doctor & Gabby; Abadzis-s; multiple covers on each. 9-Lost Dimension x-over part 3 4.00

DOCTOR WHO: THE THIRD DOCTOR (Based on the Jon Pertwee version)
Titan Comics: Oct, 2016 - No. 5, Mar, 2017 ($3.99)

1-5-Jo and The Brigadier app.; multiple covers on each 4.00

DOCTOR WHO: THE THIRTEENTH DOCTOR (Jodie Whittaker version)
Titan Comics: No. 0, Oct, 2018; No. 1, Dec, 2018 - No. 12, Oct, 2019 ($3.99)

0 - The Many Lives of Doctor Who ($7.99); short stories of each of the previous Doctors 8.00
1-12: 1-Houser-s/Stott-a; Ryan, Yasmin & Graham app. 4.00
... Holiday Special #1, (12/19, 1/20, $5.99) Houser-s/Ingranata-a 6.00
(Season 2) 2.1-2.4: 2.1-(2/20) Tenth Doctor & Martha app. 4.00

DOCTOR WHO: THE TWELFTH DOCTOR (Based on the Peter Capaldi version)
Titan Comics: Nov, 2014 - No. 15, Jan, 2016 ($3.99)

1-15: 1-The Doctor and Clara; Dave Taylor-a; multiple covers on each 4.00

DOCTOR WHO: THE TWELFTH DOCTOR YEAR TWO (Based on the Peter Capaldi version)
Titan Comics: Feb, 2016 - No. 15, Apr, 2017 ($3.99)

1-15: 1-The Doctor and Clara. 6-Intro. Hattie 4.00

DOCTOR WHO: THE TWELFTH DOCTOR YEAR THREE (The Peter Capaldi version)
Titan Comics: May, 2017 - No. 13, Apr, 2018 ($3.99)

1-13: 5-Bill Potts comic debut. 8-Lost Dimension x-over part 6; 9th & 10th Doctors app. 4.00

DOCTOR WHO: TIME LORD VICTORIOUS
Titan Comics: Oct, 2020 - No. 2, Nov, 2020 ($5.99, limited series)

1,2-The 10th Doctor and the Daleks app.; Jody Houser-s 6.00

DR. WONDER
Old Town Publishing: June, 1996 - No. 5 ($2.95, B&W)

1-5: 1-Intro & origin of Dr. Wonder; Dick Ayers-c/a; Irwin Hasen-a 3.00

DOCTOR ZERO
Marvel Comics (Epic Comics): Apr, 1988 - No. 8, Aug, 1989 ($1.25/$1.50)

1-8: 1-Sienkiewicz-c. 6,7-Spiegle-a 3.00
NOTE: ***Sienkiewicz** a-3i, 4i; c-1.*

DO-DO (Funny Animal Circus Stories)
Nation-Wide Publishers: 1950 - No. 7, 1951 (5¢, 5x7-1/4" Miniature)

	GD 2.0	VG 4.0	FN 6.0	VF 8.0	VF/NM 9.0	NM- 9.2
1 (52 pgs.)	22	44	66	132	216	300
2-7	12	24	36	69	97	125

DODO & THE FROG, THE (Formerly Funny Stuff; also see It's Game Time #2)
National Periodical Publications: No. 80, 9-10/54 - No. 88, 1-2/56; No. 89, 8-9/56; No. 90, 10-11/56; No. 91, 9/57; No. 92, 11/57 (See Comic Cavalcade and Captain Carrot)

	GD 2.0	VG 4.0	FN 6.0	VF 8.0	VF/NM 9.0	NM- 9.2
80-1st app. Doodles Duck by Sheldon Mayer	20	40	60	114	182	250
81-91: Doodles Duck by Mayer in #81,83-90	11	22	33	62	86	110
92-(Scarce)-Doodles Duck by S. Mayer	18	36	54	105	165	225

DOG DAYS OF SUMMER
DC Comics: Jul, 2019 ($9.99, one-shot, squarebound)

1-Short stories by various; Krypto, Beast Boy, Batcow, Killer Croc, Animal Man app. 10.00

DOGFACE DOOLEY
Magazine Enterprises: 1951 - No. 5, 1953

Doctor Who: The Twelfth Doctor #14 © BBC

Dollar Comics: Swamp Thing #1 © DC

Doll Man #25 © QUA

	GD 2.0	VG 4.0	FN 6.0	VF 8.0	VF/NM 9.0	NM- 9.2
1(A-1 40)	32	64	96	188	307	425
2(A-1 43), 3(A-1 49), 4(A-1 53)	20	40	60	118	192	265
5(A-1 64) Classic good girl-c	52	104	156	328	552	775
I.W. Reprint #1('64), Super Reprint #17	3	6	9	15	22	28

DOG MOON
DC Comics (Vertigo): 1996 ($6.95, one-shot)
1-Robert Hunter-scripts; Tim Truman-c/a. 7.00

DOG OF FLANDERS, A
Dell Publishing Co.: No. 1088, Mar, 1960

	GD	VG	FN	VF	VF/NM	NM-
Four Color 1088-Movie, photo-c	5	10	15	33	57	80

DOGPATCH (See Al Capp's... & Mammy Yokum)

DOGS OF WAR (Also see Warriors of Plasm #13)
Defiant: Apr, 1994 - No. 5, Aug, 1994 ($2.50)
1-5: 5-Schism x-over 4.00

DOGS-O-WAR
Crusade Comics: June, 1996 - No. 3, Jan, 1997 ($2.95, B&W, limited series)
1-3: 1,2-Photo-c 4.00

DOLLAR COMICS
DC Comics: 2019 - 2020 ($1.00, reprints with new house ads)
...: Amethyst 1 - ('20) Reprints Amethyst, Princess of Gemworld #1; Estrada & Colón-a 3.00
...: Batman 386 - ('20) Reprints intro/origin of Black Mask; Moench-s/Mandrake-a 3.00
...: Batman 428 - ('20) Reprints Death of Jason Todd; Starlin-s/Aparo-a/Mignola-c 3.00
...: Batman 497 - ('19) Reprints Bane breaking Batman's back; Moench-s/Aparo-a/Jones-c 3.00
...: Batman 567 - ('20) Reprints 1st app. of Cassandra Cain Batgirl; Damion Scott-a 3.00
...: Batman 608 - ('19) Reprints 1st issue of Hush storyline; Loeb-s/Jim Lee-a 3.00
...: Batman 613 - ('19) Reprint from Hush storyline; Harley Quinn & Catwoman app. 3.00
...: Batman 663 - ('20) Reprints Joker storybook issue; Morrison-s/Van Fleet-a 3.00
...: Batman Adventures 12 - ('19) Reprints comic book debut of Harley Quinn; Batgirl app. 3.00
...: Batman/Huntress: Cry For Blood 1 (3/20) - Rucka-s/Burchett-a; The Question app. 3.00
...: Batman: Shadow of the Bat 1 - ('20) The Last Arkham; Grant-s/Breyfogle-a 3.00
...: Birds of Prey 1 - ('19) Reprints 1st 1999 Black Canary/Oracle issue; Dixon-s/Land-a 3.00
...: Blackest Night 1 - ('19) Reprints 1st issue of series; Johns-s/Reis-a 3.00
...: Catwoman 1 - ('20) Reprints 1st issue of 2002 series; Darwyn Cooke & Mike Allred-a 3.00
...: Crisis of Infinite Earths 1 - ('19) 1st issue of series; Wolfman-s/Pérez-a; Alex Ross-c 3.00
...: Detective Comics 554 - ('20) Reprints 1st new look Black Canary 3.00
...: Detective Comics 854 - (11/19) Early Batwoman spotlight; Williams III-a; photo-c 3.00
...: Flashpoint 1 - (1/20) Reprints 1st issue of series; Johns-s/Andy Kubert-a/c 3.00
...: Green Lantern 1 - ('20) Reprints 2011 New 52 issue; Johns-s/Mahnke-a 3.00
...: Green Lantern: Rebirth 1 - ('20) Reprints 2004 issue; Johns-s/Van Sciver-a 3.00
...: Harley Quinn 1 - ('19) Reprints 1st issue of 2013 series; Conner-c 3.00
...: Infinite Crisis 1 - ('19) Reprints 1st issue of series; Johns-s/Jimenez-a/Jim Lee-c 3.00
...: JLA 1 - ('20) Reprints 1996 issue; Morrison-s/Porter-a 3.00
...: JLA: Year One 1 - ('20) Reprints 1998 issue; Waid & Augustyn-s/Kitson-a 3.00
...: Justice League 1 - ('20) Reprints 1987 issue; Giffen & DeMatteis-s/Maguire-a 3.00
...: Justice League 1 - ('20) Reprints 2011 New 52 issue; Geoff Johns-s/Jim Lee-a 3.00
...: Justice League of America 1 - ('20) Reprints 2006 issue; Meltzer-s/Benes-a 3.00
...: Luthor 1 - ('19) Reprints Lex Luthor: Man of Steel #1; Azzarello-s/Bermejo-a/c 3.00
...: New Teen Titans 2 - ('20) Reprints debut of Deathstroke; Wolfman-s/Pérez-a 3.00
...: Robin 1 - ('20) Reprints 1991 issue; Tim Drake; Dixon-s/Lyle-a 3.00
...: Sandman 23 - ('20) Lucifer loses his wings and leaves Hell; Gaiman-s/Kelley Jones-a 3.00
...: Superman 75 - ('19) Reprints Death of Superman issue from 1993 3.00
...: Swamp Thing 1 - ('19) Reprints 1st issue of 1972 series; Wein-s/Wrightson-a 3.00
...: Swamp Thing 57 - ('20) Reprints #57 from '82 series; Adam Strange app.; Moore-s 3.00
...: Tales of the Teen Titans 3 - ('19) Conclusion of The Judas Contract; Pérez-a 3.00
...: The Brave and the Bold 197 - (3/20) Golden Age Batman and Catwoman team-up 3.00
...: The Flash 1 - ('20) Reprints 1987 issue with Wally West as the Flash; Guice-a 3.00
...: The Flash 164 - ('19) Reprints 2000 issue; Johns-s/Unzueta-a/Bolland-c 3.00
...: The Flash: Rebirth 1 - ('20) Reprints 2009 issue; Johns-s/Van Sciver-a 3.00
...: The Joker 1 - ('19) Reprints 1st issue of 1975 series; O'Neil-s/Novick-a 3.00
...: Watchmen 1 - ('19) Reprints 1st issue of series; Alan Moore-s/Dave Gibbons-a 3.00

DOLLFACE & HER GANG (Betty Betz'...)
Dell Publishing Co.: No. 309, Jan, 1951

	GD	VG	FN	VF	VF/NM	NM-
Four Color 309	8	16	24	54	102	150

DOLLHOUSE
Dark Horse Comics: Mar, 2011; Jul, 2011 - No. 5, Nov, 2011 ($3.50, limited series)
1-5-Richards-a; two covers on each 4.00
...: Epitaphs (3/11, $3.50) reprints story from DVD collection; covers by Noto & Morris 4.00

DOLLHOUSE FAMILY, THE
DC Comics (Hill House Comics): Jan, 2020 - No. 6, Jun, 2020 ($3.99)
1-6-Carey-s/Gross-a; back-up serial Sea Dogs in each 4.00

DOLLMAN (Movie)
Eternity Comics: Sept, 1991 - No. 4, Dec, 1991 ($2.50, limited series)
1-4: Adaptation of film 4.00

DOLL MAN QUARTERLY, THE (Doll Man #17 on; also see Feature Comics #27 & Freedom Fighters)
Quality Comics: Fall, 1941 - No. 7, Fall, '43; No. 8, Spr, '46 - No. 47, Oct, 1953

	GD 2.0	VG 4.0	FN 6.0	VF 8.0	VF/NM 9.0	NM- 9.2
1-Dollman (by Cassone), Justin Wright begin	349	698	1047	2443	4272	6100
2-The Dragon begins; Crandall-a(5)	158	316	474	1003	1727	2450
3,4	97	194	291	621	1061	1500
5-Crandall-a	94	188	282	597	1024	1450
6,7(1943)	55	110	165	352	601	850
8(1946)-1st app. Torchy by Bill Ward	190	380	570	1207	2079	2950
9(Summer 1946)	57	114	171	362	619	875
10-20	42	84	126	265	445	625
21-26,28-30: 28-Vs. The Flame	39	78	117	240	395	550
27-Sci-fi bondage-c	45	90	135	284	480	675
31-(12/50)-Intro Elmo, the wonder dog (Dollman's faithful dog)	48	96	144	302	514	725
32-35,38,40: 32-34-Jeb Rivers app. 34-Crandall-a(p)	40	80	120	246	411	575
36-Giant shark-c	47	94	141	296	498	700
37-Origin & 1st app. Dollgirl; Dollgirl bondage-c	100	200	300	635	1093	1550
39- "Narcotics...the Death Drug" c-/story	57	114	171	382	619	875
41-47	34	68	102	199	325	450
Super Reprint #11('64, r/#20),15(r/#23),17(r/#28): 15,17-Torchy app.; Andru/Esposito-c	3	6	9	21	33	45

NOTE: ***Ward*** *Torchy in 8, 9, 11, 12, 14-24, 27; by Fox-#26, 30, 35-47.* ***Crandall*** *a-2, 5, 10, 13 & Super #11, 17, 18.* ***Crandall/Cuidera*** *c-40-42.* ***Guardineer*** *a-3. Bondage c-27, 37, 38, 39.*

DOLLY
Ziff-Davis Publ. Co.: No. 10, July-Aug, 1951 (Funny animal)

	GD	VG	FN	VF	VF/NM	NM-
10-Painted-c	14	28	42	80	115	150

DOLLY DILL
Marvel Comics/Newsstand Publ.: 1945

	GD	VG	FN	VF	VF/NM	NM-
1	40	80	120	246	411	575

DOLLZ, THE
Image Comics: Apr, 2001 - No. 2, June, 2001 ($2.95)
1,2: 1-Four covers; Sniegoski & Green-s/Green-a 3.00

DOMINATION FACTOR
Marvel Comics: Nov, 1999 - 4.8, Feb, 2000 ($2.50, interconnected mini-series)
1.1, 2.3, 3.5, 4.7-Fantastic Four; Jurgens-s/a 3.00
1.2, 2.4, 3.6, 4.8-Avengers; Ordway-s/a 3.00

DOMINIC FORTUNE
Marvel Comics (MAX): Oct, 2009 - No. 4, Jan, 2010 ($3.99, limited series)
1-4-Howard Chaykin-s/a/c 4.00

DOMINION
Image Comics: Jan, 2003 - No. 2 ($2.95)
1,2-Keith Giffen-s/a 5.00

DOMINION (Manga)
Eclipse Comics: Dec, 1990 - No. 6., July, 1990 ($2.00, B&W, limited series)
1-6 4.00

DOMINION: CONFLICT 1 (Manga)
Dark Horse Comics: Mar, 1996 - No. 6, Aug, 1996 ($2.95, B&W, limited series)
1-6: Shirow-c/a/scripts 3.00

DOMINIQUE LAVEAU: VOODOO CHILD
DC Comics (Vertigo): May, 2012 - No. 7, Nov, 2012 ($2.99, limited series)
1-7-Selwyn Seyfu Hinds-s/Denys Cowan-a 3.00

DOMINO (See X-Force)
Marvel Comics: Jan, 1997 - No. 3, Mar, 1997 ($1.95, limited series)
1-3: 2-Deathstrike-c/app. 4.00

DOMINO (See X-Force)
Marvel Comics: Jun, 2003 - No. 4, Aug, 2003 ($2.50, limited series)
1-4-Stelfreeze-c/a; Pruett-s 3.00

DOMINO (X-Force)
Marvel Comics: Jun, 2018 - No. 10, Mar, 2019 ($3.99)
1-10-Simone-s/Baldeón-a. 4-6-Shang-Chi app. 8-Morbius app. 9,10-Longshot app. 4.00

GD 2.0 | VG 4.0 | FN 6.0 | VF 8.0 | VF/NM 9.0 | NM- 9.2

Annual 1 (11/18, $4.99) Short flashback stories by various incl. Simone, Nicieza, Kirk 5.00

DOMINO CHANCE
Chance Enterprises: May-June, 1982 - No. 9, May, 1985 (B&W)

1-9: 7-1st app. Gizmo, 2 pgs. 8-1st full Gizmo story. 1-Reprint, May, 1985 4.00

DOMINO: HOTSHOTS (X-Force)
Marvel Comics: May, 2019 - No. 5, Sept, 2019 ($3.99, limited series)

1-5-Simone-s/Baldeón-a; Black Widow and Deadpool app. 4.00

DONALD AND MICKEY
IDW Publishing: Aug, 2017 - No. 4, May, 2018 ($5.99)

1-4-Reprints from European stories; 2 covers on each 6.00

DONALD AND MICKEY IN DISNEYLAND (See Dell Giants)

DONALD AND SCROOGE
Disney Comics: 1992 ($8.95, squarebound, 100 pgs.)

nn-Don Rosa reprint special; r/U.S., D.D. Advs. 1 3 4 6 8 10
1-3 (1992, $1.50)-r/D.D. Advs. (Disney) #1,22,24 & U.S. #261-263,269 3.00

DONALD AND THE WHEEL (Disney)
Dell Publishing Co.: No. 1190, Nov, 1961

Four Color 1190-Movie, Barks-c 8 16 24 56 108 160

DONALD DUCK (See Adventures of Mickey Mouse, Cheerios, Donald & Mickey, Ducktales, Dynabrite Comics, Gladstone Comic Album, Mickey & Donald, Mickey Mouse Mag., Story Hour Series, Uncle Scrooge, Walt Disney's Comics & Stories, W. D.'s Donald Duck, Wheaties & Whitman Comic Books, Wise Little Hen, The)

DONALD DUCK
Whitman Publishing Co./Grosset & Dunlap/K.K.: 1935, 1936 (All pages on heavy linen-like finish cover stock in color;1st book ever devoted to Donald Duck; see Advs. of Mickey Mouse for 1st app.) (9-1/2x13")

978(1935)-16 pgs.; Illustrated text story book 213 426 639 1363 2332 3300
nn(1936)-36 pgs.plus hard cover & dust jacket. Story completely rewritten with B&W illos added. Mickey appears and his nephews are named Morty & Monty
Book only 206 412 618 1318 2259 3200
Dust jacket only.... 40 80 120 244 402 560

DONALD DUCK (Walt Disney's) (10¢)
Whitman/K.K. Publications: 1938 (8-1/2x11-1/2", B&W, cardboard-c)
(Has D. Duck with bubble pipe on-c)

nn-The first Donald Duck & Walt Disney comic book; 1936 & 1937 Sunday strip-r(in B&W); same format as the Feature Books; 1st strips with Huey, Dewey & Louie from 10/17/37; classic bubble pipe cover 470 940 1410 3431 6066 8700

DONALD DUCK (Walt Disney's...#262 on; see 4-Color listings for titles & Four Color No. 1109 for origin story)
Dell Publ. Co./Gold Key #85-216/Whitman #217-245/Gladstone #246 on: 1940 - No. 84, Sept-Nov, 1962; No. 85, Dec, 1962 - No. 245, July, 1984; No. 246, Oct, 1986 - No. 279, May, 1990; No. 280, Sept, 1993 - No. 307, Mar,1998

Four Color 4(1940)-Daily 1939 strip-r by Al Taliaferro
2600 5200 7800 19,500 35,750 52,000
Large Feature Comic 16(1/41)-1940 Sunday strips-r in B&W
1000 2000 3000 7400 13,200 19,000
Large Feature Comic 20('41)-Comic Paint Book, r-single panels from Large Feature #16 at top of each pg. to color; daily strip-r across bottom of each pg. (Rare)
1150 2300 3450 8700 15,850 23,000
Four Color 9('42)- "Finds Pirate Gold"; 64 pgs. by Carl Barks & Jack Hannah (pgs. 1,2,5,12-40 are by Barks, his 1st Donald Duck comic book art work; © 8/17/42)
1050 2100 3150 8000 14,500 21,000
Four Color 29(9/43)- "Mummy's Ring" by Barks; reprinted in Uncle Scrooge & Donald Duck #1('65), W. D. Comics Digest #44('73) & Donald Duck Advs. #14
805 1610 2415 5877 10,389 14,900
Four Color 62(1/45)- "Frozen Gold"; 52 pgs. by Barks, reprinted in The Best of W.D. Comics & Donald Duck Advs. #4 238 476 714 1964 4432 6900
Four Color 108(1946)- "Terror of the River"; 52 pgs. by Carl Barks; reprinted in Gladstone Comic Album #2 107 214 321 856 1928 3000
Four Color 147(5/47)-in "Volcano Valley" by Barks 89 178 267 712 1606 2500
Four Color 159(8/47)-in "The Ghost of the Grotto"; 52 pgs. by Carl Barks; reprinted in Best of Uncle Scrooge & Donald Duck #1 ('66) & The Best of W.D. Comics & D.D. Advs. #9; two Barks stories 93 186 279 744 1672 2600
Four Color 178(12/47)-1st app. Uncle Scrooge by Carl Barks; reprinted in Gold Key Christmas Parade #3 & The Best of Walt Disney Comics 214 428 642 1766 3983 6200
Four Color 189(6/48)-by Carl Barks; reprinted in Best of Donald Duck & Uncle Scrooge #1('64) & D.D. Advs. #19 96 192 288 768 1734 2700
Four Color 199(10/48)-by Carl Barks; mentioned in Love and Death; r/in Gladstone Comic Album #5 93 186 279 744 1672 2600
Four Color 203(12/48)-by Barks; reprinted as Gold Key Christmas Parade #4
64 128 192 512 1156 1800
Four Color 223(4/49)-by Barks; reprinted as Best of Donald Duck #1 & Donald Duck Advs. #3
82 164 246 656 1478 2300
Four Color 238(8/49)-in "Voodoo Hoodoo" by Barks 61 122 183 488 1094 1700
Four Color 256(12/49)-by Barks; reprinted in Best of Donald Duck & Uncle Scrooge #2('67), Gladstone Comic Album #16 & W.D. Comics Digest 44('73)
52 104 156 413 932 1450
Four Color 263(2/50)-Two Barks stories; r-in D.D. #278
49 98 147 382 866 1350
Four Color 275(5/50), 282(7/50), 291(9/50), 300(11/50)-All by Carl Barks; 275, 282 reprinted in W.D. Comics Digest #44('73). #275 r/in Gladstone Comic Album #10. #291 r/in D. Duck Advs. #16 48 96 138 368 834 1300
Four Color 308(1/51), 318(3/51)-by Barks; #318-reprinted in W.D. Comics Digest #34 & D.D. Advs. #2,19 46 92 138 359 805 1250
Four Color 328(5/51)-by Carl Barks 46 92 138 340 770 1200
Four Color 339(7-8/51), 379-2nd Uncle Scrooge-c; art not by Barks.
33 66 99 238 532 825
Four Color 348(9-10/51), 356,394-Barks-c only 24 48 72 168 372 575
Four Color 367(1-2/52)-by Barks; reprinted as Gold Key Christmas Parade #2 & #8
37 74 111 274 612 950
Four Color 408(7-8/52), 422(9-10/52)-All by Carl Barks. #408-r-in Best of Donald Duck & Uncle Scrooge #1('64) & Gladstone Comic Album #13
36 72 108 266 596 925
26(11-12/52)-In "Trick or Treat" (Barks-a, 36pgs.) 1st story r-in Walt Disney Digest #16 & Gladstone C.A. #23 42 84 126 311 706 1100
27-30-Barks-c only 13 26 39 91 201 310
31-44,47-50 7 14 21 46 86 125
45-Barks-a (6 pgs.) 13 26 39 89 195 300
46- "Secret of Hondorica" by Barks, 24 pgs.; reprinted in Donald Duck #98 & 154
17 34 51 119 265 410
51-Barks-a,1/2 pg. 7 14 21 46 86 125
52- "Lost Peg-Leg Mine" by Barks, 10 pgs. 13 26 39 91 201 310
53,55-59 6 12 18 38 69 100
54- "Forbidden Valley" by Barks, 26 pgs. (10¢ & 15¢ versions exist)
15 30 45 101 223 345
60- "Donald Duck & the Titanic Ants" by Barks, 20 pgs. plus 6 more pgs.
14 28 42 98 217 335
61-67,69,70 5 10 15 34 60 85
68-Barks-a, 5 pgs. 9 18 27 62 126 190
71-Barks-r, 1/2 pg. 5 10 15 34 60 85
72-78,80,82-97,99,100: 96-Donald Duck Album 5 10 15 33 57 80
79,81-Barks-a, 1pg. 5 10 15 34 60 85
98-Reprints #46 (Barks) 5 10 15 34 60 85
101,103-111,113-135: 120-Last 12¢ issue. 134-Barks-r/#52 & WDC&S 194.
135-Barks-r/WDC&S 198, 19 pgs. 4 8 12 22 35 48
102-Super Goof. 112-1st Moby Duck 4 8 12 23 37 50
136-153,155,156,158: 149-20¢-c begin 3 6 9 14 20 26
154-Barks-r(#46) 3 6 9 16 24 32
157,159,160,164: 157-Barks-r(#45); 25¢-c begin. 159-Reprints/WDC&S #192 (10 pgs.).
160-Barks-r(#26). 164-Barks-r(#79) 3 6 9 14 20 26
161-163,165-173,175-187,189-191: 175-30¢-c begin. 187-Barks r/#68.
2 4 6 13 18 22
174,188: 174-r/4-Color #394. 3 6 9 14 19 24
175-177-Whitman variants 3 6 9 14 19 24
192-Barks-r(40 pgs.) from Donald Duck #60 & WDC&S #226,234 (52 pgs.)
3 6 9 15 22 28
193-200,202-207,209-211,213-216 2 4 6 9 13 16
201,208,212: 201-Barks-r/Christmas Parade #26, 16pgs. 208-Barks-r/#60 (6 pgs.).
212-Barks-r/WDC&S #130 2 4 6 9 13 16
217-219: 217 has 216 on-c. 219-Barks-r/WDC&S #106,107, 10 pgs. ea.
2 4 6 10 14 18
220,225-228: 228-Barks-r/F.C. #275 2 4 6 13 18 22
221,223,224: Scarce; only sold in pre-packs. 221(8/80), 223(11/80), 224(12/80)
5 10 15 35 63 90
222-(9-10/80)-(Very low distribution) 17 34 51 119 265 410
229-240: 229-Barks-r/F.C. #282. 230-Barks-r/ #52 & WDC&S #194. 236(2/82), 237(2-3/82), 238(3/82), 239(4/82), 240(5/82) 2 4 6 9 13 16
241-245: 241(4/83), 242(5/83), 243(3/84), 244(4/84), 245(7/84)(low print)
3 6 9 14 19 24
246-(1st Gladstone issue)-Barks-r/FC #422 3 6 9 15 21 26
247-249,251: 248,249-Barks-r/DD #54 & 26. 251-Barks-r/1945 Firestone
2 4 6 9 13 16
250-($1.50, 68 pgs.)-Barks-r/4-Color #9 2 4 6 10 14 18
252-277,280: 254-Barks-r/FC #328. 256-Barks-r/FC #147. 257-($1.50, 52 pgs.)-Barks-r/ Vacation Parade #1. 261-Barks-r/FC #300. 275-Kelly-r/FC #92. 280 (#1, 2nd Series)
1 2 3 5 6 8
278,279,286: 278,279 ($1.95, 68 pgs.): 278-Rosa-a; Barks-r/FC #263. 279-Rosa-c; Barks-r/MOC #4. 286-Rosa-a 1 2 3 5 7 9
281,282,284 1 2 3 4 5 7
283-Don Rosa-a, part-c & scripts 1 2 3 5 6 8
285,287-307 5.00
286 ($2.95, 68 pgs.)-Happy Birthday, Donald 6.00
Mini-Comic #1(1976)-(3-1/4x6-1/2"); r/D.D. #150 2 4 6 8 11 14

NOTE: ***Carl Barks*** *wrote all issues he illustrated, but #117, 126, 138 contain his script only. Issues 4-Color #189, 199, 203, 223, 238, 256, 263, 275, 282, 308, 348, 356, 367, 394, 408, 422, 26-30, 35, 44, 46, 52, 55, 57, 60, 65, 70-73, 77-80, 83, 101, 103, 105, 106, 111, 126, 246r, 266r, 268r, 271r, 275r, 278r(F.C. 263) all have* **Barks** *covers.* **Barks** *r-263-267, 269-278-282, 284, 285. #96 titled "Comic Album", #99-"Christmas Album". New art issues (not reprints)-106-46, 148-63, 167, 169, 170, 172, 173, 175, 178, 179, 196, 209, 223, 225, 236.* **Taliaferro** *daily newspaper strips #258-260, 264, 284, 285; Sunday strips #247, 280-283.*

DONALD DUCK (Numbering continues from Donald Duck and Friends #362)
BOOM! Studios (Kaboom!): No. 363, Feb, 2011 - No. 367, Jun, 2011 ($3.99)

363-367: 363-Barks reprints incl. "Mystery of the Loch". 364-Rosa-c 4.00

DONALD DUCK
IDW Publishing: May, 2015 - No. 21, Jun, 2017 ($3.99)

1-Legacy numbered #368; art by Scarpa and others; multiple covers 4.00
2-21-Reprints of Italian & Dutch stories; multiple covers on each. 8-Christmas issue 4.00
...'s Halloween Scream (10/15, Halloween giveaway) r/Donald Duck Advs. #7,8 (1990) 3.00

DONALD DUCK ADVENTURES (See Walt Disney's Donald Duck Adventures)

DONALD DUCK ALBUM (See Comic Album No. 1,3 & Duck Album)
Dell Publishing Co./Gold Key: 5-7/59 - F.C. No. 1239, 10-12/61; 1962; 8/63 - No. 2, Oct, 1963

Four Color 995 (#1) 7 14 21 44 82 120
Four Color 1099,1140,1239-Barks-c 7 14 21 44 82 120
Four Color 1182, 01204-207 (1962-Dell) 5 10 15 34 60 85
1(8/63-Gold Key)-Barks-c 5 10 15 34 60 85
2(10/63) 4 8 12 28 47 65

DONALD DUCK AND FRIENDS (Numbering continues from Walt Disney's ...)
BOOM! Studios: No. 347, Oct, 2009 - No. 362, Jan, 2011 ($2.99)

347-362: Two covers on most. Retitled "Donald Duck" with #363 3.00

DONALD DUCK AND THE BOYS (Also see Story Hour Series)
Whitman Publishing Co.: 1948 (5-1/4x5-1/2", 100pgs., hard-c; art & text)

845-(49) new illos by Barks based on his Donald Duck 10-pager in WDC&S #74, Expanded text not written by Barks; Cover not by Barks
50 100 150 350 600 850
(Prices vary widely on this book)

DONALD DUCK AND THE CHRISTMAS CAROL

Domino: Hotshots #2 © MAR

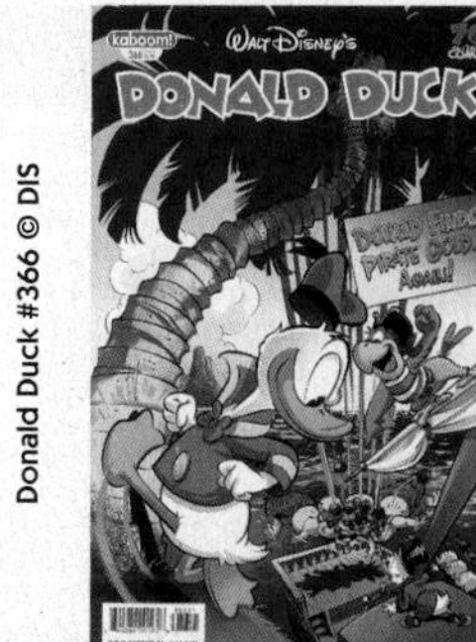

Donald Duck #366 © DIS

Doom Patrol #95 © DC

	GD	VG	FN	VF	VF/NM	NM-
	2.0	4.0	6.0	8.0	9.0	9.2

Whitman Publishing Co.: 1960 (A Little Golden Book, 6-3/8"x7-5/8", 28 pgs.)
nn-Story book pencilled by Carl Barks with the intended title "Uncle Scrooge's Christmas Carol." Finished art adapted by Norman McGary. (Rare)-Reprinted in Uncle Scrooge in Color. 20 40 60 100 185 270

DONALD DUCK BEACH PARTY (Also see Dell Giants)
Gold Key: Sept, 1965 (12¢)
1(#10158-509)-Barks-r/WDC&S #45; painted-c 6 12 18 38 69 100

DONALD DUCK BOOK (See Story Hour Series)

DONALD DUCK COMICS DIGEST
Gladstone Publishing: Nov, 1986 - No. 5, July, 1987 ($1.25/$1.50, 96 pgs.)
1,3: 1-Barks-c/a-r 1 3 4 6 8 10
2,4,5: 4,5-$1.50-c 6.00

DONALD DUCK FUN BOOK (See Dell Giants)

DONALD DUCK IN DISNEYLAND (See Dell Giants)

DONALD DUCK MARCH OF COMICS (See March of Comics #4,20,41,56,69,263)

DONALD DUCK MERRY CHRISTMAS (See Dell Giant No. 53)

DONALD DUCK PICNIC PARTY (See Picnic Party listed under Dell Giants)

DONALD DUCK TELLS ABOUT KITES (See Kite Fun Book)

DONALD DUCK, THIS IS YOUR LIFE (Disney, TV)
Dell Publishing Co.: No. 1109, Aug-Oct, 1960
Four Color 1109-Gyro flashback to WDC&S #141; origin Donald Duck (1st told) 12 24 36 81 176 270

DONALD DUCK XMAS ALBUM (See regular Donald Duck No. 99)

DONALD IN MATHMAGIC LAND (Disney)
Dell Publishing Co.: No. 1051, Oct-Dec, 1959 - No. 1198, May-July, 1961
Four Color 1051 (#1)-Movie 8 16 24 56 108 160
Four Color 1198-Reprint of above 6 12 18 37 66 95

DONALD QUEST (Donald Duck in parallel universe of Feudarnia)
IDW Publishing: Nov, 2016 - No. 5, Mar, 2017 ($3.99, limited series)
1-5-English version of Italian story; multiple covers on each. 1-Ambrosio-s/Freccero-a 4.00

DONATELLO, TEENAGE MUTANT NINJA TURTLE
Mirage Studios: Aug, 1986 ($1.50, B&W, one-shot, 44 pgs.)
1 3 6 9 17 25 36

DONDI
Dell Publishing Co.: No. 1176, Mar-May, 1961 - No. 1276, Dec, 1961
Four Color 1176 (#1)-Movie; origin, photo-c 6 12 18 37 66 95
Four Color 1276 4 8 12 28 47 65

DON FORTUNE MAGAZINE
Don Fortune Publishing Co.: Aug, 1946 - No. 6, Feb, 1947
1-Delecta of the Planets by C.C. Beck in all 34 68 102 199 325 450
2 15 30 45 94 147 200
3-6: 3-Bondage-c 15 30 45 83 124 165

DONG XOAI, VIETNAM 1965
DC Comics: 2010 ($19.95, B&W graphic novel)
SC-Joe Kubert-s/a/c; includes report of actual events that inspired the story 20.00

DONKEY KONG (See Blip #1)

DONNA MATRIX
Reactor, Inc.: Aug, 1993 ($2.95, 52 pgs.)
1-Computer generated-c/a by Mike Saenz; 3-D effects 4.00

DON NEWCOMBE
Fawcett Publications: 1950 (Baseball)
nn-Photo-c 54 108 162 343 574 825

DON ROSA'S COMICS AND STORIES
Fantagraphics Books (CX Comics): 1983 ($2.95)
1,2: 1-(68 pgs.) Reprints Rosa's The Pertwillaby Papers episodes #128-133.
2-(60 pgs.) Reprints episodes #134-138 2 4 6 11 16 20

DON SIMPSON'S BIZARRE HEROES (Also see Megaton Man)
Kitchen Sink Press/Fiasco Comics: May, 1990 - No. 17, Sept, 1996 ($2.50/$2.95, B&W)
1-(5/90, Kitchen Sink) Don Simpson-s/a 1 3 4 6 8 10
1-(5/94, Fiasco) Features Megaton Man 2 4 6 10 14 18
2-10: 9-Title changes to Bizarre Heroes 2 4 6 8 10 12
0,11-17: 0-(12/94)-Begin $2.95-c; r/Bizarre Heroes #1. 16-Indicia also reads Megaton Man vs. Forbidden Frankenstein #1. 17-(9/96)-Indicia also reads Megaton Man #0; intro Megaton Man and the Fiascoverse to new readers 1 2 3 5 6 8

DON'T GIVE UP THE SHIP
Dell Publishing Co.: No. 1049, Aug, 1959
Four Color 1049-Movie, Jerry Lewis photo-c 9 18 27 58 114 170

DON WINSLOW OF THE NAVY
Merwil Publishing Co.: Apr, 1937 - No. 2, May, 1937 (96 pgs.)(A pulp/comic book cross; stapled spine)
V1#1-Has 16 pgs. comics in color. Captain Colorful & Jupiter Jones by Sheldon Mayer; complete Don Winslow novel 690 1380 2070 5200 -- --
2-Sheldon Mayer-a 190 380 570 1450 -- --

DON WINSLOW OF THE NAVY (See Crackajack Funnies, Famous Feature Stories, Popular Comics & Super Book #5,6)
Dell Publishing Co.: No. 2, Nov, 1939 - No. 22, 1941
Four Color 2 (#1)-Rare 258 516 774 1651 2826 4000
Four Color 22 60 120 180 381 653 925

DON WINSLOW OF THE NAVY (See TV Teens; Movie, Radio, TV) (Fightin' Navy No. 74 on)
Fawcett Publications/Charlton No. 70 on: 2/43 - #64, 12/48; #65, 1/51 - #69, 9/51; #70, 3/55 - #73, 9/55
1-(68 pgs.)-Captain Marvel on cover 135 270 405 864 1482 2100
2 45 90 135 284 480 675
3 37 74 111 222 361 500
4-6: 6-Flag-c 30 60 90 177 289 400
7-10: 8-Last 68 pg. issue? 22 44 66 132 216 300
11-20 19 38 57 111 176 240
21-40 16 32 48 94 147 200
41-43,45-64: 51,60-Singapore Sal (villain) app. 64-(12/48) 15 30 45 85 130 175
44-Classic spider-c 43 86 129 271 461 650
65(1/51)-Flying Saucer attack; photo-c 23 46 69 136 223 310
66 - 69(9/51): All photo-c. 66-sci-fi story 15 30 45 85 130 175
70(3/55)-73: 70-73 r-/#26,58 & 59 10 20 30 56 76 95

DOODLE JUMP (Based on the game app)
Dynamite Entertainment: 2014 - No. 6, 2015 ($3.99, limited series)
1-6-Steve Uy-a; multiple covers on each 4.00

DOOM
Marvel Comics: Oct, 2000 - No. 3, Dec, 2000 ($2.99, limited series)
1-3-Dr. Doom; Dixon-s/Manco-a 4.00

DOOMED (Also see Teen Titans #14 (2016))
DC Comics: Aug, 2015 - No. 6, Jan, 2016 ($2.99, limited series)
1-6: 1-Lobdell-s/Fernandez-a. 3-Alpha Centurion app. 4-6-Superman app. 3.00

DOOM FORCE SPECIAL
DC Comics: July, 1992 ($2.95, 68 pgs., one-shot, mature) (X-Force parody)
1-Morrison scripts; Simonson, Steacy, & others-a; Giffen/Mignola-c 4.00

DOOM PATROL, THE (Formerly My Greatest Adventure No. 1-85; see Brave and the Bold, DC Special Blue Ribbon Digest 19, Official... Index & Showcase No. 94-96)
National Periodical Publ.: No. 86, 3/64 - No. 121, 9-10/68; No. 122, 2/73 - No. 124, 6-7/73
86-1 pg. origin (#86-121 are 12¢ issues) 36 72 108 259 580 900
87-98: 88-Origin The Chief. 91-Intro. Mento 10 20 30 64 132 200
99-Intro. Beast Boy (later becomes the Changeling in New Teen Titans) 42 84 126 311 706 1100
100-Origin Beast Boy; Robot-Maniac series begins (12/65) 14 28 42 93 204 315
101-110: 102-Challengers of the Unknown app. 104-Wedding issue. 105-Robot-Maniac series ends. 106-Negative Man begins (origin) 7 14 21 46 86 125
111-120 6 12 18 37 66 95
121-Death of Doom Patrol; Orlando-c. 13 26 39 89 195 300
122-124: All reprints 2 4 6 8 11 14

DOOM PATROL
DC Comics (Vertigo imprint #64 on): Oct, 1987 - No, 87, Feb, 1995 (75¢-$1.95, new format)
1-Wraparound-c; Lightle-a 2 4 6 10 14 18
2-18: 3-1st app. Lodestone. 4-1st app. Karma. 8,15,16-Art Adams-c(i). 18-Invasion tie-in 4.00
19-(2/89)-Grant Morrison scripts begin, ends #63; 1st app Crazy Jane; $1.50-c & new format begins. 3 6 9 14 19 24
20-30: 29-Superman app. 30-Night Breed fold-out 6.00
31-34,37-41,45-49,51-56,58-60: 39-World Without End preview 4.00
35-1st brief app. of Flex Mentallo 2 4 6 11 16 20
36-1st full app. of Flex Mentallo 2 4 6 8 11 14
42-44-Origin of Flex Mentallo. 4.00

50,57 ($2.50, 52 pgs.) 5.00
61-87: 61,70-Photo-c. 73-Death cameo (2 panels) 4.00
...And Suicide Squad 1 (3/88, $1.50, 52 pgs.)-Wraparound-c 5.00
Annual 1 (1988, $1.50, 52 pgs.) 5.00
Annual 2 (1994, $3.95, 68 pgs.)-Children's Crusade tie-in. 5.00
...: Crawling From the Wreckage TPB (2004, $19.95) r/#19-25; Morrison-s 20.00
...: Down Paradise Way TPB (2005, $19.99) r/#35-41; Morrison-s 20.00
...: Magic Bus TPB (2007, $19.99) r/#51-57; Morrison-s; new Bolland-c 20.00
...: Musclebound TPB (2006, $19.99) r/#42-50; Morrison-s; new Bolland-c 20.00
...: Planet Love TPB (2008, $19.99) r/#58-63 & Doom Force Special #1; Morrison-s 20.00
...: The Painting That Ate Paris TPB (2004, $19.95) r/#26-34; Morrison-s 20.00
NOTE: *Bisley painted c-26-48, 55-58. **Bolland** c-64, 75. **Dringenberg** a-42(p). **Steacy** a-53.*

DOOM PATROL
DC Comics: Dec, 2001 - No. 22, Sept, 2003 ($2.50)
1-Intro. new team with Robotman; Tan Eng Huat-c/a; John Arcudi-s 4.00
2-22: 4,5-Metamorpho & Elongated Man app. 13,14-Fisher-a. 20-Geary-a 3.00

DOOM PATROL (see JLA #94-99)
DC Comics: Aug, 2004 - No. 18, Jan, 2006 ($2.50)
1-18-John Byrne-s/a. 1-Green Lantern, Batman app. 3.00

DOOM PATROL
DC Comics: Oct, 2009 - No. 22, Jul, 2011 ($3.99/$2.99)
1-7: 1-Giffen-s/Clark-a; back-up Metal Men feature w/Maguire-a. 1-Two covers. 4-5-Blackest Night. 6-Negative Man origin re-told 4.00
8-22-($2.99) 11,12-Ambush Bug app. 16-Giffen-a. 21-Robotman origin retold 3.00
...: Brotherhood TPB (2011, $17.99) r/#7-13 18.00
...: We Who Are About to Die TPB (2010, $14.99) r/#1-6; cover gallery; design art 15.00

DOOM PATROL
DC Comics (Young Animal): Nov, 2016 - No. 12, Dec, 2018 ($3.99)
1-12: 1-Gerald Way-s/Nick Derington-a; main cover has peel-off gyro sticker. 8-Allred-a 4.00
1-Director's Cut (5/17, $5.99) Pencil/ink art; original script with thumbnails 6.00
.../ JLA Special 1 (4/18, $4.99) Part 5 of Milk Wars crossover; Eaglesham-a/Mann-c 5.00

DOOM PATROL (See Tangent Comics/ Doom Patrol)

DOOM PATROL: WEIGHT OF THE WORLDS
DC Comics (Young Animal): Sept, 2019 - No. 7, Sept, 2020 ($3.99)
1-7: 1-Gerald Way-s/James Harvey-a. 3-Shaner-a. 5-Cloonan-a 4.00

DOOMSDAY
DC Comics: 1995 ($3.95, one-shot)
1-Year One story by Jurgens, L. Simonson, Ordway, and Gil Kane; Superman app. 5.00

DOOMSDAY CLOCK (See Watchmen)
DC Comics: Jan, 2018 - No. 12, Feb, 2020 ($4.99/$5.99, limited series)
1-Follows end of Watchmen; intro new Rorschach; Johns-s/Frank-a; 2 covers by Frank 5.00
1-($5.99) Lenticular cover 6.00
2-11: Two covers on each. 2-Comedian returns; Nathaniel Dusk makes DCU return as fictional 1940s -'50s film noir detective. 5-7-Joker app.; origin of Marionette 5.00
12-($5.99) Superman vs. Dr. Manhattan; intro of the Metaverse 6.00

DOOMSDAY + 1 (Also see Charlton Bullseye)
Charlton Comics: July, 1975 - No. 6, June, 1976; No. 7, June, 1978 - No. 12, May, 1979
1: #1-5 are 25¢ issues 4 8 12 23 37 50
2-6: 4-Intro Lor. 5-Ditko-a(1 pg.) 6-Begin 30¢-c 2 4 6 10 14 18
V3#7-12 (reprints #1-6) 6.00
5 (Modern Comics reprint, 1977) 6.00
NOTE: ***Byrne** c/a-1-12; Painted covers-2-7.*

DOOMSDAY.1
IDW Publishing: May, 2013 - No. 4, Aug, 2013 ($3.99)
1-4-John Byrne-s/a/c 4.00

DOOMSDAY SQUAD, THE
Fantagraphics Books: Aug, 1986 - No. 7, 1987 ($2.00)
1,2,4-7: Byrne-a in all. 1,2-New Byrne-c. 4-Neal Adams-c. 5-7-Gil Kane-c 4.00
3-Usagi Yojimbo app. (1st in color); new Byrne-c 6.00

DOOM'S IV
Image Comics (Extreme): July, 1994 - No.4, Oct, 1994 ($2.50, limited series)
1-4-Liefeld story 4.00
1,2-Two alternate Liefeld-c each, 4 covers form 1 picture 5.00

DOOM: THE EMPEROR RETURNS
Marvel Comics: Jan, 2002 - No. 3, Mar, 2002 ($2.50, limited series)
1-3-Dixon-s/Manco-a; Franklin Richards app. 4.00

DOOM 2099 (See Marvel Comics Presents #118 & 2099: World of Tomorrow)
Marvel Comics: Jan, 1993 - No. 44, Aug, 1996 ($1.25/$1.50/$1.95)
1-Metallic foil stamped-c 6.00
1-2nd printing 3.00
2-24,26-44: 4-Ron Lim-c(p). 17-bound-in trading card sheet. 40-Namor & Doctor Strange app. 41-Daredevil app., Namor-c/app. 44-Intro The Emissary; story contin'd in 2099: World of Tomorrow 4.00
18-Variant polybagged with Sega Sub-Terrania poster 5.00
25 ($2.25, 52 pgs.) 5.00
25 ($2.95, 52pgs.) Foil embossed cover 6.00
29 ($3.50)-acetate-c. 5.00
No. 1 (2/20, $4.99) Zdarsky-s/Castiello-a; tie-in to 2099 specials and ASM #33-36 (2020) 5.00

DOOMWAR
Marvel Comics: Apr, 2010 - No. 6, Sept, 2010 ($3.99, limited series)
1-6-Doctor Doom invades Wakanda; Black Panther & X-Men app.; Romita Jr.-c/Eaton-a 4.00

DOORWAY TO NIGHTMARE (See Cancelled Comic Cavalcade and Madame Xanadu)
DC Comics: Jan-Feb, 1978 - No. 5, Sept-Oct, 1978
1-Madame Xanadu in all 6 12 18 38 69 100
2-5: 4-Craig-a 2 4 6 10 14 18
NOTE: ***Kaluta** covers on all. Merged into The Unexpected with No. 190.*

DOPEY DUCK COMICS (Wacky Duck No. 3) (See Super Funnies)
Timely Comics (NPP): Fall, 1945 - No. 2, Apr, 1946
1-Casper Cat, Krazy Krow 50 100 150 315 533 750
2-Casper Cat, Krazy Krow 34 68 102 204 332 460

DORK
Slave Labor: June, 1993 - No. 11 ($2.50-$3.50, B&W, mature)
1-7,9-11: Evan Dorkin-c/a/scripts in all. 1(8/95),2(1/96)-(2nd printings). 1(3/97) (3rd printing). 1-Milk & Cheese app. 3-Eltingville Club starts. 6-Reprints 1st Eltingville Club app. from Instant Piano #1 4.00
8-($3.50) 4.00
Who's Laughing Now? TPB (2001, $11.95) reprints most of #1-5 12.00
The Collected Dork, Vol. 2: Circling the Drain (6/03, $13.95) r/most of #7-10 & other-s 14.00

DOROTHY & THE WIZARD IN OZ (Adaptation of the original 1908 L. Frank Baum book) (Also see Wonderful Wizard of Oz, Marvelous Land of Oz, and Ozma of Oz)
Marvel Comics: Nov, 2011 - No. 8, Aug, 2012 ($3.99, limited series)
1-8-Eric Shanower-a/Skottie Young-a/c 4.00

DOROTHY LAMOUR (Formerly Jungle Lil)(Stage, screen, radio)
Fox Feature Syndicate: No. 2, June, 1950 - No. 3, Aug, 1950
2-Wood-a(3), photo-c 41 82 123 256 428 600
3-Wood-a(3), photo-c 34 68 102 199 325 450

DOROTHY OF OZ PREQUEL
IDW Publishing: Mar, 2012 - No. 4, Aug, 2012 ($3.99, limited series)
1-4-Tipton-s/Shedd-a 4.00

DOT DOTLAND (Formerly Little Dot Dotland)
Harvey Publications: No. 62, Sept, 1974 - No. 63, Nov, 1974
62,63 2 4 6 11 16 20

DOTTY (...& Her Boy Friends)(Formerly Four Teeners; Glamorous Romances No. 41 on)
Ace Magazines (A. A. Wyn): No. 35, June, 1948 - No. 40, May, 1949
35-Teen-age 15 30 45 86 133 180
36-40: 37-Transvestism story 11 22 33 64 90 115

DOTTY DRIPPLE (Horace & Dotty Dripple No. 25 on)
Magazine Ent.(Life's Romances)/Harvey No. 3 on: 1946 - No. 24, June, 1952 (Also see A-1 No. 1, 3-8, 10)
1 (nd) (10¢) 16 32 48 94 147 200
2 11 22 33 60 83 105
3-10: 3,4-Powell-a 7 14 21 37 46 55
11-24 6 12 18 31 38 45

DOTTY DRIPPLE AND TAFFY
Dell Publishing Co.: No. 646, Sept, 1955 - No. 903, May, 1958
Four Color 646 (#1) 6 12 18 37 66 95
Four Color 691,718,746,801,903 4 8 12 28 47 65

DOUBLE ACTION COMICS
National Periodical Publications: No. 2, Jan, 1940 (68 pgs., B&W)
2-Contains original stories(?); pre-hero DC contents; same cover as Adventure No. 37. (seven known copies, four in high grade) (not an ashcan)
4300 8600 12,900 25,800 34,400 43,000
NOTE: *The cover to this book was probably reprinted from Adventure #37. #1 exists as an ash can copy with B&W cover; contains a coverless comic on inside with 1st & last page missing. There is proof of at least limited newsstand distribution. #2 cover proof only sold in 2005 for $4,000.*

DOUBLE COMICS
Elliot Publications: 1940 - 1943 (132 pgs.)
1940 issues; Masked Marvel-c 320 640 960 2240 3920 5600
1941 issues; Masked Marvel-c & the Mad Mong vs. the White Flash-c, Tornado Tim-c (attached), Nordac-c, & Green Light covers known 284 568 852 1818 3109 4400
1942 issues 284 568 852 1818 3109 4400
1943 issues 206 412 618 1318 2259 3200
NOTE: *Double Comics consisted of an almost endless combination of pairs of remaindered, unsold issues of comics representing most publishers and usually mixed publishers in the same book; e.g., a Captain America with a Silver Streak, or a Feature with a Detective, etc., could appear inside the same cover. The actual contents would have to determine its price. Prices listed are for average contents. Any containing rare origin or first issues are worth much more. Covers also vary in same year. Value would be approximately 50 percent of contents.*

DOUBLE-CROSS (See The Crusaders)

DOUBLE-DARE ADVENTURES
Harvey Publications: Dec, 1966 - No. 2, Mar, 1967 (35¢/25¢, 68 pgs.)
1-Origin Bee-Man, Glowing Gladiator, & Magic-Master; Simon/Kirby-a
6 12 18 40 73 105
2-Torres-a; r/Alarming Adv. #3('63) 5 10 15 31 53 75
NOTE: ***Powell** a-1. **Simon/Sparling** c-1, 2.*

DOUBLE DRAGON
Marvel Comics: July, 1991 - No. 6, Dec, 1991 ($1.00, limited series)
1-6: Based on video game. 2-Art Adams-c 4.00

DOUBLE EDGE
Marvel Comics: Alpha, 1995; Omega, 1995 ($4.95, limited series)
Alpha ($4.95)- Punisher story, Nick Fury app. 5.00
Omega ($4.95)-Punisher, Daredevil, Ghost Rider app. Death of Nick Fury 5.00

DOUBLE IMAGE
Image Comics: Feb, 2001 - No. 5, July, 2001 ($2.95)
1-5: 1-Flip covers of Codeflesh (Casey-s/Adlard-a) and The Bod (Young-s). 2-Two covers. 5-"Trust in Me" begins; Chaudhary-a 3.00

DOUBLE LIFE OF PRIVATE STRONG, THE
Archie Publications/Radio Comics: June, 1959 - No. 2, Aug, 1959
1-Origin & re-intro The Shield; Simon & Kirby-c/a, their re-entry into the super-hero genre; intro./1st app. The Fly; 1st S.A. super-hero for Archie Publ.
36 72 108 259 580 900
2-S&K-c/a; Tuska-a; The Fly app. (2nd or 3rd?) 18 36 54 126 281 435

DOUBLE TROUBLE
St. John Publishing Co.: Nov, 1957 - No. 2, Jan-Feb, 1958
1,2: Tuffy & Snuffy by Frank Johnson; dubbed "World's Funniest Kids"

Doomsday Clock #2 © DC

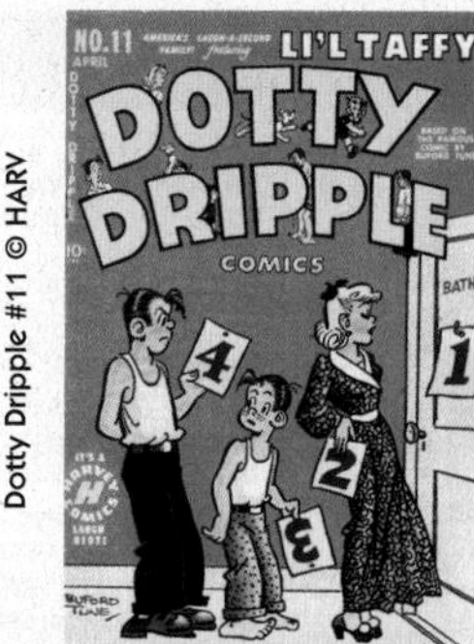

Dotty Dripple #11 © HARV

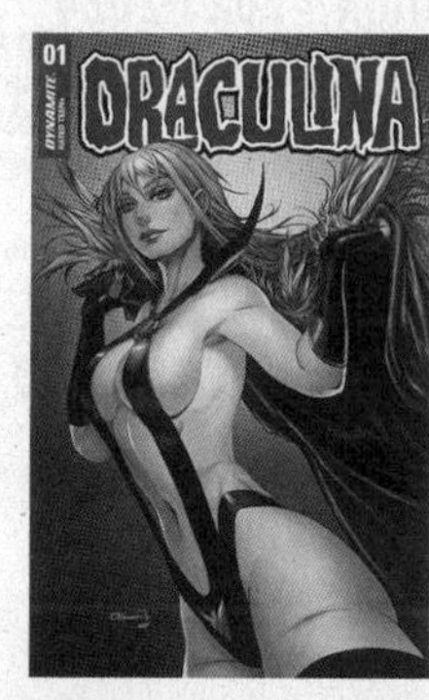

Draculina #1 © DYN

GD 2.0 | VG 4.0 | FN 6.0 | VF 8.0 | VF/NM 9.0 | NM- 9.2

9 18 27 52 69 85

DOUBLE TROUBLE WITH GOOBER
Dell Publishing Co.: No. 417, Aug, 1952 - No. 556, May, 1954

Four Color 417 5 10 15 34 60 85
Four Color 471,516,556 4 8 12 27 44 60

DOUBLE UP COMICS
Elliott Publications: 1941 (Pocket size, 192 pgs., 10¢)

1-Contains rebound copies of digest sized issues of Pocket Comics, Speed Comics, & Spitfire Comics; Japanese WWII-c 300 600 900 2070 3635 5200

DOVER & CLOVER (See All Funny & More Fun Comics #93)

DOVER BOYS (See Adventures of the...)

DOVER THE BIRD
Famous Funnies Publishing Co.: Spring, 1955

1-Funny animal; code approved (10¢-c) 11 22 33 64 90 115
1-Same cover; not code approved (6¢-c, 3 for 15¢) 10 20 30 58 79 100

DOWN
Image Comics (Top Cow): Dec, 2005 - No. 4, Mar, 2006 ($2.99)

1-4-Warren Ellis-s. 1-Tony Harris-a/c. 2-4-Cully Hamner-a 3.00
Down & Top Cow's Best of Warren Ellis TPB (6/06, $15.99) r/#1-4 & Tales of the Witchblade #3,4; Ellis-s; script for Down #1 with Harris sketch pages 16.00

DOWN WITH CRIME
Fawcett Publications: Nov, 1952 - No. 7, Nov, 1953

1 47 94 141 296 498 700
2,4,5: 2,4-Powell-a in each. 5-Bondage-c 26 52 78 154 252 350
3-Used in **POP**, pg. 106; "H is for Heroin" drug story 30 60 90 177 289 400
6,7: 6-Used in **POP**, pg. 80 26 52 78 154 252 350

DO YOU BELIEVE IN NIGHTMARES?
St. John Publishing Co.: Nov, 1957 - No. 2, Jan, 1958

1-Mostly Ditko-c/a 71 142 213 454 777 1100
2-Ayers-a 41 82 123 256 428 600

D.P. 7
Marvel Comics Group (New Universe): Nov, 1986 - No. 32, June, 1989

1-20, 3.00
21-32-Low print 4.00
Annual #1 (11/87)-Intro. The Witness 4.00
... Classic Vol. 1 TPB (2007, $24.99) r/#1-9; Mark Gruenwald-s/Paul Ryan-a in all 25.00
NOTE: *Williamson a-9i, 11i; c-9i.*

DRACULA (See Bram Stoker's Dracula, Giant-Size..., Little Dracula, Marvel Graphic Novel, Requiem for Dracula, Spider-Man Vs...., Stoker's..., Tomb of... & Wedding of...; also see Movie Classics under Universal Presents as well as Dracula)

DRACULA (See Movie Classics for #1)(Also see Frankenstein & Werewolf)
Dell Publ. Co.: No. 2, 11/66 - No. 4, 3/67; No. 6, 7/72 - No. 8, 7/73 (No #5)

2-Origin & 1st app. Dracula (11/66) (super hero) 5 10 15 33 57 80
3,4: 4-Intro. Fleeta ('67) 3 6 9 21 33 45
6-('72)-r/#2 w/origin 3 6 9 15 22 28
7,8-r/#3, #4 2 4 6 13 18 22

DRACULA (Magazine)
Warren Publishing Co.: 1979 (120 pgs., full color)

Book 1-Maroto art; Spanish material translated into English (mail order only) 6 12 18 37 66 95

DRACULA
Marvel Comics: Jul, 2010 - No. 4, Sept, 2010 ($3.99, limited series)

1-4-Colored reprint of Bram Stoker's Classic Dracula adapt. from Dracula Lives!, Legion of Monsters and Stoker's Dracula; Thomas-s/Giordano-a; J. Djurdjevic-c 4.00

DRACULA CHRONICLES
Topps Comics: Apr, 1995 - No. 3, June, 1995 ($2.50, limited series)

1-3-Linsner-c 4.00

DRACULA LIVES! (Magazine)(Also see Tomb of Dracula) (Reprinted in Stoker's Dracula)
Marvel Comics Group: 1973(no month) - No. 13, July, 1975 (75¢, B&W) (76 pgs.)

1-Boris painted-c 8 16 24 56 108 160
2 (7/73)-1st time origin Dracula; Adams, Starlin-a 5 10 15 34 60 85
3-1st app. Robert E. Howard's Soloman Kane; Adams-c/a 5 10 15 31 53 75
4,5: 4-Ploog-a. 5(V2#1)-Bram Stoker's Classic Dracula adapt. begins 4 8 12 23 37 50
6-9: 6-8-Bram Stoker adapt. 9-Bondage-c 4 8 12 23 37 50
10 (1/75)-16 pg. Lilith solo (1st?) 4 8 12 27 44 60
11-13: 11-21 pg. Lilith solo sty. 12-31 pg. Dracula sty 4 8 12 23 37 50
Annual 1(Summer, 1975, $1.25, 92 pgs.)-Morrow painted-c; 6 Dracula stys. 25 pgs. Adams-a(r) 4 8 12 25 40 55
NOTE: ***N. Adams** a-2, 3i, 10i, Annual 1r(2, 3i). **Alcala** a-9. **Buscema** a-3p, 6p, Annual 1p. **Colan** a(p)-1, 2, 5, 6, 8. **Evans** a-7. **Gulacy** a-9. **Heath** a-1r, 13. **Pakula** a-6r. Sutton a-13.**Weiss** r-Annual 1p. 4 **Dracula** stories each in 1, 609; 3 **Dracula** stories each in 2, 4, 5,, 13.*

DRACULA: LORD OF THE UNDEAD
Marvel Comics: Dec, 1998 - No. 3, Dec, 1998 ($2.99, limited series)

1-3-Olliffe & Palmer-a 4.00

DRACULA: RETURN OF THE IMPALER
Slave Labor Graphics: July, 1993 - No. 4, Oct, 1994 ($2.95, limited series)

1-4 4.00

DRACULA'S REVENGE
IDW Publishing: Apr, 2004 - No. 3 ($3.99, limited series)

1,2-Forbeck-s/Kudranski-a 4.00

DRACULA: THE COMPANY OF MONSTERS
BOOM! Studios: Aug, 2010 - No. 12, Jul, 2011 ($3.99)

1-12: 1-5-Busiek & Gregory-s/Godlewski-a. 1-Two covers by Brereton and Salas 4.00

DRACULA VERSUS ZORRO
Topps Comics: Oct, 1993 - No. 2, Nov, 1993 ($2.95, limited series)

1,2: 1-Spot varnish & red foil-c. 2-Polybagged w/16 pg. Zorro #0 4.00

DRACULA VERSUS ZORRO
Dark Horse Comics: Sept, 1998 - No. 2, Oct, 1998 ($2.95, limited series)

1,2 4.00

DRACULA: VLAD THE IMPALER (Also see Bram Stoker's Dracula)
Topps Comics: Feb, 1993 - No. 3, Apr, 1993 ($2.95, limited series)

1-3-Polybagged with 3 trading cards each; Maroto-c/a 4.00

DRACULINA (From Vampirella)
Dynamite Entertainment: 2021 - No. 6, 2022 ($3.99, limited series)

1-6-Christopher Priest-s/Michael Sta. Maria-a; multiple covers on each 4.00

DRACULINA: BLOOD SIMPLE
Dynamite Entertainment: 2023 - Present ($3.99, limited series)

1-Christopher Priest-s/Michael Sta. Maria-a; multiple covers on each 4.00

DRAFT, THE
Marvel Comics: 1988 ($3.50, one-shot, squarebound)

1-Sequel to "The Pitt" 4.00

DRAFTED: ONE HUNDRED DAYS
Devil's Due Publishing: June, 2009 ($5.99, one-shot)

1-Barack Obama on a post-galactic-war Earth; Powers-s 6.00

DRAG 'N' WHEELS (Formerly Top Eliminator)
Charlton Comics: No. 30, Sept, 1968 - No. 59, May, 1973

30 4 8 12 28 47 65
31-40-Scot Jackson begins 3 6 9 18 28 38
41-50 3 6 9 16 24 32
51-59: Scot Jackson 2 4 6 13 18 22
Modern Comics Reprint 58('78) 5.00

DRAGON, THE (Also see The Savage Dragon)
Image Comics (Highbrow Ent.): Mar, 1996 - No. 5, July, 1996 (99¢, lim. series)

1-5: Reprints Savage Dragon limited series w/new story & art. 5-Youngblood app; includes 5 pg. Savage Dragon story from 1984 4.00

DRAGON AGE (Based on the EA videogame)
IDW Publishing (EA Comics): Mar, 2010 - No. 6, Nov, 2010 ($3.99)

1-6-Orson Scott Card & Aaron Johnston-s; Ramos-c 4.00

DRAGON AGE: BLUE WRAITH (Based on the EA videogame)
Dark Horse Comics: Jan, 2020 - No. 3, Mar, 2020 ($3.99, limited series)

1-3-DeFilippis & Weir-s/Furukawa-a/Teng-c 4.00

DRAGON AGE: DECEPTION (Based on the EA videogame)
Dark Horse Comics: Oct, 2018 - No. 3, Dec, 2018 ($3.99, limited series)

1-3-DeFilippis & Weir-s/Furukawa-a/Teng-c 4.00

DRAGON AGE: DARK FORTRESS (Based on the EA videogame)
Dark Horse Comics: Mar, 2021 - No. 3, May, 2022 ($3.99, limited series)

1-3-DeFilippis & Weir-s/Furukawa-a/Teng-c 4.00

DRAGON AGE: KNIGHT ERRANT (Based on the EA videogame)

Dark Horse Comics: May, 2017 - No. 5, Sept, 2017 ($3.99, limited series)

1-5-DeFilippis & Weir-s/Furukawa-a/Teng-c 4.00

DRAGON AGE: MAGEKILLER (Based on the EA videogame)
Dark Horse Comics: Dec, 2015 - No. 5, Apr, 2016 ($3.99, limited series)

1-3-Rucka-s/Carnero-a/Teng-c 4.00

DRAGON AGE: THE MISSING (Based on the EA videogame)
Dark Horse Comics: Jan, 2023 - Present ($3.99, limited series)

1,2-Mann-s/McKeown-a 4.00

DRAGON AGE: THOSE WHO SPEAK (Based on the EA videogame)
Dark Horse Comics: Aug, 2012 - No. 3, Nov, 2012 ($3.50, limited series)

1-3-Gaider-s/Hardin-a/Palumbo-c 3.50

DRAGON ARCHIVES, THE (Also see The Savage Dragon)
Image Comics: Jun, 1998 - No. 4, Jan, 1999 ($2.95, B&W)

1-4: Reprints early Savage Dragon app. 4.00

DRAGON BALL
Viz Comics: Mar, 1998 - Part 6: #2, Feb, 2003($2.95, B&W, Manga reprints read right to left)

	GD	VG	FN	VF	VF/NM	NM-
Part 1: 1-Akira Toriyama-s/a	10	20	30	67	141	215
2	3	6	9	16	23	30
3-12	1	3	4	6	8	10
1-12 (2nd & 3rd printings)						4.00
Part 2: 1-(4/99)	2	4	6	11	16	20
2-15: 15-($3.50-c)	1	2	3	5	6	8
Part 3: 1-14						5.00
Part 4: 1-10						5.00
Part 5: 1-7						5.00
Part 6: 1,2						5.00

DRAGON BALL Z
Viz Comics: Mar, 1998 - Part 5: #10, Oct, 2002 ($2.95, B&W, Manga reprints read right to left)

	GD	VG	FN	VF	VF/NM	NM-
Part 1: 1-Akira Toriyama-s/a	6	12	18	38	69	100
2	3	6	9	14	19	24
3-9	1	3	4	6	8	10
1-9 (2nd & 3rd printings)						4.00
Part 2: 1	2	4	6	10	14	18
2-14						6.00
Part 3: 1-10						4.00
Part 4: 1-15						4.00
Part 5: 1-10						4.00

DRAGON, THE: BLOOD & GUTS (Also see The Savage Dragon)
Image Comics (Highbrow Entertainment): Mar, 1995 - No. 3, May, 1995 ($2.50, lim. series)

1-3: Jason Pearson-c/a/scripts 4.00

DRAGON CHIANG
Eclipse Books: 1991 ($3.95, B&W, squarebound, 52 pgs.)

nn-Timothy Truman-c/a(p) 4.00

DRAGONFLIGHT
Eclipse Books: Feb, 1991 - No. 3, 1991 ($4.95, 52 pgs.)

Book One - Three: Adapts 1968 novel 5.00

DRAGONFLY (See Americomics #4)
Americomics: Sum, 1985 - No. 8, 1986 ($1.75/$1.95)

1 5.00
2-8 4.00

DRAGONFLY & DRAGONFLYMAN (See The Wrong Earth)
AHOY Comics: 2019 - No. 5, 2020 ($3.99, limited series)

1-5-Each hero versus Devil Man; Peyer-s/Krause-a 4.00
1-Free Comic Book Day 2019 Edition; Russ Braun-a; back-up Captain Ginger story 3.00

DRAGONFORCE
Aircel Publishing: 1988 - No. 13, 1989 ($2.00)

1-Dale Keown-c/a/scripts in #1-12 4.00
2-13: 13-No Keown-a 3.00
...Chronicles Book 1-5 ($2.95, B&W, 60 pgs.): Dale Keown-r/Dragonring & Dragonforce 4.00

DRAGONHEART (Movie)
Topps Comics: May, 1996 - No. 2, June, 1996 ($2.95/$4.95, limited series)

1-($2.95, 24 pgs.)-Adaptation of the film; Hildebrandt Bros-c; Lim-a. 3.00
2-($4.95, 64 pgs.) 5.00

DRAGONLANCE (Also see TSR Worlds)
DC Comics: Dec, 1988 - No. 34, Sept, 1991 ($1.25/$1.50, Mando paper)

1-Based on TSR game 4.00
2-34: Based on TSR game. 30-32-Kaluta-c 3.00

DRAGONLANCE: CHRONICLES
Devil's Due Publ.: Aug, 2005 - No. 8, Mar, 2006 ($2.95)

1-8-Dabb-s/Kurth-a 3.00
...: Dragons of Autumn Twilight TPB (2006, $17.95) r/#1-8 18.00

DRAGONLANCE: CHRONICLES (Volume 2)
Devil's Due Publ.: July, 2006 - No. 4, Jan, 2007 ($4.95/$4.99, 48 pgs.)

1-4-Dragons of Winter Night; Dabb-s/Kurth-a 5.00
...: Dragons of Winter Night TPB (3/07, $18.99) r/#1-4; cover gallery 19.00

DRAGONLANCE: CHRONICLES (Volume 3)
Devil's Due Publ.: Mar, 2007 - No. 12, ($3.50)

1-11-Dragons of Spring Dawning; Dabb-s/Cope-a 3.50

DRAGONLANCE: THE LEGEND OF HUMA
Devil's Due Publ.: Jan, 2004 - No. 6, Oct, 2005 ($2.95)

1-6-Mike Miller & Rael-a 3.00

DRAGON LINES
Marvel Comics (Epic Comics/Heavy Hitters): May, 1993 - No. 4, Aug, 1993 ($1.95, lim. series)

1-($2.50)-Embossed-c; Ron Lim-c/a in all 4.00
2-4 3.00

DRAGON LINES: WAY OF THE WARRIOR
Marvel Comics (Epic Comics/ Heavy Hitters): Nov, 1993 - No. 2, Jan, 1994 ($2.25, limited series)

1,2-Ron Lim-c/a(p) 3.00

DRAGONQUEST
Silverwolf Comics: Dec, 1986 - No. 2, 1987 ($1.50, B&W, 28 pgs.)

1,2-Tim Vigil-c/a in all 5.00

DRAGON'S CLAWS
Marvel UK, Ltd.: July, 1988 - No. 10, Apr, 1989 ($1.25/$1.50/$1.75, British)

1-10: 3-Death's Head 1 pg. strip on back-c (1st app.). 4-Silhouette of Death's Head on last pg. 5-1st full app. new Death's Head 4.00

DRAGON'S LAIR: SINGE'S REVENGE (Based on the Don Bluth video game)
CrossGen Comics: Sept, 2003 - No. 3 ($2.95, limited series)

1-3-Mangels-s/Laguna-a 3.00

DRAGONSLAYER (Movie)
Marvel Comics Group: October, 1981 - No. 2, Nov, 1981

1,2-Paramount Disney movie adaptation 4.00

DRAGOON WELLS MASSACRE
Dell Publishing Co.: No. 815, June, 1957

	GD	VG	FN	VF	VF/NM	NM-
Four Color 815-Movie, photo-c	8	16	24	51	96	140

DRAGSTRIP HOTRODDERS (World of Wheels No. 17 on)
Charlton Comics: Sum, 1963; No. 2, Jan, 1965 - No. 16, Aug, 1967

	GD	VG	FN	VF	VF/NM	NM-
1	7	14	21	46	86	125
2-5	4	8	12	25	40	55
6-16	3	6	9	21	33	45

DRAIN
Image Comics: Nov, 2006 - No. 6, Mar, 2008 ($2.99)

1-6: 1-Cebulski-s/Takeda-a; two covers by Takeda and Finch 3.00
Vol. 1 TPB (2008, $16.99) r/#1-6; cover gallery and Takeda sketch art gallery 17.00

DRAKUUN
Dark Horse Comics: Feb, 1997 - No. 25, Mar, 1999 ($2.95, B&W, manga)

1-25; 1-6- Johji Manabe-s/a in all. Rise of the Dragon Princess series. 7-12-Revenge of Gustav. 13-18-Shadow of the Warlock. 19-25-The Hidden War 3.00

DRAMA
Sirius: June, 1994 ($2.95, mature)

	GD	VG	FN	VF	VF/NM	NM-
1-1st full color Dawn app. in comics	2	4	6	9	12	15
1-Limited edition (1400 copies); signed & numbered; fingerprint authenticity	3	6	9	19	30	40

NOTE: *Dawn's 1st full color app. was a pin-up in Amazing Heroes' Swimsuit Special #5.*

DRAMA OF AMERICA, THE
Action Text: 1973 ($1.95, 224 pgs.)

	GD	VG	FN	VF	VF/NM	NM-
1- "Students' Supplement to History"	2	4	6	8	10	12

DRAWING BLOOD
Kevin Eastman Studios: May, 2019 - No. 4, Aug, 2019 ($3.99, limited series)

1-4-Avallone-s/Bishop & Eastman-a 4.00

DRAWING ON YOUR NIGHTMARES
Dark Horse Comics: Oct, 2003 ($2.99, one-shot)

1-Short stories; The Goon, Criminal Macabre, Tales of the Vampires; Templesmith-c 3.00

DRAX (Guardians of the Galaxy)
Marvel Comics: Jan, 2016 - No. 11, Nov, 2016 ($3.99)

1-11-CM Punk & Cullen Bunn-s/Hepburn-a. 1-Guardians app. 4,5-Fin Fang Foom app. 4.00

DRAX THE DESTROYER (Guardians of the Galaxy)
Marvel Comics: Nov, 2005 - No. 4, Feb, 2006 ($2.99, limited series)

1-4-Giffen-s/Breitweiser-a 5.00
...: Earthfall TPB (2006, $10.99) r/#1-4; character design page 11.00

DREAD GODS
IDW Publishing: Jul, 2017 - No. 4, Oct, 2018 ($3.99)

1-4-Marz-s/Raney-a 4.00

DREADLANDS (Also see Epic)
Marvel Comics (Epic Comics): 1992 - No. 4, 1992 ($3.95, lim. series, 52 pgs.)

1-4: Stiff-c 4.00

DREADSTAR (See Epic Illustrated #3 for 1st app. and Eclipse Graphic Album Series #5)
Marvel Comics (Epic Comics)/First Comics No. 27 on: Nov, 1982 - No. 64, Mar, 1991

	GD	VG	FN	VF	VF/NM	NM-
1	2	4	6	11	16	20
2-5,8-49						4.00
6,7,51-64: 6,7-1st app. Interstellar Toybox; 8pgs. ea.; Wrightson-a. 51-64-Lower print run						5.00
50						6.00
Annual 1 (12/83)-r/The Price (Eclipse Graphic Album Series #5)						5.00

DREADSTAR
Malibu Comics (Bravura): Apr, 1994 - No. 6, Jan, 1995 ($2.50, limited series)

1-6-Peter David scripts: 1,2-Starlin-c 4.00

NOTE: *Issues 1-6 contain Bravura stamps.*

DREADSTAR AND COMPANY
Marvel Comics (Epic Comics): July, 1985 - No. 6, Dec, 1985

1-6: 1,3,6-New Starlin-a: 2-New Wrightson-c; reprints of Dreadstar series 4.00

DREAM BOOK OF LOVE (Also see A-1 Comics)
Magazine Enterprises: No. 106, June-July, 1954 - No. 123, Oct-Nov, 1954

	GD	VG	FN	VF	VF/NM	NM-
A-1 106 (#1)-Powell, Bolle-a; Montgomery Clift, Donna Reed photo-c	22	44	66	128	209	290
A-1-114 (#2)-Guardineer, Bolle-a; Piper Laurie, Victor Mature photo-c	16	32	48	92	144	195
A-1 123 (#3)-Movie photo-c	15	30	45	86	133	180

Dragon Age: The Missing #1 © EA

The Dreaming (2018) #4 © DC

Drifter #8 © Againdemon & Klein

	GD	VG	FN	VF	VF/NM	NM-
	2.0	4.0	6.0	8.0	9.0	9.2

DREAM BOOK OF ROMANCE (Also see A-1 Comics)
Magazine Enterprises: No. 92, 1954 - No. 124, Oct-Nov, 1954

A-1 92 (#5)-Guardineer-a; photo-c 20 40 60 117 189 260
A-1 101 (#6)(4-6/54)-Marlon Brando photo-c; Powell, Bolle, Guardineer-a 39 78 117 231 378 525
A-1 109,110,124: 109 (#7)(7-8/54)-Powell-a; movie photo-c. 110 (#8)(1/54)-Movie photo-c. 124 (#9)(10-11/54) 15 30 45 86 133 180

DREAMER, THE
Kitchen Sink Press: 1986 ($6.95, B&W, graphic novel)

nn-Will Eisner-s/a 20.00
DC Comics Reprint ($7.95, 6/00) 8.00

DREAMERY, THE
Eclipse Comics: Dec, 1986 - No. 14, Feb, 1989 ($2.00, B&W, Baxter paper)

1-14: 2-7-Alice In Wonderland adapt. 4.00

DREAMING, THE (See Sandman, 2nd Series)
DC Comics (Vertigo): June, 1996 - No. 60, May, 2001 ($2.50)

1-McKean-c on all.; LaBan scripts & Snejbjerg-a 4.00
2-30,32-60: 2,3-LaBan scripts & Snejbjerg-a. 4-7-Hogan scripts; Parkhouse-a. 8-Zulli-a. 9-11-Talbot-s/Taylor-a(p). 41-Previews Sandman: The Dream Hunters. 50-Hempel, Fegredo, McManus, Totleben-a 3.00
31-($3.95) Art by various 4.00
...Beyond The Shores of Night TPB ('97, $19.95) r/#1-8 20.00
...Special (7/98, $5.95, one-shot) Trial of Cain 6.00
...Through The Gates of Horn and Ivory TPB ('99, $19.95) r/#15-19,22-25 20.00

DREAMING, THE (The Sandman Universe)
DC Comics (Vertigo): Nov, 2018 - No. 20, Jun, 2020 ($3.99)

1-20: 1-Spurrier-s/Evely-a/Jae Lee-c; Lucien & Merv Pumpkinhead app. 7,8-Larson-a 4.00

DREAMING EAGLES
AfterShock Comics: Dec, 2015 - No. 6, Jun, 2016 ($3.99)

1-6-Ennis-s/Coleby-a; Tuskegee Airmen in WWII 4.00

DREAMING, THE: WAKING HOURS (The Sandman Universe)
DC Comics (Vertigo): Oct, 2020 - No. 12, Sept, 2021 ($3.99)

1-12: 1-G. Willow Wilson-s/Nick Robles-a; intro Ruin 4.00

DREAM OF LOVE
I. W. Enterprises: 1958 (Reprints)

1,2,8: 1-r/Dream Book of Love #1; Bob Powell-a. 2-r/Great Lover's Romances #10. 8-Great Lover's Romances #1; also contains 2 Jon Juan stories by Siegel & Schomburg; Kinstler-c. 3 6 9 18 27 36
9-Kinstler-c; 1pg. John Wayne interview & Frazetta illo from John Wayne Adv. Comics #2 3 6 9 18 27 36

DREAM POLICE
Marvel Comics (Icon): Aug, 2005 ($3.99)

1-Straczynski-s/Deodato-a/c 4.00

DREAM POLICE
Image Comics (Joe's Comics): Apr, 2014 - No. 12, Sept, 2016 ($2.99)

1-12-Straczynski-s/Kotian-a 3.00

DREAMS OF THE DARKCHYLDE
Darkchylde Entertainment: Oct, 2000 - No. 6, Sept, 2001 ($2.95)

1-6-Randy Queen-s in all. 1-Brandon Peterson-c/a 3.00

DREAM TEAM (See Battlezones: Dream Team 2)
Malibu Comics (Ultraverse): July, 1995 ($4.95, one-shot)

1-Pin-ups teaming up Marvel & Ultraverse characters by various artists including Allred, Romita, Darrow, Balent, Quesada & Palmiotti 5.00

DREAM THIEF
Dark Horse Comics: May, 2013 - No. 5, Sept, 2013 ($3.99, limited series)

1-5-Nitz-s/Smallwood-a. 1-Alex Ross-c. 2-Ryan Sook-c. 4-Dan Brereton-c 4.00

DREAM THIEF: ESCAPE
Dark Horse Comics: Jun, 2014 - No. 4, Sept, 2014 ($3.99, limited series)

1-4-Nitz-s/Smallwood-c. 1,2-Smallwood-a. 3,4-Galusha-a 4.00

DREAMWAVE PRODUCTIONS PREVIEW
Dreamwave Productions: May, 2002 ($1.00, one-shot)

nn-Previews Arkanium, Transformers: The War Within and other series 3.00

DRESDEN FILES (See Jim Butcher's...)

DRIFTER
Image Comics: Nov, 2014 - No. 19, Jun, 2017 ($3.50/$3.99)

1-19-Ivan Brandon-s/Nic Klein-a; multiple covers on each. 15-Start $3.99-c 4.00

DRIFT FENCE (See Zane Grey 4-Color 270)

DRIFT MARLO
Dell Publishing Co.: May-July, 1962 - No. 2, Oct-Dec, 1962 (Painted-c)

01-232-207 (#1) 5 10 15 31 53 75
2 (12-232-212) 4 8 12 27 44 60

DRISCOLL'S BOOK OF PIRATES
David McKay Publ. (Not reprints): 1934 (B&W, hardcover; 124 pgs, 7x9")

nn-"Pieces of Eight" strip by Montford Amory 27 54 81 158 259 360

DRIVER: CROSSING THE LINE (Based on the Ubisoft videogame)
DC Comics: Oct, 2011 ($2.99, one-shot)

1-David Lapham-s/Greg Scott-a/ Jock-c; bonus character design art 3.00

DROIDS (Based on Saturday morning cartoon) (Also see Dark Horse Comics)
Marvel Comics (Star Comics): April, 1986 - No. 8, June, 1987

1-R2D2 & C-3PO from Star Wars app. in all 3 6 9 19 30 40
2-8: 2,5,7,8-Williamson-a(i) 2 4 6 8 10 12
NOTE: *Romita a-3p. Sinnott a-3i.*

DROOPY (see Tom & Jerry #60)

DROOPY (Tex Avery's...)
Dark Horse Comics: Oct, 1995 - No. 3, Dec, 1995 ($2.50, limited series)

1-Characters created by Tex Avery; painted-c on all 1 3 4 6 8 10
2 4.00
3-Headlights Christmas-c 1 3 4 6 8 10

DROPSIE AVENUE: THE NEIGHBORHOOD
Kitchen Sink Press: June, 1995 ($15.95/$24.95, B&W)

nn-Will Eisner (softcover) 18.00
nn-Will Eisner (hardcover) 30.00

DROWNED GIRL, THE
DC Comics (Piranha Press): 1990 ($5.95, 52 pgs, mature)

nn 1 2 3 5 6 8

DRUG WARS
Pioneer Comics: 1989 ($1.95)

1-Grell-c 4.00

DRUID
Marvel Comics: May, 1995 - No. 4, Aug, 1995 ($2.50, limited series)

1-4: Warren Ellis scripts. 4.00

DRUM BEAT
Dell Publishing Co.: No. 610, Jan, 1955

Four Color 610-Movie, Alan Ladd photo-c 8 16 24 55 105 155

DRUMS OF DOOM
United Features Syndicate: 1937 (25¢)(Indian)(Text w/color illos.)

nn-By Lt. F.A. Methot; Golden Thunder app.; Tip Top Comics ad in comic; nice-c 47 94 141 296 498 700

DRUNKEN FIST
Jademan Comics: Aug, 1988 - No. 54, Jan, 1993 ($1.50/$1.95, 68 pgs.)

1 1 2 3 5 6 8
2-50 4.00
51-54 4.00

DUCK ALBUM (See Donald Duck Album)
Dell Publishing Co.: No. 353, Oct, 1951 - No. 840, Sept, 1957

Four Color 353 (#1)-Barks-c; 1st Uncle Scrooge-c (also appears on back-c). 13 26 39 91 201 310
Four Color 450-Barks-c 9 18 27 63 129 195
Four Color 492,531,560,586,611,649,686, 7 14 21 46 86 125
Four Color 726,782,840 6 12 18 37 66 95

DUCK AVENGER
IDW Publishing: No. 0, Aug, 2016; Oct, 2016 - No. 5, Jun, 2017 ($4.99/$5.99/$6.99)

0-Reprints of Italian Donald Duck costumed super-hero stories 6.00
1,3-($5.99) Three covers. 1-(10/16) Red Raider app. 2 4 6 8 10 12
2-($4.99) Three covers; Xadhoom app. 6.00
4,5-($6.99) 1 2 3 5 6 8

DUCKMAN
Dark Horse Comics: Sept, 1990 ($1.95, B&W, one-shot)

1-Story & art by Everett Peck 5 10 15 35 63 90

	GD	VG	FN	VF	VF/NM	NM-
	2.0	4.0	6.0	8.0	9.0	9.2

DUCKMAN
Topps Comics: Nov, 1994 - No. 5, May, 1995; No. 0, Feb, 1996 ($2.50)
0 (2/96, $2.95, B&W)-r/Duckman #1 from Dark Horse Comics 5.00
1-5: 1-w/ coupon #A for Duckman trading card. 2-w/Duckman 1st season episode guide 5.00

DUCKMAN: THE MOB FROG SAGA
Topps Comics: Nov, 1994 - No. 3, Feb, 1995 ($2.50, limited series)
1-3: 1-w/coupon #B for Duckman trading card, S. Shaw!-c 5.00

DUCKTALES
Gladstone Publ.: Oct, 1988 - No. 13, May, 1990 (1,2,9-11: $1.50; 3-8: 95¢)
1-Barks-r 3 6 9 15 22 28
2-Barks-r 2 4 6 8 10 12
3-11: 2-7,9-11-Barks-r 5.00
12,13 ($1.95, 68 pgs.)-Barks-r; 12-r/F.C. #495 6.00
Disney Presents Carl Barks' Greatest DuckTales Stories Vol. 1 (Gemstone Publ., 2006, $10.95) r/stories adapted for the animated TV series including "Back to the Klondike" 11.00
Disney Presents Carl Barks' Greatest DuckTales Stories Vol. 2 (Gemstone Publ., 2006, $10.95) r/stories adapted for the animated TV series; "Robot Robbers" app. 11.00

DUCKTALES (TV)
Disney Comics: June, 1990 - No. 18, Nov, 1991 ($1.50)
1-All new stories; Marv Wolfman-s 2 4 6 10 14 18
2-18 5.00
Disney's DuckTales by Marv Wolfman: Scrooge's Quest TPB (Gemstone, 9/07, $15.99) r/#1-7; intro. by Wolfman 16.00
Disney's DuckTales: The Gold Odyssey TPB (Gemstone, 10/08, $15.99) 16.00
The Movie nn (1990, $7.95, 68 pgs.)-Graphic novel adapting animated movie 8.00

DUCKTALES (TV)
Boom Entertainment (KABOOM!): May, 2011 - No. 6, Nov, 2011 ($3.99)
1-Three covers; Spector-s/Massaroli-a 1 2 3 5 6 8
2-6: 2-4-Three covers on each; Spector-s/Massaroli-a. 5,6-Two covers; crossover with Darkwing Duck #17,18 4.00

DUCKTALES (Based on the 2017 TV series)
IDW Publishing: No. 0, Jul, 2017; No. 1, Sept, 2017 - No. 20, Apr, 2019 ($3.99)
0-20: 0,1-Caramagna-s; multiple covers 4.00

DUCKTALES: FAIRES AND SCARES
IDW Publishing: Dec, 2019 - No. 3, Feb, 2020 ($3.99, limited series)
1-3: 1,2-Behling-s. 3-Caramagna-s 4.00

DUCKTALES: SCIENCE AND SILENCE
IDW Publishing: Aug, 2019 - No. 3, Oct, 2019 ($3.99, limited series)
1-3-Behling-s 4.00

DUDLEY (Teen-age)
Feature/Prize Publications: Nov-Dec, 1949 - No. 3, Mar-Apr, 1950
1-By Boody Rogers 30 60 90 177 289 400
2,3 15 30 45 86 133 180

DUDLEY DO-RIGHT (TV)
Charlton Comics: Aug, 1970 - No. 7, Aug, 1971 (Jay Ward)
1 8 16 24 55 105 155
2-7 6 12 18 37 66 95

DUEL MASTERS (Based on a trading card game)
Dreamwave Productions: Nov, 2003 - No. 8, Sept, 2004 ($2.95)
1-8: 1-Bagged with card; Augustyn-s 3.00

DUKE NUKEM: GLORIOUS BASTARD (Based on the video game)
IDW Publishing: Jul, 2011 - No. 4, Nov, 2011 ($3.99)
1-4: 1-Three covers; Waltz-s/Xermanico-a 4.00

DUKE OF THE K-9 PATROL
Gold Key: Apr, 1963
1 (10052-304) 4 8 12 25 40 55

DUMBO (Disney; see Movie Comics, & Walt Disney Showcase #12)
Dell Publishing Co.: No. 17, 1941 - No. 668, Jan, 1958
Four Color 17 (#1)-Mickey Mouse, Donald Duck, Pluto app. 284 568 852 1818 3109 4400
Large Feature Comic 19 ('41)-Part-r 4-Color 17 300 600 900 2010 3505 5000
Four Color 234 ('49) 15 30 45 100 220 340
Four Color 668 (12/55)-1st of two printings. Dumbo on-c with starry sky. Same-c as #234 11 22 33 73 157 240
Four Color 668 (1/58)-2nd printing. Same cover altered with Timothy Mouse added. Same contents 7 14 21 48 89 130

DUMBO COMIC PAINT BOOK (See Dumbo, Large Feature Comic No. 19)

DUNC AND LOO (#1-3 titled "Around the Block with Dunc and Loo")
Dell Publishing Co.: Oct-Dec, 1961 - No. 8, Oct-Dec, 1963
1 5 10 15 35 63 90
2 4 8 12 27 44 60
3-8 3 6 9 21 33 45
NOTE: *Written by* **John Stanley**; **Bill Williams** *art.*

DUNE (Movie)
Marvel Comics: Apr, 1985 - No. 3, June, 1985
1-r/Marvel Super Special; movie adaptation 3 6 9 17 26 35
2,3-Adaptation continues 2 4 6 8 11 14

DUNE
BOOM! Studios: Jul, 2021 - Dec, 2021 ($7.99, series of one-shots)
...: A Whisper of Caladan Seas 1 (12/21) Herbert & Anderson-s/Rebelka-a 8.00
...: Blood of the Sardaukar 1 (7/21) Herbert & Anderson-s/Gorham-a 8.00

DUNE: HOUSE ATREIDES
BOOM! Studios: Oct, 2020 - No. 12, Dec, 2021 ($4.99)
1-12-Prequel to the original novel; Brian Herbert & Kevin J. Anderson-s/Dev Pramanik-a 5.00

DUNE: HOUSE HARKONNEN
BOOM! Studios: Jan, 2023 - No. 12 ($4.99)
1-12-Prequel to the novel; Brian Herbert & Kevin J. Anderson-s/Michael Shelfer-a 5.00

DUNE: THE WATERS OF KANLY
BOOM! Studios: May, 2022 - No. 4, Aug, 2022 ($4.99)
1-4-Set during the events of the novel; Brian Herbert & Kevin J. Anderson-s/Mortarino-a 5.00

DUNGEONS & DRAGONS
IDW Publishing: No. 0, Aug, 2010 - No. 15, Jan, 2012 ($1.00/$3.99)
0-(8/10, $1.00) Five covers; previews D&D series and Dark Sun mini-series 3.00
1-15: 1-(11/10, $3.99) Di Vito-a/Rogers-s; two covers. 2-Two covers 4.00
Annual 2012: Eberron (3/12, $7.99) Crilley-s/Diaz & Rojo-a 8.00
Annual 2022 (8/22, $7.99) Zub-s/Mello & Clodfelter-a 8.00
... 100 Page Giant (9/19, $5.99) Reprints by various incl. Zub & Dunbar 6.00
... 100 Page Spectacular (1/12, $7.99) Reprints by various incl. Duursema & Morales 8.00
...: The Best of Minsc & Boo 1 (4/22, $5.99) Reprints highlighting the characters 6.00

DUNGEONS & DRAGONS: A DARKENED WISH
IDW Publishing: Feb, 2019 - No. 5, Aug, 2019 ($3.99, limited series)
1-5-B. Dave Walters-s/Tess Fowler-a; multiple covers on each 4.00

DUNGEONS & DRAGONS: AT THE SPINE OF THE WORLD
IDW Publishing: Oct, 2020 - No. 4, Jan, 2021 ($3.99, limited series)
1-4-Garcia & Mendez-s/Coccolo-a; multiple covers on each 4.00

DUNGEONS & DRAGONS: CUTTER
IDW Publishing: Apr, 2013 - No. 5, Sept, 2013 ($3.99, limited series)
1-5-R.A. & Geno Salvatore-s/Baldeon-a; 2 covers on each 4.00

DUNGEONS & DRAGONS: EVIL AT BALDUR'S GATE
IDW Publishing: Apr, 2018 - No. 5, Aug, 2018 ($3.99, limited series)
1-5: 1-Jim Zub-s/Dean Kotz-a 4.00

DUNGEONS & DRAGONS: FORGOTTEN REALMS
IDW Publishing: Apr, 2012 - No. 5, Sept, 2012 ($3.99, limited series)
1-5-Greenwood-s/Ferguson-a 4.00
... 100 Page Spectacular (4/12, $7.99) Reprints by various incl. Rags Morales 8.00

DUNGEONS & DRAGONS: FROST GIANT'S FURY
IDW Publishing: Dec, 2016 - No. 5, Apr, 2017 ($3.99, limited series)
1-5-Jim Zub-s/Netho Diaz-a 4.00

DUNGEONS & DRAGONS: INFERNAL TIDES
IDW Publishing: Nov, 2019 - No. 5 ($3.99, limited series)
1,2-Jim Zub-s/Max Dunbar-a; multiple covers on each 4.00

DUNGEONS & DRAGONS: LEGENDS OF BALDUR'S GATE
IDW Publishing: Oct, 2014 - No. 5, Feb, 2016 ($3.99, limited series)
1-5-Jim Zub-s/Max Dunbar-a 4.00
... #1 Greatest Hits Collection (4/16, $1.00) reprints #1 3.00

DUNGEONS & DRAGONS: MINDBREAKER
IDW Publishing: Oct, 2021 - No. 5, Feb, 2022 ($3.99, limited series)
1-5-Jim Zub-s/Eduardo Mello-a 4.00

DUNGEONS & DRAGONS: RAVENLOFT – ORPHAN OF AGONY ISLE
IDW Publishing: Jun, 2022 - Present ($3.99, limited series)
1-3-Quinn-s/Underwood-a 5.00

DUNGEONS & DRAGONS: SHADOWS OF THE VAMPIRE
IDW Publishing: Apr, 2016 - No. 5, Aug, 2016 ($4.99/$3.99, limited series)
1-($4.99) Jim Zub-s/Nelson Dániel-a; 4 covers 5.00
2-5-($3.99) Three covers on each 4.00

DUNGEONS & DRAGONS: THE LEGEND OF DRIZZT: NEVERWINTER TALES
IDW Publishing: Aug, 2011 - No. 5, Dec, 2011 ($3.99, limited series)
1-5-R.A. & Geno Salvatore-s/Agustin Padilla-a 4.00

DUO
DC Comics: Jul, 2022 - No. 6, Dec, 2022 ($3.99, limited series)
1-6-Greg Pak-s/Khoi Pham-a 4.00

DURANGO KID, THE (Also see Best of the West, Great Western & White Indian)
(Charles Starrett starred in Columbia's Durango Kid movies)
Magazine Enterprises: Oct-Nov, 1949 - No. 41, Oct-Nov, 1955 (All 36 pgs.)
1-Charles Starrett photo-c; Durango Kid & his horse Raider begin; Dan Brand & Tipi (origin) begin by Frazetta & continue through #16 74 148 222 470 810 1150
2-Starrett photo-c. 34 68 102 199 325 450
3-5-All have Starrett photo-c. 29 58 87 172 281 390
6-10: 7-Atomic weapon-c/story 16 32 48 94 147 200
11-16-Last Frazetta issue 14 28 42 80 115 150
17-Origin Durango Kid 16 32 48 94 147 200
18-30: 18-Fred Meagher-a on Dan Brand begins.19-Guardineer-c/a(3) begins, end #41. 23-Intro. The Red Scorpion 10 20 30 54 72 90
31-Red Scorpion returns 9 18 27 52 69 85
32-41-Bolle/Frazetta*ish*-a (Dan Brand; true in later issues?) 9 18 27 50 65 80
NOTE: *#6, 8, 14, 15 contain* **Frazetta** *art not reprinted in White Indian.* **Ayers** *c-18.* **Guardineer** *a(3)-19-41; c-19-41.* **Fred Meagher** *a-18-29 at least.*

DURANGO KID, THE
AC Comics: 1990 - #2, 1990 ($2.50,$2.75, half-color)
1,2: 1-Starrett photo front/back-c; Guardineer-r. 2-B&W)-Starrett photo-c; White Indian-r by Frazetta; Guardineer-r (50th anniversary of films) 4.00

DUSTCOVERS: THE COLLECTED SANDMAN COVERS 1989-1997
DC Comics (Vertigo): 1997 ($39.95, Hardcover)
Reprints Dave McKean's Sandman covers with Gaiman text 40.00
Softcover (1998, $24.95) 25.00

DUSTY STAR
Image Comics (Desperado Studios): No. 0, Apr, 1997 - No. 1 ($2.95, B&W)
0,1-Pruett-s/Robinson-a 3.00

Duck Tales (2017) #2 © DIS

Duo #2 © Hudlin & Cowan

Dynamo 5 #10 © Faerber & Asrar

	GD 2.0	VG 4.0	FN 6.0	VF 8.0	VF/NM 9.0	NM- 9.2

DUSTY STAR
Image Comics (Desperado Publishing): June, 2006 ($3.50)

1-Pruett-s/Robinson-s/a 3.50

DV8 (See Gen 13)
Image Comics (WildStorm Productions): Aug, 1996 - No. 25, Dec, 1998;
DC Comics (WildStorm Prod.): No. 0, Apr, 1999 - No. 32, Nov, 1999 ($2.50)

1/2 6.00
1-Warren Ellis scripts & Humberto Ramos-c/a(p) 4.00
1-(7-variant covers, w/1 by Jim Lee) ...each 4.00
2-4: 3-No Ramos-a 3.00
5-32: 14-Regular-c, 14-Variant-c by Charest. 26-(5/99)-McGuinness-c 3.00
14-($3.50) Voyager Pack w/Danger Girl preview 5.00
0-(4/99, $2.95) Two covers (Rio and McGuinness) 3.00
Annual 1 (1/98, $2.95) 4.00
Annual 1999 ($3.50) Slipstream x-over with Gen13 4.00
Rave-(7/96, $1.75)-Ramos-c; pinups & interviews 3.00
...: Neighborhood Threat TPB (2002, $14.95) r/#1-6 & #1/2; Ellis intro.; Ramos-c 15.00

DV8: GODS AND MONSTERS
DC Comics (WildStorm): June, 2010 - No. 8, Jan, 2011 ($2.99, limited series)

1-8-Wood-s/Issacs-a 3.00
TPB (2011, $17.99) r/#1-8 18.00

DV8 VS. BLACK OPS
Image Comics (WildStorm): Oct, 1997 - No. 3, Dec, 1997 ($2.50, limited series)

1-3-Bury-s/Norton-a 3.00

DWIGHT D. EISENHOWER
Dell Publishing Co.: December, 1969

01-237-912 - Life story 5 10 15 34 60 85

DYING IS EASY
IDW Publishing: Dec, 2019 - Present ($3.99)

1-3-Joe Hill-s/Martin Simmonds-a/c 4.00

DYNABRITE COMICS
Whitman Publishing Co.: 1978 - 1979 (69¢, 10x7-1/8", 48 pgs., cardboard-c)
(Blank inside covers)

11350 - Walt Disney's Mickey Mouse & the Beanstalk (4-C 157). 11350-1 - Mickey Mouse Album (4-C 1057, 1151,1246). 11351 - Mickey Mouse & His Sky Adventure (4-C 214, 343). 11354 - Goofy: A Gaggle of Giggles. 11354-1 - Super Goof Meets Super Thief. 11356 - (?). 11359 - Bugs Bunny-r. 11360 - Winnie the Pooh Fun and Fantasy (Disney-r).
each.... 2 4 6 10 14 18
11352 - Donald Duck (4-C 408, Donald Duck 45,52)-Barks-a. 11352-1 - Donald Duck (4-C 318, 10 pg. Barks/ WDC&S 125,128)-Barks-c(r). 11353 - Daisy Duck's Diary (4-C 1055,1150) Barks-a. 11355 - Uncle Scrooge (Barks-a/U.S. 12,33). 11355-1 - Uncle Scrooge (Barks-a/U.S. 13,16) - Barks-c(r). 11357 - Star Trek (r/-Star Trek 33,41). 11358 - Star Trek (r/-Star Trek 34,36). 11361 - Gyro Gearloose & the Disney Ducks (r/4-C 1047,1184)-Barks-c(r)
each.... 2 4 6 11 16 20

DYNAMIC ADVENTURES
I. W. Enterprises: No. 8, 1964 - No. 9, 1964

8-Kayo Kirby-r by Baker?/Fight Comics 53. 3 6 9 16 23 30
9-Reprints Avon's "Escape From Devil's Island"; Kinstler-c
3 6 9 17 26 35

DYNAMIC CLASSICS (See Cancelled Comic Cavalcade)
DC Comics: Sept-Oct, 1978 (44 pgs.)

1-Neal Adams Batman, Simonson Manhunter-r 2 4 6 9 12 15

DYNAMIC COMICS (No #4-7)
Harry 'A' Chesler: Oct, 1941 - No. 3, Feb, 1942; No. 8, Mar, 1944 - No. 25, May, 1948

1-Origin Major Victory by Charles Sultan (reprinted in Major Victory #1), Dynamic Man & Hale the Magician; The Black Cobra only app.; Major Victory & Dynamic Man begin
290 580 870 1856 3178 4500
2-Origin Dynamic Boy & Lady Satan; intro. The Green Knight & sidekick Lance Cooper
181 362 543 1158 1979 2800
3-1st small logo, resumes with #10 151 302 453 959 1655 2350
8-Classic-c; Dan Hastings, The Echo, The Master Key, Yankee Boy begin;
Yankee Doodle Jones app.; hypo story 1300 2600 3900 8700 13,850 19,000
9-Mr. E begins; Mac Raboy-c 142 284 426 909 1555 2200
10-Small logo begins 129 258 387 826 1413 2000
11-Classic-c 541 1082 1623 3950 6975 10,000
12-16: 15-The Sky Chief app. 16-Marijuana story 93 186 279 591 1021 1450
17(1/46)-Illustrated in **SOTI**, "The children told me what the man was going to do with the hot poker," but Wertham saw this in Crime Reporter #2
97 194 291 621 1061 1500
18-Classic Airplanehead monster-c 258 516 774 1651 2826 4000
19-Classic puppeteer-c by Gattuso 93 186 279 591 1021 1450
20-Bare-breasted woman-c 168 336 504 1075 1838 2600
21-Dinosaur-c; new logo 65 130 195 416 708 1000
22,25 55 110 165 352 601 850
23,24-(68 pgs.): 23-Yankee Girl app. 53 106 159 334 567 800
I.W. Reprint #1,8('64): 1-r/#23. 8-Exist? 3 6 9 20 31 42
NOTE: *Kinstler c-IW #1. Tuska art in many issues, #3, 9, 11, 12, 16, 19. Bondage c-16.*

DYNAMITE (Becomes Johnny Dynamite No. 10 on)
Comic Media/Allen Hardy Publ.: May, 1953 - No. 9, Sept, 1954

1-Pete Morisi-a; Don Heck-c; r-as Danger #6 50 100 150 315 533 750
2 26 52 78 154 252 350
3-Marijuana story; Johnny Dynamite (1st app.) begins by Pete Morisi(c/a); Heck text-a; man shot in face at close range 34 68 102 199 325 450
4-Injury-to-eye, prostitution; Morisi-c/a 32 64 96 188 307 425
5-9-Morisi-c/a in all. 7-Prostitute story & reprints 24 48 72 142 234 325

DYNAMO (Also see Tales of Thunder & T.H.U.N.D.E.R. Agents)
Tower Comics: Aug, 1966 - No. 4, June, 1967 (25¢)

1-Crandall/Wood, Ditko/Wood-a; Weed series begins; NoMan & Lightning cameos; Wood-c/a 8 16 24 56 108 160
2-4: Wood-c/a in all 5 10 15 35 63 90
NOTE: *Adkins/Wood a-2. Ditko a-4?. Tuska a-2, 3.*

DYNAMO 5 (See Noble Causes: Extended Family #2 for debut of Captain Dynamo)
Image Comics: Jan, 2007 - No. 25, Oct, 2009 ($3.50/$2.99)

1-Intro. the offspring of Captain Dynamo; Faerber-s/Asrar-a 8.00
2 5.00
3-7,11-24 : 5-Intro. Synergy. 13-Origin of Myriad. 21-Firebird app. 3.50
8-10-($2.99) 3.50
25-($4.99) Back-up short stories of team members 5.00
Annual #1 (4/08, $5.99) r/Captain Dynamo app. in Nobel Causes: Extended Family #2 and three new stories by Faerber & various; pin-up gallery 6.00
#0 (2/09, 99¢) short story leading into #20; text synopsis of story so far 3.00
...: Holiday Special 2010 (12/10, $3.99) Faerber-s/Takara-a 4.00
... Vol. 1: Post-Nuclear Family TPB (2007, $9.99) r/#1-7; Kirkman intro. 10.00
... Vol. 2: Moments of Truth TPB (2008, $14.99) r/#8-13 15.00

DYNAMO 5: SINS OF THE FATHER
Image Comics: Jun, 2010 - No. 5, Oct, 2010 ($3.99, limited series)

1-5-Faerber-s/Brilha-a. 2-4-Invincible app. 4.00

DYNAMO JOE (Also see First Adventures & Mars)
First Comics: May, 1986 - No. 15, Jan, 1988 (#12-15: $1.75)

1-15: 4-Cargonauts begin, Special 1(1/87)-Mostly-r/Mars 3.00

DYNOMUTT (TV)(See Scooby-Doo (3rd series))
Marvel Comics Group: Nov, 1977 - No. 6, Sept, 1978 (Hanna-Barbera)

1-The Blue Falcon, Scooby Doo in all 5 10 15 31 53 75
2-6-All newsstand only 3 6 9 17 26 35

EAGLE, THE (1st Series) (See Science Comics & Weird Comics #8)
Fox Feature Syndicate: July, 1941 - No. 4, Jan, 1942

1-The Eagle begins; Rex Dexter of Mars app. by Briefer; all issues feature German war covers 486 972 1458 3550 6275 9000
2-The Spider Queen begins (origin) 258 516 774 1651 2826 4000
3,4: 3-Joe Spook begins (origin) 232 464 696 1485 2543 3600

EAGLE COMICS (2nd Series)
Rural Home Publ.: Feb-Mar, 1945 - No. 2, Apr-May, 1945

1-Aviation stories 142 284 426 909 1555 2200
2-Lucky Aces 90 180 270 576 988 1400
NOTE: *L. B. Cole c/a in each.*

EARTH 4 (Also see Urth 4)
Continuity Comics: Dec, 1993 - No. 4, Jan, 1994 ($2.50)

1-4: 1-3 all listed as Dec, 1993 in indicia 3.00

EARTH 4 DEATHWATCH 2000
Continuity Comics: Apr, 1993 - No. 3, Aug, 1993 ($2.50)

1-3 3.00

EARTH MAN ON VENUS (An...) (Also see Strange Planets)
Avon Periodicals: 1951

nn-Wood-a (26 pgs.); Fawcette-c 271 542 813 1734 2967 4200

EARTH-PRIME (Set in the continuity of the CW television shows)
DC Comics: Jun, 2022 - No. 6, Aug, 2022 ($5.99, limited series)

...: Batwoman 1 (6/22) Takes place during season 3; Clayton Henry-a 6.00
...: Superman & Lois 2 (6/22) Grummett-a 6.00
...: Legends of Tomorrow 3 (7/22) Pelletier-a; back-up story with Booster Gold 6.00

GD VG FN VF VF/NM NM-
2.0 4.0 6.0 8.0 9.0 9.2

...: Stargirl 4 (7/22) Robinson & Sevenbergen-s/Ordway-a; The Needle app. 6.00
...: The Flash 5 (8/22) Spotlight on Impulse, XS and Kid Flash; LaFuente-a 6.00
...: Hero's Twilight 6 (8/22) Heroes vs. Magog; Robson-a; back-up with Cisco 6.00

EARTH 2
DC Comics: Jul, 2012 - No. 32, May, 2015 ($3.99/$2.99)

1-($3.99) James Robinson-s/Nicola Scott-a/Ivan Reis-c; 4.00
1-Variant-c by Hitch 6.00
2-15-($2.99) 2-New Flash. 3-New Green Lantern. 4-New Atom 3.00
15.1, 15.2 (11/13, $2.99, regular covers) 3.00
15.1 (11/13, $3.99, 3-D cover) "Desaad #1" on cover; Levitz-s/Cinar-a 5.00
15.2 (11/13, $3.99, 3-D cover) "Solomon Grundy #1" on cover; Kindt-s/Lopresti-a 5.00
16-24,26-30: 16-Superman returns. 17-Batman returns. 20-Jae Lee-c. 28-Lobo app. 3.00
25-($3.99) New Superman revealed 4.00
#0 (11/12, $2.99) Superman, Batman, Wonder Woman, Terry Sloan app.; Giorello-a 3.00
Annual 1 (7/13, $4.99) Robinson-s/Cafu-a; new Batman app. 5.00
Annual 2 (3/14, $4.99) Taylor-s/Rocha-a; origin of new Batman 5.00
...: Futures End 1 (11/14, $2.99, regular-c) Five years later; Barrows-a 3.00
...: Futures End 1 (11/14, $3.99, 3-D cover) 4.00

EARTH 2: SOCIETY
DC Comics: Aug, 2015 - No. 22, May, 2017 ($2.99)

1-22: 1-Johnny Sorrow app.; Dick Grayson as Batman. 4-Anarky app. 6-Intro. Hourman. 15-Tony Harris-a (8 pgs.) 3.00
Annual 1 (10/16, $4.99) Abnett-s/Redondo & Neves-a; The Ultra-Humanite app. 5.00

EARTH 2: WORLD'S END
DC Comics: Dec, 2014 - No. 26, Jun, 2015 ($2.99, weekly series)

1-25: 1-Prelude to Darkseid's first attack. 3,7,8,10-Constantine app. 3.00
26-($3.99) Andy Kubert-c; leads into Convergence #1 4.00

EARTHWORM JIM (TV, cartoon)
Marvel Comics: Dec, 1995 - No. 3, Feb, 1996 ($2.25)

	GD 2.0	VG 4.0	FN 6.0	VF 8.0	VF/NM 9.0	NM- 9.2
1-Based on video game and toys	5	10	15	30	50	70
2,3	2	4	6	9	12	15

EARTH X
Marvel Comics: No. 0, Mar, 1999 - No. 12, Apr, 2000 ($3.99/$2.99, lim. series)

nn- (Wizard supplement) Alex Ross sketchbook; painted-c 6.00
Sketchbook (2/99) New sketches and previews 6.00

	GD 2.0	VG 4.0	FN 6.0	VF 8.0	VF/NM 9.0	NM- 9.2
0-(3/99)-Prelude; Leon-a(p)/Ross-c	1	2	3	4	5	7
1-(4/99)-Leon-a(p)/Ross-c	1	2	3	4	5	7

1-2nd printing 4.00
2-12 4.00
#1/2 (Wizard) Nick Fury on cover; Reinhold-a 6.00
#X (6/00, $3.99) 4.00
... Trilogy Companion TPB (2008, $29.99) r/#1/2; artwork and content from the Earth X, Paradise X and Universe X series; gallery of variant covers and promotional art 30.00
HC (2005, $49.99) r/#0,1-12, #1/2, X; foreward by Joss Whedon; Ross sketch pages 50.00
TPB (12/00, $24.95) r/#0,1-12, X; foreward by Joss Whedon 25.00

EASTER BONNET SHOP (See March of Comics No. 29)

EASTER WITH MOTHER GOOSE
Dell Publishing Co.: No. 103, 1946 - No. 220, Mar, 1949

	GD 2.0	VG 4.0	FN 6.0	VF 8.0	VF/NM 9.0	NM- 9.2
Four Color 103 (#1)-Walt Kelly-a	20	40	60	138	307	475
Four Color 140 ('47)-Kelly-a	16	32	48	107	236	365
Four Color 185 ('48), 220-Kelly-a	14	28	42	96	211	325

EAST MEETS WEST
Innovation Publishing: Apr, 1990 - No. 2, 1990 ($2.50, limited series, mature)

1,2: 1-Stevens part-i; Redondo-c(i). 2-Stevens-c(i); 1st app. Cheech & Chong in comics 4.00

EAST OF WEST
Image Comics: Mar, 2013 - Present ($3.50/$3.99)

1-Hickman-s/Dragotta-a 6.00
2-26-Hickman-s/Dragotta-a 3.50
27-44-($3.99) 4.00
45-($4.99) 5.00
... : The World (12/14, $3.99) Source book for characters, events, settings, timelines 4.00

EAT THE RICH
BOOM! Studios: Aug, 2021 - No. 5, Dec, 2021 ($3.99, limited series)

1-5-Sarah Gailey-s/Pius Bak-a 4.00

EC ARCHIVES
Gemstone Publishing/Dark Horse Books: 2006 - Present ($49.95/$49.99, hardcover with dustjacket)

Crime SuspenStories Vol. 1 - Recolored reprints of #1-6; foreward by Max Allan Collins 50.00
Frontline Combat Vol. 1 - Recolored reprints of #1-6; foreward by Henry G. Franke III 50.00
Haunt of Fear Vol. 1 - Recolored reprints of #15-17,4-6; foreward by Robert Englund 50.00
Haunt of Fear Vol. 2 - Recolored reprints of #7-12; foreward by Tim Sullivan 50.00
Panic Vol. 1 - Recolored reprints of #1-6; foreward by Bob Fingerman 50.00
Shock SuspenStories Vol. 1 - Recolored reprints of #1-6; foreward by Steven Spielberg 50.00
Shock SuspenStories Vol. 2 - Recolored reprints of #7-12; foreward by Dean Kamen 50.00
Shock SuspenStories Vol. 3 - Recolored reprints of #13-18; foreward by Brian Bendis 50.00
Tales From the Crypt Vol. 1 - Recolored reprints of Crypt of Terror #17-19 and Tales From the Crypt #20-22; foreward by John Carpenter; Al Feldstein behind-the-scenes info 100.00
Tales From the Crypt Vol. 2 - Recolored reprints of #23-28; foreward by Joe Dante 50.00
Tales From the Crypt Vol. 3 - Recolored reprints of #29-34; foreward by Bob Overstreet 50.00
Tales From the Crypt Vol. 4 - (DH) Recolored reprints of #35-40; foreward by Russ Cochran 50.00
Tales From the Crypt Vol. 5 - (DH) Recolored reprints of #41-46; foreward by Bruce Campbell 50.00
Two-Fisted Tales Vol. 1 - Recolored reprints of #18-23; foreward by Stephen Geppi 50.00
Two-Fisted Tales Vol. 2 - Recolored reprints of #24-29; foreward by Rocco Versaci, Ph.D. 50.00
Two-Fisted Tales Vol. 3 - (DH) Recolored reprints of #30-35; foreward by Joe Kubert 50.00
Vault of Horror Vol. 1 - Recolored reprints of #12-17; foreward by R.L. Stine 50.00
Vault of Horror Vol. 2 - Recolored reprints of #18-23; foreward by John Landis 80.00
Vault of Horror Vol. 3 - (DH) Recolored reprints of #24-29; foreward by Mike Richardson 50.00
Vault of Horror Vol. 4 - (DH) Recolored reprints of #30-35; foreward by Jonathan Maberry 50.00
Weird Fantasy Vol. 1 - (DH) Recolored reprints of #13-17; foreward by Walt Simonson 50.00
Weird Science Vol. 1 - Recolored reprints of #1-6; foreward by George Lucas 75.00
Weird Science Vol. 2 - Recolored reprints of #7-12; foreward by Paul Levitz 50.00
Weird Science Vol. 3 - Recolored reprints of #13-18; foreward by Jerry Weist 50.00

E. C. CLASSIC REPRINTS
East Coast Comix Co.: May, 1973 - No. 12, 1976 (E.C. Comics reprinted in color minus ads)

	GD 2.0	VG 4.0	FN 6.0	VF 8.0	VF/NM 9.0	NM- 9.2
1-The Crypt of Terror #1 (Tales from the Crypt #46)	2	4	6	11	16	20
2-12: 2-Weird Science #15('52). 3-Shock SuspenStories #12. 4-Haunt of Fear #12. 5-Weird Fantasy #13('52). 6-Crime SuspenStories #25. 7-Vault of Horror #26. 8-Shock SuspenStories #6. 9-Two-Fisted Tales #34. 10-Haunt of Fear #23. 11-Weird Science 12(#1). 12-Shock SuspenStories #2	2	4	6	8	11	14

EC CLASSICS
Russ Cochran: Aug, 1985 - No. 12, 1986? (High quality paper; each-r 8 stories in color) (#2-12 were resolicited in 1990)($4.95, 56 pgs., 8x11")

	GD 2.0	VG 4.0	FN 6.0	VF 8.0	VF/NM 9.0	NM- 9.2
1-12: 1-Tales From the Crypt. 2-Weird Science. 3-Two-Fisted Tales (r/31); Frontline Combat (r/9). 4-Shock SuspenStories. 5-Weird Fantasy. 6-Vault of Horror. 7-Weird Science-Fantasy (r/23,24). 8-Crime SuspenStories (r/17,18). 9-Haunt of Fear (r/14,15). 10-Panic (r/1,2). 11-Tales From the Crypt (r/23,24). 12-Weird Science (r/20,22)	1	2	3	4	5	7

ECHO
Abstract Studio: Mar, 2008 - No. 30, May, 2011 ($3.50)

1-Terry Moore-s/a/c 8.00
2-30 3.50
Terry Moore's Echo: Moon Lake TPB (2008, $15.95) r/#1-5; Moore sketch pages 16.00

ECHOLANDS
Image Comics: Aug, 2021 - No. 6, Feb, 2022 ($4.99, printed sideways for landscape view)

1-6-JH Williams III & W. Haden Blackman-s/Williams III-a; two covers on each 5.00
...: Raw Cut Edition 1-6 (9/21 - No. 6, 2/22, $4.99) Reprints with B&W art; creator bonuses 5.00

ECHO OF FUTUREPAST
Pacific Comics/Continuity Com.: May, 1984 - No. 9, Jan, 1986 ($2.95, 52 pgs.)

1-9: Neal Adams-c/a in all? 6.00
NOTE: ***N. Adams*** *a-1-6,7i,9i; c-1-3, 5p,7i,8,9i.* ***Golden*** *a-1-6 (Bucky O'Hare); c-6.* ***Toth*** *a-6,7.*

ECLIPSE GRAPHIC ALBUM SERIES
Eclipse Comics: Oct, 1978 - 1989 (8-1/2x11") (B&W #1-5)

1-Sabre (10/78, B&W, 1st print.); Gulacy-a; 1st direct sale graphic novel 16.00
1-Sabre (2nd printing, 1/79) 8.00
1-Sabre (3rd printing, $5.95) 6.00
1-Sabre 30th Anniversary Edition (2008, $14.99, 9x6" HC) new McGregor & Gulacy intros. original script with sketch art 15.00
2,6,7: 2-Night Music (11/79, B&W)-Russell-a. 6-I Am Coyote (11/84, color)-Rogers-c/a. 7-The Rocketeer (2nd print, $7.95). 7-The Rocketeer (3rd print, 1991, $8.95) 10.00
3,4: 3-Detectives, Inc. (5/80, B&W, $6.95)-Rogers-a. 4-Stewart The Rat (1980, B&W) -G. Colan-a 10.00
5-The Price (10/81, B&W)-Starlin-a 20.00
7-The Rocketeer (9/85, color)-Dave Stevens-a (r/chapters 1-5)(see Pacific Presents & Starslayer); has 7 pgs. new-a 25.00
7-The Rocketeer, signed & limited HC 90.00
7-The Rocketeer, hardcover (1986, $19.95) 40.00
7-The Rocketeer, unsigned HC (3rd, $32.95) 33.00
8-Zorro In Old California ('86, color) 14.00
8,12-Hardcover 18.00
9,10: 9-Sacred And The Profane ('86)-Steacy-a. 10-Somerset Holmes ('86, $15.95)-Adults, soft-c 16.00
9,10,12-Hardcover ($24.95). 12-signed & #'d 25.00
11-Floyd Farland, Citizen of the Future ('87, $2.95, B&W) Chris Ware-s/a 15.00
12,28,31,35: 12-Silverheels ('87, $7.95, color). 28-Miracleman Book I ($5.95). 31-Pigeons From Hell by R. E. Howard (11/88). 35-Rael: Into The Shadow of the Sun ('88, $7.95) 10.00
13-The Sisterhood of Steel ('87, $8.95, color) 10.00
14,16,18,20,23,24: 14-Samurai, Son of Death ('87, $4.95, B&W). 16,18,20,23-See Airfighters Classics #1-4. 24-Heartbreak ($4.95, B&W) 7.00
14 (2nd pr.),17,21: 14-Samurai, Son of Death ($3.95, 2nd printing). 17-Valkyrie, Prisoner of the Past SC ('88, $3.95, color). 21-XYR-Multiple ending comic ('88, $3.95, B&W) 6.00
15,22,27: 15-Twisted Tales (11/87, color)-Dave Stevens-c. 22-Alien Worlds #1 (5/88, $3.95, 52 pgs.)-Nudity. 27-Fast Fiction (She) ($5.95, B&W) 8.00
17-Valkyrie, Prisoner of the Past S&N Hardcover ('88, $19.95) 25.00
19-Scout: The Four Monsters ('88, $14.95, color)-r/Scout #1-7; soft-c 15.00
25,30,32-34: 25-Alex Toth's Zorro Vol. 1 ,2($10.95, B&W). 30-Brought To Light; Alan Moore scripts ('89). 32-Teenaged Dope Slaves and Reform School Girls. 33-Bogie. 34-Air Fighters Classics #5 12.00
29-Real Love: Best of Simon & Kirby Romance Comics (10/88, $12.95) 15.00
30,31: Limited hardcover ed. ($29.95). 31-signed 30.00
36-Dr. Watchstop: Adventures in Time and Space ('89, $8.95) 10.00

ECLIPSE MAGAZINE (Becomes Eclipse Monthly)
Eclipse Publishing: May, 1981 - No. 8, Jan, 1983 ($2.95, B&W, magazine)

1-8: 1-1st app. Cap'n Quick and a Foozle by Rogers, Ms. Tree by Beatty, and Dope by Trina Robbins. 2-1st app. I Am Coyote by Rogers. 7-1st app. Masked Man by Boyer 4.00
NOTE: ***Colan*** *a-3, 5, 8.* ***Golden*** *c/a-2.* ***Gulacy*** *a-6, c-1, 6.* ***Kaluta*** *c/a-5.* ***Mayerik*** *a-2, 3.* ***Rogers*** *a-1-8.* ***Starlin*** *a-1.* ***Sutton*** *a-6.*

ECLIPSE MONTHLY
Eclipse Comics: Aug, 1983 - No. 10, Jul, 1984 (Baxter paper, $2.00/$1.50/$1.75)

1-10: ($2.00, 52 pgs.)-Cap'n Quick and a Foozle by Rogers, Static by Ditko, Dope by Trina Robbins, Rio by Wildey, The Masked Man by Boyer begin. 3-Ragamuffins begins 4.00
NOTE: ***Boyer*** *c-6.* ***Ditko*** *a-1-3.* ***Rogers*** *a-1-4; c-2, 4, 7.* ***Wildey*** *a-1, 2, 5, 9, 10; c-5, 10.*

ECLIPSO (See Brave and the Bold #64, House of Secrets #61 & Phantom Stranger, 1987)
DC Comics: Nov, 1992 - No. 18, Apr, 1994 ($1.25)

1-18: 1-Giffen plots/breakdowns begin. 10-Darkseid app. Creeper in #3-6,9,11-13. 18-Spectre-c/s 4.00
Annual 1 (1993, $2.50, 68 pgs.)-Intro Prism 5.00
...: The Music of the Spheres TPB (2009, $19.99) r/stories from Countdown to Mystery #1-8 20.00

ECLIPSO: THE DARKNESS WITHIN
DC Comics: July, 1992 - No. 2, Oct, 1992 ($2.50, 68 pgs.)

1,2: 1-With purple gem attached to-c, 1-Without gem; Superman, Creeper app., 2-Concludes Eclipso storyline from annuals 4.00

Earth 2 #18 © DC

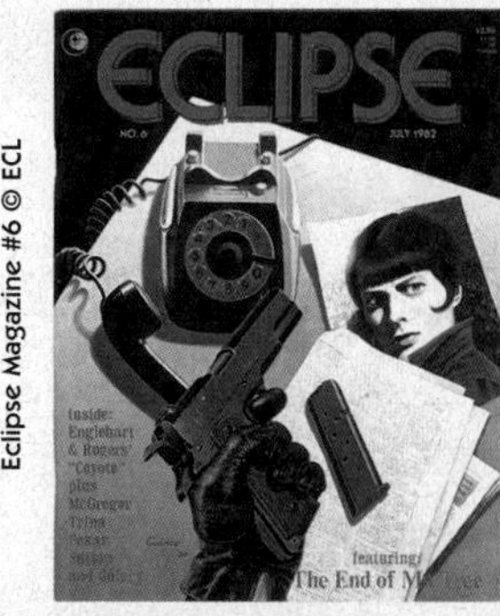

Eclipse Magazine #6 © ECL

Eden's Fall #1 © TCOW

	GD	VG	FN	VF	VF/NM	NM-
	2.0	4.0	6.0	8.0	9.0	9.2

EC SAMPLER - FREE COMIC BOOK DAY
Gemstone Publishing: May, 2008

Reprinted stories with restored color from Weird Science #6, Two-Fisted Tales #22, Crypt of Terror #17, Shock Suspenstories #6 — 3.00

E. C. 3-D CLASSICS (See Three Dimensional...)

ECTOKID (See Razorline)
Marvel Comics: Sept, 1993 - No. 9, May, 1994 ($1.75/$1.95)

1-($2.50)-Foil embossed-c; created by C. Barker — 5.00
2-9: 2-Origin. 5-Saint Sinner x-over — 4.00
...: Unleashed! 1 (10/94, $2.95, 52 pgs.) — 5.00

ED "BIG DADDY" ROTH'S RATFINK COMIX (Also see Ratfink)
World of Fandom/ Ed Roth: 1991 - No. 3, 1991 ($2.50)

1-3: Regular Ed., 1-Limited double cover — 2 4 6 11 16 20

EDDIE CAMPBELL'S BACCHUS
Eddie Campbell Comics: May, 1995 - No. 60, May, 2001 ($2.95, B&W)

1-Cerebus app. — 1 2 3 5 6 8
1-2nd printing (5/97) — 3.00
2-10: 9-Alex Ross back-c — 5.00
11-60 — 3.00
Doing The Islands With Bacchus ('97, $17.95) — 18.00
Earth, Water, Air & Fire ('98, $9.95) — 10.00
King Bacchus ('99, $12.95) — 13.00
The Eyeball Kid ('98, $8.50) — 8.50

EDDIE STANKY (Baseball Hero)
Fawcett Publications: 1951 (New York Giants)

nn-Photo-c — 41 82 123 256 428 600

EDEN
AfterShock Comics: May, 2021 ($6.99, oversized 8-1/2" x 10-7/8", one shot)

1-Cullen Bunn-s/Dalibor Talajic-a — 7.00

EDEN'S FALL (Characters from Postal, The Tithe, and Think Tank)
Image Comics (Top Cow): Aug, 2016 - No. 3 ($3.99)

1-3-Matt Hawkins & Bryan Hill-s/Atilio Rojo-a — 4.00

EDEN'S TRAIL
Marvel Comics: Jan, 2003 - No. 5, May 2003 ($2.99, unfinished lim. series, printed sideways)

1-5-Chuck Austen-s/Steve Uy-a — 3.00

EDGAR ALLAN POE'S MORELLA AND THE MURDERS IN THE RUE MORGUE
Dark Horse Comics: Jun, 2015 ($3.99, one-shot)

1-Adaptation of Poe's poems; story and art by Richard Corben — 4.00

EDGAR ALLAN POE'S SNIFTER OF BLOOD
AHOY Comics: 2020 - No. 6, 2021 ($4.99)

1-6-Short stories; adaptations and paradies of Poe by various. 2-Monster Serials — 5.00

EDGAR ALLAN POE'S SNIFTER OF DEATH
AHOY Comics: 2021 - No. 6, 2022 ($4.99)

1-6-Short stories; adaptations and paradies of Poe by various. 1-Monster Serials — 5.00

EDGAR ALLAN POE'S SNIFTER OF TERROR
AHOY Comics: 2018 - 2020 ($3.99)

1-6-Short stories; adaptations and paradies of Poe by various — 4.00
Season Two 1-6: 2-Action Comics #1 cover spoof; Russell-s. 3-Medley-s/a — 4.00

EDGAR ALLAN POE'S THE CONQUEROR WORM
Dark Horse Comics: Nov, 2012 ($3.99, one-shot)

1-Adaptation of Poe's poem; story and art by Richard Corben; Corben sketch pages — 4.00

EDGAR ALLAN POE'S THE FALL OF THE HOUSE OF USHER
Dark Horse Comics: May, 2013 - No. 2, Jun, 2013 ($3.99, limited series)

1,2-Adaptation of Poe's poem; story and art by Richard Corben; Corben sketch pages — 4.00

EDGAR ALLAN POE'S - THE FALL OF THE HOUSE OF USHER AND OTHER TALES OF HORROR
Catlan Communications Pub.: Sept. 1985 (hardcover graphic novel)

nn-Reprints of Poe story issues from Warren comic mags; all Richard Corben-a; numbered edition of 350 signed by Corben; 60 pgs. — 130.00
nn-Softcover edition — 60.00

EDGAR ALLAN POE'S THE PREMATURE BURIAL
Dark Horse Comics: Apr, 2014 ($3.99, one-shot)

1-Adaptation of The Premature Burial and The Cask of Amontillado; Corben-s/a/c — 4.00

EDGAR ALLAN POE'S THE RAVEN AND THE RED DEATH
Dark Horse Comics: Oct, 2013 ($3.99, one-shot)

1-Adaptation of The Raven and The Masque of the Red Death; Corben-s/a/c — 4.00

	GD	VG	FN	VF	VF/NM	NM-
	2.0	4.0	6.0	8.0	9.0	9.2

EDGAR BERGEN PRESENTS CHARLIE McCARTHY
Whitman Publishing Co. (Charlie McCarthy Co.): No. 764, 1938 (36 pgs.; 15x10-1/2"; color)

764 — 90 180 270 576 988 1400

EDGAR RICE BURROUGHS' CARSON OF VENUS
American Mythology Prods.: 2018 - Present ($3.99)

...Fear on Four Worlds 1 - part 1 of crossover; Mills-s/Mesarcia-a — 4.00
...: Pirates of Venus 1,2 - Reprints from Korak, Son of Tarzan #46-53; Wein-s/Kaluta-a — 4.00
...: The Flames Beyond 1-3: 1-Kaluta-c/Carey-s/Mesarcia-a — 4.00
.../ Warlord of Mars 1-Kaluta-c/Avallone-s/Mesarcia-a — 4.00

EDGAR RICE BURROUGHS' PELLUCIDAR
American Mythology Prods.: 2018 - 2019 ($3.99)

1-At the Earth's Core; Wolfer-s/Rearte-a — 4.00
1-Fear on Four Worlds; part 3 of crossover; Wolfer-s/Mesarcia-a — 4.00
1-Wings of Death; Wolfer-s/Büll-a — 4.00

EDGAR RICE BURROUGHS' TARZAN: A TALE OF MUGAMBI
Dark Horse Comics: 1995 ($2.95, one-shot)

1 — 3.00

EDGAR RICE BURROUGHS' TARZAN: IN THE LAND THAT TIME FORGOT AND THE POOL OF TIME
Dark Horse Comics: 1996 ($12.95, trade paperback)

nn-r/Russ Manning-a — 13.00

EDGAR RICE BURROUGHS' TARZAN OF THE APES
Dark Horse Comics: May, 1999 ($12.95, trade paperback)

nn-reprints — 13.00

EDGAR RICE BURROUGHS' TARZAN: THE LOST ADVENTURE
Dark Horse Comics: Jan, 1995 - No. 4, Apr, 1995 ($2.95, B&W, limited series)

1-4: ERB's last Tarzan story, adapted by Joe Lansdale — 3.00
Hardcover (12/95, $19.95) — 20.00
Limited Edition Hardcover ($99.95)-signed & numbered — 100.00

EDGAR RICE BURROUGHS' TARZAN: THE RETURN OF TARZAN
Dark Horse Comics: May, 1997 - No. 3, July, 1997 ($2.95, limited series)

1-3 — 3.00

EDGAR RICE BURROUGHS' TARZAN: THE RIVERS OF BLOOD
Dark Horse Comics: Nov, 1999 - No. 4, Feb, 2000 ($2.95, limited series)

1-4-Kordey-c/a — 3.00

EDGAR RICE BURROUGHS' THE LAND THAT TIME FORGOT
American Mythology Prods.: 2016 - No. 3, 2016 ($3.99, limited series)

1-3-Wolfer-s/Caracuzzo-a
1-Fear on Four Worlds; part 4 of crossover; Wolfer-s/Büll-a — 4.00
.../ Pellucidar: Terror From the Earth's Core 1-3 ('17, $3.99) Wolfer-s/Magora & Cuesta-a — 4.00
... See-Ta The Savage 1,2 (2017, $3.99) Wolfer-s/a — 4.00

EDGAR RICE BURROUGHS' THE MOON MAID
American Mythology Prods.: 2018 - 2019 ($3.99)

1-3-Catacombs of the Moon — 4.00
1-Fear on Four Worlds; part 2 of x-over; Mills-s/Rearte-a — 4.00

EDGE
Malibu Comics (Bravura): July, 1994 - No. 3, Apr, 1995 ($2.50/$2.95, unfinished lim.series)

1-3-S. Grant-story & Gil Kane-c/a; w/Bravura stamp. 3-($2.95-c) — 3.00

EDGE (Re-titled as Vector starting with #13)
CrossGeneration Comics: May, 2002 - No. 12, Apr, 2003 ($9.95/$11.95/$7.95, TPB)

1-3: Reprints from various CrossGen titles — 10.00
4-8-($11.95) — 12.00
9-12-($7.95, 8-1/4" x 5-1/2") digest-sized reprints — 8.00

EDGE OF CHAOS
Pacific Comics: July, 1983 - No. 3, Jan, 1984 (Limited series)

1-3-Morrow c/a; all contain nudity — 3.00

EDGE OF DOOM (Horror anthology)
IDW Publishing: Oct, 2010 - No. 5, Mar, 2011 ($3.99)

1-5-Steve Niles-s/Kelley Jones-a — 4.00

EDGE OF SPIDER-GEDDON (Leads into Spider-Geddon #0)
Marvel Comics: Oct, 2018 - No. 4, Dec, 2018 ($3.99, limited series)

1-4: 1-Anarchic Spider-Man app.; Sandoval-a. 2-Peni Parker, SP//dr app. 4-Kuder-s/a — 4.00

GD VG FN VF VF/NM NM-
2.0 4.0 6.0 8.0 9.0 9.2

EDGE OF SPIDER-VERSE (See Amazing Spider-Man 2014 series #7-14)
Marvel Comics: Nov, 2014 - No. 5, Dec, 2014 ($3.99, limited series)

1-Spider-Man Noir; Isanove-a. 2 4 6 9 13 16
2-Gwen Stacy Spider-Woman 1st app.; Robbi Rodriguez-a/c
18 36 54 122 271 420
2 Facsimile Edition (4/22, $3.99) r/#2 with original 2014 ads 4.00
3,4: 3-Weaver-s/a 1 3 4 6 8 10
5-1st app. Sp//dr & Peni Parker; Gerard Way-s 3 6 9 19 30 40

EDGE OF SPIDER-VERSE
Marvel Comics: Oct, 2022 - No. 5, Dec, 2022 ($4.99, limited series)

1-5: 1-Spider-Man Noir, Araña, Spider-Rex app. 2-Spider-Gwen, Spider-UK app. 5-Intro Web-Weaver 5.00

EDGE OF VENOMVERSE (Leads into Venomverse series)
Marvel Comics: Aug, 2017 - No. 5, Oct, 2017 ($3.99, limited series)

1-5: 1-Venom merges with X-23; Boschi-a. 2-Gwenpool/Venom; Daredevil app. 3-Ghost Rider. 4-Old Man Logan. 5-Deadpool; Stokoe-a 4.00

EDWARD SCISSORHANDS (Based on the movie)
IDW Publishing: Oct, 2014 - No. 10, Jul, 2015 ($3.99)

1-Kate Leth-s/Drew Rausch-a; multiple covers 2 4 6 8 11 14
2-10-Multiple covers on each 4.00

ED WHEELAN'S JOKE BOOK STARRING FAT & SLAT (See Fat & Slat)

EERIE (Strange Worlds No. 18 on)
Avon Per.: No. 1, Jan, 1947; No. 1, May-June, 1951 - No. 17, Aug-Sept, 1954

1(1947)-1st supernatural comic; Kubert, Fugitani-a; bondage-c
1000 2000 3000 7400 13,200 19,000
1(1951)-Reprints story from 1947 #1 168 336 504 1075 1838 2600
2-Wood-c/a; bondage-c 181 362 543 1158 1979 2800
3-Wood-c; Kubert, Wood/Orlando-a 135 270 405 864 1482 2100
4,5-Wood-c 100 200 300 635 1093 1550
6,8,13,14: 8-Kinstler-a; bondage-c; Phantom Witch Doctor story
57 114 171 362 619 875
7-Wood/Orlando-c; Kubert-a 90 180 270 576 988 1400
9-Kubert-a; Check-c 97 194 291 621 1061 1500
10,11: 10-Kinstler-a. 11-Kinstlerish-a by McCann 60 120 180 381 653 925
12-Dracula story from novel, 25 pgs. 77 154 231 493 847 1200
15-Reprints No. 1('51) minus-c(bondage) 50 100 150 315 533 750
16-Wood-a r-/No. 2 53 106 159 334 567 800
17-Wood/Orlando & Kubert-a; reprints #3 minus inside & outside Wood-c
55 110 165 352 601 850

NOTE: ***Hollingsworth** a-9-11; c-10, 11.*

EERIE
I. W. Enterprises: 1964

I.W. Reprint #1('64)-Wood-c(r); r-story/Spook #1 5 10 15 30 50 70
I.W. Reprint #2,6,8: 8-Dr. Drew by Grandenetti from Ghost #9
4 8 12 27 44 60
I.W. Reprint #9-r/Tales of Terror #1(Toby); Wood-c 5 10 15 31 53 75

EERIE (Magazine)(See Warren Presents)
Warren Publ. Co.: No. 1, Sept, 1965; No. 2, Mar, 1966 - No. 139, Feb, 1983

1-24 pgs., black & white, small size (5-1/4x7-1/4"), low distribution; cover from inside back cover of Creepy No. 2; stories reprinted from Creepy No. 7, 8. At least three different versions exist.
First Printing - B&W, 5-1/4" wide x 7-1/4" high, evenly trimmed. On page 18, panel 5, in the upper left-hand corner, the large rear view of a bald headed man blends into solid black and is unrecognizable. Overall printing quality is poor. 61 122 183 488 1094 1700
Second Printing - B&W, 5-1/4x7-1/4", with uneven, untrimmed edges (if one of these were trimmed evenly, the size would be less than as indicated). The figure of the bald headed man on page 18, panel 5 is clear and discernible. The staples have a 1/4" blue stripe. 16 32 48 110 243 375
Other unauthorized reproductions for comparison's sake would be practically worthless. One known version was probably shot off a first printing copy with some loss of detail; the finer lines tend to disappear in this version which can be determined by looking at the lower right-hand corner of page one, first story. The roof of the house is shaded with straight lines. These lines are sharp and distinct on original, but broken on this version.

NOTE: ***The Overstreet Comic Book Price Guide** recommends that, before buying a 1st issue, you consult an expert.*

2-Frazetta-c; Toth-a; 1st app. host Cousin Eerie 12 24 36 82 179 275
3-Frazetta-c & half pg. ad (rerun in #4); Toth, Williamson, Ditko-a
10 20 30 64 132 200
4,6: 4-Frazetta-a (1/2 pg. ad) 7 14 21 44 82 120
5,7-Frazetta-c. Ditko-a in all 8 16 24 52 99 145
8-Frazetta-c; Ditko-a 9 18 27 57 111 165
9-11,25: 9,10-Neal Adams-a, Ditko-a. 11-Karloff Mummy adapt.-Wood-s/a. 25-Steranko-c
7 14 21 44 82 120
12-16,18-22,24,32-35,40,45: 12,13,20-Poe-s. 12-Bloch-s. 12,15-Jones-a. 13-Lovecraft-s. 14,16-Toth-a. 16,19,24-Stoker-s. 16,32,33,43-Corben-a. 34-Early Boris-c. 35-Early Brunner-a. 35,40-Early Ploog-a. 40-Frankenstein; Ploog-a (6/72, 6 months before Marvel's series) 5 10 15 30 50 70
17-(low distribution) 22 44 66 154 340 525
23-Classic Frazetta-c; Adams-a(reprint) 32 64 96 230 515 800
26-31,36-38,43,44 4 8 12 27 44 60
39,41: 39-1st Dax the Warrior; Maroto-a. 41-(low distribution)
5 10 15 34 60 85
42,51: 42-('73 Annual, 84 pgs.) Spooktacular; Williamson-a. 51-('74 Annual, 76 pgs.) Color poster insert; Toth-a 5 10 15 30 50 70
46,48: 46-Dracula series by Sutton begins; 2pgs. Vampirella. 48-Begin "Mummy Walks" and "Curse of the Werewolf" series (both continue in #49,50,52,53)
4 8 12 27 44 60
47,49,50,52,53: 47-Lilith. 49-Marvin the Dead Thing. 50-Satanna, Daughter of Satan. 52-Hunter by Neary begins. 53-Adams-a 4 8 12 25 40 55
54,55-Color insert Spirit story by Eisner, reprints sections 12/21/47 & 6/16/46 54-Dr. Archaeus series begins 3 6 9 21 33 45
56,57,59,63,69,77,78: All have 8 pg. slick color insert. 56,57,77-Corben-a. 59-(100 pgs.) Summer Special, all Dax issue. 69-Summer Special, all Hunter issue, Neary-a. 78-All Mummy issue 3 6 9 21 33 45
58,60,62,68,72,: 8 pg. slick color insert & Wrightson-a in all. 58,60,62-Corben-a. 60-Summer Giant (9/74, $1.25) 1st Exterminator One; Wood-a. 62-Mummies Walk. 68-Summer Special (84 pgs.) 4 8 12 23 37 50
61,64-67,71: 61-Mummies Walk-s, Wood-a. 64-Corben-a. 64,65,67-Toth-a. 65,66-El Cid. 67-Hunter II. 71-Goblin-c/1st app. 3 6 9 17 26 35
70,73-75 3 6 9 14 20 26
76-1st app. Darklon the Mystic by Starlin-s/a 3 6 9 20 31 42
79,80-Origin Darklon the Mystic by Starlin 3 6 9 17 26 35
81,86,97: 81-Frazetta-c, King Kong; Corben-a. 86-(92 pgs.) All Corben issue. 97-Time Travel/Dinosaur issue; Corben,Adams-a 3 6 9 16 23 30
82-Origin/1st app. The Rook 3 6 9 18 28 38
83,85,88,89,91-93,98,99: 98-Rook (31 pgs.). 99-1st Horizon Seekers.
2 4 6 10 14 18
84,87,90,96,100: 84,100-Starlin-a. 87-Hunter 3; Nino-a. 87,90-Corben-a. 96-Summer Special (92 pgs.). 100-(92 pgs.) Anniversary issue; Rook (30 pgs.)
2 4 6 13 18 22
94,95-The Rook & Vampirella team-up. 95-Vampirella-c; 1st MacTavish
3 6 9 16 24 32
101,106,112,115,118,120,121,128: 101-Return of Hunter II, Starlin-a. 106-Hard John Nuclear Hit Parade Special, Corben-a. 112-All Maroto issue, Luana-s. 115-All José Ortiz issues. 118-1st Haggarth. 120-1st Zud Kamish. 121-Hunter/Darklon. 128-Starlin-a, Hsu-a
2 4 6 10 14 18
102-105,107-111,113,114,116,117,119,122-124,126,127,129: 103-105,109-111-Gulacy-a. 104-Beast World. 2 4 6 9 13 16
125-(10/81, 84 pgs.) all Neal Adams issue 3 6 9 14 19 24
130-(76 pgs.) Vampirella-c/sty (54 pgs.); Pantha, Van Helsing, Huntress, Dax, Schreck, Hunter, Exterminator One, Rook app. 3 6 9 16 23 30
131-(Lower distr.); all Wood issue 3 6 9 14 20 26
132-134,136: 132-Rook returns. 133-All Ramon Torrents-a issue. 134,136-Color comic insert
2 4 6 10 14 18
135-(Lower distr., 10/82, 100 pgs.) All Ditko issue 3 6 9 14 20 26
137-139 (lower distr.):137-All Super-Hero issue. 138-Sherlock Holmes. 138,139-Color comic insert 2 4 6 13 18 22
Yearbook '70-Frazetta-c 5 10 15 35 63 90
Annual '71, '72-Reprints in both 4 8 12 25 40 55
... Archives - Volume One HC (Dark Horse, 3/09, $49.95, dustjacket) r/#1-5 50.00
... Archives - Volume Two HC (Dark Horse, 9/09, $49.95, dustjacket) r/#6-10; interview with Frank Frazetta from 1985 50.00

NOTE: *The above books contain art by many good artists:* ***N. Adams, Brunner, Corben, Craig (Taycee), Crandall, Ditko, Eisner, Evans, Jeff Jones, Krenkel, McWilliams, Morrow, Orlando, Ploog, Severin, Starlin, Torres, Toth, Williamson, Wood,*** *and* ***Wrightson****; covers by* ***Bode', Corben, Davis, Frazetta, Morrow****, and* ***Orlando. Frazetta*** *c-2, 3, 7, 8, 23. Annuals from 1973-on are included in regular numbering. 1970-74 Annuals are complete reprints. Annuals from 1975-on are in the format of the regular issues.*

EERIE
Dark Horse Comics: Jul, 2012 - No. 8, Dec, 2015 ($2.99, B&W)

1-8-Sci-fi anthology by various. 2-Allred-a. 3-Wood-a(r). 4,6-Kelley Jones-a 3.00

EERIE ADVENTURES (Also see Weird Adventures)
Ziff-Davis Publ. Co.: Winter, 1951 (Painted-c)

1-Powell-a(2), McCann-a; used in **SOTI**; bondage-c; Krigstein back-c
116 232 348 742 1271 1800

NOTE: *Title dropped due to similarity to Avon's Eerie & legal action.*

EERIE TALES (Magazine)
Hastings Associates: 1959 (Black & White)

1-Williamson, Torres, Tuska-a, Powell(2), & Morrow(2)-a
25 50 75 150 245 340

EERIE TALES
Super Comics: 1963-1964

Super Reprint No. 10,11,12,18: 10('63)-r/Spook #27. Purple Claw in #11,12 ('63); #12-r/Avon's Eerie #1('51)-Kida-r 3 6 9 17 26 35
15-Wolverton-a, Spacehawk-r/Blue Bolt Weird Tales #113; Disbrow-a
5 10 15 30 50 70

EFFIGY
DC Comics (Vertigo): Mar, 2015 - No. 7, Sept, 2015 ($2.99/$3.99)

1-5: 1-Tim Seeley-s/Marley Zarcone-a 3.00
6,7-($3.99) 4.00

EGBERT
Arnold Publications/Quality Comics Group: Spring, 1946 - No. 20, Aug, 1950

1-Funny animal; intro Egbert & The Count 25 50 75 150 245 340
2 14 28 42 82 121 160
3-10 10 20 30 56 76 95
11-20 9 18 27 47 61 75

EGYPT
DC Comics (Vertigo): Aug, 1995 - No.7, Feb, 1996 ($2.50, lim. series, mature)

1-7: Milligan scripts in all. 3.00

EH! (...Dig This Crazy Comic) (From Here to Insanity No. 8 on)
Charlton Comics: Dec, 1953 - No. 7, Nov-Dec, 1954 (Satire)

1-Davis-*ish*-c/a by Ayers, Wood-*ish*-a by Giordano; Atomic Mouse app.
47 94 141 296 498 700
2-Ayers-c/a 28 56 84 165 270 375
3,5,7 26 52 78 154 252 350
4,6: Sexual innuendo-c. 6-Ayers-a 34 68 102 199 325 450

EI8GT
Dark Horse Comics: Feb, 2015 - No. 5, Jun, 2015 ($3.50)

1-Rafael Albuquerque-a/c; Mike Johnson-s 3.50

EIGHTBALL (Also see David Boring)
Fantagraphics Books: Oct, 1989 - Present ($2.75/$2.95/$3.95, semi-annually, mature)

1 (1st printing) Daniel Clowes-s/a in all 11 22 33 76 163 250
2,3 3 6 9 15 22 28
4-19: 17-(8/96) 2 4 6 8 11 14
20,21: 21-($4.95) Concludes David Boring 3-parter 2 4 6 8 10 12
22-($5.95) 29 short stories 2 4 6 8 10 12
23-($7.00, 9" x 12") The Death Ray 2 4 6 9 12 15
Twentieth Century Eightball (2002, $19.00) r/Clowes strips 20.00

Eerie (2013) #3 © NCC

Eight Billion Genies #1 © Silent E Prods.

Electric Warriors (2019) #4 © DC

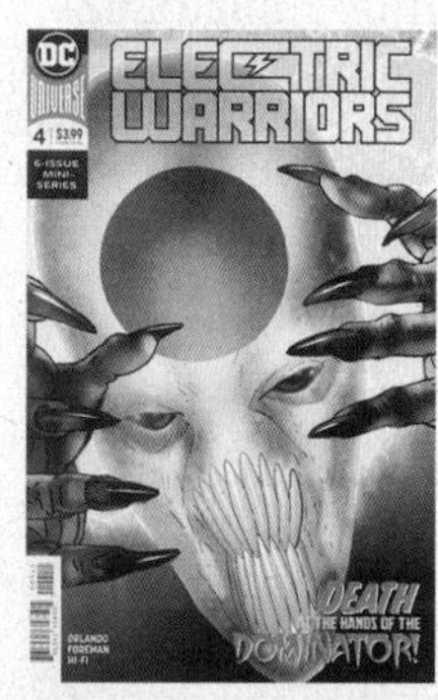

	GD	VG	FN	VF	VF/NM	NM-
	2.0	4.0	6.0	8.0	9.0	9.2

EIGHT BILLION GENIES
Image Comics: May, 2022 - No. 8 ($3.99, limited series)
1-7: Charles Soule-s/Ryan Browne-a 4.00

EIGHTH WONDER, THE
Dark Horse Comics: Nov, 1997 ($2.95, one-shot)
nn-Reprints stories from Dark Horse Presents #85-87 3.00

EIGHT IS ENOUGH KITE FUN BOOK (See Kite Fun Book 1979 in the Promotional Comics section)

EIGHT LEGGED FREAKS
DC Comics (WildStorm): 2002 ($6.95, one-shot, squarebound)
nn-Adaptation of 2002 mutant spider movie; Joe Phillips-a; intro by Dean Devlin 7.00

1872 (Secret Wars tie-in)
Marvel Comics: Sept, 2015 - No. 4, Dec, 2015 ($3.99, limited series)
1-4-Red Wolf in the western town of Timely in 1872. 4-Avengers of the West 4.00

80 PAGE GIANT (...Magazine No. 2-15)
National Periodical Publications: 8/64 - No. 15, 10/65; No. 16, 11/65 - No. 89, 7/71 (25¢) (All reprints) (#1-56: 84 pgs.; #57-89: 68 pgs.)

	GD	VG	FN	VF	VF/NM	NM-
1-Superman Annual; originally planned as Superman Annual #9 (8/64)	34	68	102	245	548	850
2-Jimmy Olsen	18	36	54	125	276	430
3,4: 3-Lois Lane. 4-Flash-G.A.-r; Infantino-a	15	30	45	103	227	350
5-Batman; has Sunday newspaper strip; Catwoman-r; Batman's Life Story-r (25th anniversary special)	15	30	45	103	227	350
6-Superman	13	26	39	91	201	310
7-Sgt. Rock's Prize Battle Tales; Kubert-c/a	26	52	78	182	404	625
8-More Secret Origins-origins of JLA, Aquaman, Robin, Atom, & Superman; Infantino-a	26	52	78	182	404	625
9-15: 9-Flash (r/Flash #106,117,123 & Showcase #14); Infantino-a. 10-Superboy. 11-Superman; all Luthor issue. 12-Batman; has Sunday newspaper strip. 13-Jimmy Olsen. 14-Lois Lane. 15-Superman and Batman; Joker-c/story	12	24	36	82	179	275

Continued as part of regular series under each title in which that particular book came out, a Giant being published instead of the regular size. Issues No. 16 to No. 89 are listed for your information. See individual titles for prices.
16-JLA #39 (11/65), 17-Batman #176, 18-Superman #183, 19-Our Army at War #164, 20-Action #334, 21-Flash #160, 22-Superboy #129, 23-Superman #187, 24-Batman #182, 25-Jimmy Olsen #95, 26-Lois Lane #68, 27-Batman #185, 28-World's Finest #161, 29-JLA #48, 30-Batman #187, 31-Superman #193, 32-Our Army at War #177, 33-Action #347, 34-Flash #169, 35-Superboy #138, 36-Superman #197, 37-Batman #193, 38-Jimmy Olsen #104, 39-Lois Lane #77, 40-World's Finest #170, 41-JLA #58, 42-Superman #202, 43-Batman #198, 44-Our Army at War #190, 45-Action #360, 46-Flash #178, 47-Superboy #147, 48-Superman #207, 49-Batman #203, 50-Jimmy Olsen #113, 51-Lois Lane #86, 52-World's Finest #179, 53-JLA #67, 54-Superman #212, 55-Batman #208, 56-Our Army at War #203, 57-Action #373, 58-Flash #187, 59-Superboy #156, 60-Superman #217, 61-Batman #213, 62-Jimmy Olsen #122, 63-Lois Lane #95, 64-World's Finest #188, 65-JLA #76, 66-Superman #222, 67-Batman #218, 68-Our Army at War #216, 69-Adventure #390, 70-Flash #196, 71-Superboy #165, 72-Superman #227, 73-Batman #223, 74-Jimmy Olsen #131, 75-Lois Lane #104, 76-World's Finest #197, 77-JLA #85, 78-Superman #232, 79-Batman #228, 80-Our Army at War #229, 81-Adventure #403, 82-Flash #205, 83-Superboy #174, 84-Superman #239, 85-Batman #233, 86-Jimmy Olsen #140, 87-Lois Lane #113, 88-World's Finest #206, 89-JLA #93.

87TH PRECINCT (TV) (Based on the Ed McBain novels)
Dell Publishing Co.: Apr-June, 1962 - No. 2, July-Sept, 1962

	GD	VG	FN	VF	VF/NM	NM-
Four Color 1309(#1)-Krigstein-a	9	18	27	60	120	180
2-Photo-c	7	14	21	43	89	130

E IS FOR EXTINCTION (Secret Wars tie-in)
Marvel Comics: Aug, 2015 - No. 4, Nov, 2015 ($4.99/$3.99, limited series)
1-($4.99) New X-Men in Mutopia; Burnham-s/Villalobos-a 5.00
2-4-($3.99) Cassandra Nova returns 4.00

EL BOMBO COMICS
Standard Comics/Frances M. McQueeny: 1946

	GD	VG	FN	VF	VF/NM	NM-
nn(1946), 1(no date)	21	42	63	122	199	275

EL CAZADOR
CrossGen Comics: Oct, 2003 - No. 6, Jun, 2004 ($2.95)
1-Dixon-s/Epting-a 5.00
2-6: 5-Lady Death preview 3.00
...: The Bloody Ballad of Blackjack Tom 1 (4/04, $2.95, one-shot) Cariello-a 3.00

EL CID
Dell Publishing Co.: No. 1259, 1961

	GD	VG	FN	VF	VF/NM	NM-
Four Color 1259-Movie, photo-c	7	14	21	46	86	125

EL DIABLO (See All-Star Western #2 & Weird Western Tales #12)
DC Comics: Aug, 1989 - No. 16, Jan, 1991 ($1.50-$1.75, color)
1 ($2.50, 52pgs.)-Masked hero 4.00
2-16 3.00

EL DIABLO
DC Comics (Vertigo): Mar, 2001 - No. 4, Jun, 2001 ($2.50, limited series)
1-4-Azzarello-s/Zezelj-a/Sale-c 3.00
TPB (2008, $12.99) r/#1-4 13.00

EL DIABLO
DC Comics: Nov, 2008 - No. 6, Apr, 2009 ($2.99, limited series)
1-6-Nitz-s/Hester-a/c. 4,5-Freedom Fighters app. 3.00

EL DORADO (See Movie Classics)

ELEANOR & THE EGRET
AfterShock Comics: Apr, 2017 - No. 5, Nov, 2017 ($3.99)
1-5-John Layman-s/Sam Kieth-a/c 4.00

ELECTRIC ANT
Marvel Comics: Jun, 2010 - No. 5, Oct, 2010 ($3.99, Baxter paper)
1-5-Based on a Philip K. Dick story; David Mack-s/Pascal Alixe-a; Paul Pope-c 4.00

ELECTRIC SUBLIME
IDW Publishing: Oct, 2016 - No. 4, Jan, 2017 ($3.99, limited series)
1-4-W. Maxwell Prince-s/Martin Morazzo-a; two covers on each 4.00

ELECTRIC UNDERTOW (See Strikeforce Morituri: Electric Undertow)

ELECTRIC WARRIOR
DC Comics: May, 1986 - No. 18, Oct, 1987 ($1.50, Baxter paper)
1-18 3.00

ELECTRIC WARRIORS
DC Comics: Jan, 2019 - No. 6, Jun, 2019 ($3.99, limited series)
1-6-Steve Orlando-s/Travel Foreman-a 4.00

ELECTROPOLIS
Image Comics: May, 2001 - No. 4, Jan, 2003 ($2.95/$5.95)
1-3-Dean Motter-s/a. 3-(12/01) 3.00
4-(1/03, $5.95, 72 pages) The Infernal Machine pts. 4-6 6.00

ELEKTRA (Also see Daredevil #319-325)
Marvel Comics: Mar, 1995 - No. 4, June, 1995 ($2.95, limited series)
1-4-Embossed-c; Scott McDaniel-a 5.00

ELEKTRA (Also see Daredevil)
Marvel Comics: Nov, 1996 - No. 19, Jun, 1998 ($1.95)
1-Peter Milligan scripts; Deodato-c/a 4.00
1-Variant-c 6.00
2-19: 4-Dr. Strange-c/app. 10-Logan-c/app. 3.00
#(-1) Flashback (7/97) Matt Murdock-c/app.; Deodato-c/a 3.00
.../Cyblade (Image, 3/97,$2.95) Devil's Reign pt. 7 3.00

ELEKTRA (Vol. 2) (Marvel Knights)
Marvel Comics: Sept, 2001 - No. 35, Jun, 2004 ($3.50/$2.99)
1-Bendis-s/Austen-a/Horn-c 4.00
2-6: 2-Two covers (Sienkiewicz and Horn) 3,4-Silver Samurai app. 3.00

	GD	VG	FN	VF	VF/NM	NM-
3-Initial printing with panel of nudity; most copies pulped	6	12	18	38	69	100

7-35: 7-Rucka-s begin. 9,10,17-Bennett-a. 19-Meglia-a. 23-25-Chen-a; Sienkiewicz-c 3.00
...Vol. 1: Introspect TPB (2002, $16.99) r/#10-15; Marvel Knights: Double Shot #3 17.00
...Vol. 2: Everything Old is New Again TPB (2003, $16.99) r/#16-22 17.00
...Vol. 3: Relentless TPB (2004, $14.99) r/#23-28 15.00
...Vol. 4: Frenzy TPB (2004, $17.99) r/#29-35 18.00

ELEKTRA (All-New Marvel Now!)
Marvel Comics: Jun, 2014 - No. 11, May, 2015 ($3.99)
1-11: 1-Blackman-s/Del Mundo-a; multiple covers. 2,6,7-Lady Bullseye app. 4.00

ELEKTRA
Marvel Comics: Apr, 2017 - No. 5, Aug, 2017 ($3.99, limited series)
1-5: Matt Owens-s/Juann Cabal-a; Arcade app. 4.00

ELEKTRA
Marvel Comics: No. 100, Jun, 2022 ($4.99, one-shot)
100-Main story by Nocenti-s/Kotian-a; Typhoid Mary app.; bonus cover gallery 5.00

ELEKTRA & WOLVERINE: THE REDEEMER
Marvel Comics: Jan, 2002 - No. 3, Mar, 2002 ($5.95, square-bound, lim. series)
1-3-Greg Rucka-s/Yoshitaka Amano-a/c 6.00
HC (5/02, $29.95, with dustjacket) r/#1-3, interview with Greg Rucka 30.00

ELEKTRA: ASSASSIN (Also see Daredevil)
Marvel Comics (Epic Comics): Aug, 1986 - No. 8, June, 1987 (Limited series, mature)

	GD	VG	FN	VF	VF/NM	NM-
1,8-Miller scripts in all; Sienkiewicz-c/a	1	3	4	6	8	10

2-7 5.00

GD 2.0 | VG 4.0 | FN 6.0 | VF 8.0 | VF/NM 9.0 | NM- 9.2

Signed & numbered hardcover (Graphitti Designs, $39.95, 2000 print run)- reprints 1-8 60.00
TPB (2000, $24.95) 25.00

ELEKTRA: BLACK, WHITE & BLOOD
Marvel Comics: Mar, 2022 - No. 4, Jul, 2022 ($4.99, B&W with red, limited series)
1-4-Short story anthology by various. 1-Art by Bagley, Romero & D'Armini 5.00

ELEKTRA: GLIMPSE & ECHO
Marvel Comics: Sept, 2002 - No. 4, Dec, 2002 ($2.99, limited series)
1-4-Scott Morse-s/painted-a 3.00

ELEKTRA LIVES AGAIN (Also see Daredevil)
Marvel Comics (Epic Comics): 1990 ($24.95, oversize, hardcover, 76 pgs.)(Produced by Graphitti Designs)
nn-Frank Miller-c/a/scripts; Lynn Varley painted-a; Matt Murdock & Bullseye app. 40.00
2nd printing (9/02, $24.99) 25.00

ELEKTRA MEGAZINE
Marvel Comics: Nov, 1996 - No. 2, Dec, 1996 ($3.95, 96 pgs., reprints, limited series)
1,2: Reprints Frank Miller's Elektra stories in Daredevil 4.00

ELEKTRA SAGA, THE
Marvel Comics Group: Feb, 1984 - No. 4, June, 1984 ($2.00, limited series, Baxter paper)
1-4-r/Daredevil #168-190; Miller-c/a 5.00

ELEKTRA: THE HAND
Marvel Comics: Nov, 2004 - No. 5, Feb, 2005 ($2.99, limited series)
1-5-Gossett-a/Sienkiewicz-c/Yoshida-s; origin of the Hand in the 16th century 3.00

ELEKTRA: THE MOVIE
Marvel Comics: Feb, 2005 ($5.99)
1-Movie adaptation; McKeever-s/Perkins-a; photo-c 6.00
TPB (2005, $12.95) r/movie adaptation, Daredevil #168, 181 & Elektra #(-1) 13.00

ELEMENTALS, THE (See The Justice Machine, Morningstar Special, and Vortex)
Comico The Comic Co. : Jun, 1984 - No. 29, Sept, 1988; V2#1, Mar, 1989 - No. 26, Apr, 1993 ($1.50/$2.50, Baxter paper); V3#1, Dec, 1995 - No. 3 ($2.95)
1-Willingham-c/a, 1-8 5.00
2-29: 9-Bissette-a(p). 10-Photo-c. 18-Prelude to Avalon mini-series 3.00
V2#1-26: 16-1st app. Strikeforce America 3.00
V3#1-3: 1-Daniel-a(p), bagged w/gaming card 3.00
Lingerie (5/96, $2.95) 3.00
Special 1,2 (3/86, 1/89)-1-Willingham-a(p) 3.00

ELEMENTALS: (Title series), **Comico**
--GHOST OF A CHANCE, 12/95 ($5.95)-graphic novel, nn-Ross-c. 6.00
--HOW THE WAR WAS WON, 6/96 - No. 2, 8/96 ($2.95) 1,2-Tony Daniel-a, & 1-Variant-c; no logo 3.00
--SEX SPECIAL, 1991 - No. 4, Feb, 1993 ($2.95, color) 2 covers for each 3.00
--SEX SPECIAL, 5/97 - No. 2, 6/97 ($2.95, B&W) 1-Tony Daniel, Jeff Moy-a, 2-Robb Phipps, Adam McDaniel-a 3.00
--SWIMSUIT SPECTACULAR 1996, 6/96 ($2.95), 1-pin-ups, 1-Variant-c; no logo 3.00
--THE VAMPIRE'S REVENGE, 6/96 - No. 2 8/96 ($2.95) 1,2-Willingham-s, 1-Variant-c; no logo 3.00

ELEPHANTMEN
Image Comics: July, 2006 - No. 80, Jan, 2018 ($2.99/$3.50/$3.99) (Flip covers on most)
1-16: 1-Starkings-s/Moritat-a/Ladronn-c. 6-Campbell flip-c. 15-Sale flip-c 4.00
17-30-($3.50) 25-Flip book preview of Marineman 4.00
31-49,51-80-($3.99) 32-Conan/Red Sonja homage. 42-44-Dave Sim-a (5 pgs.) 4.00
50-($5.99) Flip book with reprint of #1; cover gallery 6.00
...: Man and Elephantman 1 (3/11, $3.99) Three covers 4.00
... Shots (5/15, $5.99) Reprints short stories from anthologies; art by Sim, Sale, & others 6.00
...: The Pilot (5/07, $2.99) short stories and pin-ups by various incl. Sale, Jim Lee, Jae Lee 4.00
...: War Toys (11/07 - No. 3, 4/08, $2.99) 1-3-Mappo war; Starkings-s/Moritat-a/Ladronn-c 4.00
... War Toys: Yvette (7/09, $3.50) Starkings-s/Moritat-a 4.00
Giant-Size Elephantmen 1 (10/11, $5.99) r/#31,32 & Man and Elephantman; Campbell-c 6.00

1111 (ELEVEN ELEVEN)
Crusade Entertainment: Oct, 1996 ($2.95, B&W, one-shot)
1-Wrightson-c/a 4.00

ELEVEN OR ONE
Sirius: Apr, 1995 ($2.95)
1-Linsner-c/a 1 3 4 6 8 10
1-(6/96) 2nd printing 3.50

ELFLORD
Nightwind Productions: Jun, 1980 - Vol. 2 #1, 1982 (B&W, magazine-size)
1-1st Barry Blair-s/c/a in comics; B&W-c; limited print run for all
10 20 30 67 141 215
2-5-B&W-c 5 10 15 31 53 75
6-14: 9-14-Color-c 4 8 12 27 44 60
Vol. 2 #1 (1982) 4 8 12 23 37 50

ELFLORD
Aircel Publ.: 1986 - No. 6, Oct, 1989 ($1.70, B&W); V2#1- V2#31, 1995 ($2.00)
1 6.00
2-4,V2#1-20,22-30: 4-6: Last B&W. V2#1-Color-a begin. 22-New cast. 25-Begin B&W 4.00
1,2-2nd printings 3.00
21-Double size ($4.95) 5.00

ELFLORD
Warp Graphics: Jan, 1997-No.4, Apr, 1997 ($2.95, B&W, mini-series)
1-4 3.00

ELFLORD (CUTS LOOSE) (Vol. 2)
Warp Graphics: Sept, 1997 - No. 7, Apr, 1998 ($2.95, B&W, mini-series)
1-7 3.00

ELFLORD: DRAGON'S EYE
Night Wynd Enterprises: 1993 ($2.50, B&W)
1 3.00

ELFLORD: THE RETURN
Mad Monkey Press: 1996 ($6.95, magazine size)
1 7.00

ELFQUEST (Also see Fantasy Quarterly & Warp Graphics Annual)
Warp Graphics, Inc.: No. 2, Aug, 1978 - No. 21, Feb, 1985 (All magazine size)
No. 1, Apr, 1979

NOTE: **Elfquest** was originally published as one of the stories in **Fantasy Quarterly** #1. When the publisher went out of business, the creative team, Wendy and Richard Pini, formed WaRP Graphics and continued the series, beginning with **Elfquest** #2. **Elfquest** #1, which reprinted the story from **Fantasy Quarterly**, was published about the same time **Elfquest** #4 was released. Thereafter, most issues were reprinted as demand warranted, until Marvel announced it would reprint the entire series under its Epic imprint (Aug., 1985).

1(4/79)-Reprints Elfquest story from Fantasy Quarterly No. 1
1st printing ($1.00-c) 8 16 24 55 105 155
2nd printing ($1.25-c) 2 4 6 10 14 18
3rd printings ($1.50-c) 1 2 3 5 6 8
4th printing; different-c ($1.50-c) 5.00
2(8/78) 1st printing ($1.00-c) 5 10 15 31 53 75
2nd printings ($1.25-c) 6.00
3rd & 4th printings ($1.50-c)(all 4th prints 1989) 5.00
3-5: 1st printings ($1.00-c) 3 6 9 17 26 35
6-9: 1st printings ($1.25-c) 3 6 9 15 22 28
2nd & 3rd printings ($1.50-c) 5.00
10-21: ($1.50-c); 16-8pg. preview of A Distant Soil 2 4 6 11 16 20
10-14: 2nd printings ($1.50) 5.00

ELFQUEST
Marvel Comics (Epic Comics): Aug, 1985 - No. 32, Mar, 1988
1-Reprints in color the Elfquest epic by Warp Graphics 1 2 3 5 6 8
2-32 4.00

ELFQUEST
DC Comics: 2003 - 2005
Archives Vol. 1 (2003, $49.95, HC) r/#1-5 50.00
Archives Vol. 2 (2005, $49.95, HC) r/#6-10 & Epic Illustrated #1 50.00
25th Anniversary Special (2003, $2.95) r/Elfquest #1 (Apr, 1979); interview w/Pinis 4.00

ELFQUEST (Title series), Warp Graphics
'89 - No. 4, '89 ($1.50, B&W) 1-4: R-original Elfquest series 4.00

ELFQUEST (Volume 2),**Warp Graphics:** V2#1, 5/96 - No. 33, 2/99 ($4.95/$2.95, B&W)
V2#1-31: 1,3,5,8,10,12,13,18,21,23,25-Wendy Pini-c 6.00
32,33-($2.95-c) 4.00
--BLOOD OF TEN CHIEFS, 7/93 - No. 20, 9/95 ($2.00/$2.50)
1-20-By Richard & Wendy Pini 4.00
--HIDDEN YEARS, 5/92 - No. 29, 3/96 ($2.00/$2.25)1-9,9 1/2, 10-29 4.00
--JINK, 11/94 - No. 12, 2/6 ($2.25/$2.50) 1-12-W. Pini/John Byrne-back-c 4.00
--KAHVI, 10/95 - No. 6,3/96 ($2.25, B&W) 1-6 4.00
--KINGS CROSS, 11/97 - No. 2, 12/97 ($2.95, B&W) 1,2 4.00
--KINGS OF THE BROKEN WHEEL, 6/90 - No. 9, 2/92 ($2.00, B&W) (3rd Elfquest saga)
1-9: By R. & W. Pini; 1-Color insert 5.00
1-2nd printing 4.00
--METAMORPHOSIS, 4/96 ($2.95, B&W) 1 4.00
--NEW BLOOD (...Summer Special on-c #1 only), 8/92 - No. 35, 1/96 ($2.00-$2.50, color/ B&W) 1-($3.95, 68 pgs.,...Summer Special on-c)-Byrne-a/scripts (16 pgs.) 5.00
2-35: Barry Blair-a in all 4.00
1993 Summer Special ($3.95) Byrne-a/scripts 5.00
--SHARDS, 8/94 - No. 16, 3/96 ($2.25/$2.50) 1-16 4.00
--SIEGE AT BLUE MOUNTAIN, WaRP Graphics/Apple 3/87 - No. 8, 12/88 (1.75/ $1.95, B&W)
1-Staton-a(i) in all; 2nd Elfquest saga 1 2 3 5 6 8
1-3-2nd printing 4.00
2-8 5.00
--THE REBELS, 11/94 - No. 12, 3/96 ($2.25/$2.50, B&W/color) 1-12 4.00
--TWO-SPEAR, 10/95 - No. 5, 2/96 ($2.25, B&W) 1-5 4.00
--WAVE DANCERS, 12/93 - No. 6, 3/96, 1-6: 1-Foil-c & poster 4.00
Special 1 ($2.95) 4.00
--WORLDPOOL, 7/97 ($2.95, B&W) 1-Richard Pini-s/Barry Blair-a 4.00

ELFQUEST: STARGAZER'S HUNT
Dark Horse Comics: Nov, 2019 - No. 4, Oct, 2020 ($3.99)
1-4-Wendy & Richard Pini-s/Sonny Strait-a 4.00

ELFQUEST: THE DISCOVERY
DC Comics: Mar, 2006 - No. 4, Sept, 2006 ($3.99, limited series)
1-4-Wendy Pini-a/Wendy & Richard Pini-s 5.00
TPB (2006, $14.99) r/#1-4 15.00

ELFQUEST: THE FINAL QUEST
Dark Horse Comics: Oct, 2013; No. 1, Jan, 2014 - No. 24, Feb, 2018 ($3.50/$3.99)
1-14-Wendy Pini-a/Wendy & Richard Pini-s 3.50
15-24-($3.99) 4.00
... Special (10/13, $5.99) Wendy Pini-a/Wendy & Richard Pini-s; prologue to series 6.00

ELFQUEST: THE GRAND QUEST
DC Comics: 2004 - No. 14, 2006 ($9.95/$9.99, B&W, digest-size)
Vol. 1-6 ('04)1-r/Elfquest #1-5; new W. Pini-c. 2-r/#5-8. 3-r/#8-11. 4-r/#11-15. 5-r/#15-18 6-r/#18-20 10.00
Vol. 7-9 ('05) 1-r/Siege At Blue Mountain #1-3. 8-r/SABM #3-5. 9-r/SABM #6-8 10.00
Vol. 10-14 ('05) 10-r/Kings of the Broken Wheel #1-3. 11-KotBW #5-7 & Frazetta Fant. Ill. 12-r/Kings of the Broken Wheel #8&9. 13-r/Elfquest V2 #4-18. 14-r/Hidden Years #4-9 1/2 10.00

ELFQUEST: THE SEARCHER AND THE SWORD
DC Comics: 2004 ($24.95/$14.99, graphic novel)
HC (2004, $24.95, with dust jacket)-Wendy and Richard Pini-s/a/c 25.00

Elektra (2017) #3 © MAR

ElfQuest: The Final Quest #17 © Warp

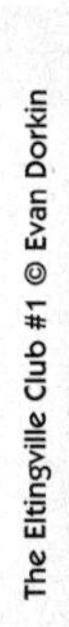

The Eltingville Club #1 © Evan Dorkin

GD 2.0 | VG 4.0 | FN 6.0 | VF 8.0 | VF/NM 9.0 | NM- 9.2

SC (2004, $14.99) 15.00

ELFQUEST: WOLFRIDER
DC Comics: 2003 - No. 2, 2003 ($9.95, digest-size)

Volume 1 ('03, $9.95, digest-size) r/Elfquest V2#19,21,23,25,27,29,31; Blood of Ten Chiefs #2; Hidden Years #5; New Blood Special #1; New Blood 1993 Special #1; new W. Pini-c 10.00
Volume 2 ('03, $9.95, digest-size) r/Elfquest V2#33; Blood of Ten Chiefs #10,11,19; Warp Graphics Annual #1 10.00

ELIMINATOR (Also see The Solution #16 & The Night Man #16)
Malibu Comics (Ultraverse): Apr, 1995 - No. 3, Jul, 1995 ($2.95/$2.50, lim. series)

0-Mike Zeck-a in all 3.00
1-3-($2.50): 1-1st app. Siren 3.00
1-($3.95)-Black cover edition 4.00

ELIMINATOR FULL COLOR SPECIAL
Eternity Comics: Oct, 1991 ($2.95, one-shot)

1-Dave Dorman painted-c 4.00

ELLA CINDERS (See Comics On Parade, Comics Revue #1,4, Famous Comics Cartoon Book, Giant Comics Editions, Sparkler Comics, Tip Top & Treasury of Comics)

ELLA CINDERS
United Features Syndicate: 1938 - 1940

	GD	VG	FN	VF	VF/NM	NM-
Single Series 3(1938)	48	96	144	302	514	725
Single Series 21(#2 on-c, #21 on inside), 28('40)	40	80	120	246	411	575

ELLA CINDERS
United Features Syndicate: Mar, 1948 - No. 5, Mar, 1949

	GD	VG	FN	VF	VF/NM	NM-
1-(#2 on cover)	18	36	54	105	165	225
2	13	26	39	72	101	130
3-5	9	18	27	52	69	85

ELLERY QUEEN
Superior Comics Ltd.: May, 1949 - No. 4, Nov, 1949

	GD	VG	FN	VF	VF/NM	NM-
1-Kamen-c; L.B. Cole-a; r-in Haunted Thrills	63	126	189	403	689	975
2-4: 3-Drug use stories(2)	43	86	129	271	461	650

NOTE: *Iger shop art in all issues.*

ELLERY QUEEN (TV)
Ziff-Davis Publishing Co.: 1-3/52 (Spring on-c) - No. 2, Summer/52 (Saunders painted-c)

	GD	VG	FN	VF	VF/NM	NM-
1-Saunders-c	54	108	162	343	574	825
2-Saunders bondage, torture-c	42	84	126	265	445	625

ELLERY QUEEN (Also see Crackajack Funnies No. 23)
Dell Publishing Co.: No. 1165, Mar-May, 1961 - No.1289, Apr, 1962

	GD	VG	FN	VF	VF/NM	NM-
Four Color 1165 (#1)	9	18	27	58	114	175
Four Color 1243 (11/61-1/62), 1289	7	14	21	48	89	130

ELMER FUDD (Also see Camp Comics, Daffy, Looney Tunes #1 & Super Book #10, 22)
Dell Publishing Co.: No. 470, May, 1953 - No. 1293, Mar-May, 1962

	GD	VG	FN	VF	VF/NM	NM-
Four Color 470 (#1)	10	20	30	67	141	215
Four Color 558,628,689('56)	6	12	18	38	69	100
Four Color 725,783,841,888,938,977,1032,1081,1131,1171,1222,1293('62)	5	10	15	33	57	80

ELMO COMICS
St. John Publishing Co.: Jan, 1948 (Daily strip-r)

	GD	VG	FN	VF	VF/NM	NM-
1-By Cecil Jensen	15	30	45	85	130	175

ELONGATED MAN (See Flash #112 & Justice League of America #105)
DC Comics: Jan, 1992 - No. 4, Apr, 1992 ($1.00, limited series)

1-4: 3-The Flash app. 3.00

ELRIC (Of Melnibone)(See First Comics Graphic Novel #6 & Marvel Graphic Novel #2)
Pacific Comics: Apr, 1983 - No. 6, Apr, 1984 ($1.50, Baxter paper)

1-6: Russell-c/a(i) in all 3.00

ELRIC
Topps Comics: 1996 ($2.95, one-shot)

0-One Life: Russell-c/a; adapts Neil Gaiman's short story "One Life--Furnished in Early Moorcock." 3.00

ELRIC, SAILOR ON THE SEAS OF FATE
First Comics: June, 1985 - No. 7, June, 1986 ($1.75, limited series)

1-7: Adapts Michael Moorcock's novel 3.00

ELRIC, STORMBRINGER
Dark Horse Comics/Topps Comics: 1997 - No. 7, 1997 ($2.95, limited series)

1-7: Russell-c/s/a; adapts Michael Moorcock's novel 3.00

ELRIC: THE BALANCE LOST
BOOM! Studios: Jul, 2011 - No. 12, Jun, 2012 ($3.99)

1-12: 1-Roberson-s/Biagini-a; four covers. 2-11-Three covers 4.00

ELRIC: THE BANE OF THE BLACK SWORD
First Comics: Aug, 1988 - No. 6, June, 1989 ($1.75/$1.95, limited series)

1-6: Adapts Michael Moorcock's novel 3.00

ELRIC: THE DREAMING CITY
Titan Comics: Sept, 2021 - No. 2, Oct, 2021 ($3.99, limited series)

1,2: Adapts Michael Moorcock's novel 4.00

ELRIC: THE VANISHING TOWER
First Comics: Aug, 1987 - No. 6, June, 1988 ($1.75, limited series)

1-6: Adapts Michael Moorcock's novel 3.00

ELRIC: WEIRD OF THE WHITE WOLF
First Comics: Oct, 1986 - No. 5, June, 1987 ($1.75, limited series)

1-5: Adapts Michael Moorcock's novel 3.00

EL SALVADOR - A HOUSE DIVIDED
Eclipse Comics: March, 1989 ($2.50, B&W, Baxter paper, stiff-c, 52 pgs.)

1-Gives history of El Salvador 4.00

ELSEWHERE
Image Comics: Aug, 2017 - No. 8, Jul, 2018 ($3.99)

1-8: 1-Jay Faerber-s/Sumeyye Kesgin-a; Amelia Earhart & DB Cooper app. 4.00

ELSEWHERE PRINCE, THE (Moebius' Airtight Garage)
Marvel Comics (Epic): May, 1990 - No. 6, Oct, 1990 ($1.95, limited series)

1-6: Moebius scripts & back-up-a in all 3.00

ELSEWORLDS 80-PAGE GIANT (See DC Comics Presents: ... for reprint)
DC Comics: Aug, 1999 ($5.95, one-shot)

	GD	VG	FN	VF	VF/NM	NM-
1-Most copies destroyed by DC over content of the "Superman's Babysitter" story; some UK shipments sold before recall	13	26	39	86	188	290

ELSEWORLD'S FINEST
DC Comics: 1997 - No. 2, 1997 ($4.95, limited series)

1,2: Elseworld's story-Superman & Batman in the 1920's 5.00

ELSEWORLD'S FINEST: SUPERGIRL & BATGIRL
DC Comics: 1998 ($5.95, one-shot)

	GD	VG	FN	VF	VF/NM	NM-
1-Haley-a	1	3	4	6	8	10

ELSIE THE COW
D. S. Publishing Co.: Oct-Nov, 1949 - No. 3, July-Aug, 1950

	GD	VG	FN	VF	VF/NM	NM-
1-(36 pgs.)	34	68	102	204	332	460
2,3	22	44	66	132	216	300

ELSON'S PRESENTS
DC Comics: 1981 (100 pgs., no cover price)

	GD	VG	FN	VF	VF/NM	NM-
Series 1-6: Repackaged 1981 DC comics; 1-DC Comics Presents #29, Flash #303, Batman #331. 2-Superman #335, Ghosts #96, Justice League of America #186. 3-New Teen Titans #3, Secrets of Haunted House #32, Wonder Woman #275. 4-Secrets of the LSH #1, Brave & the Bold #170, New Adv. of Superboy #13. 5-LSH #271, Green Lantern #136, Super Friends #40. 6-Action #515, Mystery in Space #115, Detective #498	2	4	6	11	16	20

ELTINGVILLE CLUB, THE (Characters from Dork)
Dark Horse Comics: Apr, 2014 - No. 2, Aug, 2015 ($3.99, B&W, limited series)

1,2-Evan Dorkin-s/a 4.00
HC-(2/16, $19.99) Reprints #1,2 and stories from Dork, Instant Piano, DHP 20.00

ELVEN (Also see Prime)
Malibu Comics (Ultraverse): Oct, 1994 - No. 4, Feb, 1995 ($2.50, lim. series)

0 ($2.95)-Prime app. 3.00
1-4: 2,4-Prime app. 3-Primevil app. 3.00
1-Limited Foil Edition- no price on cover 4.00

ELVIRA IN HORRORLAND
Dynamite Entertainment: 2022 - No. 5, 2022 ($3.99, limited series)

1-5-Avallone-s/Califano-a; multiple covers. 1-Elvira in Bates Motel 4.00

ELVIRA MEETS VINCENT PRICE
Dynamite Entertainment: 2021 - No. 5, 2022 ($3.99, limited series)

1-5-Avallone-s/Samu-a; multiple covers 4.00

ELVIRA MISTRESS OF THE DARK
Marvel Comics: Oct, 1988 ($2.00, B&W, magazine size)

	GD	VG	FN	VF	VF/NM	NM-
1-Movie adaptation	3	6	9	17	26	35

GD 2.0 · VG 4.0 · FN 6.0 · VF 8.0 · VF/NM 9.0 · NM- 9.2

ELVIRA MISTRESS OF THE DARK
Claypool Comics (Eclipse): May, 1993 - No. 166, Feb, 2007 ($2.50, B&W)

1-Austin-a(i). Spiegle-a 2 4 6 8 10 12
2-6: Spiegle-a 5.00
7-99,101-166-Photo-c: 4.00
100-(8/01) Kurt Busiek back-up-s; art by DeCarlo and others 4.00
TPB ($12.95) 13.00

ELVIRA MISTRESS OF THE DARK
Dynamite Entertainment: 2018 - No. 12, 2020 ($3.99)

1-12: 1-Avallone-s/Acosta-a; multiple covers; Mary Wollstonecraft app. 2-E.A. Poe app. 4.00
... Spring Special One-Shot (2019, $4.99) Ruiz & Parent-s/a 5.00

ELVIRA'S HOUSE OF MYSTERY
DC Comics: Jan, 1986 - No. 11, Jan, 1987

1,11: 11-Dave Stevens-c 3 6 9 17 25 34
2-10: 9-Photo-c, Special 1 (3/87, $1.25) 1 2 3 5 6 8

ELVIRA THE SHAPE OF ELVIRA
Dynamite Entertainment: 2019 - No. 4, 2019 ($3.99, limited series)

1-4: 1-3-Avallone-s/Strukan-a; multiple covers. 4-Qualano-a 4.00

ELVIS MANDIBLE, THE
DC Comics (Piranha Press): 1990 ($3.50, 52 pgs., B&W, mature)

nn 4.00

ELVIS PRESLEY (See Career Girl Romances #32, Go-Go, Howard Chaykin's American Flagg #10, Humbug #8, I Love You #60 & Young Lovers #18)

EL ZOMBO FANTASMA
Dark Horse Comics (Rocket Comics): Apr, 2004 - No. 3, June, 2004 ($2.99)

1-3-Wilkins-s&a/Munroe-s 3.00

E-MAN
Charlton Comics: Oct, 1973 - No. 10, Sept, 1975 (Painted-c No. 7-10)

1-Origin & 1st app. E-Man; Staton c/a in all 3 6 9 17 25 34
2-5: 2,4,5-Ditko-a. 3-Howard-a. 5-Miss Liberty Belle app. by Ditko 2 4 6 9 12 15
6-10: 6,7,9,10-Early Byrne-a (#6 is 1/75). 6-Disney parody. 8-Full-length story; Nova begins as E-Man's partner 2 4 6 11 16 20
1-4,9,10 (Modern Comics reprints, '77) 5.00
NOTE: *Killjoy app.-No. 2, 4. Liberty Belle app.-No. 5. Rog 2000 app.-No. 6, 7, 9, 10. Travis app.-No. 3.* ***Sutton*** *a-1.*

E-MAN
Comico: Sept, 1989 ($2.75, one-shot, no ads, high quality paper)

1-Staton-c/a; Michael Mauser story 4.00

E-MAN
Comico: V4#1, Jan, 1990 - No. 3, Mar, 1990 ($2.50, limited series)

1-3: Staton-c/a 4.00

E-MAN
Alpha Productions: Oct, 1993 ($2.75)

V5#1-Staton-c/a; 20th anniversary issue 4.00

E-MAN COMICS (Also see Michael Mauser & The Original E-Man)
First Comics: Apr, 1983 - No. 25, Aug, 1985 ($1.00/$1.25, direct sales only)

1-25: 2-X-Men satire. 3-X-Men/Phoenix satire. 6-Origin retold. 8-Cutey Bunny app. 10-Origin Nova Kane. 24-Origin Michael Mauser 4.00
NOTE: ***Staton*** *a-1-5, 6-25p; c-1-25.*

E-MAN RETURNS
Alpha Productions: 1994 ($2.75, B&W)

1-Joe Staton-c/a(p) 4.00

EMERALD CITY OF OZ, THE (Dorothy Gale from Wonderful Wizard of Oz)
Marvel Comics: Sept, 2013 - No. 5, Feb, 2014 ($3.99, limited series)

1-5-Eric Shanower-s/Skottie Young-a/c 4.00

EMERALD DAWN
DC Comics: 1991 ($4.95, trade paperback)

nn-Reprints Green Lantern: Emerald Dawn #1-6 1 2 3 5 6 8

EMERALD DAWN II (See Green Lantern...)

EMERGENCY (Magazine)
Charlton Comics: June, 1976 - No. 4, Jan, 1977 (B&W)

1-Neal Adams-c/a; Heath, Austin-a 4 8 12 27 44 60
2,3: 2-N. Adams-c. 3-N. Adams-a. 3 6 9 19 30 40
4-Alcala-a 3 6 9 15 22 28

EMERGENCY (TV)
Charlton Comics: June, 1976 - No. 4, Dec, 1976

1-Staton-c; early Byrne-a (22 pages) 4 8 12 25 40 55
2-4: 2-Staton-c. 2,3-Byrne text illos. 3 6 9 15 22 28

EMERGENCY DOCTOR
Charlton Comics: Summer, 1963 (one-shot)

1 3 6 9 21 33 45

EMIL & THE DETECTIVES (See Movie Comics)

EMISSARY (Jim Valentino's...)
Image Comics (Shadowline): May, 2006 - No. 6 ($3.50)

1-6: 1-Rand-s/Ferreyra-a. 4-6-Long-s 3.50

EMMA (Adaptation of the Jane Austen novel)
Marvel Comics: May, 2011 - No. 5, Sept, 2011 ($3.99)

1-5-Nancy Butler-s/Janet K. Lee-a 4.00

EMMA FROST
Marvel Comics: Aug, 2003 - No. 18, Feb, 2005 ($2.50/$2.99)

1-7-Emma in high school; Bollers-s/Green-a/Horn-c 3.00
8-18-($2.99) 3.00
... Vol. 1: Higher Learning TPB (2004, $7.99, digest size) r/#1-6 8.00
... Vol. 2: Mind Games TPB (2005, $7.99, digest size) r/#7-12 8.00
... Vol. 3: Bloom TPB (2005, $7.99, digest size) r/#13-18 8.00

EMMA PEEL & JOHN STEED (See The Avengers)

EMPEROR'S NEW CLOTHES, THE
Dell Publishing Co.: 1950 (10¢, 68 pgs., 1/2 size, oblong)

nn - (Surprise Books series) 7 14 21 37 46 55

EMPIRE
Image Comics (Gorilla): May, 2000 - No. 2, Sept, 2000 ($2.50)
DC Comics: No. 0, Aug, 2003; Sept, 2003 - No. 6, Feb, 2004 ($4.95/$2.50, limited series)

1,2: 1 (5/00)-Waid-s/Kitson-a; w/Crimson Plague prologue 3.00
0-(8/03) reprints #1,2 5.00
1-6: 1-(9/03) new Waid-s/Kitson-a/c 3.00
TPB (DC, 2004, $14.95) r/series; Kitson sketch pages; Waid intro. 15.00

EMPIRE OF THE DEAD: ACT ONE (George Romero's...)
Marvel Comics: Mar, 2014 - No. 5, Aug, 2014 ($3.99)

1-5-George Romero-s/Alex Maleev-a/c; zombies & vampires 4.00

EMPIRE OF THE DEAD: ACT TWO (George Romero's...)
Marvel Comics: Nov, 2014 - No. 5, Mar, 2015 ($3.99)

1-5-George Romero-s/Dalibor Talajic-a; zombies & vampires 4.00

EMPIRE OF THE DEAD: ACT THREE (George Romero's...)
Marvel Comics: Jun, 2015 - No. 5, Nov, 2015 ($3.99)

1-5-George Romero-s/Andrea Mutti-a; zombies & vampires 4.00

EMPIRE STRIKES BACK, THE (See Marvel Comics Super Special #16 & Marvel Special Edition)

EMPIRE: UPRISING
IDW Publishing: Apr, 2015 - No. 4, Jul, 2015 ($3.99)

1-4: Sequel to the 2003-2004 series; Waid-s/Kitson-a; two covers on each 4.00

EMPRESS
Marvel Comics (Icon): Jun, 2016 - No. 7, Jan, 2017 ($3.99/$5.99)

1-6-Millar-s/Immonen-a 4.00
7-($5.99) 6.00

EMPTY, THE
Image Comics: Feb, 2015 - No. 6, Sept, 2015 ($3.50/$3.99)

1-3-Jimmie Robinson-s/a 3.50
4-6-($3.99) 4.00

EMPTY LOVE STORIES
Slave Labor #1 & 2/Funny Valentine Press: Nov, 1994 - No. 2 ($2.95, B&W)

1,2: Steve Darnall scripts in all. 1-Alex Ross-c. 2-(8/96)-Mike Allred-c 4.00
1,2-2nd printing (Funny Valentine Press) 3.00
... 1999-Jeff Smith-c; Doran-a 4.00
..."Special" (2.95) Ty Templeton-c 4.00

EMPTY ZONE
Image Comics: Jun, 2015 - No. 10, Jul, 2016 ($3.50/$3.99)

1-8-Jason Shawn Alexander-s/a 3.50
9,10-($3.99) 4.00

EMPYRE (Also see Road to Empyre)
Marvel Comics: Sept, 2020 - No. 6 ($5.99/$4.99, weekly limited series)

1-($5.99) Ewing & Slott-s/Schiti-a; multiple covers; Fantastic Four & the Avengers app. 6.00
2-5-($4.99) 2-Carol Danvers gains the Accuser hammer. 3-Black Panther app. 5.00
6-($5.99) Ewing & Slott-s/Schiti-a; FF, Avengers, Spider-Man, Wolverine app. 6.00
...: Aftermath Avengers #1 (11/20, $4.99) Wedding of Hulkling and Wiccan 5.00
...: Fallout Fantastic Four #1 (11/20, $3.99) Slott-s/Izaakse-a; Uatu returns 4.00
...: Fantastic Four #0 (6/20, $4.99) Slott-s/Silva-a; leads into Empyre #1; The Profiteer app. 5.00
... Handbook 1 (6/20, $4.99) Profile pages of participants, teams, alien races 5.00
...: Savage Avengers 1 (9/20, $4.99) Duggan-s/Smallwood-a; Conan & Venom app. 5.00

EMPYRE: AVENGERS
Marvel Comics: No. 0, Jul, 2020; Sept, 2020 - No. 3 Oct, 2020 ($4.99/$3.99 limited series)

0-($4.99) Ewing-s/Larraz-a 5.00
1-3-($3.99) Zub-s/Magno-a; Avengers & Ka-Zar app. 4.00

EMPYRE: CAPTAIN AMERICA
Marvel Comics: Sept, 2020 - No. 3, Oct, 2020 ($3.99 limited series)

1-3-P.K. Johnson-s/Olivetti-a 4.00

EMPYRE: X-MEN
Marvel Comics: Sept, 2020 - No. 4, Oct, 2020 ($4.99 limited series)

1-4: 1-Hickman & Howard-s/Buffagni-a. 2-Werneck-a; Hordeculture app. 5.00

ENCHANTED APPLES OF OZ, THE (See First Comics Graphic Novel #5)

ENCHANTED TIKI ROOM
Marvel Comics (Disney Kingdoms): Dec, 2016 - No. 5, Apr, 2017 ($3.99)

1-5-Jon Adams-s/Horacio Domingues-a 4.00

ENCHANTER
Eclipse Comics: Apr, 1987 - No. 3, Aug. 1987 ($2.00, B&W, limited series)

1-3 3.00

ENCHANTING LOVE
Kirby Publishing Co.: Oct, 1949 - No. 6, July, 1950 (All 52 pgs.)

1-Photo-c 25 50 75 150 245 340
2-Photo-c; Powell-a 15 30 45 88 137 185
3,4,6: 3-Jimmy Stewart photo-c. 4-Photo-c 15 30 45 85 130 175
5-Ingels-a, 9 pgs.; photo-c 21 42 63 122 199 275

ENCHANTMENT VISUALETTES (Magazine)
World Editions: Dec, 1949 - No. 5, Apr, 1950 (Painted c-1)

1-Contains two romance comic strips each 28 56 84 168 274 380
2 19 38 57 112 179 245
3-5 17 34 51 98 154 210

ENDER IN EXILE (Orson Scott Card's...)
Marvel Comics: Aug, 2010 - No. 5, Dec, 2010 ($3.99, limited series)

E-Man #3 © CC

Emma #1 © MAR

E-ratic #5 © AWA

	GD	VG	FN	VF	VF/NM	NM-
	2.0	4.0	6.0	8.0	9.0	9.2

GD VG FN VF VF/NM NM- 2.0 4.0 6.0 8.0 9.0 9.2

1-5-Sequel to Ender's Game; Johnston-s/Mhan-a/Fiumara-c 4.00

ENDER'S GAME: BATTLE SCHOOL
Marvel Comics: Dec, 2008 - No. 5, Jun, 2009 ($3.99, limited series)

1-5-Adaptation of Orson Scott Card novel Ender's Game; Yost-s/Ferry-a. 1-Two covers 4.00
Ender's Game: Mazer in Prison Special (4/10, $3.99) Johnston-s/Mhan-a 4.00
Ender's Game: Recruiting Valentine (8/09, $3.99) Timothy Green-a 4.00
Ender's Game: The League War (6/10, $3.99) Aaron Johnston-s/Timothy Green-a 4.00
Ender's Game: War of Gifts Special (2/10, $4.99) Timothy Green-a 5.00

ENDER'S GAME: COMMAND SCHOOL
Marvel Comics: Nov, 2009 - No. 5, Apr, 2010 ($3.99, limited series)

1-5-Adaptation of Orson Scott Card novel Ender's Game; Yost-s/Ferry-a 4.00

ENDER'S SHADOW: BATTLE SCHOOL
Marvel Comics: Feb, 2009 - No. 5, Jun, 2009 ($3.99, limited series)

1-5-Adaptation of O.S. Card novel Ender's Shadow; Carey-s/Fiumara-a. 1-Two covers 4.00

ENDER'S SHADOW: COMMAND SCHOOL
Marvel Comics: Nov, 2009 - No. 5, Apr, 2010 ($3.99, limited series)

1-5-Adaptation of O.S. Card novel Ender's Shadow; Carey-s/Fiumara-a 4.00

END LEAGUE, THE
Dark Horse Comics: Dec, 2007 - No. 9, Nov, 2009 ($2.99/$3.99)

1-8: 1-Broome-c/a; Remender-s. 5,6-Canete-a 3.00
9-($3.99) MacDonald-a/Canete-c 4.00

END OF NATIONS
DC Comics: Jan, 2012 - No. 4, Apr, 2012 ($2.99, limited series)

1-4-Based on the Trion Worlds videogame; Sanchez-s/Guichet-a/Sprouse-c 3.00

END TIMES OF BRAM AND BEN
Image Comics: Jan, 2013 - No. 4, Apr, 2013 ($2.99, limited series)

1-4: 1-Rapture parody; Asmus & Festante-s/Broo-a. 1-Mahfood-c 3.00

ENEMY ACE SPECIAL (Also see Our Army at War #151, Showcase #57, 58 & Star Spangled War Stories #138)
DC Comics: 1990 ($1.00, one-shot)

1-Kubert-r/Our Army #151,153; c-r/Showcase 57 5.00

ENEMY ACE: WAR IDYLL
DC Comics: 1990 (Graphic novel)

Hardcover-George Pratt-s/painted-a/c 30.00
Softcover (1991, $14.95) 15.00

ENEMY ACE: WAR IN HEAVEN
DC Comics: 2001 - No. 2, 2001 ($5.95, squarebound, limited series)

1,2-Ennis-s; Von Hammer in WW2. 1-Weston & Alamy-a. 2-Heath-a 6.00
TPB (2003, $14.95) r/#1,2 & Star Spangled War Stories #139; Jim Dietz-painted-c 15.00

ENGINEHEAD
DC Comics: June, 2004 - No. 6, Nov, 2004 ($2.50, limited series)

1-6-Joe Kelly-s/Ted McKeever-a/c. 6-Metal Men app. 3.00

ENIAC
Bad Idea: Mar, 2021 - No. 4, Jun, 2021 ($3.99, limited series)

1-Kindt-s/Braithwaite-a; first printing with white logo 3 6 9 16 23 30
1-Not First Printing edition with dark title logo 4.00
2-4-Kindt-s/Braithwaite-a in all 4.00

ENIGMA
DC Comics (Vertigo): Mar, 1993 - No. 8, Oct, 1993 ($2.50, limited series)

1-8: Milligan scripts 3.00
Trade paperback ($19.95)-reprints 20.00

ENO AND PLUM (Also see Cud Comics)
Oni Press: Mar, 1998 ($2.95, B&W)

1-Terry LaBan-s/c/a 3.00

ENSIGN O'TOOLE (TV)
Dell Publishing Co.: Aug-Oct, 1963

1 4 8 12 23 37 50

ENSIGN PULVER (See Movie Classics)

ENTER: THE COMICS (Victorian Age content, see Victorian section for other Töpffer works)
University of Nebraska Press: 1965 (6-7/8 x 9-1/4", 120 pgs, hard-c)

nn - By Ellen Weisse 6 12 18 38 69 100

NOTE: Contains overview of Töpffer's life and career plus only published English translation of Töpffer's Monsieur Crepin (1837); appears to have been re-drawn by Weisse in the days before xerox machines.

ENTER THE HEROIC AGE
Marvel Comics: July, 2010 ($3.99, one-shot)

1-Short stories of Avengers Academy, Atlas, Black Widow, Thunderbolts; Hitch-c 4.00

ENTER THE HOUSE OF SLAUGHTER
BOOM! Studios: Aug, 2021 (Free Comic Book Day giveaway)

nn - Previews House of Slaughter series; Tynion IV & Brombal-s/Shehan-a 3.00

EPIC
Marvel Comics (Epic Comics): 1992 - Book 4, 1992 ($4.95, lim. series, 52 pgs.)

Book One-Four: 2-Dorman painted-c 5.00

*NOTE: Alien Legion in #3. Cholly & Flytrap by **Burden**(scripts) & **Suydam**(art) in 3, 4. Dinosaurs in #4. Dreadlands in #1. Hellraiser in #1. Nightbreed in #2. Sleeze Brothers in #2. Stalkers in #1-4. Wild Cards in #1-4.*

EPIC ANTHOLOGY
Marvel Comics (Epic Comics): Apr, 2004 ($5.99)

1-Short stories by various; debut 2nd Sleepwalker by Kirkman-s 6.00

EPIC ILLUSTRATED (Magazine)
Marvel Comics Group: Spring, 1980 - No. 34, Feb, 1986 ($2.00/$2.50, B&W/color, mature)

1-Frazetta-c; Silver Surfer/Galactus-sty; Wendy Pini-s/a; Suydam-s/a; Metamorphosis Odyssey begins (thru #9) Starlin-a 4 8 12 25 40 55
2,4-10: 2-Bissette/Veitch-a; Goodwin-s. 4-Ellison 15 pg. story w/Steacy-a; Hempel-s/a; Veitch-s/a. 5-Hildebrandts-c/interview; Jusko-a; Vess-s/a. 6-Ellison-s (26 pgs). 7-Adams-s/a(16 pgs.); BWS interview. 8-Suydam-s/a; Vess-s/a. 9-Conrad-c. 10-Marada the She-Wolf-c/sty(21 pgs.) by Claremont/Bolton 2 4 6 8 11 14
3-1st app. Dreadstar (face apps. in 1 panel in #2) 5 10 15 33 57 80
11-20: 11-Wood-a; Jusko-a. 12-Wolverton Spacehawk-r edited & recolored w/article on him; Muth-a. 13-Blade Runner preview by Williamson. 14-Elric of Melnibone by Russell; Revenge of the Jedi preview. 15-Vallejo-c & interview; 1st Dreadstar solo story (cont'd in Dreadstar #1). 16-B. Smith-c/a(2); Sim-s/a. 17-Starslammers preview. 18-Go Nagai; Williams-a. 19-Jabberwocky w/Hampton-a; Cheech Wizard-s. 20-The Sacred & the Profane begins by Ken Steacy; Elric by Gould; Williams-a 1 3 4 6 8 10
21-30: 21-Vess-s/a. 22-Frankenstein w/Wrightson-a. 26-Galactus series begins (thru #34); Cerebus the Aardvark story by Dave Sim. 27-Groo. 28-Cerebus. 29-1st Sheeva. 30-Cerebus; History of Dreadstar, Starlin-s/a; Williams-a; Vess-a
2 4 6 8 10 12
31-33: 31-Bolton-c/a. 32-Cerebus portfolio. 2 4 6 8 11 14
34-R.E.Howard tribute by Thomas-s/Plunkett-a; Moore-s/Veitch-a; Cerebus; Cholly & Flytrap w/Suydam-a; BWS-a 3 6 9 14 19 24
Sampler (early 1980 8 pg. preview giveaway) same cover as #1 with "Sampler" text 6.00

*NOTE: **N. Adams** a-7; c-6. **Austin** a-15-20i. **Bode** a-19, 23, 27r. **Bolton** a-7, 10-12, 15, 18, 22-25; c-10, 18, 22, 23. **Boris** c/a-15. **Brunner** c-12. **Buscema** a-1p, 9p, 11-13p. **Byrne/Austin** a-26-34. **Chaykin** a-2; c-8. **Conrad** a-2-5, 7-9, 25-34; c-17. **Corben** a-15; c-2. **Frazetta** c-1. **Golden** a-3r. **Gulacy** c/a-3. **Jeff Jones** c-25. **Kaluta** a-17r, 21, 24r, 26; c-4, 28. **Nebres** a-1. **Reese** a-12. **Russell** a-2-4, 9, 14, 33; c-14. **Simonson** a-17. **B. Smith** c/a-7, 16. **Starlin** a-1-9, 14, 15, 34. **Steranko** c-19. **Williamson** a-13, 27, 34. **Wrightson** a-13p, 22, 25, 27, 34; c-30.*

EPIC LITE
Marvel Comics (Epic Comics): Sept, 1991 ($3.95, 52 pgs., one-shot)

1-Bob the Alien, Normalman by Valentino 4.00

EPICURUS THE SAGE
DC Comics (Piranha Press): Vol. 1, 1991 - Vol. 2, 1991 ($9.95, 8-1/8x10-7/8")

Volume 1,2-Sam Kieth-c/a; Messner-Loebs-s 2 4 6 11 16 20
TPB (2003, $19.95) r/ #1,2, Fast Forward Rising the Sun; new story 20.00

EPILOGUE
IDW Publishing: Sept, 2008 - No. 4, Dec, 2008 ($3.99)

1-4-Steve Niles-s/Kyle Hotz-a/c 4.00

EQUILIBRIUM (Based on the 2002 movie)
American Mythology Prods.: 2016 - No. 3, 2017 ($3.99)

1-3-Pat Shand-s/Jason Craig-a; multiple covers 4.00
...: Deconstruction 1 (2017, $3.99) Moroney-s/Dela Cuesta-a 4.00
...: Gunkata Casebook 1 (2018, $3.99) Mell-s/Hilinski-a 4.00

ERADICATOR
DC Comics: Aug, 1996 - No. 3, Oct, 1996 ($1.75, limited series)

1-3: Superman app. 3.00

E-RATIC
AWA Studios: Dec, 2020 - No. 5, Apr, 2021 ($3.99, limited series)

1-5-Kaare Andrews-s/a/c. 1-Variant-c by Mike Deodato 4.00

E-RATIC: RECHARGED
AWA Studios: Sept, 2022 - No. 4, Feb, 2023 ($3.99, limited series)

1-4-Kaare Andrews-s/a/c. 1-Variant-c by Mike Deodato 4.00

ERNIE COMICS (Formerly Andy Comics #21; All Love Romances #26 on)
Current Books/Ace Periodicals: No. 22, Sept, 1948 - No. 25, Mar, 1949

nn (9/48,11/48; #22,23)-Teenage humor 16 32 48 94 147 200

	GD 2.0	VG 4.0	FN 6.0	VF 8.0	VF/NM 9.0	NM- 9.2
24,25	14	28	42	80	115	150

EROS / PSYCHE
Ablaze Publishing: 2021 - No. 5, 2021 ($3.99, limited series)
1-5-Maria Llovet-s/a; multiple covers on each 4.00

ERRAND BOYS
Image Comics: Oct, 2018 - No. 5, Feb, 2019 ($3.99, limited series)
1-5-Kirkbridge-s/Koutsis-a 4.00

ESCAPADE IN FLORENCE (See Movie Comics)

ESCAPE FROM DEVIL'S ISLAND
Avon Periodicals: 1952

	GD 2.0	VG 4.0	FN 6.0	VF 8.0	VF/NM 9.0	NM- 9.2
1-Kinstler-c; r/as Dynamic Adventures #9	50	100	150	315	533	750

ESCAPE FROM NEW YORK (Based on the Kurt Russell movie)
BOOM! Studios: Dec, 2014 - No. 16, Apr, 2016 ($3.99)
1-16: 1-8-Christopher Sebela-s/Diego Barreto-a; multiple covers on each. 9-16-Simic-a 4.00

ESCAPE FROM THE PLANET OF THE APES (See Power Record Comics)

ESCAPE TO WITCH MOUNTAIN (See Walt Disney Showcase No. 29)

ESCAPISTS, THE (See Michael Chabon Presents The Amazing Adventures of the Escapist)
Dark Horse Comics: July, 2006 - No. 6, Dec, 2006 ($1.00/$2.99, limited series)
1-($1.00) Frank Miller-c; r/Vaughan story from Michael Chabon... #8 3.00
2-6($2.99) Vaughan-s/Rolston & Alexander-a. 2-James Jean-c. 3-Cassaday-c 3.00

ESPERS (Also see Interface)
Eclipse Comics: July, 1986 - No. 5, Apr, 1987 ($1.25/$1.75, Mando paper)
1-5-James Hudnall story & David Lloyd-a. 3.00

ESPERS
Halloween Comics: V2#1, 1996 - No. 6, 1997 ($2.95, B&W) (1st Halloween Comics series)
V2#1-6: James D. Hudnall scripts 3.00
Undertow TPB ('98, $14.95) r/#1-6 15.00

ESPERS
Image Comics: V3#1, 1997 - No. 7, 1998 ($2.95, B&W, limited series)
V3#1-7: James D. Hudnall scripts 3.00
Black Magic TPB ('98, $14.95) r/#1-4 15.00

ESPIONAGE (TV)
Dell Publishing Co.: May-July, 1964

	GD 2.0	VG 4.0	FN 6.0	VF 8.0	VF/NM 9.0	NM- 9.2
1	3	6	9	21	33	45

ESSENTIAL (Title series), **Marvel Comics**

--ANT-MAN, '02 (B&W- r) V1-Reprints app. from Tales To Astonish #27, #35-69; Kirby-c 15.00

--AVENGERS, '98 (B&W- r) V1-R-Avengers #1-24; new Immonen-c 15.00
V2(6/00)-Reprints Avengers #25-46, King-Size Special #1; Immonen-c 15.00
V3(3/01)-Reprints Avengers #47-68, Annual #2; Immonen-c 15.00
V4('04)-Reprints Avengers #69-97, Incredible Hulk #140; Neal Adams-c 17.00
V5('06)-Reprints Avengers #98-119, Daredevil #99, Defenders #8-11 17.00
V6('08)-Reprints Avengers #120-140, Giant Size #1-4, Capt. Marvel #33 & FF #150 17.00

--CAPTAIN AMERICA, '00 (B&W- r) V1-Reprints stories from Tales of Suspense #59-99, Captain America #100-102; new Romita & Milgrom-c 15.00
V2(1/02)-Reprints #103-126; Steranko-c 15.00
V3('06)-Reprints #127-153 17.00
V4('07)-Reprints #157-186 17.00

--CLASSIC X-MEN, '06 (B&W- r) (See Essential Uncanny X-Men for V1)
V2-($16.99) R-X-Men #25-53 & Avengers #53; Gil Kane-c 17.00

--CONAN, '00 (B&W- r) V1-R-Conan the Barbarian#1-25; new Buscema-c 15.00

--DAREDEVIL, '02 - V4 (B&W-r)
V1-R-Daredevil #1-25 15.00
V2-($16.99) R-Daredevil #26-48, Special #1, Fantastic Four #73 17.00
V3-($16.99) R-Daredevil #49-74, Iron Man #35-38 17.00
V4-($16.99) R-Daredevil #75-101, Avengers #111 17.00

--DAZZLER, '07 (B&W- r) V1-R/#1-21, X-Men #130-131, Amaz. Spider-Man #203 17.00

--DEFENDERS, '05 (B&W-r) V1-Reprints Doctor Strange #183, Sub-Mariner #22,34,35, Incredible Hulk #126, Marvel Feature #1-3, Defenders #1-14, Avengers #115-118 17.00
V2-($16.99) R- Defenders #15-30, Giant-Size Defenders #1-4, Marvel Two-In-One #6,7, Marvel Team-Up #33-35 and Marvel Treasury Edition #12 17.00
V3-($16.99) R- Defenders #31-60 and Annual #1 17.00

--DOCTOR STRANGE, '04 - V3 (B&W-r)
V1-($15.95) Reprints Strange Tales #110,111,114-168 17.00
V1 (2nd printing)-(2006, $16.99) Reprints Strange Tales #110,111,114-168 17.00
V2-($16.99) R-Doctor Strange #169-178,180-183; Avengers #61, Sub-Mariner #22 Marvel Feature #1, Incredible Hulk #126 and Marvel Premiere #3-14 17.00
V3-($16.99) R-Doctor Strange #1-29 & Annual #1;Tomb of Dracula #44,45 17.00

--FANTASTIC FOUR, '98 - V6 (B&W-r)
V1-Reprints FF #1-20, Annual #1; new Alan Davis-c; multiple printings exist 17.00
V2-Reprints FF #21-40, Annual #2; Davis and Farmer-c 15.00
V3-Reprints FF #41-63, Annual #3,4; Davis-c 15.00
V4-Reprints FF #64-83, Annual #5,6 17.00
V5-Reprints FF #84-110 17.00
V6-Reprints FF #111-137 17.00

--GHOST RIDER, '05 (B&W-r) V1-Reprints Marvel Spotlight #5-12, Ghost Rider #1-20 and Daredevil #138 17.00
V2-Reprints Ghost Rider #21-50 17.00

--GODZILLA, '06 (B&W-r) V1-Godzilla #1-24 20.00

--HOWARD THE DUCK, '02 (B&W- r) V1-Reprints #1-27, Annual #1; plus stories from Marvel Treasury Ed. #12, Man-Thing #1, Giant-Size Man-Thing #4,5, Fear #19; Bolland-c 15.00

--HULK, '99 (B&W-r) V1-R-Incred. Hulk #1-6, Tales To Astonish stories; new Timm-c 15.00
V2-Reprints Tales To Astonish #102-117, Annual #1 15.00
V3-Reprints Incredible Hulk #118-142, Capt. Marvel #20&21, Avengers #88 17.00
V4-Reprints Incredible Hulk #143-170 17.00
V5-Reprints Incredible Hulk #171-200, Annual #5 17.00

--HUMAN TORCH, '03 (B&W-r) V1-Strange Tales #101-134 & Ann. 2; Kirby-c 15.00

--IRON MAN, '00 - V3 (B&W-r)
V1-Reprints Tales Of Suspense #39-72; new Timm-c and back-c 15.00
V2-Reprints Tales Of Suspense #73-99, Tales To Astonish #82 & Iron Man #1-11 17.00
V3-Reprints Iron Man #12-38 & Daredevil #73 17.00

--KILLRAVEN, '05 (B&W-r) V1-Reprints Amazing Adventures V2 #18-39, Marvel Team-Up #45, Marvel Graphic Novel #7, Killraven #1 (2001) 17.00

--LUKE CAGE, POWER MAN, '05 (B&W-r) V1-Hero For Hire #1-16 & Power Man #17-27 17.00
V2-Reprints Power Man #28-49 & Annual #1 17.00

--MAN-THING, '06 (B&W-r) V1-Reprints Savage Tales #1, Astonishing Tales #12-13, Adventure Into Fear #10-19, Man-Thing #1-14, Giant-Size Man-Thing #1-2 & Monsters Unleashed #5,8,9 17.00
V2-R/Man-Thing #15-22 & #1-11 ('79 series), Giant-Size Man-Thing #3-5, Rampaging Hulk #7, Marvel Team-Up #68, Marvel Two-In-One #43 & Doctor Strange #41 17.00

--MARVEL HORROR, '06 (B&W-r) V1-R/#Ghost Rider #1-2, Marvel Spotlight #12-24, Son of Satan #1-8, Marvel Two-In-One #14, Marvel Team-Up #32,80,81, Vampire Tales #2-3, Haunt of Horror #2,4,5, Marvel Premiere #27, & Marvel Preview #7 17.00

--MARVEL SAGA, '08 (B&W-r) V1-R/#1-12 17.00

--MARVEL TEAM-UP, '02 - V2 (B&W-r) V1('02, '06)-R/#1-24 17.00
V2-R/#25-51 and Marvel Two-In-One #17 17.00

--MARVEL TWO-IN-ONE, '05 - V2 (B&W-r)
V1-Reprints Marvel Feature #11&12, Marvel Two-In-One #1-20,22-25 & Annual #1, Marvel Team-Up #47 and Fantastic Four Ann. #11 17.00
V2-R/#26-52 & Annual #2,3 17.00

--MONSTER OF FRANKENSTEIN, '04 (B&W-r) V1-Reprints Monster of Frankenstein #1-5, Frankenstein Monster #6-18, Giant-Size Werewolf #2, Monsters Unleashed #2,4-10 & Legion of Monsters #1 17.00

--MOON KNIGHT, '06 (B&W-r) V1-Reprints Moon Knight #1-10 and early apps. 17.00
V2-R/#11-30 17.00

--MS. MARVEL, '07 (B&W-r) V1-Reprints Ms. Marvel #1-23, Marvel Super-Heroes Magazine #10,11, and Avengers Annual #10 17.00

--NOVA, '06 (B&W-r) V1-Reprints Nova #1-25, AS-M #171, Marvel Two-In-One Ann. #3 17.00

--OFFICIAL HANDBOOK OF THE MARVEL UNIVERSE, '06 (B&W-r) V1-Reprints #1-15 profiling Abomination through Zzzax; dead and inactive characters; weapons & hardware; wraparound-c by Byrne 17.00

--OFFICIAL HANDBOOK OF THE MARVEL UNIVERSE - DELUXE EDITION, '06 (B&W-r)
V1-Reprints #1-7 profiling Abomination through Magneto; wraparound-c by Byrne 17.00
V2-Reprints #8-14 profiling Magus through Wolverine; wraparound-c by Byrne 17.00
V3-Reprints #15-20 profiling Wonder Man through Zzzax & Book of the Dead 17.00

--OFFICIAL HANDBOOK OF THE MARVEL UNIVERSE - MASTER EDITION, '08 (B&W-r)
V1-Reprints profiling Abomination through Gargoyle 17.00
V2-Reprints profiles 17.00

--OFFICIAL HANDBOOK OF THE MARVEL UNIVERSE - UPDATE '89, '06 (B&W-r)
V1-Reprints #1-8; wraparound-c by Frenz 17.00

--PETER PARKER, THE SPECTACULAR SPIDER-MAN, '05 (B&W-r) V1-Reprints #1-31 17.00
V2-Reprints #32-53 & Annual #1,2; Amazing Spider-Man Annual #13 17.00
V3-Reprints #54-74 & Annual #3; Frank Miller-c 17.00

--POWER MAN AND IRON FIST, '07 (B&W-r) V1-R/#50-72,74-75 17.00

--PUNISHER, '04, '06 - '12 (B&W-r) V1-Reprints early app. in Amazing Spider-Man, Captain America, Daredevil, Marvel Preview and Punisher #1-5 (2 printings) 17.00
V2-Punisher #1-20, Annual #1 and Daredevil #257 17.00
V3-Punisher #21-40, Annual #2,3 17.00
V4-Punisher #41-59 17.00

--RAMPAGING HULK, '08 (B&W-r) V1-R/#1-9, The Hulk! #10-15 & Incredible Hulk #269 17.00

--SAVAGE SHE-HULK, '06 (B&W-r) V1-R/#1-25 17.00

--SILVER SURFER, '98 - Present (B&W-r)
V1-R-material from SS#1-18 and Fantastic Four Ann. #5 15.00
V2-R-SS#1(1982), SS#1-18 & Ann#1(1987), Epic Illustrated #1, Marvel Fanfare #51 17.00

--SPIDER-MAN, '96 - V8 (B&W-r)
V1-R-AF #15, Amaz. S-M #1-20, Ann. #1 (2 printings) 15.00
V2-R-Amaz. Spider-Man #21-43, Annual #2,3 15.00
V3-R-Amaz. Spider-Man #44-68 15.00
V4-R-Amaz. Spider-Man #69-89; Annual #4,5; new Timm-f&b-c 15.00
V5-R-Amaz. Spider-Man #90-113; new Romita-c 15.00
V6-R-Amaz. Spider-Man #114-137, Giant-Size Super-Heroes #1 G-S S-M #1,2 17.00
V7-R-Amaz. Spider-Man #138-160, Annual #10; Giant-Size Spider-Man #3-5 17.00
V8-R-Amaz. Spider-Man #161-185, Annual #11; G-S Spider-Man #6; Nova #12 17.00

--SPIDER-WOMAN, '05 (B&W-r) V1-Reprints Marvel Spotlight #32, Marvel Two-In-One #29-33, Spider-Woman #1-25 17.00
V2-R-Spider-Woman #26-50, Marvel Team-Up #97 & Uncanny X-Men #148 17.00

--SUPER-VILLAIN TEAM-UP, '04 (B&W-r) V1-r/S-V T-U #1-14 & 16-17, Giant-Size S-V T-U #1,2; Avengers #154-156; Champions #16, & Astonishing Tales #1-8 17.00

--TALES OF THE ZOMBIE, '06 (B&W-r) V1-($16.99) r/#1-10 & Dracula Lives #1,2 17.00

--THOR, '01 (B&W-r) V1-R-Journey Into Mystery #83-112 15.00
V2-($16.99) R-Thor #113-136 & Annual #1,2 17.00
V3-($16.99) R-Thor #137-166 17.00

--TOMB OF DRACULA, '03 - V4 (B&W-r) V1-R-Tomb of Dracula #1-25, Werewolf By Night #15, Giant-Size Chillers #1 15.00
V2-($16.99) R-Tomb of Dracula #26-49, Giant-Size Dracula #2-5, Dr. Strange #14 17.00
V3-($16.99) R-Tomb of Dracula #50-70, Tomb of Dracula Magazine #1-4 17.00
V4-($16.99) R/Stories from Tomb of Dracula Magazine #2-6, Dracula Lives! #1-13, and Frankenstein Monster #7-9 17.00

--UNCANNY X-MEN, '99 (B&W reprints) (See Essential Classic X-Men for V2)
V1-Reprints X-Men (1st series) #1-24; Timm-c 15.00

ESSENTIAL VERTIGO: SWAMP THING
DC Comics: Nov, 1996 - No. 24, Oct, 1998 ($1.95/$2.25,B&W, reprints)
1-11,13-24: 1-9-Reprints Alan Moore's Swamp Thing stories 4.00

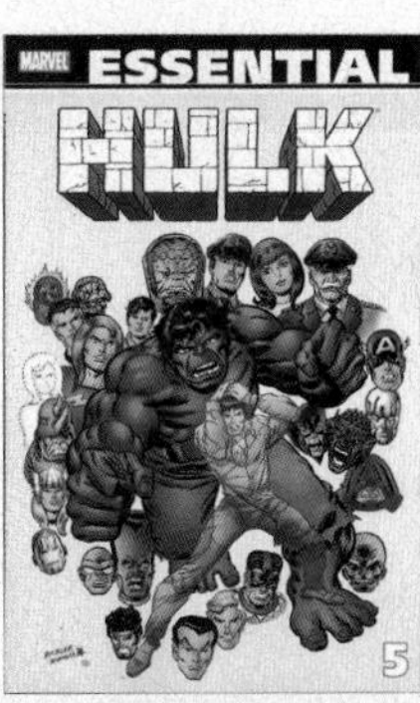

Essential Hulk Volume 5 © MAR

Eternal Soulfire #1 © Aspen MLT

Eternal Warrior (2013) #1 © VAL

GD 2.0 | VG 4.0 | FN 6.0 | VF 8.0 | VF/NM 9.0 | NM- 9.2

12-($3.50) r/Annual #2 5.00

ESSENTIAL VERTIGO: THE SANDMAN
DC Comics (Vertigo): Aug, 1996 - No. 32, Mar, 1999 ($1.95/$2.25, reprints)

1-13,15-31: Reprints Sandman, 2nd series 4.00
14-($2.95) 4.00
32-($4.50) Reprints Sandman Special #1 4.50

ESSENTIAL WEREWOLF BY NIGHT
Marvel Comics: 2005 - V2 (B&W reprints)

V1-($16.99) r/Marvel Spotlight #2-4, Werewolf By Night 1-23, Marvel Team-Up #12, Tomb of Dracula #18, Giant-Size Creatures #1 17.00
V2-R/#22-43, Giant-Size Werewolf #2-5 and Marvel Premiere #28 17.00

ESSENTIAL WOLVERINE
Marvel Comics: 1999 - V4 (B&W reprints)

V1-r/#1-23, V2-r/#24-47, V3-R/#48-69, V4-R/#70-90 17.00

ESSENTIAL X-FACTOR
Marvel Comics: 2005 - V2 (B&W reprints)

V1-($16.99) r/X-Factor #1-16 & Annual #1, Avengers #262, Fantastic Four #286, Thor #373&374 and Power Pack #27 17.00
V2-Reprints X-Factor #17-35 & Annual #2, Thor #378 17.00

ESSENTIAL X-MEN
Marvel Comics: 1996 - V8 (B&W reprints)

V1-V4: V1-R/Giant Size X-Men #1, X-Men #94-119. V2-R-X-Men #120-144. V3-R-Uncanny X-Men #145-161, Ann. #3-5. V4-Uncanny X-Men #162-179, Ann. #6 15.00
V5-($16.99) R/Uncanny X-Men #180-198, Ann. #7-8 17.00
V6-($16.99) R/Uncanny X-Men #199-213, Ann. #9, New Mutants Special Edition #1, X-Factor #9-11, New Mutants #46, Thor #373-374 and Power Pack #27 17.00
V7-($16.99) R/Uncanny X-Men #214-228, Ann. #10,11, and F.F. vs. The X-Men #1-4 17.00
V8-($16.99) R/Uncanny X-Men #229-243, Ann. #12 & X-Factor #36-39 17.00

ESTABLISHMENT, THE (Also see The Authority and The Monarchy)
DC Comics (WildStorm): Nov, 2001 - No. 13, Nov, 2002 ($2.50)

1-13-Edginton-s/Adlard-a 3.00

ET-ER (Extraterrestrial Emergency Room)
AWA Studios: Oct, 2021; Jun, 2022 ($3.99)

1,2: 1-McComsey-s/Pulido-a; Panosian-s/Crystal-a. 2-Cho-c 4.00

ETERNAL
BOOM! Studios: Dec, 2014 - No. 4, Apr, 2015 ($3.99)

1-4: 1-Harms-s/Valletta-a/Irving-c 4.00

ETERNAL, THE
Marvel Comics (MAX): Aug, 2003 - No. 6, Jan, 2004 ($2.99, mature)

1-6-Austen-s/Walker-a 3.00

ETERNAL BIBLE, THE
Authentic Publications: 1946 (Large size) (16 pgs. in color)

1 16 32 48 94 147 200

ETERNAL EMPIRE
Image Comics: May, 2017 - No. 10, Aug, 2018 ($3.99)

1-9-Sarah Vaughn & Jonathan Luna-s/Luna-a/c 4.00
10-($4.99) Conclusion 5.00

ETERNALS, THE
Marvel Comics Group: July, 1976 - No. 19, Jan, 1978

1-(Regular 25¢ edition)-Origin & 1st app. Ikaris & The Eternals
6 12 18 41 76 110
1-(30¢-c variant, limited distribution) 25 50 75 175 388 600
2-(Reg. 25¢ edition)-1st app. Ajak & The Celestials 4 8 12 28 47 65
2-(30¢-c variant, limited distribution) 17 34 51 117 259 400
3-19: 3-1st app. Sersi. 5-1st app. Makarri, Domo, Zuras, & Thena. 11-1st app. Kingo. 14,15-Cosmic powered Hulk-c/story 3 6 9 14 19 24
12-16-(35¢-c variants, limited distribution) 9 18 27 61 123 185
Annual 1(10/77) 3 6 9 14 20 25
... No. 1 Facsimile Edition (2/20, $3.99) Reprints #1 with original 1976 ads 4.00
...: Secrets From the Marvel Universe 1 (2/20, $4.99) Reprints from What If? #23-30 5.00
Eternals by Jack Kirby HC (2006, $75.00, dust jacket) r/#1-19 & Annual #1; intro by Royer; letter pages from #1,2,Annual #1; afterwords by Robert Greenberger 75.00
NOTE: *Kirby c/a(p) in all.*

ETERNALS, THE
Marvel Comics: Oct, 1985 - No. 12, Sept, 1986 (Maxi-series, mando paper)

1,12 (52 pgs.): 12-Williamson-a(i) 5.00
2-11 4.00

GD 2.0 | VG 4.0 | FN 6.0 | VF 8.0 | VF/NM 9.0 | NM- 9.2

ETERNALS
Marvel Comics: Aug, 2006 - No. 7, Mar, 2007 ($3.99, limited series)

1-7-Neil Gaiman-s/John Romita Jr.-a/Rick Berry-c 4.00
1-7-Variant covers by Romita Jr. 4.00
1-Variant cover by Coipel 4.00
... Sketchbook (2006, $1.99, B&W) character sketches and sketch pages from #1 4.00
HC (2007, $29.99, dustjacket) r/#1-7; gallery of variant covers; sketches, Gaiman interview, Gaiman's original proposal; background essay on Kirby's Eternals 30.00

ETERNALS
Marvel Comics: Aug, 2008 - No. 9, May, 2009 ($2.99)

1-9: 1-6-Acuña-a/c; Knauf-s. 2,4-Iron Man app. 7,8-Nguyen-a; X-Men app. 3.00
Annual 1 (1/09, $3.99) Alixe-a/McGuinness-c; & reprint from Eternals #7 ('77) Kirby-s/a 4.00

ETERNALS
Marvel Comics: Mar, 2021 - No. 12, Jul, 2022 ($4.99/$3.99)

1-($4.99) Kieron Gillen-s/Esad Ribic-a; Ikaris returns; Iron Man & Thanos app. 5.00
2-12-($3.99) 2-Ikaris battles Thanos. 5-12-Thanos app. 11-Vilanova-a 4.00
...: Celestia 1 (12/21, $3.99) Gillen-s/Zama-a; history of the city 4.00
... Forever 1 (12/21, $3.99) Macchio-s/Bachs-a/Nauck-c 4.00
...: Thanos Rises 1 (11/21, $3.99) Gillen-s/Weaver-a; parents of Thanos and his birth 4.00
...: The Heretic 1 (5/22, $3.99) Gillen-s/Bodenheim & Salazar-a; Uranos app. 4.00

ETERNAL SOULFIRE (Also see Soulfire)
Aspen MLT, Inc.: Jul, 2015 - No. 6, Feb, 2016 ($3.99, limited series)

1-6-Multiple covers on each. 1-Krul-s/Konat-a. 3-Tovar & Konat-a 4.00

ETERNALS: THE HEROD FACTOR
Marvel Comics: Nov, 1991 ($2.50, 68 pgs.)

1 4.00

ETERNAL WARRIOR (See Solar #10 & 11)
Valiant/Acclaim Comics (Valiant): Aug, 1992 - No. 50, Mar, 1996 ($2.25/$2.50)

1-Unity x-over; Miller-c; origin Eternal Warrior & Aram (Armstrong)
2 4 6 8 10 12
1-($2.25-c) Gold logo 3 6 9 15 22 28
1-Gold foil logo on embossed cover; no cover price 4 8 12 25 40 55
2,3,5-8: 2-Unity x-over; Simonson-c. 3-Archer & Armstrong x-over. 5-2nd full app. Bloodshot (12/92; see Rai #0). 6,7: 6-2nd app. Master Darque. 8-Flip book w/Archer & Armstrong #8 4.00
4-1st brief app. Bloodshot (last pg.); see Rai #0 for 1st full app.; Cowan-c
3 6 9 18 28 38
9-25,27-34: 9-1st Book of Geomancer. 14-16-Bloodshot app. 18-Doctor Mirage cameo. 19-Doctor Mirage app. 22-W/bound-in trading card. 25-Archer & Armstrong app.; cont'd from A&A #25 3.00
26-($2.75, 44 pgs.)-Flip book w/Archer & Armstrong 4.00
35-50: 35-Double-c; $2.50-c begins. 50-Geomancer app. 3.00
Special 1 (2/96, $2.50)-Wings of Justice; Art Holcomb script 3.00
Yearbook 1 (1993, $3.95), 2(1994, $3.95) 4.00

ETERNAL WARRIOR (Also see Wrath of the Eternal Warrior)
Valiant Entertainment: Sept, 2013 - No. 8, Apr, 2014 ($3.99)

1-8: 1-Pak-s/Hairsine-a; 2 covers. 2-Hairsine & Crain-a 4.00
...: Awakening 1 (5/17, $3.99) Venditti-s/Guedes-a 4.00

ETERNAL WARRIORS (Series of one-shots)
Acclaim Comics (Valiant Heroes)

...: Archer & Armstrong 1 (12/97, $3.95) Teranishi-a 4.00
...: Blackworks 1 (3/98, $3.95) Doug Wheatley-a 4.00
...: Digital Alchemy Vol. 2 (9/97, $3.95, 64 pgs.) Holcomb-s/Eaglesham-a(p) 4.00
...: Mog (3/98, $3.95, 64 pgs.) Holcomb-s/Morales-a(p) 4.00
...: The Immortal Enemy (6/98, $3.95, 64 pgs.) Holcomb-s/Jimenez-a(p) 4.00
...: Time and Treachery Vol. 1 (6/97, $3.95, 64 pgs.) Reintro Aram, Archer, Ivar the Timewalker, & Gilad the Warmaster; 1st app. Shalla Redburn; Holcomb script; 2 covers 4.00

ETERNAL WARRIOR: DAYS OF STEEL
Valiant Entertainment: Nov, 2014 - No. 3, Jan, 2015 ($3.99)

1-3-Milligan-s/Nord-a 4.00

ETERNAL WARRIORS: FIST AND STEEL
Acclaim Comics (Valiant): May, 1996 - No. 2, June, 1996 ($2.50, lim. series)

1,2: Geomancer app. in both. 1-Indicia reads "June." 2-Bo Hampton-a 4.00

ETERNITY (Also see Divinity)
Valiant Entertainment: Oct, 2017 - No. 4, Jan, 2018 ($3.99, limited series)

1-4: 1-Kindt-s/Hairsine-a; 5 covers 4.00

ETERNITY GIRL
DC Comics (Young Animal): May, 2018 - No. 6, Oct, 2018 ($3.99)

	GD 2.0	VG 4.0	FN 6.0	VF 8.0	VF/NM 9.0	NM- 9.2

1-6-Visaggio-s/Liew-a. 1-Intro. Caroline Sharp 4.00

ETERNITY SMITH
Renegade Press: Sept, 1986 - No. 5, May, 1987 ($1.25/$1.50, 36 pgs.)

1-5: 1st app. Eternity Smith. 5-Death of Jasmine 4.00

ETERNITY SMITH
Hero Comics: Sept, 1987 - No. 9, 1988 ($1.95)

V2#1-9: 8-Indigo begins 4.00

ETHER
Dark Horse Comics: Nov, 2016 - No. 5, Mar, 2017 ($3.99)

1-5-Matt Kindt-s/David Rubin-a 4.00

ETHER ("The Copper Golems" on cover)
Dark Horse Comics: May, 2018 - No. 5, Sept, 2018 ($3.99)

1-5-Matt Kindt-s/David Rubin-a 4.00

ETHER: THE DISAPPEARANCE OF VIOLET BELL
Dark Horse Comics: Sept, 2019 - No. 5, Jan, 2020 ($3.99)

1-5-Matt Kindt-s/David Rubin-a 4.00

ETTA KETT
King Features Syndicate/Standard: No. 11, Dec, 1948 - No. 14, Sept, 1949

	GD	VG	FN	VF	VF/NM	NM-
11-Teenage	16	32	48	94	147	200
12-14	14	28	42	76	108	140

EUTHANAUTS
IDW Publishing (Black Crown): Jul, 2018 - No. 5, Nov, 2018 ($3.99)

1-5-Tini Howard-s/Nick Robles-a 4.00

EVA: DAUGHTER OF THE DRAGON
Dynamite Entertainment: 2007 ($4.99, one-shot)

1-Two covers by Jo Chen and Edgar Salazar; Jerwa-s/Salazar-a 5.00

EVANESCENCE
Opus: Aug, 2022 - Present ($4.99, limited series)

1-3-Stories inspired by the band's music. 1-Kelly McKernan-s/a 5.00
...: My Heart is Broken 1 (2/23, $6.99) Maura McHugh-s/V.R. TenagaComics-a 7.00

EVANGELINE (Also see Primer)
Comico/First Comics V2#1 on/Lodestone Publ.: 1984 - #2, 6/84; V2#1, 5/87 - V2#12, Mar, 1989 (Baxter paper)

1,2, V2#1 (5/87) - 12, Special #1 (1986, $2.00)-Lodestone Publ. 4.00

EVA THE IMP
Red Top Comic/Decker: 1957 - No. 2, Nov, 1957

	GD	VG	FN	VF	VF/NM	NM-
1,2	8	16	24	40	50	60

EVE
BOOM! Studios: May, 2021 - No. 5, Sept, 2021 ($3.99, limited series)

1-5-Victor LaValle-s/Jo Mi-Gyeong-a; multiple covers on each 4.00

EVE: CHILDREN OF THE MOON
BOOM! Studios: Oct, 2022 - No. 5, Feb, 2023 ($3.99, limited series)

1-5-Victor LaValle-s/Jo Mi-Gyeong-a; multiple covers on each 4.00

EVEN MORE FUND COMICS (Benefit book for the Comic Book Legal Defense Fund) (Also see More Fund Comics)
Sky Dog Press: Sept, 2004 ($10.00, B&W, trade paperback)

nn-Anthology of short stories and pin-ups by various; Spider-Man-c by Cho 10.00

EVENT LEVIATHAN (See Action Comics #1007-1012 and Leviathan Dawn one-shot)
DC Comics: Aug, 2019 - No. 6, Jan, 2020 ($3.99, limited series)

1-6-Bendis-s/Maleev-a; Batman, Lois Lane, The Question, Green Arrow, Manhunter app. 4.00

E.V.E. PROTOMECHA
Image Comics (Top Cow): Mar, 2000 - No. 6, Sept, 2000 ($2.50)

	GD	VG	FN	VF	VF/NM	NM-
Preview ($5.95) Flip book w/Soul Saga preview	2	4	6	8	10	12
1-6: 1-Covers by Finch, Madureira, Garza. 2-Turner var-c						3.00
1-Another Universe variant-c						5.00
TPB (5/01, $17.95) r/#1-6 plus cover galley and sketch pages						18.00

EVERAFTER (See Fables)
DC Comics (Vertigo): Nov, 2016 - No. 12, Oct, 2017 ($3.99)

1-12: 1-Justus & Sturges-s/Travis Moore-a; Snow & Bigby app. 7-Buckingham-a 4.00

EVERQUEST: ... (Based on online role-playing game)
DC Comics (WildStorm): 2002 ($5.95, one-shots)

The Ruins of Kunark - Jim Lee & Dan Norton-a; McQuaid & Lee-s; Lee-c 6.00
Transformations - Philip Tan-a; Devin Grayson-s; Portacio-c 6.00

EVER THE WAY OUT
Abstract Studio: 2020 ($17.99, B&W, graphic novel)

GN - Terry Moore-s/a; intro. Everly; Rachel & Lilith app. 18.00

EVERYBODY'S COMICS (See Fox Giants)

EVERYMAN, THE
Marvel Comics (Epic Comics): Nov, 1991 ($4.50, one-shot, 52 pgs.)

	GD	VG	FN	VF	VF/NM	NM-
1-Mike Allred-a	1	2	3	4	5	7

EVERYTHING
Dark Horse Comics (Berger Books): Sept, 2019 - No. 5, Jan, 2020 ($3.99)

1-5-Christopher Cantwell-s/I.N.J. Culbard-a 4.00

EVERYTHING HAPPENS TO HARVEY
National Periodical Publications: Sept-Oct, 1953 - No. 7, Sept-Oct, 1954

	GD	VG	FN	VF	VF/NM	NM-
1	43	86	129	271	461	650
2	22	44	66	132	216	300
3-7	19	38	57	111	176	240

EVERYTHING'S ARCHIE
Archie Publications: May, 1969 - No. 157, Sept, 1991 (Giant issues No. 1-20)

	GD	VG	FN	VF	VF/NM	NM-
1-(68 pages)	9	18	27	59	117	175
2-(68 pages)	4	8	12	28	47	65
3-5-(68 pages)	4	8	12	25	40	55
6-13-(68 pages)	3	6	9	17	26	35
14-31-(52 pages)	2	4	6	13	18	22
32 (7/74)-50 (8/76)	2	4	6	8	10	12
51-80 (12/79),100 (4/82)	1	2	3	5	6	8
81-99						6.00
101-103,105,106,108-120						5.00
104,107-Cheryl Blossom app.	1	2	3	4	5	7
121-156: 142,148-Gene Colan-a						4.00
157-Last issue						5.00

EVERYTHING'S DUCKY (Movie)
Dell Publishing Co.: No. 1251, 1961

	GD	VG	FN	VF	VF/NM	NM-
Four Color 1251-Mickey Rooney & Buddy Hackett photo-c	7	14	21	44	82	120

EVE STRANGER
IDW Publishing (Black Crown): Apr, 2019 - No. 5, Aug, 2019 ($3.99)

1-5-David Barnett-s/Philip Bond-a/c 4.00

EVE: VALKYRIE (Based on the video game)
Dark Horse Comics: Oct, 2015 - No. 4, Jan, 2016 ($3.99, limited series)

1-4-Brian Wood-s/Eduardo Francisco-a 4.00

EVIL DEAD, THE (Movie)
Dark Horse Comics: Jan, 2008 - No. 4, Apr, 2008 ($2.99, limited series)

1-4-Adaptation of the Sam Raimi/Bruce Campbell movie; Bolton painted-a/c 4.00

EVIL DEAD 2 (Movie)
Space Goat Productions: 2016 ($3.99, one-shots)

...: Revenge of Hitler 1 - Edginton-s/Watts-a 4.00
...: Revenge of Jack the Ripper 1 - Ball-s/Mauriz-a 4.00
...: Revenge of Krampus 1 - Edginton-s/Youkovich-a 4.00

EVIL DEAD 2: BEYOND DEAD BY DAWN (Movie)
Space Goat Productions: 2015 - No. 3, 2015 ($3.99, limited series)

1-3-Sequel to the Sam Raimi/Bruce Campbell movie; Hannah-s/Bagenda & Bazaldua-a 4.00

EVIL DEAD 2: CRADLE OF THE DAMNED (Movie)
Space Goat Productions: 2016 - No. 3, 2016 ($3.99, limited series)

1-3-Hannah-s/Bagenda & Bazaldua-a 4.00

EVIL DEAD 2: DARK ONES RISING (Movie)
Space Goat Productions: 2016 - No. 3, 2016 ($3.99, limited series)

1-3-Sequel to the Sam Raimi/Bruce Campbell movie; Hannah-s/Valdes-a 4.00

EVIL DEAD 2: REVENGE OF EVIL ED (Movie)
Space Goat Productions: 2017 - No. 2, 2017 ($3.99, limited series)

1,2-Edginton-s/Riccardi-a; Hitler, Rasputin, Bin Laden & Dracula app. 4.00

EVIL ERNIE
Eternity Comics: Dec, 1991 - No. 5, 1992 ($2.50, B&W, limited series)

	GD	VG	FN	VF	VF/NM	NM-
1-1st app. Lady Death by Steven Hughes (12,000 print run); Lady Death app. in all issues	16	32	48	110	243	375
2-1st Lady Death-c (7,000 print run)	9	18	27	61	123	185
3-(7,000 print run)	5	10	15	33	57	80
4-(8,000 print run)	4	8	12	28	47	65
5	4	8	12	25	40	55
Special Edition 1	3	6	9	21	33	45
Youth Gone Wild! ($9.95, trade paperback)-r/#1-5	2	4	6	8	10	12
Youth Gone Wild! Director's Cut ($4.95)-Limited to 15,000, shows the making of the comic						6.00

EVIL ERNIE (Monthly series)
Chaos! Comics: July, 1998 - No. 10, Apr, 1999 ($2.95)

	GD	VG	FN	VF	VF/NM	NM-
1-Pulido & Nutman-s/Brewer-a	1	3	4	6	8	10
1-($10.00) Premium Ed.	2	4	6	8	10	12
2-10-Pulido & Nutman-s/Brewer-a						4.00
... Baddest Battles (1/97, $1.50) Pin-ups; 2 covers						5.00
... Pieces of Me (11/00, $2.95, B&W) Flashback story; Pulido-s/Beck-a						4.00
... Relentless (5/02, $4.99, B&W) Pulido-s/Beck, Bonk, & Brewer-a						5.00
... Returns (10/01, $3.99, B&W) Pulido-s/Beck-a						4.00

EVIL ERNIE
Dynamite Entertainment: 2012 - No. 6, 2013 ($3.99)

1-6: 1-Origin re-told; Snider-s/Craig-a; covers by Brereton, Seeley, Syaf & Bradshaw 4.00

EVIL ERNIE (Volume 2)
Dynamite Entertainment: 2014 - No. 6, 2015 ($3.99)

1-6-Tim & Steve Seeley-s/Rafael Lanhellas-a; multiple covers 4.00

EVIL ERNIE (Volume 3)
Dynamite Entertainment: 2021 - No. 5, 2022 ($3.99, limited series)

1-5-Scott Lobdell-s/Ariel Medel; multiple covers; rebirth of Ernie 4.00

EVIL ERNIE: DEPRAVED
Chaos! Comics: Jul, 1999 - No. 3, Sept, 1999 ($2.95, limited series)

1-3-Pulido-s/Brewer-a 4.00

EVIL ERNIE: DESTROYER
Chaos! Comics: Oct, 1997 - No. 9, Jun, 1998 ($2.95, limited series)

Preview ($2.50), 1-9-Flip cover 4.00

EVIL ERNIE: GODEATER
Dynamite Entertainment: 2016 - No. 5, 2016 ($3.99)

1-5-Jordan-s/Worley-a; Davidsen-s/Razek-a; multiple covers 4.00

EVIL ERNIE: IN SANTA FE
Devil's Due Publ.: Sept, 2005 - No. 4, Mar, 2006 ($2.95, limited series)

1-4-Alan Grant-s/Tommy Castillo-a/Alex Horley-c 4.00

EVIL ERNIE: REVENGE
Chaos! Comics: Oct, 1994 - No. 4, Feb, 1995 ($2.95, limited series)

Eve #1 © Victor LaValle

Evil Ernie (2015) #6 © DYN

Excalibur (2019) #13 © MAR

GD VG FN VF VF/NM NM-
2.0 4.0 6.0 8.0 9.0 9.2

1-Glow-in-the-dark-c; Lady Death app. 1-3-flip book w. Kilzone Preview (series of 3)
1 2 3 5 6 8
1-Commemorative-(4000 print run) 2 4 6 8 10 12
2-4 4.00
Trade paperback (10/95, $12.95) 13.00

EVIL ERNIE: STRAIGHT TO HELL
Chaos! Comics: Oct, 1995 - No. 5, May, 1996 ($2.95, limited series)
1-Fold-out-c 1 3 4 6 8 10
1,3:1-($19.95) Chromium Ed. 3-Chastity Chase-c-(4000 printed) 20.00
2-5 4.00
Special Edition (10,000) 20.00

EVIL ERNIE: THE RESURRECTION
Chaos! Comics: 1993 - No. 4, 1994 (Limited series)
0 5.00
1 2 4 6 8 10 12
1A-Gold 3 6 9 16 23 30
2-4 1 2 3 5 6 8

EVIL ERNIE VS. THE MOVIE MONSTERS
Chaos! Comics: Mar, 1997 ($2.95, one-shot)
1 4.00
1-Variant-"Chaos-Scope•Terror Vision" card stock-c 1 3 4 6 8 10

EVIL ERNIE VS. THE SUPER HEROES
Chaos! Comics: Aug, 1995; Sept, 1998 ($2.95)
1-Lady Death poster 4.00
1-Foil-c variant (limited to 10,000) 2 4 6 11 16 20
1-Limited Edition (1000) 2 4 6 11 16 20
2-(9/98) Ernie vs. JLA and Marvel parodies 4.00

EVIL ERNIE: WAR OF THE DEAD
Chaos! Comics: Nov, 1999 - No. 3, Jan, 2000 ($2.95, limited series)
1-3-Pulido & Kaminski-s/Brewer-a. 3-End of Evil Ernie 4.00

EVIL EYE
Fantagraphics Books: June, 1998 - No. 12, Jun, 2004 ($2.95/$3.50/$3.95, B&W)
1-7-Richard Sala-s/a 4.00
8-10-($3.50) 4.00
11,12-($3.95) 4.00

EVO (Crossover from Tomb Raider #25 & Witchblade #60)
Image Comics (Top Cow): Feb, 2003 ($2.99, one-shot)
1-Silvestri-c/a(p); Endgame x-over pt. 3; Sara Pezzini & Lara Croft app. 3.00

EWOKS (Star Wars) (TV) (See Star Comics Magazine)
Marvel Comics (Star Comics): June, 1985 - No. 14, Jul, 1987 (75¢/$1.00)
1 4 8 12 25 40 55
2-9 2 4 6 9 12 15
10-Williamson-a (From Star Wars) 5 10 15 33 57 80
11-14: 14-($1.00-c) 2 4 6 11 16 20

EXCALIBUR (Also see Marvel Comics Presents #31)
Marvel Comics: Apr, 1988; Oct, 1988 - No. 125, Oct, 1998 ($1.50/$1.75/$1.99)
Special Edition nn (The Sword is Drawn)(4/88, $3.25)-1st Excalibur comic
1 2 3 5 6 8
Special Edition nn (4/88)-no price on-c 2 4 6 8 10 12
Special Edition nn (2nd & 3rd print, 10/88, 12/89) 5.00
...The Sword is Drawn (Apr, 1992, $4.50) 5.00
1($1.50, 10/88)-X-Men spin-off; Nightcrawler, Shadowcat (Kitty Pryde), Capt. Britain, Phoenix & Meggan begin 6.00
2-4 5.00
5-10 4.00
11-49,51-70,72-74,76: 10,11-Rogers/Austin-a. 21-Intro Crusader X. 22-Iron Man x-over. 24-John Byrne app. in story. 26-Ron Lim-c/a. 27-B. Smith-a(p). 37-Dr. Doom & Iron Man app. 41-X-Men (Wolverine) app.; Cable cameo. 49-Neal Adams c-swipe. 52,57-X-Men (Cyclops, Wolverine) app. 53-Spider-Man-c/story. 58-X-Men (Wolverine, Gambit, Cyclops, etc.)-c/story. 61-Phoenix returns. 68-Starjammers-c/story 3.00
50-($2.75, 56 pgs.)-New logo 4.00
71-($3.95, 52 pgs.)-Hologram on-c; 30th anniversary 5.00
75-($3.50, 52 pgs.)-Holo-grafx foil-c 5.00
75-($2.25, 52 pgs.)-Regular edition 4.00
77-81,83-86: 77-Begin $1.95-c; bound-in trading card sheet. 83-86-Deluxe Editions and Standard Editions. 86-1st app. Pete Wisdom 3.00
82-($2.50)-Newsstand edition 4.00
82-($3.50)-Enhanced edition 5.00
87-89,91-99,101-110: 87-Return from Age of Apocalypse. 92-Colossus-c/app. 94-Days of Future Tense 95-X-Man-c/app. 96-Sebastian Shaw & the Hellfire Club app. 99-Onslaught app. 101-Onslaught tie-in. 102-w/card insert. 103-Last Warren Ellis scripts; Belasco app. 104,105-Hitch & Neary-c/a. 109-Spiral-c/app. 3.00
90,100-($2.95)-double-sized. 100-Onslaught tie-in; wraparound-c 4.00
111-124: 111-Begin $1.99-c, wraparound-c. 119-Calafiore-a 3.00
125-($2.99) Wedding of Capt. Britain and Meggan 4.00
Annual 1,2 ('93, '94, 68 pgs.)-1st app. Khaos. 2-X-Men & Psylocke app. 4.00
#(-1) Flashback (7/97) 3.00
...Air Apparent nn (12/91, $4.95)-Simonson-c 6.00
...Mojo Mayhem nn (12/89, $4.50)-Art Adams/Austin-c/a 6.00
...: The Possession nn (7/91, $2.95, 52 pgs.) 4.00
...: XX Crossing (7/92, 5/92-inside, $2.50)-vs. The X-Men 4.00
...Classic Vol. 1: The Sword is Drawn TPB (2005, $19.99) r/#1-5 & Special Edition nn (The Sword is Drawn) 20.00
...Classic Vol. 2: Two-Edged Sword TPB (2006, $24.99) r/#6-11 25.00
...Classic Vol. 3: Cross-Time Caper Book 1 TPB (2007, $24.99) r/#12-20 25.00
...Classic Vol. 4: Cross-Time Caper Book 2 TPB (2007, $24.99) r/#21-28 25.00
...Classic Vol. 5 TPB (2008, $24.99) r/#29-34 & Marvel GN Excalibur: Weird War III 25.00

EXCALIBUR
Marvel Comics: Feb, 2001 - No. 4, May, 2001 ($2.99)
1-4-Return of Captain Britain; Raimondi-a 3.00

EXCALIBUR (X-Men Reloaded title) (Leads into House of M series, then New Excalibur)
Marvel Comics: July, 2004 - No. 14, July, 2005 ($2.99)
1-14: 1-Claremont-s/Lopresti-a/Park-c; Magneto returns. 6-11-Beast app. 13,14-Prelude to House of M; Dr. Strange app. 3.00
House of M Prelude: Excalibur TPB (2005, $11.99) r/#11-14 12.00
... Vol. 1: Forging the Sword (2004, $9.99) r/#1-4 10.00
... Vol. 2: Saturday Night Fever (2005, $14.99) r/#5-10 15.00

EXCALIBUR (Follows from House of X & Powers of X series)
Marvel Comics: Dec, 2019 - No. 26, Feb, 2022 ($4.99/$3.99)
1-($4.99) Tini Howard-s/Marcus To-a; Betsy Braddock, Rogue, Gambit, Jubilee app. 5.00
2-26-($3.99): 10,11-Kitty Pryde app. 12-15-"X of Swords" tie-ins. 21-Hellfire Gala 4.00

EXCELLENCE
Image Comics (Skybound): May, 2019 - Present ($3.99)
1-12-Brandon Thomas-s/Khary Randolph-a 4.00

EXCITING COMICS
Nedor/Better Publications/Standard Comics: Apr, 1940 - No. 69, Sept, 1949
1-Origin & 1st app. The Mask, Jim Hatfield, Sgt. Bill King, Dan Williams begin; early Robot-c (see Smash #1) 514 1028 1542 3750 6625 9500
2-The Sphinx begins; The Masked Rider app.; Son of the Gods begins, ends #8
258 516 774 1651 2826 4000
3-Classic Science Fiction Robot-c 290 580 870 1856 3178 4500
4-6: All have Sci-Fi covers by Max Plaisted 206 412 618 1318 2259 3200
7,8-Schomburg jungle covers 161 322 483 1030 1765 2500
9-Origin/1st app. of The Black Terror & sidekick Tim, begin series (5/41)
(Black Terror c-9-21,23-52,54,55) 1700 3400 5100 12,700 23,850 35,000
10-2nd app. Black Terror (6/41) 411 822 1233 2877 5039 7200
11-3rd app. Black Terror (7/41) 258 516 774 1651 2826 4000
12,13-Bondage covers 194 388 582 1242 2121 3000
14-Last Sphinx, Dan Williams 158 316 474 1003 1727 2450
15-The Liberator begins (origin); WWII-c 200 400 600 1280 2190 3100
16,19,20: 20-The Mask ends 132 264 396 838 1444 2050
17,18-WWII-c 158 316 474 1003 1727 2450
21,23,24 106 212 318 673 1162 1650
22-Origin The Eaglet; The American Eagle begins 142 284 426 909 1555 2200
25-Robot-c 226 452 678 1446 2473 3500
26-Schomburg-c begin; Nazi WWII-c 232 464 696 1485 2543 3600
27,30-Japanese WWII-c 213 426 639 1363 2332 3300
28-(Scarce) Crime Crusader begins, ends #58; Nazi WWII-c
925 1850 2775 5550 9275 13,000
29-Nazi WWII-c 226 452 678 1446 2473 3500
31,35,36-Japanese WWII-c. 35-Liberator ends, not in 31-33
177 354 531 1124 1937 2750
32-34,37-Nazi WWII-c 177 354 531 1124 1937 2750
38 Gangster-c 126 252 378 806 1378 1950
39-WWII-c; Nazis giving poison candy to kids on cover; origin Kara, Jungle Princess
1440 2880 4320 9000 13,500 18,000
40,41-Last WWII covers in this title; Japanese WWII-c
171 342 513 1086 1868 2650
42-50: 42-The Scarab begins. 45-Schomburg Robot-c. 49-Last Kara, Jungle Princess. 50-Last American Eagle 93 186 279 591 1021 1450
51-Miss Masque begins (1st app.) 129 258 387 826 1413 2000

GD VG FN VF VF/NM NM-
2.0 4.0 6.0 8.0 9.0 9.2

52,54: 54-Miss Masque ends 87 174 261 553 952 1350
53-Miss Masque-c 284 568 852 1818 3109 4400
55-58: 55-Judy of the Jungle begins (origin), ends #69; 1 pg. Ingels-a; Judy of the Jungle c-56-66. 57,58-Airbrush-c 87 174 261 553 952 1350
59-Frazetta art in Caniff style; signed Frank Frazeta (one t), 9 pgs. 103 206 309 659 1130 1600
60-66: 60-Rick Howard, the Mystery Rider begins. 66-Robinson/Meskin-a 77 154 231 493 847 1200
67-69-All western covers 30 60 90 177 289 400

NOTE: ***Schomburg (Xela)** c-26-68; airbrush c-57-66. Black Terror by **R. Moreira**-#65. **Roussos** a-62. Bondage-c 9, 12, 13, 20, 23, 25, 30, 59.*

EXCITING ROMANCES
Fawcett Publications: 1949 (nd); No. 2, Spring, 1950 - No. 5, 10/50; No. 6 (1951, nd); No. 7, 9/51 -No. 12, 1/53 (Photo-c on #1-3)

1,3: 1(1949). 3-Wood-a 16 32 48 94 147 200
2,4,5-(1950) 12 24 36 67 94 120
6-12 10 20 30 54 72 90

NOTE: ***Powell** a-8-10. **Marcus Swayze** a-5, 6, 9. Photo c-1-7, 10-12.*

EXCITING ROMANCE STORIES (See Fox Giants)

EXCITING WAR (Korean War)
Standard Comics (Better Publ.): No. 5, Sept, 1952 - No. 8, May, 1953; No. 9, Nov, 1953

5 37 74 111 222 361 500
6-Flame thrower/burning body-c 65 130 195 416 708 1000
7,9 22 44 66 132 216 300
8-Toth-a 37 74 111 222 361 500

EXCITING X-PATROL
Marvel Comics (Amalgam): June, 1997 ($1.95, one-shot)

1-Barbara Kesel-s/Bryan Hitch-a 4.00

EX-CON
Dynamite Entertainment: 2014 - No. 5, 2015 ($2.99, limited series)

1-5-Swierczynski-s/Burns-a/Bradstreet-c 3.00

EXECUTIONER, THE (Don Pendleton's...)
IDW Publishing: Apr, 2008 - No. 5, Aug, 2008 ($3.99)

1-5-Mack Bolan origin re-told; Gallant-a/Wojtowicz-s 4.00

EXECUTIVE ASSISTANT: ASSASSINS
Aspen MLT: Jul, 2012 - No. 18, Feb, 2014 ($3.99)

1-18: 1-Five covers; Hernandez-s/Gunderson-a 4.00

EXECUTIVE ASSISTANT: IRIS (Also see All New Executive Assistant: Iris)
Aspen MLT: No. 0, Apr, 2009 - No. 6, Nov, 2010 ($2.50/$2.99)

0-($2.50) Wohl-s/Francisco-a; 3 covers 3.00
1-6-($2.99) Multiple covers on each 3.00
Annual 2015 (3/15, $5.99) Three stories by various; Benitez-c 6.00
... Sourcebook 1 (1/16, $4.99) Character profiles & storyline summaries 5.00

EXECUTIVE ASSISTANT: IRIS (Volume 2) (The Hit List Agenda x-over)
Aspen MLT: No. 0, Jul, 2011 - No. 5, Dec, 2011 ($2.50/$2.99/$3.50)

0-($2.50) Wohl-s/Francisco-a; sketch page art; 3 covers 3.00
1-4-($2.99) Multiple covers on each. 1-Francisco-a. 2-4-Odagawa-a 3.00
5-($3.50) Odagawa-a 3.50

EXECUTIVE ASSISTANT: IRIS (Volume 3) (See All New Executive Assistant: Iris for Vol. 4)
Aspen MLT: Dec, 2012 - No. 5, Sept, 2013 ($3.99)

1-5-Multiple covers on each. 1-Wohl-s/Lei-a 4.00

EXECUTIVE ASSISTANT: IRIS (Volume 5)
Aspen MLT: May, 2018 - No. 5, Sept, 2018 ($3.99)

1-5-Multiple covers on each. 1-Northcott-s/Tran-a 4.00
... Primer 1 (5/18, 25¢) Origin re-told; recaps of previous volumes 3.00

EXECUTIVE ASSISTANT: LOTUS (The Hit List Agenda x-over)
Aspen MLT: Aug, 2011 - No. 3, Oct, 2011 ($2.99, limited series)

1-3-Multiple covers on each. Hernandez-s/Nome-a 3.00

EXECUTIVE ASSISTANT: ORCHID (The Hit List Agenda x-over)
Aspen MLT: Aug, 2011 - No. 3, Oct, 2011 ($2.99, limited series)

1-3: 1-Lobdell-s/Gunnell-a; multiple covers 3.00

EXECUTIVE ASSISTANT: VIOLET (The Hit List Agenda x-over)
Aspen MLT: Aug, 2011 - No. 3, Oct, 2011 ($2.99, limited series)

1-3: 1-Andreyko-s/Mhan-a; multiple covers 3.00

EXILED (Part 1 of x-over with Journey Into Mystery #637,638 & New Mutants #42,43)
Marvel Comics: July, 2012 ($2.99, one-shot)

1-Thor, Loki and New Mutants app.; DiGiandomenico-a 3.00

EXILED, THE
Whatnot Publishing: Feb, 2023 ($3.99)

1-Story by Wesley Snipes, Adam Lawson & Keith Arem; Gabriel Santos-a 4.00

EXILE ON THE PLANET OF THE APES
BOOM! Studios: Mar, 2012 - No. 4 ($3.99, limited series)

1-3-Bechko & Hardman-s/Laming-a 4.00

EXILES (Also see Break-Thru)
Malibu Comics (Ultraverse): Aug, 1993 - No. 4, Nov, 1993 ($1.95)

1,2,4: 1,2-Bagged copies of each exist. 4-Team dies; story cont'd in Break-Thru #1 3.00
3-($2.50, 40 pgs.)-Rune flip-c/story by B. Smith (3 pgs.) 4.00
1-Holographic-c edition 5.00

EXILES (All New, The) (2nd Series) (Also see Black September)
Malibu Comics (Ultraverse): Sept, 1995 - V2#11, Aug, 1996 ($1.50)

Infinity (9/95, $1.50)-Intro new team including Marvel's Juggernaut & Reaper 3.00
Infinity (2000 signed), V2#1 (2000 signed) 1 3 4 6 8 10
V2 #1-(10/95, 64 pgs.)-Reprint of Ultraforce V2#1 follows lead story 4.00
V2#2-4,6-11: 2-1st app. Hellblade. 8-Intro Maxis. 11-Vs. Maxis; Ripfire app.; cont'd in Ultraforce #12 3.00

GD VG FN VF VF/NM NM-
2.0 4.0 6.0 8.0 9.0 9.2

V2#5-($2.50) Juggernaut returns to the Marvel Universe. 4.00

EXILES (Also see X-Men titles) (Leads into New Exiles series)
Marvel Comics: Aug, 2001 - No. 100, Feb, 2008 ($2.99/$2.25)

1-($2.99) Blink and parallel world X-Men; Winick-s/McKone & McKenna-a 2 4 6 10 14 18
2-10-($2.25) 2-Two covers (McKone & JH Williams III). 5-Alpha Flight app. 4.00
11-24: 22-Blink leaves; Magik joins. 23,24-Walker-a; alternate Weapon-X app. 3.00
25-99: 25-Begin $2.99-c; Inhumans app.; Walker-a. 26-30-Austen-s. 33-Wolverine app. 35-37-Fantastic Four app. 37-Sunfire dies, Blink returns. 38-40-Hyperion app. 69-71-House of M. 77,78-Squadron Supreme app. 85,86-Multiple Wolverines. 90-Claremont-s begin; Psylocke app. 97-Shadowcat joins 3.00
100-($3.99) Last issue; Blink leaves; continues in Exiles (Days of Then and Now); r/#1 4.00
Annual 1 (2/07, $3.99) Bedard-s/Raney-a/c 4.00
Exiles #1 (Days of Then and Now) (3/08, $3.99) short stories by various 4.00

EXILES
Marvel Comics: Jun, 2009 - No. 6, Nov, 2009 ($2.99/$3.99)

1,6-($3.99) Blink and parallel world Scarlet Witch, Beast and others; Bullock-c 4.00
2-5-($2.99) 3.00

EXILES
Marvel Comics: Jun, 2018 - No. 12, Mar, 2019 ($3.99)

1,4-12-Blink and parallel world Ms. Marvel, Iron Lad, Valkyrie & Wolvie; Nick Fury app. 4-The Thing & Falcon app. 8-Quinones-a 4.00
2-Intro Tessa Thompson 2 4 6 10 14 18
3-Intro Peggy Carter (Captain America) 4 8 12 23 37 50

EXILES VS. THE X-MEN (Titled All-New Exiles vs. X-Men on cover)
Malibu Comics (Ultraverse): Oct, 1995 (one-shot)

0-Limited Super Premium Edition; signed w/certificate; gold foil logo,
0-Limited Premium Edition 1 3 4 6 8 10

EXIT STAGE LEFT: THE SNAGGLEPUSS CHRONICLES
DC Comics: Mar, 2018 - No. 6, Aug, 2018 ($3.99)

1-6-Russell-s/Feehan-a; Snagglepuss as a 1950s playwright; Huckleberry Hound app. 4.00

EX MACHINA
DC Comics: Aug, 2004 - No. 50, Sept, 2010 ($2.95/$2.99)

1-Intro. Mitchell Hundred; Vaughan-s/Harris-a/c 4.00
1-Special Edition (6/10, $1.00) Reprints #1 with "What's Next?" logo on cover 3.00
2-49: 12-Intro. Automaton. 33-Mitchell meets the Pope 3.00
50-($4.99) Wraparound-c 5.00
...: The Deluxe Edition Book One HC (2008, $29.99, dustjacket) r/#1-11; Vaughan's original proposal, Harris sketch pages; Brad Meltzer intro. 30.00
...: The Deluxe Edition Book Two HC (2009, $29.99, dustjacket) r/#12-20; Special #1,2; script and pencil art for #20; Wachowski Bros. intro. 30.00
...: The Deluxe Edition Book Three HC (2010, $29.99, dustjacket) r/#21-29; Special #3 and Ex Machina: Inside the Machine 30.00
...: The Deluxe Edition Book Four HC (2010, $29.99, dustjacket) r/#30-40; cover gallery 30.00
...: The Deluxe Edition Book Five HC (2011, $29.99, dustjacket) r/#41-50; Special #4 30.00
...: Inside the Machine (4/07, $2.99) script pages and Harris art and cover process 3.00
...: Masquerade Special (#3) (10/07, $3.50) John Paul Leon-a; Harris-c 3.50
... Special 1,2 (6/06 - No. 2, 8/06, $2.99) Sprouse-a; flashback to the Great Machine 3.00
... Special 4 (5/09, $3.99) Leon-a; Great Machine flashback; covers by Harris & Leon 4.00
...: Dirty Tricks TPB (2009, $12.99) r/#35-39 and Masquerade Special #3 13.00
...: Ex Cathedra TPB (2008, $12.99) r/#30-34 13.00
...: March To War TPB (2006, $12.99) r/#17-20 and Special #1,2 13.00
...: Power Down TPB (2008, $12.99) r/#26-29 & ...: Inside the Machine 13.00
...: Ring Out the Old TPB (2010, $14.99) r/#40-44 and Special #4 15.00
...: Smoke Smoke TPB (2007, $12.99) r/#21-25 13.00
...: The First Hundred Days TPB ('05, $9.95) r/#1-5; photo reference and sketch pages 10.00
...: Tag TPB (2005, $12.99) r/#6-10; Harris sketch pages 13.00
...: Term Limits TPB (2010, $14.99) r/#45-50 15.00

EX-MUTANTS
Malibu Comics: Nov, 1992 - No. 18, Apr, 1994 ($1.95/$2.25/$2.50)

1-18: 1-Polybagged w/Skycap; prismatic cover 4.00

EXORCISTS (See The Crusaders)

EXORSISTERS
Image Comics: Oct, 2018 - Present ($3.99)

1-6-Ian Boothby-s/Gisele Lagacé-a. 1-Four covers. 2-6-Two covers 4.00

EXOSQUAD (TV)
Topps Comics: No. 0, Jan, 1994 ($1.00)

0-($1.00, 20 pgs.)-1st app.; Staton-a(p); wraparound-c 3.00

EXOTIC ROMANCES (Formerly True War Romances)
Quality Comics Group (Comic Magazines): No. 22, Oct, 1955 - No. 31, Nov, 1956

22 19 38 57 111 176 240
23-26,29 14 28 42 81 118 155
27,31-Baker-c/a 30 60 90 177 289 400
28,30-Baker-a 22 44 66 128 209 290

EXPANSE, THE (Based on the books of James S.A. Corey)
BOOM! Studios: Dec, 2020 - No. 4, Mar, 2021 ($3.99, limited series)

1-4-Bechko-s/Aragon-a 4.00

EXPENDABLES, THE (Movie)
Dynamite Entertainment: 2010 - No. 4, 2010 ($3.99, limited series)

1-4-Chuck Dixon-s/Esteve Polls-a/Lucio Parrillo-c; prelude to the 2010 movie 4.00

EXPLOITS OF DANIEL BOONE
Quality Comics Group: Nov, 1955 - No. 6, Oct, 1956

1-All have Cuidera-c(i) 20 40 60 118 192 265
2 (1/56) 14 28 42 82 121 160
3-6 13 26 39 74 105 135

EXPLOITS OF DICK TRACY (See Dick Tracy)

EXPLORER JOE

Exiles (2018) #1 © MAR

Extraordinary X-Men #8 © MAR

Fables #70 © B. Willingham & DC

	GD	VG	FN	VF	VF/NM	NM-
	2.0	4.0	6.0	8.0	9.0	9.2

Ziff-Davis Comic Group (Approved Comics): Win, 1951 - No. 2, Oct-Nov, 1952

1-Saunders painted cover	30	60	90	177	289	400
2-Krigstein-a; Saunders painted cover	18	36	54	105	165	225

EXPLORERS OF THE UNKNOWN (See Archie Giant Series #587, 599)
Archie Comics: June, 1990 - No. 6, Apr, 1991 ($1.00)

1-6: Featuring Archie and the gang 4.00

EXPOSED (...True Crime Cases; ...Cases in the Crusade Against Crime #5-9)
D. S. Publishing Co.: Mar-Apr, 1948 - No. 9, July-Aug, 1949

1	258	516	774	1651	2826	4000
2-Giggling killer story with excessive blood; two injury-to-eye panels; electrocution panel	48	96	144	302	514	725
3,8,9	21	42	63	122	199	275
4-Orlando-a	22	44	66	128	209	290
5-Breeze Lawson, Sky Sheriff by E. Good	22	44	66	128	209	290
6,7: 6-Ingels-a; used in **SOTI**, illo. "How to prepare an alibi" 7-Illo. in **SOTI**, "Diagram for housebreakers;" used by N.Y. Legis. Committee	50	100	150	315	533	750

EXTERMINATION
BOOM! Studios: Jun, 2012 - No. 8, Jan, 2013 ($1.00/$3.99)

1-($1.00) Nine covers; Spurrier-s/Jeffrey Edwards-a 4.00
2-8-($3.99) 4.00

EXTERMINATION
Marvel Comics: Oct, 2018 - No. 5, Feb, 2019 ($4.99, limited series)

1-($4.99)-Brisson-s/Larraz-a; the original five X-Men and Cable app.; Bloodstorm killed 5.00
2-4-($3.99) 4.00
5-($4.99) Brisson-s/Larraz-a; original X-Men return to their past 5.00

EXTERMINATORS, THE
DC Comics (Vertigo): Mar, 2006 - No. 30, Aug, 2008 ($2.99)

1-30: Simon Oliver-s/Tony Moore-a in most. 11,12-Hawthorne-a 3.00
...: Bug Brothers TPB (2006, $9.99) r/#1-5; intro. by screenwriter Josh Olson 10.00
...: Bug Brothers Forever TPB (2008, $14.99) r/#24-30; intro. by Simon Oliver 15.00
...: Crossfire and Collateral TPB (2008, $14.99) r/#17-23 15.00
...: Insurgency TPB (2007, $12.99) r/#6-10 13.00
...: Lies of Our Fathers TPB (2007, $14.99) r/#11-16 15.00

EXTINCT!
New England Comics Press: Wint, 1991-92 - No. 2, Fall, 1992 ($3.50, B&W)

1,2-Reprints and background info of "perfectly awful" Golden Age stories 4.00

EXTINCTION EVENT
DC Comics (WildStorm): Sept, 2003 - No. 5, Jan, 2004 ($2.50, limited series)

1-5-Booth-a/Weinberg-s 3.00

EXTRA!
E. C. Comics: Mar-Apr, 1955 - No. 5, Nov-Dec, 1955

1-Not code approved	27	54	81	216	346	475
2-5: 3-1st EC Picto-Fiction story	17	34	51	136	213	290

NOTE: ***Craig, Crandall, Severin*** *art in all.*

EXTRA!
Gemstone Publishing: Jan, 2000 - No. 5, May, 2000 ($2.50)

1-5-Reprints E.C. series 4.00

EXTRA COMICS
Magazine Enterprises: 1948 (25¢, 3 comics in one)

1-Giant; consisting of rebound ME comics. Two versions known; (1)-Funnyman by Siegel & Shuster, Space Ace, Undercover Girl, Red Fox by L.B. Cole, Trail Colt & (2)-All Funnyman	84	168	252	538	919	1300

EXTRAORDINARY X-MEN
Marvel Comics: Jan, 2016 - No. 20, May, 2017 ($4.99/$3.99)

1-($4.99) Team of Old Man Logan, Storm, Jean Grey & others; Lemire-s/Ramos-a 5.00
2-7,9-20-($3.99) 2-Mister Sinister returns. 6,7,13-16-Ibanez-a. 9-12-Apocalypse Wars 4.00
8-($4.99) Apocalypse Wars x-over; Ramos-a; back-up story with Doctor Strange 5.00
Annual 1 (11/16, $4.99) Masters-s/Barberi-a; Montclare-s/Kämpe-a; Moon Girl app. 5.00

EXTREME
Image Comics (Extreme Studios): Aug, 1993 (Giveaway)

0 3.00

EXTREME CARNAGE
Marvel Comics: Sept, 2021 - Nov, 2021 ($4.99/$3.99, 8-part series)

...: Agony 1 (11/21, $3.99) Part 7; Wong-s/Galán-a 4.00
... Alpha 1 (9/21, $4.99) Part 1; P.K. Johnson-s/Garcia-a; Flash Thompson app. 5.00
...: Lasher 1 (10/21, $3.99) Part 4; Chapman-s/Mooneyham-a 4.00
... Omega 1 (11/21, $4.99) Part 8; P.K. Johnson-s/Garcia-a 5.00
...: Phage 1 (9/21, $3.99) Part 3; Orlando-s/Sandoval-a 4.00
...: Riot 1 (10/21, $3.99) Part 5; Wong-s/Galán-a 4.00
...: Scream 1 (9/21, $3.99) Part 2; Chapman-s/Mooneyham-a 4.00
...: Toxin 1 (11/21, $3.99) Part 6; Orlando-s/Sandoval-a 4.00

EXTREME DESTROYER
Image Comics (Extreme Studios): Jan, 1996 ($2.50)

Prologue 1-Polybagged w/card; Liefeld-c, Epilogue 1-Liefeld-c 3.00

EXTREME JUSTICE
DC Comics: No. 0, Jan, 1995 - No. 18, July, 1996 ($1.50/$1.75)

0-18 3.00

EXTREMELY YOUNGBLOOD
Image Comics (Extreme Studios): Sept, 1996 ($3.50, one-shot)

1 3.50

EXTREME SACRIFICE
Image Comics (Extreme Studios): Jan, 1995 ($2.50, limited series)

Prelude (#1)-Liefeld wraparound-c; polybagged w/ trading card 3.00
Epilogue (#2)-Liefeld wraparound-c; polybagged w/trading card 3.00
Trade paperback (6/95, $16.95)-Platt-a 17.00

EXTREME SUPER CHRISTMAS SPECIAL
Image Comics (Extreme Studios): Dec, 1994 ($2.95, one-shot)

1 3.00

EXTREMIST, THE
DC Comics (Vertigo): Sept, 1993 - No. 4, Dec, 1993 ($1.95, limited series)

1-4-Peter Milligan scripts; McKeever-c/a 3.00
1-Platinum Edition 5.00

EYE OF NEWT
Dark Horse Comics: Jun, 2014 - No. 4, Sept, 2014 ($3.99, limited series)

1-4-Michael Hague-s/a/c 4.00

EYE OF THE STORM
DC Comics (WildStorm): Sept, 2003 ($4.95)

Annual 1-Short stories by various incl. Portacio, Johns, Coker, Pearson, Arcudi 5.00

FABLES
DC Comics (Vertigo): July, 2002 - No. 149, Apr, 2015; No. 151, Jul, 2022 - Present ($2.50/$2.75/$2.99/$3.99)

1-Willingham-s/Medina-a; two covers by Maleev & Jean 65.00
1: Special Edition (12/06, 25¢) r/#1 with preview of 1001 Nights of Snowfall 3.00
1: Special Edition (9/09, $1.00) r/#1 with preview of Peter & Max 3.00
1-Special Edition (8/10, $1.00) Reprints #1 with "What's Next?" logo on cover 3.00
1-Special Edition (3/16, $3.99) Reprints #1 with new cover by Dave McKean 4.00
2-Medina-a 15.00
3-5 10.00
6-37: 6-10-Buckingham-a. 11-Talbot-a. 18-Medley-a. 26-Preview of The Witching 5.00
6-RRP Edition wraparound variant-c; promotional giveaway for retailers (200 printed) 215.00
38-49,51-74,76-99,101-149: 38-Begin $2.75-c. 49-Begin $2.99-c. 57,58,76-Allred-a. 83-85-X-over with Jack of Fables & The Literals. 101-Shanower-a. 107-Terry Moore-a 113-Back-up art by Russell, Cannon, Hughes. 147-Terry Moore-a (3 pgs.) 3.00
50-($3.99) Wedding of Snow White and Bigby Wolf; preview of Jack of Fables series 5.00
75-($4.99) Geppetto surrenders; pin-up gallery by Powell, Nowlan, Cooke & others 5.00
100-(1/11, $9.99, squarebound) Buckingham-a; short stories art by Hughes & others 10.00
(#150) Fables: Farewell (2015, $17.99) Main story with Buckingham-a; numerous short stories with art by various incl. Neal Adams, Allred, Leialoha, Medina, Dodson 18.00
151-157: 151-(7/22, $3.99) Buckingham-a 4.00
Animal Farm (2003, $12.95, TPB) r/#6-10; sketch pages by Buckingham & Jean 13.00
...: Arabian Nights (And Days) (2006, $14.99, TPB) r/#42-47 15.00
...: Homelands (2005, $14.99, TPB) r/#34-41 15.00
Legends in Exile (2002, $9.95, TPB) r/#1-5; new short story Willingham-s/a 15.00
...: March of the Wooden Soldiers (2004, $17.95, TPB) r/#19-21 & ...: The Last Castle 18.00
...: 1001 Nights of Snowfall HC (2006, $19.99) short stories by Willingham with art by various incl. Bolton, Kaluta, Jean, McPherson, Thompson, Vess, Wheatley, Buckingham 20.00
...: 1001 Nights of Snowfall (2008, $14.99, TPB) short stories with art by various 15.00
...: Rose Red (2011, $17.99, TPB) r/#94-100; Buckingham design and sketch pages 18.00
...: Sons of Empire (2007, $17.99, TPB) r/#52-59 18.00
...: Storybook Love (2004, $14.95, TPB) r/#11-18 15.00
...: The Dark Ages (2009, $17.99, TPB) r/#76-82 18.00
...: The Deluxe Edition Book One HC (2009, $29.99, DJ) r/#1-10; character sketch-a 30.00
...: The Deluxe Edition Book Two HC (2010, $29.99, DJ) r/#11-18 & ...: The Last Castle 30.00
...: The Good Prince (2008, $17.99, TPB) r/#60-69 18.00
...: The Great Fables Crossover (2010, $17.99, TPB) r/#83-85, Jack of Fables #33-35 and

	GD 2.0	VG 4.0	FN 6.0	VF 8.0	VF/NM 9.0	NM- 9.2

The Literals #1-3; sneak preview of Peter & Max: A Fables Novel 18.00
...: The Last Castle (2003, $5.95) Hamilton-a/Willingham-s; prequel to title 6.00
...: The Mean Seasons (2005, $14.99, TPB) r/#22,28-33 15.00
...: War and Pieces (2008, $17.99, TPB) r/#70-75; sketch and pin-up pages 18.00
...: Witches (2010, $17.99, TPB) r/#86-93 18.00
...: Wolves (2006, $17.99, TPB) r/#48-51; script to #50 18.00

FABLES: THE WOLF AMONG US (Based on the Telltale Games video game)
DC Comics (Vertigo): Mar, 2015 - No. 16, Jun, 2016 ($3.99, printing of digital first stories)
1-16-Prequel to Fables; Sturges & Justus-s 4.00

FACE, THE (Tony Trent, the Face No. 3 on) (See Big Shot Comics)
Columbia Comics Group: 1941 - No. 2, 1943
1-The Face; Mart Bailey WWII-c 110 220 330 704 1202 1700
2-Bailey WWII-c 74 148 222 470 810 1150

FACES OF EVIL
DC Comics: Mar, 2009 ($2.99, series of one-shots)
...: Deathstroke 1 - Jeanty-a/Ladronn-c; Ravager app. 3.00
...: Kobra 1 - Jason Burr returns; Julian Lopez-a 3.00
...: Prometheus 1 - Gates-s/Dallacchio-a; origin re-told; Anima killed 3.00
...: Solomon Grundy 1 - Johns-s/Kolins-a; leads into Solomon Grundy mini-series 3.00

FACTOR X
Marvel Comics: Mar, 1995 - No. 4, July, 1995 ($1.95, limited series)
1-Age of Apocalypse 5.00
2-4 4.00

FACULTY FUNNIES
Archie Comics: June, 1989 - No. 5, May, 1990 (75¢/95¢ #2 on)
1-5: 1,2,4,5-The Awesome Foursome app. 3.00

FADE FROM GRACE
Beckett Comics: Aug, 2004 - No. 5, Mar, 2005 (99¢/$1.99)
1-(99¢) Jeff Amano-a/c; Gabriel Benson-s; origin of Fade 3.00
2-5-($1.99) 3.00
TPB (2005, $14.99) r/#1-5; cover gallery, afterword by David Mack 15.00

FADE OUT, THE
Image Comics: Aug, 2014 - No. 12, Jan, 2016 ($3.50/$3.99)
1-12-Ed Brubaker-s/Sean Phillips-a/c. 12-($3.99) 4.00

FAFHRD AND THE GREY MOUSER (Also see Sword of Sorcery & Wonder Woman #202)
Marvel Comics: Oct, 1990 - No. 4, 1991 ($4.50, 52 pgs., squarebound)
1-4: Mignola/Williamson-a; Chaykin scripts 5.00

FAGIN THE JEW
Doubleday: Oct, 2003 ($15.95, softcover graphic novel)
nn-Will Eisner-s/a; story of Fagin from Dickens' Oliver Twist 16.00

FAIREST (Characters from Fables)
DC Comics (Vertigo): May, 2012 - No. 33, Mar, 2015 ($2.99)
1-33: 1-6-Willingham-s/Jimenez-a. 1-Wraparound-c by Hughes & variant-c by Jimenez 3.00
...: In All The Land HC (2013, $24.99, dustjacket) New short stories by various; Hughes-c 25.00

FAIRLADY
Image Comics: Apr, 2019 - No. 5, Aug, 2019 ($3.99)
1-5-Brian Schirmer-s/Claudio Balboni-a 4.00

FAIRY QUEST: OUTCASTS
BOOM! Studios: Nov, 2014 - No. 2, Dec, 2014 ($3.99, limited series)
1,2-Jenkins-s/Ramos-a/c 4.00

FAIRY QUEST: OUTLAWS
BOOM! Studios: Feb, 2013 - No. 2, Mar, 2013 ($3.99, limited series)
1,2-Jenkins-s/Ramos-a/c 4.00

FAIRY TALE PARADE (See Famous Fairy Tales)
Dell Publishing Co.: June-July, 1942 - No. 121, Oct, 1946 (Most by Walt Kelly)
1-Kelly-a begins 86 172 258 688 1544 2400
2(8-9/42) 38 76 114 285 641 1000
3-5 (10-11/42 - 2-4/43) 29 58 87 196 441 685
6-9 (5-7/43 - 11-1/43-44) 22 44 66 154 340 525
Four Color 50('44), 69('45), 87('45) 21 42 63 147 324 500
Four Color 104, 114('46)-Last Kelly issue 16 32 48 112 249 385
Four Color 121('46)-Not by Kelly 10 20 30 69 147 225
NOTE: *#1-9, 4-Color #50, 69 have* ***Kelly*** *c/a; 4-Color #87, 104, 114-***Kelly*** *art only. #9 has a redrawn version of The Reluctant Dragon. This series contains all the classic fairy tales from Jack In The Beanstalk to Cinderella.*

FAIRY TALES
Ziff-Davis Publ. Co. (Approved Comics): No. 10, Apr-May, 1951 - No. 11, June-July, 1951
10,11-Painted-c 24 48 72 142 234 325

FAITH
DC Comics (Vertigo): Nov, 1999 - No. 5, Mar, 2000 ($2.50, limited series)
1-5-Ted McKeever-s/c/a 3.00

FAITH (Zephyr from Harbinger)
Valiant Entertainment: Jan, 2016 - No. 4, Apr, 2016 ($3.99, limited series)
1-4-Houser-s/Portela-a. 3,4-Torque app. 4.00

FAITH (Harbinger)
Valiant Entertainment: Jul, 2016 - No. 12, Jun, 2017 ($3.99)
1-12: 1-4-Houser-s/Pere Pérez-a. 5-Hillary Clinton app. 7-12-Eisma-a 4.00
Faith's Winter Wonderland Special 1 (12/17, $3.99) Sauvage-s/Portela & Kim-a 4.00

FAITH AND THE FUTURE FORCE (Harbinger)
Valiant Entertainment: Jul, 2017 - No. 4, Oct, 2017 ($3.99, limited series)
1-4-Houser-s. 1-Segovia & Kitson-a. 2-Kitson & Bernard-a. 3-Most Valiant heroes app. 4.00

FAITH DREAMSIDE (Harbinger)
Valiant Entertainment: Sept, 2018 - No. 4, Jan, 2019 ($3.99, limited series)
1-4-Houser-s/MJ Kim-a; Doctor Mirage app. 4.00

FAITHFUL
Marvel Comics/Lovers' Magazine: Nov, 1949 - No. 2, Feb, 1950 (52 pgs.)
1-Photo-c 30 60 90 177 289 400
2-Photo-c 17 34 51 105 165 225

FAITHLESS (Also see Heartbeat)
BOOM! Studios: Apr, 2019 - No. 6, Sept, 2019 ($3.99, limited series)
1-6-Brian Azzarello-s/Maria Llovet-a 4.00

FAITHLESS II
BOOM! Studios: Jun, 2020 - No. 6, Nov, 2020 ($3.99, limited series)
1-6-Brian Azzarello-s/Maria Llovet-a 4.00

FAITHLESS III
BOOM! Studios: Feb, 2022 - No. 6, Jul, 2022 ($3.99, limited series)
1-6-Brian Azzarello-s/Maria Llovet-a 4.00

FAKER
DC Comics (Vertigo): Sept, 2007 - No. 6, Feb, 2008 ($2.99, limited series)
1-6-Mike Carey-s/Jock-a/c 3.00
TPB (2008, $14.99) r/#1-6; Jock sketch pages 15.00

FALCON (See Marvel Premiere #49, Avengers #181 & Captain America #117 & 133)
Marvel Comics Group: Nov, 1983 - No. 4, Feb, 1984 (Mini-series)
1-Paul Smith-c/a(p) 2 4 6 9 13 16
2-4: 2-Paul Smith-c/Mark Bright-a. 3-Kupperberg-c 6.00

FALCON (Marvel Legacy)
Marvel Comics: Dec, 2017 - No. 8, Jul, 2018 ($3.99)
1-8: 1-Sam Wilson back as the Falcon after Secret Empire; Barnes-s/Cassara-a. 6-8-Misty Knight app. 7,8-Blade app. 4.00

FALCON & WINTER SOLDIER
Marvel Comics: Apr, 2020 - No. 5, Jan, 2021 ($3.99, limited series)
1-5-Derek Landy-s/Federico Vicentini-a; intro. The Natural 4.00

FALL AND RISE OF CAPTAIN ATOM, THE
DC Comics: Mar, 2017 - No. 6, Aug, 2017 ($2.99, limited series)
1-6-Bates-s/Conrad-a 3.00

FALLEN ANGEL
DC Comics: Sept, 2003 - No. 20, July, 2005 ($2.50/$2.95)
1-9-Peter David-s/David Lopez-a/Stelfreeze-c; intro. Lee 3.00
10-20: 10-Begin $2.95-c. 13,17-Kaluta-c. 20-Last issue; Pérez-c 3.00
TPB (2004, $12.95) r/#1-6; intro. by Harlan Ellison 13.00
Down to Earth TPB (2007, $14.99) r/#7-12 15.00

FALLEN ANGEL
IDW Publ.: Dec, 2005 - No. 33, Dec, 2008 ($3.99)
1-33: 1-14-Peter David-s/J.K Woodward-a. Retailer variant-c for each. 15-Donaldson-a. 17-Flip cover with Shi story; Tucci-a. 25-Wraparound-c; character gallery 4.00
... Reborn 1-4 (7/09 - No. 4, 10/09, $3.99) David-s/Woodward-a; Illyria (from Angel) app. 4.00
... Return of the Son 1-4 (1/11 - No. 4, 4/11, $3.99) David-s/Woodward-a; 4.00
...: To Serve in Heaven TPB (8/06, $19.99) r/#1-5; gallery of reg & variant covers 20.00

FALLEN ANGEL ON THE WORLD OF MAGIC: THE GATHERING
Acclaim (Armada): May, 1996 ($5.95, one-shot)
1-Nancy Collins story 6.00

FALLEN ANGELS
Marvel Comics Group: April, 1987 - No. 8, Nov, 1987 (Limited series)
1-8 4.00

FALLEN ANGELS (Follows from House of X & Powers of X series)
Marvel Comics: Jan, 2020 - No. 6, Mar, 2020 ($4.99/$3.99, limited series)
1-($4.99) Bryan Hill-s/Szymon Kudranski-a; Psylocke, Magneto, Cable, X-23 app. 5.00
2-6-($3.99) 5,6-Bling! and Husk app. 4.00

FALLEN SON: THE DEATH OF CAPTAIN AMERICA
Marvel Comics: June, 2007 - No. 5, Aug, 2007 ($2.99, limited series)
1-5: Loeb-s in all. 1-Wolverine; Yu-a/c. 2-Avengers; McGuinness-a/c. 3-Captain America; Romita Jr.-a/c; Hawkeye app. 4-Spider-Man; Finch-c/a. 5-Cassaday-c/a 3.00
1-5-Variant covers by Turner 3.00
HC (2007, $19.99, dustjacket) r/#1-5 20.00
TPB (2008, $13.99) r/#1-5 14.00

FALLEN WORLD
Valiant Entertainment: May, 2019 - No. 5, Sept, 2019 ($3.99, limited series)
1-5-Abnett-s/Pollina-a; cyborg samurai Rai in New Japan in 4002 AD 4.00

FALLING IN LOVE
Arleigh Pub. Co./National Per. Pub.: Sept-Oct, 1955 - No. 143, Oct-Nov, 1973
1 54 108 162 343 574 825
2 30 60 90 177 289 400
3-10 20 40 60 114 182 250
11-20 15 30 45 90 140 190
21-40 14 28 42 80 115 150
41-47: 47-Last 10¢ issue 13 26 39 74 105 135
48-70 6 12 18 37 66 95
71-99,108: 108-Wood-a (4 pgs., 7/69) 4 8 12 28 47 65
100 (7/68) 5 10 15 30 50 70
101-107,109-124 3 6 9 19 30 40
125-133: 52 pgs. 4 8 12 25 40 55
134-143 3 6 9 15 22 28
NOTE: ***Colan*** *c/a-75, 81. 52 pgs.-#125-133.*

FALLING MAN, THE
Image Comics: Feb, 1998 ($2.95)
1-McCorkindale-s/Hester-a 3.00

FALL OF THE HOUSE OF USHER, THE (See A Corben Special & Spirit section 8/22/48)

FALL OF THE HULKS (Also see Hulk and Incredible Hulk)
Marvel Comics: Feb, 2010 - July, 2010 ($3.99, one-shots & limited series)

The Fade Out #4 © Basement Gang

Falcon & Winter Soldier #3 © MAR

Famous First Edition C-61 © DC

GD 2.0 | VG 4.0 | FN 6.0 | VF 8.0 | VF/NM 9.0 | NM- 9.2

Alpha (2/10) Pelletier-a; The Leader, Dr. Doom, MODOK and The Thinker app. 4.00
Gamma (2/10) Romita Jr. -a; funeral for General Ross 4.00
Red Hulk (3/10 - No. 4, 6/10) 1-4: 1-A-Bomb app. 4.00
Savage She-Hulks (5/10 - No. 3, 7/10) 1-3: Cover tryptich by Campbell; Espin-a 4.00

FALL OF THE ROMAN EMPIRE (See Movie Comics)

FALL OUT TOY WORKS
Image Comics: Sept, 2009 - No. 5, Jun, 2010 ($3.99)
1-5-Co-created by Pete Wentz of the band Fall Out Boy; Basri-a. 5-Lau-c 4.00

FAMILY AFFAIR (TV)
Gold Key: Feb, 1970 - No. 4, Oct, 1970 (25¢)
1-With pull-out poster; photo-c 5 10 15 34 60 85
1-With poster missing 3 6 9 17 26 35
2-4-Photo-c 3 6 9 20 31 42

FAMILY DYNAMIC, THE
DC Comics: Oct, 2008 - No. 3, Dec, 2008 ($2.25)
1-3-J. Torres-s/Tim Levins-a 3.00

FAMILY FUNNIES
Parents' Magazine Institute: No. 9, Aug-Sept, 1946
9 8 16 24 40 50 60

FAMILY FUNNIES (Tiny Tot Funnies No. 9)
Harvey Publications: Sept, 1950 - No. 8, Apr, 1951
1-Mandrake (has over 30 King Feature strips) 12 24 36 67 94 125
2-Flash Gordon, 1 pg. 8 16 24 44 57 70
3-8: 4,5,7-Flash Gordon, 1 pg. 7 14 21 37 46 55

FAMILY GUY (TV)
Devil's Due Publ.: 2006 ($6.95)
nn-101 Ways to Kill Lois; 2-Peter Griffin's Guide to Parenting; 3-Books Don't Taste Very Good 7.00
... A Big Book o' Crap TPB (10/06, $16.95) r/nn,2,3 17.00

FAMILY MATTER
Kitchen Sink Press: 1998 ($24.95/$15.95, graphic novel)
Hardcover ($24.95) Will Eisner-s/a 25.00
Softcover ($15.95) 16.00

FAMILY TREE
Image Comics: Nov, 2019 - No. 12, Jun, 2021 ($3.99)
1-12-Jeff Lemire-s/Phil Hester-a/c 4.00

FAMOUS AUTHORS ILLUSTRATED (See Stories by...)

FAMOUS CRIMES
Fox Feature Syndicate/M.S. Dist. No. 51,52: June, 1948 - No. 19, Sept, 1950; No. 20, Aug, 1951; No. 51, 52, 1953
1-Blue Beetle app. & crime story-r/Phantom Lady #16 161 322 483 1030 1765 2500
2-Has woman dissolved in acid; lingerie-c/panels 155 310 465 992 1696 2400
3-Injury-to-eye story used in **SOTI**, pg. 112; has two electrocution stories 84 168 252 538 919 1300
4-6 34 68 102 199 325 450
7- "Tarzan, the Wyoming Killer" (**SOTI**, pg. 44) 55 110 165 352 601 850
8-20: 17-Morisi-a. 20-Same cover as #15 26 52 78 154 252 350
51 (nd, 1953) 21 42 63 122 199 275
52 (Exist?) 22 44 66 132 216 300

FAMOUS FEATURE STORIES
Dell Publishing Co.: 1938 (7-1/2x11", 68 pgs.)
1-Tarzan, Terry & the Pirates, King of the Royal Mtd., Buck Jones, Dick Tracy, Smilin' Jack, Dan Dunn, Don Winslow, G-Man, Tailspin Tommy, Mutt & Jeff, Little Orphan Annie reprints - all illustrated text 77 154 231 493 847 1200

FAMOUS FIRST EDITION (See Limited Collectors' Edition)
National Periodical Publications/DC Comics: ($1.00, 10x13-1/2", 72 pgs.) (No.6-8, 68 pgs.) 1974 - No. 8, Aug-Sept, 1975; C-61, 1979
(Hardbound editions with dust jackets are from Lyle Stuart, Inc.)
C-26-Action Comics #1; gold ink outer-c 6 12 18 40 73 105
C-26-Hardbound edition w/dust jacket 15 30 45 105 233 360
C-28-Detective #27; silver ink outer-c 6 12 18 42 79 115
C-28-Hardbound edition w/dust jacket 15 30 45 105 233 360
C-30-Sensation #1(1974); bronze ink outer-c 5 10 15 33 57 80
C-30-Hardbound edition w/dust jacket 13 26 39 89 195 300
F-4-Whiz Comics #2(#1)(10-11/74)-Cover not identical to original (dropped "Gangway for Captain Marvel" from cover); gold ink on outer-c 5 10 15 30 50 70
F-4-Hardbound edition w/dust jacket 13 26 39 89 195 300
F-5-Batman #1(F-6 inside); silver ink on outer-c 5 10 15 34 60 85
F-5-Hardbound edition w/dust jacket (exist?) 13 26 39 89 195 300
V2#F-6-Wonder Woman #1 5 10 15 35 63 90
F-6-Wonder Woman #1 Hardbound w/dust jacket 13 26 39 89 195 300
F-7-All-Star Comics #3 5 10 15 31 53 75
F-8-Flash Comics #1(8-9/75) 5 10 15 31 53 75
V8#C-61-Superman #1(1979, $2.00) 4 8 12 28 47 65
V8#C-61 (Whitman variant) 5 10 15 30 50 70
V8#C-61 (Softcover in plain grey slipcase, edition of 250 copies) Each signed by Jerry Siegel and Joe Shuster at the bottom of the inside front cover 600.00
Warning: The above books are almost **exact** reprints of the originals that they represent except for the Giant-Size format. None of the originals are Giant-Size. The first five issues and C-61 were printed with two covers. Reprint information can be found on the outside cover, but not on the inside cover which was reprinted exactly like the original (inside and out).

FAMOUS FUNNIES
Eastern Color: 1934; July, 1934 - No. 218, July, 1955

A Carnival of Comics (See Promotional Comics section)

Series 1-(Very rare)(nd-early 1934)(68 pgs.) No publisher given (Eastern Color PrintingCo.); sold in chain stores for 10¢. 35,000 print run. Contains Sunday strip reprints of Mutt & Jeff, Reg'lar Fellers, Nipper, Hairbreadth Harry, Strange As It Seems, Joe Palooka, Dixie Dugan, The Nebbs, Keeping Up With the Jones, and others. Inside front and back covers and pages 1-16 of Famous Funnies Series 1, #s 49-64 reprinted from **Famous Funnies**, **A Carnival of Comics**, and most of pages 17-48 reprinted from **Funnies on Parade**. 7500 15,000 22,500 45,000 -- --

No. 1 (Rare)(7/34-on stands 5/34) - Eastern Color Printing Co. First monthly newsstand comic book. Contains Sunday strip reprints of Toonerville Folks, Mutt & Jeff, Hairbreadth Harry, S'Matter Pop, Nipper, Dixie Dugan, The Bungle Family, Connie, Ben Webster, Tailspin Tommy, The Nebbs, Joe Palooka, & others. 3400 6800 10,200 25,500 -- --
2 (Rare, 9/34) 825 1650 2475 6200 -- --
3-Buck Rogers Sunday strip-r by Rick Yager begins, ends #218; not in #191-208; 1st comic book app. of Buck Rogers; the number of the 1st strip reprinted is pg. 190, Series No. 1 975 1950 2925 7300 -- --
4 350 700 1050 2625 -- --
5-1st Christmas-c on a newsstand comic 400 800 1200 3000 -- --
6-10 250 500 750 1900 -- --
11,12,18-Four pgs. of Buck Rogers in each issue, completes stories in Buck Rogers #1 which lacks these pages. 18-Two pgs. of Buck Rogers reprinted in Daisy Comics #1 126 252 378 806 1378 1950
13-17,19,20: 14-Has two Buck Rogers panels missing. 17-2nd Christmas-c on a newsstand comic (12/35) 93 186 279 591 1021 1450
21,23-30: 27-(10/36)-War on Crime begins (4 pgs.); 1st true crime in comics (reprints); part photo-c. 29-X-Mas-c (12/36) 71 142 213 454 777 1100
22-Four pgs. of Buck Rogers needed to complete stories in Buck Rogers #1 84 168 252 538 919 1300
31,33,34,36,37,39,40: 33-Careers of Baby Face Nelson & John Dillinger traced 50 100 150 315 533 750
32-(3/37) 1st app. the Phantom Magician (costume hero) in Advs. of Patsy 55 110 165 352 601 850
35-Two pgs. Buck Rogers omitted in Buck Rogers #2 57 114 171 362 619 875
38-Full color portrait of Buck Rogers 53 106 159 334 567 800
41-60: 41,53-X-Mas-c. 55-Last bottom panel, pg. 4 in Buck Rogers redrawn in Buck Rogers #3 39 78 117 231 378 525
61,63,64,66,67,69,70 27 54 81 158 259 360
62,65,68,73-78-Two pgs. Kirby-a "Lightnin' & the Lone Rider". 65,77-X-Mas-c 29 58 87 170 278 385
71,79,80: 80-(3/41)-Buck Rogers story continues from Buck Rogers #5 24 48 72 142 234 325
72-Speed Spaulding begins by Marvin Bradley (artist), ends #88. This series was written by Edwin Balmer & Philip Wylie (later appeared as film & book "When Worlds Collide") 25 50 75 147 241 335
81-Origin & 1st app. Invisible Scarlet O'Neil (4/41); strip begins #82, ends #167; 1st non-funny-c (Scarlet O'Neil) 129 258 387 826 1413 2000
82-Buck Rogers-c 39 78 117 240 395 550
83-87,90: 86-Connie vs. Monsters on the Moon-c (sci/fi). 87 has last Buck Rogers full page-r. 90-Bondage-c 21 42 63 122 199 275
88,89: 88-Buck Rogers in "Moon's End" by Calkins, 2 pgs.(not reprints). Beginning with #88, all Buck Rogers pgs. have rearranged panels. 89-Origin & 1st app. Fearless Flint, the Flint Man 25 50 75 150 245 340
91-93,95,96,98-99,101,103-110: 98-Hitler, Tojo and Mussolini on inside back-c. 101-Christmas cover. 105-Series 2 begins (Strip Page #1) 17 34 51 98 154 210
94-Buck Rogers in "Solar Holocaust" by Calkins, 3 pgs.(not reprints) 20 40 60 114 182 250
97-War Bond promotion, Buck Rogers by Calkins, 2 pgs.(not reprints) 18 36 54 107 169 230
100-1st comic to reach #100; 100th Anniversary cover features 11 major Famous

GD 2.0 | VG 4.0 | FN 6.0 | VF 8.0 | VF/NM 9.0 | NM- 9.2

Funnies characters, including Buck Rogers 24 48 72 142 234 325
102-Chief Wahoo vs. Hitler,Tojo & Mussolini-c (1/43) 93 186 279 591 1021 1450
111-130 (5/45): 113-X-Mas-c 14 28 42 76 108 140
131-150 (1/47): 137-Strip page No. 110 omitted; Christmas-c. 144-(7/46) 12th Anniversary cover 12 24 36 69 97 125
151-162,164-168: 162-New Year's Eve-c 11 22 33 64 90 115
163-St. Valentine's Day-c (2/48) 14 28 42 76 108 140
169,170-Two text illos. by Al Williamson, his 1st comic book work 14 28 42 80 115 150
171-190: 171-Strip pgs. 227,229,230, Series 2 omitted. 172-Strip Pg. 232 omitted. 173-Christmas-c. 190-Buck Rogers ends with start of strip pg. 302, Series 2; Oaky Doaks-c/story 11 22 33 60 83 105
191-197,199,201,203,206-208: No Buck Rogers. 191-Barney Carr, Space detective begins, ends #192. 10 20 30 58 79 100
198,200,202,205-One pg. Frazetta ads; no B. Rogers 11 22 33 60 83 105
204-Used in **POP**, pg. 79,99; war-c begin, end #208 13 26 39 74 105 135
209-211,215,216: Frazetta-c. 209-Buck Rogers begins (12/53) with strip pg. 480, Series 2; 211-Buck Rogers ads by Anderson begins, ends #217. #215-Contains B. Rogers strip pg. 515-518, series 2 followed by pgs.179-181, Series 3 300 600 900 2010 3505 5000
212-214-Frazetta-c 486 972 1458 3550 6275 9000
217-Buck Rogers-c 22 44 66 132 216 300
218-Buck Rogers ends with pg. 199, Series 3; Wee Three-c/story 11 22 33 64 90 115

NOTE: ***Rick Yager*** *did the Buck Rogers Sunday strips reprinted in Famous Funnies. The Sundays were formerly done by Russ Keaton and Lt. Dick Calkins did the dailies, but would sometimes assist Yager on a panel or two from time to time. Strip No. 169 is Yager's first full Buck Rogers page. Yager did the strip until 1958 when* ***Murphy Anderson*** *took over.* ***Tuska*** *art from 4/26/59 - 1965. Virtually every panel was rewritten for Famous Funnies. Not identical to the original Sunday page. The Buck Rogers reprints run continuously through Famous Funnies issue No. 190 (Strip No. 302) with no break in story line. The story line has no continuity after No. 190. The Buck Rogers newspaper strips came out in four series: Series 1, 3/30/30 - 9/21/41 (No. 1 - 600); Series 2, 9/28/41 -10/21/51 (No. 1 -525)(Strip No. 110-1/2 (1/2 pg.) published in only a few newspapers); Series 3, 10/28/51 -2/9/58 (No. 100-428) (No No.1-99); Series 4, 2/16/58 - 6/13/65 (No numbers, dates only).* ***Everett*** *c-85, 86.* ***Moulton*** *a-100. Chief Wahoo c-93, 97, 102, 116, 136, 139, 151. Dickie Dare c-83, 88. Fearless Flint c-89. Invisible Scarlet O'Neil c-81, 87, 95, 121(part), 132. Scorchy Smith c-84, 90.*

FAMOUS FUNNIES
Eastern Color: 1936

nn-2-color cvr/reprint of #10 w/issue #21(4/36) on inside. Blank back & interior cvrs. A CGC 5.5 copy sold in 2018 for $1920

FAMOUS FUNNIES
Super Comics: 1964

Super Reprint Nos. 15-18:17-r/Double Trouble #1. 18-Space Comics #? 2 4 6 10 14 18

FAMOUS GANGSTERS (Crime on the Waterfront No. 4)
Avon Periodicals/Realistic No. 3: Apr, 1951 - No. 3, Feb, 1952

1-3: 1-Capone, Dillinger; c-/Avon paperback #329. 2-Dillinger Machine Gun Killer; Wood-c/a (1 pg.); r/Saint #7 & retitled "Mike Strong". 3-Lucky Luciano & Murder, Inc; c-/Avon paperback #66 50 100 150 315 533 750

FAMOUS INDIAN TRIBES
Dell Publishing Co.: July-Sept, 1962; No. 2, July, 1972

12-264-209(#1) (The Sioux) 3 6 9 15 21 26
2(7/72)-Reprints above 1 3 4 6 8 10

FAMOUS STARS
Ziff-Davis Publ. Co.: Nov-Dec, 1950 - No. 6, Spring, 1952 (All have photo-c)

1-Shelley Winters, Susan Peters, Ava Gardner, Shirley Temple; Jimmy Stewart & Shelley Winters photo-c; Whitney-a 42 84 126 265 445 625
2-Betty Hutton, Bing Crosby, Colleen Townsend, Gloria Swanson; Betty Hutton photo-c; Everett-a(2) 32 64 96 188 307 425
3-Farley Granger, Judy Garland's ordeal (life story; she died 6/22/69 at the age of 47), Alan Ladd; Farley Granger photo-c; Whitney-a 37 74 111 222 361 500
4-Al Jolson, Bob Mitchum, Ella Raines, Richard Conte, Vic Damone; Jane Russell and Bob Mitchum photo-c; Crandall-a, 6pgs. 26 52 78 154 252 350
5-Liz Taylor, Betty Grable, Esther Williams, George Brent, Mario Lanza; Liz Taylor photo-c; Krigstein-a 60 120 180 381 653 925
6-Gene Kelly, Hedy Lamarr, June Allyson, William Boyd, Janet Leigh, Gary Cooper; Gene Kelly photo-c 26 52 78 154 252 350

FAMOUS STORIES (...Book No. 2)
Dell Publishing Co.: 1942 - No. 2, 1942

1,2: 1-Treasure Island. 2-Tom Sawyer 32 64 96 188 307 425

FAMOUS TV FUNDAY FUNNIES
Harvey Publications: Sept, 1961 (25¢ Giant)

1-Casper the Ghost, Baby Huey, Little Audrey 5 10 15 34 60 85

FAMOUS WESTERN BADMEN (Formerly Redskin)
Youthful Magazines: No. 13, Dec, 1952 - No. 15, Apr, 1953

13-Redskin story 15 30 45 88 137 185
14,15: 15-The Dalton Boys story 11 22 33 64 90 115

FAN BOY
DC Comics: Mar, 1999 - No. 6, Aug, 1999 ($2.50, limited series)

1-6: 1-Art by Aragonés and various in all. 2-Green Lantern-c/a by Gil Kane. 3-JLA. 4-Sgt. Rock art by Heath, Marie Severin. 5-Batman art by Sprang, Adams, Miller, Timm. 6-Wonder Woman; art by Rude, Grell 3.00
TPB (2001, $12.95) r/#1-6 13.00

FANBOYS VS. ZOMBIES
BOOM! Studios: Apr, 2012 - No. 20, Nov, 2013 ($1.00/$3.99)

1-($1.00) Eight covers; Humphries-s/Gaylord-a; zombies at San Diego Comic-Con 3.00
2-20-($3.99) 2-12-Multiple covers on each. 17-Bryan Turner-a 4.00

FANTASTIC (Formerly Captain Science; Beware No. 10 on)
Youthful Magazines: No. 8, Feb, 1952 - No. 9, Apr, 1952

8-Capt. Science by Harrison 84 168 252 538 919 1300
9-Harrison-a; decapitation, shrunken head panels 58 116 174 371 636 900

FANTASTIC ADVENTURES

GD 2.0 | VG 4.0 | FN 6.0 | VF 8.0 | VF/NM 9.0 | NM- 9.2

Super Comics: 1963 - 1964 (Reprints)

9,10,12,15,16,18: 9-r/? 10-r/He-Man #2(Toby). 11-Disbrow-a. 12-Unpublished Chesler material? 15-r/Spook #23. 16-r/Dark Shadows #2(Steinway); Briefer-a.18-r/Superior Stories #1 3 6 9 17 26 35
11-Wood-a; r/Blue Bolt #118 4 8 12 23 37 50
17-Baker-a(2) r/Seven Seas #6 4 8 12 23 37 50

FANTASTIC COMICS
Fox Feature Syndicate: Dec, 1939 - No. 23, Nov, 1941

1-Intro/origin Samson; Stardust, The Super Wizard, Sub Saunders (by Kiefer), Space Smith, Capt. Kidd begin 975 1950 2919 7100 12,550 18,000
2-Powell text illos 389 778 1167 2723 4762 6800
3-Classic Lou Fine Robot-c; Powell text illos 13,750 27,500 41,250 75,600 92,800 110,000
4-Lou Fine-c 366 732 1098 2562 4481 6400
5-Classic Lou Fine-c 486 972 1458 3550 6275 9000
6,7-Simon-c. 6-Bondage/torture-c 331 662 993 2317 4059 5800
8-Bondage/torture-c 300 600 900 1950 3375 4800
9,10: 9-Bondage-c. 10-Intro/origin David, Samson's aide 194 388 582 1242 2121 3000
11-16,18-20: 11-Bondage/torture on a bed of nails-c. 16-Stardust ends 155 310 465 992 1696 2400
17,23: 17-1st app. Black Fury & sidekick Chuck; ends #23. 23-Origin The Gladiator 168 336 504 1075 1838 2600
21-The Banshee begins(origin); ends #23; Hitler-c 432 864 1296 3154 5577 8000
22-WWII Holocaust bondage torture-c (likeness of Hitler as furnace on-c) 703 1406 2109 5132 9066 13,000

NOTE: ***Lou Fine*** *c-1-5.* ***Tuska*** *a-3-5, 8. Issue #11 has indicia to Mystery Men Comics #15. All issues feature Samson covers.*

FANTASTIC COMICS (Imagining of a 1941 issue by modern creators in Golden Age style)
Image Comics: No. 24, Jan, 2008 ($5.99, Golden Age sized, one-shot)

24-Samson, Yank Wilson, Stardust, Sub Saunders, Space Smith, Capt. Kidd app.; Larsen-c/a; art by Allred, Sienkiewicz, Yeates, Scioli, Hembeck, Ashley Wood & others 6.00

FANTASTIC COMICS (Fantastic Fears #1-9; Becomes Samson #12)
Ajax/Farrell Publ.: No. 10, Nov-Dec, 1954 - No. 11, Jan-Feb, 1955

10 (#1) 33 66 99 194 317 440
11-Robot-c 41 82 123 256 428 600

FANTASTIC FABLES
Silverwolf Comics: Feb, 1987 - No. 2, 1987 ($1.50, 28 pgs., B&W)

1,2: 1-Tim Vigil-a (6 pgs.). 2-Tim Vigil-a (7 pgs.) 4.00

FANTASTIC FEARS (Formerly Captain Jet) (Fantastic Comics #10 on)
Ajax/Farrell Publ.: No. 7, May, 1953 - No. 9, Sept-Oct, 1954

7(#1, 5/53)-Tales of Stalking Terror 103 206 309 659 1130 1600
8(#2, 7/53) 63 126 189 403 689 975
3,4 54 108 162 343 574 825
5-(1-2/54)-Ditko story (1st drawn) is written by Bruce Hamilton; r-in Weird V2#8 (1st pro work for Ditko but Daring Love #1 was published 1st) 258 516 774 1651 2826 4000
6-Decapitation-girl's head w/paper cutter (classic) 161 322 483 1030 1765 2500
7(5-6/54), 9(9-10/54) 47 94 141 296 498 700
8(7-8/54)-Contains story intended for Jo-Jo; name changed to Kaza; decapitation story 52 104 156 328 552 775

FANTASTIC FIVE
Marvel Comics: Oct, 1999 - No. 5, Feb, 2000 ($1.99)

1-5: 1-M2 Universe; recaps origin; Ryan-a. 2-Two covers 3.00
Spider-Girl Presents Fantastic Five: In Search of Doom (2006, $7.99, digest) r/#1-5 8.00

FANTASTIC FIVE
Marvel Comics: Sept, 2007 - No. 5, Nov, 2007 ($2.99, limited series)

1-5-DeFalco-s/Lim-a; Dr. Doom returns vs. the future Fantastic Five 3.00
...: The Final Doom TPB (2007, $13.99) r/#1-5; cover sketches with inks 14.00

FANTASTIC FORCE
Marvel Comics: Nov, 1994 - No. 18, Apr, 1996 ($1.75)

1-($2.50)-Foil wraparound-c; intro Fantastic Force w/Huntara, Devlor, Psi-Lord & Vibraxas 5.00
2-18: 13-She-Hulk app. 4.00

FANTASTIC FORCE (See Fantastic Four #558, Nu-World heroes from 500 years in the future)
Marvel Comics: Jun, 2009 - No. 4, Sept, 2009 ($3.99/$2.99, limited series)

1-($3.99)-Ahearne-s/Kurth-a/Hitch-c; Fantastic Four app. 4.00
2-4-($2.99) 3,4-Ego the Living Planet app. 3.00

FANTASTIC FOUR (See America's Best TV..., Fireside Book Series, Giant-Size..., Giant Size Super-Stars, Marvel Age..., Marvel Collectors Item Classics, Marvel Knights 4, Marvel Milestone Edition, Marvel's Greatest, Marvel Treasury Edition, Marvel Triple Action, Official Marvel Index to..., Power Record Comics & Ultimate...)

FANTASTIC FOUR (See Volume Three for issues #500-611)
Marvel Comics Group: Nov, 1961 - No. 416, Sept, 1996 (Created by Stan Lee & Jack Kirby)

1-Origin & 1st app. The Fantastic Four (Reed Richards: Mr. Fantastic, Johnny Storm: The Human Torch, Sue Storm: The Invisible Girl, & Ben Grimm: The Thing–Marvel's 1st super-hero group since the G.A.; 1st app. S.A. Human Torch); origin/1st app. The Mole Man. 6650 13,300 26,600 66,500 183,250 300,000
1-Golden Record Comic Set Reprint (1966)-cover not identical to original 46 92 138 340 770 1200
with Golden Record 52 104 156 411 931 1450
2-Vs. The Skrulls (last 10¢ issue); (should have a pin-up of The Thing which many copies are missing) 600 1200 1800 4950 12,475 20,000
3-Fantastic Four don costumes & establish Headquarters; brief 1pg. origin; intro. The Fantasti-Car; Human Torch drawn w/two left hands on-c 600 1200 1800 4950 12,475 20,000
4-1st S. A. Sub-Mariner app. (5/62) 660 1320 1980 5450 13,725 22,000
5-Origin & 1st app. Doctor Doom 3200 6400 9600 25,600 52,800 80,000
6-Sub-Mariner, Dr. Doom team up; 1st Marvel villain team-up (2nd S.A. Sub-Mariner app. 333 666 1000 2831 6416 10,000
7,9,10: 7-1st app. Kurrgo. 9-3rd Sub-Mariner app. 10-Stan Lee & Jack Kirby app. in story 166 332 498 1370 3085 4800
8-1st app. Puppet-Master & Alicia Masters 179 358 537 1477 3339 5200

Famous Funnies #211 © EAS

Fantastic Five #4 © MAR

Fantastic Four #112 © MAR

	GD 2.0	VG 4.0	FN 6.0	VF 8.0	VF/NM 9.0	NM- 9.2
11-Origin/1st app. The Impossible Man (2/63)	169	338	507	1394	3147	4900
12-Fantastic Four vs. The Hulk (1st meeting); 1st Hulk x-over & ties w/Amazing Spider-Man #1 as 1st Marvel x-over; (3/63)	415	830	1245	3700	9850	16,000
13-Intro. The Watcher; 1st app. The Red Ghost	317	634	951	2695	6098	9500
14,15,17,19: 14-Sub-Mariner x-over. 15-1st app. Mad Thinker. 19-Intro. Rama-Tut (Kang)	68	136	204	544	1222	1900
16-1st Ant-Man x-over (7/63); Wasp cameo	96	192	288	768	1734	2700
18-Origin/1st app. The Super Skrull	125	250	375	1000	2250	3500
20-Origin/1st app. The Molecule Man	86	172	258	688	1544	2400
21-Intro. The Hate Monger; 1st Sgt. Fury x-over (12/63)	50	100	150	400	900	1400
22-24: 22-Sue Storm gains more powers	40	80	120	296	673	1050
25-The Hulk vs. The Thing (their 1st battle); 3rd Avengers x-over (1st time w/Captain America)(cameo, 4/64); 2nd S.A. app. Cap (takes place between Avengers #4 & 5)	155	310	465	1279	2890	4500
26-The Hulk vs. The Thing (continued); 4th Avengers x-over	69	138	207	552	1251	1950
27-1st Doctor Strange x-over (6/64)	50	100	150	400	900	1400
28-Early X-Men x-over (7/64); same date as X-Men #6	61	122	183	488	1094	1700
29,30: 30-Intro. Diablo	36	72	108	259	580	900
31,32,34,35,37-40: 31-Early Avengers x-over (10/64). 35-Intro/1st app. Dragon Man. 39-Wood inks on Daredevil (early x-over)	25	50	75	175	388	600
33-1st app. Attuma; part photo-c	54	108	162	432	966	1500
36-Intro/1st app. Madam Medusa & the Frightful Four (Sandman, Wizard, Paste Pot Pete)	75	150	225	600	1350	2100
41-44: 41-43-Frightful Four app. 44-Intro. Gorgon	16	32	48	107	236	365
45-Intro/1st app. The Inhumans (c/story, 12/65); also see Incredible Hulk Special #1 & Thor #146, & 147	136	272	408	1088	2444	3800
46-1st Black Bolt-c (Kirby) & 1st full app.	71	142	213	568	1284	2000
47-3rd app. The Inhumans	23	46	69	151	356	550
48-Partial origin/1st app. The Silver Surfer & Galactus (3/66) by Lee & Kirby; Galactus brief app. in last panel; 1st of 3 part story	414	828	1242	3602	7800	12,000
49-2nd app./1st cover Silver Surfer & Galactus	234	468	702	1931	4366	6800
50-Silver Surfer battles Galactus; full S.S.-c	241	482	723	1988	4494	7000
51-Classic "This Man...This Monster" story	40	80	120	296	673	1050
52-1st app. The Black Panther (7/66)	367	734	1100	3100	7050	11,000
53-Origin & 2nd app. The Black Panther; origin/1st app. of Klaw	30	60	90	216	483	750
54-Inhumans cameo	16	32	48	110	243	375
55-Thing battles Silver Surfer; 4th app. Silver Surfer	46	92	138	359	805	1250
56-Silver Surfer cameo	17	34	51	117	259	400
57-Dr. Doom steals Silver Surfer's powers (also see Silver Surfer: Loftier Than Mortals); Dr. Doom & Silver Surfer-c	35	70	105	252	564	875
58-60: Dr. Doom with Silver Surfer's powers. 59,60-Inhumans cameo	13	26	39	89	195	300
61-63,: 61-Silver Surfer cameo; Sandman app. (new costume). 62-1st Blastaar; Sandman app. 63-Sandman & Blastaar team-up	11	22	33	76	163	250
64-1st Kree Sentry #459	15	30	45	103	227	350
65-1st app. Ronan the Accuser; 1st Kree Supreme Intelligence	32	64	96	230	515	800
66-Begin 2 part origin of Him (Warlock); does not app. (9/67)	34	68	102	245	548	850
66,67-2nd printings (1994)	3	6	9	16	23	30
67-Origin/1st brief app. Him (Warlock); 1 page; see Thor #165,166 for 1st full app.; white cover scarcer in true high grade	64	128	192	512	1156	1800
68-71	9	18	27	61	123	185
72-Silver Surfer-c/story (pre-dates Silver Surfer #1)	38	76	114	285	641	1000
73-Spider-Man, D.D., Thor x-over; cont'd from Daredevil #38	14	28	42	96	211	325
74-Silver Surfer app.	18	36	54	124	275	425
75-Galactus and Silver Surfer app.	26	52	78	182	404	625
76,77: Silver Surfer app.(#77 is same date/S.S. #1)	10	20	30	70	150	230
78-80: 78-Wizard app. 80-1st Tomazooma, the Living Totem	9	18	27	57	111	165
81,84-88: 81-Crystal joins & dons costume; vs. the Wizard. 84-87-Dr. Doom app. 88-Mole Man app.	8	16	24	54	102	150
82,83-Black Bolt & the Inhumans app.; vs. Maximus	9	18	27	58	114	170
89-93,95-98,101: 89-Mole Man app. 91-Skrulls disguised as 1930s era gangsters; 1st app. Torgo. 92-The Thing app. as a space gladiator. 93-Thing vs. Torgo. 95-1st app. the Monocle. 96-Mad-Thinker app. 98-Neil Armstrong Moon landing issue. 101-Last Kirby-a issue	7	14	21	49	92	135
94-(1/70) Intro Agatha Harkness; Frightful Four app.	31	62	93	223	499	775
99-Black Bolt & the Inhumans app.	8	16	24	54	102	150
100 (7/70) F.F. vs Thinker and Puppet-Master	10	20	30	70	150	230

	GD 2.0	VG 4.0	FN 6.0	VF 8.0	VF/NM 9.0	NM- 9.2
102-104: 102-Romita Sr-a; 102-104-Sub-Mariner & Magneto app.	7	14	21	44	82	120
105,106,108,109,111: 108-Features Kirby & Buscema-a; Kirby material produced after issue #101, his last official issue before leaving Marvel. 109-Annihilus app. 111-Hulk cameo	6	12	18	41	76	110
107-Classic Thing transformation-c; 1st John Buscema-a on FF (2/71); 1st app. Janus	8	16	24	54	102	150
110-Initial version w/green Thing and blue faces and pink uniforms on-c	46	92	138	359	805	1250
110-Corrected-c w/accurately colored faces and uniforms and orange Thing	9	18	27	58	114	170
112-Hulk Vs. Thing (7/71)	71	142	213	568	1284	2000
113-115: 113-1st app. The Overmind; Watcher app. 114-vs the Overmind. 115-Origin of the Overmind; plot by Stan Lee, Archie Goodwin script; last 15¢ issue	5	10	15	35	63	90
116 (52 pgs.) FF and Dr. Doom vs. the Overmind; the Stranger app.; Goodwin story	8	16	24	51	96	140
117-119: 117,118-Diablo app; Goodwin-s 119-Black Panther app. vs Klaw; 1st Roy Thomas FF story	5	10	15	33	57	80
120-1st app. Gabriel the Air-Walker (new herald of Galactus); Stan Lee story	14	28	42	96	211	325
121,123: 121-Silver Surfer vs. Gabriel; Galactus app. 123-Silver Surfer & Galactus app.	6	12	18	38	69	110
122-Silver Surfer & Galactus app; black cover, scarcer in higher grade	7	14	21	49	92	135
124,125,127,130,134-140: 125-Last Stan Lee-s. 127-Mole Man & Tyrannus app. 130-vs the new Frightful Four (Thundra, Sandman, Trapster and Wizard; Black Bolt & Inhumans app.). 134,135-Dragon Man app. 134-1st full Gerry Conway issue. 136-Shaper of Worlds app; Dragon Man cameo. 137-Shaper of Worlds app. 138-Return of the Miracle Man. 139-vs. Miracle Man. 140-Annihilus app.	5	10	15	30	50	70
126-Origin FF retold; cover swipe of FF #1; Roy Thomas scripts begin	5	10	15	35	63	90
128-Four page glossy insert of FF Friends & Foes; Mole Man app.	5	10	15	34	60	85
129-1st app. Thundra (super-strong Femizon) joins new Frightful Four	13	26	39	89	195	300
131-133: 131-Black Bolt, Medusa, Crystal, Quicksilver app; New Frightful Four app; Ross Andru-a; Steranko-c. 132-Black Bolt & Inhumans app.; vs. Maximus; last Roy Thomas-s (returns in issue #158). 133-Thing vs Thundra battle issue; Ramona Fradon-a; Gerry Conway script	5	10	15	35	63	90
141-146,148-149: 141-Franklin Richards 'depowered'; Annihilus app.; FF break-up; last Buscema-a. 142-1st Darkoth the Demon; Dr. Doom app; Kirbyish-a by Buckler begins. 143,144-vs. Dr. Doom. 145,146-vs. Ternak the Abominable Snowman. 148-vs. Wizard, Sandman, Trapster. 149-Sub-Mariner app.	4	8	12	27	44	60
147-Thing vs. Sub-Mariner-c/s	5	10	15	31	53	75
150-Crystal & Quicksilver's wedding; Avengers, Ultron-7 and Black Bolt & the Inhumans app; story continued from Avengers #127	5	10	15	33	57	80
151-154,158-160: 151-1st Mahkizmo the Nuclear Man; origin Thundra. 152,153-Thundra & Mahkizmo app. 154-Nick Fury app; part-r issue (Strange Tales #127). 158,159 vs. Xemu; Black Bolt & Inhumans app. 160-Arkon app.	3	6	9	17	26	35
155-157: Silver Surfer & Dr. Doom in all	4	8	12	28	47	65
161-163,168-171: 162,163-Arkon app. 168-Luke Cage, Power Man joins the FF (to replace the Thing). 169-Luke Cage app; 1st app. Thing exoskeleton. 170-Luke Cage leaves the FF; Puppet Master app. 171-1st Gorr the Golden Gorilla; Pérez-a	3	6	9	14	20	25
164-Re-intro Marvel Boy (as the Crusader); 1st George Pérez-a on FF	6	12	18	42	79	115
165-Origin of Marvel Boy & the Crusader; 1st app. Frankie Ray. Pérez-a; death of the Crusader (a new Marvel Boy appears in Captain America #217)	3	6	9	19	30	40
166,167-vs the Hulk; Pérez-a. 167-The Thing loses his powers	4	8	12	23	37	50
169-173-(30¢-c, limited distribution)(4-8/76)	6	12	18	40	73	105
172-175: 172-Galactus & High Evolutionary app. 175-Galactus vs. High Evolutionary; the Thing regains his powers	3	6	9	15	22	28
176-180: 176-Re-intro Impossible Man; Marvel artists app. 177-1st app. the Texas Twister & Captain Ultra; Impossible Man & Brute app. 178-179-Impossible Man, Tigra & Thundra app; Reed loses his stretching ability. 180-r/#101 by Kirby	3	6	9	14	19	24
181-199: 181-183-The Brute, Mad Thinker & Annihilus app; last Roy Thomas-s. 184-1st Eliminator; Len Wein-s begin. (co-plotter in #183-182) 185,186-New Salem Witches app.; part origin Agatha Harkness. 187,188-vs. Klaw & the Molecule Man. 189-G.A Human Torch app.; r-FF Annual #4. 190-1st Marv Wolfman FF. 191-FF break-up; Wolfman/Wein-s. 192-Last Pérez-a; Texas Twister app. 193,194-Diablo & Darkoth the Death Demon app. 195-Sub-Mariner app.; Wolfman begins as full plotter & scripter.						

GD 2.0 | VG 4.0 | FN 6.0 | VF 8.0 | VF/NM 9.0 | NM- 9.2

196-1st full app. of the clone of Dr. Doom. 197-vs. the Red Ghost; Reed regains his stretching ability. 198-vs Dr. Doom. 199-Origin & death of the clone of Doom; Dr. Doom app. 2 4 6 10 14 18

200-(11/78 52 pgs)-FF reunited vs. Dr. Doom 4 8 12 27 44 60

201-203,219,222-231: 202-vs. Quasimodo. 219-Sub-Mariner app.; Moench & Sienkiewicz 1st FF work. 222-Agatha Harkness & Gabriel the Devil Hunter app. 224-Contains unused alternate-c for #3 and pin-ups. 225-Thor & Odin app. 226-1st Samurai Destroyer. 229-1st Ebon-Seeker. 230-vs. Ebon Seeker; Avengers app. 231-1st Stygorr of the Negative Zone 1 3 4 6 8 10

204-1st Nova Corps (cameo); 1st app. Queen Adora of Xandar; 1st app. of Xandar; FF vs. the Skrulls 3 6 9 19 30 40

205-1st full app. Nova Corps; Xandarian/Skrull war 3 6 9 17 26 35

206-208: 206-Nova app.; story continued from Nova #25; Sphinx & Skrulls app. 207-Spider-Man app. 208-Nova & and the New Champions app. (Powerhouse, Diamondhead, the Comet & Crimebuster); Sphinx app. 2 4 6 9 12 15

209-210,213,214: 209-1st Byrne-a on FF; 1st Herbie the Robot. 210-Galactus app. 213-Galactus vs. the Sphinx; Terrax app. 2 4 6 10 14 18

211-1st app. Terrax (new Herald of Galactus) 7 14 21 46 86 125

212-Byrne-a; Galactus vs. the High Evolutionary 3 6 9 16 23 30

215-218,220-221: Byrne-a in all. 215-Blastaar app; 1st app. the Futurist. 216-Blastaar & Futurist app; last Wolfman-s. 217-Early app. Dazzler (4/80); by Byrne; vs Herbie the Robot (destroyed). 218-Spider-Man app; vs. Frightful Four; continued from Spectacular Spider-Man #42. 220-1st Byrne story on FF; origin retold; Avengers and Vindicator app. 2 4 6 8 10 12

232-Byrne story & art begins (7/81); vs. Diablo; brief Dr. Strange app; re-intro Frankie Raye 2 4 6 11 16 20

233-235,237-241,245-249,251,253-256: 233-Hammerhead app. 234,235-Ego the Living Planet. 238-Origin & 1st app. of Frankie Raye's flame powers, joins the FF. The Thing is 'devolved' into an 'uglier' version. 239-1st app. Aunt Petunia. 240-Black Bolt & the Inhumans app; Attilan (home of the Inhumans) relocated to the Moon. 241-Black Panther app. 245-Thing returns to his rocky-look. 246-Dr. Doom returns. 247-Doom and FF team-up vs. Prince Zorba; Doom regains rule of Latveria; 1st app. Kristoff. 248-Black Bolt & and the Inhumans app. 249-vs Gladiator (of the Sh'iar). 251-FF explore the Negative Zone; Annihillus app. 254-1st Mantracora. 255-Brief Daredevil app; Annihilus app. 256-FF return from the Negative Zone; vs Annihilus; Avengers, Galactus and Nova (Frankie Raye) app. 1 2 3 5 6 8

236-20th Anniversary issue (11/81, 68 pgs, $1.00)-brief origin FF; Byrne-c(p)/a; new Kirby-a; Marvel Super-Heroes & Stan Lee app. on cover; Dr. Doom and Puppet Master app.; 1st 'Liddleville' 2 4 6 9 12 15

242-vs. Terrax; Thor, Iron Man & Daredevil cameos 2 4 6 8 10 12

243-Classic Galactus-c by Byrne; Thor, Captain America, Dr. Strange, Spider-Man & Daredevil app. 4 8 12 25 40 55

244-Frankie Raye becomes Nova – the new Herald of Galactus 4 8 12 28 47 65

250,257-260: 250-(52 pgs)-Spider-Man x-over; Byrne-a; Skrulls impersonate New X-Men; Gladiator app. 257-Galactus devours the Skrull homeworld; Sue announces pregnancy; Vision & Scarlet Witch cameo. 258-Dr. Doom team-up with Terrax; Kristoff app. 259-Dr. Doom & Terrax. vs FF; Silver Surfer cameo. 260-Terrax, Silver Surfer & Sub-Mariner app.; 'death' of Dr. Doom 1 3 4 6 8 10

252-Reads sideways; Annihilus app. Contains skin 'Tattooz' decals (no 'Tattooz' were included in Canadian editions, also in Amazing Spider-Man #238)
with Tattooz 1 3 4 6 8 10
without Tattooz 1 2 3 5 6 8

261-262: The Trial of Reed Richards. 261-Silver Surfer & the Watcher app. 262-Origin Galactus; John Byrne writes himself into story; the Watcher, Odin, Eternity app. 1 2 3 5 6 8

263-285: 263-Mole Man app. Vision cameo. 264-vs Mole Man; swipes-c of FF #1. 265-Secret Wars x-over; She-Hulk replaces the Thing; Vision & Scarlet Witch app. 267-Dr. Octopus, Michael Morbius, Donald Blake & Bruce Banner app; Sue loses her baby. 268-Origin She-Hulk retold; Hulk and Dr. Octopus app. 269-1st app. Terminus; re-intro. Wyatt Wingfoot. 270-vs Terminus. 271-1st Gormuu (flashback story pre-FF #1). 272-1st app. Nathaniel Richards – the Warlord (Reed's father). 273-Nathaniel Richards app. 274-Spider-Man's alien costume app; (4th app. 1/85, 2 pgs.) the Thing app. on Battleworld. 275-She-Hulk solo story. 276-Mephisto & Dr. Strange app. 277-Split story format - the Thing returns to Earth and battles Dire Wraiths; FF battle Mephisto; Dr. Strange app. 278-Origin Dr. Doom retold; Kristoff becomes new Dr. Doom. 279-Baxter Building destroyed by Kristoff; new Hate Monger app. 280-New Hate Monger & Psycho Man app.; 1st app. Sue as Malice. 281-New Hate Monger, Malice & Psycho Man app. 282-Power Pack cameo; Secret Wars II x-over; Psycho Man app.; infinity cover. 283,284-vs. Psycho Man. 285-Secret Wars II x-over; Beyonder app. 6.00

286-2nd app. X-Factor 2 4 6 11 16 20

287-295: 287-Return of Dr. Doom. 288-Secret Wars II x-over; Dr. Doom vs. the Beyonder. 289-Blastaar app; Basilisk killed by Scourge; Nick Fury app; Annihilus returns. 290-Blastaar, Annihilus & Nick Fury app. 291-Action Comics #1 cover swipe; Nick Fury app. 292-Hitler-c; Nick Fury app. 293-West Coast Avengers app; last Byrne-a. 294-Byrne plot only (last); Ordway-a; Roger Stern script. 295-Stern-s begin (over brief Byrne plot) 6.00

296-($1.50, 64-pgs)-Barry Smith-c/a (pgs 1-10); Shooter plot; Stan Lee script; Gammil, Frenz, Milgrom, John Buscema, Silvestri and Ordway-p; Sinnott & Colletta-inks; Mole Man app; the Thing returns to the FF 1 2 3 5 6 8

297-318,321-330: 297-Roger Stern-s begins; John Buscema-a returns. 299-Black costume Spider-Man app. 300-Wedding of Johnny Storm and 'Alicia'- see issue #358. 301-Wizard & Mad-Thinker app. 303-Thundra app. 304-Steve Englehart-s begins; vs. Quicksilver; the Thing becomes leader of the FF. 305-Quicksilver & Kristoff app ; Crystal rejoins FF; Dr. Doom app; leads into FF Annual #20. 306-v.s Diablo; Black Bolt & the Inhumans app; Captain America cameo; Ms. Marvel (Sharon Ventura) app. 307-Ms. Marvel joins the FF. vs. Diablo; Reed and Sue leave the FF. 308-1st Fasaud. 309-vs Fasaud; last Buscema-a. 310-Keith Pollard-a begins; 1st mutated Thing; Ms. Marvel becomes 'She-Thing'. 311-Black Panther & Dr. Doom app. 312-Dr. Doom, Black Panther & X-Factor app. 313-Mole Man app. 314-Belasco & Master Pandemonium app. 315-Master Pandemonium & Comet Man app; Morbius the Living Vampire cameo. 316-Ka-Zar & Shanna the She-Devil app.; origin of the Savage Land. 317-Comet Man app. 318-Molecule Man & Dr. Doom app. 322-Ron Lim guest-a; She-Hulk vs. Ms. Marvel; Dragon Man app; Aron the Renegade Watcher app. 322-Inferno x-over; Graviton, Aron & Dragon Man app. 323-Inferno x-over; Mantis & Kang app. 324-Kang, Mantis & Necrodamus app; Silver Surfer cameo. 325-Mantis, Kang & Silver Surfer app. 326-vs new Frightful Four (Wizard, Hydroman, Klaw and Titania); Reed & Sue return; the Thing becomes human; Englehart-s as 'John Harkness'. 327-vs Frightful Four; Aron the Renegade Watcher & Dragon Man app. 328-1st app. Aron's evil version of the FF; Frightful Four & Dragon Man app. 329-Evil FF vs. Mole Man; Aron app. 6.00

319,320: 319-(Double-size, 39 pgs); Secret Wars III; origin of the Beyonder; Dr. Doom, Molecule Man, Shaper of Worlds, Kubik app. 320-Grey Hulk vs. Thing; Dr. Doom app; x-over w/Incredible Hulk #350 1 2 3 5 6 8

331-346, 351,352,354-357,359,360: 331-Ultron app. in dream sequence; Aron the Renegade Watcher app. 333-Avengers & Dr. Strange app. Evil FF vs real FF; Aron the Renegade Watcher app. 334-Acts of Vengeance x-over; Simonson-s begin; Buckler-a; Thor & Captain America app. 335-Acts of Vengeance x-over; Apocalypse cameo. 336-Acts of Vengeance x-over. 337-Simonson-s and art begin; Thor & Iron Man join FF's mission. 338-Iron Man & Thor app. Death's Head app. Galactus cameo. 339-Thor vs. Gladiator; Galactus & the Black Celestial app. 340-Iron Man, Thor & Galactus app; death of the Black Celestial. 341-Thor, Iron Man & Galactus app. 342-Spider-Man cameo; no Simonson-s or art. 343-President Dan Quayle app. 346-T.V.A (Time Variance Authority) app. 351-Kubik & Kosmos app; Mark Bagley-a. 352-Reed vs Dr. Doom; Kristof app; Justice Peace & the T.V.A app. 354-FF on trial by the T.V.A; Justice Peace and Mark Gruenwald (as Mr. Chairman) app. 354-Last Simonson issue. 355-vs. the Wrecker. 356-1st Tom Defalco-s & Paul Ryan-a (begin four-year run); Puppet Master & New Warriors app. 357-Alicia Masters revealed to be a Skrull (since issue #265); Puppet Master app. 6.00

347-Ghost Rider, Wolverine, Spider-Man, Hulk-c/stories thru #349; Arthur Adams-c/a(p) in each 1 3 4 6 8 10

347,348-Gold second printings 1 2 3 5 6 8

348-350: 348-349-Arthur Adams-c/a(p). 350-($1.50, 52 pgs)-The 'real' Dr. Doom returns; Kristoff app. Sharon Ventura becomes human again. Ben becomes the Thing again 1 2 3 5 6 8

353-FF on trial by the T.V.A.; Mr. Mobius app. 3 6 9 19 30 40

358-(11/91, $2.25, 88 pgs)-30th anniversary issue; gives history of the FF; die-cut-c; Art Adams back-up story-a; origin of Lyja the Skrull as Alicia Masters; 1st app. Paibok the Power Skrull 2 4 6 9 12 15

361-368, 372-373: 361-Dr. Doom & the Yancy Street gang app. 362-Spider-Man app; 1st app. of the Innerverse. 363-1st app. Occulus. 364,365-vs. Occulus; 365-Sharon Ventura returns. 366-Infinity War x-over; Magus app; Paibok & Devos team-up. 367-Infinity War x-over; Magus app. numerous super-heroes app. 368-Infinity War x-over; Magus app. Human Torch vs. X-Men doppelgangers. 372-Spider-Man, Molecule Man, Puppet Master & Aron the Renegade Watcher app.; Silver Sable & the Wild Pack cameo; Devos, Paibok & Lyja app. 373-Human Torch vs. Silver Sable & the Wild Pack; Molecule Man vs. Aron the Rogue Watcher; Dr. Doom app. (steals the power of Aron) 6.00

369,370-Infinity War x-over. 369-Thanos & Warlock and the Infinity Watch app; Aron the Renegade Watcher app.; the Magus gains the Infinity Gauntlet. 370-Warlock vs. the Magus for the Infinity Gauntlet; 1st app. Lyja the Lazer-fist 1 2 3 5 6 8

371-All-white embossed-c ($2.00); 1st new (revealing) Invisible Woman costume; Paibok, Devos & Lyja vs. Human Torch; Aron the Renegade Watcher app; Ms. Marvel (Sharon Ventura) rejoins the FF 1 2 3 5 6 8

371-All-red 2nd printing ($2.00) 6.00

374,375: 374-vs Wolverine, Dr. Strange, Ghost Rider, the Hulk and Spider-Man (as the Secret Defenders); Thing's face injured by Wolverine; Dr. Doom app; Black Bolt & the Inhumans cameo; Uatu the Watcher app. 375-($2.95, 52 pgs)-Holo-Grafx foil-c; Secret Defenders app.; Black Bolt & the Inhumans app; cosmic powered Dr. Doom app. Uatu app.; re-intro Nathaniel Richards (from issue #273); Lyja changes allegiance to the FF 6.00

376-($2.95)-Variant polybagged w/Dirt Magazine #4 and music tape; harder to find in true NM- 9.2 due to being packaged with a tape cassette 1 2 3 5 6 8

376-380,382-386: 376-Nathaniel Richards and Dr. Doom app; Franklin becomes an adult (Psi-Lord). 377-1st app. Huntara; origin Devos; Paibok, Dr. Doom & Klaw app. 378-vs. Devos, Paibok & Huntara; Avengers, Spider-Man & Daredevil app. 379-Devos, Paibok, Huntara & Dr. Doom app. 380-Dr. Doom app. 382-Contains a coupon from Kaybee Toys for an exclusive Ghost Rider issue; also has 16-pg Midnight Sons 'Siege of Darkness' insert; Devos vs. the Skrull Empire. 383-Paibok vs. Devos. 384-Scott Lang app. as Ant-Man; Psi-Lord vs. Invisible Woman. 385-Starblast x-over; Ant-Man & Sub-Mariner app.; continues in Namor the Sub-Mariner #48. 386-Starblast x-over; Ant-Man & Sub-Mariner app. 5.00

381-'Death' of Reed Richards & Dr. Doom 1 2 3 5 6 8

387-Newstand ed. ($1.25) 5.00

387-($2.95)-Collectors Ed. w/die-cut foil-c; Ant-Man app; Invisible Woman returns to her regular costume 1 2 3 5 6 8

388-393,396,397: 388-Bound in trading card sheet; Ant-Man, Sub-Mariner & Avengers app; 1st app. the Dark Raider. 389-Ant-Man, Sub-Mariner and the Collector app. 390- Ant-Man & Sub-Mariner app. Galactus & Silver Surfer app. in flashback to FF #48-50. 391-Ant-Man, Sub-Mariner, Galactus & Silver Surfer app. 392-vs. the Dark Raider. 396-Power Rangers card insert. 397-Aron the Renegade Watcher & the Dark Raider app; return of Kristoff; Ant-Man app. 5.00

394-($2.95)-Collectors Edition-polybagged w/16-pg. Marvel; Action Hour book and acetate print; pink logo; Ant-Man, Wyatt Wingfoot & She-Hulk app. 1 2 3 5 6 8

394-(Newstand Edition-$1.50; white logo 5.00

395,398,399: 395-Wolverine-c/story; Ant-Man app. 398,399-($2.50)-Rainbow foil-c; Ant-Man, Uatu, Aron & the Dark Raider app. 6.00

400-($3.95, 64-pgs)-Rainbow foil-c; Stan Lee introduction; Celestials vs. the Watchers; Kristoff joins the FF. Ant-Man app.; Avengers & Spider-Man app. in back-up story; origin of the FF retold; Uatu vs. Aron (dies) 6.00

401-404,406-415: 401-Atlantis Rising x-over; Sub-Mariner & Thor app; Black Bolt cameo. 402-Atlantis Rising x-over; Sub-Mariner vs. Black Bolt; Thor vs. the FF. 404-1st brief app. Hyperstorm (arm only). 406-Return of Dr. Doom; Hyperstorm revealed, battles FF. 407-Return of Mr. Fantastic; x-over w/FF Unlimited #12; Hyperstorm app. 408-vs Hyperstorm; Dr. Doom app. 409-Dr. Doom & FF vs. Hyperstorm; Thing's facial injury cured (since #374). 410-Gorgon of the Inhumans app. 411-Black Bolt & the Inhumans app. 412-Mr. Fantastic vs. Sub-Mariner. 413-Silver Surfer cameo; x-over w/Doom 2099 #42; Doom 2099 & Hyperstorm app; Franklin returns to being a child (Psi-Lord since #376). 414-Galactus vs. Hyperstorm; last Paul Ryan-a (since #356). 415-Onslaught tie-in; Pacheco-a; Professor X & Avengers app.; Apocalypse cameo; story continued in X-Men #55 5.00

405-Overpower card insert; scarcer in higher grades due to card indentation; new Ant-Man costume; Zarko the Tomorrow Man app; Conan cameo; 2nd app. Hyperstorm (cameo) 6.00

416-($2.50, 48 pgs)-Onslaught tie-in; Pacheco-a; Dr. Doom app; last issue; story continues in Onslaught Marvel Universe #1; Reed, Ben & Victor Von Doom app. in flashback in back-up story; Uatu the Watcher app. 6.00

#500-up (See Fantastic Four Vol. 3; series resumed original numbering after Vol. 3 #70)

Annual 1('63)-Origin of Sub-Mariner & 1st modern app. of Atlantis & the Atlanteans incl. Lady Dorma; FF origin retold; Spider-Man app. in detailed retelling of his app. from Amazing

Fantastic Four #231 © MAR

Fantastic Four Annual #11 © MAR

Fantastic Four #587 © MAR

	GD 2.0	VG 4.0	FN 6.0	VF 8.0	VF/NM 9.0	NM- 9.2
Spider-Man #1	172	344	516	1419	3210	5000
Annual 2('64)-Dr. Doom origin & c/story; FF #5-r in 2nd story; Pharaoh Rama-Tut app. in 3rd story	107	214	321	856	1928	3000
Annual 3('65)-Reed & Sue wed; r/#6,11	28	56	84	202	451	700
Special 4(11/66)-G.A. Torch x-over (1st S.A. app.) & origin retold; r/#25,26 (Hulk vs. Thing); Torch vs. Torch battle; Mad-Thinker app; 1st app Quasimodo	14	28	42	94	207	320
Special 5(11/67)-New art; Intro. Psycho-Man; early Black Panther, Inhumans & Silver Surfer (1st solo story); Black Bolt & the Inhumans app; Sue is revealed to be pregnant; Quasimodo app.	26	52	78	182	404	625
Special 6(11/68)-Intro. Annihilus; birth of Franklin Richards; new 48 pg. movie length epic; last non-reprint annual	100	200	300	800	1800	2800
Annual No. 6 Facsimile Edition (3/20, $4.99) Reprints Special #6 with original 1968 ads	2	4	6	8	10	12
Special 7(11/69)-all reprint issue; r/FF #1; r/origin of Dr. Doom from FF #5 & Dr. Doom story from FF Annual #2; Marvel staff photos seen in 'Because you Demanded it' featurette; new-c by Kirby	7	14	21	46	86	125
Special 8-10: All reprints. 8(12/70)-F.F. vs. Sub-Mariner plus gallery of F.F. foes. Special 9(12/71)-r/FF #43, Strange Tales #131 & FF Annual #3. Special 10('73)-r/FF Annual #3,4; new-c by John Buscema	4	8	12	27	44	60
Annual 11-('76)-New story & art begins; alternate Earth versions of the Invaders app; story continues into Marvel Two-in-One Annual #1; Kirby-c	3	6	9	11	16	20
Annual 12-14: Annual 12 ('78)-Black Bolt & the Inhumans app; vs. the Sphinx. Annual 13 ('78)-vs the Mole Man; Daredevil app. Annual 14 ('79)-Pérez-a; Avengers cameo; Sandman & Salem's Seven app.	2	4	6	9	13	16
Annual 15-17: 15-(80, 68 pgs.); Perez-a; Captain Marvel & Dr. Doom app. Annual 16-('81)-Ditko-a/c; 1st Dragon lord. Annual 17-('83)-Byrne-c/a; Skrulls app.	1	2	3	5	6	8
Annual 18-23: 18-('84)-Minor x-over w/X-Men #137; Wolverine cameo; wedding of Black Bolt & Medusa; the Watcher app. Annual 19-('85)-vs the Skrulls; x-over w/Avengers Annual #14. Annual 20-('87)-Dr. Doom & Mephisto app; continued from FF #305. Annual 21-('88, 64 pgs.)-Square bound; Evolutionary War x-over; Black Bolt & the Inhumans app. Aron the Watcher app. (unnamed). Annual 22-('89, 64 pgs.)-Square bound; Atlantis Attacks x-over; Avengers & Dr. Strange app. Annual 23-('90, 64 pgs.)-Squarebound; 'Days of Future Present' Pt. 1; 1st Ahab; story continues in New Mutants Annual #6 (not X-Factor Annual #5 as noted); Dr. Doom app. in back-up feature; Byrne-c						6.00
Annual 24-27 (all square bound editions): Annual 24-('91, 64 pgs.); Korvac Quest Pt.1; Guardians of the Galaxy app; story continues in Thor Annual #16; Molecule Man & Super-Skrull app. in back-up features. Annual 25-('92, 64 pgs.)-Citizen Kang Pt.3; continued from Thor Annual #17; Avengers app.; story continues in Avengers Annual #21; Moondragon vs. Mantis solo story & Kang retrospective. Annual 26-('93, 64 pgs.)-Bagged w/card featuring a new character 'Wildstreak'; vs. Dreadface; Kubik & Kosmos app. in solo story featuring the Celestials. Annual 27-('94, 64 pgs.)-Justice Peace & the T.V.A (Time Variance Authority) app.; featuring the chairman (Mark Gruenwald); Molecule Man vs. Beyonder solo story						6.00
... #1 Facsimile Edition (10/18, $3.99) reprints #1 with original 1961 ads; bonus essays and gallery of FF #1 cover swipes and homages						4.00
... #52 Facsimile Edition (1/23, $3.99) reprints #52 with original 1966 ads						4.00
Best of the Fantastic Four Vol. 1 HC (2005, $29.99) oversized reprints of classic stories from FF#1,39,40,51,100,116,176,236,267, Ann.2, V3#56,60 and more; Brevoort intro.						30.00
Maximum Fantastic Four HC (2005, $49.99, dust jacket) r/Fantastic Four #1 with super-sized art; historical background from Walter Mosley and Mark Evanier; dust jacket unfolds to a poster: giant FF#1 cover on one side, gallery of interior pages on other						50.00
...: Monsters Unleashed nn (1992, $5.95)-r/F.F. #347-349 w/new Arthur Adams-c	2	4	6	10	14	18
...: Nobody Gets Out Alive (1994, $15.95) TPB r/ #387-392						16.00
... Omnibus Vol. 1 HC (2005, $99.99) r/#1-30 & Annual 1 plus letter pages; 3 intros. and a 1974 essay by Stan Lee; original plot synopsis for FF #1; essays and Kirby art						100.00
... Omnibus Vol. 2 HC (2007, $99.99) r/#31-60, Annual 2-4 and Not Brand Echh #1 plus letter pages and essays by Stan Lee, Reginald Hudlin, Roy Thomas and others						100.00
Special Edition 1(5/84)-r/Annual #1; Byrne-c/a						5.00
...: The Lost Adventure (4/08, $4.99) Lee & Kirby story partially used in flashback in FF #108 completed with additional art by Frenz & Sinnott; plus reprint of FF #108						5.00
... Visionaries: George Pérez Vol. 1 (2005, $19.99) r/#164-167,170,176-178,184-186						20.00
... Visionaries: George Pérez Vol. 2 (2006, $19.99) r/#187-188,191-192, Annual #14-15, Marvel Two-In-One #60 and back-up story from Adventures of the Thing #3						20.00
... Visionaries (11/01, $19.95) r/#232-240 by John Byrne						20.00
... Visionaries Vol. 2 (2004, $24.99) r/#241-250 by John Byrne						25.00
... Visionaries John Byrne Vol. 3 (2004, $24.99) r/#251-257; Annual #17; Avengers #233 and Thing #2						25.00
... Visionaries John Byrne Vol. 4 (2005, $24.99) r/#258-267; Alpha Flight #4 & Thing #10						25.00
... Visionaries John Byrne Vol. 5 (2005, $24.99) r/#268-275; Annual #18 & Thing #19						25.00
... Visionaries John Byrne Vol. 6 ('06, $24.99) r/#276-284; Secret Wars II #2 & Thing #23						25.00
... Visionaries John Byrne Vol. 7 ('07, $24.99) r/#285,286, Ann. #19, Avengers #263 & Ann. #14, and X-Factor #1						25.00
... Visionaries John Byrne Vol. 8 ('07, $24.99) r/#287-295						25.00
... Visionaries: Walter Simonson Vol. 1 (2007, $19.99) r/#334-341						20.00

*NOTE: **Arthur Adams** c/a-347-349p. **Austin** c(i)-232-236, 238, 240-242, 250i, 286i. **Buckler** c-151, 168. **John Buscema** a(p)-107, 108(w/**Kirby, Sinnott & Romita**),109-130, 132, 134-141, 160, 173-175, 202, 296-309p, Annual 11, 13; c(p)-107-122, 124-129, 133-139, 202, Annual 12p, Special 10. **Byrne** a-209-218p, 220p, 221p, 232-265, 266i, 267-273, 274-293p, Annual 17, 19; c-211-214p, 220p, 232-236p, 237, 238p, 239, 240-242p, 243-249, 250p, 251-267, 269-277, 278-281p, 283p, 284, 285, 286p, 288-293, Annual 17, 18. **Ditko** a-13i, 14i(w/**Kirby**-p), Annual 16. **G. Kane** c-145p, 146p, 150p, 160p. **Kirby** a-1-102p, 108p, 180r, 189r, 236p, Special 1-10; c-1-101, 164, 167, 171-177, 180, 181, 190, 200, Annual 11, Special 1-7, 9. **Marcos** a-Annual 14i. **Mooney** a-118i, 152i. **Perez** a(p)-164-167, 170-172, 176-178, 184-188, 191p, 192p. Annual 14p, 15p; c(p)-183-188, 191, 192, 194-197. **Simonson** a-337-341, 343, 344p, 345p, 346, 350p, 352-354; c-212, 334-341, 342p, 343-346, 350, 353, 354. **Steranko** c-130-132p. **Williamson** c-357i.*

FANTASTIC FOUR (Volume Two)
Marvel Comics: V2#1, Nov, 1996 - No. 13, Nov, 1997 ($2.95/$1.95/$1.99) (Produced by WildStorm Productions)

	GD 2.0	VG 4.0	FN 6.0	VF 8.0	VF/NM 9.0	NM- 9.2
1-($2.95)-Reintro Fantastic Four; Jim Lee-c/a; Brandon Choi scripts; Mole Man app.						5.00
1-($2.95)-Variant-c	1	2	3	4	5	7
2-9: 2-Namor-c/app. 3-Avengers-c/app. 4-Two covers; Dr. Doom cameo						3.00
10,11,13: All $1.99-c. 13-"World War 3"-pt. 1, x-over w/Image						3.00
12-($2.99) "Heroes Reunited"-pt. 1						4.00
...: Heroes Reborn (7/00, $17.95, TPB) r/#1-6						18.00
Heroes Reborn: Fantastic Four (2006, $29.99, TPB) r/#1-12; Jim Lee intro.; pin-ups						30.00

FANTASTIC FOUR (Volume Three)
Marvel Comics: V3#1, Jan, 1998 - No. 588, Apr, 2011 ($2.99/$1.99/$2.25)
No. 600, Jan, 2012 - No. 611, Dec, 2012 (Issues #589-#599 do not exist, see FF series)

	GD 2.0	VG 4.0	FN 6.0	VF 8.0	VF/NM 9.0	NM- 9.2
1-($2.99)-Heroes Return; Lobdell-s/Davis & Farmer-a1	2	3	5	6	8	
1-Alternate Heroes Return-c	1	3	4	6	8	10
2-4,12: 2-Two covers. 4-Claremont-s/Larroca-a begin; Silver Surfer c/app. 12-($2.99) Wraparound-c by Larroca						5.00
5-10: 6-Heroes For Hire app. 9-Spider-Man-c/app.						4.00
11-1st app. Ayesha	2	4	6	9	12	15
13-25: 13,14-Ronan-c/app. 25-($2.99) Dr. Doom returns						4.00
26-49: 27-Dr. Doom marries Sue. 30-Begin $2.25-c. 32,42-Namor-c/app. 35-Regular cover; Pacheco-s/a begins. 37-Super-Skrull-c/app. 38-New Baxter Building						3.00
35-($3.25) Variant foil enhanced-c; Pacheco-s/a begins						4.00
50-($3.99, 64 pgs.) BWS-c; Grummett, Pacheco, Rude, Udon-a						4.00
51-53,55-59: 51-53-Bagley-a(p)/Wieringo-c; Inhumans app. 55,56-Immonen-a 57-59-Warren-s/Grant-a						3.00
54-($3.50, 100 pgs.) Birth of Valeria; r/Annual #6 birth of Franklin						4.00
60-(9¢-c) Waid-s/Wieringo-a begin						3.00
60-($2.25 newsstand edition)(also see Promotional Comics section)						3.00
61-70: 62-64-FF vs. Modulus. 65,66-Buckingham-a. 68-70-Dr. Doom app.						3.00

(After #70 [Aug, 2003] numbering reverted back to original Vol. 1 with #500, Sept, 2003)

	GD 2.0	VG 4.0	FN 6.0	VF 8.0	VF/NM 9.0	NM- 9.2
500-($3.50) Regular edition; concludes Dr. Doom app.; Dr. Strange app.; Rivera painted-c						4.00
500-($4.99) Director's Cut Edition; chromium-c by Wieringo; sketch and script pages						8.00
501-516: 501,502-Casey Jones-a. 503-508-Porter-a. 509-Wieringo-c/a resumes. 512,513-Spider-Man app. 514-516-Ha-c/Medina-a						3.00
517-537: 517-Begin $2.99-c. 519-523-Galactus app. 527-Straczynski-s begins. 537-Dr. Doom.						3.00
527-Variant Edition with different McKone-c						3.00
527-Wizard World Philadelphia Edition with B&W McKone sketch-c						3.00
536-Variant cover by Bryan Hitch						5.00
537-B&W variant cover						5.00
538-542-Civil War. 538-Don Blake reclaims Thor's hammer						4.00
543-45th Anniversary; Black Panther and Storm replace Reed and Sue; Granov-c						4.00
544-553: 544-546-Silver Surfer app.; Turner-c						3.00
554-568-Millar-s/Hitch-a/c. 558-561-Doctor Doom-c/app. 562-Funeral & proposal						3.00
554-Variant-c by Bianchi						6.00
554-Variant Skrull-c by Suydam						15.00
569-($3.99) Wraparound-c; Immonen-a; Dr. Doom app.						4.00
570-1st Council of Reeds	2	4	6	11	16	20
571-586: 570-572,575-578-Eaglesham-a. 574-Spider-Man app. 584-586-Galactus app.						3.00
587-(3/11, $3.99) Death of Human Torch; Epting-a; issue is in black polybag; Davis-c						4.00
587-Variant-c by Cassaday						10.00
588-($3.99) Last issue; Dragotta-a; preview of FF #1; back-up w/Spider-Man; Davis-c						4.00
589-599-**Do not exist**; story continues in FF series						
600-(1/12, $7.99) Avengers app.; Human Torch returns, back-up short stories; Dell'Otto-c						8.00
600-Variant-c by John Romita, Jr.						10.00
600-Variant-c by Art Adams						15.00
601-603,605,605.1, 606-611: 601-603-Johnny Storm & Avengers app. 602,603-Galactus app. 605.1-Alternate origin; Choi-a. 607,608-Black Panther app. 611-Doctor Doom app.						3.00
604-($3.99) Future Franklin and Valeria app.						4.00
...'98 Annual ($3.50) Immonen-a						4.00
...'99 Annual ($3.50) Ladronn-a						4.00
...'00 Annual ($3.50) Larocca-a; Marvel Girl back-up story						4.00

...'01 Annual ($2.99) Maguire-a; Thing back-up w/Yu-a 4.00
... Annual 32 (8/10, $4.99) Hitch-a/c 5.00
... Annual 33 (9/12, $4.99) Alan Davis-s/a/c; Dr. Strange & Clan Destine app. 5.00
... : A Death in the Family (7/06, $3.99, one-shot) Weeks-a/c; and r/F.F. #245 4.00
... By J. Michael Straczynski Vol. 1 (2005, $19.99, HC) r/#527-532 20.00
Civil War: Fantastic Four TPB (2007, $17.99) r/#538-543; 45th Anniversary Toasts 18.00
... Cosmic-Size Special 1 (2/09, $4.99) Cary Bates-s/Bing Cansino-a; r/F.F. #237 5.00
Fantastic 4th Voyage of Sinbad (9/01, $5.95) Claremont-s/Ferry-a 6.00
Flesh and Stone (8/01, $12.95, TPB) r/#35-39 13.00
... Giant-Size Adventures 1 (8/09, $3.99) Cifuentes & Coover-a; Egghead app. 4.00
... In...Ataque del M.O.D.O.K.! (11/10, $3.99) English & Spanish editions; Beland-s/Doe-a 4.00
... /Inhumans TPB (2007, $19.99) r/#51-54 and Inhumans ('00) #1-4 20.00
...: Isla De La Muerte! (2/08, $3.99) English & Spanish editions; Beland-s/Doe-a 4.00
... MGC #570 (7/11, $1.00) r/#570 with "Marvel's Greatest Comics" cover banner 3.00
... Presents: Franklin Richards 1 (11/05, $2.99) r/back-up stories from Power Pack #1-4 plus new 5 pg. story; Sumerak-s/Eliopoulos-a (Also see Franklin Richards) 3.00
...Special (2/06, $2.99) McDuffie-s/Casey Jones-a; dinner with Dr. Doom 3.00
...Tales Vol. 1 (2005, $7.99, digest) r/Marvel Age: FF Tales #1, Tales of the Thing #1-3, and Spider-Man Team-Up Special 8.00
...: The Last Stand (8/11, $4.99) r/#574, 587 & 588 (death of Johnny Storm) 5.00
...: The New Fantastic Four HC (2007, $19.99) r/#544-550; variant covers & sketch pgs. 20.00
...: The New Fantastic Four SC (2008, $15.99) r/#544-550; variant covers & sketch pgs. 16.00
... : The Wedding Special 1 (1/06, $5.00) 40th Anniversary new story & r/FF Annual #3 5.00
... Vol. 1 HC (2004, $29.99, dust jacket) oversized reprint /#60-70, 500-502; Mark Waid intro and series proposal; cover gallery 30.00
... Vol. 2 HC (2005, $29.99, d.j.) oversized r/#503-513; Waid intro.; deleted scenes 30.00
... Vol. 3 HC (2005, $29.99, d.j.) oversized r/#514-524; Waid commentaries; cover sketches 30.00
... Vol. 1: Imaginauts (2003, $17.99, TPB) r/#56,60-66; Mark Waid's series proposal 18.00
... Vol. 2: Unthinkable (2003, $17.99, TPB) r/#67-70,500-502; #500 Director's Cut extras 18.00
... Vol. 3: Authoritative Action (2004, $12.99, TPB) r/#503-508 13.00
... Vol. 4: Hereafter (2004, $11.99, TPB) r/#509-513 12.00
... Vol. 5: Disassembled (2004, $14.99, TPB) r/#514-519 15.00
... Vol. 6: Rising Storm (2005, $13.99, TPB) r/#520-524 14.00
...: The Beginning of the End TPB (2008, $14.99) r/#525,526,551-553 & Fantastic Four: Isla De La Muerte! one-shot 15.00
...: The Life Fantastic TPB (2006, $16.99) r/#533-535; The Wedding Special, Special (2/06) and A Death in the Family one-shots 17.00
Wizard #1/2 -Lim-a 10.00

FANTASTIC FOUR (Volume Four) (Marvel NOW!) (Also see FF)
Marvel Comics: Jan, 2013 - No. 16, Mar, 2014 ($2.99)

1-5-Fraction-s/Bagley-a/c 3.00
5AU-(5/13, $3.99) Age of Ultron tie-in; Fraction-s/Araújo-a/Bagley-c 4.00
6-15: 6,7-Blastaar app. 9,13-15-Dr. Doom app. 14,15-Ienco-a 3.00
16-($3.99) Fantastic Four vs. Doom, The Annihilating Conqueror; back-up w/Quinones-a 4.00

FANTASTIC FOUR (Volume Five) (All-New Marvel NOW!)
Marvel Comics: Apr, 2014 - No. 14, Feb, 2015; No. 642, Mar, 2015 - No. 645, Jun, 2015 ($3.99)

1-4-Robinson-s/Kirk-a. 3,4-Frightful Four app. 4.00
5-($4.99) Trial of the Fantastic Four; flashback-a by various incl. Starlin, Allred, Samnee 5.00
6-14: 6-8-Original Sin tie-in. 10,11-Scarlet Witch app. 11,12-Spider-Man app. 4.00
642-(3/15)-644: Heroes Reborn Avengers app. 643,644-Sleepwalker app. 4.00
645-($5.99) Psycho Man & the Frightful Four app.; Kirk-a; bonus back-up stories 6.00
Annual 1 (11/14, $4.99) Sue vs. Doctor Doom in Latveria; Grummett-a 5.00
100th Anniversary Special: Fantastic Four 1 (9/14, $3.99) Van Meter-s/Estep-a 4.00

FANTASTIC FOUR (Volume Six)
Marvel Comics: Oct, 2018 - No. 48, Dec, 2022 ($5.99/$3.99)

1-($5.99) Slott-s/Pichelli & Bianchi-a; Ben proposes to Alicia 6.00
2-4,6-11,13-20-($3.99) 4-Wrecking Crew app.; intro The Fantastix. 6-9-Doom vs. Galactus. 10-War of The Realms tie-in; Moon Girl app. 13-Thing vs. Hulk. 15-Intro. Sky 4.00
5-($7.99) Wedding of Ben and Alicia; art by Kuder, Allred (origin re-telling) and Hughes 8.00
12-($4.99) Thing battles the Immortal Hulk; Izaakse-a; Future Foundation back-up 5.00
21-24,26-31,33,34: 21-23-Tie-in to Empyre event; Wolverine and Spider-Man app. 24-Iceman app. 28-Silver Surfer app. 29,30-King in Black tie-ins 4.00
25-($5.99) She-Hulk & Doctor Doom app.; back-up story with Uatu & Nick Fury 6.00
32-($4.99) The Bride of Doom part 1; Doctor Doom and Lyja app. 5.00
35-($9.99) 60th Anniversary celebration; Romita Jr.-a; Kang, Immortus, Rama-Tut app.; back-up story retelling origin; Waid-s/Renaud-a 10.00
36-43,45-48: 38-She-Hulk app. 40-45-Reckoning War. 48 Judgment Day tie-in 4.00
...: Anniversary Tribute 1 (1/22, $6.99) Remakes 1961's FF #1 and FF Annual #3 with current
44-($4.99) Reckoning War; Silver Surfer & Doctor Doom app. 5.00
artists each redrawing a page in their style; McNiven-c swipe of FF #1 7.00
...: 4 Yancy Street 1 (10/19, $4.99) Duggan-s; the Terrible Trio app. 5.00
...: Grimm Noir 1 (4/20, $4.99) Duggan-s/Garney-a 5.00
...: Marvels Snapshots 1 (5/20, $4.99) Dorkin & Dyer-s/Dewey-a 5.00
...: Negative Zone 1 (1/20, $4.99) Carey-s/Caselli-a; Blastaar app. 5.00
...: Road Trip 1 (2/21, $4.99) Cantwell-s/Andrade-a 5.00
...: The Prodigal Sun 1 (9/19, $4.99) Davis-s/Manna-a; Ka-Zar app. 5.00
...: Wedding Special 1 (2/19, $4.99) Simone-s/Braga-a; Slott-a/Buckingham-a; Hembeck-s/a 5.00

FANTASTIC FOUR (Volume Seven)
Marvel Comics: Jan, 2023 - Present ($4.99/$3.99)

1-($4.99) North-s/Coello-a; main cover by Alex Ross 5.00
2-4-($3.99) 4.00

FANTASTIC FOUR AND POWER PACK
Marvel Comics: Sept, 2007 - No. 4, Dec, 2007 ($2.99, limited series)

1-4-Gurihiru-a/Van Lente-s; the Wizard app. 3.00
...: Favorite Son TPB (2008, $7.99, digest size) r/#1-4 8.00

FANTASTIC FOUR: ANTITHESIS
Marvel Comics: Oct, 2020 - No. 4, Jan, 2021 ($4.99, limited series)

1-4-Neal Adams-a/Mark Waid-s; Silver Surfer & Galactus app. 5.00

FANTASTIC FOUR: ATLANTIS RISING
Marvel Comics: June, 1995 - No. 2, July, 1995 ($3.95, limited series)

1,2: Acetate-c 5.00
Collector's Preview (5/95, $2.25, 52 pgs.) 4.00

FANTASTIC FOUR: BIG TOWN
Marvel Comics: Jan, 2001 - No. 4, Apr, 2001 ($2.99, limited series)

1-4:"What If?" story; McKone-a/Englehart-s 3.00

FANTASTIC FOUR: FIREWORKS
Marvel Comics: Jan, 1999 - No. 3, Mar, 1999 ($2.99, limited series)

1-3-Remix; Jeff Johnson-a 4.00

FANTASTIC FOUR: FIRST FAMILY
Marvel Comics: May, 2006 - No. 6, Oct, 2006 ($2.99, limited series)

1-6-Casey-s/Weston-a; flashback to the days after the accident 3.00
TPB (2006, $15.99) r/#1-6 16.00

FANTASTIC FOUR: FOES
Marvel Comics: Mar, 2005 - No. 6, Aug, 2005 ($2.99, limited series)

1-6-Kirkman-s/Rathburn-a. 1-Puppet Master app. 3-Super-Skrull app. 4-Mole Man app. 3.00
TPB (2005, $16.99) r/#1-6 17.00

FANTASTIC FOUR: FULL CIRCLE
Abrams ComicArts (Marvel Comics): 2022 ($24.99, hardcover with dust jacket)

nn-Silver Age version of the team goes to the Negative Zone; Alex Ross-s/a 25.00
Previews Exclusive Slipcase Edition (2022, $40.00, limited to 3,000); bonus print 40.00

FANTASTIC FOUR: GRAND DESIGN
Marvel Comics: Dec, 2019 - No. 2, Jan, 2020 ($5.99, limited series)

1,2-History of the Fantastic Four retold; Tom Scioli-s/a/c; bonus background text info. 6.00

FANTASTIC FOUR: HOUSE OF M (Reprinted in House of M: Fantastic Four/ Iron Man TPB)
Marvel Comics: Sept, 2005 - No. 3, Nov, 2005 ($2.99, limited series)

1-3: Fearsome Four, led by Doom; Scot Eaton-a 3.00

FANTASTIC FOUR INDEX (See Official...)

FANTASTIC FOUR/ IRON MAN: BIG IN JAPAN
Marvel Comics: Dec, 2005 - No. 4, Mar, 2006 ($3.50, limited series)

1-4-Seth Fisher-a/c; Zeb Wells-s; wraparound-c on each 3.50
TPB (2006, $12.99) r/#1-4 and Seth Fisher illustrated story from Spider-Man Unlimited #8 13.00

FANTASTIC FOUR: LIFE STORY
Marvel Comics: Jul, 2021 - No. 6, Apr, 2022 ($4.99, limited series)

1-6-The 1961 Fantastic Four ages in real time; Russell-s/Izaakse-a. 2-The '70s; intro Doom and Namor. 4-The '90s; Silver Surfer app. 5-The '00s; Galactus arrives 5.00

FANTASTIC FOUR: 1 2 3 4
Marvel Comics: Oct, 2001 - No. 4, Jan, 2002 ($2.99, limited series)

1-4-Morrison-s/Jae Lee-a. 2-4-Namor-c/app. 3.00
TPB (2002, $9.99) r/#1-4 10.00

FANTASTIC FOUR ROAST
Marvel Comics Group: May, 1982 (75¢, one-shot, direct sales)

1-Celebrates 20th anniversary of F.F.#1; X-Men, Ghost Rider & many others cameo; Golden, Miller, Buscema, Rogers, Byrne, Anderson art; Hembeck/Austin-c 5.00

FANTASTIC FOUR: THE END
Marvel Comics: Jan, 2007 - No. 6, May, 2007 ($2.99, limited series)

1-6-Alan Davis-s/a; last adventure of the future FF. 1-Dr. Doom-c/app. 3.00
Roughcut #1 ($3.99) B&W pencil art for full story and text script; B&W sketch cover 4.00
HC (2007, $19.99, dustjacket) r/#1-6 20.00
SC (2008, $14.99) r/#1-6 15.00

FANTASTIC FOUR: THE LEGEND
Marvel Comics: Oct, 1996 ($3.95, one-shot)

1-Tribute issue 4.00

FANTASTIC FOUR: THE MOVIE
Marvel Comics: Aug, 2005 ($4.99/$12.99, one-shot)

1-($4.99) Movie adaptation; Jurgens-a; behind the scenes feature; Doom origin; photo-c 5.00
TPB-($12.99) Movie adaptation, r/Fantastic Four #5 & 190, and FF Vol. 3 #60, photo-c 13.00

FANTASTIC FOUR: TRUE STORY
Marvel Comics: Sept, 2008 - No. 4, Jan, 2009 ($2.99, limited series)

1-4-Cornell-s/Domingues-a/Henrichon-c 3.00

FANTASTIC FOUR 2099
Marvel Comics: Jan, 1996 - No. 8, Aug, 1996 ($3.95/$1.95)

1-($3.95)-Chromium-c; X-Nation preview 5.00
2-8: 4-Spider-Man 2099-c/app. 5-Doctor Strange app. 7-Thibert-c 4.00
... No. 1 (1/20, $4.99) Karla Pacheco-s/Steven Cummings-a; H.E.R.B.I.E. app. 5.00
NOTE: *Williamson a-1i; c-1i.*

FANTASTIC FOUR UNLIMITED
Marvel Comics: Mar, 1993 - No. 12, Dec, 1995 ($3.95, 68 pgs.)

1-12: 1-Black Panther app. 4-Thing vs. Hulk. 5-Vs. The Frightful Four. 6-Vs. Namor. 7, 9-12-Wraparound-c 4.00

FANTASTIC FOUR UNPLUGGED
Marvel Comics: Sept, 1995 - No. 6, Aug 1996 (99¢, bi-monthly)

1-6 4.00

FANTASTIC FOUR - UNSTABLE MOLECULES
(Indicia for #1 reads STARTLING STORIES: ... ; #2 reads UNSTABLE MOLECULES)
Marvel Comics: Mar, 2003 - No. 4, June, 2003 ($2.99, limited series)

1-4-Guy Davis-c/a 3.00
Fantastic Four Legends Vol. 1 TPB (2003, $13.99) r/#1-4, origin from FF #1 (1963) 14.00
TPB (2005, $13.99) r/#1-4 14.00

FANTASTIC FOUR VS. X-MEN
Marvel Comics: Feb, 1987 - No. 4, June, 1987 (Limited series)

1-4: 4-Austin-a(i) 5.00

FANTASTIC FOUR: WORLD'S GREATEST COMICS MAGAZINE
Marvel Comics: Feb, 2001 - No. 12 (Limited series)

1-12: Homage to Lee & Kirby era of F.F.; s/a by Larsen & various. 5-Hulk-c/app. 10-Thor app. 3.00

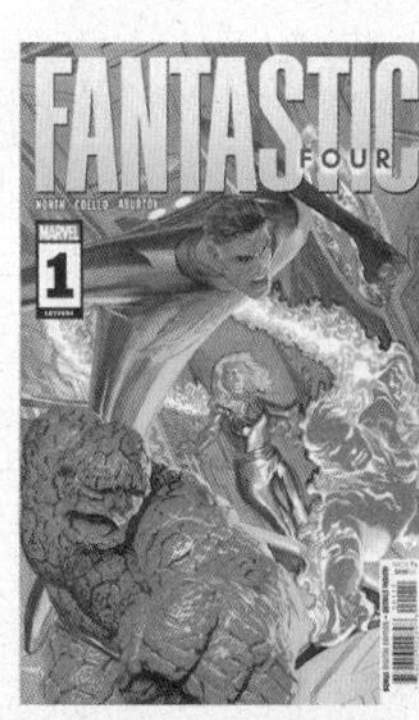

Fantastic Four (2023) #1 © MAR

Fantastic Four: Life Story #1 © MAR

Faster Than Light #4 © Anomaly

	GD 2.0	VG 4.0	FN 6.0	VF 8.0	VF/NM 9.0	NM- 9.2

FANTASTIC GIANTS (Formerly Konga #1-23)
Charlton Comics: V2#24, Sept, 1966 (25¢, 68 pgs.)

V2#24-Special Ditko issue; origin Konga & Gorgo reprinted plus two new Ditko stories 9 18 27 57 111 165

FANTASTIC TALES
I. W. Enterprises: 1958 (no date) (Reprint, one-shot)

1-Reprints Avon's "City of the Living Dead" 5 10 15 30 50 70

FANTASTIC VOYAGE (See Movie Comics)
Gold Key: Aug, 1969 - No. 2, Dec, 1969

1 (TV) 4 8 12 27 44 60
2-Cover has the text "Civilian Miniaturized Defense Force" in yellow bar at top; back cover has painted art 3 6 9 19 30 40
2-Variant cover has text "In This Issue Sweepstakes..." along top; ad on back-c 4 8 12 23 37 50

FANTASTIC VOYAGES OF SINDBAD, THE
Gold Key: Oct, 1965 - No. 2, June, 1967

1-Painted-c on both 7 14 21 46 86 125
2 5 10 15 33 57 80

FANTASTIC WORLDS
Standard Comics: No. 5, Sept, 1952 - No. 7, Jan, 1953

5-Toth, Anderson-a 50 100 150 315 533 750
6-Toth-c/a 39 78 117 231 378 525
7 32 64 96 188 307 425

FANTASY ILLUSTRATED
New Media Publ.: Spring 1982 ($2.95, B&W magazine)

1-P. Craig Russell-c/a; art by Ditko, Sekowsky, Sutton; Englehart-s 1 3 4 6 8 10

FANTASY MASTERPIECES (Marvel Super Heroes No. 12 on)
Marvel Comics Group: Feb, 1966 - No. 11, Oct, 1967; V2#1, Dec, 1979 - No. 14, Jan, 1981

1-Photo of Stan Lee (12¢-c #1,2) 9 18 27 60 120 180
2-r/1st Fin Fang Foom from Strange Tales #89 6 12 18 38 69 100
3-8: 3-G.A. Capt. America-r begin, end #11; 1st 25¢ Giant; Colan-r. 3-6-Kirby-c(p). 4-Kirby-c(p)(i). 7-Begin G.A. Sub-Mariner, Torch-r/M. Mystery. 8-Torch battles the Sub-Mariner-r/Marvel Mystery #9 6 12 18 37 66 95
9-Origin Human Torch-r/Marvel Comics #1 6 12 18 41 76 110
10,11: 10-r/origin & 1st app. All Winners Squad from All Winners #19. 11-r/origin of Toro (H.T. #1) & Black Knight #1 5 10 15 34 60 85
V2#1(12/79, 75¢, 52 pgs.)-r/origin Silver Surfer from Silver Surfer #1 with editing plus reprints cover; J. Buscema-a 2 4 6 9 12 15
2-14-Reprints Silver Surfer #2-14 w/covers 6.00

NOTE: ***Buscema*** *c-V2#7-9(in part).* ***Ditko*** *r-1-3, 7, 9.* ***Everett*** *r-1,7-9.* ***Matt Fox*** *r-9i.* ***Kirby*** *r-1-11; c(p)-3, 4i, 5, 6.* ***Starlin*** *r-8-13. Some direct sale V2#14's had a 50¢ cover price. #3-11 contain Capt. America-r/Capt. America #3-10. #7-11 contain G.A.Human Torch & Sub-Mariner-r.*

FANTASY QUARTERLY (Also see Elfquest)
Independent Publishers Syndicate: Spring, 1978 (B&W)

1-1st app. Elfquest; Dave Sim-a (6 pgs.) 14 28 42 93 204 315

FANTOMAN (Formerly Amazing Adventure Funnies)
Centaur Publications: No. 2, Aug, 1940 - No. 4, Dec, 1940

2-The Fantom of the Fair, The Arrow, Little Dynamite-r begin; origin The Ermine by Filchock; Burgos, J. Cole, Ernst, Gustavson-a 181 362 543 1158 1979 2800
3,4: Gustavson-r. 4-Red Blaze story 148 296 444 947 1624 2300

FANTOMEX MAX
Marvel Comics: Dec, 2013 - No. 4, Mar, 2014 ($3.99)

1-4-Hope-s/Crystal-a/Francavilla-c 4.00

FAR CRY: RITE OF PASSAGE (Based on the Far Cry videogame series)
Dark Horse Comics: May, 2021 - No. 3, Aug, 2021 ($3.99, limited series)

1-3-Bryan Edward Hill-s/Geraldo Borges-a 4.00

FAREWELL MOONSHADOW (See Moonshadow)
DC Comics (Vertigo): Jan, 1997 ($7.95, one-shot)

nn-DeMatteis-s/Muth-c/a 8.00

FARGO KID (Formerly Justice Traps the Guilty)(See Feature Comics #47)
Prize Publications: V11#3(#1), June-July, 1958 - V11#5, Oct-Nov, 1958

V11#3(#1)-Origin Fargo Kid, Severin-c/a; Williamson-a(2); Heath-a 18 36 54 105 165 225
V11#4,5-Severin-c/a 13 26 39 74 105 135

FARMER'S DAUGHTER, THE
Stanhall Publ./Trojan Magazines: Feb-Mar, 1954 - No. 3, June-July, 1954; No. 4, Oct, 1954

1-Lingerie, nudity panel 206 412 618 1318 2259 3200
2-4(Stanhall) 129 258 387 826 1413 2000

FARMHAND
Image Comics: Jul, 2018 - Present ($3.99)

1-20-Rob Guillory-s/a 4.00

FARSCAPE (Based on TV series)
BOOM! Studios: Nov, 2008 - No. 4, Feb, 2009 ($3.99)

1-4-O'Bannon-s/Patterson-a; multiple covers 4.00

FARSCAPE (Based on TV series)
BOOM! Studios: Nov, 2009 - No. 24, Oct, 2011 ($3.99)

1-24-O'Bannon-s/Sliney-a; multiple covers 4.00
...: D'Argo's Lament 1-4 (4/09 - No. 4, 7/09, $3.99) Edwards-a; three covers on each 4.00
...: D'Argo's Quest 1-4 (12/09 - No. 4, 3/10, $3.99) Cleveland-a; three covers on each 4.00
...: D'Argo's Trial 1-4 (8/09 - No. 4, 11/09, $3.99) Cleveland-a; multiple covers on each 4.00
...: Gone and Back 1-4 (7/09 - No. 4, 10/09, $3.99) Patterson-a; multiple covers on each 4.00
...: Scorpius 0-7 (4/10 - No. 7, 2010, $3.99) 0-3-Ruiz-a; multiple-c. 4-7-Purcell-a 4.00
...: Strange Detractors 1-4 (3/09 - No. 4, 6/09, $3.99) Sliney-a; three covers on each 4.00

FARSCAPE: WAR TORN (Based on TV series)
DC Comics (WildStorm): Apr, 2002 - No. 2, May, 2002 ($4.95, limited series)

1,2-Teranishi-a/Wolfman-s; photo-c 5.00

FAR SECTOR
DC Comics (Young Animal): Jan, 2020 - No. 12, Aug, 2021 ($3.99)

1-12: 1-Intro Green Lantern Sojourner Mullein; N.K. Jemisin-s/Jamal Campbell-a 4.00

FASHION IN ACTION
Eclipse Comics: Aug, 1986 - Feb, 1987 (Baxter paper)

Summer Special 1, Winter Special 1, each Snyder III-c/a 3.00

FASTBALL EXPRESS (Major League Baseball)
Ultimate Sports Force: 2000 ($3.95, one-shot)

1-Polybagged with poster; Johnson, Maddux, Park, Nomo, Clemens app. 4.00

FASTER THAN LIGHT
Image Comics (Shadowline): Sept, 2015 - No. 10, Sept, 2016 ($2.99)

1-10-Brian Haberlin-s/a 3.00

FASTEST GUN ALIVE, THE (Movie)
Dell Publishing Co.: No. 741, Sept, 1956 (one-shot)

Four Color 741-Photo-c 7 14 21 44 82 120

FAST FICTION (...Action) (Stories by Famous Authors Illustrated #6 on)
Seaboard Publ./Famous Authors Ill.: Oct, 1949 - No. 5, Mar, 1950 (All have Kiefer-c)(48 pgs.)

1-Scarlet Pimpernel; Jim Lavery-c/a 36 72 108 214 347 480
2-Captain Blood; H. C. Kiefer-c/a 26 52 78 152 249 345
3-She, by Rider Haggard; Vincent Napoli-a 34 68 102 199 325 450
4-(1/50, 52 pgs.)-The 39 Steps; Lavery-c/a 19 38 57 112 176 240
5-Beau Geste; Kiefer-c/a 19 38 57 112 176 240

NOTE: ***Kiefer*** *a-2, 5; c-2, 3,5.* ***Lavery*** *c/a-1, 4.* ***Napoli*** *a-3.*

FAST FORWARD
DC Comics (Piranha Press): 1992 - No. 3, 1993 ($4.95, 68 pgs.)

1-3: 1-Morrison scripts; McKean-c/a. 3-Sam Kieth-a 5.00

FAST WILLIE JACKSON
Fitzgerald Periodicals, Inc.: Oct, 1976 - No. 7, 1977

1 8 16 24 54 102 150
2-7 4 8 12 23 40 55

FAT ALBERT (...& the Cosby Kids) (TV)
Gold Key: Mar, 1974 - No. 29, Feb, 1979

1 9 18 27 57 111 165
2-10 3 6 9 16 24 32
11-29 2 4 6 11 16 20

FATALE (Also see Powers That Be #1 & Shadow State #1,2)
Broadway Comics: Jan, 1996 - No. 6, Aug, 1996 ($2.50)

1-6: J.G. Jones-c/a in all, Preview Edition 1 (11/95, B&W) 3.00

FATALE
Image Comics: Jan, 2012 - No. 24, Jul, 2014 ($3.50)

1-Brubaker-s/Phillips-a/c 5.00
1-Variant-c of Demon with machine gun 8.00
1-Second through Fifth printings 4.00
2-23-Brubaker-s/Phillips-a/c in all 3.50

24-($4.99) Story conclusion; bonus preview of The Fade Out series 5.00

FAT AND SLAT (Ed Wheelan) (Becomes Gunfighter No. 5 on)
E. C. Comics: Summer, 1947 - No. 4, Spring, 1948

1-Intro/origin Voltage, Man of Lightning; "Comics" McCormick, the World's No. 1 Comic Book Fan begins, ends #4 55 110 165 352 601 850
2-4: 4-Comics McCormick-c feature 37 74 111 222 361 500

FAT AND SLAT JOKE BOOK
All-American Comics (William H. Wise): Summer, 1944 (52 pgs., one-shot)

nn-by Ed Wheelan 37 74 111 222 361 500

FATE (See Hand of Fate & Thrill-O-Rama)

FATE
DC Comics: Oct, 1994 - No. 22, Sept, 1996 ($1.95/$2.25)

0,1-22: 8-Begin $2.25-c. 11-14-Alan Scott (Sentinel) app. 10,14-Zatanna app. 21-Phantom Stranger app. 22-Spectre app. 3.00

FATHER'S DAY
Dark Horse Comics: Oct, 2014 - No. 4, Jan, 2015 ($3.99, limited series)

1-4-Mike Richardson-s/Gabriel Guzmán-a 4.00

FATHOM
Comico: May, 1987 - No. 3, July, 1987 ($1.50, limited series)

1-3 3.00

FATHOM
Image Comics (Top Cow Prod.): Aug, 1998 - No. 14, May, 2002 ($2.50)

Preview 12.00
0-Wizard supplement 7.00
0-($6.95) DF Alternate 7.00
1/2 (Wizard) origin of Cannon; Turner-a 6.00
1/2 (3/03, $2.99) origin of Cannon 3.00
1-Turner-s/a; three covers; alternate story pages 6.00
1-Reprint Edition (8/21, $1.99) Bonus preview of Fathom: The Core #1 3.00
1-Wizard World Edition 9.00
2-14: 12-14-Witchblade app. 13,14-Tomb Raider app. 3.00
9-Green foil-c edition 15.00
9,12-Holofoil editions 18.00
12,13-DFE alternate-c 6.00
13,14-DFE Gold edition 8.00
14-DFE Blue 15.00
... Collected Edition 1 (3/99, $5.95) r/Preview & all three #1's 6.00
... Collected Edition 2-4 (3-12/99, $5.95) 2-r/#2,3. 3-r/#4,5. 4-r/#6,7 6.00
... Collected Edition 5 (4/00, $5.95) 5-r/#8,9 6.00
... Primer (6/11, $1.00) Comic style summary of Volume 1; text summaries of Vol. 2 & 3 3.00
... Swimsuit Special (5/99, $2.95) Pin-ups by various 3.00
... Swimsuit Special 2000 (12/00, $2.95) Pin-ups by various; Turner-c 3.00
Michael Turner's Fathom HC ('01, $39.95) r/#1-9, black-c w/silver foil 40.00
Michael Turner's Fathom SC ('01, $24.95) r/#1-9, new Turner-c 25.00
Michael Turner's Fathom The Definitive Edition ('08, $49.95) r/Preview, #0,1/2,1-14, Swimsuit Special 1999 & 2000; cover gallery; foreword by Geoff Johns 50.00

FATHOM (MICHAEL TURNER'S...) (Volume 2)
Aspen MLT, Inc.: No. 0, Apr, 2005 - No. 11, Dec, 2006 ($2.50/$2.99)

0-($2.50) Turnbull-a/Turner-c 3.00
1-11-($2.99) 1-Five covers. 2-Two covers. 4-Six covers 3.00
... Beginnings (2005, $1.99) Two covers; Turnbull-a 3.00
...: Killian's Vessel 1 (7/07, $2.99) 3 covers; Odagawa-a 3.00
... Prelude (6/05, $2.99) Seven covers; Garza-a 3.00

FATHOM (MICHAEL TURNER'S...) (Volume 3)
Aspen MLT, Inc.: No. 0, Jun, 2008 - No. 10, Feb, 2010 ($2.50/$2.99)

0-($2.50) Garza-a/c 3.00
1-10-($2.99) Garza-a; multiple covers on each 3.00

FATHOM (MICHAEL TURNER'S...) (Volume 4)
Aspen MLT, Inc.: No. 0, Jun, 2011 - No. 9, May, 2013 ($2.50/$2.99/$3.50)

0-($2.50) Lobdell-s/Konat-a/c; interview with Lobdell; sketch art 3.00
1-3-($2.99) 1-Five covers 3.00
4-9-($3.50) 3.50

FATHOM (MICHAEL TURNER'S...) (Volume 5)
Aspen MLT, Inc.: Jul, 2013 - No. 8, Sept, 2014 ($1.00/$3.99)

1-($1.00) Wohl-s/Konat-a; multiple covers 3.00
2-8-($3.99) Multiple covers on all 4.00
Annual 1 (6/14, $5.99) Turner-c; short stories by Turner, Wohl/Calero, Ruffino & others 6.00

FATHOM (ALL NEW MICHAEL TURNER'S...) (Volume 6)
Aspen MLT, Inc.: Feb, 2017 - No. 8, Sept, 2017 ($3.99)

1-8-Northcott-s/Renna-a; multiple covers 4.00

FATHOM (ALL NEW MICHAEL TURNER'S...) (Volume 7)
Aspen MLT: Jun, 2018 - No. 8, Apr, 2019 ($3.99)

1-8-Multiple covers on each; Ron Marz-s/Siya Oum-a 4.00
... Primer 1 (6/18, 25¢) Origin re-told; recaps of previous volumes 3.00

FATHOM (ALL NEW MICHAEL TURNER'S...) (Volume 8)
Aspen MLT: May, 2019 - No. 6, Oct, 2019 ($3.99)

1-6-Multiple covers on each; Hernandez-s/Campetella-a 4.00

FATHOM BLUE (MICHAEL TURNER'S...)
Aspen MLT, Inc.: Jun, 2015 - No. 6, Dec, 2015 ($3.99, limited series)

1-6-Hernandez-s/Avella-a; multiple covers on all 4.00

FATHOM: BLUE DESCENT (MICHAEL TURNER'S...)
Aspen MLT, Inc.: Jun, 2010 - No. 4, Feb, 2012 ($2.50/$2.99, limited series)

0-($2.50) Scott Clark-a; covers by Clark & Benitez 3.00
1-4-($2.99) Alex Sanchez-a. 1-Covers by Clark & Finch 3.00

FATHOM: CANNON HAWKE (MICHAEL TURNER'S...)
Aspen MLT, Inc.: Nov, 2005 - No. 5, Feb, 2006 ($2.99)

1-5-To-a/Turner-c 3.00
... Prelude (11/05, $2.50) Turner-c 3.00

FATHOM: DAWN OF WAR (MICHAEL TURNER'S...)
Aspen MLT, Inc.: Oct, 2004 - No. 3, Dec, 2004 ($2.99, limited series)

0-Caldwell-a 3.00
1-3-Caldwell-a 3.00
...: Cannon Hawke #0 ('04, $2.50) Turner-c 3.00
... The Complete Saga Vol. 1 (2005, $9.99) r/series with cover gallery 10.00

FATHOM: KIANI (MICHAEL TURNER'S...)
Aspen MLT, Inc.: No. 0, Feb, 2007 - No. 4, Dec, 2007 ($2.99, limited series)

0-4-Marcus To-a. 1-Six covers 3.00
Vol. 2 (4/12, $2.50) 0-Four covers 3.00
Vol. 2 (5/12 - No. 4, 11/12, $3.50) 1-4-Hernandez-s/Nome-a; multiple covers on each 3.50
Vol. 3 (3/14 - No. 4, 6/14, $3.99) 1-4-Hernandez-s/Cafaro-a; multiple covers on each 4.00
Vol. 4 (2/15 - No. 4, 5/15, $3.99) 1-4-Hernandez-s/Cafaro-a; multiple covers on each 4.00

FATHOM: KILLIAN'S TIDE
Image Comics (Top Cow Prod.): Apr, 2001 - No. 4, Nov, 2001 ($2.95)

1-4-Caldwell-a(p); two covers by Caldwell and Turner. 2-Flip-book preview of Universe 3.00
1-DFE Blue, 1-Holographic logo 12.00
4-Foil-c 12.00

FATHOM: THE CORE (Leads into Soulfire: The Core)
Aspen MLT, Inc.: Nov, 2021 - No. 2, Dec, 2021 ($3.99, limited series)

1,2-Hernandez-s/Konat-a; multiple covers 4.00

FATHOM: THE ELITE SAGA (MICHAEL TURNER'S...)
Aspen MLT, Inc.: Jun, 2013 - No. 5, Jul, 2013 ($3.99, weekly limited series)

1-5-Hernandez-s/Marion-a; multiple covers; leads into Fathom Volume 5 4.00

FATIMA...CHALLENGE TO THE WORLD (Also see Our Lady of Fatima)
Catechetical Guild: 1951, 36 pgs. (15¢)

nn (not same as 'Challenge to the World') 8 16 24 42 54 65

FATMAN, THE HUMAN FLYING SAUCER
Lightning Comics (Milson Publ. Co.): April, 1967 - No. 3, Aug-Sept, 1967 (68 pgs.) (Written by Otto Binder)

1-Origin/1st app. Fatman & Tinman by C.C. Beck; 1st app. Anti-Man; 2-pg. Fatman pin-up by Beck 7 14 21 49 92 135
2-C. C. Beck-a 5 10 15 33 57 80
3-(Scarce)-Beck-a 6 12 18 41 76 110

FAUNTLEROY COMICS (Super Duck Presents...)
Close-Up/Archie Publications: 1950; No. 2, 1951; No. 3, 1952

1-Super Duck-c/stories by Al Fagaly in all 12 24 36 69 97 125
2,3 8 16 24 40 50 60

FAUST
Northstar Publishing/Rebel Studios #7 on: 1989 - No 13, 1997 ($2.00/$2.25, B&W, mature themes)

1-Decapitation-c; Tim Vigil-c/a in all 3 6 9 19 30 40
1-2nd - 4th printings 4.00
2 2 4 6 8 11 14
2-2nd & 3rd printings, 3,5-2nd printing 4.00
3 2 4 6 8 10 12
4-10: 7-Begin Rebel Studios series 5.00
11-13-Scarce 2 4 6 8 11 14

FAWCETT MOTION PICTURE COMICS (See Motion Picture Comics)

FAWCETT MOVIE COMIC
Fawcett Publications: 1949 - No. 20, Dec, 1952 (All photo-c)

nn- "Dakota Lil"; George Montgomery & Rod Cameron (1949) 20 40 60 120 195 270
nn- "Copper Canyon"; Ray Milland & Hedy Lamarr (1950) 15 30 45 90 140 190
nn- "Destination Moon" (1950) 68 136 204 435 743 1050
nn- "Montana"; Errol Flynn & Alexis Smith (1950) 15 30 45 90 140 190
nn- "Pioneer Marshal"; Monte Hale (1950) 15 30 45 90 140 190
nn- "Powder River Rustlers"; Rocky Lane (1950) 20 40 60 117 189 260
nn- "Singing Guns"; Vaughn Monroe, Ella Raines & Walter Brennan (1950) 14 28 42 82 121 160
7- "Gunmen of Abilene"; Rocky Lane; Bob Powell-a (1950) 16 32 48 92 144 195
8- "King of the Bullwhip"; Lash LaRue; Bob Powell-a (1950) 21 42 63 126 206 285
9- "The Old Frontier"; Monte Hale; Bob Powell-a (2/51; mis-dated 2/50) 15 30 45 90 140 190
10- "The Missourians"; Monte Hale (4/51) 15 30 45 90 140 190
11- "The Thundering Trail"; Lash LaRue (6/51) 19 38 57 111 176 240
12- "Rustlers on Horseback"; Rocky Lane (8/51) 15 30 45 90 140 190
13- "Warpath"; Edmond O'Brien & Forrest Tucker (10/51) 14 28 42 80 115 150
14- "Last Outpost"; Ronald Reagan (12/51) 32 64 96 188 307 425
15-(Scarce)- "The Man From Planet X"; Robert Clark; Schaffenberger-a (2/52) 258 516 774 1651 2826 4000
16- "Ten Tall Men"; Burt Lancaster 13 26 39 74 105 135
17- "Rose of Cimarron"; Jack Buetel & Mala Powers 10 20 30 58 79 100
18- "The Brigand"; Anthony Dexter & Anthony Quinn; Schaffenberger-a 10 20 30 58 79 100
19- "Carbine Williams"; James Stewart; Costanza-a; James Stewart photo-c 11 22 33 62 86 110
20- "Ivanhoe"; Robert Taylor & Liz Taylor photo-c 18 36 54 105 165 225

FAWCETT'S FUNNY ANIMALS (No. 1-26, 80-on titled "Funny Animals"; becomes Li'l Tomboy No. 92 on?)
Fawcett Publications/Charlton Comics No. 84 on: 12/42 - #79, 4/53; #80, 6/53 - #83, 12?/53; #84, 4/54 - #91, 2/56

1-Capt. Marvel on cover; intro. Hoppy The Captain Marvel Bunny, cloned from Capt. Marvel;

Fathom V3 #3 © Aspen MLT

Fear Agent #30 © Remender & Moore

Fear Itself #3 © MAR

	GD 2.0	VG 4.0	FN 6.0	VF 8.0	VF/NM 9.0	NM- 9.2
Billy the Kid & Willie the Worm begin	65	130	195	416	708	1000
2-Xmas-c	37	74	111	222	361	500
3-5: 3(2/43)-Spirit of '43-c	26	52	78	154	252	350
6,7,9,10	15	30	45	88	137	185
8-Flag-c	16	32	48	92	144	195
11-20: 14-Cover is a 1944 calendar	12	24	36	69	97	125
21-40: 25-Xmas-c. 26-St. Valentine's Day-c	10	20	30	54	72	90
41-86,90,91	9	18	27	47	61	75
87-89(10-54-2/55)-Merry Mailman ish (TV/Radio)-part photo-c	10	20	30	54	72	90

NOTE: *Marvel Bunny in all issues to at least No. 68 (not in 49-54).*

FAZE ONE FAZERS
AC Comics: 1986 - No. 4, Sept, 1986 (Limited series)

1-4 — 3.00

F.B.I., THE
Dell Publishing Co.: Apr-June, 1965

	GD	VG	FN	VF	VF/NM	NM-
1-Sinnott-a	5	10	15	31	53	75

F.B.I. STORY, THE (Movie)
Dell Publishing Co.: No. 1069, Jan-Mar, 1960

	GD	VG	FN	VF	VF/NM	NM-
Four Color 1069-Toth-a; James Stewart photo-c	9	18	27	61	123	185

FBP: FEDERAL BUREAU OF PHYSICS (Titled Collider for issue #1)
DC Comics (Vertigo): Sept, 2013 - No. 24, Nov, 2015 ($2.99/$3.99)

Collider #1- Simon Oliver-s/Robbi Rodriguez-a/Nathan Fox-c — 3.00
2-20: 2-(10/13) — 3.00
21-24-($3.99) — 4.00

FEAR (Adventure into...)
Marvel Comics Group: Nov, 1970 - No. 31, Dec, 1975

	GD	VG	FN	VF	VF/NM	NM-
1-Fantasy & Sci-Fi-r in early issues; 68 pg. Giant size; Kirby-a(r)	9	18	27	59	117	175
2-6: 2-4-(68 pgs.). 5,6-(52 pgs.) Kirby-a(r)	5	10	15	30	50	70
7-9-Kirby-a(r)	3	6	9	20	31	42
10-Man-Thing begins (10/72, 4th app.), ends #19; see Savage Tales #1 for 1st app.; 1st solo series; Chaykin/Morrow-c/a;	12	24	36	80	173	265
11-Neal Adams-c	13	26	39	89	195	300
12,13,14,16-18: 12-Starlin/Buckler-a. 17-Origin/1st app. Wundarr	3	6	9	17	26	35
15-1st full-length Man-Thing story (8/73)	3	6	9	21	33	45
19-Intro. Howard the Duck; Val Mayerik-a (12/73)	16	32	48	110	243	375
20-Morbius, the Living Vampire begins, ends #31; has history recap of Morbius with X-Men & Spider-Man	10	20	30	64	132	200
21-23,25	3	6	9	16	24	32
24-Blade-c/sty	10	20	30	68	144	220
26-31	3	6	9	14	19	24

NOTE: ***Bolle** a-13i. **Brunner** c-15-17. **Buckler** a-11p, 12i. **Chaykin** a-10i. **Colan** a-23r. **Craig** a-10p. **Ditko** a-6-8r. **Evans** a-30. **Everett** a-9, 10i, 21r. **Gulacy** a-20p. **Heath** a-12r. **Heck** a-8r, 13r. **Gil Kane** a-21p; c(p)-20, 21, 23-28, 31. **Kirby** a-1-9r. **Maneely** a-24r. **Mooney** a-11i, 26r. **Morrow** a-11i. **Paul Reinman** a-14r. **Robbins** a(p)-25-27, 31. **Russell** a-23p, 24p. **Severin** c-8. **Starlin** c-12p.*

FEAR AGENT
Image Comics (#1-11)/Dark Horse Comics.: Oct, 2005 - No. 32, Nov, 2011 ($2.99/$3.50)

1-11: 1-Remender-s/Moore-a. 5-Opeña-a begins. 11-Francavilla-a — 3.00
... The Last Goodbye 1-4 (Dark Horse, 6/07 - No. 4, 9/07) (#12-15) — 3.00
Tales of the Fear Agent: Twelve Steps in One (#16), 17-27 — 3.00
28-32-($3.50) Hawthorne & Moore-a/Moore-c — 3.50
... Vol 1.: Re-Ignition TPB (2006, $9.99) r/#1-4 — 10.00
... Vol 2.: My War TPB (Dark Horse Books, 2007, $14.95) r/#5-10; Opeña sketch pages — 15.00

FEARBOOK
Eclipse Comics: April, 1986 ($1.75, one-shot, mature)

1-Scholastic Mag-r; Bissette-a — 6.00

FEAR CASE
Dark Horse Comics: Feb, 2021 - No. 4, May, 2021 ($3.99)

1-4-Matt Kindt-s/Tyler Jenkins-a — 4.00

FEAR EFFECT (Based on the video game)
Image Comics (Top Cow): May, 2000; March, 2001 ($2.95)

Retro Helix 1 (3/01), Special 1 (5/00) — 3.00

FEAR IN THE NIGHT (See Complete Mystery No. 3)

FEAR ITSELF
Marvel Comics: Jun, 2011 - No. 7, Dec, 2011 ($3.99/$4.99, limited series)

1-6-Fraction-s/Immonen-a/McNiven-c. 3-Bucky apparently killed — 4.00
1-Blank cover — 4.00
7-($4.99) Thor perishes; previews of ...: The Fearless, Incredible Hulk #1, Defenders #1 — 5.00
7.1 Captain America (1/12, $3.99) Brubaker-s/Guice-a; Bucky's fate — 4.00
7.2 Thor (1/12, $3.99) Fraction-s/Adam Kubert-a/c; Thor's funeral; Tanarus returns — 4.00
7.3 Iron Man (1/12, $3.99) Fraction-s/Larroca-a/c; Odin app. — 4.00
...: Black Widow (8/11, $3.99) Peter Nguyen-a; Peregrine app. — 4.00
...: Book of the Skull (5/11, $3.99) prequel to series; WWII flashback, Red Skull app. — 4.00
...: Fellowship of Fear (10/11, $3.99) profiles of hammer-wielders and fear thrivers — 4.00
...: FF (9/11, $2.99) Reed & Sue vs. Ben Grimm; Grummett-a/Dell'Otto-c — 3.00
...: Sin's Past (6/11, $4.99) r/Captain America #355-357; Sisters of Sin app. — 5.00
... Spotlight (6/11, $3.99) Interviews with Fraction and Immonen; feature articles — 4.00
...: The Monkey King (11/11, $2.99) Joshua Fialkov-s/Juan Doe-a — 3.00
...: The Worthy (9/11, $3.99) Origins of the hammer wielders; s/a by various — 4.00

FEAR ITSELF: DEADPOOL
Marvel Comics: Aug, 2011 - No. 3, Oct, 2011 ($2.99, limited series)

1-3-Hastings-s/Dazo-a — 3.00

FEAR ITSELF: FEARSOME FOUR
Marvel Comics: Aug, 2011 - No. 4, Nov, 2011 ($2.99, limited series)

1-4-Art by Bisley and others; Man-Thing, She-Hulk & Howard the Duck app. — 3.00

FEAR ITSELF: HULK VS. DRACULA
Marvel Comics: Nov, 2011 - No. 3, Dec, 2011 ($2.99, limited series)

1-3-Gischler-s/Stegman-a; Dell'Otto-c — 3.00

FEAR ITSELF: SPIDER-MAN
Marvel Comics: Jul, 2011 - No. 3, Sept, 2011 ($2.99, limited series)

1-3-Yost-s/McKone-a; Vermin app. — 3.00

FEAR ITSELF: THE DEEP
Marvel Comics: Aug, 2011 - No. 4, Nov, 2011 ($2.99, limited series)

1-4-Bunn-s/Garbett-a; Sub-Mariner vs. Attuma; Doctor Strange & Silver Surfer app. — 3.00

FEAR ITSELF: THE FEARLESS (Follows Fear Itself #7)
Marvel Comics: Dec, 2011 - No. 12, Jun, 2012 ($2.99, limited series)

1-12: 1-Fate of the Hammers; Bagley & Pelletier-a; Art Adams-c. 7-Wolverine app. — 3.00

FEAR ITSELF: THE HOME FRONT
Marvel Comics: Jun, 2011 - No. 7, Dec, 2011 ($3.99, limited series)

1-7-Short story anthology; Speedball w/Mayhew-a in all; Chaykin-a; Djurdjevic-c — 4.00

FEAR ITSELF: UNCANNY X-FORCE
Marvel Comics: Sept, 2011 - No. 3, Nov, 2011 ($2.99, limited series)

1-3-Bianchi-a/c — 3.00

FEAR ITSELF: WOLVERINE
Marvel Comics: Sept, 2011 - No. 3, Nov, 2011 ($2.99, limited series)

1-3-Boschi-a; Wolverine vs. S.T.R.I.K.E. 1-Acuña-c. 2,3-Molina-c — 3.00

FEAR ITSELF: YOUTH IN REVOLT
Marvel Comics: Jul, 2011 - No. 6, Dec, 2011 ($2.99, limited series)

1-6-Firestar and The Initiative app.; McKeever-s/Norton-a — 3.00

FEARLESS
Marvel Comics: Sept, 2019 - No. 4, Dec, 2019 ($4.99, limited series)

1-4 Stories of Captain Marvel, Storm, Invisible Woman and other female heroes — 5.00

FEARLESS DAWN MEETS HELLBOY
Albatross Funnybooks: 2020 ($3.99, one-shot)

1-Mike Mignola & Steve Mannion-s/a — 4.00

FEARLESS DEFENDERS (Marvel NOW!)
Marvel Comics: Apr, 2013 - No. 12, Feb, 2014 ($2.99/3.99)

1-4,5-7: 1-Valkyrie & Misty Knight team-up; Bunn-s/Sliney-a. 2-Dani Moonstar app. — 3.00
4AU-(7/13, $3.99) Age of Ultron tie-in; Dr. Doom & Ares app. — 4.00
8-12-($3.99) — 4.00

FEARLESS FAGAN
Dell Publishing Co.: No. 441, Dec, 1952 (one-shot)

	GD	VG	FN	VF	VF/NM	NM-
Four Color 441	5	10	15	31	53	75

FEAR OF A RED PLANET
AfterShock Comics: Nov, 2022 - Present ($4.99, limited series)

1-3-Mark Sable-s/Andrea Olimpieri-a — 5.00

FEAR THE FUNHOUSE
Archie Comics Publications: Dec, 2022 ($3.99, one-shot)

1-Short horror stories with the Archie gang — 4.00

FEATHERS
Archaia (BOOM! Studios): Jan, 2015 - No. 6, Jun, 2015 ($3.99, limited series)

GD VG FN VF VF/NM NM-
2.0 4.0 6.0 8.0 9.0 9.2

1-6-Jorge Corona-s/a 4.00

FEATURE BOOK (Dell) (See Large Feature Comic)

FEATURE BOOKS (Newspaper-r, early issues)
David McKay Publications: May, 1937 - No. 57, 1948 (B&W)
(Full color, 68 pgs. begin #26 on)

Note: See individual alphabetical listings for prices

nn-Popeye & the Jeep (#1, 100 pgs.); reprinted as Feature Books #3(Very Rare; only 3 known copies, 1-VF, 2-in low grade)
nn-Dick Tracy (#1)-Reprinted as Feature Book #4 (100 pgs.) & in part as 4-Color #1 (Rare, less than 10 known copies)

NOTE: *Above books were advertised together with different covers from Feat. Books #3 & 4.*

1-King of the Royal Mtd. (#1)
3-Popeye (7/37) by Segar;
4-Dick Tracy (8/37)-Same as nn issue but a new cover added
6-Dick Tracy (10/37)
8-Secret Agent X-9 (12/37) -Not by Raymond
9-Dick Tracy (1/38)
11-Little Annie Rooney (#1, 3/38)
13-Inspector Wade (5/38)
15-Barney Baxter (#1) (7/38)
17-Gangbusters (#1, 9/38) (1st app.)
20-Phantom (#1, 12/38)
22-Phantom
24-Lone Ranger (1941)
26-Prince Valiant (1941)-Hal Foster-c/a; newspaper strips reprinted, pgs. 1-28,30-63; color & 68 pg. issues begin; Foster cover is only original comic book artwork by him
36('43),38,40('44),42,43, 45,47-Blondie
39-Phantom
46-Mandrake in the Fire World-(58 pgs.)
48-Maltese Falcon by Dashiell Hammett('46)
51,54-Rip Kirby; Raymond-c/s; origin-#51
53,56,57-Phantom
2-Popeye (6/37) by Segar same as nn issue but a new cover added
5-Popeye (9/37) by Segar
7-Little Orphan Annie (#1, 11/37) (Rare)-Reprints strips from 12/31/34 to 7/17/35
10-Popeye (2/38)
12-Blondie (#1) (4/38) (Rare)
14-Popeye (6/38) by Segar
16-Red Eagle (8/38)
18,19-Mandrake
21-Lone Ranger
23-Mandrake
25-Flash Gordon (#1)-Reprints not by Raymond
27-29,31,34-Blondie
30-Katzenjammer Kids (#1, 1942)
32,35,41,44-Katzenjammer Kids
33(nn)-Romance of Flying; World War II photos
37-Katzenjammer Kids; has photo & biog. of Harold H. Knerr (1883-1949) who took over strip from Rudolph Dirks in 1914
49,50-Perry Mason; based on Gardner novels
52,55-Mandrake

NOTE: *All Feature Books through #25 are over-sized 8-1/2x11-3/8" comics with color covers and black and white interiors. The covers are rough, heavy stock. The page counts, including covers, are as follows: nn, #3, 4-100 pgs.; #1, 2-52 pgs.; #5-25 are all 76 pgs. #33 was found in bound set from publisher. Reprints from 1980s exist.*

FEATURE COMICS (Formerly Feature Funnies)
Quality Comics Group: No. 21, June, 1939 - No. 144, May, 1950

21-The Clock, Jane Arden & Mickey Finn continue from Feature Funnies
74 148 222 470 810 1150
22-26: 23-Charlie Chan begins (8/39, 1st app.) 50 100 150 315 533 750
26-(nn, nd)-Cover in one color, (10¢, 36 pgs.; issue No. blanked out. Two variations exist, each contain half of the regular #26) 53 106 159 334 567 800
27-(12/39, Rare)-Origin/1st app. Doll Man by Eisner (scripts) & Lou Fine (art); Doll Man begins, ends #139 838 1676 2514 6117 10,809 15,500
28-(1/40, Rare)-2nd app. Doll Man by Lou Fine 258 516 774 1651 2826 4000
29-Clock-c 135 270 405 864 1482 2100
30-1st Doll Man-c 226 452 678 1446 2473 3500
31-Last Clock & Charlie Chan issue (4/40); Charlie Chan moves to Big Shot #1 following month (5/40) 90 180 270 576 988 1400
32,34,36: Dollman covers. 32-Rusty Ryan & Samar begin. 34-Captain Fortune app.
90 180 270 576 988 1400
33,35,37: 37-Last Fine Doll Man 54 108 162 343 574 825

NOTE: *A 15¢ Canadian version of Feature Comics #37, made in the US, exists.*

38,40-Dollman covers. 38-Origin the Ace of Space. 40-Bruce Blackburn in costume
60 120 180 381 653 925
39,41: 39-Origin The Destroying Demon, ends #40; X-Mas-c.
41 82 123 256 428 600
42,46,48,50-Dollman covers. 42-USA, the Spirit of Old Glory begins. 46-Intro. Boyville Brigadiers in Rusty Ryan. 48-USA ends 45 90 135 284 480 675
43,45,47,49: 47-Fargo Kid begins 32 64 96 188 307 425
44-Doll Man by Crandall begins, ends #63; Crandall-a(2)
60 120 180 381 653 925
51,53,55,57,59: 57-Spider Widow begins 22 44 66 132 216 300
52,54,56,58,60-Dollman covers. 56-Marijuana story in Swing Sisson strip. 60-Raven begins, ends #71 33 66 99 194 317 440
61,63,65,67 20 40 60 118 192 265
62,64,66,68-Dollman covers. 68-(5/43) 29 58 87 172 281 390
69,71-Phantom Lady x-over in Spider Widow 22 44 66 132 216 300
70-Dollman-c; Phantom Lady x-over 33 66 99 194 317 440
72,74,77-80,100-Dollman covers. 72-Spider Widow ends
24 48 72 142 234 325
73,75,76 18 36 54 105 165 225
81-99-All Dollman covers 20 40 60 115 185 255
101-144: 139-Last Doll Man & last Doll Man cover. 140-Intro. Stuntman Stetson (Stuntman Stetson c-140-144) 17 34 51 100 158 215

NOTE: ***Celardo** a-37-43. **Crandall** a-44-60, 62, 63-on(most). **Gustavson** a-(Rusty Ryan)- 32-134. **Powell** a-34, 64-73. The Clock c-25, 28, 29. Doll Man c-30, 32, 34, 36, 38, 40, 42, 44, 46, 48, 50, 52, 54, 56, 58, 60, 62, 64, 66, 68, 70, 72, 74, 77-139. Joe Palooka c-21, 24, 27.*

FEATURE FILMS
National Periodical Publ.: Mar-Apr, 1950 - No. 4, Sept-Oct, 1950 (All photo-c)

1- "Captain China" with John Payne, Gail Russell, Lon Chaney & Edgar Bergen
65 130 195 416 708 1000
2- "Riding High" with Bing Crosby 69 138 207 435 735 1035
3- "The Eagle & the Hawk" with John Payne, Rhonda Fleming & D. O'Keefe
66 132 198 416 701 985
4- "Fancy Pants"; Bob Hope & Lucille Ball 72 144 216 454 770 1085

FEATURE FUNNIES (Feature Comics No. 21 on)(Earliest Quality Comics title)
Comic Favorites Inc./Quality Comics Group: Oct, 1937 - No. 20, May, 1939

1(V9#1-indicia)-Joe Palooka, Mickey Finn (1st app.), The Bungles, Jane Arden, Dixie Dugan (1st app.), Big Top, Ned Brant, Strange As It Seems, & Off the Record strip reprints begin
280 560 840 1540 2520 3500
2-The Hawk app. (11/37); Goldberg-c 129 258 387 826 1413 2000
3-Hawks of Seas begins by Eisner, ends #12; The Clock begins; Christmas-c
106 212 318 673 1162 1650
4,5 74 148 222 470 810 1150
6-12: 11-Archie O'Toole by Bud Thomas begins, ends #22
55 110 165 352 601 850
13-Espionage, Starring Black X begins by Eisner, ends #20
61 122 183 390 670 950
14-20 45 90 135 284 480 675

NOTE: *Joe Palooka covers 1, 6, 9, 12, 15, 18.*

FEATURE PRESENTATION, A (Feature Presentations Magazine #6)
(Formerly Women in Love) (Also see Startling Terror Tales #11)
Fox Feature Syndicate: No. 5, April, 1950

5(#1)-Black Tarantula (scarce) 77 154 231 493 847 1200

FEATURE PRESENTATIONS MAGAZINE (Formerly A Feature Presentation #5; becomes Feature Stories Magazine #3 on)
Fox Feature Syndicate: No. 6, July, 1950

6(#2)-Moby Dick; Wood-c 34 68 102 199 325 450

FEATURE STORIES MAGAZINE (Formerly Feature Presentations Mag. #6)
Fox Feature Syndicate: No. 3, Aug, 1950

3-Jungle Lil, Zegra stories; bondage-c 43 86 129 271 461 650

FEDERAL MEN COMICS
DC Comics: 1936

nn-Ashcan comic, not distributed to newsstands, only for in house use (no known sales)

FEDERAL MEN COMICS (See Adventure Comics #32, The Comics Magazine, New Adventure Comics, New Book of Comics, New Comics & Star Spangled Comics #91)
Gerard Publ. Co.: No. 2, 1945 (DC reprints from 1930's)

2-Siegel/Shuster-a; cover redrawn from Det. #9 52 104 156 328 552 775

FELICIA HARDY: THE BLACK CAT
Marvel Comics: July, 1994 - No. 4, Oct, 1994 ($1.50, limited series)

1-Spider-Man app. 2 4 6 11 16 20
2-4: 4-Spider-Man app. 5.00

FELIX'S NEPHEWS INKY & DINKY
Harvey Publications: Sept, 1957 - No. 7, Oct, 1958

1-Cover shows Inky's left eye with 2 pupils 14 28 42 76 108 140
2-7 8 16 24 42 54 65

NOTE: ***Messmer** art in 1-6. **Oriolo** a-1-7.*

FELIX THE CAT (See Cat Tales 3-D, The Funnies, March of Comics #24,36,51, New Funnies & Popular Comics)
Dell Publ. No. 1-19/Toby No. 20-61/Harvey No. 62-118/Dell No. 1-12:
1943 - No. 118, Nov, 1961; Sept-Nov, 1962 - No. 12, July-Sept, 1965

Four Color 15 86 172 258 688 1544 2400
Four Color 46('44) 46 92 138 359 805 1250
Four Color 77('45) 40 80 120 296 673 1050
Four Color 119('46)-All new stories begin 36 72 108 259 580 900
Four Color 135('46) 23 46 69 156 348 540
Four Color 162(9/47) 18 36 54 124 275 425
1(2-3/48)(Dell) 29 58 87 209 467 725
2 12 24 36 84 185 285
3-5 10 20 30 65 135 205
6-19(2-3/51-Dell) 8 16 24 54 102 150
20-30,32,33,36,38-61(6/55)-All Messmer issues.(Toby): 28-(2/52)-Some copies have #29 on cover, #28 on inside (Rare in high grade) 15 30 45 100 220 340
31,34,35-No Messmer-a; Messmer-c only 31,34 8 16 24 54 102 150
37-(100 pgs., 25 ¢, 1/15/53, X-Mas-c, Toby; daily & Sunday-r (rare)
36 72 108 266 596 925
62(8/55)-80,100 (Harvey) 4 8 12 28 47 65
81-99 4 8 12 25 40 55
101-118(11/61): 101-117-Reprints. 118-All new-a 3 6 9 17 26 35
12-269-211(#1, 9-11/62)(Dell)-No Messmer 4 8 12 28 47 65
2-12(7-9/65)(Dell, TV)-No Messmer 4 8 12 23 37 50
3-D Comic Book 1(1953-One Shot, 25¢)-w/glasses 39 78 117 231 378 525
Summer Annual nn ('53, 25¢, 100 pgs., Toby)-Daily & Sunday-r
50 100 150 315 533 750
Winter Annual 2 ('54, 25¢, 100 pgs., Toby)-Daily & Sunday-r
47 94 141 296 498 700

(Special note: Despite the covers on Toby 37 and the Summer Annual above proclaiming "all new stories," they were actually reformatted newspaper strips)

NOTE: ***Otto Messmer** went to work for Universal Film as an animator in 1915 and then worked for the Pat Sullivan animation studio in 1916. He created a black cat in the cartoon short, Feline Follies in 1919 that became known as Felix in the early 1920s. The Felix Sunday strip began Aug. 14, 1923 and continued until Sept. 19, 1943 whjen **Messmer** took the character to Dell (Western Publishing) and began doing Felix comic books, first adapting strips to the comic format. The first all new Felix comic was Four Color #119 in 1946 (#4 in the Dell run). The daily Felix was begun on May 9, 1927 by another artist, but by the following year, **Messmer** did it too. King Features took the daily away from **Messmer** in 1954 and he began to do some of his most dynamic art for Toby Press. The daily was continued by **Joe Oriolo** who drew it until it was discontinued Jan. 9, 1967. **Oriolo** was **Messmer's** assistant for many years and inked some of **Messmer's** pencils through the Toby run, as well as doing some of the stories by himself. Though **Messmer** continued to work for Harvey, his contiributons were limited, and no all **Messmer** stories appeared after the Toby run until some early Toby reprints were published in the 1990s Harvey revival of the title. 4-Color No. 15, 46, 77 and the Toby Annuals are all daily or Sunday newspaper reprints from the 1930's-1940's drawn by **Otto Messmer**. #101-r/#64; 102-r/#65; 103-r/#67; 104-117-r/#68-81. **Messmer**-a in all Dell/Toby/Harvey issues except #31, 34, 35, 97, 98, 100, 118. **Oriolo** a-20, 31-on.*

FELIX THE CAT (Also see The Nine Lives of...)
Harvey Comics/Gladstone: Sept, 1991 - No. 7, Jan, 1993 ($1.25/$1.50, bi-monthly)

1: 1950s-r/Toby issues by Messmer begins. 1-Inky and Dinky back-up story (produced by Gladstone) 6.00
2-7, Big Book, V2#1 (9/92, $1.95, 52 pgs.) 4.00

FELIX THE CAT AND FRIENDS
Felix Comics: 1992 - No. 5, 1993 ($1.95)

Felix the Cat #11 © DELL

Female Furies #1 © DC

50 Girls 50 #1 © Cho & Murray

GD 2.0 | VG 4.0 | FN 6.0 | VF 8.0 | VF/NM 9.0 | NM- 9.2

1-5: 1-Contains Felix trading cards 4.00

FELIX THE CAT & HIS FRIENDS (Pat Sullivan's...)
Toby Press: Dec, 1953 - No. 3, 1954 (Indicia title for #2&3 as listed)

1 (Indicia title, "Felix and His Friends," #1 only) 33 66 99 194 317 440
2-3 20 40 60 118 192 265

FELIX THE CAT DIGEST MAGAZINE
Harvey Comics: July, 1992 ($1.75, digest-size, 98 pgs.)

1-Felix, Richie Rich stories 6.00

FELIX THE CAT KEEPS ON WALKIN'
Hamilton Comics: 1991 ($15.95, 8-1/2"x11", 132 pgs.)

nn-Reprints 15 Toby Press Felix the Cat and Felix and His Friends stories in new color 16.00

FELL
Image Comics: Sept, 2005 - No. 9, Jan, 2008 ($1.99)

1-9-Warren Ellis-s/Ben Templesmith-a 3.00
..., Vol. 1: Feral City TPB (2007, $14.99) r/#1-8 15.00

FELON
Image Comics (Minotaur Press): Nov, 2001 - No. 4, Apr, 2002 ($2.95, B&W)

1-4-Rucka-s/Clark-a/c 3.00

FEMALE FURIES (See New Gods titles)
DC Comics: Apr, 2019 - No. 6, Sept, 2019 ($3.99, limited series)

1-6-Origin of the Granny Goodness & the Furies; Castellucci-s/Melo-a. 4-Simonson-c 4.00

FEM FANTASTIQUE
AC Comics: Aug, 1988 ($1.95, B&W)

V2#1-By Bill Black; Bettie Page pin-up 2 4 6 8 10 12

FEMFORCE (Also see Untold Origin of the Femforce)
Americomics: Apr, 1985 - No. 109 (1.75-/2.95, B&W #16-56)

1-Black-a in most; Nightveil, Ms. Victory begin 2 4 6 9 13 16
2-10 4.00
11-43: 25-Origin/1st app. new Ms. Victory. 28-Colt leaves. 29,30-Camilla-r by Mayo from Jungle Comics. 36-(2.95, 52 pgs.) 4.00
44,64: 44-W/mini-comic, Catman & Kitten #0. 64-Re-intro Black Phantom 5.00
45-49,51-63,65-99: 51-Photo-c from movie. 57-Begin color issues. 95-Photo-c 3.00
50 ($2.95, 52 pgs.)-Contains flexi-disc; origin retold; most AC characters app. 4.00
100-($3.95) 5.00
100-($6.90)-Polybagged 1 2 3 5 6 8
101-109-($4.95) 5.00
Special 1 (Fall, '84)(B&W, 52pgs.)-1st app. Ms. Victory, She-Cat, Blue Bulleteer, Rio Rita & Lady Luger 4.00
Bad Girl Backlash-(12/95, $5.00) 5.00
Frightbook 1 ('92, $2.95, B&W)-Halloween special, In the House of Horror 1 ('89, 2.50, B&W), Night of the Demon 1 ('90, 2.75, B&W), Out of the Asylum Special 1 ('87, B&W, $1.95), Pin-Up Portfolio 4.00
Pin-Up Portfolio (5 issues) 4.00

FEMFORCE UP CLOSE
AC Comics: Apr, 1992 - No. 11, 1995 ($2.75, quarterly)

1-11: 1-Stars Nightveil; inside f/c photo from Femforce movie. 2-Stars Stardust. 3-Stars Dragonfly. 4-Stars She-Cat 4.00

FENCE
BOOM! Studios (Boom! Box): Nov, 2017 - No. 12, Nov, 2018 ($3.99)

1-12-C.S. Pacat-s/Johanna the Mad-a 4.00

FERDINAND THE BULL (See Mickey Mouse Magazine V4#3)(Walt Disney's)
Dell Publishing Co.: 1938 (10¢, large size (9-1/2" x 10"), some color w/rest B&W)

nn 24 48 72 142 234 325

FERRET
Malibu Comics: Sept, 1992; May, 1993 - No. 10, Feb, 1994 ($1.95)

1-(1992, one-shot) 3.00
1-10: 1-Die-cut-c. 2-4-Collector's Ed. w/poster. 5-Polybagged w/Skycap 3.00
2-4-($1.95)-Newsstand Edition w/different-c 3.00

FERRYMAN
DC Comics (WildStorm): Early Dec, 2008 - No. 5, Mar, 2009 ($3.50)

1-5-Andreyko-s/Wayshak-a 3.50

FEVER RIDGE: A TALE OF MACARTHUR'S JUNGLE WAR
IDW Publishing: Feb, 2013 - No. 4, Oct, 2013 ($3.99)

1-4-Heimos-s/Runge-a/DeStefano-I; 1940s War stories on New Guinea 4.00

FF (Fantastic Four after Human Torch's death)
Marvel Comics: May, 2011 - No. 23, Dec, 2012 ($3.99)

1-Hickman-s/Epting-a; Spider-Man joins 4.00
1-Blank variant cover 4.00
1-Variant-c by Daniel Acuña 8.00
1-Variant-c by Stan Goldberg 6.00
2-23-($2.99) 2-Dr. Doom joins. 4,5-Kitson-a. 5-7-Black Bolt returns. 10,11-Avengers app. 3.00
...: Fifty Fantastic Years 1 (11/11, $4.99) Handbook format profiles of heroes and foes 5.00

FF (Marvel NOW!)
Marvel Comics: Jan, 2013 - No. 16, Mar, 2014 ($2.99)

1-15: 1-Fraction-s/Allred-a; new team forms (Ant-Man, She-Hulk, Medusa, Ms. Thing) 6,9-Quinones-a. 7,8,12-15-Dr. Doom app. 11-Impossible Man app. 3.00
16-($3.99) Ant-Man vs. Doom; back-up w/Quinones-a; Uatu & Silver Surfer app. 4.00

F5
Image Comics/Dark Horse: Jan, 2000 - No. 4, Oct, 2000 ($2.50/$2.95)

Preview (1/00, $2.50) Character bios and b&w pages; Daniel-s/a 3.00
1-($2.95, 48 pages) Tony Daniel-s/a 4.00
1-($20.00) Variant bikini-c 20.00
2-4-($2.50) 3.00
F5 Origin (Dark Horse Comics, 11/01, $2.99) w/cover gallery & sketches 3.00

FIBBER McGEE & MOLLY (Radio)(Also see A-1 Comics)
Magazine Enterprises: No. 25, 1949 (one-shot)

A-1 25 15 30 45 85 130 175

FICTION ILLUSTRATED
Byron Preiss Visual Publ./Pyramid: No. 1, Jan, 1975 - No. 4, Jan, 1977 ($1.00, #1,2 are digest size, 132 pgs.; #3,4 are graphic novels for mail order and specialty bookstores only)

1,2: 1-Schlomo Raven; Sutton-a. 2-Starfawn; Stephen Fabian-a. 2 4 6 13 18 22
3-($1.00-c, 4 3/4 x 6 1/2" digest size) Chandler; new Steranko-a 3 6 9 14 20 26
3-($4.95-c, 8 1/2 x 11" graphic novel; low print) same contents and indicia, but "Chandler" is the cover feature title 5 10 15 31 53 75
4-($4.95-c, 8 1/2 x 11" graphic novel; low print) Son of Sherlock Holmes; Reese-a 4 8 12 27 44 60

FICTION SQUAD
BOOM! Studios: Oct, 2014 - No. 6, Mar, 2015 ($3.99, limited series)

1-6-Jenkins-s/Bachs-a 4.00

FIELD, THE
Image Comics: Apr, 2014 - No. 4, Sept, 2014 ($3.50, limited series)

1-4-Brisson-s/Roy-a 3.50

FIERCE
Dark Horse Comics (Rocket Comics): July, 2004 - No. 4, Dec, 2004 ($2.99, limited series)

1-4-Jeremy Love-s/Robert Love-a 3.00

15-LOVE
Marvel Comics: Aug, 2011 - No. 3, Oct, 2011 ($4.99, limited series)

1-3-Tennis academy story; Andi Watson-s/Tommy Ohtsuka-a/c; Sho Murase-c 5.00

50 GIRLS 50
Image Comics: Jun, 2011 - No. 4, Sept, 2011 ($2.99, limited series)

1-4-Frank Cho-c; Cho & Murray-s/Medellin-a 3.00

52 (Leads into Countdown series)
DC Comics: Week One, July, 2006 - Week Fifty-Two, Jul, 2007 ($2.50, weekly series)

1-Chronicles the year after Infinite Crisis; Johns, Morrison, Rucka & Waid-s; JG Jones-c 4.00
2-10: 2-History of the DC Universe back-up thru #11. 6-1st app. The Great Ten. 7-Intro. Kate Kane. 10-Supernova 3.00
11-Batwoman debut (single panel cameo in #9) 4.00
12-52: 12-Isis gains powers; back-up 2 pg. origins begin. 15-Booster Gold killed. 17-Lobo returns. 30-Batman-c/Robin & Nightwing app. 37-Booster Gold returns. 38-The Question dies. 42-Ralph Dibny dies. 44-Isis dies. 48-Renee becomes The Question. 50-World War III. 51-Mister Mind evolves. 52-The Multiverse is re-formed; wraparound-c 3.00
...: The Companion TPB (2007, $19.99) r/solo stories of series' prominent characters 20.00
...: Volume One TPB (2007, $19.99) r/#1-13; sample of page development; cover gallery 20.00
...: Volume Two TPB (2007, $19.99) r/#14-26; creator notes and sketches; cover gallery 20.00
...: Volume Three TPB (2007, $19.99) r/#27-39; notes and sketches; cover gallery 20.00
...: Volume Four TPB (2007, $19.99) r/#40-52; creator commentary; cover gallery 20.00

52 AFTERMATH: THE FOUR HORSEMEN (Takes place during 52 Week Fifty)
DC Comics: Oct, 2007 - No. 6, Mar, 2008 ($2.99, limited series)

1-6-Giffen-s/Olliffe-a; Superman, Batman & Wonder Woman app. 2-4,6-Van Sciver-c 3.00
TPB (2008, $19.99) r/#1-6 20.00

	GD 2.0	VG 4.0	FN 6.0	VF 8.0	VF/NM 9.0	NM- 9.2

52/WWIII (Takes place during 52 Week Fifty)
DC Comics: Part One, Jun, 2007 - Part Four, Jun, 2007 ($2.50, 4 issues came out same day)

	GD	VG	FN	VF	VF/NM	NM-
Part One - Part Four: Van Sciver-c; heroes vs. Black Adam. 3-Terra dies						3.00
DC: World War III TPB (2007, $17.99) r/Part One - Four and 52 Week 50						18.00

55 DAYS AT PEKING (See Movie Comics)

FIGHT AGAINST CRIME (Fight Against the Guilty #22, 23)
Story Comics: May, 1951 - No. 21, Sept, 1954

	GD	VG	FN	VF	VF/NM	NM-
1-True crime stories #1-4	65	130	195	416	708	1000
2	39	78	117	240	395	550
3,5: 5-Frazetta-a, 1 pg.; content change to horror & suspense	39	78	117	236	388	540
4-Drug story "Hopped Up Killers"	43	86	129	271	461	650
6,7: 6-Used in **POP**, pgs. 83,84	129	258	387	826	1413	2000
8-Last crime format issue	39	78	117	231	378	525

NOTE: *No. 9-21 contain violent, gruesome stories with blood, dismemberment, decapitation, E.C. style plot twists and several E.C. swipes. Bondage c-4, 6, 18, 19.*

	GD	VG	FN	VF	VF/NM	NM-
9-11,13	65	130	195	416	708	1000
12-Morphine drug story "The Big Dope"	142	284	426	909	1555	2200
14-Tothish art by Ross Andru; electrocution-c	123	246	369	787	1344	1900
15-B&W & color illos in **POP**	74	148	222	470	810	1150
16-E.C. story swipe/Haunt of Fear #19; Tothish-a by Ross Andru; bondage-c	97	194	291	621	1061	1500
17-Wildey E.C. story swipe/Shock SuspenStories #9; knife through neck-c (1/54)	106	212	318	673	1162	1650
18,19: 19-Bondage/torture-c	71	142	213	454	777	1100
20-Decapitation cover; contains hanging, ax murder, blood & violence	1750	3500	5250	13,300	24,150	35,000
21-E.C. swipe	87	174	261	553	952	1350

NOTE: ***Cameron** a-4, 5, 8. **Hollingsworth** a-3-7, 9, 10, 13. **Wildey** a-6, 15, 16.*

FIGHT AGAINST THE GUILTY (Formerly Fight Against Crime)
Story Comics: No. 22, Dec, 1954 - No. 23, Mar, 1955

	GD	VG	FN	VF	VF/NM	NM-
22-Toth styled art by Ross Andru; Ditko-a; E.C. story swipe; electrocution-c (Last pre-code)	57	114	171	362	619	875
23-Hollingsworth-a	36	72	108	211	343	475

FIGHT CLUB 2 (Sequel to the movie)(Also see Free Comic Book Day 2015)
Dark Horse Comics: May, 2015 - No. 10, Mar, 2016 ($3.99)

	GD	VG	FN	VF	VF/NM	NM-
1-10-Chuck Palahniuk-s/Cameron Stewart-a						4.00

FIGHT CLUB 3 (Sequel to the movie)
Dark Horse Comics: Jan, 2019 - No. 12, Dec, 2019 ($3.99)

	GD	VG	FN	VF	VF/NM	NM-
1-12-Chuck Palahniuk-s/Cameron Stewart-a/David Mack-c						4.00

FIGHT COMICS
Fiction House Magazines: Jan, 1940 - No. 83, 11/52; No. 84, Wint, 1952-53; No. 85, Spring, 1953; No. 86, Summer, 1954

	GD	VG	FN	VF	VF/NM	NM-
1-Origin Spy Fighter, Starring Saber; Jack Dempsey life story; Shark Brodie & Chip Collins begin; Fine-c; Eisner-a	423	846	1269	3000	5250	7500
2-Joe Louis life story; Fine/Eisner-c	194	388	582	1242	2121	3000
3-Rip Regan, the Power Man begins (3/40); classic-c	232	464	696	1485	2543	3600
4,5: 4-Fine-c	148	296	444	947	1624	2300
6-10: 6,7-Powell-c	129	258	387	826	1413	2000
11-14: Rip Regan ends	123	246	369	787	1344	1900
15-1st app. Super American plus-c (10/41)	300	600	900	2010	3505	5000
16-Captain Fight begins (12/41); Spy Fighter ends	148	296	444	947	1624	2300
17,18: Super American ends	106	212	318	673	1162	1650
19-Japanese WWII-c; Captain Fight ends; Senorita Rio begins (6/42, origin & 1st app.); Rip Carson, Chute Trooper begins	129	258	387	826	1413	2000
20-Classic female decapitation-c	155	310	465	992	1696	2400
21-27,29,30: 21-24,26,27-Japanese WWII-c	100	200	300	635	1093	1550
28-Classic Japanese WWII torture-c	181	362	543	1158	1979	2800
31-Classic Japanese WWII decapitation-c	514	1028	1542	3750	6625	9500
32-Tiger Girl begins (6/44, 1st app.?); Nazi WWII-c	300	600	900	1950	3375	4800
33,35-39,41,42: 42-Last WWII-c (2/46)	84	168	252	538	919	1300
34-Classic Japanese WWII bondage-c	168	336	504	1075	1838	2600
40-Classic Nazi vulture bondage-c	168	336	504	1075	1838	2600
43,45-50: 48-Used in Love and Death by Legman. 49-Jungle-c begin, end #81	47	94	141	296	498	700
44-Classic bondage/torture-c; Capt. Fight returns	219	438	657	1402	2401	3400
51-Origin Tiger Girl; Patsy Pin-Up app.	45	90	135	284	480	675
52-60,62-64-Last Baker issue	31	62	93	182	296	410
61-Origin Tiger Girl retold	32	64	96	188	307	425
65-78: 78-Used in **POP**, pg. 99	26	52	78	154	252	350
79-The Space Rangers app.	30	60	90	177	289	400
80-85: 81-Last jungle-c. 82-85-War-c/stories	23	46	69	136	223	310
86-Two Tigerman stories by Evans-r/Rangers Comics #40,41; Moreira-r/Rangers Comics #45	24	48	72	142	234	325

NOTE: *Bondage covers, Lingerie, headlights panels are common. Captain Fight by **Kamen**-51-66. Kayo Kirby by **Baker**-#43-64, 67(not by Baker). Senorita Rio by **Kamen**-#57-64; by **Grandenetti**-#65, 66. Tiger Girl by **Baker**-#36-60, 62-64; **Eisner** c-1-3, 5, 10, 11. **Kamen** a-54?, 57? **Tuska** a-1, 5, 8, 10, 21, 29, 34. **Whitman** c-73-84. **Zolnerwich** c-16, 17, 22. Power Man c-5, 6, 9. Super American c-15-17. Tiger Girl c-49-81.*

FIGHT FOR LOVE
United Features Syndicate: 1952 (no month)

	GD	VG	FN	VF	VF/NM	NM-
nn-Abbie & Slats newspaper-r	14	28	42	76	108	140

FIGHT FOR TOMORROW
DC Comics (Vertigo): Nov, 2002 - No. 6, Apr, 2003 ($2.50, limited series)

	GD	VG	FN	VF	VF/NM	NM-
1-6-Denys Cowan-a/Brian Wood-s. 1-Jim Lee-c. 5-Jo Chen-c						3.00
TPB (2008, $14.99) r/#1-6						15.00

FIGHT GIRLS
AWA Studios: Jul, 2021 - No. 5, Nov, 2021 ($3.99, limited series)

	GD	VG	FN	VF	VF/NM	NM-
1-5-Frank Cho-s/a/c						4.00

FIGHTING AIR FORCE (See United States Fighting Air Force)

FIGHTIN' AIR FORCE (Formerly Sherlock Holmes?; Never Again? War and Attack #54 on)
Charlton Comics: No. 3, Feb, 1956 - No. 53, Feb-Mar, 1966

	GD	VG	FN	VF	VF/NM	NM-
V1#3	11	22	33	64	90	115
4-10	8	16	24	40	50	60
11(3/58, 68 pgs.)	9	18	27	52	69	85
12 (100 pgs.)-U.S. Nukes Russia	15	30	45	90	140	190
13-30: 13,24-Glanzman-a. 24-Glanzman-c. 27-Area 51, UFO story	3	6	9	21	33	45
31-53: 50-American Eagle begins	3	6	9	16	23	30

FIGHTING AMERICAN
Headline Publ./Prize (Crestwood): Apr-May, 1954 - No. 7, Apr-May, 1955

	GD	VG	FN	VF	VF/NM	NM-
1-Origin & 1st app. Fighting American & Speedboy (Capt. America & Bucky clones); S&K-c/a(3); 1st super hero satire series	216	432	648	1382	2366	3350
2-S&K-a(3)	106	212	318	673	1162	1650
3-5: 3,4-S&K-a(3). 5-S&K-a(2); Kirby/?-a	93	186	279	591	1021	1450
6-Origin-r (4 pgs.) plus 2 pgs. by S&K	87	174	261	553	952	1350
7-Kirby-a	81	162	243	518	884	1250

NOTE: ***Simon & Kirby** covers on all. 6 is last pre-code issue.*

FIGHTING AMERICAN
Harvey Publications: Oct, 1966 (25¢)

	GD	VG	FN	VF	VF/NM	NM-
1-Origin Fighting American & Speedboy by S&K-r; S&K-c/a(3); 1 pg. Neal Adams ad	6	12	18	37	66	95

FIGHTING AMERICAN
DC Comics: Feb, 1994 - No. 6, 1994 ($1.50, limited series)

	GD	VG	FN	VF	VF/NM	NM-
1-6						4.00

FIGHTING AMERICAN (Vol. 3)
Awesome Entertainment: Aug, 1997 - No. 2, Oct, 1997 ($2.50)

	GD	VG	FN	VF	VF/NM	NM-
Preview-Agent America (pre-lawsuit)	1	2	3	5	6	7
1-Four covers by Liefeld, Churchill, Platt, McGuinness						4.00
1-Platinum Edition, 1-Gold foil Edition						10.00
1-Comic Cavalcade Edition, 2-American Ent. Spice Ed.						4.00
2-Platt-c, 2-Liefeld variant-c						4.00

FIGHTING AMERICAN
Titan Comics: Oct, 2017 - No. 4, Jan, 2018 ($3.99)

	GD	VG	FN	VF	VF/NM	NM-
1-4-Rennie-s/Mighten-a; multiple covers; Fighting American & Speedboy trapped in 2017						4.00

FIGHTING AMERICAN: DOGS OF WAR
Awesome-Hyperwerks: Sept, 1998 - No. 3, May, 1999 ($2.50)

	GD	VG	FN	VF	VF/NM	NM-
Limited Convention Special (7/98, B&W) Platt-a						4.00
1-3-Starlin-s/Platt-a/c						4.00

FIGHTING AMERICAN: RULES OF THE GAME
Awesome Entertainment: Nov, 1997 - No. 3, Mar, 1998 ($2.50, lim. series)

	GD	VG	FN	VF	VF/NM	NM-
1-3: 1-Loeb-s/McGuinness-a/c. 2-Flip book with Swat! preview						4.00
1-Liefeld SPICE variant-c, 1-Dynamic Forces Ed.; McGuinness-c						4.00
1-Liefeld Fighting American & cast variant-c						4.00

FIGHTING AMERICAN: THE TIES THAT BIND
Titan Comics: Apr, 2018 - No. 4, Jul, 2018 ($3.99, limited series)

	GD	VG	FN	VF	VF/NM	NM-
1-4-Rennie-s/Andie Tong-a; multiple covers						4.00

FIGHTIN' ARMY (Formerly Soldier and Marine Comics) (See Captain Willy Schultz)
Charlton Comics: No. 16, 1/56 - No. 127, 12/76; No. 128, 9/77 - No. 172, 11/84

	GD	VG	FN	VF	VF/NM	NM-
16	10	20	30	56	76	95
17-19,21-23,25-30	7	14	21	37	46	55
20-Ditko-a	9	18	27	52	69	85
24 (3/58, 68 pgs.)	9	18	27	50	65	80
31-45	3	6	9	18	28	38
46-50,52-60	3	6	9	16	23	30
51-Hitler-c	3	6	9	21	33	45
61-75	3	6	9	14	19	24
76-1st The Lonely War of Willy Schultz	3	6	9	17	26	35
77-80: 77-92-The Lonely War of Willy Schultz. 79-Devil Brigade	3	6	9	14	19	24
81-88,91,93-99: 82,83-Devil Brigade	2	4	6	10	14	18
89,90,92-Ditko-a	3	6	9	14	20	26
100	2	4	6	13	18	22
101-127	2	4	6	8	11	14
128-140	1	2	3	5	7	9
141-165	1	2	3	4	5	7
166-172-Low print run	1	2	3	5	6	8
108 (Modern Comics-1977)-Reprint						5.00

NOTE: ***Aparo** c-154. **Glanzman** a-77-88. **Montes/Bache** a-48, 49, 51, 69, 75, 76, 170r.*

FIGHTING CARAVANS (See Zane Grey 4-Color 632)

FIGHTING DANIEL BOONE
Avon Periodicals: 1953

	GD	VG	FN	VF	VF/NM	NM-
nn-Kinstler-c/a, 22 pgs.	21	42	63	122	199	275
I.W. Reprint #1-Reprints #1 above; Kinstler-c/a; Lawrence/Alascia-a	3	6	9	14	19	24

FIGHTING DAVY CROCKETT (Formerly Kit Carson)
Avon Periodicals: No. 9, Oct-Nov, 1955

	GD	VG	FN	VF	VF/NM	NM-
9-Kinstler-c	12	24	36	69	97	125

FIGHTIN' FIVE, THE (Formerly Space War) (Also see The Peacemaker)
Charlton Comics: July, 1964 - No. 41, Jan, 1967; No. 42, Oct, 1981 - No. 49, Dec, 1982

	GD	VG	FN	VF	VF/NM	NM-
V2#28-Origin/1st app. Fightin' Five; Montes/Bache-a	6	12	18	42	79	115
29-39-Montes/Bache-a in all	4	8	12	27	44	60
40-Peacemaker begins (1st app.)	86	172	258	685	1544	2400
41-Peacemaker (2nd app.); Montes/Bache-a	13	26	39	86	188	290
42-49: Reprints						6.00

FIGHTING FRONTS!
Harvey Publications: Aug, 1952 - No. 5, Jan, 1953

	GD	VG	FN	VF	VF/NM	NM-
1	15	30	45	83	124	165
2-Extreme violence; Nostrand/Powell-a	15	30	45	86	133	180

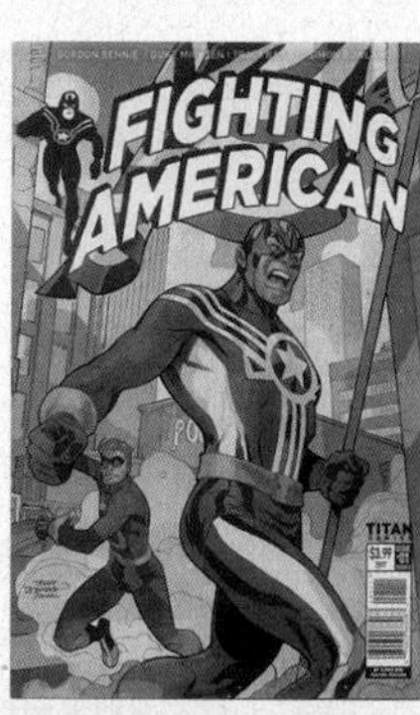

Fighting American (2017) #1 © S&K

Fightin' Navy #74 © CC

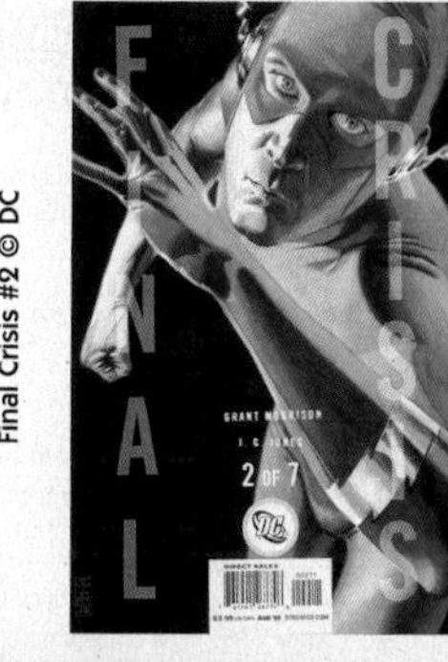

Final Crisis #2 © DC

	GD 2.0	VG 4.0	FN 6.0	VF 8.0	VF/NM 9.0	NM- 9.2
3-5: 3-Powell-a	9	18	27	47	61	75

FIGHTING INDIAN STORIES (See Midget Comics)

FIGHTING INDIANS OF THE WILD WEST!
Avon Periodicals: Mar, 1952 - No. 2, Nov, 1952

	GD 2.0	VG 4.0	FN 6.0	VF 8.0	VF/NM 9.0	NM- 9.2
1-Geronimo, Chief Crazy Horse, Chief Victorio, Black Hawk begin; Larsen-a; McCann-a(2)	24	48	72	142	234	325
2-Kinstler-c & inside-c only; Larsen, McCann-a	16	32	48	94	147	200
100 Pg. Annual (1952, 25¢)-Contains three comics rebound; Geronimo, Chief Crazy Horse, Chief Victorio; Kinstler-c	45	90	135	284	480	675

FIGHTING LEATHERNECKS
Toby Press: Feb, 1952 - No. 6, Dec, 1952

	GD 2.0	VG 4.0	FN 6.0	VF 8.0	VF/NM 9.0	NM- 9.2
1- "Duke's Diary"; full pg. pin-ups by Sparling	23	46	69	138	227	315
2-5: 2- "Duke's Diary" full pg. pin-ups. 3-5- "Gil's Gals"; full pg. pin-ups	14	28	42	80	115	150
6-(Same as No. 3-5?)	14	28	42	76	108	140

FIGHTING MAN, THE (War)
Ajax/Farrell Publications(Excellent Publ.): May, 1952 - No. 8, July, 1953

	GD 2.0	VG 4.0	FN 6.0	VF 8.0	VF/NM 9.0	NM- 9.2
1	21	42	63	122	199	275
2	14	28	42	82	121	160
3-8	11	22	33	62	86	110
Annual 1 (1952, 25¢, 100 pgs.)	61	122	183	390	670	950

FIGHTIN' MARINES (Formerly The Texan; also see Approved Comics)
St. John(Approved Comics)/Charlton Comics No. 14 on:
No. 15, 8/51 - No. 12, 3/53; No. 14, 5/55 - No. 132, 11/76; No. 133, 10/77 - No. 176, 9/84 (No #13?) (Korean War #1-3)

	GD 2.0	VG 4.0	FN 6.0	VF 8.0	VF/NM 9.0	NM- 9.2
15(#1)-Matt Baker c/a "Leatherneck Jack"; slightly large size; Fightin' Texan No. 16 & 17?	65	130	195	416	708	1000
2-1st Canteen Kate by Baker; slightly large size; partial Baker-c	103	206	309	659	1130	1600
3-9,11-Canteen Kate by Baker; Baker c-#2,3,5-11; 4-Partial Baker-c	43	86	129	271	461	650
10-Matt Baker-c	48	96	144	302	514	725
12-No Baker-a; Last St. John issue?	14	28	42	78	112	145
14 (5/55; 1st Charlton issue; formerly?)-Canteen Kate by Baker; all stories reprinted from #2	26	52	78	154	252	350
15-Baker-c	18	36	54	105	165	225
16,18-20-Not Baker-c. 16-Grey-tone-c	9	18	27	52	69	85
17-Canteen Kate by Baker	21	42	63	122	199	275
21-24	8	16	24	42	54	65
25-(68 pgs.)(3/58)-Check-a?	12	24	36	67	94	120
26-(100 pgs.)(8/58)-Check-a(5)	15	30	45	88	137	185
27-50	3	6	9	19	30	40
51-81: 78-Shotgun Harker & the Chicken series begin	3	6	9	16	23	30
82-85: 85-Last 12¢ issue	3	6	9	15	22	28
86-94: 94-Last 15¢ issue	2	4	6	11	16	20
95-100,122: 122-(1975) Pilot issue for "War" title (Fightin' Marines Presents War)	2	4	6	10	14	18
101-121	2	4	6	8	11	14
123-140: 132 Hitler-c	2	4	6	8	10	12
141-170	1	2	3	5	6	8
171-176-Low print run	1	3	4	6	8	10
120(Modern Comics reprint, 1977)	1	2	3	5	6	8

NOTE: *No. 14 & 16 (CC) reprint St. John issues; No. 16 reprints St. John insignia on cover.* ***Colan*** *a-3, 7.* ***Glanzman*** *c/a-92, 94.* ***Montes/Bache*** *a-48, 53, 55, 64, 65, 72-74, 77-83, 176r.*

FIGHTING MARSHAL OF THE WILD WEST (See The Hawk)

FIGHTIN' NAVY (Formerly Don Winslow)
Charlton Comics: No. 74, 1/56 - No. 125, 4-5/66; No. 126, 8/83 - No. 133, 10/84

	GD 2.0	VG 4.0	FN 6.0	VF 8.0	VF/NM 9.0	NM- 9.2
74	5	10	15	34	60	85
75-81	4	8	12	23	37	50
82-Sam Glanzman-a (68 pg. Giant)	5	10	15	31	53	75
83-(100 pgs.)	6	12	18	41	76	110
84-99,101: 101-UFO-c/story	3	6	9	17	26	35
100	3	6	9	18	28	38
102-105,106-125('66)	3	6	9	14	21	26
126-133 (1984)-Low print run	1	2	3	5	6	8

NOTE: ***Montes/Bache*** *a-109.* ***Glanzman*** *a-82, 92, 96, 98, 100, 131r.*

FIGHTING PRINCE OF DONEGAL, THE (See Movie Comics)

FIGHTIN' TEXAN (Formerly The Texan & Fightin' Marines?)
St. John Publishing Co.: No. 16, Sept, 1952 - No. 17, Dec, 1952

	GD 2.0	VG 4.0	FN 6.0	VF 8.0	VF/NM 9.0	NM- 9.2
16,17: Tuska-a each. 17-Cameron-c/a	14	28	42	76	108	140

FIGHTING UNDERSEA COMMANDOS (See Undersea Fighting...)
Avon Periodicals: May, 1952 - No. 5, April, 1953 (U.S. Navy frogmen)

	GD 2.0	VG 4.0	FN 6.0	VF 8.0	VF/NM 9.0	NM- 9.2
1-Cover title is Undersea Fighting... #1 only	21	42	63	124	202	280
2	14	28	42	82	121	160
3-5: 1,3-Ravielli-c. 4-Kinstler-c	13	26	39	72	101	130

FIGHTING WAR STORIES
Men's Publications/Story Comics: Aug, 1952 - No. 5, 1953

	GD 2.0	VG 4.0	FN 6.0	VF 8.0	VF/NM 9.0	NM- 9.2
1	19	38	57	111	176	240
2-5	14	28	42	76	108	140

FIGHTING YANK (See America's Best Comics & Startling Comics)
Nedor/Better Publ./Standard: Sept, 1942 - No. 29, Aug, 1949

	GD 2.0	VG 4.0	FN 6.0	VF 8.0	VF/NM 9.0	NM- 9.2
1-The Fighting Yank begins; Mystico, the Wonder Man app; bondage-c	389	778	1167	2723	4762	6800
2	219	438	657	1402	2401	3400
3,4: Nazi WWII-c. 4-Schomburg-c begin	181	362	543	1158	1979	2800
5,8,9: 5-Nazi-c. 8,9-Japan War-c	181	362	543	1158	1979	2800
6-Classic Japanese WWII-c	365	730	1095	2555	4478	6400
7-Classic Hitler special bomb-c; Grim Reaper app.	365	730	1095	2555	4478	6400
10-Nazi bondage/torture/hypo-c	314	628	942	2198	3849	5500
11,14,15: 11-The Oracle app. 15-Bondage/torture-c	100	200	300	635	1093	1550
12-Hirohito bondage Japanese WWII-c	206	412	618	1318	2259	3200
13-Last War-c (Japanese)	300	600	900	1920	3310	4700
16-20: 18-The American Eagle app.	77	154	231	493	847	1200
21-Kara, Jungle Princess app.; lingerie-c	226	452	678	1446	2473	3500
22-Schomburg Miss Masque dinosaur-c	119	238	357	762	1306	1850
23-Classic Schomburg hooded vigilante-c	519	1038	1557	3789	6695	9600
24-Miss Masque app.	90	180	270	576	988	1400
25-Robinson/Meskin-a; strangulation, lingerie panel; The Cavalier app.	87	174	261	553	952	1350
26-29: All-Robinson/Meskin-a. 28-One pg. Williamson-a	61	122	183	390	670	950

NOTE: ***Schomburg (Xela)*** *c-4-29; airbrush-c 28, 29. Bondage c-1, 4, 8, 10, 11, 12, 15, 17.*

FIGHTMAN
Marvel Comics: June, 1993 ($2.00, one-shot, 52 pgs.)

	GD 2.0	VG 4.0	FN 6.0	VF 8.0	VF/NM 9.0	NM- 9.2
1						4.00

FIGHT THE ENEMY
Tower Comics: Aug, 1966 - No. 3, Mar, 1967 (25¢, 68 pgs.)

	GD 2.0	VG 4.0	FN 6.0	VF 8.0	VF/NM 9.0	NM- 9.2
1-Lucky 7 & Mike Manly begin	5	10	15	33	57	80
2-1st Boris Vallejo comic art; McWilliams-a	4	8	12	23	37	50
3-Wood-a (1/2 pg.); McWilliams, Bolle-a	4	8	12	23	37	50

FIGMENT (Disney Kingdoms) (See Disney Kingdoms: Figment 2 for sequel)
Marvel Comics: Aug, 2014 - No. 5, Dec, 2014 ($3.99, limited series)

	GD 2.0	VG 4.0	FN 6.0	VF 8.0	VF/NM 9.0	NM- 9.2
1-5-Jim Zub-s/Filipe Andrade-a						4.00

FILM FUNNIES
Marvel Comics (CPC): Nov, 1949 - No. 2, Feb, 1950 (52 pgs.)

	GD 2.0	VG 4.0	FN 6.0	VF 8.0	VF/NM 9.0	NM- 9.2
1-Krazy Krow, Wacky Duck	27	54	81	160	263	365
2-Wacky Duck	20	40	60	115	185	255

FILM STARS ROMANCES
Star Publications: Jan-Feb, 1950 - No. 3, May-June, 1950 (True life stories of movie stars)

	GD 2.0	VG 4.0	FN 6.0	VF 8.0	VF/NM 9.0	NM- 9.2
1-Rudy Valentino & Gregory Peck stories; L. B. Cole-c; lingerie panels	57	114	171	362	619	875
2-Liz Taylor/Robert Taylor photo-c & true life story	68	136	204	435	743	1050
3-Douglas Fairbanks story; photo-c	33	66	99	194	317	440

FILTH, THE
DC Comics (Vertigo): Aug, 2002 - No. 13, Oct, 2003 ($2.95, limited series)

	GD 2.0	VG 4.0	FN 6.0	VF 8.0	VF/NM 9.0	NM- 9.2
1-13-Morrison-s/Weston & Erskine-a						3.00
TPB (2004, $19.95) r/#1-13						20.00

FINAL CRISIS
DC Comics: July, 2008 - No. 7, Mar, 2009 ($3.99, limited series)

	GD 2.0	VG 4.0	FN 6.0	VF 8.0	VF/NM 9.0	NM- 9.2
1-Grant Morrison-s/J.G. Jones-a/c; Martian Manhunter killed; 2 covers						4.00
1-Director's Cut (10/08, $4.99) B&W printing of #1 with creator commentary						5.00
2-7: 2-Barry Allen-c/cameo; intro Big Science Action; two covers. 6-Batman zapped						4.00
SC (2010, $19.99) r/#1-7, FC: Superman Beyond #1,2, FC: Submit & FC Sketchbook						20.00
...: Rage of the Red Lanterns (12/08, $3.99) Atrocitus app.; intro. Blue Lantern; 3 covers						4.00
...: Requiem (9/08, $3.99) History, death and funeral of the Martian Manhunter; 2 covers						4.00
...: Resist (12/08, $3.99) Checkmate app; Rucka & Trautman-s/Sook-a; 2 covers						4.00
...: Secret Files (2/09, $3.99) origin of Libra; Wein-s/Shasteen-a; JG Jones sketch-a						4.00
... Sketchbook (7/08, $2.99) Jones development sketches with Morrison commentary						3.00
...: Submit (12/08, $3.99) Black Lightning & Tattooed Man team up; Morrison-s; 2 covers						4.00

	GD 2.0	VG 4.0	FN 6.0	VF 8.0	VF/NM 9.0	NM- 9.2

FINAL CRISIS: DANCE (Final Crisis Aftermath)
DC Comics: Jul, 2009 - No. 6, Dec, 2009 ($2.99, limited series)
1-6-Super Young Team; Joe Casey-s/Chriscross-a/Stanley Lau-c 3.00
TPB (2009, $17.99) r/#1-6 18.00

FINAL CRISIS: ESCAPE (Final Crisis Aftermath)
DC Comics: Jul, 2009 - No. 6, Dec, 2009 ($2.99, limited series)
1-6-Nemesis & Cameron Chase app.; Ivan Brandon-s/Marco Rudy-a/Scott Hampton-c 3.00
TPB (2010, $17.99) r/#1-6 18.00

FINAL CRISIS: INK (Final Crisis Aftermath)
DC Comics: Jul, 2009 - No. 6, Dec, 2009 ($2.99, limited series)
1-6-The Tattooed Man; Eric Wallace-s/Fabrizio Florentino-a/Brian Stelfreeze-c 3.00
TPB (2010, $17.99) r/#1-6 18.00

FINAL CRISIS: LEGION OF THREE WORLDS
DC Comics: Oct, 2008 - No. 5, Sept, 2009 ($3.99, limited series)
1-Johns-s/Pérez-a; R.J. Brande killed; Time Trapper app.; two covers on each issue 5.00
2-5-Three Legions meet; two covers. 3-Bart Allen returns. 4-Superboy (Conner) returns 4.00
HC (2009, $19.99) r/#1-5; variant covers 20.00
SC (2010, $14.99) r/#1-5; variant covers 15.00

FINAL CRISIS: REVELATIONS
DC Comics: Oct, 2008 - No. 5, Feb, 2009 ($3.99, limited series)
1-5-Spectre and The Question; 2 covers on each. 1-Dr. Light killed; Rucka-s/Tan-a 4.00
HC (2009, $19.99, d.j.) r/#1-5; variant covers 20.00
SC (2010, $14.99) r/#1-5; variant covers 15.00

FINAL CRISIS: ROGUE'S REVENGE
DC Comics: Sept, 2008 - No. 3, Nov, 2008 ($3.99, limited series)
1-3-Johns-s/Kolins-a; Flash's Rogues, Zoom and Inertia app. 4.00
HC (2009, $19.99, d.j.) r/#1-3 & Flash #182,197; variant covers 20.00
SC (2010, $14.99) r/#1-3 & Flash #182,197; variant covers 15.00

FINAL CRISIS: RUN (Final Crisis Aftermath)
DC Comics: Jul, 2009 - No. 6, Dec, 2009 ($2.99, limited series)
1-6-The Human Flame on the run; Sturges-s/Williams-a/Kako-c 3.00
TPB (2010, $17.99) r/#1-6 18.00

FINAL CRISIS: SUPERMAN BEYOND
DC Comics: Oct, 2008 - No. 2, Mar, 2009 ($4.50, limited series)
1,2-Morrison-s/Mahnke-a; parallel-Earth Supermen app.; 3-D pages and glasses 4.50

FINAL NIGHT, THE (See DC related titles and Parallax: Emerald Night)
DC Comics: Nov, 1996 - No. 4, Nov, 1996 ($1.95, weekly limited series)
1-4: Kesel-s/Immonen-a(p) in all. 4-Parallax's final acts 4.00
Preview 3.00
TPB-(1998, $12.95) r/#1-4, Parallax: Emerald Night #1, and preview 13.00

FINALS (See Vertigo Resurrected:... for collected reprint)
DC Comics (Vertigo): Sept, 1999 - No. 4, Dec, 1999 ($2.95, limited series)
1-4-Will Pfeifer-s/Jill Thompson-a 4.00

FINDING NEMO (Based on the Pixar movie)
BOOM! Studios: Jul, 2010 - No. 4, Oct, 2010 ($2.99, limited series)
1-4-Michael Raicht & Brian Smith-s/Jake Myler-a.1-Three covers 4.00

FINDING NEMO: REEF RESCUE (Based on the Pixar movie)
BOOM! Studios: May, 2009 - No. 4, Aug, 2009 ($2.99, limited series)
1-4-Marie Croall-s/Erica Leigh Currey-a; 2 covers 4.00

FIN FANG FOUR RETURN!
Marvel Comics: Jul, 2009 ($3.99, one-shot)
1-Fin Fang Foom, Googam, Elektro, Gorgilla and Doc Samson app. 5.00

FIRE
Caliber Press: 1993 - No. 2, 1993 ($2.95, B&W, limited series, 52 pgs.)
1,2-Brian Michael Bendis-s/a 4.00
TPB (1999, 2001, $9.95) Restored reprints of series 10.00

FIREARM (Also see Codename: Firearm, Freex #15, Night Man #4 & Prime #10)
Malibu Comics (Ultraverse): Sept, 1993 - No. 18, Mar, 1995 ($1.95/$2.50)
0 ($14.95)-Came w/ video containing 1st half of story (comic contains 2nd half); 1st app. Duet 15.00
1,3-6: 1-James Robinson scripts begin; Cully Hamner-a; Chaykin-c; 1st app. Alec Swan. 3-Intro The Sportsmen; Chaykin-c. 4-Break-Thru x-over; Chaykin-c. 5-1st app. Ellen (Swan's girlfriend); 2 pg. origin of Prime. 6-Prime app. (story cont'd in Prime #10); Brereton-c 3.00
1-($2.50)-Newsstand edition polybagged w/card 3.50
1-Ultra Limited silver foil-c 1 2 3 5 6 8
2 ($2.50, 44 pgs.)-Hardcase app.;Chaykin-c; Rune flip-c/story by B. Smith (3 pgs.) 4.00
7-10,12-17: 12-The Rafferty Saga begins, ends #18; 1st app. Rafferty. 15-Night Man & Freex app. 17-Swan marries Ellen 3.00
11-($3.50, 68 pgs.)-Flip book w/Ultraverse Premiere #5 4.00
18-Death of Rafferty; Chaykin-c 4.00
NOTE: ***Brereton** c-6. **Chaykin** c-1-4, 14, 16, 18. **Hamner** a-1-4. **Herrera** a-12. **James Robinson** scripts-0-18.*

FIRE BALL XL5 (See Steve Zodiac & The ...)

FIREBIRDS (See Noble Causes)
Image Comics: Nov, 2004 ($5.95)
1-Faerber-s/Ponce-a/c; intro. Firebird 6.00

FIREBRAND (Also see Showcase '96 #4)
DC Comics: Feb, 1996 - No. 9, Oct, 1996 ($1.75)
1-9: Brian Augustyn scripts; Velluto-c/a in all. 9-Daredevil #319-c/swipe 3.00

FIREBREATHER
Image Comics: Jan, 2003 - No. 4, Apr, 2003 ($2.95)
1-4-Hester-s/Kuhn-a 3.00
...: The Iron Saint (12/04, $6.95, squarebound) Hester-s/Kuhn-a 7.00
TPB (7/04, $13.95) r/#1-4; foreword by Brad Meltzer; gallery and sketch pages 14.00

FIREBREATHER
Image Comics: Jun, 2008 - No. 4, Feb, 2009 ($2.99)
1-4-Hester-s/Kuhn-a 3.00

FIREBREATHER (Vol.3): HOLMGANG
Image Comics: Nov, 2010 - No. 4, ($3.99, limited series)
1,2-Hester-s/Kuhn-a 4.00

FIREFLY (Based on the 2002 TV series)(Also see Serenity)
BOOM! Studios: Nov, 2018 - No. 36, Jan, 2022 ($3.99)
1-24,26-36: 1-Greg Pak-s/Dan McDaid-a. 20-24-Blue Sun Rising 4.00
25-($4.99) Pius Bak-a; time-jumps to after the movie 5.00
...: Bad Company 1 (3/19, $7.99) Back story on Saffron; Gordon-s/Mortarino-a 8.00
...: Blue Sun Rising 0 (9/20, $7.99) Leads into Firefly #21; Greg Pak-s/Dan McDaid-a 8.00
...: Blue Sun Rising 1 (12/20, $7.99) Follows Firefly #24; Greg Pak-s/Dan McDaid-a 8.00
...: Keep Flying 1 (11/22, $7.99) Jensen-s/Izzo-a 8.00
...: River Run 1 (9/21, $7.99) River and Simon's escape from Osiris 8.00
...: The Holiday Special 1 (12/21, $7.99) Christmas Carol homage by various; Inhyuk Lee-c 8.00
...: The Outlaw Ma Reynolds 1 (1/20, $7.99) Takes place after #12; Pak-s/Gianfelice-a 8.00
...: The Sting (11/19, $19.99, HC) Saffron returns; Delilah S. Dawson-s; art by various 20.00
...: 20th Anniversary Special 1 (8/22, $7.99) Two stories 8.00

FIREFLY: BRAND NEW 'VERSE (Based on the 2002 TV series)
BOOM! Studios: Mar, 2021 - No. 6, Aug, 2021 ($4.99)
1-6-Gordon-s/Mascolo-a; Zoë and a new crew 20 years after the events of Firefly 5.00

FIRE FROM HEAVEN
Image Comics (WildStorm Productions): Mar, 1996 ($2.50)
1,2-Moore-s 3.00

FIREHAIR COMICS (Formerly Pioneer West Romances #3-6; also see Rangers Comics)
Fiction House Magazines (Flying Stories): Winter/48-49; No. 2, Wint/49-50; No. 7, Spr/51 - No. 11, Spr/52

	GD	VG	FN	VF	VF/NM	NM-
1-Origin Firehair	54	108	162	343	574	825
2-Continues as Pioneer West Romances for #3-6	22	44	66	128	209	290
7-11	22	44	66	132	216	300
I.W. Reprint 8-(nd)-Kinstler-c; reprints Rangers #57; Dr. Drew story by Grandenetti	3	6	9	18	28	38

FIRE POWER
Image Comics: Aug, 2020 - Present ($3.99)
1-11,13-24-Robert Kirkman-s/Chris Samnee-a 4.00
12-($4.99) 5.00

FIRESIDE BOOK SERIES (Hard and soft cover editions)
Simon and Schuster: 1974 - 1980 (130-260 pgs.), Square bound, color

		GD	VG	FN	VF	VF/NM	NM-
Amazing Spider-Man, The, 1979,	HC	7	14	21	48	89	130
130 pgs., $3.95, Bob Larkin-c	SC	5	10	15	33	57	80
America At War–The Best of DC War	HC	10	20	30	64	132	200
Comics, 1979, $6.95, 260 pgs, Kubert-c	SC	6	12	18	42	79	115
Best of Spidey Super Stories (Electric	HC	9	18	27	57	111	165
Company) 1978, $3.95,	SC	6	12	18	37	66	95
Bring On The Bad Guys (Origins of the	HC	7	14	21	46	86	125
Marvel Comics Villains) 1976, $6.95, 260 pgs.; Romita-c	SC	5	10	15	31	53	75
Captain America, Sentinel of Liberty,1979,	HC	7	14	21	48	89	130
130 pgs., $12.95, Cockrum-c	SC	5	10	15	33	57	80
Doctor Strange Master of the Mystic	HC	7	14	21	48	89	130
Arts, 1980, 130 pgs.	SC	5	10	15	33	57	80
Fantastic Four, The, 1979, 130 pgs.	HC	7	14	21	46	86	125
	SC	5	10	15	31	53	75
Heart Throbs–The Best of DC Romance	HC	13	26	39	86	188	290
Comics, 1979, 260 pgs., $6.95	SC	8	16	24	56	108	160
Incredible Hulk, The, 1978, 260 pgs.	HC	7	14	21	46	86	125
(8 1/4" x 11")	SC	5	10	15	31	53	75
Marvel's Greatest Superhero Battles,	HC	9	18	27	57	111	165
1978, 260 pgs., $6.95, Romita-c	SC	6	12	18	37	66	95
Mysteries in Space, 1980, $7,95,	HC	8	16	24	52	99	145
Anderson-c. r-DC sci/fi stories	SC	5	10	15	34	60	85
Origins of Marvel Comics, 1974, 260 pgs., $5.95. r-covers & origins of Fantastic Four, Hulk, Spider-Man, Thor,	HC	7	14	21	49	92	135
& Doctor Strange	SC	5	10	15	33	57	80
Silver Surfer, The, 1978, 130 pgs.,	HC	8	16	24	51	96	140
$4.95, Norem-c	SC	6	12	18	37	66	95
Son of Origins of Marvel Comics, 1975, 260 pgs., $6.95, Romita-c. Reprints covers & origins of X-Men, Iron Man,	HC	7	14	21	46	86	125
Avengers, Daredevil, Silver Surfer	SC	5	10	15	31	53	75
Superhero Women, The–Featuring the	HC	9	18	27	57	111	165
Fabulous Females of Marvel Comics, 1977, 260 pgs., $6.95, Romita-c	SC	6	12	18	37	66	95

Note: *Prices listed are for 1st printings. Later printings have lesser value.*

FIRESTAR
Marvel Comics Group: Mar, 1986 - No. 4, June, 1986 (75¢)(From Spider-Man TV series)
1,2: 1-X-Men & New Mutants app. 2-Wolverine-c (not real Wolverine?); Art Adams-a(p) 6.00
3,4: 3-Art Adams/Sienkiewicz-c. 4-B. Smith-c 4.00
X-Men: Firestar Digest (2006, $7.99, digest-size) r/#1-4; profile pages 8.00
1 (Jun, 2010, $3.99) Sean McKeever-s/Emma Rios-a 4.00

FIRESTONE (See Donald And Mickey Merry Christmas)

FIRESTORM (Also see The Fury of Firestorm, Cancelled Comic Cavalcade, DC Comics Presents, Flash #289, & Justice League of America #179)
DC Comics: March, 1978 - No. 5, Oct-Nov, 1978

	GD	VG	FN	VF	VF/NM	NM-
1-Origin & 1st app.	6	12	18	28	69	100
2,4,5: 2-Origin Multiplex. 4-1st app. Hyena	2	4	6	11	16	20
3-Origin & 1st app. Killer Frost (Crystal Frost)	4	8	12	28	47	65

...: The Nuclear Man TPB (2011, $17.99) r/#1-5 and stories from Flash #289-293, plus

Fire Power #1 © Kirkman & Sammee

Firestorm (2006) #23 © DC

First Strike #1 © Hasbro

GD VG FN VF VF/NM NM-
2.0 4.0 6.0 8.0 9.0 9.2

story from Cancelled Comic Cavalcade (uncolored) 18.00

FIRESTORM
DC Comics: July, 2004 - No. 35, June, 2007 ($2.50/$2.99)

1-24: 1-Intro. Jason Rusch; Jolley-s/ChrisCross-a. 6-Identity Crisis tie-in. 7-Bloodhound x-over. 8-Killer Frost returns. 9-Ronnie Raymond returns. 17-Villains United tie-in. 21-Infinite Crisis. 24-One Year Later; Killer Frost app. 3.00
25-35: 25-Begin $2.99-c; Mr. Freeze app. 33-35-Mister Miracle & Orion app. 3.00
...: Reborn TPB (2007, $14.99) r/#23-27 15.00

FIRESTORM, THE NUCLEAR MAN (Formerly Fury of Firestorm)
DC Comics: No. 65, Nov, 1987 - No. 100, Aug, 1990

65-99: 66-1st app. Zuggernaut; Firestorm vs. Green Lantern. 67,68-Millennium tie-ins. 71-Death of Capt. X. 83-1st new look 4.00
100-($2.95, 68 pgs.) 5.00
Annual 5 (10/87)-1st app. new Firestorm 5.00

FIRST, THE
CrossGeneration Comics: Jan, 2001 - No. 37, Jan, 2004 ($2.95)

1-10: 1-Barbara Kesel-s/Bart Sears & Andy Smith-a 4.00
11-37 3.00
Preview (11/00, free) 8 pg. intro 3.00
Two Houses Divided Vol. 1 TPB (11/01, $19.95) r/#1-7; new Moeller-c 20.00
Magnificent Tension Vol. 2 TPB (2002, $19.95) r/#8-13 20.00
Sinister Motives Vol. 3 TPB (2003, $15.95) r/#14-19 16.00
Vol. 4 Futile Endeavors (2003, $15.95) r/#20-25 16.00
Vol. 5 Liquid Alliances (2003, $15.95) r/#26-31 16.00
Vol. 6 Ragnarok (2004, $15.95) r/#32-37 16.00

FIRST AMERICANS, THE
Dell Publishing Co.: No. 843, Sept, 1957

Four Color 843-Marsh-a 8 16 24 54 102 150

FIRST BORN (See Witchblade and Darkness titles)
Image Comics (Top Cow): Aug, 2007 - No. 3 ($2.99, limited series)

... First Look (6/07, 99¢) Preview; The Darkness app.; Sejic-a; 2 covers (color & B&W) 3.00
1-3-($2.99) Two covers; Marz-s/Sejic-a. 3-Sara's baby is born 3.00
1-B&W variant Sejic cover 5.00
...: Aftermath (5/08, $3.99) short stories; Magdalena app.; two covers by Sook & Sejic 4.00

FIRST CHRISTMAS, THE (3-D)
Fiction House Magazines (Real Adv. Publ. Co.): 1953 (25¢, 8-1/4x10-1/4", oversize)(Came w/glasses)

nn-(Scarce)-Kelly Freas painted-c; Biblical theme, birth of Christ; Nativity-c
39 78 117 231 378 525

FIRST COMICS GRAPHIC NOVEL
First Comics: Jan, 1984 - No. 21? (52 pgs./176 pgs., high quality paper)

1,2: 1-Beowulf ($5.95)(both printings). 2-Time Beavers 10.00
3($11.95, 100 pgs.)-American Flagg! Hard Times (2nd printing exists) 15.00
4-Nexus ($6.95)-r/B&W 1-3 15.00
5,7: 5-The Enchanted Apples of Oz ($7.95, 52 pgs.)-Intro by Harlan Ellison (1986). 7-The Secret Island Of Oz ($7.95) 10.00
6-Elric of Melnibone ($14.95, 176 pgs.)-Reprints with new color 18.00
8,10,14,18: Teenage Mutant Ninja Turtles Book I -IV ($9.95, 132 pgs.)-8-r/TMNT #1-3 in color w/12 pgs. new-a; origin. 10-r/TMNT #4-6 in color. 14-r/TMNT #7,8 in color plus new 12 pg. story. 18-r/TMNT #10,11 plus 3 pg. fold-out 20.00
9-Time 2: The Epiphany by Chaykin (11/86, $7.95, 52 pgs. - indicia says #8) 20.00
11-Sailor On The Sea of Fate ($14.95) 16.00
nn-Time 2: The Satisfaction of Black Mariah (9/87) 10.00
12-American Flagg! Southern Comfort (10/87, $11.95) 15.00
13,16,17,21: 13-The Ice King Of Oz. 16-The Forgotten Forest of Oz ($8.95). 17-Mazinger (68 pgs., $8.95). 21-Elric, The Weird of the White Wolf; r/#1-5 10.00
15,19: 15-Hex Breaker: Badger ($7.95). 19-The Original Nexus Graphic Novel ($7.95, 104 pgs.)-Reprints First Comics Graphic Novel #4 12.00
20-American Flagg!: State of the Union ($11.95, 96 pgs.); r/A.F. #7-9 15.00
NOTE: *Most or all issues have been reprinted.*

1ST FOLIO (The Joe Kubert School Presents...)
Pacific Comics: Mar, 1984 ($1.50, one-shot)

1-Joe Kubert-c/a(2 pgs.); Adam & Andy Kubert-a 4.00

1ST ISSUE SPECIAL
National Periodical Publications: Apr, 1975 - No. 13, Apr, 1976 (Tryout series)

1,6: 1-Intro. Atlas; Kirby-c/a/script. 6-Dingbats 3 6 9 18 27 36
2,12: 2-Green Team (see Cancelled Comic Cavalcade). 12-Origin/1st app. "Blue" Starman (2nd app. in Starman, 2nd Series #3); Kubert-c 2 4 6 8 11 14
3-Metamorpho by Ramona Fradon 2 4 6 11 16 20

GD VG FN VF VF/NM NM-
2.0 4.0 6.0 8.0 9.0 9.2

4,10,11: 4-Lady Cop. 10-The Outsiders. 11-Code Name: Assassin; Grell-c
1 3 4 6 8 10
5-Manhunter; Kirby-c/a/script 3 6 9 18 27 36
7,9: 7-The Creeper by Ditko (c/a). 9-Dr. Fate; Kubert-c/Simonson-a.
2 4 6 11 16 20
8-Origin/1st app. The Warlord; Grell-c/a (11/75) 6 12 18 37 66 95
13-Return of the New Gods; Darkseid app.; 1st new costume Orion; predates New Gods #12 by more than a year 3 6 9 21 33 45

FIRST KISS
Charlton Comics: Dec, 1957 - No. 40, Jan, 1965

V1#1 5 10 15 35 63 90
V1#2-10 3 6 9 21 33 45
11-40 3 6 9 15 22 28

FIRST LOVE ILLUSTRATED
Harvey Publications(Home Comics)(True Love): 2/49 - No. 9, 6/50; No. 10, 1/51 - No. 86, 3/58; No. 87, 9/58 - No. 88, 11/58; No. 89, 11/62, No. 90, 2/63

1-Powell-a(2) 23 46 69 138 227 315
2-Powell-a 14 28 42 81 118 155
3-"Was I Too Fat To Be Loved" story 17 34 51 98 154 210
4-10 11 22 33 62 86 110
11,12,14-30: 30-Lingerie panel 9 18 27 52 69 85
13-"I Joined a Teen-age Sex Club" story 39 78 117 240 395 550
31-34,37,39-49: 49-Last pre-code (2/55) 9 18 27 47 61 75
35-Used in **SOTI**, illo "The title of this comic book is First Love"
24 48 72 142 234 325
36-Communism story, "Love Slaves" 15 30 45 83 124 165
38-Nostrand-a 10 20 30 56 76 95
50-66,71-90 8 16 24 42 54 65
67-70-Kirby-c 9 18 27 52 69 85
NOTE: ***Disbrow** a-13. **Orlando** c-87. **Powell** a-1, 3-5, 7, 10, 11, 13-17, 19-24, 26-29, 33,35-41, 43, 45, 46, 50, 54, 55, 57, 58, 61-63, 65, 71-73, 76, 79r, 82, 84, 88.*

FIRST MEN IN THE MOON (See Movie Comics)

FIRST ROMANCE MAGAZINE
Home Comics(Harvey Publ.)/True Love: 8/49 - #6, 6/50; #7, 6/51 - #50, 2/58; #51, 9/58 - #52, 11/58

1 20 40 60 115 185 255
2 12 24 36 67 94 120
3-5 10 20 30 54 72 90
6-10,28: 28-Nostrand-a(Powell swipe) 8 16 24 44 57 70
11-20 8 16 24 40 50 60
21-27,29-32: 32-Last pre-code issue (2/55) 7 14 21 37 46 55
33-40,44-52 7 14 21 35 43 50
41-43-Kirby-c 8 16 24 44 57 70
NOTE: ***Powell** a-1-5, 8-10, 14, 18, 20-22, 24, 25, 28, 36, 46, 48, 51.*

FIRST STRIKE (Hasbro heroes)
IDW Publishing: Aug, 2017 - No. 6, Oct, 2017 ($3.99, limited series)

1-6-Transformers, G.I. Joe, Rom, Micronauts and MASK app.; multiple covers on each 4.00

FIRST TRIP TO THE MOON (See Space Adventures No. 20)

FIRST WAVE (Based on Sci-Fi Channel TV series)
Andromeda Entertainment: Dec, 2000 - No. 4, Jun, 2001 ($2.99)

1-4-Kuhoric-s/Parsons-a/Busch-c 3.00

FIRST WAVE (Also see Batman/Doc Savage Special #1)
DC Comics: May, 2010 - No. 6, Mar, 2011 ($3.99, limited series)

1-6-Batman, Doc Savage and The Spirit app.; Azzarello-s/Morales-a/JG Jones-c 4.00
... Special 1 (6/11, $3.99) Winslade-a/Jones-c 4.00
HC (2011, $29.99, dustjacket) r/#1-6 & Batman/Doc Savage Special #1; sketch art 30.00

FIRST X-MEN
Marvel Comics: Oct, 2012 - No. 5, Mar, 2013 ($3.99, limited series)

1-5: 1-Neal Adams-a/c; Adams & Gage-s; Wolverine & Sabretooth 1st meet Xavier 4.00

FISH POLICE (Inspector Gill of the...#2, 3)
Fishwrap Productions/Comico V2#5-17/Apple Comics #18 on:
Dec, 1985 - No. 11, Nov, 1987 ($1.50, B&W); V2#5, April, 1988 - V2#17, May, 1989 ($1.75, color) No. 18, Aug, 1989 - No. 26, Dec, 1990 ($2.25, B&W)

1-11, 1(5/86),2-2nd print, V2#5-17-(Color): V2#5-11. 12-17, new-a, 18-26 ($2.25-c, B&W). 18-Origin Inspector Gill 3.00
Special 1($2.50, 7/87, Comico) 3.00
Graphic Novel: Hairballs (1987, $9.95, TPB) r/#1-4 in color 10.00

FISH POLICE
Marvel Comics: V2#1, Oct, 1992 - No. 6, Mar, 1993 ($1.25)

GD 2.0 | VG 4.0 | FN 6.0 | VF 8.0 | VF/NM 9.0 | NM- 9.2

V2#1-6: 1-Hairballs Saga begins; r/#1 (1985) 3.00

FISTFUL OF BLOOD
IDW Publishing: Oct, 2015 - No. 4, Jan, 2016 ($4.99, limited series)
1-4-Eastman-s/Bisley-a; remastering of series from Heavy Metal magazine 5.00

5 CENT COMICS (Also see Whiz Comics)
Fawcett Publ.: Feb, 1940 (8 pgs., reg. size, B&W)
nn - 1st app. Dan Dare. Ashcan comic, not distributed to newsstands, only for in-house use. A CGC certified 9.6 copy sold for $10,800 in 2003, and a CGC 9.4 sold for $11,500 in 2005.

5 RONIN (Marvel characters in Samurai setting)
Marvel Comics: May, 2011 - No. 5, May, 2011 ($2.99, weekly limited series)
1-Wolverine. 2-Hulk. 3-Punisher. 4-Psylocke; Mack-c. 5-Deadpool 5.00

5-STAR SUPER-HERO SPECTACULAR (See DC Special Series No. 1)

FIVE WEAPONS
Image Comics: Feb, 2013 - No. 10, Jul, 2014 ($3.50)
1-10-Jimmie Robinson-s/a/c 3.50

FIVE YEARS
Abstract Studio: 2019 - No. 10, 2020 ($3.99, B&W)
1-10-Terry Moore-s/a; characters from Strangers in Paradise, Rachel Rising, Echo app. 7-David-c/app. 4.00

FIX, THE
Image Comics: Apr, 2016 - No. 12, Jun, 2018 ($3.99)
1-12-Nick Spencer-s/Steve Lieber-a 4.00

FLAILING AT LOVE
Aardvark-Vanaheim: Sept, 2022 ($4.00, B&W, one-shot)
1-Cerebus figures placed over original Gustave Doré artwork; Falling in Love #40 c-swipe 4.00

FLAME, THE (See Big 3 & Wonderworld Comics)
Fox Feature Synd.: Sum, 1940 - No. 8, Jan, 1942 (#1,2: 68 pgs; #3-8: 44 pgs.)
1-Flame stories reprinted from Wonderworld #5-9; origin The Flame; Lou Fine-a (36 pgs.), 415 830 1245 2905 5103 7300
2-Fine-a(2); Wing Turner by Tuska; r/Wonderworld #3,10 206 412 618 1318 2259 3200
3-8: 3-Powell-a 135 270 405 864 1482 2100

FLAME, THE (Formerly Lone Eagle)
Ajax/Farrell Publications (Excellent Publ.): No. 5, Dec-Jan, 1954-55 - No. 3, April-May, 1955
5(#1)-1st app. new Flame 71 142 213 454 777 1100
2,3 48 96 144 302 514 725

FLAMING CARROT COMICS (Also see Junior Carrot Patrol)
Killian Barracks Press: Summer-Fall, 1981 ($1.95, one shot) (Lg size, 8-1/2x11")
1-Bob Burden-c/a/scripts; serially #'ed to 6500 9 18 27 62 126 190

FLAMING CARROT COMICS (See Anything Goes, Cerebus, Teenage Mutant Ninja Turtles/Flaming Carrot Crossover & Visions)
Aardvark-Vanaheim/Renegade Press #6-17/Dark Horse #18-31:
May, 1984 - No. 5, Jan, 1985; No. 6, Mar, 1985 - No. 31, Oct, 1994 ($1.70/$2.00, B&W)
1-Bob Burden story/art 6 12 18 38 69 100
2 3 6 9 17 25 34
3 2 4 6 13 18 22
4-6 2 4 6 9 12 15
7-9 1 3 4 6 8 10
10-12 6.50
13-15 4.00
15-Variant without cover price 6.00
16-(6/87) 1st app. Mystery Men 3 6 9 19 30 40
17-23,25: 18-1st Dark Horse issue. 25-Contains trading cards; TMNT app. 4.00
24-(2.50, 52 pgs.)-10th anniversary issue 5.00
26,27-Teenage Mutant Ninja Turtles x-over. 26-Begin $2.25-c. 27-McFarlane-c 6.00
28-31: 29-Begin $2.50-c 4.00
Annual 1(1/97, $5.00) 5.00
... & Reid Fleming, World's Toughest Milkman (12/02, $3.99) listed as #32 in indicia 4.00
... :Fortune Favors the Bold (1998, $16.95, TPB) r/#19-24 17.00
... :Men of Mystery (7/97, $12.95, TPB) r/#1-3, + new material 13.00
... 's Greatest Hits (4/98, $17.95, TPB) r/#12-18, + new material 18.00
... :The Wild Shall Wild Remain (1997, $17.95, TPB) r/#4-11, + new s/a 18.00

FLAMING CARROT COMICS
Image Comics (Desperado): Dec, 2004 - 2006 ($2.95/$3.50, B&W)
1-3-Bob Burden story/art 6.00
4-($3.50-c) 1 2 3 4 5 7
... Special #1 (3/06, $3.50) All Photo comic 3.50
... Vol. 6 (2006, $14.99) r/1-4 & Special #1; intro. by Brian Bolland 15.00

FLAMING CEREBUS COMICS (Cerebus in Hell)
Aardvark-Vanaheim: Mar, 2021 ($4.00, B&W)
1-Cerebus figures placed over Gustave Doré artwork of Hell; Flaming Carrot #1-c swipe 4.00

FLAMING LOVE
Quality Comics Group (Comic Magazines): Dec, 1949 - No. 6, Oct, 1950 (Photo covers #2-6) (52 pgs.)
1-Ward-c/a (9 pgs.) 55 110 165 352 601 850
2 30 60 90 177 289 400
3-Ward-a (9 pgs.); Crandall-a 39 78 117 231 378 525
4-6: 4-Gustavson-a 24 48 72 142 234 325

FLAMING WESTERN ROMANCES (Formerly Target Western Romances)
Star Publications: No. 3, Mar-Apr, 1950
3-Robert Taylor, Arlene Dahl photo on-c with biographies inside; L. B. Cole-c 55 110 165 352 601 850

FLARE (Also see Champions for 1st app. & League of Champions)
Hero Comics/Hero Graphics Vol. 2 on: Nov, 1988 - No. 3, Jan, 1989 ($2.75, color, 52 pgs); V2#1, Nov, 1990 - No. 7, Nov, 1991 ($2.95/$3.50, color, mature, 52 pgs.);V2#8, Oct, 1992 - No. 16, Feb, 1994 ($3.50/$3.95, B&W, 36 pgs.)
V1#1-3, V2#1-16: 5-Eternity Smith returns. 6-Intro The Tigress 4.00
Annual 1(1992, $4.50, B&W, 52 pgs.)-Champions-r 4.50

FLARE ADVENTURES
Hero Graphics: Feb, 1992 - No. 12, 1993? ($3.50/$3.95)
1 (90¢, color, 20 pgs.) 4.00
2-12-Flip books w/Champions Classics 4.00

FLASH, THE (See Adventure Comics, The Brave and the Bold, Crisis On Infinite Earths, DC Comics Presents, DC Special, DC Special Series, DC Super-Stars, The Greatest Flash Stories Ever Told, Green Lantern, Impulse, JLA, Justice League of America, Showcase, Speed Force, Super Team Family, Titans & World's Finest)

FLASH, THE (1st Series)(Formerly Flash Comics)(See Showcase #4,8,13,14)
National Periodical Publ./DC: No. 105, Feb-Mar, 1959 - No. 350, Oct, 1985
105-(2-3/59)-Origin Flash(retold), & Mirror Master (1st app.) 800 1600 2800 10,000 23,500 37,000
106-Origin Grodd & Pied Piper; Flash's 1st visit to Gorilla City; begin Grodd the Super Gorilla trilogy (Scarce) 367 734 1100 3100 7050 11,000
107-Grodd trilogy, part 2 141 282 423 1163 2632 4100
108-Grodd trilogy ends 125 250 375 1000 2250 3500
109-2nd app. Mirror Master 89 178 267 712 1606 2500
110-Intro/origin Kid Flash who later becomes Flash in Crisis On Infinite Earths #12; begin Kid Flash trilogy, ends #112 (also in #114,116,118); 1st app. & origin of The Weather Wizard 300 600 900 2475 5588 8700
111-2nd Kid Flash tryout; Cloud Creatures 93 186 279 744 1672 2600
112-Origin & 1st app. Elongated Man (4-5/60); also apps. in #115,119,130 107 214 321 856 1928 3000
113-Origin & 1st app. Trickster 82 164 246 656 1478 2300
114-Captain Cold app. (see Showcase #8) 62 124 186 502 1126 1750
115,116,118-120: 119-Elongated Man marries Sue Dearborn. 120-Flash & Kid Flash team-up for 1st time 46 92 138 340 770 1200
117-Origin & 1st app. Capt. Boomerang; 1st & only S.A. app. Winky Blinky & Noddy 57 114 171 456 1028 1600
121,122: 122-Origin & 1st app. The Top 33 66 99 238 532 825
123-(9/61)-Re-intro. Golden Age Flash; origins of both Flashes; 1st mention of an Earth II where DC G. A. heroes live 300 600 900 2550 5775 9000
123-(Facsimile Edition)(2020, $3.99) Reprints issue with original 1961 ads and letters 5.00
123-(Facsimile Edition)(12/22, $4.99) Reprints issue with original 1961 ads and letters 5.00
124-Last 10¢ issue 29 58 87 209 467 725
125-128,130: 127-Return of Grodd-c/story. 128-Origin & 1st app. Abra Kadabra. 130-(7/62)-1st Gauntlet of Super-Villains (Mirror Master, Capt. Cold, The Top, Capt. Boomerang & Trickster) 27 54 81 189 420 650
129-2nd G.A. Flash x-over; J.S.A. cameo in flashback (1st S.A. app. G.A. Green Lantern, Hawkman, Atom, Black Canary & Dr. Mid-Nite. Wonder Woman (1st S.A. app.?) appears) 27 54 81 194 435 675
131-134,136,138: 131-Early Green Lantern x-over (9/62). 136-1st Dexter Miles 18 36 54 121 268 415
135-1st app. of Kid Flash's yellow costume (3/63) 25 50 75 175 388 600
137-G.A. Flash x-over; J.S.A. cameo (1st S.A. app.)(1st real app. since 2-3/51); 1st S.A. app. Vandal Savage & Johnny Thunder; JSA team decides to re-form 42 84 126 311 706 1100
139-Origin & 1st app. Prof. Zoom 136 272 408 1088 2444 3800
140-Origin & 1st app. Heat Wave 24 48 72 168 372 575
141-146,148-150: 142-Trickster app. 13 26 39 87 191 295
147-2nd Prof. Zoom 21 42 63 147 324 500
151-Engagement of Barry Allen & Iris West; G.A. Flash vs. The Shade. 13 26 39 86 188 290
152-159: 159-Dr. Mid-Nite cameo 10 20 30 66 138 210
160-(80-Pg. Giant G-21); G.A. Flash & Johnny Quick-r 12 24 36 79 170 260
161-164,166,167: 167-New facts about Flash's origin 8 16 24 56 108 160
165-Barry Allen weds Iris West 9 18 27 58 114 170
168,170: 168-Green Lantern-c/app. 170-Dr. Mid-Nite, Dr. Fate, G.A. Flash x-over 8 16 24 56 108 160
169-(80-Pg. Giant G-34)-New facts about origin 9 18 27 57 111 165
171,172,174,176,177,179,180: 171-JLA, Green Lantern, Atom flashbacks. 174-Barry Allen reveals I.D. to wife. 179-(5/68)-Flash travels to Earth-Prime and meets DC editor Julie Schwartz; 1st unnamed app. Earth-Prime (See Justice League of America #123 for 1st named app. & 3rd app. overall) 7 14 21 48 89 130
173-G.A. Flash x-over 8 16 24 56 108 160
175-2nd Superman/Flash race (12/67) (See Superman #199 & World's Finest #198,199); JLA cameo; gold kryptonite used (on J'onn J'onzz impersonating Superman) 19 38 57 131 291 450
178-(80-Pg. Giant G-46) 9 18 27 57 111 165
181-186,188,189: 186-Re-intro. Sargon. 189-Last 12¢-c 5 10 15 34 60 85
187,196: (68-Pg. Giants G-58, G-70) 6 12 18 40 73 105
190-195,197-199: 198-Zatanna 1st solo story 4 8 12 27 44 60
200-(9/70) 5 10 15 33 57 80
201-204,206,207: 201-New G.A. Flash story. 206-Elongated Man begins 207-Last 15¢ issue 3 6 9 21 33 45
205-(68-Pg. Giant G-82) 6 12 18 41 76 110
208-213-(52 pg.): 211-G.A. Flash origin-r/#104; Roller Derby-c. 213-Reprints #137 4 8 12 25 40 55
214-DC 100 Page Super Spectacular DC-11; origin Metal Men-r/Showcase #37; never before published G.A. Flash story 9 18 27 58 114 170
215 (52 pgs.)-Flash-r/Showcase #4; G.A. Flash x-over, continued in #216 5 10 15 30 50 70
216,220: 220-1st app. Turtle since Showcase #4 3 6 9 17 26 35
217-219: Neal Adams-a in all. 217-Green Lantern/Green Arrow series begins (9/72); 2nd G.L. & G.A. team-up series (see Green Lantern #76). 219-Last Green Arrow 5 10 15 34 60 85
221-224,227,228,230,231: 222-G. Lantern x-over. 228-(7-8/74)-Flash writer Cary Bates travels to Earth-One & meets Flash, Iris Allen & Trickster; 2nd unnamed app. Earth-Prime (See Justice League of America #123 for 1st named app. & 3rd app. overall) 3 6 9 14 19 24
225-Professor Zoom-c/app. 6 12 18 37 66 95
226-Neal Adams-p 3 6 9 17 26 35
229,232-(100 pg. issues)-G.A. Flash-r & new-a. 229-G.A. Flash & Rag Doll app. in new story

Five Years #3 © Terry Moore

The Flash #237 © DC

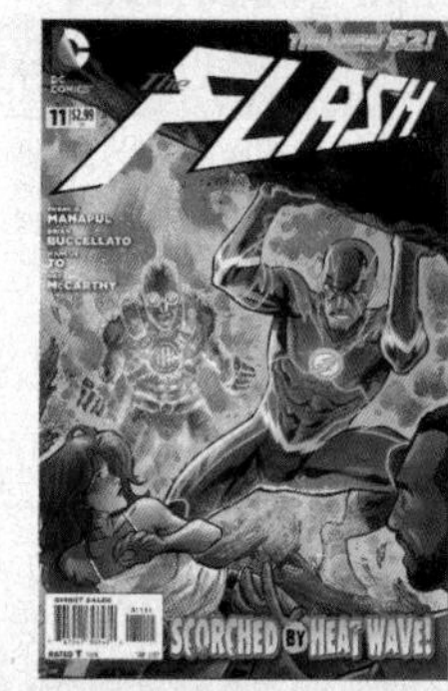

Flash (2011) #11 © DC

	GD	VG	FN	VF	VF/NM	NM-
	2.0	4.0	6.0	8.0	9.0	9.2

5 10 15 30 50 70
233-Professor Zoom-c/app. 3 6 9 21 33 45
234-236,238-250: 235-Green Lantern x-over. 243-Death of The Top. 245-Origin The Floronic Man in Green Lantern back-up, ends #246. 246-Last Green Lantern. 247-Jay Garrick app. 250-Intro Golden Glider 2 4 6 10 14 18
237-Professor Zoom-c/app. 3 6 9 18 28 38
251-274: 256-Death of The Top retold. 265-267-(44 pgs.). 267-Origin of Flash's uniform. 270-Intro The Clown 2 4 6 8 10 12
268,273,274,278,283,286-(Whitman variants; low print run; no issue #s shown on covers) 2 4 6 8 11 14
275,276-Iris Allen dies 2 4 6 13 18 22
275,276-(Whitman variants; low print run; no issue #s shown on covers) 3 6 9 16 23 30
277-288,290: 286-Intro/origin Rainbow Raider 1 3 4 6 8 10
289-1st Pérez DC art (Firestorm); new Firestorm back-up series begins (9/80), ends #304 2 4 6 8 10 12
291-299,301-305: 291-1st app. Saber-Tooth (villain). 295-Gorilla Grodd-c/story. 298-Intro & origin new Shade. 301-Atomic bomb-c. 303-The Top returns. 304-Intro/origin Colonel Computron; 305-G.A. Flash x-over 6.00
300-(8/81, 52 pgs.)-25th Anniversary issue; Flash's origin and life story retold; wraparound-c by Infantino; no ads 1 3 4 6 8 10
306-313-Dr. Fate by Giffen. 309-Origin Flash retold 6.00
314-322,325-340: 318-322-Creeper back-ups. 319-Origin of Eradicator. 328-Iris West Allen's death retold. 329-JLA app. 340-Trial of the Flash begins 5.00
323,324-Two part Flash vs. Flash story. 323-Creeper back-up. 324-Death of Reverse Flash (Professor Zoom) 4 8 12 22 35 48
341-349: 344-Origin Kid Flash 6.00
350-Double size ($1.25) Final issue 1 2 3 5 6 8
Annual 1 (10-12/63, 80 pg. Giant)-Origin Elongated Man & Kid Flash-r; origin Grodd; G.A. Flash-r 35 70 105 252 564 875
Annual 1 Replica Edition (2001, $6.95)-Reprints the entire 1963 Annual 7.00
...Chronicles SC Vol. 1 (2009, $14.99)-r/Showcase #4,8,13,14 and Flash #105,106 15.00
...Chronicles SC Vol. 2 (2010, $14.99)-r/Flash #107-112 15.00
The Flash Spectacular (See DC Special Series No. 11)
The Flash vs. The Rogues TPB (2009, $14.99) r/1st app. of classic rogues in Showcase #8 and Flash #105,106,110,113,117,122,140,155; new Van Sciver-c 15.00
The Life Story of the Flash (1997, $19.95, Hardcover) "Iris Allen's" chronicle of Barry Allen's life; comic panels w/additional text; Waid & Augustyn-s/ Kane & Staton-a/Orbik painted-c 20.00
The Life Story of the Flash (1998, $12.95, Softcover) New Orbik-c 13.00
NOTE: ***N. Adams*** *c-194, 195, 203, 204, 206-208, 211, 213, 215, 226p, 246.* ***M. Anderson*** *c-165, a(i)-195, 200-204, 206-208.* ***Austin*** *a-233i, 234i, 246i.* ***Buckler*** *a-271p, 272p; c(p)-247-250, 252, 253p, 255, 256p, 258, 262, 265-267, 269-271.* ***Giffen*** *a-306-313p; c-310p, 315.* ***Giordano*** *a-226i.* ***Sid Greene*** *a-167-174i, 229i(r).* ***Grell*** *a-237p, 238p, 240-243p; c-236.* ***Heck*** *a-198p.* ***Infantino/Anderson*** *a-135. c-135, 170-174, 192, 200, 201, 328-330.* ***Infantino/Giella*** *c-105-112, 163, 164, 166-168.* ***G. Kane*** *a-195p, 197-199p, 229r, 232r; c-197-199, 312p.* ***Kubert*** *a-108p, 215i(r); c-189-191.* ***Lopez*** *c-272.* ***Meskin*** *a-229r, 232r.* ***Perez*** *a-289-293p; c-293.* ***Starlin*** *a-294-296p.* ***Staton*** *c-263p, 264p. Green Lantern x-over-131, 143, 168, 171, 191.*

FLASH (2nd Series)(See Crisis on Infinite Earths #12 and All Flash #1)
DC Comics: June, 1987 - No. 230, Mar, 2006; No. 231, Oct, 2007 - No. 247, Feb, 2009

1-Guice-c/a begins; New Teen Titans app. 3 6 9 14 20 26
2-10: 3-Intro. Kilgore. 5-Intro. Speed McGee. 7-1st app. Blue Trinity. 8,9-Millennium tie-ins. 9-1st app. The Chunk 5.00
11-78,80: 12-Free extra 16 pg. Dr. Light story. 19-Free extra 16 pg. Flash story. 28-Capt. Cold app. 29-New Phantom Lady app. 40-Dr. Alchemy app. 50-($1.75, 52 pgs.). 62-Flash: Year One begins, ends #65. 65-Last $1.00-c. 66-Aquaman app. 69,70-Green Lantern app. 70-Gorilla Grodd story ends. 73-Re-intro Barry Allen & begin saga ("Barry Allen's" true ID revealed in #78). 76-Re-intro of Max Mercury (Quality Comics' Quicksilver), not in uniform until #77. 80-($1.25-c) Regular Edition 4.00
79,80 ($2.50): 79-(68 pgs.) Barry Allen saga ends. 80-Foil-c 5.00
81-91,93-99,101: 81,82-Nightwing & Starfire app. 84-Razer app. 94-Zero Hour. 95-"Terminal Velocity" begins, ends #100. 96,98,99-Kobra app. 97-Origin Max Mercury; Chillblaine app. 4.00
92-1st Impulse 3 6 9 21 33 45
100 ($2.50)-Newstand edition; Kobra & JLA app. 4.00
100 ($3.50)-Foil-c edition; Kobra & JLA app. 5.00
102-131: 102-Mongul app.; begin-$1.75-c. 105-Mirror Master app. 107-Shazam app. 108-"Dead Heat" begins; 1st app. Savitar. 109-"Dead Heat" Pt. 2 (cont'd in Impulse #10). 110-"Dead Heat" Pt. 4 (cont'd in Impulse #11). 111-"Dead Heat" finale; Savitar disappears into the Speed Force; John Fox cameo (2nd app.). 112-"Race Against Time" begins, ends #118; re-intro John Fox. 113-Tornado Twins app. 119-Final Night x-over. 127-129-Rogue's Gallery & Neron. 128,129-JLA-app.130-Morrison & Millar-s begin 3.50
132-149: 135-GL & GA app. 138,140-Black Flash cameos. 141-1st full app. Black Flash. 142-Wally almost marries Linda; Waid-s return. 144-Cobalt Blue origin. 145-Chain Lightning begins. 147-Professor Zoom app. 149-Barry Allen app. 3.00
150-($2.95) Final showdown with Cobalt Blue 4.00
151-162: 151-Casey-s. 152-New Flash-c. 154-New Flash ID revealed. 159-Wally marries Linda. 162-Last Waid-s. 3.00
163-169,171-187,189-196,201-206: 163-Begin $2.25-c. 164-186-Bolland-c. 183-1st app of 2nd Trickster (Axel Walker). 196-Winslade-a. 201-Dose-a begins. 205-Batman-c/app. 3.00
170-1st app. Cicada; Bolland-c 5.00
188-($2.95) Mirror Master, Weather Wizard, Trickster app. 4.00
197-Origin of Zoom (Hunter Zolomon) (6/03) 5 10 15 31 53 75
198,199-Zoom app. 1 3 4 6 8 10
200-($3.50) Flash vs. Zoom; Barry Allen & Hal Jordan app.; wraparound-c 1 2 3 5 6 8
207-230: 207-211-Turner-c/Porter-a. 209-JLA app. 210-Nightwing app. 212-Origin Mirror Master. 214-216-Identity Crisis x-over. 219-Wonder Woman app. 220-Rogue War 224-Zoom & Prof. Zoom app. 225-Twins born; Barry Allen app.; last Johns-s 3.00
231-247: 231-(10/07) Waid-s/Acuña-a. 240-Grodd app.; "Dark Side Club" 3.00
#0-(10/94) Zero Hour issue released between #94 & 95 3.00
#1,000,000 (11/98) 853rd Century x-over 3.00
Annual 1-7,9: 2-('87-'94,'96, 68 pgs), 3-Gives history of G.A.,S.A., & Modern Age Flash in text. 4-Armaggedon 2001. 5-Eclipso-c/story. 7-Elseworlds story. 9-Legends of the Dead Earth story; J.H. Williams-a(p); Mick Gray-a(i) 4.00
Annual 8 (1995, $3.50)-Year One story 4.00
Annual 10 (1997, $3.95)-Pulp Heroes stories 4.00
Annual 11,12 ('98, '99)-11-Ghosts; Wrightson-c. 12-JLApe; Art Adams-c 4.00
Annual 13 ('00, $3.50) Planet DC; Alcatena-c/a 4.00
...: Blitz (2004, $19.95, TPB)-r/#192-200; Kolins-c 20.00
...: Blood Will Run (2002, 2008; $17.95, TPB)-r/#170-176, Secret Files #3, Iron Heights 18.00
...: Crossfire (2004, $17.95, TPB)-r/#183-191 & parts of Flash Secret Files #3 18.00
Dead Heat (2000, $14.95, TPB)-r/#108-111, Impulse #10,11 15.00
...80-Page Giant (8/98, $4.95) Flash family stories by Waid, Millar and others; Mhan-c 5.00
...80-Page Giant 2 (4/99, $4.95) Stories of Flash family, future Kid Flash, original Teen Titans and XS 5.00
...: Emergency Stop (2008, $12.99, TPB)-r/#130-135; Morrison & Millar-s 13.00
...: Ignition (2005, $14.95, TPB)-r/#201-206 15.00
...: Iron Heights (2001, $5.95)-Van Sciver-c/a; 1st app. of the prison; intro. Girder, Murmur, Double Down and Blacksmith 6.00
...: Mercury Falling (2009, $14.99, TPB)-r/Impulse #62-67 15.00
...: Our Worlds at War 1 (10/01, $2.95)-Jae Lee-c; Black Racer app. 3.00
...Plus 1 (1/1997, $2.95)-Nightwing-c/app. 4.00
Race Against Time (2001, $14.95, TPB)-r/#112-118 15.00
...: Rogues (2003, $14.95, TPB)-r/#177-182 15.00
...: Rogue War (2006, $17.99, TPB)-r/#1/2,212,218,220-225; cover gallery 18.00
...Secret Files 1 (11/97, $4.95) Origin-s & pin-ups 5.00
...Secret Files 2 (11/99, $4.95) Origin of Replicant 5.00
...Secret Files 3 (11/01; $4.95) Intro. Hunter Zolomon (who later becomes Zoom) 20.00
Special 1 (1990, $2.95, 84 pgs.)-50th anniversary issue; Kubert-c; 1st Flash story by Mark Waid; 1st app. John Fox (27th Century Flash) 5.00
Terminal Velocity (1996, $12.95, TPB)-r/#95-100. 13.00
...: The Greatest Stories Ever Told (2007, $19.99, TPB) reprints; Ross-c/Waid intro. 20.00
The Return of Barry Allen (1996, $12.95, TPB)-r/#74-79 13.00
The Secret of Barry Allen (2005, $19.99, TPB)-r/#207-211,213-217; Turner sketch page 20.00
...: The Wild Wests HC (2008, $24.99, dustjacket)-r/#231-237 25.00
...: Time Flies (2002, $5.95)-Seth Fisher-c/a; Rozum-s 6.00
TV Special 1 (1991, $3.95, 76 pgs.)-Photo-c plus behind the scenes photos of TV show; Saltares-a, Byrne scripts 5.00
Wizard #1/2 (2005) prelude to Rogue Wars; Justiano-a 10.00
...: Wonderland TPB (2007, $12.99, TPB)-r/#164-169 13.00
NOTE: ***Guice*** *a-1-9p, 11p, Annual 1p; c-1-9p, Annual 1p.* ***Perez*** *c-15-17, Annual 2i.* ***Charest*** *c/a-Annual 5p.*

FLASH, THE (Brightest Day)(Leads into Flashpoint series)
DC Comics: Jun, 2010 - No. 12, Jul, 2011 ($3.99/$2.99)

1-($3.99) Barry Allen vs. the 25th Century Rogues; Johns-s/Manapul-a/c 4.00
1-Variant-c by Tony Harris 10.00
2-12-($2.99) Capt. Boomerang app. 8-Reverse Flash origin retold 3.00
2-12-Variant covers. 2-Sook. 3-Horn. 4-Kolins. 5-Sook. 6-Garza. 7-Cooke 5.00
...: Secret Files and Origins 1 (5/10, $3.99) Johns-s/Kolins-a; profiles of the Rogues 4.00
...: The Dastardly Death of the Rogues HC (2011, $19.99, dj) r/#1-7 & Secret Files 20.00

FLASH (New DC 52)
DC Comics: Nov, 2011 - No. 52, Jul, 2016 ($2.99/$3.99)

1-Manapul & Buccellato-s; Manapul-a/c 2 4 6 8 10 12
1-Special Edition (12/14, $1.00) reprints #1 with Flash TV image above cover logo 3.00
2-24: 6,7-Captain Cold app. 8,9,13-17-Grodd app. 17-24-Reverse Flash app. 18-Takara-a. 21-Kid Flash app. 3.00
23.1, 23.2, 23.3 (11/13, $2.99, regular-c) 3.00
23.1 (11/13, $3.99, 3-D cover) "Grodd #1" on cover; Batista-a/Manapul-c 1 3 4 6 8 10
23.2 (11/13, $3.99, 3-D cover) "Reverse Flash #1" on cover; origin; Hepburn-a/Manapul-c 1 3 4 6 8 10

GD VG FN VF VF/NM NM-
2.0 4.0 6.0 8.0 9.0 9.2

23.3 (11/13, $3.99, 3-D cover) "The Rogues #1" on cover; Zircher-a/Manapul-c
1 3 4 6 8 10
25-($3.99) Zero Year; Sprouse & Manapul-a; first meeting of Barry and Iris 4.00
26-39: 26-Googe-a. 27-Buccellato-s begin. 28-Deadman app. 3.00
40-49,51,52: 40-($3.99) Professor Zoom cameo. 41-47-Prof. Zoom app. 4.00
50-($4.99) The Rogues and The Riddler app.; back-up Kid Flash story 5.00
#0 (11/12, $2.99) Barry's childhood and origin re-told; Manapul-a/c 3.00
Annual #1 (10/12, $4.99) Continued from #12; origin of Glider; Kolins-a 5.00
Annual #2 (9/13, $4.99) Green Lantern app.; Basri-a 5.00
Annual #3 (6/14, $4.99) Intro. Wally West; Grodd app.; leads into Flash #31 5.00
Annual #4 (9/15, $4.99) Jensen-s/Dazo-a; background on Eobard Thawne; cont'd in #43 5.00
...: Futures End 1 (11/14, $2.99, reg.-c) Five years later; Wally West gains speed power 3.00
...: Futures End 1 (11/14, $3.99, 3-D cover) 4.00

FLASH, THE (DC Rebirth)(Reverts to legacy numbering with #750)
DC Comics: Aug, 2016 - No. 88, Early Apr, 2020; No. 750, Late Apr, 2020 - Present ($2.99/$3.99)

1-20: 1-3-Williamson-s/Di Giandomenico-a. 3-Intro Godspeed. 8-Wally becomes the new Kid Flash in costume. 9-Flash of Two Worlds cover swipe; both Wallys app. 10-12-The Shade app. 14-17-Rogues Reloaded 3.00
21,22-The Button x-over with Batman #21,22. 21-Flashpoint Thomas Wayne app.; Porter-a. 22-Reverse Flash app; Jay Garrick app.; leads into Doomsday Clock series 3.00
23,24,26-49: 23-Reverse Flash & Hal Jordan app. 28-Intro. Negative Flash. 33-Dark Nights: Metal tie-in. 36-Preview of Damage #1. 39-44-Grodd app. 42-Panosian-a. 46-Zoom app. 47-49-Flash War; the Renegades app.; Porter-a 3.00
25-($3.99) Reverse Flash origin re-told; art by Di Giandomenico, Sook & Googe 4.00
50-74-($3.99) 50-Flash War concl.; Zoom app.; Impulse returns. 59-Intro. Fuerza. 64,65-X-over with Batman #64,65; Gotham Girl app. 70-74-Year One; origin re-told 4.00
75-($4.99) Year of the Villain tie-in; Turtle app.; art by Porter, Duce & Kolins 5.00
76-88: 76-83-Year of the Villain tie-ins. 82-Acetate-c 4.00
750-($7.99, 80 pages) The Flash Age pt. 1; short stories and pin-ups by various incl. Johns, Wolfman, & Manapul; Flash Forward epilogue; multiple covers 10.00
751-774,776-794: 758-760-Tornado Twins app.; Jesse Quick & Max Mercury return. 759-762-Reverse Flash app. 763-766-Dr. Alchemy app. 767-Endless Winter pt. 2; Black Adam app. 770-Jay Garrick & The Ray app. in WWII vs. Hitler. 771-Legion of Doom app.; Maguire-a. 772,773-Heat Wave app. 776-779-Dr. Fate & Justice League Dark app. 786-Dark Crisis tie-in. 790-796-One Minute War 4.00
775-($4.99) Starbreaker and Eclipso return 5.00
Annual 1 (3/18, $4.99) Porter & Duce-a; leads into Flash War in Flash #47 5.00
Annual 2 (3/19, $4.99) Kolins-a; Godspeed & Impulse app. 5.00
Annual 3 (8/20, $4.99) Suicide Squad app.; Segovia, Peterson & Pagulayan-a 5.00
2021 Annual 1 (9/21, $5.99) Return to Sanctuary; Peterson & Pagulayan-a 6.00
2022 Annual 1 (10/21, $5.99) Linda's romance novel 6.00
...: One Minute War Special (3/23, $5.99) Tie-in with Flash #790-796 6.00
...: One Minute War: Start the Clock 1 (5/23, $5.99) Reprints Flash #790-792 6.00
...: Rebirth (8/16) Williamson-s/Di Giandomenico-a; Wally West & Batman app. 3.00
.../ Speed Buggy Special 1 (7/18, $4.99) Lobdell-s/Booth-a; Wally West & Savitar app. 5.00

FLASH, THE (See Tangent Comics/ The Flash)

FLASH AND GREEN LANTERN: THE BRAVE AND THE BOLD
DC Comics: Oct, 1999 - No. 6, Mar, 2000 ($2.50, limited series)

1-6-Waid & Peyer-s/Kitson-a. 4-Green Arrow app.; Grindberg-a(p) 4.00
TPB (2001, $12.95) r/#1-6 13.00

FLASH COMICS
DC Comics: Dec. 1939

1-Ashcan comic, not distributed to newsstands, only for in-house use. Cover art is Adventure Comics #41 and interior from All-American Comics #8. A CGC certified 9.6 sold for $11,500 in 2004. A CGC certified 9.4 sold for $6,572.50 in 2008. A CGC certified 9.6 sold for $8,513 in 2013. A CGC certified 9.4 sold for $20,315 in 2018.

FLASH COMICS (Whiz Comics No. 2 on)
Fawcett Publications: Jan, 1940 (12 pgs., B&W, regular size)
(Not distributed to newsstands; printed for in-house use)

NOTE: ***Whiz Comics** #2 was preceded by two books, **Flash Comics** and **Thrill Comics**, both dated Jan, 1940, (12 pgs, B&W, regular size) and were not distributed. These two books are identical except for the title, and were sent out to major distributors as ad copies to promote sales. It is believed that the complete 68 page issue of Fawcett's **Flash** and **Thrill Comics** #1 was finished and ready for publication with the January date. Since DC Comics was also about to publish a book with the same date and title, Fawcett hurriedly printed up the black and white version of **Flash Comics** to secure copyright before DC. The inside covers are blank, with the covers and inside pages printed on a high quality uncoated paper stock.The eight page origin story of Captain Thunder is composed of pages 1-7 and 13 of the Captain Marvel story essentially as they appeared in the first issue of **Whiz Comics**. The balloon dialogue on page thirteen was relettered to tie the story into the end of page seven in **Flash** and **Thrill Comics** to produce a shorter version of the origin story for copyright purposes. Obviously, DC acquired the copyright and Fawcett dropped **Flash** as well as **Thrill** and came out with **Whiz Comics** a month later. Fawcett never used the cover to **Flash** and **Thrill** #1, designing a new cover for **Whiz Comics**. Fawcett also must have discovered that Captain Thunder had already been used by another publisher (Captain Terry Thunder by Fiction House). All references to Captain Thunder were relettered to Captain Marvel before appearing in **Whiz**.*

1-(nn on-c, #1 on inside)-Origin & 1st app. Captain Thunder. Cover by C.C. Beck. Eight copies of Flash and three copies of Thrill exist. All 3 copies of Thrill sold in 1986 for between $4,000-$10,000 each. A NM copy of Thrill sold in 1987 for $12,000. A VG copy of Thrill sold in 1987 for $9000 cash. A CGC certified 9.0 copy of the Flash Comics version sold for $10,117.50 in 2006. A CGC certified 9.4 copy of the Flash Comics version sold for $14,340 in 2008. A CGC certified 9.0 copy of the Thrill Comics version sold for $20,315 in 2008. A CGC certified 8.0 copy sold for $12,999 in 2012. A CGC certified 4.5 copy sold for $19,750 in 2017. A CGC certified 9.0 copy of Thrill Comics sold for $41,040 in 2017. A CGC certified 9.4 copy of Flash Comics sold for $85,000 in 2019.

FLASH COMICS (The Flash No. 105 on) (Also see All-Flash)
National Periodical Publ./All-American: Jan, 1940 - No. 104, Feb, 1949

1-The Flash (origin/1st app.) by Harry Lampert, Hawkman (origin/1st app.) by Gardner Fox, The Whip, & Johnny Thunder (origin/1st app.) by Stan Asch; Cliff Cornwall by Moldoff, Flash Picture Novelets (later Minute Movies w/#12) begin; Moldoff (Shelly) cover; 1st app. Shiera Sanders who later becomes Hawkgirl, #24; reprinted in Famous First Edition (on sale 11/10/39); The Flash-c 26,800 53,600 80,400 195,600 285,300 375,000
1-Reprint, Oversize 13-1/2x10". **WARNING:** This comic is an exact reprint of the original except for its size. DC published it in 1974 with a second cover titling it as a Famous First Edition. There have been many reported cases of the outer cover being removed and the interior sold as the original edition. The reprint with the new outer cover removed is practically worthless. See Famous First Edition for value.
2-Rod Rian begins, ends #11; Hawkman-c 1800 3600 5400 11,500 20,250 29,000
3-King Standish begins (1st app.), ends #41 (called The King #16-37,39-41); E.E. Hibbard-a begins on Flash 524 1048 1572 3825 6763 9700
4-Moldoff (Shelly) Hawkman begins; The Whip-c 371 742 1113 2600 4550 6500
5-The King-c 300 600 900 2010 3505 5000
6-2nd Flash-c (alternates w/Hawkman #6 on) 892 1784 2676 6512 11,506 16,500
7-2nd Hawkman-c; 1st Moldoff Hawkman-c 676 1352 2028 4935 8718 12,500
8-New logo begins; classic Moldoff Flash-c 423 846 1269 3000 5250 7500
9,10: 9-Moldoff Hawkman-c; 10-Classic Moldoff Flash-c
415 830 1245 2905 5103 7300
11-13,15-20: 12-Les Watts begins; "Sparks" #16 on. 13-Has full page ad for All Star Comics #3. 17-Last Cliff Cornwall 265 530 795 1694 2897 4100
14-World War II cover 300 600 900 2070 3635 5200
21-Classic Hawkman-c 290 580 870 1856 3178 4500
22,23 239 478 717 1530 2615 3700
24-Shiera becomes Hawkgirl (12/41); see All-Star Comics #5 for 1st app.
290 580 870 1856 3178 4500
25-28,30: 28-Last Les Sparks. 158 316 474 1003 1727 2450
29-Ghost Patrol begins (origin/1st app.), ends #104
187 374 561 1197 2049 2900
31-Classic Hawkman dragon-c 194 388 582 1242 2121 3000
32,34,35,37-40: 158 316 474 1003 1727 2450
33-Classic Hawkman WWII-c; origin The Shade 300 600 900 2070 3635 5200
36-1st app. Rag Doll (see Flash #229) 174 348 522 1114 1907 2700
41-50 135 270 405 864 1482 2100
51-61: 52-1st computer in comics, c/s (4/44). 59-Last Minute Movies. 61-Last Moldoff Hawkman 110 220 330 704 1202 1700
62-Hawkman by Kubert begins 142 284 426 909 1555 2200
63-66,68-85: 66,68-Hop Harrigan app. 70-Mutt & Jeff app. 80-Atom begins, ends #104
100 200 300 635 1093 1550
67-Hawkman dinosaur-c; Hop Harrigan app. 142 284 426 909 1555 2200
86-Intro. The Black Canary in Johnny Thunder (8/47); see All-Star #38.
3700 7400 11,100 22,200 29,600 37,000
87,88,90: 87-Intro. The Foil. 88-Origin Ghost. 148 296 444 947 1624 2300
89-Intro villain The Thorn (scarce) 290 580 870 1856 3178 4500
91,93-99: 98-Atom & Hawkman don new costumes 155 310 465 992 1696 2400
92-1st solo Black Canary plus-c; rare in Mint due to black ink smearing on white-c
1075 2150 3225 8200 14,850 21,500
100 (10/48),103(Scarce)-52 pgs. each 300 600 900 2010 3505 5000
101,102(Scarce) 300 600 900 2070 3635 5200
104-Origin The Flash retold (Scarce) 975 1950 2919 7100 12,550 18,000
NOTE: ***Irwin Hasen** a-Wheaties Giveaway. c-97, Wheaties Giveaway. **E.E. Hibbard** c-6, 12, 20, 24, 26, 28, 30, 44, 46, 48, 50, 62, 66, 68, 69, 72, 74, 76, 78, 80, 82. **Infantino** a-86p, 90, 93-95, 99-104; c-90, 92, 93, 97, 99, 101, 103. **Kinstler** a-87, 89(Hawkman); c-87. **Chet Kozlak** c-77, 79, 81. **Krigstein** a-94. **Kubert** a-62-76, 83, 85, 86, 88-104; c-63, 65, 67, 70, 71, 73, 75, 83, 85, 86, 88, 89, 91, 94, 96, 98, 100, 104. **Moldoff** a-3; c-3, 7-11, 13-17, plus odd #'s 19-61. **Martin Naydell** c-52, 54, 56, 58, 60, 64, 84.*

FLASH DIGEST, THE (See DC Special Series #24)

FLASH FORCE 2000
DC Comics: 1984

1-5 6.00

FLASH FORWARD (See Heroes in Crisis series)
DC Comics: Nov, 2019 - No. 6, Apr, 2020 ($3.99, limited series)

1-6-Follows Wally West after Heroes in Crisis; Lobdell-s/Booth-a. 2-Jai & Iris app. 4.00

FLASH GIANT (Barry Allen)
DC Comics: 2019 - No. 7, 2019 ($4.99, 100 pgs., squarebound, Walmart exclusive)

1-New story Simone-s/Henry-a; reprints from Flash #8 ('11), Adam Strange #1 ('04), and Shazam from Justice League #7 & 8('11) 8.00
2-7: 2-New story plus Flash, Adam Strange and Shazam reprints continue 5.00

FLASH GIANT
DC Comics: 2019 - No. 4, 2020 ($4.99, 100 pgs., squarebound, Mass Market & Direct Market editions exist for each issue, with different covers)

1-4: 1-New stories vs. King Shark and Grodd; reprints. 3-The Atom app. 5.00

FLASH GORDON (See Defenders Of The Earth, Eat Right to Work..., Giant Comic Album, King Classics, King Comics, March of Comics #118, 133, 142, The Phantom #18, Street Comix & Wow Comics, 1st series)

FLASH GORDON
Dell Publishing Co.: No. 25, 1941; No. 10, 1943 - No. 512, Nov, 1953

Feature Books 25 (#1)(1941))-r-not by Raymond 187 374 561 1197 2049 2900
Four Color 10(1942)-by Alex Raymond; reprints "The Ice Kingdom"
96 192 288 768 1734 2700
Four Color 84(1945)-by Alex Raymond; reprints "The Fiery Desert"
42 84 126 311 706 1100
Four Color 173 26 52 78 182 404 625
Four Color 190-Bondage-c; "The Adventures of the Flying Saucers"; 5th Flying Saucer story (6/48)- see The Spirit 9/28/47(1st), Shadow Comics V7#10 (2nd, 1/48), Captain Midnight #60 (3rd, 2/48) & Boy Commandos #26 (4th, 3-4/48)
31 62 93 223 499 775
Four Color 204,247 19 38 57 131 291 450
Four Color 424-Painted-c 13 26 39 89 195 300
2(5-7/53-Dell)-Painted-c; Evans-a? 10 20 30 69 147 225
Four Color 512-Painted-c 10 20 30 67 141 215

FLASH GORDON (See Tiny Tot Funnies)
Harvey Publications: Oct, 1950 - No. 4, April, 1951

1-Alex Raymond-a; bondage-c; reprints strips from 7/14/40 to 12/8/40
57 114 171 362 619 875
2-Alex Raymond-a; r/strips 12/15/40-4/27/41 34 68 102 199 325 450
3,4-Alex Raymond-a; 3-bondage-c; r/strips 5/4/41-9/21/41. 4-r/strips 10/24/37-3/27/38 33 66 99 194 317 440
5-(Rare)-Small size-5-1/2x8-1/2"; B&W; 32 pgs.; Distributed to some mail subscribers only 100 200 300 635 1093 1550
(Also see All-New No. 15, Boy Explorers No. 2, and Stuntman No. 3)

FLASH GORDON
Gold Key: June, 1965

1 (1947 reprint)-Painted-c 9 18 27 59 117 175

FLASH GORDON (Also see Comics Reading Libraries in the Promotional Comics section)

The Flash (2016) #783 © DC

Flash Comics #52 © DC

Flashpoint Beyond #6 © DC

	GD 2.0	VG 4.0	FN 6.0	VF 8.0	VF/NM 9.0	NM- 9.2

King #1-11/Charlton #12-18/Gold Key #19-23/Whitman #28 on:
9/66 - #11, 12/67; #12, 2/69 - #18, 1/70; #19, 9/78 - #37, 3/82 (Painted covers No. 19-30, 34)

1-1st S.A. app Flash Gordon; Williamson c/a(2); E.C. swipe/Incredible S.F. #32; Mandrake story 8 16 24 54 102 150
1-Army giveaway(1968)("Complimentary" on cover)(Same as regular #1 minus Mandrake story & back-c) 5 10 15 30 50 70
2-8: 2-Bolle, Gil Kane-c; Mandrake story. 3-Williamson-c. 4-Secret Agent X-9 begins, Williamson-c/a(3). 5-Williamson-c/a(2). 6,8-Crandall-a. 7-Raboy-a (last in comics?). 8-Secret Agent X-9-r 4 8 12 28 47 65
9-13: 9,10-Raymond-r. 10-Buckler's 1st pro work (11/67). 11-Crandall-a. 12-Crandall-c/a. 13-Jeff Jones-a (15 pgs.) 4 8 12 27 44 60
14,15: 15-Last 12¢ issue 3 6 9 19 30 40
16,17: 17-Brick Bradford story 3 6 9 16 24 32
18-Kaluta-a (3rd pro work?)(see Teen Confessions) 3 6 9 21 33 45
19(9/78, G.K.), 20-26 2 4 6 8 10 12
27-29,34-37: 34-37-Movie adaptation 2 4 6 8 11 14
30 (10/80) (scarce, from Whitman 3-pack only, 40¢-c) 4 8 12 27 44 60
30 (7/81; re-issue, 50¢-c), 31-33-single issues 2 4 6 11 16 20
31-33 (Bagged 3-pack): Movie adaptation; Williamson-a. 60.00

NOTE: *Aparo a-8.* ***Bolle*** *a-21, 22.* ***Boyette*** *a-14-18.* ***Briggs*** *c-10.* ***Buckler*** *a-10.* ***Crandall*** *c-6.* ***Estrada*** *a-3.* ***Gene Fawcette*** *a-29, 30, 34, 37.* ***McWilliams*** *a-31-33, 36.*

FLASH GORDON
DC Comics: June, 1988 - No. 9, Holiday, 1988-'89 ($1.25, mini-series)

1-9: 1,5-Painted-c 4.00

FLASH GORDON
Marvel Comics: June, 1995 - No. 2, July, 1995 ($2.95, limited series)

1,2: Schultz scripts; Williamson-a 4.00

FLASH GORDON (The Mercy Wars)
Ardden Entertainment: Aug, 2008 - No. 6, Jul, 2009 ($3.99)

1-6: 1-Deneen-s/Green-a; two covers 4.00
...: The Mercy Wars #0 (4/09, $2.99) 3.00

FLASH GORDON
Dynamite Entertainment: 2014 ($3.99)

1-8: 1-Parker-s/Shaner-a; six covers. 2-8-Multiple covers on each 4.00
Annual 2014 ($7.99, squarebound) Short stories of the characters' pasts 8.00
Holiday Special 2014 ($5.99) Christmas-themed short stories by various 6.00

FLASH GORDON: INVASION OF THE RED SWORD
Ardden Entertainment: Jan, 2011 - No. 6, Nov, 2011 ($3.99)

1-6-Deneen-s/Garcia-a. 1-Two covers 4.00

FLASH GORDON: KINGS CROSS
Dynamite Entertainment: 2016 - No. 5, 2017 ($3.99)

1-5-Jeff Parker-s/Jesse Hamm-a; multiple covers on each; Mandrake & Phantom app. 4.00

FLASH GORDON THE MOVIE
Western Publishing Co.: 1980 (8-1/4 x 11", $1.95, 68 pgs.)

11294-Williamson-c/a; adapts movie 2 4 6 11 16 20
13743-Hardback edition 3 6 9 16 23 30

FLASH GORDON: ZEITGEIST
Dynamite Entertainment: 2011 - No. 10, 2013 ($1.00/$3.99)

1-($1.00) Flash, Dale and Zarkov head to Mongo; 4 covers by Ross, Renaud & others 4.00
2-10-($3.99) 2-8-Three covers. 9,10-Ross-c 4.00

FLASH/ GREEN LANTERN: FASTER FRIENDS (See Green Lantern/Flash...)
DC Comics: No. 2, 1997 ($4.95, continuation of Green Lantern/Flash: Faster Friends #1)

2-Waid/Augustyn-s 5.00

FLASHPOINT (Elseworlds Flash)
DC Comics: Dec, 1999 - No. 3, Feb, 2000 ($2.95, limited series)

1-3-Paralyzed Barry Allen; Breyfogle-a/McGreal-s 4.00

FLASHPOINT (Leads into DC New 52 relaunches)
DC Comics: Jul, 2011 - No. 5, Late Oct, 2011 ($3.99, limited series)

1-Johns-s/Andy Kubert-a; 2 covers on each 3 6 9 19 30 40
2-5-Johns-s/Andy Kubert-a. 2-4-Bonus design art. 5-New timeline 1 2 3 5 6 8
...: Abin Sur - The Green Lantern 1-3 (8/11 - No. 3, 10/11, $2.99) Massaferra-a/c 4.00
...: Batman Knight of Vengeance 1-3 (8/11 - No. 3, 10/11, $2.99) Risso-a/Johnson-c 1 3 4 6 8 10
...: Batman Knight of Vengeance 1 (6/22, $7.99) r/#1-3 & Flashpoint Beyond #0 8.00
...: Canterbury Cricket, The (8/11, $2.99, one-shot) Carlin-s/Morales-a 3.00
...: Citizen Cold 1-3 (8/11 - No. 3, 10/11, $2.99) Scott Kolins-s/a/c 3.00
...: Deadman and the Flying Grayson 1-3 (8/11 - No. 3, 10/11, $2.99) Chiang-c 3.00
...: Deathstroke & The Curse of the Ravager 1-3 (8/11 - No. 3, 10/11, $2.99) Bennett-a 3.00
...: Emperor Aquaman 1-3 (8/11 - No. 3, 10/11, $2.99) Bedard-s/Syaf-c 3.00
...: Frankenstein and the Creatures of the Unknown 1-3 (8/11 - No. 3, 10/11, $2.99) 3.00
...: Green Arrow Industries (8/11, $2.99, one-shot) Kalvachev-c 5.00
...: Grodd of War (8/11, $2.99, one-shot) Manapul-c 3.00
...: Hal Jordan 1-3 (8/11 - No. 3, 10/11, $2.99) 1-Oliver-a. 2,3-Richards-a 3.00
...: Kid Flash Lost 1-3 (8/11 - No. 3, 10/11, $2.99) Gates-s/Manapul-c; Brainiac app. 3.00
...: Legion of Doom 1-3 (8/11 - No. 3, 10/11, $2.99) Glass-s/Sepulveda-c 3.00
...: Lois Lane and the Resistance 1-3 (8/11 - No. 3, 10/11, $2.99) Abnett & Lanning-s 3.00
...: Outsider, The 1-3 (8/11 - No. 3, 10/11, $2.99) Robinson-s/Nowlan-c 3.00
...: Project Superman 1-3 (8/11 - No. 3, 10/11, $2.99) Gene Ha-c/a 3.00
...: Reverse Flash (8/11, $2.99, one-shot) Kolins-s/Gomez-a 1 3 4 6 8 10
...: Secret Seven 1-3 (8/11 - No. 3, 10/11, $2.99) Pérez-c on all. 1-Pérez-a. 3.00
...: Wonder Woman and The Furies 1-3 (8/11 - No. 3, 10/11, $2.99) Aquaman app. 4.00
...: World of Flashpoint 1-3 (8/11 - No. 3, 10/11, $2.99) Traci 13 app. 3.00

FLASHPOINT BEYOND
DC Comics: No. 0, Jun, 2022 - No. 6, Dec, 2022 ($5.99/$4.99/$3.99, limited series)

0-($5.99) Johns-s-Risso-a; Thomas Wayne back in the Flashpoint Universe 6.00
1-($4.99) Aquaman & Wonder Woman app.; Xermánico & Janin-a 5.00
2-6-($3.99) 2,3-Subject 1 app. 4.00

FLASH: REBIRTH
DC Comics: Jun, 2009 - No. 6, Apr, 2010 ($3.99/$2.99, limited series)

1-($3.99) Barry Allen's return; Johns-s/Van Sciver-a; Flash-c by Van Sciver 1 2 3 5 6 8
1-Variant Barry Allen-c by Van Sciver 2 4 6 9 12 15
1-Second thru fourth printings 4.00
1-Special Edition (8/10, $1.00) reprints #1 with "What's Next?" logo on cover 3.00
2-6-($2.99) 3-Max Mercury returns 3.00
2-6-Variant covers by Van Sciver 8.00
HC (2010, $19.99, dustjacket) r/#1-6; Johns original proposal; sketch art; cover gallery 20.00
SC (2011, $14.99) r/#1-6; Johns original proposal; sketch art; cover gallery 15.00

FLASH: SEASON ZERO (Based on the 2014 TV series)
DC Comics: Dec, 2014 - No. 12, Nov, 2015 ($2.99, printings of digital-first stories)

1-12-Photo-c on #1-8. 1-4,6-9-Hester-a. 5-Felicity Smoak app. 7-9-Intro. Suicide Squad 3.00

FLASH: THE FASTEST MAN ALIVE (3rd Series)(See Infinite Crisis)
DC Comics: Aug, 2006 - No. 13, Aug, 2007 ($2.99)

1-Bart Allen becomes the Flash; Lashley-a/Bilson & Demeo-s 3.00
1-Variant-c by Joe and Andy Kubert 5.00
2-12: 5-Cyborg app. 7-Inertia returns. 10-Zoom app. 3.00
13-Bart Allen dies; 2 covers 3.00
13-DC Nation Edition from the 2007 San Diego Comic-Con 8.00
...: Full Throttle TPB (2007, $12.99) r/#7-13, All-Flash #1, DCU Infinite Holiday Spec. story 13.00
...: Lightning in a Bottle TPB (2007, $12.99) r/#1-6 13.00

FLASH: THE FASTEST MAN ALIVE (Tie-in to the movie)
DC Comics: Nov, 2022 - No. 3, Jan, 2023 ($5.99, limited series)

1-3: 1-Batman & Girder app.; Barry gets the new costume. 2-Tarpit app.; Ferreyra-a 6.00

FLAT-TOP
Mazie Comics/Harvey Publ.(Magazine Publ.) No. 4 on: 11/53 - No. 3, 5/54; No. 4, 3/55 - No. 7, 9/55

1-Teenage; Flat-Top, Mazie, Mortie & Stevie begin 14 28 42 81 118 155
2,3 9 18 27 50 65 80
4-7 8 16 24 40 50 60

FLAVOR
Image Comics: May, 2018 - No. 6, Oct, 2018 ($3.99)

1-6-Joseph Keatinge-s/Wook Jin Clark-a 4.00

FLAWED
Image Comics: Sept, 2022 - Present ($3.99)

1-5-Chuck Brown-s/Prenzy-a 4.00

FLESH AND BONES
Upshot Graphics (Fantagraphics Books): June, 1986 - No. 4, Dec, 1986 (Limited series)

1-4: Alan Moore scripts (r) & Dalgoda by Fujitake 4.00

FLESH CRAWLERS
Kitchen Sink Press: Aug, 1993 - No. 3, 1995 ($2.50, B&W, limited series, mature)

1-3 4.00

FLEX MENTALLO (Man of Muscle Mystery) (See Doom Patrol, 2nd Series)
DC Comics (Vertigo): Jun, 1996 - No. 4, Sept, 1996 ($2.50, lim. series, mature)

1-4: Grant Morrison scripts & Frank Quitely-c/a in all; banned from reprints due to

	GD	VG	FN	VF	VF/NM	NM-
	2.0	4.0	6.0	8.0	9.0	9.2

Charles Atlas legal action 2 4 6 9 13 16

FLINCH (Horror anthology)
DC Comics (Vertigo): Jun, 1999 - No. 16, Jan, 2001 ($2.50)
1-16: 1-Art by Jim Lee, Quitely, and Corben. 5-Sale-c. 11-Timm-a 4.00

FLINTSTONE KIDS, THE (TV) (See Star Comics Digest)
Star Comics/Marvel Comics #5 on: Aug, 1987 - No. 11, Apr, 1989
1 1 3 4 6 8 10
2-11 5.00

FLINTSTONES, THE (TV)(See Dell Giant #48 for No. 1)
Dell Publ. Co./Gold Key No. 7 (10/62) on: No. 2, Nov-Dec, 1961 - No. 60, Sept, 1970 (Hanna-Barbera)
2-2nd app. (TV show debuted on 9/30/60); 1st app. of Cave Kids; 15¢-c thru #5
13 26 39 86 188 290
3-6(7-8/62): 3-Perry Gunnite begins. 6-1st 12¢-c 7 14 21 49 92 135
7 (10/62; 1st GK) 8 16 24 54 102 150
8-10 5 10 15 35 63 90
11-1st app. Pebbles (6/63) 9 18 27 59 117 175
12-15,17-20 4 8 12 28 47 65
16-1st app. Bamm-Bamm (1/64) 9 18 27 59 117 175
21-23,25-30,33: 26,27-2nd & 3rd app. The Grusomes. 30-1st app. Martian Mopheads (10/65). 33-Meet Frankenstein & Dracula 4 8 12 27 44 60
24-1st app. The Grusomes 6 12 18 42 79 115
31,32,35-40: 31-Xmas-c. 36-Adaptation of "the Man Called Flintstone" movie. 39-Reprints
4 8 12 23 37 50
34-1st app. The Great Gazoo 6 12 18 42 79 115
41-60: 46-Last 12¢ issue 3 6 9 20 31 42
At N. Y. World's Fair ('64)-J.W. Books (25¢)-1st printing; no date on-c (29¢ version exists, 2nd print?) Most H-B characters app.; including Yogi Bear, Top Cat, Snagglepuss and the Jetsons 6 12 18 37 66 95
At N. Y. World's Fair (1965 on-c; re-issue; Warren Pub.)
NOTE: *Warehouse find in 1984.* 2 4 6 11 16 20
Bigger & Boulder 1(#30013-211) (Gold Key Giant, 11/62, 25¢, 84 pgs.)
8 16 24 52 99 145
Bigger & Boulder 2-(1966, 25¢)-Reprints B&B No. 1 4 8 12 25 40 55
...On the Rocks (9/61, $1.00, 6-1/4x9", cardboard-c, high quality paper,116 pgs.)
B&W new material 9 18 27 59 117 175
...With Pebbles & Bamm Bamm (100 pgs., G.K.)-30028-511 (paper-c, 25¢) (11/65)
7 14 21 46 86 125
NOTE: *(See Comic Album #16, Bamm-Bamm & Pebbles Flintstone, Dell Giant 48, Golden Comics Digest, March of Comics #229, 243, 271, 289, 299, 317, 327, 341, Pebbles Flintstone, Top Comics #2-4, and Whitman Comic Book.)*

FLINTSTONES, THE (TV)(...& Pebbles)
Charlton Comics: Nov, 1970 - No. 50, Feb, 1977 (Hanna-Barbera)
1 7 14 21 44 82 120
2 4 8 12 27 44 60
3-7,9,10 3 6 9 19 30 40
8- "Flintstones Summer Vacation" (Summer, 1971, 52 pgs.)
5 10 15 31 53 75
11-20,36: 36-Mike Zeck illos (early work) 3 6 9 16 23 30
21-35,38-41,43-45 3 6 9 14 19 24
37-Byrne text illos (early work; see Nightmare #20) 3 6 9 16 23 30
42-Byrne-a (2 pgs.) 3 6 9 16 23 30
46-50 2 4 6 13 18 22
Digest nn (1972, B&W, 100 pgs.) (low print run) 3 6 9 19 30 40
(Also see Barney & Betty Rubble, Dino, The Great Gazoo, & Pebbles & Bamm-Bamm)

FLINTSTONES, THE (TV)(See Yogi Bear, 3rd series) (Newsstand sales only)
Marvel Comics Group: October, 1977 - No. 9, Feb, 1979 (Hanna-Barbera)
1,7-9: 1-(30¢-c). 7-9-Yogi Bear app. 3 6 9 19 30 40
1-(35¢-c variant, limited distribution) 9 18 27 59 117 175
2,3,5,6: Yogi Bear app. 3 6 9 15 22 28
4-The Jetsons app. 3 6 9 16 24 32

FLINTSTONES, THE (TV)
Harvey Comics: Sept, 1992 - No. 13, Jun, 1994 ($1.25/$1.50) (Hanna-Barbera)
V2#1-13 5.00
...Big Book 1,2 (11/92, 3/93; both $1.95, 52 pgs.) 2 4 6 11 16 20
...Giant Size 1-3 (10/92, 4/93, 11/93; $2.25, 68 pgs.) 1 3 4 6 8 10

FLINTSTONES, THE (TV)
Archie Publications: Sept, 1995 - No. 22, June, 1997 ($1.50)
1 1 3 4 6 8 10
2-22 4.00

FLINTSTONES, THE (TV)
DC Comics: Sept, 2016 - No. 12, Aug, 2017 ($3.99)
1-12: 1-6,8-12-Mark Russell-s/Steve Pugh-a; multiple covers. 2-Intro. Dino. 7-Leonardi-a; Great Gazoo app. 11-Jill Thompson-c. 11,12-Great Gazoo app. 4.00

FLINTSTONES AND THE JETSONS, THE (TV)
DC Comics: Aug, 1997 - No. 21, May, 1999 ($1.75/$1.95/$1.99)
1 1 3 4 6 8 10
2-21: 19-Bizarro Elroy-c 4.00

FLINTSTONES CHRISTMAS PARTY, THE (See The Funtastic World of Hanna-Barbera No. 1)

FLIP
Harvey Publications: April, 1954 - No. 2, June, 1954 (Satire)
1-Nostrand-a 25 50 75 175 388 600
2-Nostrand & Powell-a 16 32 48 112 249 385

FLIPPER (TV)
Gold Key: Apr, 1966 - No. 3, Nov, 1967 (All have photo-c)
1 6 12 18 41 76 110
2,3 4 8 12 28 47 65

FLIPPITY & FLOP
National Per. Publ. (Signal Publ. Co.): 12-1/51-52 - No. 46, 8-10/59; No. 47, 9-11/60
1-Sam dog & his pets Flippity The Bird and Flop The Cat begin; Twiddle and Twaddle begin
41 82 123 256 428 600
2 20 40 60 114 182 250
3-5 15 30 45 85 130 175
6-10 14 28 42 80 115 150
11-20: 20-Last precode (3/55) 11 22 33 64 90 115
21-47 10 20 30 56 76 95

FLOYD FARLAND (See Eclipse Graphic Album Series #11)

FLY, THE (Also see Adventures of..., Blue Ribbon Comics & Flyman)
Archie Enterprises, Inc.: May, 1983 - No. 9, Oct, 1984
1,2: 1-Mr. Justice app; origin Shield; Kirby-a; Steranko-c. 2-Ditko-a; Flygirl app. 6.00
3-5: Ditko-a in all. 4,5-Ditko-c(p) 5.00
6-9: Ditko-a in all. 6-8-Ditko-c(p) 6.00
NOTE: ***Ayers** c-9. **Buckler** a-1, 2. **Kirby** a-1. **Nebres** c-3, 4, 5i, 6, 7i. **Steranko** c-1, 2.*

FLY, THE
Impact Comics (DC): Aug, 1991 - No. 17, Dec, 1992 ($1.00)
1 5.00
2-17: 4-Vs. The Black Hood. 9-Trading card inside 4.00
Annual 1 ('92, $2.50, 68 pgs.)-Impact trading card 5.00

FLYBOY (Flying Cadets)(Also see Approved Comics #5)
Ziff-Davis Publ. Co. (Approved): Spring, 1952 - No. 2, Oct-Nov, 1952
1-Saunders painted-c 24 48 72 144 237 330
2-(10-11/52)-Saunders painted-c 16 32 48 94 147 200

FLYING ACES (Aviation stories)
Key Publications: July, 1955 - No. 5, Mar, 1956
1 13 26 39 72 101 130
2-5: 2-Trapani-a 8 16 24 44 57 70

FLYING A'S RANGE RIDER, THE (TV)(See Western Roundup under Dell Giants)
Dell Publishing Co.: #404, 6-7/52; #2, June-Aug, 1953 - #24, Aug, 1959 (All photo-c)
Four Color 404(#1)-Titled "The Range Rider" 10 20 30 68 144 220
2 6 12 18 38 69 100
3-10 5 10 15 34 60 85
11-16,18-24 5 10 15 30 50 70
17-Toth-a 5 10 15 34 60 85

FLYING CADET (WW II Plane Photos)
Flying Cadet Publ. Co.; Jan, 1943 - V2#8, Nov, 1944 (Half photos, half comics)
V1#1-Painted-c 22 44 66 132 216 300
2-Photo-c, P-47 Thunderbolt 14 28 42 76 108 140
3-9 (Two #6's, Sept. & Oct.): 4,5,6a,6b-Photo-c 13 26 39 72 101 130
V2#1-7 (1/44-9/44)(#10-16): 1,2,4-7-Photo-c 12 24 36 67 94 120
7 (#17 on cover)-Bare-breasted woman-c 55 110 165 352 601 850

FLYING COLORS 10th ANNIVERSARY SPECIAL
Flying Colors Comics: Fall 1998 ($2.95, one-shot)
1-Dan Brereton-c; pin-ups by Jim Lee and Jeff Johnson 3.00

FLYIN' JENNY
Pentagon Publ. Co./Leader Enterprises #2: 1946 - No. 2, 1947 (1945 strip-r)
nn-Marcus Swayze strip-r (entire insides) 27 54 81 158 259 360
2-Baker-c; Swayze strip reprints 58 116 174 371 636 900

FLYING MODELS
H-K Publ. (Health-Knowledge Publs.): V61#3, May, 1954 (5¢, 16 pgs.)
V61#3 (Rare) 15 30 45 86 133 180

FLYING NUN (TV)
Dell Publishing Co.: Feb, 1968 - No. 4, Nov, 1968
1-Sally Field photo-c 8 16 24 56 108 160
2-4: 2-Sally Field photo-c 5 10 15 30 50 70

FLYING NURSES (See Sue & Sally Smith...)

FLYING SAUCERS (See The Spirit 9/28/47(1st app.), Shadow Comics V7#10 (2nd, 1/48), Captain Midnight #60 (3rd, 2/48), Boy Commandos #26 (4th, 3-4/48) & Flash Gordon Four Color 190 (5th, 6/48))

FLYING SAUCERS (See Out of This World Adventures #2)
Avon Periodicals/Realistic: 1950; 1952; 1953
1(1950)-Wood-a, 21 pgs.; Fawcette-c 138 276 414 876 1513 2150
nn(1952)-Cover altered plus 2 pgs. of Wood-a not in original
74 148 222 470 810 1150
nn(1953)-Reprints above (exist?) 68 136 204 435 743 1050

FLYING SAUCERS (Comics)
Dell Publishing Co.: April, 1967 - No. 4, Nov, 1967; No. 5, Oct, 1969
1-(12¢-c) 10 20 30 69 147 225
2-5: 5-Has same cover as #1, but with 15¢ price 5 10 15 30 50 70

FLY MAN (Formerly Adventures of The Fly; Mighty Comics #40 on)
Mighty Comics Group (Radio Comics) (Archie): No. 32, July, 1965 - No. 39, Sept, 1966 (Also see Mighty Crusaders)
32,33-Comet, Shield, Black Hood, The Fly & Flygirl x-over. 33-Re-intro Wizard, Hangman (1st S.A. appearances) 5 10 15 35 63 90
34-39: 34-Shield begins. 35-Origin Black Hood. 36-Hangman x-over in Shield; re-intro. & origin of Web (1st S.A. app.). 37-Hangman, Wizard x-over in Flyman; last Shield issue. 38-Web story. 39-Steel Sterling (1st S.A. app.) 4 8 12 28 47 65

FLY, THE ; OUTBREAK (Sequel to the 1986 and 1989 movies)
IDW Publishing: Mar, 2015 - No. 5, Aug, 2015 ($3.99)
1-5-Martin Brundle's story continues; Brandon Seifert-s/Menton3-a; multiple covers 4.00

FOLKLORDS
BOOM! Studios: Nov, 2019 - No. 5 ($3.99, limited series)
1-5-Matt Kindt-s/Matt Smith-a 4.00

FOLLOW ME DOWN: A RECKLESS BOOK
Image Comics: Oct, 2022 ($24.99, HC graphic novel)
HC - Ed Brubaker-s/Sean Phillips-a; 5th book in the Reckless series 25.00

FOLLOW THE SUN (TV)

The Flintstones (2016) #1 © H-B

Foolkiller (2017) #1 © MAR

Forbidden Worlds #50 © ACG

Dell Publishing Co.: May-July, 1962 - No. 2, Sept-Nov, 1962 (Photo-c)

	GD 2.0	VG 4.0	FN 6.0	VF 8.0	VF/NM 9.0	NM- 9.2
01-280-207(No.1)	5	10	15	30	50	70
12-280-211(No.2)	4	8	12	27	44	60

FOODINI (TV)(The Great…; see Jingle Dingle & Pinhead &…)
Continental Publ. (Holyoke): March, 1950 - No. 4, Aug, 1950 (All have 52 pgs.)

	GD 2.0	VG 4.0	FN 6.0	VF 8.0	VF/NM 9.0	NM- 9.2
1-Based on TV puppet show (very early TV comic)	27	54	81	162	266	370
2-Jingle Dingle begins	15	30	45	90	140	190
3,4	14	28	42	76	108	140

FOOEY (Magazine) (Satire)
Scoff Publishing Co.: Feb, 1961 - No. 4, May, 1961

	GD 2.0	VG 4.0	FN 6.0	VF 8.0	VF/NM 9.0	NM- 9.2
1	5	10	15	35	63	90
2-4	3	6	9	21	33	45

FOOFUR (TV)
Marvel Comics (Star Comics)/Marvel No. 5 on: Aug, 1987 - No. 6, Jun, 1988

	GD 2.0	VG 4.0	FN 6.0	VF 8.0	VF/NM 9.0	NM- 9.2
1-6						5.00

FOOLKILLER (Also see The Amazing Spider-Man #225, The Defenders #73, Man-Thing #3 & Omega the Unknown #8)
Marvel Comics: Oct, 1990 - No. 10, Oct, 1991 ($1.75, limited series)

	GD 2.0	VG 4.0	FN 6.0	VF 8.0	VF/NM 9.0	NM- 9.2
1-10: 1-Origin 3rd Foolkiller; Greg Salinger app; DeZuniga-a(i) in 1-4. 8-Spider-Man x-over						3.00

FOOLKILLER
Marvel Comics: Dec, 2007 - No. 5, Jul, 2008 ($3.99, limited series)

	GD 2.0	VG 4.0	FN 6.0	VF 8.0	VF/NM 9.0	NM- 9.2
1-5-Hurwitz-s/Medina-a. 2-Origin						4.00

FOOLKILLER
Marvel Comics: Jan, 2017 - No. 5, May, 2017 ($3.99, limited series)

	GD 2.0	VG 4.0	FN 6.0	VF 8.0	VF/NM 9.0	NM- 9.2
1-5-Max Bemis-s/Dalibor Talajic-a. 4-Deadpool app. 5-The Hood app.						4.00

FOOLKILLER: WHITE ANGELS
Marvel Comics: Sept, 2008 - No. 5, Jan, 2009 ($3.99, limited series)

	GD 2.0	VG 4.0	FN 6.0	VF 8.0	VF/NM 9.0	NM- 9.2
1-5-Hurwitz-s/Azaceta-a						4.00

FOOM (Friends Of Ol' Marvel)
Marvel Comics: 1973 - No. 22, 1979 (Marvel fan magazine)

	GD 2.0	VG 4.0	FN 6.0	VF 8.0	VF/NM 9.0	NM- 9.2
1	9	18	27	63	129	195
2-Hulk-c by Steranko; Wolverine prototype	17	34	51	117	259	400
3,4	6	12	18	38	69	100
5-Deathlok preview	6	12	18	42	79	115
6-9,11: 11-Kirby-a & interview	5	10	15	34	60	85
10-Article on new X-Men that came out before Giant-Size X-Men #1; new X-Men cover by Dave Cockrum	86	172	258	688	1544	2400
12-15: 11-Star-Lord preview. 12-Vision-c. 13-Daredevil-c. 14-Conan. 15-Howard the Duck; preview of Ms. Marvel & Capt. Britain	5	10	15	34	60	85
16-20: 16-Marvel bullpen. 17-Stan Lee issue. 19-Defenders	5	10	15	31	53	75
21-Star Wars	6	12	18	37	66	95
22-Spider-Man-c; low print run final issue	6	12	18	41	76	110

FOOTBALL THRILLS (See Tops In Adventure)
Ziff-Davis Publ. Co.: Fall-Winter, 1951-52 - No. 2, Fall, 1952 (Edited by "Red" Grange)

	GD 2.0	VG 4.0	FN 6.0	VF 8.0	VF/NM 9.0	NM- 9.2
1-Powell a(2); Saunders painted-c; Red Grange, Jim Thorpe stories	36	72	108	211	343	475
2-Saunders painted-c	21	42	63	126	206	285

FOOT SOLDIERS, THE
Dark Horse Comics: Jan, 1996 - No. 4, Apr, 1996 ($2.95, limited series)

	GD 2.0	VG 4.0	FN 6.0	VF 8.0	VF/NM 9.0	NM- 9.2
1-4: Krueger story & Avon Oeming-a. in all. 1-Alex Ross-c. 4-John K. Snyder, III-c						4.00

FOOT SOLDIERS, THE (Volume Two)
Image Comics: Sept, 1997 - No. 5, May, 1998 ($2.95, limited series)

	GD 2.0	VG 4.0	FN 6.0	VF 8.0	VF/NM 9.0	NM- 9.2
1-5: 1-Yeowell-a. 2-McDaniel, Hester, Sienkiewicz, Giffen-a						3.00

FOR A NIGHT OF LOVE
Avon Periodicals: 1951

	GD 2.0	VG 4.0	FN 6.0	VF 8.0	VF/NM 9.0	NM- 9.2
nn-Two stories adapted from the works of Emile Zola; Astarita, Ravielli-a; Kinstler-c	43	86	129	271	461	650

FORBIDDEN BRIDES OF THE FACELESS SLAVES IN THE SECRET HOUSE OF THE NIGHT OF DREAD DESIRE (Neil Gaiman's...)
Dark Horse Books: 2017 ($17.99, HC graphic novel)

	GD 2.0	VG 4.0	FN 6.0	VF 8.0	VF/NM 9.0	NM- 9.2
HC-Neil Gaiman-s/Shane Oakley-a						18.00

FORBIDDEN KNOWLEDGE: ADVENTURE BEYOND THE DOORWAY TO SOULS WITH RADICAL DREAMER (Also see Radical Dreamer)
Mark's Giant Economy Size Comics: 1996 ($3.50, B&W, one-shot, 48 pgs.)

	GD 2.0	VG 4.0	FN 6.0	VF 8.0	VF/NM 9.0	NM- 9.2
nn-Max Wrighter app.; Wheatley-c/a/script; painted infinity-c						4.00

FORBIDDEN LOVE
Quality Comics Group: Mar, 1950 - No. 4, Sept, 1950 (52 pgs.)

	GD 2.0	VG 4.0	FN 6.0	VF 8.0	VF/NM 9.0	NM- 9.2
1-(Scarce)-Classic photo-c; Crandall-a	161	322	483	1030	1765	2500
2-(Scarce)-Classic photo-c	103	206	309	659	1130	1600
3-(Scarce)-Photo-c	90	180	270	576	988	1400
4-(Scarce)-Ward/Cuidera-a; photo-c	97	194	291	621	1061	1500

FORBIDDEN LOVE (See Dark Mansion of…)

FORBIDDEN PLANET
Innovation Publishing: May, 1992 - No. 4, 1992 ($2.50, limited series)

	GD 2.0	VG 4.0	FN 6.0	VF 8.0	VF/NM 9.0	NM- 9.2
1-4: Adapts movie; painted-c						4.00

FORBIDDEN TALES OF DARK MANSION (Formerly Dark Mansion of Forbidden Love #1-4)
National Periodical Publ.: No. 5, May-June, 1972 - No. 15, Feb-Mar, 1974

	GD 2.0	VG 4.0	FN 6.0	VF 8.0	VF/NM 9.0	NM- 9.2
5-(52 pgs.)	6	12	18	38	69	100
6-15: 13-Kane/Howard-a	3	6	9	17	26	35

NOTE: ***N. Adams** c-9. **Alcala** a-9-11, 13. **Chaykin** a-7,15. **Evans** a-14. **Heck** a-5. **Kaluta** a-7i, 8-12; c-7, 8, 13. **G. Kane** a-13. **Kirby** a-6. **Nino** a-8, 12, 15. **Redondo** a-14.*

FORBIDDEN WORLDS
American Comics Group: 7-8/51 - No. 34, 10-11/54; No. 35, 8/55 - No. 145, 8/67 (No. 1-5: 52 pgs.; No. 6-8: 44 pgs.)

	GD 2.0	VG 4.0	FN 6.0	VF 8.0	VF/NM 9.0	NM- 9.2
1-Williamson/Frazetta-a (10 pgs.)	190	380	570	1216	2083	2950
2	77	154	231	493	847	1200
3-Williamson/Wood-a (7 pgs.); Frazetta (1 panel)	77	154	231	493	847	1200
4	50	100	150	315	533	750
5-Krenkel/Williamson-a (8 pgs.)	57	114	171	362	619	875
6-Harrison/Williamson-a (8 pgs.)	52	104	156	328	552	775
7,8,10: 7-1st monthly issue	37	74	111	222	361	500
9-A-Bomb explosion story	39	78	117	234	385	535
11-20	26	52	78	154	252	350
21-23,25-33	21	42	63	122	199	275
24-E.C. swipe by Landau	61	122	183	390	670	950
34(10-11/54)(Scarce)(becomes Young Heroes #35 on)-Last pre-code issue; A-Bomb explosion story	26	52	78	154	252	350
35(8/55)-Scarce	22	44	66	132	216	300
36-62	14	28	42	82	121	160
63,69,76,78-Williamson-a in all; w/Krenkel #69	15	30	45	83	124	165
64,66-68,70-72,74,75,77,79-85,87-90	11	22	33	60	83	105
65- "There's a New Moon Tonight" listed in #114 as holding 1st record fan mail response	15	30	45	90	140	190
73-1st app. Herbie by Ogden Whitney	68	136	204	435	743	1050
86-Flying saucer-c by Schaffenberger	12	24	36	67	94	120
91-93,95-100	5	10	15	34	60	85
94-Herbie (2nd app.)	14	28	42	96	211	325
101-109,111-113,115,117-120	4	8	12	28	44	60
110,116-Herbie app. 116-Herbie goes to Hell; Elizabeth Tayor-c	8	16	24	56	108	160
114-1st Herbie-c; contains list of editor's top 20 ACG stories	11	22	33	76	163	250
121-123	3	6	9	21	33	45
124,127-130: 124-Magic Agent app.	4	8	12	23	37	50
125-Magic Agent app.; intro. & origin Magicman series, ends #141; Herbie app.	5	10	15	31	53	75
126-Herbie app.	4	8	12	27	44	60
131-139: 133-Origin/1st app. Dragonia in Magicman (1-2/66); returns in #138. 136-Nemesis x-over in Magicman	3	6	9	21	33	45
140-Mark Midnight app. by Ditko	4	8	12	23	37	50
141-145	3	6	9	19	30	40

NOTE: ***Buscema** a-75, 79, 81, 82, 140r. **Cameron** a-5. **Disbrow** a-10. **Ditko** a-137p, 138, 140. **Landau** a-24, 27-29, 31-34, 48, 86r, 96, 143-45. **Lazarus** a-18, 23, 24, 57. **Moldoff** a-27, 31, 139r. **Reinman** a-93. **Whitney** a-70, 115, 116, 137; c-40, 46, 57, 60, 68, 70, 78, 79, 90, 93, 94, 100, 102, 103, 106-108, 114, 129.*

FORCE, THE (See The Crusaders)

FORCE MAJEURE: PRAIRIE BAY (Also see Wild Stars)
Little Rocket Publications: May, 2002 ($2.95, B&W)

	GD 2.0	VG 4.0	FN 6.0	VF 8.0	VF/NM 9.0	NM- 9.2
1-Tierney-s/Gil-c/a						3.00

FORCE OF BUDDHA'S PALM THE
Jademan Comics: Aug, 1988 - No. 55, Feb, 1993 ($1.50/$1.95, 68 pgs.)

	GD 2.0	VG 4.0	FN 6.0	VF 8.0	VF/NM 9.0	NM- 9.2
1,55-Kung Fu stories in all						5.00
2-54						4.00

FORCE WORKS
Marvel Comics: July, 1994 - No. 22, Apr, 1996 ($1.50)

1-($3.95)-Fold-out pop-up-c; Iron Man, Wonder Man, Spider-Woman, U.S. Agent &

GD 2.0 | VG 4.0 | FN 6.0 | VF 8.0 | VF/NM 9.0 | NM- 9.2

Scarlet Witch (new costume) 4.00
2-11, 13-22: 5-Blue logo & pink logo versions. 9-Intro Dreamguard. 13-Avengers app. 3.00
5-Pink logo ($2.95)-polybagged w/ 16pg. Marvel Action Hour Preview & acetate print 4.00
12 ($2.50)-Flip book w/War Machine. 4.00

FORD ROTUNDA CHRISTMAS BOOK (See Christmas at the Rotunda)

FOREIGN INTRIGUES (Formerly Johnny Dynamite; becomes Battlefield Action #16 on)
Charlton Comics: No. 14, 1956 - No. 15, Aug, 1956

14,15-Johnny Dynamite continues 10 20 30 54 72 90

FOREMOST BOYS (See 4Most)

FOREVER DARLING (Movie)
Dell Publishing Co.: No. 681, Feb, 1956

Four Color 681-w/Lucille Ball & Desi Arnaz; photo-c 11 22 33 77 166 255

FOREVER EVIL (See Justice League #23 (2013))
DC Comics: Nov, 2013 - No. 7, Jul, 2014 ($3.99, limited series)

1-Earth Three Crime Syndicate takes over; Nightwing unmasked; Johns-s/Finch-a 4.00
1-Director's Cut 1 (12/13, $5.99) Pencil artwork with full script 6.00
2-6: 2-Luthor dons the green battlesuit. 4-Sinestro returns 4.00
7-($4.99) 5.00
... Aftermath: Batman vs. Bane 1 (6/14, $3.99) Tomasi-s/Eaton-a 4.00

FOREVER EVIL: A.R.G.U.S.
DC Comics: Dec, 2013 - No. 6, May, 2014 ($2.99, limited series)

1-6-Gates-s. Steve Trevor in search of missing heroes. 1,2-Deathstroke app. 3.00

FOREVER EVIL: ARKHAM WAR
DC Comics: Dec, 2013 - No. 6, May, 2014 ($2.99, limited series)

1-6-Tomasi-s/Eaton-a; Bane and the Arkham inmates. 4-6-The Talons app. 4.00

FOREVER EVIL: ROGUES REBELLION
DC Comics: Dec, 2013 - No. 6, May, 2014 ($2.99, limited series)

1-6-Buccellato-s/Hepburn-a/Shalvey-c. 2-Deathstorm & Power Ring app. 6-Grodd app. 3.00

FOREVER MAELSTROM
DC Comics: Jan, 2003 - No. 6, Jun, 2003 ($2.95, limited series)

1-6-Chaykin & Tischman-s/Lucas & Barreto-a 3.00

FOREVER PEOPLE, THE
National Periodical Publications: Feb-Mar, 1971 - No. 11, Oct-Nov, 1972 (Fourth World)
(#1-3, 10-11 are 36 pgs; #4-9 are 52 pgs.)

1-1st app. Forever People; Superman x-over; Kirby-c/a begins; 1st full app. Darkseid (3rd anywhere, 3 weeks before New Gods #1); Darkseid storyline begins, ends #8 (app. in 1-4,6,8; cameos in 5,11) 18 36 54 124 275 425
2-9: 4-G.A. reprints thru #9. 9,10-Deadman app. 4 8 12 28 47 65
10,11 3 6 9 22 35 45
Jack Kirby's Forever People TPB (1999, $14.95, B&W&Grey) r/#1-11 plus bonus cover gallery 15.00

NOTE: *Kirby c/a(p)-1-11; #4-9 contain Sandman reprints from Adventure #85, 84, 75, 80, 77, 74 in that order.*

FOREVER PEOPLE
DC Comics: Feb, 1988 - No. 6, July, 1988 ($1.25, limited series)

1-6 4.00

FORGE
CrossGeneration Comics: Feb, 2002 - No. 13, May, 2003 ($9.95/$11.95/$7.95, TPB)

1-3: Reprints from various CrossGen titles 10.00
4-8-($11.95) 12.00
9-13-($7.95, 8-1/4" x 5-1/2") digest-sized reprints 8.00

FOR GIRLS ONLY
Bernard Baily Enterprises: 11/53 - No. 2, 6/54 (100 pgs., digest size, 25¢)

1-25% comic book, 75% articles, illos, games 42 84 126 265 445 625
2-Eddie Fisher photo & story. 36 72 108 211 343 475

FORGOTTEN FOREST OF OZ, THE (See First Comics Graphic Novel #16)

FORGOTTEN QUEEN, THE
Valiant Entertainment: Feb, 2019 - No. 4, May, 2019 ($3.99, limited series)

1-4-Tini Howard-s/Amilcar Pinna-a 4.00

FORGOTTEN REALMS (Also see Avatar & TSR Worlds)
DC Comics: Sept, 1989 - No. 25, Sept, 1991 ($1.50/$1.75)

1, Annual 1 (1990, $2.95, 68 pgs.) 4.00
2-25: Based on TSR role-playing game. 18-Avatar story 3.00

FORGOTTEN REALMS (Based on Wizards of the Coast game)
Devil's Due Publ.: June, 2005 - No. 3, Aug, 2005 ($4.95)

1-3-Salvatore-s/Seeley-a 5.00
...Exile (11/05 - No. 3, 1/06, $4.95) 1-3-Daab-s/Seeley-a. 1-Flip cover 5.00
...: Legacy (2/08 - No. 3, 6/08, $5.50) 1-3-Daab-s/Atkins-a 5.50
The Legend of Drizzt Book II: Exile (2006, $14.95, TPB) r/#1-3 15.00
...Sojourn (3/06 - No. 3, 6/06, $4.95) 1-3-Daab-s/Seeley-a 5.00
...: Streams of Silver (12/06 - No. 3, $5.50) 1-3-Daab-s/Semeiks-a 5.50
...The Crystal Shard (8/06 - No. 3, 12/06, $4.95) 1-3-Daab-s/Semeiks-a 5.00
...The Halfling's Gem (8/07 - No. 3, 12/07, $5.50) 1-3-Daab-s/Seeley-a; two covers 5.50

FORLORN RIVER (See Zane Grey Four Color 395)

FOR LOVERS ONLY (Formerly Hollywood Romances)
Charlton Comics: No. 60, Aug, 1971 - No. 87, Nov, 1976

60 3 6 9 19 30 40
61-80,82-87: 67-Morisi-a 2 4 6 11 16 20
81-Psychedelic cover 3 6 9 16 23 30

FORMERLY KNOWN AS THE JUSTICE LEAGUE
DC Comics: Sept, 2003 - No. 6, Feb, 2004 ($2.50, limited series)

1-Giffen & DeMatteis-s/Maguire-a; Booster Gold, Blue Beetle, Captain Atom, Mary Marvel, Fire, and Elongated Man app. 4.00
2-6: 3,4-Roulette app. 6-JLA app. 3.00
TPB (2004, $12.95) r/#1-6 13.00

FORMIC WARS: BURNING EARTH
Marvel Comics: Apr, 2011 - No. 7, Sept, 2011 ($3.99, limited series)

1-7-Prequel to Orson Scott Card's novel Ender's Game. 1-Covers by Larroca & Hitch 4.00

FORMIC WARS: SILENT STRIKE (Follows Burning Earth limited series)
Marvel Comics: Feb, 2012 - No. 5, Jun, 2012 ($3.99, limited series)

1-5-Johnston-s/Caracuzzo-a/Camuncoli-c 4.00

FORTNITE X MARVEL: ZERO WAR (Polybagged with digital code)
Marvel Comics: Aug, 2022 - No. 5, Nov, 2022 ($5.99/$4.99, limited series)

1,5-($5.99) Spider-Man, Wolverine & Doctor Doom app.; Dávila-a 6.00
2-4-($4.99) 2,3-Avengers app. 5.00

FORT: PROPHET OF THE UNEXPLAINED
Dark Horse Comics: June, 2002 - No. 4, Sept, 2002 ($2.99, B&W, limited series)

1-4-Peter Lenkov-s/Frazer Irving-c/a 3.00
TPB (2003, $9.95) r/#1-4 10.00

FORTUNE AND GLORY
Oni Press: Dec, 1999 - No. 3, Apr, 2000 ($4.95, B&W, limited series)

1-3-Brian Michael Bendis in Hollywood 5.00
TPB ($14.95) 15.00

40 BIG PAGES OF MICKEY MOUSE
Whitman Publ. Co.: No. 945, Jan, 1936 (10-1/4x12-1/2", 44 pgs., cardboard-c)

945-Reprints Mickey Mouse Magazine #1, but with a different cover; ads were eliminated and some illustrated stories had expanded text. The book is 3/4" shorter than Mickey Mouse Mag. #1, but the reprints are same size (Rare) 194 388 582 1242 2121 3000

47 RONIN
Dark Horse Comics: Nov, 2012 - No. 5, Jul, 2013 ($3.99, limited series)

1-5-Mike Richardson-s/Stan Sakai-a/c; 18th century samurai legend 4.00

FOR YOUR EYES ONLY (See James Bond...)

FOUNTAIN, THE (Companion graphic novel to the Darren Aronofsky film)
DC Comics (Vertigo): 2005 ($39.99, hardcover with dust jacket)

1-Darren Aronofsky-s/Kent Williams-a 40.00

FOUR (Fantastic Four; See Marvel Knights 4 #28-30)

FOUR COLOR
Dell Publishing Co.: Sept?, 1939 - No. 1354, Apr-June, 1962
(Series I are all 68 pgs.)

NOTE: *Four Color only appears on issues #19-25, 1-99,101. Dell Publishing Co. filed these as Series I, #1-25, and Series II, #1-1354. Issues beginning with #710? were printed with and without ads on back cover. Issues without ads are worth more.*

SERIES I:

	GD 2.0	VG 4.0	FN 6.0	VF 8.0	VF/NM 9.0	NM- 9.2
1(nn)-Dick Tracy	1150	2300	3450	8750	16,625	24,500
2(nn)-Don Winslow of the Navy (#1) (Rare) (11/39?)	258	516	774	1651	2826	4000
3(nn)-Myra North (1/40)	126	252	378	806	1378	1950
4-Donald Duck by Al Taliaferro (1940)(Disney)(3/40?)	2600	5200	7800	19,500	35,750	52,000
(Prices vary widely on this book)						
5-Smilin' Jack (#1) (5/40?)	100	200	300	635	1093	1550
6-Dick Tracy (Scarce)	284	568	852	1818	3109	4400
7-Gang Busters	71	142	213	454	777	1100
8-Dick Tracy	155	310	465	992	1696	2400
9-Terry and the Pirates-r/Super #9-29	84	168	252	538	919	1300
10-Smilin' Jack	84	168	252	538	919	1300
11-Smitty (#1)	61	122	183	390	670	950
12-Little Orphan Annie; reprints strips from 12/19/37 to 6/4/38	84	168	252	538	919	1300
13-Walt Disney's Reluctant Dragon('41)-Contains 2 pgs. of photos from film; 2 pg. foreword to Fantasia by Leopold Stokowski; Donald Duck, Goofy, Baby Weems & Mickey Mouse (as the Sorcerer's Apprentice) app. (Disney)	232	464	696	1485	2543	3600
14-Moon Mullins (#1)	55	110	165	352	601	850
15-Tillie the Toiler (#1)	71	142	213	454	777	1100
16-Mickey Mouse (#1) (Disney) by Gottfredson	1500	3000	4500	19,500	--	--
17-Walt Disney's Dumbo, the Flying Elephant (#1)(1941)-Mickey Mouse, Donald Duck, & Pluto app. (Disney)	284	568	852	1818	3109	4400
18-Jiggs and Maggie (#1)(1936-38-r)	60	120	180	381	653	925
19-Barney Google and Snuffy Smith (#1)-(1st issue with Four Color on the cover)	58	116	174	371	636	900
20-Tiny Tim	47	94	141	296	498	700
21-Dick Tracy	100	200	300	635	1093	1550
22-Don Winslow	60	120	180	381	653	925
23-Gang Busters	55	110	165	352	601	850
24-Captain Easy	61	122	183	390	670	950
25-Popeye (1941)	119	238	357	762	1306	1850

SERIES II:

	GD 2.0	VG 4.0	FN 6.0	VF 8.0	VF/NM 9.0	NM- 9.2
1-Little Joe (1942)	75	150	225	600	1350	2100
2-Harold Teen	37	74	111	274	612	950
3-Alley Oop (#1)	54	108	162	432	966	1500
4-Smilin' Jack	77	154	231	493	847	1200
5-Raggedy Ann and Andy (#1)	50	100	150	400	900	1400
6-Smitty	34	68	102	245	548	850
7-Smokey Stover (#1)	27	54	81	189	420	650
8-Tillie the Toiler	28	56	84	202	451	700
9-Donald Duck Finds Pirate Gold, by Carl Barks & Jack Hannah (Disney) (© 8/17/42)	1050	2100	3150	8000	14,500	21,000
10-Flash Gordon by Alex Raymond; reprinted from "The Ice Kingdom"	96	192	288	768	1734	2700
11-Wash Tubbs	27	54	81	194	435	675
12-Walt Disney's Bambi (#1)	50	100	150	400	900	1400
13-Mr. District Attorney (#1)-See The Funnies #35 for 1st app.	36	72	108	259	580	900
14-Smilin' Jack	34	68	102	245	548	850
15-Felix the Cat (#1)	86	172	258	688	1544	2400

Forever Evil #1 © DC

47 Ronin #1 © DH

Four Color Comics #21 © Walter Lantz

	GD 2.0	VG 4.0	FN 6.0	VF 8.0	VF/NM 9.0	NM- 9.2
16-Porky Pig (#1)(1942)- "Secret of the Haunted House"	104	208	312	832	1866	2900
17-Popeye	52	104	156	416	933	1450
18-Little Orphan Annie's Junior Commandos; Flag-c; reprints strips from 6/14/42 to 11/21/42	68	136	204	435	743	1050
19-Walt Disney's Thumper Meets the Seven Dwarfs (Disney); reprinted in Silly Symphonies	50	100	150	400	900	1400
20-Barney Baxter	27	54	81	194	435	675
21-Oswald the Rabbit (#1)(1943)	46	92	138	359	805	1250
22-Tillie the Toiler	19	38	57	131	291	450
23-Raggedy Ann and Andy	35	70	105	252	564	875
24-Gang Busters	32	64	96	230	515	800
25-Andy Panda (#1) (Walter Lantz)	50	100	150	390	870	1350
26-Popeye	52	104	156	416	933	1450
27-Walt Disney's Mickey Mouse and the Seven Colored Terror	79	158	237	632	1416	2200
28-Wash Tubbs	19	38	57	131	291	450
29-Donald Duck and the Mummy's Ring, by Carl Barks (Disney) (9/43)	805	1610	2415	5877	10,389	14,900
30-Bambi's Children (1943)-Disney	44	88	132	326	738	1150
31-Moon Mullins	17	34	51	119	265	410
32-Smitty	18	36	54	124	275	425
33-Bugs Bunny "Public Nuisance #1"	125	250	375	1000	2250	3500
34-Dick Tracy	42	84	126	311	706	1100
35-Smokey Stover	17	34	51	114	252	390
36-Smilin' Jack	23	46	69	164	362	560
37-Bringing Up Father	20	40	60	138	307	475
38-Roy Rogers (#1, © 4/44)-1st western comic with photo-c (see Movie Comics #3)	155	310	465	1279	2890	4500
39-Oswald the Rabbit (1944)	29	58	87	209	467	725
40-Barney Google and Snuffy Smith	20	40	60	140	310	480
41-Mother Goose and Nursery Rhyme Comics (#1)-All by Walt Kelly	26	52	78	182	404	625
42-Tiny Tim (1934-r)	18	36	54	128	284	440
43-Popeye (1938-'42-r)	30	60	90	216	483	750
44-Terry and the Pirates (1938-r)	32	64	96	230	515	800
45-Raggedy Ann	26	52	78	182	404	625
46-Felix the Cat and the Haunted Castle	46	92	138	359	805	1250
47-Gene Autry (copyright 6/16/44)	35	70	105	252	564	875
48-Porky Pig of the Mounties by Carl Barks (7/44)	102	204	306	826	1838	2850
49-Snow White and the Seven Dwarfs (Disney)	52	104	156	413	932	1450
50-Fairy Tale Parade-Walt Kelly art (1944)	21	42	63	147	324	500
51-Bugs Bunny Finds the Lost Treasure	39	78	117	289	657	1025
52-Little Orphan Annie; reprints strips from 6/18/38 to 11/19/38	26	52	78	182	404	625
53-Wash Tubbs	15	30	45	103	227	350
54-Andy Panda	25	50	75	175	388	600
55-Tillie the Toiler	14	28	42	96	211	325
56-Dick Tracy	34	68	102	247	554	860
57-Gene Autry	30	60	90	216	483	750
58-Smilin' Jack	23	46	69	164	362	560
59-Mother Goose and Nursery Rhyme Comics-Kelly-c/a	19	38	57	131	291	450
60-Tiny Folks Funnies	17	34	51	117	259	400
61-Santa Claus Funnies(11/44)-Kelly art	25	50	75	175	388	600
62-Donald Duck in Frozen Gold, by Carl Barks (Disney) (1/45)	238	476	714	1964	4432	6900
63-Roy Rogers; color photo-all 4 covers	40	80	120	296	673	1050
64-Smokey Stover	12	24	36	84	185	285
65-Smitty	14	28	42	96	211	325
66-Gene Autry	30	60	90	216	483	750
67-Oswald the Rabbit	16	32	48	112	249	385
68-Mother Goose and Nursery Rhyme Comics, by Walt Kelly	19	38	57	131	291	450
69-Fairy Tale Parade, by Walt Kelly	21	42	63	147	324	500
70-Popeye and Wimpy	24	48	72	168	372	575
71-Walt Disney's Three Caballeros, by Walt Kelly (© 4/45)-(Disney)	69	138	207	552	1251	1950
72-Raggedy Ann	21	42	63	147	324	500
73-The Gumps (#1)	13	26	39	89	195	300
74-Marge's Little Lulu (#1)	190	380	570	1568	3534	5500
75-Gene Autry and the Wildcat	23	46	69	164	362	560
76-Little Orphan Annie; reprints strips from 2/28/40 to 6/24/40	20	40	60	144	317	490
77-Felix the Cat	40	80	120	296	673	1050
78-Porky Pig and the Bandit Twins	30	60	90	216	483	750
79-Walt Disney's Mickey Mouse in The Riddle of the Red Hat by Carl Barks (8/45)	100	200	300	800	1800	2800
80-Smilin' Jack	14	28	42	93	204	315
81-Moon Mullins	11	22	33	77	166	255
82-Lone Ranger	40	80	120	296	673	1050
83-Gene Autry in Outlaw Trail	23	46	69	164	362	560
84-Flash Gordon by Alex Raymond-Reprints from "The Fiery Desert"	42	84	126	311	706	1100
85-Andy Panda and the Mad Dog Mystery	15	30	45	103	227	350
86-Roy Rogers; photo-c	29	58	87	209	467	725
87-Fairy Tale Parade by Walt Kelly; Dan Noonan-c	21	42	63	147	324	500
88-Bugs Bunny's Great Adventure (Sci/fi)	25	50	75	175	388	600
89-Tillie the Toiler	14	28	42	96	211	325
90-Christmas with Mother Goose by Walt Kelly (11/45)	15	30	45	104	230	365
91-Santa Claus Funnies by Walt Kelly (11/45)	18	36	54	124	275	425
92-Walt Disney's The Wonderful Adventures Of Pinocchio (1945); Donald Duck by Kelly, 16 pgs. (Disney)	52	104	156	416	933	1450
93-Gene Autry in The Bandit of Black Rock	19	38	57	133	297	460
94-Winnie Winkle (1945)	13	26	39	87	191	295
95-Roy Rogers Comics; photo-c	29	58	87	209	467	725
96-Dick Tracy	23	46	69	161	356	550
97-Marge's Little Lulu (1946)	71	142	213	568	1284	2000
98-Lone Ranger, The	28	56	84	202	451	700
99-Smitty	11	22	33	73	157	240
100-Gene Autry Comics; 1st Gene Autry photo-c	22	44	66	155	345	535
101-Terry and the Pirates	20	40	60	135	300	465

NOTE: *No. 101 is last issue to carry "Four Color" logo on cover; all issues beginning with No. 100 are marked "...O. S." (One Shot) which can be found in the bottom left-hand panel on the first page; the numbers following "O. S." relate to the year/month issued.*

	GD 2.0	VG 4.0	FN 6.0	VF 8.0	VF/NM 9.0	NM- 9.2
102-Oswald the Rabbit-Walt Kelly art, 1 pg.	15	30	45	100	220	340
103-Easter with Mother Goose by Walt Kelly	20	40	60	138	307	475
104-Fairy Tale Parade by Walt Kelly	16	32	48	112	249	385
105-Albert the Alligator and Pogo Possum (#1) by Kelly (4/46)	64	128	192	512	1156	1800
106-Tillie the Toiler (5/46)	10	20	30	70	150	230
107-Little Orphan Annie; reprints strips from 11/16/42 to 3/24/43	18	36	54	128	284	440
108-Donald Duck in The Terror of the River, by Carl Barks (Disney) (© 4/16/46)	107	214	321	856	1928	3000
109-Roy Rogers Comics; photo-c	22	44	66	154	340	525
110-Marge's Little Lulu	46	92	138	359	805	1250
111-Captain Easy	14	28	42	93	204	315
112-Porky Pig's Adventure in Gopher Gulch	18	36	54	124	275	425
113-Popeye; all new Popeye stories begin	15	30	45	100	220	340
114-Fairy Tale Parade by Walt Kelly	16	32	48	112	249	385
115-Marge's Little Lulu	44	88	132	326	738	1150
116-Mickey Mouse and the House of Many Mysteries (Disney)	27	54	81	189	420	650
117-Roy Rogers Comics; photo-c	17	34	51	119	265	410
118-Lone Ranger, The	28	56	84	202	451	700
119-Felix the Cat; all new Felix stories begin	36	72	108	259	580	900
120-Marge's Little Lulu	36	72	108	266	596	925
121-Fairy Tale Parade-(not Kelly)	10	20	30	69	147	225
122-Henry (#1) (10/46)	16	32	48	110	243	375
123-Bugs Bunny's Dangerous Venture	17	34	51	117	259	400
124-Roy Rogers Comics; photo-c	17	34	51	119	265	410
125-Lone Ranger, The	19	38	57	133	297	460
126-Christmas with Mother Goose by Walt Kelly (1946)	12	24	36	82	179	275
127-Popeye	15	30	45	100	220	340
128-Santa Claus Funnies- "Santa & the Angel" by Gollub; "A Mouse in the House" by Kelly	15	30	45	103	227	350
129-Walt Disney's Uncle Remus and His Tales of Brer Rabbit (#1) (1946)-Adapted from Disney movie "Song of the South"	32	64	96	230	515	800
130-Andy Panda (Walter Lantz)	10	20	30	70	150	230
131-Marge's Little Lulu	36	72	108	266	596	925
132-Tillie the Toiler (1947)	10	20	30	70	150	230
133-Dick Tracy	18	36	54	124	275	425
134-Tarzan and the Devil Ogre; Marsh-c/a	59	118	177	472	1061	1650
135-Felix the Cat	23	46	69	156	348	540
136-Lone Ranger, The	19	38	57	133	297	460
137-Roy Rogers Comics; photo-c	17	34	51	119	265	410
138-Smitty	10	20	30	64	132	200

	GD 2.0	VG 4.0	FN 6.0	VF 8.0	VF/NM 9.0	NM- 9.2
139-Marge's Little Lulu (1947)	35	70	105	252	564	875
140-Easter with Mother Goose by Walt Kelly	16	32	48	107	236	365
141-Mickey Mouse and the Submarine Pirates (Disney)	24	48	72	168	372	575
142-Bugs Bunny and the Haunted Mountain	17	34	51	117	259	400
143-Oswald the Rabbit & the Prehistoric Egg	9	18	27	59	117	175
144-Roy Rogers Comics (1947)-Photo-c	17	34	51	119	265	410
145-Popeye	15	30	45	100	220	340
146-Marge's Little Lulu	35	70	105	252	564	875
147-Donald Duck in Volcano Valley, by Carl Barks (Disney) (5/47)	89	178	267	712	1606	2500
148-Albert the Alligator and Pogo Possum by Walt Kelly (5/47)	44	88	132	326	738	1150
149-Smilin' Jack	10	20	30	66	138	210
150-Tillie the Toiler (6/47)	10	20	30	66	138	210
151-Lone Ranger, The	16	32	48	112	249	385
152-Little Orphan Annie; reprints strips from 1/2/44 to 5/6/44	12	24	36	82	179	275
153-Roy Rogers Comics; photo-c	15	30	45	105	233	360
154-Walter Lantz Andy Panda	10	20	30	70	150	230
155-Henry (7/47)	10	20	30	70	150	230
156-Porky Pig and the Phantom	12	24	36	79	170	260
157-Mickey Mouse & the Beanstalk (Disney)	24	48	72	168	372	575
158-Marge's Little Lulu	35	70	105	252	564	875
159-Donald Duck in the Ghost of the Grotto, by Carl Barks (Disney) (8/47)	93	186	279	744	1672	2600
160-Roy Rogers Comics; photo-c	15	30	45	105	233	360
161-Tarzan and the Fires Of Tohr; Marsh-c/a	59	118	177	472	1061	1650
162-Felix the Cat (9/47)	18	36	54	124	275	425
163-Dick Tracy	16	32	48	110	243	375
164-Bugs Bunny Finds the Frozen Kingdom	17	34	51	117	259	400
165-Marge's Little Lulu	42	84	126	311	706	1100
166-Roy Rogers Comics (52 pgs.)-Photo-c	15	30	45	105	233	360
167-Lone Ranger, The	16	32	48	112	249	385
168-Popeye (10/47)	15	30	45	100	220	340
169-Woody Woodpecker (#1)- "Manhunter in the North"; drug use story	21	42	63	147	324	500
170-Mickey Mouse on Spook's Island (11/47)(Disney)-reprinted in Mickey Mouse #103	20	40	60	144	317	490
171-Charlie McCarthy (#1) and the Twenty Thieves	27	54	81	194	435	675
172-Christmas with Mother Goose by Walt Kelly (11/47)	12	24	36	82	179	275
173-Flash Gordon	26	52	78	182	404	625
174-Winnie Winkle	9	18	27	60	120	180
175-Santa Claus Funnies by Walt Kelly (1947)	15	30	45	103	227	350
176-Tillie the Toiler (12/47)	10	20	30	66	138	210
177-Roy Rogers Comics-(36 pgs.); Photo-c	15	30	45	100	220	340
178-Donald Duck "Christmas on Bear Mountain" by Carl Barks; 1st app. Uncle Scrooge (Disney)(12/47)	214	428	642	1766	3983	6200
179-Uncle Wiggily (#1)-Walt Kelly-c	16	32	48	108	239	370
180-Ozark Ike (#1)	12	24	36	83	182	280
181-Walt Disney's Mickey Mouse in Jungle Magic	20	40	60	144	317	490
182-Porky Pig in Never-Never Land (2/48)	12	24	36	79	170	260
183-Oswald the Rabbit (Lantz)	9	18	27	59	117	175
184-Tillie the Toiler	10	20	30	66	138	210
185-Easter with Mother Goose by Walt Kelly (1948)	14	28	42	96	211	325
186-Walt Disney's Bambi (4/48)-Reprinted as Movie Classic Bambi #3 (1956)	16	32	48	110	243	375
187-Bugs Bunny and the Dreadful Dragon	12	24	36	84	185	285
188-Woody Woodpecker (Lantz, 5/48)	12	24	36	82	179	275
189-Donald Duck in The Old Castle's Secret, by Carl Barks (Disney) (6/48)	96	192	288	768	1734	2700
190-Flash Gordon (6/48); bondage-c; "The Adventures of the Flying Saucers"; 5th Flying Saucer story- see The Spirit 9/28/47(1st), Shadow Comics V7#10 (2nd, 1/48),Captain Midnight #60 (3rd, 2/48) & Boy Commandos #26 (4th, 3-4/48)	31	62	93	223	499	775
191-Porky Pig to the Rescue	12	24	36	79	170	260
192-The Brownies (#1)-by Walt Kelly (7/48)	14	28	42	96	211	325
193-M.G.M. Presents Tom and Jerry (#1)(1948)	34	68	102	245	548	850
194-Mickey Mouse in The World Under the Sea (Disney)-Reprinted in Mickey Mouse #101	20	40	60	144	317	490
195-Tillie the Toiler	9	18	27	57	111	165
196-Charlie McCarthy in The Haunted Hide-Out; part photo-c	17	34	51	119	265	410
197-Spirit of the Border (#1) (Zane Grey) (1948)	12	24	36	84	185	285
198-Andy Panda	10	20	30	70	150	230
199-Donald Duck in Sheriff of Bullet Valley, by Carl Barks; Barks draws himself on wanted poster, last page; used in Love & Death (Disney) (10/48)	93	186	279	744	1672	2600
200-Bugs Bunny, Super Sleuth (10/48)	12	24	36	84	185	285
201-Christmas with Mother Goose by W. Kelly	10	20	30	66	138	210
202-Woody Woodpecker	9	18	27	59	117	175
203-Donald Duck in the Golden Christmas Tree, by Carl Barks (Disney) (12/48)	64	128	192	512	1156	1800
204-Flash Gordon (12/48)	19	38	57	131	291	450
205-Santa Claus Funnies by Walt Kelly	12	24	36	84	185	285
206-Little Orphan Annie; reprints strips from 11/10/40 to 1/11/41	8	16	24	52	99	145
207-King of the Royal Mounted (#1) (12/48)	14	28	42	94	207	320
208-Brer Rabbit Does It Again (Disney) (1/49)	12	24	36	82	179	275
209-Harold Teen	7	14	21	49	92	135
210-Tippie and Cap Stubbs	9	18	27	57	111	165
211-Little Beaver (#1)	11	22	33	73	157	240
212-Dr. Bobbs	7	14	21	49	92	135
213-Tillie the Toiler	9	18	27	57	111	165
214-Mickey Mouse and His Sky Adventure (2/49)(Disney)-Reprinted in Mickey Mouse #105	17	34	51	114	252	390

	GD 2.0	VG 4.0	FN 6.0	VF 8.0	VF/NM 9.0	NM- 9.2
215-Sparkle Plenty (Dick Tracy-r by Gould)	12	24	36	82	179	275
216-Andy Panda and the Police Pup (Lantz)	8	16	24	55	105	155
217-Bugs Bunny in Court Jester	12	24	36	84	185	285
218-Three Little Pigs and the Wonderful Magic Lamp (Disney) (3/49)(#1)	11	22	33	78	163	250
219-Swee'pea	10	20	30	64	132	200
220-Easter with Mother Goose by Walt Kelly	14	28	42	96	211	325
221-Uncle Wiggily-Walt Kelly cover in part	10	20	30	64	132	200
222-West of the Pecos (Zane Grey)	8	16	24	55	105	155
223-Donald Duck "Lost in the Andes" by Carl Barks (Disney-4/49) (square egg story)	82	164	246	656	1478	2300
224-Little Iodine (#1), by Hatlo (4/49)	13	26	39	89	195	300
225-Oswald the Rabbit (Lantz)	7	14	21	46	86	125
226-Porky Pig and Spoofy, the Spook	9	18	27	61	123	185
227-Seven Dwarfs (Disney)	13	26	39	89	195	300
228-Mark of Zorro, The (#1) (1949)	27	54	81	189	420	650
229-Smokey Stover	6	12	18	42	79	115
230-Sunset Pass (Zane Grey)	8	16	24	55	105	155
231-Mickey Mouse and the Rajah's Treasure (Disney)	17	34	51	114	252	390
232-Woody Woodpecker (Lantz, 6/49)	21	42	63	147	324	500
233-Bugs Bunny, Sleepwalking Sleuth	12	24	36	84	185	285
234-Dumbo in Sky Voyage (Disney)	15	30	45	100	220	340
235-Tiny Tim	7	14	21	48	89	130
236-Heritage of the Desert (Zane Grey) (1949)	8	16	24	55	105	155
237-Tillie the Toiler	9	18	27	57	111	165
238-Donald Duck in Voodoo Hoodoo, by Carl Barks (Disney) (8/49)	61	122	183	488	1094	1700
239-Adventure Bound (8/49)	6	12	18	41	76	110
240-Andy Panda (Lantz)	8	16	24	55	105	155
241-Porky Pig, Mighty Hunter	9	18	27	61	123	185
242-Tippie and Cap Stubbs	6	12	18	41	76	110
243-Thumper Follows His Nose (Disney)	13	26	39	89	195	300
244-The Brownies by Walt Kelly	10	20	30	68	144	220
245-Dick's Adventures (9/49)	6	12	18	41	76	110
246-Thunder Mountain (Zane Grey)	6	12	18	37	66	95
247-Flash Gordon	19	38	57	131	291	450
248-Mickey Mouse and the Black Sorcerer (Disney)	17	34	51	114	252	390
249-Woody Woodpecker in the "Globetrotter" (10/49)	9	18	27	59	117	175
250-Bugs Bunny in Diamond Daze; used in **SOTI**, pg. 309	13	26	39	89	195	300
251-Hubert at Camp Moonbeam	10	20	30	64	132	200
252-Pinocchio (Disney)-not by Kelly; origin	13	26	39	87	195	300
253-Christmas with Mother Goose by W. Kelly	10	20	30	66	138	210
254-Santa Claus Funnies by Walt Kelly; Pogo & Albert story by Kelly (11/49)	12	24	36	84	185	285
255-The Ranger (Zane Grey) (1949)	6	12	18	37	66	95
256-Donald Duck in "Luck of the North" by Carl Barks (Disney) (12/49)-Shows #257 on inside	52	104	156	413	932	1450
257-Little Iodine	9	18	27	58	114	170
258-Andy Panda and the Balloon Race (Lantz)	8	16	24	55	105	155
259-Santa and the Angel (Gollub art-condensed from #128) & Santa at the Zoo (12/49) -two books in one	9	18	27	59	117	175
260-Porky Pig, Hero of the Wild West (12/49)	9	18	27	61	123	185
261-Mickey Mouse and the Missing Key (Disney)	17	34	51	114	252	390
262-Raggedy Ann and Andy	9	18	27	57	111	165
263-Donald Duck in "Land of the Totem Poles" by Carl Barks (Disney) (2/50)-Has two Barks stories	49	98	147	382	866	1350
264-Woody Woodpecker in the Magic Lantern (Lantz)	9	18	27	59	117	175
265-King of the Royal Mounted (Zane Grey)	9	18	27	62	126	190
266-Bugs Bunny on the "Isle of Hercules" (2/50)-Reprinted in Best of Bugs Bunny #1	10	20	30	67	141	215
267-Little Beaver; Harmon-c/a	8	16	24	51	96	140
268-Mickey Mouse's Surprise Visitor (1950)(Disney)	16	32	48	108	239	370
269-Johnny Mack Brown (#1)-Photo-c	19	38	57	133	297	460
270-Drift Fence (Zane Grey) (3/50)	6	12	18	37	66	95
271-Porky Pig in Phantom of the Plains	9	18	27	61	123	185
272-Cinderella (Disney) (4/50)	14	28	42	96	211	325
273-Oswald the Rabbit (Lantz)	7	14	21	46	86	125
274-Bugs Bunny, Hare-brained Reporter	10	20	30	67	141	215
275-Donald Duck in "Ancient Persia" by Carl Barks (Disney) (5/50)	48	96	138	368	834	1300
276-Uncle Wiggily	7	14	21	49	92	135
277-Porky Pig in Desert Adventure (5/50)	9	18	27	61	123	185
278-(Wild) Bill Elliott Comics (#1)-Photo-c	13	26	39	89	195	300
279-Mickey Mouse and Pluto Battle the Giant Ants (Disney); reprinted in Mickey Mouse #102 & 245	13	26	39	86	188	290
280-Andy Panda in The Isle Of Mechanical Men (Lantz)	8	16	24	55	105	155
281-Bugs Bunny in The Great Circus Mystery	10	20	30	67	141	215
282-Donald Duck and the Pixilated Parrot by Carl Barks (Disney) (© 5/23/50)	48	96	138	368	834	1300
283-King of the Royal Mounted (7/50)	9	18	27	62	126	190
284-Porky Pig in The Kingdom of Nowhere	9	18	27	61	123	185
285-Bozo the Clown & His Minikin Circus (#1) (TV)	19	38	57	131	291	450
286-Mickey Mouse in The Uninvited Guest (Disney	13	26	39	86	188	290
287-Gene Autry's Champion in The Ghost Of Black Mountain; photo-c	11	22	33	76	163	250
288-Woody Woodpecker in Klondike Gold (Lantz)	9	18	27	59	117	175
289-Bugs Bunny in "Indian Trouble"	10	20	30	67	141	215
290-The Chief (#1) (8/50)	9	18	27	57	111	165
291-Donald Duck in "The Magic Hourglass" by Carl Barks (Disney) (9/50)	48	96	138	368	834	1300
292-The Cisco Kid Comics (#1)	23	46	69	156	348	540
293-The Brownies-Kelly-c/a	10	20	30	68	144	220
294-Little Beaver	8	16	24	51	96	140

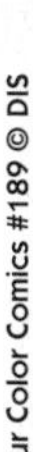

Four Color Comics #189 © DIS

Four Color Comics #224 © KFS

Four Color Comics #347 © WB

	GD 2.0	VG 4.0	FN 6.0	VF 8.0	VF/NM 9.0	NM- 9.2
295-Porky Pig in President Porky (9/50)	9	18	27	61	123	185
296-Mickey Mouse in Private Eye for Hire (Disney)	13	26	39	86	188	290
297-Andy Panda in The Haunted Inn (Lantz, 10/50)	8	16	24	55	105	155
298-Bugs Bunny in Sheik for a Day	10	20	30	67	141	215
299-Buck Jones & the Iron Horse Trail (#1)	14	28	42	93	204	315
300-Donald Duck in "Big-Top Bedlam" by Carl Barks (Disney) (11/50)	48	96	138	368	834	1300
301-The Mysterious Rider (Zane Grey)	6	12	18	37	66	95
302-Santa Claus Funnies (11/50)	8	16	24	51	96	140
303-Porky Pig in The Land of the Monstrous Flies	8	16	24	51	96	140
304-Mickey Mouse in Tom-Tom Island (Disney) (12/50)	12	24	36	79	170	260
305-Woody Woodpecker (Lantz)	9	18	27	59	117	175
306-Raggedy Ann	7	14	21	46	86	125
307-Bugs Bunny in Lumber Jack Rabbit	9	18	27	59	117	175
308-Donald Duck in "Dangerous Disguise" by Carl Barks (Disney) (1/51)	46	92	138	359	805	1250
309-Betty Betz' Dollface and Her Gang (1951)	8	16	24	54	102	150
310-King of the Royal Mounted (1/51)	7	14	21	46	86	125
311-Porky Pig in Midget Horses of Hidden Valley	8	16	24	51	96	140
312-Tonto (#1)	11	22	33	75	160	245
313-Mickey Mouse in The Mystery of the Double-Cross Ranch (#1) (Disney) (2/51)	12	24	36	79	170	260

Note: Beginning with the above comic in 1951 Dell/Western began adding #1 in small print on the covers of several long running titles with the evident intention of switching these titles to their own monthly numbers, but when the conversions were made, there was no connection. It is thought that the post office may have stepped in and decreed the sequences should commence as though the first four colors printed had each begun with number one, or the first issues sold by subscription. Since the regular series' numbers don't correctly match to the numbers of earlier issues published, it's not known whether or not the numbering was in error.

	GD 2.0	VG 4.0	FN 6.0	VF 8.0	VF/NM 9.0	NM- 9.2
314-Ambush (Zane Grey)	6	12	18	37	66	95
315-Oswald the Rabbit (Lantz)	6	12	18	40	73	105
316-Rex Allen (#1)-Photo-c; Marsh-a	14	28	42	94	207	320
317-Bugs Bunny in Hair Today Gone Tomorrow (#1)	9	18	27	59	117	175
318-Donald Duck in "No Such Varmint" by Carl Barks (#1)-Indicia shows #317 (Disney, © 1/23/51)	46	92	138	359	805	1250
319-Gene Autry's Champion; painted-c	6	12	18	41	76	110
320-Uncle Wiggily (#1)	7	14	21	49	92	135
321-Little Scouts (#1) (3/51)	6	12	18	42	79	115
322-Porky Pig in Roaring Rockets (#1 on-c)	8	16	24	51	96	140
323-Susie Q. Smith (#1) (3/51)	8	16	24	51	96	140
324-I Met a Handsome Cowboy (3/51)	8	16	24	52	99	145
325-Mickey Mouse in The Haunted Castle (#2) (Disney) (4/51)	12	24	36	79	170	260
326-Andy Panda (#1) (Lantz)	6	12	18	41	76	110
327-Bugs Bunny and the Rajah's Treasure (#2)	9	18	27	59	117	175
328-Donald Duck in Old California (#2) by Carl Barks-Peyote drug use issue (Disney) (5/51)	46	92	138	340	770	1200
329-Roy Roger's Trigger (#1)(5/51)-Painted-c	14	28	42	97	214	330
330-Porky Pig Meets the Bristled Bruiser (#2)	8	16	24	51	96	140
331-Alice in Wonderland (Disney) (1951)	18	36	54	124	275	425
332-Little Beaver	8	16	24	51	96	140
333-Wilderness Trek (Zane Grey) (5/51)	6	12	18	37	66	95
334-Mickey Mouse and Yukon Gold (Disney) (6/51)	12	24	36	79	170	260
335-Francis the Famous Talking Mule (#1, 6/51)-1st Dell non animated movie comic (all issues based on movie)	11	22	33	73	157	240
336-Woody Woodpecker (Lantz)	9	18	27	59	117	175
337-The Brownies-not by Walt Kelly	6	12	18	38	69	100
338-Bugs Bunny and the Rocking Horse Thieves	9	18	27	59	117	175
339-Donald Duck and the Magic Fountain-not by Carl Barks (Disney) (7-8/51)	33	66	99	238	532	825
340-King of the Royal Mounted (7/51)	7	14	21	46	86	125
341-Unbirthday Party with Alice in Wonderland (Disney) (7/51)	18	36	54	124	275	425
342-Porky Pig the Lucky Peppermint Mine; r/in Porky Pig #3	6	12	18	40	73	105
343-Mickey Mouse in The Ruby Eye of Homar-Guy-Am (Disney)-Reprinted in Mickey Mouse #104	10	20	30	67	141	215
344-Sergeant Preston from Challenge of The Yukon (#1) (TV)	14	28	42	94	207	320
345-Andy Panda in Scotland Yard (8-10/51) (Lantz)	6	12	18	41	76	110
346-Hideout (Zane Grey)	6	12	18	37	66	95
347-Bugs Bunny the Frigid Hare (8-9/51)	9	18	27	59	117	175
348-Donald Duck "The Crocodile Collector"; Barks-c only (Disney) (9-10/51)	24	48	72	168	372	575

	GD 2.0	VG 4.0	FN 6.0	VF 8.0	VF/NM 9.0	NM- 9.2
349-Uncle Wiggily	6	12	18	41	76	110
350-Woody Woodpecker (Lantz)	9	18	27	59	117	175
351-Porky Pig & the Grand Canyon Giant (9-10/51)	6	12	18	40	73	105
352-Mickey Mouse in The Mystery of Painted Valley (Disney)	10	20	30	67	141	215
353-Duck Album (#1)-Barks-c (Disney)	13	26	39	91	201	310
354-Raggedy Ann & Andy	7	14	21	46	86	125
355-Bugs Bunny Hot-Rod Hare	9	18	27	59	117	175
356-Donald Duck in "Rags to Riches"; Barks-c only	24	48	72	168	372	575
357-Comeback (Zane Grey)	5	10	15	33	57	80
358-Andy Panda (Lantz) (11-1/52)	6	12	18	41	76	110
359-Frosty the Snowman (#1)	11	22	33	75	160	245
360-Porky Pig in Tree of Fortune (11-12/51)	6	12	18	40	73	105
361-Santa Claus Funnies	8	16	24	51	96	140
362-Mickey Mouse and the Smuggled Diamonds (Disney)	10	20	30	67	141	215
363-King of the Royal Mounted	6	12	18	40	73	105
364-Woody Woodpecker (Lantz)	6	12	18	37	66	95
365-The Brownies-not by Kelly	6	12	18	38	69	100
366-Bugs Bunny Uncle Buckskin Comes to Town (12-1/52)	9	18	27	59	117	175
367-Donald Duck in "A Christmas for Shacktown" by Carl Barks (Disney) (1-2/52)	37	74	111	274	612	950
368-Bob Clampett's Beany and Cecil (#1)	25	50	75	175	388	600
369-The Lone Ranger's Famous Horse Hi-Yo Silver (#1); Silver's origin	11	22	33	72	154	235
370-Porky Pig in Trouble in the Big Trees	6	12	18	40	73	105
371-Mickey Mouse in The Inca Idol Case (1952) (Disney)	10	20	30	67	141	215
372-Riders of the Purple Sage (Zane Grey)	5	10	15	33	57	80
373-Sergeant Preston (TV)	9	18	27	58	114	170
374-Woody Woodpecker (Lantz)	6	12	18	37	66	95
375-John Carter of Mars (E. R. Burroughs)-Jesse Marsh-a; origin	36	72	108	259	580	900
376-Bugs Bunny, "The Magic Sneeze"	9	18	27	59	117	175
377-Susie Q. Smith	5	10	15	35	63	90
378-Tom Corbett, Space Cadet (#1) (TV)-McWilliams-a	19	38	57	133	297	460
379-Donald Duck in "Southern Hospitality"; 2nd Uncle Scrooge-c; not by Barks (Disney)	33	66	99	238	532	825
380-Raggedy Ann & Andy	7	14	21	46	86	125
381-Marge's Tubby (#1)	20	40	60	138	307	475
382-Snow White and the Seven Dwarfs (Disney)-origin; partial reprint of Four Color #49 (Movie)	12	24	36	82	179	275
383-Andy Panda (Lantz)	5	10	15	35	63	90
384-King of the Royal Mounted (3/52)(Zane Grey)	6	12	18	40	73	105
385-Porky Pig in The Isle of Missing Ships (3-4/52)	6	12	18	40	73	105
386-Uncle Scrooge (#1)-by Carl Barks (Disney) in "Only a Poor Old Man" (3/52)	195	390	585	1600	4200	6800
387-Mickey Mouse in High Tibet (Disney) (4-5/52)	10	20	30	67	141	215
388-Oswald the Rabbit (Lantz)	6	12	18	40	73	105
389-Andy Hardy Comics (#1)	7	14	21	46	86	125
390-Woody Woodpecker (Lantz)	6	12	18	37	66	95
391-Uncle Wiggily	6	12	18	41	76	110
392-Hi-Yo Silver	7	14	21	44	82	120
393-Bugs Bunny	9	18	27	59	117	175
394-Donald Duck in Malayalaya-Barks-c only (Disney)	24	48	72	168	372	575
395-Forlorn River(Zane Grey)-First Nevada (5/52)	5	10	15	33	57	80
396-Tales of the Texas Rangers(#1)(TV)-Photo-c	10	20	30	69	147	225
397-Sergeant Preston of the Yukon (TV) (5/52)	9	18	27	58	114	170
398-The Brownies-not by Kelly	6	12	18	38	69	100
399-Porky Pig in The Lost Gold Mine	6	12	18	40	73	105
400-Tom Corbett, Space Cadet (TV)-McWilliams-c/a	11	22	33	73	157	240
401-Mickey Mouse and Goofy's Mechanical Wizard (Disney) (6-7/52)	9	18	27	60	120	180
402-Mary Jane and Sniffles	10	20	30	65	135	205
403-Li'l Bad Wolf (Disney) (6/52)(#1)	9	18	27	58	114	190
404-The Range Rider (#1) (Flying A's...)(TV)-Photo-c	10	20	30	68	144	220
405-Woody Woodpecker (Lantz) (6-7/52)	6	12	18	37	66	95
406-Tweety and Sylvester (#1)	14	28	42	97	214	330
407-Bugs Bunny, Foreign-Legion Hare	8	16	24	54	102	150
408-Donald Duck and the Golden Helmet by Carl Barks (Disney) (7-8/52)	36	72	108	266	596	925
409-Andy Panda (7-9/52)	5	10	15	35	63	90

	GD 2.0	VG 4.0	FN 6.0	VF 8.0	VF/NM 9.0	NM- 9.2
410-Porky Pig in The Water Wizard (7/52)	6	12	18	40	73	105
411-Mickey Mouse and the Old Sea Dog (Disney) (8-9/52)	9	18	27	60	120	180
412-Nevada (Zane Grey)	5	10	15	33	57	80
413-Robin Hood (Disney-Movie) (8/52)-Photo-c (1st Disney movie Four Color book)	9	18	27	62	126	190
414-Bob Clampett's Beany and Cecil (TV)	14	28	42	96	211	325
415-Rootie Kazootie (#1) (TV)	10	20	30	69	147	225
416-Woody Woodpecker (Lantz)	6	12	18	37	66	95
417-Double Trouble with Goober (#1) (8/52)	5	10	15	34	60	85
418-Rusty Riley, a Boy, a Horse, and a Dog (#1)-Frank Godwin-a (strip reprints) (8/52)	8	16	24	54	102	150
419-Sergeant Preston (TV)	9	18	27	58	114	170
420-Bugs Bunny in The Mysterious Buckaroo (8-9/52)	8	16	24	54	102	150
421-Tom Corbett, Space Cadet(TV)-McWilliams-a	11	22	33	73	157	240
422-Donald Duck and the Gilded Man, by Carl Barks (Disney) (9-10/52) (#423 on inside)	36	72	108	266	596	925
423-Rhubarb, Owner of the Brooklyn Ball Club (The Millionaire Cat) (#1)-Painted cover	7	14	21	49	92	135
424-Flash Gordon-Test Flight in Space (9/52)	13	26	39	89	195	300
425-Zorro, the Return of	12	24	36	82	179	275
426-Porky Pig in The Scalawag Leprechaun	6	12	18	40	73	105
427-Mickey Mouse and the Wonderful Whizzix (Disney) (10-11/52)-Reprinted in Mickey Mouse #100	9	18	27	60	120	180
428-Uncle Wiggily	5	10	15	34	63	90
429-Pluto in "Why Dogs Leave Home" (Disney) (10/52)(#1)	12	24	36	80	173	265
430-Marge's Tubby, the Shadow of a Man-Eater	12	24	36	80	173	265
431-Woody Woodpecker (10/52) (Lantz)	6	12	18	37	66	95
432-Bugs Bunny and the Rabbit Olympics	8	16	24	54	102	150
433-Wildfire (Zane Grey) (11-1/52-53)	5	10	15	33	57	80
434-Rin Tin Tin "In Dark Danger" (#1) (TV) (11/52)-Photo-c	16	32	48	111	246	380
435-Frosty the Snowman (11/52)	7	14	21	48	89	130
436-The Brownies-not by Kelly (11/52)	5	10	15	35	63	90
437-John Carter of Mars (E.R. Burroughs)-Marsh-a	18	36	54	128	284	440
438-Annie Oakley (#1) (TV)	13	26	39	89	195	300
439-Little Hiawatha (Disney) (12/52)j(#1)	8	16	24	55	105	155
440-Black Beauty (12/52)	6	12	18	35	69	100
441-Fearless Fagan	5	10	15	31	53	75
442-Peter Pan (Disney) (Movie)	12	24	36	79	170	260
443-Ben Bowie and His Mountain Men (#1)	9	18	27	63	129	195
444-Marge's Tubby	12	24	36	80	173	265
445-Charlie McCarthy	7	14	21	44	82	120
446-Captain Hook and Peter Pan (Disney)(Movie)(1/53)	10	20	30	66	138	210
447-Andy Hardy Comics	5	10	15	30	50	70
448-Bob Clampett's Beany and Cecil (TV)	14	28	42	96	211	325
449-Tappan's Burro (Zane Grey) (2-4/53)	5	10	15	33	57	80
450-Duck Album; Barks-c (Disney)	9	18	27	63	129	195
451-Rusty Riley-Frank Godwin-a (strip-r) (2/53)	5	10	15	33	57	80
452-Raggedy Ann & Andy (1953)	7	14	21	46	86	125
453-Susie Q. Smith (2/53)	5	10	15	35	63	90
454-Krazy Kat Comics; not by Herriman	6	12	18	42	79	115
455-Johnny Mack Brown Comics(3/53)-Photo-c	6	12	18	40	73	105
456-Uncle Scrooge Back to the Klondike (#2) by Barks (3/53) (Disney)	95	190	285	760	1955	3150
457-Daffy (#1)	12	24	36	83	182	280
458-Oswald the Rabbit (Lantz)	5	10	15	35	63	90
459-Rootie Kazootie (TV)	6	12	18	41	76	110
460-Buck Jones (4/53)	6	12	18	42	79	115
461-Marge's Tubby	10	20	30	70	150	230
462-Little Scouts	5	10	15	30	50	70
463-Petunia (4/53)	5	10	15	35	63	90
464-Bozo (4/53)	9	18	27	61	123	185
465-Francis the Famous Talking Mule	6	12	18	41	76	110
466-Rhubarb, the Millionaire Cat; painted-c	6	12	18	38	69	100
467-Desert Gold (Zane Grey) (5-7/53)	5	10	15	33	57	80
468-Goofy (#1) (Disney)	12	24	36	82	179	275
469-Beetle Bailey (#1) (5/53	13	26	39	89	195	300
470-Elmer Fudd	10	20	30	67	141	215
471-Double Trouble with Goober	4	8	12	27	44	60
472-Wild Bill Elliott (6/53)-Photo-c	5	10	15	35	63	90
473-Li'l Bad Wolf (Disney) (6/53)(#2)	6	12	18	41	76	110
474-Mary Jane and Sniffles	8	16	24	51	96	140
475-M.G.M.'s The Two Mouseketeers (#1)	9	18	27	59	117	175
476-Rin Tin Tin (TV)-Photo-c	9	18	27	62	126	190
477-Bob Clampett's Beany and Cecil (TV)	14	28	42	96	211	325
478-Charlie McCarthy	7	14	21	44	82	120
479-Queen of the West Dale Evans (#1)-Photo-c	17	34	51	114	252	390
480-Andy Hardy Comics	5	10	15	30	50	70
481-Annie Oakley And Tagg (TV)	9	18	27	59	117	175
482-Brownies-not by Kelly	5	10	15	35	63	90
483-Little Beaver (7/53)	5	10	15	35	63	90
484-River Feud (Zane Grey) (8-10/53)	5	10	15	33	57	80
485-The Little People-Walt Scott (#1)	9	18	27	58	114	170
486-Rusty Riley-Frank Godwin strip-r	5	10	15	33	57	80
487-Mowgli, the Jungle Book (Rudyard Kipling's)	8	16	24	52	99	145
488-John Carter of Mars (Burroughs)-Marsh-a; painted-c	18	36	54	128	284	440
489-Tweety and Sylvester	9	18	27	59	117	175
490-Jungle Jim (#1)	9	18	27	60	120	180
491-Silvertip (#1) (Max Brand)-Kinstler-a (8/53)	8	16	24	56	108	160
492-Duck Album (Disney)	7	14	21	46	86	125
493-Johnny Mack Brown; photo-c	6	12	18	40	73	105
494-The Little King (#1)	9	18	27	61	123	185
495-Uncle Scrooge (#3) (Disney)-by Carl Barks (9/53)	60	120	180	480	1240	2000
496-The Green Hornet; painted-c	28	56	84	202	451	700
497-Zorro (Sword of...)-Kinstler-a	12	24	36	82	179	275
498-Bugs Bunny's Album (9/53)	6	12	18	41	76	110
499-M.G.M.'s Spike and Tyke (#1) (9/53)	8	16	24	55	105	155
500-Buck Jones	6	12	18	42	79	115
501-Francis the Famous Talking Mule	5	10	15	35	63	90
502-Rootie Kazootie (TV)	6	12	18	41	76	110
503-Uncle Wiggily (10/53)	5	10	15	34	63	90
504-Krazy Kat; not by Herriman	6	12	18	42	79	115
505-The Sword and the Rose (Disney) (10/53)(Movie)-Photo-c	9	18	27	58	114	170
506-The Little Scouts	5	10	15	30	50	70
507-Oswald the Rabbit (Lantz)	5	10	15	35	63	90
508-Bozo (10/53)	9	18	27	61	123	185
509-Pluto (Disney) (10/53)	8	16	24	52	99	145
510-Son of Black Beauty	5	10	15	31	53	75
511-Outlaw Trail (Zane Grey)-Kinstler-a	5	10	15	35	63	90
512-Flash Gordon (11/53)	10	20	30	67	141	215
513-Ben Bowie and His Mountain Men	5	10	15	34	60	85
514-Frosty the Snowman (11/53)	7	14	21	48	89	130
515-Andy Hardy	5	10	15	30	50	70
516-Double Trouble With Goober	4	8	12	27	44	60
517-Chip 'N' Dale (#1) (Disney)	12	24	36	79	170	260
518-Rivets (11/53)	5	10	15	34	60	85
519-Steve Canyon (#1)-Not by Milton Caniff	9	18	27	59	117	175
520-Wild Bill Elliott-Photo-c	5	10	15	35	63	90
521-Beetle Bailey (12/53)	7	14	21	49	92	135
522-The Brownies	5	10	15	35	63	90
523-Rin Tin Tin (TV)-Photo-c (12/53)	9	18	27	62	126	190
524-Tweety and Sylvester	9	18	27	59	117	175
525-Santa Claus Funnies	8	16	24	51	96	140
526-Napoleon	6	12	18	42	79	115
527-Charlie McCarthy	7	14	21	44	82	120
528-Queen of the West Dale Evans; photo-c	9	18	27	62	126	190
529-Little Beaver	5	10	15	35	63	90
530-Bob Clampett's Beany and Cecil (TV) (1/54)	14	28	42	96	211	325
531-Duck Album (Disney)	7	14	21	46	86	125
532-The Rustlers (Zane Grey) (2-4/54)	5	10	15	33	57	80
533-Raggedy Ann and Andy	7	14	21	46	86	125
534-Western Marshal (Ernest Haycox's)-Kinstler-a	7	14	21	44	82	120
535-I Love Lucy (#1) (TV) (2/54)-Photo-c	48	96	144	374	862	1350
536-Daffy (3/54)	8	16	24	52	99	145
537-Stormy, the Thoroughbred... (Disney-Movie) on top 2/3 of each page; Pluto story on bottom 1/3 of each page (2/54)	6	12	18	40	73	105
538-The Mask of Zorro; Kinstler-a	12	24	36	82	179	275
539-Ben and Me (Disney) (3/54)	5	10	15	33	57	80
540-Knights of the Round Table (3/54) (Movie)-Photo-c	6	12	18	41	76	110
541-Johnny Mack Brown; photo-c	6	12	18	40	73	105
542-Super Circus Featuring Mary Hartline (TV) (3/54)	8	16	24	56	108	160
543-Uncle Wiggily (3/54)	5	10	15	34	63	90
544-Rob Roy (Disney-Movie)-Manning-a; photo-c	9	18	27	57	111	165
545-The Wonderful Adventures of Pinocchio-Partial reprint of Four Color #92 (Disney-Movie)	9	18	27	61	123	185
546-Buck Jones	6	12	18	42	79	115
547-Francis the Famous Talking Mule	5	10	15	35	63	90
548-Krazy Kat; not by Herriman (4/54)	5	10	15	31	53	75
549-Oswald the Rabbit (Lantz)	5	10	15	35	63	90
550-The Little Scouts	5	10	15	30	50	70
551-Bozo (4/54)	9	18	27	61	123	185
552-Beetle Bailey	7	14	21	49	92	135
553-Susie Q. Smith	5	10	15	35	63	90
554-Rusty Riley (Frank Godwin strip-r)	5	10	15	33	57	80
555-Range War (Zane Grey)	5	10	15	33	57	80
556-Double Trouble With Goober (5/54)	4	8	12	27	44	60
557-Ben Bowie and His Mountain Men	5	10	15	34	60	85
558-Elmer Fudd (5/54)	6	12	18	38	69	100
559-I Love Lucy (#2) (TV)-Photo-c	30	60	90	216	483	750
560-Duck Album (Disney) (5/54)	7	14	21	46	86	125
561-Mr. Magoo (5/54)	9	18	27	60	120	180
562-Goofy (Disney)(#2)	7	14	21	46	86	125
563-Rhubarb, the Millionaire Cat (6/54)	6	12	18	38	69	100
564-Li'l Bad Wolf (Disney)(#3)	6	12	18	41	76	110
565-Jungle Jim	5	10	15	34	60	85
566-Son of Black Beauty	5	10	15	31	53	75
567-Prince Valiant (#1)-By Bob Fuje (Movie)-Photo-c	10	20	30	69	147	225
568-Gypsy Colt (Movie) (6/54)	6	12	18	42	79	115
569-Priscilla's Pop	6	12	18	42	79	115
570-Bob Clampett's Beany and Cecil (TV)	14	28	42	96	211	325
571-Charlie McCarthy	7	14	21	44	82	120
572-Silvertip (Max Brand) (7/54); Kinstler-a	5	10	15	34	60	85
573-The Little People by Walt Scott	6	12	18	37	66	95
574-The Hand of Zorro; Kinstler-a	12	24	36	82	179	275
575-Annie Oakley and Tagg (TV)-Photo-c	9	18	27	59	117	175
576-Angel (#1) (8/54)	5	10	15	34	60	85
577-M.G.M.'s Spike and Tyke	6	12	18	38	69	100
578-Steve Canyon (8/54)	5	10	15	35	63	90
579-Francis the Famous Talking Mule	5	10	15	35	63	90
580-Six Gun Ranch (Luke Short-8/54)	5	10	15	34	60	85
581-Chip 'N' Dale (#2) (Disney)	6	12	18	42	79	115
582-Mowgli Jungle Book (Kipling) (8/54)	5	10	15	34	60	85
583-The Lost Wagon Train (Zane Grey)	5	10	15	33	57	80
584-Johnny Mack Brown-Photo-c	6	12	18	40	73	105
585-Bugs Bunny's Album	6	12	18	41	76	110

Four Color Comics #516 © KFS

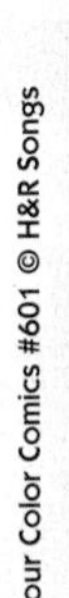

Four Color Comics #601 © H&R Songs

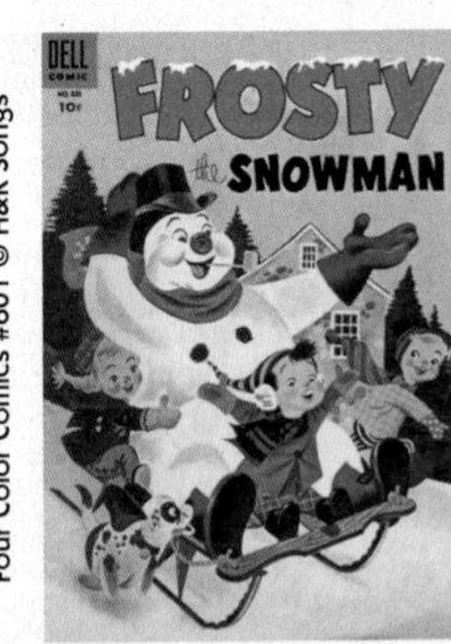

Four Color Comics #702 © DIS

	GD 2.0	VG 4.0	FN 6.0	VF 8.0	VF/NM 9.0	NM- 9.2
586-Duck Album (Disney)	7	14	21	46	86	125
587-The Little Scouts	5	10	15	30	50	70
588-King Richard and the Crusaders (Movie) (10/54) Matt Baker-a; photo-c	10	20	30	66	138	210
589-Buck Jones	6	12	18	42	79	115
590-Hansel and Gretel; partial photo-c	7	14	21	49	92	135
591-Western Marshal (Ernest Haycox's)-Kinstler-a	5	10	15	35	63	90
592-Super Circus (TV)	6	12	18	41	76	110
593-Oswald the Rabbit (Lantz)	5	10	15	35	63	90
594-Bozo (10/54)	9	18	27	61	123	185
595-Pluto (Disney)	7	14	21	46	86	125
596-Turok, Son of Stone (#1)	96	192	288	768	1734	2700
597-The Little King	6	12	18	38	69	100
598-Captain Davy Jones	6	12	18	38	69	100
599-Ben Bowie and His Mountain Men	5	10	15	34	60	85
600-Daisy Duck's Diary (#1) (Disney) (11/54)	8	16	24	55	105	155
601-Frosty the Snowman	7	14	21	48	89	130
602-Mr. Magoo and Gerald McBoing-Boing	9	18	27	60	120	180
603-M.G.M.'s The Two Mouseketeers	6	12	18	41	76	110
604-Shadow on the Trail (Zane Grey)	5	10	15	33	57	80
605-The Brownies-not by Kelly (12/54)	5	10	15	35	63	90
606-Sir Lancelot (not TV)	7	14	21	46	86	125
607-Santa Claus Funnies	8	16	24	51	96	140
608-Silvertip- "Valley of Vanishing Men" (Max Brand)-Kinstler-a	5	10	15	34	60	85
609-The Littlest Outlaw (Disney-Movie) (1/55)-Photo-c	7	14	21	44	82	120
610-Drum Beat (Movie); Alan Ladd photo-c	8	16	24	55	105	155
611-Duck Album (Disney)	7	14	21	46	86	125
612-Little Beaver (1/55)	5	10	15	34	60	85
613-Western Marshal (Ernest Haycox's) (2/55)-Kinstler-a	5	10	15	35	63	90
614-20,000 Leagues Under the Sea (Disney) (Movie) (2/55)-Painted-c	10	20	30	64	132	200
615-Daffy	8	16	24	52	99	145
616-To the Last Man (Zane Grey)	5	10	15	33	57	80
617-The Quest of Zorro	12	24	36	82	179	275
618-Johnny Mack Brown; photo-c	6	12	18	40	73	105
619-Krazy Kat; not by Herriman	5	10	15	31	53	75
620-Mowgli Jungle Book (Kipling)	5	10	15	34	60	85
621-Francis the Famous Talking Mule (4/55)	5	10	15	33	57	80
622-Beetle Bailey	7	14	21	49	92	135
623-Oswald the Rabbit (Lantz)	5	10	15	33	57	80
624-Treasure Island(Disney-Movie)(4/55)-Photo-c	9	18	27	59	117	175
625-Beaver Valley (Disney-Movie)	6	12	18	37	66	95
626-Ben Bowie and His Mountain Men	5	10	15	34	60	85
627-Goofy (Disney) (5/55)	7	14	21	46	86	125
628-Elmer Fudd	6	12	18	38	69	100
629-Lady and the Tramp with Jock (Disney)	9	18	27	62	126	190
630-Priscilla's Pop	6	12	18	42	79	115
631-Davy Crockett, Indian Fighter (#1) (Disney) (5/55) (TV)-Fess Parker photo-c	15	30	45	103	227	350
632-Fighting Caravans (Zane Grey)	5	10	15	33	57	80
633-The Little People by Walt Scott (6/55)	6	12	18	37	66	95
634-Lady and the Tramp Album (Disney) (6/55)	7	14	21	48	89	130
635-Bob Clampett's Beany and Cecil (TV)	14	28	42	96	211	325
636-Chip 'N' Dale (Disney)	6	12	18	42	79	115
637-Silvertip (Max Brand)-Kinstler-a	5	10	15	34	60	85
638-M.G.M.'s Spike and Tyke (8/55)	6	12	18	38	69	100
639-Davy Crockett at the Alamo (Disney) (7/55) (TV)-Fess Parker photo-c	12	24	36	82	179	275
640-Western Marshal (Ernest Haycox's)-Kinstler-a	5	10	15	35	63	90
641-Steve Canyon (1955)-by Caniff	5	10	15	35	63	90
642-M.G.M.'s The Two Mouseketeers	6	12	18	41	76	110
643-Wild Bill Elliott; photo-c	5	10	15	33	57	80
644-Sir Walter Raleigh (5/55)-Based on movie "The Virgin Queen"; photo-c	6	12	18	42	79	115
645-Johnny Mack Brown; photo-c	6	12	18	40	73	105
646-Dotty Dripple and Taffy (#1)	6	12	18	37	66	95
647-Bugs Bunny's Album (9/55)	6	12	18	41	76	110
648-Jace Pearson of the Texas Rangers (TV)-Photo-c	6	12	18	40	73	105
649-Duck Album (Disney)	7	14	21	46	86	125
650-Prince Valiant; by Bob Fuje	8	16	24	55	105	155
651-King Colt (Luke Short) (9/55)-Kinstler-a	5	10	15	34	60	85

	GD 2.0	VG 4.0	FN 6.0	VF 8.0	VF/NM 9.0	NM- 9.2
652-Buck Jones	5	10	15	35	63	90
653-Smokey the Bear (#1) (10/55)	10	20	30	67	141	215
654-Pluto (Disney)	7	14	21	46	86	125
655-Francis the Famous Talking Mule	5	10	15	33	57	80
656-Turok, Son of Stone (#2) (10/55)	42	84	126	311	706	1100
657-Ben Bowie and His Mountain Men	5	10	15	34	60	85
658-Goofy (Disney)	7	14	21	46	86	125
659-Daisy Duck's Diary (Disney)(#2)	6	12	18	40	73	105
660-Little Beaver	5	10	15	34	60	85
661-Frosty the Snowman	7	14	21	48	89	130
662-Zoo Parade (TV)-Marlin Perkins (11/55)	6	12	18	38	69	100
663-Winky Dink (TV)	9	18	27	60	120	180
664-Davy Crockett in the Great Keelboat Race (TV) (Disney) (11/55)-Fess Parker photo-c	11	22	33	75	160	245
665-The African Lion (Disney-Movie) (11/55)	5	10	15	35	63	90
666-Santa Claus Funnies	8	16	24	51	96	140
667-Silvertip and the Stolen Stallion (Max Brand) (12/55)-Kinstler-a	5	10	15	34	60	85
668-Dumbo (Disney) (12/55)-First of two printings. Dumbo on cover with starry sky. Reprints 4-Color #234?; same-c as #234	11	22	33	73	157	240
668-Dumbo (Disney) (1/58)-Second printing. Same cover altered, with Timothy Mouse added. Same contents as above	7	14	21	48	89	130
669-Robin Hood (Disney-Movie) (12/55)-Reprints #413 plus-c; photo-c	6	12	18	38	69	100
670-M.G.M's Mouse Musketeers (#1) (1/56)-Formerly the Two Mouseketeers	6	12	18	41	76	110
671-Davy Crockett and the River Pirates (TV) (Disney) (12/55)-Jesse Marsh-a; Fess Parker photo-c	11	22	33	75	160	245
672-Quentin Durward (1/56) (Movie)-Photo-c	6	12	18	42	79	115
673-Buffalo Bill, Jr. (#1) (TV)-James Arness photo-c	9	18	27	62	126	190
674-The Little Rascals (#1) (TV)	10	20	30	67	141	215
675-Steve Donovan, Western Marshal (#1) (TV)-Kinstler-a; photo-c	8	16	24	51	96	140
676-Will-Yum!	5	10	15	30	50	70
677-Little King	6	12	18	38	69	100
678-The Last Hunt (Movie)-Photo-c	6	12	18	42	79	115
679-Gunsmoke (#1) (TV)-Photo-c	20	40	60	136	303	470
680-Out Our Way with the Worry Wart (2/56)	5	10	15	35	63	90
681-Forever Darling (Movie) with Lucille Ball & Desi Arnaz (2/56)-; photo-c	11	22	33	77	166	255
682-The Sword & the Rose (Disney-Movie)-Reprint of #505; Renamed When Knighthood Was in Flower for the novel; photo-c	6	12	18	42	79	115
683-Hi and Lois (3/56)	6	12	18	38	69	100
684-Helen of Troy (Movie)-Buscema-a; photo-c	10	20	30	66	138	210
685-Johnny Mack Brown; photo-c	6	12	18	40	73	105
686-Duck Album (Disney)	7	14	21	46	86	125
687-The Indian Fighter (Movie)-Kirk Douglas photo-c	8	16	24	54	102	150
688-Alexander the Great (Movie) (5/56)-Buscema-a; photo-c	7	14	21	46	86	125
689-Elmer Fudd (3/56)	6	12	18	38	69	100
690-The Conqueror (Movie) - John Wayne photo-c	15	30	45	103	227	350
691-Dotty Dripple and Taffy	4	8	12	28	47	65
692-The Little People-Walt Scott	5	10	15	34	60	85
693-Song of the South (Disney) (1956)-Partial reprint of #129	10	20	30	64	132	200
694-Super Circus (TV)-Photo-c	6	12	18	41	76	110
695-Little Beaver	5	10	15	34	60	85
696-Krazy Kat; not by Herriman (4/56)	5	10	15	31	53	75
697-Oswald the Rabbit (Lantz)	5	10	15	33	57	80
698-Francis the Famous Talking Mule (4/56)	5	10	15	33	57	80
699-Prince Valiant-by Bob Fuje	8	16	24	55	105	155
700-Water Birds and the Olympic Elk (Disney-Movie) (4/56)	5	10	15	33	57	80
701-Jiminy Cricket (#1) (Disney) (5/56)	9	18	27	57	111	165
702-The Goofy Success Story (Disney)	7	14	21	46	86	125
703-Scamp (#1) (Disney)	10	20	30	64	132	200
704-Priscilla's Pop (5/56)	6	12	18	42	79	115
705-Brave Eagle (#1) (TV)-Photo-c	7	14	21	46	86	125
706-Bongo and Lumpjaw (Disney) (6/56)	6	12	18	41	76	110
707-Corky and White Shadow (Disney) (5/56)-Mickey Mouse Club (TV); photo-c	7	14	21	46	86	125
708-Smokey the Bear	6	12	18	40	73	105
709-The Searchers (Movie) - John Wayne photo-c	27	54	81	194	435	675
710-Francis the Famous Talking Mule	5	10	15	33	57	80
711-M.G.M's Mouse Musketeers	5	10	15	31	53	75

	GD 2.0	VG 4.0	FN 6.0	VF 8.0	VF/NM 9.0	NM- 9.2
712-The Great Locomotive Chase (Disney-Movie) (9/56)-Photo-c	7	14	21	46	86	125
713-The Animal World (Movie) (8/56)	5	10	15	34	60	85
714-Spin and Marty (#1) (TV) (Disney)-Mickey Mouse Club (6/56); photo-c	11	22	33	75	160	245
715-Timmy (8/56)	6	12	18	41	76	110
716-Man in Space (Disney)(A science feature from Tomorrowland)	8	16	24	56	108	160
717-Moby Dick (Movie)-Gregory Peck photo-c	9	18	27	59	117	175
718-Dotty Dripple and Taffy	4	8	12	28	47	65
719-Prince Valiant; by Bob Fuje (8/56)	8	16	24	55	105	155
720-Gunsmoke (TV)-James Arness photo-c	9	18	27	63	129	195
721-Captain Kangaroo (TV)-Photo-c	13	26	39	91	201	310
722-Johnny Mack Brown-Photo-c	6	12	18	40	73	105
723-Santiago (Movie)-Kinstler-a (9/56); Alan Ladd photo-c	10	20	30	64	132	200
724-Bugs Bunny's Album	5	10	15	34	60	85
725-Elmer Fudd (9/56)	5	10	15	33	57	80
726-Duck Album (Disney) (9/56)	6	12	18	37	66	95
727-The Nature of Things (TV) (Disney)-Jesse Marsh-a	5	10	15	33	57	80
728-M.G.M's Mouse Musketeers	5	10	15	31	53	75
729-Bob Son of Battle (11/56)	5	10	15	30	50	70
730-Smokey Stover	5	10	15	34	60	85
731-Silvertip and The Fighting Four (Max Brand)-Kinstler-a	5	10	15	34	60	85
732-Zorro, the Challenge of (10/56)	12	24	36	82	179	275
733-Buck Jones	5	10	15	35	63	90
734-Cheyenne (#1) (TV) (10/56)-Clint Walker photo-c	13	26	39	89	195	300
735-Crusader Rabbit (#1) (TV)	23	46	69	161	356	550
736-Pluto (Disney)	7	14	21	46	86	125
737-Steve Canyon-Caniff-a	5	10	15	35	63	90
738-Westward Ho, the Wagons (Disney-Movie)-Fess Parker photo-c	8	16	24	54	102	150
739-Bounty Guns (Luke Short)-Drucker-a	5	10	15	30	50	70
740-Chilly Willy (#1) (Walter Lantz)	9	18	27	59	117	175
741-The Fastest Gun Alive (Movie)(9/56)-Photo-c	7	14	21	44	82	120
742-Buffalo Bill, Jr. (TV)-Photo-c	6	12	18	37	66	95
743-Daisy Duck's Diary (Disney) (11/56)	6	12	18	40	73	105
744-Little Beaver	5	10	15	34	60	85
745-Francis the Famous Talking Mule	5	10	15	33	57	80
746-Dotty Dripple and Taffy	4	8	12	28	47	65
747-Goofy (Disney)	7	14	21	46	86	125
748-Frosty the Snowman (11/56)	5	10	15	35	63	90
749-Secrets of Life (Disney-Movie)-Photo-c	5	10	15	31	53	75
750-The Great Cat Family (Disney-TV/Movie)-Pinocchio & Alice app.	6	12	18	42	79	115
751-Our Miss Brooks (TV)-Photo-c	9	18	27	59	117	175
752-Mandrake, the Magician	12	24	36	80	173	265
753-Walt Scott's Little People (11/56)	5	10	15	34	60	85
754-Smokey the Bear	6	12	18	40	73	105
755-The Littlest Snowman (12/56)	6	12	18	37	66	95
756-Santa Claus Funnies	8	16	24	51	96	140
757-The True Story of Jesse James (Movie)-Photo-c	9	18	27	58	114	170
758-Bear Country (Disney-Movie)	5	10	15	34	60	85
759-Circus Boy (TV)-The Monkees' Mickey Dolenz photo-c (12/56)	13	26	39	87	191	295
760-The Hardy Boys (#1) (TV) (Disney)-Mickey Mouse Club; photo-c	11	22	33	72	154	235
761-Howdy Doody (TV) (1/57)	9	18	27	61	123	185
762-The Sharkfighters (Movie) (1/57); Buscema-a; photo-c	9	18	27	59	117	175
763-Grandma Duck's Farm Friends (#1) (Disney)	8	16	24	51	96	140
764-M.G.M's Mouse Musketeers	5	10	15	31	53	75
765-Will-Yum!	5	10	15	30	50	70
766-Buffalo Bill, Jr. (TV)-Photo-c	6	12	18	37	66	95
767-Spin and Marty (TV) (Disney)-Mickey Mouse Club (2/57)	9	18	27	58	114	170
768-Steve Donovan, Western Marshal (TV)-Kinstler-a; photo-c	6	12	18	38	69	100
769-Gunsmoke (TV)-James Arness photo-c	9	18	27	63	129	195
770-Brave Eagle (TV)-Photo-c	5	10	15	33	57	80
771-Brand of Empire (Luke Short)(3/57)-Drucker-a	5	10	15	30	50	70
772-Cheyenne (TV)-Clint Walker photo-c	8	16	24	54	102	150
773-The Brave One (Movie)-Photo-c	5	10	15	35	63	90
774-Hi and Lois (3/57)	5	10	15	30	50	70
775-Sir Lancelot and Brian (TV)-Buscema-a; photo-c	9	18	27	59	117	175
776-Johnny Mack Brown; photo-c	6	12	18	40	73	105
777-Scamp (Disney) (3/57)	6	12	18	42	79	115
778-The Little Rascals (TV)	6	12	18	38	69	100
779-Lee Hunter, Indian Fighter (3/57)	6	12	18	40	73	105
780-Captain Kangaroo (TV)-Photo-c	12	24	36	79	170	260
781-Fury (#1) (TV) (3/57)-Photo-c	7	14	21	49	92	135
782-Duck Album (Disney)	6	12	18	37	66	95
783-Elmer Fudd	5	10	15	33	57	80
784-Around the World in 80 Days (Movie) (2/57)-Photo-c	7	14	21	46	86	125
785-Circus Boy (TV) (4/57)-The Monkees' Mickey Dolenz photo-c	10	20	30	64	132	200
786-Cinderella (Disney) (3/57)-Partial-r of #272	8	16	24	54	102	150
787-Little Hiawatha (Disney) (4/57)(#2)	6	12	18	38	69	100
788-Prince Valiant; by Bob Fuje	7	14	21	44	82	120
789-Silvertip-Valley Thieves (Max Brand) (4/57)-Kinstler-a	5	10	15	34	60	85
790-The Wings of Eagles (Movie) (John Wayne)-Toth-a; John Wayne photo-c; 10¢ & 15¢ editions exist	13	26	39	89	195	300

	GD 2.0	VG 4.0	FN 6.0	VF 8.0	VF/NM 9.0	NM- 9.2
791-The 77th Bengal Lancers (TV)-Photo-c	7	14	21	44	82	120
792-Oswald the Rabbit (Lantz)	5	10	15	33	57	80
793-Morty Meekle	5	10	15	30	50	70
794-The Count of Monte Cristo (5/57) (Movie)-Buscema-a	8	16	24	51	96	140
795-Jiminy Cricket (Disney)(#2)	7	14	21	44	82	120
796-Ludwig Bemelman's Madeleine and Genevieve	5	10	15	35	63	90
797-Gunsmoke (TV)-Photo-c	9	18	27	63	129	195
798-Buffalo Bill, Jr. (TV)-Photo-c	6	12	18	37	66	95
799-Priscilla's Pop	6	12	18	42	79	115
800-The Buccaneers (TV)-Photo-c	6	12	18	42	79	115
801-Dotty Dripple and Taffy	4	8	12	28	47	65
802-Goofy (Disney) (5/57)	7	14	21	46	86	125
803-Cheyenne (TV)-Clint Walker photo-c	8	16	24	54	102	150
804-Steve Canyon-Caniff-a (1957)	5	10	15	35	63	90
805-Crusader Rabbit (TV)	17	34	51	119	265	410
806-Scamp (Disney) (6/57)	6	12	18	42	79	115
807-Savage Range (Luke Short)-Drucker-a	5	10	15	30	50	70
808-Spin and Marty (TV)(Disney)-Mickey Mouse Club; photo-c	9	18	27	58	114	170
809-The Little People (Walt Scott)	5	10	15	34	60	85
810-Francis the Famous Talking Mule	5	10	15	31	53	75
811-Howdy Doody (TV) (7/57)	9	18	27	61	123	185
812-The Big Land (Movie); Alan Ladd photo-c	8	16	24	52	99	145
813-Circus Boy (TV)-The Monkees' Mickey Dolenz photo-c	10	20	30	64	132	200
814-Covered Wagons, Ho! (Disney)-Donald Duck (TV) (6/57); Mickey Mouse app.	7	14	21	46	86	125
815-Dragoon Wells Massacre (Movie)-photo-c	8	16	24	51	96	140
816-Brave Eagle (TV)-photo-c	5	10	15	33	57	80
817-Little Beaver	5	10	15	34	60	85
818-Smokey the Bear (6/57)	6	12	18	40	73	105
819-Mickey Mouse in Magicland (Disney) (7/57)	7	14	21	49	92	135
820-The Oklahoman (Movie)-Photo-c	9	18	27	60	120	180
821-Wringle Wrangle (Disney)-Based on movie "Westward Ho, the Wagons"; Marsh-a; Fess Parker photo-c	7	14	21	46	86	125
822-Paul Revere's Ride with Johnny Tremain (TV) (Disney)-Toth-a	9	18	27	57	111	165
823-Timmy	5	10	15	34	60	85
824-The Pride and the Passion (Movie) (8/57)-Frank Sinatra & Cary Grant photo-c	10	20	30	66	138	210
825-The Little Rascals (TV)	6	12	18	38	69	100
826-Spin and Marty and Annette (TV) (Disney)-Mickey Mouse Club; Annette Funicello photo-c	18	36	54	126	281	435
827-Smokey Stover (8/57)	5	10	15	34	60	85
828-Buffalo Bill, Jr. (TV)-Photo-c	6	12	18	37	66	95
829-Tales of the Pony Express (TV) (8/57)-Painted-c	6	12	18	42	79	115
830-The Hardy Boys (TV) (Disney)-Mickey Mouse Club (8/57); photo-c	9	18	27	60	120	180
831-No Sleep 'Til Dawn (Movie)-Karl Malden photo-c	8	16	24	51	96	140
832-Lolly and Pepper (#1)	6	12	18	42	79	115
833-Scamp (Disney) (9/57)	6	12	18	42	79	115
834-Johnny Mack Brown; photo-c	6	12	18	40	73	105
835-Silvertip-The False Rider (Max Brand)	5	10	15	34	60	85
836-Man in Flight (Disney) (TV) (9/57)	7	14	21	44	82	120
837-Cotton Woods, (All-American Athlete...)	5	10	15	30	50	70
838-Bugs Bunny's Life Story Album (9/57)	5	10	15	34	60	85
839-The Vigilantes (Movie)	8	16	24	54	102	150
840-Duck Album (Disney) (9/57)	6	12	18	37	66	95
841-Elmer Fudd	5	10	15	33	57	80
842-The Nature of Things (Disney-Movie) ('57)-Jesse Marsh-a (TV series)	5	10	15	33	57	80
843-The First Americans (Disney) (TV)-Marsh-a	8	16	24	54	102	150
844-Gunsmoke (TV)-Photo-c	9	18	27	63	129	195
845-The Land Unknown (Movie)-Alex Toth-a	11	22	33	76	163	250
846-Gun Glory (Movie)-by Alex Toth; photo-c	8	16	24	51	96	140
847-Perri (squirrels) (Disney-Movie)-Two different covers published	6	12	18	38	69	100
848-Marauder's Moon (Luke Short)	5	10	15	30	50	70
849-Prince Valiant; by Bob Fuje	7	14	21	44	82	120
850-Buck Jones	5	10	15	35	63	90
851-The Story of Mankind (Movie) (1/58)-Hedy Lamarr & Vincent Price photo-c	8	16	24	51	96	140
852-Chilly Willy (2/58) (Lantz)	6	12	18	37	66	95
853-Pluto (Disney) (10/57)	7	14	21	46	86	125
854-The Hunchback of Notre Dame (Movie)-Photo-c	12	24	36	79	170	260
855-Broken Arrow (TV)-Photo-c	7	14	21	44	82	120
856-Buffalo Bill, Jr. (TV)-Photo-c	6	12	18	37	66	95
857-The Goofy Adventure Story (Disney) (11/57)	7	14	21	46	86	125
858-Daisy Duck's Diary (Disney) (11/57)	5	10	15	35	63	90
859-Topper and Neil (TV) (11/57)	7	14	21	44	82	120
860-Wyatt Earp (#1) (TV)-Manning-a; photo-c	11	22	33	72	154	235
861-Frosty the Snowman	5	10	15	35	63	90
862-The Truth About Mother Goose (Disney-Movie) (11/57)	7	14	21	48	89	130
863-Francis the Famous Talking Mule	5	10	15	31	53	75
864-The Littlest Snowman	6	12	18	37	66	95
865-Andy Burnett (TV) (Disney) (12/57)-Photo-c	9	18	27	57	111	165
866-Mars and Beyond (Disney-TV)(A science feature from Tomorrowland)	9	18	27	59	117	175
867-Santa Claus Funnies	8	16	24	51	96	140
868-The Little People (12/57)	5	10	15	34	60	85
869-Old Yeller (Disney-Movie)-Photo-c	6	12	18	42	73	115
870-Little Beaver (1/58)	5	10	15	34	60	85
871-Curly Kayoe	5	10	15	33	57	80
872-Captain Kangaroo (TV)-Photo-c	12	24	36	79	170	260
873-Grandma Duck's Farm Friends (Disney)	6	12	18	37	66	95

Four Color Comics #778 © Hal Roach

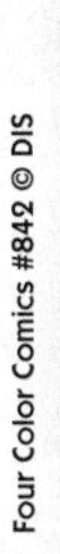

Four Color Comics #842 © DIS

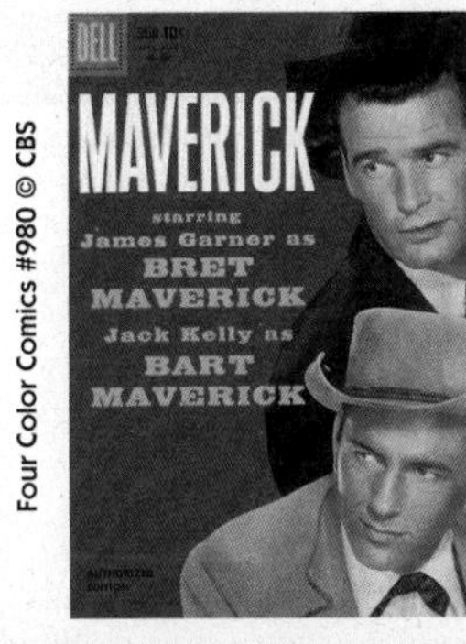

Four Color Comics #980 © CBS

	GD 2.0	VG 4.0	FN 6.0	VF 8.0	VF/NM 9.0	NM- 9.2
874-Old Ironsides (Disney-Movie with Johnny Tremain) (1/58)	8	16	24	51	96	140
875-Trumpets West (Luke Short) (2/58)	5	10	15	30	50	70
876-Tales of Wells Fargo (#1)(TV)(2/58)-Photo-c	9	18	27	59	117	175
877-Frontier Doctor with Rex Allen (TV)-Alex Toth-a; Rex Allen photo-c	9	18	27	59	117	175
878-Peanuts (#1)-Schulz-c only (2/58)	155	310	465	1279	2890	4500
879-Brave Eagle (TV) (2/58)-Photo-c	5	10	15	33	57	80
880-Steve Donovan, Western Marshal-Drucker-a (TV)-Photo-c	5	10	15	31	53	75
881-The Captain and the Kids (2/58)	5	10	15	30	50	70
882-Zorro (Disney)-1st Disney issue; by Alex Toth (TV) (2/58); photo-c	14	28	42	96	211	325
883-The Little Rascals (TV)	5	10	15	35	63	90
884-Hawkeye and the Last of the Mohicans (TV) (3/58); photo-c	7	14	21	44	82	120
885-Fury (TV) (3/58)-Photo-c	5	10	15	35	63	90
886-Bongo and Lumpjaw (Disney) (3/58)	5	10	15	31	53	75
887-The Hardy Boys (Disney) (TV)-Mickey Mouse Club (1/58)-Photo-c	9	18	27	60	120	180
888-Elmer Fudd (3/58)	5	10	15	33	57	80
889-Clint and Mac (Disney) (TV) (3/58)-Alex Toth-a; photo-c	10	20	30	67	141	215
890-Wyatt Earp (TV)-by Russ Manning; photo-c	8	16	24	52	99	145
891-Light in the Forest (Disney-Movie) (3/58)-Fess Parker photo-c	6	12	18	42	79	115
892-Maverick (#1) (TV) (4/58)-James Garner photo-c	20	40	60	144	317	490
893-Jim Bowie (TV)-Photo-c	7	14	21	44	82	120
894-Oswald the Rabbit (Lantz)	5	10	15	33	57	80
895-Wagon Train (#1) (TV) (3/58)-Photo-c	10	20	30	64	132	200
896-The Adventures of Tinker Bell (Disney)	12	24	36	82	179	275
897-Jiminy Cricket (Disney)	7	14	21	44	82	120
898-Silvertip (Max Brand)-Kinstler-a (5/58)	5	10	15	34	60	85
899-Goofy (Disney) (5/58)	5	10	15	35	63	90
900-Prince Valiant; by Bob Fuje	7	14	21	44	82	120
901-Little Hiawatha (Disney)	6	12	18	38	69	100
902-Will-Yum!	5	10	15	30	50	70
903-Dotty Dripple and Taffy	4	8	12	28	47	65
904-Lee Hunter, Indian Fighter	5	10	15	30	50	70
905-Annette (Disney) (TV) (5/58)-Mickey Mouse Club; Annette Funicello photo-c	24	48	72	168	372	575
906-Francis the Famous Talking Mule	5	10	15	31	53	75
907-Sugarfoot (#1) (TV)Toth-a; photo-c	11	22	33	73	157	240
908-The Little People and the Giant-Walt Scott (5/58)	5	10	15	34	60	85
909-Smitty	4	8	12	25	40	55
910-The Vikings (Movie)-Buscema-a; Kirk Douglas photo-c	9	18	27	59	117	175
911-The Gray Ghost (TV)-Photo-c	8	16	24	55	105	155
912-Leave It to Beaver (#1) (TV)-Photo-c	16	32	48	111	246	380
913-The Left-Handed Gun (Movie) (7/58); Paul Newman photo-c	9	18	27	62	126	190
914-No Time for Sergeants (Movie)-Andy Griffith photo-c; Toth-a	10	20	30	66	138	210
915-Casey Jones (TV)-Alan Hale photo-c	6	12	18	40	73	105
916-Red Ryder Ranch Comics (7/58)	4	8	12	28	47	65
917-The Life of Riley (TV)-Photo-c	11	22	33	73	157	240
918-Beep Beep, the Roadrunner (#1) (7/58)-Published with two different back covers	14	28	42	96	211	325
919-Boots and Saddles (#1) (TV)-Photo-c	7	14	21	48	89	130
920-Zorro (Disney) (TV) (6/58)Toth-a; photo-c	10	20	30	66	138	210
921-Wyatt Earp (TV)-Manning-a; photo-c	8	16	24	52	99	145
922-Johnny Mack Brown by Russ Manning; photo-c	7	14	21	44	82	120
923-Timmy	5	10	15	34	60	85
924-Colt .45 (#1) (TV) (8/58)-W. Preston photo-c	9	18	27	62	126	190
925-Last of the Fast Guns (Movie) (8/58)-Photo-c	6	12	18	41	76	110
926-Peter Pan (Disney)-Reprint of #442	6	12	18	40	73	105
927-Top Gun (Luke Short) Buscema-a	5	10	15	30	50	70
928-Sea Hunt (#1) (9/58) (TV)-Lloyd Bridges photo-c	12	24	36	80	173	265
929-Brave Eagle (TV)-Photo-c	5	10	15	33	57	80
930-Maverick (TV) (7/58)-James Garner photo-c	11	22	33	73	157	240
931-Have Gun, Will Travel (#1) (TV)-Photo-c	13	26	39	89	195	300
932-Smokey the Bear (His Life Story)	6	12	18	40	73	105
933-Zorro (Disney, 9/58) (TV)-Alex Toth-a; photo-c	10	20	30	66	138	210

	GD 2.0	VG 4.0	FN 6.0	VF 8.0	VF/NM 9.0	NM- 9.2
934-Restless Gun (#1) (TV)-Photo-c	10	20	30	64	132	200
935-King of the Royal Mounted	5	10	15	31	53	75
936-The Little Rascals (TV)	5	10	15	35	63	90
937-Ruff and Reddy (#1) (9/58) (TV) (1st Hanna-Barbera comic book)	12	24	36	79	170	260
938-Elmer Fudd (9/58)	5	10	15	33	57	80
939-Steve Canyon - not by Caniff	5	10	15	35	63	90
940-Lolly and Pepper (10/58)	5	10	15	30	50	70
941-Pluto (Disney) (10/58)	5	10	15	35	63	90
942-Pony Express (Tales of the ...) (TV)	5	10	15	34	60	85
943-White Wilderness (Disney-Movie) (10/58)	6	12	18	37	66	95
944-The 7th Voyage of Sinbad (Movie) (9/58)-Buscema-a; photo-c	12	24	36	81	176	270
945-Maverick (TV)-James Garner/Jack Kelly photo-c	11	22	33	73	157	240
946-The Big Country (Movie)-Photo-c	6	12	18	42	79	115
947-Broken Arrow (TV)-Photo-c (11/58)	5	10	15	33	57	80
948-Daisy Duck's Diary (Disney) (11/58)	5	10	15	35	63	90
949-High Adventure(Lowell Thomas')(TV)-Photo-c	6	12	18	40	73	105
950-Frosty the Snowman	5	10	15	35	63	90
951-The Lennon Sisters Life Story (TV)-Toth-a, 32 pgs.; photo-c	11	22	33	76	163	250
952-Goofy (Disney) (11/58)	5	10	15	35	63	90
953-Francis the Famous Talking Mule	5	10	15	31	53	75
954-Man in Space-Satellites (TV)	7	14	21	48	89	130
955-Hi and Lois (11/58)	5	10	15	30	50	70
956-Ricky Nelson (#1) (TV)-Photo-c	17	34	51	114	252	390
957-Buffalo Bee (#1) (TV)	9	18	27	59	117	175
958-Santa Claus Funnies	6	12	18	41	76	110
959-Christmas Stories-(Walt Scott's Little People) (1951-56 strip reprints)	5	10	15	34	60	85
960-Zorro (Disney) (TV) (12/58)-Toth art; photo-c	10	20	30	66	138	210
961-Jace Pearson's Tales of the Texas Rangers (TV)-Spiegle-a; photo-c	5	10	15	34	60	85
962-Maverick (TV) (1/59)-James Garner/Jack Kelly photo-c	11	22	33	73	157	240
963-Johnny Mack Brown; photo-c	6	12	18	40	73	105
964-The Hardy Boys (TV) (Disney) (1/59)-Mickey Mouse Club; photo-c	9	18	27	60	120	180
965-Grandma Duck's Farm Friends (Disney)(1/59)	5	10	15	34	60	85
966-Tonka (starring Sal Mineo; Disney-Movie)-Photo-c	8	16	24	56	108	160
967-Chilly Willy (2/59) (Lantz)	6	12	18	37	66	95
968-Tales of Wells Fargo (TV)-Photo-c	8	16	24	54	102	150
969-Peanuts (2/59)	36	72	108	259	580	900
970-Lawman (#1) (TV)-Photo-c	11	22	33	75	160	245
971-Wagon Train (TV)-Photo-c	6	12	18	41	76	110
972-Tom Thumb (Movie)-George Pal (1/59)	8	16	24	52	99	145
973-Sleeping Beauty and the Prince(Disney)(5/59)	12	24	36	82	179	275
974-The Little Rascals (TV) (3/59)	5	10	15	35	63	90
975-Fury (TV)-Photo-c	5	10	15	35	63	90
976-Zorro (Disney) (TV)-Toth-a; photo-c	10	20	30	66	138	210
977-Elmer Fudd (3/59)	5	10	15	33	57	80
978-Lolly and Pepper	5	10	15	30	50	70
979-Oswald the Rabbit (Lantz)	5	10	15	33	57	80
980-Maverick (TV) (4-6/59)-James Garner/Jack Kelly photo-c	11	22	33	73	157	240
981-Ruff and Reddy (TV) (Hanna-Barbera)	8	16	24	52	99	145
982-The New Adventures of Tinker Bell (TV) (Disney)	10	20	30	66	138	210
983-Have Gun, Will Travel (TV) (4-6/59)-Photo-c	9	18	27	62	126	190
984-Sleeping Beauty's Fairy Godmothers (Disney)	10	20	30	67	141	215
985-Shaggy Dog (Disney-Movie)-Photo-all four covers; Annette on back-c(5/59)	8	16	24	54	102	150
986-Restless Gun (TV)-Photo-c	7	14	21	49	92	135
987-Goofy (Disney) (7/59)	5	10	15	35	63	90
988-Little Hiawatha (Disney)	6	12	18	38	69	100
989-Jiminy Cricket (Disney) (5-7/59)	7	14	21	44	82	120
990-Huckleberry Hound (#1)(TV)(Hanna-Barbera); 1st app. Huck, Yogi Bear, & Pixie & Dixie & Mr. Jinks	18	36	54	128	284	440
991-Francis the Famous Talking Mule	5	10	15	31	53	75
992-Sugarfoot (TV)-Toth-a; photo-c	10	20	30	66	138	210
993-Jim Bowie (TV)-Photo-c	5	10	15	35	63	90
994-Sea Hunt (TV)-Lloyd Bridges photo-c	9	18	27	57	111	165
995-Donald Duck Album (Disney) (5-7/59)(#1)	7	14	21	44	82	120
996-Nevada (Zane Grey)	5	10	15	33	57	80

	GD 2.0	VG 4.0	FN 6.0	VF 8.0	VF/NM 9.0	NM- 9.2
997-Walt Disney Presents-Tales of Texas John Slaughter (#1) (TV) (Disney)-Photo-c; photo of W. Disney inside-c	7	14	21	46	86	125
998-Ricky Nelson (TV)-Photo-c	17	34	51	114	252	390
999-Leave It to Beaver (TV)-Photo-c	13	26	39	89	195	300
1000-The Gray Ghost (TV) (6-8/59)-Photo-c	8	16	24	55	105	155
1001-Lowell Thomas' High Adventure (TV) (8-10/59)-Photo-c	5	10	15	34	60	85
1002-Buffalo Bee (TV)	6	12	18	42	79	115
1003-Zorro (TV) (Disney)-Toth-a; photo-c	10	20	30	66	138	210
1004-Colt .45 (TV) (6-8/59)-Photo-c	7	14	21	48	89	130
1005-Maverick (TV)-James Garner/Jack Kelly photo-c	11	22	33	73	157	240
1006-Hercules (Movie)-Buscema-a; photo-c	10	20	30	69	147	225
1007-John Paul Jones (Movie)-Robert Stack photo-c	6	12	18	40	73	105
1008-Beep Beep, the Road Runner (7-9/59)	8	16	24	54	102	150
1009-The Rifleman (#1) (TV)-Photo-c	23	46	69	161	358	550
1010-Grandma Duck's Farm Friends (Disney)-by Carl Barks	11	22	33	73	157	240
1011-Buckskin (#1) (TV)-Photo-c	7	14	21	44	82	120
1012-Last Train from Gun Hill (Movie) (7/59)-Photo-c	8	16	24	52	99	145
1013-Bat Masterson (#1) (TV) (8/59)-Gene Barry photo-c	11	22	33	72	154	235
1014-The Lennon Sisters (TV)-Toth-a; photo-c	11	22	33	72	154	235
1015-Peanuts-Schulz-c	36	72	108	259	580	900
1016-Smokey the Bear Nature Stories	5	10	15	31	53	75
1017-Chilly Willy (Lantz)	6	12	18	37	66	95
1018-Rio Bravo (Movie)(6/59)-John Wayne; Toth-a; John Wayne, Dean Martin & Ricky Nelson photo-c	28	53	84	202	451	700
1019-Wagon Train (TV)-Photo-c	6	12	18	41	76	110
1020-Jungle Jim-McWilliams-a	5	10	15	33	57	80
1021-Jace Pearson's Tales of the Texas Rangers (TV)-Photo-c	5	10	15	34	60	85
1022-Timmy	5	10	15	34	60	85
1023-Tales of Wells Fargo (TV)-Photo-c	8	16	24	54	102	150
1024-Darby O'Gill and the Little People (Disney-Movie)-Toth-a; photo-c	9	18	27	59	117	175
1025-Vacation in Disneyland (8-10/59)-Carl Barks-a(24pgs.) (Disney)	15	30	45	103	227	350
1026-Spin and Marty (TV) (Disney) (9-11/59)-Mickey Mouse Club; photo-c	7	14	21	44	82	120
1027-The Texan (#1)(TV)-Photo-c	9	18	27	57	111	165
1028-Rawhide (#1) (TV) (9-11/59)-Clint Eastwood photo-c; Tufts-a	25	50	75	175	388	600
1029-Boots and Saddles (TV) (9/59)-Photo-c	5	10	15	34	60	85
1030-Spanky and Alfalfa, the Little Rascals (TV)	5	10	15	35	63	90
1031-Fury (TV)-Photo-c	5	10	15	35	63	90
1032-Elmer Fudd	5	10	15	33	57	80
1033-Steve Canyon-not by Caniff; photo-c	5	10	15	35	63	90
1034-Nancy and Sluggo Summer Camp (9-11/59)	5	10	15	30	50	70
1035-Lawman (TV)-Photo-c	8	16	24	52	99	145
1036-The Big Circus (Movie)-Photo-c	6	12	18	40	73	105
1037-Zorro (Disney) (TV)-Tufts-a; Annette Funicello photo-c	12	24	36	81	176	270
1038-Ruff and Reddy (TV)(Hanna-Barbera)(1959)	8	16	24	52	99	145
1039-Pluto (Disney) (11-1/60)	5	10	15	35	63	90
1040-Quick Draw McGraw (#1) (TV) (Hanna-Barbera) (12-2/60)	14	28	42	96	211	325
1041-Sea Hunt (TV) (10-12/59)-Toth-a; Lloyd Bridges photo-c	9	18	27	57	111	165
1042-The Three Chipmunks (Alvin, Simon & Theodore) (#1) (TV) (10-12/59)	10	20	30	66	138	210
1043-The Three Stooges (#1)-Photo-c	23	46	69	161	356	550
1044-Have Gun, Will Travel (TV)-Photo-c	9	18	27	62	126	190
1045-Restless Gun (TV)-Photo-c	7	14	21	49	92	135
1046-Beep Beep, the Road Runner (11-1/60)	8	16	24	54	102	150
1047-Gyro Gearloose (#1) (Disney)-All Barks-c/a	16	32	48	107	236	365
1048-The Horse Soldiers (Movie) (John Wayne)-Sekowsky-a; painted cover featuring John Wayne	12	24	36	80	173	265
1049-Don't Give Up the Ship (Movie) (8/59)-Jerry Lewis photo-c	9	18	27	58	114	170
1050-Huckleberry Hound (TV) (Hanna-Barbera) (10-12/59)	12	24	36	80	173	265
1051-Donald in Mathmagic Land (Disney-Movie)	8	16	24	56	108	160
1052-Ben-Hur (Movie) (11/59)-Manning-a	10	20	30	66	138	210
1053-Goofy (Disney) (11-1/60)	5	10	15	35	63	90
1054-Huckleberry Hound Winter Fun (TV) (Hanna-Barbera) (12/59)	12	24	36	80	173	265
1055-Daisy Duck's Diary (Disney)-by Carl Barks (11-1/60)	8	16	24	56	108	160
1056-Yellowstone Kelly (Movie)-Clint Walker photo-c	6	12	18	41	76	110
1057-Mickey Mouse Album (Disney)	6	12	18	42	79	115
1058-Colt .45 (TV)-Photo-c	7	14	21	48	89	130
1059-Sugarfoot (TV)-Photo-c	7	14	21	49	92	135
1060-Journey to the Center of the Earth (Movie)-Pat Boone & James Mason photo-c	12	24	36	82	179	275
1061-Buffalo Bee (TV)	6	12	18	42	79	115
1062-Christmas Stories (Walt Scott's Little People strip-r)	5	10	15	34	60	85
1063-Santa Claus Funnies	6	12	18	41	76	110
1064-Bugs Bunny's Merry Christmas (12/59)	5	10	15	34	60	85
1065-Frosty the Snowman	5	10	15	35	63	90
1066-77 Sunset Strip (#1) (TV)-Toth-a (1-3/60)-Efrem Zimbalist, Jr. & Edd "Kookie" Byrnes photo-c	9	18	27	63	129	195
1067-Yogi Bear (#1) (TV) (Hanna-Barbera)	13	26	39	89	195	300
1068-Francis the Famous Talking Mule	5	10	15	31	53	75
1069-The FBI Story (Movie)-Toth-a; James Stewart photo on-c	9	18	27	61	123	185
1070-Solomon and Sheba (Movie)-Sekowsky-a; photo-c	10	20	30	64	132	200
1071-The Real McCoys (#1) (TV) (1-3/60)-Toth-a; Walter Brennan photo-c	9	18	27	62	126	190
1072-Blythe (Marge's)	5	10	15	34	60	85
1073-Grandma Duck's Farm Friends-Barks-c/a (Disney)	11	22	33	73	157	240
1074-Chilly Willy (Lantz)	6	12	18	37	66	95
1075-Tales of Wells Fargo (TV)-Photo-c	8	16	24	54	102	150
1076-The Rebel (#1) (TV)-Sekowsky-a; photo-c	10	20	30	68	144	220
1077-The Deputy (#1) (TV)-Buscema-a; Henry Fonda photo-c	10	20	30	64	132	200
1078-The Three Stooges (2-4/60)-Photo-c	11	22	33	76	163	250
1079-The Little Rascals (TV) (Spanky & Alfalfa)	5	10	15	35	63	90
1080-Fury (TV) (2-4/60)-Photo-c	5	10	15	35	63	90
1081-Elmer Fudd	5	10	15	33	57	80
1082-Spin and Marty (Disney) (TV)-Photo-c	7	14	21	44	82	120
1083-Men into Space (TV)-Anderson-a; photo-c	6	12	18	41	76	110
1084-Speedy Gonzales	7	14	21	46	86	125
1085-The Time Machine (H.G. Wells) (Movie) (3/60)-Alex Toth-a; Rod Taylor photo-c	16	32	48	110	243	375
1086-Lolly and Pepper	5	10	15	30	50	70
1087-Peter Gunn (TV)-Photo-c	8	16	24	52	99	145
1088-A Dog of Flanders (Movie)-Photo-c	5	10	15	33	57	80
1089-Restless Gun (TV)-Photo-c	7	14	21	49	92	135
1090-Francis the Famous Talking Mule	5	10	15	31	53	75
1091-Jacky's Diary (4-6/60)	5	10	15	34	60	85
1092-Toby Tyler (Disney-Movie)-Photo-c	6	12	18	41	76	110
1093-MacKenzie's Raiders (Movie/TV)-Richard Carlson photo-c from TV show	6	12	18	40	73	105
1094-Goofy (Disney)	5	10	15	35	63	90
1095-Gyro Gearloose (Disney)-All Barks-c/a	9	18	27	59	117	175
1096-The Texan (TV)-Rory Calhoun photo-c	7	14	21	46	86	125
1097-Rawhide (TV)-Manning-a; Clint Eastwood photo-c	13	26	39	91	201	310
1098-Sugarfoot (TV)-Photo-c	7	14	21	49	92	135
1099-Donald Duck Album (Disney) (5-7/60)-Barks-c	7	14	21	44	82	120
1100-Annette's Life Story (Disney-Movie) (5/60)-Annette Funicello photo-c	18	36	54	125	276	430
1101-Robert Louis Stevenson's Kidnapped (Disney-Movie) (5/60); photo-c	6	12	18	42	79	115
1102-Wanted: Dead or Alive (#1) (TV) (5-7/60); Steve McQueen photo-c	14	28	42	96	211	325
1103-Leave It to Beaver (TV)-Photo-c	13	26	39	89	195	300
1104-Yogi Bear Goes to College (TV) (Hanna-Barbera) (6-8/60)	8	16	24	56	108	160
1105-Gale Storm (Oh! Susanna) (TV)-Toth-a; photo-c	10	20	30	69	147	225
1106-77 Sunset Strip(TV)(6-8/60)-Toth-a; photo-c	7	14	21	49	92	135
1107-Buckskin (TV)-Photo-c	6	12	18	40	73	105
1108-The Troubleshooters (TV)-Keenan Wynn photo-c	6	12	18	42	79	115
1109-This Is Your Life, Donald Duck (Disney) (TV) (8-10/60)-Gyro flashback to WDC&S #141; origin Donald Duck (1st told)	12	24	36	81	176	270
1110-Bonanza (#1) (TV) (6-8/60)-Photo-c	32	64	96	230	515	800
1111-Shotgun Slade (TV)-Photo-c	6	12	18	37	66	95
1112-Pixie and Dixie and Mr. Jinks (#1) (TV) (Hanna-Barbera) (7-9/60)	8	16	24	54	102	150
1113-Tales of Wells Fargo (TV)-Photo-c	8	16	24	54	102	150
1114-Huckleberry Finn (Movie) (7/60)-Photo-c	6	12	18	42	79	115
1115-Ricky Nelson (TV)-Manning-a; photo-c	12	24	36	82	179	275
1116-Boots and Saddles (TV) (8/60)-Photo-c	5	10	15	34	60	85
1117-Boy and the Pirates (Movie)-Photo-c	6	12	18	37	66	95
1118-The Sword and the Dragon (Movie) (6/60)-Photo-c	8	16	24	54	102	150
1119-Smokey the Bear Nature Stories	5	10	15	31	53	75
1120-Dinosaurus (Movie)-Painted-c	8	16	24	51	96	140
1121-Hercules Unchained (Movie) (8/60)-Crandall/Evans-a	9	18	27	61	123	185
1122-Chilly Willy (Lantz)	6	12	18	37	66	95
1123-Tombstone Territory (TV)-Photo-c	7	14	21	49	92	135
1124-Whirlybirds (#1) (TV)-Photo-c	7	14	21	49	92	135
1125-Laramie (#1) (TV)-Photo-c; G. Kane/Heath-a	8	16	24	66	108	160
1126-Hotel Deparee - Sundance (TV) (8-10/60)-Earl Holliman photo-c	6	12	18	42	79	115
1127-The Three Stooges-Photo-c (8-10/60)	11	22	33	76	163	250
1128-Rocky and His Friends (#1) (TV) (Jay Ward) (8-10/60)	27	54	81	194	435	675
1129-Pollyanna (Disney-Movie)-Hayley Mills photo-c	8	16	24	52	99	145
1130-The Deputy (TV)-Buscema-a; Henry Fonda photo-c	8	16	24	54	102	150
1131-Elmer Fudd (9-11/60)	5	10	15	33	57	80
1132-Space Mouse (Lantz) (8-10/60)	6	12	18	37	66	95
1133-Fury (TV)-Photo-c	5	10	15	35	63	90
1134-Real McCoys (TV)-Toth-a; photo-c	9	18	27	62	126	190
1135-M.G.M.'s Mouse Musketeers (9-11/60)	4	8	12	28	47	65
1136-Jungle Cat (Disney-Movie)-Photo-c	6	12	18	40	73	105
1137-The Little Rascals (TV)	5	10	15	35	63	90
1138-The Rebel (TV)-Photo-c	8	16	24	55	105	155
1139-Spartacus (Movie) (11/60)-Buscema-a; Kirk Douglas photo-c	11	22	33	77	166	255
1140-Donald Duck Album (Disney)-Barks-c	7	14	21	44	82	120
1141-Huckleberry Hound for President (TV) (Hanna-Barbera) (10/60)	7	14	21	46	86	125
1142-Johnny Ringo (TV)-Photo-c	7	14	21	49	92	135
1143-Pluto (Disney) (11-1/61)	5	10	15	35	63	90
1144-The Story of Ruth (Movie)-Photo-c	9	18	27	57	111	165

Four Color Comics #1049 © H.B. Wallis

Four Color Comics #1166 © Jay Ward

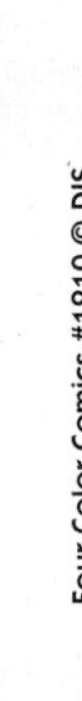

Four Color Comics #1210 © DIS

	GD 2.0	VG 4.0	FN 6.0	VF 8.0	VF/NM 9.0	NM- 9.2
1145-The Lost World (Movie)-Gil Kane-a; photo-c; 1 pg. Conan Doyle biography by Torres	9	18	27	61	123	185
1146-Restless Gun (TV)-Photo-c; Wildey-a	7	14	21	49	92	135
1147-Sugarfoot (TV)-Photo-c	7	14	21	49	92	135
1148-I Aim at the Stars-the Werner Von Braun Story (Movie) (11-1/61)-Photo-c	7	14	21	44	82	120
1149-Goofy (Disney) (11-1/61)	5	10	15	35	63	90
1150-Daisy Duck's Diary (Disney) (12-1/61) by Carl Barks	8	16	24	56	108	160
1151-Mickey Mouse Album (Disney) (11-1/61)	6	12	18	42	79	115
1152-Rocky and His Friends (TV) (Jay Ward) (12-2/61)	17	34	51	114	252	390
1153-Frosty the Snowman	5	10	15	35	63	90
1154-Santa Claus Funnies	6	12	18	41	76	110
1155-North to Alaska (Movie)-John Wayne photo-c	15	30	45	105	233	360
1156-Walt Disney Swiss Family Robinson (Movie) (12/60)-Photo-c	9	18	27	59	117	175
1157-Master of the World (Movie) (7/61)	8	16	24	55	105	155
1158-Three Worlds of Gulliver (2 issues exist with different covers) (Movie)-Photo-c	6	12	18	42	79	115
1159-77 Sunset Strip (TV)-Toth-a; photo-c	7	14	21	49	92	135
1160-Rawhide (TV)-Clint Eastwood photo-c	13	26	39	91	201	310
1161-Grandma Duck's Farm Friends (Disney) by Carl Barks (2-4/61)	11	22	33	73	157	240
1162-Yogi Bear Joins the Marines (TV) (Hanna-Barbera) (5-7/61)	8	16	24	56	108	160
1163-Daniel Boone (3-5/61); Marsh-a	5	10	15	35	63	90
1164-Wanted: Dead or Alive (TV)-Steve McQueen photo-c	10	20	30	64	132	200
1165-Ellery Queen (#1) (3-5/61)	9	18	27	58	114	175
1166-Rocky and His Friends (TV) (Jay Ward)	17	34	51	114	252	390
1167-Tales of Wells Fargo (TV)-Photo-c	7	14	21	48	89	130
1168-The Detectives (TV)-Robert Taylor photo-c	10	20	30	66	138	210
1169-New Adventures of Sherlock Holmes	12	24	36	82	179	275
1170-The Three Stooges (3-5/61)-Photo-c	11	22	33	76	163	250
1171-Elmer Fudd	5	10	15	33	57	80
1172-Fury (TV)-Photo-c	5	10	15	35	63	90
1173-The Twilight Zone (#1) (TV) (5/61)-Crandall/Evans-c/a; Crandall tribute to Ingles	23	46	69	161	356	550
1174-The Little Rascals (TV)	5	10	15	33	57	80
1175-M.G.M.'s Mouse Musketeers (3-5/61)	4	8	12	28	47	65
1176-Dondi (Movie)-Origin; photo-c	6	12	18	37	66	95
1177-Chilly Willy (Lantz) (4-6/61)	6	12	18	37	66	95
1178-Ten Who Dared (Disney-Movie) (12/60)-Painted-c; cast member photo on back-c	7	14	21	46	86	125
1179-The Swamp Fox (TV) (Disney)-Leslie Nielsen photo-c	9	18	27	62	126	190
1180-The Danny Thomas Show (TV)-Toth-a; photo-c	16	32	48	107	236	365
1181-Texas John Slaughter (TV) (Walt Disney Presents...) (4-6/61)-Photo-c	6	12	18	38	69	100
1182-Donald Duck Album (Disney) (5-7/61)	5	10	15	34	60	85
1183-101 Dalmatians (Disney-Movie) (3/61)	11	22	33	75	160	245
1184-Gyro Gearloose; All Barks-c/a (Disney) (5-7/61) Two variations exist	9	18	27	59	117	175
1185-Sweetie Pie	6	12	18	38	69	100
1186-Yak Yak (#1) by Jack Davis (2 versions - one minus 3-pg. Davis-c/a)	8	16	24	56	108	160
1187-The Three Stooges (6-8/61)-Photo-c	11	22	33	76	163	250
1188-Atlantis, the Lost Continent (Movie) (5/61)-Photo-c	9	18	27	62	126	190
1189-Greyfriars Bobby (Disney-Movie) (11/61)-Photo-c (scarce)	6	12	18	41	76	110
1190-Donald and the Wheel (Disney-Movie) (11/61); Barks-c	8	16	24	56	108	160
1191-Leave It to Beaver (TV)-Photo-c	13	26	39	89	195	300
1192-Ricky Nelson (TV)-Manning-a; photo-c	12	24	36	82	179	275
1193-The Real McCoys (TV) (6-8/61)-Photo-c	7	14	21	48	89	130
1194-Pepe (Movie) (4/61)-Photo-c	5	10	15	33	57	80
1195-National Velvet (#1) (TV)-Photo-c	6	12	18	41	76	110
1196-Pixie and Dixie and Mr. Jinks (TV) (Hanna-Barbera) (7-9/61)	5	10	15	35	63	90
1197-The Aquanauts (TV) (5-7/61)-Photo-c	8	16	24	51	96	140
1198-Donald in Mathmagic Land (Disney-Movie)-Reprint of #1051	6	12	18	37	66	95

	GD 2.0	VG 4.0	FN 6.0	VF 8.0	VF/NM 9.0	NM- 9.2
1199-The Absent-Minded Professor (Disney-Movie) (4/61)-Photo-c	7	14	21	49	92	135
1199-Shaggy Dog & The Absent-Minded Professor (Disney-Movie) (8/67)-Photo-c	7	14	21	49	92	135
1200-Hennessey (TV) (8-10/61)-Gil Kane-a; photo-c	7	14	21	48	89	130
1201-Goofy (Disney) (8-10/61)	5	10	15	35	63	90
1202-Rawhide (TV)-Clint Eastwood photo-c	13	26	39	91	201	310
1203-Pinocchio (Disney) (3/62)	7	14	21	49	92	135
1204-Scamp (Disney)	4	8	12	27	44	60
1205-David and Goliath (Movie) (7/61)-Photo-c	7	14	21	48	89	130
1206-Lolly and Pepper (9-11/61)	5	10	15	30	50	70
1207-The Rebel (TV)-Sekowsky-a; photo-c	8	16	24	55	105	155
1208-Rocky and His Friends (Jay Ward) (TV)	17	34	51	114	252	390
1209-Sugarfoot (TV)-Photo-c (10-12/61)	7	14	21	49	92	135
1210-The Parent Trap (Disney-Movie) (8/61)-Hayley Mills photo-c	10	20	30	64	132	200
1211-77 Sunset Strip (TV)-Manning-a; photo-c	7	14	21	46	86	125
1212-Chilly Willy (Lantz) (7-9/61)	6	12	18	37	66	95
1213-Mysterious Island (Movie)-Photo-c	9	18	27	58	114	170
1214-Smokey the Bear	5	10	15	31	53	75
1215-Tales of Wells Fargo (TV) (10-12/61)-Photo-c	7	14	21	48	89	130
1216-Whirlybirds (TV)-Photo-c	7	14	21	46	86	125
1218-Fury (TV)-Photo-c	5	10	15	35	63	90
1219-The Detectives (TV)-Robert Taylor & Adam West photo-c	10	20	30	66	138	210
1220-Gunslinger (TV)-Photo-c	8	16	24	52	99	145
1221-Bonanza (TV) (9-11/61)-Photo-c	15	30	45	100	220	340
1222-Elmer Fudd (9-11/61)	5	10	15	33	57	80
1223-Laramie (TV)-Gil Kane-a; photo-c	6	12	18	37	66	95
1224-The Little Rascals (TV) (10-12/61)	5	10	15	33	57	80
1225-The Deputy (TV)-Henry Fonda photo-c	8	16	24	54	102	150
1226-Nikki, Wild Dog of the North (Disney-Movie) (9/61)-Photo-c	5	10	15	33	57	80
1227-Morgan the Pirate (Movie)-Photo-c	7	14	21	46	86	125
1229-Thief of Baghdad (Movie)-Crandall/Evans-a; photo-c	6	12	18	41	76	110
1230-Voyage to the Bottom of the Sea (#1) (Movie)-Photo insert on-c	12	24	36	79	170	260
1231-Danger Man (TV) (9-11/61)-Patrick McGoohan photo-c	11	22	33	77	166	255
1232-On the Double (Movie)	6	12	18	37	66	95
1233-Tammy Tell Me True (Movie) (1961)	8	16	24	52	99	145
1234-The Phantom Planet (Movie) (1961)	8	16	24	54	102	150
1235-Mister Magoo (#1) (12-2/62)	7	14	21	48	89	130
1235-Mister Magoo (3-5/65) 2nd printing; reprint of 12-2/62 issue	5	10	15	35	63	90
1236-King of Kings (Movie)-Photo-c	8	16	24	52	99	145
1237-The Untouchables (#1) (TV)-Not by Toth; photo-c	18	36	54	124	275	425
1238-Deputy Dawg (TV)	9	18	27	63	129	195
1239-Donald Duck Album (Disney) (10-12/61)-Barks-c	7	14	21	44	82	120
1240-The Detectives (TV)-Tufts-a; Robert Taylor photo-c	8	16	24	51	96	140
1241-Sweetie Pie	5	10	15	31	53	75
1242-King Leonardo and His Short Subjects (#1) (TV) (11-1/62)	10	20	30	67	141	215
1243-Ellery Queen	7	14	21	48	89	130
1244-Space Mouse (Lantz) (11-1/62)	6	12	18	37	66	95
1245-New Adventures of Sherlock Holmes	11	22	33	75	160	245
1246-Mickey Mouse Album (Disney)	6	12	18	42	79	115
1247-Daisy Duck's Diary (Disney) (12-2/62)	5	10	15	35	63	90
1248-Pluto (Disney)	5	10	15	35	63	90
1249-The Danny Thomas Show (TV)-Manning-a; photo-c	12	24	36	80	173	265
1250-The Four Horsemen of the Apocalypse (Movie)-Photo-c	8	16	24	56	108	160
1251-Everything's Ducky (Movie) (1961)	7	14	21	44	82	120
1252-The Andy Griffith Show (TV)-Photo-c; 1st show aired 10/3/60	42	84	126	311	706	1100
1253-Space Man (#1) (1-3/62)	9	18	27	59	117	175
1254- "Diver Dan" (#1) (TV) (2-4/62)-Photo-c	10	20	30	69	147	225
1255-The Wonders of Aladdin (Movie) (1961)	6	12	18	42	79	115
1256-Kona, Monarch of Monster Isle (#1) (2-4/62)-Glanzman-a	10	20	30	66	138	210

	GD 2.0	VG 4.0	FN 6.0	VF 8.0	VF/NM 9.0	NM- 9.2
1257-Car 54, Where Are You? (#1) (TV) (3-5/62)-Photo-c	8	16	24	56	108	160
1258-The Frogmen (#1)-Evans-a	9	18	27	62	126	190
1259-El Cid (Movie) (1961)-Photo-c	7	14	21	46	86	125
1260-The Horsemasters (TV, Movie) (Disney) (12-2/62)-Annette Funicello photo-c	10	20	30	69	147	225
1261-Rawhide (TV)-Clint Eastwood photo-c	13	26	39	91	201	310
1262-The Rebel (TV)-Photo-c	8	16	24	55	105	155
1263-77 Sunset Strip (TV) (12-2/62)-Manning-a; photo-c	7	14	21	46	86	125
1264-Pixie and Dixie and Mr. Jinks (TV) (Hanna-Barbera)	5	10	15	35	63	90
1265-The Real McCoys (TV)-Photo-c	7	14	21	48	89	130
1266-M.G.M.'s Spike and Tyke (12-2/62)	4	8	12	28	47	65
1267-Gyro Gearloose; Barks-c/a, 4 pgs. (Disney) (12-2/62)	7	14	21	48	89	130
1268-Oswald the Rabbit (Lantz)	5	10	15	33	57	80
1269-Rawhide (TV)-Clint Eastwood photo-c	13	26	39	91	201	310
1270-Bullwinkle and Rocky (#1) (TV) (Jay Ward) (3-5/62)	16	32	48	112	249	385
1271-Yogi Bear Birthday Party (TV) (Hanna-Barbera) (11/61) (Given away for 1 box top from Kellogg's Corn Flakes)	6	12	18	40	73	105
1272-Frosty the Snowman	5	10	15	35	63	90
1273-Hans Brinker (Disney-Movie)-Photo-c (2/62)	6	12	18	37	66	95
1274-Santa Claus Funnies (12/61)	6	12	18	41	76	110
1275-Rocky and His Friends (TV) (Jay Ward)	17	34	51	114	252	390
1276-Dondi	4	8	12	28	47	65
1278-King Leonardo and His Short Subjects (TV)	10	20	30	67	141	215
1279-Grandma Duck's Farm Friends (Disney)	5	10	15	34	60	85
1280-Hennesey (TV)-Photo-c	6	12	18	40	73	105
1281-Chilly Willy (Lantz) (4-6/62)	6	12	18	37	66	95
1282-Babes in Toyland (Disney-Movie) (1/62); Annette Funicello photo-c	13	26	39	86	188	290
1283-Bonanza (TV) (2-4/62)-Photo-c	15	30	45	100	220	340
1284-Laramie (TV)-Heath-a; photo-c	6	12	18	37	66	95
1285-Leave It to Beaver (TV)-Photo-c	13	26	39	89	195	300
1286-The Untouchables (TV)-Photo-c	13	26	39	89	195	300
1287-Man from Wells Fargo (TV)-Photo-c	6	12	18	42	79	115
1288-Twilight Zone (TV) (4/62)-Crandall/Evans-c/a	112	24	36	79	170	260
1289-Ellery Queen	7	14	21	48	89	130
1290-M.G.M.'s Mouse Musketeers	4	8	12	28	47	65
1291-77 Sunset Strip (TV)-Manning-a; photo-c	7	14	21	46	86	125
1293-Elmer Fudd (3-5/62)	5	10	15	33	57	80
1294-Ripcord (TV)	7	14	21	46	86	125
1295-Mister Ed, the Talking Horse (#1) (TV) (3-5/62)-Photo-c	14	28	42	96	211	325
1296-Fury (TV) (3-5/62)-Photo-c	5	10	15	35	63	90
1297-Spanky, Alfalfa and the Little Rascals (TV)	5	10	15	33	57	80
1298-The Hathaways (TV)-Photo-c	5	10	15	35	63	90
1299-Deputy Dawg (TV)	9	18	27	63	129	195
1300-The Comancheros (Movie) (1961)-John Wayne photo-c	15	30	45	100	220	340
1301-Adventures in Paradise (TV) (2-4/62)	6	12	18	37	66	95
1302-Johnny Jason, Teen Reporter (2-4/62)	4	8	12	25	40	55
1303-Lad: A Dog (Movie)-Photo-c	5	10	15	33	57	80
1304-Nellie the Nurse (3-5/62)-Stanley-a	9	18	27	62	126	190
1305-Mister Magoo (3-5/62)	7	14	21	48	89	130
1306-Target: The Corruptors (#1) (TV) (3-5/62)-Photo-c	5	10	15	35	63	90
1307-Margie (TV) (3-5/62)	8	16	24	51	96	140
1308-Tales of the Wizard of Oz (TV) (3-5/62)	14	28	42	97	214	325
1309-87th Precinct (#1) (TV) (4-6/62)-Krigstein-a; photo-c	9	18	27	60	120	180
1310-Huck and Yogi Winter Sports (TV) (Hanna-Barbera) (3/62)	8	16	24	54	102	150
1311-Rocky and His Friends (TV) (Jay Ward)	17	34	51	114	252	390
1312-National Velvet (TV)-Photo-c	4	8	12	27	44	60
1313-Moon Pilot (Disney-Movie)-Photo-c	6	12	18	41	76	110
1328-The Underwater City (Movie) (1961)-Evans-a; photo-c	7	14	21	49	92	135
1329-See Gyro Gearloose #01329-207						
1330-Brain Boy (#1)-Gil Kane-a	10	20	30	69	147	225
1332-Bachelor Father (TV)	7	14	21	46	86	125
1333-Short Ribs (4-6/62)	6	12	18	38	69	100
1335-Aggie Mack (4-6/62)	6	12	18	37	66	95
1336-On Stage; not by Leonard Starr	5	10	15	34	60	85
1337-Dr. Kildare (#1) (TV) (4-6/62)-Photo-c	10	20	30	64	132	200
1341-The Andy Griffith Show (TV) (4-6/62)-Photo-c	36	72	108	266	596	925
1348-Yak Yak (#2)-Jack Davis-c/a	7	14	21	46	86	125
1349-Yogi Bear Visits the U.N. (TV) (Hanna-Barbera) (1/62)-Photo-c	8	16	24	54	102	150
1350-Comanche (Disney-Movie)(1962)-Reprints 4-Color #966 (title change from "Tonka" to "Comanche") (4-6/62)-Sal Mineo photo-c	5	10	15	35	63	90
1354-Calvin & the Colonel (#1) (TV) (4-6/62)	9	18	27	60	120	180

NOTE: *Missing numbers probably do not exist.*

4-D MONKEY, THE (Adventures of... #? on)
Leung's Publications: 1988 - No. 11, 1990 ($1.80/$2.00, 52 pgs.)

1-11: 1-Karate Pig, Ninja Flounder & 4-D Monkey (48 pgs., centerfold is a Christmas card). 2-4 (52 pgs.) 4.00

FOUR FAVORITES (Crime Must Pay the Penalty No. 33 on)
Ace Magazines: Sept, 1941 - No. 32, Dec, 1947

	GD 2.0	VG 4.0	FN 6.0	VF 8.0	VF/NM 9.0	NM- 9.2
1-Vulcan, Lash Lightning (formerly Flash Lightning in Sure-Fire), Magno the Magnetic Man & The Raven begin; flag/Hitler-c	320	640	960	2240	3920	5600
2-The Black Ace only app.; WWII flag-c	168	336	504	1075	1838	2600
3-Last Vulcan; V For Victory WWII-c	161	322	483	1030	1765	2500
4,5: 4-The Raven & Vulcan end; Unknown Soldier begins (see Our Flag), ends #28. 5-Captain Courageous begins (5/42), ends #28 (moves over from Captain Courageous #6); not in #6. 5,6-Bondage/torture-c	174	348	522	1114	1967	2700
6-8: 6-The Flag app.; Mr. Risk begins (7/42)	142	284	426	909	1555	2200
9-Kurtzman-a (Lash Lightning); robot-c	155	310	465	992	1696	2400
10-Classic Kurtzman-c/a (Magno & Davey)	343	686	1029	2400	4200	6000
11-Kurtzman-a; Hitler, Mussolini, Hirohito-c; L.B. Cole-a; Unknown Soldier by Kurtzman	354	708	1062	2478	4339	6200
12-L.B. Cole-a; Japanese WWII-c	161	322	483	1030	1765	2500
13-L.B. Cole-c (his first cover?); WWII-c	148	296	444	947	1624	2300
14,16-18,20: 18,20-Palais-c/a	81	162	243	518	884	1250
15-Japanese WWII-c	90	180	270	576	988	1400
19-Nazi WWII bondage-c	155	310	465	992	1696	2400
21-No Unknown Soldier; The Unknown app.	103	206	309	659	1130	1600
22-27: 22-Captain Courageous drops costume. 23-Unknown Soldier drops costume. 25-29-Hap Hazard app. 26-Last Magno	58	116	174	371	636	900
28,29: Hap Hazard app. in all	41	82	123	256	428	600
30-32: 30-Funny-c begin (teen humor), end #32	22	44	66	128	209	290

NOTE: ***Dave Berg** c-5. **Jim Mooney** a-6; c-1-3. **Palais** a-18-20; c-18-25.*

FOUR HORSEMEN, THE (See The Crusaders)

FOUR HORSEMEN
DC Comics (Vertigo): Feb, 2000 - No. 4, May, 2000 ($2.50, limited series)

1-4-Esad Ribic-c/a; Robert Rodi-s 3.00

FOUR HORSEMEN OF THE APOCALYPSE, THE (Movie)
Dell Publishing Co.: No. 1250, Jan-Mar, 1962 (one-shot)

	GD 2.0	VG 4.0	FN 6.0	VF 8.0	VF/NM 9.0	NM- 9.2
Four Color 1250-Photo-c	8	16	24	56	108	160

4MOST (Foremost Boys No. 32-40; becomes Thrilling Crime Cases #41 on)
Novelty Publications/Star Publications No. 37-on:
Winter, 1941-42 - V8#5(#36), 9-10/49; #37, 11-12/49 - #40, 4-5/50

	GD 2.0	VG 4.0	FN 6.0	VF 8.0	VF/NM 9.0	NM- 9.2
V1#1-The Target by Sid Greene, The Cadet & Dick Cole begin with origins retold; produced by Funnies Inc.; quarterly issues begin, end V6#3; German WWII-c	219	438	657	1402	2401	3400
2-Last Target (Spr/42); WWII cover	74	148	222	470	810	1150
3-Dan'l Flannel begins; flag-c	53	106	159	334	567	800
4-1pg. Dr. Seuss (signed) (Aut/42); fish in the face-c	57	114	171	362	619	875
V2#1-3	28	56	84	165	270	375
4-Hitler, Tojo & Mussolini app. as pumpkins on-c	74	148	222	470	810	1150
V3#1-4	20	40	60	114	182	250
V4#1-4: 2-Walter Johnson-c	15	30	45	83	124	165
V5#1-4: 1-The Target & Targeteers app.	14	28	42	76	108	140
V6#1-4	11	22	33	62	86	110
5-L.B. Cole-c	24	48	72	142	234	325
V7#1,3,5, V8#1, 37	11	22	33	60	83	105
2,4,6-L.B. Cole-c. 6-Last Dick Cole	21	42	63	122	199	275
V8#2,3,5-L.B. Cole-c/a	24	48	72	142	234	325
4-L.B. Cole-a	15	30	45	88	137	185
38-40: 38-Johnny Weismuller (Tarzan) life story & Jim Braddock (boxer) life story. 38-40-L.B. Cole-c. 40-Last White Rider	17	34	51	98	154	210
Accepted Reprint 38-40 (nd): 40-r/Johnny Weismuller life story; all have L.B. Cole-c	10	20	30	56	76	95

411
Marvel Comics: June, 2003 - No. 2, Jul, 2003 ($3.50, limited series)

1,2-Tributes to peacemakers; s/a by various. 1-Millar, Quitely, Mack, Winslade & others-s/a. 2-Harris, Phillips, Manco, Bruce Jones. 3.50

FOUR POINTS, THE
Aspen MLT Inc.: Apr, 2015 - No. 5, Aug, 2015 ($3.99)

1-5-Lobdell-s/Gunderson-a; multiple covers 4.00

FOUR-STAR BATTLE TALES
National Periodical Publications: Feb-Mar, 1973 - No. 5, Nov-Dec, 1973

	GD 2.0	VG 4.0	FN 6.0	VF 8.0	VF/NM 9.0	NM- 9.2
1-Reprints begin	3	6	9	16	24	32
2-5	2	4	6	11	16	20

NOTE: ***Drucker** r-1, 3-5. **Heath** r-2, 5; c-1. **Krigstein** r-5. **Kubert** r-4; c-2.*

FOUR STAR SPECTACULAR
National Periodical Publications: Mar-Apr, 1976 - No. 6, Jan-Feb, 1977

	GD 2.0	VG 4.0	FN 6.0	VF 8.0	VF/NM 9.0	NM- 9.2
1-Includes G.A. Flash story with new art	3	6	9	14	20	25
2-6: Reprints in all. 2-Infinity cover	2	4	6	8	11	14

NOTE: *All contain DC Superhero reprints. #1 has 68 pgs.; #2-6, 52 pgs. #1, 4-Hawkman app.; #2-Kid Flash app.; #3-Green Lantern app; #2, 4, 5-Wonder Woman, Superboy app; #5-Green Arrow, Vigilante app; #6-Blackhawk G.A.-r.*

FOUR TEENERS (Formerly Crime Must Pay The Penalty; Dotty No. 35 on)
A. A. Wyn: No. 34, April, 1948 (52 pgs.)

	GD 2.0	VG 4.0	FN 6.0	VF 8.0	VF/NM 9.0	NM- 9.2
34-Teen-age comic; Dotty app.; Curly & Jerry continue from Four Favorites	18	36	54	107	169	230

FOURTH MAN, THE
AWA Studios: Jan, 2022 - No. 4, Apr, 2022 ($3.99, limited series)

1-4-Jeff McComsly-s/Mike Deodato, Jr.-a 4.00

4001 A.D. (See Valiant 2016 FCBD edition for prelude)
Valiant Entertainment: May, 2016 - No. 4, Aug, 2016 ($3.99, limited series)

1-4-Matt Kindt-s/Clayton Crain-a. 1-David Mack-a (3 pages) 4.00
...: Bloodshot 1 (6/16, $3.99) Lemire-s/Braithwaite-a; Bloodshot reforms in 4001 A.D. 4.00
...: Shadowman 1 (7/16, $3.99) Houser & Roberts-s/Gill-a 4.00
...: War Mother 1 (8/16, $3.99) Van Lente-s/Giorello-a 4.00
...: X-O Manowar 1 (5/16, $3.99) Venditti-s/Henry-a; prelude to main series 4.00

FOURTH WORLD GALLERY, THE (Jack Kirby's...)
DC Comics: 1996 (9/96) ($3.50, one-shot)

nn-Pin-ups of Jack Kirby's Fourth World characters (New Gods, Forever People & Mister Miracle) by John Byrne, Rick Burchett, Dan Jurgens, Walt Simonson & others 4.00

FOUR WOMEN
DC Comics (Homage): Dec, 2001 - No. 5, Apr, 2002 ($2.95, limited series)

Four Color Comics #1281 © Walter Lantz

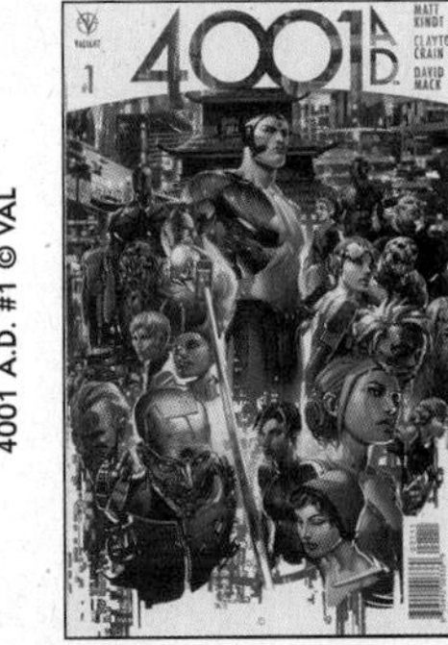

4001 A.D. #1 © VAL

The Fox: Family Values #1 © ACP

	GD 2.0	VG 4.0	FN 6.0	VF 8.0	VF/NM 9.0	NM- 9.2
1-5-Sam Kieth-s/a						3.00
TPB (2002, $17.95) r/series; foreward by Kieth						18.00

FOX, THE
Archie Comic Publications (Red Circle Comics): Dec, 2013 - No. 5, Apr, 2014 ($2.99)

	GD 2.0	VG 4.0	FN 6.0	VF 8.0	VF/NM 9.0	NM- 9.2
1-5-Dean Haspiel-a/Haspiel and Mark Waid-s. 1-Three covers. 2-Two covers						3.00

FOX, THE
Archie Comic Publications (Dark Circle Comics): Jun, 2015 - No. 5, Oct, 2015 ($3.99)

	GD 2.0	VG 4.0	FN 6.0	VF 8.0	VF/NM 9.0	NM- 9.2
1-5-Dean Haspiel-a/Haspiel and Mark Waid-s; multiple covers on each						4.00
...: Family Values 1 (7/22, $3.99. one-shot) Haspiel-s/a; reprint with Alex Toth-s/a						4.00

FOX AND THE CROW (Stanley & His Monster No. 109 on) (See Comic Cavalcade & Real Screen Comics)
National Periodical Publications: Dec-Jan, 1951-52 - No. 108, Feb-Mar, 1968

	GD 2.0	VG 4.0	FN 6.0	VF 8.0	VF/NM 9.0	NM- 9.2
1	129	258	387	826	1413	2000
2(Scarce)	57	114	171	362	619	875
3-5	37	74	111	222	361	500
6-10 (6-7/53)	26	52	78	154	252	350
11-20 (10/54)	20	40	60	114	182	250
21-30: 22-Last precode issue (2/55)	15	30	45	83	124	165
31-40	12	24	36	69	97	125
41-60	6	12	18	37	66	95
61-80	5	10	15	31	53	75
81-94: 94-(11/65)-The Brat Finks begin	4	8	12	25	40	55
95-Stanley & His Monster begins (origin & 1st app)	9	18	27	59	117	175
96-99,101-108	3	6	9	19	30	40
100 (10-11/66)	3	6	9	21	33	45

NOTE: *Many later covers by* ***Mort Drucker.***

FOX AND THE HOUND, THE (Disney)(Movie)
Whitman Publishing Co.: Aug, 1981 - No. 3, Oct, 1981

	GD 2.0	VG 4.0	FN 6.0	VF 8.0	VF/NM 9.0	NM- 9.2
11292- Golden Press Graphic Novel	2	4	6	8	10	12
1-3-Based on animated movie	1	2	3	5	7	9

FOXFIRE (See The Phoenix Resurrection)
Malibu Comics (Ultraverse): Feb, 1996 - No. 4, May, 1996 ($1.50)

	GD 2.0	VG 4.0	FN 6.0	VF 8.0	VF/NM 9.0	NM- 9.2
1-4: Sludge, Ultraforce app. 4-Punisher app.						3.00

FOX GIANTS (Also see Giant Comics Edition)
Fox Feature Syndicate: 1944 - 1950 (25¢, 132 - 196 pgs.)

	GD 2.0	VG 4.0	FN 6.0	VF 8.0	VF/NM 9.0	NM- 9.2
Album of Crime nn(1949, 132p)	74	148	222	470	810	1150
Album of Love nn(1949, 132p)	81	162	243	518	884	1250
All Famous Crime Stories nn('49, 132p)	74	148	222	470	810	1150
All Good Comics 1(1944, 132p)(R.W. Voigt)-The Bouncer, Purple Tigress,Rick Evans, Puppeteer, Green Mask; Infinity-c	97	194	291	621	1061	1500
All Great nn(1944, 132p)-Capt. Jack Terry, Rick Evans, Jaguar Man	61	122	183	390	670	950
All Great nn(Chicago Nite Life News)(1945, 132p)-Green Mask, Bouncer, Puppeteer, Rick Evans, Rocket Kelly	61	122	183	390	670	950
All-Great Confession Magazine nn(1949, 132p)	77	154	231	493	847	1200
All-Great Confessions nn(1949, 132p)	77	154	231	493	847	1200
All Great Crime Stories nn('49, 132p)	74	148	222	470	810	1150
All Great Jungle Adventures nn('49, 132p)	97	194	291	621	1061	1500
All Real Confession Magazine 3 (3/49, 132p)	77	154	231	493	847	1200
All Real Confession Magazine 4 (4/49, 132p)	77	154	231	493	847	1200
All Your Comics 1(1944, 132p)-The Puppeteer, Red Robbins, & Merciless the Sorcerer	63	126	189	403	689	975
Almanac Of Crime nn(1948, 148p)-Phantom Lady	90	180	270	576	988	1400
Almanac Of Crime 1(1950, 132p)	71	142	213	454	777	1100
Book Of Love nn(1950, 132p)	74	148	222	470	810	1150
Burning Romances 1(1949, 132p)	90	180	270	576	988	1400
Crimes Incorporated nn(1950, 132p)	68	136	204	435	743	1050
Daring Love Stories nn(1950, 132p)	74	148	222	470	810	1150
Everybody's Comics 1(1944, 50¢, 196p)-The Green Mask, The Puppeteer, The Bouncer, Rocket Kelly, Rick Evans	74	148	222	470	810	1150
Everybody's Comics 1(1946, 196p)-Green Lama, The Puppeteer	63	126	189	403	689	975
Everybody's Comics 1(1946, 196p)-Same as 1945 Ribtickler	50	100	150	315	533	750
Everybody's Comics nn(1947, 132p)-Jo-Jo, Purple Tigress, Cosmo Cat, Bronze Man	63	126	189	403	689	975
Exciting Romance Stories nn(1949, 132p)	77	154	231	493	847	1200
Famous Love nn(1950, 132p)-Photo-c	74	148	222	470	810	1150
Intimate Confessions nn(1950, 132p)	74	148	222	470	810	1150
Journal Of Crime nn(1949, 132p)	74	148	222	470	810	1150
Love Problems nn(1949, 132p)	77	154	231	493	847	1200
Love Thrills nn(1950, 132p)	74	148	222	470	810	1150
March of Crime nn('48, 132p)-Female w/rifle-c	76	152	228	486	831	1175
March of Crime nn('49, 132p)-Cop w/pistol-c	68	136	204	435	743	1050
March of Crime nn(1949, 132p)-Coffin & man w/machine-gun-c	68	136	204	435	743	1050
Revealing Love Stories nn(1950, 132p)	74	148	222	470	810	1150
Ribtickler nn(1945, 50¢, 196p)-Chicago Nite Life News; Marvel Mutt, Cosmo Cat, Flash Rabbit, The Nebbs app.	55	110	165	352	601	850
Romantic Thrills nn(1950, 132p)	74	148	222	470	810	1150
Secret Love Stories nn(1949, 132p)	77	154	231	493	847	1200
Strange Love nn(1950, 132p)-Photo-c	103	206	309	659	1130	1600
Sweetheart Scandals nn(1950, 132p)	74	148	222	470	810	1150
Teen-Age Love nn(1950, 132p)	74	148	222	470	810	1150
Throbbing Love nn(1950, 132p)-Photo-c; used in **POP**, pg. 107	100	200	300	635	1093	1550
Truth About Crime nn(1949, 132p)	74	148	222	470	810	1150
Variety Comics 1(1946, 132p)-Blue Beetle, Jungle Jo	71	142	213	454	777	1100
Variety Comics nn(1950, 132p)-Jungle Jo, My Secret Affair (w/Harrison/Wood-a), Crimes by Women & My Story	58	116	174	371	636	900
Western Roundup nn('50, 132p)-Hoot Gibson; Cody of the Pony Express app.	47	94	141	296	498	700

NOTE: *Each of the above usually contain four remaindered Fox books minus covers. Since these missing covers often had the first page of the first story, most Giants therefore are incomplete. Approximate values are listed. Books with appearances of Phantom Lady, Rulah, Jo-Jo, etc. could bring more.*

FOXHOLE (Becomes Never Again #8?)
Mainline/Charlton No. 5 on: 9-10/54 - No. 4, 3-4/55; No. 5, 7/55 - No. 7, 3/56

	GD 2.0	VG 4.0	FN 6.0	VF 8.0	VF/NM 9.0	NM- 9.2
1-Classic Kirby-c	161	322	483	1030	1765	2500
2-Kirby-c/a(2); Kirby scripts based on his war time experiences	47	94	141	296	498	700
3-5-Simon/Kirby-c only	34	68	102	204	332	460
6-Kirby-c/a(2)	42	84	126	265	445	625
7-Simon & Kirby-c	24	48	72	142	234	325
Super Reprints #10,15-17: 10-r/? 15,16-r/United States Marines #5,8. 17-r/Monty Hall #?	3	6	9	16	22	28
11,12,18-r/Foxhole #1,2,3; Kirby-c	3	6	9	19	30	40

NOTE: ***Kirby*** *a(r)-Super #11, 12.* ***Powell*** *a(r)-Super #15, 16. Stories by actual veterans.*

FOXY FAGAN COMICS (Funny Animal)
Dearfield Publishing Co.: Dec, 1946 - No. 7, Summer, 1948

	GD 2.0	VG 4.0	FN 6.0	VF 8.0	VF/NM 9.0	NM- 9.2
1-Foxy Fagan & Little Buck begin	15	30	45	90	140	190
2	9	18	27	52	69	85
3-7: 6-Rocket ship-c	9	18	27	47	61	75

FRACTION
DC Comics (Focus): June, 2004 - No. 6, Nov, 2004 ($2.50, limited series)

	GD 2.0	VG 4.0	FN 6.0	VF 8.0	VF/NM 9.0	NM- 9.2
1-6-David Tischman-s/Timothy Green II-a						3.00
SC (2011, $17.99) r/#1-6; cover gallery						18.00

FRACTURED FAIRY TALES (TV)
Gold Key: Oct, 1962 (Jay Ward)

	GD 2.0	VG 4.0	FN 6.0	VF 8.0	VF/NM 9.0	NM- 9.2
1 (10022-210)-From Bullwinkle TV show	10	20	30	64	132	200

FRAGGLE ROCK (TV)
Marvel Comics (Star Comics)/Marvel V2#1 on: Apr, 1985 - No. 8, Sept, 1986; V2#1, Apr, 1988 - No. 5, Aug, 1988

	GD 2.0	VG 4.0	FN 6.0	VF 8.0	VF/NM 9.0	NM- 9.2
1 (75¢-c)	3	6	9	14	19	24
2-6 (75¢-c)	1	3	4	6	8	10
7,8	1	2	3	5	6	8
V2#1-5-($1.00): Reprints 1st series						4.00

FRAGGLE ROCK: JOURNEY TO THE EVERSPRING, (JIM HENSON'S...)
Archaia: Oct, 2014 - No. 4, Jan, 2015 ($3.99, limited series)

	GD 2.0	VG 4.0	FN 6.0	VF 8.0	VF/NM 9.0	NM- 9.2
1-4-Kate Leth-s/Jake Myler-a. 1-Multiple covers						5.00

FRANCIS, BROTHER OF THE UNIVERSE
Marvel Comics Group: 1980 (75¢, 52 pgs., one-shot)

	GD 2.0	VG 4.0	FN 6.0	VF 8.0	VF/NM 9.0	NM- 9.2
1-John Buscema/Marie Severin-a; story of Francis Bernadone, celebrating his 800th birthday in 1982						6.00

FRANCIS THE FAMOUS TALKING MULE (All based on movie)
Dell Publishing Co.: No. 335 (#1), June, 1951 - No. 1090, March, 1960

	GD 2.0	VG 4.0	FN 6.0	VF 8.0	VF/NM 9.0	NM- 9.2
Four Color 335 (#1)	11	22	33	73	157	240
Four Color 465	6	12	18	41	76	110
Four Color 501,547,579	5	10	15	35	63	90
Four Color 621,655,698,710,745	5	10	15	33	57	80
Four Color 810,863,906,953,991,1068,1090	5	10	15	31	53	75

GD 2.0 | VG 4.0 | FN 6.0 | VF 8.0 | VF/NM 9.0 | NM- 9.2

FRANK
Nemesis Comics (Harvey): Apr (Mar inside), 1994 - No. 4, 1994 ($1.75/$2.50, limited series)
1-4-($2.50, direct sale): 1-Foil-c Edition 3.50
1-4-($1.75)-Newsstand Editions; Cowan-a in all 3.00

FRANK
Fantagraphics Books: Sept, 1996 ($2.95, B&W)
1-Woodring-c/a/scripts 3.00

FRANK BUCK (Formerly My True Love)
Fox Feature Syndicate: No. 70, May, 1950 - No. 3, Sept, 1950
70-Wood a(p)(3 stories)-Photo-c 39 78 117 240 395 550
71-Wood-a (9 pgs.); photo/painted-c 21 42 63 122 199 275
3: 3-Photo/painted-c 15 30 45 88 137 185
NOTE: *Based on "Bring 'Em Back Alive" TV show.*

FRANKEN-CASTLE (See The Punisher, 2009 series)

FRANKENSTEIN (See Dracula, Movie Classics & Werewolf)
Dell Publishing Co.: Aug-Oct, 1964; No. 2, Sept, 1966 - No. 4, Mar, 1967
1(12-283-410)(1964)(2nd printing; see Movie Classics for 1st printing)
7 14 21 48 92 135
2-Intro. & origin super-hero character (9/66) 5 10 15 35 63 90
3,4 4 8 12 27 44 60

FRANKENSTEIN (The Monster of...; also see Monsters Unleashed #2, Power Record Comics, Psycho & Silver Surfer #7)
Marvel Comics Group: Jan, 1973 - No. 18, Sept, 1975
1-Ploog-c/a begins, ends #6 11 22 33 73 157 240
2 5 10 15 35 63 90
3-5 4 8 12 23 37 50
6,7,10: 7-Dracula cameo 3 6 9 18 28 38
8,9-Dracula c/sty. 9-Death of Dracula 5 10 15 31 53 75
11-17 3 6 9 16 23 30
18-Wrightson-c(i) 3 6 9 17 26 35
NOTE: ***Adkins** c-17i. **Buscema** a-7-10p. **Ditko** a-12r. **G. Kane** c-15p. **Orlando** a-8r. **Ploog** a-1-3, 4p, 5p, 6; c-1-6. **Wrightson** c-18i.*

FRANKENSTEIN (Mary Wollstonecraft Shelley's...; A Marvel Illustrated Novel)
Marvel Pub.: 1983 ($8.95, B&W, 196 pgs., 8x11" TPB)
nn-Wrightson-a; 4 pg. intro. by Stephen King 5 10 15 33 57 80
Limited HC Edition 175.00

FRANKENSTEIN, AGENT OF S.H.A.D.E. (New DC 52)
DC Comics: Nov, 2011 - No. 16, Mar, 2013 ($2.99)
1-16: 1-Lemire-s/Ponticelli-a/J.G. Jones-c; Ray Palmer & The Creature Commandos app. 5-Crossover with OMAC #5. 13-15-Rotworld 3.00
#0 (11/12, $2.99) Kindt-s/Ponticelli-a; Frankenstein's origin 3.00

FRANKENSTEIN ALIVE, ALIVE
IDW Publishing: May, 2012 - No. 4, Jan, 2018 ($3.99, B&W)
1-3-Niles-s/Wrightson-a; interview with creators; excerpt from M.W. Shelley writings 4.00
4-($4.99) Art by Wrightson and Kelley Jones 5.00
... Reanimated Edition (4/14, $5.99) r/#1,2; silver foil cover logo 6.00
... Trio (1/18, $7.99) r/#1-3; silver foil cover logo 8.00

FRANKENSTEIN COMICS (Also See Prize Comics)
Prize Publ. (Crestwood/Feature): Sum, 1945 - V5#5(#33), Oct-Nov, 1954
1-Frankenstein begins by Dick Briefer (origin); Frank Sinatra parody
371 742 1113 2600 4550 6500
2 116 232 348 742 1271 1800
3-5 87 174 261 553 952 1350
6-10: 7-S&K a(r)/Headline Comics. 8(7-8/47)-Superman satire
74 148 222 470 810 1150
11-17(1-2/49)-11-Boris Karloff parody-c/story. 17-Last humor issue
58 116 174 371 636 900
18(3/52)-New origin, horror series begins 135 270 405 864 1482 2100
19,20(V3#4, 8-9/52) 97 194 291 621 1061 1500
21(V3#5), 22(V3#6), 23(V4#1) - #28(V4#6) 74 148 222 470 810 1150
29(V5#1) - #33(V5#5) 63 126 189 403 689 975
NOTE: ***Briefer** c/a-all. **Meskin** a-21, 29.*

FRANKENSTEIN/DRACULA WAR, THE
Topps Comics: Feb, 1995 - No. 3, May, 1995 ($2.50, limited series)
1-3 4.00

FRANKENSTEIN, JR. (...& the Impossibles) (TV)
Gold Key: Jan, 1966 (Hanna-Barbera)
1-Super hero (scarce) 12 24 36 80 173 265

FRANKENSTEIN MOBSTER
Image Comics: No. 0, Oct, 2003 - No. 7, Dec, 2004 ($2.95)
0-7: 0-Two covers by Wheatley and Hughes; Wheatley-s/a. 1-Variant-c by Wieringo 3.00

FRANKENSTEIN: NEW WORLD (From Hellboy)
Dark Horse Comics: Aug, 2022 - No. 4, Dec, 2022 ($3.99, limited series)
1-4-Mignola, Golden & Sniegoski-s/Bergting-a 4.00

FRANKENSTEIN: OR THE MODERN PROMETHEUS
Caliber Press: 1994 ($2.95, one-shot)
1 4.00

FRANKENSTEIN UNDERGROUND (From Hellboy)
Dark Horse Comics: Mar, 2015 - No. 5, Jul, 2015 ($3.50, limited series)
1-5-Mike Mignola-s/c; Ben Stenbeck-a 3.50

FRANKENSTEIN UNDONE (From Hellboy)
Dark Horse Comics: Jan, 2020 - No. 2, Apr, 2020 ($3.99, limited series)
1,2-Mike Mignola & Scott Allie-s/Ben Stenbeck-a/c 4.00

FRANK FRAZETTA FANTASY ILLUSTRATED (Magazine)
Quantum Cat Entertainment: Spring 1998 - No. 8 ($5.95, quarterly)
1-Anthology; art by Corben, Horley, Jusko 1 3 4 6 8 10
1-Linsner variant-c 15.00
2-Battle Chasers by Madureira; Harris-a 8.00
2-Madureira Battle Chasers variant-c 12.00
3-8-Frazetta-c 6.00
3-Tony Daniel variant-c 15.00
5,6-Portacio variant-c, 7,8-Alex Nino variant-c 10.00
8-Alex Ross Chicago Comicon variant-c 10.00

FRANK FRAZETTA'S DAWN ATTACK
Opus Comics: Nov, 2022 - Present ($4.99)
1,2-Yapur & McDaid-a 5.00

FRANK FRAZETTA'S DEATH DEALER
Image Comics: Mar, 2007 - No. 6, Jan, 2008 ($3.99)
1-6-Nat Jones-a; 3 covers (Frazetta, Jones, Jones sketch) 4.00

FRANK FRAZETTA'S DEATH DEALER
Opus Comics: May, 2022 - Present ($4.99)
1-9: 1-4-Iverson-s/Martino-a. 5-Gronbekk-s/Galindo-a 5.00

FRANK FRAZETTA'S...
Fantagraphics Books/Image Comics: one-shots
... Creatures 1 (Image Comics, 7/08, $3.99) Bergting-a; covers by Frazetta & Bergting
1 3 4 6 8 10
... Dark Kingdom 1-4 (Image, 4/08 - No. 4, 1/10, $3.99) Vigil-a; covers by Frazetta & Vigil
1 3 4 6 8 10
... Dracula Meets the Wolfman 1 (Image, 8/08, $3.99) Francavilla-a; 2 covers
1 3 4 6 8 10
... Moon Maid 1 (Image, 1/09, $3.99) Tim Vigil-a; covers by Frazetta & Vigil
1 3 4 6 8 10
... Neanderthal 1 (Image, 4/09, $3.99) Fotos & Vigil-a; covers by Frazetta & Fotos
1 3 4 6 8 10
... Sorcerer 1 (Image, 8/09, $3.99) Medors-a; covers by Frazetta & Medors
1 3 4 6 8 10
... Swamp Demon 1 (Image, 7/08, $3.99) Medors-a; covers by Frazetta & Medors
1 3 4 6 8 10
... Thun'da Tales 1 (Fantagraphics Books, 1987, $2.00) Frazetta-r
1 3 4 6 8 10
... Untamed Love 1 (Fantagraphics Books, 11/87, $2.00) r/1950's romance comics
1 3 4 6 8 10

FRANKIE COMICS (...& Lana No. 13-15) (Formerly Movie Tunes; becomes Frankie Fuddle No. 16 on)
Marvel Comics (MgPC): No. 4, Wint, 1946-47 - No. 15, June, 1949
4-Mitzi, Margie, Daisy app. 30 60 90 177 289 400
5-9 20 40 60 114 182 250
10-15: 13-Anti-Wertham editorial 17 34 51 98 154 210

FRANKIE DOODLE (See Sparkler, both series)
United Features Syndicate: No. 7, 1939
Single Series 7 37 74 111 222 361 500

FRANKIE FUDDLE (Formerly Frankie & Lana)
Marvel Comics: No. 16, Aug, 1949 - No. 17, Nov, 1949
16,17 15 30 45 90 140 190

FRANKLIN RICHARDS (Fantastic Four)
Marvel Comics: April, 2006 - Jun, 2009 ($2.99/$3.99, one-shots)
...: A Fantastic Year 1 (2018, $7.99) reprints various one-shots; Eliopoulos-s/a 8.00
...: April Fools (6/09, $3.99) Eliopoulos-s/a 4.00
...: Collected Chaos (2008, $8.99, digest) reprints various one-shots 9.00
...: Fall Football Fiasco (1/08, $2.99) Eliopoulos-a/Sumerak-s 3.00
...: Happy Franksgiving (1/07, $2.99) Thanksgiving stories by Eliopoulos-a/Sumerak-s 3.00
...: It's Dark Reigning Cats & Dogs (4/09, $3.99) Eliopoulos-s/a 4.00
...: Lab Brat (2007, $7.99, digest) reprints one-shots and Masked Marvel back-ups 8.00
...: March Madness (5/07, $2.99) More science gone wrong by Eliopoulos-a/Sumerak-s 3.00
...: Monster Mash (11/07, $2.99) Science mishaps by Eliopoulos-a/Sumerak-s 3.00
...: Not-So-Secret Invasion (7/08, $2.99) Skrull cover; The Wizard app. 3.00
... One Shot (4/06, $2.99) short stories by Eliopoulos-a/Sumerak-s 3.00
...: School's Out (4/09, $3.99) Eliopoulos-s/a; Katie Power app. 4.00
...: Sons of Geniuses (1/09, $3.99) parallel dimension alternate version hijinks 4.00
...: Spring Break (5/08, $2.99) short stories by Eliopoulos-a/Sumerak-s 3.00
...: Summer Smackdown (10/08, $2.99) short stories by Eliopoulos-a/Sumerak-s 3.00
...: Super Summer Spectacular (9/06, $2.99) short stories by Eliopoulos-a/Sumerak-s 3.00
...: World Be Warned (8/07, $2.99) short stories by Eliopoulos-a/Sumerak-s; Hulk app. 3.00

FRANK LUTHER'S SILLY PILLY COMICS (See Jingle Dingle...)
Children's Comics (Maltex Cereal): 1950 (10¢)
1-Characters from radio, records, & TV 14 28 42 82 121 160
NOTE: *Also printed as a promotional comic for Maltex cereal.*

FRANK MERRIWELL AT YALE (Speed Demons No. 5 on?)
Charlton Comics: June, 1955 - No. 4, Jan, 1956 (Also see Shadow Comics)
1 9 18 27 52 69 85
2-4 7 14 21 35 43 50

FRANK MILLER'S PANDORA
Frank Miller Presents: 2022 - Present ($7.99/$3.99)
1-($7.99) Created by Frank Miller; Emma Kubert-a 8.00
2-($3.99) 4.00

FRANTIC (Magazine) (See Ratfink & Zany)
Pierce Publishing Co.: Oct, 1958 - V2#2, Apr, 1959 (Satire)
V1#1 39 78 117 240 395 550
2 15 30 45 85 130 175
V2#1,2: 1-Burgos-a, Severin-c/a; Powell-a? 11 22 33 62 86 110

FRAY (Also see Buffy the Vampire Slayer "season eight" #16-19)
Dark Horse Comics: June, 2001 - No. 8, July, 2003 ($2.99, limited series)
1-Joss Whedon-s/Moline & Owens-a 1 2 3 5 6 8
1-DF Gold edition 2 4 6 9 12 15

Frankenstein Underground #1 © Mike Mignola

Frank Frazetta's Death Dealer #1 © Frazetta Girls LLC

Freedom Fighters (2019) #1 © DC

	GD 2.0	VG 4.0	FN 6.0	VF 8.0	VF/NM 9.0	NM- 9.2

2-8: 6-(3/02). 7-(4/03) — 4.00
TPB (11/03, $19.95) r/#1-8; intros by Whedon & Loeb; Moline sketch pages — 20.00

FREAK FORCE (Also see Savage Dragon)
Image Comics (Highbrow Ent.): Dec, 1993 - No. 18, July, 1995 ($1.95/$2.50)

1-18-Superpatriot & Mighty Man in all; Erik Larsen scripts in all. 4-Vanguard app. 8-Begin $2.50-c. 9-Cyberforce-c & app. 13-Variant-c — 3.00

FREAK FORCE (Also see Savage Dragon)
Image Comics: Apr, 1997 - No. 3, July, 1997 ($2.95)

1-3-Larsen-s — 3.00

FREAK OUT, USA (See On the Scene Presents...)

FREAK SHOW
Image Comics (Desperado): 2006 ($5.99, B&W, one-shot)

nn-Bruce Jones-s/Bernie Wrightson-c/a — 6.00

FREAKS OF THE HEARTLAND
Dark Horse Comics: Jan, 2004 - No. 6, Nov, 2004 ($2.99)

1-6-Steve Niles-s/Greg Ruth-a — 3.00

FRECKLES AND HIS FRIENDS (See Crackajack Funnies, Famous Comics Cartoon Book, Honeybee Birdwhistle... & Red Ryder)

FRECKLES AND HIS FRIENDS
Standard Comics/Argo: No. 5, 11/47 - No. 12, 8/49; 11/55 - No. 4, 6/56

	GD	VG	FN	VF	VF/NM	NM-
5-Reprints	18	36	54	107	169	230
6-12-Reprints. 7-9-Airbrush-c (by Schomburg?). 11-Lingerie panels	11	22	33	62	86	110

NOTE: *Some copies of No. 8 & 9 contain a printing oddity. The negatives were elongated in the engraving process, probably to conform to page dimensions on the filler pages. Those pages only look normal when viewed at a 45 degree angle.*

	GD	VG	FN	VF	VF/NM	NM-
1(Argo,'55)-Reprints (NEA Service)	7	14	21	37	46	55
2-4	5	10	14	20	24	28

FREDDY (Formerly My Little Margie's Boy Friends) (Also see Blue Bird)
Charlton Comics: V2#12, June, 1958 - No. 47, Feb, 1965

	GD	VG	FN	VF	VF/NM	NM-
V2#12-Teenage	5	10	15	30	50	70
13-15	3	6	9	17	25	34
16-47	3	6	9	14	19	24

FREDDY
Dell Publishing Co.: May-July, 1963 - No. 3, Oct-Dec, 1964

	GD	VG	FN	VF	VF/NM	NM-
1	3	6	9	19	30	40
2,3	3	6	9	15	22	28

FREDDY KRUEGER'S A NIGHTMARE ON ELM STREET
Marvel Comics: Oct, 1989 - No. 2, Dec, 1989 ($2.25, B&W, movie adaptation, magazine)

	GD	VG	FN	VF	VF/NM	NM-
1,2: Origin Freddy Krueger; Buckler/Alcala-a	3	6	9	19	30	40

FREDDY'S DEAD: THE FINAL NIGHTMARE
Innovation Publishing: Oct, 1991 - No. 3, Dec 1991 ($2.50, color mini-series, adapts movie)

	GD	VG	FN	VF	VF/NM	NM-
1-3: Dismukes (film poster artist) painted-c	2	4	6	9	12	15

FREDDY VS. JASON VS. ASH (Freddy Krueger, Friday the 13th, Army of Darkness)
DC Comics (WildStorm): Early Jan, 2008 - No. 6, May, 2008 ($2.99, limited series)

	GD	VG	FN	VF	VF/NM	NM-
1-Three covers by J. Scott Campbell; Kuhoric-s/Craig-a	3	6	9	17	26	35
1-Second printing with 3 covers combined sideways	1	3	4	6	8	10
2-6: 2-4-Eric Powell-c. 5,6-Richard Friend-c	1	3	4	6	8	10
2-4-Second printings with B&W covers						4.00
TPB (2008, $17.99) r/#1-6; creators' interviews	7	14	21	44	82	120

FREDDY VS. JASON VS. ASH: THE NIGHTMARE WARRIORS
DC Comics (WildStorm): Aug, 2009 - No. 6, Jan, 2010 ($3.99, limited series)

	GD	VG	FN	VF	VF/NM	NM-
1-Suydam-c; Katz & Kuhoric-s/Craig-a	1	3	4	6	8	10
2-6-Katz & Kuhoric-s/Craig-a						5.00
TPB (2010, $17.99) r/#1-6; cover gallery	5	10	15	30	50	70

FRED HEMBECK DESTROYS THE MARVEL UNIVERSE
Marvel Comics: July, 1989 ($1.50, one-shot)

1-Punisher app.; Staton-i (5 pgs.) — 4.00

FRED HEMBECK SELLS THE MARVEL UNIVERSE
Marvel Comics: Oct, 1990 ($1.25, one-shot)

1-Punisher, Wolverine parodies; Hembeck/Austin-c — 4.00

FREE COMIC BOOK DAY
Various publishers

2013 (Avengers/Hulk)(Marvel, 5/13) Hulk and Avengers Assemble animated series — 3.00
2014 (Guardians of the Galaxy)(Marvel, 5/14) r/#1; Thanos & Spider-Verse back-ups — 3.00
2015 (Avengers)(Marvel, 6/15) All-New Avengers and Uncanny Humans — 3.00
2015 (Dark Horse, 5/15) Previews Fight Club 2, The Goon, and The Strain — 3.00
2015 (Secret Wars #1)(Marvel, 6/15) Prelude to Secret Wars series (#0 on cover); back-up with Avengers/Attack on Titan x-over; Alex Ross wraparound-c — 3.00
2016 (Captain America #1)(Marvel, 5/16) Preview of Captain America: Steve Rogers #1 and Amazing Spider-Man "Dead No More" storyline — 3.00
2016 (Civil War II #1)(Marvel, 5/16) Preview of Civil War II #1 and All-New All-Different Avengers #9; Nadia Pym (The Wasp) app. — 3.00
2016 (Dark Horse, 5/16) Previews Serenity, Hellboy and Aliens: Defiance — 3.00
2017 (Dark Horse, 5/17) Avatar (movie) w/Doug Wheatley-a; Briggs Land story - Wood-s/ Dell'Edera-a — 3.00
2017 (All-New Guardians of the Galaxy)(Marvel, 7/17) 1-Duggan-s/Kuder-a; preview of Defenders #1; Bendis-s/Marquez-a — 3.00
2017 (Secret Empire)(Marvel, 7/17) 1-Spencer-s/Sorrentino-a/Brooks-c; Steve Rogers vs. the Avengers; back-up prelude to Peter Parker: The Spectacular Spider-Man #1; Zdarsky-s/Siqueira-a; Vulture app. — 3.00
2018 (Amazing Spider-Man/Guardians of the Galaxy)(Marvel, 5/18) Ottley-c — 3.00
2018 (Avengers/Captain America)(Marvel, 5/18) Aaron-s/Pichelli-a & Coates-s/Yu-a — 3.00
2018 (Dark Horse, 5/18) Previews Overwatch and Black Hammer; Niemczyk-c — 3.00
2019 (Dark Horse, 5/19) Previews Minecraft and Incredibles 2; Cassie Anderson-c — 3.00
2019 (Dark Horse, 5/19) Stranger Things and Black Hammer; Chun Lo-c — 3.00
2019 (Avengers/Savage Avengers)(Marvel, 7/19) Aaron-s/Caselli-a; McGuinness-c — 3.00
2019 (Spider-Man/Venom)(Marvel, 7/19) Stegman-c; previews Absolute Carnage — 3.00
2021 (Avengers/Hulk)(Marvel, 10/21) Ottley-c; previews Avengers #50 & Hulk #1 (2022) — 3.00
2021 (AWA, 8/21) Previews The Resistance: Uprising, Moths, Not All Robots — 3.00
2021 (Dark Horse, 8/21) Previews Critical Roll & The Witcher; Tyler Walpole-c — 3.00
2021 (Spider-Man/Venom)(Marvel, 10/21) Gleason-c; also previews Daredevil — 3.00
...: Dark Circle 1 (Archie Comic Pub., 6-7/15) Previews Black Hood, The Fox, The Shield — 3.00
...: R.I.P.D. and The True Lives of the Fabulous Killjoys (Dark Horse, 5/13) Flipbook with Mass Effect — 3.00

FREEDOM AGENT (Also see John Steele)
Gold Key: Apr, 1963 (12¢)

	GD	VG	FN	VF	VF/NM	NM-
1 (10054-304)-Painted-c	4	8	12	28	47	65

FREEDOM FIGHTERS (See Justice League of America #107,108)
National Periodical Publ./DC Comics: Mar-Apr, 1976 - No. 15, July-Aug, 1978

	GD	VG	FN	VF	VF/NM	NM-
1-Uncle Sam, The Ray, Black Condor, Doll Man, Human Bomb, & Phantom Lady begin (all former Quality characters)	4	8	12	23	37	50
2-9: 4,5-Wonder Woman x-over. 7-1st app. Crusaders2	4	6	9	12	15	
10-15: 10-Origin Doll Man; Cat-Man-c/story (4th app; 1st revival since Detective #325). 11-Origin The Ray. 12-Origin Firebrand. 13-Origin Black Condor. 14-Batgirl & Batwoman app. 15-Batgirl & Batwoman app.; origin Phantom Lady	2	4	6	9	13	16

NOTE: ***Buckler** c-5-11p, 13p, 14p.*

FREEDOM FIGHTERS (Also see "Uncle Sam and the Freedom Fighters")
DC Comics: Nov, 2010 - No. 9, Jul, 2011 ($2.99)

1-9-Travis Moore-a. 1-6-Dave Johnson-c — 3.00

FREEDOM FIGHTERS
DC Comics: Feb, 2019 - No. 12, Mar, 2020 ($3.99, limited series)

1-12: 1-Venditti-s/Barrows-a; intro. new Freedom Fighters on present day Earth-X — 4.00

FREEDOM FORCE
Image Comics: Jan, 2005 - No. 6, June, 2005 ($2.95)

1-6-Eric Dieter-s/Tom Scioli-a — 3.00

FREELANCERS
BOOM! Studios: Oct, 2012 - No. 6, Mar, 2013 ($1.00/$3.99)

1-($1.00) Brill-s/Covey-a; eight covers; back-up origin of Valerie & Cassie — 3.00
2-6-($3.99) Multiple covers on each — 4.00

FREEMIND
Future Comics: No. 0, Aug, 2002; Nov, 2002 - No. 7, June, 2003 ($3.50)

0-($2.25) Two covers by Giordano & Layton — 3.00
1-7 ($3.50) 1-Two covers by Giordano & Layton; Giordano-a thru #3. 4,5-Leeke-a — 3.50

FREEREALMS
DC Comics (WildStorm): Sept, 2009 - No. 12, Oct, 2010 ($3.99, limited series)

1-12-Based on the online game; Jon Buran-a — 4.00
... Book One TPB (2010, $19.99) r/#1-6 — 20.00
... Book Two TPB (2010, $19.99) r/#7-12 — 20.00

FREEX
Malibu Comics (Ultraverse): July, 1993 - No. 18, Mar, 1995 ($1.95)

1-3,5-14,16-18: 1-Polybagged w/trading card. 2-Some were polybagged w/card. 6-Nightman-c/story. 7-2 pg. origin Hardcase by Zeck. 17-Rune app. — 3.00

	GD 2.0	VG 4.0	FN 6.0	VF 8.0	VF/NM 9.0	NM- 9.2
1-Holographic-c edition						8.00
1-Ultra 5,000 limited silver ink-c						5.00
4-($2.50, 48 pgs.)-Rune flip-c/story by B. Smith (3 pgs.); 3 pg. Night Man preview						4.00
15 ($3.50)-w/Ultraverse Premiere #9 flip book; Alec Swan & Rafferty app.						4.00
Giant Size 1 (7/94, $2.50)-Prime app.						4.00

NOTE: *Simonson c-1.*

FREEZE, THE
Image Comics: Dec, 2018 - No. 4, Mar, 2019 ($3.99)

	GD	VG	FN	VF	VF/NM	NM-
1-4-Dan Wickline-s/Phillip Sevy-a						4.00

FRENEMY OF THE STATE
Oni Press: May, 2010 - No. 5, Dec, 2011 ($3.99)

	GD	VG	FN	VF	VF/NM	NM-
1-5-Rashida Jones, Christina Weir & Nunzio DeFilippis-s						4.00

FRENZY (Magazine) (Satire)
Picture Magazine: Apr, 1958 - No. 7, Jun, 1959

	GD	VG	FN	VF	VF/NM	NM-
1-Painted-c	16	32	48	94	147	200
2-7	9	18	27	52	69	85

FRESHMEN
Image Comics: Jul, 2005 - No. 6, Mar, 2006 ($2.99)

	GD	VG	FN	VF	VF/NM	NM-
1-Sterbakov-s/Kirk-a; co-created by Seth Green; covers by Pérez, Migliari, Linsner						3.00
2-6-Migliari-c						3.00
... Yearbook (1/06, $2.99) profile pages of characters; art by various incl. Chaykin, Kirk						3.00
... Vol. 1 (3/06, $16.99, TPB) r/#1-6 & Yearbook; cover gallery with concept art						17.00

FRESHMEN (Volume 2)
Image Comics: Nov, 2006 - No. 6, Aug, 2007 ($2.99)

	GD	VG	FN	VF	VF/NM	NM-
1-6: 1-Sterbakov-s/Conrad-a; 4 covers						3.00
...: Summer Vacation Special (7/08, $4.99) Sterbakov-s; bonus pin-ups by various						5.00
... Vol. 2 Fundamentals of Fear (6/07, $16.99, TPB) r/#1-6; cover gallery, journals						17.00

FRIDAY FOSTER
Dell Publishing Co.: October, 1972

	GD	VG	FN	VF	VF/NM	NM-
1-Black heroine; Jack Sparling-a	25	50	75	175	388	600

FRIDAY THE 13TH (Based on the horror movie franchise)
DC Comics (WildStorm): Feb, 2007 - No. 6, July, 2007 ($2.99, mature)

	GD	VG	FN	VF	VF/NM	NM-
1-Gray & Palmiotti-s/Archer-a; cover by Sook	3	6	9	16	23	30
1-Variant-c by Bradstreet	4	8	12	23	37	50
2-6: Gray & Palmiotti-s/Archer-a/Sook-c						6.00
...: Abuser and The Abused (6/08, $3.50) Fialkov-s/Andy B. -a	2	4	6	11	16	20
...: Bad Land 1,2 (3/08 - No. 2, 4/08, $2.99) Marz-s/Huddleston-a/McKone-c	1	3	4	6	8	10
...: How I Spent My Summer Vacation 1,2 (11/07 - No. 2, 12/07, $2.99) Aaron-s/Archer-a	2	4	6	11	16	20
...: Pamela's Tale 1,2 (9/07 - No. 2, 10/07, $2.99) Andreyko-s/Moll-a/Nguyen-c	2	4	6	11	16	20

FRIENDLY GHOST, CASPER, THE (Becomes Casper... #254 on)
Harvey Publications: Aug, 1958 - No. 224, Oct, 1982; No. 225, Oct, 1986 - No. 253, June, 1990

	GD	VG	FN	VF	VF/NM	NM-
1-Infinity-c	75	150	225	600	1350	2100
2	25	50	75	175	388	600
3-6: 6-X-Mas-c	11	22	33	76	163	250
7-10	9	18	27	61	123	185
11-20: 18-X-Mas-c	8	16	24	51	96	140
21-30	5	10	15	34	60	85
31-50	4	8	12	25	40	55
51-70,100: 54-X-Mas-c	3	6	9	19	30	40
71-99	3	6	9	16	23	30
101-131: 131-Last 12¢ issue	3	6	9	14	20	26
132-159	2	4	6	11	16	20
160-163: All 52 pg. Giants	3	6	9	14	20	26
164-199: 173,179,185-Cub Scout Specials	2	4	6	8	10	12
200	2	4	6	8	11	14
201-224	1	2	3	5	7	9
225-237: 230-X-mas-c. 232-Valentine's-c						5.00
238-253: 238-Begin $1.00-c. 238,244-Halloween-c. 243-Last new material						4.00

FRIENDLY NEIGHBORHOOD SPIDER-MAN
Marvel Comics: Dec, 2005 - No. 24, Nov, 2007 ($2.99)

	GD	VG	FN	VF	VF/NM	NM-
1-Evolve or Die pt. 1; Peter David-s/Mike Wieringo-a; Morlun app.						4.00
1-Variant Wieringo-c with regular costume						5.00
2-4: 2-New Avengers app. 3-Spider-Man dies						3.00
2-4-var-c: 2-Bag-Head Fantastic Four costume. 3-Captain Universe. 4-Wrestler						5.00
5-10: 6-Red & gold costume. 8-10-Uncle Ben app.						3.00
11-23: 17-Black costume; Sandman app.						3.00
24-($3.99) "One More Day" part 2; Quesada-a; covers by Quesada & Djurdjevic						4.00
Annual 1 (7/07, $3.99) Origin of The Sandman; back-up w/Doran-a						4.00
... Vol. 1: Derailed (2006, $14.99) r/#5-10; Wieringo sketch pages						15.00
... Vol. 2: Mystery Date (2007, $13.99) r/#11-16						14.00

FRIENDLY NEIGHBORHOOD SPIDER-MAN
Marvel Comics: Mar, 2019 - No. 14, Feb, 2020 ($4.99/$3.99)

	GD	VG	FN	VF	VF/NM	NM-
1-($4.99) Taylor-s/Cabal-a; Aunt May's diagnosis; Ferreira-a						5.00
2-14-($3.99) 2-Intro. The Rumor. 7-10-Lashley-a; Prowler app. 12,13-Fantastic Four app.						4.00

FRIEND OF THE DEVIL: A RECKLESS BOOK
Image Comics: Apr, 2021 ($24.99, HC graphic novel)

	GD	VG	FN	VF	VF/NM	NM-
HC - Ed Brubaker-s/Sean Phillips-a; 2nd book in the Reckless series						25.00

FRIENDS OF MAXX (Also see Maxx)
Image Comics (I Before E): Apr, 1996 - No. 3, Mar, 1997 ($2.95)

	GD	VG	FN	VF	VF/NM	NM-
1-3: Sam Kieth-c/a/scripts. 1-Featuring Dude Japan						3.00

FRIGHT
Atlas/Seaboard Periodicals: June, 1975 (Aug. on inside)

	GD	VG	FN	VF	VF/NM	NM-
1-Origin/1st app. The Son of Dracula; Frank Thorne-c/a	3	6	9	17	26	35

FRIGHT NIGHT
Now Comics: Oct, 1988 - No. 22, 1990 ($1.75)

	GD	VG	FN	VF	VF/NM	NM-
1-Adapts movie	2	4	6	9	12	15
2-22: 2-Movie adaptation cont. 8, 9-Evil Ed horror photo-c from movie						4.00

FRIGHT NIGHT
American Mythology Productions: 2021 - Present ($3.99)

	GD	VG	FN	VF	VF/NM	NM-
1-Based on the original novel; Kuhoric-s; art by Craig, Vokes, Geldhof & Webb						4.00

FRIGHT NIGHT II
Now Comics: 1989 ($3.95, 52 pgs.)

	GD	VG	FN	VF	VF/NM	NM-
1-Adapts movie sequel						6.00

FRINGE (Based on the 2008 FOX television series)
DC Comics (WildStorm): Oct, 2008 - No. 6, Aug, 2009 ($2.99, limited series)

	GD	VG	FN	VF	VF/NM	NM-
1-6-Anthology by various. 1-Mandrake & Coleby-a						4.00
TPB (2009, $19.99) r/#1-6; intro. by TV series co-creators Kurtzman & Orci						20.00

FRINGE: TALES FROM THE FRINGE (Based on the 2008 FOX television series)
DC Comics (WildStorm): Aug, 2010 - No. 6, Jan, 2011 ($3.99, limited series)

	GD	VG	FN	VF	VF/NM	NM-
1-6-Anthology by various; LaTorre-c. 1-Reg & photo-c						4.00
2-6-Variant covers from parallel world. 2-Death of Batman. 3-Superman/Dark Knight Returns. 4-Crisis #7 Supergirl holding dead Superman. 5-Justice League #1 w/Jonah Hex. 6-Red Lantern/Red Arrow #76						10.00
TPB (2011, $14.99) r/#1-6 with variant cover gallery and sketch art						15.00

FRISKY ANIMALS (Formerly Frisky Fables; Super Cat #56 on)
Star Publications: No. 44, Jan, 1951 - No. 55, Sept, 1953

	GD	VG	FN	VF	VF/NM	NM-
44-Super Cat; L.B. Cole	25	50	75	150	245	340
45-Classic L. B. Cole-c	37	74	111	222	361	500
46-51,53-55: Super Cat. 54-Super Cat-c begin	22	44	66	132	216	300
52-L. B. Cole-c/a, 3 1/2 pgs.; X-Mas-c	24	48	72	142	234	325

NOTE: *All have* ***L. B. Cole****-c. No. 47-No Super Cat.* ***Disbrow*** *a-49, 52.* ***Fago*** *a-51.*

FRISKY ANIMALS ON PARADE (Formerly Parade Comics; becomes Superspook)
Ajax-Farrell Publ. (Four Star Comic Corp.): Sept, 1957 - No. 3, Dec-Jan, 1957-1958

	GD	VG	FN	VF	VF/NM	NM-
1-L. B. Cole-c	20	40	60	115	185	265
2-No L. B. Cole-c	11	22	33	62	86	110
3-L. B. Cole-c	17	34	51	98	154	210

FRISKY FABLES (Frisky Animals No. 44 on)
Premium Group/Novelty Publ./Star Publ. V5#4 on: Spring, 1945 - No. 43, Oct, 1950

	GD	VG	FN	VF	VF/NM	NM-
V1#1-Funny animal; Al Fago-c/a #1-38	27	54	81	158	259	360
2,3(Fall & Winter, 1945)	15	30	45	90	140	190
V2#1(#4, 4/46) - 9,11,12(#15, 3/47): 4-Flag-c	13	26	39	72	101	130
10-Christmas-c. 12-Valentine's-c	13	26	39	74	105	135
V3#1(#16, 4/47) - 12(#27, 3/48): 4-Flag-c. 7,9-Infinity-c. 10-X-Mas-c. 12-Washington crossing the Delaware parody-c	11	22	33	64	90	115
V4#1(#28, 4/48) - 7(#34, 2-3/49)	10	20	30	58	79	100
V5#1(#35, 4-5/49) - 4(#38, 10-11/49)	10	20	30	56	76	95
39-43-L. B. Cole-c; 40-Xmas-c	22	44	66	130	213	295
Accepted Reprint No. 43 (nd); L.B. Cole-c; classic story "The Mad Artist"	11	22	33	62	86	110

FRITZI RITZ (See Comics On Parade, Single Series #5, 1(reprint), Tip Top & United Comics)

FRITZI RITZ (United Comics No. 8-26) (Also see Tip Topper for early Peanuts by Schulz)
United Features Synd./St. John No. 37-55/Dell No. 56 on:
1939; Fall, 1948; No. 3, 1949 - No. 7, 1949; No. 27, 3-4/53 - No. 36, 9-10/54; No. 37 - No. 55, 9-11/57; No. 56, 12-2/57-58 - No. 59, 9-11/58

	GD	VG	FN	VF	VF/NM	NM-
Single Series #5 (1939)	45	90	135	284	480	675
nn(1948)-Special Fall issue; by Ernie Bushmiller	27	54	81	162	266	370
3(#1)	22	44	66	128	209	290
4-7(1949): 6-Abbie & Slats app.	14	28	42	82	121	160
27(1953)-33,37-50,57-59-Early Peanuts (1-4 pgs.) by Schulz. 29-Five pg. Abbie & Slats; 1 pg. Mamie by Russell Patterson. 38(9/55)-41(4/56)-Low print run	21	42	63	122	199	275
34-36,51-56: 36-1 pg. Mamie by Patterson	12	24	36	69	97	125

NOTE: *Abbie & Slats in #6,7, 27-31. Li'l Abner in #32-36.*

FROGMAN COMICS
Hillman Periodicals: Jan-Feb, 1952 - No. 11, May, 1953

	GD	VG	FN	VF	VF/NM	NM-
1	21	42	63	122	199	275
2	13	26	39	74	105	135
3,4,6-11: 4-Meskin-a	11	22	33	62	86	110
5-Krigstein-a	12	24	36	69	97	125

FROGMEN, THE
Dell Publishing Co.: No. 1258, Feb-Apr, 1962 - No. 11, Nov-Jan, 1964-65 (Painted-c)

	GD	VG	FN	VF	VF/NM	NM-
Four Color 1258(#1)-Evans-a	9	18	27	62	126	190
2,3-Evans-a; part Frazetta inks in #2,3	5	10	15	34	60	85
4,6-11	4	8	12	25	40	55
5-Toth-a	4	8	12	28	47	65

FROM BEYOND THE UNKNOWN
National Periodical Publications: 10-11/69 - No. 25, 11-12/73

	GD	VG	FN	VF	VF/NM	NM-
1	5	10	15	35	63	90
2-6	3	6	9	21	33	45
7-11: (64 pgs.) 7-Intro Col. Glenn Merrit	4	8	12	23	37	50
12-17: (52 pgs.) 13-Wood-a(i)(r). 17-Pres. Nixon-c	3	6	9	18	28	38
18-25: Star Rovers-r begin #18,19. Space Museum in #23-25	3	6	9	14	20	25

NOTE: ***N. Adams*** *c-3, 6, 8, 9.* ***Anderson*** *c-2, 4, 5, 10, 11i, 15-17, 22; reprints-3, 4, 6-8, 10, 11, 13-16, 24, 25.* ***Infantino*** *r-1-5, 7-19, 23-25; c-11p.* ***Kaluta*** *c-18, 19.* ***Gil Kane*** *a-9r.* ***Kubert*** *c-1, 7, 12-14.* ***Toth*** *a-2r.* ***Wood*** *a-13i. Photo c-22.*

FROM BEYOND THE UNKNOWN GIANT
DC Comics: 2020 ($4.99, one-shot, 100 pgs., squarebound, Mass Market & Direct Market editions exist with different covers)

	GD	VG	FN	VF	VF/NM	NM-
1-New stories of Green Lantern, Kamandi & Legion of Super-Heroes and reprints						5.00

FROM DUSK TILL DAWN (Movie)
Big Entertainment: 1996 ($4.95, one-shot)

Friendly Neighborhood Spider-Man (2019) #1 © MAR

From Beyond the Unknown #11 © DC

Frontline Combat #9 © WMG

	GD 2.0	VG 4.0	FN 6.0	VF 8.0	VF/NM 9.0	NM- 9.2
nn-Adaptation of the film; Brereton-c	2	4	6	8	10	12
nn-($9.95)Deluxe Ed. w/ new material	2	4	6	11	16	20

FROM HELL
Mad Love/Tundra Publishing/Kitchen Sink: 1991 - No. 11, Sept, 1998 (B&W)

	GD	VG	FN	VF	VF/NM	NM-
1-Alan Moore and Eddie Campbell's Jack The Ripper story collected from the Taboo anthology series	3	6	9	16	23	30
1-(2nd printing)	2	4	6	8	10	12
1-(3rd printing)	1	2	3	4	5	7
2	1	3	4	6	8	10
2-(2nd printing)						6.00
2-(3rd printing)						4.00
3-1st Kitchen Sink Press issue	1	3	4	6	8	10
3-(2nd printing)						5.00
4-10: 10-(8/96)	1	2	3	5	6	8
11-Dance of the Gull Catchers (9/98, $4.95) Epilogue	2	4	6	10	14	18
Tundra Publishing reprintings 1-5 ('92)	1	2	3	4	5	7
HC						125.00
HC Ltd. Edition of 1,000 (signed and numbered)						230.00
TPB-1st printing (11/99)						60.00
TPB-2nd printing (3/00)						50.00
TPB-3rd printing (11/00)						40.00
TPB-4th printing (7/01) Regular and movie covers						35.00
TPB-5th printing - Regular and movie covers						35.00

FROM HERE TO INSANITY (Satire) (Formerly Eh! #1-7) (See Frantic & Frenzy)
Charlton Comics: No. 8, Feb, 1955 - V3#1, 1956

	GD	VG	FN	VF	VF/NM	NM-
8	26	52	78	154	252	350
9	22	44	66	132	216	300
10-Ditko-c/a (3 pgs.)	35	70	105	208	339	470
11-All Kirby except 4 pgs.	43	86	129	271	461	650
12-(Mag. size) Marilyn Monroe, Jackie Gleason-c; all Kirby except 4 pgs.	47	94	141	296	498	700
V3#1(1956)-Ward-c/a(2) (signed McCartney); 5 pgs. Wolverton-a; 3 pgs. Ditko-a; magazine format (cover says "Crazy, Man, Crazy" and becomes Crazy, Man, Crazy with V2#2)	81	162	243	518	884	1250

FROM THE PIT
Fantagor Press: 1994 ($4.95, one-shot, mature)

	GD	VG	FN	VF	VF/NM	NM-
1-R. Corben-a; HP Lovecraft back-up story	5	10	15	31	53	75

FRONTIER DOCTOR (TV)
Dell Publishing Co.: No. 877, Feb, 1958 (one-shot)

	GD	VG	FN	VF	VF/NM	NM-
Four Color 877-Toth-a, Rex Allen photo-c	9	18	27	59	117	175

FRONTIER FIGHTERS
National Periodical Publications: Sept-Oct, 1955 - No. 8, Nov-Dec, 1956

	GD	VG	FN	VF	VF/NM	NM-
1-Davy Crockett, Buffalo Bill (by Kubert), Kit Carson begin (Scarce)	63	126	189	403	689	975
2	42	84	126	265	445	625
3-8	39	78	117	236	388	540

NOTE: *Buffalo Bill by* ***Kubert*** *in all.*

FRONTIER ROMANCES
Avon Periodicals/I. W.: Nov-Dec, 1949 - No. 2, Feb-Mar, 1950 (Painted-c)

	GD	VG	FN	VF	VF/NM	NM-
1-Used in **SOTI**, pg. 180 (General reference) & illo. "Erotic spanking in a western comic book"	84	168	252	538	919	1300
2 (Scarce)-Woodish-a by Stallman	50	100	150	315	533	750
I.W. Reprint #1-Reprints Avon's #1	4	8	12	25	40	55
I.W. Reprint #9-Reprints ?	3	6	9	17	26	35

FRONTIER SCOUT: DAN'L BOONE (Formerly Death Valley; The Masked Raider No. 14 on)
Charlton Comics: No. 10, Jan, 1956 - No. 13, Aug, 1956; V2#14, Mar, 1965

	GD	VG	FN	VF	VF/NM	NM-
10	10	20	30	54	72	90
11-13(1956)	6	12	18	31	38	45
V2#14(3/65)	3	6	9	15	22	28

FRONTIERSMAN
Image Comics: Sept, 2021 - Present ($3.99)

	GD	VG	FN	VF	VF/NM	NM-
1-5-Kindlon-s/Ferrari-a; wraparound-c on each						4.00
...: Lock-Up Special 1 (5/22, $5.99) Kindlon-s/Assirelli-a; wraparound-c						6.00

FRONTIER TRAIL (The Rider No. 1-5)
Ajax/Farrell Publ.: No. 6, May, 1958

	GD	VG	FN	VF	VF/NM	NM-
6	6	12	18	31	38	45

FRONTIER WESTERN
Atlas Comics (PrPI): Feb, 1956 - No. 10, Aug, 1957

	GD	VG	FN	VF	VF/NM	NM-
1-The Pecos Kid rides	26	52	78	154	252	350
2,3,6-Williamson-a, 4 pgs. each	15	30	45	94	147	200
4,7,9,10: 10-Check-a	13	26	39	74	105	135
5-Crandall, Baker, Davis-a; Williamson text illos	15	30	45	86	133	180
8-Crandall, Morrow, & Wildey-a	14	28	42	76	108	140

NOTE: ***Baker*** *a-9.* ***Colan*** *a-2, 6.* ***Drucker*** *a-3, 4.* ***Heath*** *c-5.* ***Maneely*** *c/a-2, 7, 9.* ***Maurera*** *a-2.* ***Romita*** *a-7.* ***Severin*** *c-6, 8, 10.* ***Tuska*** *a-2.* ***Wildey*** *a-5, 8. Ringo Kid in No. 4.*

FRONTLINE COMBAT
E. C. Comics: July-Aug, 1951 - No. 15, Jan, 1954

	GD	VG	FN	VF	VF/NM	NM-
1-Severin/Kurtzman-a	109	218	327	872	1386	1900
2	49	98	147	392	621	850
3	39	78	117	312	494	675
4-Used in **SOTI**, pg. 257; contains "Air Burst" by Kurtzman which is his personal all-time favorite story; "Light Brigade!" story based on Tennyson's "Charge of the Light Brigade"	40	80	120	320	510	700
5-John Severin and Bill Elder bios.	31	62	93	248	399	550
6-10: 6-Kurtzman bio. 9-Civil War issue	25	50	75	200	320	440
11-15	21	42	63	168	264	360

NOTE: ***Davis*** *a-in all; c-11, 12.* ***Evans*** *a-10-15.* ***Heath*** *a-1.* ***Kubert*** *a-14.* ***Kurtzman*** *a-1-5; c-1-9.* ***Severin*** *a-5-7, 9, 13, 15.* ***Severin/Elder*** *a-2-11; c-10.* ***Toth*** *a-8, 12.* ***Wood*** *a-1-4, 6-10, 12-15; c-13-15. Special issues: No. 7 (Iwo Jima), No. 9 (Civil War), No. 12 (Air Force).*
(Canadian reprints known; see Table of Contents.)

FRONTLINE COMBAT
Russ Cochran/Gemstone Publishing: Aug, 1995 - No. 14 ($2.00/$2.50)

	GD	VG	FN	VF	VF/NM	NM-
1-14-E.C. reprints in all						4.00

FRONT PAGE COMIC BOOK
Front Page Comics (Harvey): 1945

	GD	VG	FN	VF	VF/NM	NM-
1-Kubert-a; intro. & 1st app. Man in Black by Powell; Fuje-c	194	388	582	1242	2121	3000

FROST AND FIRE (See DC Science Fiction Graphic Novel)

FROSTBITE
DC Comics (Vertigo): Nov, 2016 - No. 6, Apr, 2017 ($3.99)

	GD	VG	FN	VF	VF/NM	NM-
1-6-Joshua Williamson-s/Jason Shawn Alexander-a						4.00

FROSTY THE SNOWMAN
Dell Publishing Co.: No. 359, Nov, 1951 - No. 1272, Dec-Feb?/1961-62

	GD	VG	FN	VF	VF/NM	NM-
Four Color 359 (#1)	11	22	33	75	160	245
Four Color 435,514,601,661	7	14	21	48	89	130
Four Color 748,861,950,1065,1153,1272	5	10	15	35	63	90

FROZEN (Disney movie)
Joe Books Ltd.: Jul, 2016 - No. 5 ($2.99)

	GD	VG	FN	VF	VF/NM	NM-
1-5-Georgia Ball-s/Benedetta Barone-a						4.00

FROZEN... (Disney movie)
Dark Horse Comics: 2018 - Present ($3.99, limited series)

	GD	VG	FN	VF	VF/NM	NM-
...: Breaking Boundaries (8/18 - No. 3, 10/18) 1-3: 1-Caranagna & Nitz-s						4.00
...: Reunion Road (3/19 - No. 3, 5/19) 1-3-Caranagna-s/Francisco-a						4.00
...: The Hero Within (6/19 - No. 3, 9/19) 1-3-Caranagna-s						4.00
...: True Treasure (11/19 - No. 3, 1/20) 1-3-Caranagna-s; leads up to Frozen 2 movie						4.00

FRUITMAN SPECIAL (See Bunny #2 for 1st app.)
Harvey Publications: Dec, 1969 (68 pgs.)

	GD	VG	FN	VF	VF/NM	NM-
1-Funny super hero	4	8	12	27	44	60

F-TROOP (TV)
Dell Publishing Co.: Aug, 1966 - No. 7, Aug, 1967 (All have photo-c)

	GD	VG	FN	VF	VF/NM	NM-
1	13	26	39	91	201	310
2-7	5	10	15	34	60	85

FUGITIVES FROM JUSTICE (True Crime Stories)
St. John Publishing Co.: Feb, 1952 - No. 5, Oct, 1952

	GD	VG	FN	VF	VF/NM	NM-
1	34	68	102	199	325	450
2-Matt Baker-r/Northwest Mounties #2; Vic Flint strip reprints begin	30	60	90	177	289	400
3-Reprints panel from Authentic Police Cases that was used in **SOTI** with changes; Tuska-a	28	56	84	165	270	375
4	16	32	48	94	147	200
5-Last Vic Flint-r; bondage-c	21	42	63	122	199	275

FUGITOID
Mirage Studios: 1985 (B&W, magazine size, one-shot)

	GD	VG	FN	VF	VF/NM	NM-
1-Ties into Teenage Mutant Ninja Turtles #5	5	10	15	33	57	80

FU JITSU
AfterShock Comics: Sept, 2017 - No. 5, Feb, 2018 ($3.99)

	GD 2.0	VG 4.0	FN 6.0	VF 8.0	VF/NM 9.0	NM- 9.2
1-5-Jai Nitz-s/Wesley St. Claire-a						4.00

FULL OF FUN
Red Top (Decker Publ.)(Farrell)/I. W. Enterprises: Aug, 1957 - No. 2, Nov, 1957; 1964

	GD 2.0	VG 4.0	FN 6.0	VF 8.0	VF/NM 9.0	NM- 9.2
1(1957)-Funny animal; Dave Berg-a	9	18	27	50	65	80
2-Reprints Bingo, the Monkey Doodle Boy	5	10	15	25	31	36
8-I.W. Reprint('64)	2	4	6	10	14	18

FUN AT CHRISTMAS (See March of Comics No. 138)

FUN CLUB COMICS (See Interstate Theatres...)

FUN COMICS (Formerly Holiday Comics #1-8; Mighty Bear #13 on)
Star Publications: No. 9, Jan, 1953 - No. 12, Oct, 1953

	GD 2.0	VG 4.0	FN 6.0	VF 8.0	VF/NM 9.0	NM- 9.2
9-(25¢ Giant)-L. B. Cole X-Mas-c; X-Mas issue	28	56	84	165	270	375
10-12-L. B. Cole-c. 12-Mighty Bear-c/story	21	42	63	122	199	275

FUNDAY FUNNIES (See Famous TV..., and Harvey Hits No. 35,40)

FUN-IN (TV)(Hanna-Barbera)
Gold Key: Feb, 1970 - No. 10, Jan, 1972; No. 11, 4/74 - No. 15, 12/74

	GD 2.0	VG 4.0	FN 6.0	VF 8.0	VF/NM 9.0	NM- 9.2
1-Dastardly & Muttley in Their Flying Machines; Perils of Penelope Pitstop in #1-4; It's the Wolf in all	6	12	18	41	76	110
2-4,6-Cattanooga Cats in 2-4	3	6	9	21	33	45
5,7-Motormouse & Autocat, Dastardly & Muttley in both; It's the Wolf in #7	4	8	12	23	37	50
8,10-The Harlem Globetrotters, Dastardly & Muttley in #10	4	8	12	23	37	50
9-Where's Huddles?, Dastardly & Muttley, Motormouse & Autocat app.	4	8	12	23	37	50
11-Butch Cassidy	3	6	9	19	30	40
12-15: 12,15-Speed Buggy. 13-Hair Bear Bunch. 14-Inch High Private Eye	3	6	9	19	30	40

FUNKY PHANTOM, THE (TV)
Gold Key: Mar, 1972 - No. 13, Mar, 1975 (Hanna-Barbera)

	GD 2.0	VG 4.0	FN 6.0	VF 8.0	VF/NM 9.0	NM- 9.2
1	5	10	15	31	53	75
2-5	3	6	9	18	28	38
6-13	3	6	9	15	22	28

FUNLAND
Ziff-Davis (Approved Comics): No date (1940s) (25¢)

	GD 2.0	VG 4.0	FN 6.0	VF 8.0	VF/NM 9.0	NM- 9.2
nn-Contains games, puzzles, cut-outs, etc.	25	50	75	150	245	340

FUNLAND COMICS
Croyden Publishers: 1945

	GD 2.0	VG 4.0	FN 6.0	VF 8.0	VF/NM 9.0	NM- 9.2
1-Funny animal	21	42	63	122	199	275

FUNNIES, THE (New Funnies No. 65 on)
Dell Publishing Co.: Oct, 1936 - No. 64, May, 1942

	GD 2.0	VG 4.0	FN 6.0	VF 8.0	VF/NM 9.0	NM- 9.2
1-Tailspin Tommy, Mutt & Jeff, Alley Oop (1st app?), Capt. Easy (1st app.), Don Dixon begin	370	740	1110	2220	3810	5400
2 (11/36)-Scribbly by Mayer begins (see Popular Comics #6 for 1st app.)	170	340	510	1020	1735	2450
3	125	250	375	750	1275	1800
4,5: 4(1/37)-Christmas-c	95	190	285	570	960	1350
6-10	75	150	225	430	703	975
11-20: 16-Christmas-c	70	140	210	400	663	925
21-29: 25-Crime Busters by McWilliams(4pgs.)	55	110	165	315	520	725
30-John Carter of Mars (origin/1st app.) begins by Edgar Rice Burroughs; Jim Gary-a Warner Bros.' Bosko-c (4/39)	300	600	900	1920	3310	4700
31-34,36-44: 31,32-Gary-a. 33-John Coleman Burroughs art begins on John Carter. 34-Last funny-c. 40-John Carter of Mars-c	113	226	339	718	1234	1750
35-(9/39)-Mr. District Attorney begins; based on radio show; 1st cover app. John Carter of Mars	239	478	717	1530	2615	3700
45-Origin/1st app. Phantasmo, the Master of the World (Dell's 1st super-hero, 7/40) & his sidekick Whizzer McGee	129	258	387	826	1413	2000
46-50: 46-The Black Knight begins, ends #62	66	132	198	425	725	1025
51-56-Last ERB John Carter of Mars	53	106	159	334	567	800
57-Intro. & origin Captain Midnight (7/41)	377	754	1131	2639	4620	6600
58-60: 58-Captain Midnight-c begin, end #63	100	200	300	635	1093	1550
61-Andy Panda begins by Walter Lantz; WWII-c	148	296	444	947	1624	2300
62,63: 63-Last Captain Midnight-c; bondage-c	84	168	252	538	919	1300
64-Format change; Oswald the Rabbit, Felix the Cat, Li'l Eight Ball app.; origin & 1st app. Woody Woodpecker in Oswald; last Capt. Midnight; Oswald, Andy Panda, Li'l Eight Ball-c	300	600	900	1920	3310	4700

NOTE: ***Mayer*** *c-26, 48.* ***McWilliams*** *art in many issues on "Rex King of the Deep". Alley Oop c-17, 20. Captain Midnight c-57(i/2), 58-63. John Carter c-35-37, 40. Phantasmo c-45-56, 57(1/2), 58-61(part). Rex King c-38, 39, 42. Tailspin Tommy c-41.*

FUNNIES ANNUAL, THE
Avon Periodicals: 1959 ($1.00, approx. 7x10", B&W; tabloid-size)

	GD 2.0	VG 4.0	FN 6.0	VF 8.0	VF/NM 9.0	NM- 9.2
1-(Rare)-Features the best newspaper comic strips of the year: Archie, Snuffy Smith, Beetle Bailey, Henry, Blondie, Steve Canyon, Buz Sawyer, The Little King, Hi & Lois, Popeye, & others. Also has a chronological history of the comics from 2000 B.C. to 1959.	58	116	174	371	636	900

FUNNIES ON PARADE (See Promotional Comics section)

FUNNY ANIMALS (See Fawcett's Funny Animals)
Charlton Comics: Sept, 1984 - No. 2, Nov, 1984

	GD 2.0	VG 4.0	FN 6.0	VF 8.0	VF/NM 9.0	NM- 9.2
1,2-Atomic Mouse-r; low print						6.00

FUNNYBONE (... The Laugh-Book of Comical Comics)
La Salle Publishing Co.: 1944 (25¢, 132 pgs.)

	GD 2.0	VG 4.0	FN 6.0	VF 8.0	VF/NM 9.0	NM- 9.2
nn	39	78	117	240	395	550

FUNNY BOOK (...Magazine for Young Folks) (Hocus Pocus No. 9)
Parents' Magazine Press (Funny Book Publishing Corp.):
Dec, 1942 - No. 9, Aug-Sept, 1946 (Comics, stories, puzzles, games)

	GD 2.0	VG 4.0	FN 6.0	VF 8.0	VF/NM 9.0	NM- 9.2
1-Funny animal; Alice In Wonderland app.	20	40	60	114	182	250
2-Gulliver in Giant-Land	13	26	39	74	105	135
3-9: 4-Advs. of Robin Hood. 9-Hocus-Pocus strip	10	20	30	58	79	100

FUNNY COMICS
Modern Store Publ.: 1955 (7¢, 5x7", 36 pgs.)

	GD 2.0	VG 4.0	FN 6.0	VF 8.0	VF/NM 9.0	NM- 9.2
1-Funny animal	6	12	18	42	79	115

FUNNY COMIC TUNES (See Funny Tunes)

FUNNY FABLES
Decker Publications (Red Top Comics): Aug, 1957 - V2#2, Nov, 1957

	GD 2.0	VG 4.0	FN 6.0	VF 8.0	VF/NM 9.0	NM- 9.2
V1#1	8	16	24	42	54	65
V1#2,V2#1,2: V1#2 (11/57)-Reissue of V1#1	6	12	18	31	38	45

FUNNY FILMS (Features funny animal characters from films)
American Comics Group(Michel Publ./Titan Publ.): Sept-Oct, 1949 - No. 29, May-June, 1954 (No. 1-4: 52 pgs.)

	GD 2.0	VG 4.0	FN 6.0	VF 8.0	VF/NM 9.0	NM- 9.2
1-Puss An' Boots, Blunderbunny begin	20	40	60	118	192	265
2	12	24	36	69	97	125
3-10: 3-X-Mas-c	9	18	27	47	61	75
11-20	7	14	21	35	43	50
21-29	6	12	18	28	34	40

FUNNY FOLKS
DC Comics: Feb, 1946

nn-Ashcan comic, not distributed to newsstands, only for in house use (no known sales)

FUNNY FOLKS (Hollywood... on cover only No. 16-26; becomes Hollywood Funny Folks No. 27 on)
National Periodical Publ.: April-May, 1946 - No. 26, June-July, 1950 (52 pgs., #15 on)

	GD 2.0	VG 4.0	FN 6.0	VF 8.0	VF/NM 9.0	NM- 9.2
1-Nutsy Squirrel begins (1st app.) by Rube Grossman; Grossman-a in most issues	47	94	141	296	498	700
2	24	48	72	140	230	320
3-5: 4-1st Nutsy Squirrel-c	15	30	45	90	140	190
6-10: 6,9-Nutsy Squirrel-c begin	12	24	36	67	94	120
11-26: 15-Begin 52 pg. issues (8-9/48)	10	20	30	56	76	95

NOTE: ***Sheldon Mayer*** *a-in some issues.* ***Post*** *a-18. Christmas c-12.*

FUNNY FROLICS
Timely/Marvel Comics (SPI): Summer, 1945 - No. 5, Dec, 1946

	GD 2.0	VG 4.0	FN 6.0	VF 8.0	VF/NM 9.0	NM- 9.2
1-Sharpy Fox, Puffy Pig, Krazy Krow	36	72	108	211	343	475
2-(Fall 1945)	20	40	60	117	189	260
3,4: 3-(Spring 1946)	16	32	48	94	147	200
5-Kurtzman-a	17	34	51	100	158	215

FUNNY FUNNIES
Nedor Publishing Co.: April, 1943 (68 pgs.)

	GD 2.0	VG 4.0	FN 6.0	VF 8.0	VF/NM 9.0	NM- 9.2
1-Funny animals; Peter Porker app.	27	54	81	158	259	360

FUNNYMAN (Also see Cisco Kid Comics & Extra Comics)
Magazine Enterprises: Dec, 1947; No. 1, Jan, 1948 - No. 6, Aug, 1948

nn(12/47)-Prepublication B&W undistributed copy by Siegel & Shuster-(5-3/4x8"), 16 pgs.; Sold at auction in 1997 for $575.00

	GD 2.0	VG 4.0	FN 6.0	VF 8.0	VF/NM 9.0	NM- 9.2
1-Siegel & Shuster-a in all; Dick Ayers 1st pro work (as assistant) on 1st few issues	61	122	183	390	670	950
2	36	72	108	211	343	475
3-6	31	62	93	184	300	415

FUNNY MOVIES (See 3-D Funny Movies)

FUNNY PAGES (Formerly The Comics Magazine)
Comics Magazine Co./Ultem Publ.(Chesler)/Centaur Publications:
No. 6, Nov, 1936 - No. 42, Oct, 1940

	GD 2.0	VG 4.0	FN 6.0	VF 8.0	VF/NM 9.0	NM- 9.2
V1#6 (nn, nd)-The Clock begins (2 pgs., 1st app.), ends #11; The Clock is the 1st masked comic book hero	459	918	1377	3350	5925	8500
7-11: 11-(6/37)	194	388	582	1242	2121	3000
V2#1-V2#5: V2#1 (9/37)(V2#2 on-c; V2#1 in indicia). V2#2 (10/37)(V2#3 on-c; V2#2 in indicia). V2#3(11/37 - 5	161	322	483	1030	1765	2500
6(1st Centaur, 3/38)	181	362	543	1158	1979	2800
7-9	148	296	444	947	1624	2300
10(Scarce, 9/38)-1st app. of The Arrow by Gustavson (Blue costume)	595	1190	1785	4350	7675	11,000
11,12	187	374	561	1197	2049	2900
V3#1-Bruce Wayne prototype in "Case of the Missing Heir," by Bob Kane, 3 months before app. Batman (See Det. Pic. Stories #5)	300	600	900	2070	3635	5200
2-6,8: 6,8-Last funny covers	181	362	543	1158	1979	2800
7-1st Arrow-c (9/39)	476	952	1428	3475	6138	8800
9-Tarpe Mills jungle-c	194	388	582	1242	2121	3000
10-2nd Arrow-c (Rare)	476	952	1428	3475	6138	8800
V4#1(1/40, Arrow-c)-(Rare)-The Owl & The Phantom Rider app.; origin Mantoka, Maker of Magic by Jack Cole. Mad Ming begins, ends #42; Tarpe Mills-a	476	952	1428	3475	6138	8800
35-Classic Arrow-c (Scarce)	503	1006	1509	3672	6486	9300
36-38-Mad Ming-c	295	590	885	1888	3244	4600
39-41-Arrow-c	326	652	978	2282	3991	5700
42 (Scarce,10/40)-Arrow-c	420	840	1260	2940	5170	7400

NOTE: ***Biro*** *c-V2#9.* ***Burgos*** *c-V3#10.* ***Jack Cole*** *a-V2#3, 7, 8, 10, 11, V3#2, 6, 9, 10, V4#1, 37; c-V3#2, 4.* ***Eisner*** *a-V1#7, 8?, 10.* ***Ken Ernst*** *a-V1#7, 8.* ***Everett*** *a-V2#11 (illos).* ***Filchock*** *c-V2#10, V3#6.* ***Gill Fox*** *a-V2#11.* ***Sid Greene*** *a-39.* ***Guardineer*** *a-V2#2, 3, 5.* ***Gustavson*** *a-V2#5, 11, 12, V3#1-10, 35, 38-42; c-V3#7, 35, 39-42.* ***Bob Kane*** *a-V3#1.* ***McWilliams*** *a-V2#12, V3#1, 3-6.* ***Tarpe Mills*** *a-V3#8-10, V4#1; c-V3#9.* ***Ed Moore Jr.*** *a-V2#12.* ***Schwab*** *c-V3#1.* ***Bob Wood*** *a-V2#2, 3, 8, 11, V3#6, 9, 10; c-V2#6, 7. Arrow c-V3#7, 10, V4#1, 35, 40-42.*

FUNNY PICTURE STORIES (Comic Pages V3#4 on)
Comics Magazine Co./Centaur Publications: Nov, 1936 - V3#3, May, 1939

	GD 2.0	VG 4.0	FN 6.0	VF 8.0	VF/NM 9.0	NM- 9.2
V1#1-The Clock begins (c-feature)(see Funny Pages for 1st app.)	595	1190	1785	4350	7675	11,000
2	252	504	756	1613	2757	3900
3-6(4/37): 4-Eisner-a	194	388	582	1242	2121	3000
7-(6/37) (Rare) Racial humor-c	423	846	1269	3046	5323	7600
V2#1 (9/37; V1#10 on-c; V2#1 in indicia)-Jack Strand begins	145	290	435	921	1586	2250
2 (10/37; V1#11 on-c; V2#2 in indicia)	142	284	426	909	1555	2200
3-5,7-11(11/38): 4-Christmas-c	129	258	387	826	1413	2000
6-(1st Centaur, 3/38)	148	296	444	947	1624	2300
V3#1(1/39)-3	123	246	369	787	1344	1900

Fun-In #3 © H-B

Funny Pages V3 #6 © CEN

Fury: Peacemaker #1 © MAR

GD VG FN VF VF/NM NM-
2.0 4.0 6.0 8.0 9.0 9.2

NOTE: ***Biro*** *c-V2#1, 8, 9, 11.* ***Guardineer*** *a-V1#11; c-V2#6, V3#5.* ***Bob Wood*** *c/a-V1#11, V2#2; c-V2#3, 5.*

FUNNY STUFF (Becomes The Dodo & the Frog No. 80)
All-American/National Periodical Publications No. 7 on: Summer, 1944 - No. 79, July-Aug, 1954 (#1-7 are quarterly)

1-The Three Mouseketeers (ends #28) & The "Terrific Whatzit" begin; Sheldon Mayer-a; Grossman-a in most issues 103 206 309 659 1130 1600
2-Sheldon Mayer-a 47 94 141 296 498 700
3-5: 3-Flash parody. 5-All Mayer-a/scripts issue 32 64 96 188 307 425
6-10 10-(6/46) 20 40 60 117 189 260
11-17,19 15 30 45 90 140 190
18-The Dodo & the Frog (2/47, 1st app?) begin?; X-Mas-c 28 56 84 165 270 375
19-1st Dodo & the Frog-c (3/47) 20 40 60 117 189 260
20-2nd Dodo & the Frog-c (4/47) 15 30 45 84 127 170
21,23-30: 24-Infinity-c. 30-Christmas-c 11 22 33 62 86 110
22-Superman cameo 40 80 120 246 411 575
31-79: 62-Bo Bunny app. by Mayer. 70-Bo Bunny series begins 10 20 30 56 76 95

NOTE: ***Mayer*** *a-1-8, 55, ,57, 58, 61, 62, 64, 65, 68, 70, 72, 74-79; c-2, 5, 6, 8.*

FUNNY STUFF STOCKING STUFFER
DC Comics: Mar, 1985 ($1.25, 52 pgs.)

1-Almost every DC funny animal featured 4.00

FUNNY 3-D
Harvey Publications: December, 1953 (25¢, came with 2 pair of glasses)

1-Shows cover in 3-D on inside 13 26 39 74 105 135

FUNNY TUNES (Animated Funny Comic Tunes No. 16-22; Funny Comic Tunes No. 23, on covers only; Oscar No. 24 on)
U.S.A. Comics Magazine Corp. (Timely): No. 16, Summer, 1944 - No. 23, Fall, 1946

16-Silly Seal, Ziggy Pig, Krazy Krow begin 28 56 84 165 270 375
17 (Fall/44)-Becomes Gay Comics #18 on? 22 44 66 130 213 295
18-22: 21-Super Rabbit app. 20 40 60 120 195 270
23-Kurtzman-a 21 42 63 124 202 280

FUNNY TUNES (Becomes Space Comics #4 on)
Avon Periodicals: July, 1953 - No. 3, Dec-Jan, 1953-54

1-Space Mouse, Peter Rabbit, Merry Mouse, Spotty the Pup, Cicero the Cat begin; all continue in Space Comics 15 30 45 84 127 170
2,3 9 18 27 52 69 85

FUNNY WORLD
Marbak Press: 1947 - No. 3, 1948

1-The Berrys, The Toodles & other strip-r begin 11 22 33 60 83 105
2,3 8 16 24 40 50 60

FUNTASTIC WORLD OF HANNA-BARBERA, THE (TV)
Marvel Comics Group: Dec, 1977 - No. 3, June, 1978 ($1.25, oversized)

1-3: 1-The Flintstones Christmas Party(12/77). 2-Yogi Bear's Easter Parade(3/78). 3-Laff-a-lympics(6/78) 4 8 12 25 40 55

FUN TIME
Ace Periodicals: Spring, 1953; No. 2, Sum, 1953; No. 3(nn), Fall, 1953; No. 4, Wint, 1953-54

1-(25¢, 100 pgs.)-Funny animal 24 48 72 142 234 325
2-4 (All 25¢, 100 pgs.) 17 34 51 103 162 220

FUN WITH LITTLE ARCHIE AND FRIENDS SPECIAL
Archie Comic Publications: Jun, 2022 ($3.99, one-shot)

1-Sabrina & Salem app. 4.00

FUN WITH SANTA CLAUS (See March of Comics No. 11, 108, 325)

FURTHER ADVENTURES OF CYCLOPS AND PHOENIX (Also see Adventures of Cyclops and Phoenix, Uncanny X-Men & X-Men)
Marvel Comics: June, 1996 - No. 4, Sept, 1996 ($1.95, limited series)

1-4: Origin of Mr. Sinister; Milligan scripts; John Paul Leon-c/a(p). 2-4-Apocalypse app. 4.00
Trade Paperback (1997, $14.99) r/1-4 15.00

FURTHER ADVENTURES OF INDIANA JONES, THE (Movie) (Also see Indiana Jones and the Last Crusade & Indiana Jones and the Temple of Doom)
Marvel Comics Group: Jan, 1983 - No. 34, Mar, 1986

1-Byrne/Austin-a; Austin-c 3 6 9 14 19 24
2-34: 2-Byrne/Austin-c/a 4.00

NOTE: ***Austin*** *a-1i, 2i, 6i, 9i; c-1, 2i, 6i, 9i.* ***Byrne*** *a-1p, 2p; c-2p.* ***Chaykin*** *a-6p; c-6p, 8p-10p.* ***Ditko*** *a-21p, 25-28, 34.* ***Golden*** *c-24, 25.* ***Simonson*** *c-9. Painted c-14.*

FURTHER ADVENTURES OF NICK WILSON, THE
Image Comics: Jan, 2018 - No. 5, May 2018 ($3.99)

1-5-Gorodetsky & Andreyko-s/Sadowski-a 4.00

FURTHER ADVENTURES OF NYOKA, THE JUNGLE GIRL, THE (See Nyoka)
AC Comics: 1988 - No. 5, 1989 ($1.95, color; $2.25/$2.50, B&W)

1-5 : 1,2-Bill Black-a plus reprints. 3-Photo-c. 5-(B&W)-Reprints plus movie photos 4.00

FURY (Straight Arrow's Horse...) (See A-1 No. 119)

FURY (TV) (See March Of Comics #200)
Dell Publishing Co./Gold Key: No. 781, Mar, 1957 - Nov, 1962 (All photo-c)

Four Color 781 7 14 21 49 92 135
Four Color 885,975,1031,1080,1133,1172,1218,1296 5 10 15 35 63 90
01292-208(#1-'62), 10020-211(11/62-G.K.) 5 10 15 33 57 80

FURY
Marvel Comics: May, 1994 ($2.95, one-shot)

1-Iron Man, Red Skull, FF, Hatemonger, Logan app.; origin Nick Fury 4.00

FURY (Volume 3)
Marvel Comics (MAX): Nov, 2001 - No. 6, Apr, 2002 ($2.99, mature content)

1-6-Ennis-s/Robertson-a 4.00

FURY/ AGENT 13
Marvel Comics: June, 1998 - No. 2, July, 1998 ($2.99, limited series)

1,2-Nick Fury returns 4.00

FURY MAX (Nick Fury)("My War Gone By" on cover)
Marvel Comics (MAX): Jul, 2012 - No. 13, Aug, 2013 ($3.99, mature content)

1-13: 1-Ennis-s/Parlov-a/Johnson-c; Nick Fury in 1954 Indochina. 7-9-Frank Castle app. 4.00

FURY OF FIRESTORM, THE (Becomes Firestorm The Nuclear Man on cover with #50, in indicia with #65) (Also see Firestorm)
DC Comics: June, 1982 - No. 64, Oct, 1987 (75¢ on)

1-Intro The Black Bison; brief origin 3 6 9 18 28 38
2-6,8-22,25-40,43-64: 4-JLA x-over. 6-Masters of the Universe preview insert. 17-1st app. Firehawk. 21-Death of Killer Frost. 22-Origin. 27-Firestorm pin-up by Gil Kane. 34-1st app./origin Killer Frost II. 39-Weasel's ID revealed. 48-Intro. Moonbow. 53-Origin & 1st app. Silver Shade. 55,56-Legends x-over. 58-1st app./origin new Parasite 4.00
7-1st app. Plastique 2 4 6 9 12 15
23-(5/84) 1st app. Felicity Smoak (Byte) 3 6 9 15 22 28
24-(6/84)-1st app. Bug (origin); origin Byte; 1st app. Blue Devil in a prevue pull-out 3 6 9 16 23 30
41,42-Crisis x-over. 41-Harbinger, Psycho Pirate-c/app. 5.00
61-Test cover variant; Superman logo 4 8 12 27 44 60
Annual 1-4: 1(1983), 2(1984), 3(1985), 4(1986) 5.00

NOTE: ***Colan*** *a-19p, Annual 4p.* ***Giffen*** *a-Annual 4p.* ***Gil Kane*** *c-30.* ***Nino*** *a-37.* ***Tuska*** *a-(p)-17, 18, 32, 45.*

FURY OF FIRESTORM: THE NUCLEAR MEN (New DC 52)
DC Comics: Nov, 2011 - No. 20, Jul, 2013 ($2.99)

1-18: 1-Van Sciver & Simone-s/Cinar-a/Van Sciver-c. 7,8-Van Sciver-a. 9-JLI app. 3.00
19,20-Killer Frost app. 5.00
#0 (11/12, #2.99) Cinar-a/c 3.00

FURY OF SHIELD
Marvel Comics: Apr, 1995 - No. 4, July, 1995 ($2.50/$1.95, limited series)

1 ($2.50)-Foil-c 5.00
2-4: 4-Bagged w/ decoder 4.00

FURY: PEACEMAKER
Marvel Comics: Apr, 2006 - No. 6, Sept, 2006 ($3.50, limited series)

1-6-Flashback to WW2; Ennis-s/Robertson-a. 1-Deodato-c. 2-Texeira-c. 5-Dillon-c 3.50
TPB (2006, $17.99) r/#1-6 18.00

FURY: S.H.I.E.L.D. 50TH ANNIVERSARY
Marvel Comics: Nov, 2015 ($3.99, one-shot)

1-Walker-s/Ferguson-a/Deodato-c; Nick Fury Jr. time travels to meet 1965 Nick Fury 4.00

FUSED
Image Comics: Mar, 2002 - No. 4, Jan, 2003 ($2.95)

1-4-Steve Niles-s. 1,2-Paul Lee-a. 3-Brad Rader-a. 4-Templesmith-a 3.00

FUSED
Dark Horse Comics: Dec, 2003 - No. 4, Mar, 2004 ($2.95)

1-4-Steve Niles-s/Josh Medors-a. 1-Powell-c 3.00

FUSION
Eclipse Comics: Jan, 1987 - No. 17, Oct, 1989 ($2.00, B&W, Baxter paper)

1-17: 11-The Weasel Patrol begins (1st app.?) 3.00

FUSION
Image Comics (Top Cow): May, 2009 - No. 3, Jul, 2009 ($2.99, limited series)

1-3-Avengers, Thunderbolts, Cyberforce and Hunter-Killer meet; Kirkham-a 3.00

FUTURAMA (TV)
Bongo Comics: 2000 - No. 81, 2016 ($2.50/$2.99/$3.99, bi-monthly)

1-Based on the FOX-TV animated series; Groening/Morrison-c
5 10 15 31 53 75
1-San Diego Comic-Con Premiere Edition 6 12 18 41 76 110
2-10: 8-CGC cover spoof; X-Men parody 2 4 6 8 10 12
11-30 6.00
31-81: 40,64-Santa app. 50-55-Poster included 4.00
Annual 1 (2018, $4.99) Wacky Races spoof; Pinocchio homage 5.00
Futurama Adventures TPB (2004, $14.95) r/#5-9 15.00
Futurama Conquers the Universe TPB (2007, $14.95) r/#10-13 15.00
Futurama-O-Rama TPB (2002, $12.95) r/#1-4; sketch pages of Fry's development 15.00
...: The Time Bender Trilogy TPB (2006, $14.95) r/#16-19; cover gallery 15.00

FUTURAMA/SIMPSONS INFINITELY SECRET CROSSOVER CRISIS (TV) (See Simpsons/Futurama Crossover Crisis II for sequel)
Bongo Comics: 2002 - No. 2, 2002 ($2.50, limited series)

1-Evil Brain Spawns put Futurama crew into the Simpsons' Springfield
3 6 9 15 22 28
2 2 4 6 8 10 12

FUTURE COMICS
David McKay Publications: June, 1940 - No. 4, Sept, 1940

1-(6/40, 64 pgs.)-Origin The Phantom (1st in comics) (4 pgs.); The Lone Ranger (8 pgs.) & Saturn Against the Earth (4 pgs.) begin
314 628 942 2198 3849 5500
2 161 322 483 1030 1765 2500
3,4 123 246 369 787 1344 1900

FUTURE COP L.A.P.D. (Electronic Arts video game) (Also see Promotional Comics section)
DC Comics (WildStorm): Jan, 1999 ($4.95, magazine sized)

1-Stories & art by various 5.00

FUTURE FIGHT FIRSTS (Also see Agents of Atlas 2019 series)
Marvel Comics: Dec, 2019 - Jan, 2020 ($4.99, limited series of one-shots)

...: Crescent and Io 1 (1/20) Origin stories; Alyssa Wong-s/Jon Lam-a 5.00
...: Luna Snow 1 (12/19) Origin story; Alyssa Wong-s/Gang Hyuk Lim-a 5.00
...: White Fox 1 (12/19) Origin story; Alyssa Wong-s/Kevin Libranda & Geoffo-a 5.00

FUTURE FOUNDATION (From Fantastic Four)
Marvel Comics: Oct, 2019 - No. 5, Feb, 2020 ($3.99, limited series)

1-5-Whitley-s; Alex & Julie Power, Dragon Man, Onome, Bentley-23 app. 1-3-Robson-a 4.00

FUTURE IMPERFECT (Secret Wars tie-in)
Marvel Comics: Aug, 2015 - No. 5, Nov, 2015 ($3.99, limited series)

1-5-Peter David-s/Greg Land-a; Maestro (Hulk) and The Thing (Thaddeus Ross) app. 4.00

FUTURE QUEST
DC Comics: Jul, 2016 - No. 12, Jul, 2017 ($3.99)

1-12: 1-Jonny Quest, Space Ghost, Birdman and Dr. Zin app.; Shaner & Rude-a. 8-Olivetti-a; The Impossibles app. 4.00

FUTURE QUEST PRESENTS
DC Comics: Oct, 2017 - No. 12, Sept, 2018 ($3.99)

1-4: 1-3-Space Ghost and the Herculoids; Parker-s/Olivetti-a/c. 4-Galaxy Trio; Randall-a 4.00
5-12: 5-7-Birdman; Hester-s/Rude-a; Mentok app. 8-Mightor. 9-11-Herculoids 4.00

FUTURE SHOCK
Image Comics: 2006 (Free Comic Book Day giveaway)

...: FCBD 2006 Edition; Spawn, Invincible, Savage Dragon & others short stories 3.00

FUTURE STATE: AQUAMAN
DC Comics: Mar, 2021 - No. 2, Apr, 2021 ($3.99, limited series)

1,2-Aquaman (Jackson Hyde) & Aquawoman (Andy Curry) app.; Thomas-s/Sampere-a 4.00

FUTURE STATE: BATMAN / SUPERMAN
DC Comics: Mar, 2021 - No. 2, Apr, 2021 ($3.99, limited series)

1,2-Batman & Superman vs. False Face Society in the near future; Yang-s/Oliver-a 4.00

FUTURE STATE: CATWOMAN
DC Comics: Mar, 2021 - No. 2, Apr, 2021 ($3.99, limited series)

1,2-Catwoman (Selina Kyle) in the near future; Talia app.; Ram V-s/Schmidt-a 4.00

FUTURE STATE: DARK DETECTIVE
DC Comics: Mar, 2021 - No. 4, Late Apr, 2021 ($5.99, limited series)

1-4-Bruce Wayne in the near future; Tamaki-s/Mora-a. 1,3-Back-up with Grifter and Huntress. 2,4-Back-up with Red Hood & Ravager. 4-White Rabbit app. 6.00

FUTURE STATE: GOTHAM
DC Comics: Jul, 2021 - No. 18, Dec, 2022 ($3.99, B&W)

1-18: 1-Red Hood featured; manga-style B&W art by Milogiannis; back-up (r) w/Otomo-s/a. 2-Back-up (r) w/Coipel-a. 3-5-Punchline app. 4-Harley Quinn-a. 8,9-Cizmesija-a 4.00

FUTURE STATE: GREEN LANTERN
DC Comics: Mar, 2021 - No. 2, Apr, 2021 ($5.99, limited series)

1,2-The Corps without rings. 1-Back-up with Jessica Cruz vs. Lyssa Drak; Guy Gardner. 2-Back-ups with Hal Jordan, Mogo, Keli Quintela, & Jo Mullein 6.00

FUTURE STATE: HARLEY QUINN
DC Comics: Mar, 2021 - No. 2, Apr, 2021 ($3.99, limited series)

1,2-Harley in the near future; Black Mask app.; Stephanie Phillips-s/Simone DiMeo-a 4.00

FUTURE STATE: IMMORTAL WONDER WOMAN
DC Comics: Mar, 2021 - No. 2, Apr, 2021 ($5.99, limited series)

1,2-Diana in the far future; Darkseid app.; Bartel-a; back-up with Nubia 6.00

FUTURE STATE: JUSTICE LEAGUE
DC Comics: Mar, 2021 - No. 2, Apr, 2021 ($5.99, limited series)

1,2-Superman (Jon Kent), Batman (Tim Fox), WW (Yara Flor), Aquawoman, G.L. (Jo Mullein), and Flash team; Hyperclan app.; back-up with J.L. Dark; Doctor Fate app. 6.00

FUTURE STATE: KARA ZOR-EL, SUPERWOMAN
DC Comics: Mar, 2021 - No. 2, Apr, 2021 ($3.99, limited series)

1,2-Kara on the Moon colony; intro. Lynari; Bennett-s/Sauvage-a 4.00

FUTURE STATE: LEGION OF SUPER-HEROES
DC Comics: Mar, 2021 - No. 2, Apr, 2021 ($3.99, limited series)

1,2-Bendis-s/Rossmo-a; Legion reunites in the farther future 4.00

FUTURE STATE: NIGHTWING
DC Comics: Mar, 2021 - No. 2, Apr, 2021 ($3.99, limited series)

1,2-Nightwing & Batman (Tim Fox) vs. Peacekeepers; Nicola Scott-a/Andrew Constant-s 4.00

FUTURE STATE: ROBIN ETERNAL
DC Comics: Mar, 2021 - No. 2, Apr, 2021 ($3.99, limited series)

1,2-Tim Drake and Spoiler; Fitzmartin-s/Barrows-a 4.00

FUTURE STATE: SHAZAM! (Continues in Future State: Black Adam)
DC Comics: Mar, 2021 - No. 2, Apr, 2021 ($3.99, limited series)

1,2-Vixen, Question, Miss Martian, Powerhouse, Creeper, Giganta app.; Pansica-a 4.00

FUTURE STATE: SUICIDE SQUAD
DC Comics: Mar, 2021 - No. 2, Apr, 2021 ($5.99, limited series)

1,2-Team with Superman (Conner Kent), Batman (Talon), Martian Manhunter (Clayface), Aquaman (Fisherman), Flash (Bolt); back-up with Black Adam & Justice Legion-A 6.00

FUTURE STATE: SUPERMAN: HOUSE OF EL
DC Comics: Apr, 2021 ($5.99, one-shot)

1-P.K. Johnson-s/Scott Godlewski-a; set in the far future with Kal-El's descendants 6.00

FUTURE STATE: SUPERMAN OF METROPOLIS
DC Comics: Mar, 2021 - No. 2, Apr, 2021 ($5.99, limited series)

1,2-Jon Kent vs. Supergirl; Timms-a; back-ups with Mister Miracle and The Guardian 6.00

FUTURE STATE: SUPERMAN VS. IMPERIOUS LEX
DC Comics: Mar, 2021 - No. 3, May, 2021 ($3.99, limited series)

1-Lexor joining the United Planets; Mark Russell-s/Steve Pugh-a 4.00

FUTURE STATE: SUPERMAN / WONDER WOMAN
DC Comics: Mar, 2021 - No. 2, Apr, 2021 ($3.99, limited series)

1,2-Jon Kent & Yara Flor vs. Solaris; Watters-s/Del Duca-a 4.00

FUTURE STATE: SUPERMAN: WORLDS OF WAR (Continues in Superman: House of El)
DC Comics: Mar, 2021 - No. 2, Apr, 2021 ($7.99, limited series)

1,2-Janin-a; back-ups with Mr. Miracle, Midnighter and Black Racer 8.00

FUTURE STATE: SWAMP THING
DC Comics: Mar, 2021 - No. 2, Apr, 2021 ($3.99, limited series)

1,2-Ram V-s/Mike Perkins-a; Jason Woodrue & Obsidian app. 4.00

FUTURE STATE: TEEN TITANS (Leads into Teen Titans Academy)
DC Comics: Mar, 2021 - No. 2, Apr, 2021 ($3.99, limited series)

1,2-Sheridan-s/Sandoval-a; Red X app.; Dick Grayson as Death-Wing 4.00

FUTURE STATE: THE FLASH (Prelude to Future State: Teen Titans)
DC Comics: Mar, 2021 - No. 2, Apr, 2021 ($3.99, limited series)

1,2-Vietti-s. 1-Eaglesham-a; Flashes vs. Wally West as Famine. 2-Peterson-a 4.00

FUTURE STATE: THE NEXT BATMAN
DC Comics: Mar, 2021 - No. 4, Apr, 2021 ($7.99, limited series)

1-4-Tim Fox as Batman; Ridley-s. 1-Derington-a. 1,3-Back-ups with Outsiders, Arkham Knights. 2,4-Back-ups with Batgirls & Gotham City Sirens 8.00

FUTURE STATE: THE FLASH (Prelude to Future State: Teen Titans)
DC Comics: Mar, 2021 - No. 2, Apr, 2021 ($3.99, limited series)

1,2-Yara Flor from the Amazon Rainforest; Jöelle Jones-s/a 4.00

FUTURE WORLD COMICS
George W. Dougherty: Summer, 1946 - No. 2, Fall, 1946

1,2: H.C. Kiefer-c; preview of the World of Tomorrow 37 74 111 222 361 500

FUTURE WORLD COMIX (Warren Presents...)
Warren Publications: Sept, 1978 (B&W magazine, 84 pgs.)

1-Corben, Maroto, Morrow, Nino, Sutton-a; Todd-c/a; contains nudity panels
2 4 6 8 11 14

FUTURIANS, THE (See Marvel Graphic Novel #9)
Lodestone Publishing/Eternity Comics: Sept, 1985 - No. 3, 1985 ($1.50)

1-3: Indicia title "Dave Cockrum's..." 4.00
Graphic Novel 1 ($9.95, Eternity)-r/#1-3, plus never published #4 issue 10.00

FX
IDW Publishing: Mar, 2008 - No. 6, Aug, 2008 ($3.99)

1-6-John Byrne-a/c; Wayne Osborne-s 4.00

G-8 (Listed at G-Eight)

GABBY (Formerly Ken Shannon) (Teen humor)
Quality Comics Group: No. 11, Jul, 1953; No. 2, Sep, 1953 - No. 9, Sep, 1954

11(#1)(7/53) 14 28 42 78 112 145
2 9 18 27 52 69 85
3-9 9 18 27 47 61 75

GABBY GOB (See Harvey Hits No. 85, 90, 94, 97, 100, 103, 106, 109)

GABBY HAYES ADVENTURE COMICS
Toby Press: Dec, 1953

1-Photo-c 16 32 48 94 147 200

GABBY HAYES WESTERN (Movie star)(See Monte Hale, Real Western Hero & Western Hero)
Fawcett Publications/Charlton Comics No. 51 on: Nov, 1948 - No. 50, Jan, 1953; No. 51, Dec, 1954 - No. 59, Jan, 1957

1-Gabby & his horse Corker begin; photo front/back-c begin
42 84 126 265 445 625
2 21 42 63 124 202 280
3-5 15 30 45 88 137 185
6-10: 9-Young Falcon begins 14 28 42 78 112 145

Futurama Comics #67 © Bongo

Future State: Teen Titans #1 © DC

Gambit (2013) #15 © MAR

	GD 2.0	VG 4.0	FN 6.0	VF 8.0	VF/NM 9.0	NM- 9.2
11-20: 19-Last photo back-c	11	22	33	64	90	115
21-49: 20,22,24,26,28,29-(52 pgs.)	9	18	27	52	69	85
50-(1/53)-Last Fawcett issue; last photo-c?	10	20	30	58	79	100
51-(12/54)-1st Charlton issue; photo-c	11	22	33	60	83	105
52-59(1955-57): 53,55-Photo-c. 58-Swayze-a	8	16	24	42	54	65

GAGS
United Features Synd./Triangle Publ. No. 9 on: Jul, 1937 - V3#10, Oct, 1944 (13-3/4x10-3/4")

	GD	VG	FN	VF	VF/NM	NM-
1(7/37)-52 pgs.; 20 pgs. Grin & Bear It, Fellow Citizen	32	64	96	188	307	425
V1#9 (36 pgs.) (7/42)	14	28	42	76	108	140
V3#10	10	20	30	58	79	100

GALACTA: DAUGHTER OF GALACTUS
Marvel Comics: July, 2010 ($3.99, one-shot)
1-Adam Warren-s/Hector Sevilla-a; Warren & Sevilla-c : Wolverine and the FF app. 4.00

GALACTICA 1980 (Based on the Battlestar Galactica TV series)
Dynamite Entertainment: 2009 - No. 4, 2009 ($3.50)
1-4-Guggenheim-s/Razek-a 3.50

GALACTICA: THE NEW MILLENNIUM
Realm Press: Sept, 1999 ($2.99)
1-Stories by Shooter, Braden, Kuhoric 3.00

GALACTIC GUARDIANS
Marvel Comics: July, 1994 - No. 4, Oct, 1994 ($1.50, limited series)
1-4 4.00

GALACTIC WARS COMIX (Warren Presents... on cover)
Warren Publications: Dec, 1978 (B&W magazine, 84 pgs.)

	GD	VG	FN	VF	VF/NM	NM-
nn-Wood, Williamson-r; Battlestar Galactica/Flash Gordon photo/text stories	2	4	6	9	13	16

GALACTUS THE DEVOURER
Marvel Comics: Sept, 1999 - No. 6, Mar, 2000 ($3.50/$2.50, limited series)

	GD	VG	FN	VF	VF/NM	NM-
1-($3.50) L. Simonson-s/Muth & Sienkiewicz-a	2	4	6	8	10	12
2-5-($2.50) Buscema & Sienkiewicz-a						6.00
6-($3.50) Death of Galactus; Buscema & Sienkiewicz-a	1	2	3	5	6	8

GALAKTIKON
Albatross Funnybooks: 2017 - No. 6, 2018 ($3.99, limited series)
1-6-Brendon Small-s/Steve Mannion-a. 1-5-Eric Powell-c. 6-Mannion-c 4.00

GALAXIA (Magazine)
Astral Publ.: 1981 ($2.50, B&W, 52 pgs.)

	GD	VG	FN	VF	VF/NM	NM-
1-Buckler/Giordano-c; Texeira/Guice-a; 1st app. Astron, Sojourner, Bloodwing, Warlords; Buckler-s/a	2	4	6	11	16	20

GALAXY QUEST: GLOBAL WARNING! (Based on the 1999 movie)
IDW Publishing: Aug, 2008 - No. 5, Dec, 2008 ($3.99)
1-5-Lobdell-s/Kyriazis-a 4.00

GALAXY QUEST: THE JOURNEY CONTINUES (Based on the 1999 movie)
IDW Publishing: Jan, 2015 - No. 4, Apr, 2015 ($3.99)
1-4-Erik Burnham-s/Nacho Arranz-a 4.00

GALLANT MEN, THE (TV)
Gold Key: Oct, 1963 (Photo-c)

	GD	VG	FN	VF	VF/NM	NM-
1(1008-310)-Manning-a	3	6	9	21	33	45

GALLEGHER, BOY REPORTER (Disney, TV)
Gold Key: May, 1965

	GD	VG	FN	VF	VF/NM	NM-
1(10149-505)-Photo-c	3	6	9	17	26	35

GAMBIT (See X-Men #266 & X-Men Annual #14)
Marvel Comics: Dec, 1993 - No. 4, Mar, 1994 ($2.00, limited series)

	GD	VG	FN	VF	VF/NM	NM-
1-($2.50)-Lee Weeks-c/a in all; gold foil stamped-c	3	6	9	15	24	32
1 (Gold)	7	14	21	46	86	125
2-4						6.00

GAMBIT
Marvel Comics: Sept, 1997 - No. 4, Dec, 1997 ($2.50, limited series)

	GD	VG	FN	VF	VF/NM	NM-
1-4-Janson-a/Mackie & Kavanagh-s	1	2	3	5	6	8

GAMBIT
Marvel Comics: Feb, 1999 - No. 25, Feb, 2001 ($2.99/$1.99)

	GD	VG	FN	VF	VF/NM	NM-
1-($2.99) Five covers; Nicieza-a/Skroce-a	1	2	3	5	6	8
2-11,13-16-($1.99): 2-Two covers (Skroce & Adam Kubert)						3.00
12-($2.99)						4.00
17-24: 17-Begin $2.25-c. 21-Mystique-c/app.						3.00
25-($2.99) Leads into "Gambit & Bishop"						4.00
...1999 Annual ($3.50) Nicieza-s/McDaniel-a						4.00
...2000 Annual ($3.50) Nicieza-s/Derenick & Smith-a						4.00

GAMBIT
Marvel Comics: Nov, 2004 - No. 12, Aug, 2005 ($2.99)
1-12: 1-Jeanty-a/Land-c/Layman-s. 5-Wolverine-c/app. 9-Brother Voodoo-c/app. 3.00
... and the Champions: From the Marvel Vault 1 (10/11, $2.99) George Tuska's last art 3.00
...: Hath No Fury TPB (2005, $14.99) r/#7-12 15.00
...: House of Cards TPB (2005, $14.99) r/#1-6; Land cover sketches; unused covers 15.00

GAMBIT
Marvel Comics: Oct, 2012 - No. 17, Nov, 2013 ($2.99)
1-17: 1-Asmus-s/Mann-a; covers by Mann & Bachalo. 6,7-Pete Wisdom app. 3.00

GAMBIT
Marvel Comics: Jul, 2022 - No. 5, Jan, 2023 ($3.99)
1-5-Claremont-s/Kotian-a; untold story from era with de-aged amnesiac Storm 4.00

GAMBIT & BISHOP (... : Sons of the Atom on cover)
Marvel Comics: Feb, 2001 - No. 6, May, 2001 ($2.25, bi-weekly limited series)
Alpha (2/01) Prelude to series; Nord-a 3.00
1-6-Jeanty-a/Williams-c 3.00
Genesis (3/01, $3.50) reprints their first apps. and first meeting 4.00

GAMBIT AND THE X-TERNALS
Marvel Comics: Mar, 1995 - No. 4, July, 1995 ($1.95, limited series)
1-4-Age of Apocalypse 4.00

GAME BOY (Super Mario covers on all)
Valiant: 1990 - No. 4, 1990 ($1.95, coated-c)

	GD	VG	FN	VF	VF/NM	NM-
1	4	8	12	27	44	60
2	3	6	9	19	30	40
3,4-Layton-c. 4-Morrow-a	3	6	9	14	20	25

GAMEKEEPER (Guy Ritchie's...)
Virgin Comics: Mar, 2007 - No. 5, Sept, 2007; Mar, 2008 - No. 5, Jul, 2008 ($2.99)
1-5-Andy Diggle-s/Mukesh Singh-a; 2 covers on each 3.00
1-Extended Edition (6/07, $2.99) r/#1 with script excerpt and sketch art 3.00
Series 2 (3/08 - No. 5, 7/08) 1-5-Parker-s/Randle-a 3.00
Vol. 1 TPB (10/07, $14.99) r/#1-5; script and sketch pages; Guy Ritchie intro. 15.00

GAME OF THRONES, A (George R.R. Martin's...) (Based on A Song of Ice and Fire)
Dynamite Entertainment: 2011 - No. 24, 2014 ($3.99)

	GD	VG	FN	VF	VF/NM	NM-
1-Covers by Alex Ross and Mike Miller	3	6	9	17	26	35
2-24: 2-Covers by Alex Ross and Mike Miller						6.00

GAMERA
Dark Horse Comics: Aug, 1996 - No. 4, Nov, 1996 ($2.95, limited series)
1-4 3.00

GAMMA FLIGHT (From Immortal Hulk)
Marvel Comics: Aug, 2021 - No. 5, Dec, 2021 ($3.99, limited series)
1-5-Ewing & Frasier-s/Medina-a; Puck, Titania, Absorbing Man & Doc Sasquatch team 4.00

GAMMARAUDERS
DC Comics: Jan, 1989 - No. 10, Dec, 1989 ($1.25/$1.50/$2.00)
1-10-Based on TSR game 3.00

GAMORA (Guardians of the Galaxy)
Marvel Comics: Feb, 2017 - No. 5, Jul, 2017 ($3.99, limited series)
1-5-Perlman-s/Checchetto-a. 1,5-Thanos & Nebula app. 4.00

GAMORRA SWIMSUIT SPECIAL
Image Comics (WildStorm Productions): June, 1996 ($2.50, one-shot)
1-Campbell wraparound-c; pinups 4.00

GANDY GOOSE (Movies/TV)(See All Surprise, Giant Comics Edition #5A &10, Paul Terry's Comics & Terry-Toons)
St. John Publ. Co./Pines No. 5,6: Mar, 1953 - No. 5, Nov, 1953; No. 5, Fall, 1956 - No. 6, Sum/58

	GD	VG	FN	VF	VF/NM	NM-
1-All St. John issues are pre-code	15	30	45	85	130	175
2	9	18	27	50	65	80
3-5(1953)(St. John)	7	14	21	37	46	55
5,6(1956-58)(Pines)-CBS Television Presents...	5	10	15	24	30	35

GANG BUSTERS (See Popular Comics #38)
David McKay/Dell Publishing Co.: 1938 - 1943

	GD 2.0	VG 4.0	FN 6.0	VF 8.0	VF/NM 9.0	NM- 9.2
Feature Books 17(McKay)('38)-1st app.	93	186	279	591	1021	1450
Large Feature Comic 10('39)-(Scarce)	97	194	291	621	1061	1500
Large Feature Comic 17('41)	61	122	183	390	670	950
Four Color 7(1940)	71	142	213	454	777	1100
Four Color 23('42)	55	110	165	352	601	850
Four Color 24('43)	32	64	96	230	515	800

GANG BUSTERS (Radio/TV)(Gangbusters #14 on)
National Periodical Publ.: Dec-Jan, 1947-48 - No. 67, Dec-Jan, 1958-59 (No. 1-23: 52 pgs.)

	GD 2.0	VG 4.0	FN 6.0	VF 8.0	VF/NM 9.0	NM- 9.2
1	97	194	291	621	1061	1500
2	41	82	123	256	428	600
3-5	28	56	84	165	270	375
6-10: 9-Dan Barry-a. 9,10-Photo-c	21	42	63	122	199	275
11-13-Photo-c	17	34	51	100	158	215
14,17-Frazetta-a, 8 pgs. each. 14-Photo-c	36	72	108	211	343	475
15,16,18-20,26: 26-Kirby-a	15	30	45	85	130	175
21-25,27-30	14	28	42	76	108	140
31-44: 44-Last Pre-code (2-3/55)	12	24	36	67	94	120
45-67	10	20	30	54	72	90

NOTE: ***Barry** a-6, 8, 10. **Drucker** a-51. **Moreira** a-48, 50, 59. **Roussos** a-8.*

GANGLAND
DC Comics (Vertigo): Jun, 1998 - No. 4, Sept, 1998 ($2.95, limited series)

	GD 2.0	VG 4.0	FN 6.0	VF 8.0	VF/NM 9.0	NM- 9.2
1-4: Crime anthology by various. 2-Corben-a						3.00
TPB-(2000, $12.95) r/#1-4; Bradstreet-c						13.00

GANGSTERS AND GUN MOLLS
Avon Per./Realistic Comics: Sept, 1951 - No. 4, June, 1952 (Painted c-1-3)

	GD 2.0	VG 4.0	FN 6.0	VF 8.0	VF/NM 9.0	NM- 9.2
1-Wood-a, 1 pg; c-/Avon paperback #292	77	154	231	493	847	1200
2-Check-a, 8 pgs.; Kamen-a; Bonnie Parker story	71	142	213	454	777	1100
3-Marijuana mentioned; used in **POP**, pg. 84,85	57	114	171	362	619	875
4-Syd Shores-c	53	106	159	334	567	800

GANGSTERS CAN'T WIN
D. S. Publishing Co.: Feb-Mar, 1948 - No. 9, June-July, 1949 (All 52 pgs?)

	GD 2.0	VG 4.0	FN 6.0	VF 8.0	VF/NM 9.0	NM- 9.2
1-True crime stories	50	100	150	315	533	750
2-Skull-c	309	618	927	2163	3782	5400
3,5,6	25	50	75	150	245	340
4-Acid in face story	34	68	102	199	325	450
7-9	20	40	60	118	192	265

NOTE: ***Ingles** a-5, 6. **McWilliams** a-5, 7, 8. **Reinman** c-6.*

GANG WORLD
Standard Comics: No. 5, Nov, 1952 - No. 6, Jan, 1953

	GD 2.0	VG 4.0	FN 6.0	VF 8.0	VF/NM 9.0	NM- 9.2
5-Bondage-c	27	54	81	160	263	365
6	20	40	60	114	182	250

GARBAGE PAIL KIDS COMIC BOOK (Based on the tranding cards)
IDW Publishing: Dec, 2014 - Feb, 2015 ($3.99, series of one-shots)

	GD 2.0	VG 4.0	FN 6.0	VF 8.0	VF/NM 9.0	NM- 9.2
... Love Stinks (2/15) short stories by various incl. Haspiel, Wheeler, Bagge; 3 covers	1	2	3	5	6	8
... Puke-tacular (12/14) short stories by various incl. Bagge, Wray, Barta; 3 covers	2	4	6	9	12	15

GARBAGE PAIL KIDS: ORIGINS (Based on the tranding cards)
Dynamite Entertainment: 2022 - No. 3, 2022 ($3.99)

	GD 2.0	VG 4.0	FN 6.0	VF 8.0	VF/NM 9.0	NM- 9.2
1-3-Zapata-a. 1-Origin of Adam Bomb						4.00

GARFIELD (Newspaper/cartoon cat)(Also see Grumpy Cat)
Boom Entertainment (KaBOOM!): May, 2012 - No. 36, Apr, 2015 ($3.99)

	GD 2.0	VG 4.0	FN 6.0	VF 8.0	VF/NM 9.0	NM- 9.2
1-24-Evanier-s. 1-Two covers by Barker. 8-Christmas-c. 13,20-Pet Force app.						4.00
1-4-First Appearance Variants by Jim Davis. 1-Garfield. 2-Odie. 3-Jon. 4-Nermal						10.00
25-($4.99) Covers by George Pérez and Barker; bonus pin-ups						5.00
26-36: 30-EC-style horror cover. 33-36-His 9 Lives						4.00
... 2016 Summer Special 1 (7/16, $7.99) Evanier & Nickel-s; Batman spoof	1	2	3	5	6	8
... 2018 Vacation Times Blues 1 (5/18, $7.99) Evanier & Nickel-s; Hirsch-c	1	2	3	5	6	8
... Cheesy Holiday Special 1 (12/15, $4.99) Christmas stories; Evanier & Nickel-s						5.00
...: Pet Force Special 1 (8/13, $4.99) Cover swipe of Amazing Spider-Man #50						5.00
...: Pet Force 2014 Special (4/14, $4.99) The Pet Force multiverse; bonus sketch art						5.00
... TV or Not TV? 1 (10/18, $7.99) Halloween stories; Evanier & Nickel-s; Hirsch-c						8.00

GARFIELD: HOMECOMING (Newspaper/cartoon cat)
Boom Entertainment (KaBOOM!): Jun, 2018 - No. 4, Sept, 2018 ($3.99, limited series)

	GD 2.0	VG 4.0	FN 6.0	VF 8.0	VF/NM 9.0	NM- 9.2
1-4-Scott Nickel-s. 1-Talmadge & Alfaro-a. 2-Paroline, Lamb & Alfaro-a						4.00

GARGOYLE (See The Defenders #94)
Marvel Comics Group: June, 1985 - No. 4, Sept, 1985 (75¢, limited series)

	GD 2.0	VG 4.0	FN 6.0	VF 8.0	VF/NM 9.0	NM- 9.2
1-Wrightson-c; character from Defenders						5.00
2-4						4.00

GARGOYLES (TV cartoon)
Marvel Comics: Feb, 1995 - No. 11, Dec, 1995 ($2.50)

	GD 2.0	VG 4.0	FN 6.0	VF 8.0	VF/NM 9.0	NM- 9.2
1-11: Based on animated series						3.00
... Facsimile Edition Issue #1 (Dynamite Ent., 2023, $3.99) r/#1; preview of 2022 series						4.00

GARGOYLES (TV cartoon)
Dynamite Entertainment: 2022 - Present ($3.99)

	GD 2.0	VG 4.0	FN 6.0	VF 8.0	VF/NM 9.0	NM- 9.2
1-3-Weisman-s/Kambadais-a						4.00

GARRISON
DC Comics (WildStorm): Jun, 2010 - No. 6, Nov, 2010 ($2.99)

	GD 2.0	VG 4.0	FN 6.0	VF 8.0	VF/NM 9.0	NM- 9.2
1-6-Mariotte-s/Francavilla-a/c						3.00

GARRISON'S GORILLAS (TV)
Dell Publishing Co.: Jan, 1968 - No. 4, Oct, 1968; No. 5, Oct, 1969 (Photo-c)

	GD 2.0	VG 4.0	FN 6.0	VF 8.0	VF/NM 9.0	NM- 9.2
1	4	8	12	28	47	65
2-5: 5-Reprints #1	3	6	9	19	30	40

GARY GIANNI'S THE MONSTERMEN
Dark Horse Comics: Aug, 1999 ($2.95, one-shot)

	GD 2.0	VG 4.0	FN 6.0	VF 8.0	VF/NM 9.0	NM- 9.2
1-Gianni-s/c/a; back-up Hellboy story by Mignola						4.00

GASM (Sci-Fi, Horror, Fantasy comics magazine)(Mature content)
Stories, Layouts & Press, Inc.: Nov, 1977 - nn (No. 5), Jun, 1978 (B&W/color)

	GD 2.0	VG 4.0	FN 6.0	VF 8.0	VF/NM 9.0	NM- 9.2
1-Mark Wheatley-s/a; Gene Day-s/a; Workman-a	3	6	9	16	23	30
2 (12/77) Wheatley-a; Winnick-s/a; Workman-a	2	4	6	11	16	20
nn(#3, 2/78) Day-s/a; Wheatley-a; Workman-a	2	4	6	10	14	18
nn(#4, 4/78) Day-s/a; Wheatley-a; Corben-a	3	6	9	14	20	26
nn(#5, 6/78) Hempel-a; Howarth-a; Corben-a	3	6	9	16	23	30

GASOLINA
Image Comics (Skybound): Sept, 2017 - No. 18, May, 2019 ($3.99)

	GD 2.0	VG 4.0	FN 6.0	VF 8.0	VF/NM 9.0	NM- 9.2
1-18-Sean Mackiewicz-s/Niko Walter-a						4.00

GASOLINE ALLEY (Top Love Stories No. 3 on?)
Star Publications: Sept-Oct, 1950 - No. 2, Dec, 1950 (Newspaper-r)

	GD 2.0	VG 4.0	FN 6.0	VF 8.0	VF/NM 9.0	NM- 9.2
1-Contains 1 pg. intro. history of the strip (The Life of Skeezix); reprints 15 scenes of highlights from 1921-1935, plus an adventure from 1935 and 1936 strips; a 2-pg. filler is included on the life of the creator Frank King, with photo of the cartoonist.	24	48	72	144	237	330
2-(1936-37 reprints)-L. B. Cole-c	28	56	84	165	270	375

(See Super Book No. 21)

GASP!
American Comics Group: Mar, 1967 - No. 4, Aug, 1967 (12¢)

	GD 2.0	VG 4.0	FN 6.0	VF 8.0	VF/NM 9.0	NM- 9.2
1	5	10	15	34	60	85
2-4	3	6	9	21	33	45

GATECRASHER
Black Bull Entertainment: Mar, 2000 - No. 4, Jun, 2000 ($2.50, limited series)

	GD 2.0	VG 4.0	FN 6.0	VF 8.0	VF/NM 9.0	NM- 9.2
1,2-Waid-s/Conner & Palmiotti-c/a; 1,2-variant-c by J.G. Jones						3.00
3,4: 3-Jusko var-c. 4-Linsner-c						3.00
... Ring of Fire TPB (11/00, $12.95) r/#1-4; Hughes-c; Ennis intro.						13.00

GATECRASHER (Regular series)
Black Bull Entertainment: Aug, 2000 - No. 6, Jan, 2001 ($2.50, limited series)

	GD 2.0	VG 4.0	FN 6.0	VF 8.0	VF/NM 9.0	NM- 9.2
1-6-Waid-s/Conner & Palmiotti-c/a; 1-3-Variant-c by Fabry. 4-Hildebrandts variant-c. 5-Art Adams var-c. 6-Texeira var-c						3.00

GAY COMICS (Honeymoon No. 41)
Timely Comics/USA Comic Mag. Co. No. 18-24: Mar, 1944 (no month); No. 18, Fall, 1944 - No. 40, Oct, 1949

	GD 2.0	VG 4.0	FN 6.0	VF 8.0	VF/NM 9.0	NM- 9.2
1-Wolverton's Powerhouse Pepper; Tessie the Typist begins; 1st app. Willie (one shot)	116	232	348	742	1271	1800
18-(Formerly Funny Tunes #17?)-Wolverton-a	71	142	213	454	777	1100
19-29: Wolverton-a in all. 21,24-6 pg., 7 pg. Powerhouse Pepper; additional 2 pg. story in 24). 23-7 pg Wolverton story & 2 two pg stories (total of 11pgs.). 24,29-Kurtzman-a (24-"Hey Look"(2))	55	110	165	352	601	850
30,33,36,37-Kurtzman's "Hey Look"	30	60	90	177	289	400
31-Kurtzman's "Hey Look" (1), Giggles 'N' Grins (1-1/2)	30	60	90	177	289	400
32,35,38-40: 35-Nellie The Nurse begins?	27	54	81	160	263	365
34-Three Kurtzman's "Hey Look"	30	60	90	177	289	400

GAY COMICS (Also see Smile, Tickle, & Whee Comics)
Modern Store Publ.: 1955 (7¢, 5x7-1/4", 52 pgs.)

	GD 2.0	VG 4.0	FN 6.0	VF 8.0	VF/NM 9.0	NM- 9.2
1	7	14	21	46	86	125

GAY PURR-EE (See Movie Comics)

GCPD: THE BLUE WALL (Gotham City Police Deptartment)
DC Comics: Dec, 2022 - No. 6 ($3.99, limited series)

	GD 2.0	VG 4.0	FN 6.0	VF 8.0	VF/NM 9.0	NM- 9.2
1-5-John Ridley-s/Stefano Raffaele-a; intro. Officer Samantha Park						4.00

GEARS OF WAR (Based on the video game)
DC Comics (WildStorm): Dec, 2008 - No. 24, Aug, 2012 ($3.99/$2.99)

	GD 2.0	VG 4.0	FN 6.0	VF 8.0	VF/NM 9.0	NM- 9.2
1-15: 1-Liam Sharp-a/Joshua Ortega-s. 1-Two covers						4.00
16-24-($2.99) 16-Traviss-s/Gopez-a. 18-20-Mhan-a. 19-24-Prelude to Gears of War 3						3.00
... Reader (4/09, $3.99) r/#1 & 2 in flipbook						4.00
... Sourcebook (8/09, $3.99) character pin-ups by various; Platt-c						4.00
Book One HC (2009, $19.99, dustjacket) r/#1-6 & Sourcebook						20.00
Book One SC (2010, $14.99) r/#1-6 & Sourcebook						15.00
Book Two HC (2011, $24.99, dustjacket) r/#7-13						25.00

GEARS OF WAR: HIVEBUSTERS (Based on the video game)
IDW Publishing: Mar, 2019 - No. 4, Jun, 2019 ($3.99)

	GD 2.0	VG 4.0	FN 6.0	VF 8.0	VF/NM 9.0	NM- 9.2
1-4-Kurtis Wiebe-s, 1,2-Alan Quah-a. 3-Quah & Coccolo-a. 4-Padilla & Wagner Reis-a						4.00
Gears Pop One-Shot (7/19, $4.99) Art in the style of Funko Pop figures						5.00

GEARS OF WAR: THE RISE OF RAAM (Based on the video game)
IDW Publishing: Jan, 2018 - No. 4, Apr, 2018 ($3.99)

	GD 2.0	VG 4.0	FN 6.0	VF 8.0	VF/NM 9.0	NM- 9.2
1-4-Kurtis Wiebe-s/Max Dunbar-a						4.00

GEAR STATION, THE
Image Comics: Mar, 2000 - No. 5, Nov, 2000 ($2.50)

	GD 2.0	VG 4.0	FN 6.0	VF 8.0	VF/NM 9.0	NM- 9.2
1-Four covers by Ross, Turner, Pat Lee, Fraga						3.00
1-($6.95) DF Cover						7.00
2-5: 2-Two covers by Fraga and Art Adams						3.00

GEEK, THE (See Brother Power... & Vertigo Visions)

GEEKSVILLE (Also see 3 Geeks, The)
3 Finger Prints/ Image: Aug, 1999 - No. 6, Mar, 2001 ($2.75/$2.95, B&W)

	GD 2.0	VG 4.0	FN 6.0	VF 8.0	VF/NM 9.0	NM- 9.2
1,2,4-6-The 3 Geeks by Koslowski; Innocent Bystander by Sassaman						6.00
3-Includes "Babes & Blades" mini-comic	1	2	3	5	6	8
0-(3/00) First Image issue						3.00
(Vol. 2) 1-4-($2.95) 3-Mini-comic insert by the Geeks. 4-Steve Borock app.						3.00

GEIGER
Image Comics (Mad Ghost): Apr, 2021 - Present ($3.99)

	GD 2.0	VG 4.0	FN 6.0	VF 8.0	VF/NM 9.0	NM- 9.2
1-5-Geoff Johns-s/Gary Frank-a						4.00
6-($4.99) Junkyard Joe app.						5.00
... 80-Page Giant 1 (2/22, $7.99) Stories of the Las Vegas casinos; s-a by various incl. Johns, Frank, Hitch, Kelley Jones, Pelletier, Prado; preview of Junkyard Joe #1						8.00

Garfield #36 © PAWS Inc.

Gears of War #1 © Epic Comics

Generation Hope #4 © MAR

	GD 2.0	VG 4.0	FN 6.0	VF 8.0	VF/NM 9.0	NM- 9.2

G-8 AND HIS BATTLE ACES (Based on pulps)
Gold Key: Oct, 1966
1 (10184-610)-Painted-c 4 8 12 27 44 60

G-8 AND HIS BATTLE ACES
Blazing Comics: 1991 ($1.50, one-shot)
1-Glanzman-a; Truman-c 3.00
NOTE: *Flip book format with "The Spider's Web" #1 on other side w/***Glanzman**-a, **Truman**-c.

GEM COMICS
Spotlight Publishers: Apr, 1945 (52 pgs)
1-Little Mohee, Steve Strong app.; Jungle bondage-c
77 154 231 493 847 1200

GEMINI BLOOD
DC Comics (Helix): Sept, 1996 - No. 9, May, 1997 ($2.25, limited series)
1-9: 5-Simonson-c 3.00

GEN ACTIVE
DC Comics (WildStorm): May, 2000 - No. 6, Aug, 2001 ($3.95)
1-6: 1-Covers by Campbell and Madureira; Gen 13 & DV8 app. 5-Mahfood-a; Quitely and Stelfreeze-c. 6-Portacio-a/c 4.00

GENE AUTRY (See March of Comics No. 25, 28, 39, 54, 78, 90, 104, 120, 135, 150 in the Promotional Comics section & Western Roundup under Dell Giants)

GENE AUTRY COMICS (Movie, Radio star; singing cowboy)
Fawcett Publications: Jan, 1942 (On sale 12/17/41) - No. 10, 1943 (68 pgs.)
(Dell takes over with No. 11)
1 (Scarce)-Gene Autry & his horse Champion begin; photo back-c
343 686 1029 2400 4200 6000
2-(1942) 90 180 270 576 988 1400
3-5: 3-(11/1/42) 50 100 150 315 533 750
6-10 41 82 123 256 428 600

GENE AUTRY COMICS (...& Champion No. 102 on)
Dell Publishing Co.: No. 11, 1943 - No. 121, Jan-Mar, 1959 (TV - later issues)
11 (1943, 60 pgs.)-Continuation of Fawcett series; photo back-c; first Dell issue
32 64 96 230 515 800
12 (2/44, 60 pgs.) 28 56 84 202 451 700
Four Color 47 (1944, 60 pgs.) 35 70 105 252 564 875
Four Color 57 (11/44), 66 ('45)(52 pgs. each) 30 60 90 216 483 750
Four Color 75, 83 ('45, 36 pgs. each) 23 46 69 164 362 560
Four Color 93 ('45, 36 pgs.) 19 38 57 133 297 460
Four Color 100 ('46, 36 pgs.) First Gene Autry photo-c
22 44 66 155 345 535
1 (5-6/46, 52 pgs.) 33 66 99 238 532 825
2 (7-8/46)-Photo-c begin, end #111 14 28 42 96 211 325
3-5: 4-Intro Flapjack Hobbs 11 22 33 76 163 250
6-10 10 20 30 64 132 200
11-20: 20-Panhandle Pete begins 9 18 27 60 120 180
21-29 (36 pgs.) 8 16 24 52 99 145
30-40 (52 pgs.) 7 14 21 44 82 120
41-56 (52 pgs.) 6 12 18 38 69 100
57-66 (36 pgs.): 58-X-mas-c 5 10 15 34 60 85
67-80 (52 pgs.): 70-X-mas-c 5 10 15 34 60 85
81-90 (52 pgs.): 82-X-mas-c. 87-Blank inside-c 5 10 15 31 53 75
91-99 (36 pgs. No. 91-on). 94-X-mas-c 4 8 12 28 47 65
100 5 10 15 30 50 70
101-111-Last Gene Autry photo-c 4 8 12 27 44 60
112-121-All Champion painted-c, most by Savitt 4 8 12 25 40 55
NOTE: *Photo back covers 4-18, 20-45, 48-65.* **Manning** *a-118.* **Jesse Marsh** *art: 4-Color No. 66, 75, 93, 100, No. 1-25, 27-37, 39, 40.*

GENE AUTRY'S CHAMPION (TV)
Dell Publ. Co.: No. 287, 8/50; No. 319, 2/51; No. 3, 8-10/51 - No. 19, 8-10/55
Four Color 287(#1)('50, 52 pgs.)-Photo-c 11 22 33 76 163 250
Four Color 319(#2, '51), 3: 2-Painted-c begin, most by Sam Savitt
6 12 18 41 76 110
4-19: 19-Last painted-c 4 8 12 28 47 65

GENE COLAN TRIBUTE BOOK (Produced for The Hero Initiative)
Marvel Comics: 2008 ($9.99, one-shot)
1-Spotlighted stories from Tales of Suspense #89,90, Doctor Strange #174 and others 12.00

GENE DOGS
Marvel Comics UK: Oct, 1993 - No. 4, Jan, 1994 ($1.75, limited series)
1-($2.75)-Polybagged w/4 trading cards 5.00
2-4: 2-Vs. Genetix 4.00

GENE POOL
IDW Publishing: Oct, 2003 ($6.99, squarebound)
nn-Wein & Wolfman-s/Cummings-a 7.00

GENERAL DOUGLAS MACARTHUR
Fox Feature Syndicate: 1951
nn-True life story 21 42 63 122 199 275

GENERATION HEX
DC Comics (Amalgam): June, 1997 ($1.95, one-shot)
1-Milligan-s/ Pollina & Morales-a 4.00

GENERATION HOPE (See X-Men titles and Cable)
Marvel Comics: Jan, 2011 - No. 17, May, 2012 ($3.99/$2.99)
1-($3.99) Gillen-s/Espin-a; Coipel-c; back-up bio of Hope Summers 4.00
1-Variant-c by Greg Land 8.00
2-17-($2.99) 5,9-McKelvie-a. 10,11-Seeley-a. 11-X-Men: Schism tie-in 3.00

GENERATION M (Follows House of M x-over)
Marvel Comics: Jan, 2006 - No. 5, May, 2006 ($2.99, limited series)
1-5-Jenkins-s/Bachs-a. 1-Chamber app. 2-Jubilee app. 3-Blob-c. 4-Angel-c 3.00
Decimation: Generation M TPB (2006, $13.99) r/#1-5 14.00

GENERATION NEXT
Marvel Comics: Mar, 1995 - No. 4, June, 1995 ($1.95, limited series)
1-4-Age of Apocalypse; Scott Lobdell scripts & Chris Bachalo-c/a 4.00

GENERATIONS: (Team-ups of legacy characters after Secret Empire)
Marvel Comics: Oct, 2017 - Nov, 2017 ($4.99, series of one-shots)
... Banner Hulk & The Totally Awesome Hulk 1 (10/17) Pak-s/Buffagni-a 5.00
... Captain Marvel & Captain Mar-Vell 1 (11/17) Stohl-s/Schoonover-a; Annihilus app. 5.00
... Hawkeye & Hawkeye 1 (10/17) Thompson-s/Raffaele-a; Swordsman app. 5.00
... Iron Man & Ironheart 1 (11/17) Bendis-s; future Tony Stark as Sorceror Supreme app. 5.00
... Miles Morales Spider-Man & Peter Parker Spider-Man 1 (11/17) Bendis-s 5.00
... Ms. Marvel & Ms. Marvel 1 (11/17) Kamala meets younger Carol; Nightscream app. 5.00
... Phoenix & Jean Grey 1 (10/17) Bunn-s/Silva-a; Galactus app. 5.00
... Sam Wilson Captain America & Steve Rogers Captain America 1 (11/17) Spencer-s 5.00
... The Unworthy Thor & The Mighty Thor 1 (10/17) Aaron-s/Asrar-a; Apocalypse app. 5.00
... Wolverine & All-New Wolverine 1 (10/17) Taylor-s/Rosanas-a; Sabretooth app. 5.00

GENERATIONS... (Follows events in Dark Nights: Death Metal)
DC Comics: Mar, 2021 - Apr, 2021 ($9.99, limited series)
... Forged 1 (4/21, $9.99) Conclusion vs. Dominus; Jor-El, O.M.A.C. app.; art by various 10.00
... Shattered 1 (3/21, $9.99) Kamandi teams with Booster Gold, 1939 Batman, Steel, Sinestro, Starfire, Silver Age Superboy and Dr. Light; intro Dominus; art by various 10.00

GENERATION X (See Gen [13]/ Generation X)
Marvel Comics: Oct, 1994 - No. 75, June, 2001 ($1.50/$1.95/$1.99/$2.25)
Collectors Preview ($1.75), "Ashcan" Edition 3.00
-1(7/97) Flashback story 3.00
1/2 (San Diego giveaway) 2 4 6 8 10 12
1-($3.95)-Wraparound chromium-c; Scott Lobdell scripts & Chris Bachalo-a begins
1 3 4 6 8 10
2-($1.95)-Deluxe edition, Bachalo-a 4.00
3,4-($1.95)-Deluxe Edition; Bachalo-a 4.00
2-10: 2-4-Standard Edition. 5-Returns from "Age of Apocalypse," begin $1.95-c. 6-Bachalo-a(p) ends, returns #17. 7-Roger Cruz-a(p). 10-Omega Red-c/app. 3.00
11-24, 26-28: 13,14-Bishop-app. 17-Stan Lee app. (Stan Lee scripts own dialogue); Bachalo/Buckingham-a; Onslaught update. 18-Toad cameo. 20-Franklin Richards app; Howard the Duck cameo. 21-Howard the Duck app. 22-Nightmare app. 3.00
25-($2.99)-Wraparound-c. Black Tom, Howard the Duck app. 4.00
29-37: 29-Begin $1.99-c, "Operation Zero Tolerance". 33-Hama-s 3.00
38-49: 38-Dodson-a begins. 40-Penance ID revealed. 49-Maggott app. 3.00
50,57-($2.99): 50-Crossover w/X-Man #50 4.00
51-56, 58-62: 59-Avengers & Spider-Man app. 3.00
63-74: 63-Ellis-s begin. 64-Begin $2.25-c. 69-71-Art Adams-c 3.00
75-($2.99) Final issue; Chamber joins the X-Men; Lim-a 4.00
'95 Special-($3.95) 4.00
'96 Special-($2.95)-Wraparound-c; Jeff Johnson-c/a 4.00
'97 Special-($2.99)-Wraparound-c; 4.00
'98 Annual-($3.50)-vs. Dracula 4.00
'99 Annual-($3.50)-Monet leaves 4.00
75¢ Ashcan Edition 3.00
...Holiday Special 1 (2/99, $3.50) Pollina-a 4.00
...Underground Special 1 (5/98, $2.50, B&W) Mahfood-a 3.00

GENERATION X
Marvel Comics: Jul, 2017 - No. 9, Jan, 2018; No. 85, Feb, 2018 - No. 87, Apr, 2018 ($3.99)

GD VG FN VF VF/NM NM-
2.0 4.0 6.0 8.0 9.0 9.2

1-9: 1-Strain-s/Pinna-a 4.00
[Title switches to legacy numbering after #9 (1/18)]
85-87: 85-(2/18) Monet app.; Dodson-c 4.00

GENERATION X/ GEN 13 (Also see Gen 13/ Generation X)
Marvel Comics: 1997 ($3.99, one-shot)
1-Robinson-s/Larroca-a(p) 4.00

GENERATION ZERO (see Harbinger Wars)
Valiant Entertainment: Aug, 2016 - No. 9, Apr, 2017 ($3.99)
1-9: 1-Van Lente-s/Portela-a; multiple covers. 3-Archie-style art by Derek Charm 4.00

GENERIC COMIC, THE
Marvel Comics Group: Apr, 1984 (one-shot)
1 3.00

GENE RODDENBERRY'S LOST UNIVERSE
Tekno Comix: Apr, 1995 - No. 7, Oct, 1995 ($1.95)
1-7: 1-3-w/ bound-in game piece & trading card. 4-w/bound-in trading card 3.00

GENE RODDENBERRY'S XANDER IN LOST UNIVERSE
Tekno Comix: No. 0, Nov, 1995; No. 1, Dec, 1995 - No. 8, July, 1996 ($2.25)
0,1-8: 1-5-Jae Lee-c. 4-Polybagged. 8-Pt. 5 of The Big Bang x-over 3.00

GENESIS (See DC related titles)
DC Comics: Oct, 1997 - No. 4, Oct, 1997 ($1.95, weekly limited series)
1-4: Byrne-s/Wagner-a(p) in all. 4.00

GENESIS: THE #1 COLLECTION (WildStorm Archives)
WildStorm Productions: 1998 ($9.99, TPB, B&W)
nn-Reprints #1 issues of WildStorm titles and pin-ups 10.00

GENETIX
Marvel Comics UK: Oct, 1993 - No. 6, Mar, 1994 ($1.75, limited series)
1-($2.75)-Polybagged w/4 cards; Dark Guard app. 4.00
2-6: 2-Intro Tektos. 4-Vs. Gene Dogs 3.00

GENEXT (Next generation of X-Men)
Marvel Comics: July, 2008 - No. 5, Nov, 2008 ($3.99, limited series)
1-5: 1-Claremont-s/Scherberger-a; character profile pages 4.00

GENEXT: UNITED
Marvel Comics: July, 2009 - No. 5, Dec, 2009 ($3.99, limited series)
1-5: 1-Claremont-s/Meyers-a; Beast app. 4.00

GENIS-VELL: CAPTAIN MARVEL
Marvel Comics: Sept, 2022 - No. 5, Jan, 2023 ($4.99/$3.99)
1-($4.99) Peter David-s/Juanan Ramírez-a; Genis-Vell & Rick Jones return 5.00
2-5-($3.99) 2-Death app. 3-5-Shatterax app. 4.00

GENIS-VELL: MARVEL TALES
Marvel Comics: Jan, 2022 ($7.99, one-shot)
1-Reprints Captain Marvel #0-3 (2000); Rick Jones with Captain Marvel (Genis-Vell) 8.00

GENIUS
Image Comics (Top Cow): Aug, 2014 - No. 5, Aug, 2014 ($3.99, limited series)
1-5-Bernardin & Freeman-s/Afua Richardson-a 4.00

GEN:LOCK (Based on the animated series) (Printings of stories that first appeared online) (Issues #6 & #7 were solicited but not printed)
DC Comics (Rooster Teeth Productions): Jan, 2020 - No. 5, May, 2020 ($3.99)
1-5: 1,2,5-Kelly & Lanzing-s/Barberi-a. 3,4-Prasetya-a 4.00

GEN 12 (Also see Gen 13 and Team 7)
Image Comics (WildStorm Productions): Feb, 1998 - No. 5, June, 1998 ($2.50, lim. series)
1-5: 1-Team 7 & Gen 13 app.; wraparound-c 3.00

GEN 13 (Also see Wild C.A.T.S. #1 & Deathmate Black #2)
Image Comics (WildStorm Productions): Feb, 1994 - No. 5, July 1994 ($1.95, limited series)
0 (8/95, $2.50)-Ch. 1 w/Jim Lee-p; Ch. 4 w/Charest-p 4.00
1/2 1 2 3 4 5 7
1-($2.50)-Created by Jim Lee 1 3 4 6 8 10
1-2nd printing 3.00
1-"3-D" Edition (9/97, $4.95)-w/glasses 5.00
2-($2.50) 1 2 3 4 5 7
3-Pitt-c & story 4.00
4-Pitt-c & story; wraparound-c 4.00
5 4.00
5-Alternate Portacio-c; see Deathblow #5 6.00
...Collected Edition ('94, $12.95)-r/#1-5 13.00
...Rave ($1.50, 3/95)-wraparound-c 4.00
...: Who They Are And How They Came To Be... (2006, $14.99) r/#1-5; sketch gallery 15.00
NOTE: *Issues 1-4 contain coupons redeemable for the ashcan edition of Gen 13 #0. Price listed is for a complete book.*

GEN 13
Image Comics (WildStorm Productions): Mar, 1995 - No. 36, Dec, 1998;
DC Comics (WildStorm): No. 37, Mar, 1999 - No. 77, Jul, 2002 ($2.95/$2.50)
1-A (Charge)-Campbell/Garner-c 2 4 6 8 10 12
1-B (Thumbs Up)-Campbell/Garner-c 1 3 4 6 8 10
1-C-1-F,1-I-1-M: 1-C (Lil' GEN 13)-Art Adams-c. 1-D (Barbari-GEN)-Simon Bisley-c. 1-E (Your Friendly Neighborhood Grunge)-Cleary-c. 1-F (GEN 13 Goes Madison Ave.)-Golden-c. 1-I (That's the way we became GEN 13)-Campbell/Gibson-c. 1-J (All Dolled Up)-Campbell/McWeeney-c. 1-K (Verti-GEN)-Dunn-c. 1-L (Picto-Fiction). 1-M (Do it Yourself Cover) 1 2 3 4 5 7
1-G (Lin-GEN-re)-Michael Lopez-c 3 6 9 16 24 32
1-H (GEN-et Jackson)-Jason Pearson-c 3 6 9 19 30 40
1-Chromium-c by Campbell 4 8 12 27 44 60
1-Chromium-c by Jim Lee 5 10 15 33 57 80
1-"3-D" Edition (2/98, $4.95)-w/glasses 5.00
2 ($1.95, Newsstand)-WildStorm Rising Pt. 4; bound-in card 4.00
2-12: 2-($2.50, Direct Market)-WildStorm Rising Pt. 4, bound-in card. 6,7-Jim Lee-c/a(p). 9-Ramos-a. 10,11-Fire From Heaven Pt. 3. & Pt.9 4.00
11-($4.95)-Special European Tour Edition; chromium-c 3 6 9 14 20 25
13A,13B,13C-($1.30, 13 pgs.): 13A-Archie & Friends app. 13B-Bone-c/app.; Teenage Mutant Ninja Turtles, Madman, Spawn & Jim Lee app. 5.00
14-24: 20-Last Campbell-a 4.00
25-($3.50)-Two covers by Campbell and Charest 4.00
25-($3.50)-Voyager Pack w/Danger Girl preview 5.00
25-Foil-c 10.00
26-32,34: 26-Arcudi-s/Frank-a begins. 34-Back-up story by Art Adams 3.00
33-Flip book w/Planetary preview 4.00
35-49: 36,38,40-Two covers. 37-First DC issue. 41-Last Frank-a 3.00
50-($3.95) Two covers by Lee and Benes; art by various 4.00
51-76: 51-Moy-a; Fairchild loses her powers. 60-Warren-s/a. 66-Art by various incl. Campbell (3 pgs.). 70,75,76-Mays-a. 76-Original team dies 3.00
77-($3.50) Mays, Andrews, Warren-a 4.00
Annual 1 (1997, $2.95) Ellis-s/ Dillon-c/a. 5.00
Annual 1999 ($3.50, DC) Slipstream x-over w/ DV8 5.00
Annual 2000 ($3.50) Devil's Night x-over w/WildStorm titles; Bermejo-c 4.00
...: A Christmas Caper (1/00, $5.95, one-shot) McWeeney-s/a 6.00
... Archives (4/98, $12.99) B&W reprints of mini-series, #0,1/2,1-13ABC; includes cover gallery and sourcebook 13.00
...: Carny Folk (2/00, $3.50) Collect back-up stories 3.50
... European Vacation TPB ($6.95) r/#6,7 7.00
.../ Fantastic Four (2001, $5.95) Maguire-s/c/a(p) 6.00
...: Going West (6/99, $2.50, one-shot) Pruett-s 3.00
...: Grunge Saves the World (5/99, $5.95, one-shot) Altieri-c/a 6.00
... I Love New York TPB ($9.95) r/part #25, 26-29; Frank-c 10.00
... London, New York, Hell TPB ($6.95) r/Annual #1 & Bootleg Ann. #1 7.00
... Lost in Paradise TPB ($6.95) r/#3-5 7.00
.../ Maxx (12/95, $3.50, one-shot) Messner-Loebs-s, 1st Coker-c/a. 4.00
...: Meanwhile (2003, $17.95) r/#43,44,66-70; all Warren-s; art by various 18.00
...: Medicine Song (2001, $5.95) Brent Anderson-c/a(p)/Raab-s 6.00
... Science Friction (2001, $5.95) Haley & Lopresti-a 6.00
... Starting Over TPB ($14.95) r/#1-7 15.00
... Superhuman Like You TPB ($12.95) r/#60-65; Warren-c 13.00
... #13 A,B&C Collected Edition ($6.95, TPB) r/#13A,B&C 7.00
... 3-D Special (1997, $4.95, one-shot) Art Adams-s/a(p) 5.00
...: The Unreal World (7/96, $2.95, one-shot) Humberto Ramos-c/a 3.00
... We'll Take Manhattan TPB ($14.95) r/#45-50; new Benes-c 15.00
...: Wired (4/99, $2.50, one-shot) Richard Bennett-c/a 3.00
... Yearbook 1997 (6/97, $2.50) College-themed stories and pin-ups by various 3.00
...: 'Zine (12/96, $1.95, B&W, digest size) Campbell/Garner-c 3.00
Variant Collection-Four editions (all 13 variants w/Chromium variant-limited, signed) 100.00

GEN 13
DC Comics (WildStorm): No. 0, Sept, 2002 - No. 16, Feb, 2004 ($2.95)
0-(13¢-c) Intro. new team; includes previews of 21 Down & The Resistance 3.00
1-Claremont-s/Garza-c/a; Fairchild app. 3.00
2-16: 8-13-Bachs-a. 16-Original team returns 3.00
...: September Song TPB (2003, $19.95) r/#0-6; Garza sketch pages 20.00

GEN 13 (Volume 4)
DC Comics (WildStorm): Dec, 2006 - No. 39, Feb, 2011 ($2.99)
1-39: 1-Simone-s/Caldwell-a; re-intro the original team; Caldwell-c. 8-The Authority app. 3.00
1-Variant-c by J. Scott Campbell 5.00
...: Armageddon (1/08, $2.99) Gage-s/Meyers-a; future Gen13 app. 3.00
...: Best of a Bad Lot TPB (2007, $14.99) r/#1-6 15.00
...: 15 Minutes TPB (2008, $14.99) r/#14-20 15.00
...: Road Trip TPB (2008, $14.99) r/#7-13 15.00
...: World's End TPB (2009, $17.99) r/#21-26 18.00

GEN 13 BOOTLEG
Image Comics (WildStorm): Nov, 1996 - No. 20, Jul, 1998 ($2.50)
1-Alan Davis-a; alternate costumes-c 4.00
1-Team falling variant-c 5.00
2-7: 2-Alan Davis-a. 5,6-Terry Moore-s. 7-Robinson-s/Scott Hampton-a 4.00
8-10-Adam Warren-s/a 4.00
11-20: 11,12-Lopresti-s/a & Simonson-s. 13-Wieringo-s/a. 14-Mariotte-s/Phillips-a. 15,16-Strnad-s/Shaw-a. 18-Altieri-s/a(p)/c, 18-Variant-c by Bruce Timm 4.00
Annual 1 (2/98, $2.95) Ellis-s/Dillon-c/a 5.00
... Grunge: The Movie (12/97, $9.95) r/#8-10, Warren-c 10.00
...Vol. 1 TPB (10/98, $11.95) r/#1-4 12.00

GEN 13/ GENERATION X (Also see Generation X / Gen 13)
Image Comics (WildStorm Publications): July, 1997 ($2.95, one-shot)
1-Choi-s/ Art Adams-p/Garner-i. Variant covers by Adams/Garner and Campbell/McWeeney 4.00
1-($4.95) 3-D Edition w/glasses; Campbell-c 5.00

GEN 13 INTERACTIVE
Image Comics (WildStorm): Oct, 1997 - No. 3, Dec, 1997 ($2.50, lim. series)
1-3-Internet voting used to determine storyline 4.00
... Plus! (7/98, $11.95) r/series & 3-D Special (in 2-D) 12.00

GEN 13: MAGICAL DRAMA QUEEN ROXY
Image Comics (WildStorm): Oct, 1998 - No. 3, Dec, 1998 ($3.50, lim. series)
1-3-Adam Warren-s/c/a; manga style, 2-Variant-c by Hiroyuki Utatane 4.00
1-($6.95) Dynamic Forces Ed. w/Variant Warren-c 7.00

GEN 13/MONKEYMAN & O'BRIEN
Image Comics (WildStorm): Jun, 1998 - No. 2, July, 1998 ($2.50, lim. series)
1,2-Art Adams-s/a(p); 1-Two covers 4.00
1-($4.95) Chromium-c 5.00
1-($6.95) Dynamic Forces Ed. 7.00

GEN 13: ORDINARY HEROES
Image Comics (WildStorm Publications): Feb, 1996 - No. 2, July, 1996 ($2.50, lim. series)
1,2-Adam Hughes-c/a/scripts 4.00
TPB (2004, $14.95) r/series, Gen13 Bootleg #1&2 and Wildstorm Thunderbook; new Hughes-c and art pages 15.00

Generation X (2017) #8 © MAR

Gen 13 V4 #1 © WSP

Ghost (2012) #2 © DH

GD 2.0 | VG 4.0 | FN 6.0 | VF 8.0 | VF/NM 9.0 | NM- 9.2

GENTLE BEN (TV)
Dell Publishing Co.: Feb, 1968 - No. 5, Oct, 1969 (All photo-c)
1 4 8 12 25 40 55
2-5: 5-Reprints #1 3 6 9 16 23 30

GEOMANCER (Also see Eternal Warrior: Fist & Steel)
Valiant: Nov, 1994 - No. 8, June, 1995 ($3.75/$2.25)
1 ($3.75)-Chromium wraparound-c; Eternal Warrior app. 5.00
2-8 4.00

GEORGE OF THE JUNGLE (TV)(See America's Best TV Comics)
Gold Key: Feb, 1969 - No. 2, Oct, 1969 (Jay Ward)
1 8 16 24 56 108 160
2 5 10 15 35 63 90

GEORGE PAL'S PUPPETOONS (Funny animal puppets)
Fawcett Publications: Dec, 1945 - No. 18, Dec, 1947; No. 19, 1950
1-Captain Marvel-c 50 100 150 315 533 750
2 26 52 78 154 252 350
3-10 15 30 45 94 147 200
11-19 14 28 42 81 118 155

GEORGE PEREZ'S SIRENS
BOOM! Studios: Sept, 2014 - No. 6, Dec, 2016 ($3.99, limited series)
1-6-George Pérez-s/a; multiple covers 4.00

GEORGE R.R. MARTIN'S A CLASH OF KINGS (Based on A Song of Ice and Fire, Book 2)
Dynamite Entertainment: 2017 - No. 16, 2019; 2020 - No. 16 ($3.99)
1-16: 1-Landry Q. Walker-s/Mel Rubi-a; multiple covers 4.00
Volume 2 (2020 - No. 16) 1-16-Landry Q.Walker-s/Mel Rubi-a 4.00

GEORGIE COMICS (...& Judy Comics #20-35?; see All Teen & Teen Comics)
Timely Comics/GPI No. 1-34: Spr, 1945 - No. 39, Oct, 1952 (#1-3 are quarterly)
1-Dave Berg-a 57 114 171 362 619 875
2 34 68 102 204 332 460
3-5,7,8(11/46) 26 52 78 154 252 350
6-Georgie visits Timely Comics 33 66 99 194 317 440
9,10-Kurtzman's "Hey Look" (1 & ?); Millie the Model & Margie app.
30 60 90 177 289 400
11,12: 11-Margie, Millie app. 22 44 66 128 209 290
13-Kurtzman's "Hey Look", 3 pgs. 22 44 66 132 216 300
14-Wolverton-a(1 pg.); Kurtzman's "Hey Look" 23 46 69 136 223 310
15,16,18-20 20 40 60 118 192 265
17,29-Kurtzman's "Hey Look", 1 pg. 21 42 63 126 206 285
21-24,27,28,30-39: 21-Anti-Wertham editorial. 33-38-Hy Rosen-c
20 40 60 120 195 265
25-Painted-c by classic pin-up artist Peter Driben 119 238 357 762 1306 1850
26-Logo design swipe from Archie Comics 40 80 120 246 411 575

GERALD McBOING-BOING AND THE NEARSIGHTED MR. MAGOO (TV)
(Mr. Magoo No. 6 on)
Dell Publishing Co.: Aug-Oct, 1952 - No. 5, Aug-Oct, 1953
1 10 20 30 64 132 200
2-5 8 16 24 54 102 150

GERONIMO (See Fighting Indians of the Wild West!)
Avon Periodicals: 1950 - No. 4, Feb, 1952
1-Indian Fighter; Maneely-a; Texas Rangers-r/Cowpuncher #1; Fawcette-c
26 52 78 154 252 350
2-On the Warpath; Kit West app.; Kinstler-c/a 17 34 51 100 158 215
3-And His Apache Murderers; Kinstler-c/a(2); Kit West-r/Cowpuncher #6
17 34 51 100 158 215
4-Savage Raids of; Kinstler-c & inside front-c; Kinstlerish-a by McCann(3)
16 32 48 94 147 200

GERONIMO JONES
Charlton Comics: Sept, 1971 - No. 9, Jan, 1973
1 3 6 9 15 22 28
2-9 2 4 6 8 10 12
Modern Comics Reprint #7('78) 5.00

GETALONG GANG, THE (TV)
Marvel Comics (Star Comics): May, 1985 - No. 6, Mar, 1986
1-6: Saturday morning TV stars 5.00

GET JIRO!
DC Comics (Vertigo): 2012 ($24.99, hardcover graphic novel with dust jacket)
HC - Anthony Bourdain & Joel Rose-s/Langdon Foss-a 25.00
SC - (2013, $14.99) Anthony Bourdain & Joel Rose-s/Langdon Foss-a 15.00

GET JIRO: BLOOD AND SUSHI
DC Comics (Vertigo): 2015 ($22.99, hardcover graphic novel with dust jacket)
HC - Prequel to Get Jiro!; Anthony Bourdain & Joel Rose-s/Alé Garza-a/Dave Johnson-c 23.00

GET LOST
Mikeross Publications/New Comics: Feb-Mar, 1954 - No. 3, June-July, 1954 (Satire)
1-Andru/Esposito-a in all? 48 96 144 302 514 725
2-Andru/Esposito-c; has 4 pg. E.C. parody featuring "The Sewer Keeper"
32 64 96 188 307 425
3-John Wayne 'Hondo' parody 26 52 78 154 252 350
1,2 (10,12/87-New Comics)-B&W r-original 4.00

GET SMART (TV)
Dell Publ. Co.: June, 1966 - No. 8, Sept, 1967 (All have Don Adams photo-c)
1 10 20 30 64 132 200
2,3-Ditko-a 6 12 18 40 73 105
4-8: 8-Reprints #1 (cover and insides) 5 10 15 33 57 80

GHOST (...Comics #9)
Fiction House Magazines: 1951(Winter) - No. 11, Summer, 1954
1-Most covers by Whitman 300 600 900 2010 3505 5000
2-Ghost Gallery & Werewolf Hunter stories; classic-c
258 516 774 1651 2826 4000
3-9: 3,6,7,9-Bondage-c. 9-Abel, Discount-a 194 388 582 1242 2121 3000
10,11-Dr. Drew by Grandenetti in each, reprinted from Rangers; 11-Evans-r/
Rangers #39; Grandenetti-r/Rangers #49 155 310 465 992 1696 2400

GHOST (See Comic's Greatest World)
Dark Horse Comics: Apr, 1995 - No. 36, Apr, 1998 ($2.50/$2.95)
1-Adam Hughes-a 1 3 4 6 8 10
2,3-Hughes-a 5.00
4-24: 4-Barb Wire app. 5,6-Hughes-c. 12-Ghost/Hellboy preview. 15,21-X app.
18,19-Barb Wire app. 4.00
25-($3.50)-48 pgs. special 5.00
26-36: 26-Begin $2.95-c. 29-Flip book w/Timecop. 33-36-Jade Cathedral; Harris painted-c 4.00
Special 1 (7/94, $3.95, 48 pgs.) 1 2 3 4 5 7
Special 2 (6/98, $3.95) Barb Wire app. 5.00
Special 3 (see Ghost Volume 2)
... Black October (1/99, $14.95, trade paperback)-r/#6-9,26,27 15.00
... Nocturnes (1996, $9.95, trade paperback)-r/#1-3 & 5 10.00
... Omnibus Vol. 1 (10/08, $24.95, 9x6") r/#1-12; Special 1 and Decade of Dark Horse #2 25.00
... Stories (1995, $9.95, trade paperback)-r/Early Ghost app. 10.00

GHOST (Volume 2)
Dark Horse Comics: Sept, 1998 - No. 22, Aug, 2000 ($2.95)
1-22: 1-4-Ryan Benjamin-c/Zanier-a 3.00
Handbook (8/99, $2.95) guide to issues and characters 3.00
Special 3 (12/98, $3.95) 5.00

GHOST (3rd series)
Dark Horse Comics: No. 0, Sept, 2012 - No. 4, Mar, 2013 ($2.99)
0-4-DeConnick-s/Noto-a. 0-Frison-c. 1,2-Covers by Noto & Alex Ross 3.00

GHOST (4th series)
Dark Horse Comics: Dec, 2013 - No. 12, Feb, 2015 ($2.99)
1-12: 1,2-DeConnick & Sebela-s/Sook-a/Dodson-c. 3,4-Borges-a 3.00

GHOST AND THE SHADOW
Dark Horse Comics: Dec, 1995 ($2.95, one-shot)
1-Moench scripts 6.00

GHOST/BATGIRL
Dark Horse Comics: Aug, 2000 - No. 4, Dec, 2000 ($2.95, limited series)
1-4-Cassandra Cain Batgirl; Oracle & Bruce Wayne app.; Benjamin-c/a 4.00

GHOST/HELLBOY
Dark Horse Comics: May, 1996 - No. 2, June, 1996 ($2.50, limited series)
1,2: Mike Mignola-c/scripts & breakdowns; Scott Benefiel finished-a 5.00

GHOST BREAKERS (Also see Racket Squad in Action, Red Dragon & (CC) Sherlock Holmes Comics)
Street & Smith Publications: Sept, 1948 - No. 2, Dec, 1948 (52 pgs.)
1-Powell-c/a(3); Dr. Neff (magician) app. 53 106 159 334 567 800
2-Powell-c/a(2); Maneely-a 41 82 123 256 428 600

GHOSTBUSTERS (TV) (Also, see Real...and Slimer)
First Comics: Feb, 1987 - No. 6, Aug, 1987 ($1.25)
1-6: Based on new animated TV series 5.00

GHOSTBUSTERS
IDW Publishing: Sept, 2011 - No. 16, Dec, 2012 ($3.99)

1-16-Burnham-s/Schoening-a; multiple covers 4.00
...: 100-Page Spooktacular (10/12, $7.99) reprints of IDW stories 10.00

GHOSTBUSTERS
IDW Publishing: (one-shots)

Annual 2017 (1/17, $7.99) Burnham-s/Schoening-a and short stories by various 8.00
Annual 2018 (2/18, $7.99) Burnham-s/Schoening-a; Ghostbusters: Crossing Over prelude 8.00
Answer the Call Ghostbusters 35th Anniversary One-Shot (4/19, $3.99) Female team 4.00
...: Con-Volution (6/10, $3.99) Josh Howard-a 4.00
...: Deviations (3/16, $4.99) What If.. Ghostbusters never crossed the streams 5.00
... Funko Universe One Shot (5/17, $4.99) Story with Funko Pop-styled characters 5.00
... Halloween Comicfest 2017 (10/17, giveaway) Burnham-s/Schoening-a 3.00
...: Tainted Love (2/10, $3.99) Salgood Sam-a 4.00
... 35th Anniversary: Extreme: One Shot (4/20, $3.99) Comic team 4.00
... 35th Anniversary: Ghostbusters: One Shot (4/20, $3.99) Movie team; Schoening-a 4.00
... 35th Anniversary: Tthe Real Ghostbusters: One Shot (4/20, $3.99) Cartoon team 4.00
... 20/20 (1/19, $4.99) Set 20 years in the future; Sanctum of Slime team app. 5.00
...: What in Samhain Just Happened? (10/10, $3.99) Peter David-s/Dan Schoening-a 4.00

GHOSTBUSTERS
IDW Publishing: Feb, 2013 - No. 20, Sept, 2014 ($3.99)

1-20-Janine & the female Ghostbuster crew; Burnham-s/Schoening-a; multiple covers 4.00
Annual 2015 (11/15, $7.99) Burnham-s/Schoening-a and bonus 1-pagers by various 8.00

GHOSTBUSTERS: ANSWER THE CALL
IDW Publishing: Oct, 2017 - No. 5, Feb, 2018 ($3.99)

1-5-Female crew; Thompson-s/Howell-a 4.00

GHOSTBUSTERS: CROSSING OVER
IDW Publishing: Mar, 2018 - No. 8, Oct, 2018 ($3.99)

1-8-Meeting of movie, cartoon, comic Ghostbusters teams; Burnham-s/Schoening-a 4.00

GHOSTBUSTERS: DISPLACED AGGRESSION
IDW Publishing: Sept, 2009 - No. 4, Dec, 2009 ($3.99)

1-Lobdell-s/Kyriazis-a 1 3 4 6 8 10
2,3 4.00
Hundred Penny Press: Ghostbusters: Displaced Aggression (3/11, $1.00) r/#1 5.00

GHOSTBUSTERS: GET REAL
IDW Publishing: Jun, 2015 - No. 4, Sept, 2015 ($3.99)

1-4-Burnham-s/Schoening-a; multiple-c; Real Ghostbusters meet comic Ghostbusters 4.00

GHOSTBUSTERS: INFESTATION (Zombie x-over with Star Trek, G.I. Joe & Transformers)
IDW Publishing: Mar, 2011 - No. 2, Mar, 2011 ($3.99, limited series)

1,2-Kyle Hotz-a; covers by Hotz and Snyder III 1 2 3 5 6 8

GHOSTBUSTERS: INTERNATIONAL
IDW Publishing: Jan, 2016 - No. 11, Nov, 2016 ($3.99)

1-11-Burnham-s/Schoening-a; 2 covers on each 4.00

GHOSTBUSTERS: LEGION (Movie)
88 MPH Studios: Feb, 2004 - No. 4, May, 2004 ($2.95/$3.50)

1-Steve Kurth-a/Andrew Dabb-s 1 3 4 6 8 10
1-3-($3.50) Brereton variant-c 2 4 6 11 16 20
2-4 4.00

GHOSTBUSTERS 101
IDW Publishing: Mar, 2017 - No. 6, Aug, 2017 ($3.99, limited series)

1-6-Burnham-s/Schoening-a; multiple covers on each; original and female teams meet 4.00

GHOSTBUSTERS: THE OTHER SIDE
IDW Publishing: Oct, 2008 - No. 4, Jan, 2009 ($3.99)

1-Champagne-s/Nguyen-a 1 3 4 6 8 10
2-4 4.00

GHOSTBUSTERS II
Now Comics: Oct, 1989 - No. 3, Dec, 1989 ($1.95, mini-series)

1-3: Movie Adaptation 2 4 6 9 12 15

GHOSTBUSTERS: YEAR ONE
IDW Publishing: Jan, 2020 - No. 4, ($3.99, limited series)

1,2-Burnham-s/Schoening-a; multiple-c; first year after the events of the first movie 4.00

GHOST CASTLE (See Tales of...)

GHOSTED
Image Comics (Skybound): Jul, 2013 - No. 20, May, 2015 ($2.99)

1-20: 1-Williamson-s/Sudzuka-a/Phillips-c. 6-10-Gianfelice-a. 16-Ryp-a 3.00

GHOSTED IN L.A.
BOOM! Studios (BOOM! Box): Jul, 2019 - No. 12, Aug, 2020 ($3.99)

1-12-Sina Grace-s/Siobhan Keenan-a. 10-Grace-a 4.00

GHOST IN THE SHELL (Manga)
Dark Horse: Mar, 1995 - No. 8, Oct, 1995 ($3.95, B&W/color, lim. series)

1 6 12 18 38 69 100
2 3 6 9 19 30 40
3 3 6 9 16 23 30
4-8 2 4 6 8 11 14

GHOST IN THE SHELL 2: MAN-MACHINE INTERFACE (Manga)
Dark Horse Comics: Jan, 2003 - No. 11, Dec, 2003 ($3.50, color/B&W, lim. series)

1-Masamune Shirow-s/a in all 2 4 6 8 10 12
2-11: 5-B&W 5.00

GHOST IN YOU, THE: A RECKLESS BOOK
Image Comics: Apr, 2022 ($24.99, HC graphic novel)

HC - Ed Brubaker-s/Sean Phillips-a; 4th book in the Reckless series 25.00

GHOSTLY HAUNTS (Formerly Ghost Manor)
Charlton Comics: #20, 9/71 - #53, 12/76; #54, 9/77 - #55, 10/77; #56, 1/78 - #58, 4/78

20 4 8 12 23 37 50
21 3 6 9 14 19 24
22-25,27,31-34,36-Ditko-c/a. 27-Dr. Graves x-over. 32-New logo. 33-Back to
old logo 3 6 9 16 23 30
26,29,30,35-Ditko-c 2 4 6 13 18 22
28,37-40-Ditko-a. 39-Origin & 1st app. Destiny Fox 2 4 6 11 16 20
41,42: 41-Sutton-c; Ditko-a. 42-Newton-c/a 2 4 6 13 18 22
43-46,48,50,52-Ditko-a 2 4 6 10 14 18
47,54,56-Ditko-c/a. 56-Ditko-a(r). 3 6 9 14 19 24
49,51,53,55,57 2 4 6 8 10 12
58 (4/78) Last issue 3 6 9 14 19 24
40,41(Modern Comics-r, 1977, 1978) 6.00
NOTE: ***Ditko*** *a-22-25, 27, 28, 31-34, 36-41, 43-48, 50, 52, 54, 56r; c-22-27, 29, 30, 33-36, 47, 54, 56.* ***Glanzman*** *a-20.* ***Howard*** *a-27, 30, 35, 40-43, 48, 54, 57.* ***Kim*** *a-38, 41, 57.* ***Larson*** *a-48, 50.* ***Newton*** *c/a-42.* ***Staton*** *a-32, 35; c-28, 46.* ***Sutton*** *c-33, 37, 39, 41.*

GHOSTLY TALES (Formerly Blue Beetle No. 50-54)
Charlton Comics: No. 55, 4-5/66 - No. 124, 12/76; No. 125, 9/77 - No. 169, 10/84

55-Intro. & origin Dr. Graves; Ditko-a 9 18 27 61 123 185
56-58,60,61,70,71,72,75-Ditko-a. 70-Dr. Graves ends. 75-Last 12¢ issue
5 10 15 30 50 70
59,62-66,68 4 8 12 23 37 50
67,69,73-Ditko-c/a 5 10 15 33 57 80
74,91,98,119,123,124,127-130: 127,130-Sutton-a 2 4 6 13 18 22
76,79-82,85-Ditko-a 3 6 9 16 24 32
77,78,83,84,86-90,92-95,97,99-Ditko-c/a 4 8 12 23 37 50
96-Ditko-c 3 6 9 16 24 32
100-Ditko-c; Sutton-a 3 6 9 17 26 35
101,103-105-Ditko-a 3 6 9 14 19 24
102,109-Ditko-c/a 3 6 9 16 23 30
110,113-Sutton-c; Ditko-a 3 6 9 14 19 24
106-Ditko & Sutton-a; Sutton-c 3 6 9 14 19 24
107-Ditko, Wood, Sutton-a 3 6 9 14 20 26
108,116,117,126-Ditko-a 3 6 9 14 19 24
111,118,120-122,125-Ditko-c/a 3 6 9 16 23 30
112,114,115: 112,114-Ditko, Sutton-a. 114-Newton-a. 115-Newton, Ditko-a.
3 6 9 14 19 24
131-134,151,157,163-Ditko-c/a 2 4 6 13 18 22
135,142,145-150,153,154,156,158-160 1 2 3 5 7 9
136-141,143,144,152,155-Ditko-a 2 4 6 8 10 12
161,162,164-168-Lower print run. 162-Nudity panel 2 4 6 9 12 15
169 (10/84) Last issue; lower print run 2 4 6 11 16 20
NOTE: ***Aparo*** *a-65, 66, 68, 72, 137, 141r, 142r; c-71, 72, 74-76, 81, 146r, 149.* ***Ditko*** *a-55-58, 60, 61, 67, 69-73, 75-90, 92-95, 97, 99-118, 120-122, 125r, 126r, 131-141r, 143r, 144r, 146, 147, 149-152, 154-157, 159-161, 163; c-67, 69, 73, 77, 78, 83, 84, 86-90, 92-97, 99, 102, 109, 111, 118, 120-122, 125, 131-133, 147, 148, 151, 157-160, 163.* ***Glanzman*** *a-167.* ***Howard*** *a-95, 98, 99, 108, 117, 129, 131; c-98, 107, 120, 121, 161.* ***Larson*** *a-117, 119, 136, 159; c-136.* ***Morisi*** *a-83, 84, 86.* ***Newton*** *a-114; c-115(painted).* ***Palais*** *a-61.* ***Staton*** *a-161; c-117.* ***Sutton*** *a-106, 107, 111-114, 127, 130, 162; c-100, 106, 110, 113(painted).* ***Wood*** *a-107.*

GHOSTLY WEIRD STORIES (Formerly Blue Bolt Weird)
Star Publications: No. 120, Sept, 1953 - No. 124, Sept, 1954

120-Jo-Jo-r 174 348 522 1114 1907 2700
121,123,124: 121-Jo-Jo-r. 123-Jo-Jo; Disbrow-a(2). 124-Torpedo Man
155 310 465 992 1696 2400
122-The Mask-r/Capt. Flight #5; Rulah-r; has 1pg. story 'Death and the Devil Pills'
from Western Outlaws #17 258 516 774 1651 2826 4000
NOTE: ***Disbrow*** *a-120-124.* ***L. B. Cole*** *covers-all issues (#122 is a sci-fi cover).*

GHOST MANOR (Ghostly Haunts No. 20 on)
Charlton Comics: July, 1968 - No. 19, July, 1971

1 9 18 27 58 114 170
2-7: 7-Last 12¢ issue 4 8 12 28 47 65
8-12,17: 17-Morisi-a 3 6 9 19 30 40
13,14,16-Ditko-a 4 8 12 22 35 48
15,18,19-Ditko-c/a 4 8 12 28 47 65

GHOST MANOR (2nd Series)
Charlton Comics: Oct, 1971-No. 32, Dec, 1976; No. 33, Sept, 1977-No. 77, 11/84

1 6 12 18 38 69 100
2,3,5-7,9-Ditko-c 3 6 9 17 26 35
4,10-Ditko-c/a 3 6 9 21 33 45
8-Wood, Ditko-a; Sutton-c 3 6 9 19 30 40
11,14-Ditko-c/a 3 6 9 16 24 32
12,17,27,30 2 4 6 9 13 16
13,15,16,23-26,29: 13-Ditko-a. 15,16-Ditko-c. 23-Sutton-a. 24-26,29-Ditko-a.
26-Early Zeck-a; Boyette-c 2 4 6 13 18 22
18-(3/74) Newton 1st pro art; Ditko-a; Sutton-c 3 6 9 15 22 28
19-21: 19-Newton, Sutton-a; nudity panels. 20-Ditko-a. 21-E-Man, Blue Beetle, Capt. Atom
cameos; Ditko-a. 2 4 6 13 18 22
22-Newton-c/a; Ditko-a 3 6 9 14 19 24
25,28,31,37,38-Ditko-c/a: 28-Nudity panels 3 6 9 14 19 24
32-36,39,41,45,48-50,53: 34-Black Cat by Kim 2 4 6 8 10 12
40-Ditko-a; torture & drug use 2 4 6 13 18 22
42,43,46,47,51,52,60,62,69-Ditko-c/a 2 4 6 11 16 20
44,54,71-Ditko-a 2 4 6 8 11 14
55,56,58,59,61,63,65-68,70 1 2 3 5 7 9
57-Wood, Ditko, Howard-a 2 4 6 9 12 15
64-Ditko & Newton-a 2 4 6 8 11 14
71-76 (low print) 2 3 4 6 8 10
77-(11/84) Last issue Aparo-r/Space Adventures V3#60 (Paul Mann)
2 4 6 9 13 16
19 (Modern Comics reprint, 1977) 6.00
NOTE: ***Ditko*** *a-4, 8, 10, 11(2), 13, 14, 18, 20-22, 24-26, 28, 29, 31, 37r, 38r, 40r, 42-44r, 46r, 47, 51r, 52r, 54r, 57, 60, 62(4), 64r, 69, 71; c-2-7, 9-11, 14-16, 28, 31, 37, 38, 42, 43, 46, 47, 51, 52, 60, 62, 64.* ***Howard*** *a-4, 8, 12, 17, 19-21, 31, 41, 45, 57.* ***Newton*** *a-18-20, 22, 64; c-22.* ***Staton*** *a-13, 38, 44, 45.* ***Sutton*** *a-19, 23, 25, 45; c-8, 18.*

GHOST RACERS (Secret Wars Battleworld tie-in)
Marvel Comics: Aug, 2015 - No. 4, Nov, 2015 ($3.99, limited series)

1-4-Johnny Blaze, Danny Ketch, Robbie Reyes, Carter Slade app.; Francavilla-c 4.00

GHOST RIDER (See A-1 Comics, Best of the West, Black Phantom, Bobby Benson, Great Western, Red Mask & Tim Holt)

Ghostbusters International #1 © Columbia Picts.

Ghost Manor #5 © CC

Ghost Rider (2007) #12 © MAR

GD VG FN VF VF/NM NM-
2.0 4.0 6.0 8.0 9.0 9.2

GD VG FN VF VF/NM NM-
2.0 4.0 6.0 8.0 9.0 9.2

Magazine Enterprises: 1950 - No. 14, 1954

NOTE: *The character was inspired by Vaughn Monroe's "Ghost Riders in the Sky", and Disney's movie "The Headless Horseman".*

1(A-1 #27)-Origin Ghost Rider 155 310 465 992 1696 2400
2-5: 2(A-1 #29), 3(A-1 #31), 4(A-1 #34), 5(A-1 #37)-All Frazetta-c only 119 238 357 762 1306 1850
6,7: 6(A-1 #44)-Loco weed story, 7(A-1 #51) 55 110 165 352 601 850
8,9: 8(A-1 #57)-Drug use story, 9(A-1 #69) 41 82 123 256 428 600
10(A-1 #71)-Vs. Frankenstein 50 100 150 315 533 750
11-14: 11(A-1 #75). 12(A-1 #80)-Bondage-c; one-eyed Devil-c. 13(A-1 #84). 14(A-1 #112) 39 78 117 231 378 525

NOTE: ***Dick Ayers** art in all; c-1, 6-14.*

GHOST RIDER, THE (See Night Rider & Western Gunfighters)
Marvel Comics Group: Feb, 1967 - No. 7, Nov, 1967 (Western hero)(12¢)

1-Origin & 1st app. Ghost Rider; Kid Colt-reprints begin 44 88 132 326 738 1150
2 9 18 27 59 117 175
3-7: 6-Last Kid Colt-r; All Ayers-c/a(p) 8 16 24 55 105 155

GHOST RIDER (See The Champions, Marvel Spotlight #5, Marvel Team-Up #15, 58, Marvel Treasury Edition #18, Marvel Two-In-One #8, The Original Ghost Rider & The Original Ghost Rider Rides Again)
Marvel Comics Group: Sept, 1973 - No. 81, June, 1983 (Super-hero)

1-Johnny Blaze, the Ghost Rider begins; 1st brief app. Daimon Hellstrom (Son of Satan) 55 110 165 441 996 1550
2-1st full app. Daimon Hellstrom; gives glimpse of costume (1 panel); story continues in Marvel Spotlight #12 14 28 42 97 214 330
3-5: 3-Ghost Rider gains power to make cycle of fire; Son of Satan app. 7 14 21 44 82 120
6-9 4 8 12 28 47 65
10-Hulk on cover; reprints origin/1st app. from Marvel Spotlight #5; Ploog-a 6 12 18 37 66 95
11-16: 11-Hulk app. 3 6 9 16 23 30
17,19-(Reg. 25¢ editions)(4,8/76) 3 6 9 16 23 30
17,19-(30¢-c variants, limited distribution) 6 12 18 42 79 115
18-(Reg. 25¢ edition)(6/76). Spider-Man-c & app. 3 6 9 17 26 35
18-(30¢-c variant, limited distribution) 6 12 18 42 79 115
20-Daredevil x-over; ties into D.D. #138; Byrne-a 3 6 9 19 30 40
21-30: 22-1st app. Enforcer. 29,30-Vs. Dr. Strange 2 4 6 10 14 18
24-26-(35¢-c variants, limited distribution) 6 12 18 42 79 115
31-34,36-49: 40-Nuclear explosion-c 2 4 6 8 10 12
35-Death Race classic; Starlin-c/a/sty 3 6 9 15 22 28
50-Double size 3 6 9 14 20 25
51-76: 55-Werewolf by Night app. 68-Origin retold 1 2 3 5 6 8
77-80: 77-Origin retold. 80-Brief origin recap 1 3 4 6 8 10
81-Death of Ghost Rider (Demon leaves Blaze) 4 8 12 23 37 50
... Team Up TPB (2007, $15.99) r/#27, 50, Marvel Team-Up #91, Marvel Two-In-One #80, Avengers #214 and Marvel Premiere #28; Night Rider app.; cover gallery 16.00

NOTE: ***Anderson** c-64p. **Infantino** a(p)-43, 44, 51. **G. Kane** a-21p; c(p)-1, 2, 4, 5, 8, 9, 11-13, 19, 20, 24, 25. **Kirby** c-21-23. **Mooney** a-2-9p, 30i. **Nebres** c-26i. **Newton** a-23i. **Perez** c-26p. **Shores** a-2i. **J. Sparling** a-62p, 64p, 65p. **Starlin** a(p)-35. **Sutton** a-1p, 44i, 64i, 65i, 66, 67i. **Tuska** a-13p, 14p, 16p.*

GHOST RIDER (Volume 2) (Also see Doctor Strange/Ghost Rider Special, Marvel Comics Presents & Midnight Sons Unlimited)
Marvel Comics (Midnight Sons imprint #44 on): V2#1, May, 1990 - No. 93, Feb, 1998 ($1.50/$1.75/$1.95)

1-($1.95, 52 pgs.)-Origin/1st app. new Ghost Rider; Kingpin app. 4 8 12 27 44 60
1-2nd printing (not gold) 5.00
2-5: 3-Kingpin app. 5-Punisher app.; Jim Lee-c 6.00
5-Gold background 2nd printing 4.00
6-14,16-24,29,30,32-39: 6-Punisher app. 6,17-Spider-Man/Hobgoblin-c/story. 9-X-Factor app. 10-Reintro Johnny Blaze on the last pg. 11-Stroman-c/a(p). 12,13-Dr. Strange x-over cont'd in D.S. #28. 13-Painted-c. 14-Johnny Blaze vs. Ghost Rider; origin recap 1st Ghost Rider (Blaze). 18-Painted-c by Nelson. 29-Wolverine-c/story. 32-Dr. Strange x-over; Johnny Blaze app. 34-Williamson-a(i). 36-Daredevil app. 37-Archangel app. 4.00
15-Glow in the dark-c 1 3 4 6 8 10
25-27: 25-($2.75)-Double-size; contains pop-up scene insert. 26,27-X-Men x-over; Lee/Williams-c on both 5.00
28,31-($2.50, 52 pgs.)-Polybagged w/poster; part 1 & part 6 of Rise of the Midnight Sons storyline (see Ghost Rider/Blaze #1) 5.00
40-Outer-c is Darkhold envelope made of black parchment w/gold ink; Midnight Massacre; Demogoblin app. 6.00
41-48: 41-Lilith & Centurious app.; begin $1.75-c. 41-43-Neon ink-c. 43-Has free extra 16 pg. insert on Siege of Darkness. 44,45-Siege of Darkness parts 2 & 10. 44-Spot varnish-c. 46-Intro new Ghost Rider. 48-Spider-Man app. 4.00
49,51-60,62-74: 49-Begin $1.95-c; bound-in trading card sheet; Hulk app. 55-Werewolf by Night app. 65-Punisher app. 67,68-Gambit app. 68-Wolverine app. 73,74-Blaze, Vengeance app. 4.00
50,61: 50-($2.50, 52 pgs.)-Regular edition 5.00
50-($2.95, 52 pgs.)-Collectors Ed. die cut foil-c 5.00
75-89: 76-Vs. Vengeance. 77,78-Dr. Strange-app. 78-New costume 4.00
90-92 6.00
93-($2.99)-Last issue; Saltares & Texeira-a 4 8 12 28 47 65
(#94, see Ghost Rider Finale for unpublished story)
#(-1) Flashback (7/97) Saltares-a 4.00
Annual 1,2 ('93, '94, $2.95, 68 pgs.) 1-Bagged w/card 5.00
...And Cable 1 (9/92, $3.95, stiff-c, 68 pgs.)-Reprints Marvel Comics Presents #90-98 w/new Kieth-c 4.00
...:Crossroads (11/95, $3.95) Die cut cover; Nord-a 5.00
... Cycle of Vengeance 1 (3/12, $5.99) r/Marvel Spotlight #5, Ghost Rider (1990) #1 and Ghost Rider (2006) #1; Leinil Yu-c 6.00
... Finale (2007, $3.99) r/#93 and the story meant for the unpublished #94; Saltares-a 4.00
Highway to Hell (2001, $3.50) Reprints origin from Marvel Spotlight #5 3.50
...: Resurrected TPB (2001, $12.95) r/#1-7 13.00

NOTE: ***Andy & Joe Kubert** c/a-28-31. **Quesada** c-21. **Williamson** a(i)-33-35; c-33i.*

GHOST RIDER (Volume 3)
Marvel Comics: Aug, 2001 - No. 6, Jan, 2002 ($2.99, limited series)

1-6-Grayson-s/Kaniuga-a/c 3.00
...: The Hammer Lane TPB (6/02, $15.95) r/#1-6 16.00

GHOST RIDER
Marvel Comics: Nov, 2005 - No. 6, Apr, 2006 ($2.99, limited series)

1-6-Garth Ennis-s/Clayton Crain-a/c. 1-Origin retold 3.00
1 (Director's Cut) (2005, $3.99) r/#1 with Ennis pitch and script and Crain art process 4.00
...: Road to Damnation HC (2006, $19.99, dust jacket) r/#1-6; variant covers & concept-a 20.00
...: Road to Damnation SC (2007, $14.99) r/#1-6; variant covers & concept-a 15.00

GHOST RIDER
Marvel Comics: Sept, 2006 - No. 35, Jul, 2009 ($2.99)

1-11: 1-Daniel Way-s/Saltares & Texeira-a. 2-4-Dr. Strange app. 6,7-Corben-a 3.00
12-27,29-35: 12,13-World War Hulk; Saltares-a/Dell'Otto-c. 23-Danny Ketch returns 3.00
28-($3.99) Silvestri-c/Huat-a; back-up history of Danny Ketch 4.00
Annual 1 (1/08, $3.99) Ben Oliver-a/c/Stuart Moore-s 4.00
Annual 2 (10/08, $3.99) Spurrier-s/Robinson-a; r/Ghost Rider #35 (1979) 4.00
... Vol. 1: Vicious Cycle TPB (2007, $13.99) r/#1-5 14.00
... Vol. 2: The Life and Death of Johnny Blaze TPB (2007, $13.99) r/#6-11 14.00
... Vol. 3: Apocalypse Soon TPB (2008, $10.99) r/#12,13 & Annual #1 11.00
... Vol. 4: Revelations TPB (2008, $14.99) r/#14-19 15.00

GHOST RIDER
Marvel Comics: No. 0.1, Aug, 2011 - No. 9, May 2012 ($2.99/$3.99)

0.1-($2.99) Johnny Blaze gets rid of the Spirit of Vengeance; Matthew Clark-a 3.00
1-($3.99) Adam Kubert-c; Fear Itself tie-in; new female Ghost Rider; Mephisto app. 4.00
2-9: 2-4-($2.99) Fear Itself tie-in. 5-Garbett-a. 7,8-Hawkeye app. 3.00

GHOST RIDER (Robbie Reyes) (Also see All-New Ghost Rider)
Marvel Comics: Jan, 2017 - No. 5, May, 2017 ($3.99)

1-5-Felipe Smith-s; Hulk (Amadeus Cho) and X-23 app. 1-Intro. Pyston Nitro. 3-5-Silk app. 4.00

GHOST RIDER (Danny Ketch)
Marvel Comics: Dec, 2019 - No. 7, Sept, 2020 ($4.99/$3.99)

1-($4.99) Brisson-s/Kuder-a; Johnny Blaze, Lilith & Mephisto app. 5.00
2-7-($3.99) 2-Johnny becomes the Rider. 5-7-Punisher & Wolverine app. 6,7-Dr. Strange 4.00
...: Danny Ketch - Marvel Tales 1 (1/23, $7.99) Reprints Ghost Rider (1990) #1-3 8.00
...: Return of Vengeance 1 (2/21, $4.99) Howard Mackie-s/Javier Saltares-a 5.00

GHOST RIDER (Johnny Blaze)
Marvel Comics: Apr, 2022 - Present ($5.99/$3.99)

1-($5.99) Benjamin Percy-s/Cory Smith-a; Johnny Blaze returns 6.00
2-12-($3.99) 5,6-Wolverine app. 4.00
...: Vengeance Forever (10/22, $4.99) Percy-s/Ryp-a; stories of previous Ghost Riders 5.00

GHOST RIDER/BALLISTIC
Marvel Comics: Feb, 1997 ($2.95, one-shot)

1-Devil's Reign pt. 3 1 2 3 5 6 8

GHOST RIDER/BLAZE: SPIRITS OF VENGEANCE (Also see Blaze)
Marvel Comics (Midnight Sons imprint #17 on): Aug, 1992 - No. 23, June, 1994 ($1.75)

1-($2.75, 52 pgs.)-Polybagged w/poster; part 2 of Rise of the Midnight Sons storyline; Adam Kubert-c/a begins 1 2 3 5 6 8
2-11,14-21: 4-Art Adams & Joe Kubert-p. 5,6-Spirits of Venom parts 2 & 4 cont'd from Web

GD VG FN VF VF/NM NM-
2.0 4.0 6.0 8.0 9.0 9.2

of Spider-Man #95,96 w/Demogoblin. 14-17-Neon ink-c. 15-Intro Blaze's new costume & power. 17,18-Siege of Darkness parts 8 & 13. 17-Spot varnish-c 4.00
12-($2.95)-Glow-in-the-dark-c 6.00
13-($2.25)-Outer-c is Darkhold envelope made of black parchment w/gold ink; Midnight Massacre x-over 6.00
22,23: 22-Begin $1.95-c; bound-in trading card sheet 4.00
NOTE: ***Adam & Joe Kubert** c-7, 8. **Adam Kubert/Steacy** c-6. **J. Kubert** a-13p(6 pgs.)*

GHOST RIDER/CAPTAIN AMERICA: FEAR
Marvel Comics: Oct, 1992 ($5.95, 52 pgs.)
nn-Wraparound gatefold-c; Williamson inks 1 3 4 6 8 10

GHOST RIDER: DANNY KETCH
Marvel Comics: Dec, 2008 - No. 5, Apr, 2009 ($3.99, limited series)
1-5-Saltares-a 4.00

GHOST RIDER: HEAVEN'S ON FIRE
Marvel Comics: Oct, 2009 - No. 6, Mar, 2010 ($3.99, limited series)
1-6: 1-Jae Lee-c/Boschi-a/Aaron-s; Hellstorm app.; r/pages from Ghost Rider #1 ('73) 4.00

GHOST RIDER: TRAIL OF TEARS
Marvel Comics: Apr, 2007 - No. 6, Sept, 2007 ($2.99, limited series)
1-6-Garth Ennis-s/Clayton Crain-a/c; Civil War era tale 3.00
HC (2007, $19.99) r/series 20.00
SC (2008, $14.99) r/series 15.00

GHOST RIDER 2099
Marvel Comics: May, 1994 - No. 25, May, 1996 ($1.50/$1.95)
1 ($2.25)-Collector's Edition w/prismatic foil-c 2 4 6 9 12 15
1 ($1.50)-Regular Edition; bound-in trading card sheet 5.00
2-24: 7-Spider-Man 2099 app. 4.00
2-(Variant; polybagged with Sega Sub-Terrania poster) 5.00
25 ($2.95) 4.00
... No. 1 (2/20, $4.99) Brisson-s/Couceiro-a; tie-in with 2099 one-shots 5.00

GHOST RIDER, WOLVERINE, PUNISHER: THE DARK DESIGN
Marvel Comics: Dec, 1994 ($5.95, one-shot)
nn-Gatefold-c 6.00

GHOST RIDER; WOLVERINE; PUNISHER: HEARTS OF DARKNESS
Marvel Comics: Dec, 1991 ($4.95, one-shot, 52 pgs.)
1-Double gatefold-c; John Romita, Jr.-c/a(p) 1 3 4 6 8 10

GHOSTS (See The World Around Us #24)

GHOSTS (Ghost No. 1)
National Periodical Publications/DC Comics: Sept-Oct, 1971 - No. 112, May, 1982 (No. 1-5: 52 pgs.)
1-Aparo-a 13 26 39 89 195 300
2-Wood-a(i) 7 14 21 44 82 120
3-5-(52 pgs.) 6 12 18 38 69 100
6-10 4 8 12 27 44 60
11-20 3 6 9 14 20 25
21-39 2 4 6 9 13 16
40-(68 pgs.) 3 6 9 16 23 30
41-60 2 4 6 8 10 12
61-96 1 2 3 5 6 8
97-99-The Spectre vs. Dr. 13 by Aparo. 97,98-Spectre-c by Aparo.
2 4 6 10 14 18
100-Infinity-c 2 4 6 8 10 12
101-112 1 2 3 5 6 8
NOTE: ***B. Baily** a-77. **Buckler** c-99, 100. **J. Craig** a-108. **Ditko** a-77, 111. **Giffen** a-104p, 106p, 111p. **Glanzman** a-2. **Golden** a-88. **Infantino** a-8. **Kaluta** c-7, 93, 101. **Kubert** a-8; c-89, 105-108, 111. **Mayer** a-111. **McWilliams** a-99. **Win Mortimer** a-89, 91, 94. **Nasser/Netzer** a-97. **Newton** a-92p, 94p. **Nino** a-35, 37, 57. **Orlando** a-74i; c-80. **Redondo** a-8, 13, 45. **Sparling** a(p)-90, 93, 94. **Spiegle** a-103, 105. **Tuska** a-2i. Dr. 13, the Ghostbreaker back-ups in 95-99, 101.*

GHOSTS
DC Comics (Vertigo): Dec, 2012 ($7.99, one-shot)
1-Short stories by various incl. Johns, Lemire, Pope, Lapham; Joe Kubert's last work 8.00

GHOSTS GIANT
DC Comics: 2019 ($4.99, 100-page, squarebound)
1-Short stories; new Spectre, Constantine and Gentleman Ghost plus reprints 8.00

GHOST-SPIDER (Also see Spider-Gwen)
Marvel Comics: Oct, 2019 - No. 10, Oct, 2020 ($3.99)
1-10: 1-McGuire-s/Miyazawa-a; Gwen goes to college on Earth-616; Jackal app. 4.00
Annual 1 (11/19, $4.99) Vita Ayala-a/Pere Pérez-a; Arcade app. 5.00

GHOSTS SPECIAL (See DC Special Series No. 7)

GHOST STATION ZERO (See Codename: Baboushka)
Image Comics: Aug, 2017 - No. 4, Nov, 2017 ($3.99)
1-4-Johnston-s/Chankhamma-a 4.00

GHOST STORIES (See Amazing Ghost Stories)

GHOST STORIES
Dell Publ. Co.: Sept-Nov, 1962; No. 2, Apr-June, 1963 - No. 37, Oct, 1973
12-295-211(#1)-Written by John Stanley 7 14 21 49 92 135
2 4 8 12 28 47 65
3-10: Two No. 6's exist with different c/a(12-295-406 & 12-295-503)
#12-295-503 is actually #9 with indicia to #6 3 6 9 19 30 40
11-21: 21-Last 12¢ issue 3 6 9 16 23 30
22-37 2 4 6 13 18 22
NOTE: *#21-34, 36, 37 all reprint earlier issues.*

GHOST WHISPERER (Based on the CBS television series)
IDW Publishing: Mar, 2008 - No. 5, July, 2008 ($3.99)
1-5: 1-Two covers by Casagrande & Ho; Casagrande-a 5.00

GHOST WHISPERER: THE MUSE
IDW Publishing: Dec, 2008 - No. 4, Mar, 2009 ($3.99)
1-4-Two covers (photo & art) for each; Barbara Kesel-s/ Adriano Loyola-a 5.00

GHOUL, THE
IDW Publishing: Nov, 2009 - No. 3, Mar, 2010 ($3.99, limited series)
1-3-Niles-s/Wrightson-a 4.00

GHOUL TALES (Magazine)
Stanley Publications: Nov, 1970 - No. 5, July, 1971 (52 pgs.) (B&W)
1-Aragon pre-code reprints; Mr. Mystery as host; bondage-c
8 16 24 55 105 155
2,3: 2-(1/71)Reprint/Climax #1. 3-(3/71) 5 10 15 31 53 75
4-(5/71)Reprints story "The Way to a Man's Heart" used in **SOTI**
5 10 15 34 60 85
5-ACG reprints 4 8 12 27 44 60
NOTE: *No. 1-4 contain pre-code Aragon reprints.*

GIANT BOY BOOK OF COMICS (Also see Boy Comics)
Newsbook Publications (Gleason): 1945 (240 pgs., hard-c)
1-Crimebuster & Young Robin Hood; Biro-c 132 264 396 838 1444 2050

GIANT COMIC ALBUM
King Features Syndicate: 1972 (59¢, 11x14", 52 pgs., B&W, cardboard-c)
Newspaper reprints: Barney Google, Little Iodine, Katzenjammer Kids, Henry, Beetle Bailey, Blondie, & Snuffy Smith each... 3 6 9 19 30 40
Flash Gordon ('68-69 Dan Barry) 4 8 12 25 40 55
Mandrake the Magician ('59 Falk), Popeye 4 8 12 23 37 50

GIANT COMICS
Charlton Comics: Summer, 1957 - No. 3, Winter, 1957 (25¢, 96 pgs., not rebound material)
1-Atomic Mouse, Lil Genius, Lil Tomboy app. 32 64 96 188 307 425
2-(Fall '57) Romance 36 72 108 211 343 475
3-Christmas Book; Atomic Mouse, Atomic Rabbit, Li'l Genius, Li'l Tomboy & Atom the Cat stories 23 46 69 136 223 310

GIANT COMICS (See Wham-O Giant Comics)

GIANT COMICS EDITION (See Terry-Toons) (Also see Fox Giants)
St. John Publishing Co.: 1947 - No. 17, 1950 (25¢, 100-164 pgs.)
1-Mighty Mouse 68 136 204 435 743 1050
2-Abbie & Slats 40 80 120 246 411 575
3-Terry-Toons Album; 100 pgs. 53 106 159 334 567 800
4-Crime comics; contains Red Seal No. 16, used & illo. in **SOTI**
93 186 279 591 1021 1450
5-Police Case Book (4/49, 132 pgs.)-Contents varies; contains remaindered St. John books - some volumes contain 5 copies rather than 4, with 160 pages; Matt Baker-c
87 174 261 553 952 1350
5A-Terry-Toons Album (132 pgs.)-Mighty Mouse, Heckle & Jeckle, Gandy Goose & Dinky stories 45 90 135 284 480 675
6-Western Picture Stories; Baker-c/a(3); Tuska-a; The Sky Chief, Blue Monk, Ventrilo app., 132 pgs. 77 154 231 493 847 1200
7-Contains a teen-age romance plus 3 Mopsy comics
97 194 291 621 1061 1500
8-The Adventures of Mighty Mouse (10/49) 45 90 135 284 480 675
9-Romance and Confession Stories; Kubert-a(4); Baker-a; photo-c (132 pgs.)
187 374 561 1197 2049 2900
10-Terry-Toons Album (132 pgs.)-Mighty Mouse, Heckle & Jeckle, Gandy Goose stories
45 90 135 284 480 675
11-Western Picture Stories-Baker-c/a(4); The Sky Chief, Desperado, & Blue Monk app.; another version with Son of Sinbad by Kubert (132 pgs.)
77 154 231 493 847 1200
12-Diary Secrets; Baker prostitute-c; 4 St. John romance comics; Baker-a
1825 3650 5475 10,950 16,475 22,000
13-Romances; Baker, Kubert-a 219 438 657 1402 2401 3400
14-Mighty Mouse Album (132 pgs.) 45 90 135 284 480 675
15-Romances (4 love comics)-Baker-c 290 580 870 1856 3178 4500
16-Little Audrey; Abbott & Costello, Casper 61 122 183 390 670 950
17(nn)-Mighty Mouse Album (nn, no date, but did follow No. 16); 100 pgs. on cover but has 148 pgs. 47 94 141 296 498 700
NOTE: *The above books contain remaindered comics and contents could vary with each issue. No. 11, 12 have part photo magazine insides.*

GIANT COMICS EDITIONS
United Features Syndicate: 1940's (132 pgs.)
1-Abbie & Slats, Abbott & Costello, Jim Hardy, Ella Cinders, Iron Vic, Gordo, & Bill Bumlin 54 108 162 343 574 825
2-Jim Hardy, Ella Cinders, Elmo & Gordo 40 80 120 246 411 560
NOTE: *Above books contain rebound copies; contents can vary.*

GIANT DAYS
BOOM! Studios (BOOM! Box): Mar, 2015 - No. 54, Sept, 2019 ($3.99)
1-24,26-49,51-54: 1-6-John Allison-s/Lissa Treiman-a/c. 7-Max Sarin-a begins. 38-Madrigal-a. Allison-a. 54-Esther & Daisy's graduations 4.00
25,50-($4.99) 25-Christmas story 5.00
...: As Time Goes By 1 (10/19, $7.99) Final issue; takes place a year after #54 8.00
... 2016 Holiday Special #1 (10/16, $7.99) Treiman-a/c; back-up w/Caanan Grall-a 8.00
... 2017 Holiday Special #1 (10/16, $7.99) St-Onge-a/c 8.00
... : Where Women Glow and Men Plunder 1 (12/18, $7.99) Ed visits Australia; Allison-s/a 8.00

GIANT GRAB BAG OF COMICS (See Archie All-Star Specials under Archie Comics)

GIANTKILLER
DC Comics: Aug, 1999 - No. 6, Jan, 2000 ($2.50, limited series)
1-6-Story and painted art by Dan Brereton 3.00
...A to Z: A Field Guide to Big Monsters (8/99) 3.00
...Vol. 1 TPB (Image Comics, 2006, $14.99) r/#1-6 & A-Z; gallery of concept art 15.00

GIANTKILLERS
IDW Publishing: No. 0, Nov, 2017 ($3.99)
0-Bart Sears-s/a; Ron Marz-s/Tom Raney-a 4.00
... One-Shot (3/19, $7.99) Sears-s; art by Leonardi/Pennington & Hetrick 8.00

GIANT-MAN (Tie-in to War of the Realms event)
Marvel Comics: Jul, 2019 - No. 3, Aug, 2019 ($3.99, limited series)
1-3-Williams-s/Castiello-a; Ant-Man, Giant-Man, Goliath & Atlas app. 3-Moonstone app. 4.00

Ghost-Spider #9 © MAR

Giant Days #6 © John Allison

Giant-Size Fantastic Four #2 © MAR

GD VG FN VF VF/NM NM-
2.0 4.0 6.0 8.0 9.0 9.2

GIANTS (See Thrilling True Story of the Baseball...)

GIANTS
Dark Horse Comics: Dec, 2017 - No. 5, Apr, 2018 ($3.99)
1-5-Carlos & Miguel Valderrama-s/a 4.00

GIANT-SIZE ATOM
DC Comics: May, 2011 ($4.99, one-shot)
1-Gary Frank-c; Hawkman app.; Lemire-s/Asrar-a 5.00

GIANT-SIZE...
Marvel Comics Group: May, 1974 - Dec, 1975 (35/50¢, 52/68 pgs.)
(Some titles quarterly) (Scarce in strict NM or better due to defective cutting, gluing and binding; warping, splitting and off-center pages are common)

Avengers 1(8/74)-New-a plus G.A. H. Torch-r; 1st modern app. The Whizzer; 1st modern app. Miss America; 2nd app. Invaders; Kang, Rama-Tut, Mantis app. 8 16 24 54 102 150
Avengers 2,3,5: 2(11/74)-Death of the Swordsman; origin of Rama-Tut. 3(2/75). 5(12/75)-Reprints Avengers Special #1 5 10 15 30 50 70
Avengers 4 (6/75)-Vision marries Scarlet Witch. 8 16 24 56 108 160
Captain America 1(12/75)-r/stories T.O.S. 59-63 by Kirby (#63 reprints origin) 5 10 15 31 53 75
Captain Marvel 1(12/75)-r/Capt. Marvel #17, 20, 21 by Gil Kane (p) 5 10 15 30 50 70
Chillers 1(6/74, 52 pgs)-Curse of Dracula; origin/1st app. Lilith, Dracula's daughter; Heath-r, Colan-c/a(p); becomes Giant-Size Dracula #2 on 18 36 54 122 271 420
Chillers 1(2/75, 50¢, 68 pgs.)-Alcala-a 5 10 15 34 60 85
Chillers 2(5/75)-All-r; Everett-r from Advs. into Weird Worlds 3 6 9 20 31 42
Chillers 3(8/75)-Wrightson-c(new)/a(r); Colan, Kirby, Smith-r 4 8 12 25 40 55
Conan 1(9/74)-B. Smith-r/#3; start adaptation of Howard's "Hour of the Dragon" (ends #4); 1st app. Belit (one-panel cameo with blonde hair); new-a begins 5 10 15 33 57 80
Conan 2(12/74)-B. Smith-r/#5; Sutton-a(i)(#1 also); Buscema-c 3 6 9 19 30 40
Conan 3-5: 3(4/75)-B. Smith-r/#6; Sutton-a(i). 4(6/75)-B. Smith-r/#7. 5(1975)-B. Smith-r/#14,15; Kirby-c 3 6 9 16 24 32
Creatures 1(5/74, 52 pgs.)-Werewolf app; 1st app. Tigra (formerly Cat); Crandall-r; becomes Giant-Size Werewolf w/#2 12 24 36 82 179 275
Daredevil 1(1975)-Reprints Daredevil Annual #1 6 12 18 37 66 95
Defenders 1(7/74, 68-pgs.)-Dr. Strange, Hulk, Namor & Valkyrie app; continued from Defenders #12; mostly reprint stories, with a few pages of new material by Jim Starlin; Hulk-r from Incredible Hulk #3; Sub-Mariner-r from Sub-Mariner (Golden Age) #41; Dr. Strange-r from Strange Tales #145; Silver Surfer-r from Fantastic Four Annual #5 7 14 21 46 86 125
Defenders 2(10/74, 68-pgs.)-New G. Kane-c/a/p; Son of Satan app. vs. Asmodeus; Sub-Mariner-r from Young Men #25; Black Knight-r from Black Knight #4 (1955); Dr. Strange-r from Strange Tales #119 4 8 12 27 44 60
Defenders 3(1/75, 68-pgs.)-1st app. Korvac; Grandmaster vs. The Prime Mover; Daredevil app.; G.A. Sub-Mariner-r from Sub-Mariner #38; Dr. Strange-r from Strange Tales #120 19 38 57 131 291 450
Defenders No. 3 Facsimile Edition (2/20, $4.99) Reprints issue with original ads 1 3 4 6 8 10
Defenders 4(4/75, 68-pgs.)-Continued from Defenders #21; Yellowjacket & Wasp app; vs. Egghead, Squadron Sinister (Hyperion, Dr. Spectrum and the Whizzer; Sub-Mariner-r from Human Torch Comics #4 (technically 3rd issue); Dr. Strange-r from Strange Tales #121 4 8 12 23 37 50
Defenders 5(7/75, 68-pgs.)-Continued from Defenders #25; Guardians of the Galaxy app; (3rd app); continued from Marvel Two-in-One #5; story continued in Defenders #26; Nighthawk-r from Daredevil #62 4 8 12 23 37 50
Doc Savage 1(1975, 68 pgs.)-r/#1,2; Mooney-r 3 6 9 20 31 42
Doctor Strange 1(11/75)-Reprints stories from Strange Tales #164-168; Lawrence, Tuska-r 5 10 15 35 63 90
Dracula 2(9/74, 50¢)-Formerly Giant-Size Chillers 4 8 12 25 40 55
Dracula 3(12/74)-Fox-r/Uncanny Tales #6 3 6 9 20 31 42
Dracula 4(3/75)-Ditko-r(2) 3 6 9 20 31 42
Dracula 5(6/75)-1st Byrne art at Marvel 5 10 15 33 57 80
Fantastic Four 2,3: 2(8/74)-Formerly Giant-Size Super-Stars; Ditko-r. 2-Buscema-a. 3(11/74)-Buckler-a 4 8 12 27 44 60
Fantastic Four 4(2/75)-1st Madrox; Buscema-a 25 50 75 175 388 600
Fantastic Four 5,6: 5(5/75)-All-r; Kirby, G. Kane-r. 6(10/75)-All-r; Kirby-r 4 8 12 23 37 50
Hulk 1(1975) r/Hulk Special #1 5 10 15 31 53 75
Invaders 1(6/75, 50¢, 68 pgs.)-Origin; G.A. Sub-Mariner-r/Sub-Mariner #1; intro Master Man 6 12 18 41 76 110

GD VG FN VF VF/NM NM-
2.0 4.0 6.0 8.0 9.0 9.2

Iron Man 1(1975)-Ditko reprint 5 10 15 35 63 90
Kid Colt 1-3: 1(1/75). 2(4/75). 3(7/75)-new Ayers-a 7 14 21 48 89 130
Man-Thing 1(8/74)-New Ploog-c/a (25 pgs.); Ditko-r/Amazing Adv. #11; Kirby-r/ Strange Tales Ann. #2 & T.O.S. #15; (#1-5 all have new Man-Thing stories, pre-hero-r & are 68 pgs.) 6 12 18 38 69 100
Man-Thing 2,3: 2(11/74)-Buscema-c/a(p); Kirby, Powell-r. 3(2/75)-Alcala-a; Ditko, Kirby, Sutton-r; Gil Kane-c 3 6 9 21 33 45
Man-Thing 4,5: 4(5/75)-Howard the Duck by Brunner-c/a; Ditko-r. 5(8/75)-Howard the Duck by Brunner (p); Dracula cameo in Howard the Duck; Buscema-a(p); Sutton-a(i); G. Kane-c 5 10 15 30 50 70
Marvel Triple Action 1,2: 1(5/75). 2(7/75) 3 6 9 19 30 40
Master of Kung Fu 1(9/74)-Russell-a; Yellow Claw-r in #1-4; Gulacy-a in #1,2 5 10 15 33 57 80
Master of Kung Fu 2-4: 2-(12/74)-r/Yellow Claw #1. 3(3/75)-Gulacy-a; Kirby-a. 4(6/75)-Kirby-a 4 8 12 23 37 50
Power Man 1(1975) 4 8 12 28 47 65
Spider-Man 1(7/74)-Spider-Man /Human Torch-r by Kirby/Ditko; Byrne-r plus new-a (Dracula-c/story) 9 18 27 59 117 175
Spider-Man 2,3: 2(10/74)-Shang-Chi-c/app. 3(1/75)-Doc Savage-c/app.; Daredevil/ Spider-Man-r w/Ditko-a 5 10 15 30 50 70
Spider-Man 4(4/75)-3rd Punisher app.; Byrne, Ditko-r 12 24 36 79 170 260
Spider-Man 5,6: 5(7/75)-Man-Thing/Lizard-c. 6(9/75) 4 8 12 27 44 60
Super-Heroes Featuring Spider-Man 1(6/74, 35¢, 52 pgs.)-Spider-Man vs. Man-Wolf; Morbius, the Living Vampire app.; Ditko-r; G. Kane-a(p); Spidey villains app. 8 16 24 56 108 160
Super-Stars 1(5/74, 35¢, 52 pgs.)-Fantastic Four; Thing vs. Hulk; Kirbyish-c/a by Buckler/Sinnott; F.F. villains profiled; becomes Giant-Size Fantastic Four #2 on 6 12 18 41 76 110
Super-Villain Team-Up 1(3/75, 68 pgs.)-Craig-r(i) (Also see Fantastic Four #6 for 1st super-villain team-up) 5 10 15 30 50 70
Super-Villain Team-Up 2(6/75, 68 pgs.)-Dr. Doom, Sub-Mariner app.; Spider-Man-r from Amazing Spider-Man #8 by Ditko; Sekowsky-a(p) 3 6 9 21 33 45
Thor 1(7/75) 5 10 15 34 60 85
Werewolf 2(10/74, 68 pgs.)-Formerly Giant-Size Creatures; Ditko-r; Frankenstein app. 4 8 12 25 40 55
Werewolf 3,5: 3(1/75, 68 pgs.). 5(7/75, 68 pgs.) 3 6 9 19 30 40
Werewolf 4(4/75, 68 pgs.)-Morbius the Living Vampire app. 4 8 12 27 44 60
X-Men 1(Summer, 1975, 50¢, 68 pgs.)-1st app. new X-Men; intro. Nightcrawler, Storm, Colossus & Thunderbird; 2nd full app. Wolverine after Incredible Hulk #181 1000 2000 3000 5000 7500 10,000
X-Men No. 1 Facsimile Edition (9/19, $4.99) Reprints issue with original ads 15.00
X-Men 2 (11/75)-N. Adams-r (51 pgs) 10 20 30 66 138 210
Giant Size Marvel TPB (2005, $24.99) reprints stories from Giant-Size Avengers #1, G-S Fantastic Four #4, G-S Defenders #4, G-S Super-Heroes #1, G-S Invaders #1, G-S X-Men #1 and Giant-Size Creatures #1 25.00

GIANT-SIZE...
Marvel Comics: 2005 - 2021 ($4.99/$3.99)
Amazing Spider-Man: Chameleon Conspiracy 1 (8/21, $5.99) Follows ASM #69 (2021) 6.00
Amazing Spider-Man: King's Ransom 1 (7/21, $5.99) Follows ASM #66 (2021) 6.00
Astonishing X-Men 1 (7/08, $4.99) Concludes story from Astonishing X-Men #24; Whedon-s/ Cassaday-a/wraparound-c; Spider-Man, FF, Dr. Strange app.; variant cover gallery 5.00
Astonishing X-Men 1 (7/08, $4.99) Variant B&W cover 5.00
Avengers 1 (2/08, $4.99) new short stories and r/Avengers #58, 201; Hitch-c 5.00
Avengers/Invaders 1 ('08, $3.99) r/Avengers #71; Invaders #10, Ann. 1 & G-S #2 4.00
Black Cat: Infinity Score 1 (1/22, $4.99) Follows Black Cat V2 #10 (2021) 5.00
Gwen Stacy 1 (10/22, $9.99) r/Gwen Stacy #1,2 and unpublished stories meant for #3-5 10.00
Hulk 1 (8/06, $4.99)-2 new stories; Planet Hulk (David-s/Santacruz-a) & Hulk vs. The Champions (Pak-s/Lopresti-a; r/Incredible Hulk: The End) 5.00
Incredible Hulk 1 (7/08, $3.99)-1 new story; r/Incredible Hulk Annual #7; Frank-c 4.00
Invaders 2 ('05, $4.99)-new Thomas-s/Weeks-a; r/Invaders #1&2 & All-Winners #1&2 5.00
Marvel Adventures The Avengers (9/07, $3.99) Agents of Atlas and Kang app.; Kirk-a: reprint of 1st Namora app. from Marvel Mystery Comics #82; reprint from Venus #1 4.00
Spider-Man (7/14, $4.99) origin retold, other short stories; Scherberger-c 5.00
Spider-Woman ('05, $4.99)-new Bendis-s/Mays-a; r/Marvel Spotlight #32 & S-W #1,37,38 5.00
Wolverine (12/06, $4.99)-new Lapham-s/Aja-a; r/X-Men #6,7 5.00
X-Men 3 ('05, $4.99)-new Whedon-s/N. Adams-a; r/team-ups; Cockrum & Cassaday-c 5.00
X-Men: Fantomex 1 (10/20, $4.99) Hickman-s/Rod Reis-a; history revealed 5.00
X-Men: Jean Grey and Emma Frost 1 (4/20, $4.99) Hickman-s/Dauterman-a 5.00
X-Men: Magneto 1 (9/20, $4.99) Hickman-s/Ramón Pérez-a; Namor app. 5.00
X-Men: Nightcrawler 1 (5/20, $4.99) Hickman-s/Alan Davis-a; Magik & Lockheed app. 5.00
X-Men: Storm 1 (11/20, $4.99) Hickman-s/Dauterman-a; Cypher & Fantomex app. 5.00
X-Men: Thunderbird 1 (6/22, $4.99) John Proudstar returns in current time; new look 5.00

	GD 2.0	VG 4.0	FN 6.0	VF 8.0	VF/NM 9.0	NM- 9.2
X-Men: Tribute to Wein & Cockrum 1 (11/20, $5.99) Wein's original script re-drawn by modern artists (1 page each); bonus profiles of Wein, Cockrum & Claremont; Granov-c						6.00
X-Statix 1 (9/19, $4.99) Milligan-s/Allred-a; intro new team members						5.00

GIANT-SIZE JINGLES (Cerebus figures placed over original Gustave Doré artwork)
Aardvark-Vanaheim: 2019 ($4.00, B&W)

	GD 2.0	VG 4.0	FN 6.0	VF 8.0	VF/NM 9.0	NM- 9.2
1-"Three Giant-Size Firsts worth noting" according to the cover; G.S X-Men #1-c swipe						4.00

GIANT-SIZE LITTLE MARVEL: AVX (Secret Wars tie-in)
Marvel Comics: Aug, 2015 - No. 4, Nov, 2015 ($3.99, limited series)

	GD 2.0	VG 4.0	FN 6.0	VF 8.0	VF/NM 9.0	NM- 9.2
1-4-Skottie Young-s/a; all ages kid-version Avengers vs. X-Men spoof. 4-GOTG app.						4.00

GIANT-SIZE PUBLIC DEFENDERS (Cerebus)
Aardvark-Vanaheim: 2022 ($8.00, B&W)

	GD 2.0	VG 4.0	FN 6.0	VF 8.0	VF/NM 9.0	NM- 9.2
1-Giant-Size Defenders #1-c swipe						8.00

GIANT SPECTACULAR COMICS (See Archie All-Star Special under Archie Comics)

GIANT SUMMER FUN BOOK (See Terry-Toons...)

G. I. COMBAT
Quality Comics Group: Oct, 1952 - No. 43, Dec, 1956

	GD 2.0	VG 4.0	FN 6.0	VF 8.0	VF/NM 9.0	NM- 9.2
1-Crandall-c; Cuidera a-1-43i	271	542	813	1734	2967	4200
2	57	114	171	362	619	875
3-5,10-Crandall-c/a	52	104	156	328	552	775
6-Crandall-a	47	94	141	296	498	700
7-9	43	86	129	271	461	650
11-20	34	68	102	204	332	460
21-31,33,35-43: 41-1st S.A. issue	33	66	99	194	317	440
32-Nuclear attack-c/story "Atomic Rocket Assault"	45	90	135	284	480	675
34-Crandall-a	36	72	108	211	343	475

G. I. COMBAT (See DC Special Series #22)
National Periodical Publ./DC Comics: No. 44, Jan, 1957 - No. 288, Mar, 1987

	GD 2.0	VG 4.0	FN 6.0	VF 8.0	VF/NM 9.0	NM- 9.2
44-Grey tone-c	102	204	306	816	1833	2850
45	46	92	138	340	770	1200
46-50	37	74	111	274	612	950
51-Grey tone-c	44	88	132	326	738	1150
52-54,59,60	32	64	96	230	515	800
55-Minor Sgt. Rock prototype by Finger	36	72	108	259	580	900
56-Sgt. Rock prototype by Kanigher/Kubert	50	100	150	400	900	1400
57,58-Pre-Sgt. Rock Easy Co. stories	38	76	114	281	628	975
61-65,70-73	24	48	72	168	372	575
66-Pre-Sgt. Rock Easy Co. story	36	72	108	259	580	900
67-1st Tank Killer	46	92	138	359	805	1250
68-(1/59) "The Rock" - Sgt. Rock prototype. Part of lead-up trio to 1st definitive Sgt. Rock. Character named Jimmy referred to as "The Rock" appears as a sergeant on the cover and as a private in the story. In reprint (Our Army at War #242) DC edits Jimmy's name out; also see Our Army at War #81-84	166	332	498	1370	3085	4800
69-Grey tone-c	42	84	126	311	706	1100
74-American flag-c	30	60	90	216	483	750
75-80: 75-Grey tone-c begin, end #109	37	74	111	274	612	950
81,82,84-86-Grey tone-c	34	68	102	245	548	850
83-1st Big Al, Little Al, & Charlie Cigar; grey tone-c	46	92	138	340	770	1200
87-(4-5/61) 1st Haunted Tank; series begins; classic Heath washtone-c	197	394	591	1625	3663	5700
88-(6-7/61) 2nd Haunted Tank; Grey tone-c	54	108	162	432	966	1500
89,90: 90-Last 10¢ issue; Grey tone-c	33	66	99	238	532	825
91-(12/61-1/62)1st Haunted Tank-c; Grey tone-c	75	150	225	600	1350	2100
92-95,99-Grey tone-c. 94-Panel inspired a famous Roy Lichtenstein painting	28	56	84	202	451	700
96-98-Grey tone-c	22	44	66	154	340	525
100,108: 100-(6-7/63) Grey tone-c. 108-1st Sgt. Rock x-over	23	46	69	164	362	560
101-103,105-107-Grey tone-c	18	36	51	121	268	415
104,109-Grey tone-c	22	44	66	154	340	525
110-112,115-118,120	13	26	39	91	201	310
113-Grey tone-c	18	36	54	122	271	420
114-Origin Haunted Tank	38	76	114	285	641	1000
119-Grey tone-c	16	32	48	112	249	385
121-136: 121-1st app. Sgt. Rock's father. 125-Sgt. Rock app. 136-Last 12¢ issue	9	18	27	60	120	180
137,139,140	6	12	18	41	76	110
138-Intro. The Losers (Capt. Storm, Gunner/Sarge, Johnny Cloud) in Haunted Tank (10-11/69)	14	28	42	93	204	310
141-143	4	8	12	28	47	65
144-148 (68 pgs.)	5	10	15	33	57	80
149,151-154 (52 pgs.): 151-Capt. Storm story. 151,153-Medal of Honor series by Maurer	4	8	12	28	47	65
150- (52 pgs.) Ice Cream Soldier story (tells how he got his name); Death of Haunted Tank-c/s	5	10	15	33	57	80
155-167,169,170	3	6	9	15	22	28
168-Neal Adams-c	4	8	12	23	37	50
171-194,196-199	3	6	9	14	19	24
195-(10/76) Haunted Tank meets War That Time Forgot; Dinosaur-c/s; Kubert-a	3	6	9	16	24	32
200-(3/77) Haunted Tank-c/s; Sgt. Rock and the Losers app.; Kubert-c	3	6	9	17	25	34
201,202 ($1.00 size) Neal Adams-c	3	6	9	17	25	34
203-210 ($1.00 size)	3	6	9	15	22	28
211-230 ($1.00 size)	3	6	9	14	19	24
231-259 ($1.00 size).232-Origin Kana the Ninja. 244-Death of Slim Stryker; 1st app. The Mercenaries. 246-(76 pgs., $1.50)-30th Anniversary issue. 257-Intro. Stuart's Raiders	2	4	6	10	14	18
260-281: 260-Begin $1.25, 52 pg. issues, end #281. 264-Intro Sgt. Bullet; origin Kana. 269-Intro. The Bravos of Vietnam. 274-Cameo of Monitor from Crisis on Infinite Earths	2	4	6	8	11	14
282-288 (75¢): 282-New advs. begin	1	3	4	6	8	10

NOTE: ***N. Adams** c-168, 201, 202. **Check** a-168, 173. **Drucker** a-48, 61, 63, 66, 71, 72, 76, 134, 140, 141, 144, 147, 148, 153. **Evans** a-135, 138, 158, 164, 166, 201, 202, 204, 205, 215, 256. Giffen a-267. **Glanzman** a-most issues. **Kubert/Heath** a-most issues; **Kubert** covers most issues. **Morrow** a-159-161(2 pgs.). **Redondo** a-189, 240i, 243i. **Sekowsky** a-162p. **Severin** a-147, 152, 154. **Simonson** c-169. **Thorne** a-152, 156. **Wildey** a-153. Johnny Cloud app.-112, 115, 120. Mlle. Marie app.-123, 132, 200. Sgt. Rock app.-111-113, 115, 120, 125, 141, 146, 147, 149, 200. USS Stevens by **Glanzman**-145, 150-153, 157. **Grandenetti** c-44-48.*

G. I. COMBAT
DC Comics: Nov, 2010 ($3.99, one-shot)

	GD 2.0	VG 4.0	FN 6.0	VF 8.0	VF/NM 9.0	NM- 9.2
1-Haunted Tank and General J.E.B. Stuart app.; Sturges-s/Winslade-a/Darrow-c						4.00

G. I. COMBAT
DC Comics: Jul, 2012 - No. 7, Feb, 2013 ($3.99)

	GD 2.0	VG 4.0	FN 6.0	VF 8.0	VF/NM 9.0	NM- 9.2
1-7: 1-War That Time Forgot; Olivetti-a; Unknown Soldier; Panosian-a; two covers						4.00
#0 (11/12, $3.99) Unknown Soldiers through history; War That Time Forgot; Olivetti-a						4.00

GIDEON FALLS
Image Comics: Mar, 2018 - No. 27, Dec, 2020 ($3.99)

	GD 2.0	VG 4.0	FN 6.0	VF 8.0	VF/NM 9.0	NM- 9.2
1-26-Lemire-s/Sorrentino-a						4.00
#1 Director's Cut (9/18, $4.99) r/#1 in B&W with original script						5.00
27-($7.99, 80 pgs.) Last issue; Lemire-s/Sorrentino-a						8.00

GIDGET (TV)
Dell Publishing Co.: Apr, 1966 - No. 2, Dec, 1966

	GD 2.0	VG 4.0	FN 6.0	VF 8.0	VF/NM 9.0	NM- 9.2
1-Sally Field photo-c	9	18	27	62	126	190
2	7	14	21	49	92	135

GIFT COMICS
Fawcett Publications: 1942 - No. 4, 1949 (50¢/25¢, 324 pgs./152 pgs.)

	GD 2.0	VG 4.0	FN 6.0	VF 8.0	VF/NM 9.0	NM- 9.2
1-Captain Marvel, Bulletman, Golden Arrow, Ibis the Invincible, Mr. Scarlet, & Spy Smasher begin; not rebound, remaindered comics, printed at same time as originals; 50¢-c & 324 pgs. begin, end #3.	331	662	993	2317	4059	5800
2-Commando Yank, Phantom Eagle, others app.	213	426	639	1363	2332	3300
3-(50¢, 324 pgs.)	161	322	483	1030	1765	2500
4-(25¢, 152 pgs.)-The Marvel Family, Captain Marvel, etc.; each issue can vary in contents	103	206	309	659	1130	1600

GIFTS FROM SANTA (See March of Comics No. 137)

GIFTS OF THE NIGHT
DC Comics (Vertigo): Feb, 1999 - No. 4, May, 1999 ($2.95, limited series)

	GD 2.0	VG 4.0	FN 6.0	VF 8.0	VF/NM 9.0	NM- 9.2
1-4-Bolton-c/a; Chadwick-s						3.00

GIGANTIC
Dark Horse Comics: Nov, 2008 - No. 5, Jan, 2010 ($3.50, limited series)

	GD 2.0	VG 4.0	FN 6.0	VF 8.0	VF/NM 9.0	NM- 9.2
1-5-Remender-s/Nguyen-a; Earth as a reality show						3.50

GIGGLE COMICS (Spencer Spook No. 100) (Also see Ha Ha Comics)
Creston No.1-63/American Comics Group No. 64 on; Oct, 1943 - No. 99, Jan-Feb, 1955

	GD 2.0	VG 4.0	FN 6.0	VF 8.0	VF/NM 9.0	NM- 9.2
1-Funny animal	50	100	150	315	533	750
2	25	50	75	150	245	340
3-5: Ken Hultgren-a begins?	18	36	54	103	162	220
6-9: 9-1st Superkatt (6/44)	15	30	45	85	130	175
10-Superkatt shoots Japanese plane & fights Nazi robot	17	34	51	98	154	210
11-20	14	28	42	78	112	145
21-40: 22-Spencer Spook 2nd app. 32-Patriotic-c. 37-X-Mas-c. 39-St. Valentine-c	13	26	39	72	101	130
41-54,56-59,62-99: Spencer Spook app. in many. 44-Mussel-Man app. (Superman parody). 45-Witch Hazel 1st app. 46-Bob Hope & Bing Crosby app. 49,69-X-Mas-c.	10	20	30	58	79	100
55,60,61-Milt Gross-a. 61-X-Mas-c	13	26	39	74	105	135

G-I IN BATTLE (G-I No. 1 only)
Ajax-Farrell Publ./Four Star: Aug, 1952 - No. 9, July, 1953; Mar, 1957 - No. 6, May, 1958

	GD 2.0	VG 4.0	FN 6.0	VF 8.0	VF/NM 9.0	NM- 9.2
1	37	74	111	222	361	500
2	30	60	90	177	289	400
3-9	15	30	45	85	130	175
Annual 1(1952, 25¢, 100 pgs.)	41	82	123	256	428	600
1(1957-Ajax)	11	22	33	62	86	110
2-6	7	14	21	37	46	55

G. I. JANE
Stanhall/Merit No. 11: May, 1953 - No. 11, Mar, 1955 (Misdated 3/54)

	GD 2.0	VG 4.0	FN 6.0	VF 8.0	VF/NM 9.0	NM- 9.2
1-PX Pete begins; Bill Williams-c/a	55	110	165	352	601	850
2-7(5/54)	40	80	120	246	411	575
8-10(12/54, Stanhall)	30	60	90	177	289	400
11 (3/55, Merit)	30	60	90	177	289	400

G. I. JOE (Also see Advs. of..., Showcase #53, 54 & The Yardbirds)
Ziff-Davis Publ. Co. (Korean War): No. 10, Feb/Mar, 1951; No. 11, Apr/May, 1951 - No. 51, Jun, 1957 (52 pgs.: #10-14, V2 #6-17?)

	GD 2.0	VG 4.0	FN 6.0	VF 8.0	VF/NM 9.0	NM- 9.2
10(#1)-Saunders painted-c begin	31	62	93	182	296	410
11-14(#2-5, 10/51): 11-New logo. 12-New logo	16	32	48	94	147	200
V2#6(12/51)-17-(11/52; Last 52 pgs.?)	15	30	45	84	127	170
18-(25¢, 100 pg. Giant, 12-1/52-53)	36	72	108	211	343	475
19-30: 20-22,24,28-31-The Yardbirds app.	14	28	42	78	112	145
31-47,49-51	13	26	39	72	101	130
48-Atom bomb story	13	26	39	74	105	135

NOTE: ***Powell** a-V2#7, 8, 11. **Norman Saunders** painted c-10-14, V2#6-14, 26, 30, 31, 35, 38, 39. **Tuska** a-7. Bondage c-29, 35, 38.*

G. I. JOE (America's Movable Fighting Man)
Custom Comics: 1967 (5-1/8x8-3/8", 36 pgs.)

	GD 2.0	VG 4.0	FN 6.0	VF 8.0	VF/NM 9.0	NM- 9.2
nn-Schaffenberger-a; based on Hasbro toy	5	10	15	31	53	75

G.I. JOE
Dark Horse Comics: Dec, 1995 - No. 4, Apr, 1996 ($1.95, limited series)

	GD 2.0	VG 4.0	FN 6.0	VF 8.0	VF/NM 9.0	NM- 9.2
1-4: Mike W. Barr scripts. 1-Three Frank Miller covers with title logos in red, white and blue. 2-Breyfogle-c. 3-Simonson-c						5.00

G.I. JOE
Dark Horse Comics: V2#1, June, 1996 - V2#4, Sept, 1996 ($2.50)

	GD 2.0	VG 4.0	FN 6.0	VF 8.0	VF/NM 9.0	NM- 9.2
V2#1-4: Mike W. Barr scripts. 4-Painted-c						5.00

G.I. JOE

G. I. Combat #80 © DC

Gideon Falls #27
© 171 Studios & A. Sorrentino

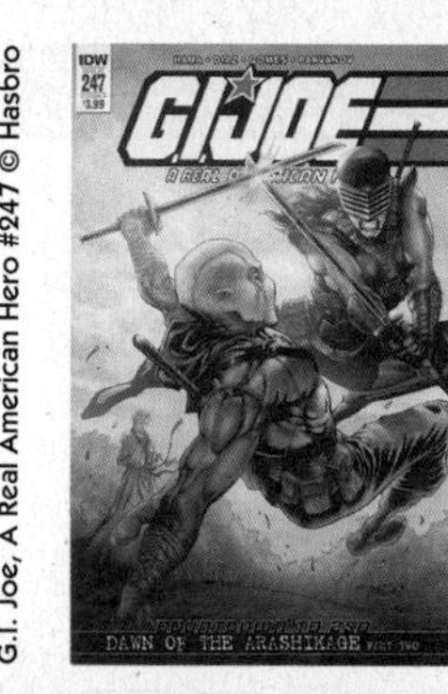

G.I. Joe, A Real American Hero #247 © Hasbro

GD VG FN VF VF/NM NM-
2.0 4.0 6.0 8.0 9.0 9.2

Image Comics/Devil's Due Publishing: 2001 - No. 43, May, 2005 ($2.95)

1-Campbell-c; back-c painted by Beck; Blaylock-s 2 4 6 8 10 12
1-2nd printing with front & back covers switched 6.00
2,3 5.00
4-($3.50) 5.00
5-20,22-41: 6-SuperPatriot preview. 18-Brereton-c. 31-33-Wraith back-up; Caldwell-a 3.00
21-Silent issue; Zeck-a; two covers by Campbell and Zeck 4.00
42,43-($4.50)-Dawn of the Red Shadows; leads into G.I. Joe Vol. 2 4.50
...: Cobra Reborn (1/04, $4.95) Bradstreet-c/Jenkins-s 5.00
...: G.I. Joe Reborn (2/04, $4.95) Bradstreet-c/Bennett & Saltares-a 5.00
...: Malfunction (2003, $15.95) r/#11-15 16.00
... M. I. A. (2002, $4.95) r/#1&2; Beck back-c from #1 on cover 5.00
...: Players & Pawns (11/04, $12.95) r/#28-33; cover gallery 13.00
...: Reborn (2004, $9.95) r/Cobra Reborn & G.I. Joe Reborn 10.00
...: Reckonings (2002, $12.95) r/#6-9; Zeck-c 13.00
...: Reinstated (2002, $14.95) r/#1-4 15.00
...: The Return of Serpentor (9/04, $12.95) r/#16,22-25; cover gallery 13.00
...Vol. 8: The Rise of the Red Shadows (1/06, $14.95) r/#42,43 & prologue pgs. from #37-41 15.00

G.I. JOE (Volume 2) (Also see Snake Eyes: Declassified)
Devil's Due Publishing: No. 0, June, 2005 - No. 36, June, 2008 (25¢/$2.95/$3.50/$4.50)

0-(25¢-c) Casey-s/Caselli-a 3.00
1-4,7-19 ($2.95): 1-Four covers; Casey-s/Caselli-a. 4-R. Black-c 3.00
5,6-($4.50) 6-Wraparound-c 4.50
20-29,31-35-($3.50) 25-Wraparound-c World War III part 1 3.50
30,36-($5.50) 30-Double-sized World War III part 6. 36-Double-sized WW III part 12 5.50
...America's Elite Vol. 1: The Newest War TPB ('06, $14.95) r/#0-5; cover gallery 15.00
...America's Elite Vol. 2: The Ties That Bind TPB (8/06, $15.95) r/#6-12; cover gallery 16.00
...America's Elite Vol. 3: In Sheep's Clothing TPB (2007, $18.99) r/#13-18; cover gallery 19.00
...America's Elite Vol. 4: Truth and Consequences TPB (9/07, $18.99) r/#19-24; covers 19.00
... Data Desk Handbook (10/05, $2.95) character profile pages 3.00
... Data Desk Handbook A-M (10/07, $5.50) character profile pages 5.50
... Data Desk Handbook N-Z (11/07, $3.50) character profile pages 3.50
...: Scarlett: Declassified (7/06, $4.95) Scarlett's childhood and training; Noto-c/a 5.00
... Special Missions (2/06, $4.95) short stories and profile pages by various 5.00
... Special Missions Antarctica (12/06, $4.95) short stories and profile pages by various 5.00
... Special Missions Brazil (4/07, $5.50) short stories and profile pages by various 5.50
... Special Missions: The Enemy (9/07, $5.50) two stories and profile pages by various 5.50
... Special Missions Tokyo (9/06, $4.95) short stories and profile pages by various 5.00
...: The Hunt For Cobra Commander (5/06, 25¢) short story and character profiles 3.00

G.I. JOE
IDW Publishing: No. 0, Oct, 2008; No. 1, Jan, 2009 - No. 27, Feb, 2011 ($1.00/$3.99)

0-($1.00) Short stories by Dixon & Hama; creator interviews and character sketches 3.00
1-27-($3.99) 1-Dixon-s/Atkins-a; covers by Johnson, Atkins and Dell'Otto 4.00
...: Cobra Commander Tribute - 100-Page Spectacular 1 (4/11, $7.99) reprints 8.00
...: Special - Helix (8/09, $3.99) Reed-s/Suitor-a 4.00

G.I. JOE, VOLUME 2 (Prelude in G.I. Joe: Cobra Civil War #0) (Season 2 in indicia)
IDW Publishing: May, 2011 - No. 21, Jan, 2013 ($3.99)

1-21: 1-Dixon-s/Saltares-a; three covers by Howard. 9-Cobra Command Part 1 4.00

G.I. JOE VOLUME 3
IDW Publishing: Feb, 2013 - No. 15, Apr, 2014 ($3.99)

1-15-Van Lente-s/Kurth-a in most; multiple covers. 6-Igle-a. 12-15-Allor-s 4.00

G.I. JOE VOLUME 4
IDW Publishing: Sept, 2014 - No. 8, Apr, 2015 ($3.99)

1-4-The Fall of G.I. Joe; Karen Traviss-s/Steve Kurth-a; multiple covers 4.00

G.I. JOE (Follows the Revolution x-over)
IDW Publishing: Jan, 2017 - No. 9, Oct, 2017 ($3.99)

1-9: 1-4-Reconstruction; Dreadnoks app.; Milonogiannis-a; multiple covers 4.00
... First Strike 1 (9/17, $3.99) Tie-in to First Strike x-over series; Kyriazis-a; 3 covers 4.00
...: Revolution 1 (10/16, $3.99) Tie-in to Revolution x-over; Sitterson-s/Milonogiannis-a 4.00

G.I. JOE
IDW Publishing: Sept, 2019 - No. 5 ($3.99)

1-5: 1-Intro. Tiger; Allor-s/Evenhuis-a; multiple covers. 4-Walter-a 4.00
...: Castle Fall (11/20, $7.99) Allor-s/Evenhuis-a 8.00

G.I. JOE AND THE TRANSFORMERS
Marvel Comics Group: Jan, 1987 - No. 4, Apr, 1987 (Limited series)

1 3 6 9 14 19 24
2-4 1 2 3 5 6 8

G.I. JOE, A REAL AMERICAN HERO (...Starring Snake-Eyes on-c #135 on)
Marvel Comics Group: June, 1982 - No. 155, Dec, 1994

1-Printed on Baxter paper; based on Hasbro toy 10 20 30 69 147 225
2-Printed on regular paper; 1st app. Kwinn 6 12 18 38 69 100
3-10: 6-1st app. Oktober Guard 3 6 9 16 23 30
11-20: 11-Intro Airborne. 13-1st Destro (cameo). 14-1st full app. Destro. 15-1st app. Major Blood. 16-1st app. Cover Girl and Trip-Wire 2 4 6 13 18 22
21-1st app. Storm Shadow; silent issue 12 24 36 82 179 275
22-1st app. Duke and Roadblock 4 8 12 27 44 60
23,24,28-30,60: 60-Todd McFarlane-a 2 4 6 8 11 14
25-1st full app. Zartan, 1st app of Cutter, Deep Six, Mutt and Junkyard, and The Dreadnoks 4 8 12 25 40 55
26,27-Origin Snake-Eyes parts 1 & 2 3 6 9 17 25 34
31-50: 31-1st Spirit Iron-Knife. 32-1st Blowtorch, Lady J, Recondo, Ripcord. 33-New headquarters. 40-1st app. of Shipwreck, Barbecue. 48-1st app. Sgt. Slaughter. 49-1st app. of Lift-Ticket, Slipstream, Leatherneck, Serpentor 1 2 3 5 6 8
51-59,61-90 6.00
91,92,94-99: 94-96-Snake Eyes Trilogy 1 2 3 5 6 8
93-Snake-Eyes' face first revealed 3 6 9 15 22 28
100,135-138: 135-138-($1.75)-Bagged w/trading card. 138-Transformers app. 2 4 6 10 14 18
101-122,124-133: 101-New Oktober Guard app. 110-1st Garney-a. 117- Debut G.I. Joe Ninja Force 2 4 6 8 10 12
123,134: 123-Cobra Commander. 134-Snake-Eyes 3 6 9 14 20 25
139-142-New Transformers app. 3 6 9 14 20 25
143,145-149: 145-Intro. G.I. Joe Star Brigade 2 4 6 10 14 18
144-Origin Snake-Eyes 3 6 9 14 20 26
150-Low print thru #155 3 6 9 21 33 45
151-154: 152-30th Anniversary (of doll) issue, original G.I. Joe General Joseph Colton app. (also app. in #151) 3 6 9 19 30 40
155-Last issue 9 18 27 62 126 190
All 2nd printings 4.00
Special #1 (2/95, $1.50) r/#60 w/McFarlane-a. Cover swipe from Spider-Man #1 10 20 30 69 147 225
Special Treasury Edition (1982)-r/#1 4 8 12 23 37 50
Volume 1 TPB (4/02, $24.95) r/#1-10; new cover by Michael Golden 35.00
Volume 2 TPB (6/02, $24.95) r/#11-20; new cover by J. Scott Campbell 35.00
Volume 3 TPB (2002, $24.99) r/#21-30; new cover by J. Scott Campbell 35.00
Volume 4 TPB (2002, $25.99) r/#31-40; new cover by J. Scott Campbell 35.00
Volume 5 TPB (2002, $24.99) r/#42-50; new cover by J. Scott Campbell 35.00
Yearbook 1-4: (3/85-3/88)-r/#1; Golden-c/back-c. 2-Golden-c/a. 3-Zeck-c; silent story 5.00
Yearbook #1 Reprint (1/21, $3.99) Reprints #1 with new cover by Netho Diaz 4.00
Yearbook #2 Reprint (6/21, $5.99) Reprints #2 by Hama-s/Golden-a 6.00
Yearbook #3 Reprint (9/21, $5.99) Reprints #3 silent story by Hama-s/Wagner-a 6.00
Yearbook #4 Reprint (12/21, $5.99) Reprints #4 by Hama-s/Trimpe-a 6.00
NOTE: ***Garney** a(p)-110. **Golden** c-23, 29, 34, 36. **Heath** a-24. **Rogers** a(p)-75, 77-82, 84, 86; c-77.*

G. I. JOE, A REAL AMERICAN HERO
IDW Publishing: No. 156, Jul, 2010 - No. 300, Nov, 2022 ($3.99)

156-199-Continuation of story from Marvel series #155 (1994); Hama-s 4.00
200-(3/14, $5.99) Multiple covers; bonus interview with artist SL Gallant 6.00
201-249,251-254,256-299: 201-214-Hama-s/Gallant-a. 213-Death of Snake Eyes. 216-218-Villanelli-a. 219-225-Cobra World Order 4.00
250-($4.99) Hama-s/Diaz-a; Dawn of the Arashikage conclusion 5.00
255-($4.99) Hama-s/Tolibao-a; IDW's 100th issue; Snake Eyes origin 5.00
300-($6.99) Hama-s/Gallant-a; wraparound main-c 7.00
Annual 2012 (2/12, $7.99) Hama-s; Frenz, Wagner & Trimpe-a 8.00
... #1 Anniversary Edition (3/18, $3.99) r/#1(1982); silver foil cover logo 4.00
...: Cobraaaa! (3/22, $7.99) Reprints of Cobra's most notorious stories; Daniel Maine-c 8.00
...: Cobra World Order Prelude (10/15, $3.99) Starts seven-part bi-weekly event 4.00
... 40th Anniversary Special 1 (4/22, $7.99) Pages of #21 redrawn by current artists, plus reprint of original 1984 story; bonus sketch pages 8.00
Hundred Penny Press: G.I. Joe: Real American Hero #1 (3/11, $1.00) r/#1 (1982) 3.00
... Yearbook 2019 (1/19, $4.99) Dawn Moreno, new Snake Eyes app.; Hama-s 5.00
...– Yo, Joe! (2/22, $7.99) Reprints of greatest adventures; Daniel Maine-c 8.00

G. I. JOE, A REAL AMERICAN HERO – SSATURDAY MORNING ADVENTURES
IDW Publishing: Feb, 2022 - No. 4, Jun, 2022 ($3.99, limited series)

1-4-Art style of the cartoon; Burnham-s/Schoening-a 4.00

G. I. JOE, A REAL AMERICAN HERO: SILENT OPTION
IDW Publishing: Sept, 2018 - No. 4, Dec, 2018 ($4.99, limited series)

1-4-Hama-s/Diaz-a; spotlight on Snake Eyes (Dawn Moreno); Agent Helix back-up story 5.00

G. I. JOE, A REAL AMERICAN HERO VS. THE SIX MILLION DOLLAR MAN
IDW Publishing: Feb, 2018 - No. 4, May, 2018 ($3.99, limited series)

1-4-Ferrier-s/Gallant-a; 5 covers 4.00

G.I. JOE: BATTLE FILES

	GD	VG	FN	VF	VF/NM	NM-
	2.0	4.0	6.0	8.0	9.0	9.2

Image Comics: 2002 - No. 3, 2002 ($5.95)
1-3-Profile pages of characters and history; Beck-c 6.00

G.I. JOE: COBRA (#5-on is continuation of G.I. Joe: Cobra II #4, not G.I. Joe: Cobra #4)
IDW Publishing: Mar, 2009 - No. 13, Feb, 2011 ($3.99)
1-4,5-13: 1-4-Gage & Costa-s/Fuso-a/covers by Chaykin & Fuso. 5-8-Carrera-a 4.00
Hundred Penny Press: G.I. Joe: Cobra #1 (4/11, $1.00) r/#1 with Chaykin-c 3.00
... Special (9/09, $3.99) Costa-s/Fuso-a 4.00
... Special 2 - Chameleon (9/10, $3.99) Costa-s/Fuso-a 4.00
... II (1/10 - No. 4, 4/10, $3.99) 1-4-Gage & Costa-s/Fuso-a/covers by Chaykin & Fuso 4.00

G.I. JOE: COBRA CIVIL WAR
IDW Publishing: No. 0, Apr, 2011 ($3.99)
0-Prelude to G.I. Joe, Cobra & Snake Eyes Civil War series; four covers 4.00
0-Muzzle Flash Edition (6/11, price not shown) r/#0 in B&W and partial color 4.00

G.I. JOE: COBRA VOLUME 2 (Prelude in G.I. Joe: Cobra Civil War #0)
IDW Publishing: May, 2011 - No. 9, Jan, 2012 ($3.99)(Re-named Cobra with #10)
1-9: Multiple covers on all. 1-4-Costa-s/Fuso-a 4.00

G. I. JOE COMICS MAGAZINE
Marvel Comics Group: Dec, 1986 - No. 13, 1988 ($1.50, digest-size)
1-G.I. Joe reprints 2 4 6 11 16 20
2-13: G.I. Joe-r 1 3 4 6 8 10

G.I. JOE DECLASSIFIED
Devil's Due Publishing: June, 2006 - No. 3 ($4.95, bi-monthly)
1-3-New "early" adventures of the team; Hama-s; Quinn & DeLandro-a; var-c for each 5.00
TPB (1/07, $18.99) r/#1-3; cover gallery 19.00

G.I. JOE: DEVIATIONS
IDW Publishing: Mar, 2016 ($4.99, one-shot)
1-Paul Allor-s/Corey Lewis-a; What If Cobra defeated G.I. Joe and ruled the world 5.00

G.I. JOE DREADNOKS: DECLASSIFIED
Devil's Due Publishing: Nov, 2006 - No. 3, Mar, 2007 ($4.95/$4.99/$5.50, bi-monthly)
1,2-Secret history of the team; Blaylock-s; var-c for each 5.00
3-($5.50) 5.50

G.I. JOE EUROPEAN MISSIONS (Action Force in indicia) (Series reprints Action Force)
Marvel Comics Ltd. (British): Jun, 1988 - No. 15, Dec, 1989 ($1.50/$1.75)
1,3-Snake Eyes & Storm Shadow-c/s 2 4 6 8 10 12
2,4-15 6.00

G.I. JOE: FRONT LINE
Image Comics: 2002 - No. 18, Dec, 2003 ($2.95)
1-18: 1-Jurgens-a/Hama-s. 1-Two covers by Dorman & Sharpe. 7,8-Harris-c 3.00
...Vol. 1 - The Mission That Never Was TPB (2003, $14.95) r/ #1-4; script pages 15.00
...Vol. 2 - Icebound TPB (3/04, $12.95) r/ #5-8 13.00
...Vol. 3 - History Repeating TPB (4/04, $9.95) r/#11-14 10.00
...Vol. 4 - One-Shots TPB (5/04, $15.95) r/#9,10,15-18 16.00

G.I. JOE: FUTURE NOIR SPECIAL
IDW Publishing: Nov, 2010 - No. 2, Dec, 2010 ($3.99, limited series, greytone art)
1,2-Schmidt-s/Bevilacqua-a 4.00

G. I. JOE: HEARTS & MINDS
IDW Publishing: May, 2010 - No. 5, Sept, 2010 ($3.99)
1-5: Short origin stories; Brooks-s; Chaykin & Fuso-a 4.00

G. I. JOE: INFESTATION (Zombie x-over with Star Trek, Ghostbusters & Transformers)
IDW Publishing: Mar, 2011 - No. 2, Mar, 2011 ($3.99, limited series)
1,2-Timpano-a; covers by Timpano and Snyder III 4.00

G.I. JOE: MASTER & APPRENTICE
Image Comics: May, 2004 - No. 4, Aug, 2004 ($2.95)
1-4-Caselli-a/Jerwa-s 3.00

G.I. JOE: MASTER & APPRENTICE 2
Image Comics: Feb, 2005 - No. 4, May, 2005 ($2.95, limited series)
1-4: Stevens & Vedder-a/Jerwa-s 3.00

G.I. JOE MOVIE PREQUEL...
IDW Publishing: Mar, 2009 - No. 4, June, 2009 ($3.99, limited series)
1-4-Two covers on each: 1-Duke. 2-Destro. 3-The Baroness. 4-SnakeEyes 4.00

G.I. JOE: OPERATION HISS
IDW Publishing: Feb, 2010 - No. 5, Jun, 2010 ($3.99, limited series)
1-5: 1-4-Reed-s/Padilla-a; covers by Corroney & Padilla. 5-Guglotta-a 4.00

G. I. JOE ORDER OF BATTLE, THE
Marvel Comics Group: Dec, 1986 - No. 4, Mar, 1987 (limited series)
1-4 6.00

G.I. JOE: ORIGINS
IDW Publishing: Feb, 2009 - No. 23, Jan, 2011 ($3.99)
1-23: 1-Origin of Snake Eyes; Hama-s. 12-Templesmith-a. 19-Benitez-a 4.00

G.I. JOE: RELOADED
Image Comics: Mar, 2004 -No. 14, Apr, 2005 ($2.95)
1-14: 1-3-Granov-c/Ney Rieber-s. 5,6-Rieber-s/Saltares-a. 8-Origin of the Baroness 4.00
Vol. 1 In the Name of Patriotism (11/04, $12.95) r/#1-6; cover gallery 13.00

G.I. JOE: RISE OF COBRA MOVIE ADAPTATION
IDW Publishing: July, 2009 - No. 4, July, 2009 ($3.99, weekly limited series)
1-4-Tipton-s/Maloney-a; two covers 4.00

G.I. JOE: SIERRA MUERTE
IDW Publishing: Feb, 2019 - No. 3, Apr, 2019 ($4.99, limited series)
1-3-Michel Fiffe-s/a 5.00

G.I. JOE SIGMA 6 (Based on the cartoon TV series)
Devil's Due Publishing: Dec, 2005 - No. 6, May, 2006 ($2.95, limited series)
1-6-Andrew Daab-s 3.00

TPB Vol. 1 (10/06, $10.95, 8-1/4" x 5-3/4") r/#1-6; cover gallery 11.00

G.I. JOE: SNAKE EYES
IDW Publishing: Oct, 2009 - No. 4, Jan, 2010 ($3.99, limited series)
1-4-Ray Park & Kevin VanHook-s/Lee Ferguson-a; two covers 4.00

G.I. JOE: SNAKE EYES, AGENT OF COBRA
IDW Publishing: Jan, 2015 - No. 5, May, 2015 ($3.99, limited series)
1-5-Costa-s/Villanelli-a 4.00

G.I. JOE: SNAKE EYES, VOLUME 2 (Continues as Snake Eyes #8)
IDW Publishing: May, 2011 - No. 7, Nov, 2011 ($3.99)
1-7: 1-Dixon-s/Atkins & Padilla-a; two covers 4.00

G. I. JOE SPECIAL MISSIONS (Indicia title: Special Missions)
Marvel Comics Group: Oct, 1986 - No. 28, Dec, 1989 ($1.00)
1 1 3 4 6 8 10
2-20 5.00
21-28 6.00

G. I. JOE: SPECIAL MISSIONS
IDW Publishing: Mar, 2013 - No. 14, Apr, 2014($3.99)
1-14: 1-4-Dixon-s/Gulacy-a; covers by Chen and Gulacy. 5-7-Rosado-a. 10-13-Gulacy-a 4.00

G. I. JOE: THE COBRA FILES
IDW Publishing: Apr, 2013 - No. 9, Dec, 2013 ($3.99)
1-9: 1-Costa-s/Fuso-a; multiple covers. 5,6-Dell'edera-a 4.00

G.I. JOE 2 MOVIE PREQUEL...
IDW Publishing: Feb, 2012 - No. 4, Apr, 2012 ($3.99, limited series)
1-4-Barber-s/Navarro & Rojo-a 4.00

G.I. JOE VS. THE TRANSFORMERS
Image Comics: Jun, 2003 - No. 6, Nov, 2003 ($2.95, limited series)
1-Blaylock-s/Mike Miller-a; three covers by Miller, Campbell & Andrews 4.00
1-2nd printing; black cover with logo; back-c by Campbell 3.00
2-6: 2-Two covers by Miller & Brooks 3.00
TPB (3/04, $15.95) r/series; sketch pages 16.00

G.I. JOE VS. THE TRANSFORMERS (Volume 2)
Devil's Due Publ.: Sept, 2004 - No. 4, Dec, 2004 ($4.95/$2.95, limited series)
1-($4.95) Three covers; Jolley-s/Su & Seeley-a 5.00
2-4-($2.95) Two covers by Su & Pollina 3.00
Vol. 2 TPB (4/05, $14.95) r/series; interview with creators; sketch pages and covers 15.00

G.I. JOE VS. THE TRANSFORMERS (Volume 3) THE ART OF WAR
Devil's Due Publ.: Mar, 2006 - No. 5, July, 2006 ($2.95, limited series)
1-5: 1-Three covers; Seeley-s/Ng-a 3.00
TPB (8/06, $14.95) r/series; cover gallery 15.00

G.I. JOE VS. THE TRANSFORMERS (Volume 4) BLACK HORIZON
Devil's Due Publ.: Jan, 2007 - No. 2, Feb, 2007 ($5.50, limited series)
1,2: 1-Three covers; Seeley-s/Wildman-a. 2-Two covers 5.50

G. I. JUNIORS (See Harvey Hits No. 86,91,95,98,101,104,107,110,112,114,116,118,120,122)

GILES SEASON 11 (From Buffy the Vampire Slayer)
Dark Horse Comics: Feb, 2018 - No. 4, May, 2018 ($3.99, limited series)
1-4-Whedon & Alexander-s/Jon Lam-a 5.00

GILGAMESH II
DC Comics: 1989 - No. 4, 1989 ($3.95, limited series, prestige format, mature)
1-4: Starlin-c/a/scripts 5.00

GIL THORP
Dell Publishing Co.: May-July, 1963
1-Caniff-*ish* art 4 8 12 23 37 50

GINGER
Archie Publications: 1951 - No. 10, Summer, 1954
1-Teenage humor; headlights-c 245 490 735 1568 2684 3800
2-(1952) 39 78 117 231 378 525
3-6: 6-(Sum/53) 22 44 66 128 209 290
7-10-Katy Keene app. 40 80 120 246 411 575

GINGER FOX (Also see The World of Ginger Fox)
Comico: Sept, 1988 - No. 4, Dec, 1988 ($1.75, limited series)
1-4: Part photo-c on all 3.00

GIRL
DC Comics (Vertigo Verite): Jul, 1996 - No. 3, 1996 ($2.50, lim. series, mature)
1-3: Peter Milligan scripts; Fegredo-c/a 3.00

GIRL COMICS (Becomes Girl Confessions No. 13 on)
Marvel/Atlas Comics(CnPC): Oct, 1949 - No. 12, Jan, 1952 (#1-4: 52 pgs.)
1-Photo-c 37 74 111 222 361 500
2-Kubert-a; photo-c 20 40 60 117 189 260
3-Everett-a; Liz Taylor photo-c 41 82 123 256 428 600
4-11: 4-Photo-c. 10-12-Sol Brodsky-c 16 32 48 96 151 205
12-Krigstein-a; Al Hartley-c 17 34 51 100 158 215

GIRL COMICS
Marvel Comics: May, 2010 - No. 3, Sept, 2010 ($4.99, limited series)
1-3-Anthology of short stories by women creators. 1-Conner-c. 2-Thompson-c. 3-Chen-c 5.00

GIRL CONFESSIONS (Formerly Girl Comics)
Atlas Comics (CnPC/ZPC): No. 13, Mar, 1952 - No. 35, Aug, 1954
13-Everett-a 20 40 60 117 189 260
14,15,19,20 16 32 48 92 144 195
16-18-Everett-a 17 34 51 100 158 215
21-35: Robinson-a 15 30 45 83 124 165

GIRL CRAZY
Dark Horse Comics: May, 1996 - No. 3, July, 1996 ($2.95, B&W, limited series)
1-3: Gilbert Hernandez-a/scripts. 3.00

G.I. Joe Origins #14 © Hasbro

Ginger #9 © ACP

Girl Comics #1 © MAR

GIRL FROM U.N.C.L.E., THE (TV) (Also see The Man From...)
Gold Key: Jan, 1967 - No. 5, Oct, 1967

	GD 2.0	VG 4.0	FN 6.0	VF 8.0	VF/NM 9.0	NM- 9.2
1-McWilliams-a; Stephanie Powers photo front/back-c & pin-ups (no ads, 12¢)	7	14	21	46	86	125
2-5-Leonard Swift-Courier No. 5. 4-Back-c pin-up	5	10	15	33	57	80

GIRL IN THE BAY, THE
Dark Horse Comics (Berger Books): Feb, 2019 - No. 4, May, 2019 ($3.99)

1-4-J.M. DeMatteis-s/Corin Howell-a 4.00

GIRLS
Image Comics: May, 2005 - No. 24, Apr, 2007 ($2.95/$2.99)

1-Luna Brothers-s/a/c 4.00
2-24 3.00
Image Firsts: Girls #1 (4/10, $1.00) r/#1 with "Image Firsts" cover logo 3.00
... Vol. 1: Conception TPB (2005, $14.99) r/#1-6 15.00
... Vol. 2: Emergence TPB (2006, $14.99) r/#7-12 15.00
... Vol. 3: Survival TPB (2006, $14.99) r/#13-18 15.00
... Vol. 4: Extinction TPB (2007, $14.99) r/#19-24 15.00

GIRLS' FUN & FASHION MAGAZINE (Formerly Polly Pigtails)
Parents' Magazine Institute: V5#44, Jan, 1950 - V5#48, Sept., 1950

	GD 2.0	VG 4.0	FN 6.0	VF 8.0	VF/NM 9.0	NM- 9.2
V5#44	9	18	27	52	69	85
45-48	8	16	24	42	54	65

GIRLS IN LOVE
Fawcett Publications: May, 1950 - No. 2, July, 1950

	GD 2.0	VG 4.0	FN 6.0	VF 8.0	VF/NM 9.0	NM- 9.2
1-Photo-c	15	30	45	85	130	175
2-Photo-c	12	24	36	67	94	120

GIRLS IN LOVE (Formerly G. I. Sweethearts No. 45)
Quality Comics Group: No. 46, Sept, 1955 - No. 57, Dec, 1956

	GD 2.0	VG 4.0	FN 6.0	VF 8.0	VF/NM 9.0	NM- 9.2
46	15	30	45	85	130	175
47-53,55,56	13	26	39	74	105	130
54- 'Commie' story	14	28	42	82	121	160
57-Matt Baker-c/a	20	40	60	118	192	265

GIRLS IN WHITE (See Harvey Comics Hits No. 58)

GIRLS' LIFE (Patsy Walker's Own Magazine For Girls!)
Atlas Comics (BFP): Jan, 1954 - No. 6, Nov, 1954

	GD 2.0	VG 4.0	FN 6.0	VF 8.0	VF/NM 9.0	NM- 9.2
1	24	48	72	142	234	325
2-Al Hartley-c	15	30	45	86	133	180
3-6	15	30	45	84	127	170

GIRLS' LOVE STORIES
National Comics (Signal Publ. No. 9-65/Arleigh No. 83-117): Aug-Sept, 1949 - No. 180, Nov-Dec, 1973 (No. 1-13: 52 pgs.)

	GD 2.0	VG 4.0	FN 6.0	VF 8.0	VF/NM 9.0	NM- 9.2
1-Toth, Kinstler-a, 8 pgs. each; photo-c	90	180	270	576	988	1400
2-Kinstler-a?	41	82	123	256	428	600
3-10: 1-9-Photo-c	27	54	81	160	263	365
11-20	21	42	63	122	199	275
21-33: 21-Kinstler-a. 33-Last pre-code (1-2/55)	15	30	45	86	133	180
34-50	12	24	36	67	94	120
51-70	10	20	30	58	79	100
71-99: 83-Last 10¢ issue	5	10	15	33	57	80
100	5	10	15	34	60	85
101-146: 113-117-April O'Day app.	3	6	9	21	33	45
147-151- "Confessions" serial. 150-Wood-a	4	8	12	22	35	48
152-160,171-179	3	6	9	17	26	34
161-170 (52 pgs.)	4	8	12	23	37	50
180 Last issue	3	6	9	21	33	45

Ashcan (8-9/49) not distributed to newsstands (a FN/VF copy sold for $836.50 in 2012)

GIRLS OF DIMENSION 13, THE
AfterShock Comics: Apr, 2021 - No. 5, Aug, 2021 ($4.99/$3.99, limited series)

1-($4.99) Graham Nolan-s/Bret Blevins-a 5.00
2-5-($3.99) 4.00

GIRLS' ROMANCES
National Periodical Publ.(Signal Publ. No. 7-79/Arleigh No. 84): Feb-Mar, 1950 - No. 160, Oct, 1971 (No. 1-11: 52 pgs.)

	GD 2.0	VG 4.0	FN 6.0	VF 8.0	VF/NM 9.0	NM- 9.2
1-Photo-c	74	148	222	470	810	1150
2-Photo-c; Toth-a	39	78	117	236	388	540
3-10: 3-6-Photo-c	26	52	78	156	256	355
11,12,14-20	19	38	57	111	176	240
13-Toth-c	20	40	60	118	192	265
21-31: 31-Last pre-code (2-3/55)	15	30	45	84	127	170
32-50	7	14	21	46	86	125
51-99: 78-Panel inspired a famous Roy Lichtenstein painting. 80-Last 10¢ issue	5	10	15	34	60	85
100	5	10	15	35	53	90
101-108,110-120: 105-Panel inspired a famous Roy Lichtenstein painting	4	8	12	23	37	50
109-Beatles-c/story	19	38	57	131	291	450
121-133,135-140	3	6	9	21	33	45
134-Neal Adams-c (splash pg. is same as-c)	6	12	18	40	73	105
141-158	3	6	9	18	28	38
159,160-52 pgs.	5	10	15	30	50	70

GIRL WHO KICKED THE HORNETS NEST, THE
DC Comics (Vertigo): 2015 ($29.99, HC graphic novel, dustjacket)

HC-Adaptation of the novel; Mina-s/Mutti & Fuso-a/Bermejo-c 30.00

GIRL WHO WOULD BE DEATH, THE
DC Comics (Vertigo): Dec, 1998 - No. 4, March, 1999 ($2.50, lim. series)

1-4-Kiernan-s/Ormston-a 3.00

GIRL WITH THE DRAGON TATTOO, THE
DC Comics (Vertigo): Book One, 2012; Book Two, 2013 ($19.99, HC graphic novels)

Book One HC-First part of the adaptation of the novel; Mina-s/Manco-a/Bermejo-c 20.00
Book Two HC-Second part of the adaptation; Mina-s/Manco-a/Bermejo-c 20.00

G. I. SWEETHEARTS (Formerly Diary Loves; Girls In Love #46 on)
Quality Comics Group: No. 32, June, 1953 - No. 45, May, 1955

	GD 2.0	VG 4.0	FN 6.0	VF 8.0	VF/NM 9.0	NM- 9.2
32	15	30	45	88	137	185
33-45: 44-Last pre-code (3/55)	12	24	36	67	94	120

G.I. TALES (Formerly Sgt. Barney Barker No. 1-3)
Atlas Comics (MCI): No. 4, Feb, 1957 - No. 6, July, 1957

	GD 2.0	VG 4.0	FN 6.0	VF 8.0	VF/NM 9.0	NM- 9.2
4-Severin-a(4)	15	30	45	88	137	185
5	13	26	39	72	101	130
6-Orlando, Powell, & Woodbridge-a	13	26	39	74	105	135

GIVE ME LIBERTY (Also see Dark Horse Presents Fifth Anniversary Special, Dark Horse Presents #100-4, Happy Birthday Martha Washington, Martha Washington Goes to War, Martha Washington Stranded In Space & San Diego Comicon Comics #2)
Dark Horse Comics: June, 1990 - No. 4, 1991 ($4.95, limited series, 52 pgs.)

1-4: 1st app. Martha Washington; Frank Miller scripts, Dave Gibbons-c/a in all 6.00

G. I. WAR BRIDES
Superior Publishers Ltd.: Apr, 1954 - No. 8, June, 1955

	GD 2.0	VG 4.0	FN 6.0	VF 8.0	VF/NM 9.0	NM- 9.2
1	20	40	60	114	182	250
2	14	28	42	80	115	150
3-8: 4-Kamenesque-a; lingerie panels	14	28	42	76	108	140

G. I. WAR TALES
National Periodical Publications: Mar-Apr, 1973 - No. 4, Oct-Nov, 1973

	GD 2.0	VG 4.0	FN 6.0	VF 8.0	VF/NM 9.0	NM- 9.2
1-Reprints in all; dinosaur-c/s	4	8	12	29	40	55
2-N. Adams-a(r)	3	6	9	14	20	26
3,4: 4-Krigstein-a(r)	3	6	9	14	19	24

NOTE: *Drucker a-3r, 4r.* ***Heath*** *a-4r.* ***Kubert*** *a-2, 3; c-4r.*

GIZMO
Mirage Studios: 1986 - No. 6, July, 1987 ($1.50, B&W)

1-6 4.00

G.L.A. (Great Lakes Avengers)(Also see GLX-Mas Special)
Marvel Comics: June, 2005 - No. 4, Sept, 2005 ($2.99, limited series)

1-4-Slott-s/Pelletier-a 3.00
...: Misassembled TPB (2005, $14.99) r/#1-4, West Coast Avengers #46 (1st app.) and Marvel Super-Heroes #8 (1st app. Squirrel Girl; Ditko-a) 15.00

GLADSTONE COMIC ALBUM
Gladstone: 1987 - No. 28, 1990 ($5.95/$9.95, 8-1/2x11")(All Mickey albums are by Gottfredson)

	GD 2.0	VG 4.0	FN 6.0	VF 8.0	VF/NM 9.0	NM- 9.2
1-25: 1-Uncle Scrooge; Barks-r; Beck-c. 2-Donald Duck; r/F.C. #108 by Barks. 3-Mickey Mouse-r by Gottfredson. 4-Uncle Scrooge; r/F.C. #456 by Barks w/unedited story. 5-Donald Duck Advs.; r/F.C. #199. 6-Uncle Scrooge-r by Barks. 7-Donald Duck-r by Barks. 8-Mickey Mouse-r. 9-Bambi; r/F.C. #186? 10-Donald Duck Advs.; r/F.C. #275. 11-Uncle Scrooge; r/U.S. #4. 12-Donald And Daisy; r/F.C. #1055, WDC&S. 13-Donald Duck Advs.; r/F.C. #408. 14-Uncle Scrooge; Barks-r/U.S #21. 15-Donald And Gladstone; Barks-r. 16-Donald Duck Advs.; r/F.C. #238. 17-Mickey Mouse strip-r (The World of Tomorrow, The Pirate Ghost Ship). 18-Donald Duck and the Junior Woodchucks; Barks-r. 19-Uncle Scrooge; r/U.S. #12; Rosa-c. 20-Uncle Scrooge; r/F.C. #386; Barks-c/a(r). 21-Donald Duck Family; Barks-c/a(r). 22-Mickey Mouse strip-r. 23-Donald Duck; Barks-r/D.D. #26 w/unedited story. 24-Uncle Scrooge; Barks-r; Rosa-c. 25-D. Duck; Barks-c/a-r/F.C. #367	1	3	4	6	8	10

GD 2.0 | VG 4.0 | FN 6.0 | VF 8.0 | VF/NM 9.0 | NM- 9.2

26-28: All have $9.95-c. 26-Mickey & Donald; Gottfredson-c/a(r). 27-Donald Duck; r/WDC&S by Barks; Barks painted-c. 28-Uncle Scrooge & Donald Duck; Rosa-c/a (4 stories) 1 3 4 6 8 10
Special 1-7: 1 ('89-'90, $9.95/13.95)-1-Donald Duck Finds Pirate Gold; r/F.C. #9. 2 ('89, $8.95)-Uncle Scrooge and Donald Duck; Barks-r/Uncle Scrooge #5; Rosa-c. 3 ('89, $8.95)-Mickey Mouse strip-r. 4 ('89, $11.95)-Uncle Scrooge; Rosa-c/a-r/Son of the Sun from U.S. #219 plus Barks-r/U.S. 5 ('90, $11.95)-Donald Duck Advs.; Barks-r/F.C. #282 & 422 plus Barks painted-c. 6 ('90, $12.95)-Uncle Scrooge; Barks-c/a-r/Uncle Scrooge. 7 ('90, $13.95)-Mickey Mouse; Gottfredson strip-r 2 4 6 9 11 14

GLADSTONE COMIC ALBUM (2nd Series)(Also see The Original Dick Tracy)
Gladstone Publishing: 1990 ($5.95, 8-1/2 x 11," stiff-c, 52 pgs.)
1,2-The Original Dick Tracy. 2-Origin of the 2-way wrist radio 6.00
3-D Tracy Meets the Mole-r by Gould ($6.95). 1 2 3 5 6 8

GLAMOROUS ROMANCES (Formerly Dotty)
Ace Magazines (A. A. Wyn): No. 41, July, 1949 - No. 90, Oct, 1956 (Photo-c 68-90)
41-Dotty app. 20 40 60 114 182 250
42-72,74-80: 44-Begin 52 pg. issues. 45,50-61-Painted-c. 80-Last pre-code (2/55) 14 28 42 82 121 160
73-L.B. Cole-r/All Love #27 15 30 45 83 124 165
81-90 13 26 39 74 105 135

GLAMOURPUSS
Aardvark-Vanaheim Inc.: Apr, 2008 - No. 26, Jul, 2012 ($3.00, B&W)
1-26: 1-Two covers; Dave Sim-s/a/c. 9,10-Gene Colan-c. 11-Heath-c. 19-Allred-c 3.00
1-Comics Industry Preview Edition (Diamond Dateline supplement) 4.00

GLOBAL FREQUENCY
DC Comics (WildStorm): Dec, 2002 - No. 12, Aug, 2004 ($2.95, limited series)
1-12-Warren Ellis-s. 1-Leach-a. 2-Fabry-a. 3-Dillon-a. 5-Muth-a. 7-Bisley-a. 12-Ha-a 3.00
1-RRP Edition variant-c; promotional giveaway for retailers (200 printed) 10.00
...: Detonation Radio TPB (2005, $14.95) r/#7-12 15.00
...: Planet Ablaze TPB (2003, $14.95) r/#1-6 15.00

GLORY
Image Comics (Extreme Studios)/Maximum Press: Mar, 1995 - No. 22, Apr, 1997 ($2.50)
0-Deodato-c/a, 1-(3/95)-Deodato-a 4.00
1A-Variant-c 5.00
2-11,13-22: 4-Variant-c by Quesada & Palmiotti. 5-Bagged w/Youngblood gaming card. 7,8-Deodato-c/a(p). 8-Babewatch x-over. 9-Cruz-c; Extreme Destroyer Pt. 5; polybagged w/card. 10-Angela-c/app. 11-Deodato-c. 3.00
12-($3.50)-Photo-c 4.00
... & Friends Christmas Special (12/95, $2.50) Deodato-c 3.00
... & Friends Lingerie Special (9/95, $2.95) Pin-ups w/photos; photo-c; variant-c exists 3.00
... /Angela: Angels in Hell (4/96, $2.50) Flip book w/Darkchylde #1 4.00
... /Avengelyne (10/95, $3.95) 1-Chromium-c, 1-Regular-c 4.00
Trade Paperback (1995, $9.95)-r/#1-4 10.00

GLORY (Continues numbering from the 1995-1997 series)
Image Comics: Feb, 2012 - No. 34, Apr, 2013 ($2.99/$3.99)
23-28-Joe Keatinge-s/Ross Campbell-a. 23-Supreme app. 3.00
29-34-($3.99) 4.00

GLORY
Awesome Comics: Mar, 1999 ($2.50)
0-Liefeld-c; story and sketch pages 3.00

GLORY (ALAN MOORE'S...)
Avatar Press: Dec, 2001 - No. 2 ($3.50)
Preview-(9/01, $1.99) B&W pages and cover art; Alan Moore-s 3.00
0-Four regular covers 3.50
1,2: 1-Alan Moore-s/Mychaels & Gebbie-a; nine covers by various. 2-Five covers 3.50

GLORY & FRIENDS BIKINI FEST
Image Comics (Extreme): Sept, 1995 - No. 2, Oct, 1995 ($2.50, limited series)
1,2: 1-Photo-c; centerfold photo; pin-ups 4.00

GLORY/CELESTINE: DARK ANGEL
Image Comics/Maximum Press (Extreme Studios): Sept, 1996 - No. 3, Nov, 1996 ($2.50)
1-3 3.00

GLOW (Gorgeous Ladies of Wrestling)(Based on the Netflix series)
IDW Publishing: Mar, 2019 - No. 4, Jun, 2019 ($3.99, limited series)
1-4-Tini Howard-s/Hannah Templer-a; multiple covers on each 4.00
...: Summer Special (7/19, $3.99) Devin Grayson-s/Lisa Sterle-a 4.00

GLOW VS THE BABYFACE (Gorgeous Ladies of Wrestling)(Based on the Netflix series)
IDW Publishing: Nov, 2019 - No. 4, Feb, 2020 ($3.99, limited series)
1-4-Garcia & Mendez-s/Templer-a; multiple covers on each 4.00

GLX-MAS SPECIAL (Great Lakes Avengers)
Marvel Comics: Feb, 2006 ($3.99, one-shot)
1-Christmas themed stories by various incl. Haley, Templeton, Grist, Wieringo 4.00

G-MAN: CAPE CRISIS
Image Comics: Aug, 2009 - No. 5, Jan, 2010 ($2.99, limited series)
1-5-Chris Giarrusso-s/a; back-up short strips by various 3.00

GNOME MOBILE, THE (See Movie Comics)

GOBBLEDYGOOK
Mirage Studios: 1984 - No. 2, 1984 (B&W)(1st Mirage comics, published at same time)
1-(24 pgs.)-(distribution of approx. 50) Teenage Mutant Ninja Turtles app. on full page back-c ad; Teenage Mutant Ninja Turtles do not appear inside. 1st app of Fugitoid 1125 2250 3375 9550 21,775 34,000
2-(24 pgs.)-Teenage Mutant Ninja Turtles on full page back-c ad 333 666 1000 2831 6416 10,000
NOTE: *Counterfeit copies exist. Originals feature both black & white covers and interiors. Signed and numbered copies do not exist.*

GOBBLEDYGOOK
Mirage Studios: Dec, 1986 ($3.50, B&W, one-shot, 100 pgs.)
1-New 8 pg. TMNT story plus a Donatello/Michaelangelo 7 pg. story & a Gizmo story; Corben-i(r)/TMNT #7 5 10 15 34 60 85

GOBLIN, THE
Warren Publishing Co.: June, 1982 - No. 3, Dec, 1982 ($2.25, B&W magazine with 8 pg. color insert comic in all)
1-The Gremlin app. Philo Photon & the Troll Patrol, Micro-Buccaneers & Wizard Wormglow begin & app. in all. Tin Man app. Golden-a(p). Nebres-c/a in all 3 6 9 14 19 24
2,3: 2-1st Hobgoblin. 3-Tin Man app. 2 4 6 10 14 18
NOTE: ***Bermejo** a-1-3. **Elias** a-1-3. **Laxamana** a-1-3. **Nino** a-3.*

GO-BOTS (Based on the Hasbro toys)
IDW Publishing: Nov, 2018 - No. 5, Mar, 2019 ($3.99, limited series)
1-5-Tom Scioli-s/a/c 3.00

GOD COMPLEX
Image Comics: Dec, 2009 - No. 7, Jun, 2010 ($2.99)
1-7-Oeming & Berman-s/Broglia-a/Oeming-c 3.00

GOD COMPLEX: DOGMA
Image Comics (Top Cow): Oct, 2017 - No. 6, Jun, 2018 ($3.99)
1-6-Jenkins-s/Prasetya-a 4.00

GOD COUNTRY
Image Comics: Jan, 2017 - No. 6, Jun, 2017 ($3.99, limited series)
1-Donny Cates-s/Geoff Shaw-a 4 8 12 23 37 50
2-6 1 2 3 5 6 8

GODDAMNED, THE
Image Comics: Nov, 2015 - No. 5, Nov, 2016 ($3.99)
1-5-Jason Aaron-s/r.m. Guéra-a; story of Cain and Noah 4.00

GODDAMNED, THE: THE VIRGIN BRIDES
Image Comics: Jul, 2020 - No. 5, May, 2021 ($3.99)
1-5-Jason Aaron-s/r.m. Guéra-a 4.00

GODDESS
DC Comics (Vertigo): Jun, 1995 - No. 8, Jan, 1996 ($2.95, limited series)
1-Garth Ennis scripts; Phil Winslade-c/a in all 5.00
2-8 4.00

GODDESS MODE
DC Comics (Vertigo): Feb, 2019 - No. 6, Jul, 2019 ($3.99)
1-6-Zoë Quinn-s/Robbi Rodriguez-a 4.00

GODFATHERS, THE (See The Crusaders)

GOD HATES ASTRONAUTS
Image Comics: Sept, 2014 - No. 10, Jul, 2015 ($3.50)
1-10-Ryan Browne-s/a. 1-Covers by Browne & Darrow 3.50

GOD IS
Spire Christian Comics (Fleming H. Revell Co.): 1973, 1975 (35-49¢)
nn-(1973) By Al Hartley 3 6 9 14 19 24
nn-(1975) 2 4 6 10 14 18

GOD IS DEAD
Avatar Press: Aug, 2013 - No. 48, Feb, 2016 ($3.99)
1-24,26-46: 1-5-Hickman & Costa-s/Amorim-a 4.00
25,48-($5.99) 25-Costa-s/DiPascale, Nobile & Urdinola-a. 48-Last issue; cover gallery 6.00
...Book of Acts Alpha (7/14, $5.99) Short stories by Alan Moore and others 6.00
...Book of Acts Omega (7/14, $5.99) Short stories by various 6.00

GODKILLERS
AfterShock Comics: Feb, 2020 - No. 5, Aug, 2020 ($3.99, limited series)
1-5-Mark Sable-s/Maan House-a 4.00

GODLAND
Image Comics: July, 2005 - Finale, Dec, 2013 ($2.99)
1-35-Joe Casey-s; Kirby-esque art by Tom Scioli. 13-Var-c by Giffen & Larsen. 33-"Dogland" on cover 3.00
16-(60¢-c) Re-cap/origin issue 3.00
36-($3.99) 4.00
... Finale (12/13, $6.99) Final issue 7.00
Image Firsts: Godland #1 (9/10, $1.00) r/#1 with "Image Firsts" cover logo 3.00
...: Celestial Edition One HC (2007, $34.99) r/#1-12 and story from Image Holiday Special; intro. by Grant Morrison; cover gallery, developmental art and original story pitches 35.00

GOD OF TREMORS
AfterShock Comics: Aug, 2021 ($6.99, over-sized 8-1/2" x 10-7/8", one-shot)
1-Peter Milligan-s/Piotr Kowalski-a 7.00

GOD OF WAR (Based on the Sony videogame)
DC Comics (WildStorm): May, 2010 - No. 6, Mar, 2011 ($3.99/$2.99, limited series)
1-6-Wolfman-s/Sorrentino-a/Park-c. 6-($2.99) 4.00

GOD OF WAR (Based on the Sony videogame)
Dark Horse Comics: Nov, 2018 - No. 4, Feb, 2019 ($3.99, limited series)
1-4-Chris Roberson-s/Tony Parker-a/E.M. Gist-c 4.00

GOD OF WAR: FALLEN GOD (Based on the Sony videogame)
Dark Horse Comics: Mar, 2021 - No. 4, Jun, 2021 ($3.99, limited series)
1-4-Chris Roberson-s/Tony Parker-a/Dave Rapoza-c 4.00

GOD SAVE THE QUEEN
DC Comics (Vertigo): 2007 ($19.99, hardcover with dustjacket, graphic novel)
HC-Mike Carey-s/John Bolton-painted art 20.00
SC-(2008, $12.99) Different painted-c by Bolton 13.00

GOD'S COUNTRY (Also see Marvel Comics Presents)
Marvel Comics: 1994 ($6.95)
nn-P. Craig Russell-a; Colossus story; r/Marvel Comics Presents #10-17 7.00

GLOW #1 © Netflix

Godland #22 © Casey & Scioli

Godzilla (2013) #13 © Toho

GD VG FN VF VF/NM NM-
2.0 4.0 6.0 8.0 9.0 9.2

GOD'S HEROES IN AMERICA
Catechetical Guild Educational Society: 1956 (nn) (25¢/35¢, 68 pgs.)
307 3 6 9 18 27 36

GOD'S SMUGGLER (Religious)
Spire Christian Comics/Fleming H. Revell Co.: 1972 (35¢/39¢/40¢)
1-Three variations exist 3 6 9 14 19 24

GODWHEEL
Malibu Comics (Ultraverse): No. 0, Jan, 1995 - No. 3, Feb, 1995 ($2.50, limited series)
0-3: 0-Flip-c. 1-1st app. Primevil; Thor cameo (1 panel). 3-Pérez-a in Ch. 3, Thor app. 3.00

GODZILLA (Movie)
Marvel Comics : August, 1977 - No. 24, July, 1979 (Based on movie series)
1-(Regular 30¢ edition)-Moench-s/Trimpe-a/Mooney-i
6 12 18 41 76 110
1-(35¢-c variant, limited distribution) 25 50 75 175 388 600
2-(Regular 30¢ edition)-Tuska-i. 3 6 9 17 26 35
2,3-(35¢-c) variant, limited distribution) 11 22 33 76 163 250
3-(30¢-c) Champions app.(w/o Ghost Rider) 3 6 9 16 24 32
4-10: 4,5-Sutton-a 2 4 6 11 16 20
11-23: 14-Shield app. 20-F.F. app. 21,22-Devil Dinosaur app.
2 4 6 9 13 16
24-Last issue 3 6 9 16 23 30

GODZILLA (Movie)
Dark Horse Comics: May, 1988 - No. 6, 1988 ($1.95, B&W, limited series) (Based on movie series)
1 3 6 9 14 19 24
2-6 1 3 4 6 8 10
...Collection (1990, $10.95)-r/1-6 with new-c 16.00
...Color Special 1 (Sum, 1992, $3.50, color, 44 pgs.)-Arthur Adams wraparound-c/a & part scripts 2 4 6 8 10 12
...King Of The Monsters Special (8/87, $1.50)-Origin; Bissette-c/a
2 4 6 11 16 20
...Vs. Barkley nn (12/93, $2.95, color)-Dorman painted-c
3 6 9 16 23 30

GODZILLA (King of the Monsters) (Movie)
Dark Horse Comics: May, 1995 - No. 16, Sept, 1996 ($2.50) (Based on movies)
0,1: 0-r/Dark Horse Comics #10,11. 1-Kevin Maguire scripts
2 4 6 9 12 15
2-16: 2,3-Maguire scripts. 3-8-Art Adams-c 5.00
...Vs. Hero Zero ($2.50) 5.00

GODZILLA
IDW Publishing: May, 2012 - Nov, 2022 ($3.99/$7.99)
1-13: 1-5,7,8,10-Swierczynski-s/Gane-a; multiple covers on each. 6-Wachter-a 4.00
... Best of Godzilla (6/22, $6.99) Reprints of 4 recent stories 7.00
... Best of Mothra (10/22, $6.99) Reprints of 4 recent stories 7.00
... Rivals Vs. Battra (8/22, $7.99) Rosie Knight-s/Oliver Ono-a; Mothra app. 8.00
... Rivals Vs. Gigan (11/22, $7.99) Davidsen-s/SidVenBlu-a 8.00
... Rivals Vs. Hedorah (6/21, $7.99) Battle in New York City in 1971; E.J. Su-a 8.00
... Rivals Vs. King Ghidorah (3/22, $7.99) Kidnapped to Mars; Adam Gorham-s/a 8.00
... Rivals Vs. Mothra (9/21, $7.99) Battle in Japan in 1984; Gallant-a 8.00
...: The IDW Era (5/14, $3.99) Plot synopses of mini-series and cover galleries 4.00

GODZILLA: CATACLYSM
IDW Publishing: Aug, 2014 - No. 5, Dec, 2014 ($3.99, limited series)
1-5-Bunn-s/Wachter-a; multiple covers on each 4.00

GODZILLA: GANGSTERS AND GOLIATHS
IDW Publishing: Jun, 2011 - No. 5, Oct, 2011 ($3.99, limited series)
1-5-Layman-s/Ponticelli-a; Mothra app. 1-Darrow-c 4.00

GODZILLA IN HELL
IDW Publishing: Jul, 2015 - No. 5, Nov, 2015 ($3.99, limited series)
1-5: Two covers on each. 1-Stokoe-s/a. 5-Wachter-s/a 4.00

GODZILLA: KINGDOM OF MONSTERS
IDW Publishing: Mar, 2011 - No. 12, Feb, 2012 ($3.99)
1-12: 1-Hester-a; covers by Ross & Powell. 2,3-Covers by Hester & Powell 4.00
...: 100 Cover Charity Spectacular (8/11, $7.99) Variant covers for Japan Disaster Relief 8.00

GODZILLA LEGENDS (Spotlight on other monsters)
IDW Publishing: Nov, 2011 - No. 5, Mar, 2012 ($3.99, limited series)
1-5-Art Adams-c. 1-Anguirus. 2-Rodan. 3-Titanosaurus. 4-Hedorah. 5-Kumonga 4.00

GODZILLA: MONSTERS AND PROTECTORS
IDW Publishing: Apr, 2021 - No. 5, Aug, 2021 ($4.99/$3.99, limited series)

GD VG FN VF VF/NM NM-
2.0 4.0 6.0 8.0 9.0 9.2

1-($4.99) Burnham-s/Schoening-a 5.00
2-5-($3.99) 2,5-Mothra app. 3,5-Biollante app. 4.00

GODZILLA: MONSTERS AND PROTECTORS ALL HAIL THE KING
IDW Publishing: Oct, 2022 - No. 5, Feb, 2023 ($3.99, limited series)
1-5-Burnham-s/Schoening-a 4.00

GODZILLA: OBLIVION
IDW Publishing: Mar, 2016 - No. 5, Jul, 2016 ($3.99, limited series)
1-5-Fialkov-s/Churilla-a; Mechagodzilla & Ghidorah app. 4.00

GODZILLA: RAGE ACROSS TIME
IDW Publishing: Aug, 2016 - No. 5, Nov, 2016 ($3.99, limited series)
1-5-Story & art by various 4.00

GODZILLA: RULERS OF EARTH
IDW Publishing: Jun, 2013 - No. 25, Jun, 2015 ($3.99, limited series)
1-24: 1-8-Chris Mowry-s/Matt Frank-a 4.00
25-($7.99) Mowry-s/Frank & Zornow-a 8.00

GODZILLA: THE HALF-CENTURY WAR
IDW Publishing: Aug, 2012 - No. 5, Feb, 2013 ($3.99, limited series)
1-5-James Stokoe-s/a 4.00

GODZILLA VS. THE MIGHTY MORPHIN POWER RANGERS
BOOM! Studios / IDW Publishing: Mar, 2022 - No. 5, Sept, 2022 ($3.99, limited series)
1-5-Cullen Bunn-s/Freddie Williams III-a 4.00

GOG (VILLAINS) (See Kingdom Come)
DC Comics: Feb, 1998 ($1.95, one-shot)
1-Waid-s/Ordway-a(p)/Pearson-c 3.00

GO GIRL!
Image Comics: Aug, 2000 - No. 5 ($3.50, B&W, quarterly)
1-5-Trina Robbins-s/Anne Timmons-a; pin-up gallery 3.50

GO-GO
Charlton Comics: June, 1966 - No. 9, Oct, 1967
1-Miss Bikini Luv begins; Rolling Stones, Beatles, Elvis, Sonny & Cher, Bob Dylan, Sinatra, parody; Herman's Hermits pin-ups; D'Agostino-c/a in #1-8
9 18 27 59 117 175
2-Ringo Starr, David McCallum & Beatles photos on cover; Beatles story and photos; Blooperman & parody of JLA heroes 9 18 27 57 111 165
3,4: 3-Blooperman, ends #6; 1 pg. Batman & Robin satire; full pg. photo pin-ups Lovin' Spoonful & The Byrds 5 10 15 33 57 80
5,7,9: 5 (2/67)-Super Hero & TV satire by Jim Aparo & Grass Green begins. 6-8-Aparo-a. 7-Photo of Brian Wilson of Beach Boys on-c & Beach Boys photo inside f/b-c. 9-Aparo-c/a
5 10 15 33 57 80
6-Parody of JLA & DC heroes vs. Marvel heroes; Aparo-a; Elvis parody; Petula Clark photo-c; first signed work by Jim Aparo 5 10 15 35 63 90
8-Monkees photo on-c & photo inside f/b-c 6 12 18 38 69 100

GO-GO AND ANIMAL (See Tippy's Friends...)

GOING STEADY (Formerly Teen-Age Temptations)
St. John Publ. Co.: No. 10, Dec, 1954 - No. 13, June, 1955; No. 14, Oct, 1955
10(1954)-Matt Baker-c/a 213 426 639 1363 2332 3300
11(2/55, last precode), 12(4/55)-Baker-c 90 180 270 576 988 1400
13(6/55)-Baker-c/a 110 220 330 704 1202 1700
14(10/55)-Matt Baker-c/a, 25 pgs. 129 258 387 826 1413 2000

GOING STEADY (Formerly Personal Love)
Prize Publications/Headline: V3#3, Feb, 1960 - V3#6, Aug, 1960; V4#1, Sept-Oct, 1960
V3#3-6, V4#1 7 14 21 48 89 130

GOING STEADY WITH BETTY (Becomes Betty & Her Steady No. 2)
Avon Periodicals: Nov-Dec, 1949 (Teen-age)
1-Partial photo-c 47 94 141 296 498 700

GOLDEN AGE, THE (TPB also reprinted in 2005 as JSA: The Golden Age)
DC Comics (Elseworlds): 1993 - No. 4, 1994 ($4.95, limited series)
1-4: James Robinson scripts; Paul Smith-c/a; gold foil embossed-c 6.00
Trade Paperback (1995, $19.95) intro by Howard Chaykin 20.00

GOLDEN AGE SECRET FILES
DC Comics: Feb, 2001 ($4.95, one-shot)
1-Origins and profiles of JSA members and other G.A. heroes; Lark-c 5.00

GOLDEN ARROW (See Fawcett Miniatures, Mighty Midget & Whiz Comics)

GOLDEN ARROW (...Western No. 6)
Fawcett Publications: Spring, 1942 - No. 6, Spring, 1947 (68 pgs.)

GD VG FN VF VF/NM NM-
2.0 4.0 6.0 8.0 9.0 9.2

1-Golden Arrow begins 52 104 156 328 552 775
2-(1943) 25 50 75 150 245 340
3-5: 3-(Win/45-46). 4-(Spr/46). 5-(Fall/46) 16 32 48 94 147 200
6-Krigstein-a 17 34 51 100 158 215
Ashcan (1942) not distributed to newsstands, only for in house use. A CGC certified 9.0 sold for $3,734.38 in 2008.

GOLDEN COMICS DIGEST
Gold Key: May, 1969 - No. 48, Jan, 1976
NOTE: *Whitman editions exist of many titles and are generally valued the same.*

1-Tom & Jerry, Woody Woodpecker, Bugs Bunny 5 10 15 33 57 80
2-Hanna-Barbera TV Fun Favorites; Space Ghost, Flintstones, Atom Ant, Jetsons, Yogi Bear, Banana Splits, others app. 6 12 18 41 76 110
3-Tom & Jerry, Woody Woodpecker 3 6 9 16 24 32
4-Tarzan; Manning & Marsh-a 4 8 12 28 47 65
5,8-Tom & Jerry, W. Woodpecker, Bugs Bunny 3 6 9 16 23 30
6-Bugs Bunny 3 6 9 16 23 30
7-Hanna-Barbera TV Fun Favorites 5 10 15 33 57 80
9-Tarzan 4 8 12 28 47 65
10,12-17: 10-Bugs Bunny. 12-Tom & Jerry, Bugs Bunny, W. Woodpecker Journey to the Sun. 13-Tom & Jerry. 14-Bugs Bunny Fun Packed Funnies. 15-Tom & Jerry, Woody Woodpecker, Bugs Bunny. 16-Woody Woodpecker Cartoon Special. 17-Bugs Bunny 3 6 9 16 23 30
11-Hanna-Barbera TV Fun Favorites 5 10 15 34 60 85
18-Tom & Jerry; Barney Bear-r by Barks 3 6 9 16 24 32
19-Little Lulu 4 8 12 25 40 55
20-22: 20-Woody Woodpecker Falltime Funtime. 21-Bugs Bunny Showtime. 22-Tom & Jerry Winter Wingding 3 6 9 16 23 30
23-Little Lulu & Tubby Fun Fling 4 8 12 25 40 55
24-26,28: 24-Woody Woodpecker Fun Festival. 25-Tom & Jerry. 26-Bugs Bunny Halloween Hulla-Boo-Loo; Dr. Spektor article, also #25. 28-Tom & Jerry 3 6 9 14 20 26
27-Little Lulu & Tubby in Hawaii 4 8 12 24 38 52
29-Little Lulu & Tubby 4 8 12 24 38 52
30-Bugs Bunny Vacation Funnies 3 6 9 14 20 26
31-Turok, Son of Stone; r/4-Color #596,656; c-r/#9 4 8 12 27 44 60
32-Woody Woodpecker Summer Fun 3 6 9 14 20 26
33,36: 33-Little Lulu & Tubby Halloween Fun; Dr. Spektor app. 36-Little Lulu & Her Friends 4 8 12 24 38 52
34,35,37-39: 34-Bugs Bunny Winter Funnies. 35-Tom & Jerry Snowtime Funtime. 37-Woody Woodpecker County Fair. 39-Bugs Bunny Summer Fun 3 6 9 14 20 26
38-The Pink Panther 3 6 9 16 24 32
40,43: 40-Little Lulu & Tubby Trick or Treat; all by Stanley. 43-Little Lulu in Paris 4 8 12 24 38 52
41,42,44,47: 41-Tom & Jerry Winter Carnival. 42-Bugs Bunny. 44-Woody Woodpecker Family Fun Festival. 47-Bugs Bunny 3 6 9 14 20 25
45-The Pink Panther 3 6 9 16 24 32
46-Little Lulu & Tubby 4 8 12 21 33 45
48-The Lone Ranger 3 6 9 17 26 35
NOTE: *#1-30, 164 pgs.; #31 on, 132 pgs..*

GOLDEN LAD
Spark/Fact & Fiction Publ.: July, 1945 - No. 5, June, 1946 (#4, 5: 52 pgs.)

1-Origin & 1st app. Golden Lad & Swift Arrow; Sandusky and the Senator begins 68 136 204 435 743 1050
2-Mort Meskin-c/a 33 66 99 194 317 440
3,4-Mort Meskin-c/a 30 60 90 177 289 400
5-Origin & 1st app. Golden Girl; Shaman & Flame app. 41 82 123 256 428 600
NOTE: *All have* **Robinson,** *and* **Roussos** *art plus* **Meskin** *covers and art.*

GOLDEN LEGACY
Fitzgerald Publishing Co.: 1966 - 1972 (Black History) (25¢)

1-12,14-16: 1-Toussaint L'Ouverture (1966), 2-Harriet Tubman (1967), 3-Crispus Attucks & the Minutemen (1967), 4-Benjamin Banneker (1968), 5-Matthew Henson (1969), 6-Alexander Dumas & Family (1969), 7-Frederick Douglass, Part 1 (1969), 8-Frederick Douglass, Part 2 (1970), 9-Robert Smalls (1970), 10-J. Cinque & the Amistad Mutiny (1970), 11-Men in Action: White, Marshall J. Wilkins (1970), 12-Black Cowboys (1972), 14-The Life of Alexander Pushkin (1971), 15-Ancient African Kingdoms (1972), 16-Black Inventors (1972) each.... 4 8 12 23 37 50
13-The Life of Martin Luther King, Jr. (1972) 5 10 15 30 50 70
1-10,12,13,15,16(1976)-Reprints 2 4 6 9 12 15

GOLDEN LOVE STORIES (Formerly Golden West Love)
Kirby Publishing Co.: No. 4, April, 1950

4-Powell-a; Glenn Ford/Janet Leigh photo-c 20 40 60 114 182 250

GOLDEN PICTURE CLASSIC, A
Western Printing Co. (Simon & Shuster): 1956-1957 (Text stories w/illustrations in color; 100 pgs. each)

CL-401: Treasure Island 11 22 33 64 90 115
CL-402,403: 402: Tom Sawyer. 403: Black Beauty 10 20 30 54 72 90
CL-404, 405: CL-404: Little Women. CL-405: Heidi 10 20 30 54 72 90
CL-406: Ben Hur 8 16 24 44 57 70
CL-407: Around the World in 80 Days 8 16 24 44 57 70
CL-408: Sherlock Holmes 9 18 27 50 65 80
CL-409: The Three Musketeers 8 16 24 44 57 70
CL-410: The Merry Advs. of Robin Hood 8 16 24 44 57 70
CL-411,412: 411: Hans Brinker. 412: The Count of Monte Cristo 9 18 27 50 65 80
(Both soft & hardcover editions are valued the same)
NOTE: *Recent research has uncovered new information. Apparently #s 1-6 were issued in 1956 and #7-12 in 1957. But they can be found in five different series listings: CL-1 to CL-12 (softbound); CL-401 to CL-412 (also softbound); CL-101 to CL-112 (hardbound); plus two new series discoveries: A Golden Reading Adventure, publ. by Golden Press; edited down to 60 pages and reduced in size to 6x9"; only #s discovered so far are #381 (CL-4), #382 (CL-6) & #387 (CL-3). They have no reorder list and some have covers different from GPC. There have also been found British hardbound editions of GPC with dust jackets. Copies of all five listed series vary from scarce to very rare. Some editions of some series have not yet been found at all.*

GOLDEN PICTURE STORY BOOK
Racine Press (Western): Dec, 1961 (50¢, Treasury size, 52 pgs.) (All are scarce)
ST-1-Huckleberry Hound (TV); Hokey Wolf, Pixie & Dixie, Quick Draw McGraw, Snooper and Blabber, Augie Doggie app. 15 30 45 103 227 350
ST-2-Yogi Bear (TV); Snagglepuss, Yakky Doodle, Quick Draw McGraw, Snooper and Blabber, Augie Doggie app. 15 30 45 103 227 350
ST-3-Babes in Toyland (Walt Disney's...)-Annette Funicello photo-c 19 38 57 131 291 450
ST-4-(...of Disney Ducks)-Walt Disney's Wonderful World of Ducks (Donald Duck, Uncle Scrooge, Donald's Nephews, Grandma Duck, Ludwig Von Drake, & Gyro Gearloose stories) 19 38 57 131 291 450

GOLDEN RECORD COMIC (See Amazing Spider-Man #1, Avengers #4, Fantastic Four #1, Journey Into Mystery #83) (Also see Superman Record Comic and Batman Record Comic in the Promotional section)

GOLDEN STORY BOOKS
Western Printing Co. (Simon & Shuster): 1949-1950 (Heavy covers, digest size, 128 pgs.) (Illustrated text in color)

7-Walt Disney's Mystery in Disneyville, a book-length adventure starring Donald and Nephews, Mickey and Nephews, and with Minnie, Daisy and Goofy. Art by Dick Moores & Manuel Gonzales (scarce) 31 62 93 182 296 410
10-Bugs Bunny's Treasure Hunt, a book-length adventure starring Bugs & Porky Pig, with Petunia Pig & Nephew, Cicero. Art by Tom McKimson (scarce) 21 42 63 122 199 275
11,12 ('50): 11-M-G-M's Tom & Jerry. 12-Walt Disney's "So Dear My Heart" 20 40 60 114 182 250

GOLDEN WEST LOVE (Golden Love Stories No. 4)
Kirby Publishing Co.: Sept-Oct, 1949 - No. 3, Feb, 1950 (All 52 pgs.)

1-Powell-a in all; Roussos-a; painted-c 25 50 75 150 245 340
2,3: Photo-c 17 34 51 105 165 225

GOLDEN WEST RODEO TREASURY (See Dell Giants)

GOLDFISH (See A.K.A. Goldfish)

GOLD GOBLIN (Spider-Man)
Marvel Comics: Jan, 2023 - Present ($3.99)

1-4-Cantwell-s/Medina-a; Norman Osborn as a hero 4.00

GOLDIE VANCE
Boom Entertainment (BOOM! Box): Apr, 2016 - No. 12, May, 2017 ($3.99)

1-12: 1-8-Hope Larson-s/Brittney Williams-a. 1-Five covers. 2-4-Two covers. 9-12-Hayes-a 4.00

GOLDILOCKS (See March of Comics No. 1)

GOLD KEY: ALLIANCE
Dynamite Entertainment: 2016 - No. 5, 2016 ($3.99, limited series)

1-5: 1-Team up of Magnus, Turok, Solar & Samson; Hester-s/Peeples-a 4.00

GOLD KEY CHAMPION
Gold Key: Mar, 1978 - No. 2, May, 1978 (50¢, 52 pgs.)

1-Space Family Robinson; half-r 2 4 6 9 13 16
2-Mighty Samson; half-r 1 3 4 6 8 10

GOLD KEY SPOTLIGHT
Gold Key: May, 1976 - No. 11, Feb, 1978

1-Tom, Dick & Harriet 2 4 6 8 11 14
2-11: 2-Wacky Advs. of Cracky. 3-Wacky Witch. 4-Tom, Dick & Harriet. 5-Wacky Advs. of Cracky. 6-Dagar the Invincible; Santos-a; origin Demonomicon. 7-Wacky Witch & Greta Ghost. 8-The Occult Files of Dr. Spektor, Simbar, Lu-sai; Santos-a. 9-Tragg. 10-O. G. Whiz. 11-Tom, Dick & Harriet 2 4 6 8 10 12

GOLD MEDAL COMICS
Cambridge House: 1945 (25¢, one-shot, 132 pgs.)

nn-Captain Truth by Fujitani as well as Stallman and Howie Post, Crime Detector, The Witch of Salem, Luckyman, others app. 42 84 126 265 445 625

GOLEM WALKS AMONG US!, THE
Dark Horse Comics: Aug, 2021 - No. 2, Sept, 2021 ($3.99, limited series)

1,2-Mignola & Golden-s/Bergting-a; set in 1938 Italy 4.00

GOMER PYLE (TV)
Gold Key: July, 1966 - No. 3, Oct, 1967

1-Photo front/back-c 10 20 30 67 141 215
2,3-Photo-c 6 12 18 37 66 95

GON
DC Comics (Paradox Press): July, 1996 - No. 4, Oct, 1996; No. 5, 1997 ($5.95, B&W, digest-size, limited series)

1-5: Misadventures of baby dinosaur; 1-Gon. 2-Gon Again. 3-Gon: Here Today, Gone Tomorrow. 4-Gon: Going, Going...Gon. 5-Gon Swimmin'. Tanaka-c/a/scripts in all 1 3 4 6 8 10

GON COLOR SPECTACULAR
DC Comics (Paradox Press): 1998 ($5.95, square-bound)

nn-Tanaka-c/a/scripts 2 4 6 10 14 18

GONERS
Image Comics: Oct, 2014 - No. 6, Mar, 2015 ($2.99)

1-6-Semahn-s/Corona-a 3.00

GON ON SAFARI
DC Comics (Paradox Press): 2000 ($7.95, B&W, digest-size)

nn-Tanaka-c/a/scripts 1 3 4 6 8 10

GON UNDERGROUND
DC Comics (Paradox Press): 1999 ($7.95, B&W, digest-size)

nn-Tanaka-c/a/scripts 1 3 4 6 8 10

GON WILD
DC Comics (Paradox Press): 1997 ($9.95, B&W, digest-size)

nn-Tanaka-c/a/scripts in all. (Rep. Gon #3,4) 2 4 6 9 12 15

GOOD ASIAN, THE

Gold Goblin #1 © MAR

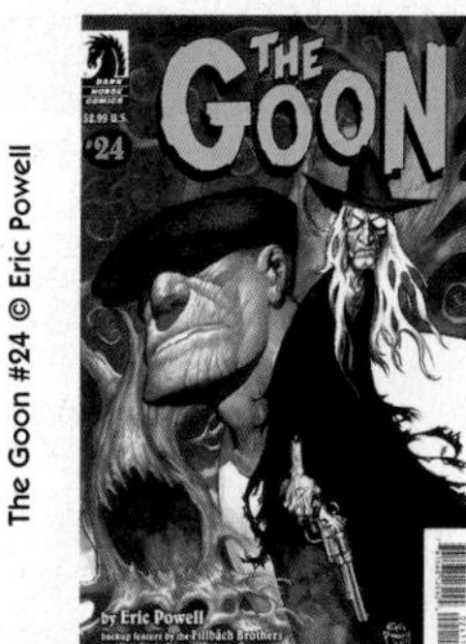

The Goon #24 © Eric Powell

Gotham Academy #5 © DC

GD 2.0 | VG 4.0 | FN 6.0 | VF 8.0 | VF/NM 9.0 | NM- 9.2

Image Comics: May, 2021 - No. 10, Apr, 2022 ($3.99)

1-10-Pornsak Pichetshote-s/Alexandre Tefenkgi-a; Chinese-Americans in 1936 San Fran. 4.00

GOODBYE, MR. CHIPS (See Movie Comics)

GOOD GIRL ART QUARTERLY
AC Comics: Summer, 1990 - No. 15, Spring, 1994; No. 19, 2001 (B&W/color, 52 pgs.)

1-($3.50)-All have one new story (often FemForce) & rest reprints by Baker, Ward & other "good girl" artists 2 4 6 9 12 15
2-($3.95), 19-(2001) FX Convention Exclusive 6.00
3-15-($3.50) 6.00

GOOD GIRL COMICS (Formerly Good Girl Art Quarterly)
AC Comics: No. 16, Summer, 1994 - No. 18, 1995 (B&W)

16-18 6.00

GOOD GUYS, THE
Defiant: Nov, 1993 - No. 9, July, 1994 ($2.50/$3.25/$3.50)

1-($3.50, 52 pgs.)-Glory x-over from Plasm 4.00
2,3,5-9: 3-Chasm app. 9-Pre-Schism issue 3.00
4-($3.25, 52 pgs.) Nudge sends Chasm to Plasm 4.00

GOOD, THE BAD AND THE UGLY, THE (Also see Man With No Name)
Dynamite Entertainment: 2009 - No. 8 ($3.50)

1-8: 1-Character from the 1966 Clint Eastwood movie; Dixon-s/Polls-a; three covers 3.50

GOOD TRIUMPHS OVER EVIL! (Also see Narrative Illustration)
M.C. Gaines: 1943 (12 pgs., 7-1/4"x10", B&W) (not a comic book) (Rare)

nn-A pamphlet, sequel to Narrative Illustration 168 336 504 1075 1838 2600
NOTE: *Print, A Quarterly Journal of the Graphic Arts Vol. 3 No. 3 (64 pg. square bound) features 1st printing of Good Triumphs Over Evil! A VG copy sold for $350 in 2005.*

GOOFY (Disney)(See Dynabrite Comics, Mickey Mouse Magazine V4#7, Walt Disney Showcase #35 & Wheaties)
Dell Publishing Co.: No. 468, May, 1953 - Sept-Nov, 1962

	GD	VG	FN	VF	VF/NM	NM-
Four Color 468 (#1)	12	24	36	82	179	275
Four Color 562,627,658,702,747,802,857	7	14	21	46	86	125
Four Color 899,952,987,1053,1094,1149,1201	5	10	15	35	63	90
12-308-211(Dell, 9-11/62)	5	10	15	31	53	75

GOOFY ADVENTURES
Disney Comics: June, 1990 - No. 17, 1991 ($1.50)

1-17: Most new stories. 2-Joshua Quagmire-a w/free poster. 7-WDC&S-r plus new-a. 9-Gottfredson-r. 14-Super Goof story. 15-All Super Goof issue. 17-Gene Colan-a(p) 3.00

GOOFY ADVENTURE STORY (See Goofy No. 857)

GOOFY COMICS (Companion to Happy Comics)(Not Disney)
Nedor Publ. Co. No. 1-14/Standard No. 14-48: June, 1943 - No. 48, 1953 (Animated Cartoons)

	GD	VG	FN	VF	VF/NM	NM-
1-Funny animal; Oriolo-c	41	82	123	256	428	600
2	22	44	66	128	209	290
3-10	16	32	48	92	144	195
11-19	14	28	42	78	112	145
20-35-Frazetta text illos in all	14	28	42	82	121	160
36-48	11	22	33	64	90	115

GOOFY SUCCESS STORY (See Goofy No. 702)

GOON, THE
Avatar Press: Mar, 1999 - No. 3, July, 1999 ($3.00, B&W)

	GD	VG	FN	VF	VF/NM	NM-
1-Eric Powell-s/a	20	40	60	138	307	475
2	5	10	15	34	60	85
3	6	12	18	37	66	95

...: Rough Stuff (Albatross, 1/03, $15.95) r/Avatar Press series #1-3 20.00
...: Rough Stuff (Dark Horse, 2/04, $12.95) r/Avatar Press series #1-3 newly colored 15.00

GOON, THE (2nd series)
Albatross Exploding Funny Books: Oct, 2002 - No. 4, Feb, 2003 ($2.95)

	GD	VG	FN	VF	VF/NM	NM-
1-Eric Powell-s/a	5	10	15	35	63	90
2-4	3	6	9	14	20	25
...Color Special 1 (8/02)	3	6	9	17	25	34

...: Nothin' But Misery Vol. 1 (Dark Horse, 7/03, $15.95, TPB) - Reprints The Goon #1-4 (Albatross series), Color Special, and story from DHP #157 18.00

GOON, THE (3rd series) (Also see Dethklok Versus the Goon)
Dark Horse Comics: June, 2003 - No. 44, Nov, 2013 ($2.99/$3.50)

	GD	VG	FN	VF	VF/NM	NM-
1-Eric Powell-s/a in all	4	8	12	23	37	50
2-4	2	4	6	8	10	12

5-31: 7-Hellboy-c/app; framing seq. by Mignola 14-Two covers 4.00
32-($3.99, 3/09) Tenth Anniversary issue; with sketch pages and pin-ups 5.00
33-44-($3.50) 33-Silent issue. 35-Dorkin-s. 39-Gimmick issue. 41-43-Buckingham-a. 44-Spanish issue 3.50
... 25¢ Edition (9/05, 25¢) 3.00
...: Chinatown and the Mystery of Mr. Wicker HC (11/07, $19.95) original GN; Powell-s/a 20.00
...: Fancy Pants Edition HC (10/05, $24.95, dust jacket) r/#1,2 of 2nd series & #1,3,5,9 of 3rd series; Powell intro.; sketch pages and cover gallery 25.00
...: Heaps of Ruination (5/05, $12.95, TPB) r/#5-8; intro. by Frank Darabont 13.00
...: My Murderous Childhood (And Other Grievous Yarns) (5/04, $13.95, TPB) r/#1-4 and short story from Drawing on Your Nightmares one-shot; intro. by Frank Cho 14.00
...: One For One (8/10, $1.00) r/#1 with red cover frame 3.00
...: One For The Road (6/14, $3.50) Jack Davis-c; EC horror hosts app. 3.50
...: Theater Bizarre (10/15, $3.99) Prelude to The Lords of Misery; Zombo app. 4.00
...: Virtue and the Grim Consequences Thereof (2/06, $16.95) r/#9-13 17.00
...: Wicked Inclinations (12/06, $14.95) r/#14-18; intro. by Mike Allred 15.00

GOON, THE (4th series)
Albatross Funnybooks: 2019 - Present ($3.99)

1-14: 1-4,13,14-Eric Powell-s/a. 5-8-Powell & Sniegoski-s/Parson-a. 9-12-Langridge-s/Norton-a 4.00

GOON NOIR, THE (Dwight T. Albatross's...)
Dark Horse Comics: Sept, 2006 - No. 3, Jan, 2007 ($2.99, B&W, limited series)

1-3-Anthology 1-Oswalt-s/Ploog-a; Sniegoski-s/Powell-a; Morrison-s/a; Niles-s/Sook-a 4.00

GOON: OCCASION OF REVENGE, THE
Dark Horse Comics: Jul, 2014 - No. 4, Dec, 2014 ($3.50, limited series)

1-4-Powell-s/a. 3-Origin of Kid Gargantuan 3.50

GOON: ONCE UPON A HARD TIME, THE
Dark Horse Comics: Feb, 2015 - No. 4, Oct, 2015 ($3.50, limited series)

1-4-Powell-s/a 3.50

GOOSE (Humor magazine)
Cousins Publ. (Fawcett): Sept, 1976 - No. 3, 1976 (75¢, 52 pgs., B&W)

1-Nudity in all 3 6 9 18 28 38
2,3: 2-(10/76) Fonz-c/s; Lone Ranger story. 3-Wonder Woman, King Kong, Six Million Dollar Man stories 3 6 9 14 20 26

GOOSEBUMPS: DOWNLOAD AND DIE!
IDW Publishing: Feb, 2018 - No. 3, Apr, 2018 ($3.99, limited series)

1-3-Jen Vaughn-s/Michelle Wong-a 4.00

GOOSEBUMPS: HORRORS OF THE WITCH HOUSE
IDW Publishing: Mar, 2019 - No. 3, May, 2019 ($3.99, limited series)

1-3-Denton J. Tipton & Matthew Dow Smith-s/Chris Fenoglio-a 4.00

GOOSEBUMPS: MONSTERS AT MIDNIGHT
IDW Publishing: Oct, 2017 - No. 3, Dec, 2017 ($3.99, limited series)

1-3-Lambert-s/Fenoglio-a 4.00

GOOSEBUMPS: SECRETS OF THE SWAMP
IDW Publishing: Sept, 2020 - No. 5, Jan, 2021 ($3.99, limited series)

1-5-Nijkamp-s/Montanez-a 4.00

GORDO (See Comics Revue No. 5 & Giant Comics Edition)

GORGO (Based on M.G.M. movie) (See Return of...)
Charlton Comics: May, 1961 - No. 23, Sept, 1965

	GD	VG	FN	VF	VF/NM	NM-
1-Ditko-a, 22 pgs.	30	60	90	216	483	750
2,3-Ditko-c/a	15	30	45	100	220	340
4-Ditko-c	10	20	30	67	141	215
5-11,13-16: 11,13-16-Ditko-a. 11-Ditko-c	8	16	24	56	108	160
12,17-23: 12-Reptisaurus x-over. 17-23-Montes/Bache-a. 20-Giordano-c	6	12	18	37	66	95
Gorgo's Revenge('62)-Becomes Return of...	7	14	21	48	89	130

GORILLA MAN (From Agents of Atlas)
Marvel Comics: Sept, 2010 - No. 3, Nov, 2010 ($3.99, limited series)

1-3-Parker-s/Caracuzzo-a. 1-Johnson-c. 3-Dell'Otto-c 4.00

GOSPEL BLIMP, THE
Spire Christian Comics (Fleming H. Revell Co.): 1974, 1975 (35¢/39¢, 36 pgs.)

	GD	VG	FN	VF	VF/NM	NM-
nn-(1974)	3	6	9	14	19	24
nn-(1975)	2	4	6	9	13	16

GOTHAM ACADEMY
DC Comics: Dec, 2014 - No. 18, Jul, 2016 ($2.99)

1-18: 1-Cloonan & Fletcher-s/Kerschl-a. 4-6-Killer Croc. 6,7-Damian Wayne app. 3.00
Annual 1 (10/16, $4.99) Art by Archer, Wildgoose, Dialynas, Msassyk; Blight app. 5.00
...: Endgame 1 (5/15, $2.99) Tie-in to Joker story in Batman titles 3.00

GOTHAM ACADEMY: SECOND SEMESTER

GD VG FN VF VF/NM NM-
2.0 4.0 6.0 8.0 9.0 9.2

DC Comics: Nov, 2016 - No. 12, Oct, 2017 ($2.99)
1-12: 1-3-Cloonan, Fletcher & Kerschl-s/Archer-a. 4-Jon Lam-a. 11-Damian app. 3.00

GOTHAM BY GASLIGHT (A Tale of the Batman)(See Batman: Master of...)
DC Comics: 1989 ($3.95, one-shot, squarebound, 52 pgs.)
nn-Mignola/Russell-a; intro by Robert Bloch 2 4 6 11 16 20

GOTHAM BY MIDNIGHT
DC Comics: Jan, 2015 - No. 12, Feb, 2016 ($2.99)
1-12: 1-5-Fawkes-s/Templesmith-a/c. 4,5,7-11-The Spectre app. 6-12-Ferreyra-a 3.00
Annual 1 (9/15, $4.99) Fawkes-s/Duce-a; The Gentleman Ghost origin 5.00

GOTHAM CENTRAL
DC Comics: Early Feb, 2003 - No. 40, Apr, 2006 ($2.50)
1-40-Stories of Gotham City Police. 1-Brubaker & Rucka-s/Lark-c/a. 10-Two-Face app. 13,15-Joker-c. 18-Huntress app. 27-Catwoman-c. 32-Poison Ivy app. 34-Teen Titans-c/app. 38-Crispus Allen killed (becomes The Spectre in Infinite Crisis #5) 3.00
... Special Edition 1 (11/14, $1.00) r/#1 with Gotham TV show banner on cover 3.00
... Book One: In the Line of Duty HC (2008, $29.99, dustjacket) r/#1-10; sketch pages 30.00
... Book One: In the Line of Duty SC (2008, $19.99) r/#1-10; sketch pages 20.00
... Book Two: Jokers and Madmen HC (2009, $29.99, dustjacket) r/#11-22 30.00
... Book Two: Jokers and Madmen SC (2011, $19.99) r/#11-22 20.00
... Book Three: On the Freak Beat HC (2010, $29.99, dustjacket) r/#23-31 30.00
... Book Four: Corrigan HC (2011, $29.99, dustjacket) r/#32-40 30.00
...: Dead Robin (2007, $17.99, TPB) r/#33-40; cover gallery 18.00
...: Half a Life (2005, $14.99, TPB) r/#6-10, Batman Chronicles #16 and Detective #747 15.00
...: In The Line of Duty (2004, $9.95, TPB) r/#1-5, cover gallery & sketch pages 10.00
...: The Quick and the Dead TPB (2006, $14.99) r/#23-25,28-31 15.00
...: Unresolved Targets (2006, $14.99, TPB) r/#12-15,19-22, cover gallery 15.00

GOTHAM CITY GARAGE
DC Comics: Dec, 2017 - No. 12, May, 2018 ($2.99, printings of stories that first appeared online)
1-12: 1-Female heroes as a biker gang; Kelly & Lanzing-s/Ching-a/Albuquerque-c 3.00

GOTHAM CITY MONSTERS
DC Comics: Nov, 2019 - No. 6, Apr, 2020 ($3.99, limited series)
1-6-Orlando-s/Nahuelpan-a; Frankenstein, Killer Croc, Orca app. 3-6-Batwoman app. 4.00

GOTHAM CITY SIRENS (Batman: Reborn)
DC Comics: Aug, 2009 - No. 26, Oct, 2011 ($2.99)
1-Catwoman, Harley Quinn and Poison Ivy; Dini-s/March-a/c
5 10 15 31 53 75
1-Variant-c by JG Jones 12 24 36 79 170 260
2-4 2 4 6 11 16 20
5-Full Harley Quinn cover 3 6 9 15 22 28
6-10 2 4 6 8 10 12
11-19 1 3 4 6 8 10
20,23-Joker, Harley Quinn cover 2 4 6 10 14 18
21-Full Harley Quinn cover 2 4 6 10 14 18
22,24-26 5.00
...: Song of the Sirens HC (2010, $19.99, dustjacket) r/#8-13 & Catwoman #83 20.00
...: Union HC (2010, $19.99, dustjacket) r/#1-7 20.00
...: Union SC (2011, $17.99) r/#1-7 18.00

GOTHAM CITY VILLAINS ANNIVERSARY GIANT
DC Comics: Jan, 2022 ($9.99, 100 pgs., squarebound, one-shot)
1-Short stories by various incl. Penguin/Catwoman by Danny DeVito-s/Mora-a; Bermejo-c 10.00

GOTHAM CITY: YEAR ONE
DC Comics: Dec, 2022 - No. 6 ($4.99, limited series)
1-5-Bruce Wayne's grandparents set in 1961; Slam Bradley app.; King-s/Hester-a 5.00

GOTHAM GAZETTE (Battle For The Cowl crossover in Batman titles)
DC Comics: May, 2009; Jul, 2009 ($2.99, one-shots)
1-Short stories of Gotham without Batman; Nguyen, March, ChrisCross & others-a 3.00
...: Batman Alive? (7/09) Vicki Vale app.; Nguyen, March, ChrisCross & others-a 3.00

GOTHAM GIRLS
DC Comics: Oct, 2002 - No. 5, Feb, 2003 ($2.25, limited series)
1-Catwoman, Batgirl, Poison Ivy, Harley Quinn from animated series; Catwoman-c
3 6 9 15 22 28
2,4,5: 2-Poison Ivy-c. 4-Montoya-c. 5-Batgirl-c 2 4 6 10 14 18
3-Harley Quinn-c 4 8 12 27 44 60

GOTHAM NIGHTS (See Batman: Gotham Nights II)
DC Comics: Mar, 1992 - No. 4, June, 1992 ($1.25, limited series)
1-4: Featuring Batman 4.00

GOTHAM UNDERGROUND
DC Comics: Dec, 2007 - No. 9, Aug, 2008 ($2.99, limited series)
1-9-Nine covers interlock for single image; Tieri-s/Calafiore-a/c. 7,8-Vigilante app. 4.00
Batman: Gotham Underground TPB (2008, $19.99) r/#1-9; interlocked image cover 20.00

GOTHIC ROMANCES (Also see My Secrets)
Atlas/Seaboard Publ.: Dec, 1974 (75¢, B&W, magazine, 76 pgs.)
1-Text w/ illos by N. Adams, Chaykin, Heath (2 pgs. ea.); painted cover from Ravenwood Gothic paperback "The Conservatory"(scarce) 34 68 102 245 548 850

GOTHIC TALES OF LOVE (Magazine)
Marvel Comics: Apr, 1975 - No. 3, 1975 (B&W, 76 pgs.)
1-3-Painted-c/a (scarce) 33 66 99 238 532 825

GOVERNOR & J. J., THE (TV)
Gold Key: Feb, 1970 - No. 3, Aug, 1970 (Photo-c)
1 4 8 12 25 40 55
2,3 3 6 9 18 28 38

GRACKLE, THE
Acclaim Comics: Jan, 1997 - No. 4, Apr, 1997 ($2.95, B&W)
1-4: Mike Baron scripts & Paul Gulacy-c/a. 1-4-Doublecross 3.00

GRAFIK MUSIK
Caliber Press: Nov, 1990 - No. 4, Aug, 1991 ($3.50/$2.50)
1-($3.50, 48 pgs., color) Mike Allred-c/a/scripts-1st app. in color of Frank Einstein (Madman)
3 6 9 18 27 36
2-($2.50, 24 pgs., color) 3 6 9 14 20 25
3,4-($2.50, 24 pgs., B&W) 2 4 6 11 16 20

GRANDMA DUCK'S FARM FRIENDS(See Walt Disney's C&S 293 & Wheaties)
Dell Publishing Co.: No. 763, Jan, 1957 - No. 1279, Feb, 1962 (Disney)
Four Color 763 (#1) 8 16 24 51 96 140
Four Color 873 6 12 18 37 66 95
Four Color 965,1279 5 10 15 34 60 85
Four Color 1010,1073,1161-Barks-a; 1073,1161-Barks-c/a
11 22 33 73 157 240

GRAND PASSION
Dynamite Entertainment: 2016 - No. 5, 2017 ($3.99, limited series)
1-5-James Robinson-s/Tom Feister-a/John Cassaday-c 4.00

GRAND PRIX (Formerly Hot Rod Racers)
Charlton Comics: No. 16, Sept, 1967 - No. 31, May, 1970
16-Features Rick Roberts 3 6 9 21 33 45
17-20 3 6 9 17 26 35
21-31 3 6 9 16 23 30

GRAPHIC FANTASY
Image Comics: Feb, 2021 - No. 2, Feb, 2021 ($9.99/$5.99, B&W)
1-Reprint of 1982 fanzine with the 1st app. of Savage Dragon by Erik Larsen 10.00
2-($5.99) Reprint of 1982 fanzine with the 2nd app. of Savage Dragon 6.00

GRAPHIQUE MUSIQUE
Slave Labor Graphics: Dec, 1989 - No. 3, May, 1990 ($2.95, 52 pgs.)
1-Mike Allred-c/a/scripts 4 8 12 23 37 50
2,3 3 6 9 19 30 45

GRASS KINGS
BOOM! Studios: Mar, 2017 - No. 15, May, 2018 ($3.99)
1-14-Matt Kindt-s/Tyler Jenkins-a 4.00
15-($4.99) Last issue; Kindt-s/Jenkins-a 5.00

GRAVESLINGER
Image Comics (Shadowline): Oct, 2007 - No. 4, Mar, 2008 ($3.50, limited series)
1-4-Denton & Mariotte-s/Cboins-a 3.50

GRAVE TALES
Hamilton Comics: Oct, 1991 - No. 3, Feb, 1992 ($3.95, B&W, mag., 52 pgs.)
1-Staton-c/a 2 3 4 6 8 10
2,3: 2-Staton-a; Morrow-c 1 2 3 5 6 8

GRAVEYARD SHIFT
Image Comics: Dec, 2014 - No. 4, Apr, 2015 ($3.50)
1-4: 1-Jay Faerber-s/Fran Bueno-a; wraparound-c 3.50

GRAVITY (Also see Beyond! limited series)
Marvel Comics: Aug, 2005 - No. 5, Dec, 2005 ($2.99, limited series)
1-5: 1-Intro. Gravity; McKeever-s/Norton-a. 2-Rhino-c/app. 5-Spider-Man app. 3.00
...: Big-City Super Hero (2005, $7.99, digest) r/#1-5 8.00

GRAY AREA, THE
Image Comics: Jun, 2004 - No. 3, Oct, 2004 ($5.95/$3.95, limited series)
1,3-($5.95) Romita, Jr.-a/Brunswick-s; sketch pages and script pages. 3-Pin-up pages 6.00
2-($3.95) 4.00
...Vol. 1: All Of This Can Be Yours (2005, $14.95) r/series & sketch,script & pin-up pages 15.00

GRAY GHOST, THE
Dell Publishing Co.: No. 911, July, 1958; No. 1000, June-Aug, 1959
Four Color 911 (#1), 1000-Photo-c each 8 16 24 55 105 155

GRAYSON (See Forever Evil) (Leads into Nightwing: Rebirth)
DC Comics: Sept, 2014 - No. 20, Jul, 2016 ($2.99/$3.99)
1-8-Dick Grayson as secret agent; Seeley & King-s/Janin-a. 1,2,6,7-Midnighter app. 3.00
9-20-($3.99): 10-Lex Luthor app. 12-Return to Gotham; Batgirl, Red Robin app. 15-"Robin War" tie-in 4.00
Annual 1 (2/15, $4.99) Mooney-a 5.00
Annual 2 (11/15, $4.99) Superman and Blockbuster app.; Alvaro Martinez-a 5.00
Annual 3 (8/16, $4.99) Harley Quinn, Constantine, Azrael, Simon Baz app. 5.00
...: Futures End 1 (11/14, $2.99, regular-c) Five years later; Mooney-a 3.00
...: Futures End 1 (11/14, $3.99, 3-D cover) 4.00

GREAT ACTION COMICS
I. W. Enterprises: 1958 (Reprints with new covers)
1-Captain Truth reprinted from Gold Medal #1 3 6 9 17 25 34
8,9-Reprints Phantom Lady #15 & 23 8 16 24 82 99 145

GREAT AMERICAN COMICS PRESENTS - THE SECRET VOICE
Peter George 4-Star Publ./American Features Syndicate: 1945 (10¢)
1-Anti-Nazi; "What Really Happened to Hitler" 81 162 243 578 884 1250

GREAT AMERICAN WESTERN, THE
AC Comics: 1987 - No. 4, 1990? ($1.75/$2.95/$3.50, B&W with some color)
1-4: 1-Western-r plus Bill Black-a. 2-Tribute to ME comics; Durango Kid photo-c 3-Tribute to Tom Mix plus Roy Rogers, Durango Kid; Billy the Kid-r by Severin; photo-c. 4- ($3.50, 52 pgs., 16 pgs. color)-Tribute to Lash LaRue; photo-c & interior photos; Fawcett-r 4.00
...Presents 1 (1991, $5.00) New Sunset Carson; film history 5.00

GREAT CAT FAMILY, THE (Disney-TV/Movie)
Dell Publishing Co.: No. 750, Nov, 1956 (one-shot)
Four Color 750-Pinocchio & Alice app. 6 12 18 42 79 115

GREAT COMICS
Great Comics Publications: Nov, 1941 - No. 3, Jan, 1942
1-Origin/1st app. The Great Zarro; Madame Strange & Guy Gorham, Wizard of Science & The Great Zarro begin 161 322 483 1030 1765 2500
2-Buck Johnson, Jungle Explorer app.; X-Mas-c 81 162 243 518 884 1250
3-Futuro Takes Hitler to Hell-c/s; "The Lost City" movie story (starring William Boyd);

Gotham By Midnight #1 © DC

Grayson #12 © DC

The Greatest Adventure #1 © ERB

GD 2.0 | VG 4.0 | FN 6.0 | VF 8.0 | VF/NM 9.0 | NM- 9.2

continues in Choice Comics #3 (scarce) 2600 5200 7800 13,000 17,500 26,000

GREAT COMICS
Novack Publishing Co./Jubilee Comics/Knockout/Barrel O' Fun: 1945

1-(Four publ. variations: Barrel O-Fun, Jubilee, Knockout & Novack)-The Defenders, Capt. Power app.; L. B. Cole-c 42 84 126 311 706 1100
1-(Jubilee)-Same cover; Boogey Man, Satanas, & The Sorcerer & His Apprentice 39 78 117 231 378 525
1-(Barrel O' Fun)-L. B. Cole-c; Barrel O' Fun overprinted in indicia; Li'l Cactus, Cuckoo Sheriff (humorous) 32 64 96 188 307 425

GREAT DOGPATCH MYSTERY (See Mammy Yokum & the...)

GREATEST ADVENTURE, THE (Edgar Rice Burroughs characters)
Dynamite Entertainment: 2017 - No. 9, 2018 ($3.99)

1-9: 1-Tarzan & Jane, Korak, Jason Gridley, John Carter & Dejah Thoris app.; Razek-a 4.00

GREATEST AMERICAN HERO (Based on the 1981-1986 TV series)
Catastrophic Comics: Dec, 2008 - No. 3, May, 2009 ($3.50/$3.95)

1-3-Origin re-told; William Katt and others-s. 3-Obama-c/app. 4.00

GREATEST BATMAN STORIES EVER TOLD, THE
DC Comics

Hardcover ($24.95) 50.00
Softcover ($15.95) "Greatest DC Stories Vol. 2" on spine 20.00
Vol. 2 softcover (1992, $16.95) "Greatest DC Stories Vol. 7" on spine 20.00

GREATEST FLASH STORIES EVER TOLD, THE
DC Comics: 1991

nn-Hardcover ($29.95); Infantino-c 45.00
nn-Softcover ($14.95) 20.00

GREATEST GOLDEN AGE STORIES EVER TOLD, THE
DC Comics: 1990 ($24.95, hardcover)

nn-Ordway-c 60.00

GREATEST HITS
DC Comics (Vertigo): Dec, 2008 - No. 6, Apr, 2009 ($2.99, limited series)

1-6-Intro. The Mates superhero team in 1967 England; Tischman-s/Fabry-a/c 3.00

GREATEST JOKER STORIES EVER TOLD, THE (See Batman)
DC Comics: 1983

Hardcover ($19.95)-Kyle Baker painted-c 50.00
Softcover ($14.95) 20.00
Stacked Deck...Expanded Edition (1992, $29.95)-Longmeadow Press Publ. 35.00

GREATEST 1950s STORIES EVER TOLD, THE
DC Comics: 1990

Hardcover ($29.95)-Kubert-c 55.00
Softcover ($14.95) "Greatest DC Stories Vol. 5" on spine 22.00

GREATEST TEAM-UP STORIES EVER TOLD, THE
DC Comics: 1989

Hardcover ($24.95)-DeVries and Infantino painted-c 55.00
Softcover ($14.95) "Greatest DC Stories Vol. 4" on spine; Adams-c 22.00

GREATEST SUPERMAN STORIES EVER TOLD, THE
DC Comics: 1987

Hardcover ($24.95) 50.00
Softcover ($15.95) 22.00

GREAT EXPLOITS
Decker Publ./Red Top: Oct, 1957

1-Krigstein-a(2) (re-issue on cover); reprints Daring Advs. #6 by Approved Comics 9 18 27 47 61 75

GREAT FOODINI, THE (See Foodini)

GREAT GAZOO, THE (The Flintstones)(TV)
Charlton Comics: Aug, 1973 - No. 20, Jan, 1977 (Hanna-Barbera)

1 4 8 12 28 47 65
2-10 3 6 9 16 23 30
11-20 2 4 6 11 16 20

GREAT GRAPE APE, THE (TV)(See TV Stars #1)
Charlton Comics: Sept, 1976 - No. 2, Nov, 1976 (Hanna-Barbera)

1 5 10 15 30 50 70
2 3 6 9 14 20 25

GREAT GRIMMAX, THE
Defiant: Aug. 1994 (8 pgs.)

GD 2.0 | VG 4.0 | FN 6.0 | VF 8.0 | VF/NM 9.0 | NM- 9.2

0-Hero Illustrated giveaway, Polgardy/Shooter story, J.G. Jones-c, Cockrum-a 4.00

GREAT LAKES AVENGERS (Also see G.L.A.)
Marvel Comics: Dec, 2016 - No. 7, Jun, 2017 ($3.99)

1-7: 1-Team reunites; Squirrel Girl cameo; Gorman-s/Robson-a. 7-Deadpool app. 4.00

GREAT LOCOMOTIVE CHASE, THE (Disney)
Dell Publishing Co.: No. 712, Sept, 1956 (one-shot)

Four Color 712-Movie, photo-c 7 14 21 46 86 125

GREAT LOVER ROMANCES (Young Lover Romances #4,5)
Toby Press: 3/51; #2, 1951(nd); #3, 1952 (nd); #6, Oct?, 1952 - No. 22, May, 1955 (Photo-c #1-5, 10 ,13, 15, 17) (no #4, 5)

1-Jon Juan story-r/Jon Juan #1 by Schomburg; Dr. Anthony King app. 28 56 84 165 270 375
2-Jon Juan, Dr. Anthony King app. 16 32 48 94 147 200
3,7,9-14,16-22: 10-Rita Hayworth photo-c. 17-Rita Hayworth & Aldo Ray photo-c 14 28 42 78 112 145
6-Kurtzman-a (10/52) 15 30 45 88 137 185
8-Five pgs. of "Pin-Up Pete" by Sparling 15 30 45 85 130 175
15-Liz Taylor photo-c (scarce) 57 114 171 362 619 875

GREAT RACE, THE (See Movie Classics)

GREAT SCOTT SHOE STORE (See Bulls-Eye)

GREAT SOCIETY COMIC BOOK, THE (Political parody)
Pocket Books Inc./Parallax Pub.: 1966 ($1.00, 36 pgs., 7"x10", one-shot)

nn-Super-LBJ-c/story; 60s politicians app. as super-heroes; Tallarico-a 3 6 9 18 28 38

GREAT TEN, THE (Characters from Final Crisis)
DC Comics: Jan, 2010 - No. 9, Sept, 2010 ($2.99, limited series)

1-9-Super team of China; Bedard-s/McDaniel-a/Stanley Lau-c 3.00

GREAT WEST (Magazine)
M. F. Enterprises: 1969 (B&W, 52 pgs.)

V1#1 2 4 6 10 14 18

GREAT WESTERN
Magazine Enterprises: No. 8, Jan-Mar, 1954 - No. 11, Oct-Dec, 1954

8(A-1 93)-Trail Colt by Guardineer; Powell Red Hawk-r/Straight Arrow begins, ends #11; Durango Kid story 18 36 54 109 172 235
9(A-1 105), 11(A-1 127)-Ghost Rider, Durango Kid app. in each. 9-Red Mask-c, but no app. 15 30 45 85 130 175
10(A-1 113)-The Calico Kid by Guardineer-r/Tim Holt #8; Straight Arrow, Durango Kid app. 12 24 36 69 97 125
I.W. Reprint #1,2 9: 1,2-r/Straight Arrow #36,42. 9-r/Straight Arrow #? 3 6 9 15 22 28
I.W. Reprint #8-Origin Ghost Rider(r/Tim Holt #11); Tim Holt app.; Bolle-a 3 6 9 16 24 32

NOTE: ***Guardineer** c-8. **Powell** a(r)-8-11 (from Straight Arrow).*

GREEK STREET
DC Comics (Vertigo): Sept, 2009 - No. 16, Dec, 2010 ($1.00/$2.99)

1-16: 1-($1.00) Milligan-s/Gianfelice-a. 2: Begin $2.99-c 3.00
...: Blood Calls For Blood SC (2010, $9.99) r/#1-5; Mike Carey intro.; sketch art 10.00
...: Cassandra Complex SC (2010, $14.99) r/#6-11 15.00

GREEN ARROW (See Action #440, Adventure, Brave & the Bold, DC Super Stars #17, Detective #521, Flash #217, Green Lantern #76, Justice League of America #4, Leading Comics, More Fun #73 (1st app.), Showcase '95 #9 & World's Finest Comics)

GREEN ARROW
DC Comics: May, 1983 - No. 4, Aug, 1983 (limited series)

1-Origin; Speedy cameo; Mike W. Barr scripts, Trevor Von Eeden-c/a 3 6 9 17 26 35
2-4 1 3 4 6 8 10

GREEN ARROW
DC Comics: Feb, 1988 - No. 137, Oct, 1998 ($1.00-$2.50) (Painted-c #1-3)

1-Mike Grell scripts begin, ends #80 2 4 6 9 12 15
2-49,51-74,76-86: 27,28-Warlord app. 35-38-Co-stars Black Canary; Bill Wray-i. 40-Grell-a. 47-Begin $1.50-c. 63-No longer has mature readers on-c. 63-66-Shado app. 81-Aparo-a begins, ends #100; Nuklon app. 82-Intro & death of Rival. 83-Huntress-c/story. 84, 85-Deathstroke app. 86-Catwoman-c/story w/Jim Balent layouts 4.00
50,75-($2.50, 52 pgs.): Anniversary issues. 75-Arsenal (Roy Harper) & Shado app. 5.00
87-96: 87-$1.95-c begins. 88-Guy Gardner, Martian Manhunter, & Wonder Woman-c/app.; Flash-c. 89-Anarky app. 90-(9/94)-Zero Hour tie-in. 91-(11/94). 93-1st app. Camorouge. 95-Hal Jordan cameo. 96-Intro new Force of July; Hal Jordan (Parallax) app; Oliver Queen learns that Connor Hawke is his son 3.00

GD 2.0 | VG 4.0 | FN 6.0 | VF 8.0 | VF/NM 9.0 | NM- 9.2

97-99,102-109: 97-Begin $2.25-c; no Aparo-a. 97-99-Arsenal app. 102,103-Underworld Unleashed x-over. 104-GL (Kyle Rayner)-c/app. 105-Robin-c/app. 107-109-Thorn app. 109-Lois Lane cameo; Weeks-c. 3.00
100-($3.95)-Foil-c; Superman app. 1 3 4 6 8 10
101-Death of Oliver Queen; Superman app. 3 6 9 16 23 30
110,111-124: 110,111-GL x-over. 110-Intro Hatchet. 114-Final Night. 115-117-Black Canary & Oracle app. 3.00
125-($3.50, 48 pgs)-GL x-over cont. in GL #92 4.00
126-136: 126-Begin $2.50-c. 130-GL & Flash x-over. 132,133-JLA app. 134,135-Brotherhood of the Fist pts. 1,5. 136-Hal Jordan-c/app. 3.00
137-Last issue; Superman app.; last panel cameo of Oliver Queen
2 4 6 9 12 15
#0 (10/94) Zero Hour; 1st app. Connor Hawke; Aparo-a(p); released between #90 & #91 3.00
#1,000,000 (11/98) 853rd Century x-over 3.00
Annual 1-6 ('88-'94, 68 pgs.)-1-No Grell scripts. 2-No Grell scripts; recaps origin Green Arrow, Speedy, Black Canary & others. 3-Bill Wray-a. 4-50th anniversary issue. 5-Batman, Eclipso app. 6-Bloodlines; Hook app. 4.00
Annual 7-('95, $3.95)-Year One story 4.00

NOTE: ***Aparo** a-0, 81-85, 86 (partial),87p, 88p, 91-95, 96i, 98-100p, 109p; c-81,98-100p. **Austin** c-96i. **Balent** layouts-86. **Burchett** c-91-95. **Campanella** a-100-108i, 110-113i; c-99i, 101-108i,110-113i. **Denys Cowan** a-39p, 41-43p, 47p, 48p, 60p; c-41-43. **Damaggio** a(p)-97p, 100-108p, 110-112p; c-97-99p, 101-108p, 110-113p. **Mike Grell** c-1-4, 10p, 11, 39, 40, 44, 45, 47-80, Annual 4, 5. **Nasser/Netzer** a-89, 96. **Sienkiewicz** a-109i. **Springer** a-67, 68. **Weeks** c-109.*

GREEN ARROW
DC Comics: Apr, 2001 - No. 75, Aug, 2007 ($2.50/$2.99)

1-Oliver Queen returns; Kevin Smith-s/Hester-a/Wagner-painted-c
2 4 6 10 14 18
1-2nd-4th printings 3.00
2-Batman cameo 1 2 3 4 5 7
2-2nd printing 3.00
3-5: 4-JLA app. 5.00
6-15: 7-Barry Allen & Hal Jordan app. 9,10-Stanley & his Monster app. 10-Oliver regains his soul. 12-Hawkman-c/app. 4.00
16-25: 16-Brad Meltzer-s begin; The Shade app. 18-Solomon Grundy-c/app. 19-JLA app. 22-Beatty-s; Count Vertigo app. 23-25-Green Lantern app.; Raab-s/Adlard-a 3.00
26-49: 26-Winick-s begin. 35-37-Riddler app. 43-Mia learns she's HIV+. 45-Mia becomes the new Speedy. 46-Teen Titans app. 49-The Outsiders app. 3.00
50-($3.50) Green Arrow's team and the Outsiders vs. The Riddler and Drakon 4.00
51-59: 51-Anarky app. 52-Zatanna-c/app. 55-59-Dr. Light app. 3.00
60-74: 60-One Year Later starts. 62-Begin $2.99-c; Deathstroke app. 69-Batman app. 3.00
75-($3.50) Ollie proposes to Dinah (see Black Canary mini-series); JLA app. 4.00
... By Jack Kirby (2001, $5.95) Collects Green Arrow stories by Kirby from the 1950s; introduction by Evanier 6.00
...: City Walls SC (2005, $17.95) r/#32, 34-39 18.00
...: Crawling Through the Wreckage SC (2007, $12.99) r/#60-65 13.00
...: Heading Into the Light SC (2006, $12.99) r/#52,54-59 13.00
...: Moving Targets SC (2006, $17.99) r/#40-50 18.00
...: Quiver HC (2002, $24.95) r/#1-10; Smith intro. 25.00
...: Quiver SC (2003, $17.95) r/#1-10; Smith intro. 18.00
...: Road to Jericho SC (2007, $17.99) r/#66-75 18.00
...Secret Files & Origins 1-(12/02, $4.95) Origin stories & profiles; Wagner-c 5.00
...: Sounds of Violence HC (2003, $19.95) r/#11-15; Hester intro. & sketch pages 20.00
...: Sounds of Violence SC (2003, $12.95) r/#11-15; Hester intro. & sketch pages 13.00
...: Straight Shooter SC (2004, $12.95) r/#26-31 13.00
...: The Archer's Quest HC (2003, $19.95) r/#16-21; pitch, script and sketch pages 20.00
...: The Archer's Quest SC (2004, $14.95) r/#16-21; pitch, script and sketch pages 15.00

GREEN ARROW (Brightest Day)
DC Comics: Aug, 2010 - No. 15, Oct, 2011 ($3.99/$2.99)

1-Oliver Queen in the Star City forest; Green Lantern app.; Neves-a/Cascioli-c 5.00
1-Variant-c by Van Sciver 8.00
2-15-($2.99) 2-Green Lantern app. 7-Mayhew-a. 8-11-The Demon app. 12-Swamp Thing 3.00
...: Into the Woods HC (2011, $22.99) r/#1-7; variant cover gallery 23.00

GREEN ARROW (DC New 52)
DC Comics: Nov, 2011 - No. 52, Jul, 2016 ($2.99)

1-Krul-s/Jurgens & Pérez-a/Wilkins-c 1 3 4 6 8 10
2-24: 4,5-Giffen-s. 13,14-Hawkman app. 17-24-Lemire-s/Sorrentino-a/c. 22-Count Vertigo app. 23,24-Richard Dragon app. 3.00
23.1 (11/13, $2.99, regular cover) "Count Vertigo #1" on cover; Sorrentino-a/c 3.00
23.1 (11/13, $3.99, 3-D cover) "Count Vertigo #1" on cover; Sorrentino-a/c 5.00
25-($3.99) Zero Year tie-in; Batman app.; back-up with Cowan-a 4.00
26-49: 26-31-Outsiders War; Lemire-s/Sorrentino-a/c. 35-40-Hitch-c; Felicity Smoak app. 3.00
50-($4.99) Kudranski-a; Deathstroke app. 5.00
51,52-Deathstroke app. 3.00
#0 (11/12) Origin story re-told; Nocenti-s/Williams II-a 3.00
Annual 1 (11/15, $4.99) Percy-s/Kudranski-a/Edwards-c 5.00
...: Futures End 1 (11/14, $2.99, regular-c) Five years later; Lemire-s/Sorrentino-a 3.00
...: Futures End 1 (11/14, $3.99, 3-D cover) 4.00

GREEN ARROW (DC Rebirth)
DC Comics: Aug, 2016 - No. 50, May, 2019 ($2.99/$3.99)

1-24: 1,2-Percy-s/Schmidt-a; Black Canary & Shado app. 3-5-Ferreyra-a. 14-Malcolm Merlyn returns. 21-24-Cheshire app. 3.00
25-($3.99) Schmidt-a; Kate Spencer app.; Moira Queen returns 4.00
26-33: 26,27-Flash app. 27-Wonder Woman app. 28-Superman app. 29-Batman app. 30,31-Green Lantern app. 32-Dark Nights: Metal tie-in 3.00
34-49-($3.99) 41,42-The Parasite app. 45-Roy Harper's funeral 4.00
50-($4.99) Nowlan-c 5.00
Annual 1 (1/18, $4.99) Count Vertigo app.; Percy-s/Carlini-a 5.00
Annual 2 (7/18, $4.99) Justice League: No Justice tie-in; Carnero-a 5.00
...: Rebirth 1 (8/16, $2.99) Percy-a/Schmidt-a; Black Canary app. 3.00

GREEN ARROW/BLACK CANARY (Titled Green Arrow for #30-32)
DC Comics: Dec, 2007 - No. 32, Jun, 2010 ($3.50/$2.99)

1-($3.50) Connor Hawke & Black Canary; follows Wedding Special; Winick-s/Chang-a 6.00
2-21-($2.99) 3-Two covers; Connor shot. 5-Dinah & Ollie's real wedding 3.00
22-30-($3.99) Back-up stories begin. 28-Origin of Cupid. 30-Blackest Night 4.00
30-Variant cover by Mike Grell 8.00
31-32-($2.99) Rise and Fall; Dallocchio-a 3.00
...: A League of Their Own TPB (2009, $17.99) r/#11-14 & G.A. Secret Files & Origins 18.00
...: Big Game TPB (2010, $19.99) r/#21-26 20.00
...: Enemies List TPB (2009, $17.99) r/#15-20 18.00
...: Family Business TPB (2008, $17.99) r/#5-10 18.00
...: Five Stages TPB (2010, $17.99) r/#27-30 18.00
...: Road To The Altar TPB (2008, $17.99) r/proposal pages from Green Arrow #75, Birds of Prey #109, Black Canary #1-4 and Black Canary Wedding Planner #1 18.00
...: The Wedding Album HC (2008, $19.99, dustjacket) r/#1-5 & Wedding Special #1 20.00
...: The Wedding Album SC (2009, $17.99) r/#1-5 & Wedding Special #1 18.00
... Wedding Special 1 (11/07, $3.99) Winick-s/Conner-a/c; Dinah & Ollie's "wedding" 10.00
... Wedding Special 1 (11/07, $3.99) 2nd printing with Ryan Sook variant-c 4.00

GREEN ARROW 80TH ANNIVERSARY 100-PAGE SUPER SPECTACULAR
DC Comics: Aug, 2021 ($9.99, squarebound, one-shot)

1-Short stories & pin-ups by various; Denny O'Neil tribute; multiple covers 10.00

GREEN ARROW: THE LONG BOW HUNTERS
DC Comics: Aug, 1987 - No. 3, Oct, 1987 ($2.95, limited series, mature)

1-Grell-c/a in all 2 4 6 8 10 12
1,2-2nd printings 4.00
2,3 6.00
Trade paperback (1989, $12.95)-r/#1-3 15.00

GREEN ARROW: THE WONDER YEAR
DC Comics: Feb, 1993 - No. 4, May, 1993 ($1.75, limited series)

1-4: Mike Grell-a(p)/scripts & Gray Morrow-a(i) 4.00

GREEN ARROW: YEAR ONE
DC Comics: Early Sept, 2007 - No. 6, Late Nov, 2007 ($2.99, bi-weekly limited series)

1-6-Origin re-told; Diggle-s/Jock-a 3.00
1-Special Edition (12/14, $1.00) Reprints #1; Arrow TV show banner atop cover 3.00
HC (2008, $24.99) r/#1-6; intro. by Brian K. Vaughan; script and sketch pages 25.00
SC (2009, $14.99) r/#1-6; intro. by Brian K. Vaughan; script and sketch pages 15.00

GREEN BERET, THE (See Tales of...)

GREEN DANTE / GREEN VIRGIL
Aardvark-Vanaheim: Apr, 2020 ($4.00, B&W)

1-Cerebus figures with original Gustave Doré artwork; Green Lantern #76-c swipe 4.00

GREEN GIANT COMICS (Also see Colossus Comics)
Pelican Publ. (Funnies, Inc.): 1940 (No price on cover; distributed in New York City only)

1-Dr. Nerod, Green Giant, Black Arrow, Mundoo & Master Mystic app.; origin Colossus (Rare)
1625 3250 4875 11,800 23,400 35,000

NOTE: *The idea for this book came from George Kapitan. Printed by Moreau Publ. of Orange, N.J. as an experiment to see if they could profitably use the idle time of their 40-page Hoe color press. The experiment failed due to the difficulty of obtaining good quality color registration and Mr. Moreau believes the book never reached the stands. The book has no price or date which lends credence to this. Contains five pages reprinted from Motion Picture Funnies Weekly.*

GREEN GOBLIN
Marvel Comics: Oct, 1995 - No. 13, Oct, 1996 ($2.95/$1.95)

1-($2.95)-Scott McDaniel-c/a begins, ends #7; foil-c 5.00
2-13: 2-Begin $1.95-c. 4-Hobgoblin-c/app; Thing app. 6-Daredevil-c/app. 8-Robertson-a; McDaniel-c. 12,13-Onslaught x-over. 13-Green Goblin quits; Spider-Man app. 3.00

GREENHAVEN
Aircel Publishing: 1988 - No. 3, 1988 ($2.00, limited series, 28 pgs.)

1-3 3.00

GREEN HORNET, THE (TV)
Dell Publishing Co./Gold Key: Sept, 1953; Feb, 1967 - No. 3, Aug, 1967

Four Color 496-Painted-c. 28 56 84 202 451 700
1-Bruce Lee photo-c and back-c pin-up 25 50 75 175 388 600
2,3-Bruce Lee photo-c 13 26 39 89 195 300

GREEN HORNET, THE (Also see Kato of the... & Tales of the...)
Now Comics: Nov, 1989 - No. 14, Feb, 1991 ($1.75)
V2#1, Sept, 1991 - V2#40, Jan, 1995 ($1.95)

1 ($2.95, double-size)-Steranko painted-c; G.A. Green Hornet 6.00
1,2: 1-2nd printing ('90, $3.95)-New Butler-c 4.00
3-14: 5-Death of original ('30s) Green Hornet. 6-Dave Dorman painted-c. 11-Snyder-c 4.00
V2#1-11,13-21,24-26,28-30,32-37: 1-Butler painted-c. 9-Mayerik-c 4.00
12-($2.50)-Color Green Hornet button polybagged inside 4.00
22,23-($2.95)-Bagged w/color hologravure card 5.00
27-($2.95)-Newsstand ed. polybagged w/multi-dimensional card (1993 Anniversary Special on cover), 27-($2.95)-Direct Sale ed. polybagged w/multi-dimensional card; cover variations 4.00
31,38: 31-($2.50)-Polybagged w/trading card 4.00
39,40-Low print run 6.00
1-($2.50)-Polybagged w/button (same as #12) 5.00
2,3-($1.95)-Same as #13 & 14 4.00
Annual 1 (12/92, $2.50), Annual 1994 (10/94, $2.95) 5.00

GREEN HORNET (Becomes Green Hornet: Legacy with #34)
Dynamite Entertainment: 2010 - No. 33, 2013 ($3.99)

1-Kevin Smith-s/Jonathan Lau-a; multiple covers by Alex Ross, Cassaday, Campbell and Segovia 4.00
2-33-Multiple covers by Ross and others on each. 11-Hester-s begins 4.00
Annual 1 (2010, $5.99) Hester-s/Netzer & Rafael-a 6.00
Annual 2 (2012, $4.99) Hester-c/Rahner-s/Cliquet-a; back-up r/G.H. Comics #1 (1940) 5.00
... FCBD Edition; 5 previews of various new Green Hornet series; Cassaday-c 3.00

GREEN HORNET
Dynamite Entertainment: 2013 - No. 13, 2014 ($3.99)

1-13: 1-Set in 1941; Mark Waid-s/Daniel Indro-a; 2 covers by Alex Ross & Paolo Rivera 4.00
... One Night in Bangkok (2023, $4.99) Denton-s/Morales-a 5.00

GREEN HORNET: AFTERMATH
Dynamite Entertainment: 2011 - No. 4, 2011 ($1.99/$3.99, limited series)

1-Nitz-s/Raynor-a; Green Hornet & Kato after the 2011 movie 3.00

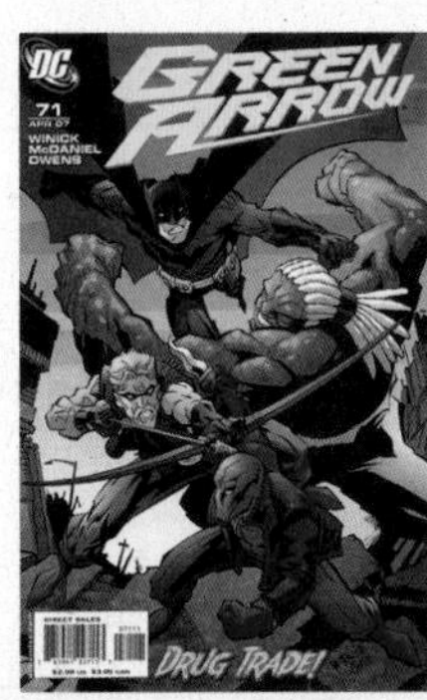

Green Arrow (2007) #71 © DC

Green Lama #3 © Spark

Green Lantern #21 © DC

GD VG FN VF VF/NM NM-
2.0 4.0 6.0 8.0 9.0 9.2

2-4-($3.99) 4.00

GREEN HORNET: BLOOD TIES
Dynamite Entertainment: 2010 - No. 4, 2011 ($3.99)
1-4-Ande Parks-s/Johnny Desjardins-a; original Green Hornet & Kato 4.00

GREEN HORNET COMICS (...Racket Buster #44) (Radio, movies)
Helnit Publ. Co.(Holyoke) No. 1-6/Family Comics(Harvey) No. 7-on:
Dec, 1940 - No. 47, Sept, 1949 (See All New #13,14)(Early issues: 68 pgs.)

1-1st app. Green Hornet & Kato; text origin of Green Hornet on inside front-c; intro the Black Beauty (Green Hornet's car); painted-c 950 1900 2850 6900 13,350 19,800
2-(3/41) Early issues based on radio adventures 284 568 852 1818 3109 4400
3 181 362 543 1158 1979 2800
4-6: 6-(8/41) 161 322 483 1030 1765 2500
7 (6/42)-1st app. of the Green Hornet villain The Murdering Clown; origin The Zebra & begins; Robin Hood, Spirit of '76, Blonde Bomber & Mighty Midgets begin; new logo 181 362 543 1158 1979 2800
8-Classic horror bondage killer dwarf-c 245 490 735 1568 2684 3800
9-Kirby-c 181 362 543 1158 1979 2800
10-(12/42) Hornet vs. The Murdering Clown-c/sty 142 284 426 909 1555 2200
11-Mr. Q app. 129 258 387 826 1413 2000
12-1st WWII cover for this title; Mr. Q app. 129 258 387 826 1413 2000
13-1st Nazi-c; shows Hitler poster on-c 290 580 870 1856 3178 4500
14-Bondage-c; Mr. Q app. 113 226 339 723 1237 1750
15-Nazi WWII-c 142 284 426 909 1555 2200
16-Nazi WWII prisoner of war cable car cover 142 284 426 909 1555 2200
17-Nazi WWII-c 135 270 405 864 1482 2100
18,19-Japanese WWII-c 135 270 405 864 1482 2100
20-Classic Japanese WWII-c 148 296 444 947 1624 2300
21-23-Japanese WWII-c 103 206 309 659 1130 1600
24-Classic Japanese poison rockets Sci-Fi-c 148 296 444 947 1624 2300
25,27,28,30 54 108 162 343 574 825
26-(9/45) Japanese WWII-c 61 122 183 390 670 950
29-Jerry Robinson skull-c 58 116 174 371 636 900
31-The Man in Black Called Fate begins (11-12/45, early app.) 57 114 171 362 619 875
32-36 37 74 111 222 361 500
37,38: Shock Gibson app. by Powell. 37-S&K Kid Adonis reprinted from Stuntman #3. 38-Kid Adonis app. 37 74 111 222 361 500
39-Stuntman story by S&K 41 82 123 256 428 600
40-47: 42-47-Kerry Drake in all. 45-Boy Explorers on-c only. 46- "Case of the Marijuana Racket" cover/story; Kerry Drake app. 29 58 87 172 281 390

NOTE: ***Fuje** a-23, 24, 26. **Henkle** c-7-9. **Kubert** a-20, 30. **Powell** a-7-10, 12, 14, 16-21, 30, 31(2), 32(3), 33, 34(3), 35, 36, 37(2), 38. **Robinson** a-27. **Schomburg** c-17-23. Kirbyish c-7, 15. Bondage c-8, 11, 14, 18, 26, 36.*

GREEN HORNET: DARK TOMORROW
Now Comics: Jun, 1993 - No. 3, Aug, 1993 ($2.50, limited series)
1-3: Future Green Hornet 4.00

GREEN HORNET: GOLDEN AGE RE-MASTERED
Dynamite Entertainment: 2010 - No. 8, 2011 ($3.99)
1-8-Re-colored reprints of 1940's Green Hornet Comics; new Rubenstein-c 4.00

GREEN HORNET: LEGACY (Numbering continues from Green Hornet 2010-2013 series)
Dynamite Entertainment: No. 34, 2013 - No. 42, 2013 ($3.99)
34-42: 34-Jai Nitz-s/Jethro Morales-a 4.00

GREEN HORNET: PARALLEL LIVES
Dynamite Entertainment: 2010 - No. 5, 2010 ($3.99, limited series)
1-5-Jai Nitz-s/Nigel Raynor-a; semi-prequel to the 2011 movie; Kato's origin 4.00

GREEN HORNET: REIGN OF THE DEMON
Dynamite Entertainment: 2016 - No. 4, 2017 ($3.99, limited series)
1-4-David Liss-s/Kewber Baal-a 4.00

GREEN HORNET '66 MEETS THE SPIRIT: VOLUME 1
Dynamite Entertainment: 2017 - No. 5, 2017 ($3.99, limited series)
1-5-Fred VanLente-s/Bob Q-a; The Octopus app. 4.00

GREEN HORNET: SOLITARY SENTINEL, THE
Now Comics: Dec, 1992 - No. 3, 1993 ($2.50, limited series)
1-3 4.00

GREEN HORNET STRIKES!
Dynamite Entertainment: 2010 - No. 10, 2012 ($3.99, limited series)
1-10: 1-Matthews-s/Padilla-a/Cassaday-c; future Green Hornet 4.00

GREEN HORNET, VOLUME 2
Dynamite Entertainment: 2018 - No. 5, 2018 ($3.99)
1-5-Amy Chu-s/German Erramouspe-a; new female Green Hornet 4.00

GREEN HORNET, VOLUME 3
Dynamite Entertainment: 2020 - No. 5, 2020 ($3.99, B&W & green tint)
1-5-Lobdell-s/Marques & Bone-a; regular Green Hornet & Kato 4.00

GREEN HORNET: YEAR ONE
Dynamite Entertainment: 2010 - No. 12, 2011 ($3.99, limited series)
1-12-Matt Wagner-s/Aaron Campbell-a; 1940s' Green Hornet & Kato. 1-5-Cassaday-c 4.00
...: Special 1 (2013, $4.99) Crosby-s/Menna-a/Chen-c 5.00

GREEN JET COMICS, THE (See Comic Books, Series 1 in the Promotional Comics section)

GREEN LAMA (Also see Comic Books, Series 1, Daring Adventures #17 & Prize Comics #7)
Spark Publications/Prize No. 7 on: Dec, 1944 - No. 8, Mar, 1946

1-Intro. Lt. Hercules & The Boy Champions; Mac Raboy-c/a #1-8 145 290 435 928 1589 2250
2-Lt. Hercules borrows the Human Torch's powers for one panel 90 180 270 576 988 1400
3-5,8: 4-Dick Tracy take-off in Lt. Hercules story by H. L. Gold (science fiction writer); Japanese WWII-c; Emperor Hirohito app. 5-Nazi WWII-c; Hitler story; Lt. Hercules story; Little Orphan Annie, Smilin' Jack & Snuffy Smith take-off (5/45) 58 116 174 371 636 900
6-Classic Raboy swastika-c 103 206 309 659 1130 1600
7-Christmas-c; Raboy craft tint-c/a (note: a small quantity of NM copies surfaced) 34 68 102 199 325 450
... Archives Featuring the Art of Mac Raboy Vol. 1 HC (Dark Horse Books, 4/08, $49.95) r/#1-4 including back-up features; foreward by Chuck Rozanski 50.00
... Archives Featuring the Art of Mac Raboy Vol. 2 HC (Dark Horse Books, 1/09, $49.95) r/#5-8; foreward by Chuck Rozanski 50.00

NOTE: ***Robinson** a-3-5, 8. Roussos a-8. Formerly a pulp hero who began in 1940.*

GREEN LANTERN (1st Series) (See All-American, All Flash Quarterly, All Star Comics, The Big All-American & Comic Cavalcade)
National Periodical Publications/All-American: Fall, 1941 - No. 38, May-June, 1949 (#1-18 are quarterly)

1-Origin retold; classic Purcell-c 3550 7100 10,650 28,400 51,900 95,000
2-1st book-length story 757 1514 2271 5526 9763 14,000
3-Classic German war-c by Mart Nodell 784 1568 2352 5723 10,112 14,500
4-Green Lantern & Doiby Dickles join the Army 411 822 1233 2877 5039 7200
5-WWII-c 354 708 1062 2478 4339 6200
6,8: 8-Hop Harrigan begins; classic-c 300 600 900 1980 3440 4900
7-Classic robot-c 314 628 942 2198 3849 5500
9-School for Vandals-s 252 504 756 1613 2757 3900
10-Origin/1st app. Vandal Savage 326 652 978 2282 3991 5700
11,13-15 194 388 582 1242 2121 3000
12-Origin/1st app. Gambler 200 400 600 1280 2190 3100
16-Classic jungle-c (scarce in high grade) 200 400 600 1280 2190 3100
17,19,20 145 290 435 921 1586 2250
18-Christmas-c 190 380 570 1207 2079 2950
21-26 142 284 426 909 1555 2200
27-Origin/1st app. Sky Pirate 181 362 543 1158 1979 2800
28-1st Sportsmaster (Crusher Crock) 161 322 483 1030 1765 2500
29-All Harlequin issue; classic Harlequin-c 252 504 756 1613 2757 3900
30-Origin/1st app. Streak the Wonder Dog by Toth (2-3/48) (Rare) 486 972 1458 3550 6275 9000
31-Harlequin-c/app. 181 362 543 1158 1979 2800
32-35: 35-Kubert-c. 35-38-New logo 129 258 387 826 1413 2000
36-38: 37-Sargon the Sorcerer app. 158 316 474 1011 1731 2450

NOTE: *Book-length stories #2-7. **Mayer/Moldoff** c-9. **Mayer/Purcell** c-8. **Purcell** c-1. **Mart Nodell** c-2, 3, 7. **Paul Reinman** c-11, 12, 15-22. **Toth** a-28, 30, 31, 34-38; c-28, 30, 34p, 36-38p. Cover to #8 says Fall while the indicia says Summer Issue. Streak the Wonder Dog c-30 (w/Green Lantern), 34, 36, 38.*

GREEN LANTERN (See Action Comics Weekly, Adventure Comics, Brave & the Bold, Day of Judgment, DC Special, DC Special Series, Flash, Guy Gardner, Guy Gardner Reborn, JLA, JSA, Justice League of America, Parallax: Emerald Night, Showcase, Showcase '93 #12 & Tales of The...Corps)

GREEN LANTERN (2nd Series)(Green Lantern Corps #206 on) (See Showcase #22-24)
National Periodical Publ./DC Comics: Jul/Aug. 1960 - No. 89, Apr/May 1972; No. 90, Aug/Sept. 1976 - No. 205, Oct, 1986

1-(7-8/60)-Origin retold; Gil Kane-c/a continues; 1st app. Guardians of the Universe 490 980 1470 4550 11,775 19,000
2-1st Pieface 100 200 300 800 1800 2800
3-Contains readers poll 59 118 177 472 1061 1650
4,5: 5-Origin/1st app. Hector Hammond 46 92 138 359 805 1250
6-Intro Tomar-Re the alien G.L. 44 88 132 326 738 1150
7-Origin/1st app. Sinestro (7-8/61) 132 264 396 1056 2378 3700

	GD 2.0	VG 4.0	FN 6.0	VF 8.0	VF/NM 9.0	NM- 9.2
8-1st 5700 A.D. story; grey tone-c	46	92	138	340	770	1200
9-1st Sinestro-c; 1st Jordan Brothers; last 10¢-c	50	100	150	400	900	1400
10	38	76	114	285	641	1000
11,12	23	46	69	161	356	550
13-Flash x-over	38	76	111	274	612	975
14,15,17-20: 14-Origin/1st app. Sonar. 20-Flash app.	19	38	57	131	291	450
16-Origin & 1st app. (Silver Age) Star Sapphire	50	100	150	400	900	1400
21,22,25-28,30: 21-Origin & 1st app. Dr. Polaris	13	26	39	89	195	300
23-1st Tattooed Man	15	30	45	105	233	360
24-Origin & 1st app. Shark	27	54	81	194	435	675
29-JLA cameo; 1st Blackhand	21	42	63	147	324	500
31-39: 37-1st app. Evil Star (villain)	11	22	33	76	163	250
40-Origin of Infinite Earths (10/65); 2nd solo G.A. Green Lantern in Silver Age (see Showcase #55); origin The Guardians; Doiby Dickles app.	48	96	138	368	834	1300
41-44,46-50: 42-Zatanna x-over. 43-Flash x-over	10	20	30	64	132	200
45-2nd S.A. app. G.A. Green Lantern in title (6/66)	14	28	42	94	207	320
51,53-58	8	16	24	54	102	150
52-G.A. Green Lantern x-over; Sinestro app.	11	22	33	76	163	250
59-1st app. Guy Gardner (3/68)	46	92	138	359	805	1250
60,62-69: 69-Wood inks; last 12¢ issue	6	12	18	41	76	110
61-G.A. Green Lantern x-over	7	14	21	49	92	135
70-75	5	10	15	35	63	90
76-(4/70)-Begin Green Lantern/Green Arrow series (by Neal Adams #76-89) ends #122 (see Flash #217 for 2nd series)	96	192	288	768	1734	2700
77-Neal Adams-c/a	12	24	36	82	179	275
78-80-Neal Adams-c/a	10	20	30	67	141	215
81-84: 82-Wrightson-i(1 pg.). 83-G.L. reveals i.d. to Carol Ferris. 84-N. Adams/Wrightson-a (22 pgs.); last 15¢-c; partial photo-c	9	18	27	59	117	175
85,86-(52 pgs.) Classic anti-drug covers/stories; Speedy as a heroin junkie. 86-G.A. Green Lantern-r; Toth-a	11	22	33	76	163	250
87-(52 pgs.) 1st app. John Stewart (12-1/71-72) (becomes 3rd Green Lantern in #182); 2nd app. Guy Gardner (cameo)	54	108	162	432	966	1500
88-(2-3/72, 52 pgs.)-Unpubbed G.A. Green Lantern story; Green Lantern-r/Showcase #23. N. Adams-c/a (1 pg.)	9	18	27	59	117	175
89-(4-5/72, 52 pgs.)-G.A. Green Lantern-r; Green Lantern & Green Arrow move to Flash #217 (2nd team-up series)	8	16	24	56	108	160
90 (8-9/76)-Begin 3rd Green Lantern/Green Arrow team-up series; Mike Grell-c/a begins, ends #111	3	6	9	19	30	40
91-99	2	4	6	10	16	20
100-(1/78, Giant)-1st app. Air Wave II	3	6	9	19	30	40
101-107,111,113-115,117-119: 107-1st Tales of the G.L. Corps story	2	4	6	8	11	14
108-110-(44 pgs)-G.A. Green Lantern back-ups in each. 111-Origin retold; G.A. Green Lantern app.	2	4	6	10	14	18
112-G.A. Green Lantern origin retold	3	6	9	16	23	30
116-1st app. Guy Gardner as a G.L. (5/79)	4	8	12	28	47	65
116-Whitman variant; issue # on cover	5	10	15	33	57	80
117-119,121-(Whitman variants; low print run; none have issue # on cover)	2	4	6	10	14	18
120,121,123-140,142-150: 123-Last Green Lantern/Green Arrow team-up. 130-132-Tales of the G.L. Corps. 132-Adam Strange series begins, ends147. 136,137-1st app. Citadel; Space Ranger app. 142,143-Omega Men app.;Perez-c. 144-Omega Men cameo. 148-Tales of the G.L. Corps begins, ends #173. 150-Anniversary issue, 52 pgs.; no G.L. Corps	1	2	3	5	7	9
122-2nd app. Guy Gardner as Green Lantern; Flash & Hawkman brief app.	3	6	9	15	22	28
141-1st app. Omega Men (6/81)	4	8	12	27	44	60
151-180,183,184,186,187: 159-Origin Evil Star. 160,161-Omega Men app. 172-Gibbons-c/a begins. 175-No issue number shown on cover						6.00
181,182,185,188,191: 181-Hal Jordan resigns as G.L. 182-John Stewart becomes new G.L.; origin recap of Hal Jordan as G.L. 185-Origin new G.L. (John Stewart).188-I.D. revealed; 1st app. Mogo; Alan Moore back-up scripts. 191-Re-intro Star Sapphire (cameo)	1	2	3	5	6	8
189,190,193,196-199,202-205: 194,198-Crisis x-over. 199-Hal Jordan returns as a member of G.L. Corps (3 G.L.s now).						5.00
192-Re-intro & origin of Star Sapphire (1st full app.)	2	4	6	9	13	16
194-Hal Jordan/Guy Gardner battle; Guardians choose Guy Gardner to become new Green Lantern	1	2	3	5	6	8
195-Guy Gardner becomes Green Lantern; Crisis on Infinite Earths x-over	2	4	6	10	13	18
200-Double-size	1	2	3	5	6	8
201-Green Lantern Corps begins (is cover title, says premiere issue); intro. Kilowog	3	6	9	20	31	42
Annual 1 (Listed as Tales Of The Green Lantern Corps Annual 1)						
Annual 2,3 (See Green Lantern Corps Annual #2,3)						5.00
... No. 1 (Facsimile Edition)(2020, $3.99) r/#1 with original 1960 ads and letter column						4.00
... No. 85 (Facsimile Edition)(2019, $3.99) r/#85 with original ads and letter column						4.00
Special 1 (1988), 2 (1989)-(Both $1.50, 52 pgs.)						5.00
... Chronicles TPB (2009, $14.99) r/Showcase #22-24 & Green Lantern #1-3						15.00
... Chronicles Vol. 2 TPB (2009, $14.99) r/Green Lantern #4-9						15.00
... Chronicles Vol. 3 TPB (2010, $14.99) r/Green Lantern #10-14 and Flash #131						15.00

NOTE: ***N. Adams** a-76, 77-87p, 89; c-63, 76-89. **M. Anderson** a-137i. **Austin** a-93i, 94i, 171i. **Chaykin** c-196. **Greene** a-39-49i, 58-63i; c-54-58i. **Grell** a-90-100, 106, 108-111; c-90-106, 108-112. **Heck** a-120-122p. **Infantino** a-137p, 145-147p, 151, 152p. **Gil Kane** a-1-49p, 50-57, 58-61p, 68-75p, 85p(r), 87p(r), 88p(r), 156, 177, 184p; c-1-52, 54-61p, 67-75, 123, 154, 156, 165-171, 177, 184. **Newton** a-148p, 149p, 181. **Perez** c-132p, 141-144. **Sekowsky** a-65p, 170p. **Simonson** c-200. **Sparling** a-63p. **Starlin** c-129, 133. **Staton** a-117p, 123-127p, 128, 129-131p, 132-139, 140p, 141-146, 147p, 148-150, 151-155p; c-107p, 117p, 135(i), 136p, 145p, 146, 147, 148-152p, 155p. **Toth** a-86r, 171p. **Tuska** a-166-168p, 170p.*

GREEN LANTERN (3rd Series)
DC Comics: June, 1990 - No. 181, Nov, 2004 ($1.00/$1.25/$1.50/$1.75/$1.95/$1.99/$2.25)

	GD 2.0	VG 4.0	FN 6.0	VF 8.0	VF/NM 9.0	NM- 9.2
1-Hal Jordan, John Stewart & Guy Gardner return; Batman & JLA app.	1	3	4	6	8	10
2-18,20-26: 9-12-Guy Gardner solo story. 13-(52 pgs.). 18-Guy Gardner solo story. 25-($1.75, 52 pgs.)-Hal Jordan/Guy Gardner battle						5.00
19-($1.75, 52 pgs.)-50th anniversary issue; Mart Nodell (original G.A. artist) part-p on G.A. Green Lantern; G. Kane-c						6.00
27-45,47: 30,31-Gorilla Grodd-c/story(see Flash #69). 38,39-Adam Strange-c/story. 42-Deathstroke-c/s. 47-Green Arrow x-over						4.00
46,48,49,50: 46-Superman app. cont'd in Superman #82. 48-Emerald Twilight part 1. 50-($2.95, 52 pgs.)-Glow-in-the-dark-c						6.00
51-62: 51-1st app. New Green Lantern (Kyle Rayner) with new costume. 53-Superman-c/story. 55-(9/94)-Zero Hour; leads into issue #0. 56-(11/94)						4.00
63,64-Kyle Rayner vs. Hal Jordan.						4.00
65-80,82-92: 63-Begin $1.75-c. 65-New Titans app. 66,67-Flash app. 71-Batman & Robin app. 72-Shazam!-c/app. 73-Wonder Woman-c/app. 73-75-Adam Strange app. 76,77-Green Arrow x-over. 80-Final Night. 87-JLA app. 91-Genesis x-over. 92-Green Arrow x-over						4.00
81-(Regular Ed.)-Memorial for Hal Jordan (Parallax); most DC heroes app.						5.00
81-($3.95, Deluxe Edition)-Embossed prism-c						6.00
93-99: 93-Begin $1.95-c; Deadman app. 94-Superboy app. 95-Starlin-a(p). 98,99-Legion of Super-Heroes-c/app.						4.00
100-($2.95) Two covers (Jordan & Rayner); vs. Sinestro						6.00
101-106: 101-106-Hal Jordan-c/app. 103-JLA-c/app. 104-Green Arrow app. 105,106-Parallax app.						4.00
107-126: 107-Jade becomes a Green Lantern. 119-Hal Jordan/Spectre app. 125-JLA app.						3.00
127-149: 127-Begin $2.25-c. 129-Winick-s begin. 134-136-JLA-c/app. 143-Joker: Last Laugh; Lee-c. 145-Kyle becomes The Ion. 149-Superman-c/app.						3.00
150-($3.50) Jim Lee-c; Kyle becomes Green Lantern again; new costume						4.00
151-181: 151-155-Jim Lee-c. 154-Terry attacked. 155-Spectre-c/app. 162-164-Crossover with Green Arrow #23-25. 165-Raab-s begin. 169-Kilowog returns						3.00
#0 (10/94) Zero Hour; published between #55 & #56						3.00
#1,000,000 (11/98) 853rd Century x-over; Hitch & Neary-a/c						3.00
Annual 1-3: ('92-'94, 68 pgs.)-1-Eclipso app. 2 -Intro Nightblade. 3-Elseworlds story						5.00
Annual 4 (1995, $3.50)-Year One story						5.00
Annual 5,7,8 ('96, '98, '99, $2.95): 5-Legends of the Dead Earth. 7-Ghosts; Wrightson-c. 8-JLApe; Art Adams-c						5.00
Annual 6 (1997, $3.95)-Pulp Heroes story						5.00
Annual 9 (2000, $3.50) Planet DC						4.00
...80 Page Giant (12/98, $4.95) Stories by various						5.00
...80 Page Giant 2 (6/99, $4.95) Team-ups						5.00
...80 Page Giant 3 (8/00, $5.95) Darkseid vs. the GL Corps						6.00
...: 1001 Emerald Nights (2001, $6.95) Elseworlds; Guay-a/c; LaBan-s						7.00
...3-D #1 (12/98, $3.95) Jeanty-a						4.00
...: A New Dawn TPB (1998, $9.95)-r/#50-55						10.00
...: Baptism of Fire TPB (1999, $12.95)-r/#59,66,67,70-75						13.00
...: Brother's Keeper (2003, $12.95)-r/#151-155; Green Lantern Secret Files #3						13.00
...: Emerald Allies TPB (2000, $14.95)-r/GL/GA team-ups						15.00
...: Emerald Knights TPB (1998, $12.95)-r/Hal Jordan's return						13.00
...: Emerald Twilight nn (1994, $5.95)-r/#48-50						6.00
...: Emerald Twilight/New Dawn TPB (2003, $19.95)-r/#48-55						20.00
...: Ganthet's Tale nn (1992, $5.95, 68 pgs.)-Silver foil logo; Niven scripts; Byrne-c/a						6.00
.../Green Arrow Vol. 1 (2004, $12.95) -r/GL #76-82; intro. by O'Neil						13.00
.../Green Arrow Vol. 2 (2004, $12.95) -r/GL #83-87,89 & Flash #217-219, 226; cover gallery with 1983-84 GL/GA covers #1-7; intro. by Giordano						13.00
.../Green Arrow Collection, Vol. 2-r/GL #84-87,89 & Flash #217-219 & GL/GA #5-7 by O'Neil/Adams/Wrightson						13.00
...: New Journey, Old Path TPB (2001, $12.95)-r/#129-136						13.00
... : Our Worlds at War (8/01, $2.95) Jae Lee-c; prelude to x-over						3.00
...: Passing The Torch (2004, $12.95, TPB) r/#156,158-161 & GL Secret Files #2						13.00
...Plus 1 (12/1996, $2.95)-The Ray & Polaris-c/app.						4.00
...Secret Files 1-3 (7/98-7/02, $4.95)1-Origin stories & profiles. 2-Grell-c						5.00
.../Superman: Legend of the Green Flame (2000, $5.95) 1988 unpub. Neil Gaiman story of Hal Jordan with new art by various; Frank Miller-c						6.00
...: The Power of Ion (2003, $14.95, TPB) r/#142-150						15.00
...The Road Back nn (1992, $8.95)-r/1-8 w/covers						9.00
...: Traitor TPB (2001, $12.95) r/Legends of the DCU #20,21,28,29,37,38						13.00
...: Willworld (2001, $24.95, HC) Seth Fisher-a/J.M. DeMatteis-s; Hal Jordan						25.00
...: Willworld (2003, $17.95, SC) Seth Fisher-a/J.M. DeMatteis-s; Hal Jordan						18.00

NOTE: ***Staton** a(p)-9-12; c-9-12.*

GREEN LANTERN (See Tangent Comics/ Green Lantern)

GREEN LANTERN (4th Series) (Follows Hal Jordan's return in Green Lantern: Rebirth)
DC Comics: July, 2005 - No. 67, Aug, 2011 ($3.50/$2.99)

	GD 2.0	VG 4.0	FN 6.0	VF 8.0	VF/NM 9.0	NM- 9.2
1-($3.50) Two covers by Pacheco and Ross; Johns-s/Van Sciver and Pacheco-a						5.00
2-20-($2.99) 2-4-Manhunters app. 6-Bianchi-a. 7,8-Green Arrow app. 8-Bianchi-c. 9-Batman app.; two covers by Bianchi and Van Sciver. 10,11-Reis-a. 17-19-Star Sapphire returns. 18-Acuna-a; Sinestro Corps back-ups begin						3.00
8-Variant-c by Neal Adams						8.00
21-Sinestro Corps War pt. 2						5.00
21-2nd printing with variant green hued background-c						3.00
22-24: 22-Sinestro Corps War pt. 4; green hued-c. 23-Part 6. 24-Part 8						4.00
22,23-2nd printings. 22-Yellow hued-c. 23-B&W Hal Jordan with colored rings						3.00
25-($4.99) Sinestro Corps War conclusion; Ivan Reis-c						6.00
25-($4.99) Variant cover by Gary Frank; Sinestro Corps War conclusion						8.00
26-28,30-43: 26-Alpha Lanterns. 30-35-Childhood & origin re-told; Sinestro app. 41-Origin Larfleeze. 43-Prologue to Blackest Night, origin of Black Hand; Mahnke-a						3.00
29-Childhood & origin re-told						5.00
29-Special Edition (6/10, $1.00) reprints #29 with "What's Next?" logo on cover						3.00
29-Special Edition (2010 San Diego Comic-Con giveaway) reprints #29 with new Van Sciver cover and Geoff Johns intro on inside front cover						3.00
39-43-Variant covers: 39,40-Migliari. 41-42-Barrows						12.00
44-49,51,52-Blackest Night. 44-Flash app. 46-Sinestro vs. Mongul. 47-Black Lantern Abin Sur. 49-Art by Benes & Ordway; Atom and Mera app. 51-Nekron app.						3.00
44-49,51-Variant covers: 44-Tan. 45-Manapul. 46. Andy Kubert. 47-Benes. 48-Morales. 49-Migliari. 51-Horn. 52-Shane Davis						8.00
50-($3.99)-Black Lantern Spectre & Parallax app.; Mahnke-a/c						4.00
50-Variant-c by Jim Lee						12.00
53-67: 53-62-Brightest Day. 54,55-Lobo app. 58-60-Flash app. 60-Krona returns. 64-67-War of the Green Lanterns x-over. 67-Sinestro becomes a Green Lantern						3.00
FCBD 2011 Green Lantern Flashpoint Special Edition (6/11, giveaway) r/#30 and previews Flashpoint x-over; Andy Kubert-a						3.00
...: Larfleeze Christmas Special 1 (2/11, $3.99) Johns-s/Booth-a/Ha-c						4.00
.../Plastic Man: Weapons of Mass Deception (2/11, $4.99) Brent Anderson-a						5.00
...Secret Files and Origins 2005 (6/05, $4.99) Johns-s/Cooke & Van Sciver-a; profiles with art by various incl. Chaykin, Gibbons, Gleason, Igle; Pacheco-c						5.00

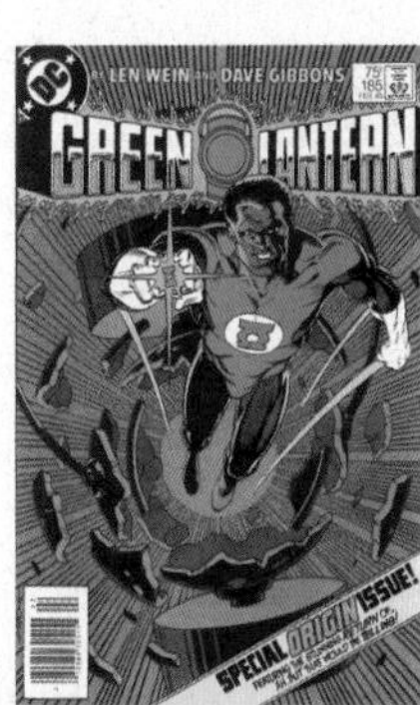

Green Lantern (1960) #185 © DC

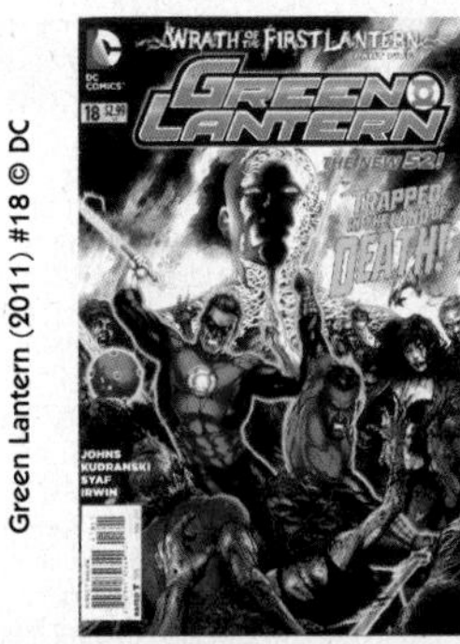

Green Lantern (2011) #18 © DC

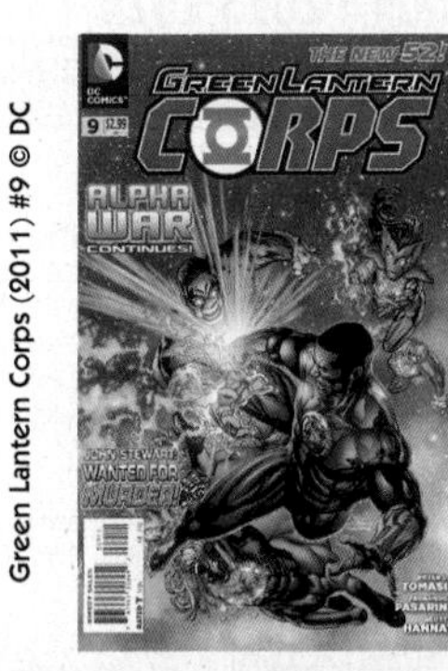

Green Lantern Corps (2011) #9 © DC

GD VG FN VF VF/NM NM-
2.0 4.0 6.0 8.0 9.0 9.2

.../Sinestro Corps: Secret Files 1 (2/08, $4.99) Profiles of Green Lanterns and Corps info 5.00
...: Agent Orange HC (2009, $19.99) r/#38-42 & Blackest Night #0; sketch art 20.00
...: Agent Orange SC (2010, $14.99) r/#38-42 & Blackest Night #0; sketch art 15.00
Blackest Night: Green Lantern HC (2010, $24.99) r/#43-52; variant covers; sketch art 25.00
Blackest Night: Green Lantern SC (2011, $19.99) r/#43-52; variant covers; sketch art 20.00
...: Brightest Day HC (2011, $22.99) r/#53-62; variant cover gallery 23.00
...: In Brightest Day SC (2008, $19.99) r/stories selected by Geoff Johns w/commentary 20.00
...: No Fear HC (2006, $24.99) r/#1-6 & Secret Files and Origins 25.00
...: No Fear SC (2008, $12.99) r/#1-6 & Secret Files and Origins 13.00
...: Rage of the Red Lanterns HC (2009, $24.99) r/#26-28,36-38 & Final Crisis: Rage... 25.00
...: Rage of the Red Lanterns SC (2010, $14.99) r/#26-28,36-38 & Final Crisis: Rage... 15.00
...: Revenge of the Green Lanterns HC (2006, $19.99) r/#7-13; variant cover gallery 20.00
...: Revenge of the Green Lanterns SC (2008, $12.99) r/#7-13; variant cover gallery 13.00
...: Secret Origin HC (2008, $19.99) r/#29-35 20.00
...: Secret Origin (New Edition) HC (2010, $19.99) r/#29-35; intro. by Ryan Reynolds 20.00
...: Secret Origin SC (2008, $14.99) r/#29-35 15.00
...: Secret Origin (New Edition) SC (2011, $14.99) r/#29-35; intro. by Ryan Reynolds; photo-c of Reynolds from movie; movie preview photo gallery 15.00
... Super Spectacular (1/12, $7.99, magazine-size) r/Blackest Night #0,1, Green Lantern #76 from 1970 and Brave and the Bold #30 from 2009 8.00
...: Tales of the Sinestro Corps HC (2008, $29.99, d.j.) r/back-up stories from #18-20, Tales of the Sinestro Corps series, Green Lantern: Sinestro Corps Special and Sinestro Corps: Secret Files 30.00
...: Tales of the Sinestro Corps SC (2009, $14.99) same contents as HC 15.00
...: The Sinestro Corps War Vol. 1 HC (2008, $24.99, d.j.) r/#21-23, Green Lantern Corps #14-15 and Green Lantern: Sinestro Corps Special 25.00
...: The Sinestro Corps War Vol. 1 SC (2009, $14.99) same contents as HC 15.00
...: The Sinestro Corps War Vol. 2 HC (2008, $24.99, d.j.) r/#24,25, Green Lantern Corps #16-19; interview with the creators and sketch art 25.00
... - Wanted: Hal Jordan HC (2007, $19.99) r/#14-20 without Sinestro Corps back-ups 20.00
... - Wanted: Hal Jordan SC (2008, $14.99) r/#14-20 without Sinestro Corps back-ups 15.00

GREEN LANTERN (DC New 52)
DC Comics: Nov, 2011 - No. 52, Jul, 2016 ($2.99/$3.99)

1-19: 1-Sinestro as Green Lantern; Johns-s/Mahnke-a/Reis-c (1st & 2nd print). 6-Choi-a. 9-Origin of the Indigo tribe. 14-Justice League app. 17-19-Wrath of the First Lantern 3.00
1-9-Variant-c. 1-Capullo. 2-Finch. 3-Van Sciver. 4-Manapul. 5-Choi. 6-Reis. 8-Keown 4.00
8-Combo pack ($3.99) polybagged with digital code 4.00
20-($7.99, squarebound) Conclusion of "Wrath of the First Lantern"; last Johns-s 8.00
21-23: 21-Venditti-s/Tan-a begin 3.00
23.1, 23.2, 23.3, 23.4 (11/13, $2.99, regular covers) 3.00
23.1 (11/13, $3.99, 3-D cover) "Relic #1" on cover; origin of Relic; Morales-a 6.00
23.2 (11/13, $3.99, 3-D cover) "Mongul #1" on cover; origin; Starlin-s/Porter-a 5.00
23.3 (11/13, $3.99, 3-D cover) "Black Hand #1" on cover; Soule-s/Ponticelli-a 5.00
23.4 (11/13, $3.99, 3-D cover) "Sinestro #1" on cover; origin; Kindt-s/Eaglesham-a 5.00
24-27,29-34: 24-Lights Out pt. 1; Relic app.; Central Battery destroyed 3.00
28-Flip-book with Red Lanterns #28; Red Lantern Supergirl app. 3.00
35-40: 35-37-Godhead x-over; New Gods, Orion & Metron app. 36,37-Black Hand app. 3.00
41-49,51,52-($3.99) 42,43,45,46-Black Hand app. 43-Relic returns. 47-Parallax app. 4.00
50-($4.99) Parallax app.; Sienkiewicz-c 5.00
#0 (11/12, $2.99) Simon Baz becomes a Green Lantern; Mahnke-a 3.00
Annual 1 (10/12, $4.99) 1st print w/black-c; Rise of the Third Army prologue 5.00
Annual 2 (12/13, $4.99) Lights Out pt. 5; Sean Chen-a 5.00
Annual 3 (2/15, $4.99) Godhead conclusion; Van Sciver-c 5.00
Annual 4 (11/15, $4.99) Venditti-s/Alixe-a 5.00
...: Futures End 1 (11/14, $2.99, regular-c) Five years later; Relic app. 3.00
...: Futures End 1 (11/14, $3.99, 3-D cover) 4.00
.../New Gods: Godhead 1 (12/14, $4.99) Part 1 to Godhead x-over; Highfather app. 5.00

GREEN LANTERN, THE
DC Comics: Jan, 2019 - No. 12, Dec, 2019 ($4.99/$3.99)

1-($4.99) Grant Morrison-s/Liam Sharp-a 5.00
2-11-($3.99) 2-Evil Star app. 5,6-Adam Strange app. 8-Green Arrow app. 4.00
12-($4.99) Leads into Green Lantern: Blackstars #1 5.00
Annual 1 (9/19, $4.99) Air Wave app.; Morrison-s/Camuncoli-a 5.00

GREEN LANTERN
DC Comics: Jun, 2021 - No. 12, Jun, 2022 ($4.99)

1-12: 1-Teen Lantern & John Stewart featured; Thorne-s/Soy-a. 3-7-Raney-a; Jo Mullein app. 8-ChrisCross-a. 12-John Stewart becomes the Emerald Knight 5.00
2021 Annual 1 (11/21, $5.99) Sinestro Corps app.; Cady-s/Basri & Derenick-a 6.00

GREEN LANTERN ANNUAL NO. 1, 1963
DC Comics: 1998 ($4.95, one-shot)

1-Reprints Golden Age & Silver Age stories in 1963-style 80 pg. Giant format; new Gil Kane sketch art 5.00

GD VG FN VF VF/NM NM-
2.0 4.0 6.0 8.0 9.0 9.2

GREEN LANTERN: BLACKSTARS
DC Comics: Jan, 2020 - No. 3, Mar, 2020 ($3.99, limited series)

1-3-Morrison-s/Xermanico-a; Mongul app. 4.00

GREEN LANTERN: BRIGHTEST DAY; BLACKEST NIGHT
DC Comics: 2002 ($5.95, squarebound, one-shot)

nn-Alan Scott vs. Solomon Grundy in 1944; Snyder III-c/a; Seagle-s
1 2 3 5 6 8

GREEN LANTERN: CIRCLE OF FIRE
DC Comics: Early Oct, 2000 - No. 2, Late Oct, 2000 (limited series)

1-($4.95) Intro. other Green Lanterns 5.00
2-($3.75) 4.00
Green Lantern (x-overs)- .../Adam Strange; .../Atom; .../Firestorm; ... /Green Lantern, Winick-s; .../Power Girl (all $2.50-c) 3.00
TPB (2002, $17.95) r/#1,2 & x-overs 18.00

GREEN LANTERN CORPS, THE (Formerly Green Lantern; see Tales of...)
DC Comics: No. 206, Nov, 1986 - No. 224, May, 1988

206-223: 212-John Stewart marries Katma Tui. 220,221-Millennium tie-ins 4.00
224-Double-size last issue 5.00
...Corps Annual 2,3- (12/86,8/87) 1-Formerly Tales of ...Annual #1; Alan Moore scripts. 3-Indicia says Green Lantern Annual #3; Moore scripts; Byrne-a 5.00
NOTE: ***Austin*** *a-Annual 3i.* ***Gil Kane*** *a-223, 224p; c-223, 224, Annual 2.* ***Russell*** *a-Annual 3i.* ***Staton*** *a-207-213p, 217p, 221p, 222p, Annual 3; c-207-213p, 217p, 221p, 222p.* ***Willingham*** *a-213p, 219p, 220p, 218p, 219p, Annual 2, 3p; c-218p, 219p.*

GREEN LANTERN CORPS
DC Comics: Aug, 2006 - No. 63, Oct, 2011 ($2.99)

1,14-19: 1-Gibbons-s. 14-19-Sinestro Corps War pts. 3,5,7,9,10, Epilogue 4.00
2-13: 2-6,10,11-Gibbons-s. 9-Darkseid app. 3.00
20-38: 20-Mongul app. 3.00
20-Second printing with sketch-c 3.00
34-38: 34-37-Variant covers by Migliari. 38-Fabry var-c 10.00
39-45-Blackest Night. 43-45-Red Lantern Guy Gardner 3.00
39-45-Variant covers: 39-Jusko. 40-Tucci. 41,42,44-Horn. 43-Ladronn. 45 Bolland 8.00
46,47-($3.99) 46-Blackest Night. 47-Brightest Day 4.00
48-61-($2.99) 48-Migliari-c; Ganthet joins the Corps. 49-52-Cyborg Superman app. 58-60-War of the Green Lanterns x-over. 60-Mogo destroyed 3.00
Blackest Night: Green Lantern Corps HC (2010, $24.99, d.j.) r/#39-47, cover gallery 25.00
Blackest Night: Green Lantern Corps SC (2011, $19.99) r/#39-47, cover gallery 20.00
...: Emerald Eclipse HC (2009, $24.99) r/#33-39; gallery of variant covers 25.00
...: Emerald Eclipse SC (2010, $14.99) r/#33-39; gallery of variant covers 15.00
...: Revolt of the Alpha-Lanterns HC (2011, $22.99) r/#21,22,48-52 23.00
...: Ring Quest TPB (2008, $14.99) r/#19,20,23-26 15.00
...: The Dark Side of Green TPB (2007, $12.99) r/#7-13 13.00
...: To Be a Lantern TPB (2007, $12.99) r/#1-6 13.00

GREEN LANTERN CORPS (DC New 52)
DC Comics: Nov, 2011 - No. 40, May, 2015 ($2.99)

1-23: 1-Tomasi-s/Pasarin-a/Mahnke-c; John Stewart & Guy Gardner. 4-6-Andy Kubert-c 3.00
24-39: 24-Lights Out pt. 2; Oa destroyed. 25-Year Zero. 35-37-Godhead x-over 3.00
40-($3.99) Chang-a 4.00
#0 (11/12, $2.99) Origin of Guy Gardner; Tomasi-s/Pasarin-a 3.00
Annual 1 (3/13, $4.99) Rise of the Third Army conclusion; Mogo returns 5.00
Annual 2 (3/14, $4.99) Villains United; Evil Star, Bolphunga, Kanjar Ro app. 5.00
...: Futures End 1 (11/14, $2.99, regular-c) Five years later; Indigo Tribe app. 3.00
...: Futures End 1 (11/14, $3.99, 3-D cover) 4.00

GREEN LANTERN CORPS: EDGE OF OBLIVION
DC Comics: Mar, 2016 - No. 6, Aug, 2016 ($2.99, limited series)

1-6: 1-3-Taylor-s/Van Sciver-a. 4,5-Syaf-a 3.00

GREEN LANTERN CORPS QUARTERLY
DC Comics: Summer, 1992 - No. 8, Spring, 1994 ($2.50/$2.95, 68 pgs.)

1-G.A. Green Lantern story; Staton-a(p) 5.00
2-8: 2-G.A. G.L.-c/story; Austin-c(i); Gulacy-a(p). 3-G.A. G.L. story. 4-Austin-i. 7-Painted-c; Tim Vigil-a. 8-Lobo-c/s 4.00

GREEN LANTERN CORPS: RECHARGE
DC Comics: Nov, 2005 - No. 5, Mar, 2006 ($3.50/$2.99, limited series)

1-($3.50) Kyle Rayner, Guy Gardner & Kilowog app.; Gleason-a 4.00
2-5-($2.99) 3.00
TPB (2006, $12.99) r/series 13.00

GREEN LANTERN: DRAGON LORD
DC Comics: 2001 - No. 3, 2001 ($4.95, squarebound, limited series)

1-3: A G.L. in ancient China; Moench-s/Gulacy-c/a 5.00

GREEN LANTERN: EARTH ONE
DC Comics: Mar, 2018 (Graphic novel)
Volume One HC ($24.95) Hardman & Bechko-s/Hardman-a; re-imagined origin 25.00

GREEN LANTERN 80TH ANNIVERSARY 100-PAGE SUPER SPECTACULAR
DC Comics: Aug, 2020 ($9.99, squarebound, one-shot)
1-Short stories and pin-ups by various incl. Johns, O'Neil, Grell, Reis; multiple covers 10.00

GREEN LANTERN: EMERALD DAWN (Also see Emerald Dawn)
DC Comics: Dec, 1989 - No. 6, May, 1990 ($1.00, limited series)
1-Origin retold; Giffen plots in all 6.00
2-6: 4-Re-intro. Tomar-Re 4.00

GREEN LANTERN: EMERALD DAWN II (Emerald Dawn II #1 & 2)
DC Comics: Apr, 1991 - No. 6, Sept, 1991 ($1.00, limited series)
1-6 4.00
TPB (2003, $12.95) r/#1-6; Alan Davis-c 13.00

GREEN LANTERN: EMERALD WARRIORS
DC Comics: Oct, 2010 - No. 13, Oct, 2011 ($3.99/$2.99)
1-5-($3.99) Guy Gardner's exploits; Migliari-c. 1-Bermejo variant-c. 2-5-Massaferra var-c 4.00
6-13-($2.99) 6,7-Covers by Migliari & Massaferra. 8-10-War of the Green Lanterns x-over 3.00

GREEN LANTERN: EVIL'S MIGHT (Elseworlds)
DC Comics: 2002 - No. 3 ($5.95, squarebound, limited series)
1-3-Kyle Rayner in 19th century NYC; Rogers-a; Chaykin & Tischman-s 6.00

GREEN LANTERN: FEAR ITSELF
DC Comics: 1999 (Graphic novel)
Hardcover ($24.95) Ron Marz-s/Brad Parker painted-a 25.00
Softcover ($14.95) 15.00

GREEN LANTERN/FLASH: FASTER FRIENDS (See Flash/Green Lantern...)
DC Comics: 1997 ($4.95, limited series)
1-Marz-s 5.00

GREEN LANTERN GALLERY
DC Comics: Dec, 1996 ($3.50, one-shot)
1-Wraparound-c; pin-ups by various 4.00

GREEN LANTERN/GREEN ARROW (Also see The Flash #217)
DC Comics: Oct, 1983 - No. 7, April, 1984 (52-60 pgs.)
1- Reprints Green Lantern #76, 77 2 4 6 8 10 12
2-7-Reprints from Green Lantern #78-89 5.00
NOTE: ***Neal Adams** r-1-7; c-1-4. **Wrightson** r-4, 5.*

GREEN LANTERN/HUCKLEBERRY HOUND SPECIAL
DC Comics: Dec, 2018 ($4.99, one-shot)
1-John Stewart and Huckleberry Hound meet in 1972; Russell-s/Leonardi-a 5.00

GREEN LANTERN · LEGACY: THE LAST WILL & TESTAMENT OF HAL JORDAN
DC Comics: 2002 ($24.95, hardcover graphic novel)
Hardcover-Anderson & Sienkiewicz-a/c; Kelly-s; Return of Oa 25.00
Softcover (2004, $17.95) 18.00

GREEN LANTERN: LOST ARMY
DC Comics: Aug, 2015 - No. 6, Jan, 2016 ($2.99)
1-6: 1-Bunn-s/Saiz-a; featuring John Stewart, Guy Gardner, Kilowog, Arisia, Krona 3.00

GREEN LANTERN: MOSAIC (Also see Cosmic Odyssey #2)
DC Comics: June, 1992 - No. 18, Nov, 1993 ($1.25)
1-18: Featuring John Stewart. 1-Painted-c by Cully Hamner 3.00

GREEN LANTERN MOVIE PREQUEL (2011 movie)
DC Comics: July, 2011; Oct, 2011 ($2.99, one-shots)
...: Abin Sur 1 - Green-s/Gleason-a; movie photo-c 3.00
...: Hal Jordan 1 - Johns & Berlanti-s/Ordway-a; movie photo-c; Sinestro & Tomar-Re app. 3.00
...: Kilowog 1 - Tomasi-s/Ferreira-a; movie photo-c 3.00
...: Sinestro 1 (10/11) - Johns-s/Tolibao, Richards & Ordway-a; movie photo-c 3.00
...: Tomar-Re 1 - Guggenheim-s/Richards-a; movie photo-c 3.00

GREEN LANTERN: NEW GUARDIANS (DC New 52)
DC Comics: Nov, 2011 - No. 40, May, 2015 ($2.99)
1-Bedard-s/Kirkham-a/c; Kyle origin flashback; Fatality app. 6.00
2-23: 13-16-Third Army. 21-Relic freed. 22,23-Kyle vs. Relic. 23-Blue Lanterns destroyed 3.00
24-34: 24-Lights Out pt. 3. 3.00
35-39: 35-37-Godhead x-over; Highfather app. 38,39-Oblivion returns 3.00
40-($3.99) Oblivion app.; the start of the White Lantern Corps 4.00
#0 (11/12, $2.99) Bedard-s/Kuder-a; Zamarons app. 3.00
Annual 1 (3/13, $4.99) Giffen-s/Kolins-a/c 5.00
Annual 2 (6/14, $4.99) Segovia-a; takes place between #30 & #31 5.00
...: Futures End 1 (11/14, $2.99, regular-c) Five years later; intro. Saysoran 3.00
...: Futures End 1 (11/14, $3.99, 3-D cover) 4.00

GREEN LANTERN: REBIRTH
DC Comics: Dec, 2004 - No. 6, May, 2005 ($2.95, limited series)
1-Johns-s/Van Sciver-a; Hal Jordan as The Spectre on-c 8.00
1-2nd printing; Hal Jordan as Green Lantern on-c 4.00
1-3rd printing; B&W-c version of 1st printing 3.00
1 Special Edition (9/09, $1.00) r/#1 with "After Watchmen" cover frame 3.00
2-Guy Gardner becomes a Green Lantern again; JLA app. 5.00
2-2nd & 3rd printings 3.00
3-6: 3-Sinestro returns. 4-6-JLA & JSA app. 3.00
HC (2005, $24.99, dust jacket) r/series & Wizard preview; intro. by Brad Meltzer 25.00
SC (2007, 2010, $14.99) r/series & Wizard preview; intro. by Brad Meltzer 15.00

GREEN LANTERNS (DC Rebirth) (Also see Hal Jordan and the Green Lantern Corps)
DC Comics: Aug, 2016 - No. 57, Dec, 2018 ($2.99/$3.99)
1-24: 1-Simon Baz and Jessica Cruz team up; Humphries-s/Rocha-a. 6-1st app. the Phantom Ring. 8-Dominators app.; Benes-a. 9-14-Phantom Lantern. 16,17-Batman app. 3.00
25-($3.99) Lanterns vs. Volthoom; Rocha-a 4.00
26-49: 28-31-The Ancient Lanterns app. 35-Intro. Singularity Jain. 35,36-Bolphunga app. 3.00
50-57-($3.99) 50,51,55-57-Perkins-a. 53-57-Cyborg Superman app. 4.00
Annual 1 (7/18, $4.99) Diggle-s/Perkins-a 5.00
...: Rebirth 1 (8/16, $2.99) Van Sciver & Benes-a; Hal Jordan & Atrocitus app. 3.00

GREEN LANTERN SEASON TWO, THE (Follows Green Lantern: Blackstars series)
DC Comics: Apr, 2020 - No. 12, May, 2021 ($4.99/$3.99)
1-($4.99) Grant Morrison-s/Liam Sharp-a; intro Young Guardians; Hal returns to Earth 5.00
2-11-($3.99) 4-The Flash app. 11-Hector Hammond app. 4.00
12-($4.99) Hector Hammond app. 5.00

GREEN LANTERN/SENTINEL: HEART OF DARKNESS
DC Comics: Mar, 1998 - No. 3, May, 1998 ($1.95, limited series)
1-3-Marz-s/Pelletier-a 4.00

GREEN LANTERN/SILVER SURFER: UNHOLY ALLIANCES
DC Comics: 1995 ($4.95, one-shot)(Prelude to DC Versus Marvel)
nn-Hal Jordan app. 2 4 6 8 11 14

GREEN LANTERN SINESTRO CORPS SPECIAL (Continues in Green Lantern #21)
DC Comics: Aug, 2007 ($4.99, one-shot)
1-Kyle Rayner becomes Parallax; Cyborg Superman & Earth-Prime Superboy app.; Johns-s; Van Sciver-a/c; back-up story origin of Sinestro; Gibbons-a; Sinestro on cover 2 4 6 8 10 12
1-(2nd printing) Kyle Rayner as Parallax on cover 6.00
1-(3rd printing) Sinestro cover with muted colors 5.00

GREEN LANTERN/ SPACE GHOST SPECIAL
DC Comics: May, 2017 ($4.99, one-shot)
1-Tynion IV-s/Olivetti-a/c; back-up Ruff 'n' Ready re-intro. by Chaykin-s/a 5.00

GREEN LANTERN: THE ANIMATED SERIES (Based on the Cartoon Network series)
DC Comics: No. 0, Jan, 2012 - No. 14, Sept, 2013 ($2.99)
0,1: 0-Baltazar & Franco-s/Brizuela-a; Kilowog and Red Lanterns app. 5.00
2-14: 13-Lobo app. 4.00

GREEN LANTERN: THE GREATEST STORIES EVER TOLD
DC Comics: 2006 ($19.99, TPB)
SC-Reprints Showcase #22; G.L. #1,31,74,87,172; ('90 series) #3, and others; Ross-c 20.00

GREEN LANTERN: THE NEW CORPS
DC Comics: 1999 - No. 2, 1999 ($4.95, limited series)
1,2-Kyle recruits new GLs; Eaton-a 5.00

GREEN LANTERN VS. ALIENS
Dark Horse Comics: Sept, 2000 - No. 4, Dec, 2000 ($2.95, limited series)
1-4: 1-Hal Jordan and GL Corps vs. Aliens; Leonardi-p. 2-4-Kyle Rayner 3.00

GREEN MASK, THE (See Mystery Men)
Summer, 1940 - No. 9, 2/42; No. 10, 8/44 - No. 11, 11/44;
Fox Feature Syndicate: V2#1, Spring, 1945 - No. 6, 10-11/46
V1#1-Origin The Green Mask & Domino; reprints/Mystery Men #1-3,5-7;
Lou Fine-c 300 600 900 1980 3440 4900
2-Zanzibar The Magician by Tuska 135 270 405 864 1482 2100
3-Powell-a; Marijuana story 103 206 309 659 1130 1600
4-Navy Jones begins, ends #6 84 168 252 538 919 1300
5 63 126 189 403 689 975
6-The Nightbird begins, ends #9; Good Girl bondage/torture-c
258 516 774 1651 2826 4000
7,9: 9(2/42)-Becomes The Bouncer #10(nn) on? & Green Mask #10 on
54 108 162 343 574 825
8-Classic Good Girl torture/bondage-c 290 580 870 1856 3178 4500
10,11: 10-Origin One Round Hogan & Rocket Kelly
40 80 120 246 411 575
V2#1 32 64 96 188 307 425
2-6 25 50 75 150 245 340

GREEN PLANET, THE
Charlton Comics: 1962 (one-shot) (12¢)
nn-Giordano-c; sci-fi 10 20 30 67 141 215

GREEN TEAM (See Cancelled Comic Cavalcade & 1st Issue Special)

GREEN TEAM: TEEN TRILLIONAIRES
DC Comics: Jul, 2013 - No. 8, Mar, 2014 ($2.99)
1-8-Baltazar & Franco-s/Guara-a. 1-3-Conner-c. 3-Deathstroke app. 8-Teen Titans app. 3.00
1-Variant-c by Chiang 3.00

GREEN VALLEY
Image Comics (Skybound): Oct, 2016 - No. 9, Jun, 2017 ($2.99/$3.99)
1-8-Max Landis-s/Giuseppe Camuncoli-a 3.00
9-($3.99) 4.00

GREEN WOMAN, THE
DC Comics (Vertigo): 2010 ($24.99, HC graphic novel)
HC-John Bolton-a/Peter Straub & Michael Easton-s 25.00

GREETINGS FROM SANTA (See March of Comics No. 48)

GRENDEL (Also see Primer #2, Mage and Comico Collection)
Comico: Mar, 1983 - No. 3, Feb, 1984 ($1.50, B&W)(#1 has indicia to Skrog #1)
1-Origin Hunter Rose 12 24 36 80 173 265
2,3: 2-Origin Argent 8 16 24 56 108 160

GRENDEL
Comico: Oct, 1986 - No. 40, Feb, 1990 ($1.50/$1.95/$2.50, mature)
1 2 4 6 10 14 18
1,2: 2nd printings 3.00
2,3,5-15: 13-15-Ken Steacy-c. 4.00
4,16: 4-Dave Stevens-c(i). 16-Re-intro Mage (series begins, ends #19) 6.00
17-40: 24-25,27-28,30-31-Snyder-c/a 3.00
Devil by the Deed (Graphic Novel, 10/86, $5.95, 52 pgs.)-r/Grendel back-ups/
Mage 6-14; Alan Moore intro. 1 3 4 6 8 10
Devil's Legacy ($14.95, 1988, Graphic Novel) 2 4 6 9 12 15
Devil's Vagary (10/87, B&W & red)-No price; included in Comico Collection

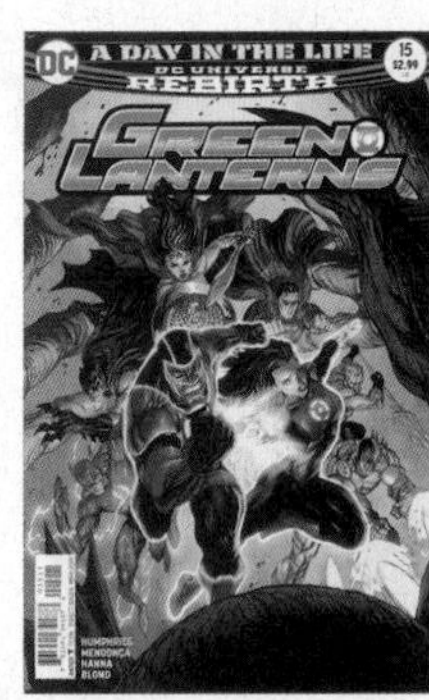

Green Lanterns #15 © DC

Grendel: Behold the Devil #1 © Matt Wagner

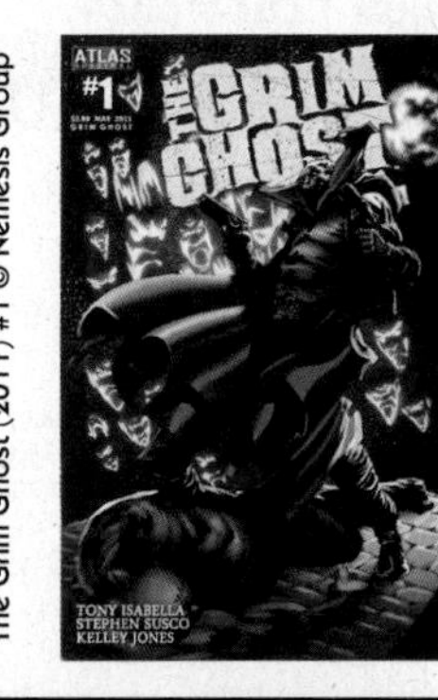

The Grim Ghost (2011) #1 © Nemesis Group

	GD 2.0	VG 4.0	FN 6.0	VF 8.0	VF/NM 9.0	NM- 9.2
	2	4	6	8	10	12

GRENDEL (Title series): **Dark Horse Comics**

--ARCHIVES, 5/07 ($14.95, HC) r/1st apps. in Primer #2 and Grendel #1-3; Wagner intro. 15.00

--BEHOLD THE DEVIL, No. 0, 7/07 - No. 8, 6/08 ($3.50/50¢, B&W&Red)
0-(50¢-c) Prelude to series; Matt Wagner-s/a; interview with Wagner 3.00
1-8-Matt Wagner-s/a/c in all 3.50

--BLACK, WHITE, AND RED, 11/98 - No. 4, 2/99 ($3.95, anthology)
1-Wagner-s in all. Art by Sale, Leon and others 5.00
2-4: 2-Mack, Chadwick-a. 3-Allred, Kristensen-a. 4-Pearson, Sprouse-a 4.00

--CLASSICS, 7/95 - 8/95 ($3.95, mature) 1,2-reprints; new Wagner-c 4.00

--CYCLE, 10/95 ($5.95) 1-nn-history of Grendel by M. Wagner & others 6.00

--DEVIL BY THE DEED, 7/93 ($3.95, varnish-c) 1-nn-M. Wagner-c/a/scripts; r/Grendel back-ups from Mage #6-14 6.00
Reprint (12/97, $3.95) w/pin-ups by various 4.00
Hardcover (2007, $12.95) reprint recolored to B&W&red; includes covers and intros from previously reprinted editions 13.00

--DEVIL CHILD, 6/99 - No. 2, 7/99 ($2.95, mature) 1,2-Sale & Kristiansen-a/Schutz-s 3.00

--DEVIL QUEST, 11/95 ($4.95) 1-nn-Prequel to Batman/Grendel II; M. Wagner story & art; r/back-up story from Grendel Tales series. 5.00

--DEVILS AND DEATHS, 10/94 - 11/94 ($2.95, mature) 1,2 3.00

: DEVIL'S LEGACY, 3/00 - No. 12, 2/01 ($2.95, reprints 1986 series, recolored)
1-12-Wagner-s/c; Pander Bros.-a 3.00

: DEVIL'S ODYSSEY, 10/19 - No. 8, 7/21 ($3.99) 1-8-Wagner-s/a; Grendel Prime returns 4.00

: DEVIL'S REIGN, 5/04 - No. 7, 12/04 ($3.50, repr. 1989 series #34-40, recolored)
1-7-Sale-c/a. 3.50

: GOD AND THE DEVIL, No. 0, 1/03 - No. 10, 12/03 ($3.50/$4.99, repr. 1986 series, recolored)
0-9: 0-Sale-c/a; r/#23. 1-9-Snyder-c 3.50
10-($4.99) Double-sized; Snyder-c 5.00

--RED, WHITE & BLACK, 9/02 - No. 4, 12/02 ($4.99, anthology)
1-4-Wagner-s in all. 1-Art by Thompson, Sakai, Mahfood and others. 2-Kelley Jones, Watson, Brereton, Hester & Parks-a. 3-Oeming, Noto, Cannon, Ashley Wood, Huddleston-a 4-Chiang, Dalrymple, Robertson, Snyder III and Zulli-a 5.00
TPB (2005, $19.95) r/#1-4; cover gallery, artist bios 20.00

--TALES: DEVIL'S CHOICES, 3/95 - 6/95 ($2.95, mature) 1-4 3.00

--TALES: FOUR DEVILS, ONE HELL, 8/93 - 1/94 ($2.95, mature)
1-6-Wagner painted-c 3.00
TPB (12/94, $17.95) r/#1-6 18.00

--TALES: HOMECOMING, 12/94 - 2/95 ($2.95, mature) 1-3 3.00

--TALES: THE DEVIL IN OUR MIDST, 5/94 - 9/95 ($2.95, mature) 1-5-Wagner painted-c 3.00

--TALES: THE DEVIL MAY CARE, 12/95 - No. 6, 5/96 ($2.95, mature)
1-6-Terry LaBan scripts. 5-Batman/Grendel II preview 3.00

--TALES: THE DEVIL'S APPRENTICE, 9/97 - No. 3, 11/97 ($2.95, mature)
1-3 3.00

--TALES: THE DEVIL'S HAMMER, 2/94 - No. 3, 4/94 ($2.95, mature)
1-3-Rob Walton-s/a; back-up stories by Wagner 3.00

: THE DEVIL INSIDE, 9/01 - No. 3, 11/01 ($2.99)
1-3-r/#13-15 with new Wagner-c 3.00

VS. THE SHADOW, 9/14 - No. 3, 11/14 ($5.99, squarebound)
Matt Wagner-s/a/c; Grendel time-travels to The Shadow's era 6.00

: WAR CHILD, 8/92 - No. 10, 6/93 ($2.50, lim. series, mature)
1-9: 1-4-Bisley painted-c; Wagner-i & scripts in all 3.00
10-($3.50, 52 pgs.) Wagner-c 4.00
Limited Edition Hardcover ($99.95) 100.00

GRENDEL, KENTUCKY
AWA Studios: Sept, 2020 - No. 4, Dec, 2020 ($3.99, limited series)
1-4-Jeff McComsey-s/Tommy Lee Edwards-a 4.00

GREYFRIARS BOBBY (Disney)(Movie)
Dell Publishing Co.: No. 1189, Nov, 1961 (one-shot)
Four Color 1189-Photo-c 6 12 18 41 76 110

GREYLORE
Sirius: 12/85 - No. 5, Sept, 1986 ($1.50/$1.75, high quality paper)
1-5: Bo Hampton-a in all 3.00

GREYSHIRT: INDIGO SUNSET (Also see Tomorrow Stories)
America's Best Comics: Dec, 2001 - No. 6, Aug, 2002 ($3.50, limited series)
1-6-Veitch-s/a. 4-Back-up w/John Severin-a. 6-Cho-a 3.50
TPB (2002, $19.95) r/#1-6; preface by Alan Moore 20.00

GRIDIRON GIANTS
Ultimate Sports Ent.: 2000 - No. 2 ($3.95, cardstock covers)
1,2-NFL players Sanders, Marino, Plummer, T. Davis battle evil 4.00

GRIFFIN, THE
DC Comics: 1991 - No. 6, 1991 ($4.95, limited series, 52 pgs.)
Book 1-6: Matt Wagner painted-c 5.00

GRIFTER (Also see Team 7 & WildC.A.T.S)
Image Comics (WildStorm Prod.): May, 1995 - No. 10, Mar, 1996 ($1.95)
1 ($1.95, Newsstand)-WildStorm Rising Pt. 5 3.00
1-10:1 ($2.50, Direct)-WildStorm Rising Pt. 5, bound-in trading card 3.00
...: One Shot (1/95, $4.95) Flip-c 5.00

GRIFTER
Image Comics (WildStorm Prod.): V2#1, July, 1996 - No. 14, Aug, 1997 ($2.50)
V2#1-14: Steven Grant scripts 3.00

GRIFTER (DC New 52)
DC Comics: Nov, 2011 - No. 16, Mar, 2013 ($2.99)
1-16: 1-Grifter in the new DC universe; Edmonson-s/Cafu-a/c. 4-Green Arrow app. 3.00
#0 (11/12, $2.99) Liefeld-s/c; Clark-a 3.00

GRIFTER & MIDNIGHTER
DC Comics (WildStorm Prod.): May, 2007 - No. 6, Oct, 2007 ($2.99, limited series)
1-6-Dixon-s/Benjamin-a/c. 1,3-The Authority app. 3.00
TPB (2008, $17.99) r/#1-6 18.00

GRIFTER AND THE MASK
Dark Horse Comics: Sept, 1996 - No. 2, Oct, 1996 ($2.50, limited series)
(1st Dark Horse Comics/Image x-over)
1,2: Steve Seagle scripts 3.00

GRIFTER/BADROCK (Also see WildC.A.T.S & Youngblood)
Image Comics (Extreme Studios): Oct, 1995 - No.2, Nov, 1995 ($2.50, unfinished lim. series)
1,2: 2-Flip book w/Badrock #2 3.00

GRIFTER/SHI
Image Comics (WildStorm Productions): Apr, 1996 - No. 2, May, 1996 ($2.95, limited series)
1,2: 1-Jim Lee-c/a(p); Travis Charest-a(p). 2-Billy Tucci-c/a(p); Travis Charest-a(p) 3.00

GRIM
BOOM! Studios: May, 2022 - Present ($3.99)
1-8-Stephanie Phillips-s/Flaviano-a 4.00

GRIM GHOST, THE
Atlas/Seaboard Publ.: Jan, 1975 - No. 3, July, 1975
1-3: Fleisher-s in all. 1-Origin. 2-Son of Satan; Colan-a. 3-Heath-c
2 4 6 13 18 22

GRIM GHOST
Ardden Entertainment (Atlas Comics): Mar, 2011 - No. 6, Nov, 2011 ($2.99)
1-6-Isabella & Susco-s/Kelley Jones-a. 1-Re-intro. Matthew Dunsinane 3.00
... Issue Zero - NY Comicon Edtion (10/10, $2.99) Qing Ping Mui-a; prequel to #1 3.00

GRIMJACK (Also see Demon Knight & Starslayer)
First Comics: Aug, 1984 - No. 81, Apr, 1991 ($1.00/$1.95/$2.25)
1-John Ostrander scripts & Tim Truman-c/a begins 1 2 3 5 6 8
2-25: 20-Sutton-c/a begins. 22-Bolland-a. 3.00
26-2nd color Teenage Mutant Ninja Turtles 2 4 6 8 10 12
27-74,76-81 (Later issues $1.95, $2.25): 30-Dynamo Joe x-over; 31-Mandrake-c/a begins. 73,74-Kelley Jones-a 3.00
75-($5.95, 52 pgs.)-Fold-out map; coated stock 6.00
The Legend of Grimjack Vol. 1 (IDW Publishing, 2004, $19.99) r/Starslayer #10-18; 8 new pages & art 20.00
The Legend of Grimjack Vol. 2 (IDW, 2005, $19.99) r/#1-7; unpublished art 20.00
The Legend of Grimjack Vol. 3 (IDW, 2005, $19.99) r/#8-14; cover gallery 20.00
The Legend of Grimjack Vol. 4 (IDW, 2005, $24.99) r/#15-21; cover gallery 25.00
The Legend of Grimjack Vol. 5 (IDW, 5/06, $24.99) r/#22-30; cover gallery 25.00
The Legend of Grimjack Vol. 6 (IDW, 1/07, $24.99) r/#31-37; cover gallery 25.00
The Legend of Grimjack Vol. 7 (IDW, 4/07, $24.99) r/#38-46; covers; "Rough Trade" 25.00
NOTE: *Truman c/a-1-17.*

GRIMJACK CASEFILES
First Comics: Nov, 1990 - No. 5, Mar, 1991 ($1.95, limited series)
1-5 Reprints 1st stories from Starslayer #10 on 3.00

	GD 2.0	VG 4.0	FN 6.0	VF 8.0	VF/NM 9.0	NM- 9.2
GRIMJACK: KILLER INSTINCT						
IDW Publ.: Jan, 2005 - No. 6, June, 2005 ($3.99, limited series)						
1-6-Ostrander-s/Truman-a						4.00
GRIMJACK: THE MANX CAT						
IDW Publ.: Aug, 2009 - No. 6, Jan, 2010 ($3.99, limited series)						
1-6-Ostrander-s/Truman-a						4.00
GRIMM (Based on the NBC TV series)						
Dynamite Entertainment.: 2013 - No. 12, 2014 ($3.99)						
1-11: 1-Two covers (Alex Ross & photo). 2-11-Pararillo & photo-c on each						4.00
12-($4.99) Gaffen & McVey-s/Rodolfo-a; Pararillo & photo-c						5.00
#0 (2013, Free Comic Book Day giveaway) Prequel to issue #1; Portacio-c						3.00
... Portland, WU (2014, $7.99) Gaffen & McVey-s/Govar-a/c						8.00
...: The Warlock 1-4 (2013 - No. 4, 2014, $3.99) Nitz-s/Malaga-a						4.00
GRIMM VOLUME 2 (Based on the NBC TV series)						
Dynamite Entertainment.: 2016 - No. 5, 2017 ($3.99)						
1-5-Kittredge-s/Sanapo-a; two covers						4.00
GRIMM FAIRY TALES						
Zenescope Entertainment: Jun, 2005 - No. 125, Aug, 2016 ($2.99/$3.99)						
1-Al Rio-c; Little Red Riding Hood app.; multiple variant covers	6	12	18	38	69	100
2-Multiple variant covers	3	6	9	19	30	40
3-6-Multiple variant covers	2	4	6	10	14	18
7-12: Multiple covers on each						6.00
13-74,76-84,86-99,101,102: Multiple covers on each						3.00
75-(7/12, $5.99) Covers by Campbell, Sejic, Michaels and others						6.00
85-(5/13, $5.99) Unleashed part 2						6.00
100-(7/14, $5.99) Age of Darkness; covers by Neal Adams and others						6.00
103-124-($3.99)						4.00
125-(8/16, $9.99) Five covers						10.00
#0 Free Comic Book Day Special Edition (4/14, giveaway) Age of Darkness tie-in						3.00
2016 Annual (10/16, $5.99) Spotlight on Skylar; art by various; 4 covers						6.00
... Animated One Shot (10/12, $3.99) Schnepp-c; bonus design art						4.00
Grimm Tales of Terror 2016 Holiday Special (11/16, $5.99) 4 covers						6.00
Grimm Tales of Terror 2019 Halloween Special (10/19, $5.99) 5 covers						6.00
Grimm Universe Presents Fall 2019 (8/19, $7.99) 5 covers						8.00
... Halloween Special 1,2, 2013, 2014, 2015, 2016 (10/09, 10/10, 10/13, 10/14, 9/15, 10/16, $5.99) Multiple covers on each						6.00
... Holiday Edition (11/14, $5.99) The story of Krampus; multiple covers						6.00
... Presents Wounded Warriors (7/13, $6.99) Multiple military-themes covers						7.00
... The Dark Queen One Shot (1/14, $5.99) Sharma-a; 4 covers						6.00
GRIMM FAIRY TALES (Volume 2)						
Zenescope Entertainment: Dec, 2016 - Present ($3.99)						
1-24,26-49,51-69: 1-3-Brusha-s/Silva-a; multiple covers. 37-Leads into 2020 Annual						4.00
25-($5.99) The War of the Grail; continues in Annual 2019; Goetten-a						6.00
50-($5.99) A Dark Conclusion; gatefold wraparound-c						6.00
... 2017 Halloween Special (10/17, $5.99) Short stories by various; 4 covers						6.00
...: 2019 Annual (1/19, $5.99) Casallos-a; 4 covers						6.00
...: 2019 Giant-Size (2/19, $5.99) Casallos-a; 5 covers; continues in #26						6.00
...: 2019 Holiday Special (11/19, $5.99) Short stories by various; 5 covers						6.00
...: 2020 Annual (6/20, $5.99) Abrera-a; 4 covers; Skye vs. Merlin; follows #37						6.00
...: 2020 Holiday Special (12/20, $5.99) Short stories by various; 5 covers						6.00
...: 2022 Annual (8/22, $7.99) Abrera-a; 4 covers; follows #62						8.00
...: Universus One-Shot (3/20, $4.99) Franchini-s/Garcia-a; two covers; includes cards						5.00
GRIMM FAIRY TALES PRESENTS ALICE IN WONDERLAND						
Zenescope Entertainment: Jan, 2012 - No. 6, May, 2012 ($2.99)						
1-Multiple variant covers	3	6	9	15	22	28
2-6: Multiple covers on each	1	2	3	5	6	8
GRIMM FAIRY TALES MYTHS & LEGENDS						
Zenescope Entertainment: Jan, 2011 - No. 25, Feb, 2013 ($2.99)						
1-Campbell-c; multiple variant covers	2	4	6	9	12	15
2-5						6.00
6-24						3.00
25-(2/13, $5.99) Multiple variant covers						6.00
GRIMM FAIRY TALES PRESENTS WONDERLAND (Title changes to Wonderland with #43)						
Zenescope Entertainment: Jul, 2012 - Finale, Sept, 2016 ($2.99)						
1-Campbell-c; multiple variant covers	2	4	6	9	12	15
2,3						6.00
4-18						3.00
19-24,26-49-($3.99)						4.00
25-(7/14, $5.99) Multiple variant covers						6.00
50-(8/16, $5.99) Multiple variant covers						6.00
... Finale (9/16, $5.99) Last issue; 4 covers; Shand-s/Follini-a						6.00
Free Comic Book Day 2015 Special Edition (5/15, giveaway) Brescini-a						3.00
GRIMMISS ISLAND (Issue #1 titled Itty Bitty Comics #5: Grimmiss Island)						
Dark Horse Comics: Mar, 2015 - No. 4, Jun, 2015 ($2.99, limited series)						
1-4-All-ages humor story by Art Baltazar & Franco						3.00
GRIMM'S GHOST STORIES (See Dan Curtis)						
Gold Key/Whitman No. 55 on: Jan, 1972 - No. 60, June, 1982 (Painted-c #1-42,44,46-56)						
1	5	10	15	30	50	70
2-5,8: 5,8-Williamson-a	3	6	9	14	20	25
6,7,9,10	2	4	6	11	16	20
11-20	2	4	6	8	11	14
21-42,45-54: 32,34-Reprints. 45-Photo-c	1	3	4	6	8	10
43,44,55-60: 43,44-(52 pgs.). 43-Photo-c. 58(2/82). 59(4/82)-Williamson-a(r/#8). 60(6/82)	2	4	6	8	11	14
Mini-Comic No. 1 (3-1/4x6-1/2", 1976)	1	3	4	6	8	10

NOTE: *Reprints-#32?, 34?, 39, 43, 44, 47?, 53; 56-60(1/3).* **Bolle** *a-8, 17, 22-25, 27, 29(2), 33, 35, 41, 43r, 45(2), 48(2), 50, 52, 57.* **Celardo** *a-17, 26, 28p, 30, 31, 43(2), 45.* **Lopez** *a-24, 25.* **McWilliams** *a-33, 44r, 48, 54(2), 57, 58.* **Win Mortimer** *a-31, 33, 49, 51, 55, 56, 58(2), 59, 60.* **Roussos** *a-25, 30.* **Sparling** *a-23, 24, 28, 30, 31, 33, 43r, 44, 45, 51(2), 52, 56-58, 59(2), 60.* **Spiegle** *a-44.*

	GD 2.0	VG 4.0	FN 6.0	VF 8.0	VF/NM 9.0	NM- 9.2
GRIN (The American Funny Book) (Satire)						
APAG House Pubs: Nov, 1972 - No. 3, April, 1973 (Magazine, 52 pgs.)						
1-Parodies-Godfather, All in the Family	3	6	9	17	26	35
2,3	2	4	6	13	18	22
GRIN & BEAR IT (See Gags)						
Dell Publishing Co.: No. 28, 1941						
Large Feature Comic 28	22	44	66	128	209	290
GRINDHOUSE: DOORS OPEN AT MIDNIGHT						
Dark Horse Comics: Oct, 2013 - No. 8, May, 2014 ($3.99)						
1-8: 1-Francavilla-c/DeCampi-s. 1,2-Bee Vixens From Mars. 3,4-Prison Ship Antares						4.00
GRINDHOUSE: DRIVE IN, BLEED OUT						
Dark Horse Comics: Nov, 2014 - No. 8, Aug, 2015 ($3.99)						
1-8: 1,2-Slay Ride; DeCampi-s/Guéra-a. 7,8-Nebulina. 8-Manara-c						4.00
GRIPS (Extreme violence)						
Silverwolf Comics: Sept, 1986 - No. 4, Dec, 1986 ($1.50, B&W, mature)						
1-Tim Vigil-c/a in all						6.00
2-4						4.00
GRIP: THE STRANGE WORLD OF MEN						
DC Comics (Vertigo): Jan, 2002 - No. 5, May, 2002 ($2.50, limited series)						
1-4-Gilbert Hernandez-s/a						3.00
GRIT GRADY (See Holyoke One-Shot No. 1)						
GROO (Also see Sergio Aragonés' Groo...)						
GROO (Sergio Aragonés'...)						
Image Comics: Dec, 1994 - No. 12, Dec, 1995 ($1.95)						
1-12: 2-Indicia reads #1, Jan, 1995; Aragonés-c/a in all						4.00
GROO (Sergio Aragonés'...)						
Dark Horse Comics: Jan, 1998 - No. 4, Apr, 1998 ($2.95)						
1-4: Aragonés-c/a in all						4.00
...: One For One (9/10, $1.00) reprints #1 with red cover frame						3.00
GROO CHRONICLES, THE (Sergio Aragonés)						
Marvel Comics (Epic Comics): June, 1989 - No. 6, Feb, 1990 ($3.50)						
Book 1-6: Reprints early Pacific issues						5.00
GROO: FRAY OF THE GODS (Sergio Aragonés'...)						
Dark Horse Comics: Jul, 2016 - No. 4, Jan, 2017 ($3.99, limited series)						
1-4-Aragonés-c/a; Evanier-s						4.00
GROO: FRIENDS AND FOES (Sergio Aragonés'...)						
Dark Horse Comics: Jan, 2015 - No. 12, Jan, 2016 ($3.99)						
1-12-Aragonés-c/a in all; spotlights on various characters. 1-Spotlight on Captain Ahax						4.00
GROO: GODS AGAINST GROO (Sergio Aragonés'...)						
Dark Horse Comics: Dec, 2022 - No. 4, Mar, 2023 ($3.99, limited series)						
1-4-Aragonés-c/a; Evanier-s						4.00
GROO MEETS TARZAN (Sergio Aragonés'...)						
Dark Horse Comics: Jul, 2021 - No. 4, Nov, 2021 ($3.99, limited series)						
1-4-Aragonés & Evanier-s/Aragonés-a(Groo) & Thomas Yeates (Tarzan)						4.00
GROO: PLAY OF THE GODS (Sergio Aragonés'...)						
Dark Horse Comics: Jul, 2017 - No. 4, Oct, 2017 ($3.99, limited series)						
1-4-Aragonés-c/a; Evanier-s						4.00
GROO SPECIAL						
Eclipse Comics: Oct, 1984 ($2.00, 52 pgs., Baxter paper)						
1-Aragonés-c/a	3	6	9	16	23	30
GROOT (Guardians of the Galaxy)						
Marvel Comics: Aug, 2015 - No. 6, Jan, 2016 ($3.99)						
1-4,6: 1-Loveness-s/Kesinger-a; Rocket Raccoon app. 2-Flashback to Groot meeting Rocket. 3-Silver Surfer app.						4.00
5-Baby Groot app.	2	4	6	9	12	15
GROO THE WANDERER (See Destroyer Duck #1 & Starslayer #5)						
Pacific Comics: Dec, 1982 - No. 8, Apr, 1984						
1-Aragonés-c/a(p)/Evanier-s in all; Aragonés bio.	3	6	9	21	33	45
2-5: 5-Deluxe paper (1.00-c)	2	4	6	9	13	16
6-8	2	4	6	10	14	18
GROO THE WANDERER (Sergio Aragonés'...) (See Marvel Graphic Novel #32)						
Marvel Comics (Epic Comics): March, 1985 - No. 120, Jan, 1995						
1-Aragonés-c/a in all	3	6	9	16	23	30
2-10	1	2	3	5	6	8
11-20,50-($1.50, double size)						5.00
21-49,51-99: 87-direct sale only, high quality paper						4.00
100-($2.95, 52 pgs.)						5.00
101-120						4.00
Groo Carnival, The (12/91, $8.95)-r/#9-12						11.00
Groo Garden, The (4/94, $10.95)-r/#25-28						11.00
GROO VS. CONAN (Sergio Aragonés'...)						
Dark Horse Comics: Jul, 2014 - No. 4, Oct, 2014 ($3.50, limited series)						
1-4: Aragonés & Evanier-s/Aragonés-c/a in all; Thomas Yeates on Conan art						3.50
GROOVY (Cartoon Comics - not CCA approved)						
Marvel Comics Group: March, 1968 - No. 3, July, 1968						
1-Monkees, Ringo Starr, Sonny & Cher, Mamas & Papas photos	9	18	27	59	117	175
2,3	6	12	18	37	66	95
GROSS POINT						
DC Comics: Aug, 1997 - No. 14, Aug, 1998 ($2.50)						
1-14: 1-Waid/Augustyn-s						3.00
GROUNDED						

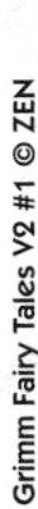
Grimm Fairy Tales V2 #1 © ZEN

Groo vs. Conan #1 © Aragonés & CPI

Guardians of the Galaxy #29 © MAR

	GD	VG	FN	VF	VF/NM	NM-
	2.0	4.0	6.0	8.0	9.0	9.2

Image Comics: July, 2005 - No. 6, May, 2006 ($2.95/$2.99, limited series)
1-6-Mark Sable-s/Paul Azaceta-a. 1-Mike Oeming-c 3.00
Vol. 1: Powerless TPB (2006, $14.99) r/#1-6; sketch pages and creator bios 15.00

GRRL SCOUTS (Jim Mahfood's...) (Also see 40 oz. Collected)
Oni Press: Mar,1999 - No. 4, Dec, 1999 ($2.95, B&W, limited series)
1-4-Mahfood-s/c/a 3.00
TPB (2003, $12.95) r/#1-4; pin-ups by Warren, Winick, Allred, Fegredo and others 13.00

GRRL SCOUTS: MAGIC SOCKS
Image Comics: May, 2017 - No. 6, Oct, 2017 ($3.99, limited series)
1-6-Mahfood-s/c/a 4.00

GRRL SCOUTS: STONE GHOST
Image Comics: Nov, 2021 - No. 6, Apr, 2022 ($3.99, limited series)
1-6-Mahfood-s/c/a 4.00

GRRL SCOUTS: WORK SUCKS
Image Comics: Feb, 2003 - No. 4, May, 2003 ($2.95, B&W, limited series)
1-4-Mahfood-s/c/a 3.00
TPB (2004, $12.95) r/#1-4; pin-ups by Oeming, Dwyer, Tennapel and others 13.00

GRUMBLE
Albatross Funnybooks: 2018 - Present ($3.99)
1-10-Rafer Roberts-s/Mike Norton-a 4.00
...: Memphis & Beyond the Infinite 1-5 (2020 - No 5, 2020, $3.99) Roberts-s/Norton-a 4.00
... vs. The Goon (2019, Free Comic Book Day giveaway) Mike Norton & Eric Powell-a 3.00

GRUMPY CAT
Dynamite Entertainment: 2015 - No. 3, 2015 ($3.99, limited series)
1-3-Short stories; Ben McCool & Ben Fisher-s/Steve Uy & Michelle Nguyen-a 4.00
..., Free Comic Book Day 2016 (giveaway) Short stories by various 3.00

GRUMPY CAT AND POKEY
Dynamite Entertainment: 2016 - No. 6, 2016 ($3.99, limited series)
1-6-Short stories. 1-McCool & Fisher-s/Uy, Haeser & Garbowska-a; multiple covers 4.00

GRUMPY CAT / GARFIELD
Dynamite Entertainment: 2017 - No. 3, 2017 ($3.99, limited series)
1-3-Mark Evanier-s/Steve Uy-a; multiple covers 4.00

GUADALCANAL DIARY (See American Library)

GUARDIAN ANGEL
Image Comics: May, 2002 - No. 2, July, 2002 ($2.95)
1,2-Peterson-s/Wiesenfeld-a 3.00

GUARDIANS
Marvel Comics: Sept, 2004 - No. 5, Dec, 2004 ($2.99, limited series)
1-5-Sumerak-s/Casey Jones-a 3.00

GUARDIANS OF INFINITY
Marvel Comics: Feb, 2016 - No. 8, Sept, 2016 ($4.99)
1-8-Guardians of the Galaxy & 31st century Guardians. 1-Back-up story with The Thing 5.00

GUARDIANS OF KNOWHERE (Secret Wars tie-in)
Marvel Comics: Sept, 2015 - No. 4, Nov, 2015 ($3.99, limited series)
1-4-Bendis-s/Deodato-a; Guardians of the Galaxy, Angela & Mantis app. 4.00
1-Variant Gwenom (Gwen/Venom) cover by Guillory 8.00

GUARDIANS OF METROPOLIS
DC Comics: Nov, 1995 - Feb, 1995 ($1.50, limited series)
1-4: 1-Superman & Granny Goodness app. 4.00

GUARDIANS OF THE GALAXY (Also see The Defenders #26, Marvel Presents #3, Marvel Super-Heroes #18, Marvel Two-In-One #5)
Marvel Comics: June, 1990 - No. 62, July, 1995 ($1.00/$1.25)
1-Valentino-c/a(p) begin; 1st app. Taserface 3 6 9 21 33 45
2-5: 2-Zeck-c(i). 5-McFarlane-c(i) 1 3 4 6 8 10
6-15: 7-Intro Malevolence (Mephisto's daughter); Perez-c(i). 8-Intro Rancor (descendant of Wolverine) in cameo. 9-1st full app. Rancor; Rob Liefeld-c(i). 10-Jim Lee-c(i). 13,14-1st app. Spirit of Vengeance (futuristic Ghost Rider). 14-Spirit of Vengeance vs. The Guardians. 15-Starlin-c(i) 4.00
16-($1.50, 52 pgs.)-Starlin-c(i) 5.00
17-24,26-38,40-47: 17-20-31st century Punishers storyline. 20-Last $1.00-c. 21-Rancor app. 22-Reintro Starhawk. 24-Silver Surfer-c/story; Ron Lim-c. 26-Origin retold. 27-28-Infinity War x-over; 27-Inhumans app. 43-Intro Wooden (son of Thor) 4.00
25-($2.50)-Prism foil-c; Silver Surfer/Galactus-c/s 5.00
25-($2.50)-Without foil-c; newsstand edition 4.00
39-($2.95, 52 pgs.)-Embossed & holo-grafx foil-c; Dr. Doom vs. Rancor 5.00

	GD	VG	FN	VF	VF/NM	NM-
	2.0	4.0	6.0	8.0	9.0	9.2

48,49,51-56: 48-bound-in trading card sheet 4.00
50-($2.00, 52 pgs.)-Newsstand edition 5.00
50-($2.95, 52 pgs.)-Collectors ed. w/foil embossed-c 6.00
57-61 1 2 3 5 6 8
62 2 4 6 10 14 18
Annual 1-4: ('91-'94, 68 pgs.)-1-Origin. 2-Spirit of Vengeance-c/story. 3,4-Bagged w/card 5.00

GUARDIANS OF THE GALAXY (See Annihilation series)
Marvel Comics: July, 2008 - No. 25, Jun, 2010 ($2.99)
1-Continued from Annihilation Conquest #6; origin of the new Guardians: Star-Lord, Drax, Warlock, Rocket Raccoon, Quasar (female version: Phyla-Vell) and Gamora; Mantis and Groot appear but not official members; Cosmo the talking dog and Nova (Richard Rider) app.; Abnett & Lanning-s/Pelletier-a 6 12 18 38 69 100
1-Second printing; variant-c 3 6 9 14 20 25
2,3: 2-Vance Astro (Major Victory) app.; full-size Groot on the cover but still growing (potted plant-size) in story. 3-Starhawk app; Guardians vs. the Universal Church of Truth 2 4 6 10 14 18
3-Variant cover 2 4 6 11 16 20
4,5-Secret Invasion x-overs; Skrulls app. 1 3 4 6 8 10
5-Monkey variant-c by Nic Klein 2 4 6 9 12 15
6-Secret Invasion x-over; Warlock, Gamora, Quasar and Star-Lord leave the team 1 3 4 6 8 10
7-Original Guardians app: Vance Astro, Charlie-27, Martinex & Yondu app; Groot, Mantis and Bug (from the Micronauts) join Rocket Raccoon, Vance Astro (Major Victory) and a re-grown Groot as the Guardians; Blastaar app. 2 4 6 8 10 12
7-Variant-c by Jim Valentino 2 4 6 11 16 20
8-War of Kings x-over; Blastaar & Ronan the Accuser app. 1 3 4 6 8 10
8-Variant-c; Thanos with the Infinity Gauntlet by Brandon Peterson 3 6 9 19 30 40
9-12: 9-War of Kings x-over; Star-Lord and Jack Flagg vs. Blastaar at the super-villain prison in the Negative Zone. 10-War of Kings x-over; Blastaar & Reed Richards app. Star-Lord reunited with the Guardians. 11-Drax and Quasar (Phyla-Vell) story; Maelstrom & Dragon of the Moon app. 12-Moondragon returns; Quasar (Wendell Vaughn) regains the Quantum-bands becomes Protector of the Universe; Maelstrom & Oblivion app; Phyla-Vell becomes new Avatar of Death 1 3 4 6 8 10
13-War of Kings x-over; Phyla-Vell changes name to 'Martyr'; Moondragon & Jack Flagg join the Guardians; Warlock, Drax & Gamora return to Guardians; Black Bolt & the Inhumans, Vulcan, ruler of the Shi'ar Empire and the Starjammers app.; story continues on War of Kings #3 2 4 6 8 10 12
14-20: 14-War of Kings x-over; Warlock vs. Vulcan; Guardians vs. the Inhumans. 15-War of Kings x-over; Guardians vs. the Sh'iar; Black Bolt & the Inhumans app. 16-War of Kings x-over; Star-Lord, Bug, Jack Flagg, Mantis & Cosmo vs. the Badoon; original Guardians: Martinex, Youndu, Charlie-27, Starhawk and Major Victory app. 17-War of Kings x-over; 'death' of Warlock & Martyr; return of the Magus. 18-Star-Lord, Mantis, Cosmo, Bug & Jack Flagg in alternate future 3000AD; Killraven & Hollywood (Wonder Man) app.; vs. the Martians; original Guardians app.; Starhawk, Charlie-27 & Nikki. 19-Kang app.; 'death' of Martyr & Warlock again; 'death' of Major Victory, Gamora, Cosmo & Mantis. 20-Realm of Kings x-over; Star-Lord, Groot, Rocket Raccoon, Bug, Jack Flagg, Drax & Moondragon appear as the Guardians 1 3 4 6 8 10
17-Variant 70th Anniversary Frame-c by Perkins 2 4 6 11 16 20
21-Realm of Kings x-over; brief appearance of the Cancerverse 2 4 6 8 10 12
22,23: 23-Realm of Kings x-over; the Magus returns. 23-Martyr, Gamora, Cosmo, Mantis & Major Victory return to life; Magus app. 2 4 6 9 12 15
23-Deadpool Variant-c by Alex Garner 3 6 9 17 26 35
24-Realm of Kings x-over; Thanos returns, kills Martyr; Maelstrom app. 3 6 9 14 20 25
25-Last issue; Guardians vs. Thanos; leads into Thanos Imperative #1 3 6 9 16 23 30
25-Variant-c by Skottie Young 2 4 6 11 16 20

GUARDIANS OF THE GALAXY (Marvel NOW!) (Also see the 2013 Nova series) (See Incredible Hulk #271, Iron Man #55, Marvel Preview #4,7, Strange Tales #180 and Tales to Astonish #13 for 1st app. of 2014 movie characters)
Marvel Comics: No. 0.1, Apr, 2013; No. 1, May, 2013 - No. 27, Jul, 2015 ($3.99)
0.1-(4/13) Origin of Star-Lord; Bendis-s/McNiven-a 5.00
1-Bendis-s/McNiven-a; Iron Man app.; at least 15 variant covers exist 2 4 6 8 10 12
2-4: Iron Man app. 1 2 3 5 6 8
5-Angela & Thanos app. 5.00
6-13: 8,9-Infinity tie-in; Francavilla-a/c. 10-Maguire-a. 11-13-Trial of Jean Grey 4.00
14-($4.99) Venom and Captain Marvel app.; Bradshaw-a; Guardians of 3014 app. 5.00
15-24,26,27: 16,17-Angela app. 18-20-Original Sin tie-in; Thanos app. 23-Origin of the Symbiotes. 24-Black Vortex crossover 4.00
25-($4.99)-Black Vortex crossover; Kree homeworld destroyed 5.00

	GD 2.0	VG 4.0	FN 6.0	VF 8.0	VF/NM 9.0	NM- 9.2

Annual 1 (2/15, $4.99) Bendis-s/Cho-a; Nick Fury, Dum Dum, Skrulls app. 5.00
...: Best Story Ever 1 (6/15, $3.99) Tim Seeley-s; Nebula & Thanos app. 4.00
...: Galaxy's Most Wanted 1 (9/14, $3.99) Rocket & Groot; DiVito-a; r/Thor #314 Drax app. 4.00
100th Anniversary Special: Guardians of the Galaxy (9/14, $3.99) Future Guardians 4.00
...: Tomorrow's Avengers 1 (9/13, $4.99) Short stories; art by various 5.00
Marvel's Guardians of the Galaxy Prelude 1,2 (6/14 - No. 2, 7/14, $2.99) 1-Gamora & Nebula app. 2-Rocket & Groot 3.00

GUARDIANS OF THE GALAXY
Marvel Comics: Dec, 2015 - No. 19, Jun, 2017 ($3.99)

1-18: 1-Rocket, Groot, Drax, Venom, The Thing and Kitty Pryde team; Bendis-s. 12,13-Civil War II tie-ins. 12-Avengers app. 14-Spider-Man app.; Maguire-a 4.00
19-($4.99) Thanos and Annihilus app.; Schiti, Noto, Pichelli, Bagley & others-a 5.00
1.MU (Monsters Unleashed) (5/17, $4.99) Baldeón-a/Walsh-c 5.00
... Dream On 1 (6/17, $3.99) Death's Head app.; r/1st Taserface from GOTG #1 (1990) 4.00
... Mission Breakout 1 (7/17, $4.99) Hastings-s/Salazar-a; The Collector app. 5.00

GUARDIANS OF THE GALAXY (Marvel Legacy)
Marvel Comics: No. 146, Jan, 2018 - No. 150, Mar, 2018 ($3.99)

146-149: 146-Ant-Man joins; Nova Corps app.; Duggan-s/To-a 4.00
150-($4.99) Lenticular-c by Ross; Adam Warlock returns 5.00

GUARDIANS OF THE GALAXY
Marvel Comics: Mar, 2019 - No. 12, Feb, 2020 ($4.99/$3.99)

1-($4.99) Cates-s/Shaw-a; Cosmic Ghost Rider, Silver Surfer, Beta Ray Bill & others join 5.00
2-11-($3.99) 2-Hela & The Collector app. 4.00
12-($4.99) Donny Cates-s/Cory Smith-a 5.00
Annual 1 (8/19, $4.99) Takes place before issue #7; Cosmo, Quasar, Adam Warlock app. 5.00
...: Marvel Presents No. 3 Facsimile Ed. (3/19, $3.99) r/Marvel Presents #3 w/original ads 4.00
...: The Prodigal Sun 1 (11/19, $4.99) Peter David-s/Francesco Manna-a 5.00

GUARDIANS OF THE GALAXY
Marvel Comics: Mar, 2020 - No. 18, Nov, 2021 ($4.99/$3.99)

1-($4.99) Al Ewing-s/Juann Cabal-a; Nova (Richard Rider) and Marvel Boy app. 5.00
2-12,14-18-($3.99) 3-5-Blackjack O'Hare app. 10-King in Black tie-in 4.00
13-($4.99) Legacy issue #175; Doctor Doom cameo 5.00
...: Cosmic Rewind 1 (1/23, $3.99) Kevin Shinick-s/Gerardo Sandoval-a 4.00

GUARDIANS OF THE GALAXY ADAPTATION ("... Vol. 2 Prelude" on cover)
Marvel Comics: Mar, 2017 - No. 2, Apr, 2017 ($3.99, limited series)

1,2-Adaptation of the 2014 movie; Corona Pilgrim-s/Chris Allen-a 4.00

GUARDIANS OF THE GALAXY & X-MEN: THE BLACK VORTEX
Marvel Comics: Alpha, Apr, 2015 - Omega, Jun, 2015 ($4.99, bookends for crossover)

... Alpha (4/15) Part 1 of crossover; McGuinness-a 5.00
... Omega (6/15) Part 13 of crossover; Ronan app.; McGuinness-a 5.00

GUARDIANS OF THE GALAXY: MOTHER ENTROPY
Marvel Comics: Jul, 2017 - No. 5, Jul, 2017 ($3.99, weekly limited series)

1-5-Starlin-s/Alan Davis-a; Pip the Troll app. 4-Gladiator app. 4.00

GUARDIANS OF THE GALAXY: TELLTALE GAMES (Based on the videogame)
Marvel Comics: Sept, 2017 - No. 5, Jan, 2018 ($3.99, limited series)

1-5: 1-Van Lente-s/Espin-a. 2-5-Cosmo app. 5-Thanos app. 4.00

GUARDIANS TEAM-UP
Marvel Comics: May, 2015 - No. 10, Oct, 2015 ($3.99)

1-10: 1-Bendis-s/Art Adams-a. 1,2-The Avengers & Nebula app. 3-Black Vortex crossover. 4-Gamora & She-Hulk. 7-Drax & Ant-Man. 9-Spider-Man & Star-Lord; Pulido-s/a. 10-Deadpool & Rocket 4.00

GUARDIANS 3000
Marvel Comics: Dec, 2014 - No. 8, Jul, 2015 ($3.99)

1-8: 1-Abnett-s/Sandoval-a; Alex Ross-c; Guardians vs. Badoon in 3014 A.D. 1-6-Ross-c. 6-Guardians meet the 2015 Guardians 4.00

GUARDING THE GLOBE (See Invincible)
Image Comics: Aug, 2010 - No. 6, Oct, 2011 ($3.50)

1-6-Kirkman & Cereno-s/Getty-a. 1-Back-c swipe of Avengers #4 w/Obama 3.50

GUARDING THE GLOBE (2nd series) (See Invincible Universe)
Image Comics: Sept, 2012 - No. 6, Feb, 2013 ($2.99)

1-6: 1-Wraparound-c; Hester-s/Nauck-a 3.00

GUERRILLA WAR (Formerly Jungle War Stories)
Dell Publishing Co.: No. 12, July-Sept, 1965 - No. 14, Mar, 1966

12-14 3 6 9 16 23 30

GUIDEBOOK TO THE MARVEL CINEMATIC UNIVERSE
Marvel Comics: Dec, 2015 - Feb, 2017 ($3.99)

... - Marvel's Agents of S.H.I.E.L.D. Season One (8/16, $3.99) Profile pages 4.00
... - Marvel's Agents of S.H.I.E.L.D. Season Two/Marvel's Agent Carter Season One (12/16, $3.99) Flipbook with character profile pages; both covers by Marcos Martin 4.00
... - Marvel's Agents of S.H.I.E.L.D. Season Three/Marvel's Agent Carter Season Two (2/17, $3.99) Flipbook with character profile pages; covers by Del Mundo & Johnson 4.00
... - Marvel's Avengers: Age of Ultron (11/16, $3.99) Profile pages of characters 4.00
... - Marvel's Captain America: Civil War (3/17, $3.99) Profile pages 4.00
... - Marvel's Captain America: The First Avenger (3/16, $3.99) Profile pages 4.00
... - Marvel's Captain America: The Winter Soldier/Marvel's Ant-Man (7/16, $3.99) Flipbook 4.00
... - Marvel's Doctor Strange (5/17, $3.99) Profile pages of characters, weapons, locations 4.00
... - Marvel's Guardians of the Galaxy (9/16, $3.99) Profile pages of characters, locations 4.00
... - Marvel's Incredible Hulk/Marvel's Iron Man 2 (1/16, $3.99) Flipbook; profile pages 4.00
... - Marvel's Iron Man (12/15, $3.99) Profile pages of characters, weapons, locations 4.00
... - Marvel's Iron Man 3/Marvel's Thor: The Dark World (6/16, $3.99) Flipbook profiles 4.00
... - Marvel's The Avengers (4/16, $3.99) Profile pages of characters, weapons 4.00
... - Marvel's Thor (2/16, $3.99) Profile pages of characters, weapons, locations 4.00

GUILD, THE (Based on the web-series)
Dark Horse Comics: Mar, 2010 - No. 3, May, 2010 ($3.50, limited series)

1-3-Felicia Day-s/Jim Rugg-a; two covers on each 3.50
... Bladezz 1 (6/11, $3.50) Currie-a/Kerschl-c; variant-c by Dalrymple 3.50
... Clara 1 (9/11, $3.50) Chan-a/Chaykin-c; variant-c by Aronowitz 3.50
... Fawkes 1 (5/12, $3.50) Day & Wheaton-s/McKelvie-a; variant-c by Rios 3.50
... Tink 1 (3/11, $3.50) art by Donaldson, Warren, Seeley & others; variant-c by Bagge 3.50
... Vork 1 (12/10, $3.50) Robertson-a/c; variant-c by Hernandez 3.50
... Zaboo 1 (12/11, $3.50) Cloonan-a/Dorkin-c; variant-c by Jeanty 3.50

GUILTY (See Justice Traps the Guilty)

GULLIVER'S TRAVELS (See Dell Jr. Treasury No. 3)
Dell Publishing Co.: Sept-Nov, 1965

1 5 10 15 31 53 75

GUMBY
Wildcard Ink: July, 2006 - No. 3 ($3.99)

1-3-Bob Burden & Rick Geary-s&a 4.00

GUMBY'S SUMMER FUN SPECIAL
Comico: July, 1987 ($2.50)

1-Art Adams-c/a; B. Burden scripts 6.00

GUMBY'S WINTER FUN SPECIAL
Comico: Dec, 1988 ($2.50, 44 pgs.)

1-Art Adams-c/a 6.00

GUMPS, THE (See Merry Christmas..., Popular & Super Comics)
Dell Publ. Co./Bridgeport Herald Corp.: No. 73, 1945; Mar-Apr, 1947 - No. 5, Nov-Dec, 1947

Four Color 73 (Dell)(1945) 13 26 39 89 195 300
1 (3-4/47) 19 38 57 112 179 245
2-5 12 24 36 67 94 120

GUN CANDY (Also see The Ride)
Image Comics: July, 2005 - No. 2 ($5.99)

1,2-Stelfreeze-c/a; flip book with The Ride (1-Pearson-c. 2-Noto-c) 6.00

GUNFIGHTER (Fat & Slat #1-4) (Becomes Haunt of Fear #15 on)
E. C. Comics (Fables Publ. Co.): No. 5, Sum, 1948 - No. 14, Mar-Apr, 1950

5,6-Moon Girl in each 103 206 309 659 1130 1600
7-14: 13,14-Bondage-c 53 106 159 334 567 800

NOTE: *Craig & H. C. Kiefer art in most issues.* ***Craig*** *c-5, 6, 13, 14.* ***Feldstein/Craig*** *a-10.* ***Feldstein*** *a-7-11.* ***Harrison/Wood*** *a-13, 14.* ***Ingels*** *a-5-14; c-7-12.*

GUNFIGHTERS, THE
Super Comics (Reprints): 1963 - 1964

10-12,15,16,18: 10,11-r/Billy the Kid #s? 12-r/The Rider #5(Swift Arrow). 15-r/Straight Arrow #42; Powell-r. 16-r/Billy the Kid #?(Toby). 18-r/The Rider #3; Severin-c 2 4 6 10 14 18

GUNFIGHTERS, THE (Formerly Kid Montana)
Charlton Comics: No. 51, 10/66 - No. 52, 10/67; No. 53, 6/79 - No. 85, 7/84

51,52 2 4 6 11 16 20
53,54,56:53,54-Williamson/Torres-r/Six Gun Heroes #47,49. 56-Williamson/Severin-c; Severin-r/Sheriff of Tombstone #1 1 3 4 6 8 10
55,57-80 6.00
81-84-Lower print run 1 2 3 5 6 8
85-S&K-r/1955 Bullseye 1 3 4 6 8 10

GUNFIRE (See Deathstroke Annual #2 & Showcase 94 #1,2)
DC Comics: May, 1994 - No. 13, June, 1995 ($1.75/$2.25)

1-13: 2-Ricochet-c/story. 5-(9/94). 6-(11/94) 3.00
#0-(10/94) Zero Hour tie-in, released between #5 & #6 3.00

GUN GLORY (Movie)
Dell Publishing Co.: No. 846, Oct, 1957 (one-shot)

Four Color 846-Toth-a, photo-c. 8 16 24 51 96 140

GUNHAWK, THE (Formerly Whip Wilson)(See Wild Western and Two-Gun Western #5)
Marvel Comics/Atlas (MCI): No. 12, Nov, 1950 - No. 18, Dec, 1951

12 23 46 69 138 227 315
13-18: 13-Tuska-a. 16-Colan-a. 18-Maneely-c 16 32 48 96 151 205

GUNHAWKS (Gunhawk No. 7)
Marvel Comics Group: Oct, 1972 - No. 7, October, 1973

1,6: 1-Reno Jones, Kid Cassidy; Shores-c/a(p). 6-Kid Cassidy dies 4 8 12 23 37 50
2-5,7: 7-Reno Jones solo 2 4 6 13 18 22

GUNHAWKS, THE (Marvel 80th Anniversary salute to western comics)
Marvel Comics: Apr, 2019 ($3.99, one shot)

1-David & Maria Lapham-s/Luca Pizzari-a 4.00

GUN HONEY
Titan Comics: Oct, 2021 - No. 4, Jan, 2022 ($3.99, limited series)

1-4-Charles Ardai-s/Ang Hor Kheng-a; multiple covers on each 4.00

GUN HONEY: BLOOD FOR BLOOD
Titan Comics: Sept, 2022 - No. 4, Jan, 2023 ($3.99, limited series)

1-4-Charles Ardai-s/Ang Hor Kheng-a; multiple covers on each 4.00

GUNMASTER (Becomes Judo Master #89 on)
Charlton Comics: 9/64 - No. 4, 1965; No. 84, 7/65 - No. 88, 3-4/66; No. 89, 10/67

V1#1 5 10 15 30 50 70
2-4, V5#84-86: 84-Formerly Six-Gun Heroes 3 6 9 15 22 28
V5#87-89 2 4 6 11 16 20

NOTE: *Vol. 5 was originally cancelled with #88 (3-4/66). #89 on, became Judo Master, then later in 1967, Charlton issued #89 as a Gunmaster one-shot.*

GUNNING FOR HITS
Image Comics: Jan, 2019 - No. 6, Jun, 2019 ($3.99)

1-6-Jeff Rougvie-s/Moritat-a 4.00

GUN RUNNER
Marvel Comics UK: Oct, 1993 - No. 6, Mar, 1994 ($1.75, limited series)

1-($2.75)-Polybagged w/4 trading cards; Spirits of Vengeance app. 5.00
2-6: 2-Ghost Rider & Blaze app. 4.00

GUNS AGAINST GANGSTERS (True-To-Life Romances #8 on)

Guardians of the Galaxy (2019) #4 © MAR

Gun Honey #3 © Winterfall LLC

Gunslinger Spawn #9 © TMP

Curtis Publications/Novelty Press: Sept-Oct, 1948 - No. 6, July-Aug, 1949; V2#1, Sept-Oct, 1949

	GD 2.0	VG 4.0	FN 6.0	VF 8.0	VF/NM 9.0	NM- 9.2
1-Toni & Greg Gayle begins by Schomburg; L.B. Cole-c	58	116	174	371	636	900
2-L.B. Cole-c	39	78	117	240	395	550
3-5	36	72	108	211	343	475
6-Giant shark and Toni Gayle-c by Cole	129	258	387	826	1413	2000
V2#1	34	68	102	199	325	450

NOTE: ***L. B. Cole** c-1-6, V2#1, 2; a-1, 2, 3(2), 4-6.*

GUNSLINGER
Dell Publishing Co.: No. 1220, Oct-Dec, 1961 (one-shot)

	GD 2.0	VG 4.0	FN 6.0	VF 8.0	VF/NM 9.0	NM- 9.2
Four Color 1220-Photo-c	8	16	24	52	99	145

GUNSLINGER (Formerly Tex Dawson...)
Marvel Comics Group: No. 2, Apr, 1973 - No. 3, June, 1973

	GD 2.0	VG 4.0	FN 6.0	VF 8.0	VF/NM 9.0	NM- 9.2
2,3	2	4	6	13	18	22

GUNSLINGERS
Marvel Comics: Feb, 2000 ($2.99)

	GD 2.0	VG 4.0	FN 6.0	VF 8.0	VF/NM 9.0	NM- 9.2
1-Reprints stories of Two-Gun Kid, Rawhide Kid and Caleb Hammer						3.00

GUNSLINGER SPAWN
Image Comics (Todd McFarlane Prods.): Oct, 2021 - Present ($5.99/$2.99)

	GD 2.0	VG 4.0	FN 6.0	VF 8.0	VF/NM 9.0	NM- 9.2
1-($5.99) Todd McFarlane-s/Brett Booth-a; back-up by Ales Kot-s/Philip Tan-a						6.00
2-17-($2.99) McFarlane-s/Booth-a. 3-6-Clown returns						3.00

GUNSMITH CATS: (Title series), **Dark Horse Comics**

	GD 2.0	VG 4.0	FN 6.0	VF 8.0	VF/NM 9.0	NM- 9.2
--BAD TRIP (Manga), 6/98 - No. 6, 11/98 ($2.95, B&W) 1-6						3.00
--BEAN BANDIT (Manga), 1/99 - No. 9 ($2.95, B&W, limited series) 1-9						3.00
--GOLDIE VS. MISTY (Manga), 11/97 - No. 7, 5/98 ($2.95, B&W) 1-7						3.00
--KIDNAPPED (Manga), 11/99 - No. 10, 8/00 ($2.95, B&W) 1-10						3.00
--MISTER V (Manga), 10/00 - No. 11, 8/01 ($3.50/$2.99), B&W) 1-11						3.50
--THE RETURN OF GRAY (Manga), 8/96 - No. 7, 2/97 ($2.95, B&W) 1-7						3.00
--SHADES OF GRAY (Manga), 5/97 - No. 5, 9/97 ($2.95, B&W) 1-5						3.00
--SPECIAL (Manga) Nov, 2001 ($2.99, B&W, one-shot)						3.00

GUNSMOKE (Blazing Stories of the West)
Western Comics (Youthful Magazines): Apr-May, 1949 - No. 16, Jan, 1952

	GD 2.0	VG 4.0	FN 6.0	VF 8.0	VF/NM 9.0	NM- 9.2
1-Gunsmoke & Masked Marvel begin by Ingels; Ingels bondage-c	58	116	174	371	636	900
2-Ingels-c/a(2)	37	74	111	222	361	500
3-Ingels bondage-c/a	33	66	99	194	317	440
4-6: Ingels-c	25	50	75	150	245	340
7-10	16	32	48	98	154	210
11-16: 15,16-Western/horror stories	15	30	45	94	147	200

NOTE: ***Stallman** a-11, 14. **Wildey** a-15, 16.*

GUNSMOKE (TV)
Dell Publishing Co./Gold Key (All have James Arness photo-c): No. 679, Feb, 1956 - No. 27, Feb, 1969 - No. 6, Feb, 1970

	GD 2.0	VG 4.0	FN 6.0	VF 8.0	VF/NM 9.0	NM- 9.2
Four Color 679(#1)	20	40	60	136	303	470
Four Color 720,769,797,844 (#2-5),6(11-1/57-58)	9	18	27	63	129	195
7,8,9,11,12-Williamson-a in all, 4 pgs. each	8	16	24	54	102	150
10-Williamson/Crandall-a, 4 pgs.	8	16	24	54	102	150
13-27	7	14	21	44	82	120
1 (Gold Key)	7	14	21	44	82	120
2-6('69-70)	4	8	12	23	37	50

GUNSMOKE TRAIL
Ajax-Farrell Publ./Four Star Comic Corp.: June, 1957 - No. 4, Dec, 1957

	GD 2.0	VG 4.0	FN 6.0	VF 8.0	VF/NM 9.0	NM- 9.2
1	11	22	33	64	90	115
2-4	7	14	21	35	43	50

GUNSMOKE WESTERN (Formerly Western Tales of Black Rider)
Atlas Comics No. 32-35(CPS/NPI); Marvel No. 36 on: No. 32, Dec, 1955 - No. 77, July, 1963

	GD 2.0	VG 4.0	FN 6.0	VF 8.0	VF/NM 9.0	NM- 9.2
32-Baker & Drucker-a	27	54	81	158	259	360
33,35,36-Williamson-a in each: 5,6 & 4 pgs. plus Drucker-a #33. 33-Kinstler-a?	19	38	57	111	176	240
34-Baker-a, 4 pgs.; Severin-c	20	40	60	114	182	250
37-Davis-a(2); Williamson text illo	15	30	45	90	140	190
38,39: 39-Williamson text illo (unsigned)	14	28	42	82	121	160
40-Williamson/Mayo-a (4 pgs.)	15	30	45	84	127	170
41,42,45,46,48,49,52-54,57,58,60: 49,52-Kid from Texas story. 57-1st Two Gun Kid by Severin. 60-Sam Hawk app. in Kid Colt	13	26	39	74	105	135
43,44-Torres-a	13	26	39	74	105	135
47,51,59,61: 47,51,59-Kirby-a. 61-Crandall-a	14	28	42	80	115	150
50-Kirby, Crandall-a	15	30	45	84	127	170
55,56-Matt Baker-a	15	30	45	86	133	180
62-67,69,71-73,77-Kirby-a. 72-Origin Kid Colt	8	16	24	51	96	140
68,70,74-76: 68-(10¢-c)	7	14	21	46	86	125
68-(10¢ cover price blacked out, 12¢ printed on)	13	26	39	89	195	310

NOTE: ***Colan** a-35-37, 39, 72, 76. **Davis** a-37, 52, 54, 55; c-50, 54. **Ditko** a-66; c-56p. **Drucker** a-.32-34. **Heath** c-33. **Jack Keller** a-34, 35, 40, 51, 53, 55, 56, 60, 61, 65, 68, 69, 71, 72, 74, 75, 77; c-72. **Kirby** a-47, 50, 51, 59, 62(3), 63-67, 69, 71, 73, 77; c-56(w/**Ditko**), 57, 58, 60, 61(w/**Ayers**), 62, 63, 65, 66, 68, 69, 71-77. **Maneely** a-53; c-45. **Robinson** a-35. **Severin** a-35, 59-61; c-34, 35, 39, 42, 43. **Tuska** a-34. **Wildey** a-10, 37, 42, 56, 57. Kid Colt in all. Two-Gun Kid in No. 57, 59, 60-63. Wyatt Earp in No. 45, 48, 49, 51-56, 58.*

GUNS OF FACT & FICTION (Also see A-1 Comics)
Magazine Enterprises: No. 13, 1948 (one-shot)

	GD 2.0	VG 4.0	FN 6.0	VF 8.0	VF/NM 9.0	NM- 9.2
A-1 13-Used in **SOTI,** pg. 19; Ingels & J. Craig-a	36	72	108	211	343	475

GUNS OF THE DRAGON
DC Comics: Oct, 1998 - No. 4, Jan, 1999 ($2.50, limited series)

	GD 2.0	VG 4.0	FN 6.0	VF 8.0	VF/NM 9.0	NM- 9.2
1-4-DCU in the 1920's; Enemy Ace & Bat Lash app.						3.00

GUNWITCH, THE : OUTSKIRTS OF DOOM (See The Nocturnals)
Oni Press: June, 2001 - No. 3, Oct, 2001 ($2.95, B&W, limited series)

	GD 2.0	VG 4.0	FN 6.0	VF 8.0	VF/NM 9.0	NM- 9.2
1-3-Brereton-s/painted-c/Naifeh-s						3.00

GUY GARDNER (Guy Gardner: Warrior #17 on)(Also see Green Lantern #59)
DC Comics: Oct, 1992 - No. 44, July, 1996 ($1.25/$1.50/$1.75)

	GD 2.0	VG 4.0	FN 6.0	VF 8.0	VF/NM 9.0	NM- 9.2
1-Staton-c/a(p) begins						4.00
2-24,26-30: 6-Guy vs. Hal Jordan. 8-Vs. Lobo-c/story. 15-JLA x-over, begin $1.50-c. 18-Begin 4-part Emerald Fallout story; splash page x-over GL #50. 18-21-Vs. Hal Jordan. 24-(9/94)-Zero Hour						3.00
25 (11/94, $2.50, 52 pgs.)						4.00
29 ($2.95)-Gatefold-c						4.00
29-Variant-c (Edward Hopper's Nighthawks)						3.00
31-44: 31-$1.75-c begins. 40-Gorilla Grodd-c/app. 44-Parallax-app. (1 pg.)						3.00
#0-(10/94) Zero Hour tie-in; released between #24 & #25						3.00
Annual 1 (1995, $3.50)-Year One story						4.00
Annual 2 (1996, $2.95)-Legends of the Dead Earth story						4.00

GUY GARDNER: COLLATERAL DAMAGE
DC Comics: 2006 - No. 2 ($5.99, square-bound, limited series)

	GD 2.0	VG 4.0	FN 6.0	VF 8.0	VF/NM 9.0	NM- 9.2
1,2-Howard Chaykin-s/a						6.00

GUY GARDNER REBORN
DC Comics: 1992 - Book 3, 1992 ($4.95, limited series)

	GD 2.0	VG 4.0	FN 6.0	VF 8.0	VF/NM 9.0	NM- 9.2
1-3: Staton-c/a(p). 1-Lobo-c/cameo. 2,3-Lobo-c/s						6.00

GWAR: ORGASMAGEDDON (Based on the band GWAR)
Dynamite Entertainment: 2017 - No. 4, 2017 ($3.99, limited series)

	GD 2.0	VG 4.0	FN 6.0	VF 8.0	VF/NM 9.0	NM- 9.2
1-4-Matt Maguire & Matt Miner-s/Sawyer & Maguire-a; multiple covers						4.00

GWENPOOL (Also see Unbelievable Gwenpool)
Marvel Comics: Feb, 2016; Feb, 2017 ($5.99, one-shots)

	GD 2.0	VG 4.0	FN 6.0	VF 8.0	VF/NM 9.0	NM- 9.2
... Holiday Special: Merry Mix-Up (2/17, $5.99) 1-Deadpool, Squirrel Girl, Punisher app.						6.00
... Special (2/16, $5.99) 1-Christmas-themed short stories; She-Hulk, Deadpool app.						6.00

GWENPOOL STRIKES BACK
Marvel Comics: Oct, 2019 - No. 5, Feb, 2020 ($3.99, limited series)

	GD 2.0	VG 4.0	FN 6.0	VF 8.0	VF/NM 9.0	NM- 9.2
1-5-Leah Williams-s/David Baldeón-a. 1-Spider-Man app. 3-5-Ms. Marvel app. 5-Photo-c						4.00

GWEN STACY (See Giant-Size Gwen Stacy for all 5 chapters)
Marvel Comics: Apr, 2020 - No. 2, May, 2020 ($4.99/$3.99, unfinished 5-issue series)

	GD 2.0	VG 4.0	FN 6.0	VF 8.0	VF/NM 9.0	NM- 9.2
1-($4.99) Gage-s/Nauck-a; main cover by Adam Hughes; Gwen in high school						5.00
2-($3.99) Norman Osborn app.						4.00

GYPSY COLT
Dell Publishing Co.: No. 568, June, 1954 (one-shot)

	GD 2.0	VG 4.0	FN 6.0	VF 8.0	VF/NM 9.0	NM- 9.2
Four Color 568-Movie	6	12	18	42	79	115

GYRO GEARLOOSE (See Dynabrite Comics, Walt Disney's C&S #140 & Walt Disney Showcase #18)
Dell Publishing Co.: No. 1047, Nov-Jan/1959-60 - May-July, 1962 (Disney)

	GD 2.0	VG 4.0	FN 6.0	VF 8.0	VF/NM 9.0	NM- 9.2
Four Color 1047 (No. 1)-All Barks-c/a	16	32	48	107	236	365
Four Color 1095,1184-All by Carl Barks	9	18	27	59	117	175
Four Color 1267-Barks c/a, 4 pgs.	7	14	21	48	89	130
01329-207 (#1, 5-7/62)-Barks-c only (intended as 4-Color 1329?)	5	10	15	35	63	90

HACKER FILES, THE
DC Comics: Aug, 1992 - No. 12, July, 1993 ($1.95)

	GD 2.0	VG 4.0	FN 6.0	VF 8.0	VF/NM 9.0	NM- 9.2
1-12: 1-Sutton-a(p) begins; computer generated-c						3.00

GD VG FN VF VF/NM NM-
2.0 4.0 6.0 8.0 9.0 9.2

HACK/SLASH
Devil's Due Publishing: Apr. 2004 - No. 32, Mar, 2010 ($3.25/$4.95)

1-Seeley-s/Caselli-a/c 4 8 12 28 47 65
...: (The Series) 1-5,7-24,26,27,29-32 (5/07-No. 32, 3/10, $3.50) Flashack to Cassie's childhood and origin. 12-Milk & Cheese cameo. 15-Re-Animator app. 5.00
6,28-Archie parodies 2 4 6 11 16 20
25-($5.50) Double sized issue; Baugh-a; two covers 5.50
...: Comic Book Carnage (3/05) Manfredi-a/Seeley-s; Robert Kirkman & Steve Niles app. 1 3 4 6 8 10
...: First Cut TPB (10/05, $14.95) r/one-shots with sketch pages, designs, interviews 15.00
...: Girls Gone Dead (10/04, $4.95) Manfredi-a 1 3 4 6 8 10
...: Land of Lost Toys 1-3 (11/05 - No. 3, 1/06, $3.25) Crossland-a/Seeley-s 5.00
...: New Reader Halloween Treat #1 (10/08, $3.50) origin retold; Cassie's diary pages 5.00
...: The Final Revenge of Evil Ernie (6/05, $4.95) Salman-a/Seeley-s; two covers 1 2 3 5 6 8
...: Trailers (2/05, $3.25) short stories by Seeley; art by various; three covers 6.00
...: Slice Hard (12/05, $4.95) Seeley-s 5.00
...: Slice Hard Pre-Sliced 25¢ Special (2/06, 25¢) origin story by Seeley; sketch pages 3.00
...: Vs Chucky (3/07, $5.50) Seeley-s/Merhoff-a; 3 covers 1 3 4 6 8 10
...: Vol. 2 Death By Sequel TPB (1/07, $18.99) r/Land of Lost Toys #1-3, Trailers, Slice Hard 19.00
...: Vol. 3 Friday the 31st TPB (10/07, $18.99) r/The Series #1-4 & ... Vs Chucky 19.00

HACK/SLASH
Image Comics: Feb, 2011 - No. 25, Mar, 2013 ($3.50)

1-Seeley-s/Leister-a 2 4 6 8 10 12
2-25: 5-Esquejo-c. 9-11-Bomb Queen app. 5.00
... Annual 2010: Murder Messiah (10/10, $5.99) Seeley-s/Morales-a 1 3 4 6 8 10
... Annual 2011: Hatchet/Slash (11/11, $5.99) 6.00
.../ Eva: Monster's Ball 1-4 (Dynamite Ent., 2011 - No. 4, 2011, $3.99) Jerwa-s/Razek-a 5.00
... 15th Anniversary Celebration (12/19, $5.99) Cassie appears in the real world; pin-ups 6.00
... Hot Shorts 1 (10/22, $3.99) Seeley-s; art by Seeley, Terry & Leister 5.00
...: Me Without You (1/11, $3.50) Leister-a/Seeley-s; 2 covers 1 3 4 6 8 10
.../ Nailbiter 1 (3/15, $4.99) Flip book with Nailbiter / Hack/Slash 1 5.00
...: Trailers #2 (11/10, $6.99) short stories; story & art by various; Seeley-c 7.00
Image Firsts: Hack/Slash #1 (10/10, $1.00) r/#1 (2004) with "Image Firsts" cover frame 4.00

HACK SLASH: MY FIRST MANIAC
Image Comics: Jun, 2010 - No. 4, Sept, 2010 ($3.99)

1-Leister-a/Seeley-s 1 3 4 6 8 10
2-4 5.00

HACK SLASH: RESURRECTION
Image Comics: Oct, 2017 - No. 12, Oct, 2018 ($3.99)

1-12-Tini Howard-s/Celor-a. 3-Vlad returns. 8-11-Vampirella app. 4.00

HACK SLASH: SON OF SAMHAIN
Image Comics: Jul, 2014 - No. 5, Nov, 2014 ($3.99)

1-Laiso-a/Moreci & Seeley-s 2 4 6 8 10 12
2-5 5.00

HACK/SLASH VS. CHAOS
Dynamite Entertainment: 2018 - No. 5, 2019 ($3.99)

1-5-Seeley-s; multiple covers; Evil Ernie, Chastity, Purgatori app. 1-Lobosco-a 4.00

HACK/SLASH VS. VAMPIRELLA
Dynamite Entertainment: 2017 - No. 5, 2018 ($3.99)

1-5-Aldridge-s/Lobosco-a; multiple covers 4.00

HACKTIVIST
Archaia Black Label: Jan, 2014 - No. 4, Apr, 2014 ($3.99)

1-4-Kelly & Lanzing-s/To-a; created by Alyssa Milano 4.00
... Volume 2 (BOOM! Ent.; 7/15 - No. 6, 12/15, $3.99) 1-6-Kelly & Lanzing-s/To-a 4.00

HAGAR THE HORRIBLE (See Comics Reading Libraries in the Promotional Comics section)

HA HA COMICS (Teepee Tim No. 100 on; also see Giggle Comics)
Scope Mag.(Creston Publ.) No. 1-80/American Comics Group: Oct, 1943 - No. 99, Jan, 1955

1-Funny animal 43 86 129 271 461 650
2 24 48 72 142 234 325
3-5: Ken Hultgren-a begins? 19 38 57 109 172 235
6-10 15 30 45 85 130 175
11-20: 14-Infinity-c 14 28 42 76 108 140
21-40 12 24 36 67 94 120
41-43,45-94,97-99: 49,61-X-Mas-c 10 20 30 58 79 100
44-1st Tee-Pee Tim app.; begin series; Little Black Sambo app. 12 24 36 67 94 120
95,96-3-D effect-c/story 20 40 60 115 185 255

HAIL HYDRA (Secret Wars tie-in)
Marvel Comics: Sept, 2015 - No. 4, Jan, 2016 ($3.99, limited series)

1-4-Nomad (Ian Rogers) vs. Hydra; Remender-s/Boschi-a; Venom app. 4.00

HAIR BEAR BUNCH, THE (TV) (See Fun-In No. 13)
Gold Key: Feb, 1972 - No. 9, Feb, 1974 (Hanna-Barbera)

1 4 8 12 23 37 50
2-9 3 6 9 16 24 32

HALCYON
Image Comics: Nov, 2010 - No. 5, May, 2011 ($2.99)

1-5-Guggenheim & Butters-s/Bodenheim-a 3.00

HALF PAST DANGER
IDW Publishing: May, 2013 - No. 6, Oct, 2013 ($3.99, limited series)

1-6: Dinosaurs and Nazis in 1943; Stephen Mooney-s/a/c 4.00

HALF PAST DANGER 2
IDW Publishing: Sept, 2017 - No. 5, Jan, 2018 ($3.99, limited series)

1-5-Nazis in 1943; Stephen Mooney-s/a/c 4.00

HAL JORDAN AND THE GREEN LANTERN CORPS (DC Rebirth) (Also see Green Lanterns)
DC Comics: Sept, 2016 - No. 50, Early Oct, 2018 ($2.99)

1-24: 1-Venditti-s/Sandoval-a; Sinestro app.; GL Corps returns. 4,5,17,22-24-Van Sciver-a. 10-12-Larfleeze app. Kyle becomes a Green Lantern again 3.00
25-($3.99) Van Sciver-a 4.00
26-49: 26,27-Orion of the New Gods app. 30,31-Superman app. 32-Dark Nights: Metal. 37-41-Zod app. 42-Darkstars return. 42,45-Van Sciver-a 3.00
50-($3.99) Sandoval-a; Zod app.
...: Rebirth 1 (9/16, $2.99) Venditti-s/Van Sciver-a; Sinestro & Lyssa app. 3.00

HALLELUJAH TRAIL, THE (See Movie Classics)

HALL OF FAME FEATURING THE T.H.U.N.D.E.R. AGENTS
JC Productions(Archie Comics Group): May, 1983 - No. 3, Dec, 1983

1-3: Thunder Agents-r(Crandall, Kane, Tuska, Wood-a). 2-New Ditko-c 4.00

HALLOWEEN (Movie)
Chaos! Comics: Nov, 2000; Apr, 2001 ($2.95/$2.99, one-shots)

1-Brewer-a; Michael Myers childhood at the Sanitarium 4.00
...II: The Blackest Eyes (4/01, $2.99) Beck-a 4.00
...III: The Devil's Eyes (11/01, $2.99) Justiniano-a 4.00

HALLOWEEN (Halloween Nightdance on cover)(Movie)
Devils Due Publishing: Mar, 2008 - No. 4, May, 2008 ($3.50, limited series)

1-4-Seeley-a/Hutchinson-s; multiple covers on each 3.50
...: 30 Years of Terror (8/08, $5.50) short stories by various incl. Seeley 5.50

HALLOWEEN EVE
Image Comics: Oct, 2012 ($3.99, one-shot)

One-Shot - Brandon Montclare-s/Amy Reeder-a; two covers by Reeder 4.00

HALLOWEEN HORROR
Eclipse Comics: Oct, 1987 (Seduction of the Innocent #7)($1.75)

1-Pre-code horror-r 5.00

HALLOWEEN MEGAZINE
Marvel Comics: Dec, 1996 ($3.95, one-shot, 96 pgs.)

1-Reprints Tomb of Dracula 4.00

HALLOWEEN PARTY
Image Comics: Oct, 2022 ($4.99, one-shot)

1-Scotch McTiernan returns; Duggan & Posehn-s/Koblish-a 5.00

HALLOWS' EVE
Marvel Comics: May, 2023 - Present ($3.99, limited series)

1-Janine Godbe from Amazing Spider-Man; Schultz-s/Dowling-a 4.00

HALO GRAPHIC NOVEL (Based on video game)
Marvel Publishing Inc.: 2006 ($24.99, hardcover with dust jacket)

HC-Anthology set in the Halo universe; art by Bisley, Moebius and others; pin-up gallery by various incl. Darrow, Pratt, Williams and Van Fleet; Phil Hale painted-c 25.00

HALO: BLOOD LINE (Based on video game)
Marvel Comics: Feb, 2010 - No. 5, Jul, 2010 ($3.99, limited series)

1-5-Van Lente-s/Portela-a 4.00

HALO: COLLATERAL DAMAGE (Based on video game)
Dark Horse Comics: Jun, 2018 - No. 3, Aug, 2018 ($3.99)

1-3-Alex Irvine-s/Dave Crossland-a 4.00

HALO: ESCALATION (Based on video game)
Dark Horse Comics: Dec, 2013 - No. 24, Nov, 2015 ($3.99)

1-24: 1-4-Chris Schlerf-s/Sergio Ariño-a 4.00

HALO: FALL OF REACH - BOOT CAMP (Based on video game)
Marvel Comics: Nov, 2010 - No. 4, Apr, 2011 ($3.99, limited series)

1-4-Reed-s/Ruiz-a 4.00

HALO: FALL OF REACH - COVENANT (Based on video game)
Marvel Comics: Jun, 2011 - No. 4, Dec, 2011 ($3.99, limited series)

1-4-Reed-s/Ruiz-a 4.00

HALO: FALL OF REACH - INVASION (Based on video game)
Marvel Comics: Mar, 2012 - No. 4, Aug, 2012 ($3.99, limited series)

1-4-Reed-s/Ruiz-a 4.00

HALO: HELLJUMPER (Based on video game)
Marvel Comics: Sept, 2009 - No. 5, Jan, 2010 ($3.99, limited series)

1-5-Peter David-s/Eric Nguyen-a 4.00

HALO: INITIATION (Based on video game)
Dark Horse Comics: Aug, 2013 - No. 3, Oct, 2013 ($3.99, limited series)

1-3-Brian Reed-s/Marco Castiello-a 4.00

HALO: LONE WOLF (Based on video game)
Dark Horse Comics: Jan, 2019 - No. 4, Apr, 2019 ($3.99, limited series)

1-4-Toole-s/McKeown-a; spotlight on Linda-058 4.00

HALO: RISE OF ATRIOX (Based on video game)
Marvel Comics: Aug, 2017 - No. 5, Jan, 2018 ($3.99, limited series)

1-5: 1-Cullen Bunn-s/Eric Nguyen-a. 2-Houser-s/Gonzalez-a. 3-John Jackson Miller-s 4.00

HALO: UPRISING (Based on video game) (Also see Marvel Spotlight: Halo)
Marvel Comics: Oct, 2007 - No. 4, Jun, 2009 ($3.99, limited series)

1-4-Bendis-s/Maleev-a; takes place between the *Halo 2* and *Halo 3* video games 4.00

HALO JONES (See The Ballad of...)

HAMMER, THE
Dark Horse Comics: Oct, 1997 - No. 4, Jan, 1998 ($2.95, limited series)

1-4-Kelley Jones-s/c/a, ...: Uncle Alex (8/98, $2.95) 3.00

HAMMER, THE: THE OUTSIDER
Dark Horse Comics: Feb, 1999 - No. 3, Apr, 1999 ($2.95, limited series)

Hack / Slack #25 © Hack / Slack Inc.

Hal Jordan and the Green Lantern Corps #17 © DC

Han Solo #2 © Lucasfilm

	GD	VG	FN	VF	VF/NM	NM-
	2.0	4.0	6.0	8.0	9.0	9.2

1-3-Kelley Jones-s/c/a 3.00

HAMMERLOCKE
DC Comics: Sept, 1992 - No. 9, May, 1993 ($1.75, limited series)
1-($2.50, 52 pgs.)-Chris Sprouse-c/a in all 4.00
2-9 3.00

HAMMER OF GOD (Also see Nexus)
First Comics: Feb, 1990 - No. 4, May, 1990 ($1.95, limited series)
1-4 3.00

HAMMER OF GOD: BUTCH
Dark Horse Comics: May, 1994 - No. 4, Aug, 1994 ($2.50, limited series)
1-3 3.00

HAMMER OF GOD: PENTATHLON
Dark Horse Comics: Jan, 1994 ($2.50, one shot)
1-Character from Nexus 3.00

HAMMER OF GOD: SWORD OF JUSTICE
First Comics: Feb 1991 - Mar 1991 ($4.95, lim. series, squarebound, 52 pgs.)
V2#1,2 5.00

HAMMER OF THE GODS
Insight Studio Groups: 2001 - No. 5, 2001 ($2.95, limited series)
1-Michael Oeming & Mark Wheatley-s/a; Frank Cho-c 6.00
1-(IDW, 7/11, $1.00) reprints #1 with "Hundred Penny Press" logo on Oeming cover 3.00
2-5: 3-Hughes-c. 5-Dave Johnson-c 3.00
The Color Saga (2002, $4.95) r/"Enemy of the Gods" internet strip 5.00
Mortal Enemy TPB (2002, $18.95) r/#1-5; intro. by Peter David; afterword by Raven 19.00

HAMMER OF THE GODS: HAMMER HITS CHINA
Image Comics: Feb, 2003 - No. 3, Sept, 2003 ($2.95, limited series)
1-3-Oeming & Wheatley-s/a; Oeming-c. 2-Frankenstein Mobster by Wheatley 3.00

HANDBOOK OF THE CONAN UNIVERSE, THE (Reprinted in The Official... Anniversary Ed.)
Marvel Comics: June, 1985; Jan, 1986 ($1.25, one-shot)
1-(6/85) Kaluta-c (2 printings) 6.00
1-(1/86) Kaluta-c 6.00
nn-(no date, circa '87-88, B&W, 36 pgs.) reprints '86 with changes; new painted cover
1 2 3 5 6 8

HAND OF FATE (Formerly Men Against Crime)
Ace Magazines: No. 8, Dec, 1951 - No. 25, Dec, 1954 (Weird/horror stories) (Two #25's)
8-Surrealistic text story 60 120 180 381 653 925
9,10,21-Necronomicon sty; drug belladonna used 41 82 123 256 428 600
11-18,20,22,23 36 72 108 211 343 475
19-Bondage, hypo needle scenes 43 86 129 271 461 650
24-Electric chair-c 50 100 150 315 533 750
25a(11/54), 25b(12/54)-Both have Cameron-a 36 72 108 211 343 475
NOTE: ***Cameron** a-9, 10, 19-25a, 25b; c-13. **Sekowsky** a-8, 9, 13, 14.*

HAND OF FATE
Eclipse Comics: Feb, 1988 - No. 3, Apr, 1988 ($1.75/$2.00, Baxter paper)
1-3; 3-B&W 4.00

HANDS OF THE DRAGON
Seaboard Periodicals (Atlas): June, 1975
1-Origin/1st app.; Craig-a(p)/Mooney inks 3 6 9 14 19 24

HANGMAN, THE
Archie Comic Publications: Dec, 2015 - No. 4, Dec, 2016 ($3.99)
1-4-Tieri-s/Ruiz-a; new Hangman recruited; multiple covers 4.00

HANGMAN COMICS (Special Comics No. 1; Black Hood No. 9 on)
(Also see Flyman, Mighty Comics, Mighty Crusaders & Pep Comics)
MLJ Magazines: No. 2, Spring, 1942 - No. 8, Fall, 1943
2-The Hangman, Boy Buddies begin 420 840 1260 2940 5170 7400
3-Beheading splash pg.; Nazi war-c; classic-c 622 1244 1866 4541 8021 11,500
4-Classic Nazi WWII hunchback torture-c 459 918 1377 3350 5925 8500
5-1st Japan war-c; bondage/torture-c 300 600 900 1950 3375 4800
6-Horror-c 290 580 870 1856 3178 4500
7,8: 8-2nd app. Super Duck (ties w/Jolly Jingles #11)
265 530 795 1694 2897 4100
NOTE: ***Fuje** a-7(3), 8(3); c-3. **Reinman** c/a-3. Bondage c-3. **Sahle** c-6.*

HANK
Pentagon Publishing Co.: 1946
nn-Coulton Waugh's newspaper reprint 12 24 36 69 97 125

HANK HOWARD, PIZZA DETECTIVE IN CALIGULA'S SAFE
Bad Idea: May, 2021 ($1.00, one-shot)
1-Venditti-s/Lapham-a 5.00

HANK JOHNSON, AGENT OF HYDRA (Secret Wars tie-in)
Marvel Comics: Oct, 2015 ($3.99, one-shot)
1-Mandel-s/Walsh-a; Steranko cover swipe by Conner 4.00

HANNA-BARBERA (See Golden Comics Digest No. 2, 7, 11)

HANNA-BARBERA ALL-STARS
Archie Publications: Oct, 1995 - No. 4, Apr, 1996 ($1.50, bi-monthly)
1-4 4.00

HANNA-BARBERA BANDWAGON (TV)
Gold Key: Oct, 1962 - No. 3, Apr, 1963
1-Giant, 84 pgs. 1-Augie Doggie app.; 1st app. Lippy the Lion, Touché Turtle & Dum Dum, Wally Gator, Loopy de Loop, 11 22 33 73 157 240
2-Giant, 84 pgs.; Mr. & Mrs. J. Evil Scientist (1st app.) in Snagglepuss story; Yakky Doodle, Ruff and Reddy and others app. 8 16 24 51 96 140
3-Regular size; Mr. & Mrs. J. Evil Scientist app. (pre-#1), Snagglepuss, Wally Gator and others app. 6 12 18 40 73 105

HANNA-BARBERA GIANT SIZE
Harvey Comics: Oct, 1992 - No. 3 ($2.25, 68 pgs.)
V2#1-3:Flintstones, Yogi Bear, Magilla Gorilla, Huckleberry Hound, Quick Draw McGraw, Yakky Doodle & Chopper, Jetsons & others 6.00

HANNA-BARBERA HI-ADVENTURE HEROES (See Hi-Adventure...)

HANNA-BARBERA PARADE (TV)
Charlton Comics: Sept, 1971 - No. 10, Dec, 1972
1 6 12 18 41 76 110
2,4-10 4 8 12 25 40 55
3-(52 pgs.)- "Summer Picnic" 5 10 15 33 57 80
NOTE: *No. 4 (1/72) went on sale late in 1972 with the January 1973 issues.*

HANNA-BARBERA PRESENTS
Archie Publications: Nov, 1995 - No. 8 ($1.50, bi-monthly)
1-8: 1-Atom Ant & Secret Squirrel. 2-Wacky Races. 3-Yogi Bear. 4-Quick Draw McGraw & Magilla Gorilla. 5-A Pup Named Scooby-Doo. 6-Superstar Olympics. 7-Wacky Races. 8-Frankenstein Jr. & the Impossibles 4.00

HANNA-BARBERA SPOTLIGHT (See Spotlight)

HANNA-BARBERA SUPER TV HEROES (TV)
Gold Key: Apr, 1968 - No. 7, Oct, 1969 (Hanna-Barbera)
1-The Birdman, The Herculoids (ends #6; not in #3), Moby Dick, Young Samson & Goliath (ends #2,4), and The Mighty Mightor begin; Spiegle-a in all
13 26 39 89 195 300
2-The Galaxy Trio app.; Shazzan begins; 12¢ & 15¢ versions exist
9 18 27 59 117 175
3,6,7-The Space Ghost app. 8 16 24 51 96 140
4,5 7 14 21 44 82 120
NOTE: *Birdman in #1,2,4,5. Herculoids in #2,4-7. Mighty Mightor in #1,2,4-7. Moby Dick in all. Shazzan in #2-5. Young Samson & Goliath in #1,3.*

HANNA-BARBERA TV FUN FAVORITES (See Golden Comics Digest #2,7,11)

HANNA-BARBERA (TV STARS) (See TV Stars)

HANS BRINKER (Disney)
Dell Publishing Co.: No. 1273, Feb, 1962 (one-shot)
Four Color 1273-Movie, photo-c 6 12 18 37 66 95

HANS CHRISTIAN ANDERSEN
Ziff-Davis Publ. Co.: 1953 (100 pgs., Special Issue)
nn-Danny Kaye (movie)-Photo-c; fairy tales 20 40 60 114 182 250

HANSEL & GRETEL
Dell Publishing Co.: No. 590, Oct, 1954 (one-shot)
Four Color 590-Partial photo-c 7 14 21 49 92 135

HANSI, THE GIRL WHO LOVED THE SWASTIKA
Spire Christian Comics (Fleming H. Revell Co.): 1973, 1976 (39¢/49¢)
1973 edition with 39¢-c 11 22 33 77 166 255
1976 edition with 39¢-c 9 18 27 63 129 195
1976 edition with 49¢-c 14 28 42 96 211 325

HAN SOLO (Star Wars)
Marvel Comics: Aug, 2016 - No. 5, Jan, 2017 ($3.99, limited series)
1-5-Marjorie Liu-s/Mark Brooks-a/Lee Bermejo-c; takes place between Episodes 4 & 5 4.00

HAP HAZARD COMICS (Real Love No. 25 on)

GD 2.0 | VG 4.0 | FN 6.0 | VF 8.0 | VF/NM 9.0 | NM- 9.2

Ace Magazines (Readers' Research): Summer, 1944 - No. 24, Feb, 1949
(#1-6 are quarterly issues)
1 20 40 60 118 192 265
2 12 24 36 69 97 125
3-10 10 20 30 56 76 95
11,12,15,16,20-24 9 18 27 52 69 85
13,17-19-Good Girl covers 39 78 117 240 395 550
14-(4/47) Feldstein-c; Cary Grant, Frank Sinatra, Van Johnson, Guy Madison, Alan Ladd and Robert Taylor app. 43 86 129 271 461 650

HAP HOPPER (See Comics Revue No. 2)

HAPPIEST MILLIONAIRE, THE (See Movie Comics)

HAPPI TIM (See March of Comics No. 182)

HAPPY
Image Comics: Sept, 2012 - No. 4, Feb, 2013 ($2.99, limited series)
1-4-Grant Morrison-s/Darick Robertson-a. 1-Covers by Robertson & Allred 5.00

HAPPY BIRTHDAY MARTHA WASHINGTON (Also see Give Me Liberty, Martha Washington Goes To War, & Martha Washington Stranded In Space)
Dark Horse Comics: Mar, 1995 ($2.95, one-shot)
1-Miller script; Gibbons-c/a 4.00

HAPPY COMICS (Happy Rabbit No. 41 on)
Nedor Publ./Standard Comics (Animated Cartoons): Aug, 1943 - No. 40, Dec, 1950
(Companion to Goofy Comics)
1-Funny animal 39 78 117 240 395 550
2 20 40 60 118 192 265
3-10 15 30 45 85 130 175
11-19 13 26 39 78 112 145
20-31,34-37-Frazetta text illos in all (2 in #34&35, 3 in #27,28,30). 27-Al Fago-a 15 30 45 83 124 165
32-Frazetta-a, 7 pgs. plus 2 text illos; Roussos-a 27 54 81 158 259 360
33-Frazetta-a(2), 6 pgs. each (Scarce) 36 72 108 211 343 475
38-40 12 24 36 69 97 125

HAPPYDALE: DEVILS IN THE DESERT
DC Comics (Vertigo): 1999 - No. 2, 1999 ($6.95, limited series)
1,2-Andrew Dabb-s/Seth Fisher-a 7.00

HAPPY DAYS (TV)(See Kite Fun Book)
Gold Key: Mar, 1979 - No. 6, Feb, 1980
1-Photo-c of TV cast; 35¢-c 5 10 15 30 50 70
2-6-(40¢-c) 2 4 6 10 14 18

HAPPY HOLIDAY (See March of Comics No. 181)

HAPPY HORROR DAYS
Archie Comic Publications: Feb, 2023 ($3.99, one-shot)
1-Short Christmas-themed horror stories; Krampus app. 4.00

HAPPY HOULIHANS (Saddle Justice No. 3 on; see Blackstone, The Magician Detective)
E. C. Comics: Fall, 1947 - No. 2, Winter, 1947-48
1-Origin Moon Girl (same date as Moon Girl #1) 106 212 318 673 1162 1650
2 40 80 120 244 402 560

HAPPY HOUR
AHOY Comics: 2020 - No. 6, 2021 ($3.99, limited series)
1-6-Peter Milligan-s/Michael Montenat-a 4.00

HAPPY JACK
Red Top (Decker): Aug, 1957 - No. 2, Nov, 1957
V1#1,2 7 14 21 35 43 50

HAPPY JACK HOWARD
Red Top (Farrell)/Decker: 1957
nn-Reprints Handy Andy story from E. C. Dandy Comics #5, renamed "Happy Jack" 6 12 18 31 38 45

HAPPY RABBIT (Formerly Happy Comics)
Standard Comics (Animated Cartoons): No. 41, Feb, 1951 - No. 48, Apr, 1952
41-Funny animal 11 22 33 64 90 115
42-48 9 18 27 50 65 80

HARBINGER (Also see Unity)
Valiant: Jan, 1992 - No. 41, June, 1995 ($1.95/$2.50)
0-Prequel to the series; available by redeeming coupons in #1-6; cover image has pink sky; title logo is blue 5 10 15 31 53 75
0-(2nd printing) cover has blue sky & red logo 1 3 4 6 8 10
1-1st app. (with coupon) 6 12 18 38 69 100
2-4: 4-Low print run 3 6 9 14 19 24
5,6: 5-Solar app. 6-Torque dies 2 4 6 9 12 15
7-10: 8,9-Unity x-overs. 8-Miller-c. 9-Simonson-c. 10-1st app. H.A.R.D Corps (10/92) 1 2 3 5 6 8
11-24,26-41: 14-1st app. Stronghold. 18-Intro Screen. 19-1st app. Stunner. 22-Archer & Armstrong app. 24-Cover similar to #1. 26-Intro New Harbingers. 29-Bound-in trading card. 30-H.A.R.D. Corps app. 32-Eternal Warrior app. 33-Dr. Eclipse app. 4.00
25-($3.50, 52 pgs.)-Harada vs. Sting 5.00
...: Acts of God 1 (1/98, $3.95) Paco Diaz-a 4.00
...Files 1,2 (8/94,2/95 $2.50) 4.00
...: The Beginning HC (2007, $24.95) recolored reprints #0-7 and Story of Harada from coupons from #1-6; new "Origin of Harada" story by Shooter and Bob Hall 30.00
Trade paperback nn (11/92, $9.95)-Reprints #1-4 & comes polybagged with a copy of Harbinger #0 w/new-c. Price for TPB only 15.00
NOTE: *Issues 1-6 have coupons with origin of Harada and are redeemable for Harbinger #0.*

HARBINGER
Valiant Entertainment: Jun, 2012 - No. 25, Jul, 2014 ($3.99)(#0 released between #8 & #9)
1-Dysart-s/Khari Evans-a; covers by Lozzi and Suayan (Pullbox variant) 4.00
1-Variant cover by Braithwaite 10.00
1-QR voice variant cover by Jelena Djurdjevic 45.00
2-24-Two covers on each (standard & pullbox). 2-Origin continues. 11-14-Harbinger Wars tie-in. 23-Flamingo dies 4.00
25-($4.99) Back-up story by Tiwary & Larosa; bonus features and cover gallery 5.00
#0 (2/13, $3.99) Origin of Harada; Suayan & Pere Pérez-a; covers by Crain & Suayan 4.00
#0-Variant gatefold-c by Lewis Larosa 15.00
... Bleeding Monk #0 (3/14, $3.99) Dysart-s; art by Evans, Suayan, Segovia & LaRosa 4.00
... Faith #0 (12/14, $3.99) Dysart-s; Robert Gill-a 4.00

HARBINGER, THE
Valiant Entertainment: Oct, 2021 - No. 8, May, 2022 ($3.99)
1-8-Kelly & Lansing-s/Rodriguez-a; Pete Stanchek returns. 4-Faith cameo 4.00

HARBINGER: OMEGAS
Valiant Entertainment: Jul, 2014 - No. 3, Oct, 2014 ($3.99, limited series)
1-3-Dysart-s/Sandoval-a 4.00

HARBINGER RENEGADE
Valiant Entertainment: Nov, 2016 - No. 8, Oct, 2017; No. 0 Nov, 2017 ($3.99, limited series)
1-8: 1-Rafer Roberts-s/Darick Robertson-a; intro Alexander Solomon. 6-Ryp-a 4.00
#0-(11/17) Follows #8; Ryp-a; H.A.R.D. Corps app. 4.00

HARBINGER WARS
Valiant Entertainment: Apr, 2013 - No. 4, Jul, 2013 ($3.99, limited series)
1-4: 1-Dysart-s/Henry, Crain & Suayan-a; covers by Larosa & Henry (Pullbox) 4.00
1-Variant cover by Crain 10.00
1-Variant cover by Zircher 50.00

HARBINGER WARS 2
Valiant Entertainment: May, 2018 - No. 4, Aug, 2018 ($3.99, limited series)
1-4-Kindt-s/Giorello-a; Bloodshot, Ninjak, X-O Manowar, Live Wire app. 4.00
...: Aftermath 1 (9/18, $3.99) Kindt-s/Pollina-a; X-O Manowar & Live Wire app. 4.00
...: Prelude (5/18, $3.99) Heisserer-s/Allén-a 4.00

HARD BOILED
Dark Horse Comics: Sept, 1990 - No. 3, Mar, 1992 ($4.95/$5.95, 8 1/2x11", lim. series)
1-Frank Miller-s/Darrow-c/a in all; sexually explicit & violent 3 6 9 14 19 24
2,3 2 4 6 8 10 12
TPB (5/93, $15.95) 20.00
Big Damn Hard Boiled (12/97, $29.95, B&W) r/#1-3 4 8 12 23 37 50

HARDCASE (See Break Thru, Flood Relief & Ultraforce, 1st Series)
Malibu Comics (Ultraverse): June, 1993 - No. 26, Aug, 1995 ($1.95/$2.50)
1-Intro Hardcase; Dave Gibbons-c; has coupon for Ultraverse Premiere #0; Jim Callahan-a(p) begin, ends #3 4.00
1-With coupon missing 2.00
1-Platinum Edition 6.00
1-Holographic Cover Edition; 1st full-c holograph tied w/Prime 1 & Strangers 1 8.00
1-Ultra Limited silver foil-c 6.00
2,3-Callahan-a, 2-($2.50)-Newsstand edition bagged w/trading card 3.00
4,6-15, 17-19: 4-Strangers app. 7-Break-Thru x-over. 8-Solution app. 9-Vs. Turf. 12-Silver foil logo, wraparound-c. 17-Prime app. 3.00
5-($2.50, 48 pgs.)-Rune flip-c/story by B. Smith (3 pgs.) 4.00
16 ($3.50, 68 pgs.)-Rune pin-up 4.00
20-26: 23-Loki app. 3.00
NOTE: *Perez a-8(2); c-20i.*

HARDCORE
Image Comics: May, 2012 ($2.99)
1-Kirkman-s/Stelfreeze-a/Silvestri-c 2 4 6 8 10 12

HARDCORE
Image Comics (Skybound): Dec, 2018 - No. 5, Apr, 2019 ($3.99)
1-5-Diggle-s/Vitti-a/Panosian-c 4.00

HARDCORE: RELOADED
Image Comics (Skybound): Dec, 2019 - No. 5, Jun, 2020 ($3.99)
1-5-Brandon Thomas-s/Francis Portela-a/Nic Klein-c 4.00

HARDCORE STATION
DC Comics: July, 1998 - No. 6, Dec, 1998 ($2.50, limited series)
1-6-Starlin-s/a(p). 3-Green Lantern-c/app. 5,6-JLA-c/app. 3.00

H.A.R.D. CORPS, THE (See Harbinger #10)
Valiant: Dec, 1992 - No. 30, Feb, 1995 ($2.25) (Harbinger spin-off)
1-($2.50)-Gatefold-c by Jim Lee & Bob Layton 5.00
1-Gold variant 15.00
2-30: 5-Bloodshot-c/story cont'd from Bloodshot #3. 5-Variant edition; came w/Comic Defense System. 10-Turok app. 17-vs. Armorines. 18-Bound-in trading card. 20-Harbinger app. 3.00

HARD TIME
DC Comics (Focus): Apr, 2004 - No. 12, Mar, 2005 ($2.50)
1-12-Gerber-s/Hurtt-a; 1-Includes previews of other DC Focus series 3.00
...: 50 to Life (2004, $9.95, TPB) r/#1-6; cover gallery with sketches 10.00

HARD TIME: SEASON TWO
DC Comics: Feb, 2006 - No. 7, Aug, 2006 ($2.50/$2.99)
1-5-Gerber-s/Hurtt-a 3.00
6,7-($2.99) 7-Ethan paroled in 2053 3.00

HARDWARE
DC Comics (Milestone): Apr, 1993 - No. 50, Apr, 1997 ($1.50/$1.75/$2.50)
1-($2.95)-Collector's Edition polybagged w/poster & trading card (direct sale only) 6.00
1-Platinum Edition 7 14 21 46 86 125
1-Regular edition 1 3 4 6 8 10
2-15,17-19: 11-Shadow War x-over. 11,14-Simonson-c. 12-Buckler-a(p). 17-Worlds Collide Pt. 2. 18-Simonson-c; Worlds Collide Pt. 9. 15-1st Humberto Ramos DC work 3.00
16,25: 16-($2.50, 52 pgs.)-Newsstand Ed. 25-($2.95, 52 pgs.) 4.00
16,50-($3.95, 52 pgs.)-16-Collector's Edition w/gatefold 2nd cover by Byrne; new armor; Icon app. 6.00
20-24,26-48 3.00

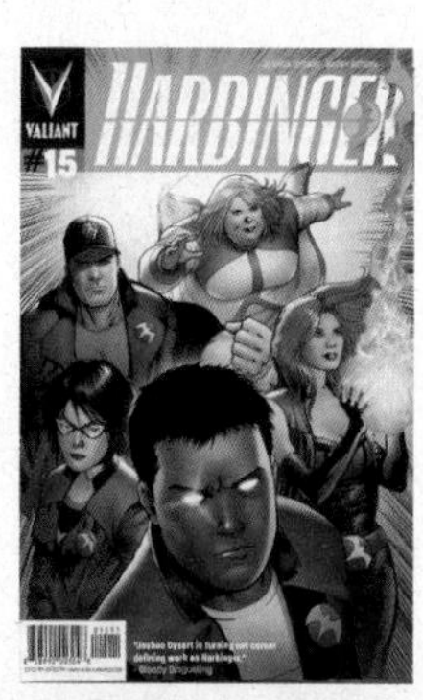

Harbinger (2013) #15 © VAL

Hardware: Season One #6 © Milestone

Harley Quinn (2016) #50 © DC

GD VG FN VF VF/NM NM-
2.0 4.0 6.0 8.0 9.0 9.2

49-Moebius-c 5 10 15 35 63 90
...: The Man in the Machine TPB (2010, $19.99) r/#1-8 20.00

HARDWARE: SEASON ONE (Milestone Returns)
DC Comics: Oct, 2021 - No. 6, Jul, 2022 ($3.99, limited series)

1-6-Brandon Thomas-s/Denys Cowan-a 4.00

HARDY BOYS, THE (Disney)
Dell Publ. Co.: No. 760, Dec, 1956 - No. 964, Jan, 1959 (Mickey Mouse Club)

Four Color 760 (#1)-Photo-c 11 22 33 72 154 235
Four Color 830(8/57), 887(1/58), 964-Photo-c 9 18 27 60 120 180

HARDY BOYS, THE (TV)
Gold Key: Apr, 1970 - No. 4, Jan, 1971

1 4 8 12 27 44 60
2-4 3 6 9 17 26 35

HARLAN ELLISON'S DREAM CORRIDOR
Dark Horse Comics: Mar, 1995 - No. 5, July, 1995 ($2.95, anthology)

1-5: Adaptation of Ellison stories. 1-4-Byrne-a. 4.00
Special (1/95, $4.95) 6.00
Trade paperback-(1996, $18.95, 192 pgs)-r/#1-5 & Special #1 19.00

HARLAN ELLISON'S DREAM CORRIDOR QUARTERLY
Dark Horse Comics: V2#1, Aug, 1996 ($5.95, anthology, squarebound)

V2#1-Adaptations of Ellison's stories w/new material; Neal Adams-a 6.00
Volume 2 TPB (3/07, $19.95) r/V2#1 and unpublished material incl. last Swan-a 20.00

HARLEEN
DC Comics (Black Label): Nov, 2019 - No. 3, Feb, 2020 ($7.99, 10-3/4" x 8-1/2", lim. series)

1-3-Retelling of Harley Quinn's origin with the Joker; Stjepan Sejic-s/a 8.00

HARLEM GLOBETROTTERS (TV) (See Fun-In No. 8, 10)
Gold Key: Apr, 1972 - No. 12, Jan, 1975 (Hanna-Barbera)

1 5 10 15 30 50 70
2-5 3 6 9 15 22 28
6-12 2 4 6 13 18 22

NOTE: *#4, 8, and 12 contain 16 extra pages of advertising.*

HARLEQUIN VALENTINE
Dark Horse Comics: Nov, 2001 ($10.95, hardcover, one-shot)

nn-Neil Gaiman-s; painted-a/c by John Bolton 11.00

HARLEY & IVY MEET BETTY & VERONICA (Archie Comics)
DC Comics: Dec, 2017 - No. 6, May, 2018 ($3.99, limited series)

1-6: 1-Harvey & Ivy go to Riverdale; Dini & Andreyko-s/Braga-a. 1-Conner-c. 2-Zatanna app. 3,4-The Joker app. 4.00
1-Variant-c by Adam Hughes 5.00

HARLEY QUINN (See Batman Adventures #12 for 1st app.)(Also see Gotham City Sirens, Old Lady Harley, and Suicide Squad)
DC Comics: Dec, 2000 - No. 38, Jan, 2004 ($2.95/$2.25/$2.50)

1-Joker and Poison Ivy app.; Terry & Rachel Dodson-a/c
5 10 15 33 57 80
2,3-($2.25): 2-Two-Face-c/app. 3-Slumber party 2 4 6 11 16 20
4-9,11-($2.25). 6,7-Riddler app. 1 3 4 6 8 10
10-Batgirl-c/s 2 4 6 10 14 18
12-($2.95) Batman app. 2 4 6 10 14 18
13,17-19: 13-Joker: Last Laugh. 17,18-Bizarro-c/app. 19-Superman-c
2 4 6 11 16 20
14-16,20-24,26-31,33-37: 23-Begin $2.50-c. 23,24-Martian Manhunter app.
1 2 3 5 6 8
25-Classic Joker-c/s 3 6 9 16 23 30
32-Joker-c/app. 2 4 6 11 16 20
38-Last issue; Adlard-a/Morse-c 3 6 9 14 20 25
Harley & Ivy: Love on the Lam (2001, $5.95) Winick-s/Chiodo-c/a
3 6 9 14 20 26
...: Our Worlds at War (10/01, $2.95) Jae Lee-c; art by various
2 4 6 10 14 18

HARLEY QUINN (DC New 52)
DC Comics: No. 0, Jan, 2014 - No. 30, Sept, 2016 ($2.99/$3.99)

0-Conner & Palmiotti-s; art by Conner & various; Conner-c
2 4 6 10 14 18
0-Variant-c by Stephane Roux 3 6 9 14 20 25
1-(2/14) Chad Hardin-a; Conner-c 3 6 9 17 25 34
1-Variant-c by Adam Hughes 13 26 39 89 195 300
1-Halloween Fest Special Edition (12/15, free) r/#1 with "Halloween ComicFest" logo 5.00
2-Poison Ivy app. 2 4 6 9 12 15
3-5: 4-Roux-a 1 2 3 5 6 8
6-16: 6,7-Poison Ivy app. 11-13-Power Girl app. 16-Intro. of The Gang of Harleys 4.00
17-30-($3.99) 17-19-Capt Strong app. 20,21-Deadshot app. 25-Joker app. 26-28-Red Tool app. 30-Charretier-a; Poison Ivy app. 4.00
Annual 1 (12/14, $5.99) Polybagged with "Rub 'N Smell" pages 6.00
... & The Suicide Squad April Fools' Special 1 (6/16, $4.99) Rob Williams-s/Jim Lee-a 5.00
...Director's Cut #0 (8/14, $4.99) With commentary by Conner & Palmiotti; cover gallery 5.00
...: Futures End 1 (11/14, $2.99, regular-c) Five years later; Joker app. 5.00
...: Futures End 1 (11/14, $3.99, 3-D cover) 1 3 4 6 8 10
... Holiday Special (2/15, $4.99) Christmas-themed stories; back-up Darwyn Cooke-a
1 3 4 6 8 10
... Invades Comic-Con International: San Diego 1 (9/14, $4.99) Wraparound-c
1 3 4 6 8 10
... Road Trip Special (11/15, $5.99) Harley, Catwoman & Poison Ivy road trip; Conner-c
1 2 3 5 6 8
... Valentine's Day Special (4/15, $4.99) Bruce Wayne and Poison Ivy app.
1 2 3 5 6 8

HARLEY QUINN (DC Rebirth)
DC Comics: Oct, 2016 - No. 75, Oct, 2020 ($2.99/$3.99)

1-Conner & Palmiotti-s/Hardin-a; Poison Ivy & Red Tool app.
1 2 3 5 6 8
2-6: 4-Linsner-a. 6-Joker flashback w/Jill Thompson-a (4 pgs.) 4.00
7-24: 9-Kaluta-a (4 pgs.). 10-Linsner & Moritat-a. 15,16-Power Girl & Atlee app. 17-Back-up stories by Dini & Palmiotti-s/Blevins-a begin, thru #25; Joker app. 3.00
25-($3.99) Back-up story w/Joker continues in Harley Loves Joker #1 4.00
26-46: 27-Tieri-s/Carlini-a/Thompson-c. 29-Kaluta-a (5 pgs.) 34-Last Palmiotti & Conner-s. 35-39-Tieri-s. 36,37-Penguin app. 42-Old Lady Harley. 45,46-Granny Goodness & Female Furies app. 3.00
47-49,51-74 ($3.99) 47-Harley on Apokolips. 48,49-Lord Death Man app. 51,52-Capt. Triumph app. 57,58-Batman app. 71-74-Booster Gold app. 4.00
50-($4.99) Jonni DC app.; art by various; Conner infinity-c; Captain Triumph returns 5.00
63-($4.99) Variant Year of the Villain painted-c by Frank Cho 5.00
75-($5.99) Roast of Harley Quinn; back up story tie-in to Joker War; Punchline app. 6.00
... Batman Day Special Edition (10/17, giveaway) r/#7; Joker app. 5.00
...: Be Careful What You Wish For Special Edition 1 (3/18, $4.99) Reprints story from Loot Crate edition plus 18 new pages; art by Conner, Hardin, Schmidt & Caldwell 5.00
.../Gossamer 1 (10/18, $4.99) Looney Tunes monster; Conner-c/Brito-a 5.00
... 25th Anniversary Special 1 (11/17, $4.99) Short stories by various incl. Dini, Conner, Palmiotti, Zdarsky, Quinones, Hardin; 2 covers by Conner & Dodson 5.00
Harley Quinn's Greatest Hits TPB (2016, $9.99) r/Batman Advs. #12 & other stories 10.00
Harley Quinn's Villain of the Year (2019, $4.99) Russell-s/Norton-a/Conner-c 5.00

HARLEY QUINN (Infinite Frontier)
DC Comics: May, 2021 - Present ($3.99)

1-24: 1-Phillips-s/Rossmo-a. 7-9-"Fear State" tie-ins. 10-Braga-a. 23-Robin (Damian) app. 4.00
25-($4.99) Old Lady Harley and a multiverse of Harleys app. 5.00
26,27-Batwoman app. 4.00
... 30th Anniversary Special 1 (11/22, $9.99) Short stories by various; multiple covers 10.00
... Uncovered 1 (11/22, $5.99) Gallery of recent variant covers by Chew, Hughes, others 6.00
2021 Annual 1 (11/21, $5.99) Phillips-s/Lafuente & Sommariva-a; Joker app. 6.00
2022 Annual 1 (10/22, $5.99) Phillips-s/Buonfantino & Duarte-a; Task Force XX app. 6.00

HARLEY QUINN AND HER GANG OF HARLEYS
DC Comics: Jun, 2016 - No. 6, Nov, 2016 ($3.99, limited series)

1-6-Palmiotti & Tieri-s/Mauricet-a/Conner-c; intro. Harley Sinn. 5-Origin of Harley Sinn 4.00

HARLEY QUINN & POISON IVY
DC Comics: Nov, 2019 - No. 6, Apr, 2020 ($3.99, limited series)

1-6-Houser-s/Melo-a. 1,2-Floronic Man app. 2,3-Mad Hatter app. 5-Batwoman app. 4.00

HARLEY QUINN AND POWER GIRL
DC Comics: Aug, 2015 - No. 6, Feb, 2016 ($3.99, limited series)

1-6-Takes place during Harley Quinn #11-13; Vartox app.; Roux-a 4.00

HARLEY QUINN & THE BIRDS OF PREY
DC Comics (Black Label): Apr, 2020 - No. 4, Mar, 2021 ($5.99, 8-1/2" x 10-3/4", lim. series)

1-4-Conner & Palmiotti-s/Conner-a; Power Girl, Huntress & Cassandra Cain app. 6.00

HARLEY QUINN: HARLEY LOVES JOKER
DC Comics: Early Jul, 2018 - No. 2, Jul, 2018 ($3.99, limited series)

1,2-Dini-s/Blevins-a; covers by Conner & Cho; original costume Harley; intro The Grison 4.00

HARLEY QUINN: THE ANIMATED SERIES
DC Comics: Oct, 2022 (Series of one-shots)

... The Real Sidekicks of New Gotham Special 1 (10/22, $9.99)-Short stories; Sarin-c 10.00

HARLEY QUINN: THE ANIMATED SERIES: LEGION OF BATS! (Follows Season 3)

DC Comics: Dec, 2022 - No. 6, ($3.99)

	GD 2.0	VG 4.0	FN 6.0	VF 8.0	VF/NM 9.0	NM- 9.2
1-5: 1-Tee Franklin-s/Shae Beagle-a; Harley joins the Bat-family						4.00

HARLEY QUINN: THE ANIMATED SERIES: THE EAT. BANG! KILL. TOUR (Follows Season 2)
DC Comics: Nov, 2021 - No. 6, Apr, 2022 ($3.99)

	GD 2.0	VG 4.0	FN 6.0	VF 8.0	VF/NM 9.0	NM- 9.2
1-6-Tee Franklin-s/Max Sarin-a; Poison Ivy, Catwoman & Vixen app.						4.00

HARLEY'S LITTLE BLACK BOOK (Harley Quinn team-up book)
DC Comics: Feb, 2016 - No. 6, May, 2017 ($4.99, bi-monthly)

	GD 2.0	VG 4.0	FN 6.0	VF 8.0	VF/NM 9.0	NM- 9.2
1-4,6: 1-Palmiotti & Conner-s; Wonder Woman app.; Conner-c. 2-Green Lantern app. 3-Zatanna app.; Linsner-a. 4-DC Bombshells app.; Tucci-a. 6-Lobo app.; Bisley-a						5.00
1-Polybagged variant-c by Campbell (3 versions: sketch, B&W, and color)	1	2	3	5	6	8
5-Neal Adams-a; homage to "Superman vs. Muhammad Ali"						5.00

HAROLD TEEN (See Popular Comics, & Super Comics)
Dell Publishing Co.: No. 2, 1942 - No. 209, Jan, 1949

	GD 2.0	VG 4.0	FN 6.0	VF 8.0	VF/NM 9.0	NM- 9.2
Four Color 2	37	74	111	274	612	950
Four Color 209	7	14	21	49	92	135

HARROW COUNTY (Also see Tales From Harrow County)
Dark Horse Comics: May, 2015 - No. 32, Jun, 2018 ($3.99)

	GD 2.0	VG 4.0	FN 6.0	VF 8.0	VF/NM 9.0	NM- 9.2
1-31: 1-8-Cullen Bunn-s/Tyler Crook-a. 9,17-Carla Speed McNeil-a						4.00
1-Halloween ComicFest Edition (10/16, no price) r/#1						3.00
32-($4.99) Last issue; Bunn-s/Crook-a						5.00

HARROWERS, THE (See Clive Barker's...)

HARSH REALM (Inspired 1999 TV series)
Harris Comics: 1993- No. 6, 1994 ($2.95, limited series)

	GD 2.0	VG 4.0	FN 6.0	VF 8.0	VF/NM 9.0	NM- 9.2
1-6: Painted-c. Hudnall-s/Paquette & Ridgway-a						4.00
TPB (2000, $14.95) r/series						15.00

HARVESTER, THE
Legendary Comics: Feb, 2015 - No. 6, Jul, 2015 ($3.99)

	GD 2.0	VG 4.0	FN 6.0	VF 8.0	VF/NM 9.0	NM- 9.2
1-6-Brandon Seifert-s/Eric Battle-a/c						4.00

HARVEY
Marvel Comics: Oct, 1970; No. 2, 12/70; No. 3, 6/72 - No. 6, 12/72

	GD 2.0	VG 4.0	FN 6.0	VF 8.0	VF/NM 9.0	NM- 9.2
1-Teenage	10	20	30	66	138	210
2-6	7	14	21	46	86	125

HARVEY COLLECTORS COMICS (Titled Richie Rich Collectors Comics on cover of #6-on)
Harvey Publ.: Sept, 1975 - No. 15, Jan, 1978; No. 16, Oct, 1979 (52 pgs.)

	GD 2.0	VG 4.0	FN 6.0	VF 8.0	VF/NM 9.0	NM- 9.2
1-Reprints Richie Rich #1,2	2	4	6	13	18	22
2-10: 7-Splash pg. shows cover to Friendly Ghost Casper #1	2	4	6	8	11	14
11-16: 16-Sad Sack-r	1	2	3	5	7	9

NOTE: *All reprints: Casper-#2, 7, Richie Rich-#1, 3, 5, 6, 8-15, Sad Sack-#16. Wendy-#4.*

HARVEY COMICS HITS (Formerly Joe Palooka #50)
Harvey Publications: No. 51, Oct, 1951 - No. 62, Apr, 1953

	GD 2.0	VG 4.0	FN 6.0	VF 8.0	VF/NM 9.0	NM- 9.2
51-The Phantom	41	82	123	256	428	600
52-Steve Canyon's Air Power(Air Force sponsored)	13	26	39	72	101	130
53-Mandrake the Magician	20	40	60	118	192	265
54-Tim Tyler's Tales of Jungle Terror	13	26	39	74	105	135
55-Love Stories of Mary Worth	12	24	36	69	97	125
56-The Phantom; bondage-c	32	64	96	188	307	425
57-Rip Kirby Exposes the Kidnap Racket; entire book by Alex Raymond	16	32	48	98	154	210
58-Girls in White (nurses stories)	14	28	42	82	121	160
59-Tales of the Invisible featuring Scarlet O'Neil	17	34	51	100	158	215
60-Paramount Animated Comics #1 (9/52) (3rd app. Baby Huey); 2nd Harvey app. Baby Huey & Casper the Friendly Ghost (1st in Little Audrey #25 (8/52)); 1st app. Herman & Catnip (c/story) & Buzzy the Crow	71	142	213	454	777	1100
61-Casper the Friendly Ghost #6 (3rd Harvey Casper, 10/52)-Casper-c	60	120	180	381	653	925
62-Paramount Animated Comics #2; Herman & Catnip, Baby Huey & Buzzy the Crow	20	40	60	117	189	260

HARVEY COMICS LIBRARY
Harvey Publications: Apr, 1952 - No. 2, 1952

	GD 2.0	VG 4.0	FN 6.0	VF 8.0	VF/NM 9.0	NM- 9.2
1-Teen-Age Dope Slaves as exposed by Rex Morgan, M.D.; drug propaganda story; used in **SOTI**, pg. 27	459	918	1377	3350	5925	8500
2-Dick Tracy Presents Sparkle Plenty in "Blackmail Terror"	26	52	78	154	252	350

HARVEY COMICS SPOTLIGHT
Harvey Comics: Sept, 1987 - No. 4, Mar, 1988 (75¢/$1.00)

	GD 2.0	VG 4.0	FN 6.0	VF 8.0	VF/NM 9.0	NM- 9.2
1-New material; begin 75¢-c, ends #3; Sad Sack						5.00
2-4: 2,4-All new material. 2-Baby Huey. 3-Little Dot; contains reprints w/5 pg. new story. 4-$1.00-c; Little Audrey						4.00

NOTE: No. 5 was advertised but not published.

HARVEY HITS (Also see Tastee-Freez Comics in the Promotional Comics section)
Harvey Publications: Sept, 1957 - No. 122, Nov, 1967

	GD 2.0	VG 4.0	FN 6.0	VF 8.0	VF/NM 9.0	NM- 9.2
1-The Phantom	35	70	105	252	564	875
2-Rags Rabbit (10/57)	7	14	21	44	82	120
3-Richie Rich (11/57)-r/Little Dot; 1st book devoted to Richie Rich; see Little Dot for 1st app.	155	310	465	1279	2890	4500
4-Little Dot's Uncles (12/57)	17	34	51	117	259	400
5-Stevie Mazie's Boy Friend (1/58)	5	10	15	34	60	85
6-The Phantom (2/58); 2pg. Powell-a	20	40	60	135	300	465
7-Wendy the Good Little Witch (3/58, pre-dates Wendy #1; 1st book devoted to Wendy)	57	114	171	456	1028	1600
8-Sad Sack's Army Life; George Baker-c	9	18	27	59	117	175
9-Richie Rich's Golden Deeds; (2nd book devoted to Richie Rich) reprints Richie Rich story from Tastee-Freez #1	86	172	258	688	1544	2400
10-Little Lotta's Lunch Box	12	24	36	82	179	275
11-Little Audrey Summer Fun (7/58)	9	18	27	59	117	175
12-The Phantom; 2pg. Powell-a (8/58)	16	32	48	108	239	370
13-Little Dot's Uncles (9/58); Richie Rich 1pg.	11	22	33	73	157	240
14-Herman & Katnip (10/58, TV/movies)	5	10	15	31	53	75
15-The Phantom (12/58)-1 pg. origin	17	34	51	114	252	390
16-Wendy the Good Little Witch (1/59); Casper app.	14	28	42	96	211	325
17-Sad Sack's Army Life (2/59)	5	10	15	34	66	85
18-Buzzy & the Crow	4	8	12	25	40	55
19-Little Audrey (4/59)	5	10	15	34	60	85
20-Casper & Spooky	7	14	21	44	82	120
21-Wendy the Witch	7	14	21	44	82	120
22-Sad Sack's Army Life	4	8	12	28	47	65
23-Wendy the Witch (8/59)	7	14	21	44	82	120
24-Little Dot's Uncles (9/59); Richie Rich 1pg.	8	16	24	54	102	150
25-Herman & Katnip (10/59)	3	6	9	21	33	45
26-The Phantom (11/59)	12	24	36	80	173	265
27-Wendy the Good Little Witch (12/59)	6	12	18	42	79	115
28-Sad Sack's Army Life (1/60)	4	8	12	25	40	55
29-Harvey-Toon (No.1)('60); Casper, Buzzy	5	10	15	31	53	75
30-Wendy the Witch (3/60)	7	14	21	44	82	120
31-Herman & Katnip (4/60)	3	6	9	19	30	40
32-Sad Sack's Army Life (5/60)	3	6	9	21	33	45
33-Wendy the Witch (6/60)	6	12	18	40	73	105
34-Harvey-Toon (7/60)	4	8	12	23	37	50
35-Funday Funnies (8/60)	3	6	9	19	30	40
36-The Phantom (1960)	11	22	33	76	163	250
37-Casper & Nightmare	6	12	18	37	66	95
38-Harvey-Toon	4	8	12	23	37	50
39-Sad Sack's Army Life (12/60)	3	6	9	20	31	42
40-Funday Funnies (1/61)	3	6	9	16	24	32
41-Herman & Katnip	3	6	9	16	24	32
42-Harvey-Toon (3/61)	3	6	9	18	28	38
43-Sad Sack's Army Life (4/61)	3	6	9	18	28	38
44-The Phantom (5/61)	11	22	33	72	154	235
45-Casper & Nightmare	5	10	15	30	50	70
46-Harvey-Toon (7/61)	3	6	9	16	24	32
47-Sad Sack's Army Life (8/61)	3	6	9	16	24	32
48-The Phantom (9/61)	11	22	33	72	154	235
49-Stumbo the Giant (1st app. in Hot Stuff)	8	16	24	56	108	160
50-Harvey-Toon (11/61)	3	6	9	16	23	30
51-Sad Sack's Army Life (12/61)	3	6	9	16	23	30
52-Casper & Nightmare	4	8	12	28	47	65
53-Harvey-Toons (2/62)	3	6	9	16	23	30
54-Stumbo the Giant	5	10	15	33	57	80
55-Sad Sack's Army Life (4/62)	3	6	9	16	23	30
56-Casper & Nightmare	4	8	12	25	40	55
57-Stumbo the Giant	5	10	15	33	57	80
58-Sad Sack's Army Life	3	6	9	16	23	30
59-Casper & Nightmare (7/62)	4	8	12	25	40	55
60-Stumbo the Giant (9/62)	5	10	15	31	53	75
61-Sad Sack's Army Life	3	6	9	15	22	28
62-Casper & Nightmare	4	8	12	22	35	48
63-Stumbo the Giant	4	8	12	27	44	60
64-Sad Sack's Army Life (1/63)	3	6	9	15	22	28
65-Casper & Nightmare	4	8	12	22	35	48
66-Stumbo The Giant (3/63)	4	8	12	27	44	60
67-Sad Sack's Army Life (4/63)	3	6	9	15	22	28
68-Casper & Nightmare	4	8	12	22	35	48
69-Stumbo the Giant (6/63)	4	8	12	27	44	60
70-Sad Sack's Army Life (7/63)	3	6	9	15	22	28
71-Casper & Nightmare (8/63)	3	6	9	20	31	42
72-Stumbo the Giant	4	8	12	27	44	60
73-Little Sad Sack (10/63)	3	6	9	15	22	28
74-Sad Sack's Muttsy... (11/63)	3	6	9	15	22	28
75-Casper & Nightmare	3	6	9	18	28	38
76-Little Sad Sack	3	6	9	15	22	28
77-Sad Sack's Muttsy...	3	6	9	15	22	28
78-Stumbo the Giant (3/64); JFK caricature	4	8	12	28	44	60
79-87: 79-Little Sad Sack (4/64). 80-Sad Sack's Muttsy... (5/64). 81-Little Sad Sack. 82-Sad Sack's Muttsy... 83-Little Sad Sack(8/64). 84-Sad Sack's Muttsy... 85-Gabby Gob (#1) (10/64). 86-G. I. Juniors (#1)(11/64). 87-Sad Sack's Muttsy... (12/64)	3	6	9	15	22	28
88-Stumbo the Giant (1/65)	4	8	12	27	44	60
89-122: 89-Sad Sack's Muttsy... 90-Gabby Gob. 91-G. I. Juniors. 92-Sad Sack's Muttsy... (5/65). 93-Sadie Sack (6/65). 94-Gabby Gob. 95-G. I. Juniors (8/65). 96-Sad Sack's Muttsy... (9/65). 97-Gabby Gob (10/65). 98-G. I. Juniors (11/65). 99-Sad Sack's Muttsy... (12/65). 100-Gabby Gob(1/66). 101-G. I. Juniors (2/66). 102-Sad Sack's Muttsy... (3/66). 103-Gabby Gob. 104- G. I. Juniors. 105-Sad Sack's Muttsy... 106-Gabby Gob (7/66). 107-G. I. Juniors (8/66). 108-Sad Sack's Muttsy...109-Gabby Gob. 110-G. I. Juniors (11/66). 111-Sad Sack's Muttsy... (12/66). 112-G. I. Juniors. 113-Sad Sack's Muttsy... 114-G. I. Juniors. 115-Sad Sack's Muttsy... 116-G. I. Juniors (5/67). 117-Sad Sack's Muttsy... 118-G. I. Juniors. 119-Sad Sack's Muttsy... (8/67). 120-G. I. Juniors (9/67). 121-Sad Sack's Muttsy... (10/67). 122-G. I. Juniors (11/67)	2	4	6	10	14	18

HARVEY HITS COMICS
Harvey Publications: Nov, 1986 - No. 6, Oct, 1987

	GD 2.0	VG 4.0	FN 6.0	VF 8.0	VF/NM 9.0	NM- 9.2
1-Little Lotta, Little Dot, Wendy & Baby Huey	1	2	3	4	5	7
2-6: 3-Xmas-c						4.50

HARVEY POP COMICS (Rock Happening) (Teen Humor)
Harvey Publications: Oct, 1968 - No. 2, Nov, 1969 (Both are 68 pg. Giants)

	GD 2.0	VG 4.0	FN 6.0	VF 8.0	VF/NM 9.0	NM- 9.2
1-The Cowsills	5	10	15	34	60	85
2-Bunny	5	10	15	31	53	75

HARVEY 3-D HITS (See Sad Sack)

HARVEY-TOON (...S) (See Harvey Hits No. 29, 34, 38, 42, 46, 50, 53)

HARVEY WISEGUYS (...Digest #? on)
Harvey Comics: Nov, 1987; #2, Nov, 1988; #3, Apr, 1989 - No. 4, Nov, 1989 (98 pgs., digest-size, $1.25/$1.75)

	GD 2.0	VG 4.0	FN 6.0	VF 8.0	VF/NM 9.0	NM- 9.2
1-Hot Stuff, Spooky, etc.	2	3	4	6	8	10

Harrow County #28 © Bunn & Crook

Haunt #9 © TMP

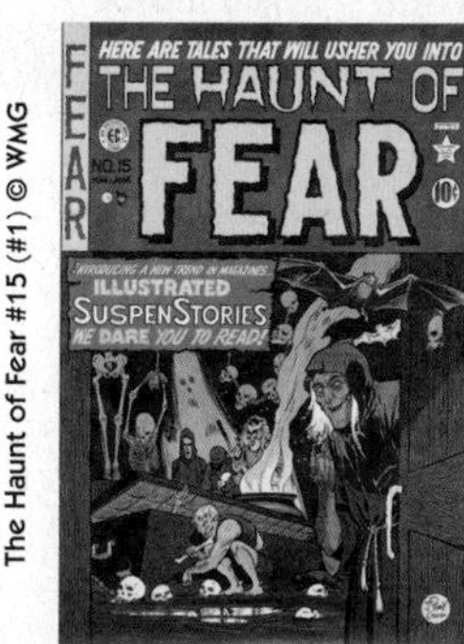

The Haunt of Fear #15 (#1) © WMG

GD 2.0 | VG 4.0 | FN 6.0 | VF 8.0 | VF/NM 9.0 | NM- 9.2

2-4: 2 (68 pgs.) 1 2 3 4 5 7

HASBRO HEROES SOURCEBOOK 2017
IDW Publishing: May, 2017 - No. 3, Jul, 2017 ($4.99, limited series)

1-3-Profile pages of characters from Transformers, G.I. Joe, Micronauts, Rom, M.A.S.K. 5.00

HASBRO TOYBOX QUARTERLY
IDW Publishing: Dec, 2017 ($5.99, one-shot)

1-Short stories of My Little Pony, Equestria Girls and Hanazuki by various; pin-ups 6.00

HASHTAG: DANGER (Also see back-ups in High Heaven and Captain Ginger)
IDW Publishing: 2019 - No. 5, 2019 ($3.99, limited series)

1-5-Peyer-s/Giarrusso-a; Snelson back-ups by Constant-s/Harper-a 4.00

HATARI (See Movie Classics)

HATCHET (Based on the 2007 movie)(Also see Victor Crowley's ...)
American Mythology Productions: No. 0, 2017 - No. 3, 2018 ($3.99)

0-3-Kuhoric-s/Mangum-a; Victor Crowley app. 4.00

HATCHET: VENGEANCE (Based on the 2007 movie)
American Mythology Productions: 2018 - No. 3, 2021 ($3.99)

1-3-Kuhoric-s/Calzada-a; prelude to the first movie 4.00

HATE
Fantagraphics Books: Spr, 1990 - No. 30, 1998 ($2.50/$2.95, B&W/color)

1 2 4 6 8 10 12
2-3 6.00
4-10 5.00
11-20: 16- color begins 4.00
21-29 3.00
30-($3.95) Last issue 4.00
Annual 1 (2/01, $3.95) Peter Bagge-s/a 5.00
Annual 2-9 (12/01 - No. 9, Spr, 2011; $4.95) Peter Bagge-s/a 5.00
Buddy Bites the Bullet! (2001, $16.95) r/Buddy stories in color 17.00
Buddy Go Home! (1997, $16.95) r/Buddy stories in color 17.00
Hate-Ball Special Edition ($3.95, giveaway)-reprints 4.00
Hate Jamboree (10/98, $4.50) old & new cartoons 4.50

HATHAWAYS, THE (TV)
Dell Publishing Co.: No. 1298, Feb-Apr, 1962 (one-shot)

Four Color 1298-Photo-c 5 10 15 35 63 90

HAUNT
Image Comics: Oct, 2009 - No. 28, Dec, 2012 ($2.99)

1-McFarlane & Kirkman-s/Capullo & Ottley-a/McFarlane-a(i)/c; two variant-c 6.00
2-28: 2-Two covers. 13-($1.99). 19-Casey-s/Fox-a begins 3.00
Image Firsts: Haunt #1 (10/10, $1.00) r/#1 with "Image First" cover logo 3.00

HAUNTED (See This Magazine Is Haunted)

HAUNTED (Baron Weirwulf's Haunted Library on-c #21 on)
Charlton Comics: 9/71 - No. 30, 11/76; No. 31, 9/77 - No. 75, 9/84

1-All Ditko issue 7 14 21 44 82 120
2-7-Ditko-c/a 3 6 9 21 33 45
8,12,28-Ditko-a 2 4 6 13 18 22
9,19 2 4 6 8 11 14
10,20,15,18: 10,20-Sutton-a. 15-Sutton-c 2 4 6 8 11 14
11,13,14,16-Ditko-c/a 3 6 9 16 23 30
17-Sutton-c/a; Newton-a 2 4 6 9 12 15
21-Newton-c/a; Sutton-a; 1st Baron Weirwulf 3 6 9 16 24 32
22-Newton-c/a; Sutton-a 2 4 6 9 13 16
23,24-Sutton-c; Ditko-a 2 4 6 9 13 16
25-27,29,32,33 1 3 4 6 8 10
30,41,47,49-52,60,74-Ditko-c/a: 51-Reprints #1 2 4 6 11 16 20
31,35,37,38-Sutton-a 1 3 4 6 8 10
34,36,39,40,42,57-Ditko-a 2 4 6 8 10 12
43-46,48,53-56,58,59,61-73: 59-Newton-a. 64-Sutton-c. 71-73-Low print
1 2 3 5 6 8
75-(9/84) Last issue; low print 2 4 6 9 13 16

NOTE: ***Aparo** c-45. **Ditko** a-1-8, 11-16, 18, 23, 24, 28, 30, 34r, 36r, 39-42r, 47r, 49-52r, 57, 60, 74. c-1-7, 11, 13, 14, 16, 30, 41, 47, 49-52, 74. **Howard** a-6, 9, 18, 22, 25, 32. **Kim** a-9, 19. **Morisi** a-13. **Newton** a-17, 21, 59r; c-21, 22(painted). **Staton** a-11, 12, 18, 21, 22, 30, 33, 35, 38; c-18, 33, 38. **Sutton** a-10, 17, 20-22, 31, 35, 37, 38; c-15, 17, 18, 23(painted), 24(painted), 27, 64r. #49 reprints Tales of the Mysterious Traveler #4.*

HAUNTED, THE
Chaos! Comics: Jan, 2002 - No. 4, Apr, 2002 ($2.99, limited series)

1-4-Peter David-s/Nat Jones-a 3.00
...: Gray Matters (7/02, $2.99) David-s/Jones-a 3.00

HAUNTED CITY
Aspen MLT: No. 0, Aug, 2011 - No. 2 ($2.50/$3.50)

0-($2.50)-Taylor & Johnson-s/Michael Ryan-a; four covers 3.00
1,2-($3.50) 1-Taylor & Johnson-s/Michael Ryan-a; four covers 3.50

HAUNTED LOVE
Charlton Comics: Apr, 1973 - No. 11, Sept, 1975

1-Tom Sutton-a (16 pgs.) 7 14 21 48 89 130
2,3,6,7,10,11 3 6 9 19 30 40
4,5-Ditko-a 3 6 9 23 37 50
8,9-Newton-c 3 6 9 20 31 42
Modern Comics #1(1978) 2 3 4 6 8 10

NOTE: ***Howard** a-8i. **Kim** a-7-9. **Newton** c-8, 9. **Staton** a-1-6. **Sutton** a-1, 3-5, 10, 11.*

HAUNTED MANSION, THE (Disney Kingdoms)
Marvel Comics: May, 2016 - No. 5, Sept, 2016 ($3.99, limited series)

1-5-Joshua Williamson-s/Jorge Coelho-a/E.M. Gist-c 4.00
... No. 1 Halloween Comic Fest 2016 (giveaway, 12/16) r/#1 3.00

HAUNTED TANK, THE
DC Comics (Vertigo): Feb, 2009 - No. 5, June, 2009 ($2.99, limited series)

1-5-Marraffino-s/Flint-a. 1-Two covers by Flint and Joe Kubert 3.00
TPB (2010, $14.99) r/#1-5 15.00

HAUNTED THRILLS (Tales of Horror and Terror)
Ajax/Farrell Publications: June, 1952 - No. 18, Nov-Dec, 1954

1-r/Ellery Queen #1 110 220 330 704 1202 1700
2-L. B. Cole-a r-/Ellery Queen #1 71 142 213 454 777 1100
3,4: 3-Drug use story 58 116 174 371 636 900
5-Classic skull-c 423 846 1269 3000 5250 7500
6-8,10,12: 7-Hitler story. 61 122 183 390 670 950
9-Classic decapitated heads-c 181 362 543 1158 1979 2800
11-Nazi death camp story 181 362 543 1158 1979 2800
13-18: 14-Jesus Christ apps. in story by Webb. 15-Jo-Jo-r. 18-Lingerie panels; skull-c
54 108 162 343 574 825

NOTE: ***Kamenish** art in most issues. **Webb** a-12.*

HAUNT OF FEAR (Formerly Gunfighter)
E. C. Comics: No. 15, May-June, 1950 - No. 28, Nov-Dec, 1954

15(#1, 1950)(Scarce) 429 858 1287 3432 5466 7500
16-1st app. "The Witches Cauldron" & the Old Witch (by Kamen); begin series as hostess of Haunt of Fear (also see Yellowjacket #7-10) 183 366 549 1464 2332 3200
17-Origin of Crypt of Terror, Vault of Horror, & Haunt of Fear; used in **SOTI**, pg. 43; last pg. Ingels-a used by N.Y. Legis. Comm.; story "Monster Maker" based on Frankenstein. Old Witch by Feldstein 183 366 549 1464 2332 3200
4-Ingels becomes regular artist for Old Witch. 1st Vault Keeper & Crypt Keeper app. in HOF; begin series 109 218 327 872 1386 1900
5-Injury-to-eye panel, pg. 4 of Wood story 97 194 291 776 1238 1700
6,7,9,10: 6-Crypt Keeper by Feldstein begins. 9-Crypt Keeper by Davis begins. 10-Ingels biog. 74 148 222 592 946 1300
8-Classic Feldstein Shrunken Head-c 109 218 327 872 1386 1900
11,12: Classic Ingels-c; 11-Kamen biog. 12-Feldstein biog.; "Poetic Justice" story adapted for the 1972 Tales From the Crypt film 74 148 222 592 946 1300
13,15,16,20: 16-Ray Bradbury adaptation. 20-Feldstein-r/Vault of Horror #12
57 114 171 456 728 1000
14-Origin Old Witch by Ingels; classic-Ingels-c 97 194 291 776 1238 1700
17-Classic Ingels-c and "Horror We? How's Bayou?" story, considered ECs best horror story
126 252 378 1008 1604 2200
18-Old Witch-c; Ray Bradbury adaptation & biography
89 178 267 712 1131 1550
19-Used in **SOTI**, ill. "A comic book baseball game" & Senate investigation on juvenile delinq. bondage/decapitation-c 86 172 258 688 1094 1500
21-27: 22-"Wish You Were Here" story inspired by "The Monkey's Paw" by W.W. Jacobs, which is referenced in story; adapted for the 1972 Tales From the Crypt film; Snow White satire. 23-EC version of the Hansel and Gretel story; **SOTI**, pg. 241 discusses the original Grimm tale in relation to comics. 24-Used in Senate Investigative Report, pg.8. 26-Contains anti-censorship editorial, 'Are you a Red Dupe?' 27-Cannibalism story; Vault Keeper shown reading **SOTI;** brief text reference to unpublished 4th EC horror title The Crypt of Terror
44 88 132 352 564 775
28-Low distribution 71 142 213 568 909 1250

NOTE: *(Canadian reprints known; see Table of Contents). **Craig** a-15-17, 5, 7, 10, 12, 13; c-15-17, 5-7. **Crandall** a-20, 21, 26, 27. **Davis** a-4-26, 28. **Evans** a-15-19, 22-25, 27. **Feldstein** a-15-17, 20; c-4, 8-10. **Ingels** a-16, 17, 4-28; c-11-28. **Kamen** a-16, 4, 6, 7, 9-11, 13-19, 21-28. **Krigstein** a-28. **Kurtzman** a-15(#1), 17(#3). **Orlando** a-9, 12. **Wood** a-15, 16, 4-6.*

HAUNT OF FEAR, THE
Gladstone Publishing: May, 1991 - No. 2, July, 1991 ($2.00, 68 pgs.)

1,2: 1-Ghastly Ingels-c(r); 2-Craig-c(r) 4.00

	GD	VG	FN	VF	VF/NM	NM-
	2.0	4.0	6.0	8.0	9.0	9.2

HAUNT OF FEAR
Russ Cochran/Gemstone Publ.: Sept, 1991 - No. 5, 1992 ($2.00, 68 pgs.); Nov, 1992 - No. 28, Aug, 1998 ($1.50/$2.00/$2.50)

1-28: 1-Ingels-c(r). 1-3-r/HOF #15-17 with original-c. 4,5-r/HOF #4,5 with original-c 4.00
Annual 1-5: 1- r/#1-5. 2- r/#6-10. 3- r/#11-15. 4- r/#16-20. 5- r/#21-25 14.00
Annual 6-r/#26-28 9.00

HAUNT OF HORROR, THE (Digest)
Marvel Comics: Jun, 1973 - No. 2, Aug, 1973 (164 pgs.; text and art)

1-Morrow painted skull-c; stories by Ellison, Howard, and Leiber; Brunner-a
4 8 12 28 47 65
2-Kelly Freas painted bondage-c; stories by McCaffrey, Goulart, Leiber, Ellison; art by Simonson, Brunner, and Buscema 3 6 9 18 27 36

HAUNT OF HORROR, THE (Magazine)
Cadence Comics Publ. (Marvel): May, 1974 - No. 5, Jan, 1975 (75¢) (B&W)

1,2: 2-Origin & 1st app. Gabriel the Devil Hunter; Satana begins
4 8 12 23 37 50
3-5: 4-Neal Adams-a. 5-Evans-a(2) 4 8 12 25 40 55
NOTE: *Alcala a-2. Colan a-2p. Heath r-1. Krigstein r-3. Reese a-1. Simonson a-1.*

HAUNT OF HORROR: EDGAR ALLAN POE
Marvel Comics (MAX): July, 2006 - No. 3, Sept, 2006 ($3.99, B&W, limited series)

1-3- Poe-inspired/adapted stories with Richard Corben-a 4.00
HC (2006, $19.99) r/series; cover sketches 20.00

HAUNT OF HORROR: LOVECRAFT
Marvel Comics (MAX): Aug, 2008 - No. 3, Oct, 2008 ($3.99, B&W, limited series)

1-3-Lovecraft-inspired/adapted stories with Richard Corben-a 4.00

HAVE GUN, WILL TRAVEL (TV)
Dell Publishing Co.: No. 931, 8/58 - No. 14, 7-9/62 (All Richard Boone photo-c)

Four Color 931 (#1) 13 26 39 89 195 300
Four Color 983,1044 (#2,3) 9 18 27 62 126 190
4 (1-3/60) - 10 7 14 21 46 86 125
11-14 7 14 21 44 82 120

HAVEN: THE BROKEN CITY (See JLA/Haven: Arrival and JLA/Haven: Anathema)
DC Comics: Feb, 2002 - No. 9, Oct, 2002 ($2.50, limited series)

1-9-Olivetti-c/a: 1- JLA app. Series concludes in JLA/Haven: Anathema 3.00

HAVOK & WOLVERINE - MELTDOWN (See Marvel Comics Presents #24)
Marvel Comics (Epic Comics): Mar, 1989 - No. 4, Oct, 1989 ($3.50, mini-series, squarebound, mature)

1-4: Art by Kent Williams & Jon J. Muth; story by Walt & Louise Simonson 6.00

HAWAIIAN DICK (Also see Aloha, Hawaiian Dick)
Image Comics: Dec, 2002 - No. 3, Feb, 2003 ($2.95, limited series)

1-3-B. Clay Moore-s/Steven Griffin-a 3.00
...: Byrd of Paradise TPB (8/03, $14.95) r/#1-3, script & sketch pages 15.00

HAWAIIAN DICK: SCREAMING BLACK THUNDER
Image Comics: Nov, 2007 - No. 5, Oct, 2008 ($2.99, limited series)

1-5-B. Clay Moore-s/Scott Chantler-a 3.00

HAWAIIAN DICK: THE LAST RESORT
Image Comics: Aug, 2004 - No. 4, June, 2006 ($2.95/$2.99, limited series)

1-4-B. Clay Moore-s/Steven Griffin-a 3.00
Vol. 2 TPB (10/06, $14.99) r/#1-4 & the original series pitch 15.00

HAWAIIAN EYE (TV)
Gold Key: July, 1963 (Troy Donahue, Connie Stevens photo-c)

1 (10073-307) 5 10 15 34 60 85

HAWAIIAN ILLUSTRATED LEGENDS SERIES
Hogarth Press: 1975 (B&W)(Cover printed w/blue, yellow, and green)

1-Kalelealuaka, the Mysterious Warrior 5.00

HAWK, THE (Also see Approved Comics #1, 7 & Tops In Adventure)
Ziff-Davis/St. John Publ. Co. No. 4 on: Wint/51 - No. 3, 11-12/52; No. 4, 1-2/53; No. 8, 9/54 - No. 12, 5/55 (Painted c-1-4)(#5-7 don't exist)

1-Anderson-a 33 66 99 194 317 440
2 (Sum, '52)-Kubert, Infantino-a 19 38 57 111 176 240
3-4 14 28 42 82 121 160
8-12: 8(9/54)-Reprints #3 w/different-c by Baker. 9-Baker-c/a; Kubert-a(r)/#2. 10-Baker-c/a; r/one story from #2. 11-Baker-c; Buckskin Belle & The Texan app. 12-Baker-c/a; Buckskin Belle app. 43 86 129 271 461 650
3-D 1(11/53, 25¢)-Came w/glasses; Baker-c 39 78 117 240 395 550
NOTE: *Baker c-8-12. Larsen a-10. Tuska a-1, 9, 12. Painted c-1, 4, 7.*

HAWK AND THE DOVE, THE (See Showcase #75 & Teen Titans) (1st series)
National Periodical Publications: Aug-Sept, 1968 - No. 6, June-July, 1969

1-Ditko-c/a 8 16 24 56 108 160
2-6: 5-Teen Titans cameo 5 10 15 31 53 75
NOTE: *Ditko c/a-1, 2. Gil Kane a-3p, 4p, 5, 6p; c-3-6.*

HAWK AND DOVE (2nd Series)
DC Comics: Oct, 1988 - No. 5, Feb, 1989 ($1.00, limited series)

1-Rob Liefeld-c/a(p) in all; 1st app. Dawn Granger as Dove 6.00
2-5 3.00
Trade paperback ('93, $9.95)-Reprints #1-5 12.00

HAWK AND DOVE
DC Comics: June, 1989 - No. 28, Oct, 1991 ($1.00)

1-28 4.00
Annual 1,2 ('90, '91; $2.00) 1-Liefeld pin-up. 2-Armageddon 2001 x-over 5.00

HAWK AND DOVE
DC Comics: Nov, 1997 - No. 5, Mar, 1998 ($2.50, limited series)

1-5-Baron-s/Zachary & Giordano-a 4.00

HAWK AND DOVE (DC New 52)
DC Comics: Nov, 2011 - No. 8, Jun, 2012 ($2.99)

1-8: 1-Gates-s/Liefeld-a/c; Deadman app. 6-Batman & Robin app.; Liefeld-s/a/c 3.00

HAWK AND WINDBLADE (See Elflord)
Warp Graphics: Aug, 1997 - No.2, Sept, 1997 ($2.95, limited series)

1,2-Blair-s/Chan-c/a 3.00

HAWKEN: MELEE (Based on the computer game Hawken)
Archaia Black Label: Dec, 2013 - No. 5 ($3.99, limited series)

1,2: 1-Abnett-s/Dallocchio-a. 2-Jim Mahfood-s/a 4.00

HAWKEYE (See The Avengers #16 & Tales Of Suspense #57)
Marvel Comics Group: Sept, 1983 - No. 4, Dec, 1983 (limited series)

1-Mark Gruenwald-a/scripts in all; origin Hawkeye 3 6 9 19 30 40
2-4: 3-Origin Mockingbird. 4-Hawkeye & Mockingbird elope
2 4 6 9 12 15

HAWKEYE
Marvel Comics: Jan, 1994 - No. 4, Apr, 1994 ($1.75, limited series)

1 1 3 4 6 8 10
2-4 5.00

HAWKEYE (Volume 2)
Marvel Comics: Dec, 2003 - No. 8, Aug, 2004 ($2.99)

1-8: 1-6-Nicieza-s/Raffaele-a. 7,8-Bennett-a; Black Widow app. 4.00

HAWKEYE (Also see All-New Hawkeye)
Marvel Comics: Oct, 2012 - No. 22, Sept, 2015 ($2.99)

1-Fraction-s/Aja-a; Kate Bishop app. 3 6 9 17 25 34
2,3 1 3 4 6 8 10
4-8: 7-Lieber & Hamm-a 6.00
9-21: 10,12-Francavilla-a. 11-Dog issue. 16-Released before #15 4.00
22-($4.99) Aja-a 5.00
Annual 1 (9/13, $4.99) Pulido-a; Kate Bishop in L.A.; Madame Mask app. 5.00

HAWKEYE (Kate Bishop as Hawkeye)
Marvel Comics: Feb, 2017 - No. 16, May, 2018 ($3.99)

1-16: 1-5,7-11-Thompson-s/Romero-a. 5,6-Jessica Jones app. 4.00

HAWKEYE AND MOCKINGBIRD (Avengers) (Leads into Widowmaker mini-series)
Marvel Comics: Aug, 2010 - No. 6, Jan, 2011 ($3.99/$2.99)

1-($3.99) Heroic Age; Jim McCann-s/David Lopez-a; history of the characters 4.00
2-6-($2.99) Phantom Rider, Dominic Fortune & Crossfire app. 3.00

HAWKEYE & THE LAST OF THE MOHICANS (TV)
Dell Publishing Co.: No. 884, Mar, 1958 (one-shot)

Four Color 884-Lon Chaney Jr. photo-c 7 14 21 44 82 120

HAWKEYE: BLINDSPOT (Avengers)
Marvel Comics: Apr, 2011 - No. 4, Jul, 2011 ($2.99, limited series)

1-4: 1-McCann-s/Diaz-a; Zemo app. 2-Diaz & Dragotta-a 3.00

HAWKEYE: EARTH'S MIGHTIEST MARKSMAN
Marvel Comics: Oct, 1998 ($2.99, one-shot)

1-Justice and Firestar app.; DeFalco-s 5.00

HAWKEYE: FREEFALL
Marvel Comics: Mar, 2020 - No. 6, Nov, 2020 ($3.99, limited series)

1-6-Rosenberg-s/Schmidt-a; The Hood app. 4-Daredevil app. 4.00

HAWKEYE: KATE BISHOP
Marvel Comics: Jan, 2022 - No. 5, May, 2022 ($3.99)

1-5-Marieke Nijkamp-s/Enid Balám-a 4.00

HAWKEYE VS. DEADPOOL
Marvel Comics: No. 0, Nov, 2014 - No. 4, Mar, 2015 ($4.99/$3.99, limited series)

0-($4.99) Duggan-s/Lolli-a; Black Cat app. 3 6 9 14 19 24
1-($3.99) Covers by Harren & Pearson; Kate Bishop & Typhoid Mary app.
1 3 4 6 8 10
2-4 4.00

HAWKGIRL (Title continued from Hawkman #49, Apr, 2006)
DC Comics: No. 50, May, 2006 - No. 66, Sept, 2007 ($2.50/$2.99)

50-66: 50-Chaykin-a/Simonson-s begin; One Year Later. 52-Begin $2.99-c. 57,58-Bennett-a. 59-Blackfire app. 63-Batman app. 64-Superman app. 3.00
...: Hath-Set TPB (2008, $17.99) r/#61-66 18.00
...: Hawkman Returns TPB (2007, $17.99) r/#57-60 & JSA Classified #21,22 18.00
...: The Maw TPB (2007, $17.99) r/#50-56 18.00

HAWKMAN (See Atom & Hawkman, The Brave & the Bold, DC Comics Presents, Detective Comics, Flash Comics, Hawkworld, JSA, Justice League of America #31, Legend of the Hawkman, Mystery in Space, Savage Hawkman, Shadow War Of..., Showcase, & World's Finest #256)

HAWKMAN (1st Series) (Also see The Atom #7 & Brave & the Bold #34-36, 42-44, 51)
National Periodical Publications: Apr-May, 1964 - No. 27, Aug-Sept, 1968

1-(4-5/64)-Anderson-c/a begins, ends #21 64 128 192 512 1156 1800
2 20 40 60 141 313 485
3,5: 5-2nd app. Shadow Thief 13 26 39 89 195 300
4-Origin & 1st app. Zatanna (10-11/64) 185 370 555 1480 2840 4200
6 10 20 30 66 138 210
7 9 18 27 62 126 190
8-10: 9-Atom cameo; Hawkman & Atom learn each other's I.D.; 3rd app. Shadow Thief
8 16 24 54 102 150
11-15 6 12 18 40 73 105
16-27: 18-Adam Strange x-over (cameo #19). 25-G.A. Hawkman-r by Moldoff. 26-Kirby-a(r). 27-Kubert-c 5 10 15 34 60 85

HAWKMAN (2nd Series)
DC Comics: Aug, 1986 - No. 17, Dec, 1987

1-Shadow-Thief app. 1 2 3 5 6 8
2-17: 10-Byrne-c, Special #1 (1986, $1.25) 4.00
Trade paperback (1989, $19.95)-r/Brave and the Bold #34-36,42-44 by Kubert; Kubert-c 20.00

HAWKMAN (4th Series)(See both Hawkworld limited & ongoing series)
DC Comics: Sept, 1993 - No. 33, July, 1996 ($1.75/$1.95/$2.25)

Hawk & Dove (2011) #6 © DC

Hawkeye: Kate Bishop #5 © MAR

Headline Comics #23 © Prize

GD 2.0	VG 4.0	FN 6.0	VF 8.0	VF/NM 9.0	NM- 9.2

1-($2.50)-Gold foil embossed-c; storyline cont'd from Hawkworld ongoing series; new costume & powers. 1 2 3 5 6 8
2-33: 2-Green Lantern x-over. 3-Airstryke app. 4,6-Wonder Woman app. 13-(9/94)-Zero Hour. 15-Aquaman-c & app. 23-Wonder Woman app. 25-Kent Williams-c. 29,30-Chaykin-c. 32-Breyfogle-c 4.00
#0-(10/94) Zero Hour tie-in; released between #13 & #14 4.00
Annual 1 (1993, $2.50, 68 pgs.)-Bloodlines Earthplague 5.00
Annual 2 (1995, $3.95)-Year One story 5.00

HAWKMAN (Title continues as Hawkgirl #50-on) (See JSA #23 for return)
DC Comics: May, 2002 - No. 49, Apr, 2006 ($2.50)

1-Johns & Robinson-s/Morales-a 5.00
1-2nd printing 3.00
2-40: 2-4-Shadow Thief app. 5,6-Green Arrow-c/app. 8-Atom-c/app. 13-Van Sciver-a. 14-Gentleman Ghost app. 15-Hawkwoman app. 16-Byth returns. 23-25-Black Reign x-over with JSA #56-58. 26-Byrne-c/a. 29,30-Land-c. 37-Golden Eagle returns 3.00
41-49: 41-Hawkman killed. 43-Golden Eagle origin. 46-49-Adam Kubert-c 3.00
...: Allies & Enemies TPB (2004, $14.95) r/#7-14 & pages from Secret Files and Origins 15.00
...: Endless Flight TPB (2003, $12.95) r/#1-6 & Secret Files and Origins 13.00
...: Rise of the Golden Eagle TPB (2006, $17.99) r/#37-45 18.00
... Secret Files and Origins (10/02, $4.95) profiles and pin-ups by various 5.00
... Special 1 (10/08, $3.50) Tie-in to Rann-Thanagar Holy War series; Starlin-s/a(p) 3.50
...: Wings of Fury TPB (2005, $17.99) r/#15-22 18.00

HAWKMAN
DC Comics: Aug, 2018 - No. 29, Jan, 2021 ($3.99)

1-29: 1-12-Venditti-s/Hitch-a. 1,9-12-Madame Xanadu app. 4-6-The Atom app. 13-Conrad-a 14-18-Year of the Villain tie-in. 14-17-Shadow Thief app. 18-22-The Infected. 27-Justice Society app. 4.00

HAWKMAN: FOUND (See Dark Nights: Metal series and other tie-ins)
DC Comics: Feb, 2018 ($3.99, one-shot)

1-Lemire-s/Hitch-a; foil-c 4.00

HAWKMOON: THE JEWEL IN THE SKULL
First Comics: May, 1986 - No. 4, Nov, 1986 ($1.75, limited series, Baxter paper)

1-4: Adapts novel by Michael Moorcock 3.00

HAWKMOON: THE MAD GOD'S AMULET
First Comics: Jan, 1987 - No. 4, July, 1987 ($1.75, limited series, Baxter paper)

1-4: Adapts novel by Michael Moorcock 3.00

HAWKMOON: THE RUNESTAFF
First Comics: Jun, 1988 -No. 4, Dec, 1988 ($1.75-$1.95, lim. series, Baxter paper)

1-4: ($1.75) Adapts novel by Michael Moorcock. 3,4 ($1.95) 3.00

HAWKMOON: THE SWORD OF DAWN
First Comics: Sept, 1987 - No. 4, Mar, 1988 ($1.75, lim. series, Baxter paper)

1-4: Dorman painted-c; adapts Moorcock novel 3.00

HAWKS OF THE SEAS (WILL EISNER'S...)
Dark Horse Comics: July, 2003 ($19.95, B&W, hardcover)

nn-Reprints 1937-1939 weekly Pirate serial by Will Eisner; Williamson intro. 20.00

HAWKWORLD
DC Comics: 1989 - No. 3, 1989 ($3.95, prestige format, limited series)

Book 1-3: 1-Tim Truman story & art in all; Hawkman dons new costume; reintro Byth 5.00
TPB (1991, $16.95) r/#1-3 17.00

HAWKWORLD (3rd Series)
DC Comics: June, 1990 - No. 32, Mar, 1993 ($1.50/$1.75)

1-Hawkman spin-off; story cont'd from limited series. 4.00
2-32: 15,16-War of the Gods x-over. 22-J'onn J'onzz app. 3.00
Annual 1-3 ('90-'92, $2.95, 68 pgs.), 2-2nd printing with silver ink-c 4.00
NOTE: ***Truman** a-30-32; c-27-32, Annual 1.*

HAYWIRE
DC Comics: Oct, 1988 - No. 13, Sept, 1989 ($1.25, mature)

1-13 3.00

HAZARD
Image Comics (WildStorm Prod.): June, 1996 - No. 7, Nov, 1996 ($1.75)

1-7: 1-Intro Hazard; Jeff Mariotte scripts begin; Jim Lee-c(p) 3.00

HAZEL & CHA CHA SAVE CHRISTMAS: TALES FROM THE UMBRELLA ACADEMY
Dark Horse Comics: Nov, 2019 ($4.99, one-shot)

1-Gerald Way & Scott Allie-s/Tommy Lee Edwards-a; covers by Edwards & Mahfood 2 4 6 8 10 12

HEADLINE COMICS
DC Comics: Jan. 1942

nn - Ashcan comic, not distributed to newsstands, only for in-house use. Cover art is More Fun Comics #73, interior being Star Spangled Comics #2 (a FN copy sold for $2270.50 in 2012)

HEADLINE COMICS (...For the American Boy) (...Crime No. 32-39)
Prize Publ./American Boys' Comics: Feb, 1943 - No. 22, Nov-Dec, 1946; No. 23, 1947 - No. 77, Oct, 1956

1-WWII-c/sty.; Junior Rangers-c/stories begin; Yank & Doodle x-over in Junior Rangers (Junior Rangers are Uncle Sam's nephews) 116 232 348 742 1271 1800
2-Japanese WWII-c; Junior Rangers "Nip the Nippons!"-c 71 142 213 454 777 1100
3-Junior Rangers vs. Hitler sty.; 1st app. Invisible Boy; German WWII-c; used in **POP**, pg. 84 (scarce) 68 136 204 435 743 1050
4-Junior Rangers vs. Hitler, Mussolini, Hirohito & Dr. Schmutz (1st app.); German WWII-c; (scarce) 68 136 204 435 743 1050
5-7,9: 5-Junior Rangers invade Italy; WWII-c/sty. 6,7-Nazi WWII-c/sty. 7-1st app. Kinker Kinkaid (ends #12). 9-WWII Halloween-c/sty 61 122 183 390 670 950
8-Classic Hitler-c 2725 5450 8175 16,500 23,250 30,000
10-Hitler story 71 142 213 454 777 1000
11-Classic Mad Japanese scientist WWII-c 486 972 1458 3550 6275 9000
12,13,15: 13,15-Blue Streak app. 31 62 93 184 300 415
14-Japanese WWII-c 45 90 135 284 480 675
16-Origin & 1st app. Atomic Man (11-12/45) 39 78 117 240 395 550
17,18-Atomic Man-c/sty. 30 60 90 177 289 400
19-Atomic Man-c/sty.; S&K-a 53 106 159 334 567 800
20,21: 21-Atomic Man ends (9-10/46) 24 48 72 140 230 320
22-Last Junior Rangers; Kiefer-c 20 40 60 118 192 265
23,24: (All S&K-a). 23-Valentine's Day Massacre story; content changes to true crime. 24-Dope-crazy killer story 39 78 117 231 378 525
25-35-S&K-c/a. 25-Powell-a 34 68 102 199 325 450
36-S&K-a; photo-c begin 29 58 87 172 281 390
37-1 pg. S&K, Severin-a; rare Kirby photo-c app. 52 104 156 328 552 775
38,40-Meskin-a 17 34 51 98 154 210
39,41-43,46-56: 41-J. Edgar Hoover 26th Anniversary Issue with photo on-c. 43,49-Meskin-a. 48-Meskin-c 15 30 45 86 133 180
44,45-S&K-c; Severin/Elder, Meskin-a 21 42 63 122 199 275
57-77: 70-Roller Derby-c. 72-Meskin-c/a(i) 14 28 42 82 121 160
NOTE: ***Hollingsworth** a-30. Photo c-36-43. **H. C. Kiefer** c-12-16, 22. Atomic Man c-17-19.*

HEAP, THE
Skywald Publications: Sept, 1971 (52 pgs.)

1-Kinstler-r/Strange Worlds #8; new-s w/Sutton-a 5 10 15 33 57 80

HEART AND SOUL
Mikeross Publications: April-May, 1954 - No. 2, June-July, 1954

1,2 14 28 42 80 115 150

HEART ATTACK
Image Comics (Skybound): Nov, 2019 - No. 6, Jun, 2020 ($3.99)

1-6-Shawn Kittelsen-s/Eric Zawadzki-a 4.00

HEARTBEAT (Also see Faithless)
BOOM! Studios: Nov, 2019 - No 5, Mar, 2020 ($3.99, limited series)

1-5-Maria Llovet-s/a 4.00

HEARTBREAKERS (Also see Dark Horse Presents)
Dark Horse Comics: Apr, 1996 - No. 4, July, 1996 ($2.95, limited series)

1-4: 1-With paper doll & pin-up. 2-Alex Ross pin-up. 3-Evan Dorkin pin-ups. 4-Brereton-c; Matt Wagner pin-up 3.00
...Superdigest (7/98, $9.95, digest-size) new stories 10.00

HEARTLAND (See Hellblazer)
DC Comics (Vertigo): Mar, 1997 ($4.95, one-shot, mature)

1-Garth Ennis-s/Steve Dillon-c/a 5.00

HEART OF EMPIRE
Dark Horse Comics: Apr, 1999 - No. 9, Dec, 1999 ($2.95, limited series)

1-9-Bryan Talbot-s/a 3.00

HEART OF THE BEAST, THE
DC Comics (Vertigo): 1994 ($19.95, hardcover, mature)

1-Dean Motter scripts 20.00

HEARTS OF DARKNESS (See Ghost Rider; Wolverine; Punisher: Hearts of...)

HEART THROBS (Love Stories No. 147 on)
Quality Comics/National Periodical #47(4-5/57) on (Arleigh #48-101): 8/49 - No. 8, 10/50; No. 9, 3/52 - No. 146, Oct, 1972

1-Classic Ward-c, Gustavson-a, 9 pgs. 57 114 171 362 619 875

GD VG FN VF VF/NM NM-
2.0 4.0 6.0 8.0 9.0 9.2

2-Ward-c/a (9 pgs); Gustavson-a 36 72 108 211 343 475
3-Gustavson-a 20 40 60 114 182 250
4,6,8-Ward-a, 8-9 pgs. 22 44 66 132 216 300
5,7 16 32 48 94 147 200
9-Robert Mitchum, Jane Russell photo-c 19 38 57 112 179 245
10,15-Ward-a 19 38 57 112 179 245
11-14,16-20: 12 (7/52) 14 28 42 80 115 150
21-Ward-c 18 36 54 107 169 230
22,23-Ward-a(p) 15 30 45 84 127 170
24-33: 33-Last pre-code (3/55) 14 28 42 78 112 145
34-39,41-44,46 (12/56; last Quality issue) 13 26 39 74 105 135
40-Ward-a; r-7 pgs./#21 14 28 42 82 121 160
45-Baker-a 9 18 27 59 117 175
47-(4-5/57; 1st DC issue) 26 52 78 182 404 625
48-60, 100 10 20 30 64 132 200
61-70 7 14 21 49 92 135
71-99: 74-Last 10 cent issue 7 14 21 44 82 120
101-The Beatles app. on-c 19 38 57 131 291 450
102-119: 102-123-(Serial)-Three Girls, Their Lives, Their Loves
5 10 15 33 57 80
120-(6-7/69) Neal Adams-c 6 12 18 42 79 115
121-132,143-146 4 8 12 27 44 60
133-142-(52 pgs.) 5 10 15 31 53 75

NOTE: *Gustavson a-8. Tuska a-128. Photo c-4, 5, 8-10, 15, 17.*

HEART THROBS - THE BEST OF DC ROMANCE COMICS (See Fireside Book Series)

HEART THROBS
DC Comics (Vertigo): Jan, 1999 - No. 4, Apr, 1999 ($2.95, lim. series)

1-4-Romance anthology. 1-Timm-c. 3-Corben-a 4.00

HEATHCLIFF (See Star Comics Magazine)
Marvel Comics (Star Comics)/Marvel Comics No. 23 on: Apr, 1985 - No. 56, Feb, 1991 (#16-on, $1.00)

1-Post-a most issues 2 4 6 9 12 15
2-10,47: 47-Batman parody (Catman vs. the Soaker) 5.00
11-46,48-56: 43-X-Mas issue 4.00
Annual 1 ('87) 5.00

HEATHCLIFF'S FUNHOUSE
Marvel Comics (Star Comics)/Marvel No. 6 on: May, 1987 - No. 10, 1988

1 5.00
2-10 4.00

HEATHENS, THE
AfterShock Comics: Nov, 2021 - No. 5, Mar, 2022 ($4.99/$3.99, limited series)

1-($4.99) Cullen Bunn & Heath Amodio-s/Sami Kivelä-a 5.00
2-5-($3.99) 4.00

HEAVY HITTERS
Marvel Comics (Epic Comics): 1993 ($3.75, 68 pgs.)

1-Bound w/trading card; Lawdog, Feud, Alien Legion, Trouble With Girls, & Spyke 4.00

HEAVY LIQUID
DC Comics (Vertigo): Oct, 1999 - No. 5, Feb, 2000 ($5.95, limited series)

1-5-Paul Pope-s/a; flip covers 6.00
TPB (2001, $29.95) r/#1-5 30.00
TPB (2009, $24.95) r/#1-5; development sketches and cover gallery; new cover 25.00
HC (2008, $39.99, dustjacket) r/#1-5; development sketches and cover gallery 40.00

HEAVY VINYL (Title changed from Hi-Fi Fight Club after #3)
Boom Entertainment (BOOM! Box): No. 4, Nov, 2017 ($3.99)

4-Carly Usdin-s/Nina Vakueva-a 4.00

HECKLE AND JECKLE (Paul Terry's...)(See Blue Ribbon, Giant Comics Edition #5A & 10, Paul Terry's, Terry-Toons Comics)
St. John Publ. Co. No. 1-24/Pines No. 25 on: No. 3, 2/52 - No. 24, 10/55; No. 25, Fall/56 - No. 34, 6/59

3(#1)-Funny animal 28 56 84 165 270 375
4(6/52), 5 14 28 42 82 121 160
6-10(4/53) 10 20 30 54 72 90
11-20 8 16 24 40 50 60
21-34: 25-Begin CBS Television Presents on-c 7 14 21 35 43 50

HECKLE AND JECKLE (TV) (See New Terrytoons)
Gold Key/Dell Publ. Co.: 11/62 - No. 4, 8/63; 5/66; No. 2, 10/66; No. 3, 8/67

1 (11/62; Gold Key) 6 12 18 37 66 95
2-4 3 6 9 21 33 45
1 (5/66; Dell) 4 8 12 25 40 55
2,3 3 6 9 18 28 38

(See March of Comics No. 379, 472, 484)

HECKLE AND JECKLE 3-D
Spotlight Comics: 1987 - No. 2?, 1987 ($2.50)

1,2 5.00

HECKLER, THE
DC Comics: Sept, 1992 - No. 6, Feb, 1993 ($1.25)

1-6-T&M Bierbaum-s/Keith Giffen-c/a 4.00

HECTIC PLANET
Slave Labor Graphics 1998 ($12.95/$14.95)

Book 1,2-r-Dorkin-s/a from Pirate Corp$ Vol. 1 & 2 15.00

HECTOR COMICS (The Keenest Teen in Town)
Key Publications: Nov, 1953 - No. 3, 1954

1-Teen humor 12 24 36 69 97 125
2,3 8 16 24 42 54 65

HECTOR HEATHCOTE (TV)
Gold Key: Mar, 1964

1 (10111-403) 6 12 18 41 76 110

HECTOR THE INSPECTOR (See Top Flight Comics)

HEDGE KNIGHT, THE
Image Comics: Aug, 2003 - No. 6, Apr, 2004 ($2.95, limited series)

1-6-George R.R. Martin-s/Mike S. Miller-a. 1-Two covers by Kaluta and Miller 3.00
George R.R. Martin's The Hedge Knight HC (Marvel, 2006, $19.99) r/series; 2 covers 20.00
George R.R. Martin's The Hedge Knight SC (Marvel, 2007, $14.99) r/series 15.00
TPB (2004, $14.95) r/series plus new short story 15.00

HEDGE KNIGHT II: SWORN SWORD
Marvel Comics (Dabel Brothers): Jun, 2007 - No. 6, Jun, 2008 ($2.99, limited series)

1-6-George R.R. Martin-s/Mike Miller-a. 1-Two covers by Yu & Miller, plus Miller B&W-c 3.00
... HC (2008, $19.99) r/series; 2 covers 20.00

HEDY DE VINE COMICS (Formerly All Winners #21? or Teen #22?(6/47); Hedy of Hollywood #36 on; also see Annie Oakley & Venus)
Marvel Comics (RCM): No. 22, Aug, 1947 - No. 35, Oct, 1949

22-1st app. Hedy De Vine (also see Joker #32) 97 194 291 621 1061 1500
23,24,27-30: 23-Wolverton-a, 1 pg; Kurtzman's "Hey Look", 2 pgs. 24,27-30- "Hey Look" by Kurtzman, 1-3 pgs. 54 108 162 343 574 825
25-Classic "Hey Look" by Kurtzman, "Optical Illusion"
61 122 183 390 670 950
26- "Giggles 'n' Grins" by Kurtzman 47 94 141 296 498 700
31-34: 32-Anti-Wertham editorial 36 72 108 211 343 475
35-Four pgs. "Rusty" by Kurtzman 39 78 117 231 378 525

HEDY-MILLIE-TESSIE COMEDY (See Comedy Comics)

HEDY OF HOLLYWOOD (Formerly Hedy Devine Comics)
Marvel Comics (RCM)/Atlas #50: No. 36, Feb, 1950 - No. 50, Sept, 1952

36(#1) 50 100 150 315 533 750
37-50 37 74 111 222 361 500

HEDY WOLFE (Also see Patsy & Hedy & Miss America Magazine V1#2)
Atlas Publishing Co. (Emgee): Aug, 1957

1-Patsy Walker's rival; Al Hartley-c 36 72 108 211 343 475

HEE HAW (TV)
Charlton Press: July, 1970 - No. 7, Aug, 1971

1 5 10 15 30 50 70
2-7 3 6 9 21 33 45

HEIDI (See Dell Jr. Treasury No. 6)

HEIDI SAHA (AN ILLUSTRATED HISTORY OF...)
Warren Publishing: 1973 (500 printed)

nn-Photo-c; an early Vampirella model for Warren (a FN/VF copy sold in 2011 for $776.75)

HELEN OF TROY (Movie)
Dell Publishing Co.: No. 684, Mar, 1956 (one-shot)

Four Color 684-Buscema-a, photo-c 10 20 30 66 138 210

HELL
Dark Horse Comics: July, 2003 - No. 4, Mar, 2004 ($2.99, limited series)

1-4-Augustyn-s/Demong-a/Meglia-c 3.00

HELLBLAZER (John Constantine) (See Saga of Swamp Thing #37 & 2013 Constantine title) (Also see Books of Magic limited series and Sandman Universe Presents)
DC Comics (Vertigo #63 on): Jan, 1988 - No. 300, Apr, 2013 ($1.25-$2.99)

1-(44 pgs.)-John Constantine; McKean-c thru #21; 1st app. Papa Midnite
5 10 15 34 60 85
1-Special Edition (7/10, $1.00) r/#1 with "What's Next?" cover logo 5.00
2-5 1 2 3 5 7 9
6-8,10: 10-Swamp Thing cameo 6.00
9,19: 9-X-over w/Swamp Thing #76. 19-Sandman app.
1 2 3 5 6 8
11-18,20 6.00
21-26,28-30: 22-Williams-c. 24-Contains bound-in Shocker movie poster. 25,26-Grant Morrison scripts. 5.00
27-Neil Gaiman scripts; Dave McKean-a; low print run
3 6 9 21 33 45
31-39: 36-Preview of World Without End. 5.00
40-($2.25, 52 pgs.)-Dave McKean-a & colors; preview of Kid Eternity 6.00
41-Ennis scripts begin; ends #83 5.00
42-49,51-74,76-99,101-119: 44,45-Sutton-a(i). 52-Glenn Fabry painted-c begin. 62-Special Death insert by McKean. 63-Silver metallic ink on-c. 77-Totleben-c. 84-Sean Phillips-c/a begins; Delano story. 85-88-Eddie Campbell story. 89-Paul Jenkins scripts begin 4.00
50,75,100,120: 50-($3.00, 52 pgs.). 75-($2.95, 52 pgs.). 100,120 ($3.50,48 pgs.) 5.00
121-199, 201-249, 251-274,276-299: 129-Ennis-s. 141-Bradstreet-a. 146-150-Corben-a. 151-Azzarello-s begin. 175-Carey-s begin; Dillon-a. 176-Begin $2.75-c. 182,183-Bermejo-a. 216-Mina-s begins. 220-Begin $2.99-c. 229-Carey-s/Leon-a. 234-Initial printing (white title logo) has missing text; corrected printing has lt. blue title logo. 265,266,271-274-Bisley-a. 268-271-Shade the Changing Man app. 4.00
200-($4.50) Carey-s/Dillon, Frusin, Manco-a 5.00
250-($3.99) Short stories by various; art by Lloyd, Phillips, Milligan; Bermejo-c 4.00
275-($4.99) Constantine's wedding; Bisley-c 5.00
300-($4.99) Last issue; Bisley-c 5.00
Annual 1 (1989, $2.95, 68 pgs.)-Bryan Talbot's 1st work in American comics 6.00
Annual 1 (Annual 2011 on cover, 2/12, $4.99)-Milligan-s/Bisley-a/c 5.00
Special 1 (1993, $3.95, 68 pgs.)-Ennis story; w/pin-ups. 5.00
...Black Flowers (2005, $14.99, TPB) r/#181-186 15.00
...Bloodlines (2007, $19.99, TPB) r/#47-50,52-55,59-61 20.00
...Damnation's Flame (1999, $16.95, TPB) r/#72-77 17.00
...Dangerous Habits (1997, $14.95, TPB) r/#41-46 15.00
...Fear and Loathing (1997, $14.95, TPB) r/#62-67 18.00
...Fear and Loathing (2nd printing, $17.95) 18.00
...: Freezes Over (2003, $14.95, TPB) r/#157-163 15.00
...Good Intentions (2002, $12.95, TPB) r/#151-156 13.00
...Hard Time (2001, $9.95, TPB) r/#146-150 10.00
...Haunting (2003, $12.95, TPB) r/#134-139 13.00
...Highwater (2004, $19.95, TPB) r/#164-174 20.00

Heathcliff #12 © MAR

Hellblazer #232 © DC

Hellboy in Hell #10 © Mike Mignola

GD 2.0 | VG 4.0 | FN 6.0 | VF 8.0 | VF/NM 9.0 | NM- 9.2

John Constantine Hellblazer: All His Engines HC (2005, $24.95, with dustjacket) new graphic novel; Mike Carey-s/Leonardo Manco-a 25.00
John Constantine Hellblazer: All His Engines SC (2006, $14.99) new graphic novel 15.00
John Constantine Hellblazer: Bloody Carnations SC (2011, $19.99) r/#267-275 20.00
John Constantine Hellblazer: Empathy is the Enemy SC (2006, $14.99) r/#216-222 15.00
John Constantine Hellblazer: Hooked SC (2010, $14.99) r/#256-260 15.00
John Constantine Hellblazer: India SC (2010, $14.99) r/#261-266 15.00
John Constantine Hellblazer: Joyride SC (2008, $14.99) r/#230-237 15.00
John Constantine Hellblazer: Pandemonium HC (2010, $24.99, with dustjacket) new graphic novel; Jamie Delano-s/Jock-a 25.00
John Constantine Hellblazer: Pandemonium SC (2011, $17.99) new graphic novel 18.00
John Constantine Hellblazer: Scab SC (2009, $14.99) r/#250-255 15.00
John Constantine Hellblazer: The Devil You Know SC (2007, $19.99) r/#10-13, Annual #1 and The Horrorist miniseries #1,2 20.00
John Constantine Hellblazer: The Family Man SC (2008, $19.99, TPB) r/#23,24,28-33 20.00
John Constantine Hellblazer: The Fear Machine SC (2008, $19.99, TPB) r/#14-22 20.00
John Constantine Hellblazer: The Red Right Hand SC (2007, $14.99) r/#223-228 15.00
John Const. Hellblazer: The Roots of Coincidence SC ('09, $14.99) r/#243,244,247-249 15.00
...Original Sins (1993, $19.95, TPB) r/#1-9 20.00
...Original Sins (2011, $19.99, TPB) r/#1-9 20.00
...Rake at the Gates of Hell (2003, $19.95, TPB) r/#78-83; Heartland #1 20.00
...: Rare Cuts (2005, $14.95, TPB) r/#11,25,26,35,56,84 & Vertigo Secret Files: Hellblazer 15.00
...: Reasons To Be Cheerful (2007, $14.99, TPB) r/#201-206 15.00
...: Red Sepulchre (2005, $12.99, TPB) r/#175-180 13.00
...: Setting Sun (2004, $12.95, TPB) r/#140-143 13.00
...: Son of Man (2004, $12.95, TPB) r/#129-133 13.00
...: Stations of the Cross (2006, $14.99, TPB) r/#194-200 15.00
...: Staring At The Wall (2005, $14.99, TPB) r/#187-193 15.00
...Tainted Love (1998, $16.95, TPB) r/#68-71, Vertigo Jam #1 and Hellblazer Special #1 17.00

NOTE: ***Alcala** a-8i, 9i, 18-22i. **Gaiman** scripts-27. **McKean** a-27,40; c-1-21. **Sutton** a-44i, 45i. **Talbot** a-Annual 1.*

HELLBLAZER (DC Rebirth)
DC Comics: Oct, 2016 - No. 24, Sept, 2018 ($2.99/$3.99)

1-8: 1-4-Simon Oliver-s/Moritat-a; Swamp Thing app. 5-7-Cassaday-c 3.00
9-24-($3.99): 9-12-Fabbri-a. 11,12-Lotay-c. 15-Justice League app. 20-24-Huntress app. 4.00
...: Rebirth 1 (9/16, $2.99) Oliver-s/Moritat-a; Swamp Thing, Wonder Woman app. 3.00

HELLBLAZER: CITY OF DEMONS
DC Comics (Vertigo): Early Dec, 2010 - No. 5, Feb, 2011 ($2.99, limited series)

1-5-Si Spencer-s/Sean Murphy-a/c 3.00
TPB (2011, $14.99) r/#1-5 & story from Vertigo Winter's Edge #3 15.00

HELLBLAZER: RISE AND FALL
DC Comics (Black Label): Nov, 2020 - No. 2, Jan, 2021 ($6.99, limited series, over-sized 10-7/8" x 8-1/2")

1,2-Tom Taylor-s/Darick Robertson-a; 2 covers on each 7.00

HELLBLAZER SPECIAL: BAD BLOOD
DC Comics (Vertigo): Sept, 2000 - No. 4, Dec, 2000 ($2.95, limited series)

1-4-Delano-s/Bond-a; Constantine in 2025 London 3.00

HELLBLAZER SPECIAL: CHAS
DC Comics (Vertigo): Sept, 2008 - No. 5, Jan, 2009 ($2.99, limited series)

1-5-Story of Constantine's cab driver; Oliver-s/Sudzuka-a/Fabry-c 3.00
... - The Knowledge TPB (2009, $14.99) r/#1-5 15.00

HELLBLAZER SPECIAL: LADY CONSTANTINE
DC Comics (Vertigo): Feb, 2003 - No. 4, May, 2003 ($2.95, limited series)

1-4-Story of Johanna Constantine in 1785; Diggle-s/Sudzuka-a/Noto-c 3.00

HELLBLAZER/THE BOOKS OF MAGIC
DC Comics (Vertigo): Dec, 1997 - No. 2, Jan, 1998 ($2.50, limited series)

1,2-John Constantine and Tim Hunter 4.00

HELLBOY (Also see Batman/Hellboy/Starman, Danger Unlimited #4, Dark Horse Presents, Gen[13] #13B, Ghost/Hellboy, John Byrne's Next Men, San Diego Comic Con #2, Savage Dragon, & Young Hellboy)

HELLBOY
Dark Horse Comics: Apr, 2008

... : Free Comic Book Day; Three short stories; Mignola-c; art by Fegredo, Davis, Azaceta 4.00

HELLBOY: ALMOST COLOSSUS
Dark Horse Comics (Legend): Jun, 1997 - No. 2, Jul, 1997 ($2.95, lim. series)

1,2-Mignola-s/a 1 3 4 6 8 10

HELLBOY AND THE B.P.R.D.
Dark Horse Comics: Dec, 2014 - No. 5, Apr, 2015 ($3.50, limited series)

1-5-Mignola & Arcudi-s/Maleev-a/c; Hellboy's first mission; set in 1952 3.50
...: Her Fatal Hour and The Sending (12/20, $3.99) Mignola-s/Trevallion-a 4.00
...: Long Night at Goloski Station (10/19, $3.99) Mignola-s/Matt Smith-a/Mignola-c 4.00
...: Night of the Cyclops (5/22, $3.99) Mignola-s/Vatine-a/c 4.00
...: 1953 - Beyond the Fences 1-3 (2/16 - No. 3, 4/16, $3.50) Paolo Rivera-a/c 3.50
...: 1953 - The Phantom Hand & The Kelpie (10/15, $3.50) Mignola-s/c; Stenbeck-a 3.50
...: 1953 - The Witch Tree & Rawhead and Bloody Bones (11/15, $3.50) Mignola-s/c; Stenbeck-a 3.50
...: 1953 - The Witch Tree & Rawhead and Bloody Bones, Halloween Comics Fest (10/17, giveaway) Mignola-s/c; Stenbeck-a 3.00
...: 1954 - Black Sun 1,2 (9/16 - No. 2, 10/16, $3.99) Stephen Green-a/c 4.00
...: 1954 - Ghost Moon 1,2 (3/17 - No. 2, 4/17, $3.99) Mignola & Roberson-s/Churilla-a 4.00
...: 1954 - The Unreasoning Beast (11/16, $3.99) Mignola & Roberson-s/Reynolds-a 4.00
...: 1955 - Burning Season (2/18, $3.99) Mignola & Roberson-s/Rivera-a 4.00
...: 1955 - Occult Intelligence 1-3 (9/17 - No. 3, 11/17, $3.99) Churilla-a 4.00
...: 1955 - Secret Nature (8/16, $3.99) Mignola & Roberson-s/Martinbrough-a 4.00
...: 1956 1-5 (11/18 - No. 5, 3/19, $3.99) Mignola & Roberson-s/Norton, Li & Oeming-a 4.00
...: 1957 - Falling Sky (8/22, $3.99) Mignola & Roberson-s/Martinbrough-a 4.00
...: 1957 - Family Ties (9/21, $3.99) Mignola & Roberson-s/Campbell-a 4.00
...: 1957 - Forgotten Lives (2/22, $3.99) Mignola & Roberson-s/Green-a 4.00
...: Old Man Whittier (6/22, $3.99) Mignola-s/Walta-a/c 4.00
...: Saturn Returns 1-3 (8/19 - No. 3, 10/19, $3.99) Mignola & Allie-s/Mitten-a 4.00
...: The Beast of Vargu (6/19, $3.99) Mignola-s/Fegredo-a/c 4.00
...: The Return of Effie Kolb 1,2 (2/20 - No. 2, 10/20, $3.99) Mignola-s/Zach Howard-a 4.00
...: The Secret of Chesbro House 1,2 (7/21 - No. 2, 8/21, $3.99) McManus-a 4.00
...: The Seven Wives Club (11/20, $4.99) Mignola-s/Hughes-a; covers by Mignola & Hughes 4.00
...: Time is a River (7/22, $3.99) Mignola-s/László-a/c 4.00

HELLBOY/BEASTS OF BURDEN
Dark Horse Comics: Oct, 2010 ($3.50, one-shot)

... Sacrifice - Dorkin & Mignola-s/Jill Thompson-a 1 3 4 6 8 10

HELLBOY: BEING HUMAN
Dark Horse Comics: May, 2011 ($3.50, one-shot)

nn-Mignola-s; Richard Corben-a/c; Roger app. 2 4 6 8 10 12

HELLBOY: BOX FULL OF EVIL
Dark Horse Comics: Aug, 1999 - No. 2, Sept, 1999 ($2.95, lim. series)

1,2-Mignola-s/a; back-up story w/ Matt Smith-a 2 4 6 8 10 12

HELLBOY: BUSTER OAKLEY GETS HIS WISH
Dark Horse Comics: Apr, 2011 ($3.50, one-shot)

nn-Mignola-s; Kevin Nowlan-a; two covers by Mignola & Nowlan 1 3 4 6 8 10

HELLBOY CHRISTMAS SPECIAL
Dark Horse Comics: Dec, 1997 ($3.95, one-shot)

nn-Christmas stories by Mignola, Gianni, Darrow 3 6 9 14 19 24

HELLBOY: CONQUEROR WORM
Dark Horse Comics: May, 2001 - No. 4, Aug, 2001 ($2.99, limited series)

1-4-Mignola-s/a/c 2 4 6 8 10 12

HELLBOY: DARKNESS CALLS
Dark Horse Comics: Apr, 2007 - No. 6, Nov, 2007 ($2.99, limited series)

1-6-Mignola-s/Fegredo-a 1 2 3 5 6 8

HELLBOY: DOUBLE FEATURE OF EVIL
Dark Horse Comics: Nov, 2010 ($3.50, one-shot)

1-Mignola-s; Corben-a/c 1 2 3 5 6 8

HELLBOY: HOUSE OF THE LIVING DEAD
Dark Horse Comics: Nov, 2011 ($14.99, hardcover graphic novel)

1-Mignola-s; Corben-a/c; Hellboy and Lucha Libre 15.00

HELLBOY IN HELL (Follows Hellboy's death in Hellboy: The Fury)
Dark Horse Comics: Dec, 2012 - No. 10, Jun, 2016 ($2.99)

1-Mignola-s/a/c in all 1 3 4 6 8 10
1-Variant "Year in Monsters" cover 16.00
2-6 1 2 3 5 6 8
7-10 4.00

HELLBOY IN LOVE
Dark Horse Comics: Oct, 2022 - No. 5 ($3.99, limited series)

1-3-Christopher Golden-s/Matt Smith-a; set in 1979 4.00

HELLBOY IN MEXICO
Dark Horse Comics: May, 2010 ($3.50, one-shot)

1-Mignola-s; Corben-a/c; Mexican wrestlers vs. monsters 1 3 4 6 8 10

HELLBOY: IN THE CHAPEL OF MOLOCH

	GD	VG	FN	VF	VF/NM	NM-
	2.0	4.0	6.0	8.0	9.0	9.2

Dark Horse Comics: Oct, 2008 ($2.99, one-shot)
nn-Mignola-s/a/c 1 2 3 5 6 8

HELLBOY: INTO THE SILENT SEA
Dark Horse Comics: Apr, 2017 ($14.99, HC graphic novel)
nn-Mignola-s/c; Gianni-a 15.00

HELLBOY, JR.
Dark Horse Comics: Oct, 1999 - No. 2, Nov, 1999 ($2.95, limited series)
1,2-Stories and art by various 6.00
TPB (1/04, $14.95) r/#1&2, Halloween; sketch pages; intro. by Steve Niles; Bill Wray-c 15.00

HELLBOY, JR., HALLOWEEN SPECIAL
Dark Horse Comics: Oct, 1997 ($3.95, one-shot)
nn-"Harvey" style renditions of Hellboy characters; Bill Wray, Mike Mignola & various-s/a; wraparound-c by Wray 1 3 4 6 8 10

HELLBOY: KRAMPUSNACHT
Dark Horse Comics: Dec, 2017 ($3.99, one-shot)
nn-Krampus app.; Mike Mignola-s/Adam Hughes-a; covers by Mignola & Hughes 4.00

HELLBOY: MAKOMA, OR A TALE TOLD...
Dark Horse Comics: Feb, 2006 - No. 2, Mar, 2006 ($2.99, lim. series)
1,2-Mignola-s/c; Mignola & Corben-a 6.00

HELLBOY PREMIERE EDITION
Dark Horse Comics (Wizard): 2004 (no price, one-shot)
nn- Two covers by Mignola & Davis; Mignola-s/a; BPRD story w/Arcudi-s/Davis-a 2 4 6 9 12 15
Wizard World Los Angeles-Movie photo-c; Mignola-s/a; BPRD story w/Arcudi-s/Davis-a 2 4 6 9 13 16

HELLBOY: SEED OF DESTRUCTION (First Hellboy series)
Dark Horse Comics (Legend): Mar, 1994 - No. 4, Jun, 1994 ($2.50, lim. series)
1-Mignola-c/a w/Byrne scripts; Monkeyman & O'Brien back-up story (origin) by Art Adams. 5 10 15 30 50 70
2-1st app. Abe Sapien & Liz Sherman 3 6 9 19 30 40
3,4 2 4 6 10 14 18
Hellboy: One for One (8/10, $1.00) r/#1 Hellboy story with red cover frame 6.00
Trade paperback (1994, $17.95)-collects all four issues plus r/Hellboy's 1st app. in San Diego Comic Con #2 & pin-ups 18.00
Limited edition hardcover (1995, $99.95)-includes everything in trade paperback plus additional material. 100.00

HELLBOY STRANGE PLACES
Dark Horse Books: Apr, 2006 ($17.95, TPB)
SC - Reprints Hellboy: The Third Wish #1,2 and Hellboy: The Island #1,2; sketch pages 18.00

HELLBOY: THE BONES OF GIANTS
Dark Horse Comics: Nov, 2021 - No. 4, Feb, 2022 ($3.99, lim. series)
1-4-Mignola & Golden-s/Matt Smith-a 4.00

HELLBOY: THE BRIDE OF HELL
Dark Horse Comics: Dec, 2009 ($3.50, one-shot)
1-Mignola-s/c; Corben-a; preview of The Marquis: Inferno 1 2 3 5 6 8

HELLBOY: THE CHAINED COFFIN AND OTHERS
Dark Horse Comics (Legend): Aug, 1998 ($17.95, TPB)
nn-Mignola-c/a/s; reprints out-of-print one shots; pin-up gallery 18.00

HELLBOY: THE COMPANION
Dark Horse Books: May, 2008 ($14.95, 9"x6", TPB)
nn-Overview of Hellboy history, characters, stories, mythology; text with Mignola panels 15.00

HELLBOY: THE CORPSE
Dark Horse Comics: Mar, 2004 (25¢, one-shot)
nn-Mignola-c/a/scripts; reprints "The Corpse" serial from Capitol City's Advance Comics catalog; development sketches and photos of the Corpse from the Hellboy movie 5.00

HELLBOY: THE CORPSE AND THE IRON SHOES
Dark Horse Comics (Legend): Jan, 1996 ($2.95, one-shot)
nn-Mignola-c/a/scripts; reprints "The Corpse" serial w/new story 1 3 4 6 8 10

HELLBOY: THE CROOKED MAN
Dark Horse Comics: Jul, 2008 - No. 3, Sept, 2008 ($2.99, lim. series)
1-3-Mignola-s/Corben-a/c 1 2 3 5 6 8

HELLBOY: THE FURY
Dark Horse Comics: Jun, 2011 - No. 3, Aug, 2011 ($2.99, lim. series)
1-3-Mignola-s/c; Fegredo-a. 1-Variant-c by Fegredo. 3-Hellboy dies 1 2 3 5 6 8
3-Retailer Incentive Variant 16 32 48 110 243 375

HELLBOY: THE GOLDEN ARMY
Dark Horse Comics: Jan, 2008 (no cover price)
nn-Prelude to the 2008 movie; Del Toro & Mignola-s/Velasco-a; 3 photo covers 1 3 4 6 8 10

HELLBOY: THE ISLAND
Dark Horse Comics: June, 2005 - No. 2, July, 2005 ($2.99, lim. series)
1,2: Mignola-c/a & scripts 1 2 3 5 6 8

HELLBOY: THE MIDNIGHT CIRCUS
Dark Horse Books: Oct, 2013 ($14.99, hardcover graphic novel)
nn-Mignola-s/c; Fegredo-a; young Hellboy runs away from BPRD in 1948 15.00

HELLBOY: THE RIGHT HAND OF DOOM
Dark Horse Comics (Legend): Apr, 2000 ($17.95, TPB)
nn-Mignola-c/a/s; reprints 18.00

HELLBOY: THE SILVER LANTERN CLUB
Dark Horse Comics: Oct, 2021 - No. 5, Mar, 2022 ($3.99, limited series)
1-5-Mignola & Roberson-s/Mitten & Stenbeck-a 4.00

HELLBOY: THE SLEEPING AND THE DEAD
Dark Horse Comics: Dec, 2010 - No. 2, Feb, 2011 ($3.50, lim. series)
1,2-Mignola-s/Scott Hampton-a 1 2 3 5 6 8

HELLBOY: THE STORM
Dark Horse Comics: Jul, 2010 - No. 3, Sept, 2010 ($2.99, lim. series)
1-3-Mignola-s/Fegredo-a 1 2 3 5 6 8

HELLBOY: THE THIRD WISH
Dark Horse Comics (Maverick): July, 2002 - No. 2, Aug, 2002 ($2.99, limited series)
1,2-Mignola-c/a/s 1 3 4 6 8 10

HELLBOY THE TROLL WITCH AND OTHERS
Dark Horse Books: Nov, 2007 ($17.95, TPB)
SC - Reprints Hellboy: Makoma, Hellboy Premiere Edition and stories from Dark Horse Book of Hauntings, DHB of Witchcraft, DHB of the Dead, DHB of Monsters 18.00

HELLBOY: THE WILD HUNT
Dark Horse Comics: Dec, 2008 - No. 8, Nov, 2009 ($2.99, lim. series)
1-8: Mignola-c/s; Fegredo-a 1 2 3 5 6 8

HELLBOY: THE WOLVES OF ST. AUGUST
Dark Horse Comics (Legend): 1995 ($4.95, squarebound, one-shot)
nn-Mignola--c/a/scripts; r/Dark Horse Presents #88-91 with additional story 2 4 6 8 10 12

HELLBOY VS. LOBSTER JOHNSON: THE RING OF DEATH
Dark Horse Comics: May, 2019 ($3.99, one-shot)
1-Mignola & Roberson-s; art by Norton & Grist; Paolo Rivera-c 4.00

HELLBOY: WAKE THE DEVIL (Sequel to Seed of Destruction)
Dark Horse Comics (Legend): Jun, 1996 - No. 5, Oct, 1996 ($2.95, lim. series)
1-5: Mignola-c/a & scripts; The Monstermen back-up story by Gary Gianni 2 4 6 8 10 12
TPB (1997, $17.95) r/#1-5 18.00

HELLBOY: WEIRD TALES
Dark Horse Comics: Feb, 2003 - No. 8, Apr, 2004 ($2.99, limited series, anthology)
1-8-Hellboy stories from other creators. 1-Cassaday-c/s/a; Watson-s/a. 6-Cho-c 1 2 3 5 6 8
... Vol. 1 (2004, 17.95) r/#1-4 18.00
... Vol. 2 (2004, 17.95) r/#5-8 and Lobster Johnson serial from #1-8 18.00

HELLBOY WINTER SPECIAL
Dark Horse Comics: Jan, 2016; Jan, 2017; Dec, 2018; Jan, 2020 ($3.99, one-shots)
1-Short stories by Mignola, Sale, Oeming, Allie, Roberson and others; Sale-c 4.00
nn (1/17)-Short stories; Mignola & Roberson-s, Mitten, Grist & Fiumara-a; Fiumara-c 4.00
... 2018 (12/18) Short stories; Mignola-s/Stenbeck-a; Bá & Moon-s/a; Zonjic-s/a 4.00
... 2019 (1/20) Short stories; Mignola-s/László-a; Roberson-s/Del Duca-a; Mutti-a 4.00

HELLCAT
Marvel Comics: Sept, 2000 - No. 3, Nov, 2000 ($2.99)
1-3-Englehart-s/Breyfogle-a; Hedy Wolfe app. 3.00

HELLCOP
Image Comics (Avalon Studios): Aug, 1998 - No. 4, Mar, 1999 ($2.50)
1-4: 1-(Oct. on-c) Casey-s 3.00

HELLCOP
Image Comics (Shadowline): Oct, 2021 - No. 10, Aug, 2022 ($3.99)
1-10-Brian Haberlin-s/a 4.00
...: Halloween Special 1 (10/21, $7.99, bagged with 3-D glasses) r/#1 with 3-D effects 8.00

HELL ETERNAL
DC Comics (Vertigo Verité): 1998 ($6.95, squarebound, one-shot)
1-Delano-s/Phillips-a 7.00

HELLGATE: LONDON (Based on the video game)
Dark Horse Comics: No. 0, May 2006 - No. 3, Mar, 2007 ($2.99)
0-3-Edginton-s/Pugh-a/Briclot-c 3.00

HELLHOUNDS (...: Panzer Cops #3-6)
Dark Horse Comics: 1994 - No. 6, July, 1994 ($2.50, B&W, limited series)
1-6: 1-Hamner-c. 2-Joe Phillips-c. 3-(4/94) 4.00

HELLHOUND, THE REDEMPTION QUEST
Marvel Comics (Epic Comics): Dec, 1993 - No. 4, Mar, 1994 ($2.25, lim. series, coated stock)
1-4 4.00

HELLIONS (See 2020 X-Men titles)
Marvel Comics: May, 2020 - No. 18, Feb, 2022 ($4.99/$3.99)
1-($4.99) Havok, Mr. Sinister, Psylocke, Scalphunter app.; Wells-s/Segovia-a 5.00
2-17-($3.99) 2-Scalphunter renamed Greycrow. 5,6-"X of Swords" tie-in. 12-Hellfire Gala 4.00
18-($4.99) Last issue; Wells-s/Carlos & Segovia-a 5.00

HELL IS A SQUARED CIRCLE
AfterShock Comics: Sept, 2022 ($7.99, oversized 8-1/2" x 10-7/8", one shot)
1-Chris Condon-s/Francesco Biagini-a 8.00

HELLMOUTH (Crossover with Buffy the Vampire Slayer and Angel)
BOOM! Studios: Oct, 2019 - No. 5, Feb, 2020 ($3.99, limited series)
1-5-Bellaire & Lambert-s/Carlini-a 4.00

HELLO BUDDIES
Harvey Publications: 1953 (25¢, small size)
1 5 10 15 33 57 80

HELL 'O DALI (Cerebus)
Aardvark-Vanaheim: Oct, 2022 ($4.00, B&W)
1-X-Men #42-c swipe 4.00

HELLO, I'M JOHNNY CASH
Spire Christian Comics (Fleming H. Revell Co.): 1976 (39¢/49¢)

Hellions #2 © MAR

Hell Sonja #1 © RS LLC

He-Man: The Eternity War #10 © Mattel

	GD 2.0	VG 4.0	FN 6.0	VF 8.0	VF/NM 9.0	NM- 9.2

nn-(39¢-c) 3 6 9 18 28 38
nn-(49¢-c) 3 6 9 15 22 28

HELL ON EARTH (See DC Science Fiction Graphic Novel)

HELLO PAL COMICS (Short Story Comics)
Harvey Publications: Jan, 1943 - No. 3, May, 1943 (Photo-c)
1-Rocketman & Rocketgirl begin; Yankee Doodle Jones app.; Mickey Rooney photo-c
68 136 204 435 743 1050
2-Charlie McCarthy photo-c (scarce) 56 112 168 349 595 840
3-Bob Hope photo-c (scarce) 60 120 180 384 660 935

HELLRAISER (See Clive Barker's...)

HELLRAISER/NIGHTBREED – JIHAD (Also see Clive Barker's...)
Epic Comics (Marvel Comics): 1991 - Book 2, 1991 ($4.50, 52 pgs.)
Book 1,2 1 3 4 6 8 10

HELL-RIDER (Motorcycle themed magazine)
Skywald Publications: Aug, 1971 - No. 2, Oct, 1971 (B&W, 68 pgs.)
1-Origin & 1st app.; Butterfly & the Wild Bunch begin; 1st Hell-Rider by Andru, Esposito and Friedrich 9 18 27 57 111 165
2-Andru, Ayers, Buckler, Shores-a 5 10 15 34 60 85
NOTE: *#3 advertised in Psycho #5 but did not come out.* **Buckler** *a-1, 2.* **Rosenbaum** *c-1,2.*

HELL'S ANGEL (Becomes Dark Angel #6 on)
Marvel Comics UK: July, 1992 - No. 5, Nov, 1993 ($1.75)
1-5: X-Men (Wolverine, Cyclops)-c/stories. 1-Origin. 3-Jim Lee cover swipe 4.00

HELLSHOCK
Image Comics: July, 1994 - No. 4, Nov, 1994 ($1.95, limited series)
1-4-Jae Lee-c/a & scripts. 4-Variant-c. 4.00

HELLSHOCK
Image Comics: Jan, 1997 - No. 3, Jan, 1998 ($2.95/$2.50, limited series)
1-($2.95)-Jae Lee-c/s/a, Villarrubia-painted-a 5.00
2-($2.50) 4.00
Book 3: The Science of Faith (1/98, $2.50) Jae Lee-c/s/a, Villarrubia-painted-a 4.00
Vol. 1 HC (2006, $49.99) r/#1-3 re-colored, with unpublished 22 pg. conclusion; cover gallery and sketches; alternate opening art; intro. by Jim Lee 50.00

HELL SONJA
Dynamite Entertainment: 2021 - No. 5, 2022 ($3.99, limited series)
1-5: 1-4-Hastings-s/Qualano-a; multiple covers on each; the alternate Sonjas app. 4.00

HELLSPAWN
Image Comics: Aug, 2000 - No. 16, Apr, 2003 ($2.50)
1-Bendis-s/Ashley Wood-c/a; Spawn & Clown app. 1 2 3 5 6 8
2-9: 6-Last Bendis-s; Mike Moran (Miracleman app.). 7-Niles-s 4.00
10-15-Templesmith-a 4.00
16-Final issue; Templesmith-a 1 3 4 6 8 10
...: The Ashley Wood Collection Vol. 1 (4/06, $24.95, TPB) r/#1-10; sketch & cover gallery 25.00

HELLSTORM: PRINCE OF LIES (See Ghost Rider #1 & Marvel Spotlight #12)
Marvel Comics: Apr, 1993 - No. 21, Dec, 1994 ($2.00)
1-($2.95)-Parchment-c w/red thermographic ink 4.00
2-21: 14-Bound-in trading card sheet. 18-P. Craig Russell-c 3.00

HELLSTORM: SON OF SATAN
Marvel Comics (MAX): Dec, 2006 - No. 5, Apr, 2007 ($3.99, limited series)
1-5-Suydam-c/Irvine-s/Braun & Janson-a 4.00
... - Equinox TPB (2007, $17.99) r/#1-5; interviews with the creators 18.00

HELLSTROM: MARVEL TALES
Marvel Comics: Jan, 2021 ($7.99, one-shot)
1-Reprints notable apps. in Ghost Rider #1, Son of Satan #1, Marvel Fanfare #59 and Hellstorm, Prince of Lies #1; Ralph Macchio intro. 8.00

HELL TO PAY
Image Comics: Nov, 2022 - Present ($3.99)
1-3-Soule-s/Sliney-a 4.00

HELMET OF FATE, THE (Series of one-shots following Doctor Fate's helmet)
DC Comics: Mar, 2007 - May 2007 ($2.99, one-shots)
...: Black Alice (5/07) Simone-s/Rouleau-a/c 3.00
...: Detective Chimp (3/07) Willingham-s/McManus-a/Bolland-c 3.00
...: Ibis the Invincible (3/07) Williams-s/Winslade-a; the Ibistick returns 3.00
...: Sargon the Sorcerer (4/07) Niles-s/Scott Hampton-s; debut new Sargon 3.00
...: Zauriel (4/07) Gerber-s/Snejbjerg-a/Kaluta-c; leads into new Doctor Fate series 3.00
TPB (2007, $14.99) r/one-shots 15.00

HELM GREYCASTLE
Image Comics (Top Cow): Apr, 2021 - No. 4, Sept, 2021 ($3.99, limited series)
1-4-Barajas-s/Handoko-a; bonus Role Playing Game pages in each 4.00

HELP US! GREAT WARRIOR
BOOM! Studios (BOOM! Box): Feb, 2015 - No. 6, Jul, 2015 ($3.99)
1-6-Madeleine Flores-s/a 4.00

HE-MAN (See Masters Of The Universe)

HE-MAN (Also see Tops In Adventure)
Ziff-Davis Publ. Co. (Approved Comics): Fall, 1952
1-Kinstler painted-c; Powell-a 20 40 60 118 192 265

HE-MAN
Toby Press: May, 1954 - No. 2, July, 1954 (Painted-c by B. Safran)
1-Gorilla-c 19 38 57 109 172 235
2-Shark-c 17 34 51 100 158 215

HE-MAN AND THE MASTERS OF THE UNIVERSE
DC Comics: Sept, 2012 - No. 6, Mar, 2013 ($2.99)
1-James Robinson-s/Philip Tan-a/c; Skeletor app. 2 4 6 8 10 12
2-6: 5-Adam gets the sword 5.00

HE-MAN AND THE MASTERS OF THE UNIVERSE
DC Comics: Jun, 2013 - No. 19, Jan, 2015 ($2.99)
1-Giffen-s/Mhan-a/Benes-c 1 3 4 6 8 10
2-12,15-17: 7,8-Abnett-s/Kayanan-a 5.00
13,14-Origin of She-Ra begins 3 6 9 14 20 25
18-Full app. of She-Ra 4 8 12 27 44 60
19-Origin of Skeletor 3 6 9 16 23 30

HE-MAN AND THE MASTERS OF THE MULTIVERSE
DC Comics: Jan, 2020 - No. 6, Jul, 2020 ($3.99, limited series)
1-6: 1-3-Seeley-s/Fraga-a; He-Man of Hellskull app. 4-6-Derenick-a 4.00

HE-MAN: THE ETERNITY WAR
DC Comics: Feb, 2015 - No. 15, Apr, 2016 ($2.99)
1-Abnett-s/Mhan-a; Hordak invades; origin of Grayskull
1 3 4 6 8 10
2-15 3.00

HE-MAN / THUNDERCATS
DC Comics: Dec, 2016 - No. 6, May, 2017 ($3.99, limited series)
1-Freddie Williams II-a; Mumm-Ra & Skeletor app. 3 6 9 16 23 30
2-6 5.00

HENNESSEY (TV)
Dell Publishing Co.: No. 1200, Aug-Oct, 1961 - No. 1280, Mar-May, 1962
Four Color 1200-Gil Kane-a, photo-c 7 14 21 48 89 130
Four Color 1280-Photo-c 6 12 18 40 73 105

HENRY (Also see Little Annie Rooney)
David McKay Publications: 1935 (52 pgs.) (Daily B&W strip reprints)(10"x10" cardboard-c)
1-By Carl Anderson 43 86 129 271 461 650

HENRY (See King Comics & Magic Comics)
Dell Publishing Co.: No. 122, Oct, 1946 - No. 65, Apr-June, 1961
Four Color 122-All new stories begin 16 32 48 110 243 375
Four Color 155 (7/47), 1 (1-3/48)-All new stories 10 20 30 70 150 230
2 6 12 18 40 73 105
3-10 5 10 15 34 60 85
11-20: 20-Infinity-c 5 10 15 30 50 70
21-30 4 8 12 25 40 55
31-40 3 6 9 21 33 45
41-65 3 6 9 17 26 35

HENRY (See Giant Comic Album and March of Comics No. 43, 58, 84, 101, 112, 129, 147, 162, 178, 189)

HENRY ALDRICH COMICS (TV)
Dell Publishing Co.: Aug-Sept, 1950 - No. 22, Sept-Nov, 1954
1-Part series written by John Stanley; Bill Williams-a
9 18 27 60 120 180
2 5 10 15 35 63 90
3-5 5 10 15 31 53 75
6-10 4 8 12 27 44 60
11-22 4 8 12 23 37 50

HENRY BREWSTER
Country Wide (M.F. Ent.): Feb, 1966 - V2#7, Sept, 1967 (All 25¢ Giants)
1 3 6 9 19 30 40

GD 2.0 | VG 4.0 | FN 6.0 | VF 8.0 | VF/NM 9.0 | NM 9.2

2-6(12/66), V2#7-Powell-a in most 3 6 9 14 20 25

HEPCATS
Antarctic Press: Nov, 1996 - No. 12 ($2.95, B&W)
0-12-Martin Wagner-c/s/a: 0-color 3.00
0-($9.95) CD Edition 10.00

HERALDS
Marvel Comics: Aug, 2010 - No. 5, Aug, 2010 ($2.99, weelky limited series)
1-5-Kathryn Immonen-s/Zonjic & Harren-a; She-Hulk, Hellcat, Emma Frost, Photon app. 3.00

HERBIE (See Forbidden Worlds #73,94,110,114,116 & Unknown Worlds #20)
American Comics Group: April-May, 1964 - No. 23, Feb, 1967 (All 12¢)
1-Whitney-c/a in most issues 19 38 57 131 291 450
2-4 8 16 24 56 108 160
5-Beatles parody (10 pgs.), Dean Martin, Frank Sinatra app. (10-11/64)
9 18 27 61 123 185
6,7,9,10 7 14 21 48 89 130
8-Origin & 1st app. The Fat Fury 8 16 24 55 105 155
11-23: 14-Nemesis & Magicman app. 17-r/2nd Herbie from Forbidden Worlds
#94. 23-r/1st Herbie from F.W. #73 6 12 18 37 66 95
... Archives Volume One HC (Dark Horse, 8/08, $49.95, dust jacket) r/earliest apps. in
Forbidden Worlds, Unknown Worlds, and Herbie #1-5; Scott Shaw intro. 50.00

HERBIE
Dark Horse Comics: Oct, 1992 - No. 12, 1993 ($2.50, limited series)
1-Whitney-r plus new-c/a in all; Byrne-c/a & scripts 4.00
2-6: 3-Bob Burden-c/a. 4-Art Adams-c 3.00

HERBIE GOES TO MONTE CARLO, HERBIE RIDES AGAIN (See Walt Disney Showcase No. 24, 41)

HERC (Hercules from the Avengers)
Marvel Comics: Jun, 2011 - No. 10, Jan, 2012 ($2.99)
1-6, (6.1), 7-10: 1-Pak & Van Lente-s; Hobgoblin app. 3-6-Fear Itself tie-in. 6.1-Grell-a
7,8-Spider-Island tie-in; Herc gets Spider-powers. 10-Elektra app. 3.00

HERCULES (See Hit Comics #1-21, Journey Into Mystery Annual, Marvel Graphic Novel #37, Marvel Premiere #26 & The Mighty...)

HERCULES (See Charlton Classics)
Charlton Comics: Oct, 1967 - No. 13, Sept, 1969; Dec, 1968
1-Thane of Bagarth begins; Glanzman-a in all 5 10 15 30 50 70
2-13: 1-5,7-10-Aparo-a. 8-(12¢-c) 4 8 12 23 37 50
4-Magazine format (low distribution) 8 16 24 54 102 150
8-Magazine format (low distribution)(12/68, 35¢, B&W); new Hercules story plus-r story/#1;
Thane-r/#1-3 5 10 15 33 57 80
Modern Comics reprint 10('77), 11('78) 6.00

HERCULES (Prince of Power) (Also see The Champions)
Marvel Comics Group: V1#1, Sept, 1982 - V1#4, Dec, 1982;
V2#1, Mar, 1984 - V2#4, Jun, 1984 (color, both limited series)
1-4, V2#1-4: Layton-c/a. 4-Death of Zeus. 4.00
NOTE: *Layton a-1, 2, 3p, 4p, V2#1-4; c-1-4, V2#1-4.*

HERCULES
Marvel Comics: Jun, 2005 - No. 5, Sept, 2005 ($2.99, limited series)
1-5-Texeira-a/c; Tieri-s. 4-Capt. America, Wolverine and New Avengers app. 3.00
...: New Labors of Hercules TPB (2005, $13.99) r/#1-5 14.00

HERCULES
Marvel Comics: Jan, 2016 - No. 6, Jun, 2016 ($3.99)
1-6: 1-Dan Abnett-s/Luke Ross-a; Gilgamesh app. 4.00

HERCULES: FALL OF AN AVENGER (Continues in Heroic Age: Prince of Power)
Marvel Comics: May, 2010 - No. 2, June, 2010 ($3.99, limited series)
1,2-Follows Hercules' demise in Incredible Hercules #141; Olivetti-c/a 4.00

HERCULES: HEART OF CHAOS
Marvel Comics: Aug, 1997 - No. 3, Oct, 1997 ($2.50, limited series)
1-3-DeFalco-s, Frenz-a 3.00

HERCULES: OFFICIAL COMICS MOVIE ADAPTION
Acclaim Books: 1997 ($4.50, digest size)
nn-Adaptation of the Disney animated movie 4.50

HERCULES: THE LEGENDARY JOURNEYS (TV)
Topps Comics: June, 1996 - No. 5, Oct, 1996 ($2.95)
1-2: 1-Golden-c 4.00
3-Xena-c/app. 2 4 6 8 10 12
3-Variant-c 2 4 6 11 16 20
4,5: Xena-c/app. 5.00

HERCULES UNBOUND
National Periodical Publications: Oct-Nov, 1975 - No. 12, Aug-Sept, 1977
1-García-López-a/Wood-i begins 2 4 6 12 16 20
2-12: 2-6-García-López-a. 7-Adams ad. 10-Atomic Knights x-over
1 3 4 6 8 10
NOTE: *Buckler c-7p. Layton inks-No. 9, 10. Simonson a-7-10p, 11, 12; c-8p, 9-12. Wood a-1-8i; c-7i, 8i.*

HERCULES (...Unchained #1121) (Movie)
Dell Publishing Co.: No. 1006, June-Aug, 1959 - No.1121, Aug, 1960
Four Color 1006-Buscema-a, photo-c 10 20 30 69 147 225
Four Color 1121-Crandall/Evans-a 9 18 27 61 123 185

HERCULES: TWILIGHT OF A GOD
Marvel Comics: Aug, 2010 - No. 4, Nov, 2010 ($3.99, limited series)
1-4-Layton-s/a(i); Lim-a; Galactus app. 4.00

HERCULIAN
Image Comics: Mar, 2011 ($4.99, oversized, one-shot)
1-Golden Age style superhero stories and humor pages; Erik Larsen-s/a/c 5.00

HERE COMES SANTA (See March of Comics No. 30, 213, 340)

HERE'S HOWIE COMICS
National Periodical Publications: Jan-Feb, 1952 - No. 18, Nov-Dec, 1954
1 42 84 126 265 445 625
2 22 44 66 128 209 290
3-5: 5-Howie in the Army issues begin (9-10/52) 16 32 48 98 154 210
6-10 15 30 45 86 133 180
11-18 15 30 45 84 127 170
Ashcan (1,2/51) not distributed to newsstands (a FN copy sold for $836.50 in 2012)

HERETIC, THE
Dark Horse (Blanc Noir): Nov, 1996 - No. 4, Mar, 1997 ($2.95, lim. series)
1-4:-w/back-up story 3.00

HERITAGE OF THE DESERT (See Zane Grey, 4-Color 236)

HERMAN & KATNIP (See Harvey Comics Hits #60 & 62, Harvey Hits #14,25,31,41 & Paramount Animated Comics #1)

HERMANN
Aardvark-Vanaheim: Dec, 2020 ($4.00, B&W)
1-Cerebus figures with original Gustave Doré artwork; homage to Watchmen's Rorschach 4.00

HERMES VS. THE EYEBALL KID
Dark Horse Comics: Dec, 1994 - No. 3,Feb, 1995 ($2.95, B&W, limited series)
1-3: Eddie Campbell-c/a/scripts 3.00

H-E-R-O (Dial H For HERO)
DC Comics: Apr, 2003 - No. 22, Jan, 2005 ($2.50)
1-Will Pfeiffer-s/Kano-a/Van Fleet-c 3.50
2-22: 2-6-Kano-a. 7,8-Gleason-a. 12-14-Kirk-a. 15-22-Robby Reed app. 3.00
...: Double Feature (6/03, $4.95) r/#1&2 5.00
...: Powers and Abilities (2003, $9.95) r/#1-6; intro. by Geoff Johns 10.00

HERO (Warrior of the Mystic Realms)
Marvel Comics: May, 1990 - No. 6, Oct, 1990 ($1.50, limited series)
1-6: 1-Portacio-i 3.00

HERO ALLIANCE, THE
Sirius Comics: Dec, 1985 - No. 2, Sept, 1986 (B&W)
1,2: 2-($1.50), Special Edition 1 (7/86, color) 3.00

HERO ALLIANCE
Wonder Color Comics: May, 1987 ($1.95)
1-Ron Lim-a 3.00

HERO ALLIANCE
Innovation Publishing: V2#1, Sept, 1989 - V2#17, Nov, 1991 ($1.95, 28 pgs.)
V2#1-17: 1,2-Ron Lim-a 3.00
Annual 1 (1990, $2.75, 36 pgs.)-Paul Smith-c/a 3.00
Special 1 (1992, $2.50, 32 pgs.)-Stuart Immonen-a (10 pgs.) 3.00

HERO ALLIANCE: END OF THE GOLDEN AGE
Innovation Publ.: July, 1989 - No. 3, Aug, 1989 ($1.75, bi-weekly lim. series)
1-3: Bart Sears & Ron Lim-c/a; reprints & new-a 3.00

HEROBEAR AND THE KID
Boom Entertainment (KaBOOM!)
... 2013 Annual 1 (10/13, $3.99) Halloween-themed story 4.00
... 2016 Fall Special 1 (10/16, $5.99) Saving Time: Part Two 6.00
... Special (6/13, $3.99) Mike Kunkel-s/a/c 4.00
...: The Inheritance (8/13 - No. 5, 12/13, $3.99) 1-5-Mike Kunkel-s/a/c; origin re-told 4.00

HERO COMICS (Hero Initiative benefit book)
IDW Publishing: 2009 - Present ($3.99)
1-Short story anthology by various incl. Colan, Chaykin; covers by Wagner & Campbell 4.00
2011-Covers by Campbell & Hughes; Gaiman-s/Kieth-a; Chew & Elephantmen app. 4.00
2012-Cover by Campbell; TMNT by Eastman; art by Heath, Sim, Kupperberg, & others 4.00
2014-Covers by Campbell & Kieth; Sable by Grell; art by Kieth, Goldberg & others 4.00
...: A Hero Initiative Benefit Book SC (5/16, $19.99) reprints from previous editions 20.00

HEROES
Marvel Comics: Dec, 2001 ($3.50, magazine-size, one-shot)
1-Pin-up tributes to the rescue workers of the Sept. 11 tragedy; art and text by
various; cover by Alex Ross 6.00
1-2nd and 3rd printings 4.00

HEROES (Also see Shadow Cabinet & Static)
DC Comics (Milestone): May, 1996 - No. 6, Nov, 1996 ($2.50, limited series)
1-Intro Heroes (Iota, Donner, Blitzen, Starlight, Payback & Static) 6.00
2-6 4.00

HEROES (Based on the NBC TV series)
DC Comics (WildStorm): 2007; 2009 ($29.99, hardcover with dustjacket)
Vol. 1 - Collects 34 installments of the online graphic novel; art by various; two covers by
Jim Lee and Alex Ross; intro. by Masi Oka; Jeph Loeb interview 30.00
Vol. 2 - (2009) Collects 46 installments of the online graphic novel; art by various incl.
Gaydos, Grummett, Gunnell, Odagawa; two covers by Tim Sale and Gene Ha 30.00

HER-OES
Marvel Comics: Jun, 2010 - No. 4, Sept, 2010 ($2.99, limited series)
1-4-Randolph-s/Rousseau-a; Wasp, She-Hulk, Namora as teenagers 3.00

HEROES AGAINST HUNGER
DC Comics: 1986 ($1.50; one-shot for famine relief)
1-Superman, Batman app.; Neal Adams-c(p); includes many artists work;
Jeff Jones assist (2 pg.) on B. Smith-a; Kirby-a 6.00

HEROES ALL CATHOLIC ACTION ILLUSTRATED
Heroes All Co.: 1943 - V6#5, Mar 10, 1948 (paper covers)
V1#1-(16 pgs., 8x11") 24 48 72 142 234 325
V1#2-(16 pgs., 8x11") 19 38 57 111 176 240
V2#1(1/44)-3(3/44)-(16 pgs., 8x11") 15 30 45 94 147 200
V3#1(1/45)-10(12/45)-(16 pgs., 8x11") 15 30 45 85 130 175
V4#1-35 (12/20/46)-(16 pgs.) 14 28 42 80 115 150
V5#1(1/10/47)-8(2/28/47)-(16 pgs.), V5#9(3/7/47)-20(11/25/47)-(32 pgs.),
V6#1(1/10/48)-5(3/10/48)-(32 pgs.) 12 24 36 69 97 125

Hercules (2016) #1 © MAR

Heroes in Crisis #5 © DC

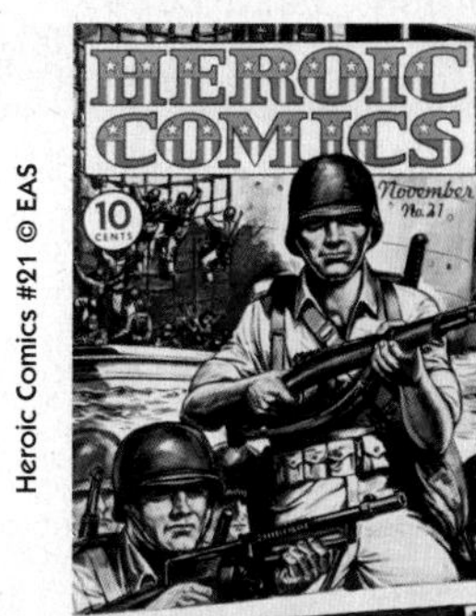

Heroic Comics #21 © EAS

GD 2.0 | VG 4.0 | FN 6.0 | VF 8.0 | VF/NM 9.0 | NM- 9.2

HEROES ANONYMOUS
Bongo Comics: 2003 - No. 6, 2004 ($2.99, limited series)
1-6-($2.99)-Bill Morrison-c. 2-Guerra-a. 3-Pepoy-a 3.00

HEROES AT HOME
Marvel Comics: 2020 ($9.99, 5" x 5", one-shot)
1-Zeb Wells-s/Gurihiru-a; humor strips of Marvel heroes quarantined at home 10.00

HEROES FOR HIRE
Marvel Comics: July, 1997 - No. 19, Jan, 1999 ($2.99/$1.99)
1-($2.99)-Wraparound cover 6.00
2-19: 2-Variant cover. 7-Thunderbolts app. 9-Punisher-c/app. 10,11-Deadpool-c/app. 18,19-Wolverine-c/app. 4.00
.../Quicksilver '98 Annual ($2.99) Siege of Wundagore pt.5 5.00

HEROES FOR HIRE
Marvel Comics: Oct, 2006 - No. 15, Dec, 2007 ($2.99)
1-5-Tucci-a/c; Black Cat, Shang-Chi, Tarantula, Humbug & Daughters of the Dragon app. 3.00
6-15: 6-8-Sparacio-c. 9,10-Golden-c. 11-13-World War Hulk x-over. 13-Takeda-c 3.00
... Vol. 1: Civil War (2007, $13.99) r/#1-5 14.00
... Vol. 2: Ahead of the Curve (2007, $13.99) r/#6-10 14.00
... Vol. 3: World War Hulk (2008, $13.99) r/#11-15 14.00

HEROES FOR HIRE
Marvel Comics: Feb, 2011 - No. 12, Nov, 2011 ($3.99/$2.99)
1-($3.99) Abnett & Lanning-s/Walker-a; back-up history of the various teams 4.00
2-12-($2.99) 2-Silver Sable & Ghost Rider app. 5-Punisher app. 9-11-Fear Itself tie-in 3.00

HEROES FOR HOPE STARRING THE X-MEN
Marvel Comics Group: Dec, 1985 ($1.50, one-shot, 52 pgs., proceeds donated to famine relief)
1-Stephen King scripts; Byrne, Miller, Corben-a; Wrightson/J. Jones-a (3 pgs.); Art Adams-c; Starlin back-c 1 3 4 6 8 10

HEROES: GODSEND (Based on the NBC TV series)(Prelude to the 2015 revival)
Titan Comics: Apr, 2016 - No. 5, Aug, 2016 ($3.99, limited series)
1-5: 1-Origin of Farah Nazan; Roy Allan Martinez-a; multiple covers on each 4.00

HEROES, INC. PRESENTS CANNON
Wally Wood/CPL/Gang Publ.: 1969 - No. 2, 1976 (Sold at Army PXs)
nn-Ditko, Wood-a; Wood-c; Reese-a(p) 3 6 9 14 20 25
2-Wood-c; Ditko, Byrne, Wood-a; 8-1/2x10-1/2"; B&W; $2.00 3 6 9 19 30 40
NOTE: *First issue not distributed by publisher; 1,800 copies were stored and 900 copies were stolen from warehouse. Many copies have surfaced in recent years.*

HEROES IN CRISIS
DC Comics: Nov, 2018 - No. 9, Jul, 2019 ($3.99, limited series)
1-9: 1-Tom King-s/Clay Mann-a; murder of Wally West, Arsenal and others 4.00

HEROES OF THE WILD FRONTIER (Formerly Baffling Mysteries)
Ace Periodicals: No. 27, Jan, 1956 - No. 2, Apr, 1956
27(#1),2-Davy Crockett, Daniel Boone, Buffalo Bill 6 12 18 32 39 46

HEROES REBORN (one-shots)
Marvel Comics: Jan, 2000 ($1.99)
...:Ashema; ...:Doom; ...:Doomsday; ...:Masters of Evil; ...:Rebel; ...:Remnants; ...:Young Allies 3.00

HEROES REBORN
Marvel Comics: Jul, 2021 - No. 7, Aug, 2021 ($5.99/$4.99, weekly limited series)
1-($5.99) Squadron Supreme replaces the Avengers; Blade app.; Aaron-s/McGuinness-a 6.00
2-7-($4.99) 2-Captain America returns. 4-Stokoe-a. 7-Leads into Heroes Return #1 5.00
...: American Knights 1 (8/21, $4.99) Spotlight on Luke Cage & Nighthawk; Grist-s/Allen-a 5.00
...: Hyperion & The Imperial Guard 1 (7/21, $4.99) Gady-s/Bandini-a 5.00
...: Magneto & The Mutant Force 1 (7/21, $4.99) Orlando-s/Chang-a 5.00
...: Marvel Double Action 1 (8/21, $4.99) Nighthawk & Falcon in '70s style team-up; Jurgens-a 5.00
...: Night-Gwen 1 (8/21, $4.99) Ayala-s/Karami-a; Misty Knight app. 5.00
...: Peter Parker, The Amazing Shutterbug 1 (7/21, $4.99) Lim & De Latorre-a 5.00
...: Siege Society 1 (7/21, $4.99) Ziglar-s/Medina-a; Hawkeye, Black Widow & others 5.00
...: Weapon X & Final Flight 1 (8/21, $4.99) Wolverine & Sasquatch app.; Boschi-a 5.00
...: Young Squadron 1 (7/21, $4.99) Kid Spectrum, Girl Power, Falcon & Deadpool app. 5.00

HEROES REBORN: THE RETURN (Also see Avengers, Fantastic Four, Iron Man & Captain America titles for issues and TPBs)
Marvel Comics: Dec, 1997 - No. 4, Dec, 1997 ($2.50, weekly mini-series)
1-4-Avengers, Fantastic Four, Iron Man & Captain America rejoin regular Marvel Universe; Peter David-s/Larocca-c/a 4.00
1-4-Variant-c for each 6.00
Wizard 1/2 1 2 3 5 7 9
Return of the Heroes TPB ('98, $14.95) r/#1-4 15.00

HEROES RETURN
Marvel Comics: Aug, 2021 ($5.99, conclusion to Heroes Reborn)
1-($5.99) Squadron Supreme vs. the Avengers & Blade; Aaron-s/McGuinness-a 6.00

HEROES: VENGEANCE (Based on the NBC TV series)(Prelude to the 2015 revival)
Titan Comics: Nov, 2015 - No. 5, Mar, 2016 ($3.99, limited series)
1-5: 1-Origin of El Vengador; Rubine-a; multiple covers on each 4.00

HERO FOR HIRE (Power Man No. 17 on; also see Cage)
Marvel Comics Group: June, 1972 - No. 16, Dec, 1973
1-Origin & 1st app. Luke Cage; Tuska-a(p) 71 142 213 588 1284 2000
2-Tuska-a(p); 1st app. Claire Temple 7 14 21 48 89 130
3,4: 3-1st app. Mace. 4-1st app. Phil Fox of the Bugle 5 10 15 33 57 80
5-1st app. Black Mariah 5 10 15 35 63 90
6-10: 8,9-Dr. Doom app. 9-F.F. app. 10-1st app. Mr. Death 4 8 12 25 40 55
11-16: 14-Origin retold. 15-Everett Sub-Mariner-r('53). 16-Origin Stilletto; death of Rackham 3 6 9 20 31 42

HERO HOTLINE (1st app. in Action Comics Weekly #637)
DC Comics: April, 1989 - No. 6, Sept, 1989 ($1.75, limited series)
1-6: Super-hero humor; Schaffenberger-i 3.00

HEROIC ADVENTURES (See Adventures)

HEROIC AGE
Marvel Comics: Nov, 2010 ($3.99, limited series)
... Heroes 1 (11/10, $3.99) profile of heroes, bios, pros, cons, "power grid"; Raney-c 4.00
... Villains 1 (1/11, $3.99) profile of villains, bios, pros, cons, "power grid"; Jae Lee-c 4.00
... X-Men 1 (2/11, $3.99) profile of members in Steve Rogers journal entries,; Jae Lee-c 4.00

HEROIC AGE: PRINCE OF POWER (Continued from Hercules: Fall of an Avenger)
Marvel Comics: Jul, 2010 - No. 4, Oct, 2010 ($3.99, limited series)
1-4-Van Lente & Pak-s; Thor app.; leads into Chaos War #1 4.00

HEROIC COMICS (Reg'lar Fellers...#1-15; New Heroic #41 on)
Eastern Color Printing Co./Famous Funnies (Funnies, Inc. No. 1):
Aug, 1940 - No. 97, June, 1955
1-Hydroman (origin) by Bill Everett, The Purple Zombie (origin) & Mann of India by Tarpe Mills begins (all 1st apps.) 245 490 735 1568 2684 3800
2 103 206 309 659 1130 1600
3,4 57 114 171 362 619 875
5,6 50 100 150 315 533 750
7-Origin & 1st app. Man O'Metal (1 pg.) 52 104 156 328 552 775
8-10: 10-Lingerie panels 39 78 117 234 385 535
11,13 37 74 111 222 361 500
12-Music Master (origin/1st app.) begins by Everett, ends No. 31; last Purple Zombie & Mann of India 41 82 123 256 428 600
14,15-Hydroman x-over in Rainbow Boy. 14-Origin & 1st app. Rainbow Boy (super hero). 15-1st app. Downbeat 37 74 111 222 361 500
16-20: 16-New logo. 17-Rainbow Boy x-over in Hydroman. 19-Rainbow Boy x-over in Hydroman & vice versa 26 52 78 154 252 350
21-30:25-Rainbow Boy x-over in Hydroman. 28-Last Man O'Metal. 29-Last Hydroman 20 40 60 114 182 250
31,34,38 9 18 27 50 65 80
32,36,37-Toth-a (3-4 pgs. each) 10 20 30 56 76 95
33,35-Toth-a (8 & 9 pgs.) 10 20 30 58 79 100
39-42-Toth, Ingels-a 10 20 30 58 79 100
43,46,47,49-Toth-a (2-4 pgs.). 47-Ingels-a 10 20 30 54 72 90
44,45,50-Toth-a (6-9 pgs.) 10 20 30 56 76 95
48,53,54 9 18 27 47 61 75
51-Williamson-a 10 20 30 56 76 95
52-Williamson-a (3 pg. story) 9 18 27 50 65 80
55-Toth-a 10 20 30 54 72 90
56-60: 60-Everett-a 9 18 27 50 65 80
61-Everett-a 9 18 27 47 61 75
62,64-Everett-c/a 10 20 30 54 72 90
63-Everett-c 9 18 27 52 69 85
65-Williamson/Frazetta-a; Evans-a (2 pgs.) 13 26 39 72 101 130
66,75,94-Frazetta-a (2 pgs. each) 9 18 27 52 69 85
67,73-Frazetta-a (4 pgs. each) 11 22 33 60 83 105
68,74,76-80,84,85,88-93,95-97: 95-Last pre-code 9 18 27 47 61 75
69,72-Frazetta-a (6 & 8 pgs. each); 1st (?) app. Frazetta Red Cross ad 13 26 39 72 101 130

GD VG FN VF VF/NM NM-
2.0 4.0 6.0 8.0 9.0 9.2

70,71,86,87-Frazetta, 3-4 pgs. each; 1 pg. ad by Frazetta in #70 10 20 30 56 76 95
81,82-Frazetta art (1 pg. each): 81-1st (?) app. Frazetta Boy Scout ad (tied w/ Buster Crabbe #9 9 18 27 50 65 80
83-Frazetta-a (1/2 pg.) 9 18 27 50 65 80
NOTE: **Evans** a-64, 65. **Everett** a-(Hydroman-c/a-No. 1-9), 44, 60-64; c-1-9, 62-64. **Harvey Fuller** c-28-35. **Sid Greene** a-38-43, 46. **Guardineer** a-42(3), 43, 44, 45(2), 49(3), 50, 60, 61(2), 65, 67(2) 70-72. **Ingels** c-41. **Kiefer** a-46, 48; c-19-22, 24, 44, 46, 48, 51-53, 65, 67-69, 71-74, 76, 77, 79, 80, 82, 85, 86, 88, 89, 94, 95. **Mort Lawrence** a-45. **Tarpe Mills** a-2(2), 3(2), 10. **Ed Moore** a-49, 52-54, 56-63, 65-69, 72-74, 76, 77. **H.G. Peter** a-58-74, 76, 77, 87. **Paul Reinman** a-49. **Rico** a-31. Captain Tootsie by **Beck**-31, 32. Painted-c #16 on. Hydroman c-1-11. Music Master c-12, 13, 15. Rainbow Boy c-14.

HERO INITIATIVE: MIKE WIERINGO BOOK (Also see Hero Comics)
Marvel Comics: Aug, 2008 ($4.99)
1-The "What If" Fantastic Four story with Wieringo-a (7 pgs.) finished by other artists after his passing; art by Davis, Immonen, Ramos, Kitson and others; written tributes 5.00

HERO TRADE, THE (1st Bad Idea title)
Bad Idea: Sept, 2020 ($3.00, B&W, one-shot)
1-Matt Kindt-s/David Lapham-a 17 54 51 117 259 400

HERO TRADE: A BRIEF CASE (Bonus mailed with only 50 orders of Hero Trade)
Bad Idea: Feb, 2021 (limited edition of 50, B&W, one-shot)
1-Kindt-s/Lapham-a; r/story pages from Eniac #1 38 76 114 285 641 1000

HERO TRADE: PASSIVE / AGGRESSIVE
Bad Idea: Aug, 2021 ($5.99, same cover with 2 different lead stories)
Aggressive version-(noted on inside front cover) Kindt-s/Lapham-a; distributed to Eastern U.S. 1 3 4 6 8 10
Passive version-(noted on inside front cover) Kindt-s/Lapham-a; distributed to Western U.S. (more rare than the Aggressive version) 2 4 6 9 12 15

HERO WORSHIP
Avatar Press: Jun, 2012 - No. 6, Nov, 2012 ($3.99)
1-6: 1-Zak Penn & Scott Murphy-s/Michael DiPascale-a; 2 covers 4.00

HERO ZERO (Also see Comics' Greatest World & Godzilla Versus Hero Zero)
Dark Horse Comics: Sept, 1994 ($2.50)
0 3.00

HE WHO FIGHTS WITH MONSTERS
Ablaze Publishing: 2021 - No. 5, 2022 ($3.99, limited series)
1-5-Francesco Artibani-s/Werther Dell'Edra-a; multiple covers on each 4.00

HEX (Replaces Jonah Hex)
DC Comics: Sept, 1985 - No. 18, Feb, 1987 (Story cont'd from Jonah Hex # 92)
1-Hex in post-atomic war world; origin 6.00
2-10,14-18: 6-Origin Stiletta 4.00
11-13: All contain future Batman storyline. 13-Intro The Dogs of War (origin #15) 6.00
NOTE: **Giffen** a(p)-15-18; c(p)-15,17,18. **Texeira** a-1, 2p, 3p, 5-7p, 9p, 11-14p; c(p)-1, 2, 4-7, 12.

HEXBREAKER (See First Comics Graphic Novel #15)

HEXED
BOOM! Studios: Aug, 2014 - No. 12, Aug, 2015 ($3.99)
1-12: 1-Michael Alan Nelson-s/Dan Mora-s; 3 covers 4.00

HEXWARE
Image Comics: Dec, 2022 - Present ($3.99)
1-3-Tim Seeley-s/Zulema Scotto Lavina-a 4.00

HEX WIVES
DC Comics (Vertigo): Dec, 2018 - No. 6, May, 2019 ($3.99)
1-6: 1-Ben Blacker-s/Mirka Andolfo-a/Joëlle Jones-c. 5-Lotay-c 4.00

HEY KIDS! COMICS!
Image Comics: Aug, 2018 - No. 5, Dec, 2018 ($3.99, limited series)
1-5-Howard Chaykin-s/a 4.00

HEY KIDS! COMICS! VOL. 2, PROPHETS & LOSS
Image Comics: May, 2021 - No. 6, Oct, 2021 ($3.99, limited series)
1-6-Howard Chaykin-s/a 4.00

HEY THERE, IT'S YOGI BEAR (See Movie Comics)

HI-ADVENTURE HEROES (TV)
Gold Key: May, 1969 - No. 2, Aug, 1969 (Hanna-Barbera)
1-Three Musketeers, Gulliver, Arabian Knights 5 10 15 30 50 70
2-Three Musketeers, Micro-Venture, Arabian Knights 4 8 12 27 44 60

HI AND LOIS
Dell Publishing Co.: No. 683, Mar, 1956 - No. 955, Nov, 1958
Four Color 683 (#1) 6 12 18 38 69 100
Four Color 774(3/57),955 5 10 15 30 50 70

HI AND LOIS
Charlton Comics: Nov, 1969 - No. 11, July, 1971
1 3 6 9 14 20 25
2-11 2 4 6 9 12 15

HICKORY (See All Humor Comics)
Quality Comics Group: Oct, 1949 - No. 6, Aug, 1950
1-Sahl-c/a in all; Feldstein?-a 33 66 99 194 317 440
2 21 42 63 122 199 275
3-6-Good Girl covers 55 110 165 352 601 850

HIDDEN CREW, THE (See The United States Air Force Presents:...)

HIDDEN SOCIETY
Dark Horse Comics: Feb, 2020 - No. 4, Oct, 2020 ($3.99, limited series)
1-4-Rafael Scavone-s/Rafael Albuquerque-a; two covers 4.00

HIDE-OUT (See Zane Grey, Four Color No. 346)

HIDING PLACE, THE
Spire Christian Comics (Fleming H. Revell Co.): 1973 (39¢/49¢)
nn 3 6 9 17 26 35

HI-FI FIGHT CLUB (Title changes to Heavy Vinyl for #4)
Boom Entertainment (BOOM! Box): Aug, 2017 - No. 3, Oct, 2017 ($3.99)
1-3-Carly Usdin-s/Nina Vakueva-a 4.00

HIGH ADVENTURE
Red Top(Decker) Comics (Farrell): Oct, 1957
1-Krigstein-r from Explorer Joe (re-issue on-c) 6 12 18 31 38 45

HIGH ADVENTURE (TV)
Dell Publishing Co.: No. 949, Nov, 1958 - No. 1001, Aug-Oct, 1959 (Lowell Thomas)
Four Color 949 (#1)-Photo-c 6 12 18 40 73 105
Four Color 1001-Lowell Thomas'...(#2) 5 10 15 34 60 85

HIGH CHAPPARAL (TV)
Gold Key: Aug, 1968 (Photo-c)
1 (10226-808)-Tufts-a 6 12 18 38 69 100

HIGH HEAVEN
Ahoy Comics: 2018 - No. 5, 2019 ($3.99)
1-5-Tom Peyer-s/Greg Scott-a; back-up w/Giarusso-a 4.00

HIGHLANDER
Dynamite Entertainment: No. 0, 2006 - No. 12, 2007 (25¢/$2.99)
0-(25¢-c) Takes place after the first movie; photo-c and Dell'Otto painted-c 3.00
1-12: 1-($2.99) Three covers; Moder-a/Jerwa & Oeming-s. 2-Three covers 3.00
... Origins: The Kurgan 1,2 (2009 - No. 2, 2009, $4.99) Three covers; Rafael-a 5.00
...: Way of the Sword (2007 - No. 4, 2008, $3.50) Two interlocking covers for each 3.50

HIGHLANDER: THE AMERICAN DREAM
IDW Publishing: Feb, 2017 - No. 5, Jun, 2017 ($3.99)
1-5-Brian Ruckley-s/Andrea Mutti-a; multiple covers; MacLeod in 1985 New York 4.00

HIGH LEVEL
DC Comics (Vertigo): Apr, 2019 - No. 6, Nov, 2019 ($3.99)
1-6-Sheridan-s/Bagenda-a 4.00

HIGH ROADS
DC Comics (Cliffhanger): June, 2002 - No. 6, Nov, 2002 ($2.95, limited series)
1-6-Leinil Yu-c/a; Lobdell-s 3.00
TPB (2003, $14.95) r/#1-6; sketch pages 15.00

HIGH SCHOOL CONFIDENTIAL DIARY (Confidential Diary #12 on)
Charlton Comics: June, 1960 - No. 11, Mar, 1962
1 5 10 15 33 57 80
2-11 3 6 9 19 30 40

HIGHWAYMEN
DC Comics (WildStorm): Aug, 2007 - No. 5, Dec, 2007 ($2.99)
1-5-Bernardin & Freeman-s/Garbett-a 3.00
TPB (2008, $17.99) r/#1-5 18.00

HIGH WAYS, THE
IDW Publishing: Dec, 2012 - No. 4, Apr, 2013 ($3.99, limited series)
1-4-John Byrne-s/a/c 4.00

HI HI PUFFY AMIYUMI (Based on Cartoon Network animated series)
DC Comics: Apr, 2006 - No. 3, June, 2006 ($2.25, limited series)
1-3-Phil Moy-a 3.00

HI-HO COMICS
Four Star Publications: nd (2/46?) - No. 3, 1946
1-Funny Animal; L.B. Cole-c 43 86 129 271 461 650
2,3: 2-L. B. Cole-c 31 62 93 184 300 415

HI-JINX (Teen-age Animal Funnies)
La Salle Publ. Co./B&I Publ. Co. (American Comics Group)/Creston: 1945; July-Aug, 1947 - No. 7, July-Aug, 1948
nn-(© 1945, 25 cents, 132 Pgs.)(La Salle) 36 72 108 211 343 475
1-Teen-age, funny animal 23 46 69 136 223 310
2,3 15 30 45 86 133 180
4-7-Milt Gross. 4-X-Mas-c 22 44 66 128 209 290

HI-LITE COMICS
E. R. Ross Publishing Co.: Fall, 1945
1-Miss Shady 27 54 81 158 259 360

HILLBILLY
Albatross Funnybooks: 2016 - No. 12, 2018 ($3.99)
1-12-Eric Powell-s/c; Powell-a in #1-7. 2-The Buzzard app. 5-Back-up with Mannion-a. 8-Di Meo-a 4.00

HILLBILLY (Red Eyed Witchery From Beyond on cover)
Albatross Funnybooks: 2018 - No. 4, 2019 ($3.99)
1-4-Eric Powell-s/c; Simone Di Meo-a 4.00

HILLBILLY COMICS
Charlton Comics: Aug, 1955 - No. 4, July, 1956 (Satire)
1-By Art Gates 15 30 45 90 140 190
2-4 12 24 36 69 97 125

HILL HOUSE COMICS 2019 SAMPLER
DC Comics (Hill House Comics): Oct, 2019 (no price, promotional giveaway)
nn-Previews Basketful of Heads, The Dollhouse Family, and The Low, Low Woods 3.00

HILLY ROSE'S SPACE ADVENTURES
Astro Comics: May, 1995 - No. 9 ($2.95, B&W)
1 1 2 3 5 7 9
2-9 5.00
Trade Paperback (1996, $12.95)-r/#1-5 13.00

HINTERKIND
DC Comics (Vertigo): Dec, 2013 - No. 18, Jul, 2015 ($2.99)

Hi-Fi Fight Club #1 © Scheme Machine

Hillbilly #4 © Eric Powell

Hit Monkey #1 © MAR

GD VG FN VF VF/NM NM-
2.0 4.0 6.0 8.0 9.0 9.2

1-18: 1-Ian Edginton-s/Francesco Trifogli-a/Greg Tocchini-c 3.00

HIP FLASK (Also see Elephantmen)
Active Images/Image Comics
...: Ouroborous (12/12, $4.99) Starkings-s/Ladronn-a 5.00
... Unnatural Selection (9/02, $2.99) Casey & Starkings-s/Ladronn-a; var.-c by Madureira, Campbell, Churchill 3.00

HIP-IT-TY HOP (See March of Comics No. 15)

HIRE, THE (BMWfilms.com's...)
Dark Horse Comics: July, 2004 - No. 6 ($2.99)
1-4: 1-Matt Wagner-s/Wagner & Velasco-a. 2-Bruce Campbell-s/Plunkett-a. 3-Waid-s 3.00
TPB (4/06, $17.95) r/#1-4 18.00

HI-SCHOOL ROMANCE (...Romances No. 41 on)
Harvey Publ./True Love(Home Comics): Oct, 1949 - No. 5, June, 1950; No. 6, Dec, 1950 - No. 73, Mar, 1958; No. 74, Sept, 1958 - No. 75, Nov, 1958
1-Photo-c 19 38 57 111 176 240
2-Photo-c 12 24 36 69 97 125
3-9: 3-5-Photo-c 10 20 30 56 76 95
10-Rape story 17 34 51 100 158 215
11-20 9 18 27 47 61 75
21-31 8 16 24 40 50 60
32- "Unholy passion" story 11 22 33 64 90 115
33-36: 36-Last pre-code (2/55) 7 14 21 37 46 55
37-53,59-72,74,75 6 12 18 32 39 46
54-58,73-Kirby-c 8 16 24 40 50 60
NOTE: ***Powell*** *a-1-3, 5, 8, 12-16, 18, 21-23, 25-27, 30-34, 36, 37, 39, 45-48, 50-52, 57, 58, 60, 64, 65, 67, 69.*

HI-SCHOOL ROMANCE DATE BOOK
Harvey Publications: Nov, 1962 - No. 3, Mar, 1963 (25¢ Giants)
1-Powell, Baker-a 6 12 18 41 76 110
2,3 3 6 9 21 33 45

HIS NAME IS SAVAGE (Magazine format)
Adventure House Press: June, 1968 (35¢, 52 pgs.)
1-Gil Kane-a 5 10 15 31 53 75

HI-SPOT COMICS (Red Ryder No. 1 & No. 3 on)
Hawley Publications: No. 2, Nov, 1940
2-David Innes of Pellucidar; art by J. C. Burroughs; written by Edgar Rice Burroughs
300 600 900 1950 3375 4800

HISTORY OF THE DC UNIVERSE (Also see Crisis on Infinite Earths)
DC Comics: Sept, 1986 - No. 2, Nov, 1986 ($2.95, limited series)
1,2: 1-Perez-c/a 5.00
Limited Edition hardcover 4 8 12 26 41 55
Softcover (2002, $9.95) new Alex Ross wraparound-c 13.00
Softcover (2009, $12.99) Alex Ross wraparound-c 13.00

HISTORY OF THE MARVEL UNIVERSE
Marvel Comics: Sept, 2019 - No. 6, Feb, 2020 ($4.99, limited series)
1-6-Mark Waid-s/Javier Rodríguez-a chronological Marvel history & bonus annotations 5.00

HISTORY OF VIOLENCE, A (Inspired the 2005 movie)
DC Comics (Paradox Press) 1997 ($9.95, B&W graphic novel)
nn-Paperback ($9.95) John Wagner-s/Vince Locke-a 3 6 9 14 20 25

HIT
BOOM! Studios: Sept, 2013 - No. 4, Dec, 2013 ($3.99, limited series)
1-4-Bryce Carlson-s/Vanesa R. Del Ray-a/Ryan Sook-c 4.00
...: 1957 (3/15 - No. 4, 7/15, $3.99) 1-4-Bryce Carlson-s/Vanesa R. Del Ray-a/c 4.00

HITCHHIKERS GUIDE TO THE GALAXY (See Life, the Universe and Everything & Restaurant at the End of the Universe)
DC Comics: 1993 - No. 3, 1993 ($4.95, limited series)
1-3: Adaptation of Douglas Adams book 5.00
TPB (1997, $14.95) r/#1-3 15.00

HIT COMICS
Quality Comics Group: July, 1940 - No. 65, July, 1950
1-Origin/1st app. Neon, the Unknown & Hercules; intro. The Red Bee; Bob & Swab, Blaze Barton, the Strange Twins, X-5 Super Agent, Casey Jones & Jack & Jill (ends #7) begin
1000 2000 3000 7400 13,200 19,000
2-The Old Witch begins, ends #14 (scarce) 377 754 1131 2639 4620 6600
3-Casey Jones ends; transvestism story "Jack & Jill"
360 720 1080 2520 4410 6300
4-Super Agent (ends #17), & Betty Bates (ends #65) begin; X-5 ends
314 628 942 2198 3849 5500

GD VG FN VF VF/NM NM-
2.0 4.0 6.0 8.0 9.0 9.2

5-Classic Lou Fine cover 1100 2200 3300 8400 15,200 22,000
6,8-10: 10-Old Witch by Crandall (4 pgs.); 1st work in comics (4/41)
284 568 852 1818 3109 4400
7-Skull bondage-c 432 864 1296 3154 5577 8000
11-Classic cover 371 742 1113 2600 4550 6500
12-16: 13-Blaze Barton ends 187 374 561 1197 2049 2900
17-Last Neon; Crandall Hercules in all; last Lou Fine-c; skeleton-c
290 580 870 1856 3178 4500
18-Origin & 1st app. Stormy Foster, the Great Defender (12/41); The Ghost of Flanders begins; Crandall-c 226 452 678 1446 2473 3500
19,20 148 296 444 947 1624 2300
21-24: 21-Last Hercules. 24-Last Red Bee & Strange Twins
135 270 405 864 1482 2100
25-Origin & 1st app. Kid Eternity and begins by Moldoff (12/42); 1st app. The Keeper (Kid Eternity's aide) 265 530 795 1694 2897 4100
26-Blackhawk x-over in Kid Eternity 123 246 369 787 1344 1900
27-29 55 110 165 352 601 850
30,31- "Bill the Magnificent" by Kurtzman, 11 pgs. in each
50 100 150 315 533 750
32-40: 32-Plastic Man x-over. 34-Last Stormy Foster
34 68 102 199 325 450
41-50 24 48 72 140 230 320
51-60-Last Kid Eternity 22 44 66 132 216 300
61-63-Crandall-c/a; 61-Jeb Rivers begins 23 46 69 138 227 315
64,65-Crandall-a 22 44 66 132 216 300
NOTE: ***Crandall*** *a-11-17(Hercules), 23, 24(Stormy Foster); c-18-20, 23, 24.* ***Fine*** *c-1-14, 16, 17(most).* ***Ward*** *c-33. Bondage c-7, 64. Hercules c-3, 10-17. Jeb Rivers c-61-65. Kid Eternity c-25-60 (w/ Keeper-28-34, 36, 39-43, 45-55). Neon the Unknown c-2, 4, 8, 9. Red Bee c-1, 5-7. Stormy Foster c-18-24.*

HIT-GIRL (Also see Kick-Ass)
Marvel Comics (Icon): Aug, 2012 - No. 5, Apr, 2013 ($2.99, limited series)
1-Takes place between Kick-Ass & Kick Ass 2 series; Millar-s/Romita Jr.-a/c
1 2 3 5 6 8
2-5 3.00

HIT-GIRL (Also see Kick-Ass)
Image Comics: Feb, 2018 - No. 12, Jan, 2019 ($3.99)
1-12: 1-4-Millar-s/Ortiz-a. 5-8-In Canada; Lemire-s/Risso-a. 9-12-Albuquerque-s/a 4.00

HIT-GIRL SEASON TWO (Also see Kick-Ass)
Image Comics: Feb, 2019 - No. 12, Jan, 2020 ($3.99)
1-12: 1-4-Kevin Smith-s/Pernille Orum-a. 5-8-Hong Kong; Parlov-a. 9-12-India 4.00

HITLER'S ASTROLOGER (See Marvel Graphic Novel #35)

HITMAN (Also see Bloodbath #2, Batman Chronicles #4, Demon #43-45 & Demon Annual #2)
DC Comics: May, 1996 - No. 60, Apr, 2001 ($2.25/$2.50)
1-Garth Ennis-s & John McCrea-c/a begin; Batman app.
2 4 6 10 14 18
2-Joker-c;Two Face, Mad Hatter, Batman app. 1 2 3 5 6 8
3-5: 3-Batman-c/app.; Joker app. 4-1st app. Nightfist 5.00
6-20: 8-Final Night x-over. 10-GL cameo. 11-20: 11,12-GL-c/app. 15-20-"Ace of Killers". 16-18-Catwoman app. 17-19-Demon-app. 4.00
21-59: 34-Superman-c/app. 3.00
60-($3.95) Final issue; includes pin-ups by various 4.00
#1,000,000 (11/98) Hitman goes to the 853rd Century 3.00
Annual 1 (1997, $3.95) Pulp Heroes 5.00
.../Lobo: That Stupid Bastich (7/00, $3.95) Ennis-s/Mahnke-a 4.00
TPB-(1997, $9.95) r/#1-3, Demon Ann. #2, Batman Chronicles #4 10.00
Ace of Killers TPB ('00/'11, $17.95/$17.99) r/#15-22 18.00
Local Heroes TPB ('99, $17.95) r/#9-14 & Annual #1 18.00
10,000 Bullets TPB ('98, $9.95) r/#4-8 10.00
Ten Thousand Bullets TPB ('10, $17.99) r/#4-8 & Annual #1; intro, by Kevin Smith 18.00
Who Dares Wins TPB ('01, $12.95) r/#23-28 13.00

HIT-MONKEY (See Deadpool)
Marvel Comics: Apr, 2010; Sept, 2010 - No. 3, Nov, 2010 ($3.99/$2.99)
1-(4/10, $3.99) Printing of story from Marvel Digital Comics; Frank Cho-c; origin revealed 4.00
1-3-Daniel Way-s/Talajic-a/Johnson-c; Bullseye app. 3.00

HI-YO SILVER (See Lone Ranger's Famous Horse... and The Lone Ranger; and March of Comics No. 215 in the Promotional Comics section)

HOBBIT, THE
Eclipse Comics: 1989 - No. 3, 1990 ($4.95, squarebound, 52 pgs.)
Book 1-Adapts novel; Wenzel-a 3 6 9 17 26 35
Book 1-Second printing 5.00
Book 2,3-Adaptation continues 2 4 6 8 11 14
Graphic Novel (1990, Ballantine)-r/#1-3 25.00

GD VG FN VF VF/NM NM-
2.0 4.0 6.0 8.0 9.0 9.2

HOCUS POCUS (See Funny Book #9)

HOGAN'S HEROES (TV) (Also see Wild!)
Dell Publishing Co.: June, 1966 - No. 8, Sept, 1967; No. 9, Oct, 1969

1: Photo-c on #1-7 9 18 27 58 114 170
2,3-Ditko-a(p) 6 12 18 40 73 105
4-9: 9-Reprints #1 5 10 15 31 53 75

HOKUM & HEX (See Razorline)
Marvel Comics (Razorline): Sept, 1993 - No. 9, May, 1994 ($1.75/$1.95)

1-($2.50)-Foil embossed-c; by Clive Barker 5.00
2-9: 5-Hyperkind x-over 4.00

HOLIDAY COMICS
Fawcett Publications: 1942 (25¢, 196 pgs.)

1-Contains three Fawcett comics plus two page portrait of Captain Marvel; Capt. Marvel, Jungle Girl #1, & Whiz. Not rebound, remaindered comics; printed at the same time as originals (scarce in high grade) 325 650 975 2300 4550 6800

HOLIDAY COMICS (Becomes Fun Comics #9-12)
Star Publications: Jan, 1951 - No. 8, Oct, 1952

1-Funny animal contents (Frisky Fables) in all; L. B. Cole X-Mas-c
43 86 129 271 461 650
2-Classic L. B. Cole-c 39 78 117 240 395 550
3-8: 5,8-X-Mas-c; all L.B. Cole-c 22 44 66 132 216 300
Accepted Reprint 4 (nd)-L.B. Cole-c 12 24 36 67 94 120

HOLIDAY DIGEST
Harvey Comics: 1988 ($1.25, digest-size)

1 1 2 3 5 7 9

HOLIDAY PARADE (Walt Disney's...)
W. D. Publications (Disney): Winter, 1990-91(no year given) - No. 2, Winter, 1990-91 ($2.95, 68 pgs.)

1-Reprints 1947 Firestone by Barks plus new-a 5.00
2-Barks-r plus other stories 4.00

HOLIDAY PARTY (Scotch McTiernan's)
Image Comics: Jan, 2023 ($3.99, one-shot)

1-Duggan & Posehn-s/Koblish-a 4.00

HOLI-DAY SURPRISE (Formerly Summer Fun)
Charlton Comics: V2#55, Mar, 1967 (25¢ Giant)

V2#55 4 8 12 27 44 60

HOLLYWOOD COMICS
New Age Publishers: Winter, 1944 (52 pgs.)

1-Funny animal 24 48 72 142 234 325

HOLLYWOOD CONFESSIONS
St. John Publishing Co.: Oct, 1949 - No. 2, Dec, 1949

1-Kubert-c/a (entire book) 50 100 150 315 533 750
2-Kubert-c/a (entire book) (Scarce) 53 106 159 334 567 800

HOLLYWOOD DIARY
Quality Comics Group: Dec, 1949 - No. 5, July-Aug, 1950

1-No photo-c 34 68 102 204 332 460
2-Photo-c 21 42 63 122 199 275
3-5-Photo-c. 3-Betty Carlin photo-c. 5-June Allyson/Peter Lawford photo-c
19 38 57 109 172 235

HOLLYWOOD FILM STORIES
Feature Publications/Prize: April, 1950 - No. 4, Oct, 1950 (All photo-c; "Fumetti" type movie comic)

1-June Allyson photo-c 27 54 81 158 259 360
2-4: 2-Lizabeth Scott photo-c. 3-Barbara Stanwick photo-c. 4-Betty Hutton photo-c
19 38 57 111 176 240

HOLLYWOOD FUNNY FOLKS (Formerly Funny Folks; Becomes Nutsy Squirrel #61 on)
National Periodical Publ.: No. 27, Aug-Sept, 1950 - No. 60, July-Aug, 1954

27-Nutsy Squirrel continues 14 28 42 81 118 155
28-40 10 20 30 58 79 100
41-60 9 18 27 52 69 85
NOTE: *Rube Grossman a-most issues. Sheldon Mayer a-27-35, 37-40, 43-46, 48-51, 53, 56, 57, 60.*

HOLLYWOOD LOVE DOCTOR (See Doctor Anthony King...)

HOLLYWOOD PICTORIAL (...Romances on cover)
St. John Publishing Co.: No. 3, Jan, 1950

3-Matt Baker-a; photo-c 45 90 135 284 480 675
(Becomes a movie magazine - Hollywood Pictorial Western with No. 4.)

HOLLYWOOD ROMANCES (Formerly Brides In Love; becomes For Lovers Only #60 on)
Charlton Comics: V2#46, 11/66; #47, 10/67; #48, 11/68;V3#49,11/69-V3#59, 6/71

V2#46-Rolling Stones-c/story 10 20 30 64 132 200
V2#47-V3#59: 56- "Born to Heart Break" begins 3 6 9 17 26 35

HOLLYWOOD SECRETS
Quality Comics Group: Nov, 1949 - No. 6, Sept, 1950

1-Ward-c/a (9 pgs.) 52 104 156 328 552 775
2-Crandall-a, Ward-c/a (9 pgs.) 42 84 126 265 445 625
3-6: All photo-c. 5-Lex Barker (Tarzan)-c 20 40 60 117 189 260
...of Romance, I.W. Reprint #9; r/#2 above w/Kinstler-c
3 6 9 14 19 24

HOLLYWOOD SUPERSTARS
Marvel Comics (Epic Comics): Nov, 1990 - No. 5, Apr, 1991 ($2.25)

1-($2.95, 52 pgs.)-Spiegle-c/a in all; Aragonés-a, inside front-c plus 2-4 pgs. 4.00
2-5 ($2.25) 3.00

HOLO-MAN (See Power Record Comics)

HOLYOKE ONE-SHOT
Holyoke Publishing Co. (Tem Publ.): 1944 - No. 10, 1945 (All reprints)

1,2: 1-Grit Grady (on cover only), Miss Victory, Alias X (origin)-All reprints from Captain Fearless. 2-Rusty Dugan (Corporal); Capt. Fearless (origin), Mr. Miracle (origin) app.
39 78 117 231 378 525
3-Miss Victory; r/Crash #4; Cat Man (origin), Solar Legion by Kirby app.; Miss Victory on cover only (1945) 57 114 171 362 619 875
4,6,8: 4-Mr. Miracle; The Blue Streak app.; reprints early Cat-Man story. 6-Capt. Fearless, Alias X, Capt. Stone (splash used as-c to #10); Diamond Jim & Rusty Dugan (splash from cover of #2). 8-Blue Streak, Strong Man (story matches cover to #7)-Crash reprints
32 64 96 188 307 425
5,7: 5-U.S. Border Patrol Comics (Sgt. Dick Carter of the...), Miss Victory (story matches cover to #3), Citizen Smith, & Mr. Miracle app. 7-Secret Agent Z-2, Strong Man, Blue Streak (story matches cover to #8); Reprints from Crash #2
33 66 99 194 317 440
9-Citizen Smith, The Blue Streak, Solar Legion by Kirby & Strongman, the Perfect Human app.; reprints from Crash #4 & 5; Citizen Smith on cover only-from story in #5 (1944-before #3) 36 72 108 211 343 475
10-Captain Stone; r/Crash; Solar Legion by S&K 36 72 108 211 343 475

HOLY TERROR
Legendary Comics: Sept, 2011 ($29.95, HC graphic novel, 12-1/4" wide x 9-1/4" tall)

HC-Frank Miller-s/a/c; B&W art with spot color; The Fixer vs. Al-Qaeda in Empire City 30.00

HOME (Based on the DreamWorks movie)
Titan Comics: Aug, 2015 - No. 4, Nov, 2015 ($3.99)

1-4: 1-Davison-s/Hebb-a 4.00

HOMECOMING
Aspen MLT: Aug, 2012 - No. 4, Sept, 2013 ($3.99)

1-4: 1-Wohl-s/Laiso-a; covers by Michael Turner and Mike DeBalfo 4.00

HOMER COBB (See Adventures of...)

HOMER HOOPER
Atlas Comics: July, 1953 - No. 4, Dec, 1953

1-Teenage humor 18 36 54 105 165 225
2-4 14 28 42 76 108 140

HOMER, THE HAPPY GHOST (See Adventures of...)
Atlas(ACI/PPI/WPI)/Marvel: 3/55 - No. 22, 11/58; V2#1, 11/69 - V2#4, 5/70

V1#1-Dan DeCarlo-c/a begins, ends #22 39 78 117 240 395 550
2-1st code approved issue 22 44 66 128 209 290
3-10 20 40 60 118 192 265
11-20,22 19 38 57 111 176 240
21-Sci-fi cover 37 74 111 222 361 500
V2#1 (11/69) 13 26 39 86 188 290
2-4 8 16 24 54 102 150

HOME RUN (Also see A-1 Comics)
Magazine Enterprises: No. 89, 1953 (one-shot)

A-1 89 (#3)-Powell-a; Stan Musial photo-c 20 40 60 117 189 260

HOMICIDE (Also see Dark Horse Presents)
Dark Horse Comics: Apr, 1990 ($1.95, B&W, one-shot)

1-Detective story 3.00

HOMIES
Dynamite Entertainment: 2016 - No. 4, 2017 ($3.99)

1-4-Gonzales & Serrano-s/Huerta-a 4.00

HONEYMOON (Formerly Gay Comics)
A Lover's Magazine(USA) (Marvel): No. 41, Jan, 1950

41-Photo-c; article by Betty Grable 19 38 57 111 176 240

HONEYMOONERS, THE (TV)
Lodestone: Oct, 1986 ($1.50)

1-Photo-c 6.00

HONEYMOONERS, THE (TV)
Triad Publications: Sept, 1987 - No. 13? ($2.00)

1-13 5.00

HONEYMOON ROMANCE
Artful Publications (Canadian): Apr, 1950 - No. 2, July, 1950 (25¢, digest size)

1,2-(Rare) 350 700 1050 1750 2625 3500

HONEY WEST (TV)
Gold Key: Sept, 1966 (Photo-c)

1 (10186-609) 9 18 27 62 126 190

HONEY WEST (TV)
Moonstone: 2010 - No. 4 ($5.99/$3.99)

1-($5.99) Trina Robbins-s/Cynthia Martin-a; two art covers & two photo covers 6.00
2-4-($3.99) 4.00

HONG KONG PHOOEY (TV)
Charlton Comics: June, 1975 - No. 9, Nov, 1976 (Hanna-Barbera)

1 7 14 21 44 82 120
2 3 6 9 19 30 40
3-9 3 6 9 15 22 28

HONG ON THE RANGE
Image/Flypaper Press: Dec, 1997 - No. 3, Feb, 1998 ($2.50, lim. series)

1-3: Wu-s/Lafferty-a 3.00

HOOD, THE
Marvel Comics (MAX): Jul, 2002 - No. 6, Dec, 2002 ($2.99, limited series)

1-6-Vaughan-s/Hotz-c/a 3.00
Vol. 1 Blood From Stones HC (2007, $19.99, dustjacket) r/#1-6; production sketch art 20.00
Vol. 1 Blood From Stones TPB (2003, $14.99) r/#1-6 15.00

HOODED HORSEMAN, THE (Formerly Blazing West)
American Comics Group (Michel Publ.): No. 21, 1-2/52 - No. 27, 1-2/54; No. 18, 12-1/54-55 - No. 22, 8-9/55

21(1-2/52)-Hooded Horseman, Injun Jones cont. 18 36 54 105 165 225

Home #4 © Dreamworks

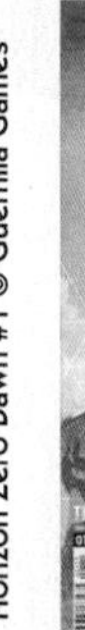

Horizon Zero Dawn #1 © Guerrilla Games

Horrific #11 © CM

	GD 2.0	VG 4.0	FN 6.0	VF 8.0	VF/NM 9.0	NM- 9.2
22	19	38	57	111	176	240
23,24,27(1-2/54)	10	20	30	58	79	100
25 (9-10/53)-Cowboy Sahib on cover only; Hooded Horseman i.d. revealed	11	22	33	62	86	110
26-Origin/1st app. Cowboy Sahib by L. Starr	13	26	39	74	105	135
18(12-1/54-55)(Formerly Out of the Night)	11	22	33	62	86	110
19,21,22: 19-Last precode (1-2/55)	9	18	27	50	65	80
20-Origin Johnny Injun	10	20	30	54	72	90

NOTE: *Whitney c/a-21('52), 20-22.*

HOODED MENACE, THE (Also see Daring Adventures)
Realistic/Avon Periodicals: 1951 (one-shot)

	GD	VG	FN	VF	VF/NM	NM-
nn-Based on a band of hooded outlaws in the Pacific Northwest, 1900-1906; reprinted in Daring Advs. #15	232	464	696	1485	2543	3600

HOODS UP (See the Promotional Comics section)

HOOK (Movie)
Marvel Comics: Early Feb, 1992 - No. 4, Late Mar, 1992 ($1.00, limited series)

	GD	VG	FN	VF	VF/NM	NM-
1-4: Adapts movie; Vess-c; 1-Morrow-a(p)						4.00
nn (1991, $5.95, 84 pgs.)-Contains #1-4; Vess-c						6.00
1 (1991, $2.95, magazine, 84 pgs.)-Contains #1-4; Vess-c (same cover as nn issue)						4.00

HOOK JAW
Titan Comics: Jan, 2017 - No. 5, May, 2017 ($3.99)

	GD	VG	FN	VF	VF/NM	NM-
1-5-Inspired by a 1976 British comic strip; Si Spurrier-s/Conor Boyle-a; multiple covers						4.00

HOOT GIBSON'S WESTERN ROUNDUP (See Western Roundup under Fox Giants)

HOOT GIBSON WESTERN (Formerly My Love Story)
Fox Feature Syndicate: No. 5, May, 1950 - No. 3, Sept, 1950

	GD	VG	FN	VF	VF/NM	NM-
5,6(#1,2): 5-Photo-c. 6-Photo/painted-c	21	42	63	123	197	270
3-Wood-a; painted-c	22	44	66	131	211	290

HOPALONG CASSIDY (Also see Bill Boyd Western, Master Comics, Real Western Hero, Six Gun Heroes & Western Hero; Bill Boyd starred as Hopalong Cassidy in movies, radio & TV)
Fawcett Publications: Feb, 1943; No. 2, Summer, 1946 - No. 85, Nov, 1953

	GD	VG	FN	VF	VF/NM	NM-
1 (1943, 68 pgs.)-H. Cassidy & his horse Topper begin (on sale 1/8/43)-Captain Marvel app. on-c	194	388	582	1242	2121	3000
2-(Sum, '46)	41	82	123	256	428	600
3,4: 3-(Fall, '46, 52 pgs. begin)	20	40	60	114	182	250
5- "Mad Barber" story mentioned in **SOTI**, pgs. 308,309; photo-c	21	42	63	122	199	275
6-10: 8-Photo-c	16	32	48	94	147	200
11-19: 11,13-19-Photo-c	14	28	42	80	115	150
20-29 (52 pgs.)-Painted/photo-c	12	24	36	69	97	125
30,31,33,34,37-39,41 (52 pgs.)-Painted-c	11	22	33	60	83	105
32,40 (36pgs.)-Painted-c	10	20	30	54	72	90
35,42,43,45-47,49-51,53,54,56 (52 pgs.)-Photo-c	10	20	30	56	76	95
36,44,48 (36 pgs.)-Photo-c	9	18	27	52	69	85
52,55,57-70 (36 pgs.)-Photo-c	9	18	27	47	61	75
71-84-Photo-c	8	16	24	42	54	65
85-Last Fawcett issue; photo-c	9	18	27	52	69	85

NOTE: *Line-drawn c-1-4, 6, 7, 9, 10, 12.*

	GD	VG	FN	VF	VF/NM	NM-
... & The 5 Men of Evil (AC Comics, 1991, $12.95) r/newspaper strips and Fawcett story "Signature of Death"						13.00

HOPALONG CASSIDY
National Periodical Publications: No. 86, Feb, 1954 - No. 135, May-June, 1959 (All-36 pgs.)

	GD	VG	FN	VF	VF/NM	NM-
86-Gene Colan-a begins, ends #117; photo covers continue	36	72	108	216	351	485
87	20	40	60	118	189	260
88-91: 91-1 pg. Superboy-sty (7/54)	15	30	45	83	124	165
92-99 (98 has #93 on-c; last precode issue, 2/55). 95-Reversed photo-c to #52. 98-Reversed photo-c to #61. 99-Reversed photo-c to #60	14	28	42	76	108	140
100-Same cover as #50	15	30	45	83	124	165
101-108: 105-Same photo-c as #54. 107-Same photo-c as #51. 108-Last photo-c	6	12	18	38	69	100
109-130: 118-Gil Kane-a begins. 123-Kubert-a (2 pgs.). 124-Grey tone-c	5	10	15	35	63	90
131-135	6	12	18	37	66	95

HOPELESS SAVAGES (Also see Too Much Hopeless Savages)
Oni Press: Aug, 2001 - No. 4, Nov, 2001 ($2.95, B&W, limited series)

	GD	VG	FN	VF	VF/NM	NM-
1-4-Van Meter-s/Norrie-a/Clugston-Major-a/Watson-c						3.00
Free Comic Book Day giveaway (5/02) r/#1 with "Free Comic Book Day" banner on-c						3.00
TPB (2002, $13.95, 8" x 5.75") r/#1-4; plus color stories; Watson-c						14.00

HOPELESS SAVAGES: GROUND ZERO
Oni Press: June, 2002 - No. 4, Oct, 2002 ($2.95, B&W, limited series)

	GD	VG	FN	VF	VF/NM	NM-
1-4-Van Meter-s/O'Malley-a/Dodson-c. 1-Watson-a						3.00
TPB (2003, $11.95, 8" x 5.75") r/#1-4; Dodson-c						12.00

HOPE SHIP
Dell Publishing Co.: June-Aug, 1963

	GD	VG	FN	VF	VF/NM	NM-
1	3	6	9	15	22	28

HOPPY THE MARVEL BUNNY (See Fawcett's Funny Animals)
Fawcett Publications: Dec, 1945 - No. 15, Sept, 1947

	GD	VG	FN	VF	VF/NM	NM-
1	34	68	102	199	325	450
2	15	30	45	90	140	190
3-15: 7-Xmas-c	14	28	42	76	108	140

HORACE & DOTTY DRIPPLE (Dotty Dripple No. 1-24)
Harvey Publications: No. 25, Aug, 1952 - No. 43, Oct, 1955

	GD	VG	FN	VF	VF/NM	NM-
25-43	5	10	15	23	29	36

HORIZONTAL LIEUTENANT, THE (See Movie Classics)

HORIZON ZERO DAWN (Based on the Guerrilla Games videogame)
Titan Comics: Sept, 2020 - No. 4, Nov, 2020; Aug, 2021 - No. 2.4, Feb, 2022 ($3.99)

	GD	VG	FN	VF	VF/NM	NM-
1-4-Anne Toole-s/Ann Maulina-a; multiple covers						4.00
(Volume 2, 8/21 - 2/22) 2.1-2.4: 2.1-2.3-Elmer Damaso-a. 2.4-Maulina-a						4.00

HOROBI
Viz Premiere Comics: 1990 - No. 8, 1990 ($3.75, B&W, mature readers, 84 pgs.) V2#1, 1990 - No. 7, 1991 ($4.25, B&W, 68 pgs.)

	GD	VG	FN	VF	VF/NM	NM-
1-8: Japanese manga, Part Two, #1-7						5.00

HORRIFIC (Terrific No. 14 on)
Artful/Comic Media/Harwell/Mystery: Sept, 1952 - No. 13, Sept, 1954

	GD	VG	FN	VF	VF/NM	NM-
1	290	580	870	1856	3178	4500
2	155	310	465	992	1696	2400
3-Bullet in head-c	343	686	1029	2400	4200	6000
4,5,7,9,10: 4-Shrunken head-c. 7-Guillotine-c	103	206	309	659	1130	1600
6-Jack The Ripper story	126	252	378	806	1378	1950
8-Origin & 1st app. The Teller (E.C. parody)	194	388	582	1242	2121	3000
11-13: 11-Swipe/Witches Tales #6,27; Devil-c	65	130	195	416	708	1000

NOTE: ***Don Heck** a-8; c-3-13. **Hollingsworth** a-4. **Morisi** a-8. **Palais** a-5, 7-12.*

HORRORCIDE
IDW Publishing: Sept, 2004 ($6.99)

	GD	VG	FN	VF	VF/NM	NM-
1-Steve Niles short stories; art by Templesmith, Medors and Chee						7.00

HORROR FROM THE TOMB (Mysterious Stories No. 2 on)
Premier Magazine Co.: Sept, 1954

	GD	VG	FN	VF	VF/NM	NM-
1-Woodbridge/Torres, Check-a; The Keeper of the Graveyard is host	295	590	885	1888	3244	4600

HORRORIST, THE (Also see Hellblazer)
DC Comics (Vertigo): Dec, 1995 - No. 2, Jan, 1996 ($5.95, lim. series, mature)

	GD	VG	FN	VF	VF/NM	NM-
1,2: Jamie Delano scripts, David Lloyd-c/a; John Constantine (Hellblazer) app.						6.00

HORROR OF COLLIER COUNTY
Dark Horse Comics: Oct, 1999 - No. 5, Feb, 2000 ($2.95, B&W, limited series)

	GD	VG	FN	VF	VF/NM	NM-
1-5-Rich Tommaso-s/a						3.00

HORRORS, THE (Formerly Startling Terror Tales #10)
Star Publications: No. 11, Jan, 1953 - No. 15, Apr, 1954

	GD	VG	FN	VF	VF/NM	NM-
11-Horrors of War; Disbrow-a(2)	84	168	252	538	919	1300
12-Horrors of War; color illo in **POP**	65	130	195	416	708	1000
13-Horrors of Mystery; crime stories	226	452	678	1446	2473	3500
14,15-Horrors of the Underworld; crime stories	65	130	195	416	708	1000

NOTE: *All have **L. B. Cole** covers; a-12. **Hollingsworth** a-13. **Palais** a-13r.*

HORROR TALES (Magazine)
Eerie Publications: V1#7, 6/69 - V6#6, 12/74; V7#1, 2/75; V7#2, 5/76 - V8#5, 1977; V9#1-3, 8/78; V10#1(2/79) (V1-V6: 52 pgs.; V7, V8#2: 112 pgs.; V8#4 on: 68 pgs.) (No V5#3, V8#1,3)

	GD	VG	FN	VF	VF/NM	NM-
V1#7	9	18	27	59	117	175
V1#8,9	7	14	21	46	86	125
V2#1-6('70), V3#1-6('71), V4#1-3,5-7('72)	6	12	18	40	73	105
V4#4-LSD story reprint/Weird V3#5	7	14	21	46	86	125
V5#1,2,4,5(6/73),5(10/73),6(12/73),V6#1-6('74),V7#1,2,4('76),V7#3('76)-Giant issue, V8#2,4,5('77)	6	12	18	37	66	95
V9#1-3(11/78, $1.50), V10#1(2/79)	6	12	18	38	69	100

NOTE: *Bondage-c-V6#1, 3, V7#2.*

HORSE FEATHERS COMICS
Lev Gleason Publ.: Nov, 1945 - No. 4, July(Summer on-c), 1948 (52 pgs.) (#2,3 are oversized)

	GD	VG	FN	VF	VF/NM	NM-
1-Wolverton's Scoop Scuttle, 2 pgs.	22	44	66	132	216	300
2	14	28	42	78	112	145

	GD 2.0	VG 4.0	FN 6.0	VF 8.0	VF/NM 9.0	NM- 9.2
3,4: 3-(5/48)	10	20	30	56	76	95

HORSEMAN
Crusade Comics/Kevlar Studios: Mar, 1996 - No. 3, Nov, 1997 ($2.95)

	GD 2.0	VG 4.0	FN 6.0	VF 8.0	VF/NM 9.0	NM- 9.2
0-1st Kevlar Studios issue, 1-(3/96)-Crusade issue; Shi-c/app., 1-(11/96)-3-(11/97)-Kevlar Studios						4.00

HORSEMASTERS, THE (Disney)(TV, Movie)
Dell Publishing Co.: No. 1260, Dec-Feb, 1961/62

	GD 2.0	VG 4.0	FN 6.0	VF 8.0	VF/NM 9.0	NM- 9.2
Four Color 1260-Annette Funicello photo-c	10	20	30	69	147	225

HORSE SOLDIERS, THE
Dell Publishing Co.: No. 1048, Nov-Jan, 1959/60 (John Wayne movie)

	GD 2.0	VG 4.0	FN 6.0	VF 8.0	VF/NM 9.0	NM- 9.2
Four Color 1048-Painted-c, Sekowsky-a	12	24	36	80	173	265

HORSE WITHOUT A HEAD, THE (See Movie Comics)

HOT DOG
Magazine Enterprises: June-July, 1954 - No. 4, Dec-Jan, 1954-55

	GD 2.0	VG 4.0	FN 6.0	VF 8.0	VF/NM 9.0	NM- 9.2
1(A-1 #107)	13	26	39	74	105	135
2,3(A-1 #115),4(A-1 #136)	9	18	27	47	61	75

HOT DOG (See Jughead's Pal, Hotdog)

HOTEL DEPAREE - SUNDANCE (TV)
Dell Publishing Co.: No. 1126, Aug-Oct, 1960 (one-shot)

	GD 2.0	VG 4.0	FN 6.0	VF 8.0	VF/NM 9.0	NM- 9.2
Four Color 1126-Earl Holliman photo-c	6	12	18	42	79	115

HOTELL
AWA Studios: Mar, 2020 - No. 4, Aug, 2020 ($3.99, limited series)

	GD 2.0	VG 4.0	FN 6.0	VF 8.0	VF/NM 9.0	NM- 9.2
1-4-John Lees-s/Dalibor Talajic-a						4.00

HOTELL VOL. 2
AWA Studios: Dec, 2021 - No. 5, Apr, 2022 ($3.99, limited series)

	GD 2.0	VG 4.0	FN 6.0	VF 8.0	VF/NM 9.0	NM- 9.2
1-5-John Lees-s/Dalibor Talajic-a						4.00

HOT ROD AND SPEEDWAY COMICS
Hillman Periodicals: Feb-Mar, 1952 - No. 5, Apr-May, 1953

	GD 2.0	VG 4.0	FN 6.0	VF 8.0	VF/NM 9.0	NM- 9.2
1	32	64	96	188	307	425
2-Krigstein-a	20	40	60	120	195	270
3-5	13	26	39	74	105	135

HOT ROD COMICS (...Featuring Clint Curtis) (See XMas Comics)
Fawcett Publications: Nov, 1951 (no month given) - V2#7, Feb, 1953

	GD 2.0	VG 4.0	FN 6.0	VF 8.0	VF/NM 9.0	NM- 9.2
nn (V1#1)-Powell-c/a in all	36	72	108	211	343	475
2 (4/52)	20	40	60	114	182	250
3-6, V2#7	15	30	45	83	124	165

HOT ROD KING (Also see Speed Smith the Hot Rod King)
Ziff-Davis Publ. Co.: Fall, 1952

	GD 2.0	VG 4.0	FN 6.0	VF 8.0	VF/NM 9.0	NM- 9.2
1-Giacoia-a; Saunders painted-c	36	72	108	211	343	475

HOT ROD RACERS (Grand Prix No. 16 on)
Charlton Comics: Dec, 1964 - No. 15, July, 1967

	GD 2.0	VG 4.0	FN 6.0	VF 8.0	VF/NM 9.0	NM- 9.2
1	8	16	24	52	99	145
2-5	5	10	15	30	50	70
6-15	4	8	12	23	37	50

HOT RODS AND RACING CARS
Charlton Comics (Motor Mag. No. 1): Nov, 1951 - No. 120, June, 1973

	GD 2.0	VG 4.0	FN 6.0	VF 8.0	VF/NM 9.0	NM- 9.2
1-Speed Davis begins; Indianapolis 500 story	36	72	108	211	343	475
2	19	38	57	111	176	240
3-10	12	24	36	69	97	125
11-20	10	20	30	54	72	90
21-33,36-40	8	16	24	44	57	70
34, 35 (? & 6/58, 68 pgs.)	11	22	33	60	83	105
41-60	7	14	21	37	46	55
61-80	3	6	9	19	30	40
81-100	3	6	9	16	23	30
101-120	3	6	9	14	19	24

HOT SHOT CHARLIE
Hillman Periodicals: 1947 (Lee Elias)

	GD 2.0	VG 4.0	FN 6.0	VF 8.0	VF/NM 9.0	NM- 9.2
1	17	34	51	100	158	215

HOT SHOTS: AVENGERS
Marvel Comics: Oct, 1995 ($2.95, one-shot)

	GD 2.0	VG 4.0	FN 6.0	VF 8.0	VF/NM 9.0	NM- 9.2
nn-pin-ups						4.00

HOTSPUR
Eclipse Comics: Jun, 1987 - No. 3, Sep, 1987 ($1.75, lim. series, Baxter paper)

	GD 2.0	VG 4.0	FN 6.0	VF 8.0	VF/NM 9.0	NM- 9.2
1-3						3.00

HOT STUFF (See Stumbo Tinytown)
Harvey Comics: V2#1, Sept, 1991 - No. 12, June, 1994 ($1.00)

	GD 2.0	VG 4.0	FN 6.0	VF 8.0	VF/NM 9.0	NM- 9.2
V2#1-Stumbo back-up story						5.00
2-12 ($1.50)						4.00
...Big Book 1 (11/92), 2 (6/93) (Both $1.95, 52 pgs.)						5.00

HOT STUFF CREEPY CAVES
Harvey Publications: Nov, 1974 - No. 7, Nov, 1975

	GD 2.0	VG 4.0	FN 6.0	VF 8.0	VF/NM 9.0	NM- 9.2
1	4	8	12	23	37	50
2-7	3	6	9	15	21	26

HOT STUFF DIGEST
Harvey Comics: July, 1992 - No. 5, Nov, 1993 ($1.75, digest-size)

	GD 2.0	VG 4.0	FN 6.0	VF 8.0	VF/NM 9.0	NM- 9.2
V2#1-Hot Stuff, Stumbo, Richie Rich stories						6.00
2-5						4.00

HOT STUFF GIANT SIZE
Harvey Comics: Oct, 1992 - No. 3, Oct, 1993 ($2.25, 68 pgs.)

	GD 2.0	VG 4.0	FN 6.0	VF 8.0	VF/NM 9.0	NM- 9.2
V2#1-Hot Stuff & Stumbo stories						5.00
2,3						4.00

HOT STUFF SIZZLERS
Harvey Publications: July, 1960 - No. 59, Mar, 1974; V2#1, Aug, 1992

	GD 2.0	VG 4.0	FN 6.0	VF 8.0	VF/NM 9.0	NM- 9.2
1- 84 pgs. begin, ends #5; Hot Stuff, Stumbo begin	16	32	48	107	236	365
2-5	8	16	24	52	99	145
6-10: 6-68 pgs. begin, ends #45	5	10	15	35	63	90
11-20	4	8	12	27	44	60
21-45	3	6	9	19	30	40
46-52: 52 pgs. begin	3	6	9	16	23	30
53-59	2	4	6	10	14	18
V2#1-(8/92, $1.25)-Stumbo back-up						5.00

HOT STUFF, THE LITTLE DEVIL (Also see Devil Kids & Harvey Hits)
Harvey Publications (Illustrated Humor): 10/57 - No. 141, 7/77; No. 142, 2/78 - No. 164, 8/82; No. 165, 10/86 - No. 171, 11/87; No. 172, 11/88; No. 173, Sept, 1990 - No. 177, 1/91

	GD 2.0	VG 4.0	FN 6.0	VF 8.0	VF/NM 9.0	NM- 9.2
1-1st app. Hot Stuff; UFO story	166	332	498	1370	3085	4800
2-Stumbo-like giant 1st app. (12/57)	38	76	114	285	641	1000
3-Stumbo the Giant debut (2/58)	19	38	57	133	297	460
4,5	17	34	51	117	259	400
6-10	10	20	30	66	138	210
11-20	8	16	24	51	96	140
21-40	5	10	15	34	60	85
41-60	4	8	12	25	40	55
61-80	3	6	9	19	30	40
81-105	3	6	9	15	22	28
106-112: All 52 pg. Giants	3	6	9	17	26	35
113-125	2	4	6	9	12	15
126-141	1	2	3	5	7	9
142-177: 172-177-($1.00)						6.00
Harvey Comics Classics Vol. 3 TPB (Dark Horse Books, 3/08, $19.95) Reprints Hot Stuff's earliest appearances in this title and Devil Kids, mostly B&W with some color stories; history, early concept drawings; foreword by Mark Arnold						20.00

HOT WHEELS (TV)
National Periodical Publications: Mar-Apr, 1970 - No. 6, Jan-Feb, 1971

	GD 2.0	VG 4.0	FN 6.0	VF 8.0	VF/NM 9.0	NM- 9.2
1	11	22	33	73	157	240
2,4,5	6	12	18	37	66	95
3-Neal Adams-c	7	14	21	48	89	130
6-Neal Adams-c/a	8	16	24	55	105	155

NOTE: *Toth a-1p, 2-5; c-1p, 5.*

HOURMAN (Justice Society member, see Adventure Comics #48)

HOURMAN (See JLA and DC One Million)
DC Comics: Apr, 1999 - No. 25, Apr, 2001 ($2.50)

	GD 2.0	VG 4.0	FN 6.0	VF 8.0	VF/NM 9.0	NM- 9.2
1-25: 1-JLA app.; McDaniel-c. 2-Tomorrow Woman-c/app. 6,7-Amazo app. 11-13-Justice Legion A app. 16-Silver Age flashback. 18,19-JSA-c/app. 22-Harris-c/a. 24-Hourman Vs. Rex Tyler						4.00

HOUSE OF CEREBUS
Aardvark-Vanaheim: Jan, 2020 ($4.00, B&W)

	GD 2.0	VG 4.0	FN 6.0	VF 8.0	VF/NM 9.0	NM- 9.2
1-Swamp Thing parady; Dave Sim-s/a; House of Secrets #92-c swipe						4.00

HOUSE OF FUN
Dark Horse Comics: Dec, 2012 ($3.50)

	GD 2.0	VG 4.0	FN 6.0	VF 8.0	VF/NM 9.0	NM- 9.2
0-Reprints Evan Dorkin humor strips from Dark Horse Presents #10-12						3.50

HOUSE OF GOLD AND BONES
Dark Horse Comics: Apr, 2013 - No. 4, Jul, 2013 ($3.99, limited series)

	GD 2.0	VG 4.0	FN 6.0	VF 8.0	VF/NM 9.0	NM- 9.2
1-4-Corey Taylor-s/Richard Clark-a; 2 covers on each						4.00

HOUSE OF HEM
Marvel Comics: 2015 ($7.99, one-shot)

	GD 2.0	VG 4.0	FN 6.0	VF 8.0	VF/NM 9.0	NM- 9.2
1-Reprints Fred Hembeck's Marvel highlights incl. Fantastic Four Roast; wraparound-c						8.00

HOUSE OF LOST HORIZONS, THE (A Sarah Jewell Mystery)
Dark Horse Comics: May, 2021 - No. 5, Sept, 2021 ($3.99, limited series)

	GD 2.0	VG 4.0	FN 6.0	VF 8.0	VF/NM 9.0	NM- 9.2
1-5-Chris Roberson-s/Leila Del Duca-a						4.00

HOUSE OF M (Also see miniseries with Fantastic Four, Iron Man and Spider-Man)
Marvel Comics: Aug, 2005 - No. 8, Dec, 2005 ($2.99, limited series)

	GD 2.0	VG 4.0	FN 6.0	VF 8.0	VF/NM 9.0	NM- 9.2
1-Bendis-s/Coipel-a/Ribic-c; Scarlet Witch changes reality; Quesada variant-c						5.00
2-8-Variant covers for each. 3-Hawkeye returns						3.00
... MGC #1 (6/11, $1.00) r/#1 with "Marvel's Greatest Comics" logo on cover						3.00
Secrets Of The House Of M (2005, $3.99, one-shot) profile pages and background info						4.00
... Sketchbook (6/05) B&W preview sketches by Coipel, Davis, Hairsine, Quesada						3.00
TPB (2006, $24.99) r/#1-8 and The Pulse: House of M Special Edition newspaper						25.00
...: Fantastic Four/ Iron Man TPB (2006, $13.99) r/ both House of M mini-series						14.00
...: World of M Featuring Wolverine TPB (2006, $13.99) r/2005 x-over issues Wolverine #33-35, Black Panther #7, Captain America #10 and The Pulse #10						14.00
HC (2008, $29.99, oversized with d.j.) r/#1-8, The Pulse: House of M Special Edition newspaper and Secrets Of The House Of M one-shot; script pages; cover gallery						30.00

HOUSE OF M (Secret Wars tie-in)
Marvel Comics: Oct, 2015 - No. 4, Dec, 2015 ($3.99, limited series)

	GD 2.0	VG 4.0	FN 6.0	VF 8.0	VF/NM 9.0	NM- 9.2
1-4: 1,2-Hopeless & Bunn-s/Failla-a; Magneto & the House of Magnus. 3,4-Anindito-a						4.00

HOUSE OF M: AVENGERS
Marvel Comics: Jan, 2008 - No. 5, Apr, 2008 ($2.99, limited series)

	GD 2.0	VG 4.0	FN 6.0	VF 8.0	VF/NM 9.0	NM- 9.2
1-5-Gage-s/Perkins-a; Luke Cage, Iron Fist, Hawkeye, Tigra, Misty Knight, Shang-Chi						3.00

HOUSE OF M: MASTERS OF EVIL
Marvel Comics: Oct, 2009 - No. 4, Jan, 2010 ($3.99, limited series)

	GD 2.0	VG 4.0	FN 6.0	VF 8.0	VF/NM 9.0	NM- 9.2
1-4-Gage-s/Garcia-a/Perkins-c; The Hood app.						4.00

HOUSE OF MYSTERY
DC Comics: Dec/Jan. 1951

nn - Ashcan comic, not distributed to newsstands, only for in-house use. Cover art is Danger Trail #3 with interior being Star Spangled Comics #109. A VG+ copy sold for $2,357.50 in 2002.

HOUSE OF MYSTERY (See Brave and the Bold #93, Elvira's House of Mystery, Limited Collectors' Edition & Super DC Giant)

HOUSE OF MYSTERY, THE
National Periodical Publications/DC Comics: Dec-Jan, 1951-52 - No. 321, Oct, 1983 (No. 194-203: 52 pgs.)

Hot Stuff Sizzlers #36 © HARV

House of Hem #1 © MAR

House of Mystery #223 © DC

	GD 2.0	VG 4.0	FN 6.0	VF 8.0	VF/NM 9.0	NM- 9.2
1-DC's first horror comic	300	600	900	1970	3410	4850
2	135	270	405	864	1482	2100
3	77	154	231	493	847	1200
4,5	65	130	195	416	708	1000
6-10	58	116	174	371	636	900
11-15	50	100	150	315	533	750
16(7/53)-25	40	80	120	246	411	575
26-35(2/55)-Last pre-code issue; 30-Woodish-a	34	68	102	204	332	460
36-50: 50-Text story of Orson Welles' War of the Worlds broadcast	18	36	54	122	271	420
51-60: 55-1st S.A. issue	15	30	45	105	233	360
61,63,65,66,69,70,72,76,79,85-Kirby-a	17	34	51	117	259	400
62,64,67,68,71,73-75,77,78,80-83,86-99: 92-Grey tone-c	15	30	45	100	220	340
84-Prototype of Negative Man (Doom Patrol)	28	56	84	202	451	700
100 (7/60)	15	30	45	105	233	360
101-116: 109-Toth, Kubert-a. 116-Last 10¢ issue	11	22	33	77	166	255
117-130: 117-Swipes-c to HOS #20. 120-Toth-a	10	20	30	67	141	215
131-142	9	18	27	60	120	180
143-J'onn J'onzz, Manhunter begins (6/64), ends #173; story continues from Detective #326; intro. Idol-Head of Diabolu	20	40	60	135	300	465
144	9	18	27	57	111	165
145-155,157-159: 149-Toth-a. 155-The Human Hurricane app. (12/65), Red Tornado prototype. 158-Origin Diabolu Idol-Head	6	12	18	37	66	95
156-Robby Reed begins (origin/1st app.), ends #173	13	26	39	89	195	300
160-(7/66)-Robby Reed becomes Plastic Man in this issue only; 1st S.A. app. Plastic Man; intro Marco Xavier (Martian Manhunter) & Vulture Crime Organization; ends #173	18	36	54	124	275	425
161-173: 169-Origin/1st app. Gem Girl	5	10	15	31	53	75
174-Mystery format begins.	25	50	75	175	388	600
175-1st app. Cain (House of Mystery host); Adams-c	16	32	48	107	236	365
176,177-Neal Adams-c	10	20	30	64	132	200
178-Neal Adams-c/a (2/69)	10	20	30	70	150	230
179-Neal Adams/Orlando, Wrightson-a (1st pro work, 3 pgs.); Adams-c	20	40	60	138	307	475
180,181,183: Wrightson-a (3,10, & 3 pgs.); Adams-c. 180-Last 12¢ issue; Kane/Wood-a(2). 183-Wood-a	9	18	27	60	120	180
182,184-Adams-c. 182-Toth-a. 184-Kane/Wood, Toth-a	7	14	21	48	89	130
185-Williamson/Kaluta-a; Howard-a (3 pgs.); Adams-c	8	16	24	51	96	140
186-N. Adams-c/a; Wrightson-a (10 pgs.)	9	18	27	59	117	175
187,190: Adams-c. 187-Toth-a. 190-Toth-a(r)	6	12	18	40	73	105
188-Wrightson-a (8 & 3pgs.); Adams-c	8	16	24	52	99	145
189,192,197: Adams-c on all. 189-Wood-a(i). 192-Last 15¢-c	6	12	18	40	73	105
191-Wrightson-a (8 & 3pgs.); Adams-c	7	14	21	49	92	135
193-Wrightson-c	6	12	18	40	73	105
194-Wrightson-c; 52 pgs begin, end #203; Toth,Kirby-a	8	16	24	51	96	140
195-Wrightson-c. Swamp creature story by Wrightson similar to Swamp Thing (10 pgs.)(10/71)	11	22	33	73	157	240
196,198	5	10	15	35	63	90
199-Adams-c; Wood-a(8pgs.); Kirby-a	6	12	18	42	79	115
200-(25¢, 52 pgs.)-One third-r (3/72)	6	12	18	41	76	110
201-203-(25¢, 52 pgs.)-One third-r	5	10	15	33	57	80
204-Wrightson-c/a, 9 pgs.	6	12	18	38	69	100
205,206,208,210,212,215,216,218	4	8	12	23	37	50
207-Wrightson-c/a; Starlin, Redondo-a	6	12	18	38	69	100
209,211,213,214,217,219-Wrightson-c	5	10	15	31	53	75
220,222,223	3	6	9	21	33	45
221-Wrightson/Kaluta-a(8 pgs.); Wrightson-c	6	12	18	37	66	95
224-229: 224-Wrightson-r from Spectre #9; Dillin/Adams-r from House of Secrets #82; begin 100 pg. issues; Phantom Stranger-r. 225,227-(100 pgs.): 225-Spectre app. 226-Wrightson/Redondo-a Phantom Stranger-r. 228-N. Adams inks; Wrightson-r. 229-Wrightson-a(r); Toth-r; last 100 pg. issue	5	10	15	35	63	90
230,232-235,237-250: 230-UFO-c	3	6	9	16	23	30
231-Classic Wrightson-c	6	12	18	41	76	110
236-Wrightson-c; Ditko-a(p); N. Adams-i	5	10	15	35	63	90
251-254-(84 pgs.)-Adams-c. 251-Wood-a	4	8	12	27	44	60
255,256-(84 pgs.)-Wrightson-c	4	8	12	27	44	60
257-259-(84 pgs.)	3	6	9	18	28	38
260-289: 282-(68 pgs.)-Has extra story "The Computers That Saved Metropolis" Radio Shack giveaway by Jim Starlin	2	4	6	8	10	12
290-1st "I, Vampire"	8	16	24	51	96	140
291-299: 291,293,295-299- "I, Vampire"	2	4	6	11	16	20
300,319-"I, Vampire". 319-Death of Andrew Bennett	3	6	9	14	19	24
301-318,320: 301-318-"I, Vampire"	2	4	6	11	16	20
321-Final issue; Joe Orlando & Karen Berger app.	3	6	9	17	25	34
Welcome to the House of Mystery (7/98, $5.95) reprints stories with new framing story by Gaiman and Aragonés						6.00

NOTE: ***Neal Adams*** *a-236i; c-175-192, 197, 199, 251-254.* ***Alcala*** *a-209, 217, 219, 224, 227.* ***M. Anderson*** *a-212; c/a-37.* ***Aparo*** *a-209.* ***Aragones*** *a-185, 186, 194, 196, 200, 202, 229, 251.* ***Baily*** *a-279p.* ***Cameron*** *a-76, 79.* ***Colan*** *a-202r.* ***Craig*** *a-263, 275, 295, 300.* ***Dillin/Adams*** *r-224.* ***Ditko*** *a-236p, 247, 254, 258, 276; c-277.* ***Drucker*** *a-37.* ***Evans*** *c-218.* ***Fradon*** *a-251.* ***Giffen*** *a-284.* ***Giunta*** *a-199, 227r.* ***Golden*** *a-257, 259.* ***Heath*** *a-194r; c-203.* ***Howard*** *a-182, 185, 187, 196, 229r, 247i, 254, 279i.* ***Kaluta*** *a-195, 200, 250r; c-200-202, 210, 212, 233, 260, 261, 263, 265, 267, 268, 273, 276, 284, 287, 288, 293-295, 300, 302, 304, 305, 309-319, 321.* ***Bob Kane*** *a-84.* ***Gil Kane*** *a-196p, 253p, 300p.* ***Kirby*** *a-194r, 199r; c-65, 76, 78, 79, 85.* ***Kubert*** *c-282, 283, 285, 286, 289-292, 297-299, 301, 303, 306-308.* ***Maneely*** *a-68, 227r.* ***Mayer*** *a-317p.* ***Meskin*** *a-52-144 (most), 195r, 224r, 229r; c-63, 66, 124, 127.* ***Mooney*** *a-24, 159, 160.* ***Moreira*** *a-3, 4, 20-50, 58, 59, 62, 68, 77, 79, 90, 108, 113, 123, 201r, 228; c-4-28, 44, 47, 50, 54, 59, 62, 64, 68, 70, 73.* ***Morrow*** *a-192, 196, 255, 320i.* ***Mortimer*** *a-204(3 pgs.).* ***Nasser*** *a-276.* ***Newton*** *a-259, 272.* ***Nino*** *a-204, 212, 213, 220, 224, 225, 245, 250, 252-256, 283.* ***Orlando*** *a-175(2 pgs.), 178, 240i; c-240, 258p, 262, 264p, 270p, 271, 272, 274, 275, 278, 296i.* ***Redondo*** *a-194, 195, 197, 202, 203, 207, 211, 214, 217, 219, 226, 227, 229, 235, 241, 287(layout), 302p, 303i, 308; c-229.* ***Reese*** *a-195, 200, 205i.* ***Rogers*** *a-254, 274, 277.* ***Roussos*** *a-65, 84, 224i.* ***Sekowsky*** *a-282p.* ***Sparling*** *a-203.* ***Starlin*** *a-207(2 pgs.), 282p; c-281.* ***Leonard Starr*** *a-9.* ***Staton*** *a-300p.* ***Sutton*** *a-189, 271, 290, 291, 293, 295, 297-299, 302, 303, 306-309, 310-313i, 314.* ***Tuska*** *a-293p, 294p, 316p.* ***Wrightson*** *c-193-195, 204, 207, 209, 211, 213, 214, 217, 219, 221, 231, 236, 255, 256; r-224.*

HOUSE OF MYSTERY
DC Comics (Vertigo): Jul, 2008 - No. 42, Dec, 2011 ($2.99)

	GD 2.0	VG 4.0	FN 6.0	VF 8.0	VF/NM 9.0	NM- 9.2
1-Cain & Abel app.; Rossi-a/Weber-c	2	4	6	9	12	15
1-Variant-c by Bernie Wrightson	3	6	9	17	26	35
2-12,14-42: 9-Wrightson-a (6 pgs.). 16-Corben-a						3.00
13-Art by Neal Adams, Ralph Reese, Eric Powell, Sergio Aragonés						3.00
13-Variant-c by Neal Adams						5.00
... Halloween Annual #1 (12/09, $4.99) 1st app. I, Zombie in 7 pg. preview; short stories by various incl. Nowlan, Wagner, Willingham	3	6	9	14	20	25
... Halloween Annual #2 (12/10, $4.99) short stories by various incl. Carey, Allred, Gross						6.00
...: Love Stories for Dead People TPB (2009, $14.99) r/#6-10						15.00
...: Room and Boredom TPB (2008, $9.99) r/#1-5						10.00
...: Safe as Houses TPB (2011, $14.99) r/#26-30						15.00
...: The Beauty of Decay TPB (2010, $17.99) r/#16-20 & Halloween Annual #1						18.00
...: The Space Between TPB (2010, $14.99) r/#11-15; sketch pages						15.00
...: Under New Management TPB (2011, $14.99) r/#20-25						15.00

HOUSE OF NIGHT (Based on the series of novels by P.C. Cast and Kristin Cast)
Dark Horse Comics: Nov, 2011 - No. 5, Mar, 2012 ($1.00/$2.99, limited series)

	GD 2.0	VG 4.0	FN 6.0	VF 8.0	VF/NM 9.0	NM- 9.2
1-($1.00) Cast, Cast & Dalian-s/Joëlle Jones & Kerschl-a; Frison-c						3.00
1-($1.00) Variant-c by Steve Morris						4.00
2-5-($2.99) Jones-a; two covers by Jones & Ryan Hill on each						3.00

HOUSE OF PENANCE
Dark Horse Comics: Apr, 2016 - No. 5, Aug, 2016 ($3.99)

	GD 2.0	VG 4.0	FN 6.0	VF 8.0	VF/NM 9.0	NM- 9.2
1-5: 1-Peter J. Tomasi-s/Ian Bertram-a						4.00

HOUSE OF SECRETS (Combined with The Unexpected after #154)
National Periodical Publications/DC Comics: 11-12/56 - No. 80, 9-10/66; No. 81, 8-9/69 - No. 140, 2-3/76; No. 141, 8-9/76 - No. 154, 10-11/78

	GD 2.0	VG 4.0	FN 6.0	VF 8.0	VF/NM 9.0	NM- 9.2
1-Drucker-a; Moreira-c	148	296	444	1221	2761	4300
2-Moreira-a	48	96	144	368	834	1300
3-Kirby-c/a	46	92	138	340	770	1200
4-Kirby-a	34	68	102	245	548	850
5-7	25	50	75	175	388	600
8-Kirby-a	27	54	81	189	420	650
9-11: 11-Lou Cameron-a (unsigned); Kirby-a	24	48	72	168	372	575
12-Kirby-c/a; Lou Cameron-a	25	50	75	175	388	600
13-15: 14-Flying saucer-c	17	34	51	117	259	400
16-20	16	32	48	110	243	375
21,22,24-30	14	28	42	96	211	325
23-1st app. Mark Merlin & begin series (8/59)	20	40	60	138	307	475
31-50: 48-Toth-a. 50-Last 10¢ issue	12	24	36	82	179	275
51-60: 58-Origin Mark Merlin	10	20	30	64	132	200
61-First Eclipso (7-8/63) and begin series	66	132	198	528	1189	1850
62	9	18	27	59	117	175
63-65-Toth-a on Eclipso (see Brave and the Bold #64)	7	14	21	48	89	130
66-1st Eclipso-c (also #67,70,78,79); Toth-a	10	20	30	67	141	214
67,73: 67-Toth-a on Eclipso. 73-Mark Merlin becomes Prince Ra-Man (1st app.)	7	14	21	44	82	120
68-72,74-80: 76-Prince Ra-Man vs. Eclipso. 80-Eclipso, Prince Ra-Man end	6	12	18	38	69	100
81-Mystery format begins; 1st app. Abel (House Of Secrets host); (cameo in DC Special #4)	24	48	72	168	372	575
82-84: 82-Neal Adams-c(i)	8	16	24	54	102	150

GD 2.0 | VG 4.0 | FN 6.0 | VF 8.0 | VF/NM 9.0 | NM- 9.2

85,90: 85-N. Adams-a(i). 90-Buckler (early work)/N. Adams-a(i)
8 16 24 55 105 155
86,88,89,91 7 14 21 48 89 130
87-Wrightson & Kaluta-a 8 16 24 55 105 155
92-1st app. Swamp Thing-c/story (8 pgs.)(6-7/71) by Berni Wrightson(p) with ink assists by Jeff Jones, Kaluta & Weiss; classic-c 420 840 1680 3360 5030 6700
92 (Facsimile Edition)(2019, $3.99) r/#92 w/original ads and letter column
2 4 6 9 12 15
93,94,96-(52 pgs.)-Wrightson-c. 94-Wrightson-a(i); 96-Wood-a
8 16 24 55 105 155
95,97,98-(52 pgs.) 6 12 18 37 66 95
99-Wrightson splash pg. 5 10 15 35 63 90
100-Classic Wrightson-c 8 16 24 55 105 155
101,102,104,105,108-111,113-120 3 6 9 19 30 40
103,106,107-Wrightson-c 5 10 15 34 60 85
112-Grey tone-c 4 8 12 25 40 55
121-133 2 4 6 11 16 20
134-Wrightson-a 3 6 9 17 26 35
135,136,139-Wrightson-a/c 3 6 9 20 31 42
137,138,141-153 2 4 6 8 10 12
140-1st solo origin of the Patchworkman (see Swamp Thing #3)
3 6 9 16 23 30
154 (10-11/78, 44 pgs.) Last issue 2 4 6 9 13 16

NOTE: ***Neal Adams*** *c-81, 82, 84-88, 90, 91.* ***Alcala*** *a-104-107.* ***Anderson*** *a-91. Aparo a-93, 97, 105.* ***B. Bailey*** *a-107.* ***Cameron*** *a-13, 15.* ***Colan*** *a-63.* ***Ditko*** *a-139p, 148.* ***Elias*** *a-58.* ***Evans*** *a-118.* ***Finlay*** *a-7r(Real Fact?).* ***Glanzman*** *a-91.* ***Golden*** *a-151.* ***Heath*** *a-31.* ***Heck*** *a-85.* ***Kaluta*** *a-87, 98, 99; c-98, 99, 101, 102, 105, 149, 151, 154.* ***Bob Kane*** *a-18, 21.* ***G. Kane*** *a-85p.* ***Kirby*** *c-3, 11, 12.* ***Kubert*** *a-39.* ***Meskin*** *a-2-68 (most), 94r; c-55-60.* ***Moreira*** *a-7, 8, 51, 54, 102-104, 106, 108, 113, 116, 118, 121, 123, 127; c-1, 2, 4-10, 13-20.* ***Morrow*** *a-86, 89, 90; c-89, 146-148.* ***Nino*** *a-101, 103, 106, 109, 115, 117, 126, 128, 131, 147, 153.* ***Redondo*** *a-95, 99, 102, 104p, 113, 116, 134, 136, 139, 140.* ***Reese*** *a-85.* ***Severin*** *a-91.* ***Starlin*** *c-150.* ***Sutton*** *a-154.* ***Toth*** *a-63-67, 83, 93r, 94r, 96r-98r, 123.* ***Tuska*** *a-90, 104.* ***Wrightson*** *a-134; c-92-94, 96, 100, 103, 106, 107, 135, 136, 139.*

HOUSE OF SECRETS
DC Comics (Vertigo): Oct, 1996 - No. 25, Dec, 1998 ($2.50) (Creator-owned series)

1-Steven Seagle-s/Kristiansen-c/a. 5.00
2-25: 5,7-Kristiansen-c/a. 6-Fegrado-a 4.00
TPB-(1997, $14.95) r/1-5 15.00

HOUSE OF SECRETS: FACADE
DC Comics (Vertigo): 2001 - No. 2, 2001 ($5.95, limited series)

1,2-Steven Seagle-s/Teddy Kristiansen-c/a. 6.00

HOUSE OF SLAUGHTER (See Something is Killing the Children & Enter the House of Slaughter)
BOOM! Studios: Oct, 2021 - Present ($3.99, limited series)

1-12: 1-4-Tynion IV & Brombal-s/Shehan-a. 6-10-Cadonici-a 4.00

HOUSE OF TERROR (3-D)
St. John Publishing Co.: Oct, 1953 (25¢, came w/glasses)

1-Kubert, Baker-a 32 64 96 188 307 425

HOUSE OF WHISPERS (The Sandman Universe)(Issues #21 & #22 were only released digitally)
DC Comics (Vertigo): Nov, 2018 - No. 20, Jun, 2020 ($3.99)

1-20: 1-Hopkinson-s/Stanton-a; Abel & Goldie app. 4.00

HOUSE OF X (Weekly series alternating with Powers of X #1-6)
Marvel Comics: Sept, 2019 - No. 6, Dec, 2019 ($5.99/$4.99)

1-($5.99) Hickman-s/Larraz-a; Fantastic Four app. 6.00
2-6-($4.99) 2-Moira MacTaggart new origin. 3-Bonus Krakoan alphabet translation guide 5.00

HOUSE OF YANG, THE (See Yang)
Charlton Comics: July, 1975 - No. 6, June, 1976; 1978

1-Sanho Kim-a in all 2 4 6 13 18 22
2-6 2 4 6 8 10 12
Modern Comics #1,2(1978) 6.00

HOUSE ON THE BORDERLAND
DC Comics (Vertigo): 2000 ($29.95, hardcover, one-shot)

HC-Adaptation of William Hope Hodgson book; Corben-a 30.00
SC (2003, $19.95) 20.00

HOUSE II: THE SECOND STORY
Marvel Comics: Oct, 1987 (One-shot)

1-Adapts movie 4.00

HOWARD CHAYKIN'S AMERICAN FLAGG (See American Flagg!)
First Comics: V2#1, May, 1988 - V2#12, Apr, 1989 ($1.75/$1.95, Baxter paper)

V2#1-9,11,12-Chaykin-c(p) in all 3.00
10-Elvis Presley photo-c 4.00

HOWARD THE DUCK (See Bizarre Adventures #34, Crazy Magazine, Fear, Man-Thing, Marvel Treasury Edition & Sensational She-Hulk #14-17)
Marvel Comics Group: Jan, 1976 - No. 31, May, 1979; No. 32, Jan, 1986; No. 33, Sept, 1986

1-Brunner-c/a; Spider-Man x-over (low distr.) 8 16 24 55 105 155
2-Brunner-c/a 3 6 9 16 24 32
3,4-(Regular 25¢ edition). 3-Buscema-a(p), (7/76) 3 6 9 14 20 26
3,4-(30¢-c, limited distribution) 6 12 18 37 60 95
5 2 4 6 10 14 18
6-11: 8-Howard The Duck for president. 9-1st Sgt. Preston Dudley of RCMP. 10-Spider-Man-c/sty 1 3 4 6 8 10
12-1st brief app. Kiss (3/77) 4 8 12 27 44 60
13-(30¢-c) 1st full app. Kiss (6/77); Daimon Hellstrom app. plus cameo of Howard as Son of Satan 4 8 12 28 47 65
13-(35¢-c, limited distribution) 10 20 30 67 141 215
14-32: 14-17-(Regular 30¢-c). 14-Howard as Son of Satan-c/story; Son of Satan app. 16-Album issue; 3 pgs. comics. 22,23-Man-Thing-c/stories; Star Wars parody. 30,32-P. Smith-a 1 2 3 5 6 8
14-17-(35¢-c, limited distribution) 7 14 21 46 86 125
33-Last issue; low print run 2 4 6 9 12 15
Annual 1(1977, 52 pgs.)-Mayerik-a 2 4 6 10 14 18
... No. 1 Facsimile Ed. (8/19, $3.99) r/#1 w/original ads 4.00
... Omnibus HC (2008, $99.99, dustjacket) r/#1-33 & Annual #1, Adventure Into Fear #19, Man-Thing #1, Giant-Size Man-Thing #4&5, Marvel Treasury Ed. #12, Marvel Team-Up #96 and FOOM #15; Gerber foreword; creator interviews; bonus art; 2 covers 100.00

NOTE: ***Austin*** *c-29i.* ***Bolland*** *c-33.* ***Brunner*** *a-1p, 2p; c-1, 2.* ***Buckler*** *c-3p.* ***Buscema*** *a-3p.* ***Colan*** *a(p)-4-15, 17-20, 24-27, 30, 31; c(p)-4-31, Annual 1p.* ***Leialoha*** *a-1-13i; c(i)-3-5, 8-11.* ***Mayerik*** *a-22, 23, 33.* ***Paul Smith*** *a-30p, 32. Man-Thing app. in #22, 23.*

HOWARD THE DUCK (Magazine)
Marvel Comics Group: Oct, 1979 - No. 9, Mar, 1981 (B&W, 68 pgs.)

1-Art by Colan, Janson, Golden. Kidney Lady app. 3 6 9 16 24 32
2,3,6-9 (nudity in most): 2-Mayerick-c. 3-Xmas issue; Jack Davis-c; Duck World flashback. 6-1st Street People back-up story. 7-Has pin-up by Byrne; Man-Thing-c/s (46 pgs.). 8-Batman parody w/Marshall Rogers-a; Dave Sim-a (1 pg.). 9-Marie Severin-a; John Pound painted-c 2 4 6 8 10 12
4,5: 4-Beatles, John Lennon, Elvis, Kiss & Devo cameos; Hitler app. 5-Undead Duck, Dracula app. 2 4 6 10 14 18

NOTE: ***Buscema*** *a-4p.* ***Colan*** *a-1-5p, 7-9p.* ***Jack Davis*** *c-3.* ***Golden*** *a(p)-1, 5, 6(51pgs.).* ***Rogers*** *a-7, 8.* ***Simonson*** *a-7.*

HOWARD THE DUCK (Volume 2)
Marvel Comics: Mar, 2002 - No. 6, Aug, 2002 ($2.99)

1-Gerber-s/Winslade-a/Fabry-c 6.00
2-6: 2,4-6-Gerber-s/Winslade-a/Fabry-c. 3-Fabry-a/c 4.00
TPB (9/02, $14.99) r/#1-6 15.00

HOWARD THE DUCK (Volume 3)
Marvel Comics: Dec, 2007 - No. 4, Feb, 2008 ($2.99, limited series)

1-4-Templeton-s/Bobillo-a/c; She-Hulk app. 4.00
...: Media Duckling TPB (2008, $11.99) r/#1-4; Howard the Duck #1 (1/76) and pages from Civil War: Choosing Sides 12.00

HOWARD THE DUCK (Volume 4)
Marvel Comics: May 2015 - No. 5, Oct, 2015 ($3.99)

1-5-Zdarsky-s/Quinones-a. 1-Spider-Man app. 2-Guardians of the Galaxy app. 4.00

HOWARD THE DUCK (Volume 5)
Marvel Comics: Jan, 2016 - No. 11, Dec, 2016 ($4.99/$3.99)

1-($4.99) Zdarsky-s/Quinones-a; back-up with Gwenpool in #1-3
3 6 9 14 19 24
2-3-($4.99): 2-Fish-a 6.00
4-11-($3.99) 4,5-Silver Surfer, Galactus & the Guardians of the Galaxy app. 6-Squirrel Girl x-over. 7-Maguire-a. 8-Beverly app. 9-Lea Thompson app. 9-11-Mojo app. 4.00

HOWARD THE DUCK HOLIDAY SPECIAL
Marvel Comics: Feb, 1997 ($2.50, one-shot)

1-Wraparound-c; Hama-s 1 2 3 5 6 8

HOWARD THE DUCK: THE MOVIE
Marvel Comics Group: Dec, 1986 - No. 3, Feb, 1987 (Limited series)

1-3: Movie adaptation; r/Marvel Super Special 5.00

HOWARD THE HUMAN (Secret Wars tie-in)
Marvel Comics: Oct, 2015 ($3.99, one-shot)

1-Howard the Duck as human in an all-animal world; Skottie Young-s/Jim Mahfood-a 4.00

HOW BOYS AND GIRLS CAN HELP WIN THE WAR
The Parents' Magazine Institute: 1942 (10¢, one-shot)

1-All proceeds used to buy war bonds 41 82 123 256 428 600

HOWDY DOODY (TV)(See Jackpot of Fun-- & Poll Parrot)(Some have stories by John Stanley)
Dell Publishing Co.: 1/50 - No. 38, 7-9/56; No. 761, 1/57; No. 811, 7/57

1-(Scarce)-Photo-c; 1st TV comic 79 158 237 632 1416 2200
2-Photo-c 34 68 102 241 541 840
3-5: All photo-c 19 38 57 133 297 460
6-Used in **SOTI**, pg. 309; classic-c; painted covers begin
25 50 75 175 388 600
7-10 12 24 36 84 185 285
11-20: 13-X-Mas-c 10 20 30 70 150 230
21-38, Four Color 761,811 9 18 27 61 123 185

HOW IT BEGAN
United Features Syndicate: No. 15, 1939 (one-shot)

Single Series 15 39 78 117 240 395 550

HOWLING COMMANDOS OF S.H.I.E.L.D.
Marvel Comics: Dec, 2015 - No. 6, May, 2016 ($3.99)

1-6: 1-Barbiere-s/Schoonover-a; Dum Dum Dugan, Orrgo, Man-Thing, Hit-Monkey app. 4.00

HOW SANTA GOT HIS RED SUIT (See March of Comics No. 2)

HOW THE WEST WAS WON (See Movie Comics)

HOW TO DRAW FOR THE COMICS
Street and Smith: No date (1942?) (10¢, 64 pgs., B&W & color, no ads)

nn-Art by Robert Winsor McCay (recreating his father's art), George Marcoux (Supersnipe artist), Vernon Greene (The Shadow artist), Jack Binder (with biog.), Thorton Fisher, Jon Small, & Jack Farr; has biographies of each artist
42 84 126 265 445 625

H. P. LOVECRAFT'S CTHULHU
Millennium Publications: Dec, 1991 - No. 3, May, 1992 ($2.50, limited series)

1-3: 1-Contains trading cards on thin stock 4.00

H. R. PUFNSTUF (TV) (See March of Comics #360)
Gold Key: Oct, 1970 - No. 8, July, 1972

1-Photo-c 10 20 30 64 132 200
2-8-Photo-c on all. 6-8-Both Gold Key and Whitman editions exist
7 14 21 46 86 125

HUBERT AT CAMP MOONBEAM
Dell Publishing Co.: No. 251, Oct, 1949 (one shot)

Four Color 251 10 20 30 64 132 200

HUCK
Image Comics: Nov, 2015 - No. 6, Apr, 2016($3.50/$3.99)

1-5-Millar-s/Albuquerque-a; 2 covers on each 3.50
6-($3.99) 4.00

House of Slaughter #6 © Tynion & Dell'Edera

Howard the Duck (2007) #1 © MAR

Hulk (2012) #47 © MAR

	GD 2.0	VG 4.0	FN 6.0	VF 8.0	VF/NM 9.0	NM- 9.2

HUCK & YOGI JAMBOREE (TV)
Dell Publishing Co.: Mar, 1961 ($1.00, 6-1/4x9", 116 pgs., cardboard-c, high quality paper) (B&W original material)
nn (scarce) 9 18 27 59 117 175

HUCK & YOGI WINTER SPORTS (TV)
Dell Publishing Co.: No. 1310, Mar, 1962 (Hanna-Barbara) (one-shot)
Four Color 1310 8 16 24 54 102 150

HUCK FINN (See The New Adventures of... & Power Record Comics)

HUCKLEBERRY FINN (Movie)
Dell Publishing Co.: No. 1114, July, 1960
Four Color 1114-Photo-c 6 12 18 42 79 115

HUCKLEBERRY HOUND (See Dell Giant #31,44, Golden Picture Story Book, Kite Fun Book, March of Comics #199, 214, 235, Spotlight #1 & Whitman Comic Books)

HUCKLEBERRY HOUND (TV)
Dell/Gold Key No. 18 (10/62) on: No. 990, 5-7/59 - No. 43, 10/70 (Hanna-Barbera)
Four Color 990(#1)-1st app. Huckleberry Hound, Yogi Bear, & Pixie & Dixie & Mr. Jinks
18 36 54 128 284 440
Four Color 1050,1054 (12/59) 12 24 36 80 173 265
3(1-2/60) - 7 (9-10/60), Four Color 1141 (10/60) 7 14 21 46 86 125
8-10 6 12 18 37 66 95
11,13-17 (6-8/62) 5 10 15 30 50 70
12-1st Hokey Wolf & Ding-a-Ling 5 10 15 33 57 80
18,19 (84pgs.; 18-20 titled ...Chuckleberry Tales) 7 14 21 44 82 120
20-Titled Chuckleberry Tales 4 8 12 28 47 65
21-30: 28-30-Reprints 4 8 12 23 37 50
31-43: 31,32,35,37-43-Reprints 3 6 9 19 30 40

HUCKLEBERRY HOUND (TV)
Charlton Comics: Nov, 1970 - No. 8, Jan, 1972 (Hanna-Barbera)
1 5 10 15 33 57 80
2-8 3 6 9 17 26 35

HUEY, DEWEY, & LOUIE (See Donald Duck, 1938 for 1st app. Also see Mickey Mouse Magazine V4#2, V5#7 & Walt Disney's Junior Woodchucks Limited Series)

HUEY, DEWEY, & LOUIE BACK TO SCHOOL (See Dell Giant #22, 35, 49 & Dell Giants)

HUEY, DEWEY, AND LOUIE JUNIOR WOODCHUCKS (Disney)
Gold Key No. 1-61/Whitman No. 62 on: Aug, 1966 - No. 81, July, 1984
(See Walt Disney's Comics & Stories #125)
1 8 16 24 54 102 150
2,3(12/68) 4 8 12 23 37 50
4,5(4/70)-r/two WDC&S D.Duck stories by Barks 3 6 9 19 30 40
6-17 3 6 9 17 26 35
18,27-30 3 6 9 15 21 26
19-23,25-New storyboarded scripts by Barks, 13-25 pgs. per issue
3 6 9 18 28 38
24,26: 26-r/Barks Donald Duck WDC&S stories 3 6 9 16 23 30
31-57,60,61: 35,41-r/Barks J.W. scripts 2 4 6 8 11 14
58,59: 58-r/Barks Donald Duck WDC&S stories 2 4 6 9 13 16
62-64 (Whitman) 2 4 6 9 13 16
65-(9/80), 66 (Pre-pack? scarce) 4 8 12 25 40 55
67 (1/81),68 2 4 6 9 13 16
67-40¢ cover variant 4 8 12 17 21 24
69-74: 72(2/82), 73(2-3/82), 74(3/82) 2 4 6 8 11 14
75-81 (all #90183; pre-pack; nd, nd code; scarce): 75(4/83), 76(5/83), 77(7/83), 78(8/83), 79(4/84), 80(5/84), 81(7/84) 3 6 9 16 23 30

HUGGA BUNCH (TV)
Marvel Comics (Star Comics): Oct, 1986 - No. 6, Aug, 1987
1-6 6.00

HULK (Magazine)(Formerly The Rampaging Hulk)(Also see The Incredible Hulk)
Marvel Comics: No. 10, Aug., 1978 - No. 27, June, 1981 ($1.50)
10-16,18: 10-Bill Bixby interview. 11-Moon Knight begins. 12-15,18-Moon Knight stories. 12-Lou Ferrigno interview. 3 6 9 14 20 25
17-Moon Knight story with 1st Randall Spector 7 14 21 46 86 125
19-27: 20-Moon Knight story. 23-Last full color issue; Banner is attacked. 24-Part color, Lou Ferrigno interview. 25-Part color. 26,27-are B&W
2 4 6 11 16 20

NOTE: #10-20 have fragile spines which split easily. ***Alcala*** *a(i)-15, 17-20, 22, 24-27.* ***Buscema*** *a-23; c-26.* ***Chaykin*** *a-21-25.* ***Colan*** *a(p)-11, 19, 24-27.* ***Jusko*** *painted c-12.* ***Nebres*** *a-16.* ***Severin*** *a-19i. Moon Knight by* ***Sienkiewicz*** *in 13-15, 17, 18, 20.* ***Simonson*** *a-27; c-23. Dominic Fortune appears in #21-24.*

HULK (Becomes Incredible Hulk Vol. 2 with issue #12) (Also see Marvel Age Hulk)
Marvel Comics: Apr, 1999 - No. 11, Feb, 2000 ($2.99/$1.99)
1-($2.99) Byrne-s/Garney-a 1 2 3 5 6 8
1-Variant-c 2 4 6 8 10 12
1-DFE Remarked-c 50.00
1-Gold foil variant 10.00
2-7-($1.99): 2-Two covers. 5-Art by Jurgens, Buscema & Texeira. 7-Avengers app. 4.00
8-Hulk battles Wolverine 2 4 6 9 12 15
9-11: 11-She-Hulk app. 3.00
1999 Annual ($3.50) Chapter One story; Byrne-s/Weeks-a 4.00
Hulk Vs. The Thing (12/99, $3.99, TPB) reprints their notable battles 4.00

HULK (Also see Fall of the Hulks and King-Size Hulk) (Becomes Red She-Hulk with #58)
Marvel Comics: Mar, 2008 - No. 57, Oct, 2012 ($2.99/$3.99)
1-Red Hulk app.; Abomination killed; Loeb-s/McGuinness-a/c
4 8 12 28 47 65
1-Variant-c by Acuña 4 8 12 28 47 65
1-Variant-c with Incredible Hulk #1 cover swipe by McGuinness 70.00
1,2-2nd printings with wraparound McGuinness variant-c 3.00
2-22: 2-Iron Man app.; Rick Jones becomes the new Abomination. 4,6-Red Hulk vs. green Hulk; two covers (each Hulk); Thor app. 7-9-Art Adams & Cho-a (2 covers) 10-Defenders re-form. 14,15-X-Force, Elektra & Deadpool app. 15-Red She-Hulk app. 19-21-Fall of the Hulks x-over. 19-FF app. 22-World War Hulks 4.00
2-9: 2-Variant-c by Djurdjevic. 3-Var-c by Finch. 5-Var-c by Coipel. 6,7-Var-c by Turner 8-Var-c by Sal Buscema. 9-Two covers w/Hulks as Santa 6.00
23-($4.99) Origin of the Red Hulk; art by Sale, Romita, Deodato, Trimpe, Yu, others 5.00
24-31-($3.99): 24-World war Hulks. 25,26-Iron Man app. 26-Thor app. 4.00
30.1, 32-49 ($2.99): 34-Planet Red Hulk begins. 37-38-Fear Itself tie-in 3.00
50-($3.99) Haunted Hulk; Dr. Strange app.; back-up w/Brereton-a; Pagulayan-c 4.00
50-Variant covers by Art Adams, Humberto Ramos & Walt Simonson 15.00
51-57: 53-57-Eaglesham-a; Alpha Flight app. 3.00
... Family: Green Genes 1 (2/09, $4.99) new She-Hulk, Scorpion, Skaar & Mr. Fixit stories
1 2 3 5 6 8
... Let the Battle Begin 1 (5/10, $3.99) Snider-s/Kurth-a; Del Mundo-c; McGuinness-a 4.00
... MGC #1 (6/10, $1.00) r/#1 with "Marvel's Greatest Comics" logo on cover
1 3 4 6 8 10
... Monster-Size Special (12/08, $3.99) monster-themed stories by Niles, David & others 4.00
...: Raging Thunder 1 (8/08, $3.99) Hulk vs. Thundra; Breitweiser-a; r/FF #133; Land-c
2 4 6 9 12 15
Hulk-Sized Mini-Hulks ('11, $2.99) Red, Green & Blue Hulks all-ages humor; Giarrusso-a
1 3 4 6 8 10
... Vs. Fin Fang Foom (2/08, $3.99) new re-telling of first meeting; r/Strange Tales #89
1 2 3 5 6 8
... Vs. Hercules (6/08, $3.99) Djurdjevic-c; new story w/art by various; r/Tales To Ast. #79
1 2 3 5 6 8
...: Winter Guard (2/10, $3.99) Darkstar, Crimson Dynamo app. Steve Ellis-a/c
1 3 4 6 8 10
Hulk 100 Project (2008, $10.00, SC, charity book for the HERO Initiative) collection of 100 variant covers by Adams, Romita Sr. & Jr., Cho, McGuinness and more 10.00

HULK (Follows Indestructible Hulk series)
Marvel Comics: Jun, 2014 - No. 16, Jul, 2015 ($3.99)
1-15: 1-4-Waid-s/Bagley-a. 3,4-Avengers app. 5-Alex Ross-c. 6-15-Duggan-s. 13,14-Deadpool app. 14-15-Hulk vs. Red Hulk 4.00
16-($4.99) Avengers app.; Duggan-s/Bagley-a; leads into Secret Wars 5.00
Annual 1 (11/14, $4.99) Monty Nero-s; art by Luke Ross, Goddard & Laming 5.00

HULK (Jennifer Walters as Hulk; follows events of Civil War II)(Continues as She-Hulk #159)
Marvel Comics: Feb, 2017 - No. 11, Dec, 2017 ($3.99)
1-11: 1-6-Mariko Tamaki-s/Nico Leon-a. 3,11-Hellcat app. 4.00

HULK (Follows Immortal Hulk series)
Marvel Comics: Jan, 2022 - Present ($4.99/$3.99)
1-($4.99) Donny Cates-s/Ryan Ottley-a 5.00
2-12-($3.99) 2-Alternate dimension Wolverine app. 7,8-Iron Man & Thor app. 4.00

HULK AND POWER PACK (All ages series)
Marvel Comics: May, 2007 - No. 4, Aug, 2007 ($2.99, limited series)
1-4-Sumerak-s. 1,2,4-Williams-a. 1-Absorbing Man app. 3-Kuhn-a; Abomination app. 3.00
...: Pack Smash! (2007, $6.99, digest) r/#1-4 7.00

HULK & THING: HARD KNOCKS
Marvel Comics: Nov, 2004 - No. 4, Feb, 2005 ($3.50, limited series)
1-4-Bruce Jones-s/Jae Lee-a/c 3.50
TPB (2005, $13.99) r/#1-4 and Giant-Size Super-Stars #1 14.00

HULK: BROKEN WORLDS
Marvel Comics: May, 2009 -No. 2, July, 2009 ($3.99, limited series)
1,2-Short stories of alternate world Hulks by various, incl. Trimpe, David, Warren 4.00

GD 2.0 | VG 4.0 | FN 6.0 | VF 8.0 | VF/NM 9.0 | NM- 9.2

HULK CHRONICLES: WWH
Marvel Comics: Oct, 2008 - No. 6, Mar, 2009 ($4.99, limited series)
1-6-Reprints stories from World War Hulk x-over. 1-R/Inc. Hulk #106 & WWH Prologue 5.00

HULK: DESTRUCTION
Marvel Comics: Sept, 2005 - No. 4, Dec, 2005 ($2.99, limited series)
1-4-Origin of the Abomination; Peter David-s/Jim Muniz-a 3.00

HULKED-OUT HEROES
Marvel Comics: Jun, 2010 - No. 2, Jun, 2010 ($3.99, limited series)
1,2-World War Hulks tie-in; Deadpool app.; Ramos-a 4.00

HULK: FUTURE IMPERFECT
Marvel Comics: Jan, 1993 - No. 2, Dec, 1992 (In error) ($5.95, 52 pgs., squarebound, limited series)
1,2: Embossed-c; Peter David story & George Perez-c/a. 1-1st app. Maestro.
3 6 9 14 20 25

HULK: GRAND DESIGN
Marvel Comics: May, 2022 - Jun, 2022 ($5.99, limited series)
... - Madness 1 (6/22, $5.99) Jim Rugg-s/a; revisits events from Inc. Hulk #301-474 6.00
... - Monster 1 (5/22, $5.99) Jim Rugg-s/a; revisits highlights from Inc. Hulk #1-300 6.00

HULK: GRAY
Marvel Comics: Dec, 2003 - No. 6, Apr, 2004 ($3.50, limited series)
1-6-Hulk's origin & early days; Loeb-s/Sale-a/c 4.00
HC (2004, $21.99, with dust jacket) oversized r/#1-6 22.00
SC (2005, $19.99) r/#1-6 20.00

HULKLING & WICCAN
Marvel Comics: Aug, 2022 ($5.99, one-shot)
1-Trujillo-s/Nishijima-a 6.00

HULK: NIGHTMERICA
Marvel Comics: Aug, 2003 - No. 6, May, 2004 ($2.99, limited series)
1-6-Brian Ashmore painted-a/c 4.00

HULK/ PITT
Marvel Comics: 1997 ($5.99, one-shot)
1-David-s/Keown-c/a 1 3 4 6 8 10

HULK: SEASON ONE
Marvel Comics: 2012 ($24.99, hardcover graphic novel)
HC - Origin and early days; Van Lente-s/Fowler-a/Tedesco painted-c 25.00

HULK SMASH
Marvel Comics: Mar, 2001 - No. 2, Apr, 2001 ($2.99, limited series)
1,2-Ennis-s/McCrea & Janson-a/Nowlan painted-c 3.00

HULK SMASH AVENGERS
Marvel Comics: Jul, 2012 - No. 5, July, 2012 ($2.99, weekly limited series)
1-5-Hulk vs. Avengers from various points in Marvel History. 1-Frenz-a. 5-Oeming-a 3.00

HULK: THE MOVIE
Marvel Comics
...Adaptation (8/03, $3.50) Bruce Jones-s/Bagley-a/Keown-c 4.00
TPB (2003, $12.99) r/Adaptation, Ultimates #5, Inc. Hulk #34, Ult. Marvel Team-Up #2&3 13.00

HULK 2099
Marvel Comics: Dec, 1994 - No. 10, Sept, 1995 ($1.50/$1.95)
1-($2.50)-Green foil-c 1 2 3 5 6 8
2-10: 2-A. Kubert-c 4.00

HULKVERINES
Marvel Comics: Apr, 2019 - No. 3, Jun, 2019 ($4.99)
1-3-Hulk, Weapon H, Wolverine and The Leader app.; Pak-s/Anindito-a 4.00

HULK VS. THOR: BANNER OF WAR ALPHA (Tie-in to Hulk #7,8, Thor #25,26 x-over)
Marvel Comics: Jun, 2022 ($4.99, one-shot)
1-Part 1 of x-over; Cates-s/Coccolo-a; The Watcher app.; continues in Thor #25 5.00

HULK/WOLVERINE: 6 HOURS
Marvel Comics: Mar, 2003 - No. 4, May, 2003 ($2.99, limited series)
1-4-Bruce Jones-s/Scott Kolins-a; Bisley-c 3.00
Hulk Legends Vol. 1: Hulk/Wolverine: 6 Hours (2003, $13.99, TPB) r/#1-4 & 1st Wolverine app. from Incredible Hulk #181 14.00

HUMAN BOMB
DC Comics: Feb, 2013 - No. 4, May, 2013 ($2.99, limited series)
1-4: 1-Re-intro/origin; Gray & Palmiotti-s/Ordway-a/c 3.00

HUMAN DEFENSE CORPS
DC Comics: Jul, 2003 - No. 6, Dec, 2003 ($2.50, limited series)
1-6-Ty Templeton-s/Sauve, Jr & Vlasco-a. 1-Lois Lane app. 3.00

HUMAN FLY
I.W. Enterprises/Super: 1963 - 1964 (Reprints)
I.W. Reprint #1-Reprints Blue Beetle #44('46) 3 6 9 15 22 28
Super Reprint #10-R/Blue Beetle #46('47) 3 6 9 15 22 28

HUMAN FLY, THE
Marvel Comics Group: Sept, 1977 - No. 19, Mar, 1979
1-(Regular 30¢-c) Origin; Spider-Man x-over 3 6 9 21 33 45
1-(35¢-c, limited distribution) 10 20 30 64 132 200
2-(Regular 30¢-c)-Ghost Rider app. 2 4 6 11 16 20
2-(35¢-c, limited distribution) 6 12 18 41 76 110
3-8,10-18 5.00
9,19: 9-Daredevil x-over; Byrne-c(p). 19-Last issue 2 4 6 8 10 12
NOTE: *Austin c-4i, 9i.* ***Elias*** *a-1, 3p, 4p, 7p, 10-12p, 15p, 18p, 19p.* ***Layton*** *c-19.*

HUMANKIND
Image Comics (Top Cow): Sept, 2004 - No. 5, Mar, 2005 ($2.99, limited series)
1-5-Tony Daniel-a. 1-Three covers by Daniel, Silvestri, and Land 3.00

HUMAN RACE, THE
DC Comics: May, 2005 - No. 7, Nov, 2005 ($2.99, limited series)
1-7-Raab-s/Justiniano-a/c 3.00

HUMAN TARGET
DC Comics (Vertigo): Apr, 1999 - No. 4, July, 1999 ($2.95, limited series)
1-4-Milligan-s/Bradstreet-c/Biukovic-a 3.00
1-Special Edition (6/10, $1.00) r/#1 with "What's Next?" logo on cover 3.00
TPB (2000, $12.95) new Bradstreet-c 13.00
...: Chance Meetings TPB (2010, $14.99) r/#1-4 and Human Target: Final Cut GN 15.00

HUMAN TARGET
DC Comics (Vertigo): Oct, 2003 - No. 21, June, 2005 ($2.95)
1-21: 1-5-Milligan-s/Pulido-a/c. 6-Chiang-a 3.00
...: Living in Amerika TPB (2004, $14.95) r/#6-10; Chiang sketch pages 15.00
...: Second Chances TPB (2011, $19.99) r/#1-10; Chiang sketch pages 20.00
...: Strike Zones TPB (2004, $9.95) r/#1-5 10.00

HUMAN TARGET (Based on the Fox TV series)
DC Comics: Apr, 2010 - No. 6, Sept, 2010 ($2.99, limited series)
1-6-Wein-s/Redondo-a; back-up stories by various. 1-Bermejo-c. 5-Sook-c 3.00
TPB (2010, $17.99) r/#1-6 18.00

HUMAN TARGET, THE (Also see Tales of the Human Target)
DC Comics (Black Label): Jan, 2022 - No. 12, Apr, 2023 ($4.99, limited series)
1-12-Tom King-s/Greg Smallwood-a; Ice app. 3,6-Guy Gardner app. 8-Rocket Red app. 5.00

HUMAN TARGET: FINAL CUT
DC Comics (Vertigo): 2002 ($29.95/$19.95, graphic novel)
Hardcover (2002, $29.95) Milligan-s/Pulido-a/c 30.00
Softcover (2003, $19.95) 20.00

HUMAN TARGET SPECIAL (TV)
DC Comics: Nov, 1991 ($2.00, 52 pgs., one-shot)
1 4.00

HUMAN TORCH, THE (Red Raven #1)(See All-Select, All Winners, Marvel Mystery, Men's Adventures, Mystic Comics (2nd series), Sub-Mariner, USA & Young Men)
Timely/Marvel Comics (TP 2,3/TCI 4-9/SePI 10/SnPC 11-25/CnPC 26-35/Atlas Comics (CPC 36-38)): No. 2, Fall, 1940 - No. 15, Spring, 1944; No. 16, Fall, 1944 - No. 35, Mar, 1949 (Becomes Love Tales #36 on); No. 36, April, 1954 - No. 38, Aug, 1954
2(#1)-Intro & Origin Toro; The Falcon, The Fiery Mask, Mantor the Magician, & Microman only app.; Human Torch by Burgos, Sub-Mariner by Everett begin (origin of each in text); WWII-c 3000 6000 9000 21,000 49,500 80,000
3(#2)-40 pg. H.T. story; H.T. & S.M. battle over who is best artist in text-Everett or Burgos 811 1622 2433 5920 10,460 15,000
4(#3)-Origin The Patriot in text; last Everett Sub-Mariner; Sid Greene-a 595 1190 1785 4350 7675 11,000
5(#4)-The Patriot app; Angel x-over in Sub-Mariner (Summer, 1941); 1st Nazi war-c this title; back-c ad for Young Allies #1 with diff. cover-a 486 972 1458 3550 6275 9000
5-Human Torch battles Sub-Mariner (Fall, '41); 60 pg. story 730 1460 2190 5329 9415 13,500
6-Schomburg hooded villain bondage-c 420 840 1260 2940 5170 7400
7-1st Japanese war-c 432 864 1296 3154 5577 8000
8-Human Torch battles Sub-Mariner; 52 pg. story; Wolverton-a, 1 pg.; Nazi WWII-c 703 1406 2109 5132 9066 13,000
9-Classic Human Torch vs. Gen. Rommel, "The Desert Rat"; Nazi WWII-c 459 918 1377 3350 5925 8500
10-Human Torch battles Sub-Mariner, 45 pg. story; Wolverton-a, 1 pg.; Nazi WWII-c 486 972 1458 3550 6275 9000
11,14,15: 11-Nazi WWII-c. 14-Nazi WWII-c; 1st Atlas Globe logo (Winter, 1943-44; see All Winners #11 also) 354 708 1062 2478 4339 6200
12-Classic Japanese WWII-c, Torch melts Japanese soldier's arm 1400 2800 4200 9800 18,900 28,000
13-Classic Schomburg Japanese WWII bondage-c 400 800 1200 2800 4900 7000
16-20: 16-18,20-Japanese WWII-c. 19-Bondage-c. 20-Last War issue 290 580 870 1856 3178 4500
21,22,24-30: 27-2nd app. (1st-c) Asbestos Lady (see Capt. America Comics #63 for 1st app.) 219 438 657 1402 2401 3400
23 (Sum/46)-Becomes Junior Miss 24? Classic Schomburg Robot-c 371 742 1113 2600 4550 6500
31,32: 31-Namora x-over in Sub-Mariner (also #30); last Toro. 32-Sungirl, Namora app.; Sungirl-c 194 388 582 1242 2121 3000
33-Capt. America x-over 239 478 717 1530 2615 3700
34-Sungirl solo 194 388 582 1242 2121 3000
35-Captain America & Sungirl app. (1949) 194 388 582 1242 2121 3000
36-38(1954)-Sub-Mariner in all 161 322 483 1030 1765 2500
NOTE: *Ayers Human Torch in 36(3).* ***Brodsky*** *c-25, 31-33?, 37, 38.* ***Burgos*** *c-36.* ***Everett*** *a-1-3, 27, 28, 30, 37, 38.* ***Powell*** *a-36(Sub-Mariner).* ***Schomburg*** *c-1-3, 5-8, 10-23.* ***Sekowsky*** *c-28, 34?, 35?* ***Shores*** *c-24, 26, 27, 29, 30.* ***Mickey Spillane*** *text 4-6. Bondage c-2, 12, 19.*

HUMAN TORCH, THE (Also see Avengers West Coast, Fantastic Four, The Invaders, Saga of the Original... & Strange Tales #101)
Marvel Comics Group: Sept, 1974 - No. 8, Nov, 1975
1: 1-8-r/stories from Strange Tales #101-108 6 12 18 37 66 95
2-8: 1st H.T. title since G.A. 7-vs. Sub-Mariner 3 6 9 16 23 30
NOTE: *Golden Age & Silver Age Human Torch-r #1-8.* ***Ayers*** *r-6, 7.* ***Kirby/Ayers*** *r-1-5, 8.*

HUMAN TORCH (From the Fantastic Four)
Marvel Comics: June, 2003 - No. 12, Jun, 2004 ($2.50/$2.99)
1-7-Skottie Young-c/a; Karl Kesel-s 3.00
8-12-($2.99) 8,10-Dodd-a. 9-Young-a. 11-Porter-a. 12-Medina-a 3.00
... Vol. 1: Burn TPB (2005, $7.99, digest size) r/#1-6 8.00

HUMAN TORCH COMICS 70TH ANNIVERSARY SPECIAL
Marvel Comics: July, 2009 ($3.99, one-shot)
1-Covers by Granov and Martin; new story and r/1st app Toro from Human Torch #2 5.00

HUMBUG (Satire by Harvey Kurtzman)
Humbug Publications: Aug, 1957 - No. 9, May, 1958; No. 10, June, 1958; No. 11, Oct, 1958
1-Wood-a (intro pgs. only) 28 56 84 165 270 375

Human Target (2021) #9 © DC

Huntress (2011) #1 © DC

Hyperion #1 © MAR

	GD 2.0	VG 4.0	FN 6.0	VF 8.0	VF/NM 9.0	NM- 9.2
2	15	30	45	85	130	175
3-9: 8-Elvis in Jailbreak Rock	14	28	42	76	108	140
10,11-Magazine format. 10-Photo-c	15	30	45	90	140	190
Bound Volume(#1-9)(extremely rare)	65	130	195	416	708	1000

NOTE: *Davis a-1-11. Elder a-2-4, 6-9, 11. Heath a-2, 4-8, 10. Jaffee a-2, 4-9. Kurtzman a-11.*

HUMDINGER (Becomes White Rider and Super Horse #3 on?)
Novelty Press/Premium Group: May-June, 1946 - V2#2, July-Aug, 1947

	GD 2.0	VG 4.0	FN 6.0	VF 8.0	VF/NM 9.0	NM- 9.2
1-Jerkwater Line, Mickey Starlight by Don Rico, Dink begin	39	78	117	231	378	525
2	16	32	48	98	154	210
3-6, V2#1,2	13	26	39	74	105	135

HUMONGOUS MAN
Alternative Press (Ikon Press): Sept, 1997 -No. 3 ($2.25, B&W)

1-3-Stepp & Harrison-c/s/a. 3.00

HUMOR (See All Humor Comics)

HUMPHREY COMICS (Joe Palooka Presents...; also see Joe Palooka)
Harvey Publications: Oct, 1948 - No. 22, Apr, 1952

	GD 2.0	VG 4.0	FN 6.0	VF 8.0	VF/NM 9.0	NM- 9.2
1-Joe Palooka's pal (r); (52 pgs.)-Powell-a	16	32	48	94	147	200
2,3: Powell-a	10	20	30	54	72	90
4-Boy Heroes app.; Powell-a	10	20	30	58	79	100
5-8,10: 5,6-Powell-a. 7-Little Dot app.	8	16	24	42	54	65
9-Origin Humphrey	9	18	27	50	65	80
11-22	8	16	24	40	50	60

HUNCHBACK OF NOTRE DAME, THE
Dell Publishing Co.: No. 854, Oct, 1957 (one shot)

	GD 2.0	VG 4.0	FN 6.0	VF 8.0	VF/NM 9.0	NM- 9.2
Four Color 854-Movie, photo-c	12	24	36	79	170	260

HUNGER (See Age of Ultron and Cataclysm titles)
Marvel Comics: Sept, 2013 - No. 4, Dec, 2013 ($3.99, limited series)

1-4-Fialkov-s/Kirk-a/Granov-c; Galactus in the Ultimate Universe. 2-4-Silver Surfer app. 4.00
1-Variant-c by Neal Adams 18.00

HUNGER, THE
Speakeasy Comics: May, 2005 ($2.99)

1-Andy Bradshaw-s/a; Eric Powell-c 3.00

HUNGER DOGS, THE (See DC Graphic Novel #4)

HUNGRY GHOSTS
Dark Horse Comics (Berger Books): Jan, 2018 - No. 4, Apr, 2018 ($3.99, limited series)

1-4-Anthony Bourdain & Joel Rose-s/Paul Pope-c. 1-Ponticelli & Del Rey-a. 2-Manco & Santolouco-a. 3-Cabrol & Paul Pope-a. 4-Francavilla & Koh-a 4.00

HUNK
Charlton Comics: Aug, 1961 - No. 11, 1963

	GD 2.0	VG 4.0	FN 6.0	VF 8.0	VF/NM 9.0	NM- 9.2
1	4	8	12	23	37	50
2-11	3	6	9	14	20	25

HUNT, THE
Image Comics (Shadowline): Jul, 2016 - No. 5, Dec, 2016 ($3.99)

1-5-Colin Lorimer-s/a 4.00

HUNTED (Formerly My Love Memoirs)
Fox Feature Syndicate: No. 13, July, 1950; No. 2, Sept, 1950

	GD 2.0	VG 4.0	FN 6.0	VF 8.0	VF/NM 9.0	NM- 9.2
13(#1)-Used in **SOTI**, pg. 42 & illo. "Treating police contemptuously" (lower left); Hollingsworth bondage-c	71	142	213	454	777	1100
2	25	50	75	150	245	340

HUNTER-KILLER
Image Comics (Top Cow): Nov, 2004 - No. 12, Mar, 2007 ($2.99)

0-(11/04, 25¢) Prelude with Silvestri sketch page and Waid afterword 3.00
1-12: 1-(3/05, $2.99) Waid-s/Silvestri-a; four covers. 2-Linsner variant-c 3.00
... Collected Edition Vol. 1 (9/05, $4.99) r/#0-3 5.00
...Dossier 1 (9/05, $2.99) character profiles with art by various; Migliari-c 3.00
... Volume 1 TPB (1/08, $24.99) r/#0-12; Dossier and Script Book; variant covers 25.00

HUNTER: THE AGE OF MAGIC (See Books of Magic)
DC Comics (Vertigo): Sept, 2001 - No. 25, Sept, 2003 ($2.50/$2.75)

1-25: Horrocks-s/Case-a. 1-8-Bolton-c. 14-Begin $2.75-c. 19-Bachalo-c 3.00

HUNT FOR WOLVERINE (Leads into Return of Wolverine series)
Marvel Comics: Jun, 2018 ($5.99)

1-Soule-s; Logan's removal from the statue; X-Men, Tony Stark, Daredevil app. 6.00
...: Dead Ends 1 (10/18, $4.99) Soule-s/Rosanas-a; conclusion to story 5.00

HUNT FOR WOLVERINE: ADAMANTIUM AGENGA
Marvel Comics: Jul, 2018 - No. 4, Oct, 2018 ($3.99, limited series)

1-4-Iron Man, Spider-Man, Jessica Jones & Luke Cage app.; Taylor-s/Silva-a 4.00

HUNT FOR WOLVERINE: CLAWS OF A KILLER
Marvel Comics: Jul, 2018 - No. 4, Oct, 2018 ($3.99, limited series)

1-4-Sabretooth, Daken & Lady Deathstrike app.; Tamaki-s/Guice-a 4.00

HUNT FOR WOLVERINE: MYSTERY IN MADRIPOOR
Marvel Comics: Jul, 2018 - No. 4, Oct, 2018 ($3.99, limited series)

1-4-Psylocke, Storm, Rogue, Jubilee, Kitty Pryde & Domino app.; Zub-s/Silas-a 4.00

HUNT FOR WOLVERINE: WEAPON LOST
Marvel Comics: Jul, 2018 - No. 4, Oct, 2018 ($3.99, limited series)

1-4-Daredevil, Misty Knight & Cypher app.; Soule-s/Buffagni-a 4.00

HUNTRESS, THE (See All-Star Comics #69, Batman Family, DC Super Stars #17, Detective #652, Infinity, Inc. #1 & Wonder Woman #271)
DC Comics: Apr, 1989 - No. 19, Oct, 1990 ($1.00, mature)

	GD 2.0	VG 4.0	FN 6.0	VF 8.0	VF/NM 9.0	NM- 9.2
1-Staton-c/a(p) in all	2	4	6	9	12	15
2-19: 17-19-Batman-c/stories						4.00
...: Darknight Daughter TPB (2006, $19.99) r/origin & early apps. in DC Super Stars #17, Batman Family #18-20 & Wonder Woman #271-287,289,290,294,295; Bolland-c						20.00

HUNTRESS, THE
DC Comics: June, 1994 - No. 4, Sept, 1994 ($1.50, limited series)

1-4-Netzer-c/a: 2-Batman app. 4.00

HUNTRESS (Leads into 2012 World's Finest series)
DC Comics: Dec, 2011 - No. 6, May, 2012 ($2.99, limited series)

1-6-Levitz-s/To-a/March-c 3.00

HUNTRESS: YEAR ONE
DC Comics: Early July, 2008 - No. 6, Late Sept, 2008 ($2.99, limited series)

1-6-Origin re-told; Cliff Richards-a/Ivory Madison-s 3.00
TPB (2009, $17.99) r/#1-6; intro. by Paul Levitz 18.00

HURRICANE COMICS
Cambridge House: 1945 (52 pgs.)

	GD 2.0	VG 4.0	FN 6.0	VF 8.0	VF/NM 9.0	NM- 9.2
1-(Humor, funny animal)	34	68	102	199	325	450

HYBRIDS
Continunity Comics: Jan, 1994 ($2.50, one-shot)

1-Neal Adams-c(p) & part-a(i); embossed-c. 4.00

HYBRIDS DEATHWATCH 2000
Continuity Comics: Apr, 1993 - No. 3, Aug, 1993 ($2.50)

0-(Giveaway)-Foil-c; Neal Adams-c(i) & plots (also #1,2) 4.00
1-3: 1-Polybagged w/card; die-cut-c. 2-Thermal-c. 3-Polybagged w/card; indestructible-c; Adams plot 4.00

HYBRIDS ORIGIN
Continunity Comics: 1993 - No. 5, Jan, 1994 ($2.50)

1-5: 2,3-Neal Adams-c. 4,5-Valeria the She-Bat app. Adams-c(i) 4.00

HYDE
IDW Publ.: Oct, 2004 ($7.49, one-shot)

1-Steve Niles-s/Nick Stakal 7.50

HYDE-25
Harris Publications: Apr, 1995 ($2.95, one-shot)

0-Coupon for poster; r/Vampirella's 1st app. 3.00

HYDROMAN (See Heroic Comics)

HYPERION (Squadron Supreme)
Marvel Comics: May, 2016 - No. 6, Oct, 2016 ($3.99)

1-6: 1-4,6-Wendig-s/Virella-a. 5-Anindito-a. 5,6-Iron Man & Thundra app. 4.00

HYPERKIND (See Razorline)
Marvel Comics: Sept, 1993 - No. 9, May, 1994 ($1.75/$1.95)

1-($2.50)-Foil embossed-c; by Clive Barker 4.00
2-9 3.00
...Unleashed 1 (8/94, $2.95, 52 pgs., one-shot) 4.00

HYPER MYSTERY COMICS
Hyper Publications: May, 1940 - No. 2, June, 1940 (68 pgs.)

	GD 2.0	VG 4.0	FN 6.0	VF 8.0	VF/NM 9.0	NM- 9.2
1-Hyper, the Phenomenal begins; Calkins-a	300	600	900	1950	3375	4800
2-H.G. Peter-a	181	362	543	1158	1979	2800

HYPERNATURALS
BOOM! Studios: Jul, 2012 - No. 12, Jun, 2013 ($3.99)

1-12: 1-Abnett & Lanning-s/Walker & Guinaldo-a; at least eight covers. 2-Two printings 4.00

GD VG FN VF VF/NM NM-
2.0 4.0 6.0 8.0 9.0 9.2

... Free Comic Book Day Edition (5/12) Prelude to issue #1 3.00

HYPERSONIC
Dark Horse Comics: Nov, 1997 - No. 4, Feb, 1998 ($2.95, limited series)
1-4: Abnett & White-s/Erskine-a 3.00

I AIM AT THE STARS (Movie)
Dell Publishing Co.: No. 1148, Nov-Jan/1960-61 (one-shot)
Four Color 1148-The Werner Von Braun Sty-photo-c 7 14 21 44 82 120

I AM AN AVENGER (See Avengers, Young Avengers and Pet Avengers)
Marvel Comics: Nov, 2010 - No. 5, Mar, 2011 ($3.99, limited series)
1-5-Short stories by various. 1-Yu-c. 2-Land-c. 2-4-Mayhew-a. 3-Noto-c. 4-Acuña-c 4.00

I AM BATMAN (Jace Fox from Future State)(Story continued from The Next Batman; Second Son)
DC Comics: No. 0, Oct, 2021 - No. 18, Apr, 2023 ($4.99/$3.99)
0-($4.99) John Ridley-s/Travel Foreman-a 5.00
1-18-($3.99) Ridley-s. 1-4-Segovia-a. 13,14-The Question app. 15-Sinestro app. 4.00

I AM CAPTAIN AMERICA
Marvel Comics: Jan, 2012 ($3.99, one-shot)
1-Collection of Captain America-themed 70th Anniversary covers with artist profiles 4.00

I AM COYOTE (See Eclipse Graphic Album Series & Eclipse Magazine #2)

I AM GROOT (Guardians of the Galaxy)
Marvel Comics: Jul, 2017 - No. 5, Nov, 2017 ($3.99, limited series)
1-Hastings-s/Flaviano-a; Guardians of the Galaxy app.
1 3 4 6 8 10
2-5: 5-Guardians of the Galaxy app. 4.00

I AM IRON MAN
Marvel Comics: May, 2023 - Present ($3.99)
1-Murewa Ayodele-s/Dotun Akande-a 4.00

I AM LEGEND
Eclipse Books: 1991 - No. 4, 1991 ($5.95, B&W, squarebound, 68 pgs.)
1-4: Based on 1954 novel by Richard Matheson 1 2 3 5 6 8

I AM LEGION (English version of French graphic novel Je Suis Légion)
Devils Due Publishing: Jan, 2009 - No. 6, July, 2009 ($3.50)
1-6-John Cassaday-a/Fabien Nury-s; two covers 3.50

IBIS, THE INVINCIBLE (See Fawcett Miniatures, Mighty Midget & Whiz)
Fawcett Publications: 1942 (Fall?); #2, Mar.,1943; #3, Wint, 1945 - #5, Fall, 1946; #6, Spring, 1948
1-Origin Ibis; Raboy-c; on sale 1/2/43 271 542 813 1734 2967 4200
2-Bondage-c (on sale 2/5/43) 113 226 339 718 1234 1750
3-Wolverton-a #3-6 (4 pgs. each) 77 154 231 493 847 1200
4-6: 5-Bondage-c 53 106 159 334 567 800
NOTE: *Mac Raboy c(p)-3-5. Schaffenberger c-6.*

I-BOTS (See Isaac Asimov's I-BOTS)

I CAN SELL YOU A BODY
IDW Publ.: Dec, 2019 - No. 4, Mar, 2020 ($3.99)
1-4-Ryan Ferrier-s/George Kambadais-a 4.00

ICE AGE ON THE WORLD OF MAGIC: THE GATHERING (See Magic The Gathering)

ICE CREAM MAN (Horror anthology)
Image Comics: Jan, 2018 - Present ($3.99)
1-Prince-s/Morazzo-a; 1st app. of the Ice Cream Man
9 18 27 59 117 175
1-2nd printing 5 10 15 33 57 80
2 4 8 12 23 37 50
3-15 2 4 6 10 14 18
16-24,26-34: 17-Action Comics #1 cover swipe. 20-Dr. Seuss homage (10 pgs.) 4.00
25-($4.99) Bonus back-up story 5.00
... Presents Quarantine Comix Special 1 (9/20, $5.99) Printing of online mini-comics
2 4 6 10 14 18

ICE KING OF OZ, THE (See First Comics Graphic Novel #13)

ICEMAN (Also see The Champions & X-Men #94)
Marvel Comics Group: Dec, 1984 - No. 4, June, 1985 (Limited series)
1,2,4: Zeck covers on all 4.00
3-The Defenders, Champions (Ghost Rider) & the original X-Men x-over 5.00

ICEMAN (X-Men)
Marvel Comics: Dec, 2001 - No. 4, Mar, 2002 ($2.50, limited series)
1-4-Abnett & Lanning-s/Kerschl-a 3.00

ICEMAN (X-Men)
Marvel Comics: Aug, 2017 - No. 11, May, 2018 ($3.99)
1-11: 1-Grace-s/Vitti-a. 2-Kitty Pryde app. 5-Juggernaut app. 4.00

ICEMAN (X-Men)
Marvel Comics: Nov, 2018 - No. 5, Mar, 2019 ($3.99, limited series)
1-5: 1-Grace-s/Stockman-a. 2-White Queen app. 4,5-Mr. Sinister app. 4.00

ICEMAN AND ANGEL (X-Men)
Marvel Comics: May, 2011 ($2.99, one-shot)
1-Brian Clevinger-s/Juan Doe-a; Goom & Googam app. 3.00

ICON
DC Comics (Milestone): May, 1993 - No. 42, Feb, 1997 ($1.50/$1.75/$2.50)
1-($2.95)-Collector's Edition polybagged w/poster & trading card (direct sale only)
2 4 6 11 16 20
1-Regular edition 2 4 6 9 12 15
2-24,30-42: 9-Simonson-c. 15,16-Worlds Collide Pt. 4 & 11. 15-Superboy app.
16-Superman-c/story. 40-Vs. Blood Syndicate 4.00
25-($2.95, 52 pgs.) 6.00
... A Hero's Welcome SC (2009, $19.99) r/#1-8; intro. by Reginald Hudlin
3 6 9 21 33 45
...: Mothership Connection SC (2010, $24.99) r/#13,19-22,24-27,30 25.00

GD VG FN VF VF/NM NM-
2.0 4.0 6.0 8.0 9.0 9.2

ICON & ROCKET: SEASON ONE
DC Comics: Sept, 2021 - No. 6, May, 2022 ($3.99)
1-6-Hudlin-s/Braithwaite-a. 5,6-Static app. 4.00

ICON VS. HARDWARE
DC Comics: Apr, 2023 - Present ($4.99)
1-Hudlin & Chills-s/Cowan & Montanez-a 4.00

IDAHO
Dell Publishing Co.: June-Aug, 1963 - No. 8, July-Sept, 1965
1 3 6 9 18 27 36
2-8: 5-7-Painted-c 2 4 6 9 13 16

IDEAL (... a Classical Comic) (2nd Series) (Love Romances No. 6 on)
Timely Comics: July, 1948 - No. 5, March, 1949 (Feature length stories)
1-Antony & Cleopatra 42 84 126 265 445 625
2-The Corpses of Dr. Sacotti 36 72 108 211 343 475
3-Joan of Arc; used in **SOTI**, pg. 310 'Boer War' 33 66 99 194 317 440
4-Richard the Lion-hearted; titled "...the World's Greatest Comics";
The Witness story 45 90 135 284 480 675
5-Ideal Love & Romance; change to love; photo-c 22 44 66 132 216 300

IDEAL COMICS (1st Series) (Willie Comics No. 5 on)
Timely Comics (MgPC): Fall, 1944 - No. 4, Spring, 1946
1-Funny animal; Super Rabbit in all 47 94 141 296 498 700
2 24 48 72 142 234 325
3,4 21 42 63 126 206 285

IDEAL LOVE & ROMANCE (See Ideal, A Classical Comic)

IDEAL ROMANCE (Formerly Tender Romance)
Key Publ.: No. 3, April, 1954 - No. 8, Feb, 1955 (Diary Confessions No. 9 on)
3-Bernard Baily-c 14 28 42 80 115 150
4-8: 4-6-B. Baily-c 10 20 30 56 76 95

IDEALS (Secret Stories)
Ideals Publ., USA: 1981 (68 pgs, graphic novels, 7x10", stiff-c)
Captain America - Star Spangled Super Hero 3 6 9 19 30 40
Fantastic Four - Cosmic Quartet 3 6 9 19 30 40
Incredible Hulk - Gamma Powered Goliath 3 6 9 19 30 40
Spider-Man - World Famous Wall Crawler 4 8 12 23 37 50

IDENTITY CRISIS
DC Comics: Aug, 2004 - No. 7, Feb, 2005 ($3.95, limited series)
1-Meltzer-s/Morales-a/Turner-c in all; Sue Dibny murdered 5.00
1-(Second printing) black-c with white sketch lines 5.00
1-(3rd & 4th) 3rd-Bloody broken photo glass image-c by Morales. 4th-Turner red-c 4.00
1-Diamond Retailer Summit Edition with sketch-c 30.00
1-Special Edition (6/09, $1.00) r/#1 with "After Watchmen" cover frame 3.00
2-7: 2-4-Deathstroke app. 5-Firestorm, Jack Drake, Capt. Boomerang killed 4.00
2-(Second printing) new Morales sketch-c 4.00
Final printings for all issues with red background variant covers 4.00
HC (2005, $24.99, dust jacket) r/series; Director's Cut extras; cover gallery; Whedon intro.;
2 covers: Direct Market-c by Turner, Bookstore-c with Morales-a 25.00
SC (2006, $14.99) r/series; Director's Cut extras; cover gallery; Whedon intro 15.00

IDENTITY DISC
Marvel Comics: Aug, 2004 - No. 5, Dec, 2004 ($2.99, limited series)
1-5-Sabretooth, Bullseye, Sandman, Vulture, Deadpool, Juggernaut app.; Higgins-a 4.00
TPB (2004, $13.99) r/#1-5 14.00

IDES OF BLOOD
DC Comics (WildStorm): Oct, 2010 - No. 6, Mar, 2011 ($3.99/$2.99, limited series)
1-6-Stuart Paul-s/Christian Duce-a/Michael Geiger-c; Roman Empire vampires 4.00

I DIE AT MIDNIGHT (Vertigo V2K)
DC Comics (Vertigo): 2000 ($6.95, prestige format, one-shot)
1-Kyle Baker-s/a 7.00

IDOL
Marvel Comics (Epic Comics): 1992 - No. 3, 1992 ($2.95, mini-series, 52 pgs.)
Book 1-3 4.00

IDOLIZED
Aspen MLT: No. 0, Jun, 2012 - No. 5, Apr, 2013 ($2.50/$3.99)
0-($2.50) Schwartz-s/Gunnell-a; regular & photo covers; Superhero Idol background 3.00
1-5-($3.99) 1-Art Adams & photo covers; origin of Joule 4.00

I DREAM OF JEANNIE (TV)
Dell Publishing Co.: Apr, 1966 - No. 2, Dec, 1966 (Photo-c)
1-Barbara Eden photo-c, each 22 44 66 154 340 525
2 10 20 30 66 138 210

I FEEL SICK
Slave Labor Graphics: Aug, 1999 - No. 2, May, 2000 ($3.95, limited series)
1,2-Jhonen Vasquez-s/a 4.00

IGNITED
Humanoids, Inc.: 2019 - Present ($3.99)
1-8: 1-Waid & Osajvefo-s/Briones-a 4.00

I HATE FAIRYLAND (Also see I Hate Image, FCBD Special)
Image Comics: Oct, 2015 - No. 20, Jul, 2018 ($3.50/$3.99)
1-10-Skottie Young-s/a/c; each has variant cover with "F*** Fairyland" title 3.50
11-20-($3.99) 12-Lone Wolf & Cub homage-c. 13-Rankine-a. 20-Finale 4.00
...: I Hate Image Special Edition (10/17, $5.99) r/I Hate Image FCBD Special with 4 new pages; bonus script and sketch art; 2 covers 6.00

I HATE FAIRYLAND (Volume 2)
Image Comics: Nov, 2022 - Present ($3.99)
1-4-Skottie Young-s/Brett Bean-a; Gert as a young adult 4.00

I HATE GALLANT GIRL
Image Comics (Shadowline): Nov, 2008 - No. 3, Jan, 2009 ($3.50, limited series)

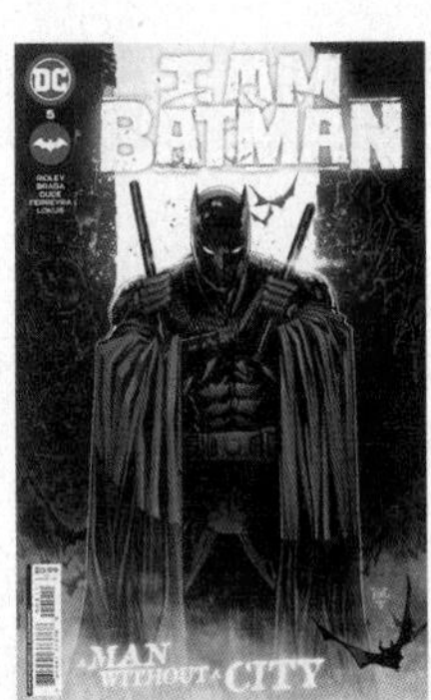

I Am Batman #5 © DC

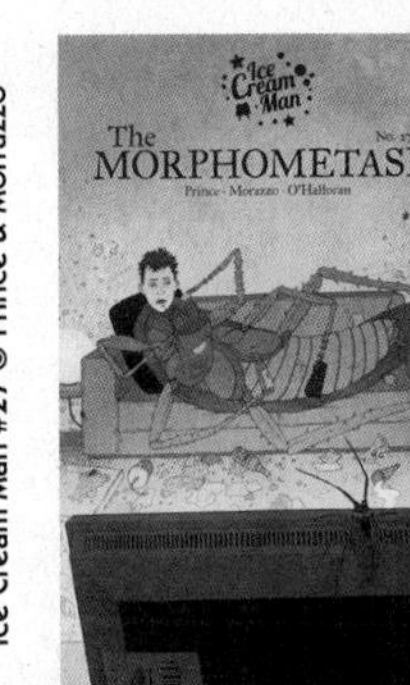

Ice Cream Man #27 © Prince & Morrazzo

I Love Lucy #10 © Desilu

GD 2.0 | VG 4.0 | FN 6.0 | VF 8.0 | VF/NM 9.0 | NM- 9.2

1-3-Kat Cahill-s/Seth Damoose-a 3.50

I HATE IMAGE, FCBD SPECIAL
Image Comics: May, 2017 (free giveaway)

1-Gert from I Hate Fairyland vs. Image characters from Walking Dead, Bitch Planet, Saga, Paper Girls, Chew, Spawn and others; Skottie Young-s/a/c 3.00

I (heart) MARVEL
Marvel Comics: Apr, 2006; May, 2006 ($2.99, one-shots)

...: Marvel AI 1 (4/06) Cebulski-s; manga art by various; Vision, Daredevil, Elektra app. 3.00
...: Masked Intentions 1 (5/06) Squirrel Girl, Speedball, Firestar, Justice app.; Nicieza-s 4.00
...: My Mutant Heart 1 (4/06) Wolverine, Cannonball, Doop app. 3.00
...: Outlaw Love 1 (4/06) Bullseye, The Answer, Ruby Thursday app.; Nicieza-s 3.00
...: Web of Romance 1 (4/06) Spider-Man, Mary Jane, The Avengers app. 3.00

ILLEGITIMATES, THE
IDW Publishing: Dec, 2013 - No. 6, May, 2014 ($3.99)

1-6: 1-Taran Killam & Marc Andreyko-a/Kevin Sharpe-a; covers by Ordway & Willingham 4.00

ILLUMUNATI
Marvel Comics: Jan, 2016 - No. 7, Jul, 2016 ($3.99)

1-7: 1-Williamson-s/Crystal-a; The Hood, Titania and others team. 4-Thor app. 4.00

ILLUMINATOR
Marvel Comics/Nelson Publ.: 1993 - No. 4, 1993 ($4.99/$2.95, 52 pgs.)

1,2-($4.99) Religious themed 5.00
3,4 4.00

ILLUSTRATED GAGS
United Features Syndicate: No. 16, 1940

Single Series 16 24 48 72 142 234 325

ILLUSTRATED LIBRARY OF..., AN (See Classics Illustrated Giants)

ILLUSTRATED STORIES OF THE OPERAS
Baily (Bernard) Publ. Co.: 1943 (16 pgs.; B&W) (25 cents) (covers are black & red ink on white or yellow paper, with scarcer editions having B&W with red)

nn-(Rare)(4 diff. issues)-Faust (part-r in Cisco Kid #1, 2 cover versions: 25¢ & no price) nn-Aida, nn-Carmen; Baily-a, nn-Rigoletto 87 174 261 553 952 1350

ILLUSTRATED STORY OF ROBIN HOOD & HIS MERRY MEN, THE (See Classics Giveaways, 12/44)

ILLUSTRATED TARZAN BOOK, THE (See Tarzan Book)

I LOVED (Formerly Rulah; Colossal Features Magazine No. 33 on)
Fox Feature Syndicate: No. 28, July, 1949 - No. 32, Mar, 1950

28 25 50 75 150 245 340
29-32 19 38 57 111 176 240

I LOVE LUCY
Eternity Comics : 6/90 - No. 6, 1990;V2#1, 11/90 - No. 6, 1991 ($2.95, B&W, mini-series)

1-6: Reprints 1950s comic strip; photo-c 4.00
Book II #1-6: Reprints comic strip; photo-c 4.00
...In Full Color 1 (1991, $5.95, 52 pgs.)-Reprints I Love Lucy Comics #4,5,8,16; photo-c with embossed logo (2 versions exist, one with pgs. 18 & 19 reversed, the other corrected) 1 2 3 5 6 8
...In 3-D 1 (1991, $3.95, w/glasses)-Reprints I Love Lucy Comics; photo-c; bagged 6.00

I LOVE LUCY COMICS (TV) (Also see The Lucy Show)
Dell Publishing Co.: No. 535, Feb, 1954 - No. 35, Apr-June, 1962 (Lucille Ball photo-c on all)

Four Color 535(#1) 48 96 144 374 862 1350
Four Color 559(#2, 5/54) 30 60 90 216 483 750
3 (8-10/54) - 5 17 34 51 114 252 390
6-10 13 26 39 87 191 295
11-20 10 20 30 68 144 220
21-35 9 18 27 59 117 175

I LOVE NEW YORK
Linsner.com: 2002 ($2.95, B&W, one-shot)

1-Linsner-s/a; benefit book for the Sept. 11 charities 3.00

I LOVE YOU
Fawcett Publications: June, 1950 (one-shot)

1-Photo-c 19 38 57 111 176 240

I LOVE YOU (Formerly In Love)
Charlton Comics: No. 7, 9/55 - No. 121, 12/76; No. 122, 3/79 - No. 130, 5/80

7-Kirby-c; Powell-a 9 18 27 63 129 195
8-10 5 10 15 34 60 85
11-16,18-20 5 10 15 31 53 75
17-(68 pg. Giant) 7 14 21 49 92 135
21-50: 26-No Torres-a 4 8 12 25 40 55
51-59 3 6 9 21 33 45
60-(1/66)-Elvis Presley line drawn c/story 17 34 51 114 252 390
61-85 3 6 9 16 23 30
86-90,92-98,100-110 2 4 6 8 11 14
91-(5/71) Ditko-a (5 pgs.) 3 6 9 14 19 24
99-David Cassidy pin-up 2 4 6 11 16 20
111-113,115-130 2 4 6 8 10 12
114-Psychedelic cover 3 6 9 18 28 38

I, LUSIPHUR (Becomes Poison Elves, 1st series #8 on)
Mulehide Graphics: 1991 - No. 7, 1992 (B&W, magazine size)

1-Drew Hayes-c/a/scripts 7 14 21 46 86 125
2,4,5 3 6 9 14 20 25
3-Low print run 4 8 12 27 44 60
6,7 2 4 6 8 11 14
Poison Elves: Requiem For An Elf (Sirius Ent., 6/96, $14.95, trade paperback) -Reprints I, Lusiphur #1,2 as text, and 3-6 15.00

I'M A COP
Magazine Enterprises: 1954 - No. 3, 1954

1(A-1 #111)-Powell-c/a in all 19 38 57 111 176 240
2(A-1 #126), 3(A-1 #128) 13 26 39 74 105 135

IMAGE COMICS HARDCOVER
Image Comics: 2005 ($24.99, hardcover with dust jacket)

Vol. 1-New Spawn by McFarlane-s/a; Savage Dragon origin by Larsen; CyberForce by Silvestri; ShadowHawk by Valentino; intro by Marder; Image timeline 25.00

IMAGE COMICS SUMMER SPECIAL
Image Comics: July, 2004 (Free Comic Book Day giveaway)

1-New short stories of Spawn, Invincible, Savage Dragon and Witchblade 3.00

IMAGE FIRST
Image Comics: 2005 ($6.99, TPB)

Vol. 1 (2005) r/Strange Girl #1, Sea of Red #1, The Walking Dead #1 and Girls #1 3 6 9 14 20 25

IMAGE FIRSTS (Reprints of first issues)
Image Comics: Feb, 2021 ($1.00, series of one-shots)

...: Ascender #1 - Lemire-s/Nguyen-a 3.00
...: Bitter Root #1 - Walker & Brown-s/Greene-a 3.00
...: Die #1 - Gillen-s/Hans-a 3.00
...: Killadelphia #1 - Barnes-s/Alexander-a 3.00
...: Mercy #1 - Mirka Andolfo-a 3.00
...: The Old Guard #1 - Rucka-s/Fernández-a 3.00
...: Undiscovered Country #1 - Snyder & Soule-s/Camuncoli-a 3.00

IMAGE GRAPHIC NOVEL
Image Int.: 1984 ($6.95)(Advertised as Pacific Comics Graphic Novel #1)

1-The Seven Samuroid; Brunner-c/a 12.00

IMAGE HOLIDAY SPECIAL 2005
Image Comics: 2005 ($9.99, TPB)

nn-Holiday-themed short stories by various incl. Walking Dead by Kirkman; Larsen, Kurtz, Valentino; Frank Cho-c 3 6 9 14 20 25

IMAGE INTRODUCES...
Image Comics: Oct, 2001 - June, 2002 ($2.95, anthology)

Believer #1-Schamberger-s/Thurman & Molder-a; Legend of Isis preview 3.00
Cryptopia #1-Raab-s/Quinn-a 3.00
Dog Soldiers #1-Hunter-s/Pachoumis-a 3.00
Legend of Isis #1-Valdez-a 3.00
Primate #1-Two covers; Beau Smith & Bernhardt-s/Byrd-a 3.00

IMAGES OF A DISTANT SOIL
Image Comics: Feb, 1997 ($2.95, B&W, one-shot)

1-Sketches by various 3.00

IMAGES OF SHADOWHAWK (Also see Shadowhawk)
Image Comics: Sept, 1993 - No. 3, 1994 ($1.95, limited series)

1-3: Keith Giffen-c/a; Trencher app. 3.00

IMAGE! 30TH ANNIVERSARY ANTHOLOGY
Image Comics: Apr, 2022 - No. 12 ($5.99, squarebound)

1-10: Short story anthology featuring Image characters; some serialized stories 6.00

IMAGE 20 (FREE COMIC BOOK DAY 2012...)
Image Comics: May, 2012 (giveaway, one-shot)

GD 2.0 | VG 4.0 | FN 6.0 | VF 8.0 | VF/NM 9.0 | NM- 9.2

nn-Previews of Revival, Guarding the Globe, It-Girl and the Atomics, Near Death 3.00

IMAGE TWO-IN-ONE
Image Comics: Mar, 2001 ($2.95, 48 pgs., B&W, one-shot)
1-Two stories; 24 pages produced in 24 hrs. by Larsen and Eliopoulos 4.00

IMAGE UNITED
Image Comics: No. 0, Mar, 2010; Nov, 2009 - No. 6 ($3.99, limited series)
0-(3/10, $2.99) Fortress and Savage Dragon app. 3.00
1-3-($3.99) Image character crossover; Kirkman-s; art by Larsen, Liefeld, McFarlane, Portacio, Silvestri and Valentino; Spawn, Witchblade, Savage Dragon, Youngblood, Cyberforce and Shadowhawk app. Multiple covers on each 4.00
1-Jim Lee variant-c 8.00

IMAGE ZERO
Image Comics: 1993 (Received through mail w/coupons from Image books)
0-Savage Dragon, StormWatch, Shadowhawk, Strykeforce; 1st app. Troll; 1st app. McFarlane's Freak, Blotch, Sweat and Bludd 5.00

IMAGINARIES, THE
Image Comics: Mar, 2005 - No. 4, June, 2005 ($2.95, limited series)
1-4-Mike S. Miller & Ben Avery-s; Miller & Titus-a 3.00

IMAGINARY FIENDS
DC Comics (Vertigo): Jan, 2018 - No. 6, Jun, 2016 ($3.99, limited series)
1-6-Tim Seeley-s/Stephen Molnar-a/Richard Pace-c 4.00

IMAGINE AGENTS
BOOM! Studios: Oct, 2013 - No. 4, Jan, 2014 ($3.99, limited series)
1-4-Brian Joines-s/Bachan-a 4.00

I'M DICKENS - HE'S FENSTER (TV)
Dell Publishing Co.: May-July, 1963 - No. 2, Aug-Oct, 1963 (Photo-c)
1 5 10 15 33 57 80
2 5 10 15 30 50 70

I MET A HANDSOME COWBOY
Dell Publishing Co.: No. 324, Mar, 1951
Four Color 324 8 16 24 52 99 145

IMMORAL X-MEN
Marvel Comics: Apr 2023 - Present ($4.99)
1-Sins of Sinister part 4; Gillen-s/Medina-a 5.00

IMMORTAL BROTHERS: THE TALE OF THE GREEN KNIGHT
Valiant Entertainment: Apr, 2017 ($4.99, one-shot)
1-Van Lente-s/Nord & Henry-a; Archer & Faith app.; bonus preview of Rapture 5.00

IMMORTAL DOCTOR FATE, THE
DC Comics: Jan, 1985 - No. 3, Mar, 1985 ($1.25, limited series)
1-3: 1-Reprints; Simonson-c/a. 2-R/back-ups from Flash #306-313; Giffen-c/a(p) 6.00

IMMORTAL HULK
Marvel Comics: Aug, 2018 - No. 50, Dec, 2021 ($4.99/$3.99)
1-($4.99) Bruce Banner returns; intro Jackie McGee; Ewing-s/Bennett-a
3 6 9 16 23 30
2-($3.99) Intro Dr. Frye 3 6 9 21 33 45
3-15: 4,5-Sasquatch app. 6,7-Avengers app. 9-13-Absorbing Man app. 13,14-Betty app. 14-Kyle Hotz-a 2 4 6 11 16 20
16-Joe Fixit returns 1 3 4 6 8 10
17-24-($3.99) 4.00
25-($5.99) Hulk as the Breaker of Worlds; Germán García-a 6.00
26-32,34-49: 26-Amadeus Cho app. 30-32-Xemnu app. 34-The Leader's origin retold. 46,47-Avengers app. 4.00
33-($5.99) 750th Legacy issue; Xemnu app.; art by Bennett & Pitarra 6.00
50-($9.99, squarebound) Fantastic Four app. 10.00
#0-(11/20, $4.99) Reprints Incredible Hulk #312 & #(-1) with new framing story; De Iulis-a 5.00
...: Flatline 1 (4/21, $4.99) Declan Shalvey-s/a 5.00
...: Great Power 1 (4/20, $4.99) Spider-Man gets Hulk powers; Fantastic Four app. 5.00
...: The Best Defense 1 (2/19, $4.99) Ewing-s/Di Meo-a; see Defenders: The Best Defense 5.00
...: The Threshing Place 1 (11/19, $4.99) Lemire-s/Del Mundo-a/c 5.00
...: Time of Monsters 1 (7/21, $4.99) Ewing & Paknadel-s/Ferreyra-a/c; back-up w/Nowlan-a 5.00

IMMORTAL HULK DIRECTOR'S CUT
Marvel Comics: Oct, 2019 - No. 6, Dec, 2019 ($5.99/$4.99)
1-($5.99) Reprints #1 with bonus pencil art, variant cover gallery; creator interviews 6.00
2-6-($4.99) Reprints with bonus pencil art and/or scripts and interviews 5.00

IMMORTAL IRON FIST, THE (Also see Iron Fist)
Marvel Comics: Jan, 2007 - No. 27, Aug, 2009 ($2.99/$3.99)
1-Brubaker & Fraction-s/Aja-c/a; origin retold; intro. Orson Randall
1 3 4 6 8 10
1-Variant-c by Dell'Otto 3 6 9 17 26 35
1-Director's Cut ($3.99) r/#1 and 8-page story from Civil War: Choosing Sides; script excerpt; character designs; sketch and inks art; cover variant and concepts 4.00
2,3 1 2 3 5 6 8
4-7,9-13,15-26: 6,17-20-Flashback-a by Heath. 21-Green-a 3.00
8-1st Immortal weapons & Fat Cobra 2 4 6 9 12 15
14,27: 14-($3.99) Heroes For Hire app. 27-Last issue; 2 covers; Foreman & Lapham-a 4.00
Annual 1 (11/07, $3.99) Brubaker & Fraction-s/Chaykin, Brereton & J. Djurdjevic-a 4.00
... Orson Randall and the Death Queen of California (11/08, $3.99) art by Camuncoli 4.00
... Orson Randall and the Green Mist of Death (4/08, $3.99) art by Heath and various 4.00
...: The Origin of Danny Rand (2008, $3.99) r/Marvel Premiere #15-16 recolored 4.00
... Vol. 1: The Last Iron Fist Story HC (2007, $19.99, dustjacket) r/#1-6, story from Civil War: Choosing Sides; sketch pages 20.00
... Vol. 1: The Last Iron Fist Story SC (2007, $14.99) same content as HC 15.00
... Vol. 2: The Seven Capital Cities HC (2008, $24.99, dustjacket) r/#8-14 & Annual #1 25.00

IMMORTALIS (See Mortigan Goth: Immortalis)

IMMORTAL MEN, THE (Follows events of Dark Nights: Metal)
DC Comics: Jun, 2018 - No. 6, Nov, 2018 ($2.99)
1-6: 1-Jim Lee & Ryan Benjamin-a/Tynion IV-s; Batman Who Laughs cameo 4.00

IMMORTAL RED SONJA
Dynamite Entertainment: 2022 - No. 10, 2022 ($3.99)
1-10: 1-Abnett-s/Miracolo-a. 2,3-Pinna-a 4.00

IMMORTAL SHE-HULK
Marvel Comics: Nov, 2020 ($4.99, one-shot)
1-Ewing-s/Davis-Hunt-a; origin re-told, Wolverine, Thor, The Leader app. 5.00

IMMORTAL WEAPONS (Also see Immortal Iron Fist)
Marvel Comics: Sept, 2009 - No. 5, Jan, 2010 ($3.99, limited series)
1-5: Back-up Iron Fist stories in all. 1-Origin of Fat Cobra. 2-Brereton-a 4.00

IMMORTAL X-MEN
Marvel Comics: May 2022 - No. 10, Mar, 2023 ($5.99/$3.99)
1-Gillen-s/Werneck-a; wraparound-c 6.00
2-10-($3.99) 4.00

IMOGEN OF THE WYRDING WAY (Tales From the Outerverse)
Dark Horse Comics: Jun, 2021 ($3.99, one-shot)
1-Mignola & Golden-s/Bergting-a 4.00

IMPACT
E. C. Comics: Mar-Apr, 1955 - No. 5, Nov-Dec, 1955
1-Not code approved; classic Holocaust story 40 80 120 320 510 700
1-Variant printed by Charlton. Title logo is white instead of yellow and print quality is inferior. Distributed to newsstands before being destroyed & reprinted (scarce)
43 86 129 344 547 750
2 19 38 57 152 246 340
3-5: 4-Crandall-a 16 32 48 128 202 275
NOTE: *Crandall a-1-4. Davis a-2-4; c-1-5. Evans a-1, 4, 5. Ingels a-in all. Kamen a-3. Krigstein a-1, 5. Orlando a-2, 5.*

IMPACT
Gemstone Publishing: Apr, 1999 - No. 5, Aug, 1999 ($2.50)
1-5-Reprints E.C. series 4.00

IMPACT CHRISTMAS SPECIAL (!mpact W!nter Special on cover)
DC Comics (Impact Comics): 1991 ($2.50, 68 pgs.)
1-Gift of the Magi by Infantino/Rogers; The Black Hood, The Fly, The Jaguar, & The Shield stories 4.00

IMPACT WINTER SPECIAL (See Impact Christmas Special, the title used in the indicia)

IMPERIAL GUARD
Marvel Comics: Jan, 1997 - No. 3, Mar, 1997 ($1.95, limited series)
1-3: Augustyn-s in all; 1-Wraparound-c 3.00

IMPERIUM
Valiant Entertainment: Mar, 2015 - No. 16, May, 2016 ($3.99)
1-16: 1-4-Dysart-s/Braithwaite-a. 5-8-Eaton-a. 9-12-The Vine Imperative; Cafu-a 4.00

IMPOSSIBLE MAN SUMMER VACATION SPECTACULAR, THE
Marvel Comics: Aug, 1990; No. 2, Sept, 1991 ($2.00, 68 pgs.) (See Fantastic Four#11)
1-Spider Man, Quasar, Dr. Strange, She-Hulk, Punisher & Dr. Doom stories; Barry Crain, Guice-a; Art Adams-c(i) 4.00
2-Ka Zar & Thor app.; Cable Wolverine-c app. 4.00

IMPULSE (See Flash #92, 2nd Series for 1st app.) (Also see Young Justice)
DC Comics: Apr, 1995 - No. 89, Oct, 2002 ($1.50/$1.75/$1.95/$2.25/$2.50)
1-Mark Waid scripts & Humberto Ramos-c/a(p) begin; brief retelling of origin 6.00
2-12: 9-XS from Legion (Impulse's cousin) comes to the 20th Century, returns to the 30th Century in #12. 10-Dead Heat Pt. 3 (cont'd in Flash #110). 11-Dead Heat Pt. 4 (cont'd in Flash #111); Johnny Quick dies. 4.00
13-25: 14-Trickster app. 17-Zatanna-c/app. 21-Legion-c/app. 22-Jesse Quick-c/app. 24-Origin; Flash app. 25-Last Ramos-a. 3.00
26-55: 26-Rousseau-a begins. 28-1st new Arrowette (see World's Finest #113). 30-Genesis x-over. 47-Superman-c/app. 50-Batman & Joker-c/app. Van Sciver-a begins 3.00
56-62: 56-Young Justice app. 3.00
63-89: 63-Begin $2.50-c. 66-JLA,JSA-c/app. 68,69-Adam Strange, GL app. 77-Our Worlds at War x-over; Young Justice-c/app. 85-World Without Young Justice x-over pt. 2. 3.00
#1,000,000 (11/98) John Fox app. 3.00
Annual 1 (1996, $2.95)-Legends of the Dead Earth; Parobeck-a 4.00
Annual 2 (1997, $3.95)-Pulp Heroes stories; Orbik painted-c 4.00
.../Atom Double-Shot 1(2/98, $1.95) Jurgens-s/Mhan-a 3.00
...: Bart Saves the Universe (4/99, $5.95) JSA app. 6.00
...Plus (9/97, $2.95) w/Gross Out (Scare Tactics)-c/app. 4.00
...Reckless Youth (1997, $14.95, TPB) r/Flash #92-94, Impulse #1-6 15.00

INCAL, THE
Marvel Comics (Epic): Nov, 1988 - No. 3, Jan, 1989 ($10.95/$12.95, mature)
1-Moebius-c/a in all; sexual content 4 8 12 27 44 60
2,3 2 4 6 11 16 20

INCOGNEGRO
DC Comics (Vertigo): 2008 ($19.99, B&W, hardcover graphic novel with dustjacket)
HC-Mat Johnson-s/Warren Pleece-a 20.00

INCOGNEGRO: RENAISSANCE
Dark Horse Comics (Berger Books): Feb, 2018 - No. 5, Jun, 2018 ($3.99, B&W, lim. series)
1-5-Mat Johnson-s/Warren Pleece-a 5.00

INCOGNITO
Marvel Comics (Icon): Dec, 2008 - No. 6, Aug, 2009 ($3.50/$3.99, limited series)
1-5-Brubaker-s/Phillips-a/c; pulp noir-style 3.50
6-($3.99) Bonus history of the Zeppelin pulps 4.00
...: Bad Influences (10/10 - No. 5, 4/11, $3.50) 1-5 Brubaker-s/Phillips-a/c 3.50

INCOMING
Marvel Comics: Feb, 2020 ($9.99, one-shot)
1-Leads into the Empyre event; Masked Raider app.; connecting short stories by various 10.00

INCOMPLETE DEATH'S HEAD (Also see Death's Head)
Marvel Comics UK: Jan, 1993 - No. 12, Dec, 1993 ($1.75, limited series)

Immortal Hulk #41 © MAR

Imperium #5 © VAL

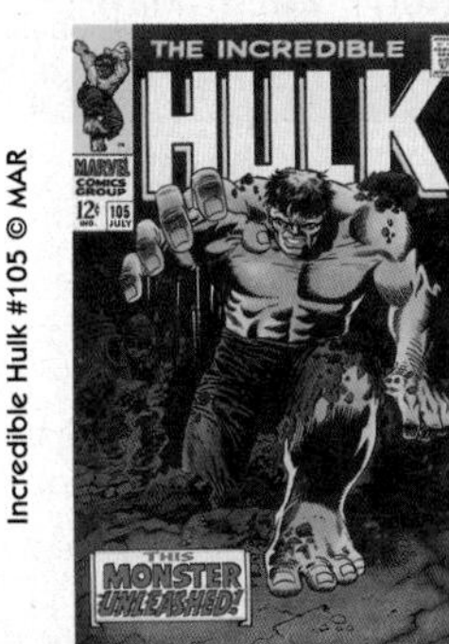

Incredible Hulk #105 © MAR

GD VG FN VF VF/NM NM-
2.0 4.0 6.0 8.0 9.0 9.2

1-($2.95, 56 pgs.)-Die-cut cover 4.00
2-11: 2-Re-intro original Death's Head. 3-Original Death's Head vs. Dragon's Claws 3.00
12-($2.50, 52 pgs.)-She Hulk app. 4.00

INCORRUPTIBLE (Also see Irredeemable)
BOOM! Studios: Dec, 2000 - No. 30, May, 2012 ($3.99)

1-30: 1-Waid-s/Diaz-a; 3 covers 4.00
1-Artist Edition (12/11, $3.99) r/#1 in B&W with bonus sketch and design art 4.00

INCREDIBLE HERCULES (Continued from Incredible Hulk #112, Jan, 2008)
Marvel Comics: No. 113, Feb, 2008 - No. 141, Apr, 2010 ($2.99/$3.99)

113-125: 113-Ares and Wonder Man app.; Art Adams-c. 116-Romita Jr-c; Eternals app. 3.00
113-Variant-c by Pham 5.00
126-($3.99) Hercules origin retold; back-up story w/Miyazawa-a 4.00
127-137: 128-Dark Avengers app. 132-Replacement Thor. 136-Thor app. 3.00
138-141-($3.99) Assault on New Olympus; Avengers app. 4.00

INCREDIBLE HULK, THE (See Aurora, The Avengers #1, The Defenders #1, Giant-Size..., Hulk, Marvel Collectors Item Classics, Marvel Comics Presents #26, Marvel Fanfare, Marvel Treasury Edition, Power Record Comics, Rampaging Hulk, She-Hulk, 2099 Unlimited & World War Hulk)

INCREDIBLE HULK, THE
Marvel Comics: May, 1962 - No. 6, Mar, 1963; No. 102, Apr, 1968 - No. 474, Mar, 1999

1-Origin & 1st app. (skin is grey colored); Kirby pencils begin, end #5
7100 14,200 24,850 75,800 237,900 400,000
2-1st green skinned Hulk; Kirby/Ditko-a 730 1460 2190 6200 14,100 22,000
3-Origin retold; 1st app. Ringmaster (9/62) 286 572 858 2360 5330 8300
4-Brief origin retold 221 442 663 1823 4112 6400
5-1st app of Tyrannus 262 524 786 2162 4881 7600
6-(3/63) Intro. Teen Brigade; all Ditko-a 224 448 672 1848 4174 6500
102-(4/68) (Continued from Tales to Astonish #101)-Origin retold; Hulk in Asgard; Enchantress & Executioner app; Gary Friedrich-s begin 38 76 114 285 641 1000
103-1st Space Parasite 12 24 36 83 182 280
104-Hulk vs. the Rhino 14 28 42 96 211 325
105-1st Missing Link 14 28 42 96 211 325
106-110: 106-vs. Missing Link; Nick Fury & SHIELD app; Trimpe pencils begin (continues through issue #193). 107,108-vs. the Mandarin. 108-Nick Fury & SHIELD app.; Stan Lee-s (continues through issue #120). 109,110-Ka-Zar app.
9 18 27 58 114 170
111-117: 111-Ka-Zar app.; 1st Galaxy Master. 112-Origin of the Galaxy Master. 113-vs. Sandman. 114-Sandman & Mandarin vs. the Hulk. 115-117-vs. the Leader
7 14 21 44 82 120
118-Hulk vs. Sub-Mariner 10 20 30 67 141 215
119,120,123-125: 119-Maximus (of the Inhumans) app. 120-Last Stan Lee plot, Roy Thomas script; Maximus app. 123,124-vs. The Leader. 124-1st Sal Buscema-p (as a fill-in). 125-vs. the Absorbing Man 5 10 15 35 63 90
121-Roy Thomas-s begin; 1st app. and origin of the Glob
7 14 21 49 92 135
122-Hulk battles Thing (12/69); Fantastic Four app. 12 24 36 79 170 260
126-1st Barbara Norriss (becomes Valkyrie in Defenders #4); story continued from Sub-Mariner #22 (see Dr. Strange #183 for pt.1); Dr. Strange gives up being Sorcerer Supreme 7 14 21 44 82 120
127,129,130,132-139: 127-Tryannus & the Mole Man app; 1st app. Mogol. 129-Leader revives the Glob. 130-(story continues from Captain Marvel #21); 132-HYDRA app. 134-1st Golem. 135-Kang & Phantom Eagle app. 136-1st Xeron the Starslayer; Abomination cameo. 137-Xeron app. Hulk vs. Abomination. 138-Sandman app. 139-Leader app; Hulk story continues in Avengers #88 5 10 15 30 50 70
128-Avengers app. 6 12 18 37 66 95
131-1st Jim Wilson; Iron Man app. 6 12 18 40 73 105
140-Written by Harlan Ellison; 1st Jarella (Hulk's love); story continues from Avengers #88; battles Psyklop 7 14 21 46 86 125
140-2nd printing 2 4 6 8 11 14
141-1st app. Doc Samson (7/71) 23 46 69 156 348 540
142-2nd Valkyrie app. (Samantha Parrington) (see Avengers #82 for 1st Marvel Valkyrie); Enchantress app. 7 14 21 46 86 125
143,144-Doctor Doom app. 6 12 18 38 69 100
145-(52-pgs)-Origin retold 6 12 18 37 66 95
146-151: 146,147-Richard Nixon & The Leader app. 148-Jarella app. 149-1st app. The Inheritor. 150-Havok app. 151-Has minor Ant-Man app.
4 8 12 25 40 55
152,153: Hulk on trial; Daredevil, Fantastic Four, Avengers app.
4 8 12 28 47 65
154-Ant-Man app; story coincides with Ant-Man's re-intro in Marvel Feature #4; Hydra & the Chameleon app. 4 8 12 27 44 60
155-160: 155-1st Shaper of Worlds. 156-Jarella app. 157,158-the Leader & Rhino app. 158-Counter-Earth & the High Evolutionary app. 159-Steve Englehart-s begin; Hulk vs. Abomination. 160-vs. Tiger Shark app. 4 8 12 22 35 48

GD VG FN VF VF/NM NM-
2.0 4.0 6.0 8.0 9.0 9.2

161-The Mimic dies; Beast app. 6 12 18 37 66 95
162-1st app. The Wendigo (4/73) Beast app. 17 34 51 117 259 400
163-165,170,173,174,179: 163-1st app. The Gremlin. 164-1st Capt. Omen & Colonel John D. Armbuster. 165-Capt. Omen app; 1st Aquon. 173,174-vs the Cobalt Man. 179-Return of the Missing Link; 1st Len Wein-s 3 6 9 17 25 34
166-169,171: 166-1st Zzzax; Hawkeye app.; story continues into Defenders #7. 167-Hulk vs. MODOK. 168-1st Harpy (transformed Betty Ross; also seen briefly in nudity panels) 169-1st Bi-Beast; MODOK and A.I.M app; Harpy transformed back into Betty. 171-vs. Abomination; last Englehart-s 3 6 9 18 27 36
172-X-Men cameo; origin Juggernaut retold 6 12 18 41 76 110
175-Black Bolt/Inhumans c/story 4 8 12 23 37 50
176-Hulk on Counter-Earth; Man-Beast app; Warlock cameo (2 panels only)
4 8 12 25 40 55
177-1st actual death of Warlock (last panel only); Man-Beast app.
6 12 18 41 76 110
178-Rebirth of Warlock (story continues in Strange Tales #178)
7 14 21 46 86 125
180-(10/74)-1st brief app. Wolverine (last pg.) 89 178 367 712 1606 2500
181-(11/74)-1st full Wolverine story; Trimpe-a 1200 2400 3600 6000 9000 12,000
182-Wolverine cameo; see Giant-Size X-Men #1 for next app.; 1st Crackajack Jackson
25 50 75 175 388 600
183-Zzzax app. 4 8 12 23 37 50
184-vs. Warlord Kraa 3 6 9 18 27 36
185-192,194-196,199: 185-Death of Col. Armbuster. 186-1st Devastator. 187-188-vs. the Gremlin, Nick Fury app. 189-Mole Man app. 190-1st Glorian; Shaper of Worlds app. 191-vs. the Toad Men; Glorian & Shaper of Worlds app. 194-vs. the Locust; 1st Sal Buscema-p (through #309). 195-Abomination & Hulk team-up. 196-Hulk vs. Abomination. 199-Hulk vs. SHIELD & Doc Samson; Nick Fury app.
3 6 9 15 22 28
193-vs. Doc Samson c/story; last regular Trimpe-p 4 8 12 23 37 50
197-Collector, Man-Thing & Glob app; Wrightson-c 7 14 21 44 82 120
198-Collector, Man-Thing & Glob app. 3 6 9 19 30 40
198,199, 201,202-(30¢-c variants, lim. distribution) 8 16 24 56 108 160
200-(25¢-c) Silver Surfer app. (illusion only); anniversary issue
4 8 12 27 44 60
200-(30¢-c variant, limited distribution)(6/76) 8 16 24 51 96 140
201-(25¢-c)-Conan swipe-c/sty (vs. Bronak the Barbarian)
3 6 9 16 23 30
202-205,208-211,213,215-220: 202-Jarella app.; Psyklop cameo. 203-Jarella app.; death of Psyklop. 204-Trimpe-p; alternate Hulk origin. 205-Death of Jarella; vs. the Crypto Man. 208-Absorbing Man app. 209-Hulk vs. Absorbing Man. 210,211-Hulk team-up with Dr. Druid vs. the Maha Yogi. 213-1st Quintronic Man. 215,216-vs. the second Bi-Beast. 218-Doc Samson vs. the Rhino (no Hulk in story). 219-220-vs. Captain Barracuda
2 4 6 10 14 18
206,207-Defenders app. 3 6 9 14 19 24
212,214: 212-1st app. The Constrictor. 214-Hulk vs. Jack of Hearts (1st app. outside of B&W magazines) 3 6 9 14 19 24
212-216-(35¢-c variant, limited distribution) 12 24 36 82 179 275
221-227,230-231: 221-Stingray app. 222-Last Wein-s; Jim Starlin co-plot and (p). 223-The Leader returns; Roger Stern-s begin. 224-225-vs. The Leader. 227-Original Avengers app. (in dream sequence) 2 4 6 8 10 12
228-1st female Moonstone (Karla Sofen) (10/78) 5 10 15 31 53 75
229-2nd app. new Moonstone 2 4 6 10 14 18
232,233: 232-Captain America x-over from Captain America #230; vs. Moonstone, Vamp and 'the Corporation'; Marvel Man (Quasar) app. 233-Marvel Man app. (Quasar)
2 4 6 8 11 14
234-(4/79)-Marvel Man formally changes his name to Quasar
5 10 15 34 60 85
235-249: 235-237-Machine Man app. 238-President Jimmy Carter app. 241-243-vs. Tyrannus. 243-Last Stern-s. 244-vs. It the Living Colossus. 245-1st Mantlo-s (through #313); 1st app. The Super-Mandroid (Col. Talbot); Captain Mar-Vell cameo. 246-Captain Mar-Vell app.; Hulk vs. Super-Mandroid. 247-Minor Captain Mar-Vell app. 248-vs. the Gardener. 249-Steve Ditko-p 2 4 6 8 10 12
250-Giant-Size (square-bound, 48-pgs)-Silver Surfer app.
5 10 15 31 53 75
251-253,256-270: 251-3-D Man app. 252,253-Woodgod app. 256-1st Sabra (Israeli super-hero). 257-1st Arabian Knight. 258,259-Soviet Super-Soldiers, Red Guardian & the Presence app. 260-Death of Col. Talbot. 261-Absorbing Man app. 263-Landslide & Avalanche app. 264-Death of the Night Flyer; Corruptor app. 265-1st app. The Rangers (Firebird, Shooting Star, Night Rider, Red Wolf & Lobo, Texas Tornado); Corruptor app. 266-High Evolutionary app. 267-Glorian & the Shaper of Worlds app. 268-Pariah-c/s; origin of Rick Jones retold. 269-1st Marvel Universe app. of Bereet; 1st Hulk-Hunters (Amphibion, Torgo, Dark Crawler). 270-Hulk Hunters, Bereet & Galaxy Master app. 1 3 4 6 8 10
254-1st app. the U-Foes (evil versions of the Fantastic Four)
3 6 9 16 23 30

GD 2.0 | VG 4.0 | FN 6.0 | VF 8.0 | VF/NM 9.0 | NM- 9.2

255-Hulk vs. Thor 3 6 9 15 22 28
271-(5/82)-2nd app. & 1st full app. Rocket Raccoon (see Marvel Preview #7 for debut) 12 24 36 79 170 260
272-3rd app Rocket Raccoon; Sasquatch & Wendigo app; Wolverine & Alpha Flight cameo in flashback; Bruce Banner's mind takes control of the Hulk 4 8 12 27 44 60
273-277,280-299: 273-Sasquatch app. 275-vs. Megalith; U-Foes app. 276,277-U-foes app. 280,281-The Leader returns. 282-She-Hulk app. 283,284-Avengers app; vs. the Leader. 285-Zzzax app. 287-290-MODOK & Abomination app. 292-Circus of Crime & Dragon Man app. 293-Fantastic Four app. (in a dream). 294,295-Boomerang app. 296-Rom app. 297-299-Dr. Strange & Nightmare app. 1 3 4 6 8 10
278,279-Most Marvel characters app. (Wolverine in both). 279-X-Men & Alpha Flight cameos 1 3 4 6 8 10
300-(11/84, 52 pgs)-Spider-Man app. in new black costume on-c & 2 pg. cameo; Hulk reverts to savagery; Thor, Daredevil, Power Man & Iron Fist, Human Torch app; Dr. Strange banishes the Hulk from Earth 3 6 9 19 30 40
301-313: 301-Hulk banished to the 'Crossroads' (through #313); Dr. Strange app. 302-Mignola-c. 304-U-Foes cameo; Mignola-c (through issue #309). 305-vs the U-Foes. 306-Return of Xeron the Starslayer. 307-Death of Xeron. 308-vs N'Garia demons. 309-Last Sal Buscema-a. 310-Blevins-a. 311-Mignola-c/a. 312-Secret Wars II x-over; Mignola-c/a; origin retold w/further details regarding physical abuse at the hands of his father. 313-Crossover w/Alpha Flight #29; Mignola-c/a 1 2 3 5 6 8
314-Byrne-c/a begins; ends #319; Hulk returns to Earth; vs. Doc Samson 1 3 4 6 8 10
315-319: 315-Hulk & Banner separated. 316-vs Hercules, Sub-Mariner, Wonder Man & Iron Man of the Avengers. 317-1st app. the new Hulkbusters; Hulk vs. Doc Samson. 318-Doc Samson vs. Hulkbusters. 319-Banner and Betty Ross wed 1 2 3 5 6 8
320,325,327-329: 320-Al Milgrom story & art begin. 325-vs. Zzzax. 327-Zzzax app. 328-1st Peter David-s. 329-1st app. The Outcasts 6.00
321-323: 321-Avengers vs. Hulk. 322-Avengers & West Coast Avengers app. 323-East & West Coast Avengers app. 1 2 3 5 6 8
324-Return of the Grey Hulk (Banner & Hulk rejoined) first since #1 (c-swipe of #1) 3 6 9 19 30 40
326-Grey vs. Green (Rick Jones) Hulk 2 4 6 8 11 14
330-1st McFarlane-c/p; last Milgrom-s; Thunderbolt Ross 'dies' 3 6 9 20 31 42
331-Peter David begins as regular plotter; McFarlane-p 3 6 9 17 25 34
332-Grey Hulk & Leader vs. Green Hulk (Rick Jones) 2 4 6 8 11 14
333-334,338-339: 338-1st app. Mercy. 339-The Leader app. 1 2 3 4 8 10
335-No McFarlane-a 1 2 3 5 6 8
336,337-X-Factor app. 1 3 4 6 8 10
340-Classic Hulk vs. Wolverine-c by McFarlane 10 20 30 69 147 225
341-344,346: 341-vs. The Man-Bull; McFarlane begins pencils and inks. 342-The Leader app. 343-1st app. Rock & Redeemer. 344-McFarlane (p) only; vs. The Leader, Rock & Redeemer; Betty revealed to be pregnant. 346-The Leader app. Last McFarlane-p (co-penciled with Erik Larsen) 1 2 3 4 8 12
345-($1.50, 52 pgs) vs. The Leader; Gamma-Bomb explosion; World thinks the Hulk is dead; McFarlane (p) only 3 6 9 21 33 45
347-349,351-366: 347-1st app. The Hulk as 'Mr. Fixit'; relocated to Las Vegas; 1st app. Marlo; Absorbing Man app. 348-vs. Absorbing Man. 349-Spider-Man app; Dr. Doom cameo. 351-How the Hulk survived the Gamma-Bomb is revealed. 355-Glorian app. 356-Glorian & Shaper of Worlds app. 359-Wolverine-c (illusion) by John Byrne. 360-Nightmare & D'spayre app; Betty loses her baby. 361-Iron Man app. 362-Werewolf by Night app. 363-Acts of Vengeance tie-in; Dr. Doom & Grey Gargoyle app. 364-vs Abomination; 1st app. Madman. 365-Fantastic Four app. 366-Leader & Madman app. 6.00
350-Hulk/Thing battle 2 4 6 8 11 14
367-1st Dale Keown-a on Hulk (3/90) Leader & Madman app. 1 2 3 5 6 8
368-371,373-375: 368-Sam Kieth-c/a; 1st app. Pantheon. 369-Keown-a (becomes regular artist through #398); vs. the Freedom Force. 370,371-Dr. Strange & Namor app. (Defenders reunion). 374,375-vs. the Super-Skrull. 6.00
372-Green Hulk returns 1 2 3 5 6 8
376-Green vs. Grey Hulk; 1st app. Agamemnon of the Pantheon 2 4 6 10 14 18
377-(1/91, $1.00) 1st all new Hulk; fluorescent green background-c 3 6 9 19 30 40
377-($1.00) 2nd printing; black background-c 3 6 9 14 20 25
377-($1.75) 3rd printing from 1994; low print run; muted green background-c 15 30 45 103 227 350
378-392,394-399: 378,380,389-No Keown-a. 379-Contined from issue #377; new direction for the Hulk; 1st app. of Delphi, Ajax, Achilles, Paris & Hector of the Pantheon. 380-Doc Samson app. 381,382-Pantheon app. 383-Infinity Gauntlet x-over; Abomination app. 384-Infinity Gauntlet tie-in; Abomination app. 385-Infinity Gauntlet tie-in. 386,387-Sabra app. 388-1st app. Speedfreak. 390-X-Factor cameo. 391,392-X-Factor app.394-1st app. Trauma; no Keown-a. 395,396-Punisher app. 397-399; Leader & U-Foes app. 398-Last Keown-a. 5.00
393-($2.50, 72 pgs) 6.00
393-2nd print; silver-ink background 5.00
400-($2.50, 68-pgs)-Holo-grafx foil-c & r/TTA #63 6.00
400-2nd print; yellow logo 5.00
401-403,405-416: 401-U-Foes app. 402-Return of Doc Samson; Juggernaut & Red Skull app. 403-Gary Frank-a begins; Juggernaut & Red Skull app. 405-1st app. Piecemeal. 406-Captain America app. 407-vs. Piecemeal & Madman. 408-vs. Piecemeal & Madman; Motormouth & Killpower (Marvel UK characters) app. 409-vs. Madman; Motormouth & Killpower app. 410-Nick Fury & SHIELD app. 411-Pantheon vs. SHIELD; Nick Fury app. 412-Hulk & She-Hulk vs. Bi-Beast. 413-Trauma app; Pt. 1 (of 4) of the Troyjan War. 414-vs. Trauma; Silver Surfer app. 415-Silver Surfer & Starjammers app. 416-Final of the Troyjan War; death of Trauma. 5.00
404-Avengers vs. Juggernaut & the Hulk; Red Skull app. 6.00
417,419-424: 417-Begins $1.50-c; Rick Jones Bachelor party; many heroes from Avengers & Fantastic Four app; Hulk returns from "Future Imperfect". 419-No Frank-a. 420-Special AIDS awareness issue; death of Jim Wilson. 421-Hulk & the Pantheon in Asgard. 423-Hela app. 4.00
418-($2.50)-Collectors Edition w/Gatefold die-cut-c; the wedding of Rick Jones & Marlo; includes cameo apps. of various Marvel characters as well as DC''s Death & Peter David 5.00
418-($1.50, Regular Edition) 4.00
425-($2.25, 52 pgs); Last Frank-a; Liam Sharp-a begins; death of Achilles 5.00
425-($3.50, 52 pgs)-Holographic-c 1 2 3 5 6 8
426-433,442: 426-Nick Fury app. 427,428-Man-Thing app. 430-Speedfreak app. 431,432-Abomination app. 432-Last Sharp-a. 433-Punisher app; title becomes part of the 'Marvel Edge' titles (through #439). 442-She-Hulk & Doc Samson team-up; no Hulk app. 4.00
434-Funeral for Nick Fury; Wolverine, Dr. Strange, Avengers app; Marvel Overpower card insert (harder to find above 9.2 due to card indentations) 5.00
435-($2.50)-Rhino app; excerpt from "What Savage Beast" 5.00
436-439: 436-"Ghosts of the Future" Pt.1 (of 5); Leader app. 439-Maestro app. 5.00
440-"Ghosts of the Future" Pt. 5; Hulk vs. Thor 6.00
441-She-Hulk-c/s; "Pulp Fiction" parody-c 3 6 9 21 33 45
443,446-448: 443-Begin $1.50-c; re-app. of Hulk. 446-w/card insert. 447-Begin Deodato-c/a 4.00
444,445: 444-Cable-c/app; Onslaught x-over. 445-Onslaught x-over; Avengers app. 5.00
447-Variant-c 5.00
449-1st app. Thunderbolts (1/97); Citizen V, Songbird, Mach-1, Techno, Atlas & Meteorite 7 14 21 46 86 125
450-($2.95)-Thunderbolts app. 2 stories; Heroes Reborn versions of Hulk, Dr. Strange, Mr. Fantastic & Iron Man app. 6.00
451-453, 458-470: 452-Heroes Reborn Hulk app. 453-Hulk vs. Heroes Reborn Hulk. 458-Mr. Hyde app. 459-Abomination app. 461-Maestro app. 463-Silver Surfer cameo. 464-Silver Surfer app. 465-Mr. Fantastic & Tony Stark app. 466-'Death' of Betty Banner. 467-Last Peter David issue. 468-Casey-s/Puilido-a begin. 469-Super-Adaptoid & Ringmaster app. 470-Ringmaster & the Circus of Crime app. 4.00
454-Wolverine & Ka-Zar app; Adam Kubert-a 6.00
455-Wolverine, Storm, Cannonball & Cyclops of the X-Men app.; Adam Kubert-a 6.00
456-Apocalypse enlists the Hulk as 'War'; Juggernaut app. 6.00
457-Hulk (as Horseman of the Apocalypse 'War' vs. Juggernaut. Apocalypse app. 1 3 4 6 8 10
471-473: 471-Circus of Crime app. 473-Watcher app; Abomination revealed as Betty's killer. 5.00
474-($2.99) Last issue; Abomination app; c-homage to issue #1 2 4 6 8 10 12
#(-1) Flashback (7/97) Kubert-a 5.00
Special 1 (10/68, 25¢, 68 pg.)-New 51 pg. story; Hulk battles the Inhumans (early app) 46 92 138 359 805 1250
Special 2 (10/69, 25¢, 68 pg.)-Origin retold (from issue #3) r-TTA #62-66 7 14 21 48 89 130
Special 3,4: 3-(1/71, 25¢, 68 pg.)-r/TTA #70-74. 4-(1/72, 52 pg.)-r/TTA 75-77 & Not Brand Echh #5 4 8 12 28 47 65
Annual 5 (1976) 2nd app. Groot 8 16 24 56 108 160
Annual 6 (1977)-1st app. Paragon (later becomes Her, then later Ayesha); Dr. Strange app. 5 10 15 31 53 75
Annual 7 ('78)-Byrne/Layton-c/a; Iceman & Angel app; vs. the Mastermold 3 6 9 19 30 40
Annual 8 ('79)-Byrne/Stern-s; Hulk vs. Sasquatch 2 4 6 8 11 14
Annual 9,10: 9-('80)-Ditko-p. 10-('81)-Captain Universe app. 1 2 3 5 6 8
Annual 11 ('82)-Doc Samson back-up by Miller-(p)(5 pg); Spider-Man & Avengers app. 1 3 4 6 8 10
Annual 12-14: 12-('83)-Trimpe-a. 13-('84)-Story takes place at the 'Crossroads' (after Hulk was banished from Earth); takes place between Incredible Hulk #301-302. 14-Byrne-s; takes place between pages of Incredible Hulk #314 6.00
Annual 15-('86)-Zeck-c; Abomination & Tryannus app. 6.00
Annual 16-20: 16-('90, $2.00, 68 pgs. "Lifeform" Pt. 3; continued from Daredevil Annual #6, continued in Silver Surfer Annual #3; She-Hulk app. in back-up story. 17-('91, $2.00)-"Subterranean Wars" Pt. 2; continued from Avengers Annual #20; continued in Namor the Sub-Mariner Annual #1. 18-('92)-"Return of the Defenders" Pt.1; continued in Namor the Sub-Mariner Annual #2. 19-('93)-Bagged w/card; 1st app. Lazarus 6.00
...'97 ($2.99) Pollina-c 1 2 3 5 6 8
...And Wolverine 1 (10/86, $2.50)-r/1st app. (#180-181) 3 6 9 17 26 35
...: Beauty and the Behemoth ('98, $19.95, TPB) r/Bruce & Betty stories 20.00
...Ground Zero ('95, $12.95) r/#340-346 15.00
...Hercules Unleashed (10/96, $2.50) David-s/Deodato-c/a 4.00
... No. 1 Facsimile Edition (12/19, 12/23, $3.99) r/#1 with original 1962 ads 4.00
... No. 180 Facsimile Edition (3/20, $3.99) r/#180 with original ads and letter column 1 3 4 6 8 10
... No. 181 Facsimile Edition (5/19, $3.99) r/#181 with original ads and letter column 2 4 6 9 12 15
... No. 182 Facsimile Edition (5/19, $3.99) r/#182 with original ads and letter column 1 2 3 5 6 8
... No. 347 Facsimile Edition (3/23, $3.99) r/#1 with original 1988 ads 4.00
... Omnibus Vol. 1 HC (2008, $99.99, dustjacket) r/#1-6 & 102, Tales To Astonish #59-101 bonus art, cover reprints; afterword by Peter David; Kirby cover from #1 180.00
... Omnibus Vol. 1 HC (2008, $99.99, dustjacket) Variant-c swipe of #1 by Alex Ross 140.00
.../Sub-Mariner '98 Annual ($2.99) 6.00
...Versus Quasimodo 1 (3/83, one-shot)-Based on Saturday morning cartoon 2 4 6 9 12 15
...Vs. Superman 1 (7/99, $5.95, one-shot)-painted-c by Rude 3 6 9 14 19 24
...Versus Venom 1 (4/94, $2.50, one-shot)-Embossed-c; red foil logo 40.00
... Visionaries: Peter David Vol. 1 (2005, $19.99) r/#331-339 written by Peter David 25.00
... Visionaries: Peter David Vol. 2 (2005, $19.99) r/#340-348 20.00
... Visionaries: Peter David Vol. 3 (2006, $19.99) r/#349-354, Web of Spider-Man #44, and Fantastic Four #320 20.00
... Visionaries: Peter David Vol. 4 (2007, $19.99) r/#355-363 and Marvel Comics Presents #26,45 40.00
... Visionaries: Peter David Vol. 5 (2008, $19.99) r/#364-372 and Annual #16 40.00
Wizard #1 Ace Edition - Reprints #1 with new Andy Kubert-c 14.00
Wizard #181 Ace Edition - Reprints #181 with new Chen-c 25.00

(Also see titles listed under **Hulk**)

NOTE: ***Adkins** a-111-116i.* ***Austin** a(i)-350, 351, 353, 354; c-302i, 350i.* ***Ayers** a-3-5i.* ***Buckler** a-Annual 5; c-252.* ***John Buscema** c-202p.* ***Byrne** a-314-319p; c-314-316, 318, 319, 359, Annual 14i.* ***Colan** c-363.* ***Ditko** a-2i, 6,*

Incredible Hulks #626 © MAR

Incredible Science Fiction #33 © WMG

Indestructible Hulk #1 © MAR

GD 2.0 | VG 4.0 | FN 6.0 | VF 8.0 | VF/NM 9.0 | NM- 9.2

249, Annual 2r(5), 3r, 9p; c-2i, 6, 235, 249. ***Everett*** *c-133i.* ***Golden*** *c-248, 251.* ***Kane*** *c(p)-193, 194, 196, 198.* ***Dale Keown*** *a(p)-367, 369-377, 379, 381-388, 390-393, 395-398; c-369-377p, 381, 382p, 384, 385, 386, 387p, 388, 390p, 391-393, 395p, 396, 397p, 398.* ***Kirby*** *a-1-5p, Special 2, 3p, Annual 5p; c-1-5, Annual 5.* ***McFarlane*** *a-330-334p, 336-339p, 340-343, 344-346p; c-330p, 340p, 341-343, 344p, 345, 346p.* ***Mignola*** *c-302, 305, 313.* ***Miller*** *c-258p, 261, 264, 268.* ***Mooney*** *a-230p, 287i, 288i.* ***Powell*** *a-Special 3r(2).* ***Romita*** *a-Annual 17p.* ***Severin*** *a(i)-108-110, 131-133, 141-151, 153-155; c(i)-109, 110, 132, 142, 144-155.* ***Simonson*** *c-283, 364-367.* ***Starlin*** *a-222p; c-217.* ***Staton*** *a(i)-187-189, 191-209.* ***Tuska*** *a-102i, 105i, 106i, 218p.* ***Williamson*** *a-310i; c-310i, 311i.* ***Wrightson*** *c-197.*

INCREDIBLE HULK (Vol. 2) (Formerly Hulk #1-11; becomes Incredible Hercules with #113) (Re-titled Incredible Hulks #612-on)(Also see World War Hulk)
Marvel Comics: No. 12, Mar, 2000 - No. 112, Jan, 2008 ($1.99-$3.50)
No. 600, Sept, 2009 - No. 625, Oct, 2011 ($3.99/$4.99)

12-Jenkins-s/Garney & McKone-a 6.00
13,14-($1.99) Garney & Buscema-a 1 2 3 5 6 8
15-24,26-32: 15-Begin $2.25-c. 21-Maximum Security x-over. 24-($1.99-c) 3.00
25-($2.99) Hulk vs. The Abomination; Romita Jr.-a 4.00
33-($3.50, 100 pgs.) new Bogdanove-a/Priest-s; reprints 4.00
34-Bruce Jones-s begin; Romita Jr.-a 5.00
35-49,51-54: 35-39-Jones-s/Romita Jr.-a. 40-43-Weeks-a. 44-49-Immonen-a 3.00
50-($3.50) Deodato-a begins; Abomination app. thru #54 4.00
55-74,77-91: 55(25¢-c) Absorbing Man returns; Fernandez-a. 60-65,70-72-Deodato-a. 66-69-Braithwaite-a. 71-74-Iron Man app. 77-($2.99-c) Peter David-s begin/Weeks-a. 80-Wolverine-c. 82-Jae Lee-c/a. 83-86-House of M x-over. 87-Scorpion app. 3.00
75,76-($3.50) The Leader app. 75-Robertson-a/Frank-c. 76-Braithwaite-a 4.00
92-Planet Hulk begins; Ladronn-c 5.00
92-2nd printing with variant-c by Bryan Hitch 4.00
93-99,101-105 Planet Hulk; Ladronn-c 3.00
100-($3.99) Planet Hulk continues; back-up w/Frank-a; r/#152,153; Ladronn-c 5.00
100-($3.99) Green Hulk variant-c by Michael Turner 10.00
100-($3.99) Gray Hulk variant-c by Michael Turner 30.00
106-World War Hulk begins; Gary Frank-a/c 6.00
106-2nd printing with new cover of Hercules and Angel 3.00
107-112: 107-Hercules vs. Hulk. 108-Rick Jones app. 112-Art Adams-c 3.00
600-(9/09, $4.99) Covers by Ross, Sale and wraparound-c by McGuinness; back-up with Stan Lee-s; r/Hulk: Gray #1; cover gallery 5.00
601-611-($3.99): 601-605-Olivetti-a. 603-Wolverine app. 606-608-Fall of the Hulks 4.00
(Title becomes Incredible Hulks with #612, Nov, 2010)
612-621: 612-617-Dark Son. 618-620-Chaos War. 621-Hercules app. 4.00
622-634-($2.99) 623-625-Ka-Zar app.; Eaglesham-a. 626-629-Grummett-a 3.00
635-($3.99) Fin Fang Foom & Dr. Strange app.; Greg Pak interview 4.00
Annual 2000 ($3.50) Texeira-a/Jenkins-s; Avengers app. 4.00
Annual 2001 ($2.99) Thor-c/app.; Larsen-s/Williams III-c 4.00
Annual 1 (8/11, $3.99) Identity Wars; Spider-Man and Deadpool app.; Barrionuevo-a 4.00
... & The Human Torch: From the Marvel Vault 1 (8/11, $2.99) unpublished story w/Ditko-a 3.00
... : Boiling Point (Volume 2, 2002, $8.99, TPB) r/#40-43; Andrews-c 9.00
Dogs of War (6/01, $19.95, TPB) r/#12-20 20.00
House of M (2006, $13.99) r/House of M tie-in issues Incredible Hulk #83-87 14.00
Hulk: Planet Hulk HC (2007, $39.99, dustjacket) oversized r/#92-105, Planet Hulk: Gladiator Guidebook, stories from Amazing Fantasy (2004) #15 and Giant-Size Hulk #1 40.00
Hulk: Planet Hulk SC (2008, $34.99) same content as HC 35.00
Planet Hulk: Gladiator Guidebook (2006, $3.99) bios of combatants and planet history 4.00
...: Prelude to Planet Hulk (2006, $13.99, TPB) r/#88-91 & Official Handbook: Hulk 2004 14.00
...: Return of the Monster (7/02, $12.99, TPB) r/#34-39 13.00
...: The End (8/02, $5.95) David-s/Keown-a; Hulk in the far future 6.00
...: The End HC (2008, $19.99, dustjacket) r/The End and Hulk: Future Imperfect #1-2 20.00
...Volume 1 HC (2002, $29.99, oversized) r/#34-43 & Startling Stories: Banner #1-4 30.00
...Volume 2 HC (2003, $29.99, oversized) r/#44-54; sketch pages and cover gallery 30.00
Volume 3: Transfer of Power (2003, $12.99, TPB) r/#44-49 13.00
Volume 4: Abominable (2003, $11.99, TPB) r/#50-54; Abomination app.; Deodato-a 12.00
Volume 5: Hide in Plain Sight (2003, $11.99, TPB) r/#55-59; Fernandez-a 12.00
Volume 6: Split Decisions (2004, $12.99, TPB) r/#60-65; Deodato-a 13.00
Volume 7: Dead Like Me (2004, $12.99, TPB) r/#66-69 & Hulk Smash #1&2 13.00
Volume 8: Big Things (2004, $17.99, TPB) r/#70-76; Iron Man app. 18.00
Volume 9: Tempest Fugit (2005, $14.99, TPB) r/#77-82 15.00

INCREDIBLE HULK (Also see Indestructible Hulk)
Marvel Comics: Dec, 2011 - No. 15, Dec, 2012 ($3.99)

1-Aaron-s/Silvestri-a; bonus interview with Aaron; cover by Silvestri 4.00
1-Variant covers by Neal Adams, Whilce Portacio & Ladronn 8.00
2-7: 2-Silvestri, Portacio & Tan-a. 7-Hulk & Banner merge; Portacio-a 4.00
7.1-(7/12, $2.99) Palo-a/Komarck-c; Red She-Hulk app. 3.00
8-15: 8-Punisher app.; Dillon-a. 12-Wolverine & The Thing app. 4.00

INCREDIBLE HULK (Marvel Legacy)(Continued from Totally Awesome Hulk #23)
Marvel Comics: No. 709, Dec, 2017 - No. 717, Jul, 2018 ($3.99)

709-717: 709-713-"Return to Planet Hulk"; Hulk goes to Sakaar; Pak-s/Land-a. 717-Cho-c 4.00
...: Last Call 1 (8/19, $4.99) Peter David-s/Dale Keown-a; Mister Hyde app. 5.00

INCREDIBLE HULKS: ENIGMA FORCE
Marvel Comics: Nov, 2010 - No. 3, Jan, 2011 ($3.99, limited series)

1-3-Reed-s/Munera-a/Pagulayan-c; Bug app. 4.00

INCREDIBLE MR. LIMPET, THE (See Movie Classics)

INCREDIBLES, THE
Image Comics: Nov, 2004 - No. 4, Feb, 2005 ($2.99, limited series)

1-4-Adaptation of 2004 Pixar movie; Ricardo Curtis-a 3.00
TPB (2005, $12.95) r/#1-4; cover gallery 13.00

INCREDIBLES, THE (Pixar characters)
BOOM! Studios: No. 0, Jul, 2009 - No. 15, Oct, 2010 ($2.99)

0-15: 0-3-City of Incredibles; Waid & Walker-s. 0,1-Wagner-c. 8-15-Walker-s 3.00
...: Family Matters 1-4 (3/09 - No. 4, 6/09) Waid-s/Takara-a. 1-Five covers 3.00

INCREDIBLES 2: CRISIS IN MID-LIFE! & OTHER STORIES (Pixar characters)
Dark Horse Comics: Jul, 2018 - No. 3, Sept, 2018 ($3.99, limited series)

1-3-Short stories by Gage, Gurihiru, Bone, Walker and Greppi 4.00

INCREDIBLES 2: SECRET IDENTITIES (Pixar characters)
Dark Horse Comics: Apr, 2019 - No. 3, Jun, 2019 ($3.99, limited series)

1-3-Christos Gage-s/Jean-Claudio Vinci-a 4.00

INCREDIBLES 2: SLOW BURN (Pixar characters)
Dark Horse Comics: Feb, 2020 - No. 3 ($3.99, limited series)

1-3-Christos Gage-s/Jean-Claudio Vinci-a; Jack loses his speed powers 4.00

INCREDIBLE SCIENCE FICTION (Formerly Weird Science-Fantasy)
E. C. Comics: No. 30, July-Aug, 1955 - No. 33, Jan-Feb, 1956

Issue	GD 2.0	VG 4.0	FN 6.0	VF 8.0	VF/NM 9.0	NM- 9.2
30-Davis-c begin, end #32	57	114	171	456	728	1000
31-Williamson/Krenkel-a, Wood-a(2)	50	100	150	400	638	875
32-"Food For Thought" by Williamson/Krenkel	51	102	153	408	654	900
33-Classic Wood-c; "Judgment Day" story-r/Weird Fantasy #18; final issue & last E.C. comic book	69	138	207	552	876	1200

NOTE: ***Davis*** *a-30, 32, 33; c-30-32.* ***Krigstein*** *a-in all.* ***Orlando*** *a-30, 32, 33.* ***Wood*** *a-30, 31, 33; c-33.*

INCREDIBLE SCIENCE FICTION (Formerly Weird Science-Fantasy)
Russ Cochran/Gemstone Publ.: No. 8, Aug, 1994 - No. 11, May, 1995 ($2.00)

8-11: Reprints #30-33 of E.C. series 4.00

INCURSION
Valiant Entertainment: Feb, 2019 - No. 4, May, 2019 ($3.99, limited series)

1-4: 1-Diggle & Paknadel-s/Braithwaite-a; Geomancer app.; Punk Mambo preview 4.00

INDEPENDENCE DAY (Movie)
Marvel Comics: No. 0, June, 1996 - No. 2, Aug, 1996 ($1.95, limited series)

0-Special Edition; photo-c 5.00
0-2 3.00

INDEPENDENCE DAY (Movie)
Titan Comics: Mar, 2016 - No. 5, Jul, 2016 ($3.99, limited series)

1-5: 1-Victor Gischler-s/Steve Scott-a; four covers. 2-5-Two covers 4.00

INDESTRUCTIBLE
IDW (Darby Pop): Dec, 2013 - No. 10, Dec, 2014 ($3.99)

1-10: 1-Kline-s/Garron & Garcia-a 4.00
...: Stingray One Shot (5/15, $3.99) Marsick-s/Reguzzoni-a 4.00

INDESTRUCTIBLE HULK (Marvel NOW!)(Follows Incredible Hulk 2011-2012 series)
Marvel Comics: Jan, 2013 - No. 20, May, 2014 ($3.99)

1-Waid-s/Yu-a; Banner hired by SHIELD; Maria Hill app. 4.00
2-20: 2-Iron Man app. 4,5-Attuma app. 6-8-Thor app.; Simonson-a/c. 9,10-Daredevil app. 12-Two-Gun Kid, Kid Colt, and Rawhide Kid app. 17,18-Iron Man app. 4.00
Annual 1 (2/14, $4.99) Parker-s/Asrar-a; Iron Man app. 5.00
... Special 1 (12/13, $4.99) Original X-Men and Superior Spider-Man app. 5.00

INDIANA JONES (Title series), **Dark Horse Comics**

--ADVENTURES, 6/08 ($6.95, digest-sized) Vol. 1 - new all-ages adventures; Beavers-a 7.00
--AND THE ARMS OF GOLD, 2/94 - 5/94 ($2.50) 1-4 3.00
--AND THE FATE OF ATLANTIS, 3/91 - 9/91 ($2.50) 1-4-Dorman painted-c on all; contain trading cards (#1 has a 2nd printing, 10/91) 3.00
--AND THE GOLDEN FLEECE, 6/94 - 7/94 ($2.50) 1,2 3.00
--AND THE IRON PHOENIX, 12/94 - 3/95 ($2.50) 1-4 3.00

INDIANA JONES AND THE KINGDOM OF THE CRYSTAL SKULL
Dark Horse Comics: May, 2008 - No. 2, May, 2008 ($5.99, limited series, movie adaptation)

1,2-Luke Ross-a/John Jackson Miller-adapted-s; two covers by Struzan & Fleming 6.00

GD VG FN VF VF/NM NM-
2.0 4.0 6.0 8.0 9.0 9.2

TPB (5/08, $12.95) r/#1,2; Struzan-c 13.00

INDIANA JONES AND THE LAST CRUSADE
Marvel Comics: 1989 - No. 4, 1989 ($1.00, limited series, movie adaptation)
1-4: Williamson-i assist 3.00
1-(1989, $2.95, B&W mag., 80 pgs.) 4.00

--AND THE SHRINE OF THE SEA DEVIL: Dark Horse, 9/94 ($2.50, one shot)
1-Gary Gianni-a 3.00

--AND THE SARGASSO PIRATES: Dark Horse, 12/95 - 3/96 ($2.50) 1-4: 1,2-Ross-c 3.00

--AND THE SPEAR OF DESTINY: Dark Horse, 4/95 - 8/95 ($2.50) 1-4 3.00

--AND THE TOMB OF THE GODS, 6/08 - No. 4, 3/09 ($2.99) 1-4: 1-Tony Harris-c 3.00

--THUNDER IN THE ORIENT: Dark Horse, 9/93 - '94 ($2.50)
1-6: Dan Barry story & art in all; 1-Dorman painted-c 3.00

INDIANA JONES AND THE TEMPLE OF DOOM
Marvel Comics Group: Sept, 1984 - No. 3, Nov, 1984 (Movie adaptation)
1-3-r/Marvel Super Special; Guice-a 5.00

INDIANA JONES OMNIBUS
Dark Horse Books: Feb, 2008; June 2008; Feb, 2009 ($24.95, digest-size)
Volume One - Reprints Indiana Jones and the Fate of Atlantis, Indiana Jones: Thunder in the Orient; and Indiana Jones and the Arms of Gold mini-series 25.00
Volume Two - Reprints I.J. and the Golden Fleece, I.J. and the Shrine of the Sea Devil, I.J. and the Iron Phoenix, I.J. and the Spear of Destiny, I.J. and the Sargasso Pirates 25.00
The Further Adventures Volume One - (2/09) r/Raiders of the Lost Ark #1-3 & The Further Adventures of Indiana Jones #1-12 25.00

INDIAN BRAVES (Baffling Mysteries No. 5 on)
Ace Magazines: March, 1951 - No. 4, Sept, 1951
1-Green Arrowhead begins, apps. in all 28 56 84 165 270 375
2 11 22 33 64 90 115
3,4 9 18 27 47 61 75
I.W. Reprint #1 (nd)-r/Indian Braves #4 2 4 6 9 13 16

INDIAN CHIEF (White Eagle...) (Formerly The Chief, Four Color 290)
Dell Publ. Co.: No. 3, July-Sept, 1951 - No. 33, Jan-Mar, 1959 (All painted-c)
3 5 10 15 34 60 85
4-11: 6-White Eagle app. 4 8 12 28 47 65
12-1st White Eagle (10-12/53)-Not same as earlier character
5 10 15 33 57 80
13-29 4 8 12 23 37 50
30-33-Buscema-a 4 8 12 25 40 55

INDIAN CHIEF (See March of Comics No. 94, 110, 127, 140, 159, 170, 187)

INDIAN FIGHTER, THE (Movie)
Dell Publishing Co.: No. 687, May, 1956 (one-shot)
Four Color 687-Kirk Douglas photo-c 8 16 24 54 102 150

INDIAN FIGHTER
Youthful Magazines: May, 1950 - No. 11, Jan, 1952
1 22 44 66 132 216 300
2-Wildey-a/c(bondage) 14 28 42 82 121 160
3-11: 3,4-Wildey-a. 6-Davy Crockett story 11 22 33 62 86 110
NOTE: *Hollingsworth a-5.* ***Walter Johnson*** *c-1, 3, 4, 6.* ***Palais*** *a-10.* ***Stallman*** *a-5-8.* ***Wildey*** *a-2-4; c-2, 5.*

INDIAN LEGENDS OF THE NIAGARA (See American Graphics)

INDIANS
Fiction House Magazines (Wings Publ. Co.): Spring, 1950 - No. 17, Spr, 1953 (1-8: 52 pgs.)
1-Manzar The White Indian, Long Bow & Orphan of the Storm begin
35 70 105 208 339 470
2-Starlight begins 17 34 51 100 158 215
3-5: 5-17-Most-c by Whitman 15 30 45 85 130 175
6-10 14 28 42 80 115 150
11-17 13 26 39 74 105 135

INDIANS OF THE WILD WEST
I. W. Enterprises: Circa 1958? (no date) (Reprints)
9-Kinstler-c; Whitman-a; r/Indians #? 3 6 9 14 19 24

INDIANS ON THE WARPATH
St. John Publishing Co.: 1950 (no month) (132 pgs.)
nn-Matt Baker-c; contains St. John comics rebound. Many combinations possible
54 108 162 343 574 825

INDIAN TRIBES (See Famous Indian Tribes)

INDIAN WARRIORS (Formerly White Rider and Super Horse; becomes Western Crime Cases #9)
Star Publications: No. 7, June, 1951 - No. 8, Sept, 1951
7-White Rider & Superhorse continue; "Last of the Mohicans" serial begins;
L.B. Cole-c 23 46 69 136 223 310
8-L.B. Cole-c 21 42 63 122 199 275
3-D 1(12/53, 25¢)-Came w/glasses; L.B. Cole-c 37 74 111 218 354 490
Accepted Reprint(nn)(inside cover shows White Rider & Superhorse #11)-r/cover to #7;
origin White Rider &...; L.B. Cole-c 8 16 24 44 57 70
Accepted Reprint #8 (nd); L.B. Cole-c (r-cover to #8) 8 16 24 44 57 70

INDOORS-OUTDOORS (See Wisco)

INDUSTRIAL GOTHIC
DC Comics (Vertigo): Dec, 1995 - No. 5, Apr, 1996 ($2.50, limited series)
1-5: Ted McKeever-c/a/scripts 3.00

INFAMOUS (Based on the Sony videogame)
DC Comics: Early May, 2011 - No. 6, Late July, 2011 ($2.99, limited series)
1-6: 1-William Harms-s/Eric Nguyen-a/Doug Mahnke-c. 3-6-Benes-c 3.00

INFAMOUS IRON MAN (Doctor Doom as Iron Man)
Marvel Comics: Dec, 2016 - No. 12, Nov, 2017 ($3.99)
1-12: 1-Bendis-s/Maleev-a; Diablo app. 1-9-The Thing app. 5-Doom's mother returns 4.00

INFECTED, THE (Year of the Villain tie-ins)
DC Comics: Feb, 2020 ($3.99, series of one-shots)
...: Deathbringer (2/20) Donna Troy corrupted by The Batman That Laughs; Teen Titans app. 4.00
...: King Shazam (1/20) Billy Batson corrupted; Marvel Family app.; Bennett-a 4.00
...: Scarab (2019) Jaime Reyes Blue Beetle corrupted; Williams II-a 4.00
...: The Commissioner (2/20) Jim Gordon corrupted; Batgirl app.; Herbert-a 4.00

INFERIOR FIVE, THE (Inferior 5 #11, 12) (See Showcase #62, 63, 65)
National Periodical Publications (#1-10: 12¢): 3-4/67 - No. 10, 9-10/68; No. 11, 8-9/72 - No. 12, 10-11/72
1-(3-4/67)-Sekowsky-a(p); 4th app. 6 12 18 37 66 95
2-5: 2-Plastic Man, F.F. app. 4-Thor app. 3 6 9 21 33 45
6-9: 6-Stars DC staff 3 6 9 16 23 30
10-Superman x-over; F.F., Spider-Man & Sub-Mariner app.
4 8 12 25 40 55
11,12: Orlando-c/a; both r/Showcase #62,63 2 4 6 11 16 20

INFERIOR FIVE
DC Comics: Nov, 2019 - No. 4, Feb, 2020 ($3.99, limited series originally planned for 12 issues)
1-4-Giffen & Lemire-s&a; back-up with Peacemaker 4.00

INFERNAL MAN-THING (Sequel to story in Man-Thing #12 [1974])
Marvel Comics: Sept, 2012 - No. 3, Oct, 2012 ($3.99, limited series)
1-3-Gerber-s; painted-a by Nowlan; Art Adams-c. 1,2-Bonus reprint of Man-Thing #12 4.00

INFERNO (See Legion of Super-Heroes)
DC Comics: Oct, 1997 - No. 4, Feb, 1998 ($2.50, limited series)
1-Immonen-s/c/a in all 4.00
2-4 3.00

INFERNO (Secret Wars tie-in)
Marvel Comics: Jul, 2015 - No. 5, Nov, 2015 ($3.99, limited series)
1-5-Hopeless-s/Garrón-a; Magik, Colossus, Nightcrawler, Madelyne Pryor app. 4.00

INFERNO (X-Men on Krakoa)
Marvel Comics: Nov, 2021 - No. 4, Mar, 2022 ($5.99, limited series)
1-4-Hickman-s/Schiti & Caselli-a; Moira MacTaggert's role in building Krakoa 6.00

INFERNO GIRL RED (See Radiant Black)
Image Comics: Jan, 2023 - No. 3 ($5.99, limited series)
1,2-D'Urso-a/Groom-s 6.00

INFERNO: HELLBOUND
Image Comics (Top Cow): Jan, 2002 - No. 3 ($2.50/$2.99)
1,2: 1-Seven covers; Silvestri-a/Silvestri and Wohl-s 3.00
3-($2.99) Tan-a 3.00
#0 (7/02, $3.00) Tan-a 3.00
Wizard #0- Previews series; bagged with Wizard Top Cow Special mag 3.00

INFESTATION (Zombie crossover with G.I. Joe, Star Trek, Transformers and Ghostbusters)
IDW Publishing: Jan, 2011 - No. 2, Apr, 2011 ($3.99, limited series)
1,2-Abnett & Lanning-s/Messina-a; two covers by Messina & Snyder III 4.00
...: Outbreak 1-4 (6/11 - No. 4, 9/11, $3.99) Messina-a; Covert Vampiric Operations app. 4.00

INFESTATION 2 (IDW characters vs. H.P. Lovecraft's Elder Gods)
IDW Publishing: Jan, 2012 - No. 2, Apr, 2012 ($3.99, limited series)
1,2-Swierczynski-s/Messina-a; three covers by Garner, Ramondelli & Messina 4.00
...: Dungeons & Dragons 1,2 (2/12 - No. 2, 2/12, $3.99) 3 covers 4.00
...: G.I. Joe 1,2 (3/12 - No. 2, 3/12, $3.99) Raicht-s/De Landro-a; 3 covers 4.00
...: Team-Up 1 (2/12, $3.99) Ryall-s/Robinson-a; covers by Powell & Morrison 4.00
...: Teenage Mutant Ninja Turtles 1,2 (3/12 - No. 2, 3/12, $3.99) Mark Torres-a; 3 covers 4.00
...: 30 Days of Night 1 (4/12, $3.99) Swierczynski-s/Sayger-a; 3 covers 4.00
...: Transformers 1,2 (2/12 - No. 2, 2/12, $3.99) Dixon-s/Guidi-a; 3 covers 4.00

INFIDEL
Image Comics: Mar, 2018 - No. 5, Jul, 2018 ($3.99, limited series)
1-5-Pornsak Pichetshote-s/Aaron Campbell-a 4.00

INFINITE, THE
Image Comics (SkyBound): Aug, 2011 - No. 4, Nov, 2011 ($2.99)
1-4: 1-Robert Kirkman-s/Rob Liefeld-a; at least 11 covers. 2-Six covers 3.00

INFINITE CRISIS
DC Comics: Dec, 2005 - No. 7, Jun, 2006 ($3.99, limited series)
1-Johns-s/Jimenez-a; two covers by Jim Lee and George Pérez
1 3 4 6 8 10
1-RRP Edition with Jim Lee sketch-c 100.00
2,4,6,7: 4-New Spectre; Earth-2 returns. 6-Superboy killed, new Earth formed. 7-Earth-2 Superman dies 5.00
3-1st app. Jaime Reyes 1 3 4 6 8 10
5-1st Jaime Reyes as new Blue Beetle; Earth-2 Lois Lane dies
3 6 9 19 30 40
HC (2006, $24.99, dustjacket) r/#1-7; DiDio intro.; sketch cover gallery; interview/commentary with Johns, Jimenez and editors; sketch art 25.00
... Companion TPB (2006, $14.99) r/Day of Vengeance: Infinite Crisis Special #1, Rann-Thanagar War: ICS #1, The Omac Project: ICS #1, Villains United: ICS #1 15.00
... Secret Files 2006 (4/06, $5.99) tie-in story with Earth-2 Lois and Superman, Earth-Prime Superboy and Alexander Luthor; art by various; profile pages 6.00

INFINITE CRISIS AFTERMATH (See Crisis Aftermath:...)

INFINITE CRISIS: FIGHT FOR THE MULTIVERSE (Based on the video game)
DC Comics: Sept, 2014 - No. 12, Aug, 2015 ($3.99, limited series)
1-12: 1-Abnett-s; art by various. 2-6-Polybagged 4.00

INFINITE DARK
Image Comics: Oct, 2018 - No. 8, Jul, 2019 ($3.99)
1-8-Ryan Cady-s/Andrea Mutti-a 4.00

INFINITE FRONTIER
DC Comics: No. 0, May, 2021 - No. 6 ($5.99/$4.99)
0-($5.99) Short stories previewing the new DC Multiverse; Wonder Woman returns 6.00
1-6-($4.99) Justice Incarnate app. (Calvin Ellis Superman, Flashpoint Batman, Mary Marvel, Captain Carrot, Aquawoman, Machinehead) 5.00

Infernal Man-Thing #1 © MAR

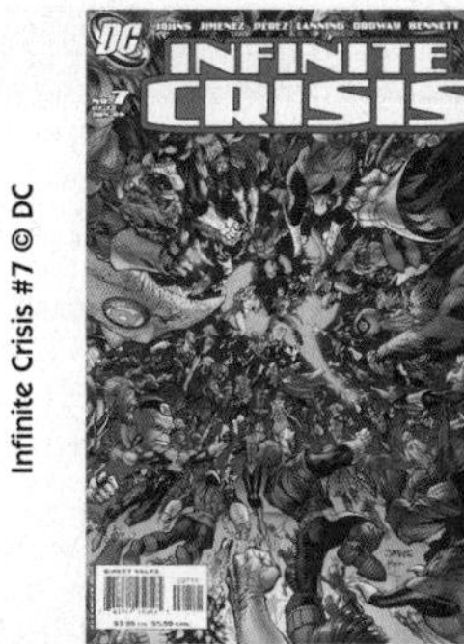
Infinite Crisis #7 © DC

Infinity Wars (2018) #2 © MAR

GD VG FN VF VF/NM NM-
2.0 4.0 6.0 8.0 9.0 9.2

...: Secret Files 1 (8/21, $9.99) Short stories featuring Director Bones, Calvin Ellis, Roy Harper, Jade, Psycho Pirate 10.00

INFINITE LOOP
IDW Publishing: Apr, 2015 - No. 6, Sept, 2015 ($3.99)
1-6-Pierrick Colinet-s/Elsa Charretier-a 4.00

INFINITE LOOP, VOLUME 2
IDW Publishing: Sept, 2017 - No. 4, Dec, 2017 ($3.99)
1-4-Colinet & Charretier-s/Di Nicuolo-a 4.00

INFINITE VACATION
Image Comics (Shadowline): Jan, 2011 - No. 5, Jan, 2013 ($3.50/$5.99)
1-4-Nick Spencer-s/Christian Ward-a/c 3.50
5-($5.99) Conclusion; gatefold centerfold 6.00

INFINITY (Crossover with the Avengers titles)
Marvel Comics: Oct, 2013 - No. 6, Jan, 2014 ($4.99/$3.99/$5.99, limited series)
1-($4.99) Avengers, Inhumans and Thanos app.; Hickman-s/Cheung-a/Adam Kubert-c 5.00
2-5-($3.99) Opeña-a. 3-Terragen bomb triggered 4.00
6-($5.99) Cheung-a 6.00
Free Comic Book Day 2013 (Infinity) 1 (5/13, giveaway) Previews series; Cheung-a 3.00

INFINITY ABYSS (Also see Marvel Universe: The End)
Marvel Comics: Aug, 2002 - No. 6, Oct, 2002 ($2.99, limited series)
1-5-Starlin-s/a; Thanos, Captain Marvel, Spider-Man, Dr. Strange app. 4.00
6-($3.50) 4.00
Thanos Vol. 2: Infinity Abyss TPB (2003, $17.99) r/ #1-6 25.00

INFINITY COUNTDOWN
Marvel Comics: May, 2018 - No. 5, Sept, 2018 ($4.99, limited series with one-shots)
1-5-Duggan-s/Kuder-a; Guardians of the Galaxy app.; Groot restored 5.00
... Adam Warlock 1 (4/18, $4.99) Prelude to series; Duggan-s/Allred-a 5.00
... Black Widow 1 (8/18, $4.99) Duggan-s/Virella-a; Jamie Braddock app. 5.00
... Captain Marvel 1 (7/18, $4.99) McCann-s/Olortegui-a; alternate Capt. Marvels app. 5.00
... Champions 1,2 (8/18, 9/18, $4.99) 1-Zub-s/Laiso-a; Warbringer & Thanos app. 5.00
... Daredevil 1 (7/18, $4.99) Duggan-s/Sprouse, Noto & Ferguson-a 5.00
... Darkhawk 1-4 (7/18 - No. 4, 9/18, $4.99) Bowers & Sims-s/Gang Lim-a 5.00
... Prime 1 (4/18, $4.99) Prelude; Duggan-s/Deodato-a; Wolverine, Magus, Ultron app. 5.00

INFINITY CRUSADE
Marvel Comics: June, 1993 - No. 6, Nov, 1993 ($3.50/$2.50, limited series, 52 pgs.)
1-6: By Jim Starlin & Ron Lim. 1-($3.50). 2-6-($2.99) 6.00

INFINITY ENTITY, THE (Concludes in Thanos: The Infinity Entity GN)
Marvel Comics: May, 2016 - No. 4, Jun, 2016 ($3.99, limited series)
1-4: Jim Starlin-s/Alan Davis-a. 1-Rebirth of Adam Warlock. 4-Mephisto app. 4.00

INFINITY GAUNTLET (The... #2 on; see Infinity Crusade, The Infinity War & Warlock & the Infinity Watch)
Marvel Comics: July, 1991 - No. 6, Dec, 1991 ($2.50, limited series)
1-Thanos-c/stories in all; Starlin scripts in all 4 8 12 27 44 60
2-6: 5,6-Ron Lim-c/a 2 4 6 11 16 20
TPB (4/99, $24.95) r/#1-6 30.00
NOTE: ***Lim*** *a-3p(part), 5p, 6p; c-5i, 6i.* ***Perez*** *a-1-3p, 4p(part); c-1(painted), 2-4, 5i, 6i.*

INFINITY GAUNTLET (Secret Wars tie-in)
Marvel Comics: Jul, 2015 - No. 5, Jan, 2016 ($3.99, limited series)
1-5-Duggan & Weaver-s/Weaver-a; Thanos & The Guardians of the Galaxy app. 4.00

INFINITY: HEIST (Tie-in to the Infinity crossover)
Marvel Comics: Nov, 2013 - No. 4, Feb, 2014 ($3.99, limited series)
1-4-Tieri-s/Barrionuevo-a; Spymaster, Titanium Man, Whirlwind app. 4.00

INFINITY, INC. (See All-Star Squadron #25)
DC Comics: Mar, 1984 - No. 53, Aug, 1988 ($1.25, Baxter paper, 36 pgs.)
1-Brainwave, Jr., Fury, The Huntress, Jade, Northwind, Nuklon, Obsidian, Power Girl, Silver Scarab & Star Spangled Kid begin 5.00
2-13,38-49,51-53: 2-Dr. Midnite, G.A. Flash, W. Woman, Dr. Fate, Hourman, Green Lantern, Wildcat app. 5-Nudity panels. 13-Re-intro Rose and Thorn. 46,47-Millennium tie-ins. 49-Hector Hall becomes The Sandman (1970s Kirby) 3.00
14-Todd McFarlane-a (5/85, 2nd full story) 3 6 9 17 26 35
15,17-37-McFarlane-a (20,23,24: 5 pgs. only; 33: 2 pgs.); 18-24-Crisis x-over. 21-Intro new Hourman & Dr. Midnight. 26-New Wildcat app. 31-Star Spangled Kid becomes Skyman. 32-Green Fury becomes Green Flame. 33-Origin Obsidian. 35-1st modern app. G.A. Fury 4.00
16-Mr. Bones debut 1 3 4 6 8 10
50 ($2.50, 52 pgs.) 4.00
Annual 1,2: 1(12/85)-Crisis x-over. 2('88, $2.00), Special 1 ('87, $1.50) 4.00

GD VG FN VF VF/NM NM-
2.0 4.0 6.0 8.0 9.0 9.2

...: The Generations Saga Volume One HC (2011, $39.99) r/#1-4, All-Star Squadron #25,26 & All-Star Squadron Annual #2 40.00
NOTE: ***Kubert*** *r-4.* ***McFarlane*** *a-14-37p, Annual 1p; c(p)-14-19, 22, 25, 26, 31-33, 37, Annual 1.* ***Newton*** *a-12p, 13p(last work 4/85).* ***Tuska*** *a-11p. JSA app. 3-10.*

INFINITY, INC. (See 52)
DC Comics: Nov, 2007 - No. 12, Oct, 2008 ($2.99)
1-12: 1-Milligan-s; Steel app. 3.00
...: Luthor's Monsters TPB (2008, $14.99) r/#1-5 15.00
...: The Bogeyman TPB (2008, $14.99) r/#6-10 15.00

INFINITY MAN AND THE FOREVER PEOPLE
DC Comics: Aug, 2014 - No. 9, May, 2015 ($2.99)
1-9: 1-DiDio-s/Giffen-a. 2,5,6-Grummett-a. 3-Starlin-a. 4-6-Guy Gardner app. 9-Giffen-a 3.00
...: Futures End 1 (11/14, $2.99, regular-c) Five years later; Philip Tan-a 3.00
...: Futures End 1 (11/14, $3.99, 3-D cover) 4.00

INFINITY: THE HUNT (Tie-in to the Infinity crossover)
Marvel Comics: Nov, 2013 - No. 4, Jan, 2014 ($3.99, limited series)
1-4-Kindt-s/Sanders-a; Avengers Academy, Wolverine & She-Hulk app. 4.00

INFINITY WAR, THE (Also see Infinity Gauntlet & Warlock and the Infinity...)
Marvel Comics: June, 1992 - No. 6, Nov, 1992 ($2.50, mini-series)
1-Starlin scripts, Lim-c/a(p), Thanos app. in all 1 3 4 6 8 10
2-6: All have wraparound gatefold covers 6.00
TPB (2006, $29.99) r/#1-6, Marvel Comics Presents #108-111, Warlock and the Infinity Watch #7-10; cover gallery and synopses of Infinity War crossovers 30.00

INFINITY WARS (Also see Infinity Countdown)
Marvel Comics: Oct, 2018 - No. 6 ($5.99/$4.99, limited series)
1-($5.99) Duggan-s/Deodato-a; Guardians of the Galaxy, Dr. Strange, Loki app. 6.00
2-5-($4.99) 3-Infinity Warps created; Deodato-a 5.00
6-($5.99) Duggan-s/Deodato-a; Adam Warlock app. 6.00
...: Fallen Guardian 1 (2/19, $4.99) MacDonald-a; takes place after #6 5.00
... Infinity 1 (3/19, $3.99) Duggan-s/Bagley-a; The fate of the Time Stone; Loki app. 4.00
... Prime 1 (9/18, $4.99) Duggan-s/Deodato-a; prelude to series; Thanos killed 5.00

INFINITY WARS: ARACHKNIGHT
Marvel Comics: Dec, 2018 - No. 2, Jan, 2019 ($3.99, limited series)
1,2-Origin of Spider-Man/Moon Knight combo; Hopeless-s/Garza-a 4.00

INFINITY WARS: GHOST PANTHER
Marvel Comics: Jan, 2019 - No. 2, Feb, 2019 ($3.99, limited series)
1,2-Origin of Ghost Rider/Black Panther combo; MacKay-s/Palo-a; Killraven app. 4.00

INFINITY WARS: INFINITY WARPS
Marvel Comics: Jan, 2019 - No. 2, Feb, 2019 ($3.99, limited series)
1,2-Short stories of Observer-X, Moon Squirrel and Tippysaur, Green Widow and others 4.00

INFINITY WARS: IRON HAMMER
Marvel Comics: Nov, 2018 - No. 2, Dec, 2018 ($3.99, limited series)
1,2-Origin of Iron Man/Thor combo; Ewing-s/Rosanas-a 4.00

INFINITY WARS: SLEEPWALKER
Marvel Comics: Dec, 2018 - No. 4, Feb, 2019 ($3.99, limited series)
1-4-Bowers & Sims-s/Nauck-a 4.00

INFINITY WARS: SOLDIER SUPREME
Marvel Comics: Nov, 2018 - No. 2, Dec, 2018 ($3.99, limited series)
1,2: 1-Origin of Captain America/Doctor Strange combo; Duggan-s/Adam Kubert-a 4.00

INFINITY WARS: WEAPON HEX
Marvel Comics: Dec, 2018 - No. 2, Jan, 2019 ($3.99, limited series)
1,2-Origin of X-23/Scarlet Witch combo; Acker & Blacker-s/Sandoval-a 4.00

INFORMER, THE
Feature Television Productions: April, 1954 - No. 5, Dec, 1954
1-Sekowsky-a begins 20 40 60 114 182 250
2 10 20 30 58 79 100
3-5 9 18 27 50 65 80

IN HIS STEPS
Spire Christian Comics (Fleming H. Revell Co.): 1973, 1977 (39/49¢)
nn 2 4 6 11 16 20

INHUMAN (Also see Uncanny Inhumans)
Marvel Comics: Jun, 2014 - No. 14, Jun, 2015 ($3.99)
1-14: 1-3-Soule-s/Madureira-a; Medusa app. 4-7,9-11-Stegman-a. 10-Spider-Man app. 4.00
Annual 1 (7/15, $4.99) Soule-s/Stegman-a; continues from #14; Ms. Marvel app. 5.00
... Special 1 (6/15, $4.99) Crossover with Amaz. Spider-Man & All-New Capt. America 5.00

INHUMANITY
Marvel Comics: Feb, 2014 - No. 2, Mar, 2014 ($3.99)

1,2: 1-After the fall of Attilan, origin of the Inhumans retold; Fraction-s/Coipel-a 4.00
...: Superior Spider-Man 1 (3/14, $3.99) Gage-s/Hans-a/c 4.00
...: The Awakening 1,2 (2/14 - No. 2, 3/14, $3.99) Kindt-s/Davidson-a 4.00

INHUMANOIDS, THE (TV)
Marvel Comics (Star Comics): Jan, 1987 - No. 4, July 1987

1-4: Based on Hasbro toys 4.00

INHUMANS, THE (See Amazing Adventures, Fantastic Four #54 & Special #5, Incredible Hulk Special #1, Marvel Graphic Novel & Thor #146)
Marvel Comics Group: Oct, 1975 - No. 12, Aug, 1977

1: #1-4,6 are 25¢ issues 6 12 18 41 76 110
2-4-Peréz-a 3 6 9 14 20 25
5-12: 9-Reprints Amazing Adventures #1,2('70). 12-Hulk app.
2 4 6 10 14 18
4-(30¢-c variant, limited distribution)(4/76) Pérez-a 4 8 12 27 44 60
6-(30¢-c variant, limited distribution)(8/76) 4 8 12 27 44 60
11,12-(35¢-c variants, limited distribution) 6 12 18 41 76 110
Special 1(4/90, $1.50, 52 pgs.)-F.F. cameo 5.00
...: The Great Refuge (5/95, $2.95) 4.00
NOTE: ***Buckler** c-2-4p, 5. **Gil Kane** a-5-7p; c-1p, 7p, 8p. **Kirby** a-9r. **Mooney** a-11i. **Perez** a-1-4p, 8p.*

INHUMANS (Marvel Knights)
Marvel Comics: Nov, 1998 - No. 12, Oct, 1999 ($2.99, limited series)

1-Jae Lee-c/a; Paul Jenkins-s 3 6 9 15 22 28
1-($6.95) DF Edition; Jae Lee variant-c 3 6 9 17 26 35
2-Two covers by Lee and Darrow 6.00
3,4,6-12 4.00
5-1st app. Yelena Belova (Black Widow) 6 12 18 38 69 100
TPB (10/00, $24.95) r/#1-12 25.00

INHUMANS (Volume 3)
Marvel Comics: Jun, 2000 - No. 4, Oct, 2000 ($2.99, limited series)

1-4-Ladronn-c/Pacheco & Marin-s. 1-3-Ladronn-a. 4-Lucas-a 3.00

INHUMANS (Volume 6)
Marvel Comics: Jun, 2003 - No. 12, Jun, 2004 ($2.50/$2.99)

1-12: 1-6-McKeever-s/Clark-a/JH Williams III-c. 7-Begin $2.99-c. 7,8-Teranishi-a 3.00
Vol. 1: Culture Shock (2005, $7.99, digest) r/#1-6; story pitch and sketch pages 8.00

INHUMANS: ATTILAN RISING (Secret Wars tie-in)
Marvel Comics: Jul, 2015 - No. 5, Nov, 2015 ($3.99, limited series)

1-5-Soule-s/Timms-a/Johnson-c 4.00

INHUMANS: JUDGMENT DAY
Marvel Comics: Mar, 2018 ($4.99, one-shot)

1-Follows from Royals #12; Al Ewing-s/Del Mundo & Libranda-a; Acuna-c 5.00

INHUMANS: ONCE AND FUTURE KINGS
Marvel Comics: Oct, 2017 - No. 5, Feb, 2018 ($3.99, limited series)

1-5: 1-Priest-s/Noto-a; young Black Bolt, Maximus & Medusa. 4-Spider-Man app. 4.00

INHUMANS PRIME
Marvel Comics: May, 2017 ($4.99, one-shot)

1-Follows IVX series; leads into Royals #1; Al Ewing-s/Ryan Sook & Chris Allen-a 5.00

INHUMANS 2099
Marvel Comics: Nov, 2004 ($2.99, one-shot)

1-Kirkman-s/Rathburn-a/Pat Lee-c 3.00

INHUMANS VS. X-MEN (See IVX)

INJECTION
Image Comics: May, 2015 - No. 15, Nov, 2017 ($2.99/$3.99)

1-10-Warren Ellis-s/Declan Shalvey-a 3.00
11-15-($3.99) 4.00

INJUSTICE: GODS AMONG US (Based on the video game)
DC Comics: Mar, 2013 - No. 12, Feb, 2014 ($3.99)

1-Lois Lane dies; Joker app. 3 6 9 19 30 40
1-Variant-c 4 8 12 23 37 50
1-Second printing 6.00
2-Joker killed 10.00
3-12: 6-Nightwing dies 4.00
Annual 1 (1/14, $4.99) Harley Quinn & Lobo app.; Ryp-c 5.00

INJUSTICE (Gods Among Us:) **YEAR TWO** (Based on the video game)
DC Comics: Mar, 2014 - No. 12, Late Nov, 2014 ($2.99)

1-Sinestro app. 1 2 3 5 6 8
2-12: 2-6,9-12-Sinestro app. 7-11-Harley Quinn app. 4.00
Annual 1 (12/14, $4.99) Stories of Oracle, Green Lantern & Sinestro; Raapack-c 5.00

INJUSTICE: GODS AMONG US: YEAR THREE (Based on the video game)
DC Comics: Early Dec, 2014 - No. 12, Late May, 2015 ($2.99, printings of digital-first stories)

1-12: 1-Constantine joins the fight. 5-New Deadman app. 3.00
Annual 1 (6/15, $4.99) Prequel to Year Three; Constantine app.; Titans vs. Superman 5.00

INJUSTICE: GODS AMONG US: YEAR FOUR (Based on the video game)
DC Comics: Early Jul, 2015 - No. 12, Late Dec, 2015 ($2.99, printings of digital-first stories)

1-12: 1-The Olympus Gods join the fight. 10-Harley Quinn cover 3.00

INJUSTICE: GODS AMONG US: YEAR FIVE (Based on the video game)
DC Comics: Early Mar, 2016 - No. 20, Late Dec, 2016 ($2.99, printings of digital-first stories)

1-20: 1-Doomsday & Bane app. 6-Solomon Grundy app. 7-Damian becomes Nightwing. 12-Alfred killed by Zsasz. 18-Deathstroke app. 3.00
Annual 1 (1/17, $4.99) Harley Quinn app.; leads into Injustice: Ground Zero 5.00

INJUSTICE: GROUND ZERO (Follows Year Five)
DC Comics: Early Feb, 2016 - No. 12, Jul, 2017 ($2.99, printings of digital-first stories)

1-12: 1-Mhan & Derenick-a; Harley & Joker app. 12-Superman vs. Superman 3.00

INJUSTICE 2 (Follows Ground Zero)(Prequel to the Injustice 2 video game)
DC Comics: Early Jul, 2017 - No. 36, Dec, 2018 ($2.99, printings of digital-first stories)

1-36: 1-Taylor-s/Redondo-a; Harley joins the Suicide Squad. 3-Intro. Athanasia. 6-Intro/origin Supergirl 3.00
Annual 1 (1/18, $4.99) Origin of Wonder Woman; back-up with Harley Quinn; Mhan-a 5.00
Annual 2 (1/19, $4.99) Follows #36; Ma & Pa Kent app.; Redondo-a 5.00

INJUSTICE VS. MASTERS OF THE UNIVERSE (Injustice: Gods Among Us)
DC Comics: Sept, 2018 - No. 6, Mar, 2019 ($3.99, limited series)

1-Seeley-s/Williams II-a; Justice Leaguers & He-Man vs. Darkseid & Skeletor
1 2 3 5 6 8
1-Variant-c by Tim Seeley 2 4 6 8 10 12
2-6 4.00

INKBLOT
Image Comics: Sept, 2020 - Present ($3.99)

1-15-Emma Kubert & Rusty Gladd-s/a 4.00

INKY & DINKY (See Felix's Nephews...)

IN LOVE (...Magazine on-c; I Love You No. 7 on)
Mainline/Charlton No. 5 (5/55)-on: Aug-Sept, 1954 - No. 6, July, 1955 ('Adult Reading' on-c)

1-Simon & Kirby-a; book-length novel in all issues 68 136 204 435 743 1050
2,3-S&K-a. 3-Last pre-code (12-1/54-55) 39 78 117 240 395 550
4-S&K-a.(Rare) 41 82 123 256 428 600
5-S&K-c only 23 46 69 136 223 310
6-No S&K-a 15 30 45 86 133 180

IN SEARCH OF THE CASTAWAYS (See Movie Comics)

INSEXTS
AfterShock Comics: Dec, 2015 - No. 13, Sept, 2017 ($3.99, mature)

1-13-Marguerite Bennett-s/Ariela Kristantina-a 4.00

INSIDE CRIME (Formerly My Intimate Affair)
Fox Feature Syndicate (Hero Books): No. 3, July, 1950 - No. 2, Sept, 1950

3-Wood-a (10 pgs.); L. B. Cole-c 39 78 117 240 395 550
2-Used in **SOTI**, pg. 182,183; r/Spook #24 29 58 87 172 281 390
nn (nd, M.S. Dist. Pub.) Wally Wood-c 14 28 42 80 115 150

INSPECTOR, THE (TV) (Also see The Pink Panther)
Gold Key: July, 1974 - No. 19, Feb, 1978

1 3 6 9 18 28 38
2-5 2 4 6 13 18 22
6-9 2 4 6 10 14 18
10-19: 11-Reprints 2 4 6 8 10 12

INSPECTOR, THE Volume 2 (The Pink Panther)
American Mythology: 2016 ($3.99, one-shot)

1-The Pink Files; new stories by Fridolfs & Gallagher; reprints 4.00

INSPECTOR GILL OF THE FISH POLICE (See Fish Police)

INSPECTOR WADE
David McKay Publications: No. 13, May, 1938

Feature Books 13 39 78 117 240 395 550

INSTANT PIANO
Dark Horse Comics: Aug, 1994 - No. 4, Feb, 1995 ($3.95, B&W, bimonthly, mature)

1-4 4.00

INSUFFERABLE
IDW Publishing: May, 2015 - No. 8, Dec, 2015 ($3.99)

1-8-Waid-s/Krause-a 4.00

INSUFFERABLE: HOME FIELD ADVANTAGE
IDW Publishing: Oct, 2016 - No. 4, Jan, 2017 ($3.99)

1-4-Waid-s/Krause-a 4.00

INSUFFERABLE: ON THE ROAD
IDW Publishing: Feb, 2016 - No. 6, Jul, 2016 ($3.99)

1-6-Waid-s/Krause-a 4.00

INSURGENT
DC Comics: Mar, 2013 - No. 3, May, 2013 ($2.99, limited series)

1-3-DeSanto & Farmer-s/Dallocchio-a 3.00

INTERFACE
Marvel Comics (Epic Comics): Dec, 1989 - No. 8, Dec, 1990 ($1.95, mature, coated paper)

1-8: Cont. from 1st ESPers series; painted-c/a 3.00
Espers: Interface TPB ('98, $16.95) r/#1-6 17.00

INTERNATIONAL COMICS (...Crime Patrol No. 6)
E. C. Comics: Spring, 1947 - No. 5, Nov-Dec, 1947

1-Schaffenberger-a begins, ends #4 142 284 426 909 1555 2200
2 65 130 195 416 708 1000
3-5 55 110 165 352 601 850

INTERNATIONAL CRIME PATROL (Formerly International Comics #1-5; becomes Crime Patrol No. 7 on)
E. C. Comics: No. 6, Spring, 1948

6-Moon Girl app. 271 542 813 1721 2961 4200

INTERNATIONAL IRON MAN
Marvel Comics: May, 2016 - No. 7, Nov, 2016 ($3.99)

1-7-Bendis-s/Maleev-a. 1-4-Flashback to college years in London. 5-Intro. Amanda Armstrong. 6,7-Flashback to Stark's real parents meeting 4.00

INTERSECT
Image Comics: Nov, 2014 - No. 6, Apr, 2015 ($3.50)

1-6-Ray Fawkes-s/a. 1-Lemire-c. 2-Kindt-c 3.50

IN THE DAYS OF THE MOB (Magazine)
Hampshire Dist. Ltd. (National): Fall, 1971 (B&W)

1-Kirby-a; John Dillinger wanted poster inside (1/2 value if poster is missing)
7 14 21 48 89 130

Injustice 2 #25 © DC

Invader Zim #37 © Viacom

Invincible #41 © Kirkman & Walker

GD VG FN VF VF/NM NM-
2.0 4.0 6.0 8.0 9.0 9.2

IN THE PRESENCE OF MINE ENEMIES
Spire Christian Comics/Fleming H. Revell Co.: 1973 (35/49¢)
nn 3 6 9 15 22 28

IN THE SHADOW OF EDGAR ALLAN POE
DC Comics (Vertigo): 2002 (Graphic novel)
Hardcover (2002, $24.95) Fuqua-s/Phillips and Parke photo-a 25.00
Softcover (2003, $17.95) 18.00

INTIMATE
Charlton Comics: Dec, 1957 - No. 3, May, 1958
1 37 74 111 222 361 500
2,3 14 28 42 80 115 150

INTIMATE CONFESSIONS (See Fox Giants)

INTIMATE CONFESSIONS
Country Press Inc.: 1942
nn-Ashcan comic, not distributed to newsstands, only for in house use. A VF copy sold for $1,000 in 2007, and a VF+ copy sold for $1,525 in 2007.

INTIMATE CONFESSIONS
Realistic Comics: July-Aug, 1951 - No. 7, Aug, 1952; No. 8, Mar, 1953 (All painted-c)
1-Kinstler-a; c/Avon paperback #222 232 464 696 1485 2543 3600
2 57 114 171 362 619 875
3-c/Avon paperback #250; Kinstler-c/a 58 116 174 371 636 900
4-8: 4-c/Avon paperback #304; Kinstler-c. 6-c/Avon paperback #120. 8-c/Avon paperback #375; Kinstler-a 50 100 150 315 533 750

INTIMATE CONFESSIONS
I. W. Enterprises/Super Comics: 1964
I.W. Reprint #9,10, Super Reprint #10,12,18 3 6 9 15 22 28

INTIMATE LOVE
Standard Comics: No. 5, 1950 - No. 28, Aug, 1954
5-8: 6-8-Severin/Elder-a 15 30 45 85 130 175
9 13 26 39 72 101 130
10-Jane Russell, Robert Mitchum photo-c 18 36 54 105 165 225
11-18,20,23,25,27,28 12 24 36 67 94 120
19,21,22,24,26-Toth-a 13 26 39 74 105 135
NOTE: *Celardo a-8, 10. **Colletta** a-23. **Moreira** a-13(2). Photo-c-6, 7, 10, 12, 14, 15, 18-20, 24, 26, 27.*

INTIMATES, THE
DC Comics (WildStorm): Jan, 2005 - No. 12, Dec, 2005 ($2.95/$2.99)
1-12: 1-Joe Casey-s/Jim Lee-c/Lee and Giuseppe Camuncoli-a 3.00

INTIMATE SECRETS OF ROMANCE
Star Publications: Sept, 1953 - No. 2, Apr, 1954
1,2-L. B. Cole-c 28 56 84 165 270 375

INTRIGUE
Quality Comics Group: Jan, 1955
1-Horror; Jack Cole reprint/Web of Evil 45 90 135 284 480 675

INTRIGUE
Image Comics: Aug, 1999 - No. 3, Feb, 2000 ($2.50/$2.95)
1,2: 1-Two covers (Andrews, Wieringo); Shum-s/Andrews-a 3.00
3-($2.95) 3.00

INTRUDER
TSR, Inc.: 1990 - No. 10, 1991 ($2.95, 44 pgs.)
1-10 4.00

INVADERS, THE (TV)(Aliens From a Dying Planet)
Gold Key: Oct, 1967 - No. 4, Oct, 1968 (All have photo-c)
1-Spiegle-a in all 9 18 27 60 120 180
2-4: 2-Pin-up on back-c. 3-Has variant 15¢-c with photo back-c 6 12 18 37 66 95

INVADERS, THE (Also see The Avengers #71, Giant-Size Invaders, and All-New Invaders)
Marvel Comics Group: August, 1975 - No. 40, May, 1979; No. 41, Sept, 1979
1-Captain America & Bucky, Human Torch & Toro, & Sub-Mariner begin; cont'd. from Giant Size Invaders #1; #1-7 are 25¢ issues 7 14 21 44 82 120
2-5: 2-1st app. Brain-Drain. 3-Battle issue; Cap vs. Namor vs. Torch; intro U-Man 3 6 9 19 30 40
6,9,10: 6-(Regular 25¢ edition). 6-(7/76) Liberty Legion app. 9-Origin Baron Blood. 10-G.A. Capt. America-r/C.A #22 2 4 6 11 16 20
6-(30¢-c variant, limited distribution) 6 12 18 38 69 100
7-(Reg. 25¢ edition) Intro Baron Blood & intro/1st app. Union Jack; Human Torch origin retold 6 12 18 41 76 110

GD VG FN VF VF/NM NM-
2.0 4.0 6.0 8.0 9.0 9.2

7-(30¢-c variant, limited distribution) 11 22 33 73 157 240
8-Union Jack-c/story 4 8 12 27 44 60
11,13-16,19: 11-Origin Spitfire; intro The Blue Bullet. 14-1st app. The Crusaders. 16-Re-intro The Destroyer. 19-Hitler-c/story 2 4 6 9 13 16
12-1st Jacqueline as Spitfire 5 10 15 31 53 75
17,18-(Regular 30¢-c): 17-Intro Warrior Woman. 18-Re-intro The Destroyer w/new origin 3 6 9 21 33 45
17-19,21-(35¢-c variants, limited distribution) 11 22 33 75 160 245
20-(Regular 30¢-c) Reprints origin/1st app. Sub-Mariner from Motion Picture Funnies Weekly with color added & brief write-up about MPFW; 1st app. new Union Jack II 5 10 15 31 53 75
20-(35¢-c variant, limited distribution) 12 24 36 80 173 265
21-(Regular 30¢ edition)-r/Marvel Mystery #10 (battle issue) 2 4 6 9 13 16
22-30,34-40: 22-New origin Toro. 24-r/Marvel Mystery #17 (team-up issue; all-r). 25-All new-a begins. 28-Intro new Human Top & Golden Girl. 29-Intro Teutonic Knight. 34-Mighty Destroyer joins. 35-The Whizzer app. 1 3 4 6 8 10
31-33: 31-Frankenstein-c/sty. 32,33-Thor app. 2 4 6 8 11 14
41-Double size last issue 3 6 9 16 23 30
Annual 1 (9/77)-Schomburg, Rico stories (new); Schomburg-c/a (1st for Marvel in 30 years); Avengers app.; re-intro The Shark & The Hyena 5 10 15 33 57 80
... Classic Vol. 1 TPB (2007, $24.99) r/#1-9, Giant-Size Invaders #1 and Marvel Premiere #29,30; cover pencils and cover inks 25.00
NOTE: ***Buckler** a-5. **Everett** r-20('39), 21(1940), 24, Annual 1. **Gil Kane** c(p)-13, 17, 18, 20-27. **Kirby** c(p)-3-12, 14-16, 32, 33. **Mooney** a-5i, 16, 22. **Robbins** a-1-4, 6-9, 10(3 pg.), 11-15, 17-21, 23, 25-28; c-28.*

INVADERS (See Namor, the Sub-Mariner #12)
Marvel Comics Group: May, 1993 - No. 4, Aug, 1993 ($1.75, limited series)
1-4 4.00

INVADERS (2004 title - see New Invaders)

INVADERS
Marvel Comics: Mar, 2019 - No. 12, Feb, 2020 ($4.99/$3.99)
1-($4.99) Zdarsky-s/Magno & Guice-a; Captain America, Namor & Winter Soldier 5.00
2-12-($3.99) 2-Hydro-Man app. 5-7-Avengers app. 4.00

INVADERS FROM HOME
DC Comics (Piranha Press): 1990 - No. 6, 1990 ($2.50, mature)
1-6 3.00

INVADERS NOW! (See Avengers/Invaders and The Torch series)
Marvel Comics: Nov, 2010 - No. 5, Mar, 2011 ($3.99, limited series)
1-5-Alex Ross-c; Steve Rogers, Bucky, Human Torch & Toro, Sub-Mariner app. 4.00

INVADER ZIM
Oni Press: Jul, 2015 - Present ($3.99)
1-Jhonen Vasquez-s/Aaron Alexovich-a; multiple covers 4.00
2-49: 40-Multiverse Zims; short stories by various 4.00
50-($6.99) Vasquez & Trueheart-s/Wucinich-a 7.00
... #1 Square One Edition (2/17, $1.00) r/#1 3.00
...: Free Comic Book Day Edition (5/18, giveaway) r/#20; Floopsy & Shmoopsy app. 3.00
...: Oni 25th Anniversary Edition (11/22, $9.99) r/#1; silver foil cover enhancements 10.00

INVADER ZIM QUARTERLY
Oni Press: Jun, 2020 - Present ($5.99)
...Dib's Dilemma 1 (9/20, $5.99) Logan-s/Wucinich-a; multiple covers 6.00
...Gir's Big Day 1 (6/20, $5.99) Eric Trueheart-s/Aaron Alexovich-a; multiple covers 6.00

INVASION
DC Comics: Holiday, 1988-'89 - No. 3, Jan, 1989 ($2.95, lim. series, 84 pgs.)
1-3: 1-McFarlane/Russell-a. 2-McFarlane/Russell & Giffen/Gordon-a 5.00
Invasion! TPB (2008, $24.99) r/#1-3 25.00

INVINCIBLE (Also see The Pact #4)
Image Comics: Jan, 2003 - No. 144, Feb, 2018 ($2.95/$2.99)
1-Kirkman-s/Walker-a 38 76 114 285 641 1000
2-Kirkman-s/Walker-a 10 20 30 64 132 200
3-Kirkman-s/Walker-a 4 8 12 25 40 55
4-8: 4-Preview of The Moth 2 4 6 11 16 20
9,12-14: 14-Cho-c 2 4 6 8 10 12
10 3 6 9 21 33 45
11-Origin of Omni-Man 8 16 24 51 96 140
15-24,26-41,43-49: 33-Tie-in w/Marvel Team-Up #14 6.00
25-($4.95) Science Dog app.; back-up stories w/origins of Science Dog and teammates 6.00
42-($1.99) Includes re-cap of the entire series 5.00
50-(6/08, $4.99) Two covers; back-up origin of Cecil Stedman; Science Dog app. 1 3 4 6 8 10
51-59,61-74: 51-Jim Lee-c; new costumes. 57-Continues in Astounding Wolf-Man #11.

	GD 2.0	VG 4.0	FN 6.0	VF 8.0	VF/NM 9.0	NM- 9.2

71-74-Viltrumite War 4.00
76-99,101-109,111-117: 89-Intro. Zandale. 97-Origin of Bulletproof. 112-Baby born 3.00
60-($3.99) Invincible War; Witchblade, Savage Dragon, Spawn, Youngblood app. 1 2 3 5 6 8
75-($5.99) Viltrumite War; Science Dog back-up; 2 covers 1 3 4 6 8 10
100-(1/13, $3.99) "The Death of Everyone" conclusion; multiple covers 5.00
110-Rape issue 6.00
118-141: 118-(25¢-c). 124-126-Reboot. 132-Oliver dies. 133-(25¢-c) Mark & Eve wedding 3.00
142-143-($3.99) 4.00
144-($5.99) Last issue; art by Ottley & Walker 6.00
#0-(4/05, 50¢) Origin of Invincible; Ottley-a 3.00
#1 Facsimile Edition-(1/23, $3.99) Reprints #1 4.00
Image Firsts: Invincible #1 (4/10, $1.00) r/#1 with "Image Firsts" cover logo 3.00
Official Handbook of the Invincible Universe 1,2 (11/06, 1/07, $4.99) profile pages 5.00
Official Handbook of the Invincible Universe Vol. 1 (2007, $12.99) r/#1-2; sketch pages 13.00
... Presents Atom Eve 1,2 (12/07, 3/08, $2.99) origin of Atom Eve; Bellegarde-a 3.00
... Presents Atom Eve & Rex Splode 1-3 (10/09 - 2/10, $2.99) origin of Rex 3.00
... Returns (4/10, $3.99) Leads into Viltrumite War in #71; 4 covers 4.00
... Undeluxe #1-(1/23, $3.99) Reprints #1 in B&W with bonus sketch art 4.00
... Universe Primer 1 (5/08, $5.99) r/Invincible #1, Brit #1, Astounding Wolf-Man #1 6.00
The Complete Invincible Library Vol. 1 Slipcase HC (2006, $125.00) oversized r/#1-24, #0 and story from Image Comics Summer Special (FCBD 2004); sketch pages; script for #1 125.00
..., Ultimate Collection Vol. 1 HC (2005, $34.95) oversized r/#1-13; sketch pages 35.00
..., Ultimate Collection Vol. 2 HC (2006, $34.99) oversized r/#14-24, #0 and story from Image Comics Summer Special (FCBD 2004); sketch pages and script for #23; intro by Damon Lindelof; afterword by Robert Kirkman 35.00
..., Ultimate Collection Vol. 3 HC (2007, $34.95) oversized r/#25-35 & The Pact #4; sketch pages and script for #28; afterword by Robert Kirkman 35.00
..., Ultimate Collection Vol. 4 HC (2008, $34.99) oversized r/#36-47; sketch & script pgs. 35.00
Vol. 1: Family Matters TPB (8/03, $12.95) r/#1-4; intro. by Busiek; sketch pages 13.00
Vol. 2: Eight in Enough TPB (3/04, $12.95) r/#5-8; intro. by Larsen; sketch pages 13.00
Vol. 3: Perfect Strangers TPB (2004, $12.95) r/#9-12; intro. by Brevoort; sketch pages 13.00
Vol. 4: Head of the Class TPB (1/05, $14.95) r/#14-19; intro. by Waid; sketch pages 15.00
Vol. 5: The Facts of Life TPB (2005, $14.99) r/#0,20-24; intro. by Wieringo; sketch pages 15.00
Vol. 6: A Different World TPB (2006, $14.99) r/#25-30; intro. by Brubaker; sketch pages 15.00
Vol. 7: Three's Company TPB (2006, $14.99) r/#31-35 & The Pact #4; sketch pages 15.00
Vol. 8: My Favorite Martian TPB (2007, $14.99) r/#36-41; sketch pages 15.00
Vol. 9: Out of This World TPB (2008, $14.99) r/#42-47; sketch pages 15.00

INVINCIBLE FOUR OF KUNG FU & NINJA
Leung Publications: April, 1988 - No. 6, 1989 ($2.00)

1-($2.75) 4.00
2-6: 2-Begin $2.00-c 3.00

INVINCIBLE IRON MAN
Marvel Comics: July, 2008 - No. 33, Feb, 2011;
No. 500, Mar, 2011 - No. 527, Dec, 2012 ($2.99/$3.99)

1-Fraction-s/Larroca-a; covers by Larroca & Quesada 5.00
1-Downey movie photo wraparound 6.00
1-Secret Movie Variant white-c with movie cast 30.00
2-18: 2-War Machine and Thor app. 7-Spider-Man app. 8-10-Dark Reign. 11-War Machine app.; Pepper gets her armor suit. 12-Namor app. 3.00
19,20-($3.99) 20-Stark Disassembled starts; back-up synopsis of recent storylines 4.00
21-24-Covers by Larocca and Zircher: 21-Thor & Capt. America app. 22-Dr. Strange app. 3.00
25-($3.99) Fraction-s/Larroca-a; new armor 4.00
26-31-($2.99) 29-New Rescue armor 3.00
32,33-($3.99)-War Machine app.; back-up w/McKelvie-a 4.00

(After #33, numbering reverts to original Vol. 1 as #500)

500-(3/11, $4.99) Two covers by Larroca; Mandarin & Spider-Man app.; cover gallery 5.00
500-Variant-c by Romita Jr. 10.00
500.1 (4/11, $2.99) History re-told; Fraction-s/Larroca-a/c 3.00
501-527-($3.99) 501-503-Doctor Octopus app. 503-Back-up w/Chaykin-a. 504-509-Fear Itself tie-in; Grey Gargoyle app. 517-New War Machine armor 4.00
Annual 1 (8/10, $4.99) Larroca-c; history of the Mandarin; Di Giandomenico-a 5.00
...MGC #1 (4/10, free) r/#1 with "Marvel's Greatest Comics" cover logo 3.00

INVINCIBLE IRON MAN
Marvel Comics: Dec, 2015 - No. 14, Dec, 2016 ($3.99)

1-6,8,10-14: 1-Bendis-s/Marquez-a; Doctor Doom & Madame Masque app. 6-14-Deodato-a. 8-Spider-Man app. 11-14-Civil War II tie-in 4.00
7-1st app. Riri Williams (cameo); Spider-Man app. 6 12 18 41 76 110
9-1st full app. of Riri Williams 6 12 18 41 76 110

INVINCIBLE IRON MAN (Riri Williams as Ironheart)
Marvel Comics: Jan, 2017 - No. 11, Nov, 2017 ($3.99)

1-11: 1-Bendis-s/Caselli-a; Riri Williams childhood origin; Animax app. 4.00

INVINCIBLE IRON MAN (Marvel Legacy)(Also continued from Infamous Iron Man)
Marvel Comics: No. 593, Dec, 2017 - No. 600, Jul, 2018 ($3.99)

593-599-Bendis-s/Caselli & Maleev-a; Ironheart & Doctor Doom app. 4.00
600-($5.99) James Rhodes returns; leads into Tony Stark: Iron Man series 6.00

INVINCIBLE RED SONJA, THE
Dynamite Entertainment: 2021 - No. 10, 2022 ($3.99)

1-10-Palmiotti & Conner-s/Moritat-a 4.00

INVINCIBLE UNIVERSE (Characters from Invincible)
Image Comics: Apr, 2013 - No. 12, Apr, 2014 ($2.99)

1-12-Hester-s/Nauck-a. 1-Wraparound-c 3.00

INVISIBLE BOY (See Approved Comics)

INVISIBLE KINGDOM
Dark Horse Comics (Berger Books): Mar, 2019 - Present ($3.99)

1-10-G. Willow Wilson-s/Christian Ward-a 4.00

INVISIBLE MAN, THE (See Superior Stories #1 & Supernatural Thrillers #2)

INVISIBLE PEOPLE
Kitchen Sink Press: 1992 (B&W, lim. series)

Book One: Sanctum; Book Two: "The Power": Will Eisner-s/a in all 4.00
Book Three: "Mortal Combat" 4.00
Hardcover ($34.95) 35.00
TPB (DC Comics, 9/00, $12.95) reprints series 13.00

INVISIBLE REPUBLIC
Image Comics: Feb, 2015 - No. 15, Mar, 2017 ($2.99/$3.99)

1-10-Hardman & Bechko-s/Hardman-a 3.00
11-15-($3.99) 4.00

INVISIBLES, THE (1st Series)
DC Comics (Vertigo): Sept, 1994 - No. 25, Oct, 1996 ($1.95/$2.50, mature)

1-($2.95, 52 pgs.)-Intro King Mob, Ragged Robin, Boy, Lord Fanny & Dane (Jack Frost); Grant Morrison scripts in all 2 4 6 9 12 15
2-8: 4-Includes bound-in trading cards. 5-1st app. Orlando; brown paper-c 4.00
9-25: 10-Intro Jim Crow. 13-15-Origin Lord Fanny. 19-Origin King Mob; polybagged. 20-Origin Boy. 21-Mister Six revealed. 25-Intro Division X 3.00
Apocalipstick (2001, $19.95, TPB)-r/#9-16; Bolland-c 20.00
Entropy in the U.K. (2001, $19.95, TPB)-r/#17-25; Bolland-c 20.00
Say You Want A Revolution (1996, $17.50, TPB)-r/#1-8 18.00
NOTE: ***Buckingham*** *a-25p.* ***Rian Hughes*** *c-1, 5.* ***Phil Jimenez*** *a-17p-19p.* ***Paul Johnson*** *a-16, 21.* ***Sean Phillips*** *c-2-4, 6-25.* ***Weston*** *a-10p.* ***Yeowell*** *a-1p-4p, 22p-24p.*

INVISIBLES, THE (2nd Series)
DC Comics (Vertigo): V2#1, Feb, 1997 - No. 22, Feb, 1999 ($2.50, mature)

1-Intro Jolly Roger; Grant Morrison scripts, Phil Jimenez-a, & Brian Bolland-c begins 6.00
2-22: 9,14-Weston-a 4.00
Bloody Hell in America TPB ('98, $12.95) r/#1-4 13.00
Counting to None TPB ('99, $19.95) r/#5-13 20.00
Kissing Mr. Quimper TPB ('00, $19.95) r/#14-22 20.00

INVISIBLES, THE (3rd Series) (Issue #'s go in reverse from #12 to #1)
DC Comics (Vertigo): V3#12, Apr, 1999 - No. 1, June, 2000 ($2.95, mature)

1-12-Bolland-c; Morrison-s on all. 1-Quitely-a. 2-4-Art by various. 5-8-Phillips-a. 9-12-Phillip Bond-a. 4.00
The Invisible Kingdom TPB ('02, $19.95) r/#12-1; new Bolland-c 20.00

INVISIBLE SCARLET O'NEIL (Also see Famous Funnies #81 & Harvey Comics Hits #59)
Famous Funnies (Harvey): Dec, 1950 - No. 3, Apr, 1951 (2-3 pgs. of Powell-a in each issue.)

1 27 54 81 158 259 360
2,3 20 40 60 114 182 250

INVISIBLE WOMAN (Fantastic Four)
Marvel Comics: Sept, 2019 - No. 5, Jan, 2020 ($3.99, limited series)

1-5-Mark Waid-s/Mattia De Iulis-a; main cover by Adam Hughes; Black Widow app. 4.00

ION (Green Lantern Kyle Rayner) (See Countdown)
DC Comics: Jun, 2006 - No. 12, May, 2007 ($2.99)

1-12: 1-Marz-s/Tocchini-a. 3-Mogo app. 9,10-Tangent Green Lantern app. 12-Monitor app. 3.00
...: The Torchbearer TPB (2007, $14.99) r/#1-6 15.00

I, PAPARAZZI
DC Comics (Vertigo): 2001 ($29.95, HC, digitally manipulated photographic art)

nn-Pat McGreal-s/Steven Parke-digital-a/Stephen John Phillips-photos 30.00

IRON AGE
Marvel Comics: Aug, 2011 - No. 3, Oct, 2011 ($4.99, limited series)

1-3-Iron Man time travels. 1-Avengers. 2-Fantastic Four. 3-Dazzler & X-Men 5.00
...: Alpha (8/11, $2.99) First part of the series; Dark Phoenix app.; Issacs-a 3.00
...: Omega (10/11, $2.99) Conclusion of the series; Olivetti-c/Issacs-a 3.00

IRON AND THE MAIDEN
Aspen MLT: Sept, 2007 - No. 4, Dec, 2007 ($3.99)

1-4: 1-Two covers by Manapul and Madureira/Matsuda; Jason Rubin-s 4.00
...: Brutes, Bims and the City (2/08, $2.99) character backgrounds/development art 3.00

IRON CAT
Marvel Comics: Aug, 2022 - No. 5, Dec, 2022 ($4.99/$3.99, limited series)

1-($4.99)-Jed MacKay-s Pere Pérez-a; Black Cat app. 5.00
2-5-($3.99) Madame Menace app. 4.00

IRON CORPORAL, THE (See Army War Heroes #22)
Charlton Comics: No. 23, Oct, 1985 - No. 25, Feb, 1986

23-25: Glanzman-a(r); low print 6.00

IRON FIST (See Immortal Iron Fist, Deadly Hands of Kung Fu, Marvel Premiere & Power Man)
Marvel Comics: Nov, 1975 - No. 15, Sept, 1977

	GD 2.0	VG 4.0	FN 6.0	VF 8.0	VF/NM 9.0	NM- 9.2
1-Iron Fist battles Iron Man (#1-6: 25¢)	10	20	30	64	132	200
2	4	8	12	28	47	65
3-10: 4-6-(Regular 25¢ edition)(4-6/76). 8-Origin retold	3	6	9	19	30	40
4-6-(30¢-c variant, limited distribution)	6	12	18	41	76	110
11,13: 13-(30¢-c)	3	6	9	16	24	32
12-Capt. America app.	6	12	18	38	69	100
13-(35¢-c variant, limited distribution)	16	32	48	110	243	375
14-1st app. Sabretooth (8/77)(see Power Man)	38	76	114	285	641	1000
14-(35¢-c variant, limited distribution)	162	324	486	1337	3019	4700
15-(Regular 30¢ ed.) X-Men app., Byrne-a	8	16	24	54	102	150
15-(35¢-c variant, limited distribution)	61	122	183	488	1094	1700

NOTE: ***Adkins*** *a-8p, 10i, 13i; c-8i.* ***Byrne*** *a-1-15p; c-8p, 15p.* ***G. Kane*** *c-4-6p.* ***McWilliams*** *a-1i.*

IRON FIST
Marvel Comics: Sept, 1996 - No. 2, Oct, 1996 ($1.50, limited series)

1,2 5.00

IRON FIST
Marvel Comics: Jul, 1998 - No. 3, Sept, 1998 ($2.50, limited series)

1-3: Jurgens-s/Guice-a 4.00

IRON FIST (Also see Immortal Iron Fist)
Marvel Comics: May, 2004 - No. 6, Oct, 2004 ($2.99)

1-6: 1-4,6-Kevin Lau-c/a. 5-Mays-c/a 4.00

Invincible Iron Man (2015) #4 © MAR

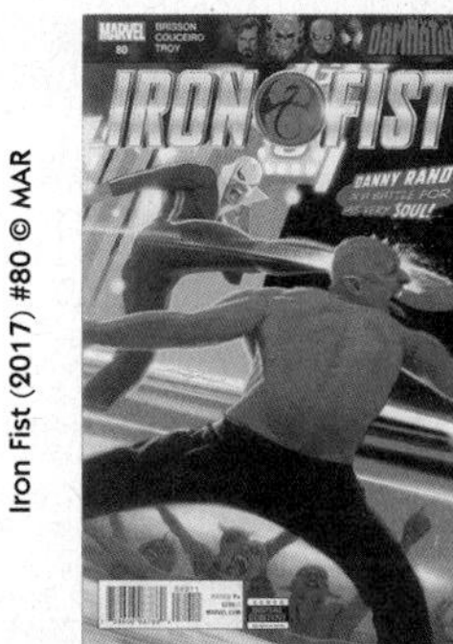

Iron Fist (2017) #80 © MAR

Iron Man #17 © MAR

GD 2.0 | VG 4.0 | FN 6.0 | VF 8.0 | VF/NM 9.0 | NM- 9.2

IRON FIST
Marvel Comics: May, 2017 - No. 7, Nov, 2017; No. 73, Dec, 2017 - No. 80, Jun, 2018 ($3.99)
1-7: 1-Brisson-s/Perkins-a. 4.00
[Title switches to legacy numbering after #7 (11/17)]
73-80: 73-77-Sabretooth app. 78-80-Damnation x-over; Orson Randall app. 4.00

IRON FIST
Marvel Comics: Apr, 2022 - No. 5, Oct, 2022 ($3.99)
1-5: 1-Intro. Lin Lie, the new Iron Fist; Danny Rand app. 5-Loki app. 4.00

IRON FIST: HEART OF THE DRAGON
Marvel Comics: Mar, 2021 - No. 6, Aug, 2021 ($3.99)
1-6-Hama-s/Wachter-a; Luke Cage, Taskmaster, and Lady Bullseye app. 4.00

IRON FIST: PHANTOM LIMB (Printing of digital-first story)
Marvel Comics: 2018 ($19.99, square-bound TPB)
nn-Chapman-s/Sanna-a; Luke Cage app. 20.00

IRON FIST: THE LIVING WEAPON
Marvel Comics: Jun, 2014 - No. 12, Jul, 2015 ($3.99)
1-12-Kaare Andrews-s/a/c; origin re-told in flashbacks 4.00

IRON FIST: WOLVERINE
Marvel Comics: Nov, 2000 - No. 4, Feb, 2001 ($2.99, limited series)
1-4-Igle-c/a; Kingpin app. 2-Iron Man app. 3,4-Capt. America app. 4.00

IRON GHOST
Image Comics: Apr, 2005 - No. 6, Mar, 2006 ($2.95/$2.99, limited series)
1-6-Chuck Dixon-s/Sergio Cariello-a; flip cover on each 3.00

IRONHAND OF ALMURIC (Robert E. Howard's...)
Dark Horse Comics: Aug, 1991 - No. 4, 1991 ($2.00, B&W, mini-series)
1-4: 1-Conrad painted-c 3.00

IRONHEART (Riri Williams) (See Invincible Iron Man #7)
Marvel Comics: Jan, 2019 - No. 12, Jan, 2020 ($4.99/$3.99)
1-($4.99) Eve L. Ewing-s/Libranda & Vecchio-a; Clash app. 5.00
2-12-($3.99) 6-Miles (Spider-Man) app. 7,8-Nadia (Wasp) app. 8-Dr. Strange app. 4.00

IRON HORSE (TV)
Dell Publishing Co.: March, 1967 - No. 2, June, 1967
1-Dale Robertson photo covers on both 3 6 9 17 26 35
2 3 6 9 15 21 26

IRONJAW (Also see The Barbarians)
Atlas/Seaboard Publ.: Jan, 1975 - No. 4, July, 1975
1,2-Neal Adams-c. 1-1st app. Iron Jaw; Sekowsky-a(p); Fleisher-s
3 6 9 16 24 32
3,4-Marcos. 4-Origin 2 4 6 9 13 16

IRON LANTERN
Marvel Comics (Amalgam): June, 1997 ($1.95, one-shot)
1-Kurt Busiek-s/Paul Smith & Al Williamson-a 4.00

IRON MAIDEN LEGACY OF THE BEAST
Heavy Metal Inc.: Oct, 2017 - No. 5 ($3.99, limited series)
1-Llexi Leon & Edginton-s/West-a/Casas-c; Eddie app. 4.00

IRON MAN (Also see The Avengers #1, Giant-Size..., Marvel Collectors Item Classics, Marvel Double Feature, Marvel Fanfare, Tales of Suspense #39 & Uncanny Tales #52)
Marvel Comics: May, 1968 - No. 332, Sept, 1996
1-Origin; Colan-c/a(p); story continued from Iron Man & Sub-Mariner #1
250 500 750 1500 2300 3100
2 16 32 48 107 236 365
3-Iron Man vs. The Freak 12 24 36 82 179 275
4,5: 4-Unicorn app. 10 20 30 64 132 200
6-10: 7,8-Gladiator app. 9-Iron Man battles green Hulk-like android. 9,10-The Mandarin app.
8 16 24 52 99 145
11-15: 10,11-Mandarin app. 12-1st app. Controller. 15-Last 12c issue; vs Unicorn and the Red Ghost 7 14 21 44 82 120
16,18-20: 16-Vs. Unicorn and the Red Ghost. 18-Avengers app. 19-Captain America app. 5 10 15 34 60 85
17-1st Madame Masque & Midas (Mordecai Midas) 10 20 30 68 144 220
21-24,26-30: 21-Crimson Dynamo app. 22-Death of Janice Cord; Crimson Dynamo app. 27-Intro Firebrand. 28-Controller app. 4 8 12 28 47 65
25-Iron Man battles Sub-Mariner 7 14 21 44 82 120
31-42: 33-1st app. Spymaster. 35-Daredevil & Nick Fury vs. Zodiak; x-over w/Daredevil #73. 36-Daredevil & Nick Fury vs Zodiak. 39-Avengers app. 42-Last 15c issue
4 8 12 25 40 55
43-Intro the Guardsman (25¢ Giant, 52 pgs); Giant-Man back-up (r) from TTA #52
7 14 21 44 82 120
44-46,48-53: 44-Capt. America app; back-up Ant-Man w/Andru-a. 46-The Guardsman dies. 48-Firebrand app. 49-Super-Adaptoid app. 50-Princess Python app. 53-1st Black Lama; Starlin part pencils 4 8 12 23 37 50
47-Origin retold; Barry Smith-a(p) 12 24 36 79 170 260
54-Iron Man battles Sub-Mariner; 1st app. Moondragon (1/73) as Madame MacEvil; Everett part-c 21 42 63 147 324 500
55-1st app. Thanos, Drax the Destroyer, Mentor, Starfox & Kronos (2/73); Starlin-c/a
160 320 480 960 1480 2000
56-Starlin-a 5 10 15 35 63 90
57-63: 57,58-Mandarin and Unicorn app. 59-Firebrand app. 60,61-Vs. the Masked Marauder. 62-Whiplash app. 63-Vs. Dr. Spectrum 3 6 9 17 26 35
64,65,67-70: 64,65-Dr. Spectrum app; origin is #65; Thor brief app. 67-Last 20c issue. 68-Sunfire, Mandarin and Unicorn app. 69,70-Mandarin, Yellow Claw & Ultimo app.
3 6 9 15 22 28
66-Iron Man vs. Thor. 5 10 15 35 63 90
71-84: 71-Yellow Claw & Black Lama app. 72-Black Lama app; Iron Man at the San Diego Comic Con. 73-Vs. Crimson Dynamo & Radioactive Man; Stark Industries renamed Stark International. 74-Modok vs. Mad-Thinker; Black Lama app in "War of the Super-Villains". 75-Black Lama & Yellow Claw app. 76-r/#9. 77-Conclusion of the "War of the Super-Villains"; Black Lama app. 80-Origin of Black Lama. 81-Black Lama & Firebrand app. 82,83-Red Ghost app. 2 4 6 11 16 20
85-89-(Regular 25¢ editions): 86-1st app. Blizzard. 87-Origin Blizzard. 88-Brief Thanos cameo. 89-Daredevil app.; last 25¢-c 2 4 6 11 16 20
85-89-(30¢-c variants, limited distribution)(4-8/76) 6 12 18 40 73 105
90-99: 90,91-Blood Brothers & Controller app. 92-Vs. Melter. 95-Ultimo app. 96-1st new Guardsman (Michael O' Brien). 98,99-Mandarin & Sunfire app.
2 4 6 10 14 18
99,101-103-(35¢-c variants, limited dist.) 12 24 36 86 188 290
100-(7/77)-Starlin-c; Iron Man vs. The Mandarin 5 10 15 33 57 80
100-(35¢-c variant, limited dist.) 27 54 81 194 435 675
101-Intro DreadKnight; Frankenstein app. 3 6 9 16 23 30
102-2nd DreadKnight 2 4 6 11 16 20
103-117: 103-Jack of Hearts app; guest stars through issue #113. 104-107-Vs. Midas. 109-1st app. New Crimson Dynamo; 1st app. Vanguard. 110-Origin Jack of Hearts retold; death of Count Nefaria. 113,114-Unicorn and Titanium Man app. 114,115-Avengers app; 1st John Romita Jr. pencils on Iron Man (10/78). 116-1st David Michelinie & Bob Layton issue 2 4 6 9 12 15
118-Byrne-a(p); 1st app. Jim Rhodes 6 12 18 41 76 110
119,122-124,127: 122-Origin. 123-128-Tony treated for alcohol problem. 123,124-Vs. Blizzard, Melter & Whiplash; Justin Hammer app. 127-Vs. Justin Hammer's "Super-Villain army"
3 6 9 14 19 24
120,121,126: 120,121-Sub-Mariner app. 126-Classic Tony becoming Iron Man-c
3 6 9 15 22 28
125-Avengers & Ant-Man (Scott Lang) app. 3 6 9 17 25 34
128-(11/79) Classic Tony Stark alcoholism cover 10 20 30 67 141 215
129,130,134-149: 134,135-Titanium Man app. 137-139-Spymaster app. 142-Intro. Space Armor. 143-1st app. Sunturion. 146 Backlash app. (formally Whiplash). 148-Captain America app. 149-Dr. Doom app. 2 4 6 8 10 12
131-133: 131,132-Hulk x-over. 133-Hulk/Ant Man-c 2 4 6 10 14 18
150-Double size; Dr. Doom; Merlin & Camelot 6 12 18 37 66 95
151-168: 151-Ant-Man (Scott Lang) app. 152-1st app stealth armor. 153-Living Laser app; last Layton co-plot (returns in #215). 154-Unicorn app. 156-Intro the Mauler; last Michelinie plot (returns in issue #215); last Romita Jr. art (p). 159-Paul Smith-a(p); Fantastic Four app. 160-Serpent Squad app. 161-Moon Knight app. 163-Intro. Obadiah Stane (hand only). 166-1st full app. Obadiah Stane. 167-Tony Stark alcohol problem resurfaces. 168-Machine Man app. 1 3 4 6 8 10
169-New Iron Man (Jim Rhodes replaces Tony Stark) 2 4 6 10 14 18
170-199: 172-Captain America x-over. 180-181-Vs. Mandarin. 191-198-Tony Stark returns as original Iron Man. 197-Secret Wars II x-over; Byrne-c 1 2 3 5 6 8
200-(11/85, $1.25, 52 pgs.)-Tony Stark returns as new Iron Man (red & white armor) thru #230 3 6 9 16 23 30
201-213,215-224: 206-Hawkeye & Mockingbird app. 219-Intro. The Ghost. 220-Spymaster & Ghost app. 224-Vs. Beetle, Backlash, Blizzard & Justin Hammer 5.00
214-Spider-Woman (Julia Carpenter) app. in new black costume (1/87) 6.00
225-(12/87, $1.25, 40 pgs)- Armor Wars begins; Ant-Man app.
2 4 6 8 10 12
226-227,229-230: Armor Wars in all. 226-West Coast Avengers app. 227-Beetle app.; Iron Man vs SHIELD Mandroids. 229-Vs. Crimson Dynamo & Titanium Man. 230-Armor Wars conclusion; vs Firepower 5.00
228-Armor Wars; Iron Man vs. Captain America (as the Captain) 6.00
231,234,247: 231-Intro. new Iron Man armor. 234-Spider-Man x-over. 247-Hulk x-over 5.00
232,233,235-243,245,246,248,249: 232-Barry Windsor Smith co-plot and (p). 233-Ant-Man app. 235,236-Vs. Grey Gargoyle. 238-Rhino & Capt. America app. 239,240-Vs. Justin Hammer.

241,242-Mandarin app. 243-Tony Stark loses use of legs. 249-Dr. Doom app. 4.00
244-($1.50, 52 pgs.)-New Armor makes him walk 5.00
250-($1.50, 52 pgs.)-Dr. Doom-c/story; Acts of Vengeance x-over; last Michelinie/Layton issue 5.00
251-274,276-281,283,285-287,289,292-299: 255-Intro new Crimson Dynamo (Valenyine Shatalov). 258-Byrne script & Romita Jr.-a(p) begins. 261-264-Mandarin & Fin Fang Foom app. 290-James Rhodes retains the War Machine armor. 292-Capt. America app. 295-Infinity Crusade x-over. 296,297-Omega Red app. 298,299-Return of Ultimo 4.00
275-($1.50, 52 pgs.) Mandarin & Fin Fang Foom app. 5.00
282-1st full app. War Machine (7/92) 6 12 18 41 76 110
284-Death of Iron Man (Tony Stark); James Rhodes becomes War Machine 1 2 3 5 6 8
288-($2.50, 52pg.)-Silver foil stamped-c; Iron Man's 350th app. in comics 5.00
290-($2.95, 52pg.)-Gold foil stamped-c; 30th ann. 5.00
291-Iron Man & War Machine team-up 5.00
300-($3.95, 68 pgs.)-Collector's Edition w/embossed foil-c; anniversary issue; War Machine-c/story 5.00
300-($2.50, 68 pgs.)-Newsstand Edition 5.00
301,303: 301-Venom cameo. 303-Captain America app. 5.00
302-Venom-c/story; Captain America app. 2 4 6 8 10 12
304-Thunderstrike app; begin $1.50-c; bound-in-trading card sheet 3 6 9 17 26 35
305-Hulk-c/story 3 6 9 16 23 30
306-309-Mandarin app. 309-War Machine app. 4.00
310-($2.95) Polybagged w/16 pg Marvel Action Hour preview & acetate print 6.00
310-($1.50) Regular edition; white logo; "Hands of the Mandarin" x-over w/Force Works and War Machine 5.00
311,312- "Hands of the Mandarin" x-over w/Force Works and War Machine. 312-w/bound-in Power Ranger card 4.00
313,315,316,318: 315-316-Black Widow app. 316-Crimson Dynamo & Titanium Man app. 5.00
314-Crossover w/Captain America; Henry Pym app. 6.00
317-($2.50)-Flip book; Black Widow app; death of Titanium Man; Hawkeye, War Machine & USAgent app. 6.00
319-Intro. new Iron Man armor; Force Works app; prologue to "The Crossing" story 6.00
320-325: 321-w/Overpower card insert. 322-324-Avengers app; x-over w/Avengers and Force Works. 325-($2.95)-Wraparound-c; Tony Stark Iron Man vs "Teen" Tony Iron Man; Avengers & Force Works x-over; continued in Avengers #395 5.00
326- "Teen" Tony app. as Iron Man thru #332; Avengers, Thor & Cap America x-over 6.00
327-330: 330-War Machine & Stockpile app; return of Morgan Stark 4.00
331-War Machine app; leads into the "Onslaught" x-over 5.00
332-(9/96) Onslaught x-over; last issue 6.00
Special 1 (8/70)-Sub-Mariner x-over; Everett-c 7 14 21 44 82 120
Special 2 (11/71, 52 pgs.)-r/TOS #81,82,91 (all-r) 3 6 9 21 33 45
Annual 3 (1976)-Man-Thing app. 3 6 9 15 22 28
King Size 4 (8/77)-The Champions (w/Ghost Rider) app.; Newton-a(i) 3 6 9 14 20 26
Annual 5 ('82) Black Panther & Mandarin app. 2 4 6 10 14 18
Annual 6-9: ('83-'86) 6-New Iron Man (J. Rhodes) app. 8-X-Factor app. 6.00
Annual 10 ('89) Atlantis Attacks x-over; P. Smith-a; Layton/Guice-a; Sub-Mariner app. 6.00
Annual 11-15 ('90-'94): 11-Terminus Factor pt. 2; origin of Mrs. Arbogast by Ditko (p&i). 12-1 pg. origin recap; Ant-Man back-up-s; Subterranean Wars Pt. 4. 13-Darkhawk & Avengers West Coast app.; Colan/Williamson-a. 14-Bagged w/card; 1st app. Face Thief 15- Iron Man vs. the Controller 6.00
...: Armor Wars TPB (2007, $24.99) r/#225-232; Michelinie intro. 25.00
Manual 1 (1993, $1.75)-Operations handbook 5.00
Graphic Novel: Crash (1988, $12.95, Adults, 72 pgs.)-Computer generated art & color; violence & nudity 13.00
...Collector's Preview 1(11/94, $1.95)-wraparound-c; text & illos-no comics 4.00
...: Demon in a Bottle HC (2008, $24.99) r/#120-128; two covers 25.00
...: Demon in a Bottle TPB (2006, $24.99) r/#120-128 25.00
...: Many Armors of Iron Man (2008, $24.99) r/#47, 142-144, 152-153, 200, 218 25.00
...Vs. Dr. Doom (12/94, $12.95)-r/#149-150, 249,250. Julie Bell-c 13.00
...Vs. Dr. Doom: Doomquest HC (2008, $19.99, dustjacket)-r/#149-150, 249,250; new Michelinie intro.; bonus art 20.00
...: War Machine TPB (2008, $29.99) r/#280-291 30.00
The Invincible Iron Man Omnibus Vol. 1 HC (2008, $99.99, dustjacket) r/Iron Man stories from Tales of Suspense #39-83 & Tales To Astonish #82; 1992 intro. by Stan Lee; 1975 essay by Lee; 2008 essay by Layton; gallery of original art and covers; creator bios 100.00

NOTE: **Austin** c-105i, 109-111i, 151i. **Byrne** a-118p; c-109p, 197, 253. **Colan** a-1p, 253, Special 1p(3); c-1p. **Craig** a-1i, 2-4, 5-13i, 14, 15-19i, 24p, 25p, 26-28i; c-2-4. **Ditko** a-160p. **Everett** c-29. **Guice** a-233-241p. **G. Kane** c(p)-52-54, 63, 67, 72-75, 77-79, 88, 98. **Kirby** a-Special 1p; 80p, 90, 92-95. **Mooney** a-40i, 43i, 47i. **Perez** c-103p. **Simonson** c-Annual 8. **B. Smith** a-232p, 243i; c-232. **P. Smith** a-159p, 245p, Annual 10p; c-159. **Starlin** a-53p(part), 55p, 56p; c-55p, 160, 163. **Tuska** a-5-13p, 15-23p, 24i, 32p, 38-46p, 48-54p, 57-61p, 63-69p, 70-72p, 78p, 86-92p, 95-106p, Annual 4p. **Wood** a-Special 1i.

IRON MAN (The Invincible...) (Volume Two)
Marvel Comics: Nov, 1996 - No. 13, Nov, 1997 ($2.95/$1.95/$1.99)
(Produced by WildStorm Productions)

V2#1-3-Heroes Reborn begins; Scott Lobdell scripts & Whilce Portacio-c/a begin; new origin Iron Man & Hulk. 2-Hulk app. 3-Fantastic Four app. 5.00
1-Variant-c 6.00
4-11: 4-Two covers. 6-Fantastic Four app.; Industrial Revolution; Hulk app. 7-Return of Rebel. 11-($1.99) Dr. Doom-c/app. 4.00
12-($2.99) "Heroes Reunited"-pt. 3; Hulk-c/app. 5.00
13-($1.99) "World War 3"-pt. 3, x-over w/Image 4.00
Heroes Reborn: Iron Man (2006, $29.99, TPB) r/#1-12; Heroes Reborn #1/2; pin-ups 30.00

IRON MAN (The Invincible...) (Volume Three)
Marvel Comics: Feb, 1998 - No. 89, Dec, 2004 ($2.99/$1.99/$2.25)

V3#1-($2.99)-Follows Heroes Return; Busiek scripts & Chen-c/a begin; Deathsquad app. 6.00
1-Alternate Ed. 1 2 3 5 7 9
2-12: 2-Two covers. 6-Black Widow-c/app. 7-Warbird-c/app. 8-Black Widow app. 9-Mandarin returns 4.00
13-($2.99) battles the Controller 5.00
14-24: 14-Fantastic Four-c/app. 3.00
25-($2.99) Iron Man and Warbird battle Ultimo; Avengers app. 4.00
26-30-Quesada-s. 28-Whiplash killed. 29-Begin $2.25-c. 3.00
31-45,47-49,51-54: 35-Maximum Security x-over; FF-c/app. 41-Grant-a begins. 44-New armor debut. 48-Ultron-c/app. 3.00
46-($3.50, 100 pgs.) Sentient armor returns; r/V1#78,140,141 4.00
50-($3.50) Grell-s begin; Black Widow app. 4.00
55-($3.50) 400th issue; Asamiya-c; back-up story Stark reveals ID; Grell-a 4.00
56-66: 56-Reis-a. 57,58-Ryan-a. 59-61-Grell-c/a. 62,63-Ryan-a. 64-Davis-a; Thor-c/app. 3.00
67-89: 67-Begin $2.99-c; Gene Ha-c. 75-83-Granov-c. 84-Avengers Disassembled prologue 85-89-Avengers Disassembled. 85-88-Harris-a. 86-89-Pat Lee-c. 87-Rumiko killed 3.00
.../Captain America '98 Annual ($3.50) vs. Modok 4.00
1999, 2000 Annual ($3.50) 4.00
2001 Annual ($2.99) Claremont-s/Ryan-a 4.00
Avengers Disassembled: Iron Man TPB (2004, $14.99) r/#84-89 15.00
Mask in the Iron Man (5/01, $14.95, TPB) r/#26-30, #1/2 15.00

IRON MAN (The Invincible...)
Marvel Comics: Jan, 2005 - No. 35, Jan, 2009 ($3.50/$2.99)

1-($3.50-c) Warren Ellis-s/Adi Granov-c/a; start of Extremis storyline 5.00
2-6-($2.99): 5-Flashback to origin; Stark gets new abilities 4.00
7-14: 7-Knauf-s/Zircher-a. 13,14-Civil War 3.00
15-24,26,27,29-35: 15-Stark becomes Director of S.H.I.E.L.D. 19,20-World War Hulk. 33-Secret Invasion; War Machine app. 34,35-War Machine title logo 3.00
25,28-($3.99) 25-Includes movie preview & armor showcase. 28-Red & white armor 4.00
All-New Iron Manual (2/08, $4.99) Handbook-style guide to characters & armor suits 5.00
... By Design 1 (11/10, $3.99) Gallery of 2010 variant covers with artist commentary 4.00
.../Captain America: Casualities of War (2/07, $3.99) two covers; flashbacks 4.00
...: Director of S.H.I.E.L.D. Annual 1 (1/08, $3.99) Madame Hydra app.; Cheung-c 4.00
Free Comic Book Day 2010 (Iron Man: Supernova) #1 (5/10, 9-1/2" x 6-1/4") Nova app. 3.00
Free Comic Book Day 2010 (Iron Man/Thor) #1 (5/10, 9-1/2" x 6-1/4") Romita Jr.-a/c 3.00
...Golden Avenger 1 (11/08, $2.99) Santacruz-a; movie photo-c 3.00
.../Hulk/Fury 1 (2/09, $3.99) crossover of movie-version characters 4.00
Indomitable Iron Man (4/10, $3.99) B&W stories; Chaykin-s/a; Rosado-a; Parrillo-c 4.00
Iron Manual Mark 3 (6/10, $3.99) Handbook-format profiles of characters 4.00
...: Iron Protocols (12/09, $3.99) Olivetti-c/Nelson-a 4.00
...: Kiss and Kill (8/10, $3.99) Black Widow and Wolverine app. 4.00
Marvel Halloween Ashcan 2007 (8-1/2" x 5-3/8") updated origin; Michael Golden-c 3.00
...: Requiem (2009, $4.99) r/TOS #39, Iron Man #144 (1981); armor profiles 5.00
...: The End (1/09, $4.99) future Tony Stark retires; Michelinie-s/Chang & Layton-a 5.00
...: Titanium! 1 (12/10, $4.99) short stories by various; Yardin-c 5.00
Civil War: Iron Man TPB (2007, $11.99) r/#13,14, .../Captain America: Casualities of War, and Civil War: The Confession 12.00
HC (2006, $19.99, dust jacket) r/#1-6 and Granov covers from Iron Man V3 #75-83 20.00
...: Director of S.H.I.E.L.D. TPB (2007, $14.99) r/#15-18; Strange Tales #135 (1965) and Iron Man #129; profile pages for Iron Man and S.H.I.E.L.D.; creator interviews 15.00
...: Extremis SC (2007, $14.99) r/#1-6 and Granov covers from Iron Man V3 #75-83 15.00
...: Execute Program SC (2007, $14.99) r/#7-12; cover layouts and sketches 15.00

IRON MAN (Marvel Now!)(Leads into Superior Iron Man)
Marvel Comics: Jan, 2013 - No. 28, Aug, 2014 ($3.99)

1-28: 1-8-Gillen-s/Land-c/a. 5-Stark heads out to space. 9-17-Secret Origin of Tony Stark. 9-12-Eaglesham-a. 17-Arno Stark revealed. 23-26-Malekith app. 4.00
20.INH (3/12, $3.99) Inhumanity tie-in; origin The Exile; Padilla-a 4.00
Annual 1 (4/14, $4.99) Gillen-s/Martinez, Padilla & Marz-a 5.00
... Special 1 (9/14, $4.99) Cont'd from Uncanny X-Men Special #1; Ryan-s/Handoko-a 5.00

IRON MAN (The Armor Wars)
Marvel Comics: No. 258.1, Jul, 2013 - No. 258.4, Jul, 2013 ($3.99, weekly limited series)

258.1-258.4 - Set after Iron Man #258 (1990); Michelinie-s/Dave Ross & Bob Layton-a 4.00

IRON MAN (Follows the Iron Man 2020 series)(Continues in Invincible Iron Man #1)
Marvel Comics: Nov, 2020 - No. 25, Jan, 2023 ($4.99/$3.99)

1-($4.99) Cantwell-s/Cafu-a; main wraparound cover by Alex Ross; Patsy Walker app. 5.00
2-24-($3.99) Hellcat app. 2-Crusher Creel app. 8-Moondragon app. 16-Doctor Doom app. 4.00
25-($5.99) Legacy issue #650; back-up with Thor app. & faux reprint in early '70s style 6.00
Annual 1 (8/21, $4.99) MacKay-s/Roberson-a; Miles Morales app. 5.00
.../Hellcat Annual 1 (8/22, $4.99) Chris Cantwell-s/Ruairí Coleman-a; Hedy Wolfe app. 5.00

IRON MAN
Marvel Comics: Feb, 2023 - Present ($4.99/$3.99)

1-($4.99) Duggan-sFrigeri-a 5.00
2,3-($3.99) 2-Ironheart app. 3-War Machine app. 4.00

IRON MAN AND POWER PACK
Marvel Comics: Jan, 2008 - No. 4, Apr, 2008 ($2.99, limited series)

1-4-Gurihiru-c/Sumerak-s; Puppet Master app.; Mini Marvels back-ups in each 3.00
...: Armored and Dangerous TPB (2008, $7.99, digest size) r/series 8.00

IRON MAN & SUB-MARINER
Marvel Comics Group: Apr, 1968 (12¢, one-shot) (Pre-dates Iron Man #1 & Sub-Mariner #1)

1-Iron Man story by Colan/Craig continued from Tales of Suspense #99 & continued in Iron Man #1; Sub-Mariner story by Colan continued from Tales to Astonish #101 & continued in Sub-Mariner #1; Colan/Everett-c 38 76 114 285 641 1000

IRON MAN AND THE ARMOR WARS
Marvel Comics: Oct, 2009 - No. 4, Jan, 2010 ($2.99, limited series)

1-4-Rousseau-a; Crimson Dynamo & Omega Red app. 3.00

IRON MAN: ARMORED ADVENTURES
Marvel Comics: Sept, 2009 ($3.99, one-shot)

1-Based on the 2009 cartoon; Brizuela-a; Nick Fury & Living Laser app. 4.00

IRON MAN: BAD BLOOD
Marvel Comics: Sept, 2000 - No. 4, Dec, 2000 ($2.99, limited series)

1-4-Micheline-s/Layton-a 3.00

IRON MAN: ENTER THE MANDARIN
Marvel Comics: Nov, 2007 - No. 6, Apr, 2008 ($2.99, limited series)

1-6-Casey-s/Canete-a; retells first meeting 3.00
TPB (2008, $14.99) r/#1-6 15.00

IRON MAN: EXTREMIS DIRECTOR'S CUT
Marvel Comics: Jun, 2010 - No. 6, Sept, 2010 ($3.99, limited series)

1-6-Reprints Iron Man #1-6 (2005 series) with script pages and design art 4.00

IRON MAN: FATAL FRONTIER

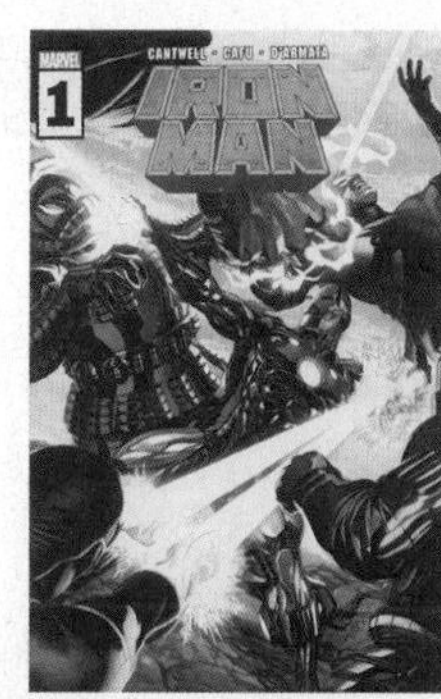

Iron Man (2020) #1 © MAR

Iron Man: Legacy #6 © MAR

Irredeemable #1 © BOOM

	GD 2.0	VG 4.0	FN 6.0	VF 8.0	VF/NM 9.0	NM- 9.2

Marvel Comics: 2014 ($34.99, hardcover)
HC - Printing of digital comic #1-13 and r/Iron Man Annual #1 (4/14) 35.00

IRON MAN: HONG KONG HEROES
Marvel Comics: May, 2018 ($3.99, one-shot)
1-Howard Wong-s/Justice Wong-a; Hulk & Black Panther app.; intro Arwyn Wong 4.00

IRON MAN: HOUSE OF M (Also see House of M and related x-overs)
(Reprinted in House of M: Fantastic Four/ Iron Man TPB)
Marvel Comics: Sept, 2005 - No. 3, Nov, 2005 ($2.99, limited series)
1-3-Pat Lee-a/c; Greg Pak-s 3.00

IRON MAN: HYPERVELOCITY
Marvel Comics: Mar, 2007 - No. 6, Aug, 2007 ($2.99, limited series)
1-6-Adam Warren-s/Brian Denham-a/c 3.00
TPB (2007, $14.99) r/#1-6; layout pages and armor design sketches 15.00

IRON MAN: I AM IRON MAN
Marvel Comics: Mar, 2010 - No. 2, Apr, 2010 ($3.99, limited series)
1,2-Adaptation of the first movie; Peter David-s/Sean Chen-a/Adi Granov-c 4.00

IRON MAN: INEVITABLE
Marvel Comics: Feb, 2006 - No. 6, July, 2006 ($2.99, limited series)
1-6-Joe Casey-s/Frazer Irving; Spymaster and the Living Laser app. 3.00
TPB (2006, $14.99) r/#1-6; cover sketches 15.00

IRON MAN: LEGACY
Marvel Comics: Jun, 2010 - No. 11, Apr, 2011 ($3.99/$2.99)
1-Van Lente-s/Kurth-a; Dr. Doom app.; back-up r/debut in Tales of Suspense #39 4.00
2-11-($2.99) 4-Titanium Man & Crimson Dynamo app. 6-The Pride app. 3.00

IRON MAN: LEGACY OF DOOM
Marvel Comics: Jun, 2008 - No. 4, Sept, 2008 ($2.99, limited series)
1-4-Michelinie-s/Lim & Layton-a; Dr. Doom app. 3.00

IRON MAN NOIR
Marvel Comics: Jun, 2010 - No. 4, Sept, 2010 ($3.99, limited series)
1-4-Pulp-style set in 1939; Snyder-s/Garcia-a 4.00

IRON MAN: RAPTURE
Marvel Comics: Jan, 2011 - No. 4, Feb, 2011 ($3.99, limited series)
1-4-Irvine-s/Medina-a/Bradstreet-c. 3,4-War Machine app. 4.00

IRON MAN: SEASON ONE
Marvel Comics: 2013 ($24.99, hardcover graphic novel)
HC - Origin story and early days; Chaykin-s/Parel-a/Tedesco painted-c 25.00

IRON MAN: THE COMING OF THE MELTER
Marvel Comics: Jul, 2013 ($3.99, one-shot)
1-Movie version; Ron Lim-a; back-up reprint of Iron Man #72 (1/75); 3 covers 4.00

IRON MAN: THE IRON AGE
Marvel Comics: Aug, 1998 - No. 2, Sept, 1998 ($5.99, limited series)
1,2-Busiek-s; flashback story from gold armor days 6.00

IRON MAN: THE LEGEND
Marvel Comics: Sept, 1996 ($3.95, one-shot)
1-Tribute issue 5.00

IRON MAN/ THOR
Marvel Comics: Jan, 2011 - No. 4, Apr, 2011 ($3.99, limited series)
1-4-Eaton-a; Crimson Dynamo & Diablo app. 4.00

IRON MANTICORE (Reprints from Cerebus in Hell)
Aardvark-Vanaheim: Sept, 2019 ($4.00, B&W)
1-Cerebus figures placed over original Doré artwork of Hell; Iron Man #128-c swipe 4.00

IRON MAN 2: ... (Follows the first movie)
Marvel Comics: Jun, 2010 - Nov, 2010 ($3.99, limited series)
Agents of S.H.I.E.L.D. 1 (11/10, $3.99) Nick Fury, Agent Coulson & Black Widow app. 4.00
Public Identity (6/10 - No. 3, 7/10, $3.99) 1-3-Kitson & Lim-a/Granov-c 4.00
Spotlight (4/10, $3.99) Interviews with Granov, Guggenheim, Fraction, Ellis, Michelinie 4.00

IRON MAN 2 ADAPTATION, (MARVEL'S...)
Marvel Comics: Jan, 2013 - No. 2, Feb, 2013 ($2.99, limited series)
1,2-Photo-c; Rosanas-a 3.00

IRON MAN 2.0
Marvel Comics: Apr, 2011 - No. 12, Feb, 2012 ($3.99/$2.99)
1-($3.99) Spencer-s/Kitson-c; back-up history of War Machine 4.00
1-Variant-c by Djurdjevic 6.00
2-7,(7.1),8-12-($2.99) 2,3-Kitson, Kano & Di Giandomenico-a. 5-7-Fear Itself tie-in 3.00
...: Modern Warfare 1 (10/11, $4.99) r/#1-3 with variant covers 5.00

IRON MAN 3 PRELUDE, (MARVEL'S...)
Marvel Comics: Mar, 2013 - No. 2, Apr, 2013 ($2.99, limited series)
1,2-Photo-c; Gage-s/Kurth-a; War Machine app. 3.00

IRON MAN 2020 (Also see Machine Man limited series)
Marvel Comics: June, 1994 ($5.95, one-shot)
nn 6.00

IRON MAN 2020
Marvel Comics: Mar, 2020 - No. 6, Oct, 2020 ($4.99, limited series)
1-6-Slott & Gage-s/Woods-a; Arno Stark as Iron Man; Machine Man app. 5.00

IRON MAN: VIVA LAS VEGAS
Marvel Comics: Jul, 2008 - No. 2 ($3.99, unfinished limited series)
1,2-Jon Favreau-s/Adi Granov-a/c 4.00

IRON MAN VS WHIPLASH
Marvel Comics: Jan, 2010 - No. 4, Apr, 2010 ($3.99, limited series)
1-4-Briones-a/Peterson-c; origin of new Whiplash 4.00

IRON MAN/X-O MANOWAR: HEAVY METAL (See X-O Manowar/Iron Man: In Heavy Metal)
Marvel Comics: Sept, 1996 ($2.50, one-shot) (1st Marvel/Valiant x-over)
1-Pt. II of Iron Man/X-O Manowar x-over; Fabian Nicieza scripts; 1st app. Rand Banion 4.00

IRON MARSHALL
Jademan Comics: July, 1990 - No. 32, Feb, 1993 ($1.75, plastic coated-c)
1,32: Kung Fu stories. 1-Poster centerfold 5.00
2-31-Kung Fu stories in all 4.00

IRON PATRIOT (Marvel Now!)
Marvel Comics: May, 2014 - No. 5, Sept, 2014 ($3.99)
1-5-James Rhodes in the armor; Ales Kot-s/Garry Brown-a/c 4.00

IRON VIC (See Comics Revue No. 3 & Giant Comics Editions)
United Features Syndicate/St. John Publ. Co.: 1940

	GD 2.0	VG 4.0	FN 6.0	VF 8.0	VF/NM 9.0	NM- 9.2
Single Series 22	40	80	120	246	411	575

IRONWOLF
DC Comics: 1986 ($2.00, one shot)
1-r/Weird Worlds #8-10; Chaykin story & art 4.00

IRONWOLF: FIRES OF THE REVOLUTION (See Weird Worlds #8-10)
DC Comics: 1992 ($29.95, hardcover)
nn-Chaykin/Moore story, Mignola-a w/Russell inks. 30.00

IRREDEEMABLE (Also see Incorruptible)
BOOM! Studios: Apr, 2009 - No. 37, May, 2012 ($3.99)
1-37: 1-Waid-s/Krause-a; 3 covers; Grant Morrison afterword. 2-32-Three covers 4.00
1-Artist Edition (12/11, $3.99) r/#1 in B&W with bonus sketch and design art 4.00
... Special 1 (4/10, $3.99) Art by Azaceta, Rios & Chaykin; three covers 4.00

IRREDEEMABLE ANT-MAN, THE
Marvel Comics: Dec, 2006 - No. 12, Nov, 2007 ($2.99)
1-12-Kirkman-s/Hester-a/c; intro. Eric O'Grady as the new Ant-Man. 7-Ms. Marvel app. 10-World War Hulk x-over 3.00
... Vol. 1: Lowlife (2007, $9.99, digest) r/#1-6 10.00
... Vol. 2: Small-Minded (2007, $9.99, digest) r/#7-12 10.00

ISAAC ASIMOV'S I-BOTS
Tekno Comix: Dec, 1995 - No. 7, May, 1996 ($1.95)
1-7: 1-6-Perez-c/a. 2-Chaykin variant-c exists. 3-Polybagged. 7-Lady Justice-c/app. 4.00

ISAAC ASIMOV'S I-BOTS
BIG Entertainment: V2#1, June, 1996 - No. 9, Feb, 1997 ($2.25)
V2#1-9: 1-Lady Justice-c/app. 6-Gil Kane-c 4.00

ISIS (TV) (Also see Shazam)
National Per.l Publ./DC Comics: Oct-Nov, 1976 - No. 8, Dec-Jan, 1977-78

	GD 2.0	VG 4.0	FN 6.0	VF 8.0	VF/NM 9.0	NM- 9.2
1-Wood inks	5	10	15	31	53	75
2-8: 5-Isis new look. 7-Origin	2	4	6	9	13	16

ISLAND AT THE TOP OF THE WORLD (See Walt Disney Showcase #27)

ISLAND OF DR. MOREAU, THE (Movie)
Marvel Comics Group: Oct, 1977 (52 pgs.)

	GD 2.0	VG 4.0	FN 6.0	VF 8.0	VF/NM 9.0	NM- 9.2
1-Gil Kane-c	1	3	4	6	8	10

ISLAND OF DR. MOREAU, THE (Adaptation of the novel)

	GD 2.0	VG 4.0	FN 6.0	VF 8.0	VF/NM 9.0	NM- 9.2

IDW Publishing: Jul, 2019 - No. 2, Aug, 2019 ($4.99, limited series)

	GD	VG	FN	VF	VF/NM	NM-
1,2-Ted Adams & Gabriel Rodríguez-s/Rodríguez-a						5.00

ISOLA
Image Comics: Apr, 2018 - Present ($3.99)

	GD	VG	FN	VF	VF/NM	NM-
1-10-Brenden Fletcher & Karl Kerschl-s/Kerschl & Msassyk-a						4.00
... Prologue (1/19, no cover price) reprints pages from Motor Crush #1-5						3.00

I SPY (TV)
Gold Key: Aug, 1966 - No. 6, Sept, 1968 (All have photo-c)

	GD	VG	FN	VF	VF/NM	NM-
1-Bill Cosby, Robert Culp photo covers	12	24	36	79	170	260
2-6: 3,4-McWilliams-a. 5-Last 12¢-c	6	12	18	38	69	100

IT! (See Astonishing Tales No. 21-24 & Supernatural Thrillers No. 1)

ITCHY & SCRATCHY COMICS (The Simpsons TV show)
Bongo Comics: 1993 - No. 3, 1993 ($1.95)

	GD	VG	FN	VF	VF/NM	NM-
1-3: 1-Bound-in jumbo poster. 3-w/decoder screen trading card	2	4	6	9	13	16
Holiday Special ('94, $1.95)	2	4	6	8	10	12

IT GIRL (Also see Atomics, and Madman Comics)
Oni Press: May, 2002 ($2.95, one-shot)

	GD	VG	FN	VF	VF/NM	NM-
1-Allred-s/Clugston-Major-c/a; Atomics and Madman app.						3.00

IT GIRL! AND THE ATOMICS (Also see Atomics, and Madman Comics)
Image Comics: Aug, 2012 - No. 12, Jul, 2013 ($2.99)

	GD	VG	FN	VF	VF/NM	NM-
1-12: 1-Rich-s/Norton-a/Allred-c. 2-Two covers (Allred & Cooke). 6-Clugston Flores-a						3.00

IT REALLY HAPPENED
William H. Wise No. 1,2/Standard (Visual Editions): 1944 - No. 11, Oct, 1947

	GD	VG	FN	VF	VF/NM	NM-
1-Kit Carson & Ben Franklin stories	34	68	102	204	332	460
2,3-Nazi WWII-c	18	36	54	105	165	225
4,6,9,11: 4-D-Day story. 6-Ernie Pyle WWII-c; Joan of Arc story. 9-Captain Kidd & Frank Buck stories	14	28	42	82	121	160
5-Lou Gehrig & Lewis Carroll stories	20	40	60	118	192	265
7-Teddy Roosevelt story	15	30	45	88	137	185
8-Story of Roy Rogers	19	38	57	111	176	240
10-Honus Wagner & Mark Twain stories	17	34	51	100	158	215

NOTE: ***Guardineer** a-7(2), 8(2), 10, 11. **Schomburg** c-1-7, 9-11.*

IT RHYMES WITH LUST (Also see Bold Stories & Candid Tales)
St. John Publishing Co.: 1950 (Digest size, 128 pgs., 25¢)

	GD	VG	FN	VF	VF/NM	NM-
nn (Rare)-Matt Baker & Ray Osrin-a	383	766	1149	2681	4691	6700

IT'S A BIRD...
DC Comics: 2004 ($24.95, hardcover with dust jacket)

	GD	VG	FN	VF	VF/NM	NM-
HC-Semi-autobiographical story of Steven Seagle writing Superman; Kristiansen-a						25.00
SC-($17.95)						18.00

IT'S ABOUT TIME (TV)
Gold Key: Jan, 1967

	GD	VG	FN	VF	VF/NM	NM-
1 (10195-701)-Photo-c	4	8	12	28	47	65

IT'S A DUCK'S LIFE
Marvel Comics/Atlas(MMC): Feb, 1950 - No. 11, Feb, 1952

	GD	VG	FN	VF	VF/NM	NM-
1-Buck Duck, Super Rabbit begin	22	44	66	128	209	290
2	14	28	42	80	115	150
3-11	13	26	39	72	101	130

IT'S GAMETIME
National Periodical Publications: Sept-Oct, 1955 - No. 4, Mar-Apr, 1956

	GD	VG	FN	VF	VF/NM	NM-
1-(Scarce)-Infinity-c; Davy Crockett app. in puzzle	119	238	357	762	1306	1850
2,3 (Scarce): 2-Dodo & The Frog	77	154	231	493	847	1200
4 (Rare)	87	174	261	553	952	1350

IT'S LOVE, LOVE, LOVE
St. John Publishing Co.: Nov, 1957 - No. 2, Jan, 1958 (10¢)

	GD	VG	FN	VF	VF/NM	NM-
1,2	10	20	30	54	72	90

IT! THE TERROR FROM BEYOND SPACE
IDW Publishing: Jul, 2010 - No. 3, Sept, 2010 ($3.99, limited series)

	GD	VG	FN	VF	VF/NM	NM-
1-3-Naraghi-s/Dos Santos-a/Mannion-c						4.00

ITTY BITTY COMICS (Issue #5, see Grimmiss Island; title changes to Grimmiss Island)
Dark Horse Comics: Nov, 2014 - No. 4, Feb, 2015 ($2.99, limited series)

	GD	VG	FN	VF	VF/NM	NM-
1-4-All-ages humor stories of kid-version Mask by Art Baltazar & Franco						3.00

ITTY BITTY COMICS: THE MASK
Dark Horse Comics: Nov, 2014 - No. 4, Feb, 2015 ($2.99, limited series)

	GD	VG	FN	VF	VF/NM	NM-
1-4-All-ages humor stories of kid-version Mask by Art Baltazar & Franco						3.00

ITTY BITTY HELLBOY
Dark Horse Comics: Aug, 2013 - No. 5, Dec, 2013 ($2.99, limited series)

	GD	VG	FN	VF	VF/NM	NM-
1-5-All-ages humor stories of kid-version Hellboy characters by Art Baltazar & Franco						3.00

ITTY BITTY HELLBOY: THE SEARCH FOR THE WERE-JAGUAR
Dark Horse Comics: Nov, 2015 - No. 4, Feb, 2016 ($2.99, limited series)

	GD	VG	FN	VF	VF/NM	NM-
1-4-All-ages humor stories of kid-version Hellboy characters by Art Baltazar & Franco						3.00

I, VAMPIRE (DC New 52)
DC Comics: Nov, 2011 - No. 19, Jun, 2013 ($2.99)

	GD	VG	FN	VF	VF/NM	NM-
1-Fialkov-s/Sorrentino-a/Frison-c						6.00
2-19: 4-Constantine app. 5-7-Batman app. 7,8-Crossover with Justice League Dark #7,8. 12-Stormwatch app. 16-19-Constantine app.						4.00
#0-(11/12, $2.99) Origin of Andrew Bennett; Fialkov-s/Sorrentino-a/Crain-c						3.00

IVANHOE (See Fawcett Movie Comics No. 20)

IVANHOE
Dell Publishing Co.: July-Sept, 1963

	GD	VG	FN	VF	VF/NM	NM-
1 (12-372-309)	3	6	9	20	31	42

IVAR, TIMEWALKER
Valiant Entertainment: Jan, 2015 - No. 12, Dec, 2015 ($3.99)

	GD	VG	FN	VF	VF/NM	NM-
1-12: 1-4-Fred Van Lente-s/Clayton Henry-a. 5-8-Portela-a. 9-Pere Perez-a						4.00

IVX (Inhumans vs X-Men) (Also see Death of X)
Marvel Comics: No. 0, Jan, 2017 - No. 6, May, 2017 ($3.99/$4.99/$5.99)

	GD	VG	FN	VF	VF/NM	NM-
0-($4.99) Soule-s/Rocafort-a; Beast, Medusa, Emma Frost, Magneto app.						5.00
1-($5.99) Soule & Lemire-s/Yu-a; multiple covers						6.00
2-5-($3.99) 2-Yu-a. 3-5-Garrón-a						4.00
6-($4.99) Yu-a; leads into Inhumans Prime #1, X-Men Prime #1 & Unc. Inhumans #20						5.00

IWO JIMA (See Spectacular Features Magazine)

IXTH GENERATION (See Ninth Generation)

I, ZOMBIE (Inspired the 2015 TV show)(See House of Mystery Halloween Annual #1 for 1st app.)
DC Comics (Vertigo): July, 2010 - No. 28, Oct, 2012 ($1.00/$2.99)

	GD	VG	FN	VF	VF/NM	NM-
1-($1.00) Allred-a/Roberson-s; 2 covers by Allred & Cooke	3	6	9	16	23	30
2-28-($2.99) Allred-c/a in most. 12-Gilbert Hernandez-a. 18-Jay Stephens-a. 25-Rugg-a						4.00
... Special Edition 1 (5/15, $1.00) r/#1; new inteview with Allred						4.00
...: Dead to the World TPB (2011, $14.99) r/#1-5 & House of Mystery Hall. Ann. #1						15.00

JACE PEARSON OF THE TEXAS RANGERS (Radio/TV)(4-Color #396 is titled Tales of the Texas Rangers; ...'s Tales of ... #11-on)(See Western Roundup under Dell Giants)
Dell Publishing Co.: No. 396, 5/52 - No. 1021, 8-10/59 (No #10) (All-Photo-c)

	GD	VG	FN	VF	VF/NM	NM-
Four Color 396 (#1)	10	20	30	69	147	225
2(5-7/53) - 9(2-4/55)	6	12	18	40	73	105
Four Color 648(#10, 9/55)	6	12	18	40	73	105
11(11-2/55-56) - 14,17-20(6-8/58)	5	10	15	33	57	80
15,16-Toth-a	5	10	15	34	60	85
Four Color 961,1021: 961-Spiegle-a	5	10	15	34	60	85

NOTE: *Joel McCrea photo c-1-9, F.C. 648 (starred on radio show only); Willard Parker photo c-11-on (starred on TV series).*

JACK ARMSTRONG (Radio)(See True Comics)
Parents' Institute: Nov, 1947 - No. 9, Sept, 1948; No. 10, Mar, 1949 - No. 13, Sept, 1949

nn (6/47) Ashcan edition; full color slick cover (a FN/VF sold for $485 in 2011)

	GD	VG	FN	VF	VF/NM	NM-
1-(Scarce) (odd size) Cast intro. inside front-c; Vic Hardy's Crime Lab begins	50	100	150	315	533	750
2	21	42	63	126	206	285
3-5	15	30	45	90	140	190
6-13	14	28	42	81	118	155

JACK CROSS
DC Comics: Oct, 2005 - No. 4, Jan, 2006 ($2.50)

	GD	VG	FN	VF	VF/NM	NM-
1-4-Warren Ellis-s/Gary Erskine-a						3.00
DC Comics Presents: Jack Cross #1 (12/10, $7.99, squarebound) r/#1-4						8.00

JACKED
DC Comics (Vertigo): Jan, 2016 - No. 6, Jun, 2016 ($3.99)

	GD	VG	FN	VF	VF/NM	NM-
1-6-Eric Kripke-s/John Higgins-a/Glenn Fabry-c						4.00

JACKIE CHAN'S SPARTAN X
Topps Comics: May, 1997 - No. 3 ($2.95, limited series)

	GD	VG	FN	VF	VF/NM	NM-
1-3-Michael Golden-s/a; variant photo-c						3.00

JACKIE CHAN'S SPARTAN X: HELL BENT HERO FOR HIRE
Image Comics (Little Eva Ink): Mar, 1998 - No. 3 ($2.95, B&W)

	GD	VG	FN	VF	VF/NM	NM-
1-3-Michael Golden-s/a: 1-variant photo-c						3.00

JACKIE GLEASON (TV) (Also see The Honeymooners)
St. John Publishing Co.: Sept, 1955 - No. 4, Dec, 1955?

	GD	VG	FN	VF	VF/NM	NM-
1(1955)(TV)-Photo-c	87	174	261	553	952	1350
2-4	54	108	162	343	574	825

JACKIE GLEASON AND THE HONEYMOONERS (TV)
National Periodical Publications: June-July, 1956 - No. 12, Apr-May, 1958

	GD	VG	FN	VF	VF/NM	NM-
1-1st app. Ralph Kramden	161	322	483	1030	1765	2500
2	84	168	252	538	919	1300
3-11: 8-Statue of Liberty-c	57	114	171	362	619	875
12 (Scarce)	81	162	243	518	884	1250

JACKIE JOKERS (Became Richie Rich &...)
Harvey Publications: March, 1973 - No. 4, Sept, 1973 (#5 was advertised, but not published)

	GD	VG	FN	VF	VF/NM	NM-
1-1st app.	3	6	9	16	23	30
2-4: 2-President Nixon app.	2	4	6	8	11	14

JACKIE ROBINSON (Famous Plays of...) (Also see Negro Heroes #2 & Picture News #4)
Fawcett Publications: May, 1950 - No. 6, 1952 (Baseball hero) (All photo-c)

	GD	VG	FN	VF	VF/NM	NM-
nn	110	220	330	704	1202	1700
2	57	114	171	362	619	875
3-6	48	96	144	302	514	725

JACK IN THE BOX (Formerly Yellowjacket Comics #1-10; becomes Cowboy Western Comics #17 on)
Frank Comunale/Charlton Comics No. 11 on: Feb, 1946; No. 11, Oct, 1946 - No. 16, Nov-Dec, 1947

	GD	VG	FN	VF	VF/NM	NM-
1-Stitches, Marty Mouse & Nutsy McKrow	27	54	81	158	259	360
11-Yellowjacket (early Charlton comic)	29	58	87	172	281	390
12,14,15	18	36	54	105	165	225
13-Wolverton-a	39	78	117	231	378	525
16-12 pg. adapt. of Silas Marner; Kiefer-a	19	38	57	111	176	240

JACK KIRBY OMNIBUS, THE
DC Comics: 2011; 2013 ($49.99, hardcover with dustjacket)

	GD	VG	FN	VF	VF/NM	NM-
Vol. 1 ('11) Recolored reprints of Kirby's DC work from 1946, 1957-1959; Evanier intro.						50.00
Vol. 2 ('13) Recolored reprints of Kirby's DC work from 1973-1987; Morrow intro.						50.00

JACK KIRBY'S FOURTH WORLD (See Mister Miracle & New Gods, 3rd Series)
DC Comics: Mar, 1997 - No. 20, Oct, 1998 ($1.95/$2.25)

	GD	VG	FN	VF	VF/NM	NM-
1-20: 1-Byrne-a/scripts & Simonson-c begin; story cont'd from New Gods, 3rd Series #15; retells "The Pact" (New Gods, 1st Series #7); 1st brief DC app. Thor. 2-Thor vs. Big Barda; "Apokolips Then" back-up begins; Kirby-c/swipe (Thor #126) 8-Genesis x-over. 10-Simonson-s/a 13-Simonson back-up story. 20-Superman-c/app.						4.00

Ivar, Timewalker #7 © VAL

Jack of Fables #39 © BW & DC

James Bond: 007 #2 © Fleming Prod.

GD 2.0 | VG 4.0 | FN 6.0 | VF 8.0 | VF/NM 9.0 | NM- 9.2

JACK KIRBY'S FOURTH WORLD OMNIBUS
DC Comics: 2007 - Vol. 4, 2008 ($49.99, hardcovers with dustjackets)
Vol. 1 ('07) Recolored reprints in chronological order of Superman's Pal, Jimmy Olsen #133-139, Forever People #1-3, New Gods #1-3, and Mister Miracle #1-3; Morrison intro, bonus art 150.00
Vol. 2 ('07) r/Jimmy Olsen #141-145, F.P. #4-6, N.G. #4-6 & M.M. #4-6; bonus art 80.00
Vol. 3 ('07) r/Jimmy Olsen #146-148, F.P. #7-10, N.G. #7-10 & M.M. #7-9; bonus art 50.00
Vol. 4 ('08) r/F.P. #11, M.M. #10-18, N.G. #11 & reprint series #6, & DC Graphic Novel #6 (The Hunger Dogs); Levitz intro.; Evanier afterword; character profile pages 50.00

JACK KIRBY'S GALACTIC BOUNTY HUNTERS
Marvel Comics (Icon): July, 2006 - No. 6, Nov, 2007 ($3.99)
1-6-Based on a Kirby concept; Mike Thibodeaux-a; Lisa Kirby, Thibodeaux and others-s 4.00
HC (2007, $24.99) r/series; pin-ups and supplemental art and interviews 25.00

JACK KIRBY'S SECRET CITY SAGA
Topps Comics (Kirbyverse): No. 0, Apr, 1993; No. 1, May, 1993 - No. 4, Aug, 1993 ($2.95, limited series)
0-(No cover price, 20 pgs.)-Simonson-c/a 4.00
0-Red embossed-c (limited ed.) 5.00
0-Gold foil-c (limited ed.) 1 3 4 6 8 10
1-4-Bagged w/3 trading cards; Ditko-c/a: 1-Ditko/Art Adams-c. 2-Ditko/Byrne-c; has coupon for Pres. Clinton holo-foil trading card. 3-Dorman poster; has coupon for Gore holo-foil trading card. 4-Ditko/Perez-c 4.00
NOTE: *Issues #1-4 contain coupons redeemable for Kirbychrome version of #1*

JACK KIRBY'S SILVER STAR (Also see Silver Star)
Topps Comics (Kirbyverse): Oct, 1993 ($2.95)(Intended as a 4-issue limited series)
1-Silver ink-c; Austin-c/a(i); polybagged w/3 cards 4.00

JACK KIRBY'S TEENAGENTS (See Satan's Six)
Topps Comics (Kirbyverse): Aug, 1993 - No. 4, Nov, 1993 ($2.95, limited series)
1-4: Bagged with/3 trading cards; Busiek-s/Austin-c(i): 3-Liberty Project app. 4.00

JACK KRAKEN
Dark Horse Comics: May, 2014 ($3.99, one-shot)
1-Tim Seeley-s; art by Ross Campbell & Jim Terry 4.00

JACK OF FABLES (See Fables)
DC Comics (Vertigo): Sept, 2006 - No. 50, Apr, 2011 ($2.99)
1-49: 1-Willingham & Sturges-s/Akins-a. 33-35-Crossover with Fables and The Literals 3.00
50-($4.99) Akins & Braun-a; Bolland-c 5.00
1-Special Edition (8/10, $1.00) r/#1 with "What's Next?" logo on cover 3.00
...: Americana TPB (2008, $14.99) r/#17-21 15.00
...: Jack of Hearts TPB (2007, $14.99) r/#6-11 15.00
...: The Bad Prince TPB (2008, $14.99) r/#12-16 15.00
...: The Big Book of War TPB (2009, $14.99) r/#28-32 15.00
...: The End TPB (2011, $17.99) r/#46-50 18.00
...: The Fulminate Blade TPB (2011, $14.99) r/#41-45 15.00
...: The (Nearly) Great Escape TPB (2007, $14.99) r/#1-5; Akins sketch pages 15.00
...: The New Adventures of Jack and Jack TPB (2010, $14.99) r/#36-40 15.00
...: Turning Pages TPB (2009, $14.99) r/#22-27 15.00

JACK OF HEARTS (Also see The Deadly Hands of Kung Fu #22 & Marvel Premiere #44)
Marvel Comics Group: Jan, 1984 - No. 4, Apr, 1984 (60¢, limited series)
1-4 4.00

JACKPOT!
AfterShock Comics: Apr, 2016 - No. 6, Jun, 2017 ($3.99)
1-6-Ray Fawkes-s/Brian Stelfreeze-c. 1-4-Marco Failla-a. 5,6-Georges Duarte-a 4.00

JACKPOT COMICS (Jolly Jingles #10 on)
MLJ Magazines: Spring, 1941 - No. 9, Spring, 1943
1-The Black Hood, Mr. Justice, Steel Sterling & Sgt. Boyle begin; WWII sunburst-c by Biro 411 822 1233 2877 5039 7200
2-S. Cooper-c 181 362 543 1158 1979 2800
3-Hubbell-c; bondage -c 181 362 543 1158 1979 2800
4-Archie begins; (his face appears on cover in small circle) (Win/41; on sale 12/41)-(also see Pep Comics #22); 1st app. Mrs. Grundy, the principal; Novick-c 3900 7800 11,700 22,200 29,600 37,000
5-Hitler, Tojo, Mussolini-c by Montana; 1st definitive Mr. Weatherbee; 1st brief app. Reggie in 1 panel 838 1676 2514 6117 10,809 15,500
6,7-Bondage-c by Novick 300 600 900 2070 3635 5200
8,9-Sahle-c. 8-WWII-c. 9-WWII bondage-c 284 568 852 1818 3109 4400

JACK Q FROST (See Unearthly Spectaculars)

JACK STAFF (Vol. 2; previously published in Britain)
Image Comics: Feb, 2003 - No. 20, May, 2009 ($2.95/$3.50)
1-5-Paul Grist-s/a 3.50
6-20-($3.50) 6-Flashback to the WW2 Freedom Fighters 3.50
... Special 1 (1/08, $3.50) Molachi the Immortal app. 3.50
The Weird World of Jack Staff King Size Special 1 (7/07, $5.99, B&W) r/story serialized in Comics International magazine; afterword by Grist 6.00
Vol. 1: Everything Used to Be Black and White TPB (12/03, $19.95) r/British issues 20.00
Vol. 2: Soldiers TPB (2005, $15.95) r/#1-5; cover gallery 16.00
Vol. 3: Echoes of Tomorrow TPB (2006, $16.99) r/#6-12; cover gallery 17.00

JACK THE GIANT KILLER (See Movie Classics)

JACK THE GIANT KILLER (New Adventures of...)
Bimfort & Co.: Aug-Sept, 1953
V1#1-H. C. Kiefer-c/a 34 68 102 199 325 450

JACKY'S DIARY
Dell Publishing Co.: No. 1091, Apr-June, 1960 (one-shot)
Four Color 1091 5 10 15 34 60 85

JADEMAN COLLECTION
Jademan Comics: Dec, 1989 - No. 3, 1990 ($2.50, plastic coated-c, 68 pgs.)
1-3: 1-Wraparound-c w/fold-out poster 4.00

JADEMAN KUNG FU SPECIAL
Jademan Comics: 1988 ($1.50, 64 pgs.)
1 4.00

JADE WARRIORS (Mike Deodato's...)
Image Comics (Glass House Graphics): Nov, 1999 - No. 3, 2000 ($2.50)
1-3-Deodato-a 3.00
1-Variant-c 3.00

JAGUAR, THE (Also see The Adventures of...)
Impact Comics (DC): Aug, 1991 - No. 14, Oct, 1992 ($1.00)
1-14: 4-The Black Hood x-over. 7-Sienkiewicz-c. 9-Contains Crusaders trading card 4.00
Annual 1 (1992, $2.50, 68 pgs.)-With trading card 5.00

JAGUAR GOD
Verotik: Mar, 1995 - No. 7, June, 1997 ($2.95, mature)
0 (2/96, $3.50)-Embossed Frazetta-c; Bisley-a; w/pin-ups. 5.00
1-Frazetta-c. 5.00
2-7: 2-Frazetta-c. 3-Bisley-c. 4-Emond-c. 7-($2.95)-Frazetta-c 4.00

JAKE THRASH
Aircel Publishing: 1988 - No. 3, 1988 ($2.00)
1-3 3.00

JAM, THE (...Urban Adventure)
Slave Labor Nos. 1-5/Dark Horse Comics Nos. 6-8/Caliber Comics No. 9 on: Nov, 1989 - No. 14, 1997 ($1.95/$2.50/$2.95, B&W)
1-14: Bernie Mireault-c/a/scripts. 6-1st Dark Horse issue. 9-1st Caliber issue 3.00

JAMBOREE COMICS
Round Publishing Co.: Feb, 1946(no month given) - No. 3, Apr, 1946
1-Funny animal 21 42 63 122 199 275
2,3 15 30 45 85 130 175

JAMES BOND
Dynamite Entertainment: 2015 - No. 12, 2016 ($3.99)
1-12-Warren Ellis-s/Jason Masters-a; multiple covers on each. 1-6-Vargr. 7-12-Eidolon 4.00
...: M (2018, $4.99) Shalvey-s/c; Holden-a 5.00
...: Moneypenny (2016, $4.99) Houser-s/Edgar-a/Lotay-c 5.00
...: Service (2017, $7.99) Kieron Gillen-s/Antonio Fuso-a/Jamie McKelvie-c 8.00
...: Solstice (2017, $4.99) Ibrahim Moustafa-s/a 5.00

JAMES BOND (Volume 2)
Dynamite Entertainment: 2017 - No. 6, 2017 ($3.99)
1-6-Black Box; Percy-s/Lobosco-a. 1-Five covers. 2-6-Multiple covers on each 4.00

JAMES BOND (Volume 3)
Dynamite Entertainment: 2019 - No. 6, 2020 ($3.99)
1-6: 1-Ayala & Lore-s/Gapstur-a 4.00

JAMES BOND: AGENT OF SPECTRE
Dynamite Entertainment: 2021 - No. 5, 2021 ($3.99, limited series)
1-5-Gage-s/Casalanguida-a; Blofeld app.; multiple covers on each 4.00

JAMES BOND 007
Dynamite Entertainment: 2018 - No. 12, 2019 ($3.99, limited series)
1-12: 1-3-Greg Pak-s/Marc Laming-a; Oddjob app. 4-6-Stephen Mooney-a; Goldfinger app. 4.00

	GD 2.0	VG 4.0	FN 6.0	VF 8.0	VF/NM 9.0	NM- 9.2

JAMES BOND: 007
Dynamite Entertainment: 2022 - No. 6, 2023 ($3.99)
1-6-Philip Kennedy Johnson-s/Marco Finnegan-a 4.00

JAMES BOND 007: A SILENT ARMAGEDDON
Dark Horse Comics/Acme Press: Mar, 1993 - Apr 1993 (limited series)
1,2 5.00

JAMES BOND 007: GOLDENEYE (Movie)
Topps Comics: Jan, 1996 ($2.95, unfinished limited series of 3)
1-Movie adaptation; Stelfreeze-c 1 2 3 5 6 8

JAMES BOND 007: SERPENT'S TOOTH
Dark Horse Comics/Acme Press: July 1992 - Aug 1992 ($4.95, limited series)
1-3-Paul Gulacy-c/a 5.00

JAMES BOND 007: SHATTERED HELIX
Dark Horse Comics: Jun 1994 - July 1994 ($2.50, limited series)
1,2 5.00

JAMES BOND 007: THE QUASIMODO GAMBIT
Dark Horse Comics: Jan 1995 - May 1995 ($3.95, limited series)
1-3 4.50

JAMES BOND: FELIX LEITER
Dynamite Entertainment: 2017 - No. 6, 2017 ($3.99)
1-6-James Robinson-s/Aaron Campbell-a 4.00

JAMES BOND FOR YOUR EYES ONLY
Marvel Comics Group: Oct, 1981 - No. 2, Nov, 1981
1,2-Movie adapt.; r/Marvel Super Special #19 6.00

JAMES BOND: HAMMERHEAD
Dynamite Entertainment: 2016 - No. 6, 2016 ($3.99)
1-6-Diggle-s/Casalanguida-a. 1-Three covers 4.00

JAMES BOND: HIMEROS
Dynamite Entertainment: 2021 - No. 5, 2022 ($3.99, limited series)
1-5: 1-Barnes-s/Fuso-a; covers by Francavilla & Guice. 3-Minotti-a 4.00

JAMES BOND JR. (TV)
Marvel Comics: Jan, 1992 - No. 12, Dec, 1992 (#1: $1.00, #2-on: $1.25)
1-12: Based on animated TV show 4.00

JAMES BOND: KILL CHAIN
Dynamite Entertainment: 2017 - No. 6, 2017 ($3.99)
1-6-Diggle-s/Casalanguida-a. 1-Three covers. 2-Felix Leiter app. 4.00

JAMES BOND: LICENCE TO KILL (See Licence To Kill)

JAMES BOND: ORIGIN
Dynamite Entertainment: 2018 - No. 12, 2019 ($3.99)
1-12: 1-Parker-s/Bob Q-a; multiple covers; young James Bond in 1941 WWII England 4.00

JAMES BOND: PERMISSION TO DIE
Eclipse Comics/ACME Press: 1989 - No. 3, 1991 ($3.95, lim. series, squarebound, 52 pgs.)
1-3: Mike Grell-c/a/scripts in all. 3-($4.95) 5.00

JAMES BOND: THE BODY
Dynamite Entertainment: 2018 - No. 6, 2018 ($3.99)
1-6: 1-Kot-s/Casalanguida-a. 2-Fuso-a 4.00

JAM, THE: SUPER COOL COLOR INJECTED TURBO ADVENTURE #1 FROM HELL!
Comico: May, 1988 ($2.50, 44 pgs., one-shot)
1 4.00

JANE ARDEN (See Feature Funnies & Pageant of Comics)
St. John (United Features Syndicate): Mar, 1948 - No. 2, June, 1948
1-Newspaper reprints 18 36 54 107 169 230
2 14 28 42 82 121 160

JANE FOSTER & THE MIGHTY THOR
Marvel Comics: Aug, 2022 - No. 5, Dec, 2022 ($3.99, limited series)
1-5-Gronbekk-s/Dowling-a; Sif & The Enchantress app. 4.00

JANE WIEDLIN'S LADY ROBOTIKA
Image Comics: Jul, 2010 - No. 2, Aug, 2010 ($3.50, unfinished limited series)
1,2-Wiedlin & Bill Morrison-s. 1-Morrison & Rodriguez-a. 2-Moy-a 3.50

JANN OF THE JUNGLE (Jungle Tales No. 1-7)
Atlas Comics (CSI): No. 8, Nov, 1955 - No. 17, June, 1957
8(#1) 48 96 144 302 514 725
9,11-15 29 58 87 172 281 390
10-Williamson/Colletta-c 34 68 102 199 325 450
16,17-Williamson/Mayo-a(3), 5 pgs. each 31 62 93 186 303 420
NOTE: *Everett c-15-17.* ***Heck*** *a-8, 15, 17.* ***Maneely*** *c-11.* ***Shores*** *a-8.*

JASON & THE ARGOBOTS
Oni Press: Aug, 2002 - No. 4, Dec, 2002 ($2.95, B&W, limited series)
1-4-Torres-s/Norton-c/a 3.00
Vol. 1 Birthquake TPB (6/03, $11.95, digest size) r/#1-4, Sunday comic strips 12.00
Vol. 2 Machina Ex Deus TPB (9/03, $11.95, digest size) new story 12.00

JASON & THE ARGONAUTS (See Movie Classics)

JASON GOES TO HELL: THE FINAL FRIDAY (Movie)
Topps Comics: July, 1993 - No. 3, Sept, 1993 ($2.95, limited series)
1-Adaptation of film. 1-Glow-in-the-dark-c 3 6 9 18 27 36
2,3-Adaptation continues 2 4 6 9 12 15

JASON'S QUEST (See Showcase #88-90)

JASON VS. LEATHERFACE
Topps Comics: Oct, 1995 - No. 3, Jan, 1996 ($2.95, limited series)
1-Collins scripts; Bisley-c on all 3 6 9 17 26 35
2,3 2 4 6 11 16 20

JAWS 2 (See Marvel Comics Super Special, A)

JAY & SILENT BOB (See Clerks, Oni Double Feature, and Tales From the Clerks)
Oni Press: July, 1998 - No. 4, Oct, 1999 ($2.95, B&W, limited series)
1-Kevin Smith-s/Fegredo-a; photo-c & Quesada/Palmiotti-c
2 4 6 9 12 15
1-San Diego Comic Con variant covers (2 different covers, came packaged with action figures) 10.00
1-2nd & 3rd printings, 2-4: 2-Allred-c. 3-Flip-c by Jaime Hernandez 5.00
Chasing Dogma TPB (1999, $11.95) r/#1-4; Alanis Morissette intro. 13.00
Chasing Dogma TPB (2001, $12.95) r/#1-4 in color; Morissette intro. 13.00
Chasing Dogma HC (1999, $69.95, S&N) r/#1-4 in color; Morissette intro. 70.00

JCP FEATURES
J.C. Productions (Archie): Feb, 1982-c; Dec, 1981-indicia ($2.00, one-shot, B&W magazine)
1-T.H.U.N.D.E.R. Agents; Black Hood by Morrow & Neal Adams; Texeira-a; 2 pgs. S&K-a from Fly #1 2 4 6 10 14 18

JEAN GREY (X-Men) (Also see Phoenix Resurrection: The Return of Jean Grey)
Marvel Comics: Jul, 2017 - No. 11, Mar, 2018 ($3.99)
1-10: 1-Hopeless-s/Ibáñez-a. 4-Thor app. 6-Dr. Strange app. 7-Scarlet Witch app. 4.00
11-($4.99) Follows Phoenix Resurrection #5; leads into X-Men: Red #1 5.00

JEANIE COMICS (Formerly All Surprise; Cowgirl Romances #28)
Marvel Comics/Atlas(CPC): No. 13, April, 1947 - No. 27, Oct, 1949
13-Mitzi, Willie begin 41 82 123 256 428 600
14,15 28 56 84 165 270 375
16-Used in Love and Death by Legman; Kurtzman's "Hey Look"
36 72 108 211 343 475
17-19,21,22-Kurtzman's "Hey Look" (1-3 pgs. each) 23 46 69 136 223 310
20,23-27 21 42 63 124 202 280

JEEP COMICS (Also see G.I. Comics and Overseas Comics)
R. B. Leffingwell & Co.: Winter, 1944, No. 2, Spring, 1945 - No. 3, Mar-Apr, 1948
1-Capt. Power, Criss Cross & Jeep & Peep (costumed) begin
93 186 279 591 1021 1450
2- Jeep & Peep-c 53 106 159 334 567 800
3-L. B. Cole dinosaur-c 68 136 204 435 743 1050

JEEPERS CREEPERS (Based on the 2001 horror movie)
Dynamite Entertainment: 2018 - No. 5, 2018 ($3.99, limited series)
1-5-Marc Andreyko-s/Kewber Baal-a; multiple covers on each 4.00

JEFF JORDAN, U.S. AGENT
D. S. Publishing Co.: Dec, 1947 - Jan, 1948
1 21 42 63 126 206 285

JEFF STEINBERG: CHAMPION OF EARTH
Oni Press: Aug, 2016 - No. 6, Mar, 2017 ($4.99)
1-6: 1-Fialkov-s/Fleecs-a; covers by Fleecs & Burnham 5.00

JEM & THE HOLOGRAMS
IDW Publishing: Mar, 2015 - No. 26, Apr, 2017 ($3.99)
1-25: 1-Origin re-told; multiple covers 4.00
26-($4.99) Thompson-s/Lagace-a; previews Infinite x-over series; cover gallery 5.00
Annual 2017 (1/17, $7.99) Thompson-s; art by Lagace and others; 2 covers 8.00
... Holiday Special (12/15, $3.99) Mebberson-a 4.00
IDW Greatest Hits: Jem and the Holograms #1 (7/16, $1.00) r/#1 3.00
... 20/20 #1 (1/19, $4.99) Set 20 years in the future; Sina Grace-s/Siobhan Keenan-a 5.00
... Valentine Special (2/16, $3.99) Thompson-s/Bartel-a 4.00

JEM AND THE HOLOGRAMS: DIMENSIONS
IDW Publishing: Nov, 2017 - No. 4, Feb, 2018 ($3.99, limited series)
1-4-Anthology by various; multiple covers on each. 1-Leth-s/Ford-a 4.00

JEM AND THE HOLOGRAMS: INFINITE
IDW Publishing: Jun, 2017 - No. 3, Aug, 2017 ($3.99, limited series)
1-3-Part 1,3,5 of the x-over with Jem and the Holograms: The Misfits: Infinite 4.00

JEM AND THE HOLOGRAMS: THE MISFITS: INFINITE
IDW Publishing: Jun, 2017 - No. 3, Aug, 2017 ($3.99, limited series)
1-3-Part 2,4,6 of the x-over with Jem and the Holograms: Infinite 4.00

JEMM, SON OF SATURN
DC Comics: Sept, 1984 - No. 12, Aug, 1985 (Maxi-series, mando paper)
1-12: 3-Origin. 4-Superman app. 4.00
NOTE: ***Colan*** *a-1-12p; c-1-5, 7-12p.*

JEM: THE MISFITS (From Jem and the Holograms)
IDW Publishing: Dec, 2016 - No. 5, Apr, 2017 ($3.99)
1-5-Kelly Thompson-s/Jenn St-Onge-a 4.00

JENNIFER BLOOD
Dynamite Entertainment: 2011 - No. 36, 2014 ($3.99)
1-36: 1-3-Garth Ennis-s/Adriano Batista-a; four covers on each. 4-The Ninjettes app. 4.00
Annual 1 (2012, $4.99) Al Ewing-s/Igor Vitorino-a/Sean Chen-c; origin 5.00
... Presents Giulietta Romeo: Hitwoman 1 (2022, $4.99) Van Lente-s/Carey-a 5.00

JENNIFER BLOOD: BORN AGAIN
Dynamite Entertainment: 2014 - No. 5, 2014 ($3.99)
1-5-Steven Grant-s/Kewber Baal-a/Stephen Segovia-c 4.00

JENNIFER BLOOD: FIRST BLOOD
Dynamite Entertainment: 2011 - No. 6, 2013 ($3.99)
1-6-Mike Carroll-s/Igor Vitorino-a/Mike Mayhew-c; origin & training 4.00

JENNIFER BLOOD, VOLUME 2
Dynamite Entertainment: 2021 - No. 10, 2022 ($3.99)
1-10: 1-Fred Van Lente-s/Vincenzo Federici-a; multiple covers on each 4.00

JENNIFER'S BODY (Based on the 2009 movie)
BOOM! Studios: Aug, 2009 ($24.99, hardcover graphic novel)
HC-Short stories of Jennifer and her victims; Spears-s/art by various; pin-up art 25.00

Jem and the Holograms #1 © Hasbro

Jennifer Blood: Born Again #1 © Spitfire

Jessica Jones #13 © MAR

	GD 2.0	VG 4.0	FN 6.0	VF 8.0	VF/NM 9.0	NM- 9.2
JENNY FINN						
Oni Press: June, 1999 - No. 2, Sept, 1999 ($2.95, B&W, unfinished lim. series)						
1,2-Mignola & Nixey-s/Nixey-a/Mignola-c						3.00
...: Doom (Atomeka, 2005, $6.99, TPB) r/#1 & 2 with new supplemental material						7.00
JENNY SPARKS: THE SECRET HISTORY OF THE AUTHORITY						
DC Comics (WildStorm): Aug, 2000 - No. 5, Mar, 2001 ($2.50, limited series)						
1-Millar-s/McCrea & Hodgkins-a/Hitch & Neary-c						4.00
1-Variant-c by McCrea	1	3	4	6	8	10
2-5: 2-Apollo & Midnighter. 3-Jack Hawksmoor. 4-Shen. 5-Engineer						3.00
TPB (2001, $14.95) r/#1-5; Ellis intro.						15.00
JERICHO (Based on the TV series)						
Devil's Due Publishing/IDW Publishing: Oct, 2009 - Jan, 2014 ($3.99)						
... Redux (IDW, 2/11, $7.99) r/Season 3: Civil War #1-3						8.00
... Season 3: Civil War 1-4: 1-Story by the show's writing staff						4.00
... Season 4: 1-5: 1-(7/12) Photo-c & Bradstreet-c						4.00
JERRY DRUMMER (Boy Heroes of the Revolutionary War) (Formerly Soldier & Marine V2#9)						
Charlton Comics: V3#10, Apr, 1957 - V3#12, Oct, 1957						
V3#10-12: 11-Whitman-c/a	6	12	18	33	41	48
JERRY IGER'S... (All titles, Blackthorne/First)(Value: cover or less)						
JERRY LEWIS (See The Adventures of...)						
JERSEY GODS						
Image Comics: Feb, 2009 - No. 12, May, 2010 ($3.50)						
1-11: 1-Brunswick-s/McDaid-a; two covers by McDaid and Allred						3.50
12-($4.99) Wraparound cover swipe of Superman #252 by Allred						5.00
JESSE JAMES (The True Story Of..., also seeThe Legend of...)						
Dell Publishing Co.: No. 757, Dec, 1956 (one shot)						
Four Color 757-Movie, photo-c	9	18	27	58	114	170
JESSE JAMES (See Badmen of the West & Blazing Sixguns)						
Avon Periodicals: 8/50 - No. 9, 11/52; No. 15, 10/53 - No. 29, 8-9/56						
1-Kubert Alabam-r/Cowpuncher #1	26	52	78	152	249	345
2-Kubert-a(3)	19	38	57	111	176	240
3-Kubert Alabam-r/Cowpuncher #2	16	32	48	98	154	210
4,9-No Kubert	14	28	42	76	108	140
5,6-Kubert Jesse James-a(3); 5-Wood-a(1pg.)	17	34	51	100	158	215
7-Kubert Jesse James-a(2)	15	30	45	90	140	190
8-Kinstler-a(3)	14	28	42	80	115	150
15-Kinstler-r/#3	12	24	36	69	97	125
16-Kinstler-r/#3 & story-r/Butch Cassidy #1	13	26	39	72	101	130
17-19,21: 17-Jesse James-r/#4; Kinstler-c idea from Kubert splash in #6. 18-Kubert Jesse James-r/#5. 19-Kubert Jesse James-r/#6. 21-Two Jesse James-r/#4, Kinstler-r/#4	11	22	33	64	90	115
20-Williamson/Frazetta-a; r/Chief Vic. Apache Massacre; Kubert Jesse James-r/#6; Kit West story by Larsen	17	34	51	105	165	225
22-29: 22,23-No Kubert. 24-New McCarty strip by Kinstler; Kinstler-r. 25-New McCarty Jesse James strip by Kinstler; Jesse James-r/#7,9. 26,27-New McCarty Jesse James strip plus a Kinstler/McCann Jesse James-r. 28-Reprints most of Red Mountain, Featuring Quantrells Raiders	11	22	33	64	90	115
Annual nn (1952; 25¢, 100 pgs.)- "...Brings Six-Gun Justice to the West"- 3 earlier issues rebound; Kubert, Kinstler-a(3)	39	78	117	231	378	525

NOTE: *Mostly reprints #10 on.* ***Fawcette** c-1, 2.* ***Kida** a-5.* ***Kinstler** a-3, 4, 7-9, 15r, 16r(2), 21-27; c-3, 4, 9, 17-27. Painted c-5-8. 22 has 2 stories r/Sheriff Bob Dixon's Chuck Wagon #1 with name changed to Sheriff Bob Trent.*

	GD 2.0	VG 4.0	FN 6.0	VF 8.0	VF/NM 9.0	NM- 9.2
JESSE JAMES						
Realistic Publications: July, 1953						
nn-Reprints Avon's #1; same-c, colors different	14	28	42	76	108	140
JESSICA JONES (Also see Alias)						
Marvel Comics: Dec, 2016 - No. 18, May, 2018 ($3.99)						
1-18-Bendis-s/Gaydos-a; Luke Cage app. 1-Misty Knight app. 13-17-Purple Man app.						4.00
...: Purple Daughter (2019, $19.99, square-bound) Printing of digital-first story; De Julis-a						20.00
JESSICA JONES: BLIND SPOT						
Marvel Comics: Mar, 2020 - No. 6, May, 2020 ($3.99, printing of digital-first story)						
1-6-Kelly Thompson-s/Mattia De Iulis-a. 2,3-Elsa Bloodstone app. 4-Spider-Man app.						4.00
JEST (Formerly Snap; becomes Kayo #12)						
Harry 'A' Chesler: No. 10, 1944; No. 11, 1944						
10-Johnny Rebel & Yankee Boy app. in text	28	56	84	168	274	380
11-Little Nemo in Adventure Land	25	50	75	150	245	340
JESTER						
Harry 'A' Chesler: No. 10, 1945						
10	24	48	72	142	234	325
JESUS						
Spire Christian Comics (Fleming H. Revell Co.): 1979 (49¢)						
nn	2	4	6	11	16	20
JET (See Jet Powers)						
JET (Crimson from Wildcore & Backlash)						
DC Comics (WildStorm): Nov, 2000 - No. 4, Feb, 2001 ($2.50, limited series)						
1-4-Nguyen-a/Abnett & Lanning-s						3.00
JET ACES						
Fiction House Magazines: 1952 - No. 4, 1953						
1- Sky Advs. of American War Aces (on sale 6/20/52)	24	48	72	142	234	325
2-4	15	30	45	85	130	175
JETCAT CLUBHOUSE (Also see Land of Nod, The)						
Oni Press: Apr, 2001 - No. 3, Aug, 2001 ($3.25)						
1-3-Jay Stephens-s/a. 1-Wraparound-c						3.25
TPB (8/02, $10.95, 8 3/4" x 5 3/4") r/#1-3 & stories from Nickelodeon mag. & other						11.00
JET DREAM (...and Her Stunt-Girl Counterspies)(See The Man from Uncle #7)						
Gold Key: June, 1968 (12¢)						
1-Painted-c	4	8	12	27	44	60
JET FIGHTERS (Korean War)						
Standard Magazines: No. 5, Nov, 1952 - No. 7, Mar, 1953						
5,7-Toth-a. 5-Toth-c	18	36	54	105	165	225
6-Celardo-a	14	28	42	81	118	155
JET POWER						
I.W. Enterprises: 1963						
I.W. Reprint 1,2-r/Jet Powers #1,2	3	6	9	17	26	35
JET POWERS (American Air Forces No. 5 on)						
Magazine Enterprises: 1950 - No. 4, 1951						
1(A-1 #30)-Powell-c/a begins	43	86	129	271	461	650
2(A-1 #32) Classic Powell dinosaur-c/a	43	86	129	271	461	650
3(A-1 #35)-Williamson/Evans-a	45	90	135	284	480	675
4(A-1 #38)-Williamson/Wood-a; "The Rain of Sleep" drug story	47	94	141	296	498	700
JET PUP (See 3-D Features)						
JETSONS, THE (TV) (See March of Comics #276, 330, 348 & Spotlight #3)						
Gold Key: Jan, 1963 - No. 36, Oct, 1970 (Hanna-Barbera)						
1-1st comic book app.	46	92	138	340	770	1200
2	11	22	33	73	157	240
3-10: 9-Flintstones x-over	8	16	24	56	108	160
11-22	7	14	21	44	82	120
23-36-Reprints: 23-(7/67)	5	10	15	30	50	70
JETSONS, THE (TV) (Also see Golden Comics Digest)						
Charlton Comics: Nov, 1970 - No. 20, Dec, 1973 (Hanna-Barbera)						
1	9	18	27	61	123	185
2	4	8	12	28	47	65
3-10: Flintstones x-over	3	6	9	20	31	42
11-20	3	6	9	16	24	32
nn (1973, digest, 60¢, 100 pgs.) B&W one page gags	4	8	12	23	37	50
JETSONS, THE (TV)						
Harvey Comics: V2#1, Sept, 1992 - No. 5, Nov, 1993 ($1.25/$1.50) (Hanna-Barbera)						
V2#1-5						5.00
...Big Book V2#1,2,3 ($1.95, 52 pgs.): 1-(11/92). 2-(4/93). 3-(7/93)						5.00
...Giant Size 1,2,3 ($2.25, 68 pgs): 1-(10/92). 2-(4/93). 3-(10/93)						5.00
JETSONS, THE (TV)						
Archie Comics: Sept, 1995 - No. 8, Apr, 1996 ($1.50)						
1-8						4.00
JETSONS, THE (TV)						
DC Comics: Jan, 2018 - No. 6, Mar, 2018 ($3.99, limited series)						
1-6: 1-Palmiotti-s/Brito-a; covers by Conner & Dave Johnson						4.00
JETTA OF THE 21ST CENTURY						
Standard Comics: No. 5, Dec, 1952 - No. 7, Apr, 1953 (Teen-age Archie type)						
5-Dan DeCarlo-a	103	206	309	659	1130	1600
6-Robot-c	77	154	231	493	847	1200
7	61	122	183	390	670	950

GD 2.0 | VG 4.0 | FN 6.0 | VF 8.0 | VF/NM 9.0 | NM- 9.2

TPB (Airwave Publ., 2006, $9.99) B&W reprint of series; Bill Morrison intro./back-c 10.00

JEW GANGSTER
DC Comics: 2005 ($14.99, SC graphic novel)
SC-Joe Kubert-s/a 15.00

JEZEBEL JADE (Hanna-Barbara)
Comico: Oct, 1988 - No. 3, Dec, 1988 ($2.00, mini-series)
1-3: Johnny Quest spin-off; early Adam Kubert-a 3.00

JEZEBELLE (See Wildstorm 2000 Annuals)
DC Comics (WildStorm): Mar, 2001 - No. 6, Aug, 2001 ($2.50, limited series)
1-6-Ben Raab-s/Steve Ellis-a 3.00

JIGGS & MAGGIE
Dell Publishing Co.: No. 18, 1941 (one shot)
Four Color 18 (#1)-(1936-38-r) 60 120 180 381 653 925

JIGGS & MAGGIE
Standard Comics/Harvey Publications No. 22 on: No. 11, 1949 (June) - No. 21, 2/53; No. 22, 4/53 - No. 27, 2-3/54
11 20 40 60 114 182 250
12-15,17-21 14 28 42 76 108 140
16-Wood text illos. 14 28 42 78 112 145
22-24-Little Dot app. 12 24 36 69 97 125
25,27 11 22 33 60 83 105
26-Four pgs. partially in 3-D 15 30 45 83 124 165
NOTE: *Sunday page reprints by McManus loosely blended into story continuity. Based on Bringing Up Father strip. Advertised on covers as "All New."*

JIGSAW (Big Hero Adventures)
Harvey Publ. (Funday Funnies): Sept, 1966 - No. 2, Dec, 1966 (36 pgs.)
1-Origin & 1st app.; Crandall-a (5 pgs.) 4 8 12 23 37 50
2-Man From S.R.A.M. 3 6 9 16 23 30

JIGSAW OF DOOM (See Complete Mystery No. 2)

JIM BOWIE (Formerly Danger?; Black Jack No. 20 on)
Charlton Comics: No. 16, Mar, 1956 - No. 19, Apr, 1957
16 8 16 24 44 57 70
17-19: 18-Giordano-c 6 12 18 29 36 42

JIM BOWIE (TV, see Western Tales)
Dell Publishing Co.: No. 893, Mar, 1958 - No. 993, May-July, 1959
Four Color 893 (#1) 7 14 21 44 82 120
Four Color 993-Photo-c 5 10 15 35 63 90

JIM BUTCHER'S THE DRESDEN FILES: DOG MEN (Based on the Dresden Files novels)
Dynamite Entertainment: 2017 - No. 6, 2017 ($3.99, limited series)
1-6: 1-Jim Butcher & Mark Powers-s/Diego Galindo-a/c 4.00

JIM BUTCHER'S THE DRESDEN FILES: DOWN TOWN (Based on the Dresden Files novels)
Dynamite Entertainment: 2015 - No. 6, 2015 ($3.99, limited series)
1-6: 1-Jim Butcher & Mark Powers-s/Carlos Gomez-a/Stjepan Sejic-c 4.00

JIM BUTCHER'S THE DRESDEN FILES: FOOL MOON
Dynamite Entertainment: 2011 - No. 8, 2012 ($3.99, limited series)
1-8: 1-Jim Butcher & Mark Powers-s/Chase Conley-a/Brett Booth-c 4.00

JIM BUTCHER'S THE DRESDEN FILES: GHOUL GOBLIN
Dynamite Entertainment: 2012 - No. 6, 2013 ($3.99, limited series)
1-6: 1-Jim Butcher & Mark Powers-s/Joseph Cooper-a; Syaf-c 4.00

JIM BUTCHER'S THE DRESDEN FILES: STORM FRONT (Based on the Dresden Files novels)
Dabel Bros. Productions: Oct, 2008 (Nov. on-c) - No. 4, Apr, 2009 ($3.99, limited series)
1-4-Jim Butcher & Mark Powers-s/Ardian Syaf-a; covers by Syaf & Tsai 4.00
Vol. 2: 1,2 (7/09 - No. 4) 4.00

JIM BUTCHER'S THE DRESDEN FILES: WAR CRY
Dynamite Entertainment: 2014 - No. 5, 2014 ($3.99/$4.99, limited series)
1-4: 1-Jim Butcher & Mark Powers-s/Carlos Gomez-a; Sejic-c 4.00
5-($4.99) Wraparound-c by Sejic 5.00

JIM BUTCHER'S THE DRESDEN FILES: WELCOME TO THE JUNGLE
Dabel Bros. Productions: Mar, 2008 (Apr. on-c) - No. 4, Jul, 2008 ($3.99, limited series)
1-Jim Butcher-s/Ardian Syaf-a; Ardian Syaf-c 5.00
1-Variant-c by Chris McGrath 8.00
1-New York Comic-Con 2008 variant-c 15.00
1-Second printing 4.00
2-4-Two covers on each 4.00
HC (2008, $19.95, dustjacket) r/#1-4; Butcher intro.; concept art pages 20.00

JIM BUTCHER'S THE DRESDEN FILES: WILD CARD
Dynamite Entertainment: 2016 - No. 6, 2016 ($3.99, limited series)
1-6-Jim Butcher & Mark Powers-s/Carlos Gomez-a/c 4.00

JIM DANDY
Dandy Magazine (Lev Gleason): May, 1956 - No. 3, Sept, 1956 (Charles Biro)
1-Jim Dandy adventures w/Cup, an alien & his flying saucer (both invisible) from the planet Zikalug begins; ends #3. Biro-c. 1,2-Bammy Boozle app.
15 30 45 85 130 175
2,3: 2-Two pg. actual flying saucer reports 11 22 33 60 83 105

JIM HARDY (See Giant Comics Eds., Sparkler & Treasury of Comics #2 & 5)
United Features Syndicate/Spotlight Publ.: 1939; 1942; 1947 - No. 2, 1947
Single Series 6 ('39) 52 104 156 328 552 775
Single Series 27('42) 40 80 120 244 402 560
1('47)-Spotlight Publ. 18 36 54 105 165 225
2 12 24 36 67 94 120

JIM HARDY
Spotlight/United Features Synd.: 1944 (25¢, 132 pgs.) (Tip Top, Sparkler-r)
nn-Origin Mirror Man; Triple Terror app. 43 86 129 271 401 650

JIM HENSON'S BENEATH THE DARK CRYSTAL
BOOM! Studios (Archaia): Jul, 2018 - No. 12, Aug, 2019 ($3.99, limited series)
1-12-Adam Smith-s/Alexandria Huntington-a 4.00

JIM HENSON'S LABYRINTH: CORONATION
BOOM! Studios (Archaia): Feb, 2018 - No. 12, Mar, 2019 ($3.99, limited series)
1-12: 1-Spurrier-s/Bayliss-a/Staples-c; Jareth before becoming the Goblin King 4.00

JIM HENSON'S LABYRINTH: UNDER THE SPELL
BOOM! Studios (Archaia): Nov, 2018 ($7.99, one-shot)
1-Short stories; Vidaurri-s/Webb-a; Grace-s/Sun-a; Dialynaš-s/a; Issacs-c 8.00

JIM HENSON'S THE DARK CRYSTAL: AGE OF RESISTANCE
BOOM! Studios (Archaia): Sept, 2019 - No. 12, Oct, 2020 ($3.99, limited series)
1-12: 1-6,8-Addis & Matthews-s/Andelfinger-a. 7-Carlomagno-a. 9-12-Migyeong-a 4.00

JIM HENSON'S THE STORYTELLER: DRAGONS (Also see The Storyteller)
BOOM! Studios (Archaia): Dec, 2015 - No. 4, Mar, 2016 ($3.99, limited series)
1-4: 2-Pride-s/a 4.00

JIM HENSON'S THE STORYTELLER: GHOSTS
BOOM! Studios (Archaia): Mar, 2019 - No. 4, Aug, 2020 ($3.99, limited series)
1-4: 1-Márk László-s/a. 2-Jennifer Rostowsky-s/a. 3-Michael Walsh-s/a 4-VER-s/a 4.00

JIM HENSON'S THE STORYTELLER: SHAPESHIFTERS
BOOM! Studios (Archaia): Mar, 2022 - No. 4, Jun, 2022 ($3.99, limited series)
1-4 4.00

JIM HENSON'S THE STORYTELLER: TRICKSTERS
BOOM! Studios (Archaia): Mar, 2021 - No. 4, Jun, 2021 ($3.99, limited series)
1-4-Momoko main-c on all. 1-Rivera-s/Zhang-a. 2-Ifueko-s/Kubo-a 4.00

JIM HENSON'S THE STORYTELLER: WITCHES
BOOM! Studios (Archaia): Sept, 2014 - No. 4, Dec, 2014 ($3.99, limited series)
1-4: 1-Vidaurri-s/a. 2-Vanderklugt-s/a. 3-Matthew Dow Smith-s/a. 4-Stokely-s/a 4.00

JIMINY CRICKET (Disney,, see Mickey Mouse Mag. V5#3 & Walt Disney Showcase #37)
Dell Publishing Co.: No. 701, May, 1956 - No. 989, May-July, 1959
Four Color 701 9 18 27 57 111 165
Four Color 795, 897, 989 7 14 21 44 82 120

JIM LEE SKETCHBOOK
DC Comics (WildStorm): 2002 (no price, 16 pgs.)
nn-Various DC and WildStorm character sketches by Lee 8.00

JIMMY CORRIGAN (See Acme Novelty Library)

JIMMY DURANTE (Also see A-1 Comics)
Magazine Enterprises: No. 18, Oct, 1949 - No. 20, Winter 1949-50
A-1 18,20-Photo-c (scarce) 52 104 156 328 552 775

JIMMY OLSEN (See Superman's Pal...)

JIMMY OLSEN
DC Comics: May, 2011 ($5.99, one-shot)
1-Reprints back-up feature from Action Comics #893-896 plus new material; Conner-c 6.00

JIMMY OLSEN: ADVENTURES BY JACK KIRBY
DC Comics: 2003, 2004 ($19.95, TPB)
nn-(2003) Reprints Jack Kirby's early issues of Superman's Pal Jimmy Olsen #133-139,141; Mark Evanier intro.; cover by Kirby and Steve Rude 20.00
Vol. 2 (2004) Reprints #142-148; Evanier intro.; cover gallery and sketch pages 20.00

JIMMY'S BASTARDS
AfterShock Comics: Jun, 2017 - No. 9, Jul, 2018 ($3.99)
1-9: 1-Garth Ennis-s/Russ Braun-a/Dave Johnson-c; intro. Secret Agent Jimmy Regent 4.00

JIMMY WAKELY (Cowboy movie star)
National Per. Publ.: Sept-Oct, 1949 - No. 18, July-Aug, 1952 (1-13: 52pgs.)
1-Photo-c, 52 pgs. begin; Alex Toth-a; Kit Colby Girl Sheriff begins
45 90 135 284 480 675
2-Toth-a 18 36 54 107 169 230
3,4,6,7-Frazetta-a in all, 3 pgs. each; Toth-a in all. 7-Last photo-c. 4-Kurtzman "Pot-Shot Pete", 1 pg; Toth-a 21 42 63 122 199 275
5,8-15-Toth-a; 12,14-Kubert-a (3 & 2 pgs.) 16 32 48 94 147 200
16-18 15 30 45 83 124 165
NOTE: *Gil Kane c-10-18p.*

JIM RAY'S AVIATION SKETCH BOOK
Vital Publishers: Mar-Apr, 1946 - No. 2, May-June, 1946 (15¢)
1-Picture stories of planes and pilots; atomic explosion panel
40 80 120 246 411 575
2-Story of General "Nap" Arnold 27 54 81 160 263 365

JIM SOLAR (See Wisco/Klarer in the Promotional Comics section)

JINGLE BELLE (Paul Dini's...)
Oni Press/Top Cow: Nov, 1999 - No. 2, Dec, 1999 ($2.95, B&W, limited series)
1,2-Paul Dini-s. 2-Alex Ross flip-c 4.00
Jingle Belle: Dash Away All (12/03, $11.95, digest-size) Dini-s/Garibaldi-a 12.00
Jingle Belle: Gift-Wrapped (Top Cow, 12/11, $3.99) Dini-s/Gladden-a 4.00
Jingle Belle: Santa Claus vs. Frankenstein (Top Cow, 12/08, $2.99) Dini-s/Gladden-a 3.00
Jingle Belle's Cool Yule (11/02, $13.95,TPB) r/All-Star Holiday Hullabaloo, The Mighty Elves, and Jubilee; internet strips and a color section w/DeStefano-a 14.00
Jingle Belle: The Homemade's Tale (IDW, 11/18, $4.99) Dini-s/Baldari-a/Buscema-c 5.00
Paul Dini's Jingle Belle Jubilee (11/01, $2.95) Dini-s; art by Rolston, DeCarlo, Morrison and Bone; pin-ups by Thompson and Aragonés 3.00
Paul Dini's Jingle Belle's All-Star Holiday Hullabaloo (11/00, $4.95) stories by various including Dini, Aragonés, Jeff Smith, Bill Morrison; Frank Cho-c 5.00
Paul Dini's Jingle Belle: The Fight Before Christmas (12/05, $2.99) Dini-s/Bone & others-a 3.00
Paul Dini's Jingle Belle: The Mighty Elves (7/01, $2.95) Dini-s/Bone-a 3.00
Paul Dini's Jingle Belle Winter Wingding (11/02, $2.95) Dini-s/Clugston-Major-c 3.00
The Bakers Meet Jingle Belle (12/06, $2.99) Dini-s/Kyle Baker-a 3.00
TPB (10/00, $8.95) r/#1&2, and app. from Oni Double Feature #13 9.00

JINGLE BELLE (Paul Dini's...)

Jimmy's Bastards #2 © Spitfire

Jinny Hex Special #1 © DC

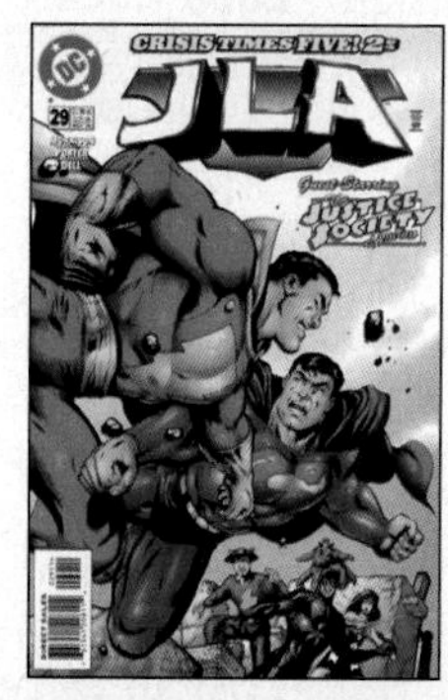

JLA #29 © DC

	GD	VG	FN	VF	VF/NM	NM-
	2.0	4.0	6.0	8.0	9.0	9.2

Dark Horse Comics: Nov, 2004 - No. 4, Apr, 2005 ($2.99, limited series)
1-4-Paul Dini-s/Jose Garibaldi-a 3.00
TPB (9/05, $12.95) r/#1-4 13.00

JINGLE BELLS (See March of Comics No. 65)

JINGLE DINGLE CHRISTMAS STOCKING COMICS (See Foodini #2)
Stanhall Publications: V2#1, 1951 (no date listed) (25¢, 100 pgs.; giant-size) (Publ. annually)

	GD	VG	FN	VF	VF/NM	NM-
V2#1-Foodini & Pinhead, Silly Pilly plus games & puzzles	28	56	84	168	274	380

JINGLE JANGLE COMICS (Also see Puzzle Fun Comics)
Eastern Color Printing Co.: Feb, 1942 - No. 42, Dec, 1949

	GD	VG	FN	VF	VF/NM	NM-
1-Pie-Face Prince of Old Pretzleburg, Jingle Jangle Tales by George Carlson, Hortense, & Benny Bear begin	55	110	165	352	601	850
2-4: 2,3-No Pie-Face Prince. 4-Pie-Face Prince-c	25	50	75	150	245	340
5 (10/42)	21	42	63	126	206	285
6-10: 8-No Pie-Face Prince	16	32	48	94	147	200
11-15	14	28	42	80	115	150
16-30: 17,18-No Pie-Face Prince. 24,30-XMas-c	11	22	33	62	86	110
31-42: 36,42-Xmas-c	10	20	30	56	76	95

NOTE: ***George Carlson** a-(2) in all except No. 2, 3, 8; c-1-6. **Carlson** 1 pg. puzzles in 9, 10, 12-15, 18, 20. **Carlson** illustrated a series of Uncle Wiggily books in 1930's.*

JING PALS
Victory Publishing Corp.: Feb, 1946 - No. 4, Aug?, 1946 (Funny animal)

	GD	VG	FN	VF	VF/NM	NM-
1-Wishing Willie, Puggy Panda & Johnny Rabbit begin	20	40	60	118	192	265
2-4	14	28	42	80	115	150

JINKS, PIXIE, AND DIXIE (See Kite Fun Book & Whitman Comic Books)

JINNY HEX SPECIAL (From Young Justice 2019 series)
DC Comics: Feb, 2021 ($4.99, one shot)
1-Visaggio-s/Melnikov-a/Derington-c; Jonah Hex and Superman cameos 5.00

JINX
Caliber Press: 1996 - No. 7, 1996 ($2.95, B&W, 32 pgs.)
1-7: Brian Michael Bendis-c/a/scripts. 2-Photo-c 3.00

JINX (Volume 2)
Image Comics: 1997 - No. 5, 1998 ($2.95, B&W, bi-monthly)
1-4: Brian Michael Bendis-c/a/scripts. 3.00
5-($3.95) Brereton-c 4.00
...Buried Treasures ('98, $3.95) short stories, ...Confessions ('98, $3.95) short stories, ...Pop Culture Hoo-Hah ('98, $3.95) humor shorts 4.00
TPB (1997, $10.95) r/Vol 1,#1-4 11.00
...: The Definitive Collection ('01, $24.95) remastered #1-5, sketch pages, art gallery, script excerpts, Mack intro. 25.00

JINX: TORSO
Image Comics: 1998 - No. 6, 1999 ($3.95/$4.95, B&W)
1-6-Based on Eliot Ness' pursuit of America's first serial killer; Brian Michael Bendis & Marc Andreyko-s/Bendis-a. 3-6-($4.95) 5.00
Softcover (2000, $24.95) r/#1-6; intro. by Greg Rucka; photo essay of the actual murders and police documents 25.00
Hardcover (2000, $49.95) signed & numbered 50.00

JINXWORLD SAMPLER
DC Comics: 2018 ($1.00)
nn-Reprints Scarlet #1, United States of Murder, Inc. #1 & Powers #1; Bendis-s 3.00

JIRNI
Aspen MLT: Apr, 2013 - No. 5, Oct, 2013 ($1.00/$3.99)
1-($1.00) J.T. Krul-s/Paolo Pantalena-a; multiple covers 3.00
2-5-($3.99) Multiple covers on each 4.00
Vol. 2 #1 (6/14, $3.99) Krul-s/Pantalena-a 4.00
Vol. 2 #1-5 (8/15 - No. 5, 12/15, $3.99) Krul-s/Marion-a; multiple covers on each 4.00
Vol. 3 #1-5 (3/18 - No. 5, 7/18, $3.99) Krul-s/Maria-a; multiple covers on each 4.00
... Primer (3/18, 25¢) Origin re-told with re-cap of Vol. 1 & 2; sketch art 4.00

JLA (See Justice League of America and Justice Leagues)
DC Comics: Jan, 1997 - No. 125, Apr, 2006 ($1.95/$1.99/$2.25/$2.50)

	GD	VG	FN	VF	VF/NM	NM-
1-Morrison-s/Porter & Dell-a. The Hyperclan app.	2	4	6	9	12	15
2	1	3	4	6	8	10
3,4	1	2	3	5	7	9

5-Membership drive; Tomorrow Woman app. 6.00
6-9: 6-1st app. Zauriel. 8-Green Arrow joins. 6.00
10-21: 10-Rock of Ages begins. 11-Joker and Luthor-c/app. 12-Intro. Hourman from the 853rd century. 14-Darkseid app. 15-($2.95) Rock of Ages concludes; intro. Superman One Million. 16-New members join; Prometheus app. 17,20-Jorgensen-a. 18-21-Waid-s. 20,21-Adam Strange c/app. 5.00
22-40: 22-Begin $1.99-c; Sandman (Daniel) app. 23-1st app. Justice Legion A. 27-Amazo app. 28-31-JSA app. 35-Hal Jordan/Spectre app. 36-40-World War 3 4.00
41-($2.99) Conclusion of World War 3; last Morrison-s 5.00
42-49,51-74: 43-Waid-s; Ra's al Ghul app. 44-Begin $2.25-c. 46-Batman leaves. 47-Hitch & Neary-a begins; JLA battles Queen of Fables. 52-55-Hitch-a. 59-Joker: Last Laugh. 61-68-Kelly-s/Mahnke-a. 69-73-Hunt for Aquaman; bi-monthly with alternating art by Mahnke and Guichet 4.00
50-($3.75) JLA vs. Dr. Destiny; art by Hitch & various 5.00
75-(1/03, $3.95) leads into Aquaman (4th series) #1 5.00
76-99: 76-Firestorm app. 77-Banks-a. 79-Kanjar Ro app. 91-93-O'Neil-s/Huat-a. 94-99-Byrne & Ordway-a/Claremont-s; Doom Patrol app. 4.00
100-($3.50) Intro. Vera Black; leads into Justice League Elite #1 5.00
101-125: 101-106-Austen-s/Garney-a/c. 107-114-Crime Syndicate app.; Busiek-s. 115-Begin $2.50-c; Johns & Heinberg-s; Secret Society of Super-Villains app. 4.00
#1,000,000 (11/98) 853rd Century x-over 4.00
Annual 1 (1997, $3.95) Pulp Heroes; Augustyn-s/Olivetti & Ha-a 5.00
Annual 2 (1998, $2.95) Ghosts; Wrightson-c 5.00
Annual 3 (1999, $2.95) JLApe; Art Adams-c 5.00
Annual 4 (2000, $3.50) Planet DC x-over; Steve Scott-c/a 5.00
... American Dreams (1998, $7.95, TPB) r/#5-9 8.00
...: Crisis of Conscience TPB (2006, $12.99) r/#115-119 13.00
.../ Cyberforce (DC/Top Cow, 2005, $5.99) Kelly-s/Mahnke-a/Silvestri-c 6.00
Divided We Fall (2001, $17.95, TPB) r/#47-54 18.00
...80-Page Giant 1 (7/98, $4.95) stories & art by various 6.00
...80-Page Giant 2 (11/99, $4.95) Green Arrow & Hawkman app. Hitch-c 6.00
...80-Page Giant 3 (10/00, $5.95) Pariah & Harbinger; intro. Moon Maiden 6.00
...Foreign Bodies (1999, $5.95, one-shot) Kobra app.; Semeiks-a 6.00
...Gallery (1997, $2.95) pin-ups by various; Quitely-c 4.00
...God & Monsters (2001, $6.95, one-shot) Benefiel-a/c 7.00
Golden Perfect (2003, $12.95, TPB) r/#61-65 13.00
.../ Haven: Anathema (2002, $6.95) Concludes the Haven: The Broken City series 7.00
.../ Haven: Arrival (2001, $6.95) Leads into the Haven: The Broken City series 7.00
...In Crisis Secret Files 1 (11/98, $4.95) recap of JLA in DC x-overs 5.00
...: Island of Dr. Moreau, The (2002, $6.95, one-shot) Elseworlds; Pugh-c/a; Thomas-s 7.00
.../ JSA Secret Files & Origins (1/03, $4.95) prelude to JLA/JSA: Virtue & Vice; short stories and pin-ups by various; Pacheco-c 5.00
.../ JSA: Virtue and Vice HC (2002, $24.95) Teams battle Despero & Johnny Sorrow; Goyer & Johns-s/Pacheco-a/c 25.00
.../ JSA: Virtue and Vice SC (2003, $17.95) 18.00
Justice For All (1999, $14.95, TPB) r/#24-33 15.00
New World Order (1997, $5.95, TPB) r/#1-4 6.00
...: Obsidian Age Book One, The (2003, $12.95) r/#66-71 13.00
...: Obsidian Age Book Two, The (2003, $12.95) r/#72-76 13.00
One Million (2004, $19.95, TPB) r/#DC One Million #1-4 and other #1,000,000 x-overs 20.00
...: Our Worlds at War (9/01, $2.95) Jae Lee-c; Aquaman presumed dead 4.00
...: Pain of the Gods (2005, $12.99) r/#101-106 13.00
...Primeval (1999, $5.95, one-shot) Abnett & Lanning-s/Olivetti-a 6.00
...: Riddle of the Beast HC (2001, $24.95) Grant-s/painted-a by various; Sweet-c 25.00
...: Riddle of the Beast SC (2003, $14.95) Grant-s/painted-a by various; Kaluta-c 15.00
Rock of Ages (1998, $9.95, TPB) r/#10-15 10.00
Rules of Engagement (2004, $12.95, TPB) r/#77-82 13.00
...: Seven Caskets (2000, $5.95, one-shot) Brereton-s/painted-c/a 6.00
...: Shogun of Steel (2002, $6.95, one-shot) Elseworlds; Justiniano-c/a 7.00
...Showcase 80-Page Giant (2/00, $4.95) Hitch-c 5.00
Strength in Numbers (1998, $12.95, TPB) r/#16-23, Secret Files #2 and Prometheus #1 13.00
...Superpower (1999, $5.95, one-shot) Arcudi-s/Eaton-a; Mark Antaeus joins 6.00
Syndicate Rules (2005, $17.99, TPB) r/#107-114, Secret Files #4 18.00
Terror Incognita (2002, $12.95, TPB) r/#55-60 13.00
...: The Deluxe Edition Vol. 1 HC (2008, $29.99, dustjacket) oversized r/#1-9 and JLA Secret Files #1 30.00
...: The Deluxe Edition Vol. 2 HC (2009, $29.99, dustjacket) oversized r/#10-17, JLA/Wildcats, and Prometheus #1 30.00
...: The Deluxe Edition Vol. 3 HC (2010, $29.99, dustjacket) oversized r/#22-26, 28-31 & #1,000,000 30.00
...: The Deluxe Edition Vol. 4 HC (2010, $34.99, dustjacket) oversized r/#34, 36-41, JLA Classified #1-3 and JLA: Earth 2 GN 35.00
The Tenth Circle (2004, $12.95, TPB) r/#94-99 13.00
...: The Greatest Stories Ever Told TPB (2006, $19.99) r/Justice League of America #19,71, 122,166-168,200, Justice League #1, JLA Secret Files #1 and JLA #61; Alex Ross-c 20.00
Tower of Babel (2001, $12.95, TPB) r/#42-46, Secret Files #3, 80-Page Giant #1 15.00
Trial By Fire (2004, $12.95, TPB) r/#84-89 13.00
...Vs. Predator (DC/Dark Horse, 2000, $5.95, one-shot) Nolan-c/a 10.00
...: Welcome to the Working Week (2003, $6.95, one-shot) Patton Oswalt-s 7.00

GD VG FN VF VF/NM NM-
2.0 4.0 6.0 8.0 9.0 9.2

...: World War III (2000, $12.95, TPB) r/#34-41 13.00
...: World Without a Justice League (2006, $12.99, TPB) r/#120-125 13.00
...: Zatanna's Search (2003, $12.95, TPB) rep. Zatanna's early app. & origin; Bolland-c 50.00

JLA: ACT OF GOD
DC Comics: 2000 - No. 3, 2001 ($4.95, limited series)
1-3-Elseworlds; metahumans lose their powers; Moench-s/Dave Ross-a 5.00

JLA: AGE OF WONDER
DC Comics: 2003 - No. 2, 2003 ($5.95, limited series)
1,2-Elseworlds; Superman and the League of Science during the Industrial Revolution 6.00

JLA: A LEAGUE OF ONE
DC Comics: 2000 (Graphic novel)
Hardcover ($24.95) Christopher Moeller-s/painted-a 25.00
Softcover (2002, $14.95) 15.00

JLA/AVENGERS (See Avengers/JLA for #2 & #4)
Marvel Comics: Sept, 2003; No. 3, Dec, 2003 ($5.95, limited series)
1-Busiek-s/Pérez-a; wraparound-c; Krona, Starro, Grandmaster, Terminus app.
3 6 9 14 20 25
3-Busiek-s/Pérez-a; wraparound-c; Phantom Stranger app.
3 6 9 16 23 30
SC (2008, $19.99) r/4-issue series; cover gallery; intros by Stan Lee & Julius Schwartz
9 16 24 54 102 150

JLA: BLACK BAPTISM
DC Comics: May, 2001 - No. 4, Aug, 2001 ($2.50, limited series)
1-4-Saiz-a(p)/Bradstreet-c; Zatanna app. 4.00

JLA: CLASSIFIED
DC Comics: Jan, 2005 - No. 54, May, 2008 ($2.95/$2.99)
1-3-Morrison-s/McGuinness-a/c; Ultramarines app. 3.00
4-9-"I Can't Believe It's Not The Justice League," Giffen & DeMatteis-s/Maguire-a 3.00
10-31,33-54: 10-15-New Maps of Hell; Ellis-s/Guice-a. 16-21-Garcia-Lopez-a. 22-25-Detroit League & Royal Flush Gang app.; Englehart-s. 26-28-Chaykin-s. 37-41-Kid Amazo. 50-54-Byrne-a/Middleston-c 3.00
32-($3.99) Dr. Destiny app.; Jurgens-a 4.00
I Can't Believe It's Not The Justice League TPB (2005, $12.99) r/#4-9 13.00
...: Kid Amazo TPB (2007, $12.99) r/#37-41 13.00
...: New Maps of Hell TPB (2006, $12.99) r/#10-15 13.00
...: That Was Now, This Is Then TPB (2008, $14.99) r/#50-54 15.00
...: The Hypothetical Woman TPB (2008, $12.99) r/#16-21 13.00
...: Ultramarine Corps TPB (2007, $14.99) r/#1-3, JLA/WildC.A.T.s #1 and JLA Secret Files 2004 #1 15.00

JLA CLASSIFIED: COLD STEEL
DC Comics: 2005 - No. 2, 2006 ($5.99, limited series, prestige format)
1,2-Chris Moeller-s/a; giant robot Justice League 6.00

JLA: CREATED EQUAL
DC Comics: 2000 - No. 2, 2000 ($5.95, limited series, prestige format)
1,2-Nicieza-s/Maguire-a; Elseworlds-Superman as the last man on Earth 6.00

JLA: DESTINY
DC Comics: 2002 - No. 4, 2002 ($5.95, prestige format, limited series)
1-4-Elseworlds; Arcudi-s/Mandrake-a 6.00

JLA / DOOM PATROL SPECIAL (Milk Wars DC/Young Animal crossover)
DC Comics: Mar, 2018 ($4.99, one-shot)
1-Part 1 of crossover; Orlando & Way-s/Aco-a/Quitely-c; Lord Manga Khan app. 5.00

JLA: EARTH 2
DC Comics: 2000 (Graphic novel)
Hardcover ($24.95) Morrison-s/Quitely-a; Crime Syndicate app. 25.00
Softcover ($14.95) 15.00

JLA: GATEKEEPER
DC Comics: 2001 - No. 3, 2001 ($4.95, prestige format, limited series)
1-3-Truman-s/a 5.00

JLA: HEAVEN'S LADDER
DC Comics: 2000 ($9.95, Treasury-size one-shot)
nn-Bryan Hitch & Paul Neary-c/a; Mark Waid-s 10.00

JLA/HITMAN (Justice League/Hitman in indicia)
DC Comics: Nov, 2007 - No. 2, Dec, 2007 ($3.99, limited series)
1,2-Ennis-s/McCrea-a; Bloodlines creatures return 4.00

JLA: INCARNATIONS
DC Comics: Jul, 2001 - No. 7, Feb, 2002 ($3.50, limited series)
1-7-Ostrander-s/Semeiks-a; different eras of the Justice League 4.00

JLA: LIBERTY AND JUSTICE
DC Comics: Nov, 2003 ($9.95, Treasury-size one-shot)
nn-Alex Ross-c/a; Paul Dini-s; story of the classic Justice League 10.00

JLA PARADISE LOST
DC Comics: Jan, 1998 - No. 3, Mar, 1998 ($1.95, limited series)
1-3-Millar-s/Olivetti-a 4.00

JLA: SCARY MONSTERS
DC Comics: May, 2003 - No. 6, Oct, 2003 ($2.50, limited series)
1-6-Claremont-s/Art Adams-c 4.00

JLA SECRET FILES
DC Comics: Sept, 1997 - 2004 ($4.95)
1-Standard Ed. w/origin-s & pin-ups 5.00
1-Collector's Ed. w/origin-s & pin-ups; cardstock-c 6.00
2,3: 2-(8/98) origin-s of JLA #16's newer members. 3-(12/00) 5.00
... 2004 (11/04) Justice League Elite app.; Mahnke & Byrne-a; Crime Syndicate app. 5.00

JLA: SECRET ORIGINS
DC Comics: Nov, 2002 ($7.95, Treasury-size one-shot)
nn-Alex Ross 2-page origins of Justice League members; text by Paul Dini 8.00

JLA: SECRET SOCIETY OF SUPER-HEROES
DC Comics: 2000 - No. 2, 2000 ($5.95, limited series, prestige format)
1,2-Elseworlds JLA; Chaykin and Tischman-s/McKone-a 6.00

JLA /SPECTRE: SOUL WAR
DC Comics: 2003 - No. 2, 2003 ($5.95, limited series, prestige format)
1,2-DeMatteis-s/Banks & Neary-a 6.00

JLA: THE NAIL (Elseworlds) (Also see Justice League of America: Another Nail)
DC Comics: Aug, 1998 - No. 3, Oct, 1998 ($4.95, prestige format)
1-3-JLA in a world without Superman; Alan Davis-s/a(p) 5.00
TPB ('98, $12.95) r/series w/new Davis-c 13.00

JLA / TITANS
DC Comics: Dec, 1998 - No. 3, Feb, 1999 ($2.95, limited series)
1-3-Grayson-s; P. Jimenez-c/a 3.00
...:The Technis Imperative ('99, $12.95, TPB) r/#1-3; Titans Secret Files 13.00

JLA: TOMORROW WOMAN (Girlfrenzy)
DC Comics: June, 1998 ($1.95, one-shot)
1-Peyer-s; story takes place during JLA #5 3.00

JLA / WILDC.A.T.S
DC Comics: 1997 ($5.95, one-shot, prestige format)
1-Morrison-s/Semeiks & Conrad-a 6.00

JLA /WITCHBLADE
DC Comics/Top Cow: 2000 ($5.95, prestige format, one-shot)
1-Pararillo-c/a 6.00

JLA / WORLD WITHOUT GROWN-UPS (See Young Justice)
DC Comics: Aug, 1998 - No. 2, Sept, 1998 ($4.95, prestige format)
1,2-JLA, Robin, Impulse & Superboy app.; Ramos & McKone-a 6.00
TPB ('98, $9.95) r/series & Young Justice: The Secret #1 10.00

JLA: YEAR ONE
DC Comics: Jan, 1998 - No. 12, Dec, 1998 ($2.95/$1.95, limited series)
1-($2.95)-Waid & Augustyn-s/Kitson-a 5.00
1-Platinum Edition 12.00
2-12-($1.95): 5-Doom Patrol-c/app. 7-Superman app. 4.00
TPB ('99,'09; $19.95/$19.99) r/#1-12; Busiek intro. 20.00

JLA-Z
DC Comics: Nov, 2003 - No. 3, Jan, 2004 ($2.50, limited series)
1-3-Pin-ups and info on current and former JLA members and villains; art by various 4.00

JLX
DC Comics (Amalgam): Apr, 1996 ($1.95, one-shot)
1-Mark Waid scripts 5.00

JLX UNLEASHED
DC Comics (Amalgam): June, 1997 ($1.95, one-shot)
1-Priest-s/Oscar Jimenez & Rodriguez-a 4.00

JOAN OF ARC (Also see A-1 Comics, Classics Illustrated #78, and Ideal a Classical Comic)
Magazine Enterprises: No. 21, 1949 (one shot)
A-1 21-Movie adaptation; Ingrid Bergman photo-covers & interior photos; Whitney-a 32 64 96 188 307 425

JOE COLLEGE
Hillman Periodicals: Fall, 1949 - No. 2, Wint, 1950 (Teen-age humor, 52 pgs.)
1-Powell-a; Briefer-a 18 36 54 105 165 225
2-Powell-a 13 26 39 72 101 130

JOE FIXIT (See Incredible Hulk #347)
Marvel Comics: Mar, 2023 - Present ($3.99)
1,2-Set during Banner's Vegas era; Peter David-s/Yildiray Cinar-a 4.00

JOE FRANKENSTEIN
IDW Publishing: Feb, 2015 - No. 4, May, 2015 ($3.99)
1-4-Chuck Dixon & Graham Nolan-s/Graham Nolan-a 4.00

JOE GOLEM
Dark Horse Comics: Nov, 2015 - No. 5, Mar, 2016 ($3.50)
1-5-Mignola & Golden-s/Reynolds-a 4.00

JOE GOLEM: THE CONJURORS
Dark Horse Comics: May, 2019 - No. 5, Oct, 2019 ($3.99)
1-5-Mignola & Golden-s/Bergting-a 4.00

JOE GOLEM: THE DROWNING CITY
Dark Horse Comics: Sept, 2018 - No. 5, Jan, 2019 ($3.99)
1-5-Mignola & Golden-s/Bergting-a 4.00

JOE GOLEM: THE OUTER DARK
Dark Horse Comics: May, 2017 - No. 5, Jan, 2018 ($3.99)
1-5-Mignola & Golden-s/Reynolds-a. 4,5-Titled Joe Golem: Flesh and Blood #1,2 4.00

JOE JINKS
United Features Syndicate: No. 12, 1939
Single Series 12 36 72 108 211 343 475

JOE KUBERT PRESENTS
DC Comics: Dec, 2012 - No. 6, May, 2013 ($4.99, limited series)
1-6: Anthology of short stories by Kubert, Buniak & Glanzman. 1-Hawkman app. 5.00

JOE LOUIS (See Fight Comics #2, Picture News #6 & True Comics #5)
Fawcett Publications: Sept, 1950 - No. 2, Nov, 1950 (Photo-c) (Boxing champ) (See Dick Cole #10)
1-Photo-c; life story 63 126 189 403 689 975
2-Photo-c 45 90 135 284 480 675

JOE PALOOKA (1st Series)(Also see Big Shot Comics, Columbia Comics & Feature Funnies)

JLA Classified #50 © DC

Joe Fixit #1 © MAR

John Carter, Warlord of Mars #2 © ERB

	GD	VG	FN	VF	VF/NM	NM-
	2.0	4.0	6.0	8.0	9.0	9.2

Columbia Comic Corp. (Publication Enterprises): 1942 - No. 4, 1944

1-1st to portray American president; gov't permission required 135 270 405 864 1482 2100
2 (1943)-Hitler-c 126 252 378 806 1378 1950
3-Nazi Sub-c 55 110 165 352 601 850
4 43 86 129 271 461 650

JOE PALOOKA (2nd Series) (Battle Adv. #68-74; ...Advs. #75, 77-81, 83-85, 87; Champ of the Comics #76, 82, 86, 89-93) (See All-New)
Harvey Publications: Nov, 1945 - No. 118, Mar, 1961

1-By Ham Fisher 63 126 189 403 689 975
2 33 66 99 194 317 440
3,4,6,7-1st Flyin' Fool, ends #25 19 38 57 111 176 240
5-Boy Explorers by S&K (7-8/46) 22 44 66 128 209 290
8-10 14 28 42 82 121 160
11-14,16,18-20: 14-Black Cat text-s(2). 18-Powell-a.; Little Max app. 19-Freedom Train-c 12 24 36 69 97 125
15-Origin & 1st app. Humphrey (12/47); Super-heroine Atoma app. by Powell 16 32 48 94 147 200
17-Humphrey vs. Palooka-c/s; 1st app. Little Max 15 30 45 90 140 190
21-26,29,30: 22-Powell-a. 30-Nude female painting 10 20 30 56 76 95
27-Little Max app.; Howie Morenz-s 10 20 30 58 79 100
28-Babe Ruth 4 pg. sty. 10 20 30 58 79 100
31,39,51: 31-Dizzy Dean 4 pg. sty. 39-(12/49) Humphrey & Little Max begin; Sonny Baugh football-s; Sherlock Max-s. 51-Babe Ruth 2 pg. sty; Jake Lamotta 1/2 pg. sty 9 18 27 50 65 80
32-38,40-50,52-61: 35-Little Max-c/story(4 pgs.); Joe Louis 1 pg. sty. 36-Humphrey story. 41-Bing Crosby photo on-c. 44-Palooka marries Ann Howe. 50-(11/51)-Becomes Harvey Comics Hits #51 8 16 24 44 57 70
62-S&K Boy Explorers-r 9 18 27 50 65 80
63-65,73-80,100: 79-Story of 1st meeting with Ann 8 16 24 40 50 60
66,67-'Commie' torture story "Drug-Diet Horror" 14 28 42 81 118 155
68,70-72: 68,70-Joe vs. "Gooks"-c. 71-Bloody bayonets-c. 72-Tank-c 14 28 42 78 112 145
69-1st "Battle Adventures" issue; torture & bondage 15 30 45 84 127 170
81-99,101-115: 104,107-Humphrey & Little Max-s 7 14 21 37 46 55
116-S&K Boy Explorers-r (Giant, '60) 9 18 27 47 61 75
117-(84 pg. Giant) r/Commie issues #66,67; Powell-a 9 18 27 52 69 85
118-(84 pg. Giant) Jack Dempsey 2 pg. sty, Powell-a 9 18 27 47 61 75
...**Visits the Lost City** nn (1945)(One Shot)(50¢)-164 page continuous story strip reprint. Has biography & photo of Ham Fisher; possibly the single longest comic book story published in that era (159 pgs.?) (scarce) 242 484 726 1537 2644 3750

NOTE: ***Nostrand/Powell** a-73. **Powell** a-7, 8, 10, 12, 14, 17, 19, 26-45, 47-53, 70, 73 at least. Black Cat text stories #8, 12, 13, 19.*

JOE PALOOKA
IDW Publishing: Dec, 2012 - No. 6, May, 2013 ($3.99, limited series)

1-6: 1-Bullock-s/Peniche-a; Joe Palooka updated as a MMA fighter 4.00

JOE PSYCHO & MOO FROG
Goblin Studios: 1996 - No. 5, 1997 ($2.50, B&W)

1-5: 4-Two covers 3.00
...Full Color Extravagarbonzo ($2.95, color) 3.00

JOE THE BARBARIAN
DC Comics (Vertigo): Mar, 2010 - No. 8, May, 2011 ($1.00/$2.99/$3.99)

1-($1.00) Grant Morrison-s/Sean Murphy-a 3.00
2-7-($2.99) 3.00
8-($3.99) 4.00

JOE YANK (Korean War)
Standard Comics (Visual Editions): No. 5, Mar, 1952 - No. 16, 1954

5-Toth, Celardo, Tuska-a 15 30 45 84 127 170
6-Toth, Severin/Elder-a 14 28 42 78 112 145
7-Pinhead Perkins by Dan DeCarlo (in all?) 11 22 33 62 86 110
8-Toth-c 13 26 39 72 101 130
9-16: 9-Andru-c. 12-Andru-a 11 22 33 62 86 110

JOHN BOLTON'S HALLS OF HORROR
Eclipse Comics: June, 1985 - No. 2, June, 1985 ($1.75, limited series)

1,2-British-r; Bolton-c/a 5.00

JOHN BOLTON'S STRANGE WINK
Dark Horse Comics: Mar, 1998 - No. 3, May, 1998 ($2.95, B&W, limited series)

1-3-Anthology; Bolton-s/c/a 5.00

JOHN BYRNE'S NEXT MEN (See Dark Horse Presents #54)
Dark Horse Comics (Legend imprint #19 on): Jan, 1992 - No. 30, Dec, 1994 ($2.50, mature)

1-Silver foil embossed-c; Byrne-c/a/scripts in all 1 3 4 6 8 10
1-4: 1-2nd printing with gold ink logo 3.00
0-(2/92)-r/chapters 1-4 from DHP w/new Byrne-c 4.00
5-20,22-30: 7-10-MA #1-4 mini-series on flip side. 16-Origin of Mark IV. 17-Miller-c. 19-22-Faith storyline. 23-26-Power storyline. 27-30-Lies storyline Pt. 1-4 4.00
21-(12/93) 2nd Hellboy; cover and Hellboy pages by Mike Mignola; Byrne other pages (see San Diego Comic Con Comics #2 for 1st app.) 8 16 24 54 102 150
...Parallel, Book 2 ($16.95)-TPB; r/#7-12 17.00
...Fame, Book 3($16.95)-TPB r/#13-18 17.00
...Faith, Book 4($14.95)-TPB r/#19-22 15.00

NOTE: *Issues 1 through 6 contain certificates redeemable for an exclusive Next Men trading card set by Byrne. Prices are for complete books. **Cody** painted c-23-26. **Mignola** a-21(part); c-21.*

JOHN BYRNE'S NEXT MEN (Continues in Next Men: Aftermath #40)
IDW Publishing: Dec, 2010 - No. 9, Aug, 2011 ($3.99)

1-9-John Byrne-s/a/c in all. 1-Origin retold. 6,7-Abraham Lincoln app. 4.00

JOHN BYRNE'S 2112
Dark Horse Comics (Legend): Oct, 1991 ($9.95, TPB)

1-Byrne-c/a/s 10.00

JOHN CARTER OF MARS (See The Funnies & Tarzan #207)
Dell Publishing Co.: No. 375, Mar-May, 1952 - No. 488, Aug-Oct, 1953
(Edgar Rice Burroughs)

Four Color 375 (#1)-Origin; Jesse Marsh-a 36 72 108 259 580 900
Four Color 437, 488-Painted-c 18 36 54 128 284 440

JOHN CARTER OF MARS
Gold Key: Apr, 1964 - No. 3, Oct, 1964

1(10104-404)-r/4-Color #375; Jesse Marsh-a 8 16 24 54 102 150
2(407), 3(410)-r/4-Color #437 & 488; Marsh-a 5 10 15 35 63 90

JOHN CARTER OF MARS
House of Greystroke: 1970 (10-1/2x16-1/2", 72 pgs., B&W, paper-c)

1941-42 Sunday strip-r; John Coleman Burroughs-a 4 8 12 23 37 50

JOHN CARTER OF MARS
Dynamite Entertainment: 2022 - No. 5, 2022 ($3.99)

1-5-Chuck Brown-s/George Kambadais-a; multiple covers 4.00

JOHN CARTER OF MARS: A PRINCESS OF MARS
Marvel Comics: Nov, 2011 - No. 5, Mar, 2012 ($2.99, limited series)

1-5: 1-Langridge-s/Andrade-a; covers by Young and Andrade. 2-4-Young-c 3.00

JOHN CARTER: THE END
Dynamite Entertainment: 2017 - No. 5, 2017 ($3.99)

1-5-Brian Wood-s/Alex Cox-a; multiple covers 4.00

JOHN CARTER: THE GODS OF MARS
Marvel Comics: May, 2012 - No. 5, Sept, 2012 ($3.99, limited series)

1-5-Sam Humphries-s/Ramón Pérez-a; Carter's 2nd trip to Mars 4.00

JOHN CARTER: THE WORLD OF MARS
Marvel Comics: Dec, 2011 - No. 4, Mar, 2012 ($3.99, limited series)

1-4-Movie prequel; Peter David-s/Luke Ross-a. 1-Ribic-c. 4-Olivetti-c 4.00

JOHN CARTER, WARLORD OF MARS (Also see Tarzan #207-209 and Weird Worlds)
Marvel Comics: June, 1977 - No. 28, Oct, 1979

1,18: 1-Origin. 18-Frank Miller-a(p)(1st publ. Marvel work) 4 8 12 23 37 50
1-(35¢-c variant, limited dist.) 10 20 30 70 150 230
2-5-(35¢-c variants, limited dist.) 7 14 21 48 89 130
2-17,19-28: 11-Origin Dejah Thoris 2 4 6 9 12 15
Annuals 1-3: 1(1977). 2(1978). 3(1979)-All 52 pgs. with new book-length stories 1 3 4 6 8 10
Edgar Rice Burroughs' John Carter of Mars: Weird Worlds TPB (Dark Horse Books, Jan. 2011, $14.99) r/stories from Tarzan #207-209 and Weird Worlds #1-7; Marv Wolfman intro. 15.00

NOTE: ***Austin** c-24i. **Gil Kane** a-1-10p; c-1p, 2p, 3, 4-9p, 10, 15p, Annual 1p. **Layton** a-17i. **Miller** c-25, 26p. **Nebres** a-2-4i, 8-16i; c(i)-6-9, 11-22, 25, Annual 1. **Perez** c-24p. **Simonson** a-15p. **Sutton** a-7i.*

JOHN CARTER, WARLORD OF MARS
Dynamite Entertainment: 2014 - No. 14, 2015 ($3.99)

1-14: 1-5-Marz-s/Malsuni-a; multiple covers on all 4.00
... 2015 Special ($4.99) Napton-s/Rodolfo-a/Parillo-c 5.00

JOHN CONSTANTINE: HELLBLAZER
DC Comics (Black Label): Jan, 2020 - No. 12, Jan, 2021 ($3.99)

1-12: Simon Spurrier-s. 1-3,6-8-Aaron Campbell-a. 4,5,9-Matias Bergara-a 4.00

JOHN CONSTANTINE - HELLBLAZER SPECIAL: PAPA MIDNITE
DC Comics (Vertigo): April, 2005 - No. 5, Aug, 2005 ($2.95/$2.99, limited series)

	GD 2.0	VG 4.0	FN 6.0	VF 8.0	VF/NM 9.0	NM- 9.2
1-5-Origin of Papa Midnite; Akins-a/Johnson-s						5.00

JOHN F. KENNEDY, CHAMPION OF FREEDOM
Worden & Childs: 1964 (no month) (25¢)

nn-Photo-c	9	18	27	61	123	185

JOHN F. KENNEDY LIFE STORY
Dell Publishing Co.: Aug-Oct, 1964; Nov, 1965; June, 1966 (12¢)

12-378-410-Photo-c	9	18	27	59	117	175
12-378-511 (reprint, 11/65)	4	8	12	23	37	50
12-378-606 (reprint, 6/66)	3	6	9	20	31	42

JOHN FORCE (See Magic Agent)

JOHN HIX SCRAP BOOK, THE
Eastern Color Printing Co. (McNaught Synd.): Late 1930's (no date) (10¢, 68 pgs., regular size)

1-Strange As It Seems (resembles Single Series books)	48	96	144	302	514	725
2-Strange As It Seems	34	68	102	199	325	450

JOHN JAKES' MULLKON EMPIRE
Tekno Comix: Sept, 1995 - No. 6, Feb, 1996 ($1.95)

1-6						3.00

JOHN LAW DETECTIVE (See Smash Comics #3)
Eclipse Comics: April, 1983 ($1.50, Baxter paper)

1-Three Eisner stories originally drawn in 1948 for the never published John Law #1; original cover pencilled in 1948 & inked in 1982 by Eisner						4.00

JOHN McCAIN (See Presidential Material: John McCain)

JOHNNY APPLESEED (See Story Hour Series)

JOHNNY CASH (See Hello, I'm...)

JOHNNY DANGER (See Movie Comics, 1946)
Toby Press: 1950 (Based on movie serial)

1-Photo-c; Sparling-a	27	54	81	158	259	360

JOHNNY DANGER PRIVATE DETECTIVE
Toby Press: Aug, 1954 (Reprinted in Danger #11 by Super)

1-Photo-c; Opium den story	23	46	69	136	223	310

JOHNNY DYNAMITE (Formerly Dynamite #1-9; Foreign Intrigues #14 on)
Charlton Comics: No. 10, June, 1955 - No. 12, Oct, 1955

10-12	15	30	45	88	137	185

JOHNNY DYNAMITE
Dark Horse Comics: Sept, 1994 - Dec, 1994 ($2.95, B&W & red, limited series)

1-4: Max Allan Collins scripts in all; Terry Beatty-a						3.00
...: Underworld GN (AiT/Planet Lar, 3/03, $12.95, B&W) r/#1-4 in B&W without red						13.00

JOHNNY HAZARD
Best Books (Standard Comics) (King Features): No. 5, Aug, 1948 - No. 8, May, 1949; No. 35, date?

5-Strip reprints by Frank Robbins (c/a)	20	40	60	118	192	265
6,8-Strip reprints by Frank Robbins	17	34	51	103	162	220
7,35: 7-New art, not Robbins	14	28	42	78	112	145

JOHNNY JASON (...Teen Reporter)
Dell Publishing Co.: Feb-Apr, 1962 - No. 2, June-Aug, 1962

Four Color 1302, 2(01380-208)	4	8	12	25	40	55

JOHNNY LAW, SKY RANGER
Good Comics (Lev Gleason): Apr, 1955 - No. 3, Aug, 1955; No. 4, Nov, 1955

1-Edmond Good-c/a	14	28	42	78	112	145
2-4	10	20	30	54	72	90

JOHNNY MACK BROWN (Western star; see Western Roundup under Dell Giants)
Dell Publishing Co.: No. 269, Mar, 1950 - No. 963, Feb, 1959 (All Photo-c)

Four Color 269(#1)(3/50, 52pgs.)-Johnny Mack Brown & his horse Rebel begin; photo front/back-c begin; Marsh-a in #1-9	19	38	57	133	297	460
2(10-12/50, 52pgs.)	10	20	30	66	138	210
3(1-3/51, 52pgs.)	8	16	24	54	102	150
4-10 (9-11/52)(36pgs.), Four Color 455,493,541,584,618,645,685,722,776,834,963	6	12	18	40	73	105
Four Color 922-Manning-a	7	14	21	44	82	120

JOHNNY PERIL (See Comic Cavalcade #15, Danger Trail #5, Sensation Comics #107 & Sensation Mystery)

JOHNNY RINGO (TV)
Dell Publishing Co.: No. 1142, Nov-Jan, 1960/61 (one shot)

Four Color 1142-Photo-c	7	14	21	49	92	135

JOHNNY STARBOARD (See Wisco)

JOHNNY THE HOMICIDAL MANIAC (Also see Squee)
Slave Labor Graphics: Aug, 1995 - No. 7, Jan, 1997 ($2.95, B&W, lim. series)

1-Jhonen Vasquez-c/s/a (1995)	9	18	27	60	120	180
1-Special Signed & numbered edition of 2,000 (1996)	5	10	15	33	57	80
2,3: 2-(11/95). 3-(2/96)	1	3	4	6	8	10
4-7: 4-(5-96). 5-(8/96)						5.00
Hardcover-($29.95) r/#1-7						35.00
TPB-($19.95)						25.00

JOHNNY THUNDER
National Periodical Publications: Feb-Mar, 1973 - No. 3, July-Aug, 1973

1-Johnny Thunder & Nighthawk-r. in all	3	6	9	17	26	35
2,3: 2-Trigger Twins app.	2	4	6	8	11	14

NOTE: *All contain 1950s DC reprints from All-American Western.* ***Drucker*** *r-2, 3.* ***G. Kane*** *r-2, 3.* ***Moreira*** *r-1.* ***Toth*** *r-1, 3; c-1r, 3r. Also see All-American, All-Star Western, Flash Comics, Western Comics, World's Best & World's Finest.*

JOHN PAUL JONES
Dell Publishing Co.: No. 1007, July-Sept, 1959 (one-shot)

Four Color 1007-Movie, Robert Stack photo-c	6	12	18	40	73	105

JOHN ROMITA JR. 30TH ANNIVERSARY SPECIAL
Marvel Comics: 2006 ($3.99, one-shot)

nn-r/1st story in Amazing Spider-Man Annual #11; timeline, sketch pages, interviews						4.00

JOHN STEED & EMMA PEEL (See The Avengers, Gold Key series)

JOHN STEELE SECRET AGENT (Also see Freedom Agent)
Gold Key: Dec, 1964

1-Freedom Agent	6	12	18	41	76	110

JOHN STEWART: THE EMERALD KNIGHT (Green Lantern)
DC Comics: Feb, 2023 ($5.99, one-shot)

1-Geoffrey Thorne-s/Marco Santucci-a						6.00

JOHN WAYNE ADVENTURE COMICS (Movie star; See Big Tex, Oxydol-Dreft, Tim McCoy, & With The Marines...#1)
Toby Press: Winter, 1949-50 - No. 31, May, 1955 (Photo-c: 1-12,17,25-on)

1 (36pgs.)-Photo-c begin (1st time in comics on-c)	265	530	795	1694	2597	4100
2-4: 2-(4/50, 36pgs.)-Williamson/Frazetta-a(2) 6 & 2 pgs. (one story-r/Billy the Kid #1); photo back-c. 3-(36pgs.)-Williamson/Frazetta-a(2), 16 pgs. total; photo back-c. 4-(52pgs.)-Williamson/Frazetta-a(2), 16 pgs. total	84	168	252	538	919	1300
5 (52pgs.)-Kurtzman-a-(Alfred "L" Newman in Potshot Pete)	65	130	195	416	708	1050
6 (52pgs.)-Williamson/Frazetta-a (10 pgs.); Kurtzman-a "Pot-Shot Pete", (5 pgs.); & "Genius Jones", (1 pg.)	76	152	228	486	831	1175
7 (52pgs.)-Williamson/Frazetta-a (10 pgs.)	66	132	198	419	722	1025
8 (36pgs.)-Williamson/Frazetta-a(2) (12 & 9 pgs.)	77	154	231	493	847	1200
9-11: Photo western-c	43	86	129	268	454	640
12,14-Photo war-c. 12-Kurtzman-a(2 pg.) "Genius"	43	86	129	271	461	650
13,15: 13,15-Line-drawn-c begin, end #24	39	78	117	236	388	540
16-Williamson/Frazetta-r/Billy the Kid #1	40	80	120	248	414	580
17-Photo-c	40	80	120	248	414	580
18-Williamson/Frazetta-a (r/#4 & 8, 19 pgs.)	43	86	129	268	454	640
19-24: 23-Evans-a?	36	72	108	214	347	480
25-Photo-c resume; end #31; Williamson/Frazetta-r/Billy the Kid #3	43	86	129	268	454	640
26-28,30-Photo-c	39	78	117	236	388	540
29,31-Williamson/Frazetta-a in each (r/#4, 2)	41	82	123	256	428	600

NOTE: *Williamsonish art in later issues by* ***Gerald McCann.***

JOHN WICK (Based on the Keanu Reeves movies)
Dynamite Entertainment: 2018 - No. 5, 2019 ($3.99)

1-Pak-s/Valletta-a; four covers	3	6	9	21	33	45
2-Three covers	2	4	6	9	12	15
3-5-Gaudio-a; three covers						5.00

JOIN THE FUTURE
AfterShock Comics: Mar, 2020 - No. 5, Sept, 2020 ($4.99/$3.99)

1-($4.99) Zack Kaplan-s/Piotr Kowalski-a						5.00
2-5-($3.99)						4.00

JO-JO COMICS (...Congo King #7-29; My Desire #30 on)(Also see Fantastic Fears and Jungle Jo)
Fox Feature Syndicate: 1945 - No. 29, July, 1949 (Two No.7's; no #13)

nn(1945)-Funny animal, humor	30	60	90	177	289	400
2(Sum,'46)-6(4-5/47): Funny animal. 2-Ten pg. Electro story (Fall/46)	19	38	57	111	176	240
7(7/47)-Jo-Jo, Congo King begins (1st app.); Bronze Man & Purple Tigress app.	110	220	330	704	1202	1700
7(#8) (9/47)	84	168	252	538	919	1300
8(#9) Classic Kamen mountain of skulls-c; Tanee begins	129	258	387	826	1413	2000
9,10(#10,11)	71	142	213	454	777	1100
11,12(#12,13),14,16: 11,16-Kamen bondage-c	60	120	180	381	653	925
15-Cited by Dr. Wertham in 5/47 Saturday Review of Literature	61	122	183	390	670	950
17-Kamen bondage-c	116	232	348	742	1271	1800
18-20	58	116	174	371	636	900
21-24,26-29: 21-Hollingsworth-a (4 pgs.; 23-1 pg.)	50	100	150	315	533	750
25-Classic bondage-c by Matt Baker	622	1244	1866	4541	8021	11,500

NOTE: *Many bondage-c/a by* ***Baker/Kamen/Feldstein/Good.*** *No. 7's have Princesses Gwenna, Geesa, Yolda, & Safra before settling down on Tanee.*

JOKEBOOK COMICS DIGEST ANNUAL (...Magazine No. 5 on)
Archie Publications: Oct, 1977 - No. 13, Oct, 1983 (Digest Size)

1(10/77)-Reprints; Neal Adams-a	2	4	6	13	18	22
2(4/78)-5	2	4	6	9	12	15
6-13	1	3	4	6	8	10

JOKER
DC Comics: 2008 ($19.99, hardcover graphic novel with dustjacket)

HC-Joker is released from Arkham; Azzarello-s/Bermejo-a						20.00

JOKER, THE (See Batman #1, Batman: The Killing Joke, Brave & the Bold, Detective, Greatest Joker Stories & Justice League Annual #2)
National Periodical Publications: May, 1975 - No. 9, Sept-Oct, 1976

1-Two-Face app.	11	22	33	76	163	250
2-Willie the Weeper app.	6	12	18	41	76	110
3,4: 3-The Creeper app. 4-Green Arrow-c/sty	5	10	15	33	57	80
5-9: 6-Sherlock Holmes-c/sty. 7-Lex Luthor-c/story. 8-Scarecrow-c/story. 9-Catwoman-c/story	4	8	12	26	44	60
...: The Greatest Stories Ever Told TPB (2008, $19.99) r/Batman #1 and other apps.						20.00

JOKER, THE (See Tangent Comics/ The Joker)

JOKER, THE
DC Comics: May, 2021 - No. 15, Sept, 2022 ($4.99/$5.99)

1-($4.99) Tynion IV-s/March-a; back-up Punchline story in all issues						5.00
2-14-($5.99) 2-Intro Vengeance (daughter of Bane). 5,10-Francavilla-a						6.00
15-($6.99) Bane and Vengeance app.						7.00

John Stewart: The Emerald Knight #1 © DC

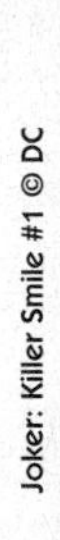
Joker: Killer Smile #1 © DC

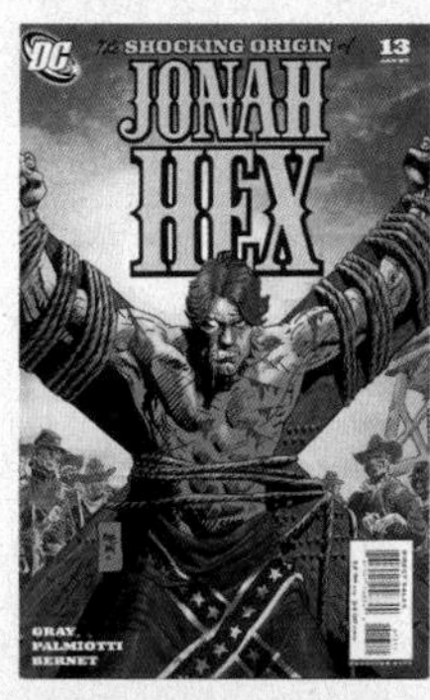

Jonah Hex (2006) #15 © DC

GD VG FN VF VF/NM NM-
2.0 4.0 6.0 8.0 9.0 9.2

2021 Annual 1-(1/22, $5.99) Tynion IV & Rosenberg-s/Francavilla-a; Catman app. 6.00

JOKER COMICS (Adventures Into Terror No. 43 on)
Timely/Marvel Comics No. 36 on (TCI/CDS): Apr, 1942 - No. 42, Aug, 1950

1-(Rare)-Powerhouse Pepper (1st app.) begins by Wolverton; Stuporman app. from Daring Comics 349 698 1047 2443 4272 6100
2-Wolverton-a; 1st app. Tessie the Typist & begin series 161 322 483 1030 1765 2500
3-5-Wolverton-a 103 206 309 659 1130 1600
6-10-Wolverton-a. 6-Tessie-c begin 58 116 174 371 636 900
11-20-Wolverton-a 54 108 162 343 574 825
21,22,24-27,29,30-Wolverton cont'd. & Kurtzman's "Hey Look" in #23-27 48 96 144 302 514 725
23-1st "Hey Look" by Kurtzman; Wolverton-a 52 104 156 328 552 775
28,32,34,37-41: 28-Millie the Model begins. 32-Hedy begins. 41-Nellie the Nurse app. 27 54 81 160 263 365
31-Last Powerhouse Pepper; not in #28 42 84 126 265 445 625
33,35,36-Kurtzman's "Hey Look" 28 56 84 165 270 375
42-Only app. 'Patty Pinup,' clone of Millie the Model 28 56 84 165 270 375

JOKER / DAFFY DUCK
DC Comics: Oct, 2018 ($4.99, one-shot)

1-Lobdell-s/Booth-a/c; Daffy Duck as a Joker henchman; Batman app. 6.00
1-Variant-c by Sanford Greene 2 4 6 8 10 12

JOKER: DEVIL'S ADVOCATE
DC Comics: 1996 ($24.95/$12.95, one-shot)

nn-(Hardcover)-Dixon scripts/Nolan & Hanna-a 35.00
nn-(Softcover) 20.00

JOKER 80TH ANNIVERSARY 100-PAGE SUPER SPECTACULAR
DC Comics: Jun, 2020 ($9.99, squarebound, one-shot)

1-Short stories and pin-ups by various; origin Punchline; multiple covers 10.00

JOKER / HARLEY: CRIMINAL SANITY
DC Comics (Black Label): Dec, 2019 - No. 9 ($5.99, 10-3/4" x 8-1/2", lim. series)

1-7: 1,2-Kami Garcia-s/Mico Suayan & Mike Mayhew-a. 1-Three covers. 2-7-Two covers 6.00
... Secret Files 1 (9/20, $5.99) Covers by Mack & Sienkiewicz; art by Mack and others 6.00

JOKER: KILLER SMILE (See Batman: The Smile Killer one-shot for epilogue)
DC Comics (Black Label): Dec, 2019 - No. 3, Apr, 2020 ($5.99, 10-3/4" x 8-1/2", lim. series)

1-3-Jeff Lemire-s/Andrea Sorrentino-a; two covers by Sorrentino & Kaare Andrews 6.00

JOKER: LAST LAUGH (See Batman: The Joker's Last Laugh for TPB)
DC Comics: Dec, 2001 - No. 6, Jan, 2002 ($2.95, weekly limited series)

1-6: 1,6-Bolland-c 4.00
...Secret Files (12/01, $5.95) Short stories by various; Simonson-c 1 2 3 5 6 8

JOKER / MASK
Dark Horse Comics: May, 2000 - No. 4, Aug, 2000 ($2.95, limited series)

1-Batman, Harley Quinn, Poison Ivy app. 3 6 9 14 20 25
2-4 2 4 6 9 12 15

JOKER PRESENTS: A PUZZLEBOX, THE
DC Comics: Oct, 2021 - No. 7, Apr, 2022 ($4.99, printing of digital-first series)

1-7: 1-Rosenberg-s/Merino-a; main-c by Zdarsky; Riddler murdered 5.00

JOKER'S ASYLUM
DC Comics: Sept, 2008 ($2.99, weekly limited series of one-shots)

...: Joker - Andy Kubert-c, Sanchez-a; ...: Penguin - Pearson-c/a; ...: Poison Ivy - Guillem March-c/a; ...: Scarecrow - Juan Doe-c/a; ...: Two-Face - Andy Clarke-c/a 5.00
Batman: The Joker's Asylum TPB (2008, $14.99) r/one-shots 15.00

JOKER'S ASYLUM II
DC Comics: Aug, 2010 ($2.99, weekly limited series of one-shots)

...: Clayface - Kelley Jones-c/a; ; ...: Killer Croc - Mattina-c; Mad Hatter - Giffen & Sienkiewicz-a, Sienkiewicz-c; ...: Riddler - Van Sciver-c 1 2 3 5 6 8
...: Harley Quinn - Quinones-a 3 6 9 15 22 28
Batman: The Joker's Asylum Volume 2 TPB (2011, $14.99) r/one-shots 15.00

JOKER, THE: THE MAN WHO STOPPED LAUGHING
DC Comics: Dec, 2022 - Present ($5.99, limited series)

1-6-Rosenberg-s/DiGiandomenico & Francavilla-a. 4-Joker pregnancy story 6.00

JOKER, THE: YEAR OF THE VILLAIN
DC Comics: 2019 ($4.99, one-shot)

1-John Carpenter & Anthony Burch-s/Philip Tan-a; Enchantress app. 5.00

JOLLY CHRISTMAS, A (See March of Comics No. 269)

JOLLY COMICS: Four Star Publishing Co.: 1947 (Advertised, not published)

JOLLY COMICS
No publisher: No date (1930s-40s)(10¢, cover is black/red ink on yellow paper, blank inside-c)

nn-Snuffy Smith & Katzenjamer Kids on-c only. Buck Rogers, Dickey Dare, Napoleon & others app. Reprints Ace Comics #8-c. A GD copy sold in 2014 for $358.50 245 490 735 1568 2684 3800

JOLLY JINGLES (Formerly Jackpot Comics)
MLJ Magazines: No. 10, Sum, 1943 - No. 16, Wint, 1944/45

10-Super Duck begins (origin & 1st app.); Woody The Woodpecker begins (not same as Lantz character) 71 142 213 454 777 1100
11 (Fall, '43)-2nd Super Duck (see Hangman #8) 37 74 111 222 361 500
12-Hitler-c 123 246 369 787 1344 1900
13-16: 13-Sahle-c. 15,16-Vigoda-c 27 54 81 158 259 360

JONAH HEX (See All-Star Western, Hex and Weird Western Tales)
National Periodical Pub./DC Comics: Mar-Apr, 1977 - No. 92, Aug, 1985

1-Garcia-Lopez-c/a 9 18 27 59 117 175
2-1st app. El Papagayo 5 10 15 33 57 80
3,4,9: 9-Wrightson-c. 5 10 15 30 50 70
5,6,10: 5-Rep 1st app. from All-Star Western #10 4 8 12 28 47 65
7,8-Explains Hex's face disfigurement (origin) 5 10 15 33 57 80
11-20: 12-Starlin-c 3 6 9 17 26 35
21-32: 23-Intro. Mei Ling. 31,32-Origin retold 2 4 6 13 18 22
33-50 2 4 6 8 11 14
51-80 1 2 3 5 7 9
81-91: 89-Mark Texeira-a. 91-Cover swipe from Superman #243 (hugging a mystery woman) 2 4 6 8 10 12
92-Story cont'd in Hex #1 3 6 9 19 30 40

NOTE: ***Ayers** a(p)-35-37, 40, 41, 44-53, 56, 58-82. **Buckler** a-11; c-11, 13-16. **Kubert** c-43-46. **Morrow** a-90-92; c-10. **Spiegle(Tothish)** a-34, 38, 40, 49, 52. **Texeira** a-89p. Batlash back-ups in 49, 52. El Diablo back-ups in 48, 56-60, 73-75. Scalphunter back-ups in 40, 41, 45-47.*

JONAH HEX (Also see All Star Western [2011 DC New 52 title])
DC Comics: Jan, 2006 - No. 70, Oct, 2011 ($2.99)

1-Justin Gray & Jimmy Palmiotti-s/Luke Ross-a/Quitely-c 5.00
1-Special Edition (7/10, $1.00) r/#1 with "What's Next?" logo on cover 3.00
2-49,51-70: 3-Bat Lash app. 10,16,17,19,20,22-Noto-a. 11-El Diablo app.; Beck-a. 13-15-Origin retold. 21,23,27,30,32,37,38,42,52,54,57,59,61,63,67-Bernet-a. 33-Darwyn Cooke-a/c. 34-Sparacio-a. 51-Giordano-c. 53-Tucci-c/a. 62-Risso-a 3.00
50-($3.99) Darwyn Cooke-a/c 4.00
...: Bullets Don't Lie TPB (2009, $14.99) r/#31-36 15.00
...: Counting Corpses TPB (2010, $14.99) r/#43,50-54 15.00
...: Face Full of Violence TPB (2006, $12.99) r/#1-6 13.00
...: Guns of Vengeance TPB (2007, $12.99) r/#7-12 13.00
...: Lead Poisoning TPB (2009, $14.99) r/#37-42 15.00
...: Luck Runs Out TPB (2008, $12.99) r/#25-30 13.00
...: No Way Back HC (2010, $19.99) new GN; Gray & Palmiotti-s/DeZuniga-a 20.00
...: No Way Back SC (2011, $14.99) new GN; Gray & Palmiotti-s/DeZuniga-a 15.00
...: Only the Good Die Young TPB (2008, $12.99) r/#19-24 13.00
...: Origins TPB (2007, $12.99) r/#13-18 13.00
...: Tall Tales TPB (2011, $14.99) r/#55-60 15.00
...: The Six Gun War TPB (2010, $14.99) r/#44-49 15.00
...: Welcome to Paradise TPB (2010, $17.99) r/debut in All-Star Western #10 plus early apps. in Weird Western Tales and Jonah Hex #2,4 (1977 series) 18.00

JONAH HEX AND OTHER WESTERN TALES (Blue Ribbon Digest)
DC Comics: Sept-Oct, 1979 - No. 3, Jan-Feb, 1980 (100 pgs.)

1-3: 1-Origin Scalphunter-r, Ayers/Evans, Neal Adams-a.; painted-c. 2-Weird Western Tales-r; Neal Adams, Toth, Aragonés-a. 3-Outlaw-r, Scalphunter-r; Gil Kane, Wildey-a 2 4 6 11 16 20

JONAH HEX: RIDERS OF THE WORM AND SUCH
DC Comics (Vertigo): Mar, 1995 - No. 5, July, 1995 ($2.95, limited series)

1-5-Lansdale story, Truman-a 4.00

JONAH HEX: SHADOWS WEST
DC Comics (Vertigo): Feb, 1999 - No. 3, Apr, 1999 ($2.95, limited series)

1-3-Lansdale-s/Truman-a 4.00

JONAH HEX SPECTACULAR (See DC Special Series No. 16)

JONAH HEX: TWO-GUN MOJO
DC Comics (Vertigo): Aug, 1993 - No. 5, Dec, 1993 ($2.95, limited series)

1-Lansdale scripts in all; Truman/Glanzman-a in all w/Truman-c 6.00
1-Platinum edition with no price on cover 20.00
2-5 4.00
TPB-(1994, $12.95) r/#1-5 13.00

GD 2.0 | VG 4.0 | FN 6.0 | VF 8.0 | VF/NM 9.0 | NM- 9.2

JONAH HEX/ YOSEMITE SAM
DC Comics: Aug, 2017 ($4.99, one-shot)
1-Palmiotti-s/Teixeira-a; Foghorn Leghorn app. 5.00

JONESES, THE
AWA Studios: Apr, 2022 - No. 5, Aug, 2022 ($3.99, limited series)
1-5-Moreci-s/Vitti-a 4.00

JONESY (Formerly Crack Western)
Comic Favorite/Quality Comics Group: No. 85, Aug, 1953; No. 2, Oct, 1953 - No. 8, Oct, 1954
85(#1)-Teen-age humor 13 26 39 74 105 135
2 8 16 24 44 57 70
3-8 7 14 21 37 46 55

JONESY
BOOM! Studios (BOOM! Box): Feb, 2016 - No. 12, Apr, 2017 ($3.99, originally a 4-part series)
1-12-Sam Humphries-s/Caitlin Rose Boyle-a. 1-Multiple covers 4.00

JON JUAN (Also see Great Lover Romances)
Toby Press: Spring, 1950
1-All Schomburg-a (signed Al Reid on-c); written by Siegel; used in **SOTI**, pg. 38 (Scarce)
90 180 270 576 988 1400

JONNI THUNDER (...A.K.A. Thunderbolt)
DC Comics: Feb, 1985 - No. 4, Aug, 1985 (75¢, limited series)
1-4: 1-Origin & 1st app. 4.00

JONNY DOUBLE
DC Comics (Vertigo): Sept, 1998 - No. 4, Dec, 1998 ($2.95, limited series)
1-4-Azzarello-s 3.00
TPB (2002, $12.95) r/#1-4; Chiarello-c 13.00

JONNY QUEST (TV)
Gold Key: Dec, 1964 (Hanna-Barbera)
1 (10139-412) 38 76 114 281 628 975

JONNY QUEST (TV)
Comico: June 1986 - No. 31, Dec, 1988 ($1.50/$1.75)(Hanna-Barbera)
1,3,5: 3,5-Dave Stevens-c 6.00
2,4,6-31: 30-Adapts TV episode 4.00
Special 1(9/88, $1.75), 2(10/88, $1.75) 4.00
NOTE: ***M. Anderson*** *a-9.* ***Mooney*** *a-Special 1.* ***Pini*** *a-2.* ***Quagmire*** *a-31p.* ***Rude*** *a-1; c-2i.* ***Sienkiewicz*** *c-11.* ***Spiegle*** *a-7, 12, 21; c-21* ***Staton*** *a-2i, 11p.* ***Steacy*** *c-8.* ***Stevens*** *a-4i; c-3,5.* ***Wildey*** *a-1, c-1, 7, 12.* ***Williamson*** *a-4i; c-4i.*

JONNY QUEST CLASSICS (TV)
Comico: May, 1987 - No. 3, July, 1987 ($2.00) (Hanna-Barbera)
1-3: Wildey-c/a; 3-Based on TV episode 4.00

JON SABLE, FREELANCE (Also see Mike Grell's Sable & Sable)
First Comics: 6/83 - No. 56, 2/88 (#1-17, $1; #18-33, $1.25, #34-on, $1.75)
1-Mike Grell-c/a/scripts 5.00
2-56: 3-5-Origin, parts 1-3. 6-Origin, part 4. 11-1st app. of Maggie the Cat. 14-Mando paper begins. 16-Maggie the Cat. app. 25-30-Shatter app. 34-Deluxe format begins ($1.75) 3.00
The Complete Jon Sable, Freelance: Vol. 1 (IDW, 2005, $19.99) r/#1-6 20.00
The Complete Jon Sable, Freelance: Vol. 2 (IDW, 2005, $19.99) r/#7-11 20.00
The Complete Jon Sable, Freelance: Vol. 3 (IDW, 2005, $19.99) r/#12-16 20.00
The Complete Jon Sable, Freelance: Vol. 4 (IDW, 2005, $19.99) r/#17-21 20.00
NOTE: ***Aragones*** *a-33; c-33(part).* ***Grell*** *a-1-43;c-1-52, 53p, 54-56.*

JON SABLE, FREELANCE
IDW Publ.: (Limited series)
...: Ashes of Eden 1-5 (2009 - No. 5, 2/10, $3.99) Mike Grell-c/a/scripts 4.00
...: Bloodtrail 1-6 (4/05 - No. 6, 11/05, $3.99) Mike Grell-c/a/scripts 4.00
...: Bloodtrail TPB (4/06, $19.99) r/#1-6; cover gallery 20.00

JOOK JOINT
Image Comics: Oct, 2018 - No. 5 ($3.99, limited series)
1,2-Tee Franklin-s/Alitha Martinez-a 4.00

JOSEPH & HIS BRETHREN (See The Living Bible)

JOSIE (She's... #1-16) (...& the Pussycats #45 on) (See Archie's Pals 'n' Gals #23 for 1st app.) (Also see Archie Giant Series Magazine #528, 540, 551, 562, 571, 584, 597, 610, 622)
Archie Publ./Radio Comics: Feb, 1963; No. 2, Aug, 1963 - No. 106, Oct, 1982
1 71 142 213 568 1284 2000
2 18 36 54 124 275 425
3-5 10 20 30 69 147 225
6-10: 6-(5/64) Book length Haunted Mansion-c/s. 7-(8/64) 1st app. Alexandra Cabot?
7 14 21 49 92 135
11-20 5 10 15 34 60 85
21, 23-30 5 10 15 30 50 70
22 (9/66)-Mighty Man & Mighty (Josie Girl) app. 5 10 15 33 57 80
31-44 4 8 12 25 40 55
45 (12/69)-Josie and the Pussycats begins (Hanna Barbera TV cartoon); 1st app. of the Pussycats 42 84 126 311 706 1100
46-2nd app./1st cover Pussycats 13 26 39 89 195 300
47-3rd app. of the Pussycats 8 16 24 54 102 150
48,49-Pussycats band-c/s 8 16 24 56 108 160
50-J&P-c; go to Hollywood, meet Hanna & Barbera 9 18 27 57 111 165
51-54 4 8 12 23 37 50
55-74 (2/74)(52 pg. issues). 73-Pussycats band-c 4 8 12 23 37 50
75-90(8/76) 3 6 9 14 20 26
91-99 2 4 6 11 16 20
100 (10/79) 3 6 9 14 19 24
101-106: 103-Pussycats band-c 2 4 6 13 18 22

JOSIE & THE PUSSYCATS (TV)
Archie Comics: 1993 - No. 2, 1994 ($2.00, 52 pgs.)(Published annually)
1,2-Bound-in pull-out poster in each. 2-(Spr/94) 1 2 3 5 6 8

JOSIE AND THE PUSSYCATS
Archie Comic Publications: Nov, 2016 - No. 9, Oct, 2017 ($3.99)
1-9: 1-Bennett & Deordio-s/Audrey Mok-a; multiple covers; back-up classic reprints. 5,6-Riverdale TV previews. 9-Shannon-a 4.00

JOURNAL OF CRIME (See Fox Giants)

JOURNEY
Aardvark-Vanaheim #1-14/Fantagraphics Books #15-on: 1983 - No. 14, Sept, 1984; No. 15, Apr, 1985 - No. 27, July, 1986 (B&W)
1 1 3 4 6 8 10
2-27: 20-Sam Kieth-a 4.00

JOURNEY INTO FEAR
Superior-Dynamic Publications: May, 1951 - No. 21, Sept, 1954
1-Baker-r(2) 155 310 465 992 1696 2400
2 71 142 213 454 777 1100
3,4 54 108 162 343 574 825
5-10,15: 15-Used in **SOTI**, pg. 389 47 94 141 296 498 700
11-14,16-21 43 86 129 271 461 650
NOTE: *Kamenish 'headlight'-a most issues.* ***Robinson*** *a-10.*

JOURNEY INTO MYSTERY (1st Series) (Thor Nos. 126-502)
Atlas(CPS No. 1-48/AMI No. 49-68/Marvel No. 69 (6/61) on): 6/52 - No. 48, 8/57; No. 49, 11/58 - No. 125, 2/66; 503, 11/96 - No. 521, June, 1998
1-Weird/horror stories begin 1700 3400 5100 11,900 17,950 24,000
2 258 516 774 1651 2826 4000
3,4 206 412 618 1318 2259 3200
5,7-11 187 374 561 1197 2049 2900
6-Classic Everett-c 258 516 774 1651 2826 4000
12-20,22: 15-Atomic explosion panel. 22-Davis*esque*-a; last pre-code issue (2/55)
119 238 357 762 1306 1850
21-Kubert-a; Tothish-a by Andru 126 252 378 806 1378 1950
23-32,35-38,40: 24-Torres?-a. 38-Ditko-a 900 180 270 576 988 1400
33-Williamson-a; Ditko-a (his 1st for Atlas?) 116 232 348 742 1271 1800
34,39: 34-Krigstein-a. 39-1st S.A. issue; Wood-a 97 194 291 621 1061 1500
41-Crandall-a; Frazetta*esque*-a by Morrow 46 92 138 350 788 1225
42,46,48: 42,48-Torres-a. 46-Torres & Krigstein-a 44 88 132 326 738 1150
43,44-Williamson/Mayo-a in both. 43-Invisible Woman prototype
48 96 144 379 865 1350
45,47 42 84 126 311 706 1100
49-Matt Fox, Check-a 50 100 1050 400 900 1400
50,52-54: Ditko/Kirby-a. 50-Davis-a. 54-Williamson-a
50 100 1050 400 900 1400
51-Kirby/Wood-a 62 124 186 496 1123 1750
55-61,63-65,67-69,71,72,74,75: 74-Contents change to Fantasy. 75-Last 10¢ issue
42 84 126 311 706 1100
62-Prototype ish. (The Hulk); 1st app. Xemnu (Titan) called "The Hulk"
104 208 312 832 1866 2900
66-Prototype ish. (The Hulk)-Return of Xemnu "The Hulk"
79 158 237 632 1416 2200
70-Prototype ish. (The Sandman)(7/61); similar to Spidey villain
55 110 165 440 995 1550
73-Story titled "The Spider" where a spider is exposed to radiation & gets powers of a human and shoots webbing; a reverse prototype of Spider-Man's origin
79 158 237 632 1416 2200
76,77,80,81: 80-Anti-communist propaganda story 36 72 108 266 596 925
76-(10¢ cover price blacked out, 12¢ printed on) 61 122 183 488 1094 1700
78-The Sorceror (Dr. Strange prototype) app. (3/62) 66 132 198 528 1189 1850
79-Prototype issue. (Mr. Hyde) 48 96 144 379 865 1350
82-Prototype ish. (Scorpion) 44 88 132 326 738 1150
83-Origin & 1st app. The Mighty Thor by Kirby (8/62) and begin series; Thor-c also begin
2650 5300 9275 26,500 75,750 120,000
83-Reprint from the Golden Record Comic Set 27 54 81 194 435 675
With the record (1966) 38 76 114 281 628 975
84-2nd app. Thor 400 800 1200 3400 7700 12,000
85-1st app. Loki & Heimdall; 1st brief app. Odin (1 panel); 1st app. Asgard
2000 4000 6000 12,000 19,000 26,000
86-1st full app. Odin 114 228 342 912 2056 3200
87-Prisoner of the Reds 100 200 300 800 1800 2800
88-2nd Loki-c 111 222 333 888 1994 3100
89-Origin Thor retold; classic Thor-c 155 310 465 1279 2890 4500
90-No Kirby-a 71 142 213 568 1284 2000
91,92,94,96-Sinnott-a 52 104 156 416 933 1450
93,97-Kirby-a; Tales of Asgard series begins #97 (origin which concludes in #99); origin & 1st app. Lava Man. 97-1st app. Surtur (1 panel) 54 108 162 432 966 1500
95-Sinnott-a; Thor vs. Thor 62 124 186 496 1123 1750
98,99-Kirby/Heck-a. 98-Origin/1st app. The Human Cobra. 99-1st app. Mr. Hyde; Surtur app.
42 84 126 311 706 1100
100-Kirby/Heck-a; Thor battles Mr. Hyde 40 80 120 296 673 1050
101,108: 101-(2/64)-2nd Avengers x-over (w/o Capt. America); see Tales Of Suspense #49 for 1st x-over. 108-(9/64)-Early Dr. Strange & Avengers x-over; ten extra pgs. Kirby-a
28 56 84 202 451 700
102-(3/64) 1st app. Sif, Balder and Hela 61 122 183 488 1094 1700
103-1st app. Enchantress 125 250 375 1000 2250 3500
104-107,110: 105-109-Ten extra pgs. Kirby-a in each. 107-1st app. Grey Gargoyle. 110,111-Two part battle vs. The Human Cobra & Mr. Hyde
27 54 81 194 435 675
109-Magneto-c & app. (1st x-over, 10/64) 48 96 144 384 867 1350
111,113: 113-Origin Loki 20 40 60 138 307 475
112-Thor Vs. Hulk (1/65); Origin Loki 75 150 225 600 1350 2100
114-Origin/1st app. Absorbing Man 42 84 126 311 706 1100
115-Detailed origin of Loki 26 52 78 182 404 625
116,117,120-123,125 16 32 48 110 243 375
118-1st app. Destroyer 33 66 99 238 532 825
119-Intro Hogun, Fandral, Volstagg; 2nd Destroyer 25 50 75 175 388 600
124-Hercules-c/story 17 34 51 114 252 390
503-521: 503-(11/96, $1.50)-The Lost Gods begin; Tom DeFalco scripts & Deodato Studios-c/a. 505-Spider-Man-c/app. 509-Loki-c/app. 514-516-Shang-Chi 4.00
#(-1) Flashback (7/97) Tales of Asgard Donald Blake app. 6.00
Annual 1(1965, 25¢, 72 pgs.)-New Thor vs. Hercules(1st app.)-c/story (see Incredible Hulk #3);

Josie #1 © ACP

Journey Into Mystery #644 © MAR

JSA #26 © DC

GD VG FN VF VF/NM NM-
2.0 4.0 6.0 8.0 9.0 9.2

Kirby-c/a; r/#85,93,95,97 141 282 423 1142 2571 4000

NOTE: **Ayers** a-14, 39, 64i, 71i, 74i, 80i. **Bailey** a-43. **Briefer** a-5, 12. **Cameron** a-35. **Check** a-17. **Colan** a-23, 81; c-14. **Ditko** a-33, 38, 50-96; c-58, 67, 71, 88i. **Kirby/Ditko** a-50-83. **Everett** a-20, 48; c-4-7, 9, 36, 37, 39-42, 44, 45, 47. **Forte** a-19, 35, 40, 53. **Heath** a-4-6, 11, 14; c-1, 8, 11, 15, 51. **Heck** a-53, 58, 73. **Kirby** a(p)-51, 52, 56, 57-60, 62-64, 66, 67, 69-89, 93, 97, 98, 100(w/**Heck**), 101-125; c-50-57, 59-66, 68-70, 72-82, 88(w/**Ditko**), 83 & 84 (w/**Sinnott**), 85-96(w/**Ayers**), 97-125p. **Leiber/Fox** a-93, 98-102. **Maneely** c-20-22. **Morisi** a-42. **Morrow** a-41, 42. **Orlando** a-30, 45, 57. **Mac Pakula** (Tothish) a-9, 35, 41. **Powell** a-20, 27, 34. **Reinman** a-39, 70, 87, 92, 96i. **Robinson** a-9. **Roussos** a-39. **Robert Sale** a-14. **Severin** a-27; c-30. **Sinnott** a-41; c-50. **Tuska** a-11. **Wildey** a-16.

JOURNEY INTO MYSTERY (Series and numbering continue from Thor #621)
Marvel Comics: No. 622, Jun, 2011 - No. 655, Oct, 2013 ($3.99/$2.99)

622-Reincarnated young Loki; Thor app.; Braithwaite-a; Hans-c 4.00
622-Variant covers by Art Adams and Lee Weeks 6.00
623-626, 626.1, 627-630-($2.99) Fear Itself tie-in. 628,629-Portacio-a 3.00
631-655: 631-Portacio-a; Aftermath. 632-Hellstrom app. 637,638-Exiled x-over with New Mutants #41-43. 642-644-Crossover with Mighty Thor #19-21. 646-Features Sif 3.00

JOURNEY INTO MYSTERY (2nd Series)
Marvel Comics: Oct, 1972 - No. 19, Oct, 1975

1-Robert Howard adaptation; Starlin/Ploog-a 5 10 15 35 63 90
2-5: 2,3,5-Bloch adapt. 4-H. P. Lovecraft adapt. 3 6 9 18 28 38
6-19: Reprints 3 6 9 17 25 34

NOTE: **N. Adams** a-2i. **Ditko** r-7, 10, 12, 14, 15, 19; c-10. **Everett** r-9, 14. **G. Kane** a-1p, 2p; c-1-3p. **Kirby** r-7, 13, 15, 18, 19; c-7. **Mort Lawrence** r-2. **Maneely** r-3. **Orlando** r-16. **Reese** a-1, 2i. **Starlin** a-1p, 3p. **Torres** r-16. **Wildey** r-9, 14.

JOURNEY INTO MYSTERY: THE BIRTH OF KRAKOA
Marvel Comics: Nov, 2018 ($4.99, one-shot)

1-Nick Fury and the Howling Commandos app.; Hopeless-s/Morissette-Phan-a 5.00

JOURNEY INTO UNKNOWN WORLDS (Formerly Teen)
Atlas Comics (WFP): No. 36, Sept, 1950 - No. 38, Feb, 1951;
No. 4, Apr, 1951 - No. 59, Aug, 1957

36(#1)-Science fiction/weird; "End Of The Earth" c/story
275 550 825 1750 3275 4800
37(#2)-Science fiction; "When Worlds Collide" c/story; Everett-c/a; Hitler story
135 270 405 864 1482 2100
38(#3)-Science fiction 116 232 348 742 1271 1800
4-6,8,10-Science fiction/weird 74 148 222 470 810 1150
7-Wolverton-a "Planet of Terror", 6 pgs; electric chair c-inset/story
110 220 330 704 1202 1700
9-Giant eyeball story 97 194 291 621 1061 1500
11,12-Krigstein-a 53 106 159 334 567 800
13,16,17,20 47 94 141 296 498 700
14-Wolverton-a "One of Our Graveyards Is Missing", 4 pgs; Tuska-a
87 174 261 553 952 1350
15-Wolverton-a "They Crawl by Night", 5 pgs.; 2 pg. Maneely s/f story
90 180 270 576 988 1400
18,19-Matt Fox-a 54 108 162 343 574 825
21-33: 21-Decapitation-c. 24-Sci/fic story. 26-Atom bomb panel. 27-Sid Check-a. 33-Last pre-code (2/55) 40 80 120 246 411 575
34-Kubert, Torres-a 36 72 108 211 343 475
35-Torres-a 34 68 102 199 325 450
36-45,48,50,53,55,59: 43-Krigstein-a. 44-Davis-a. 45,55,59-Williamson-a in all; with Mayo #55,59. 55-Crandall-a. 48,53-Crandall-a (4 pgs. #48). 48-Check-a. 50-Davis, Crandall-a
31 62 93 186 303 420
46,47,49,52,54,56-58: 54-Torres-a 29 58 87 172 281 390
51-Ditko, Wood-a 34 68 102 204 332 460

NOTE: **Ayers** a-24, 43, **Berg** a-38(#3), 43. **Lou Cameron** a-33. **Colan** a-37(#2), 6, 17, 19, 20, 23, 39. **Ditko** a-45, 51. **Drucker** a-35, 58. **Everett** a-37(#2), 11, 14, 41, 55, 56; c-37(#2), 11, 13, 14, 17, 22, 47, 48, 50, 53-55, 59. **Forte** a-49. **Fox** a-21i. **Heath** a-36(#1), 4, 6-8, 17, 20, 22, 36i; c-18. **Keller** a-15. **Mort Lawrence** a-38, 39. **Maneely** a-7, 8, 15, 16, 22, 49, 58; c-8, 19, 25, 52. **Morrow** a-48. **Orlando** a-44, 57. **Pakula** a-36. **Powell** a-42, 53, 54. **Reinman** a-8. **Rico** a-21. **Robert Sale** a-24, 49. **Sekowsky** a-4, 5, 9. **Severin** a-38, 51; c-38, 48i, 56. **Sinnott** a-9, 21, 24. **Tuska** a-38(#3), 14. **Wildey** a-25, 43, 44.

JOURNEY INTO UNKNOWN WORLDS (Marvel 80th Anniversary salute to science fiction)
Marvel Comics: Mar, 2019 ($3.99, one-shot)

1-Bunn-s/Sanna-a; Chapman-s/Manna-a; McKone-c 4.00

JOURNEY TO STAR WARS: THE FORCE AWAKENS - SHATTERED EMPIRE
Marvel Comics: Nov, 2015 - No. 4, Dec, 2015 ($3.99, weekly limited series)

1-4-Rucka-s; takes place just after Episode 6 Battle of Endor; multiple covers on each 4.00

JOURNEY TO STAR WARS: THE LAST JEDI - CAPTAIN PHASMA
Marvel Comics: Nov, 2017 - No. 4, Dec, 2017 ($3.99, weekly limited series)

1-4-Checchetto-a/Renaud-c; takes place at the end of Episode 7 and just after 4.00

JOURNEY TO STAR WARS: THE RISE OF SKYWALKER - ALLEGIANCE
Marvel Comics: Dec, 2019 - No. 4, Dec, 2020 ($4.99/$3.99, weekly limited series)

1-($4.99) Ethan Sacks-s/Luke Ross-a; follows events after Episode 8 5.00

GD VG FN VF VF/NM NM-
2.0 4.0 6.0 8.0 9.0 9.2

2-4-($3.99) Sacks-s/Ross-a; interlocking covers with #1 4.00

JOURNEY TO THE CENTER OF THE EARTH (Movie)
Dell Publishing Co.: No. 1060, Nov-Jan, 1959/60 (one-shot)

Four Color 1060-Pat Boone & James Mason photo-c 12 24 36 82 179 275

JOY OPERATIONS
Dark Horse Comics: Nov, 2021 - No. 5, Mar, 2022 ($3.99)

1-5-Bendis-s/Stephen Byrne-a/c. 1-Variant-c by Mack. 2-Variant-c by Oeming 4.00

JOYRIDE
BOOM! Studios: Apr, 2016 - No. 12, Apr, 2017 ($3.99, originally planned as a 4-part series)

1-12-Jackson Lanzing & Collin Kelly-s/Marcus To-a. 1-Multiple covers 4.00

JSA (Justice Society of America) (Also see All Star Comics)
DC Comics: Aug, 1999 - No. 87, Sept, 2006 ($2.50/$2.99)

1-Robinson and Goyer-s; funeral of Wesley Dodds 2 4 6 8 10 12
2-5: 4-Return of Dr. Fate 6.00
6-24: 6-Black Adam-c/app. 11,12-Kobra. 16-20-JSA vs. Johnny Sorrow. 19,20-Spectre app. 22-Hawkgirl origin. 23-Hawkman returns 4.00
25-($3.75) Hawkman rejoins the JSA 1 2 3 5 7 9
26-36, 38-49: 27-Capt. Marvel app. 29-Joker: Last Laugh. 31,32-Snejbjerg-a. 33-Ultra-Humanite. 34-Intro. new Crimson Avenger and Hourman. 42-G.A. Mr. Terrific and the Freedom Fighters app. 46-Eclipso returns 3.00
37-($3.50) Johnny Thunder merges with the Thunderbolt; origin new Crimson Avenger4.00
50-($3.95) Wraparound-c by Pacheco; Sentinel becomes Green Lantern again 4.00
51-74,76-82: 51-Kobra killed. 54-JLA app. 55-Ma Hunkle (Red Tornado) app. 56-58-Black Reign x-over with Hawkman #23-25. 64-Sand returns. 67-Identity Crisis tie-in; Gibbons-a. 68,69,72-81-Ross-c. 73,74-Day of Vengeance tie-in. 76-OMAC tie-in. 82-Infinite Crisis x-over; Levitz-s/Pérez-a 3.00
75-($2.99) Day of Vengeance tie-in; Alex Ross Spectre-c 4.00
83-87: One Year Later; Pérez-c. 83-85,87-Morales-a; Gentleman Ghost app. 85-Begin $2.99-c; Earth-2 Batman, Atom, Sandman, Mr. Terrific app. 86,87-Ordway-a. 3.00
Annual 1 (10/00, $3.50) Planet DC; intro. Nemesis 4.00
...: Black Reign TPB (2005, $12.99) r/#56-58, Hawkman #23-25; Watson cover gallery 13.00
...: Black Vengeance TPB (2006, $19.99) r/#66-75 20.00
...: Darkness Falls TPB (2002, $19.95) r/#6-15 20.00
...: Fair Play TPB (2003, $14.95) r/#26-31 & Secret Files #2 15.00
...: Ghost Stories TPB (2006, $14.99) r/#82-87 15.00
...: Justice Be Done TPB (2000, $14.95) r/Secret Files & #1-5 15.00
...: Lost TPB (2005, $19.99) r/#59-67 20.00
...: Mixed Signals TPB (2006, $14.99) r/#76-81 15.00
...: Our Worlds at War 1 (9/01, $2.95) Jae Lee-c; Saltares-a 3.00
... Presents Green Lantern TPB (2008, $14.99) r/JSA Classified #25,32,33 and Green Lantern: Brightest Day, Blackest Night 15.00
...: Princes of Darkness TPB (2005, $19.95) r/#46-55 20.00
...: Savage Times TPB (2004, $14.95) r/#39-45 15.00
... Secret Files 1 (8/99, $4.95) Origin stories and pin-ups; death of Wesley Dodds (G.A. Sandman); intro new Hawkgirl 2 4 6 11 16 20
... Secret Files 2 (9/01, $4.95) Short stories and profile pages
1 2 3 5 6 8
...: Stealing Thunder TPB (2003, $14.95) r/#32-38; JSA vs. The Ultra-Humanite 15.00
...: The Golden Age TPB (2005, $19.99) r/"The Golden Age" Elseworlds mini-series 20.00
...: The Return of Hawkman TPB (2002, $19.95) r/#16-26 & Secret Files #1 20.00

JSA: ALL STARS
DC Comics: July, 2003 - No. 8, Feb, 2004 ($2.50/$3.50, limited series, back-up stories in Golden Age style)

1-3,5,6,8-Goyer & Johns-s/Cassaday-c. 1-Velluto-a; intro. Legacy. 2-Hawkman by Loeb/Sale 3-Dr. Fate by Cooke. 5-Hourman by Chaykin. 6-Dr. Mid-nite by Azzarello/Risso 3.00
4-Starman by Robinson/Harris; 1st app. Courtney Whitmore as Stargirl 3.00
7-($3.50) Mr. Terrific back-up story by Chabon; Lark-a 4.00
TPB (2004, $14.95) r/#1-8 15.00

JSA: ALL STARS
DC Comics: Feb, 2010 - No. 18, Jul, 2011 ($3.99/$2.99)

1-13-Younger JSA members form team. 1-Covers by Williams and Sook 4.00
14-18-($2.99) 3.00
...: Constellations TPB (2010, $14.99) r/#1-6 and sketch art 15.00
...: Glory Days TPB (2011, $17.99) r/#7-13 18.00

JSA: CLASSIFIED (Issues #1-4 reprinted in Power Girl TPB)
DC Comics: Sept, 2005 - No. 39, Aug, 2008 ($2.50/$2.99)

1-(1st printing) Conner-c/a; origin of Power Girl 1 3 4 6 8 10
1-(1st printing) Adam Hughes variant-c 3 6 9 16 23 30
1-(2nd & 3rd printings) 2nd-Hughes B&W sketch-c. 3rd-Close-up of Conner-c 6.00
2-11: 2-LSH app. 4-Leads into Infinite Crisis #2. 5-7-Injustice Society app. 10-13-Vandal

GD 2.0 | VG 4.0 | FN 6.0 | VF 8.0 | VF/NM 9.0 | NM- 9.2

Savage origin retold; Gulacy-a/c 3.00
12-39: 12-Begin $2.99-c. 17,18-Bane app. 19,20-Morales-a. 21,22-Simonson-s/a 3.00
...: Honor Among Thieves TPB (2007, $14.99) r/#5-9 15.00

JSA LIBERTY FILES: THE WHISTLING SKULL
DC Comics: Feb, 2013 - No. 6, Jul, 2013 ($2.99, limited series)
1-6-Dr. Mid-Nite and Hourman in 1940; B. Clay Moore-s/Tony Harris-c/a 3.00

JSA STRANGE ADVENTURES
DC Comics: Oct, 2004 - No. 6, Mar, 2005 ($3.50, limited series)
1-6-Johnny Thunder as pulp writer; Kitson-a/Watson-c/ Kevin Anderson-s 3.50
TPB (2010, $14.99) r/#1-6 15.00

JSA: THE LIBERTY FILE (Elseworlds)
DC Comics: Feb, 2000 - No. 2, Mar, 2000 ($6.95, limited series)
1,2-Batman, Dr. Mid-Nite and Hourman vs. WW2 Joker; Tony Harris-c/a 7.00
JSA: The Liberty Files TPB (2004, $19.95) r/The Liberty File and The Unholy Three series 20.00

JSA: THE UNHOLY THREE (Elseworlds)(Sequel to JSA: The Liberty File)
DC Comics: 2003 - No. 2, 2003 ($6.95, limited series)
1,2-Batman, Superman and Hourman; Tony Harris-c/a 7.00

JSA VS. KOBRA
DC Comics: Aug, 2009 - No. 6, Jan, 2010 ($2.99, limited series)
1-6-Kramer-a/Ha-c; Jason Burr app. 3.00
TPB (2010, $14.99) r/#1-6; cover gallery 15.00

J2 (Also see A-Next and Juggernaut)
Marvel Comics: Oct, 1998 - No. 12, Sept, 1999 ($1.99)
1-12:1-Juggernaut's son; Lim-a. 2-Two covers; X-People app. 3-J2 battles the Hulk 3.00
Spider-Girl Presents Juggernaut Jr. Vol.1: Secrets & Lies (2006, $7.99, digest) r/#1-6 8.00

JUBILEE (X-Men)
Marvel Comics: Nov, 2004 - No. 6, Apr, 2005 ($2.99)
1-6: 1-Jubilee in a Los Angeles high school; Kirkman-s; Casey Jones-c 3.00

JUDAS
BOOM! Studios: Dec, 2017 - No. 4, Mar, 2018 ($3.99, limited series)
1-4-Judas' time with Jesus and in the Afterlife; Lucifer app.; Loveness-s/Rebelka-a 4.00

JUDAS COIN, THE
DC Comics: 2012 ($22.99, hardcover graphic novel with dust jacket)
HC-Walt Simonson-s/a/c; Batman, Two-Face, Golden Gladiator, Viking Prince, Captain Fear, Bat Lash, Manhunter 2070 app.; bonus sketch gallery 23.00

JUDENHASS
Aardvark-Vanaheim Press: 2008 ($4.00, B&W, squarebound)
nn-Dave Sim-writer/artist; The Shoah and Jewish persecution through history 4.00

JUDE, THE FORGOTTEN SAINT
Catechetical Guild Education Soc.: 1954 (16 pgs.; 8x11"; full color; paper-c)
nn 6 12 18 28 34 40

JUDGE COLT
Gold Key: Oct, 1969 - No. 4, Sept, 1970 (Painted cover)
1 3 6 9 16 23 30
2-4 2 4 6 9 13 16

JUDGE DREDD (...Classics #62 on; also see Batman - Judge Dredd, The Law of Dredd & 2000 A.D. Monthly)
Eagle Comics/IPC Magazines Ltd./Quality Comics #34-35, V2#1-37/ Fleetway #38 on: Nov, 1983 - No. 35, 1986; V2#1, Oct, 1986 - No. 77, 1993
1-Bolland-c/a 6 12 18 37 66 95
2-5 2 4 6 9 12 15
6-35 6.00
V2#1-('86)-New look begins 6.00
2-10 5.00
11-77: 20-Begin $1.50-c. 21/22, 23/24-Two issue numbers in one. 28-1st app. Megaman (super-hero). 39-Begin $1.75-c. 51-Begin $1.95-c. 53-Bolland-a. 57-Reprints 1st published Judge Dredd story 4.00
Special 1 5.00
NOTE: ***Bolland** a-1-6, 8, 10; c-1-10, 15. **Guice** c-V2#23/24, 26, 27.*

JUDGE DREDD (3rd Series)
DC Comics: Aug, 1994 - No. 18, Jan, 1996 ($1.95)
1-18: 12-Begin $2.25-c 4.00
nn ($5.95)-Movie adaptation, Sienkiewicz-c 6.00

JUDGE DREDD
IDW Publishing: Nov, 2012 - No. 30, May, 2015 ($3.99)
1-30: 1-Swierczynski-s; six covers 4.00

JUDGE DREDD
IDW Publishing: Dec, 2015 - No. 12, Nov, 2016 ($3.99)
1-12: 1-Farinas & Freitas-s/McDaid-a; multiple covers 4.00
Annual 1 (2/17, $7.99) Farinas & Freitas-s/McDaid-a; two covers 8.00
...: Cry of the Werewolf (3/17, $5.99) Reprint from 2000 AD; Steve Dillon-a/c; new pin-ups 6.00
...: Deviations (3/17, $4.99) McCrea-s/a; What If Dredd stayed a werewolf; bonus pin-ups 5.00
... Funko Universe (4/17, $4.99) Short stories w/characters styled like Pop! Vinyl figures 5.00
...: Mega-City Zero 1 (5/18, $1.00) reprints #1 3.00
...: 100-Page Giant (2/20, $5.99) Reprints stories from recent mini-series 6.00

JUDGE DREDD: ANDERSON, PSI-DIVISION
IDW Publishing: Aug, 2014 - No. 4, Dec, 2014 ($3.99)
1-4-Matt Smith-s/Carl Critchlow-a; three covers on each 4.00

JUDGE DREDD CLASSICS (Reprints)
IDW Publishing: Jul, 2013 - No. 6 ($3.99)
1-6-Wagner & Grant-s 4.00
Free Comic Book Day 2013 (5/13, free) Judge Death app.; Walter the Wobot back-ups 3.00
...: The Dark Judges 1-5 (1/15 - No. 5, 5/15, $3.99) Wagner & Grant-s/Bolland-a 4.00

JUDGE DREDD: LEGENDS OF THE LAW
DC Comics: Dec, 1994 - No. 13, Dec, 1995 ($1.95)
1-13: 1-5-Dorman-c 4.00

JUDGE DREDD: MEGA-CITY TWO
IDW Publishing: Jan, 2014 - No. 5, May, 2014 ($3.99)
1-5-Wolk-s/Farinas-a 4.00

JUDGE DREDD'S CRIME FILE
Eagle Comics: Aug, 1985 - No. 6, Feb, 1986 ($1.25, limited series)
1-6: 1-Byrne-a 5.00

JUDGE DREDD: THE BLESSED EARTH
IDW Publishing: Apr, 2017 - No. 8, Nov, 2017 ($3.99)
1-8-Farinas & Freitas-a; multiple covers on each 4.00

JUDGE DREDD: THE EARLY CASES
Eagle Comics: Feb, 1986 - No. 6, Jul, 1986 ($1.25, Mega-series, Mando paper)
1-6: 2000 A.D.-r 5.00

JUDGE DREDD: THE JUDGE CHILD QUEST (Judge Child in indicia)
Eagle Comics: Aug, 1984 - No. 5, Oct, 1984 ($1.25, Lim. series, Baxter paper)
1-5: 2000A.D.-r; Bolland-c/a 6.00

JUDGE DREDD: THE MEGAZINE
Fleetway/Quality: 1991 - No. 3 ($4.95, stiff-c, squarebound, 52 pgs.)
1-3 5.00

JUDGE DREDD: TOXIC
IDW Publishing: Oct, 2018 - No. 4, Jan, 2019 ($3.99)
1-4-Paul Jenkins-s/Marco Castiello-a 4.00

JUDGE DREDD: UNDER SIEGE
IDW Publishing: May, 2018 - No. 4, Aug, 2018 ($3.99)
1-4-Mark Russell-s/Max Dunbar-a 4.00

JUDGE DREDD VS. ALIENS: INCUBUS
Dark Horse Comics: March, 2003 - No. 4, June, 2003 ($2.99, limited series)
1-4-Flint-a/Wagner & Diggle-s 3.00

JUDGE DREDD: YEAR ONE
IDW Publishing: Mar, 2013 - No. 4, Jul, 2013 ($3.99)
1-4-Matt Smith-s/Simon Coleby-a 4.00

JUDGE PARKER
Argo: Feb, 1956 - No. 2, 1956
1-Newspaper strip reprints 8 16 24 44 57 70
2 6 12 18 31 38 45

JUDGMENT DAY
Awesome Entertainment: June, 1997 - No. 3, Oct, 1997 ($2.50, limited series)
1-3: 1 Alpha-Moore-s/Liefeld-c/a(p) flashback art by various in all. 2 Omega. 3 Final Judgment. All have a variant cover by Dave Gibbons 4.00
...Aftermath-($3.50) Moore-s/Kane-a; Youngblood, Glory, New Men, Maximage, Allies and Spacehunter short stories. Also has a variant cover by Dave Gibbons 4.00
TPB (Checker Books, 2003, $16.95) r/series 17.00

JUDO JOE
Jay-Jay Corp.: Aug, 1953 - No. 3, Dec, 1953 (Judo lessons in each issue)
1-Drug ring story 18 36 54 105 165 225
2,3: 3-Hypo needle story 12 24 36 67 94 120

JUDOMASTER (Gun Master #84-89) (Also see Crisis on Infinite Earths, Sarge Steel #6, Special War Series, & Thunderbolt)
Charlton Comics: No. 89, May-June, 1966 - No. 98, Dec, 1967 (Two No. 89's)
89-3rd app. Judomaster 4 8 12 28 47 65
90-Origin of Thunderbolt 4 8 12 25 40 55
91-Sarge Steel begins 4 8 12 22 35 48
92-98: 93-Intro. Tiger 3 6 9 21 33 45
93,94,96,98 (Modern Comics reprint, 1977) 1 2 3 5 6 8
NOTE: ***Morisi** Thunderbolt #90. #91 has 1 pg. biography on writer/artist Frank McLaughlin.*

JUDY CANOVA (Formerly My Experience) (Stage, screen, radio)
Fox Feature Syndicate: No. 23, May, 1950 - No. 3, Sept, 1950
23(#1)-Wood-c,a(p)? 30 60 90 177 289 400
24-Wood-a(p) 28 56 84 165 270 375
3-Wood-c; Wood/Orlando-a 31 62 93 184 300 415

JUDY GARLAND (See Famous Stars)

JUDY JOINS THE WAVES
Toby Press: 1951 (For U.S. Navy)
nn 10 20 30 58 79 100

JUGGERNAUT (See X-Men)
Marvel Comics: Apr, 1997, Nov, 1999 ($2.99, one-shots)
1-(4/97) Kelly-s/ Rouleau-a 4.00
1-(11/99) Casey-s; Eighth Day x-over; Thor, Iron Man, Spidey app. 4.00

JUGGERNAUT (X-Men)
Marvel Comics: Nov, 2020 - Present ($3.99)
1-5-Nicieza-s/Garney-a. 2-Hulk app. 4,5-Arnim Zola app. 4.00

JUGHEAD (Formerly Archie's Pal...)
Archie Publications: No. 126, Nov, 1965 - No. 352, June, 1987
126-130: 129-LBJ on cover 3 6 9 18 28 38
131,133,135-160(9/68) 3 6 9 16 23 30
132,134: 132-Shield-c; The Fly & Black Hood app.; Shield cameo. 134-Shield-c 5 10 15 30 50 70
161-180 2 4 6 13 19 24
181-199 2 4 6 9 13 16
200(1/72) 2 4 6 11 16 20
201-240(5/75) 2 4 6 8 10 12
241-270(11/77) 1 2 3 5 7 9
271-299 1 2 3 4 5 7
300(5/80)-Anniversary issue; infinity-c 1 2 3 5 6 8

Judge Dredd (2015) #1 © Rebellion

Juggernaut (2020) #1 © MAR

Jughead (2015) #2 © ACP

	GD 2.0	VG 4.0	FN 6.0	VF 8.0	VF/NM 9.0	NM- 9.2
301-320(1/82)						5.00
321-324,326-352						4.00
325-(10/82) Cheryl Blossom app. (not on cover); same month as intro. (cover & story) in Archie's Girls, Betty & Veronica #320; Jason Blossom app.; DeCarlo-a	10	20	30	67	149	215

JUGHEAD (2nd Series)(Becomes Archie's Pal Jughead Comics #46 on)
Archie Enterprises: Aug, 1987 - No. 45, May, 1993 (.75/$1.00/$1.25)

	GD 2.0	VG 4.0	FN 6.0	VF 8.0	VF/NM 9.0	NM- 9.2
1	1	2	3	4	5	7
2-10						4.00
11-45: 4-X-Mas issue. 17-Colan-c/a						3.00

JUGHEAD (Volume 3)
Archie Comic Publications: Nov, 2015 - No. 16, Aug, 2017 ($3.99)

1-16-Multiple covers and classic back-up reprints. 1-6-Chip Zdarsky-s/Erica Henderson-a. 5,6-Jughead as Captain Hero. 7-13-Derek Charm-a. 9-13-Ryan North-s; Sabrina app. 4.00

JUGHEAD AND ARCHIE DOUBLE DIGEST (Becomes Jughead & Archie Comics Digest)
Archie Comic Publ.: Jun, 2014 - No. 27, Oct, 2017 ($3.99-$6.99, digest-size)

	NM- 9.2
1-3: 1-Reprints; That Wilkin Boy app.	4.00
4,7-9,11-14,16,19,26-($4.99)	5.00
5,10,15,21,23,25-($6.99, 320 pgs.) Titled Jughead & Archie Jumbo Comics Digest	7.00
6,17,18,20,22,24,27-($5.99, 192 pgs.) Titled Jughead & Archie Comics Annual. 24-Winter Annual	6.00

JUGHEAD & FRIENDS DIGEST MAGAZINE
Archie Publ.: Jun, 2005 - No. 38, Aug, 2010 ($2.39/$2.49/$2.69, digest-size)

1-38: 1-That Wilkin Boy app. 3.00

JUGHEAD AS CAPTAIN HERO (See Archie as Pureheart the Powerful, Archie Giant Series Magazine #142 & Life With Archie)
Archie Publications: Oct, 1966 - No. 7, Nov, 1967

	GD 2.0	VG 4.0	FN 6.0	VF 8.0	VF/NM 9.0	NM- 9.2
1-Super hero parody	9	18	27	57	111	165
2	5	10	15	34	60	85
3-7	4	8	12	28	47	65

JUGHEAD COMICS, NIGHT AT GEPPI'S ENTERTAINMENT MUSEUM
Archie Comic Publ. Inc: 2008

Free Comic Book Day giveaway - New story; Archie gang visits GEM; Steve Geppi app. 3.00

JUGHEAD JONES COMICS DIGEST, THE (...Magazine No. 10-64; Jughead Jones Digest Magazine #65)
Archie Publ.: June, 1977 - No. 100, May, 1996 ($1.35/$1.50/$1.75, digest-size, 128 pgs.)

	GD 2.0	VG 4.0	FN 6.0	VF 8.0	VF/NM 9.0	NM- 9.2
1-Neal Adams-a; Capt. Hero-r	4	8	12	25	40	55
2(9/77)-Neal Adams-a	3	6	9	16	23	30
3-6,8-10	2	4	6	11	16	20
7-Origin Jaguar-r; N. Adams-a.	2	4	6	13	18	22
11-20: 13-r/1957 Jughead's Folly	2	4	6	8	10	12
21-50	1	2	3	4	5	7
51-70						5.00
71-100						3.00

JUGHEAD'S BABY TALES
Archie Comics: Spring, 1994 - No. 2, Wint. 1994 ($2.00, 52 pgs.)

1,2: 1-Bound-in pull-out poster 4.00

JUGHEAD'S DINER
Archie Comics: Apr, 1990 - No. 7, Apr, 1991 ($1.00)

	NM- 9.2
1	5.00
2-7	4.00

JUGHEAD'S DOUBLE DIGEST (...Magazine #5)
Archie Comics: Oct, 1989 - No. 200, Apr, 2014 ($2.25 - $3.99/$5.99)

	GD 2.0	VG 4.0	FN 6.0	VF 8.0	VF/NM 9.0	NM- 9.2
1	2	4	6	8	10	12
2-10: 2,5-Capt. Hero stories	1	2	3	5	6	8
11-25						5.00
26-195: 58-Begin $2.99-c. 66-Begin $3.19-c. 91-Begin $3.59-c. 138-Reprints entire Jughead #1 (1949). 139-142-"New Look" Jughead; Staton-a. 148-Begin $3.99-c						4.00
196-200-($5.99) Titled "Jughead's Double Double Digest"						6.00
Archie New Look Series Book 2, Jughead "The Matchmakers" TPB (2009, $10.95) r/new look series in #139-142; new cover by Staton & Milgrom						11.00

JUGHEAD'S EAT-OUT COMIC BOOK MAGAZINE (See Archie Giant Series Magazine No. 170)

JUGHEAD'S FANTASY
Archie Publications: Aug, 1960 - No. 3, Dec, 1960

	GD 2.0	VG 4.0	FN 6.0	VF 8.0	VF/NM 9.0	NM- 9.2
1	26	52	78	182	404	625
2	14	28	42	96	211	325
3	12	24	36	79	170	260

JUGHEAD'S FOLLY
Archie Publications (Close-Up): 1957 (36 pgs.)(one-shot)

	GD 2.0	VG 4.0	FN 6.0	VF 8.0	VF/NM 9.0	NM- 9.2
1-Jughead a la Elvis (Rare) (1st reference to Elvis in comics?)	90	180	270	576	988	1400

JUGHEAD'S JOKES
Archie Publications: Aug, 1967 - No. 78, Sept, 1982
(No. 1-8, 38 on: reg. size; No. 9-23: 68 pgs.; No. 24-37: 52 pgs.)

	GD 2.0	VG 4.0	FN 6.0	VF 8.0	VF/NM 9.0	NM- 9.2
1	8	16	24	54	102	150
2	5	10	15	30	50	70
3-8	3	6	9	17	26	35
9,10 (68 pgs.)	3	6	9	19	30	40
11-23(4/71) (68 pgs.)	3	6	9	16	23	30
24-37(1/74) (52 pgs.)	2	4	6	11	16	20
38-50(9/76)	1	3	4	6	8	10
51-78						6.00

JUGHEAD'S PAL HOT DOG (See Laugh #14 for 1st app.)
Archie Comics: Jan, 1990 - No. 5, Oct, 1990 ($1.00)

	NM- 9.2
1	5.00
2-5	4.00

JUGHEAD'S SOUL FOOD
Spire Christian Comics (Fleming H. Revell Co.): 1979 (49¢/59¢)

	GD 2.0	VG 4.0	FN 6.0	VF 8.0	VF/NM 9.0	NM- 9.2
nn-Low print run	3	6	9	15	22	28

JUGHEAD'S TIME POLICE
Archie Comics: July, 1990 - No. 6, May, 1991 ($1.00, bi-monthly)

	NM- 9.2
1	5.00
2-6: Colan-a-3-6p; c-3-6	4.00

JUGHEAD'S TIME POLICE
Archie Comic Publications: Aug, 2019 - No. 5, Dec, 2019 ($3.99, limited series)

1-5-Sina Grace-s/Derek Charm-a; multiple covers on each; January McAndrews app. 4.00

JUGHEAD: THE HUNGER (Continues in Jughead The Hunger vs Vampironica)
Archie Comic Publications: Dec, 2017 - No. 13, May, 2019 ($3.99)

	NM- 9.2
1-13-Tieri-s; Jughead as a werewolf. 1-8-Pat & Tim Kennedy-a; 2-13-Eisma-a (partial)	4.00
Jughead The Hunger, One-Shot (5/17, $4.99) Tieri-s/Walsh-a; prelude to issue #1	5.00

JUGHEAD: THE HUNGER VS VAMPIRONICA
Archie Comic Publications: Jun, 2019 - No. 5, Dec, 2019 ($3.99, limited series)

1-5-Tieri-s/Pat & Tim Kennedy-a; Eisma-a (partial); multiple covers. 3-5 Sabrina app. 4.00

JUGHEAD WITH ARCHIE DIGEST (...Plus Betty & Veronica & Reggie Too No. 1,2; ...Magazine #33-?, 101-on; ...Comics Digest Mag.)
Archie Pub.: Mar, 1974 - No. 200, May, 2005 ($1.00-$2.39)

	GD 2.0	VG 4.0	FN 6.0	VF 8.0	VF/NM 9.0	NM- 9.2
1	5	10	15	34	60	85
2	4	8	12	23	37	50
3-10	3	6	9	17	26	35
11-13,15-17,19,20: Capt. Hero-r in #14-16; Capt. Pureheart #17,19	2	4	6	10	14	18
14,18,21,22-Pureheart the Powerful in #18,21,22	2	4	6	11	16	20
23-30: 29-The Shield-r. 30-The Fly-r	1	3	4	6	8	10
31-50,100	1	2	3	5	6	8
51-99	1	2	3	4	5	7
101-121						4.00
122-200: 156-Begin $2.19-c. 180-Begin $2.39-c						3.00

JUICE SQUEEZERS
Dark Horse Comics: Jan, 2014 - No. 4, Apr, 2014 ($3.99, limited series)

1-4-David Lapham-s/a/c 4.00

JUKE BOX COMICS
Famous Funnies: Mar, 1948 - No. 6, Jan, 1949

	GD 2.0	VG 4.0	FN 6.0	VF 8.0	VF/NM 9.0	NM- 9.2
1-Toth-c/a; Hollingsworth-a	41	82	123	256	428	600
2-Transvestism story	27	54	81	158	259	360
3-6: 3-Peggy Lee story. 4-Jimmy Durante line drawn-c. 6-Features Desi Arnaz plus Arnaz line drawn-c	20	40	60	117	189	260

JULES VERNE'S LIGHTHOUSE
Image Comics: Apr, 2021 - No. 5, Sept, 2021 ($4.99/$3.99, limited series)

	NM- 9.2
1-($4.99) David Hine & Brian Haberlin-s/Haberlin-a	5.00
2-5-($3.99)	4.00

JUMBO COMICS (Created by S.M. Iger)
Fiction House Magazines (Real Adv. Publ. Co.): Sept, 1938 - No. 167, Mar, 1953 (No. 1-3: 68 pgs.; No. 4-8: 52 pgs.)(No. 1-8 oversized-10-1/2x14-1/2"; black & white)

1-(Rare)-Sheena Queen of the Jungle(1st app.) by Meskin, Hawks of the Seas (The Hawk

#10 on; see Feature Funnies #3) by Eisner, The Hunchback by Dick Briefer (ends #8), Wilton of the West (ends #24), Inspector Dayton (ends #67) & ZX-5 (ends #140) begin; 1st comic art by Jack Kirby (Count of Monte Cristo & Wilton of the West); Mickey Mouse appears (1 panel) with brief biography of Walt Disney; 1st app. Peter Pupp by Bob Kane. Note: Sheena was created by Iger for publication in England as a newspaper strip. The early issues of Jumbo contain Sheena strip-r; multiple panel-c 1,2,7 4400 8800 13,200 35,200 -- --
2-(Rare)-Origin Sheena. Diary of Dr. Hayward by Kirby (also #3) plus 2 other stories; contains strip from Universal Film featuring Edgar Bergen & Charlie McCarthy plus-c (preview of film) 1500 3000 4500 12,000 -- --
3-Last Kirby issue 1050 2100 3150 8400 -- --
4-(Scarce)-Origin The Hawk by Eisner; Wilton of the West by Fine (ends #14)(1st comic work); Count of Monte Cristo by Fine (ends #15); The Diary of Dr. Hayward by Fine (cont'd #8,9) 975 1950 2925 7800 -- --
5-Christmas-c 900 1800 2700 7200 -- --
6-8-Last B&W issue. #8 was a 1939 N. Y. World's Fair Special Edition; Frank Buck's Jungleland story 790 1580 2370 6300 -- --
9-Stuart Taylor begins by Fine (ends #140); Fine-c; 1st color issue (8-9/39)-1st Sheena (jungle) cover; 8-1/4x10-1/4" (oversized in width only) 1190 2380 3570 9500 -- --
10-Regular size 68 pg. issues begin; Sheena dons new costume w/origin costume; Stuart Taylor sci/fi-c; classic Lou Fine-c. 541 1082 1623 3950 6975 10,000
11-13: 12-The Hawk-c by Eisner. 13-Eisner-c 258 516 774 1651 2826 4000
14-Intro. Lightning (super-hero) on-c only 258 516 774 1651 2826 4000
15-1st Lightning story and begins, ends #41 174 348 522 1114 1907 2700
16-Lightning-c 194 388 582 1242 2121 3000
17,18,20: 17-Lightning part-c 148 296 444 947 1624 2300
19-Classic Sheena Giant Ape-c by Powell 187 374 561 1197 2049 2900
21-30: 22-1st Tom, Dick & Harry; origin The Hawk retold. 25-Midnight the Black Stallion begins, ends #65 106 212 318 673 1162 1650
31-(9/41)-1st app. Mars God of War in Stuart Taylor story (see Planet Comics #15.) (scarce) 366 732 1098 2562 4481 6400
32-40: 35-Shows V2#11 (correct number does not appear) 87 174 281 553 952 1350
41-50: 42-Ghost Gallery begins, ends #167 54 108 162 343 574 825
51-60: 52-Last Tom, Dick & Harry 43 86 129 271 461 650
61-70: 68-Sky Girl begins, ends #130; not in #79 39 78 117 231 378 525
71-93,95-99: 89-ZX5 becomes a private eye. 32 64 96 188 307 425
94-Used in Love and Death by Legman 36 72 108 211 343 475
100 33 66 99 194 317 440
101-121 27 54 81 160 263 365
121-140,150-158: 155-Used in **POP**, pg. 98 24 48 72 142 234 325
141-149-Two Sheena stories. 141-Long Bow, Indian Boy begins, ends #160 25 50 75 147 241 335
159-163: Space Scouts serial in all. 160-Last jungle-c (6/52). 161-Ghost Gallery covers begin, end #167. 163-Suicide Smith app. 28 56 84 165 270 375
164-The Star Pirate begins, ends #165 58 116 174 371 636 900
165-167: 165,167-Space Rangers app. 52 104 156 328 552 775

NOTE: *Bondage covers, negligee panels, torture, etc. are common in this series. Hawks of the Seas, Inspector Dayton, Spies in Action, Sports Shorts, & Uncle Otto by Eisner, #1-7. Hawk by* ***Eisner****-#10-15.* ***Eisner*** *c-1-8, 12-14. 1pg. Patsy pin-ups in 92-97, 99-101. Sheena by* ***Meskin****-#1, 4; by* ***Powell****-#2, 3, 5-28;* ***Powell*** *c-14, 16, 17, 19.* ***Powell/Eisner*** *c-15. Sky Girl by* ***Matt Baker****-#69-78, 80-130. ZX-5 & Ghost Gallery by* ***Kamen****-#90-130.* ***Bailey*** *a-3-8.* ***Briefer*** *a-1-8, 10.* ***Fine*** *a-14; c-9-11.* ***Kamen*** *a-101, 105, 123, 132; c-105, 121-145.* ***Bob Kane*** *a-1-8.* ***Whitman*** *c-146-167(most). Jungle c-9, 13, 15, 17 on.*

JUMPER: JUMPSCARS
Oni Press: Jan, 2008 ($14.95, graphic novel)

SC-Prelude to 2008 movie Jumper; Brian Hurtt-a/c 15.00

JUNGLE ACTION
Atlas Comics (IPC): Oct, 1954 - No. 6, Aug, 1955

1-Leopard Girl begins by Al Hartley (#1,3); Jungle Boy by Forte; Maneely-a in all 57 114 171 362 619 875
2-(3-D effect cover) 48 96 144 302 514 725
3-6: 3-Last precode (2/55) 34 68 102 204 332 460

NOTE: ***Maneely*** *c-1, 2, 5, 6.* ***Romita*** *a-3, 6.* ***Shores*** *a-3, 6; c-3, 4?.*

JUNGLE ACTION (...& Black Panther #18-21?)
Marvel Comics Group: Oct, 1972 - No. 24, Nov, 1976

1-Lorna, Jann-r (All reprints in 1-4) 5 10 15 33 57 80
2-4 3 6 9 17 25 34
5-Black Panther begins (r/Avengers #62) 12 24 36 82 179 275
6-New solo Black Panther stories begin; 1st app. Erik Killmonger 30 60 90 216 483 750
7,9,10: 9-Contains pull-out centerfold ad by Mark Jewelers 5 10 15 33 57 80
8-Origin Black Panther 7 14 21 46 86 125
11-18,23,24: 18-1st app. Madame Slay (Erik Killmonger's girlfriend). 23-r/#22. 24-1st Wind Eagle; story cont'd in Marvel Premiere #51-#53 3 6 9 17 26 35
19,20-Black Panther vs. the Klan (cont'd in #21,22) 5 10 15 35 63 90
21(Regular 25¢ edition)(5/76) The Klan app. 10 20 30 64 132 200
21-(30¢-c variant, limited distribution) 13 26 39 89 195 300
22-(Regular 25¢ edition)(7/76) 5 10 15 33 57 80
22-(30¢-c variant, limited distribution) 10 20 30 69 147 225

NOTE: ***Buckler*** *a-6-9p, 22; c-8p, 12p.* ***Buscema*** *a-5p; c-22.* ***Byrne*** *c-23.* ***Gil Kane*** *a-8p; c-2, 4, 10p, 11p, 13-17, 19, 24.* ***Kirby*** *c-18.* ***Maneely*** *r-1.* ***Russell*** *a-13i.* ***Starlin*** *c-3p.*

JUNGLE ADVENTURES
Super Comics: 1963 - 1964 (Reprints)

10,12,15,17,18: 10-r/Terrors of the Jungle #4 & #10(Rulah). 12-r/Zoot #14(Rulah).15-r/Kaanga from Jungle #152 & Tiger Girl. 17-All Jo-Jo-r. 18-Reprints/White Princess of the Jungle #1; no Kinstler-a; origin of both White Princess & Cap'n Courage 3 6 9 19 30 40

JUNGLE ADVENTURES
Skywald Comics: Mar, 1971 - No. 3, June, 1971 (25¢, 52 pgs.) (Pre-code reprints & new-s)

1-Zangar origin; reprints of Jo-Jo, Blue Gorilla(origin)/White Princess #3, Kinstler-r/White Princess #2 3 6 9 19 30 40
2,3: 2-Zangar, Sheena-r/Sheena #17 & Jumbo #162, Jo-Jo, origin Slave Girl-r. 3-Zangar, Jo-Jo, White Princess, Rulah-r 3 6 9 15 22 28

JUNGLE BOOK (See King Louie and Mowgli, Movie Comics, Mowgli..., Walt Disney Showcase #45 & Walt Disney's The Jungle Book)

JUNGLE CAT (Disney)
Dell Publishing Co.: No. 1136, Sept-Nov, 1960 (one shot)

Four Color 1136-Movie, photo-c 6 12 18 40 73 105

JUNGLE COMICS
Fiction House Magazines: 1/40 - No. 157, 3/53; No. 158, Spr, 1953 - No. 163, Summer, 1954

1-Origin The White Panther, Kaanga, Lord of the Jungle, Tabu, Wizard of the Jungle; Wambi, the Jungle Boy, Camilla & Capt. Terry Thunder begin (all 1st app.). Lou Fine-c 676 1352 2028 4935 8718 12,500
2-Fantomah, Mystery Woman of the Jungle begins, ends #51; The Red Panther begins, ends #26 245 490 735 1568 2684 3800
3,4 174 348 522 1114 1907 2700
5-Classic Eisner-c 232 469 696 1485 2543 3600
6-10: 7,8-Powell-c 103 206 309 659 1130 1600
11-Classic dinosaur-c 219 438 657 1402 2401 3400
12-20: 13-Tuska-c 74 148 222 470 810 1150
21-30: 25-Shows V2#1 (correct number does not appear). #27-New origin Fantomah, Daughter of the Pharoahs; Camilla dons new costume 58 116 174 371 636 900
31-40 45 90 135 284 480 675
41,43-50 41 82 123 258 428 600
42-Kaanga by Crandall, 12 pgs. 55 110 165 352 601 850
51-60 37 74 111 222 361 500
61-70: 67-Cover swipes Crandall splash pg. in #42 33 66 99 194 317 440
71-80: 79-New origin Tabu 28 56 84 165 270 375
81-97,99 27 54 81 158 259 360
98-Used in **SOTI**, pg. 185 & illo "In ordinary comic books, there are pictures within pictures for children who know how to look;" used by N.Y. Legis. Comm. 41 82 123 256 428 600
100 31 62 93 186 303 420
101-110: 104-In Camilia story, villain is Dr. Wertham 26 52 78 154 252 350
111-120: 118-Clyde Beatty app. 24 48 72 144 237 330
121-130 23 46 69 136 223 310
131-163: 135-Desert Panther begins in Terry Thunder (origin), not in #137; ends (dies) #138. 139-Last 52 pg. issue. 141-Last Tabu. 143,145-Used in **POP**, pg. 99. 151-Last Camilla & Terry Thunder. 152-Tiger Girl begins. 158-Last Wambi; Sheena app. 21 42 63 126 206 285
I.W. Reprint #1,9: 1-r/? 9-r/#151 3 6 9 19 30 40

NOTE: *Bondage covers, negligee panels, torture, etc. are common to this series. Camilla by* ***Fran Hopper****-#70-92; by* ***Baker****-#69, 100-113, 115, 116; by* ***Lubbers****-#97-99 by* ***Tuska****-#63, 65. Kaanga by* ***John Celardo****-#80-113; by* ***Larsen****-#71, 75-79; by* ***Moreira****-#58, 60, 61, 63-70, 72-74; by* ***Tuska****-#37, 62; by* ***Whitman****-#114-163. Tabu by* ***Larsen****-#59-75, 82-92; by* ***Whitman****-#93-115. Terry Thunder by* ***Hopper****-#71, 72; by* ***Celardo****-#78, 79; by* ***Lubbers****-#80-85. Tiger Girl-r by* ***Baker****-#152, 153, 155-157, 159. Wambi by* ***Baker****-#62-67, 74.* ***Astarita*** *c-45, 46.* ***Celardo*** *a-78; c-98-113.* ***Crandall*** *c-67 from splash pg.* ***Eisner*** *c-2, 5, 6.* ***Fine*** *c-1.* ***Larsen*** *a-65, 66, 71, 72, 74, 75, 79, 83, 84, 87-90.* ***Moreira*** *c-43, 44.* ***Morisi*** *a-51.* ***Powell*** *c-7, 8.* ***Sultan*** *c-3, 4.* ***Tuska*** *c-13.* ***Whitman*** *c-132-163(most).* ***Zolnerowich*** *c-11, 12, 18-41.*

JUNGLE COMICS
Blackthorne Publishing: May, 1988 - No. 4 ($2.00, B&W/color)

1-Dave Stevens-c; B. Jones scripts in all 3 6 9 14 20 26
2-4: 2-B&W-a begins 6.00

JUNGLE GIRL (See Lorna, the...)

JUNGLE GIRL (Nyoka, Jungle Girl No. 2 on)
Fawcett Publications: Fall, 1942 (one-shot)(No month listed)

1-Bondage-c; photo of Kay Aldridge who played Nyoka in movie serial app. on-c. Adaptation of the classic Republic movie serial Perils of Nyoka. 1st comic to devote entire contents to a movie serial adaptation 148 296 444 947 1624 2300

JUNGLE GIRL
Dynamite Entertainment: No. 0, 2007 - 2009 (25¢/$2.99/$3.50)

0-(25¢-c) Eight page preview; preview of Superpowers w/Alex Ross-a 3.00
1-5-Frank Cho-plot/cover; Batista-a/variant-c 3.00
... Season 2 ($3.50) 1-5-Two covers by Cho & Batista 3.50
... Season 3 ($3.99) 1-4-Cho-c/Jadson-a/Murray-s 4.00

JUNGLE JIM (Also see Ace Comics)
Standard Comics (Best Books): No. 11, Jan, 1949 - No. 20, Apr, 1951

11 15 30 45 90 140 190
12-20 11 22 33 62 86 110

JUNGLE JIM
Dell Publishing Co.: No. 490, 8/53 - No. 1020, 8-10/59 (Painted-c)

Four Color 490(#1) 9 18 27 60 120 180
Four Color 565(#2, 6/54) 5 10 15 34 60 85
3(10-12/54)-5 4 8 12 27 44 60
6-19(1-3/59) 4 8 12 25 40 55
Four Color 1020(#20) 5 10 15 33 57 80

JUNGLE JIM
King Features Syndicate: No. 5, Dec, 1967

5-Reprints Dell #5; Wood-c 2 4 6 10 14 18

JUNGLE JIM (Continued from Dell series)
Charlton Comics: No. 22, Feb, 1969 - No. 28, Feb, 1970 (#21 was an overseas edition only)

22-Dan Flagg begins; Ditko/Wood-a 3 6 9 21 33 45
23-26: 23-Last Dan Flagg; Howard-c. 24-Jungle People begin 3 6 9 15 21 26
27,28: 27-Ditko/Howard-a. 28-Ditko-a 3 6 9 16 24 32

NOTE: *Ditko cover of #22 reprints story panels*

JUNGLE JO
Fox Feature Syndicate (Hero Books): Mar, 1950 - No. 3, Sept, 1950

nn-Jo-Jo blanked out in titles of interior stories, leaving Congo King; came out after Jo-Jo #29 (intended as Jo-Jo #30?) 68 136 204 435 743 1050
1-Tangi begins; part Wood-a 74 148 222 470 810 1150
2,3 53 106 159 334 567 800

JUNGLE LIL (Dorothy Lamour #2 on; also see Feature Stories Magazine)

Jungle Action #19 © MAR

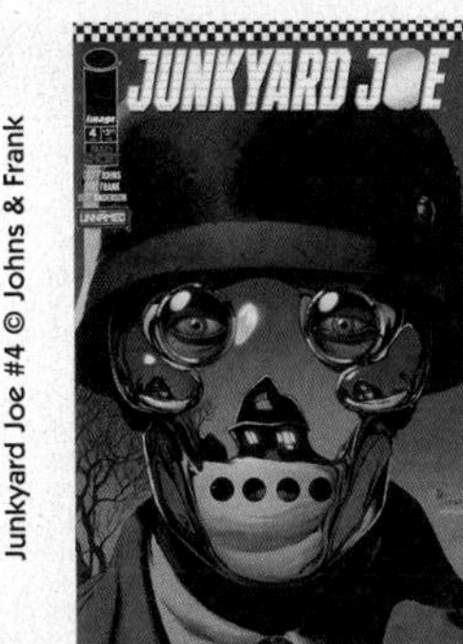

Junkyard Joe #4 © Johns & Frank

Jupiter's Legacy #1 © Millar & Quitely

	GD 2.0	VG 4.0	FN 6.0	VF 8.0	VF/NM 9.0	NM- 9.2
Fox Feature Syndicate (Hero Books): April, 1950						
1	61	122	183	390	670	950
JUNGLE TALES (Jann of the Jungle No. 8 on)						
Atlas Comics (CSI): Sept, 1954 - No. 7, Sept, 1955						
1-Jann of the Jungle	53	106	159	334	567	800
2-7: 3-Last precode (1/55)	37	74	111	222	361	500
NOTE: *Heath c-5. Heck a-6, 7. Maneely a-2; c-1, 3. Shores a-5-7; c-4, 6. Tuska a-2.*						
JUNGLE TALES OF TARZAN						
Charlton Comics: Dec, 1964 - No. 4, July, 1965						
1	5	10	15	35	63	90
2-4	4	8	12	25	40	55
NOTE: *Giordano c-3p. Glanzman a-1-3. Montes/Bache a-4.*						
JUNGLE TERROR (See Harvey Comics Hits No. 54)						
JUNGLE THRILLS (Formerly Sports Thrills; Terrors of the Jungle #17 on)						
Star Publications: No. 16, Feb, 1952; Dec, 1953; No. 7, 1954						
16-Phantom Lady & Rulah story-reprint/All Top No. 15; used in **POP**, pg. 98,99; L. B. Cole-c	71	142	213	454	777	1100
3-D 1(12/53, 25¢)-Came w/glasses; Jungle Lil & Jungle Jo appear; L. B. Cole-c	54	108	162	343	574	825
7-Titled 'Picture Scope Jungle Adventures;' (1954, 36 pgs, 15¢)-3-D effect c/stories; story & coloring book; Disbrow-a/script; L.B. Cole-c	57	114	171	362	619	875
JUNGLE TWINS, THE (Tono & Kono)						
Gold Key/Whitman No. 18: Apr, 1972 - No. 17, Nov, 1975; No. 18, May, 1982						
1-All painted covers	3	6	9	16	23	30
2-5	2	4	6	9	12	15
6-18: 18(Whitman, 5/82)-Reprints	1	3	4	6	8	10
NOTE: *UFO c/story No. 13. Painted-c No. 1-17. Spiegle c-18.*						
JUNGLE WAR STORIES (Guerrilla War No. 12 on)						
Dell Publishing Co.: July-Sept, 1962 - No. 11, Apr-June, 1965 (Painted-c)						
01-384-209 (#1)	4	8	12	27	44	60
2-11	3	6	9	17	25	34
JUNIE PROM (Also see Dexter Comics)						
Dearfield Publishing Co.: Winter, 1947-48 - No. 7, Aug, 1949						
1-Teen-age	42	84	126	265	445	625
2	30	60	90	177	289	400
3-7	24	48	72	142	234	325
JUNIOR						
Fantagraphics Books: June, 2000 - No. 5, Jan, 2001 ($2.95, B&W)						
1-5-Peter Bagge-s/a						3.00
JUNIOR CARROT PATROL (Jr. Carrot Patrol #2)						
Dark Horse Comics: May, 1989; No. 2, Nov, 1990 ($2.00, B&W)						
1,2-Flaming Carrot spin-off. 1-Bob Burden-c(i)						4.00
JUNIOR COMICS (Formerly Li'l Pan; becomes Western Outlaws with #17)						
Fox Feature Syndicate: No. 9, Sept, 1947 - No. 16, July, 1948						
9-Feldstein-c/a; headlights-c	213	426	639	1363	2332	3300
10-16: 10-12,14-16-Feldstein-c/a; headlights-c	194	388	582	1242	2121	3000
JUNIOR FUNNIES (Formerly Tiny Tot Funnies No. 9)						
Harvey Publ. (King Features Synd.): No. 10, Aug, 1951 - No. 13, Feb, 1952						
10-Partial reprints in all; Blondie, Dagwood, Daisy, Henry, Popeye, Felix, Katzenjammer Kids	8	16	24	42	54	65
11-13	7	14	21	37	46	55
JUNIOR HOPP COMICS						
Stanmor Publ.: Feb, 1952 - No. 3, July, 1952						
1-Teenage humor	23	46	69	136	223	310
2,3: 3-Dave Berg-a	15	30	45	90	140	190
JUNIOR MEDICS OF AMERICA, THE						
E. R. Squire & Sons: No. 1359, 1957 (15¢)						
1359	6	12	18	33	41	48
JUNIOR MISS						
Timely/Marvel (CnPC): Wint, 1944; No. 24, Apr, 1947 - No. 39, Aug, 1950						
1-Frank Sinatra & June Allyson life story	50	100	150	315	533	750
24-Formerly The Human Torch #23?	25	50	75	150	245	340
25-38: 29,31,32,34-Cindy-c/stories (others?)	18	36	54	105	165	225
39-Kurtzman-a	19	38	57	111	176	240
NOTE: *Painted-c 35-37. 35, 37-all romance. 36, 38-mostly teen humor. Louise Alston c-36.*						
JUNIOR PARTNERS (Formerly Oral Roberts' True Stories)						

	GD 2.0	VG 4.0	FN 6.0	VF 8.0	VF/NM 9.0	NM- 9.2
Oral Roberts Evangelistic Assn.: No. 120, Aug, 1959 - V3#12, Dec, 1961						
120(#1)	4	8	12	25	40	55
2(9/59)	3	6	9	17	26	35
3-12(7/60)	2	4	6	13	18	22
V2#1(8/60)-5(12/60)	2	4	6	9	13	16
V3#1(1/61)-12	2	4	6	8	10	12
JUNIOR TREASURY (See Dell Junior...)						
JUNIOR WOODCHUCKS GUIDE (Walt Disney's...)						
Danbury Press: 1973 (8-3/4"x5-3/4", 214 pgs., hardcover)						
nn-Illustrated text based on the long-standing J.W. Guide used by Donald Duck's nephews Huey, Dewey & Louie by Carl Barks. The guidebook was a popular plot device to enable the nephews to solve problems facing their uncle or Scrooge McDuck (scarce)	5	10	15	31	53	75
JUNIOR WOODCHUCKS LIMITED SERIES (Walt Disney's...)						
W. D. Publications (Disney): July, 1991 - No. 4, Oct, 1991 ($1.50, limited series; new & reprint-a)						
1-The Beagle Boys app.; Barks-r	1	3	4	6	8	10
2-4						4.00
JUNIOR WOODCHUCKS (See Huey, Dewey & Louie...)						
JUNKYARD JOE						
Image Comics (Mad Ghost): Oct, 2022 - Present ($4.99/$3.99)						
1-Junkyard Joe in 1972 Vietnam War; Geoff Johns-s/Gary Frank-a; multiple covers						5.00
2-5-Jumps to modern times; focus on Muddy Davis						4.00
JUPITER'S CIRCLE (Prequel to Jupiter's Legacy)						
Image Comics: Apr, 2015 - No. 6, Sept, 2015 ($3.50/$3.99)						
1-6-Mark Millar-s/Frank Quitely-a/c. 1-Three covers. 1-3,6-Torres-a. 4,5-Gianfelice-a						4.00
Volume 2 (11/15 - No. 6, 5/16) 1-6-Covers by Quitely & Sienkiewicz. 1,2,6-Torres-a. 3-5-Spouse-a						4.00
JUPITER'S LEGACY						
Image Comics: Apr, 2013 - No. 5, Jan, 2015 ($2.99/$4.99)						
1-4-Mark Millar-s/Frank Quitely-a/c						3.00
1-Variant-c by Hitch						4.00
5-($4.99) Covers by Hitch and Fegredo; bonus pin-ups and cosplay photos						5.00
1-Studio Edition (12/13, $4.99) Quitely's B&W art and Millar's script; design art						5.00
JUPITER'S LEGACY REQUIEM						
Image Comics: Jun, 2021 - No. 6, Dec, 2021 ($5.99/$3.99)						
1,6-($5.99)-Mark Millar-s. 1-Edwards-a. 6-Matt Smith-a						6.00
2-5-($3.99) 2-4-Edwards-a. 5-Matt Smith-a						4.00
JUPITER'S LEGACY 2						
Image Comics: Jan, 2016 - No. 5, Jul, 2017 ($3.99)						
1-5-Mark Millar-s/Frank Quitely-a/c						4.00
JURASSIC LEAGUE						
DC Comics: Jul, 2022 - No. 6 ($3.99, limited series)						
1-5-Gedeon & Johnson-s/Gedeon-a; Justice League as dinosaurs in prehistoric era						4.00
JURASSIC PARK						
Topps Comics: June, 1993 - No. 4, Aug, 1993; No. 5, Oct, 1994 - No. 10, Feb, 1995						
1-($2.50)-Newsstand Edition; Kane/Perez-a in all; 1-4: movie adaptation	2	4	6	10	14	18
1-($2.95)-Collector's Ed.; polybagged w/3 cards	3	6	9	14	20	25
1-Amberchrome Edition w/no price or ads	8	16	24	54	102	150
2-4-($2.50)-Newsstand Edition						5.00
2,3-($2.95)-Collector's Ed.; polybagged w/3 cards	1	3	4	6	8	10
4-10: 4-($2.95)-Collector's Ed.; polybagged w/1 of 4 different action hologram trading card; Gil Kane/Pérez-a. 5-becomes Advs. of						5.00
Annual 1 ($3.95, 5/95)	1	3	4	6	8	10
Trade paperback (1993, $9.95)-r/#1-4; bagged w/#0	3	6	9	14	20	25
JURASSIC PARK						
IDW Publishing: Jun, 2010 - No. 5, Oct, 2010 ($3.99, limited series)						
1-5: Takes place 13 years after the first movie; Schreck-s. 1-Covers by Yeates & Miller						5.00
JURASSIC PARK: DANGEROUS GAMES						
IDW Publishing: Sept, 2011 - No. 5, Jan, 2012 ($3.99, limited series)						
1-5-Erik Bear-s/Jorge Jimenez-a, 1-Covers by Darrow & Zornow						4.00
JURASSIC PARK: RAPTOR						
Topps Comics: Nov, 1993 - No. 2, Dec, 1993 ($2.95, limited series)						
1,2: 1-Bagged w/3 trading cards & Zorro #0; Golden c-1,2						6.00
JURASSIC PARK: RAPTORS ATTACK						

Topps Comics: Mar, 1994 - No. 4, June, 1994 ($2.50, limited series)
1-4-Michael Golden-c/frontispiece 6.00

JURASSIC PARK: RAPTORS HIJACK
Topps Comics: July, 1994 - No. 4, Oct, 1994 ($2.50, limited series)
1-4: Michael Golden-c/frontispiece 5.00

JURASSIC PARK: THE DEVILS IN THE DESERT
IDW Publishing: Jan, 2011 - No. 4, Apr, 2011 ($3.99, limited series)
1-4-John Byrne-s/a/c 4.00

JUST A PILGRIM
Black Bull Entertainment: May, 2001 - No. 5, Sept, 2001 ($2.99)
Limited Preview Edition (12/00, $7.00) Ennis & Ezquerra interviews 7.00
1-Ennis-s/Ezquerra-a; two covers by Texeira & JG Jones 3.00
2-5: 2-Fabry-c. 3-Nowlan-c. 4-Sienkiewicz-c 3.00
TPB (11/01, $12.99) r/#1-5; Waid intro. 13.00

JUST A PILGRIM: GARDEN OF EDEN
Black Bull Entertainment: May, 2002 - No. 4, Aug, 2002 ($2.99, limited series)
Limited Preview Ed. (1/02, $7.00) Ennis & Ezquerra interviews; Jones-c 7.00
1-4-Ennis-s/Ezquerra-a 3.00
TPB (11/02, $12.99) r/#1-4; Gareb Shamus intro. 13.00

JUSTICE
Marvel Comics Group (New Universe): Nov, 1986 - No. 32, June, 1989
1-32: 26-32-$1.50-c (low print run) 3.00

JUSTICE
DC Comics: Oct, 2005 - No. 12, Aug, 2007 ($2.99/$3.50/$3.99, bi-monthly maxi-series)
1-Classic Justice League vs. The Legion of Doom; Alex Ross & Doug Braithwaite-a; Jim Krueger-s; two covers by Ross; Ross sketch pages 5.00
1-2nd & 3rd printings 4.00
2-($3.50) 4.00
2 (2nd printing), 3-11-($3.50) 3.50
12-($3.99) Two covers (Heroes & Villains) 4.00
Absolute Justice HC (2009, $99.99, slipcased book with dustjacket) oversized r/#1-12; afterwords by creators; Ross sketch and design art; photo gallery of action figures 100.00
HC (2011, $39.99, dustjacket) r/#1-12 40.00
... Volume One HC (2006, $19.99, dustjacket) r/#1-4; Krueger intro.; sketch pages 20.00
... Volume One SC (2008, $14.99) r/#1-4; Krueger intro.; sketch pages 15.00
... Volume Two HC (2007, $19.99, dustjacket) r/#5-8; Krueger intro.; sketch pages 20.00
... Volume Two SC (2008, $14.99) r/#5-8; Krueger intro.; sketch pages 15.00
... Volume Three HC (2007, $19.99, dustjacket) r/#9-12; Ross intro.; sketch pages 20.00
... Volume Three SC (2007, $14.99) r/#9-12; Ross intro.; sketch pages 15.00

JUSTICE COMICS (Formerly Wacky Duck; Tales of Justice #53 on)
Marvel/Atlas Comics (NPP 7-9,4-19/CnPC 20-23/MjMC 24-38/Male 39-52:
No. 7, Fall/47 - No. 9, 6/48; No. 4, 8/48 - No. 52, 3/55

	GD 2.0	VG 4.0	FN 6.0	VF 8.0	VF/NM 9.0	NM- 9.2
7(#1, 1947)	43	86	129	271	461	650
8(#2)-Kurtzman-a "Giggles 'n' Grins" (3)	29	58	87	172	281	390
9(#3, 6/48)	24	48	72	142	234	325
4	21	42	63	122	199	275
5(9/48)-9: 8-Anti-Wertham editorial	19	38	57	111	176	240
10-15-Photo-c	16	32	48	92	144	195
16-30	15	30	45	86	133	180
31-40,42-52: 35-Gene Colan-a. 48-Last precode; Pakula & Tuska-a. 50-Ayers-a	15	30	45	84	127	170
41-Electrocution-c	28	56	84	165	270	375

NOTE: ***Hartley** a-48. **Heath** a-24. **Maneely** c-44, 52. **Pakula** a-43, 45, 47, 48. **Louis Ravielli** a-39, 47. **Robinson** a-22, 25, 28, 41. **Sale** c-45. **Shores** c-7(#1), 8(#2)? **Tuska** a-41, 48. **Wildey** a-52.*

JUSTICE: FOUR BALANCE
Marvel Comics: Sept, 1994 - No. 4, Dec, 1994 ($1.75, limited series)
1-4: 1-Thing & Firestar app. 3.00

JUSTICE, INC. (The Avenger) (Pulp)
National Periodical Publications: May-June, 1975 - No. 4, Nov-Dec, 1975

	GD 2.0	VG 4.0	FN 6.0	VF 8.0	VF/NM 9.0	NM- 9.2
1-McWilliams-a, Kubert-c; origin	2	4	6	11	16	20
2-4: 2-4-Kirby-a(p), c-2,3p. 4-Kubert-c	2	4	6	11	16	20

NOTE: *Adapted from Kenneth Robeson novel, creator of Doc Savage.*

JUSTICE, INC. (Pulp)
DC Comics: 1989 - No. 2, 1989 ($3.95, 52 pgs., squarebound, mature)
1,2: Re-intro The Avenger; Andrew Helfer scripts & Kyle Baker-c/a 5.00

JUSTICE, INC. (Pulp)
Dynamite Entertainment: 2014 - No. 6, 2015 ($3.99/$5.99)
1-5-The Shadow, Doc Savage and The Avenger app; Uslan-s/Timpano-a; multiple covers 4.00
6-($5.99) Covers by Ross, Francavilla, Hardman and Syaf 6.00

JUSTICE, INC.: THE AVENGER (Pulp)
Dynamite Entertainment: 2015 - No. 6, 2015 ($3.99)
1-6: 1-Waid-s/Freire-a; multiple covers incl. 1975 series #1 cover swipe by Ross 4.00

JUSTICE, INC.: THE AVENGER VOLUME 1 (Pulp)
Dynamite Entertainment: 2017 - No. 4, 2017 ($3.99)
1-4-Higgins & Gentile-s/Shibao-a. 1-Covers by Mandrake & Shibao 4.00

JUSTICE LEAGUE (...International #7-25; ...America #26 on)
DC Comics: May, 1987 - No. 113, Aug, 1996 (Also see Legends #6)

	GD 2.0	VG 4.0	FN 6.0	VF 8.0	VF/NM 9.0	NM- 9.2
1-Batman, Green Lantern (Guy Gardner), Blue Beetle, Mr. Miracle, Capt. Marvel & Martian Manhunter begin; 1st app. Maxwell Lord	3	6	9	15	22	28
2,3: 3-Regular-c (white background)						6.00
3-Limited-c (yellow background, Superman logo)	5	10	15	30	50	70

4-6,8-10: 4-Booster Gold joins. 5-Origin Gray Man; Batman vs. Guy Gardner; Creeper app. 9,10-Millennium x-over 5.00
7-($1.25, 52 pgs.)-Capt. Marvel & Dr. Fate resign; Capt. Atom & Rocket Red join 6.00
11-17,22,23,25-49,51-68,71-82: 16-Bruce Wayne-c/story. 31,32-J. L. Europe x-over. 58-Lobo app. 61-New team begins; swipes-c to J.L. of A. #1('60). 70-Newsstand version w/o outer-c. 71-Direct sales version w/black outer-c. 71-Newsstand version w/o outer-c. 80-Intro new Booster Gold. 82,83-Guy Gardner-c/stories 4.00
18-21,24,50: 18-21-Lobo app. 24-($1.50)-1st app. Justice League Europe. 50-($1.75, 52 pgs.) 5.00

	GD 2.0	VG 4.0	FN 6.0	VF 8.0	VF/NM 9.0	NM- 9.2
69-Doomsday tie-in; takes place between Superman: The Man of Steel #18 & Superman #74	2	4	6	10	14	18

69,70-2nd printings 3.00
70-Funeral for a Friend part 1; red 3/4 outer-c 5.00
83-99,101-113: 92-(9/94)-Zero Hour x-over; Triumph app. 113-Green Lantern, Flash & Hawkman app. 4.00
100 ($3.95)-Foil-c; 52 pgs. 5.00
100 ($2.95)-Newstand 4.00
#0-(10/94) Zero Hour (published between #92 & #93); new team begins (Hawkman, Flash, Wonder Woman, Metamorpho, Nuklon, Crimson Fox, Obsidian & Fire) 4.00
Annual 1-8,10 ('87-'94, '96, 68 pgs.): 2-Joker-c/story; Batman cameo. 5-Armageddon 2001 x-over; Silver ink 2nd print. 7-Bloodlines x-over. 8-Elseworlds story. 10-Legends of the Dead Earth 5.00
Annual 9 (1995, $3.50)-Year One story 5.00
Special 1,2 ('90,'91, 52 pgs.): 1-Giffen plots. 2-Staton-a(p) 5.00
Spectacular 1 (1992, $1.50, 52 pgs.)-Intro new JLI & JLE teams; ties into JLI #61 & JLE #37; two interlocking covers by Jurgens 5.00
A New Beginning Trade Paperback (1989, $12.95)-r/#1-7 13.00
... International Vol. 1 HC (2008, $24.99) r/#1-7; new intro. by Giffen 25.00
... International Vol. 1 SC (2009, $17.99) r/#1-7; new intro. by Giffen 18.00
... International Vol. 2 HC (2008, $24.99) r/#8-13, Annual #1 and Suicide Squad #13 25.00
... International Vol. 2 SC (2009, $17.99) r/#8-13, Annual #1 and Suicide Squad #13 18.00
... International Vol. 3 SC (2009, $19.99) r/#14-22 20.00
... International Vol. 4 SC (2010, $17.99) r/#23-30 18.00
... International Vol. 5 SC (2011, $19.99) r/#Annual #2,3 & Justice League Europe #1-6 20.00
... International Vol. 6 SC (2011, $24.99) r/#31-35 & Justice League Europe #7-11 25.00
NOTE: ***Anderson** c-61i. **Austin** a-1i, 60i; c-1i. **Giffen** a-13; c-21p. **Guice** a-62i. **Maguire** a-1-12, 16-19, 22, 23. **Russell** a-Annual 1i; c-54i. **Willingham** a-30p, Annual 2.*

JUSTICE LEAGUE (DC New 52)
DC Comics: Oct, 2011 - No. 52, Aug, 2016 ($3.99)

	GD 2.0	VG 4.0	FN 6.0	VF 8.0	VF/NM 9.0	NM- 9.2
1-Johns-s/Jim Lee-a/c; Batman, Green Lantern & Superman app.; orange background-c	2	4	6	13	18	22
1-Combo-Pack edition ($4.99) polybagged with digital download code; blue background-c	1	3	4	6	8	10

1-Variant-c by Finch 25.00
1-Second printing 25.00
2-11,13-23: 3-Wonder Woman & Aquaman arrive. 4-Darkseid arrives. 6-Pandora back-up. 7-Gene Ha-a; back-up Shazam origin begins; Frank-a. 8-D'Anda-a. 13,14-Cheetah app. 15-17-Throne of Atlantis. 22,23-Trinity War. 23-Crime Syndicate arrives 4.00
12-Superman/Wonder Woman kiss-c 4.00
23.1, 23.2, 23.3, 23.4 (11/13, $2.99, regular-c) 3.00
23.1 (11/13, $3.99, 3-D cover) "Darkseid #1" on cover; origin; Kaiyo app.; Reis-c 5.00
23.2 (11/13, $3.99, 3-D cover) "Lobo #1" on cover; Bennett-s/Oliver-a/Kuder-c 5.00
23.3 (11/13, $3.99, 3-D cover) "Dial E #1" on cover; Miéville-s; art by various 5.00
23.4 (11/13, $3.99, 3-D cover) "Secret Society #1" on cover; Owlman app.; Kudranski-a 5.00
24-29-Forever Evil. 24-Origin of Ultraman. 25-Origin of Owlman. 27-Cyborg upgraded. 28,29-Metal Men return 4.00
30-39: 30-Lex Luthor app.; intro Jessica Cruz. 31-33-Doom Patrol app. 33-Luthor joins. 35-Amazo virus unleashed; intro Lena Luthor 4.00
40-Darkseid War prologue, continues in DC's 2015 FCBD edition; intro. Grail (cameo) 4.00
41-($4.99) Darkseid War pt 1; Mister Miracle & the Anti-Monitor app.; intro Myrina Black 5.00
42-49-Darkseid War; Darkseid vs. the Anti-Monitor. 45,46-Manapul-a 4.00
48-Coloring Book variant-c by Kolins 4.00

	GD 2.0	VG 4.0	FN 6.0	VF 8.0	VF/NM 9.0	NM- 9.2
50-($5.99) Conclusion to Darkseid War; Jessica Cruz becomes a Green Lantern; first mention of the "3 Jokers"	3	6	9	14	20	25

51,52: 51-Flashback with Robin; Pelletier-a. Lex Luthor as Superman; Grummett-a 4.00
#0-(11/12, $3.99) Origin of Shazam; back-up with Pandora 4.00
...: Darkseid War: Batman (12/15, $3.99) Pasarin-a; Batman on Mobius chair; Joe Chill app. 4.00
...: Darkseid War: Flash (1/16, $3.99) Merino-a; Flash vs. the Black Racer 4.00
...: Darkseid War: Green Lantern (1/16, $3.99) Shaner-a; Hal Jordan becomes God of Light 4.00
...: Darkseid War: Lex Luthor (2/16, $3.99) Dazo-a; The God of Apocalypse 4.00
...: Darkseid War: Shazam (1/16, $3.99) Kolins-a 4.00
...: Darkseid War Special (6/16, $3.99) Reis, Jimenez & Pelletier-a; Grail's origin 4.00
...: Darkseid War: Superman (1/16, $3.99) Dazo-a; The God of Steel 4.00
...: Futures End 1 (11/14, $2.99, regular-c) Cont'd from Justice League United: FE #1 3.00
...: Futures End 1 (11/14, $3.99, 3-D cover) 4.00
...: Trinity War Director's Cut 1 (10/13, $5.99) r/#22 pencil art and script 6.00

JUSTICE LEAGUE (DC Rebirth)
DC Comics: Sept, 2016 - No. 43, Jun, 2018 ($2.99)
1-11: 1-Hitch-s/Daniel-a. 4-Merino-a. 6-Clark & Derenick-a. 11-Amazo app. 3.00
1 Director's Cut (12/16, $5.99) r/#1 with B&W art; original script; variant cover gallery 6.00
12-24,26-43: 12,13: Justice League vs. Suicide Squad tie-ins. 12-Max Lord returns. 20,21-Hitch-a. 24-Mera app. 26-Intro. Justice League's children. 32,33-Dark Nights: Metal 41-43-Deathstroke app. 3.00
25-($3.99) Hitch-s/Derenick-a; Mera app. 4.00
... Day Special Edition 1 (1/18, giveaway) r/Justice League #1 (2011) new Reis-c 3.00
...: Rebirth 1 (9/16, $2.99) Hitch-s/a; pre-New 52 Superman joins 3.00

JUSTICE LEAGUE (Follows Justice League: No Justice series)
DC Comics: Early Aug, 2018 - No. 75, Jun, 2022 ($3.99/$4.99)
1-24: 1-Snyder-s/Cheung-a; Legion of Doom app. 2-4-Jimenez-a. 5-Tynion IV-s/Mahnke-a. 7,8-Batman Who Laughs and Starman (Will Payton) app. 10,11-Manapul-a. 11,12-Drowned Earth x-over with Aquaman. 19-24-Mr. Mxyzptlk app. 4.00
25-($4.99) Year of the Villain prelude 5.00
26-49,51-58: 27-Amazo app. 30-37-Kamandi and the JSA app. 40-42-Madame Xanadu app. 45-The Spectre app. 48,49-Spurrier-s. 53-57-Death Metal tie-ins. 58-Endless Winter 4.00
50-($5.99) Conclusion of "The Rule of War"; Lopresti-a 6.00
59-74-($4.99): 59-Bendis-s/Marquez-a begins; Naomi app.; back-up JL Dark in all 5.00
75-($6.99) Death of the Justice League; acetate outer cover; prelude to Dark Crisis #1 7.00
Annual 1 (3/19, $4.99) New Gods & Green Lantern Corps app.; Sampere-a/Paquette-c 5.00
Annual 2 (11/20, $4.99) JLA vs. The Hall of Justice; Venditti-s/Lopresti-a 5.00
2022 Annual 1 (4/22, $5.99) Bendis-s/Sanford Greene-a; OMAC app. 6.00
... /Aquaman: Drowned Earth 1 (12/18, $4.99) Porter-a; continues in Justice League #11 5.00
...: Road to Dark Crisis 1 (7/22, $5.99) Follows events of Justice League #75 6.00

Justice #9 © DC

Justice League (2018) #1 © DC

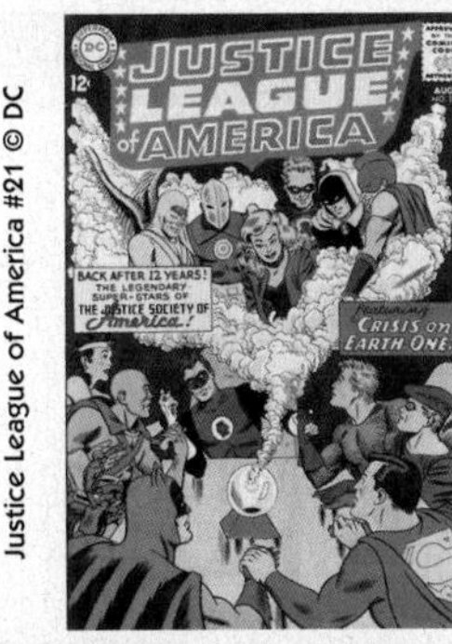

Justice League of America #21 © DC

GD VG FN VF VF/NM NM-
2.0 4.0 6.0 8.0 9.0 9.2

GD VG FN VF VF/NM NM-
2.0 4.0 6.0 8.0 9.0 9.2

JUSTICE LEAGUE ADVENTURES (Based on Cartoon Network series)
DC Comics: Jan, 2002 - No. 34, Oct, 2004 ($1.99/$2.25)

1-Timm & Ross-c 4.00
2-32: 3-Nicieza-s. 5-Starro app. 10-Begin $2.25-c. 14-Includes 16 pg. insert for VERB with Haberlin CG-art. 15,29-Amancio-a. 16-McCloud-s. 20-Psycho Pirate app. 25,26-Adam Strange-c/app. 28-Legion of Super-Heroes app. 30-Kamandi app. 3.00
Free Comic Book Day giveaway - (5/02) r/#1 with "Free Comic Book Day" banner on-c 3.00
TPB (2003, $9.95) r/#1,3,6,10-13; Timm/Ross-c from #1 10.00
...Vol. 1: The Magnificent Seven (2004, $6.95) digest-size reprints #3,6,10-12 7.00
...Vol. 2: Friends and Foes (2004, $6.95) digest-size reprints #13,14,16,19,20 7.00

JUSTICE LEAGUE: A MIDSUMMER'S NIGHTMARE
DC Comics: Sept, 1996 - No. 3, Nov, 1996 ($2.95, limited series, 38 pgs.)

1-3: Re-establishes Superman, Batman, Green Lantern, The Martian Manhunter, Flash, Aquaman & Wonder Woman as the Justice League; Mark Waid & Fabian Nicieza co-scripts; Jeff Johnson & Darick Robertson-a(p); Kevin Maguire-c 5.00
TPB-(1997, $8.95) r/1-3 9.00

JUSTICE LEAGUE: CRY FOR JUSTICE
DC Comics: Sept, 2009 - No. 7, Apr, 2010 ($3.99, limited series)

1-7-James Robinson-s/Mauro Cascioli-a/c. 1-Two covers; Congorilla origin 4.00
HC (2010, $24.99, d.j.) r/#1-7, Face of Evil: Prometheus 25.00
SC (2011, $19.99) r/#1-7, Face of Evil: Prometheus 20.00

JUSTICE LEAGUE DARK (DC New 52)
DC Comics: Nov, 2011 - No. 40, May, 2015 ($2.99/$3.99)

1-23: 1-Milligan-s; Deadman, Madame Xanadu, Zatanna, Shade, John Constantine app. 7,8-Crossover with I,Vampire #6,7. 7-Batgirl app. 9-Black Orchid joins. 11,12-Tim Hunter app. 13-Leads into J.L. Dark Annual #1. 19-21-Flash app. 22,23-Trinity War 3.00
23.1, 23.2 (11/13, $2.99, regular-c) 3.00
23.1 (11/13, $3.99, 3-D cover) "The Creeper #1" on cover; origin; Nocenti-s/Janin-c 5.00
23.2 (11/13, $3.99, 3-D cover) "Eclipso #1" on cover; origin; Tan-a/Janin-c 5.00
24-40: 24-29-Forever Evil tie-ins. 40-Constantine returns 4.00
#0-(11/12, $2.99) Constantine and Zatanna's 1st meeting; Garbett-a/Sook-c 3.00
Annual #1 (12/12, $4.99) Continued from #13; Frankenstein & Amethyst app. 5.00
Annual #2 (12/14, $4.99) Janson-a/March-c; House of Wonders app. 5.00
...: Futures End 1 (11/14, $2.99, regular-c) Five years later; Etrigan app. 3.00
...: Futures End 1 (11/14, $3.99, 3-D cover) 4.00

JUSTICE LEAGUE DARK (See back-up stories in Justice League #59-70)
DC Comics: Sept, 2018 - No. 29, Feb, 2021 ($3.99)

1-12: 1-Tynion IV-s; Wonder Woman, Zatanna, Swamp Thing, Detective Chimp app. 4.00
13-29: 13-18-Year of The Villain tie-ins. 13-Buckingham-a; origin Dr. Fate. 20-23-Animal Man app. 20,23-Hotz-a. 29-Endless Winter part 7 4.00
Annual 1 (9/19, $4.99) Jason Woodrue and Circe app. 5.00
2021 Annual 1 (1/22, $5.99) Ram V & Watters-s/Mitten-a; Yuga Khan & Merlin app. 6.00
... and Wonder Woman: The Witching Hour 1 (12/18, $4.99) Black Orchid app.; Merino-a 5.00

JUSTICE LEAGUE ELITE (See JLA #100 and JLA Secret Files 2004)
DC Comics: Sept, 2004 - No. 12, Aug, 2005 ($2.50)

1-12-Flash, Green Arrow, Vera Black and others; Kelly-s/Mahnke-a. 5,6-JSA app. 3.00
JL Elite TPB (2005, $19.99) r/#1-4, Action #775, JLA #100, JLA Secret Files 2004 20.00
... Vol. 2 TPB (2007, $19.99) r/#5-12 20.00

JUSTICE LEAGUE EUROPE (Justice League International #51 on)
DC Comics: Apr, 1989 - No. 68, Sept., 1994 (75¢/ $1.00/$1.25/$1.50)

1-Giffen plots in all, breakdowns in #1-8,13-30; Justice League #1-c/swipe 5.00
2-10: 7-9-Batman app. 7,8-JLA x-over. 8,9-Superman app. 4.00
11-49: 12-Metal Men app. 20-22-Rogers-c/a(p). 33,34-Lobo vs. Despero. 37-New team begins; swipes-c to JLA #9; see JLA Spectacular 4.00
50-($2.50, 68 pgs.)-Battles Sonar 4.00
51-68: 68-Zero Hour x-over; Triumph joins Justice League Task Force (See JLTF #17) 3.00
Annual 1-5 ('90-'94, 68 pgs.)-1-Return of the Global Guardians; Giffen plots/breakdowns. 2-Armageddon 2001; Giffen-a(p); Rogers-a(p); Golden-a(i). 5-Elseworlds story 5.00
NOTE: *Phil Jimenez a-68p. Rogers c/a-20-22. Sears a-1-12, 14-19, 23-29; c-1-10, 12, 14-19, 23-29.*

JUSTICE LEAGUE: GENERATION LOST (Brightest Day)
DC Comics: Early July, 2010 - No. 24, Early Jun, 2011 ($2.99, bi-weekly limited series)

1-23: 1-Maxwell Lord's return; Winick & Giffen-s. 1-5,7-Harris-c. 13-Magog killed 3.00
24-($4.99) Wonder Woman vs. Omac Prime; Lopresti-a/Nguyen-c 5.00
... Volume One HC (2010, $39.99, dustjacket) r/#1-12; cover gallery 40.00

JUSTICE LEAGUE GIANT (See Wonder Woman Giant #1 for continued JL & Aquaman)
(See reprint of new stories in Wonder Woman: Come Back to Me)
DC Comics: 2018 - No. 7, 2019 ($4.99, 100 pgs., squarebound, Walmart exclusive)

1-New Wonder Woman story Seeley-s/Leonardi-a; reprints Justice League ('11), The Flash ('11), and Aquaman ('11) in all 8.00
2-7: 2-New WW by Seeley-s/Watanabe-a. 3-New WW by Palmiotti & Conner-s/Hardin-a begins. 4-7-Jonah Hex app. in new WW story 5.00

JUSTICE LEAGUE: GODS & MONSTERS (Tie-in to 2015 animated film)
DC Comics: Oct, 2015 - No. 3, Oct, 2015 ($3.99, weekly limited series)

1-3-DeMatteis & Timm-s/Silas-a; alternate Superman, Batman & Wonder Woman 4.00
... - Batman 1 (9/15, $3.99) origin of the Kirk Langstrom Batman; Matthew Dow Smith-a 4.00
... - Superman 1 (9/15, $3.99) origin of the Hernan Guerra Superman; Moritat-a 4.00
... - Wonder Woman 1 (9/15, $3.99) origin of Bekka of New Genesis; Leonardi-a 4.00

JUSTICE LEAGUE INCARNATE (Story continues in 2022's Justice League #75)
DC Comics: Jan, 2022 - No. 5, May, 2022 ($4.99, limited series)

1-5-Earth-23 Superman, Flashpoint Batman, Capt. Carrot, Doctor Multiverse app. 5.00

JUSTICE LEAGUE INFINITY (Style of the Justice League 2001 animated series)
DC Comics: Sept, 2021 - No. 7, Mar, 2022 ($3.99, limited series)

1-7: 1-Amazo returns. 2-Overman app. 3,4-Darkseid app. 5-7 Justice Alliance app. 4.00

JUSTICE LEAGUE INTERNATIONAL (See Justice League Europe)

JUSTICE LEAGUE INTERNATIONAL (DC New 52)
DC Comics: Nov, 2011 - No. 12, Oct, 2012 ($2.99)

1-12: 1-Jurgens-s/Lopresti-a/c; Batman, Booster Gold, Guy Gardner, Vixen, Fire, Ice. 8-Batwing joins; OMAC app. 3.00
Annual 1 (10/12, $4.99) Fabok-a/c; JLI vs. OMAC; Blue Beetle joins 5.00

JUSTICE LEAGUE: LAST RIDE
DC Comics: Jul, 2021 - No. 7, Jan, 2022 ($3.99, limited series)

1-7-Zdarsky-s/Mendonca-a; set in the future; Darkseid, Brainiac, Cyborg Superman app. 4.00

JUSTICE LEAGUE: NO JUSTICE
DC Comics: Jul, 2018 - No. 4, Jul, 2018 ($3.99, weekly limited series)

1-4: 1-Brainiac app.; Justice League, Teen Titans, Titans, Suicide Squad team ups. 1,2,4-Manapul-a. 2-Vril Dox app. 3-Rossmo-a 4.00

JUSTICE LEAGUE ODYSSEY
DC Comics: Nov, 2018 - No. 25, Dec, 2020 ($3.99)

1-10: 1-Williamson-s/Sejic-a; Cyborg, Starfire, Jessica Cruz and Azrael vs. Darkseid 4.00
11-25: 11-15-Year of The Villain tie-ins. 16-Intro Gamma Knife 4.00

JUSTICE LEAGUE OF AMERICA (See Brave & the Bold #28-30, Mystery In Space #75 & Official... Index) (See Crisis on Multiple Earths TPBs for reprints of JLA/JSA crossovers)
National Periodical Publ./DC Comics: Oct-Nov, 1960 - No. 261, Apr, 1987 (#91-99,139-157: 52 pgs.)

1-(10-11/60)-Origin & 1st app. Despero; Aquaman, Batman, Flash, Green Lantern, J'onn J'onzz, Superman & Wonder Woman continue from Brave and the Bold 650 1300 2600 8450 20,475 32,500
2 125 250 375 1000 2250 3500
3-Origin/1st app. Kanjar Ro (see Mystery in Space #75)(scarce in high grade due to black-c) 121 242 363 968 2184 3400
4-Green Arrow joins JLA 82 164 246 656 1478 2300
5-Origin & 1st app. Dr. Destiny 64 128 192 512 1156 1800
6-8,10: 6-Origin & 1st app. Prof. Amos Fortune. 7-(10-11/61)-Last 10¢ issue. 10-(3/62)-Origin & 1st app. Felix Faust; 1st app. Lord of Time 46 92 138 359 805 1250
9-(2/62)-Origin JLA (1st origin) 53 106 159 424 950 1475
11-15: 12-(6/62)-Origin & 1st app. Dr. Light. 13-(8/62)-Speedy app. 14-(9/62)-Atom joins JLA. 29 58 87 209 467 725
16-20: 17-Adam Strange flashback 24 48 72 168 372 575
21-(8/63)-"Crisis on Earth-One"; re-intro. of JSA in this title (see Flash #129) (1st S.A. app. Hourman & Dr. Fate) 54 108 162 432 966 1500
22- "Crisis on Earth-Two"; JSA x-over (story continued from #21) 38 76 114 285 641 1000
23-28: 24-Adam Strange app. 27-Robin app. 17 34 51 117 259 400
29-"Crisis on Earth-Three"; JSA x-over; 1st app. Crime Syndicate of America (Ultraman, Owlman, Superwoman, Power Ring, Johnny Quick); 1st S.A. app. Starman 36 72 108 259 580 900
30-JSA x-over; Crime Syndicate app. 20 40 60 138 307 475
31-Hawkman joins JLA, Hawkgirl cameo (11/64) 15 30 45 105 233 360
32,34: 32-Intro & Origin Brain Storm. 34-Joker-c/sty 11 22 33 72 154 235
33,35,36,40,41: 40-3rd S.A. Penguin app. 41-Intro & origin The Key 10 20 30 66 138 210
37-39: 37,38-JSA x-over. 37-1st S.A. app. Mr. Terrific; Batman cameo. 38-"Crisis on Earth-A". 39-Giant G-16; r/B&B #28,30 & JLA #5 12 24 36 83 182 280
42-45: 42-Metamorpho app. 43-Intro. Royal Flush Gang 8 16 24 56 108 160
46-JSA x-over; 1st S.A. app. Sandman; 3rd S.A. app. of G.A. Spectre (8/66) 14 28 42 96 211 325
47-JSA x-over; 4th S.A. app of G.A. Spectre. 10 20 30 66 138 210
48-Giant G-29; r/JLA #2,3 & B&B #29 9 18 27 59 117 175
49,50,52-54,57,59,60 7 14 21 46 86 125

	GD 2.0	VG 4.0	FN 6.0	VF 8.0	VF/NM 9.0	NM- 9.2
51-Zatanna app.	10	20	30	69	147	225
55-Intro. Earth 2 Robin (1st G.A. Robin in S.A.)	10	20	30	66	138	210
56-JLA vs. JSA (1st G.A. Wonder Woman in S.A.)	9	18	27	63	129	195
58-Giant G-41; r/JLA #6,8,1	9	18	27	57	111	165
61-63,66,68-72: 69-Wonder Woman quits. 71-Manhunter leaves. 72-Last 12¢ issue	5	10	15	35	63	90
64-(8/68)-JSA story; origin/1st app. S.A. Red Tornado	10	20	30	66	138	210
65-JSA story continues	6	12	18	38	69	100
67-Giant G-53; r/JLA #4,14,31	8	16	24	52	99	145
73-1st S.A. app. of G.A. Superman	8	16	24	51	96	140
74-Black Canary joins; Larry Lance dies; 1st meeting of G.A. & S.A. Superman; Neal Adams-c	10	20	30	67	141	215
75-2nd app. Green Arrow in new costume (see Brave & the Bold #85)	36	72	108	259	580	900
76-Giant G-65	6	12	18	42	79	115
77-80: 78-Re-intro Vigilante (1st S.A. app?)	4	8	12	28	47	65
81-90: 82-1st S.A. app. of G.A. Batman (cameo). 83-Apparent death of The Spectre. 87-Zatanna app. 90-Last 15¢ issue	4	8	12	27	44	60
91,92: 91-1st meeting of the G.A. & S.A. Robin; begin 25¢, 52 pgs. issues, ends #99. 92-S.A. Robin tries on costume that is similar to that of G.A. Robin in All Star Comics #58	4	8	12	28	47	65
93-(Giant G-77,G-89; 68 pgs.)	6	12	18	41	76	110
94-1st app. Merlyn (Green Arrow villain); reprints 1st Sandman story (Adv. #40) & origin/1st app. Starman (Adv. #61); Deadman x-over; N. Adams-a (4 pgs.)	8	16	24	54	102	150
95,96: 95-Origin Dr. Fate & Dr. Midnight -r/ More Fun #67, All-American #25). 96-Origin Hourman (Adv. #48); Wildcat-r	5	10	15	30	50	70
97-99: 97-Origin JLA retold; Sargon, Starman-r. 98-G.A. Sargon, Starman-r. 99-G.A. Sandman, Atom-r; last 52 pg. issue	4	8	12	27	44	60
100-(8/72)-1st meeting of G.A. & S.A. W. Woman	7	14	21	44	82	120
101,102: JSA x-overs. 102-Red Tornado destroyed	4	8	12	28	47	65
103-106,109: 103-Rutland Vermont Halloween x-over; Phantom Stranger joins. 105-Elongated Man joins. 106-New Red Tornado joins. 109-Hawkman resigns	3	6	9	19	30	40
107,108-JSA x-over; 1st revival app. of G.A. Uncle Sam, Black Condor, The Ray, Dollman, Phantom Lady & The Human Bomb	4	8	12	28	47	65
110,112-116: All 100 pgs. 112-Amazo app; Crimson Avenger, Vigilante-r; origin Starman-r/ Adv. #81. 115-Martian Manhunter app.	5	10	15	33	57	80
111-JLA vs. Injustice Gang; intro. Libra (re-appears in 2008's Final Crisis); Shining Knight, Green Arrow-r	5	10	15	34	60	85
117-122,125-134: 117-Hawkman rejoins. 120,121-Adam Strange app. 125,126-Two-Face-app. 128-Wonder Woman rejoins. 129-Destruction of Red Tornado	3	6	9	16	23	30
123-(10/75),124: JLA/JSA x-over. DC editor Julie Schwartz & JLA writers Cary Bates & Elliot S! Maggin appear in story as themselves. 1st named app. Earth-Prime (3rd app. after Flash; 1st Series #179 & 228)	3	6	9	21	33	45
135-136: 135-137-G.A. Bulletman, Bulletgirl, Spy Smasher, Mr. Scarlet, Pinky & Ibis x-over, 1st appearances since G.A.	3	6	9	17	26	35
137-(12/76) Superman battles G.A. Captain Marvel	5	10	15	33	57	80
138-Adam Strange app. w/c by Neal Adams; 1st app. Green Lantern of the 73rd Century	4	8	12	25	40	55
139-157: 139-157-(52 pgs.): 139-Adam Strange app. 144-Origin retold; origin J'onn J'onzz. 145-Red Tornado resurrected. 147,148-Legion of Super-Heroes x-over	2	4	6	10	14	18
158-160-(44 pgs.)	2	4	6	8	11	14
158,160-162,169,171,172,173,176,179,181-(Whitman variants; low print run, none show issue # on cover)	2	4	6	10	14	18
161-165,169-182: 161-Zatanna joins & new costume. 171,172-JSA x-over. 171-Mr. Terrific murdered. 178-Cover similar to #1; J'onn J'onzz app. 179-Firestorm joins. 181-Green Arrow leaves JLA	1	2	3	5	6	8
166-168- "Identity Crisis (2004)" precursor; JSA app. vs. Secret Society of Super-Villains	3	6	9	16	23	30
166-168-Whitman variants (no issue # on covers)	4	8	12	23	37	50
183-185-JSA/New Gods/Darkseid/Mr. Miracle x-over	2	4	6	10	14	18
186-194,198,199: 192,193-Real origin Red Tornado. 193-1st app. All-Star Squadron as free 16 pg. insert	1	2	3	5	6	8
195-197-JSA app. vs. Secret Society of Super-Villains	1	3	4	6	8	10
200 ($1.50, Anniversary issue, 76 pgs.)-JLA origin retold; Green Arrow rejoins; Bolland, Aparo, Giordano, Gil Kane, Infantino, Kubert-a; Pérez-c/a	2	4	6	9	12	15
201-206,209-243,246-259: 203-Intro/origin new Royal Flush Gang. 219,220-True origin Black Canary. 228-Re-intro Martian Manhunter. 228-230-War of the Worlds storyline; JLA Satellite destroyed by Martians. 233-Story cont'd from Annual #2. 243-Aquaman leaves. 250-Batman rejoins. 253-Origin Despero. 258-Death of Vibe. 258-261-Legends x-over						6.00
207,208-JSA, JLA, & All-Star Squadron team-up	1	2	3	5	6	8
244,245-Crisis x-over						6.00
260-Death of Steel	1	2	3	5	6	8
261-Last issue	1	3	4	6	8	10
Annual 1-3 ('83-'85), 2-Intro new J.L.A. (Aquaman, Martian Manhunter, Steel, Gypsy, Vixen, Vibe, Elongated Man & Zatanna). 3-Crisis x-over	1	2	3	5	6	8
... Hereby Elects (2006, $14.99, TPB) reprints issues where new members joined; JLofA #4,75,105,106,146,161,173 &174; roster of various incarnations; Ordway-c						15.00

NOTE: ***Neal Adams** c-63, 66, 67, 70, 74, 79, 81, 82, 86-89, 91, 92, 94, 96-98, 138, 139. **M. Anderson** c-1-4, 6, 7, 10, 12-14. **Aparo** a-200. **Austin** a-200i. **Baily** a-96r. **Bolland** a-200. **Buckler** c-158, 163, 164. **Burnley** r-94, 98, 99. **Greene** a-46-61i, 64-73i, 110i(r). **Grell** c-117, 122. **Kaluta** c-154p. **Gil Kane** a-200. **Krigstein** a-96(r/Sensation #84). **Kubert** a-200; c-72, 73. **Nino** a-228i, 230i. **Orlando** c-151i. **Perez** a-184-186p, 192-197p, 200p; c-184p, 186, 192-195, 196p, 197p, 199, 200, 201p, 202, 203-205p, 207-209, 212-215, 217, 219, 220. **Reinman** r-97. **Roussos** a-62i. **Sekowsky** a-37, 38, 44-63p, 110-112p(r); c-46-48p, 51p. **Sekowsky/Anderson** c-5, 8, 9, 11, 15. **B. Smith** c-185i. **Starlin** c-178-180, 183, 185p. **Staton** a-244p; c-157p, 244p. **Toth** r-110. **Tuska** a-153, 228p, 241-243p. JSA x-overs-21, 22, 29, 30, 37, 38, 46, 47, 55, 56, 64, 65, 73, 74, 82, 83, 91, 92, 100, 101, 102, 107, 108, 110, 113, 115, 123, 124, 135-137, 147, 148, 159, 160, 171, 172, 183-185, 195-197, 207-209, 219, 220, 231, 232, 244.*

JUSTICE LEAGUE OF AMERICA
DC Comics: No. 0, Sept, 2006 - No. 60, Oct, 2011 ($2.99/$3.99)

	NM- 9.2
0-Meltzer-s; history of the JLA; art by various incl. Lee, Giordano, Benes; Turner-c	5.00
0-Variant-c by Campbell	15.00
1-($3.99) Two interlocking covers by Benes; Benes-a	5.00
1-Variant-c by Turner	8.00
1-RRP Edition; sideways composite of both Benes covers	50.00
1-Second printing; Benes cover image between black bars	4.00
2-5-($2.99) Turner-c	4.00
2-5: Variant-c: 2-Jimenez. 3-Sprouse. 4-JG Jones. 5-Art Adams	5.00
6,7-($3.50) 6-JLA vs. Amazo; covers by Turner and Hughes. 7-Roster picked, new HQs; two Benes covers and Turner cover.	4.00
8-11,13-24,26-38-($2.99) 8-11-JLA/JSA team-up; covers by Turner & Jimenez. 10-Wally West returns. 13-Two covers. 13-15-Injustice Gang. 16-Tangent Flash. 20-Queen Bee app. 21-Libra app.; leads into Final Crisis #1. 35,36-Royal Flush Gang app. 38-Bagley-a begins	3.00
12-($3.50) Two Ross covers; origin retold with Wight-a; Benes-a	4.00
25-($3.99) McDuffie-s/art by various; Benes-c	4.00
39-49,51,52-($3.99) 39,40-Blackest Night. 41-New team; 2 covers. 44-48-Justice Society app. 44-Jade returns.	4.00
50-($4.99) Crime Syndicate app.; Bagley-a; wraparound-c by Van Sciver	5.00
50-Variant-c by Bagley, swipe of Quitely's JLA: Earth 2 cover	8.00
50-Variant-c by Jim Lee; swipe of Brave and the Bold #28 Starro cover	120.00
53-60-($2.99) 54-Booth-a; Eclipso returns. 55-Doomsday app.	3.00
... 80 Page Giant (11/09, $5.99) Anacleto-c; short stories by various; Ra's al Ghul app.	6.00
... 80 Page Giant 2011 (6/11, $5.99) Lau-c; chapters by various; JLA goes to Hell	6.00
Free Comic Book Day giveaway - (2007) r/#0 with "Free Comic Book Day" banner on-c	3.00
Justice League Wedding Special 1 (11/07, $3.99) McKone-a; Injustice League forms	4.00
...: Dark Things HC (2011, $24.99, dustjacket) r/#44-48 & J.S.A. #41,42	25.00
...: The Injustice Gang HC (2008, $19.99, dustjacket) r/#13-16; Wedding Special	20.00
...: The Lightning Saga HC (2008, $24.99, dustjacket) r/#0,8-12 & Justice Society of America #5,6; intro. by Patton Oswalt	25.00
...: The Lightning Saga SC (2008, $17.99) r/#0,8-12 & J.S.A. #5,6; intro. by Oswalt	18.00
...: Sanctuary SC (2009, $14.99) r/#17-21	15.00
...: Second Coming HC (2009, $19.99, dustjacket) r/#22-26	20.00
...: Second Coming SC (2010, $17.99) r/#22-26	18.00
...: Team History HC (2010, $19.99, dustjacket) r/#38-43	20.00
...: The Tornado's Path HC (2007, $24.99, dustjacket) r/#1-7; variant cover gallery; Lindelof intro.; commentary by Meltzer & Benes	25.00
...: The Tornado's Path SC (2008, $17.99) r/#1-7; variant cover gallery; Lindelof intro.; commentary by Meltzer & Benes	18.00
...: When Worlds Collide HC (2009, $24.99, dustjacket) r/#27,28,30-34	25.00
...: When Worlds Collide SC (2010, $14.99) r/#27,28,30-34	15.00

JUSTICE LEAGUE OF AMERICA (DC New 52)(Leads into Justice League United)
DC Comics: Apr, 2013 - No. 14, Jul, 2014 ($3.99)

	NM- 9.2
1-14: 1-Johns-s/Finch-a/c; Green Arrow, Catwoman, Martian Manhunter, Katana & others team; variant covers with U.S. flag and each of the 50 state flags plus DC and Puerto Rico. 2-Covers by Finch and Ryp. 3-7: 3-5-Martian Manhunter back-up. 4,5-Shaggy Man app. 6,7-Trinity War. 8-14-Forever Evil. 10-Stargirl origin. 11,12-Despero app.	4.00
7.1, 7.2, 7.3, 7.4 (11/13, $2.99, regular-c)	3.00
7.1 (11/13, $3.99, 3-D cover) "Deadshot #1" on cover; origin; Kindt-s/Daniel-c	5.00
7.2 (11/13, $3.99, 3-D cover) "Killer Frost #1" on cover; origin; Gates-s/Santacruz-a	5.00
7.3 (11/13, $3.99, 3-D cover) "Shadow Thief #1" on cover; origin; Hardin-a/Daniel-c	5.00
7.4 (11/13, $3.99, 3-D cover) "Black Adam #1" on cover; Black Adam returns	5.00

JUSTICE LEAGUE OF AMERICA
DC Comics: Aug, 2015 - No. 10, Jan, 2017 ($5.99/$3.99)

	NM- 9.2
1-($5.99) Bryan Hitch-s/a; the Parasite app.	6.00
2-10-($3.99) 2-4-Hitch-s/a. 5-Martian Manhunter spotlight; Kindt & Williams-s/Tan-a	4.00

JUSTICE LEAGUE OF AMERICA (DC Rebirth)
DC Comics: Apr, 2017 - No. 29, Jun, 2018 ($2.99)

	NM- 9.2
1-24,26-29: 1-Orlando-s/Reis-a; team of Batman, Black Canary, Lobo, Vixen, Killer Frost, The Atom & The Ray; Lord Havok app. 14-17-Ray Palmer app. 18-20-Prometheus app. 21-Intro new Aztek. 22-24-Queen of Fables app. 23,24-Promethea app.	3.00
25-($3.99) Lord Havok app.	4.00
Annual 1 (1/18, $4.99) Lobo & Black Canary team-up; Kelley Jones-a	5.00
...: Killer Frost - Rebirth 1 (3/17, $2.99) Orlando-s/Andolfo-a; Amanda Waller app.	3.00
...: Rebirth 1 (4/17, $2.99) Orlando-s/Reis-a; team assembles	3.00
...: The Atom - Rebirth 1 (3/17, $2.99) Orlando-s; Ryan Choi as the new Atom	3.00
...: The Ray - Rebirth 1 (3/17, $2.99) Orlando-s; Stephen Byrne-a; origin	3.00
...: Vixen - Rebirth 1 (3/17, $2.99) Orlando & Houser-s; Jamal Campbell-a; origin retold	3.00

JUSTICE LEAGUE OF AMERICA : ANOTHER NAIL (Elseworlds) (Also see JLA: The Nail)
DC Comics: 2004 - No. 3, 2004 ($5.95, prestige format)

	NM- 9.2
1-3-Sequel to JLA: The Nail; Alan Davis-s/a(p)	6.00
TPB (2004, $12.95) r/series	13.00

JUSTICE LEAGUE OF AMERICA SUPER SPECTACULAR
DC Comics: 1999 ($5.95, mimics format of DC 100 Page Super Spectaculars)

	NM- 9.2
1-Reprints Silver Age JLA and Golden Age JSA	6.00

JUSTICE LEAGUE OF AMERICA'S VIBE (DC New 52)
DC Comics: Apr, 2013 - No. 10, Feb, 2014 ($2.99)

	NM- 9.2
1-10: 1,2-Johns & Kreisberg-s/Woods-a/Finch-c; origin. 5-Suicide Squad app.	3.00

JUSTICE LEAGUE OF AMERICA/ THE 99
DC Comics: Dec, 2010 - No. 6, May, 2011 ($3.99/$2/99, limited series)

	NM- 9.2
1-3-($3.99) Derenick-a/Massaferra-c; JLA meets Teshkeel Comics characters	4.00
4-6-($2.99) Starro app.	3.00

JUSTICE LEAGUE/ POWER RANGERS
DC Comics: Mar, 2017 - No. 6, Nov, 2017 ($3.99, limited series)

	NM- 9.2
1-6-Tom Taylor-s/Stephen Byrne-a; Lord Zedd app.; Power Rangers in JLA dimension	4.00

JUSTICE LEAGUE QUARTERLY (...International Quarterly #6 on)
DC Comics: Winter, 1990-91 - No. 17, Winter, 1994 ($2.95/$3.50, 84 pgs.)

	NM- 9.2
1-12,14-17: 1-Intro The Conglomerate (Booster Gold, Praxis, Gypsy, Vapor, Echo, Maxi-Man, & Reverb); Justice League #1-c/swipe. 1,2-Giffen plots/breakdowns. 3-Giffen plot; 72 pgs. 4-Rogers/Russell-a in back-up. 5,6-Mark Waid scripts. 8,17-Global Guardians app.	4.00
13-Linsner-c	6.00

NOTE: ***Phil Jimenez** a-17p. **Sprouse** a-1p.*

JUSTICE LEAGUE: RISE AND FALL
DC Comics: 2010, 2011

	NM- 9.2
Justice League: The Rise and Fall Special #1 (5/10, $3.99) Hunt for Green Arrow	4.00

Justice League of America #207 © DC

Justice League of America (2015) #1 © DC

Justice Society of America (2007) #3 © DC

GD 2.0 | VG 4.0 | FN 6.0 | VF 8.0 | VF/NM 9.0 | NM- 9.2

HC-(2011, $24.99) Reprints Justice League of America #43, Justice League: The Rise and Fall Special #1, Green Arrow #31,32 and Justice League: The Rise of Arsenal #1-4 25.00

JUSTICE LEAGUES...
DC Comics: Mar, 2001 ($2.50, limited series)

JL?, Justice League of Amazons, Justice League of Atlantis, Justice League of Arkham, Justice League of Aliens, JLA: JLA split by the Advance Man; Perez-c in all; s&a by various 3.00

JUSTICE LEAGUE TASK FORCE
DC Comics: June, 1993 - No. 37, Aug, 1996 ($1.25/$1.50/$1.75)

1-37: Aquaman, Nightwing, Flash, J'onn J'onzz, & Gypsy form team. 5,6-Knight-quest tie-ins (new Batman cameo #5, 1 pg.). 15-Triumph cameo. 16-(9/94)-Zero Hour x-over; Triumph app.; leads into issue #0. 17-(11/94)-Triumph becomes part of Justice League Task Force (See JLE #68). 26-Impulse app. 35-Warlord app. 37-Triumph quits team 4.00
#0 (10/94) Zero Hour; released between #16 & #17 3.00

JUSTICE LEAGUE: THE NEW FRONTIER SPECIAL (Also see DC: The New Frontier)
DC Comics: May, 2008 ($4.99, one-shot)

1-Short stories by Darwyn Cooke, J. Bone and Dave Bullock; bonus movie storyboards 5.00

JUSTICE LEAGUE: THE RISE OF ARSENAL (Follows Justice League: Cry For Justice)
DC Comics: May, 2010 - No. 4, Aug, 2010 ($3.99, limited series)

1-4-Horn-c/Borges-a/Krul-s. 2,3-Cheshire app. 4.00

JUSTICE LEAGUE 3000
DC Comics: Feb, 2014 - No. 15, May, 2015 ($2.99)

1-15-Justice League of the 31st century. 1-Giffen & DeMatteis-s/Porter-a/c. 10-Etrigan app. 11-Blue Beetle and Booster Gold cameo. 12-14-Blue Beetle and Booster Gold app. 14-Kamandi app.; Kuhn-a 14,15-Etrigan app. 15-Fire returns 3.00

JUSTICE LEAGUE 3001
DC Comics: Aug, 2015 - No. 12, Jul, 2016 ($2.99)

1-12: 1-Giffen & DeMatteis-s/Porter-a/c; Supergirl app. 4-Kolins-a. 5,6-Harley Quinn app. 3.00

JUSTICE LEAGUE UNITED (DC New 52)
DC Comics: No. 0, Jun, 2014 - No. 16, Feb, 2016 ($3.99)

0-16: 0-Lemire-s/McKone-a; Adam Strange, Lobo & Byth app. 3-Hawkman killed. 6-10-Legion of Super-Heroes app. 11-13,15-Harris-c. 13-15-Sgt Rock app. 4.00
Annual #1 (12/14, $4.99) Legion of Super-Heroes app.; continued in #6 5.00
...: Futures End 1 (11/14, $2.99, reg-c) 5 years later; 2-parter with Justice League: FE #1 3.00
...: Futures End 1 (11/14, $3.99, 3-D cover) 4.00

JUSTICE LEAGUE UNLIMITED (Based on Cartoon Network animated series)
DC Comics: Nov, 2004 - No. 46, Aug, 2008 ($2.25)

1-46: 1-Zatanna app. 2,23,42-Royal Flush Gang app. 4-Adam Strange app. 10-Creeper app. 17-Freedom Fighters app. 18-Space Cabby app. 27-Black Lightning app. 34-Zod app. 41-Harley Quinn-c/app. 3.00
Free Comic Book Day giveaway (5/06) r/#1 with "Free Comic Book Day" banner on-c 3.00
Jam Packed Action (2005, $7.99, digest) adaptations of two TV episodes 8.00
... Vol. 1: United They Stand (2005, $6.99, digest) r/#1-5 7.00
... Vol. 2: World's Greatest Heroes (2006, $6.99, digest) r/#6-10 7.00
... Vol. 3: Champions of Justice (2006, $6.99, digest) r/#11-15 7.00
...: Heroes (2009, $12.99, full-size) r/#23-29 13.00
...: The Ties That Bind (2008, $12.99, full-size) r/#16-22 13.00

JUSTICE LEAGUE VS. SUICIDE SQUAD (Leads into Justice League of America '17 series)
DC Comics: Feb, 2017 - No. 6, Mar, 2017 ($3.99, weekly limited series)

1-6: 1-Max Lord & Lobo app.; Fabok-a. 2-Daniel-a. 4-6-Eclipso app. 6-Porter-a 4.00

JUSTICE LEAGUE VS. THE LEGION OF SUPER-HEROES
DC Comics: Mar, 2022 - No. 6, Nov, 2022 ($3.99, limited series)

1-6-Bendis-s/Godlewski-a; teams face The Great Darkness 4.00

JUSTICE MACHINE, THE
Noble Comics: June, 1981 - No. 5, Nov, 1983 ($2.00, nos. 1-3 are mag. size)

	GD	VG	FN	VF	VF/NM	NM-
1-Byrne-c(p)	3	6	9	15	21	26
2-Austin-c(i)	2	4	6	9	12	15
3	1	3	4	6	8	10

4,5, Annual 1: Ann. 1-(1/84, 68 pgs.)(published by Texas Comics); 1st app. The Elementals; Golden-c(p); new Thunder Agents story (43 pgs.) 6.00

JUSTICE MACHINE (Also see The New Justice Machine)
Comico/Innovation Publishing: Jan, 1987 - No. 29, May 1989 ($1.50/$1.75)

1-29 3.00
Annual 1(6/89, $2.50, 36 pgs.)-Last Comico ish. 3.00
Summer Spectacular 1 ('89, $2.75)-Innovation Publ.; Byrne/Gustovich-c 3.00

JUSTICE MACHINE, THE
Innovation Publishing: 1990 - No. 4, 1990 ($1.95/$2.25, deluxe format, mature)

1-4: Gustovich-c/a in all 3.00

JUSTICE MACHINE FEATURING THE ELEMENTALS
Comico: May, 1986 - No. 4, Aug, 1986 ($1.50, limited series)

1-4 3.00

JUSTICE RIDERS
DC Comics: 1997 ($5.95, one-shot, prestige format)

1-Elseworlds; Dixon-s/Williams & Gray-a 6.00

JUSTICE SOCIETY
DC Comics: 2006; 2007 ($14.99, TPB)

Vol. 1 - Rep. from 1976 revival in All Star Comics #58-67 & DC Special #29; Bolland-c 15.00
Vol. 2 - R/All Star Comics #68-74 & Adventure Comics #461-466; new Bolland-c 15.00

JUSTICE SOCIETY OF AMERICA (See Adventure #461 & All-Star #3)
DC Comics: April, 1991 - No. 8, Nov, 1991 ($1.00, limited series)

1-8: 1-Flash. 2-Black Canary. 3-Green Lantern. 4-Hawkman. 5-Flash/Hawkman. 6-Green Lantern/Black Canary. 7-JSA 4.00

JUSTICE SOCIETY OF AMERICA (Also see Last Days of the... Special)
DC Comics: Aug, 1992 - No. 10, May, 1993 ($1.25)

1-10: 1-1st app. Jesse Quick 4.00

JUSTICE SOCIETY OF AMERICA (Follows JSA series)
DC Comics: Feb, 2007 - No. 54, Oct, 2011 ($3.99/$2.99)

	GD	VG	FN	VF	VF/NM	NM-
1-($3.99) New team selected; intro. Maxine Hunkle; Alex Ross-c	2	4	6	9	12	15
1-Variant-c by Eaglesham	2	4	6	10	14	18

2-22,24-49,51-54: 1-Covers by Ross & Eaglesham. 3,4-Vandal Savage app. 5,6-JLA/JSA team-up. 9-22-Kingdom Come Superman app.18-Magog app. 22-Superman returns to Kingdom Come Earth; Ross partial art. 23-25-Ordway-a. 26-Triptych cover by Ross. 33-Team splits. 34,35-Mordru app. 41,42-Justice League x-over. 52-54-Challengers of the Unknown app. 54-Darwyn Cooke-c 3.00
23-Black Adam-c/app. 6.00
50-($4.99) Degaton app.; art by Derenick, Chaykin, Williams II, and Pérez; Massafera-c 5.00
JSA Annual 1 (9/08, $3.99) Power Girl on Earth-2; Ross-c/Ordway-a 5.00
JSA Annual 2 (4/10, $4.99) All Star team app.; Magog quits; Williams-a 5.00
... 80 Page Giant (1/10, $5.99) short stories by various incl. Ordway, S. Hampton 6.00
... 80 Page Giant 2010 (12/10, $5.99) short stories by various 6.00
... 80 Page Giant 2011 (8/11, $5.99) short stories by various incl. Chaykin, Hampton 6.00
... Special (11/10, $4.99) Scott Kolins-s/a; spotlight on Magog 5.00
...: Axis of Evil SC (2010, $14.99) r/#34-40 15.00
...: Black Adam and Isis HC (2009, $19.99, d.j.) r/#23-28 20.00
...: Black Adam and Isis SC (2010, $14.99) r/#23-28 15.00
... Kingdom Come Special: Magog (1/09, $3.99) Pasarin-a; origin re-told; 2 covers 4.00
... Kingdom Come Special: Superman (1/09, $3.99) Lois' death re-told; Alex Ross-s/a/c; thumbnails, photo references, sketch art 4.00
... Kingdom Come Special: Superman (1/09, $3.99) Eaglesham variant cover 8.00
... Kingdom Come Special: The Kingdom (1/09, $3.99) Pasarin-a; 2 covers 4.00
...: The Bad Seed SC (2010, $14.99) r/#29-33 15.00
...: The Next Age SC (2008, $14.99) r/#1-4; Ross and Eaglesham sketch pages 15.00
...: Thy Kingdom Come Part One HC (2008, $19.99, d.j.) r/#7-12; Ross sketch pages 20.00
...: Thy Kingdom Come Part One SC (2009, $14.99) r/#7-12; Ross sketch pages 15.00
...: Thy Kingdom Come Part Two HC (2008, $24.99, d.j.) r/#13-18 & Annual #1; Ross sketch pages 25.00
...: Thy Kingdom Come Part Two SC (2009, $19.99) r/#13-18 & Ann. #1; Ross sketch-a 20.00
...: Thy Kingdom Come Part Three HC (2009, $24.99, d.j.) r/#19-22 & K.C. Specials - Superman, Magog and The Kingdom; Ross sketch pages 25.00
...: Thy Kingdom Come Part Three SC (2010, $19.99) same contents as HC 20.00

JUSTICE SOCIETY OF AMERICA (Follows The New Golden Age one-shot)
DC Comics: Jan, 2023 - Present ($3.99)

1-3-Johns-s/Janin-a. 2-Huntress meets the 1940 JSA 4.00

JUSTICE SOCIETY OF AMERICA 100-PAGE SUPER SPECTACULAR
DC Comics: 2000 ($6.95, mimics format of DC 100 Page Super Spectaculars)

1-"1975 Issue" reprints Flash team-up and Golden Age JSA 7.00

JUSTICE SOCIETY RETURNS, THE (See All Star Comics (1999) for related titles)
DC Comics: 2003 ($19.95, TPB)

TPB-Reprints 1999 JSA x-over from All-Star Comics #1,2 and related one-shots 20.00

JUSTICE TRAPS THE GUILTY (Fargo Kid V11#3 on)
Prize/Headline Publications: Oct-Nov, 1947 - V11#2(#92), Apr-May, 1958 (True FBI Cases)

	GD	VG	FN	VF	VF/NM	NM-
V2#1-S&K-c/a; electrocution-c	97	194	291	621	1061	1500
2-S&K-c/a	43	86	129	271	461	650
3-5-S&K-c/a	39	78	117	231	378	525

GD VG FN VF VF/NM NM-
2.0 4.0 6.0 8.0 9.0 9.2

6-S&K-c/a; Feldstein-a 43 86 129 271 461 650
7,9-S&K-c/a. 7-9-V2#1-3 in indicia; #7-9 on-c 34 68 102 204 332 460
8-Krigstein-a; S&K-c; lie detector machine-c 32 64 96 188 307 425
10-Krigstein-a; S&K-c/a 34 68 102 204 332 460
11,18,19-S&K-c 20 40 60 118 192 265
12,14-17,20-No S&K. 14-Severin/Elder-a (8pg.) 14 28 42 80 115 150
13-Used in **SOTI**, pg. 110-111 16 32 48 92 144 195
21,30-S&K-c/a 21 42 63 122 199 275
22,23-S&K-c 15 30 45 90 140 190
24-26,27,29,31-50: 32-Meskin story 14 28 42 76 108 140
28-Kirby-c 15 30 45 86 133 180
51-55,57,59-70 12 24 36 67 94 120
56-Ben Oda, Joe Simon, Joe Genola, Mort Meskin & Jack Kirby app. in police line-up on classic-c 24 48 72 142 234 325
58-Illo. in **SOTI**, "Treating police contemptuously" (top left); text on heroin 36 72 108 211 343 475
71-92: 76-Orlando-a 10 20 30 54 72 90
NOTE: ***Bailey*** *a-12, 13.* ***Elder*** *a-8.* ***Kirby*** *a-19p.* ***Meskin*** *a-22, 27, 63, 64; c-45, 46.* ***Robinson/Meskin*** *a-5, 19.* ***Severin*** *a-8, 11p. Photo c-12, 15-17.*

JUST IMAGINE STAN LEE WITH... (Stan Lee re-invents DC icons)
DC Comics: 2001 - 2002 ($5.95, prestige format, one-shots)
(Adam Hughes back-c on all)(Michael Uslan back-up stories in all, diff. artists)
Scott McDaniel Creating **Aquaman**- Back-up w/Ramona Fradon-a 6.00
Joe Kubert Creating **Batman**- Back-up w/Michael Kaluta-a 6.00
Chris Bachalo Creating **Catwoman**- Back-up w/Darwyn Cooke & Mike Allred-a 2 4 6 8 10 12
John Cassaday Creating **Crisis**- no back-up story 6.00
Kevin Maguire Creating **The Flash**- Back-up w/Sergio Aragonés-a 6.00
Dave Gibbons Creating **Green Lantern**- Back-up w/Dick Giordano-a 6.00
Jerry Ordway Creating **JLA** 6.00
John Byrne Creating **Robin**- Back-up w/John Severin-a 6.00
Walter Simonson Creating **Sandman**- Back-up w/Richard Corben-a 6.00
Gary Frank Creating **Shazam!**- Back-up w/Kano-a 1 2 3 5 6 8
John Buscema Creating **Superman**- Back-up w/Kyle Baker-a 2 4 6 8 10 12
Jim Lee Creating **Wonder Woman**- Back-up w/Gene Colan-a 2 4 6 8 11 14
Secret Files and Origins #1 (3/02, $4.95) Crisis prologue; Jurgens-a 5.00
TPB -Just Imagine Stan Lee Creating the DC Universe: Book One (2002, $19.95) r/Batman, Wonder Woman, Superman, Green Lantern 20.00
TPB -Just Imagine Stan Lee Creating the DC Universe: Book Two (2003, $19.95) r/Flash, JLA, Secret Files and Origins, Robin, Shazam; sketch pages 20.00
TPB -Just Imagine Stan Lee Creating the DC Universe: Book Three (2004, $19.95) r/Aquaman, Catwoman, Sandman, Crisis; profile pages 20.00

JUST MARRIED
Charlton Comics: January, 1958 - No. 114, Dec, 1976
1 9 18 27 63 129 195
2 5 10 15 30 50 70
3-10 4 8 12 23 37 50
11-30 3 6 9 16 23 30
31-50 2 4 6 11 16 20
51-70 2 4 6 9 13 16
71-78,80-89 2 4 6 8 11 14
79-Ditko-a (7 pages) 2 4 6 10 14 18
90-Susan Dey and David Cassidy full page poster 2 4 6 11 16 20
91-114 2 4 6 8 10 12

KA'A'NGA COMICS (...Jungle King)(See Jungle Comics)
Fiction House Magazines (Glen-Kel Publ. Co.): Spring, 1949 - No. 20, Summer, 1954
1-Ka'a'nga, Lord of the Jungle begins 68 136 204 435 743 1050
2 (Winter, '49-'50) 35 70 105 208 339 470
3,4 28 56 84 165 270 375
5-Camilla app. 28 56 84 165 270 375
6-10: 7-Tuska-a. 9-Tabu, Wizard of the Jungle app. 10-Used in **POP**, pg. 99 19 38 57 111 176 240
11-15: 15-Camilla-r by Baker/Jungle #106 15 30 45 85 130 175
16-Sheena app. 15 30 45 88 137 185
17-20 14 28 42 82 121 160
I.W. Reprint #1,8: 1-r/#18; Kinstler-c. 8-r/#10 3 6 9 15 22 28
NOTE: ***Celardo*** *c-1.* ***Whitman*** *c-8-20(most).*

KABOOM
Awesome Entertainment: Sept, 1997 - No. 3, Nov, 1997 ($2.50)
1-3: 1-Matsuda-a/Loeb-s; 4 covers exist (Matsuda, Sale, Pollina and McGuinness), 1-Dynamic Forces Edition, 2-Regular, 2-Alicia Watcher variant-c, 2-Gold logo variant-c, 3-Two covers by Liefeld & Matsuda, 3-Dynamic Forces Ed., Prelude Ed. 3.00
Prelude Gold Edition 4.00

KABOOM (2nd series)
Awesome Entertainment: July, 1999 - No. 3, Dec, 1999 ($2.50)
1-3: 1-Grant-a(p); at least 4 variant covers 3.00

KABOOM! SUMMER BLAST FREE COMIC BOOK DAY EDITION
Boom Entertainment (KaBOOM!): May 2013; May 2014 (free giveaways)
nn-(5/13) Short stories of Adventure Time, Regular Show, Herobear, Garfield, Peanuts 3.00
nn-(5/14) Adventure TIme, Regular Show, Steven Universe, Uncle Grandpa and others 3.00

KABUKI
Caliber: Nov, 1994 ($3.50, B&W, one-shot)
nn-(Fear The Reaper) 1st app.; David Mack-c/a/s 1 2 3 5 6 8
Color Special (1/96, $2.95)-Mack-c/a/scripts; pin-ups by Tucci, Harris & Quesada 4.00
Gallery (8/95, $2.95)- pinups from Mack, Bradstreet, Paul Pope & others 3.00

KABUKI
Image Comics: Oct, 1997 - No. 9, Mar, 2000 ($2.95, color)
1-David Mack-c/s/a 5.00
1-($10.00)-Dynamic Forces Edition 1 3 4 6 8 10
2-5 4.00
6-9 3.00
#1/2 (9/01, $2.95) r/Wizard 1/2; Eklipse Mag. article; bio 3.00
...Classics (2/99, $3.95) Reprints Fear the Reaper 4.00
...Classics 2 (3/99, $3.95) Reprints Dance of Dance 4.00
...Classics 3-5 (3-6/99, $4.95) Reprints Circle of Blood-Acts 1-3 5.00
...Classics 6-12 (7/99-3/00, $3.25) Various reprints 3.25
...Images (6/98, $4.95) r/#1 with new pin-ups 5.00
...Images 2 (1/99, $4.95) r/#1 with new pin-ups 5.00
...Metamorphosis TPB (10/00, $24.95) r/#1-9; Sienkiewicz intro.; 2nd printing exists 25.00
...Reflections 1-4 (7/98-5/02; $4.95) new story plus art techniques 5.00
... The Ghost Play (11/02, $2.95) new story plus interview 3.00

KABUKI
Marvel Comics (Icon): July, 2004 - No. 9, Sept, 2007 ($2.99, color)
1-9: 1-David Mack-c/s/a in all; variant-c by Alex Maleev. 4-Variant-c by Adam Hughes. 6-Variant-c by Mignola. 8-Variant-c by Kent Williams. 9-Allred var-c 3.00
...: The Alchemy HC (2008, $29.99, dust jacket) oversized r/#1-9; bonus art & content 30.00
... Reflections 5-15 (7/05-10/09, $5.99) paintings & sketches of recent work; photos 6.00

KABUKI AGENTS (SCARAB)
Image Comics: Aug, 1999 - No. 8, Aug, 2001 ($2.95, B&W)
1-8-David Mack-s/Rick Mays-a 3.00

KABUKI: CIRCLE OF BLOOD
Caliber Press: Jan, 1995 - No. 6, Nov, 1995 ($2.95, B&W)
1-David Mack story/a in all 5.00
2-6: 3-#1 on inside indicia. 3.00
6-Variant-c 3.00
TPB ($16.95) r/#1-6, intro. by Steranko 17.00
TPB (1997, $17.95) Image Edition-r/#1-6, intro. by Steranko 18.00
TPB ($24.95) Deluxe Edition 25.00

KABUKI: DANCE OF DEATH
London Night Studios: Jan, 1995 ($3.00, B&W, one-shot)
1-David Mack-c/a/scripts 1 2 3 5 6 8

KABUKI: DREAMS
Image Comics: Jan, 1998 ($4.95, TPB)
nn-Reprints Color Special & Dreams of the Dead 5.00

KABUKI: DREAMS OF THE DEAD
Caliber: July, 1996 ($2.95, one-shot)
nn-David Mack-c/a/scripts 3.00

KABUKI FAN EDITION
Gemstone Publ./Caliber: Feb, 1997 (mail-in offer, one-shot)
nn-David Mack-c/a/scripts 4.00

KABUKI: MASKS OF THE NOH
Caliber: May, 1996 - No. 4, Feb, 1997 ($2.95, limited series)
1-4: 1-Three-c (1A-Quesada, 1B-Buzz, &1C-Mack). 3-Terry Moore pin-up 3.00
TPB-(4/98, $10.95) r/#1-4; intro by Terry Moore 11.00

KABUKI: SKIN DEEP
Caliber Comics: Oct, 1996 - No. 3, May, 1997 ($2.95)
1-3:David Mack-c/a/scripts. 2-Two-c (1-Mack, 1-Ross) 3.00
TPB-(5/98, $9.95) r/#1-3; intro by Alex Ross 10.00

KAMANDI: AT EARTH'S END
DC Comics: June, 1993 - No. 6, Nov, 1993 ($1.75, limited series)
1-6: Elseworlds storyline 3.00

KAMANDI CHALLENGE, THE (Commemoration for Jack Kirby's 100th birthday)
DC Comics: Mar, 2017 - No. 12, Feb, 2018 ($4.99/$3.99, limited series)
1-($4.99) DiDio-s/Giffen-a; Abnett-s/Eaglesham-a; Timm-c 5.00
2-11-($3.99) 2-Neal Adams-a; Tomasi-s; covers by Adams & Rocafort. 3-Palmiotti-s/Conner-a. 8-Giffen-s/Rude-a; Jim Lee-c. 10-Shane Davis-a. 11-Simonson-a 4.00
12-($4.99) Gail Simone-s; art by Jill Thompson and Ryan Sook; afterword by Paul Levitz 5.00
... Special 1 (3/17, $7.99) r/#1,32 and unpubl'd #60,61 from Cancelled Comic Cavalcade 8.00

KAMANDI, THE LAST BOY ON EARTH (Also see Alarming Tales #1, Brave and the Bold #120 & 157, Cancelled Comic Cavalcade & Wednesday Comics)
National Periodical Publ./DC Comics: Oct-Nov, 1972 - No. 59, Sept-Oct, 1978
1-Origin & 1st app. Kamandi; intro Ben Boxer 7 14 21 46 86 125
2,3 4 8 12 28 47 65
4,5: 4-Intro. Prince Tuftan of the Tigers. 5-Intro. Flower 4 8 12 25 40 55
6-10 3 6 9 18 28 38
11-20 3 6 9 15 22 28
21-28,30,31,33-40: 24-Last 20¢ issue. 31-Intro Pyra. 2 4 6 13 18 22
29,32: 29-Superman x-over. 32-(68 pgs.)-r/origin from #1 plus one new story; 4 pg. biog. of Jack Kirby with B&W photos 3 6 9 14 20 26
41-57: 50 Kamandi becomes an OMAC 2 4 6 10 14 18
58-Karate Kid x-over from LSH (see Karate Kid #15) 3 6 9 14 19 24
59-(44 pgs.)-Story cont'd in Brave and the Bold #157; The Return of Omac back-up by Starlin-c/a(p) cont'd in Warlord #37 3 6 9 16 23 30
NOTE: ***Ayers*** *a(p)-48-59 (most).* ***Giffen*** *a-44p, 45p.* ***Kirby*** *a-1-40p; c-1-33.* ***Kubert*** *c-34-41.* ***Nasser*** *a-45p, 46p.* ***Starlin*** *a-59p; c-57, 59p.*

KAMEN RIDER ZERO ONE
Titan Comics: Dec, 2022 - Present ($3.99)
1-Easton-s/Prasetya-a 4.00

KAMUI (Legend Of...#2 on)
Eclipse Comics/Viz Comics: May 12, 1987 - No. 37, Nov. 15, 1988 ($1.50, B&W, bi-weekly)
1-37: 1-3 have 2nd printings 3.00

KANAN - THE LAST PADAWAN (Star Wars)
Marvel Comics: Jun, 2015 - No. 12, May, 2016 ($3.99)
1-12: 1-Weisman-s/Larraz-a; takes place after Episode 3; flashbacks to the Clone Wars. 9-11-General Grievous app. 4.00

Kabuki V7 #6 © David Mack

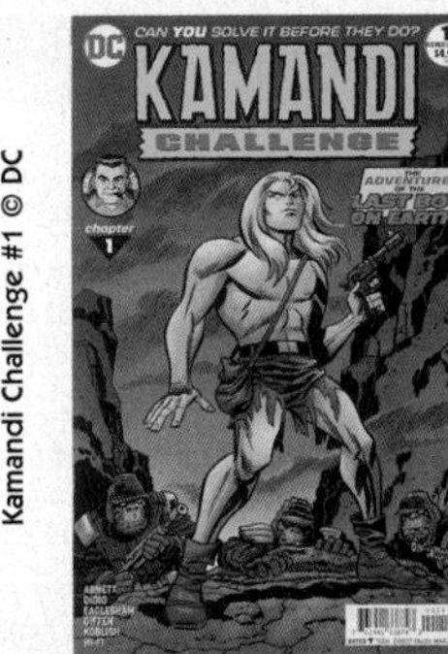

Kamandi Challenge #1 © DC

Kang the Conqueror #5 © MAR

	GD 2.0	VG 4.0	FN 6.0	VF 8.0	VF/NM 9.0	NM- 9.2

KANE & LYNCH (Based on the video games)
DC Comics (WildStorm): Oct, 2010 - No. 6, Apr, 2011 ($3.99/$2.99, limited series)

1-4-($3.99) Templesmith-c/Edginton-s/Mitten-a						4.00
5,6-($2.99)						3.00
TPB (2011, $17.99) r/#1-6; cover gallery						18.00

KANG THE CONQUEROR (Leads into Timeless #1)
Marvel Comics: Oct, 2021 - No. 5, Feb, 2022 ($4.99/$3.99)

1-($4.99) Lanzing & Kelly-s/Magno-a; origin of young Kang (Nathaniel Richards)						5.00
2-5-($3.99) 2-Rama-Tut app. 3-Doctor Doom & the Avengers app.						4.00

KAOS MOON (Also see Negative Burn #34)
Caliber Comics: 1996 - No. 4, 1997 ($2.95, B&W)

1-4-David Boller-s/a						3.00
3,4-Limited Alternate-c						4.00
3,4-Gold Alternate-c, Full Circle TPB ($5.95) r/#1,2						6.00

KAPTARA
Image Comics: Apr, 2015 - No. 5, Nov, 2015 ($3.50)

1-5-Chip Zdarsky-s/Kagan McLeod-a						3.50

KARATE KID (See Action, Adventure, Legion of Super-Heroes, & Superboy)
National Periodical Publications/DC Comics: Mar-Apr, 1976 - No. 15, July-Aug, 1978 (Legion of Super-Heroes spin-off)

1-Meets Iris Jacobs; Estrada/Staton-a	4	8	12	23	37	50
2-14: 2-Major Disaster app. 14-Robin x-over	2	3	4	6	8	10
15-Continued into Kamandi #58	2	4	6	11	16	20

NOTE: ***Grell** c-1-4, 7, 8, 5p, 6p, **Staton** a-1-9i. Legion x-over-No. 1, 2, 4, 6, 10, 12, 13. Princess Projectra x-over-#8, 9.*

KARMEN
Image Comics: Mar, 2021 - No. 5, Jul, 2021 ($3.99, lim. series, English version of French comic)

1-5-Guillem March-s/a/c. 1-Variant-c by Manara						4.00

KARNAK (Inhumans)
Marvel Comics: Dec, 2015 - No. 6, Apr, 2017 ($3.99)

1-6: 1,2-Warren Ellis-s/Gerardo Zaffino-a. 3-6-Roland Boschi-a						4.00

KATANA (DC New 52) (From Justice League Of America 2013 series)
DC Comics: Apr, 2013 - No. 10, Feb, 2014 ($2.99)

1-10: 1,2-Nocenti-s/Sanchez-a/Finch-c; origin. 2-Steve Trevor app. 3-6-Creeper app.						3.00

KATHY
Standard Comics: Sept, 1949 - No. 17, Sept, 1955

1-Teen-age	43	86	129	271	461	650
2-Schomburg-c	20	40	60	118	192	265
3-5	15	30	45	84	127	170
6-17: 17-Code approved	14	28	42	82	121	160

KATHY (The Teenage Tornado)
Atlas Comics/Marvel (ZPC): Oct, 1959 - No. 27, Feb, 1964 (most issues contain paper dolls and pin-up pages)

1-The Teen-age Tornado; Goldberg-c/a in all	37	74	111	218	354	490
2	20	40	60	117	189	260
3-15	18	36	54	105	165	225
16-23,25,27: 22-(4/63) Elvis Presley & Ricky Nelson app. in story "A Song in Her Heart"	15	30	45	85	130	175
24-(8/63) Frank Sinatra, Cary Grant, Ed Sullivan & Liz Taylor-c	20	40	60	120	195	270
26-(12/63) Kathy becomes a model; Millie app.	15	30	45	90	140	190

KAT KARSON
I. W. Enterprises: No date (Reprint)

1-Funny animals	2	4	6	11	16	18

KATO (Also see The Green Hornet)
Dynamite Entertainment: 2010 - No. 14, 2011 ($3.99)

1-14: 1-Kato and daughter origin; Garza-a/Parks-s. 2-10 Bernard-a						4.00
Annual 1 (2011, $4.99) Parks-s/Salazar-a						5.00

KATO OF THE GREEN HORNET (Also see The Green Hornet)
Now Comics: Nov, 1991 - No. 4, Feb, 1992 ($2.50, mini-series)

1-4: Brent Anderson-c/a						5.00

KATO OF THE GREEN HORNET II (Also see The Green Hornet)
Now Comics: Nov, 1992 - No. 2, Dec, 1993 ($2.50, mini-series)

1,2-Baron-s/Mayerik & Sherman-a						5.00

KATO ORIGINS (Also see The Green Hornet: Year One)
Dynamite Entertainment: 2010 - No. 11, 2011 ($3.99)

1-11-Kato in 1942; Jai Nitz-s/Colton Worley-a; covers by Worley & Francavilla						4.00

KATY KEENE (Also see Kasco Komics, Laugh, Pep, Suzie, & Wilbur)
Archie Publ./Close-Up/Radio Comics: 1949 - No. 4, 1951; No. 5, 3/52 - No. 62, Oct, 1961 (50-53-Adventures of...on-c) (Cut and missing pages are common)

1-Bill Woggon-c/a begins; swipes-c to Mopsy #1	265	530	795	1694	2897	4100
2-(1950)	87	174	261	553	952	1350
3-5: 3-(1951). 4-(1951). 5-(3/52)	63	126	189	403	689	975
6-10	45	90	135	284	480	675
11,13-21: 21-Last pre-code issue (3/55)	39	78	117	231	378	525
12-(Scarce)	45	90	135	284	480	675
22-40	28	56	84	165	270	375
41-60: 54-Wedding Album plus wedding pin-up	22	44	66	128	209	290
61-Sci-fi-c	29	58	87	172	281	390
62-Classic Robot-c	57	114	171	362	619	875
Annual 1('54, 25¢)-All new stories; last pre-code	66	132	198	419	722	1025
Annual 2-6('55-59, 25¢)-All new stories	37	74	111	222	361	500
3-D 1(1953, 25¢, large size)-Came w/glasses	43	86	129	271	401	650
Charm 1(9/58)-Woggon-c/a; new stories, and cut-outs	37	74	111	222	361	500
Glamour 1(1957)-Puzzles, games, cut-outs	37	74	111	218	354	490
Spectacular 1('56)	37	74	111	222	361	500

NOTE: *Debby's Diary in #45, 47-49, 52, 57.*

KATY KEENE COMICS DIGEST MAGAZINE
Close-Up, Inc. (Archie Ent.): 1987 - No. 10, July, 1990 ($1.25/$1.35/$1.50, digest size)

1	3	6	9	14	19	24
2-10	1	3	4	6	8	10

NOTE: *Many used copies are cut-up inside.*

KATY KEENE FASHION BOOK MAGAZINE
Radio Comics/Archie Publications: 1955 - No. 13, Sum, '56 - N. 23, Wint, '58-59 (nn 3-10) (no #11,12)

1-Bill Woggon-c/a	66	132	198	419	722	1025
2	37	74	111	218	354	490
13-18: 18-Photo Bill Woggon	28	56	84	165	270	375
19-23	23	46	69	138	227	315

KATY KEENE HOLIDAY FUN (See Archie Giant Series Magazine No. 7, 12)

KATY KEENE MODEL BEHAVIOR
Archie Comic Publications: 2008 ($10.95, TPB)

Vol. 1 - New story and reprinted apps./pin-ups from Archie & Friends #101-112						11.00

KATY KEENE PINUP PARADE
Radio Comics/Archie Publications: 1955 - No. 15, Summer, 1961 (25¢) (Cut-out & missing pages are common)

1-Cut-outs in all?; last pre-code issue	65	130	195	416	708	1000
2-(1956)	35	70	105	208	339	470
3-5: 3-(1957). 5-(1959)	30	60	90	177	289	400
6-10,12-14: 8-Mad parody. 10-Bill Woggon photo	25	50	75	150	245	340
11-Story of how comics get CCA approved, narrated by Katy	32	64	96	188	307	425
15(Rare)-Photo artist & family	47	94	141	296	498	700

KATY KEENE SPECIAL (Katy Keene #7 on; see Laugh Comics Digest)
Archie Ent.: Sept, 1983 - No. 33, 1990 (Later issues published quarterly)

1-10: 1-Woggon-r; new Woggon-c. 3-Woggon-r	1	3	4	6	8	10
11-25: 12-Spider-Man parody	1	2	3	5	6	8
26-32-(Low print run)	2	4	6	8	10	12
33	2	4	6	8	11	14

KATZENJAMMER KIDS, THE (See Captain & the Kids & Giant Comic Album)
David McKay Publ./Standard No. 12-21(Spring/'50 - 53)/Harvey No. 22, 4/53 on: 1945-1946; Summer, 1947 - No. 27, Feb-Mar, 1954

Feature Books 30	21	42	63	126	206	285
Feature Books 32,35('45),41,44('46)	19	38	57	112	179	245
Feature Book 37-Has photos & biography of Harold Knerr	20	40	60	115	190	260
1(1947)-All new stories begin	20	40	60	115	190	260
2-5	12	24	36	69	97	125
6-11	10	20	30	56	76	95
12-14(Standard)	9	18	27	47	61	75
15-21(Standard)	8	16	24	44	57	70
22-25,27(Harvey): 22-24-Henry app.	7	14	21	35	43	50
26-Half in 3-D	16	32	48	98	154	210

KAYO (Formerly Bullseye & Jest; becomes Carnival Comics)
Harry 'A' Chesler: No. 12, Mar, 1945

	GD 2.0	VG 4.0	FN 6.0	VF 8.0	VF/NM 9.0	NM- 9.2

12-Green Knight, Capt. Glory, Little Nemo (not by McCay) 36 72 108 211 343 475

KA-ZAR (Also see Marvel Comics #1, Savage Tales #6 & X-Men #10)
Marvel Comics Group: Aug, 1970 - No. 3, Mar, 1971 (Giant-Size, 68 pgs.)

1-Reprints earlier Ka-Zar stories; Avengers x-over in Hercules; Daredevil, X-Men app.; hidden profanity-c 5 10 15 34 60 85
2,3-Daredevil-r. 2-r/Daredevil #13 w/Kirby layouts; Ka-Zar origin, Angel-r from X-Men by Tuska. 3-Romita & Heck-a (no Kirby) 3 6 9 21 33 45
NOTE: *Buscema r-2. Colan a-1p(r). Kirby c/a-1, 2. #1-Reprints X-Men #10 & Daredevil #24.*

KA-ZAR
Marvel Comics Group: Jan, 1974 - No. 20, Feb, 1977 (Regular Size)

1 4 8 12 25 40 55
2-10 2 4 6 8 11 14
11-14,16,18-20: 16-Only a 30 ¢ edition exists 1 2 3 5 6 8
15,17-(Regular 25¢ edition)(8/76) 1 2 3 5 6 8
15,17-(30¢-c variants, limited distribution) 4 8 12 23 37 50
NOTE: *Alcala a-6i, 8i. Brunner c-4. J. Buscema a-6-10p; c-1, 5, 7. Heath a-12. G. Kane c(p)-3, 5, 8-11, 15, 20. Kirby c-12p. Reinman a-1p.*

KA-ZAR (Volume 2)
Marvel Comics: May, 1997 - No. 20, Dec, 1998 ($1.95/$1.99)

1-Waid-s/Andy Kubert-c/a. thru #4 5.00
1-2nd printing; new cover 4.00
2,4: 2-Two-c 4.00
3-Alpha Flight #1 preview 5.00
5-13,15-20: 8-Includes Spider-Man Cybercomic CD-ROM. 9-11-Thanos app. 15-Priest-s/Martinez & Rodriguez-a begin; Punisher app. 4.00
14-($2.99) Last Waid/Kubert issue; flip book with 2nd story previewing new creative team of Priest-s/Martinez & Rodriguez-a 5.00
'97 Annual ($2.99)-Wraparound-c 5.00

KA-ZAR
Marvel Comics: Aug, 2011 - No. 5, Dec, 2011 ($2.99, limited series)

1-5-Jenkins-s/Alixe-a/c 3.00

KA-ZAR LORD OF THE SAVAGE LAND (Follows Empyre: Avengers #1-3)
Marvel Comics: Nov, 2021 - Present ($3.99)

1-4: 1-Zac Thompson-s/Germán García-a 4.00

KA-ZAR: MARVEL TALES
Marvel Comics: Nov, 2021 ($7.99, one-shot)

1-Reprints Marvel Tales (1982) #1-4; X-Men app.; intro. by Ralph Macchio 8.00

KA-ZAR OF THE SAVAGE LAND
Marvel Comics: Feb, 1997 ($2.50, one-shot)

1-Wraparound-c 4.00

KA-ZAR: SIBLING RIVALRY
Marvel Comics: July, 1997 ($1.95, one-shot)

(# -1) Flashback story w/Alpha Flight #1 preview 4.00

KA-ZAR THE SAVAGE (See Marvel Fanfare)
Marvel Comics Group: Apr, 1981 - No. 34, Oct, 1984 (Regular size)(Mando paper #10 on)

1-Bruce Jones-s begin 1 3 4 6 8 10
2-20,24,27,28,30-34: 11-Origin Zabu. 12-One of two versions with panel missing on pg. 10. 20-Kraven the Hunter-c/story (also apps. in #21) 4.00
12-Version with panel on pg. 10 (1600 printed) 1 3 4 6 8 10
21-23, 25,26-Spider-Man app. 26-Photo-c. 4.00
29-Double size; Ka-Zar & Shanna wed 5.00
NOTE: *B. Anderson a-1-15p, 18, 19; c-1-17, 18p, 20(back). G. Kane a(back-up)-11, 12, 14.*

KEEN DETECTIVE FUNNIES (Formerly Detective Picture Stories?)
Centaur Publications: No. 8, July, 1938 - No. 24, Sept, 1940

V1#8-The Clock continues-r/Funny Picture Stories #1; Roy Crane-a (1st?) 400 800 1200 2800 4900 7000
9-Tex Martin by Eisner; The Gang Buster app. 300 600 900 2040 3570 5100
10,11: 11-Dean Denton story (begins?) 290 580 870 1856 3178 4500
V2#1,2-The Eye Sees by Frank Thomas begins; ends #23(Not in V2#3&5). 2-Jack Cole-a 194 388 582 1242 2121 3000
3-6: 3-TNT Todd begins. 4-Gabby Flynn begins. 5,6-Dean Denton story 168 336 504 1075 1838 2600
7-The Masked Marvel by Ben Thompson begins (7/39, 1st app.)(scarce) 331 662 993 2317 4059 5800
8-Nudist ranch panel w/four girls 232 464 696 1485 2543 3600
9-11 155 310 465 992 1696 2400
12(12/39)-Origin The Eye Sees by Frank Thomas; death of Masked Marvel's sidekick ZL 194 388 582 1242 2121 3000
V3#1 148 296 444 947 1624 2300
18-Bondage/torture-c 219 438 657 1402 2401 3400
19,21,22 148 296 444 947 1624 2300
20-Classic Eye Sees-c by Thomas 314 628 942 2198 3849 5500
23-Air Man begins (intro); Air Man-c 206 412 618 1318 2259 3200
24-(scarce) Air Man-c 232 464 696 1485 2543 3600
NOTE: *Burgos a-V2#2. Jack Cole a-V2#2. Eisner a-10, V2#6r. Ken Ernst a-V2#4-7, 9, 10, 19, 21; c-V2#4. Everett a-V2#6, 7, 9, 11, 12, 20. Guardineer a-V2#5, 66. Gustavson a-V2#4-6. Simon c-V3#1. Thompson c-V2#7, 9, 10, 22.*

KEEN KOMICS
Centaur Publications: V2#1, May, 1939 - V2#3, Nov, 1939

V2#1(Large size)-Dan Hastings (s/f), The Big Top, Bob Phantom the Magician, The Mad Goddess app. 371 742 1113 2600 4550 6500
V2#2(Reg. size)-The Forbidden Idol of Machu Picchu; Cut Carson by Burgos begins 161 322 483 1030 1765 2500
V2#3-Saddle Sniffl by Jack Cole, Circus Pays, Kings Revenge app. 135 270 405 864 1482 2100
NOTE: *Binder a-V2#2. Burgos a-V2#2, 3. Ken Ernst a-V2#3. Gustavson a-V2#2. Jack Cole a-V2#3.*

KEEN TEENS (Girls magazine)
Life's Romances Publ./Leader/Magazine Ent.: 1945; nn, 1946; No. 3, Feb-Mar, 1947 - No. 6, Aug-Sept, 1947

nn (#1)-14 pgs. Claire Voyant (cont'd. in other nn issue) movie photos, Dotty Dripple, Gertie O'Grady & Sissy; Van Johnson, Sinatra photo-c 61 122 183 390 670 950
nn (#2, 1946)-16 pgs. Claire Voyant & 16 pgs. movie photos 40 80 120 246 411 575
3-6: 4-Glenn Ford photo-c. 5-Perry Como-c 21 42 63 124 202 280

KELLYS, THE (Formerly Rusty Comics; Spy Cases No. 26 on)
Marvel Comics (HPC): No. 23, Jan, 1950 - No. 25, June, 1950 (52 pgs.)

23-Teenage 22 44 66 128 209 290
24,25: 24-Margie app. 15 30 45 86 133 180

KEN MAYNARD WESTERN (Movie star)(See Wow Comics, 1936)
Fawcett Publ.: Sept, 1950 - No. 8, Feb, 1952 (All 36 pgs; photo front/back-c)

1-Ken Maynard & his horse Tarzan begin 29 58 87 172 281 390
2 17 34 51 98 154 210
3-8: 6-Atomic bomb explosion panel 14 28 42 76 108 140

KENNEL BLOCK BLUES
BOOM! Studios: Feb, 2016 - No. 4, May, 2016 ($3.99, limited series)

1-4-Ryan Ferrier-s/Daniel Bayliss-a 4.00

KEN SHANNON (Becomes Gabby #11 on) (Also see Police Comics #103)
Quality Comics Group: Oct, 1951 - No. 10, Apr, 1953 (A private eye)

1-Crandall-a 54 108 162 343 574 825
2-Crandall c/a(2) 41 82 123 256 428 600
3-Horror-c; Crandall-a 48 96 144 302 514 725
4,5-Crandall-a 32 64 96 188 307 425
6-Crandall-c/a; "The Weird Vampire Mob"-c/s 54 108 162 343 574 825
7-"The Ugliest Man Alive"-c; Crandall-a 43 86 129 271 461 650
8,9: 8-Opium den drug use story 27 54 81 158 259 360
10-Crandall-c 27 54 81 162 266 370
NOTE: *Crandall/Cuidera c-1-10. Jack Cole a-1-9. #1-15 published after title change to Gabby.*

KEN STUART
Publication Enterprises: Jan, 1949 (Sea Adventures)

1-Frank Borth-c/a 15 30 45 88 137 185

KENT BLAKE OF THE SECRET SERVICE (Spy)
Marvel/Atlas Comics (20CC): May, 1951 - No. 14, July, 1953

1-Injury to eye, bondage, torture; Brodsky-c 40 80 120 246 411 575
2-Drug use w/hypo scenes; Brodsky-c 22 44 66 128 209 290
3-14: 8-R.Q. Sale-a (2 pgs.) 15 30 45 88 157 185
NOTE: *Heath c-5, 7, 8. Infantino c-12. Maneely c-3. Sinnott a-2(3). Tuska a-8(3pg.).*

KENT MENACE
Brilliant Entertainment/American Mythology Prods.: Autumn 2020; May, 2021 ($5.00/$3.99)

#0 ($5.00) Intro. story with Braden-s/Malbrough-a; bonus pin-ups 5.00
#0: The Director's Cut (AMP, 5/21, $3.99) r/#0 with new story with Braden-s/Malbrough-a; 2 new text stories by Meggan Groves Robinson & Marty Grosser 4.00
Gods and Monsters Promotional Edition (11/22, $3.99) Short stories and text stories 4.00

KENTS, THE
DC Comics: Aug, 1997 - No. 12, July, 1998 ($2.50, limited series)

1-12-Ostrander-s/art by Truman and Bair (#1-8), Mandrake (#9-12) 4.00
TPB ($19.95) r/#1-12 20.00

KERRY DRAKE (Also see A-1 Comics)
Argo: Jan, 1956 - No. 2, March, 1956

1,2-Newspaper-r 9 18 27 50 65 80

KERRY DRAKE DETECTIVE CASES (...Racket Buster No. 32,33)
(Also see Chamber of Clues & Green Hornet Comics #42-47)
Life's Romances/Compix/Magazine Ent. No.1-5/Harvey No.6 on: 1944 - No. 5, 1944; No. 6, Jan, 1948 - No. 33, Aug, 1952

nn(1944)(A-1 Comics)(slightly over-size) 39 78 117 231 378 525
2 22 44 66 132 216 300
3,4(1944) 19 38 57 111 176 240
5(1944)-Bondage headlight-c 66 132 198 419 722 1025
6,8(1948): Lady Crime by Powell. 8-Bondage-c 15 30 45 84 127 170
7-Kubert-a; biog of Andriola (artist) 15 30 45 86 133 180
9,10-Two-part marijuana story; Kerry smokes marijuana in #10 19 38 57 111 176 240
11-15 13 26 39 74 105 135
16-33 10 20 30 56 76 95
NOTE: *Andiola c-6-9. Berg a-5. Powell a-10-23, 28, 29.*

KEVIN KELLER (Also see Veronica #202 for 1st app. & #207-210 for first mini-series)
Archie Comics Publications: Apr, 2012 - No. 15, Nov, 2014 ($2.99)

1-14-Two covers on each. 5-Action #1 swipe-c. 6-George Takei app. 3.00
15-($3.99) The Equalizer app.; 3 covers incl. Sensation #1 and X-Men #141 swipes 4.00

KEWPIES
Will Eisner Publications: Spring, 1949

1-Feiffer-a; Kewpie Doll ad on back cover; used in **SOTI**, pg. 35 77 154 231 493 847 1200

KEY COMICS
Consolidated Magazines: Jan, 1944 - No. 5, Aug, 1946

1-The Key, Will-O-The-Wisp begin 61 122 183 390 670 950
2 (3/44) 34 68 102 204 332 460
3,4: 3 (Winter 45/46). 4-(5/46)-Origin John Quincy The Atom (begins); Walter Johnson c-3-5 30 60 90 177 289 400
5-4pg. Faust Opera adaptation; Kiefer-a; back-c advertises "Masterpieces Illustrated" by Lloyd Jacquet after he left Classic Comics (no copies of Masterpieces Illustrated known) 37 74 111 222 361 500

KEY OF Z
BOOM! Studios: Oct, 2011 - No. 4, Jan, 2012 ($3.99, limited series)

1-4: 1-Claudio Sanchez & Chondra Echert-s/Aaron Kuder-a; covers by Fox & Moore 4.00

KEY RING COMICS
Dell Publishing Co.: 1941 (16 pgs.; two colors) (sold 5 for 10¢)

1-Sky Hawk, 1-Features Sleepy Samson, 1-Origin Greg Gilday; r/War Comics #2

Ka-Zar V2 #1 © MAR

Kent Menace Gods and Monsters Promo #1 © Braden & Malbrough

Kick-Ass #8 © Millar & Romita Jr.

GD VG FN VF VF/NM NM-
2.0 4.0 6.0 8.0 9.0 9.2

19 38 57 111 176 240
1-Radior (Super hero) 20 40 60 120 195 270
1-Viking Carter (WWII Nazi-c) 20 40 60 117 189 260
NOTE: *Each book has two holes in spine to put in binder.*

KICK-ASS
Marvel Comics (Icon): April, 2008 - No. 8, Mar, 2010 ($2.99)

1-Mark Millar-s/John Romita Jr.-a/c 24.00
1-Red variant cover by McNiven 25.00
1-2nd printing 4.00
1-Director's Cut (8/08, $3.99) r/#1 with script and sketch pages; Millar afterword 5.00
2 8.00
3-8: 3-1st app. Hit-Girl. 5-Intro. Red Mist 4.00
NOTE: *Multiple printings exist for most issues.*

KICK-ASS
Image Comics: Feb, 2018 - No. 18, Oct, 2019 ($3.99)

1-18: 1-6-Mark Millar-s/John Romita Jr.-a/c. 1-Intro. Patience Lee. 7-18-Niles-s/Frusin-a 4.00

KICK-ASS 2
Marvel Comics (Icon): Dec, 2010 - No. 7, May, 2012 ($2.99/$4.99)

1-6-Mark Millar-s/John Romita Jr.-a/c. 1-Five printings 3.00
1-6-Variant covers. 1-Edwards. 2-Yu. 5-Photo & Hitch. 6-Photo-c 5.00
7-($4.99) Extra-sized finale; bonus preview of Secret Service #1 5.00
7-($4.99) Variant photo-c 7.00

KICK-ASS 3
Marvel Comics (Icon): Jul, 2013 - No. 8, Oct, 2014 ($2.99/$3.99/$4.99/$5.99)

1-5-($2.99) Mark Millar-s/John Romita Jr.-a/c 3.00
1-5-Variant covers. 1-Hughes. 2-Fegredo. 3-Mack. 5-Bond 5.00
6-($4.99) Secret origin of Hit-Girl 5.00
7-($3.99) 4.00
8-($5.99) 6.00

KICK-ASS VS. HIT-GIRL
Image Comics: Nov, 2020 - No. 5, Mar, 2021 ($3.99)

1-5-Patience Lee vs. Mindy McCready; Niles-s/Frusin-a 4.00

KID CARROTS
St. John Publishing Co.: September, 1953

1-Funny animal 13 26 39 74 105 135

KID COLT ONE-SHOT
Marvel Comics: Sept, 2009 ($3.99)

1-DeFalco-s/Burchett-a/Luke Ross-c 4.00

KID COLT OUTLAW (Kid Colt #1-4; ...Outlaw #5-on)(Also see All Western Winners, Best Western, Black Rider, Giant-Size..., Two-Gun Kid, Two-Gun Western, Western Winners, Wild Western, Wisco)
Marvel Comics(LCC) 1-16; Atlas(LMC) 17-102; Marvel 103-on: 8/48 - No. 139, 3/68; No. 140, 11/69 - No. 229, 4/79

1-Kid Colt & his horse Steel begin. 276 552 828 1753 3027 4300
2 106 212 318 673 1162 1650
3-5: 4-Anti-Wertham editorial; Tex Taylor app. 5-Blaze Carson app.
68 136 204 435 743 1050
6-8: 6-Tex Taylor app; 7-Nimo the Lion begins, ends #10
42 84 126 265 445 625
9,10 (52 pgs.) 45 90 135 284 480 675
11-Origin (10/50) 47 94 141 296 498 700
12-20 29 58 87 170 278 385
21-32 24 48 72 140 230 320
33-45: Black Rider in all 20 40 60 120 195 270
46,47,49,50 19 38 57 112 179 245
48-Kubert-a 20 40 60 115 185 255
51-53,55,56 17 34 51 103 162 220
54-Williamson/Maneely-c 19 38 57 111 176 240
57-60,66: 4-pg. Williamson-a in all 10 20 30 70 150 230
61-63,67-78,80-86: 69,73-Maneely-c. 70-Severin-c. 86-Kirby-a(r).
10 20 30 68 144 220
64,65-Crandall-a 11 22 33 76 163 250
79,87: 79-Origin retold. 87-Davis-a(r) 10 20 30 70 150 230
88,89-Williamson-a in both (4 pgs.). 89-Redrawn Matt Slade #2
10 20 30 70 150 230
90-99,101-106,108,109: 91-Kirby/Ayers-c. 95-Kirby/Ayers-c/story. 102-Last 10¢ issue
12 24 36 83 182 280
100 17 34 51 117 259 400
107-Only Kirby sci-fi cover of title 46 92 138 340 770 1200
110-(5/63)-1st app. Iron Mask (Iron Man type villain) 16 32 48 110 243 375
111-113,115-120 9 18 27 62 126 190
114-(1/64)-2nd app. Iron Mask 12 24 36 84 185 285
121-129,133-139: 121-Rawhide Kid x-over. 125-Two-Gun Kid x-over. 139-Last 12¢ issue
6 12 18 42 79 115
130-132 (68 pgs.)-one new story each. 130-Origin 8 16 24 51 96 140
140-155: 140-Reprints begin (later issues mostly-r). 155-Last 15¢ issue
3 6 9 16 24 32
156-Giant; reprints (52 pgs.) 4 8 12 22 35 48
157-180,200: 170-Origin retold. 3 6 9 15 22 28
181-199 3 6 9 14 19 24
201-229: 201-New material w/Rawhide Kid app; Kane-c. 229-Rawhide Kid-r
2 4 6 11 16 20
205-209-(30¢-c variants, limited dist.) 12 24 36 82 179 275
218-220-(35¢-c variants, limited dist.) 22 44 66 154 340 525
...Album (no date; 1950's; Atlas Comics)-132 pgs.; cardboard cover,
B&W stories; (Rare) 174 348 522 1114 1907 2700
NOTE: ***Ayers** a-many. **Colan** a-52, 53, 84, 112, 114; c(p)-223, 228, 229. **Crandall** a-140r, 167r. **Everett** a-90, 137i, 225i(r). **Heath** a-8(2); c-34, 35, 39, 44, 46, 48, 49, 57, 64. **Heck** a-135, 139. **Jack Keller** a-25(2), 26-68(3-4), 73, 78, 82, 84, 85, 88, 92, 94p, 98, 99, 101, 102, 106-130, 132, 140-150r. **Kirby** a-86r, 93, 96, 119, 176(part); c-87, 92-95, 97, 99-112, 114-117, 121-123, 197r; w/**Ditko** c-89. **Maneely** a-12, 68, 81; c-9, 17, 19, 40-43, 47, 52, 53, 62, 65, 68, 73, 78, 81, 142r, 150r. **Morrow** a-173r, 216r. **Rico** a-13, 18. **Severin** c-55, 58, 59, 84, 143, 148, 149i. **Shores** a-39, 41-43, 143r; c-1-10(most), 24. **Sutton** a-136, 137p, 225p(r). **Wildey** a-47, 54, 82, 144r. **Williamson** r-147, 170, 172, 216. **Woodbridge** a-64, 81. Black Rider in #33-45, 74, 86. Iron Mask in #110, 114, 121, 127. Sam Hawk in #80, 84, 101, 111, 121, 146, 174, 181, 188.*

KID COWBOY (Also see Approved Comics #4 & Boy Cowboy)
Ziff-Davis Publ./St. John (Approved Comics) #11,14: 1950 - No. 11, Wint, '52-'53; No. 13, April 1953; No. 14, June, 1954 (No #12) (Painted covers #1-10,13,14)

1-Lucy Belle & Red Feather begin 24 48 72 140 230 320
2-Maneely-c 15 30 45 84 127 170
3-11,13,14: (#3, spr. '51). 5-Berg-a. 14-Code approved
14 28 42 80 115 150

KID DEATH & FLUFFY HALLOWEEN SPECIAL
Event Comics: Oct, 1997 ($2.95, B&W, one-shot)

1-Variant-c by Cebollero & Quesada/Palmiotti 4.00

KID DEATH & FLUFFY SPRING BREAK SPECIAL
Event Comics: July, 1996 ($2.50, B&W, one-shot)

1-Quesada & Palmiotti-c/scripts 4.00

KIDDIE KAPERS
Kiddie Kapers Co., 1945/Decker Publ. (Red Top-Farrell): 1945?(nd); Oct, 1957; 1963 - 1964

1(nd, 1945-46?, 36 pgs.)-Infinity-c; funny animal 13 26 39 72 101 130
1(10/57)(Decker)-Little Bit-r from Kiddie Karnival 5 10 15 24 30 35
Super Reprint #7, 10('63), 12, 14('63), 15,17('64), 18('64): 10, 14-r/Animal Adventures #1. 15-Animal Advs. #? 17-Cowboys 'N' Injuns #? 2 4 6 9 13 16

KIDDIE KARNIVAL
Ziff-Davis Publ. Co. (Approved Comics): 1952 (25¢, 100 pgs.) (One Shot)

nn-Rebound Little Bit #1,2; painted-c 39 78 117 240 395 550

KID ETERNITY (Becomes Buccaneers) (See Hit Comics)
Quality Comics Group: Spring, 1946 - No. 18, Nov, 1949

1 90 180 270 576 988 1400
2 40 80 120 246 411 575
3-Mac Raboy-a 41 82 123 256 428 600
4-10 26 52 78 154 252 350
11-18 20 40 60 115 185 255

KID ETERNITY
DC Comics: 1991 - No. 3, Nov, 1991 ($4.95, limited series)

1-3: Grant Morrison scripts/Duncan Fegredo-a/c 6.00
TPB (2006, $14.99) r/#1-3 15.00

KID ETERNITY
DC Comics (Vertigo): May, 1993 - No. 16, Sept, 1994 ($1.95, mature)

1-16: 1-Gold ink-c. 6-Photo-c. All Sean Phillips-c/a except #15 (Phillips-c/i only) 3.00

KID FROM DODGE CITY, THE
Atlas Comics (MMC): July, 1957 - No. 2, Sept, 1957

1-Don Heck-c 18 36 54 107 169 230
2-Everett-c 13 26 39 78 112 145

KID FROM TEXAS, THE (A Texas Ranger)
Atlas Comics (CSI): June, 1957 - No. 2, Aug, 1957

1-Powell-a; Severin-c 16 32 48 96 151 205
2 12 24 36 69 97 125

KID KOKO

	GD	VG	FN	VF	VF/NM	NM-
	2.0	4.0	6.0	8.0	9.0	9.2

I. W. Enterprises: 1958

Reprint #1,2-(r/M.E.'s Koko & Kola #4, 1947)	4	7	10	14	17	20

KID KOMICS (Kid Movie Komics No. 11)
Timely Comics (USA 1,2/FCI 3-10): Feb, 1943 - No. 10, Spring, 1946

1-Origin Captain Wonder & sidekick Tim Mullrooney, & Subbie; intro the Sea-Going Lad, Pinto Pete, & Trixie Trouble; Knuckles & Whitewash Jones (from Young Allies) app.; Wolverton-a (7 pgs.)	725	1450	2175	5300	9650	14,000
2-The Young Allies, Red Hawk, & Tommy Tyme begin; last Captain Wonder & Subbie; Schomburg Japanese WWII bondage-c	300	600	900	2070	3635	5200
3-The Vision, Daredevils & Red Hawk app.	232	464	696	1485	2543	3600
4-The Destroyer begins; Sub-Mariner app.; Red Hawk & Tommy Tyme end; classic Schomburg WWII human meat grinder-c	295	590	885	1888	3244	4600
5,6: 5-Tommy Tyme begins, ends #10	148	296	444	947	1624	2300
7-10: 7,10-The Whizzer app. Destroyer not in #7,8. 10-Last Destroyer, Young Allies & Whizzer	123	246	369	787	1344	1900

NOTE: *Brodsky c-5. Schomburg c-2-4, 6-10. Shores c-1. Captain Wonder c-1, 2. The Young Allies c-3-10.*

KID LOBOTOMY
IDW Publishing (Black Crown): Oct, 2017 - No. 6, Mar, 2018 ($3.99)

1-6: 1-Milligan-s/Fowler-a; covers by Fowler & Quitely 4.00

KID MONTANA (Formerly Davy Crockett Frontier Fighter; The Gunfighters No. 51 on)
Charlton Comics: V2#9, Nov, 1957 - No. 50, Mar, 1965

V2#9 (#1)	4	8	12	28	47	65
10	3	6	9	19	30	40
11,12,14-20	3	6	9	15	22	28
13-Williamson-a	3	6	9	19	30	40
21-35: 25,31-Giordano-c. 32-Origin Kid Montana. 34-Geronimo-c/s. 35-Snow Monster-c/s	2	4	6	11	16	20
36-50: 36-Dinosaur-c/s. 37,48-Giordano-c	2	4	6	9	12	15

NOTE: *Title change to Montana Kid on cover only #44 & 45; remained Kid Montana on inside.* ***Chasal*** *a-29,30.* ***Giordano*** *c-25,31,37,48.* ***Giordano/Alascia*** *c-12.* ***Mastroserio*** *a-9,11,13,14,22; c-11,14.* ***Masulli/Mastroserio*** *c-13.* ***Montes/Bache*** *c-42.* ***Morisi*** *c-16,32-34,36?,40,41,44,46; a-13,15;16,31-50.* ***Nicholas/Alascia*** *a-44,48.*

KID MOVIE KOMICS (Formerly Kid Komics; Rusty Comics #12 on)
Timely Comics: No. 11, Summer, 1946

11-Silly Seal & Ziggy Pig; 2 pgs. Kurtzman "Hey Look" plus 6 pg. "Pigtales" story	37	74	111	218	354	490

KIDNAPPED (See Marvel Illustrated: Kidnapped)

KIDNAPPED (Robert Louis Stevenson's...also see Movie Comics)(Disney)
Dell Publishing Co.: No. 1101, May, 1960

Four Color 1101-Movie, photo-c	6	12	18	42	79	115

KIDNAP RACKET (See Harvey Comics Hits No. 57)

KID SLADE, GUNFIGHTER (Formerly Matt Slade...)
Atlas Comics (SPI): No. 5, Jan, 1957 - No. 8, July, 1957

5-Maneely, Roth, Severin-a in all; Maneely-c	15	30	45	90	140	190
6,8-Severin-c	12	24	36	69	97	125
7-Williamson/Mayo-a, 4 pgs.; Maneely-c	14	28	42	80	115	150

KID SUPREME (See Supreme)
Image Comics (Extreme Studios): Mar, 1996 - No. 3, July, 1996 ($2.50)

1-3: Fraga-a/scripts. 3-Glory-c/app. 3.00

KID ZOO COMICS
Street & Smith Publications: July, 1948 (52 pgs.)

1-Funny Animal	36	72	108	211	343	475

KILLADELPHIA
Image Comics: Nov, 2019 - Present ($3.99)

1-28-Philadelphia vampires; Rodney Barnes-s/Jason Shawn Alexander-a/c 4.00

KILL ALL PARENTS
Image Comics: June, 2008 ($3.99, one-shot)

1-Marcelo Di Chiara-a/Mark Andrew Smith-s 4.00

KILLAPALOOZA
DC Comics (WildStorm): July, 2009 - No. 6, Dec, 2009 ($2.99, limited series)

1-6: 1-Beechen-s/Hairsine-a/c 3.00
TPB (2010, $19.99) r/#1-6 20.00

KILLER (...Tales By Timothy Truman)
Eclipse Comics: March, 1985 ($1.75, one-shot, Baxter paper)

1-Timothy Truman-c/a 4.00

KILLER INSTINCT (Video game)
Acclaim Comics: June, 1996 - No. 6 ($2.50, limited series)

1-6: 1-Bart Sears-a(p). 4-Special #1. 5-Special #2. 6-Special #3 4.00

KILLER INSTINCT (Video game)
Dynamite Entertainment: 2017 - No. 6, 2018 ($3.99, limited series)

1-6: 1,2-Ian Edginton-s/Cam Adams-a; multiple covers. 3-6-Ediano Silva-a 4.00

KILLER QUEENS
Dark Horse Comics: Aug, 2021 - No. 4, Nov, 2021 ($3.99, limited series)

1-4-David M. Booher-s/Claudia Balboni-a; 3 covers on each 4.00

KILLERS
Valiant Entertainment: Jul, 2019 - No. 5, Nov, 2019 ($3.99, limited series)

1-5-B. Clay Moore-s/Fernando Dagnino-a; origin of KI-6 4.00

KILLERS, THE
Magazine Enterprises: 1947 - No. 2, 1948 (No month)

1-Mr. Zin, the Hatchet Killer; mentioned in **SOTI**, pgs. 179,180; used by N.Y. Legis. Comm.; L. B. Cole-c	206	412	618	1318	2259	3200
2-(Scarce)-Hashish smoking story; "Dying, Dying, Dead" drug story; Whitney, Ingels-a; Whitney hanging-c	174	348	522	1114	1907	2700

KILLING GIRL
Image Comics: Aug, 2007 - No. 5, Dec, 2007 ($2.99, limited series)

1-5: 1-Frank Espinosa-a/Glen Brunswick-s; covers by Espinosa and Frank Cho 3.00

KILLING JOKE, THE (See Batman: The Killing Joke under Batman one-shots)

KILLING RED SONJA, VOLUME 1 (Follows Red Sonja Volume 5 #12)
Dynamite Entertainment: 2020 - No. 5, 2020 ($3.99)

1-5-Russell & Ingman-s/Rousseau-a. 4-Sorcerors of Wigur-Nomadene app. 4.00

KILL LOCK, THE
IDW Publishing: Dec, 2019 - No. 6, May, 2020 ($3.99)

1-3-Livio Ramondelli-s/a 4.00

KILL LOCK, THE: THE ARTISAN WRAITH
IDW Publishing: Mar, 2022 - No. 6, Aug, 2022 ($3.99/$7.99)

1-5-Livio Ramondelli-s/a 4.00
6-($7.99) Double size finale 8.00

KILLMONGER (From Black Panther)
Marvel Comics: Feb, 2019 - No. 5, May, 2019 ($4.99/$3.99, limited series)

1-($4.99) Bryan Hill-s/Juan Ferreyra-a; N'Jadaka's rise to Killmonger; Kingpin app. 5.00
2-5-($3.99) 2,3-Bullseye app. 3-5-Black Widow app. 4.00

KILL OR BE KILLED
Image Comics: Aug, 2016 - No. 20, Jun, 2018 ($3.99)

1-20-Ed Brubaker-s/Sean Phillips-a 4.00

KILLPOWER: THE EARLY YEARS
Marvel Comics UK: Sept, 1993 - No. 4, Dec, 1993 ($1.75, mini-series)

1-($2.95)-Foil embossed-c 4.00
2-4: 2-Genetix app. 3-Punisher app. 3.00

KILLRAVEN (See Amazing Adventures #18 (5/73))
Marvel Comics: Feb, 2001 ($2.99, one-shot)

1-Linsner-s/a/c 3.00

KILLRAVEN
Marvel Comics: Dec, 2002 - No. 6, May, 2003 ($2.99, limited series)

1-6-Alan Davis-s/a(p)/Mark Farmer-i 3.00
HC (2007, $19.99) r/#1-6; cover gallery, pencil art; foreward by Alan Davis 20.00

KILLRAZOR
Image Comics (Top Cow Productions): Aug, 1995 ($2.50, one-shot)

1 3.00

KILL WHITEY DONOVAN
Dark Horse Comics: Dec, 2019 - No. 5, Apr, 2020 ($3.99, limited series)

1-5-Sydney Duncan-s/Natalie Barahona-a; 2 covers by Pearson and Barahona 4.00

KILL YOUR BOYFRIEND
DC Comics (Vertigo): June, 1995 ($4.95, one-shot)

1-Grant Morrison story 6.00
1 ($5.95, 1998) 2nd printing 6.00

KILROY (Volume 2)
Caliber Press: 1998 ($2.95, B&W)

1-Pruett-s 3.00

KILROY IS HERE
Caliber Press: 1995 ($2.95, B&W)

1-10 3.00

KILROYS, THE
B&I Publ. Co. No. 1-19/American Comics Group: June-July, 1947 - No. 54, June-July, 1955

1	30	60	90	177	289	400
2	15	30	45	92	144	195
3-5: 5-Gross-a	15	30	45	83	124	165
6-10: 8-Milt Gross's Moronica (1st app.)	12	24	36	69	97	125
11-20: 14-Gross-a	10	20	30	56	76	95
21-30	9	18	27	52	69	85
31-47,50-54	9	18	27	47	61	75
48,49-(3-D effect-c/stories)	19	38	57	112	179	245

KILROY: THE SHORT STORIES
Caliber Press: 1995 ($2.95, B&W)

1 3.00

KIM REAPER
Oni Press: Apr, 2017 - No. 4, Jul, 2017 ($3.99, limited series)

1-4-Sarah Graley-s/a/c 4.00

KIM REAPER: VAMPIRE ISLAND
Oni Press: Sept, 2018 - No. 4, Nov, 2018 ($3.99, limited series)

1-4-Sarah Graley-s/a/c 4.00

KIN
Image Comics (Top Cow): Mar, 2000 - No. 6, Sept, 2000 ($2.95)

1-5-Gary Frank-s/c/a 3.00
1-($6.95) DF Alternate footprint cover 7.00
6-($3.95) 4.00
... Descent of Man TPB (2002, $19.95) r/ #1-6 20.00

KINDRED, THE
Image Comics (WildStorm Productions): Mar, 1994 - No. 4, July, 1995 ($1.95, lim. series)

1-($2.50)-Grifter & Backlash app. in all; bound-in trading card 4.00
2-4 3.00
2,3: 2-Variant-c. 3-Alternate-c by Portacio, see Deathblow #5 4.00
Trade paperback (2/95, $9.95) 10.00

NOTE: ***Booth*** *c/a-1-4. The first four issues contain coupons redeemable for a Jim Lee Grifter/Backlash print.*

KINDRED II, THE
DC Comics (WildStorm): Mar, 2002 - No. 4, June, 2002 ($2.50, limited series)

1-4-Booth-s/Booth & Regla-a 3.00

KINETIC
DC Comics (Focus): May, 2004 - No. 8, Dec, 2004 ($2.50)

1-8-Puckett-s/Pleece-a/c 3.00

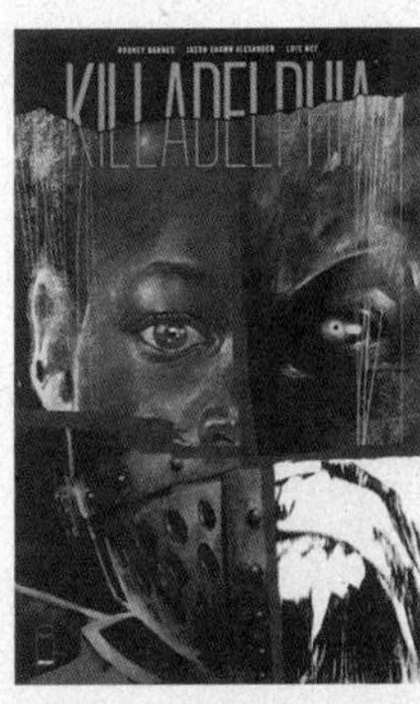
Killadelphia #9 © Barnes & Alexander

King Conan (2022) #1 © CPI

King in Black: Namor #1 © MAR

GD VG FN VF VF/NM NM-
2.0 4.0 6.0 8.0 9.0 9.2

TPB (2005, $9.99) r/#1-8; cover gallery and sketch pages 10.00

KING (Magazine)
Skywald Publ.: Mar, 1971 - No. 2, July, 1971

1-Violence; semi-nudity; Boris Vallejo-a (2 pgs.) 5 10 15 31 53 75
2-Photo-c 3 6 9 21 33 45

KING ARTHUR AND THE KNIGHTS OF JUSTICE
Marvel Comics UK: Dec, 1993 - No. 3, Feb, 1994 ($1.25, limited series)

1-3: TV adaptation 3.00

KING CLASSICS
King Features : 1977 (36 pgs., cardboard-c) (Printed in Spain for U.S. distr.)

1-Connecticut Yankee, 2-Last of the Mohicans, 3-Moby Dick, 4-Robin Hood, 5-Swiss Family Robinson, 6-Robinson Crusoe, 7-Treasure Island, 8-20,000 Leagues, 9-Christmas Carol, 10-Huck Finn, 11-Around the World in 80 Days, 12-Davy Crockett, 13-Don Quixote, 14-Gold Bug, 15-Ivanhoe, 16-Three Musketeers, 17-Baron Munchausen, 18-Alice in Wonderland, 19-Black Arrow, 20-Five Weeks in a Balloon, 21-Great Expectations, 22-Gulliver's Travels, 23-Prince & Pauper, 24-Lawrence of Arabia (Originals, 1977-78)
each.... 2 4 6 10 14 18
Reprints (1979; HRN-24) 2 4 6 8 10 12

NOTE: *The first eight issues were not numbered. Issues No. 25-32 were advertised but not published. The 1977 originals have HRN 32a; the 1978 originals have HRN 32b.*

KING COLT (See Luke Short's Western Stories)

KING COMICS (Strip reprints)
David McKay Publications/Standard #156-on: 4/36 - No. 155, 11-12/49; No. 156, Spr/50 - No. 159, 2/52 (Winter on-c)

	GD	VG	FN	VF	VF/NM	NM-
1-1st app. Flash Gordon by Alex Raymond; Brick Bradford (1st app.), Popeye, Henry (1st app.) & Mandrake the Magician (1st app.) begin; Popeye-c begin	1690	3380	5070	13,500	--	--
2	375	750	1125	2060	3180	4300
3	260	520	780	1560	2330	3100
4	200	400	600	1100	1725	2350
5	145	290	435	800	1250	1700
6-10: 9-X-Mas-c	105	210	315	580	890	1200
11-20	77	154	231	420	660	900
21-30: 21-X-Mas-c	58	116	174	320	498	675
31-40: 33-Last Segar Popeye	47	94	141	260	425	590
41-50: 46-Text illos by Marge Buell contain characters similar to Lulu, Alvin & Tubby. 50-The Lone Ranger begins	37	74	111	218	354	490
51-60: 52-Barney Baxter begins?	34	68	102	199	325	450
61-The Phantom begins	36	72	108	211	343	475
62-80: 76-Flag-c. 79-Blondie begins	20	40	60	114	182	250
81-99	15	30	45	85	130	175
100	19	38	57	109	172	235
101-114: 114-Last Raymond issue (1 pg.); Flash Gordon by Austin Briggs begins, ends #155	14	28	42	76	108	140
115-145: 117-Phantom origin retold	10	20	30	56	76	95
146,147-Prince Valiant in both	9	18	27	50	65	80
148-155: 155-Flash Gordon ends (11-12/49)	9	18	27	50	65	80
156-159: 156-New logo begins (Standard)	9	18	27	47	61	75

NOTE: *Marge Buell text illos in No. 24-46 at least.*

KING CONAN (Conan The King No. 20 on)
Marvel Comics Group: Mar, 1980 - No. 19, Nov, 1983 (52 pgs.)

1 3 6 9 14 19 24
2-19: 4-Death of Thoth Amon. 7-1st Paul Smith-a, 1 pg. pin-up (9/81) 5.00

NOTE: ***J. Buscema** a-1-9p, 17p; c(p)-1-5, 7-9, 14, 17. **Kaluta** c-19. **Nebres** a-17i, 18, 19i. **Severin** c-18. **Simonson** c-6.*

KING CONAN
Marvel Comics: Feb, 2022 - No. 6, Sept, 2022 ($4.99/$3.99)

1-($4.99) Jason Aaron-s/Mahmud Asrar-a; Thoth-Amon app. 5.00
2-6-($3.99) 5-Thoth-Amon origin re-told 4.00

KING CONAN: THE CONQUEROR
Dark Horse Comics: Feb, 2014 - No. 6, Jul, 2014 ($3.50, limited series)

1-6-Truman-s/Giorello-a/c 3.50

KING CONAN: THE HOUR OF THE DRAGON
Dark Horse Comics: May, 2013 - No. 6, Oct, 2013 ($3.50, limited series)

1-6-Truman-s/Giorello-a/Parel-c 3.50

KING CONAN: THE PHOENIX ON THE SWORD
Dark Horse Comics: Jan, 2012 - No. 4, Apr, 2012 ($3.50, limited series)

1-4-Truman-s/Giorello-a/Robinson-c. 1-Variant-c by Parel 3.50

KING CONAN: THE SCARLET CITADEL
Dark Horse Comics: Feb, 2011 - No. 4, May, 2011 ($3.50, limited series)

1-4-Truman-s/Giorello-a/Robertson-c. 1-Variant-c by Parel 3.50

KING CONAN: WOLVES BEYOND THE BORDER
Dark Horse Comics: Dec, 2015 - No. 4, Mar, 2016 ($3.99, limited series)

1-4-Truman-s/Giorello-a/c. 1-Kull app. 4-Bran Mak Morn app. 4.00

KING DAVID
DC Comics (Vertigo): 2002 ($19.95, 8 1/2" x 11")

nn-Story of King David; Kyle Baker-s/a 20.00

KINGDOM, THE
DC Comics: Feb, 1999 - No. 2, Feb, 1999 ($2.95/$1.99, limited series)

1,2-Waid-s; sequel to Kingdom Come; introduces Hypertime 1 3 4 6 8 10
...: Kid Flash 1 (2/99, $1.99) Waid-s/Pararillo-a, ...: Nightstar 1 (2/99, $1.99) Waid-s/Haley-a, ...: Offspring 1 (2/99, $1.99) Waid-s/Quitely-a, ...: Planet Krypton 1 (2/99, $1.99) Waid-s/Kitson-a, ...: Son of the Bat 1 (2/99, $1.99) Waid-s/Apthorp-a 3.00

KINGDOM COME (Also see Justice Society of America #9-22)
DC Comics: 1996 - No. 4, 1996 ($4.95, painted limited series)

1-Mark Waid scripts & Alex Ross-painted c/a in all; tells the last days of the DC Universe; 1st app. Magog 3 6 9 14 19 24
2-Superman forms new Justice League 3 6 9 14 19 24
3-Return of Captain Marvel 2 4 6 8 10 12
4-Final battle of Superman and Captain Marvel 2 4 6 8 11 14
Deluxe Slipcase Edition-($89.95) w/Revelations companion book, 12 new story pages, foil stamped covers, signed and numbered 120.00
Hardcover Edition-($29.95)-Includes 12 new story pages and artwork from Revelations, new cover artwork with gold foil inlay 40.00
Hardcover 2nd printing 30.00
Softcover Ed.-($14.95)-Includes 12 new story pgs. & artwork from Revelations, new c-artwork 20.00
Softcover Ed.-(2008, $17.99)-New wraparound gatefold cover by Ross 18.00

KING: FLASH GORDON
Dynamite Entertainment: 2015 - No. 4, 2015 ($3.99)

1-4: 1-Acker & Blacker-s/Ferguson-a/Cooke-c; variant-c by Liefeld. 2-Zdarsky-c 4.00

KING IN BLACK (See Venom and Knull: Marvel Tales)
Marvel Comics: Feb, 2021 - No. 5, Jun, 2021 ($5.99/$4.99)

1-($5.99) Cates-s/Stegman-a; Knull arrives on Earth; Venom & the Avengers app. 6.00
2-4-($4.99) 2-Namor & Spider-Man app. 3-Thor returns. 4-Enigma Force app. 5.00
5-($5.99) Cates-s/Stegman-a; Silver Surfer, Venom & the Avengers app. 6.00
...: Black Knight 1 (4/21, $4.99) Spurrier-s/Saiz-a 5.00
...: Black Panther 1 (4/21, $4.99) Thorne-s/Peralta-a; Shuri & Storm app. 5.00
...: Captain America 1 (5/21, $4.99) Lore-s/Colak & Leon-a; Falcon & Winter Soldier app. 5.00
...: Ghost Rider 1 (5/21, $4.99) Brisson-s/Frigeri-a; Mephisto app. 5.00
... Handbook 1 (5/21, $4.99) Profiles for the symbiotes and major characters 5.00
...: Immortal Hulk 1 (2/21, $4.99) Ewing-s/Kuder-a; Savage Hulk vs. symbiotes 5.00
...: Iron Man/Doom 1 (2/21, $3.99) Cantwell-s/Larroca-a; battle a symbiote Santa Claus 4.00
...: Marauders 1 (4/21, $4.99) Gerry Duggan-s/Luke Ross-a 5.00
...: Scream 1 (5/21, $4.99) Clay Chapman-s/Garry Brown-a 5.00
...: Spider-Man 1 (5/21, $4.99) MacKay-s/Bandini-a; Reptil app. 5.00
...: Wiccan and Hulkling 1 (5/21, $4.99) Tini Howard-s/Luciano Vecchio-a 5.00

KING IN BLACK: GWENOM VS. CARNAGE
Marvel Comics: Mar, 2021 - No. 3, May, 2021 ($3.99, limited series)

1-3-McGuire-s/Flaviano-a; Ghost-Spider & Mary Jane Watson app. 4.00

KING IN BLACK: NAMOR
Marvel Comics: Feb, 2021 - No. 5, Jun, 2021 ($3.99, limited series)

1-5-Busiek-s/Dewey-a; flashback to Namor's youth 4.00

KING IN BLACK: PLANET OF THE SYMBIOTES
Marvel Comics: Mar, 2021 - No. 3, Jun, 2021 ($3.99, limited series)

1-3-Scream app.; Knull attacks Ravencroft; Misty Knight & John Jameson app. 4.00

KING IN BLACK: RETURN OF THE VALKYRIES
Marvel Comics: Feb, 2021 - No. 4, May, 2021 ($3.99, limited series)

1-4-Aaron & Gronbekk-s/Vakueva-a; Jane Foster, The Sentry & Dani Moonstar app. 4.00

KING IN BLACK: THUNDERBOLTS
Marvel Comics: Mar, 2021 - No. 3, May, 2021 ($3.99, limited series)

1-3-Rosenberg-s/Ferreyra-a; Star, Rhino, Batroc, Taskmaster app. 4.00

KING: JUNGLE JIM
Dynamite Entertainment: 2015 - No. 4, 2015 ($3.99)

1-4: 1-Tobin-s/Jarrell-a/Cooke-c; variant-c by Liefeld. 2-Zdarsky-c 4.00

KING KONG (See Movie Comics)

KING KONG: THE 8TH WONDER OF THE WORLD (Adaptation of 2005 movie)

	GD	VG	FN	VF	VF/NM	NM-
	2.0	4.0	6.0	8.0	9.0	9.2

Dark Horse Comics: Dec, 2005 ($3.99, planned limited series completed in TPB)
1-Photo-c; Dustin Weaver-a/Christian Gossett-s 1 3 4 6 8 10
TPB (11/06, $12.95) r/#1 and unpublished parts 2&3; photo-c; Dorman paintings 13.00

KING LEONARDO & HIS SHORT SUBJECTS (TV)
Dell Publishing Co./Gold Key: Nov-Jan, 1961-62 - No. 4, Sept, 1963
Four Color 1242,1278 10 20 30 67 141 215
01390-207(5-7/62)(Dell) 8 16 24 52 99 145
1 (10/62) 9 18 27 60 120 180
2-4 7 14 21 48 89 130

KING LOUIE & MOWGLI (See Jungle Book under Movie Comics)
Gold Key: May, 1968 (Disney)
1 (#10223-805)-Characters from Jungle Book 4 8 12 23 37 50

KING: MANDRAKE THE MAGICIAN
Dynamite Entertainment: 2015 - No. 4, 2015 ($3.99)
1-4: 1-Langridge-s/Treece-a/Cooke-c; variant-c by Liefeld. 2-Zdarsky-c 4.00

KING OF DIAMONDS (TV)
Dell Publishing Co.: July-Sept, 1962
01-391-209-Photo-c 4 8 12 27 44 60

KING OF KINGS (Movie)
Dell Publishing Co.: No. 1236, Oct-Nov, 1961
Four Color 1236-Photo-c 8 16 24 52 99 145

KING OF NOWHERE
BOOM! Studios: Mar, 2020 - No. 5, Sept, 2020 ($3.99, limited series)
1-5-W. Maxwell Prince-s/Tyler Jenkins-a 4.00

KING OF SPIES
Image Comics: Dec, 2021 - No. 4, Mar, 2022 ($4.99/$3.99, limited series)
1-($4.99) Mark Millar-s/Matteo Scalera-a; intro. Roland King 5.00
2,3-($3.99) 4.00
4-($5.99) 6.00

KING OF THE BAD MEN OF DEADWOOD
Avon Periodicals: 1950 (See Wild Bill Hickok #16)
nn-Kinstler-c; Kamen/Feldstein-r/Cowpuncher #2 22 44 66 132 216 300

KING OF THE ROYAL MOUNTED (See Famous Feature Stories, King Comics, Red Ryder #3 & Super Book #2, 6)

KING OF THE ROYAL MOUNTED (Zane Grey's...)
David McKay/Dell Publishing Co.: No. 1, May, 1937; No. 9, 1940; No. 207, Dec, 1948 - No. 935, Sept-Nov, 1958
Feature Books 1 (5/37)(McKay) 110 220 330 704 1202 1700
Large Feature Comic 9 (1940) 54 108 162 343 574 825
Four Color 207(#1, 12/48) 14 28 42 94 207 320
Four Color 265,283 9 18 27 62 126 190
Four Color 310,340 7 14 21 46 86 125
Four Color 363,384, 8(6-8/52)-10 6 12 18 40 73 105
11-20 5 10 15 31 53 75
21-28(3-5/58) 4 8 12 27 44 60
Four Color 935(9-11/58) 5 10 15 31 53 75
NOTE: *4-Color No. 207, 265, 283, 310, 340, 363, 384 are all newspaper reprints with* ***Jim Gary*** *art. No. 8 on are all Dell originals. Painted c-No. 9-on.*

KINGPIN
Marvel Comics: Nov, 1997 ($5.99, squarebound, one-shot)
nn-Spider-Man & Daredevil vs. Kingpin; Stan Lee-s/ John Romita Sr.-a 6.00

KINGPIN
Marvel Comics: Aug, 2003 - No. 7, Jan, 2004 ($2.50/$2.99, limited series)
1-6-Bruce Jones-s/Sean Phillips & Klaus Janson-a 3.00
7-($2.99) 3.00

KINGPIN
Marvel Comics: Apr, 2017 - No. 5, Aug, 2017 ($3.99, limited series)
1-Wilson Fisk goes legit; Matthew Rosenberg-s/Ben Torres-a. 2-5-Tombstone app. 4.00

KING: PRINCE VALIANT
Dynamite Entertainment: 2015 - No. 4, 2015 ($3.99)
1-4: 1-Cosby-s/Salasl-a/Cooke-c; variant-c by Liefeld. 2-Zdarsky-c 4.00

KING RICHARD & THE CRUSADERS
Dell Publishing Co.: No. 588, Oct, 1954
Four Color 588-Movie, Matt Baker-a, photo-c 10 20 30 66 138 210

KING-SIZE CABLE SPECTACULAR (Takes place between Cable (2008 series) #6 & #7)
Marvel Comics: Nov, 2008 ($4.99, one-shot)
1-Lashley-a; Deadpool #1 preview; cover gallery of variants from 2008 series 5.00

KING-SIZE CONAN
Marvel Comics: Feb, 2021 ($6.99, one-shot)
1-Short stories by various incl. Roy Thomas, Eastman, Busiek, McNiven, Woods 7.00

KING-SIZE HULK (Takes place between Hulk (2008 series) #3 & #4)
Marvel Comics: July, 2008 ($4.99, one-shot)
1-Art Adams, Frank Cho, & Herb Trimpe-a; double-c by Cho & Adams; Red Hulk, She-Hulk & Wendigo app.; origin Abomination; r/Incr. Hulk #180,181 & Avengers #83
2 4 6 9 12 15

KING-SIZE SPIDER-MAN SUMMER SPECIAL
Marvel Comics: Oct, 2008 ($4.99, one-shot)
1-Short stories by various; Falcon app.; Burchett, Giarrusso & Coover-a 5.00

KINGSMEN: THE RED DIAMOND (Sequel to Secret Service)(Inspired Kingsmen movies)
Image Comics: Sept, 2017 - No. 6, Feb, 2018 ($3.99, limited series)
1-6-Rob Willliams-s/Simon Fraser-a. 1-Multiple covers 4.00

KINGS OF THE NIGHT
Dark Horse Comics: 1990 - No. 2, 1990 ($2.25, limited series)
1,2-Robert E. Howard adaptation; Bolton-c 3.00

KING SOLOMON'S MINES (Movie)
Avon Periodicals: 1951
nn (#1 on 1st page) 53 106 159 334 567 800

KING SPAWN
Image Comics: Aug, 2021 - Present ($5.99/$2.99)
1-($5.99) Sean Lewis-s/Javi Fernandez-a; back-ups with Haunt, Nightmare, Gunslinger Spawn; stories by McFarlane; art by various; multiple covers 6.00
2-20-($2.99) 4-She-Spawn app. 9,13-15-Nachlik-a. 18-Mack-c 3.00

KINGS QUEST
Dynamite Entertainment: 2016 - No. 5, 2016 ($3.99, limited series)
1-5-Flash Gordon, Mandrake, Prince Valiant, The Phantom team; multiple-c on each 4.00

KING'S ROAD
Dark Horse Comics: Feb, 2016 - No. 3, Apr, 2016 ($3.99, limited series)
1-3-Peter Hogan-s/Phil Winslade & Staz Johnson-a; Johnson-c 4.00

KINGS WATCH
Dynamite Entertainment: 2013 - No. 5, 2014 ($3.99)
1-5-Flash Gordon, Mandrake and The Phantom team up; Parker-s/Laming-a 4.00

KINGSWAY WEST
Dark Horse Comics: Aug, 2016 - No. 4, Feb, 2017 ($3.99)
1-4-Greg Pak-s/Mirko Colak-a/c 4.00

KING TANK GIRL
Albatross Funnybooks: 2020 - No. 5, 2021 ($3.99, limited series)
1-5-Alan Martin-s/Brett Parson-a; Tank Girl and crew go to England 4.00

KING: THE PHANTOM
Dynamite Entertainment: 2015 - No. 4, 2015 ($3.99)
1-4: 1-Clevinger-s/Schoonover-a/Cooke-c; var-c by Liefeld; Mandrake app. 2-Zdarsky-c 4.00

KING THOR
Marvel Comics: Nov, 2019 - No. 4, Feb, 2020 ($3.99/$5.99, limited series)
1-3-($3.99) Jason Aaron-s/Esad Ribic-a; set in the far future; Frigg, Ellisiv & Atli app. 4.00
4-($5.99) Leads into 2020 Thor series; art by Ribic, Del Mundo, Coipel & others 6.00

KING TIGER
Dark Horse Comics: Aug, 2015 - No. 4, Nov, 2015 ($3.99, limited series)
1-4-Randy Stradley-s/Doug Wheatley-a/c 4.00

KIPLING, RUDYARD (See Mowgli, The Jungle Book)

KIRBY: GENESIS
Dynamite Entertainment: No. 0, 2011 - No. 8, 2012 ($1.00/$3.99)
0-($1.00) Busiek-s; art by Alex Ross & Jack Herbert; series preview, sketch-a 3.00
1-8-($3.99) Ross & Herbert-a. 1-Seven covers. 2-8-Covers by Ross & Sook 4.00

KIRBY: GENESIS - CAPTAIN VICTORY
Dynamite Entertainment: 2011 - No. 6, 2012 ($3.99)
1-6: 1-Origin retold; four covers; Sterling Gates-s/Wagner Reis-a 4.00

KIRBY: GENESIS - DRAGONSBANE
Dynamite Entertainment: 2012 - No. 4, 2013 ($3.99, unfinished limited series)
1-4-Rodi & Ross-s/Casas-a; covers by Ross and Herbert 4.00

KIRBY: GENESIS - SILVER STAR
Dynamite Entertainment: 2011 - No. 6, 2012 ($3.99)
1-6-Jai Nitz-s/Johnny Desjardins-a. 1-Four covers. 2-6-Three covers 4.00

KISS (See Crazy Magazine, Howard the Duck #12, 13, Marvel Comics Super Special #1, 5, Rock Fantasy Comics #10 & Rock N' Roll Comics #9)

KISS
Dark Horse Comics: June, 2002 - No. 13, Sept, 2003 ($2.99, limited series)
1-Photo-c and J. Scott Campbell-c; Casey-s 6.00
2-13: 2-Photo-c and J. Scott Campbell-c. 3-Photo-c and Leinil Yu-c 4.00
...: Men and Monsters TPB (9/03, $12.95) r/#7-10 13.00
...: Rediscovery TPB (2003, $9.95) r/#1-3 10.00
...: Return of the Phantom TPB (2003, $9.95) r/#4-6 10.00
...: Unholy War TPB (2004, $9.95) r/#11-13 10.00

KISS
IDW Publishing: June, 2012 - No. 8, Jan, 2013 ($3.99)
1-8-Multiple covers on each. 1,2-Ryall-s/Igle-a 4.00

KISS (Volume 1)
Dynamite Entertainment: 2016 - No. 10, 2017 ($3.99)
1-10-Amy Chu-s/Kewber Baal-a; multiple covers 4.00
...: Blood and Stardust 1-5 (2018 - No. 5, 2019, $3.99) Bryan Hill-s/Rodney Buscemi-a 4.00
...: Forever (2017, $7.99, squarebound) Burnham-s/Daniel HDR-a/Cinar-c 8.00
...: The Demon 1-4 (2017, $3.99) prequel to 2016 series; Chu & Burnham-s/Casallos-a 4.00

KISS 4K
Platinum Studios Comics: May, 2007 - No. 6, Apr, 2008 ($3.99/$2.99)
1-Sprague-s/Crossley & Campos-a/Migliari-c 4.00
1-B&W sketch-c 6.00
1-Destroyer Edition ($50.00, 30"x18", edition of 5000) 50.00
2-6-($2.99) 3.00
KISSMAS (12/07, $4.99) Christmas-themed issue; re-cap of issues #1-4 5.00

KISSING CHAOS
Oni Press: Sept, 2001 - No. 8, Mar, 2002 ($2.25, B&W, 6" x 9", limited series)
1-8-Arthur Dela Cruz-s/a 3.00
...: Nine Lives (12/03, $2.99, regular comic-sized) 3.00
...: 1000 Words (7/03, $2.99, regular comic-sized) 3.00
TPB (9/02, $17.95) r/#1-8 18.00

KISSING CHAOS: NONSTOP BEAUTY
Oni Press: Oct, 2002 - No. 4, March, 2003 ($2.95, B&W, 6" x 9", limited series)
1-4-Arthur Dela Cruz-s/a 3.00

King of Spies #2 © Netflix

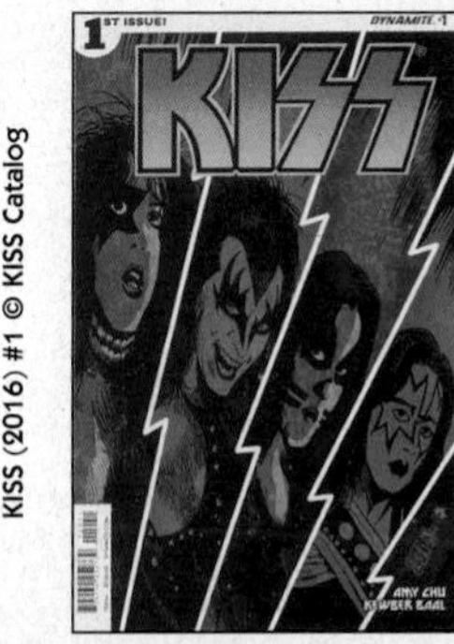

KISS (2016) #1 © KISS Catalog

Klaws of the Panther #1 © MAR

	GD 2.0	VG 4.0	FN 6.0	VF 8.0	VF/NM 9.0	NM- 9.2
TPB (9/03, $11.95) r/#1-4						12.00

KISS KIDS
IDW Publishing: Aug, 2013 - No. 4, Nov, 2013 ($3.99, limited series)
1-4-Short stories of KISS members as grade-school kids; Ryall & Waltz-s 4.00

KISS KISS BANG BANG
CrossGen Comics: Feb, 2004 - No. 5, Jun, 2004 ($2.95)
1-5-Bedard-s/Perkins-a 3.00

KISS ME, SATAN
Dark Horse Comics: Sept, 2013 - No. 5, Jan, 2014 ($3.99, limited series)
1-5-Gischler-s/Ferreyra-a; Dave Johnson-c 4.00

KISS: PHANTOM OBSESSION
Dynamite Entertainment: 2021 - No. 5, 2021 ($3.99)
1-5-Edginton-s/Celor-a; multiple covers 4.00

KISS SOLO
IDW Publishing: Mar, 2013 - No. 4, Jun, 2013 ($3.99, limited series)
1-4-Multiple covers on each. 1-Ryall-s/Medina-a. 2-Waltz-s/Rodriguez-a 4.00

KISS THE ARMY OF DARKNESS
Dynamite Entertainment: 2018 ($3.99, one-shot)
1-Bowers & Sims-s/Coleman-a; multiple covers; KISS meets Ash 4.00

KISS: THE END
Dynamite Entertainment: 2019 - No. 5, 2019 ($3.99, limited series)
1-5-Amy Chu-s/Edu Menna-a; multiple covers. 2-Flashback to 1973 4.00

KISS: THE PSYCHO CIRCUS
Image Comics: Aug, 1997 - No. 31, June, 2000 ($1.95/$2.25/$2.50)

	GD	VG	FN	VF	VF/NM	NM-
1-Holguin-s/Medina-a(p)	2	4	6	8	10	12
1-2nd & 3rd printings						3.00
2						6.00
3,4: 4-Photo-c						5.00
5-8: 5-Begin $2.25-c						4.00
9-29						4.00
30,31: 30-Begin $2.50-c						4.00
Book 1 TPB ('98, $12.95) r/#1-6						13.00
Book 2 Destroyer TPB (8/99, $9.95) r/#10-13						10.00
Book 3 Whispered Scream TPB ('00, $9.95) r/#7-9,18						10.00
...Magazine 1 ($6.95) r/#1-3 plus interviews						7.00
...Magazine 2-5 ($4.95) 2-r/#4,5 plus interviews. 3-r/#6,7. 4-r/#8,9						5.00
Wizard Edition ('98, supplement) Bios, tour preview and interviews						3.00

KISS / VAMPIRELLA
Dynamite Entertainment: 2017 - No. 5, 2017 ($3.99)
1-5-Sebela-s/Martello-a; multiple covers; Vampirella meets KISS in 1974 4.00

KISSYFUR (TV)
DC Comics: 1989 (Sept.) ($2.00, 52 pgs., one-shot)
1-Based on Saturday morning cartoon 4.00

KISS: ZOMBIES
Dynamite Entertainment: 2019 - No. 5, 2020 ($3.99, limited series)
1-5-Ethan Sacks-s/Rodney Buchemi-a; multiple covers; KISS in the zombie future 4.00

KIT CARSON (Formerly All True Detective Cases No. 4; Fighting Davy Crockett No. 9; see Blazing Sixguns & Frontier Fighters)
Avon Periodicals: 1950; No. 2, 8/51 - No. 3, 12/51; No. 5, 11-12/54 - No. 8, 9/55 (No #4)

	GD	VG	FN	VF	VF/NM	NM-
nn(#1) (1950)- "...Indian Scout" ; r-Cowboys 'N' Injuns #?	16	32	48	96	151	205
2(8/51)	14	28	42	78	112	145
3(12/51)- "...Fights the Comanche Raiders"	12	24	36	69	97	125
5-6,8(11-12/54-9/55): 5-Formerly All True Detective Cases (last pre-code); titled "...and the Trail of Doom"	11	22	33	60	83	105
7-McCann-a?	11	22	33	60	83	105
I.W. Reprint #10('63)-r/Kit Carson #1; Severin-c	2	4	6	11	16	20

NOTE: ***Kinstler** c-1-3, 5-8.*

KIT CARSON & THE BLACKFEET WARRIORS
Realistic: 1953

	GD	VG	FN	VF	VF/NM	NM-
nn-Reprint; Kinstler-c	14	28	42	78	112	145

KITCHEN, THE
DC Comics (Vertigo): Jan, 2015 - No. 8, Aug, 2015 ($2.99, limited series)
1-8-Masters-s/Doyle-a/Cloonan-c 3.00

KIT KARTER
Dell Publishing Co.: May-July, 1962

	GD	VG	FN	VF	VF/NM	NM-
1	3	6	9	19	30	40

KITTY
St. John Publishing Co.: Oct, 1948

	GD	VG	FN	VF	VF/NM	NM-
1-Teenage; Lily Renee-c/a	25	50	75	150	245	340

KITTY PRYDE, AGENT OF S.H.I.E.L.D. (Also see Excalibur and Mekanix)
Marvel Comics: Dec, 1997 - No. 3, Feb, 1998 ($2.50, limited series)
1-3-Hama-s 4.00

KITTY PRYDE AND WOLVERINE (Also see Uncanny X-Men & X-Men)
Marvel Comics Group: Nov, 1984 - No. 6, Apr, 1985 (Limited series)

	GD	VG	FN	VF	VF/NM	NM-
1-Characters from X-Men	2	4	6	11	16	20
2-6						5.00
X-Men: Kitty Pryde and Wolverine HC (2008, $19.99) r/series						20.00

KLARER GIVEAWAYS (See Wisco in the Promotional Comics section)

KLARION (The Witchboy)
DC Comics: Dec, 2014 - No. 6, May, 2015 ($2.99)
1-6: 1-3-Nocenti-s/McCarthy-a. 4-Fiorentino-a 3.00

KLAUS
BOOM! Studios: Nov, 2015 - No. 7, Aug, 2016 ($3.99)

	NM-
1-7: 1-Origin of Santa Claus; Grant Morrison-s/Dan Mora-a; multiple covers	4.00
... and the Crisis in Xmasville 1 (12/17, $7.99) Morrison-s/Mora-a; Snowmaiden app.	8.00
... and the Crying Snowman 1 (12/18, $7.99) Morrison-s/Mora-a;	8.00
... and the Life & Times of Joe Christmas 1 (12/19, $7.99) Morrison-s/Mora-a; calendar printed sideways showing Joe Christmas from 1930-2001	8.00
... and the Witch of Winter 1 (12/16, $7.99) Morrison-s/Mora-a; Geppetto app.	8.00

KLAWS OF THE PANTHER (Also see Black Panther)
Marvel Comics: Dec, 2010 - No. 4, Feb, 2011 ($3.99, limited series)

	GD	VG	FN	VF	VF/NM	NM-
1-Maberry-s/Gugliotta-a/Del Mundo-c; Ka-Zar & Shanna app.	3	6	9	14	20	25
2-4: 3-Spider-Man app.	1	2	3	5	6	8

KNIGHT AND SQUIRE (Also see Batman #667-669)
DC Comics: Dec, 2010 - No. 6, May, 2011 ($2.99, limited series)
1-6-Cornell-s/Broxton-a. 1-Two covers by Paquette & Tucci. 5,6-Joker app. 4.00
TPB (2011, $14.99) r/#1-6; sketch and design art 15.00

KNIGHT AND THE LADY OF PLAY, THE
Image Comics: Nov, 2022 ($3.99, one-shot)
1-Jonathan Luna-s/a 4.00

KNIGHTED
AWA Studios: Nov, 2021 - No. 5, Apr, 2022 ($3.99, limited series)
1-5-Gregg Hurwitz-s/Mark Texeira-a 4.00

KNIGHTHAWK
Acclaim Comics (Windjammer): Sept, 1995 - No. 6, Nov, 1995 ($2.50, lim. series)
1-6: 6-origin 4.00

KNIGHTMARE
Image Comics (Extreme Studios): Feb, 1995 - No. 5, June, 1995 ($2.50)
0 ($3.50) 4.00
1-5: 4-Quesada & Palmiotti variant-c, 5-Flip book w/Warcry 3.00

KNIGHTS 4 (See Marvel Knights 4)

KNIGHTS OF PENDRAGON, THE (Also see Pendragon)
Marvel Comics Ltd.: July, 1990 - No. 18, Dec, 1991 ($1.95)
1-18: 1-Capt. Britain app. 2,8-Free poster inside. 9,10-Bolton-c. 11,18-Iron Man app. 3.00

KNIGHTS OF THE ROUND TABLE
Dell Publishing Co.: No. 540, Mar, 1954

	GD	VG	FN	VF	VF/NM	NM-
Four Color 540-Movie, photo-c	6	12	18	41	76	110

KNIGHTS OF THE ROUND TABLE
Pines Comics: No. 10, April, 1957

	GD	VG	FN	VF	VF/NM	NM-
10-Features Sir Lancelot	6	12	18	28	34	40

KNIGHTS OF THE ROUND TABLE
Dell Publishing Co.: Nov-Jan, 1963-64

	GD	VG	FN	VF	VF/NM	NM-
1 (12-397-401)-Painted-c	3	6	9	20	31	42

KNIGHTS OF X (X-Men)
Marvel Comics: Jun, 2022 - No. 5, Oct, 2022 ($4.99/$3.99)
1-($4.99) Tini Howard-s/Bob Quinn-a; Captain Britain, Gambit, King Arthur app. 5.00
2-5-($3.99) 4.00

	GD 2.0	VG 4.0	FN 6.0	VF 8.0	VF/NM 9.0	NM- 9.2

KNIGHTS TEMPORAL
AfterShock Comics: Jul, 2019 - No. 5, Jan, 2020 ($3.99, limited series)
1-5-Cullen Bunn-s/Fran Galán-a 4.00

KNIGHTSTRIKE (Also see Operation: Knightstrike)
Image Comics (Extreme Studios): Jan, 1996 ($2.50)
1-Rob Liefeld & Eric Stephenson story; Extreme Destroyer Part 6. 3.00

KNIGHT WATCHMAN (See Big Bang Comics & Dr. Weird)
Image Comics: June, 1998 - No. 4, Oct, 1998 ($2.95/$3.50, B&W, lim. series)
1-4-Ben Torres-c/a in all. 4-($3.50) 4.00

KNIGHT WATCHMAN: GRAVEYARD SHIFT
Caliber Press: 1994 ($2.95, B&W)
1,2-Ben Torres-a 4.00

KNOCK EM DEAD
AfterShock Comics: Dec, 2020 - No. 5, Apr, 2021 ($4.99/$3.99)
1-($4.99) Eliot Rahal-s/Mattia Monaco-a 5.00
2-5-($3.99) 4.00

KNOCK KNOCK (...Who's There?)
Dell Publ./Gerona Publications: No. 801, 1936 (52 pgs.) (8x9", B&W)
801-Joke book; Bob Dunn-a 16 32 48 94 147 200

KNOCKOUT ADVENTURES
Fiction House Magazines: Winter, 1953-54
1-Reprints Fight Comics #53 w/Rip Carson-c/s 16 32 48 94 147 200

KNUCKLES (Spin-off of Sonic the Hedgehog)
Archie Publications: Apr, 1997 - No. 32, Feb, 2000 ($1.50/$1.75/$1.79)
1 2 4 6 8 10 12
2-32 4.00

KNUCKLES' CHAOTIX
Archie Publications: Jan, 1996 ($2.00, annual)
1 2 4 6 8 10 12

KNULL
Marvel Comics: Feb, 2021 ($7.99, one-host)
1-Reprints Venom (2018) #3,4,25 & Web of Venom: Carnage Born #1 8.00

KOBALT
DC Comics (Milestone): June, 1994 - No. 16, Sept, 1995 ($1.75/$2.50)
1-15: 1-Byrne-c. 4-Intro Page 3.00
16-Kent Williams-c 2 4 6 9 12 15

KOBRA (Unpublished #8 appears in DC Special Series No. 1)
National Periodical Publications: Feb-Mar, 1976 - No. 7, Mar-Apr, 1977
1-1st app.; Kirby-a redrawn by Marcos; only 25¢-c 3 6 9 18 28 38
2-7: (All 30¢ issues) 3-Giffen-a 1 3 4 6 8 10
...: Resurrection TPB (2010, $19.99) r/#1, DC Special Series No. 1 and later apps. in Checkmate #23-25, Faces of Evil: Kobra #1 and various Who's Who issues 20.00
NOTE: ***Austin** a-3i. **Buckler** a-5p; c-5p. **Kubert** c-4. **Nasser** a-6p, 7; c-7.*

KOKEY KOALA (...and the Magic Button)
Toby Press: May, 1952
1-Funny animal 17 34 51 100 158 215

KOKO AND KOLA (Also see A-1 Comics #16 & Tick Tock Tales)
Com/Magazine Enterprises: Fall, 1946 - No. 5, May, 1947; No. 6, 1950
1-Funny animal 19 38 57 111 176 240
2-X-Mas-c 14 28 42 76 108 140
3-6: 6(A-1 28) 11 22 33 62 86 110

KO KOMICS
Gerona Publications: Oct, 1945 (scarce)
1-The Duke of Darkness & The Menace (hero); Kirby-c 106 212 318 678 1164 1650

KOLCHAK: THE NIGHT STALKER (TV)
Moonstone: 2002 - 2007 ($6.50/$6.95)
1-($6.50) Jeff Rice-s/Gordon Purcell-a 6.50
... Black & White & Read All Over (2005, $4.95) short stories by various; 2 covers 5.00
... Devil in the Details (2003, $6.95) Trevor Von Eeden-a 7.00
... Eve of Terror (2005, $5.95) Gentile-s/Figueroa-a/Beck-c 6.00
... Fever Pitch (2002, $6.95) Christopher Jones-a 7.00
... Get of Belial (2002, $6.95) Art Nichols-a 7.00
... Lambs to the Slaughter (2003, $6.95) Trevor Von Eeden-a 7.00
... Pain Most Human (2004, $6.95) Greg Scott-a 7.00
... Tales: The Frankenstein Agenda 1 (2007 - No. 3, $3.50) Michelinie-s 3.50
... Tales of the Night Stalker 1-7 (2003 - No. 7, $3.50) two covers by Moore & Ulanski 3.50
TPB (2004, $17.95) r/#1, Get of Belial & Fever Pitch 18.00
Vol. 2: Terror Within TPB (2006, $16.95) r/Pain Most Human, Pain Without Tears & Devil in the Details 17.00

KOMIC KARTOONS
Timely Comics (EPC): Fall, 1945 - No. 2, Winter, 1945
1,2-Andy Wolf, Bertie Mouse 37 74 111 222 361 500

KOMIK PAGES (Formerly Snap; becomes Bullseye #11)
Harry 'A' Chesler, Jr. (Our Army, Inc.): Apr, 1945 (All reprints)
10(#1 on inside)-Land O' Nod by Rick Yager (2 pgs.), Animal Crackers, Foxy GrandPa, Tom, Dick & Mary, Cheerio Minstrels, Red Starr plus other 1-2 pg. strips; Cole-a 30 60 90 177 289 400

KONA (...Monarch of Monster Isle)
Dell Publishing Co.: Feb-Apr, 1962 - No. 21, Jan-Mar, 1967 (Painted-c)
Four Color 1256 (#1) 10 20 30 66 138 210
2-10: 4-Anak begins. 6-Gil Kane-c 5 10 15 34 60 85
11-21 4 8 12 28 47 65
NOTE: ***Glanzman** a-all issues.*

KONGA (Fantastic Giants No. 24) (See Return of...)
Charlton Comics: 1960; No. 2, Aug, 1961 - No. 23, Nov, 1965
1(1960)-Based on movie; Giordano-c 27 54 81 194 435 675
2-5: 2-Giordano-c; no Ditko-a 11 22 33 73 157 240
6-9-Ditko-c/a 9 18 27 60 120 180
10-15 8 16 24 56 108 160
16-23 6 12 18 37 66 95
NOTE: ***Ditko** a-1, 3-15; c-4, 6-9, 11. **Glanzman** a-12. **Montes & Bache** a-16-23.*

KONGA'S REVENGE (Formerly Return of...)
Charlton Comics: No. 2, Summer, 1963 - No. 3, Fall, 1964; Dec, 1968
2,3: 2-Ditko-c/a 7 14 21 49 92 135
1(12/68)-Reprints Konga's Revenge #3 3 6 9 16 24 32

KONG: GODS OF SKULL ISLAND
BOOM! Studios: Oct, 2017 ($7.99, one-shot)
1-Phillip Kennedy Johnson-s/Chad Lewis-a 8.00

KONG OF SKULL ISLAND
BOOM! Studios: Jul, 2016 - No. 12, Jun, 2017 ($3.99, limited series)
1-12-James Asmus-s/Carlos Magno-a; multiple covers on each 4.00
... 2018 Special 1 (5/18, $7.99) Paul Allor-s/Carlos Magno-a 8.00

KONG ON THE PLANET OF THE APES
BOOM! Studios: Nov, 2017 - No. 6, Apr, 2018 ($3.99, limited series)
1-6-Ryan Ferrier-s/Carlos Magno-a; multiple covers on each 4.00

KONG THE UNTAMED
National Periodical Publications: June-July, 1975 - V2#5, Feb-Mar, 1976
1-1st app. Kong; Wrightson-c; Alcala-a 3 6 9 16 23 30
2-Wrightson-c; Alcala-a 2 4 6 11 16 20
3-5: 3-Alcala-a 1 3 4 6 8 10

KOOKABURRA K
Marvel Comics (Soleil): 2009 - No. 3, 2010 ($5.99, limited series)
1-3-Humberto Ramos-a/c 6.00

KOOKIE
Dell Publishing Co.: Feb-Apr, 1962 - No. 2, May-July, 1962 (15 cents)
1-Written by John Stanley; Bill Williams-a 7 14 21 46 86 125
2 6 12 18 41 76 110

KOOSH KINS
Archie Comics: Oct, 1991 - No. 3, Feb, 1992 ($1.00, bi-monthly, limited series)
1-3 4.00
NOTE: *No. 4 was planned, but cancelled.*

KORAK, SON OF TARZAN (Edgar Rice Burroughs)(See Tarzan #139)
Gold Key: Jan, 1964 - No. 45, Jan, 1972 (Painted-c No. 1-?)
1-Russ Manning-a 9 18 27 60 120 180
2-5-Russ Manning-a 5 10 15 33 57 80
6-11-Russ Manning-a 5 10 15 30 50 70
12-23: 12,13-Warren Tufts-a. 14-Jon of the Kalahari ends. 15-Mabu, Jungle Boy begins. 21-Manning-a. 23-Last 12¢ issue 4 8 12 27 44 60
24-30 3 6 9 21 33 45
31-45 3 6 9 17 26 35

KORAK, SON OF TARZAN (Tarzan Family #60 on; see Tarzan #230)
National Periodical Publications: V9#46, May-June, 1972 - V12#56, Feb-Mar, 1974; No. 57, May-June, 1975 - No. 59, Sept-Oct, 1975 (Edgar Rice Burroughs)
46-(52 pgs.)-Carson of Venus begins (origin), ends #56; Pellucidar feature; Weiss-a 3 6 9 15 22 28
47-59: 49-Origin Korak retold 2 4 6 8 11 14
NOTE: *All have covers by **Joe Kubert**. **Manning** strip reprints-No. 57-59. **Murphy Anderson** a-52,56. **Michael Kaluta** a-46-56. **Frank Thorne** a-46-51.*

KORE
Image Comics: Apr, 2003 - No. 5, Sept, 2003 ($2.95)
1-5: 1-Two covers by Capullo and Seeley; Seeley-a (p) 3.00

KORG: 70,000 B. C. (TV)
Charlton Publications: May, 1975 - No. 9, Nov, 1976 (Hanna-Barbera)
1,2: 1-Boyette-c/a. 2-Painted-c; Byrne text illos 2 4 6 13 18 22
3-9 2 4 6 8 11 14

KORNER KID COMICS: Four Star Publications: 1947 (Advertised, not pub.)

KORVAC SAGA (Secret Wars tie-in)
Marvel Comics: Aug, 2015 - No. 4, Nov, 2015 ($3.99, limited series)
1-4-Guardians 3000, Avengers and Wonder Man app.; Abnett-s/Schmidt-a 4.00

KOSHCHEI IN HELL
Dark Horse Comics: Nov, 2022 - No. 4 ($3.99, limited series)
1-3-Mignola-s/c; Stenbeck-a 4.00

KOSHCHEI THE DEATHLESS
Dark Horse Comics: Dec, 2017 - No. 6, Jun, 2018 ($3.99, limited series)
1-6-Mignola-s/c; Stenbeck-a; Hellboy app. 4.00

KRAMPUS
Image Comics: Dec, 2013 - No. 5, May, 2014 ($2.99)
1-5-Sinterklaas' assistant; Joines-s/Kotz-a 3.00

KRAZY KAT
Holt: 1946 (Hardcover)
Reprints daily & Sunday strips by Herriman 57 114 171 362 619 875
dust jacket only 42 84 126 265 450 635

KRAZY KAT (See Ace Comics & March of Comics No. 72, 87)

KRAZY KAT COMICS (...& Ignatz the Mouse early issues)
Dell Publ. Co./Gold Key: May-June, 1951 - F.C. #696, Apr, 1956; Jan, 1964 (None by Herriman)
1(1951) 10 20 30 67 141 215
2-5 (#5, 8-10/52) 5 10 15 35 63 90

Kong of Skull Island #1 © DeVito Artworks

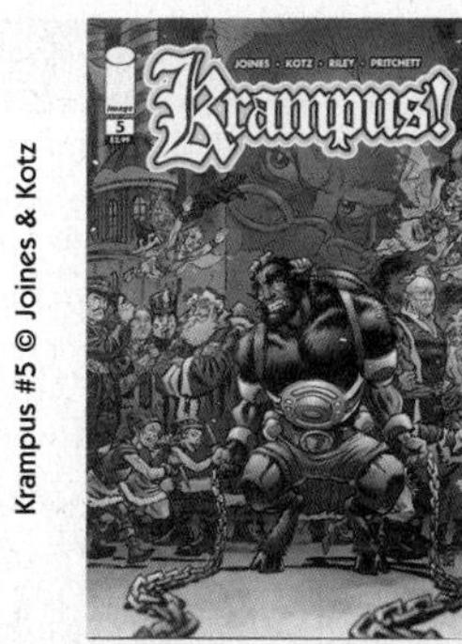

Krampus #5 © Joines & Kotz

Kung Fu Panda #5 © Dreamworks

	GD 2.0	VG 4.0	FN 6.0	VF 8.0	VF/NM 9.0	NM- 9.2
Four Color 454,504	6	12	18	42	79	115
Four Color 548,619,696 (4/56)	5	10	15	31	53	75
1(10098-401)(1/64-Gold Key)(TV)	4	8	12	25	40	55

KRAZY KOMICS (1st Series) (Cindy Comics No. 27 on) (Also see Ziggy Pig)
Timely Comics (USA No. 1-21/JPC No. 22-26): July, 1942 - No. 26, Spr, 1947

	GD	VG	FN	VF	VF/NM	NM-
1-Toughy Tomcat, Ziggy Pig (by Jaffee) & Silly Seal begin	155	310	465	992	1696	2400
2	55	110	165	352	601	850
3-8,10	39	78	117	240	395	550
9-Hitler parody-c	148	296	444	947	1624	2300
11,13,14	28	56	84	165	270	375
12-Timely's entire art staff drew themselves into a Creeper story	42	84	126	265	445	625
15-(8-9/44)-Has "Super Soldier" by Pfc. Stan Lee	30	60	90	177	289	400
16-24,26: 16-(10-11/44). 26-Super Rabbit-c/story	23	46	69	136	223	310
25-Wacky Duck-c/story & begin; Kurtzman-a (6pgs.)	30	60	90	177	289	400

KRAZY KOMICS (2nd Series)
Timely/Marvel Comics: Aug, 1948 - No. 2, Nov, 1948

	GD	VG	FN	VF	VF/NM	NM-
1-Wolverton (10 pgs.) & Kurtzman (8 pgs.)-a; Eustice Hayseed begins (Li'l Abner swipe)	68	136	204	435	743	1050
2-Wolverton-a (10 pgs.); Powerhouse Pepper cameo	47	94	141	296	498	700

KRAZY KROW (Also see Dopey Duck, Film Funnies, Funny Frolics & Movie Tunes)
Marvel Comics (ZPC): Summer, 1945 - No. 3, Wint, 1945/46

	GD	VG	FN	VF	VF/NM	NM-
1	37	74	111	218	354	490
2,3	23	46	69	136	223	310
I.W. Reprint #1('57), 2('58), 7	3	6	9	15	22	28

KRAZYLIFE (Becomes Nutty Life #2)
Fox Feature Syndicate: 1945 (no month)

	GD	VG	FN	VF	VF/NM	NM-
1-Funny animal	32	64	96	188	307	425

KREE/SKRULL WAR STARRING THE AVENGERS, THE
Marvel Comics: Sept, 1983 - No. 2, Oct, 1983 ($2.50, 68 pgs., Baxter paper)

1,2 — 6.00

*NOTE: **Neal Adams** p-1r, 2. **Buscema** a-1r, 2r. **Simonson** a-1p; c-1p.*

KROFFT SUPERSHOW (TV)
Gold Key: Apr, 1978 - No. 6, Jan, 1979

	GD	VG	FN	VF	VF/NM	NM-
1-Photo-c	3	6	9	17	26	35
2-6: 6-Photo-c	3	6	9	14	19	24

KRRSANTAN: STAR WARS TALES
Marvel Comics: Jul, 2022 ($7.99, squarebound, one-shot)

1-Reprints early apps. in Star Wars (2015) #14,15,20 and Star Wars: Doctor Aphra Annual #1 — 5.00

KRULL
Marvel Comics Group: Nov, 1983 - No. 2, Dec, 1983

1,2-Adaptation of film; r/Marvel Super Special. 1-Photo-c from movie — 5.00

KRUSTY COMICS (TV)(See Simpsons Comics)
Bongo Comics: 1995 - No. 3, 1995 ($2.25, limited series)

1-3 — 5.00

KRYPTON CHRONICLES
DC Comics: Sept, 1981 - No. 3, Nov, 1981

1-3: 1-Buckler-c(p) — 4.00

KRYPTO THE SUPERDOG (TV)
DC Comics: Nov, 2006 - No. 6, Apr, 2007 ($2.25)

1-6-Based on Cartoon Network series. 1-Origin retold — 3.00

KULL
Dark Horse Comics: Nov, 2008 - No. 6, May, 2009 ($2.99)

1-6: 1-Nelson-s/Conrad-a; two covers by Andy Brase and Joe Kubert — 3.00

KULL AND THE BARBARIANS
Marvel Comics: May, 1975 - No. 3, Sept, 1975 ($1.00, B&W, magazine)

	GD	VG	FN	VF	VF/NM	NM-
1-(84 pgs.) Andru/Wood-r/Kull #1; 2 pgs. Neal Adams; Gil Kane(p), Marie & John Severin-a(r); Krenkel text illo.	4	8	12	22	35	48
2,3: 2-(84 pgs.) Red Sonja by Chaykin begins; Solomon Kane by Weiss/Adams; Gil Kane-a; Solomon Kane pin-up by Wrightson. 3-(76 pgs.) Origin Red Sonja by Chaykin; Adams-a; Solomon Kane app.	3	6	9	17	26	35

KULL: ETERNAL
IDW Publsihing: Jun, 2017 - No. 3, Apr, 2018 ($3.99, limited series)

1-3-Waltz-s/Pizzari-a; multiple covers on each; Kull travels through history — 4.00

KULL: THE CAT AND THE SKULL
Dark Horse Comics: Oct, 2011 - No. 4, Jan, 2012 ($3.50, limited series)

1-4-Lapham-s/Guzman-a/Chen-c. 1-Variant-c by Hans — 3.50

KULL THE CONQUEROR (...the Destroyer #11 on; see Conan #1, Creatures on the Loose #10, Marvel Preview, Monsters on the Prowl)
Marvel Comics Group: June, 1971 - No. 2, Sept, 1971; No. 3, July, 1972 - No. 15, Aug, 1974; No. 16, Aug, 1976 - No. 29, Oct, 1978

	GD	VG	FN	VF	VF/NM	NM-
1-Andru/Wood-a; 2nd app. & origin Kull; 15¢ issue	6	12	18	42	79	115
2-5: 2-3rd Kull app. Last 15¢ iss. 3-13: 20¢ issues. 3-Thulsa Doom-c/app.	3	6	9	19	30	40
6-10: 7-Thulsa Doom-c/app	2	4	6	10	14	18
11-15: 11-15-Ploog-a. 14,15: 25¢ issues	2	4	6	8	11	14
16-(Regular 25¢ edition)(8/76)	2	3	4	6	8	10
16-(30¢-c variant, limited distribution)	3	6	9	19	30	40
17-29: 21-23-(Reg. 30¢ editions)	2	3	4	6	8	10
21-23-(35¢-c variants, limited distribution)	10	20	30	70	150	230

*NOTE: No. 1, 2, 7-9, 11 are based on Robert E. Howard stories. **Alcala** a-17p, 18-20i; c-24. **Ditko** a-12r, 15r. **Gil Kane** c-15p, 21. **Nebres** a-22i-27i; c-25i, 27i. **Ploog** c-11, 12p, 13. **Severin** a-2-9i; c-2-10i, 19. **Starlin** c-14.*

KULL THE CONQUEROR
Marvel Comics Group: Dec, 1982 - No. 2, Mar, 1983 (52 pgs., Baxter paper)

1,2: 1-Buscema-a(p) — 4.00

KULL THE CONQUEROR (No. 9,10 titled "Kull")
Marvel Comics Group: 5/83 - No. 10, 6/85 (52 pgs., Baxter paper)

V3#1-10: Buscema-a in #1-3,5-10 — 4.00

NOTE: Bolton a-4. Golden painted c-3-8. Guice a-4p. Sienkiewicz a-4; c-2.

KULL: THE HATE WITCH
Dark Horse Comics: Nov, 2010 - No. 4, Feb, 2011 ($3.50)

1-4-Lapham-s/Guzman-a/Fleming-c — 3.50

KUNG FU (See Deadly Hands of..., & Master of...)

KUNG FU FIGHTER (See Richard Dragon...)

KUNG FU PANDA
Titan Comics: Nov, 2015 -No. 4, Jan, 2016 ($3.99, limited series)

1-4-Simon Furman-s. 1,2-Lee Robinson-a — 4.00

KUNG FU PANDA 2
Ape Entertainment: 2011 - No. 6, 2012 ($3.95/$3.99, limited series)

1-6-Short stories by various — 4.00

KURT BUSIEK'S ASTRO CITY (Limited series) (Also see Astro City: Local Heroes)
Image Comics (Juke Box Productions): Aug, 1995 - No. 6, Jan, 1996 ($2.25)

	GD	VG	FN	VF	VF/NM	NM-
1-Kurt Busiek scripts, Brent Anderson-a & Alex Ross front & back-c begins; 1st app. Samaritan & Honor Guard (Cleopatra, MHP, Beautie, The Black Rapier, Quarrel & N-Forcer)	3	6	9	14	19	24
2-6: 2-1st app. The Silver Agent, The Old Soldier, & the "original" Honor Guard (Max O'Millions, Starwoman, the "original" Cleopatra, the "original" N-Forcer, the Bouncing Beatnik, Leopardman & Kitkat). 3-1st app. Jack-in-the-Box & The Deacon. 4-1st app. Winged Victory (cameo), The Hanged Man & The First Family. 5-1st app. Crackerjack, The Astro City Irregulars, Nightingale & Sunbird. 6-Origin Samaritan; 1st full app. Winged Victory	1	3	4	6	8	10

Life In The Big City-(8/96, $19.95, trade paperback)-r/Image Comics limited series w/sketchbook & cover gallery; Ross-c — 20.00
Life In The Big City-(8/96, $49.95, hardcover, 1000 print run)-r/Image Comics limited series w/sketchbook & cover gallery; Ross-c — 50.00

KURT BUSIEK'S ASTRO CITY (1st Homage Comics series)
Image Comics (Homage Comics): V2#1, Sept, 1996 - No. 15, Dec, 1998;
DC Comics (Homage Comics): No. 16, Mar, 1999 - No. 22, Aug, 2000 ($2.50)

	GD	VG	FN	VF	VF/NM	NM-
1/2-(10/96)-The Hanged Man story; 1st app. The All-American & Slugger, The Lamplighter, The Time-Keeper & Eterneon	1	3	4	6	8	10
1/2-(1/98) 2nd printing w/new cover						3.00
1- Kurt Busiek scripts, Alex Ross-c, Brent Anderson-p & Will Blyberg-i begin; intro The Gentleman, Thunderhead & Helia.	1	2	3	5	6	8
1-(12/97, $4.95) "3-D Edition" w/glasses						5.00
2-Origin The First Family; Astra story	1	2	3	4	5	7
3-5: 4-1st app. The Crossbreed, Ironhorse, Glue Gun & The Confessor (cameo)						6.00
6-10						5.00
11-22: 14-20-Steeljack story arc. 16-(3/99) First DC issue						3.00
TPB-($19.95) Ross-c, r/#4-9, #1/2 w/sketchbook						20.00
Family Album TPB ($19.95) r/#1-3,10-13						20.00
The Tarnished Angel HC ($29.95) r/#14-20; new Ross dust jacket; sketch pages by Anderson & Ross; cover gallery with reference photos						30.00

	GD 2.0	VG 4.0	FN 6.0	VF 8.0	VF/NM 9.0	NM- 9.2

The Tarnished Angel SC ($19.95) r/#14-20; new Ross-c 20.00

KURTZ VS. KURTZ (Cerebus)
Aardvark-Vanaheim: Aug, 2022 ($4.00, B&W)
1-Two-Fisted Tales #18-c swipe 4.00

LABMAN
Image Comics: Nov, 1996 ($3.50, one-shot)
1-Allred-c 4.00

LAB RATS
DC Comics: June, 2002 - No. 8, Jan, 2003 ($2.50)
1-8-John Byrne-s/a. 5,6-Superman app. 3.00

LABYRINTH
Marvel Comics Group: Nov, 1986 - No. 3, Jan, 1987 (Limited series)
1-3: David Bowie movie adaptation; r/Marvel Super Special #40 3 6 9 17 23 35

LABYRINTH (Jim Henson's...)
Boom Entertainment (Archaia): (one-shots)
... Masquerade 1 (12/21, $7.99)-Donnelly-s/Bak, Dodge, & Carlomagno-a 2 4 6 9 12 15
... 30th Anniversary Special 1 (8/16, $9.99)-Short stories by various; multiple covers 3 6 9 14 20 25
... 2017 Special 1 (11/17, $7.99) Short stories by various incl. Katie Cook & Landridge 2 4 6 8 10 12

LA COSA NOSTROID (See Scud: The Disposible Assassin)
Fireman Press: Mar, 1996 - No. 9, 1998 ($2.95, B&W)
1-9-Dan Harmon-s/Rob Schrab-c/a 3.00

LAD: A DOG (Movie)
Dell Publishing Co.: 1961 - No. 2, July-Sept, 1962
Four Color 1303 5 10 15 33 57 80
2 4 8 12 23 37 50

LA DIABLA (Prelude to The Lords of Misery)
Albatross Funnybooks: 2020 ($3.99, one-shot)
1-Eric Powell-s/a; various origins of La Diabla 4.00

LADY AND THE TRAMP (Disney, See Dell Giants & Movie Comics)
Dell Publishing Co.: No. 629, May, 1955 - No. 634, June, 1955
Four Color 629 (#1)-..with Jock 9 18 27 62 126 190
Four Color 634-...Album 7 14 21 48 89 130

LADY BALTIMORE
Dark Horse Comics: Mar, 2021 - No. 5, Oct, 2021 ($3.99, limited series)
1-5-Mike Mignola & Christopher Golden-s/Bridgit Connell-a 4.00

LADY CASTLE
BOOM! Studios: Jan, 2017 - No. 4, May, 2017 ($3.99, limited series)
1-4: 1-Delilah Dawson-s/Ashley Woods-a. 2-4-Farrow-a 4.00

LADY COP (See 1st Issue Special)

LADY DEADPOOL
Marvel Comics: Sept, 2010 ($3.99, one-shot)
1-Land-c/Lashley-a 2 4 6 11 16 20

LADY DEATH (See Evil Ernie)
Chaos! Comics: Jan, 1994 - No. 3, Mar, 1994 ($2.75, limited series)
1/2-Steven Hughes-c/a in all 1 3 6 6 8 10
1/2 Gold 1 3 4 6 8 10
1/2 Signed Limited Edition 2 4 6 8 10 12
1/2 Velvet 3 6 9 14 19 24
1-($3.50)-Chromium-c 2 4 6 11 16 20
1-Commemorative 2 4 6 10 14 18
1-(9/96, $2.95) "Encore Presentation"; r/#1 5.00
2 1 3 4 6 8 10
3 5.00
... And Jade (4/02, $2.99) Augustyn-s/Reis-a 3.00
...And The Women of Chaos! Gallery #1 (11/96, $2.25) pin-ups by various 3.00
.../Bad Kitty (9/01, $2.99) Mota-c/a 3.00
.../Bedlam (6/02, $2.99) Augustyn-s/Reis-c 3.00
...By Steven Hughes (6/00, $2.95) Tribute issue to Steven Hughes 3.00
...By Steven Hughes Deluxe Edition(6/00, $15.95) 16.00
.../Chastity (1/02, $2.99) Mota-c/a; Augustyn-s 3.00
...Death Becomes Her #0 (11/97, $2.95) Hughes-c/a 3.00
...FAN Edition: All Hallow's Eve #1 (1/97, mail-in) 5.00
...In Lingerie #1 (8/95, $2.95) pin-ups, wraparound-c 3.00
...In Lingerie #1-Leather Edition (10,000) 12.00
...In Lingerie #1-Micro Premium Edition; Lady Demon-c (2,000) 35.00
...: Love Bites (3/01, $2.99) Kaminski-s/Luke Ross-a 3.00
.../Medieval Witchblade (8/01, $3.50) covers by Molenaar and Silvestri 3.50
.../Medieval Witchblade Preview Ed. (8/01, $1.99) Molenaar-c 3.00
...: Mischief Night (11/01, $2.99) Ostrander-s/Reis-a 3.00
...: Re-Imagined (7/02, $2.99) Gossett-c 3.00
...: River of Fear (4/01, $2.99) Bennett-a(p)/Cleavenger-c 3.00
...Swimsuit Special #1-($2.50)-Wraparound-c 3.00
...Swimsuit Special #1-Red velvet-c 14.00
...Swimsuit 2001 #1-(2/01, $2.99)-Reis-c; art by various 3.00
...: The Reckoning (7/94, $6.95)-r/#1-3 7.00
...: The Reckoning (8/95, $12.95)- new printing including Lady Death 1/2 & Swimsuit Special #1 13.00
.../Vampirella (3/99, $3.50) Hughes-c/a 3.50
.../Vampirella 2 (3/00, $3.50) Deodato-c/a 3.50
... Vs. Purgatori (12/99, $3.50) Deodato-a 3.50
... Vs. Vampirella Preview (2/00, $1.00) Deodato-a/c 3.00

LADY DEATH (Ongoing series)
Chaos! Comics: Feb, 1998 - No. 16, May, 1999 ($2.95)
1-Pulido-s/Steven Hughes-c/a 2 4 6 9 12 15
2-16: 2-4: Pulido-s/Hughes-c/a. 5-8,13-16-Deodato-a. 9-11-Hughes-a 4.00
...Retribution (8/98, $2.95) Jadsen-a 4.00
...Retribution Premium Ed. 6.00

LADY DEATH
Boundless Comics: No. 0, Nov, 2010 - No. 26 ($3.99)
0-26-Pulido & Wolfer-s/Mueller-a on most; multiple covers on all. 25-Borstel-a 4.00
... Free Comic Book Day 2012 (5/12, free) "The Beginning" on cover; Mueller-a 3.00
... Origins Annual 1 (8/11, $4.99) Martin-a/Pulido-s 5.00
... Premiere (7/10, free) previews series; five covers 3.00

LADY DEATH...
Coffin Comics (One-shots)
... #1 - 25th Anniversary Edition (2/19, $4.99) remastered reprint of Lady Death #1 ('94) 5.00
... Chaos Rules 1 (5/16, $7.99) Pulido & Augustyn-s/Verma-a 8.00
... Hellraiders 1 (1/19, $4.99) Pulido & Maclean-s/Verma-a; multiple covers 5.00
... Merciless Onslaught 1 (8/17, $7.99) Pulido & Maclean-s/Verma-a; multiple covers 8.00
... Oblivion Kiss 1 (4/17, $7.99) Pulido & Maclean-s/Verma-a; multiple covers 8.00
... Revelations 1 (2/17, $3.99) Pin-up gallery of covers 4.00
... Zodiac 1 (12/16, $3.99) 12 pin-up images of the 12 zodiac signs by Nei Ruffino 4.00

LADY DEATH: ALIVE
Chaos! Comics: May, 2001 - No. 4, Aug, 2001 ($2.99, limited series)
1-4-Ivan Reis-a; Lady Death becomes mortal 3.00

LADY DEATH: A MEDIEVAL TALE (Brian Pulido's...)
CG Entertainment: Mar, 2003 - No. 12, Apr, 2004 ($2.95)
1-12: 1-Brian Pulido-s/Ivan Reis-a; Lady Death in the CrossGen Universe 3.00
Vol.1 TPB (2003, $9.95) digest-sized reprint of #1-6 10.00

LADY DEATH: APOCALYPSE
Boundless Comics: Jan, 2015 - No. 6, Jun, 2015 ($4.99)
1-6: 1-4-Wolfer-s/Borstel-a; multiple covers. 5,6-Wickline-s/Mueller-a 5.00
#0 (8/15, $6.99) Pulido-s/Valenzuela-a; bonus art gallery 7.00

LADY DEATH: APOCALYPTIC ABYSS
Coffin Comics: Feb, 2019 - No. 2, Apr, 2019 ($4.99, limited series)
1,2-Pulido & Maclean-s/Verma-a 5.00

LADY DEATH: BLASPHEMY ANTHEM
Coffin Comics: Dec, 2020 - No. 2, Feb, 2021 ($4.99, limited series)
1,2-Pulido & Maclean-s/Bernard-a; The Trinity app. 5.00

LADY DEATH: CATACLYSMIC MAJESTY
Coffin Comics: Feb, 2022 - No. 2, Apr, 2022 ($4.99, limited series)
1,2-Pulido & Maclean-s/Bernard-a 5.00

LADY DEATH: DARK ALLIANCE
Chaos! Comics: July, 2002 - No. 5, ($2.99, limited series)
1-3-Reis-a/Ostrander-s 3.00

LADY DEATH: DARK MILLENNIUM
Chaos! Comics: Feb, 2000 - No. 3, Apr, 2000 ($2.95, limited series)
Preview (6/00, $5.00) 5.00
1-3-Ivan Reis-a 3.00

LADY DEATH: GODDESS RETURNS
Chaos! Comics: Jun, 2002 - No. 2, Aug, 2002 ($2.99, limited series)
1,2-Mota-a/Ostrander-s 3.00

LADY DEATH: HEARTBREAKER
Chaos! Comics: Mar, 2002 - No. 4, ($2.99, limited series)
1-Molenaar-a/Ostrander-s 3.00

LADY DEATH: JUDGEMENT WAR
Chaos! Comics: Nov, 1999 - No. 3, Jan, 2000 ($2.95, limited series)
Prelude (10/99) two covers 4.00
1-3-Ivan Reis-a 4.00

LADY DEATH: LAST RITES
Chaos! Comics: Oct, 2001 - No. 4, Feb, 2001 ($2.99, limited series)
1-4-Ivan Reis-a/Ostrander-s 3.00

LADY DEATH: MALEVOLENT DECIMATION
Coffin Comics: Apr, 2021 - No. 2, May, 2021 ($4.99, limited series)
1,2-Pulido & Maclean-s/Bernard-a 5.00

LADY DEATH: NECROTIC GENESIS
Coffin Comics: Jan 2023 - No. 2, ($5.99, limited series)
1,2-Pulido & Maclean-s/Bernard-a 6.00

LADY DEATH: NIGHTMARE SYMPHONY
Coffin Comics: Nov, 2018 - No. 2, Dec, 2019 ($4.99, limited series)
1,2-Pulido & Maclean-s/Spay-a 5.00

LADY DEATH ORIGINS: CURSED
Boundless Comics: Mar, 2012 - No. 3, May, 2012 ($4.99/$3.99, limited series)
1-($4.99)-Pulido-s/Guzman-a; multiple covers 5.00
2,3-($3.99) 4.00

LADY DEATH: SACRIFICIAL ANNIHILATION
Coffin Comics: Jun, 2022 - No. 2, Aug, 2022 ($5.99, limited series)
1,2-Pulido & Maclean-s/Bernard-a 6.00

LADY DEATH: SCORCHED EARTH
Coffin Comics: Feb, 2020 - No. 2, Nov, 2020 ($4.99, limited series)
1,2-Pulido & Maclean-s/Bernard-a 5.00

LADY DEATH: THE CRUCIBLE
Chaos! Comics: Nov, 1996 - No. 6, Oct, 1997 ($3.50/$2.95, limited series)
1/2 4.00
1/2 Cloth Edition 8.00
1-Wraparound silver foil embossed-c 5.00

Lady Death (2011) #5 © Avatar

Lady Demon (2014) #4 © DYN

Lady Rawhide (2013) #1 © Zorro Prods.

	GD 2.0	VG 4.0	FN 6.0	VF 8.0	VF/NM 9.0	NM- 9.2
2-6-($2.95)						4.00

LADY DEATH: THE GAUNTLET
Chaos! Comics: Apr, 2002 - No. 2, May, 2002 ($2.99, limited series)

1,2: 1-J. Scott Campbell-c/redesign of Lady Death's outfit; Mota-a 4.00

LADY DEATH: THE ODYSSEY
Chaos! Comics: Apr, 1996 - No. 4, Aug, 1996 ($3.50/$2.95)

	GD	VG	FN	VF	VF/NM	NM-
1-($1.50)-Sneak Peek Preview						4.00
1-($1.50)-Sneak Peek Preview Micro Premium Edition (2500 print run)	2	4	6	9	12	15
1-($3.50)-Embossed, wraparound goil foil-c						5.00
1-Black Onyx Edition (200 print run)	5	10	15	33	57	80
1-($19.95)-Premium Edition (10,000 print run)						20.00
2-4-($2.95)						3.00

LADY DEATH: THE RAPTURE
Chaos! Comics: Jun, 1999 - No. 4, Sept, 1999 ($2.95, limited series)

1-4-Ivan Reis-c/a; Pulido-s 4.00

LADY DEATH: THE WILD HUNT (Brian Pulido's...)
CG Entertainment: Apr, 2004 - No. 2, May, 2005 ($2.95)

1-2: 1-Brian Pulido-s/Jim Cheung-a 3.00

LADY DEATH: TREACHEROUS INFAMY
Coffin Comics: Jul, 2021 - No. 2, Sept, 2021 ($4.99, limited series)

1,2-Pulido & Maclean-s/Bernard-a 5.00

LADY DEATH: TRIBULATION
Chaos! Comics: Dec, 2000 - No. 4, Mar, 2001 ($2.95, limited series)

1-4-Ivan Reis-a; Kaminski-s 3.00

LADY DEATH II: BETWEEN HEAVEN & HELL
Chaos! Comics: Mar, 1995 - No. 4, July, 1995 ($3.50, limited series)

	GD	VG	FN	VF	VF/NM	NM-
1-Chromium wraparound-c; Evil Ernie cameo	1	2	3	5	6	8
1-Commemorative (4,000), 1-Black Velvet-c	2	4	6	10	14	18
1-Gold	1	3	4	6	8	10
1-"Refractor" edition (5,000)	2	4	6	11	16	20
2-4						3.50
4-Lady Demon variant-c	1	2	3	5	7	9
Trade paperback-($12.95)-r/#1-4						13.00

LADY DEATH: UNHOLY RUIN
Coffin Comics: Apr, 2018 - No. 2, Jun, 2018 ($4.99, limited series)

1,2-Pulido & Maclean-s/Verma-a 5.00

LADY DEMON
Chaos! Comics: Mar, 2000 - No. 3, May, 2000 ($2.95, limited series)

1-3-Kaminski-s/Brewer-a 3.00

LADY DEMON
Dynamite Entertainment: 2014 - No. 4, 2015 ($3.99)

1-4: 1-3-Gillespie-s/Andolfo-a; multiple covers. 1-Origin retold. 4-Ramirez-a 4.00

LADY FOR A NIGHT (See Cinema Comics Herald)

LADY HEL
Dynamite Entertainment: 2022 - No. 4, 2022 ($3.99)

1-4-Burnham-s/Tasbolatov-a; multiple covers; Purgatori app. 4.00

LADY JUSTICE (See Neil Gaiman's...)

LADY KILLER
Dark Horse Comics: Jan, 2015 - No. 5, May, 2015 ($3.50)

1-5-Joëlle Jones-a/Jones and Jamie Rich-s 3.50

LADY KILLER 2
Dark Horse Comics: Aug, 2016 - No. 5, Sept, 2017 ($3.99)

1-5-Joëlle Jones-s/a 4.00

LADY LUCK (Formerly Smash #1-85) (Also see Spirit Sections #1)
Quality Comics Group: No. 86, Dec, 1949 - No. 90, Aug, 1950

	GD	VG	FN	VF	VF/NM	NM-
86(#1)	155	310	465	992	1696	2400
87-90	93	186	279	591	1021	1450

LADY MECHANIKA
Aspen MLT: No. 0, Oct, 2010 - No. 5, Mar, 2015 ($2.50/$2.99)

	NM-
0-Joe Benitez-s/a; two covers; Benitez interview and sketch pages	3.00
0-(Benitez Productions, 8/15, $1.00)	3.00
1-(1/11, $2.99) Multiple covers	10.00
2-5-Multiple covers on each. 5-($4.99)	5.00
... FCBD Vol. 1 Issue 1 (5/16, giveaway) r/#0; excerpt from mini-series	3.00
... FCBD 2019 Vol. 1 Issue 1 (5/19, giveaway) r/#0; excerpts from mini-series	3.00

LADY MECHANIKA: LA BELLE DAME SANS MERCI
Benitez Productions: Jul, 2018 - No. 3, Oct, 2018 ($3.99, limited series)

1-3-Joe Benitez-a/s; M.M. Chen-s; multiple covers on each 4.00

LADY MECHANIKA: LA DAMA DE LA MUERTE
Benitez Productions: Sept, 2016 - No. 3, Dec, 2016 ($3.99, limited series)

1-3-Joe Benitez-a/s; M.M. Chen-s; multiple covers on each 4.00

LADY MECHANIKA: SANGRE
Benitez Productions: Jun, 2019 - No. 5, Jan, 2020 ($3.99, limited series)

1-5-Joe Benitez-a/s; M.M. Chen-s; Brian Ching-a; multiple covers on each 4.00

LADY MECHANIKA: THE CLOCKWORK ASSASSIN
Benitez Productions: Jul, 2017 - No. 3, Oct, 2017 ($3.99, limited series)

1-3-Joe Benitez-a/M.M. Chen-s; multiple covers on each 4.00

LADY MECHANIKA: THE LOST BOYS OF WEST ABBEY
Benitez Productions: May, 2016 - No. 2, Jun, 2016 ($3.99, limited series)

1,2-Joe Benitez-a/M.M. Chen-s; multiple covers on each 4.00

LADY MECHANIKA: THE MONSTER OF THE MINISTRY OF HELL
Benitez Productions: Dec, 2021 - No. 4, May, 2022 ($3.99, limited series)

1-4-Joe Benitez-s/a; multiple covers on each 4.00

LADY MECHANIKA: THE TABLET OF DESTINIES
Benitez Productions: Apr, 2015 - No. 6, Oct, 2015 ($3.99, limited series)

1-6-Joe Benitez-s/a; multiple covers on each 4.00

LADY PENDRAGON
Maximum Press: Mar, 1996 ($2.50)

1-Matt Hawkins script 3.00

LADY PENDRAGON
Image Comics: Nov, 1998 - No. 3, Jan, 1999 ($2.50, mini-series)

	NM-
Preview (6/98) Flip book w/ Deity preview	3.00
1-3: 1-Matt Hawkins-s/Stinsman-a	3.00
1-($6.95) DF Ed. with variant-c by Jusko	7.00
2-($4.95)Variant edition	5.00
0-(3/99) Origin; flip book	3.00

LADY PENDRAGON (Volume 3)
Image Comics: Apr, 1999 - No. 9, Mar, 2000 ($2.50, mini-series)

	NM-
1,2,4-6,8-10: 1-Matt Hawkins-s/Stinsman-a. 2-Peterson-c	3.00
3-Flip book w/Alley Cat preview (1st app.)	4.00
7-($3.95) Flip book; Stinsman-a/Cleavenger painted-a	4.00
Gallery Edition (10/99, $2.95) pin-ups	3.00
...Merlin (1/00, $2.95) Stinsman-a	3.00
.../ More Than Mortal (5/99, $2.50) Scott-s/Norton-a; 2 covers by Norton & Finch	3.00
.../ More Than Mortal Preview (2/99) Diamond Dateline supplement	3.00
Pilot Season: Lady Pendragon (5/08, $3.99) Hawkins-s/Eru-a; wraparound-c by Struzan	4.00

LADY RAWHIDE
Topps Comics: July, 1995 - No. 5, Mar, 1996 ($2.95, bi-monthly, limited series)

	NM-
1-5: Don McGregor scripts & Mayhew-a. in all. 2-Stelfreeze-c. 3-Hughes-c. 4-Golden-c. 5-Julie Bell-c.	3.00
It Can't Happen Here TPB (8/99, $16.95) r/#1-5	17.00
Mini Comic 1 (7/95) Maroto-a; Zorro app.	3.00
Special Edition 1 (6/95, $3.95)-Reprints	4.00

LADY RAWHIDE (Volume 2)
Topps Comics: Oct, 1996 - No. 5, June, 1997 ($2.95, limited series)

1-5: 1-Julie Bell-c. 3.00

LADY RAWHIDE (Volume 1)
Dynamite Entertainment: 2013 - No. 5, 2014 ($3.99)

1-5-Trautmann-s/Estevam-a/Linsner-c 4.00

LADY RAWHIDE / LADY ZORRO
Dynamite Entertainment: 2015 - No. 4, 2015 ($3.99, limited series)

1-4-Denton-s/Villegas-a. 1-Mayhew-c. 2-4-Chin-c 4.00

LADY RAWHIDE OTHER PEOPLE'S BLOOD (ZORRO'S ...)
Image Comics: Mar, 1999 - No. 5, July, 1999 ($2.95, B&W)

1-5-Reprints Lady Rawhide series in B&W 3.00

LADY SUPREME (See Asylum)(Also see Supreme & Kid Supreme)
Image Comics (Extreme): May, 1996 - No. 2, June, 1996 ($2.50, limited series)

GD VG FN VF VF/NM NM-
2.0 4.0 6.0 8.0 9.0 9.2

1,2-Terry Moore -s: 1-Terry Moore-c. 2-Flip book w/Newmen preview 3.00

LADY ZORRO
Dynamite Entertainment: 2014 - No. 4, 2014 ($3.99, limited series)
1-4-de Campi-s/Villegas-a/Linsner-c 4.00

LADY ZORRO (Also see Zorro: Galleon of the Dead)
American Mythology Prods.: 2020 ($3.99, one-shot)
1-Pat Shand-s/Vincenzo Carratu-a; origin of Muat 4.00

LAFF-A-LYMPICS (TV)(See The Funtastic World of Hanna-Barbera)
Marvel Comics: Mar, 1978 - No. 13, Mar, 1979 (Newsstand sales only)
1-Yogi Bear, Scooby Doo, Pixie & Dixie, etc. 3 6 9 21 33 45
2-8 3 6 9 14 19 24
9-13: 11-Jetsons x-over; 1 pg. illustrated bio of Mighty Mightor, Herculoids, Shazzan, Galaxy Trio & Space Ghost 3 6 9 16 23 30

LAFFY-DAFFY COMICS
Rural Home Publ. Co.: Feb, 1945 - No. 2, Mar, 1945
1-Funny animal 15 30 45 84 127 170
2-Funny animal 12 24 36 69 97 125

LAGUARDIA
Dark Horse Comics (Berger Books): Dec, 2018 - No. 4, Mar, 2019 ($4.99, limited series)
1-4-Nnedi Okorafor-s/Tana Ford-a 5.00

LAKE OF FIRE
Image Comics: Aug, 2016 - No. 5, Dec, 2016 ($3.99)
1-5-Nathan Fairbairn-s/Matt Smith-a 4.00

LA MUERTA...
Coffin Comics (One-shots)
...: Ascension 1 (1019 $7.99) Maclean-s/Gomez-a 8.00
...: Descent 1 (7/16, $7.99) Maclean-s/Gomez-a; origin 8.00
...: Last Rites 1 (9/16, $7.99) Maclean-s/Gomez-a 8.00
...: Onslaught 1 (5/22, $7.99) Maclean-s/Gomez-a 8.00
...: Vengeance 1 (9/17, $7.99) Maclean-s/Gomez-a 8.00

LA MUERTA: RETRIBUTION
Coffin Comics: Sept, 2018 - No. 2, Sept, 2018 ($4.99, limited series)
1,2-Mike Maclean-s/Joel Gomez-a 5.00

LANA (Little Lana No. 8 on)
Marvel Comics (MjMC): Aug, 1948 - No. 7, Aug, 1949 (Also see Annie Oakley)
1-Rusty, Millie begin 68 136 204 435 743 1050
2-Kurtzman's "Hey Look" (1); last Rusty 34 68 102 204 332 460
3-7: 3-Nellie begins 25 50 75 150 245 340

LANCELOT & GUINEVERE (See Movie Classics)

LANCELOT LINK, SECRET CHIMP (TV)
Gold Key: Apr, 1971 - No. 8, Feb, 1973 (All photo-c)
1 5 10 15 35 63 90
2-8 4 8 12 23 37 50

LANCELOT STRONG (See The Shield)

LANCE O'CASEY (See Mighty Midget & Whiz Comics)
Fawcett Publications: Spring, 1946 - No. 3, Fall, 1946; No. 4, Summer, 1948
1-Captain Marvel app. on-c 32 64 96 188 307 425
2 19 38 57 111 176 240
3,4 15 30 45 85 130 175
NOTE: *The cover for the 1st issue was done in 1942 but was not published until 1946. The cover shows 68 pages but actually has only 36 pages.*

LANCER (TV)(Western)
Gold Key: Feb, 1969 - No. 3, Sept, 1969 (All photo-c)
1 4 8 12 25 40 55
2,3 3 6 9 17 26 35

LANDO (Star Wars)
Marvel Comics: Sept, 2015 - No. 5, Dec, 2015 ($3.99, limited series)
1-5-Soule-s/Maleev-a; Lobot & Emperor Palpatine app. 4.00

LAND OF NOD, THE
Dark Horse Comics: July, 1997 - No. 3, Feb, 1998 ($2.95, B&W)
1-3-Jetcat; Jay Stephens-s/a 3.00

LAND OF OZ
Arrow Comics: 1998 - No. 9 ($2.95, B&W)
1-9-Bishop-s/Bryan-s/a 3.00

LAND OF THE DEAD (George A. Romaro's...)
IDW Publishing: Aug, 2005 - No. 5 ($3.99, limited series)
1-4-Adaptation of 2005 movie; Ryall-s/Rodriguez-a 4.00
TPB (3/06, $19.99) r/#1-5; cover gallery 20.00

LAND OF THE GIANTS (TV)
Gold Key: Nov, 1968 - No. 5, Sept, 1969 (All have photo-c)
1 6 12 18 42 79 115
2-5 4 8 12 28 47 65

LAND OF THE LOST COMICS (Radio)
E. C. Comics: July-Aug, 1946 - No. 9, Spring, 1948
1 48 96 144 302 514 725
2 31 62 93 182 296 410
3-9 24 48 72 144 237 330

LAND THAT TIME FORGOT, THE (Movie)
Amercan Mythology Productions: 2019 - No. 2, 2019 ($3.99, B&W)
1,2-Reprints movie adaptation from Marvel Movie Premiere #1; Wolfman-s/Cardy-c 4.00

LAND THAT TIME FORGOT, THE : FEARLESS
Amercan Mythology Productions: 2020 - No. 3, 2021 ($3.99)
1-3-Wolfer-s/Casas-a 4.00

LAND UNKNOWN, THE (Movie)
Dell Publishing Co.: No. 845, Sept, 1957
Four Color 845-Alex Toth-a 11 22 33 76 163 250

LANTERN CITY (TV)
BOOM! Studios (Archaia): May, 2015 - No. 12, Apr, 2016 ($3.99)
1-12: 1-Jenkins & Daley-s/Magno-a. 3-Daley & Scott-s 4.00

LA PACIFICA
DC Comics (Paradox Press): 1994/1995 ($4.95, B&W, limited series, digest size, mature)
1-3 5.00

LARA CROFT AND THE FROZEN OMEN (Also see Tomb Raider titles)
Dark Horse Comics: Oct, 2015 - No. 5, Feb, 2016 ($3.99)
1-5: 1-Corinna Bechko-s/Randy Green-a 4.00

LARAMIE (TV)
Dell Publishing Co.: Aug, 1960 - July, 1962 (All photo-c)
Four Color 1125-Gil Kane/Heath-a 8 16 24 66 108 160
Four Color 1223,1284, 01-418-207 (7/62) 6 12 18 37 66 95

LAREDO (TV)
Gold Key: June, 1966
1 (10179-606)-Photo-c 3 6 9 21 33 45

LARFLEEZE (Orange Lantern) (Story continued from back-ups in Threshold #1-5)
DC Comics: Aug, 2013 - No. 12, Aug, 2014 ($2.99)
1-12: 1-Giffen & DeMatteis-s/Kolins-a/Porter-c; origin told 3.00

LARGE FEATURE COMIC (Formerly called Black & White in previous guides)
Dell Publishing Co.: 1939 - No. 13, 1943

Note: See individual alphabetical listings for prices

1 (Series I)-Dick Tracy Meets the Blank
3-Heigh-Yo Silver! The Lone Ranger (text & ill.)(76 pgs.); also exists as a Whitman #710; based on radio
6-Terry & the Pirates & The Dragon Lady; reprints dailies from 1936
8-Dick Tracy the Racket Buster
9-King of the Royal Mounted (Zane Grey's...)
10-(Scarce)-Gang Busters (No. appears on inside front cover); first slick cover (based on radio program)
13-Dick Tracy and Scottie of Scotland Yard
15-Dick Tracy and the Kidnapped Princes
17-Gang Busters (1941)
18-Phantasmo (see The Funnies #45)
20-Donald Duck Comic Paint Book (rarer than #16) (Disney)
21,22: 21-Private Buck. 22-Nuts & Jolts
24-Popeye in "Thimble Theatre" by Segar
26-Smitty
28-Grin and Bear It
30-Tillie the Toiler
2-Winnie Winkle (#1)
3-Dick Tracy
4-Tiny Tim (#1)
6-Terry and the Pirates; Caniff-a
8-Bugs Bunny (#1)('42)
9-Bringing Up Father
10-Popeye (Thimble Theatre)
11-Barney Google and Snuffy Smith
13-(nn)-1001 Hours Of Fun; puzzles & games; by A. W. Nugent. This book was bound as #13 with Large Feature Comics in publisher's files
2-Terry and the Pirates (#1)
4-Dick Tracy Gets His Man
5-Tarzan of the Apes (#1) by Harold Foster (origin); reprints 1st Tarzan dailies from 1929
7-(Scarce, 52 pgs.)-Hi-Yo Silver the Lone Ranger to the Rescue; also exists as a Whitman #715, based on radio program
11-Dick Tracy Foils the Mad Doc Hump
12-Smilin' Jack; no number on-c
14-Smilin' Jack Helps G-Men Solve a Case!
16-Donald Duck; 1st app. Daisy Duck on back cover (6/41-Disney)
19-Dumbo Comic Paint Book (Disney); partial-r from 4-Color #17
23-The Nebbs
25-Smilin' Jack-1st issue to show title on-c
27-Terry and the Pirates; Caniff-c/a
29-Moon Mullins
1 (Series II)-Peter Rabbit by Harrison Cady; arrival date-3/27/42
5-Toots and Casper
7-Pluto Saves the Ship (#1) (Disney)-Written by Carl Barks, Jack Hannah, & Nick George (Barks' 1st comic book work)
12-Private Buck

NOTE: *The Black & White Feature Books are oversized 8-1/2x11-3/8" comics with color covers and black and white interiors. The first nine issues all have rough, heavy stock covers and, except for #7, all have 76 pages, including covers. #7 and #10-on all have 52 pages. Beginning with #10 the covers are slick and thin and, because of their size, are difficult to handle without damaging. For this reason, they are seldom found in fine to mint condition. The paper stock, unlike Wow #1 and Capt. Marvel #1, is itself not unstable ...just thin. Many issues were reprinted in the early 1980s, identical except for the copyright notice on the first page.*

LARRY DOBY, BASEBALL HERO
Fawcett Publications: 1950 (Cleveland Indians)
nn-Bill Ward-a; photo-c 87 174 261 553 952 1350

LARRY HARMON'S LAUREL AND HARDY (...Comics)
National Periodical Publ.: July-Aug, 1972 (Digest advertised, not published)
1-Low print run 9 18 27 59 117 175

LARS OF MARS
Ziff-Davis Publishing Co.: No. 10, Apr-May, 1951 - No. 11, July-Aug, 1951 (Painted-c) (Created by Jerry Siegel, editor)
10-Origin; Anderson-a(3) in each; classic robot-c 129 258 387 826 1413 2000
11-Gene Colan-a; classic-c 97 194 291 621 1061 1500

LARS OF MARS 3-D
Eclipse Comics: Apr, 1987 ($2.50)
1-r/Lars of Mars #10,11 in 3-D plus new story 5.00
2-D limited edition (B&W, 100 copies) 20.00

LASER ERASER & PRESSBUTTON (See Axel Pressbutton & Miracle Man 9)
Eclipse Comics: Nov, 1985 - No. 6, 1987 (95¢/$2.50, limited series)
1-6: 5,6-(95¢) 3.00
...In 3-D 1 (8/86, $2.50) 4.00
2-D 1 (B&W, limited to 100 copies signed & numbered) 20.00

LASH LARUE WESTERN (Movie star; King of the bullwhip)(See Fawcett Movie Comic, Motion Picture Comics & Six-Gun Heroes)

Lake of Fire #1 © Fairbairn & Smith

Lassie #38 © DELL

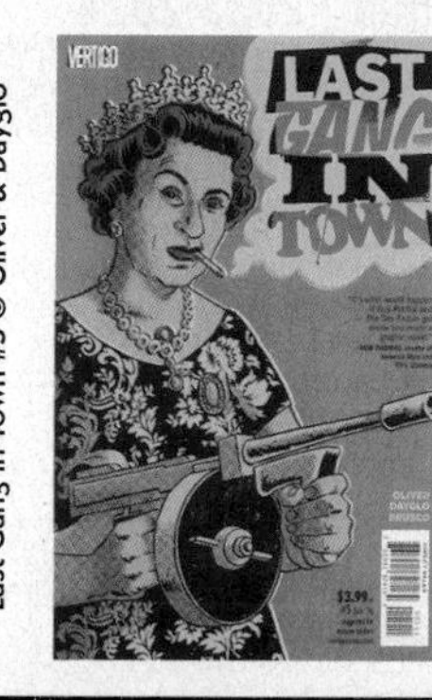

Last Gang in Town #5 © Oliver & Dayglo

	GD 2.0	VG 4.0	FN 6.0	VF 8.0	VF/NM 9.0	NM- 9.2
Fawcett Publications: Sum, 1949 - No. 46, Jan, 1954 (36 pgs., 1-6,9,13,16-on)						
1-Lash & his horse Black Diamond begin; photo front/back-c begin	58	116	174	371	636	900
2(11/49)	29	58	87	172	281	390
3-5	22	44	66	130	213	295
6,9: 6-Last photo back-c; intro. Frontier Phantom (Lash's twin brother)	19	38	57	109	172	235
7,8,10 (52pgs.)	20	40	60	114	182	250
11,12,14,15 (52pgs.)	15	30	45	84	127	170
13,16-20 (36pgs.)	14	28	42	80	115	150
21-30: 21-The Frontier Phantom app.	12	24	36	69	97	125
31-45	11	22	33	60	83	105
46-Last Fawcett issue & photo-c	11	22	33	64	90	115

LASH LARUE WESTERN (Continues from Fawcett series)
Charlton Comics: No. 47, Mar-Apr, 1954 - No. 84, June, 1961

	GD	VG	FN	VF	VF/NM	NM-
47-Photo-c	14	28	42	80	115	150
48	11	22	33	60	83	105
49-60, 67,68-(68 pgs.). 68-Check-a	9	18	27	52	69	85
61-66,69,70: 52-r/#8; 53-r/#22	9	18	27	47	61	75
71-83	8	16	24	40	50	60
84-Last issue	9	18	27	47	61	75

LASH LARUE WESTERN
AC Comics: 1990 ($3.50, 44 pgs) (24 pgs. of color, 16 pgs. of B&W)
1-Photo covers; r/Lash #6; r/old movie posters 4.00
Annual 1 (1990, $2.95, B&W, 44 pgs.)-Photo covers 4.00

LASSIE (TV)(M-G-M's... #1-36; see Kite Fun Book)
Dell Publ. Co./Gold Key No. 59 (10/62) on: June, 1950 - No. 70, July, 1969

	GD	VG	FN	VF	VF/NM	NM-
1 (52 pgs.)-Photo-c; inside lists One Shot #282 in error	26	52	78	182	404	625
2-Painted-c begin	8	16	24	56	108	160
3-10	6	12	18	37	66	95
11-19: 12-Rocky Langford (Lassie's master) marries Gerry Lawrence. 15-1st app. Timbu	5	10	15	30	50	70
20-22-Matt Baker-a	5	10	15	33	57	80
23-38: 33-Robinson-a.	4	8	12	28	47	65
39-1st app. Timmy as Lassie picks up her TV family; photo-c	5	10	15	35	63	90
40-50-Photo-c on all	4	8	12	28	47	65
51-58-Photo-c on all	4	8	12	27	44	60
59 (10/62)-1st Gold Key	4	8	12	28	47	65
60-70: 63-Last Timmy (10/63). 64-r/#19. 65-Forest Ranger Corey Stuart begins, ends #69. 70-Forest Rangers Bob Ericson & Scott Turner app. (Lassie's new masters)	4	8	12	25	40	55
11193(1978, $1.95, 224 pgs., Golden Press)-Baker-r (92 pgs.)	4	8	12	25	40	55

NOTE: *Also see March of Comics #210, 217, 230, 254, 266, 278, 296, 308, 324,334, 346, 358, 370, 381, 394, 411, 432.*

LAST AMERICAN, THE
Marvel Comics (Epic): Dec, 1990 - No. 4, March, 1991 ($2.25, mini-series)
1-4: Alan Grant scripts 3.00

LAST ANNIHILATION, THE
Marvel Comics: Nov, 2021 ($4.99, series of one-shots)
...: Wakanda 1 (11/21) Peralta-a; M'Baku, Shuri, Manifold & Vibraxas app. 5.00
...: Wiccan & Hulkling 1 (11/21) Bazaldua-a; Dormammu app. 5.00

LAST AVENGERS STORY, THE (Last Avengers #1)
Marvel Comics: Nov, 1995 - No. 2, Dec, 1995 ($5.95, painted, limited series) (Alterniverse)
1,2: Peter David story; acetate-c in all. 1-New team (Hank Pym, Wasp, Human Torch, Cannonball, She-Hulk, Hotshot, Bombshell, Tommy Maximoff, Hawkeye & Mockingbird) forms to battle Ultron 59, Kang the Conqueror, The Grim Reaper & Oddball 6.00
...: Marvel Tales 1 (2/22, $7.99) Reprints #1,2; intro. by Ralph Macchio 8.00

LAST BARBARIANS, THE
Image Comics: Feb, 2023 - Present ($3.99)
1-Brian Haberlin-s/a 4.00

LAST BATTLE, THE
Image Comics: Dec, 2011 ($7.99, square-bound, one-shot)
1-Facari-s/Brereton-painted art/c; Roman gladiator story; bonus Brereton sketch pages 8.00

LAST CHRISTMAS, THE
Image Comics: May, 2006 - No. 5, Oct, 2006 ($2.99, limited series)
1-5-Gerry Duggan & Brian Posehn-s/Rick Remender & Hilary Barta-a 3.00
TPB (2006, $14.99) r/#1-5; Patton Oswalt intro.; sketch pages and art 15.00

LAST CONTRACT, THE
BOOM! Studios: Jan, 2016 - No. 4, Apr, 2016 ($3.99, limited series)
1-4-Brisson-s/Estherren-a/c 4.00

LAST DAY IN VIETNAM
Dark Horse Books: July, 2000 ($10.95, graphic novel)
nn-Will Eisner-s/a/c 11.00

LAST DAYS OF ANIMAL MAN, THE
DC Comics: July, 2009 - No. 6, Dec, 2009 ($2.99, limited series)
1-6: 1-Conway-s/Batista-a/Bolland-c. 3,4-Starfire app. 5,6-Future Justice League app. 3.00
TPB (2010, $17.99) r/#1-6 18.00

LAST DAYS OF THE JUSTICE SOCIETY SPECIAL
DC Comics: 1986 ($2.50, one-shot, 68 pgs.)
1-62 pg. JSA story plus unpubbed G.A. pg. 2 4 6 8 10 12

LAST DEFENDERS, THE
Marvel Comics: May, 2008 - No. 6, Oct, 2008 ($2.99, limited series)
1-6-Nighthawk, She-Hulk, Colossus, and Blazing Skull; Muniz-a. 2-Deodato-c 3.00

LAST FANTASTIC FOUR STORY, THE
Marvel Comics: Oct, 2007 ($4.99, one-shot)
1-Stan Lee-s/John Romita, Jr.-a/c; Galactus app. 5.00

LAST GANG IN TOWN
DC Comics (Vertigo): Feb, 2016 - No. 6, Aug, 2016 ($3.99, limited series)
1-6: 1-Simon Oliver-s/Rufus Dayglo-a/Rob Davis-c 4.00

LAST GENERATION, THE
Black Tie Studios: 1986 - No. 5, 1989 ($1.95, B&W, high quality paper)
1-5 3.00
Book 1 (1989, $6.95)-By Caliber Press 7.00

LAST GOD, THE
DC Comics (Black Label): Dec, 2019 - No. 12, Mar, 2021 ($4.99)
1-12-Phillip Kennedy Johnson-s/Riccardo Federici-a 5.00
...: Songs of Lost Children 1 (12/20, $4.99) Dan Watters-s/Steve Beach-a 5.00
...: Tales From the Book of Ages 1 (8/20, $4.99) Roleplaying sourcebook 5.00

LAST HERO STANDING (Characters from Spider-Girl's M2 universe)
Marvel Comics: Aug, 2005 - No. 5, Aug, 2005 ($2.99, weekly limited series)
1-5: 1-DeFalco-s/Olliffe-a. 4-Thor app. 5-Capt. America dies 3.00
TPB (2005, $13.99) r/#1-5 14.00

LAST HUNT, THE
Dell Publishing Co.: No. 678, Feb, 1956
Four Color 678-Movie, photo-c 6 12 18 42 79 115

LAST KISS
ACME Press (Eclipse): 1988 ($3.95, B&W, squarebound, 52 pgs.)
1-One story adapts E.A. Poe's The Black Cat 4.00

LAST OF THE COMANCHES (Movie) (See Wild Bill Hickok #28)
Avon Periodicals: 1953
nn-Kinstler-c/a, 21pgs.; Ravielli-a 22 44 66 128 209 290

LAST OF THE ERIES, THE (See American Graphics)

LAST OF THE FAST GUNS, THE
Dell Publishing Co.: No. 925, Aug, 1958
Four Color 925-Movie, photo-c 6 12 18 41 76 110

LAST OF THE MOHICANS (See King Classics & White Rider and...)

LAST OF THE VIKING HEROES, THE (Also see Silver Star #1)
Genesis West Comics: Mar, 1987 - No. 12 ($1.50/$1.95)
1-4,5A,5B,6-12: 4-Intro The Phantom Force, 1-Signed edition ($1.50), 5A-Kirby/Stevens-c. 5B,6 ($1.95). 7-Art Adams-c. 8-Kirby back-c. 4.00
Summer Special 1-3: 1-(1988)-Frazetta-c & illos. 2 (1990, $2.50)-A TMNT app. 3 (1991, $2.50)-Teenage Mutant Ninja Turtles 4.00
Summer Special 1-Signed edition (sold for $1.95) 4.00
NOTE: ***Art Adams** c-7. **Byrne** c-3. **Kirby** c-1p, 5p. **Perez** c-2i. **Stevens** c-5Ai.*

LAST ONE, THE
DC Comics (Vertigo): July, 1993 - No. 6, Dec, 1993 ($2.50, lim. series, mature)
1-6 3.00

LAST PHANTOM, THE (Lee Falk's Phantom)
Dynamite Entertainment: 2010 - No. 12, 2012 ($3.99)

GD 2.0 | VG 4.0 | FN 6.0 | VF 8.0 | VF/NM 9.0 | NM- 9.2

1-12-Beatty-s/Ferigato-a; 1-Two covers by Alex Ross; Neves & Prado var. covers 4.00
Annual 1 (2011, $4.99) Beatty-s/Desjardins-a; two covers by Desjardins & Ross 5.00

LAST PLANET STANDING
Marvel Comics: July, 2006 - No. 5, Sept, 2006 ($2.99, limited series)
1-5-Galactus threatens Spider-Girl & Fantastic Five's M2 Earth; Avengers app.; Olliffe-a 3.00
TPB (2006, $13.99) r/series 14.00

LAST RONIN, THE (See TMNT: The Last Ronin)

LAST SHADOWHAWK, THE
Image Comics: Aug, 2022 ($3.99)
1-Philip Tan-s/a 4.00
... 3D #1 (9/22, $7.99)-Printed with 3D effects; bagged with 3D glasses 8.00

LAST SHOT
Image Comics: Aug, 2001 - No. 4, Mar, 2002 ($2.95, limited series)
1-4: 1-Wraparound-c; by Studio XD 3.00
...: First Draw (5/01, $2.95) Introductory one-shot 3.00

LAST SIEGE, THE
Image Comics: May, 2018 - No. 8, Jan, 2019 ($3.99)
1-8-Landry Q. Walker-s/Justin Greenwood-a 4.00

LAST SONS OF AMERICA
BOOM! Studios: Nov, 2015 - No. 4, Apr, 2016 ($3.99, limited series)
1-4-Phillip Johnson-s/Matthew Dow Smith-a 4.00

LAST SPACE RACE, THE
AfterShock Comics: Oct, 2018 - No. 5, Jul, 2019 ($3.99, limited series)
1-5-Peter Calloway-s/Alex Shibao-a 4.00

LAST STARFIGHTER, THE
Marvel Comics Group: Oct, 1984 - No. 3, Dec, 1984 (75¢, movie adaptation)
1-3: r/Marvel Super Special; Guice-c 4.00

LAST STOP ON THE RED LINE
Dark Horse Comics: May, 2019 - No. 4, Oct, 2019 ($3.99, limited series)
1-4-Paul Maybury-s/Sam Lotfi-a 4.00

LAST TEMPTATION, THE
Marvel Comics: 1994 - No. 3, 1994 ($4.95, limited series)
1-3-Alice Cooper story; Neil Gaiman scripts; McKean-c; Zulli-a: 1-Two covers 5.00
HC (Dark Horse Comics, 2005, $14.95) r/#1-3; Gaiman intro. 15.00

LAST TRAIN FROM GUN HILL
Dell Publishing Co.: No. 1012, July, 1959
Four Color 1012-Movie, photo-c 8 16 24 52 99 145

LAST TRAIN TO DEADSVILLE: A CAL McDONALD MYSTERY (See Criminal Macabre)
Dark Horse Comics: May, 2004 - No. 4, Sept, 2004 ($2.99, limited series)
1-4-Steve Niles-s/Kelley Jones-a/c 3.00
TPB (2005, $14.95) r/series 15.00

LATEST ADVENTURES OF FOXY GRANDPA (See Foxy Grandpa)

LATEST COMICS (Super Duper No. 3?)
Spotlight Publ./Palace Promotions (Jubilee): Mar, 1945 - No. 2, 1945?
1-Super Duper 22 44 66 132 216 300
2-Bee-29 (nd); Jubilee in indicia blacked out 16 32 48 94 147 200

LAUGH
Archie Enterprises: June, 1987 - No. 29, Aug, 1991 (75¢/$1.00)
V2#1 5.00
2-10,14,24: 5-X-Mas issue. 14-1st app. Hot Dog. 24-Re-intro Super Duck 4.00
11-13,15-23,25-29: 19-X-Mas issue 3.00

LAUGH COMICS (Teenage) (Formerly Black Hood #9-19) (Laugh #226 on)
Archie Publications (Close-Up): No. 20, Fall, 1946 - No. 400, Apr, 1987
20-Archie begins; Katy Keene & Taffy begin by Woggon; Suzie & Wilbur also begin;
Archie covers begin 181 362 543 1158 1979 2800
21-23,25 71 142 213 454 777 1100
24- "Pipsy" by Kirby (6 pgs.) 77 154 231 493 847 1200
26-30 47 94 141 296 498 700
31-40 39 78 117 231 378 525
41-60: 41,54-Debbi by Woggon 27 54 81 158 259 360
61-80: 67-Debbi by Woggon 19 38 57 109 172 235
81-99 9 18 27 62 126 190
100 10 20 30 66 138 210
101-105,110,112,114-126: 125-Debbi app. 7 14 21 49 92 135
106-109,111,113-Neal Adams-a (1 pg.) in each 8 16 24 51 96 140
127-144: Super-hero app. in all (see note) 8 16 24 56 108 160
145-(4/63) Josie by DeCarlo begins 9 18 27 59 117 175
146-149-early Josie app. by DeCarlo 6 12 18 38 69 100
150,162,163,165,167,169,170-No Josie 4 8 12 28 47 65
151-161,164,168-Josie app. by DeCarlo 5 10 15 33 57 80
166-Beatles-c (1/65) 9 18 27 57 111 165
171-180, 200 (11/67) 4 8 12 23 37 50
181-199 3 6 9 15 22 28
201-240(3/71) 2 4 6 11 16 20
241-280(7/74) 2 4 6 9 13 16
281-299 2 4 6 8 10 12
300(3/76) 2 4 6 8 11 14
301-340 (7/79) 1 2 3 5 7 9
341-370 (1/82) 1 2 3 4 5 7
371-379,385-399 5.00
380-Cheryl Blossom app. 2 4 6 11 16 20
381-384,400: 381-384-Katy Keene app.; by Woggon-381,382 6.00
NOTE: *The Fly app. in 128, 129, 132, 134, 138, 139. Flygirl app. in 136, 137, 143. Flyman app. in 137. The Jaguar app. in 127, 130, 131, 133, 135, 140-142, 144. Josie app. in 145-149, 151-161, 164, 168. Katy Keene app. in 20-125, 129, 130, 133. Horror/Sci-Fi covers on 128-135, 137, 139. Many issues contain paper dolls.* ***Al Fagaly*** *c-20-29.* ***Montana*** *c-33, 36, 37, 42.* ***Bill Vigoda*** *c-30, 50.*

LAUGH COMICS DIGEST (...Magazine #23-89; Laugh Digest Mag. #90 on)
Archie Publ. (Close-Up No. 1, 3 on): 8/74; No. 2, 9/75; No. 3, 3/76 - No. 200, Apr, 2005 (Digest-size) (Josie and Sabrina app. in most issues)
1-Neal Adams-a 5 10 15 31 53 75
2,7,8,19-Neal Adams-a 3 6 9 19 30 40
3-6,9,10 3 6 9 15 22 28
11-18,20 2 4 6 11 16 20
21-40 2 4 6 9 13 16
41-60 1 3 4 6 8 10
61-80 1 2 3 5 6 8
81-99 5.00
100 6.00
101-138 4.00
139-200: 139-Begin $1.95-c. 148-Begin $1.99-c. 156-Begin $2.19-c. 180-Begin $2.39-c 3.00
NOTE: *Katy Keene in 23, 25, 27, 32-38, 40, 45-48, 50. The Fly-r in 19, 20. The Jaguar-r in 25, 27. Mr. Justice-r in 21. The Web-r in 23.*

LAUGH COMIX (Laugh Comics inside)(Formerly Top Notch Laugh; Suzie Comics No. 49 on)
MLJ Magazines: No. 46, Summer, 1944 - No. 48, Winter, 1944-45
46-Wilbur & Suzie in all; Harry Sahle-c 41 82 123 256 428 600
47,48: 47-Sahle-c. 48-Bill Vigoda-c 29 58 87 172 281 390

LAUGH-IN MAGAZINE (TV)(Magazine)
Laufer Publ. Co.: Oct, 1968 - No. 12, Oct, 1969 (50¢) (Satire)
V1#1 5 10 15 30 50 70
2-12 3 6 9 21 33 45

LAUREL & HARDY (See Larry Harmon's... & March of Comics No. 302, 314)

LAUREL AND HARDY (...Comics)
St. John Publ. Co.: 3/49 - No. 3, 9/49; No. 26, 11/55 - No. 28, 3/56 (No #4-25)
1 110 220 330 704 1202 1700
2 47 94 141 296 498 700
3 39 78 117 240 395 550
26-28 (Reprints) 19 38 57 111 176 240

LAUREL AND HARDY (TV)
Dell Publishing Co.: Oct, 1962 - No. 4, Sept-Nov, 1963
12-423-210 (8-10/62) 6 12 18 42 79 115
2-4 (Dell) 4 8 12 28 47 65

LAUREL AND HARDY (Larry Harmon's...)
Gold Key: Jan, 1967 - No. 2, Oct, 1967
1-Photo back-c 5 10 15 30 50 70
2 4 8 12 21 33 45

LAUREL AND HARDY
American Mythology Productions: 2019 - No. 2, 2019 ($3.99)
1,2-New stories and reprints 4.00
... Christmas Follies 1 (2020, $3.99) New stories; Check-s/Tapié-a; Pacheco-s/a 4.00
... Gold Key Edition #1 (2019, $3.99) Reprints #1 from Jan, 1967 4.00
.../ The Three Stooges 1 (2020, $3.99) New story; Check & Kuhoric-s/Tapié-a 4.00

L.A.W., THE (LIVING ASSAULT WEAPONS)
DC Comics: Sept, 1999 - No. 6, Feb, 2000 ($2.50, limited series)
1-6-Blue Beetle, Question, Judomaster, Capt. Atom app.; Giordano-a. 5-JLA app. 3.00

LAW AGAINST CRIME (Law-Crime on cover)
Essenkay Publishing Co.: April, 1948 - No. 3, Aug, 1948 (Real Stories from Police Files)
1-(#1-3 are half funny animal, half crime stories)-L. B. Cole-c/a in all; electrocution-c
300 600 900 2070 3635 5200
2-L. B. Cole-c/a 135 270 405 864 1482 2100
3-Used in **SOTI**, pg. 180,181 & illo "The wish to hurt or kill couples in lovers' lanes;"
reprinted in All-Famous Crime #9 168 336 504 1075 1838 2600

LAW AND ORDER
Maximum Press: Sept, 1995 - No. 2, 1995 ($2.50, unfinished limited series)
1,2 3.00

LAWBREAKERS (...Suspense Stories No. 10 on)
Law and Order Magazines (Charlton): Mar, 1951 - No. 9, Oct-Nov, 1952
1 50 100 150 315 533 750
2 31 62 93 182 296 410
3,5,6,8,9: 6-Anti-Wertham editorial 25 50 75 150 245 340
4- "White Death" junkie story 37 74 111 218 354 490
7- "The Deadly Dopesters" drug story 39 78 117 240 395 550

LAWBREAKERS ALWAYS LOSE!
Marvel Comics (CBS): Spring, 1948 - No. 10, Oct, 1949
1-2pg. Kurtzman-a, "Giggles 'n' Grins" 48 96 144 302 514 725
2 27 54 81 160 263 365
3-5: 4-Vampire story 20 40 60 118 192 265
6(2/49)-Has editorial defense against charges of Dr. Wertham
22 44 66 128 209 290
7-Used in **SOTI**, illo "Comic-book philosophy" 42 84 126 265 445 625
8-10: 9,10-Photo-c 19 38 57 111 176 240
NOTE: ***Brodsky*** *c-4, 5.* ***Shores*** *c-1-3, 6-8.*

LAWBREAKERS SUSPENSE STORIES (Formerly Lawbreakers; Strange Suspense Stories No. 16 on)
Capitol Stories/Charlton Comics: No. 10, Jan, 1953 - No. 15, Nov, 1953
10 65 130 195 416 708 1000
11 (3/53)-Severed tongues-c/story & woman negligee scene
465 930 1395 3395 5998 8600
12-14: 13-Giordano-c begin, end #15 45 90 135 284 480 675
15-Acid-in-face-c/story; hands dissolved in acid story
142 284 426 909 1555 2200

LAW-CRIME (See Law Against Crime)

LAWDOG
Marvel Comics (Epic Comics): May, 1993 - No. 10, Feb, 1993
1-10 3.00

Laugh Comics #358 © ACP

Lazarus Planet: Alpha #1 © DC

Leave It to Binky #42 © DC

GD 2.0 | VG 4.0 | FN 6.0 | VF 8.0 | VF/NM 9.0 | NM- 9.2

LAWDOG/GRIMROD: TERROR AT THE CROSSROADS
Marvel Comics (Epic Comics): Sept, 1993 ($3.50)

1 — 4.00

LAWMAN (TV)
Dell Publishing Co.: No. 970, Feb, 1959 - No. 11, Apr-June, 1962 (All photo-c)

Four Color 970(#1) John Russell, Peter Brown photo-c — 11 22 33 75 160 245
Four Color 1035('60), 3(2-4/60)-Toth-a — 8 16 24 52 99 145
4-11 — 6 12 18 37 66 95

LAW OF DREDD, THE (Also see Judge Dredd)
Quality Comics/Fleetway #8 on: 1989 - No. 33, 1992 ($1.50/$1.75)

1-33: Bolland a-1-6,8,10-12,14(2 pg),15,19 — 3.00

LAWRENCE (See Movie Classics)

LAZARUS (Also see Lazarus: X +66)
Image Comics: Jun, 2013 - Present ($2.99/$3.50/$3.99)

1-9-Rucka-s/Lark-a/c — 3.50
10-21-($3.50) 19-Bonus preview of Black Magic #1 — 3.50
22-28-($3.99) — 4.00
Image Firsts Lazarus #1 (11/15, $1.00) reprints #1; afterword by Rucka; Lark sketch art — 3.00
... Sourcebook, Volume 1: Carlyle (4/16, $3.99) Dossier of politics, locations, weapons — 4.00
... Sourcebook, Volume 2: Hock (5/17, $3.99) Dossier of politics, locations, weapons — 4.00
... Sourcebook, Volume 3: Vassalovka (2/18, $3.99) Dossier of politics, locations — 4.00

LAZARUS CHURCHYARD
Tundra Publishing: June, 1992 - No. 3, 1992 ($3.95/$4.50, 44 pgs., coated stock)

1-3 — 5.00
The Final Cut (Image, 1/01, $14.95, TPB) Reprints Ellis/D'Israeli strips — 15.00

LAZARUS FIVE
DC Comics: July, 2000 - No. 5, Nov, 2000 ($2.50, limited series)

1-5-Harris-c/Abell-a(p) — 3.00

LAZARUS PLANET
DC Comics: Mar, 2023 - Apr, 2023 ($4.99/$5.99, series of one-shots)

...: Alpha (3/23, $5.99) Heroes vs. King Fire Bull; Waid-s/Federici-a — 6.00
...: Assault on Krypton (3/23, $4.99) Dreamer, Power Girl, Mercy Graves app. — 5.00
...: Dark Fate (4/23, $4.99) Huntress & Doom Patrol app. — 5.00
...: Legends Reborn (3/23, $4.99) Titans, Firestorm, City Boy & The Question app. — 5.00
...: Next Evolution (4/23, $4.99) The Vigil, Flatline, Deadeye, Red Canary, Sideways app. — 5.00
...: Omega (4/23, $5.99) Black Alice, Monkey Prince, Zatanna app.; back-up w/Darkseid — 6.00
...: We Once Were Gods (3/23, $4.99) Aquaman, Wonder Woman, Shazam family app. — 5.00

LAZARUS PLANET: REVENGE OF THE GODS
DC Comics: May, 2023 - No. 4 ($4.99, limited series)

1-Wonder Woman, Shazam family app. — 5.00

LAZARUS: RISEN (Characters from Lazarus)
Image Comics: Mar, 2019 - Present ($7.99, squarebound, limited series)

1-7-Rucka-s/Lark-a; takes place in the year X +68 — 8.00

LAZARUS: X +66 (Characters from Lazarus)
Image Comics: Jul, 2017 - No. 6, Feb, 2018 ($3.99, limited series)

1-6: 1-Lieber-a; how Casey became a Dagger. 2-Chater-a. 5-Evely-a — 4.00

LCSD 2021 FRIDAY (Local Comic Shop Day edition)
Image Comics: Nov, 2021 ($3.99, one-shot)

1-Ed Brubaker-s/Marcos Martin-a — 4.00

LEADING COMICS
DC Comics: Jan. 1942

nn - Ashcan comic, not distributed to newsstands, only for in-house use. Cover art is Detective Comics #57, interior of Star Spangled Comics #2 (a FN+ copy sold for $1015.75 in 2012)

LEADING COMICS (...Screen Comics No. 42 on)
National Periodical Publications: Winter, 1941-42 - No. 41, Feb-Mar, 1950

1-Origin The Seven Soldiers of Victory; Green Arrow & Speedy, Crimson Avenger, Shining Knight, The Vigilante, Star Spangled Kid & Stripesy begin; The Dummy (Vigilante villain) 1st app.; 1st Green Arrow-c — 459 918 1377 3350 5925 8500
2-Meskin-a; Fred Ray-c — 148 296 444 947 1624 2300
3 — 110 220 330 704 1202 1700
4,5 — 74 148 222 470 810 1150
6-10 — 54 108 162 343 574 825
11,12,14(Spring, 1945) — 42 84 126 265 445 625
13-Classic robot-c — 123 246 369 787 1344 1900
15-(Sum,'45)-Contents change to funny animal — 29 58 87 172 281 390
16-22,24-30: 16-Nero Fox-c begin, end #22 — 15 30 45 84 127 170
23-1st app. Peter Porkchops by Otto Feuer & begins — 29 58 87 172 281 390
31,32,34-41: 34-41-Leading Screen... on-c only — 14 28 42 76 108 140
33-(Scarce) — 21 42 63 122 199 275

NOTE: *Otto Feuer-a most #15-on; Rube Grossman-a most #15-on;c-15-41. Post a-23-37, 39, 41.*

LEADING MAN
Image Comics: June, 2006 - No. 5, Feb, 2007 ($3.50, limited series)

1-5-B. Clay Moore-s/Jeremy Haun-a — 3.50
TPB (2/07, $14.95) r/#1-5; sketch gallery — 15.00

LEADING SCREEN COMICS (Formerly Leading Comics)
National Periodical Publ.: No. 42, Apr-May, 1950 - No. 77, Aug-Sept, 1955

42-Peter Porkchops-c/stories continue — 14 28 42 76 108 140
43-77 — 12 24 36 69 97 125

NOTE: *Grossman a-most. Mayer a-45-48, 50, 54-57, 60, 62-74, 75(3), 76, 77.*

LEAGUE OF CHAMPIONS, THE (Also see The Champions)
Hero Graphics: Dec, 1990 - No. 12, 1992 ($2.95, 52 pgs.)

1-12: 1-Flare app. 2-Origin Malice — 4.00

LEAGUE OF EXTRAORDINARY CEREBI, THE (Cerebus in Hell)
Aardvark-Vanaheim: Oct, 2018 ($4.00, B&W)

1-Cerebus figures placed over original Gustave Doré artwork of Hell — 4.00

LEAGUE OF EXTRAORDINARY CORONA, THE (Cerebus in Hell)
Aardvark-Vanaheim: Nov, 2021 ($4.00, B&W)

1-Cerebus figures placed over original Gustave Doré artwork of Hell — 4.00

LEAGUE OF EXTRAORDINARY GENTLEMEN, THE
America's Best Comics: Mar, 1999 - No. 6, Sept, 2000 ($2.95, limited series)

1-Alan Moore-s/Kevin O'Neill-a — 3 6 9 14 20 26
1-DF Edition ($10.00) O'Neill-c — 3 6 9 16 24 32
2,3 — 6.00
4-6: 5-Revised printing with "Amaze 'Whirling Spray' Syringe" parody ad — 4.00
5-Initial printing recalled because of "Marvel Co. Syringe" parody ad — 14 28 42 93 204 315
... Compendium 1,2: 1-r/#1,2. 2-r/#3,4 — 6.00
Hardcover (2000, $24.95) r/#1-6 plus cover gallery — 25.00

LEAGUE OF EXTRAORDINARY GENTLEMEN, THE (Volume 2)
America's Best Comics: Sept, 2002 - No. 6, Nov, 2003 ($3.50, limited series)

1-6-Alan Moore-s/Kevin O'Neill-a — 5.00
... Bumper Compendium 1,2: 1-r/#1,2. 2-r/#3,4 — 6.00
... Black Dossier (HC, 2007, $29.99) new graphic novel; 3-D section with glasses; extras — 30.00

LEAGUE OF EXTRAORDINARY GENTLEMEN
Top Shelf Productions/Knockabout Comics: 2009; 2011; 2012 ($7.95/$9.95, squarebound)

... Century: 1910 (2009, $7.95) Alan Moore-s/Kevin O'Neill-a — 8.00
... Century #2 "1969" (2011, $9.95) Alan Moore-s/Kevin O'Neill-a — 10.00
... Century #3 "2009" (2012, $9.95) Alan Moore-s/Kevin O'Neill-a — 10.00

LEAGUE OF EXTRAORDINARY GENTLEMEN VOLUME 4: THE TEMPEST
Top Shelf Productions: Jun, 2018 - No. 6, Jun, 2019 ($4.99, limited series)

1-6-Alan Moore-s/Kevin O'Neill-a. 3-Includes 3-D pages and glasses — 5.00

LEAGUE OF JUSTICE
DC Comics (Elseworlds): 1996 - No. 2, 1996 ($5.95, 48 pgs., squarebound)

1,2: Magic-based alternate DC Universe story; Giordano-i — 6.00

LEATHERFACE
Arpad Publishing: May (April on-c), 1991 - No. 4, May, 1992 ($2.75, painted-c)

1-Based on Texas Chainsaw movie; Dorman-c — 3 6 9 16 23 30
2-4-Dorman-c on all — 2 4 6 8 10 12

LEATHERNECK THE MARINE (See Mighty Midget Comics)

LEAVE IT TO BEAVER (TV)
Dell Publishing Co.: No. 912, June, 1958; May-July, 1962 (All photo-c)

Four Color 912 — 16 32 48 111 246 380
Four Color 999,1103,1191,1285, 01-428-207 — 13 26 39 89 195 300

LEAVE IT TO BINKY (Binky No. 72 on) (Super DC Giant) (No. 1-22: 52 pgs.)
National Periodical Publs.: 2-3/48 - #60, 10/58; #61, 6-7/68 - #71, 2-3/70 (Teen-age humor)

1-Lucy wears Superman costume — 53 106 159 334 567 800
2 — 25 50 75 150 245 340
3,4 — 19 38 57 111 176 240
5-Superman cameo — 22 44 66 128 209 290
6-10 — 15 30 45 84 127 170
11-14,16-22: Last 52 pg. issue — 13 26 39 72 101 130

15-Scribbly story by Mayer 14 28 42 80 115 150
23-28,30-45: 45-Last pre-code (2/55) 10 20 30 58 79 100
29-Used in **POP**, pg. 78 11 22 33 62 86 110
46-60: 60-(10/58) 6 12 18 37 66 95
61 (6-7/68) 1950's reprints with art changes 5 10 15 35 63 90
62-69: 67-Last 12¢ issue 4 8 12 28 47 65
70-7pg. app. Bus Driver who looks like Ralph from Honeymooners
5 10 15 31 53 75
71-Last issue 5 10 15 30 50 70
NOTE: ***Aragones**-a-61, 62, 67. **Drucker** a-28. **Mayer** a-1, 2, 15. Created by **Mayer**.*

LEAVE IT TO CHANCE
Image Comics (Homage Comics): Sept, 1996 - No. 11, Sept, 1998; No. 13, July, 2002
DC Comics (Homage Comics): No. 12, Jun, 1999 ($2.50/$2.95/$4.95)

1-3: 1-Intro Chance Falconer & St. George; James Robinson scripts & Paul Smith-c/a 5.00
4-12: 12-(6/99) 3.00
13-(7/02, $4.95) includes sketch pages and pin-ups 5.00
Free Comic Book Day Edition (2003) - James Robinson-s/Paul Smith-a 3.00
Shaman's Rain TPB (1997, $9.95) r/#1-4 10.00
Shaman's Rain HC (2002, $14.95, over-sized 8 1/4" x 12") r/#1-4 15.00
Trick or Threat TPB (1997, $12.95) r/#5-8 13.00
Trick or Threat HC (2002, $14.95, over-sized 8 1/4" x 12") r/#5-8 15.00
Vol. 3: Monster Madness and Other Stories HC (2003, $14.95, 8 1/4" x 12") r/#9-11 15.00

LEAVING MEGALOPOLIS: SURVIVING MEGALOPOLIS
Dark Horse Comics: Jan, 2016 - No. 6, Sept, 2016 ($3.99)

1-6-Gail Simone-s/Jim Calafiore-a 4.00

LEE HUNTER, INDIAN FIGHTER
Dell Publishing Co.: No. 779, Mar, 1957; No. 904, May, 1958

Four Color 779 (#1) 6 12 18 40 73 105
Four Color 904 5 10 15 30 50 70

LEFT-HANDED GUN, THE (Movie)
Dell Publishing Co.: No. 913, July, 1958

Four Color 913-Paul Newman photo-c 9 18 27 62 126 190

LEGACY
Majestic Entertainment: Oct, 1993 - No. 2, Nov, 1993; No. 0, 1994 ($2.25)

1-2,0: 1-Glow-in-the-dark-c. 0-Platinum 3.00

LEGACY
Image Comics: May, 2003 - No. 4, Feb, 2004 ($2.95)

1-4: 1-Francisco-a/Treffiletti-s 3.00

LEGACY OF KAIN (Based on the Eidos video game)
Top Cow Productions: Oct, 1999; Jan, 2004 ($2.99)

...Defiance 1 (1/04, $2.99) Cha-c; Kirkham-a 2 4 6 9 12 15
...Soul Reaver 1 (10/99, Diamond Dateline supplement) Benitez-c
2 4 6 9 12 15

LEGACY OF LUTHER STRODE, THE (Also see Legend of Luther Strode)
Image Comics: Apr, 2015 - No. 6, May, 2016 ($3.99/$3.50)

1-($3.99) Justin Jordan-s/Tradd Moore-a 4.00
2-6-($3.50) 3.50

LEGEND
DC Comics (WildStorm): Apr, 2005 - No. 4, July, 2005 ($5.95/$5.99, limited series)

1-4-Howard Chaykin-s/Russ Heath-a; inspired by Philip Wylie's novel "Gladiator" 6.00

LEGENDARY STAR-LORD (Guardians of the Galaxy)
Marvel Comics: Sept, 2014 - No. 12, Jul, 2015 ($3.99)

1-12: 1-Humphries-s/Medina-a. 4-Thanos app. 9-11-Black Vortex x-over 4.00

LEGENDARY TALESPINNERS
Dynamite Entertainment: 2010 - No. 3, 2010 ($3.99)

1-3-Kuhoric-s/Bond-a; two covers 4.00

LEGENDERRY: A STEAMPUNK ADVENTURE
Dynamite Entertainment: 2014 - No. 7, 2014 ($3.99)

1-7-Willingham-s/Davila-a/Benitez-c. 4.00

LEGENDERRY: GREEN HORNET
Dynamite Entertainment: 2015 - No. 5, 2015 ($3.99)

1-5-Gregory-s/Peeples-a; multiple covers 4.00

LEGENDERRY: RED SONJA
Dynamite Entertainment: 2015 - No. 5, 2015 ($3.99)

1-5: 1-Andreyko-s/Aneke-a; multiple covers; Steampunk Sonja; Bride of Frankenstein app. 4.00

LEGENDERRY: RED SONJA (Volume 2)
Dynamite Entertainment: 2018 - No. 5, 2018 ($3.99)

1-5-Andreyko-s/Lima-a; multiple covers; Kulan Gath app. 4.00

LEGENDERRY: VAMPIRELLA
Dynamite Entertainment: 2015 - No. 5, 2015 ($3.99)

1-5-Avallone-s/Cabrera-a; Steampunk Vampirella 4.00

LEGEND OF CUSTER, THE (TV)
Dell Publishing Co.: Jan, 1968

1-Wayne Maunder photo-c 3 6 9 17 26 35

LEGEND OF ISIS
Alias Entertainment: May, 2005 - No. 5 ($2.99)

1-5: 1-Three covers; Ottney-s/Fontana-a 3.00
...: Beginnings TPB (5/05, $9.99) Ottney-s 10.00

LEGEND OF JESSE JAMES, THE (TV)
Gold Key: Feb, 1966

10172-602-Photo-c 3 6 9 19 30 40

LEGEND OF KAMUI, THE (See Kamui)

LEGEND OF LOBO, THE (See Movie Comics)

LEGEND OF LUTHER STRODE, THE (Sequel to Strange Talent of Luther Strode)
Image Comics: Dec, 2012 - No. 6, Aug, 2013 ($3.50, limited series)

1-5: Justin Jordan-s/Tradd Moore-a 3.50

LEGEND OF OZ: TIK-TOK AND THE KALIDAH
Aspen MLT: Apr, 2016 - No. 3, Jul, 2016 ($3.99)

1-3-Rob Anderson-s/Renato Rei-a. 1-Three covers. 2,3-Two covers 4.00

LEGEND OF OZ: THE WICKED WEST
Big Dog Press: Oct, 2011 - No. 6, Aug, 2012; Oct, 2012 - No. 18, May 2014 ($3.50)

1-6-Multiple covers on all 3.50
Vol. 2 1-18-Multiple covers on all 3.50

LEGEND OF OZ: THE WICKED WEST
Aspen MLT: Oct, 2015 - No. 6, Mar, 2016 ($3.99)

1-6-Reprints 2011 series 4.00

LEGEND OF SHANG-CHI, THE
Marvel Comics: Apr, 2021 ($3.99, one-shot)

1-Alyssa Wong-s/Andie Tong-a; Lady Deathstrike app. 4.00

LEGEND OF SUPREME
Image Comics (Extreme): Dec, 1994 - No. 3, Feb, 1995 ($2.50, limited series)

1-3 3.00

LEGEND OF THE ELFLORD
DavDez Arts: July, 1998 - No. 2, Sept, 1998 ($2.95)

1,2-Barry Blair & Colin Chin-s/a 3.00

LEGEND OF THE HAWKMAN
DC Comics: 2000 - No. 3, 2000 ($4.95, limited series)

1-3-Raab-s/Lark-c/a 5.00

LEGEND OF THE SHADOW CLAN
Aspen MLT: Feb, 2013 - No. 5, Jul, 2013 ($1.00/$3.99)

1-($1.00) David Wohl-s/Cory Smith-a; mutiple covers 3.00
2-5-($3.99) 4.00

LEGEND OF THE SHIELD, THE
DC Comics (Impact Comics): July, 1991 - No. 16, Oct, 1992 ($1.00)

1-16: 6,7-The Fly x-over. 12-Contains trading card 4.00
Annual 1 (1992, $2.50, 68 pgs.)-Snyder-a; w/trading card 4.00

LEGEND OF THE SWAMP THING HALLOWEEN SPECTACULAR
DC Comics: Dec, 2020 ($5.99, one-shot)

1-Six short stories by various; art by Perkins, Timms, Stanton, Ward, Rios; Perkins-c 6.00

LEGEND OF WONDER WOMAN, THE
DC Comics: May, 1986 - No. 4, Aug, 1986 (75¢, limited series)

1 2 4 6 8 10 12
2-4 1 3 4 6 8 10

LEGEND OF WONDER WOMAN, THE (Printing of digital-first stories)
DC Comics: Mar, 2016 - No. 9, Oct, 2016 ($3.99)

1-9: Childhood/origin flashbacks of Diana; Renae de Liz-s/a. 2-Steve Trevor app. 4.00

LEGEND OF YOUNG DICK TURPIN, THE (Disney)(TV)
Gold Key: May, 1966

1 (10176-605)-Photo/painted-c 3 6 9 19 30 40

LEGEND OF ZELDA, THE (Link: The Legend... in indicia)
Valiant Comics: 1990 - No. 4, 1990 ($1.95, coated stiff-c) V2#1, 1990 - No. 5, 1990 ($1.50)

1 10 20 30 64 132 200
2-4: 4-Layton-c(i) 3 6 9 16 24 32
V2#1-5 2 4 6 8 10 12

LEGENDS
DC Comics: Nov, 1986 - No. 6, Apr, 1987 (75¢, limited series)

1-Byrne-c/a(p) in all; 1st app. Amanda Waller and the new Captain Marvel
3 6 9 14 20 25
2,4,5 6.00
3-1st app. new Suicide Squad; death of Blockbuster 3 6 9 17 26 35
6-1st app. new Justice League 2 4 6 9 13 16

LEGENDS OF DANIEL BOONE, THE (...Frontier Scout)
National Periodical Publications: Oct-Nov, 1955 - No. 8, Dec-Jan, 1956-57

1 (Scarce)-Nick Cardy c-1-8 60 120 180 381 653 925
2 (Scarce) 47 94 141 296 498 700
3-8 (Scarce) 37 74 111 222 361 500

LEGENDS OF NASCAR, THE
Vortex Comics: Nov, 1990 - No. 14, 1992? (#1 3rd printing (1/91) says 2nd printing inside)

1-Bill Elliott biog.; Trimpe-a ($1.50) 5.00
1-2nd printing (11/90, $2.00) 3.00
1-3rd print; contains Maxx racecards ($3.00) 3.00
2-14: 2-Richard Petty. 3-Ken Schrader (7/91). 4-Bobby Allison; Spiegle-a(p); Adkins part-i. 5-Sterling Marlin. 6-Bill Elliott. 7-Junior Johnson; Spiegle-c/a. 8-Benny Parsons; Heck-a 3.00
1-13-Hologram cover versions. 2-Hologram shows Bill Elliott's car by mistake (all are numbered & limited) 5.00
2-Hologram corrected version 5.00
Christmas Special ($5.95) 6.00

LEGENDS OF RED SONJA
Dynamite Entertainment: 2013 - No. 5, 2014 ($3.99)

1-5-Short stories by various incl. Simone, Grayson; covers by Anacleto & Thorne 4.00

LEGENDS OF THE DARK CLAW
DC Comics (Amalgam): Apr, 1996 ($1.95)

1-Jim Balent-c/a 1 3 4 6 8 10

LEGENDS OF THE DARK KNIGHT (See Batman: ...)

LEGENDS OF THE DARK KNIGHT
DC Comics: Dec, 2012 - No. 13, Dec, 2013 ($3.99, printings of digital first stories)

Legendary Star-Lord #1 © MAR

Legion (2018) #5 © MAR

Legion of Super-Heroes #294 © DC

GD	VG	FN	VF	VF/NM	NM-
2.0	4.0	6.0	8.0	9.0	9.2

1-13: 1-Lindelof-s. 2-4-Joker app. 5-Hester-a 4.00
... 100 Page Super Spectacular 1-5 (2/14 - No. 5, 3/15, quarterly, $9.99) 1-(2/14) 10.00

LEGENDS OF THE DARK KNIGHT
DC Comics: Jul, 2021 - No. 8, Feb, 2022 ($3.99, printings of digital first stories)

1-8: 1-3-Darick Robertson-s/a. 1,2-Joker app. 7-Azrael app. 4.00

LEGENDS OF THE DC UNIVERSE
DC Comics: Feb, 1998 - No. 41, June, 2001 ($1.95/$1.99/$2.50)

1-13,15-21: 1-3-Superman; Robinson-s/Semeiks-a/Orbik-painted-c. 4,5-Wonder Woman; Deodato-a/Rude painted-c. 8-GL/GA, O'Neil-s. 10,11-Batgirl; Dodson-a. 12,13-Justice League. 15-17-Flash. 18-Kid Flash; Guice-a. 19-Impulse; prelude to JLApe Annuals. 20,21-Abin Sur 4.00
14-($3.95) Jimmy Olsen; Kirby-esque-c by Rude 5.00
22-27,30: 22,23-Superman; Rude-c/Ladronn-a. 26,27-Aquaman/Joker 3.00
28,29: Green Lantern & the Atom; Gil Kane-a; covers by Kane and Ross 3.00
31,32: 32-Begin $2.50-c; Wonder Woman; Texeira-c 3.00
33-36-Hal Jordan as The Spectre; DeMatteis-s/Zulli-a; Hale painted-c 3.00
37-41: 37,38-Kyle Rayner. 39-Superman. 40,41-Atom; Harris-c 3.00
... Crisis on Infinite Earths 1 (2/99, $4.95) Untold story during and after Crisis on Infinite Earths #4; Wolfman-s/Ryan-a/Orbik-c 5.00
... 80 Page Giant 1 (9/98, $4.95) Stories and art by various incl. Ditko, Perez, Gibbons, Mumy; Joe Kubert-c 5.00
... 80 Page Giant 2 (1/00, $4.95) Stories and art by various incl. Challengers by Art Adams; Sean Phillips-c 5.00
... 3-D Gallery (12/98, $2.95) Pin-ups w/glasses 4.00

LEGENDS OF THE LEGION (See Legion of Super-Heroes)
DC Comics: Feb, 1998 - No. 4, May, 1998 ($2.25, limited series)

1-4:1-Origin-s of Ultra Boy. 2-Spark. 3-Umbra. 4-Star Boy 4.00

LEGENDS OF THE STARGRAZERS (See Vanguard Illustrated #2)
Innovation Publishing: Aug, 1989 - No. 6, 1990 ($1.95, limited series, mature)

1-6: 1-Redondo part inks 3.00

LEGENDS OF THE WORLD'S FINEST (See World's Finest)
DC Comics: 1994 - No. 3, 1994 ($4.95, squarebound, limited series)

1-3: Simonson scripts; Brereton-c/a; embossed foil logos 6.00
TPB-(1995, $14.95) r/#1-3 15.00

LEGENDS OF TOMORROW
DC Comics: May, 2016 - No. 6, Oct, 2016 ($7.99, squarebound)

1-6: Short stories of Firestorm, Metal Men, Metamorpho and Sugar & Spike. 6-Legion of Super-Heroes app. 8.00

LEGION (David Haller from X-Men)
Marvel Comics: Mar, 2018 - No. 5, Jul, 2018 ($3.99)

1-5: 1-3-MIlligan-s/Torres-a. 4-Ferguson-a 4.00

L.E.G.I.O.N. (The # to right of title represents year of print)(Also see Lobo & R.E.B.E.L.S.)
DC Comics: Feb, 1989 - No. 70, Sept, 1994 ($1.50/$1.75)

1-Giffen plots/breakdowns in #1-12,28 6.00
2-22,24-47: 3-Lobo app. #3 on. 4-1st Lobo-c this title. 5-Lobo joins L.E.G.I.O.N. 13-Lar Gand app. 16-Lar Gand joins L.E.G.I.O.N., leaves #19. 31-Capt. Marvel app. 35-L.E.G.I.O.N. '92 begins 4.00
23,70-($2.50, 52 pgs.)-L.E.G.I.O.N. '91 begins. 70-Zero Hour 5.00
48,49,51-69: 48-Begin $1.75-c. 63-L.E.G.I.O.N. '94 begins; Superman x-over 4.00
50-($3.50, 68 pgs.) 5.00
Annual 1-5 ('90-94, 68 pgs.): 1-Lobo, Superman app. 2-Alan Grant scripts. 5-Elseworlds story; Lobo app. 5.00
NOTE: *Alan Grant scripts in #1-39, 51, Annual 1, 2.*

LEGION, THE (Continued from Legion Lost & Legion Worlds)
DC Comics: Dec, 2001 - No. 38, Oct, 2004 ($2.50)

1-Abnett & Lanning-s; Coipel & Lanning-c/a 4.00
2-24: 3-8-Ra's al Ghul app. 5-Snejbjerg-a. 9-DeStefano-a. 12-Legion vs. JLA. 16-Fatal Five app.; Walker-a 17,18-Ra's al Ghul app. 20-23-Universo app. 3.00
25-($3.95) Art by Harris, Cockrum, Rivoche; teenage Clark Kent app.; Harris-c 4.00
26-38-Superboy in classic costume. 26-30-Darkseid app. 31-Giffen-a. 35-38-Jurgens-a 3.00
...Secret Files 3003 (1/04, $4.95) Kirk-a, Harris-c/a; Superboy app. 5.00
...Foundations TPB (2004, $19.95) r/#25-30 & Secret Files 3003; Harris-c 20.00

LEGION LOST (Continued from Legion of Super-Heroes [4th series] #125)
DC Comics: May, 2000 - No. 12, Apr, 2001 ($2.50, limited series)

1-Abnett & Lanning-s. Coipel & Lanning-c/a 1 2 3 4 5 7
2-12-Abnett & Lanning-s. Coipel & Lanning-c/a in most. 4,9-Alixe-a 3.00
HC (2011, $39.99, dustjacket) r/#1-12 40.00

LEGION LOST (DC New 52)

GD	VG	FN	VF	VF/NM	NM-
2.0	4.0	6.0	8.0	9.0	9.2

DC Comics: Nov, 2011 - No. 16, Mar, 2013 ($2.99)

1-16: 1-Nicieza-s/Woods/a/c; Legionnaires trapped in the 21st century. 7,8-DeFalco-s. 8-Prelude to The Culling; Ravagers app. 9-The Culling x-over with Teen Titans. 14-16-Superboy & the Ravagers app. 3.00
#0 (11/12, $2.99) Origin of Timber Wolf; DeFalco-s/Woods-a 3.00

LEGIONNAIRES (See Legion of Super-Heroes #40, 41 & Showcase 95 #6)
DC Comics: Apr, 1992 - No. 81, Mar, 2000 ($1.25/$1.50/$2.25)

1-49,51-77: 1-(4/92)-Chris Sprouse-c/a; polybagged w/SkyBox trading card. 11-Kid Quantum joins. 18-(9/94)-Zero Hour; leads into #0. 19(11/94). 37-Valor (Lar Gand) becomes M'onel. 43-Legion tryouts; reintro Princess Projectra, Shadow Lass & others. 47-Forms one cover image with LSH #91. 60-Karate Kid & Kid Quantum join. 61-Silver Age & 70's Legion app. 76-Return of Wildfire. 79,80-Coipel-c/a; Legion vs. the Blight 3.00
50-($3.95) Pullout poster by Davis/Farmer 4.00
#0-(10/94)-Zero Hour restart of Legion; released between #18 & #19 3.00
#1,000,000 (11/98) Sean Phillips-a 3.00
Annual 1,3 ('94,'96 $2.95)-1-Elseworlds-s. 3-Legends of the Dead Earth-s 4.00
Annual 2 (1995, $3.95)-Year One-s 4.50

LEGIONNAIRES THREE
DC Comics: Jan, 1986 - No. 4, May, 1986 (75¢, limited series)

1-4 4.00

LEGION OF MONSTERS (Also see Marvel Premiere #28 & Marvel Preview #8)
Marvel Comics Group: Sept, 1975 ($1.00, B&W, magazine, 76 pgs.)

1-Origin & 1st app. Legion of Monsters; Neal Adams-c; Morrow-a; origin & only app. The Manphibian; Frankenstein by Mayerik; Bram Stoker's Dracula adaptation; Reese-a; painted-c (#2 was advertised with Morbius & Satana, but was never published) 12 24 36 80 173 265

LEGION OF MONSTERS (One-shots)
Marvel Comics: Apr, 2007 - Sept, 2007 ($2.99)

... Man-Thing (5/07) Huston-s/Janson-a/Land-c; Simon Garth: Zombie by Ted McKeever 2 4 6 9 12 15
... Morbius (9/07) Cahill-s/Gaydos-a/Land-c; Dracula w/Finch-a/Cebulski-s 2 4 6 9 12 15
... Satana (8/07) Furth-s/Andrasofszky-a/Land-c; Living Mummy by Hickman 2 4 6 9 12 15
... Werewolf By Night (4/07) Carey-s/Land-a/c; Monster of Frankenstein by Skottie Young 2 4 6 9 12 15
HC (2007, $24.99, dustjacket) oversized r/series and classic stories; sketch pages 32.00

LEGION OF MONSTERS
Marvel Comics: Dec, 2011 - No. 4, Mar, 2012 ($3.99, limited series)

1-Hopeless-s/Doe-a/c; Morbius, Manphibian, Elsa Bloodstone app. 2 4 6 11 16 20
2-4 4.00

LEGION OF NIGHT, THE
Marvel Comics: Oct, 1991 - No. 2, Oct, 1991 ($4.95, 52 pgs.)

1,2-Whilce Portacio-c/a(p) 5.00

LEGION OF SUBSTITUTE HEROES SPECIAL (See Adventure Comics #306)
DC Comics: July, 1985 ($1.25, one-shot, 52 pgs.)

1-Giffen-c/a(p) 4.00

LEGION OF SUPER-HEROES (See Action Comics, Adventure, All New Collectors Edition, Legionnaires, Legends of the Legion, Limited Collectors Edition, Secrets of the..., Superboy & Superman)
National Periodical Publications: Feb, 1973 - No. 4, July-Aug, 1973

1-Legion & Tommy Tomorrow reprints begin 3 6 9 21 33 45
2-4: 2-Forte-r. 3-r/Adv. #340. Action #240. 4-r/Adv. #341, Action #233; Mooney-r 2 4 6 13 18 22

LEGION OF SUPER-HEROES, THE (Formerly Superboy and...; Tales of The Legion #314 on)
DC Comics: No. 259, Jan, 1980 - No. 313, July, 1984

259(#1)-Superboy leaves Legion 2 4 6 8 11 14
260-270: 265-Contains 28 pg. insert "Superman & the TRS-80 computer"; origin Tyroc; Tyroc leaves Legion 6.00
261,263,264,266-(Whitman variants; low print run; no cover #'s) 2 4 6 8 11 14
271-289: 272-Blok joins; origin; 20 pg. insert-Dial 'H' For Hero. 277-Intro. Reflecto. 280-Superboy re-joins Legion. 282-Origin Reflecto. 283-Origin Wildfire 6.00
290-294-Great Darkness saga. 294-Double size (52 pgs.) 1 2 3 5 7 9
295-299,301-313: 297-Origin retold. 298-Free 16 pg. Amethyst preview. 306-Brief origin Star Boy (Swan art). 311-Colan-a 4.00
300-(68 pgs., Mando paper)-Anniversary issue; has c/a by almost everyone at DC 5.00

	GD	VG	FN	VF	VF/NM	NM-
	2.0	4.0	6.0	8.0	9.0	9.2

Annual 1-3(82-84, 52 pgs.)-1-Giffen-c/a; 1st app./origin new Invisible Kid who joins Legion. 2-Karate Kid & Princess Projectra wed & resign 5.00
...The Great Darkness Saga (1989, $17.95, 196 pgs.)-r/LSH #287,290-294 & Annual #3; Giffen-c/a 4 8 12 23 37 50
...The Great Darkness Saga The Deluxe Edition HC (2010, $39.99, dj)-r/LSH #284-296 & Annual #1; new intro. by Levitz, script for #290, Giffen design sketches 5 10 15 30 50 70

NOTE: ***Aparo*** *c-282, 283, 300(part).* ***Austin*** *c-268i.* ***Buckler*** *c-273p, 274p, 276p.* ***Colan*** *a-311p.* ***Ditko*** *a(p)-267, 268, 272, 274, 276, 281.* ***Giffen*** *a-285-313p, Annual 1p; c-287p, 288p, 289, 290p, 291p, 292, 293, 294-299p, 300, 301-313p, Annual 1p, 2p.* ***Perez*** *c-268p, 277-280, 281p.* ***Starlin*** *a-265.* ***Staton*** *a-259p, 260p, 280.* ***Tuska*** *a-308p.*

LEGION OF SUPER-HEROES (3rd Series) (Reprinted in Tales of the Legion)
DC Comics: Aug, 1984 - No. 63, Aug, 1989 ($1.25/$1.75, deluxe format)

1-Silver ink logo 1 3 4 6 8 10
2-36,39-44,46-49,51-62: 4-Death of Karate Kid. 5-Death of Nemesis Kid. 12-Cosmic Boy, Lightning Lad, & Saturn Girl resign. 14-Intro new members: Tellus, Sensor Girl, Quislet. 15-17-Crisis tie-ins. 18-Crisis x-over. 25-Sensor Girl i.d. revealed as Princess Projectra. 35-Saturn Girl rejoins. 42,43-Millennium tie-ins. 44-Origin Quislet 3.00
37,38-Death of Superboy 2 4 6 9 13 16
45,50: 45 ($2.95, 68 pgs.)-Anniversary ish. 50-Double size ($2.50-c) 4.00
63-Final issue 4.00
Annual 1-4 (10/85-'88, 52 pgs.)-1-Crisis tie-in 4.00
...: An Eye For An Eye TPB (2007, $17.99)-r/#1-6; intro by Paul Levitz; cover gallery 18.00
...: The More Things Change TPB (2008, $17.99)-r/#7-13; cover gallery 18.00

NOTE: ***Byrne*** *c-36p.* ***Giffen*** *a(p)-1, 2, 50-55, 57-63, Annual 1p, 2; c-1-5p, 54p, Annual 1.* ***Orlando*** *a-6p.* ***Steacy*** *c-45-50, Annual 3.*

LEGION OF SUPER-HEROES (4th Series)
DC Comics: Nov, 1989 - No. 125, Mar, 2000 ($1.75/$1.95/$2.25)

1-Giffen-c/a(p)/scripts begin (4 pg.-a only #18) 6.00
2-20,26-49,51-53,55-58: 4-Mon-El (Lar Gand) destroys Time Trapper, changes reality. 5-Alt. reality story where Mordru rules all; Ferro Lad app. 6-1st app. of Laurel Gand (Lar Gand's cousin). 8-Origin. 13-Free poster by Giffen showing new costumes. 15-(2/91)-1st reference of Lar Gand as Valor. 17-Tornado Twins app. 26-New map of headquarters. 34-Six pg. preview of Timber Wolf mini-series. 40-Minor Legionnaires app. 41-(3/93)-SW6 Legion renamed Legionnaires w/new costumes and some new code-names 4.00
21-25: 21-24-Lobo & Darkseid storyline. 24-Cameo SW6 younger Legion duplicates. 25-SW6 Legion full intro. 5.00
50-($3.50, 68 pgs.) 5.00
54-($2.95)-Die-cut & foil stamped-c 5.00
59-99: 61-(9/94)-Zero Hour. 62-(11/94). 75-XS travels back to the 20th Century (cont'd in Impulse #9). 77-Origin of Brainiac 5. 81-Reintro Sun Boy. 85-Half of the Legion sent to the 20th century, Superman-c/app. 86-Final Night. 87-Deadman-c/app. 88-Impulse-c/app. Adventure Comics #247 cover swipe. 91-Forms one cover image with Legionnaires #47. 96-Wedding of Ultra Boy and Apparition. 99-Robin, Impulse, Superboy app. 3.00
100-($5.95, 96 pgs.)-Legionnaires return to the 30th Century; gatefold-c; 5 stories-art by Simonson, Davis and others 1 2 3 4 5 7
101-121: 101-Armstrong-a(p) begins. 105-Legion past & present vs. Time Trapper. 109-Moder-a. 110-Thunder joins. 114,115-Bizarro Legion. 120,121-Fatal Five. 3.00
122-124: 122,123-Coipel-c/a. 124-Coipel-c 4.00
125-Leads into "Legion Lost" maxi-series; Coipel-c 5.00
#0-(10/94)-Zero Hour restart of Legion; released between #61 & #62 3.00
#1,000,000 (11/98) Giffen-a 3.00
Annual 1-5 (1990-1994, $3.50, 68 pgs.): 4-Bloodlines. 5-Elseworlds story 4.00
Annual 6 (1995,$3.95)-Year One story 4.00
Annual 7 (1996, $3.50, 48 pgs.)-Legends of the Dead Earth story; intro 75th Century Legion of Super-Heroes; Wildfire app. 4.00
Legion: Secret Files 1 (1/98, $4.95) Retold origin & pin-ups 5.00
Legion: Secret Files 2 (6/99, $4.95) Story and profile pages 5.00
The Beginning of Tomorrow TPB ('99, $17.95) r/post-Zero Hour reboot 18.00

NOTE: ***Giffen*** *a-1-24; breakdowns-26-32, 34-36; c-1-7, 8(part), 9-24.* ***Brandon Peterson*** *a(p)-15(1st for DC), 16, 18, Annual 2(54 pgs.); c-Annual 2p.* ***Swan/Anderson*** *c-8(part).*

LEGION OF SUPER-HEROES (5th Series) (Title becomes Supergirl and the Legion of Super-Heroes #16-36) (Intro. in Teen Titans/Legion Special)
DC Comics: Feb, 2005 - No. 15, Apr, 2006; No. 37, Feb, 2008 - No. 50, Mar, 2009 ($2.95/$2.99)

1-15: 1-Waid-s/Kitson-a/c. 4-Kirk & Gibbons-a. 9-Jeanty-a. 15-Dawnstar, Tyroc, Blok-c 3.00
37-50: 37-Shooter-s/Manapul-a begin; two interlocking covers. 50-Wraparound cover 3.00
44-Variant-c by Neal Adams 5.00
... Death of a Dream TPB ('06, $14.99) r/#7-13 15.00
... Enemy Manifest HC ('09, $24.99, dustjacket) r/#45-50 25.00
... Enemy Manifest SC ('10, $14.99) r/#45-50 15.00
... Enemy Rising HC ('08, $19.99, dustjacket) r/#37-44 20.00
... Enemy Rising SC ('09, $14.99) r/#37-44 15.00
...: 1050 Years of the Future TPB ('08, $19.99) r/greatest tales of their 50 year history 20.00
... Teenage Revolution TPB ('05, $14.99) r/#1-6 & Teen Titans/Legion Spec.; sketch pages 15.00

LEGION OF SUPER-HEROES (6th Series)
DC Comics: Jul, 2010 - No. 16, Oct, 2011 ($3.99/$2.99)

1-9: 1-Earth-Man app.; Titan destroyed; Levitz-s/Cinar-a/c. 6-Jimenez back-up-a 4.00
1-6-Variant covers by Jim Lee 8.00
10-16-($2.99) 12-16-Legion of Super-Villains app. 3.00
Annual 1 (2/11, $4.99) New Emerald Empress; Levitz-s/Giffen-a 5.00
...: The Choice HC (2011, $24.99, dustjacket) r/#1-6; variant-c gallery and Cinar art 25.00

LEGION OF SUPER-HEROES (DC New 52)(Also see Legion Lost)
DC Comics: Nov, 2011 - No. 23, Oct, 2013 ($2.99)

1-23: 1-4-Levitz-s/Portela-a. 5-Simonson-c/a. 8-Lightle-a. 17-Giffen-a. 23-Maguire-a 3.00
#0 (11/12, $2.99) Story of Brainiac 5 joining the Legion; Levitz-s/Kolins-a 3.00

LEGION OF SUPER-HEROES (See Superman (2018 series) #14,15)
DC Comics: Jan, 2020 - Present ($3.99)

1-12: 1-Bendis-s/Sook-a; Superboy (Jon Kent) joins the Legion; Mordru app. 3-Robin app. 4,5-Origin retold. 4-Sook & Janin-a. 5-Sook & Godlewski-a. 6-Intro Gold Lantern & Dr. Fate. 8,9-Different artist each page; 8-Mack, Allred, Maleev. 9-Grell, Nowlan, Romita, Jr. 4.00
...: Millennium 1,2 ($4.99, 11/19 - No. 2, 12/19) Bendis-s; Rose & Thorn, Kamandi app. 5.00

LEGION OF SUPER-HEROES/BUGS BUNNY SPECIAL
DC Comics: Aug, 2017 ($4.99, one-shot)

1-Humphries-s/Grummett-a/c; Bugs Bunny in the 31st century; Supergirl & Validus app. 5.00

LEGION OF SUPER-HEROES IN THE 31ST CENTURY (Based on the animated series)
DC Comics: June, 2007 - No. 20, Jan, 2009 ($2.25)

1-20: 1-Chynna Clugston-a; Fatal Five app. 6-Green Lantern Corps app. 15-Impulse app. 3.00
1-(6/07) Free Comic Book Day giveaway 3.00
...: Tomorrow's Heroes (2008, $14.99) r/#1-7; cover gallery 15.00

LEGION OF SUPER-VILLAINS
DC Comics: May, 2011 ($4.99, one-shot)

1-Levitz-s/Portela-a; Saturn Queen, Lightning Lord, Sun-Killer, Micro Lad app. 5.00

LEGION OF X (Legion and the X-Men)
Marvel Comics: Jun, 2022 - No. 10, Apr, 2023 ($4.99/$3.99)

1-($4.99) Spurrier-s/Bazaldua-a 5.00
2-10-($3.99) 2-Banshee app. 6-Judgment Day tie-in 4.00

LEGION: PROPHETS (Prelude to 2010 movie)
IDW Publishing: Nov, 2009 - No. 4, Dec, 2009 ($3.99, limited series)

1-4: Stewart & Waltz-s. 1-Muriel-a. 2-Holder-a. 3-Paronzini-a. 4-Gaydos-a 4.00

LEGION: SCIENCE POLICE (See Legion of Super-Heroes)
DC Comics: Aug, 1998 - No. 4, Nov, 1998 ($2.25, limited series)

1-4-Ryan-a 3.00

LEGION: SECRET ORIGIN (Legion of Super-Heroes)
DC Comics: Dec, 2011 - No. 6, May, 2012 ($2.99, limited series)

1-6-Levitz-s/Batista-a; formation of the Legion retold 3.00

LEGION WORLDS (Follows Legion Lost series)
DC Comics: Jun, 2001 - No. 6, Nov, 2001 ($3.95, limited series)

1-6-Abnett & Lanning-s; art by various. 5-Dillon-a. 6-Timber Wolf app. 4.00

LEGO NINJAGO: GARMADON
Image Comics: Apr, 2022 - No. 5, Oct, 2022 ($3.99, limited series)

1-5-Lego-style story; Tri Vuong-s/a 4.00

LEMONADE KID, THE (See Bobby Benson's B-Bar-B Riders)
AC Comics: 1990 ($2.50, 28 pgs.)

1-Powell-c(r); Red Hawk-r by Powell; Lemonade Kid-r/Bobby Benson by Powell (2 stories) 3.00

LENNON SISTERS LIFE STORY, THE
Dell Publishing Co.: No. 951, Nov, 1958 - No. 1014, Aug, 1959

Four Color 951 (#1)-Toth-a, 32pgs, photo-c 11 22 33 76 163 250
Four Color 1014-Toth-a, photo-c 11 22 33 72 154 235

LENORE
Slave Labor Graphics/Titan Comics: Feb, 1998 - Present ($2.95/$3.95, B&W, color #13-on)

1-12: 1-Roman Dirge-s/a, 1,2-2nd printing 4.00
13-($3.95, color) 4.00
Vol. 2 (8/09 - No. 11) 1-11: 1-1st and 2nd printings; Lenore's origin 4.00
Vol. 3 (9/19, $3.99) 1-Two covers 4.00
...: Cooties TPB (3/06, $13.95) r/#9-12; pin-ups by various 14.00
...: Noogies TPB ($11.95) r/#1-4 12.00
...: Pink Bellies HC (Titan, 3/15, $17.99) Vol. 2 #8-11 18.00
...: Purple Nurples HC (8/13, $17.95) Vol. 2 #4-7 18.00
...: Swirlies HC (8/12, $17.95) r/#13 & Vol. 2 #1-3 18.00
...: Wedgies TPB (2000, $13.95) r/#5-8 14.00

LEONARD NIMOY'S PRIMORTALS
Tekno Comix: Mar, 1995 - No. 15, May, 1996 ($1.95)

1-15: Concept by Leonard Nimoy & Isaac Asimov 1-3-w/bound-in game piece & trading card. 4-w/Teknophage Steel Edition coupon. 13,14-Art Adams-c. 15-Simonson-c 4.00

LEONARD NIMOY'S PRIMORTALS
BIG Entertainment: V2#0, June, 1996 - No. 8, Feb, 1997 ($2.25)

V2#0-8: 0-Includes Pt. 9 of "The Big Bang" x-over. 0,1-Simonson-c. 3-Kelley Jones-c 4.00

LEONARD NIMOY'S PRIMORTALS ORIGINS
Tekno Comix: Nov, 1995 - No. 2, Dec, 1995 ($2.95, limited series)

1,2: Nimoy scripts; Art Adams-c; polybagged 4.00

LEONARDO (Also see Teenage Mutant Ninja Turtles)
Mirage Studios: Dec, 1986 ($1.50, B&W, one-shot)

1 4 8 12 27 44 60

LEONIDE THE VAMPYR
Dark Horse Comics: Oct, 2022; Dec, 2022 ($3.99, one-shots)

...: A Christmas For Crows (12/22); Mike Mignola-s/Rachele Aragno-a 4.00
...: Miracle at the Crows Head (10/22); Mike Mignola-s/Rachele Aragno-a 4.00

LEO THE LION
I. W. Enterprises: No date (1960s) (10¢)

1-Reprint 2 4 6 9 13 16

LEROY (Teen-age)
Standard Comics: Nov, 1949 - No. 6, Nov, 1950

1 23 46 69 136 223 310
2-Frazetta text illo. 16 32 48 94 147 200
3-6: 3-Lubbers-a 14 28 42 78 112 145

LESTER OF THE LESSER GODS
Albatross Funnybooks: 2021 ($3.99, one-shot)

1-Eric Powell, Lucky Yates & Mac Cushing/Gideon Kendall-a 4.00

LETHAL (Also see Brigade)
Image Comics (Extreme Studios): Feb, 1996 ($2.50, unfinished limited series)

1-Marat Mychaels-c/a. 3.00

LETHAL FOES OF SPIDER-MAN (Sequel to Deadly Foes of Spider-Man)
Marvel Comics: Sept, 1993 - No. 4, Dec, 1993 ($1.75, limited series)

1-4 4.00

LETHARGIC LAD

Legion of Super-Heroes (2011) #22 © DC

Lenore V2 #7 © Roman Dirge

Liberty Comics #1 © CBLDF

GD VG FN VF VF/NM NM-
2.0 4.0 6.0 8.0 9.0 9.2

Crusade Ent.: June, 1996 - No. 3, Sept, 1996 ($2.95, B&W, limited series)

1,2 3.00
3-Alex Ross-c/swipe (Kingdom Come) 4.00
...Jumbo Sized Annual #1 (Summer 2002, $3.99) prints comic stories from internet 4.00

LETHARGIC LAD ADVENTURES
Crusade Ent./Destination Ent.#3 on: Oct, 1997 - No. 12, Sept./Oct. 1999 ($2.95, B&W)

1-12-Hyland-s/a. 9-Alex Ross sketch page & back-c 3.00

LET ME IN: CROSSROADS (Based on the 2010 movie Let Me In)
Dark Horse Comics: Dec, 2010 - No. 4, Mar, 2011 ($3.99, limited series)

1-4-Prelude to the film; Andreyko-s/Reynolds-a/Phillips-c 4.00
1-4 Variant photo-c 8.00

LET'S PRETEND (CBS radio)
D. S. Publishing Co.: May-June, 1950 - No. 3, Sept-Oct, 1950

1 22 44 66 128 209 290
2,3 16 32 48 94 147 200

LET'S READ THE NEWSPAPER
Charlton Press: 1974

nn-Features Quincy by Ted Sheares 1 3 4 6 8 10

LET'S TAKE A TRIP (TV) (CBS Television Presents)
Pines Comics: Spring, 1958

1-Marv Levy-c/a 6 12 18 27 33 38

LETTER 44
Oni Press: Oct, 2013 - No. 35, Aug, 2017 ($1.00/$3.99)

1-($1.00)-Soule-a/Alberto Alburquerque-a 5.00
2-35-($3.99) 7-Joëlle Jones-a. 14-Drew Moss-a. 28-Gluskova-a 4.00
... #1 Square One Edition (2/17, $1.00) r/#1 3.00

LETTERS TO SANTA (See March of Comics No. 228)

LEV GLEASON PRESENTS
Comic House: Apr, 2021 - Present ($9.99)

1,2: 1-New stories of Silver Streak, Captain Canuck. 2-Golden Age Daredevil 10.00

LEVIATHAN DAWN (Also see Event Leviathan)
DC Comics: 2020 ($4.99, one-shot)

1-Follows Event Leviathan series; Bendis-s/Maleev-a 5.00

LEX LUTHOR: MAN OF STEEL
DC Comics: May, 2005 - No. 5, Sept, 2005 ($2.99, limited series)

1-5: 1-Azzarello-s/Bermejo-a/c in all. 3-Batman-c/app. 3.00
TPB (2005, $12.99) r/series 13.00
Luthor HC (2010, $19.99, d.j.) r/#1-5 with 10 new story pages; cover gallery & sketch-a 20.00

LEX LUTHOR/PORKY PIG
DC Comics: Oct, 2018 ($4.99, one-shot)

1-Mark Russell-s/Brad Walker-a/Ben Oliver-c; back-up story in classic cartoon style 5.00

LEX LUTHOR: THE UNAUTHORIZED BIOGRAPHY
DC Comics: 1989 ($3.95, 52 pgs., one-shot, squarebound)

1-Painted-c; Clark Kent app. 6.00

LEX LUTHOR: YEAR OF THE VILLAIN
DC Comics: 2019 ($4.99, one-shot)

1-Latour-s/Hitch-a; multiverse of Luthors app. 5.00

LGBTQ ETC PEOPLE (Reprints from Cerebus in Hell)
Aardvark-Vanaheim: Jun, 2019 ($4.00, B&W)

1-Cerebus figures placed over original Gustave Doré artwork of Hell; X-Men #1-c swipe 4.00

LIBERTY COMICS (Miss Liberty No. 1)
Green Publishing Co.: No. 5, May, 1945 - No. 15, July, 1946 (MLJ & other-r)

5 (5/45)-The Prankster app; Starr-a 36 72 108 211 343 475
10-Hangman & Boy Buddies app.; reprints 3 Hangman stories, incl. Hangman #8
41 82 123 256 428 600
11 (V2#2, 1/46)-Wilbur in women's clothes 19 38 57 111 176 240
12 (V2#4)-Black Hood & Suzie app.; classic Skull-c 258 516 774 1651 2826 4000
14,15-Patty of Airliner; Starr-a in both 29 58 87 172 281 390

LIBERTY COMICS (The CBLDF Presents...)
Image Comics: July, 2008; Oct, 2009 ($3.99/$4.99, Comic Book Legal Defense Fund benefit)

1-Two covers by Campbell & Mignola; art by Cooke, Aragones, A. Adams & others 4.00
1-(12/08) Second printing with Thor-c by Simonson 4.00
2-(10/09, $4.99) two covers by Romita Jr. & Sale; art by Allred, Templesmith, Jim Lee 5.00
Liberty Annual 2010 (10/10, $4.99) Covers by Gibbons & Robertson 5.00
Liberty Annual 2011 (10/11, $4.99) Covers by Wagner & Cassaday 5.00
Liberty Annual 2012 (10/12, $4.99) Covers by Dodson & Bá; Walking Dead story 5.00
Liberty Annual 2013 (10/13, $4.99) Covers by Corben & Marquez 5.00
Liberty Annual 2014 (10/14, $4.99) Covers by Allred, Simonson, & Charm 5.00
Liberty Annual 2015 (10/15, $4.99) Covers by Fegredo, Fowler & Del Rey 5.00
Liberty Annual 2016 (11/16, $4.99) Stories by Guinan, Pope, Wimberly, Schkade & others 5.00

LIBERTY COMICS
Heroic Publishing: Sept, 2007 ($4.50)

1-Mark Sparacio-c 4.50

LIBERTY GIRL
Heroic Publishing: Aug, 2006 - No. 3, May, 2007 ($3.25/$2.99)

1-3-Mark Sparacio-c/a 3.25

LIBERTY GUARDS
Chicago Mail Order: 1942 (Centaur Publ.)

nn-Reprints Man of War #1 with cover of Liberty Scouts #1; Nazi subs pulling into the harbor in front of the Capitol building & Washington Monument cover by Gustavson
194 388 582 1242 2121 3000

LIBERTY MEADOWS
Insight Studios Group/Image Comics #27 on: 1999 - No. 37 ($2.95, B&W)

1-Frank Cho-s/a; reprints newspaper strips 3 6 9 17 26 35
1-2nd & 3rd printings 1 2 3 4 5 7
2,3 2 4 6 8 11 14
4-10 1 2 3 4 5 7
11-25,27-37: 20-Adam Hughes-c. 22-Evil Brandy vs. Brandy. 27-1st Image issue, printed sideways 3.00
..., Cover Girl HC (Image, 2006, $24.99, with dustjacket) r/color covers of #1-19,21-37 along with B&W inked versions, sketches and pin-up art 25.00
...: Eden Book 1 SC (Image, 2002, $14.95) r/#1-9; sketch gallery 15.00
...: Eden Book 1 SC 2nd printing (Image, 2004, $19.95) r/#1-9; sketch gallery 20.00
...: Eden Book 1 HC (Image, 2003, $24.95, with dustjacket) r/#1-9; sketch gallery 25.00
...: Creature Comforts Book 2 HC (Image, 2004, $24.95, with d.j.) r/#10-18; sketch gallery 25.00
...: Creature Comforts Book 2 SC (Image, 12/04, $14.95) r/#10-18; sketch gallery 15.00
...Book 3: Summer of Love HC (Image, 12/04, $24.95) r/#19-27; sketch gallery 25.00
...Book 3: Summer of Love SC (Image, 7/05, $14.95) r/#19-27; sketch gallery 15.00
...Book 4: Cold, Cold Heart HC (Image, 9/05, $24.95) r/#28-36; sketch gallery 25.00
...Book 4: Cold, Cold Heart SC (Image, 2006, $14.99) r/#28-36; sketch gallery 15.00
Image Firsts: Liberty Meadows #1 (9/10, $1.00) r/#1 3.00
... Sourcebook (5/04, $4.95) character info and unpublished strips 5.00
... Wedding Album (#26) (2002, $2.95) 3.00

LIBERTY PROJECT, THE
Eclipse Comics: June, 1987 - No. 8, May, 1988 ($1.75, color, Baxter paper)

1-8: 6-Valkyrie app. 3.00

LIBERTY SCOUTS (See Liberty Guards & Man of War)
Centaur Publications: No. 2, June, 1941 - No. 3, Aug, 1941

2(#1)-Origin The Fire-Man, Man of War; Vapo-Man & Liberty Scouts begin; intro Liberty Scouts; Gustavson-c/a in both 194 388 582 1242 2121 3000
3(#2)-Origin & 1st app. The Sentinel 187 374 561 1197 2049 2900

LIBRARIANS, THE (Based on the TV series)
Dynamite Entertainment: 2017 - No. 4, 2018 ($3.99)

1-4-Pfeiffer-s/Buchemi-a; multiple covers 4.00

LICENCE TO KILL (James Bond 007) (Movie)
Eclipse Comics: 1989 ($7.95, slick paper, 52 pgs.)

nn-Movie adaptation; Timothy Dalton photo-c 1 3 4 6 8 10
Limited Hardcover ($24.95) 25.00

LIDSVILLE (TV)
Gold Key: Oct, 1972 - No. 5, Oct, 1973

1-Photo-c on all 5 10 15 31 53 75
2-5 3 6 9 21 33 45

LIEUTENANT, THE (TV)
Dell Publishing Co.: April-June, 1964

1-Photo-c 3 6 9 17 26 35

LIEUTENANT BLUEBERRY (Also see Blueberry)
Marvel Comics (Epic Comics): 1991 - No. 3, 1991 (Graphic novel)

1-($8.95)-Moebius-a in all 4 8 12 27 44 60
2-($8.95) 3 6 9 19 30 40
3-($14.95) 4 8 12 27 44 60

LT. ROBIN CRUSOE, U.S.N. (See Movie Comics & Walt Disney Showcase #26)

GD 2.0 | VG 4.0 | FN 6.0 | VF 8.0 | VF/NM 9.0 | NM- 9.2

LIFE AND DEATH OF TOYO HARADA, THE
Valiant Entertainment: Mar, 2019 - No. 6, Jul, 2019 ($3.99, limited series)
1-6-Dysart-s/Cafu-a. 2-Flashback-a by Guice. 3-Albert Einstein app. 4.00

LIFE EATERS, THE
DC Comics (WildStorm): 2003 ($29.95, hardcover with dust jacket)
HC-David Brin-s; Scott Hampton-painted-a/c; Norse Gods team with the Nazis 30.00
SC-(2004, $19.95) 20.00

LIFE IS STRANGE (Based on the Square Enix video game)
Titan Comics: Dec, 2018 - No. 12, Feb, 2020 ($3.99)
1-12-Emma Vieceli-s/Claudia Leonardi-a 4.00

LIFE IS STRANGE (Based on the Square Enix video game)
Titan Comics: Nov, 2020 - No. 2.4 ($3.99)
2.1-2.4-Emma Vieceli-s/Claudia Leonardi-a 4.00

LIFE IS STRANGE: COMING HOME (Based on the Square Enix video game)
Titan Comics: Aug, 2021 - No. 2, Sept, 2021 ($5.99, limited series)
1,2-Emma Vieceli-s/Claudia Leonardi-a 6.00

LIFE IS STRANGE: SETTLING DUST (Based on the Square Enix video game)
Titan Comics: Oct, 2021 - No. 4, Apr, 2022 ($3.99, limited series)
1-4-Emma Vieceli-s/Claudia Leonardi-a 4.00

LIFE OF CAPTAIN MARVEL, THE
Marvel Comics Group: Aug, 1985 - No. 5, Dec, 1985 ($2.00, Baxter paper)
1-5: 1-All reprint Starlin issues of Iron Man #55, Capt. Marvel #25-34 plus Marvel Feature #12 (all with Thanos). 4-New Thanos back-c by Starlin 6.00

LIFE OF CAPTAIN MARVEL, THE (Carol Danvers)
Marvel Comics: Sept, 2018 - No. 5, Feb, 2019 ($4.99/$3.99, limited series)
1-($4.99) Childhood flashbacks; Stohl-s/Pacheco & Sauvage-a 5.00
2-5-($3.99) 4-Origin of Carol's mother 4.00

LIFE OF CHRIST, THE
Catechetical Guild Educational Society: No. 301, 1949 (35¢, 100 pgs.)
301-Reprints from Topix(1949)-V5#11,12 10 20 30 58 79 100

LIFE OF CHRIST: THE CHRISTMAS STORY, THE
Marvel Comics/Nelson: Feb, 1993 ($2.99, slick stock)
nn 5.00

LIFE OF CHRIST: THE EASTER STORY, THE
Marvel Comics/Nelson: 1993 ($2.99, slick stock)
nn 5.00

LIFE OF CHRIST VISUALIZED
Standard Publishers: 1942 - No. 3, 1943
1-3: All came in cardboard case, each.... 9 18 27 50 65 80
Case only..... 10 20 30 54 72 90

LIFE OF CHRIST VISUALIZED
The Standard Publ. Co.: 1946? (48 pgs. in color)
nn 7 14 21 37 46 55

LIFE OF ESTHER VISUALIZED
The Standard Publ. Co.: No. 2062, 1947 (48 pgs. in color)
2062 7 14 21 37 46 55

LIFE OF JOSEPH VISUALIZED
The Standard Publ. Co.: No. 1054, 1946 (48 pgs. in color)
1054 7 14 21 37 46 55

LIFE OF PAUL (See The Living Bible)

LIFE OF POPE JOHN PAUL II, THE
Marvel Comics Group: Jan, 1983 ($1.50/$1.75)
1 3 6 9 14 19 24

LIFE OF RILEY, THE (TV)
Dell Publishing Co.: No. 917, July, 1958
Four Color 917-William Bendix photo-c 11 22 33 73 157 240

LIFE ON ANOTHER PLANET
Kitchen Sink Press: 1978 (B&W, graphic novel, magazine size)
nn-Will Eisner-s/a 20.00
Reprint (DC Comics, 5/00, $12.95) 13.00

LIFE'S LIKE THAT
Croyden Publ. Co.: 1945 (25¢, B&W, 68 pgs.)
nn-Newspaper Sunday strip-r by Neher 8 16 24 44 57 70

LIFE STORIES OF AMERICAN PRESIDENTS (See Dell Giants)

LIFE STORY
Fawcett Publications: Apr, 1949 - V8#46, Jan, 1953; V8#47, Apr, 1953 (All have photo-c?)
V1#1 20 40 60 114 182 250
2 12 24 36 67 94 120
3-6, V2#7-12 (3/50) 10 20 30 54 72 90
V3#13-Wood-a (4/50) 15 30 45 94 147 200
V3#14-18, V4#19-24, V5#25-30, V6#31-35 9 18 27 50 65 80
V6#36- "I sold drugs" on-c 15 30 45 85 130 175
V7#37,40-42, V8#44,45 9 18 27 47 61 75
V7#38, V8#43-Evans-a 9 18 27 50 65 80
V7#39-Drug Smuggling & Junkie story 14 28 42 76 108 140
V8#46,47 (Scarce) 11 22 33 62 86 110
NOTE: *Powell a-13, 23, 24, 26, 28, 30, 32, 39. Marcus Swayze a-1-3, 10-12, 15, 16, 20, 21, 23-25, 31, 35, 37, 40, 44, 46.*

LIFE, THE UNIVERSE AND EVERYTHING (See Hitchhikers Guide to the Galaxy & Restaurant at the End of the Universe)
DC Comics: 1996 - No. 3, 1996 ($6.95, squarebound, limited series)
1-3: Adaptation of novel by Douglas Adams. 1 2 3 4 5 7

LIFE WITH ARCHIE
Archie Publications: Sept, 1958 - No. 286, Sept, 1991
1 79 158 237 632 1416 2200
2-(9/59) 34 68 102 245 548 850
3-5: 3-(7/60) 18 36 54 128 284 440
6-8,10 13 26 39 86 188 290
9,11-Horror/SciFi-c 18 36 54 124 275 425
12-20 9 18 27 58 114 170
21(7/63)-30 8 16 24 54 102 150
31-34,36-38,40,41 7 14 21 46 86 125
35,39-Horror/Sci-Fi-c 10 20 30 64 132 200
42-Pureheart begins (1st app.-c/s, 10/65) 14 28 42 96 211 325
43,44 8 16 24 51 96 140
45(1/66) 1st Man From R.I.V.E.R.D.A.L.E. 9 18 27 57 111 165
46-Origin Pureheart 8 16 24 54 102 150
47-49 6 12 18 41 76 110
50-United Three begin: Pureheart (Archie), Superteen (Betty), Captain Hero (Jughead) 9 18 27 61 123 185
51-59: 59-Pureheart ends 5 10 15 35 63 90
60-Archie band begins, ends #66 6 12 18 41 76 110
61-66: 61-Man From R.I.V.E.R.D.A.L.E.-c/s 5 10 15 31 53 75
67-80 4 8 12 25 40 55
81-99 3 6 9 21 33 45
100 (8/70), 113-Sabrina & Salem app. 4 8 12 27 44 60
101-112, 114-130(2/73), 139(11/73)-Archie Band c/s 3 6 9 14 20 25
131,134-138,140-146,148-161,164-170(6/76) 2 4 6 11 16 20
132,133,147,163-all horror-c/s 3 6 9 17 25 34
162-UFO c/s 3 6 9 16 23 30
171,173-175,177-184,186,189,191-194,196 2 4 6 8 10 12
172,185,197 : 172-(9/77)-Bi-Cent. spec. ish, 185-2nd 24th cent.-c/s, 197-Time machine/SF-c/s 2 4 6 8 11 14
176(12/76)-1st app. Capt. Archie of Starship Rivda, in 24th century c/s; 1st app. Stella the Robot 3 6 9 16 23 30
187,188,195,198,199-all horror-c/s 2 4 6 11 16 20
190-1st Dr. Doom-c/s 3 6 9 14 19 24
200 (12/78) Maltese Pigeon-s 2 4 6 10 14 18
201-203,205-237,239,240(1/84): 208-Reintro Veronica 1 3 4 6 8 10
204-Flying saucer-c/s 2 4 6 8 10 12
238-(9/83)-25th anniversary issue; Ol' Betsy (jalopy) replaced 1 3 4 6 8 10
241-278,280-285: 250-Comic book convention-s 5.00
279,286: 279-Intro Mustang Sally ($1.00, 7/90) 6.00
NOTE: *Gene Colan a-272-279, 285, 286. Horror/Sci-Fi-c 9, 11, 35, 39, 162.*

LIFE WITH ARCHIE (The Married Life) (Magazine)
Archie Publications: Sept, 2010 - No. 37, Sept, 2014 ($3.99, magazine-size)
1-Continuation of Married Life stories from Archie #600-605; articles/interviews 1 3 4 6 8 10
2-10 5.00
11-15,17-34 4.00
16-Kevin Keller gay wedding 10.00
36-($4.99, comic-size) Death of Archie; 5 covers by Allred, Francavilla, Hughes, Ramon Perez & Staples 1 2 3 5 6 8
37-($4.99, comic-size) One Year Later aftermath; 5 covers by Chiang, Edwards, Alex Ross, Simonson & Thompson 5.00
...: The Death of Archie: A Life Celebrated Commemorative Issue (2014, $9.99) reprints #36 & #37 in magazine size; afterword by Jon Goldwater; cover gallery w/artist quotes 10.00

LIFE WITH MILLIE (Formerly A Date With Millie) (Modeling With Millie #21 on)
Atlas/Marvel Comics Group: No. 8, Dec, 1960 - No. 20, Dec, 1962
8-Teenage 13 26 39 96 188 290
9-11 10 20 30 64 132 200
12-20 9 18 27 60 120 180

LIFE WITH SNARKY PARKER (TV)
Fox Feature Syndicate: Aug, 1950
1-Early TV comic; photo-c from TV puppet show 34 68 102 199 325 450

LIFE ZERO
Ablaze Publishing: 2022 - No. 6, 2022 ($3.99)
1-5-Stefano Vietti-s/Marco Checchetto-a 4.00

LIGHT AND DARKNESS WAR, THE
Marvel Comics (Epic Comics): Oct, 1988 - No. 6, Dec, 1989 ($1.95, lim. series)
1-6 3.00

LIGHT BRIGADE, THE
DC Comics: 2004 - No. 4, 2004 ($5.95, limited series)
1-4-Archangels in World War II; Tomasi-s/Snejbjerg-a 6.00
TPB (2005, 2009, $19.99) r/series; cover galery 20.00

LIGHT FANTASTIC, THE (Terry Pratchett's)
Innovation Publishing: June, 1992 - No. 4, Sept, 1992 ($2.50, mini-series)
1-4: Adapts 2nd novel in Discworld series 3.00

LIGHTHOUSE (See Jules Verne's Lighthouse)

LIGHT IN THE FOREST (Disney)
Dell Publishing Co.: No. 891, Mar, 1958
Four Color 891-Movie, Fess Parker photo-c 6 12 18 42 79 115

LIGHTNING COMICS (Formerly Sure-Fire No. 1-3)
Ace Magazines: No. 4, Dec, 1940 - No. 13(V3#1), June, 1942
4-Characters continue from Sure-Fire 245 490 735 1568 2684 3800
5,6: 6-Dr. Nemesis begins 181 362 543 1158 1979 2800
V2#1-6: 2- "Flash Lightning" becomes "Lash..." 135 270 405 864 1482 2100
V3#1-Intro. Lightning Girl & The Sword 135 270 405 864 1482 2100
NOTE: *Anderson a-V2#6. Mooney c-V1#5, 6, V2#1-6, V3#1. Bondage c-V2#6. Lightning-c on all.*

LIGHTNING COMICS PRESENTS
Lightning Comics: May, 1994 ($3.50)
1-Red foil-c distr. by Diamond Distr., 1-Black/yellow/blue-c distrib. by Capital Distr.,

Life of Captain Marvel (2018) #1 © MAR

Life With Archie (2010) #37 © ACP

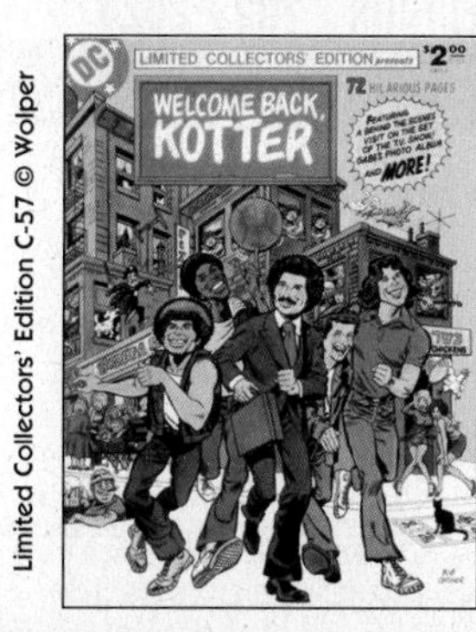

Limited Collectors' Edition C-57 © Wolper

	GD	VG	FN	VF	VF/NM	NM-
	2.0	4.0	6.0	8.0	9.0	9.2

1-Red/yellow-c distributed by H. World, 1-Platinum 3.50

LIGHTSTEP
Dark Horse Comics (Eipix Comics): Nov, 2018 - No. 5, Apr, 2019 ($3.99, limited series)
1-5-Milos Slavkovic-s/a; Mirko Topalski-s 4.00

LI'L ... (These titles are listed under Little ...)

LILI
Image Comics: No. 0, 1999 ($4.95, B&W)
0-Bendis & Yanover-s 5.00

LILLITH (See Warrior Nun...)
Antarctic Press: Sept, 1996 - No. 3, Feb, 1997 ($2.95, limited series)
1-3: 1-Variant-c 5.00

LIMITED COLLECTORS' EDITION (See Famous First Edition, Marvel Treasury #28, Rudolph The Red-Nosed Reindeer, & Superman Vs. The Amazing Spider-Man; becomes All-New Collectors' Edition)
National Periodical Publications/DC Comics:
(#21-34,51-59: 84 pgs.; #35-41: 68 pgs.; #42-50: 60 pgs.)
C-21, Summer, 1973 - No. C-59, 1978 ($1.00) (10x13-1/2")

(Rudolph...C-20 (implied), 12/72)-See Rudolph The Red-Nosed Reindeer
C-21: Shazam (TV); r/Captain Marvel Jr. #11 by Raboy; C.C. Beck-c, biog. & photo 3 6 9 21 33 45
C-22: Tarzan; complete origin reprinted from #207-210; all Kubert-c/a; Joe Kubert biography & photo inside 3 6 9 17 26 35
C-23: House of Mystery; Wrightson, N. Adams/Orlando, G. Kane/Wood, Toth, Aragones, Sparling reprints 4 8 12 25 40 55
C-24: Rudolph The Red-Nosed Reindeer 6 12 18 40 73 105
C-25: Batman; Neal Adams-c/a(r); G.A. Joker-r; Batman/Enemy Ace-r; Novick-a(r); has photos from TV show 4 8 12 27 44 60
C-26: See Famous First Edition C-26 (same contents)
C-27,C-29,C-31: C-27: Shazam (TV); G.A. Capt. Marvel & Mary Marvel-r; Beck-r. C-29: Tarzan; reprints "Return of Tarzan" from #219-223 by Kubert; Kubert-c. C-31: Superman; origin-r; Giordano-a; photos of George Reeves from 1950s TV show on inside b/c; Burnley, Boring-r 3 6 9 16 23 30
C-32: Ghosts (new-a) 3 6 9 21 33 45
C-33: Rudolph The Red-Nosed Reindeer(new-a) 5 10 15 35 63 90
C-34: Christmas with the Super-Heroes; unpublished Angel & Ape story by Oksner & Wood; Batman & Teen Titans-r 3 6 9 16 23 30
C-35: Shazam (TV); photo cover features TV's Captain Marvel, Jackson Bostwick; Beck-r; TV photos inside b/c 3 6 9 15 22 28
C-36: The Bible; all new adaptation beginning with Genesis by Kubert, Redondo & Mayer; Kubert-c 3 6 9 15 22 28
C-37: Batman; r-1946 Sundays; inside b/c photos of Batman TV show villains (all villain issue; r/G.A. Joker, Catwoman, Penguin, Two-Face, & Scarecrow stories plus 1946 Sundays-r) 3 6 9 18 28 38
C-38: Superman; 1 pg. N. Adams; part photo-c; photos from TV show on inside back-c 3 6 9 16 23 30
C-39: Secret Origins of Super-Villains; N. Adams-i(r); collection reprints 1950's Joker origin, Luthor origin from Adv. Comics #271, Captain Cold origin from Showcase #8 among others; G.A. Batman-r; Beck-r 3 6 9 16 23 30
C-40: Dick Tracy by Gould featuring Flattop; newspaper-r from 12/21/43 - 5/17/44; biog. of Chester Gould 3 6 9 15 22 28
C-41: Super Friends (TV); JLA-r(1965); Toth-c/a 3 6 9 16 24 32
C-42: Rudolph 4 8 12 27 44 60
C-43-C-47: C-43: Christmas with the Super-Heroes; Wrightson, S&K, Neal Adams-a. C-44: Batman; N. Adams-p(r) & G.A.-r; painted-c. C-45: More Secret Origins of Super-Villains; Flash-r/#105; G.A. Wonder Woman & Batman/Catwoman-r. C-46: Justice League of America(1963-r); 3 pgs. Toth-a C-47: Superman Salutes the Bicentennial (Tomahawk interior); 2 pgs. new-a 3 6 9 14 20 26
C-48,C-49: C-48: Superman Vs. The Flash (Superman/Flash race); swipes-c to Superman #199; r/Superman #199 & Flash #175; 6 pgs. Neal Adams-a. C-49: Superboy & the Legion of Super-Heroes 3 6 9 16 23 30
C-50: Rudolph The Red-Nosed Reindeer; contains poster attached at the centerfold with a cardstock flap (1/2 price if poster is missing) 4 8 12 27 44 60
C-51: Batman; Neal Adams-c/a 3 6 9 18 28 38
C-52,C-57: C-52: The Best of DC; Neal Adams-c/a; Toth, Kubert-a. C-57: Welcome Back, Kotter-r(TV)(5/78) includes unpublished #11 3 6 9 16 23 30
C-53 thru C-56, C-58, C-60 thru C-62 (See All-New Collectors' Edition)
C-59: Batman's Strangest Cases; N. Adams-r; Wrightson-r/Swamp Thing #7; N. Adams/Wrightson-c 3 6 9 16 23 30

NOTE: *All-r with exception of some special features and covers.* ***Aparo*** *a-52r; c-37.* ***Grell*** *c-49.* ***Infantino*** *a-25, 39, 44, 45, 52.* ***Bob Kane*** *r-25.* ***Robinson*** *r-25, 44.* ***Sprang*** *r-44. Issues #21-31, 35-39, 45, 48 have back cover cut-outs.*

LINDA (Everybody Loves...) (Phantom Lady No. 5 on)
Ajax-Farrell Publ. Co.: Apr-May, 1954 - No. 4, Oct-Nov, 1954
1-Kamenish-a 22 44 66 132 216 300
2-Lingerie panel 15 30 45 90 140 190
3,4 14 28 42 80 115 150

LINDA CARTER, STUDENT NURSE (Also see Night Nurse)
Atlas Comics (AMI): Sept, 1961 - No. 9, Jan, 1963
1-Al Hartley-c; 1st app. character who becomes Night Nurse in Daredevil V2 #58 (2004) 187 374 561 1197 2049 2900
2-9 30 60 90 177 289 400

LINDA LARK
Dell Publishing Co.: Oct-Dec, 1961 - No. 8, Aug-Oct, 1963
1 3 6 9 21 33 45
2-8 3 6 9 14 19 24

LINE OF DEFENSE 3000AD (Based on the video game)
DC Comics: No. 0, 2012 (no price)
0-Brian Ching-a 3.00

LINUS, THE LIONHEARTED (TV)
Gold Key: Sept, 1965
1 (10155-509) 6 12 18 38 69 100

LION, THE (See Movie Comics)

LION & THE EAGLE, THE
AfterShock Comics: Feb, 2022 - No. 4, Jun, 2022 ($7.99, 8-1/2" x 10-7/8", limited series)
1-4-Garth Ennis-s/PJ Holden-a 8.00

LIONHEART
Awesome Comics: Sept, 1999 - No. 2, Dec, 1999 ($2.99/$2.50)
1-Ian Churchill-story/a, Jeph Loeb-s; Coven app. 5.00
2-Flip book w/Coven #4 4.00

LION OF SPARTA (See Movie Classics)

LIPPY THE LION AND HARDY HAR HAR (TV)
Gold Key: Mar, 1963 (12¢) (See Hanna-Barbera Band Wagon #1)
1 (10049-303) 7 14 21 46 86 125

LISA COMICS (TV)(See Simpsons Comics)
Bongo Comics: 1995 ($2.25)
1-Lisa in Wonderland 1 3 4 6 8 10

LITERALS, THE (See Fables and Jack of Fables)
DC Comics (Vertigo): June, 2009 - No. 3, Aug, 2009 ($2.99)
1-3-Crossover with Fables #83-85 and Jack of Fables #33-35; Buckingham-c/a 3.00

LI'L ABNER (See Comics on Parade, Sparkle, Sparkler Comics, Tip Top Comics & Tip Topper)
United Features Syndicate: 1939 - 1940
Single Series 4 ('39) 90 180 270 576 988 1400
Single Series 18 ('40) (#18 on inside, #2 on-c) 68 136 204 435 743 1050

LI'L ABNER (Al Capp's; continued from Comics on Parade #58)
Harvey Publ. No. 61-69 (2/49)/Toby Press No. 70 on: No. 61, Dec, 1947 - No. 97, Jan, 1955
(See Oxydol-Dreft in Promotional Comics section)
61(#1)-Wolverton & Powell-a 28 56 84 165 270 375
62-65: 63-The Wolf Girl app. 65-Powell-a 16 32 48 92 144 195
66,67,69,70 15 30 45 86 133 180
68-Full length Fearless Fosdick-c/story 17 34 51 98 154 210
71-74,76,80 13 26 39 74 105 135
75,77-79,86,91-All with Kurtzman art; 86-Sadie Hawkins Day. 91-r/#77 15 30 45 83 124 165
81-85,87-90,92-94,96,97: 83-Evil-Eye Fleegle & Double Whammy app. 88-Cousin Weakeyes goes hunting. 94-Six lessons from Adam Lazonga. 96-Football issue 12 24 36 69 97 125
95-Full length Fearless Fosdick story 14 28 42 76 108 140

LI'L ABNER
Toby Press: 1951
1 19 38 57 112 179 245

LI'L ABNER'S DOGPATCH (See Al Capp's...)

LITTLE AL OF THE F.B.I.
Ziff-Davis Publications: No. 10, 1950 (no month) - No. 11, Apr-May, 1951 (Saunders painted-c)
10(1950) 22 44 66 132 216 300
11(1951) 17 34 51 98 154 210

LITTLE AL OF THE SECRET SERVICE
Ziff-Davis Publications: No. 10, 7-8/51; No, 2, 9-10/51; No. 3, Winter, 1951 (Saunders painted-c)
10(#1) 20 40 60 118 192 265

	GD 2.0	VG 4.0	FN 6.0	VF 8.0	VF/NM 9.0	NM- 9.2
2,3	16	32	48	92	144	185

LITTLE AMBROSE
Archie Publications: September, 1958

	GD 2.0	VG 4.0	FN 6.0	VF 8.0	VF/NM 9.0	NM- 9.2
1-Bob Bolling-c	20	40	60	115	185	255

LITTLE ANGEL
Standard (Visual Editions)/Pines: No. 5, Sept, 1954; No. 6, Sept, 1955 - No. 16, Sept, 1959

	GD 2.0	VG 4.0	FN 6.0	VF 8.0	VF/NM 9.0	NM- 9.2
5-Last pre-code issue	9	18	27	50	65	80
6-16	7	14	21	35	43	50

LITTLE ANNIE ROONEY (Also see Henry)
David McKay Publ.: 1935 (25¢, B&W dailies, 48 pgs.)(10"x10", cardboard-c)

	GD 2.0	VG 4.0	FN 6.0	VF 8.0	VF/NM 9.0	NM- 9.2
Book 1-Daily strip-r by Darrell McClure	39	78	117	231	378	525

LITTLE ANNIE ROONEY (See King Comics & Treasury of Comics)
David McKay/St. John/Standard: 1938; Aug, 1948 - No. 3, Oct, 1948

	GD 2.0	VG 4.0	FN 6.0	VF 8.0	VF/NM 9.0	NM- 9.2
Feature Books 11 (McKay, 1938)	39	78	117	236	388	540
1 (St. John)	16	32	48	92	144	195
2,3	10	20	30	54	72	90

LITTLE ARCHIE (The Adventures of... #13-on) (See Archie Giant Series Mag. #527, 534, 538, 545, 549, 556, 560, 566, 570, 583, 594, 596, 607, 609, 619)
Archie Publications: 1956 - No. 180, Feb, 1983 (Giants No. 3-84)

	GD 2.0	VG 4.0	FN 6.0	VF 8.0	VF/NM 9.0	NM- 9.2
1-(Scarce)	141	282	423	1142	2571	4000
2 (1957)	46	92	138	368	834	1300
3-5: 3-(1958)-Bob Bolling-c & giant issues begin	25	50	75	175	388	600
6-10	18	36	54	122	271	420
11-17,19,21 (84 pgs.)	13	26	39	86	188	290
18,20,22 (84 pgs.)-Horror/Sci-Fi-c	19	38	57	128	284	440
23-39 (68 pgs.)	8	16	24	56	108	160
40 (Fall/66)-Intro. Little Pureheart-c/s (68 pgs.)	9	18	27	59	117	175
41,44-Little Pureheart (68 pgs.)	7	14	21	44	82	120
42-Intro The Little Archies Band, ends #66 (68 pgs.)	7	14	21	48	89	130
43-1st Boy From R.I.V.E.R.D.A.L.E. (68 pgs.)	7	14	21	46	86	125
45-58 (68 pgs.)	5	10	15	35	63	90
59 (68 pgs.)-Little Sabrina begins	8	16	24	56	108	160
60-66 (68 pgs.)	5	10	15	30	50	70
67(9/71)-84: 84-Last 52pg. Giant-Size (2/74)	3	6	9	19	30	40
85-99	3	6	9	14	19	24
100	3	6	9	14	20	26
101-112,114-116,118-129	2	4	6	9	13	16
113,117,130: 113-Halloween Special issue(12/76). 117-Donny Osmond-c cameo 130-UFO cover (5/78)	2	4	6	11	16	20
131-150(1/80), 180(Last issue, 2/83)	2	4	6	8	10	12
151-179	1	3	4	6	8	10
...In Animal Land 1 (1957)	32	64	96	230	515	800
...In Animal Land 17 (Winter, 1957-58)-19 (Summer,1958)-Formerly Li'l Jinx	13	26	39	86	188	290
Archie Classics - The Adventures of Little Archie Vol. 1 TPB (2004, $10.95) reprints						11.00
Vol. 2 TPB (2008, $9.95) reprints plus new 22 pg. story with Bolling-s/a						10.00

NOTE: *Little Archie Band app. 42-66. Little Sabrina in 59-78,80-180*

LITTLE ARCHIE CHRISTMAS SPECIAL (See Archie Giant Series #581)

LITTLE ARCHIE COMICS DIGEST ANNUAL (...Magazine #5 on)
Archie Publications: 10/77 - No. 48, 5/91 (Digest-size, 128 pgs., later issues $1.35-$1.50)

	GD 2.0	VG 4.0	FN 6.0	VF 8.0	VF/NM 9.0	NM- 9.2
1(10/77)-Reprints	3	6	9	19	30	40
2(4/78,3(11/78)-Neal Adams-a. 3-The Fly-r by S&K	3	6	9	14	20	26
4(4/79) - 10	2	4	6	10	14	18
11-20	2	4	6	8	10	12
21-30: 28-Christmas-c	1	2	3	5	6	8
31-48: 40,46-Christmas-c						5.00

NOTE: *Little Archie, Little Jinx, Little Jughead & Little Sabrina in most issues.*

LITTLE ARCHIE DIGEST MAGAZINE
Archie Comics: July, 1991 - No. 21, Mar, 1998 ($1.50/$1.79/$1.89, digest size, bi-annual)

	GD 2.0	VG 4.0	FN 6.0	VF 8.0	VF/NM 9.0	NM- 9.2
V2#1						6.00
2-10						4.00
11-21						3.00

LITTLE ARCHIE MYSTERY
Archie Publications: Aug, 1963 - No. 2, Oct, 1963 (12¢ issues)

	GD 2.0	VG 4.0	FN 6.0	VF 8.0	VF/NM 9.0	NM- 9.2
1	18	36	54	124	275	425
2	9	18	27	62	126	190

LITTLE ARCHIE, ONE SHOT
Archie Comic Publications: May, 2017 ($4.99, one-shot)

	GD 2.0	VG 4.0	FN 6.0	VF 8.0	VF/NM 9.0	NM- 9.2
nn-Art Baltazar & Franco-s/a; 3 covers; Sabrina app.						5.00

LITTLE ASPIRIN (See Little Lenny & Wisco)
Marvel Comics (CnPC): July, 1949 - No. 3, Dec, 1949 (52 pgs.)

	GD 2.0	VG 4.0	FN 6.0	VF 8.0	VF/NM 9.0	NM- 9.2
1-Oscar app.; Kurtzman-a (4 pgs.)	22	44	66	132	216	300
2-Kurtzman-a (4 pgs.)	14	28	42	82	121	160
3-No Kurtzman-a	10	20	30	58	79	100

LITTLE AUDREY (Also see Playful...)
St. John Publ.: Apr, 1948 - No. 24, May, 1952

	GD 2.0	VG 4.0	FN 6.0	VF 8.0	VF/NM 9.0	NM- 9.2
1-1st app. Little Audrey	161	322	483	1030	1765	2500
2	47	94	141	296	498	700
3-5	28	56	84	165	270	375
6-10	20	40	60	115	190	260
11-20: 16-X-Mas-c	15	30	45	85	130	175
21-24	14	28	42	80	115	150

LITTLE AUDREY (See Harvey Hits #11, 19)
Harvey Publications: No. 25, Aug, 1952 - No. 53, April, 1957

	GD 2.0	VG 4.0	FN 6.0	VF 8.0	VF/NM 9.0	NM- 9.2
25-(Paramount Pictures Famous Star... on-c); 1st Harvey Casper and Baby Huey (1 month earlier than Harvey Comic Hits #60(9/52))	29	58	87	209	467	725
26-30: 26-28-Casper app.	9	18	27	60	120	180
31-40: 32-35-Casper app.	7	14	21	44	82	120
41-53	5	10	15	33	57	80
...Clubhouse 1 (9/61, 68 pg. Giant)-New stories & reprints	9	18	27	57	111	165

LITTLE AUDREY
Harvey Comics: Aug, 1992 - No. 8, July, 1994 ($1.25/$1.50)

	GD 2.0	VG 4.0	FN 6.0	VF 8.0	VF/NM 9.0	NM- 9.2
V2#1						5.00
2-8						4.00

LITTLE AUDREY (...Yearbook)
St. John Publishing Co.: 1950 (50¢, 260 pgs.)

	GD 2.0	VG 4.0	FN 6.0	VF 8.0	VF/NM 9.0	NM- 9.2
Contains 8 complete 1949 comics rebound; Casper, Alice in Wonderland, Little Audrey, Abbott & Costello, Pinocchio, Moon Mullins, Three Stooges (from Jubilee), Little Annie Rooney app. (Rare)	200	400	600	1280	2190	3100

(Also see All Good & Treasury of Comics)
NOTE: *This book contains remaindered St. John comics; many variations possible.*

LITTLE AUDREY & MELVIN (Audrey & Melvin No. 62)
Harvey Publications: May, 1962 - No. 61, Dec, 1973

	GD 2.0	VG 4.0	FN 6.0	VF 8.0	VF/NM 9.0	NM- 9.2
1	9	18	27	63	129	195
2-5	4	8	12	25	40	55
6-10	3	6	9	21	33	45
11-20	3	6	9	16	23	30
21-40: 22-Richie Rich app.	2	4	6	13	18	22
41-50,55-61	2	4	6	9	13	16
51-54: All 52 pg. Giants	2	4	6	13	18	22

LITTLE AUDREY TV FUNTIME
Harvey Publ.: Sept, 1962 - No. 33, Oct, 1971 (#1-31: 68 pgs.; #32,33: 52 pgs.)

	GD 2.0	VG 4.0	FN 6.0	VF 8.0	VF/NM 9.0	NM- 9.2
1-Richie Rich app.	9	18	27	63	129	195
2,3: Richie Rich app.	4	8	12	27	44	60
4,5: 5-25¢ & 35¢ issues exist	4	8	12	23	37	50
6-10	3	6	9	17	26	35
11-20	3	6	9	14	19	24
21-33	2	4	6	11	16	20

LITTLE BAD WOLF (Disney; see Walt Disney's C&S #52, Walt Disney Showcase #21 & Wheaties)
Dell Publishing Co.: No. 403, June, 1952 - No. 564, June, 1954

	GD 2.0	VG 4.0	FN 6.0	VF 8.0	VF/NM 9.0	NM- 9.2
Four Color 403 (#1)	9	18	27	58	114	190
Four Color 473 (6/53), 564	6	12	18	41	76	110

LI'L BATTLESTAR GALACTICA (Classic 1978 TV series)
Dynamite Entertainment: 2014 ($3.99, one-shot)

	GD 2.0	VG 4.0	FN 6.0	VF 8.0	VF/NM 9.0	NM- 9.2
1-Kid version spoof by Franco & Art Baltazar; covers by Baltazar & Garbowska						4.00

LITTLE BEAVER
Dell Publishing Co.: No. 211, Jan, 1949 - No. 870, Jan, 1958 (All painted-c)

	GD 2.0	VG 4.0	FN 6.0	VF 8.0	VF/NM 9.0	NM- 9.2
Four Color 211('49)-All Harman-a	11	22	33	73	157	240
Four Color 267,294,332(5/51)	8	16	24	51	96	140
3(10-12/51)-8(1-3/53)	5	10	15	31	53	75
Four Color 483(8-10/53),529	5	10	15	35	63	90
Four Color 612,660,695,744,817,870	5	10	15	34	60	85

LI'L BIONIC KIDS (Six Million Dollar Man and Bionic Woman)
Dynamite Entertainment: 2014 ($3.99, one-shot)

	GD 2.0	VG 4.0	FN 6.0	VF 8.0	VF/NM 9.0	NM- 9.2
1-Kid version spoof; Bigfoot app.; Jerwa-s/McGinty-a; covers by Baltazar & Garbowska						4.00

LITTLE BIT
Jubilee/St. John Publishing Co.: Mar, 1949 - No. 2, June, 1949

	GD 2.0	VG 4.0	FN 6.0	VF 8.0	VF/NM 9.0	NM- 9.2
1-Kid humor	15	30	45	84	127	170
2	10	20	30	58	79	100

LI'L DEPRESSED BOY
Image Comics: Feb, 2011 - No. 16, Apr, 2013 ($2.99/$3.99)

	GD 2.0	VG 4.0	FN 6.0	VF 8.0	VF/NM 9.0	NM- 9.2
1-12-S. Steven Struble-s/Sina Grace-a. 5-Guillory-c. 6-Adlard-c. 10-Childish Gambino app.						3.00
13-16-($3.99)						4.00
Vol. 0 (12/11, $9.99) reprints earlier stories from webcomics & anthologies; various-a						10.00

LI'L DEPRESSED BOY: SUPPOSED TO BE THERE TOO
Image Comics: Oct, 2014 - No. 5, Jun, 2015 ($3.99)

	GD 2.0	VG 4.0	FN 6.0	VF 8.0	VF/NM 9.0	NM- 9.2
1-5-S. Steven Struble-s/Sina Grace-a						4.00

LITTLE DOT (See Humphrey, Li'l Max, Sad Sack, and Tastee-Freez Comics)
Harvey Publications: Sept, 1953 - No. 164, Apr, 1976

	GD 2.0	VG 4.0	FN 6.0	VF 8.0	VF/NM 9.0	NM- 9.2
1-Intro./1st app. Richie Rich & Little Lotta	1000	2000	3000	7300	12,900	18,500
2-1st app. Freckles & Pee Wee (Richie Rich's poor friends)	181	362	543	1158	1979	2800
3	106	212	318	678	1164	1650
4	94	188	282	597	1025	1450
5-Origin dots on Little Dot's dress	106	212	318	678	1164	1650
6-Richie Rich, Little Lotta, & Little Dot all on cover; 1st Richie Rich cover featured	245	490	735	1568	2684	3800
7-10: 9-Last pre-code issue (1/55)	71	142	213	454	777	1100
11-20	39	78	117	231	378	525
21-30	18	36	54	107	169	230
31-40	14	28	42	80	115	150
41-50	11	22	33	62	86	110
51-60	9	18	27	52	69	85
61-80	4	8	12	27	44	60
81-100	3	6	9	19	30	40
101-141: 122-Richie Rich, Little Lotta, & Little Dot birthday-c. 134-Richie Rich, Little Lotta, Little Audrey & Little Dot lemonade-c	3	6	9	16	23	30
142-145: All 52 pg. Giants	3	6	9	17	26	35
146-164	2	4	6	11	16	20

NOTE: *Richie Rich & Little Lotta in all.*

LITTLE DOT
Harvey Comics: Sept, 1992 - No. 7, June, 1994 ($1.25/$1.50)

	GD 2.0	VG 4.0	FN 6.0	VF 8.0	VF/NM 9.0	NM- 9.2
V2#1-Little Dot, Little Lotta, Richie Rich in all						5.00
2-7 ($1.50)						4.00

LITTLE DOT DOTLAND (Dot Dotland No. 62, 63)

Little Audrey #8 © STJ

Little Eva #15 © STJ

Little Lenny #1 © MAR

Harvey Publications: July, 1962 - No. 61, Dec, 1973

	GD 2.0	VG 4.0	FN 6.0	VF 8.0	VF/NM 9.0	NM- 9.2
1-Richie Rich begins	12	24	36	81	176	270
2,3	7	14	21	44	82	120
4,5	5	10	15	35	63	90
6-10	5	10	15	30	50	70
11-20	4	8	12	23	37	50
21-30	3	6	9	17	26	35
31-50	3	6	9	16	23	30
51-54: All 52 pg. Giants	3	6	9	17	26	35
55-61	2	4	6	11	16	20

LITTLE DOT'S UNCLES & AUNTS (See Harvey Hits No. 4, 13, 24)
Harvey Enterprises: Oct, 1961; No. 2, Aug, 1962 - No. 52, Apr, 1974

	GD 2.0	VG 4.0	FN 6.0	VF 8.0	VF/NM 9.0	NM- 9.2
1-Richie Rich begins; 68 pgs. begin	15	30	45	103	227	350
2,3	8	16	24	51	96	140
4,5	5	10	15	35	63	90
6-10	5	10	15	31	53	75
11-20	4	8	12	23	37	50
21-37: Last 68 pg. issue	3	6	9	18	28	38
38-52: All 52 pg. Giants	3	6	9	16	23	30

LITTLE DRACULA
Harvey Comics: Jan, 1992 - No. 3, May, 1992 ($1.25, quarterly, mini-series)

	GD 2.0	VG 4.0	FN 6.0	VF 8.0	VF/NM 9.0	NM- 9.2
1-3						4.00

LITTLE ENDLESS STORYBOOK, THE (See The Sandman titles and Delirium's Party)
DC Comics: 2001 ($5.95, Prestige format, one-shot)

	GD 2.0	VG 4.0	FN 6.0	VF 8.0	VF/NM 9.0	NM- 9.2
nn-Jill Thompson-s/painted-a/c; puppy Barnabas searches for Delirium						10.00
HC (2011, $14.99) r/story plus original character sketches and merchandise design						15.00

LI'L ERNIE (Evil Ernie)
Dynamite Entertainment: 2014 ($3.99, one-shot)

	GD 2.0	VG 4.0	FN 6.0	VF 8.0	VF/NM 9.0	NM- 9.2
1-Kid version spoof; Roger Langridge-s/a; covers by Baltazar & Garbowska						4.00

LITTLE EVA
St. John Publishing Co.: May, 1952 - No. 31, Nov, 1956

	GD 2.0	VG 4.0	FN 6.0	VF 8.0	VF/NM 9.0	NM- 9.2
1	22	44	66	128	209	290
2	14	28	42	78	112	145
3-5	10	20	30	56	76	95
6-10	9	18	27	47	61	75
11-31	8	16	24	42	54	65
3-D 1,2(10/53, 11/53, 25¢)-Both came w/glasses. 1-Infinity-c	18	36	54	107	169	230
I.W. Reprint #1-3,6-8: 1-r/Little Eva #28. 2-r/Little Eva #29. 3-r/Little Eva #24	2	4	6	8	11	14
Super Reprint #10,12('63),14,16,18('64): 18-r/Little Eva #25.	2	4	6	8	11	14

LI'L GENIUS (Formerly Super Brat; Summer Fun No. 54) (See Blue Bird & Giant Comics #3)
Charlton Comics: No. 6, 1954 - No. 52, 1/65; No. 53, 10/65; No. 54, 10/85 - No. 55, 1/86

	GD 2.0	VG 4.0	FN 6.0	VF 8.0	VF/NM 9.0	NM- 9.2
6 (#1)	11	22	33	62	86	110
7-10	7	14	21	37	46	55
11-1st app. Li'l Tomboy (10/56); same month as 1st issue of Li'l Tomboy (V14#92)	8	16	24	40	50	60
12-15,19,20	6	12	18	29	36	42
16,17-(68 pgs.)	8	16	24	40	50	60
18-(100 pgs., 10/58)	11	22	33	60	83	105
21-35: 34-Atomic bomb explosion	3	6	9	15	22	28
36-53	2	4	6	10	14	18
54,55 (Low print)						6.00

LI'L GHOST
St. John Publ. Co./Fago No. 1 on: 2/58; No. 2,1/59 - No. 3, Mar, 1959

	GD 2.0	VG 4.0	FN 6.0	VF 8.0	VF/NM 9.0	NM- 9.2
1(St. John)	13	26	39	72	101	130
2,3	8	16	24	44	57	70

LITTLE GIANT COMICS
Centaur Publications: 7/38 - No. 3, 10/38; No. 4, 2/39 (132 pgs.) (6-3/4x4-1/2")

	GD 2.0	VG 4.0	FN 6.0	VF 8.0	VF/NM 9.0	NM- 9.2
1-B&W with color-c; stories, puzzles, magic	295	590	885	1888	3244	4600
2,3-B&W with color-c	226	452	678	1446	2473	3500
4 (6-5/8x9-3/8")(68 pgs., B&W inside)	226	452	678	1446	2473	3500

NOTE: ***Filchock** c-2, 4. **Gustavson** a-1. **Pinajian** a-4. **Bob Wood** a-1.*

LITTLE GIANT DETECTIVE FUNNIES
Centaur Publ.: Oct, 1938; No. 4, Jan, 1939 (6-3/4x4-1/2", 132 pgs., B&W)

	GD 2.0	VG 4.0	FN 6.0	VF 8.0	VF/NM 9.0	NM- 9.2
1-B&W with color-c	300	600	900	1920	3310	4700
4(1/39, B&W; color-c; 68 pgs., 6-1/2x9-1/2")-Eisner-r	239	478	717	1530	2615	3700

LITTLE GIANT MOVIE FUNNIES
Centaur Publ.: Aug, 1938 - No. 2, Oct, 1938 (6-3/4x4-1/2", 132 pgs., B&W)

	GD 2.0	VG 4.0	FN 6.0	VF 8.0	VF/NM 9.0	NM- 9.2
1-Ed Wheelan's "Minute Movies" reprints	265	530	795	1694	2897	4100
2-Ed Wheelan's "Minute Movies" reprints	200	400	600	1280	2190	3100

LITTLE GROUCHO (...the Red-Headed Tornado; ...Grouchy No. 2)
Reston Publ. Co.: No. 16; Feb-Mar, 1955 - No. 2, June-July, 1955 (See Tippy Terry)

	GD 2.0	VG 4.0	FN 6.0	VF 8.0	VF/NM 9.0	NM- 9.2
16, 1 (2-3/55)	11	22	33	62	86	110
2(6-7/55)	8	16	24	44	57	70

LITTLE HIAWATHA (Disney; see Walt Disney's C&S #143)
Dell Publishing Co.: No. 439, Dec, 1952 - No. 988, May-July, 1959

	GD 2.0	VG 4.0	FN 6.0	VF 8.0	VF/NM 9.0	NM- 9.2
Four Color 439 (#1)	8	16	24	55	105	155
Four Color 787 (4/57), 901 (5/58), 988	6	12	18	38	69	100

LITTLE IKE
St. John Publishing Co.: April, 1953 - No. 4, Oct, 1953

	GD 2.0	VG 4.0	FN 6.0	VF 8.0	VF/NM 9.0	NM- 9.2
1-Kid humor	14	28	42	82	121	160
2	9	18	27	47	61	75
3,4	8	16	24	40	50	60

LITTLE IODINE (See Giant Comic Album)
Dell Publ. Co.: No. 224, 4/49 - No. 257, 1949; 3-5/50 - No. 56, 4-6/62 (1-4-52pgs.)

	GD 2.0	VG 4.0	FN 6.0	VF 8.0	VF/NM 9.0	NM- 9.2
Four Color 224-By Jimmy Hatlo	13	26	39	89	195	300
Four Color 257	9	18	27	58	114	170
1(3-5/50)	10	20	30	66	138	210
2-5	5	10	15	35	63	90
6-10	5	10	15	30	50	70
11-20	4	8	12	27	44	60
21-30: 27-Xmas-c	4	8	12	23	37	50
31-40	3	6	9	21	33	45
41-56	3	6	9	19	30	40

LITTLE JACK FROST
Avon Periodicals: 1951

	GD 2.0	VG 4.0	FN 6.0	VF 8.0	VF/NM 9.0	NM- 9.2
1	15	30	45	94	147	200

LI'L JINX (Little Archie in Animal Land #17) (Also see Pep Comics #62)
Archie Publications: No. 1(#11), Nov, 1956 - No. 16, Sept, 1957

	GD 2.0	VG 4.0	FN 6.0	VF 8.0	VF/NM 9.0	NM- 9.2
1(#11)-By Joe Edwards; "First Issue" on cover	21	42	63	126	206	285
12(1/57)-16	14	28	42	80	115	150

LI'L JINX (See Archie Giant Series Magazine No. 223)

LI'L JINX CHRISTMAS BAG (See Archie Giant Series Mag. No. 195, 206, 219)

LI'L JINX GIANT LAUGH-OUT (See Archie Giant Series Mag. No. 176, 185)
Archie Publications: No. 33, Sept, 1971 - No. 43, Nov, 1973 (52 pgs.)

	GD 2.0	VG 4.0	FN 6.0	VF 8.0	VF/NM 9.0	NM- 9.2
33-43 (52 pgs.)	2	4	6	13	18	22

LITTLE JOE (See Popular Comics & Super Comics)
Dell Publishing Co.: No. 1, 1942

	GD 2.0	VG 4.0	FN 6.0	VF 8.0	VF/NM 9.0	NM- 9.2
Four Color 1	75	150	225	600	1350	2100

LITTLE JOE
St. John Publishing Co.: Apr, 1953

	GD 2.0	VG 4.0	FN 6.0	VF 8.0	VF/NM 9.0	NM- 9.2
1	10	20	30	58	79	100

LI'L KIDS (Also see Li'l Pals)
Marvel Comics Group: 8/70 - No. 2, 10/70; No. 3, 11/71 - No. 12, 6/73

	GD 2.0	VG 4.0	FN 6.0	VF 8.0	VF/NM 9.0	NM- 9.2
1	8	16	24	55	105	155
2-9	4	8	12	28	47	65
10-12-Calvin app.	5	10	15	30	50	70

LITTLE KING
Dell Publishing Co.: No. 494, Aug, 1953 - No. 677, Feb, 1956

	GD 2.0	VG 4.0	FN 6.0	VF 8.0	VF/NM 9.0	NM- 9.2
Four Color 494 (#1)	9	18	27	61	123	185
Four Color 597, 677	6	12	18	38	69	100

LITTLE LANA (Formerly Lana)
Marvel Comics (MjMC): No. 8, Nov, 1949; No. 9, Mar, 1950

	GD 2.0	VG 4.0	FN 6.0	VF 8.0	VF/NM 9.0	NM- 9.2
8,9	21	42	63	126	206	285

LITTLE LENNY
Marvel Comics (CDS): June, 1949 - No. 3, Nov, 1949

	GD 2.0	VG 4.0	FN 6.0	VF 8.0	VF/NM 9.0	NM- 9.2
1-Little Aspirin app.	18	36	54	105	165	225
2,3	12	24	36	67	94	120

LITTLE LIZZIE
Marvel Comics (PrPI)/Atlas (OMC): 6/49 - No. 5, 4/50; 9/53 - No. 3, Jan, 1954

	GD 2.0	VG 4.0	FN 6.0	VF 8.0	VF/NM 9.0	NM- 9.2
1-Kid humor	20	40	60	118	192	265

	GD 2.0	VG 4.0	FN 6.0	VF 8.0	VF/NM 9.0	NM- 9.2
2-5	12	24	36	67	94	120
1 (9/53, 2nd series by Atlas)-Howie Post-c	13	26	39	74	105	135
2,3	10	20	30	54	72	90

LITTLE LOTTA (See Harvey Hits No. 10)
Harvey Publications: 11/55 - No. 110, 11/73; No. 111, 9/74 - No. 120, 5/76
V2#1, Oct, 1992 - No. 4, July, 1993 ($1.25)

	GD	VG	FN	VF	VF/NM	NM-
1-Richie Rich (r) & Little Dot begin	64	128	192	512	1156	1800
2,3	18	36	54	128	284	440
4,5	10	20	30	69	147	225
6-10	7	14	21	46	86	125
11-20	5	10	15	35	63	90
21-40	4	8	12	23	37	50
41-60	3	6	9	18	28	38
61-80: 62-1st app. Nurse Jenny	3	6	9	15	22	28
81-99	2	4	6	11	16	20
100-103: All 52 pg. Giants	3	6	9	14	19	24
104-120	2	4	6	8	10	12
V2#1-4 (1992-93)						4.00

NOTE: *No. 121 was advertised, but never released.*

LITTLE LOTTA FOODLAND
Harvey Publications: 9/63 - No. 14, 10/67; No. 15, 10/68 - No. 29, Oct, 1972

	GD	VG	FN	VF	VF/NM	NM-
1-Little Lotta, Little Dot, Richie Rich, 68 pgs. begin	11	22	33	73	157	240
2,3	6	12	18	38	69	100
4,5	5	10	15	30	50	70
6-10	4	8	12	23	37	50
11-20	3	6	9	16	23	30
21-26: 26-Last 68 pg. issue	3	6	9	14	20	25
27,28: Both 52 pgs.	2	4	6	11	16	20
29-(36 pgs.)	2	4	6	8	11	14

LITTLE LULU (Formerly Marge's Little Lulu)
Gold Key 207-257/Whitman 258 on: No. 207, Sept, 1972 - No. 268, Mar, 1984

	GD	VG	FN	VF	VF/NM	NM-
207,209,220-Stanley-r. 207-1st app. Henrietta	2	4	6	13	18	22
208,210-219: 208-1st app. Snobbly, Wilbur's butler	2	4	6	9	13	16
221-240,242-249, 250(r/#166), 251-254(r/#206)	2	4	6	8	10	12
241,263-Stanley-r	2	4	6	8	11	14
255-257(Gold Key): 256-r/#212	1	3	4	6	8	10
258,259,262(50¢-c),264(2/82),265(3/82) (Whitman)	2	4	6	11	16	20
260-(9/80)(Whitman pre-pack only - low distribution)	15	30	45	103	227	350
261-(11/80)(Whitman pre-pack only)	7	14	21	44	82	120
262-(1/81) Variant 40¢-c price error (reg. ed. 50¢-c)	3	6	9	15	22	28
266-268 (All #90028 on-c; no date, no date code; 3-pack): 266(7/83). 267(8/83). 268(3/84)-Stanley-r	3	6	9	17	26	35

LITTLE MARY MIXUP (See Comics On Parade)
United Features Syndicate: No. 10, 1939, - No. 26, 1940

	GD	VG	FN	VF	VF/NM	NM-
Single Series 10, 26	37	74	111	222	361	500

LITTLE MAX COMICS (Joe Palooka's Pal; see Joe Palooka)
Harvey Publications: Oct, 1949 - No. 73, Nov, 1961

	GD	VG	FN	VF	VF/NM	NM-
1-Infinity-c; Little Dot begins; Joe Palooka on-c	31	62	93	182	296	410
2-Little Dot app.; Joe Palooka on-c	15	30	45	84	127	170
3-Little Dot app.; Joe Palooka on-c	10	20	30	58	79	100
4-10: 5-Little Dot app., 1pg.	9	18	27	47	61	75
11-20	8	16	24	40	50	60
21-40: 23-Little Dot app. 38-r/#20	6	12	18	31	38	45
41-62,66	3	6	9	17	26	35
63-65,67-73-Include new five pg. Richie Rich stories. 70-73-Little Lotta app.	3	6	9	18	28	38

LI'L MENACE
Fago Magazine Co.: Dec, 1958 - No. 3, May, 1959

	GD	VG	FN	VF	VF/NM	NM-
1-Peter Rabbit app.	11	22	33	60	83	105
2-Peter Rabbit (Vincent Fago's)	8	16	24	40	50	60
3	6	12	18	31	38	45

LITTLE MERMAID, THE (Walt Disney's...; also see Disney's...)
W. D. Publications (Disney): 1990 (no date given)($5.95, no ads, 52 pgs.)

	GD	VG	FN	VF	VF/NM	NM-
nn-Adapts animated movie	1	3	4	6	8	10
nn-Comic version ($2.50)	1	2	3	5	6	8

LITTLE MERMAID, THE (Also see Disney's The Little Mermaid Limited Series)
Disney Comics: 1992 - No. 4, 1992 ($1.50, mini-series)

	GD	VG	FN	VF	VF/NM	NM-
1-Based on movie						6.00
2-4						4.00
1-4: 2nd printings sold at Wal-Mart w/different-c						4.00
Set of #1-4 in unopened 4-issue Collector's Pack						60.00

LITTLE MERMAID, THE
Disney Comics: Oct, 2019 - No. 3, Feb, 2020 ($3.99, limited series)

	GD	VG	FN	VF	VF/NM	NM-
1-3-Adapts the movie; Castellucci-s/Lavina-a/c						4.00

LITTLE MISS MUFFET
Best Books (Standard Comics)/King Features Synd.: No. 11, Dec, 1948 - No. 13, March, 1949

	GD	VG	FN	VF	VF/NM	NM-
11-Strip reprints; Fanny Cory-c/a	14	28	42	80	115	150
12,13-Strip reprints; Fanny Cory-c/a	9	18	27	52	69	85

LITTLE MISS SUNBEAM COMICS
Magazine Enterprises/Quality Bakers of America: June-July, 1950 - No. 4, Dec-Jan, 1950-51

	GD	VG	FN	VF	VF/NM	NM-
1	20	40	60	117	189	265
2-4	13	26	39	74	105	135
...Advs. In Space ('55)	8	16	24	42	54	65

LITTLE MONSTERS, THE (See March of Comics #423, Three Stooges #17)
Gold Key: Nov, 1964 - No. 44, Feb, 1978

	GD	VG	FN	VF	VF/NM	NM-
1	6	12	18	37	66	95
2	3	6	9	20	31	42
3-10	3	6	9	16	24	32
11-20	3	6	9	15	21	26
21-30: 19-21-Reprints	2	4	6	11	16	20
31-44: 34-39,43-Reprints	2	4	6	8	11	14

LITTLE MONSTERS (Movie)
Now Comics: 1989 - No. 6, June, 1990 ($1.75)

	GD	VG	FN	VF	VF/NM	NM-
1-6: Photo-c from movie						5.00

LITTLE MONSTERS
Image Comics: Mar, 2022 - Present ($3.99)

	GD	VG	FN	VF	VF/NM	NM-
1-10-Jeff Lemire-s/Dustin Nguyen-a/c						4.00

LITTLE NEMO (See Cocomalt, Future Comics, Help, Jest, Kayo, Punch, Red Seal, & Superworld; most by Winsor McCay Jr., son of famous artist) (Other McCay books: see Little Sammy Sneeze & Dreams of the Rarebit Fiend)

LITTLE NEMO (...in Slumberland)
McCay Features/Nostalgia Press('69): 1945 (11x7-1/4", 28 pgs., B&W)

	GD	VG	FN	VF	VF/NM	NM-
1905 & 1911 reprints by Winsor McCay	13	26	39	72	101	130
1969-70 (Exact reprint)	2	4	6	9	12	15

LITTLE NEMO: RETURN TO SLUMBERLAND
IDW Publishing: Aug, 2014 - No. 4, Feb, 2015 ($3.99)

	GD	VG	FN	VF	VF/NM	NM-
1-4-New stories in McCay style; Shanower-s/Rodriguez-a in all. 1-Multiple covers						4.00

LITTLE ORPHAN ANNIE (See Annie, Famous Feature Stories, Marvel Super Special, Merry Christmas..., Popular Comics, Super Book #7, 11, 23 & Super Comics)

LITTLE ORPHAN ANNIE
David McKay Publ./Dell Publishing Co.: No. 7, 1937 - No. 3, Sept-Nov, 1948; No. 206, Dec, 1948

	GD	VG	FN	VF	VF/NM	NM-
Feature Books(McKay) 7-(1937) (Rare)	135	270	405	864	1482	2100
Four Color 12(1941)	84	168	252	538	919	1300
Four Color 18(1943)-Flag-c	68	136	204	435	743	1050
Four Color 52(1944)	26	52	78	182	404	625
Four Color 76(1945)	20	40	60	144	317	490
Four Color 107(1946)	18	36	54	128	284	440
Four Color 152(1947)	12	24	36	82	179	275
1(3-5/48)-r/strips from 5/7/44 to 7/30/44	12	24	36	81	176	270
2-r/strips from 7/21/40 to 9/9/40	9	18	27	57	111	165
3-r/strips from 9/10/40 to 11/9/40	8	16	24	55	105	155
Four Color 206(12/48)	8	16	24	52	99	145

LI'L PALS (Also see Li'l Kids)
Marvel Comics Group: Sept, 1972 - No. 5, May, 1973

	GD	VG	FN	VF	VF/NM	NM-
1	8	16	24	54	102	150
2-5: 5-Super Rabbit story	5	10	15	30	50	70

LI'L PAN (Formerly Rocket Kelly; becomes Junior Comics with #9)(Also see Wotalife Comics)
Fox Feature Syndicate: No. 6, Dec-Jan, 1946-47 - No. 8, Apr-May, 1947

	GD	VG	FN	VF	VF/NM	NM-
6	15	30	45	88	137	185
7,8: 7-Atomic bomb story; robot-c	14	28	42	78	112	145

LITTLE PEOPLE (Also see Darby O'Gill & the...)
Dell Publishing Co.: No. 485, Aug-Oct, 1953 - No. 1062, Dec, 1959 (Walt Scott's)

	GD	VG	FN	VF	VF/NM	NM-
Four Color 485 (#1)	9	18	27	58	114	170
Four Color 573(7/54), 633(6/55)	6	12	18	37	66	95
Four Color 692(3/56),753(11/56),809(7/57),868(12/57),908(5/58),959(12/58),1062	5	10	15	34	60	85

LITTLE RASCALS
Dell Publishing Co.: No. 674, Jan, 1956 - No. 1297, Mar-May, 1962

	GD	VG	FN	VF	VF/NM	NM-
Four Color 674 (#1)	10	20	30	67	141	215
Four Color 778(3/57),825(8/57)	6	12	18	38	69	100
Four Color 883(3/58),936(9/58),974(3/59),1030(9/59),1079(2-4/60),1137(9-11/60)	5	10	15	35	63	90
Four Color 1174(3-5/61),1224(10-12/61),1297	5	10	15	33	57	80

LI'L RASCAL TWINS (Formerly Nature Boy)
Charlton Comics: No. 6, 1957 - No. 18, Jan, 1960

	GD	VG	FN	VF	VF/NM	NM-
6-Li'l Genius & Tomboy in all	7	14	21	35	43	50
7-18: 7-Timmy the Timid Ghost app.	4	8	12	18	22	25

LITTLE RED HOT: (CHANE OF FOOLS)
Image Comics: Feb, 1999 - No. 3, Apr, 1999 ($2.95/$3.50, B&W, limited series)

	GD	VG	FN	VF	VF/NM	NM-
1-3-Dawn Brown-s/a. 2,3-($3.50-c)						4.00
The Foolish Collection TPB ($12.95) r/#1-3						13.00

LITTLE RED HOT: BOUND
Image Comics: July, 2001 - No. 3, Nov, 2001 ($2.95, color, limited series)

	GD	VG	FN	VF	VF/NM	NM-
1-3-Dawn Brown-s/a.						4.00

LITTLE ROQUEFORT COMICS (See Paul Terry's Comics #105)
St. John Publishing Co.(all pre-code)/Pines No. 10: June, 1952 - No. 9, Oct, 1953; No. 10, Summer, 1958

	GD	VG	FN	VF	VF/NM	NM-
1-By Paul Terry; Funny Animal	15	30	45	85	130	175
2	9	18	27	47	61	75
3-10: 10-CBS Television Presents on-c	7	14	21	37	46	55

LITTLE SAD SACK (See Harvey Hits No. 73, 76, 79, 81, 83)
Harvey Publications: Oct, 1964 - No. 19, Nov, 1967

	GD	VG	FN	VF	VF/NM	NM-
1-Richie Rich app. on cover only	5	10	15	34	60	85
2-10	3	6	9	17	26	35
11-19	3	6	9	15	22	28

LITTLE SCOUTS
Dell Publishing Co.: No. 321, Mar, 1951 - No. 587, Oct, 1954

	GD	VG	FN	VF	VF/NM	NM-
Four Color 321 (#1, 3/51)	6	12	18	42	79	115
2(10-12/51) - 6(10-12/52)	4	8	12	25	40	55
Four Color 462,506,550,587	5	10	15	30	50	70

LITTLE SHOP OF HORRORS SPECIAL (Movie)
DC Comics: Feb, 1987 ($2.00, 68 pgs.)

	GD	VG	FN	VF	VF/NM	NM-
1-Colan-c/a	2	4	6	11	16	20

LI'L SONJA (Red Sonja)

Little Mermaid (2019) #1 © DIS

Li'l Vampi #1 © DYN

Lobo (2015) #10 © DC

GD VG FN VF VF/NM NM-
2.0 4.0 6.0 8.0 9.0 9.2

Dynamite Entertainment: 2014 ($3.99, one-shot)
1-Kid version spoof; Jim Zub-s/Joel Carroll-a; covers by Baltazar & Garbowska 4.00

LITTLE SPUNKY
I. W. Enterprises: No date (1958) (10¢)
1-r/Frisky Fables #1 2 4 6 11 16 20

LITTLE STAR
Oni Press: Feb, 2005 - No. 6, Dec, 2005 ($2.99, B&W, limited series)
1-6-Andi Watson-s/a 3.00
TPB (4/06, $19.95) r/#1-6 20.00

LITTLE STOOGES, THE (The Three Stooges' Sons)
Gold Key: Sept, 1972 - No. 7, Mar, 1974
1-Norman Maurer cover/stories in all 3 6 9 18 28 38
2-7 2 4 6 13 18 22

LITTLEST OUTLAW (Disney)
Dell Publishing Co.: No. 609, Jan, 1955
Four Color 609-Movie, photo-c 7 14 21 44 82 120

LITTLEST PET SHOP (Based on the Hasbro toys)
IDW Publishing: May, 2014 - No. 5, Sept, 2014 ($3.99)
1-5: 1-Ball-s/Peña-a; multiple covers. 2-5-Two covers on each 4.00
... Spring Cleaning (4/15, $7.99) Four short stories; Ball-s; art by various 8.00

LITTLEST SNOWMAN, THE
Dell Publishing Co.: No. 755, 12/56; No. 864, 12/57; 12-2/1963-64
Four Color 755,864, 1(1964) 6 12 18 37 66 95

LI'L TOMBOY (Formerly Fawcett's Funny Animals; see Giant Comics #3)
Charlton Comics: V14#92, Oct, 1956; No. 93, Mar, 1957 - No. 107, Feb, 1960
V14#92-Ties as 1st app. with Li'l Genius #11 7 14 21 35 43 50
93-107: 97-Atomic Bunny app. 5 10 15 24 29 34

LI'L VAMPI (Vampirella)
Dynamite Entertainment: 2014 ($3.99, one-shot)
1-Kid version spoof; Trautmann-s/Garbowska-a; covers by Baltazar & Garbowska 4.00

LI'L WILLIE COMICS (Formerly & becomes Willie Comics #22 on)
Marvel Comics (MgPC): No. 20, July, 1949 - No. 21, Sept, 1949
20,21: 20-Little Aspirin app. 17 34 51 105 165 225

LITTLE WOMEN (See Power Record Comics)

LIVE IT UP
Spire Christian Comics (Fleming H. Revell Co.): 1973, 1974,1976 (39-49 cents)
nn-1973 Edition 2 4 6 13 18 22
nn-1974,1976 Editions 2 4 6 8 11 14

LIVEWIRE
Valiant Entertainment: Dec, 2018 - No. 12, Nov, 2019 ($3.99)
1-12: 1-4-Vita Ayala-s/Raúl Allén-a. 5-8-Kano-a. 9-12-Tana Ford-a 4.00

LIVEWIRES
Marvel Comics: Apr, 2005 - No. 6, Sept, 2005 ($2.99, limited series)
1-6-Adam Warren-s/c; Rick Mays-a 3.00
...: Clockwork Thugs, Yo (2005, $7.99, digest) r/#1-6 8.00

LIVING BIBLE, THE
Living Bible Corp.: Fall, 1945 - No. 3, Spring, 1946
1-The Life of Paul; all have L. B. Cole-c 50 100 150 315 533 750
2-Joseph & His Brethren; Jonah & the Whale 36 72 108 211 343 475
3-Chaplains At War (classic-c) 53 106 159 334 567 800

LIVING WITH THE DEAD
Dark Horse Comics: Oct, 2007 - No. 3, Nov, 2007 ($2.99, limited series)
1-3-Zombies; Mike Richardson-s/Ben Stenbeck-a/Richard Corben-c 3.00

LOADED BIBLE
Image Comics: Apr, 2006; May, 2007; Feb, 2008 ($4.99)
...: Jesus vs. Vampires (4/06) Tim Seeley-s/Nate Bellegarde-a 5.00
...2: Blood of Christ (5/07) Seeley-s/Mike Norton-a. ...3: Communion (2/08) 5.00

LOADED BIBLE: BLOOD OF MY BLOOD
Image Comics: Mar, 2022 - No. 6, Jul, 2022 ($3.99, limited series)
1-6-Tim Seeley & Steve Orlando-s/Giuseppe Cafaro-a 4.00

LOBO
Dell Publishing Co.: Dec, 1965; No. 2, Oct, 1966
1-1st black character to have his own title 46 92 138 368 834 1300
2 23 46 69 161 356 550

LOBO (Also see Action #650, Adventures of Superman, Demon (2nd series), Justice League, L.E.G.I.O.N., Mister Miracle, Omega Men #3 & Superman #41)
DC Comics: Nov, 1990 - No. 4, Feb, 1991 ($1.50, color, limited series)
1-(99¢)-Giffen plots/Breakdowns in all 2 4 6 11 16 20
1-2nd printing 4.00
2-4: 2-Legion '89 spin-off. 1-4 have Bisley painted covers & art 6.00
...: Blazing Chain of Love 1 (9/92, $1.50)-Denys Cowan-c/a; Alan Grant scripts, ...Convention Special 1 (1993, $1.75), ...: Portrait of a Victim 1 (1993, $1.75) 4.00
... Paramilitary Christmas Special 1 (1991, $2.39, 52 pgs.) Bisley-c/a 5.00
...: Portrait of a Bastich TPB (2008, $19.99) r/#1-4 & Lobo's Back #1-4 20.00

LOBO (Also see Showcase '95 #9)
DC Comics: Dec, 1993 - No. 64, Jul, 1999 ($1.75/$1.95/$2.25/$2.50, mature)
1 ($2.95)-Foil enhanced-c; Alan Grant scripts begin 1 3 4 6 8 10
2-64: 2-7-Alan Grant scripts. 50-Lobo vs. the DCU. 58-Giffen-a 4.00
#0-(10/94)-Origin retold; published between #9 & #10 4.00
#1,000,000 (11/98) 853rd Century x-over 4.00
Annual 1 (1993, $3.50, 68 pgs.)-Bloodlines x-over 5.00
Annual 2 (1994, $3.50)-21 artists (20 listed on-c); Alan Grant script; Elseworlds story 5.00
Annual 3 (1995, $3.95)-Year One story 5.00
.../Authority: Holiday Hell TPB (2006, $17.99) r/Lobo Paramilitary Christmas Special; Authority/Lobo: Jingle Hell and Spring Break Massacre; WildStorm Winter Special 18.00
...Big Babe Spring Break Special (Spr, '95, $1.95)-Balent-a 6.00
...Bounty Hunting for Fun and Profit ('95)-Bisley-c 6.00
... Chained (5/97, $2.50)-Alan Grant story 5.00
.../Deadman: The Brave And The Bald (2/95, $3.50) 5.00
.../Demon: Helloween (12/96, $2.25)-Giarrano-a 4.00
...Fragtastic Voyage 1 ('97, $5.95)-Mejia painted-c/a 1 3 4 6 8 10
...Gallery (9/95, $3.50)-pin-ups. 1 3 4 6 8 10
...In the Chair 1 (8/94, $1.95, 36 pgs.), ...I Quit-(12/95, $2.25) 4.00
.../Judge Dredd ('95, $4.95). 5.00
...Lobocop 1 (2/94, $1.95)-Alan Grant scripts; painted-c 4.00

LOBO (Younger version from New 52 Justice League #23.2)
DC Comics: Dec, 2014 - No. 13, Feb, 2016 ($2.99)
1-Bunn-s/Brown-a 6.00
2-13: 2-5-Bunn-s/Brown-a. 4-Superman app. 10,11-Sinestro app. 13-Hal Jordan app. 4.00
Annual 1 (9/15, $4.99) Bunn-s/Rocha-a; the Sinestro Corps app.; leads into Lobo #10 5.00

LOBO: (Title Series), DC Comics
--A CONTRACT ON GAWD, 4/94 - 7/94 (mature) 1-4: Alan Grant scripts. 3-Groo cameo 4.00
--DEATH AND TAXES, 10/96 - No. 4, 1/97, 1-4-Giffen/Grant scripts 4.00
--GOES TO HOLLYWOOD, 8/96 ($2.25), 1-Grant scripts 6.00
--HIGHWAY TO HELL, 1/10 - No. 2, 2/10 ($6.99), 1,2-Scott Ian-s/Sam Kieth-a/c 7.00
TPB (2010, $19.99) r/#1,2; intro. by Scott Ian; Kieth B&W art pages 20.00
--INFANTICIDE, 10/92 - 1/93 ($1.50, mature), 1-4-Giffen-c/a; Grant scripts 4.00
--/ MASK, 2/97 - No. 2, 3/97 ($5.95), 1,2 1 3 4 6 8 10
--/ ROAD RUNNER, 8/17 ($4.99), 1-Bill Morrison-s/Kelley Jones-a/c; Wile E. Coyote app. 1 3 4 6 8 10
--'S BACK, 5/92 - No. 4, 11/92 ($1.50, mature), 1-4: 1-Has 3 outer covers. Bisley painted-c 1,2; a-1-3. 3-Sam Kieth-c; all have Giffen plots/breakdown & Grant scripts 4.00
Trade paperback (1993, $9.95)-r/1-4 10.00
--THE DUCK, 6/97 ($1.95), 1-A. Grant-s/V. Semeiks & R. Kryssing-a 1 3 4 6 8 10
--UNAMERICAN GLADIATORS, 6/93 - No. 4, 9/93 ($1.75, mature), 1-4-Mignola-c; Grant/Wagner scripts 4.00
--UNBOUND, 8/03 - No. 6, 5/04 ($2.95), 1-6-Giffen-s/Horley-c/a. 4-6-Ambush Bug app. 4.00

LOBSTER JOHNSON (One-shots) (See B.P.R.D. and Hellboy titles)
Dark Horse Comics
...: A Chain Forged in Life (7/15, $3.50) Mignola & Arcudi-s; Nixey & Nowlan-a 4.00
...: Caput Mortuum (9/12, $3.50) Mignola & Arcudi-s; Zonjic-c/a 4.00
...: Garden of Bones (1/17, $3.99) Mignola & Arcudi-s; Stephen Green-a/Zonjic-c 4.00
...: Mangekyo (8/17, $3.99) Mignola & Arcudi-s; Stenbeck-a/Zonjic-c 4.00
...: Satan Smells a Rat (5/13, $3.50) Mignola & Arcudi-s; Nowlan-c/a 4.00
...: The Forgotten Man (4/16, $3.50) Mignola & Arcudi-s; Snejbjerg-a/Zonjic-c 4.00
...: The Glass Mantis (12/15, $3.50) Mignola & Arcudi-s; Fejzula-a/Zonjic-c 4.00

LOBSTER JOHNSON: A SCENT OF LOTUS (See B.P.R.D. and Hellboy titles)
Dark Horse Comics: Jul, 2013 - No. 2, Aug, 2013 ($3.50, limited series)
1,2-Mignola & Arcudi-s; Fiumara-a/Zonjic-c 4.00

GD VG FN VF VF/NM NM-
2.0 4.0 6.0 8.0 9.0 9.2

LOBSTER JOHNSON: GET THE LOBSTER
Dark Horse Comics: Feb, 2014 - No. 5, Aug, 2014 ($3.99, limited series)
1-5-Mignola & Arcudi-s; Zonjic-a/c 4.00

LOBSTER JOHNSON: METAL MONSTERS OF MIDTOWN
Dark Horse Comics: May, 2016 - No. 3, Jul, 2016 ($3.50/$3.99, limited series)
1-3-Mignola & Arcudi-s; Zonjic-a/c. 1-$3.50. 2,3-$3.99 4.00

LOBSTER JOHNSON: THE BURNING HAND
Dark Horse Comics: Jan, 2012 - No. 5, May, 2012 ($3.50, limited series)
1-5-Mignola & Arcudi-s; Zonjic-a. 1-Two covers by Dave Johnson & Mignola 4.00

LOBSTER JOHNSON: THE IRON PROMETHEUS
Dark Horse Comics: Sept, 2007 - No. 5, Jan, 2008 ($2.99, limited series)
1-Mignola-s/c; Armstrong-a 1 3 4 6 8 10
2-5-Mignola-s/c; Armstrong-a 5.00

LOBSTER JOHNSON: THE PIRATE'S GHOST
Dark Horse Comics: Mar, 2017 - No. 3, May, 2017 ($3.99, limited series)
1-3-Mignola & Arcudi-s; Zonjic-a/c 4.00

LOCAL MAN
Image Comics: Feb, 2023 - Present ($3.99)
1-Seeley-s/Fleecs-a; flip-cover by Seeley 4.00

LOCKE & KEY
IDW Publ.: Feb, 2008 - No. 6, July, 2008 ($3.99, limited series)
1-Joe Hill-s/Gabriel Rodriguez-a 5 10 15 30 50 70
1-Second printing 2 4 6 8 10 12
2 2 4 6 9 13 16
3-6 1 3 4 6 8 10
...: Free Comic Book Day Edition (5/11) r/story from Crown of Shadows 4.00
...: Grindhouse (8/12, $3.99) EC-style; Hill-s/Rodriguez-a; bonus Guide to the Keyhouse 2 4 6 11 16 20
...: Guide to the Known Keys (1/12, $3.99) Key to the Moon; bonus Guide to the Keys 2 4 6 9 12 15
...: Welcome to Lovecraft Legacy Edition #1 (8/10, $1.00) r/#1; synopsis of later issues 4.00
...: Welcome to Lovecraft Special Edition #1 SC (9/09, $5.99) Hill-s/Rodriguez-a; script; back-up story with final art from Seth Fisher 1 3 4 6 8 10

LOCKE & KEY: ALPHA
IDW Publ.: Aug, 2013 - No. 2, Oct, 2013 ($7.99, limited series)
1,2-Series conclusion; Joe Hill-s/Gabriel Rodriguez-a 8.00

LOCKE & KEY: CLOCKWORKS
IDW Publ.: Jun, 2011 - No. 6, Apr, 2012 ($3.99, limited series)
1-6: 1-Hill-s/Rodriguez-a; set in 1776 4.00

LOCKE & KEY: CROWN OF SHADOWS
IDW Publ.: Nov, 2009 - No. 6, Apr, 2010 ($3.99, limited series)
1-6-Joe Hill-s/Gabriel Rodriguez-a 6.00

LOCKE & KEY: DOG DAYS
IDW Publ.: Oct, 2019 ($4.99, one-shot)
nn - Joe Hill-s/Gabriel Rodriguez-a; bonus preview of Dying is Easy #1 5.00

LOCKE & KEY: HEAD GAMES
IDW Publ.: Jan, 2009 - No. 6, Jun, 2009 ($3.99, limited series)
1-6-Joe Hill-s/Gabriel Rodriguez-a. 3-EC style-c 6.00

LOCKE & KEY: ...IN PALE BATTALIONS GO...
IDW Publ.: Aug, 2020 - No. 3, Oct, 2020 ($3.99, limited series)
1-3-Joe Hill-s/Gabriel Rodriguez-a 4.00

LOCKE & KEY: KEYS TO THE KINGDOM
IDW Publ.: Sept, 2010 - No. 6, Mar, 2011 ($3.99, limited series)
1-6-Joe Hill-s/Gabriel Rodriguez-a 4.00

LOCKE & KEY: OMEGA
IDW Publ.: Nov, 2012 - No. 5, May, 2013 ($3.99, limited series)
1-5-Next to Final series; Joe Hill-s/Gabriel Rodriguez-a 4.00

LOCKE & KEY: SMALL WORLD
IDW Publ.: Dec, 2016 ($4.99, one-shot)
1-Set in early 1900s; Joe Hill-s/Gabriel Rodriguez-a; multiple covers 5.00

LOCKE & KEY / THE SANDMAN UNIVERSE
IDW Publ.: No. 0, Oct, 2020 - Nov, 2021 ($3.99/$6.99)
0-"Open the Moon" by Joe Hill-s/Gabriel Rodriguez-a; r/Sandman #1 4.00
...: Hell & Gone 1 (IDW, 4/21, $6.99) Hill-s/Rodriguez-a; the imprisoned Dream app. 7.00
...: Hell & Gone 2 (DC, 11/21, $6.99) Hill-s/Rodriguez-a 7.00

LOCKJAW (From the Inhumans)
Marvel Comics: Apr, 2018 - No. 4, Jul, 2018 ($3.99, limited series)
1-4-Kibblesmith-s/Villa-a; D-Man app. 1,2-Ka-Zar app. 3-Spider-Ham app. 4.00

LOCKJAW AND THE PET AVENGERS (Also see Tails of the Pet Avengers)
Marvel Comics: July, 2009 - No. 4, Oct, 2009 ($2.99, limited series)
1-4-Lockheed, Frog Thor, Zabu, Lockjaw and Redwing team up; 2 covers on each 3.00

LOCKJAW AND THE PET AVENGERS UNLEASHED
Marvel Comics: May, 2010 - No. 4, Aug, 2010 ($2.99, limited series)
1-4-Eliopoulos-s/Guara-a; 2 covers on each 3.00

LOCO (Magazine) (Satire)
Satire Publications: Aug, 1958 - V1#3, Jan, 1959
V1#1-Chic Stone-a 9 18 27 50 65 80
V1#2,3-Severin-a, 2 pgs. Davis; 3-Heath-a 7 14 21 37 46 55

LODGER
IDW Publishing (Black Crown): Oct, 2018 - No. 5, Feb, 2019 ($3.99, B&W)
1-5-Davis & Maria Lapham-s/David Lapham-a. 1-Covers by Lapham & Sienkiewicz 4.00

LOGAN (Wolverine)
Marvel Comics: May, 2008 - No. 3, Jul, 2008 ($3.99, limited series)
1-3-Vaughan-s/Risso-a/c; regular & B&W editions for each 4.00

LOGAN: PATH OF THE WARLORD
Marvel Comics: Feb, 1996 ($5.95, one-shot)
1-John Paul Leon-a 1 2 3 5 6 8

LOGAN: SHADOW SOCIETY
Marvel Comics: 1996 ($5.95, one-shot)
1 6.00

LOGAN'S RUN
Marvel Comics Group: Jan, 1977 - No. 7, July, 1977
1: 1-5-Based on novel & movie 3 6 9 14 20 26
2-5,7: 6,7-New stories adapted from novel 2 4 6 8 10 12
6-1st Thanos solo story (back-up) by Zeck (6/77)(See Iron Man #55 for debut) 4 8 12 28 47 65
6-(35¢-c variant, limited distribution) 14 28 42 96 211 325
7-(35¢-c variant, limited distribution) 10 20 30 69 147 225
NOTE: **Austin** *a-6i.* **Gulacy** *c-6.* **Kane** *c-7p.* **Perez** *a-1-5p; c-1-5p.* **Sutton** *a-6p, 7p.*

LOIS & CLARK, THE NEW ADVENTURES OF SUPERMAN
DC Comics: 1994 ($9.95, one-shot)
1-r/Man of Steel #2, Superman Ann. 1, Superman #9 & 11, Action #600 & 655, Adventures of Superman #445, 462 & 466 1 3 4 6 8 10

LOIS LANE (Also see Daring New Adventures of Supergirl, Showcase #9,10 & Superman's Girlfriend...)
DC Comics: Aug, 1986 - No. 2, Sept, 1986 ($1.50, 52 pgs.)
1,2-Morrow-c/a in each 4.00

LOIS LANE
DC Comics: Sept, 2019 - No. 12, Sept, 2020 ($3.99)
1-12: 1-Rucka-s/Perkins-a; The Question (Renee) app. 3-The Question (Charlie) app. 6-Event Leviathan tie-in 4.00

LOKI (Thor)(Also see Vote Loki)
Marvel Comics: Sept, 2004 - No. 4, Nov, 2004 ($3.50)
1-Rodi-s/Ribic-a/c in all 2 4 6 8 10 12
2-4 4.00
HC (2005, $17.99, with dustjacket) oversized r/#1-4; original proposal and sketch pages 18.00
SC (2007, $12.99) r/#1-4; original proposal and sketch pages 13.00

LOKI (Thor)
Marvel Comics: Dec, 2010 - No. 4, May, 2011 ($3.99, limited series)
1-4-Aguirre-Sacasa-s/Fiumara-a. 2-Balder dies 4.00

LOKI (Thor)
Marvel Comics: Sept, 2019 - No. 5, Jan, 2020 ($3.99, limited series)
1-5: 1-4-Kibblesmith-s/Bazaldua-a. 2,4-Tony Stark app. 5-Wolverine app. 4.00

LOKI: AGENT OF ASGARD (Thor)
Marvel Comics: Apr, 2014 - No. 17, Oct, 2015 ($2.99/$3.99)
1-5: 1-Ewing-s/Garbett-a/Frison-c; Avengers app. 3.00
6-17-($3.99) 6-9-Axis tie-ins. 6,7-Doctor Doom app. 14-17-Secret Wars tie-ins 4.00

LOKI: RAGNAROK AND ROLL (not the character from Thor)
BOOM! Studios: Feb, 2014 - No. 4, Jun, 2014 ($3.99, limited series)
1,2-Esquivel-s/Gaylord-a/Ziritt-c 4.00

LOLA XOXO
Aspen MLT: Apr, 2014 - No. 6, Mar, 2015 ($3.99)
1-6-Siya Oum-s/a; multiple covers 4.00
The Art of Lolo XOXO 1 (9/16, $5.99) Siya Oum sketch pages and cover gallery 6.00

LOLA XOXO VOLUME 2
Aspen MLT: Jul, 2017 - No. 6, Jan, 2018 ($3.99)
1-6-Siya Oum-s/a; multiple covers 4.00

LOLA XOXO VOLUME 3
Aspen MLT: Jul, 2019 - No. 6, Aug, 2020 ($3.99)
1-6-Siya Oum-s/a; multiple covers 4.00

LOLA XOXO: WASTELAND MADAM
Aspen MLT: Apr, 2015 - No. 4, Feb, 2016 ($3.99)
1-4-Vince Hernandez-s/Siya Oum-a; multiple covers 4.00

LOLLIPOP KIDS, THE
AfterShock Comics: Oct, 2018 - No. 5, Apr, 2019 ($3.99)
1-5-Adam Glass-s/Diego Yapur-a/Robert Hack-c 4.00

LOLLY AND PEPPER
Dell Publishing Co.: No. 832, Sept, 1957 - July, 1962
Four Color 832(#1) 6 12 18 42 79 115
Four Color 940,978,1086,1206 5 10 15 30 50 70
01-459-207 (7/62) 3 6 9 18 28 38

LOMAX (See Police Action)

LONE
Dark Horse Comics: Sept, 2003 - No. 6, Mar, 2004 ($2.99)
1-6-Stuart Moore-s/Jerome Opeña-a/Templesmith-c 3.00

LONE EAGLE (The Flame No. 5 on)
Ajax/Farrell Publications: Apr-May, 1954 - No. 4, Oct-Nov, 1954
1 15 30 45 90 140 190
2-4: 3-Bondage-c 10 20 30 56 76 95

LONE GUNMEN, THE (From the X-Files)
Dark Horse Comics: June, 2001 ($2.99, one-shot)
1-Paul Lee-a; photo-c 3.00

LONELY HEART (Formerly Dear Lonely Hearts; Dear Heart #15 on)
Ajax/Farrell Publ. (Excellent Publ.): No. 9, Mar, 1955 - No. 14, Feb, 1956

Locke & Key: Clockworks #6 © Joe Hill & IDW

Loki: Agent of Asgard #9 © MAR

Lone Ranger V2 #12 © Classic Media

	GD 2.0	VG 4.0	FN 6.0	VF 8.0	VF/NM 9.0	NM- 9.2

9-Kamen-*esque*-a; (Last precode) 17 34 51 98 154 210
10-14 13 26 39 74 105 135

LONELY RECEIVER
AfterShock Comics: Sept, 2020 - No. 5, Jan, 2021 ($4.99/$3.99)
1-($4.99) Zac Thompson-s/Jen Hickman-a/c 5.00
2-5-($3.99) 4.00

LONE RANGER, THE (See Ace Comics, Aurora, Dell Giants, Future Comics, Golden Comics Digest #48, King Comics, Magic Comics & March of Comics #165, 174, 193, 208, 225, 238, 310, 322, 338, 350)

LONE RANGER, THE
Dell Publishing Co.: No. 3, 1939 - No. 167, Feb, 1947
Large Feature Comic 3(1939)-Heigh-Yo Silver; text with illus. by Robert Weisman; also exists as a Whitman #710 (scarce) 284 568 852 1818 3109 4400
Large Feature Comic 7(1939)-Illustr. by Henry Vallely; Hi-Yo Silver the Lone Ranger to the Rescue; also exists as Whitman #715 (scarce) 265 530 795 1694 2897 4100
Feature Book 21(1940), 24(1941) 106 212 318 673 1162 1650
Four Color 82(1945) 40 80 120 296 673 1050
Four Color 98(1945),118(1946) 28 56 84 202 451 700
Four Color 125(1946),136(1947) 19 38 57 133 297 460
Four Color 151,167(1947) 16 32 48 112 249 385

LONE RANGER, THE (Movie, radio & TV; Clayton Moore starred as Lone Ranger in the movies; No. 1-37: strip reprints)(See Dell Giants)
Dell Publishing Co.: Jan-Feb, 1948 - No. 145, May-July, 1962
1 (36 pgs.)-The Lone Ranger, his horse Silver, companion Tonto & his horse Scout begin 71 142 213 568 1284 2000
2 (52 pgs. begin, end #41) 27 54 81 194 435 675
3-5 22 44 66 154 340 525
6,7,9,10 16 32 48 112 249 385
8-Origin retold; Indian back-c begin, end #35 19 38 57 131 291 450
11-20: 11- "Young Hawk" Indian boy serial begins, ends #145 12 24 36 80 173 265
21,22,24-31: 51-Reprint. 31-1st Mask logo 10 20 30 64 132 200
23-Origin retold 12 24 36 80 173 265
32-37: 32-Painted-c begin. 36-Animal photo back-c begin, end #49. 37-Last newspaper-r issue; new outfit; red shirt becomes blue; most known copies show the blue shirt on-c & inside 9 18 27 58 114 170
37-Variant issue; Long Ranger wears a red shirt on-c and inside. A few copies of the red shirt outfit were printed before catching the mistake and changing the color to blue (rare) 16 32 48 110 243 375
38-41 (All 52 pgs.) 38-Paul S. Newman-s (wrote most of the stories #38-on) 8 16 24 54 102 150
42-50 (36 pgs.) 7 14 21 46 86 125
51-74 (52 pgs.): 56-One pg. origin story of Lone Ranger & Tonto. 71-Blank inside-c 6 12 18 42 79 115
75,77-99: 79-X-mas-c 6 12 18 40 73 105
76-Classic flag-c 7 14 21 44 82 120
100 7 14 21 46 86 125
101-111: Last painted-c 6 12 18 37 66 95
112-Clayton Moore photo-c begin, end #145 15 30 45 103 227 350
113-117: 117-10¢ &15¢-c exist 9 18 27 60 120 180
118-Origin Lone Ranger, Tonto, & Silver retold; Dan Reid origin; Special Silver anniversary issue 19 38 57 131 291 450
119-140: 139-Fran Striker-s 8 16 24 56 108 160
141-145 9 18 27 58 114 170
NOTE: ***Hank Hartman*** *painted c(signed)-65, 66, 70, 75, 82; unsigned-64?, 67-69?, 71, 72, 73?, 74?, 76-78, 80, 81, 83-91, 92?, 93-111.* ***Ernest Nordli*** *painted c(signed)-42, 50, 52, 53, 56, 59, 60; unsigned-39-41, 44-49, 51, 54, 55, 57, 58, 61-63?*

LONE RANGER, THE
Gold Key (Reprints in #13-20): 9/64 - No. 16, 12/69; No. 17, 11/72; No. 18, 9/74 - No. 28, 3/77
1-Retells origin 7 14 21 46 86 125
2 3 6 9 21 33 45
3-10: Small Bear-r in #6-12. 10-Last 12¢ issue 3 6 9 19 30 40
11-17 3 6 9 15 22 28
18-28 2 4 6 11 16 20
Golden West 1(30029-610, 10/66)-Giant; r/most Golden West #3 including Clayton Moore photo front/back-c 6 12 18 40 73 105

LONE RANGER
Dynamite Entertainment: 2006 - No. 25, 2011 ($2.99/$3.50/$3.99)
1-Retells origin; Carriello-a/Matthews-s; badge cover by Cassaday 4.00
1-Variant mask cover by Cassaday 5.00
1-Baltimore Comic-Con 2006 variant cover with masked face and horse silhouette 12.00
1-Directors' Cut ($4.99) r/#1 with comments at page bottoms, script and sketches 5.00
2-23: 2-Origin continues; Tonto app. 3.50
24-($3.99) 4.00
25-($4.99) Carriello-a 5.00
... and Tonto 1-4 (200-2010, $4.99) Cassaday-c 5.00
... Volume 1: Now and Forever TPB (2007, $19.99) r/#1-6; sketch pages 20.00

LONE RANGER: VOLUME 1
Dynamite Entertainment: 2018 - No. 5, 2019 ($3.99, limited series)
1-5-Mark Russell-s/Bob Q-a. 1-Cover by Cassaday, Allred & Francavilla 4.00

LONE RANGER, THE (Volume 2)
Dynamite Entertainment: 2012 - No. 25, 2014 ($3.99)
1-25: 1-Parks-s/Polls-a; two covers by Ross & Francavilla. 2-21-Francavilla-c 4.00
Annual 2013 ($4.99) Denton-s/Triano-a/Worley-c 5.00

LONE RANGER AND TONTO, THE
Topps Comics: Aug, 1994 - No. 4, Nov, 1994 ($2.50, limited series)
1-4: 3-Origin of Lone Ranger; Tonto leaves; Lansdale story, Truman-c/a in all. 3.00
1-4: Silver logo. 1-Signed by Lansdale and Truman 6.00
Trade paperback (1/95, $9.95) 10.00

LONE RANGER AND ZORRO: THE DEATH OF ZORRO, THE
Dynamite Entertainment: 2011 - No. 5, 2011 ($3.99, limited series)
1-5: 1-Four covers by Alex Ross and others; Parks-s/Polls-a 4.00

LONE RANGER GREEN HORNET
Dynamite Entertainment: 2016 - No. 5, 2016 ($3.99, limited series)
1-5-Uslan-s/Timpano-a. 3-Jesse Owens as the new Lone Ranger 4.00

LONE RANGER'S COMPANION TONTO, THE (TV)
Dell Publishing Co.: No. 312, Jan, 1951 - No. 33, Nov-Jan/58-59 (All painted-c)
Four Color 312(#1, 1/51) 11 22 33 75 160 245
2(8-10/51),3: (#2 titled "Tonto") 6 12 18 42 79 115
4-10 5 10 15 35 63 90
11-20 5 10 15 31 53 75
21-33 4 8 12 28 47 65
NOTE: ***Ernest Nordli*** *painted c(signed)-2, 7; unsigned-3-6, 8-11, 12?, 13, 14, 18?, 22-24?*
See Aurora Comic Booklets.

LONE RANGER'S FAMOUS HORSE HI-YO SILVER, THE (TV)
Dell Publishing Co.: No. 369, Jan, 1952 - No. 36, Oct-Dec, 1960 (All painted-c, most by Sam Savitt) (Lone Ranger appears in most issues)
Four Color 369(#1)-Silver's origin as told by The Lone Ranger 11 22 33 72 154 235
Four Color 392(#2, 4/52) 7 14 21 44 82 120
3(7-9/52)-10(4-6/52) 5 10 15 31 53 75
11-36 4 8 12 27 44 60

LONE RANGER, THE : SNAKE OF IRON
Dynamite Entertainment: 2012 - No. 4, 2013 ($3.99, limited series)
1-4: 1-Dixon-s/Polls-a/Calero-c 4.00

LONE RANGER, THE : VINDICATED
Dynamite Entertainment: 2014 - No. 4, 2015 ($3.99, limited series)
1-4-Justin Gray-s/Rey Villegas-a. 1-Cassaday-c. 2-4-Laming-c 4.00

LONE RIDER (Also see The Rider)
Superior Comics(Farrell Publ.): Apr, 1951 - No. 26, Jul, 1955 (#3-on: 36 pgs.)
1 (52 pgs.)-The Lone Rider & his horse Lightnin' begin; Kamen-*ish*-a begins 39 78 117 231 378 525
2 (52 pgs.)-The Golden Arrow begins (origin) 20 40 60 117 189 260
3-6: 6-Last Golden Arrow 19 38 57 109 172 235
7-Golden Arrow becomes Swift Arrow; origin of his shield 20 40 60 114 182 250
8-Origin Swift Arrow 18 36 54 107 169 230
9,10 12 24 36 69 97 125
11-14 10 20 30 54 72 90
15-Golden Arrow origin-r from #2, changing name to Swift Arrow 12 24 36 67 94 120
16-20,22-26: 23-Apache Kid app. 9 18 27 50 65 80
21-3-D effect-c 18 36 54 105 165 225

LONERS, THE
Marvel Comics: June, 2007 - No. 6, Jan, 2008 ($2.99, limited series)
1-6-Cebulski-s/Moline-a/Pearson-c; Lightspeed, Spider-Woman, Ricochet app. 3.00
...: The Secret Lives of Super Heroes TPB (2008, $14.99) r/#1-6; sketch pages 15.00

LONE WOLF AND CUB
First Comics: May, 1987 - No. 45, Apr, 1991 ($1.95-$3.25, B&W, deluxe size)
1-Frank Miller-c & intro.; reprints manga series by Koike & Kojima

GD 2.0 | VG 4.0 | FN 6.0 | VF 8.0 | VF/NM 9.0 | NM- 9.2

3 6 9 14 19 24
1-2nd print, 3rd print, 2-2nd print 4.00
2-12: 6-72 pgs. origin issue 1 3 4 6 8 10
13-38,40: 40-Ploog-c 6.00
39-($5.95, 120 pgs.)-Ploog-c 1 2 3 5 6 8
41-44: 41-($3.95, 84 pgs.)-Ploog-c. 42-Ploog-c 6.00
45-Last issue; low print 3 6 9 16 23 30
Deluxe Edition ($19.95, B&W) 20.00
NOTE: *Sienkiewicz c-13-24. Matt Wagner c-25-30.*

LONE WOLF AND CUB (Trade paperbacks)
Dark Horse Comics: Aug, 2000 - No. 28 ($9.95, B&W, 4" x 6", approx. 300 pgs.)
1-Collects First Comics reprint series; Frank Miller-c 18.00
1-(2nd printing) 12.00
1-(3rd-5th printings) 10.00
2,3-(1st printings) 12.00
2,3-(2nd printings) 10.00
4-28 10.00

LONE WOLF 2100 (Also see Reveal)
Dark Horse Comics: May, 2002 - No. 11, Dec, 2003 ($2.99, color)
1-New homage to Lone Wolf and Cub; Kennedy-s/Velasco-a 4.00
2-11 3.00
...: The Red File (1/03, $2.99) character and story background files 3.00
... Vol. 1 - Shadows on Saplings TPB (2003, $12.95, 6" x 9") r/#1-4 13.00
... Vol. 2 - The Language of Chaos TPB (2003, $12.95, 6" x 9") r/#5-8, Dirty Tricks short story from Reveal 13.00

LONE WOLF 2100: CHASE THE SETTING SUN
Dark Horse Comics: Jan, 2016 - No. 4, Apr, 2016 ($3.99, color)
1-4-Heisserer-s/Sepulveda-a 4.00

LONG BOW (...Indian Boy)(See Indians & Jumbo Comics #141)
Fiction House Mag. (Real Adventures Publ.): 1951 - No. 8, Fall, 1952; No. 9, Spring, 1953
1-Most covers by Maurice Whitman 21 42 63 124 202 280
2 12 24 36 69 97 125
3-9 10 20 30 58 79 100

LONG HOT SUMMER, THE
DC Comics (Milestone): Jul, 1995 - No. 3, Sept, 1995 ($2.95/$2.50, lim. series)
1-3: 1-($2.95-c). 2,3-($2.50-c) 1 3 4 6 8 10

LONG JOHN SILVER & THE PIRATES (Formerly Terry & the Pirates)
Charlton Comics: No. 30, Aug, 1956 - No. 32, March, 1957 (TV)
30-32: Whitman-c 13 26 39 72 101 130

LONGSHOT (Also see X-Men, 2nd Series #10)
Marvel Comics: Sept, 1985 - No. 6, Feb, 1986 (60¢, limited series)
1-Art Adams/Whilce Portacio-c/a in all 4 8 12 27 44 60
2-5: 4-Spider-Man app. 2 4 6 11 16 20
6-Double size 3 6 9 14 20 26
Trade Paperback (1989, $16.95)-r/#1-6 17.00

LONGSHOT
Marvel Comics: Feb, 1998 ($3.99, one-shot)
1-DeMatteis-s/Zulli-a 4.00

LONGSHOT SAVES THE MARVEL UNIVERSE
Marvel Comics: Jan, 2014 - No. 4, Feb, 2014 ($2.99, limited series)
1-4-Hastings-s/Camagni-a/Nakayama-c. 3,4-Superior Spider-Man app. 3.00

LOOKING GLASS WARS: HATTER M
Image Comics (Desperado): Dec, 2005 - No. 4, Nov, 2006 ($3.99)
1-4-Templesmith-a/c 4.00

LOONEY TUNES (2nd Series) (TV)
Gold Key/Whitman: April, 1975 - No. 47, June, 1984
1-Reprints 3 6 9 21 33 45
2-10: 2,4-reprints 2 4 6 13 18 22
11-20: 16-reprints 2 4 6 9 12 15
21-30 2 3 4 6 8 10
31,32,36-42(2/82) 1 2 3 5 6 8
33-(8/80)-35 (Whitman pre-pack only, scarce) 3 6 9 21 33 45
43(4/82),44(6/83) (low distribution) 2 4 6 9 13 16
45-47 (All #90296 on-c; nd, nd code, pre-pack) 45(8/83), 46(3/84), 47(6/84)
3 6 9 14 20 26

LOONEY TUNES (3rd Series) (TV)
DC Comics: Apr, 1994 - Present ($1.50/$1.75/$1.95/$1.99/$2.25/$2.50/$2.99)
1-10,120: 1-Marvin Martian-c/sty; Bugs Bunny, Roadrunner, Daffy begin. 120-($2.95-C) 4.00
11-119,121-187: 23-34-($1.75-c). 35-43-($1.95-c). 44-Begin $1.99-c. 93-Begin $2.25-c. 100-Art by various incl. Kyle Baker, Marie Severin, Darwyn Cooke, Jill Thompson 3.00
188-271: 188-Begin $2.99-c; Scooby-Doo spoof. 193-Christmas-c. 237-Duck Dodgers 3.00
...Back In Action Movie Adaptation (12/03, $3.95) photo-c 4.00

LOONEY TUNES AND MERRIE MELODIES COMICS ("Looney Tunes" #166(8/55) on)
(Also see Porky's Duck Hunt)
Dell Publishing Co.: 1941 - No. 246, July-Sept, 1962
1-Porky Pig, Bugs Bunny, Daffy Duck, Elmer Fudd, Mary Jane & Sniffles, Pat Patsy and Pete begin (1st comic book app. of each). Bugs Bunny story by Win Smith (early Mickey Mouse artist) 1300 2600 3900 9900 20,950 32,000
2 (11/41) 197 394 591 1625 3663 5700
3-Kandi the Cave Kid begins by Walt Kelly; also in #4-6,8,11,15
132 264 396 1056 2378 3700
4-Kelly-a 125 250 375 1000 2250 3500
5-Bugs Bunny The Super-Duper Rabbit story (1st funny animal super hero, 3/42; also see Coo Coo); Kelly-a 96 192 288 768 1734 2700
6,8: 8-Kelly-a 75 150 225 600 1350 2100
7,9,10: 9-Painted-c. 10-Flag-c 52 104 156 416 933 1450
11,15-Kelly-a; 15-Christmas-c 52 104 156 416 933 1450
12-14,16-19 38 76 114 285 641 1000
20-25: Pat, Patsy & Pete by Walt Kelly in all. 20-War Bonds-c
32 64 96 230 515 800
26-30 23 46 69 161 356 550
31-40: 33-War Bonds-c. 39-Christmas-c 18 36 54 128 284 440
41-50: 45-War Bonds-c 14 28 42 96 211 325
51-60: 51-Christmas-c 11 22 33 76 163 250
61-80 8 16 24 56 108 160
81-99: 87,99-Christmas-c 7 14 21 49 92 135
100-New Year's-c 8 16 24 55 105 155
101-120 9 18 27 58 114 170
121-150: 124-New Year's-c. 133-Tattoo-c 5 10 15 35 63 90
151-200: 159-Christmas-c 5 10 15 33 57 80
201-240 5 10 15 31 53 75
241-246 5 10 15 33 57 80

LOONY SPORTS (Magazine)
3-Strikes Publishing Co.: Spring, 1975 (68 pgs.)
1-Sports satire 2 4 6 8 11 14

LOOSE CANNON (Also see Action Comics Annual #5 & Showcase '94 #5)
DC Comics: June, 1995 - No. 4, Sept, 1995 ($1.75, limited series)
1-4: Adam Pollina-a. 1-Superman app. 3.00

LOOY DOT DOPE
United Features Syndicate: No. 13, 1939
Single Series 13 35 70 105 208 339 470

LORD JIM (See Movie Comics)

LORD OF THE JUNGLE
Dynamite Entertainment: 2012 - No. 15, 2013 ($1.00/$3.99)
1-($1.00) Retelling of Tarzan's origin; Nelson-s/Castro-a; four covers 3.00
2-15-($3.99) 2-6-Three covers. 7-13-Two covers 4.00
Annual 1 (2012, $4.99) Rahner-s/Davila-a/Parrillo-c 5.00

LORD OF THE JUNGLE VOLUME 3
Dynamite Entertainment: 2022 - Present ($3.99)
1-3-Dan Jurgens-s/Benito Gallego-a; retelling of Tarzan's origin 4.00

LORD PUMPKIN
Malibu Comics (Ultraverse): Oct, 1994 ($2.50, one-shot)
0-Two covers 3.00

LORD PUMPKIN/NECROMANTRA
Malibu Comics (Ultraverse): Apr, 1995 - No. 4, July, 1995 ($2.95, limited series, flip book)
1-4 3.00

LORDS OF AVALON: KNIGHT OF DARKNESS
Marvel Comics: Jan, 2008 - No. 6, July, 2009 ($3.99, limited series)
1-6-($3.99)-Kenyon & Furth-s; Ohtsuka-a/c 4.00

LORDS OF AVALON: SWORD OF DARKNESS
Marvel Comics: Apr, 2008 - No. 6, Sept, 2008 ($3.99/$2.99, limited series)
1-($3.99)-Adaptation of Sherrilyn Kenyon's Arthurian fantasy; Ohtsuka-a/c 4.00
2-6-($2.99) 3.00
HC (2008, $19.99) r/#1-6; two covers 20.00

LORDS OF EMPYRE (Tie-in to Empyre series)
Marvel Comics: Sept, 2020 - Oct, 2020 ($4.99, series of one-shots)
...: Celestial Messiah 1 (10/20) Paknadel-s/Lins-a; leads into Empyre #3 5.00
...: Emperor Hulkling 1 (9/20) Zdarsky & Oliveira-s/Garcia-a; prelude to events of Empyre 5.00
...: Swordsman 1 (10/20) Paknadel-s/Nachlik-a 5.00

LORDS OF MARS
Dynamite Entertainment: 2013 - No. 6, 2014 ($3.99, limited series)
1-6-Tarzan and Jane meet John Carter on Mars; Nelson-s/Castro-a; multiple covers 4.00

LORDS OF THE JUNGLE
Dynamite Entertainment: 2016 - No. 6, 2016 ($3.99, limited series)
1-6-Tarzan and Sheena app.; Bechko-s/Castro-a; covers by Castro & Massafera 4.00

LORNA, RELIC WRANGLER
Image Comics: Mar, 2011 ($3.99, one-shot)
1-Micah Harris-s; J. Bone-c 4.00

LORNA THE JUNGLE GIRL (...Jungle Queen #1-5)
Atlas Comics (NPI 1/OMC 2-11/NPI 12-26): July, 1953 - No. 26, Aug, 1957
1-Origin & 1st app. 63 126 189 403 689 975
2-Intro. & 1st app. Greg Knight 34 68 102 204 332 460
3-5 31 62 93 182 296 410
6-11: 11-Last pre-code (1/55) 27 54 81 158 259 360
12-17,19-26: 14-Colletta & Maneely-c 24 48 72 142 234 325
18-Williamson/Colletta-c 25 50 75 147 241 335
NOTE: *Brodsky c-1-3, 5, 9. Everett c-21, 23-26. Heath c-6, 7. Maneely c-12, 15. Romita a-18, 20, 22, 24, 26. Shores a-14-16, 18, 24, 26; c-11, 13, 16. Tuska a-6.*

LOSERS (Inspired the 2010 movie)
DC Comics (Vertigo): Aug, 2003 - No. 32, Mar, 2006 ($2.95/$2.99)
1-Andy Diggle-s/Jock-a 2 4 6 11 16 20
1-Special Edition (6/10, $1.00) r/#1 with "What's Next?" logo on cover
1 2 3 5 6 8
2-32: 15-Bagged with Sky Captain CD. 20-Oliver-a. 27-Wilson-a 3.00
...: Ante Up TPB (2004, $9.95) r/#1-6 10.00
...: Book Two TPB (2010, $24.99) r/#13-32; Ian Rankin intro.; preliminary art pages 25.00
...: Close Quarters TPB (2005, $14.99) r/#20-25 15.00
...: Double Down TPB (2004, $12.95) r/#7-12 13.00
...: Endgame TPB (2006, $14.99) r/#26-32 15.00
...: Trifecta TPB (2005, $14.99) r/#13-19 15.00
...: Volumes One and Two TPB (2010, $19.99) r/#1-12; new intro. by Diggle 20.00

LOSERS SPECIAL (See Our Fighting Forces #123)(Also see G.I. Combat & Our Fighting Forces)
DC Comics: Sept, 1985 ($1.25, one-shot)

Looney Tunes #159 © WB

The Lost Boys #1 © WB

Love and Rockets #8 © Fantagraphics

GD VG FN VF VF/NM NM-
2.0 4.0 6.0 8.0 9.0 9.2

1-Capt. Storm, Gunner & Sarge; Crisis on Infinite Earths x-over 1 3 4 6 8 10

LOST, THE
Chaos! Comics: Dec, 1997 - No. 3 ($2.95, B&W, unfinished limited series)
1-3-Andreyko-script: 1-Russell back-c 3.00

LOST BOYS, THE (Sequel to the 1987 vampire movie)
DC Comics (Vertigo): Dec, 2016 - No. 6, May, 2017 ($3.99)
1-6-Tim Seeley-s/Scott Godlewski-a/Tony Harris-c; Frog Bros. app. 4.00

LOST BOYS: REIGN OF FROGS (Based on the 1987 vampire movie)
DC Comics (WildStorm): Jul, 2008 - No. 4, Oct, 2008 ($3.50, limited series)
1-4-Rodionoff-s/Gomez-a; Edgar Frog app. 3.50
TPB (2009, $12.99) r/#1-4 13.00

LOST CITY EXPLORERS
AfterShock Comics: Jun, 2018 - No. 5, Oct, 2018 ($3.99, limited series)
1-5-Zack Kaplan-s/Alvaro Sarraseca-a 4.00

LOST CONTINENT
Eclipse Int'l: Sept, 1990 - No. 6, 1991 ($3.50, B&W, squarebound, 60 pgs.)
1-6: Japanese story translated to English 4.00

LOST IN SPACE (Movie)
Dark Horse Comics: Apr, 1998 - No. 3, July, 1998 ($2.95, limited series)
1-3-Continuation of 1998 movie; Erskine-c 4.00

LOST IN SPACE (TV)(Also see Space Family Robinson)
Innovation Publishing: Aug, 1991 - No. 12, Jan, 1993 ($2.50, limited series)
1-Bill Mumy (Will Robinson) script 1 2 3 5 6 8
1,2-Special Ed.; r/#1,2 plus new art & new-c 3.00
2-12: 9-Perez-c; Mumy script 3.00
Annual 1 (1991, $2.95, 52 pgs.) Good Girl bondage-c 3 6 9 14 19 24
Annual 2 (1992, $2.95, 52 pgs.) 4.00
...: Project Robinson (11/93, $2.50) 1st & only part of intended series 3.00

LOST IN SPACE: COUNTDOWN TO DANGER (Based on the 2018 Netflix series)
Legendary Comics: Oct, 2018 ($17.95, hardcover, one-shot)
HC-Short stories occuring before and during events of the series; Zid-a 18.00

LOST IN SPACE: THE LOST ADVENTURES (IRWIN ALLEN'S...) (TV)
American Gothic Press: Mar, 2016 - No. 6, Nov, 2016 ($3.99, limited series)
1-6-Adaptation of unused scripts. 1-3-The Curious Galactics. 4-6-Malice in Wonderland 6.00

LOST IN SPACE: VOYAGE TO THE BOTTOM OF THE SOUL
Innovation Publishing: No. 13, Aug, 1993 - No. 18, 1994 ($2.50, limited series)
13(V1#1, $2.95)-Embossed silver logo edition; Bill Mumy scripts begin; painted-c 1 3 4 6 8 10
13(V1#1, $4.95)-Embossed gold logo edition bagged w/poster 4 8 12 23 37 50
14-18: Painted-c 1 2 3 5 6 8
NOTE: *Originally intended to be a 12 issue limited series.*

LOST PLANET
Eclipse Comics: 5/87 - No. 5, 2/88; No. 6, 3/89 (Mini-series, Baxter paper)
1-6-Bo Hampton-c/a in all 3.00

LOST SOLDIERS
Image Comics: Jul, 2020 - No. 5, Dec, 2020 ($3.99, limited series)
1-5-Alex Kot-s/Luca Casalanguida-a 4.00

LOST WAGON TRAIN, THE (See Zane Grey Four Color 583)

LOST WORLD, THE
Dell Publishing Co.: No. 1145, Nov-Jan, 1960-61
Four Color 1145-Movie, Gil Kane-a, photo-c; 1pg. Conan Doyle biography by Torres 9 18 27 61 123 185

LOST WORLD, THE (See Jurassic Park)
Topps Comics: May, 1997 - No. 4, Aug, 1997 ($2.95, limited series)
1-Movie adaptation 3 6 9 14 20 25
2-4-Movie adaptation continues 1 3 4 6 8 10

LOST WORLDS (Weird Tales of the Past and Future)
Standard Comics: No. 5, Oct, 1952 - No. 6, Dec, 1952
5- "Alice in Terrorland" by Alex Toth; J. Katz-a 65 130 195 416 708 1000
6-Toth-a 45 90 135 284 480 675

LOT, THE
Bad Idea: Jul, 2021 - No. 4, Oct, 2021 ($5.99, limited series)

GD VG FN VF VF/NM NM-
2.0 4.0 6.0 8.0 9.0 9.2

1-4-Lead story with Marguerite Bennett-s/Renato Guedes-a; back-ups by various 6.00

LOTS 'O' FUN COMICS
Robert Allen Co.: 1940s? (5¢, heavy stock, blue covers)
nn-Contents can vary; Felix, Planet Comics known; contents would determine value. Similar to Up-To-Date Comics. Remainders - re-packaged.

LOT 13
DC Comics: Dec, 2012 - No. 5, Apr, 2013 ($2.99, limited series)
1-5-Niles-s/Fabry-a/c 3.00

LOU GEHRIG (See The Pride of the Yankees)

LOVE ADVENTURES (Actual Confessions #13)
Marvel (IPS)/Atlas Comics (MPI): Oct, 1949; No. 2, Jan, 1950; No. 3, Feb, 1951 - No. 12, Aug, 1952
1-Photo-c 32 64 96 188 307 425
2-Powell-a; Tyrone Power, Gene Tierney photo-c 24 48 72 140 230 320
3-8,10-12: 8-Robinson-a 16 32 48 94 147 200
9-Everett-a 17 34 51 98 154 210

LOVE AND AARDVARKS (Reprints from Cerebus in Hell)
Aardvark-Vanaheim: Apr, 2018 ($4.00, B&W)
1-Cerebus figures placed over original Doré artwork; Love and Rockets #1 cover swipe 4.00

LOVE AND MARRIAGE
Superior Comics Ltd. (Canada): Mar, 1952 - No. 16, Sept, 1954
1 25 50 75 150 245 340
2 15 30 45 84 127 170
3-10 14 28 42 81 118 155
11-16 13 26 39 72 101 130
I.W. Reprint #1,2,8,11,14: 8-r/Love and Marriage #3. 11-r/Love and Marriage #11 3 6 9 14 20 25
Super Reprint #10('63),15,17('64):15-Love and Marriage #? 3 6 9 14 20 25
NOTE: *All issues have* ***Kamenish*** *art.*

LOVE AND ROCKETS
Fantagraphics Books: 1981 - No. 50, May, 1996 ($2.95/$2.50/$4.95, B&W, mature)
1-B&W-c (1981, $1.00; publ. by Hernandez Bros.)(800 printed) 13 26 39 86 188 290
1 (Fall '82; Fantagraphics, color-c) 9 18 27 60 120 180
1-2nd & 3rd printing, 2-11,29-31: 2nd printings 2 4 6 9 12 15
2 3 6 9 19 30 40
3-10 2 4 6 8 10 12
11-49: 30 ($2.95, 52 pgs.) 5.00
50-($4.95) 6.00

LOVE AND ROCKETS (Volume 2)
Fantagraphics Books: Spring, 2001 - No. 20, Summer, 2007 ($3.95-$7.99, B&W, mature)
1-Gilbert, Jaime and Mario Hernandez-s/a 1 3 4 6 8 10
2-9 5.00
10-($5.95) 6.00
11-19-($4.50) 4.50
20-($7.99) 8.00
...: Stories • Free Comic Book Day 2016 Edition (giveaway) 3.00

LOVE AND ROMANCE
Charlton Comics: Sept, 1971 - No. 24, Sept, 1975
1 3 6 9 21 33 45
2-5,7-10 2 4 6 10 14 18
6-David Cassidy pin-up; grey-tone cover 3 6 9 14 19 24
11,13-24 2 4 6 8 10 12
12-Susan Dey poster 2 4 6 10 14 18

LOVE AT FIRST SIGHT
Ace Magazines (RAR Publ. Co./Periodical House): Oct, 1949 - No. 43, Nov, 1956 (Photo-c: 18-42)
1-Painted-c 39 78 117 240 395 550
2-Painted-c 20 40 60 117 189 260
3-10: 4,7-Painted-c 17 34 51 98 154 210
11-20 15 30 45 85 130 175
21-33: 33-Last pre-code 15 30 45 83 124 165
34-43 14 28 42 78 112 145

LOVE BUG, THE (See Movie Comics)

LOVEBUNNY AND MR. HELL
Devil's Due Publ./Image Comics: 2002 - 2004 ($2.95, B&W, one-shots)
1-Tim Seeley-s 6.00

	GD 2.0	VG 4.0	FN 6.0	VF 8.0	VF/NM 9.0	NM- 9.2
...: A Day in the Lovelife (Image, 2003) Blaylock-a						3.00
...: Savage Love (Image, 2003) Seeley-s/a; Savage Dragon app.; Seeley & Larsen-c						3.00
TPB (4/04, $9.95, digest-sized) reprints						10.00

LOVE CLASSICS
A Lover's Magazine/Marvel: Nov, 1949 - No. 2, Feb, 1950 (Photo-c, 52 pgs.)

	GD 2.0	VG 4.0	FN 6.0	VF 8.0	VF/NM 9.0	NM- 9.2
1,2: 2-Virginia Mayo photo-c; 30 pg. story "I Turned Into a Small-Town Flirt"	36	72	108	211	343	475

LOVE CONFESSIONS
Quality Comics: Oct, 1949 - No. 54, Dec, 1956 (Photo-c: 3,4,6,7,9,11-18,21,24,25)

	GD 2.0	VG 4.0	FN 6.0	VF 8.0	VF/NM 9.0	NM- 9.2
1-Ward-c/a, 9 pgs; Gustavson-a	50	100	150	315	533	750
2-Gustavson-a; Ward-c	25	50	75	150	245	340
3	19	38	57	111	176	240
4-Crandall-a	20	40	60	114	182	250
5-Ward-a, 7 pgs.	20	40	60	120	195	270
6,7,9,11-13,15,16,18: 7-Van Johnson photo-c. 8-Robert Mitchum & Jane Russell photo-c	15	30	45	88	137	185
8,10-Ward-a (2 stories in #10)	20	40	60	117	189	260
14,17,19,22-Ward-a; 17-Faith Domerque photo-c	20	40	60	114	182	250
20-Ward-a(2)	20	40	60	117	189	260
21,23-28,30-38,40-42: Last precode, 4/55	15	30	45	83	124	165
29-Ward-a	18	36	54	105	165	225
39,53-Matt Baker-a	16	32	48	96	151	205
43,44,46,47,50-52,54: 47-Ward-c?	14	28	42	81	118	155
45,48-Ward-a	16	32	48	94	147	200
49-Baker-c/a	24	48	72	142	234	325

LOVECRAFT
DC Comics: 2003 (graphic novel)

	GD 2.0	VG 4.0	FN 6.0	VF 8.0	VF/NM 9.0	NM- 9.2
Hardcover ($24.95) Rodionoff & Giffen-s/Breccia-a; intro. by John Carpenter						25.00
Softcover ($17.95)						18.00

LOVE DIARY
Our Publishing Co./Toytown/Patches: July, 1949 - No. 48, Oct, 1955 (Photo-c: 1-30) (52 pgs. #1-11?)

	GD 2.0	VG 4.0	FN 6.0	VF 8.0	VF/NM 9.0	NM- 9.2
1-Krigstein-a	37	74	111	222	361	500
2,3-Krigstein & Mort Leav-a in each	22	44	66	128	209	290
4-8	18	36	54	105	165	225
9,10-Everett-a	19	38	57	111	176	240
11-15,17-20	16	32	48	94	147	200
16- Mort Leav-a, 3 pg. Baker-sty. Leav-a	18	36	54	105	165	225
21-30,32-48: 45-Leav-a. 47-Last precode(12/54)	15	30	45	90	140	190
31-John Buscema headlights-c	26	52	78	154	252	350

LOVE DIARY (Diary Loves #2 on; title change due to previously published title)
Quality Comics Group: Sept, 1949

	GD 2.0	VG 4.0	FN 6.0	VF 8.0	VF/NM 9.0	NM- 9.2
1-Ward-c/a, 9 pgs.	53	106	159	334	567	800

LOVE DIARY
Charlton Comics: July, 1958 - No. 102, Dec, 1976

	GD 2.0	VG 4.0	FN 6.0	VF 8.0	VF/NM 9.0	NM- 9.2
1	14	28	42	82	121	160
2	9	18	27	50	65	80
3-5,7-10	8	16	24	40	50	60
6-Torres-a	8	16	24	42	54	65
11-20	4	8	12	23	37	50
21-40	3	6	9	16	23	30
41-60	3	6	9	14	19	24
61-78,80,100-102	2	4	6	10	14	18
79-David Cassidy pin-up	3	6	9	14	19	24
81,83,84,86-99	2	4	6	8	11	14
82,85: 82-Partridge Family poster. 85-Danny poster	2	4	6	11	16	20

LOVE DOCTOR (See Dr. Anthony King...)

LOVE DRAMAS (True Secrets No. 3 on?)
Marvel Comics (IPS): Oct, 1949 - No. 2, Jan, 1950

	GD 2.0	VG 4.0	FN 6.0	VF 8.0	VF/NM 9.0	NM- 9.2
1-Jack Kamen-a; photo-c	32	64	96	188	307	425
2-Photo-c	20	40	60	118	192	265

LOVE EVERLASTING
Image Comics: Aug, 2022 - Present ($3.99)

	GD 2.0	VG 4.0	FN 6.0	VF 8.0	VF/NM 9.0	NM- 9.2
1-5-Romance stories; Tom King-s/Elsa Charretier-a						4.00

LOVE EXPERIENCES (Challenge of the Unknown No. 6)
Ace Periodicals (A.A. Wyn/Periodical House): Oct, 1949 - No. 5, June, 1950; No. 6, Apr, 1951 - No. 38, June, 1956

	GD 2.0	VG 4.0	FN 6.0	VF 8.0	VF/NM 9.0	NM- 9.2
1-Painted-c	36	72	108	211	343	475
2	19	38	57	111	176	240
3-5: 5-Painted-c	16	32	48	92	144	195
6-10	15	30	45	86	133	180
11-30: 30-Last pre-code (2/55)	15	30	45	83	124	165
31-38: 38-Indicia date-6/56; c-date-8/56	14	28	42	80	115	150

NOTE: ***Anne Brewster** a-15. Photo c-4, 15-35, 38.*

LOVE FIGHTS
Oni Press: June, 2003 - No. 12, Aug, 2004 ($2.99, B&W)

	GD 2.0	VG 4.0	FN 6.0	VF 8.0	VF/NM 9.0	NM- 9.2
1-12-Andi Watson-s/a						3.00
Vol. 1 TPB (4/04, $14.95, digest-size) r/#1-6						15.00

LOVE IS LOVE
IDW Publishing/DC Comics: 2016 ($9.99, TPB)

	GD 2.0	VG 4.0	FN 6.0	VF 8.0	VF/NM 9.0	NM- 9.2
SC-Anthology to benefit the survivors of the Orlando Pulse shooting; Charretier-c	3	6	9	14	19	24

LOVE JOURNAL
Our Publishing Co.: No. 10, Oct, 1951 - No. 25, July, 1954

	GD 2.0	VG 4.0	FN 6.0	VF 8.0	VF/NM 9.0	NM- 9.2
10-Woman on-c "Branded"	142	284	426	909	1555	2200
11-15,17-25: 19-Mort Leav-a	34	68	102	199	325	450
16-Buscema headlight-c	41	82	123	256	428	600

LOVELAND
Mutual Mag./Eye Publ. (Marvel): Nov, 1949 - No. 2, Feb, 1950 (52 pgs.)

	GD 2.0	VG 4.0	FN 6.0	VF 8.0	VF/NM 9.0	NM- 9.2
1,2-Photo-c	22	44	66	128	209	290

LOVELESS
DC Comics: Dec, 2005 - No. 24, Jun, 2008 ($2.99)

	GD 2.0	VG 4.0	FN 6.0	VF 8.0	VF/NM 9.0	NM- 9.2
1-24: 1-Azzarello-s/Frusin-a. 6-8,15,22,23,24-Zezelj-a. 11,12,16-21-Dell'Edera-a						3.00
...: A Kin of Homecoming TPB (2006, $9.99) r/#1-5						10.00
...: Blackwater Falls TPB (2008, $19.99) r/#13-24						20.00
...: Thicker Than Blackwater TPB (2007, $14.99) r/#6-12						15.00

LOVE LESSONS
Harvey Comics/Key Publ. No. 5: Oct, 1949 - No. 5, June, 1950

	GD 2.0	VG 4.0	FN 6.0	VF 8.0	VF/NM 9.0	NM- 9.2
1-Metallic silver-c printed over the cancelled covers of Love Letters #1; indicia title is "Love Letters"	21	42	63	122	199	275
1-Non-metallic version	19	38	57	111	176	240
2-Powell-a; photo-c	13	26	39	72	101	130
3-5: 3,4-Photo-c	10	20	30	56	76	95

LOVE LETTERS (10/49, Harvey; advertised but never published; covers were printed before cancellation and were used as the cover to Love Lessons #1)

LOVE LETTERS (Love Secrets No. 32 on)
Quality Comics: 11/49 - #6, 9/50; #7, 3/51 - #31, 6/53; #32, 2/54 - #51, 12/56

	GD 2.0	VG 4.0	FN 6.0	VF 8.0	VF/NM 9.0	NM- 9.2
1-Ward-c, Gustavson-a	39	78	117	231	378	525
2-Ward-c, Gustavson-a	29	58	87	172	281	390
3-Gustavson-a	20	40	60	117	189	260
4-Ward-a, 9 pgs.; photo-c	24	48	72	142	234	325
5-8,10	15	30	45	86	133	180
9-One pg. Ward "Be Popular with the Opposite Sex"; Robert Mitchum photo-c	16	32	48	92	144	195
11-Ward-r/Broadway Romances #2 & retitled	16	32	48	92	144	195
12-15,18-20	15	30	45	83	124	165
16,17-Ward-a; 16-Anthony Quinn photo-c. 17-Jane Russell photo-c	20	40	60	117	189	260
21-29	14	28	42	82	121	160
30,31(6/53)-Ward-a	15	30	45	86	133	180
32(2/54)-39: 37-Ward-a. 38-Crandall-a. 39-Last precode (4/55)	14	28	42	78	112	145
40-48	13	26	39	74	105	135
49-51: 49,50-Baker-a. 51-Baker-c	19	38	57	111	176	240

NOTE: *Photo-c on most 3-28.*

LOVE LIFE
P. L. Publishing Co.: Nov, 1951

	GD 2.0	VG 4.0	FN 6.0	VF 8.0	VF/NM 9.0	NM- 9.2
1	17	34	51	98	154	210

LOVELORN (Confessions of the Lovelorn #52 on)
American Comics Group (Michel Publ./Regis Publ.): Aug-Sept, 1949 - No. 51, July, 1954 (No. 1-26: 52 pgs.)

	GD 2.0	VG 4.0	FN 6.0	VF 8.0	VF/NM 9.0	NM- 9.2
1	27	54	81	158	259	360
2	16	32	48	94	147	200
3-10	14	28	42	82	121	160
11-20,22-48: 18-Drucker-a(2 pgs.). 46-Lazarus-a	14	28	42	78	112	145
21-Prostitution story	18	36	54	105	165	225
49-51-Has 3-D effect-c/stories	22	44	66	132	216	300

LOVE MEMORIES
Fawcett Publications: 1949 (no month) - No. 4, July, 1950 (All photo-c)

	GD 2.0	VG 4.0	FN 6.0	VF 8.0	VF/NM 9.0	NM- 9.2
1	21	42	63	122	199	275
2-4: 2-(Win/49-50)	14	28	42	76	108	140

LOVE ME TENDERLOIN: A CAL McDONALD MYSTERY
Dark Horse Comics: Jan, 2004 ($2.99, one-shot)

	GD 2.0	VG 4.0	FN 6.0	VF 8.0	VF/NM 9.0	NM- 9.2
1-Niles-s/Templesmith-a/c						3.00

LOVE MYSTERY
Fawcett Publications: June, 1950 - No. 3, Oct, 1950 (All photo-c)

	GD 2.0	VG 4.0	FN 6.0	VF 8.0	VF/NM 9.0	NM- 9.2
1-George Evans-a	28	56	84	165	270	375
2,3-Evans-a. 3-Powell-a	19	38	57	111	176	240

LOVE PROBLEMS (See Fox Giants)

LOVE PROBLEMS AND ADVICE ILLUSTRATED (see True Love...)

LOVE ROMANCES (Formerly Ideal #5)
Timely/Marvel/Atlas(TCI No. 7-71/Male No. 72-106): No. 6, May, 1949 - No. 106, July, 1963

	GD 2.0	VG 4.0	FN 6.0	VF 8.0	VF/NM 9.0	NM- 9.2
6-Photo-c	32	64	96	189	307	425
7-Photo-c; Kamen-a	19	38	57	111	176	240
8-Kubert-a; photo-c	19	38	57	111	176	240
9-20: 9-12-Photo-c	16	32	48	96	151	205
21,24-Krigstein-a	18	36	54	105	165	225
22,23,25-35,37,39,40	16	32	48	92	144	195
36,38-Krigstein-a	16	32	48	94	147	200
41-44,46,47: Last precode (2/55)	15	30	45	90	140	190
45,57-Matt Baker-a	19	38	57	112	179	245
48,50-52,54-56,58-74	9	18	27	58	114	170
49,53-Toth-a, 6 & ? pgs.	9	18	27	60	120	180
75,77,82-Matt Baker-a	11	22	33	75	160	245
76,78-81,86,88-90,92-95: 80-Heath-c. 95-Last 10¢-c?	10	20	30	67	141	215
83,84,87,91,106-Kirby-c. 83-Severin-a	13	26	39	86	188	290
85,96,99-105-Kirby-c/a	15	30	45	100	220	340
97-10¢ cover price blacked out, 12¢ printed on cover; Kirby-c/a	25	50	75	175	388	600
98-Kirby-c/a	16	32	48	110	243	375

NOTE: ***Anne Brewster** a-67, 72. **Colletta** a-37, 40, 42, 44, 46, 67(2); c-42, 44, 46, 49, 54, 80. **Everett** c-70. **Hartley** c-20, 21, 30, 31. **Heath** a-87. **Kirby** c-80, 85, 88. **Robinson** a-29.*

LOVE ROMANCES (Marvel 80th Anniversary salute to romance comics)
Marvel Comics: Apr, 2019 ($3.99, one-shot)

	GD 2.0	VG 4.0	FN 6.0	VF 8.0	VF/NM 9.0	NM- 9.2
1-Short stories by various incl. Simone, Antonio, Hopeless, Martello, Jon Adams						4.00

LOVERS (Formerly Blonde Phantom)

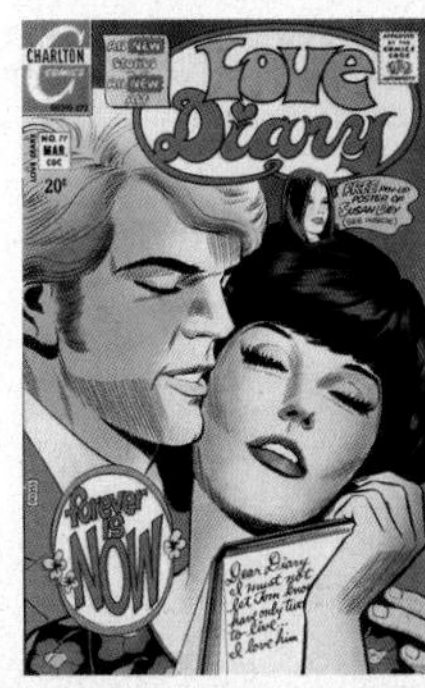

Love Diary #77 © CC

Love Everlasting #2 © BHLA & CKTK

Lucifer (2016) #10 © DC

Marvel Comics No. 23,24/Atlas No. 25 on (ANC): No. 23, May, 1949 - No. 86, Aug?, 1957

	GD 2.0	VG 4.0	FN 6.0	VF 8.0	VF/NM 9.0	NM- 9.2
23-Photo-c begin, end #29	32	94	96	188	307	425
24-Toth-*ish* plus Robinson-a	18	36	54	105	165	225
25,30-Kubert-a; 7, 10 pgs.	19	38	57	111	176	240
26-29,31-36,39,40: 35-Maneely-c	15	30	45	90	140	190
37,38-Krigstein-a	17	34	51	98	154	210
41-Everett-a(2)	17	34	51	98	154	210
42,44-65: 65-Last pre-code (1/55)	15	30	45	83	124	165
43-Frazetta 1 pg. ad	15	30	45	84	127	170
66,68-80,82-86	14	28	42	82	121	160
67-Toth-a	15	30	45	84	127	170
81-Baker-a	15	30	45	90	140	190

NOTE: ***Anne Brewster** a-86. **Colletta** a-54, 59, 62, 64, 65, 69, 85; c-61, 64, 65, 75. **Hartley** c-37, 53, 54. **Heath** a-61. **Maneely** a-57. **Powell** a-27, 30. **Robinson** a-42, 54, 56.*

LOVERS' LANE
Lev Gleason Publications: Oct, 1949 - No. 41, June, 1954 (No. 1-18: 52 pgs.)

	GD 2.0	VG 4.0	FN 6.0	VF 8.0	VF/NM 9.0	NM- 9.2
1-Biro-c	24	48	72	142	234	325
2-Biro-c	15	30	45	85	130	175
3-20: 3,4-Painted-c. 20-Frazetta 1 pg. ad	14	28	42	78	112	145
21-38,40,41	12	24	36	69	97	125
39-Story narrated by Frank Sinatra	15	30	45	85	130	175

NOTE: ***Briefer** a-6, 13, 21. **Esposito** a-5. **Fuje** a-4, 16; c-many. **Guardineer** a-1, 3. **Kinstler** c-41. **Sparling** a-3. **Tuska** a-6. Painted c-3-18. Photo c-19-22, 26-28.*

LOVE SCANDALS
Quality Comics: Feb, 1950 - No. 5, Oct, 1950 (Photo-c #2-5) (All 52 pgs.)

	GD 2.0	VG 4.0	FN 6.0	VF 8.0	VF/NM 9.0	NM- 9.2
1-Ward-c/a, 9 pgs.	39	78	117	240	395	550
2,3: 2-Gustavson-a	19	38	57	111	176	240
4-Ward-a, 18 pgs; Gil Fox-a	29	58	87	172	281	390
5-C. Cuidera-a; tomboy story "I Hated Being a Woman"	22	44	66	132	216	300

LOVE SECRETS
Marvel Comics(IPC): Oct, 1949 - No. 2, Jan, 1950 (52 pgs., photo-c)

	GD 2.0	VG 4.0	FN 6.0	VF 8.0	VF/NM 9.0	NM- 9.2
1	25	50	75	150	245	340
2	18	36	54	105	165	225

LOVE SECRETS (Formerly Love Letters #31)
Quality Comics Group: No. 32, Aug, 1953 - No. 56, Dec, 1956

	GD 2.0	VG 4.0	FN 6.0	VF 8.0	VF/NM 9.0	NM- 9.2
32	20	40	60	114	182	250
33,35-39	15	30	45	83	124	165
34-Ward-a	18	36	54	105	165	225
40-Matt Baker-c	20	40	60	115	185	255
41-43: 43-Last precode (3/55)	15	30	45	83	124	165
44,47-50,53,54	14	28	42	80	115	150
45-Ward-a	15	30	45	88	137	185
46-Ward-a; Baker-a	17	34	51	100	158	215
51,52-Ward(r). 52-r/Love Confessions #17	15	30	45	83	124	165
55-Baker-a	16	32	48	94	147	200
56-Baker-c	20	40	60	117	189	260

LOVE STORIES (See Top Love Stories)

LOVE STORIES (Formerly Heart Throbs)
National Periodical Publ.: No. 147, Nov, 1972 - No. 152, Oct-Nov, 1973

	GD 2.0	VG 4.0	FN 6.0	VF 8.0	VF/NM 9.0	NM- 9.2
147-152	3	6	9	16	23	30

LOVE STORIES OF MARY WORTH (See Harvey Comics Hits #55 & Mary Worth)
Harvey Publications: Sept, 1949 - No. 5, May, 1950

	GD 2.0	VG 4.0	FN 6.0	VF 8.0	VF/NM 9.0	NM- 9.2
1-1940's newspaper reprints-#1-4	12	24	36	69	97	125
2-5: 3-Kamen/Baker-a?	9	18	27	50	65	80

LOVE TALES (Formerly The Human Torch #35)
Marvel/Atlas Comics (ZPC No. 36-50/MMC No. 67-75): No. 36, 5/49 - No. 58, 8/52; No. 59, date? - No. 75, Sept, 1957

	GD 2.0	VG 4.0	FN 6.0	VF 8.0	VF/NM 9.0	NM- 9.2
36-Photo-c	30	60	90	177	289	400
37	17	34	51	100	158	215
38-44,46-50: 39-41-Photo-c. 48-Maneely-c	15	30	45	90	140	190
45,51,52,69: 45-Powell-a. 51,69-Everett-a. 52-Krigstein-a	16	32	48	92	144	195
53-60: 60-Last pre-code (2/55)	15	30	45	84	127	170
61-68,70-75: 75-Brewster, Cameron, Colletta-a	14	28	42	82	121	160

LOVE THRILLS (See Fox Giants)

LOVE TRAILS (Western romance)
A Lover's Magazine (CDS)(Marvel): Dec, 1949 - No. 2, Mar, 1950 (52 pgs.)

	GD 2.0	VG 4.0	FN 6.0	VF 8.0	VF/NM 9.0	NM- 9.2
1,2: 1-Photo-c	22	44	66	128	209	290

LOW
Image Comics: Aug, 2014 - No. 26, Feb, 2021 ($3.99/$3.50)

	GD 2.0	VG 4.0	FN 6.0	VF 8.0	VF/NM 9.0	NM- 9.2
1,11-26-($3.99) Remender-s/Tocchini-a						4.00
2-10-($3.50) Remender-s/Tocchini-a						3.50

LOWELL THOMAS' HIGH ADVENTURE (See High Adventure)

LOWLIFES
IDW Publishing: Jun, 2018 - No. 4, Sept, 2018 ($3.99, limited series)

	GD 2.0	VG 4.0	FN 6.0	VF 8.0	VF/NM 9.0	NM- 9.2
1-3-Buccellato-s/Sentenac-a						4.00

LOW, LOW WOODS, THE
DC Comics (Hill House Comics): Feb, 2020 - No. 6, Aug, 2020 ($3.99)

	GD 2.0	VG 4.0	FN 6.0	VF 8.0	VF/NM 9.0	NM- 9.2
1-6-Carmen Machado-s/Dani-a						4.00

LT. (See Lieutenant)

LUCAS STAND
BOOM! Studios: Jun, 2016 - No. 6, Nov, 2016 ($3.99, limited series)

	GD 2.0	VG 4.0	FN 6.0	VF 8.0	VF/NM 9.0	NM- 9.2
1-6-Kurt Sutter & Caitlin Kittredge-s/Jesús Hervás-a. 1-Multiple covers						4.00

LUCAS STAND: INNER DEMONS
BOOM! Studios: Feb, 2018 - No. 4, May, 2018 ($3.99, limited series)

	GD 2.0	VG 4.0	FN 6.0	VF 8.0	VF/NM 9.0	NM- 9.2
1-4-Kurt Sutter & Caitlin Kittredge-s/Jesús Hervás-a						4.00

LUCIFER (See The Sandman #4)
DC Comics (Vertigo): Jun, 2000 - No. 75, Aug, 2006 ($2.50/$2.75)

	GD 2.0	VG 4.0	FN 6.0	VF 8.0	VF/NM 9.0	NM- 9.2
1-Carey-s/Weston-a/Fegredo-c	4	8	12	28	47	65
2,3-Carey-s/Weston-a/Fegredo-c	1	3	4	6	8	10
4-10: 4-Pleece-a. 5-Gross-a						4.00
11-49,51-73: 16-Moeller-c begin. 25,26-Death app. 45-Naifeh-a. 53-Kaluta-c begin. 62-Doran-a. 63-Begin $2.75-c						3.00
50-($3.50) P. Craig Russell-a; Mazikeen app.						4.00
74-($2.99) Kaluta-c						3.00
75-($3.99) Last issue; Lucifer's origins retold; Morpheus app.; Gross-a/Moeller-c						4.00
Preview-16 pg. flip book w/Swamp Thing Preview						3.00
Vertigo Essentials: Lucifer #1 Special Edition (3/16, $1.00) Flipbook with GN promos						3.00
...: A Dalliance With the Damned TPB ('02, $14.95) r/#14-20						15.00
...: Children and Monsters TPB ('01, $17.95) r/#5-13						18.00
...: Crux TPB (2006, $14.99) r/#55-61						15.00
...: Devil in the Gateway TPB ('01, $14.95) r/#1-4 & Sandman Presents:..#1-3						15.00
...: Evensong TPB (2007, $14.99) r/#70-75 & Lucifer: Nirvana one-shot						15.00
...: Exodus TPB (2005, $14.95) r/#42-44,46-49						15.00
...: Inferno TPB (2003, $14.95) r/#29-35						15.00
...: Mansions of the Silence TPB (2004, $14.95) r/#36-41						15.00
...: Morningstar TPB (2006, $14.99) r/#62-69						15.00
...: Nirvana (2002, $5.95) Carey-s/Muth-painted-c/a; Daniel app.						6.00
...: The Divine Comedy TPB (2003, $17.95) r/#21-28						18.00
...: The Wolf Beneath the Tree TPB (2005, $14.99) r/#45,50-54						15.00

LUCIFER (See The Sandman #4)
DC Comics (Vertigo): Feb, 2016 - No. 19, Aug, 2017 ($3.99)

	GD 2.0	VG 4.0	FN 6.0	VF 8.0	VF/NM 9.0	NM- 9.2
1-19: 1-Holly Black-s/Lee Garbett-a/Dave Johnson-c. 6-Stephanie Hans-a						4.00

LUCIFER (The Sandman Universe)
DC Comics (Vertigo): Dec, 2018 - No. 18, May, 2020 ($3.99)

	GD 2.0	VG 4.0	FN 6.0	VF 8.0	VF/NM 9.0	NM- 9.2
1-18: 1-Dan Watters-s/Max & Sebastian Fiumara-a/Jock-c. 9-Kelley Jones-a						4.00

LUCIFER'S HAMMER (Larry Niven & Jerry Pournelle's...)
Innovation Publishing: Nov, 1993 - No. 6, 1994 ($2.50, painted, limited series)

	GD 2.0	VG 4.0	FN 6.0	VF 8.0	VF/NM 9.0	NM- 9.2
1-6: Adaptatin of novel, painted-c & art						3.00

LUCKY COMICS
Consolidated Magazines: Jan, 1944; No. 2, Sum, 1945 - No. 5, Sum, 1946

	GD 2.0	VG 4.0	FN 6.0	VF 8.0	VF/NM 9.0	NM- 9.2
1-Lucky Starr & Bobbie begin	52	104	156	328	552	775
2-4	30	60	90	177	289	400
5-Devil-c by Walter Johnson	39	78	117	240	395	550

LUCKY DEVIL
Dark Horse Comics: Aug, 2021 - No. 4, Nov, 2021 ($3.99, limited series)

	GD 2.0	VG 4.0	FN 6.0	VF 8.0	VF/NM 9.0	NM- 9.2
1-4-Cullen Bunn-s/Fran Galán-a						4.00

LUCKY DUCK
Standard Comics (Literary Ent.): No. 5, Jan, 1953 - No. 8, Sept, 1953

	GD 2.0	VG 4.0	FN 6.0	VF 8.0	VF/NM 9.0	NM- 9.2
5-Funny animal; Irving Spector-a	15	30	45	83	124	165
6-8-Irving Spector-a	12	24	36	69	97	125

NOTE: *Harvey Kurtzman tried to hire Spector for Mad #1.*

LUCKY "7" COMICS
Howard Publishers Ltd.: 1944 (No date listed)

	GD	VG	FN	VF	VF/NM	NM-
	2.0	4.0	6.0	8.0	9.0	9.2

1-Pioneer, Sir Gallagher, Dick Royce, Congo Raider, Punch Powers; bondage-c
68 136 204 435 743 1050

LUCKY STAR (Western)
Nation Wide Publ. Co.: 1950 - No. 7, 1951; No. 8, 1953 - No. 14, 1955 (5x7-1/4"; full color, 5¢)
nn (#1)-(5¢, 52 pgs.)-Davis-a 20 40 60 120 195 270
2,3-(5¢, 52 pgs.)-Davis-a 14 28 42 80 115 150
4-7-(5¢, 52 pgs.)-Davis-a 14 28 42 76 108 140
Given away with Lucky Star Western Wear by the Juvenile Mfg. Co. (SanTone)
7 14 21 35 43 50

LUCY CLAIRE: REDEMPTION
Image Comics: Dec, 2019 - Present ($3.99)
1-4-John Upchurch-s/a 4.00

LUCY SHOW, THE (TV) (Also see I Love Lucy)
Gold Key: June, 1963 - No. 5, June, 1964 (Photo-c: 1,2)
1 12 24 36 81 176 270
2 6 12 18 41 76 110
3-5: Photo back c-1,2,4,5 6 12 18 37 66 95

LUCY, THE REAL GONE GAL (Meet Miss Pepper #5 on)
St. John Publishing Co.: June, 1953 - No. 4, Dec, 1953
1-Negligee panels 41 82 123 256 428 600
2 22 44 66 128 209 290
3,4: 3-Drucker-a 21 42 63 122 199 275

LUDOCRATS, THE
Image Comics: Apr, 2020 - Present ($3.99)
1-5-Kieron Gillen & Jim Rossignol-s/Jeff Stokely-a 4.00

LUDWIG BEMELMAN'S MADELEINE & GENEVIEVE
Dell Publishing Co.: No. 796, May, 1957
Four Color 796 5 10 15 35 63 90

LUDWIG VON DRAKE (TV)(Disney)(See Walt Disney's C&S #256)
Dell Publishing Co.: Nov-Dec, 1961 - No. 4, June-Aug, 1962
1 6 12 18 38 69 100
2-4 5 10 15 30 50 70

LUFTWAFFE: 1946 (Volume 1)
Antarctic Press: July, 1996 - No. 4, Jan, 1997 ($2.95, B&W, limited series)
1-4-Ben Dunn & Ted Nomura-s/a, ...Special Ed. 3.00

LUFTWAFFE: 1946 (Volume 2)
Antarctic Press: Mar, 1997 - No. 18 ($2.95/$2.99, B&W, limited series)
1-18: 8-Reviews Tigers of Terra series 3.00
Annual 1 (4/98, $2.95)-Reprints early Nomura pages 4.00
...Color Special (4/98) 3.00
...Technical Manual 1,2 (2/98, 4/99) 4.00

LUGER
Eclipse Comics: Oct, 1986 - No. 3, Feb, 1987 ($1.75, miniseries, Baxter paper)
1-3: Bruce Jones scripts; Yeates-c/a 3.00

LUKE CAGE (Also see Cage & Hero for Hire)
Marvel Comics: Jul, 2017 - No. 5, Nov, 2017; No. 166, Dec, 2017 - No. 170, Apr, 2018 ($3.99)
1-5-Walker-s/Blake-a; Warhawk app. 4.00
[Title switches to legacy numbering after #5 (11/17)]
166-170: 166-Sanna-a; The Ringmaster app.; bonus origin re-cap w/Bagley-a 4.00

LUKE CAGE NOIR
Marvel Comics: Oct, 2009 - No. 4, Jan, 2010 ($3.99, limited series)
1-4-Glass & Benson-a/Martinbrough-a; covers by Bradstreet and Calero 4.00

LUKE SHORT'S WESTERN STORIES
Dell Publishing Co.: No. 580, Aug, 1954 - No. 927, Aug, 1958
Four Color 580(8/54), 651(9/55)-Kinstler-a 5 10 15 34 60 85
Four Color 739,771,807,848,875,927 5 10 15 30 50 70

LUMBERJANES
BOOM! Box: Apr, 2014 - Present ($3.99/$6.99)
1-Noelle Stevenson & Grace Ellis-s/Brooke Allen-a; multiple covers 10.00
2 6.00
3-24,26-49,51-72 4.00
25-($4.99) Two covers by Allen & Wiedle; preview of Lumberjanes/Gotham Academy 5.00
50-($4.99) Four covers by Leyh and Fish 5.00
73-75-($6.99) 7.00
...: A Midsummer Night's Scheme 1 (8/18, $7.99) Andelfinger-s/Gonzalez-a 8.00
...: Beyond Bay Leaf (10/15, $4.99) Faith Erin Hicks-s/Rosemary Valero-O'Connell-a 5.00
...: End of Summer (12/20, $6.99) Watters & Leyh-s/Bosy & Bryant-a 7.00
...: Faire and Square 2017 Special 1 (6/17, $7.99) Black-s/Julia-a; 3 covers 8.00
...: Making the Ghost of It 2016 Special 1 (5/16, $7.99) Wang-s/Norrie-a; Ganucheau-a 8.00
...: Somewhere That's Green 1 (5/19, $7.99) McGuire-s/Bosy-a 8.00
...: The Shape of Friendship GN (11/19, $14.99, SC) Lilah Sturges-s/Polterink-a 15.00
...: The Shape of Friendship Free Comic Book Day Special 2019 (5/19, giveaway) 3.00

LUMBERJANES / GOTHAM ACADEMY
BOOM! Box: Jun, 2016 - No. 6, Nov, 2016 ($3.99)
1-6: 1-Chynna Clugston Flores-s/Rosemary Valero-O'Connell-a; multiple covers 4.00

LUNA
BOOM! Studios: Feb, 2021 - No. 5, Jun, 2021 ($3.99, limited series)
1-5-Maria Llovet-s/a 4.00

LUNA MOON-HUNTER
WaterWalker Studios: Jul, 2012 - No. 2, Aug, 2012 ($5.95, limited series)
1,2-Rob Hughes-s/Jeff Slemons-a. 1-Posada-c. 2-Buzz-c 6.00
SC-($24.95, 180 pgs.) Painted-c by Buzz & Parrillo; art by Slemons, Buzz & LaRocque 25.00
HC-($49.95, limited edition of 1000) Signed by Hughes & Slemons; 2 bonus articles 50.00

LUNATIC FRINGE, THE
Innovation Publishing: July, 1989 - No. 2, 1989 ($1.75, deluxe format)
1,2 3.00

LUNATICKLE (Magazine) (Satire)
Whitstone Publ.: Feb, 1956 - No. 2, Apr, 1956
1,2-Kubert-a (scarce) 10 20 30 56 76 90

LUNATIK
Marvel Comics: Dec, 1995 - No. 3, Feb, 1996 ($1.95, limited series)
1-3 3.00

LURKERS, THE
IDW Publ.: Oct, 2004 - No. 4, Jan, 2005 ($3.99)
1-4-Niles-s/Casanova-a 4.00

LUST FOR LIFE
Slave Labor Graphics: Feb, 1997 - No. 4, Jan, 1998 ($2.95, B&W)
1-4: 1-Jeff Levin-s/a 3.00

LUTHOR (See Lex Luthor: Man of Steel)

LYCANTHROPE LEO
Viz Communications: 1994 - No. 7($2.95, B&W, limited series, 44 pgs.)
1-7 4.00

LYNCH (See Gen 13)
Image Comics (WildStorm Productions): May, 1997 ($2.50, one-shot)
1-Helmut-c/app. 3.00

LYNCH MOB
Chaos! Comics: June, 1994 - No. 4, Sept, 1994 ($2.50, limited series)
1-4 5.00
1-Special edition full foil-c 1 2 3 5 6 8

LYNDON B. JOHNSON
Dell Publishing Co.: Mar, 1965
12-445-503-Photo-c 4 8 12 23 37 50

M
Eclipse Books: 1990 - No. 4, 1991 ($4.95, painted, 52 pgs.)
1-Adapts movie; contains flexi-disc ($5.95) 6.00
2-4 5.00

MACE GRIFFIN BOUNTY HUNTER (Based on video game)
Image Comics (Top Cow): May, 2003 ($2.99, one-shot)
1-Nocon-a 3.00

MACGYVER: FUGITIVE GAUNTLET (Based on TV series)
Image Comics: Oct, 2012 - No. 5, Feb, 2013 ($3.50, limited series)
1-5-Lee Zlotoff & Tony Lee-s/Will Sliney-a 3.50

MACHETE (Based on the Robert Rodriguez movie)
IDW Publishing: No. 0, Sept, 2010 ($3.99)
0-Origin story; Rodriguez & Kaufman-s/Sayger-a; 3 covers 4.00

MACHINE, THE
Dark Horse Comics: Nov, 1994 - No. 4, Feb, 1995 ($2.50, limited series)
1-4 3.00

MACHINE GUN WIZARDS (See Tommy Gun Wizards)

MACHINE MAN (Also see 2001, A Space Odyssey)
Marvel Comics Group: Apr, 1978 - No. 9, Dec, 1978; No. 10, Aug, 1979 - No. 19, Feb, 1981
1-Jack Kirby-c/a/scripts begin; end #9 3 6 9 21 33 46
2-9-Kirby-c/a/s. 9-(12/78) 2 4 6 9 12 15
10-17: 10-(8/79) Marv Wolfman scripts & Ditko-a begins
1 3 4 6 8 10
18-Wendigo, Alpha Flight-ties into X-Men #140 3 6 9 17 26 35
19-Intro/1st app. Jack O'Lantern (Macendale), later becomes 2nd Hobgoblin
5 10 15 30 50 70
NOTE: *Austin c-7i, 19i. **Buckler** c-17p, 18p. **Byrne** c-14p. **Ditko** a-10-19; c-10-13, 14i, 15, 16. **Kirby** a-1-9p; c-1-5, 7-9p. **Layton** c-7i. **Miller** c-19p. **Simonson** c-6.*

MACHINE MAN (Also see X-51)
Marvel Comics Group: Oct, 1984 - No. 4, Jan, 1985 (limited series)
1-4-Barry Smith-c/a(i) & colors in all; Jocasta app. 1-3-Trimpe-a(p). 2-1st app. Arno Stark (Iron Man 2020) 5.00
TPB (1988, $6.95) r/ #1-4; Barry Smith-c 10.00
.../Bastion '98 Annual ($2.99) wraparound-c 4.00

MACHINE MAN 2020 (Also see 2020 Machine Man)
Marvel Comics: Aug, 1994 - No. 2, Sept, 1994 ($2.00, 52 pgs., limited series)
1,2: Reprints Machine Man limited series; Barry Windsor-Smith-c/i(r) 4.00

MACHINE TEEN
Marvel Comics: July, 2005 - No. 5, Nov, 2005 ($2.99, limited series)
1-5-Sumerak-s/Hawthorne-a. 1-James Jean-c 3.00
...: History (2005, $7.99, digest) r/#1-5 8.00

MACK BOLAN: THE EXECUTIONER (Don Pendleton's...)
Innovation Publishing: July, 1993 ($2.50)
1-3-($2.50) 3.00
1-($3.95)-Indestructible Cover Edition 4.00
1-($2.95)-Collector's Gold Edition; foil stamped 4.00
1-($3.50)-Double Cover Edition; red foil outer-c 4.00

MACKENZIE'S RAIDERS (Movie, TV)
Dell Publishing Co.: No. 1093, Apr-June, 1960
Four Color 1093-Richard Carlson photo-c from TV show
6 12 18 40 73 105

MACROSS (Becomes Robotech: The Macross Saga #2 on)
Comico: Dec, 1984 ($1.50)(Low print run)
1-Early manga app. 6 12 18 38 69 100

MACROSS II
Viz Select Comics: 1992 - No. 10, 1993 ($2.75, B&W, limited series)

Luna #5 © Maria Llovet

Machine Man #14 © MAR

Mad #9 © WMG

GD 2.0 | VG 4.0 | FN 6.0 | VF 8.0 | VF/NM 9.0 | NM- 9.2

1-10: Based on video series 4.00

MAD (Tales Calculated to Drive You...)
E. C. Comics (Educational Comics): Oct-Nov, 1952 - No. 550, Apr, 2018
(No. 24-on are magazine format) (Kurtzman editor No. 1-28, Feldstein No. 29 - No. ?)

1-Wood, Davis, Elder start as regulars 514 1028 1542 4112 6556 9000
2-Dick Tracy cameo 117 234 351 936 1493 2050
3,4: 3-Stan Lee mentioned. 4-Reefer mention story "Flob Was a Slob" by Davis; Superman parody 89 178 267 712 1131 1550
5-W.M. Gaines biog. 183 366 549 1464 2332 3200
6-11: 6-Popeye cameo. 7,8- "Hey Look" reprints by Kurtzman. 11-Wolverton-a; Davis story was-r/Crime Suspenstories #12 w/new Kurtzman dialogue 63 126 189 504 802 1100
12-15: 12-Archie parody. 15,18-Pot Shot Pete-r by Kurtzman 50 100 150 400 638 875
16-23(5/55): 18-Alice in Wonderland by Jack Davis. 21-1st app. Alfred E. Neuman on-c in fake ad. 22-All by Elder plus photo-montages by Kurtzman. 23-Special cancel announcement 41 82 123 328 527 725
24(7/55)-1st magazine issue (25¢); Kurtzman logo & border on-c; 1st "What? Me Worry?" on-c; 2nd printing exists 94 188 282 752 1201 1650
25-Jaffee starts as regular writer 44 88 132 352 564 775
26,27: 27-Jaffee starts as story artist; new logo 39 78 117 312 499 685
28-Last issue edited by Kurtzman; (three cover variations exist with different wording on contents banner on lower right of cover; value of each the same) 39 78 117 240 395 550
29-Kamen-a; Don Martin starts as regular; Feldstein editing begins 36 72 108 216 351 485
30-1st A. E. Neuman cover by Mingo; last Elder-a; Bob Clarke starts as regular; Disneyland & Elvis Presley spoof 57 114 171 362 619 875
31-Freas starts as regular; last Davis-a until #99 34 68 102 204 332 460
32,33: 32-Orlando, Drucker, Woodbridge start as regulars; Wood back-c. 33-Orlando back-c 27 54 81 162 266 370
34-Berg starts as regular 22 44 66 132 216 300
35-Mingo wraparound-c; Crandall-a 22 44 66 132 216 300
36-40 (7/58): 39-Beall-c 18 36 54 105 165 225
41-50: 42-Danny Kaye-s. 44-Xmas-c. 47-49-Sid Caesar-s. 48-Uncle Sam-c. 50 (10/59)-Peter Gunn-s 15 30 45 90 140 190
51-59: 52-Xmas-c; 77 Sunset Strip. 53-Rifleman-s. 54-Jaffee-a begins. 55-Sid Caesar-s. 59-Strips of Superman, Flash Gordon, Donald Duck & others. 59-Halloween/Headless Horseman-c 14 28 42 80 115 150
60 (1/61)-JFK/Nixon flip-c; 1st Spy vs. Spy by Prohias, who starts as regular 15 30 45 94 147 200
61-70: 64-Rickard starts as regular. 65-JFK-s. 66-JFK-c. 68-Xmas-c by Martin. 70-Route 66-s 6 12 18 41 76 110
71-75,77-80 (7/63): 72-10th Anniv. special; 1/3 pg. strips of Superman, Tarzan & others. 73-Bonanza-s. 74-Dr. Kildare-s 5 10 15 31 53 75
76-Aragonés starts as regular 6 12 18 37 66 95
81-85: 81-Superman strip. 82-Castro-c. 85-Lincoln-c 4 8 12 28 47 65
86-1st Fold-in; commonly creased back covers makes these and later issues scarcer in NM 5 10 15 34 60 85
87,88 5 10 15 31 53 75
89,90: 89-One strip by Walt Kelly; Frankenstein-c; Fugitive-s. 90-Ringo back-c by Frazetta; Beatles app. 5 10 15 34 60 85
91,94,96,100: 94-King Kong-c. 96-Man From U.N.C.L.E. 100-(1/66)-Anniversary issue 4 8 12 28 47 65
92,93,95,97-99: 99-Davis-a resumes 4 8 12 27 44 60
101,104,106,108,114,115,119,121: 101-Infinity-c; Voyage to the Bottom of the Sea-s. 104-Lost in Space-s. 106-Tarzan back-c by Frazetta; 2 pg. Batman by Aragonés. 108-Hogan's Heroes by Davis. 114-Rat Patrol-s. 115-Star Trek. 119-Invaders (TV). 121-Beatles-c; Ringo pin-up; flip-c of Sik-Teen; Flying Nun-s 3 6 9 20 31 42
102,103,107,109-113,116-118,120(7/68): 118-Beatles cameo 3 6 9 18 28 38
105-Batman-c/s, TV show parody (9/66) 5 10 15 34 60 85
122,124,126,128,129,131-134,136,137,139,140: 122-Ronald Reagan photo inside; Drucker & Mingo-c. 126-Family Affair-s. 128-Last Orlando. 131-Reagan photo back-c. 132-Xmas-c. 133-John Wayne/True Grit. 136-Room 222 3 6 9 15 22 28
123-Four different covers 3 6 9 16 24 32
125,127,130,135,138: 125-2001 Space Odyssey; Hitler back-c. 127-Mod Squad-c/s. 130-Land of the Giants-s; Torres begins as reg. 135-Easy Rider-c by Davis. 138-Snoopy-c; MASH-s 3 6 9 16 24 32
141-149,151-156,158-165,167-170: 141-Hawaii Five-0. 147-All in the Family-s. 153-Dirty Harry-s. 155-Godfather-c/s. 156-Columbo-s. 159-Clockwork Orange-c/s. 161-Tarzan-s. 164-Kung Fu (TV)-s. 165-James Bond-s; Dean Martin-c. 169-Drucker-c; McCloud-s. 170-Exorcist-s 3 6 9 14 19 24
150-(4/72) Partridge Family-s 3 6 9 15 21 26
157-(3/73) Planet of the Apes-c/s 3 6 9 16 23 30
166-(4/74) Classic finger-c 3 6 9 17 26 35
171-185,187,189-192,194,195,198,199: 172-Six Million Dollar Man-s; Hitler back-c. 178-Godfather II-c/s. 180-Jaws-c/s (1/76). 182-Bob Jones starts as regular. 185-Starsky & Hutch-s. 187-Fonz/Happy Days-c/s; Harry North starts as regular. 189-Travolta/Kotter-c/s. 190-John Wayne-c/s. 192-King Kong-c/s. 194-Rocky-c/s; Laverne & Shirley-s. 199-James Bond-s 2 4 6 10 14 18
186,188,197,200: 186-Star Trek-c/s. 188-Six Million Dollar Man/ Bionic Woman. 197-Spock-s; Star Wars-s. 200-Close Encounters 3 6 9 14 20 25
193,196: 193-Farrah/Charlie's Angels-c/s. 196-Star Wars-c/s 3 6 9 16 23 30
201,203,205,220: 201-Sat. Night Fever-c/s. 203-Star Wars. 205-Travolta/Grease. 220-Yoda-c, Empire Strikes Back-s 2 4 6 9 13 16
202,204,206,207,209,211-219,221-227,229,230: 204-Hulk TV show. 206-Tarzan. 208-Superman movie. 209-Mork & Mindy. 212-Spider-Man-s; Alien (movie)-s. 213-James Bond, Dracula, Rocky II-s 216-Star Trek. 219-Martin-c. 221-Shining-s. 223-Dallas-c/s. 225-Popeye. 226-Superman II. 229-James Bond. 230-Star Wars 1 3 4 6 8 10
208,228: 208-Superman movie-c/s; Battlestar Galactica-s. 228-Raiders of the Lost Ark-c/s 2 4 6 10 14 18
210-Lord of the Rings 2 4 6 10 14 18
231-235,237-241,243-249,251-260: 233-Pac-Man-c. 234-MASH-c/s. 235-Flip-c with Rocky III & Conan; Boris-a. 239-Mickey Mouse-c. 241-Knight Rider-s. 243-Superman III. 245- Last Rickard-a. 247-Seven Dwarfs-c. 253-Supergirl movie-s; Prince/Purple Rain-s. 254-Rock stars-s. 255-Reagan-c; Cosby-s. 256-Last issue edited by Feldstein; Dynasty, Bev. Hills Cop. 259-Rambo. 260-Back to the Future-c/s; Honeymooners-s 1 2 3 5 6 8
236,242,250: 236-E.T.-c/s;Star Trek II-s. 242-Star Wars/A-Team-c/s. 250-Temple of Doom-c/s; Tarzan-s 1 2 3 5 7 9
261-267,269-276,278-288,290-297: 261-Miami Vice. 262-Rocky IV-c/s, Leave It To Beaver-s. 263-Young Sherlock Holmes-s. 264-Hulk Hogan-c; Rambo-s. 267-Top Gun. 271-Star Trek IV-c/s. 272-ALF-c; Get Smart-s. 273-Pee Wee Herman-c/s. 274-Last Martin-a. 281-California Raisins-c. 282-Star Trek:TNG-s; ALF-s. 283-Rambo III-c/s. 284-Roger Rabbit-c/s. 285-Hulk Hogan-c. 287-3 pgs. Eisner-a. 291-TMNT-c; Indiana Jones-s. 292-Super Mario Bros.-c; Married with Children-s. 295-Back to the Future II. 297-Mike Tyson-c 1 2 3 4 5 7
268,277,289,298-300: 268-Aliens-c/s. 277-Michael Jackson-c/s; Robocop-s. 289-Batman movie parody. 298-Gremlins II-c/s; Robocop II. Batman-s. 299-Simpsons-c/story; Total Recall-s. 300(1/91) Casablanca-s, Dick Tracy-s, Wizard of Oz-s, Gone With The Wind-s 1 2 3 5 6 8
300-303 (1/91-6/91)-Special Hussein Asylum Editions; only distributed to the troops in the Middle East (see Mad Super Spec.) 3 6 9 16 23 30
301-310,312,313,315-320,322,324,326-334,337-349: 303-Home Alone-c/s. 305-Simpsons-s. 306-TMNT II movie. 308-Terminator II. 315-Tribute to William Gaines. 316-Photo-c. 319-Dracula-c/s. 320-Disney's Aladdin-s. 322-Batman Animated series. 327-Seinfeld-s; X-Men-s. 331-Flintstones-c/s. 332-O.J. Simpson-c/s; Simpsons app. in Lion King. 334-Frankenstein-c/s. 338-Judge Dredd-c by Frazetta. 341-Pocahontas-s. 345-Beatles app. (1 pg.) 347-Broken Arrow & Mission Impossible 5.00
311,314,321,323,325,335,336,350,354,358: 311-Addams Family-c/story, Home Improvement-s. 314-Batman Returns-c/story. 321-Star Trek DS9-c/s. 323-Jurassic Park-c/s. 325,336-Beavis & Butthead-c/s. 335-X-Files-s; Pulp Fiction-s; Interview with the Vampire-s. 336-Lois & Clark-s. 350-Polybagged w/CD Rom. 354-Star Wars; Beavis & Butthead-s. 358-X-Files 6.00
351-353,355-357,359-500 5.00
501-550-($5.99) 6.00
Mad About Super Heroes (2002, $9.95) r/super hero app.; Alex Ross-c 10.00

NOTE: ***Aragones*** *c-210, 293.* ***Beall*** *c-39.* ***Davis*** *c-2, 27, 135, 139, 173, 178, 212, 213, 219, 246, 260, 296, 308.* ***Drucker*** *a-35-62; c-122, 169, 176, 225, 234, 264, 266, 274, 280, 285, 297, 299, 303, 314, 315, 321.* ***Elder*** *c-5, 259, 261, 268.* ***Elder/Kurtzman*** *a-258-274.* ***Jules Feiffer*** *a(r)-42.* ***Freas*** *c-40-59, 62-67, 69-70, 72, 74.* ***Heath*** *a-14, 27.* ***Jaffee*** *c-199, 217, 224, 258.* ***Kamen*** *a-29.* ***Krigstein*** *a-12, 17, 24, 26.* ***Kurtzman*** *c-1, 3, 4, 6-10, 13, 16, 18.* ***Martin*** *a-29-62; c-68, 165, 229.* ***Mingo*** *c-30-37, 61, 71, 75-80, 82-114, 117-124, 126, 129, 131, 133, 134, 136, 140, 143-148, 150-162, 164, 166-168, 171, 172, 174, 175, 177, 179, 181, 183, 185, 198, 206, 209, 211, 214, 218, 221, 222, 300.* ***John Severin*** *a-1-6, 9, 10.* ***Wolverton*** *c-11; a-11, 17, 29, 31, 36, 40, 82, 137.* ***Wood*** *a-1-21, 23-62; c-26, 28, 29.* ***Woodbridge*** *a-35-62. Issues 1-23 are 36 pgs.; 24-28 are 58 pgs.; 29 on are 52 pgs.*

MAD (See Mad Follies, ...Special, More Trash from..., and The Worst from...)

MAD ABOUT MILLIE (Also see Millie the Model)
Marvel Comics Group: April, 1969 - No. 16, Nov, 1970

1-Giant issue 11 22 33 76 163 250
2,3 (Giants) 7 14 21 48 89 130
4-10 5 10 15 35 63 90
11-16: 16-r 5 10 15 34 60 85
Annual 1(11/71, 52 pgs.) 6 12 18 41 76 110

MADAME FRANKENSTEIN
Image Comics: May, 2014 - No. 7, Nov, 2014 ($2.99, B&W, limited series)

1-7-Jamie Rich-s/Megan Levens-a/Joëlle Jones-c. 1-Variant-c by Mittens 3.00

GD 2.0 | VG 4.0 | FN 6.0 | VF 8.0 | VF/NM 9.0 | NM- 9.2

MADAME MIRAGE
Image Comics (Top Cow): June, 2007 - No. 6, May, 2008 ($2.99)

1-6: 1-Paul Dini-s/Kenneth Rocafort-a; two covers by Horn and Rocafort 3.00
... First Look (5/07, 99¢) preview of series; Dini interview; cover gallery 3.00
Volume 1 TPB (7/08, $14.99) r/#1-6; cover gallery; cover and design sketches 15.00

MADAME XANADU
DC Comics: July, 1981 ($1.00, no ads, 36 pgs.)

1-Marshall Rogers-a (25 pgs.); Kaluta-c/a (2pgs.); pin-up
2 4 6 10 14 18

MADAME XANADU (Also see Doorway to Nightmare)
DC Comics (Vertigo): Aug, 2008 - No. 29, Jan, 2011 ($2.99)

1-Matt Wagner-s/Amy Reeder Hadley-a/c; Phantom Stranger app. 4.00
1,2-Variant covers. 1-Wagner. 2-Kaluta 5.00
2-29: 2-10-Amy Reeder Hadley-a/c; Phantom Stranger app. 6-Death (from The Sandman) app.; covers by Hadley & Quitely. 9-Zatara app. 10-Jim Corrigan becomes The Spectre. 11-15-Kaluta-a. 14,15-Sandman (Wesley Dodds) app. 16-18-Hadley-a; Det. Jones app. 3.00
...: Broken House of Cards TPB (2011, $17.99) r/#16-23 and story from House of Mystery Halloween Annual #1 18.00
...: Disenchanted TPB (2009, $12.99) r/#1-10; James Robinson intro.; Hadley sketch-a 13.00
...: Exodus TPB (2010, $12.99) r/#11-15; Chris Roberson intro. 13.00
...: Extra-Sensory TPB (2011, $17.99) r/#24-29 18.00

MADAM SATAN (From Chilling Adventures of Sabrina)
Archie Comics: Dec, 2020 ($3.99, one-shot)

1-Eliot Rahal-s/Julius Ohta-a; Madam Satan before becoming Greendale High principal 4.00

MADBALLS
Star Comics/Marvel Comics #9 on: Sept, 1986 - No. 3, Nov, 1986; No. 4, June, 1987 - No. 10, June, 1988

1-10: Based on toys. 9-Post-a 5.00

MADBALLS VS. GARBAGE PAIL KIDS
Dynamite Entertainment: 2022 - No. 4, 2022 ($3.99, limited series)

1-4-Sholly Fisch-s/Jason Crosby-a 4.00

MADBALLS VS. GARBAGE PAIL KIDS: TIME AGAIN, SLIME AGAIN
Dynamite Entertainment: 2023 - Present ($3.99, limited series)

1-Sholly Fisch-s/Jason Crosby-a 4.00

MAD DISCO
E.C. Comics: 1980 (one-shot, 36 pgs.)

1-Includes 30 minute flexi-disc of Mad disco music 3 6 9 14 19 24

MAD-DOG
Marvel Comics: May, 1993 - No. 6, Oct, 1993 ($1.25)

1-6-Flip book w/2nd story "created" by Bob Newhart's character from his TV show "Bob" set at a comic book company; actual s/a-Ty Templeton 3.00

MAD DOGS
Eclipse Comics: Feb, 1992 - No. 3, July, 1992 ($2.50, B&W, limited series)

1-3 3.00

MAD 84 (Mad Extra)
E.C. Comics: 1984 (84 pgs.)

1 1 3 4 6 8 10

MADE IN KOREA
Image Comics: May, 2021 - No. 6, Dec, 2021 ($3.99, limited series)

1-6-Jeremy Holt-s/George Schall-a 4.00

MAD FOLLIES (Special)
E. C. Comics: 1963 - No. 7, 1969

nn(1963)-Paperback book covers 21 42 63 147 324 500
2(1964)-Calendar 16 32 48 107 236 365
3(1965)-Mischief Stickers 11 22 33 76 163 250
4(1966)-Mobile; Frazetta-r/back-c Mad #90 9 18 27 57 111 165
5,6: 5(1967)-Stencils. 6(1968)-Mischief Stickers 7 14 21 44 82 120
7(1969)-Nasty Cards 7 14 21 44 82 120
(If bonus is missing, issue is half price)
NOTE: *Clarke c-4. **Frazetta** r-4, 6 (1 pg. ea.). **Mingo** c-1-3. **Orlando** a-5.*

MAD HATTER, THE (Costumed Hero)
O. W. Comics Corp.: Jan-Feb, 1946; No. 2, Sept-Oct, 1946

1-Freddy the Firefly begins; Giunta-c/a 81 162 243 518 884 1250
2-Has ad for E.C.'s Animal Fables #1 47 94 141 296 498 700

MADHOUSE
Ajax/Farrell Publ. (Excellent Publ./4-Star): 3-4/54 - No. 4, 9-10/54; 6/57 - No. 4, Dec?, 1957

1(1954) 42 84 126 265 445 625
2,3 24 48 72 142 234 325
4-Surrealistic-c 33 66 99 194 317 440
1(1957, 2nd series) 19 38 57 111 176 240
2-4 (#4 exist?) 14 28 42 76 108 140

MAD HOUSE (Formerly Madhouse Glads; ...Comics #104? on)
Red Circle Productions/Archie Publications: No. 95, 9/74 - No. 97, 1/75; No. 98, 8/75 - No. 130, 10/82

95,96-Horror stories through #97; Morrow-c 3 6 9 14 19 24
97-Intro. Henry Hobson; Morrow-a/c, Thorne-a 2 4 6 10 16 20
98,99,101-120-Satire/humor stories. 110-Sabrina app.,1pg.
2 4 6 8 10 12
100 2 4 6 8 11 14
121-129 2 4 6 8 11 14
130 2 4 6 10 14 18
Annual 8(1970-71)-Formerly Madhouse Ma-ad Annual; Sabrina app. (6 pgs.)
4 8 12 28 47 65
Annual 9-12(1974-75): 11-Wood-a(r) 3 6 9 15 22 28
...Comics Digest 1('75-76) r/1st & 2nd Sabrina app. 2 4 6 11 16 20
2-8(8/82)(...Mag. #5 on)-Sabrina in many 2 4 6 9 13 16
NOTE: *B. Jones a-96. McWilliams a-97. Wildey a-95, 96. See Archie Comics Digest #1, 13.*

MADHOUSE GLADS (Formerly ...Ma-ad; Madhouse #95 on)
Archie Publ.: No. 73, May, 1970 - No. 94, Aug, 1974 (No. 78-92: 52 pgs.)

73-77,93,94: 74-1 pg. Sabrina 2 4 6 9 13 16
78-92 (52 pgs.) 2 4 6 11 16 20

MADHOUSE MA-AD (...Jokes #67-70; ...Freak-Out #71-74)
(Formerly Archie's Madhouse) (Becomes Madhouse Glads #73 on)
Archie Publications: No. 67, April, 1969 - No. 72, Jan, 1970

67-71: 70-1 pg. Sabrina 3 6 9 16 23 30
72-6 pgs. Sabrina 4 8 12 28 47 65
...Annual 7(1969-70)-Formerly Archie's Madhouse Annual; becomes Madhouse Annual; 6 pgs. Sabrina 5 10 15 30 50 70

MADMAN (See Creatures of the Id #1)
Tundra Publishing: Mar, 1992 - No. 3, 1992 ($3.95, duotone, high quality, lim. series, 52 pgs.)

1-Mike Allred-c/a in all 2 4 6 9 13 16
1-2nd printing 4.00
2,3 6.00

MADMAN ADVENTURES
Tundra Publishing: 1992 - No. 3, 1993 ($2.95, limited series)

1-Mike Allred-c/a in all 1 3 4 6 8 10
2,3 5.00
TPB (Oni Press, 2002, $14.95) r/#1-3 & first app. of Frank Einstein from Creatures of the Id in color; gallery pages 15.00

MADMAN ATOMIC COMICS (Also see The Atomics)
Image Comics: Apr, 2007 - No. 17, Sept, 2009 ($2.99/$3.50)

1-12-Mike Allred-s/c/a. 1-Origin re-told; pin-ups by Rivoche and Powell. 3-Sale back-c 3.50
13-17-($3.50) Wraparound-c. 14-Back up w/Darwyn Cooke-a 3.50
All-New Giant-Size Super Ginchy Special (4/11, $5.99) Allred-s/a; back-ups/pin-ups 6.00
Madman In Your Face 3D Special (11/14, $9.99) Classic stories converted to 3D plus a new short story by Mike Allred and pin-ups by various; glasses included 10.00
... Vol. 1 (2008, $19.99) r/#1-7; bonus art; Jamie Rich intro. 20.00

MADMAN COMICS (Also see The Atomics)
Dark Horse Comics (Legend No. 2 on): Apr, 1994 - No. 20, Dec, 2000 ($2.95/$2.99)

1-Allred-c/a; F. Miller back-c. 1 3 4 6 8 10
2-3: 3-Alex Toth back-c. 5.00
4-11: 4-Dave Stevens back-c. 6,7-Miller/Darrow's Big Guy app. 6-Bruce Timm back-c. 7-Darrow back-c. 8-Origin?; Bagge back-c. 10-Allred/Ross-c; Ross back-c. 11-Frazetta back-c 4.00
12-16: 12-(4/99) 3.50
17-20: 17-The G-Men From Hell #1 on cover; Brereton back-c. 18-(#2). 19,20-($2.99-c). 20-Clowes back-c 3.50
... Boogaloo TPB (6/99, $8.95) r/Nexus Meets Madman & Madman/The Jam 9.00
... Gargantua! (2007, $125.00, HC with dustjacket) r/Madman#1-3, Madman Adventures #1-3, Madman Comics #1-20 and Madman King-Size Super Groovy Special; pin-ups 125.00
Image Firsts: Madman #1 (10/10, $1.00) r/#1 3.00
Ltd. Ed. Slipcover (1997, $99.95, signed and numbered) w/Vol.1 & Vol. 2. Vol.1- reprints #1-5; Vol. 2- reprints #6-10 100.00
The Complete Madman Comics: Vol. 2 (11/96, $17.95, TPB) r/#6-10 plus new material 18.00
Madman King-Size Super Groovy Special (Oni Press, 7/03, $6.95) new short stories by Allred, Derington, Krall and Weissman 7.00
Madman Picture Exhibition No. 1-4 (4-7/02, $3.95) pin-ups by various 4.00
Madman Picture Exhibition Limited Edition (10/02, $29.95) Hardcover collects MPE #1-4 30.00
... Volume 2 SC (2007, $17.99) r/#1-11; Erik Larsen intro. 18.00
... Volume 3 SC (2007, $17.99) r/#12-20 and story from King-Size Groovy; Allred intro. 18.00
Yearbook '95 (1996, $17.95, TPB)-r/#1-5, intro by Teller 18.00

MADMAN / THE JAM
Dark Horse Comics: Jul, 1998 - No. 2, Aug, 1998 ($2.95, mini-series)

1,2-Allred & Mireault-s/a 4.00

MAD MAX: FURY ROAD (Based on the 2015 movie)
DC Comics (Vertigo): Jul, 2015 - Oct, 2015 ($4.99, series of one-shots)

...:Furiosa (8/15, $4.99) Origin of Furiosa; Tristan Jones-a; Edwards-c 5.00
...: Max 1,2 (9/15, 10/15, $4.99) Recap of Max's history & prelude to movie 5.00
...: Nux & Immortan Joe (7/15, $4.99) Origins of Nux & Immortan Joe; Edwards-c 5.00

MAD MONSTER PARTY (See Movie Classics)

MADNESS IN MURDERWORLD
Marvel Comics: 1989 (Came with computer game from Paragon Software)

V1#1-Starring The X-Men 3 6 9 16 23 30

MADRAVEN HALLOWEEN SPECIAL
Hamilton Comics: Oct, 1995 ($2.95, one-shot)

nn-Morrow-a 4.00

MADROX (from X-Factor)
Marvel Comics (Marvel Knights): Nov, 2004 - No. 5, Mar, 2005 ($2.99)

1-5-Peter David-s/Pablo Raimondi-a; Strong Guy app. 3.00
...: Multiple Choice TPB (2005, $13.99) r/#1-5 14.00
X-Factor: Madrox - Multiple Choice HC (2008, $19.99) r/#1-5 20.00

MAD SPECIAL (...Super Special)
E. C. Publications, Inc.: Fall, 1970 - No. 141, Nov, 1999 (84 - 116 pgs.)
(If bonus is missing, issue is one half price)

Fall 1970(#1)-Bonus-Voodoo Doll; contains 17 pgs. new material
9 18 27 63 129 195
Spring 1971(#2)-Wall Nuts; 17 pgs. new material 5 10 15 33 57 80
3-Protest Stickers 5 10 15 33 57 80
4-8: 4-Mini Posters. 5-Mad Flag. 6-Mad Mischief Stickers. 7-Presidential candidate posters, Wild Shocking Message posters. 8-TV Guise 5 10 15 30 50 70
9(1972)-Contains Nostalgic Mad #1 (28 pgs.) 4 8 12 27 44 60
10-13: 10-Nonsense Stickers (Don Martin). 13-Sickie Stickers; 3 pgs. Wolverton-r/Mad #137. 11-Contains 33-1/3 RPM record. 12-Contains Nostalgic Mad #2 (36 pgs.); Davis, Wolverton-a 3 6 9 19 30 40
14,16-21,24: 4-Vital Message posters & Art Depreciation paintings. 16-Mad-hesive Stickers. 17-Don Martin posters. 20-Martin Stickers. 18-Contains Nostalgic Mad #4 (36 pgs.).

Madame Xanadu (2008) #29 © DC

Madman Atomic Comics #1 © Mike Allred

Magdalena V3 #6 © TCOW

	GD 2.0	VG 4.0	FN 6.0	VF 8.0	VF/NM 9.0	NM- 9.2
21,24-Contains Nostalgic Mad #5 (28 pgs.) & #6 (28 pgs.)	3	6	9	16	23	30
15-Contains Nostalgic Mad #3 (28 pgs.)	3	6	9	16	24	32
22,23,25,27-29,30: 22-Diplomas. 23-Martin Stickers. 25-Martin Posters. 27-Mad Shock-Sticks. 28-Contains Nostalgic Mad #7 (36 pgs.). 29-Mad Collectable-Connectables Posters. 30-The Movies	2	4	6	9	13	16
26-Has 33-1/3 RPM record	2	4	6	13	18	22
31,33-35,37-50	2	4	6	8	11	14
32-Contains Nostalgic Mad #8. 36-Has 96 pgs. of comic book & comic strip spoofs: titles "The Comics" on-c	2	4	6	9	13	16
51-70	1	3	4	6	8	10
71-88,90-100: 71-Batman parodies-r by Wood, Drucker. 72-Wolverton-c r-from 1st panel in Mad #11; Wolverton-s r/new dialogue. 83-All Star Trek spoof issue	1	2	3	5	6	8
76-(Fall, 1991)-Special Hussein Asylum Edition; distributed only to the troops in the Middle East (see Mad #300-303)	2	4	6	13	18	22
89-($3.95)-Polybaged w/1st of 3 Spy vs. Spy hologram trading cards (direct sale only issue) (other cards came w/card set)	1	3	4	6	8	10
101-141: 117-Sci-Fi parodies-r.						4.00

NOTE: *#28-30 have no number on cover.* **Freas** *c-76.* **Mingo** *c-9, 11, 15, 19, 23.*

MAE
Dark Horse Comics/Lion Forge #7-on: May, 2016 - Present ($3.99)

1-Gene Ha-s/a/c; intro. by Bill Willingham; bonus pin-ups by Graham & Conner 5.00
2-9: 2-5-Ha-s/a/c. 3-Pin-up by Katie Cook. 6-Ha-s/Ganucheau-a. 8-Waid-s. 9-Kremer-s 4.00

MAESTRO
Marvel Comics: Oct, 2020 - No. 5, Feb, 2021 ($4.99/$3.99)

1-($4.99)-Origin of future Hulk; Peter David-s/Germán Peralta; M.O.D.O.K. app. 1 2 3 5 6 8
2-5-($3.99) Hercules app. 4.00

MAESTRO: FUTURE IMPERFECT – MARVEL TALES
Marvel Comics: Oct, 2020 ($7.99, one-shot)

1-Reprints intro. of Maestro in Hulk: Future Imperfect #1,2; Peter David-s/George Pérez-a 8.00

MAESTROS
Image Comics: Oct, 2017 - No. 7, Aug, 2018 ($3.99)

1-7-Steve Skroce-s/a 4.00

MAESTRO: WAR AND PAX (Follows Maestro series)
Marvel Comics: Mar, 2021 - No. 5, Jul, 2021 ($4.99/$3.99)

1-($4.99)-Future Hulk; Peter David-s/Javier Pina; Machine Man app. 5.00
2-5-($3.99) Doctor Doom app. 4.00

MAESTRO: WORLD WAR M (Follows Maestro: War and Pax series)
Marvel Comics: Apr, 2022 - No. 5, Sept, 2022 ($4.99/$3.99)

1-($4.99)-Future Hulk; Peter David-s/German Peralta-a; The Abomination app. 5.00
2-5-($3.99) Sub-Mariner app. 3,4-Giganto returns. 5-Cabrol-a 4.00

MAGDALENA, THE (See The Darkness #15-18)
Image Comics (Top Cow): Apr, 2000 - No. 3, Jan, 2001 ($2.50)

Preview Special ('00, $4.95) Flip book w/Blood Legacy preview 5.00
1-Benitez-c/a; variant covers by Silvestri & Turner 3.00
2,3: 2-Two covers 3.00
.../Angelus #1/2 (11/01, $2.95) Benitez-c/Ching-a 3.00
...Blood Divine (2002, $9.95) r/#1-3 & #1/2; cover gallery 10.00
.../Vampirella (7/03, $2.99) Wohl-s/Benitez-a; two covers 3.00

MAGDALENA, THE (Volume 2)
Image Comics (Top Cow): Aug, 2003 - No. 4, Dec, 2003 ($2.99)

Preview (6/03) B&W preview; Wizard World East logo on cover 3.00
1-4-Holguin-s/Basaldua-a 3.00
1-Variant-c by Jim Silke benefitting ACTOR charity 5.00
TPB Volume 1 (12/06, $19.99) r/both series, Darkness #15-18 & Magdalena/Angelus 20.00
.../Daredevil (5/08, $3.99) Phil Hester-s/a; Hester & Sejic-c 4.00
.../Vampirella (12/04, $2.99) Kirkman-s/Manapul-a; two covers by Manapul and Bachalo 3.00
... Vs. Dracula Monster War 2005 (6/05, $2.99) four covers; Joyce Chin-a 3.00

MAGDALENA, THE (Volume 3)
Image Comics (Top Cow): Apr, 2010 - No. 12, May, 2012 ($3.99)

1-12: 1-Marz-s/Blake-a/Sook-c. 7,8-Keu Cha-a 4.00
... Seventh Sacrament 1 (12/14, $3.99) Tini Howard-s/Aileen Oracion-a 4.00

MAGDALENA (Volume 4)
Image Comics (Top Cow): Mar, 2017 - No. 4, Jun, 2017 ($3.99, limited series)

1-4-Howard & Cady-s/DiBari-a 4.00

MAGE (The Hero Discovered...; also see Grendel #16)
Comico: Feb, 1984 (no month) - No. 15, Dec, 1986 ($1.50, Mando paper)

	GD 2.0	VG 4.0	FN 6.0	VF 8.0	VF/NM 9.0	NM- 9.2
1-Comico's 1st color comic	3	6	9	14	20	26
2-5: 3-Intro Edsel						6.00
6-Grendel begins (1st in color)	3	6	9	17	26	35
7-1st new Grendel story	2	4	6	8	10	12
8-14: 13-Grendel dies. 14-Grendel story ends						6.00
15-($2.95) Double size w/pullout poster	1	2	3	5	6	8
Image Firsts: Mage - The Hero Discovered #1 (10/10, $1.00) r/#1 w/"Image Firsts" logo						3.00
TPB Volume 1-4 (Image, $5.95) 1- r/#1,2. 2- r/#3,4. 3- r/#5,6. 4- r/#7,8						7.00
TPB Volume 5-7 (Image, $6.95) 5- r/#9,10. 6- r/#11,12. 7- r/#13,14						7.00
TPB Volume 8 (Image, 9/99, $7.50) r/#15						7.50
..., Vol. 1 TPB (Image, 2004, $29.99) r/#1-15; cover gallery, promo artwork, bonus art						30.00

MAGE (The Hero Defined) (Volume 2)
Image Comics: July, 1997 - No. 15, Oct, 1999 ($2.50)

0-(7/97, $5.00) American Ent. Ed. 5.00
1-14: Matt Wagner-c/s/a in all. 13-Three covers 3.00
1-"3-D Edition" (2/98, $4.95) w/glasses 5.00
15-($5.95) Acetate cover 6.00
Volume 1,2 TPB ('98,'99, $9.95) 1- r/#1-4. 2-r/#5-8 10.00
Volume 3 TPB ('00, $12.95) r/#9-12 13.00
Volume 4 TPB ('01, $14.95) r/#13-15 15.00
Hardcover Vol. 2 (2005, $49.95) r/#1-15; cover gallery, character design & sketch pages 50.00

MAGE, BOOK THREE: THE HERO DENIED
Image Comics: No. 0 July, 2017 - No. 15, Feb, 2019 ($1.99/$3.99)

0-(7/17, $1.99) Return of Kevin Matchstick 3.00
1-14-Matt Wagner-c/s/a 4.00
15-($7.99) Finale of the trilogy 8.00

MAGE KNIGHT: STOLEN DESTINY (Based on the fantasy game Mage Knight)
Idea + Design Works: Oct, 2002 - No. 5, Feb, 2003 ($3.50, limited series)

1-5: 1-J. Scott Campbell-c; Cabrera-a/Dezago-s, 2-Dave Johnson-c 3.50

MAGGIE AND HOPEY COLOR SPECIAL (See Love and Rockets)
Fantagraphics Books: May, 1997 ($3.50, one-shot)

1 4.00

MAGGIE THE CAT (Also see Jon Sable, Freelance #11 & Shaman's Tears #12)
Image Comics (Creative Fire Studio): Jan, 1996 - No. 2, Feb, 1996 ($2.50, unfinished limited series)

1,2: Mike Grell-c/a/scripts 3.00

MAGIC (Magic the Gathering)
BOOM! Studios: Apr, 2021 - Present ($4.99)

1-24: 1-MacKay-s/Guara-a 5.00
...: Ajani Goldmane 1 (8/22, $8.99) McGuire-s/Olivetti-c 9.00
...: Master of Metal 1 (11/21, $8.99) Scott-s/Carlomagno & Coelho-a 9.00
...: Nahiri the Lithomancer 1 (11/22, $8.99) McGuire-s/Lobo-a 9.00

MAGICA DE SPELL GIANT HALLOWEEN HEX (Also see Walt Disney Showcase #30)
IDW Publisihing: No. 2, Sept, 2018 ($5.99, numbering continues from Disney Giant Halloween Hex)

2-Reprints from Italian & Danish editions; art by Cavazzano & Alfonso 6.00

MAGIC AGENT (See Forbidden Worlds & Unknown Worlds)
American Comics Group: Jan-Feb, 1962 - No. 3, May-June, 1962

	GD 2.0	VG 4.0	FN 6.0	VF 8.0	VF/NM 9.0	NM- 9.2
1-Origin & 1st app. John Force	5	10	15	30	50	70
2,3	3	6	9	21	33	45

MAGIC COMICS
David McKay Publications: Aug, 1939 - No. 123, Nov-Dec, 1949

	GD 2.0	VG 4.0	FN 6.0	VF 8.0	VF/NM 9.0	NM- 9.2
1-Mandrake the Magician, Henry, Popeye, Blondie, Barney Baxter, Secret Agent X-9 (not by Raymond), Bunky by Billy DeBeck & Thornton Burgess text stories illustrated by Harrison Cady begin; Henry covers begin	372	744	1116	2195	3798	5400
2	138	276	414	814	1407	2000
3	103	206	309	608	1054	1500
4	76	152	228	448	774	1100
5	64	128	192	378	652	925
6-11: 8-11-Mandrake/Henry funny covers	50	100	150	315	533	750
12-16,18,20: 12-20,22-24-Serious Mandrake mystery covers	68	136	204	435	743	1050
17-The Lone Ranger begins (scarce)	100	200	300	590	1020	1450
19-Classic robot-c (scarce)	180	360	540	1060	1830	2600
21-Mandrake/Henry funny cover	40	80	120	246	411	575
22-24	52	104	156	328	552	775
25-1st Blondie-c	42	84	126	265	445	625
26-30: 26-Dagwood-c begin	30	60	90	177	289	400
31-40: 36-Flag-c	21	42	63	122	199	275

GD VG FN VF VF/NM NM-
2.0 4.0 6.0 8.0 9.0 9.2

41-50 16 32 48 94 147 200
51-60 14 28 42 80 115 150
61-70 12 24 36 67 94 120
71-99, 107,108-Flash Gordon app; not by Raymond 10 20 30 54 72 90
100 11 22 33 60 83 105
101-106,109-123: 123-Last Dagwood-c 9 18 27 50 65 80

MAGIC FLUTE, THE (See Night Music #9-11)

MAGICIAN: APPRENTICE
Dabel Brothers/Marvel Comics (Dabel Brothers) #3 on: Mar, 2007 - No. 12, Dec, 2007 ($2.95/$2.99)
1-12-Adaptation of the Raymond E. Feist Riftwar Saga series 3.00
1,2-($5.95) 1-Wraparound variant-c by Maitz. 2-Wraparound variant-c by Booth 6.00
Collected Edition (10/06, $3.99) r/#1&2 4.00
Vol. 1 HC (2007, $19.99, dustjacket) r/#1-6; foreword by Feist 20.00
Vol. 1 SC (2007, $15.99) r/#1-6; foreword by Feist 16.00
Vol. 2 HC (2008, $19.99, dustjacket) r/#7-12 20.00

MAGICIANS, THE (Based on the series of novels by Lev Grossman)
Archaia: Nov, 2019 - No. 5, Mar, 2020 ($3.99, limited series)
1-5-Lilah Sturges-s/Pius Bak-a 4.00

MAGIC ORDER, THE
Image Comics: Jun, 2018 - No. 6, Feb, 2019 ($3.99, limited series)
1-6-Mark Millar-s/Olivier Coipel-a/c 4.00

MAGIC ORDER 2, THE
Image Comics: Oct, 2021 - No. 6, Mar, 2022 ($3.99/$4.99, limited series)
1-5-Mark Millar-s/Stuart Immonen-a/c 4.00
6-($4.99) 5.00

MAGIC ORDER 3, THE
Image Comics: Jul, 2022 - No. 6, Dec, 2022 ($3.99/$4.99, limited series)
1-5-Mark Millar-s/Gigi Cavenago-a/c 4.00
6-($4.99) 5.00

MAGIC ORDER 4, THE
Image Comics: Jan, 2023 - No. 6, ($4.99/$3.99, limited series)
1-($4.99)-Mark Millar-s/Dike Ruan-a/c 5.00
2-($3.99) 4.00

MAGIC PICKLE
Oni Press: Sept, 2001 - No. 4, Dec, 2001 ($2.95, limited series)
1-4-Scott Morse-s/a; Mahfood-a (2 pgs.) 3.00

MAGIC SWORD, THE (See Movie Classics)

MAGIC THE GATHERING (Title Series), **Acclaim Comics (Armada)**
...ANTIQUITIES WAR,11/95 - 2/96 ($2.50), 1-4-Paul Smith-a(p) 4.00
...ARABIAN NIGHTS, 12/95 - 1/96 ($2.50), 1,2 1 3 4 6 8 10
...COLLECTION ,'95 ($4.95), 1,2-polybagged 5.00
...CONVOCATIONS, '95 ($2.50), 1-nn-pin-ups 4.00
...ELDER DRAGONS ,'95 ($2.50), 1,2-Doug Wheatley-a
1 3 4 6 8 10
...FALLEN ANGEL ,'95 ($5.95), nn 1 2 3 5 6 8
...FALLEN EMPIRES ,9/95 - 10/95 ($2.75), 1,2 4.00
...Collection ($4.95)-polybagged 1 3 4 6 8 10
...HOMELANDS ,'95 ($5.95), nn-polybagged w/card; Hildebrandts-c
1 3 4 6 8 10
... ICE AGE (On The World of...) ,7/5 -11/95 ($2.50), 1-4: 1,2-bound-in Magic Card. 3,4-bound-in insert 5.00
...LEGEND OF JEDIT OJANEN, '96 ($2.50), 1,2 5.00
...NIGHTMARE, '95 ($2.50, one shot), 1 5.00
...THE SHADOW MAGE, 7/95 - 10/95 ($2.50), 1-4-bagged w/Magic The Gathering card
3 6 9 14 20 25
...Collection 1,2 (1995, $4.95)-Trade paperback; polybagged
1 3 4 6 8 10
...SHANDALAR ,'96 ($2.50), 1,2 1 3 4 6 8 10
...WAYFARER ,11/95 - 2/96 ($2.50), 1-5 5.00

MAGIC: THE GATHERING
IDW Publishing: Dec, 2011 - No. 4, Mar, 2012 ($3.99, limited series)
1-4-Forbeck-s/Cóccolo-a 4.00

MAGIC: THE GATHERING: CHANDRA
IDW Publishing: Nov, 2018 - No. 4, Feb, 2019 ($3.99, limited series)
1-4-Ayala-s/Tolibao-a 4.00

MAGIC: THE GATHERING: GERRARD'S QUEST
Dark Horse Comics: Mar, 1998 - No. 4, June, 1998 ($2.95, limited series)
1-4: Grell-s/Mhan-a 5.00

MAGIC: THE GATHERING - PATH OF VENGEANCE
IDW Publishing: Oct, 2012 - No. 4, Feb, 2013 ($4.99, limited series, bagged with card)
1-4-Forbeck-s/Cóccolo-a 5.00

MAGIC: THE GATHERING - THEROS
IDW Publishing: Oct, 2013 - No. 5 ($4.99, limited series, bagged with card)
1-5-Ciaramella-s/Cóccolo-a 5.00

MAGIC: THE GATHERING - THE SPELL THIEF
IDW Publishing: May, 2012 - No. 4, Aug, 2012 ($4.99, limited series, bagged with card)
1-4-Forbeck-s/Cóccolo-a 5.00

MAGIC: THE HIDDEN PLANESWALKER (Magic the Gathering)
BOOM! Studios: Apr, 2022 - No. 4, Jul, 2022 ($4.99)
1-4-Mairghread Scott-s/Fabiana Mascolo-a 5.00

MAGIK (Illyana and Storm Limited Series)
Marvel Comics Group: Dec, 1983 - No. 4, Mar, 1984 (60¢, limited series)
1-4: 1-Characters from X-Men; Inferno begins; X-Men cameo (Buscema pencils in #1,2; c-1p. 2-4: 2-Nightcrawler app. & X-Men cameo 5.00

MAGIK (See Black Sun mini-series)
Marvel Comics: Dec, 2000 - No. 4, Mar, 2001 ($2.99, limited series)
1-4-Liam Sharp-a/Abnett & Lanning-s; Nightcrawler app. 3.00

MAGILLA GORILLA (TV) (See Kite Fun Book)
Gold Key: May, 1964 - No. 10, Dec, 1968 (Hanna-Barbera)
1-1st comic app. 10 20 30 69 147 225
2-4: 3-Vs. Yogi Bear for President. 4-1st Punkin Puss & Mushmouse, Ricochet Rabbit & Droop-a-Long 5 10 15 34 60 85
5-10: 10-Reprints 5 10 15 30 50 70

MAGILLA GORILLA (TV)(See Spotlight #4)
Charlton Comics: Nov, 1970 - No. 5, July, 1971 (Hanna-Barbera)
1 7 14 21 44 82 120
2-5 3 6 9 21 33 45

MAGNETIC MEN FEATURING MAGNETO
Marvel Comics (Amalgam): June, 1997 ($1.95, one-shot)
1-Tom Peyer-s/Barry Kitson & Dan Panosian-a 5.00

MAGNETO (See X-Men #1)
Marvel Comics: nd (Sept, 1993) (Giveaway) (one-shot)
0-Embossed foil-c by Sienkiewicz; r/Classic X-Men #19 & 12 by Bolton 5.00

MAGNETO
Marvel Comics: Nov, 1996 - No. 4, Feb, 1997 ($1.95, limited series)
1-4: Peter Milligan scripts & Kelley Jones-a(p) 4.00

MAGNETO
Marvel Comics: Mar, 2011 ($2.99, one-shot)
1-Howard Chaykin-s/a; Roger Cruz-c 3.00

MAGNETO
Marvel Comics: May, 2014 - No. 21, Oct, 2015 ($3.99)
1-21: 1-Bunn-s/Walta-a/Rivera-c. 9-12-AXIS tie-ins. 18-21-Secret Wars tie-ins 4.00

MAGNETO AND THE MAGNETIC MEN
Marvel Comics (Amalgam): Apr, 1996 ($1.95, one-shot)
1-Jeff Matsuda-a(p) 4.00

MAGNETO ASCENDANT
Marvel Comics: May, 1999 ($3.99, squarebound one-shot)
1-Reprints early Magneto appearances 4.00

MAGNETO: DARK SEDUCTION
Marvel Comics: Jun, 2000 - No. 4, Sept, 2000 ($2.99, limited series)
1-4: Nicieza-s/Cruz-a. 3,4-Avengers-c/app. 3.00

MAGNETO: NOT A HERO (X-Men Regenesis)
Marvel Comics: Jan, 2012 - No. 4, Apr, 2012 ($2.99, limited series)
1-4-Skottie Young-s/Clay Mann-a; Joseph returns 3.00

MAGNETO REX
Marvel Comics: Apr, 1999 - No. 3, July, 1999 ($2.50, limited series)
1-3-Rogue, Quicksilver app.; Peterson-a(p) 4.00

MAGNIFICENT MS. MARVEL
Marvel Comics: May, 2019 - Present ($3.99)
1-17: 1-Saladin Ahmed-s/Minkyu Jung-a. 5-New costume. 10-Intro. Stormranger 13-Intro. Amulet. 15,17-Dum Dum Dugan app. 4.00
18-($4.99) 75th issue of Ms. Marvel; battles Stormranger 5.00
Annual 1 (9/19, $4.99) Visaggio-s/Lam-a; The Super-Skrull app. 5.00

MAGNUS (Robot Fighter)(Volume 1)
Dynamite Entertainment: 2017 - No. 5, 2017 ($3.99)
1-5-Higgins-s/Fornés-a. 1,2-Turok back-up. 3-5-Doctor Spektor back-up 4.00

MAGNUS, ROBOT FIGHTER (...4000 A.D.)(See Doctor Solar)
Gold Key: Feb, 1963 - No. 46, Jan, 1977 (All painted covers except #5,30,31)
1-Origin & 1st app. Magnus; Aliens (1st app.) series begins
86 172 258 688 1544 2400
2,3 14 28 42 94 207 320
4-10: 10-Simonson fan club illo (5/65, 1st-a?) 8 16 24 52 99 145
11-20 5 10 15 34 60 85
21,24-28: 28-Aliens ends 4 8 12 27 44 60
22,23: 22-Origin-r/#1; last 12¢ issue 4 8 12 28 47 65
29-46-Mostly reprints 3 6 9 15 22 28
...: One For One (Dark Horse Comics, 9/10, $1.00) r/#1 3.00
Russ Manning's Magnus Robot Fighter - Vol. 1 HC (Dark Horse, 2004, $49.95) r/#1-7 100.00
Russ Manning's Magnus Robot Fighter - Vol. 2 HC (DH, 6/05, $49.95) r/#8-14; forward by Steve Rude 50.00
Russ Manning's Magnus Robot Fighter - Vol. 3 HC (Dark Horse, 10/06, $49.95) r/#15-21 60.00
NOTE: *Manning* a-1-22, 28-43(r). *Spiegle* a-23, 44r.

MAGNUS ROBOT FIGHTER (Also see Vintage Magnus)
Valiant/Acclaim Comics: May, 1991 - No. 64, Feb, 1996 ($1.75/$1.95/$2.25/$2.50)
1-Nichols/Layton-c/a; 1-8 have trading cards 3 6 9 14 19 24
2-4,6,8: 4-Rai cameo. 6-1st Solar x-over. 1 3 4 6 8 10
5-Origin & 1st full app. Rai (10/91); #5-8 are in flip book format and back-c & half of book are Rai #1-4 mini-series 3 6 9 16 23 30
7-Magnus vs. Rai-c/story; 1st X-O Armor 2 4 6 11 16 20
0-Origin issue; Layton-a; ordered through mail w/coupons from 1st 8 issues plus 50¢; B. Smith trading card 3 6 9 19 30 40
0-Sold thru comic shops without trading card 3 6 9 14 19 24
9-11 6.00
12-(3.25, 44 pgs.)-Turok-c/story (1st app. in Valiant universe, 5/92); has 8 pg. Magnus story insert 3 6 9 17 26 35
13-24,26-48: 14-1st app. Isak. 15,16-Unity x-overs. 15-Miller-c. 16-Birth of Magnus.

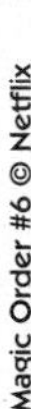

Magic Order #6 © Netflix

Magnus, Robot Fighter (2010) #1 © RH

Major X #4 © MAR

	GD 2.0	VG 4.0	FN 6.0	VF 8.0	VF/NM 9.0	NM- 9.2
21-New direction & new logo.24-Story cont'd in Rai & the Future Force #9. 33-Timewalker app. 36-Bound-in trading cards. 37-Rai, Starwatchers & Psi-Lords app. 44-Bound-in sneak peek card						4.00
21-Gold ink variant	2	4	6	11	16	20
25-($2.95)-Embossed silver foil-c; new costume						5.00
49-63						4.00
64-($2.50): 64-Magnus dies?	2	4	6	11	16	20
...Invasion (1994, $9.95)-r/Rai #1-4 & Magnus #5-8						16.00
Magnus Steel Nation (1994, $9.95) r/#1-4						16.00
Yearbook (1994, $3.95, 52 pgs.)	1	2	3	5	6	8

NOTE: ***Ditko/Reese** a-18. **Layton** a(i)-5; c-6-9i, 25; back(i)-5-8. **Reese** a(i)-22, 25, 28; c(i)-22, 24, 28. **Simonson** c-16. Prices for issues 1-8 are for trading cards and coupons intact.*

MAGNUS ROBOT FIGHTER
Acclaim Comics (Valiant Heroes): V2#1, May, 1997 - No. 18, Jun, 1998 ($2.50)

1-18: 1-Reintro Magnus; Donavon Wylie (X-O Manowar) cameo; Tom Peyer scripts & Mike McKone-c/a begin; painted variant-c exists — 4.00

MAGNUS ROBOT FIGHTER
Dark Horse Comics: Aug, 2010 - No. 4, May, 2011 ($3.50)

1-4: 1-Shooter-s/Reinhold-a; covers by Swanland & Reinhold; back-up r/#1 (1963) — 3.50

MAGNUS ROBOT FIGHTER
Dynamite Entertainment: 2014 - No. 12, 2015 ($3.99)

1-12: 1-8-Fred Van Lente-s/Cory Smith-a; multiple covers on each — 4.00
#0 (2014, $3.99) Takes place between #2 & #3; Roberto Castro-a — 4.00

MAGNUS ROBOT FIGHTER/NEXUS
Valiant/Dark Horse Comics: Dec, 1993 - No. 2, Apr, 1994 ($2.95, lim. series)

1,2: Steve Rude painted-c & pencils in all — 4.00

MAGOG (See Justice Society of America 2007 series)(Continues in Justice Society Special #1)
DC Comics: Nov, 2009 - No.12, Ot. 2010 ($2.99)

1-12: 1-Giffen-s/Porter-a/Fabry-c; variant-c by Porter. 7-Zatanna app. — 3.00
...: Lethal Force TPB (2010, $14.99) r/#1-5 — 15.00

MAID OF THE MIST (See American Graphics)

MAI, THE PSYCHIC GIRL
Eclipse Comics: May, 1987 - No. 28, July, 1989 ($1.50, B&W, bi-weekly, 44pgs.)

1-28, 1,2-2nd print — 4.00

MAJESTIC (Mr. Majestic from WildCATS)
DC Comics: Oct, 2004 - No. 4, Jan, 2005 ($2.95, limited series)

1-4-Kerschl-a/Abnett & Lanning-s. 1-Superman app.; Superman #1 cover swipe — 3.00
...: Strange New Visitor TPB (2005, $14.99) r/#1-4 & Action #811, Advs. of Superman #624 & Superman #201 — 15.00

MAJESTIC (Mr. Majestic from WildCATS)
DC Comics (WildStorm): Mar, 2005 - No. 17, July, 2006 ($2.95/$2.99)

1-17: 1-Googe-a/Abnett & Lanning-s; Superman app. 9-Jeanty-a; Zealot app. — 3.00
...: Meanwhile, Back on Earth... TPB (2006, $14.99) r/#8-12 — 15.00
...: The Final Cut TPB (2007, $14.99) r/#13-17 & story fro WildStorm Winter Special — 15.00
...: While You Were Out TPB (2006, $12.99) r/#1-7 — 13.00

MAJOR BUMMER
DC Comics: Aug, 1997 - No. 15, Oct, 1998 ($2.50)

1-15: 1-Origin and 1st app. Major Bummer — 3.00

MAJOR HOOPLE COMICS (See Crackajack Funnies)
Nedor Publications: nd (Jan, 1943)

	GD 2.0	VG 4.0	FN 6.0	VF 8.0	VF/NM 9.0	NM- 9.2
1-Mary Worth, Phantom Soldier app. by Moldoff	40	80	120	246	411	575

MAJOR VICTORY COMICS (Also see Dynamic Comics)
H. Clay Glover/Service Publ./Harry 'A' Chesler: 1944 - No. 3, Summer, 1945

	GD 2.0	VG 4.0	FN 6.0	VF 8.0	VF/NM 9.0	NM- 9.2
1-Origin Major Victory (patriotic hero) by C. Sultan (reprint from Dynamic #1); 1st app. Spider Woman; Nazi WWII-c	155	310	465	992	1696	2400
2-Dynamic Boy app.; WWII-c	84	168	252	538	919	1300
3-Rocket Boy app.; WWII-c	71	142	213	454	777	1100

MAJOR X
Marvel Comics: Jun, 2019 - No. 6, Aug, 2019 ($4.99/$3.99)

1-($4.99) Rob Liefeld-s/a; Cable, Domino, Deadpool, Wolverine app. — 5.00
2-6-($3.99) 2,4,5-Liefeld-s/Peeples-a. 3-Portacio-a. 6-Rob Liefeld-s/a — 4.00
No. 0 (10/19, $4.99) r/Wolverine #154,155 with new framing pages; Liefeld-s/a — 5.00

MALIBU ASHCAN: RAFFERTY (See Firearm #12)
Malibu Comics (Ultraverse): Nov, 1994 (99¢, B&W w/color-c; one-shot)

1-Previews "The Rafferty Saga" storyline in Firearm; Chaykin-c — 4.00

MALTESE FALCON
David McKay Publications: No. 48, 1946

	GD 2.0	VG 4.0	FN 6.0	VF 8.0	VF/NM 9.0	NM- 9.2
Feature Books 48-by Dashiell Hammett	103	206	309	659	1130	1600

MALU IN THE LAND OF ADVENTURE
I. W. Enterprises: 1964 (See White Princess of Jungle #2)

	GD 2.0	VG 4.0	FN 6.0	VF 8.0	VF/NM 9.0	NM- 9.2
1-r/Avon's Slave Girl Comics #1; Severin-c	5	10	15	31	53	75

MAMMOTH COMICS
Whitman Publishing Co.(K. K. Publ.): 1938 (84 pgs.) (B&W, 8-1/2x11-1/2")

	GD 2.0	VG 4.0	FN 6.0	VF 8.0	VF/NM 9.0	NM- 9.2
1-Alley Oop, Terry & the Pirates, Dick Tracy, Little Orphan Annie, Wash Tubbs, Moon Mullins, Smilin' Jack, Tailspin Tommy, Don Winslow, Dan Dunn, Smokey Stover & other reprints (scarce)	265	530	795	1694	2897	4100

MAN AGAINST TIME
Image Comics (Motown Machineworks): May, 1996 - No. 4, Aug, 1996 ($2.25, lim. series)

1-4: 1-Simonson-c. 2,3-Leon-c. 4-Barreto & Leon-c — 3.00

MAN AMONG YE, A
Image Comics (Top Cow): Jun, 2020 - No. 8, Feb, 2022 ($3.99)

1-8-Stephanie Phillips-s/Craig Cermak-a; Caribbean pirates in 1720 — 4.00

MAN AND SUPERMAN 100-PAGE SUPER SPECTACULAR
DC Comics: Apr, 2019 ($9.99, squarebound, one-shot)

1-Wolfman-s/Castellini-a; Clark Kent's first days in Metropolis re-told — 10.00

MAN-BAT (See Batman Family, Brave & the Bold, & Detective #400)
National Periodical Publ./DC Comics: Dec-Jan, 1975-76 - No. 2, Feb-Mar, 1976; Dec, 1984

	GD 2.0	VG 4.0	FN 6.0	VF 8.0	VF/NM 9.0	NM- 9.2
1-Ditko-a(p); Aparo-c; Batman app.; 1st app. She-Bat?; 1st app. Baron Tyme	3	6	9	21	33	45
2-Aparo-c	2	4	6	10	14	18
1 (12/84)-N. Adams-r(3)/Det.(Vs. Batman on-c)	1	2	3	5	6	8

MAN-BAT
DC Comics: Feb, 1996 - No. 3, Apr, 1996 ($2.25, limited series)

1-3: Dixon scripts in all. 2-Killer Croc-c/app. — 4.00

MAN-BAT
DC Comics: Jun, 2006 - No. 5, Oct, 2006 ($2.99, limited series)

1-5: Bruce Jones-s/Mike Huddleston-a/c. 1-Hush app. — 3.00

MAN-BAT
DC Comics: Apr, 2021 - No. 5, Aug, 2021 ($3.99, limited series)

1-5: 1-Dave Wielgosz-s/Sumit Kumar-a; covers by Hotz & Nowlan. 1-3-Task Force X — 4.00

MAN CALLED A-X, THE
Malibu Comics (Bravura): Nov, 1994 - No. 4, Jun, 1995 ($2.95, limited series)

0-4: Marv Wolfman scripts & Shawn McManus-c/a. 0-(2/95). 1-"1A" on cover — 3.00

MAN CALLED A-X, THE
DC Comics: Oct, 1997 - No. 8, May, 1998 ($2.50)

1-8: Marv Wolfman scripts & Shawn McManus-c/a. — 3.00

MAN CALLED KEV, A (See The Authority)
DC Comics (WildStorm): Sept, 2006 - No. 5, Feb, 2007 ($2.99, limited series)

1-5-Ennis-s/Ezquerra-a/Fabry-c — 3.00
TPB (2007, $14.99) r/#1-5; cover gallery — 15.00

MAN COMICS
Marvel/Atlas Comics (NPI): Dec, 1949 - No. 28, Sept, 1953 (#1-6: 52 pgs.)

	GD 2.0	VG 4.0	FN 6.0	VF 8.0	VF/NM 9.0	NM- 9.2
1-Tuska-a	41	82	123	256	428	600
2-Tuska-a	22	44	66	128	209	290
3-6	17	34	51	103	162	220
7,8	16	32	48	96	151	205
9-13,15: 9-Format changes to war	16	32	48	96	151	205
14-Henkel (3 pgs.); Pakula-a	18	36	54	105	165	225
16-21,23-28: 28-Crime issue (Bob Brant)	15	30	45	92	144	195
22-Krigstein-a, 5 pgs.	19	38	57	111	176	240

NOTE: ***Berg** a-14, 15, 19. **Colan** a-9, 13, 21, 23. **Everett** a-8, 22; c-22, 25. **Heath** a-11, 13, 16, 17, 21. **Henkel** a-7. Kubertish a-by **Bob Brown**-3. **Maneely** a-5, 11-13; c-5, 10, 11, 16. **Reinman** a-11. **Robinson** a-7, 10, 14. **Robert Sale** a-9, 11. **Sinnott** a-22, 23. **Tuska** a-14, 23.*

MANDRAKE THE MAGICIAN (See Defenders Of The Earth, 123, 46, 52, 55, Giant Comic Album, King Comics, Magic Comics, The Phantom #21, Tiny Tot Funnies & Wow Comics, '36)

MANDRAKE THE MAGICIAN (See Harvey Comics Hits #53)
David McKay Publ./Dell/King Comics (All 12¢): 1938 - 1948; Sept, 1966 - No. 10, Nov, 1967

	GD 2.0	VG 4.0	FN 6.0	VF 8.0	VF/NM 9.0	NM- 9.2
Feature Books 18,19,23 (1938)	123	246	369	787	1344	1900
Feature Books 46	71	142	213	454	777	1100
Feature Books 52,55	57	114	171	362	619	875
Four Color 752 (11/56)	12	24	36	80	173	265
1-Begin S.O.S. Phantom, ends #3	8	16	24	56	108	160

GD VG FN VF VF/NM NM-
2.0 4.0 6.0 8.0 9.0 9.2

2-7,9: 4-Girl Phantom app. 5-Flying Saucer-c/story. 5,6-Brick Bradford app. 7-Origin Lothar.
9-Brick Bradford app. 4 8 12 25 40 55
8-Jeff Jones-a (4 pgs.) 4 8 12 27 44 60
10-Rip Kirby app.; Raymond-a (14 pgs.) 5 10 15 30 50 70

MANDRAKE THE MAGICIAN
Marvel Comics: Apr, 1995 - No. 2, May, 1995 ($2.95, unfinished limited series)
1,2: Mike Barr scripts 3.00

MAN-EATERS
Image Comics: Sept, 2018 - No. 12, May, 2019 ($3.99)
1-12-Chelsea Cain-s/Kate Niemczyk-a 4.00
...: Tomorrow Belongs to You! (3/20, $4.99) 5.00

MAN-EATERS: THE CURSED
Image Comics: Jul, 2021 - No. 5, Nov, 2021 ($3.99)
1-5-Chelsea Cain-s/Kate Niemczyk & Lia Miternique-a 4.00

MAN-EATING COW (See Tick #7,8)
New England Comics: July, 1992 - No. 10, 1994? ($2.75, B&W, limited series)
1-10 3.00
Man-Eating Cow Bonanza (6/96, $4.95, 128 pgs.)-r/#1-4. 5.00

MAN FROM ATLANTIS (TV)
Marvel Comics: Feb, 1978 - No. 7, Aug, 1978
1-(84 pgs.)-Sutton-a(p), Buscema-c; origin & cast photos
3 6 9 15 22 28
2-7 6.00

MAN FROM PLANET X, THE
Planet X Productions: 1987 (no price; probably unlicensed)
1-Reprints Fawcett Movie Comic 4.00

MAN FROM U.N.C.L.E., THE (TV) (Also see The Girl From Uncle)
Gold Key: Feb, 1965 - No. 22, Apr, 1969 (All photo-c)
1 14 28 42 96 211 325
2-Photo back c-2-8 7 14 21 44 82 120
3-10: 7-Jet Dream begins (1st app., also see Jet Dream) (all new stories)
5 10 15 33 57 80
11-22: 19-Last 12¢ issue. 21,22-Reprint #10 & 7 5 10 15 30 50 70

MAN FROM U.N.C.L.E., THE (TV)
Entertainment Publishing: 1987 - No. 11 ($1.50/$1.75, B&W)
1-7 ($1.50), 8-11 ($1.75) 4.00

MAN FROM WELLS FARGO (TV)
Dell Publishing Co.: No. 1287, Feb-Apr, 1962 - May-July, 1962 (Photo-c)
Four Color 1287, #01-495-207 6 12 18 42 79 115

MANGA DARKCHYLDE (Also see Darkchylde titles)
Dark Horse Comics: Feb, 2005 - No. 5 ($2.99, limited series)
1,2-Randy Queen-s/a; manga-style pre-teen Ariel Chylde 3.00

MANGA SHI (See Tomoe)
Crusade Entertainment: Aug, 1996 ($2.95)
1-Printed back to front (manga-style) 3.00

MANGA SHI 2000
Crusade Entertainment: Feb, 1997 - No. 3, June, 1997 ($2.95, mini-series)
1-3: 1-Two covers 3.00

MANHATTAN PROJECTS, THE
Image Comics: Mar, 2012 - No. 25, Nov, 2014 ($3.50)
1-Hickman-s/Pitarra-a; intro. Robert and Joseph Oppenheimer 35.00
2 20.00
3 10.00
4-6 8.00
7-25: 10,15,19-Browne-a 4.00

MANHATTAN PROJECTS, THE : THE SUN BEYOND THE STARS
Image Comics: Mar, 2015 - No. 4, Feb, 2016 ($3.50)
1-4-Hickman-s/Pitarra-a 3.50

MANHUNT! (Becomes Red Fox #15 on)
Magazine Enterprises: 10/47 - No. 11, 8/48; No. 12 (no date); No. 13,14, 1953
1-Red Fox by L. B. Cole, Undercover Girl by Whitney, Space Ace begin (1st app.);
negligee panels 161 322 483 1030 1765 2500
2-Electrocution-c 290 580 870 1856 3178 4500
3-5 65 130 195 416 708 1000
6-Bondage, torture-c 271 542 813 1734 2967 4200
7-10: 7-Space Ace ends. 8-Trail Colt begins (intro/1st app., 5/48) by Guardineer; Trail Colt-c.
10-G. Ingels-a 53 106 159 334 567 800
11(8/48)-Frazetta-a, 7 pgs.; The Duke, Scotland Yard begin
71 142 213 454 777 1100
12 (no indicia, no date) Same content as Trail Colt nn (A-1 #24); 7 pg. Frazetta-a which were reprinted in Manhunt! #13; Undercover Girl app.; The Red Fox by L.B. Cole; Whitney-c/a;
published in Canada 486 972 1458 3550 6275 9000
13(A-1 #63)-Frazetta, r-/Trail Colt #1, 7 pgs. 60 120 180 381 653 925
14(A-1 #77)-Bondage/hypo-c; last L. B. Cole Red Fox; Ingels-a
300 600 900 1980 3440 4900

NOTE: ***Guardineer** a-1-5; c-8. **Paul Parker** c-9, 11. **Whitney** a-2-14; c-1-6, 10, 12. Red Fox by **L. B. Cole**-#1-14. #15 was advertised but came out as Red Fox #15.*

MANHUNTER (See Adventure #58, 73, Brave & the Bold, Detective Comics, 1st Issue Special, House of Mystery #143 and Justice League of America)
DC Comics: 1984 ($2.50, 76 pgs; high quality paper)
1-Simonson-c/a(r)/Detective; Batman app. 5.00

MANHUNTER
DC Comics: July, 1988 - No. 24, Apr, 1990 ($1.00)
1-24: 8,9-Flash app. 9-Invasion. 17-Batman-c/sty 4.00

MANHUNTER
DC Comics: No. 0, Nov, 1994 - No. 12, Nov, 1995 ($1.95/$2.25)
0-12 4.00

MANHUNTER (Also see Batman: Streets of Gotham)
DC Comics: Oct, 2004 - No. 38, Mar, 2009 ($2.50/$2.99)
1-21: 1-Intro. Kate Spencer; Saiz-a/Jae Lee-c/Andreyko-s. 2,3 Shadow Thief app.
13,14-Omac x-over. 20-One Year Later 3.00
22-30: 22-Begin $2.99-c. 23-Sandra Knight app. 27-Chaykin-c. 28-Batman app. 3.00
31-38: 31-(8/08) Gaydos-a. 33,34-Suicide Squad app. 3.00
...: Forgotten (2009, $17.99) r/#31-38 18.00
...: Origins (2007, $17.99) r/#15-23 18.00
...: Street Justice (2005, $12.99) r/#1-5; Andreyko intro. 13.00
...: Trial By Fire (2007, $17.99) r/#6-14 18.00
...: Unleashed (2008, $17.99) r/#24-30 18.00

MANHUNTER: ...
DC Comics: 1979, 1999
The Complete Saga TPB (1979) Reprints stories from Detective Comics #437-443 by
Goodwin and Simonson 40.00
The Special Edition TPB (1999, $9.95) r/stories from Detective Comics #437-443 12.00

MANHUNTER SPECIAL (Jack Kirby 100th Birthday tribute)
DC Comics: Oct, 2017 ($4.99, one-shot)
1-Paul Kirk Manhunter & Sandman and Sandy app.; Giffen-s/Buckingham-a; Demon back-up w/Rude-a; bonus Kirby reprint from Tales of the Unexpected #13; Bruce Timm-c 5.00

MANIAC OF NEW YORK
AfterShock Comics: Feb, 2021 - No. 5, Jun, 2021 ($4.99/$3.99)
1-($4.99) Elliott Kalan-s/Andrea Mutti-a 5.00
2-5-($3.99) 4.00

MANIAC OF NEW YORK: VOLUME 2 (The Bronx is Burning)
AfterShock Comics: Dec, 2021 - No. 4, Mar, 2022 ($4.99)
1-4-Elliott Kalan-s/Andrea Mutti-a 5.00

MANIAC OF NEW YORK: VOLUME 3 (Don't Call It a Comeback)
AfterShock Comics: Jan, 2023 - Present ($4.99)
1-Elliott Kalan-s/Andrea Mutti-a 5.00

MANIFEST DESTINY
Image Comics (Skybound): Nov, 2013 - No. 48, Dec, 2022 ($2.99/$3.99)
1-Lewis & Clark in 1804 American Frontier encountering zombies & other creatures;
Chris Dingess-s/Matthew Roberts-a 3 6 9 16 24 32
2 1 3 4 6 8 10
3-30: 25-Back-up Sacagawea story 3.00
31-48-($3.99) 4.00

MANIFEST ETERNITY
DC Comics: Aug, 2006 - No. 6, Jan, 2007 ($2.99)
1-6-Lobdell-s/Nguyen-a/c 3.00

MAN IN BLACK (See Thrill-O-Rama) (Also see All New Comics, Front Page, Green Hornet #31, Strange Story & Tally-Ho Comics)
Harvey Publications: Sept, 1957 - No. 4, Mar, 1958
1-Bob Powell-c/a 21 42 63 122 199 275
2-4: Powell-c/a 15 30 45 85 130 175

MAN IN BLACK
Lorne-Harvey Publications (Recollections): 1990 - No. 2, July, 1991 (B&W)
1,2 4.00

MAN IN FLIGHT (Disney, TV)
Dell Publishing Co.: No. 836, Sept, 1957
Four Color 836 7 14 21 44 82 120

MAN IN SPACE (Disney, TV, see Dell Giant #27)
Dell Publishing Co.: No. 716, Aug, 1956 - No. 954, Nov, 1958
Four Color 716-A science feat. from Tomorrowland 8 16 24 56 108 160
Four Color 954-Satellites 7 14 21 48 89 130

MANKIND (WWF Wrestling)
Chaos Comics: Sept, 1999 ($2.95, one-shot)
1-Regular and photo-c 5.00
1-Premium Edition ($10.00) Dwayne Turner & Danny Miki-c 10.00

MANN AND SUPERMAN
DC Comics: 2000 ($5.95, prestige format, one-shot)
nn-Michael T. Gilbert-s/a 6.00

MANN'S WORLD
AWA Studios: Jan, 2021 - No. 4, Apr, 2021 ($3.99, limited series)
1-4-Victor Gischler-s/Niko Walter-a 4.00

MAN OF STEEL, THE (Also see Superman: The Man of Steel)
DC Comics: 1986 (June release) - No. 6, 1986 (75¢, limited series)
1-6: 1-Silver logo; Byrne-c/a/scripts in all; origin, 1-Alternate-c for newsstand sales,1-Distr. to toy stores by So Much Fun, 2-6: 2-Intro. Lois Lane, Jimmy Olsen. 3-Intro/origin Magpie;
Batman-c/story. 4-Intro. new Lex Luthor 1 2 3 5 6 8
1-6-Silver Editions (1993, $1.95)-r/1-6 3.00
...The Complete Saga nn (SC)-Contains #1-6, given away in contest; limited edition
4 8 12 28 47 65

NOTE: *Issues 1-6 were released between Action #583 (9/86) & Action #584 (1/87) plus Superman #423 (9/86) & Advs. of Superman #424 (1/87).*

MAN OF STEEL, THE (Also see Action Comics #1000)(Leads into Superman #1)
DC Comics: Jul, 2018 - No. 6, Sept, 2018 ($3.99, weekly limited series)
1-6-Bendis-s; Rogol Zaar app.; interlocking covers by Reis. 1-Reis-a; intro. Melody Moore.
2-Shaner & Rude-a. 3-Sook-a. 4-Maguire-a. 5-Hughes-a. 6-Fabok-a 4.00

MAN OF THE ATOM (See Solar, Man of the Atom Vol. 2)

MAN OF WAR (See Liberty Guards & Liberty Scouts)
Centaur Publications: Nov, 1941 - No. 2, Jan, 1942
1-The Fire-Man, Man of War, The Sentinel, Liberty Guards, & Vapo-Man begin;
Gustavson-c/a; Flag-c 232 464 696 1485 2543 3600

Manifest Destiny #48 © Skybound

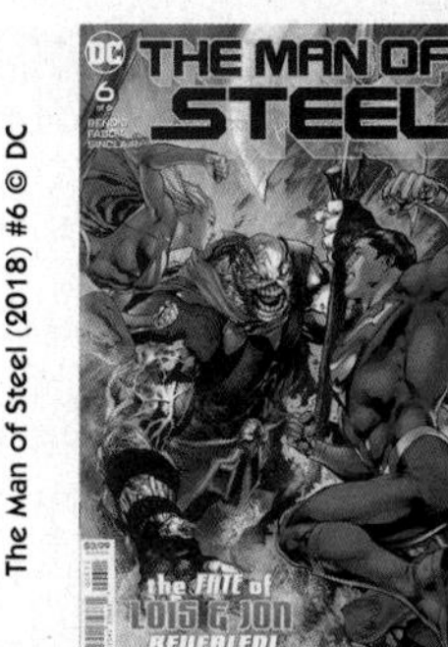

The Man of Steel (2018) #6 © DC

Man Without Fear #3 © MAR

	GD 2.0	VG 4.0	FN 6.0	VF 8.0	VF/NM 9.0	NM- 9.2
2-Intro The Ferret; Gustavson-c/a	181	362	543	1158	1979	2800

MAN OF WAR
Eclipse Comics: Aug, 1987 - No. 3, Feb, 1988 ($1.75, Baxter paper)

1-3: Bruce Jones scripts 3.00

MAN OF WAR (See The Protectors)
Malibu Comics: 1993 - No, 8, Feb, 1994 ($1.95/$2.50/$2.25)

1-5 ($1.95)-Newsstand Editions w/different-c 3.00
1-8: 1-5-Collector's Edi. w/poster. 6-8 ($2.25): 6-Polybagged w/Skycap. 8-Vs. Rocket Rangers 4.00

MAN O' MARS
Fiction House Magazines: 1953; 1964

	GD 2.0	VG 4.0	FN 6.0	VF 8.0	VF/NM 9.0	NM- 9.2
1-Space Rangers; Whitman-c	155	310	465	992	1696	2400
I.W. Reprint #1-r/Man O'Mars #1 & Star Pirate; Murphy Anderson-a	8	16	24	55	105	155

MANOR BLACK
Dark Horse Comics: Jul, 2019 - No. 4, Oct, 2019 ($3.99, limited series)

1-4-Cullen Bunn & Brian Hurtt-s/Tyler Crook-a 4.00

MANOR BLACK: FIRE IN THE BLOOD
Dark Horse Comics: Feb, 2022 - No. 4, Jul, 2022 ($3.99, limited series)

1-4-Cullen Bunn & Brian Hurtt-s/Brian Hurtt-a 4.00

MANTECH ROBOT WARRIORS
Archie Enterprises, Inc.: Sept, 1984 - No. 4, Apr, 1985 (75¢)

1-4: Ayers-c/a(p). 1-Buckler-c(i) 4.00

MAN-THING (See Fear, Giant-Size..., Marvel Comics Presents, Marvel Fanfare, Monsters Unleashed, Power Record Comics & Savage Tales)
Marvel Comics Group: Jan, 1974 - No. 22, Oct, 1975; V2#1, Nov, 1979 - V2#11, July, 1981

	GD 2.0	VG 4.0	FN 6.0	VF 8.0	VF/NM 9.0	NM- 9.2
1-Howard the Duck (2nd app.) cont'd/Fear #19	14	28	42	94	207	320
2	4	8	12	25	40	55
3-1st app. original Foolkiller	3	6	9	17	26	35
4-Origin Foolkiller; last app. 1st Foolkiller	3	6	9	16	24	32
5-11-Ploog-a. 11-Foolkiller cameo (flashback)	3	6	9	16	23	30
12-22: 19-1st app. Scavenger. 20-Spidey cameo. 21-Origin Scavenger, Man-Thing. 22-Howard the Duck cameo	2	4	6	10	14	18
V2#1(1979)	2	4	6	13	18	22

V2#2-11: 4-Dr. Strange-c/app. 11-Mayerik-a 6.00

NOTE: ***Alcala** a-14. **Brunner** c-1. J. **Buscema** a-12p, 13p, 16p. **Gil Kane** c-4p, 10p, 12-20p, 21. **Mooney** a-17, 18, 19p, 20-22, V2#1-3p. **Ploog** Man-Thing-5p, 6p, 7, 8, 9-11p; c-5, 6, 8, 9, 11. **Sutton** a-13i. No. 19 says #10 in indicia.*

MAN-THING (Volume Three, continues in Strange Tales #1 (9/98))
Marvel Comics: Dec, 1997 - No. 8, July, 1998 ($2.99)

1-8-DeMatteis-s/Sharp-a. 2-Two covers. 6-Howard the Duck-c/app. 5.00

MAN-THING (Prequel to 2005 movie)
Marvel Comics: Sept, 2004 - No. 3, Nov, 2004 ($2.99, limited series)

1-3-Hans Rodionoff-s/Kyle Hotz-a 3.00
...: Whatever Knows Fear... (2005, $12.99, TPB) r/#1-3, Savage Tales #1, Adv. Into Fear #16 13.00

MAN-THING
Marvel Comics: May, 2017 - No. 5, Aug, 2017 ($3.99, limited series)

1-5-R.L. Stein-s/German Peralta-a; back-up horror short stories; Stein-s. 1-Origin re-told 4.00

MANTLE
Image Comics: May, 2015 - No. 5, Sept, 2015 ($3.99, limited series)

1-5-Brisson-s/Level-a 4.00

MANTRA
Malibu Comics (Ultraverse): July, 1993 - No. 24, Aug, 1995 ($1.95/$2.50)

1-Polybagged w/trading card & coupon 5.00
1-Newsstand edition w/o trading card or coupon 3.00

	GD 2.0	VG 4.0	FN 6.0	VF 8.0	VF/NM 9.0	NM- 9.2
1-Full cover holographic edition	2	4	6	8	11	14
1-Ultra-limited silver foil-c	1	3	4	6	8	10

2,3,5-9,11-24: 2-($2.50-Newsstand edition bagged w/card. 3-Intro Warstrike & Kismet. 6-Break-Thru x-over. 7-Prime app.; origin Prototype by Jurgens/Austin (2 pgs.). 11-New costume. 17-Intro NecroMantra & Pinnacle; prelude to Godwheel 3.00
4-($2.50, 48 pgs.)-Rune flip-c/story by B. Smith (3 pgs.) 4.00
10-($3.50, 68 pgs.)-Flip-c w/Ultraverse Premiere #2 4.00
Giant Size 1 (7/94, $2.50, 44 pgs.) 4.00
...Spear of Destiny 1,2 (4/95, $2.50, 36pgs.) 3.00

MANTRA (2nd Series) (Also See Black September)
Malibu Comics (Ultraverse): Infinity, Sept, 1995 - No. 7, Apr, 1996 ($1.50)

Infinity (9/95, $1.50)-Black September x-over, Intro new Mantra 3.00
1-7: 1-(10/95). 5-Return of Eden (original Mantra). 6,7-Rush app. 3.00

MAN WHO F#&%ED UP TIME, THE
AfterShock Comics: Feb, 2020 - No. 5, Aug, 2020 ($3.99, limited series)

1-5-John Layman-s/Karl Mostert-a 4.00

MAN WITH NO NAME, THE (Based on the Clint Eastwood gunslinger character)
Dynamite Entertainment: 2008 - No. 11, 2009 ($3.50)

1-11: 1-Gage-s/Dias-a/Isanove-c. 7-Bernard-a 3.50

MAN WITHOUT FEAR (Follows Daredevil #612)
Marvel Comics: Mar, 2019 - No. 5, Mar, 2019 ($3.99, weekly limited series)

1-5-Jed McKay-s/Kyle Hotz-c. 1,5-Beyruth-a. 3-Defenders app. 4-Kingpin app. 4.00

MAN WITH THE SCREAMING BRAIN (Based on screenplay by Bruce Campbell & David Goodman)
Dark Horse Comics: Apr, 2005 - No. 4, July, 2005 ($2.99, limited series)

1-4-Campbell & Goodman-s; Remender-a/c. 1-Variant-c by Noto. 3-Powell var-c. 4-Mignola var-c 3.00
TPB (11/05, $13.95) r/#1-4; David Goodman intro.; cover gallery 14.00

MAN WITH THE X-RAY EYES, THE (See X,... under Movie Comics)

MANY DEATHS OF LAILA STARR, THE
BOOM! Studios: Apr, 2021 - No. 5, Sept, 2021 ($3.99, limited series)

1-5-Ram V-s/Filipe Andrade-a 4.00

MANY GHOSTS OF DR. GRAVES, THE (Doctor Graves #73 on)
Charlton Comics: 5/67 - No. 60, 12/76; No. 61, 9/77 - No. 62, 10/77; No. 63, 2/78 - No. 65, 4/78; No. 66, 6/81 - No. 72, 5/82

	GD 2.0	VG 4.0	FN 6.0	VF 8.0	VF/NM 9.0	NM- 9.2
1-Ditko-a; Palais-a; early issues 12¢-c	9	18	27	61	123	185
2-6,8,10	3	6	9	21	33	45
7,9-Ditko-a	4	8	12	25	40	55
11-13,16-18-Ditko-c/a	3	6	9	20	31	42
14,19,23,25	2	4	6	11	16	20
15,20,21-Ditko-a	3	6	9	15	22	28
22,24,26,27,29-35,38,40-Ditko-c/a	3	6	9	16	23	30
28-Ditko-c	3	6	9	15	22	28
36,46,56,57,59,61,66,67,69,71	2	4	6	8	11	14
37,41,43,51,60-Ditko-a	2	4	6	9	13	16
39,58-Ditko-c. 39-Sutton-a. 58-Ditko-a	2	4	6	9	13	16
42,44,53-Sutton-c; Ditko-a. 42-Sutton-a	2	4	6	9	13	16
45-(5/74) 2nd Newton comic work (8 pgs.); new logo; Sutton-c	2	4	6	11	16	20
47-Newton, Sutton, Ditko-a	2	4	6	10	14	18
48-Ditko, Sutton-a	2	4	6	9	13	16
49-Newton-c/a; Sutton-a.	2	4	6	8	11	14
50-Sutton-a	2	4	6	8	10	12
52-Newton-c; Ditko-a	2	4	6	9	13	16
54-Early Byrne-c; Ditko-a	2	4	6	10	14	18
55-Ditko-c; Sutton-a	2	4	6	9	13	16
62-65,68-Ditko-c/a. 65-Sutton-a	2	4	6	11	16	20
70,72-Ditko-a	2	4	6	10	14	18

Modern Comics Reprint 12,25 (1978) 6.00

NOTE: ***Aparo** a-4, 5, 7, 8, 66r, 69r; c-8, 14, 19, 66r, 67r. **Byrne** c-54. **Ditko** a-1, 7, 9, 11-13, 15-18, 20-22, 24, 26, 27, 29, 30-35, 37, 38, 40-44, 47, 48, 51-54, 58, 60r-65r, 70, 72; c-11-13, 16-18, 22, 24, 26-35, 38, 40, 55, 58, 62-65. **Howard** a-38, 39, 45i, 65; c-48. **Kim** a-36, 46, 52. **Larson** a-58. **Morisi** a-13, 14, 23, 26. **Newton** a-45, 47p, 49p; c-49, 52. **Staton** a-36, 37, 41, 43. **Sutton** a-39, 42, 47-50, 55, 65; c-42, 44, 45; painted c-53. **Zeck** a-56, 59.*

MANY LOVES OF DOBIE GILLIS (TV)
National Periodical Publications: May-June, 1960 - No. 26, Oct, 1964

	GD 2.0	VG 4.0	FN 6.0	VF 8.0	VF/NM 9.0	NM- 9.2
1-Most covers by Bob Oskner	29	58	87	209	467	725
2-5	16	32	48	110	243	375
6-10: 10-Last 10¢-c	11	22	33	75	160	245
11-26: 20-Drucker-a. 24-(3-4/64). 25-(9/64)	10	20	30	65	135	205

MANY WORLDS OF TESLA STRONG, THE (Also see Tom Strong)
America's Best Comics: July, 2003 ($5.95, one-shot)

1-Two covers by Timm & Art Adams; art by various incl. Campbell, Cho, Noto, Hughes 6.00

MARA
Image Comics: Dec, 2012 - No. 6, Oct, 2013 ($2.99)

1-6-Brian Wood-s/Ming Doyle-a 3.00

MARAUDERS
Marvel Comics: Dec, 2019 - No. 27, Mar, 2022 ($4.99/$3.99)

1-($4.99) Duggan-s/Lolli-a; Kitty Pryde, Storm, Iceman, Emma Frost, Pyro app. 5.00
2-12-($3.99) 2-Kate becomes the Red Queen. 3-Shinobi Shaw returns 4.00
13-($4.99) "X of Swords" tie-in; Black Panther and Shuri app. 5.00
14-20,22-26: 14,15- "X of Swords" tie-ins 4.00

GD 2.0 | VG 4.0 | FN 6.0 | VF 8.0 | VF/NM 9.0 | NM- 9.2

21-($4.99) Hellfire Gala; bonus reprint of Classic X-Men #7 5.00
27-($4.99) Duggan-s/Lolli & Noto-a 5.00
Annual 1-(3/22, $4.99) Orlando-s/Creees Lee-a; Daken app. 5.00

MARAUDERS
Marvel Comics: Jun, 2022 - Present ($4.99/$3.99)
1-($4.99) Orlando-s/Carlini-a; Kate Pryde, Bishop, Psylocke, Daken, Aurora app. 5.00
2-11-($3.99) 6-Judgment Day tie-in 4.00

MARAUDER'S MOON (See Luke Short, Four Color #848)

MARCH OF COMICS (See Promotional Comics section)

MARCH OF CRIME (Formerly My Love Affair #1-6) (See Fox Giants)
Fox Feature Synd.: No. 7, July, 1950 - No. 2, Sept, 1950; No. 3, Sept, 1951
7(#1)(7/50)-True crime stories; Wood-a 50 100 150 315 533 750
2(9/50)-Wood-a (exceptional) 47 94 141 296 498 700
3(9/51) 27 54 81 158 259 360

MARCO POLO (Also see Classic Comics #27
Charlton Comics Group: 1962 (Movie classic)
nn (Scarce)-Glanzman-c/a (25 pgs.) 12 24 36 79 170 260

MARC SILVESTRI SKETCHBOOK
Image Comics (Top Cow): Jan, 2004 ($2.99, one-shot)
1-Character sketches, concept artwork, storyboards of Witchblade, Darkness & others 5.00

MARC SPECTOR: MOON KNIGHT (Also see Moon Knight)
Marvel Comics: June, 1989 - No. 60, Mar, 1994 ($1.50/$1.75, direct sales)
1 3 6 9 16 23 30
2,3,5-10: 8,9-Punisher app. 1 3 4 6 8 10
4-Intro new Midnight 2 4 6 11 16 20
11-24,26-34,37-49,51-54: 15-Silver Sable app. 19-21-Spider-Man & Punisher app. 32,33-Hobgoblin II (Macendale) & Spider-Man (in black costume) app. 35-38-Punisher story. 42-44-Infinity War x-over. 46-Demogoblin app. 51,53-Gambit app. 6.00
25,50: 25-(52 pgs.)-Ghost Rider app. 50-(56 pgs.)-Special die-cut-c
2 4 6 10 14 18
35-Randall Spector app. (1st app. in Hulk magazine #17); Punisher app.
2 4 6 11 16 20
36-Shadow Knight app.; Punisher app. 3 6 9 14 20 25
55-New look; Platt-c/a 6 12 18 37 66 95
56-Platt-c/a 3 6 9 19 30 40
57-Spider-Man-c/app.; Platt-c/a 6 12 18 38 69 100
58,59-Platt-c 2 4 6 11 16 20
60-Platt-c/a; Moon Knight dies 2 4 6 13 18 22
...: Divided We Fall ($4.95, 52 pgs.) 2 4 6 11 16 20
Special 1 (1992, $2.50) 1 2 3 5 6 8
NOTE: *Cowan c(p) 20-23. Guice c-20. Heath c/a-4. Platt-a 55-57,60; c-55-60.*

MARGARET O'BRIEN (See The Adventures of...)

MARGE'S LITTLE LULU (Continues as Little Lulu from #207 on)
Dell Publishing Co./Gold Key #165-206: No. 74, 6/45 - No. 164, 7-9/62; No. 165, 10/62 - No. 206, 8/72

Marjorie Henderson Buell, born in Philadelphia, Pa., in 1904, created Little Lulu, a cartoon character that appeared weekly in the Saturday Evening Post from Feb. 23, 1935 through Dec. 30, 1944. She was not responsible for any of the comic books. **John Stanley** did pencils only on all Little Lulu comics through at least #135 (1959). He did pencils and inks on Four Color #74 & 97. **Irving Tripp** began inking stories from #1 on, and remained the comic's illustrator throughout its entire run. **Stanley** did storyboards (layouts), pencils, and scripts in all cases and inking only on covers. His word balloons were written in cursive. **Tripp** and occasionally other artists at Western Publ. in Poughkeepsie, N.Y. blew up the pencilled pages, inked the blowups, and lettered them. **Arnold Drake** did storyboards, pencils and scripts starting with #197 (1970) on, amidst reprinted issues. **Buell** sold her rights exclusively to Western Publ. in Dec., 1971. The earlier issues had to be approved by **Buell** prior to publication.

Four Color 74('45)-Intro Lulu, Tubby & Alvin 190 380 570 1568 3534 5500
Four Color 97(2/46) 71 142 213 568 1284 2000
(Above two books are all John Stanley - cover, pencils, and inks.)
Four Color 110('46)-1st Alvin Story Telling Time; 1st app. Willy; variant cover exists
46 92 138 359 805 1250
Four Color 115-1st app. Boys' Clubhouse 44 88 132 326 738 1150
Four Color 120, 131: 120-1st app. Eddie 36 72 108 266 596 925
Four Color 139('47),146,158 35 70 105 252 564 875
Four Color 165 (10/47)-Smokes doll hair & has wild hallucinations. 1st Tubby detective story
42 84 126 311 706 1100
1(1-2/48)-Lulu's Diary feature begins 75 150 225 600 1350 2100
2-1st app. Gloria; 1st app. Miss Feeny 31 62 93 223 499 775
3-5 27 54 81 194 435 675
6-10: 7-1st app. Annie; Xmas-c 21 42 63 150 330 510
11-20: 18-X-Mas-c. 19-1st app. Wilbur. 20-1st app. Mr. McNabbem
17 34 51 114 252 390
21-30: 26-r/F.C. 110. 30-Xmas-c 15 30 45 100 220 340
31-38,40: 35-1st Mumday story 12 24 36 81 176 270
39-Intro. Witch Hazel in "That Awful Witch Hazel" 12 24 36 82 179 275
41-60: 42-Xmas-c. 45-2nd Witch Hazel app. 49-Gives Stanley & others credit
10 20 30 69 147 225
61-80: 63-1st app. Chubby (Tubby's cousin). 68-1st app. Prof. Cleff. 78-Xmas-c. 80-Intro. Little Itch (2/55) 9 18 27 57 111 165
81-99: 90-Xmas-c 7 14 21 46 86 125
100 7 14 21 49 92 135
101-130: 123-1st app. Fifi 6 12 18 37 66 95
131-164: 135-Last Stanley-p 5 10 15 33 57 80
165-Giant; ...in Paris ('62) 9 18 27 61 123 185
166-Giant; ...Christmas Diary (1962 - '63) 9 18 27 61 123 185
167-169 4 8 12 28 47 65
170,172,175,176,178-196,198-200-Stanley-r. 182-1st app. Little Scarecrow Boy
3 6 9 17 26 35
171,173,174,177,197 3 6 9 16 23 30
201,203,206-Last issue to carry Marge's name 3 6 9 14 20 26
202,204,205-Stanley-r 3 6 9 16 23 30
...Summer Camp 1(8/67-G.K.-Giant) '57-58-r 5 10 15 35 63 90
...Trick 'N' Treat 1(12¢)(12/62-Gold Key) 6 12 18 40 73 105
Marge's Lulu and Tubby in Japan (15¢)(5-7/62) 01476-207
8 16 24 51 96 140
NOTE: *See Dell Giant Comics #23, 29, 36, 42, 50, & Dell Giants for annuals. All Giants not by Stanley from L.L. on Vacation (7/54) on. Irving Tripp a-#1-on. Christmas c-7, 18, 30, 42, 78, 90, 126, 166, 250. Summer Camp issues #173, 177, 181, 189, 197, 201, 206.*

MARGE'S LITTLE LULU (See Golden Comics Digest #19, 23, 27, 29, 33, 36, 40, 43, 46, & March of Comics #251, 267, 275, 293, 307, 323, 335, 349, 355, 369, 385, 406, 417, 427, 439, 456, 468, 475, 488)

MARGE'S TUBBY (Little Lulu)(See Dell Giants)
Dell Publishing Co./Gold Key: No. 381, Aug, 1952 - No. 49, Dec-Feb, 1961-62
Four Color 381(#1)-Stanley script; Irving Tripp-a 20 40 60 138 307 475
Four Color 430,444-Stanley-a 12 24 36 80 173 265
Four Color 461 (4/53)-1st Tubby & Men From Mars story; Stanley-a
10 20 30 70 150 230
5 (7-9/53)-Stanley-a 8 16 24 54 102 150
6-10 7 14 21 44 82 120
11-20 5 10 15 34 60 85
21-30 5 10 15 30 50 70
31-49 4 8 12 27 44 60
...& the Little Men From Mars No. 30020-410(10/64-G.K.)-25¢, 68 pgs.
7 14 21 44 82 120
NOTE: ***John Stanley** did all storyboards & scripts through at least #35 (1959). **Lloyd White** did all art except F.C. 381, 430, 444, 461 & #5.*

MARGIE (See My Little...)

MARGIE (TV)
Dell Publ. Co.: No. 1307, Mar-May, 1962 - No. 2, July-Sept, 1962 (Photo-c)
Four Color 1307(#1) 8 16 24 51 96 140
2 5 10 15 31 53 75

MARGIE COMICS (Formerly Comedy Comics; Reno Browne #50 on)
(Also see Cindy Comics & Teen Comics)
Marvel Comics (ACI): No. 35, Winter, 1946-47 - No. 49, Dec, 1949
35 39 78 117 231 378 525
36-38,42,45,47-49 20 40 60 118 192 265
39,41,43(2),44,46-Kurtzman's "Hey Look" 21 42 63 126 206 285
40-Three "Hey Looks", three "Giggles 'n' Grins" by Kurtzman
22 44 66 130 213 295

MARINEMAN (Ian Churchill's...)
Image Comics: Dec, 2010 - No. 6, Jun, 2011 ($3.99/$4.99)
1-5-Ian Churchill-s/a/c 4.00
6-($4.99) Origin revealed 5.00

MARINES (See Tell It to the...)

MARINES ATTACK
Charlton Comics: Aug, 1964 - No. 9, Feb-Mar, 1966
1-Glanzman-a begins 4 8 12 28 47 65
2-9: 8-1st Vietnam war-c/story 3 6 9 18 28 38

MARINES AT WAR (Formerly Tales of the Marines #4)
Atlas Comics (OPI): No. 5, Apr, 1957 - No. 7, Aug, 1957
5-7 17 34 51 100 158 215
NOTE: *Colan a-5. **Drucker** a-5. **Everett** a-5. **Maneely** a-5. **Orlando** a-7. **Severin** c-5.*

MARINES IN ACTION
Atlas News Co.: June, 1955 - No. 14, Sept, 1957
1-Rock Murdock, Boot Camp Brady begin 25 50 75 150 245 340
2-14 17 34 51 98 154 210
NOTE: ***Berg** a-2, 8, 9, 11, 14. **Heath** c-2, 9. **Maneely** c-1, 3. **Severin** a-4; c-7-11, 14.*

MARINES IN BATTLE
Atlas Comics (ACI No. 1-12/WPI No. 13-25): Aug, 1954 - No. 25, Sept, 1958
1-Heath-c; Iron Mike McGraw by Heath; history of U.S. Marine Corps. begins
43 86 129 271 461 650
2-Heath-c 22 44 66 128 209 290
3-6,8-10: 4-Last precode (2/55); Romita-a 17 34 51 100 158 215
7-Kubert/Moskowitz-a (6 pgs.) 18 36 54 105 165 225
11-16,18-21,24 16 32 48 92 144 195
17-Williamson-a (3 pgs.) 18 36 54 107 169 230
22,25-Torres-a 15 30 45 85 130 195
23-Crandall-a; Mark Murdock app. 16 32 48 94 147 200
NOTE: ***Berg** a-22. **G. Colan** a-22, 23. **Drucker** a-6. **Everett** a-4, 15; c-21. **Heath** c-1, 2, 4. **Maneely** c-23, 24. **Orlando** a-14. **Pakula** a-6, 23. **Powell** a-16. **Severin** a-22; c-12. **Sinnott** a-23. **Tuska** a-15.*

MARINE WAR HEROES (Charlton Premiere #19 on)
Charlton Comics: Jan, 1964 - No. 18, Mar, 1967
1-Montes/Bache-c/a 5 10 15 30 50 70
2-16,18: 11-Vietnam sty w/VC tunnels & moles.14,18-Montes/Bache-a
3 6 9 17 25 34
17-Tojo's plan to bomb Pearl Harbor & 1st Atomic bomb blast on Japan
5 10 15 33 57 80

MARJORIE FINNEGAN, TEMPORAL CRIMINAL
Artists, Writers & Artisans: May, 2021 - No. 8, Dec, 2021 ($3.99, limited series)
1-8-Garth Ennis-s/Goran Sudzuka-a/Andy Clarke-c 4.00

MARK, THE (Also see Mayhem)
Dark Horse Comics: Dec, 1993 - No. 4, Mar, 1994 ($2.50, limited series)
1-4 3.00

MARKED, THE
Image Comics (Shadowline): Oct, 2019 - Present ($3.99, limited series)
1-10: 1-Hine & Haberline-s/Haberline-a 4.00
...: Halloween Special 1 (10/22, $5.99) Hine & Haberline-s/Haberline-a 6.00

MARK HAZZARD: MERC
Marvel Comics Group: Nov, 1986 - No. 12, Oct, 1987 (75¢)
1-Morrow-a 2 4 6 8 10 12
2-12: Morrow-a 3.00
Annual 1 (11/87, $1.25) 4.00

MARK OF CHARON (See Negation)
CG Entertainment: Apr, 2003 - No. 5, Aug, 2003 ($2.95, limited series)
1-5-Bedard-s/Bennett-a 3.00

Marauders (2022) #1 © MAR

Marines in Action #13 © MAR

Mars Attacks / Red Sonja #1 © Topps & RS LLC

	GD	VG	FN	VF	VF/NM	NM-
	2.0	4.0	6.0	8.0	9.0	9.2

MARK OF ZORRO (See Zorro, Four Color #228)

MARK OF ZORRO, THE
American Mythology Prods.: 2019 ($3.99, one-shot)

1-Reprints Four Color #228 (5/49); Bill Ely-a 4.00

MARK 1 COMICS (Also see Shaloman)
Mark 1 Comics: Apr, 1988 - No. 3, Mar, 1989 ($1.50)

1-3: Early Shaloman app. 2-Origin 3.00

MARKSMAN, THE (Also see Champions)
Hero Comics: Jan, 1988 - No. 5, 1988 ($1.95)

1-5: 1-Rose begins. 1-3-Origin The Marksman 3.00
Annual 1 ('88, $2.75, 52 pgs.)-Champions app. 4.00

MARK TRAIL
Standard Magazines (Hall Syndicate)/Fawcett Publ. No. 5: Oct, 1955; No. 5, Summer, 1959

	GD	VG	FN	VF	VF/NM	NM-
1(1955)-Sunday strip-r	9	18	27	47	61	75
5(1959) By Ed Dodd	5	10	15	24	30	35
...Adventure Book of Nature 1 (Summer, 1958, 25¢, Pines)-100 pg. Giant; Special Camp Issue; contains 78 Sunday strip-r by Ed Dodd	10	20	30	54	72	90

MARMADUKE MONK
I. W. Enterprises/Super Comics: No date; 1963 (10¢)

	GD	VG	FN	VF	VF/NM	NM-
I.W. Reprint 1 (nd)	2	4	6	8	11	14
Super Reprint 14 (1963)-r/Monkeyshines Comics #?	2	4	6	8	10	12

MARMADUKE MOUSE
Quality Comics Group (Arnold Publ.): Spring, 1946 - No. 65, Dec, 1956 (Early issues: 52 pgs.)

	GD	VG	FN	VF	VF/NM	NM-
1-Funny animal	22	44	66	128	209	290
2	14	28	42	78	112	145
3-10	10	20	30	58	79	100
11-30	8	16	24	44	57	70
31-65: Later issues are 36 pgs.	7	14	21	37	46	55
Super Reprint #14(1963)	2	4	6	10	14	18

MARQUIS, THE
Oni Press

...: A Sin of One ($2.99, 5/03) Guy Davis-s/a; Michael Gaydos-c 3.00
...: Intermezzo TPB ($11.95, 12/03) r/A Sin of One and Hell's Courtesan #1,2 12.00

MARQUIS, THE: DANSE MACABRE
Oni Press: May, 2000 - No. 5, Feb, 2001 ($2.95, B&W, limited series)

1-5-Guy Davis-s/a. 1-Wagner-c. 2-Mignola-c. 3-Vess-c. 5-K. Jones-c 3.00
TPB (8/2001, $18.95) r/1-5 & Les Preludes; Seagle intro. 19.00

MARQUIS, THE: DEVIL'S REIGN: HELL'S COURTESAN
Oni Press: Feb, 2002 - No. 2, Apr, 2002 ($2.95, B&W, limited series)

1,2-Guy Davis-s/a 3.00

MARRIAGE OF HERCULES AND XENA, THE
Topps Comics: July, 1998 ($2.95, one-shot)

1-Photo-c; Lopresti-a; Alex Ross pin-up, 1-Alex Ross painted-c 3.00
1-Gold foil logo-c 5.00

MARRIED ... WITH CHILDREN (TV)(Based on Fox TV show)
Now Comics: June, 1990 - No. 7, Feb, 1991(12/90 inside) ($1.75)
V2#1, Sept, 1991 - No. 7, Apr, 1992 ($1.95)

	GD	VG	FN	VF	VF/NM	NM-
1	2	4	6	9	13	16
2-7: 2-Photo-c, 1,2-2nd printing, V2#2-7: 1,4,6-Photo-c						5.00
V2#1	1	3	4	6	8	10
...Buck's Tale (6/94, $1.95)	1	2	3	5	6	8
...1994 Annual nn (2/94, $2.50, 52 pgs.)-Flip book format						5.00
Special 1 (7/92, $1.95)-Kelly Bundy photo-c/poster	1	3	4	6	8	10

MARRIED ... WITH CHILDREN: KELLY BUNDY
Now Comics: Aug, 1992 - No. 3, Oct, 1992 ($1.95, limited series)

1-3: Kelly Bundy photo-c & poster in each 6.00

MARRIED ... WITH CHILDREN: QUANTUM QUARTET
Now Comics: Oct, 1993 - No. 4, 1994, ($1.95, limited series)

1-4: Fantastic Four parody 6.00

MARRIED ... WITH CHILDREN: 2099
Now Comics: June, 1993 - No. 3, Aug, 1993 ($1.95, limited series)

	GD	VG	FN	VF	VF/NM	NM-
1,2	1	3	4	6	8	10
3-Star Wars parody	2	4	6	11	16	20

MARS
First Comics: Jan, 1984 - No. 12, Jan, 1985 ($1.00, Mando paper)

1-12: Marc Hempel & Mark Wheatley story & art. 2-The Black Flame begins. 10-Dynamo Joe begins 3.00
TPB (IDW Publ., 8/05, $39.99) r/#1-12, creator commentary; bonus art; new Hempel-c 40.00

MARS & BEYOND (Disney, TV)
Dell Publishing Co.: No. 866, Dec, 1957

	GD	VG	FN	VF	VF/NM	NM-
Four Color 866-A Science feat. from Tomorrowland	9	18	27	59	117	175

MARS ATTACKS
Topps Comics: May, 1994 - No. 5, Sept, 1994 ($2.95, limited series)

	GD	VG	FN	VF	VF/NM	NM-
1-5-Giffen story; flip books	2	4	6	8	10	12
Gold Edition (5/94)	3	6	9	16	23	30
Special Edition (5/94)	2	4	6	9	12	15
Trade paperback (12/94, $12.95)-r/limited series plus new 8 pg. story						15.00

MARS ATTACKS
Topps Comics: V2#1, 8/95 - V2#3, 10/95; V2#4, 1/96 - No. 7, 5/96($2.95, bi-monthly #6 on)

V2#1-7: 1-Counterstrike storyline begins. 4-(1/96). 5-(1/96). 5,7-Brereton-c. 6-(3/96)-Simonson-c. 7-Story leads into Baseball Special #1 5.00
Baseball Special 1 (6/96, $2.95)-Bisley-c. 5.00

MARS ATTACKS
IDW Publishing: Jun, 2012 - No. 10, May, 2013 ($3.99, issues #6-10 polybagged with card)

1-10: 1-Layman-s/McCrea-a; 58 covers including all 54 cards from 1962 set 4.00
... #1 IDW's Greatest Hits Edition (3/16, $1.00) reprints #1 3.00
... Art Gallery (9/14, $3.99) Trading card style art by various 4.00
...: Classics Obliterated (6/13, $7.99) Spoofs of Moby Dick, Jekyll & Hyde, Robinson Crusoe 8.00
... KISS (1/13, $3.99) Ryall-s/Robinson-a; 2 variant-c with Judge Dredd & Star Slammers 4.00
... Popeye (1/13, $3.99) Beatty-a; 2 variant-c with Miss Fury & Opus 4.00
... The Holidays (10/12, $7.99) short stories for Halloween-Christmas; 5 covers 8.00
... The Real Ghostbusters (1/13, $3.99) Holder-a; 2 variant-c with Chew & Madman 4.00
... : The Transformers (1/13, $3.99) 2 variant-c with Spike & Strangers in Paradise 4.00
... Zombie vs. Robots (1/13, $3.99) Ryall-s; 2 variant-c with Rog-2000 & Cerebus 4.00

MARS ATTACKS
Dynamite Entertainment: 2018 - No. 5, 2019 ($3.99, limited series)

1-5-Kyle Starks-s/Chris Schweizer-a; multiple covers on each 4.00

MARS ATTACKS FIRST BORN
IDW Publishing: May, 2014 - No. 4, Aug, 2014 ($3.99, limited series)

1-4-Chris Ryall-s/Sam Kieth-a; multiple covers on each 4.00

MARS ATTACKS HIGH SCHOOL
Topps Comics: May, 1997 - No. 2, Sept, 1997 ($2.95, B&W, limited series)

1,2-Stelfreeze-c 4.00

MARS ATTACKS JUDGE DREDD
IDW Publishing: Sept, 2013 - No. 4, Dec, 2013 ($3.99, limited series)

1-4-Al Ewing-s/John McCrea-a/Greg Staples-c 4.00

MARS ATTACKS IMAGE
Topps Comics: Dec, 1996 - No. 4, Mar, 1997 ($2.50, limited series)

1-4-Giffen-s/Smith & Sienkiewicz-a 4.00

MARS ATTACKS: OCCUPATION
IDW Publishing: Mar, 2016 - No. 5, Jul, 2016 ($3.99, limited series)

1-5-John Layman-s/Andy Kuhn-a; multiple covers 4.00

MARS ATTACKS / RED SONJA
Dynamite Entertainment: 2020 - No. 5, 2020 ($3.99, limited series)

1-5-John Layman-s/Fran Strukan-a; multiple covers. 3-Intro. Green Sonja 4.00

MARS ATTACKS THE SAVAGE DRAGON
Topps Comics: Dec, 1996 - No. 4, Mar, 1997 ($2.95, limited series)

1-4: 1-w/bound-in card 4.00

MARSHAL BLUEBERRY (See Blueberry)
Marvel Comics (Epic Comics): 1991 ($14.95, graphic novel)

	GD	VG	FN	VF	VF/NM	NM-
1-Moebius-a	4	8	12	25	40	55

MARSHAL LAW (Also see Crime And Punishment: Marshall Law...)
Marvel Comics (Epic Comics): Oct, 1987 - No. 6, May, 1989 ($1.95, mature)

1-6 3.00

M.A.R.S. PATROL TOTAL WAR (Formerly Total War #1,2)
Gold Key: No. 3, Sept, 1966 - No. 10, Aug, 1969 (All-Painted-c except #7)

	GD	VG	FN	VF	VF/NM	NM-
3-Wood-a; aliens invade USA	6	12	18	38	69	100
4-10	4	8	12	23	37	50
Wally Wood's M.A.R.S. Patrol Total War TPB (Dark Horse, 9/04, $12.95) r/#3 & Total War #1&2; foreward by Batton Lash; afterword by Dan Adkins						13.00

GD VG FN VF VF/NM NM-
2.0 4.0 6.0 8.0 9.0 9.2

MARTHA WASHINGTON (Also see Dark Horse Presents Fifth Anniversary Special, Dark Horse Presents #100-4, Give Me Liberty, Happy Birthday Martha Washington & San Diego Comicon Comics #2)

MARTHA WASHINGTON... (one-shots)
Dark Horse Comics (Legend): ($2.95/$3.50, one-shots)

... Dies (7/07, $3.50) Miller-s/Gibbons-a; r/Miller's original outline for Give Me Liberty 4.00
... Stranded in Space (11/95, $2.95) Miller-s/Gibbons-a; Big Guy app. 5.00

MARTHA WASHINGTON GOES TO WAR
Dark Horse Comics (Legend): May, 1994 - No. 5, Sep, 1994 ($2.95, lim. series)

1-5-Miller scripts; Gibbons-c/a 5.00
TPB ($17.95) r/#1-5 18.00

MARTHA WASHINGTON SAVES THE WORLD
Dark Horse Comics: Dec, 1997 - No. 3, Feb, 1998 ($2.95/$3.95, lim. series)

1,2-Miller scripts; Gibbons-c/a in all 5.00
3-($3.95) 5.00

MARTHA WAYNE (See The Story of...)

MARTIAN MANHUNTER (See Detective Comics & Showcase '95 #9)
DC Comics: May, 1988 - No. 4, Aug,. 1988 ($1.25, limited series)

1-4: 1,4-Batman app. 2-Batman cameo 4.00
Special 1-(1996, $3.50) 4.00

MARTIAN MANHUNTER (See JLA)
DC Comics: No. 0, Oct, 1998 - No. 36, Nov, 2001 ($1.99)

0-(10/98) Origin retold; Ostrander-s/Mandrake-c/a 3.00
1-36: 1-(12/98). 6-9-JLA app. 18,19-JSA app. 24-Mahnke-a 3.00
#1,000,000 (11/98) 853rd Century x-over 3.00
Annual 1,2 (1998,1999; $2.95) 1-Ghosts; Wrightson-c. 2-JLApe 4.00

MARTIAN MANHUNTER (See DCU Brave New World)
DC Comics: Oct, 2006 - No. 8, May, 2007 ($2.99, limited series)

1-8-Lieberman-s/Barrionuevo-a/c 3.00
...: The Others Among Us TPB (2007, $19.99) r/#1-8 & story from DCU Brave New World 20.00

MARTIAN MANHUNTER
DC Comics: Aug, 2015 - No. 12, Jul, 2016 ($2.99)

1-12: 1-Rob Williams-s/Eddy Barrows-a. 1-3-JLA app. 10-Origin 3.00

MARTIAN MANHUNTER
DC Comics: Feb, 2019 - No. 12, Apr, 2020 ($3.99)

1-12: 1-Orlando-s/Rossmo-a; Earth detective and flashbacks to Mars. 3-Origin retold 4.00

MARTIAN MANHUNTER: AMERICAN SECRETS
DC Comics: 1992 - Book Three, 1992 ($4.95, limited series, prestige format)

1-3: Barreto-a 5.00

MARTIAN MANHUNTER/ MARVIN THE MARTIAN SPECIAL
DC Comics: Aug, 2017 ($4.99, one-shot)

1-Orlando & Barbiere-s/Lopresti-a; covers by Lopresti & DeStefano 5.00

MARTIN KANE (William Gargan as... Private Eye)(Stage/Screen/Radio/TV)
Fox Feature Syndicate (Hero Books): No. 4, June, 1950 - No. 2, Aug, 1950 (Formerly My Secret Affair)

4(#1)-True crime stories; Wood-c/a(2); used in **SOTI**, pg. 160; photo back-c 41 82 123 256 428 600
2-Wood/Orlando story, 5 pgs; Wood-a(2) 31 62 93 182 296 410

MARTIN LUTHER KING AND THE MONTGOMERY STORY (See Promotional Comics section)

MARTIN MYSTERY
Dark Horse (Bonelli Comics): Mar, 1999 - No. 6, Aug, 1999 ($4.95, B&W, digest size)

1-6-Reprints Italian series in English; Gibbons-c on #1-3 5.00

MARTY MOUSE
I. W. Enterprises: No date (1958?) (10¢)

1-Reprint 3 6 9 15 22 28

MARVEL
Marvel Comics: May, 2020 - No. 6, May, 2021 ($4.99)

1-6-Short story anthology; Alex Ross-s/a. 1-Busiek-s/Rude-a. 2-Powell-s/a; Brereton-s/a 3-Weiss-s/a; Sienkiewicz-s/a. 4-Acuña-s/a; Barta-s/a, Dr. Droom app. 5-Hughes-s/a 5.00

MARVEL ACTION: AVENGERS (All ages)(Title changed from Avengers after #5)
IDW Publishing: No. 6, May, 2019 - No. 9, Sept, 2019 ($3.99)

6-9-Iron Man, Captain America, Thor, Hawkeye, Black Widow, Black Panther & Hulk app. 4.00

MARVEL ACTION: CAPTAIN MARVEL (All ages)
IDW Publishing: Aug, 2019 - No. 3, Oct, 2019 ($3.99)

1-3-Spider-Woman app.; Sam Maggs-s/Sweeney Boo-a 4.00

MARVEL ACTION: CAPTAIN MARVEL (2nd series)(All ages)
IDW Publishing: Jan, 2021 - No. 5, May, 2021 ($3.99)

1-5: 1,2-Ghost-Spider app.; Sam Maggs-s 4.00

MARVEL ACTION: CHILLERS (All ages)
IDW Publishing: Oct, 2020 - No. 4, Dec, 2020 ($3.99)

1-4-Iron Man, Ironheart & Dr. Strange app. 2-Elsa Bloodstone app. 3-Venom app. 4.00

MARVEL ACTION CLASSICS (All ages)
IDW Publishing: May, 2019 - Present ($4.99)

... Ant-Man 1 (11/19, $4.99) Ant-Man reprints; Van Lente-s/Lolli-a; Clayton Henry-c 5.00
... Avengers Featuring Doctor Strange 1 (1/20, $4.99) Reprints; Spider-Man app. 5.00
... Hulk 1 (7/19, $4.99) Reprints; Doctor Strange, Iron Man and Spider-Man app. 5.00
... Spider-Man 1 (5/19, $4.99) Reprints; Doctor Strange and Thor app. 5.00
... Spider-Man Two-In-One 2-4 (12/19 - No. 4, 10/21, $4.99) Reprints 5.00

MARVEL ACTION HOUR FEATURING IRON MAN (TV cartoon)
Marvel Comics: Nov, 1994 - No. 8, June, 1995 ($1.50/$2.95)

1-8: Based on cartoon series 4.00
1 ($2.95)-Polybagged w/16 pg Marvel Action Hour Preview & acetate print 5.00

MARVEL ACTION HOUR FEATURING THE FANTASTIC FOUR (TV cartoon)
Marvel Comics: Nov, 1994 - No. 8, June, 1995 ($1.50/$2.95)

1-8: Based on cartoon series 4.00
1-($2.95)-Polybagged w/ 16 pg. Marvel Action Hour Preview & acetate print 5.00

MARVEL ACTION: ORIGINS (All ages stories)
IDW Publishing (Marvel): Dec, 2020 - No. 4, Oct, 2021 ($3.99)

1-Origins of Spider-Man & Thanos. 2-Captain Marvel. 3-Incredible Hulk & Venom. 4-Miles Morales Spider-Man 4.00

MARVEL ACTION: SPIDER-MAN (All ages stories)
IDW Publishing (Marvel): Nov, 2018 - No. 12, Nov, 2019 ($3.99)

1-12: 1-3-Dawson-s/Ossio-a; teen-age Peter Parker, Miles and Spider-Gwen app. 4.00
Volume 2 (1/20 - No. 3, 7/20) 1-3-Teen-age Peter Parker, Miles and Spider-Gwen app. 4.00
Volume 3 (3/21 - No. 5, 8/21) 1-5-Teen-age Peter Parker. 1,2-Scorpion app. 4.00

MARVEL ACTION UNIVERSE (TV cartoon)
Marvel Comics: Jan, 1989 ($1.00, one-shot)

1-r/Spider-Man And His Amazing Friends 4.00

MARVEL ADVENTURES
Marvel Comics: Apr, 1997 - No. 18, Sept, 1998 ($1.50)

1-18-"Animated style": 1,4,7-Hulk-c/app. 2,11-Spider-Man. 3,8,15-X-Men. 5-Spider-Man & X-Men. 6-Spider-Man & Human Torch. 9,12-Fantastic Four. 10,16-Silver Surfer. 13-Spider-Man & Silver Surfer. 14-Hulk & Dr. Strange. 18-Capt. America 4.00

MARVEL ADVENTURES...
Marvel Comics: 2007, 2008 (Free Comic Book Day giveaways)

... Free Comic Book Day 2007 (6/07) 1-Iron Man, Hulk and Franklin Richards app. 3.00
... Free Comic Book Day 2008 - Iron Man, Hulk, Ant-Man and Spider-Man app. 3.00

MARVEL ADVENTURES FANTASTIC FOUR (All ages title)
Marvel Comics: No. 0, July, 2005 - No. 48, July, 2009 ($1.99/$2.50/$2.99)

0-($1.99) Movie version characters; Dr. Doom app.; Eaton-a 3.00
1-10-($2.50) 1-Skrulls app.; Pagulayan-a. 7-Namor app. 3.00
11-48-($2.99) 12,42-Dr. Doom app. 24-Namor app. 26,28-Silver Surfer app. 3.00
... Vol. 1: Family of Heroes (2005, $6.99, digest) r/#1-4 7.00
... Vol. 2: Fantastic Voyages (2006, $6.99, digest) r/#5-8 7.00
... Vol. 3: World's Greatest (2006, $6.99, digest) r/#9-12 7.00
... Vol. 4: Cosmic Threats (2006, $6.99, digest) r/#13-16 7.00
... Vol. 5: All 4 One, 4 For All (2007, $6.99, digest) r/#17-20 7.00
... Vol. 6: Monsters & Mysteries (2007, $6.99, digest) r/#21-24 7.00
... Vol. 7: The Silver Surfer (2007, $6.99, digest) r/#25-28 7.00
... Vol. 8: Monsters, Moles, Cowboys & Coupons (2008, $7.99, digest) r/#29-32 8.00

MARVEL ADVENTURES FLIP MAGAZINE (All ages title)
Marvel Comics: Aug, 2005 - No. 26, Sept, 2007 ($3.99/$4.99)

1-11: 1-10-Rep. Marvel Advs. Fantastic Four and Marvel Advs. Spider-Man in flip format 4.00
12-14-($4.99) Reprints Marvel Advs. Spider-Man & X-Men/Power Pack in flip format 5.00
15-26-Rep. Marvel Advs. Fantastic Four and Marvel Advs. Spider-Man in flip format 5.00

MARVEL ADVENTURES HULK (All ages title)
Marvel Comics: Sept, 2007 - No. 16, Dec, 2008 ($2.99)

1-16: 1-New version of Hulk's origin; Pagulayan-c. 2-Jamie Madrox app. 13-Mummies 3.00
... Vol. 1: Misunderstood Monster (2007, $6.99, digest) r/#1-4 7.00

MARVEL ADVENTURES IRON MAN (All ages title)
Marvel Comics: July, 2007 - No. 13, Jul, 2008 ($2.99)

1-13: 1-4-Michael Golden-c. 1-New version of Iron Man's origin. 2-Intro. the Mandarin 3.00
... Vol. 1: Heart of Steel (2007, $6.99, digest) r/#1-4 7.00
... Vol. 2: Iron Armory (2008, $7.99, digest) r/#5-8 8.00

MARVEL ADVENTURES SPIDER-MAN (All ages title)
Marvel Comics: May, 2005 - No. 61, May, 2010 ($2.50/$2.99)

1-13-Lee & Ditko stories retold with new art. 13-Conner-c 3.00
14-48: 14-Begin $2.99-c. 14-16-Conner-c. 22,23-Black costume. 35-Venom app. 3.00
50-($3.99) Sinister Six app.; back-up w/Sonny Liew-a 4.00
51-61: 53-Emma Frost becomes a regular; intro. Chat; Skottie Young-c begin 3.00
... Vol. 1 HC (2006, $19.99, with dustjacket) r/#1-8; plot for #7; sketch pages from #6,8 20.00
... Vol. 1: The Sinister Six (2005, $6.99, digest) r/#1-4 7.00
... Vol. 2: Power Struggle (2005, $6.99, digest) r/#5-8 7.00
... Vol. 3: Doom With a View (2006, $6.99, digest) r/#9-12 7.00
... Vol. 4: Concrete Jungle (2006, $6.99, digest) r/#13-16 7.00
... Vol. 5: Monsters on the Prowl (2007, $6.99, digest) r/#17-20 7.00
... Vol. 6: The Black Costume (2007, $6.99, digest) r/#21-24 7.00
... Vol. 7: Secret Identity (2007, $6.99, digest) r/#25-28 7.00
... Vol. 8: Forces of Nature (2008, $7.99, digest) r/#29-32 8.00
... Vol. 9: Fiercest Foes (2008, $7.99, digest) r/#33-36 8.00

MARVEL ADVENTURES SPIDER-MAN (All ages title)
Marvel Comics: June, 2010 - No. 24, May, 2012 ($3.99/$2.99)

1-($3.99) Tobin-s; Franklin Richards back-up 4.00
2-23-($2.99): 3,7-Wolverine app. 3,4-Bullseye app. 6-Doctor Octopus app. 3.00

MARVEL ADVENTURES STARRING DAREDEVIL (...Adventure #3 on)
Marvel Comics Group: Dec, 1975 - No. 6, Oct, 1976

1 3 6 9 15 22 28
2-6-r/Daredevil #22-27 by Colan. 3-5-(25¢-c) 1 3 4 6 8 10
3-5-(30¢-c variants, limited distribution)(4,6,8/76) 6 12 18 38 69 100

MARVEL ADVENTURES SUPER HEROES (All ages title)
Marvel Comics: Sept, 2008 - No. 21, May, 2010 ($2.99)

1-21: 1-4: Spider-Man, Hulk and Iron Man team-ups. 1-Hercules app. 5-Dr. Strange app. 6-Ant-Man origin re-told. 7-Thor. 8,12-Capt. America. 17-Avengers begin 3.00

MARVEL ADVENTURES SUPER HEROES (All ages title)
Marvel Comics: June, 2010 - No. 24, May, 2012 ($3.99/$2.99)

1-($3.99) Iron Man and Avengers vs. Magneto 4.00
2-24-($2.99) 4-Deadpool app. 5-Rhino app. 11,12,22-Hulk app. 13,14,19-Thor 3.00

MARVEL ADVENTURES THE AVENGERS (All ages title)
Marvel Comics: July, 2006 - No. 39, Oct, 2009 ($2.99)

1-39-Spider-Man, Wolverine, Hulk, Iron Man, Capt. America, Storm, Giant-Girl app. 3.00
... Vol. 1: Heroes Assembled (2006, $6.99, digest) r/#1-4 7.00

Martian Manhunter (2015) #7 © DC

Marvel #6 © MAR

Marvel Action: Origins #2 © MAR

	GD	VG	FN	VF	VF/NM	NM-
	2.0	4.0	6.0	8.0	9.0	9.2

... Vol. 2: Mischief (2007, $6.99, digest) r/#5-8 7.00
... Vol. 3: Bizarre Adventures (2007, $6.99, digest) r/#9-12 7.00
... Vol. 4: The Dream Team (2007, $6.99, digest) r/#13-15 & Giant-Size #1 7.00
... Vol. 5: Some Assembling Required (2008, $7.99, digest) r/#16-19 8.00

MARVEL ADVENTURES TWO-IN-ONE
Marvel Comics: Oct, 2007 - No. 18 ($4.99, bi-weekly)

1-18: 1-9-Reprints Marvel Adventures Spider-Man and Fantastic Four stories. 10-Hulk 5.00

MARVEL AGE (The Official Marvel News Magazine)
(A low priced news Magazine in comic format to promote coming issues)
Marvel Publications: Apr, 1983 - No. 140, Sept, 1994

1-Saga of Crystar-c/s 2 4 6 8 11 14
2-5,9,11,14,15 5.00
6-Beta Ray Bill preview (9/83) 3 6 9 14 20 25
7-Spider-Ham preview 1 3 4 6 8 10
8-Stan Lee/Jim Shooter-c/interviews 2 4 6 8 11 14
10-Star Wars-c, preview Spider-Man vs. Hobgoblin 2 4 6 8 10 12
12-(3/84) 2 pg. preview/1st app. of Spider-Man in Alien Venom black costume, 2 months before Amazing Spider-Man #252 5 10 15 34 60 85
13,16: 16-New Mutants-c/s 6.00
17-Transformers preview (8/84) 2 4 6 9 13 16
18-24,26-28,30,32-37,39,40 4.00
25(4/85)-Rocket Raccoon-c/preview art one month before Rocket Raccoon #1 6.00
29-Longshot preview (8/85) 2 4 6 9 12 15
31-Thundercats preview (10/85) 2 4 6 11 16 20
38-He-Man & Masters of the Universe-c/preview 2 4 6 8 12 15
41(8/86)-Classic Stan Lee-c/sty 4 8 12 28 47 65
42-66: 53-Girls of Marvel swimsuits-c 4.00
67-Jim Lee-c, Wolverine/punisher/Sub-Mariner-c/s 6.00
68-86,88,89: 76-She-Hulk swimsuit-c by John Byrne 5.00
87-Danny Ketch as Ghost Rider 2 4 6 11 16 20
90(7/90)-Spider-Man-c by Todd McFarlane; Jim Lee Interview 3 6 9 16 23 30
91-Thanos and Silver Surfer-c 2 4 6 8 11 14
92-94,96,98,101-103,105-137,139 4.00
95-Captain America 50th Anniversary-c/issue 6.00
97(2/91)-Darkhawk-c/preview; Infinity Gauntlet 4 8 12 25 40 55
99(4/91)-Black Panther Returns-c 2 4 6 9 12 15
100-Sleepwalker 1 3 4 6 8 10
104-Wolverine-c by Jim Lee; Psylocke cameo 3 6 9 19 30 40
138(7/94)-Deadpool, Cable-c 2 4 6 11 16 20
140-Last issue 1 3 4 6 8 10
Annual 1(9/85) 2 4 6 8 10 12
Annual 2, 3(9/87) 5.00
Annual 4(6/88)-1st app. Damage Control 2 4 6 8 11 14

MARVEL AGE FANTASTIC FOUR (All ages title)
Marvel Comics: Jun, 2004 - No. 12, Mar, 2005 ($2.25)

1-12-Lee & Kirby stories retold with new art by various. 11-Impossible Man app. 3.00
...Tales (4/05, $2.25) retells first meeting with the Black Panther; O'Hare & Lim-a 3.00
Vol. 1: All For One TPB (2004, $5.99, digest size) r/#1-4 6.00
Vol. 2: Doom TPB (2004, $5.99, digest size) r/#5-8 6.00
Vol. 3: The Return of Doctor Doom TPB (2005, $5.99, digest size) r/#9-12 6.00

MARVEL AGE HULK (All ages title)
Marvel Comics: Nov, 2004 - No. 4, Feb, 2005 ($1.75)

1-3-Lee & Kirby stories retold with new art by various 3.00
Vol. 1: Incredible TPB (2005, $5.99, digest size) r/#1-4 6.00
Vol. 2: Defenders (2008, $7.99, digest) r/#5-8 8.00

MARVEL AGE SPIDER-MAN (All ages title)
Marvel Comics: May, 2004 - No. 20, Mar, 2005 ($2.25)

1-20-Lee & Ditko stories retold with new art. 4-Doctor Doom app. 5-Lizard app. 3.00
1-(Free Comic Book Day giveaway, 8/04) Spider-Man vs. The Vulture; Brooks-a 3.00
Vol. 1 TPB (2004, $5.99, digest) 1-r/#1-4 6.00
Vol. 2: Everyday Hero TPB (2004, $5.99, digest) r/#5-8 6.00
Vol. 3: Swingtime TPB (2004, $5.99, digest) r/#9-12 6.00
Spidey Strikes Back TPB (2005, 5.99, digest) r/#17-20 6.00

MARVEL AGE SPIDER-MAN TEAM-UP (Marvel Adventures on cover)
Marvel Comics: June, 2005 (Free Comic Book Day giveaway)

1-Spider-Man meets the Fantastic Four 3.00

MARVEL AGE TEAM-UP (All ages Spider-Man team-ups) (Also see Free Comic Book Day edition in the Promotional Comics section)
Marvel Comics: Nov, 2004 - No. 5, Apr, 2005 ($1.75)

1-5-Stories retold with new art by various. 1-Fantastic Four app. 3-Kitty Pryde app. 3.00
... Vol. 1: A Little Help From My Friends (2005, $7.99, digest) r/#1-5 8.00

MARVEL AND DC PRESENT FEATURING THE UNCANNY X-MEN AND THE NEW TEEN TITANS
Marvel Comics/DC Comics: 1982 ($2.00, 68 pgs., one-shot, Baxter paper)

1-3rd app. Deathstroke the Terminator; Darkseid app.; Simonson/Austin-c/a 3 6 9 21 33 45

MARVEL APES
Marvel Comics: Nov, 2008 - No. 4, Dec, 2008 ($3.99, limited series)

1-4: 1-Kesel-s/Bachs-a; back-up history story with Peyer-s/Kitson-a; two covers 4.00
1-($10.00) Hero Initiative edition with Daredevil gorilla cover by Mike Wieringo 10.00
#0-(2008, $3.99) r/Amazing Spider-Man #110,111; gallery of Marvel Apes variant covers 4.00
...: Amazing Spider-Monkey Special 1 (6/09, $3.99) Sandmonk and the Apevengers app. 4.00
...: Grunt Line 1 (7/09, $3.99) Kesel-s; Charles Darwin app. 4.00
...: Speedball Special 1 (5/09, $3.99) Bachs & Hardin-a 4.00

MARVEL ASSISTANT-SIZED SPECTACULAR
Marvel Comics: Jun, 2009 - No. 2, Jun, 2009 ($3.99, limited series)

1,2-Short stories by various incl. Isanove, Giarrusso, Nauck, Wyatt Cenak, Warren 4.00

MARVEL ATLAS (Styled after the Official Marvel Handbooks)
Marvel Comics: 2007 - No. 2, 2008 ($3.99, limited series)

1,2-Profiles and maps of countries in the Marvel Universe 4.00

MARVEL BOY (Astonishing #3 on; see Marvel Super Action #4)
Marvel Comics (MPC): Dec, 1950 - No. 2, Feb, 1951

1-Origin Marvel Boy by Russ Heath 213 426 639 1363 2332 3300
2-Everett-a; Washington DC under attack 174 348 522 1114 1907 2700

MARVEL BOY (Marvel Knights)
Marvel Comics: Aug, 2000 - No. 6, Mar, 2001 ($2.99, limited series)

1-Intro. Marvel Boy; Morrison-s/J.G. Jones-c/a 4.00
1-DF Variant-c 5.00
2-6 3.00
TPB (6/01, $15.95) 16.00

MARVEL BOY: THE URANIAN (Agents of Atlas)
Marvel Comics: Mar, 2010 - No. 3, May, 2010 ($3.99, limited series)

1-3-Origin re-told; back-up reprints from 1950s; Heath & Everett-a 4.00

MARVEL CHILLERS (Also see Giant-Size Chillers)
Marvel Comics Group: Oct, 1975 - No. 7, Oct, 1976 (All 25¢ issues)

1-Intro. Modred the Mystic, ends #2; Kane-c(p) 8 16 24 52 99 145
2-2nd Modred 3 6 9 17 26 35
3-Tigra, the Were-Woman begins (origin), ends #7 (see Giant-Size Creatures #1). Chaykin/Wrightson-c. 6 12 18 41 76 110
4,5,7: 4-Kraven app. 5,6-Red Wolf app. 7-Kirby-c; Tuska-p 2 4 6 11 16 20
4-6-(30¢-c variants, limited distribution)(4-8/76) 5 10 15 34 60 85
6-Byrne-a(p); Buckler-c(p) 3 6 9 14 20 26

NOTE: *Bolle a-1. Buckler c-2. Kirby c-7.*

MARVEL CLASSICS COMICS SERIES FEATURING...
(Also see Pendulum Illustrated Classics)
Marvel Comics Group: 1976 - No. 36, Dec, 1978 (52 pgs., no ads)

1-Dr. Jekyll and Mr. Hyde 2 4 6 13 18 22
2-10,28: 28-1st Golden-c/a; Pit and the Pendulum 2 4 6 8 11 14
11-27,29-36 1 3 4 6 8 10

NOTE: ***Adkins** c-1i, 4i, 12i. **Alcala** a-34i; c-34. **Bolle** a-35. **Buscema** c-17p, 19p, 26p. **Golden** c/a-28. **Gil Kane** c-1-16p, 21p, 22p, 24p, 32p. **Nebres** a-5; c-24i. **Nino** a-2, 8, 12. **Redondo** a-1, 9. No. 1-12 were reprinted from Pendulum Illustrated Classics.*

MARVEL COLLECTIBLE CLASSICS: AVENGERS
Marvel Comics: 1998 ($10.00, reprints with chromium wraparound-c)

1-Reprints Avengers Vol.3, #1; Perez-c 3 6 9 16 24 32

MARVEL COLLECTIBLE CLASSICS: SPIDER-MAN
Marvel Comics: 1998 ($10.00, reprints with chromium wraparound-c)

1-Reprints Amazing Spider-Man #300; McFarlane-c 72 144 216 360 505 650
2-Reprints Spider-Man #1; McFarlane-c 29 58 87 145 203 260

MARVEL COLLECTIBLE CLASSICS: X-MEN
Marvel Comics: 1998 ($10.00, reprints with chromium wraparound-c)

1-Reprints (Uncanny) X-Men #1 & 2; Adam Kubert-c 3 6 9 21 33 45
2-6: 2-Reprints Uncanny X-Men #141 & 142; Byrne-c. 3-Reprints (Uncanny) X-Men #137; Larroca-c. 4-Reprints X-Men #25; Andy Kubert-c. 5-Reprints Giant Size X-Men #1; Gary Frank-c. 6-Reprints X-Men V2#1; Ramos-c 3 6 9 16 24 32

GD	VG	FN	VF	VF/NM	NM-
2.0	4.0	6.0	8.0	9.0	9.2

MARVEL COLLECTOR'S EDITION
Marvel Comics: 1992 (Ordered thru mail with Charleston Chew candy wrapper)

1-Flip-book format; Spider-Man, Silver Surfer, Wolverine (by Sam Keith), & Ghost Rider stories; Wolverine back-c by Kieth 2 4 6 8 10 12

MARVEL COLLECTORS' ITEM CLASSICS (Marvel's Greatest #23 on)
Marvel Comics Group(ATF): Feb, 1965 - No. 22, Aug, 1969 (25¢, 68 pgs.)

1-Fantastic Four, Spider-Man, Thor, Hulk, Iron Man-r begin
15 30 45 100 220 340
2 (4/66) 7 14 21 46 86 125
3,4 5 10 15 37 66 95
5-10 5 10 15 34 60 85
11-22: 22-r/The Man in the Ant Hill/TTA #27 5 10 15 30 50 70
NOTE: *All reprints;* ***Ditko, Kirby*** *art in all.*

MARVEL COMICS (Marvel Mystery Comics #2 on)
Timely Comics (Funnies, Inc.): Oct, Nov, 1939

NOTE: The first issue was originally dated October 1939. Most copies have a black circle stamped over the date (on cover and inside) with "November" printed over it. However, some copies do not have the November overprint and could have a higher value. Most No. 1's have printing defects, i.e., tilted pages which caused trimming into the panels usually on right side and bottom. Covers exist with and without gloss finish.

1-Origin Sub-Mariner by Bill Everett(1st newsstand app.); 1st 8 pgs. were produced for Motion Picture Funnies Weekly #1 which was probably not distributed outside of advance copies; intro Human Torch by Carl Burgos, Kazar the Great (1st Tarzan clone), & Jungle Terror(only app.); intro. The Angel by Gustavson, The Masked Raider & his horse Lightning (ends #12); cover by sci/fi pulp illustrator Frank R. Paul
68,000 136,000 204,000 408,000 642,600 1,200,000

MARVEL COMICS
Marvel Comics: 1990 ($17.95, hardcover)

1-Reprint of entire Marvel Comics #1 2 4 6 10 14 18

MARVEL COMICS
Marvel Comics

... No. 1 Halloween Comic Fest 2014 (giveaway) Re-colored reprint of Human Torch and Sub-Mariner stories from Marvel Comics #1; cover swipe by Jelena Djurdjevic 3.00
... 70th Anniversary Special (10/09, $4.99) Re-colored reprint of entire Marvel Comics #1; cover swipe by Jelena Djurdjevic 6.00

MARVEL COMICS
Marvel Comics: No. 1000, Oct, 2019 - No. 1001, Dec, 2019 ($9.99/$4.99)

1000-($9.99, square-bound) Single page stories tied in to each year of Marvel from 1939-2020; intro. The Eternity Mask; s/a by various; main cover by Alex Ross 10.00
1001-($4.99) Single page stories; s/a by various 5.00

MARVEL COMICS DIGEST (All-ages Marvel reprint stories printed by Archie Comics)
Archie Comics Publications: Jul, 2017 - No. 8, Oct, 2018 ($6.99, digest-size)

1-8: 1-Spider-Man reprints. 2,6-Avengers. 3-Thor. 4-X-Men. 5-Avengers/Black Panther. 7-Avengers/Ant-Man. 8-Spider-Man & Venom 7.00

MARVEL COMICS PRESENTS
Marvel Comics (Midnight Sons imprint #143 on): Early Sept, 1988 - No. 175, Feb, 1995 ($1.25/$1.50/$1.75, bi-weekly)

1-Wolverine by Buscema in #1-10 3 6 9 16 23 30
2-5 1 3 4 6 8 10
6-10: 6-Sub-Mariner app. 10-Colossus begins 5.00
11-18,20-47,51-71: 17-Cyclops begins. 24-Havok begins. 25-Origin/1st app. Nth Man. 26-Hulk begins by Rogers. 29-Quasar app. 31-Excalibur begins by Austin (i). 32-McFarlane-a(p). 33-Capt. America; Jim Lee-a. 37-Devil-Slayer app. 38-Wolverine begins by Buscema; Hulk app. 39-Spider-Man app. 46-Liefeld Wolverine-c. 51-53-Wolverine by Rob Liefeld. 54-61-Wolverine/Hulk story: 54-Werewolf by Night begins; The Shroud by Ditko. 58-Iron Man by Ditko. 59-Punisher. 62-Deathlok & Wolverine stories 63-Wolverine. 64-71-Wolverine/Ghost Rider 8-part story. 70-Liefeld Ghost Rider/ Wolverine-c 4.00
19-1st app. Damage Control 2 4 6 8 10 12
48-50-Wolverine & Spider-Man team-up by Erik Larsen-c/a. 48-Wasp app. 49,50-Savage Dragon prototype app. by Larsen. 50-Silver Surfer. 50-53-Comet Man; Mumy scripts 6.00
72-Begin 13-part Weapon-X story (Wolverine origin) by B. Windsor-Smith (prologue)
3 6 9 17 25 34
73-Weapon-X part 1; Black Knight, Sub-Mariner 2 4 6 8 11 14
74-84: 74-Weapon-X part 2; Black Knight, Sub-Mariner. 76-Death's Head story. 77-Mr. Fantastic story. 78-Iron Man by Steacy. 80,81-Capt. America by Ditko/Austin. 81-Daredevil by Rogers/Williamson. 82-Power Man. 83-Human Torch by Ditko(a&scripts); $1.00-c direct, $1.25 newsstand. 84-Last Weapon-X (24 pg. conclusion) 4.00
85-Begin 8-part Wolverine story by Sam Kieth (c/a); 1st Kieth-a on Wolverine; begin 8-part Beast story by Jae Lee(p) with Liefeld part pencils #85,86; 1st Jae Lee-a (assisted w/Liefeld, 1991) 5.00
86-90: 86-89-Wolverine, Beast stories continue. 90-Begin 8-part Ghost Rider & Cable story, ends #97; begin flip book format w/two-c 4.00
91-174: 93-Begin 6-part Wolverine story, ends #98. 98-Begin 2-part Ghost Rider story. 99-Spider-Man story. 100-Full-length Ghost Rider/Wolverine story by Sam Keith w/Tim Vigil assists; anniversary issue, non flip-book. 101-Begin 6-part Ghost Rider/Dr. Strange story & begin 8-part Wolverine/Nightcrawler story by Colan/Williamson; Punisher story. 107-Begin 6-part Ghost Rider/Werewolf by Night story. 109-Begin 8 part Wolverine/Typhoid Mary story. 111-Iron Fist. 113-Begin 6-part Giant-Man & begin 6-part Ghost Rider/Iron Fist stories. 117-Preview of Ravage 2099 (1st app.); begin 6 part Wolverine/Venom story w/Kieth-a. 118-Preview of Doom 2099 (1st app.). 119-Begin Ghost Rider/Cloak & Dagger by Colan. 120,136,138-Spider-Man. 123-Begin 8-part Ghost Rider/Typhoid Mary story; begin 4-part She Hulk story; begin 8-part Wolverine/Lynx story. 125-Begin 6-part Iron Fist story. 130-Begin 6-part Ghost Rider/ Cage story. 136-Daredevil. 137-Begin 6-part Wolverine story & 6-part Ghost Rider story. 147-Begin 2-part Vengeance-c/story w/new Ghost Rider. 149-Vengeance-c/story w/new Ghost Rider. 150-Silver ink-c; begin 2-part Bloody Mary story w/Typhoid Mary,Wolverine, Daredevil, new Ghost Rider; intro Steel Raven. 152-Begin 4-part Wolverine, 4-part War Machine, 4-part Vengeance, 3-part Moon Knight stories; same date as War Machine #1. 143-146: Siege of Darkness parts 3,6,11,14; all have spot-varnished-c. 143-Ghost Rider/Scarlet Witch; intro new Werewolf. 144-Begin 2-part Morbius story. 145-Begin 2-part Nightstalkers story. 153-155-Bound-in Spider-Man trading card sheet. 172-Flip-book; intro new Lunatik, Giffen-c/a. 173-Flip-book; Lunatik story; Fabry-c/Giffen-a. 174-Lunatik story, Giffen-a 4.00

GD	VG	FN	VF	VF/NM	NM-
2.0	4.0	6.0	8.0	9.0	9.2

175-Flip-book with New Genix-c; Lunatik story, Giffen-a
2 4 6 10 14 18
...Colossus: God's Country (1994, $6.95) r/#10-17 1 2 3 4 5 7
....: Wolverine Vol. 1 TPB (2005, $12.99) r/Wolverine stories from #1-10 13.00
....: Wolverine Vol. 2 TPB (2006, $12.99) r/from #39-50 and Marvel Age Annual #4 13.00
....: Wolverine Vol. 3 TPB (2006, $12.99) r/from #51-61 13.00
....: Wolverine Vol. 4 TPB (2006, $12.99) r/from #62-71 13.00
NOTE: ***Austin*** *a-31-37i; c(i)-48, 50, 99, 122.* ***Buscema*** *a-1-10, 38-47; c-6.* ***Byrne*** *a-79; c-71.* ***Colan*** *a(p)-36, 37.* ***Colan/Williamson*** *a-101-108.* ***Ditko*** *a-7p, 10, 56p, 58, 80, 81, 83.* ***Guice*** *a-62.* ***Sam Kieth*** *a-85-92, 117-122; c-85-98, 99p, 100-108, 117, 118, 120-122; back c-109-113, 117.* ***Jae Lee*** *c-129(back).* ***Liefeld*** *a-51, 52, 53p(2), 85p; c-46, 70.* ***McFarlane*** *c-32.* ***Mooney*** *a-73.* ***Rogers*** *a-26, 38, 46i, 81p.* ***Russell*** *a-10-14,16,17i; c-4,19, 30,31i.* ***Saltares*** *a-8p(early), 38-45p.* ***Simonson*** *c-1.* ***B. Smith*** *a-72-84; c-72-84.* ***P. Smith*** *c-34.* ***Sparling*** *a-33.* ***Starlin*** *a-89i.* ***Staton*** *a-74.* ***Steacy*** *a-78.* ***Sutton*** *a-101-105.* ***Williamson*** *c-62i. Two Gun Kid by* ***Gil Kane*** *in #116, 122.*

MARVEL COMICS PRESENTS
Marvel Comics: Nov, 2007 - No. 12, Oct, 2008 ($3.99)

1-12-Short stories by various. 1-Wraparound-c by Campbell 4.00

MARVEL COMICS PRESENTS
Marvel Comics: Mar, 2019 - No. 9, Nov, 2019 ($4.99)

1-9: 1-Wolverine serialized story begins; Namor & Capt. America stories. 2-Gorilla Man app. 3-Crusher Hogan app. 4-Moon Knight. 5-Venom app. 6-Intro. Wolverine's daughter Rien 8-White Fox 5.00

MARVEL COMICS SUPER SPECIAL, A (Marvel Super Special #5 on)
Marvel Comics: Sept, 1977 - No. 41(?), Nov, 1986 (nn 7) ($1.50, magazine)

1-Kiss, 40 pgs. comics plus photos & features; John Buscema-a(p); also see Howard the Duck #12; ink contains real KISS blood; Dr. Doom, Spider-Man, Avengers, Fantastic Four, Mephisto app. 19 38 57 131 291 450
2-Conan (1978) 3 6 9 21 33 45
3-Close Encounters of the Third Kind (1978); Simonson-a
3 6 9 15 22 28
4-The Beatles Story (1978)-Perez/Janson-a; has photos & articles
7 14 21 49 92 135
5-Kiss (1978)-Includes poster 13 26 39 86 188 290
6-Jaws II (1978) 3 6 9 18 27 36
7-Sgt. Pepper; Beatles movie adaptation; withdrawn from U.S. distribution (French ed. exists)
8-Battlestar Galactica; tabloid size ($1.50, 1978); adapts TV show
3 6 9 14 19 24
8-Modern-r of tabloid size 2 4 6 11 16 20
8-Battlestar Galactica; publ. in regular magazine format; low distribution ($1.50, 8-1/2x11")
3 6 9 15 22 28
9-Conan 3 6 9 16 24 32
10-Star-Lord (1st color story) 5 10 15 30 50 70
11-13-Weirdworld begins #11; 25 copy special press run of each with gold seal and signed by artists (Proof quality), Spring-June, 1979 9 18 27 57 111 165
11-14: 11-13-Weirdworld (regular issues): 11-Fold-out centerfold. 14-Miller-c(p); adapts movie "Meteor." 2 4 6 8 10 12
15-Star Trek with photos & pin-ups ($1.50-c) 3 6 9 15 22 28
15-With $2.00 price; the price was changed at tail end of a 200,000 press run
3 6 9 16 24 32
16-Empire Strikes Back adaptation; Williamson-a 10 20 30 64 132 200
17-20 (Movie adaptations): 17-Xanadu. 18-Raiders of the Lost Ark. 19-For Your Eyes Only (James Bond). 20-Dragonslayer 1 2 3 5 6 8
21,23,25,26,28-30 (Movie adaptations): 21-Conan. 23-Annie. 25-Rock and Rule-w/photos; artwork is from movie. 26-Octopussy (James Bond). 28-Krull; photo-c. 29-Tarzan of the Apes (Greystoke movie). 30-Indiana Jones and the Temple of Doom
1 3 4 6 8 10
22-Blade Runner; Williamson-a/Steranko-c 6 12 18 41 76 110
24-The Dark Crystal 3 6 9 14 19 24
27-Return of the Jedi 6 12 18 41 76 110
31-39,41: 31-The Last Star Fighter. 32-The Muppets Take Manhattan. 33-Buckaroo Banzai. 34-Sheena. 35-Conan The Destroyer. 36-Dune. 37-2010. 38-Red Sonja. 39-Santa Claus:The Movie. 41-Howard The Duck
2 4 6 8 10 12
40-Labyrinth 5 10 15 34 60 85
NOTE: ***J. Buscema*** *a-1, 2, 9, 11-13, 18p, 21, 35, 40; c-11(part), 12.* ***Chaykin*** *a-9, 19p; c-18, 19.* ***Colan*** *a(p)-6, 10, 14.* ***Morrow*** *a-34; c-1i, 34.* ***Nebres*** *a-11.* ***Spiegle*** *a-29.* ***Stevens*** *a-27.* ***Williamson*** *a-27. #22-28 contain photos from movies.*

MARVEL COMICS: 2001
Marvel Comics: 2001 (no cover price, one-shot)

1-Previews new titles for Fall 2001; Wolverine-c 3.00

MARVEL DABEL BROTHERS SAMPLER
Marvel Comics: Dec, 2006 (no cover price, one-shot)

1-Profiles and sample pages of Anita Blake, Magician: Apprentice, Red Prophet, Ptolus 3.00

MARVEL DIVAS
Marvel Comics: Sept, 2009 - No. 4, Dec, 2009 ($3.99, limited series)

1-4-Black Cat, Firestar, Hellcat and Photon app. 1-Campbell-c 4.00

MARVEL DOUBLE FEATURE
Marvel Comics Group: Dec, 1973 - No. 21, Mar, 1977

1-Capt. America, Iron Man-r/T.O.S. begin 5 10 15 31 53 75
2-10: 3-Last 20¢ issue 2 4 6 10 14 18
11-17,20,21:17-Story-r/Iron Man & Sub-Mariner #1; last 25¢ issue
2 4 6 8 10 12
15-17-(30¢-c variants, limited distribution)(4,6,8/76) 5 10 15 30 50 70
18,19-Colan/Craig-r from Iron Man #1 in both 2 4 6 8 11 14
NOTE: ***Colan*** *r-1-19p.* ***Craig*** *r-17-19i.* ***G. Kane*** *r-15p; c-15p.* ***Kirby*** *r-1-16p, 20, 21; c-17-20.*

MARVEL DOUBLE SHOT
Marvel Comics: Jan, 2003 - No. 4, April, 2003 ($2.99, limited series)

1-4: 1-Hulk by Haynes; Thor w/Asamiya-a; Jusko-c. 2-Dr. Doom by Rivera; Simpsons-style Avengers by Bill Morrison 3.00

MARVEL FAMILY (Also see Captain Marvel Adventures No. 18)
Fawcett Publications: Dec, 1945 - No. 89, Jan, 1954

1-Origin Captain Marvel, Captain Marvel Jr., Mary Marvel, & Uncle Marvel retold; origin/1st app. Black Adam 2250 4500 6750 15,000 25,000 35,000
2-The 3 Lt. Marvels & Uncle Marvel app. 87 174 261 533 952 1350

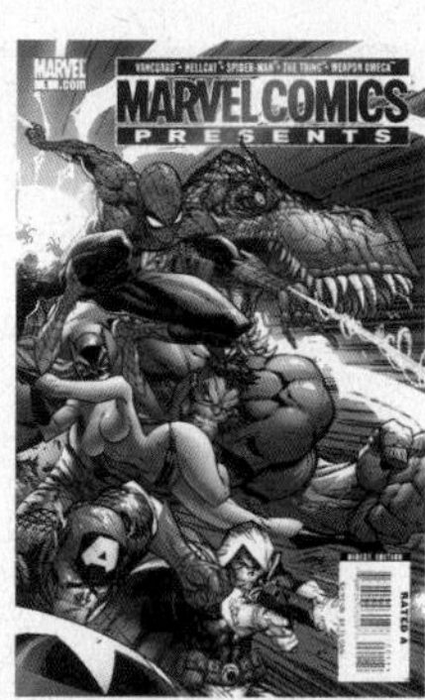

Marvel Comics Presents (2007) #1 © MAR

Marvel Family #9 © FAW

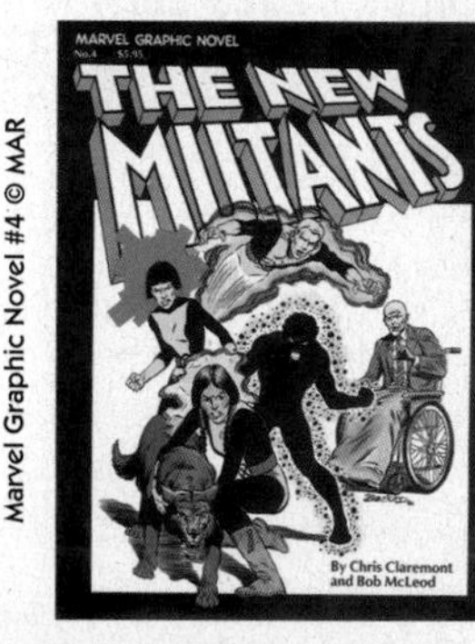

Marvel Graphic Novel #4 © MAR

	GD 2.0	VG 4.0	FN 6.0	VF 8.0	VF/NM 9.0	NM- 9.2
3	57	114	171	362	619	875
4,5	50	100	150	315	533	750
6-10: 6-Classic portrait-c with Uncle Marvel. 7-Shazam app.	40	80	120	246	411	575
11-20	33	66	99	194	317	440
21-30	29	58	87	172	281	390
31-40	25	50	75	150	245	340
41-46,48-50	24	48	72	140	230	320
47-Flying Saucer-c/story (5/50)	32	64	96	188	307	425
51-76	22	44	66	132	216	300
77-Communist Threat-c	47	94	141	296	498	700
78,81-Used in **POP**, pg. 92,93.	25	50	75	150	245	340
79,80,82-88: 79-Horror satire-c	24	48	72	144	237	330
89-Last issue; last Fawcett Captain Marvel app. (low distribution)	47	94	141	296	498	700

MARVEL FAMILY
DC Comics: Oct, 2022 ($3.99, one-shot)

	GD 2.0	VG 4.0	FN 6.0	VF 8.0	VF/NM 9.0	NM- 9.2
1-Reprint of the full 1945 issue with original ads; r/origin & 1st app. Black Adam						4.00

MARVEL FANFARE (1st Series)
Marvel Comics Group: Mar, 1982 - No. 60, Jan, 1992 ($1.25/$2.25, slick paper, direct sales)

	GD 2.0	VG 4.0	FN 6.0	VF 8.0	VF/NM 9.0	NM- 9.2
1-Spider-Man/Angel team-up; 1st Paul Smith-a (1st full story; see King Conan #7); Daredevil app. (many copies were printed missing the centerfold)	2	4	6	11	16	20
2-Spider-Man, Ka-Zar, The Angel. F.F. origin retold	2	4	6	8	10	12
3,4-X-Men & Ka-Zar. 4-Deathlok, Spidey app.	1	3	4	6	8	10
5-14: 5-Dr. Strange, Capt. America. 6-Spider-Man, Scarlet Witch. 7-Incredible Hulk; D.D. back-up(also 15). 8-Dr. Strange; Wolf Boy begins. 9-Man-Thing. 10-13-Black Widow. 14-The Vision						6.00
15,24,33: 15-The Thing by Barry Smith, c/a. 24-Weirdworld; Wolverine back-up. 33-X-Men, Wolverine app.; Punisher pin-up	1	2	3	5	6	8
16-23,25-32,34-44,46-50: 16,17-Skywolf. 16-Sub-Mariner back-up. 17-Hulk back-up. 18-Capt. America by Miller. 19-Cloak and Dagger. 20-Thing/Dr. Strange. 21-Thing/Dr. Strange /Hulk. 22,23-Iron Man vs. Dr. Octopus. 25,26-Weirdworld. 27-Daredevil/Spider-Man. 28-Alpha Flight. 29-Hulk. 30-Moon Knight. 31,32-Captain America. 34-37-Warriors Three. 38-Moon Knight/Dazzler. 39-Moon Knight/Hawkeye. 40-Angel/Rogue & Storm. 41-Dr. Strange. 42-Spider-Man. 43-Sub-Mariner/Human Torch. 44-Iron Man vs. Dr. Doom by Ken Steacy. 46-Fantastic Four. 47-Hulk. 48-She-Hulk/Vision. 49-Dr. Strange/Nick Fury. 50-X-Factor						5.00
45-All pin-up issue by Steacy, Art Adams & others	2	4	6	8	10	12
51-($2.95, 52 pgs.)-Silver Surfer; Fantastic Four & Capt. Marvel app.; 51,52-Colan/Williamson back-up (Dr. Strange)						6.00
52,53,56-60: 52,53-Black Knight; 53-Iron Man back up. 56-59-Shanna the She-Devil. 58-Vision & Scarlet Witch back-up. 60-Black Panther/Rogue/Daredevil stories						4.00
54,55-Wolverine back-ups. 54-Black Knight. 55-Power Pack						5.00
... No. 10 Facsimile Edition (12/20, $3.99) Reprints #10 with original ads						4.00
... Vol. 1 TPB (2008, $24.99) r/#1-7						25.00

NOTE: ***Art Adams*** *c-13.* ***Austin*** *a-1i, 4i, 33i, 38i; c-8i, 33i.* ***Buscema*** *a-51p.* ***Byrne*** *a-1p, 29, 48; c-29.* ***Chiodo*** *painted c-56-59.* ***Colan*** *a-51p.* ***Cowan/Simonson*** *c/a-60.* ***Golden*** *a-1, 2, 4p, 47; c-1, 2, 47.* ***Infantino*** *c/a(p)-8.* ***Gil Kane*** *a-8-11p.* ***Miller*** *a-18; c-1(Back-c), 18.* ***Perez*** *a-10, 11p, 12, 13p; c-10-13p.* ***Rogers*** *a-5p; c-5p.* ***Russell*** *a-5i, 6i, 8-11i, 43i; c-5i, 6.* ***Paul Smith*** *a-1p, 4p, 32, 60; c-4p. Staton c/a-50(p).* ***Williamson*** *a-30i, 51i.*

MARVEL FANFARE (2nd Series)
Marvel Comics: Sept, 1996 - No. 6, Feb, 1997 (99¢)

	GD 2.0	VG 4.0	FN 6.0	VF 8.0	VF/NM 9.0	NM- 9.2
1-6: 1-Capt. America & The Falcon-c/story; Deathlok app. 2-Wolverine & Hulk-c/app. 3-Ghost Rider & Spider-Man-c/app. 5-Longshot-c/app. 6-Sabretooth, Power Man, & Iron Fist-c/app						4.00

MARVEL FEATURE (See Marvel Two-In-One)
Marvel Comics Group: Dec, 1971 - No. 12, Nov, 1973 (1,2: 25¢, 52 pg. giants) (#1-3: quarterly)

	GD 2.0	VG 4.0	FN 6.0	VF 8.0	VF/NM 9.0	NM- 9.2
1-Origin/1st app. The Defenders (Sub-Mariner, Hulk & Dr. Strange); see Sub-Mariner #34,35 for prequel; Dr. Strange solo story (predates Dr. Strange #1) plus 1950s Sub-Mariner-r; Neal Adams-c	36	72	108	259	580	900
2-2nd app. Defenders; 1950s Sub-Mariner-r. Rutland, Vermont Halloween x-over	10	20	30	64	132	200
3-Defenders ends	6	12	18	40	73	105
4-Re-intro Antman (1st app. since 1960s), begin series; brief origin; Spider-Man app.	8	16	24	54	102	150
5-7,9,10: 6-Wasp app. & begins team-ups. 9-Iron Man app. 10-Last Antman	4	8	12	23	37	50
8-Origin Antman & Wasp-r/TTA #44; Kirby-a	4	8	12	27	44	60
11-Thing vs. Hulk; 1st Thing solo book (9/73); origin Fantastic Four retold	8	16	24	56	108	160
12-Thing/Iron Man; early Thanos app.; occurs after Capt. Marvel #33; Starlin-a(p)	5	10	15	35	63	90

NOTE: ***Bolle*** *a-9i.* ***Everett*** *a-1i, 3i.* ***Hartley*** *r-10.* ***Kane*** *c-3p, 7p.* ***Russell*** *a-7-10p.* ***Starlin*** *a-8, 11, 12; c-8.*

MARVEL FEATURE (Also see Red Sonja)
Marvel Comics: Nov, 1975 - No. 7, Nov, 1976 (Story cont'd in Conan #68)

	GD 2.0	VG 4.0	FN 6.0	VF 8.0	VF/NM 9.0	NM- 9.2
1-Red Sonja begins (pre-dates Red Sonja #1); adapts Howard short story; Adams-r/Savage Sword of Conan #1	5	10	15	30	50	70
2	3	6	9	14	20	25
3-6: Thorne-c/a in #2-7. 4,5-(Regular 25¢ edition)(5,7/76)	2	4	6	8	10	12
4,5-(30¢-c variants, limited distribution)	6	12	18	37	66	95
7-Red Sonja battles Conan	4	8	12	23	37	50

MARVEL FRONTIER COMICS UNLIMITED
Marvel Frontier Comics: Jan, 1994 ($2.95, 68 pgs.)

	GD 2.0	VG 4.0	FN 6.0	VF 8.0	VF/NM 9.0	NM- 9.2
1-Dances with Demons, Immortalis, Children of the Voyager, Evil Eye, The Fallen stories						4.00

MARVEL FUMETTI BOOK
Marvel Comics Group: Apr, 1984 ($1.00, one-shot)

	GD 2.0	VG 4.0	FN 6.0	VF 8.0	VF/NM 9.0	NM- 9.2
1-All photos; Stan Lee photo-c; Art Adams touch-ups						5.00

MARVEL FUN & GAMES
Marvel Comics Group: 1979/80 (color comic for kids)

	GD 2.0	VG 4.0	FN 6.0	VF 8.0	VF/NM 9.0	NM- 9.2
1,11: 1-Games, puzzles, etc. 11-X-Men-c	2	4	6	8	10	12
2-10,12,13: (beware marked pages)	1	2	3	4	5	7

MARVEL GIRL
Marvel Comics: Apr, 2011 ($2.99, one-shot)

	GD 2.0	VG 4.0	FN 6.0	VF 8.0	VF/NM 9.0	NM- 9.2
1-Early X-Men days of Jean Grey; Fialkov-s/Plati-a/Cruz-c						3.00

MARVEL GRAPHIC NOVEL
Marvel Comics Group (Epic Comics): 1982 - No. 38, 1990? ($5.95/$6.95)

	GD 2.0	VG 4.0	FN 6.0	VF 8.0	VF/NM 9.0	NM- 9.2
1-Death of Captain Marvel (2nd Marvel graphic novel); Capt. Marvel battles Thanos by Jim Starlin (c/a/scripts)	6	12	18	41	76	110
1 (2nd & 3rd printings)	2	4	6	13	18	22
2-Elric: The Dreaming City	3	6	9	14	19	24
3-Dreadstar; Starlin-c/a, 52 pgs.	3	6	9	14	20	25
4-Origin/1st app. The New Mutants (1982)	9	18	27	59	117	175
4,5-2nd printings	2	4	6	11	16	20
5-X-Men; book-length story (1982)	5	10	15	31	53	75
6-15,20,25,30,31: 6-The Star Slammers. 7-Killraven. 8-Super Boxers; Byrne scripts. 9-The Futurians. 10-Heartburst. 11-Void Indigo. 12-Dazzler. 13-Starstruck. 14-The Swords Of The Swashbucklers. 15-The Raven Banner (a Tale of Asgard). 20-Greenberg the Vampire. 25-Alien Legion. 30-A Sailor's Story. 31-Wolfpack	2	4	6	8	11	14
16,17,21,29: 16-The Aladdin Effect (Storm, Tigra, Wasp, She-Hulk). 17-Revenge Of The Living Monolith (Spider-Man, Avengers, FF app.). 21-Marada the She-Wolf. 29-The Big Chance (Thing vs. Hulk)	2	4	6	10	14	18
18-She Hulk	4	8	12	25	40	55
19,26-28: 19-Witch Queen of Acheron (Conan). 26-Dracula. 27-Avengers (Emperor Doom). 28-Conan the Reaver	2	4	6	11	16	20
22-Amaz. Spider-Man in Hooky by Wrightson	3	6	9	17	26	35
23,24: 23-Dr. Strange. 24-Love and War (Daredevil); Miller scripts	3	6	9	14	19	24
32-Death of Groo	3	6	9	14	19	24
32-2nd printing ($5.95)	2	4	6	8	10	12
33,34,36,37: 33-Thor. 34-Predator & Prey (Cloak & Dagger). 36-Willow (movie adapt.). 37-Hercules	2	4	6	8	10	12
35-Hitler's Astrologer (The Shadow, $12.95, HC)	2	4	6	11	16	20
35-Soft-c reprint (1990, $10.95)	2	4	6	9	12	15
38-Silver Surfer (Judgement Day)($14.95, HC)	2	4	6	13	18	22
38-Soft-c reprint (1990, $10.95)	2	4	6	9	12	15
nn-Abslom Daak: Dalek Killer (1990, $8.95) Dr. Who	2	4	6	9	12	15
nn-Arena by Bruce Jones (1989, $5.95) Dinosaurs	2	4	6	8	10	12
nn- A-Team Storybook Comics Illustrated (1983) r/ A-Team mini-series #1-3	2	4	6	8	10	12
nn-Ax (1988, $5.95) Ernie Colan-s/a	2	4	6	8	10	12
nn-Black Widow Coldest War (4/90, $9.95)	2	4	6	9	12	15
nn-Chronicles of Genghis Grimtoad (1990, $8.95)-Alan Grant-s	2	4	6	8	10	12
nn-Conan the Barbarian in the Horn of Azoth (1990, $8.95)	2	4	6	8	11	16
nn-Conan of Isles ($8.95)	2	4	6	8	11	16
nn-Conan Ravagers of Time (1992, $9.95) Kull & Red Sonja app.	2	4	6	8	11	16
nn-Conan -The Skull of Set	2	4	6	8	11	16
nn-Doctor Strange and Doctor Doom Triumph and Torment (1989, $17.95, HC)	2	4	6	13	18	22
nn-Dreamwalker (1989, $6.95)-Morrow-a	2	4	6	8	10	12

GD 2.0 | VG 4.0 | FN 6.0 | VF 8.0 | VF/NM 9.0 | NM- 9.2

nn-Excalibur Weird War III (1990, $9.95) 2 4 6 8 10 12
nn-G.I. Joe - The Trojan Gambit (1983, 68 pgs.) 2 4 6 9 12 15
nn-Harvey Kurtzman Strange Adventures (Epic, $19.95, HC) Aragonés, Crumb 3 6 9 14 20 25
nn-Hearts and Minds (1990, $8.95) Heath-a 2 4 6 8 10 12
nn-Inhumans (1988, $7.95)-Williamson-i 3 6 9 14 20 25
nn-Jhereg (Epic, 1990, $8.95) 2 4 6 8 10 12
nn-Kazar-Guns of the Savage Land (7/90, $8.95) 2 4 6 8 10 12
nn-Kull-The Vale of Shadow ('89, $6.95) 2 4 6 8 10 12
nn-Last of the Dragons (1988, $6.95) Austin-a(i) 2 4 6 8 10 12
nn-Nightraven: House of Cards (1991, $14.95) 2 4 6 10 14 18
nn-Nightraven: The Collected Stories (1990, $9.95) Bolton-r/British Hulk mag.; David Lloyd-c/a 2 4 6 8 10 12
nn-Original Adventures of Cholly and Flytrap (Epic, 1991, $9.95) Suydam-s/c/a 2 4 6 10 14 18
nn-Rick Mason Agent (1989, $9.95) 2 4 6 8 10 12
nn-Roger Rabbit In The Resurrection Of Doom (1989, $8.95) 2 4 6 9 12 15
nn-A Sailor's Story Book II: Winds, Dreams and Dragons ('86, $6.95, softcover) Glansman-s/c/a 2 4 6 8 10 12
nn-Squadron Supreme: Death of a Universe (1989, $9.95) Gruenwald-s; Ryan & Williamson-a 3 6 9 14 20 25
nn-Who Framed Roger Rabbit (1989, $6.95) 2 4 6 9 12 15

NOTE: ***Aragones** a-27, 32. **Buscema** a-38. **Byrne** c/a-18. **Heath** a-35i. **Kaluta** a-13, 35p; c-13. **Miller** a-24p. **Simonson** a-6; c-6. **Starlin** c/a-1,3. **Williamson** a-34. **Wrightson** c-29i.*

MARVEL HEARTBREAKERS
Marvel Comics: Apr, 2010 ($3.99, one-shot)

1-Romance short stories; Spider-Man, MJ & Gwen app.; Casagrande-a; Beast app. 4.00

MARVEL - HEROES & LEGENDS
Marvel Comics: Oct, 1996; 1997 ($2.95)

nn-Wraparound-c, ...1997 ($2.99) -Original Avengers story 6.00

MARVEL HEROES FLIP MAGAZINE
Marvel Comics: Aug, 2005 - No. 26, Sept, 2007 ($3.99/$4.99)

1-11-Reprints New Avengers and Captain America (2005 series) in flip format thru #13 4.00
12-26: 14-19-Reprints New Avengers and Young Avengers in flip format. 20-Ghost Rider 5.00

MARVEL HOLIDAY SPECIAL
Marvel Comics: No. 1, 1991 - 2011

1-($2.25, 84 pgs.) X-Men, Fantastic Four, Punisher, Thor, Capt. America, Ghost Rider, Capt. Ultra, Spidey stories; Art Adams-c/a 1 3 4 6 8 10
nn (1992, 1/93 on-c)-Wolverine, Thanos (by Starlin/Lim/Austin) 4.00
nn (1993, 1/94 on-c)-Spider-Man vs. Mephisto; Nick Fury by Chaykin; Hulk app. 4.00
nn (1994)-Capt. America, X-Men, Silver Surfer 4.00
... 1996-Spider-Man by Waid & Olliffe; X-Men, Silver Surfer 4.00
... 2004-Spider-Man by DeFalco & Miyazawa; X-Men, Fantastic Four 4.00
... 2004 TPB ($15.99) r/M.H.S. 2004 & past Christmas-themed stories 16.00
1 (1/06, $3.99) new Christmas-themed stories by various; Immonen-c 4.00
... 2006 (2/07, $3.99) Fin Fang Foom, Hydra, AIM app.; gallery of past covers; Irving-c 4.00
... 2007 (2/08, $3.99) Spider-Man & Wolverine stories; Hembeck-a 4.00
... 2011 (2/12, $3.99) Seeley-c; Spider-Man, Wolverine, Nick Fury, The Thing app. 4.00
Marvel Holiday (2006, $7.99, digest) reprints from M.H.S. 2004, 2006 & TPB 8.00
Marvel Holiday Spectacular Magazine (2009, $9.99, magazine) reprints from M.H.S. '93, '94, & Amazing Spider-Man #166; and new material w/Doe, Semeiks & Nauck-a 10.00

NOTE: ***Art Adams** a-'92. **Golden** a-'93. **Kaluta** c-'93. **Perez** c-'94.*

MARVEL ILLUSTRATED...
Marvel Comics: 2007 ($2.99)

...Jungle Book - reprints from Marvel Fanfare #8-11; Gil Kane-s/a(p); P. Craig Russell-i 3.00

MARVEL ILLUSTRATED: KIDNAPPED (Title changes to Kidnapped with #5)
Marvel Comics: Jan, 2009 - No. 5, May, 2009 ($3.99, limited series)

1-5-Adaptation of the Stevenson novel; Roy Thomas-s/Mario Gully-a/Parel-c 4.00

MARVEL ILLUSTRATED: LAST OF THE MOHICANS
Marvel Comics: July, 2007 - No. 6, Dec, 2007 ($2.99, limited series)

1-6-Adaptation of the Cooper novel; Roy Thomas-s/Steve Kurth-a. 1-Jo Chen-c 3.00
HC (2008, $19.99) r/#1-6 20.00

MARVEL ILLUSTRATED: MOBY DICK
Marvel Comics: Apr, 2008 - No. 6, Sept, 2008 ($2.99, limited series)

1-6-Adaptation of the Melville novel; Roy Thomas-s/Alixe-a/Watson-c 3.00

MARVEL ILLUSTRATED: PICTURE OF DORIAN GRAY
Marvel Comics: Jan, 2008 - No 6, July, 2008 ($2.99, limited series)

1-6-Adaptation of the Wilde novel; Roy Thomas-s/Fiumara-a. 1-Parel-c 3.00

MARVEL ILLUSTRATED: SWIMSUIT ISSUE (Also see Marvel Swimsuit Special)
Marvel Comics: 1991 ($3.95, magazine, 52 pgs.)

V1#1-Parody of Sports Illustrated swimsuit issue; Mary Jane Parker centerfold pin-up by Jusko; 2nd print exists 3 6 9 14 20 25

MARVEL ILLUSTRATED: THE ILIAD
Marvel Comics: Feb, 2008 - No. 8, Sept, 2008 ($2.99, limited series)

1-8-Adaptation of Homer's Epic Poem; Roy Thomas-s/Sepulveda-a/Rivera-c 3.00

MARVEL ILLUSTRATED: THE MAN IN THE IRON MASK
Marvel Comics: Sept, 2007 - No. 6, Feb, 2008 ($2.99, limited series)

1-6-Adaptation of the Dumas novel; Roy Thomas-s/Hugo Petrus-a. 1-Djurdjevic-c 3.00
HC (2008, $19.99) r/#1-6 20.00

MARVEL ILLUSTRATED: THE ODYSSEY (Title changes to The Odyssey with #7)
Marvel Comics: Nov, 2008 - No. 8, June, 2009 ($3.99, limited series)

1-8-Adaptation of Homer's Epic Poem; Roy Thomas-s/Greg Tocchini-a/c 4.00

MARVEL ILLUSTRATED: THE THREE MUSKETEERS
Marvel Comics: Aug, 2008 - No. 6, Jan, 2009 ($3.99, limited series)

1-6-Adaptation of the Dumas novel; Roy Thomas-s/Hugo Petrus-a/Parel-c 4.00

MARVEL ILLUSTRATED: TREASURE ISLAND
Marvel Comics: Aug, 2007 - No. 6, Jan, 2008 ($2.99, limited series)

1-6-Adaptation of the Stevenson novel; Roy Thomas-s/Mario Gully-a/Greg Hildebrandt-c 3.00
HC (2008, $19.99) r/#1-6 20.00

MARVEL KNIGHTS (See Black Panther, Daredevil, Inhumans, & Punisher)
Marvel Comics: 1998 (Previews for upcoming series)

Sketchbook-Wizard suppl.; Quesada & Palmiotti-c 4.00
Tourbook-($2.99) Interviews and art previews 4.00

MARVEL KNIGHTS
Marvel Comics: July, 2000 - No. 15, Sept, 2001 ($2.99)

1-Daredevil, Punisher, Black Widow, Shang-Chi, Dagger app. 4.00
2-15: 2-Two covers by Barreto & Quesada 3.00
.../Marvel Boy Genesis Edition (6/00) Sketchbook preview 3.00
...: Millennial Visions (2/02, $3.99) Pin-ups by various; Harris-c 4.00

MARVEL KNIGHTS (Volume 2)
Marvel Comics: May, 2002 - No. 6, Oct, 2002 ($2.99)

1-6-Daredevil, Punisher, Black Widow app.; Ponticelli-a 3.00

MARVEL KNIGHTS: DOUBLE SHOT
Marvel Comics: June, 2002 - No. 4, Sept, 2002 ($2.99, limited series)

1-4: 1-Punisher by Ennis & Quesada; Daredevil by Haynes; Fabry-c 3.00

MARVEL KNIGHTS 4 (Fantastic Four) (Issues #1&2 are titled **Knights 4**) (#28-30 titled **Four**)
Marvel Comics: Apr, 2004 - No. 30, July, 2006 ($2.99)

1-30: 1-7-McNiven-c/a; Aguirre-Sacasa-a. 8,9-Namor app. 13-Cho-c. 14-Land-c. 21-Flashback meeting with Black Panther. 30-Namor app. 3.00
...Vol. 1: The Wolf at the Door (2004, $16.99, TPB) r/#1-7 17.00
...Vol. 2: The Stuff of Nightmares (2005, $13.99, TPB) r/#8-12 14.00
...Vol. 3: Divine Time (2005, $14.99, TPB) r/#13-18 15.00
...Vol. 4: Impossible Things Happen Every Day (2006, $14.99, TPB) r/#19-24 15.00
Fantastic Four: The Resurrection of Nicholas Scratch TPB (2006, $14.99) r/#25-30 15.00

MARVEL KNIGHTS: HULK
Marvel Comics: Feb, 2014 - No. 4, May, 2104 ($3.99, limited series)

1-4-Keatinge-s/Kowalski-a; Banner in Paris 4.00

MARVEL KNIGHTS MAGAZINE
Marvel Comics: May, 2001 - No. 6, Oct, 2001 ($3.99, magazine size)

1-6-Reprints of recent Daredevil, Punisher, Black Widow, Inhumans 4.00

MARVEL KNIGHTS SPIDER-MAN (Title continues in Sensational Spider-Man #23)
Marvel Comics: Jun, 2004 - No. 22, Mar, 2006 ($2.99)

1-Wraparound-c by Dodson; Millar-s/Dodson-a; Green Goblin app. 4.00
2-12: 2-Avengers app. 2,3-Vulture & Electro app. 5,8-Cho-c/a. 6-8-Venom app. 3.00
13-18-Reginald Hudlin-s/Billy Tan-a. 13,14,18-New Avengers app. 15-Punisher app. 3.00
19-22-The Other x-over pts. 2,5,8,11; Pat Lee-a 3.00
19-22-var-c: 19-Black costume. 20-Scarlet Spider. 21-Spider-Armor. 22-Peter Parker 5.00
... Vol. 1 HC (2005, $29.99, over-sized with d.j.) r/#1-12; Stan Lee intro.; Dodson & Cho sketch pages 30.00
... Vol. 1: Down Among the Dead Men (2004, $9.99, TPB) r/#1-4 10.00
... Vol. 2: Venomous (2005, $9.99, TPB) r/#5-8 10.00
... Vol. 3: The Last Stand (2005, $9.99, TPB) r/#9-12 10.00
... Vol. 4: Wild Blue Yonder (2005, $14.99, TPB) r/#13-18 15.00

MARVEL KNIGHTS: SPIDER-MAN
Marvel Comics: Dec, 2013 - No. 5, Apr, 2014 ($3.99, limited series)

1-5-Matt Kindt-s/Marco Rudy-a; Arcade app. 4.00

MARVEL KNIGHTS 20TH
Marvel Comics: Jan, 2019 - No. 6, Mar, 2019 ($4.99/$3.99, bi-weekly limited series)

1,6-($4.99) Cates-s/Foreman-a; Daredevil, Frank Castle, Kingpin & Doctor Doom app. 5.00
2-5-($3.99) 2-Henrichon-a. 3-Couceiro-a. 4,5-Black Panther app. 4.00

MARVEL KNIGHTS 2099
Marvel Comics: 2005 ($13.99, TPB)

nn-Reprints one shots: Daredevil 2099, Punisher 2099, Black Panther 2099, Inhumans 2099 and Mutant 2099; Pat Lee-c 14.00

MARVEL KNIGHTS: X-MEN
Marvel Comics: Jan, 2014 - No. 5, May, 2014 ($3.99, limited series)

1-4-Brahm Revel-s/Cris Peter-a; Sabretooth app. 4.00

MARVEL LEGACY
Marvel Comics: Nov, 2017 ($5.99, one-shot)

1-Leads into Marvel's Legacy title re-boot following Secret Empire; Aaron-s/Ribic & McNiven main art, plus art by various; wraparound gatefold front-c by Quesada 6.00

MARVEL LEGACY: ...
Marvel Comics: 2006, 2007 ($4.99, one-shots)

... The 1960s Handbook - Profiles of 1960s iconic and minor characters; info thru 1969 5.00
... The 1970s Handbook - Profiles of 1970s iconic and minor characters; info thru 1979 5.00
... The 1980s Handbook - Profiles of 1980s iconic and minor characters; info thru 1989 5.00
... The 1990s Handbook - Profiles of 1990s iconic and minor characters; Lim-c 5.00
...: The 1960s-1990s Handbook TPB (2007, $19.99) r/one-shots 20.00

MARVELMAN CLASSIC
Marvel Comics: 2010 ($34.99, B&W)

HC-(2010, $34.99) Reprints of 1950s British Marvelman stories; character history 35.00
... Primer (8/10, $3.99) Character history; Mick Anglo interview; Quesada-c 4.00

MARVELMAN FAMILY'S FINEST
Marvel Comics: 2010 - No. 6, Jan, 2011 ($3.99, B&W, limited series)

1-6-Reprints of 1950s Marvelman, Young Marvelman and Marvelman Family stories 4.00

MARVEL MANGAVERSE:... (one-shots)
Marvel Comics: March, 2002 ($2.25, manga-inspired one-shots)

Avengers Assemble! - Udon Studio-s/a 3.00
Eternity Twilight ($3.50) - Ben Dunn-s/a/wrap-around-c 4.00
Fantastic Four - Adam Warren-s/Keron Grant-a 3.00
Ghost Riders - Chuck Austen-s/a 3.00
Punisher - Peter David-s/Lea Hernandez-a 3.00
Spider-Man - Kaare Andrews-s/a 3.00

Marvel Knights: X-Men #1 © MAR

Marvel Legacy #1 © MAR

Marvel Mystery Comics #20 © MAR

GD 2.0 VG 4.0 FN 6.0 VF 8.0 VF/NM 9.0 NM- 9.2

X-Men - C.B. Cebulski-s/Jeff Matsuda-a 3.00

MARVEL MANGAVERSE (Manga series)
Marvel Comics: June, 2002 - No. 6, Nov., 2002 ($2.25)

1-6: 1-Ben Dunn-s/a; intro. manga Captain Marvel 3.00
Vol. 1 TPB (2002, $24.95) r/one-shots 25.00
Vol. 2 TPB (2002, $12.99) r/#1-6 13.00
Vol. 3: Spider-Man-Legend of the Spider-Clan (2003, $11.99, TPB) r/series 12.00

MARVEL MASTERPIECES COLLECTION, THE
Marvel Comics: May, 1993 - No. 4, Aug, 1993 ($2.95, coated paper, lim. series)

1-4-Reprints Marvel Masterpieces trading cards w/ new Jusko paintings in each; Jusko painted-c/a 4.00

MARVEL MASTERPIECES 2 COLLECTION, THE
Marvel Comics: July, 1994 - No. 3, Sept, 1994 ($2.95, limited series)

1-3: 1-Kaluta-c; r/trading cards; new Steranko centerfold 4.00

MARVEL MILESTONE EDITION
Marvel Comics: 1991 - 1999 ($2.95, coated stock)(r/originals with original ads w/silver ink-c)

...: Amazing Fantasy #15 (3/92); ....:Hulk #181 (8/99, $2.99)
3 6 9 17 25 34
...: Amazing Spider-Man #1 (1/93), ...: Amazing Spider-Man #1 (1/93) variation- no price on-c, ...: Amazing Spider-Man #3 (3/95, $2.95), ...: Amazing Spider-Man #129 (11/92), ...: Avengers #1 (9/93), ...:Avengers #4 (3/95, $2.95), ...: Captain America #1 (3/95, $3.95), ...: Fantastic Four #1 (11/91), ...: Fantastic Four #5 (11/92), ...: Giant Size X-Men #1 (1991, $3.95, 68 pgs.), ...: Incredible Hulk #1 (3/92, says 3/91 by error), ...: Iron Man #55 (11/92), ...: Strange Tales-r/Dr. Strange stories from #110, 111, 114, & 115; ...: Tales of Suspense #39 (3/93), ...: X-Men #1-Reprints X-Men #1 (1991)
2 4 6 8 11 14
...: Amazing Spider-Man #149 (11/94, $2.95), ...: Avengers #16 (10/93), ...: X-Men #9 (10/93), ...:X-Men #28 (11/94, $2.95) 1 2 3 5 6 8
...: Iron Fist #14 (11/92) 2 4 6 8 10 12

MARVEL MILESTONES
Marvel Comics: 2005 - 2006 ($3.99, coated stock)(r/originals w/silver ink-c)

...: Beast & Kitty Pryde-r/from Amazing Adventures #11 & Uncanny X-Men #153 5.00
...: Black Panther, Storm & Ka-Zar-r/from Black Panther #26, Marvel Team-Up #100 and Marvel Mystery Comics #7 5.00
...: Blade, Man-Thing & Satana-r/from Tomb of Dracula #10, Adv. Into Fear #16 and Vampire Tales #2 5.00
...: Captain Britain, Psylocke & Sub-Mariner-r/from Spect. Spidey #114, Uncanny X-Men #213 and Human Torch #2 5.00
...: Doom, Sub-Mariner & Red Skull -r/from FF Ann. #2, Sub-Mariner Comics #1, Captain America Comics #1 5.00
...: Dragon Lord, Speedball and The Man in the Sky -r/from Marvel Spotlight #5, Speedball #1 and Amazing Adult Fantasy #14; Ditko-a on all 5.00
...: Dr. Strange, Silver Surfer, Sub-Mariner, & Hulk -r/from Marvel Premiere #3, FF Ann. #5, Marvel Comics #1, Incredible Hulk #3 5.00
...: Ghost Rider, Black Widow & Iceman -r/from Marvel Spotlight #5, Daredevil #81, X-Men #47 5.00
...: Iron Man, Ant-Man & Captain America -r/from TOS #39,40, TTA #27, Capt. America #1 5.00
...: Legion of Monsters, Spider-Man and Brother Voodoo -r/Marvel Premiere #28 & others 5.00
...: Millie the Model & Patsy Walker-r/from Millie the Model #100, Defenders #65 5.00
...: Onslaught -r/Onslaught: Marvel; wraparound-c 5.00
...: Rawhide Kid & Two-Gun Kid-r/Two-Gun Kid #60 and Rawhide Kid #17 5.00
...: Special: Bloodstone, X-51 & Captain Marvel II ($4.99) -r/from Marvel Presents #1, Machine Man #1, Amazing Spider-Man Ann. #19, and Bloodstone #1 6.00
...: Star Brand & Quasar -r/from Star Brand #1 & Quasar #1 5.00
...: Ultimate Spider-Man, Ult. X-Men, Microman & Mantor -r/from Ultimate Spider-Man #1/2, Ultimate X-Men #1/2 and Human Torch #2 5.00
...: Venom & Hercules -r/Marvel S-H Secret Wars #8, Journey Into Mystery Ann. #1 5.00
...: Wolverine, X-Men & Tuk: Caveboy -r/from Marvel Comics Presents #1, Uncanny X-Men #201, Capt. America Comics #1,2 5.00
...: (Jim Lee and Chris Claremont) X-Men and the Starjammers Pt. 1 -r/Unc. X-Men #275 5.00
...: X-Men and the Starjammers Pt. 2 -r/Unc. X-Men #276,277 5.00

MARVEL MINI-BOOKS (See Promotional Comics section)

MARVEL MONSTERS:... (one-shots)
Marvel Comics: Dec, 2005; Oct, 2019 ($3.99/$4.99)

...Devil Dinosaur 1 - Hulk app.; Eric Powell-c/a; Sniegoski-s; r/Journey Into Mystery #62 5.00
...Fin Fang Four 1 - FF app.; Powell-c; Langridge-s/Gray-a; r/Strange Tales #89 5.00
...From the Files of Ulysses Bloodstone 1 - Guide to classic Marvel monsters; Powell-c 5.00
...Monsters on the Prowl 1 - Niles-s/Fegredo-a/Powell-c; Thing, Hulk, Giant-Man & Beast app. 5.00
...Where Monsters Dwell 1 - Giffen-s/a; David-s/Pander-a; Parker-s/Braun-s; Powell-c 5.00
HC (2006, $20.99, dust jacket) r/one-shots 21.00
... No. 1 (10/19, $4.99) Bunn-s/Hepburn-a; monster pin-ups & profiles by various 5.00

GD 2.0 VG 4.0 FN 6.0 VF 8.0 VF/NM 9.0 NM- 9.2

MARVEL MOVIE PREMIERE (Magazine)
Marvel Comics Group: Sept, 1975 (B&W, one-shot)

1-Burroughs' "The Land That Time Forgot" adapt. 3 6 9 15 22 28

MARVEL MOVIE SHOWCASE FEATURING STAR WARS
Marvel Comics Group: Nov, 1982 - No. 2, Dec, 1982 ($1.25, 68 pgs.)

1-Star Wars movie adaptation; reprints Star Wars #1-3 by Chaykin; reprints-c to Star Wars #1
6 12 18 37 65 95
2-Reprints Star Wars #4-6; Stevens-r 4 8 12 29 37 50

MARVEL MOVIE SPOTLIGHT FEATURING RAIDERS OF THE LOST ARK
Marvel Comics Group: Nov, 1982 ($1.25, 68 pgs.)

1-Edited-r/Raiders of the Lost Ark #1-3; Buscema-c/a(p); movie adapt. 6.00

MARVEL MUST HAVES (Reprints of recent sold-out issues)
Marvel Comics: Dec, 2001 - 2005 ($2.99/$3.99/$4.99)

1,2,4-6: 1-r/Wolverine: Origin #1, Startling Stories: Banner #1, Tangled Web #4 and Cable #97. 2-Amazing Spider-Man #36 and others. 4-Truth #1, Capt. America V4 #1, and The Ultimates #1. 5-r/Ultimate War #1, Ult. X-Men #26, Ult Spider-Man #33. 6-Ult. Spider-Man #33-36 4.00
3-r/Call of Duty: The Brotherhood #1 & Daredevil #32,33 3.00
Amazing Spider-Man #30-32; Incredible Hulk #34-36; The Ultimates #1-3; Ultimate Spider-Man #1-3; Ultimate X-Men #1-3; (New) X-Men #114-116 each.... 4.00
NYX #1-3 3 6 9 19 30 40
NYX #4-5 with sketch & cover gallery; Ultimates 2 #1-3 each...
2 4 6 10 14 18
Spider-Man and the Black Cat #1-3; preview of #4 5.00

MARVEL MYSTERY COMICS (Formerly Marvel Comics) (Becomes Marvel Tales No. 93 on)
Timely /Marvel Comics (TP #2-17/TCI #18-54/MCI #55-92): No. 2, Dec, 1939 - No. 92, June, 1949 (Some material from #8-10 reprinted in 2004's Marvel 65th Anniversary Special #1)

2-(Rare)-American Ace begins, ends #3; Human Torch (blue costume) by Burgos, Sub-Mariner by Everett continue; 2 pg. origin recap of Human Torch; Angel-c
4200 8400 12,600 31,500 70,750 110,000
3-New logo from Marvel pulp begins; 1st app. of television in comics? in Human Torch story (1/40); Angel-c 3150 6300 9450 23,600 46,800 70,000
4-Intro. Electro, the Marvel of the Age (ends #19), The Ferret, Mystery Detective (ends #9); 1st Sub-Mariner-c by Schomburg; 2nd German swastika on-c of a comic (2/40); one month after Top-Notch Comics #2 3700 7400 11,100 27,800 54,900 82,000
5 Classic Schomburg Torch-c, his 1st ever (Scarce)
4150 8300 12,450 30,700 64,350 98,000
6-Angel-c; Gustavson Angel story 1400 2800 4200 10,600 19,300 28,000
7-Sub-Mariner attacks N.Y. city & Torch joins police force setting up battle in #8-10. Classic Schomburg Torch-c, his 2nd ever 1500 3000 4500 11,400 20,700 30,000
8-1st Human Torch & Sub-Mariner battle(6/40) 1700 3400 5100 12,700 27,350 42,000
9-(Scarce)-Human Torch & Sub-Mariner battle (cover/story); classic-c by Schomburg
5400 10,800 16,200 40,000 79,500 119,000
10-Human Torch & Sub-Mariner battle, conclusion, 1 pg.; Terry Vance, the Schoolboy Sleuth begins, ends #57 1490 2980 4470 11,100 23,800 36,500
11-Schomburg Torch-c, his 3rd ever 568 1136 1704 4146 7323 10,500
12-Classic Angel-c by Kirby 541 1082 1623 3950 6975 10,000
13-Intro. of The Vision by S&K (11/40); Sub-Mariner dons new costume, ends #15; Schomburg's 4th Human Torch-c 1100 2200 3300 8400 15,200 22,000
14-16: 14-Shows-c to Human Torch #1 on-c (12/40). 15-S&K Vision, Gustavson Angel story
476 952 1428 3475 6138 8800
17-Human Torch/Sub-Mariner team-up by Burgos/Everett; Human Torch pin-up on back-c; shows-c to Human Torch #2 on-c 530 1060 1590 3869 6835 9800
18-1st app. villain "The Cat's Paw" 454 908 1362 3314 5857 8400
19,20: 19-Origin Toro in text; shows-c to Sub-Mariner #1 on-c. 20-Origin The Angel in text
432 864 1296 3154 5577 8000
21-The Patriot begins, (intro. in Human Torch #4 (#3)); not in #46-48; Sub-Mariner pin-up on back-c; Gustavson Angel story (7/41) 459 918 1377 3350 5925 8500
22-25: 23-Last Gustavson Angel; origin The Vision in text. 24-Injury-to-eye story
423 846 1269 3088 5777 7800
26-29: 27-Ka-Zar ends; last S&K Vision who battles Satan. 28-Jimmy Jupiter in the Land of Nowhere begins, ends #48; Sub-Mariner vs. The Flying Dutchman
423 846 1269 3067 5384 7700
30-"Remember Pearl Harbor" Japanese war-c 551 1102 1653 4022 7111 10,200
31,32-"Remember Pearl Harbor" Japanese war-c. 31-Sub-Mariner by Everett ends, resumes #84. 32-1st app. The Boboes 423 846 1269 3067 5384 7700
33,35,36,38,39: 36-Nazi invasion of NYC cover. 39-WWII Nazi-c
420 840 1260 2940 5170 7400
34-Everett, Burgos, Martin Goodman, Funnies, Inc. office appear in story & battles Hitler; last Burgos Human Torch 423 846 1269 3088 5444 7800
37-Classic Hitler-c 514 1028 1542 3750 6625 9500
40-Classic Zeppelin-c 1750 3500 5250 13,300 24,150 35,000

GD 2.0 | VG 4.0 | FN 6.0 | VF 8.0 | VF/NM 9.0 | NM- 9.2

41-Hirohito & Tojo-c 459 918 1377 3350 5925 8500
42,43,47 406 812 1218 2842 4971 7100
44-Classic Super Plane-c 2250 4500 6750 17,100 31,050 45,000
45-Red Skull, Nazi hooded Vigilante war-c 649 1298 1947 4738 8369 12,000
46-Classic Hitler-c 2400 4800 7200 18,200 33,100 48,000
48-Last Vision; flag-c 432 864 1296 3154 5577 8000
49-Origin Miss America 432 864 1296 3154 5577 8000
50-Mary becomes Miss Patriot (origin) 423 846 1269 3000 5250 7500
51-60: 54-Bondage-c 320 640 960 2240 3920 5600
61,62,64-Last German war-c 300 600 900 2010 3505 5000
63-Classic Hitler War-c; The Villainess Cat-Woman only app. 541 1082 1623 3950 6975 10,000
65,66-Last Japanese War-c 300 600 900 2010 3505 5000
67-78: 74-Last Patriot. 75-Young Allies begin. 76-Ten Chapter Miss America serial begins, ends #85 194 388 582 1242 2121 3000
79-New cover format; Super Villains begin on cover; last Angel 213 426 639 1363 2332 3300
80-1st app. Capt. America in Marvel Comics 245 490 735 1568 2684 3800
81-Captain America app. 206 412 618 1318 2259 3200
82-Origin & 1st app. Namora (5/47); 1st Sub-Mariner/Namora team-up; Captain America app. 486 972 1458 3550 6275 9000
83,85: 83-Last Young Allies. 85-Last Miss America; Blonde Phantom app. 187 374 561 1197 2049 2900
84-Blonde Phantom begins (on-c of #84,88,89); Sub-Mariner by Everett begins; Captain America app.; Everett-c 245 490 735 1568 2684 3800
86-Blonde Phantom i.d. revealed; Captain America app.; last Bucky app. 194 388 582 1242 2121 3000
87-1st Capt. America/Golden Girl team-up; last Toro app. (8/48) 200 400 600 1280 2190 3100
88-Golden Girl, Namora, & Sun Girl (1st in Marvel Comics) x-over; Captain America, Blonde Phantom app. 271 542 813 1734 2967 4200
89-1st Human Torch/Sun Girl team-up; 1st Captain America solo; Blonde Phantom app. 200 400 600 1280 2190 3100
90,91: 90-Blonde Phantom un-masked; Captain America app. 91-Capt. America app.; Blonde Phantom & Sub-Mariner end; early Venus app. (4/49) (scarce) 245 490 735 1568 2684 3800
92-Feature story on the birth of the Human Torch and the death of Professor Horton (his creator); 1st app. The Witness in Marvel Comics; Captain America app. (scarce) 423 846 1269 3088 5444 7800
132 Pg. issue, B&W, 25¢ (1943-44)-printed in N. Y.; square binding, blank inside covers); has Marvel No. 33-c in color; contains Capt. America #18 & Marvel Mystery Comics #33; same contents as Captain America Annual 8000 16,000 24,000 50,000 -- --
132 Pg. issue (with variant contents), B&W, 25¢ (1942-'43)- square binding, blank inside covers; has same Marvel No. 33-c in color but contains Capt. America #22 & Marvel Mystery Comics #41 instead 8000 16,000 24,000 50,000 -- --

NOTE: ***Brodsky** c-49, 72, 86, 88-92. **Crandall** a-26i. **Everett** c-9, 27, 84. **Gabrielle** c-30-32. **Schomburg** c-3-11, 13-29, 33-36, 39-48, 50-59, 63-69, 74, 76, 132 pg. issue. **Shores** c-37, 38, 75p, 77, 78p, 79p, 80, 81p, 82-84, 85p, 87p. **Sekowsky** c-73. Bondage covers-3, 4, 7, 12, 28, 29, 49, 50, 52, 56, 57, 58, 59, 65. Angel c-2, 3, 8, 12. Remember Pearl Harbor issues-#30-32.*

MARVEL MYSTERY COMICS
Marvel Comics: Dec, 1999 ($3.95, reprints)

1-Reprints original 1940s stories; Schomburg-c from #74 5.00

MARVEL MYSTERY COMICS 70th ANNIVERARY SPECIAL
Marvel Comics: Jul, 2009 ($3.99, one-shot)

1-Rivera-c; new Sub-Mariner/Human Torch team-up set in 1941; reps. from #4 & 5 5.00

MARVEL MYSTERY HANDBOOK: 70th ANNIVERARY SPECIAL
Marvel Comics: 2009 ($4.99, one-shot)

1-Official Handbook-style profile pages of characters from Marvel's first year 5.00

MARVEL NEMESIS: THE IMPERFECTS (EA Games characters)
Marvel Comics: July, 2005 - No. 6, Dec, 2005 ($2.99, limited series)

1-6-Jae Lee-c/Greg Pak-s/Renato Arlem-a; Spider-Man, Thing, Wolverine, Elektra app 3.00
Digest (2005, $7.99) r/#1-6 8.00

MARVEL 1985
Marvel Comics: July, 2008 - No. 6, Dec, 2008 ($3.99, limited series)

1-6: 1-Marvel villains come to the real world; Millar-s/Edwards-a; three covers 4.00
HC (2009, $24.99) r/#1-6; intro. by Lindelof; Edwards production art 25.00

MARVEL NO-PRIZE BOOK, THE (The Official... on-c)
Marvel Comics Group: Jan, 1983 (one-shot, direct sales only)

1-Stan Lee as Doctor Doom cover by Golden; Kirby-a 2 4 6 10 14 18

MARVEL NOW! POINT ONE
Marvel Comics: Dec, 2012 ($5.99, one-shot)

1-Short story lead-ins to new Marvel Now! series; Nick Fury, Nova, Star-Lord, Ant-Man & others app.; s/a by various; Granov-c and baby variant-c by Skottie Young 6.00

MARVEL: NOW WHAT?!
Marvel Comics: Dec, 2013 ($3.99, one-shot)

1-Short story spoofs; Doc Octopus, X-Men, Avengers; s/a by various; Skottie Young-c 4.00

MARVELOUS ADVENTURES OF GUS BEEZER
Marvel Comics: May, 2003; Feb, 2004 ($2.99, one-shots)

...: Gus Beezer & Spider-Man 1 - (5/03) Gurihiru-a 3.00
...: Hulk 1 - (5/03) Simone-s/Lethcoe-a; She-Hulk app. 3.00
...: Spider-Man 1 - (5/03) Simone-s/Lethcoe-a; The Lizard & Dr. Doom app. 3.00
...: X-Men 1 - (5/03) Simone-s/Lethcoe-a 3.00

MARVELOUS LAND OF OZ (Sequel to Wonderful Wizard of Oz)
Marvel Comics: Jan, 2010 - No. 8, Sept, 2010 ($3.99, limited series)

1-8-Eric Shanower-a/Skottie Young-a/c. 1-Two covers by Young 4.00
1-Variant Pumpkinhead/Saw-Horse cover by McGuinness 6.00

MARVEL PETS HANDBOOK (Also see "Lockjaw and the Pet Avengers")
Marvel Comics: 2009 ($3.99, one-shot)

1-Official Handbook-style profile pages of animal characters 4.00

MARVEL PREMIERE
Marvel Comics Group: April, 1972 - No. 61, Aug, 1981 (A tryout book for new characters)

1-Origin Warlock (pre-#1) by Gil Kane/Adkins; origin Counter-Earth; Hulk & Thor cameo (#1-14 are 20¢-c) 36 72 108 259 580 900
2-Warlock ends; Kirby Yellow Claw-r 6 12 18 38 69 100
3-Dr. Strange series begins (pre #1, 7/72), Stan Lee-s/B. Smith-c/a(p) 10 20 30 69 147 225
4-Barry Smith-a; Roy Thomas brings the world of Robert E. Howard into the Marvel Universe (via serpent people) 5 10 15 33 57 80
5-9: 5-1st app. Sligguth; 1st mention of Shuma-Gorath. 6-Brunner-a; 1st N'Gabthoth (Shambler from the sea). 7-1st Dagoth; P. Craig Russell-a. 8-Starlin-(p). 9-Englehart-s; Brunner-a(p) begin 3 6 9 19 30 40
10-Death of the Ancient One; 1st app. Shuma-Gorath 25 50 75 175 388 600
11-14: 11-Three pages of original material; mostly reprint of origin from Strange Tales #115 with Ditko-a. 13-Baron Mordo app; 1st app. Cagliostro & Sise-Neg. 14-Sise-Neg & Shuma-Gorath app.14-Last Dr. Strange (3/74), gets own title 3 months later 3 6 9 15 22 28
15-Origin/1st app. Iron Fist (5/74), ends #25 32 64 96 230 515 800
16,25: 16-2nd app. Iron Fist; origin cont'd from #15; Hama's 1st Marvel-a. 25-1st Byrne Iron Fist (moves to own title next) 6 12 18 37 66 95
17,18,20,22-24: Iron Fist in all 4 8 12 23 37 50
19-1st app. Colleen Wing; Iron Fist app. 10 20 30 64 132 200
21-1st app. Misty Knight; Iron Fist app. 7 14 21 46 86 125
26-Hercules. 2 4 6 11 16 20
27-Satana 5 10 15 35 63 90
28-Legion of Monsters (Ghost Rider, Man-Thing, Morbius, Werewolf) 23 46 69 161 356 550
29-46: 29,30-The Liberty Legion. 29-1st modern app. Patriot. 31-1st app. Woodgod; last 25¢ issue. 32-1st app. Monark Starstalker. 33,34-1st color app. Solomon Kane (Robert E. Howard adaptation "Red Shadows".) 35-Origin/1st app. 3-D Man. 36,37-3-D Man. 38-1st Weirdworld. 39,40-Torpedo. 41-1st Seeker 3000! 42-Tigra. 43-Paladin. 44-Jack of Hearts (1st solo book, 10/78). 45,46-Man-Wolf 1 3 4 6 8 10
29-31-(30¢-c variants, limited distribution)(4,6,8/76) 5 10 15 31 53 75
36-38-(35¢-c variants, limited distribution)(6,8,10/77) 6 12 18 41 76 110
47-Origin/1st app. new Ant-Man (Scott Lang); Byrne-a 10 20 30 68 138 210
48-Ant-Man; Byrne-a 4 8 12 25 40 55
49-The Falcon (1st solo book, 8/79) 3 6 9 17 25 34
50-1st app. Alice Cooper; co-plotted by Alice 5 10 15 31 53 75
51-53-Black Panther vs. KKK 4 8 12 23 37 50
54-56: 54-1st Caleb Hammer. 55-Wonder Man. 56-1st color app. Dominic Fortune 1 3 4 6 8 10
57-Dr. Who (2nd U.S. app.-see Movie Classics) 4 8 12 25 40 55
58-60-Dr. Who 2 4 6 8 10 12
61-Star Lord 2 4 6 11 16 20

NOTE: ***N. Adams** (Crusty Bunkers) part inks-10, 12, 13. **Austin** a-50i, 56i; c-46i, 50i, 56i, 58. **Brunner** a-4i, 6p, 9-14p; c-9-14. **Byrne** a-47p, 48p. **Chaykin** a-32-34; c-32, 33, 56. **Giffen** a-31p, 44p; c-44. **Gil Kane** a(p)-1, 2, 15; c(p)-1, 2, 15, 16, 22-24, 27, 36, 37. **Kirby** c-26, 29-31, 35. **Layton** a-47i, 48i; c-47. **McWilliams** a-25i. **Miller** c-49p, 53p, 58p. **Nebres** a-44i; c-38i. **Nino** a-38i. **Perez** c/a-38p, 45p, 46p. **Ploog** a-38; c-5-7. **Russell** a-7p. **Simonson** a-60(2pgs.); c-57. **Starlin** a-8p; c-8. **Sutton** a-41, 43, 50p, 61; c-50p, 61. #57-60 publ'd w/two different prices on-c.*

MARVEL PRESENTS
Marvel Comics: October, 1975 - No. 12, Aug, 1977 (#1-6 are 25¢ issues)

1-Origin & 1st app. Bloodstone 6 12 18 42 79 115
2-Origin Bloodstone continued; Buckler-c 2 4 6 11 16 20
3-Guardians of the Galaxy (1st solo book, 2/76) begins, ends #12 6 12 18 38 69 100
4-7,9-12: 9,10-Origin Starhawk 2 4 6 8 11 14
4-6-(30¢-c variants, limited distribution)(4-8/76) 5 10 15 30 50 70
8-r/story from Silver Surfer #2 plus 4 pgs. new-a 3 6 9 14 20 26
11,12-(35¢-c variants, limited distribution)(6,8/77) 8 16 24 54 102 150

NOTE: ***Austin** a-6i. **Buscema** r-8p. **Chaykin** a-5p. **Kane** c-1p. **Starlin** layouts-10.*

MARVEL PREVIEW (Magazine) (Bizarre Adventures #25 on)
Marvel Comics: Feb (no month), 1975 - No. 24, Winter, 1980 (B&W) ($1.00)

1-Man-Gods From Beyond the Stars; Crusty Bunkers (Neal Adams)-a(i) & cover; Nino-a 4 8 12 23 37 50
2-1st origin The Punisher (see Amaz. Spider-Man #129 & Classic Punisher); 1st app. Dominic Fortune; Morrow-c 17 34 51 117 259 400
3,8,10: 3-Blade the Vampire Slayer. 8-Legion of Monsters; Morbius app. 10-Thor the Mighty; Starlin frontispiece 4 8 12 25 40 55
4-Star-Lord & Sword in the Star (origins & 1st app.); Morrow-c 20 40 60 138 307 475
5-Sherlock Holmes 3 6 9 15 22 28
6,9: 6-Sherlock Holmes; N. Adams frontispiece. 9-Man-God; origin Star Hawk, ends #20 3 6 9 14 19 24
7-(Summer/76) Debut of Rocket Raccoon (called Rocky Raccoon) in Sword in the Star story (see Incredible Hulk #271 (5/82) for next app.); Satana on cover 33 66 99 238 532 825
11,14,15,18-Star-Lord. 11-Byrne-a; Starlin frontispiece; 2 versions: with and w/o white Heinlein text at lower right corner of front-c; 1st app. Spartax. 14-Starlin painted-c. 18-Sienkiewicz-a; Veitch & Bissette-a 5 10 15 33 57 80
12-Haunt of Horror 5 10 15 34 60 85
13,17,20,22,24: 17-Blackmark by G. Kane (see Savage Sword of Conan #1-3). 20-Bizarre Advs. 22-King Arthur. 24-Debut Paradox 1 3 4 6 8 10
16,19,21,23: 16-Masters of Terror. 19-Kull. 21-Moon Knight (Spr/80)- Predates Moon Knight #1; The Shroud by Ditko. 23-Bizarre Advs.; Miller-a 2 4 6 8 11 14

NOTE: ***N. Adams** (C. Bunkers) r-20i. **Buscema** a-22, 23. **Byrne** a-11. **Chaykin** a-20r; c-20 (new). **Colan** a-8, 16p(3), 18p, 23p; c-16p. **Elias** a-18. **Giffen** a-7. **Infantino** a-14p. **Kaluta** a-12; c-15. **Miller** a-23. **Morrow** a-8i; c-2-4. **Perez** a-20p. **Ploog** a-8. **Starlin** c-13, 14. Nudity in some issues.*

MARVEL RIOT
Marvel Comics: Dec, 1995 ($1.95, one-shot)

1-"Age of Apocalypse" spoof; Lobdell script 4.00

MARVEL RISING
Marvel Comics: Jun, 2018 - Nov, 2018; May, 2019 - No. 5, Sept, 2019 ($5.99/$4.99, lim. series)

0-(6/18, free) Grayson-s/Failla-a; preview of Marvel Super Hero Adventures titles 3.00
1-5: 1-(5/19, $3.99) Capt. Marvel, Ms. Marvel, Squirrel Girl, America & Spider-Gwen app. 4.00

Marvelous Land of Oz #1 © MAR

Marvel Rising: Alpha #1 © MAR

Marvel's Doctor Strange Prelude #1 © MAR

	GD 2.0	VG 4.0	FN 6.0	VF 8.0	VF/NM 9.0	NM- 9.2

...: Alpha 1 (8/18, $4.99) Part 1; Squirrel Girl & Ms. Marvel team-up; Grayson-s/Duarte-a 5.00
...: Ms. Marvel/Squirrel Girl 1 (10/18, $5.99) Part 3; America Chavez app. 6.00
...: Omega 1 (11/18, $4.99) Part 4 conclusion; Arcade app. 5.00
...: Squirrel Girl/Ms. Marvel 1 (9/18, $5.99) Part 2; battle Emulator 6.00

MARVEL ROMANCE
Marvel Comics: 2006 ($19.99, TPB)

nn-Reprints romance stories from 1960-1972; art by Kirby, Buscema, Colan, Romita 20.00

MARVEL ROMANCE REDUX (Humor stories using art reprinted from Marvel romance comics)
Marvel Comics: Apr, 2006 - Aug, 2006 ($2.99, one-shots)

...: But I Thought He Loved Me Too (4/06) art by Kirby, Colan, Buscema & Romita; Giffen-c 3.00
...: Guys & Dolls (5/06) art by Starlin, Heck, Colan & Buscema; Conner-c 3.00
...: I Should Have Been a Blonde (7/06) art by Brodsky Colletta & Colan; Cho-c 3.00
...: Love is a Four Letter Word (8/06) art by Kirby, Buscema, Colan & Heck; Land-c 3.00
...: Restraining Orders are For Other Girls (6/06) art by Giordano, Kirby; Kyle Baker-c 3.00
...: Another Kind of Love TPB (2007, $13.99) r/one-shots 14.00

MARVELS (Also see Marvels: Eye of the Camera)
Marvel Comics: Jan, 1994 - No. 4, Apr, 1994 ($5.95, painted lim. series)
No. 1 (2nd Printing), Apr, 1996 - No. 4 (2nd Printing), July, 1996 ($2.95)

1-4: Kurt Busiek scripts & Alex Ross painted-c/a in all; double-c w/acetate overlay
2 4 6 8 10 12
Marvel Classic Collectors Pack ($11.90)-Issues #1 & 2 boxed (1st printings).
2 4 6 9 13 16
0-(8/94, $2.95)-no acetate overlay. 5.00
1-4-(2nd printing): r/original limited series w/o acetate overlay 3.00
... Annotated 1-4 (4/19 - No. 4, 8/19, $7.99) reprints with original script, commentary, sketch and unlettered painted art; additional extras 8.00
... Epilogue 1 (9/19, $4.99) Phil Sheldon & family during events of X-Men #98; Busiek-s/Ross-a; new interview with creators; MAD-style spoof (2 pgs.); sketch deign pages 5.00
Hardcover (1994, $59.95)-r/#0-4; w/intros by Stan Lee, John Romita, Sr., Kurt Busiek & Scott McCloud. 60.00
...: 10th Anniversary Edition (2004, $49.99, hardcover w/dustjacket) r/#0-4; scripts and commentaries; Ross sketch pages, cover gallery, behind the scenes art 50.00
Trade paperback ($19.95) 20.00

MARVELS, THE
Marvel Comics: Jun, 2021 - No. 12, Sept, 2022 ($4.99/$3.99, limited series)

1-($4.99) Kurt Busiek-s/Yildiray Cinar-a/Alex Ross-c; intro. Kevin Schumer 5.00
2-12-($3.99) 3-Winter Soldier app. 4-Spider-Man app. 5-Intro Warbird 4.00

MARVEL SAGA, THE
Marvel Comics Group: Dec, 1985 - No. 25, Dec, 1987

1-25 4.00
NOTE: *Williamson a(i)-9, 10; c(i)-7, 10-12, 14, 16.*

MARVEL'S ANT-MAN AND THE WASP PRELUDE (For the 2018 movie)
Marvel Comics: May, 2018 - No. 2, Jun, 2018 ($3.99, limited series)

1,2-Will Corona Pilgrim-s/Chris Allen-a; adaptation of Ant-Man movie 4.00

MARVEL'S ANT-MAN PRELUDE (For the 2015 movie)
Marvel Comics: Apr, 2015 - No. 2, May, 2015 ($2.99, limited series)

1,2-Will Corona Pilgrim-s/Sepulveda-a; photo-c on both; Agent Carter app. 3.00

MARVEL'S AVENGERS (Based on the Marvel's Avengers video game)
Marvel Comics: Feb, 2020 - May, 2020 ($3.99, series of one-shots)

...: Black Widow 1 (5/20) Gage-s/Bandini-a; Taskmaster app. 4.00
...: Captain America 1 (5/20) Allor-s/Jeanty-a; Batroc app. 4.00
...: Hulk 1 (4/20) Jim Zub-s/Ariel Olivetti-a 4.00
...: Iron Man 1 (4/20) Zub-s/Paco Diaz-a; Avengers & Titania app. 4.00
...: Thor 1 (4/20) Zub-s/Robert Gill-a; Loki app. 4.00

MARVEL'S AVENGERS: INFINITY WAR PRELUDE (For the 2018 movie)
Marvel Comics: Mar, 2018 - No. 2, Apr, 2018 ($3.99, limited series)

1,2-Will Corona Pilgrim-s; photo-c on both. 1-Tigh Walker-a. 2-Jorge Fornés-a 4.00

MARVEL'S AVENGERS: UNTITLED PRELUDE (Issue #1 released before final title revealed)
MARVEL'S AVENGERS: ENDGAME PRELUDE (Adaptation of Avengers: Inifinity War)
Marvel Comics: Feb, 2019 - No. 3, Apr, 2019 ($3.99, limited series)

1-3-Will Corona Pilgrim-s/Paco Diaz-a; photo-c on each 4.00

MARVEL'S BLACK PANTHER PRELUDE (For the 2018 movie)
Marvel Comics: Dec, 2017 - No. 2, Jan, 2018 ($3.99, limited series)

1,2-Will Corona Pilgrim-s/Annapaola Martello-a; photo-c on both 4.00

MARVEL'S BLACK WIDOW PRELUDE (For the 2021 movie)
Marvel Comics: Dec, 2017 - No. 2, Jan, 2018 ($3.99, limited series)

1,2-Peter David-s/C.F. Villa-a; photo-c on both; recaps her history with the Avengers 4.00

MARVEL'S CAPTAIN AMERICA: CIVIL WAR PRELUDE (For the 2016 movie)
Marvel Comics: Feb, 2016 - No. 4, Mar, 2016 ($2.99, limited series)

1-4: 1,2-Adaptation of Iron Man 3 movie; Pilgrim-s/Kudranski-a. 3,4-Adapts Captain America: The Winter Soldier movie; Ferguson-a 3.00

MARVEL'S CAPTAIN MARVEL PRELUDE (For the 2019 movie)
Marvel Comics: Jan, 2019 ($3.99, one-shot)

1-Will Corona Pilgrim-s/Andrea Di Vito-a; Fury & Hill's events during Capt. A. Civil War 4.00

MARVELS COMICS: ... (Marvel-type comics read in the Marvel Universe)
Marvel Comics: Jul, 2000 ($2.25, one-shots)

...Captain America #1 -Frenz & Sinnott-a; ...Daredevil #1 -Isabella-s/Newell-a; ...Fantastic Four #1 -Kesel-s/Paul Smith-a; Spider-Man #1 -Oliff-a; ...Thor #1 -Templeton-s/Aucoin-a 3.00
...X-Men #1 -Millar-s/ Sean Phillips & Duncan Fegredo-a 3.00
The History of Marvels Comics (no cover price)-Faux history; previews titles 3.00

MARVEL'S DOCTOR STRANGE PRELUDE (2016 movie)
Marvel Comics: Sept, 2016 - No. 2, Oct, 2016 ($3.99, limited series)

1,2-Corona Pilgrim-s/Fornés-a; photo-c 4.00

MARVEL SELECT FLIP MAGAZINE
Marvel Comics: Aug, 2005 - No. 24 ($3.99/$4.99)

1-11-Reprints Astonishing X-Men and New X-Men: Academy X in flip format 4.00
12-24-($4.99) Reprints recent X-Men mini-series in flip format 5.00

MARVEL SELECTS:
Marvel Comics: Jan, 2000 - No. 6, June, 2000 ($2.75/$2.99, reprints)

...Fantastic Four 1-6: Reprints F.F. #107-112; new Davis-c 3.00
...Spider-Man 1,2,4-6: Reprints AS-M #100,101,103,104,93; Wieringo-c 3.00
...Spider-Man 3 ($2.99): Reprints AS-M #102; new Wieringo-c 3.00

MARVEL 75TH ANNIVERSARY CELEBRATION
Marvel Comics: Dec, 2014 ($5.99, one-shot)

1-Short stories by various incl. Stan Lee, Timm, Bendis, Stan Goldberg; Rivera-c 6.00

MARVELS: EYE OF THE CAMERA (Sequel to Marvels)
Marvel Comics: Feb, 2009 - No. 6, Apr, 2010 ($3.99, limited series)

1-6-Kurt Busiek-s/Jay Anacleto-a; continuing story of photographer Phil Sheldon 4.00
1-6-B&W edition 4.00

MARVEL'S GREATEST COMICS (Marvel Collectors' Item Classics #1-22)
Marvel Comics Group: No. 23, Oct, 1969 - No. 96, Jan, 1981

	GD	VG	FN	VF	VF/NM	NM-
23-34 (Giants). Begin Fantastic Four-r/#30s?-116	3	6	9	17	26	35
35-37-Silver Surfer-r/Fantastic Four #48-50	2	4	6	11	16	20
38-50: 42-Silver Surfer-r/F.F.(others?)	2	4	6	9	13	16
51-70: 63,64-(25¢ editions)	2	4	6	8	10	12
63,64-(30¢-c variants, limited distribution)(5,7/76)	5	10	15	30	50	70
71-96: 71-73-(30¢ editions)	1	2	3	5	6	8
71-73-(35¢-c variants, limited distribution)(7,9-10/77)	7	14	21	44	82	120

...: Fantastic Four #52 (2006, $2.99) reprints entire comic with ads and letter column 6.00
NOTE: *Dr. Strange, Fantastic Four, Iron Man, Watcher-#23, 24. Capt. America, Dr. Strange, Iron Man, Fantastic Four-#25-28. Fantastic Four-#38-96.* ***Buscema*** *r-85-92; c-87-92r.* ***Ditko*** *r-23-28.* ***Kirby*** *r-23-82; c-75, 77p, 80p. #81 reprints Fantastic Four #100.*

MARVEL'S GREATEST CREATORS...
Marvel Comics: Jul, 2019 ($1.00, one-shot reprints)

... Avengers – The Origin of Mantis 1 - Reprints Avengers #123; Englehart-s/Brown-a 3.00
... Hulk – The Wedding of Rick Jones 1 - Reprints Inc. Hulk #418; David-s/Frank-a 3.00
... Invaders 1 - Reprints Invaders #1; Roy Thomas-s/Frank Robbins-a 3.00
... Iron Fist – Colleen Wing 1 - Reprints Marvel Premiere #19; Moench-s/Hama-a 3.00
... Iron Fist – Misty Knight 1 - Reprints Marvel Premiere #21; Isabella-s/Arvell Jones-a 3.00
... Luke Cage, Power Man – Piranha 1 - Reprints Power Man #30; McGregor-s 3.00
... Power Pack 1 - Reprints Power Pack #1; Louise Simonson-s/June Brigman-a 3.00
... Silver Surfer – Rude Awakening 1 - Reprints Silver Surfer #51; Marz-s/Lim-a 3.00
... Spider-Man – Kraven's Last Hunt 1 - Reprints Web of Spider-Man #31; Zeck-a 3.00
... What If? – Spider-Girl 1 - Reprints What If? #105; DeFalco-s/Frenz-a 3.00

MARVEL'S GREATEST SUPERHERO BATTLES (See Fireside Book Series)

MARVEL: SHADOWS AND LIGHT
Marvel Comics: Feb, 1997 ($2.95, B&W, one-shot)

1-Tony Daniel-c 4.00

MARVEL 1602
Marvel Comics: Nov, 2003 - No. 8, June, 2004 ($3.50/$3.99, limited series)

1-7-Neil Gaiman-s; Andy Kubert & Richard Isanove-a 3.50
8-($3.99) 4.00
... MGC #1 (7/10, $1.00) r/#1 with "Marvel's Greatest Comics" logo on cover 3.00
HC (2004, $24.99) r/series; script pages for #1, sketch pages and Gaiman afterword 25.00
SC (2005, $19.99) 20.00

MARVEL 1602: FANTASTICK FOUR
Marvel Comics: Nov, 2006 - No. 5, Mar, 2007s ($3.50, limited series)

1-5-Peter David-s/Pascal Alixe-a/Leinil Yu-c 3.50
TPB (2007, $14.99) r/#1-5; sketch page 15.00

MARVEL 1602: NEW WORLD
Marvel Comics: Oct, 2005 - No. 5, Jan, 2006 ($3.50, limited series)

1-5-Greg Pak-s/Greg Tocchini-a; "Hulk" and "Iron Man" app. 3.50
TPB (2006, $14.99) r/#1-5 15.00

MARVEL 65TH ANNIVERSARY SPECIAL
Marvel Comics: 2004 ($4.99, one-shot)

1-Reprints Sub-Mariner & Human Torch battle from Marvel Mystery Comics #8-10 6.00

MARVELS OF SCIENCE
Charlton Comics: March, 1946 - No. 4, June, 1946

1-A-Bomb story 29 58 87 172 281 390
2-4 16 32 48 96 151 205

MARVEL SPECIAL EDITION FEATURING... (Also see Special Collectors' Ed.)
Marvel Comics Group: 1975 - 1978 (84 pgs.) (Oversized)

1-The Spectacular Spider-Man ($1.50); r/Amazing Spider-Man #6,35, Annual 1; Ditko-a(r) 3 6 9 19 30 40
1,2-Star Wars ('77,'78) r/Star Wars #1-3 & #4-6; regular edition 3 6 9 14 20 25
1,2-Star Wars ('77,'78) Whitman variant 3 6 9 19 30 40
3-Star Wars ('78, $2.50, 116 pgs.); r/S. Wars #1-6; regular edition and Whitman variant exist 3 6 9 14 20 26
3-Close Encounters of the Third Kind (1978, $1.50, 56 pgs.)-Movie adaptation; Simonson-a(p) 2 4 6 10 14 18
V2#2(Spring, 1980, $2.00, oversized)- "Star Wars: The Empire Strikes Back"; r/Marvel Comics Super Special #16 3 6 9 17 26 35
NOTE: ***Chaykin** c/a(r)-1(1977), 2, 3. **Stevens** a(r)-2i, 3i. **Williamson** a(r)-V2#2.*

MARVEL SPECTACULAR
Marvel Comics Group: Aug, 1973 - No. 19, Nov, 1975

1-Thor-r from mid-sixties begin by Kirby 3 6 9 17 25 34
2-19 2 4 6 8 10 12

MARVELS: PORTRAITS
Marvel Comics: Mar, 1995 - No. 4, June, 1995 ($2.95, limited series)

1-4: Different artists renditions of Marvel characters 4.00

MARVEL SPOTLIGHT (...& Son of Satan #19, 20, 23, 24)
Marvel Comics Group: Nov, 1971 - No. 33, Apr, 1977; V2#1, July, 1979 - V2#11, Mar, 1981
(A try-out book for new characters)

1-Origin Red Wolf (western hero)(1st solo book, pre-#1); Wood inks, Neal Adams-c; only 15¢ issue 9 18 27 57 111 165
2-(25¢, 52 pgs.)-Venus-r by Everett; origin/1st app. Werewolf By Night (begins) by Ploog; N. Adams-c 71 142 213 568 1284 2000
3-Werewolf By Night 13 26 39 86 188 290
4-1st app. of the Darkhold book; Werewolf By Night ends (6/72); gets own title 9/72 17 34 51 117 259 400
5-Origin/1st app. Ghost Rider (8/72) & begins 300 600 900 2550 5775 9000
6-8: 6-Origin G.R. retold. 8-Last Ploog issue 9 18 27 57 111 165
9-11-Last Ghost Rider (gets own title next mo.) 6 12 18 41 76 110
12-Origin & 2nd full app. The Son of Satan (10/73); story cont'd from Ghost Rider #2 & into #3; series begins, ends #24 9 18 27 62 126 190
13-24: 13-Partial origin Son of Satan. 14-Last 20¢ issue. 22-Ghost Rider-c & cameo (5 panels). 24-Last Son of Satan (10/75); gets own title 12/75 2 4 6 11 16 20
25,27,30,31: 27-(Regular 25¢-c), Sub-Mariner app. 30-The Warriors Three. 31-Nick Fury 2 4 6 8 10 12
26-Scarecrow 3 6 9 15 22 28
27-(30¢-c variant, limited distribution) 5 10 15 33 57 80
28-(Regular 25¢-c) 1st solo Moon Knight app. 21 42 63 147 324 500
28-(30¢-c variant, limited distribution) 36 72 108 259 580 900
29-(Regular 25¢-c) (8/76) Moon Knight app.; last 25¢ issue 6 12 18 42 79 115
29-(30¢-c variant, limited distribution) 8 16 24 56 108 160
32-1st app./partial origin Spider-Woman (2/77); Nick Fury app. 14 28 42 96 211 325
33-Deathlok; 1st app. Devil-Slayer (see Demon-Hunter #1) 3 6 9 19 30 40
V2#1-Captain Marvel & Drax app. 2 4 6 10 14 18
1-Variant copy missing issue #1 on cover 4 8 12 28 47 65
2-5,9-11: 2-4-Captain Marvel. 2-Drax app. 4-Ditko-c/a. 5-Dragon Lord. 9-11-Captain Universe (see Micronauts #8) 1 3 4 6 8 10
6-Star-Lord origin 6 12 18 38 69 100
7-Star-Lord; Miller-c 4 8 12 23 37 50
8-Capt. Marvel; Miller-c/a(p) 2 4 6 10 14 18
NOTE: ***Austin** c-V2#2i, 8. **J. Buscema** c/a-30p. **Chaykin** a-31; c-26, 31. **Colan** a-18p, 19p. **Ditko** a-V2#4, 5, 9-11; c-V2#4, 9-11. **Kane** c-21p, 32p. **Kirby** c-29p. **McWilliams** a-20i. **Miller** a-V2#8p; c(p)-V2#2, 5, 7, 8. **Mooney** a-8i, 10i, 14p, 15, 16p, 17p, 24p, 27, 32i. **Nasser** a-33p. **Ploog** a-2-5, 6-8p; c-3-9. **Romita** c-13. **Sutton** a-9-11p, V2#6, 7. #29-25¢ & 30¢ issues exist.*

MARVEL SPOTLIGHT (Most issues spotlight one Marvel artist and one Marvel writer)
Marvel Comics: 2005 - Apr, 2010 ($2.99/$3.99)

...Brian Bendis/Mark Bagley; Daniel Way/Olivier Coipel; David Finch/Roberto Aguirre-Sacasa; Ed Brubaker/Billy Tan; John Cassaday/Sean McKeever; Joss Whedon/Michael Lark; Laurell K. Hamilton/George R.R. Martin; Neil Gaiman/Salvador Larroca; Robert Kirkman/ Greg Land; Stan Lee/Jack Kirby; Warren Ellis/Jim Cheung each... 3.00
...Steve McNiven/Mark Millar - Civil War 10.00
...: Captain America (2009) interviews with Brubaker & Hitch; Reborn preview 3.00
...: Captain America Remembered (2007) character features; creator interviews 3.00
...: Civil War Aftermath (2007) Top 10 Moments, casualty list, previews of upcoming series 3.00
...: Dark Reign (2009) features on the Avengers, Fury and others; creator interview 4.00
...: Dark Tower (2007) previews the Stephen King adaptation; creator interviews 5.00
...: Deadpool (2009) character features; interviews with Kelly, Way, Medina & Benson 3.00
...: Fantastic Four and Silver Surfer (2007) character features; creator interviews 3.00
...: Ghost Rider (2007) character and movie features; creator interviews 3.00
...: Halo (2007) a World of Halo feature; Bendis & Maleev interviews 3.00
...: Heroes Reborn/Onslaught Reborn (2006) 3.00
...: Hulk Movie (2008) character and movie features; comic & movie creator interviews 3.00
...: Iron Man Movie (2008) character and movie features; Terrence Howard interview 3.00
...: Iron Man 2 (4/10) movie preview; Granov, Fraction interviews; Whiplash profile 4.00
...: Marvel Knights 10th Anniversary (2008) Quesada interview; series synopsies 3.00
...: Marvel Zombies/Mystic Arcana (2008) character features; creator interviews 3.00
...: Marvel Zombies Return (2009) character features; creator interviews 3.00
...: New Mutants (2009) character features; Claremont & McLeod interviews 3.00
...: Punisher Movie (2008) character and movie features; creator interviews 3.00
...: Secret Invasion (2008) features on the Skrulls; Bendis, Reed & Yu interviews 3.00
...: Secret Invasion Aftermath (2008) Skrull profiles; Bendis, Reed & Diggle interviews 4.00
...: Spider-Man (2007) character features; creator interviews; Ditko art showcase 3.00
...: Spider-Man - Brand New Day (2008) storyline features; Romitas interviews 3.00
...: Spider-Man-One More Day/Brand New Day (2008) storyline features; interviews 3.00
...: Summer Events (2009, $3.99) 2009 title previews; creator interviews 4.00
...: Thor (2007) character features; Straczynski interview; Romita Jr. art showcase 3.00
...: Ultimates 3 (2008) character features; Loeb & Madureira interviews 3.00
...: Ultimatum (2008) previews the limited series; Loeb & Bendis interviews 3.00
...: Uncanny X-Men 500 Issues Celebration (2008) creator interviews; timeline 3.00
...: War of Kings (2009) character features; Abnett, Lanning, Pelletier interviews 3.00
...: Wolverine (2009, $3.99) preview of 2009 Wolverine stories; creator interviews 4.00
...: World War Hulk (2007) character features; creator interviews; early art showcase 3.00
...: X-Men: Messiah Complex (2008) X-Men crossover features; creator interviews 3.00

MARVELS PROJECT, THE
Marvel Comics: Oct, 2009 - No. 8, July, 2010 ($3.99, limited series)

1-8-Emergence of Marvel heroes in 1939-40; Brubaker-s/Epting-a; Epting & McNiven-c 4.00
1-8-Variant covers by Parel 5.00

MARVELS SNAPSHOTS (See Sub-Mariner: ...)

MARVEL'S SPIDER-MAN: CITY AT WAR (Based on the 2018 videogame)
Marvel Comics (Gamerverse): May, 2019 - No. 6, Oct, 2019 ($3.99, limited series)

1-6: 1-Hallum-s/Bandini-a/Crain-c; gets the new costume; Mr. Negative app. 4.00

MARVEL'S SPIDER-MAN: HOMECOMING PRELUDE
Marvel Comics: May, 2017 - No. 2, Jun, 2017 ($3.99, limited series)

1,2-Adaptation from Captain America: Civil War movie; Pilgrim-s/Nauck-a; photo covers 4.00

MARVEL'S SPIDER-MAN: THE BLACK CAT STRIKES (Based on the 2018 videogame)
Marvel Comics (Gamerverse): Mar, 2020 - No. 5, Nov, 2020 ($3.99, limited series)

1-5: 1-Hallum-s/Maresca-a/Takeda-c 4.00

MARVEL'S SPIDER-MAN: VELOCITY (Titled Gamerverse Spider-Man: Velocity for #1)
Marvel Comics (Gamerverse): Oct, 2020 - No. 5, Feb, 2020 ($3.99, limited series)

1-5-Hallum-s/Laiso-a/Skan-c 4.00

MARVEL'S THE AVENGERS
Marvel Comics: Feb, 2015 - No. 2, Mar, 2015 ($2.99, limited series)

1,2-Adaptation of 2012 movie; Pilgrim-s/Bennett-a; photo covers 3.00

MARVEL'S THE AVENGERS: BLACK WIDOW STRIKES
Marvel Comics: Jul, 2012 - No. 3, Aug, 2012 ($2.99, limited series)

1-3-Prelude to 2012 movie; Van Lente-s. 1,3-Photo-c. 2-Granov-c 3.00

MARVEL'S THE AVENGERS PRELUDE
Marvel Comics: May, 2012 - No. 4, Jun, 2012 ($2.99, limited series)

1-4: 1-Prelude to 2012 movie; Luke Ross & Daniel HDR-a 3.00

MARVEL'S THE AVENGERS: THE AVENGERS INITIATIVE
Marvel Comics: Jul, 2012 ($2.99, one-shot)

1-Prelude to 2012 movie; Van Lente-s/Lim-a 3.00

MARVEL'S THOR: RAGNAROK PRELUDE
Marvel Comics: Sept, 2017 - No. 4, Oct, 2017 ($3.99, limited series)

1-4: 1,2-Adapts The Incredible Hulk movie. 3,4-Adapts Thor: The Dark World movie 4.00

MARVEL SUPER ACTION (Magazine)
Marvel Comics Group: Jan, 1976 (B&W, 76 pgs.)

1-2nd app. Dominic Fortune (see Marvel Preview); early Punisher app.; Weird World & The Huntress; Evans, Ploog-a 9 18 27 58 114 170

MARVEL SUPER ACTION
Marvel Comics Group: May, 1977 - No. 37, Nov, 1981

1-Reprints Capt. America #100 by Kirby 3 6 9 21 33 45
2-13: 2,3,5-13 reprint Capt. America #101,102,103-111. 4-Marvel Boy-r(origin)/M. Boy #1. 11-Origin-r. 12,13-Classic Steranko-c/a(r). 2 4 6 9 13 16
2,3-(35¢-c variants, limited distribution)(6,8/77) 11 22 33 73 157 240
14-20: r/Avengers #55,56, Annual 2, others 2 4 6 8 10 12
21-37: 30-r/Hulk #6 from U.K. 1 3 4 6 8 10
NOTE: ***Buscema** a(r)-14p, 15p; c-18-20, 22, 35r-37. **Everett** a-4. **Heath** a-4r. **Kirby** r-1-3, 5-11. **B. Smith** a-27r, 28r. **Steranko** a(r)-12p, 13p; c-12r, 13r.*

MARVEL SUPER HERO ADVENTURES (All ages title)
Marvel Comics: Jun, 2018 - Jun, 2019 ($3.99, series of one-shots)

...: Captain Marvel - First Day of School 1 (11/18) Spider-Man and Capt. Marvel team-up 4.00
...: Captain Marvel - Frost Giants Among Us! 1 (2/19) Avengers & Squirrel Girl app. 4.00
...: Captain Marvel - Halloween Spooktacular 1 (12/18) Spider-Man app. 4.00
...: Captain Marvel - Mealtime Mayhem 1 (1/19) Spider-Gwen & Venom app. 4.00
...: Inferno 1 (10/18) Spider-Man and Inferno team-up; Venom & Medusa app. 4.00
...: Ms. Marvel and the Teleporting Dog 1 (9/18) Lockjaw and The Serpent Society app. 4.00
...: Spider-Man - Across the Super-Verse 1 (3/19) Grandmaster and other Spiders app. 4.00
...: Spider-Man and the Stolen Vibranium 1 (6/18) Spider-Man & Black Panther team-up 4.00
...: Spider-Man - Spider-Sense of Adventure 1 (5/19) Ghost-Spider and Arcade app. 4.00
...: Spider-Man - Web Designers 1 (6/19) Mysterio app. 4.00
...: Spider-Man - Web of Intrigue 1 (3/19) Miles, Gwen & Sinister Six app. 4.00
...: The Spider-Doctor 1 (7/18) Spider-Man and Doctor Strange team-up; Hela app. 4.00
...: Webs and Arrows and Ants, Oh My! 1 (8/18) Kate Bishop & Ant-Man app. 4.00

MARVEL SUPER HERO CONTEST OF CHAMPIONS
Marvel Comics Group: June, 1982 - No. 3, Aug, 1982 (Limited series)

Marvel's Spider-Man: City at War #1 © MAR

Marvel Super-Heroes #70 © MAR

Marvel's Voices #1 © MAR

GD VG FN VF VF/NM NM-
2.0 4.0 6.0 8.0 9.0 9.2

1-Features nearly all Marvel characters currently appearing in their comics;
1st Marvel limited series 4 8 12 23 37 50
2,3 3 6 9 14 19 24

MARVEL SUPER HEROES
Marvel Comics Group: October, 1966 (25¢, 68 pgs.) (1st Marvel one-shot)
1-r/origin Daredevil from D.D. #1; r/Avengers #2; G.A. Sub-Mariner-r/Marvel Mystery #8
(Human Torch app.). Kirby-a 10 20 30 67 141 215

MARVEL SUPER-HEROES (Formerly Fantasy Masterpieces #1-11)
(Also see Giant-Size Super Heroes) (#12-20: 25¢, 68 pgs.)
Marvel Comics: No. 12, 12/67 - No. 31, 11/71; No. 32, 9/72 - No. 105, 1/82
12-Origin & 1st app. Capt. Marvel of the Kree; G.A. Human Torch, Destroyer, Capt. America,
Black Knight, Sub-Mariner-r (#12-20 all contain new stories and reprints)
29 58 87 209 467 725
13-2nd app. Capt. Marvel; 1st app. of Carol Danvers (later becomes Ms. Marvel);
Golden Age Black Knight, Human Torch, Vision, Capt. America, Sub-Mariner-r
79 158 237 632 1416 2200
14-Amazing Spider-Man (5/68, new-a by Andru/Everett); G.A. Sub-Mariner, Torch, Mercury
(1st Kirby-a at Marvel), Black Knight, Capt. America reprints
10 20 30 66 138 210
15-Black Bolt cameo in Medusa (new-a); Black Knight, Sub-Mariner, Black Marvel,
Capt. America-r 8 16 24 52 99 145
16-Origin & 1st app. S. A. Phantom Eagle; G.A. Torch, Capt. America, Black Knight,
Patriot, Sub-Mariner-r 5 10 15 35 63 90
17-Origin Black Knight (new-a); G.A. Torch, Sub-Mariner-r; reprint from All-Winners Squad #21
(cover & story) 21 42 63 147 324 500
18-Origin/1st app. Guardians of the Galaxy (1/69); G.A. Sub-Mariner, All-Winners Squad-r
68 136 204 544 1222 1900
19-Ka-Zar (new-a); G.A. Torch, Marvel Boy, Black Knight, Sub-Mariner reprints; Smith-c(p);
Tuska-a(r) 5 10 15 31 53 75
20-Doctor Doom (5/69); r/Young Men #24 w/-c 39 78 114 285 641 1000
21-31: All-r issues. 21-X-Men, Daredevil, Iron Man-r begin, end #31. 31-Last Giant issue
3 6 9 19 30 40
32-50: 32-Hulk/Sub-Mariner-r begin from TTA. 2 4 6 8 11 14
51-70,100: 56-r/origin Hulk/Inc. Hulk #102; Hulk-r begin
2 4 6 8 10 12
57,58-(30¢-c variants, limited distribution)(5,7/76) 5 10 15 34 60 85
65,66-(35¢-c variants, limited distribution)(7,9/77) 8 16 24 51 96 140
71-99,101-105 1 3 4 6 8 10
NOTE: ***Austin** a-104. **Colan** a(p)-12, 13, 15, 18; c-12, 13, 15, 18. **Everett** a-14i(new); r-14, 15i, 18, 19, 33; c-85(r). New **Kirby** c-22, 27, 54. **Maneely** r-14, 15, 19. **Severin** r-83-85i, 100-102; c-100-102r. **Starlin** c-47. **Tuska** a-19p. Black Knight-r by **Maneely** in 12-16, 19. Sub-Mariner-r by **Everett** in 12-20.*

MARVEL SUPER-HEROES
Marvel Comics: May, 1990 - V2#15, Oct, 1993 ($2.95/$2.50, quart., 68-84 pgs.)
1-Moon Knight, Hercules, Black Panther, Magik, Brother Voodoo, Speedball (by Ditko)
& Hellcat; Hembeck-a 1 3 4 6 8 10
2,4,5,V2#3,6,7,9,13-15: 2-Summer Special(7/90); Rogue, Speedball (by Ditko), Iron Man, Falcon, Tigra & Daredevil. 4-Spider-Man/Nick Fury, Daredevil,Speedball, Wonder Man, Spitfire & Black Knight; Byrne-c. 5-Thor, Dr. Strange, Thing & She-Hulk; Speedball by Ditko(p). V2#3-Retells origin Capt. America w/new facts; Blue Shield, Capt. Marvel, Speedball, Wasp; Hulk by Ditko/Rogers V2#6-9: 6,7-($2.25-c) X-Men, Cloak & Dagger, The Shroud (by Ditko) & Marvel Boy in each. 9-West Coast Avengers, Iron Man app.; Kieth-c(p). V2#13-15 ($2.75, 84 pgs.): 13-All Iron Man 30th anniversary.
15-Iron Man/Thor/Volstagg/Dr. Druid 5.00
V2#8-1st app. Squirrel Girl; X-Men, Namor & Iron Man (by Ditko); Larsen-c
6 12 18 38 69 100
V2#10-Ms. Marvel/Sabretooth-c/story (intended for Ms. Marvel #24; shows-c to #24);
Namor, Vision, Scarlet Witch stories; $2.25-c 2 4 6 8 10 12
V2#11-Original Ghost Rider-c/story; Giant-Man, Ms. Marvel stories
2 4 6 11 16 20
V2#12-Dr. Strange, Falcon, Iron Man 4.00

MARVEL SUPER-HEROES MEGAZINE
Marvel Comics: Oct, 1994 - No. 6, Mar, 1995 ($2.95, 100 pgs.)
1-6: 1-r/FF #232, DD #159, Iron Man #115, Incred. Hulk #314 6.00

MARVEL SUPER-HEROES SECRET WARS (See Secret Wars II)
Marvel Comics Group: May, 1984 - No. 12, Apr, 1985 (limited series)
1 5 10 15 35 63 90
1-3-(2nd printings, sold in multi-packs) 4.00
2 2 4 6 9 13 16
3-6,9-11: 6-The Wasp dies 1 3 4 6 8 10
7,12: 7-Intro. new Spider-Woman. 12-($1.00, 52 pgs.)2 4 6 11 16 20
8-Spider-Man's new black costume explained as alien costume (1st app. Venom as
alien costume) 10 20 30 67 141 215
10-Doctor Doom cover 3 6 9 19 30 40
Secret Wars Omnibus HC (2008, $99.99, dustjacket) r/#1-12, Thor #383, She-Hulk (2004) #10
and What If? (1989) #4 & #114; photo gallery of related toys; pencil-a from #1 100.00
NOTE: ***Zeck** a-1-3,6-12; c-1,3,8-12. Additional artists (Romita Sr., Art Adams and others) had uncredited art in #12.*

MARVEL SUPER HERO SPECTACULAR (All ages)
Marvel Comics: Dec, 2015 ($3.99, one-shot)
1-Avengers, Guardians of the Galaxy and Spider-Man app.; bonus puzzle pages 4.00

MARVEL SUPER HERO SQUAD (All ages)
Marvel Comics: Mar, 2009; Nov, 2009 - No. 4, Feb, 2010 ($3.99/$2.99)
1-4-Based on the animated series; back-up humor strips and pin-ups 3.00
...Hero Up! (3/09, $3.99) Collects humor strips from MarvelKids.com; 2 covers 4.00

MARVEL SUPER HERO SQUAD (All ages)
Marvel Comics: Mar, 2010 - No. 12, Feb, 2011 ($2.99)
1-12-Based on the animated series. 1-Wraparound-c 3.00
Super Hero Squad Spectacular 1 (4/11, $3.99) The Beyonder app. 4.00

MARVEL SUPER SPECIAL, A (See Marvel Comics Super...)

MARVEL'S VOICES (Inspired by the Marvel's Voices podcast)
Marvel Comics: Apr, 2020 - Present ($4.99/$5.99/$9.99)
1-(4/20) Short stories & essays from various creators of color; intro. by Angélique Roché 5.00
1-(1/21) Expanded version of first edition; Miles Morales mask-c 5.00
... Comunidades 1 (11/22, $5.99) Short stories celebrating Latin & Latinx heritage 6.00
... Identity 1 (11/22, $5.99) Short stories celebrating Asian/Pacific Island heroes 6.00
... Indigenous Voices 1 (1/21, $4.99) Short stories by Native American creators 5.00
...: Legacy 1 (4/21, $4.99) Short stories by African American creators; afterword by Roché 5.00
...: Legacy 1 (4/22, $5.99) Short stories by African American creators; Crisscross-c 6.00
...: Pride 1 (8/22, $9.99) Short stories celebrating LGBTQIA+ heroes; bonus Handbook bios 10.00
...: Wakanda Forever (4/23, $5.99) Spotlight on Wakandan characters by Black creators 6.00

MARVEL SWIMSUIT SPECIAL (Also see Marvel Illustrated...)
Marvel Comics: 1992 - No. 4, 1995 ($3.95/$4.50, magazine, 52 pgs.)
1,3,4: 1-Silvestri-c; pin-ups by diff. artists. 3-Hughes-c 2 4 6 10 14 18
2-Rogue-c by Jusko 3 6 9 14 20 25

MARVELS X (Prequel to Earth X, Paradise X and Universe X series)
Marvel Comics: Mar, 2020 - No. 6, Dec, 2020 ($4.99)
1-6-Jim Krueger & Alex Ross-s/Well-Bee-a; covers by Ross and others 5.00

MARVEL TAILS STARRING PETER PORKER THE SPECTACULAR SPIDER-HAM
(Also see Peter Porker... and Spider-Ham)(Appears in Spider-Man: Into the Spider-Verse movie)
Marvel Comics Group: Nov, 1983 (one-shot)
1-1st app. Peter Porker, the Spectacular Spider-Ham; Captain Americat, Goose Rider,
Hulk Bunny app. 5 10 15 31 53 75

MARVEL TALES (Formerly Marvel Mystery Comics #1-92)
Marvel/Atlas Comics (MCI): No. 93, Aug, 1949 - No. 159, Aug, 1957
93-Horror/weird stories begin 300 600 900 1980 3440 4900
94-Everett-a 181 362 543 1158 1979 2800
95-New logo; classic Sci-Fi cover 314 628 942 2198 3849 5500
96,99,101,103,105 93 186 279 591 1021 1450
97-Sun Girl, 2 pgs; Kirbyish-a; one story used in N.Y. State Legislative document
110 220 330 704 1202 1700
98,100: 98-Krigstein-a 81 162 243 518 884 1250
102-Wolverton-a "The End of the World", (6 pgs.) 100 200 300 635 1093 1550
104-Wolverton-a "Gateway to Horror", (6 pgs.) 116 232 348 742 1271 1800
106,107-Krigstein-a. 106-Decapitation story 68 136 204 435 743 1050
108-120: 116-(7/53) Werewolf By Night story. 118-Hypo-c/panels in End of World story.
120-Jack Katz-a 57 114 171 362 619 875
121,123-131: 128-Flying Saucer-c. 131-Last precode (2/55)
48 96 144 302 514 725
122-Kubert-a 53 106 159 334 567 800
132,133,135-141,143,145 40 80 120 246 411 575
134-Krigstein, Kubert-a; flying saucer-c 45 90 135 284 480 675
142-Krigstein-a 40 80 120 246 411 575
144-Williamson/Krenkel-a, 3 pgs. 40 80 120 246 411 575
146,148-151,154-156,158: 150-1st S.A. issue. 156-Torres-a
36 72 108 211 343 475
147,152: 147-Ditko-a. 152-Wood, Morrow-a 39 78 117 231 378 525
153-Everett End of World c/story 43 86 129 271 461 650
157,159-Krigstein-a 37 74 111 218 354 490
NOTE: ***Andru** a-103. **Briefer** a-118. **Check** a-147. **Colan** a-102, 105, 107, 118, 120, 121, 127, 131. **Drucker** a-127, 135, 141, 146, 150. **Everett** a-98, 104, 106(2), 108(2), 131, 148, 151, 153, 155; c-107, 109, 111, 112, 114, 117, 127, 143, 147-151, 153, 155, 156. **Forte** a-119, 125, 130, 158. **Heath** a-110, 113, 118, 119; c-104-106, 110, 130. **Gil Kane** a-117. **Lawrence** a-130. **Maneely** a-111, 126, 129; c-108, 116, 120, 129, 152. **Mooney** a-114. **Morisi** a-153. **Morrow** a-150, 152, 156. **Orlando** a-149, 151, 157. **Pakula** a-119, 121, 133, 135, 144, 150, 152, 156. **Powell** a-136, 137, 150, 154. **Ravielli** a-117, 123. **Rico** a-97, 99. **Romita** a-108. **Sekowsky** a-96-98. **Shores***

GD VG FN VF VF/NM NM-
2.0 4.0 6.0 8.0 9.0 9.2

a-110; c-96. ***Sinnott*** *a-105, 116, 144.* ***Tuska*** *a-114.* ***Whitney*** *a-107.* ***Wildey*** *a-126, 138.*

MARVEL TALES (...Annual #1,2; ...Starring Spider-Man #123 on)
Marvel Comics Group (NPP earlier issues): 1964 - No. 291, Nov, 1994 (No. 1-32: 72 pgs.)
(#1-3 have Canadian variants; back & inside-c are blank, same value)

1-Reprints origins of Spider-Man/Amazing Fantasy #15, Hulk/Inc. Hulk#1, Ant-Man/T.T.A. #35, Giant Man/T.T.A. #49, Iron Man/T.O.S. #39,48, Thor/J.I.M. #83 & r/Sgt. Fury #1 — 54 108 162 432 966 1500
2 ('65)-r/X-Men #1(origin), Avengers #1(origin), origin Dr. Strange-r/Strange Tales #115 & origin Hulk(Hulk #3) — 11 22 33 76 163 250
3 (7/66)-Spider-Man, Strange Tales (H. Torch), Journey into Mystery (Thor), Tales to Astonish (Ant-Man)-r begin (r/Strange Tales #101) — 7 14 21 48 89 130
4,5 — 5 10 15 33 57 80
6-8,10: 10-Reprints 1st Kraven/Amaz. S-M #15 — 4 8 12 25 37 50
9-r/Amazing Spider-Man #14 w/cover — 4 8 12 28 47 65
11-33: 11-Spider-Man battles Daredevil-r/Amaz. Spider-Man #16. 13-Origin Marvel Boy-r from M. Boy #1. 22-Green Goblin-c/story-r/Amaz. Spider-Man #27. 30-New Angel story (x-over w/Ka-Zar #2,3). 32-Last 72 pg. iss. 33-(52 pgs.) Kraven-r — 3 6 9 17 25 34
34-50: 34-Begin regular size issues — 2 4 6 8 10 12
51-65 — 1 3 4 6 8 10
66-70-(Regular 25¢ editions)(4-8/76) — 1 3 4 6 8 10
66-70-(30¢-c variants, limited distribution) — 5 10 15 31 53 75
71-105: 75-Origin Spider-Man-r. 77-79-Drug issues-r/Amaz. Spider-Man #96-98. 98-Death of Gwen Stacy-r/Amaz. Spider-Man #121 (Green Goblin). 99-Death Green Goblin-r/Amaz. Spider-Man #122. 100-(52 pgs.)-New Hawkeye/Two Gun Kid story.
101-105-All Spider-Man-r — 1 2 3 5 6 8
80-84-(35¢-c variants, limited distribution)(6-10/77) — 6 12 18 41 76 110
106-r/1st Punisher-Amazing Spider-Man #129 — 7 14 21 44 82 120
107-136: 107-133-All Spider-Man-r. 111,112-r/Spider-Man #134,135 (Punisher). 113,114-r/Spider-Man #136,137(Green Goblin). 126-128-r/clone story from Amazing Spider-Man #149-151. 134-136-Dr. Strange-r begin; SpM stories continue. 134-Dr. Strange-r/Strange Tales #110 — 6.00
137-Origin-r Dr. Strange; shows original unprinted-c & origin Spider-Man/Amazing Fantasy #15 — 3 6 9 16 23 30
137-Nabisco giveaway — 3 6 9 14 20 25
138-Reprints all Amazing Spider-Man #1; begin reprints of Spider-Man with covers similar to originals — 3 6 9 15 22 28
139-144: r/Amazing Spider-Man #2-7 — 1 2 3 5 6 8
145-149,151-190,193-199: Spider-Man-r continue w/#8 on. 149-Contains skin "Tattooz" decals. 153-r/1st Kraven/Spider-Man #15. 155-r/2nd Green Goblin/Spider-Man #17. 161,164,165-Gr. Goblin-c/stories-r/Spider-Man #23,26,27. 178,179-Green Goblin-c/story-r/ Spider-Man #39,40. 187,189-Kraven-r. 193-Byrne-r/Marvel Team-Up begin w/scripts — 6.00
150,191,192,200: 150-($1.00, 52pgs.)-r/Spider-Man Annual #1(Kraven app.). 191-($1.50, 68 pgs.)-r/Spider-Man #96-98. 192-($1.25, 52 pgs.)-r/Spider-Man #121,122. 200-Double size ($1.25)-Miller-c & r/Annual #14 — 1 2 3 5 6 8
201-249,251,252,254-257: 208-Last Byrne-r. 210,211-r/Spidey #134,135. 212,213-r/Giant-Size Spidey #4. 213-r/1st solo Silver Surfer story/F.F. Annual #5. 214,215-r/Spidey #161,162. 222-Reprints origin Punisher/Spect. Spider-Man #83; last Punisher reprint. 209-Reprints 1st app. The Punisher/Amazing Spider-Man #129; Punisher reprints begin, end #222. 223-McFarlane-c begins, end #239. 233-Spider-Man/X-Men team-ups begin; r/X-Men #35. 234-r/Marvel Team-Up #4. 235,236-r/M. Team-Up Annual #1. 237,238-r/M. Team-Up #150. 239,240-r/M. Team-Up #38,90(Beast). 242-r/M.Team-Up #89. 243-r/M. Team-Up #117 (Wolverine). 251-r/Spider-Man #100 (Green Goblin-c/story). 252-r/1st app. Morbius/Amaz. Spider-Man #101. 254-r/M. Team-Up #15(Ghost Rider); new painted-c. 255,256-Spider-Man & Ghost Rider-r/Marvel Team-Up #58,91. 257-Hobgoblin-r begin (r/ASM #238) — 4.00
250,253: 250-($1.50, 52 pgs.)-r/1st Karma/M. Team-Up #100. 253-($1.50, 52 pgs.) -r/Amaz. S-M #102 — 5.00
258-291: 258-261-r/A. Spider-Man #239,249-251(Hobgoblin). 262,263-r/Marv. Team-Up #53,54. 262-New X-Men vs. Sunstroke story. 263-New Woodgod origin story. 264,265-r/Amazing Spider-Man Annual 5. 266-273-Reprints alien costume stories/A. S-M 252-259. 277-r/1st Silver Sable/A. S-M 265. 283-r/A. S-M 275 (Hobgoblin). 284-r/A. S-M 276 (Hobgoblin) — 5.00
285-variant w/Wonder-Con logo on c-no price-giveaway — 5.00
286-($2.95)-p/bagged w/16 page insert & animation print — 1 2 3 5 6 8

NOTE: *All contain reprints; some have new art. #89-97-r/Amazing Spider-Man #110-118; #98-136-r/#121-159; #137-150-r/Amazing Fantasy #15, #1-12 & Annual 1; #151-167-r/#13-28 & Annual 2; #168-186-r/#29-46.* ***Austin*** *a-100i; c-272i, 273i.* ***Byrne*** *a(r)-193-198p, 201-208p.* ***Ditko*** *a-1-30, 83, 100, 137-155.* ***G. Kane*** *a-71, 81, 98-101p, 249r; c-125-127p, 130p, 137-155.* ***Sam Kieth*** *c-255, 262, 263.* ***Ron Lim*** *c-266p-281p, 283p-285p.* ***McFarlane*** *c-223-239.* ***Mooney*** *a-63, 95-97i, 103(i).* ***Nasser*** *a-100p.* ***Nebres*** *a-242i.* ***Perez*** *c-259-261.* ***Rogers*** *c-240, 241, 243-252.*

MARVEL TALES
Marvel Comics: Mar, 2019 - Nov, 2020 ($7.99)

...: Annihilation 1 (2/20) reprints Marvel Two-In-One #53, Daredevil #105 and Darkhawk #6; Inhyuk Lee-c; intro. by Macchio; features Quasar, Moondragon & Darkhawk — 8.00
...: Avengers 1 (7/19) reprints Avengers #16,57,264; Bartel-c; intro. by Macchio — 8.00
...: Black Panther 1 (11/19) reprints notable appearances; Bartel-c; intro. by Macchio — 8.00
...: Black Widow 1 (4/19) reprints notable appearances; Bartel-c; intro. by Macchio — 8.00
...: Captain America 1 (9/19) reprints notable appearances; Bartel-c; intro. by Macchio — 8.00
...: Captain Britain 1 (11/20) reprints Captain Britain #1-2, Marvel Team-up #65-66, and Excalibur #1; Inhyuk Lee-c; intro. by Macchio — 8.00
...: Doctor Strange 1 (1/20) reprints notable appearances; Inhyuk Lee-c; intro. by Macchio — 8.00
...: Fantastic Four 1 (3/19) reprints FF #4, Annual #6, #245; Bartel-c; intro. by Macchio — 8.00
...: Ghost Rider 1 (12/19) reprints notable appearances; Inhyuk Lee-c; intro. by Macchio — 8.00
...: Hulk 1 (9/19) reprints notable appearances; Bartel-c; intro. by Macchio — 8.00
...: Iron Man 1 (7/19) reprints TOS #39,45 & Iron Man #150; Bartel-c; intro. by Macchio — 8.00
...: Ravencroft 1 (3/20) reprints notable stories; Inhyuk Lee-c; intro. by Macchio — 8.00
...: Silver Surfer 1 (12/19) r/Thor #193 & Sub-Mariner #34,35; Lee-c; intro. by Macchio — 8.00
...: Spider-Man 1 (8/19) reprints ASM #66, Marvel Spotlight #32 & Peter Parker #90 — 8.00
...: Thanos 1 (6/19) reprints Warlock #10, Silver Surfer #45, Warlock & Infinity Watch #8 — 8.00
...: Thor 1 (5/19) reprints JIM #85 & notable appearances; Bartel-c; intro. by Macchio — 8.00
...: Venom 1 (4/19) reprints ASM #316, 361 and Peter Parker Spec. S-M #119; Bartel-c; intro. by Macchio — 8.00
...: Wolverine 1 (4/20) reprints notable appearances; Inhyuk Lee-c; intro. by Macchio — 8.00
...: X-Men 1 (10/19) reprints notable stories; Bartel-c; intro. by Macchio — 8.00

MARVEL TALES FLIP MAGAZINE
Marvel Comics: Sept, 2005 - No. 25, Sept, 2007 ($3.99/$4.99)

1-6-Reprints Amazing Spider-Man #30-up and Amazing Fantasy (2004) in flip format — 4.00
7-10-Reprints Amazing Spider-Man #36-up and Runaways Vol. 2 in flip format — 4.00
11-25-($4.99) Reprints Amazing Spider-Man #36-up and Runaways Vol. 2 in flip format — 5.00

MARVEL TAROT, THE
Marvel Comics: 2007 ($3.99, one-shot)

1-Marvel characters featured in Tarot deck images; Djurdjevic-c — 4.00

MARVEL TEAM-UP (See Marvel Treasury Edition #18 & Official Marvel Index To...)
(Replaced by Web of Spider-Man)
Marvel Comics Group: March, 1972 - No. 150, Feb, 1985
NOTE: *Spider-Man team-ups in all but Nos. 18, 23, 26, 29, 32, 35, 97, 104, 105, 137.*

1-Human Torch — 22 44 66 154 340 525
2-Human Torch — 7 14 21 44 82 120
3-Spider-Man/Human Torch vs. Morbius (part 1); 3rd app. of Morbius (7/72) — 8 16 24 56 108 160
4-Spider-Man/X-Men vs. Morbius (part 2 of story); 4th app. of Morbius — 8 16 24 52 99 145
5-10: 5-Vision. 6-Thing. 7-Thor. 8-The Cat (4/73, came out between The Cat #3 & 4). 9-Iron Man. 10-Human Torch — 4 8 12 22 35 48
11-Inhumans — 4 8 12 23 37 50
12-Werewolf (By Night) (8/73) — 5 10 15 31 53 75
13,14,16-20: 13-Capt. America. 14-Sub-Mariner. 16-Capt. Marvel. 17-Mr. Fantastic. 18-Human Torch/Hulk. 19-Ka-Zar. 20-Black Panther; last 20¢ issue — 3 6 9 14 20 25
15-1st Spider-Man/Ghost Rider team-up (11/73) — 10 20 30 64 132 200
21,23-30: 21-Dr. Strange. 23-H-T/Iceman (X-Men cameo). 24-Brother Voodoo. 25-Daredevil. 26-H-T/Thor. 27-Hulk. 28-Hercules. 29-H-T/Iron Man. 30-Falcon — 2 4 6 8 11 14
22-Hawkeye — 3 6 9 17 26 35
31-45,47-50: 31-Iron Fist. 32-H-T/Son of Satan. 33-Nighthawk. 34-Valkyrie. 35-H-T/Dr. Strange. 36-Frankenstein. 37-Man-Wolf. 38-Beast. 39-H-T. 40-Sons of the Tiger/H-T. 41-Scarlet Witch. 42-The Vision. 43-Dr. Doom; retells origin. 44-Moondragon. 45-Killraven. 47-Thing. 48-Iron Man; last 25¢ issue. 49-Dr. Strange; Iron Man app. 50-Iron Man; Dr. Strange app. — 2 4 6 8 10 12
44-48-(30¢-c variants, limited distribution)(4-8/76) — 7 14 21 44 82 120
46-Spider-Man/Deathlok team-up — 2 4 6 11 16 20
51,52,56,57: 51-Iron Man; Dr. Strange app. 52-Capt. America. 56-Daredevil. 57-Black Widow; 2nd app. Silver Samurai — 2 4 6 8 10 12
53-Hulk; Woodgod & X-Men app., 1st Byrne-a on X-Men (1/77) — 5 10 15 30 50 70
54,55,58-60: 54,59,60: 54-Hulk; Woodgod app. 59-Yellowjacket/The Wasp. 60-The Wasp (Byrne-a in all). 55-Warlock-c/story; Byrne-a. 58-Ghost Rider — 2 4 6 8 11 14
58-62-(35¢-c variants, limited distribution)(6-10/77) — 10 20 30 64 132 200
61-64,67-70: All Byrne-a; 61-H-T. 62-Ms. Marvel; last 30¢ issue. 63-Iron Fist. 64-Daughters of the Dragon. 67-Tigra; Kraven the Hunter app. 68-Man-Thing. 69-Havok (from X-Men). 70-Thor — 2 4 6 8 11 14
65-Capt. Britain (1st U.S. app.) — 8 16 24 54 102 150
66-Capt. Britain; 1st app. Arcade — 3 6 9 18 28 38
71-74,76-78,80: 71-Falcon. 72-Iron Man. 73-Daredevil. 74-Not Ready for Prime Time Players (Belushi). 76-Dr. Strange. 77-Ms. Marvel. 78-Wonder Man. 80-Dr. Strange/Clea; last 35¢ issue — 1 3 4 6 8 10
75,79,81: Byrne-a(p). 75-Power Man; Cage app. 79-Mary Jane Watson as Red Sonja; Clark Kent cameo (1 panel, 3/79). 81-Death of Satana — 2 4 6 8 11 14
82-85,87-94,96-99: 82-Black Widow. 83-Nick Fury. 84-Shang-Chi. 89-Nightcrawler (X-Men). 91-Ghost Rider. 92-Hawkeye. 93-Werewolf by Night. 94-Spider-Man vs. The Shroud. 96-Howard the Duck; last 40¢ issue. 97-Spider-Woman/ Hulk. 98-Black Widow. 99-Machine Man. 85-Shang-Chi/Black Widow/Nick Fury. 87-Black Panther. 88-Invisible Girl. 90-Beast — 1 2 3 5 6 8
86-Guardians of the Galaxy — 2 4 6 11 16 20
95-Mockingbird (intro.); Nick Fury app. — 6 12 18 37 66 95
100-(Double-size)-Spider-Man & Fantastic Four story with origin/1st app. Karma, one of the New Mutants; X-Men & Professor X cameo; Miller-c/a(p); Storm & Black Panther story; brief origins; Byrne-a(p) — 3 6 9 18 27 36
101,102,104-116,118-140,142-149: 101-Nighthawk(Ditko-a). 102-Doc Samson. 104-Hulk/Ka-Zar. 105-Hulk/Power Man/Iron Fist. 106-Capt. America. 107-She-Hulk. 108-Paladin; Dazzler cameo. 109-Dazzler; Paladin app. 110-Iron Man. 111-Devil-Slayer. 112-King Kull; last 50¢ issue. 113-Quasar. 114-Falcon. 115-Thor. 116-Valkyrie. 118-Professor X; Wolverine app. (4 pgs.); X-Men cameo. 119-Gargoyle. 120-Dominic Fortune. 121-Human Torch. 122-Man-Thing. 123-Daredevil. 124-The Beast. 125-Tigra. 126-Hulk & Powerman/Son of Satan. 127-The Watcher. 128-Capt. America; Spider-Man/ Capt. America photo-c. 129-Vision. 130-Scarlet Witch. 131-Frogman. 132-Mr. Fantastic. 133-Fantastic Four. 134-Jack of Hearts. 135-Kitty Pryde; X-Men cameo. 136-Wonder Man. 137-Aunt May/Franklin Richards. 138-Sandman. 139-Nick Fury. 140-Black Widow. 142-Capt. Marvel. 143-Starfox. 144-Moon Knight. 145-Iron Man. 146-Nomad. 147-Human Torch; Spider-Man back to old costume. 148-Thor. 149-Cannonball — 6.00
103-Ant-Man — 3 6 9 14 20 25
117-Wolverine-c/story — 3 6 9 17 26 35
141-Daredevil; SpM/Black Widow app. (Spidey in new black costume; ties w/ Amazing Spider-Man #252 for 1st black costume) — 8 16 24 54 102 150
150-X-Men ($1.00, double-size); B. Smith-c — 3 6 9 14 19 24
Annual 1 (1976)-Spider-Man/X-Men (early app.) — 5 10 15 35 63 90
Annual 2 (1979)-Spider-Man/Hulk — 2 4 6 10 14 18
Annuals 3,4: 3 (1980)-Hulk/Power Man/Machine Man/Iron Fist; Miller-c(p). 4 (1981)-Spider-Man /Daredevil/Moon Knight/Power Man/Iron Fist; brief origins of each; Miller-c; Miller scripts on Daredevil — 1 3 4 6 8 10
Annuals 5-7: 5 (1982)-SpM/The Thing/Scarlet Witch/Dr. Strange/Quasar. 6 (1983)-Spider-Man/ New Mutants (early app.), Cloak & Dagger. 7(1984)-Alpha Flight; Byrne-c(i) — 1 2 3 5 6 8

NOTE: ***Art Adams*** *c-141p.* ***Austin*** *a-79i; c-76i, 79i, 96i, 101i, 112i, 130i.* ***Bolle*** *a-9i.* ***Byrne*** *a(p)-53-55, 59-70, 75, 79, 100; c-68p, 70p, 72p, 75, 76p, 79p, 129i, 133i.* ***Colan*** *a-87p.* ***Ditko*** *a-101.* ***Kane*** *a(p)-4-6, 13, 14, 16-19, 23; c(p)-4, 13, 14, 17-19, 23, 25, 26, 32-35, 37, 41, 44, 45, 47, 53, 54.* ***Miller*** *a-100p; c-95p, 99p, 100p, 102p, 106.* ***Mooney*** *a-2i, 7i, 8, 10p, 11p, 16i, 24-31p, 72, 93i, Annual 5i.* ***Nasser*** *a-89p; c-101p.* ***Simonson*** *c-99i, 148.* ***Paul Smith*** *c-131, 132.* ***Starlin*** *c-27.* ***Sutton*** *a-93p. "H-T" means Human Torch; "SpM" means Spider-Man; "S-M" means Sub-Mariner.*

MARVEL TEAM-UP (2nd Series)
Marvel Comics: Sept, 1997 - No. 11, July, 1998 ($1.99)

Marvel Tales #100 © MAR

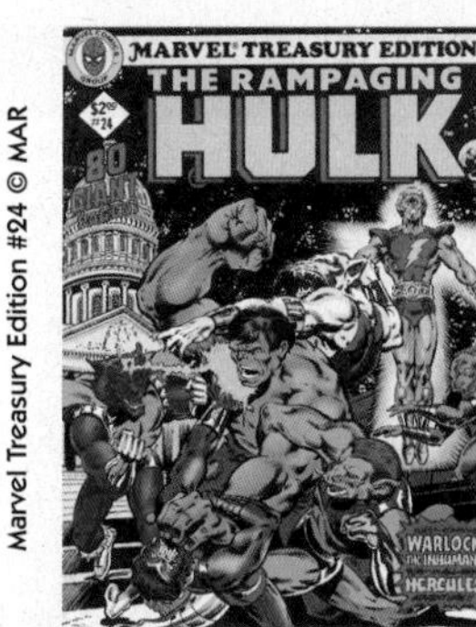

Marvel Treasury Edition #24 © MAR

Marvel 2-In-One #1 © MAR

GD VG FN VF VF/NM NM-
2.0 4.0 6.0 8.0 9.0 9.2

1-11: 1-Spider-Man team-ups begin, Generation x-app. 2-Hercules-c/app.; two covers. 3-Sandman. 4-Man-Thing. 7-Blade. 8-Namor team-ups begin, Dr. Strange app. 9-Capt. America. 10-Thing. 11-Iron Man 4.00

MARVEL TEAM-UP
Marvel Comics: Jan, 2005 - No. 25, Dec, 2006 ($2.25/$2.99)

1-7,9: 1,2-Spider-Man & Wolverine; Kirkman-s/Kolins-a. 5,6-X-23 app. 3.00
8,10-25 ($2.99-c) 10-Spider-Man & Daredevil. 12-Origin of Titannus. 14-Invincible app. 15-2nd app. of 2nd Sleepwalker 3.00
... Vol. 1: The Golden Child TPB (2005, $12.99) r/#1-6 13.00
... Vol. 2: Master of the Ring TPB (2005, $17.99) r/#7-13 18.00
... Vol. 3: League of Losers TPB (2006, $13.99) r/#14-18 14.00
... Vol. 4: Freedom Ring TPB (2007, $17.99) r/#19-25 18.00

MARVEL TEAM-UP (Ms. Marvel Team-Up in indicia for #1)
Marvel Comics: Jun, 2019 - No. 6, Nov, 2019 ($3.99, limited series)

1-6: 1-3-Ms. Marvel & Spider-Man team-up. 1-Flip book. 4-6-Ms. Marvel/Captain Marvel 4.00

MARVEL: THE LOST GENERATION
Marvel Comics: No. 12, Mar, 2000 - No. 1, Feb, 2001 ($2.99, issue #s go in reverse)

1-12-Stern-s/Byrne-s/a; untold story of The First Line. 5-Thor app. 3.00

MARVEL/ TOP COW CROSSOVERS
Image Comics (Top Cow): Nov, 2005 ($24.99, TPB)

Vol. 1-Reprints crossovers with Wolverine, Witchblade, Hulk, Darkness; Devil's Reign 25.00

MARVEL TREASURY EDITION
Marvel Comics Group/Whitman #17,18: 1974; #2, Dec, 1974 - #28, 1981 ($1.50/$2.50, 100 pgs., oversized, new-a &-r)(Also see Amazing Spider-Man, The, Marvel Spec. Ed. Feat.--, Savage Fists of Kung Fu, Superman Vs. , & 2001, A Space Odyssey)

1-Spectacular Spider-Man; story-r/Marvel Super-Heroes #14; Romita-c/a(r); G. Kane, Ditko-r; Green Goblin/Hulk-r 6 12 18 40 73 105
1-1,000 numbered copies signed by Stan Lee & John Romita on front-c & sold thru mail for $5.00; these were the 1st 1,000 copies off the press 13 26 39 89 195 300
2-10,12: 2-Fantastic Four-r/F.F. 6,11,48-50(Silver Surfer). 3-The Mighty Thor-r/Thor #125-130. 4-Conan the Barbarian; Barry Smith-c/a(r)/Conan #11. 5-The Hulk (origin-r/Hulk #3). 6-Dr. Strange. 7-Mighty Avengers. 8-Giant Superhero Holiday Grab-Bag; Spider-Man, Hulk, Nick Fury. 9-Giant; Super-hero Team-up. 10-Thor; r/Thor #154-157. 12-Howard the Duck (r/#H. the Duck #1 & G.S. Man-Thing #4,5) plus new Defenders story. 3 6 9 21 33 45
11,13-20: 11-Fantastic Four. 13-Giant Super-Hero Holiday Grab-Bag. 14-The Sensational Spider-Man; r/1st Morbius from Amazing S-M #101,102 plus #100 & r/Not Brand Echh #6. 15-Conan; B. Smith, Neal Adams-i; r/Conan #24. 16-The Defenders (origin) & Valkyrie; r/Defenders #1,4,13,14. 17-Incredible Hulk; Blob, Havok, Rhino and The Leader app. 18-The Astonishing Spider-Man; r/Spider-Man's 1st team-ups with Iron Fist, The X-Men, Ghost Rider & Werewolf by Night; inside back-c has photos from 1978 Spider-Man TV show. 19-Conan the Barbarian. 20-Hulk 3 6 9 16 23 30
21-24,27: 21-Fantastic Four. 22-Spider-Man. 23-Conan. 24-Rampaging Hulk. 27-Spider-Man 3 6 9 16 23 30
25-Spider-Man vs. The Hulk new story 4 8 12 23 37 50
26-The Hulk; 6 pg. new Wolverine/Hercules-s 3 6 9 21 33 45
28-Spider-Man/Superman; (origin of each) 5 10 15 34 60 85

NOTE: *Reprints-2, 3, 5, 7-9, 13, 14, 16, 17.* ***Neal Adams*** *a(i)-6, 15.* ***Brunner*** *a-6, 12; c-6.* ***Buscema*** *a-15, 19, 28; c-28.* ***Colan*** *a-6r; c-12p.* ***Ditko*** *a-1, 6.* ***Gil Kane*** *c-16p.* ***Kirby*** *a-1-3, 5, 7, 9-11; c-7.* ***Perez*** *a-26.* ***Romita*** *c-1, 5.* ***B. Smith*** *a-4, 15, 19; c-4, 19.*

MARVEL TREASURY OF OZ FEATURING THE MARVELOUS LAND OF OZ
Marvel Comics Group: 1975 ($1.50, oversized) (See MGM's Marvelous...)

1-Roy Thomas-s/Alfredo Alcala-a; Romita-c & bk-c 3 6 9 21 33 45

MARVEL TREASURY SPECIAL (Also see 2001: A Space Odyssey)
Marvel Comics Group: 1974; 1976 ($1.50, oversized, 84 pgs.)

Vol. 1-Spider-Man, Torch, Sub-Mariner, Avengers "Giant Superhero Holiday Grab-Bag"; Wood, Colan/Everett, plus 2 Kirby-r; reprints Hulk vs. Thing from Fantastic Four #25,26 3 6 9 19 30 40
Vol. 1-... Featuring Captain America's Bicentennial Battles (6/76)-Kirby-a; B. Smith inks, 11 pgs. 3 6 9 21 33 45

MARVEL TRIPLE ACTION (See Giant-Size...)
Marvel Comics Group: Feb, 1972 - No. 24, Mar, 1975; No. 25, Aug, 1975 - No. 47, Apr, 1979

1-(25¢ giant, 52 pgs.)-Dr. Doom, Silver Surfer, The Thing begin, end #4 ('66 reprints from Fantastic Four) 5 10 15 31 53 75
2-5 2 4 6 11 16 20
6-10 2 4 6 8 11 14
11-47: 45-r/X-Men #45. 46-r/Avengers #53(X-Men) 2 4 6 8 10 12
29,30-(30¢-c variants, limited distribution)(5,7/76) 5 10 15 33 57 80
36,37-(35¢-c variants, limited distribution)(7,9/77) 8 16 24 56 106 160

GD VG FN VF VF/NM NM-
2.0 4.0 6.0 8.0 9.0 9.2

NOTE: *#5-44, 46, 47 reprint Avengers #11 thru ?. #40-r/Avengers #48(1st Black Knight).* ***Buscema*** *a(r)-35p, 36p, 38p, 39p, 41, 42, 43p, 44p, 46p, 47p.* ***Ditko*** *a-2r; c-47.* ***Kirby*** *a(r)-1-4p; c-9-19, 22, 24, 29.* ***Starlin*** *c-7.* ***Tuska*** *a(r)-40p, 43i, 46i, 47i. #2 through #17 are 20¢-c.*

MARVEL TRIPLE ACTION
Marvel Comics: May, 2009 - No. 2, Jun, 2009 ($5.99, limited series)

1,2-Reprints stories from Wolverine First Class, Marvel Adventures Avengers & Marvel Super Heroes 6.00

MARVEL TSUM TSUM
Marvel Comics: Oct, 2016 - No. 4, Jan, 2017 ($3.99, limited series)

1-4-Based on Japanese stackable plush toys. 1-Spider-Man and the Avengers app. 4.00

MARVEL TV: GALACTUS - THE REAL STORY
Marvel Comics: Apr, 2009 ($3.99, one-shot)

1-The "hoax" of Galactus, Tieri-s/Santacruz-a; r/Fantastic Four #50 4.00

MARVEL TWO-IN-ONE (...Featuring ... #82 on; also see The Thing)
Marvel Comics Group: January, 1974 - No. 100, June, 1983

1-Thing team-ups begin; Man-Thing 7 14 21 48 89 130
2,3: 2-Sub-Mariner; last 20¢ issue. 3-Daredevil 3 6 9 21 33 45
4,6: 4-Capt. America. 6-Dr. Strange (11/74) 3 6 9 16 23 30
5-Guardians of the Galaxy (9/74, 2nd app.) 5 10 15 30 50 70
7,9,10 2 4 6 11 16 20
8-Early Ghost Rider app. (3/75) 3 6 9 17 26 35
11-14,19,20: 13-Power Man. 14-Son of Satan (early app.) 2 4 6 8 10 12
15-18-(Regular 25¢ editions)(5-7/76) 17-Spider-Man 2 4 6 8 10 12
15-18-(30¢-c variants, limited distribution) 4 8 12 27 44 60
21-29: 27-Deathlok. 29-Master of Kung Fu; Spider-Woman cameo 1 3 4 6 8 10
28,29,31-(35¢-c variants, limited distribution) 5 10 15 34 60 85
30-2nd full app. Spider-Woman (see Marvel Spotlight #32 for 1st app.) 3 6 9 17 26 35
30-(35¢-c variant, limited distribution)(8/77) 9 18 27 62 126 190
31-33-Spider-Woman app. 2 4 6 8 10 12
34-40: 39-Vision 1 2 3 5 6 8
41,42,44,45,47-49: 42-Capt. America. 45-Capt. Marvel 1 2 3 4 5 7
43,50,53,55-Byrne-a(p). 53-Quasar(7/79, 2nd app.) 1 3 4 6 8 10
46-Thing battles Hulk-c/story 2 4 6 10 14 18
51-The Beast, Nick Fury, Ms. Marvel; Miller-a/c 1 3 4 6 8 10
52-Moon Knight app.; 1st app. Crossfire 3 6 9 19 30 40
54-Death of Deathlok; Byrne-a 4 8 12 25 40 55
56-60,64-68,70-74,76-79,81,82: 60-Intro. Impossible Woman. 68-Angel. 71-1st app. Maelstrom. 76-Iceman 5.00
61-63: 61-Starhawk (from Guardians); "The Coming of Her" storyline begins, ends #63; cover similar to F.F. #67 (Him-c). 62-Moondragon; Thanos & Warlock cameo in flashback; Starhawk app. 63-Warlock revived shortly; Starhawk & Moondragon app. 2 4 6 8 10 12
69-Guardians of the Galaxy 2 4 6 9 12 15
75-Avengers (52 pgs.) 6.00
80,90,100: 80-Ghost Rider. 90-Spider-Man. 100-Double size, Byrne-s 6.00
83-89,91-99: 83-Sasquatch. 84-Alpha Flight app. 93-Jocasta dies. 96-X-Men-c & cameo 5.00
Annual 1 (1976, 52 pgs.)-Thing/Liberty Legion; Kirby-c 3 6 9 15 22 28
Annual 2 (1977, 52 pgs.)-Thing/Spider-Man; 2nd death of Thanos; end of Thanos saga; Warlock app.; Starlin-c/a 6 12 18 47 79 115
Annual 3,4 (1978-79, 52 pgs.): 3-Nova. 4-Black Bolt 1 2 3 5 6 8
Annual 5-7 (1980-82, 52 pgs.): 5-Hulk. 6-1st app. American Eagle. 7-The Thing/Champion; Sasquatch, Colossus app.; X-Men cameo (1 pg.) 6.00

NOTE: ***Austin*** *c(i)-42, 54, 56, 58, 61, 63, 66.* ***John Buscema*** *a-30p, 45; c-30p.* ***Byrne*** *(p)-43, 50, 53-55; c-43, 53p, 56p, 98i, 99i.* ***Gil Kane*** *a-1p, 2p; c(p)-1-3, 9-11, 14, 28.* ***Kirby*** *c-12, 19p, 20, 25, 27.* ***Mooney*** *a-18i, 38i, 90i.* ***Nasser*** *a-70p.* ***Perez*** *a(p)-56-58, 60, 64, 65; c(p)-32, 33, 42, 50-52, 54, 55, 57, 58, 61-66, 70.* ***Roussos*** *a-Annual 1i.* ***Simonson*** *c-43i, 97p, Annual 6i.* ***Starlin*** *c-6, Annual 1.* ***Tuska*** *a-6p.*

MARVEL TWO-IN-ONE
Marvel Comics: Sept, 2007 - No. 17, Jan, 2009 ($4.99, 64 pgs.)

1-8,13-16-Reprints Marvel Adventures Avengers and X-Men: First Class stories 5.00
9-12,17-Reprints Marvel Adventures Iron Man and Avengers stories 5.00

MARVEL 2-IN-ONE
Marvel Comics: Feb, 2018 - No. 12, Jan, 2019 ($3.99)

1-12: 1-Human Torch & The Thing team-up; Zdarsky-s/Cheung-a; Doctor Doom app. 4.00
Annual 1 (8/18, $4.99) Spotlight on Infamous Iron Man; Zdarsky-s/Shalvey-a 5.00

MARVEL UNIVERSE (See Official Handbook Of The...)

MARVEL UNIVERSE (Title on variant covers for newsstand editions of some 2001 Marvel titles. See indicia for actual titles and issue numbers)

MARVEL UNIVERSE

Marvel Comics: June, 1998 - No. 7, Dec, 1998 ($2.99/$1.99)

1-($2.99)-Invaders stories from WW2; Stern-s 5.00
2-7-($1.99): 2-Two covers. 4-7-Monster Hunters; Manley-a/Stern-s 4.00

MARVEL UNIVERSE AVENGERS AND ULTIMATE SPIDER-MAN
Marvel Comics: 2012 (no price, Halloween giveaway)

1-Reprints from Marvel Universe Ultimate Spider-Man #1 & Avengers E.M.H #1 4.00

MARVEL UNIVERSE AVENGERS ASSEMBLE (Based on the Disney XD animated series) (Titled Avengers Assemble for #1,2)
Marvel Comics: Dec, 2013 - No. 12, Nov, 2014 ($3.99/$2.99)

1-($3.99) Red Skull app.; bonus Lego-style story 4.00
2-12-($2.99) 5-Dracula app. 7-Hyperion app. 12-Impossible Man app. 3.00

MARVEL UNIVERSE AVENGERS ASSEMBLE: CIVIL WAR
Marvel Comics: May, 2016 - No. 4, Aug, 2016 ($2.99)

1-4: 1,2,4-Ultron app. 3.00

MARVEL UNIVERSE AVENGERS ASSEMBLE SEASON TWO
Marvel Comics: Jan, 2015 - No. 16, Apr, 2016 ($3.99/$2.99)

1-($3.99) Red Skull & Thanos app. 4.00
2-16-($2.99) 2-Thanos & The Watcher app. 4-Winter Soldier app. 9-Ant-Man joins 3.00

MARVEL UNIVERSE AVENGERS: ULTRON REVOLUTION
Marvel Comics: Sept, 2016 - No. 12, Oct, 2017 ($2.99)

1-12-Ultron returns; A.I.M. app. 11-Ms. Marvel joins. 12-Captain Marvel app. 3.00

MARVEL UNIVERSE GUARDIANS OF THE GALAXY (Disney XD animated series)
Marvel Comics: Apr, 2015 - No. 4, Jul, 2015 ($2.99)

1-4: 1-Back-up story with Star-Lord origin 3.00

MARVEL UNIVERSE GUARDIANS OF THE GALAXY (Disney XD animated series)
Marvel Comics: Dec, 2015 - No. 23, Dec, 2017 ($3.99/$2.99)

1-($3.99) Cosmo & Korath app.; bonus Lego story 4.00
2-23-($2.99) 3-Fin Fang Foom app. 4-Grandmaster app. 13-Loki app. 20-Thanos app.3.00

MARVEL UNIVERSE HULK: AGENTS OF S.M.A.S.H (Disney XD animated series)
Marvel Comics: Dec, 2013 - No. 4, Mar, 2014 ($2.99)

1-4: 1-Hulk, A-Bomb, She-Hulk, Red Hulk and Skaar team-up 3.00

MARVEL UNIVERSE: MILLENNIAL VISIONS
Marvel Comics: Feb, 2002 ($3.99, one-shot)

1-Pin-ups by various; wraparound-c by JH Williams & Gray 4.00

MARVEL UNIVERSE: THE END (Also see Infinity Abyss)
Marvel Comics: May, 2003 - No. 6, Aug, 2003 ($3.50/$2.99, limited series)

1-($3.50)-Thanos, X-Men, FF, Avengers, Spider-Man, Daredevil app.; Starlin-s/a(p) 4.00
2-6-($2.99) Akhenaten, Eternily, Living Tribunal app. 3.00
Thanos Vol. 3: Marvel Universe - The End (2003, $16.99) r/#1-6 17.00

MARVEL UNIVERSE ULTIMATE SPIDER-MAN (Based on the animated series)
Marvel Comics: Jun, 2012 - No. 31, Dec, 2014 ($2.99)

1-31: 1-Agent Coulson app. 13-Iron Man app. 16,19-Venom app. 29-Spider-Ham app. 3.00

MARVEL UNIVERSE ULTIMATE SPIDER-MAN: CONTEST OF CHAMPIONS
Marvel Comics: May, 2016 - No. 4, Aug, 2016 ($2.99, limited series)

1-4-The Collector & Grandmaster app. 1-Iron Man, Hulk & Kraven app. 3.00

MARVEL UNIVERSE ULTIMATE SPIDER-MAN SPIDER-VERSE
Marvel Comics: Jan, 2016 - No. 4, Apr, 2016 ($3.99/$2.99)

1-($3.99) 1-Spider-Man 2099 and Spider-Girl app. 4.00
2-4-($2.99) 3,4-Miles Morales app. 3.00

MARVEL UNIVERSE ULTIMATE SPIDER-MAN VS. THE SINISTER SIX
Marvel Comics: Sept, 2016 - No. 11, Sept, 2017 ($2.99)

1-11: 1,2-Doctor Octopus & Scarlet Spider app. 3-Dr. Strange app. 6-Venom app. 3.00

MARVEL UNIVERSE ULTIMATE SPIDER-MAN: WEB WARRIORS
Marvel Comics: Jan, 2015 - No. 12, Dec, 2015 ($3.99/$2.99)

1-($3.99) Captain America & Doctor Doom app.; back-up with Iron Spider 4.00
2-12-($2.99) 2-Hawkeye app. 3-Iron Man app. 8-Deadpool app. 12-Howling Commandos 3.00
.../Avengers Assemble Halloween ComicFest 2015 #1 (giveaway) reprints 3.00

MARVEL UNIVERSE VS. THE AVENGERS
Marvel Comics: Dec, 2012 - No. 4, Mar, 2013 ($3.99, limited series)

1-4-Avengers vs. Marvel Zombies; Maberry-s/Fernandez-a/Kuder-c 4.00

MARVEL UNIVERSE VS. THE PUNISHER
Marvel Comics: Oct, 2010 - No. 4, Nov, 2010 ($3.99, limited series)

1-4-Punisher vs. Marvel Zombies; Maberry-s/Parlov-a/c 4.00

MARVEL UNIVERSE VS. WOLVERINE
Marvel Comics: Aug, 2011 - No. 4, Nov, 2011 ($3.99, limited series)

1-4-Wolverine vs. Marvel Zombies; Maberry-s/Laurence Campbell-a/c 4.00

MARVEL UNLIMITED (Title on variant covers for newsstand editions of some 2001 Daredevil issues. See indicia for actual titles and issue numbers)

MARVEL VALENTINE SPECIAL
Marvel Comics: Mar, 1997 ($2.99, one-shot)

1-Valentine stories w/Spider-Man, Daredevil, Cyclops, Phoenix
2 4 6 10 14 18

MARVEL VERSUS DC (See DC Versus Marvel) (Also see Amazon, Assassins, Bruce Wayne: Agent of S.H.I.E.L.D., Bullets & Bracelets, Doctor Strangefate, JLX, Legend of the Dark Claw, Magneto & The Magnetic Men, Speed Demon, Spider-Boy, Super Soldier, & X-Patrol)
Marvel Comics: No. 2, 1996 - No. 3, 1996 ($3.95, limited series)

2,3: 2-Peter David script. 3-Ron Marz script; Dan Jurgens-a(p). 1st app. of Super Soldier, Spider-Boy, Dr. Doomsday, Doctor Strangefate, The Dark Claw, Nightcreeper, Amazon, Wraith & others. Storyline continues in Amalgam books. 5.00

MARVEL VISIONARIES
Marvel Comics: 2002 - 2007 (various prices, HC and TPB)

...: Chris Claremont (2005, $29.99) r/X-Men #137, Uncanny X-Men #153,205,268 & Ann. #12, Iron Fist #14, Wolverine #3, New Mutants #21 and other highlights 30.00
...: Gil Kane (8/02, $24.95) r/Amazing Spider-Man #99, Marvel Premiere #1,#15, TOA #76 & others; plus sketch pages and a cover gallery 25.00
...: Jack Kirby HC (2004, $29.99) r/career highlights- Red Raven Comics #1 (1st work), Captain America Comics #1, Avengers #4, Fantastic Four #48-50 and more 30.00
...: Jack Kirby Vol. 2 HC (2006, $34.99) r/career highlights- Captain America, Two-Gun Kid, Fantastic Four, Thor, Fin Fang Foom, Devil Dinosaur, romance and more 35.00
...: Jim Steranko (9/02, $14.95) r/Captain America #110,111,113; X-Men #50,51 and stories from Tower of Shadows #1 and Our Love Story #5; plus a cover gallery 15.00
...: John Buscema (2007, $34.99) r/career highlights-Avengers, Silver Surfer, Thor, FF, Hulk, Wolverine and others; Roy Thomas intro.; sketch pages and pin-up art 35.00
...: John Romita Jr. (2005, $29.99) r/various stories 1977-2002; debut in AS-M Ann. #11; Iron Man #128, AS-M V2 #36, issues of Hulk, Daredevil: The Man Without Fear, Punisher; sketch pages; intro. by John Romita Sr. 30.00
...: John Romita Sr. (2005, $29.99) r/various stories 1951-1997 including Young Men #24&26, Daredevil #16, ASM #39,42,50; sketch pages; intro. by John Romita Jr. 30.00
...: Roy Thomas (2006, $34.99) r/career highlights; intro. by Stan Lee 35.00
...: Steve Ditko (2005, $29.99) r/various stories 1961-1992; intro. by Blake Bell 30.00
...: Stan Lee HC (2005, $29.99) r/career highlights- Captain America Comics #3 (1st work), and various Spider-Man, FF, Thor, Daredevil stories; 1940-1995; Roy Thomas intro. 30.00

MARVEL VOICES (Also see Marvel's Voices:...)
Marvel Comics: Aug, 2021 - Present (series of one-shots)

...: Community 1 (12/21, $9.99) Stories celebrating Latin & Latinx characters & creators 10.00
...: Heritage (3/22, $4.99) Spotlight on Indigenous characters & creators 5.00
...: Identity (10/21, $5.99) Asian American & Pacific Islander characters & creators 6.00
...: Pride (8/21, $9.99) Spotlight on LGBTQ+ characters & creators 5.00

MARVEL WEDDINGS
Marvel Comics: 2005 ($19.99, TPB)

TPB-Reprints weddings of Peter & Mary Jane, Reed & Sue, Scott & Jean, and others 20.00

MARVEL WESTERNS: ...
Marvel Comics: 2006 ($3.99, one-shots)

... Kid Colt and the Arizona Girl 1 (9/06) 2 short stories & 3 Kirby/Ayers reps.; Powell-c 4.00
... Outlaw Files-Profiles and essays about Marvel western characters 4.00
... Strange Westerns Starring The Black Rider 1 (10/06) Englehart-s/Rogers-a & 2 Kirby Rawhide Kid reprints; Rogers-c 4.00
... The Two-Gun Kid 1 (8/06) 2 short stories & a Kirby/Ayers reprint; Powell-c 4.00
... Western Legends 1 (9/06) 2 short stories & r/Rawhide Kid origin by Kirby; Powell-c 4.00
HC (2006, $20.99, dustjacket) r/one-shots 21.00

MARVEL X-MEN COLLECTION, THE
Marvel Comics: Jan, 1994 - No. 3, Mar, 1994 ($2.95, limited series)

1-3-r/X-Men trading cards by Jim Lee 4.00

MARVEL - YEAR IN REVIEW (Magazine)
Marvel Comics: 1989 - No. 3, 1991 (52 pgs.)

1-3: 1-Spider-Man-c by McFarlane. 2-Capt. America-c. 3-X-Men/Wolverine-c 6.00

MARVEL: YOUR UNIVERSE
Marvel Comics: 2008; May, 2009 - No. 3, July, 2009 ($5.99)

1-3-Reprints of 5 recent comics (Ms. Marvel, Nova, Immortal Iron Fist & others) 6.00
...Saga (2008, no cover price) - Re-caps of crossovers (Secret War thru Secret Invasion) 3.00

MARVEL ZOMBIE (Simon Garth)
Marvel Comics: Dec, 2018 ($4.99, one-shot)

1-Prince-s/Raffaele-a; Spider-Man, Moon Girl, Daredevil, others in zombie apocalypse 5.00

MARVEL ZOMBIES (See Ultimate Fantastic Four #21-23, 30-32)
Marvel Comics: Feb, 2006 - No. 5, June, 2006 ($2.99, limited series)

1-Zombies vs. Magneto; Kirkman-s/Phillips-a/Suydam-c swipe of A.F. #15
4 8 12 23 37 50
1-(2nd printing) Variant Suydam-c swipe of Spider-Man #1
2 4 6 11 16 20
1-(3rd-4th printings) Variant Suydam-c swipes of Amazing Spider-Man #50 and Incredible Hulk #1 6.00
2-Avengers #4 cover swipe by Suydam 2 4 6 9 12 15
3-Inc. Hulk #340 c-swipe 3 6 9 16 23 30
3-5-(2nd printings) 3-Daredevil #179 c-swipe. 4-AS-M #39 c-swipe. 5-Silver Surfer #1 4.00
4,5: 4-X-Men #1 c-swipe. 5-AS-M Ann. #21 c-swipe 1 2 3 5 6 8
...: Dead Days (7/07, $3.99) Early days of the plaque; Kirkman-s/Phillips-a/Suydam-c 5.00
...: Dead Days HC (2008, $29.99, oversized) r/Dead Days one-shot, Ultimate Fantastic Four #21-23, 30-32, and Black Panther #28-30 30.00
...: Evil Evolution (1/10, $4.99) Apes vs. Zombies; Marcos Martin-c
1 2 3 5 6 8
... Halloween (12/12, $3.99) Van Lente-s/Vitti-a/Francavilla-c 6.00
... MGC #1 (7/10, $1.00) r/#1 with "Marvel's Greatest Comics" logo on cover 3.00
...: The Book of Angels, Demons and Various Monstrosities (2007, $3.99) profile pages 5.00
...: The Covers HC (2007, $19.99, d.j.) Suydam's covers with originals and commentary 20.00
HC (2006, $19.99) r/#1-5; Kirkman foreword; cover gallery with variants 20.00

MARVEL ZOMBIES 2
Marvel Comics: Dec, 2007 - No. 5, Apr, 2008 ($2.99, limited series)

1-5-Kirkman-s/Phillips-a/Suydam zombie-fied cover swipes 5.00
HC (2008, $19.99) r/#1-5; cover swipe gallery 20.00

MARVEL ZOMBIES 3
Marvel Comics: Dec, 2008 - No. 4, Mar, 2009 ($3.99, limited series)

1-4-Van Lente-s/Walker-a/Land-c; Machine Man, Jocasta and Morbius app. 5.00

MARVEL ZOMBIES 4
Marvel Comics: Jun, 2009 - No. 4, Sept, 2009 ($3.99, limited series)

1-4-Van Lente-s/Walker-a/Land-c; Zombie Deadpool head app. 4.00

MARVEL ZOMBIES 5
Marvel Comics: Jun, 2010 - No. 5, Sept, 2010 ($3.99, limited series)

1-5-Van Lente-s; Machine Man and Howard the Duck app. 3-Kaluta-a 4.00

MARVEL ZOMBIES (Secret Wars tie-in)
Marvel Comics: Aug, 2015 - No. 4, Dec, 2015 ($3.99, limited series)

Marvel Voices: Pride #1 © MAR

Marvel Zombies #3 © MAR

Mary Jane & Black Cat #1 © MAR

	GD 2.0	VG 4.0	FN 6.0	VF 8.0	VF/NM 9.0	NM- 9.2

1-4-Spurrier-s/Walker-a; Elsa Bloodstone vs. zombies. 2,3-Deadpool app. 4.00

MARVEL ZOMBIES / ARMY OF DARKNESS
Marvel Comics/Dynamite Entertainment: May, 2007 - No. 5, Aug, 2007($2.99, limited series)

1-Zombies vs. Ash during the start of the plaque; Layman-s/Neves-a/Suydam-c 7.00
1-Second printing with Suydam zombie-fied Captain America Comics #1 cover swipe 4.00
2-5-Suydam zombie-fied cover swipes on all 5.00
HC (2007, $19.99) r/#1-5; cover gallery with variants and non-zombied original covers 20.00

MARVEL ZOMBIES CHRISTMAS CAROL ("Zombies Christmas Carol" on cover)
Marvel Comics: Aug, 2011 - No. 5, Oct, 2011 ($3.99, limited series)

1-5-Adaptation of the Dickens classic with zombies; Kaluta-c/Baldeon-a 4.00

MARVEL ZOMBIES DESTROY!
Marvel Comics: Jul, 2012 - No. 5, Sept, 2012 ($3.99, limited series)

1-5-Howard the Duck, Dum Dum Dugan vs. zombies; Del Mundo-c 4.00

MARVEL ZOMBIES: RESURRECTION
Marvel Comics: Dec, 2019; Nov, 2020 - No. 4, No. 4, Jan, 2021 ($5.99/$3.99)

1-(12/19, $4.99) Phillip Kennedy Johnson-s/Leonard Kirk-a/Inhyuk Lee-c 5.00
1-(11/20, $5.99) Johnson-s/Kirk-a/Inhyuk Lee-c; story continues; Blade app. 6.00
2-4-($3.99) 2-Viv Vision app. 3-Logan & Silver Surfer app. 5.00

MARVEL ZOMBIES RETURN
Marvel Comics: Nov, 2009 - No. 5, Nov, 2009 ($3.99, weekly limited series)

1-5-Suydam-c. 1-Zombie Spider-Man eats the Earth-Z Sinister Six; Dragotta-a 4.00

MARVEL ZOMBIES SUPREME
Marvel Comics: May, 2011 - No. 5, Aug, 2011 ($3.99, limited series)

1-5-Zombies in Squadron Supreme dimension; Blanco-a/Komarck-c; Jack of Hearts app. 4.00

MARVILLE
Marvel Comics: Nov, 2002 - No. 7, Jul, 2003 ($2.25, limited series)

1-6-Satire on DC/AOL-Time-Warner; Jemas-a/Bright-a/Horn-c 3.00
1-($3.95) Variant foil cover by Udon Studios; bonus sketch pages and Jemas afterword 4.00
7-($2.99) Intro. to Epic Comics line with submission guidelines 3.00

MARVIN MOUSE
Atlas Comics (BPC): September, 1957

1-Everett-c/a; Maneely-a 19 38 57 111 176 240

MARY JANE (Spider-Man) (Also see Amazing Mary Jane and Spider-Man Loves Mary Jane)
Marvel Comics: Aug, 2004 - No. 4, Nov, 2004 ($2.25, limited series)

1-4-Marvel Age series with teen-age MJ Watson; Miyazawa-c/a; McKeever-s 3.00
... Vol. 1: Circle of Friends (2004, $5.99, digest-size) r/#1-4 6.00

MARY JANE & BLACK CAT (Dark Web tie-in)
Marvel Comics: Feb, 2023 - Present ($4.99/$3.99)

1-($4.99) MacKay-s/Carratu-a; Belasco app. 5.00
2,3-($3.99) 4.00

MARY JANE & BLACK CAT: BEYOND (Spider-Man)
Marvel Comics: Mar, 2022 ($4.99, one-shot)

1-MacKay-s/Villa-a; The Hood, Count Nefaria, & Tombstone app. 5.00

MARY JANE & SNIFFLES (See Looney Tunes)
Dell Publishing Co.: No. 402, June, 1952 - No. 474, June, 1953

Four Color 402 (#1) 10 20 30 65 135 205
Four Color 474 8 16 24 51 96 140

MARY JANE: HOMECOMING (Spider-Man)
Marvel Comics: May, 2005 - No. 4, Aug, 2005 ($2.99, limited series)

1-4-Teen-age MJ Watson in high school; Miyazawa-c/a; McKeever-s 3.00
... Vol. 2 (2005, $6.99, digest-size) r/#1-4 7.00

MARY MARVEL COMICS (Monte Hale #29 on) (Also see Captain Marvel #18, Marvel Family, Shazam, & Wow Comics)
Fawcett Publications: Dec, 1945 - No. 28, Sept, 1948

1-Captain Marvel introduces Mary on-c; intro/origin Georgia Sivana
194 388 582 1242 2121 3000
2 84 168 252 538 919 1300
3,4: 3-New logo 55 110 165 352 601 850
5-8: 8-Bulletgirl x-over; classic Christmas-c 45 90 135 284 480 675
9,10 40 80 120 246 411 575
11-20 30 60 90 177 289 400
21-28: 28-Western-c 27 54 81 162 266 370

MARY POPPINS (See Movie Comics & Walt Disney Showcase No. 17)

MARY SHELLEY MONSTER HUNTER
AfterShock Comics: Apr, 2019 - No. 5, Aug, 2019 ($3.99, limited series)

1-5-Adam Glass & Olivia Cuartero-Briggs-s/Hayden Sherman-a 4.00

MARY SHELLEY'S FRANKENSTEIN
Topps Comics: Oct, 1994 - Jan, 1995 ($2.95, limited series)

1-4-polybagged w/3 trading cards 5.00
1-4 ($2.50)-Newstand ed. 4.00

MARY WORTH (See Harvey Comics Hits #55 & Love Stories of...)
Argo: March, 1956 (Also see Romantic Picture Novelettes)

1-Senator's mistress makes wife jealous-s 10 20 30 54 72 90

MASK (TV)
DC Comics: Dec, 1985 - No. 4, Mar, 1986; Feb, 1987 - No. 9, Oct, 1987

1-Saturday morning TV show 3 6 9 18 27 35
2-4 1 3 4 6 8 10
1-9 (2nd series) 5.00

MASK, THE (Also see Mayhem)
Dark Horse Comics: Aug, 1991 - No. 4, Oct, 1991; No. 0, Dec, 1991 ($2.50, 36 pgs., limited series)

1-1st app. Lt. Kellaway as The Mask (see Dark Horse Presents #10 for 1st app.)
4 8 12 23 37 50
2-4 1 3 4 6 8 10
0-(12/91, B&W, 56 pgs.)-r/Mayhem #1-4 1 3 4 6 8 10
...Omnibus Vol. 1 (8/08, $24.95) r/#1-4, Mask Returns and Mask Strikes Back series 50.00
...Omnibus Vol. 2 (4/09, $24.95) r/#1-4, The Hunt For Green October, World Tour, Southern Discomfort, Toys in the Attic series and short stories from DHP 40.00

...: HUNT FOR GREEN OCTOBER July, 1995 - Oct, 1995 ($2.50, lim. series)
1-4-Evan Dorkin scripts 4.00

...: I PLEDGE ALLEGIANCE TO THE MASK Oct, 2019 - No. 4, Jan, 2020 ($3.99, lim. series)
1-4-Christopher Cantwell-s/Patric Reynolds-a 4.00

.../ MARSHAL LAW Feb, 1998 - No. 2, Mar, 1998 ($2.95, lim. series)
1,2-Mills-s/O'Neill-a 2 4 6 11 16 20

...: OFFICIAL MOVIE ADAPTATION July, 1994 - Aug, 1994 ($2.50, lim. series)
1,2 6.00

... RETURNS Oct, 1992 - No. 4, Mar, 1993 ($2.50, limited series)
1-4 4.00

... SOUTHERN DISCOMFORT Mar, 1996 - No. 4, July, 1996 ($2.50, lim. series)
1-4 4.00

... STRIKES BACK Feb, 1995 - No. 5, Jun, 1995 ($2.50, limited series)
1-5 4.00

... SUMMER VACATION July, 1995 ($10.95, one shot, hard-c)
1-nn-Rick Geary-c/a 11.00

... TOYS IN THE ATTIC Aug, 1998 - No. 4, Nov, 1998 ($2.95, limited series)
1-4-Fingerman-s 4.00

... VIRTUAL SURREALITY July, 1997 ($2.95, one shot)
nn-Mignola, Aragonés, and others-s/a 4.00

... WORLD TOUR Dec, 1995 - No. 4, Mar, 1996 ($2.50, limited series)
1-4: 3-X & Ghost-c/app. 4.00

MASK COMICS
Rural Home Publ.: Feb-Mar, 1945 - No. 2, Apr-May, 1945; No. 2, Fall, 1945

1-Classic L. B. Cole Satan-c/a; Palais-a 3000 6000 9000 22,800 41,400 60,000
2-(Scarce)-Classic L. B. Cole Satan-c; Black Rider, The Boy Magician, & The Collector app.
1100 2200 3300 8360 15,180 22,000
2-(Fall, 1945)-No publ.-same as regular #2; L. B. Cole-c
1000 2000 3000 7400 13,200 19,000

MASKED BANDIT, THE
Avon Periodicals: 1952

nn-Kinstler-a 23 46 69 136 223 310

MASKED MAN, THE
Eclipse Comics: 12/84 - #10, 4/86; #11, 10/87; #12, 4/88 ($1.75/$2.00, color/B&W #9 on, Baxter paper)

1-12: 1-Origin retold. 3-Origin Aphid-Man; begin $2.00-c 3.00

MASKED MARVEL (See Keen Detective Funnies)
Centaur Publications: Sept, 1940 - No. 3, Dec, 1940

1-The Masked Marvel begins 219 438 657 1402 2401 3400
2,3: 2-Gustavson, Tarpe Mills-a 161 322 483 1030 1765 2500

MASKED RAIDER, THE (Billy The Kid #9 on; Frontier Scout, Daniel Boone #10-13) (Also see Blue Bird)
Charlton Comics: June, 1955 - No. 8, July, 1957; No. 14, Aug, 1958 - No. 30, June, 1961

GD 2.0 | VG 4.0 | FN 6.0 | VF 8.0 | VF/NM 9.0 | NM- 9.2

1-Masked Raider & Talon the Golden Eagle begin; painted-c 21 42 63 124 202 280
2 10 20 30 58 79 100
3-8,15: 8-Billy The Kid app. 15-Williamson-a, 7 pgs. 8 16 24 44 57 70
14,16-30: 22-Rocky Lane app. 7 14 21 37 46 55

MASKED RANGER
Premier Magazines: Apr, 1954 - No. 9, Aug, 1955

1-The Masked Ranger, his horse Streak, & The Crimson Avenger (origin) begin, end #9; Woodbridge/Frazetta-a 50 100 150 315 533 750
2,3 19 38 57 111 176 240
4-8-All Woodbridge-a. 5-Jesse James by Woodbridge. 6-Billy The Kid by Woodbridge. 7-Wild Bill Hickok by Woodbridge. 8-Jim Bowie's Life Story 20 40 60 114 182 250
9-Torres-a; Wyatt Earp by Woodbridge; Says Death of Masked Ranger on-c 20 40 60 120 195 270
NOTE: *Check a-1. Woodbridge c/a-1, 4-9.*

MASKERADE
Dark Horse Comics (Secret Stash Press): Sept, 2022 - Present ($3.99)

1-4-Kevin Smith & Andy McElfresh-s/John Sprengelmeyer-a 4.00

M.A.S.K.: MOBILE ARMORED STRIKE KOMMAND (Hasbro toy)
IDW Publishing: Nov, 2016 - No. 10, Aug, 2017 ($3.99)

1-10: 1,2-Easton-s/Vargas-a. 3,6,7-Samu-a 4.00
Annual 2017 (2/17, $7.99, squarebound) Griffith-a; bonus character profiles 8.00
M.A.S.K. First Strike 1 (10/17, $3.99) G.I. Joe & Cobra app.; 3 covers; Kyriazis-a 4.00
...: Revolution 1 (9/16, $3.99) Easton-s/Vargas-a 4.00

MASK OF DR. FU MANCHU, THE (See Dr. Fu Manchu)
Avon Periodicals: 1951

1-Sax Rohmer adapt.; Wood-c/a (26 pgs.); Hollingsworth-a 142 284 426 909 1555 2200

MASK OF ZORRO, THE
Image Comics: Aug, 1998 - No. 4, Dec, 1998 ($2.95, limited series)

1-4-Movie adapt. Photo variant-c 3.00

MASKS
Dynamite Entertainment: 2012 - No. 8, 2013 ($3.99)

1-Team-up of the Shadow, Green Hornet, Spider; Alex Ross-a; multiple covers 5.00
2-8: 2-Miss Fury and Green Lama app.; Calero-a. 3-Black Terror app. 4.00

MASKS 2
Dynamite Entertainment: 2015 - No. 8, 2015 ($3.99)

1-8-Pulp hero team-up; Bunn-s/Casallos-a; multiple covers on each 4.00

MASKS: TOO HOT FOR TV!
DC Comics (WildStorm): Feb, 2004 ($4.95)

1-Short stories by various incl. Thompson, Brubaker, Mahnke, Conner; Fabry-c 5.00

MASQUE OF THE RED DEATH (See Movie Classics)

MASQUERADE (See Project Superpowers)
Dynamite Entertainment: 2009 - No. 4, 2009 ($3.50, limited series)

1-4-Alex Ross & Phil Hester-s/Carlos Paul-a; covers by Ross & others 3.50

MASS EFFECT: DISCOVERY (Based on the EA video game)
Dark Horse Comics: May, 2017 - No. 4, Oct, 2017 ($3.99, limited series)

1-4-Barlow-s/Guzmán-a 4.00

MASS EFFECT: EVOLUTION (2nd series based on the EA video game)
Dark Horse Comics: Jan, 2011 - No. 4, Apr, 2011 ($3.50, limited series)

1-4-Walters & Jackson Miller-s/Carnevale-c 3.50

MASS EFFECT: FOUNDATION (Based on the EA video game)
Dark Horse Comics: Jul, 2013 - No. 13, Jul, 2014 ($3.99, limited series)

1-13: 1-Walters-s/Francia-a. 2-4-Parker-a 4.00

MASS EFFECT: HOMEWORLDS (Based on the EA video game)
Dark Horse Comics: Apr, 2012 - No. 4, Aug, 2012 ($3.50, limited series)

1-4: 1-Walters-s/Francisco-a 3.50

MASS EFFECT: INVASION (3rd series based on the EA video game)
Dark Horse Comics: Oct, 2011 - No. 4, Jan, 2012 ($3.50, limited series)

1-4-Walters & Jackson Miller-s/Carnevale-c 3.50

MASS EFFECT: REDEMPTION (Based on the EA video game)
Dark Horse Comics: Jan, 2010 - No. 4, Apr, 2010 ($3.50, limited series)

1-4-Walters & Jackson Miller-s/Francia-a 3.50

MASSIVE, THE
Dark Horse Comics: Jun, 2012 - No. 30, Dec, 2014 ($3.50)

1-30: 1-Brian Wood-s/Kristian Donaldson-a. 4-9,25-30-Brown-a. 10-Erskine-a 3.50
...: Ninth Wave 1-6 ($3.99, 12/15 - No. 6, 5/16) Prequel to series; Wood-s/Brown-a 4.00

MASTER COMICS (Combined with Slam Bang Comics #7 on)
Fawcett Publications: Mar, 1940 - No. 133, Apr, 1953 (No. 1-6: oversized issues) (#1-3: 15¢, 52 pgs.; #4-6: 10¢, 36 pgs.; #7-Begin 68 pg. issues)

1-Origin & 1st app. Master Man; The Devil's Dagger, El Carim, Master of Magic, Rick O'Say, Morton Murch, White Rajah, Shipwreck Roberts, Frontier Marshal, Streak Sloan, Mr. Clue begin (all features end #6) 1000 2000 3000 7600 13,800 20,000
2 (Rare) 303 606 909 2121 3711 5300
3-6: 6-Last Master Man (Rare) 265 530 795 1694 2897 4100
NOTE: *#1-6 rarely found in near mint or very fine condition due to large-size format.*
7-(10/40)-Bulletman, Zoro, the Mystery Man (ends #22), Lee Granger, Jungle King, & Buck Jones begin; only app. The War Bird & Mark Swift & the Time Retarder; Zoro, Lee Granger, Jungle King & Mark Swift all continue from Slam Bang; Bulletman moves from Nickel 300 600 900 2025 3463 4900
8-The Red Gaucho (ends #13), Captain Venture (ends #22) & The Planet Princess begin 174 348 522 1114 1907 2700
9,10: 10-Lee Granger ends 151 302 453 959 1655 2350
11-Origin & 1st app. Minute-Man (2/41) 295 590 885 1888 3244 4600
12 138 276 414 876 1513 2150
13-Origin & 1st app. Bulletgirl; Hitler-c 284 568 852 1818 3109 4400
14-16: 14-Companions Three begins, ends #31 126 252 378 806 1378 1950
17-20: 17-Raboy-a on Bulletman begins. 20-Captain Marvel cameo app. in Bulletman 119 238 357 762 1306 1850
21-(12/41; Scarce)-Captain Marvel & Bulletman team up against Capt. Nazi; origin & 1st app. Capt. Marvel Jr's most famous nemesis Captain Nazi who will cause creation of Capt. Marvel Jr. in Whiz #25. Part I of trilogy origin of Capt. Marvel Jr.; 1st Mac Raboy-c for Fawcett; Capt. Nazi-c 1000 2000 3000 7600 13,800 20,000
22-(1/42)-Captain Marvel Jr. moves over from Whiz #25 & teams up with Bulletman against Captain Nazi; part III of trilogy origin of Capt. Marvel Jr. & his 1st cover and adventure 811 1622 2433 5920 10,460 15,000
23-Capt. Marvel Jr. c/stories begin (1st solo story); fights Capt. Nazi by himself. 320 640 960 2240 3920 5600
24,25 145 290 435 921 1586 2250
26,28,30-Captain Marvel Jr. vs. Capt. Nazi. 28-Liberty Bell-c. 30-Flag-c 138 276 414 887 1519 2150
27-Captain Marvel Jr. "V For Victory"-c; Capt. Nazi app. 206 412 618 1318 2259 3200
29-Hitler & Hirohito-c 366 732 1098 2562 4481 6400
31,32,35: 31-Captain Marvel & Spy Smasher Comix Cards on back-c. 32-Last El Carim & Buck Jones; intro Balbo, the Boy Magician in El Carim story; classic Eagle-c by Raboy 119 238 357 762 1306 1850
33-Capt. Marvel Jr. smashing swastika-c; Balbo, the Boy Magician (ends #47), Hopalong Cassidy (ends #49) begins 194 388 582 1242 2121 3000
34-Capt. Marvel Jr. vs. Capt. Nazi-c/story; 1st mention of Capt. Nippon 174 348 522 1114 1907 2700
36-Statue of Liberty-c 119 238 357 762 1306 1850
37-39 90 180 270 576 988 1400
40-Classic flag-c 168 336 504 1075 1838 2600
41-(8/43)-Bulletman, Capt. Marvel Jr. & Bulletgirl x-over in Minute-Man; only app. Crime Crusaders Club (Capt. Marvel Jr., Minute-Man, Bulletman & Bulletgirl) 100 200 300 635 1093 1550
42-46,49: 46-Hitler story. 49-Last Minute-Man 58 116 174 371 636 900
47-Hitler becomes Corpl. Hitler Jr. 65 130 195 416 708 1000
48-Intro. Bulletboy; Capt. Marvel cameo in Minute-Man 65 130 195 416 708 1000
50-Intro Radar & Nyoka the Jungle Girl & begin series (5/44); Radar also intro in Captain Marvel #35 (same date); Capt. Marvel x-over in Radar; origin Radar; Capt. Marvel & Capt. Marvel, Jr. introduce Radar on-c 55 110 165 352 601 850
51-58 34 68 102 204 332 460
59-62: Nyoka serial "Terrible Tiara" in all; 61-Capt. Marvel Jr. 1st meets Uncle Marvel 36 72 108 214 347 480
63-80 26 52 78 154 252 350
81,83-87,89-91,95-99: 88-Hopalong Cassidy begins (ends #94). 95-Tom Mix begins (cover only in #123, ends #133) 23 46 69 136 223 310
82,88,92-94-Krigstein-a 24 48 72 140 230 320
100 25 50 75 150 245 340
101-106-Last Bulletman (not in #104) 22 44 66 132 216 300
107-120: 118-Mary Marvel 22 44 66 128 209 290
121-131-(lower print run): 123-Tom Mix-c only 23 46 69 136 223 310
132-B&W and color illos in **POP**; last Nyoka 25 50 75 147 241 325
133-Bill Battle app. 31 62 93 182 296 410
NOTE: ***Mac Raboy** a-15-39, 40(part), 42, 58. c-21-49, 51, 52, 54, 56, 58, 68(part), 69(part). **Bulletman** c-7-11, 13(half), 15, 18(part), 19, 20, 21(w/Capt. Marvel & Capt. Nazi), 22(w/Capt. Marvel, Jr.). **Capt. Marvel, Jr.** c-23-133. **Master Man** c-1-6. **Minute Man** c-12, 13(half), 14, 16, 17, 18(part).*

MASTER DARQUE
Acclaim Comics (Valiant): Feb, 1998 ($3.95)

1-Manco-a/Christina Z.-s 4.00

MASTER DETECTIVE
Super Comics: 1964 (Reprints)

17-r/Criminals on the Loose V4 #2; r/Young King Cole #?; McWilliams-r 2 4 6 11 16 20

MASTER OF KUNG FU (Formerly Special Marvel Edition; see Deadly Hands of Kung Fu & Giant-Size...)
Marvel Comics Group: No. 17, April, 1974 - No. 125, June, 1983

17-Starlin-a; intro Black Jack Tarr; 3rd Shang-Chi (ties w/Deadly Hands #1) 7 14 21 44 82 120
18,20 3 6 9 17 25 34
19-Man-Thing-c/story 4 8 12 23 37 50
21-23,25-30 2 4 6 11 16 20
24-Starlin, Simonson-a 2 4 6 13 18 22
31-50: 33-1st Leiko Wu. 43-Last 25¢ issue 2 4 6 8 10 12
39-43-(30¢-c variants, limited distribution)(5-7/76) 7 14 21 44 82 120
51-75 1 2 3 5 6 8
53-57-(35¢-c variants, limited distribution)(6-10/77) 8 16 24 52 99 145
76-99 6.00
100,118,125-Double size 1 2 3 5 6 8
101-117,119-124 5.00
Annual 1(4/76)-Iron Fist app. 5 10 15 31 53 75
NOTE: ***Austin** c-63i, 74i. **Buscema** c-44p. **Gulacy** a(p)-18-20, 22, 25, 29-31, 33-35, 38, 39, 40(p&i), 42-50, 53r(#20); c-51, 55, 64, 67. **Gil Kane** c(p)-20, 38, 39, 42, 45, 59, 63. **Nebres** c-73i. **Starlin** a-17p, 24; c-54. **Sutton** a-42i. #53 reprints #20.*

MASTER OF KUNG FU (Secret Wars tie-in)
Marvel Comics: Jul, 2015 - No. 4, Oct, 2015 ($3.99, limited series)

1-4-Blackman-s/Talajic-a/Francavilla-c; Shang-Chi & Iron Fist app. 4.00

MASTER OF KUNG FU (Marvel Legacy)
Marvel Comics: No. 126, Jan, 2018 ($3.99, one-shot)

126-CM Punk-s/Talajic-a 4.00

MASTER OF KUNG-FU: BLEEDING BLACK
Marvel Comics: Feb, 1991 ($2.95, 84 pgs., one-shot)

1-The Return of Shang-Chi 4.00

MASTER OF KUNG-FU, SHANG-CHI:... (2002 series, see Shang Chi:...)

MASTER OF THE WORLD

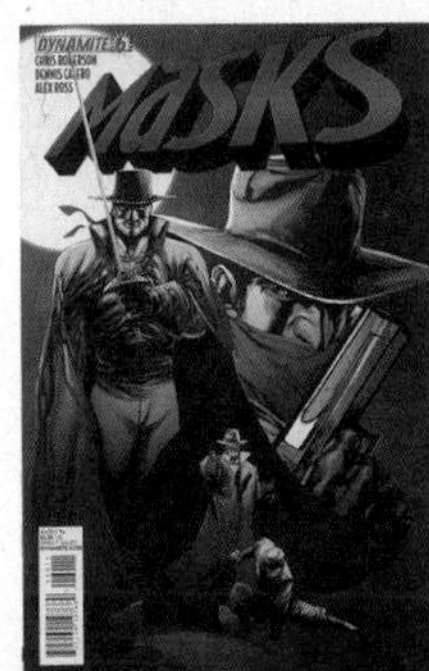

Masks #6 © DYN

Master Comics #120 © FAW

Mata Hari #4 © Beeby & Kristantina

	GD 2.0	VG 4.0	FN 6.0	VF 8.0	VF/NM 9.0	NM- 9.2

Dell Publishing Co.: No. 1157, July, 1961

Four Color 1157-Movie based on Jules Verne's "Master of the World" and "Robur the Conqueror" novels; with Vincent Price & Charles Bronson 8 16 24 55 105 155

MASTERS OF TERROR (Magazine)
Marvel Comics Group: July, 1975 - No. 2, Sept, 1975 (B&W) (All reprints)

1-Brunner, Barry Smith-a; Morrow/Steranko-c; Starlin-a(p); Gil Kane-a 4 8 12 27 44 50
2-Reese, Kane, Mayerik-a; Adkins/Steranko-c 3 6 9 15 22 28

MASTERS OF THE UNIVERSE (See DC Comics Presents #47 for 1st app.)
DC Comics: Dec, 1982 - No. 3, Feb, 1983 (Mini-series)

1 6 12 18 37 66 95
2,3: 2-Origin He-Man & Ceril 3 6 9 14 20 26
NOTE: *Alcala a-1i,, 2i. Tuska a-1-3p; c-1-3p. #2 has 75 & 95 cent cover price.*

MASTERS OF THE UNIVERSE (Comic Album)
Western Publishing Co.: 1984 (8-1/2x11", $2.95, 64 pgs.)

11362-Based on Mattel toy & cartoon 3 6 9 18 28 38

MASTERS OF THE UNIVERSE
Star Comics/Marvel #7 on: May 1986 - No. 13, May, 1988 (75¢/$1.00)

1 5 10 15 33 57 80
2-9,11: 8-Begin $1.00-c 2 4 6 8 10 12
10 3 6 9 14 20 25
12-Death of He-Man (1st Marvel app.) 5 10 15 35 63 90
13-Return of He-Man & death of Skeletor 5 10 15 34 60 85
The Motion Picture (11/87, $2.00)-Tuska-p 3 6 9 21 33 45

MASTERS OF THE UNIVERSE
Image Comics: Nov, 2002 - No. 4, March, 2003 ($2.95, limited series)

1-($2.95) Two covers by Santalucia and Campbell; Santalucia-a 2 4 6 10 14 18
1-($5.95) Variant-c by Norem w/gold foil logo 2 4 6 9 12 15
2-4($2.95) 2-Two covers by Santalucia and Manapul. 3,4-Two covers 6.00
TPB (CrossGen, 2003, $9.95, 8-1/4" x 5-1/2") digest-sized reprints #1-4 10.00

MASTERS OF THE UNIVERSE (Volume 2)
Image Comics: March, 2003 - No. 6, Aug, 2003 ($2.95)

1-6-($2.95) 1-Santalucia-c. 2-Two covers by Santalucia & JJ Kirby 1 3 4 6 8 10
1-($5.95) Wraparound variant-c by Struzan w/silver foil logo 2 4 6 8 10 12
3,4-($5.95) Wraparound variant holofoil-c. 3-By Edwards 4-By Boris Vallejo & Julie Bell 6.00
Volume 2 Dark Reflections TPB (2004, $18.95) r/#1-6 19.00

MASTERS OF THE UNIVERSE (Volume 3)
MVCreations: Apr, 2004 - No. 8, Dec, 2004 ($2.95)

1-Santalucia-c 1 2 3 5 6 8
2-8 4.00

MASTERS OF THE UNIVERSE...
CrossGen Comics

...Rise of the Snake-Men (Nov, 2003 - No. 3, $2.95) Meyers-a 6.00
...The Power of Fear (12/03, $2.95, one-shot) Santalucia-a 6.00

MASTERS OF THE UNIVERSE, ICONS OF EVIL
Image Comics/CrossGen Comics: 2003 ($4.95, one-shots)

...Beastman -(Image) Origin of Beast Man; Tony Moore-a 5.00
...Mer-Man -(CrossGen) 5.00
...Trapjaw -(CrossGen) 5.00
...Tri-Klops -(CrossGen) Walker-c 5.00
TPB (3/04, $18.95, MVCreations) r/one-shots; sketch pages 19.00

MASTERS OF THE UNIVERSE: ...
DC Comics: Dec, 2012; Mar, 2013; Jul, 2013 ($2.99, one-shots)

... Origin Of He-Man (3/13) Fialkov-s; Ben Oliver-a/c; Prince Adam finds the sword 3.00
... Origin Of Hordak (7/13) Giffen & Keene-s/Giffen-a/c 3.00
... The Origin Of Skeletor (12/12) Fialkov-s; Fraser Irving-a/c; Keldor becomes Skeletor 3.00

MASTERS OF THE UNIVERSE: MASTERVERSE
Dark Horse Comics: Feb, 2023 - Present ($3.99, limited series)

1-Anthology of multiverse stories by various incl. Kelley Jones, Aragonés, Seeley 4.00

MASTERS OF THE UNIVERSE: REVELATION
Dark Horse Comics: Jul, 2021 - No. 4, Oct, 2021 ($3.99, limited series)

1-4-Prequel to the Netflix animated series; Kevin Smith & Rob David-s/Mindy Lee-a 4.00

MASTERWORKS SERIES OF GREAT COMIC BOOK ARTISTS, THE
Sea Gate Dist./DC Comics: May, 1983 - No. 3, Dec, 1983 (Baxter paper)

1-3: 1,2-Shining Knight by Frazetta r-/Adventure. 2-Tomahawk by Frazetta-r. 3-Wrightson-c/a(r) 6.00

MATADOR
DC Comics (WildStorm): July, 2005 - No. 6, May, 2006 ($2.99, limited series)

1-6-Devin Grayson-s/Brian Stelfreeze-a/c 3.00

MATA HARI
Dark Horse Comics (Berger Books): Feb, 2018 - No. 5, Sept, 2018 ($3.99, limited series)

1-5-Beeby-s/Kristantina-a/c; story of the World War 1 spy 4.00

MATRIX COMICS, THE (Movie)
Burlyman Entertainment: 2003; 2004 ($21.95, trade paperback)

nn-Short stories by various incl. Wachowskis, Darrow, Gaiman, Sienkiewicz, Bagge 22.00
...Volume One Preview (7/03, no cover price) bios of creators; Chadwick-s/a 3.00
Volume 2-(2004) Short stories by various incl. Wachowskis, Sale, McKeever, Dorman 22.00

MATT SLADE GUNFIGHTER (Kid Slade Gunfighter #5 on; See Western Gunfighters)
Atlas Comics (SPI): May, 1956 - No. 4, Nov, 1956

1-Intro Matt & horse Eagle; Williamson/Torres-a 32 64 96 188 307 425
2-Williamson-a 17 34 51 105 165 225
3,4 14 28 42 82 121 160
NOTE: *Maneely a-1, 3, 4; c-1, 2, 4. Roth a-2-4. Severin a-1, 3, 4. Maneely c/a-1. Issue #s stamped on cover after printing.*

MAUS: A SURVIVOR'S TALE (First graphic novel to win a Pulitzer Prize)
Pantheon Books: 1986, 1991 (B&W)

Vol. 1-(...: My Father Bleeds History)(1986) Art Spiegelman-s/a; recounts stories of Spiegelman's father in 1930s-40s Nazi-occupied Poland; collects first six stories serialized in Raw Magazine from 1980-1985 30.00
Vol. 2-(...: And Here My Troubles Began)(1991) 25.00
Complete Maus Survivor's Tale -HC Vols. 1& 2 w/slipcase 35.00
Hardcover Vol. 1 (1991) 30.00
Hardcover Vol. 2 (1991) 30.00
TPB (1992, $14.00) Vols. 1& 2 18.00

MAVERICK (TV)
Dell Publishing Co.: No. 892, 4/58 - No. 19, 4-6/62 (All have photo-c)

Four Color 892 (#1)-James Garner photo-c begin 20 40 60 144 317 490
Four Color 930,945,962,980,1005 (6-8/59): 945-James Garner/Jack Kelly photo-c begin 11 22 33 73 157 240
7 (10-12/59) - 14: 11-Variant edition has "Time For Change" comic strip on back-c. 14-Last Garner/Kelly-c 8 16 24 56 108 160
15-18: Jack Kelly/Roger Moore photo-c 7 14 21 44 82 120
19-Jack Kelly photo-c (last issue) 7 14 21 46 86 125

MAVERICK (See X-Men)
Marvel Comics: Jan, 1997 ($2.95, one-shot)

1-Hama-s 5.00

MAVERICK (See X-Men)
Marvel Comics: Sept, 1997 - No. 12, Aug, 1998 ($2.99/$1.99)

1,12: 1-($2.99)-Wraparound-c. 12-($2.99) Battles Omega Red 5.00
2-11: 2-Two covers. 4-Wolverine app. 6,7-Sabretooth app. 4.00

MAVERICK MARSHAL
Charlton Comics: Nov, 1958 - No. 7, May, 1960

1 7 14 21 35 43 50
2-7 5 10 15 24 30 35

MAW
BOOM! Studios: Sept, 2021 - No. 5, Jan, 2022 ($3.99, limited series)

1-5-Jude Ellison S. Doyle-s/A.L. Kaplan-a 4.00

MAX BRAND (See Silvertip)

MAX HAMM FAIRY TALE DETECTIVE
Nite Owl Comix: 2002 - 2004 ($4.95, B&W, 6 1/2" x 8")

1-(2002) Frank Cammuso-s/a 5.00
Vol. 2 #1-3 (2003-2004) Frank Cammuso-s/a 5.00

MAXIMAGE
Image Comics (Extreme Studios): Dec, 1995 - No. 7, June 1996 ($2.50)

1-7: 1-Liefeld-c. 2-Extreme Destroyer Pt. 2; polybagged w/card. 4-Angela & Glory-c/app. 4.00

MAXIMO
Dreamwave Prods.: Jan, 2004 ($3.95, one-shot)

1-Based on the Capcom video game 4.00

MAXIMUM SECURITY (Crossover)
Marvel Comics: Oct, 2000 - No. 3, Jan, 2001 ($2.99)

GD VG FN VF VF/NM NM-
2.0 4.0 6.0 8.0 9.0 9.2

1-3-Busiek-s/Ordway-a; Ronan the Accuser, Avengers app. 3.00
...Dangerous Planet 1: Busiek-s/Ordway-a; Ego, the Living Planet 3.00
Thor vs. Ego (11/00, $2.99) Reprints Thor #133,160,161; Kirby-a 3.00

MAX RIDE: FINAL FLIGHT (Based on the James Patterson novel Maximum Ride)
Marvel Comics: Nov, 2016 - No. 5, Mar, 2017 ($3.99, limited series)
1-5-Jody Houser-s/Marco Failla-a. 1-Two covers (Nakamura & Oum) 4.00

MAX RIDE: FIRST FLIGHT (Based on the James Patterson novel Maximum Ride)
Marvel Comics: Jun, 2015 - No. 5, Oct, 2015 ($3.99, limited series)
1-5-Marguerite Bennett-s/Alex Sanchez-a. 1-Three covers 4.00

MAX RIDE: ULTIMATE FLIGHT (Based on the James Patterson novel Maximum Ride)
Marvel Comics: Jan, 2016 - No. 5, May, 2016 ($3.99, limited series)
1-5-Jody Houser-s/RB Silva-a. 1-Two covers 4.00

MAXX (Also see Darker Image, Primer #5, & Friends of Maxx)
Image Comics (I Before E): Mar, 1993 - No. 35, Feb, 1998 ($1.95)
1/2 2 4 6 8 11 14
1/2 (Gold) 20.00
1-Sam Kieth-c/a/scripts 5.00
1-Glow-in-the-dark variant 2 4 6 11 16 20
1-"3-D Edition" (1/98, $4.95) plus new back-up story 5.00
2-12: 6-Savage Dragon cameo(1 pg.). 7,8-Pitt-c & story 3.00
13-16 3.00
17-35: 21-Alan Moore-s 3.00
Volume 1 TPB (DC/WildStorm, 2003, $17.95) r/#1-6 18.00
Volume 2 TPB (DC/WildStorm, 2004, $17.95) r/#7-13 18.00
Volume 3 TPB (DC/WildStorm, 2004, $17.95) r/#14-20 18.00
Volume 4 TPB (DC/WildStorm, 2005, $17.95) r/#21-27 18.00
Volume 5 TPB (DC/WildStorm, 2005, $19.99) r/#28-35 20.00
Volume 6 TPB (DC/WildStorm, 2006, $19.99) r/Friends of Maxx #1-3 & The Maxx 3-D 20.00

MAXX: MAXXIMIZED
IDW Publishing: Nov, 2013 - No. 35, Sept, 2016 ($3.99)
1-35-Remastered, recolored reprint of the original Maxx issues 4.00

MAYA (See Movie Classics)
Gold Key: Mar, 1968
1 (10218-803)(TV) Photo-c 3 6 9 16 24 32

MAYHEM
Dark Horse Comics: May, 1989 - No. 4, Sept, 1989 ($2.50, B&W, 52 pgs.)
1-Four part Stanley Ipkiss/Mask story begins; Mask-c
4 8 12 25 40 55
2-4: 2-Mask 1/2 back-c. 4-Mask-c 1 3 4 6 8 10

MAYHEM (Tyrese Gibson's...)
Image Comics: Aug, 2009 - No. 3, Oct, 2009 ($2.99, limited series)
1-3-Tyrese Gibson co-writer; Tone Rodriguez-a/c 3.00

MAZE AGENCY, THE
Comico/Innovation Publ. #8 on: Dec, 1988 - No. 23, Aug, 1991 ($1.95-$2.50, color)
1-23: 1-5,8,9,12-Adam Hughes-c/a. 9-Ellery Queen app. 7 ($2.50)-Last Comico issue 3.00
Annual 1 (1990, $2.75)-Ploog-c; Spirit tribute ish 4.00
Special 1 (1989, $2.75)-Staton-p (Innovation) 4.00
TPB (IDW Publ., 11/05, $24.99) r/#1-5 25.00

MAZE AGENCY, THE (Vol. 2)
Caliber Comics: July, 1997 - No. 3, 1998 ($2.95, B&W)
1-3: 1-Barr-s/Gonzales-a(p). 3-Hughes-c 3.00

MAZE AGENCY, THE
IDW Publishing: Nov, 2005 - No. 3, Jan, 2006 ($3.99, limited series)
1-3-Barr-s/Padilla-a(p)/c 4.00

MAZEBOOK
Dark Horse Comics: Sept, 2021 - No. 5, Jan, 2022 ($5.99, limited series)
1-5-Jeff Lemire-s/a/c 6.00

MAZE RUNNER: THE SCORCH TRIALS (Based on the Maze Runner movies)
BOOM! Studios: Jun, 2015 ($14.99, squarebound SC)
...Official Graphic Novel Prelude - Short stories about the characters; s/a by various 15.00

MAZIE (...& Her Friends) (See Flat-Top, Mortie, Stevie & Tastee-Freez)
Mazie Comics(Magazine Publ.)/Harvey Publ. No. 13-on: 1953 - #12, 1954; #13, 12/54 - #22, 9/56; #23, 9/57 - #28, 8/58
1-(Teen-age)-Stevie's girlfriend 16 32 48 94 147 200
2 10 20 30 58 79 100
3-10 9 18 27 47 61 75
11-28 8 16 24 42 54 65

MAZIE
Nation Wide Publishers: 1950 - No. 7, 1951 (5¢) (5x7-1/4"-miniature)(52 pgs.)
1-Teen-age 23 46 69 138 227 315
2-7 16 32 48 92 144 195

MAZINGER (See First Comics Graphic Novel #17)

'MAZING MAN
DC Comics: Jan, 1986 - No. 12, Dec, 1986
1-11: 7,8-Hembeck-a 4.00
12-Dark Knight part-c by Miller 5.00
Special 1 ('87), 2 (4/88), 3 ('90)-All $2.00, 52pgs. 5.00

McCANDLESS & COMPANY
Mandalay Books/American Mythology
...: Dead Razor (2001, $7.95) J.C. Vaughn-s/Busch & Sheehan-a; 3 covers 8.00
...: Insecuritues (American Myth., 10/16, $4.99) Vaughn-s/Gonzales-a/Oeming-c 5.00
Crime Scenes: A McCandless & Company Reader TPB (Spring 2006, $17.95) Vaughn-s 18.00

McHALE'S NAVY (TV) (See Movie Classics)
Dell Publ. Co.: May-July, 1963 - No. 3, Nov-Jan, 1963-64 (All have photo-c)
1 8 16 24 54 102 150
2,3 5 10 15 34 60 85

McKEEVER & THE COLONEL (TV)
Dell Publishing Co.: Feb-Apr, 1963 - No. 3, Aug-Oct, 1963
1-Photo-c 5 10 15 34 60 85
2,3-Photo-c 4 8 12 28 47 65

McLINTOCK (See Movie Comics)

MD
E. C. Comics: Apr-May, 1955 - No. 5, Dec-Jan, 1955-56
1-Not approved by code; Craig-c 24 48 72 192 309 425
2-5 15 30 45 120 190 260
NOTE: *Crandall, Evans, Ingels, Orlando* art in all issues; *Craig* c-1-5.

MD
Russ Cochran/Gemstone Publishing: Sept, 1999 - No. 5, Jan, 2000 ($2.50)
1-5-Reprints original EC series 4.00
Annual 1 (1999, $13.50) r/#1-5 14.00

MEASLES
Fantagraphics Books: Christmas 1998 - No. 8 ($2.95, B&W, quarterly)
1-8-Anthology: 1-Venus-s by Hernandez 3.00

MECHA (Also see Mayhem)
Dark Horse Comics: June, 1987 - No. 6, 1988 ($1.50/$1.95, color/B&W)
1-6: 1,2 ($1.95, color), 3,4-($1.75, B&W), 5,6-($1.50, B&W) 3.00

MECHANIC, THE
Image Comics: 1998 ($5.95, one-shot, squarebound)
1-Chiodo-painted art; Peterson-s 6.00
1-($10.00) DF Alternate Cover Ed. 10.00

MECHANISM
Image Comics (Top Cow): Jul, 2016 - No. 5, Nov, 2016 ($3.99)
1-5-Raffaele Ienco-s/a 4.00

MECHA SPECIAL
Dark Horse Comics: May, 1995 ($2.95, one-shot)
1 3.00

MECH CADET YU
BOOM! Studios: Aug, 2017 - No. 12, Sept, 2018 ($3.99)
1-12-Greg Pak-s/Takeshi Miyazawa-a 4.00

MECH DESTROYER
Image Comics: Apr, 2001 - No. 4, Sept, 2001 ($2.95, limited series)
1-4-Jae Kim-c/a; Robert Chong-s 3.00

MECH STRIKE: MONSTER HUNTERS (Follow up to Avengers Mech Strike)
Marvel Comics: Aug, 2022 - No. 5, Dec, 2022 ($3.99, limited series)
1-5-Christos Gage-s/Paco Diaz-a; Doctor Doom, Loki, Venom and Green Goblin app. 4.00

MEDAL FOR BOWZER, A (See Promotional Comics section)

MEDAL OF HONOR COMICS
A. S. Curtis: Spring, 1946
1-War stories 20 40 60 117 189 260

MEDAL OF HONOR SPECIAL
Dark Horse Comics: 1994 ($2.50, one-shot)
1-Kubert-c/a (first story) 3.00

MEDIA STARR
Innovation Publ.: July, 1989 - No. 3, Sept, 1989 ($1.95, mini-series, 28 pgs.)
1-3: Deluxe format 3.00

MEDIEVAL SPAWN/WITCHBLADE
Image Comics (Top Cow Productions): May, 1996 - No. 3, June, 1996 ($2.95, limited series)
1-Garth Ennis scripts 2 4 6 8 10 12
1-Platinum foil-c (500 copies from Pittsburgh Con) 35.00
1-Gold 2 4 6 9 12 15
1-ETM Exclusive Edition; gold foil logo 2 4 6 8 10 12
2-3-Garth Ennis scripts in all 6.00
TPB ($9.95) r/#1-3 10.00

MEDIEVAL SPAWN & WITCHBLADE
Image Comics: May, 2018 - No. 4, Aug, 2018 ($2.99, limited series)
1-4-Haberlin & Holguin-s/Haberlin-a 3.00

MEET ANGEL (Formerly Angel & the Ape)
National Periodical Publications: No. 7, Nov-Dec, 1969
7-Wood-a(i) 4 8 12 25 40 55

MEET CORLISS ARCHER (Radio/Movie)(My Life #4 on)
Fox Feature Syndicate: Mar, 1948 - No. 3, July, 1948
1-(Teen-age)-Feldstein-c/a; headlight-c 155 310 465 992 1696 2400
2-Feldstein-c/a 74 148 222 470 810 1150
3-Feldstein-c/a 63 126 189 403 689 975
NOTE: *No. 1-3 used in Seduction of the Innocent, pg. 39.*

MEET HERCULES (See Three Stooges)

MEET MERTON
Toby Press: Dec, 1953 - No. 4, June, 1954
1-(Teen-age)-Dave Berg-c/a 24 48 72 142 234 325
2-Dave Berg-c/a 15 30 45 84 127 170
3,4-Dave Berg-c/a 14 28 42 81 118 155
I.W. Reprint #9, Super Reprint #11('63), 18 2 4 6 11 16 20

MEET MISS BLISS (Becomes Stories Of Romance #5 on)
Atlas Comics (LMC): May, 1955 - No. 4, Nov, 1955
1-Al Hartley-c/a 81 162 243 518 884 1250
2-4 36 72 108 211 343 470

MEET MISS PEPPER (Formerly Lucy, The Real Gone Gal)
St. John Publishing Co.: No. 5, April, 1954 - No. 6, June, 1954

Mazie #18 © HARV

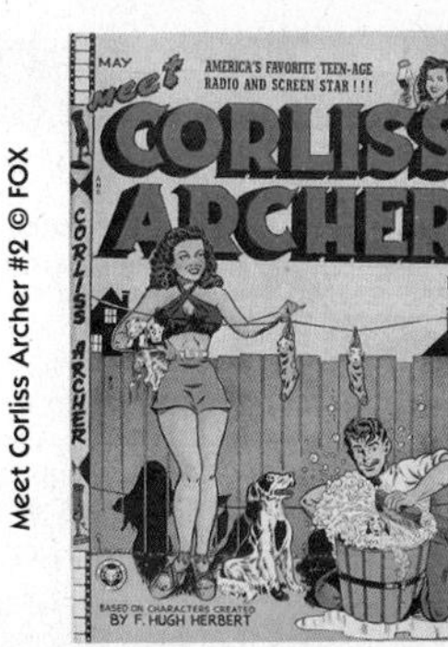

Meet Corliss Archer #2 © FOX

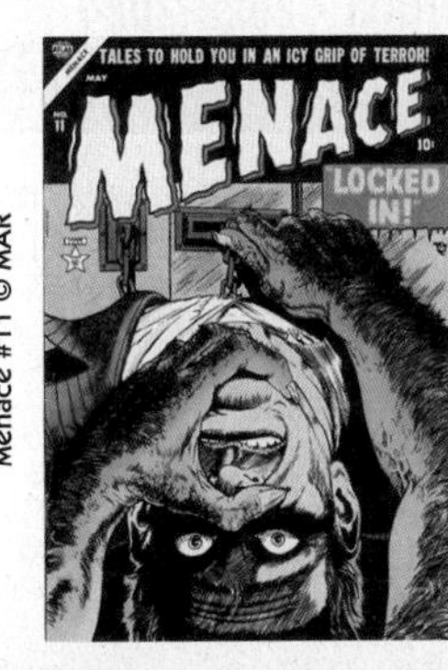

Menace #11 © MAR

GD 2.0 | VG 4.0 | FN 6.0 | VF 8.0 | VF/NM 9.0 | NM- 9.2

5-Kubert/Maurer-a 43 86 129 271 461 650
6-Kubert/Maurer-a; Kubert-c 36 72 108 211 343 475

MEET THE SKRULLS
Marvel Comics: May, 2019 - No. 5, Aug, 2019 ($3.99, limited series)
1-5-Robbie Thompson-s/Niko Henrichon-a 4.00

MEGAGHOST
Albatross Funnybooks: 2018 - No. 5, 2019 ($3.99)
1-5-Gabe Soria-s/Gideon Kendall-a 4.00

MEGALITH (Megalith Deathwatch 2000 #1,2 of second series)
Continuity: 1989 - No. 9, Mar, 1992; No, 0, Apr, 1993 - No. 7, Jan, 1994
1-($2.00-c) Neal Adams & Mark Texiera-c/Texiera & Nebres-a
1 2 3 5 6 8
2-9-($2.00-c) 4.00
2nd series: 0-(4/93)-Foil-c; no c-price, giveaway; Adams plot 3.00
1-7: 1-3-Bagged w/card: 1-Gatefold-c by Nebres; Adams plot. 2-Fold-out-c; Adams plot. 3-Indestructible-c. 4-7-Embossed-c: 4-Adams/Nebres-c; Adams part-i. 5-Sienkiewicz-i. 6-Adams part-i. 7-Adams-c(p); Adams plot 3.00

MEGAMAN
Dreamwave Productions: Sept, 2003 - No. 4, Dec, 2003 ($2.95)
1-4-Brian Augustyn-s/Mic Fong-a 3.00
1-($5.95) Chromium wraparound variant-c 6.00

MEGA MAN (Based on the Capcom video game character)
Archie Comics Publications: Jul, 2011 - No. 55, Feb, 2016 ($2.99/$3.99)
1-39 1-Spaziante-a. 20-39-Multiple covers. 24-Worlds Collide x-over begins 3.00
40-49,51-55 ($3.99) Two covers on most. 51,52-Three covers 4.00
50-($4.99) Six covers; "Worlds Unite" Sonic/Mega Man x-over pt. 4 5.00
Free Comic Book Day Edition (2012, giveaway) Origin re-told 3.00
...: Worlds Unite Battles 1 (8/15, $3.99) Sonic/Mega Man x-over; 3 wraparound covers 4.00

MEGA MAN: FULLY CHARGED (Capcom video game character)
BOOM! Studios: Aug, 2020 - No. 6, Jan, 2021 ($4.99)
1-6-Marchisello & Rinehart-s/Simeone-a 5.00

MEGAMIND: BAD. BLUE. BRILLIANT (DreamWorks'...) (Based on the 2010 movie)
Ape Entertainment: 2010 - No. 4, 2011 ($3.95, limited series)
1-4: 1-High school flashback 4.00
nn-($6.95, 9x6") Prequel to the movie; Joe Kelly-s 7.00

MEGA MORPHS
Marvel Comics: Oct, 2005 - No. 4, Dec, 2005 ($2.99, limited series)
1-4-Giant robots based on action figures; McKeever-s; Kang-a 3.00
Digest (2006, $7.99) r/#1-4 plus mini-comics 8.00

MEGATON (A super hero)
Megaton Publ.: Nov, 1983; No. 2, Oct, 1985 - No. 8, Aug, 1987 (B&W)
1-($2.00, 68 pgs.)-Erik Larsen's 1st pro work; Vanguard by Larsen begins (1st app.), ends #4; 1st app. Megaton, Berzerker, & Ethrian; Guice-c/a(p); Gustovich-a(p) in #1,2
5 10 15 34 60 85
2-($2.00, 68 pgs.)-1st brief app. The Dragon (1 pg.) by Larsen (later The Savage Dragon in Image Comics); Guice-c/a(p) 3 6 9 14 19 24
3-(44 pgs.)-1st full app. Savage Dragon-c/story by Larsen; (earlier apps. were in the 1982 fanzine Graphic Fantasy); 1st comic book work by Angel Medina (pin-up)
5 10 15 31 53 75
4-(52 pgs.)-2nd full app. Savage Dragon by Larsen; 4,5-Wildman by Grass Green
2 4 6 8 11 14
5-1st Liefeld published-a (inside f/c, 6/86) 1 3 4 6 8 10
6,7: 6-Larsen-c 1 2 3 5 6 8
8-1st Liefeld story-a (7 pg. super hero story) plus 1 pg. Youngblood ad
3 6 9 14 19 24
...Explosion (6/87, 16 pg. color giveaway)-1st app. Youngblood by Rob Liefeld (2 pg. spread); shows Megaton heroes 5 10 15 35 63 90
...Holiday Special 1 (1994, $2.95, color, 40 pgs., publ. by Entity Comics)-Gold foil logo; bagged w/Kelley Jones card; Vanguard, Megaton plus shows unpublished-c to 1987 Youngblood #1 by Liefeld/Ordway 1 2 3 5 6 8
NOTE: *Copies of Megaton Explosion were also released in early 1992 all signed by Rob Liefeld and were made available to retailers.*

MEGATON MAN (See Don Simpson's Bizarre Heroes)
Kitchen Sink Enterprises: Nov, 1984 - No. 10, 1986
1-10, 1-2nd printing (1989) 4.00
...Meets The Uncategorizable X-Thems 1 (4/89, $2.00) 4.00

MEGATON MAN: BOMB SHELL
Image Comics: Jul, 1999 - No. 2 ($2.95, B&W, mini-series)
1-Reprints stories from Megaton Man internet site 4.00

MEGATON MAN: HARD COPY
Image Comics: Feb, 1999 - No. 2, Apr, 1999 ($2.95, B&W, mini-series)
1,2-Reprints stories from Megaton Man internet site 4.00

MEGATON MAN VS. FORBIDDEN FRANKENSTEIN (Double titled as Don Simpson's Bizarre Heroes #16)
Fiasco Comics: Apr, 1996 ($2.95, B&W, one-shot)
1-Intro The Tomb Team (Forbidden Frankenstein, Drekula, Bride of the Monster, & Moon Wolf). 1 3 4 6 8 10

MEK (See Reload/Mek flipbook for TPB reprint)
DC Comics (Homage): Jan, 2003 - No. 3, Mar, 2003 ($2.95, limited series)
1-3-Warren Ellis-s/Steve Rolston-a 4.00

MEKANIX (See X-Men titles) (See X-Treme X-Men Vol. 4 for TPB)
Marvel Comics: Dec, 2002 - No. 6, May, 2003 ($2.99, limited series)
1-6-Kitty Pryde in college; Claremont-s/Bobillo & Sosa-a 4.00

MEL ALLEN SPORTS COMICS (The Voice of the Yankees)
Standard Comics: No. 5, Nov, 1949; No. 6, June, 1950
5(#1 on inside)-Tuska-a 23 46 69 136 223 310
6(#2)-Lou Gehrig story 16 32 48 94 147 200

MELVIN MONSTER
Dell Publishing Co.: Apr-June, 1965 - No. 10, Oct, 1969
1-By John Stanley 6 12 18 40 73 105
2-10-All by Stanley. #10-r/#1 5 10 15 30 50 70

MELVIN THE MONSTER (See Peter, the Little Pest & Dexter The Demon #7)
Atlas Comics (HPC): July, 1956 - No. 6, July, 1957
1-Maneely-c/a 19 38 57 111 176 240
2-6: 4-Maneely-c/a 14 28 42 76 108 140

MENACE
Atlas Comics (HPC): Mar, 1953 - No. 11, May, 1954
1-Horror & sci/fi stories begin; Everett-c/a 271 542 813 1734 2967 4200
2-Post-atom bomb disaster by Everett; anti-Communist propaganda/torture scenes; Sinnott sci/fi story "Rocket to the Moon" 187 374 561 1197 2049 2900
3,4,6-Everett-a. 4-Sci/fi story "Escape to the Moon". 6-Romita sci/fi story "Science Fiction"
129 258 387 826 1413 2000
5-Origin & 1st app. The Zombie by Everett (reprinted in Tales of the Zombie #1)(7/53); 5-Sci/fi story "Rocket Ship" 443 886 1329 3234 5717 8200
7,8,10,11: 7-Frankenstein story. 8-End of world story; Heath 3-D art(3 pgs.). 10-H-Bomb panels 110 220 330 704 1202 1700
9-Everett-a r-in Vampire Tales #1 295 590 885 1888 3244 4600
NOTE: ***Brodsky** c-7, 8, 11. **Colan** a-6; c-9. **Everett** a-1-6, 9; c-1-6. **Heath** a-1-8; c-10. **Katz** a-11. **Maneely** a-3-5, 7-9. **Powell** a-11. **Romita** a-3, 6, 8, 11. **Shelly** a-10. **Shores** a-7. **Sinnott** a-2, 7. **Tuska** a-1, 2, 5.*

MENACE
Awesome-Hyperwerks: Nov, 1998 ($2.50)
1-Jada Pinkett Smith-s/Fraga-a 3.00

MEN AGAINST CRIME (Formerly Mr. Risk; Hand of Fate #8 on)
Ace Magazines: No. 3, Feb, 1951 - No. 7, Oct, 1951
3-Mr. Risk app. 16 32 48 94 147 200
4-7: 4-Colan-a; entire book-r as Trapped! #4. 5-Meskin-a
13 26 39 72 101 130

MEN, GUNS, & CATTLE (See Classics Illustrated Special Issue)

MEN IN ACTION (Battle Brady #10 on)
Atlas Comics (IPS): April, 1952 - No. 9, Dec, 1952 (War stories)
1-Berg, Reinman-a 39 78 117 240 395 550
2,3: 3-Heath-c/a 20 40 60 120 195 270
4-6,8,9 19 38 57 111 176 240
7-Krigstein-a; Heath-c 20 40 60 120 195 270
NOTE: ***Brodsky** a-3; c-1, 4-6. **Maneely** a-4; c-5. **Pakula** a-1, 6. **Robinson** c-8. **Shores** c-9. **Sinnott** a-6.*

MEN IN ACTION
Ajax/Farrell Publications: Apr, 1957 - No. 6, Jun, 1958
1 14 28 42 82 121 160
2 9 18 27 50 65 80
3-6 8 16 24 44 57 70

MEN IN BLACK, THE (1st series)
Aircel Comics (Malibu): Jan, 1990 - No. 3 Mar, 1990 ($2.25, B&W, lim. series)
1-Cunningham-s/a in all 7 14 21 49 92 135
2,3 3 6 9 21 33 45
Graphic Novel (Jan, 1991) r/#1-3 3 6 9 17 26 35

	GD	VG	FN	VF	VF/NM	NM-
	2.0	4.0	6.0	8.0	9.0	9.2

MEN IN BLACK (2nd series)
Aircel Comics (Malibu): May, 1991 - No. 3, Jul, 1991 ($2.50, B&W, lim. series)
1-Cunningham-s/a in all 3 6 9 20 31 42
2,3 2 4 6 13 18 22

MEN IN BLACK: FAR CRY
Marvel Comics: Aug, 1997 ($3.99, color, one-shot)
1-Cunningham-s 1 3 4 6 8 10

MEN IN BLACK: RETRIBUTION
Marvel Comics: Dec, 1997 ($3.99, color, one-shot)
1-Cunningham-s; continuation of the movie 1 3 4 6 8 10

MEN IN BLACK: THE MOVIE
Marvel Comics: Oct, 1997 ($3.99, one-shot, movie adaptation)
1-Cunningham-s 2 4 6 8 10 12

MEN INTO SPACE
Dell Publishing Co.: No. 1083, Feb-Apr, 1960
Four Color 1083-Anderson-a, photo-c 6 12 18 41 76 110

MEN OF BATTLE (Also see New Men of Battle)
Catechetical Guild: V1#5, March, 1943 (Hardcover)
V1#5-Topix reprints 8 16 24 42 54 65

MEN OF WAR
DC Comics, Inc.: August, 1977 - No. 26, March, 1980 (#9,10: 44 pgs.)
1-Enemy Ace, Gravedigger (origin #1,2) begin 3 6 9 21 33 45
2-4,8-10,12-14,19,20: All Enemy Ace stories. 4-1st Dateline Frontline. 9-Unknown Soldier app. 2 4 6 11 16 20
5-7,11,15-18,21-25: 17-1st app. Rosa 2 4 6 9 13 16
26-Sgt. Rock & Easy Co.-c/s 3 6 9 14 20 26
NOTE: *Chaykin a-9, 10, 12-14, 19, 20.* ***Evans*** *c-25.* ***Kubert*** *c-2-23, 24p, 26.*

MEN OF WAR (DC New 52)
DC Comics: Nov, 2011 - No. 8, Jun, 2012 ($3.99)
1-8: 1-Sgt. Rock's grandson in modern times; Derenick-a; Navy Seals back-up; Winslade-a 6-Back-up w/Corben-a. 8-Frankenstein & G.I. Robot app. 4.00

MEN OF WRATH
Marvel Comics (ICON): Oct, 2014 - No. 5, Feb, 2015 ($3.50, limited series)
1-5-Jason Aaron-s/Ron Garney-a; two covers on each. 5-Alex Ross var-c 3.50

MEN'S ADVENTURES (Formerly True Adventures)
Marvel/Atlas Comics (CCC): No. 4, Aug, 1950 - No. 28, July, 1954
4(#1)(52 pgs.) 43 86 129 271 461 650
5-Flying Saucer story 29 58 87 172 281 390
6-8: 7-Buried alive story. 8-Sci/fic story 27 54 81 158 259 360
9-20: All war format 20 40 60 117 189 260
21,22,24,26: All horror format 45 90 135 284 480 675
23-Crandall-a; Fox-a(i); horror format 47 94 141 296 498 700
25-Shrunken head-c 110 220 330 704 1202 1700
27,28-Human Torch & Toro-c/stories; Captain America & Sub-Mariner stories in each (also see Young Men #24-28) 181 362 543 1158 1979 2800
NOTE: ***Ayers*** *a-20, 27(H. Torch).* ***Berg*** *a-15, 16.* ***Brodsky*** *c-4-9, 11, 12, 16-18, 24.* ***Burgos*** *c-27, 28 (Human Torch).* ***Colan*** *a-13, 14, 19.* ***Everett*** *a-10, 14, 22, 25, 28; c-14, 21-23.* ***Hartley*** *a-12.* ***Heath*** *a-8, 11, 24; c-13, 20, 26.* ***Lawrence*** *a-23; 27(Captain America).* ***Maneely*** *a-24; c-10, 15.* ***Mac Pakula*** *a-15, 25.* ***Post*** *a-23.* ***Powell*** *a-27(Sub-Mariner).* ***Reinman*** *a-10-12, 16.* ***Robinson*** *c-19.* ***Romita*** *a-22.* ***Sale*** *a-12-14.* ***Shores*** *c-25.* ***Sinnott*** *a-13, 21.* ***Tuska*** *a-24. Adventure-#4-8; War-#9-20; Weird/Horror-#21-26.*

MENZ INSANA
DC Comics (Vertigo): 1997 ($7.95, one-shot)
nn-Fowler-s/Bolton painted art 1 2 3 5 6 8

MEPHISTO VS... (See Silver Surfer #3)
Marvel Comics Group: Apr, 1987 - No. 4, July, 1987 ($1.50, mini-series)
1-4: 1-Fantastic Four; Austin-i. 2-X-Factor. 3-X-Men. 4-Avengers 4.00

MERA: QUEEN OF ATLANTIS (Leads into Aquaman #38)
DC Comics: Apr, 2018 - No. 6, Sept, 2018 ($3.99, limited series)
1-6: 1-Abnett-s/Medina-a; origin retold; Ocean Master app. 4.00

MERC (See Mark Hazzard: Merc)

MERCENARIES (Based on the Pandemic video game)
Dynamite Entertainment: 2007 - No. 3, 2008 ($3.99, limited series)
1-3-Michael Turner-c; Brian Reed-s/Edgar Salazar-a 4.00

MERCHANTS OF DEATH
Acme Press (Eclipse): Jul, 1988 - No. 4, Nov, 1988 ($3.50, B&W/16 pgs. color, 44 pg. mag.)
1-4: 4-Toth-c 4.00

MERCILESS: THE RISE OF MING (Also see Flash Gordon: Zeitgeist)
Dynamite Entertainment: 2012 - No. 4, 2012 ($3.99, limited series)
1-4 Ming the Merciless' rise to power; Alex Ross-c; Beatty-c/Adrian-a 4.00

MERCY (Mirka Andolfo's...)
Image Comics: Mar, 2020 - No. 6, Sept, 2020 ($3.99, limited series)
1-6-Mirka Andolfo-s/a. 1-Five covers 4.00

MERCY THOMPSON (Patricia Briggs'...)
Dynamite Entertainment: 2014 - No. 6, 2015 ($3.99, limited series)
1-6-Patricia Briggs & Rik Hoskin-s/Tom Garcia-a 4.00

MERIDIAN
CrossGeneration Comics: Jul, 2000 - No. 44, Apr, 2004 ($2.95)
1-44: Barbara Kesel-s 3.00
Flying Solo Vol. 1 TPB (2001, $19.95) r/#1-7; cover by Steve Rude 20.00
Going to Ground Vol. 2 TPB (2002, $19.95) r/#8-14 20.00
Taking the Skies Vol. 3 TPB (2002, $15.95) r/#15-20 16.00
Vol. 4: Coming Home (12/02, $15.95) r/#21-26 16.00
Vol. 5: Minister of Cadador (7/03, $15.95) r/#27-32 16.00
Vol. 6: Changing Course (1/04, $15.95) r/#33-38 16.00
Traveler Vol. 1-4 ($9.95): Digest-size reprints of TPBs 10.00

MERLIN JONES AS THE MONKEY'S UNCLE (See Movie Comics and The Misadventures of... under Movie Comics)

MERRILL'S MARAUDERS (See Movie Classics)

MERRY CHRISTMAS (See A Christmas Adventure, Donald Duck..., Dell Giant #39, & March of Comics #153 in the Promotional Comics section)

MERRY COMICS
Carlton Publishing Co.: Dec, 1945 (10¢)
nn-Boogeyman app. 29 58 87 172 281 390

MERRY COMICS: Four Star Publications: 1947 (Advertised, not published)

MERRY-GO-ROUND COMICS
LaSalle Publ. Co./Croyden Publ./Rotary Litho.: 1944 (25¢, 132 pgs.); 1946; 9-10/47 - No. 2, 1948
nn(1944)(LaSalle)-Funny animal; 29 new features 25 50 75 150 245 340
21 (Publisher?) 13 26 39 74 105 135
1(1946)(Croyden)-Al Fago-c; funny animal 15 30 45 84 127 170
V1#1,2(1947-48; 52 pgs.)(Rotary Litho. Co. Ltd., Canada); Ken Hultgren-a 12 24 36 69 97 125

MERRY MAILMAN (See Fawcett's Funny Animals #87-89)

MERRY MOUSE (Also see Funny Tunes & Space Comics)
Avon Periodicals: June, 1953 - No. 4, Jan-Feb, 1954
1-1st app.; funny animal; Frank Carin-c/a 14 28 42 82 121 160
2-4 9 18 27 50 65 80

MERRY X-MEN HOLIDAY SPECIAL
Marvel Comics: Feb, 2019 ($4.99, one-shot)
1-Holiday short stories by various; Nakayama-c 4.00

MERV PUMPKINHEAD, AGENT OF D.R.E.A.M. (See The Sandman)
DC Comics (Vertigo): 2000 ($5.95, one-shot)
1-Buckingham-a(p); Nowlan painted-c 6.00

META-4
First Comics: Feb, 1991 - No. 4, 1991 ($2.25)
1-($3.95, 52pgs.) 4.00
2-4 3.00

METAL GEAR SOLID (Based on the video game)
IDW Publ.: Sept, 2004 - No. 12, Aug, 2005 ($3.99)
1-12: 1-Two covers; Ashley Wood-a/Kris Oprisko-s 4.00
1-Retailer edition with foil cover 20.00

METAL GEAR SOLID: SONS OF LIBERTY
IDW Publ.: Sept, 2005 - No. 12, Sept, 2007 ($3.99)
#0 (9/05) profile pages on characters; Ashley Wood-a 4.00
1-12: 1-Two covers; Ashley Wood-a/Alex Garner-s 4.00

METALLIX
Future Comics: Dec, 2002 - No. 6, June, 2003 ($3.50)
0-6-Ron Lim-a. 0-(6/03) Origin. 1-Layton-c 3.50
1-Collector's Edition with variant cover by Lim 3.50
1-Free Comic Book Day Edition (4/03) Layton-c 3.00

METAL MEN (See Brave & the Bold, DC Comics Presents, and Showcase #37-40)
National Periodical Publications/DC Comics: 4-5/63 - No. 41, 12-1/69-70; No. 42, 2-3/73 - No. 44, 7-8/73; No. 45, 4-5/76 - No. 56, 2-3/78
1-(4-5/63)-5th app. Metal Men 59 118 177 472 1061 1650
2 20 40 60 144 317 490
3-5 13 26 39 89 195 300
6-10 9 18 27 59 117 175
11-20: 12-Beatles cameo (2-3/65) 7 14 21 46 86 125
21-Batman, Robin & Flash x-over 6 12 18 41 76 110
22-26,28-30 5 10 15 34 60 85
27-Origin Metal Men retold 6 12 18 42 79 115
31-41(1968-70): 38-Last 12¢ issue. 41-Last 15¢ 5 10 15 31 53 75
42-44(1973)-Reprints 2 4 6 10 14 18
45('76)-49-Simonson-a in all: 48,49-Re-intro Eclipso 2 4 6 10 14 18
50-56: 50-Part-r. 54,55-Green Lantern x-over 2 4 6 9 12 15
NOTE: ***Andru/Esposito*** *c-1-30.* ***Aparo*** *c-53-56.* ***Giordano*** *c-45, 46.* ***Kane/Esposito*** *a-30, 31; c-31.* ***Simonson*** *a-45-49; c-47-52.* ***Staton*** *a-50-56.*

METAL MEN (Also see Tangent Comics/ Metal Men)
DC Comics: Oct, 1993 - No. 4, Jan, 1994 ($1.25, mini-series)
1-($2.50)-Multi-colored foil-c 5.00
2-4: 2-Origin 4.00

METAL MEN (Also see 52)
DC Comics: Oct, 2007 - No. 8, Jul, 2008 ($2.99, limited series)
1-8-Duncan Rouleau-s/a; origin re-told. 3-Chemo returns 3.00
HC (2008, $24.99, dustjacket) r/#1-8; cover gallery and sketch pages 25.00
SC (2009, $14.99) r/#1-8; cover gallery and sketch pages 15.00

METAL MEN
DC Comics: Dec, 2019 - No. 12, Feb, 2021 ($3.99, limited series)
1-12-Dan DiDio-s/Shane Davis-a. 1-Intro. Nth Metal Man. 3-Devil Ray monster returns. 7-Intro. Animal Gas Gang. 7-9-Chemo app. 10-Origin of Nth Metal Man 4.00

METAL SOCIETY
Image Comics (Top Cow): May, 2022 - No. 5, Sept, 2022 ($3.99, limited series)
1-5-Zack Kaplan-s/Guilherme Balbi-a 4.00

METAMORPHO (See Action Comics #413, Brave & the Bold #57,58, 1st Issue Special, & World's Finest #217)
National Periodical Publications: July-Aug, 1965 - No. 17, Mar-Apr, 1968 (All 12¢ issues)
1-(7-8/65)-3rd app. Metamorpho 16 32 48 107 236 365
2,3 7 14 21 46 86 125
4-6,10: 10-Origin & 1st app. Element Girl (1-2/67) 6 12 18 37 66 95
7-9 5 10 15 33 57 80
11-17: 17-Sparling-c/a 5 10 15 30 50 70
NOTE: ***Ramona Fradon*** *a-B&B 57, 58, 1-4.* ***Orlando*** *a-5, 6; c-5-9, 11.* ***Trapani*** *a(p)-7-16; i-16.*

Men of War (2011) #8 © DC

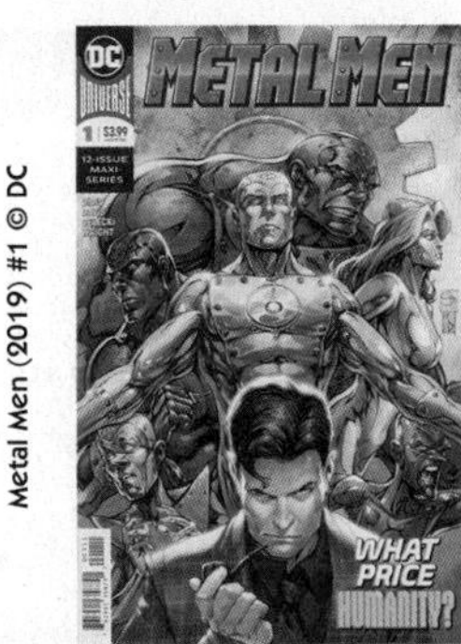

Metal Men (2019) #1 © DC

Mice Templar #1 © Oeming & Glass

GD 2.0 | VG 4.0 | FN 6.0 | VF 8.0 | VF/NM 9.0 | NM- 9.2

METAMORPHO
DC Comics: Aug, 1993 - No. 4, Nov, 1993 ($1.50, mini-series)
1-4 4.00

METAMORPHO: YEAR ONE
DC Comics: Early Dec, 2007 - No. 6, Late Feb, 2008 ($2.99, limited series)
1-6-Origin re-told; Jurgens-s/Jurgens & Delperdang-a/Nowlan-c. 6-Justice League app. 3.00
TPB ('08, $14.99) r/#1-6 15.00

METAPHYSIQUE
Malibu Comics (Bravura): Apr, 1995 - No. 6, Oct, 1995 ($2.95, limited series)
1-6: Norm Breyfogle-c/a/scripts 3.00

METEOR COMICS
L. L. Baird (Croyden): Nov, 1945
1-Captain Wizard, Impossible Man, Race Wilkins app.; origin Baldy Bean, Capt. Wizard's sidekick; bare-breasted mermaids story 63 126 189 403 689 975

METEOR MAN
Marvel Comics: Aug, 1993 - No. 6, Jan, 1994 ($1.25, limited series)
1-6: 1-Regular unbagged. 4-Night Thrasher-c/story. 6-Terry Austin-c(i) 3.00
1-Polybagged w/button & rap newspaper 4.00
...: The Movie (4/93 [7/93 on cover], $2.25) movie adaptation 3.00

METROPOL (See Ted McKeever's...)

METROPOL A.D. (See Ted McKeever's...)

METROPOLIS S.C.U. (Also see Showcase '96 #1)
DC Comics: Nov, 1995 - No. 4, Feb, 1996 ($1.50, limited series)
1-4: 1-Superman-c & app. 4.00

ME YOU LOVE IN THE DARK, THE
Image Comics: Aug, 2021 - No. 5, Dec, 2021 ($3.99, limited series)
1-5-Skottie Young-s/Jorge Corona-a 4.00

MEZZ: GALACTIC TOUR 2494 (Also See Nexus)
Dark Horse Comics: May, 1994 ($2.50, one-shot)
1 3.00

MGM'S MARVELOUS WIZARD OF OZ (See Marvel Treasury of Oz)
Marvel Comics Group/National Periodical Publications: 1975 ($1.50, 84 pgs.; oversize)
1-Adaptation of MGM's movie; J. Buscema-a 4 8 12 27 44 60

M.G.M'S MOUSE MUSKETEERS (Formerly M.G.M.'s The Two Mouseketeers)
Dell Publishing Co.: No. 670, Jan, 1956 - No. 1290, Mar-May, 1962
Four Color 670 (#4) 6 12 18 41 76 110
Four Color 711,728,764 5 10 15 31 53 75
8 (4-6/57) - 21 (3-5/60) 4 8 12 27 44 60
Four Color 1135,1175,1290 4 8 12 28 47 65

M.G.M.'S SPIKE AND TYKE (also see Tom & Jerry #79)
Dell Publishing Co.: No. 499, Sept, 1953 - No. 1266, Dec-Feb, 1961-62
Four Color 499 (#1) 8 16 24 55 105 155
Four Color 577,638 6 12 18 38 69 100
4(12-2/55-56)-10 4 8 12 27 44 60
11-24(12-2/60-61) 4 8 12 23 37 50
Four Color 1266 4 8 12 28 47 65

M.G.M.'S THE TWO MOUSKETEERS
Dell Publishing Co.: No. 475, June, 1953 - No. 642, July, 1955
Four Color 475 (#1) 9 18 27 59 117 175
Four Color 603 (11/54), 642 6 12 18 41 76 110

MIAMI VICE REMIX
IDW Publishing (Lion Forge): Mar, 2015 - No. 5, Jul, 2015 ($3.99, limited series)
1-5-Joe Casey-s/Jim Mahfood-a; re-imagined Crockett & Tubbs 4.00

MICE TEMPLAR, THE
Image Comics: Sept, 2007 - No. 6, Oct, 2008 ($3.99/$2.99)
1-($3.99)-Bryan Glass-s/Michael Avon Oeming-a/c 4.00
2-6-($2.99) 3.00

MICE TEMPLAR, THE , VOLUME 2: DESTINY
Image Comics: July, 2009 - No. 9, May, 2010 ($3.99/$2.99/$4.99)
1,2-($3.99) 1-Bryan Glass-s/Oeming & Santos-a; 2 covers. 2-Santos-a 4.00
3-8-($2.99)-Santos-a; 2 covers by Oeming & Santos 3.00
9-($4.99) 5.00

MICE TEMPLAR, THE , VOLUME 3: A MIDWINTER NIGHT'S DREAM
Image Comics: Dec, 2010 - No. 8, Mar, 2012 ($3.99/$2.99)
1,8-($3.99) 1-Bryan Glass-s/Oeming & Santos-a; 2 covers 4.00
2-7-($2.99)-Santos-a; 2 covers by Oeming & Santos 3.00

MICE TEMPLAR, THE , VOLUME 4: LEGEND
Image Comics: Mar, 2013 - No. 14, Oct, 2014 ($3.99/$2.99/$4.99)
1-($3.99)-Bryan Glass-s/Victor Santos-a; 2 covers 4.00
2-7-($2.99)-Santos-a; 2 covers by Oeming & Santos 3.00
8-($4.99) 5.00
9-13-($3.99) 4.00
14-($5.99) Bonus back-up Hammer of the Gods by Oeming & Wheatley 6.00

MICE TEMPLAR, THE , VOLUME 5: NIGHT'S END
Image Comics: Mar, 2015 - No. 5, Sept, 2015 ($3.99/$5.99)
1,3,5-($3.99)-Bryan Glass-s/Victor Santos-a; 2 covers by Oeming & Santos 4.00
2,4-($5.99)-Bonus back-up Hammer of the Gods 6.00

MICHAELANGELO CHRISTMAS SPECIAL (See Teenage Mutant Ninja Turtles Christmas Special)

MICHAELANGELO, TEENAGE MUTANT NINJA TURTLE
Mirage Studios: 1986 (One shot) ($1.50, B&W)
1-Christmas-c/story 4 8 12 28 47 65
1-2nd printing ('89, $1.75)-Reprint plus new-a 6.00

MICHAEL CHABON PRESENTS THE AMAZING ADVENTURES OF THE ESCAPIST
Dark Horse Comics: Feb, 2004 - No. 8, Nov, 2005 ($8.95, squarebound)
1-5,7,8-Short stories by Chabon and various incl. Chaykin, Starlin, Brereton, Baker 9.00
6-Includes 6 pg. Spirit & Escapist story (Will Eisner's last work); Spirit on cover 9.00
... Vol. 1 (5/04, $17.95, digest-size) r/#1&2; wraparound-c by Chris Ware 18.00
... Vol. 2 (11/04, $17.95, digest-size) r/#3&4; wraparound-c by Matt Kindt 18.00
... Vol. 3 (4/06, $14.95, digest-size) r/#5&6; Tim Sale-c 15.00

MICHAEL MOORCOCK'S ELRIC: THE MAKING OF A SORCEROR
DC Comics: 2004 - No. 4, 2006 ($5.95, prestige format, limited series)
1-4-Moorcock-s/Simonson-a 6.00
TPB (2007, $19.99) r/#1-4 20.00

MICHAEL MOORCOCK'S MULTIVERSE
DC Comics (Helix): Nov, 1997 - No. 12, Oct, 1998 ($2.50, limited series)
1-12: Simonson, Reeve & Ridgway-a 3.00
TPB (1999, $19.95) r/#1-12 20.00

MICHAEL TURNER, A TRIBUTE TO...
Aspen MLT: 2008 ($8.99, squarebound)
nn-Pin-ups and tributes from Turner's colleagues and friends; Turner & Ross-c 9.00
Michael Turner Legacy Vol. 1 #1 (6/18, $5.99) Pin-ups and tributes 6.00

MICHAEL TURNER PRESENTS: ASPEN (See Aspen)

MICKEY AND DONALD (See Walt Disney's...)

MICKEY AND DONALD CHRISTMAS PARADE
IDW Publishing: Dec, 2015 - No. 5, Nov, 2019 ($5.99/$6.99, squarebound, annual)
1,2-($5.99) English translations of Dutch, Italian and Swedish Disney Christmas stories 6.00
3-5-($6.99) English translations of Dutch & Italian Christmas stories. 3-r/Four Color #62 7.00

MICKEY AND DONALD IN VACATIONLAND (See Dell Giant No. 47)

MICKEY & THE BEANSTALK (See Story Hour Series)

MICKEY & THE SLEUTH (See Walt Disney Showcase #38, 39, 42)

MICKEY FINN (Also see Big Shot Comics #74 & Feature Funnies)
Eastern Color 1-4/McNaught Synd. #5 on (Columbia)/Headline V3#2:
Nov?, 1942 - V3#2, May, 1952
1 35 70 105 208 339 470
2 18 36 54 105 165 225
3-Charlie Chan story 14 28 42 80 115 150
4 12 24 36 67 94 120
5-10 10 20 30 54 72 90
11-15(1949): 12-Sparky Watts app. 9 18 27 47 61 75
V3#1,2(1952) 8 16 24 40 50 60

MICKEY MALONE
Hale Nass Corp.: 1936 (Color, punchout-c) (B&W-a on back)
nn - 1pg. of comics 425 850 1700 -- -- --

MICKEY MANTLE (See Baseball's Greatest Heroes #1)

MICKEY MOUSE (See Adventures of Mickey Mouse, The Best of Walt Disney Comics, Cheerios giveaways, Donald and ..., Dynabrite Comics, 40 Big Pages..., Gladstone Comic Album, Merry Christmas From..., Walt Disney's Mickey and Donald, Walt Disney's Comics & Stories, Walt Disney's..., & Wheaties)

MICKEY MOUSE (...Secret Agent #107-109; Walt Disney's... #148-205?)
(See Dell Giants for annuals) (#204 exists from both G.K. & Whitman)
Dell Publ. Co./Gold Key #85-204/Whitman #204-218/Gladstone #219 on:

GD VG FN VF VF/NM NM- / 2.0 4.0 6.0 8.0 9.0 9.2

#16, 1941 - #84, 7-9/62; #85, 11/62 - #218, 6/84; #219, 10/86 - #256, 4/90

Four Color 16(1941)-1st Mickey Mouse comic book; "...vs. the Phantom Blot" by Gottfredson 1500 3000 4500 19,500 -- --
Four Color 27(1943)- "7 Colored Terror" 79 158 237 632 1416 2200
Four Color 79(1945)-By Carl Barks (1 story) 100 200 300 800 1800 2800
Four Color 116(1946) 27 54 81 189 420 650
Four Color 141,157(1947) 24 48 72 168 372 575
Four Color 170,181,194('48) 20 40 60 144 317 490
Four Color 214('49),231,248,261 17 34 51 114 252 390
Four Color 268-Reprints/WDC&S #22-24 by Gottfredson ("Surprise Visitor") 16 32 48 108 239 370
Four Color 279,286,296 13 26 39 86 188 290
Four Color 304,313(#1),325(#2),334 12 24 36 79 170 260
Four Color 343,352,362,371,387 10 20 30 67 141 215
Four Color 401,411,427(10-11/52) 9 18 27 60 120 180
Four Color 819-Mickey Mouse in Magicland 7 14 21 49 92 135
Four Color 1057,1151,1246(1959-61)-Album; #1057 has 10¢ & 12¢ editions; back covers are different 6 12 18 42 79 115
28(12-1/52-53)-32,34 7 14 21 46 86 125
33-(Exists with 2 dates, 10-11/53 & 12-1/54) 7 14 21 46 86 125
35-50 6 12 18 37 66 95
51-73,75-80 5 10 15 33 57 80
74-Story swipe "The Rare Stamp Search" from 4-Color #422- "The Gilded Man" 6 12 18 37 66 95
81-105: 93,95-titled "Mickey Mouse Club Album". 100-105: Reprint 4-Color #427,194,279, 170,343,214 in that order 4 8 12 25 40 55
106-120 3 6 9 19 30 40
121-130 3 6 9 16 23 30
131-146 3 6 9 14 20 25
147,148: 147-Reprints "The Phantom Fires" from WDC&S #200-202.148-Reprints "The Mystery of Lonely Valley" from WDC&S #208-210 3 6 9 14 20 25
149-158 2 4 6 10 14 18
159-Reprints "The Sunken City" from WDC&S #205-207 2 4 6 10 14 18
160-178: 162-165,167-170-r 2 4 6 10 14 18
167-Whitman edition 2 4 6 10 14 18
179-(52 pgs.) 2 4 6 11 16 20
180-203: 200-r/Four Color #371 2 4 6 8 10 12
204-(Whitman or G.K.), 205,206 2 4 6 9 13 16
207(8/80), 209(pre-pack?) 6 12 18 38 69 100
208-(8-12/80)-Only distr. in Whitman 3-pack 10 20 30 69 147 225
210(2/81),211-214 2 4 6 9 13 16
215-218: 215(2/82), 216(4/82), 217(3/84), 218(misdated 8/82; actual date 7/84) 2 4 6 10 14 18
219-1st Gladstone issue; The Seven Ghosts serial-r begins by Gottfredson 2 4 6 11 16 20
220,221 2 3 4 6 8 10
222-225: 222-Editor-in Grief strip-r 5.00
226-230 5.00
231-243,246-254: 240-r/March of Comics #27. 245-r/F.C. #279. 250-r/F.C. #248 4.00
244 (1/89, $2.95, 100 pgs.)-Squarebound 60th anniversary issue; gives history of Mickey 5.00
245,255,256: 245-r/F.C. #279. 255,256-($1.95, 68 pgs.) 5.00

NOTE: *Reprints #195-197, 198(2/3), 199(1/3), 200-208, 211(1/2), 212, 213, 215(1/3), 216-on.* **Gottfredson** *Mickey Mouse serials in #219-239, 241-244, 246-249, 251-253, 255.*

Album 01-518-210(Dell), 1(10082-309)(9/63-Gold Key) 3 6 9 21 33 45
...Club 1(1/64-Gold Key)(TV) 4 8 12 22 35 48
Mini Comic 1(1976)(3-1/4x6-1/2")-Reprints 158 1 2 3 5 6 8
Surprise Party 1(30037-901, G.K.)(1/69)-40th Anniversary (see Walt Disney Showcase #47) 3 6 9 20 31 42
Surprise Party 1(1979)-r/1969 issue 1 2 3 5 6 8

MICKEY MOUSE (Continued from Mickey Mouse and Friends)
BOOM! Studios: No. 304, Jan, 2011 - No. 309, Jun, 2011 ($3.99)

304-309: 304-Peg-Leg Pete app. 309-Continues in Walt Disney's C&S #720 4.00

MICKEY MOUSE
IDW Publishing: Jun, 2015 - No. 21, Jun, 2017 ($3.99)

1-Legacy numbered #310; art by Cavazzano and others; multiple covers 4.00
2-21-Classic Disney and foreign reprints; multiple covers on each. 21-(Legacy #330) 4.00

MICKEY MOUSE ADVENTURES
Disney Comics: June, 1990 - No. 18, Nov, 1991 ($1.50)

1,8,9: 1-Bradbury, Murry-r/M.M. #45,73 plus new-a. 8-Byrne-c. 9-Fantasia 50th ann. issue w/new adapt. of movie 4.00
2-7,10-18: 2-Begin all new stories. 10-r/F.C. #214 3.00

MICKEY MOUSE AND FRIENDS (Continued from Walt Disney's Mickey Mouse and Friends) (Title continues as Mickey Mouse #304-on)
BOOM! Studios: No. 296, Sept, 2009 - No. 303, Dec, 2010 ($2.99/$3.99)

296-299,301-303: 296-299-Wizards of Mickey stories. 301-Conclusion to story in #300 3.00
300-($3.99, 9/10) Petrucha-s/Pelaez-a; back-up Tanglefoot story w/Gottfredson-a 4.00
300 Deluxe Edition ($6.99) Variant cover by Daan Jippes 7.00

MICKEY MOUSE CLUB FUN BOOK
Golden Press: 1977 (1.95, 228 pgs.)(square bound)

11190-1950s-r; 20,000 Leagues, M. Mouse Silly Symphonys, The Reluctant Dragon, etc. 4 8 12 28 47 65

MICKEY MOUSE CLUB MAGAZINE (See Walt Disney...)

MICKEY MOUSE COMICS DIGEST
Gladstone: 1986 - No. 5, 1987 (96 pgs.)

1 ($1.25-c) 1 2 3 5 6 8
2-5: 3-5 ($1.50-c) 5.00

MICKEY MOUSE IN COLOR
Another Rainbow/Pantheon: 1988 (Deluxe, 13"x17", hard-c, $250.00) (Trade, 9-7/8"x11-1/2", hard-c, $39.95)

Deluxe limited edition of 3,000 copies signed by Floyd Gottfredson and Carl Barks, designated as the "Official Mickey Mouse 60th Anniversary" book. Mickey Sunday and daily reprints, plus Barks "Riddle of the Red Hat" from Four Color #79. Comes with 45 r.p.m. record interview with Gottfredson and Barks. 240 pgs. 12 24 36 82 179 275
Deluxe, limited to 100 copies, as above, but with a unique colored pencil original drawing of Mickey Mouse by Carl Barks. 900.00
Pantheon trade edition, edited down & without Barks, 192 pgs. 3 6 9 19 30 40

MICKEY MOUSE MAGAZINE (Becomes Walt Disney's Comics & Stories)(Also see 40 Big Pages of Mickey Mouse)
K. K. Publ./Western Publishing Co.: Summer, 1935 (June-Aug, indicia) - V5#12, Sept, 1940; V1#1-5, V3#11,12, V4#1-3 are 44 pgs; V2#3-100 pgs; V5#12-68 pgs; rest are 36 pgs.(No V3#1, V4#6)

V1#1 (Large size, 13-1/4x10-1/4"; 25¢)-Contains puzzles, games, cels, stories & comics of Disney characters. Promotional magazine for Disney cartoon movies and paraphernalia 1540 3080 4620 9930 20,500 --

Note: *Some copies were autographed by the editors & given away with all early one year subscriptions.*

2 (Size change, 11-1/2x8-1/2"; 10/35; 10¢)-High quality paper begins; Messmer-a 353 706 1059 3000 -- --
3,4: 3-Messmer-a 212 424 636 1800 -- --
5-1st Donald Duck solo-c; 2nd cover app. ever; last 44 pg. & high quality paper issue 412 824 1236 3500 -- --
6-9: 6-36 pg. issues begin; Donald becomes editor. 8-2nd Donald solo-c. 9-1st Mickey/Minnie-c 176 352 528 1500 -- --
10-12, V2#1,2: 11-1st Pluto/Mickey-c; Donald fires himself and appoints Mickey as editor 165 330 495 1400 -- --
V2#3-Special 100 pg. Christmas issue (25¢); Messmer-a; Donald becomes editor of Wise Quacks 494 988 1482 4200 -- --
4-Mickey Mouse Comics & Roy Ranger (adventure strip) begin; both end V2#9; Messmer-a 147 294 441 1250 -- --
5-9: 5-Ted True (adventure strip, ends V2#9) & Silly Symphony Comics (ends V3#3) begin. 6-1st solo Minnie-c. 6-9-Mickey Mouse Movies cut-out in each 68 136 204 435 743 1050
6-Variant (3/37) Rare; distributed with "Mickey Mouse Birthday Party March 6th 1937" invitation outer cover attached to book. Only one example is known. Value will be based on future recorded sales
10-1st full color issue; Mickey Mouse (by Gottfredson; ends V3#12) & Silly Symphony (ends V3#3) full color Sunday-r, Peter The Farm Detective (ends V5#8) & Ole Of The North (ends V3#3) begins 119 238 357 762 1306 1850
11-13: 12-Hiawatha-c & feature story 61 122 183 390 670 950
V3#2-Big Bad Wolf Halloween-c 81 162 243 518 884 1250
3 (12/37)-1st app. Snow White & The Seven Dwarfs (before release of movie) (possibly 1st in print); Mickey X-Mas-c 148 296 444 947 1624 2300
4 (1/38)-Snow White & The Seven Dwarfs serial begins (on stands before release of movie); Ducky Symphony (ends V3#11) begins 103 206 309 659 1130 1600
5-1st Snow White & Seven Dwarfs-c (St. Valentine's Day) 132 264 396 838 1444 2050
6-Snow White serial ends; Lonesome Ghosts app. (2 pp.) 77 154 231 493 847 1200
7-Seven Dwarfs Easter-c 71 142 213 454 777 1100
8-10: 9-Dopey-c. 10-1st solo Goofy-c 54 108 162 343 574 825
11,12 (44 pgs; 8 more pgs. color added). 11-Mickey the Sheriff serial (ends V4#3) & Donald Duck strip-r (ends V3#12) begin. Color feature on Snow White's Forest Friends 60 120 180 381 653 925
V4#1 (10/38; 44 pgs.)-Brave Little Tailor-c/feature story, nominated for Academy Award; Bobby & Chip by Otto Messmer (ends V4#2) & The Practical Pig (ends V4#2) begin 60 120 180 381 653 925
2 (44 pgs.)-1st Huey, Dewey & Louie-c 68 136 204 435 743 1050
3 (12/38, 44 pgs.)-Ferdinand The Bull-c/feature story, Academy Award winner; Mickey Mouse & The Whalers serial begins, ends V4#12 61 122 183 390 670 950
4-Spotty, Mother Pluto strip-r begin, end V4#8 57 114 171 362 619 875
5-St. Valentine's day-c. 1st Pluto solo-c 68 136 204 435 743 1050
7 (3/39)-The Ugly Duckling-c/feature story, Academy Award winner 57 114 171 362 619 875
7 (4/39)-Goofy & Wilbur The Grasshopper classic-c/feature story from 1st Goofy solo cartoon movie; Timid Elmer begins, ends V5#5 60 120 180 381 653 925
8-Big Bad Wolf-c from Practical Pig movie poster; Practical Pig feature story 57 114 171 362 619 875
9-Donald Duck & Mickey Mouse Sunday-r begin; The Pointer feature story, nominated for Academy Award 57 114 171 362 619 875
10-Classic July 4th drum & fife-c; last Donald Sunday-r 135 270 405 864 1482 2100
11-1st slick-c; last over-sized issue 57 114 171 362 619 875
12 (9/39; format change, 10-1/4x8-1/4")-1st full color, cover to cover issue; Donald's Penguin-c/feature story 61 122 183 390 670 950
V5#1-Black Pete-c; Officer Duck-c/feature story; Autograph Hound feature story; Robinson Crusoe serial begins 90 180 270 576 988 1400
2-Goofy-c; 1st brief app. Pinocchio 103 206 309 659 1130 1600
3 (12/39)-Pinocchio Christmas-c (Before movie release). 1st app. Jiminy Cricket; Pinocchio serial begins 123 246 369 787 1344 1900
4,5: 5-Jiminy Cricket-c; Pinocchio serial ends; Donald's Dog Laundry feature story 61 122 183 390 670 950
6,7: 6-Tugboat Mickey feature story; Rip Van Winkle feature begins, ends V5#8. 7-2nd Huey, Dewey & Louie-c 60 120 180 381 653 925
8-Last magazine size issue; 2nd solo Pluto-c; Figaro & Cleo feature story 63 126 189 403 689 975
9-11: 9 (6/40; change to comic book size)-Jiminy Cricket feature story; Donald-c & Sunday-r begin. 10-Special Independence Day issue. 11-Hawaiian Holiday & Mickey's Trailer feature stories; last 36 pg. issue 71 142 213 454 777 1100
12 (Format change)-The transition issue (68 pgs.) becoming a comic book. With only a title change to follow, becomes Walt Disney's Comics & Stories #1 with the next issue 486 972 1456 3550 6275 9000

NOTE: **Otto Messmer**-*a is in many issues of the first two-three years. The following story titles and issues have gags created by* **Carl Barks:** *V4#3(12/38)-'Donald's Better Self' & 'Donald's Golf Game;' V4#4(1/39)-*

Mickey Mouse #308 © DIS

Micronauts (2016) #1 © Hasbro

Midnighter (2015) #1 © DC

	GD	VG	FN	VF	VF/NM	NM-
	2.0	4.0	6.0	8.0	9.0	9.2

'Donald's Lucky Day;' V4#7(3/39)-'Hockey Champ;' V4#7(4/39)-'Donald's Cousin Gus;' V4#9(6/39)-'Sea Scouts;' V4#12(9/39)-'Donald's Penguin;' V5#9 (6/40)-'Donald's Vacation;' V5#10(7/40)-'Bone Trouble;' V5#12(9/40)-'Window Cleaners.'

MICKEY MOUSE MAGAZINE (Russian Version)
May 16, 1991 (1st Russian printing of a modern comic book)
1-Bagged w/gold label commemoration in English 2 4 6 10 14 18

MICKEY MOUSE MARCH OF COMICS (See March of Comics #8,27,45,60,74)

MICKEY MOUSE SHORTS: SEASON ONE
IDW Publishing: Jul, 2016 - No. 4, Oct, 2016 ($3.99, limited series)
1-4-Adaptations of new Disney cartoon shorts 4.00

MICKEY MOUSE'S SUMMER VACATION (See Story Hour Series)

MICKEY MOUSE SUMMER FUN (See Dell Giants)

MICKEY SPILLANE'S MIKE DANGER
Tekno Comix: Sept, 1995 - No. 11, May, 1996 ($1.95)
1-11: 1-Frank Miller-c. 7-polybagged; Simonson-c. 8,9-Simonson-c 3.00

MICKEY SPILLANE'S MIKE DANGER
Big Entertainment: V2#1, June, 1996 - No. 10, Apr, 1997 ($2.25)
V2#1-10: Max Allan Collins scripts 3.00

MICKEY SPILLANE'S MIKE HAMMER
Titan Comics: Jul, 2018 - No. 4, Oct, 2018 ($3.99, limited series)
1-4-Max Allan Collins-s/Marcelo Salaza & Marcio Freire-a 4.00

MICKEY'S TWICE UPON A CHRISTMAS (Disney)
Gemstone Publishing: 2004 ($3.95, square-bound, one-shot)
nn-Christmas short stories with Mickey, Minnie, Donald, Uncle Scrooge, Goofy and others 4.00

MICROBOTS, THE
Gold Key: Dec, 1971 (one-shot)
1 (10271-112) Painted-c 3 6 9 15 22 28

MICRONAUTS (Toys)
Marvel Comics Group: Jan, 1979 - No. 59, Aug, 1984 (Mando paper #53 on)
1-Intro/1st app. Baron Karza 3 6 9 20 31 42
2-7,9,10,35,37,57: 7-Man-Thing app.9-1st app. Cilicia. 35-Double size; origin Microverse; intro Death Squad; Dr. Strange app. 37-Nightcrawler app.; X-Men cameo (2 pgs.).
57-(52 pgs.) 1 2 3 5 6 8
8-1st app. Capt. Universe (8/79) 4 8 12 25 40 55
11-34,36,38-56,58,59: 13-1st app. Jasmine. 15-Death of Microtron. 15-17-Fantastic Four app. 17-Death of Jasmine. 20-Ant-Man app. 21-Microverse series begins. 25-Origin Baron Karza. 25-29-Nick Fury app. 27-Death of Biotron. 34-Dr. Strange app. 38-First direct sale. 40-Fantastic Four app. 48-Early Guice-a begins. 59-Golden painted-c 5.00
Annual 1,2 (12/79,10/80)-Ditko-c/a 6.00
NOTE: *#38-on distributed only through comic shops.* **N. Adams** *c-7i.* **Chaykin** *a-13-18p.* **Ditko** *a-39p.* **Giffen** *a-36p, 37p(part).* **Golden** *a-1-12p; c-2-7p, 8-23, 24p, 38, 39, 59.* **Guice** *a-48-58p; c-49-58.* **Gil Kane** *a-38, 40-45p; c-40-45.* **Layton** *c-33-37.* **Miller** *c-31.*

MICRONAUTS (Micronauts: The New Voyages on cover)
Marvel Comics Group: Oct, 1984 - No. 20, May, 1986
V2#1-20 4.00
NOTE: **Kelley Jones** *a-1; c-1, 6.* **Guice** *a-4p; c-2p.*

MICRONAUTS
Image Comics: 2002 - No. 11, Sept, 2003 ($2.95)
2002 Convention Special (no cover price, B&W) previews series 3.00
1-11: 1-3-Hanson-a; Dave Johnson-c. 4-Su-a; 2 covers by Linsner & Hanson 3.00
...Vol. 1: Revolution (2003, $12.95, digest size) r/#1-5 13.00

MICRONAUTS (Volume 2)
Devil's Due Publishing: Mar, 2004 - No. 3, May, 2004 ($2.95)
1-3-Jolley-s/Broderick-a 3.00

MICRONAUTS
IDW Publishing: Apr, 2016 - No. 11, Mar, 2017 ($4.99/$3.99)
1-($4.99) Cullen Bunn-s/David Baldeón-a; multiple covers; Baron Karza app. 5.00
2-11-($3.99) Max Dunbar-a. 5-Revolution tie-in 4.00
Annual #1 (1/17, $7.99) Bunn-s/Ferreira-a; future Micronauts app. 8.00
... First Strike 1 (9/17, $3.99) Rom app.; leads into Rom First Strike; Gage-s/Panda-a 4.00
...: Revolution 1 (9/16, $3.99) Tie-in w/Transformers, G.I. Joe, M.A.S.K.,Action Man, Rom 4.00

MICRONAUTS: KARZA
Image Comics: Feb, 2003 - No. 4, May, 2003 ($2.95)
1-4-Krueger-s/Kurth-a 3.00

MICRONAUTS SPECIAL EDITION
Marvel Comics Group: Dec, 1983 - No. 5, Apr, 1984 ($2.00, limited series, Baxter paper)
1-5: r-/original series 1-12; Guice-c(p)-all 4.00

MICRONAUTS: WRATH OF KARZA (Leads into First Strike #1)
IDW Publishing: Apr, 2017 - No. 5, Aug, 2017 ($3.99)
1-5-Cullen Bunn & Jimmy Johnston-s/Andrew Griffith-a; multiple covers 4.00

MIDDLEWEST
Image Comics: Nov, 2018 - No. 18 ($3.99)
1-18-Skottie Young-s/Jorge Corona-a. 1-Three covers 4.00

MIDGET COMICS (Fighting Indian Stories)
St. John Publishng Co.: Feb, 1950 - No. 2, Apr, 1950 (5-3/8x7-3/8", 68 pgs.)
1-Fighting Indian Stories; Matt Baker-c 39 78 117 240 395 550
2-Tex West, Cowboy Marshal (also in #1) 18 36 54 105 165 225

MIDNIGHT (See Smash Comics #18)

MIDNIGHT
Ajax/Farrell Publ. (Four Star Comic Corp.): Apr, 1957 - No. 6, June, 1958
1-Reprints from Voodoo & Strange Fantasy with some changes 21 42 63 122 199 275
2-6 14 28 42 82 121 160

MIDNIGHTER (See The Authority)
DC Comics (WildStorm): Jan, 2007 - No. 20, Aug, 2008 ($2.99)
1-20: 1-Ennis-s/Sprouse-a/c. 6-Fabry-a. 7-Vaughan-s. 8-Gage-s. 9-Stelfreeze-a 3.00
1-4-Variant covers. 1-Michael Golden. 2-Art Adams 3-Jason Pearson. 4-Glenn Fabry 4.00
...: Anthem TPB (2008, $14.99) r/#7,10-15 15.00
...: Armageddon (12/07, $2.99) Gage-s/Coleby-a/McKone-c 3.00
...: Assassin8 TPB (2009, $14.99) r/#16-20 15.00
...: Killing Machine TPB (2008, $14.99) r/#1-6 15.00

MIDNIGHTER (See The Authority)
DC Comics: Aug, 2015 - No. 12, Jul, 2016 ($2.99)
1-12: 1-Orlando-s/Aco-a. 3-5-Grayson app. 9-12-Harley Quinn & Suicide Squad app. 3.00
2021 Annual 1 (10/21, $5.99) Cloonan & Conrad-s/Oeming-a; Mister Miracle app. 6.00

MIDNIGHTER AND APOLLO (The Authority)
DC Comics: Dec, 2016 - No. 6, May, 2017 ($3.99, limited series)
1-6-Orlando-s/Blanco-a. 1,2-Henry Bendix app. 2-6-Neron app. 4.00

MIDNIGHT MASS
DC Comics (Vertigo): Jun, 2002 - No. 8, Jan, 2003 ($2.50)
1-8-Rozum-s/Saiz & Palmiotti-a 3.00

MIDNIGHT MASS: HERE THERE BE MONSTERS
DC Comics (Vertigo): March, 2004 - No. 6, Aug, 2004 ($2.95, limited series)
1-6-Rozum-s/Paul Lee-a 3.00

MIDNIGHT MEN
Marvel Comics (Epic Comics/Heavy Hitters): June, 1993 - No. 4, Sept, 1993 ($2.50/$1.95, limited series)
1-($2.50)-Embossed-c; Chaykin-c/a & scripts in all 4.00
2-4 3.00

MIDNIGHT MYSTERY
American Comics Group: Jan-Feb, 1961 - No. 7, Oct, 1961
1-Sci/Fi story 10 20 30 64 132 200
2-7: 7-Gustavson-a 5 10 15 35 63 90
NOTE: **Reinman** *a-1, 3.* **Whitney** *a-1, 4-6; c-1-3, 5, 7.*

MIDNIGHT NATION
Image Comics (Top Cow): Oct, 2000 - No. 12, July, 2002 ($2.50/$2.95)
1-Straczynski-s/Frank-a; 2 covers 3.50
2-11: 9-Twin Towers cover 3.00
12-($2.95) Last issue 3.00
Wizard #1/2 (2001) Michael Zulli-a; two covers by Frank 3.00
Vol. 1 ('03, $29.99, TPB) r/#1-12 & Wizard #1/2; cover gallery; afterword by Straczynski 30.00

MIDNIGHT OF THE SOUL
Image Comics: Jun, 2016 - No. 5, Oct, 2016 ($3.50, limited series)
1-5-Howard Chaykin-s/a/c; set in 1950s New York City 3.50

MIDNIGHT SOCIETY: THE BLACK LAKE
Dark Horse Comics: Jun, 2015 - No. 4, Oct, 2015 ($3.99)
1-4-Drew Johnson-s/a/c 4.00

MIDNIGHT SONS UNLIMITED
Marvel Comics (Midnight Sons imprint #4 on): Apr, 1993 - No. 9, May, 1995 ($3.95, 68 pgs.)
1-9: Blaze, Darkhold (by Quesada #1), Ghost Rider, Morbius & Nightstalkers in all. 1-Painted-c. 3-Spider-Man app. 4-Siege of Darkness part 17; new Dr. Strange & new

Ghost Rider app.; spot varnish-c 4.00
NOTE: *Sears a-2.*

MIDNIGHT SUNS
Marvel Comics: Nov, 2022 - No. 5, Mar, 2023 ($3.99, limited series)
1-5-Wolverine, Magik, Blade, Spirit Rider, Agatha Harkness app. 4.00

MIDNIGHT TALES
Charlton Press: Dec, 1972 - No. 18, May, 1976
V1#1 3 6 9 19 30 40
2-10 2 4 6 10 14 18
11-18: 11-14-Newton-a(p) 2 4 6 8 11 14
12,17(Modern Comics reprint, 1977) 6.00
NOTE: *Adkins a-12i, 13i.* ***Ditko*** *a-12.* ***Howard*** *(Wood imitator) a-1-15, 17, 18; c-1-18.* ***Don Newton*** *a-11-14p.* ***Staton*** *a-1, 3-11, 13.* ***Sutton*** *a-3-10.*

MIDNIGHT VISTA
AfterShock Comics: Sept, 2019 - No. 5, Jan, 2020 ($3.99, limited series)
1-5-Eliot Rahal-s/Clara Meath-a/Juan Doe-c 4.00

MIGHTY, THE
DC Comics: Apr, 2009 - No. 12, Mar, 2010 ($2.99)
1-12: Tomasi & Champagne-s/Dave Johnson-c. 1-4-Snejbjerg-a. 5-12-Samnee-a 3.00
...: Volume 1 TPB (2009, $17.99) r/#1-6 18.00
...: Volume 2 TPB (2010, $17.99) r/#7-12 18.00

MIGHTY ATOM, THE (...& the Pixies #6) (Formerly The Pixies #1-5)
Magazine Enterprises: No. 6, 1949; Nov, 1957 - No. 6, Aug-Sept, 1958
6(1949-M.E.)-no month (1st Series) 8 16 24 42 54 65
1-6(2nd Series)-Pixies-r 5 10 15 22 26 30
I.W. Reprint #1(nd) 2 4 6 9 13 16

MIGHTY AVENGERS
Marvel Comics: May, 2007 - No. 36, Jun, 2010 ($3.99/$2.99)
1-($3.99) Iron Man, Ms. Marvel select new team; Bendis-s/Cho-a/c; Mole Man app. 5.00
2-20: 2-6-($2.99) Ultron returns. 7-15: 7-Bagley-a begins; Venom on-c. 9-11-Dr. Doom app. 12-20-Secret Invasion. 12,13-Maleev-a. 15-Romita Jr.-a. 16-Elektra. 20-Wasp funeral 3.00
21-($3.99) Dark Reign; Scarlet Witch returns; new team assembled; Pham-a 4.00
22-36: 25,26-Fantastic Four app. 35,36-Siege; Ultron returns 3.00
...: Most Wanted Files (2007, $3.99) profiles of members, accomplices & adversaries 4.00
... Vol. 1: The Ultron Initiative HC (2008, $19.99) r/#1-6; variant covers and sketch art 20.00
... Vol. 2: Venom Bomb HC (2008, $19.99) r/#7-11; B&W cover art 20.00

MIGHTY AVENGERS (Continues in Captain America and the Mighty Avengers)
Marvel Comics: Nov, 2013 - No. 14, Nov, 2014 ($3.99)
1-14: 1-Luke Cage, White Tiger, Power Man, Spectrum & Superior Spider-Man team; Land-a. 4-Falcon app. 5-She-Hulk app. 6-8-Schiti-a. 9-Ronin unmasked. 10-12-Original Sin 4.00

MIGHTY BEAR (Formerly Fun Comics; becomes Unsane #15)
Star Publ. No. 13,14/Ajax-Farrell (Four Star): No. 13, Jan, 1954 - No. 14, Mar, 1954; 9/57 - No. 3, 2/58
13,14-L. B. Cole-c 20 40 60 114 182 250
1-3('57-58)Four Star; becomes Mighty Ghost #4 8 16 24 42 54 65

MIGHTY CAPTAIN MARVEL, THE (Follows Civil War II)(Continues in Captain Marvel #125)
Marvel Comics: No. 0, Feb, 2017 - No. 9, Nov, 2017 ($3.99)
0-Stohl-s/Laiso-a; Alpha Flight app. 4.00
1-9: 1-(3/17) Stohl-s/Rosanas-a. 5-8-Secret Empire tie-ins 4.00

MIGHTY COMICS (...Presents) (Formerly Flyman)
Radio Comics (Archie): No. 40, Nov, 1966 - No. 50, Oct, 1967 (All 12¢ issues)
40-Web 5 10 15 30 50 70
41-50: 41-Shield, Black Hood. 42-Black Hood. 43-Shield, Web & Black Hood. 44-Black Hood, Steel Sterling & The Shield. 45-Shield & Hangman; origin Web retold. 46-Steel Sterling, Web & Black Hood. 47-Black Hood & Mr. Justice. 48-Shield & Hangman; Wizard x-over in Shield. 49-Steel Sterling & Fox; Black Hood x-over in Steel Sterling. 50-Black Hood & Web; Inferno x-over in Web 4 8 12 28 47 65
NOTE: ***Paul Reinman*** *a-40-50.*

MIGHTY CRUSADERS, THE (Also see Adventures of the Fly, The Crusaders & Fly Man)
Mighty Comics Group (Radio Comics): Nov, 1965 - No. 7, Oct, 1966 (All 12¢)
1-Origin The Shield 8 16 24 52 99 145
2-Origin Comet 4 8 12 28 47 65
3,5-7: 3-Origin Fly-Man. 5-Intro. Ultra-Men (Fox, Web, Capt. Flag) & Terrific Three (Jaguar, Mr. Justice, Steel Sterling). 7-Steel Sterling feature; origin Fly-Girl
4 8 12 27 44 60
4-1st S.A. app. Fireball, Inferno & Fox; Firefly, Web, Bob Phantom, Blackjack, Hangman, Zambini, Kardak, Steel Sterling, Mr. Justice, Wizard, Capt. Flag, Jaguar x-over
5 10 15 30 50 70
Volume 1: Origin of a Super Team TPB (2003, $12.95) r/#1 & Fly Man #31-33 13.00
NOTE: ***Reinman*** *a-6.*

MIGHTY CRUSADERS, THE (All New Advs. of...#2)
Red Circle Prod./Archie Ent. No. 6 on: Mar, 1983 - No. 13, Sept, 1985 ($1.00, 36 pgs, Mando paper)
1-Origin Black Hood, The Fly, Fly Girl, The Shield, The Wizard, The Jaguar, Pvt. Strong & The Web; return of MLJ heroes 1 2 3 4 5 7
2-10: 2-Mister Midnight begins. 4-Darkling replaces Shield. 5-Origin Jaguar, Shield begins. 7-Untold origin Jaguar. 10-Veitch-a 5.00
11-13-Lower print run 6.00
NOTE: ***Buckler*** *a-1-3, 4i, 5p, 7p, 8i, 9i; c-1-10p.*

MIGHTY CRUSADERS, THE (Also see The Shield, The Web and The Red Circle)
DC Comics: Sept, 2010 - No. 6, Feb, 2011 ($3.99, limited series)
1-6-The Shield, The Web, Fly-Girl, Inferno, War Eagle & The Comet team-up 4.00
... Special 1 (7/10, $4.99) Prequel to series; Pina-a/Lau-c 5.00

MIGHTY CRUSADERS, THE (Volume 3)
Archie Comic Publications (Dark Circle): Jan, 2018 - No. 4, May, 2018 ($3.99)
1-4-The Shield, Jaguar, Firefly, Darkling, Steel Sterling, The Comet & The Web team-up 4.00
...: The Shield 1 (8/21, $3.99) Rob Liefeld-s/a; multiple covers 4.00

MIGHTY GHOST (Formerly Mighty Bear #1-3)
Ajax/Farrell Publ.: No. 4, June, 1958
4 8 16 24 42 54 65

MIGHTY HERCULES, THE (TV)
Gold Key: July, 1963 - No. 2, Nov, 1963
1 (10072-307) 12 24 36 82 179 275
2 (10072-311) 12 24 36 80 173 240

MIGHTY HEROES, THE (TV) (Funny)
Dell Publishing Co.: Mar, 1967 - No. 4, July, 1967
1-Also has a 1957 Heckle & Jeckle-r 10 20 30 69 147 225
2-4: 4-Has two 1958 Mighty Mouse-r 7 14 21 48 89 130

MIGHTY HEROES
Spotlight Comics: 1987 (B&W, one-shot)
1-Heckle & Jeckle backup 5.00

MIGHTY HEROES
Marvel Comics: Jan, 1998 ($2.99, one-shot)
1-Origin of the Mighty Heroes 3.00

MIGHTY LOVE
DC Comics: 2003 ($24.99/$17.95, graphic novel)
HC-($24.95) Howard Chaykin-s/a; intro. Skylark and the Iron Angel 25.00
SC-($17.95) 18.00

MIGHTY MAN (From Savage Dragon titles)
Image Comics: Dec, 2004 ($7.95, one-shot)
1-Reprints the serialized back-ups from Savage Dragon #109-118 8.00

MIGHTY MAN (From Savage Dragon)
Image Comics: Apr, 2017 ($3.99, one-shot)
1-Larsen-s/Koutsis-a; Superpatriot, Malcolm Dragon, Horridus, Barbaric, Ricochet app. 4.00

MIGHTY MARVEL TEAM-UP THRILLERS
Marvel Comics: 1983 ($5.95, trade paperback)
1-Reprints team-up stories 3 6 9 21 33 45

MIGHTY MARVEL WESTERN, THE
Marvel Comics Group (LMC earlier issues): Oct, 1968 - No. 46, Sept, 1976 (#1-14: 68 pgs.; #15,16: 52 pgs.)
1-Begin Kid Colt, Rawhide Kid, Two-Gun Kid-r 8 16 24 51 96 140
2-5: (2-14 are 68 pgs.) 4 8 12 28 47 65
6-16: (15,16 are 52 pgs.) 4 8 12 22 35 48
17-20 3 6 9 14 19 24
21-30,32,37: 24-Kid Colt-r end. 25-Matt Slade-r begin. 32-Origin-r/Rawhide Kid #23; Williamson-r/Kid Slade #7. 37-Williamson, Kirby-r/Two-Gun Kid 51
2 4 6 10 14 18
31,33-36,38-46: 31-Baker-r. 2 4 6 9 13 16
45-(30¢-c variant, limited distribution)(6/76) 9 18 27 63 129 195
NOTE: ***Jack Davis*** *a(r)-21-24.* ***Keller*** *r-1-13, 22.* ***Kirby*** *a(r)-1-3, 6, 9, 12-14, 16, 25-29, 32-38, 40, 41, 43-46; c-29.* ***Maneely*** *a(r)-22.* ***Severin*** *c-3i, 9. No Matt Slade-#43.*

MIGHTY MIDGET COMICS, THE (Miniature)
Samuel E. Lowe & Co.: No date; circa 1942-1943 (Sold 2 for 5¢, B&W and red, 36 pgs, approx. 5x4")
Bulletman #11(1943)-r/cover/Bulletman #3 16 32 48 94 147 200
Captain Marvel Adventures #11 16 32 48 94 147 200
Captain Marvel #11 (Same as above except for full color ad on back cover; this issue was glued to cover of Captain Marvel #20 and is not found in fine-mint condition)
345 690 1035 -- -- --
Captain Marvel Jr. #11 (Same-c as Master #27 16 32 48 94 147 200
Captain Marvel Jr. #11 (Same as above except for full color ad on back-c; this issue was glued to cover of Captain Marvel #21 and is not found in fine-mint condition)
345 690 1035 -- -- --
Golden Arrow #11 15 30 45 90 140 190
Golden Arrow #11 (Same as above except for full color ad on back-c; this issue was glued to cover of Captain Marvel #21 and is not found in fine-mint condition)
285 570 855 -- -- --
Ibis the Invincible #11(1942)-Origin; reprints cover to Ibis #1 (Predates Fawcett's Ibis the Invincible #1). 18 36 54 105 165 225
Spy Smasher #11(1942) 16 32 48 94 147 200
NOTE: *The above books came in a box called "box full of books" and was distributed with other Samuel Lowe puzzles, paper dolls, coloring books, etc. They are not titled Mighty Midget Comics. All have a war bond seal on back cover which is otherwise blank. These books came in a "Mighty Midget" flat cardboard counter display rack.*
Balbo, the Boy Magician #12 (1943)-1st book devoted entirely to character.
10 20 30 54 72 90
Bulletman #12 12 24 36 69 97 125
Commando Yank #12 (1943)-Only comic devoted entirely to character.
10 20 30 56 76 95
Dr. Voltz the Human Generator (1943)-Only comic devoted entirely to character.
10 20 30 54 72 90
Lance O'Casey #12 (1943)-1st comic devoted entirely to character (Predates Fawcett's Lance O'Casey #1). 10 20 30 54 72 90
Leatherneck the Marine (1943)-Only comic devoted entirely to character.
10 20 30 54 72 90
Minute Man #12 12 24 36 67 94 120
Mister "Q" (1943)-Only comic devoted entirely to character.
10 20 30 54 72 90
Mr. Scarlet and Pinky #12 (1943)-Only comic devoted entirely to character.
10 20 30 58 79 100
Pat Wilton and His Flying Fortress (1943)-1st comic devoted entirely to character. 10 20 30 54 72 90
The Phantom Eagle #12 (1943)-Only comic devoted entirely to character.
10 20 30 54 72 90
State Trooper Stops Crime (1943)-Only comic devoted entirely to character.
10 20 30 54 72 90
Tornado Tom (1943)-Origin, r/from Cyclone #1-3; only comic devoted entirely to character.
10 20 30 54 72 90

MIGHTY MORPHIN (Mighty Morphin' Power Rangers)

Mighty Avengers #3 © MAR

Mighty Morphin Power Rangers #31 © SCG PR

Mighty Thor #15 © MAR

GD 2.0 | VG 4.0 | FN 6.0 | VF 8.0 | VF/NM 9.0 | NM- 9.2

BOOM! Studios: Nov, 2020 - No. 22, Aug, 2022 ($4.99)

1-($4.99) Parrott-s/Renna-a; multiple covers 5.00
2-22-($3.99) 4-Green Ranger unmasks 4.00

MIGHTY MORPHIN POWER RANGERS (Also see Saban's Mighty Morphin' Power Rangers)
BOOM! Studios: No. 0, Jan, 2016; Mar, 2016 - No. 55, Oct, 2020; (title skips #56-#99) No. 100, Sept, 2022 - Present ($3.99)

0-Higgins-s/Prasetya-a; Rita Repulsa & Scorpina app.; multiple covers 4.00
1-24,26-49,51-55: 1-4,6-9,11-Higgins-s/Prasetya-a. 5-Silas-a. 10-Lam-a 4.00
25,50-($4.99) 25-Sold in black polybag; Tommy dies 5.00
100-(9/22, $9.99) Legacy issue #100; Death Rangers app.; art by various 10.00
101-105: 101-Rita Repulsa returns 4.00
2016 Annual 1 (8/16, $7.99) Short stories; art by Guillory, Terry Moore, Kochalka 8.00
2017 Annual 1 (5/17, $7.99) Short stories; art by Mora, Irving, Montes; 3 covers 8.00
2018 Annual 1 (4/18, $7.99) Shattered Grid; short stories; 3 covers 8.00
... FCBD 2018 Special (5/18, giveaway) Shattered Grid; Galindo-a 3.00
... Shattered Grid 1 (8/18, $7.99) Di Nicuolo & Galindo-a 8.00
... 25th Anniversary Special 1 (6/18, $7.99) Short stories; art by Quinones & others 8.00

MIGHTY MORPHIN POWER RANGERS: PINK
BOOM! Studios: Jun, 2016 - No. 6, Jan, 2017 ($3.99, limited series)

1-6-Fletcher & Thompson-s/DiNicuolo-a; multiple covers 4.00

MIGHTY MORPHIN POWER RANGERS / TEENAGE MUTANT NINJA TURTLES
BOOM! Studios: Dec, 2019 - No. 5, Jun, 2020 ($4.99/$3.99, limited series)

1-($4.99) Ryan Parrott-s/Simone di Meo-a; Shredder app.; multiple covers 5.00
2-5-($3.99) Rita Repulsa, BeBop & Rocksteady app. 4.00

MIGHTY MORPHIN POWER RANGERS / TEENAGE MUTANT NINJA TURTLES II
BOOM! Studios: Dec, 2022 - No. 5, ($4.99, limited series)

1-3-Parrott-s/Mora-a; multiple covers 5.00

MIGHTY MORPHIN' POWER RANGERS: THE MOVIE (Also see Saban's Mighty Morphin' Power Rangers)
Marvel Comics: Sept, 1995 ($3.95, one-shot)

nn-Adaptation of movie 3 6 9 14 19 24

MIGHTY MOUSE (See Adventures of..., Dell Giant #43, Giant Comics Edition, March of Comics #205, 237, 247, 257, 447, 459, 471, 483, Oxydol-Dreft, Paul Terry's, & Terry-Toons Comics)

MIGHTY MOUSE (1st Series)
Timely/Marvel Comics (20th Century Fox): Fall, 1946 - No. 4, Summer, 1947

1 213 426 639 1363 2332 3300
2 76 152 228 486 831 1175
3,4 50 100 150 315 533 750

MIGHTY MOUSE (2nd Series) (Paul Terry's... #62-71)
St. John Publishing Co./Pines No. 68 (3/56) on (TV issues #72 on):
Aug, 1947 - No. 67, 11/55; No. 68, 3/56 - No. 83, 6/59

5(#1) 74 148 222 470 810 1150
6-10: 10-Over-sized issue 26 52 78 156 256 350
11-19 15 30 45 90 140 190
20 (11/50) - 25-(52 pg. editions) 14 28 42 76 108 140
20-25-(36 pg. editions) 12 24 36 67 94 120
26-37: 35-Flying saucer-c 11 22 33 62 86 110
38-45-(100 pgs.) 20 40 60 120 195 270
46-83: 62-64,67-Painted-c. 82-Infinity-c 10 20 30 58 79 100
Album nn (nd, 1952/53?, St. John)(100 pgs.)(Rebound issues w/new cover)
28 56 84 165 270 375
Album 1(10/52, 25¢, 100 pgs., St. John)-Gandy Goose app.
36 72 108 216 351 485
Album 2,3(11/52 & 12/52, St. John) (100 pgs.) 27 54 81 158 259 360
Fun Club Magazine 1(Fall, 1957-Pines, 25¢, 100 pgs.) (CBS TV)-Tom Terrific, Heckle & Jeckle, Dinky Duck, Gandy Goose 20 40 60 120 195 270
Fun Club Magazine 2-6(Winter, 1958-Pines) 12 24 36 67 94 120
3-D 1-(1st printing-9/53, 25¢)(St. John)-Came w/glasses; stiff covers; says World's First! on-c; 1st 3-D comic 29 58 87 170 278 385
3-D 1-(2nd printing-10/53, 25¢)-Came w/glasses; slick, glossy covers, slightly smaller
20 40 60 114 182 250
3-D 2,3(11/53, 12/53, 25¢)-(St. John)-With glasses 20 40 60 114 182 250

MIGHTY MOUSE (TV)(3rd Series)(Formerly Adventures of Mighty Mouse)
Gold Key/Dell Publ. Co. No. 166-on: No. 161, Oct, 1964 - No. 172, Oct, 1968

161(10/64)-165(9/65)-(Becomes Adventures of... No. 166 on)
4 8 12 28 47 65
166(3/66), 167(6/66)-172 3 6 9 20 31 42

MIGHTY MOUSE (TV)
Spotlight Comics: 1987 - No. 2, 1987 ($1.50, color)

1,2-New stories 4.00
...And Friends Holiday Special (11/87, $1.75) 4.00

MIGHTY MOUSE (TV)
Marvel Comics: Oct, 1990 - No. 10, July, 1991 ($1.00)(Based on Sat. cartoon)

1-10: 1-Dark Knight-c parody. 2-10: 3-Intro Bat-Bat; Byrne-c. 4,5-Crisis-c/story parodies w/Perez-c. 6-Spider-Man-c parody. 7-Origin Bat-Bat 3.00

MIGHTY MOUSE (TV)
Dynamite Entertainment: 2017 - No. 5, 2017 ($3.99)

1-5: 1-Multiple covers incl. Alex Ross & Neal Adams; Mighty Mouse in the real world 4.00

MIGHTY MOUSE ADVENTURE MAGAZINE
Spotlight Comics: 1987 ($2.00, B&W, 52 pgs., magazine size, one-shot)

1-Deputy Dawg, Heckle & Jeckle backup stories 5.00

MIGHTY MOUSE ADVENTURES (Adventures of... #2 on)
St. John Publishing Co.: November, 1951

1 43 86 129 271 461 650

MIGHTY MOUSE ADVENTURE STORIES (Paul Terry's... on-c only)
St. John Publishing Co.: 1953 (50¢, 384 pgs.)

nn-Rebound issues 63 126 189 403 689 975

MIGHTY MUTANIMALS (See Teenage Mutant Ninja Turtles Adventures #19)
May, 1991 - No. 3, July, 1991 ($1.00, limited series)
Archie Comics: Apr, 1992 - No. 9, June, 1993 ($1.25)

1-3: 1-Story cont'd from TMNT Advs. #19. 1 2 3 5 6 8
1-4 (1992) 1 2 3 5 6 8
5-9: 7-1st app. Merdude 2 4 6 8 10 12

MIGHTY SAMSON (Also see Gold Key Champion)
Gold Key/Whitman #32: July, 1964 - No. 20, Nov, 1969; No. 21, Aug, 1972; No. 22, Dec, 1973 - No. 31, Mar, 1976; No. 32, Aug, 1982 (Painted-c #1-31)

1-Origin/1st app.; Thorne-a begins 9 18 27 62 126 190
2-5 5 10 15 30 50 70
6-10: 7-Tom Morrow begins, ends #20 3 6 9 21 33 45
11-20 3 6 9 17 25 34
21-31: 21,22-r 2 4 6 13 18 22
32(Whitman, 8/82)-r 2 4 6 8 11 14

MIGHTY SAMSON
Dark Horse Comics: Dec, 2010 - No. 4, Oct, 2011 ($3.50)

1-4: 1-Origin retold; Shooter & Vaughn-s/Olliffe-a/Swanland-c; r/1st app. from 1964 3.50
1-Variant-c by Olliffe 4.00

MIGHTY THOR, THE (Continues in Thor; God of Thunder)
Marvel Comics: Jun, 2011 - No. 22, Dec, 2012 ($3.99)

1-Fraction-s/Coipel-a; Silver Surfer app.; bonus concept art from the movie 4.00
1-Variant-c by Charest 6.00
1-Variant-c by Simonson 10.00
2-22: 3-6-Galactus app. 7-Fear Itself tie-in; Odin's 1st battle vs. the Serpent. 8-Tanarus. 13-17-Simonson-c. 18-21-Alan Davis-a 4.00
12.1 (6/12, $2.99) Kitson-a/Coipel-c; flashbacks from Volstagg & Sif 3.00
Annual 1 (8/12, $4.99) Silver Surfer & Galactus app.; DeMatteis-s/Elson-a 5.00

MIGHTY THOR (Jane Foster as Thor)
Marvel Comics: Jan, 2016 - No. 23, Nov, 2017; No. 700, Dec, 2017 - No. 706, Jun, 2018 ($4.99/$3.99)

1-($4.99) Tri-fold cover; Aaron-s/Dauterman-a; Loki app. 5.00
2-23-($3.99) 3-Multiple Lokis app. 12-Origin of Mjolnir; Frazer Irving-a. 14-Epting-a. 20-Volstagg becomes the War Thor 4.00
[Title switches to legacy numbering after #23 (11/17)]
700-(12/17, $5.99) Aaron-s; art by various incl. Dauterman, Simonson, Acuna, Coipel 6.00
701-706: 701-Mangog vs. War Thor; Harren-a. 703-706-Dauterman-a 4.00
...: At the Gates of Valhalla 1 (7/18, $4.99) Intro Goddesses of Thunder; Bartel-a 5.00
... 3D #1 (6/19, $7.99, polybagged with 3D glasses) r/#1 in 3D; wraparound-c 8.00

MIGHTY VALKYRIES, THE
Marvel Comics: Jun, 2021 - No. 5, Nov, 2021 ($4.99/$3.99, limited series)

1-($4.99) Aaron & Gronbekk-s/De Iulis & D'Urso-a; Jane Foster, Loki and Hela app. 5.00
2-5-($3.99) Kraven the Hunter app. 4.00

MIKE BARNETT, MAN AGAINST CRIME (TV)
Fawcett Publications: Dec, 1951 - No. 6, Oct, 1952

1 25 50 75 150 245 340
2 15 30 45 88 137 185
3,4,6 14 28 42 81 118 155
5- "Market for Morphine" cover/story 19 38 57 111 176 240

	GD	VG	FN	VF	VF/NM	NM-
	2.0	4.0	6.0	8.0	9.0	9.2

MIKE DANGER (See Mickey Spillane's...)

MIKE DEODATO'S...
Caliber Comics: 1996, ($2.95, B&W)

...**FALLOUT 3000** #1, ...**JONAS** (mag. size) #1,...**PRIME CUTS** (mag. size) #1, ...**PROTHEUS** #1,2, ...**RAMTHAR** #1,...**RAZOR NIGHTS** #1 3.00

MIKE GRELL'S SABLE (Also see Jon Sable & Sable)
First Comics: Mar, 1990 - No. 10, Dec, 1990 ($1.75)

1-10: r/Jon Sable Freelance #1-10 by Grell 3.00

MIKE MIST MINUTE MIST-ERIES (See Ms. Tree/Mike Mist in 3-D)
Eclipse Comics: April, 1981 ($1.25, B&W, one-shot)

1 3.00

MIKE SHAYNE PRIVATE EYE
Dell Publishing Co.: Nov-Jan, 1962 - No. 3, Sept-Nov, 1962

	GD	VG	FN	VF	VF/NM	NM-
1	4	8	12	27	44	60
2,3	3	6	9	16	24	32

MILES MORALES & MOON GIRL (Continues in Avengers & Moon Girl)
Marvel Comics: Aug, 2022 ($4.99, one-shot)

1-Mashigo-s/Guara-a; Devil Dinosaur goes missing; Taskmaster app. 5.00

MILES MORALES: SPIDER-MAN
Marvel Comics: Feb, 2019 - No. 42, Nov, 2022 ($3.99)

	GD	VG	FN	VF	VF/NM	NM-
1-Ahmed-s/Garrón-a; Rhino app.	4	8	12	28	47	65
2,4,8,9,11,12,14-24,26-29: 20,21-Captain America app. 23-"King in Black" tie-in. 26-29-Clone Saga. 29-New costume on last page						4.00
3-1st Snatcher; Captain America app.	2	4	6	11	16	20
5-Starling cameo	3	6	9	14	21	26
6-Starling 1st full app.	4	8	12	23	37	50
7-1st Quantum	3	6	9	17	25	34
10-1st Ultimatum	3	4	6	11	16	20
13-Rhino app.; Billie Morales born	3	6	9	19	30	40
25-($4.99) The Clone Saga begins; Peter Parker app.; back-up with Bustos-a						5.00
30-($4.99) New costume; Taskmaster app.; back-up by Lord & Miller-s/Pichelli-a						5.00
31-41: 31,32-Taskmaster app. 36-Spider-Ham app.						4.00
42-($4.99) Rhino app.						5.00
Miles Morales: The End 1 (3/20, $4.99) Damion Scott-a; future Miles' last adventure						5.00

MILES MORALES: SPIDER-MAN
Marvel Comics: Feb, 2023 - Present ($3.99)

1-($4.99) Ziglar-s/Vincentini-a 5.00
2,3-($3.99) 2-Scorpion app. 4.00

MILES MORALES: ULTIMATE SPIDER-MAN
Marvel Comics: Jul, 2014 - No. 12, Jun, 2015 ($3.99)

	GD	VG	FN	VF	VF/NM	NM-
1-Bendis-s/Marquez-a; Peter Parker & Norman Osborn return	4	8	12	23	37	50
2-11: 11-Dr. Doom app.						6.00
12-Doctor Doom and the Ultimates app.; leads into Secret Wars #1	1	2	3	5	6	8

MILES TO GO
AfterShock Comics: Sept, 2020 - No. 5, Sept, 2021 ($3.99)

1-5-B. Clay Moore-s/Stephen Molnar-a 4.00

MILESTONE FOREVER
DC Comics: Apr, 2010 - No. 2, May, 2010 ($5.99, squarebound, limited series)

	GD	VG	FN	VF	VF/NM	NM-
1-McDuffie-s/Leon & Bright-a; Icon, Blood Syndicate, Hardware and Static app.	2	4	6	9	12	15
2-McDuffie-s/Leon & Bright-a						6.00

MILESTONE RETURNS: INFINITE EDITION
DC Comics: No. 0, Jul, 2021 ($4.99, one-shot)

0-Hudlin-s/Cowan & ChrisCross-a; Cowan-c 5.00

MILESTONES IN HISTORY
DC Comics: Aug, 2022 ($9.99, one-shot)

1-Short stories highlighting black achievements in history; s/a by various 10.00

MILITARY COMICS (Becomes Modern Comics #44 on)
Quality Comics Group: Aug, 1941 - No. 43, Oct, 1945

	GD	VG	FN	VF	VF/NM	NM-
1-Origin/1st app. Blackhawk by C. Cuidera (Eisner scripts); Miss America, The Death Patrol by Jack Cole (also #2-7,27-30), & The Blue Tracer by Guardineer; X of the Underground, The Yankee Eagle, Q-Boat & Shot & Shell, Archie Atkins, Loops & Banks by Bud Ernest (Bob Powell)(ends #13) begin	514	1028	1542	3750	6625	9500
2-Secret War News begins (by McWilliams #2-16); Cole-a; new uniform with yellow circle & hawk's head for Blackhawk	161	322	483	1030	1765	2500
3-Origin/1st app. Chop Chop (9/41)	129	258	387	826	1413	2000
4	106	212	318	678	1164	1650
5-The Sniper begins; Miss America in costume #4-7	97	194	291	621	1061	1500
6-9: 8-X of the Underground begins (ends #13). 9-The Phantom Clipper begins (ends #16)	74	148	222	470	810	1150
10-Classic Eisner-c	103	206	309	659	1130	1600
11-Flag-c	77	154	231	493	847	1200
12-Blackhawk by Crandall begins, ends #22	77	154	231	493	847	1200
13-15: 14-Private Dogtag begins (ends #83)	60	120	180	381	653	925
16-20: 16-Blue Tracer ends. 17-P.T. Boat begins	54	108	162	343	574	825
21-31: 22-Last Crandall Blackhawk. 23-Shrunken head-c. 27-Death Patrol revived. 28-True story of Mussolini	48	96	144	302	514	725
32-43	42	84	126	265	445	625

NOTE: *Berg a-6.* *Al Bryant c-31-34, 38, 40-43.* *J. Cole a-1-3, 27-32.* *Crandall a-12-22; c-13-20.* *Cuidera c-2-9. Eisner c-1, 2(part), 9, 10.* *Kotsky c-21-29, 35, 37, 39.* *McWilliams a-2-16.* *Powell a-1-13.* *Ward Blackhawk-30, 31(15 pgs. each); c-30.*

MILK AND CHEESE (Also see Cerebus Bi-Weekly #20)
Slave Labor: 1991 - No. 7, Jan, 1997 ($2.50, B&W)

	GD	VG	FN	VF	VF/NM	NM-
1-Evan Dorkin story & art in all	5	10	15	35	63	90
1-2nd-6th printings						5.00
2-"Other #1"	3	6	9	16	24	32
2-reprint						3.00
3-"Third #1"	2	4	6	11	16	20
4-"Fourth #1", 5-"First Second Issue"	1	3	4	6	8	10
6,7: 6-"#666"						5.00

NOTE: *Multiple printings of all issues exist and are worth cover price unless listed here.*

MILKMAN MURDERS, THE
Dark Horse Comics: Jun, 2004 - No. 4, Aug, 2004 ($2.99, limited series)

1-4-Casey-s/Parkhouse-a 3.00

MILLARWORLD (Mark Millar characters)
Image Comics: Jul, 2016; Sept, 2017 ($2.99)

...Annual 2016 1 (7/16) Short stories of Kick-Ass, Hit-Girl, Chrononauts and others 3.00
...Annual 2017 1 (9/17) Short stories of Kick-Ass, Superior, Huck, Nemesis and others 3.00

MILLENNIUM
DC Comics: Jan, 1988 - No. 8, Feb, 1988 (Weekly limited series)

1-Englehart-s/Staton c/a(p) 4.00
2-8 3.00
TPB (2008, $19.99) r/#1-8 20.00

MILLENNIUM (TV, spin-off from The X-Files)
IDW Publishing: Jan, 2015 - No. 5, May, 2015 ($3.99, limited series)

1-5: 1-Frank Black & Agent Mulder app.; Joe Harris-s/Colin Lorimer-a; three covers 4.00

MILLENNIUM EDITION:... (Reprints of classic DC issues, plus some WildStorm and non-DC issues with characters now published by DC)
DC Comics: Feb, 2000 - Feb, 2001 (gold foil cover stamps)

Action Comics #1, Adventure Comics #61, All Star Comics #3, All Star Comics #8, Batman #1, Detective Comics #1, Detective Comics #27, Detective Comics #38, Flash Comics #1, Military Comics #1, More Fun Comics #73, Police Comics #1, Sensation Comics #1, Superman #1, Whiz Comics #2, Wonder Woman #1 -($3.95-c) 5.00
Action Comics #252, Adventure Comics #247, Brave and the Bold #28, Brave and the Bold #85, Crisis on Infinite Earths #1, Detective #225, Detective #327, Detective #359, Detective #395, Flash #123, Gen13 #1, Green Lantern #76, House of Mystery #1, House of Secrets #92, JLA #1, Justice League #1, Mad #1, Man of Steel #1, Mysterious Suspense #1, New Gods, #1, New Teen Titans #1, Our Army at War #81, Plop! #1, Saga of the Swamp Thing #21, Shadow #1, Showcase #4, Showcase #9, Showcase #22, Superman #233, Superman (2nd) #75, Superman's Pal Jimmy Olsen #1, Watchmen #1, WildC.A.T.s #1, Wonder Woman (2nd) #1, World's Finest #71 -($2.50-c) 4.00
All-Star Western #10, Hellblazer #1, More Fun Comics #101, Preacher #1, Sandman #1, Spirit #1, Superboy #1, Superman #76, Young Romance #1-($2.95-c) 4.00
Batman: The Dark Knight Returns #1, Kingdom Come #1 -($5.95-c) 6.00
All Star Comics #3, Batman #1, Justice League #1: Chromium cover 12.00
Crisis on Infinite Earths #1 Chromium cover 20.00

MILLENNIUM FEVER
DC Comics (Vertigo): Oct, 1995 - No.4, Jan, 1996 ($2.50, limited series)

1-4: Duncan Fegredo-c/a 3.00

MILLENNIUM: THE GIRL WHO DANCED WITH DEATH
Titan Comics: Sept, 2018 - No. 3, Nov, 2018 ($5.99, limited series)

1-3-Adaptation of the Stieg Larsson novel; Runberg-s/Ortega-a 6.00

MILLENNIUM: THE GIRL WHO KICKED THE HORNET'S NEST
Titan Comics: Jan, 2018 - No. 2, Feb, 2018 ($5.99, limited series)

1,2-Adaptation of the Stieg Larsson novel; Runberg-s. 1-Homs-a. 2-Carot-a 6.00

MILLENNIUM: THE GIRL WHO PLAYED WITH FIRE
Titan Comics: Oct, 2017 - No. 2, Nov, 2017 ($5.99, limited series)

1,2-Adaptation of the Stieg Larsson novel; Runberg-s. 1-Gonzalez-a. 2-Carot-a 6.00

MILLENNIUM: THE GIRL WITH THE DRAGON TATTOO
Titan Comics: Jul, 2017 - No. 2, Aug, 2017 ($5.99, limited series)

1,2-Adaptation of the Stieg Larsson novel; Runberg-s/Homs-a 6.00

MILLENNIUM 2.5 A.D.
ACG Comics: No. 1, 2000 ($2.95)

1-Reprints 1934 Buck Rogers daily strips #1-48 3.00

MILLIE, THE LOVABLE MONSTER
Dell Publishing Co.: Sept-Nov, 1962 - No. 6, Jan, 1973

	GD	VG	FN	VF	VF/NM	NM-
12-523-211-Bill Woggon c/a in all	5	10	15	31	53	75
2(8-10/63)	4	8	12	28	47	65
3(8-10/64)	4	8	12	25	40	55
4(7/72), 5(10/72), 6(1/73)	3	6	9	14	19	24

NOTE: *Woggon a-3-6; c-3-6. 4 reprints 1; 5 reprints 2; 6 reprints 3.*

MILLIE THE MODEL (See Comedy Comics, A Date With..., Joker Comics #28, Life With..., Mad About..., Marvel Mini-Books, Misty & Modeling With...)
Marvel/Atlas/Marvel Comics(CnPC #1)(SPI/Male/VPI):1945 - No. 207, Dec, 1973

	GD	VG	FN	VF	VF/NM	NM-
1-Origin	383	766	1149	2681	4691	6700
2 (10/46)-Millie becomes The Blonde Phantom to sell Blonde Phantom perfume; a pre-Blonde Phantom app. (see All-Select #11, Fall, 1946)	181	362	543	1158	1979	2800
3-8,10: 4-7-Willie app. 7-Willie smokes extra strong tobacco. 8,10-Kurtzman's "Hey Look". 8-Willie & Rusty app.	60	120	180	381	653	925
9-Powerhouse Pepper by Wolverton, 4 pgs.	84	168	252	538	919	1300
11-Kurtzman-a, "Giggles 'n' Grins"	43	86	129	271	461	650
12,15,17,19,20: 12-Rusty & Hedy Devine app.	41	82	123	256	428	600
13,14,16,18: 13,14,16-Kurtzman's "Hey Look". 13-Hedy Devine app. 18-Dan DeCarlo-a begins	36	72	108	211	343	475
21-30	33	66	99	194	317	440
31-40	18	36	54	125	276	430
41-60: 47-Millie's 3-D poses	17	34	51	117	259	400
61-80	15	30	45	105	233	360
81-99: 93-Last DeCarlo issue?	12	24	36	79	170	260
100	12	24	36	83	182	280
101-106,108-130	8	16	24	51	96	140
107-Jack Kirby app. in story	8	16	24	54	102	150

Miles Morales: Spider-Man #17 © MAR

Mind MGMT #13 © Matt Kindt

Miracleman #23 © ECL

	GD 2.0	VG 4.0	FN 6.0	VF 8.0	VF/NM 9.0	NM- 9.2
131-134,136,138-153: 141-Groovy Gears-c/s	5	10	15	35	63	90
135-(2/66) 1st app. Groovy Gears	7	14	21	44	82	120
137-2nd app. Groovy Gears	6	12	18	38	69	100
154-New Millie begins (10/67)	7	14	21	49	92	135
155-190	5	10	15	35	63	90
191,193-199,201-206	5	10	15	33	57	80
192-(52 pgs.)	5	10	15	35	63	90
200,207(Last issue)	5	10	15	35	63	90
(Beware: cut-up pages are common in all Annuals)						
Annual 1(1962)-Early Marvel annual (2nd?)	38	76	114	285	641	1000
Annual 2(1963)	20	40	60	144	317	490
Annual 3-5 (1964-1966)	10	20	30	64	132	200
Annual 6-10(1967-11/71)	8	16	24	54	102	150
Queen-Size 11(9/74), 12(1975)	7	14	21	48	89	130

NOTE: *Dan DeCarlo a-18-93.*

MILLION DOLLAR DIGEST (Richie Rich... #23 on; also see Richie Rich...)
Harvey Publications: 11/86 - No. 7, 11/87; No. 8, 4/88 - No. 34, Nov, 1994 ($1.25/$1.75, digest size)

	GD 2.0	VG 4.0	FN 6.0	VF 8.0	VF/NM 9.0	NM- 9.2
1	1	2	3	5	6	8
2-8: 8-(68 pgs.)						6.00
9-20: 9-Begin $1.75-c. 14-May not exist	1	2	3	4	5	7
21-34	1	3	4	6	8	10

MILT GROSS FUNNIES (Also see Picture News #1)
Milt Gross, Inc. (ACG?): Aug, 1947 - No. 2, Sept, 1947

	GD 2.0	VG 4.0	FN 6.0	VF 8.0	VF/NM 9.0	NM- 9.2
1	31	62	93	186	303	420
2	21	42	63	122	199	275

MILTON THE MONSTER & FEARLESS FLY (TV)
Gold Key: May, 1966

	GD 2.0	VG 4.0	FN 6.0	VF 8.0	VF/NM 9.0	NM- 9.2
1 (10175-605)	9	18	27	57	111	165

MINDFIELD
Aspen MLT: No. 0, May, 2010 - No. 6, Sept, 2011 ($2.50/$2.99)

	NM- 9.2
0-($2.50) Krul-s/Konat-a; 3 covers	3.00
1-6-($2.99) Multiples covers on each	3.00

MIND MGMT
Dark Horse Comics: May, 2012 - No. 35, Jul, 2015 ($3.99)

	NM- 9.2
1-Matt Kindt-s/a/c	30.00
2-6	10.00
7-35	4.00
#0 (11/12, $2.99) Prints background stories from Mind MGMT Secret Files digital site	3.00
New MGMT#1/Mind Mgmt #36 (8/15, $3.99) Series conclusion	4.00

MIND MGMT: BOOTLEG
Dark Horse Comics: Jul, 2022 - No. 4, Oct, 2022 ($3.99)

	NM- 9.2
1-4-Matt Kindt-s. 1-Dalrymple-a. 2-Lesniewski-a. 3-Dave Rubin-a. 4-Jill Thompson-a	4.00

MIND THE GAP
Image Comics: May, 2012 - No. 17, May, 2014 ($2.99)

	NM- 9.2
1-17: 1-8,10-McCann-s/Esquejo-a/c. 9-McDaid-a. 11,12-Basri-a	3.00

MINIMUM CARNAGE
Marvel Comics: Dec, 2012 - Jan, 2013 ($3.99, limited series)

	NM- 9.2
...: Alpha (12/12) Venom, Carnage and Scarlet Spider app.; Medina-a/Crain-c	4.00
...: Omega (1/13) The Enigma Force in the Microverse app.	4.00

MINIMUM WAGE
Fantagraphics Books: V1#1, July, 1995 ($9.95, B&W, graphic novel, mature)
V2#1, 1995 - 1997 ($2.95, B&W, mature)

	GD 2.0	VG 4.0	FN 6.0	VF 8.0	VF/NM 9.0	NM- 9.2
V1#1-Bob Fingerman story & art	1	3	4	6	8	10
V2#1-9($2.95): Bob Fingerman story & art. 2-Kevin Nowlan back-c. 4-w/pin-ups. 5-Mignola back-c						3.00
Book Two TPB ('97, $12.95) r/V2#1-5						13.00

MINIMUM WAGE
Image Comics: Jan, 2014 - No. 6, Jun, 2014 ($3.50, B&W&Green, mature)

	NM- 9.2
1-6-Bob Fingerman story & art; story resumes in May 2000	3.50

MINIMUM WAGE: SO MANY BAD DECISIONS
Image Comics: May, 2015 - No. 6, Oct, 2015 ($3.99, B&W&Green/color pages, mature)

	NM- 9.2
1-6-Bob Fingerman story & art. 3-Marc Maron app.	4.00

MINIONS (From Despicable Me movies)
Titan Comics: Jul, 2015 - No. 2, Aug, 2015 ($3.99, limited series)

	NM- 9.2
1,2-Short stories and one-page gags; Ah-Koon-s/Collin-a	4.00

MINIONS: MINI BOSS (From Despicable Me movies)
Titan Comics: May, 2022 - No. 2, Jun, 2022 ($3.99, limited series)

	NM- 9.2
1,2-Minions and young Gru; short stories and one-page gags; Lapuss-s/Collin-a	4.00

MINIONS PAELLA! (From Despicable Me movies)
Titan Comics: Nov, 2019 - No. 2, Dec, 2019 ($3.99, limited series)

	NM- 9.2
1,2-Short stories and one-page gags; Lapuss-s/Collin-a	4.00

MINIONS SPORTS! (From Despicable Me movies)
Titan Comics: Apr, 2020 - No. 2, May, 2021 ($3.99, limited series)

	NM- 9.2
1,2-Short stories and one-page gags; Lapuss-s/Collin-a	4.00

MINIONS VIVA LE BOSS! (From Despicable Me movies)
Titan Comics: Nov, 2018 - No. 2, Jan, 2018 ($3.99, limited series)

	NM- 9.2
1,2-Short stories and one-page gags; Lapuss-s/Collin-a	4.00

MINISTRY OF SPACE
Image Comics: Apr, 2001 - No. 3, Apr, 2004 ($2.95, limited series)

	NM- 9.2
1-3-Warren Ellis-s/Chris Weston-a	3.00
...Vol. 1 Omnibus (3/04, $4.95) r/1&2	5.00
TPB (12/04, $12.95) r/series; sketch & design pages; intro by Mark Millar	13.00

MINKY WOODCOCK: THE GIRL WHO ELECTRIFIED TESLA
Titan Comics: May, 2021 - No. 4, Aug, 2021 ($3.99, limited series)

	NM- 9.2
1-4-Cynthia Von Buhler-s/a; multiple covers on each	4.00

MINKY WOODCOCK: THE GIRL WHO HANDCUFFED HOUDINI
Titan Comics: Nov, 2017 - No. 4, May, 2018 ($3.99, limited series)

	NM- 9.2
1-4-Cynthia Von Buhler-s/a. 1-Covers by Mack, McGinnis, Von Buhler & photo	4.00

MINOR MIRACLES
DC Comics: 2000 ($12.95, B&W, squarebound)

	NM- 9.2
nn-Will Eisner-s/a	13.00

MINOR THREATS
Dark Horse Comics: Aug, 2022 - No. 4, Feb, 2023 ($4.99, limited series)

	NM- 9.2
1-4-Patton Oswalt & Jordan Blum-s/Scott Hepburn-a	5.00

MINUTE MAN (See Master Comics & Mighty Midget Comics)
Fawcett Publications: Summer, 1941 - No. 3, Spring, 1942 (68 pgs.)

	GD 2.0	VG 4.0	FN 6.0	VF 8.0	VF/NM 9.0	NM- 9.2
1	239	478	717	1530	2615	3700
2-Japanese invade NYC Statue of Liberty WWII-c	174	348	522	1114	1907	2700
3	135	270	405	864	1482	2100

MINX, THE
DC Comics (Vertigo): Oct, 1998 - No. 8, May, 1999 ($2.50, limited series)

	NM- 9.2
1-8-Milligan-s/Phillips-c/a	3.00

MIRACLE COMICS
Hillman Periodicals: Feb, 1940 - No. 4, Mar, 1941

	GD 2.0	VG 4.0	FN 6.0	VF 8.0	VF/NM 9.0	NM- 9.2
1-Sky Wizard Master of Space, Dash Dixon, Man of Might, Pinkie Parker, Dusty Doyle, The Kid Cop, K-7, Secret Agent, The Scorpion, & Blandu, Jungle Queen begin; Masked Angel only app. (all 1st app.)	343	686	1029	2400	4200	6000
2-Classic Sky Wizard-c	239	478	717	1530	2615	3700
3,4: 3-Devil-c; Bill Colt, the Ghost Rider begins. 4-The Veiled Prophet & Bullet Bob (by Burnley) app.	168	336	504	1075	1838	2600

MIRACLEMAN
Eclipse Comics: Aug, 1985 - No. 15, Nov, 1988; No. 16, Dec, 1989 - No. 24, Aug, 1993

	GD 2.0	VG 4.0	FN 6.0	VF 8.0	VF/NM 9.0	NM- 9.2
1-r/British Marvelman series; Alan Moore scripts in #1-16	3	6	9	19	30	40
1-Gold variant (edition of 400, same as regular comic, but signed by Alan Moore, came with signed & #'d gold certificate of authenticity)	38	76	114	285	641	1000
1-Blue variant (edition of 600, comic came with signed blue certificate of authenticity)	34	68	102	245	548	850
2-8,10: 8-Airboy preview. 6,9,10-Origin Miracleman. 10-Snyder-c	1	2	3	5	6	8
9-Shows graphic scenes of childbirth	2	4	6	8	10	12
11-14(5/87-4/88) Totleben-a	2	4	6	11	16	20
15-($1.75-c, low print) death of Kid Miracleman	7	14	21	44	82	120
16-Last Alan Moore-s; 1st $1.95-c (low print)	3	6	9	17	25	34
17-22: 17-"The Golden Age" begins, ends #22. Dave McKean-c begins, end #22; Neil Gaiman scripts in #17-24	2	4	6	11	16	20
23-"The Silver Age" begins; Barry W. Smith-c	3	6	9	19	30	40
24-Last issue; Smith-c	3	6	9	19	30	40
3-D #1 (12/85)	2	4	6	8	10	12
3-D #1 Blue variant (edition of 99)	3	6	9	21	33	45
3-D #1 Gold variant (edition of 199)	3	6	9	16	23	30

NOTE: *Miracleman 3-D #1 (12/85) (2D edition) Interior is the same as the 3-D version except in non 3-D format. Indicia are the same for both versions of the book with only the non 3-D art distinguishing this book from the standard 3-D version. Standard 3-D edition has house ad mentioning the non 3-D edition. Two known copies exist, one in the Michigan State University Special Collection Department. (No known sales)*

Book One: A Dream of Flying (1988, $9.95, TPB) r/#1-5; Leach-c 25.00
Book One: A Dream of Flying-Hardcover (1988, $29.95) r/#1-5 70.00
Book Two: The Red King Syndrome (1990, $12.95, TPB) r/#6-10; Bolton-c 30.00
Book Two: The Red King Syndrome-Hardcover (1990, $30.95) r/#6-10 85.00
Book Three: Olympus (1990, $12.95, TPB) r/#11-16 130.00
Book Three: Olympus-Hardcover (1990, $30.95) r/#11-16 250.00
Book Four: The Golden Age (1992, $15.95, TPB) r/#17-22 30.00
Book Four: The Golden Age Hardcover (1992, $33.95) r/#17-22 50.00
Book Four: The Golden Age (1993, $12.99, TPB) new McKean-c 15.00

NOTE: Eclipse archive copies exist for #4,5,8,17,23. Each has a small Miracleman image foil-stamped on the cover. ***Chaykin*** *c-3.* ***Gulacy*** *c-7.* ***McKean*** *c-17-22.* ***B. Smith*** *c-23, 24.* ***Starlin*** *c-4.* ***Totleben*** *a-11-13; c-9, 11-13.* ***Truman*** *c-6.*

MIRACLEMAN
Marvel Comics: Mar, 2014 - No. 16, May, 2015 ($5.99/$4.99)

1-($5.99) Remastered reprints of Miracleman #1 and stories from Warrior #1&2; interview with Mick Anglo; reprints of 1950s Marvelman stories; Quesada-c 6.00
2-15: 2-($4.99) R/Warrior #3-5 and Kid Marvelman debut (1955) 5.00
16-($5.99) End of Book Three; bonus pencil art and design sketches 6.00
All-New Miracleman Annual 1 (2/15, $4.99) New stories; Morrison-s/Quesada-a and Milligan-s/Allred-a; bonus script and art pages 5.00

MIRACLEMAN
Marvel Comics: No. 0, Dec, 2022 ($5.99)

0-($5.99) Short stories by Gaiman/Buckingham, Stegman, Momoko, Aaron/Yu 6.00

MIRACLEMAN: APOCRYPHA
Eclipse Comics: Nov, 1991 - No. 3, Feb, 1992 ($2.50, limited series)

1-3: 1-Stories by Neil Gaiman, Mark Buckingham, Alex Ross & others. 3-Stories by James Robinson, Kelley Jones, Matt Wagner, Neil Gaiman, Mark Buckingham & others
1 2 3 4 5 7
TPB (12/92, $15.95) r/#1-3; Buckingham-c 20.00

MIRACLEMAN BY GAIMAN & BUCKINGHAM (The Golden Age)
Marvel Comics: Nov, 2015 - No. 6, Mar, 2016 ($4.99)

1-6-Remastered reprints of Miracleman #17-22 with bonus script and art pages 5.00

MIRACLEMAN BY GAIMAN & BUCKINGHAM: THE SILVER AGE
Marvel Comics: Dec, 2022 - Present ($4.99)

1-4: 1-Remastered Miracleman #23 with bonus script and art pages. 2-Remastered #24. 3,4-Continuation of story 5.00

MIRACLEMAN FAMILY
Eclipse Comics: May, 1988 - No. 2, Sept, 1988 ($1.95, lim. series, Baxter paper)

1,2: 2-Gulacy-c 5.00

MIRACLE OF THE WHITE STALLIONS, THE (See Movie Comics)

MIRROR'S EDGE (Based on the EA video game)
DC Comics (WildStorm): Dec, 2008 - No. 6, Jun, 2009 ($3.99, limited series)

1-6: 1-Origin of Faith; Rhianna Pratchett-s/Matthew Dow Smith-a 4.00
TPB (2009, $19.99) r/#1-6 20.00

MIRROR'S EDGE: EXORDIUM (Based on the EA video game)
Dark Horse Comics: Sept, 2015 - No. 6, Feb, 2016 ($3.99, limited series)

1-6: 1-Emgård-s/Häggström & Sammelin-a 4.00

MISADVENTURES OF ADAM WEST, THE
Bluewater Comics: Jul, 2011 - Feb, 2012 ($3.99)

1-4: 1-Two covers; co-created by Adam West 4.00
Second series 1-3 (1/12 - No. 3, 2/12) 4.00

MISADVENTURES OF MERLIN JONES, THE (See Movie Comics & Merlin Jones as the Monkey's Uncle under Movie Comics)

MISFIT CITY
BOOM! Studios (BOOM! Box): May, 2017 - No. 8, Dec, 2017 ($3.99)

1-8-Kirsten Smith & Kurt Lustgarten-s/Naomi Franquiz-a 4.00

MISPLACED
Image Comics: May, 2003 - No. 4, Dec, 2004 ($2.95)

1-4: 1-Three covers by Blaylock, Green and Clugston-Major; Blaylock-s/a 3.00
... @17 (12/04, $4.95) Nara from "Dead @17 " app.; Blaylock-s/a 5.00

MISS AMERICA COMICS (Miss America Magazine #2 on; also see Blonde Phantom & Marvel Mystery Comics)
Marvel Comics (20CC): 1944 (one-shot)

1-2 pgs. pin-ups 423 846 1269 3000 5250 7500

MISS AMERICA COMICS 70th ANNIVERARY SPECIAL
Marvel Comics: Aug, 2009 ($3.99, one-shot)

1-Eaglesham-c; new Miss America & Whizzer story; reps. from All Winners #9-11 5.00

MISS AMERICA MAGAZINE (Formerly Miss America; Miss America #51 on)
Miss America Publ. Corp./Marvel/Atlas (MAP): V1#2, Nov, 1944 - No. 93, Nov, 1958

V1#2-Photo-c of teenage girl in Miss America costume; Miss America, Patsy Walker (intro.) comic stories plus movie reviews & stories; intro. Buzz Baxter & Hedy Wolfe; 1 pg. origin Miss America 371 742 1113 2600 4550 6500
3-5-Miss America & Patsy Walker stories 116 232 348 742 1271 1800
6-Patsy Walker only 71 142 213 454 777 1100
V2#1(4/45)-6(9/45)-Patsy Walker continues 29 58 81 172 281 390
V3#1(10/45)-6(4/46) 22 44 66 132 216 300
V4#1(5/46),2,5(9/46) 20 40 60 115 185 255
V4#3(7/46)-Liz Taylor photo-c 54 108 162 343 574 825
V4#4 (8/46; 68 pgs.), V4#6 (10/46; 92 pgs.) 24 48 72 144 237 330
V5#1(11/46)-6(4/47), V6#1(5/47)-3(7/47) 18 36 54 105 165 225
V7#1(8/47)-23(#56, 6/49) 17 34 51 100 158 215
V7#24(#57, 7/49)-Kamen-a (becomes Best Western #58 on?) 18 36 54 105 165 225
V7#25(8/49), 27-44(3/52), VII,nn(5/52) 16 32 48 96 151 205
V7#26(9/49)-All comics 18 36 54 105 165 225
V1,nn(7/52)-V1,nn(1/53)(#46-49), V7#50(Spring '53), V1#51-V7?#54(7/53), 55-93 16 32 48 92 144 195

NOTE: Photo-c #1, 4, V2#1, 4, 5, V3#5, V4#3, 4, 6, V7#15, 16, 24, 26, 34, 37, 38. Painted c-3. ***Powell*** *a-V7#31.*

MISS BEVERLY HILLS OF HOLLYWOOD (See Adventures of Bob Hope)
National Periodical Publ.: Mar-Apr, 1949 - No. 9, July-Aug, 1950 (52 pgs.)

1 (Meets Alan Ladd) 77 154 231 493 847 1200
2-William Holden photo on-c 53 106 159 334 567 800
3-5: 2-9-Part photo-c. 5-Bob Hope photo on-c 43 86 129 271 461 650
6,7,9: 6-Lucille Ball photo on-c 40 80 120 246 411 575
8-Reagan photo on-c 45 90 135 284 480 675

NOTE: Beverly meets Alan Ladd in #1, Eve Arden #2, Betty Hutton #4, Bob Hope #5.

MISS CAIRO JONES
Croyden Publishers: 1945

1-Bob Oksner daily newspaper-r (1st strip story); lingerie panels 41 82 123 256 428 600

MISS FURY
Adventure Comics: 1991 - No. 4, 1991 ($2.50, limited series)

1-4: 1-Origin; granddaughter of original Miss Fury 5.00
1-Limited ed. ($4.95) 6.00

MISS FURY
Dynamite Entertainment: 2013 - No. 11, 2014 ($3.99)

1-11: 1-Multiple covers on all; Herbert-a; origin 4.00

MISS FURY (VOLUME 2)
Dynamite Entertainment: 2016 - No. 5, 2016 ($3.99, limited series)

1-5-Corinna Bechko-s/Jonathan Lau-a; covers by Lotay & Lau 4.00

MISS FURY COMICS (Newspaper strip reprints)
Timely Comics (NPI 1/CmPI 2/MPC 3-8): Winter, 1942-43 - No. 8, Winter, 1946 (Published twice a year)

1-Origin Miss Fury by Tarpe' Mills (68 pgs.) in costume w/paper dolls with cut-out costumes 622 1244 1866 4541 8021 11,500
2-(60 pgs.)-In costume w/paper dolls; hooded Nazi-c 326 652 978 2282 3991 5100
3-(60 pgs.)-In costume w/paper dolls; Hitler-c 290 580 870 1856 3178 4500
4-(52 pgs.)-Classic Nazi WWII-c with giant swastika, Tojo, Mussolini & Hitler photo on wall; in costume, 2 pgs. w/paper dolls 232 464 696 1485 2543 3600
5-(52 pgs.)-In costume w/paper dolls; Japanese WWII-c 181 362 543 1158 1979 2800
6-(52 pgs.)-Not in costume in inside stories, w/paper dolls 155 310 465 992 1696 2400
7,8-(36 pgs.)-In costume 1 pg. each; no paper dolls 123 246 369 787 1344 1900

NOTE: ***Schomburg*** *c-1, 5, 6.*

MISS FURY DIGITAL FIRST
Dynamite Entertainment: 2013 - No. 2, 2013 ($3.99, limited series)

1,2-Prints online stories. 1-Reis, Desjardins, Casas-a. 2-Casas-a 4.00

MISSION IMPOSSIBLE (TV) (Also see Wild!)
Dell Publ. Co.: May, 1967 - No. 4, Oct, 1968; No. 5, Oct, 1969 (All have photo-c)

1 9 18 27 61 123 185
2-5: 5-Reprints #1 5 10 15 35 63 90

MISSION IMPOSSIBLE (Movie) (1st Paramount Comics book)
Marvel Comics (Paramount Comics): May, 1996 ($2.95, one-shot)

1-Liefeld-c & back-up story 4.00

MISS LIBERTY (Becomes Liberty Comics)
Burten Publishing Co.: 1945 (MLJ reprints)

1-The Shield & Dusty, The Wizard, & Roy, the Super Boy app.; r/Shield-Wizard #13 43 86 129 271 461 650

MISS MELODY LANE OF BROADWAY (See The Adventures of Bob Hope)
National Periodical Publ.: Feb-Mar, 1950 - No. 3, June-July, 1950 (52 pgs.)

1-Movie stars photos app. on all-c. 97 194 291 621 1061 1500
2,3: 3-Ed Sullivan photo on-c. 47 94 141 296 498 700

MISS PEACH
Dell Publishing Co.: Oct-Dec, 1963; 1969

1-Jack Mendelsohn-a/script 7 14 21 44 82 120
...Tells You How to Grow (1969; 25¢)-Mel Lazarus-a; also given away (36 pgs.) 5 10 15 30 50 70

MISS PEPPER (See Meet Miss Pepper)

MISS SUNBEAM (See Little Miss...)

MISS VICTORY (See Captain Fearless #1,2, Holyoke One-Shot #3, Veri Best Sure Fire & Veri Best Sure Shot Comics)

MR. & MRS. BEANS
United Features Syndicate: No. 11, 1939

Single Series 11 39 78 117 240 395 550

MR. & MRS. J. EVIL SCIENTIST (TV)(See The Flintstones & Hanna-Barbera Band Wagon #3)
Gold Key: Nov, 1963 - No. 4, Sept, 1966 (Hanna-Barbera, all 12¢)

1 7 14 21 49 92 135
2-4 4 8 12 23 37 50

MR. AND MRS. X (Gambit and Rogue)
Marvel Comics: Sept, 2018 - No. 12, Aug, 2019 ($3.99)

1-12: 1-Thompson-s/Bazaldua-a; the wedding. 2,3-Deadpool app. 4-Starjammers app. 4.00

MR. ANTHONY'S LOVE CLINIC (Based on radio show)
Hillman Periodicals: Nov, 1949 - No. 5, Apr-May, 1950 (52 pgs.)

1-Photo-c on all 28 56 84 165 270 375
2 16 32 48 96 151 205
3-5 15 30 45 83 124 165

MISTER BLANK
Amaze Ink: No. 0, Jan, 1996 - No. 14, May, 2000 ($1.75/$2.95, B&W)

0-($1.75, 16 pgs.) Origin of Mr. Blank 3.00

Mirror's Edge #4 © EA Digital

Miss Peach #1 © DELL

Mister Miracle #20 © DC

	GD 2.0	VG 4.0	FN 6.0	VF 8.0	VF/NM 9.0	NM- 9.2
1-14-($2.95) Chris Hicks-s/a						3.00

MR. DISTRICT ATTORNEY (Radio/TV)
National Per. Publ.: Jan-Feb, 1948 - No. 67, Jan-Feb, 1959 (1-23: 52 pgs.)

	GD 2.0	VG 4.0	FN 6.0	VF 8.0	VF/NM 9.0	NM- 9.2
1-Howard Purcell c-5-23 (most)	123	246	369	787	1344	1900
2	47	94	141	296	498	700
3-5	33	66	99	194	317	440
6-10: 8-Rise & fall of Lucky Lynn	26	52	78	154	252	350
11-20	20	40	60	114	182	250
21-43: 43-Last pre-code (1-2/55)	15	30	45	85	130	175
44-67: 55-UFO story	14	28	42	78	112	145

MR. DISTRICT ATTORNEY (SeeThe Funnies #35)
Dell Publishing Co.: No. 13, 1942

	GD 2.0	VG 4.0	FN 6.0	VF 8.0	VF/NM 9.0	NM- 9.2
Four Color 13-See The Funnies #35 for 1st app.	36	72	108	259	580	900

MISTER E (Also see Books of Magic limited series)
DC Comics: Jun, 1991- No. 4, Sept, 1991($1.75, limited series)

1-4-Snyder III-c/a; follow-up to Books of Magic limited series 3.00

MISTER ED, THE TALKING HORSE (TV)
Dell Publishing Co./Gold Key: Mar-May, 1962 - No. 6, Feb, 1964 (All photo-c; photo back-c: 1-6)

	GD 2.0	VG 4.0	FN 6.0	VF 8.0	VF/NM 9.0	NM- 9.2
Four Color 1295	14	28	42	96	211	325
1(11/62) (Gold Key)-Photo-c	9	18	27	63	109	195
2-6: Photo-c	5	10	15	35	63	90

(See March of Comics #244, 260, 282, 290)

MR. GUM (From The Atomics)
Oni Press: April, 2003 ($2.99, one-shot)

1-Mike Allred-s/J. Bone-a; Madman & The Atomics app. 3.00

MR. HERO, THE NEWMATIC MAN (See Neil Gaiman's...)

MR. MAGOO (TV) (The Nearsighted..., ...& Gerald McBoing Boing 1954 issues; formerly Gerald McBoing-Boing And ...)
Dell Publishing Co.: No. 6, Nov-Jan, 1953-54; 5/54 - 3-5/62; 9-11/63 - 3-5/65

	GD 2.0	VG 4.0	FN 6.0	VF 8.0	VF/NM 9.0	NM- 9.2
6	9	18	27	60	120	180
Four Color 561(5/54),602(11/54)	9	18	27	60	120	180
Four Color 1235(#1, 12-2/62),1305(#2, 3-5/62)	7	14	21	48	89	130
3(9-11/63) - 5	6	12	18	42	79	115
Four Color 1235(12-536-505)(3-5/65)-2nd Printing	5	10	15	35	63	90

MR. MAJESTIC (See WildC.A.T.S.)
DC Comics (WildStorm): Sept, 1999 - No. 9, May, 2000 ($2.50)

1-9: 1-McGuinness-a/Casey & Holguin-s. 2-Two covers 3.00
TPB (2002, $14.95) r/#1-6 & Wildstorm Spotlight #1 15.00

MISTER MIRACLE (1st series) (See Cancelled Comic Cavalcade)
National Periodical Publications/DC Comics: 3-4/71 - V4#18, 2-3/74; V5#19, 9/77 - V6#25, 8-9/78; 1987 (Fourth World)

	GD 2.0	VG 4.0	FN 6.0	VF 8.0	VF/NM 9.0	NM- 9.2
1-1st app. Mr. Miracle (#1-3 are 15¢)	16	32	48	111	246	380
2,3: 2-Intro. Granny Goodness. 3-Last 15¢ issue	6	12	18	37	66	95
4-Intro. Barda; Boy Commandos-r begin; (52 pgs.)	15	30	45	103	227	350
5-8: All 52 pgs.	5	10	15	33	57	80
9-18: 9-Origin Mr. Miracle; Darkseid cameo. 15-Intro/1st app. Shilo Norman. 18-Barda & Scott Free wed; New Gods app. & Darkseid cameo; Last Kirby issue.	3	6	9	17	26	35
19-25 (1977-78)	2	4	6	8	11	14
Special 1(1987, $1.25, 52 pgs.)	1	3	4	6	8	10

Jack Kirby's Fourth World TPB ('01, $12.95) B&W&Grey-toned reprint of #11-18; Mark Evanier intro. 13.00
Jack Kirby's Mister Miracle TPB ('98, $12.95) B&W&Grey-toned reprint of #1-10; David Copperfield intro. 13.00

NOTE: ***Austin** a-19i. **Ditko** a-6r. **Golden** a-23-25p; c-25p. **Heath** a-24i, 25i; c-25i. **Kirby** a(p)/c-1-18. **Nasser** a-19i. **Rogers** a-19-22p; c-19, 20p, 21p, 22-24. 4-8 contain **Simon & Kirby** Boy Commandos reprints from Detective 82,76, Boy Commandos 1, 3 & Detective 64 in that order.*

MISTER MIRACLE (2nd Series) (See Justice League)
DC Comics: Jan, 1989 - No. 28, June, 1991 ($1.00/$1.25)

1-28: 13,14-Lobo app. 22-1st new Mr. Miracle w/new costume 4.00

MISTER MIRACLE (3rd Series)
DC Comics: Apr, 1996 - No. 7, Oct, 1996 ($1.95)

1-7: 2-Vs. JLA. 6-Simonson-c 4.00

MISTER MIRACLE (4th Series)
DC Comics: Oct, 2017 - No. 12, Jan, 2019 ($3.99, limited series)

1-Tom King-s/Mitch Gerads-a; covers by Derington & Gerads 22.00
1-Director's Cut (4/18, $5.99) r/#1 B&W art; bonus script 6.00
2-12-King-s/Gerads-a. 7-Jacob born 5.00

MR. MIRACLE (See Capt. Fearless #1 & Holyoke One-Shot #4)

MISTER MIRACLE: THE SOURCE OF FREEDOM
DC Comics: Jul, 2021 - No. 6, Jan, 2022 ($3.99, limited series)

1-6-Shilo Norman as Mister Miracle; Easton-s/Ossio-a. 1-Intro N'Vir Free. 5-Orion app. 4.00

MR. MONSTER (1st Series)(Doc Stearn... #7 on; See Airboy-Mr. Monster Special, Dark Horse Presents, Super Duper Comics & Vanguard Illustrated #7)
Eclipse Comics: Jan, 1985 - No. 10, June, 1987 ($1.75, Baxter paper)

	GD 2.0	VG 4.0	FN 6.0	VF 8.0	VF/NM 9.0	NM- 9.2
1,3: 1-1st story-r from Vanguard Ill. #7(1st app.). 3-Alan Moore scripts; Wolverton-r/Weird Mysteries #5.						5.00
2-Dave Stevens-c	2	4	6	8	11	14
4-10: 6-Ditko-r/Fantastic Fears #5 plus new Giffen-a. 10- "6-D" issue						4.00

MR. MONSTER
Dark Horse Comics: Feb, 1988 - No. 8, July, 1991 ($1.75, B&W)

1-7 3.00
8-($4.95, 60 pgs.)-Origins conclusion 5.00

MR. MONSTER ATTACKS! (Doc Stearn...)
Tundra Publ.: Aug, 1992 - No. 3, Oct, 1992 ($3.95, limited series, 32 pgs.)

1-3: Michael T. Gilbert-a/scripts; Gilbert/Dorman painted-c 4.00

MR. MONSTER PRESENTS (CRACK-A-BOOM!)
Caliber Comics: 1997 - No. 3, 1997 ($2.95, B&W&Red, limited series)

1-3: Michael T. Gilbert-a/scripts: 1-Wraparound-c 3.00

MR. MONSTER'S GAL FRIDAY...KELLY!
Image Comics: Jan, 2000 - No. 3, May, 2004 ($3.50, B&W)

1-3-Michael T. Gilbert-c; story & art by various. 3-Alan Moore-s 3.50

MR. MONSTER'S SUPER-DUPER SPECIAL
Eclipse Comics: May, 1986 - No. 8, July, 1987

	GD 2.0	VG 4.0	FN 6.0	VF 8.0	VF/NM 9.0	NM- 9.2
1-(5/86)...3-D High Octane Horror #1						5.00
1-(5/86)...2-D version, 100 copies	2	4	6	11	16	20
2-(8/86)...High Octane Horror #1, 3-(9/86)...True Crime #1, 4-(11/86)...True Crime #2, 5-(1/87)...Hi-Voltage Super Science #1, 6-(3/87)...High Shock Schlock #1, 7-(5/87)...High Shock Schlock #2, 8-(7/87)...Weird Tales Of The Future #1						4.00

NOTE: ***Jack Cole** r-3, 4. **Evans** a-2r. **Kubert** a-1r. **Powell** a-5r. **Wolverton** a-2r, 7r, 8r.*

MR. MONSTER VS. GORZILLA
Image Comics: July, 1998 ($2.95, one-shot)

1-Michael T. Gilbert-a 3.00

MR. MONSTER: WORLDS WAR TWO
Atomeka Press: 2004 ($6.99, one-shot)

nn-Michael T. Gilbert-s/George Freeman-a; two covers by Horley & Dorman 7.00

MR. MUSCLES (Formerly Blue Beetle #18-21)
Charlton Comics: No. 22, Mar, 1956; No. 23, Aug, 1956

	GD 2.0	VG 4.0	FN 6.0	VF 8.0	VF/NM 9.0	NM- 9.2
22,23	13	26	39	74	105	135

MR. MXYZPTLK (VILLAINS)
DC Comics: Feb, 1998 ($1.95, one-shot)

1-Grant-s/Morgan-a/Pearson-c 3.00

MISTER MYSTERY (Tales of Horror and Suspense)
Mr. Publ. (Media Publ.) No. 1-3/SPM Publ./Stanmore (Aragon): Sept, 1951 - No. 19, Oct, 1954

	GD 2.0	VG 4.0	FN 6.0	VF 8.0	VF/NM 9.0	NM- 9.2
1-Kurtzman-*esque* horror story	265	530	795	1694	2897	4100
2,3-Kurtzman-*esque* story. 3-Anti-Wertham edit.	90	180	270	576	988	1400
4-Bondage-c	135	270	405	864	1482	2100
5,8,10	87	174	261	553	952	1350
6-Classic torture-c	423	846	1269	3000	5250	7500
7- "The Brain Bats of Venus" by Wolverton; partially re-used in Weird Tales of the Future #7	411	822	1233	2877	5039	7200
9-Nostrand-a	129	258	387	826	1413	2000
11-(5-6/53) Wolverton "Robot Woman" story/Weird Mysteries #2, cut up, rewritten, retitled "Beauty & the Beast"" & partially redrawn; girl in "Beauty & the Beast", splash pg. redrawn from cover of Weird Tales of the Future #4 (11/52); woman on pg. 6 taken from cover of Weird Tales of the Future #2 (6/52)	649	1298	1947	4738	8369	12,000
12-Classic injury to eye-c	975	1950	2919	7100	12,550	18,000
13-16,19: 15- "Living Dead" junkie story. 16-Bondage-c. 19-Reprints	71	142	213	454	777	1100
17-Severed heads-c	142	284	426	909	1555	2200
18- "Robot Woman" by Wolverton reprinted from Weird Mysteries #2; decapitation, bondage-c	206	412	618	1318	2259	3200

NOTE: ***Andru** a-1, 2p, 3p. **Andru/Esposito** c-1-3. **Baily** c-10-18(most). **Mortellaro** c-5-7. Bondage c-7, 16. Some issues have graphic dismemberment scenes.*

	GD 2.0	VG 4.0	FN 6.0	VF 8.0	VF/NM 9.0	NM- 9.2

MR. PEABODY AND SHERMAN (Based on the 2014 Dreamworks movie)
IDW Publishing: Nov, 2013 - No. 4, Jan, 2014 ($3.99)
1-4: 1-Fisch-s/Monlongo-a; 3 covers. 2-Three covers. 3,4-Two covers 4.00

MR. PUNCH
DC Comics (Vertigo): 1994 ($24.95, one-shot)
nn (Hard-c)-Gaiman scripts; McKean-c/a 40.00
nn (Soft-c) 18.00

MISTER Q (See Mighty Midget Comics & Our Flag Comics #5)

MR. RISK (Formerly All Romances; Men Against Crime #3 on)(Also see Our Flag Comics & Super-Mystery Comics)
Ace Magazines: No. 7, Oct, 1950; No. 2, Dec, 1950
7,2 16 32 48 94 147 200

MR. SCARLET & PINKY (See Mighty Midget Comics)

MR. T
APComics: May, 2005 ($3.50)
1-Chris Bunting-s/Neil Edwards-a 3.50

MR. T AND THE T-FORCE
Now Comics: June, 1993 - No. 10, May, 1994 ($1.95, color)
1-10-Newsstand editions: 1-7-polybagged with photo trading card in each. 1,2-Neal Adams-c/a(p). 3-Dave Dorman painted-c 5.00
1-10-Direct Sale editions polybagged w/line drawn trading cards. 1-Contains gold foil trading card by Neal Adams 6.00

MISTER TERRIFIC (DC New 52)(Leads into Earth 2 series)
DC Comics: Nov, 2011 - No. 8, Jun, 2012 ($2.99)
1-8: 1-Wallace-s/Gugliotta-a/JG Jones-c; origin re-told. 2-Intro. Brainstorm 3.00

MISTER UNIVERSE (Professional wrestler)
Mr. Publications Media Publ. (Stanmor, Aragon): July, 1951; No. 2, Oct, 1951 - No. 5, April, 1952
1 30 60 90 177 289 400
2- "Jungle That Time Forgot", (24 pg. story); Andru/Esposito-c 18 36 54 103 162 220
3-Marijuana story 18 36 54 105 165 225
4,5-"Goes to War" cover/stories (Korean War) 15 30 45 83 124 165

MISTER X (See Vortex)
Mr. Publications/Vortex Comics/Caliber V3#1 on: 6/84 - No. 14, 8/88 ($1.50/$2.25, direct sales, coated paper);V2#1, Apr, 1989 - V2#12, Mar, 1990 ($2.00/$2.50, B&W, newsprint) V3#1, 1996 - No. 4, 1996 ($2.95, B&W)
1-14: 11-Dave McKean story & art (6 pgs.) 4.00
V2 #1-12: 1-11 (Second Coming, B&W): 1-Four diff.-c. 10-Photo-c 3.00
V3 #1-4 3.00
Return of... ($11.95, graphic novel)-r/V1#1-4 12.00
Return of... ($34.95, hardcover limited edition)-r/1-4 35.00
Special (no date, 1990?) 3.00

MISTER X
Dark Horse Comics: Mar, 2013 ($2.99, one-shot)
...: Hard Candy (3/13) Dean Motter-s/a 3.00

MISTER X: CONDEMNED
Dark Horse Comics: Dec, 2008 - No. 4, Mar, 2009 ($3.50, limited series)
1-4-Dean Motter-s/a 3.50

MISTER X: EVICTION
Dark Horse Comics: May, 2013 - No. 3, Jul, 2013 ($3.99, limited series)
1-3-Dean Motter-s/a 4.00

MISTER X: RAZED
Dark Horse Comics: Feb, 2015 - No. 4, May, 2015 ($3.99, limited series)
1-4-Dean Motter-s/a 4.00

MISTY
Marvel Comics (Star Comics): Dec, 1985 - No. 6, May, 1986 (Limited series)
1-6: Millie The Model's niece 4.00

MITZI COMICS (Becomes Mitzi's Boy Friend #2-7)(See All Teen)
Timely Comics: Spring, 1948 (one-shot)
1-Kurtzman's "Hey Look" plus 3 pgs. "Giggles 'n' Grins" 74 148 222 470 810 1150

MITZI'S BOY FRIEND (Formerly Mitzi Comics; becomes Mitzi's Romances)
Marvel Comics (TCI): No. 2, June, 1948 - No. 7, April, 1949
2 32 64 96 188 307 425
3-7 22 44 66 132 216 300

MITZI'S ROMANCES (Formerly Mitzi's Boy Friend)
Timely/Marvel Comics (TCI): No. 8, June, 1949 - No. 10, Dec, 1949
8-Becomes True Life Tales #8 (10/49) on? 23 46 69 138 227 315
9,10: 10-Painted-c 20 40 60 115 185 255

MNEMOVORE
DC Comics (Vertigo): Jun, 2005 - No. 6, Nov, 2005 ($2.99, limited series)
1-6-Rodionoff & Fawkes-s/Huddleston-a/c 3.00

MOBY DICK (See Feature Presentations #6, King Classics, and Classic Comics #5)
Dell Publishing Co.: No. 717, Aug, 1956
Four Color 717-Movie, Gregory Peck photo-c 9 18 27 59 117 175

MOBY DUCK (See Donald Duck #112 & Walt Disney Showcase #2,11)
Gold Key (Disney): Oct, 1967 - No. 11, Oct, 1970; No. 12, Jan, 1974 - No. 30, Feb, 1978
1-Three Little Pigs app. 4 8 12 23 37 50
2-5: 2-Beagle Boys app. 5-Captain Hook app. 2 4 6 11 16 20
6-11: 6-Huey, Dewey & Louie app. 2 4 6 9 13 16
12-30: 21,30-r 1 3 4 6 8 10

MOCKINGBIRD (From S.H.I.E.L.D.)
Marvel Comics: May, 2016 - No. 8, Dec, 2016 ($3.99)
1-8: 1-4-Chelsea Cain-s/Kate Niemczyk-a/Joëlle Jones-c. 5-Moustafa-a. 6-Civil War II tie-in 4.00
... S.H.I.E.L.D. 50th Anniversary (11/15, $3.99) Joëlle Jones-a; back-up with Red Widow 4.00

MOCKING DEAD, THE
Dynamite Entertainment: 2013 - No. 5, 2014 ($3.99, B&W, limited series)
1-5: 1-Fred Van Lente-s/Max Dunbar-a 4.00

MODEL FUN (With Bobby Benson)
Harle Publications: No. 2, Fall, 1954 - No. 5, July, 1955
2-Bobby Benson 8 16 24 42 54 65
3-5-Bobby Benson 5 10 15 25 31 36

MODELING WITH MILLIE (Formerly Life With Millie)
Atlas/Marvel Comics (Male Publ.): No. 21, Feb, 1963 - No. 54, June, 1967
21 10 20 30 67 141 215
22-30 7 14 21 44 82 120
31-53 6 12 18 37 66 95
54-Last issue; Gears-c & 6 pg. story; Beatles swipe imitators; FF #63 comic appears in story; "Millie the Marvel" 6 pg. story as super-hero 6 12 18 38 69 100

MODELS, INC.
Marvel Comics: Oct, 2009 - No. 4, Jan, 2010 ($3.99, limited series)
1-4-Millie the Model, Patsy Walker, Mary Jane Watson app.; Land-c. 1-Tim Gunn app. 4.00

MODERN COMICS (Formerly Military Comics #1-43)
Quality Comics Group: No. 44, Nov, 1945 - No. 102, Oct, 1950
44-Blackhawk continues 57 114 171 362 619 875
45-52: 49-1st app. Fear, Lady Adventuress 39 78 117 231 378 525
53-Torchy by Ward begins (9/46) 48 96 144 302 514 725
54-60: 55-J. Cole-a 34 68 102 199 325 450
61-Classic-c 41 82 123 256 428 600
62-64,66-77,79,80: 73-J. Cole-a 32 64 96 188 307 425
65-Classic Grim Reaper Skull-c 68 136 204 435 743 1050
78-1st app. Madame Butterfly 37 74 111 222 361 500
81-99,101: 82,83-One pg. J. Cole-a. 83-Last 52 pg. issue
99-Blackhawks on the moon-c/story 32 64 96 188 307 425
100 34 68 102 206 336 465
102-(Scarce)-J. Cole-a; Spirit by Eisner app. 40 80 120 246 411 575

NOTE: ***Al Bryant** c-44-51, 54, 55, 66, 69. **Jack Cole** a-55, 73. **Crandall** Blackhawk-#46, 47, 50, 51, 54, 56, 58-60, 64, 67-70, 73, 74, 76-78, 80-83; c-60-65, 67, 68, 70-95. **Crandall/Cuidera** c-56-59, 96-102. **Gustavson** a-47, 49. **Ward** Blackhawk-#52, 53, 55 (15 pgs. each), Torchy in #53-102; by **Ward** only in #53-89(9/49); by **Gil Fox** #92, 93, 102.*

MODERN FANTASY
Dark Horse Comics: Jun, 2018 - No. 4, Sept, 2018 ($3.99, limited series)
1-4-Rafer Roberts-s/Kristen Gudsnuk-a 4.00

MODERN LOVE
E. C. Comics: June-July, 1949 - No. 8, Aug-Sept, 1950
1-Feldstein, Ingels-a 161 322 483 1030 1765 2500
2-Craig/Feldstein-c/s 103 206 309 659 1130 1600
3 77 154 231 493 847 1200
4-6 (Scarce): 4-Bra/panties panels 100 200 300 635 1093 1550
7 74 148 222 470 810 1150
8-Bill Gaines/Al Feldstein app. in comic industry parody sty. 97 194 291 621 1061 1500

NOTE: ***Craig** a-3. **Feldstein** a-in most issues; c-1, 2i, 3-8. **Harrison** a-4. **Iger** a-6-8. **Ingels** a-1, 2, 4-7. **Palais** a-5. **Wood** a-7. **Wood/Harrison** a-5-7. (Canadian reprints known; see Table of Contents.)*

MODERN WARFARE 2: GHOST (Based on the videogame)
DC Comics (WildStorm): Jan, 2010 - No. 6, Sept, 2010 ($3.99, limited series)
1-6: 1-Two covers; Lapham-s/West-a 4.00
TPB (2010, $17.99) r/#1-6; cover sketches and sketch art 18.00

MOD LOVE
Western Publishing Co.: 1967 (50¢, 36 pgs.)
1-(Low print) 9 18 27 63 129 195

MODNIKS, THE
Gold Key: Aug, 1967 - No. 2, Aug, 1970
10206-708(#1) 4 8 12 23 37 50
2 3 6 9 15 22 28

M.O.D.O.K. ASSASSIN (Secret Wars tie-in)
Marvel Comics: Jul, 2015 - No. 5, Nov, 2015 ($3.99, limited series)
1-5-Yost-s/Pinna-a; Angela app. 1-Bullseye, Baron Mordo & Clea app. 4.00

M.O.D.O.K.: HEAD GAMES
Marvel Comics: Feb, 2021 - No. 4, Jun, 2021 ($3.99, limited series)
1-4-Blum & Oswalt-s/Hepburn-a; Monica Rappaccini app. 2-Tony Stark app. 3-Gwenpool app. 4-TV family cameos 4.00

M.O.D.O.K.: REIGN DELAY
Marvel Comics: Nov, 2009 ($3.99, one-shot)
1-M.O.D.O.K. cartoony humor stories from Marvel Digital Comics; Ryan Dunlavey-s/a 4.00

MOD SQUAD (TV)
Dell Publishing Co.: Jan, 1969 - No. 3, Oct, 1969 - No. 8, April, 1971
1-Photo-c 8 16 24 54 102 150
2-4: 2-4-Photo-c 4 8 12 28 47 65
5-8: 8-Photo-c; Reprints #2 4 8 12 23 37 50

MOD WHEELS
Gold Key: Mar, 1971 - No. 19, Jan, 1976
1 4 8 12 25 40 55
2-9 3 6 9 16 23 30
10-19: 11,15-Extra 16 pgs. ads 3 6 9 14 19 24

MOE & SHMOE COMICS
O. S. Publ. Co.: Spring, 1948 - No. 2, Summer, 1948
1 13 26 39 74 105 135
2 8 16 24 44 57 70

Mister X: Eviction #2 © Dean Motter

Monica Rambeau: Photon #1 © MAR

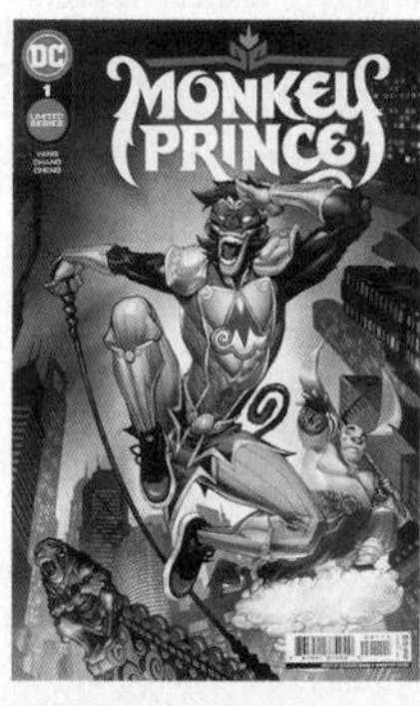

Monkey Prince #1 © DC

	GD 2.0	VG 4.0	FN 6.0	VF 8.0	VF/NM 9.0	NM- 9.2
MOEBIUS (Graphic novel)						
Marvel Comics (Epic Comics): Oct, 1987 - No. 6, 1988; No. 7, 1990; No. 8, 1991; No. 9, 1994 ($9.95, 8x11", mature)						
1	4	8	12	28	47	65
2	5	10	15	34	60	85
3-(1st & 2nd printings, $12.95)	7	14	21	46	86	125
4-6,8	4	8	12	23	37	50
7,0: 0 (1990, $12.95)	4	8	12	28	47	65
9-(1994) Printed 3 years after #8	8	16	24	51	96	140
Moebius I-Signed & #'d hard-c ($45.95, Graphitti Designs, 1,500 copies printed)-r/#1-3	10	20	30	67	141	215
MOEBIUS COMICS						
Caliber: May, 1996 - No. 6 ($2.95, B&W)						
1,5,6-Moebius-c/a on all; William Stout-a	3	6	9	14	20	25
2-4-Moebius-c/a	2	4	6	9	12	15
MOEBIUS: THE MAN FROM CIGURI						
Dark Horse Comics: 1996 ($7.95, digest-size)						
nn-Moebius-c/a	4	8	12	23	37	50
MOLLY MANTON'S ROMANCES (Romantic Affairs #3)						
Marvel Comics (SePI): Sept, 1949 - No. 2, Dec, 1949 (52 pgs.)						
1-Photo-c (becomes Blaze the Wonder Collie #2 (10/49) on? & Molly Manton's Romances #2	28	56	84	165	270	375
2-Titled "Romances of..."; photo-c	19	38	57	111	176	240
MOLLY O'DAY (Super Sleuth)						
Avon Periodicals: February, 1945 (1st Avon comic)						
1-Molly O'Day, The Enchanted Dagger by Tuska (r/Yankee #1), Capt'n Courage, Corporal Grant app.	93	186	279	591	1021	1450
MOMENT OF SILENCE						
Marvel Comics: Feb, 2002 ($3.50, one-shot)						
1-Tributes to the heroes and victims of Sept. 11; s/a by various						3.50
M.O.M. MOTHER OF MADNESS						
Image Comics: Jul, 2021 - No. 3, Oct, 2021 ($5.99/$4.99, limited series)						
1-($5.99) Emilia Clarke & Marguerite Bennett-s/Leila Leiz-a						6.00
2,3-($4.99)						5.00
MONARCHY, THE (Also see The Authority and StormWatch)						
DC Comics (WildStorm): Apr, 2001 - No. 12, May, 2002 ($2.50)						
1-12: 1-McCrea & Leach-a/Young-s						3.00
Bullets Over Babylon TPB (2001, $12.95) r/#1-4, Authority #21						13.00
MONICA RAMBEAU: PHOTON						
Marvel Comics: Feb, 2023 - Present ($3.99)						
1-3: 1-Eve Ewing-s/Luca Maresca-a; Doctor Strange and Spider-Man app.						4.00
MONKEES, THE (TV)(Also see Circus Boy, Groovy, Not Brand Echh #3, Teen-Age Talk, Teen Beam & Teen Beat)						
Dell Publishing Co.: March, 1967 - No. 17, Oct, 1969						
1-Photo-c	14	28	42	96	211	325
2-17: All photo-c. 17-Reprints #1	7	14	21	44	82	120
MONKEY AND THE BEAR, THE						
Atlas Comics (ZPC): Sept, 1953 - No. 3, Jan, 1954						
1-Howie Post-c/a in all; funny animal	15	30	45	85	130	175
2,3	10	20	30	58	79	100
MONKEYMAN AND O'BRIEN (Also see Dark Horse Presents #80, 100-5, Gen13/..., Hellboy: Seed of Destruction, & San Diego Comic Con #2)						
Dark Horse Comics (Legend): Jul, 1996 - No. 3, Sept, 1996 ($2.95, lim. series)						
1-3: New stories; Art Adams-c/a/scripts						4.00
nn-(2/96, $2.95)-r/back-up stories from Hellboy: Seed of Destruction; Adams-c/a/scripts						4.00
MONKEY PRINCE						
DC Comics: Apr, 2022 - Present ($3.99)						
1-12-Gene Luen Yang-s/Bernard Chang-a. 1-4-Batman & Robin app. 7,8-Aquaman app. 9,10-Supergirl and the Ultra-Humanite app. 10,11-Lazarus Planet tie-ins						4.00
MONKEYSHINES COMICS						
Ace Periodicals/Publishers Specialists/Current Books/Unity Publ.: Summer, 1944 - No. 27, July, 1949						
1-Funny animal	20	40	60	118	192	265
2-(Aut/44)	14	28	42	78	112	145
3-10: 3-(Win/44)	11	22	33	64	90	115
11-18,20-27: 23,24-Fago-c/a	10	20	30	54	72	90

	GD 2.0	VG 4.0	FN 6.0	VF 8.0	VF/NM 9.0	NM- 9.2
19-Frazetta-a	12	24	36	69	97	125
MONKEY'S UNCLE, THE (See Merlin Jones As... under Movie Comics)						
MONOLITH, THE						
DC Comics: Apr, 2004 - No. 12, Mar, 2005 ($3.50/$2.95)						
1-($3.50) Palmiotti & Gray-s/Winslade-a						3.50
2-12-($2.95): 6-8-Batman app.; Coker-a						3.00
...: Volume One HC (Image Comics, 2012, $17.99) r/#1-4; intro. by Jim Steranko						18.00
MONROES, THE (TV)						
Dell Publishing Co.: Apr, 1967						
1-Photo-c	3	6	9	17	26	35
MONSTER						
Fiction House Magazines: 1953 - No. 2, 1953						
1-Dr. Drew by Grandenetti; reprint from Rangers Comics #48; Whitman-c	93	186	279	591	1021	1450
2-Whitman-c	77	154	231	493	847	1200
MONSTER CRIME COMICS (Also see Crime Must Stop)						
Hillman Periodicals: Oct, 1952 (15¢, 52 pgs.)						
1 (Scarce)	271	542	813	1734	2967	4200
MONSTER HOUSE (Companion to the 2006 movie)						
IDW Publishing: June, 2006 ($7.99, one-shot)						
nn-Two stories about Bones and Skull by Joshua Dysart and Simeon Wilkins						8.00
MONSTER HOWLS (Magazine)						
Humor-Vision: December, 1966 (Satire) (35¢, 68 pgs.)						
1-John Severin-a	5	10	15	34	60	85
MONSTER HUNTERS						
Charlton Comics: Aug, 1975 - No. 9, Jan, 1977; No. 10, Oct, 1977 - No. 18, Feb, 1979						
1-Howard-a; Newton-c; 1st Countess Von Bludd and Colonel Whiteshroud	3	6	9	19	30	40
2-Sutton-c/a; Ditko-a	3	6	9	14	19	24
3,4,5,7: 4-Sutton-c/a	2	4	6	9	12	15
6,8,10: 6,8,10-Ditko-a	2	4	6	10	14	18
9,11,12	1	3	4	6	8	10
13,15,18-Ditko-c/a. 18-Sutton-a	2	4	6	10	14	18
14-Special all-Ditko issue	3	6	9	16	24	32
16,17-Sutton-a	2	3	4	6	8	10
1,2 (Modern Comics reprints, 1977)						6.00
NOTE: *Ditko a-2, 6, 8, 10, 13-15r, 18r; c-13-15, 18.* ***Howard*** *a-1, 3, 17; r-13.* ***Morisi*** *a-1.* ***Staton*** *a-1, 13.* ***Sutton*** *a-2, 4; c-2, 4; r-16-18.* ***Zeck*** *a-4-9. Reprints in #12-18.*						
MONSTER KILL SQUAD						
Bad Idea: Sept, 2021 - No. 4, Dec, 2021 ($6.99, limited series)						
1-4-Lead story with Christos Gage-s/Tomas Giorello-a; back-ups by various						7.00
MONSTER MADNESS (Magazine)						
Marvel Comics: 1972 - No. 3, 1973 (60¢, B&W)						
1-3: Stories by "Sinister" Stan Lee. 1-Frankenstein photo-c. 2-Son of Frankenstein photo-c. 3-Bride of Frankenstein photo-c	4	8	12	27	44	60
MONSTER MAN						
Image Comics (Action Planet): Sept, 1997 ($2.95, B&W)						
1-Mike Manley-c/s/a						3.00
MONSTER MASTERWORKS						
Marvel Comics: 1989 ($12.95, TPB)						
nn-Reprints 1960's monster stories; art by Kirby, Ditko, Ayers, Everett						20.00
MONSTER MATINEE						
Chaos! Comics: Oct, 1997 - No. 3, Oct, 1997 ($2.50, limited series)						
1-3: pin-ups						3.00
MONSTER MENACE						
Marvel Comics: Dec, 1993 - No. 4, Mar, 1994 ($1.25, limited series)						
1-4: Pre-code Atlas horror reprints.						6.00
NOTE: ***Ditko**-r &* ***Kirby**-r in all.*						
MONSTER OF FRANKENSTEIN (See Frankenstein and Essential Monster of Frankenstein)						
MONSTER PILE-UP						
Image Comics: Aug, 2008 ($1.99)						
1-New short stories of Astounding Wolf-Man, Firebreather, Perhapanauts, Proof						3.00
MONSTERS ATTACK (Magazine)						
Globe Communications Corpse: Sept, 1989 - No. 5, Dec, 1990 (B&W)						
1-5-Ditko, Morrow, J. Severin-a. 5-Toth, Morrow-a	1	2	3	4	5	7

MONSTERS, INC. (Based on the Disney/Pixar movie)
BOOM! Studios: Jun, 2009 - No. 4, Nov, 2009 ($2.99, limited series)

	GD 2.0	VG 4.0	FN 6.0	VF 8.0	VF/NM 9.0	NM- 9.2
...: Laugh Factory 1-4: 1,3-Three covers. 2,4-Two covers						3.00

MONSTERS, INC. (Based on the Disney/Pixar movie)
Marvel Worldwide Inc.: Feb, 2013 - No. 2 ($2.99, limited series)

	GD 2.0	VG 4.0	FN 6.0	VF 8.0	VF/NM 9.0	NM- 9.2
1,2-Movie adaptation						3.00
...: A Perfect Date (2013, $2.99)						3.00
...: The Humanween Party (4/13, $2.99)						3.00

MONSTERS ON THE PROWL (Chamber of Darkness #1-8)
Marvel Comics Group (No. 13,14: 52 pgs.): No. 9, 2/71 - No. 27, 11/73; No. 28, 6/74 - No. 30, 10/74

	GD 2.0	VG 4.0	FN 6.0	VF 8.0	VF/NM 9.0	NM- 9.2
9-Barry Smith inks	5	10	15	35	63	90
10-12,15: 12-Last 15¢ issue	4	8	12	23	37	50
13,14-(52 pgs.)	4	8	12	25	40	55
16-(4/72)-King Kull 4th app.; Severin-c	4	8	12	25	40	55
17-30	3	6	9	18	28	38

NOTE: ***Ditko** r-9, 14, 16. **Kirby** r-10-17, 21, 23, 25, 27, 28, 30; c-9, 25. **Kirby/Ditko** r-14, 17-20, 22, 24, 26, 29. **Marie/John Severin** a-16(Kull). 9-13, 15 contain one new story. Woodish art by **Reese**-11. King Kull created by Robert E. Howard.*

MONSTERS TO LAUGH WITH (Magazine) (Becomes Monsters Unlimited #4)
Marvel Comics Group: 1964 - No. 3, 1965 (B&W)

	GD 2.0	VG 4.0	FN 6.0	VF 8.0	VF/NM 9.0	NM- 9.2
1-Humor by Stan Lee	8	16	24	55	105	155
2,3: 3-Frankenstein photo-c	5	10	15	34	60	85

MONSTERS UNLEASHED (Magazine)
Marvel Comics Group: July, 1973 - No. 11, Apr, 1975; Summer, 1975 (B&W)

	GD 2.0	VG 4.0	FN 6.0	VF 8.0	VF/NM 9.0	NM- 9.2
1-Soloman Kane sty; Werewolf app.	7	14	21	46	86	125
2-4: 2-The Frankenstein Monster begins, ends #10. 3-Neal Adams-c/a; The Man-Thing begins (origin-r); Son of Satan preview. 4-Werewolf app.	4	8	12	28	47	65
5-7: Werewolf in all. 5-Man-Thing. 7-Williamson-a(r)	3	6	9	21	33	45
8-11: 8-Man-Thing; N. Adams-r. 9-Man-Thing; Wendigo app. 10-Origin Tigra	3	6	9	21	33	45
Annual 1 (Summer,1975, 92 pgs.)-Kane-a	4	8	12	25	40	55

NOTE: ***Boris** c-2, 6. **Brunner** a-2; c-11. **J. Buscema** a-2p, 4p, 5p. **Colan** a-1, 4r. **Davis** a-3r. **Everett** a-2r. **G. Kane** a-3. **Krigstein** r-4. **Morrow** a-3; c-1. **Perez** a-8. **Ploog** a-6. **Reese** a-1, 2. **Tuska** a-3p. **Wildey** a-1r.*

MONSTERS UNLEASHED
Marvel Comics: Mar, 2017 - No. 5, May, 2017 ($4.99, limited series with tie-ins)

	GD 2.0	VG 4.0	FN 6.0	VF 8.0	VF/NM 9.0	NM- 9.2
1-5: 1-Cullen Bunn-s/Steve McNiven-a; Avengers, X-Men, Guardians of the Galaxy, Inhumans & Champions app. 2-Land-a. 3-Leinil Yu-a. 4-Larroca-a. 5-Adam Kubert-a						5.00

MONSTERS UNLEASHED (Ongoing series)
Marvel Comics: Jun, 2017 - No. 12, May, 2018 ($3.99)

	GD 2.0	VG 4.0	FN 6.0	VF 8.0	VF/NM 9.0	NM- 9.2
1-12: 1-Bunn-s/Baldeón-a; Elsa Bloodstone & Mole Man app. 7,8-Fin Fang Foom app.						4.00

MONSTERS UNLIMITED (Magazine) (Formerly Monsters To Laugh With)
Marvel Comics Group: No. 4, 1965 - No. 7, 1966 (B&W)

	GD 2.0	VG 4.0	FN 6.0	VF 8.0	VF/NM 9.0	NM- 9.2
4-7: 4,7-Frankenstein photo-c	5	10	15	34	60	85

MONSTER WORLD
DC Comics (WildStorm): Jul, 2001 - No. 4, Oct, 2001 ($2.50, limited series)

	GD 2.0	VG 4.0	FN 6.0	VF 8.0	VF/NM 9.0	NM- 9.2
1-4-Lobdell-s/Meglia-c/a						3.00

MONSTER WORLD
American Gothic Press: Dec, 2015 - No. 4, May, 2016 ($3.99)

	GD 2.0	VG 4.0	FN 6.0	VF 8.0	VF/NM 9.0	NM- 9.2
1-4-Philip Kim & Steve Niles-s/Piotr Kowalski-a						4.00

MONSTRESS
Image Comics: Nov, 2015 - Present ($4.99/$3.99)

	GD 2.0	VG 4.0	FN 6.0	VF 8.0	VF/NM 9.0	NM- 9.2
1-($4.99) Marjorie Liu-s/Sana Takeda-a	3	6	9	21	33	45
2	2	4	6	9	12	15
3,4						6.00
5-43-($3.99)						4.00

MONSTRESS: TALK-STORIES
Image Comics: Nov, 2020 - No. 2, Dec, 2020 ($3.99)

	GD 2.0	VG 4.0	FN 6.0	VF 8.0	VF/NM 9.0	NM- 9.2
1,2-Marjorie Liu-s/Sana Takeda-a; spotlight on Kippa						4.00

MONSTRO MECHANICA
AfterShock Comics: Dec, 2017 - No. 5, Apr, 2018 ($3.99)

	GD 2.0	VG 4.0	FN 6.0	VF 8.0	VF/NM 9.0	NM- 9.2
1-5-Paul Allor-s/Chris Evenhuis-a; Leonardo Da Vinci and his robot in 1472						4.00

MONTANA KID, THE (See Kid Montana)

MONTE HALE WESTERN (Movie star; Formerly Mary Marvel #1-28; also see Fawcett Movie Comic, Motion Picture Comics, Picture News #8, Real Western Hero, Six-Gun Heroes, Western Hero & XMas Comics)
Fawcett Publ./Charlton No. 83 on: No. 29, Oct, 1948 - No. 88, Jan, 1956

	GD 2.0	VG 4.0	FN 6.0	VF 8.0	VF/NM 9.0	NM- 9.2
29-(#1, 52 pgs.)-Photo-c begin, end #82; Monte Hale & his horse Pardner begin	26	52	78	154	252	350
30-(52 pgs.)-Big Bow and Little Arrow begin, end #34; Captain Tootsie by Beck	14	28	42	80	115	150
31-36,38-40-(52 pgs.): 34-Gabby Hayes begins, ends #80. 39-Captain Tootsie by Beck	12	24	36	67	94	120
37,41,45,49-(36 pgs.)	10	20	30	54	72	90
42-44,46-48,50-(52 pgs.): 47-Big Bow & Little Arrow app.	10	20	30	58	79	100
51,52,54-56,58,59-(52 pgs.)	9	18	27	52	69	85
53,57-(36 pgs.): 53-Slim Pickens app.	8	16	24	44	57	70
60-81: 36 pgs. #60-on. 80-Gabby Hayes ends	8	16	24	42	54	65
82-Last Fawcett issue (6/53)	9	18	27	52	69	85
83-1st Charlton issue (2/55); B&W photo back-c begin. Gabby Hayes returns, ends #86	10	20	30	58	79	100
84 (4/55)	8	16	24	44	57	70
85-86	8	16	24	42	54	65
87,88: 87-Wolverton-r, 1/2 pg. 88-Last issue	8	16	24	44	57	70

NOTE: ***Gil Kane** a-33?, 34? Rocky Lane -1 pg. (Carnation ad)-38, 40, 41, 43, 44, 46, 55.*

MONTY HALL OF THE U.S. MARINES (See With the Marines...)
Toby Press: Aug, 1951 - No. 11, Apr, 1953

	GD 2.0	VG 4.0	FN 6.0	VF 8.0	VF/NM 9.0	NM- 9.2
1	18	36	84	105	165	225
2	11	22	33	62	86	110
3-5	9	18	27	52	69	85
6-11	9	18	27	47	61	75

NOTE: *Full page pin-ups (Pin-Up Pete) by **Jack Sparling** in #1-9.*

MOON, A GIRL...ROMANCE, A (Becomes Weird Fantasy #13 on; formerly Moon Girl #1-8)
E. C. Comics: No. 9, Sept-Oct, 1949 - No. 12, Mar-Apr, 1950

	GD 2.0	VG 4.0	FN 6.0	VF 8.0	VF/NM 9.0	NM- 9.2
9-Moon Girl cameo	161	322	483	1030	1765	2500
10,11	135	270	405	864	1482	2100
12-(Scarce)	219	438	657	1402	2401	3400

NOTE: ***Feldstein, Ingels** art in all. **Feldstein** c-9-12. **Wood/Harrison** a-10-12. Canadian reprints known; see Table of Contents.*

MOON GIRL AND DEVIL DINOSAUR
Marvel Comics: Jan, 2016 - No. 47, Nov, 2019 ($3.99)

	GD 2.0	VG 4.0	FN 6.0	VF 8.0	VF/NM 9.0	NM- 9.2
1-47: 1-Reeder & Montclare-s/Bustos-a; intro. Lunella Lafayette. 4-Hulk app. 9-11-Ms. Marvel app. 14-Thing & Hulk (Cho) app. 15-Ironheart app. 19-Intro. Girl-Moon. 22,23-Ego the Living Planet app. 25-30-The Thing and Human Torch app.						4.00

MOON GIRL AND DEVIL DINOSAUR
Marvel Comics: Feb, 2023 - Present ($3.99)

1-3: 1-Jordan Ifueko-s/Alba Glez-a

MOON GIRL AND THE PRINCE (#1) (Moon Girl #2-6; Moon Girl Fights Crime #7, 8; becomes A Moon, A Girl, Romance #9 on)(Also see Animal Fables #7, Int. Crime Patrol #6, Happy Houlihans & Tales From The Crypt #22)
E. C. Comics: Fall, 1947 - No. 8, Summer, 1949

	GD 2.0	VG 4.0	FN 6.0	VF 8.0	VF/NM 9.0	NM- 9.2
1-Origin Moon Girl (see Happy Houlihans #1). Intro Santana, Queen of the Underworld	271	542	813	1734	2967	4200
2-Moon Girl battles Futureman	135	270	405	864	1482	2100
3,4: 3-Santana, Queen of the Underworld returns. 4-Moon Girl vs. a vampire	103	206	309	659	1130	1600
5-E.C.'s 1st horror story, "Zombie Terror"	314	628	942	2198	3849	5500
6-8 (Scarce): 7-Origin Star (Moongirl's sidekick)	123	246	369	787	1344	1900

NOTE: ***Craig** a-2, 5; c-1, 2. **Moldoff** a-1-8; c-3-8 (Shelly). **Wheelan's** Fat and Slat app. in #3, 4, 6. #2 & #3 are 52 pgs., #4 on, 36 pgs. Canadian reprints known; (see Table of Contents.)*

MOON KNIGHT (Also see The Hulk, Marc Spector..., Marvel Preview #21, Marvel Spotlight & Werewolf by Night #32)
Marvel Comics Group: Nov, 1980 - No. 38, Jul, 1984 (Mando paper #33 on)

	GD 2.0	VG 4.0	FN 6.0	VF 8.0	VF/NM 9.0	NM- 9.2
1-Origin resumed in #4; Moench-s/Sienkiewicz-a	5	10	15	33	57	80
2	2	4	6	11	16	20
3-1st Midnight Man	3	6	9	19	30	40
4-Werewolf By Night app.	3	6	9	14	20	26
5-15,25,35: 25-Double size. 35-($1.00, 52 pgs.)-X-Men app.; F.F. cameo	1	2	3	5	6	8
16-22: 16-The Thing app.						6.00
23,24,26-28,31-34,36-38	2	4	6	11	16	20
29-Werewolf By Night app.	3	6	9	21	33	45
30-Werewolf By Night app.	3	6	9	14	20	26
... No. 1 Facsimile Edition (7/22, $3.99) Reprints #1 with original 1980 ads						4.00

NOTE: ***Austin** c-27i, 31i. **Cowan** a-16; c-16, 17. **Kaluta** c-36-38; back c-35. **Miller** c-9, 12p, 13p, 15p, 27p. **Ploog** back c-35. **Sienkiewicz** a-1-15, 17-20, 22-26, 28-30, 33i, 36(4), 37; c-1-5, 7, 8, 10, 11, 14-16, 18-26, 28-30, 31p, 33, 34.*

MOON KNIGHT
Marvel Comics Group: June, 1985 - V2#6, Dec, 1985

	GD 2.0	VG 4.0	FN 6.0	VF 8.0	VF/NM 9.0	NM- 9.2
V2#1-Double size; new costume	2	4	6	11	16	20
V2#2-Khonshu & Harrow app.	4	8	12	23	37	50
V2#3-6: 6-Sienkiewicz painted-c	1	2	3	5	6	8

MOON KNIGHT
Marvel Comics: Jan, 1998 - No. 4, Apr, 1998 ($2.50, limited series)

	GD 2.0	VG 4.0	FN 6.0	VF 8.0	VF/NM 9.0	NM- 9.2
1-Moench-s/Edwards-c/a	1	3	4	6	8	10
2-4-Moench-s/Edwards-c/a						5.00

MOON KNIGHT (Volume 3)
Marvel Comics: Jan, 1999 - No. 4, Feb, 1999 ($2.99, limited series)

	GD 2.0	VG 4.0	FN 6.0	VF 8.0	VF/NM 9.0	NM- 9.2
1-Moench-s/Texeira-a(p)	1	3	4	6	8	10
2-4						5.00

MOON KNIGHT (Fourth series) (Leads into Vengeance of the Moon Knight)
Marvel Comics: June, 2006 - No. 30, Jul, 2009 ($2.99)

	GD 2.0	VG 4.0	FN 6.0	VF 8.0	VF/NM 9.0	NM- 9.2
1-Finch-a/c; Huston-s	2	4	6	10	14	18
1-B&W sketch variant-c	3	6	9	14	19	24
2-19,21-26: 7-Spider-Man app. 9,10-Punisher app. 13-Suydam-c begin. 23-25-Bullseye						3.00
20-($3.99) Deodato-a; back-up r/1st app. in Werewolf By Night #32,33	2	4	6	13	18	22
Annual 1 (1/08, $3.99) Swierczynski-s/Palo-a						6.00
... Saga (2009, free) synopsis of origin and major storylines						4.00
...: Silent Knight 1 (1/09, $3.99) Milligan-s/Laurence Campbell-a/Crain-c	3	6	9	17	26	35

MOON KNIGHT (Fifth series)
Marvel Comics: Jul, 2011 - No. 12, Jun, 2012 ($3.99, limited series)

	GD 2.0	VG 4.0	FN 6.0	VF 8.0	VF/NM 9.0	NM- 9.2
1-Bendis-s/Maleev-a/c; Wolverine, Spider-Man and Capt. America "app."	1	2	3	5	6	8
2-12: 2-Echo returns. 3-Bullseye-c						4.00

MOON KNIGHT (Sixth series)
Marvel Comics: May, 2014 - No. 17, Sept, 2015 ($3.99)

	GD 2.0	VG 4.0	FN 6.0	VF 8.0	VF/NM 9.0	NM- 9.2
1-Ellis-s/Shalvey-a	3	6	9	14	20	25
2-17: 2-6-Ellis-s/Shalvey-a. 7-12-Wood-s/Smallwood-a. 13-17-Bunn						4.00

MOON KNIGHT (Seventh series)
Marvel Comics: Jun, 2016 - No. 14, Jul, 2017 ($4.99/$3.99)

	GD 2.0	VG 4.0	FN 6.0	VF 8.0	VF/NM 9.0	NM- 9.2
1-($4.99)-Lemire-s/Smallwood-a	2	4	6	11	16	20
2-($3.99)-Lemire-s/Smallwood-a	1	2	3	5	6	8
3-14-($3.99) 5-9-Art by Smallwood, Stokoe, Torres, and Francavilla						4.00

MOON KNIGHT (Marvel Legacy, Eighth series)
Marvel Comics: No. 188, Jan, 2018 - No. 200, Dec, 2018 ($3.99)

Monsters Unleashed (2017) #1 © MAR

Moon Knight (2011) #1 © MAR

More Fun Comics #12 © DC

	GD 2.0	VG 4.0	FN 6.0	VF 8.0	VF/NM 9.0	NM- 9.2
188-Intro. Sun King; Bemis-s/Burrows-a	3	6	9	21	33	45
189-Intro. The Truth	2	4	6	9	12	15
190-199						4.00
200-($4.99) Davidson-a						5.00
Annual 1 (11/19, $4.99) Acts of Evil; Moustafa & Horak-a; Kang the Conqueror app.						5.00

MOON KNIGHT (Ninth series)
Marvel Comics: Sept, 2021 - Present ($4.99/$3.99)

	GD	VG	FN	VF	VF/NM	NM-
1-($4.99)-MacKay-s/Cappuccio-a						5.00
2-19-($3.99) 4,6,7-Tigra app.						4.00
20-($4.99) Back-up story with Blade						5.00
Annual 1 (12/22, $4.99) Werewolf By Night app.; MacKay-s/Sabbatini-a						5.00

MOON KNIGHT: BLACK, WHITE & BLOOD
Marvel Comics: Jul, 2022 - No. 4, Oct, 2022 ($4.99, B&W&red, limited series)

	GD	VG	FN	VF	VF/NM	NM-
1-4: Short stories by various. 1-Hickman-s/Bachalo-a. 3-Frank Cho-c						5.00

MOON KNIGHT: DIVIDED WE FALL
Marvel Comics: 1992 ($4.95, 52 pgs.)

	GD	VG	FN	VF	VF/NM	NM-
nn-Denys Cowan-c/a(p)	3	6	9	14	19	24

MOON KNIGHT SPECIAL
Marvel Comics: Oct, 1992 ($2.50, 52 pgs.)

	GD	VG	FN	VF	VF/NM	NM-
1-Shang Chi, Master of Kung Fu-c/story						6.00

MOON KNIGHT SPECIAL EDITION
Marvel Comics Group: Nov, 1983 - No. 3, Jan, 1984 ($2.00, limited series, Baxter paper)

	GD	VG	FN	VF	VF/NM	NM-
1-Reprints from Hulk mag. by Sienkiewicz in all	3	6	9	14	19	24
2-3	1	3	4	6	8	10

MOON MULLINS (See Popular Comics, Super Book #3 & Super Comics)
Dell Publishing Co.: 1941 - 1945

	GD	VG	FN	VF	VF/NM	NM-
Four Color 14(1941)	55	110	165	352	601	850
Large Feature Comic 29(1941)	39	78	117	231	378	525
Four Color 31(1943)	17	34	51	119	265	410
Four Color 81(1945)	11	22	33	77	166	255

MOON MULLINS
Michel Publ. (American Comics Group)#1-6/St. John #7,8: Dec-Jan, 1947-48 - No. 8, Mar-May, 1949 (52 pgs)

	GD	VG	FN	VF	VF/NM	NM-
1-Alternating Sunday & daily strip-r	29	58	87	172	281	390
2	17	34	51	98	154	210
3-8: 7,8-St. John Publ. 7,8-...Featuring Kayo on-c	16	32	48	92	144	195

NOTE: ***Milt Gross** a-2-6, 8. **Frank Willard** r-all.*

MOON PILOT
Dell Publishing Co.: No. 1313, Mar-May, 1962

	GD	VG	FN	VF	VF/NM	NM-
Four Color 1313-Movie, photo-c	6	12	18	41	76	110

MOONSHADOW (Also see Farewell, Moonshadow)
Marvel Comics (Epic Comics): 5/85 - #12, 2/87 ($1.50/$1.75, mature)
(1st fully painted comic book)

	GD	VG	FN	VF	VF/NM	NM-
1-Origin; J. M. DeMatteis scripts & Jon J. Muth painted-c/a.						6.00
2-12: 11-Origin						4.00
Trade paperback (1987?)-r/#1-12						14.00
Signed & #ed HC ($39.95, 1,200 copies)-r/#1-12	4	8	12	27	44	60

MOONSHADOW
DC Comics (Vertigo): Oct, 1994 - No. 12, Aug, 1995 ($2.25/$2.95)

	GD	VG	FN	VF	VF/NM	NM-
1-11: Reprints Epic series.						3.00
12 ($2.95)-w/expanded ending						4.00
The Complete Moonshadow TPB ('98, $39.95) r/#1-12 and Farewell Moonshadow; new Muth painted-c						40.00

MOONSHINE
Image Comics: Oct, 2016 - No. 28, Nov, 2021 ($2.99/$3.99)

	GD	VG	FN	VF	VF/NM	NM-
1-6-Brian Azzarello-s/Eduardo Risso-a. 1-Covers by Risso & Frank Miller						3.00
7-28-($3.99) Azzarello-s/Risso-a						4.00

MOON-SPINNERS, THE (See Movie Comics)

MOONSTONE MONSTERS
Moonstone: 2003 - 2005 ($2.95, B&W)

	GD	VG	FN	VF	VF/NM	NM-
...: Demons ($2.95) - Short stories by various; Frenz-c						3.00
...: Ghosts ($2.95) - Short stories by various; Frenz-c						3.00
...: Sea Creatures ($2.95) - Short stories by various; Frenz-c						3.00
...: Witches ($2.95) - Short stories by various; Frenz-c						3.00
...: Zombies ($2.95) - Short stories by various; Frenz-c						3.00
Volume 1 (2004, $16.95, TPB) r/short stories from series; Wolak-c						17.00

MOONSTONE NOIR
Moonstone: 2003 - 2004 ($2.95/$4.95/$5.50, B&W)

	GD	VG	FN	VF	VF/NM	NM-
...: Bulldog Drummond (2004, $4.95) - Messner-Loebs-s/Barkley-a						5.00
...: Johnny Dollar ($4.95) - Gallaher-s/Theriault-a						5.00
...: Mr. Keen, Tracer of Lost Persons 1,2 ($2.95, limited series) - Ferguson-a						3.00
...: Mysterious Traveler (2003, $5.50) - Trevor Von Eeden-a/Joe Gentile-s						5.50
...: Mysterious Traveler Returns (2004, $4.95) - Trevor Von Eeden-a/Joe Gentile-s						5.00
...: The Lone Wolf ($4.95) - Jolley-s/Croall-a						5.00

MOPSY (See Pageant of Comics & TV Teens)
St. John Publ. Co.: Feb, 1948 - No. 19, Sept, 1953

	GD	VG	FN	VF	VF/NM	NM-
1-Part-r; reprints "Some Punkins" by Neher	52	104	156	323	549	775
2	20	40	60	120	195	270
3-10(1953): 8-Lingerie panels	18	36	54	105	165	225
11-19: 19-Lingerie-c	16	32	48	94	147	200

NOTE: *#1-7, 13, 18, 19 have paper dolls.*

MORBIUS
Marvel Comics: Jan, 2020 - No. 5, May, 2020 ($3.99)

	GD	VG	FN	VF	VF/NM	NM-
1-5-Ayala-s/Ferreira-a. 1-Intro. Elizabeth; the Melter app. 2-5-Spider-Man app.						4.00

MORBIUS: BOND OF BLOOD
Marvel Comics: Apr, 2021 ($3.99, one-shot)

	GD	VG	FN	VF	VF/NM	NM-
1-Ralph Macchio-s/Tom Reilly-a; origin told in flashback; Mister Hyde app.						4.00

MORBIUS REVISITED
Marvel Comics: Aug, 1993 - No. 5, Dec, 1993 ($1.95, mini-series)

	GD	VG	FN	VF	VF/NM	NM-
1-5-Reprints Fear #27-31						4.00

MORBIUS: THE LIVING VAMPIRE (Also see Amazing Spider-Man #101,102, Fear #20, Marvel Team-Up #3, 4, Midnight Sons Unl. & Vampire Tales)
Marvel Comics (Midnight Sons imprint #16 on): Sep, 1992 - No. 32, Apr, 1995 ($1.75/$1.95)

	GD	VG	FN	VF	VF/NM	NM-
1-($2.75, 52 pgs.)-Polybagged w/poster; Ghost Rider & Johnny Blaze x-over (part 3 of Rise of the Midnight Sons)	2	4	6	10	14	18
2	2	4	6	8	10	12
3-11,13-24,26-32: 3,4-Vs. Spider-Man-c/s.15-Ghost Rider app. 16-Spot varnish-c. 16,17-Siege of Darkness, parts 5 &13. 18-Deathlok app. 21-Bound-in Spider-Man trading card sheet; Spider-Man app.						5.00
12-($2.25)-Outer-c is a Darkhold envelope made of black parchment w/gold ink; Midnight Massacre x-over	1	3	4	6	8	10
25-($2.50, 52 pgs.)-Gold foil logo						6.00

MORBIUS: THE LIVING VAMPIRE (Marvel NOW!)
Marvel Comics: Mar, 2013 - No. 9, Nov, 2013 ($2.99)

	GD	VG	FN	VF	VF/NM	NM-
1-9: 1-Keatinge-s/Elson-a/Dell'Otto-c. 6,7-Superior Spider-Man app.						4.00

MORE FUN COMICS (Formerly New Fun Comics #1-6)
National Periodical Publs: No. 7, Jan, 1936 - No. 127, Nov-Dec, 1947 (No. 7,9-11: paper-c)

	GD	VG	FN	VF	VF/NM	NM-
7(1/36)-Oversized, paper-c; 1 pg. Kelly-a	1125	2250	3375	9000	--	--
8(2/36)-Oversized (10x12"), paper-c; 1 pg. Kelly-a; Sullivan-c	1125	2250	3375	9000	--	--
9(3-4/36)(Very rare, 1st standard-sized comic book with original material)-Last multiple panel-c	1563	3126	4689	12,500	--	--
10,11(7/36): 10-Last Henri Duval by Siegel & Shuster. 11-1st "Calling All Cars" by Siegel & Shuster; new classic logo begins	800	1600	2400	6400	--	--
12(8/36)-Slick-c begin	588	1176	1764	4700	--	--
V2#1(9/36, #13) 1 pg. Fred Astaire photo/bio	538	1076	1614	4300	--	--
2(10/36, #14)-Dr. Occult in costume (1st in color)(Superman prototype; 1st DC appearance) continues from The Comics Magazine, ends #17	2075	4150	6225	16,600	--	--
V2#3(11/36, #15), 17(V2#5)	838	1676	2514	6700	--	--
16(V2#4)-Cover numbering begins; ties with New Comics #11 as 1st DC Christmas-c; last Superman tryout issue	950	1900	2850	7600	--	--
18-20(V2#8, 5/37)	400	800	1200	3200	--	--
21(V2#9)-24(V2#12, 9/37)	258	516	774	1651	2826	4000
25(V3#1, 10/37)-27(V3#3, 12/37): 27-Xmas-c	258	516	774	1651	2826	4000
28-30: 30-1st non-funny cover	252	504	756	1613	2757	3900
31-Has ad for Action Comics #1	320	640	960	2240	3920	5600
32-35: 32-Last Dr. Occult	232	464	696	1485	2543	3600
36-40: 36-(10/38)-The Masked Ranger & sidekick Pedro begins; Ginger Snap by Bob Kane (2 pgs.; 1st-a?). 39-Xmas-c	219	438	657	1402	2401	3400
41-50: 41-Last Masked Ranger. 43-Beany (1 pg.) and Ginger Snap centerfold by Bob Kane	206	412	618	1318	2259	3200
51-The Spectre app. (in costume) in one panel ad at end of Buccaneer story	541	1082	1623	3950	6975	10,000
52-(2/40)-Origin/1st app. The Spectre (in costume splash panel only), part 1 by Bernard Baily (parts 1 & 2 written by Jerry Siegel; Spectre's costume changes color from purple & blue to green & grey; last Wing Brady; Spectre-c	16,700	33,400	50,100	117,000	208,500	300,000

GD 2.0 | VG 4.0 | FN 6.0 | VF 8.0 | VF/NM 9.0 | NM- 9.2

53-Origin The Spectre (in costume at end of story), part 2; Capt. Desmo begins; Spectre-c 3550 7100 10,650 24,800 58,400 92,000
54-The Spectre in costume; last King Carter; classic-Spectre-c 3170 6340 9510 22,200 43,600 65,000
55-(Scarce, 5/40)-Dr. Fate begins (1st app.); last Bulldog Martin; Spectre-c 3170 6340 9510 22,200 43,600 65,000
56-1st Dr. Fate-c (classic), origin continues. Congo Bill begins (6/40), 1st app.; 1200 2400 3600 9000 16,500 24,000
57-60-All Spectre-c 530 1060 1590 3869 6835 9800
61,65: 61-Classic Dr. Fate-c. 65-Classic Spectre-c 497 994 1491 3628 6414 9200
62-64,66: 63-Last Lt. Bob Neal. 64-Lance Larkin begins; all Spectre-c 389 778 1167 2723 4762 6800
67-(5/41)-Origin (1st) Dr. Fate; last Congo Bill & Biff Bronson (Congo Bill continues in Action Comics #37, 6/41)-Spectre-c 1000 2000 3000 7600 13,800 20,000
68-70: 68-Clip Carson begins. 70-Last Lance Larkin; all Dr. Fate-c 349 698 1047 2443 4272 6100
71-Origin & 1st app. Johnny Quick by Mort Weisinger (9/41); classic sci/fi Dr. Fate-c 486 972 1458 3550 6275 9000
72-Dr. Fate's new helmet; last Sgt. Carey, Sgt. O'Malley & Captain Desmo; German submarine-c (Nazi war-c) 314 628 942 2198 3849 5500
73-Origin & 1st app. Aquaman (11/41) by Paul Norris; intro. Green Arrow & Speedy; Dr. Fate-c 15,300 30,600 45,900 99,500 137,750 176,000
74-2nd Aquaman; 1st Percival Popp, Supercop; Dr. Fate-c 919 1838 2757 6709 11,855 17,000
75,76: 75-New origin Spectre; Nazi spy ring cover w/Hitler's photo. 76-Last Dr. Fate-c; Johnny Quick (by Meskin #76-97) begins, ends #107; last Clip Carson 309 618 927 2163 3782 5400
77-Green Arrow-c begin 290 580 870 1856 3178 4500
78-80 194 388 582 1242 2121 3000
81-83,85,88,90: 81-Last large logo. 82-1st small logo. 129 258 387 826 1413 2000
84-Green Arrow Japanese war-c 155 310 465 992 1696 2400
86,87-Johnny Quick-c. 87-Last Radio Squad 129 258 387 826 1413 2000
89-Origin Green Arrow & Speedy Team-up 155 310 465 992 1696 2400
91-97,99: 91-1st bi-monthly issue. 93-Dover & Clover begin (1st app., 9-10/43). 97-Kubert-a 97 194 291 621 1061 1500
98-Last Dr. Fate (scarce) 119 238 357 762 1306 1850
100 (11-12/44)-Johnny Quick-c 106 212 318 673 1162 1650
101-Origin & 1st app. Superboy (1-2/45)(not by Siegel & Shuster); last Spectre issue; Green Arrow-c 1025 2050 3075 7800 14,150 20,500
102-2nd Superboy app; 1st Dover & Clover-c 174 348 522 1114 1907 2700
103-3rd Superboy app; last Green Arrow-c 126 252 378 806 1378 1950
104-1st Superboy-c w/Dover & Clover 142 284 426 909 1555 2200
105,106-Superboy-c 123 246 369 787 1344 1900
107-Last Johnny Quick & Superboy 93 186 279 591 1021 1450
108-120: 108-Genius Jones begins; 1st c-app. (3-4/46; cont'd from Adventure Comics #102) 31 62 93 182 246 410
121-124,126: 121-123,126-Post funny animal (Jimminy & the Magic Book)-c 28 56 84 168 274 380
125-Superman c-app.w/Jimminy 106 212 318 673 1162 1650
127-(Scarce)-Post-c/a 53 106 159 334 567 800

NOTE: *All issues are scarce to rare. Cover features: The Spectre-#52-55, 57-60, 62-67. Dr. Fate-#56, 61, 68-76. The Green Arrow & Speedy-#77-85, 88-97, 99, 101 (w/Dover & Clover-#98, 103). Johnny Quick-#86, 87, 100. Dover & Clover-#102, (104, 106 w/Superboy), 107, 108(w/Genius Jones), 110, 112, 114, 117, 119. Genius Jones-#109, 111, 113, 115, 116, 118, 120.* ***Baily*** *a-45, 52-on; c-52-55, 57-60, 62-67.* ***Al Capp*** *a-45(signed Koppy).* ***Ellsworth*** *c-7.* ***Creig Flessel*** *c-30, 31, 35-48(most).* ***Guardineer*** *c-47, 49, 50.* ***Kiefer*** *a-20.* ***Meskin*** *c-86, 87, 100?* ***Moldoff*** *c-51.* ***George Papp*** *c-77-85.* ***Post*** *c-121-127.* ***Vincent Sullivan*** *c-8-28, 32-34.*

MORE FUND COMICS (Benefit book for the Comic Book Legal Defense Fund) (Also see Even More Fund Comics)
Sky Dog Press: Sept, 2003 ($10.00, B&W, trade paperback)

nn-Anthology of short stories and pin-ups by various; Hulk-c by Pérez 10.00

MORE SEYMOUR (See Seymour My Son)
Archie Publications: Oct, 1963

1-DeCarlo-a? 3 6 9 21 33 45

MORE THAN MORTAL (Also see Lady Pendragon/...)
Liar Comics: June, 1997 - No. 4, Apr, 1998 ($2.95, limited series)
Image Comics: No. 5, Dec, 1999 - No. 6, Mar, 2000 ($2.95)

1-Blue forest background-c, 1-Variant-c 4.00
1-White-c 6.00
1-2nd printing; purple sky cover 3.00
2-4: 3-Silvestri-c; 4-Two-c, one by Randy Queen 3.00
5,6: 5-1st Image Comics issue 3.00

MORE THAN MORTAL: OTHERWORLDS
Image Comics: July, 1999 - No. 4, Dec, 1999 ($2.95, limited series)

1-4-Firchow-a. 1-Two covers 3.00

MORE THAN MORTAL SAGAS
Liar Comics: Jun, 1998 - No. 3, Dec, 1998 ($2.95, limited series)

1,2-Painted art by Romano. 2-Two-c, one by Firchow 3.00
1-Variant-c by Linsner 5.00

MORE THAN MORTAL TRUTHS AND LEGENDS
Liar Comics: Aug, 1998 - No. 6, Apr, 1999 ($2.95)

1-6-Firchow-a(p) 3.00
1-Variant-c by Dan Norton 4.50

MORE TRASH FROM MAD (Annual)
E. C. Comics: 1958 - No. 12, 1969
(Note: Bonus missing = half price)

nn(1958)-8 pgs. color Mad reprint from #20 18 36 54 126 281 435
2(1959)-Market Product Labels 11 22 33 76 163 250
3(1960)-Text book covers 10 20 30 69 147 225
4(1961)-Sing Along with Mad booklet 10 20 30 69 147 225
5(1962)-Window Stickers; r/from Mad #39 8 16 24 54 102 150
6(1963)-TV Guise booklet 8 16 24 54 102 150
7(1964)-Alfred E. Neuman commemorative stamps 7 14 21 44 82 120
8(1965)-Life size poster-Alfred E. Neuman 5 10 15 35 63 90
9-12: 9,10(1966-67)-Mischief Sticker. 11(1968)-Campaign poster & bumper sticker. 12(1969)-Pocket medals 5 10 15 35 63 90

NOTE: ***Kelly Freas*** *c-1, 2, 4.* ***Mingo*** *c-3, 5-9, 12.*

MORGAN THE PIRATE (Movie)
Dell Publishing Co.: No. 1227, Sept-Nov, 1961

Four Color 1227-Photo-c 7 14 21 46 86 125

MORLOCKS
Marvel Comics: June, 2002 - No. 4, Sept, 2002 ($2.50, limited series)

1-4-Johns-s/Martinbrough-c/a. 1-1st app. Angel Dust 3.00

MORLOCK 2001
Atlas/Seaboard Publ.: Feb, 1975 - No. 3, July, 1975

1,2: 1-(Super-hero)-Origin & 1st app.; Milgrom-c 2 4 6 11 16 20
3-Ditko/Wrightson-a; origin The Midnight Man & The Mystery Men 3 6 9 15 22 28

MORNING GLORIES
Image Comics: Aug, 2010 - Present ($3.99/$3.50/$2.99)

1-($3.99) Nick Spencer-s/Joe Eisma-a/Rodin Esquejo-c; group cover 12.00
1-Second-Fourth printings 4.00
2-($3.50) Regular cover and white background 2nd printing 5.00
3-6-Regular covers and white background 2nd printings 4.00
7-23-($2.99) 3.00
24,25,27,28-($3.99) 4.00
26-($1.00) Start of Season Two 3.00
29-48-($3.50) 3.50
49-($4.99) Spencer-s/Eisma-a 5.00
50-(7/16, $5.99) 6.00
...Vol. 1 TPB (2/11, $9.99) r/#1-6 10.00

MORNINGSTAR SPECIAL
Comico: Apr, 1990 ($2.50)

1-From the Elementals; Willingham-c/a/scripts 3.00

MORTAL KOMBAT
Malibu Comics: July, 1994 - No. 6, Dec, 1994 ($2.95)

1-Two diff. covers exist 2 4 6 10 14 18
1-Limited edition gold foil embossed-c 3 6 9 16 23 30
2-6 6.00
0 (12/94), Special Edition 1 (11/94) 3 6 9 16 23 30
Tournament Edition I12/94, $3.95), II('95)($3.95) 2 4 6 13 18 22
...: **BARAKA** ,June, 1995 ($2.95, one-shot) #1; ...**BATTLEWAVE** ,2/95 - No. 6, 7/95 , #1-6; ...**GORO, PRINCE OF PAIN** ,9/94 - No. 3, 11/94, #1-3; ...**KITANA AND MILEENA** ,8/95 , ...**KUNG LAO** ,7/95 , #1; ... **RAYDON & KANO** ,3/95 - No. 3, 5/95, #1-3: ...(all $2.95-c) 2 4 6 9 12 15
...: **U.S. SPECIAL FORCES** (1/95 - No. 2, $3.50), 1,2 2 4 6 9 12 15

MORTAL KOMBAT X
DC Comics: Mar, 2015 - No. 12, Jan, 2016 ($3.99, printings of digital-first stories)

1-Kittelsen-s/Soy-a/Reis-c 2 4 6 9 12 15
2-6 1 2 3 5 6 8
7-12: 9-12-Jae Lee-c 5.00

MORTIE (Mazie's Friend; also see Flat-Top)
Magazine Publishers: Dec, 1952 - No. 4, June, 1953?

1 14 28 42 82 121 160
2-4 8 16 24 44 57 70

MORTIGAN GOTH: IMMORTALIS (See Marvel Frontier Comics Unlimited)
Marvel Comics: Sept, 1993 - No. 4, Mar, 1994 ($1.95, mini-series)

1-($2.95)-Foil-c 4.00
2-4 3.00

MORT THE DEAD TEENAGER
Marvel Comics: Nov, 1993 - No. 4, Mar, 1994 ($1.75, mini-series)

1-4 3.00

MORTY MEEKLE
Dell Publishing Co.: No. 793, May, 1957

Four Color 793 5 10 15 30 50 70

MOSAIC
Marvel Comics: Dec, 2016 - No. 8, Jul, 2017 ($4.99/$3.99)

1-($4.99) Geoffrey Thorne-s/Khary Randolph-a; intro. Morris Sackett 5.00
2-8-($3.99) 3,4-Spider-Man app. 6-Inhumans app. 8-Diablo app. 4.00

MOSES & THE TEN COMMANDMENTS (See Dell Giants)

MOSTLY WANTED
DC Comics (WildStorm): Jul, 2000 - No. 4, Nov, 2000 ($2.50, limited series)

1-4-Lobdell-s/Flores-a 3.00

MOTEL HELL (Based on the 1980 movie)
IDW Publishing: Oct, 2010 - No. 3, Dec, 2010 ($3.99, limited series)

1-3-Matt Nixon-s/Chris Moreno-a. 1,2-Bradstreet-c. 3-Moreno-c 4.00

MOTH, THE
Dark Horse Comics: Apr, 2004 - No. 4, Aug, 2004 ($2.99)

1-4-Steve Rude-c/a; Gary Martin-s 3.00
... Special (3/04, $4.95) 5.00
TPB (5/05, $12.95) r/#1-4 and Special; gallery of extras 13.00

MOTH, THE
Rude Dude Productions: May 2008 (Free Comic Book Day giveaway)

... Special Edition - Steve Rude-s/a; sketch pages 3.00

MOTH & WHISPER
AfterShock Comics: Sept, 2018 - No. 5, Jan, 2019 ($3.99, limited series)

1-5-Ted Anderson-s/Jen Hickman-a 4.00

MOTHER GOOSE AND NURSERY RHYME COMICS (See Christmas With Mother Goose)

Morning Glories #1 © Spencer & Eisma

Mother Panic #1 © DC

Motor Girl #6 © Terry Moore

Dell Publishing Co.: No. 41, 1944 - No. 862, Nov, 1957

	GD 2.0	VG 4.0	FN 6.0	VF 8.0	VF/NM 9.0	NM- 9.2
Four Color 41-Walt Kelly-c/a	26	52	78	182	404	625
Four Color 59, 68-Kelly c/a	19	38	57	131	291	450
Four Color 862-The Truth About..., Movie (Disney)	7	14	21	48	89	130

MOTHERLANDS
DC Comics (Vertigo): Mar, 2018 - No. 6, Aug, 2018 ($3.99, limited series)

	GD 2.0	VG 4.0	FN 6.0	VF 8.0	VF/NM 9.0	NM- 9.2
1-6-Spurrier-s/Stott-a/Canete-c						4.00

MOTHER PANIC
DC Comics (Young Animal): Jan, 2017 - No. 12, Dec, 2017 ($3.99)

	GD 2.0	VG 4.0	FN 6.0	VF 8.0	VF/NM 9.0	NM- 9.2
1-12: 1-Houser-s/Edwards-a; Batman cameo. 3-Batman & Batwoman app. 7-9-Leon-a						4.00
.../ Batman Special 1 (4/18, $4.99) Part 2 of Milk Wars crossover; Templeton-a/Quitely-c						5.00

MOTHER PANIC: GOTHAM A.D.
DC Comics (Young Animal): May, 2018 - No. 6, Oct, 2018 ($3.99)

	GD 2.0	VG 4.0	FN 6.0	VF 8.0	VF/NM 9.0	NM- 9.2
1-6: 1-Houser-s/Moustafa-a/Edwards-c. 1-Joker cameo. 2-Catwoman app.						4.00

MOTHER TERESA OF CALCUTTA
Marvel Comics Group: 1984

	GD 2.0	VG 4.0	FN 6.0	VF 8.0	VF/NM 9.0	NM- 9.2
1-(52 pgs.) No ads	2	4	6	9	12	15

MOTHS (Also see The Resistance)
Artists, Writers & Artisans, Inc.: Jun, 2021 - No. 6, Nov, 2021 ($3.99, limited series)

	GD 2.0	VG 4.0	FN 6.0	VF 8.0	VF/NM 9.0	NM- 9.2
1-6-J. Michael Straczynski-s/Mike Choi-a						4.00

MOTION PICTURE COMICS (See Fawcett Movie Comics)
Fawcett Publications: No. 101, 1950 - No. 114, Jan, 1953 (All-photo-c)

	GD 2.0	VG 4.0	FN 6.0	VF 8.0	VF/NM 9.0	NM- 9.2
101- "Vanishing Westerner"; Monte Hale (1950)	16	32	48	98	154	210
102- "Code of the Silver Sage"; Rocky Lane (1/51)	15	30	45	83	124	165
103- "Covered Wagon Raid"; Rocky Lane (3/51)	15	30	45	83	124	165
104- "Vigilante Hideout"; Rocky Lane (5/51)-Book length Powell-a	15	30	45	83	124	165
105- "Red Badge of Courage"; Audie Murphy; Bob Powell-a (7/51)	20	40	60	114	182	250
106- "The Texas Rangers"; George Montgomery (9/51)	15	30	45	83	124	165
107- "Frisco Tornado"; Rocky Lane (11/51)	14	28	42	80	115	150
108- "Mask of the Avenger"; John Derek	12	24	36	69	97	125
109- "Rough Rider of Durango"; Rocky Lane	14	28	42	80	115	150
110- "When Worlds Collide"; George Evans-a (5/52); Williamson & Evans drew themselves in story; (also see Famous Funnies No. 72-88)	81	162	243	518	884	1250
111- "The Vanishing Outpost"; Lash LaRue	15	30	45	90	140	190
112- "Brave Warrior"; Jon Hall & Jay Silverheels	12	24	36	67	94	120
113- "Walk East on Beacon"; George Murphy; Schaffenberger-a	10	20	30	54	72	90
114- "Cripple Creek"; George Montgomery (1/53)	10	20	30	58	79	100

MOTION PICTURE FUNNIES WEEKLY (See Promotional Comics section)

MOTOR CRUSH
Image Comics: Dec, 2016 - No. 11, Apr, 2018 ($3.99)

	GD 2.0	VG 4.0	FN 6.0	VF 8.0	VF/NM 9.0	NM- 9.2
1-11-Fletcher & Stewart-s/Tarr-a; covers by Tarr & Stewart. 6-Stewart-a						4.00

MOTOR GIRL
Abstract Studio: 2016 - No. 10, 2017 ($3.99, B&W)

	GD 2.0	VG 4.0	FN 6.0	VF 8.0	VF/NM 9.0	NM- 9.2
1-10-Terry Moore-s/a/c						4.00

MOTORHEAD (See Comic's Greatest World)
Dark Horse Comics: Aug, 1995 - No. 6, Jan, 1996 ($2.50)

	GD 2.0	VG 4.0	FN 6.0	VF 8.0	VF/NM 9.0	NM- 9.2
1-6: Bisley-c on all. 1-Predator app.						3.00
Special 1 (3/94, $3.95, 52pgs.)-Jae Lee-c; Barb Wire, The Machine & Wolf Gang app.						4.00

MOTORMOUTH (... & Killpower #7? on)
Marvel Comics UK: June, 1992 - No. 12, May, 1993 ($1.75)

	GD 2.0	VG 4.0	FN 6.0	VF 8.0	VF/NM 9.0	NM- 9.2
1-13: 1,2-Nick Fury app. 3-Punisher-c/story. 5,6-Nick Fury & Punisher app. 6-Cable cameo. 7-9-Cable app.						3.00

MOUNTAIN MEN (See Ben Bowie)

MOUSE MUSKETEERS (See M.G.M.'s...)

MOUSE ON THE MOON, THE (See Movie Classics)

MOVEMENT, THE
DC Comics: Jul, 2013 - No. 12, Jul. 2014 ($2.99)

	GD 2.0	VG 4.0	FN 6.0	VF 8.0	VF/NM 9.0	NM- 9.2
1-12: 1-Gail Simone-s/Freddie Williams-a/Amanda Conner-c. 2-4-Rainmaker app. 9,10-Batgirl app.						3.00

MOVIE CARTOONS
DC Comics: Dec, 1944 (cover only ashcan)

nn-Ashcan comic, not distributed to newsstands, only for in house use. Covers were produced, but not the rest of the book. A copy sold in 2006 for $500.

MOVIE CLASSICS
Dell Publishing Co.: Apr, 1956; May-Jul, 1962 - Dec, 1969

(Before 1963, most movie adaptations were part of the 4-Color series)
(Disney movie adaptations after 1970 are in Walt Disney Showcase)

	GD 2.0	VG 4.0	FN 6.0	VF 8.0	VF/NM 9.0	NM- 9.2
Around the World Under the Sea 12-030-612 (12/66)	4	8	12	23	37	50
Bambi 3(4/56)-Disney; r/4-Color #186	5	10	15	33	57	80
Battle of the Bulge 12-056-606 (6/66)	3	6	9	20	31	42
Beach Blanket Bingo 12-058-509	7	14	21	46	86	125
Bon Voyage 01-068-212 (12/62)-Disney; photo-c	3	6	9	21	33	45
Castilian, The 12-110-401	3	6	9	19	30	40
Cat, The 12-109-612 (12/66)	3	6	9	20	31	42
Cheyenne Autumn 12-112-506 (4-6/65)	5	10	15	31	53	75
Circus World, Samuel Bronston's 12-115-411; John Wayne app.; John Wayne photo-c	9	18	27	58	114	170
Countdown 12-150-710 (10/67)-James Caan photo-c	3	6	9	20	31	42
Creature, The 1 (12-142-302) (12-2/62-63)	29	58	87	209	467	725
Creature, The 12-142-410 (10/64)	7	14	21	46	86	125
David Ladd's Life Story 12-173-212 (10-12/62)-Photo-c	6	12	18	40	73	105
Die, Monster, Die 12-175-603 (3/66)-Photo-c	6	12	18	37	66	95
Dirty Dozen 12-180-710 (10/67)	5	10	15	34	60	85
Dr. Who & the Daleks 12-190-612 (12/66)-Peter Cushing photo-c; 1st U.S. app. of Dr. Who	25	50	75	175	388	600
Dracula 12-231-212 (10-12/62)	10	20	30	69	147	225
El Dorado 12-240-710 (10/67)-John Wayne; photo-c	12	24	36	82	179	275
Ensign Pulver 12-257-410 (8-10/64)	3	6	9	18	28	38
Frankenstein 12-283-305 (3-5/63)(see Frankenstein 8-10/64 for 2nd printing)	10	20	30	69	147	225
Great Race, The 12-299-603 (3/66)-Natallie Wood, Tony Curtis photo-c	5	10	15	30	50	70
Hallelujah Trail, The 12-307-602 (2/66) (Shows 1/66 inside); Burt Lancaster, Lee Remick photo-c	5	10	15	31	53	75
Hatari 12-340-301 (1/63)-John Wayne	7	14	21	48	89	130
Horizontal Lieutenant, The 01-348-210 (10/62)	3	6	9	18	28	38
Incredible Mr. Limpet, The 12-370-408; Don Knotts photo-c	5	10	15	31	53	75
Jack the Giant Killer 12-374-301 (1/63)	7	14	21	48	89	130
Jason & the Argonauts 12-376-310 (8-10/63)-Photo-c	9	18	27	62	126	190
Lancelot & Guinevere 12-416-310 (10/63)	5	10	15	30	50	70
Lawrence 12-426-308 (8/63)-Story of Lawrence of Arabia; movie ad on back-c; not exactly like movie	5	10	15	30	50	70
Lion of Sparta 12-439-301 (1/63)	4	8	12	23	37	50
Mad Monster Party 12-460-801 (9/67)-Based on Kurtzman's screenplay	9	18	27	63	129	195
Magic Sword, The 01-496-209 (9/62)	5	10	15	33	57	80
Masque of the Red Death 12-490-410 (8-10/64)-Vincent Price photo-c	7	14	21	44	82	120
Maya 12-495-612 (12/66)-Clint Walker & Jay North part photo-c	4	8	12	25	40	55
McHale's Navy 12-500-412 (10-12/64)	4	8	12	27	44	60
Merrill's Marauders 12-510-301 (1/63)-Photo-c	3	6	9	18	28	38
Mouse on the Moon, The 12-530-312 (10/12/63)-Photo-c	3	6	9	21	33	45
Mummy, The 12-537-211 (9-11/62) 2 versions with different back-c	20	40	60	138	307	475
Music Man, The 12-538-301 (1/63)	3	6	9	19	30	40
Naked Prey, The 12-545-612 (12/66)-Photo-c	5	10	15	31	53	75
Night of the Grizzly, The 12-558-612 (12/66)-Photo-c	4	8	12	23	37	50
None But the Brave 12-565-506 (4-6/65)	5	10	15	31	53	75
Operation Bikini 12-597-310 (10/63)-Photo-c	4	8	12	23	37	50
Operation Crossbow 12-590-512 (10-12/65)	3	6	9	19	30	40
Prince & the Pauper, The 01-654-207 (5-7/62)-Disney	4	8	12	23	37	50
Raven, The 12-680-309 (9/63)-Vincent Price photo-c	6	12	18	38	69	100
Ring of Bright Water 01-701-910 (10/69) (inside shows #12-701-909)	3	6	9	21	33	45
Runaway, The 12-707-412 (10-12/64)	3	6	9	18	28	38
Santa Claus Conquers the Martians #? (1964)-Photo-c	12	24	36	82	179	275
Santa Claus Conquers the Martians 12-725-603 (3/66, 12¢)-Reprints 1964 issue; photo-c	8	16	24	51	96	140

GD 2.0 | VG 4.0 | FN 6.0 | VF 8.0 | VF/NM 9.0 | NM- 9.2

Another version given away with a Golden Record, SLP 170, nn, no price
(3/66)-Complete with record 11 22 33 75 160 245
Six Black Horses 12-750-301 (1/63)-Photo-c 3 6 9 19 30 40
Ski Party 12-743-511 (9-11/65)-Frankie Avalon photo-c; photo inside-c; Adkins-a
4 8 12 28 47 65
Smoky 12-746-702 (2/67) 3 6 9 18 28 38
Sons of Katie Elder 12-748-511 (9-11/65); John Wayne app.; photo-c
10 20 30 68 144 220
Tales of Terror 12-793-302 (2/63)-Evans-a 5 10 15 35 63 90
Three Stooges Meet Hercules 01-828-208 (8/62)-Photo-c
9 18 27 63 129 195
Tomb of Ligeia 12-830-506 (4-6/65) 5 10 15 31 53 75
Treasure Island 01-845-211 (7-9/62)-Disney; r/4-Color #624
3 6 9 19 30 40
Twice Told Tales (Nathaniel Hawthorne) 12-840-401 (11-1/63-64);
Vincent Price photo-c 5 10 15 34 60 85
Two on a Guillotine 12-850-506 (4-6/65) 3 6 9 21 33 45
Valley of Gwangi 01-880-912 (12/69) 8 16 24 55 105 155
War Gods of the Deep 12-900-509 (7-9/65) 3 6 9 19 30 40
War Wagon, The 12-533-709 (9/67); John Wayne app.
8 16 24 51 96 140
Who's Minding the Mint? 12-924-708 (8/67) 3 6 9 18 28 38
Wolfman, The 12-922-308 (6-8/63) 10 20 30 67 141 215
Wolfman, The 1(12-922-410)(8-10/64)-2nd printing; r/#12-922-308
5 10 15 30 50 70
Zulu 12-950-410 (8-10/64)-Photo-c 7 14 21 44 82 120

MOVIE COMICS (See Cinema Comics Herald & Fawcett Movie Comics)

MOVIE COMICS
National Periodical Publications/Picture Comics: April, 1939 - No. 6, Sept-Oct, 1939 (Most all photo-c)

1- "Gunga Din", "Son of Frankenstein", "The Great Man Votes", "Fisherman's Wharf", & "Scouts to the Rescue" part 1; Wheelan "Minute Movies" begin
366 732 1098 2562 4481 6400
2- "Stagecoach", "The Saint Strikes Back", "King of the Turf","Scouts to the Rescue" part 2, "Arizona Legion", Andy Devine photo-c 274 548 822 1754 3027 4300
3- "East Side of Heaven", "Mystery in the White Room", "Four Feathers", "Mexican Rose" with Gene Autry, "Spirit of Culver", "Many Secrets", "The Mikado" (1st Gene Autry photo cover) 206 412 618 1318 2259 3200
4- "Captain Fury", Gene Autry in "Blue Montana Skies", "Streets of N.Y." with Jackie Cooper, "Oregon Trail" part 1 with Johnny Mack Brown, "Big Town Czar" with Barton MacLane, & "Star Reporter" with Warren Hull 152 304 456 965 1658 2350
5- "The Man in the Iron Mask", "Five Came Back", "Wolf Call", "The Girl & the Gambler", "The House of Fear", "The Family Next Door", "Oregon Trail" part 2
165 330 495 1056 1803 2550
6- "The Phantom Creeps", "Chumps at Oxford", & "The Oregon Trail" part 3; 2nd Robot-c
271 542 813 1734 2967 4200

NOTE: *Above books contain many original movie stills with dialogue from movie scripts. All issues are scarce.*

MOVIE COMICS
Fiction House Magazines: Dec, 1946 - No. 4, 1947

1-Big Town (by Lubbers), Johnny Danger begin; Celardo-a; Mitzi of the Movies by Fran Hopper 45 90 135 284 480 675
2-(2/47)- "White Tie & Tails" with William Bendix; Mitzi of the Movies begins; Matt Baker-a 35 70 105 208 339 470
3-(6/47)-Andy Hardy starring Mickey Rooney 35 70 105 208 339 470
4-Mitzi In Hollywood by Matt Baker; Merton of the Movies with Red Skelton; Yvonne DeCarlo & George Brent in "Slave Girl" 40 80 120 246 411 575

MOVIE COMICS
Gold Key/Whitman: Oct, 1962 - 1984

Alice in Wonderland 10144-503 (3/65)-Disney; partial reprint of 4-Color #331
4 8 12 25 40 55
Alice In Wonderland #1 (Whitman pre-pack, 3/84) 2 4 6 13 18 22
Aristocats, The 1 (30045-103)(3/71)-Disney; with pull-out poster (25¢)
(No poster = half price) 6 12 18 40 73 105
Bambi 1 (10087-309)(9/63)-Disney; r/4-C #186 4 8 12 28 47 65
Bambi 2 (10087-607)(7/66)-Disney; r/4-C #186 4 8 12 22 35 48
Beneath the Planet of the Apes 30044-012 (12/70)-with pull-out poster; photo-c
(No poster = half price) 10 20 30 64 132 200
Big Red 10026-211 (11/62)-Disney; photo-c 3 6 9 19 30 40
Big Red 10026-503 (3/65)-Disney; reprints 10026-211; photo-c
3 6 9 16 23 30
Blackbeard's Ghost 10222-806 (6/68)-Disney 3 6 9 18 28 38
Bullwhip Griffin 10181-706 (6/67)-Disney; Spiegle-a; photo-c
3 6 9 21 33 45
Captain Sindbad 10077-309 (9/63)-Manning-a; photo-c
5 10 15 35 63 90
Chitty Chitty Bang Bang 1 (30038-902)(2/69)-with pull-out poster; Disney; photo-c
(No poster = half price) 7 14 21 44 82 120
Cinderella 10152-508 (8/65)-Disney; r/4-C #786 5 10 15 30 50 70
Darby O'Gill & the Little People 10251-001(1/70)-Disney; reprints 4-Color #1024 (Toth-a);
photo-c 4 8 12 28 47 65
Dumbo 1 (10090-310)(10/63)-Disney; r/4-C #668 4 8 12 25 40 55
Emil & the Detectives 10120-502 (11/64)-Disney; photo-c & back-c photo pin-up
3 6 9 19 30 40
Escapade in Florence 1 (10043-301)(1/63)-Disney; starring Annette Funicello
7 14 21 48 89 130
Fall of the Roman Empire 10118-407 (7/64); Sophia Loren photo-c
4 8 12 23 37 50
Fantastic Voyage 10178-702 (2/67)-Wood/Adkins-a; photo-c
6 12 18 37 66 95
55 Days at Peking 10081-309 (9/63)-Photo-c 3 6 9 19 30 40
Fighting Prince of Donegal, The 10193-701 (1/67)-Disney
3 6 9 18 28 38
First Men in the Moon 10132-503 (3/65)-Fred Fredericks-a; photo-c
4 8 12 27 44 60
Gay Purr-ee 30017-301(1/63, 84 pgs.) 5 10 15 31 53 75

Gnome Mobile, The 10207-710 (10/67)-Disney; Walter Brennan photo-c & back-c photo pin-up
4 8 12 23 37 50
Goodbye, Mr. Chips 10246-006 (6/70)-Peter O'Toole photo-c
3 6 9 19 30 40
Happiest Millionaire, The 10221-804 (4/68)-Disney 3 6 9 21 33 45
Hey There, It's Yogi Bear 10122-409 (9/64)-Hanna-Barbera
6 12 18 37 66 95
Horse Without a Head, The 10109-401 (1/64)-Disney 3 6 9 18 28 38
How the West Was Won 10074-307 (7/63)-Based on the L'Amour novel; Tufts-a
4 8 12 27 44 60
In Search of the Castaways 10048-303 (3/63)-Disney; Hayley Mills photo-c
6 12 18 37 66 95
Jungle Book, The 1 (6022-801)(1/68-Whitman)-Disney; large size (10x13-1/2"); 59¢
6 12 18 38 69 100
Jungle Book, The 1 (30033-803)(3/68, 68 pgs.)-Disney; same contents as Whitman #1
4 8 12 23 37 50
Jungle Book, The 1 (6/78, $1.00 tabloid) 3 6 9 16 23 30
Jungle Book (7/84)-r/Giant; Whitman pre-pack 2 4 6 10 14 18
Kidnapped 10080-306 (6/63)-Disney; reprints 4-Color #1101; photo-c
4 8 12 23 37 50
King Kong 30036-809(9/68-68 pgs.)-painted-c 8 16 24 54 102 150
King Kong nn-Whitman Treasury($1.00, 68 pgs.,1968), same cover as Gold Key issue
7 14 21 44 82 120
King Kong 11299(#1-786, 10x13-1/4", 68 pgs., $1.00, 1978)
3 6 9 20 31 42
Lady and the Tramp 10042-301 (1/63)-Disney; r/4-Color #629
6 12 18 38 69 100
Lady and the Tramp 1 (1967-Giant; 25¢)-Disney; reprints part of Dell #1
5 10 15 35 63 90
Lady and the Tramp 2 (10042-203)(3/72)-Disney; r/4-Color #629
3 6 9 21 33 45
Legend of Lobo, The 1 (10059-303)(3/63)-Disney; photo-c
3 6 9 16 23 30
Lt. Robin Crusoe, U.S.N. 10191-610 (10/66)-Disney; Dick Van Dyke photo-c & back-c photo
pin-up 3 6 9 17 26 35
Lion, The 10035-301 (1/63)-Photo-c 3 6 9 16 24 32
Lord Jim 10156-509 (9/65)-Photo-c 3 6 9 16 24 32
Love Bug, The 10237-906 (6/69)-Disney; Buddy Hackett photo-c
4 8 12 27 44 60
Mary Poppins 10136-501 (1/65)-Disney; photo-c 5 10 15 33 57 80
Mary Poppins 30023-501 (1/65-68 pgs.)-Disney; photo-c
7 14 21 48 89 130
McLintock 10110-403 (3/64); John Wayne app.; John Wayne & Maureen O'Hara photo-c
10 20 30 69 147 225
Merlin Jones as the Monkey's Uncle 10115-510 (10/65)-Disney; Annette Funicello
front/back photo-c 5 10 15 34 60 85
Miracle of the White Stallions, The 10065-306 (6/63)-Disney
3 6 9 18 28 38
Misadventures of Merlin Jones, The 10115-405 (5/64)-Disney; Annette Funicello
photo front/back-c 5 10 15 34 60 85
Moon-Spinners, The 10124-410 (10/64)-Disney; Hayley Mills photo-c
6 12 18 37 66 95
Mutiny on the Bounty 1 (10040-302)(2/63)-Marlon Brando photo-c
3 6 9 21 33 45
Nikki, Wild Dog of the North 10141-412 (12/64)-Disney; reprints 4-Color #1226
3 6 9 16 23 30
Old Yeller 10168-601 (1/66)-Disney; reprints 4-Color #869; photo-c
3 6 9 16 23 30
One Hundred & One Dalmations 1 (10247-002) (2/70)-Disney; reprints Four Color #1183
3 6 9 21 33 45
Peter Pan 1 (10086-309)(9/63)-Disney; reprints Four Color #442
4 8 12 23 37 50
Peter Pan 2 (10086-909)(9/69)-Disney; reprints Four Color #442
3 6 9 18 28 38
Peter Pan 1 (3/84)-r/4-Color #442; Whitman pre-pack 3 6 9 14 19 24
P.T. 109 10123-409 (9/64)-John F. Kennedy 5 10 15 30 50 70
Rio Conchos 10143-503(3/65) 3 6 9 21 33 45
Robin Hood 10163-506 (6/65)-Disney; reprints Four Color #413
3 6 9 16 24 32
Shaggy Dog & the Absent-Minded Professor 30032-708 (8/67-Giant, 68 pgs.) Disney;
reprints 4-Color #985,1199 5 10 15 30 50 70
Sleeping Beauty 1 (30042-009)(9/70)-Disney; reprints Four Color #973; with pull-out poster
(No poster = half price) 7 14 21 44 82 120
Snow White & the Seven Dwarfs 1 (10091-310)(10/63)-Disney; reprints Four Color #382
4 8 12 27 44 60
Snow White & the Seven Dwarfs 10091-709 (9/67)-Disney; reprints Four Color #382
3 6 9 21 33 45
Snow White & the Seven Dwarfs 90091-204 (2/84)-Reprints Four Color #382;
Whitman pre-pack 2 4 6 11 16 20
Son of Flubber 1 (10057-304)(4/63)-Disney; sequel to "The Absent-Minded Professor"
3 6 9 21 33 45
Summer Magic 10076-309 (9/63)-Disney; Hayley Mills photo-c; Manning-a
6 12 18 38 69 100
Swiss Family Robinson 10236-904 (4/69)-Disney; reprints Four Color #1156; photo-c
4 8 12 25 40 55
Sword in the Stone, The 30019-402 (2/64-Giant, 68 pgs.)-Disney (see March of Comics #258
& Wart and the Wizard 6 12 18 42 79 115
That Darn Cat 10171-602 (2/66)-Disney; Hayley Mills photo-c
6 12 18 38 69 100
Those Magnificent Men in Their Flying Machines 10162-510 (10/65); photo-c
3 6 9 19 30 40
Three Stooges in Orbit 30016-211 (11/62-Giant, 32 pgs.)-All photos from movie; stiff-photo-c
9 18 27 60 120 180
Tiger Walks, A 10117-406 (6/64)-Disney; Torres?, Tufts-a; photo-c
4 8 12 23 37 50
Toby Tyler 10142-502 (2/65)-Disney; reprints Four Color #1092; photo-c
3 6 9 17 26 35

Movie Comics #3 © FH

MPH #1 © Millarworld & Fegredo

Ms. Marvel (2014) #7 © MAR

GD VG FN VF VF/NM NM-
2.0 4.0 6.0 8.0 9.0 9.2

Treasure Island 1 (10200-703)(3/67)-Disney; reprints Four Color #624; photo-c
3 6 9 16 23 30
20,000 Leagues Under the Sea 1 (10095-312)(12/63)-Disney; reprints Four Color #614
3 6 9 19 30 40
Wonderful Adventures of Pinocchio, The 1 (10089-310)(10/63)-Disney; reprints Four Color #545
(see Wonderful Advs. of...) 4 8 12 23 37 50
Wonderful Adventures of Pinocchio, The 10089-109 (9/71)-Disney; reprints Four Color #545
3 6 9 16 24 32
Wonderful World of the Brothers Grimm 1 (10008-210)(10/62)
5 10 15 30 50 70
X, the Man with the X-Ray Eyes 10083-309 (9/63)-Ray Milland photo on-c
7 14 21 48 89 130
Yellow Submarine 35000-902 (2/69-Giant, 68 pgs.)-With pull-out poster;
The Beatles cartoon movie; Paul S. Newman-s 28 56 84 202 451 700
Without poster 10 20 30 64 132 200

MOVIE FABLES
DC Comics: Dec, 1944 (cover only ashcan)

nn-Ashcan comic, not distributed to newsstands, only for in house use. Covers were produced, but not the rest of the book. A copy sold in 2006 for $500.

MOVIE GEMS
DC Comics: Dec, 1944 (cover only ashcan)

nn-Ashcan comic, not distributed to newsstands, only for in house use. Covers were produced, but not the rest of the book. A copy sold in 2006 for $500.

MOVIE LOVE (Also see Personal Love)
Famous Funnies: Feb, 1950 - No. 22, Aug, 1953 (All photo-c)

1-Dick Powell, Evelyn Keyes, & Mickey Rooney photo-c
27 54 81 158 259 360
2-Myrna Loy photo-c 15 30 45 90 140 190
3-7,9: 6-Ricardo Montalban photo-c. 9-Gene Tierney, John Lund, Glenn Ford, & Rhonda Fleming photo-c. 14 28 42 81 118 155
8-Williamson/Frazetta-a, 6 pgs. 60 120 180 381 653 925
10-Frazetta-a, 6 pgs. 60 120 180 381 653 925
11,14-16: 14-Janet Leigh photo-c 14 28 42 80 115 150
12-Dean Martin & Jerry Lewis photo-c (12/51, pre-dates Advs. of Dean Martin & Jerry Lewis comic) 30 60 90 177 289 400
13-Ronald Reagan photo-c with 1 pg. biog. 37 74 111 218 354 490
17-Leslie Caron & Ralph Meeker photo-c; 1 pg. Frazetta ad
14 28 42 78 112 145
18-22: 19-John Derek photo-c. 20-Donald O'Connor & Debbie Reynolds photo-c. 21-Paul Henreid & Patricia Medina photo-c. 22-John Payne & Coleen Gray photo-c
13 26 39 74 105 135
NOTE: *Each issue has a full-length movie adaptation with photo covers.*

MOVIE MONSTERS (Magazine)
Atlas/Seaboard: Dec, 1974 - No. 4, Aug, 1975 (B&W; Film, photo & article magazine)

1-(84 pages) Planet of the Apes, King Kong, Sindbad & Harryhausen, Christopher Lee Dracula, Star Trek, Werewolf, Creature from the Black Lagoon, Hammer's Mummy, Gorgo, & Exorcist 4 8 12 28 47 65
2-(2/1975) 2001: Planet of the Apes-c; 2001: A Space Odyssey; Doc Savage; Frankenstein; Rodan; One Million Years BC; (lower print run) 4 8 12 28 47 65
3-(4/1975) Phantom of the Opera-c; Wolfman, Godzilla, Boris Karloff, Batman, Forbidden Planet, Jack the Giant Killer 4 8 12 27 44 60
4-(8/1975) Thing, Flash Gordon, Lon Chaney Jr., Lost Worlds, Loch Ness Monster, Day the Earth Stood Still, Star Trek 4 8 12 27 44 60

MOVIE THRILLERS (Movie)
Magazine Enterprises: 1949

1-Adaptation of "Rope of Sand" w/Burt Lancaster; Burt Lancaster photo-c
30 60 90 177 289 400

MOVIE TOWN ANIMAL ANTICS (Formerly Animal Antics; becomes Raccoon Kids #52 on)
National Periodical Publ.: No. 24, Jan-Feb, 1950 - No. 51, July-Aug, 1954

24-Raccoon Kids continue 12 24 36 67 94 120
25-51 10 20 30 54 72 90
NOTE: ***Sheldon Mayer** a-28-33, 35, 37-41, 43, 44, 47, 49-51.*

MOVIE TUNES COMICS (Formerly Animated...; Frankie No. 4 on)
Marvel Comics (MgPC): No. 3, Fall, 1946

3-Super Rabbit, Krazy Krow, Silly Seal & Ziggy Pig 20 40 60 115 188 260

MOWGLI JUNGLE BOOK (Rudyard Kipling's...)
Dell Publ. Co.: No. 487, Aug-Oct, 1953 - No. 620, Apr, 1955

Four Color 487 (#1) 8 16 24 52 99 145
Four Color 582 (8/54), 620 5 10 15 34 60 85

MPH

GD VG FN VF VF/NM NM-
2.0 4.0 6.0 8.0 9.0 9.2

Image Comics: May, 2014 - No. 5, Feb, 2015 ($2.99/$4.99)

1-4-($2.99) Mark Millar-s/Duncan Fegredo-a; multiple covers on each 3.00
5-($4.99) Two covers 5.00

MR. (See Mister)

MRS. DEADPOOL AND THE HOWLING COMMANDOS (Secret Wars tie-in)
Marvel Comics: Aug, 2015 - No. 4, Nov, 2015 ($3.99, limited series)

1-4-Duggan-s/Espin-a; Dracula and Ghost Deadpool app. 4.00

M. REX
Image Comics: July, 1999 - No. 2, Dec, 1999 ($2.95)

Preview ($5.00) B&W pages and sketchbook; Rouleau-a 5.00
1,2-($2.95) 1-Joe Kelly-s/Rouleau-a/Anacleto-c. 2-Rouleau-c 3.00

MS. MARVEL (Also see The Avengers #183)
Marvel Comics Group: Jan, 1977 - No. 23, Apr, 1979

1-1st app. Ms. Marvel; Scorpion app. in #1,2 8 16 24 54 102 150
2-Origin 4 8 12 23 37 50
3-10: 5-Vision app. 6-10-(Reg. 30¢-c). 9-1st Deathbird. 10-Last 30¢ issue
3 6 9 14 19 24
6-10-(35¢-c variants, limited dist.)(6/77) 15 30 45 103 227 350
11-15,19-22: 19-Capt. Marvel app. 20-New costume 2 4 6 11 16 20
16-1st brief app. Mystique (Raven Darkholme) 6 12 18 41 76 110
17-Brief app. Mystique, disguised as Nick Fury 5 10 15 31 53 75
18-1st full app. Mystique; Avengers x-over 14 28 42 96 211 325
23-Vance Astro (leader of the Guardians) app. 3 6 9 18 27 36
NOTE: ***Austin** c-14i, 16i, 17i, 22i. **Buscema** a-1-3p; c(p)-2, 4, 6, 7, 15. **Infantino** a-14p, 19p. **Gil Kane** c-8. **Mooney** a-4-8p, 13p, 15-18p. **Starlin** c-12.*

MS. MARVEL (Also see New Avengers)
Marvel Comics: May, 2006 - No. 50, Apr, 2010 ($2.99)

1-Cho-c/Reed-s/De La Torre-a; Stilt-Man app. 3 6 9 17 25 34
1-Variant cover by Michael Turner 3 6 9 19 30 40
2-24: 4,5-Dr. Strange app. 6,7-Araña app. 4.00
25-($3.99) Two covers by Horn and Dodson; Secret Invasion 5.00
26-49: 26-31-Secret Invasion. 34-Spider-Man app. 35-Dark Reign. 37-Carol explodes. 39,40,46,48,49-Takeda-a. 40-Deadpool app. 41-Carol returns. 47-Spider-Man app. 3.00
50-($3.99) Mystique and Captain Marvel app.; Takeda & Oliver-a 5.00
... Annual 1 (11/08, $3.99) Spider-Man app.; Horn-c 4.00
... Special (3/07, $2.99) Reed-s/Camuncoli-a/c 3.00
... Storyteller (1/09, $2.99) Reed-s/Camuncoli-a/c 3.00
... Vol. 1: Best of the Best HC (2006, $19.99) r/#1-5 & Giant-Size Ms. Marvel #1 20.00
... Vol. 1: Best of the Best SC (2007, $14.99) r/#1-5 & Giant-Size Ms. Marvel #1 15.00
... Vol. 2: Civil War HC (2007, $19.99) r/#6-10 & Ms. Marvel Special #1 20.00
... Vol. 2: Civil War SC (2007, $14.99) r/#6-10 & Ms. Marvel Special #1 15.00
... Vol. 3: Operation Lightning Storm HC (2007, $19.99) r/#11-17 20.00
... Vol. 4: Monster Smash HC (2008, $19.99) r/#18-24 20.00

MS. MARVEL (Kamala Khan)(See Captain Marvel [2012-2014] #14&17 for cameo 1st apps.)
Marvel Comics: Apr, 2014 - No. 19, Dec, 2015 ($2.99)

1-Intro. Kamala Khan; G. Willow Wilson-s/Adrian Alphona-a; Pichelli-c
5 10 15 31 53 75
2-McKelvie-c 2 4 6 9 12 15
3-7: 3-5-Alphona-a. 3-McKelvie-c. 6,7-Wolverine app.; Wyatt-a 5.00
8-15: 8-11-Alphona-a. 9-Medusa app. 12-Loki app.; Bondoc-a. 13-15-Miyazawa-a 3.00
16-19-Secret Wars tie-ins; Captain Marvel app.; Alphona-a 3.00
...: Marvel Tales 1 (12/21, $7.99) Reprints early app. in Captain Marvel #17, All-New Marvel Now! Point One #1 and Ms. Marvel #1,2 8.00

MS. MARVEL (Kamala Khan)(Follows events of Secret Wars)
Marvel Comics: Jan, 2016 - No. 38, Apr, 2019 ($4.99/$3.99)

1-($4.99) Wilson-s/Miyazawa & Alphona-a; Chiang-c 1 2 3 5 6 8
2-11,13-30,32-38-($3.99) 2,3-Dr. Faustus app. 4-6-Nico Leon-a. 8-11-Civil War II tie-in. 4.00
12-($4.99) Andolfo-a; back-up Red Widow story 5.00
31-($4.99) 50th issue special; Wilson, Ahmed, Minhaj & Rowell-s; art by Leon & various 5.00
... & Moon Knight 1 (10/22, $4.99) Part 2; Houser-s/Roberson-a; Hunter's Moon app. 5.00
... & Venom 1 (11/22, $4.99) Part 3 of story; Houser-s/Wachter-a; Wolverine app. 5.00
... & Wolverine 1 (11/22, $4.99) Part 1 of story; Houser-s/Carlos-a; X-Men app. 5.00

MS. MARVEL: BEYOND THE LIMIT (Kamala Khan)
Marvel Comics: Feb, 2022 - No. 5, Jun, 2022 ($3.99, limited series)

1-5-Samira Ahmed-s/Andrés Genolet-a 4.00

MS. MYSTIC
Pacific Comics: Oct, 1982 - No. 2, Feb, 1984 ($1.00/$1.50)

1,2: Neal Adams-c/a/script. 1-Origin; intro Erth, Ayre, Fyre & Watr 5.00

MS. MYSTIC

	GD	VG	FN	VF	VF/NM	NM-
	2.0	4.0	6.0	8.0	9.0	9.2

Continuity Comics: 1988 - No. 9, May, 1992 ($2.00)

1-9: 1,2-Reprint Pacific Comics issues 4.00

MS. MYSTIC
Continunity Comics: V2#1, Oct, 1993 - V2#4, Jan, 1994 ($2.50)

V2#1-4: 1-Adams-c(i)/part-i. 2-4-Embossed-c. 2-Nebres part-i. 3-Adams-c(i)/plot. 4-Adams-c(p)/plot 3.00

MS. MYSTIC DEATHWATCH 2000 (Ms. Mystic #3)
Continuity: May, 1993 - No. 3, Aug, 1993 ($2.50)

1-3-Bagged w/card; Adams plots 3.00

MS. TREE QUARTERLY / SPECIAL
DC Comics: Summer, 1990 -No. 10, 1992 ($3.95/$3.50, 84 pgs, mature)

1-10: 1-Midnight story; Batman text story, Grell-a. 2,3-Midnight stories; The Butcher text stories 4.00

NOTE: *Cowan c-2.* ***Grell*** *c-1, 6.* ***Infantino*** *a-8.*

MS. TREE'S THRILLING DETECTIVE ADVENTURES (Ms. Tree #4 on; also see The Best of Ms. Tree)(Baxter paper #4-9) (See Eclipse Magazine #1 for 1st app.)
Eclipse Comics/Aardvark-Vanaheim 10-18/Renegade Press 19 on: 2/83 - #9, 7/84; #10, 8/84 - #18, 5/85; #19, 6/85 - #50, 6/89

1 4.00
2-49: 2-Schythe begins. 9-Last Eclipse & last color issue. 10,11-two-tone 3.00
50-Contains flexi-disc ($3.95, 52 pgs.) 4.00
Ms. Tree 3-D 1 (Renegade, 8/85)-With glasses; Mike Mist app. 3.00
Summer Special 1 (8/86) 3.00
1950s Three-Dimensional Crime (7/87, no glasses)-Johnny Dynamite in 3-D 3.00

NOTE; ***Miller*** *pin-up 1-4. Johnny Dynamite-r begin #36 by* ***Morisi.***

MS. VICTORY SPECIAL(Also see Capt. Paragon & Femforce)
Americomics: Jan, 1985 (nd)

1 4.00

MUCHA LUCHA (Based on Kids WB animated TV show)
DC Comics: Jun, 2003 - No. 3, Aug, 2003 ($2.25, limited series)

1-3-Rikochet, Buena Girl and The Flea app. 4.00

MUDMAN
Image Comics: Nov, 2011 - No. 6 ($3.50)

1-6-Paul Grist-s/a 3.50

MUGGSY MOUSE (Also see Tick Tock Tales)
Magazine Enterprises: 1951 - No. 3, 1951; No. 4, 1954 - No. 5, 1954; 1963

	GD	VG	FN	VF	VF/NM	NM-
1(A-1 #33)	15	30	45	88	137	185
2(A-1 #36)-Racist-c	24	48	72	142	234	325
3(A-1 #39), 4(A-1 #95), 5(A-1 #99)	10	20	30	56	76	95
Super Reprint #14(1963), I.W. Reprint #1,2 (nd)	3	6	9	14	19	24

MUGGY-DOO, BOY CAT
Stanhall Publ.: July, 1953 - No. 4, Jan, 1954

	GD	VG	FN	VF	VF/NM	NM-
1-Funny animal; Irving Spector-a	14	28	42	78	112	145
2-4	8	16	24	40	50	60
Super Reprint #12('63), 16('64)	2	4	6	11	16	20

MULAN: REVELATIONS
Dark Horse Comics: Jun, 2015 - No. 4, Nov, 2015 ($3.99)

1-4-Andreyko-s/Kaneshiro-a; Mulan in 2125 Shanghai 4.00

MULTIPLE MAN (Jamie Madrox from X-Factor)
Marvel Comics: Aug, 2018 - No. 5, Dec, 2018 ($3.99, limited series)

1-5: 1-Rosenberg-s/MacDonald-a; New Mutants & Beast app. 4.00

MULTIVERSITY, THE
DC Comics: Oct, 2014 - No. 2, Jun, 2015 ($4.99/$5.99)

1-($4.99) Morrison-s/Reis-a; Earth-23 Superman, Capt. Carrot, alternate Earth heroes gather 5.00
2-($5.99) Morrison-s/Reis-a/c 6.00
... 1&2 Director's Cut (2/16, $7.99, squarebound) reprints #1&2 with original B&W pencil art plus Morrison's original story proposals 8.00
...: Guidebook (3/15, $7.99) Legion of Sivanas, Kamandi app.; Multiverse map 8.00
...: Mastermen (4/15, $4.99) Earth-10 Overman & The Freedom Fighters; Jim Lee-a 5.00
...: Pax Americana 1 (1/15, $4.99) Earth-4 Charlton heroes; Quitely-a 5.00
...: Pax Americana Director's Cut 1 (7/15, $9.99) Quitely pencil art and Morrison's script excerpts; polybagged with large folded Multiverse map 10.00
...: The Just 1 (12/14, $4.99) Earth-16 Super-Sons and Justice League offspring; Oliver-a 5.00
...: The Society of Super-Heroes: Conquerors of the Counter-World 1 (11/14, $4.99) Earth-40 Dr. Fate, Green Lantern, Blackhawks, The Atom vs. Vandal Savage; Sprouse-a 5.00
...: Thunderworld Adventures 1 (2/15, $4.99) Earth-5 Shazam Family; Cam Stewart-c 5.00
...: Ultra Comics 1 (5/15, $4.99) Earth-33 Ultra; Mahnke-a 5.00

MULTIVERSITY: TEEN JUSTICE
DC Comics: Aug, 2022 - No. 6, Jan, 2023 ($3.99, limited series)

1-6-Gender-swapped team from Earth-11; Cohen & Lore-s/Failia-a 4.00

MUMMY, THE (See Universal Presents... under Dell Giants & Movie Classics)

MUMMY, THE: PALIMPSEST
Titan Comics (Hammer Comics): Dec, 2016 - No. 5, May, 2017 ($3.99)

1-5-Peter Milligan-s/Ronilson Freire-a 4.00

MUMMY, THE: THE RISE AND FALL OF XANGO'S AX (Based on the Brendan Fraser movies)
IDW Publishing: Apr, 2008 - No. 4, July, 2008 ($3.99, limited series)

1-4-Prequel to '08 movie The Mummy: Tomb of the Dragon Emperor; Stephen Mooney-a 4.00

MUNCHKIN
BOOM! Studios (BOOM! Box): Jan, 2015 - No. 25, Jan, 2017 ($3.99)

1-24-Short stories of characters from the card game; each issue contains a card 4.00
25-($4.99) Covers by McGinty & Fridolfs 5.00
...: Deck the Dungeons (12/15, $4.99) Katie Cook-s/Mike Luckas-a; 2 covers 5.00

MUNDEN'S BAR ANNUAL
First Comics: Apr, 1988; 1989 ($2.95/$5.95)

1-($2.95)-r/from Grimjack; Fish Police story; Ordway-c 4.00

	GD	VG	FN	VF	VF/NM	NM-
2-($5.95)-Teenage Mutant Ninja Turtles app.	2	4	6	10	14	18

MUNSTERS, THE (TV)
Gold Key: Jan, 1965 - No. 16, Jan, 1968 (All photo-c)

	GD	VG	FN	VF	VF/NM	NM-
1 (10134-501)	28	56	84	202	451	700
2	13	26	39	86	188	290
3-5	10	20	30	65	135	205
6-16	9	18	27	61	123	185

MUNSTERS, THE (TV)
TV Comics!: Aug, 1997 - No. 4 ($2.95, B&W)

	GD	VG	FN	VF	VF/NM	NM-
1-4-All have photo-c	1	3	4	6	8	10
1,4-($7.95)-Variant-c	2	4	6	10	14	18
2-Variant-c w/Beverly Owens as Marilyn	1	3	4	6	8	10
Special Comic Con Ed. (7/97, $9.95)						10.00

MUPPET... (TV)
BOOM! Studios

... King Arthur 1-4 (12/09 - No. 4, 3/10, $2.99) Benjamin & Storck-s/Alvarez-a; 2 covers 3.00
... Peter Pan 1-4 (8/09 - No. 4, 11/09, $2.99) Randolph-s/Mebberson-a; multiple covers 3.00
... Robin Hood 1-4 (4/09 - No. 4, 7/09, $2.99) Beedle-s/Villavert Jr.-a; multiple covers 3.00
... Sherlock Holmes 1-4 (8/10 - No. 4, 11/10, $2.99) Storck-s/Mebberson-a/c 3.00
... Snow White 1-4 (4/10 - No. 4, 7/10, $2.99) Snider & Storck-s/Paroline-a; 2 covers 3.00

MUPPET BABIES, THE (TV)(See Star Comics Magazine)
Marvel Comics (Star Comics)/Marvel #18 on: Aug, 1985 - No. 26, July, 1989 (Children's book)

	GD	VG	FN	VF	VF/NM	NM-
1	3	6	9	16	23	30
2-10	1	3	4	6	8	10
11-26						5.00

MUPPETS (The Four Seasons)
Marvel Worldwide: Sept, 2012 - No. 4, Dec, 2012 ($2.99, limited series)

1-4-Roger Landridge-s/a 3.00

MUPPET SHOW, THE (TV)
BOOM! Studios: Mar, 2009 - No. 4, Jun, 2009 ($2.99, limited series)

1-4-Roger Landridge-s/a; multiple covers 3.00
...: The Treasure of Peg Leg Wilson (7/09 - No. 4, 10/09) 1-4-Landridge-s/a; multiple-c 3.00

MUPPET SHOW COMIC BOOK, THE (TV)
BOOM! Studios: No. 0, Nov, 2009 - No. 11, Oct, 2010 ($2.99)

0-11: 0-3-Roger Landridge-s/a; multiple covers. 0-Paroline-a; Pigs in Space 3.00

MUPPETS TAKE MANHATTAN, THE
Marvel Comics (Star Comics): Nov, 1984 - No. 3, Jan, 1985

1-3-Movie adapt. r-/Marvel Super Special 5.00

MURCIELAGA, SHE-BAT
Heroic Publishing: Jan, 1993 - No. 2, 1993 (B&W)

1-($1.50, 28 pgs.) 3.00
2-($2.95, 36 pgs.)-Coated-c 3.00

MURDER CAN BE FUN
Slave Labor Graphics: Feb, 1996 - No. 12 ($2.95, B&W)

1-12: 1-Dorkin-c. 2-Vasquez-c. 3.00

MURDER INCORPORATED (My Private Life #16 on)
Fox Feature Syndicate: 1/48 - No. 15, 12/49; (2 No.9's); 6/50 - No. 3, 8/51

	GD	VG	FN	VF	VF/NM	NM-
1 (1st Series); 1,2 have 'For Adults Only' on-c	200	400	600	1280	2190	3100
2-Electrocution story	63	126	189	403	689	975
3,5-7,9(4/49),10(5/49),11-15	39	78	117	240	395	550
4-Classic lingerie-c	265	530	795	1694	2897	4100
8-Used in **SOTI**, pg. 160	55	110	165	352	601	850
9(3/49)-Possible use in **SOTI**, pg. 145; r/Blue Beetle #56('48)	65	130	195	416	708	1000
5(#1, 6/50)(2nd Series)-Formerly My Desire #4; bondage-c.	30	60	90	177	289	400
2(8/50)-Morisi-a	27	54	81	160	263	365
3(8/51)-Used in **POP**, pg. 81; Rico-a; lingerie-c/panels	35	70	105	208	339	470

MURDERLAND
Image Comics: Aug, 2010 - No. 3, Nov, 2010 ($2.99)

1-3-Stephen Scott-s/David Haun-a 3.00

MURDER ME DEAD
El Capitán Books: July, 2000 - No. 9, Oct, 2001 ($2.95/$4.95, B&W)

1-8-David Lapham-s/a 3.00
9-($4.95) 5.00

MURDEROUS GANGSTERS
Avon Per./Realistic No. 3 on: Jul, 1951; No. 2, Dec, 1951 - No. 4, Jun, 1952

	GD	VG	FN	VF	VF/NM	NM-
1-Pretty Boy Floyd, Leggs Diamond; 1 pg. Wood-a	155	310	465	992	1696	2400
2-Baby-Face Nelson; 1 pg. Wood-a; classic painted-c	129	258	387	826	1413	2000
3-Painted-c	55	110	165	352	601	850
4- "Murder by Needle" drug story; Mort Lawrence-a; Kinstler-c	65	130	195	416	708	1000

MURDER MYSTERIES (Neil Gaiman's...)
Dark Horse Comics: 2002 ($13.95, HC, one-shot)

HC-Adapts Gaiman story; P. Craig Russell-script/art 14.00

MURDER TALES (Magazine)
World Famous Publications: V1#10, Nov, 1970 - V1#11, Jan, 1971 (52 pgs.)

	GD	VG	FN	VF	VF/NM	NM-
V1#10-One pg. Frazetta ad	7	14	21	48	89	130
11-Guardineer-r; bondage-c	5	10	15	34	60	85

MURDERWORLD
Marvel Comics: Jan, 2023 - May, 2023 ($3.99, series of one-shots)

...: Avengers (1/23) Part 1; Arcane app.; Jim Zub & Ray Fawkes-s/Jethro Morales-a 4.00

Multiversity #2 © DC

Murderworld: Spider-Man #1 © MAR

My Date With Monsters #1 © Tobin & MacDonald

	GD	VG	FN	VF	VF/NM	NM-
	2.0	4.0	6.0	8.0	9.0	9.2

...: Game Over (5/23) Part 5; Jim Zub & Ray Fawkes-s/Tammetta-a 4.00
...: Moon Knight (4/23) Part 4; Jim Zub & Ray Fawkes-s/Pizzari-a 4.00
...: Spider-Man (2/23) Part 2; Jim Zub & Ray Fawkes-s/Karami-a 4.00
...: Wolverine (3/23) Part 5; Jim Zub & Ray Fawkes-s/Nieto-a 4.00

MUSHMOUSE AND PUNKIN PUSS (TV)
Gold Key: September, 1965 (Hanna-Barbera)
1 (10153-509) 8 16 24 55 105 155

MUSIC BOX (Jennifer Love Hewitt's...)
IDW Publishing: Nov, 2009 - No. 5, Apr, 2010 ($3.99, lim. series)
1-5-Anthology; Scott Lobdell-s/art by various. 1-Gaydos-a. 3-Archer-a 4.00

MUSIC MAN, THE (See Movie Classics)

MUTANT CHRONICLES (Video game)
Acclaim Comics (Armada): May, 1996 - No. 4, Aug, 1996 ($2.95, lim. series)
1-4: Simon Bisley-c on all, Sourcebook (#5) 4.00

MUTANT EARTH (Stan Winston's...)
Image Comics: April, 2002 - No. 4, Jan, 2003 ($2.95)
1-4-Flip book w/Realm of the Claw 3.00
Trakk...His Adventures in Mutant Earth TPB (2003, $16.95) r/#1-4; Winston interview 17.00

MUTANT MISADVENTURES OF CLOAK AND DAGGER, THE
(Becomes Cloak and Dagger #14 on)
Marvel Comics: Oct, 1988 - No. 19, Aug, 1991 ($1.25/$1.50)
1-8,10-15: 1-X-Factor app. 10-Painted-c. 12-Dr. Doom app. 14-Begin new direction 4.00
9,16-19: 9-(52 pgs.) The Avengers x-over; painted-c. 16-18-Spider-Man x-over. 18-Infinity Gauntlet x-over; Thanos cameo; Ghost Rider app. 19-(52 pgs.) Origin Cloak & Dagger 5.00
NOTE: *Austin a-12i; c(i)-4, 12, 13; scripts-all. **Russell** a-2i. **Williamson** a-14i-16i; c-15i.*

MUTANTS & MISFITS
Silverline Comics (Solson): 1987 - No. 3, 1987 ($1.95)
1-3 3.00

MUTANTS VS. ULTRAS
Malibu Comics (Ultraverse): Nov, 1995 ($6.95, one-shot)
1-r/Exiles vs. X-Men, Night Man vs. Wolverine, Prime vs. Hulk 7.00

MUTANT, TEXAS: TALES OF SHERIFF IDA RED (Also see Jingle Belle)
Oni Press: May, 2002 - No. 4, Nov, 2002 ($2.95, B&W, limited series)
1-4-Paul Dini-s/J. Bone-c/a 3.00
TPB (2003, $11.95) r/#1-4; intro. by Joe Lansdale 12.00

MUTANT 2099
Marvel Comics (Marvel Knights): Nov, 2004 ($2.99, one-shot)
1-Kirkman-s/Pat Lee-c 3.00

MUTANT X (See X-Factor)
Marvel Comics: Nov, 1998 - No. 32, June, 2001 ($2.99/$1.99/$2.25)
1-($2.99) Alex Summers with alternate world's X-Men 4.00
2-11,13-19-($1.99): 2-Two covers. 5-Man-Spider-c/app. 3.00
12,25-($2.99): 12-Pin-up gallery by Kaluta, Romita, Byrne 4.00
20-24,26-32: 20-Begin $2.25-c. 28-31-Logan-c/app. 32-Last issue 3.00
Annual '99, '00 (5/99,'00, $3.50) '00-Doran-a(p) 4.00
Annual 2001 ($2.99) Story occurs between #31 & #32; Dracula app. 4.00

MUTANT X (Based on TV show)
Marvel Comics: May, 2002; June, 2002 ($3.50)
...: Dangerous Decisions (6/02) -Kuder-s/Immonen-a 3.50
...: Origin (5/02) -Tischman & Chaykin-s/Ferguson-a 3.50

MUTATIS
Marvel Comics (Epic Comics): 1992 - No. 3, 1992 ($2.25, mini-series)
1-3: Painted-c 3.00

MUTIES
Marvel Comics: Apr, 2002 - No. 6, Sept, 2002 ($2.50)
1-6: 1-Bollars-s/Ferguson-a. 2-Spaziante-a. 3-Haspiel-a. 4-Kanuiga-a 3.00

MUTINY (Stormy Tales of the Seven Seas)
Aragon Magazines: Oct, 1954 - No. 3, Feb, 1955
1-Backlash torture bondage-c 21 42 63 122 199 275
2,3: 2-Capt. Mutiny. 3-Lashing torture bondage-c 16 32 48 92 144 195

MUTINY ON THE BOUNTY (See Classics Illustrated #100 & Movie Comics)

MUTOPIA X (Also see House of M and related titles)
Marvel Comics: Sept, 2005 - No. 5, Jan, 2006 ($2.99, limited series)
1-5-Medina-a/Hine-s 3.00
House of M: Mutopia X (2006, $13.99, TPB) r/series 14.00

	GD	VG	FN	VF	VF/NM	NM-
	2.0	4.0	6.0	8.0	9.0	9.2

MUTT AND JEFF (See All-American, All-Flash #18, Cicero's Cat, Comic Cavalcade, Famous Feature Stories, The Funnies, Popular & Xmas Comics)
All American/National 1-103(6/58)/Dell 104(10/58)-115 (10-12/59)/Harvey 116(2/60)-148: Summer, 1939 (nd) - No. 148, Nov, 1965
1(nn)-Lost Wheels 206 412 618 1318 2259 3200
2(nn)-Charging Bull (Summer, 1940, nd; on sale 6/20/40)
90 180 270 576 988 1400
3(nn)-Bucking Broncos (Summer, 1941, nd) 60 120 180 381 653 925
4(Winter, '41), 5(Summer, '42) 54 108 162 343 574 825
6-10: 6-Includes Minute Man Answers the Call 32 64 96 188 307 425
11-20: 20-X-Mas-c 21 42 63 126 206 285
21-30 16 32 48 94 147 200
31-50: 32-X-Mas-c 14 28 42 82 121 160
51-75-Last Fisher issue. 53-Last 52 pgs. 12 24 36 67 94 120
76-99,101-103: 76-Last pre-code issue(1/55) 5 10 15 35 63 90
100 6 12 18 37 66 95
104-115,132-148 5 10 15 30 48 65
116-131-Richie Rich app. 5 10 15 32 51 70
...Jokes 1-3(8/60-61, Harvey)-84 pgs.; Richie Rich in all; Little Dot in #2,3; Lotta in #2
5 10 15 30 48 65
...New Jokes 1-4(10/63-11/65, Harvey)-68 pgs.; Richie Rich in #1-3; Stumbo in #1
4 8 12 24 37 50
NOTE: *Most all issues by **Al Smith**. Issues from 1963 on have **Fisher** reprints. Clarification: early issues signed by Fisher are mostly drawn by Smith.*

MY BAD
AHOY Comics: 2021 - No. 5, 2022 ($3.99)
1-5-Mark Russell-s/Bryce Ingman-a; intro The Chandelier, Emperor King, Rush Hour 4.00

MY BAD (Volume 2)
AHOY Comics: 2022 - No. 5, 2023 ($3.99)
1-5-Mark Russell-s/Bryce Ingman-a 4.00

MY BROTHERS' KEEPER
Spire Christian Comics (Fleming H. Revell Co.): 1973 (35/49¢, 36 pgs.)
nn 2 4 6 13 18 22

MY CONFESSIONS (My Confession #7&8; formerly Western True Crime; A Spectacular Feature Magazine #11)
Fox Feature Syndicate: No. 7, Aug, 1949 - No. 10, Jan-Feb, 1950
7-Wood-a (10 pgs.) 90 180 270 576 988 1400
8,9: 8-Harrison/Wood-a (19 pgs.). 9-Wood-a 41 82 123 256 428 600
10 27 54 81 158 259 360

MYCROFT HOLMES AND THE APOCALYPSE HANDBOOK
Titan Comics: Sept, 2016 - No. 5, Mar, 2017 ($3.99)
1-5-Sherlock Holmes' older brother; Kareem Abdul-Jabbar & Raymond Obstfeld-s 4.00

MY DATE COMICS (Teen-age)
Hillman Periodicals: July, 1947 - V1#4, Jan, 1948 (2nd Romance comic; see Young Romance)
1-S&K-c/a 71 142 213 454 777 1100
2-4-S&K-c/a; Dan Barry-a 37 74 111 222 361 500

MY DATE WITH MONSTERS
AfterShock Comics: Nov, 2021 - No. 5, Mar, 2022 ($4.99/$3.99, limited series)
1-($4.99) Paul Tobin-s/Andy MacDonald-a 5.00
2,3-($3.99) 4.00

MY DESIRE (Formerly Jo-Jo Comics; becomes Murder, Inc. #5 on)
Fox Feature Syndicate: No. 30, Aug, 1949 - No. 4, April, 1950
30 (#1) 34 68 102 199 325 450
31 (#2, 10/49),3(2/50),4 22 44 66 132 216 300
31 (Canadian edition) 15 30 45 85 130 175
32(12/49)-Wood-a 37 74 111 222 361 500

MY DIARY (Becomes My Friend Irma #3 on?)
Marvel Comics (A Lovers Mag.): Dec, 1949 - No. 2, Mar, 1950
1,2-Photo-c 25 50 75 150 245 340

MY EXPERIENCE (Formerly All Top; becomes Judy Canova #23 on)
Fox Feature Syndicate: No. 19, Sept, 1949 - No. 22, Mar, 1950
19,21: 19-Wood-a. 21-Wood-a(2) 39 78 117 240 395 550
20 22 44 66 128 209 290
22-Wood-a (9 pgs.) 36 72 108 211 343 475

MY FAITH IN FRANKIE
DC Comics (Vertigo): March, 2004 - No. 4, June, 2004 ($2.95, limited series)
1-4-Mike Carey-s/Sonny Liew & Marc Hempel-a 3.00
TPB (2004, $6.95, digest-size) r/series in B&W; Dead Boy Detectives preview 7.00

	GD 2.0	VG 4.0	FN 6.0	VF 8.0	VF/NM 9.0	NM- 9.2

MY FAVORITE MARTIAN (TV)
Gold Key: 1/64; No.2, 7/64 - No. 9, 10/66 (No. 1,3-9 have photo-c)

	GD 2.0	VG 4.0	FN 6.0	VF 8.0	VF/NM 9.0	NM- 9.2
1-Russ Manning-a	12	24	36	80	173	265
2	6	12	18	42	79	115
3-9	5	10	15	35	63	90

MY FRIEND IRMA (Radio/TV) (Formerly My Diary? and/or Western Life Romances?)
Marvel/Atlas Comics (BFP): No. 3, June, 1950 - No. 47, Dec, 1954; No. 48, Feb, 1955

	GD 2.0	VG 4.0	FN 6.0	VF 8.0	VF/NM 9.0	NM- 9.2
3-Dan DeCarlo-a in all; 52 pgs. begin, end ?	97	194	291	621	1061	1500
4-Kurtzman-a (10 pgs.)	41	82	123	256	428	600
5- "Egghead Doodle" by Kurtzman (4 pgs.)	27	54	81	158	259	360
6,8-10: 9-Paper dolls, 1 pg; Millie app. (5 pgs.)	20	40	60	120	195	270
7-One pg. Kurtzman-a	21	42	63	124	202	280
11-23: 23-One pg. Frazetta-a	16	32	48	96	151	205
24-48: 41,48-Stan Lee & Dan DeCarlo app.	15	30	45	90	140	190

MY GIRL PEARL
Atlas Comics: 4/55 - #4, 10/55; #5, 7/57 - #6, 9/57; #7, 8/60 - #11, ?/61

	GD 2.0	VG 4.0	FN 6.0	VF 8.0	VF/NM 9.0	NM- 9.2
1-Dan DeCarlo-c/a in #1-6	97	194	291	621	1061	1500
2	43	86	129	271	461	650
3-6	36	72	108	211	343	475
7-11	16	32	48	107	236	365

MY GREATEST ADVENTURE (Doom Patrol #86 on)
National Periodical Publications: Jan-Feb, 1955 - No. 85, Feb, 1964

	GD 2.0	VG 4.0	FN 6.0	VF 8.0	VF/NM 9.0	NM- 9.2
1-Before CCA	155	310	465	1279	2890	4500
2	61	122	183	488	1094	1700
3-5	42	84	126	311	706	1100
6-10: 6-Science fiction format begins	34	68	102	245	548	850
11-14: 12-1st S.A. issue	26	52	78	182	404	625
15-17: Kirby-a in all	28	56	84	202	451	700
18-Kirby-c/a	30	60	90	216	483	750
19,23-25	22	44	66	154	340	525
20,21,28-Kirby-a	26	52	78	182	404	625
22-Space Ranger prototype (7-8/58)(see Showcase #15 for Space Ranger debut)	25	50	75	175	388	600
26,27,29,30	18	36	54	124	275	425
31-40	15	30	45	101	223	345
41,42,44-57,59	13	26	39	89	195	300
43-Kirby-a	14	28	42	96	211	325
58,60,61-Toth-a; Last 10¢ issue	13	26	39	91	201	310
62-76,78,79: 79-Promotes "Legion of the Strange" for next issue; renamed Doom Patrol for #80	11	22	33	73	157	240
77-Toth-a; Robotman prototype	12	24	36	82	179	275
80-(6/63)-Intro/origin Doom Patrol and begin series; origin & 1st app. Negative Man, Elasti-Girl & S.A. Robotman	152	304	456	1254	2827	4400
81,85-Toth-a	25	50	75	175	388	600
82-84	22	44	66	154	340	525

NOTE: ***Anderson** a-42. **Cameron** a-24. **Colan** a-77. **Meskin** a-25, 26, 32, 39, 45, 50, 56, 57, 61, 64, 70, 73, 74, 76, 79; c-76. **Moreira** a-11, 12, 15, 17, 20, 23, 25, 27, 37, 40-43, 46, 48, 55-57, 59, 60, 62-65, 67, 69, 70; c-1-4, 7-10. **Roussos** c/a-71-73. **Wildey** a-32.*

MY GREATEST ADVENTURE (Also see 2011 Weird Worlds series)
DC Comics: Dec, 2011 - No. 6, May, 2012 ($3.99, limited series)

1-6-Short stories of Tanga, Robotman, and Garbage Man; Lopresti-s/a, Maguire-s/a 4.00

MY GREAT LOVE (Becomes Will Rogers Western #5)
Fox Feature Syndicate: Oct, 1949 - No. 4, Apr, 1950

	GD 2.0	VG 4.0	FN 6.0	VF 8.0	VF/NM 9.0	NM- 9.2
1	32	64	96	188	307	425
2-4	18	36	54	105	165	225

MY INTIMATE AFFAIR (Inside Crime #3)
Fox Feature Syndicate: Mar, 1950 - No. 2, May, 1950

	GD 2.0	VG 4.0	FN 6.0	VF 8.0	VF/NM 9.0	NM- 9.2
1	39	78	117	240	395	550
2	19	38	57	111	176	240

MY LIFE (Formerly Meet Corliss Archer)
Fox Feature Syndicate: No. 4, Sept, 1948 - No. 15, July, 1950

	GD 2.0	VG 4.0	FN 6.0	VF 8.0	VF/NM 9.0	NM- 9.2
4-Used in **SOTI**, pg. 39; Kamen/Feldstein-a	71	142	213	454	777	1100
5-Kamen-a	41	82	123	256	428	600
6-Kamen/Feldstein-a	43	86	129	271	461	650
7-Wood-a; wash cover	45	90	135	284	480	675
8,9,11-15	22	44	66	132	216	300
10-Wood-a	34	68	102	204	332	460

MY LITTLE MARGIE (TV)
Charlton Comics: July, 1954 - No. 54, Nov, 1964

	GD 2.0	VG 4.0	FN 6.0	VF 8.0	VF/NM 9.0	NM- 9.2
1-Photo front/back-c	41	82	123	256	428	600
2-Photo front/back-c	22	44	66	128	209	290
3-7,10	14	28	42	82	121	160
8,9-Infinity-c	14	28	42	82	121	160
11-14: Part-photo-c (#13, 8/56). 14-UFO cover	13	26	39	72	101	130
15-19	12	24	36	67	94	120
20-(25¢, 100 pg. issue)	17	34	51	100	158	215
21-40: 40-Last 10¢ issue	5	10	15	35	63	90
41-53	5	10	15	33	57	80
54-(11/64) Beatles on cover; lead story spoofs the Beatle haircut craze of the 1960's; Beatles app. (scarce)	20	40	60	140	310	480

NOTE: *Doll cut-outs in 32, 33, 40, 45, 50.*

MY LITTLE MARGIE'S BOY FRIENDS (TV) (Freddy V2#12 on)
Charlton Comics: Aug, 1955 - No. 11, Apr?, 1958

	GD 2.0	VG 4.0	FN 6.0	VF 8.0	VF/NM 9.0	NM- 9.2
1-Has several Archie swipes	19	38	57	111	176	240
2	12	24	36	67	94	120
3-11	10	20	30	54	72	90

MY LITTLE MARGIE'S FASHIONS (TV)
Charlton Comics: Feb, 1959 - No. 5, Nov, 1959

	GD 2.0	VG 4.0	FN 6.0	VF 8.0	VF/NM 9.0	NM- 9.2
1	21	42	63	126	206	285
2-5	10	20	30	58	79	100

MY LITTLE PHONY: A BRONY ADVENTURE
Dynamite Entertainment: 2014 ($5.99, one-shot)

1-My Little Pony fandom parody; Moreci & Seeley-a/Haeser & Baal-a; 2 covers 6.00

MY LITTLE PONY
IDW Publishing

... Annual #1: Equestria Girls (10/13, $7.99) Price & Fleecs-a; multiple covers 8.00
... Annual 2014 (9/14, $7.99) Anderson-s/Bates-a; two covers 8.00
... Annual 2017 (2/17, $7.99) Short stories by Whitley, Rice, Price & others; two covers 8.00
... Art Gallery (11/13, $3.99) Pin-ups by Sara Richard & others 4.00
... Cover Gallery (8/13, $3.99) Gallery of regular and variant covers 4.00
... Halloween Comicfest 2016 (10/16, giveaway) reprints Friends Forever #4 3.00
... Holiday Special (12/15, $3.99) Cook-s/Hickey, Garbowska, Price, Cook-a; 3 covers 4.00
... Holiday Special 2017 (12/17, $4.99) Asmus-s/Hickey-a; 3 covers 5.00
... Holiday Special (11/19, $4.99) Asmus-s/Price & Forstner-a; 3 covers 5.00

MY LITTLE PONY
IDW Publishing: May, 2022 - Present ($3.99)

1-10: 1-Bronfman-s/Mebberson-a 4.00

MY LITTLE PONY: CLASSICS REIMAGINED - LITTLE FILLIES
IDW Publishing: Nov, 2022 - Present ($3.99, limited series)

1,2-Megan Brown-s/Jenna Ayoub-a 4.00

MY LITTLE PONY: FEATS OF FRIENDSHIP
IDW Publishing: Aug, 2019 - No. 3, Oct, 2019 ($3.99, limited series)

1-3-Ian Flynn-s/Tony Fleecs-a 4.00

MY LITTLE PONY: FIENDS FOREVER
IDW Publishing: Apr, 2015 - No. 5, May, 2015 ($3.99, weekly mini-series)

1-5-Spotlight on Equestria's villains. 1-Whitley-s/Hickey-a. 3-Garbowska-a 4.00

MY LITTLE PONY: FRIENDS FOREVER
IDW Publishing: Jan, 2014 - No. 38, Mar, 2017 ($3.99)

1-38: 1-de Campi-s/McNeil-a; multiple covers. 3,6,10,13,14,21,27,30,34,37-Garbowska-a. 8-Katie Cook-s 4.00
... - Halloween Fest 2014 (10/14, giveaway) reprints #2 3.00

MY LITTLE PONY: FRIENDSHIP IS MAGIC
IDW Publishing: Nov, 2012 - No. 102, Sept, 2021 ($3.99)

1-Katie Cook-s/Andy Price-a; 7 covers 5.00
1-Subscription variant cover by Jill Thompson 5.00
2-49,51-74,76-99,101-Multiple covers on each. 18,19-Interlocking covers 4.00
50-($5.99) Anderson-s/Price-a; Whitley-s/Fosgitt-a 6.00
75-($7.99) Katie Cook-s/Andy Price-s/a; four covers 8.00
100-($7.99) Jeremy Whitley-s/Andy Price-s/a; four covers; bonus pin-ups 8.00
102-($5.99) Jeremy Whitley-s/Andy Price-s/a; last issue; three covers; bonus pin-ups 6.00
... #1 Greatest Hits (8/16, $1.00) reprints #1 3.00
... #1 Hundred Penny Press (2/14, $1.00) reprints #1 3.00
... Deviations 1 (3/17, $4.99) Cook-s/Garbowska-a; 3 covers; Prince Blueblood app. 5.00
... 10th Anniversary Edition (12/22, $7.99) Reprints #1 8.00
... 20/20 (1/19, $4.99) Ponies meet their future selves; Anderson-s/Kuusisto-a 5.00

MY LITTLE PONY: GENERATIONS
IDW Publishing: Oct, 2021 - No. 5, Feb, 2022 ($3.99)

1-5-Gilly-s/Cacciatore-a 4.00

MY LITTLE PONY: LEGENDS OF MAGIC
IDW Publishing: Apr, 2017 - No. 12, Mar, 2018 ($3.99)

1-12: 1-6-Whitley-s/Hickey-a. 7-12-Fleecs-a 4.00
Annual 2018 (4/18, $7.99) Whitley-s/Hickey-a 8.00

MY LITTLE PONY MICRO-SERIES
IDW Publishing: Feb, 2013 - No. 10, Dec, 2013 ($3.99)

1-Twilight Sparkle - Zahler-s/a 5.00
2-10: 2-Rainbow Dash. 3-Rarity. 4-Fluttershy 4.00

MY LITTLE PONY: NIGHTMARE KNIGHTS
IDW Publishing: Oct, 2018 - No. 5, Feb, 2019 ($3.99, limited series)

1-5-Whitley-s/Fleecs-a 4.00

MY LITTLE PONY: PONYVILLE MYSTERIES
IDW Publishing: May, 2018 - Aug, 2018 ($3.99, limited series)

1-4-Christina Rice-s/Agnes Garbowska-a 4.00

MY LITTLE PONY: SPIRIT OF THE FOREST
IDW Publishing: May, 2019 - No. 3, Jul, 2019 ($3.99, limited series)

1-3-Whitley-s/Hickey-a 4.00

MY LITTLE PONY: THE MOVIE PREQUEL
IDW Publishing: Jun, 2017 - No. 4, Sept, 2017 ($3.99, limited series)

1-4-Ted Anderson-s/Andy Price-a; The Storm King app. 4.00

MY LITTLE PONY / TRANSFORMERS
IDW Publishing: Apr, 2021 - No. 4, Jul, 2021 ($3.99, limited series)

1-4-Anthology of short stories by various 4.00

MY LOVE (Becomes Two Gun Western #5 (11/50) on?)
Marvel Comics (CLDS): July, 1949 - No. 4, Apr, 1950 (All photo-c)

	GD 2.0	VG 4.0	FN 6.0	VF 8.0	VF/NM 9.0	NM- 9.2
1	28	56	84	165	270	375
2,3	19	38	57	109	172	235
4-Bettie Page photo-c (see Cupid #2)	58	116	174	371	636	900

MY LOVE
Marvel Comics Group: Sept, 1969 - No. 39, Mar, 1976

	GD 2.0	VG 4.0	FN 6.0	VF 8.0	VF/NM 9.0	NM- 9.2
1	10	20	30	64	132	200
2-9: 4-6-Colan-a	5	10	15	35	63	90
10-Williamson-r/My Own Romance #71; Kirby-a	6	12	18	37	66	95
11-13,15-19	5	10	15	30	50	70
14-(52 pgs.)-Woodstock-c/sty; Morrow-c/a; Kirby/Colletta-r	11	22	33	73	157	240
20-Starlin-a	5	10	15	30	50	70

My Girl Pearl #5 © MAR

My Little Pony: Friends Forever #34 © Hasbro

My Secret Life #25 © CC

	GD 2.0	VG 4.0	FN 6.0	VF 8.0	VF/NM 9.0	NM- 9.2
21,22,24-27,29-38: 38-Reprints	4	8	12	25	40	55
23-Steranko-r/Our Love Story #5	4	8	12	28	47	65
28-Kirby-a	4	8	12	27	44	60
39-Last issue; reprints	4	8	12	28	47	65
Special 1 (12/71)(52 pgs.)	6	12	18	37	66	95

NOTE: ***John Buscema** a-1-7, 10, 18-21, 22r(2), 24r, 25r, 29r, 34r, 36r, 37r, Spec. (r)(4); c-13, 15, 25, 27, Spec. **Colan** a-4, 5, 6, 8, 9, 16, 17, 20, 21, 22, 24r, 27r, 30r, 35r, 39r. **Colan/Everett** a-13, 15, 16, 27(r/#13). **Kirby** a-(r)-10, 14, 26, 28. **Romita** a-1-3, 19, 20, 25, 34, 38; c-1-3, 15.*

MY LOVE AFFAIR (March of Crime #7 on)
Fox Feature Syndicate: July, 1949 - No. 6, May, 1950

	GD	VG	FN	VF	VF/NM	NM-
1	40	80	120	246	411	575
2	20	40	60	114	182	250
3-6-Wood-a. 5-(3/50)-Becomes Love Stories #6	33	66	99	194	317	440

MY LOVE LIFE (Formerly Zegra)
Fox Feature Synd.: No. 6, June, 1949 - No. 13, Aug, 1950; No. 13, Sept, 1951

	GD	VG	FN	VF	VF/NM	NM-
6-Kamenish-a	36	72	108	211	343	475
7-13	19	38	57	111	176	240
13 (9/51)(Formerly My Story #12)	18	36	54	103	162	220

MY LOVE MEMOIRS (Formerly Women Outlaws; Hunted #13 on)
Fox Feature Syndicate: No. 9, Nov, 1949 - No. 12, May, 1950

	GD	VG	FN	VF	VF/NM	NM-
9,11,12-Wood-a	36	72	108	211	343	475
10	19	38	57	111	176	240

MY LOVE SECRET (Formerly Phantom Lady; Animal Crackers #31)
Fox Feature Syndicate/M. S. Distr.: No. 24, June, 1949 - No. 30, June, 1950; No. 53, 1954

	GD	VG	FN	VF	VF/NM	NM-
24-Kamen/Feldstein-a	36	72	108	211	343	475
25-Possible caricature of Wood on-c?	22	44	66	128	209	290
26,28-Wood-a	33	66	99	194	317	440
27,29,30: 30-Photo-c	20	40	60	115	185	255
53-(Reprint, M.S. Distr.) 1954? nd given; formerly Western Thrillers; becomes Crimes by Women #54; photo-c	14	28	42	76	108	140

MY LOVE STORY (Hoot Gibson Western #5 on)
Fox Feature Syndicate: Sept, 1949 - No. 4, Mar, 1950

	GD	VG	FN	VF	VF/NM	NM-
1	32	64	96	188	307	425
2	19	38	57	11	176	240
3,4-Wood-a	34	68	102	199	325	450

MY LOVE STORY
Atlas Comics (GPS): April, 1956 - No. 9, Aug, 1957

	GD	VG	FN	VF	VF/NM	NM-
1	22	44	66	128	209	290
2	15	30	45	83	124	165
3,7: Matt Baker-a. 7-Toth-a	18	36	54	105	165	225
4-6,8,9	14	28	42	80	115	150

NOTE: ***Brewster** a-3. **Colletta** a-1(2), 3, 4(2), 5; c-3.*

MYLO XYLOTO COMICS
Bongo Comics: 2013 - No. 6, 2013 ($3.99, limited series)

	GD	VG	FN	VF	VF/NM	NM-
1-6-Mark Osborne & Coldplay-s/Fuentes-a						4.00

MY NAME IS BRUCE
Dark Horse Comics: Sept, 2008 ($3.50, one-shot)

	GD	VG	FN	VF	VF/NM	NM-
nn-Adaptation of the Bruce Campbell movie; Cliff Richards-a/Bart Sears-c						3.50

MY NAME IS HOLOCAUST
DC Comics: May, 1995 - No. 5, Sept, 1995 ($2.50, limited series)

	GD	VG	FN	VF	VF/NM	NM-
1-5	1	2	3	4	5	7

MY ONLY LOVE
Charlton Comics: July, 1975 - No. 9, Nov, 1976

	GD	VG	FN	VF	VF/NM	NM-
1	3	6	9	16	24	32
2,4-9	2	4	6	9	13	16
3-Toth-a	2	4	6	11	16	20

MY OWN ROMANCE (Formerly My Romance; Teen-Age Romance #77 on)
Marvel/Atlas (MjPC/RCM No. 4-59/ZPC No. 60-76): No. 4, Mar, 1949 - No. 76, July, 1960

	GD	VG	FN	VF	VF/NM	NM-
4-Photo-c	28	56	84	168	274	380
5-10: 5,6,8-10-Photo-c	18	36	54	105	165	225
11-20: 14-Powell-a	15	30	45	88	137	185
21-42,55: 42-Last precode (2/55). 55-Toth-a	15	30	45	85	130	175
43-54,56-60	8	16	24	56	108	160
61-70,72,73,75,76	8	16	24	54	102	150
71-Williamson-a	9	18	27	57	111	165
74-Kirby-a	9	18	27	57	111	165

NOTE: ***Brewster** a-59. **Colletta** a-45(2), 48, 50, 55, 57(2), 59; c-58i, 59, 61. **Everett** a-25; c-58p. **Kirby** c-71, 75, 76. **Maneely** c-18. **Morisi** a-18. **Orlando** a-61. **Romita** a-36. **Tuska** a-10.*

MY PAL DIZZY (See Comic Books, Series I)

MY PAST (...Confessions) (Formerly Western Thrillers)
Fox Feature Syndicate: No. 7, Aug, 1949 - No. 11, Apr, 1950 (Crimes Inc. #12)

	GD	VG	FN	VF	VF/NM	NM-
7	33	66	99	194	317	440
8-10	19	38	57	111	176	240
11-Wood-a	33	66	99	194	317	440

MY PERSONAL PROBLEM
Ajax/Farrell/Steinway Comic: 11/55; No. 2, 2/56; No. 3, 9/56 - No. 4, 11/56; 10/57 - No. 3, 5/58

	GD	VG	FN	VF	VF/NM	NM-
1	15	30	45	85	130	175
2-4	9	18	27	50	65	80
1-3('57-'58)-Steinway	8	16	24	42	54	65

MY PRIVATE LIFE (Formerly Murder, Inc.; becomes Pedro #18)
Fox Feature Syndicate: No. 16, Feb, 1950 - No. 17, April, 1950

	GD	VG	FN	VF	VF/NM	NM-
16,17	22	44	66	132	216	300

MYRA NORTH (See The Comics, Crackajack Funnies & Red Ryder)
Dell Publishing Co.: No. 3, Jan, 1940

	GD	VG	FN	VF	VF/NM	NM-
Four Color 3	126	252	378	806	1378	1950

MY REAL LOVE
Standard Comics: No. 5, June, 1952 (Photo-c)

	GD	VG	FN	VF	VF/NM	NM-
5-Toth-a, 3 pgs.; Tuska, Cardy, Vern Greene-a	19	38	57	112	176	245

MY ROMANCE (Becomes My Own Romance #4 on)
Marvel Comics (RCM): Sept, 1948 - No. 3, Jan, 1949

	GD	VG	FN	VF	VF/NM	NM-
1	32	64	96	188	307	425
2,3: 2-Anti-Wertham editorial (11/48)	20	40	60	117	189	260

MY ROMANTIC ADVENTURES (Formerly Romantic Adventures)
American Comics Group: No. 72, 12/56 - No. 115, 12/60; No. 116, 7/61 - No. 138, 3/64

	GD	VG	FN	VF	VF/NM	NM-
72	12	24	36	69	97	125
73-85	8	16	24	42	54	65
86-Three pg. Williamson-a (2/58)	9	18	27	52	69	85
87-100	4	8	12	25	40	55
101-138	3	6	9	19	30	40

NOTE: ***Whitney** art in most issues.*

MY SECRET (Becomes Our Secret #4 on)
Superior Comics, Ltd.: Aug, 1949 - No. 3, Oct, 1949

	GD	VG	FN	VF	VF/NM	NM-
1	25	50	75	150	245	340
2,3	18	36	54	105	165	225

MY SECRET AFFAIR (Becomes Martin Kane #4)
Hero Book (Fox Feature Syndicate): Dec, 1949 - No. 3, April, 1950

	GD	VG	FN	VF	VF/NM	NM-
1-Harrison/Wood-a (10 pgs.)	40	80	120	246	411	575
2,3-Wood-a	34	68	102	204	332	460

MY SECRET CONFESSION
Sterling Comics: September, 1955

	GD	VG	FN	VF	VF/NM	NM-
1-Sekowsky-a	15	30	45	83	124	165

MY SECRET LIFE (Formerly Western Outlaws; Romeo Tubbs #26 on)
Fox Feature Syndicate: No. 22, July, 1949 - No. 27, July, 1950; No. 27, 9/51

	GD	VG	FN	VF	VF/NM	NM-
22	25	50	75	150	245	340
23,26-Wood-a, 6 pgs.	34	68	102	204	332	460
24,25,27	20	40	60	114	182	250
27 (9/51)	17	34	51	100	158	215

NOTE: *The title was changed to Romeo Tubbs after #25 even though #26 & 27 did come out.*

MY SECRET LIFE (Formerly Young Lovers; Sue & Sally Smith #48)
Charlton Comics: No. 19, Aug, 1957 - No. 47, Sept, 1962

	GD	VG	FN	VF	VF/NM	NM-
19	5	10	15	30	50	70
20-35	3	6	9	18	28	38
36-47: 44-Last 10¢ issue. 47-1st app. Sue & Sally Smith	3	6	9	16	24	32

MY SECRET MARRIAGE
Superior Comics, Ltd.: May, 1953 - No. 24, July, 1956 (Canadian)

	GD	VG	FN	VF	VF/NM	NM-
1	24	48	72	142	234	325
2	14	28	42	81	118	155
3-24	13	26	39	74	105	135
I.W. Reprint #9	3	6	9	14	19	24

NOTE: *Many issues contain **Kamen-ish** art.*

MY SECRET ROMANCE (Becomes A Star Presentation #3)
Hero Book (Fox Feature Syndicate): Jan, 1950 - No. 2, March, 1950

	GD	VG	FN	VF	VF/NM	NM-
1	31	62	93	184	300	415

GD 2.0 | VG 4.0 | FN 6.0 | VF 8.0 | VF/NM 9.0 | NM- 9.2

GD 2.0 | VG 4.0 | FN 6.0 | VF 8.0 | VF/NM 9.0 | NM- 9.2

2-Wood-a 34 68 102 199 325 450

MY SECRETS (Magazine) (Also see Gothic Romances)
Atlas/Seaboard: Feb, 1975 (50¢, B&W, 68 pgs.)

Vol. 1 #1 17 34 51 117 259 400

MY SECRET STORY (Formerly Captain Kidd #25; Sabu #30 on)
Fox Feature Syndicate: No. 26, Oct, 1949 - No. 29, April, 1950

26 25 50 75 150 245 340
27-29 18 36 54 103 162 220

MYSPACE DARK HORSE PRESENTS
Dark Horse Books: Sept, 2008 - Feb, 2011 ($19.95/$19.99, TPB)

Vol. 1 - Short stories previously appearing on Dark Horse's MySpace.com webpage; s/a by various incl. Whedon, Bá, Bagge, Mignola, Moon, Nord, Trimpe, Warren, Way 20.00
Vol. 2 - Collects stories from online #7-12; s/a by Way, Niles, Dorkin, Hotz & others 20.00
Vol. 3 - Collects stories from online #13-19; s/a by Mignola, Cloonan & others 20.00
Vol. 4 - Collects stories from online #20-24; s/a by Whedon, Chen & others 20.00
Vol. 5 - Collects stories from online #25-30; s/a by Thompson, Aragonés & others 20.00
Vol. 6 - Collects stories from online #31-36; s/a by Sakai, Dorkin & others 20.00

MYSTERIES (...Weird & Strange)
Superior/Dynamic Publ. (Randall Publ. Ltd.): May, 1953 - No. 11, Jan, 1955

1-All horror stories 135 270 405 864 1482 2100
2-A-Bomb blast story 71 142 213 454 777 1100
3-11: 10-Kamenish-c/a reprinted from Strange Mysteries #2; cover is from a panel in Strange Mysteries #2 43 86 129 271 461 650

MYSTERIES IN SPACE (See Fireside Book Series)

MYSTERIES OF LOVE IN SPACE
DC Comics: Mar, 2019 ($9.99, square-bound, one shot)

1-Anthology by various; Superman, Lois, Darkseid, Bizarro, Space Cabbie, Crush app. 10.00

MYSTERIES OF SCOTLAND YARD (Also see A-1 Comics)
Magazine Enterprises: No. 121, 1954 (one shot)

A-1 121-Reprinted from Manhunt (5 stories) 20 40 60 118 192 265

MYSTERIES OF UNEXPLORED WORLDS (See Blue Bird)(Becomes Son of Vulcan V2#49 on)
Charlton Comics: Aug, 1956; No. 2, Jan, 1957 - No. 48, Sept, 1965

1 41 82 123 256 428 600
2-No Ditko 21 42 63 122 199 275
3,4,8,9 Ditko-a. 3-Diko c/a (4). 4-Ditko c/a (2). 34 68 102 204 332 460
5,6,10,11: 5,6-Ditko-c/a (all). 10-Ditko-c/a(4). 11-Ditko-c/a(3); signed J. Kotdi 36 72 108 214 347 480
7-(2/58, 68 pgs.) 4 stories w/Ditko-a 39 78 117 236 388 540
12-Ditko sty (3); Baker story "The Charm Bracelet" 34 68 102 204 332 460
13-18,20 13 26 39 72 101 130
19,21-24,26-Ditko-a 27 54 81 158 259 360
25,27-30: 28-Communist A-bomb story w/Khrushchev 6 12 18 37 66 95
31-45: 43-Atomic bomb panel 5 10 15 31 53 75
46(5/65)-Son of Vulcan begins (origin/1st app.) 5 10 15 33 57 80
47,48 4 8 12 28 47 65

NOTE: *Ditko c-3-6, 10, 11, 19, 21-24. Covers to #19, 21-24 reprint story panels.*

MYSTERIOUS ADVENTURES
Story Comics: Mar, 1951 - No. 24, Mar, 1955; No. 25, Aug, 1955

1-All horror stories 116 232 348 742 1271 1800
2-(6/51) 61 122 183 390 670 950
3,4,6,10 55 110 165 352 601 850
5-Severed heads/bondage-c 219 438 657 1402 2401 3400
7-Dagger in eye panel; dismemberment stories 142 284 426 909 1555 2200
8-Eyeball story 90 180 270 576 988 1400
9-Extreme violence (8/52) 71 142 213 454 777 1100
11-(12/52)-Used in **SOTI**, pg. 84 61 122 183 390 670 950
12,14: 14-E.C. Old Witch swipe 58 116 174 371 636 900
13-Classic skull-c 730 1460 2190 5329 9415 13,500
15-21: 18-Used in Senate Investigative report, pgs. 5,6; E.C. swipe/TFTC #35; The Coffin-Keeper & Corpse (hosts). 20-Electric chair-c; used by Wertham in the Senate hearings. 21-Bondage/beheading-c; extreme violence 103 206 309 659 1130 1600
22- "Cinderella" parody 61 122 183 390 670 950
23-Disbrow-a (6 pgs.); E.C. swipe "The Mystery Keeper's Tale" (host) and "Mother Ghoul's Nursery Tale" 58 116 174 371 636 900
24,25 50 100 150 315 533 750

NOTE: ***Tothish** art by **Ross Andru**-#22, 23. **Bache** a-8. **Cameron** a-5-7. **Harrison** a-12. **Hollingsworth** a-3-8, 12. **Schaffenberger** a-24, 25. **Wildey** a-15, 17.*

MYSTERIOUS ISLAND (Also see Classic Comics #34)
Dell Publishing Co.: No. 1213, July-Sept, 1961

Four Color 1213-Movie, photo-c 9 18 27 58 114 170

MYSTERIOUS ISLE
Dell Publishing Co.: Nov-Jan, 1963/64 (Jules Verne)

1-Painted-c 3 6 9 21 33 45

MYSTERIOUS RIDER, THE (See Zane Grey, 4-Color 301)

MYSTERIOUS STORIES (Formerly Horror From the Tomb #1)
Premier Magazines: No. 2, Dec-Jan, 1954-1955 - No. 7, Dec, 1955

2-Woodbridge-c; last pre-code issue 61 122 183 390 670 950
3-Woodbridge-c/a 42 84 126 265 445 625
4-7: 5-Cinderella parody. 6-Woodbridge-c 40 80 120 246 411 575

NOTE: ***Hollingsworth** a-2, 4.*

MYSTERIOUS STRANGER
DC Comics: Aug/Sept. 1952

nn-Ashcan comic, not distributed to newsstands, only for in-house use. Cover art is All Star Western #60 with interior being Sensation Comics #100. A FN/VF copy sold for $2,357.50 in 2002.

MYSTERIOUS SUSPENSE (Also see Blue Beetle #1 (1967))
Charlton Comics: Oct, 1968 (12¢)

1-Return of the Question by Ditko (c/a) 10 20 30 69 147 225

MYSTERIOUS TRAVELER (See Tales of the...)

MYSTERIOUS TRAVELER COMICS (Radio)
Trans-World Publications: Nov, 1948

1-Powell-c/a(2); Poe adaptation, "Tell Tale Heart" 90 180 270 576 988 1400

MYSTERIUS
DC Comics (WildStorm): Mar, 2009 - No. 6, Aug, 2009 ($2.99, limited series)

1-6-Jeff Parker-a/Tom Fowler-a 3.00
TPB (2010, $17.99) r/#1-6 18.00

MYSTERY COMICS
William H. Wise & Co.: 1944 - No. 4, 1944 (No months given)

1-The Magnet, The Silver Knight, Brad Spencer, Wonderman, Dick Devins, King of Futuria, & Zudo the Jungle Boy begin (all 1st app.); Schomburg-c on all 219 438 657 1402 2401 3400
2-Bondage-c 142 284 426 909 1555 2200
3,4: 3-Lance Lewis, Space Detective begins (1st app.); Robot-c. 4-(V2#1 inside); KKK-c 129 258 387 826 1413 2000

MYSTERY COMICS DIGEST
Gold Key/Whitman?: Mar, 1972 - No. 26, Oct, 1975

1-Ripley's Believe It or Not; reprint of Ripley's #1 origin Ra-Ka-Tep the Mummy; Wood-a 4 8 12 26 41 55
2-9: 2-Boris Karloff Tales of Mystery; Wood-a; 1st app. Werewolf Count Wulfstein. 3-Twilight Zone (TV); Crandall, Toth & George Evans-a; 1st app. Tragg & Simbar the Lion Lord; (2) Crandall/Frazetta-r/Twilight Zone #1 4-Ripley's Believe It or Not; 1st app. Baron Tibor, the Vampire. 5-Boris Karloff Tales of Mystery; 1st app. Dr. Spektor. 6-Twilight Zone (TV); 1st app. U.S. Marshal Reid & Sir Duane; Evans-r. 7-Ripley's Believe It or Not; origin The Lurker in the Swamp; 1st app. Duroc. 8-Boris Karloff Tales of Mystery; McWilliams-r; Orlando-r. 9-Twilight Zone (TV); Williamson, Crandall, McWilliams-a; 2nd Tragg app.;Torres, Evans, Heck/Tuska-r 3 6 9 20 30 40
10-26: 10,13-Ripley's Believe It or Not: 13-Orlando-r. 11,14-Boris Karloff Tales of Mystery. 14-1st app. Xorkon. 12,15-Twilight Zone (TV). 16,19,22,25-Ripley's Believe It or Not. 17-Boris Karloff Tales of Mystery; Williamson-r; Orlando-r. 18,21,24-Twilight Zone (TV). 20,23,26-Boris Karloff Tales of Mystery 3 6 9 16 23 30

NOTE: *Dr. Spektor app.-#5, 10-12, 21. Durak app.-#15. Duroc app.-#14 (later called Durak). King George 1st app.-#8.*

MYSTERY GIRL
Dark Horse Comics: Dec, 2015 - No. 4, Mar, 2016 ($3.99)

1-4-Tobin-s/Albuquerque-a 4.00

MYSTERY IN SPACE (Also see Fireside Book Series and Pulp Fiction Library: ...)
National Periodical Pub.: 4-5/51 - No. 110, 9/66; No. 111, 9/80 - No. 117, 3/81 (#1-3: 52 pgs.)

1-Frazetta-a, 8 pgs.; Knights of the Galaxy begins, ends #8 286 572 858 2381 5391 8400
2 104 208 312 832 1866 2900
3 64 128 192 512 1156 1800
4,5 55 110 165 440 995 1550
6-10: 7-Toth-a 46 92 138 340 770 1200
11-15 36 72 108 259 580 900
16-18,20-25: Interplanetary Insurance feature by Infantino in all. 21-1st app. Space Cabbie. 24-Last pre-code issue 32 64 96 230 515 800
19-Virgil Finlay-a 38 76 114 281 628 975
26-40: 26-Space Cabbie feature begins. 34-1st S.A. issue. 36,40-Grey-tone-c 25 50 75 175 388 600
41-52: 45,46-Grey-tone-c. 47-Space Cabbie ends 18 36 54 128 284 440
53-Adam Strange begins (8/59, 10pg. sty); robot-c 159 318 477 1312 2956 4600
54 46 92 138 340 770 1200
55-Grey tone-c 46 92 138 340 770 1200
56-60: 59-Kane/Anderson-a 25 50 75 175 388 600
61-71: 61-1st app. Adam Strange foe Ulthoon. 62-1st app. A.S. foe Mortan. 63-Origin Vandor. 66-Star Rovers begin (1st app.). 68-1st app. Dust Devils (6/61). 69-1st Mailbag. 70-2nd app. Dust Devils. 71-Last 10¢ issue 20 40 60 136 303 470
72-74,76-80 14 28 42 93 204 315
75-JLA x-over in Adam Strange (5/62)(sequel to J.L.A. #3, 2nd app. of Kanjar Ro) 22 44 66 152 336 520
75 (Facsimile Edition) (2020, $3.99) Reprints #75 with original 1962 ads & letter column 4.00
81-86 10 20 30 68 144 220
87-(11/63)-Adam Strange/Hawkman double feat begins; 3rd Hawkman tryout series 17 34 51 114 252 390
88-Adam Strange & Hawkman stories 15 30 45 105 233 360
89-Adam Strange & Hawkman stories 14 28 42 96 211 325
90-Book-length Adam Strange & Hawkman story; 1st team-up (3/64); Hawkman moves to own title next month; classic-c 16 32 48 110 243 375
91-102: 91-End Infantino art on Adam Strange; double-length Adam Strange story. 92-Space Ranger begins (6/64), ends #103. 92-94,96,98-Space Ranger-c. 94,98-Adam Strange/ Space Ranger team-up. 102-Adam Strange ends (no Space Ranger) 8 16 24 51 96 140
103-Origin Ultra, the Multi-Alien; last Space Ranger 7 14 21 44 82 120
104-110: 110-(9/66)-Last 12¢ issue 5 10 15 31 53 75
V17#111(9/80)-117: 117-Newton-a(3 pgs.) 2 4 6 9 13 16

NOTE: ***Anderson** a-2, 4, 8-10, 12-17, 19, 45-48, 51, 57, 59i, 61-64, 70, 76, 87-91; c-9, 10, 15-25, 87, 89, 105-108, 110. **Aparo** a-111. **Austin** a-112i. **Bolland** a-115. **Craig** a-114, 116. **Ditko** a-111, 114-116. **Drucker** a-13, 14. **Elias** a-98, 102, 103. **Golden** a-113p. **Sid Greene** a-78, 91. **Infantino** a-1-8, 11, 14-25, 27-46, 48, 49, 51, 53-91, 103, 117; c-60-86, 88, 90, 91, 105, 107. **Gil Kane** a-14p, 15p, 18p, 19p, 26p, 29-59p(most), 100-102; c-52, 101. **Kubert** a-113; c-111-115. **Moreira** c-27, 28. **Rogers** a-111. **Sekowsky** a-52. **Simon & Kirby** a-4(2 pgs.). **Spiegle** a-111, 114. **Starlin** c-116. **Sutton** a-112. **Tuska** a-115p, 117p.*

MYSTERY IN SPACE
DC Comics: Nov, 2006 - No. 8, Jul, 2007 ($3.99, limited series)

1-8: 1-Captain Comet's rebirth; Starlin-s/Shane Davis-a; The Weird by Starlin 4.00
1-Variant cover by Neal Adams 10.00
Volume One TPB (2007, $17.99) r/#1-5 18.00
Volume Two TPB (2007, $17.99) r/#6-8 and The Weird from #1-4 18.00

MYSTERY IN SPACE
DC Comics (Vertigo): Jul, 2012 ($7.99, one-shot)

Mystery In Space (2006) #1 © DC

Mystery Men #3 © MAR

Mystic Arcana #1 © MAR

	GD 2.0	VG 4.0	FN 6.0	VF 8.0	VF/NM 9.0	NM- 9.2

1-Short sci-fi stories by various incl. Kaluta, Allred, Baker, Diggle, Gianfelice; Sook-c 8.00

MYSTERY MEN
Marvel Comics: Aug, 2011 - No. 5, Nov, 2011 ($2.99, limited series)

1-5-Zircher-a/c; Liss-s; Pulp-era characters in 1932 3.00

MYSTERY MEN COMICS
Fox Feature Syndicate: Aug, 1939 - No. 31, Feb, 1942

	GD	VG	FN	VF	VF/NM	NM-
1-Intro. & 1st app. The Blue Beetle, The Green Mask, Rex Dexter of Mars by Briefer, Zanzibar by Tuska, Lt. Drake, D-13-Secret Agent by Powell, Chen Chang, Wing Turner, & Captain Denny Scott	2160	4320	6480	16,200	28,100	40,000
2-Robot & sci/fi-c (2nd Robot-c w/Movie #6)	514	1028	1542	3750	6625	9500
3 (10/39)-Classic Lou Fine-c	1100	2200	3300	8350	15,175	22,000
4,5: 4-Capt. Savage begins (11/39)	400	800	1200	2800	4900	7000
6-Tuska-c	365	730	1095	2555	4478	6400
7-1st Blue Beetle-c app.	420	840	1260	2940	5170	7400
8-Lou Fine bondage-c	371	542	1113	2600	4550	6500
9-The Moth begins; Lou Fine-c	290	580	870	1856	3178	4500
10-Wing Turner by Kirby; Simon bondage-c	300	600	900	1920	3310	4700
11,12: Both Joe Simon-c. 11-Intro. Domino	271	542	813	1734	2967	4200
13-Intro. Lynx & sidekick Blackie (8/40)	200	400	600	1280	2190	3100
14-18: 16-Bondage/Hypo needle-c	181	362	543	1158	1979	2800
19-Intro. & 1st app. Miss X (ends #21)	206	412	618	1318	2259	3200
20-31: 26-The Wraith begins	168	336	504	1075	1838	2600

NOTE: *Briefer a-1-15, 20, 24; c-9. Cuidera a-22. Lou Fine c-1-5,8,9. Powell a-1-15, 24. Simon c-10-12. Tuska a-1-16, 22, 24, 27; c-6. Bondage-c 1, 3, 7, 8, 10, 16, 25, 27-29, 31. Blue Beetle c-7, 8, 10-31. D-13 Secret Agent c-6. Green Mask c-1, 3-5. Rex Dexter of Mars c-2, 9.*

MYSTERY MEN MOVIE ADAPTION
Dark Horse Comics: July, 1999 - No. 2, Aug, 1999 ($2.95, mini-series)

1,2-Fingerman-s; photo-c 3.00

MYSTERY PLAY, THE
DC Comics (Vertigo): 1994 ($19.95, one-shot)

nn-Hardcover-Morrison-s/Muth-painted art 25.00
Softcover ($9.95)-New Muth cover 10.00

MYSTERY SCIENCE THEATER 3000: THE COMIC
Dark Horse Comics: Sept, 2018 - No. 6, May, 2019 ($3.99)

1-6-Hodgson and others-s. 1-Nauck & Manley-a. 5,6-Black Cat app. 4.00

MYSTERY SOCIETY
IDW Publishing: May, 2010 - No. 5, Oct, 2010 ($3.99, limited series)

1-5-Niles-s/Staples-a 4.00
... Special (3/13, $3.99) Niles-s/Ritchie-a/c 4.00

MYSTERY TALES
Atlas Comics (20CC): Mar, 1952 - No. 54, Aug, 1957

	GD	VG	FN	VF	VF/NM	NM-
1-Horror/weird stories in all	232	464	696	1485	2543	3600
2-Krigstein-a	126	252	378	806	1378	1950
3-10: 6-A-Bomb panel. 10-Story similar to "The Assassin" from Shock SuspenStories	106	212	318	673	1162	1650
11,13-21: 14-Maneely s/f story. 20-Electric chair issue. 21-Matt Fox-a; decapitation story	68	136	204	435	743	1050
12,22: 12-Matt Fox-a. 22-Forte/Matt Fox-c; a(i)	71	142	213	454	777	1100
23-26 (2/55)-Last precode issue	60	120	180	381	653	925
27,29-35,37,38,41-43,48,49: 43-Morisi story contains Frazetta art swipes from Untamed Love	50	100	150	315	533	750
28,36,39,40,45: 28-Jack Katz-a. 36,39-Krigstein-a. 40,45-Ditko-a (#45 is 3 pgs. only)	48	96	144	302	514	725
44-Labyrinth-c/s; Williamson/Krenkel-a	58	116	174	371	636	900
46,51-Williamson/Krenkel-a. 46-Crandall text illos	52	104	156	328	552	775
47-Crandall, Ditko, Powell-a	52	104	156	328	552	775
50,52,53: 50-Torres, Morrow-a	50	100	150	315	533	750
54-Crandall, Check-a	48	96	144	302	514	725

NOTE: *Ayers a-18, 49, 52. Berg a-17, 51. Colan a-1, 3, 18, 35, 43. Colletta a-18. Drucker a-41. Everett a-2, 29, 33, 35, 41; c-8-11, 14, 38, 39, 41, 43, 44, 46, 48-51, 53. Fass a-16. Forte a-21, 22, 45, 46. Matt Fox a-12?, 21, 22; c-22. Heath a-3; c-3, 15, 17, 26. Heck a-25. Kinstler a-15. Mort Lawrence a-26, 32, 34. Maneely a-1, 9, 14, 22; c-12, 23, 24, 27. Mooney a-3, 40. Morisi a-43, 49, 52. Morrow a-50. Orlando a-51. Pakula a-16. Powell a-21, 29, 37, 38, 47. Reinman a-1, 14, 17. Robinson a-7p, 42. Romita a-37. Roussos a-4, 44. R.Q. Sale a-45, 46, 49. Severin c-52. Shores a-17, 45. Tuska a-10, 12, 14. Whitney a-2. Wildey a-37.*

MYSTERY TALES
Super Comics: 1964

	GD	VG	FN	VF	VF/NM	NM-
Super Reprint #16,17('64): 16-r/Tales of Horror #2. 17-r/Eerie #14(Avon), 18-Kubert-r/Strange Terrors #4	3	6	9	16	24	32

MYSTERY TRAIL
DC Comics: Feb/Mar 1950

nn - Ashcan comic, not distributed to newsstands, only for in-house use. Cover art is Danger Trail #3 with interior being Star Spangled Comics #109. A FN/VF copy sold for $2,357.50 in 2002.

	GD 2.0	VG 4.0	FN 6.0	VF 8.0	VF/NM 9.0	NM- 9.2

MYSTIC (3rd Series)
Marvel/Atlas Comics (CLDS 1/CSI 2-21/OMC 22-35/CSI 35-61): March, 1951 - No. 61, Aug, 1957

	GD	VG	FN	VF	VF/NM	NM-
1-Atom bomb panels; horror/weird stories in all	161	322	483	1030	1765	2500
2	81	162	243	518	884	1250
3-Eyes torn out	77	154	231	493	847	1200
4- "The Devil Birds" by Wolverton (6 pgs.)	119	238	357	762	1306	1850
5,7-10	55	110	165	352	601	850
6- "The Eye of Doom" by Wolverton (7 pgs.)	113	226	339	718	1234	1750
11-17,19,20: 16-Bondage/torture c/story	50	100	150	315	533	750
18-Classic Everett skeleton-c	271	542	813	1734	2967	4200
21-25,27-36-Last precode (3/55). 25-E.C. swipe	42	84	126	265	445	625
26-Atomic War story; severed head story/cover	57	114	171	362	619	875
37-51,53-56,61	39	78	117	231	378	525
52-Wood-a; Crandall-a?	40	80	120	246	411	575
57-Story "Trapped in the Ant-Hill" (1957) is very similar to "The Man in the Ant Hill" in TTA #27	55	110	165	352	601	850
58,59-Krigstein-a	37	74	111	222	361	500
60-Williamson/Mayo-a (4 pgs.)	39	78	117	240	395	550

NOTE: *Andru a-23, 25. Ayers a-35, 53; c-8. Berg a-49. Cameron a-49, 51. Check a-31, 60. Colan a-3, 7, 12, 21, 37, 60. Colletta a-29. Drucker a-46, 52, 56. Everett a-8, 9, 17, 40, 44, 57; c-13, 18, 21, 42, 47, 49, 51-55, 57-59, 61. Forte a-35, 52, 58. Fox a-24i. Al Hartley a-35. Heath a-10; c-10, 20, 22, 23, 25, 30. Infantino a-12. Kane a-8, 24p. Jack Katz a-31, 33. Mort Lawrence a-19, 37. Maneely a-22, 24, 58; c-7, 15, 28, 29, 31. Moldoff a-29. Morisi a-48, 49, 52. Morrow a-51. Orlando a-57, 61. Pakula a-52, 57, 59. Powell a-52, 54-56. Robinson a-5. Romita a-11, 15. R.Q. Sale a-35, 53, 58. Sekowsky a-1, 2, 4, 5. Severin c-56, 60. Tuska a-15. Whitney a-33. Wildey a-28, 30. Ed Win a-17, 20. Canadian reprints known-title 'Startling.'*

MYSTIC (Also see CrossGen Chronicles)
CrossGeneration Comics: Jul, 2000 - No. 43, Jan, 2004 ($2.95)

1-43: 1-Marz-s/Peterson & Dell-a. 15-Cameos by DC & Marvel characters 3.00

MYSTIC (CrossGen characters)
Marvel Comics: Oct, 2011 - No. 4, Jan, 2012 ($2.99, limited series)

1-4-G. Willow Wilson-s/David López-a/Amanda Conner-c 3.00

MYSTICAL TALES
Atlas Comics (CCC 1/EPI 2-8): June, 1956 - No. 8, Aug, 1957

	GD	VG	FN	VF	VF/NM	NM-
1-Everett-c/a	84	168	252	538	919	1300
2-4: 2-Berg-a. 3,4-Crandall-a.	40	80	120	246	411	575
5-Williamson-a (4 pgs.)	43	86	129	271	461	650
6-Torres, Krigstein-a	40	80	120	246	411	575
7-Bolle, Forte, Torres, Orlando-a	37	74	111	222	361	500
8-Krigstein, Check-a	39	78	117	231	378	525

NOTE: *Ayers a-6. Everett a-1; c-1-4, 6, 7. Orlando a-1, 2, 7. Pakula a-3. Powell a-1, 4. Sale a-5. Sinnott a-6.*

MYSTIC ARCANA
Marvel Comics: Aug, 2007 - Jan, 2008 ($2.99)

1-Magik on-c; art by Scott and Nguyen; Ian McNee and Dani Moonstar app. 3.00
(#2)...: Black Knight 1 (9/07, $2.99) Djurdjevic-c/Grummett & Hanna-a; origin retold 3.00
3-("Scarlet Witch" on cover)(10/07, $2.99) Djurdjevic-c/Santacruz-a; childhood 3.00
(#4)...: Sister Grimm 1 (1/08, $2.99) Nico Minoru from Runaways; Djurdjevic-c/Noto-a 3.00
...: The Book of Marvel Magic ('07, $3.99) Official Handbook profiles of the magic-related 4.00
HC (2007, $24.99, d.j.) r/series and ...: The Book of Marvel Magic 25.00

MYSTIC COMICS (1st Series)
Timely Comics (TPI 1-5/TCI 8-10): March, 1940 - No. 10, Aug, 1942

	GD	VG	FN	VF	VF/NM	NM-
1-Origin The Blue Blaze, The Dynamic Man, & Flexo the Rubber Robot; Zephyr Jones, 3X's & Deep Sea Demon app.; The Magician begins (all 1st app.); c-from Spider pulp V18#1, 6/39	1800	3600	5400	14,400	30,700	47,000
2-The Invisible Man & Master Mind Excello begin; Space Rangers, Zara of the Jungle, Taxi Taylor app. (scarce)	975	1950	2919	7100	12,550	18,000
3-Origin Hercules, who last appears in #4	519	1038	1557	3789	6695	9600
4-Origin The Thin Man & The Black Widow; Merzak the Mystic app.; last Flexo, Dynamic Man, Invisible Man & Blue Blaze (some issues have date sticker on cover; others have July w/August overprint in silver color); Roosevelt assassination-c	1000	2000	3000	7600	13,800	20,000
5-(3/41)-Origin The Black Marvel, The Blazing Skull, The Sub-Earth Man, Super Slave & The Terror; The Moon Man & Black Widow app.; 5-German war-c begin, end #10	486	972	1458	3550	6275	9000
6-(10/41)-Origin The Challenger & The Destroyer (1st app.?; also see All-Winners #2, Fall, 1941)	1200	2400	3600	9100	16,550	24,000
7-The Witness begins (12/41, origin & 1st app.); origin Davey & the Demon; last Black Widow; Hitler opens his trunk of terror-c by Simon & Kirby (classic-c)	1000	2000	3000	7600	13,800	20,000

8,10: 8-Classic Destroyer WWII Nazi bondage/torture-c. 10-Father Time, World of Wonder,

GD 2.0 | VG 4.0 | FN 6.0 | VF 8.0 | VF/NM 9.0 | NM- 9.2

& Red Skeleton app.; last Challenger & Terror 757 1514 2271 5526 9763 14,000
9-Gary Gaunt app.; last Black Marvel, Mystic & Blazing Skull; Hitler-c
1000 2000 3000 7400 13,200 19,000

NOTE: ***Gabrielle** c-8-10. **Rico** a-9(2). **Schomburg** a-1-4; c-1-6. **Sekowsky** a-9. **Sekowsky/Klein** a-8 (Challenger). Bondage c-1, 2, 9.*

MYSTIC COMICS (2nd Series)
Timely Comics (ANC): Oct, 1944 - No. 3, Win, 1944-45; No. 4, Mar, 1945

1-The Angel, The Destroyer, The Human Torch, Terry Vance the Schoolboy Sleuth,
& Tommy Tyme begin 383 766 1149 2681 4691 6700
2-(Fall/44)-Last Human Torch & Terry Vance; bondage/hypo-c
258 516 774 1651 2826 4000
3-Last Angel (two stories) & Tommy Tyme 194 388 582 1242 2121 3000
4-The Young Allies-c & app.; Schomburg-c 181 362 543 1158 1979 2800

MYSTIC COMICS 70th ANNIVERARY SPECIAL
Marvel Comics: Oct, 2009 ($3.99, one-shot)

1-New story of The Vision; r/G.A. Vision app. from Marvel Myst. Comics #13 & 16 5.00

MYSTIC HANDS OF DR. STRANGE
Marvel Comics: May, 2010 ($3.99, B&W, one-shot)

1-Short stories; art by Irving, Brunner, McKeever & Marcos Martin; Parrillo-c 4.00

MYSTIK U
DC Comics: Jan, 2018 - No. 3, Mar, 2018 ($5.99, limited series)

1-3: 1-Teenage Zatanna, Enchantress at magic college; intro. Plop; Kwitney-s/Norton-a 6.00

MYSTIQUE (See X-Men titles)
Marvel Comics: June, 2003 - No. 24, Apr, 2005 ($2.99)

1-24: 1-6-Linsner-c/Vaughan-s/Lucas-a. 7-Ryan-a begins. 8-Horn-c. 9-24-Mayhew-c
23-Wolverine & Rogue app. 3.00
... Vol. 1: Drop Dead Gorgeous TPB (2004, $14.99) r/#1-6 15.00
... Vol. 2: Tinker, Tailor, Mutant, Spy TPB (2004, $17.99) r/#7-13 18.00
... Vol. 3: Unnatural TPB (2004, $13.99) r/#14-18 14.00

MYSTIQUE & SABRETOOTH (Sabretooth and Mystique on-c)
Marvel Comics: Dec, 1996 - No. 4, Mar, 1997 ($1.95, limited series)

1-4: Characters from X-Men 4.00

MY STORY (...True Romances in Pictures #5,6; becomes My Love Life #13) (Formerly Zago)
Hero Books (Fox Feature Syndicate): No. 5, May, 1949 - No. 12, Aug, 1950

5-Kamen/Feldstein-a 55 110 165 352 601 850
6-8,11,12: 12-Photo-c 24 48 72 142 234 325
9,10-Wood-a 36 72 108 211 343 475

MYTHIC
Image Comics: May, 2015 - No. 8, 2016 ($1.99/$2.99/$3.99)

1-3: 1-($1.99) Phil Hester-s/John McCrea-a. 2,3-($2.99) 3.00
4-8-($3.99) 4.00

MYTHOS
Marvel Comics: Mar, 2006 - Dec, 2007 ($3.99)

1-Retelling of X-Men #1 with painted-a by Paolo Rivera; Paul Jenkins-s 4.00
...: Captain America 1 (8/08) Retelling of origin; painted-a by Rivera; Jenkins-s 4.00
...: Fantastic Four 1 (12/07) Retelling of Fantastic Four #1; painted-a by Rivera; Jenkins-s 4.00
...: Ghost Rider 1 (3/07) Retelling of Marvel Spotlight #5; painted-a by Rivera; Jenkins-s 4.00
...: Hulk 1 (10/06) Retelling of Incredible Hulk #1; painted-a by Rivera; Jenkins-s 4.00
...: Spider-Man 1 (8/07) Retelling of Amazing Fantasy #15; painted-a by Rivera; Jenkins-s 4.00

MYTHOS: THE FINAL TOUR
DC Comics/Vertigo: Dec, 1996 - No. 3, Feb, 1997 ($5.95, limited series)

1-3: 1-Ney Rieber-s/Amaro-a. 2-Snejbjerg-a; Constantine-app. 3-Kristiansen-a;
Black Orchid-app. 6.00

MYTHSTALKERS
Image Comics: Mar, 2003 - No. 8, Mar, 2004 ($2.95)

1-8-Jiro-a 3.00

MY TRUE LOVE (Formerly Western Killers #64; Frank Buck #70 on)
Fox Feature Syndicate: No. 65, July, 1949 - No. 69, March, 1950

65 33 66 99 194 317 440
66,68,69: 69-Morisi-a 22 44 66 128 209 290
67-Wood-a 33 66 99 194 317 440

NAIL, THE
Dark Horse Comics: June, 2004 - No. 4, Oct, 2004 ($2.99, limited series)

1-4-Rob Zombie & Steve Niles-s/Nat Jones-a/Simon Bisley-c 3.00
TPB (2005, $12.95) r/series 13.00

NAILBITER
Image Comics: May, 2014 - No. 30, Mar, 2017 ($2.99)

1-29: 1-Williamson-s/Henderson-a. 7-Brian Bendis appears as a character. 13-Archie style
cover 3.00
30-($3.99) Final issue 4.00
.../ Hack/Slash 1 (3/15, $4.99) Flip book with Hack/Slash / Nailbiter 1 5.00

NAILBITER RETURNS
Image Comics: Apr, 2020 - No. 10, Feb, 2021 ($3.99)

1-10-Williamson-s/Henderson-a 4.00

NAKED BRAIN (Marc Hempel's...)
Insight Studios Group: 2002 - No. 3, 2002 ($2.95, B&W, limited series)

1-3-Marc Hempel cartoons and sketches; Tug & Buster app. 3.00

NAKED PREY, THE (See Movie Classics)

'NAM, THE (See Savage Tales #1, 2nd series & Punisher Invades...)
Marvel Comics Group: Dec, 1986 - No. 84, Sept, 1993

1-Golden a(p)/c begins, ends #13 2 4 6 10 14 18
1 (2nd printing) 3.00
2-7,9-25,27-66,70-74: 7-Golden-a (2 pgs.). 32-Death R. Kennedy. 52,53-Frank Castle
(The Punisher) app. 52,53-Gold 2nd printings. 58-Silver logo. 65-Heath-c/a.
70-Lomax scripts begin 3.00
8-1st app. Fudd Verzyl, Tunnel Rat 1 3 4 6 8 10
26-2nd app. Fudd Verzyl, Tunnel Rat 4.00
67-69-Punisher 3 part story 4.00
75-($2.25, 52 pgs.) 6.00
76-84 3.00
Trade Paperback 1,2: 1-r/#1-4. 2-r/#5-8 1 2 3 5 6 8
TPB ('99, $14.95) r/#1-4; recolored 15.00

'NAM MAGAZINE, THE
Marvel Comics: Aug, 1988 - No. 10, May, 1989 ($2.00, B&W, 52pgs.)

1-10: Each issue reprints 2 issues of the comic 4.00

NAMELESS
Image Comics: Feb, 2015 - No. 6, Dec, 2015 ($2.99)

1-6-Morrison-s/Burnham-a 3.00

NAMELESS, THE
Image Comics: May, 1997 - No. 5, Sept, 1997 ($2.95, B&W)

1-5: Pruett/Hester-s/a 3.00
...: The Director's Cut TPB (2006, $15.99) r/#1-5; original proposal by Pruett 16.00

NAMES, THE
DC Comics (Vertigo): Nov, 2014 - No. 9, Jul, 2015 ($2.99, limited series)

1-9-Peter Milligan-s/Leandro Fernandez-a 3.00

NAMESAKE
BOOM! Studios: Nov, 2016 - No. 4, Feb, 2017 ($3.99, limited series)

1-4-Orlando-s/Rebelka-a 4.00

NAMES OF MAGIC, THE (Also see Books of Magic)
DC Comics (Vertigo): Feb, 2001 - No. 5, June, 2001 ($2.50, limited series)

1-5: Bolton painted-c on all; Case-a; leads into Hunter: The Age of Magic 3.00
TPB (2002, $14.95) r/#1-5 15.00

NAME OF THE GAME, THE
DC Comics: 2001 ($29.95, graphic novel)

Hardcover ($29.95) Will Eisner-s/a 30.00

NAMOR (Volume 2)
Marvel Comics: June, 2003 - No. 12, May, 2004 (25¢/$2.25/$2.99)

1-(25¢-c)Young Namor in the 1920s; Larroca-c/a 3.00
2-6-($2.25) Larroca-a 3.00
7-12-($2.99): 7-Olliffe-a begins 3.00

NAMORA (See Marvel Mystery Comics #82 & Sub-Mariner Comics)
Marvel Comics (PrPl): Fall, 1948 - No. 3, Dec, 1948

1-Sub-Mariner x-over in Namora; Namora by Everett(2), Sub-Mariner by
Rico (10 pgs.) 400 800 1200 2800 4900 7000
2-The Blonde Phantom & Sub-Mariner story; Everett-a
252 504 756 1613 2757 3900
3-(Scarce)-Sub-Mariner app.; Everett-a 300 600 900 2010 3505 5000

NAMORA (See Agents of Atlas)
Marvel Comics: Aug, 2010 ($3.99, one-shot)

1-Parker-s/Pichelli-a 4.00

NAMOR: CONQUERED SHORES
Marvel Comics: Dec, 2022 - No. 4, Apr, 2023 ($4.99, limited series)

1-5- Cantwell-s/Ferry-a; post-apocalyptic future; Luke Cage app. 5.00

NAMOR: THE BEST DEFENSE (Also see Immortal Hulk, Doctor Strange, Silver Surfer)
Marvel Comics: Feb, 2019 ($4.99, one-shot)

1-Chip Zdarsky-s/Carlos Magno-a; Ron Garney-c 5.00

NAMOR: THE FIRST MUTANT (Curse of the Mutants x-over with X-Men titles)
Marvel Comics: Oct, 2010 - No. 11, Aug, 2011 ($3.99/$2.99)

1-($3.99) Olivetti-a/Stuart Moore-s/Jae Lee-c; back-up retelling of origin and history 4.00
2-11-($2.99) 2-Emma Frost app. 5-Mayhew-c. 6-10-Noto-c 3.00
... Annual 1 (7/11, $3.99) Part 3 of "Escape From the Negative Zone" x-over; Fiumara-a 4.00

NAMOR, THE SUB-MARINER (See Prince Namor & Sub-Mariner)
Marvel Comics: Apr, 1990 - No. 62, May, 1995 ($1.00/$1.25/$1.50)

1-Byrne-c/a/scripts in 1-25 (scripts only #26-32) 2 4 6 10 14 18
2-5: 5-Iron Man app. 5.00
6-11,13-23,25,27-36,38-49,51-62: 16-Re-intro Iron Fist (8-cameo only). 18-Punisher cameo
(1 panel); 21-23,25-Wolverine cameos. 22,23-Iron Fist app. 28-Iron Fist-c/story.
31-Dr. Doom-c/story. 33,34-Iron Fist cameo. 35-New Tiger Shark-c/story.
48-The Thing app. 4.00
12,24: 12-(52pgs.)-Re-intro. The Invaders. 24-Namor vs. Wolverine 5.00
26-Namor w/new costume; 1st Jae Lee-c/a this title (5/92) & begins
1 3 4 6 8 10
37-Aqua holografx foil-c 5.00
50-($1.75, 52 pgs.)-Newsstand ed.; w/bound-in S-M trading card sheet (both versions) 5.00
50-($2.95, 52 pgs.)-Collector edition w/foil-c 5.00
Annual 1-4 ('91-94, 68 pgs.): 1-3 pg. origin recap. 2-Return/Defenders. 3-Bagged w/card.
4-Painted-c 5.00

NOTE: ***Jae Lee** a-26-30p, 31-37, 38p, 39, 40; c-26-40.*

'NAMWOLF
Albatross Funnybooks: 2017 - No. 4, 2017 ($3.99, limited series)

1-4-Fabian Rangel Jr.-s/Logan Faerber-a; werewolf in 1970 Viet Nam 4.00

NANCY AND SLUGGO (See Comics On Parade & Sparkle Comics)
United Features Syndicate: No. 16, 1949 - No. 23, 1954

16(#1) 12 24 36 67 94 120
17-23 8 16 24 42 54 65

NANCY & SLUGGO (Nancy #146-173; formerly Sparkler Comics)
St. John/Dell #146-187/Gold Key #188 on: No. 121, Apr, 1955-No. 192, Oct, 1963

121(4/55)(St. John) 10 20 30 56 76 95
122-145(7/57)(St. John) 9 18 27 47 61 75
146(9/57)-Peanuts begins, ends #192 (Dell) 9 18 27 59 117 175
147-161 (Dell) Peanuts in all 7 14 21 48 89 130
162-165,177-180-John Stanley-a 7 14 21 48 89 130

Mythos: Hulk #1 © MAR

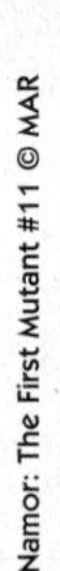

Namor: The First Mutant #11 © MAR

National Comics #21 © QUA

	GD 2.0	VG 4.0	FN 6.0	VF 8.0	VF/NM 9.0	NM- 9.2
166-176-Oona & Her Haunted House series; Stanley-a	8	16	24	52	99	145
181-187(3-5/62)(Dell)	5	10	15	35	63	90
188(10/62)-192 (Gold Key)	5	10	15	35	63	90
Four Color 1034(9-11/59)-Summer Camp	5	10	15	30	50	70

(See Dell Giant #34, 45 & Dell Giants)

NANCY DREW
Dynamite Entertainment: 2018 - No. 5, 2018 ($3.99, limited series)

1-5-Kelly Thompson-s/Jenn St-Onge-a; Hardy Boys app. 4.00

NANCY DREW AND THE HARDY BOYS: THE BIG LIE
Dynamite Entertainment: 2017 - No. 6, 2017 ($3.99, limited series)

1-6-Anthony Del Col-s/Werther Dell'Edera-a; multiple-c on each; Bobbsey twins app. 4.00

NANCY DREW: THE DEATH OF NANCY DREW
Dynamite Entertainment: 2020 - No. 6, 2020 ($3.99, limited series)

1-6-Anthony Del Col-s/Joe Eisma-a; Hardy Boys app. 4.00

NANNY AND THE PROFESSOR (TV)
Dell Publishing Co.: Aug, 1970 - No. 2, Oct, 1970 (Photo-c)

	GD	VG	FN	VF	VF/NM	NM-
1-(01-546-008)	5	10	15	30	50	70
2	4	8	12	25	40	55

NAOMI
DC Comics (Wonder Comics): Mar, 2019 - No. 6, Sept, 2019 ($3.99)

1-6-Brian Bendis & David F. Walker-s/Jamal Campbell-a. 1-Superman app. 3-6-Origin 4.00

NAOMI: SEASON TWO
DC Comics: May, 2022 - No. 6, Oct, 2022 ($3.99)

1-6-Brian Bendis & David F. Walker-s/Jamal Campbell-a. 3,5-Cyborg app. 4.00

NAPOLEON
Dell Publishing Co.: No. 526, Dec, 1953

	GD	VG	FN	VF	VF/NM	NM-
Four Color 526	6	12	18	42	79	115

NAPOLEON & SAMANTHA (See Walt Disney Showcase No. 10)

NAPOLEON & UNCLE ELBY (See Clifford McBride's...)
Eastern Color Printing Co.: July, 1942 (68 pgs.) (One Shot)

	GD	VG	FN	VF	VF/NM	NM-
1	48	96	194	302	514	725
1945-American Book-Strafford Press (128 pgs.) (8x10-1/2"; B&W reprints; hardcover)	15	30	45	86	133	190

NAPOLEON DYNAMITE (Based on the 2004 movie)
IDW Publishing: Sept, 2019 - No. 4, Dec, 2019 ($3.99, limited series)

1-4-Sequel to movie; Monlongo-a; multiple covers on each 4.00
... Valentine's Day Special (2/20, $3.99) Megan Brown-s/Christine Larsen-a; 3 covers 4.00

NARCOS (Based on the 2015-2017 TV series)
IDW Publishing: Dec, 2019 - Present ($3.99)

1,2-Ferrier-s/Malhotra-a. 1-Three covers. 2-Two covers 4.00

NARRATIVE ILLUSTRATION, THE STORY OF THE COMICS (Also see Good Triumphs Over Evil!)
M.C. Gaines: Summer, 1942 (32 pgs., 7-1/4"x10", B&W w/color inserts)

nn-16 pgs. text with illustrations of ancient art, strips and comic covers; 4 pg. WWII War Bond promo, "The Minute Man Answers the Call" color comic drawn by Shelly and a special 8-page color comic insert of "The Story of Saul" (from Picture Stories from the Bible #10 or soon to appear in PS #10) or "Noah and His Ark" or "The Story of Ruth". Insert has special title page indicating it was part of a Sunday newspaper supplement insert series that had already run in a New England "Sunday Herald." Another version exists with insert from Picture Stories from the Bible #7.
(very rare) Estimated value... 1900.00

NOTE: *Print, A Quarterly Journal of the Graphic Arts Vol. 3 No. 2 (88 pg., square bound) features the 1st printing of Narrative Illustration, The Story of The Comics. A VG+ copy sold for $750 in 2005.*

NASCAR HEROES
Starbridge Media: 2007 - No. 3 ($3.95)

1-3: 1-Origin of fictional racer Jimmy Dash. 3-Origin of the Daytona 500; DeStefano-s 4.00
nn-(2008, Free Comic Book Day giveaway) The Mystery of Driver Z 3.00

NASH (WCW Wrestling)
Image Comics: July, 1999 - No. 2, July, 1999 ($2.95)

1,2-Regular and photo-c 3.00
1-($6.95) Photo-split-cover Edition 7.00

NATHANIEL DUSK
DC Comics: Feb, 1984 - No. 4, May, 1984 ($1.25, mini-series, direct sales, Baxter paper)

1-4: 1-Intro/origin; Gene Colan-c/a in all 3.00

NATHANIEL DUSK II
DC Comics: Oct, 1985 - No. 4, Jan, 1986 ($2.00, mini-series, Baxter paper)

1-4: Gene Colan-c/a in all 3.00

NATIONAL COMICS
Quality Comics Group: July, 1940 - No. 75, Nov, 1949

	GD	VG	FN	VF	VF/NM	NM-
1-Uncle Sam begins (1st app.); origin sidekick Buddy by Eisner; origin Wonder Boy & Kid Dixon; Merlin the Magician (ends #45); Cyclone, Kid Patrol, Sally O'Neil Policewoman, Pen Miller (by Klaus Nordling; ends #22), Prop Powers (ends #26), & Paul Bunyan (ends #22) begin	865	1730	2595	6315	11,158	16,000
2	300	600	900	1980	3440	4900
3-Last Eisner Uncle Sam	239	478	717	1530	2615	3700
4-Last Cyclone	181	362	543	1158	1979	2800
5-(11/40)-Quicksilver begins (1st app.; 3rd w/lightning speed?; re-intro'd by DC in 1993 as Max Mercury in Flash #76, 2nd series); origin Uncle Sam; bondage-c	354	708	1062	2478	4339	6200
6,8-11: 8-Jack & Jill begins (ends #22). 9-Flag-c	174	348	522	1114	1907	2700
7-Classic Lou Fine-c	530	1060	1590	3869	6835	9800
12-15-Lou Fine-a	135	270	405	864	1482	2100
16-Classic skeleton-c; Lou Fine-a	459	918	1377	3350	5925	8500
17,19-22: 21-Classic Nazi swastika cover. 22-Last Pen Miller (moves to Crack #23)	110	220	330	704	1202	1700
18-(12/41)-Shows Asians attacking Pearl Harbor; on stands one month before actual event	300	600	900	2040	3570	5100
23-The Unknown & Destroyer 171 begin	106	212	318	673	1162	1650
24-Japanese War-c	116	232	348	742	1271	1800
25-30: 25-Nazi drug usage/hypodermic needle in story. 26-Wonder Boy ends. 27- G-2 the Unknown begins (ends #46). 29-Origin The Unknown	74	148	222	470	810	1150
31-33: 33-Chic Carter begins (ends #47)	68	136	204	435	743	1050
34-37,40: 35-Last Kid Patrol	60	120	180	381	653	925
38-Hitler, Tojo, Mussolini-c	116	232	348	742	1271	1800
39-Hitler-c	135	270	405	864	1482	2100
41-Classic Uncle Sam American Eagle WWII-c	71	142	213	454	777	1100
42-The Barker begins (1st app?, 5/44); The Barker covers begin	45	90	135	284	480	675
43-50: 48-Origin The Whistler	32	64	96	188	307	425
51-Sally O'Neil by Ward, 8 pgs. (12/45)	33	66	99	194	317	440
52-60	23	46	69	136	223	310
61-67: 67-Format change; Quicksilver app.	18	36	54	105	165	225
68-75: The Barker ends	16	32	48	94	147	200

NOTE: *Cole Quicksilver-13; Barker-43; c-43, 46, 47, 49-51.* ***Crandall*** *Uncle Sam-11-13 (with* ***Fine****), 25, 26; c-24-26, 30-33, 43.* ***Crandall*** *Paul Bunyan-10-13.* ***Fine*** *Uncle Sam-13 (w/****Crandall****), 17, 18; c-1-14, 16, 18, 21.* ***Gill Fox*** *c-69-74.* ***Guardineer*** *Quicksilver-27, 35.* ***Gustavson*** *Quicksilver-14-26.* ***McWilliams*** *a-23-28, 55, 57. Uncle Sam c-1-41. Barker c-42-75.*

NATIONAL COMICS (Also see All Star Comics 1999 crossover titles)
DC Comics: May, 1999 ($1.99, one-shot)

1-Golden Age Flash and Mr. Terrific; Waid-s/Lopresti-a 4.00

NATIONAL COMICS
DC Comics: Sept, 2012 ($3.99, one-shots)

... Eternity 1 (9/12) Re-intro of Kid Eternity; Lemire-s/Hamner-a/c 4.00
... Looker 1 (10/12) Vampire supermodel; Edginton-s/Mike S. Miller-a/March-c 4.00
... Madame X 1 (12/12) Rob Williams-s/Trevor Hairsine-a/Fiona Staples-c 4.00
... Rose & Thorn 1 (11/12) Taylor-s/Googe-a/Sook-c 4.00

NATIONAL CRUMB, THE (Magazine-Size)
Mayfair Publications: August, 1975 (52 pgs., B&W) (Satire)

	GD	VG	FN	VF	VF/NM	NM-
1-Grandenetti-c/a, Ayers-a	2	4	6	11	16	20

NATIONAL VELVET (TV)
Dell Publishing Co./Gold Key: May-July, 1961 - No. 2, Mar, 1963 (All photo-c)

	GD	VG	FN	VF	VF/NM	NM-
Four Color 1195 (#1)	6	12	18	41	76	110
Four Color 1312, 01-556-207, 12-556-210 (Dell)	4	8	12	27	44	60
1,2: 1(12/62) (Gold Key). 2(3/63)	4	8	12	27	44	60

NATION OF SNITCHES
Piranha Press (DC): 1990 ($4.95, color, 52 pgs.)

nn 5.00

NATION X (X-Men on the Utopia island)
Marvel Comics: Feb, 2010 - No. 4, May, 2010 ($3.99, limited series)

1-4-Short stories by various. 1,4-Allred-a. 2-Choi, Cloonan-a. 4-Doop app. 4.00
...: X-Factor (3/10, $3.99) David-s/DeLandro-a 4.00

NATURE BOY (Formerly Danny Blaze; Li'l Rascal Twins #6 on)
Charlton Comics: No. 3, March, 1956 - No. 5, Feb, 1957

3-1st app./origin; Blue Beetle story (last Golden Age app.); Buscema-c/a

	GD 2.0	VG 4.0	FN 6.0	VF 8.0	VF/NM 9.0	NM- 9.2
	28	56	84	165	270	375
4,5	19	38	57	11	176	240

NOTE: ***John Buscema** a-3, 4p, 5; c-3. **Powell** a-4.*

NATURE OF THINGS (Disney, TV/Movie)
Dell Publishing Co.: No. 727, Sept, 1956 - No. 842, Sept, 1957

	GD 2.0	VG 4.0	FN 6.0	VF 8.0	VF/NM 9.0	NM- 9.2
Four Color 727 (#1), 842-Jesse Marsh-a	5	10	15	33	57	80

NAUGHTY LIST
AfterShock Comics: Apr, 2022 - No. 4, Jul, 2022 ($4.99, limited series)

	NM- 9.2
1-4-Retelling the legend of Santa Claus; Santora-s/Ferguson-a	5.00

NAUSICAA OF THE VALLEY OF WIND
Viz Comics: 1988 - No. 7, 1989; 1989 - No. 4, 1990 ($2.50, B&W, 68pgs.)

	GD 2.0	VG 4.0	FN 6.0	VF 8.0	VF/NM 9.0	NM- 9.2
Book 1-Contains Moebius poster	2	4	6	9	12	15
Book 2-7						7.00
Part II, Book 1-4 ($2.95)						5.00

NAVY ACTION (Sailor Sweeney #12-14)
Atlas Comics (CDS): Aug, 1954 - No. 11, Apr, 1956; No. 15, 1/57 - No. 18, 8/57

	GD 2.0	VG 4.0	FN 6.0	VF 8.0	VF/NM 9.0	NM- 9.2
1-Powell-a	48	96	144	302	514	725
2-Lawrence-a; RQ Sale-a	29	58	87	172	281	390
3-11: 4-Last precode (2/55)	22	44	66	132	216	300
15-18	21	42	63	122	199	275

NOTE: ***Berg** a-7, 9. **Colan** a-8. **Drucker** a-7, 17. **Everett** a-3, 7, 16; c-16, 17. **Heath** c-1, 2, 5, 6. **Maneely** a-5, 7, 8, 18; c-9, 11. **Pakula** a-2, 3, 9. **Reinman** a-17.*

NAVY COMBAT
Atlas Comics (MPI): June, 1955 - No. 20, Oct, 1958

	GD 2.0	VG 4.0	FN 6.0	VF 8.0	VF/NM 9.0	NM- 9.2
1-Torpedo Taylor begins by Don Heck; Heath-c	47	94	141	296	498	700
2	28	56	84	165	270	375
3-10	22	44	66	128	209	290
11,13-16,18-20: 14-Torres-a	20	40	60	117	189	260
12-Crandall-a	21	42	63	126	206	285
17-Williamson-a, 4 pgs.; Torres-a	21	42	63	126	206	285

NOTE: ***Ayers** a-15. **Berg** a-10, 11. **Colan** a-11. **Drucker** a-7. **Everett** a-3, 20; c-8 & 9 w/**Tuska**, 10, 13-16. **Forte** a-15, 18. **Heck** a-11(2), 15, 19. **Maneely** c-1, 5, 6, 11, 17. **Morisi** a-8. **Pakula** a-7, 18. **Powell** a-20. **Reinman** a-18.*

NAVY HEROES
Almanac Publishing Co.: 1945

	GD 2.0	VG 4.0	FN 6.0	VF 8.0	VF/NM 9.0	NM- 9.2
1-Heavy in propaganda	26	52	78	154	252	350

NAVY PATROL
Key Publications: May, 1955 - No. 4, Nov, 1955

	GD 2.0	VG 4.0	FN 6.0	VF 8.0	VF/NM 9.0	NM- 9.2
1	13	26	39	74	105	135
2-4	8	16	24	44	57	70

NAVY TALES
Atlas Comics (CDS): Jan, 1957 - No. 4, July, 1957

	GD 2.0	VG 4.0	FN 6.0	VF 8.0	VF/NM 9.0	NM- 9.2
1-Everett-c; Berg, Powell-a	40	80	120	246	411	575
2-Williamson/Mayo-a(5 pgs); Crandall-a	25	50	75	150	245	340
3,4-Reinman-a; Severin-c. 4-Crandall-a	20	40	60	118	192	265

NOTE: ***Colan** a-4. **Maneely** c-2. **Reinman** a-2-4. **Sinnott** a-4.*

NAVY TASK FORCE
Stanmor Publications/Aragon Mag. No. 4-8: Feb, 1954 - No. 8, April, 1956

	GD 2.0	VG 4.0	FN 6.0	VF 8.0	VF/NM 9.0	NM- 9.2
1	15	30	45	84	127	170
2	9	18	27	52	69	85
3-8: 8-r/Navy Patrol #1; defeat of the Japanese Navy	8	16	24	42	54	65

NAVY WAR HEROES
Charlton Comics: Jan, 1964 - No. 7, Mar-Apr, 1965

	GD 2.0	VG 4.0	FN 6.0	VF 8.0	VF/NM 9.0	NM- 9.2
1	4	8	12	23	37	50
2-7	3	6	9	15	22	28

NAZA (Stone Age Warrior)
Dell Publishing Co.: Nov-Jan, 1963-64 - No. 9, March, 1966

	GD 2.0	VG 4.0	FN 6.0	VF 8.0	VF/NM 9.0	NM- 9.2
12-555-401 (#1)-Painted-c	6	12	18	37	66	95
2-9: 2-4-Painted-c	4	8	12	27	44	60

NEBBS, THE (Also see Crackajack Funnies)
Dell Publishing Co./Croydon Publishing Co.: 1941; 1945

	GD 2.0	VG 4.0	FN 6.0	VF 8.0	VF/NM 9.0	NM- 9.2
Large Feature Comic 23(1941)	27	54	81	158	259	360
1(1945, 36 pgs.)-Reprints	14	28	42	81	118	155

NEBULA (Guardians of the Galaxy)
Marvel Comics: Apr, 2020 - Present ($3.99)

	NM- 9.2
1,2-Vita Ayala-s/Claire Roe-a	4.00

NECESSARY EVIL
Desperado Publishing: Oct, 2007 - No. 9, Nov, 2008 ($3.99)

	NM- 9.2
1-9: 1-Joshua Williamson-s/Marcus Harris-a/Dustin Nguyen-c	4.00

NECROMANCER
Image Comics (Top Cow): Sept, 2005 - No. 6, July 2006 ($2.99)

	NM- 9.2
1-6: 1-Manapul-a/Ortega-s; three covers by Manapul, Horn & Bachalo	3.00
... Pilot Season Vol. 1 #1 (11/07, $2.99) Ortega-s/Meyers-a/Manapul-c	3.00

NECROMANCER: THE GRAPHIC NOVEL
Marvel Comics (Epic Comics): 1989 ($8.95)

	NM- 9.2
nn	9.00

NECROWAR
Dreamwave Productions: July, 2003 - No. 3, Sept, 2003 ($2.95)

	NM- 9.2
1-3-Furman-s/Granov-digital art	3.00

NEGAN LIVES! (The Walking Dead)
Image Comics: Jul, 2020 ($4.99, one-shot)

	NM- 9.2
1-Kirkman-s/Adlard-a; takes place between Walking Dead #174-193	8.00
1-2nd printing with blue title logo	5.00
1-Variant with Gold foil title logo	55.00
1-Variant with Silver foil title logo	30.00
1-2nd printing with Bronze foil title logo	8.00

NEGATION
CrossGeneration Comics: Dec, 2001 - No. 27, Mar, 2004 ($2.95)

	NM- 9.2
Prequel (12/01)	3.00
1-27: 1-(1/02) Pelletier-a/Bedard & Waid-s	3.00
... Lawbringer (11/02, $2.95) Nebres-a	3.00
Vol. 1: Bohica! (10/02, $19.95, TPB) r/ Prequel & #1-6	20.00
Vol. 2: Baptism of Fire (5/03, $15.95, TPB) r/#7-12	16.00
Vol. 3: Hounded (12/03, $15.95, TPB) r/#13-18	16.00

NEGATION WAR
CrossGeneration Comics: Apr, 2004 - No. 6 ($2.95)

	NM- 9.2
1-4-Bedard-s/Pelletier-a	3.00

NEGATIVE BURN
Caliber: 1993 - No. 50, 1997 ($2.95, B&W, anthology)

	GD 2.0	VG 4.0	FN 6.0	VF 8.0	VF/NM 9.0	NM- 9.2
1,2,4-12,14-29,31-47: Anthology by various including Bolland, Burden, Doran, Gaiman, Moebius, Moore, & Pope						4.00
3,13: 3-Bone story. 13-Strangers in Paradise story	2	4	6	8	10	12
30-Budd Root, Frankenstein, Cavewoman	2	4	6	11	16	20
48,49-($4.95)						5.00
50-($6.95, 96 pgs.)-Gaiman, Robinson, Bolland						7.00
...Summer Special 2005 (Image, 2005, $9.99) new short stories by various						10.00
...: The Best From 1993-1998 (Image, 1/05, $19.95) r/short stories by various						20.00
...Winter Special 2005 (Image, 2005, $9.95) new short stories by various						10.00

NEGATIVE BURN
Image Comics (Desperado): May, 2006 - No. 21 ($5.99, B&W, anthology)

	NM- 9.2
1-21: 1-Art by Bolland, Powell, Luna, Smith, Hester. 2-Milk & Cheese by Dorkin	6.00

NEGRO (See All-Negro)

NEGRO HEROES (Calling All Girls, Real Heroes, & True Comics reprints)
Parents' Magazine Institute: Spring, 1947 - No. 2, Summer, 1948

	GD 2.0	VG 4.0	FN 6.0	VF 8.0	VF/NM 9.0	NM- 9.2
1	194	388	582	1242	2121	3000
2-Jackie Robinson-c/story	171	342	513	1095	1873	2650

NEGRO ROMANCE (Negro Romances #4)
Fawcett Publications: June, 1950 - No. 3, Oct, 1950 (All photo-c)

	GD 2.0	VG 4.0	FN 6.0	VF 8.0	VF/NM 9.0	NM- 9.2
1-Evans-a (scarce)	265	530	795	1694	2897	4100
2,3 (scarce)	219	438	657	1402	2401	3400

NEGRO ROMANCES (Formerly Negro Romance; Romantic Secrets #5 on)
Charlton Comics: No. 4, May, 1955

	GD 2.0	VG 4.0	FN 6.0	VF 8.0	VF/NM 9.0	NM- 9.2
4-Reprints Fawcett #2 (scarce)	245	490	735	1568	2684	3800

NEIL GAIMAN AND CHARLES VESS' STARDUST
DC Comics (Vertigo): 1997 - No. 4, 1998 ($5.95/$6.95, square-bound, lim. series)

	NM- 9.2
1-4: Gaiman text with Vess paintings in all	7.00
Hardcover (1998, $29.95) r/series with new sketches	35.00
Softcover (1999, $19.95) oversized; new Vess-c	20.00

NEIL GAIMAN'S LADY JUSTICE
Tekno Comix: Sept, 1995 - No. 11, May, 1996 ($1.95/$2.25)

	NM- 9.2
1-11: 1-Sienkiewicz-c; pin-ups. 1-5-Brereton-c. 7-Polybagged. 11-The Big Bang Pt. 7	3.00
Free Comic Book Day (Super Genius, 2015, giveaway) r/#1	3.00

NEIL GAIMAN'S LADY JUSTICE
BIG Entertainment: V2#1, June, 1996 - No. 9, Feb, 1997 ($2.25)

	NM- 9.2
V2#1-9: Dan Brereton-c on all. 6-8-Dan Brereton script	3.00

NEIL GAIMAN'S MIDNIGHT DAYS
DC Comics (Vertigo): 1999 ($17.95, trade paperback)

	NM- 9.2
nn-Reprints Gaiman's short stories; new Swamp Thing w/ Bissette-a	18.00

NEIL GAIMAN'S MR. HERO-THE NEWMATIC MAN
Tekno Comix: Mar, 1995 - No. 17, May, 1996 ($1.95/$2.25)

	NM- 9.2
1-17: 1-Intro Mr. Hero & Teknophage; bound-in game piece and trading card. 4-w/Steel edition Neil Gaiman's Teknophage #1 coupon. 13-Polybagged	3.00

NEIL GAIMAN'S MR. HERO-THE NEWMATIC MAN
BIG Entertainment: V2#1, June, 1996 ($2.25)

	NM- 9.2
V2#1-Teknophage destroys Mr. Hero; includes The Big Bang Pt. 10	3.00

NEIL GAIMAN'S NEVERWHERE
DC Comics (Vertigo): Aug, 2005 - No. 9, Sept, 2006 ($2.99, limited series)

	NM- 9.2
1-9-Adaptation of Gaiman novel; Carey-s/Fabry-a/c	3.00
TPB (2007, $19.99) r/series; intro. by Carey	20.00

NEIL GAIMAN'S PHAGE-SHADOWDEATH
BIG Entertainment: June, 1996 - No. 6, Nov, 1996 ($2.25, limited series)

	NM- 9.2
1-6: Bryan Talbot-c & scripts in all. 1-1st app. Orlando Holmes	3.00

NEIL GAIMAN'S TEKNOPHAGE
Tekno Comix: Aug, 1995 - No. 10, Mar, 1996 ($1.95/$2.25)

	NM- 9.2
1-6-Rick Veitch scripts & Bryan Talbot-c/a.	3.00
1-Steel Edition	4.00
7-10: Paul Jenkins scripts in all. 8-polybagged	3.00

NEIL GAIMAN'S WHEEL OF WORLDS
Tekno Comix: Apr, 1995 - No. 1, May, 1996 ($2.95/$3.25)

	NM- 9.2
0-1st app. Lady Justice; 48 pgs.; bound-in poster	5.00
0-Regular edition	4.00
1 ($3.25, 5/96)-Bruce Jones scripts; Lady Justice & Teknophage app.; CGI photo-c	4.00

NEIL THE HORSE (See Charlton Bullseye #2)
Aardvark-Vanaheim #1-10/Renegade Press #11 on: 2/83 - No. 10, 12/84; No. 11, 4/85 - #15, 1985 (B&W)

	NM- 9.2
1($1.40)	4.00
1-2nd print	3.00
2-12: 11-w/paperdolls	3.00
13-15: Double size ($3.00). 13-w/paperdolls. 15 is a flip book(2-c)	4.00

NEIL YOUNG'S GREENDALE
DC Comics (Vertigo): 2010 ($19.99, hardcover graphic novel)

Navy Action #2 © MAR

Nemesis Reloaded #1 © Netflix

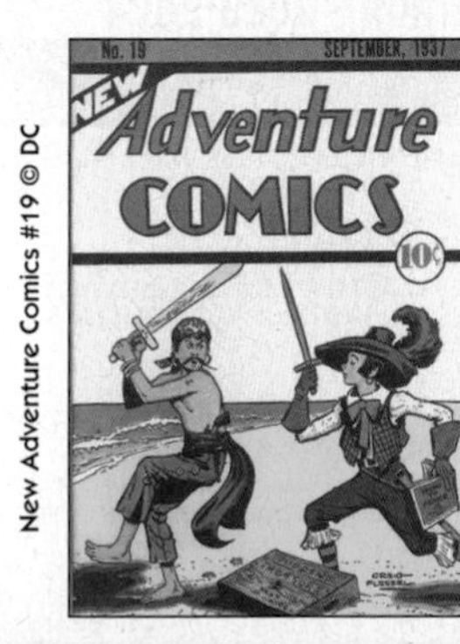

New Adventure Comics #19 © DC

	GD	VG	FN	VF	VF/NM	NM-
	2.0	4.0	6.0	8.0	9.0	9.2

HC-Story based on the Neil Young album; Dysart-s/Chiang-a; intro. by Neil Young						20.00

NELLIE THE NURSE (Also see Gay Comics & Joker Comics)
Marvel/Atlas Comics (SPI/LMC): 1945 - No. 36, Oct, 1952; 1957

1-(1945)	155	310	465	992	1696	2400
2-(Spring/46)	47	94	141	296	498	700
3,4: 3-New logo (9/46)	37	74	111	222	361	500
5-Kurtzman's "Hey Look" (3); Georgie app.	36	72	108	214	347	480
6-8,10: 7,8-Georgie app. 10-Millie app.	31	62	93	182	296	410
9-Wolverton-a (1 pg.); Mille the Model app.	34	68	102	199	325	450
11,14-16,18-Kurtzman's "Hey Look"	32	64	96	188	307	425
12- "Giggles 'n' Grins" by Kurtzman	31	62	93	182	296	410
13,17,19,20: 17-Annie Oakley app.	25	50	75	150	245	340
21-30: 28-Mr. Nexdoor-r (3 pgs.) by Kurtzman/Rusty #22	22	44	66	128	209	290
31-36: 36-Post-c	20	40	60	120	195	270
1('57)-Leading Mag. (Atlas)-Everett-a, 20 pgs	39	78	117	231	378	525

NELLIE THE NURSE
Dell Publishing Co.: No. 1304, Mar-May, 1962

Four Color 1304-Stanley-a	9	18	27	62	126	190

NEMESIS (Millar & McNiven's...)
Marvel Comics (Icon): May, 2010 - No. 4, Feb, 2011 ($2.99)

1-4-Millar-s/McNiven-a						3.00
1,2-Variant covers: 1-Yu. 2-Cassaday						8.00

NEMESIS ARCHIVES (Listed with Adventures Into the Unknown)

NEMESIS RELOADED (Reboot of the Millar & McNiven series)
Image Comics: Jan, 2023 - No. 5 ($3.99, limited series)

1,2-Millar-s/Jiménez-a						4.00

NEMESIS: THE IMPOSTERS
DC Comics: May, 2010 - No. 4, Aug, 2010 ($2.99, limited series)

1-4-Richards-a/Luvisi-c. 1-Joker app. 2-4-Batman app.						3.00

NEMESIS THE WARLOCK (Also see Spellbinders)
Eagle Comics: Sept, 1984 - No. 7, Mar, 1985 (limited series, Baxter paper)

1-7: 2000 A.D. reprints						3.00

NEMESIS THE WARLOCK
Quality Comics/Fleetway Quality #2 on: 1989 - No. 19, 1991 ($1.95, B&W)

1-19						3.00

NEMO (The League of Extraordinary Gentlemen)
Top Shelf Productions: ($14.95, hardcover, one-shots)

...: Heart of Ice HC (2/13) Alan Moore-s/Kevin O'Neill-a						15.00
...: River of Ghosts HC (2015) Alan Moore-s/Kevin O'Neill-a						15.00
...: Roses of Berlin HC (3/14) Alan Moore-s/Kevin O'Neill-a						15.00

NEON FUTURE (Steve Aoki Presents...)
Impact Theory, LLC: Oct, 2018 - No. 6, Aug, 2019 ($3.99)

1-6: 1-Neil Edwards & Jheremy Raapack-a						4.00

NEON JOE, WEREWOLF HUNTER (Based on Adult Swim TV series)
DC Comics: 2015 (no price, one-shot)

nn - Origin of Neon Joe; Glaser-s/Mandrake & Duursema-a/Panosian-c						3.00

NEUTRO
Dell Publishing Co.: Jan, 1967

1-Jack Sparling-c/a (super hero); UFO-s	5	10	15	30	50	70

NEVADA (See Zane Grey's Four Color 412, 996 & Zane Grey's Stories of the West #1)

NEVADA (Also see Vertigo Winter's Edge #1)
DC Comics (Vertigo): May, 1998 - No. 6, Oct, 1998 ($2.50, limited series)

1-6-Gerber-s/Winslade-c/a						3.00
TPB-(1999, $14.95) r/#1-6 & Vertigo Winter's Edge preview						15.00

NEVER AGAIN (War stories; becomes Soldier & Marine V2#9)
Charlton Comics: Aug, 1955; No. 8, July, 1956 (No #2-7)

1-WWII	14	28	42	81	118	155
8-(Formerly Foxhole?)	9	18	27	50	65	80

NEVERBOY
Dark Horse Comics: Mar, 2015 - No. 6, Aug, 2015 ($3.99)

1-6-Shaun Simon-s/Tyler Jenkins-a						4.00

NEVERMEN, THE (See Dark Horse Presents #148-150)
Dark Horse Comics: May, 2000 - No. 4, Aug, 2000 ($2.95, limited series)

1-4-Phil Amara-s/Guy Davis-a						3.00

NEVERMEN, THE: STREETS OF BLOOD
Dark Horse Comics: Jan, 2003 - No. 3, Apr, 2003 ($2.99, limited series)

1-3-Phil Amara-s/Guy Davis-a						3.00
TPB (7/03, $9.95) r/#1-3; Paul Jenkins intro.; Davis sketch pages						10.00

NEW ADVENTURE COMICS (Formerly New Comics; becomes Adventure Comics #32 on; V1#12 indicia says NEW COMICS #12)
National Periodical Publications: V1#12, Jan, 1937 - No. 31, Oct, 1938

V1#12-Federal Men by Siegel & Shuster continues; Jor-L mentioned; Whitney Ellsworth-c begin, end #14	735	1470	2205	5900	-	-
V2#1(2/37, #13)-(Rare)	735	1420	2205	5900	-	-
V2#2 (#14)	615	1230	1845	4900	-	-
15(V2#3)-20(V2#8): 15-1st Adventure logo; Creig Flessel-c begin, end #31. 16-1st non-funny cover. 17-Nadir, Master of Magic begins, ends #30	470	940	1410	2590	4345	6100
21(V2#9),22(V2#10, 2/37): 22-X-Mas-c	400	800	1200	2220	3700	5200
23-25,28-31	370	740	1110	2000	3400	4800
26(5/38) (rare) has house ad for Action Comics #1 showing B&W image of cover (early published image of Superman)(prices vary widely on this book)	5130	10,260	15,390	37,200	-	-
27(6/38) has house ad for Action Comics #1 showing B&W image of cover (rare) (early published image of Superman)	2450	4900	7350	14,000	21,000	28,000

NEW ADVENTURES OF ABRAHAM LINCOLN, THE
Image Comics (Homage): 1998 ($19.95, one-shot)

1-Scott McCloud-s/computer art						20.00

NEW ADVENTURES OF CHARLIE CHAN, THE (TV)
National Periodical Publications: May-June, 1958 - No. 6, Mar-Apr, 1959

1 (Scarce)-John Broome-s/Sid Greene-a in all	97	194	291	621	1061	1500
2 (Scarce)	65	130	195	416	708	1000
3-6 (Scarce)-Greene/Giella-a	55	110	165	352	601	850

NEW ADVENTURES OF CHOLLY AND FLYTRAP, THE
Epic Comics: Dec, 1990 - No. 3, Feb, 1991 ($4.95, limited series)

1-3-Arthur Suydam-s/a/c; painted covers						5.00

NEW ADVENTURES OF HUCK FINN, THE (TV)
Gold Key: December, 1968 (Hanna-Barbera)

1- "The Curse of Thut"; part photo-c	3	6	9	21	33	45

NEW ADVENTURES OF PINOCCHIO (TV)
Dell Publishing Co.: Oct-Dec, 1962 - No. 3, Sept-Nov, 1963

12-562-212(#1)	7	14	21	48	89	130
2,3	6	12	18	38	69	100

NEW ADVENTURES OF ROBIN HOOD (See Robin Hood)

NEW ADVENTURES OF SHERLOCK HOLMES (Also see Sherlock Holmes)
Dell Publishing Co.: No. 1169, Mar-May, 1961 - No. 1245, Nov-Jan, 1961/62

Four Color 1169(#1)	12	24	36	82	179	275
Four Color 1245	11	22	33	75	160	245

NEW ADVENTURES OF SPEED RACER
Now Comics: Dec, 1993 - No. 7, 1994? ($1.95)

1-7						3.00
0-(Premiere)-3-D cover						3.00

NEW ADVENTURES OF SUPERBOY, THE (Also see Superboy)
DC Comics: Jan, 1980 - No. 54, June, 1984

1	2	4	6	9	13	16
2-6,8-10						5.00
11-49,51-54: 11-Superboy gets new power. 14-Lex Luthor app. 15-Superboy gets new parents. 28-Dial "H" For Hero begins, ends #49. 45-47-1st app. Sunburst. 48-Begin 75¢-c.						4.00
1,2,5,6,8 (Whitman variants; low print run; no issue # shown on cover)	3	6	9	16	23	30
7,50: 7-Has extra story "The Computers That Saved Metropolis" by Starlin (Radio Shack giveaway w/indicia). 50-Legion app.						5.00

NOTE: ***Buckler*** *a-9p; c-36p.* ***Giffen*** *a-50; c-50. 40i.* ***Gil Kane*** *c-32p, 33p, 35, 39, 41-49.* ***Miller*** *c-51.* ***Starlin*** *a-7. Krypto back-ups in 17, 22. Superbaby in 11, 14, 19, 24.*

NEW ADVENTURES OF THE PHANTOM BLOT, THE (See The Phantom Blot)

NEW AMERICA
Eclipse Comics: Nov, 1987 - No. 4, Feb, 1988 ($1.75, Baxter paper)

1-4: Scout limited series						3.00

NEW ARCHIES, THE (TV)

GD 2.0 | VG 4.0 | FN 6.0 | VF 8.0 | VF/NM 9.0 | NM- 9.2

Archie Comic Publications: Oct, 1987 - No. 22, May, 1990 (75¢)

1 5.00
2-10: 3-Xmas issue 4.00
11-22: 17-22 (95¢-$1.00): 21-Xmas issue 3.00

NEW ARCHIES DIGEST (TV)(...Comics Digest Magazine #4?-10; ...Digest Magazine #11 on)
Archie Comics: May, 1988 - No. 14, July, 1991 ($1.35/$1.50, quarterly)

1 6.00
2-14: 6-Begin $1.50-c 3.50

NEW AVENGERS, THE (Also see Promotional section for military giveaway)
Marvel Comics: Jan, 2005 - No. 64, Jun, 2010 ($2.25/$2.50/$2.99/$3.99)

1-Bendis-s/Finch-a; Spider-Man app.; re-intro The Sentry; 4 covers by McNiven, Quesada & Finch; variants from #1-6 combine for one team image
1 3 4 6 8 10
1-Director's Cut ($3.99) includes alternate covers, script, villain gallery 6.00
1-MGC (6/10 $1.00) r/#1 with "Marvel's Greatest Comics" cover logo 3.00
2-6,8-20: 2-6-Finch-a. 4-1st app. Maria Hill. 5-Wolverine app. 8-10-Origin of the Sentry; McNiven-a. 11-Debut of Ronin. 14,15-Cho-c/a. 17-20-Deodato-a 3.00
7-1st app. The Illuminati; origin of the Sentry begins; McNiven-a
3 6 9 21 33 45
21-48: 21-26-Civil War. 21-Chaykin-a/c. 26-Maleev-a. 27-31-Yu-a; Echo & "Elektra" app. 33-37-The Hood app. 38-Gaydos-a. 39-Mack-a. 40-47-Secret Invasion 3.00
49-($3.99) Dark Reign 4.00
50-($4.99) Dark Reign; Tan, Hitch, McNiven, Yu, Horn & others-a; Tan wraparound-c 5.00
50-($4.99) Adam Kubert variant-c 6.00
51-64-($3.99) Dark Reign. 51,52-Tan & Bachalo-a. 54-Brother Voodoo becomes Sorceror Supreme. 56-Wrecking Crew app. 61-64-Siege; Steve Rogers app. 4.00
51-54-Variant covers by Bachalo 7.00
56,57-Variant covers. 56-70th Anniversary frame. 57-Super Hero Squad 6.00
Annual 1 (6/06, $3.99) Wedding of Luke Cage and Jessica Jones; Bendis-s/Coipel-a 4.00
Annual 2 (2/08, $3.99) Avengers vs. The Hood's gang; Bendis-s/Pagulayan-a 4.00
Annual 3 (2/10, $4.99) Mayhew-c/a; Dark Avengers app.; Siege preview 5.00
... Finale (6/10, $4.99) Follows Siege #4; Bendis-s/Hitch-a/c; Count Nefaria app. 5.00
...: Illuminati (5/06, $3.99) Bendis-s/Maleev-a; leads into Planet Hulk; Civil War preview 4.00
... Most Wanted Files (2006, $3.99) profile pages of Avenger villains 4.00
... Volume 1 HC (2007, $29.99) oversized r/#1-10, ... Most Wanted Files, and ... Guest Starring the Fantastic Four (militiary giveaway); new intro. by Bendis; script & sketch pages 30.00
... Volume 2 HC (2008, $29.99) oversized r/#11-20, ... Annual #1, and story from Giant-Size Spider-Woman; variant covers & sketch pages 30.00

NEW AVENGERS (The Heroic Age)
Marvel Comics: Aug, 2010 - No. 34, Jan, 2013 ($3.99)

1-Bendis-s/Immonen-a/c; Luke Cage forms new team; back-up text Avengers history 4.00
1-Variant-c by Djurdjevic 6.00
2-16: Hellstrom & Doctor Voodoo app.; back-up text Avengers history. 6-Doctor Voodoo killed. 9-13-Nick Fury flashback w/Chaykin-a. 10-Intro. Avengers 1959. 14-16-Fear Itself. 16-Daredevil joins 4.00
16.1 (11/11, $2.99) Neal Adams-a/c; Bendis-s; Norman Osborn app. 3.00
17-23-($3.99) 17-Norman Osborn attacks; Iron Man app.; Deodato-a 4.00
24-33: 24-30-Avengers vs. X-Men tie-in. 26,27-DaVinci app. 31-Gaydos-a. 32-Pacheco-a 4.00
34-($4.99) Dr. Strange become Sorcerer Supreme again; Deodato-a; gallery of Bendis-era Avengers covers 5.00
Annual 1 (11/11, $4.99) Dell'Otto-a; Wonder Man app.; continues in Avengers Annual #1 5.00

NEW AVENGERS (Marvel NOW!)
Marvel Comics: Mar, 2013 - No. 33, Jun, 2015 ($3.99)

1-7: 1-Hickman-s/Epting-a; Black Panther and the Illuminati. 4-Galactus app. 4.00
8-23: 8-12-Infinity tie-ins; Deodato-a. 13-Inhumanity; Bianchi-a. 17-21-Great Society app. 4.00
24-($4.99) Doctor Doom, Thanos and the Cabal app. 5.00
25-32: 27-Kudranski-a. 28,32-Deodato-a 4.00
33-($4.99) Doctor Doom & Molecule Man app.; leads into Secret Wars x-over; Deodato-a 5.00
Annual 1 (8/14, $4.99) Spotlight on Doctor Strange; Marco Rudy-a 5.00

NEW AVENGERS (Follows events of Secret Wars)(See U.S.Avengers)
Marvel Comics: Dec, 2015 - No. 18, Jan, 2017 ($3.99)

1-18: 1-Ewing-s/Sandoval-a; Squirrel Girl app. 5,6-Avengers of 20XX app. 8-10-Standoff tie-in; Marcus To-a. 12-17-Civil War II tie-in. 12-16-Interlocking covers 4.00

NEW AVENGERS: ILLUMINATI (Also see Civil War and Secret Invasion)
Marvel Comics: Feb, 2007 - No. 5, Jan, 2008 ($2.99, limited series)

1-5-Bendis & Reed-s/Cheung-a. 3-Origin of The Beyonder. 5-Secret Invasion 3.00
HC (2008, $19.99, dustjacket) r/#1-5; cover sketch art 20.00
SC (2008, $14.99) r/#1-5; cover sketch art 15.00

NEW AVENGERS: LUKE CAGE
Marvel Comics: Jun, 2010 - No. 3, Aug, 2010 ($3.99, limited series)

1-3-Arcudi-s/Canete-a; Spider-Man & Ronin app. 4.00

NEW AVENGERS: THE REUNION
Marvel Comics: May, 2009 - No. 4, Aug, 2009 ($3.99, limited series)

1-4-Mockingbird and Ronin (Hawkeye); McCann-s/López-a/Jo Chen-c 4.00

NEW AVENGERS/TRANSFORMERS
Marvel Comics: Sept, 2007 - No. 4, Dec, 2007 ($2.99, limited series)

1-4-Kirkham-a; Capt. America app. 1-Cheung-c. 2-Pearson-c 3.00
TPB (2008, $10.99) r/#1-4 11.00

NEW AVENGERS: ULTRON FOREVER
Marvel Comics: Jun, 2015 ($4.99)(Continues in Uncanny Avengers: Ultron Forever)

1-Part 2 of 3-part crossover with Avengers and Uncanny Avengers; Ewing-s/Alan Davis-a; team-up of past, present and future Avengers vs. Ultron 5.00

NEW BOOK OF COMICS (Also see Big Book Of Fun)
National Periodical Publ.: 1937; No. 2, Spring, 1938 (100 pgs. each) (Reprints)

1(Rare)-1st regular size comic annual; 2nd DC annual; contains r/New Comics #1-4 & More Fun #9; r/Federal Men (8 pgs.), Henri Duval (1 pg.), & Dr. Occult in costume (1 pg.) by Siegel & Shuster; Moldoff, Sheldon Mayer (15 pgs.)-a
1900 3800 5700 12,350 21,675 31,000
2-Contains-r/More Fun #15 & 16; r/Dr. Occult in costume (a Superman prototype), & Calling All Cars (4 pgs.) by Siegel & Shuster 1046 2092 3138 6800 11,900 17,000

NEWBURN
Image Comics: Nov, 2021 - No. 8, Jun, 2022 ($3.99)

1-8-Chip Zdarsky-s/Jacob Phillips-a 4.00

NEW CHALLENGERS (Challengers of the Unknown)(Follows events of Dark Nights: Metal)
DC Comics: Jul, 2018 - No. 6, Dec, 2018 ($2.99)

1-5: 1-New team recruited; Snyder & Gillespie-s/Andy Kubert-a/c. 2-Original team returns. 4-6-Marion-a 3.00

NEW CHAMPION OF SHAZAM!, THE (Continues in Lazarus Planet: We Once Were Gods)
DC Comics: Oct, 2022 - No. 4, Mar, 2023 ($3.99, limited series)

1-4-Mary receives all the power of Shazam!; Hoppy app.; Josie Campbell-s/Doc Shaner-a 4.00

NEW COMICS (New Adventure #12 on)
National Periodical Publ.: 12/35 - No. 11, 12/36 (No. 1-6: paper cover) (No. 1-5: 84 pgs.)

V1#1-Billy the Kid, Sagebrush 'n' Cactus, Jibby Jones, Needles, The Vikings, Sir Loin of Beef, Now-When I Was a Boy, & other 1-2 pg. strips; 2 pgs. Kelly art(1st)-(Gulliver's Travels); Sheldon Mayer-a(1st)(2 2pg. strips); Vincent Sullivan-c(1st)
2460 4920 7380 15,500 – –
2-1st app. Federal Men by Siegel & Shuster & begins (also see The Comics Magazine #2); Mayer, Kelly-a (Rare)(1/36) 1425 2850 4275 9000 – –
3-6: 3,4-Sheldon Mayer-a which continues in The Comics Magazine #1. 3-Vincent Sullivan-c. 4-Dickens' "A Tale of Two Cities" adaptation begins. 5-Junior Federal Men Club; Kiefer-a. 6- "She" adaptation begins 1000 2000 3000 6100 – –
7-10 650 1300 1950 4000 – –
11-Ties with More Fun #16 as DC's 1st Christmas-c 733 1466 2199 4500 – –
NOTE: *#1-6 rarely occur in mint condition.* ***Whitney Ellsworth*** *c-4-11.*

NEW CRUSADERS (Rise of the Heroes)
Archie Comics (Red Circle Comics): Oct, 2012 - No. 6, Mar, 2013 ($2.99)

1-6-The Shield and the offspring of the Mighty Crusaders 3.00

NEW DEADWARDIANS, THE
DC Comics (Vertigo): May, 2012 - No. 8, Dec, 2012 ($2.99, limited series)

1-8-Abnett-s/Culbard-a 3.00

NEW DEFENDERS (See Defenders)

NEW DNAGENTS, THE (Formerly DNAgents)
Eclipse Comics: V2#1, Oct, 1985 - V2#17, Mar, 1987 (Whole #s 25-40; Mando paper)

V2#1-17: 1-Origin recap. 7-Begin 95 cent-c. 9,10-Airboy preview 3.00
3-D 1 (1/86, $2.25) 3.00
2-D 1 (1/86)-Limited ed. (100 copies) 10.00

NEW DYNAMIX
DC Comics (WildStorm): May, 2008 - No. 5, Sept, 2008 ($2.99, limited series)

1-5-Warner-s/J.J. Kirby-a/c. 1-Variant-c by Jim Lee. 1-Convention Ed. with Lee-c 3.00

NEW ETERNALS: APOCALYPSE NOW (Also see Eternals, The)
Marvel Comics: Feb, 2000 ($3.99, one-shot)

1-Bennett & Hanna-a; Ladronn-c 4.00

NEW EXCALIBUR
Marvel Comics: Jan, 2006 - No. 24, Dec, 2007 ($2.99)

1-24: 1-Claremont-s/Ryan-a; Dazzler app. 3-Juggernaut app. 4-Lionheart app. 3.00
... Vol. 1: Defenders of the Realm TPB (2006, $17.99) r/#1-7 18.00
... Vol. 2: Last Days of Camelot TPB (2007, $19.99) r/#8-15 20.00
... Vol. 3: Battle for Eternity TPB (2007, $24.99) r/#16-24; sketch pages 25.00

NEW EXILES (Continued from Exiles #100 and Exiles - Days of Then and Now)
Marvel Comics: Mar, 2008 - No. 18, Apr, 2009 ($2.99)

1-18: 1-Claremont-s/Grummett-a; 2 covers by Land & Golden; new team 3.00
1-2nd printing with Grummett-c 3.00
Annual 1 (2/09, $3.99) Claremont-s/Grummett-a 4.00

NEW FANTASTIC FOUR
Marvel Comics: Aug, 2022 - No. 5, Dec, 2022 ($4.99/$3.99)

1-($4.99)-Spider-Man, Wolverine, Ghost Rider & Joe Fixit team; David-s/Robinson-a 5.00
2-5-($3.99) Regular Fantastic Four app. 4.00
...: Marvel Tales 1 (8/22, $7.99) Reprints Fantastic Four #347-349; bonus art 8.00

NEW 52: FUTURE'S END
DC Comics: No 0, Jun, 2014 - No. 48, Jun, 2015 ($2.99, weekly limited series)

... FCBD Special Edition #0 (6/14, giveaway) Part 1; 35 years in the future 3.00
1-36: 1-Set 5 years in the future; Azzarello, Lemire, Jurgens & Giffen-s. 29-New Firestorm. 33-Kid Deathstroke-c. 44-Brainiac steals New York (Convergence) 3.00

NEWFORCE (Also see Newmen)
Image Comics (Extreme Studios): Jan, 1996-No. 4, Apr, 1996 ($2.50, lim. series)

1-4: 1-"Extreme Destroyer" Pt. 8; polybagged w/gaming card. 4-Newforce disbands 3.00

NEW FUN COMICS (More Fun #7 on; see Big Book of Fun Comics)
National Periodical Publications: Feb, 1935 - No. 6, Oct, 1935 (10x15", No. 1-4,: slick-c) (No. 1-5: 36 pgs; 40 pgs. No. 6)

V1#1 (1st DC comic); 1st app. Oswald The Rabbit; Jack Woods (cowboy) begins
8850 17,700 26,550 62,000 – –
2(3/35)-(Very Rare) 4450 8900 13,350 31,200 – –
3-5(8/35): 3-Don Drake on the Planet Soro-c/story (sci/fi, 4/35); early (maybe 1st) DC letter column. 5-Soft-c 2850 5700 8550 20,000 – –
6(10/35)-1st Dr. Occult by Siegel & Shuster (Leger & Reuths); last "New Fun" title. "New Comics" #1 begins in Dec. which is reason for title change to More Fun; Henri Duval (ends #10) by Siegel & Shuster begins; paper-c
4600 9200 13,800 32,200 – –

NEW FUNNIES (The Funnies #1-64; Walter Lantz...#109 on; New TV... #259, 260, 272, 273; TV Funnies #261-271)
Dell Publishing Co.: No. 65, July, 1942 - No. 288, Mar-Apr, 1962

65(#1)-Andy Panda in a world of real people, Raggedy Ann & Andy, Oswald the Rabbit (with Woody Woodpecker x-overs), Li'l Eight Ball & Peter Rabbit begin; Bugs Bunny and Elmer app. 104 208 312 832 1866 2900
66-70: 66-Felix the Cat begins. 67-Billy & Bonny Bee by Frank Thomas begins. 69-Kelly-a

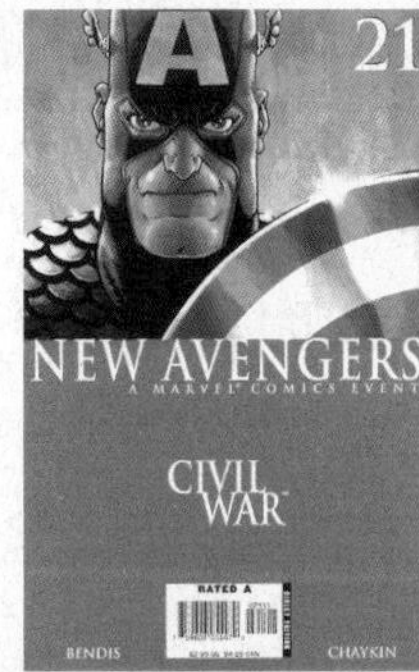

New Avengers #21 © MAR

New 52: Future's End #1 © DC

New Gods #9 © DC

	GD	VG	FN	VF	VF/NM	NM-
	2.0	4.0	6.0	8.0	9.0	9.2

(2 pgs.); The Brownies begin (not by Kelly); Halloween-c 33 66 99 238 532 825

71-75: 71-Christmas-c. 72-Kelly illos. 75-Brownies by Kelly? 21 42 63 146 318 490

76-Andy Panda (Carl Barks & Pabian-a); Woody Woodpecker x-over in Oswald ends 54 108 162 432 966 1500

77,78: 77-Kelly-c. 78-Andy Panda in a world with real people ends 16 32 48 110 243 375

79-81 10 20 30 69 147 225

82-Brownies by Kelly begins 11 22 33 76 163 250

83-85-Brownies by Kelly in ea. 83-X-mas-c; Homer Pigeon begins. 85-Woody Woodpecker, 1 pg. strip begins 11 22 33 72 154 235

86-90: 87-Woody Woodpecker stories begin 9 18 27 57 111 165

91-99 8 16 24 51 96 140

100 (6/45) 8 16 24 54 102 150

101-120: 119-X-Mas-c 7 14 21 46 86 125

121-150: 131,143-X-Mas-c 6 12 18 40 73 105

151-200: 155-X-Mas-c. 167-X-Mas-c. 182-Origin & 1st app. Knothead & Splinter. 191-X-Mas-c 5 10 15 35 63 90

201-240 5 10 15 35 57 80

241-288: 270,271-Walter Lantz c-app. 281-1st story swipes/WDC&S #100 5 10 15 30 50 70

NOTE: *Early issues written by* ***John Stanley.***

NEW GODS, THE (1st Series)(New Gods #12 on)(See Adventure #459, DC Graphic Novel #4, 1st Issue Special #13 & Super-Team Family)
National Periodical Publications/DC Comics: 2-3/71 - V2#11, 10-11/72; V3#12, 7/77 - V3#19, 7-8/78 (Fourth World)

1-Intro/1st app. Orion; 4th app. Darkseid (cameo; 3 weeks after Forever People #1) (#1-3 are 15¢ issues) 13 26 39 91 201 310

2-Darkseid-c/story (2nd full app., 4-5/71) 7 14 21 44 82 120

3-1st app. Black Racer; last 15¢ issue 6 12 18 41 76 110

4-6,8,9: (25¢, 52 pg. giants): 4-Darkseid cameo; origin Manhunter-r. 5,8-Young Gods feature. 9-1st app. Forager 4 8 12 27 44 60

7-1st app. Steppenwolf (2-3/72); Darkseid app.; origin Orion; 1st origin of all New Gods as a group; Young Gods feature 9 18 27 59 117 175

10,11: 11-Last Kirby issue. 3 6 9 21 33 45

12-19: Darkseid storyline w/minor apps. 12-New costume Orion (see 1st Issue Special #13 for 1st new costume). 19-Story continued in Adventure Comics #459,460 2 4 6 8 11 14

Jack Kirby's New Gods TPB ('98, $11.95, B&W&Grey) r/#1-11 plus cover gallery of original series and "84 reprints 12.00

NOTE: *#4-9(25¢, 52 pgs.) contain Manhunter-r by* ***Simon*** *&* ***Kirby*** *from Adventure #73, 74, 75, 76, 77, 78 with covers in that order.* ***Adkins*** *i-12-14, 17-19.* ***Buckler*** *a(p)-15.* ***Kirby*** *c/a-1-11p.* ***Newton*** *a(p)-12-14, 16-19.* ***Starlin*** *c-17.* ***Staton*** *c-19p.*

NEW GODS (Also see DC Graphic Novel #4)
DC Comics: June, 1984 - No. 6, Nov, 1984 ($2.00, Baxter paper)

1-New Kirby-c; r/New Gods #1,2 1 3 4 6 8 10

2-5: New Kirby-c; r/New Gods #3-10. 5.00

6-Reprints New Gods #11 w/48 pgs of new Kirby story & art; leads into DC Graphic Novel #4 2 4 6 8 10 12

NEW GODS (2nd Series)
DC Comics: Feb, 1989 - No. 28, Aug, 1991 ($1.50)

1-28: 1,5-28-Evanier-s. 2-4-Starlin-s. 13-History of New Gods 20th anniv. 4.00

NEW GODS (3rd Series) (Becomes Jack Kirby's Fourth World) (Also see Showcase '94 #1 & Showcase '95 #7)
DC Comics: Oct, 1995 - No. 15, Feb, 1997 ($1.95)

1-11,13-15: 9-Giffen-a(p). 10,11-Superman app. 13-Takion, Mr. Miracle & Big Barda app. 13-15-Byrne-a(p)/scripts & Simonson-c. 15-Apokolips merged w/ New Genesis; story cont'd in Jack Kirby's Fourth World 4.00

12-(11/96, 99¢)-Byrne-a(p)/scripts & Simonson-c begin; Takion cameo; indicia reads October 1996 4.00

...Secret Files 1 (9/98, $4.95) Origin-s 5.00

NEW GODS SPECIAL, THE (Jack Kirby's 100th Birthday tribute)
DC Comics: Oct, 2017 ($4.99, one-shot)

1-Spotlight on Orion; Shane Davis-s/a; back-up by Walt Simonson-s/a; short reprints 5.00

NEW GOLDEN AGE, THE (Leads into Justice Society of America 2023 series)
DC Comics: Jan, 2023 ($4.99, one-shot)

1-Per Degaton vs. various eras of the JSA & Huntress; Johns-s; profile pgs of missing 13 5.00

NEW GUARDIANS, THE
DC Comics: Sept, 1988 - No. 12, Sept, 1989 ($1.25)

1-($2.00, 52 pgs)-Staton-c/a in #1-9 5.00

	GD	VG	FN	VF	VF/NM	NM-
	2.0	4.0	6.0	8.0	9.0	9.2

2-12 4.00

NEW HEROIC (See Heroic)

NEW INVADERS (Titled Invaders for #0 & #1) (See Avengers V3#83,84)
Marvel Comics: No. 0, Aug, 2004 - No. 9, June, 2005 ($2.99)

0-9-Roster of U.S. Agent, Sub-Mariner, Blazing Skull and others. 0-Avengers app. 3.00

NEW JUSTICE MACHINE, THE (Also see The Justice Machine)
Innovation Publishing: 1989 - No. 3, 1989 ($1.95, limited series)

1-3 4.00

NEW KIDS ON THE BLOCK, THE (Also see Richie Rich and...)
Harvey Comics: Dec, 1990 - No. 8, Dec, 1991 ($1.25)

1-8 5.00

...**Back Stage Pass** 1(12/90) - 7(11/91) **Chillin'** 1(12/90) - 7(12/91): 1-Photo-c ...**Comic Tour** '90/91 1 (12/90) - 7(12/91) **Digest** 1(1/91) - 5(1/92) **Hanging Tough** 1 (2/91) **Magic Summer Tour** 1 (Fall/90) **Magic Summer Tour** nn (Fall/90, sold at concerts) **Step By Step** 1 (Fall/90, one-shot) **Valentine Girl** 1 (Fall/90, one-shot)-Photo-c 5.00

NEW LINE CINEMA'S TALES OF HORROR (Anthology)
DC Comics (WildStorm): Nov, 2007 ($2.99, one-shot)

1-Freddy Krueger and Leatherface app.; Darick Robertson-c 3.00

NEW LOVE (See Love & Rockets)
Fantagraphics Books: Aug, 1996 - No. 6, Dec, 1997 ($2.95, B&W, lim. series)

1-6: Gilbert Hernandez-s/a 3.00

NEWMAN
Image Comics (Extreme Studios): Jan, 1996 - No. 4, Apr, 1996 ($2.50, lim. series)

1-4: 1-Extreme Destroyer Pt. 3; polybagged w/card. 4-Shadowhunt tie-in; Eddie Collins becomes new Shadowhawk 3.00

NEW MANGVERSE (Also see Marvel Mangaverse)
Marvel Comics: Mar, 2006 - No. 5, July, 2006 ($2.99, lim. series)

1-5: Cebulski-s/Ohtsuka-a; The Hand and Elektra app. 3.00

...: The Rings of Fate (2006, $7.99, digest) r/#1-5 8.00

NEWMEN (becomes The Adventures Of The...#22)
Image Comics (Extreme Studios): Apr, 1994 - No. 20, Nov, 1995; No. 21, Nov, 1996 ($1.95/$2.50)

1-21: 1-5: Matsuda-c/a. 10-Polybagged w/trading card. 11-Polybagged. 20-Has a variant-c; Babewatch! x-over. 21-(11/96)-Series relaunch; Chris Sprouse-a begins; pin-up. 16-Has a variant-c by Quesada & Palmiotti 3.00

TPB-(1996, $12.95) r/#1-4 w/pin-ups 13.00

NEW MEN OF BATTLE, THE
Catechetical Guild: 1949 (nn) (Carboard-c)

nn(V8#1-3,5,6)-192 pgs.; contains 6 issues of Topix rebound 12 24 36 69 97 125

nn(V8#7-V8#11)-160 pgs.; contains 5 iss. of Topix 10 20 30 56 76 95

NEW MGMT (See Mind MGMT)

NEW MUTANTS, THE (See Marvel Graphic Novel #4 for 1st app.)(Also see X-Force & Uncanny X-Men #167)
Marvel Comics Group: Mar, 1983 - No. 100, Apr, 1991

1-Claremont-s/McLeod-a 3 6 9 21 33 45

2-,8,10: 3,4-Ties into X-Men #167. 10-1st app. Magma 1 3 4 6 8 10

9-1st app. Selene, the Black Queen 2 4 6 11 16 20

11-15,17,19,20: 13-Kitty Pryde app. 5.00

16-1st app. Warpath (w/out costume); see Uncanny X-Men #193 3 6 9 15 22 28

18-Intro. new Warlock 3 6 9 14 20 25

21-Double size; origin new Warlock; newsstand version has cover price written in by Sienkiewicz 2 4 6 11 16 20

22-24,27-30: 23-25-Cloak & Dagger app. 5.00

25-1st brief app. Legion (David Haller) 3 6 9 17 25 34

26-1st full Legion app. 3 6 9 19 30 40

31-49,51-58: 35-Magneto intro'd as new headmaster. 43-Portacio-i. 58-Contains pull-out mutant registration form 5.00

50,73: 50-Double size. 73-(52 pgs.). 6.00

59-61: Fall of The Mutants series. 60-(52 pgs.) 6.00

62-72,74-85: 68-Intro Spyder. 63-X-Men & Wolverine clones app. 76-X-Factor & X-Terminator app. 85-Liefeld-c begin 5.00

86-Rob Liefeld-a begins; McFarlane-c(i) swiped from Ditko splash pg.; 1st brief app. Cable (last page teaser) 3 6 9 17 26 35

87-1st full app. Cable (3/90) 9 18 27 59 117 175

87-2nd printing; gold metallic ink-c ($1.00) 3 6 9 16 23 30

GD VG FN VF VF/NM NM-
2.0 4.0 6.0 8.0 9.0 9.2

88-2nd app. Cable 2 4 6 10 14 18
92-No Liefeld-a; Liefeld-c 5.00
89,90,91,93-97,99: 89-3rd app. Cable. 90-New costumes. 90,91-Sabretooth app. 93,94-Cable vs. Wolverine. 95-97-X-Tinction Agenda x-over. 95-Death of new Warlock. 97-Wolverine & Cable-c, but no app. 99-1st app. of Feral (of X-Force); 2nd app. Shatterstar (cameo); Byrne-c/swipe (X-Men, 1st Series #138) 6.00
95,100-Gold 2nd printing. 100-Silver ink 3rd printing 6.00
98-1st app. Deadpool, Gideon & Domino (2/91); Liefeld-c/a 16 32 48 110 243 375
100-(52 pgs.)-1st brief app. X-Force; 1st full app. of Shatterstar 3 6 9 16 23 30
Annual 1 (1984) 3 6 9 14 19 24
Annual 2 (1986, $1.25)-1st Psylocke 6 12 18 38 69 100
Annual 3,4,6,7 ('87, '88,'90,'91, 68 pgs.): 4-Evolutionary War x-over. 6-1st new costumes by Liefeld (3 pgs.); 1st brief app. Shatterstar (of X-Force). 7-Liefeld pin-up only; X-Terminators back-up story; 2nd app. X-Force (cont'd in New Warriors Annual #1) 5.00
Annual 5 (1989, $2.00, 68 pgs.)-Atlantis Attacks; 1st Liefeld-a on New Mutants 6.00
... Classic Vol. 1 TPB (2006, $24.99) r/#1-7, Marvel Graphic Novel #4, Uncanny X-Men #167 25.00
... Classic Vol. 2 TPB (2007, $24.99) r/#8-17 25.00
... Classic Vol. 3 TPB (2008, $24.99) r/#18-25 & Annual #1 25.00
... No. 98 Facsimile Edition (9/19, $3.99) Reprints #98 with original 1991 ads and letters 4.00
... No. 98 Facsimile Edition (1/23, $3.99) Reprints #98 with original 1991 ads and letters 4.00
Special 1-Special Edition ('85, 68 pgs.)-Ties in w/X-Men Alpha Flight limited series; cont'd in X-Men Annual #9; Art Adams/Austin-a 2 4 6 10 14 18
Summer Special 1(Sum/90, $2.95, 84 pgs.) 5.00
NOTE: ***Art Adams** c-38, 39. **Austin** c-57i. **Byrne** c/a-75p. **Liefeld** a-86-91p, 93-96p, 98-100, Annual 5p, 6(3 pgs.); c-85-91p, 92, 93p, 94, 95, 96p, 97-100, Annual 5, 6p. **McFarlane** c-85-89i, 93i. **Portacio** a(i)-43. **Russell** a-48i. **Sienkiewicz** a-18-31, 35-38i; c-17-31, 35i, 37i, Annual 1. **Simonson** c-11p. **B. Smith** c-36, 40-48. **Williamson** a(i)-69, 71-73, 78-80, 82, 83; c(i)-69, 72, 73, 78i.*

NEW MUTANTS (Continues as New X-Men (Academy X))
Marvel Comics: July, 2003 - No. 13, June, 2004 ($2.50/$2.99)

1-13: 1-6-Josh Middleton-c. 7-11-Bachalo-c. 8-Begin $2.99 3.00
... Vol. 1: Back To School TPB (2005, $16.99) r/#1-6; new Middleton-c 17.00

NEW MUTANTS
Marvel Comics: July, 2009 - No. 50, Dec, 2012 ($3.99/$2.99)

1-($3.99) Neves-a; Legion app.; covers by Ross, Adam Kubert, McLeod, Benjamin 4.00
2-24-($2.99) 2-10-Adam Kubert-c. 11-Siege; Dodson-c. 12-14-Second Coming 3.00
25-($3.99) Fernandez-a; wraparound-c by Djurdjevic; Nate Grey returns 4.00
26-50: 29-32-Fear Itself tie-in. 33-Regenesis. 34-Blink returns. 42,43-Exiled x-over with Exiled #1 & Journey Into Mystery #637,638 3.00
... Saga (2009, giveaway) New Mutants character profiles and story synopsies; Neves-c 3.00

NEW MUTANTS
Marvel Comics: Jan, 2020 - No. 33, Feb, 2023 ($4.99/$3.99)

1-($4.99) Brisson & Hickman-s/Rod Reis-a; Starjammers app. 5.00
2-24,26-29,31-33-($3.99) 13- "X of Swords" tie-in 4.00
25-($4.99) Reis-a; flashback art by Jan Duursema 5.00
30-($5.99) Celebration of 40 years; short stories by various; Deadpool app. 6.00
...: War Children 1 (11/19, $4.99) Claremont-s/Sienkiewicz-a/c 5.00

NEW MUTANTS: DEAD SOULS
Marvel Comics: May, 2018 - No. 6, Oct, 2018 ($3.99, limited series)

1-6-Rosenberg-s/Gorham-a; Rictor, Boom Boom, Magik, Strong Guy & Wolfsbane app. 4.00

NEW MUTANTS FOREVER
Marvel Comics: Oct, 2010 - No. 5, Feb, 2011 ($3.99, limited series)

1-5-Claremont-s/Rio & McLeod-a; Red Skull app. 1-Back-up history of New Mutants 4.00

NEW MUTANTS, THE: TRUTH OR DEATH
Marvel Comics: Nov, 1997 - No. 3, Jan, 1998 ($2.50, limited series)

1-3-Raab-s/Chang-a(p) 3.00

NEW PEOPLE, THE (TV)
Dell Publishing Co.: Jan, 1970 - No. 2, May, 1970

1 3 6 9 17 25 34
2-Photo-c 3 6 9 15 21 26

NEW ROMANCER
DC Comics (Vertigo): Feb, 2016 - No. 6, Jul, 2016 ($3.99, limited series)

1-6-Milligan-s/Parson-a; Lord Byron & Casanova in present day 4.00

NEW ROMANCES
Standard Comics: No. 5, May, 1951 - No. 21, May, 1954

5-Photo-c 23 46 69 136 223 310
6-9: 6-Barbara Bel Geddes, Richard Basehart "Fourteen Hours" photo-c. 7-Ray Milland & Joan Fontaine photo-c. 9-Photo-c from '50s movie 15 30 45 90 140 190
10,14,16,17-Toth-a 16 32 48 94 147 200
11-Toth-a; Liz Taylor, Montgomery Clift photo-c 41 82 123 256 428 600
12,13,15,18-21 15 30 45 83 124 165
NOTE: *Celardo a-9. **Moreira** a-6. **Tuska** a-7, 20. **Photo** c-5-16.*

NEWSBOY LEGION AND THE BOY COMMANDOS SPECIAL, THE (Jack Kirby's 100th Birthday tribute)
DC Comics: Oct, 2017 ($4.99, one-shot)

1-Howard Chaykin-s/a/c; reprint from Star Spangled Comics #29; Simon-s/Kirby-a 5.00

NEWSBOY LEGION BY JOE SIMON AND JACK KIRBY, THE
DC Comics: 2010 ($49.99, hardcover with dustjacket)

Vol. 1 - Reprints apps. in Star Spangled Comics #7-32; new intro. by Joe Simon 50.00

NEW SHADOWHAWK, THE (Also see Shadowhawk & Shadowhunt)
Image Comics (Shadowline Ink): June, 1995 - No. 7, Mar, 1996 ($2.50)

1-7: Kurt Busiek scripts in all 3.00

NEWSTRALIA
Innovation Publ.: July, 1989 - No. 5, 1989 ($1.75, color)(#2 on, $2.25, B&W)

1-5: 1,2: Timothy Truman-c/a; Gustovich-i 3.00

NEW SUICIDE SQUAD (DC New 52)
DC Comics: Sept, 2014 - No. 22, Sept, 2016 ($2.99)

1-New team of Harley Quinn, Joker's Daughter, Black Manta, Deathstroke, Deadshot 3 6 9 17 26 35
2,3 1 2 3 5 6 8
4-10 4.00
11-22: 22-Cliquet-a 3.00
Annual 1 (11/15, $4.99) Continues story from #12; Briones-a 5.00
...: Futures End 1 (11/14, $2.99, regular-c) Five years later; Coelho-a 3.00
...: Futures End 1 (11/14, $3.99, 3-D cover) 4.00

NEW SUPER-MAN (DC Rebirth)(See Batman/Superman #32 for 1st app.)
DC Comics: Sept, 2016 - No. 19, Mar, 2018 ($2.99/$3.99)

1-9: 1-Kong Kenan as China's Superman; origin; Gene Luen Yang-s/Bogdanovic-a. 7-9-Master I-Ching app. 8-Ching Lung (from Detective Comics #1) app. 9-Luthor app. 3.00
10-19-($3.99) 10-Superman app. 15-Suicide Squad app. 17,18-Justice League app. 4.00

NEW SUPER-MAN & THE JUSTICE LEAGUE OF CHINA
DC Comics: No. 20, Apr, 2018 - No. 24, Aug, 2018 ($3.99)

20-24-Yang-s/Peeples-a 4.00

NEW TALENT SHOWCASE (Talent Showcase #16 on)
DC Comics: Jan, 1984 - No. 19, Oct, 1985 (Direct sales only)

1-19: Features new strips & artists. 18-Williamson-c(i) 3.00

NEW TALENT SHOWCASE
DC Comics: Jan, 2017 ($7.99, one-shot)

1-Janson-c; short stories by various; Wonder Woman, Harley Quinn, Deadman app. 8.00
... 2017 #1 (1/18, $7.99) Short stories by various; Wonder Woman, Red Hood, Duke, Katana, Deadshot, Poison Ivy and Dr. Fate app. 8.00
... 2018 #1 (2/19, $7.99) Short stories by various; Batman, Catwoman, Wonder Woman, Constantine, John Stewart and Zatanna app. 8.00

NEW TEEN TITANS, THE (See DC Comics Presents #26, Marvel and DC Present & Teen Titans; Tales of the Teen Titans #41 on)
DC Comics: Nov, 1980 - No. 40, Mar, 1984

1-Robin, Kid Flash, Wonder Girl, The Changeling (1st app.), Starfire, The Raven, Cyborg begin; partial origin 6 12 18 41 76 110
2-1st app. Deathstroke the Terminator 11 22 33 76 163 250
3,4: 3-Origin Starfire; Intro The Fearsome Five. 4-Origin continues; J.L.A. app. 3 6 9 14 20 25
5-9: 6-Origin Raven. 7-Cyborg origin. 8-Origin Kid Flash retold. 9-Minor app. Deathstroke on last pg. 2 4 6 10 14 18
10-2nd app. Deathstroke the Terminator (see Marvel & DC Present for 3rd app.); origin Changeling retold 3 6 9 14 20 25
11-20: 13-Return of Madame Rouge & Capt. Zahl; Robotman revived. 14-Return of Mento; origin Doom Patrol. 15-Death of Madame Rouge & Capt. Zahl; intro. new Brotherhood of Evil. 16-1st app. Captain Carrot (free 16 pg. preview). 18-Return of Starfire. 19-Hawkman teams-up 1 3 4 6 8 10
21,22: 21-Intro Night Force in free 16 pg. insert; intro Brother Blood. 22-1st app. Bethany Snow 2 4 6 13 18 22
23-25,27-33,35-40: 23-1st app. Vigilante (not in costume), & Blackfire; bondage-c. 24-Omega Men app. 25-Omega Men cameo; free 16 pg. preview Masters of the Universe. 27-Free 16 pg. preview Atari Force. 29-The New Brotherhood of Evil & Speedy app. 30-Terra joins the Titans. 37-Batman & The Outsiders x-over. 38-Origin Wonder Girl. 39-Last Dick Grayson as Robin; Kid Flash quits 1 2 3 5 6 8
26-1st app. Terra 2 4 6 10 14 18
34-4th app. Deathstroke the Terminator 2 4 6 9 13 16
Annual 1(11/82)-Omega Men app. 2 4 6 9 13 16
Annual V2#2(9/83)-1st app. Vigilante in costume; 1st app. Lyla 4 8 12 23 37 50
Annual 3 (See Tales of the Teen Titans Annual #3)
...: Games GN (2011, $24.99, HC) Wolfman-s/Pérez-a/c; original GN started in 1988, finished in 2011; '80s NTT roster; afterword by Pérez; Wolfman's original plot 25.00
...: Games GN (2013, $16.99, SC) same contents as HC 17.00
...: Terra Incognito TPB (2006, $19.99) r/#26,28-34 & Annual #2 20.00
...: The Judas Contract TPB (2003, $19.95) r/#39,40 plus Tales of the Teen Titans #41-44 & Annual #3 20.00
...: Who is Donna Troy? TPB (2005, $19.99) r/#38,Tales of the Teen Titans #50, New Titans #50-55 and Teen Titans/Outsiders Secret Files 2003 20.00
NOTE: ***Pérez** a-1-4p, 6-34p, 37-40p, Annual 1p, 2p; c-1-12, 13-17p, 18-21, 22p, 23p, 24-37, 38, 39(painted), 40, Annual 1, 2.*

NEW TEEN TITANS, THE (Becomes The New Titans #50 on)
DC Comics: Aug, 1984 - No. 49, Nov, 1988 ($1.25/$1.75; deluxe format)

1-New storyline; Pérez-c/a begins 2 4 6 10 14 18
2,3: 2-Re-intro Lilith 6.00
4-10: 5-Death of Trigon. 7-9-Origin Lilith. 8-Intro Kole. 10-Kole joins 5.00
11-49: 13,14-Crisis x-over. 20-Robin (Jason Todd) joins; original Teen Titans return. 38-Infinity, Inc. x-over. 47-Origin of all Titans; Titans (East & West) pin-up by Pérez 4.00
Annual 1-4 (9/85-'88): 1-Intro. Vanguard. 2-Byrne c/a(p); origin Brother Blood; intro new Dr. Light. 3-Intro. Danny Chase. 4-Pérez-c 4.00
...: The Terror of Trigon TPB (2003, $17.95) r/#1-5; new cover by Phil Jimenez 18.00
NOTE: ***Buckler** c-10. **Kelley Jones** a-47, Annual 4. **Erik Larsen** a-33. **Orlando** c-33p. **Perez** a-1-5; c-1-7, 19-23, 43. **Steacy** c-47.*

NEW TERRYTOONS (TV)
Dell Publishing Co./Gold Key: 6-8/60 - No. 8, 3-5/62; 10/62 - No. 54, 1/79

1(1960-Dell)-Deputy Dawg, Dinky Duck & Hashimoto-San begin (1st app. of each) 10 20 30 68 144 220
2-8(1962) 6 12 18 41 76 110
1(30010-210)(10/62-Gold Key, 84 pgs.)-Heckle & Jeckle begins 9 18 27 58 114 170
2(30010-301)-84 pgs. 7 14 21 49 92 135
3-5 4 8 12 27 44 60
6-10 4 8 12 21 33 45
11-20 3 6 9 15 22 28
21-30 2 4 6 9 13 16
31-43 1 3 4 6 8 10
44-54: Mighty Mouse-c/s in all 2 4 6 8 11 14
NOTE: *Reprints: #4-12, 38, 40, 47. (See March of Comics #379, 393, 412, 435)*

NEW TESTAMENT STORIES VISUALIZED

New Mutants (2010) #23 © MAR

New Teen Titans #31 © DC

New X-Men #45 © MAR

	GD	VG	FN	VF	VF/NM	NM-
	2.0	4.0	6.0	8.0	9.0	9.2

Standard Publishing Co.: 1946 - 1947
"New Testament Heroes–Acts of Apostles Visualized, Book I"
"New Testament Heroes–Acts of Apostles Visualized, Book II"
"Parables Jesus Told" Set.... 18 36 54 105 165 225
NOTE: *All three are contained in a cardboard case, illustrated on front and info about the set.*

NEWTHINK
AWA Studios: Jun, 2022 - No. 5, Oct, 2022 ($3.99)
1-5-Hurwitz-s. 1-Deodato Jr.-a. 2-Rosanas-a. 3-Keron Grant-a. 4-Mike Choi-a. 5-Conrad-a 4.00

NEW THUNDERBOLTS (Continues in Thunderbolts #100)
Marvel Comics: Jan, 2005 - No. 18, Apr, 2006 ($2.99)
1-18: 1-Grummett-a/Nicieza-s. 1-Captain Marvel app. 2-Namor app. 4-Wolverine app. 3.00
... Vol. 1: One Step Forward (2005, $14.99) r/#1-6 15.00
... Vol. 2: Modern Marvels (2005, $14.99) r/#7-12 15.00
... Vol. 3: Right of Power (2006, $17.99) r/#13-18 & Thunderbolts #100 18.00

NEW TITANS, THE (Formerly The New Teen Titans)
DC Comics: No. 50, Dec, 1988 - No. 130, Feb, 1996 ($1.75/$2.25)
50-Perez-c/a begins; new origin Wonder Girl 6.00
51-59: 50-55-Painted-c. 55-Nightwing (Dick Grayson) forces Danny Chase to resign; Batman app. in flashback, Wonder Girl becomes Troia 4.00
60,61: 60-A Lonely Place of Dying Part 2 continues from Batman #440; new Robin tie-in; Timothy Drake app. 61-A Lonely Place of Dying Part 4 4.00
62-70,72-99,101-124,126-130: 62-65: Deathstroke the Terminator app. 65-Tim Drake (Robin) app. 70-1st Deathstroke solo cover/sty. 72-79-Deathstroke in all: 74-Intro. Pantha. 79-Terra brought back to life; 1 panel cameo Team Titans (1st app.). Deathstroke in #80-84,86. 80-2nd full app. Team Titans. 83,84-Deathstroke kills his son, Jericho. 85-Team Titans app. 86-Deathstroke vs. Nightwing-c/story; last Deathstroke app. 87-New costume Nightwing. 90-92-Parts 2,5,8 Total Chaos (Team Titans). 99-1st app. Arsenal. 115-(11/94) 3.00
71-(44 pgs.)-10th anniversary issue; Deathstroke cameo 4.00
100-($3.50, 52 pgs.)-Holo-grafx foil-c 4.00
125 (3.50)-wraparound-c 4.00
#0-(10/94) Zero Hour, released between #114 & 115 3.00
Annual 5-10 ('89-'94, 68 pgs.. 7-Armaggedon 2001 x-over; 1st full app. Teen (Team) Titans (new group). 8-Deathstroke app.; Eclipso app. (minor). 10-Elseworlds story 4.00
Annual 11 (1995, $3.95)-Year One story 4.00
NOTE: ***Perez** a-50-55p, 57,60p, 58,59,61(layouts); c-50-61, 62-67i, Annual 5i; co-plots-66.*

NEW TV FUNNIES (See New Funnies)

NEW TWO-FISTED TALES, THE
Dark Horse Comics/Byron Preiss:1993 ($4.95, limited series, 52 pgs.)
1-Kurtzman-r & new-a 5.00
NOTE: ***Eisner** c-1i. **Kurtzman** c-1p, 2.*

NEWUNIVERSAL
Marvel Comics: Feb, 2007 - No. 6, July, 2007 ($2.99)
1-6-Warren Ellis-s/Salvador Larroca-a. 1,2-Variant covers by Ribic 3.00
...: 1959 (9/08, $3.99) Aftermath of the White Event of 1953; Tony Stark app. 4.00
...: Conqueror (10/08, $3.99) The White Event of 2689 B.C.; Eric Nguyen-a 4.00
... : Everything Went White HC (2007, $19.99) r/#1-6; sketch pages 20.00
... : Everything Went White SC (2008, $14.99) r/#1-6; sketch pages 15.00

NEWUNIVERSAL: SHOCKFRONT
Marvel Comics: Jul, 2008 - No. 2 ($2.99)
1,2-Warren Ellis-s/Steve Kurth-a 3.00

NEW WARRIORS, THE (See Thor #411,412)
Marvel Comics: July, 1990 - No. 75, 1996 ($1.00/$1.25/$1.50)
1-Williamson-i; Bagley-c/a(p) in #1-13, (1st printing has red cover) 3 6 9 16 23 32
1-Gold 2nd printing (7/91) 1 2 3 5 6 8
2-5: 1,3-Guice-c(i). 2-Williamson-c/a(i). 5.00
6-24,26-49,51-75: 7-Punisher cameo (last pg.). 8,9-Punisher app. 14-Darkhawk & Namor x-over. 17-Fantastic Four & Silver Surfer x-over. 19-Gideon (of X-Force) app. 28-Intro Turbo & Cardinal. 31-Cannonball & Warpath app. 42-Nova vs. Firelord. 46-Photo-c. 47-Bound-in S-M trading card sheet. 52-12 pg. ad insert. 62-Scarlet Spider-c/app. 70-Spider-Man-c/app. 72-Avengers-c/app. 4.00
25-($2.50, 52 pgs.)-Die-cut cover 5.00
40,60: 40-($2.25)-Gold foil collector's edition 5.00
50-($2.95, 52 pgs.)-Glow in the dark-c 5.00
Annual 1-4('91-'94,68 pgs.)-1-Origins all members; 3rd app. X-Force (cont'd from New Mutants Ann. #7 & cont'd in X-Men Ann. #15); x-over before X-Force #1; Bagley-c/a(p); Williamson-i. 3-Bagged w/card 5.00

NEW WARRIORS, THE
Marvel Comics: Oct, 1999 - No. 10, July, 2000 ($2.99/$2.50)
0-Wizard supplement; short story and preview sketchbook 3.00
1-($2.99) 4.00
2-10: 2-Two covers. 5-Generation X app. 9-Iron Man-c 3.00

NEW WARRIORS (See Civil War #1)
Marvel Comics: Aug, 2005 - No. 6, Feb, 2006 ($2.99, limited series)
1-6-Scottie Young-a 3.00
...: Reality Check TPB (2006, $14.99) r/#1-6 15.00

NEW WARRIORS (The Initiative)
Marvel Comics: Aug, 2007 - No. 20, Mar, 2009 ($2.99)
1-19: 1-Medina-a; new team is formed. 2-Jubilee app. 14-16-Secret Invasion 3.00
20-($3.99) 4.00
...: Defiant TPB (2008, $14.99) r/#1-6 15.00

NEW WARRIORS (All-New Marvel Now)
Marvel Comics: Apr, 2014 - No. 12, Jan, 2015 ($3.99)
1-12: 1-Nova, Speedball, Justice, Sun Girl, Scarlet Spider team; Yost-s/To-a 4.00

NEW WAVE, THE
Eclipse Comics: 6/10/86 - No. 13, 3/87 (#1-8: bi-weekly, 20pgs; #9-13: monthly)
1-13:1-Origin, concludes #5. 6-Origin Megabyte. 8,9-The Heap returns. 13-Snyder-c 3.00
...Versus the Volunteers 3-D #1,2(4/87): 1-Snyder-c 3.00

NEW WEST, THE
Black Bull Comics: Mar, 2005 - No. 2, Jun, 2005 ($4.99, limited series)
1,2-Phil Noto-a/c; Jimmy Palmiotti-s 5.00

NEW WORLD (See Comic Books, series I)

NEW WORLD, THE
Image Comics: Jul, 2018 - No. 5, Nov, 2018 ($4.99/$3.99, limited series)
1-($4.99) Ales Kot-s/Tradd Moore-a 5.00
2-5-($3.99) 4.00

NEW WORLDS
Caliber: 1996 - No. 6 ($2.95/$3.95, 80 pgs., B&W, anthology)
1-6: 1-Mister X & other stories 4.00

NEW X-MEN (See X-Men *2nd series* #114-156)

NEW X-MEN (Academy X) (Continued from New Mutants)
Marvel Comics: July, 2004 - No. 46, Mar, 2008 ($2.99)
1-46: 1,2-Green-c/a. 16-19-House of M. 20,21-Decimation. 40-Endangered Species back-ups begin. 44-46-Messiah Complex x-over; Ramos-a 3.00
Yearbook 1 (12/05, $3.99) new story and profile pages 4.00
...: Childhood's End Vol. 1 TPB (2006, $10.99) r/#20-23 11.00
...: Childhood's End Vol. 2 TPB (2006, $10.99) r/#24-27 11.00
...: Childhood's End Vol. 3 TPB (2006, $10.99) r/#28-32 11.00
...: Childhood's End Vol. 4 TPB (2007, $10.99) r/#33-36 11.00
...: Childhood's End Vol. 5 TPB (2007, $17.99) r/#37-43 18.00
House of M: New X-Men TPB (2006, $13.99) r/#16-19 and selections from Secrets Of The House of M one-shot 14.00
... Vol. 1: Choosing Sides TPB (2004, $14.99) r/#1-6 15.00
... Vol. 2: Haunted TPB (2005, $14.99) r/#7-12 15.00
... Vol. 3: X-Posed TPB (2006, $14.99) r/#12-15 & Yearbook Special 15.00

NEW X-MEN: HELLIONS
Marvel Comics: July, 2005 - No. 4, Oct, 2005 ($2.99, limited series)
1-4-Henry-a/Weir & DeFilippis-s 3.00
TPB (2006, $9.99) r/#1-4 10.00

NEW YEAR'S EVIL
DC Comics: Feb, 2020 ($9.99, squarebound one-shot)
1-Short Holiday stories featuring DC villains; Harley Quinn app.; Cheung-c 10.00

NEW YORK FIVE, THE
DC Comics (Vertigo): Mar, 2011 - No. 4, Jun, 2011 ($2.99, B&W, limited series)
1-4-Brian Wood-s/Ryan Kelly-a 3.00

NEW YORK GIANTS (See Thrilling True Story of the Baseball Giants)

NEW YORK STATE JOINT LEGISLATIVE COMMITTEE TO STUDY THE PUBLICATION OF COMICS, THE
N.Y. State Legislative Document: 1951, 1955
This document was referenced by Wertham for **Seduction of the Innocent.** Contains numerous repros from comics showing violence, sadism, torture, and sex. 1955 version (196p, No. 37, 2/23/55) - Sold for $180 in 1986.

NEW YORK, THE BIG CITY
Kitchen Sink Press: 1986 ($10.95, B&W); **DC Comics:** July, 2000 ($12.95, B&W)
nn-(1986, $10.95) Will Eisner-s/a 25.00
nn-(2000, $12.95) new printing 13.00

GD VG FN VF VF/NM NM-
2.0 4.0 6.0 8.0 9.0 9.2

NEW YORK WORLD'S FAIR (Also see Big Book of Fun & New Book of Fun)
National Periodical Publ.: 1939, 1940 (100 pgs.; cardboard covers)
(DC's 4th & 5th annuals)

1939-Scoop Scanlon, Superman (blond haired Superman on-c), Sandman, Zatara, Slam Bradley, Ginger Snap by Bob Kane begin; 1st published app. The Sandman (see Adventure #40 for his 1st drawn story); Vincent Sullivan-c; cover background by Guardineer 1900 3800 5700 14,200 32,500 –
1940-Batman, Hourman, Johnny Thunderbolt, Red, White & Blue & Hanko (by Creig Flessel) app.; Superman, Batman & Robin-c (1st time they all appear together); early Robin app.; 1st Burnley-c/a (per Burnley) 1100 2200 3300 8150 18,000 –

NOTE: *The 1939 edition was published 4/29/39 and released 4/30/39, the day the fair opened, at 25¢, and was first sold only at the fair. Since all other comics were 10¢, it didn't sell. Remaining copies were advertised beginning in the August issues of most DC comics for 25¢, but soon the price was dropped to 15¢. Everyone that sent a quarter through the mail for it received a free Superman #1 or a #2 to make up the dime difference. 15¢ stickers were placed over the 25¢ price. Four variations on the 15¢ stickers are known. The 1940 edition was published 5/11/40 and was priced at 15¢. It was a precursor to World's Best #1.*

NEW YORK: YEAR ZERO
Eclipse Comics: July, 1988 - No. 4, Oct, 1988 ($2.00, B&W, limited series)
1-4 3.00

NEXT, THE
DC Comics: Sept, 2006 - No. 6, Feb, 2007 ($2.99, limited series)
1-6-Tad Williams-s/Dietrich Smith-a; Superman app. 3.00

NEXT BATMAN, THE : SECOND SON (From Future State: The Next Batman)
DC Comics: Jun, 2021 - No. 4, Sept, 2021 ($4.99, limited series)
1-4-Ridley-s; Tim Fox as Batman; Grifter app. 4-Katana app. 5.00

NEXT MEN (See John Byrne's...)

NEXT MEN: AFTERMATH (Continued from John Byrne's Next Men 2010-2011 series)
IDW Publishing: No. 40, Feb, 2012 - No. 44, Jun, 2012 ($3.99)
40-44-John Byrne-s/a/c 4.00

NEXT NEXUS, THE
First Comics: Jan, 1989 - No. 4, April, 1989 ($1.95, limited series, Baxter paper)
1-4: Mike Baron scripts & Steve Rude-c/a. 3.00
TPB (10/89, $9.95) r/series 10.00

NEXTWAVE: AGENTS OF H.A.T.E
Marvel Comics: Mar, 2006 - No. 12, Mar, 2007 ($2.99)
1-12-Warren Ellis-s/Stuart Immonen-a. 2-Fin Fang Foom app. 12-Devil Dinosaur app. 3.00
Vol. 1 - This Is What They Want HC (2006, $19.99) r/#1-6; Ellis original pitch 20.00
Vol. 1 - This Is What They Want SC (2007, $14.99) r/#1-6; Ellis original pitch 15.00
Vol. 2 - I Kick Your Face HC (2007, $19.99) r/#7-12 20.00
Vol. 2 - I Kick Your Face SC (2008, $14.99) r/#7-12 15.00

NEXUS (See First Comics Graphic Novel #4, 19 & The Next Nexus)
Capital Comics/First Comics No. 7 on: June, 1981 - No. 6, Mar, 1984; No. 7, Apr, 1985 - No. 80?, May, 1991 (Direct sales only, 36 pgs.; V2#1('83)-printed on Baxter paper)
1-B&W version; mag. size; w/double size poster 3 6 9 21 33 45
1-B&W 1981 limited edition; 500 copies printed and signed; same as above except this version has a 2-pg. poster & a pencil sketch on paperboard by Steve Rude 7 14 21 46 86 125
2-B&W, magazine size 2 4 6 13 18 22
3-B&W, magazine size; Brunner back-c; contains 33-1/3 rpm record ($2.95 price) 2 4 6 9 13 16
V2#1-Color version 2 4 6 9 12 15
2-49,51-80: 2-Nexus' origin begins. 67-Snyder-c/a 3.00
50-($3.50, 52 pgs.) 4.00
Hardcover Volume One (Dark Horse Books, 11/05, $49.95) r/#1-3 & V2 #1-4; creator bios 50.00
HC Volume Two (Dark Horse Books, 3/06, $49.95) r/V2 #5-11; creator bios 50.00
HC Volume Three (Dark Horse Books, 5/06, $49.95) r/V2 #12-18; Marz forward 50.00
HC Volume Four (Dark Horse Books, 8/06, $49.95) r/V2 #19-25; Powell forward 50.00
HC Volume Five (Dark Horse Books, 2/07, $49.95) r/V2 #26-32; Brubaker forward 50.00
HC Volume Six (Dark Horse Books, 2/07, $49.95) r/V2 #33-39; Evanier forward 50.00
HC Volume Seven (Dark Horse Books, 2/08, $49.95) r/V2 #40-46; Brunning forward 50.00
HC Volume Eight (Dark Horse Books, 1/09, $49.95) r/V2 #47-52 and The Next Nexus #1; interview with original publishers John Davis and Milton Griepp 50.00
HC Volume Nine (Dark Horse Books, 8/09, $49.95) r/V2 #53-57 & The Next Nexus #2-4 50.00
NOTE: ***Bissette** c-V2#29. **Giffen** c/a-V2#23. **Gulacy** c-1 (B&W), 2(B&W). **Mignola** c/a-V2#28. **Rude** c-3(B&W), V2#1-22, 24-27, 30-36, 39-42, 45-48, 50, 58-60, 75; a-1-3, V2#1-7, 8-16p, 18-22p, 24-27p, 33-36p, 39-42p, 45-48p, 50, 58, 59p, 60. **Paul Smith** a-V2#37, 38, 43, 44, 51-55p; c-V2#37, 38, 43, 44, 51-55.*

NEXUS
Rude Dude Productions: No. 99, July, 2007 - No. 102, Jun, 2009 ($2.99)
99-Mike Baron scripts & Steve Rude-c/a 3.00
100-($4.99) Part 2 of Space Opera; back-up feature: History of Nexus 5.00
101/102-(6/09, $4.95) Combined issue 5.00
..., Free Comic Book Day 2007 - Excerpts from previous issues and preview of #99 3.00
... Greatest Hits (8/07, $1.99) same content as Free Comic Book Day 2007 3.00
...: The Origin (11/07, $3.99) reprints the 7/96 one-shot 4.00

NEXUS: ALIEN JUSTICE
Dark Horse Comics: Dec, 1992 - No. 3, Feb, 1993 ($3.95, limited series)
1-3: Mike Baron scripts & Steve Rude-c/a 4.00

NEXUS: EXECUTIONER'S SONG
Dark Horse Comics: June, 1996 - No. 4, Sept, 1996 ($2.95, limited series)
1-4: Mike Baron scripts & Steve Rude-c/a 3.00

NEXUS FILES
First Comics: 1989 ($4.50, color/16pgs. B&W, one-shot, squarebound, 52 pgs.)
1-New Rude-a; info on Nexus 4.50

NEXUS: GOD CON
Dark Horse Comics: Apr, 1997 - No. 2, May, 1997 ($2.95, limited series)
1,2-Baron-s/Rude-c/a 3.00

NEXUS LEGENDS
First Comics: May, 1989 - No. 23, Mar, 1991 ($1.50, Baxter paper)
1-23: R/1-3(Capital) & early First Comics issues w/new Rude covers #1-6,9,10 3.00

GD VG FN VF VF/NM NM-
2.0 4.0 6.0 8.0 9.0 9.2

NEXUS MEETS MADMAN (...Special)
Dark Horse Comics: May, 1996 ($2.95, one-shot)
nn-Mike Baron & Mike Allred scripts, Steve Rude-c/a. 3.00

NEXUS: NIGHTMARE IN BLUE
Dark Horse Comics: July, 1997 - No. 4, Oct, 1997 ($2.95, limited series)
1-4: 1,2,4-Adam Hughes-c 3.00

NEXUS: THE LIBERATOR
Dark Horse Comics: Aug, 1992 - No. 4, Nov, 1992 ($2.95, limited series)
1-4 3.00

NEXUS: THE ORIGIN
Dark Horse Comics: July, 1996 ($3.95, one-shot)
nn-Mike Baron- scripts, Steve Rude-c/a. 4.00

NEXUS: THE WAGES OF SIN
Dark Horse Comics: Mar, 1995 - No. 4, June, 1995 ($2.95, limited series)
1-4 3.00

NFL RUSH ZONE: SEASON OF THE GUARDIANS
Action Lab Comics: Feb, 2013 - No. 4 ($3.99)
1-4: 1-Matt Ryan & Roddy White app. 4.00
Free Comic Book Day edition (2013, giveaway) 3.00

NFL SUPERPRO
Marvel Comics: Oct, 1991 - No. 12, Sept, 1992 ($1.00)
1-12: 1-Spider-Man-c/app. 3.00
Special Edition (9/91, $2.00) Jusko painted-c 4.00
Super Bowl Edition (3/91, squarebound) Jusko painted-c 4.00

NICE HOUSE ON THE LAKE, THE
DC Comics (Black Label): Aug, 2021 - No. 12, Feb, 2023 ($3.99)
1-12-James Tynion IV-s/Álvaro Martínez Bueno 4.00

NICK CALM, AGENT OF C.O.D.P.I.E.C.E. (Reprints from Cerebus in Hell)
Aardvark-Vanaheim: Aug, 2018 ($4.00, B&W)
1-Cerebus figures placed over original Gustave Doré artwork; Nick Fury #4-c swipe 4.00

NICKEL COMICS
Dell Publishing Co.: 1938 (Pocket size - 7-1/2x5-1/2")(68 pgs.)
1- "Bobby & Chip" by Otto Messmer, Felix the Cat artist. Contains some English reprints 93 186 279 591 1021 1450

NICKEL COMICS
Fawcett Publications: Feb 1940
nn - Ashcan comic, not distributed to newsstands, only for in-house use. A CGC certified 9.6 copy sold for $7,200 in 2003. In 2008, a CGC certified 8.5 sold for $2,390 and an uncertified Near Mint copy sold for $3,100.

NICKEL COMICS
Fawcett Publications: May, 1940 - No. 8, Aug, 1940 (36 pgs.; Bi-Weekly; 5¢)
1-Origin/1st app. Bulletman 420 840 1260 2940 5170 7400
2 142 284 426 909 1555 2200
3 103 206 309 659 1130 1600
4-The Red Gaucho begins 87 174 261 553 952 1350
5-7 84 168 252 538 919 1300
8-World's Fair-c; Bulletman moved to Master Comics #7 in October (scarce) 106 212 318 673 1162 1650
NOTE: ***Beck** c-5-8. **Jack Binder** c-1-4. Bondage c-5. Bulletman c-1-8.*

NICK FURY
Marvel Comics: Jun, 2017 - No. 6, Nov, 2017 ($3.99, limited series)
1-6-James Robinson-s/Aco-a; Nick Fury Jr. vs. Hydra; Frankie Noble app. 4.00

NICK FURY, AGENT OF SHIELD (See Fury, Marvel Spotlight #31 & Shield)
Marvel Comics Group: 6/68 - No. 15, 11/69; No. 16, 11/70 - No. 18, 3/71
1 21 42 63 147 324 500
2,3 8 16 24 55 105 155
4-Origin retold 14 28 42 93 204 315
5-Classic-c 9 18 27 62 126 190
6,7: 7-Salvador Dali painting swipe 8 16 24 51 96 140
8-11,13: 9-Hate Monger begins, ends #11. 10-Smith layouts/pencil. 11-Smith-c. 13-1st app. Super-Patriot; last 12¢ issue 5 10 15 30 50 70
12-Smith-c/a 5 10 15 31 53 75
14-Begin 15¢ issues 4 8 12 27 44 60
15-1st app. & death of Bullseye-c/story(11/69); Nick Fury shot & killed; last 15¢ issue 8 16 24 52 99 145
16-18-(25¢, 52 pgs.)-r/Str. Tales #135-143 3 6 9 21 33 45
TPB (May 2000, $19.95) r/ Strange Tales #150-168 20.00
...: Who is Scorpio? TPB (11/00, $12.95) r/#1-3,5; Steranko-c 13.00
NOTE: ***Adkins** a-3i. **Craig** a-10i. **Sid Greene** a-12i. **Kirby** a-16-18r. **Springer** a-4, 6, 7, 8p, 9, 10p, 11; c-8, 9. **Steranko** a(p)-1-3, 5; c-1-7.*

NICK FURY AGENT OF SHIELD (Also see Strange Tales #135)
Marvel Comics: Dec, 1983 - No. 2, Jan, 1984 (2.00, 52 pgs., Baxter paper)
1,2-r/Nick Fury #1-4; new Steranko-c 1 3 4 6 8 10

NICK FURY, AGENT OF S.H.I.E.L.D.
Marvel Comics: Sept, 1989 - No. 47, May, 1993 ($1.50/$1.75)
V2#1 5.00
2-26,30-47: 10-Capt. America app. 13-Return of The Yellow Claw. 15-Fantastic Four app. 30,31-Deathlok app. 36-Cage app. 37-Woodgod c/story. 38-41-Flashes back to pre-Shield days after WWII. 44-Capt. America-c/s. 45-Viper-c/s. 46-Gideon x-over 3.00
27-29-Wolverine-c/stories 4.00
NOTE: ***Alan Grant** scripts-11. **Guice** a(p)-20-23, 25, 26; c-20-28.*

NICK FURY'S HOWLING COMMANDOS
Marvel Comics: Dec, 2005 - No. 6, May, 2006 ($2.99)
1-6: 1-Giffen-s/Francisco-a 3.00
1-Director's Cut ($3.99) r/#1 with original script and sketch design pages 4.00

NICK FURY VS. S.H.I.E.L.D.

Next Batman: Second Son #1 © DC

Nick Fury, Agent of SHIELD #1 © MAR

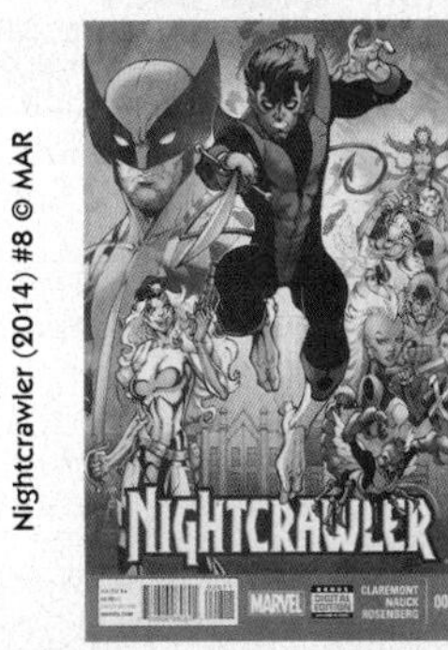

Nightcrawler (2014) #8 © MAR

GD VG FN VF VF/NM NM-
2.0 4.0 6.0 8.0 9.0 9.2

GD VG FN VF VF/NM NM-
2.0 4.0 6.0 8.0 9.0 9.2

Marvel Comics: June, 1988 - No. 6, Nov, 1988 ($3.50, 52 pgs, deluxe format)
1,2: 1-Steranko-c. 2-(Low print run) Sienkiewicz-c 6.00
3-6 5.00

NICK HALIDAY (Thrill of the Sea)
Argo: May, 1956
1-Daily & Sunday strip-r by Petree 12 24 36 67 94 120

NIGHT AND THE ENEMY (Graphic Novel)
Comico: 1988 (8-1/2x11") ($11.95, color, 80 pgs.)
1-Harlan Ellison scripts/Ken Steacy-c/a; r/Epic Illustrated & new-a (1st & 2nd printings) 12.00
1-Limited edition ($39.95) 40.00

NIGHT BEFORE CHRISTMAS, THE (See March of Comics No. 152 in the Promotional Comics section)

NIGHT BEFORE CHRISTMASK, THE
Dark Horse Comics: Nov, 1994 ($9.95, one-shot)
nn-Hardcover book; The Mask; Rick Geary-c/a 10.00

NIGHTBREED (See Clive Barker's Nightbreed)

NIGHT CLUB
Image Comics: Apr, 2005 - No. 4, Dec, 2006 ($2.95/$2.99, limited series)
1-4: 1-Mike Baron-s/Mike Norton-a 3.00

NIGHT CLUB
Image Comics: Dec, 2022 - No. 6 ($1.99, limited series)
1-3-Vampire story; Mark Millar-s/Juanan Ramírez-a 3.00

NIGHTCRAWLER (X-Men)
Marvel Comics Group: Nov, 1985 - No. 4, Feb, 1986 (Mini-series from X-Men)
1-4: 1-Cockrum-c/a 6.00

NIGHTCRAWLER (Volume 2)
Marvel Comics: Feb, 2002 - No. 4, May, 2002 ($2.50, limited series)
1-4-Matt Smith-a 3.00

NIGHTCRAWLER
Marvel Comics: Nov, 2004 - No. 12, Jan, 2006 ($2.99)
1-12: 1-6-Robertson-a/Land-c. 2-Magik app. 8-Wolverine app. 10-Man-Thing app. 3.00
...: The Devil Inside TPB (2005, $14.99) r/#1-6 15.00
...: The Winding Way TPB (2006, $14.99) r/#7-12 15.00

NIGHTCRAWLER
Marvel Comics: Jun, 2014 - No. 12, May, 2015 ($3.99)
1-12: 1-Claremont-s/Nauck-a. 7-Death of Wolverine tie-in 4.00

NIGHTCRAWLERS (Tie-in series to the Sins of Sinister event)
Marvel Comics: Apr, 2023 - No. 3 ($3.99, limited series)
1-Spurrier-s/Medina-a 4.00

NIGHTFALL: THE BLACK CHRONICLES
DC Comics (Homage): Dec, 1999 - No. 3, Feb, 2000 ($2.95, limited series)
1-3-Coker-a/Gilmore-s 3.00

NIGHT FORCE, THE (See New Teen Titans #21)
DC Comics: Aug, 1982 - No. 14, Sept, 1983 (60¢)
1 4.00
2-14: 13-Origin Baron Winter. 14-Nudity panels 3.00
NOTE: ***Colan*** *c/a-1-14p.* ***Giordano*** *c-1i, 2i, 4i, 5i, 7i, 12i.*

NIGHT FORCE
DC Comics: Dec, 1996 - No. 12, Nov, 1997 ($2.25)
1-12: 1-3-Wolfman-s/Anderson-a(p). 8-"Convergence" part 2 3.00

NIGHT FORCE
DC Comics: May, 2012 - No. 7, Nov, 2012 ($2.99, limited series)
1-7-Wolfman-s/Mandrake-a/Manco-c 3.00

NIGHT GLIDER
Topps Comics (Kirbyverse): April, 1993 ($2.95, one-shot)
1-Kirby c-1, Heck-a; polybagged w/Kirbychrome trading card 4.00

NIGHTHAWK
Marvel Comics: Sept, 1998 - No. 3, Nov, 1998 ($2.99, mini-series)
1-3-Krueger-s; Daredevil app. 3.00

NIGHTHAWK (From Squadron Supreme)
Marvel Comics: Jul, 2016 - No. 6, Dec, 2016 ($3.99)
1-6: 1-Walker-s/Villalobos-a/Cowan-c. 3-Morazzo-a 4.00

NIGHTINGALE, THE
Henry H. Stansbury Once-Upon-A-Time Press, Inc.: 1948 (10¢, 7-1/4x10-1/4", 14 pgs., 1/2 B&W)
(Very Rare)-Low distribution; distributed to Westchester County & Bronx, N.Y. only; used in **Seduction of the Innocent**, pg. 312,313 as the 1st and only "good" comic book ever published. Ill. by Dong Kingman; 1,500 words of text, printed on high quality paper & no word balloons. Copyright registered 10/22/48, distributed week of 12/5/48. Only 5000 copies printed, 6 currently known to still exist. (By Hans Christian Andersen)
Estimated value........ 450.00

NIGHT MAN, THE (See Sludge #1)
Malibu Comics (Ultraverse): Oct, 1993 - No. 23, Aug, 1995 ($1.95/$2.50)
1-($2.50, 48 pgs.)-Rune flip-c/story by B. Smith (3 pgs.) 5.00
1-Ultra-Limited silver foil-c 1 3 4 6 8 10
2-15, 17: 3-Break-Thru x-over; Freex app. 4-Origin Firearm (2 pgs.) by Chaykin. 6-TNTNT app. 8-1st app. Teknight 4.00
16 ($3.50)-flip book (Ultraverse Premiere #11) 5.00
...:The Pilgrim Conundrum Saga (1/95, $3.95, 68 pgs.)-Strangers app. 5.00
18-23: 22-Loki-c/app. 4.00
Infinity ($1.50) 4.00
...Vs. Wolverine #0-Kelley Jones-c; mail in offer 1 3 4 6 8 10
NOTE: ***Zeck*** *a-16.*

NIGHT MAN, THE
Malibu Comics (Ultraverse): Sept, 1995 - No.4, Dec, 1995 ($1.50, lim. series)
1-4: Post Black September storyline 3.00

NIGHT MAN, THE /GAMBIT
Malibu Comics (Ultraverse): Mar, 1996 - No. 3, May, 1996 ($1.95, lim. series)
0-Limited Premium Edition 4.00
1-3: David Quinn scripts in all. 3-Rhiannon discovered to be The Night Man's mother 3.00

NIGHTMARE
Ziff-Davis (Approved Comics)/St. John No. 3: Summer, 1952 - No. 3, Winter, 1952, 53 (Painted-c)
1-1 pg. Kinstler-a; Tuska-a(2) 81 162 243 518 884 1250
2-Kinstler-a-Poe's "Pit & the Pendulum" 63 126 189 403 689 975
3-Kinstler-a 57 114 171 362 619 875

NIGHTMARE (Weird Horrors #1-9) (Amazing Ghost Stories #14 on)
St. John Publishing Co.: No. 10, Dec, 1953 - No. 13, Aug, 1954
10-Reprints Ziff-Davis Weird Thrillers #2 w/new Kubert-c plus 2 pgs. Kinstler-a; Anderson, Colan & Toth-a 77 154 231 493 847 1200
11-Krigstein-a; painted-c; Poe adapt., "Hop Frog" 57 114 171 362 619 875
12-Kubert bondage-c; adaptation of Poe's "The Black Cat"; Cannibalism story 55 110 165 352 601 850
13-Reprints Z-D Weird Thrillers #3 with new cover; Powell-a(2), Tuska-a; Baker-c 271 542 813 1734 2967 4200

NIGHTMARE (Magazine) (Also see Psycho)
Skywald Publishing Corp.: Dec, 1970 - No. 23, Feb, 1975 (B&W, 68 pgs.)
1-Everett-a; Heck-a; Shores-a 11 22 33 73 157 240
2-5,8,9: 2,4-Decapitation story. 5-Nazi-s; Boris Karloff 4 pg. photo/text-s. 8-Features E.C. movie "Tales From The Crypt"; reprints some E.C. comics panels. 9-Wrightson-a; bondage-c; 1st Lovecraft Saggoth Chronicles/Cthulhu 6 12 18 38 69 100
6-Kaluta-a; Jeff Jones-c, photo & interview; 1st Living Gargoyle; Love Witch-s w/nudity; Boris Karloff-s 7 14 21 48 89 130
7 5 10 15 33 57 80
10-Wrightson-a (1 pg.); Princess of Earth-c/s; Edward & Mina Sartyros, the Human Gargoyles series continues from Psycho #8 6 12 18 38 69 100
11-19: 12-Excessive gore, severed heads. 13-Lovecraft-s. 15-Dracula-c/s. 17-Vampires issue; Autobiography of a Vampire series begins 4 8 12 28 47 65
20-John Byrne's 1st artwork (2 pgs.)(8/74); severed head-c; Hitler app. 9 18 27 59 117 175
21-23: 21-(1974 Summer Special)-Kaluta-a. 22-Tomb of Horror issue. 23-(1975 Winter Special) 5 10 15 31 53 75
Annual 1(1972)-Squarebound; B. Jones-a 5 10 15 33 57 80
Winter Special 1(1973)-All new material 4 8 12 28 47 65
Yearbook nn(1974)-B. Jones, Reese, Wildey-a 4 8 12 28 47 65
NOTE: ***Adkins*** *a-5.* ***Boris*** *c-2, 3, 5 (#4 is not by Boris).* ***Buckler*** *a-3, 15.* ***Byrne*** *a-20p.* ***Everett*** *a-1, 2, 4, 5, 12.* ***Jeff Jones*** *a-6, 21r(Psycho #6); c-6.* ***Katz*** *a-3, 5, 21.* ***Reese*** *a-4, 5.* ***Wildey*** *a-4, 5, 6, 21, '74 Yearbook.* ***Wrightson*** *a-9, 10.*

NIGHTMARE (Alex Nino's)
Innovation Publishing: 1989 ($1.95)
1-Alex Nino-a 3.00

NIGHTMARE
Marvel Comics: Dec, 1994 - No. 4, Mar, 1995 ($1.95, limited series)
1-4 3.00

NIGHTMARE & CASPER (See Harvey Hits #71) (Casper & Nightmare #6 on) (See Casper The Friendly Ghost #19)

GD VG FN VF VF/NM NM-
2.0 4.0 6.0 8.0 9.0 9.2

Harvey Publications: Aug, 1963 - No. 5, Aug, 1964 (25¢)
1-All reprints? 8 16 24 52 99 145
2-5: All reprints? 5 10 15 31 53 75

NIGHTMARE ON ELM STREET, A (Also see Freddy Krueger's...)
DC Comics (WildStorm): Dec, 2006 - No. 8, Aug, 2007 ($2.99)
1-8: 1-Two covers by Harris & Bradstreet; Dixon-s/West-a
1 3 4 6 8 10

NIGHTMARES (See Do You Believe in Nightmares)

NIGHTMARES
Eclipse Comics: May, 1985 - No. 2, May, 1985 ($1.75, Baxter paper)
1,2 5.00

NIGHTMARE THEATER
Chaos! Comics: Nov, 1997 - No. 4, Nov, 1997 ($2.50, mini-series)
1-4-Horror stories by various; Wrightson-a 4.00

NIGHTMASK
Marvel Comics Group: Nov, 1986 - No. 12, Oct, 1987
1-12 3.00

NIGHT MASTER
Silverwolf: Feb, 1987 ($1.50, B&W)
1-Tim Vigil-c/a 2 4 6 9 12 15

NIGHTMASTER (See Shadowpact)
DC Comics: Jan, 2011 ($2.99, one-shot)
1-Wrightson-c/Beechen-s/Dwyer-a; Shadowpact app. 3.00

NIGHT MUSIC (See Eclipse Graphic Album Series, The Magic Flute)
Eclipse Comics: Dec, 1984 - No. 11, 1990 ($1.75/$3.95/$4.95, Baxter paper)
1-7: 3-Russell's Jungle Book adapt. 4,5-Pelleas And Melisande (double titled) 6-Salomé (double titled). 7-Red Dog #1 3.00
8-($3.95) Ariane and Bluebeard 4.00
9-11-($4.95) The Magic Flute; Russell adapt. 5.00

NIGHT NURSE (Also see Linda Carter, Student Nurse)
Marvel Comics Group: Nov, 1972 - No. 4, May, 1973
1 36 72 108 259 580 900
2-4 11 22 33 77 166 255

NIGHT NURSE
Marvel Comics: Jul, 2015 ($7.99, one-shot)
1-Reprints 1972 series #1-4 and Daredevil V2 #80; Siya Oum-c
2 4 6 10 14 18

NIGHT OF MYSTERY
Avon Periodicals: 1953 (no month) (one-shot)
nn-1 pg. Kinstler-a, Hollingsworth-c 90 180 270 576 988 1400

NIGHT OF THE GHOUL
Dark Horse Comics: Oct, 2022 - No. 3, Dec, 2022 ($4.99, limited series)
1-3-Scott Snyder-s/Francesco Francavilla-a 5.00

NIGHT OF THE GRIZZLY, THE (See Movie Classics)

NIGHT OF THE LIVING DEADPOOL
Marvel Comics: Mar, 2014 - No. 4, May, 2014 ($3.99, limited series)
1-4-Bunn-s/Rosanas-a; Deadpool in a zombie apocalypse 4.00

NIGHT OF THE LIVING DEAD: REVENANCE
American Mythology Prods.: 2022 ($3.99)
1-S.A. Check & James Kuhoric-s/Giancarlo Caracuzo-a 4.00

NIGHTRAVEN (See Marvel Graphic Novel)

NIGHT RIDER (Western)
Marvel Comics Group: Oct, 1974 - No. 6, Aug, 1975
1: 1-6 reprint Ghost Rider #1-6 (#1-origin) 6 12 18 38 69 100
2-6 3 6 9 14 20 26

NIGHT'S CHILDREN: THE VAMPIRE
Millenium: July, 1995 - No. 2, Aug, 1995 ($2.95, B&W)
1,2: Wendy Snow-Lang story & art 3.00

NIGHTSIDE
Marvel Comics: Dec, 2001 - No. 4, Mar, 2002 ($2.99)
1-4: 1-Weinberg-s/Derenick-a; intro Sydney Taine 3.00

NIGHTS INTO DREAMS (Based on video game)
Archie Comics: Feb, 1998 -No. 6, Oct, 1998 ($1.75, limited series)
1-6 3.00

NIGHTSTALKERS (Also see Midnight Sons Unlimited)
Marvel Comics (Midnight Sons #14 on): Nov, 1992 - No. 18, Apr, 1994 ($1.75)
1-($2.75, 52 pgs.)-Polybagged w/poster; part 5 of Rise of the Midnight Sons storyline; Garney/Palmer-c/a begins; Hannibal King, Blade & Frank Drake begin
2 4 6 9 13 16
2-9,11-18: 5-Punisher app. 7-Ghost Rider app. 8,9-Morbius app. 14-Spot varnish-c. 14,15-Siege of Darkness Pts 1 & 9 3.00
10-($2.25)-Outer-c is a Darkhold envelope made of black parchment w/gold ink; Midnight Massacre part 1 6.00

NIGHT TERRORS,THE
Chanting Monks Studios: 2000 ($2.75, B&W)
1-Bernie Wrightson-c; short stories, one by Wrightson-s/a 6.00

NIGHT THRASHER (Also see The New Warriors)
Marvel Comics: Aug, 1993 - No. 21, Apr, 1995 ($1.75/$1.95)
1-($2.95, 52 pgs.)-Red holo-grafx foil-c; origin 4.00
2-21: 2-Intro Tantrum. 3-Gideon (of X-Force) app. 10-Bound-in trading card sheet; Iron Man app. 15-Hulk app. 3.00

NIGHT THRASHER: FOUR CONTROL
Marvel Comics: Oct, 1992 - No. 4, Jan, 1993 ($2.00, limited series)
1-4: 2-Intro Tantrum. 3-Gideon (of X-Force) app. 3.00

NIGHT TRIBES
DC Comics (WildStorm): July, 1999 ($4.95, one-shot)
1-Golden & Sniegoski-s/Chin-a 5.00

NIGHTVEIL (Also see Femforce)
Americomics/AC Comics: Nov, 1984 - No. 7, 1987 ($1.75)
1-7 3.00
...'s Cauldron Of Horror 1 (1989, B&W)-Kubert, Powell, Wood-r plus new Nightveil story 3.00
...'s Cauldron Of Horror 2 (1990, $2.95, B&W)-Pre-code horror-r by Kubert & Powell 3.00
...'s Cauldron Of Horror 3 (1991) 3.00
Special 1 ('88, $1.95)-Kaluta-c 3.00
One Shot ('96, $5.95)-Flip book w/ Colt 6.00

NIGHTWATCH
Marvel Comics: Apr, 1994 - No. 12, Mar, 1995 ($1.50)
1-($2.95)-Collectors edition; foil-c; Ron Lim-c/a begins; Spider-Man app. 6.00
1-12-Regular edition. 2-Bound-in S-M trading card sheet; 5,6-Venom-c & app. 7,11-Cardiac app. 3.00

NIGHTWING (Also see New Teen Titans, New Titans, Showcase '93 #11,12, Tales of the New Teen Titans & Teen Titans Spotlight)
DC Comics: Sept, 1995 - No. 4, Dec, 1995 ($2.25, limited series)
1-Dennis O'Neil story/Greg Land-a in all 2 4 6 11 16 20
2-4 5.00
...: Alfred's Return (7/95, $3.50) Giordano-a 6.00
...Ties That Bind (1997, $12.95, TPB) r/mini-series & Alfred's Return 13.00

NIGHTWING
DC Comics: Oct, 1996 - No. 153, Apr, 2009 ($1.95/$1.99/$2.25/$2.50/$2.99)
1-Chuck Dixon scripts & Scott McDaniel-c/a 4 8 12 23 37 50
2,3 1 3 4 6 8 10
4-10: 6-Robin-c/app. 5.00
11-20: 13-15-Batman app. 19,20-Cataclysm pts. 2,11 4.00
21-49,51-64: 23-Green Arrow app. 26-29-Huntress-c/app. 30-Superman-c/app. 35-39-No Man's Land. 41-Land/Geraci-a begins. 46-Begin $2.25-c. 47-Texiera-c. 52-Catwoman-c/app. 54-Shrike app. 3.00
50-($3.50) Nightwing battles Torque 4.00
65-74,76-99: 65,66-Bruce Wayne: Murderer x-over pt. 3,9. 68,69: B.W.: Fugitive pt. 6,9. 70-Last Dixon-s. 71-Devin Grayson-s begin. 81-Batgirl vs. Deathstroke. 93-Blockbuster killed. 94-Copperhead app. 96-Bagged w/CD. 96-98-War Games 3.00
75-(1/03, $2.95) Intro. Tarantula 4.00
100-(2/05, $2.95) Tarantula app. 4.00
101-117: 101-Year One begins. 103-Jason Todd & Deadman app. 107-110-Hester-a. 109-Begin $2.50-c. 109,110-Villains United tie-ins. 112-Deathstroke app. 3.00
118-One Year Later; Jason Todd as 2nd Nightwing 2 4 6 8 10 12
119-149,151-153: 120-Begin $2.99-c. 138,139-Resurrection of Ra's al Ghul x-over. 138-2nd printing. 147-Two-Face app. 3.00
150-($3.99) Batman R.I.P. x-over; Nightwing vs. Two-Face; Tan-c 4.00
#1,000,000 (11/98) teams with future Batman 3.00
Annual 1(1997, $3.95) Pulp Heroes 4.00
Annual 2 (6/07, $3.99) Dick Grayson and Barbara Gordon's shared history 4.00
...Eighty Page Giant 1 (12/00, $5.95) Intro. of Hella; Dixon-s/Haley-c 6.00
...: Big Guns (2004, $14.95, TPB) r/#47-50; Secret Files 1, Eighty Page Giant 1 15.00
...: Brothers in Blood (2007, $14.99, TPB) r/#118-124 15.00
...: A Darker Shade of Justice (2001, $19.95, TPB) r/#30-39, Secret Files #1 20.00
...: Freefall (2008, $17.99, TPB) r/#140-146 18.00
...: A Knight in Blüdhaven (1998, $14.95, TPB) r/#1-8 15.00
...: Love and Bullets (2000, $17.95, TPB) r/#1/2, 19,21,22,24-29 18.00
...: Love and War (2007, $14.99, TPB) r/#125-132 15.00
...: On the Razor's Edge (2005, $14.99, TPB) r/#52,54-60 15.00
...: Our Worlds at War (9/01, $2.95) Jae Lee-c 3.00
...: Renegade TPB (2006, $17.95) r/#112-117 18.00
...: Rough Justice (1999, $17.95, TPB) r/#9-18 18.00
Secret Files 1 (10/99, $4.95) Origin-s and pin-ups 5.00
...: The Great Leap (2009, $19.99) r/#147-153 20.00
...: The Hunt for Oracle (2003, $14.95, TPB) r/#41-46 & Birds of Prey #20,21 15.00
...: The Lost Year (2008, $14.99) r/#133-137 & Annual #2 15.00
...: The Target (2001, $5.95) McDaniel-c/a 6.00
Wizard 1/2 (Mail offer) 5.00
...: Year One (2005, $14.99) r/#101-106 15.00

NIGHTWING (DC New 52)(Leads into Grayson series)
DC Comics: Nov, 2011 - No. 30, Jul, 2014 ($2.99)
1-Dick Grayson in black/red costume; Higgins-s/Barrows-a/c 20.00
1-2nd printing with red background-c 10.00
2,3 1 2 3 5 6 8
4-7,10-14: 2-4-Batgirl app. 13,14-Lady Shiva app. 14-Joker cameo 4.00
8,9: 8-Night of the Owls prelude. 9-Night of the Owls x-over 5.00
15-Die-cut cover with Joker mask; Death of the Family tie-in 5.00
16-18: 16-Death of the Family tie-in. 18-Requiem; Tony Zucco returns 4.00
19-24,26-29: 19-24-Prankster app. 26,27-Mad Hatter app. 28,29-Mr. Zsasz app. 3.00
25-($3.99) Zero Year flashback to Haly's Circus days; Higgins-s/Conrad & Richards-a 4.00
30-($3.99) Aftermath of Forever Evil series; Grayson joins Spyral 4.00
#0-(11/12, $2.99) Origin re-told/updated; Lady Shiva app.; DeFalco-s/Barrows-a 4.00
Annual #1 (12/13, $4.99) Batgirl Wanted! tie-in; Firefly app. 5.00

NIGHTWING (DC Rebirth)
DC Comics: Sept, 2016 - Present ($2.99/$3.99)
1-Seeley-s/Fernandez-a; intro. Raptor 2 4 6 8 10 12
2-24: 5,6-Night of the Monster Men x-over. 17-20-Deathwing & Prof. Pyg app. 21-Flash (Wally) app. 22-24-Blockbuster app. 3.00
25-($3.99) Blockbuster & Tiger Shark app. 4.00
26-43: 26-28-Huntress app. 29-Dark Nights: Metal tie-in 3.00
44-49: 44-($3.99) Mooneyham-a. 49-Silencer app. 4.00
50-($4.99) Follows Grayson's shooting in Batman #55; flashback art by Janson 5.00
51-74,76,77: 51-Foil-c. 53-56-Scarecrow app. 57,58-Joker's Daughter app. 62-69-Talon app.

Night of the Ghoul #1 © Snyder & Francavilla

Nightwing (2016) #87 © DC

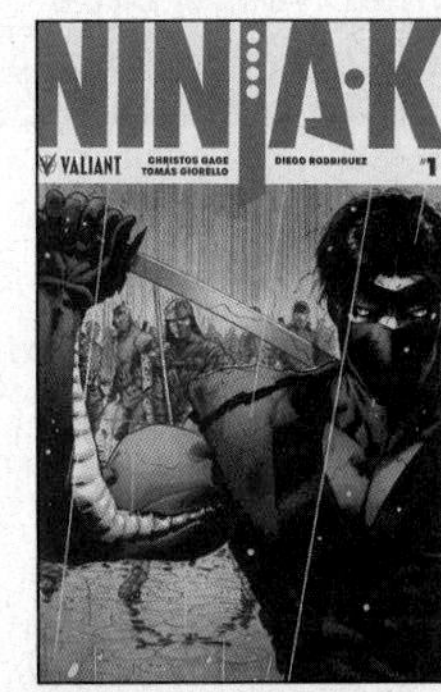

Ninja•K #1 © VAL

	GD	VG	FN	VF	VF/NM	NM-
	2.0	4.0	6.0	8.0	9.0	9.2

70,71-Joker app. 72-74-Punchline app. 73,74-Joker War tie-in 4.00
75-($5.99) Joker War tie-in; Nightwing regains real memory; KGBeast app. 6.00
78-Infinite Frontier; Taylor-s begins; intro. Bitewing the dog 12.00
79-99: 79,80-Heartless app. 84-86-Fear State tie-ins. 88-Titans app. 90,91-Flash app. 4.00
100-(3/23, $6.99) Titans app.; art by various 7.00
101-($4.99) Neron and the Titans app. 5.00
Annual 1 (10/18, $4.99) Percy-s/Schmidt-a; Vicki Vale app. 5.00
Annual 2 (12/19, $4.99) Jurgens-s/Moore-a; follows shooting in Batman #55 5.00
Annual 3 (8/20, $4.99) Jurgens-s/Miranda-a; Condor Red app.; takes place after #68 5.00
2021 Annual 1 (1/22, $5.99) Red Hood app.; Taylor-s/Tormey & HDR-a 6.00
2022 Annual 1 (1/23, $5.99) Origin of Heartless; Bitewing Year One 6.00
.../Magilla Gorilla Special 1 (12/18, $4.99) Grape Ape app.; Secret Squirrel back-up 5.00
...: Rebirth (9/16, $2.99) Seeley-s/Paquette-a; Damian app.; back in Nightwing costume 3.00

NIGHTWING (See Tangent Comics/ Nightwing)

NIGHTWING AND HUNTRESS
DC Comics: May, 1998 - No. 4, Aug, 1998 ($1.95, limited series)

1-4-Grayson-s/Land & Sienkiewicz-a 3.00
TPB (2003, $9.95) r/#1/4; cover gallery 10.00

NIGHTWINGS (See DC Science Fiction Graphic Novel)

NIGHTWING: THE NEW ORDER
DC Comics: Oct, 2017 - No. 6, Mar, 2018 ($3.99, limited series)

1-6-Higgins-s/McCarthy-a; future Nightwing in 2040. 4,5-Titans app. 5-Superman app. 4.00

NIGHTWORLD
Image Comics: Aug, 2014 - No. 4, Nov, 2014 ($3.99, limited series)

1-4-McGovern-s/Leandri-a/c 4.00

NIKKI, WILD DOG OF THE NORTH (Disney, see Movie Comics)
Dell Publishing Co.: No. 1226, Sept, 1961

Four Color 1226-Movie, photo-c 5 10 15 33 57 80

9-11 - ARTISTS RESPOND
Dark Horse Comics: 2002 ($9.95, TPB, proceeds donated to charities)

Volume 1-Short stories about the September 11 tragedies by various Dark Horse, Chaos! and Image writers and artists; Eric Drooker-c 10.00

9-11: EMERGENCY RELIEF
Alternative Comics: 2002 ($14.95, TPB, proceeds donated to the Red Cross)

nn-Short stories by various inc. Pekar, Eisner, Hester, Oeming, Noto; Cho-c 15.00

9-11 - THE WORLD'S FINEST COMIC BOOK WRITERS AND ARTISTS TELL STORIES TO REMEMBER
DC Comics: 2002 ($9.95, TPB, proceeds donated to charities)

Volume 2-Short stories about the September 11 tragedies by various DC, MAD, and WildStorm writers and artists ; Alex Ross-c 10.00

NINE RINGS OF WU-TANG
Image Comics: July, 1999 - No. 5, July, 2000 ($2.95)

Preview (7/99, $5.00, B&W) 5.00
1-5: 1-(11/99, $2.95) Clayton Henry-a 3.00
Tower Records Variant-c 5.00
Wizard #0 Prelude 3.00
TPB (1/01, $19.95) r/#1-5, Preview & Prelude; sketchbook & cover gallery 20.00

1963
Image Comics (Shadowline Ink): Apr, 1993 - No. 6, Oct, 1993 ($1.95, lim. series)

1-6: Alan Moore scripts; Veitch, Bissette & Gibbons-a(p) 3.00
1-Gold 4.00

*NOTE: **Bissette** a-2-4; **Gibbons** a-1i, 2i, 6i; c-2.*

1984 (Magazine) (1994 #11 on)
Warren Publishing Co.: June, 1978 - No. 10, Jan, 1980 ($1.50, B&W with color inserts, mature content with nudity; 84 pgs. except #4 has 92 pgs.)

1-Nino-a in all; Mutant World begins by Corben 3 6 9 16 23 30
2-10: 4-Rex Havoc begins. 7-1st Ghita of Alizarr by Thorne. 9-1st Starfire 2 4 6 10 14 18

NOTE: ***Alcala** a-1-3,5,7i. **Corben** a-1-8; c-1,2. **Nebres** a-1-8,10. **Thorne** a-7,8,10. **Wood** a-1,2,5i.*

1994 (Formerly 1984) (Magazine)
Warren Publishing Co.: No. 11, Feb, 1980 - No. 29, Feb, 1983 (B&W with color; mature; #11-(84 pgs.); #12-16,18-21,24-(76 pgs.); #17,22,23,25-29-(68 pgs.)

11,17,18,20,22,23,29: 11,17-8 pgs. color insert. 18-Giger-c. 20-1st Diana Jacklighter Manhuntress by Maroto. 22-1st Sigmund Pavlov by Nino; 1st Ariel Hart by Hsu. 23-All Nino issue 2 4 6 8 11 14
12-16,19,21,24-28: 21-1st app. Angel by Nebres. 27-The Warhawks return 1 3 4 6 8 10

NOTE: ***Corben** c-26. **Maroto** a-20, 21, 24-28. **Nebres** a-11-13, 15, 16, 18, 21, 22, 25, 28. **Nino** a-11-19, 20(2), 21, 25, 26, 28; c-21. **Redondo** c-20. **Thorne** a-11-14, 17-21, 24-26, 28, 29.*

	GD	VG	FN	VF	VF/NM	NM-
	2.0	4.0	6.0	8.0	9.0	9.2

NINJA BOY
DC Comics (WildStorm): Oct, 2001 - No. 6, Mar, 2002 ($3.50/$2.95)

1-($3.50) Ale Garza-a/c 3.50
2-6-($2.95) 3.00
...: Faded Dreams TPB (2003, $14.95) r/#1-6; sketch pages 15.00

NINJA HIGH SCHOOL (1st series)
Antarctic Press: 1986 - No. 3, Aug, 1987 (B&W)

1-Ben Dunn-s/c/a; early Manga series 2 4 6 11 16 20
2,3 2 4 6 8 10 12

NINJAK (See Bloodshot #6, 7 & Deathmate)
Valiant/Acclaim Comics (Valiant) No. 16 on: Feb, 1994 - No. 26, Nov. 1995 ($2.25/$2.50)

1 ($3.50)-Chromium-c; Quesada-c/a(p) in #1-3 6.00
1-Gold 3 6 9 19 30 40
2-13: 3-Batman, Spawn & Random (from X-Factor) app. as costumes at party (cameo). 4-w/bound-in trading card. 5,6-X-O app. 4.00
0,00,14-26: 14-(4/95)-Begin $2.50-c. 0-(6/95, $2.50). 00-(6/95, $2.50) 3.00
... Black Water HC (2013, $24.99) r/#1-6, #0, #00; bonus Quesada sketch-a 25.00
Yearbook 1 (1994, $3.95) 4.00

NINJAK
Acclaim Comics (Valiant Heroes): V2#1, Mar, 1997 -No. 12, Feb, 1998 ($2.50)

V2#1-Intro new Ninjak; 1st app. Brutakon; Kurt Busiek scripts begin; painted variant-c exists 2 4 6 9 12 15
V2#2-12: 2-1st app. Karnivor & Zeer. 3-1st app. Gigantik, Shurikai, & Nixie. 4-Origin; 1st app. Yasuiti Motomiya; intro The Dark Dozen; Colin King cameo. 9-Copycat-c 3.00

NINJAK (See Rapture)
Valiant Entertainment: Mar, 2015 - No. 27, May, 2017 ($3.99)

1-27-Multiple covers on each: 1-Kindt-s/Guice and Mann-a. 4-Origin of Roku; Ryp-a 4.00

NINJAK
Valiant Entertainment: Jul, 2021 - No. 4, Oct, 2021 ($3.99)

1-4-Jeff Parker-s/Javier Pulido-a 4.00

NINJA·K
Valiant Entertainment: No. 0, Sept, 2017; No. 1, Nov, 2017 - No. 14, Dec, 2018 ($3.99)

0-Kindt-s/Portela-a; recaps origin 4.00
1-14: 1-5-Gage-s/Giorello-a. 1-History of Ninja-A in 1917. 6-9-Ryp-a 4.00
... One Dollar Debut (5/19, $1.00) r/#1 3.00

NINJAK VS. THE VALIANT UNIVERSE
Valiant Entertainment: Jan, 2018 - No. 4, Apr, 2018 ($3.99, limited series)

1-4-Rahal-s/Bennett-a 4.00

NINJA SCROLL
DC Comics (WildStorm): Nov, 2006 - No. 12, Oct, 2007 ($2.99)

1-12: 1-J. Torres-s/Michael Chang Ting Yu-a/c. 11-Puckett-s/Meyers-a 3.00
1-3-Variant covers by Jim Lee 5.00
TPB (2007, $19.99) r/#1-3,5-7 20.00

NINJETTES (See Jennifer Blood #4)
Dynamite Entertainment: 2012 - No. 6, 2012 ($3.99, limited series)

1-6-Origin of the team; Ewing-s/Casallos-a. 6-Jennifer Blood app. 4.00

NINJETTES (See Jennifer Blood #4)
Dynamite Entertainment: 2022 - No. 5, 2022 ($3.99, limited series)

1-5-Training camp for the recruits; Van Lente-s/Cooper-a 4.00

NINTENDO COMICS SYSTEM (Also see Adv. of Super Mario Brothers)
Valiant Comics: Feb, 1990 - No. 9, Oct, 1991 ($4.95, card stock-c, 68 pgs.)

1-Featuring Game Boy, Super Mario, Clappwall 4 8 12 28 47 65
2 3 6 9 16 23 30
3-9: 3-Layton-c. 5-8-Super Mario Bros. 9-Dr. Mario 1st app. 2 4 6 9 13 16

(Ninth) **IXTH GENERATION** (See Aphrodite IX & Poseidon IX)
Image Comics (Top Cow): Jan, 2015 - No. 8, Mar, 2016 ($3.99)

1-8: 1-4-Hawkins-s/Sejic-a; Aphrodite IX app. 5-7-Atilio Rojo-a 4.00
... Hidden Files 1 (4/15, $3.99) Short story and guide to the cities; Hawkins-s/Rojo-a 4.00

NITA HAWES' NIGHTMARE BLOG
Image Comics: Oct, 2021 - No. 12, Feb, 2023 ($3.99)

1-12: 1-Rodney Barnes-s/Jason Shawn Alexander-a. 4-12-Kudranski-a 4.00

NOAH (Adaptation of the 2014 movie)
Image Comics: Mar, 2014 (HC, $29.99, 8-3/4" x 11-1/2")

GD 2.0 | VG 4.0 | FN 6.0 | VF 8.0 | VF/NM 9.0 | NM- 9.2

HC-Darren Aronofsky & Ari Handel-s/Niko Henrichon-a 30.00

NOAH'S ARK
Spire Christian Comics/Fleming H. Revell Co.: 1973,1975 (35/49¢)
nn-By Al Hartley 2 4 6 11 16 20

NOBLE CAUSES
Image Comics: July, 2001; Jan, 2002 - No. 4, May, 2002 ($2.95)
...First Impressions (7/01) Intro. the Noble family; Faerber-s 3.00
1-4: 1-(1/02) Back-up-s with Conner-a. 2-Igle back-up-a. 2-4-Two covers 3.00
...: Extended Family (5/03, $6.95) short stories by various 7.00
...: Extended Family 2 (6/04, $7.95) short stories by various 8.00
Vol. 1: In Sickness and in Health (2003, $12.95) r/#1-4 & ...First Impresssions 13.00

NOBLE CAUSES (Volume 3)
Image Comics: July, 2004 - No. 40, Mar, 2009 ($3.50)
1-24,26-40-Faerber-s. 1-Two covers. 2-Venture app. 5-Invincible app. 3.50
25-($4.99) Art by various; Randolph-c 5.00
Vol. 4: Blood and Water (2005, $14.95) r/#1-6 15.00
Vol. 5: Betrayals (2006, $14.99) r/#7-12 & The Pact V2 #2 15.00
Vol. 6: Hidden Agendas (2006, $15.99) r/#13-18 and Image Holiday Spec. 2005 story 16.00
Vol. 7: Powerless (2007, $15.99) r/#19-25; Wieringo sketch page 16.00

NOBLE CAUSES: DISTANT RELATIVES
Image Comics: Jul, 2003 - No. 4, Oct, 2003 ($2.95, B&W, limited series)
1-4-Faerber-s/Richardson & Ponce-a 3.00
Vol. 3: Distant Relatives (1/05, $12.95) r/#1-4; intro. by Joe Casey 13.00

NOBLE CAUSES: FAMILY SECRETS
Image Comics: Oct, 2002 - No. 4, Jan, 2003 ($2.95, limited series)
1,2,4-Faerber-s/Oeming-c. 1-Variant cover by Walker. 2-Valentino var-c. 4-Hester var-c 3.00
3-1st app. of Invincible (cameo & Valentino var-c) 4 8 12 23 37 50
3-1st app. of Invincible (cameo); regular Oeming-c 3 6 9 14 20 25
Vol. 2: Family Secrets (2004, $12.95) r/#1-4; sketch pages 13.00

NOBODY (Amado, Cho & Adlard's...)
Oni Press: Nov, 1998 - No. 4, Feb, 1999 ($2.95, B&W, mini-series)
1-4 3.00

NOCTERRA
Image Comics: Mar, 2021 - Present ($3.99)
1-11-Scott Snyder-s/Tony S. Daniel-a 4.00
... Blacktop Bill Special 1 (1/22, $3.99) Snyder & Daniel-s/Denys Cowan-a 4.00
... Val Special 1 (12/22, $3.99) Snyder & Daniel-s/Manapul-a 4.00

NOCTURNALS, THE
Malibu Comics (Bravura): Jan, 1995 - No. 6, Aug, 1995 ($2.95, limited series)
1-6: Dan Brereton painted-c/a & scripts 3.00
1-Glow-in-the-Dark premium edition 5.00

NOCTURNALS, THE
Dark Horse Comics/Image Comics/Oni Press: one-shots and trade paperbacks
Black Planet TPB (Oni Press, 1998, $19.95) r/#1-6 (Malibu Comics series) 20.00
Black Planet and Other Stories HC (Olympian Publ.; 7/07, $39.95) r/Black Planet & Witching Hour contents; cover & sketch gallery with Brereton interviews 40.00
Carnival of Beasts (Image, 7/08, $6.99) short stories; Brereton-s/Brereton & others-a 7.00
Sinister Path (Big Wow! Art, 2017) original GN; Brereton-s/a 16.00
Troll Bridge (Oni Press, 2000, $4.95, B&W & orange) Brereton-s/painted-c; art by Brereton, Chin, Art Adams, Sakai, Timm, Warren, Thompson, Purcell, Stephens and others 5.00
Unhallowed Eve TPB (Oni Press, 10/02, $9.95) r/Witching Hour & Troll Bridge one-shots 10.00
Witching Hour (Dark Horse, 5/98, $4.95) Brereton-s/a; reprints DHP stories + 8 new pgs. 5.00

NOCTURNALS: THE DARK FOREVER
Oni Press: Jul, 2001 -No. 3, Feb, 2002 ($2.95, limited series)
1-3-Brereton-s/painted-a/c 3.00
TPB (5/02, $9.95) r/#1-3; afterword & pin-ups by Alex Ross 10.00

NOCTURNE
Marvel Comics: June, 1995 - No. 4, Sept. 1995 ($1.50, limited series)
1-4 3.00

NO ESCAPE (Movie)
Marvel Comics: June, 1994 - No. 3, Aug, 1994 ($1.50)
1-3: Based on movie 3.00

NO HONOR
Image Comics (Top Cow): Feb, 2001 - No. 4, July, 2001 ($2.50)
Preview (12/00, B&W) Silvestri-c 3.00
1-4-Avery-s/Crain-a 3.00
TPB (8/03, $12.99) r/#1-4; intro. by Straczynski 13.00

NOIR
Dynamite Entertainment: 2013 - No. 5, 2014 ($3.99, limited series)
1-5: 1-Miss Fury, Black Sparrow & The Shadow app.; Gischler-s/Mutti-a 5.00

NOMAD (See Captain America #180)
Marvel Comics: Nov, 1990 - No. 4, Feb, 1991 ($1.50, limited series)
1-4: 1,4-Captain America app. 3.00

NOMAD
Marvel Comics: V2#1, May, 1992 - No. 25, May, 1994 ($1.75)
V2#1-25: 1-Has gatefold-c w/map/wanted poster. 4-Deadpool x-over. 5-Punisher vs. Nomad-c/story. 6-Punisher & Daredevil-c/story cont'd in Punisher War Journal #48. 7-Gambit-c/story. 10-Red Wolf app. 21-Man-Thing-c/story. 25-Bound-in trading card sheet 3.00

NOMAD: GIRL WITHOUT A WORLD (Rikki Barnes from Captain America V2 Heroes Reborn)
Marvel Comics: Nov, 2009 - No. 4, Feb, 2010 ($3.99, limited series)
1-4-McKeever-s. 2-Falcon app. 4-Young Avengers app. 4.00

NOMAN (See Thunder Agents)
Tower Comics: Nov, 1966 - No. 2, March, 1967 (25¢, 68 pgs.)
1-Wood/Williamson-c; Lightning begins; Dynamo cameo; Kane-a(p) & Whitney-a
9 18 27 57 111 165
2-Wood-c only; Dynamo x-over; Whitney-a 5 10 15 35 63 90

NOMEN OMEN
Image Comics: Oct, 2019 - No. 15, May, 2021 ($3.99)
1-15-Bucci-s/Camagni-a; 3 covers 4.00

NO MERCY
Image Comics: Apr, 2015 - No. 14, Mar, 2017 ($2.99/$3.99)
1-4-Alex de Campi-s/Carla Speed McNeil-a 3.00
5-14-($3.99) 6-EC-style cover 4.00

NONE BUT THE BRAVE (See Movie Classics)

NON-HUMANS
Image Comics: Oct, 2012 - No. 4, Jul, 2013 ($2.99)
1-4-Brunswick-s/Portacio-a/c 3.00

NON-STOP SPIDER-MAN (Leads into Savage Spider-Man series)
Marvel Comics: May, 2021 - No. 5, Nov, 2021 ($4.99/$3.99)
1-($4.99) Joe Kelly-s/Chris Bachalo-a; back-up story with Baron Zemo 5.00
2-5-($3.99) Baron Zemo app. 4.00

NOODNIK COMICS (See Pinky the Egghead)
Comic Media/Mystery/Biltmore: Dec, 1953; No. 2, Feb, 1954 - No. 5, Aug, 1954
3-D(1953, 25¢; Comic Media)(#1)-Came w/glasses 36 72 108 211 347 475
2-5 13 26 39 74 105 135

NO ONE LEFT TO FIGHT
Dark Horse Comics: Jul, 2019 - No. 5, Nov, 2019 ($3.99)
1-5-Aubrey Sitterson-s/Fico Ossio-a 4.00

NO ONE LEFT TO FIGHT II
Dark Horse Comics: Oct, 2021 - No. 5, Feb, 2022 ($3.99)
1-5-Aubrey Sitterson-s/Fico Ossio-a 4.00

NORMALMAN (See Cerebus the Aardvark #55, 56)
Aardvark-Vanaheim/Renegade Press #6 on: Jan, 1984 - No. 12, Dec, 1985 ($1.70/$2.00)
1-12: 1-Jim Valentino-c/a in all. 6-12 ($2.00, B&W): 10-Cerebus cameo; Sim-a (2 pgs.) 3.00
...- Megaton Man Special 1 (Image Comics, 8/94, $2.50) 3.00
...3-D 1 (Annual, 1986, $2.25) 3.00
...Twentieth Anniversary Special (7/04, $2.95) 3.00

NORMALS
AfterShock Comics: May, 2017 - No. 6, Oct, 2017 ($3.99, limited series)
1-6-Adam Glass-s/Dennis Calero-a 4.00

NORSE MYTHOLOGY
Dark Horse Comics: Oct, 2020 - No. 6, Mar, 2021 ($3.99, limited series)
1-6-Neil Gaiman & P. Craig Russell-s. 1-Art by Russell, Mignola, & Ordway. 2-Ordway-a 4.00

NORSE MYTHOLOGY II
Dark Horse Comics: Jun, 2021 - No. 6, Nov, 2021 ($3.99, limited series)
1-6-Gaiman & Russell-s. 1,2-Horak-a. 3,4-Buckingham-a. 5,6-Walta-a 4.00

NORSE MYTHOLOGY III
Dark Horse Comics: Feb, 2022 - No. 6, Jul, 2022 ($3.99, limited series)
1-6-Gaiman & Russell-s. 1,2-Rubin-a. 2,3-Doran-a. 3-6-Showman-a 4.00

NORTHANGER ABBEY (Adaptation of the Jane Austen novel)
Marvel Comics: Jan, 2012 - No. 5, May, 2012 ($3.99, mini-series)
1-5-Nancy Butler-s/Janet K. Lee-a/Julian Tedesco-c 4.00

NORTH AVENUE IRREGULARS (See Walt Disney Showcase #49)

NORTH FORCE
Image Comics: No. 0, Jun, 2021 ($3.99, one-shot)
0-Canada's Premier Super-Team; Savage Dragon app.; Erik Larsen-s/a 4.00

NORTH 40
DC Comics (WildStorm): Sept, 2009 - No. 6, Feb, 2010 ($2.99)
1-6-Aaron Williams-s/Fiona Staples-a 3.00
TPB (2010, $17.99) r/#1-6 18.00

NORTHLANDERS
DC Comics (Vertigo): Feb, 2008 - No. 50, Jun, 2012 ($2.99)
1-50: 1-Vikings in 980 A.D.; Wood-s/Gianfelice-a; covers by Carnivale. 35-Cloonan-a 3.00
1-3-Variant covers. 1-Adam Kubert. 2-Andy Kubert. 3-Dave Gibbons 5.00
...: Blood in the Snow TPB (2010, $14.99) r/#9,10,17-20 15.00
...: Metal and Other Stories TPB (2011, $17.99) r/#29-36 18.00
...: Sven the Returned TPB (2008, $9.99) r/#1-8; cover gallery 10.00
...: The Cross + The Hammer TPB (2009, $14.99) r/#11-16 15.00
...: The Plague Widow TPB (2010, $16.99) r/#21-28 17.00

NORTHSTAR
Marvel Comics: Apr, 1994 - No. 4, July, 1994 ($1.75, mini-series)
1-4: Character from Alpha Flight 3.00

NORTH TO ALASKA
Dell Publishing Co.: No. 1155, Dec, 1960
Four Color 1155-Movie, John Wayne photo-c 15 30 45 105 233 360

NORTHWEST MOUNTIES (Also see Approved Comics #12)
Jubilee Publications/St. John: Oct, 1948 - No. 4, July, 1949
1-Rose of the Yukon by Matt Baker; Walter Johnson-a; Lubbers-c
58 116 174 371 636 900
2-Baker-a; Lubbers-c. Ventrilo app. 45 90 135 284 480 675
3-Bondage-c, Baker-a; Sky Chief, K-9 app. 48 96 144 302 514 725
4-Baker-c/a(2 pgs.); Blue Monk & The Desperado app.
58 116 174 371 636 900

NOSFERATU WARS
Dark Horse Comics: Mar, 2014 ($3.99, one-shot)
1-Reprints serial story from Dark Horse Presents #26-29; Niles-s/Menton3-a 4.00

NO SLEEP 'TIL DAWN
Dell Publishing Co.: No. 831, Aug, 1957

Nocterra #4 © Snyder & Daniel

Non-Stop Spider-Man #1 © MAR

Nova (2007) #7 © MAR

	GD	VG	FN	VF	VF/NM	NM-
	2.0	4.0	6.0	8.0	9.0	9.2

Four Color 831-Movie, Karl Malden photo-c 8 16 24 51 96 140

NOSTALGIA ILLUSTRATED
Marvel Comics: Nov, 1974 - V2#8, Aug, 1975 (B&W, 76 pgs.)

V1#1 3 6 9 21 33 45
V1#2, V2#1-8 3 6 9 15 22 28

NOT ALL ROBOTS
Artists, Writers & Artisans, Inc.: Aug, 2021 - No. 5, Dec, 2021 ($3.99, limited series)

1-5-Russell-s/Deodato, Jr-a 4.00

NOT BRAND ECHH (Brand Echh #1-4; See Crazy, 1973)
Marvel Comics Group (LMC): Aug, 1967 - No. 13, May, 1969; No. 14, Jan, 2018
(1st Marvel parody book)

1: 1-8 are 12¢ issues 8 16 24 56 108 160
2-8: 3-Origin Thor, Hulk & Capt. America; Monkees, Alfred E. Neuman cameo. 4-X-Men app. 5-Origin/intro. Forbush Man. 7-Origin Fantastical-4 & Stuporman. 8-Beatles cameo; X-Men satire; last 12¢-c 4 8 12 28 47 65
9-13 (25¢, 68 pgs., all Giants) 9-Beatles cameo. 10-All-r; The Old Witch, Crypt Keeper & Vault Keeper cameos. 12,13-Beatles cameo 5 10 15 33 57 80
14-(1/18, $3.99) Forbush Man app.; s/a by Zdarsky, Spencer & others; Nakamura-c 4.00
NOTE: ***Colan*** *a(p)-4, 5, 8, 9, 13.* ***Everett*** *a-1i.* ***Kirby*** *a(p)-1, 3, 5-7, 10r; c-1p.* ***J. Severin*** *a-1; c-3, 6-8, 11.* ***M. Severin*** *a-1-13; c-2, 9, 10, 12, 13.* ***Sutton*** *a-3, 4, 5i, 6i, 8, 9, 10r, 11-13; c-5. Archie satire in #9. Avengers satire in #8, 12.*

NOTHING CAN STOP THE JUGGERNAUT
Marvel Comics: 1989 ($3.95)

1-r/Amazing Spider-Man #229 & 230 1 2 3 5 6 8

NO TIME FOR SERGEANTS (TV)
Dell Publ. Co.: No. 914, July, 1958; Feb-Apr, 1965 - No. 3, Aug-Oct, 1965

Four Color 914 (Movie)-Toth-a; Andy Griffith photo-c 10 20 30 66 138 210
1(2-4/65) (TV): Photo-c 5 10 15 35 63 90
2,3 (TV): Photo-c 4 8 12 28 47 65

NOVA (The Man Called... No. 22-25)(See New Warriors)
Marvel Comics Group: Sept, 1976 - No. 25, May, 1979

1-Origin/1st app. Nova (Richard Rider) Marv Wolfman-s; John Buscema-a
12 24 36 84 185 285
2,3: 2-1st app. Condor & Powerhouse. 3-1st app. Diamondhead; Sal Buscema-p begin
3 6 9 19 30 40
4,12: 4-Thor x-over; 1st app. The Corrupter; Kirby-c. 12-Spider-Man x-over w/Amazing Spider-Man #171 3 6 9 21 33 45
5-11: 5-Nova vs. Tyrannus; Kirby-c; Marvel Bullpen app (incl. Stan Lee) 6-1st app. The Sphinx & Megaman. 7-Sphinx, Condor, Powerhouse & Diamondhead app. 8-Origin Megaman. 9-Megaman app. 10-Sphinx, Condor, Powerhouse & Diamondhead app. 11-vs. Sphinx 2 4 6 8 11 14
10,11-(35¢-c variants, limited distribution)(6,7/77) 10 20 30 64 132 200
12-(35¢-c variant, limited distribution)(8/77) 11 22 33 76 163 250
13,14-(Regular 30¢ editions)(9/77) 13-Intro Crime-Buster; Sandman app. 14-vs. Sandman
2 4 6 9 13 16
13,14-(35¢-c variants, limited distribution) 10 20 30 66 138 210
15-24: 15-Infantino-a begins. 16-18-vs. Yellow Claw; Nick Fury and SHIELD app. 19-Wally West (Kid Flash) cameo; 1st app Blackout. 20-1st Project X (Sherlock Holmes robot). 21-Richard reveals his Nova I.D to parents; vs Corrupter. 22-1st app the Comet (in costume). 23-Dr. Sun app. (origin) from Tomb of Dracula; Sphinx cameo. 24-Origin Powerhouse, Diamondhead, Crime-Buster, Comet Man, Sphinx & Dr. Sun app.
1 3 4 6 8 10
25-Last issue; Powerhouse, Diamondhead, Crime-Buster, Comet Man, Sphinx & Dr. Sun app. story continues in Fantastic Four #204-214 3 6 9 14 20 26
NOTE: ***Austin*** *c-21i, 23i.* ***John Buscema*** *a(p)-1-3, 8, 21; c-1p, 2, 15.* ***Infantino*** *a(p)-15-20, 22-25; c-17-20, 21p, 23p, 24p.* ***Kirby*** *c-4p, 5, 7.* ***Nebres*** *c-25i.* ***Simonson*** *a-23i.*

NOVA
Marvel Comics: Jan, 1994 - June, 1995 ($1.75/$1.95) (Started as 4-part mini-series)

1-($2.95, 52 pgs.)-Collector's Edition w/gold foil-c; new Nova costume; Nicieza-s/Marrinan-a; continued from New Warriors #42; re-intro Richard Rider's supporting cast – Ginger Jaye, Bernie Dillon & Roger 'Caps' Cooper; origin & history recap; vs. Gladiator of the Shi'ar Imperial Guard; Queen Adora app. 1 3 4 6 8 10
1-($2.25, 52 pgs.)-Newsstand Edition w/o foil-c 5.00
2-5: 2-1st app. Tailhook; Speedball app. 3-vs. Spider-Man; Corrupter app; 1st app Nova 00. 4-Vs. Nova 00; contains Rock Video Monthly insert (centerfold). 5-Re-intro Condor; Sphinx cameo; leads into New Warriors #47; contains centerfold insert for Marvel 'Masterprints' 3.00
6,7: 6-'Time and Time Again', pt.3; story continued from Night Thrasher #11; Rage & Firestar solo stories; continues in New Warriors #48. 7- 'Time and Time Again' pt.6; continued from Night Thrasher #12; Rage & Firestar solo stories; Cloak and Dagger app; continues in New Warriors #49; last Nicieza-s 4.00
8-12: 8-1st app. Shatterforce. 9-Vs. Shatterforce. 10-Vs. Diamondhead & Rhino; New Warriors and Corrupter app. 11-She-Hulk, the Thing & Ant-Man guest star; Nick Fury cameo; contains two inserts – a Marvel Subscription offer and a centerfold insert for a personalized X-Men/Captain Universe comic. 12-Vs. Nova 00; Nick Fury, Black Bolt & the Inhumans app. 13-'Deathstorm' T-Minus 3; Firestar, Night Thrasher & Nick Fury app. 14-'Deathstorm' T-Minus 2; Nova 00, Darkhawk & the New Warriors app. 15-'Deathstorm' T-Minus 1; 1st app. Kraa (brother of Zorr from Nova #1, 1976) 3.00
16-18: 16-'Deathstorm' conclusion; vs. Kraa; Nova-Corps app; death of Nova 00. 17-vs. Supernova (Garthan Saal); Richard is stripped of his rank; Queen Adora app. 18-Last issue; Richard Rider de-powered; Supernova becomes Nova-Prime; Dire Wraith Queen app; story continues in New Warriors #60 6.00

NOVA
Marvel Comics: May, 1999 - No. 7, Nov, 1999 ($2.99/$1.99)

1-($2.99, 38 pgs.) –Larsen-s/Bennett-a; wraparound-c by Larsen; origin retold; Nebula app; reveals her father to be Zorr (from issue #1, 1976); She-Hulk, Spider-Man, Speedball, Namorita app. 5.00
2-6: 2-Two covers; vs. Diamondhead; Captain America app.; Namorita's skin returns to normal. 3-Savage Dragon app.; (as a Skrull); New Warriors, Thor, Fantastic Four & the Condor app.; return of the Sphinx. 4-vs. Condor; Fantastic Four app; Red Raven cameo. 5-Spider-Man app. 6-vs. the Sphinx; Venom cameo 3.00
7-Last issue; Red Raven & Bi-Beast app. vs. Venom 4.00

NOVA (See Secret Avengers and The Thanos Imperative)
Marvel Comics: June, 2007 - No. 36, Jun, 2010 ($2.99)

1-Abnett/Lanning-s; Chen-a; Granov-c; continued from Annihilation #6; brief Iron Man app.
3 6 9 16 24 32
2-The Initiative x-over; Nova returns to Earth; vs. Diamondhead; Iron Man & the Thunderbolts (Penance, Radioactive Man, Venom & Moonstone) app.
1 3 4 6 8 10
3-The Initiative x-over; vs. the Thunderbolts; Iron Man app.; Nova leaves Earth
1 2 3 5 6 8
4-7,9: Annihilation Conquest x-overs. 4-Phalanx and Gamora app. 5-Nova infected with the Phalanx virus; Gamora app. 6-Gamora-c by Granov; Drax app. 7-Gamora and Drax app; last Chen-a. 9-Cosmo, Gamora and Drax app. 7.00
8-1st app. Cosmo - the Russian telepathic dog; 1st app. Knowhere – a space station formed out of the severed head of a Celestial (as seen in the GOTG movie); 1st app. of the Luminals; 1st Wellington Alves-a; brief Peter Quill (Star-Lord) app.
4 8 12 23 37 50
10-14: 10-Nova and Gamora solo story; Drax app.; leads into Nova Annual #1. 11-Gamora, Drax & Warlock of the New Mutants app; Pelletier-a begins. 12-Warlock of the New Mutants app. Nova, Gamora & Drax cured of the Phalanx virus; leads into Annihilation Conquest #6. 13-Galactus & Silver Surfer app.; contains 5-pg preview of the new Eternals series; Alves-a. 14-Galactus app.; Nova vs. Silver Surfer. 15-Galactus & Silver Surfer app. 6.00
16-18: Secret Invasion x-over. 16-Super-Skrull app.; Nova returns to Earth. 17-Team up w/Darkhawk at Project Pegasus vs. the Skrulls; Quasar (Wendell Vaughn) returns. 18-Quasar & Darkhawk app; vs. the Skrulls; return of the Nova Corps 5.00
18-Zombie 1:10 variant-c by Wellington Alves 6.00
19-Darkhawk app.; Robbie Rider joins the Nova-Corps; Serpent Society app. 20-New Warriors flashback; Justice & Firestar app; Ego the Living Planet app. 21-Fantastic Four app; Ego the Living Planet becomes new base for the Nova Corps; Nova's powers are taken away. 22-Quasar app.; Andrea Divito-a begins 4.00
20-Villain 'Sphinx' variant-c by Mike Deodato Jr. 1 2 3 5 6 8
23-28: War of Kings x-over. 23-Richard Rider dons the Quantum Bands – becomes the new Quasar. 24-Gladiator & the Shi'ar Imperial Guard app. 25-Richard regains his Nova powers; Wendell Vaughn (Quasar) regains the Quantum Bands; Emperor Vulcan app. 26-Lord Ravenous app. 27-Blastaar & Lord Ravenous app. 28-War of Kings ends; Robbie Rider officially joins the Nova Corps. Quasar app. 6.00
25-'Dirty Dancing' 1980s decade 1:10 variant by Alina Urusov 5.00
28-Marvel Comics 70th Anniversary frame variant 6.00
29,30: 'Starstalker' parts 1-2. 29-1st Marvel Universe app. of Monark Starstalker (previously from Marvel Premiere #32). 30-vs. Ego the Living Planet 3.00
31-Darkhawk app. 5.00
32-34: Realm of Kings x-over; 32,33-Reed Richards, Black Bolt, Darkhawk, Namorita & the Sphinx app. 33-Moonstone, Man-Wolf, Bloodstone, Basilisk app. 34-'Death' of Black Bolt; Nova vs. Moonstone, Reed Richards vs. Bloodstone, Namorita vs. Man-Wolf, Darkhawk vs. Gyre the Raptor; contains 6 pg. preview of the New Ultimates series
1 2 3 5 6 8
34-Deadpool variant-c 2 4 6 8 12 15
35-Realm of Kings x-over; Reed Richards, Darkhawk, Namorita vs. Sphinx; Namorita brought back to current continuity 1 3 4 6 8 10
36-Last issue; Darkhawk & Quasar app.; leads into Thanos Imperative Ignition
2 4 6 10 14 18
Annual #1 (4/08, $3.99); Slightly altered origin retold; Annihilation Conquest tie-in; Quasar app.; takes place between Nova issues #10-11 1 2 3 5 6 8

	GD 2.0	VG 4.0	FN 6.0	VF 8.0	VF/NM 9.0	NM- 9.2

...: Origin of Richard Rider (2009, $4.99) origin retold from Nova #1 & 4 ('76) 5.00
... Vol. 1: Annihilation - Conquest TPB (2007, $17.99) r/#1-7; cover sketches 18.00

NOVA (Marvel NOW!)
Marvel Comics: Apr, 2013 - No. 31, Jul, 2015 ($3.99)

1-Loeb-s/McGuinness-a/c; Rocket Raccoon & Gamora app.; multiple variant covers 6.00
2-9: 2,3-Rocket Raccoon & Gamora app. 7-Superior Spider-Man app. 8,9-Infinity tie-in 4.00
10-($4.99) "Issue #100"; Speedball & Justice app.; cover gallery 5.00
11-24,26-31: 12-16-Beta Ray Bill app. 18-20-Original Sin tie-in. 19,20-Rocket Raccoon app. 23,24-Axis tie-in. 28-Black Vortex crossover 4.00
25-($4.99) Axis tie-in; Sam joins the Avengers 5.00
Annual 1 (5/15, $4.99) The Hulk app.; Duggan-s/Baldeon-a 5.00
... Special 1 (10/14, $4.99) Part 3 of x-over with Iron Man & Uncanny X-Men 5.00

NOVA
Marvel Comics: Jan, 2016 - No. 11, Nov, 2016 ($3.99)

1,2,5-11: 1-Sean Ryan-s/Cory Smith-a. 8,9-Civil War II tie-in. 10,11-Richard Rider returns 4.00
3,4-Ms. Marvel & Spider-Man (Miles) app. 1 2 3 5 6 8

NOVA
Marvel Comics: Feb, 2017 - No. 7, Aug, 2017 ($3.99)

1-7: 1-Ramón Pérez-a; Richard Rider & Ego app. 4-Gamora app. 4.00

NOW AGE ILLUSTRATED (See Pendulum Illustrated Classics)

NOW AGE BOOKS ILLUSTRATED (See Pendulum Illustrated Classics)

NOWHERE MAN
Dynamite Entertainment: 2011 - No. 4, 2011 ($3.99)

1-4-Marc Guggenheim-s/Jeevan J. Kang-a 4.00

NOWHERE MEN
Image Comics: Nov, 2012 - No. 11, Sept, 2016 ($2.99)

1-Stephenson-s/Bellegarde-a 15.00
1-2nd thru 5th printings 4.00
2 6.00
3-11 4.00

NO WORLD
Aspen MLT: Apr, 2017 - No. 6, Oct, 2017 ($3.99, limited series)

1-6-Lobdell-s/Gunderson-a; multiple covers on each 4.00

NTH MAN THE ULTIMATE NINJA (See Marvel Comics Presents #25)
Marvel Comics: Aug, 1989 - No. 16, Sept, 1990 ($1.00)

1-16-Ninja mercenary. 8-Dale Keown's 1st Marvel work (1/90, pencils) 3.00

NUBIA & THE AMAZONS (From Wonder Woman)
DC Comics: Dec, 2021 - No. 6, May, 2022 ($3.99, limited series)

1-6-Stephanie Williams-s/Alitha Martinez-a 5.00

NUBIA & THE JUSTICE LEAGUE SPECIAL (From Wonder Woman)
DC Comics: Jan, 2023 ($5.99, limited series)

1-Firefly and Parasite app.; takes place before Justice League #75 6.00

NUBIA: CORONATION SPECIAL (Prelude to Nubia: Queen of the Amazons series)
DC Comics: Jul, 2022 ($5.99, one-shot)

1-Stephanie Williams & Vita Ayala-s; art by Sauvage, Doran, Thompson, Banks, Martinez 6.00

NUBIA: QUEEN OF THE AMAZONS (From Wonder Woman)
DC Comics: Aug, 2022 - No. 4, Nov, 2022 ($3.99, limited series)

1-4-Stephanie Williams-s/Alitha Martinez-a. 1-Justice League app. 4.00

NUCLEAR FAMILY (Based on the short story Breakfast at Twilight by Philip K. Dick)
AfterShock Comics: Feb, 2021 - No. 5, Jun, 2021 ($4.99/$3.99, limited series)

1-($4.99) Stephanie Phillips-s/Tony Shasteen-a 5.00
2-5-($3.99) 4.00

NUCLEUS (Also see Cerebus)
Heiro-Graphic Publications: May, 1979 ($1.50, B&W, adult fanzine)

1-Contains "Demonhorn" by Dave Sim; early app. of Cerebus The Aardvark (4 pg. story) 5 10 15 34 60 85

NUKLA
Dell Publishing Co.: Oct-Dec, 1965 - No. 4, Sept, 1966

1-Origin & 1st app. Nukla (super hero)	5	10	15	33	57	80
2,3	3	6	9	21	33	45
4-Ditko-a, c(p)	4	8	12	25	40	55

NUMBER OF THE BEAST
DC Comics (WildStorm): June, 2008 - No. 8, Sept, 2008 ($2.99, limited series)

1-8-Beatty-s/Sprouse-a/c. 1-Variant-c by Mahnke. 6-The Authority app. 3.00
TPB (2008, $19.99) r/#1-8; character dossiers 20.00

NURSE BETSY CRANE (Formerly Teen Secret Diary) (Also see Registered Nurse for reprints)
Charlton Comics: V2#12, Aug, 1961 - V2#27, Mar, 1964 (See Soap Opera Romances)

V2#12-27 5 10 15 34 60 85

NURSE HELEN GRANT (See The Romances of...)

NURSE LINDA LARK (See Linda Lark)

NURSERY RHYMES
Ziff-Davis Publ. Co. (Approved Comics): No. 10, July-Aug, 1951 - No. 2, Winter, 1951 (Painted-c)

10 (#1), 2: 10-Howie Post-a 21 42 63 126 206 285

NURSES, THE (TV)
Gold Key: April, 1963 - No. 3, Oct, 1963 (Photo-c: #1,2)

1	5	10	15	33	57	80
2,3	3	6	9	19	30	40

NUTS! (Satire)
Premiere Comics Group: March, 1954 - No. 5, Nov, 1954

1-Hollingsworth-a	39	78	117	240	395	550
2,4,5: 5-Capt. Marvel parody	26	52	78	154	252	350
3-Drug "reefers" mentioned; Marilyn Monroe & Joe DiMaggio parody-c	28	56	84	168	274	380

NUTS (Magazine) (Satire)
Health Knowledge: Feb, 1958 - No. 2, April, 1958

1	10	20	30	58	79	100
2	8	16	24	40	50	60

NUTS & JOLTS
Dell Publishing Co.: No. 22, 1941

Large Feature Comic 22 23 46 69 136 223 310

NUTSY SQUIRREL (Formerly Hollywood Funny Folks)(See Comic Cavalcade)
National Periodical Publications: #61, 9-10/54 - #69, 1-2/56; #70, 8-9/56 - #71, 10-11/56; #72, 11/57

61-Mayer-a; Grossman-a in all	15	30	45	85	130	175
62-72: Mayer a-62,65,67-72	11	22	33	62	86	110

NUTTY COMICS
Fawcett Publications: Winter, 1946

1-Capt. Kidd story; 1 pg. Wolverton-a 15 30 45 88 137 185

NUTTY COMICS
Home Comics (Harvey Publications): 1945; No. 4, May-June, 1946 - No. 8, June-July, 1947 (No #2,3)

nn-Helpful Hank, Bozo Bear & others (funny animal)	10	20	30	56	76	95
4	8	16	24	42	54	65
5-Rags Rabbit begins(1st app.); infinity-c	9	18	27	50	65	80
6-8	7	14	21	37	46	55

NUTTY LIFE (Formerly Krazy Life #1; becomes Wotalife Comics #3 on)
Fox Feature Syndicate: No. 2, Summer, 1946

2 25 50 75 150 245 340

NU WAY
Aspen MLT: Jul, 2018 - No. 5, Jan, 2019 ($3.99, limited series)

1-5-Krul-s/Konat-a; multiple covers on each 4.00

NYOKA, THE JUNGLE GIRL (Formerly Jungle Girl; see The Further Adventures of..., Master Comics #50 & XMas Comics)
Fawcett Publications: No. 2, Winter, 1945 - No. 77, June, 1953 (Movie serial)

2	68	136	204	435	743	1050
3	39	78	117	240	395	550
4,5-Bondage covers	34	68	102	204	332	460
6-11,13,14,16-18-Krigstein-a: 17-Sam Spade ad by Lou Fine	21	42	63	122	199	275
12,15,19,20	20	40	60	115	185	255
21-30: 25-Clayton Moore photo-c?	14	28	42	81	118	155
31-40	12	24	36	69	97	125
41-50	11	22	33	62	86	110
51-60	10	20	30	54	72	90
61-77	9	18	27	50	65	80

NOTE: *Photo-c from movies 25, 30-70, 72, 75-77. Bondage c-4, 5, 7, 8, 14, 24.*

NYOKA, THE JUNGLE GIRL (Formerly Zoo Funnies; Space Adventures #23 on)
Charlton Comics: No. 14, Nov, 1955 - No. 22, Nov, 1957

14	14	28	42	76	108	140
15-22	10	20	30	58	79	100

NYX (Also see X-23 title)
Marvel Comics: Nov, 2003 - No. 7, Oct, 2005 ($2.99)

1-Quesada-s/Middleton-a/c; intro. Kiden Nixon	3	6	9	16	23	30
2	2	4	6	11	16	20
3-1st app. X-23	24	48	72	168	372	575
4-2nd app X-23	6	12	18	38	69	100
5,6-Teranishi-a	2	4	6	9	13	16
7-($3.99) Teranishi-a	2	4	6	8	10	12

NYX X-23 (2005, $34.99, oversized with d.j.) r/X-23 #1-6 & NYX #1-7; intro by Craig Kyle; sketch pages, development art and unused covers 45.00
...: Wannabe TPB (2006, $19.99) r/#1-7; development art and unused covers 20.00

NYX: NO WAY HOME
Marvel Comics: Oct, 2008 - No. 6, Apr, 2009 ($3.99)

1-6: 1-Andrasofszky-a/Liu-s/Urusov-c; sketch pages, character and cover design art 5.00

NYX, VOLUME 1
Dynamite Entertainment: 2021 - No. 10, 2022 ($3.99)

1-10-Christos Gage-s/Marc Borstel-a; multiple covers on each. 3,8-Vampirella app. 4.00

OAKLAND PRESS FUNNYBOOK, THE
The Oakland Press: 9/17/78 - 4/13/80 (16 pgs.) (Weekly)
Full color in comic book form; changes to tabloid size 4/20/80-on

Contains Tarzan by Manning, Marmaduke, Bugs Bunny, etc. (low distribution); 9/23/79 - 4/13/80 contain Buck Rogers by Gray Morrow & Jim Lawrence 5.00

OAKY DOAKS (See Famous Funnies #190)
Eastern Color Printing Co.: July, 1942 (One Shot)

1 39 78 117 240 395 550

OBERGEIST: RAGNAROK HIGHWAY
Image Comics (Top Cow/Minotaur): May, 2001 - No. 6, Nov, 2001 ($2.95, limited series)

Preview ('01, B&W, 16 pgs.) Harris painted-c 3.00
1-6-Harris-c/a/Jolley-s. 1-Three covers 3.00
... :The Directors' Cut (2002, $19.95, TPB) r/#1-6; Bruce Campbell intro. 20.00
... :The Empty Locket (3/02, $2.95, B&W) Harris & Snyder-a 3.00

OBERON
AfterShock Comics: Feb, 2019 - No. 5, Jul, 2019 ($3.99)

1-5-Ryan Parrott-s/Milos Slavkovic-a 4.00

OBIE
Store Comics: 1953 (6¢)

1 9 18 27 52 69 85

Nubia: Queen of the Amazons #1 © DC

NYX, Volume 1 #9 © DYN

Obi-Wan and Anakin #1 © Lucasfilm

	GD	VG	FN	VF	VF/NM	NM-
	2.0	4.0	6.0	8.0	9.0	9.2

OBI-WAN AND ANAKIN (Star Wars)
Marvel Comics: Mar, 2016 - No. 5, Jul, 2016 ($3.99)

1-5-Takes place a few years after Episode One; Soule-s/Checchetto-a/c 4.00

OBJECTIVE FIVE
Image Comics: July, 2000 - No. 6, Jan, 2001 ($2.95)

1-6-Lizalde-a 3.00

OBLIVION
Comico: Aug, 1995 - No. 3, May, 1996 ($2.50)

1-3: 1-Art Adams-c. 2-(1/96)-Bagged w/gaming card. 3-(5/96)-Darrow-c 3.00

OBLIVION SONG
Image Comics: Mar, 2018 - No. 36, Jun, 2022 ($3.99)

1-24,26-35-Kirkman-s/De Felici-a 4.00
25-($4.99) Flip book with Science Dog #25 - Kirkman-s/Cory Walker-a 5.00
36-($5.99) Last issue 6.00

OBNOXIO THE CLOWN (Character from Crazy Magazine)
Marvel Comics Group: April, 1983 (one-shot)

1-Vs. the X-Men 5.00

OCCULT CRIMES TASKFORCE
Image Comics: July, 2006 - No. 4, May, 2007 ($2.99, limited series)

1-4-Rosario Dawson & David Atchison-s/Tony Shasteen-a 3.00
... Vol. 1 TPB (2007, $14.99) r/#1-4; sketch and cover development art 15.00

OCCULTIST, THE
Dark Horse Comics: Dec, 2010 ($3.50, one-shot)

1-Richardson & Seeley-s/Drujiniu-a/Morris-c 3.50

OCCULTIST, THE
Dark Horse Comics: Nov, 2011 - No. 3, Jan, 2012 ($3.50, limited series)

1-3-Seeley-s/Drujiniu-a/Morris-c. 1-Variant-c by Frison 3.50

OCCULTIST, THE
Dark Horse Comics: Oct, 2013 - No. 5, Feb, 2014 ($3.50, limited series)

1-5-Seeley-s/Norton-a/Morris-c. 1-Variant-c by Rivera 3.50

OCCULT FILES OF DR. SPEKTOR, THE
Gold Key/Whitman No. 25: Apr, 1973 - No. 24, Feb, 1977; No. 25, May, 1982 (Painted-c #1-24)

	GD	VG	FN	VF	VF/NM	NM-
1-1st app. Lakota; Baron Tibor begins	6	12	18	38	69	100
2-5: 3-Mummy-c/s. 5-Jekyll & Hyde-c/s	4	8	12	23	37	50
6-10: 6,9-Frankenstein. 8,9-Dracula c/s. 9.-Jekyll & Hyde c/s. 9,10-Mummy-c/s	3	6	9	16	23	30
11-13,15-17,19-22,24: 11-1st app. Spektor as Werewolf. 11-13-Werewolf-c/s. 12,16-Frankenstein c/s. 17-Zombie/Voodoo-c. 19-Sea monster-c/s. 20-Mummy-s. 21-Swamp monster-c/s. 24-Dragon-c/s	2	4	6	11	16	20
14-Dr. Solar app.	3	6	9	16	24	32
18,23-Dr. Solar cameo	2	4	6	13	18	22
22-Return of the Owl-c/s	3	6	9	14	20	25
25(Whitman, 5/82)-r/#1 with line drawn-c	2	4	6	9	13	16

NOTE: *Also see Dan Curtis, Golden Comics Digest 33, Gold Key Spotlight, Mystery Comics Digest 5, & Spine Tingling Tales.*

OCCUPY AVENGERS (Follows Civil War II)
Marvel Comics: Jan, 2017 - No. 9, Sept, 2017 ($3.99)

1-4-Hawkeye and Red Wolf team; Pacheco-a. 3,4-Nighthawk & Nick Fury LMD app. 8,9-Secret Empire tie-ins. 9-Leads into Secret Empire #7 4.00

OCCUPY COMICS
Black Mask Studios: 2013 - No. 3, 2013 ($3.50)

1-3-Short stories and essays about the Occupy movement; s/a by various. 1-Allred-c 3.50

OCEAN
DC Comics (WildStorm): Dec, 2005 - No. 6, Sept, 2006 ($2.95/$2.99/$3.99, limited series)

1-5-Warren Ellis-s/Chris Sprouse-a 3.00
6-($3.99) Conclusion 4.00

OCEAN MASTER: YEAR OF THE VILLAIN
DC Comics: 2019 ($4.99, one-shot)

1-Watters-s/Mendonca-a; Apex Lex and Marine Marauder app. 5.00

OCTOBER FACTION, THE
IDW Publishing: Oct, 2014 - No. 18, Jul, 2016 ($3.99)

1-18-Steve Niles-s/Damien Worm-a/c 4.00
... #1 Special Edition (9/19, $3.99) r/#1 with added Netflix logo on cover 4.00

OCTOBER FACTION, THE: DEADLY SEASON
IDW Publishing: Oct, 2016 - No. 5, Feb, 2017 ($3.99, limited series)

1-5-Steve Niles-s/Damien Worm-a/c 4.00

OCTOBER FACTION: SUPERNATURAL DREAMS
IDW Publishing: Mar, 2018 - No. 5, Jul, 2018 ($3.99, limited series)

1-5-Steve Niles-s/Damien Worm-a/c 4.00

ODDLY NORMAL
Image Comics: Sept, 2014 - No. 10, Sept, 2015 ($2.99)

1-10-Otis Frampton-s/a 3.00

ODELL'S ADVENTURES IN 3-D (See Adventures in 3-D)

ODIN'S EYE
Bad Idea: Dec, 2021 - No. 5, Dec, 2021 ($9.99/$7.99, weekly limited series)

	GD	VG	FN	VF	VF/NM	NM-
1-($9.99) Dysart-s/Giorello-a	2	4	6	11	16	20
2-5	1	2	3	5	6	8

ODY-C
Image Comics: Nov, 2014 - No. 12, Oct, 2016 ($3.99)

1-12: 1-Matt Fraction-s/Christian Ward-a; 8-page gatefold 4.00

ODYSSEY, THE (See Marvel Illustrated: The Odyssey)

ODYSSEY OF THE AMAZONS
DC Comics: Mar, 2017 - No. 6, Aug, 2017 ($3.99, limited series)

1-6-Early history of the Amazons; Kevin Grevioux-s/Ryan Benjamin-a 4.00

OFFCASTES
Marvel Comics (Epic Comics/Heavy Hitters): July, 1993 - No. 3, Sept, 1993 ($1.95, limited series)

1-3: Mike Vosburg-c/a/scripts in all 3.00

OFFICIAL CRISIS ON INFINITE EARTHS INDEX, THE
Independent Comics Group (Eclipse): Mar, 1986 ($1.75)

1 5.00

OFFICIAL CRISIS ON INFINITE EARTHS CROSSOVER INDEX, THE
Independent Comics Group (Eclipse): July, 1986 ($1.75)

1-Pérez-c. 5.00

OFFICIAL DOOM PATROL INDEX, THE
Independent Comics Group (Eclipse): Feb, 1986 - No. 2, Mar, 1986 ($1.50, limited series)

1,2: Byrne-c. 4.00

OFFICIAL HANDBOOK OF THE CONAN UNIVERSE ANNIVERSARY EDITION
Marvel Comics: Dec, 2020 ($5.99, one-shot)

1-Reprints The Handbook of the Conan Universe ('85,'86); Kaluta wraparound-c 6.00

OFFICIAL HANDBOOK OF THE MARVEL UNIVERSE, THE
Marvel Comics Group: Jan, 1983 - No. 15, May, 1984 (Limited series)

1-Lists Marvel heroes & villains (letter A) 6.00
2-15: 2 (B-C, 3-(C-D). 4-(D-G). 5-(H-J), 6-(K-L). 7-(M). 8-(N-P); Punisher-c. 9-(Q-S), 10-(S). 11-(S-U). 12-(V-Z); Wolverine-c. 13,14-Book of the Dead. 15-Weaponry catalogue 5.00

NOTE: ***Bolland** a-8. **Byrne** c/a(p)-1-14; c-15p. **Grell** a-6, 9. **Kirby** a-1, 3. **Layton** a-2, 5, 7. **Mignola** a-3, 4, 5, 6, 8, 12. **Miller** a-4-6, 8, 10. **Nebres** a-3, 4, 8. **Redondo** a-3, 4, 8, 13, 14. **Simonson** a-1, 4, 6-13. **Paul Smith** a-1-12. **Starlin** a-5, 7, 8, 10, 13, 14. **Steranko** a-8p. **Zeck**-2-14.*

OFFICIAL HANDBOOK OF THE MARVEL UNIVERSE, THE
Marvel Comics Group: Dec, 1985 - No. 20, Feb, 1988 ($1.50, maxi-series)

V2#1-Byrne-c 5.00
2-20: 2,3-Byrne-c 4.00

	GD	VG	FN	VF	VF/NM	NM-
Trade paperback Vol. 1-10 ($6.95)	1	3	4	6	8	10

NOTE: ***Art Adams** a-7, 8, 11, 12, 14. **Bolland** a-8, 10, 13. **Buckler** a-1, 3, 5, 10. **Buscema** a-1, 5, 8, 9, 10, 13, 14. **Byrne** a-1-14; c-1-11. **Ditko** a-1, 2, 4, 6, 7, 11, 13. a-7, 11. **Mignola** a-2, 4, 9, 11, 13. **Miller** a-2, 4, 12. **Simonson** a-1, 2, 4-13, 15. **Paul Smith** a-1-5, 7-12, 14. **Starlin** a-6, 8, 9, 12, 16. **Zeck** a-1-4, 6, 7, 9-14, 16.*

OFFICIAL HANDBOOK OF THE MARVEL UNIVERSE, THE
Marvel Comics: July, 1989 - No. 8, Mid-Dec, 1990 ($1.50, lim. series, 52 pgs.)

V3#1-8: 1-McFarlane-a (2 pgs.) 4.00

OFFICIAL HANDBOOK OF THE MARVEL UNIVERSE, THE (Also see Spider-Man)
Marvel Comics: 2004 - Present ($3.99, one-shots)

...: Alternate Universes 2005 - Profile pages of 1602, MC2, 2099, Earth X, Mangaverse, Days of Future Past, Squadron Supreme, Spider-Ham's Larval Earth and others 4.00
...: Avengers 2004 - Profile pages; art by various; lists of character origins and 1st apps. 4.00
...: Avengers 2005 - Profile pages and info for New Avengers, Young Avengers & others 4.00
...: Book of the Dead 2004 - Profile pages of deceased Marvel characters; art by various; 4.00
...: Daredevil 2004 - Profile pages; art by various; lists of character origins and 1st apps. 4.00
...: Fantastic Four 2005 - Profile pages of members, friends & enemies 4.00
...: Golden Age 2005 - Profile pages; art by various; lists of character origins and 1st apps. 4.00
...: Horror 2005 - Profile pages; art by various; lists of character origins and 1st apps. 4.00
...: Hulk 2004 - Profile pages; art by various; lists of character origins and 1st apps. 4.00

GD VG FN VF VF/NM NM-
2.0 4.0 6.0 8.0 9.0 9.2

...: Marvel Knights 2005 - Profile pages of characters from Marvel Knights line 4.00
...: Spider-Man 2004 - Profile pages; art by various; lists of character origins and 1st apps. 4.00
...: Spider-Man 2005 - Profile pages of Spidey's friends and foes, emphasizing the recent 4.00
...: Wolverine 2004 - Profile pages; art by various; lists of character origins and 1st apps. 4.00
...: Teams 2005 - Profile pages of Avengers, X-Men and other teams 4.00
...: Women of Marvel 2005 - Profile pages; art by various; Greg Land-c 4.00
...: X-Men 2004 - Profile pages; art by various; lists of character origins and 1st apps. 4.00
...: X-Men 2005 - Profile pages; art by various; lists of character origins and 1st apps. 4.00
...: X-Men - The Age of Apocalypse 2005 - Profile pages of characters plus Exiles 4.00

OFFICIAL HANDBOOK OF THE MARVEL UNIVERSE A-Z UPDATE
Marvel Comics: Apr, 2010 - No. 5, 2010 ($3.99, limited series)
1-5-Profile pages; Andrasofszky-c 4.00

OFFICIAL HANDBOOK OF THE ULTIMATE MARVEL UNIVERSE, THE
Marvel Comics: 2005 ($3.99, one-shots)
... 2005: The Fantastic Four and Spider-Man - Profile pages; art by various 4.00
... The Ultimates and X-Men 2005 - Profile pages; art by various; Bagley-c 4.00

OFFICIAL HAWKMAN INDEX, THE
Independent Comics Group: Nov, 1986 - No. 2, Dec, 1986 ($2.00)
1,2 4.00

OFFICIAL IMAGE COMICS TIMELINE, THE
Image Comics: Feb, 2022 ($7.99, squarebound, one-shot)
1-History of Image Comics; lists of awards, crossovers, photo gallery of creators 8.00

OFFICIAL INDEX TO THE MARVEL UNIVERSE (Also see "Avengers, Thor...")
Marvel Comics: 2009 - No. 14, April, 2010 ($3.99)
1-14-Each issue has chronological synopsies, creator credits, character lists for 40-50 issues of apps. for Iron Man, Spider-Man and the X-Men starting with 1st apps. in issue #1 4.00

OFFICIAL JUSTICE LEAGUE OF AMERICA INDEX, THE
Independent Comics Group (Eclipse): April, 1986 - No. 8, Mar, 1987 ($2.00, Baxter paper)
1-8: 1,2-Perez-c. 6.00

OFFICIAL LEGION OF SUPER-HEROES INDEX, THE
Independent Comics Group (Eclipse): Dec, 1986 - No. 5, 1987 ($2.00, limited series)
(No Official in Title #2 on)
1-5: 4-Mooney-c 6.00

OFFICIAL MARVEL INDEX TO MARVEL TEAM-UP
Marvel Comics Group: Jan, 1986 - No. 6, 1987 ($1.25, limited series)
1-6 4.00

OFFICIAL MARVEL INDEX TO THE AMAZING SPIDER-MAN
Marvel Comics Group: Apr, 1985 - No. 9, Dec, 1985 ($1.25, limited series)
1 ($1.00)-Byrne-c. 5.00
2-9: 5,6,8,9-Punisher-c. 4.00

OFFICIAL MARVEL INDEX TO THE AVENGERS, THE
Marvel Comics: Jun, 1987 - No. 7, Aug, 1988 ($2.95, limited series)
1-7 5.00

OFFICIAL MARVEL INDEX TO THE AVENGERS, THE
Marvel Comics: V2#1, Oct, 1994 - V2#6, 1995 ($1.95, limited series)
V2#1-#6 4.00

OFFICIAL MARVEL INDEX TO THE FANTASTIC FOUR
Marvel Comics Group: Dec, 1985 - No. 12, Jan, 1987 ($1.25, limited series)
1-12: 1-Byrne-c. 1,2-Kirby back-c (unpub. art) 4.00

OFFICIAL MARVEL INDEX TO THE X-MEN, THE
Marvel Comics: May, 1987 - No. 7, July, 1988 ($2.95, limited series)
1-7 5.00

OFFICIAL MARVEL INDEX TO THE X-MEN, THE
Marvel Comics: V2#1, Apr, 1994 - V2#5, 1994 ($1.95, limited series)
V2#1-5: 1-Covers X-Men #1-51. 2-Covers #52-122,Special #1,2,Giant-Size #1,2. 3-Byrne-c; covers #123-177, Annuals 3-7, Spec. Ed. #1. 4-Covers Uncanny X-Men #178-234, Annuals 8-12. 5-Covers #235-287, Annuals 13-15 4.00

OFFICIAL SOUPY SALES COMIC (See Soupy Sales)

OFFICIAL TEEN TITANS INDEX, THE
Indep. Comics Group (Eclipse): Aug, 1985 - No. 5, 1986 ($1.50, lim. series)
1-5 4.00

OFFICIAL TRUE CRIME CASES (Formerly Sub-Mariner #23; All-True Crime Cases #26 on)
Marvel Comics (OCI): No. 24, Fall, 1947 - No. 25, Winter, 1947-48
24(#1)-Burgos-a; Syd Shores-c 37 74 111 222 361 500
25-Syd Shores-c; Kurtzman's "Hey Look" 24 48 72 142 234 325

OF SUCH IS THE KINGDOM
George A. Pflaum: 1955 (15¢, 36 pgs.)
nn-Reprints from 1951 Treasure Chest 5 10 14 20 24 28

O.G. WHIZ (See Gold Key Spotlight #10)
Gold Key: 2/71 - No. 6, 5/72; No. 7, 5/78 - No. 11, 1/79 (No. 7: 52 pgs.)
1-John Stanley script 5 10 15 31 53 75
2-John Stanley script 4 8 12 23 37 50
3-6(1972) 3 6 9 17 26 35
7-11(1978-79)-Part-r: 9-Tubby issue 2 4 6 9 12 15

OH, BROTHER! (Teen Comedy)
Stanhall Publ.: Jan, 1953 - No. 5, Oct, 1953
1-By Bill Williams 20 40 60 115 185 255
2-5 14 28 42 80 115 150

OH MY GODDESS! (Manga)
Dark Horse Comics: Aug, 1994 - No. 112 ($2.50-$3.99, B&W)
1-6-Kosuke Fujishima-s/a in all 3.00
... PART II 2/95 - No. 9, 9/95 ($2.50, B&W, lim.series) #1-9 3.00
... PART III 11/95 - No. 11, 9/96 ($2.95, B&W, lim. series) #1-11 3.00
... PART IV 12/96 - No. 8, 7/97 ($2.95, B&W, lim. series) #1-8 3.00
... PART V 9/97 - No. 12, 8/98 ($2.95, B&W, lim. series)
1,2,5,8: 5-Ninja Master pt. 1 3.00
3,4,6,7,10-12-($3.95, 48 pgs.) 10-Fallen Angel. 11-Play The Game 4.00
9-($3.50) "It's Lonely At The Top" 3.50
... PART VI 10/98 - No. 5, 3/99 ($3.50/$2.95, B&W, lim. series)
1-($3.50) 3.50
2-6-($2.95)-6-Super Urd one-shot 3.00
... PART VII 5/99 - No. 8, 12/99 ($2.95, B&W, lim. series) #1-3 3.00
4-8-($3.50) 3.50
... PART VIII 1/00 - No. 6, 6/00 ($3.50, B&W, lim. series) #1-3,5,7 3.50
4-($2.95) "Hail To The Chief" begins 3.00
... PART IX 7/00 - No. 7, 1/01 ($3.50/$2.99) #1-4: 3-Queen Sayoko 3.50
5-7-($2.99) 3.00
... PART X 2/01 - No. 5, 6/01 ($3.50) #1-5 3.50
... PART XI 10/01 - No. 10, 3/02 ($3.50) #1,2,7,8 3.50
3-6,9-($2.99) Mystery Child 3.00
10-($3.99) 4.00
(Series adapts new numbering) 88-90-($3.50) Learning to Love 3.50
91-94,96-103,105,107-110: 91-94 ($2.99) Traveler. 96-98-The Phantom Racer 3.00
95,104,106-($3.50) 95-Traveler pt. 5 3.50
111,112-($3.99) 4.00

OH SUSANNA (TV)
Dell Publishing Co.: No. 1105, June-Aug, 1960 (Gale Storm)
Four Color 1105-Toth-a, photo-c 10 20 30 69 147 225

OKAY COMICS
United Features Syndicate: July, 1940
1-Captain & the Kids & Hawkshaw the Detective reprints 55 110 165 352 601 850

O.K. COMICS
Hit Publications: May, 1940 (ashcan)
nn-Ashcan comic, not distributed to newsstands, only for in house use. A CGC certified 8.0 copy sold in 2003 for $1,000.

O.K. COMICS
United Features Syndicate/Hit Publications: July, 1940 - No. 2, Oct, 1940
1-Little Giant (w/super powers), Phantom Knight, Sunset Smith, & The Teller Twins begin 87 174 261 553 952 1350
2 (Rare)-Origin Mister Mist by Chas. Quinlan 93 186 279 591 1021 1450

OKLAHOMA KID
Ajax/Farrell Publ.: June, 1957 - No. 4, 1958
1 11 22 33 62 86 110
2-4 7 14 21 37 46 55

OKLAHOMAN, THE
Dell Publishing Co.: No. 820, July, 1957
Four Color 820-Movie, photo-c 9 18 27 60 120 180

OKTANE
Dark Horse Comics: Aug, 1995 - Nov, 1995 ($2.50, color, limited series)
1-4-Gene Ha-a 3.00

OKTOBERFEST COMICS
Now & Then Publ.: Fall 1976 (75¢, Canadian, B&W, one-shot)
1-Dave Sim-s/a; Gene Day-a; 1st app. Uncle Hans & Natter P. Bombast; The Beavers sty; 1st Cap'n Riverrat, Sim-s/Day-a 3 6 9 16 23 30

OLD GLORY COMICS
DC Comics: 1941
nn - Ashcan comic, not distributed to newsstands, only for in-house use. Cover art is Flash Comics #12 with interior being Action Comics #37 (no known sales)

OLD GUARD, THE (Inspired the 2020 Netflix movie)
Image Comics: Feb, 2017 - No. 5, Jun, 2017 ($3.99)
1-5-Greg Rucka-s/Leandro Fernández-a 4.00

OLD GUARD, THE: FORCE MULTIPLIED
Image Comics: Dec, 2019 - No. 5, Jul, 2020 ($3.99)
1-5-Greg Rucka-s/Leandro Fernández-a 4.00

OLD GUARD, THE: TALES THROUGH TIME
Image Comics: Apr, 2021 - No. 6, Sept, 2021 ($3.99)
1-6-Short stories by various creators: 1,6-Rucka-s/Fernández-a. 2-Bendis-s/Oeming-a 4.00

OLD HAUNTS
AWA Studios: Jun, 2020 - No. 5 ($3.99)
1-5-Ollie Masters & Rob Williams-s/Laurence Campbell-a 4.00

OLD IRONSIDES (Disney)
Dell Publishing Co.: No. 874, Jan, 1958
Four Color 874-Movie w/Johnny Tremain 8 16 24 51 96 140

OLD LADY HARLEY (See Harley Quinn #42)
DC Comics: Dec, 2018 - No. 5, Apr, 2019 ($3.99, limited series)
1-5-Tieri-s/Miranda-a/Conner-c; future Harley, Joker, Red Tool and Catwoman app. 4.00

OLD MAN HAWKEYE
Marvel Comics: Mar, 2018 - No. 12, Feb, 2019 ($3.99)
1-12-Sacks-s/Checchetto-a; takes place 5 years before the original Old Man Logan 4.00

OLD MAN LOGAN (Secret Wars tie-in)
Marvel Comics: Jul, 2015 - No. 5, Dec, 2015 ($4.99/$3.99, limited series)
1-($4.99) Bendis-s/Sorrentino-a; future Logan from Wolverine V3 #66; Emma Frost app. 5.00
2-5-($3.99) 2-Sabretooth app. 3-Apocalypse app. 5-X-Men app. 4.00

OLD MAN LOGAN (Follows Secret Wars)(Continues in Dead Man Logan)
Marvel Comics: Mar, 2016 - No. 50, Dec, 2018 ($4.99/$3.99)
1-($4.99) Lemire-s/Sorrentino-a; future Logan in current Marvel Universe 5.00
2-49-($3.99) 2-Amadeus Cho Hulk app. 4-Steve Rogers app. 7-Lady Deathstrike app.

Old Haunts #1 © AWA

Old Lady Harley #5 © DC

Once & Future #1 © Kieron Gillen

GD 2.0 | VG 4.0 | FN 6.0 | VF 8.0 | VF/NM 9.0 | NM- 9.2

14,15-Dracula app.; Andrade-a. 21-24-Past Lives. 25-30-Maestro app. 25-32-Deodato-a
31-35-Scarlet Samurai. 36-38,43-45-Bullseye app. 41,42-Kraven app. 4.00
50-($4.99) Brisson-s/Roberson & Edwards-a; Maestro app. 5.00
Annual 1 (11/18, $4.99) Frank Castle app.; Brisson-s/Di Meo-a/Shane Davis-c 5.00

OLD MAN QUILL
Marvel Comics: Apr, 2019 - No. 12, Feb, 2020 ($3.99)
1-12: 1-Sacks-s/Gill-a; Star-Lord with Guardians of the Galaxy 45+ years in the future. 6,11,12-Galactus app. 4.00

OLD YELLER (Disney, see Movie Comics, and Walt Disney Showcase #25)
Dell Publishing Co.: No. 869, Jan, 1958
Four Color 869-Movie, photo-c 6 12 18 42 73 115

OLIVER
Image Comics: Jan, 2019 - Present ($3.99)
1-4-Gary Whitta-s/Darick Robertson-a. 1-Covers by Robertson & Fabry 4.00

OLIVIA TWIST
Dark Horse Comics (Berger Books): Sept, 2018 - No. 4, Jan, 2019 ($4.99, limited series)
1-4-Darin Strauss & Adam Dalva-s/Emma Vieceli-a. 3-Tula Lotay-c. 4-Sana Takeda-c 5.00

OLYMPUS: REBIRTH
DC Comics: Oct, 2022 ($5.99, one-shot)
1-Hippolyta joins the Olympian gods; Conrad & Cloonan-s/Yarsky-a 6.00

OMAC (One Man Army; ...Corps. #4 on; also see Kamandi #59 & Warlord) (See Cancelled Comic Cavalcade)
National Periodical Publications: Sept-Oct, 1974 - No. 8, Nov-Dec, 1975
1-Origin 5 10 15 34 60 85
2-8: 8-2 pg. Neal Adams ad 3 6 9 17 26 35
Jack Kirby's Omac: One Man Army Corps HC (2008, $24.99, d.j.) r/#1-8; Evanier intro. 25.00
NOTE: ***Kirby** a-1-8p; c-1-7p. **Kubert** c-8.*

OMAC (See DCU Brave New World)
DC Comics: Sept, 2006 - No. 8, Apr, 2007 ($2.99, limited series)
1-8: 1-Bruce Jones-s/Renato Guedes-a. 1-3-Firestorm & Cyborg app. 8-Superman app. 3.00

O.M.A.C. (DC New 52)
DC Comics: Nov, 2011 - No. 8, Jun, 2012 ($2.99)
1-8: 1-DiDio-s/Giffen-a/c; Dubbilex and Brother Eye app. 2-Max Lord & Sarge Steel app. 5-Crossover with Frankenstein, Agent of SHADE #5. 6-Kolins-a 3.00

OMAC: ONE MAN ARMY CORPS
DC Comics: 1991 - No. 4, 1991 ($3.95, B&W, mini-series, mature, 52 pgs.)
Book One - Four: John Byrne-c/a & scripts 5.00

OMAC PROJECT, THE
DC Comics: June, 2005 - No. 6, Nov, 2005 ($2.50, limited series)
1-6-Prelude to Infinite Crisis x-over; Rucka-s/Saiz-a 3.00
...: Infinite Crisis Special 1 (5/06, $4.99) Rucka-s/Saiz-a; follows destruction of satellite 5.00
TPB (2005, $14.99) r/#1-6, Countdown to Infinite Crisis, Wonder Woman #219 15.00

O'MALLEY AND THE ALLEY CATS
Gold Key: April, 1971 - No. 9, Jan, 1974 (Disney)
1 3 6 9 16 23 30
2-9 2 4 6 9 13 16

OMEGA ELITE
Blackthorne Publishing: 1987 ($1.25)
1-Starlin-c 4.00

OMEGA FLIGHT
Marvel Comics: Jun, 2007 - No. 5, Oct, 2007 ($2.99, limited series)
1-Oeming-s/Kolins-a; Wrecking Crew app. 4.00
1-Second printing with Sasquatch variant-c 3.00
2-5: 5-Beta Ray Bill app. 3.00
...: Alpha to Omega TPB ('07, $13.99) r/#1-5, USAgent story/Civil War: Choosing Sides 14.00

OMEGA MEN, THE (See Green Lantern #141)
DC Comics: Dec, 1982 - No. 38, May, 1986 ($1.00/$1.25/$1.50; Baxter paper)
1-Giffen-c/a 2 4 6 8 10 12
2,4-9,11-19,21-25,28-30,32,33,36,38: 2-Origin Broot. 5,9-2nd & 3rd app. Lobo (cameo, 2 pgs. each). 7-Origin The Citadel. 19-Lobo cameo. 30-Intro new Primus 4.00
3-1st app. Lobo (5 pgs.)(6/83); Lobo-c 5 10 15 35 63 90
10-1st full Lobo story 2 4 6 11 16 20
20: 20-2nd full Lobo story 5.00
26,27,31,34,35: 26,27-Alan Moore scripts. 31-Crisis x-over. 34,35-Teen Titans x-over 4.00
37-1st solo Lobo story (8 pg. back-up by Giffen) 6.00
Annual 1(11/84, 52 pgs.), 2(11/85) 5.00
NOTE: ***Giffen** c/a-1-6p. **Morrow** a-24r. **Nino** c/a-16, 21; a-Annual 1i.*

OMEGA MEN, THE
DC Comics: Dec, 2006 - No. 6, May, 2007 ($2.99, limited series)
1-6: 1-Superman, Wonder Girl, Green Lantern app.; Flint-a/Gabrych-s 3.00

OMEGA MEN, THE
DC Comics: Aug, 2015 - No. 12, Jul, 2016 ($2.99)
1-12: 1-Tom King-s/Barnaby Bagenda-a; Kyle Rayner app. 4-Cypress-a 3.00

OMEGA THE UNKNOWN
Marvel Comics Group: March, 1976 - No. 10, Oct, 1977
1-1st app. Omega 3 6 9 21 33 45
2,3-(Regular 25¢ editions). 2-Hulk-c/story. 3-Electro-c/story. 2 4 6 9 12 15
2,3-(30¢-c variants, limited distribution) 4 8 12 28 47 65
4-10: 8-1st brief app. 2nd Foolkiller (Greg Salinger), 1 panel only. 9,10-(Reg. 30¢ editions). 9-1st full app. 2nd Foolkiller 1 3 4 6 8 10
9,10-(35¢-c variants, limited distribution) 7 14 21 44 82 120
... Classic TPB (2005, $29.99) r/#1-10 30.00
NOTE: ***Kane** c(p)-3, 5, 8, 9. **Mooney** a-1-3, 4p, 5, 6p, 7, 8i, 9, 10.*

OMEGA: THE UNKNOWN
Marvel Comics: Dec, 2007 - No. 10, Sept, 2008 ($2.99, limited series)
1-10-Jonathan Lethem-s/Farel Dalrymple-a 3.00

OMEN
Northstar Publishing: 1989 - No. 3, 1989 ($2.00, B&W, mature)
1-Tim Vigil-c/a in all 1 2 3 5 7 9
1, (2nd printing) 3.00
2,3 6.00

OMEN, THE
Chaos! Comics: May, 1998 - No. 5, Sept, 1998 ($2.95, limited series)
1-5: 1-Six covers, ...: Vexed (10/98, $2.95) Chaos! characters appear 3.00

OMNI MEN
Blackthorne Publishing: 1987 - No. 3, 1987 ($1.25)
1-3 3.00
Graphic Novel (1989, $3.50) 4.00

ONCE & FUTURE
BOOM! Studios: Aug, 2019 - No. 30, Oct, 2022 ($3.99)
1-Kieron Gillen-s/Dan Mora-a in all 2 4 6 11 16 20
2 1 3 4 6 8 10
3-8 5.00
9-24,26-29: 9-12-Beowulf and Grendel app. 4.00
25,30: 25-($4.99) Bonus preview of Grim #1. 30-Last issue 5.00

ONCE UPON A TIME: OUT OF THE PAST (TV)
Marvel Comics: 2015 ($24.99, hardcover with dustjacket)
HC-Sequel to Shadow of the Queen HC; Bechko & Vazquez-s; Stacy Lee-c 25.00

ONCE UPON A TIME: SHADOW OF THE QUEEN (TV)
Marvel Comics: 2013 ($19.99, hardcover with dustjacket)
HC-Regina and the Huntsman; Bechko-s; art by Del Mundo, Lolos, Henderson, & Kaluta 20.00

ONE, THE
Marvel Comics (Epic Comics): July, 1985 - No. 6, Feb, 1986 (Limited series, mature)
1-6: Post nuclear holocaust super-hero. 2-Intro The Other 3.00

ONE-ARM SWORDSMAN, THE
Victory Prod./Lueng's Publ. #4 on: 1987 - No. 12, 1990 ($2.75/$1.80, 52 pgs.)
1-3 ($2.75) 4.00
4-12: 4-6-$1.80-c. 7-12-$2.00-c 4.00

ONE-HIT WONDER
Image Comics: Feb, 2014 - No. 5, Apr, 2015 ($3.50)
1-5: 1-4-Sapolsky-s/Olivetti-a/c. 5-Thompson & Fiorelli-a/Roux-a 3.50

ONE HUNDRED AND ONE DALMATIANS (Disney, see Cartoon Tales, Movie Comics, and Walt Disney Showcase #9, 51)
Dell Publishing Co.: No. 1183, Mar, 1961
Four Color 1183-Movie 11 22 33 75 160 245

101 DALMATIONS (Movie)
Disney Comics: 1991 (52 pgs., graphic novel)
nn-($4.95, direct sales)-r/movie adaptation & more 1 2 3 5 6 8
1-($2.95, newsstand edition) 5.00

	GD	VG	FN	VF	VF/NM	NM-
	2.0	4.0	6.0	8.0	9.0	9.2

101 WAYS TO END THE CLONE SAGA (See Spider-Man)
Marvel Comics: Jan, 1997 ($2.50, one-shot)
1 4.00

100 BULLETS
DC Comics (Vertigo): Aug, 1999 - No. 100, Jun, 2009 ($2.50/$2.75/$2.99)
1-Azzarello-s/Risso-a/Dave Johnson-c 4 8 12 23 37 50
2-5 6.00
6-49,51-61: 26-Series summary; art by various. 45-Preview of Losers 4.00
50-($3.50) History of the Trust 5.00
62-71: 62-Begin $2.75-c. 64-Preview of Loveless 3.00
72-99: 72-Begin $2.99-c 3.00
100-($4.99) Final issue 1 3 4 6 8 10
...#1/Crime Line Sampler Flip-Book (9/09, $1.00) r/#1 with previews of upcoming GNs 3.00
...: A Foregone Tomorrow TPB (2002, $17.95) r/#20-30 18.00
...: Decayed TPB (2006, $14.99) r/#68-75; Darwyn Cooke intro. 15.00
...: First Shot, Last Call TPB (2000, $9.95) r/#1-5, Vertigo Winter's Edge #3 10.00
...: Hang Up on the Hang Low TPB (2001, $9.95) r/#15-19; Jim Lee intro. 10.00
...: Once Upon a Crime TPB (2007, $12.99) r/#76-83 13.00
...: Samurai TPB (2003, $12.95) r/#43-49 13.00
...: Six Feet Under the Gun TPB (2003, $12.95) r/#37-42 13.00
...: Split Second Chance TPB (2001, $14.95) r/#6-14 15.00
...: Strychnine Lives TPB (2006, $14.99) r/#59-67; Manuel Ramos intro. 15.00
...: The Counterfifth Detective TPB (2003, $12.95) r/#31-36 13.00
...: The Hard Way TPB (2005, $14.99) r/#50-58 15.00
...: Wilt TPB (2009, $19.99) r/#89-100; Azzarello intro. 20.00

100 BULLETS: BROTHER LONO
DC Comics (Vertigo): Aug, 2013 - No. 8, Apr, 2014 ($3.99/$2.99, limited series)
1-($3.99) Azzarello-s/Risso-a/Dave Johnson-c 4.00
2-8-($2.99) Azzarello-s/Risso-a/Dave Johnson-c on all 3.00

100 GREATEST MARVELS OF ALL TIME
Marvel Comics: Dec, 2001 ($7.50/$3.50, limited series)
1-5-Reprints top #6-#25 stories voted by poll for Marvel's 40th ann. 7.50
6-($3.50) (#5 on-c) Reprints X-Men (2nd series) #1 4.00
7-($3.50) (#4 on-c) Reprints Giant-Size X-Men #1 4.00
8-($3.50) (#3 on-c) Reprints (Uncanny) X-Men #137 (Death of Jean Grey) 4.00
9-($3.50) (#2 on-c) Reprints Fantastic Four #1 4.00
10-($3.50) (#1 on-c) Reprints Amazing Fantasy #15 (1st app. Spider-Man) 4.00

100 PAGES OF COMICS
Dell Publishing Co.: 1937 (Stiff covers, square binding)
101(Found on back cover)-Alley Oop, Wash Tubbs, Capt. Easy, Og Son of Fire, Apple Mary, Tom Mix, Dan Dunn, Tailspin Tommy, Doctor Doom
172 344 516 1092 1871 2650

100 PAGE SUPER SPECTACULAR (See DC 100 Page Super Spectacular)

100%
DC Comics (Vertigo): Aug, 2002 - No. 5, July, 2003 ($5.95, B&W, limited series)
1-5-Paul Pope-s/a 6.00
HC (2009, $39.99, dustjacket) r/#1-5; sketch pages and background info 40.00
TPB (2005, $24.99) r/#1-5; sketch pages and background info 25.00
TPB (2009, $29.99) r/#1-5; sketch pages and background info 30.00

100% TRUE?
DC Comics (Paradox Press): Summer 1996 - No. 2 ($4.95, B&W)
1,2-Reprints stories from various Paradox Press books. 5.00

$1,000,000 DUCK (See Walt Disney Showcase #5)

ONE MILLION YEARS AGO (Tor #2 on)
St. John Publishing Co.: Sept, 1953
1-Origin & 1st app. Tor; Kubert-c/a; Kubert photo inside front cover
25 50 75 150 245 340

ONE MONTH TO LIVE ("Heroic Age: ..." in indicia)
Marvel Comics: Nov, 2010 - No. 5, Nov, 2010 ($2.99, weekly limited series)
1-5-Remender-s; Spider-Man and the Fantastic Four app. 3.00

ONES, THE
Dark Horse Comics: Nov, 2022 - No. 4, Feb, 2023 ($4.99, limited series)
1-4-Brian Michael Bendis-s/Jacob Edgar-a 5.00

ONE SHOT (See Four Color...)

ONE-STAR SQUADRON
DC Comics: Feb, 2022 - No. 6, Jul, 2022 ($3.99, limited series)
1-6-Mark Russell-s/Steve Lieber-a; Red Tornado, Power Girl, The Heckler app. 4.00

1001 HOURS OF FUN
Dell Publishing Co.: No. 13, 1943
Large Feature Comic 13 (nn)-Puzzles & games; by A.W. Nugent. This book was bound as #13 w/Large Feature Comics in publisher's files 39 78 117 231 378 525

ONE TRICK RIP OFF, THE (See Dark Horse Presents)

ONI (Adaption of video game)
Dark Horse Comics: Feb, 2001 - No. 3, Apr, 2001 ($2.99, limited series)
1-3-Sunny Lee-a(p) 3.00

ONIBA: SWORDS OF THE DEMON
Aspen MLT: No. 0, Oct, 2015 ($2.50)
0-Hernandez-s/Pantalena-a; two covers 3.00

ONI DOUBLE FEATURE (See Clerks: The Comic Book and Jay & Silent Bob)
Oni Press: Jan, 1998 - No. 13, Sept, 1999 ($2.95, B&W)
1-Jay & Silent Bob; Kevin Smith-s/Matt Wagner-a 1 3 4 6 8 10
1-2nd printing 3.00
2-11,13: 2,3-Paul Pope-s/a. 3,4-Nixey-s/a. 4,5-Sienkewicz-s/a. 6,7-Gaiman-s. 9-Bagge-c. 13-All Paul Dini-s; Jingle Belle 3.00
12-Jay & Silent Bob as Bluntman & Chronic; Smith-s/Allred-a 5.00

ONI PRESS COLOR SPECIAL
Oni Press: Jun, 2001; Jul, 2002 ($5.95, annual)
...2001-Oeming "Who Killed Madman?" cover; stories & art by various 6.00
...2002-Allred wraparound-c; stories & art by various 6.00

ONSLAUGHT: EPILOGUE
Marvel Comics: Feb, 1997 ($2.95, one-shot)
1-Hama-s/Green-a; Xavier-c; Bastion-app. 4.00

ONSLAUGHT: MARVEL
Marvel Comics: Oct, 1996 ($3.95, one-shot)
1-Conclusion to Onslaught x-over; wraparound-c 2 4 6 8 10 12

ONSLAUGHT REBORN
Marvel Comics: Jan, 2007 - No. 5, Feb, 2008 ($2.99, limited series)
1-5-Loeb-s/Liefeld-a; female Bucky app. 2-Variant-c by Joe Madureira. 3-McGuiness var-c. 4-Campbell var-c. 5-Bianchi var-c; female Bucky goes to regular Marvel Universe 3.00
1-Variant-c by Michael Turner 4.00
HC (2008, $19.99) r/#1-5; sketch pages; foreword by Liefeld 20.00

ONSLAUGHT UNLEASHED
Marvel Comics: Apr, 2011 - No. 4, Jul, 2011 ($3.99, limited series)
1-4-McKeever-s/Andrade-a/Ramos-c; Secret Avengers & Young Allies app. 4.00

ONSLAUGHT: X-MEN
Marvel Comics: Aug, 1996 ($3.95, one-shot)
1-Waid & Lobdell script; Fantastic Four & Avengers app.; Xavier as Onslaught
1 3 4 6 8 10
1-Variant-c 3 6 8 11 13 15
1-Gold Edition 6 12 18 38 69 100

ON STAGE
Dell Publishing Co.: No. 1336, Apr-June, 1962
Four Color 1336-Not by Leonard Starr 5 10 15 34 60 85

ON THE DOUBLE (Movie)
Dell Publishing Co.: No. 1232, Sept-Nov, 1961
Four Color 1232 6 12 18 37 66 95

ON THE ROAD TO PERDITION (Movie)
DC Comics (Paradox Press): 2003 - Book 3, 2004 ($7.95, 8"x5 1/2", B&W, limited series)
...: Oasis, Book 1-Max Allan Collins-s/José Luis García-López-a/David Beck-c 8.00
...: Sanctuary, Book 2-Max Allan Collins-s/Steve Lieber-a/José Luis García-López-c 8.00
...: Detour, Book 3-Max Allan Collins-s/José Luis García-López-a/Steve Lieber-c/a(i) 8.00
Road to Perdition 2: On the Road (2004, $14.95) r/series; Collins intro. 15.00

ON THE ROAD WITH ANDRAE CROUCH
Spire Christian Comics (Fleming H. Revell): 1973, 1974 (39¢)
nn-1973 Edition 2 4 6 13 18 22
nn-1974 Edition 2 4 6 9 13 16

ON THE SCENE PRESENTS:...
Warren Publishing Co.: Oct, 1966 - No. 2, 1967 (B&W magazine, two #1 issues)
#1 "Super Heroes" (68 pgs.) Batman 1966 movie photo-c/s; has articles/photos/comic art from serials on Superman, Flash Gordon, Capt. America, Capt. Marvel and The Phantom
5 10 15 31 53 75
#1 "Freak Out, USA" (Fall/1966, 60 pgs.) (lower print run) articles on musicians like Zappa, Jefferson Airplane, Supremes 5 10 15 33 57 80
#2 "Freak Out, USA" (2/67, 52 pgs.) Beatles, Country Joe, Doors/Jim Morrison, Bee Gees
5 10 15 33 57 80

ON THE SPOT (Pretty Boy Floyd...)
Fawcett Publications: Fall, 1948
nn-Pretty Boy Floyd photo on-c; bondage-c 43 86 129 271 461 650

ONYX
IDW Publishing: Jul, 2015 - No. 4, Oct, 2015 ($3.99)
1-4-Gabriel Rodriguez & Chris Ryall-s&a. 1-Three covers 4.00

ONYX OVERLORD
Marvel Comics (Epic): Oct, 1992 - No. 4, Jan, 1993 ($2.75, mini-series)
1-4: Moebius scripts 3.00

OPEN SPACE
Marvel Comics: Mid-Dec, 1989 - No. 4, Aug, 1990 ($4.95, bi-monthly, 68 pgs.)
1-4: 1-Bill Wray-a; Freas-c 5.00
0-(1999) Wizard supplement; unpubl. early Alex Ross-a; new Ross-c 3.00

OPERATION BIKINI (See Movie Classics)

OPERATION: BROKEN WINGS, 1936
BOOM! Studios: Nov, 2011 - No. 3, Jan, 2012 ($3.99, limited series)
1-3-Hanna-s/Hairsine-a; English translation of French comic 4.00

OPERATION BUCHAREST (See The Crusaders)

OPERATION CROSSBOW (See Movie Classics)

OPERATION: KNIGHTSTRIKE (See Knightstrike)
Image Comics (Extreme Studios): May, 1995 - No.3, July, 1995 ($2.50)
1-3 3.00

OPERATION PERIL
American Comics Group (Michel Publ.): Oct-Nov, 1950 - No. 16, Apr-May, 1953 (#1-5: 52 pgs.)
1-Time Travelers, Danny Danger (by Leonard Starr) & Typhoon Tyler (by Ogden Whitney) begin 48 96 144 302 514 725
2-War-c 28 56 84 165 270 375
3-War-c; horror story 27 54 81 158 259 360
4,5-Sci/fi-c/story 55 110 165 352 601 850
6-10: 6,8,9,10-Sci/fi-c. 6-Tank vs. T-Rex-c. 7-Sabretooth-c
23 46 69 138 227 315
11,12-War-c; last Time Travelers 15 30 45 88 137 185
13-16: All war format 12 24 36 69 97 125
NOTE: *Starr a-2, 5. Whitney a-1, 2, 5-10, 12; c-1, 3, 5, 8, 9.*

OPERATION: S.I.N.

100 Bullets #86 © Azzarello & Risso

Optimus Prime #8 © Hasbro

The Order #9 © MAR

GD 2.0 | VG 4.0 | FN 6.0 | VF 8.0 | VF/NM 9.0 | NM- 9.2

Marvel Comics: Mar, 2015 - No. 5, Jul, 2015 ($3.99, limited series)
1-5-Peggy Carter & Howard Stark in 1952; Kathryn Immonen-s/Rich Ellis-a 4.00

OPERATION: STORMBREAKER
Acclaim Comics (Valiant Heroes): Aug, 1997 ($3.95, one-shot)
1-Waid/Augustyn-s, Braithwaite-a; Nazi-c 5.00

OPTIC NERVE
Drawn and Quarterly: Apr, 1995 - Present ($2.95-$3.95, bi-annual)
1-7: Adrian Tomine-c/a/scripts in all 3.00
8-11: 8-($3.50). 9-11-($3.95) 4.00
12,13-($5.95) Half front-c. 12-Amber Sweet story 6.00
14-($6.95) Half front-c 7.00
32 Stories-($9.95, trade paperback)-r/Optic Nerve mini-comics 10.00
32 Stories-($29.95, hardcover)-r/Optic Nerve mini-comics; signed & numbered 30.00

OPTIMUS PRIME (Transformers)
IDW Publishing: Nov, 2016 - No. 18, Oct, 2018 ($3.99)
1-Follows Revolution x-over; Barber-s/Zama-a; multiple covers
1 2 3 5 6 8
2-25-Multiple covers on each. 2,3-Barber-s/Zama-a. 4-Milne-a 4.00
Annual 2018 (2/18, $7.99) Barber-s/Tramontano & Griffith-a 8.00
... First Strike 1 (9/17, $3.99) Barber-s/Guidi & Wycough-a; part of Hasbro x-over 4.00

ORACLE: THE CURE
DC Comics: May, 2009 - No. 3, Jul, 2009 ($2.99, limited series)
1-3-Guillem March-c; Calculator app. 3.00
TPB (2010, $17.99) r/#1-3 and Birds of Prey #126,127 18.00

ORAL ROBERTS' TRUE STORIES (Junior Partners #120 on)
TelePix Publ. (Oral Roberts' Evangelistic Assoc./Healing Waters): 1956 (no month) - No. 119, 7/59 (15¢)(No. 102: 25¢)
V1#1(1956)-(Not code approved)- "The Miracle Touch"
20 40 60 114 182 250
102-(Only issue approved by code, 10/56) "Now I See"
13 26 39 74 105 135
103-119: 115-(114 on inside) 10 20 30 54 72 90
NOTE: *Also see Happiness & Healing For You.*

ORANGE BIRD, THE
Walt Disney Educational Media Co.: No date (1980) (36 pgs.; in color; slick cover)
nn-Included with educational kit on foods, ...in Nutrition Adventures nn (1980)
...and the Nutrition Know-How Revue nn (1983) 3.00

ORB (Magazine)
Orb Publishing: 1974 - No. 6, Mar/Apr 1976 (B&W/color)
1-1st app. Northern Light & Kadaver, both series begin
5 10 15 30 50 70
2,3 (72 pgs.) 3 6 9 16 23 30
4-6 (60 pgs.): 4,5-origin Northern Light 2 4 6 10 14 18
NOTE: ***Allison** a-1-3. **Gene Day** a-1-6. **P. Hsu** a-4-6. **Steacy** s/a-3,4.*

ORBIT
Eclipse Books: 1990 - No. 3, 1990 ($4.95, 52 pgs., squarebound)
1-3: Reprints from Isaac Asimov's Science Fiction Magazine; 1-Dave Stevens-c, Bolton-a. 3-Bolton-c/a, Yeates-a 5.00

ORBITER
DC Comics (Vertigo): 2003 ($24.95, hardcover with dust jacket)
HC-Warren Ellis-s/Colleen Doran-a 25.00
SC-(2004, $17.95) Warren Ellis-s/Colleen Doran-a 18.00

ORCHID
Dark Horse Comics: Oct, 2011 - No. 12, Jan, 2013 ($1.00/$3.50)
1-Tom Morello-s/Scott Hepburn-a; covers by Carnevale & Fairey 3.00
2-12-($3.50) Carnevale-c 3.50

ORCS!
BOOM! Studios (kaboom!): Feb, 2021 - No. 6, Jul, 2021 ($4.99)
1-6-Christine Larsen-s/a 5.00

ORCS IN SPACE (Issues #9-on only released digitally)
Oni Press: Apr, 2021 - No. 8, Feb, 2022 ($6.99/$4.99)
#1 & #2: 2 in 1 ($6.99) Justin Roiland co-writer/Vigneault-a 7.00
3-8-($3.99) 4.00

ORCS!: THE CURSE
BOOM! Studios (kaboom!): Jun, 2022 - No. 4, Nov, 2022 ($5.99, limited series)
1-4-Christine Larsen-s/a 6.00

GD 2.0 | VG 4.0 | FN 6.0 | VF 8.0 | VF/NM 9.0 | NM- 9.2

ORDER, THE (cont'd from Defenders V2#12)
Marvel Comics: Apr, 2002 - No. 6, Sept, 2002 ($2.25, limited series)
1-6: 1-Haley-a/Duffy & Busiek-s. 3-Avengers-c/app. 4-Jurgens-a 3.00

ORDER, THE (The Initiative following Civil War)
Marvel Comics: Sept, 2007 - No. 10, Jun, 2008 ($2.99)
1-10-California's Initiative team; Fraction-s/Kitson-a/c 3.00
... Vol. 1: The Next Right Thing TPB (2008, $14.99) r/#1-7 15.00

ORDINARY GODS
Image Comics: Jul, 2021 - Present ($3.99)
1-10: 1-8-Higgins-s/Watanabe-a. 9,10-Daniel HDR-a 4.00

ORIENTAL HEROES
Jademan Comics: Aug, 1988 - No. 55, Feb, 1993 ($1.50/$1.95, 68 pgs.)
1,55 5.00
2-54 4.00

ORIGINAL ADVENTURES OF CHOLLY & FLYTRAP, THE
Image Comics: Feb, 2006 - No. 2, June, 2006 ($5.99, limited series)
1,2-Arthur Suydam-s/a; interview with Suydam and art pages 6.00

ORIGINAL ASTRO BOY, THE
Now Comics: Sept, 1987 - No. 20, Jun, 1989 ($1.50/$1.75)
1-All have Ken Steacy painted-c/a 1 3 4 6 8 10
2-20 5.00

ORIGINAL BLACK CAT, THE
Recollections: Oct. 6, 1988 - No. 9, 1992 ($2.00, limited series)
1-9: Elias-r; 1-Bondage-c. 2-Murphy Anderson-c 5.00

ORIGINAL DICK TRACY, THE
Gladstone Publishing: Sept, 1990 - No. 5, 1991 ($1.95, bi-monthly, 68pgs.)
1-5: 1-Vs. Pruneface. 2-& the Evil influence; begin $2.00-c 4.00
NOTE: *#1 reprints strips 7/16/43 - 9/30/43. #2 reprints strips 12/1/46 - 2/2/47. #3 reprints 8/31/46 - 11/14/46. #4 reprints 9/17/45 - 12/23/45. #5 reprints 6/10/46 - 8/28/46.*

ORIGINAL DOCTOR SOLAR, MAN OF THE ATOM, THE
Valiant: Apr, 1995 ($2.95, one-shot)
1-Reprints Doctor Solar, Man of the Atom #1,5; Bob Fugitani-r; Paul Smith-c; afterword by Seaborn Adamson 4.00

ORIGINAL E-MAN AND MICHAEL MAUSER, THE
First Comics: Oct, 1985 - No. 7, April, 1986 ($1.75/$2.00, Baxter paper)
1-6: 1-Has r-/Charlton's E-Man, Vengeance Squad. 2-Shows #4 in indicia by mistake 3.00
7-($2.00, 44 pgs.)-Staton-a 4.00

ORIGINAL GHOST RIDER, THE
Marvel Comics: July, 1992 - No. 20, Feb, 1994 ($1.75)
1-20: 1-7-r/Marvel Spotlight #5-11 by Ploog w/new-c. 3-New Phantom Rider (former Night Rider) back-ups begin by Ayers. 4-Quesada-c(p). 8-Ploog-c. 8,9-r/Ghost Rider #1,2. 10-r/Marvel Spotlight #12. 11-18,20-r/Ghost Rider #3-12. 19-r/Marvel Two-in-One #8 3.00

ORIGINAL GHOST RIDER RIDES AGAIN, THE
Marvel Comics: July, 1991 - No. 7, Jan, 1992 ($1.50, limited series, 52 pgs.)
1-7: 1-r/Ghost Rider #68(origin),69 w/covers. 2-7: R/ G.R. #70-81 w/covers 4.00

ORIGINAL MAGNUS ROBOT FIGHTER, THE
Valiant: Apr, 1995 ($2.95, one-shot)
1-Reprints Magnus, Robot Fighter 4000 #2; Russ Manning-r; Rick Leonardi-c; afterword by Seaborn Adamson 5.00

ORIGINAL MARVEL ZOMBIES, THE: MARVEL TALES
Marvel Comics: Dec, 2020 ($7.99, one-shot)
1-Reprints Ultimate Fantastic Four #21-23 and Marvel Zombies #1; Macchio foreword 8.00

ORIGINAL NEXUS GRAPHIC NOVEL (See First Comics Graphic Novel #19)

ORIGINALS, THE
DC Comics (Vertigo): 2004 ($24.95/$17.99, B&W graphic novel)
HC (2004, $24.95) Dave Gibbons-s/a 25.00
SC (2005, $17.99) 18.00

ORIGINAL SHIELD, THE
Archie Enterprises, Inc.: Apr, 1984 - No. 4, Oct, 1984
1-4: 1,2-Origin Shield; Ayers p-1-4, Nebres c-1,2 5.00

ORIGINAL SIN
Marvel Comics: No. 0, Jun, 2014 - No. 8, Nov, 2014 ($4.99/$3.99, limited series)
0-($4.99) Origin of the Watcher re-told; Nova (Sam Alexander) app.; Waid-s/Cheung-a 5.00
1-($4.99) The Watcher is murdered; Aaron-s/Deodato-a 5.00

GD 2.0 | VG 4.0 | FN 6.0 | VF 8.0 | VF/NM 9.0 | NM- 9.2

2-7-($3.99) 5-Nick Fury's origin. 7-Thor loses use of his hammer 4.00
8-($4.99) Murderer revealed; new Watcher begins 5.00
Annual 1 (12/14, $4.99) Fury and Howard Stark in 1958; Cisic-a/Tedesco-c 5.00
#3.1 - #3.4 (Hulk vs. Iron Man) ($3.99, 8/14 - 10/14) Flashback to the Gamma bomb 4.00
#5.1 - #5.5 (Thor & Loki: The Tenth Realm) ($3.99, 9/14 - 11/14) Angela revealed as Thor's sister; Aaron & Ewing-s 4.00

ORIGINAL SINS (Secrets from the Watcher's Eyes unleashed in Original Sin #3)
Marvel Comics: Aug, 2014 - No. 5, Oct, 2014 ($3.99, limited series)

1-5-Short stories; Young Avengers in all issue; The Hood apps. 1-Deathlok prelude. 5-Secret of Dum Dum Dugan 4.00

ORIGINAL SWAMP THING SAGA, THE (See DC Special Series #2, 14, 17, 20)

ORIGINAL TUROK, SON OF STONE, THE
Valiant: Apr, 1995 - No. 2, May, 1995 ($2.95, limited series)

1,2: 1-Reprints Turok, Son of Stone #24,25,42; Alberto Gioletti-r; Rags Morales-c; afterword by Seaborn Adamson. 2-Reprints Turok, Son of Stone #24,33; Gioletti-r; McKone-c 4.00

ORIGIN OF GALACTUS (See Fantastic Four #48-50)
Marvel Comics: Feb, 1996 ($2.50, one-shot)

1-Lee & Kirby reprints w/pin-ups 1 3 4 6 8 10

ORIGIN OF THE DEFIANT UNIVERSE, THE
Defiant Comics: Feb, 1994 ($1.50, 20 pgs., one-shot)

1-David Lapham, Adam Pollina & Alan Weiss-a; Weiss-c 5.00
NOTE: *The comic was originally published as Defiant Genesis and was distributed at the 1994 Philadelphia ComicCon.*

ORIGINS
BOOM! Studios: Nov, 2020 - No. 6, Apr, 2021 ($3.99, limited series)

1-6-Clay McLeod Chapman-s/Jakub Rebelka-a 4.00

ORIGINS OF MARVEL COMICS (Also see Fireside Book Series)
Marvel Comics: July, 2010 ($3.99, one-shot)

1-Single page origins of prominent Marvel characters; text and art by various 4.00
...: Marvel Tales 1 (2/23, $7.99) Reprints Fantastic Four #1, Amazing Fantasy #15, X-Men #1 and Avengers #1; intro by Ralph Macchio 8.00
...: X-Men (11/10, $3.99) single page origins of X-Men and other mutants; s/a-various 4.00

ORIGIN II (Sequel to Wolverine: The Origin)
Marvel Comics: Feb, 2014 - No. 5, Jun, 2014 ($4.99/$3.99, limited series)

1-($4.99) Gillen-s/Adam Kubert-a/c; acetate overlay on cover; set in 1907 5.00
2-5-($3.99) Sabretooth app. 4.00

ORION (Manga)
Dark Horse Comics: Sept, 1992 - No. 6, July, 1993 ($2.95/$3.95, B&W, bimonthly, lim. series)

1-6: 1,2,6-Squarebound: 1-Masamune Shirow-c/a/s in all 4.00

ORION (See New Gods)
DC Comics: June, 2000 - No. 25, June, 2002 ($2.50)

1-14-Simonson-s/a. 3-Back-up story w/Miller-a. 4-Gibbons-a back-up. 7-Chaykin back-up. 8-Loeb/Liefeld back-up. 10-A. Adams back-up-a 12-Jim Lee back-up-a. 13-JLA-c/app.; Byrne-a 3.00
15-($3.95) Black Racer app.; back-up story w/J.P. Leon-a 4.00
16-24-Simonson-s/a: 19-Joker: Last Laugh x-over 3.00
25-($3.95) Last issue; Mister Miracle-c/app. 4.00
The Gates of Apocalypse (2001, $12.95, TPB) r/#1-5 & various short-s 13.00

ORORO: BEFORE THE STORM (Storm from X-Men)
Marvel Comics: Aug, 2005 - No. 4, Nov, 2005 ($2.99, limited series)

1-4-Barberi-a/Sumerak-s; young Storm in Egypt 3.00
... Digest (2006, $6.99) r/#1-4 7.00

ORPHAN AGE
AfterShock Comics.: Apr, 2019 - No. 5, Aug, 2019 ($3.99)

1-5-Ted Anderson-s/Nuno Plati-a 4.00

ORPHAN AND THE FIVE BEASTS
Dark Horse Comics.: Mar, 2021 - No. 4 ($3.99, limited series)

1-4-James Stokoe-s/a/c 4.00

ORPHAN BLACK (Based on the BBC TV show)
IDW Publishing: Feb, 2015 - No. 5, Jun, 2015 ($3.99)

1-6: Multiple covers on all. 1-Kudranski-a; spotlight on Sarah. 2-Spotlight on Helena. 3-Alison. 4-Cosima. 5-Rachel 4.00
... #1: IDW's Greatest Hits (6/18, $1.00) r/#1 3.00

ORPHAN BLACK: CRAZY SCIENCE
IDW Publishing: Jun, 2018 ($3.99, unfinished limited series)

1-Heli Kennedy-s/Fico Ossio-a; 3 covers 4.00

ORPHAN BLACK: DEVIATIONS
IDW Publishing: Mar, 2017 - No. 6, Aug, 2017 ($4.99/$3.99)

1-($4.99) Kennedy-s/Nichols-a; what if Beth wasn't hit by the train; multiple covers 5.00
2-6-($3.99) Kennedy-s/Nichols-a 4.00

ORPHAN BLACK: HELSINKI
IDW Publishing: Nov, 2015 - No. 5, Mar, 2016 ($3.99)

1-5: Multiple covers on all. 1-Alan Quah-a 4.00

ORVILLE, THE (Based on the 2017 sci-fi TV show)
Dark Horse Comics: Jul, 2019 - No. 4, Oct, 2019 ($3.99, limited series)

1-4: 1,2-New Beginnings; Goodman-s/Cabeza-a. 3,4-The Word of Avis; the Krill app. 4.00

ORVILLE, THE (Based on the 2017 sci-fi TV show)
Dark Horse Comics: Sept, 2020 - No. 4, Dec, 2020 ($3.99, limited series)

1-4: 1,2-Launch Day; Goodman-s/Cabeza-a; the Krill app. 3,4-Heroes 4.00

ORVILLE, THE: ARTIFACTS
Dark Horse Comics: Oct, 2021 - No. 2, Nov, 2021 ($3.99, limited series)

1,2-Goodman-s/Cabeza-a 4.00

ORVILLE, THE: DIGRESSIONS
Dark Horse Comics: May, 2021 - No. 2, Jun, 2021 ($3.99, limited series)

1,2-Goodman-s/Cabeza-a; takes place in Kelly Grayson's alternate timeline 4.00

OSBORN (Green Goblin)
Marvel Comics: Jan, 2011 - No. 5, Jun, 2011 ($3.99, limited series)

1-5-Deconnick-s/Rios-a/Oliver-c 4.00

OSBORN JOURNALS (See Spider-Man titles)
Marvel Comics: Feb, 1997 ($2.95, one-shot)

1-Hotz-c/a 3.00

OSCAR COMICS (Formerly Funny Tunes; Awful...#11 & 12) (Also see Cindy Comics)
Marvel Comics: No. 24, Spring, 1947 - No. 10, Apr, 1949; No. 13, Oct, 1949

24(#1, Spring, 1947) 33 66 99 194 317 440
25(#2, Sum, 1947)-Wolverton-a plus Kurtzman's "Hey Look" 34 68 102 199 325 450
26(#3)-Same as regular #3 except #26 was printed over in black ink with #3 appearing on-c below the over print 22 44 66 132 216 300
3-9,13: 8-Margie app. 22 44 66 132 216 300
10-Kurtzman's "Hey Look" 24 48 72 142 234 325

OSWALD THE RABBIT (Also see New Fun Comics #1)
Dell Publishing Co.: No. 21, 1943 - No. 1268, 12-2/61-62 (Walter Lantz)

Four Color 21(1943) 46 92 138 359 805 1250
Four Color 39(1943) 29 58 87 209 467 725
Four Color 67(1944) 16 32 48 112 249 385
Four Color 102(1946)-Kelly-a, 1 pg. 15 30 45 100 220 340
Four Color 143,183 9 18 27 59 117 175
Four Color 225,273 7 14 21 46 86 125
Four Color 315,388 6 12 18 40 73 105
Four Color 458,507,549,593 5 10 15 35 63 90
Four Color 623,697,792,894,979,1268 5 10 15 33 57 80

OSWALD THE RABBIT (See The Funnies, March of Comics #7, 38, 53, 67, 81, 95, 111, 126, 141, 156, 171, 186, New Funnies & Super Book #8, 20)

OTHER DEAD, THE
IDW Publishing: Sept, 2013 - No. 6, Feb, 2014 ($3.99)

1-6-Zombie animals; Ortega-s/Mui-a. 1-Variant-c by Dorman. 2-6-Pres. Obama app. 4.00

OTHER HISTORY OF THE DC UNIVERSE, THE
DC Comics (Black Label): Jan, 2021 - No. 5, Sept, 2021 ($6.99, 10-3/4" x 8-1/2", lim. series)

1-5-Ridley-s/Camuncoli & Cucchi-a; two covers by Camuncoli & Jamal Campbell. 1-Black Lightning origin & history. 2-Mal Duncan & Bumblebee. 3-Katana. 4-Renee Montoya 7.00

OTHER SIDE, THE
DC Comics (Vertigo): Dec, 2006 - No. 5, Apr, 2007 ($2.99, limited series)

1-5-Soldiers from both sides of the Vietnam War; Aaron-s/Stewart-a/c 3.00
TPB (2007, $12.99) r/#1-5; sketch pages, Stewart's travelogue to Saigon 13.00

OTHERWORLD
DC Comics (Vertigo): May, 2005 - No. 7, Nov, 2005 ($2.99)

1-7-Phil Jimenez-s/a(p) 3.00
...: Book One TPB (2006, $19.99) r/#1-7; cover gallery 20.00

OUR ARMY AT WAR (Becomes Sgt. Rock #302 on; also see Army At War)
National Periodical Publications: Aug, 1952 - No. 301, Feb, 1977

1 286 572 858 2402 5451 8500
2 121 242 363 968 2184 3400
3,4: 4-Krigstein-a 82 164 246 656 1478 2300
5-7 59 118 177 472 1061 1650
8-11,14-Krigstein-a 55 110 165 440 995 1550
12,15-20 46 92 138 368 834 1300
13-Krigstein-c/a; flag-c 61 122 183 488 1094 1700
21-31: Last precode (2/55) 35 70 105 252 564 875
32-40 31 62 93 223 499 775
41-60: 51-1st S.A. issue. 57,60-Grey tone-c 27 54 81 194 435 675
61-70: 61-(8/57) Pre-Sgt. Rock Easy Co.-c/s. 67-Minor Sgt. Rock prototype 25 50 75 175 388 600
71-80 23 46 69 164 362 560
81-(4/59) "The Rock of Easy" - Sgt. Rock prototype. Part of lead-up trio to 1st definitive Sgt. Rock. Story features a character named "Sgt. Rocky" as a "4th grade rate" sergeant (three stripes/chevrons) who is referred to as "The Rock of Easy". Editor also promises more stories of "...Rock-like Sergeant". Andru & Esposito-a/Haney-s 367 734 1100 3100 7050 11,000
82-(5/59) "Hold up Easy"- 1st app. of a Sgt. Rock. Part of lead-up trio to 1st definitive Sgt. Rock. Character named Sgt. Rock appears in a supporting "motivator" role as a "4th grade rate" sergeant (three stripes/chevrons) in six panels in six page story; Haney-s/Drucker-a 141 282 423 1142 2571 4000
83-(6/59) "The Rock and Wall" - 1st true appearance of Sgt. Rock. Sgt. Rock finally introduced as a Master Sergeant (three chevrons and three rockers) and is main character of story. 1st specific narration that defines the "Rock of Easy" as Sgt. Rock. 1st actual "Sgt. Rock" collaboration between creators Robert Kanigher and Joe Kubert 1015 2030 3045 8630 19,815 31,000
84-(7/59) "Laughter on Snakehead Hill" - 2nd appearance of Sgt. Rock. Story advances true Sgt. Rock continuity in 13-page title story featuring Sgt. Rock and Easy Co.; Kanigher-s/Novick-a/Kubert-c 100 200 300 800 1800 2800
85-Origin & 1st app. Ice Cream Soldier 75 150 225 600 1350 2100
86,87-Early Sgt. Rock; Kubert-a 55 110 165 444 997 1550
88-1st Sgt. Rock-c; Kubert-c/a 72 144 216 583 1267 1950
89-"No Shot From Easy!" story; Heath-c 46 92 138 359 805 1250
90-Kubert-c/a; How Rock got his stripes 80 160 240 648 1399 2150
91-All-Sgt. Rock issue; Grandenetti-c/Kubert-a 123 246 369 984 2217 3450
92,94,96-99: 97-Regular Kubert-c begin 35 70 105 252 564 875
93-1st Zack Nolan 39 78 117 289 657 1025
95-1st app. Bulldozer 46 92 138 340 770 1200
100 48 96 144 384 867 1350
101,108,113: 101-1st app. Buster. 113-1st app. Wildman & Jackie Johnson 28 56 84 202 451 700
102-104,106,107,109,110,114,116-120: 104-Nurse Jane-c/s. 109-Pre Easy Co. Sgt. Rock-s. 118-Sunny injured 26 52 78 182 404 625
105-1st app. Junior 33 66 99 238 532 825

Orphan Black #1 © Orphan Black Prods.

Our Army at War #86 © DC

Our Fighting Forces #49 © DC

	GD 2.0	VG 4.0	FN 6.0	VF 8.0	VF/NM 9.0	NM- 9.2
111-1st app. Wee Willie & Sunny	36	72	108	259	580	900
112-Classic Easy Co. roster-c	75	150	225	600	1350	2100
115-Rock revealed as orphan; 1st x-over Mlle. Marie. 1st Sgt. Rock's battle family	33	66	99	238	532	825
121-125	18	36	54	122	271	420
126-1st app. Canary; grey tone-c	27	54	81	194	435	675
127-2nd all-Sgt. Rock issue; 1st app. Little Sure Shot	29	58	87	209	467	725
128-Training & origin Sgt. Rock; 1st Sgt. Krupp	40	80	120	296	673	1050
129-139: 138-1st Sparrow. 141-1st Shaker	16	32	48	110	243	375
140-3rd all-Sgt. Rock issue	18	36	54	128	284	440
141-150: 147,148-Rock becomes a General	12	24	36	82	179	275
151-Intro. Enemy Ace by Kubert (2/65), black-c	46	92	138	368	834	1300
152-4th all-Sgt. Rock issue	15	30	45	103	227	350
153-2nd app. Enemy Ace (4/65)	21	42	63	147	324	500
154,156,157,159-161,165-167: 157-2 pg. centerfold spread pin-up as part of story. 159-1st Nurse Wendy Winston-c/s. 165-2nd Iron Major	10	20	30	69	147	225
155-3rd app. Enemy Ace (6/65)(see Showcase)	14	28	42	96	211	325
158-Book-length Sgt. Rock story; origin & 1st app. Iron Major(9/65), formerly Iron Captain; flashback to death of Rock's brother Josh	12	24	36	79	170	260
162,163-Viking Prince x-over in Sgt. Rock	11	22	33	75	160	245
164-Giant G-19	16	32	48	107	236	365
168-1st Unknown Soldier app.; referenced in Star-Spangled War Stories #157; (Sgt. Rock x-over) (6/66)	34	68	102	245	548	850
169,170	8	16	24	56	108	160
171-176,178-181: 171-1st Mad Emperor	8	16	24	54	102	150
177-(80 pg. Giant G-32)	10	20	30	64	132	200
182,183,186-Neal Adams-a. 186-Origin retold	9	18	27	59	117	175
184-Wee Willie dies	9	18	27	63	129	195
185,187,188,193-195,197-199	7	14	21	44	82	120
189,191,192,196: 189-Intro. The Teen-age Underground Fighters of Unit 3. 196-Hitler cameo	7	14	21	46	86	125
190-(80 pg. Giant G-44)	9	18	27	58	114	170
200-12 pg. Rock story told in verse; Evans-a	7	14	21	48	89	130
201,202,204-207: 201-Krigstein-r/#14. 204,205-All reprints; no Sgt. Rock. 207-Last 12¢ cover	5	10	15	35	63	90
203-(80 pg. Giant G-56)-All-r, Sgt. Rock story	8	16	24	51	96	140
208-215	4	8	12	28	47	65
216,229-(80 pg. Giants G-68, G-80): 216-Has G-58 on-c by mistake	6	12	18	41	76	110
217-219: 218-1st U.S.S. Stevens	4	8	12	27	44	60
220-Classic dinosaur/Sgt. Rock-c/s	5	10	15	33	57	80
221-228,230-234: 231-Intro/death Rock's brother. 234-Last 15¢ issue	4	8	12	23	37	50
235-239,241: 52 pg. Giants	4	8	12	28	47	65
240-Neal Adams-a; 52 pg. Giant	5	10	15	33	57	80
242-Also listed as DC 100 Page Super Spectacular #9	9	18	27	62	126	190
243-246: (All 52 pgs.) 244-No Adams-a	4	8	12	27	44	60
247-250,254-268,270: 247-Joan of Arc	3	6	9	16	23	30
251-253-Return of Iron Major	3	6	9	17	25	34
269,275-(100 pgs.)	5	10	15	33	57	80
271,272,274,276-279	3	6	9	14	19	24
273-Crucifixion-c	3	6	9	16	24	32
280-(68 pgs.)-200th app. Sgt. Rock; reprints Our Army at War #81,83	4	8	12	22	35	48
281-299,301: 295-Bicentennial cover	2	4	6	13	18	22
300-Sgt. Rock-s by Kubert (2/77)	3	6	9	15	22	28

NOTE ***Alcala** a-251. **Drucker** a-27, 67, 68, 79, 82, 83, 96, 164, 177, 203, 212, 243r, 244, 269r, 275r, 280r. **Evans** a-165-175, 200, 266, 269, 270, 274, 276, 278, 280. **Glanzman** a-218, 220, 222, 223, 225, 227, 230-232, 238-241, 244, 247, 248, 256-259, 261, 265-267, 271, 282, 283, 298. **Grandenetti** c-91,120. **Grell** a-287. **Heath** a-44, 50, 164, & most 176-281. **Kubert** a-38, 59, 67, 68 & most issues from 83-165, 171, 233, 236, 267, 275, 300; c-84, 280. **Maurer** a-233, 237, 239, 240, 45, 280, 284, 288, 290, 291, 295. **Severin** a-236, 252, 265, 267, 269r, 272. **Toth** a-235, 241, 254. **Wildey** a-283-285, 287p. **Wood** a-249.*

OUR ARMY AT WAR
DC Comics: Nov, 2010 ($3.99, one-shot)

	GD 2.0	VG 4.0	FN 6.0	VF 8.0	VF/NM 9.0	NM- 9.2
1-Joe Kubert-c; Mike Marts-s/Victor Ibáñez-a						4.00
TPB (2011, $14.99) r/#1 and other 2010 war one-shots Weird War Tales #1, Our Fighting Forces #1, G.I. Combat #1 and Star-Spangled War Stories #1						15.00

OUR FIGHTING FORCES
National Per. Publ./DC Comics: Oct-Nov, 1954 - No. 181, Sept-Oct, 1978

	GD 2.0	VG 4.0	FN 6.0	VF 8.0	VF/NM 9.0	NM- 9.2
1-Grandenetti-c/a	152	304	456	1254	2827	4400
2	62	124	186	500	1125	1750
3-Kubert-c; last precode issue (3/55)	46	92	138	359	805	1250
4,5	38	76	114	285	641	1000
6-9: 7-1st S.A. issue	31	62	93	223	499	775
10-Wood-a	34	68	102	245	548	850
11-19	27	54	81	189	420	650
20-Grey tone-c (4/57)	36	72	108	266	596	925
21-30	22	44	66	154	340	525
31-40	19	38	57	131	291	450
41-Unknown Soldier tryout	26	52	78	182	404	625
42-44	18	36	54	128	284	440
45-1st app. of Gunner & Sarge, app. thru #94	62	124	186	496	1123	1750
46	28	56	84	202	451	700
47	20	40	60	138	307	475
48,50	16	32	48	110	243	375
49-1st Pooch	30	60	90	216	483	750
51-Grey tone-c	29	58	87	209	467	725
52-64: 64-Last 10¢ issue	13	26	39	89	195	300
65-70: 66-Panel inspired a famous Roy Lichtenstein painting	10	20	30	68	144	220
71-Classic grey tone-c; Pooch fires machine gun; panel inspired a famous Roy Lichtenstein painting	27	54	81	189	420	650
72-80	9	18	27	60	120	180
81-90	8	16	24	51	96	140
91-98: 95-Devil-Dog begins, ends #98.	6	12	18	41	76	110
99-Capt. Hunter begins, ends #106	7	14	21	49	92	135
100	6	12	18	41	76	110
101-105,107-120: 116-Mlle. Marie app. 120-Last 12¢ issue	5	10	15	31	53	75
106-Hunters Hellcats begin	5	10	15	33	57	80
121,122: 121-Intro. Heller	4	8	12	28	47	65
123-The Losers (Capt. Storm, Gunner & Sarge, Johnny Cloud) begin	10	20	30	66	138	210
124-132: 132-Last 15¢ issue	4	8	12	25	40	55
133-137 (Giants). 134-Toth-a	4	8	12	28	47	65
138-145,147-150: 149-Frank Thorne-c	3	6	9	17	25	34
146-Classic "Burma Sky" story; Toth-a/Goodwin-s	3	6	9	18	28	38
151-162-Kirby a(p)	3	6	9	20	31	42
163-180	3	6	9	14	20	26
181-Last issue	3	6	9	17	25	34
... (War One-Shot) 1 (11/10, $3.99) The Losers app.; B. Clay Moore-s/Chad Hardin-a						4.00

NOTE: ***N. Adams** c-147. **Drucker** a-28, 37, 39, 42-44, 49, 53, 133r. **Evans** a-149, 164-174, 177-181. **Glanzman** a-125-128, 132, 134, 138-141, 143, 144. **Heath** a-2, 16, 18, 28, 41, 44, 49, 50, 59, 64, 114, 135-138r; c-51. **Kirby** a-151-162p; c-152-159. **Kubert** c/a in many issues. **Maurer** a-135. **Redondo** a-166. **Severin** a-123-130, 131i, 132-150.*

OUR FIGHTING FORCES GIANT
DC Comics: 2020 ($4.99, one-shot, 100 pgs., squarebound, Mass Market & Direct Market editions exist with different covers)

	GD 2.0	VG 4.0	FN 6.0	VF 8.0	VF/NM 9.0	NM- 9.2
1-New stories of The Unknown Soldier, Batwoman, and Batman w/Jim Lee-a and reprints from Men of War #4-7; art by Corben, Winslade, Kolins and others						5.00

OUR FIGHTING MEN IN ACTION (See Men In Action)

OUR FLAG COMICS
Ace Magazines: Aug, 1941 - No. 5, April, 1942

	GD 2.0	VG 4.0	FN 6.0	VF 8.0	VF/NM 9.0	NM- 9.2
1-Captain Victory, The Unknown Soldier (intro.) & The Three Cheers begin	300	600	900	2010	3505	5000
2-Origin The Flag (patriotic hero); 1st app?	219	438	657	1402	2401	3400
3-5: 5-Intro & 1st app. Mr. Risk	194	388	582	1242	2121	3000

NOTE: ***Anderson** a-1, 4. **Mooney** a-1, 2; c-2.*

OUR GANG COMICS (With Tom & Jerry #39-59; becomes Tom & Jerry #60 on; based on film characters)
Dell Publishing Co.: Sept-Oct, 1942 - No. 59, June, 1949

	GD 2.0	VG 4.0	FN 6.0	VF 8.0	VF/NM 9.0	NM- 9.2
1-Our Gang & Barney Bear by Kelly, Tom & Jerry, Pete Smith, Flip & Dip, The Milky Way begin (all 1st app.)	114	228	342	912	2056	3200
2-Benny Burro begins (#2 by Kelly)	46	92	138	368	834	1300
3-5	25	50	75	175	388	600
6-Bumbazine & Albert only app. by Kelly	31	62	93	223	499	775
7-No Kelly story	17	34	51	119	265	410
8-Benny Burro begins by Barks	42	84	126	311	706	1100
9-Barks-a(2): Benny Burro & Happy Hound; no Kelly story	38	76	114	281	628	975
10-Benny Burro by Barks	27	54	81	189	420	650
11-1st Barney Bear & Benny Burro by Barks (5-6/44); Happy Hound by Barks	34	68	102	242	541	840
12-20	16	32	48	110	243	375
21-30: 30-X-Mas-c	11	22	33	77	166	255
31-36-Last Barks issue	9	18	27	63	129	195
37-40	7	14	21	44	82	120
41-50	6	12	18	38	69	100

	GD 2.0	VG 4.0	FN 6.0	VF 8.0	VF/NM 9.0	NM- 9.2
51-57	6	12	18	37	66	95
58,59-No Kelly art or Our Gang stories	5	10	15	35	63	90
Our Gang Volume 1 (Fantagraphics Books, 2006, $12.95, TPB) r/Our Gang stories written and by Walt Kelly from #1-8; Leonard Maltin intro.; Jeff Smith-c						13.00
Our Gang Volume 2 (Fantagraphics Books, 2007, $12.95, TPB) r/Our Gang stories written and by Walt Kelly from #9-15; Steve Thompson intro.; Jeff Smith-c						13.00
Our Gang Volume 3 (Fantagraphics Books, 2008, $14.99, TPB) r/Our Gang stories written and by Walt Kelly from #16-23; Steve Thompson intro.; Jeff Smith-c						15.00

NOTE: **Barks** art in part only. **Barks** did not write Barney Bear stories #30-34. (See March of Comics #3, 26). Early issues have photo back-c.

OUR LADY OF FATIMA (Also see Fatima...)
Catechetical Guild Educational Society: 3/11/55 (15¢) (36 pgs.)

	GD	VG	FN	VF	VF/NM	NM-
395	6	12	18	31	38	45

OUR LOVE (True Secrets #3 on? or Romantic Affairs #3 on?)
Marvel Comics (SPC): Sept, 1949 - No. 2, Jan, 1950

	GD	VG	FN	VF	VF/NM	NM-
1-Photo-c	32	64	96	188	307	425
2-Photo-c	19	38	57	111	176	240

OUR LOVE STORY
Marvel Comics Group: Oct, 1969 - No. 38, Feb, 1976

	GD	VG	FN	VF	VF/NM	NM-
1	13	26	39	86	188	290
2	7	14	21	49	92	135
3,4,6-8,10,11	6	12	18	38	69	100
5-Steranko-a	12	24	36	80	173	265
9,12-Kirby-a	6	12	18	38	69	100
13-(10/71, 52 pgs.)	6	12	18	38	69	100
14-New story by Gary Fredrich & Tarpe' Mills	5	10	15	34	60	85
15-20,27:27-Colan/Everett-a(r?); Kirby/Colletta-r	4	8	12	27	44	60
21-26,28-37	4	8	12	25	40	55
38-Last issue	4	8	12	28	47	65

NOTE: **J. Buscema** a-1-3, 5-7, 9, 13r, 16r, 19r(2), 21r, 22r(2), 23r, 34r, 35r; c-11, 13, 16, 22, 23, 24, 27, 35. **Colan** a-3-6, 21r(#6), 22r, 23r(#3), 24r(#4), 27; c-19. **Katz** a-17. **Maneely** a-13r. **Romita** a-13r; c-1, 2, 4-6. **Weiss** a-16, 17, 29r(#17).

OUR MEN AT WAR
DC Comics: Aug/Sept 1952

nn - Ashcan comic, not distributed to newsstands, only for in-house use. Cover art is All Star Western #60, interior being Detective Comics #181 (a FN/VF copy sold for $1195 in 2012)

OUR MISS BROOKS
Dell Publishing Co.: No. 751, Nov, 1956

	GD	VG	FN	VF	VF/NM	NM-
Four Color 751-Photo-c	9	18	27	59	117	175

OUR SECRET (Exciting Love Stories)(Formerly My Secret)
Superior Comics Ltd.: No. 4, Nov, 1949 - No. 8, Jun, 1950

	GD	VG	FN	VF	VF/NM	NM-
4-Kamen-a; spanking scene	37	74	111	222	361	500
5,6,8	17	34	51	98	154	210
7-Contains 9 pg. story intended for unpublished Ellery Queen #5; lingerie panels	19	38	57	111	176	240

OUT
Artists, Writers & Artisans, Inc.: Oct, 2021 - No. 5, Feb, 2022 ($3.99, limited series)

	GD	VG	FN	VF	VF/NM	NM-
1-Rob Williams-s/Will Conrad-a; vampire in a Nazi POW fortress						4.00

OUTCAST, THE
Valiant: Dec, 1995 ($2.50, one-shot)

	GD	VG	FN	VF	VF/NM	NM-
1-Breyfogle-a						3.00

OUTCAST BY KIRKMAN & AZACETA
Image Comics: Jun, 2014 - No. 48, Apr, 2021 ($2.99/$3.99)

	GD	VG	FN	VF	VF/NM	NM-
1-Kirkman-s/Azaceta-a/c						10.00
2						5.00
3-47: 25-(25¢-c)						4.00
48-($4.99) Last issue						5.00

OUTCASTS
DC Comics: Oct, 1987 - No. 12, Sept, 1988 ($1.75, limited series)

	GD	VG	FN	VF	VF/NM	NM-
1-12: John Wagner & Alan Grant scripts in all						3.00

OUTER DARKNESS
Image Comics (Skybound): Nov, 2018 - Present ($3.99)

	GD	VG	FN	VF	VF/NM	NM-
1-12-John Layman-s/Afu Chan-a						4.00
.../ Chew (3/20 - Present, $3.99) 1-3-Tony Chu brought to the future						4.00

OUTER LIMITS, THE (TV)
Dell Publishing Co.: Jan-Mar, 1964 - No. 18, Oct, 1969 (Most painted-c)

	GD	VG	FN	VF	VF/NM	NM-
1	13	26	39	91	201	310
2-5	7	14	21	49	92	135
6-10	6	12	18	40	73	105
11-18: 17-Reprints #1. 18-r/#2	5	10	15	34	60	85

OUTER SPACE (Formerly This Magazine Is Haunted, 2nd Series)
Charlton Comics: No. 17, May, 1958 - No. 25, Dec, 1959; Nov, 1968

	GD	VG	FN	VF	VF/NM	NM-
17-Williamson/Wood-a	16	32	48	92	144	195
18-20-Ditko-a	28	56	84	165	270	375
21-Ditko-c	22	44	66	130	213	295
22-25	15	30	45	88	137	185
V2#1(11/68)-Ditko-a, Boyette-c	5	10	15	35	63	90

OUT FOR BLOOD
Dark Horse: Sept, 1999 - No. 4, Dec, 1999 ($2.95, B&W, limited series)

	GD	VG	FN	VF	VF/NM	NM-
1-4-Kelley Jones-c; Erskine-a						3.00

OUTLANDERS (Manga)
Dark Horse Comics: Dec, 1988 - No. 33, Sept,1991 ($2.00-$2.50, B&W, 44 pgs.)

	GD	VG	FN	VF	VF/NM	NM-
1-33: Japanese Sci-fi manga						4.00

OUTLAW (See Return of the...)

OUTLAWED
Marvel Comics: May, 2020 ($4.99, one-shot)

	GD	VG	FN	VF	VF/NM	NM-
1-Eve L. Ewing-s/Kim Jacinto-a; teen heroes banned; leads into Champions #1 (2020)	1	3	4	6	8	10

OUTLAW FIGHTERS
Atlas Comics (IPC): Aug, 1954 - No. 5, Apr, 1955

	GD	VG	FN	VF	VF/NM	NM-
1-Tuska-a	19	38	57	112	179	245
2-5: 5-Heath-c/a, 7 pgs.	14	28	42	80	115	150

NOTE: **Colan** a-4. **Hartley** a-3. **Heath** c/a-5. **Maneely** c-2, 4. **Pakula** a-2. **Reinman** a-2, 4. **Tuska** a-1-3.

OUTLAW KID, THE (1st Series; see Wild Western)
Atlas Comics (CCC No. 1-11/EPI No. 12-29): Sept, 1954 - No. 19, Sept, 1957

	GD	VG	FN	VF	VF/NM	NM-
1-Origin; The Outlaw Kid & his horse Thunder begin; Black Rider app.	41	82	123	256	428	600
2-Black Rider app.	19	38	57	111	176	240
3-7,9: 3-Wildey-a(3)	15	30	45	85	130	175
8-Williamson/Woodbridge-a, 4 pgs.	15	30	45	86	133	180
10-Williamson-a	15	30	45	86	133	180
11-17,19: 13-Baker text illo. 15-Williamson text illo (unsigned)	13	26	39	72	101	130
18-Williamson/Mayo-a	14	28	42	76	108	140

NOTE: **Berg** a-4, 7, 13. **Maneely** c-1-3, 5-8, 11-13, 15, 16, 18. **Pakula** a-3. **Severin** c-10, 17, 19. **Shores** a-1. **Wildey** a-1(3), 2-8, 10, 11, 12(4), 13(4), 15-19(4 each); c-4.

OUTLAW KID, THE (2nd Series)
Marvel Comics Group: Aug, 1970 - No. 30, Oct, 1975

	GD	VG	FN	VF	VF/NM	NM-
1-Reprints; 1-Orlando-r, Wildey-r(3)	4	8	12	28	47	65
2,3,9: 2-Reprints. 3,9-Williamson-a(r)	2	4	6	13	18	22
4-7: 7-Last 15¢ issue	2	4	6	11	16	20
8-Double size (52 pgs.); Crandall-r	3	6	9	16	24	32
10-Origin	3	6	9	19	30	40
11-20: new-a in #10-16	2	4	6	13	18	22
21-30: 27-Origin-r/#10	2	4	6	9	13	16

NOTE: **Ayers** a-10, 27r. **Berg** a-7, 25r. **Everett** a-2(2 pgs.). **Gil Kane** c-10, 11, 15, 27r, 28. **Roussos** a-10i, 27i(r). **Severin** c-1, 9, 20, 25. **Wildey** r-1-4, 6-9, 19-22, 25, 26. **Williamson** a-28r. **Woodbridge/Williamson** a-9r.

OUTLAW NATION
DC Comics (Vertigo): Nov, 2000 - No. 19, May, 2002 ($2.50)

	GD	VG	FN	VF	VF/NM	NM-
1-19-Fabry painted-c/Delano-s/Sudzuka-a						3.00
TPB (Image Comics, 11/06, $15.99) B&W reprint of #1-19; Delano intro.						16.00

OUTLAW PRINCE, THE
Dark Horse Books: 2011 ($12.99, SC, 80 pgs.)

	GD	VG	FN	VF	VF/NM	NM-
SC-Adaptation of ERB's The Outlaw of Torn; Rob Hughes-s/Thomas Yeates painted-a; origin/1st app. Norman of Torn; intro. & death of Lady Maud						13.00
Deluxe HC Limited Edition ($49.99, 112 pgs.) Bonus 2 articles (approx. 200 signed)						50.00

OUTLAWS
D. S. Publishing Co.: Feb-Mar, 1948 - No. 9, June-July, 1949

	GD	VG	FN	VF	VF/NM	NM-
1-Violent & suggestive stories	40	80	120	246	411	575
2-Ingels-a; Baker-a	42	84	126	265	445	625
3,5,6: 3-Not Frazetta. 5-Sky Sheriff by Good app. 6-McWilliams-a	20	40	60	117	189	260
4-Orlando-a	21	42	63	122	199	275
7,8-Ingels-a in each	29	58	87	172	281	390
9-(Scarce)-Frazetta-a (7 pgs.)	61	122	183	390	670	950

NOTE: *Another #3 was printed in Canada with* **Frazetta** *art "Prairie Jinx," 7 pgs.*

OUTLAWS, THE (Formerly Western Crime Cases)
Star Publishing Co.: No. 10, May, 1952 - No. 13, Sep, 1953; No. 14, Apr, 1954

	GD	VG	FN	VF	VF/NM	NM-
10-L.B. Cole-c	28	56	84	165	270	375
11-14-L.B. Cole-c. 14-Reprints Western Thrillers #4 (Fox) w/new L.B. Cole-c; Kamen, Feldstein-r	21	42	63	122	199	275

OUTLAWS
DC Comics: Sept, 1991 - No. 8, Apr, 1992 ($1.95, limited series)

	GD	VG	FN	VF	VF/NM	NM-
1-8: Post-apocalyptic Robin Hood.						3.00

OUTLAWS OF THE WEST (Formerly Cody of the Pony Express #10)
Charlton Comics: No. 11, 7/57 - No. 81, 5/70; No. 82, 7/79 - No. 88, 4/80

	GD	VG	FN	VF	VF/NM	NM-
11	9	18	27	47	61	75
12,13,15-17,19,20	6	12	18	27	33	38
14-(68 pgs., 2/58)	9	18	27	50	65	80
18-Ditko-a	10	20	30	56	76	95
21-30	3	6	9	16	23	30
31-50: 34-Gunmaster app.	2	4	6	13	18	22
51-63,65,67-70: 54-Kid Montana app.	2	4	6	10	14	18
64,66: 64-Captain Doom begins (1st app.). 68-Kid Montana series begins	2	4	6	13	18	22
71-79: 73-Origin & 1st app. The Sharp Shooter, last app. #74. 75-Last Capt. Doom	2	4	6	9	12	15
80,81-Ditko-a	2	4	6	13	18	22
82-88						6.00
64,79(Modern Comics-r, 1977, '78)						6.00

OUTLAWS OF THE WILD WEST
Avon Periodicals: 1952 (25¢, 132 pgs.) (4 rebound comics)

	GD	VG	FN	VF	VF/NM	NM-
1-Wood back-c; Kubert-a (3 Jesse James-r)	43	86	129	271	461	650

OUTLAW TRAIL (See Zane Grey 4-Color 511)

OUT OF BODY
AfterShock Comics: Jun, 2021 - No. 5, Oct, 2021 ($4.99/$3.99)

	GD	VG	FN	VF	VF/NM	NM-
1-($4.99) Peter Milligan-s/Inaki Miranda-a						5.00
2-5-($3.99)						4.00

OUT OF SANTA'S BAG (See March of Comics #10 in the Promotional Comics section)

OUT OF THE NIGHT (The Hooded Horseman #18 on)
Amer. Comics Group (Creston/Scope): Feb-Mar, 1952 - No. 17, Oct-Nov, 1954

	GD	VG	FN	VF	VF/NM	NM-
1-Williamson/LeDoux-a (9 pgs.); ACG's 1st editor's page	239	478	717	1530	2615	3700
2-Williamson-a (5 pgs.)	65	130	195	416	708	1000
3,5-10: 9-Sci/Fic story	41	82	123	256	428	600
4-Williamson-a (7 pgs.)	57	114	171	362	619	875

Outcast #4 © Robert Kirkman

Outpost Zero #8 © Skybound

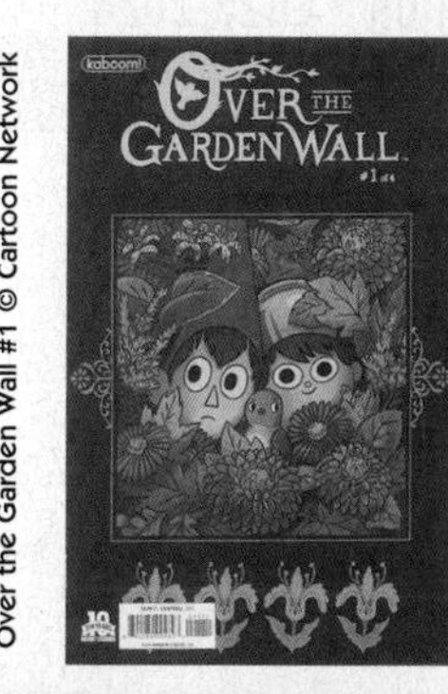

Over the Garden Wall #1 © Cartoon Network

GD 2.0 | VG 4.0 | FN 6.0 | VF 8.0 | VF/NM 9.0 | NM- 9.2

11-17: 13-Nostrand-a? 17-E.C. Wood swipe 35 70 105 208 339 470
NOTE: *Landau a-14, 16, 17. Shelly a-12.*

OUT OF THE SHADOWS
Standard Comics/Visual Editions: No. 5, July, 1952 - No. 14, Aug, 1954

5-Toth-p; Moreira, Tuska-a; Roussos-c 106 212 318 673 1162 1650
6-Toth/Celardo-a; Katz-a(2) 54 108 162 343 574 825
7,9: 7-Jack Katz-c/a(2). 9-Crandall-a(2) 48 96 144 302 514 725
8-Katz shrunken head-c 206 412 618 1318 2259 3200
10-Spider-c; Sekowsky-a 135 270 405 864 1482 2100
11-Toth-a, 2 pgs.; Katz-a; Andru-c 48 96 144 302 514 725
12-Toth/Peppe-a(2); Katz-a 61 122 183 390 670 950
13-Cannabalism story; Sekowsky-a; Roussos-c 65 130 195 416 708 1000
14-Toth-a 50 100 150 315 533 750

OUT OF THE VORTEX (Comics' Greatest World:... #1-4)
Dark Horse Comics: Oct., 1993 - No. 12, Oct, 1994 ($2.00, limited series)

1-12: 1-Foil logo. 4-Dorman-c(p). 6-Hero Zero x-over. 12-$2.50-c 3.00
NOTE: ***Art Adams** c-7. **Golden** c-8. **Mignola** c-2. **Simonson** c-3. **Zeck** c-10.*

OUT OF THIS WORLD
Charlton Comics: Aug, 1956 - No. 16, Dec, 1959

1 41 82 123 256 428 600
2 20 40 60 117 189 260
3-6-Ditko-c/a (3) each 37 74 111 222 361 500
7-(2/58, 15¢, 68 pgs.)-Ditko-c/a(4) 39 78 117 240 395 550
8-(5/58, 15¢, 68 pgs.)-Ditko-a(2) 39 78 117 240 395 550
9,10,12,16-Ditko-a 27 54 81 162 266 370
11-Ditko c/a (3) 36 72 108 214 347 480
13,15 15 30 45 85 130 175
14-Matt Baker-a, 7 pg. story 17 34 51 98 154 210
NOTE: ***Ditko** c-3-12, 16. **Reinman** a-10.*

OUT OF THIS WORLD
Avon Periodicals: June, 1950; Aug, 1950

1-Kubert-a(2) (one reprinted/Eerie #1, 1947) plus Crom the Barbarian by Gardner Fox & John Giunta (origin); Fawcette-c 168 336 504 1075 1838 2600
1-(8/50) Reprint; no month on cover 84 168 252 538 919 1300

OUT OF THIS WORLD ADVENTURES
Avon Periodicals: July, 1950 - No. 2, Apr, 1951 (25¢ sci-fi pulp magazine with 32-page color comic insert)

1-Kubert-a(2); Crom the Barbarian by Fox & Giunta; text stories by Cummings, Van Vogt, del Rey, Chandler 110 220 330 704 1202 1700
2-Kubert-a plus The Spider God of Akka by Gardner Fox & John Giunta pulp magazine w/comic insert; Wood-a (21 pgs.); mentioned in **SOTI,** page 120 65 130 195 416 708 1000

OUT OUR WAY WITH WORRY WART
Dell Publishing Co.: No. 680, Feb, 1956

Four Color 680 5 10 15 35 63 90

OUTPOSTS
Blackthorne Publishing: June, 1987 - No. 4, 1987 ($1.25)

1-4: 1-Kaluta-c(p) 3.00

OUTSIDERS, THE
DC Comics: Nov, 1985 - No. 28, Feb, 1988

1 4.00
2-28: 18-26-Batman returns. 21-Intro. Strike Force Kobra; 1st app. Clayface IV. 22-E.C. parody; Orlando-a. 21- 25-Atomic Knight app. 27,28-Millennium tie-ins 3.00
Annual 1 (12/86, $2.50), Special 1 (7/87, $1.50) 4.00
NOTE: ***Aparo** a-1-7, 9-14, 17-22, 25, 26; c-1-7, 9-14, 17, 19-26. **Byrne** a-11. **Bolland** a-6, 18; c-16. **Ditko** a-13p. **Erik Larsen** a-24, 27 28; c-27, 28. **Morrow** a-12.*

OUTSIDERS
DC Comics: Nov, 1993 - No. 24, Nov, 1995 ($1.75/$1.95/$2.25)

1-11,0,12-24: 1-Alpha; Travis Charest-c. 1-Omega; Travis Charest-c. 5-Atomic Knight app. 8-New Batman-c/story. 11-(9/94)-Zero Hour. 0-(10/94).12-(11/94). 21-Darkseid cameo. 22-New Gods app. 3.00

OUTSIDERS (See Titans/Young Justice: Graduation Day)(Leads into Batman and the Outsiders)
DC Comics: Aug, 2003 - No. 50, Nov, 2007 ($2.50/$2.99)

1-Nightwing, Arsenal, Metamorpho app.; Winick-s/Raney-a 5.00
2-Joker and Grodd app. 4.00
3-33: 3-Joker-c. 5,6-ChrisCross-a. 8-Huntress app. 9,10-Capt. Marvel Jr. app. 24,25-X-over with Teen Titans. 26,27-Batman & old Outsiders 3.00
34-50: 34-One Year Later. 36-Begin $2.99-c. 37-Superman app. 44-Red Hood app. 3.00
Annual 1 (6/07, $3.99) McDaniel-a; Black LIghtning app. 4.00
.../Checkmate: Checkout TPB (2008, $14.99) r/#47-49 & Checkmate #13-15 15.00
... Double Feature (10/03, $4.95) r/#1,2 5.00
...: Crisis Intervention TPB (2006, $12.99) r/#29-33 13.00
...: Looking For Trouble TPB (2004, $12.95) r/#1-7 & Teen Titans/Outsiders Secret Files & Origins 2003; intro. by Winick 13.00
...: Pay As You Go TPB (2007, $14.99) r/#42-46 & Annual #1 15.00
...: Sum of All Evil TPB (2004, $14.95) r/#8-15 15.00
...: The Good Fight TPB (2006, $14.99) r/#34-41 15.00
...: Wanted TPB (2005, $14.99) r/#16-23 15.00

OUTSIDERS, THE (See Batman and the Outsiders for #1-14 and #40)
DC Comics: No. 15, Apr, 2009 - No. 39, Jun, 2011 ($2.99)

15-23,26-39: 15-Alfred assembles a new team; Garbett-a. 17-19-Deathstroke app. 3.00
24,25-($3.99) Blackest Night; Terra rises as a Black Lantern 4.00
...: The Deep TPB (2009, $14.99) r/#15-20 & Batman and the Outsiders Special #1 15.00
...: The Great Divide TPB (2011, $17.99) r/#32-40; cover gallery 18.00
...: The Hunt TPB (2010, $14.99) r/#21-25 15.00
...: The Road to Hell TPB (2010, $14.99) r/#26-31 15.00

OUTSIDERS: FIVE OF A KIND (Bridges Outsiders #49 & 50)
DC Comics: Oct, 2007 ($2.99, weekly limited series)

...Katana/Shazam! (part 2 of 5) - Barr-s/Sharpe-a 3.00
...Metamorpho/Aquaman (part 4 of 5) - Wilson-s/Middleton-a 3.00
...Nightwing/Captain Boomerang (part 1 of 5) - DeFilippis & Weir-s/Willams-a 3.00
...Thunder/Martian Manhunter (part 3 of 5) - Bedard-s/Turnbull-a; Grayven app. 3.00
...Wonder Woman/Grace (part 5 of 5) - Andreyko-s/Richards-a 3.00
TPB (2008, $14.99) r/series & Outsiders #50 15.00

OUT THERE
DC Comics(Cliffhanger): July, 2001 - No. 18, Aug, 2003 ($2.50/$2.95)

1-Humberto Ramos-c/a; Brian Augustyn-s 3.00
1-Variant-c by Carlos Meglia 4.00
2-18: 3-Variant-c by Bruce Timm. 9-Begin $2.95-c 3.00
...: The Evil Within TPB (2002, $12.95) r/#1-6; Ramos sketch pages 13.00

OVERKILL: WITCHBLADE/ ALIENS/ DARKNESS/ PREDATOR
Image Comics/Dark Horse Comics: Dec, 2000 - No. 2, 2001 ($5.95)

1,2-Jenkins-s/Lansing, Ching & Benitez-a 6.00

OVERTAKEN
Aspen/MLT: Aug, 2013 - No. 5, Jan, 2018 ($1.00/$3.99)

1-5-Mastromauro-s/Lorenzana-a; multiple covers on each. 1-($1.00-c). 2-(3/16) 4.00

OVER THE EDGE
Marvel Comics: Nov, 1995 - No. 10, Aug, 1996 (99¢)

1-10: 1,6,10-Daredevil-c/story. 2,7-Dr. Strange-c/story. 3-Hulk-c/story. 4,9-Ghost Rider-c/story. 5-Punisher-c/story. 8-Elektra-c/story 3.00

OVER THE GARDEN WALL (Based on the Cartoon Network mini-series)
Boom Entertainment (KaBOOM!): Aug, 2015 - No. 4, Nov, 2015 ($3.99, limited series)

1-4-Pat McHale-s/Jim Campbell-a; multiple covers on each 4.00
Special 1 (11/14, $4.99)-Prequel to the Cartoon Network mini-series; McHale-s/Campbell-a 5.00

OVER THE GARDEN WALL: HOLLOW TOWN (Cartoon Network)
Boom Entertainment (KaBOOM!): Sept, 2018 - No. 5, Jan, 2019 ($3.99, limited series)

1-5-Celia Lowenthal-s/Jorge Monlongo-a; multiple covers on each 4.00

OVER THE GARDEN WALL ONGOING (Cartoon Network)
Boom Entertainment (KaBOOM!): Apr, 2016 - No. 20, Nov, 2018 ($3.99, limited series)

1-20: 1-4-Two stories in each; Campbell-s/Burgos-a & Levari-s/McGee-a; multiple covers 4.00
... 2017 Special 1 (9/17, $7.99) Three stories; covers by Mercado & Derek Kim 8.00

OVER THE GARDEN WALL: SOULFUL SYMPHONIES (Cartoon Network)
Boom Entertainment (KaBOOM!): Aug, 2019 - No. 5, Dec, 2019 ($3.99, limited series)

1-5-Birdie Willis-s/Rowan MacColl-a; multiple covers on each 4.00

OVERWATCH: NEW BLOOD (Based on the video game)
Dark Horse Comics: Jul, 2022 - No. 5, Nov, 2022 ($3.99, limited series)

1-5-Ray Fawkes-s/Irene Koh-a 4.00

OVERWATCH: TRACER – LONDON CALLING (Based on the video game)
Dark Horse Comics: Dec, 2020 - No. 5, Apr, 2021 ($3.99, limited series)

1-5-Mariko Tamaki-s/Babs Tarr-a 4.00

OWL, THE (See Crackajack Funnies #25, Popular Comics #72 and Occult Files of Dr. Spektor #22)
Gold Key: April, 1967; No. 2, April, 1968

1-Written by Jerry Siegel; '40s super hero 5 10 15 34 60 85
2 4 8 12 28 47 65

GD VG FN VF VF/NM NM-
2.0 4.0 6.0 8.0 9.0 9.2

OWL, THE (See Project Superpowers)
Dynamite Entertainment: 2013 - No. 4, 2013 ($3.99, limited series)
1-4-Golden Age hero in modern times; Krul-s/H.K. Michael-a; covers by Ross & Syaf 4.00

OZ (See First Comics Graphic Novel, Marvel Treaury Of Oz & MGM's Marvelous...)

OZ
Caliber Press: 1994 - 1997 ($2.95, B&W)
0,1: 0-Released between #10 & #11 1 2 3 5 6 8
1 ($5.95)-Limited Edition; double-c 1 3 4 6 8 10
2-20 3.00
...Specials: Freedom Fighters. Lion. Scarecrow. Tin Man 5.00

OZARK IKE
Dell Publishing Co./Standard Comics B11 on: Feb, 1948; Nov, 1948 - No. 24, Dec, 1951; No. 25, Sept, 1952
Four Color 180(1948-Dell) 12 24 36 83 182 280
B11, B12, 13-15 15 30 45 83 124 165
16-25 14 28 42 76 108 140

OZ: DAEMONSTORM
Caliber Press: 1997 ($3.95, B&W, one-shot)
1 4.00

OZMA OF OZ (Dorothy Gale from Wonderful Wizard of Oz)
Marvel Comics: Jan, 2011 - No. 8, Sept, 2011 ($3.99, limited series)
1-6-Eric Shanower-s/Skottie Young-a/c 4.00
Oz Primer (5/11, $3.99) creator interviews and character profiles 4.00

OZ: ROMANCE IN RAGS
Caliber Press: 1996 ($2.95, B&W, limited series)
1-3, ..Special 3.00

OZ SQUAD
Brave New Worlds/Patchwork Press: 1992 - No. 4, 1994 ($2.50/$2.75, B&W)
1-4-Patchwork Press 3.00

OZ SQUAD
Patchwork Press: Dec, 1995 - No. 10, 1996 ($3.95/$2.95, B&W)
1-($3.95) 4.00
2-10 3.00

OZ: STRAW AND SORCERY
Caliber Press: 1997 ($2.95, B&W, limited series)
1-3 3.00

OZ-WONDERLAND WARS, THE
DC Comics: Jan, 1986 - No. 3, March, 1986 (Mini-series)(Giants)
1-3-Capt. Carrot app.; funny animals 6.00

OZZIE & BABS (TV Teens #14 on)
Fawcett Publications: Dec, 1947 - No. 13, Fall, 1949
1-Teen-age 17 34 51 100 158 215
2 11 22 33 62 86 110
3-13 10 20 30 54 72 90

OZZIE AND HARRIET (The Adventures of... on cover) (Radio)
National Periodical Publications: Oct-Nov, 1949 - No. 5, June-July, 1950
1-Photo-c 116 232 348 742 1271 1800
2 54 108 162 343 574 825
3-5 45 90 135 284 480 675

OZZY OSBOURNE (Todd McFarlane Presents)
Image Comics (Todd McFarlane Prod.): June, 1999 ($4.95, magazine-sized)
1-Bio, interview and comic story; Ormston painted-a; Ashley Wood-c
1 2 3 5 6 8

PACIFIC COMICS GRAPHIC NOVEL (See Image Graphic Novel)

PACIFIC PRESENTS (Also see Starslayer #2, 3)
Pacific Comics: Oct, 1982 - No. 2, Apr, 1983; No. 3, Mar, 1984 - No. 4, Jun, 1984
1-Chapter 3 of The Rocketeer; Stevens-c/a; Bettie Page model
3 6 9 16 23 30
2-Chapter 4 of The Rocketeer (4th app.); nudity; Stevens-c/a
2 4 6 13 18 22
3,4: 3-1st app. Vanity 4.00
NOTE: ***Conrad** a-3, 4; c-3. **Ditko** a-1-3; c-1(1/2). **Dave Stevens** a-1, 2; c-1(1/2), 2.*

PACIFIC RIM: AFTERMATH
Legendary Comics: Jan, 2018 - No. 5, May, 2018 ($3.99)
1-5-Cavan Scott-s 4.00

PACIFIC RIM: TALES FROM THE DRIFT
Legendary Comics: Nov, 2015 - No. 4, Apr, 2016 ($3.99)
1-4-Beachum & Fialkov-s/Marz-a 4.00

PACIFIC RIM: TALES FROM YEAR ZERO
Legendary Comics: Jun, 2013 ($24.99, HC graphic novel)
HC - Prequel to the 2013 movie; Beacham-s/Alex Ross-c; art by various 25.00

PACT, THE
Image Comics: Feb, 1994 - No. 3, June, 1994 ($1.95, limited series)
1-3: Valentino co-scripts & layouts 3.00

PACT, THE
Image Comics: Apr, 2005 - No. 4, Jan, 2006 ($2.99/$2.95)
1-4: Invincible, Shadowhawk, Firebreather & Zephyr team-up. 1-Valentino-s/a 3.00

PAGEANT OF COMICS (See Jane Arden & Mopsy)
Archer St. John: Sept, 1947 - No. 2, Oct, 1947
1-Mopsy strip-r 25 50 75 150 245 340
2-Jane Arden strip-r 15 30 45 88 137 185

PAINKILLER JANE
Event Comics: June, 1997 - No. 5, Nov, 1997 ($3.95/$2.95)
1-Augustyn/Waid-s/Leonardi/Palmiotti-a, variant-c 4.00
2-5: Two covers (Quesada, Leonardi) 3.00
0-(1/99, $3.95) Retells origin; two covers 4.00
Essential Painkiller Jane TPB (2007, $19.99) r/#0-5; cover gallery and pin-ups 20.00

PAINKILLER JANE
Dynamite Entertainment: 2006 - No. 3, 2006 ($2.99)
1-3-Quesada & Palmiotti-s/Moder-a. 1-Four covers by Q&P, Moder, Tan and Conner 3.00
Volume #1 TPB (2007, $9.99) r/#1-3; cover gallery and Palmiotti interview 10.00

PAINKILLER JANE
Dynamite Entertainment: No. 0, 2007 - No. 5, 2007 ($3.50)
0-(25¢) Quesada & Palmiotti-s/Moder-a 3.00
1-5-($3.50) 1-Continued from #0; 5 covers. 4,5-Crossover with Terminator 2 #6,7 3.50
Volume #2 TPB (2007, $11.99) r/#0-3; cover gallery 12.00

PAINKILLER JANE / DARKCHYLDE
Event Comics: Oct, 1998 ($2.95, one-shot)
Preview-($6.95) DF Edition, 1-($6.95) DF Edition 7.00
1-Three covers; J.G. Jones-a 3.00

PAINKILLER JANE / HELLBOY
Event Comics: Aug, 1998 ($2.95, one-shot)
1-Leonardi & Palmiotti-a 5.00

PAINKILLER JANE: THE PRICE OF FREEDOM
Marvel Comics (ICON): Nov, 2013 - No. 4, Jan, 2014 ($3.99/$2.99, limited series)
1-($3.99) Palmiotti-s/Santacruz & Lotfi-a; covers by Amanda Conner & Dave Johnson 4.00
2-4-($2.99) Santacruz-a/Conner-c 3.00

PAINKILLER JANE: THE 22 BRIDES
Marvel Comics (ICON): May, 2014 - No. 3, Oct, 2014 ($4.99/$3.99, limited series)
1-($4.99) Palmiotti-s/Santacruz & Fernandez-a; covers by Christian & Conner 5.00
2,3-($3.99) Santacruz-a2-Photo-c. 3-Conner-c 4.00

PAINKILLER JANE VS. THE DARKNESS
Event Comics: Apr, 1997 ($2.95, one-shot)
1-Ennis-s; four variant-c (Conner, Hildebrandts, Quesada, Silvestri) 3.50

PAKLIS
Image Comics: May, 2017 - No. 5 ($5.99/$3.99/$4.99)
1,2,5-($5.99) Serialized anthology by Dustin Weaver-s/a/c 6.00
3-($3.99) Dustin Weaver-s/a/c 4.00
4-($4.99) Dustin Weaver-s/a/c 5.00

PANCHO VILLA
Avon Periodicals: 1950
nn-Kinstler-c 34 68 102 199 325 450

PANDEMICA
IDW Publishing: Sept, 2019 - No. 5, Jan, 2020 ($3.99)
1-5-Jonathan Maberry-s/Alex Sanchez-a 4.00

PANHANDLE PETE AND JENNIFER (TV) (See Gene Autry #20)
J. Charles Laue Publishing Co.: July, 1951 - No. 3, Nov, 1951
1 14 28 42 82 121 160
2,3: 2-Interior photo-cvrs 10 20 30 54 72 90

PANIC (Companion to Mad)
E. C. Comics (Tiny Tot Comics): Feb-Mar, 1954 - No. 12, Dec-Jan, 1955-56
1-Used in Senate Investigation hearings; Elder draws entire E. C. staff; Santa Claus & Mickey Spillane parody 53 106 159 424 675 925
2-Atomic bomb-c 31 62 93 248 399 550
3,4: 3-Senate Subcommittee parody; Davis draws Gaines, Feldstein & Kelly, 1 pg.; Old King Cole smokes marijuana. 4-Infinity-c; John Wayne parody
20 40 60 160 255 350
5-11: 8-Last pre-code issue (5/55). 9-Superman, Smilin' Jack & Dick Tracy app. on-c; has photo of Walter Winchell on-c. 11-Wheedies cereal box-c
18 36 54 144 230 315
12 (Low distribution; thousands were destroyed) 26 52 78 208 334 460
NOTE: ***Davis** a-1-12; c-12. **Elder** a-1-12. **Feldstein** c-1-3, 5. **Kamen** a-1. **Orlando** a-1-9. **Wolverton** c-4, panel-3. **Wood** a-2-9, 11, 12.*

PANIC (Magazine) (Satire)
Panic Publ.: July, 1958 - No. 6, July, 1959; V2#10, Dec, 1965 - V2#12, 1966
1 14 28 42 80 115 150
2-6 9 18 27 50 65 80
V2#10-12: Reprints earlier issues 3 6 9 17 26 35
NOTE: ***Davis** a-3(2 pgs.), 4, 5, 10; c-10. **Elder** a-5. **Powell** a-V2#10, 11. **Torres** a-1-5. **Tuska** a-V2#11.*

PANIC
Gemstone Publishing: March, 1997 - No. 12, Dec, 1999 ($2.50, quarterly)
1-12: E.C. reprints 4.00

PANTHA (See Vampirella-The New Monthly #16,17)

PANTHA (Also see Prophecy)
Dynamite Entertainment: 2012 - No. 6, 2013 ($3.99)
1-6: 1-Jerwa-s/Rodrix-a; covers by Sean Chen & Texiera. 2-6-Texiera-c 4.00

PANTHA: HAUNTED PASSION (Also see Vampirella Monthly #0)
Harris Comics: May, 1997 ($2.95, B&W, one-shot)
1-r/Vampirella #30,31 3.00

PANTHA: VOLUME 2
Dynamite Entertainment: 2022 - Present ($3.99)
1-5-Sniegoski & Acheson-s/Lima-a 4.00

PANTHEON
IDW Publishing: Apr, 2010 - No. 5, Aug, 2010 ($3.99)
1-5-Andreyko-s/Molnar-a; co-created by Michael Chiklis 4.00

PAPA MIDNITE (See John Constantine - Hellblazer Special:...)

PAPER GIRLS

Ozma of Oz #4 © MAR

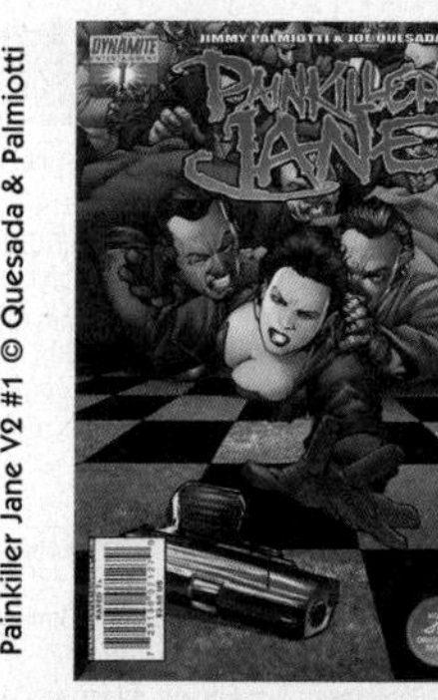

Painkiller Jane V2 #1 © Quesada & Palmiotti

Paper Girls #4 © Vaughn & Chiang

	GD	VG	FN	VF	VF/NM	NM-
	2.0	4.0	6.0	8.0	9.0	9.2

Image Comics: Oct, 2015 - No. 30, Jul, 2019 ($2.99/$3.99)
1-20-Brian K. Vaughn-s/Cliff Chiang-a 3.00
21-29-($3.99) 4.00
30-($4.99) Last issue 5.00

PARADE (See Hanna-Barbera...)

PARADE COMICS (See Frisky Animals on Parade)

PARADE OF PLEASURE
Derric Verschoyle Ltd., London, England: 1954 (192 pgs.) (Hardback book)
By Geoffrey Wagner. Contains section devoted to the censorship of American comic books with illustrations in color and black and white. (Also see **Seduction of the Innocent**). Distributed in USA by Library Publishers, N. Y. 163 326 489 652 814 975
with dust jacket.... 333 666 1000 1332 1666 2000

PARADISE TOO!
Abstract Studios: 2000 - No. 14, 2003 ($2.95, B&W)
1-14-Terry Moore's unpublished newspaper strips and sketches 3.00
Complete Paradise Too TPB (2010, $29.95) r/#1-14 with bonus material 30.00
...: Checking For Weirdos TPB (4/03, $14.95) r/#8-12 15.00
...: Drunk Ducks! TPB (7/02, $15.95) r/#1-7 16.00

PARADISE X (Also see Earth X and Universe X)
Marvel Comics: Apr, 2002 - No. 12, Aug, 2003 ($4.50/$2.99)
0-Ross-c; Braithwaite-a 4.50
1-12-($2.99) Ross-c; Braithwaite-a. 7-Punisher on-c. 10-Kingpin on-c 3.00
...:A (10/03, $2.99) Braithwaite-a; Ross-c 3.00
...:Devils (11/02, $4.50) Sadowski-a; Ross-c 4.50
...:Ragnarok 1,2 (3/02, 4/03; $2.99) Yeates-a; Ross-c 3.00
...:X (11/03, $2.99) Braithwaite-a; Ross-c; conclusion of story 3.00
...:Xen (7/02, $4.50) Yeowell & Sienkiewicz-a; Ross-c 4.50
Earth X Vol. 4: Paradise X Book 1 (2003, $29.99, TPB) r/#0,1-5, ...: Xen; Heralds #1-3 30.00
Vol. 5: Paradise X Book 2 (2004, $29.99, TPB) r/#6-12, Ragnarok #1&2; Devils, A & X 30.00

PARADISE X: HERALDS (Also see Earth X and Universe X)
Marvel Comics: Dec, 2001 - No. 3, Feb, 2002 ($3.50)
1-3-Prelude to Paradise X series; Ross-c; Pugh-a 3.50
Special Edition (Wizard preview) Ross-c 3.00

PARADOX
Dark Visions Publ: June, 1994 - No. 2, Aug, 1994 ($2.95, B&W, mature)
1,2: 1-Linsner-c. 2-Boris-c. 3.00

PARALLAX: EMERALD NIGHT (See Final Night)
DC Comics: Nov, 1996 ($2.95, one-shot, 48 pgs.)
1-Final Night tie-in; Green Lantern (Kyle Rayner) app. 4.00

PARAMOUNT ANIMATED COMICS (See Harvey Comics Hits #60, 62)
Harvey Publications: No. 3, Jun, 1953 - No. 22, Jul, 1956
3-Baby Huey, Herman & Katnip, Buzzy the Crow begin
36 72 108 211 343 475
4-6 16 32 48 92 144 195
7-Baby Huey becomes permanent cover feature; cover title becomes Baby Huey with #9
29 58 87 172 281 390
8-10: 9-Infinity-c 14 28 42 82 121 160
11-22 12 24 36 67 94 120

PARASOMNIA
Dark Horse Comics: Jun, 2021 - No. 4, Sept, 2021 ($3.99, limited series)
1-4-Cullen Bunn-s/Andrea Mutti-a 4.00

PARASOMNIA: THE DREAMING GOD
Dark Horse Comics: Aug, 2022 - No. 4, Nov, 2022 ($3.99, limited series)
1-4-Cullen Bunn-s/Andrea Mutti-a 4.00

PARENT TRAP, THE (Disney)
Dell Publishing Co.: No. 1210, Oct-Dec, 1961
Four Color 1210-Movie, Hayley Mills photo-c 10 20 30 64 132 200

PARIAH (Aron Warner's...)
Dark Horse Comics: Feb, 2014 - No. 8, Sept, 2014 ($3.99)
1-8-Aron Warner & Philip Gelatt-s/Brett Weldele-a 4.00

PARKER GIRLS (Characters from Strangers in Paradise)
Abstract Studio: 2022 - Present ($3.99, limited series)
1-5-Terry Moore-s/a; Katchoo & Tambi app. 4.00

PARLIAMENT OF JUSTICE
Image Comics: Mar, 2003 ($5.95, B&W, one-shot, square-bound)
1-Michael Avon Oeming-c/s; Neil Vokes-a 6.00

PARODY
Armour Publishing: Mar, 1977 - No. 3, Aug, 1977 (B&W humor magazine)
1 3 6 9 17 23 35
2,3: 2-King Kong, Happy Days. 3-Charlie's Angels, Rocky
2 4 6 10 14 18

PAROLE BREAKERS
Avon Periodicals/Realistic #2 on: Dec, 1951 - No. 3, July, 1952
1(#2 on inside)-r-c/Avon paperback #283 (painted-c)
66 132 198 419 722 1025
2-Kubert-a; r-c/Avon paperback #114 (photo-c) 52 104 156 328 552 775
3-Kinstler-c 42 84 126 265 445 625

PARTRIDGE FAMILY, THE (TV)(Also see David Cassidy)
Charlton Comics: Mar, 1971 - No. 21, Dec, 1973
1-(2 versions: B&W photo-c & tinted color photo-c) 8 16 24 54 102 150
2-4,6-10 5 10 15 30 50 70
5-Partridge Family Summer Special (52 pgs.); The Shadow, Lone Ranger, Charlie McCarthy, Flash Gordon, Hopalong Cassidy, Gene Autry & others app.
8 16 24 56 108 160
11-21 4 8 12 25 40 55

PARTS OF A HOLE
Caliber Press: 1991 ($2.50, B&W)
1-Short stories & cartoons by Brian Michael Bendis 3.00

PARTS UNKNOWN
Eclipse Comics/FX: July, 1992 - No. 4, Oct, 1992 ($2.50, B&W, mature)
1-4: All contain FX gaming cards 3.00

PARTS UNKNOWN
Image Comics: May, 2000 - Sept, 2000 ($2.95, B&W)
...: Killing Attractions 1 (5/00) Beau Smith-s/Brad Gorby-a 3.00
...: Hostile Takeover 1-4 (6-9/00) 3.00

PASSION, THE
Catechetical Guild: No. 394, 1955
394 9 18 27 52 69 85

PASSOVER (See Avengelyne)
Maximum Press: Dec, 1996 ($2.99, one-shot)
1 3.00

PAST AWAYS
Dark Horse Comics: Mar, 2015 - No. 9, Mar, 2016 ($3.99)
1-9: 1-Matt Kindt-s/Scott Kolins-a; two covers by Kolins & Kindt 4.00

PAT BOONE (TV)(Also see Superman's Girlfriend Lois Lane #9)
National Per. Publ.: Sept-Oct, 1959 - No. 5, May-Jun, 1960 (All have photo-c)
1 43 86 129 271 461 650
2-5: 3-Fabian, Connie Francis & Paul Anka photos on-c. 4-Previews "Journey To The Center Of The Earth". 4-Johnny Mathis & Bobby Darin photos on-c. 5-Dick Clark & Frankie Avalon photos on-c 35 70 105 208 339 470

PATCHES
Rural Home/Patches Publ. (Orbit): Mar-Apr, 1945 - No. 11, Nov, 1947
1-L. B. Cole-c 54 108 162 343 574 825
2 22 44 66 132 216 300
3,4,6,8-11: 6-Henry Aldrich story. 8-Smiley Burnette-c/s (6/47); pre-dates Smiley Burnette #1. 9-Mr. District Attorney story (radio). Leav/Keigstein-a (16 pgs.). 9-11-Leav-c. 10-Jack Carson (radio) c/story; Leav-c. 11-Red Skelton story 16 38 57 112 179 245
5-Danny Kaye-c/story; L.B. Cole-c. 24 48 72 142 234 325
7-Hopalong Cassidy-c/story 22 44 66 132 216 300

PATH, THE (Also see Negation War)
CrossGeneration Comics: Apr, 2002 - No. 23, Apr, 2004 ($2.95)
1-23: 1-Ron Marz-s/Bart Sears-a. 13-Matthew Smith-a begins 3.00

PATHFINDER (Based on the Pathfinder roleplaying game)
Dynamite Entertainment: 2012 - No. 12, 2013 ($3.99)
1-12: 1-Jim Zub-s/Andrew Huerta-a; four covers. 2-12-Multiple covers on each 4.00
... Special 2013 ($4.99, 40 pgs.) Jim Zub-s/Kevin Stokes-a 5.00

PATHFINDER: CITY OF SECRETS (Based on the Pathfinder roleplaying game)
Dynamite Entertainment: 2014 - No. 6, 2014 ($4.99)
1-6-Zub-s/Oliveira-a; Bound-in poster; multiple covers on each 5.00

PATHFINDER: GOBLINS! (Based on the Pathfinder roleplaying game)

GD VG FN VF VF/NM NM-
2.0 4.0 6.0 8.0 9.0 9.2

Dynamite Entertainment: 2013 - No. 5, 2013 ($3.99)
1-5: Short stories by various; multiple covers on each 4.00

PATHFINDER: HOLLOW MOUNTAIN (Based on the Pathfinder roleplaying game)
Dynamite Entertainment: 2015 - No. 6, 2016 ($4.99)
1-6: 1-Sutter-s/Garcia-a; multiple covers 5.00

PATHFINDER: ORIGINS (Based on the Pathfinder roleplaying game)
Dynamite Entertainment: 2015 - No. 6, 2015 ($4.99)
1-6: 1-Spotlight on Valeros; multiple-c. 2-Kyra. 3-Seoni. 4-Merisiel. 5-Harsk. 6-Ezren 5.00

PATHFINDER: RUNESCARS (Based on the Pathfinder roleplaying game)
Dynamite Entertainment: 2017 - No. 5, 2017 ($3.99/$4.99)
1-($3.99) Schneider-s/Silva-a; multiple covers 4.00
2-5-($4.99) 2,4,5-Sutter-s. 3,5-Schneider-s 5.00

PATHFINDER: SPIRAL OF BONES (Based on the Pathfinder roleplaying game)
Dynamite Entertainment: 2018 - No. 5, 2018 ($4.99)
1-5: 1-Frasier-s/Garcia-a; multiple covers; encounter map included in each 5.00

PATHFINDER: WORLDSCAPE (Based on the Pathfinder roleplaying game)
Dynamite Entertainment: 2016 - No. 6, 2017 ($4.99)
1-6-Red Sonja, John Carter and Tarzan app.; Jonathan Lau-a 5.00

PATHWAYS TO FANTASY
Pacific Comics: July, 1984
1-Barry Smith-c/a; Jeff Jones-a (4 pgs.) 4.00

PATORUZU (See Adventures of...)

PATRIOTS, THE
DC Comics (WildStorm): Jan, 2000 - No. 10, Oct, 2000 ($2.50)
1-10-Choi and Peterson-s/Ryan-a 3.00

PATSY & HEDY (Teenage)(Also see Hedy Wolfe)
Atlas Comics/Marvel (GPI/Male): Feb, 1952 - No. 110, Feb, 1967

	GD 2.0	VG 4.0	FN 6.0	VF 8.0	VF/NM 9.0	NM- 9.2
1-Patsy Walker & Hedy Wolfe; Al Jaffee-c	103	206	309	659	1130	1600
2	27	54	81	160	263	365
3-10: 3,7,8,9-Al Jaffee-c	23	46	69	136	223	310
11-20: 17,19,20-Al Jaffee-c	19	38	57	112	179	245
21-40	17	34	51	98	154	210
41-50	9	18	27	58	114	170
51-60	8	16	24	56	108	160
61-80,100: 88-Lingerie panel	8	16	24	51	96	140
81-87,89-99,101-110	7	14	21	48	89	130
Annual 1(1963)-Early Marvel annual	13	26	39	86	188	290

PATSY & HER PALS (Teenage)
Atlas Comics (PPI): May, 1953 - No. 29, Aug, 1957

	GD 2.0	VG 4.0	FN 6.0	VF 8.0	VF/NM 9.0	NM- 9.2
1-Patsy Walker	43	86	129	271	461	650
2	22	44	66	128	209	290
3-10	20	40	60	114	182	250
11-29: 24-Everett-c	16	32	48	92	144	195

PATSY WALKER (See All Teen, A Date With Patsy, Girls' Life, Miss America Magazine, Patsy & Hedy, Patsy & Her Pals & Teen Comics)
Marvel/Atlas Comics (BPC): 1945 (no month) - No. 124, Dec, 1965

	GD 2.0	VG 4.0	FN 6.0	VF 8.0	VF/NM 9.0	NM- 9.2
1-Teenage	423	846	1269	3088	5444	7800
2	55	110	165	352	601	850
3,4,6-10	40	80	120	246	411	575
5-Injury-to-eye-c	48	96	144	302	514	725
11,12,15,16,18	27	54	81	162	266	370
13,14,17,19-22-Kurtzman's "Hey Look"	29	58	87	172	281	390
23,24	22	44	66	132	216	300
25-Rusty by Kurtzman; painted-c	30	60	90	177	289	400
26-29,31: 26-31: 52 pgs.	20	40	60	118	192	265
30(52 pgs.)-Egghead Doodle by Kurtzman (1 pg.)	21	42	63	122	199	275
32-57: Last precode (3/55)	19	38	57	109	172	235
58-80,100	9	18	27	63	129	195
81-98: 92,98-Millie x-over	9	18	27	59	117	175
99-Linda Carter x-over	13	26	39	89	195	300
101-124	8	16	24	51	96	140
Fashion Parade 1(1966, 68 pgs.) (Beware cut-out & marked pages)	12	24	36	82	179	275

NOTE: *Painted c-25-28. Anti-Wertham editorial in #21. Georgie app. in #8, 11, 17. Millie app. in #10, 92, 98. Mitzi app. in #11. Rusty app. in #12, 25. Willie app. in #12.* ***Al Jaffee*** *c-44, 47, 49, 51, 57, 58.*

PATSY WALKER, A.K.A. HELLCAT
Marvel Comics: Feb, 2016 - No. 17, Jun, 2017 ($3.99)
1-17: 1-Kate Leth-s/Brittney Williams-a; She-Hulk and Tom Hale app. 2-Hedy Wolfe app. 6-Natasha Allegri-a. 6,7-Jessica Jones app. 8-Civil War II tie-in 4.00

PATSY WALKER: HELLCAT
Marvel Comics: Sept, 2008 - No. 5, Feb, 2009 ($2.99, limited series)
1-5-Lafuente-a/Kathryn Immonen-s/Stuart Immonen-c; Hellcat joins The Initiative 3.00

PAT THE BRAT (Adventures of Pipsqueak #34 on)
Archie Publications (Radio): June, 1953; Summer, 1955 - No. 4, 5/56; No. 15, 7/56 - No. 33, 7/59

	GD 2.0	VG 4.0	FN 6.0	VF 8.0	VF/NM 9.0	NM- 9.2
nn(6/53)	21	42	63	126	206	285
1(Summer, 1955)	19	38	57	111	176	240
2-4-(5/56) (#5-14 not published). 3-Early Bolling-a	10	20	30	58	79	100
15-(7/56)-33: 18-Early Bolling-a	5	10	15	34	60	85

PAT THE BRAT COMICS DIGEST MAGAZINE
Archie Publications: October, 1980 (95¢)
1-Li'l Jinx & Super Duck app. 2 4 6 10 14 18

PATTY CAKE
Permanent Press: Mar, 1995 - No. 9, Jul, 1996 ($2.95, B&W)
1-9: Scott Roberts-s/a 3.00

PATTY CAKE
Caliber Press (Tapestry): Oct, 1996 - No. 3, Apr, 1997 ($2.95, B&W)
1-3: Scott Roberts-s/a, ...Christmas (12/96) 3.00

PATTY CAKE & FRIENDS
Slave Labor Graphics: Nov, 1997 - Nov, 2000 ($2.95, B&W)
Here There Be Monsters (10/97), 1-14: Scott Roberts-s/a 3.00
Volume 2 #1 (11/00, $4.95) 5.00

PATTY POWERS (Formerly Della Vision #3)
Atlas Comics: No. 4, Oct, 1955 - No. 7, Oct, 1956

	GD 2.0	VG 4.0	FN 6.0	VF 8.0	VF/NM 9.0	NM- 9.2
4	22	44	66	128	209	290
5-7	17	34	51	98	154	210

PAT WILTON (See Mighty Midget Comics)

PAUL
Spire Christian Comics (Fleming H. Revell Co.): 1978 (49¢)
nn 2 4 6 10 14 18

PAULINE PERIL (See The Close Shaves of...)

PAUL IS DEAD (The Beatles)
Image Comics: Apr, 2020 ($16.99, graphic novel)
nn-Speculative fiction about the legend of Paul McCartney's 1966 death 17.00

PAUL REVERE'S RIDE (TV, Disney, see Walt Disney Showcase #34)
Dell Publishing Co.: No. 822, July, 1957
Four Color 822-w/Johnny Tremain, Toth-a 9 18 27 57 111 165

PAUL TERRY (See Heckle and Jeckle)

PAUL TERRY'S ADVENTURES OF MIGHTY MOUSE (See Adventures of...)

PAUL TERRY'S COMICS (Formerly Terry-Toons Comics; becomes Adventures of Mighty Mouse No. 126 on)
St. John Publishing Co.: No. 85, Mar, 1951 - No. 125, May, 1955

	GD 2.0	VG 4.0	FN 6.0	VF 8.0	VF/NM 9.0	NM- 9.2
85,86-Same as Terry-Toons #85, & 86 with only a title change; published at same time?; Mighty Mouse, Heckle & Jeckle & Gandy Goose continue from Terry-Toons	14	28	42	80	115	150
87-99	10	20	30	56	76	95
100	11	22	33	62	86	110
101-104,107-125: 121,122,125-Painted-c	10	20	30	54	72	90
105,106-Giant Comics Edition (25¢, 100 pgs.) (9/53 & ?). 105-Little Roquefort-c/story	20	40	60	118	192	265

PAUL TERRY'S MIGHTY MOUSE (See Mighty Mouse)

PAUL TERRY'S MIGHTY MOUSE ADVENTURE STORIES (See Mighty Mouse Adventure Stories)

PAUL THE SAMURAI (See The Tick #4)
New England Comics: July, 1992 - No. 6, July, 1993 ($2.75, B&W)
1-6 3.00

PAWNEE BILL
Story Comics (Youthful Magazines?): Feb, 1951 - No. 3, July, 1951

	GD 2.0	VG 4.0	FN 6.0	VF 8.0	VF/NM 9.0	NM- 9.2
1-Bat Masterson, Wyatt Earp app.	17	34	51	98	154	210
2,3: 3-Origin Golden Warrior; Cameron-a	10	20	30	58	79	100

PAYBACKS, THE
Dark Horse Comics: Sept, 2015 - No. 4, Dec, 2015 ($3.99)
1-4: 1-Cates & Rahal-s/Shaw-a 4.00

PAY-OFF (This Is the..., ...Crime, ...Detective Stories)
D. S. Publishing Co.: July-Aug, 1948 - No. 5, Mar-Apr, 1949 (52 pgs.)

	GD 2.0	VG 4.0	FN 6.0	VF 8.0	VF/NM 9.0	NM- 9.2
1-True Crime Cases #1,2	45	90	135	284	480	675
2	24	48	72	140	230	320
3-5-Thrilling Detective Stories	18	36	54	103	162	220

PEACEMAKER, THE (Also see Fightin' Five)
Charlton Comics: V3#1, Mar, 1967 - No. 5, Nov, 1967 (All 12¢ cover price)

	GD 2.0	VG 4.0	FN 6.0	VF 8.0	VF/NM 9.0	NM- 9.2
1-Fightin' Five begins	46	92	138	368	834	1300
2,3,5	5	10	15	34	60	85
4-Origin The Peacemaker	5	10	15	30	50	70
1,2(Modern Comics reprint, 1978)	1	3	4	6	8	10

PEACEMAKER (Also see Crisis On Infinite Earths & Showcase '93 #7,9,10)
DC Comics: Jan, 1988 - No. 4, Apr, 1988 ($1.25, limited series)
1-Paul Kupperberg-s/Tod Smith-a 3 6 9 15 20 25
2-4 6.00

PEACEMAKER: DISTURBING THE PEACE
DC Comics (Black Label): Mar, 2022 ($5.99, one-shot)
1-Garth Ennis-s/Garry Brown-a; revisits childhood and past missions 6.00

PEANUTS (Charlie Brown) (See Tip Top #173 and United Comics #21 for Peanuts 1st comic book app.)(Also see Fritzi Ritz, Nancy & Sluggo, Sparkle & Sparkler, Tip Top, Tip Topper & United Comics)
United Features Syndicate/Dell Publishing Co./Gold Key: 1953-54; No. 878, 2/58 - No. 13, 5-7/62; 5/63 - No. 4, 2/64

	GD 2.0	VG 4.0	FN 6.0	VF 8.0	VF/NM 9.0	NM- 9.2
1(U.F.S.)(1953-54)-Reprints United Features' Strange As It Seems, Willie, Ferdnand (scarce)	1100	2200	3300	8360	15,180	22,000
Four Color 878(#1) (Dell) Schulz-s/a, with assistance from Dale Hale and Jim Sasseville thru #4	155	310	465	1279	2890	4500
Four Color 969,1015('59)	36	72	108	259	580	900
4(2-4/60) Schulz-s/a; one story by Anthony Pocrnich, Schulz's assistant cartoonist	19	38	57	131	291	450
5-13-Schulz-c only; s/a by Pocrnich	16	32	48	110	243	375
1(Gold Key, 5/63)	35	70	105	252	564	875
2-4	14	28	42	96	211	325

PEANUTS (Charlie Brown)
BOOM! Entertainment: No. 0, Nov, 2011 - No. 4, Apr, 2012; V2 No. 1, Aug, 2012 - No. 32, Apr, 2016 ($1.00/$3.99)
0-(11/11, $1.00) New short stories and Sunday page reprints 3.00
1-4: 1-(1/12, $3.99) New short stories and Sunday page reprints; Snoopy sled cover 4.00
1-4-Variant-c with first appearance image. 1-Charlie Brown. 2-Lucy. 3-Linus. 4-Snoopy 6.00

Patsy Walker, AKA Hellcat #10 © MAR

Peanuts V2 #5 © Peanuts WW

Penny Dreadful #5 © SHO

	GD 2.0	VG 4.0	FN 6.0	VF 8.0	VF/NM 9.0	NM- 9.2

(Volume 2)

1-32: 1-(8/12, "#1 of 4" on-c)						4.00
1-12-Variant-c with first appearance image. 1-Schroeder. 2-Pig-Pen. 4-Woodstock						10.00
... Free Comic Book Day Edition (5/12) Giveaway flip book with Adventure Time						3.00
...: Friends Forever 2016 Special (7/16, $7.99) New and classic short stories						8.00
Happiness is a Warm Blanket, Charlie Brown HC (Boom Entertainment, 3/11, $19.99) adaptation of new animated special						20.00
It's Tokyo, Charlie Brown (10/12, $13.99, squarebound GN) Vicki Scott-s/a; bonus art						14.00
...: Scotland Bound, Charlie Brown (4/21, $9.99, squarebound GN) adapted from a Schulz story meant for an unproduced animated special; bonus storyboards & art						10.00
...: The Snoopy Special 1 (11/15, $4.99) New and classic Snoopy short stories						5.00
...: Where Beagles Dare! GN (9/15, $9.99, SC) Jason Cooper-s/Vicki Scott-a						10.00

PEANUTS HALLOWEEN
Fantagraphics Books: Sept, 2008 (8-1/2" x 5-3/8" ashcan giveaway)

nn-Halloween themed reprints in color and B&W — 3.00

PEARL
DC Comics (Jinxworld): Oct, 2018 - No. 12, Oct, 2019 ($3.99)

1-12-Bendis-s/Gaydos-a. 1-Bonus reprint of 1st Bendis Batman-s (Batman Chrons. #21) — 4.00

PEARL
Dark Horse Comics: May, 2022 - No. 6, Oct, 2022 ($3.99)

1-6-Bendis-s/Gaydos-a — 4.00

PEBBLES & BAMM BAMM (TV) (See Cave Kids #7, 12)
Charlton Comics: Jan, 1972 - No. 36, Dec, 1976 (Hanna-Barbera)

	GD	VG	FN	VF	VF/NM	NM-
1-From the Flintstones; "Teen Age..." on cover	5	10	15	33	57	80
2-10	3	6	9	16	24	32
11-20	2	4	6	13	18	22
21-36	2	4	6	9	13	16
nn (1973, digest, 100 pgs.) B&W one page gags	3	6	9	18	30	40

PEBBLES & BAMM BAMM (TV)
Harvey Comics: Nov, 1993 - No. 3, Mar, 1994 ($1.50) (Hanna-Barbera)

V2#1-3 — 3.00
...Giant Size 1 (10/93, $2.25, 68 pgs.)("Summer Special" on-c) — 4.00

PEBBLES FLINTSTONE (TV) (See The Flintstones #11)
Gold Key: Sept, 1963 (Hanna-Barbera)

	GD	VG	FN	VF	VF/NM	NM-
1 (10088-309)-Early Pebbles app.	9	18	27	60	120	180

PEDRO (Formerly My Private Life #17; also see Romeo Tubbs)
Fox Feature Syndicate: No. 18, June, 1950 - No. 2, Aug, 1950?

	GD	VG	FN	VF	VF/NM	NM-
18(#1)-Wood-c/a(p)	28	56	84	165	270	375
2-Wood-a?	19	38	57	112	179	240

PEE-WEE PIXIES (See The Pixies)

PELLEAS AND MELISANDE (See Night Music #4, 5)

PENALTY (See Crime Must Pay the...)

PENANCE: RELENTLESS (See Civil War, Thunderbolts and related titles)
Marvel Comics: Nov, 2007 - No. 5 ($2.99)

1-5-Speedball/Penance; Jenkins-s/Gulacy-a. 3-Wolverine app. — 3.00
TPB (2008, $13.99) r/#1-5 — 14.00

PENDRAGON (Knights of... #5 on; also see Knights of...)
Marvel Comics UK, Ltd.: July, 1992 - No. 15, Sept, 1993 ($1.75)

1-15: 1-4-Iron Man app. 6-8-Spider-Man app. — 3.00

PENDULUM ILLUSTRATED BIOGRAPHIES
Pendulum Press: 1979 (B&W)

19-355x-George Washington/Thomas Jefferson, 19-3495-Charles Lindbergh/Amelia Earhart, 19-3509-Harry Houdini/Walt Disney, 19-3517-Davy Crockett/Daniel Boone-Redondo-a, 19-3525-Elvis Presley/Beatles, 19-3533-Benjamin Franklin/Martin Luther King Jr, 19-3541-Abraham Lincoln/Franklin D. Roosevelt, 19-3568-Marie Curie/Albert Einstein-Redondo-a, 19-3576-Thomas Edison/Alexander Graham Bell-Redondo-a, 19-3584-Vince Lombardi/Pele, 19-3592-Babe Ruth/Jackie Robinson, 19-3606-Jim Thorpe/Althea Gibson

	GD	VG	FN	VF	VF/NM	NM-
Softback						5.00
Hardback	1	2	3	4	5	7

PENDULUM ILLUSTRATED CLASSICS (Now Age Illustrated)
Pendulum Press: 1973 - 1978 (75¢, 62pp, B&W, 5-3/8x8")
(Also see Marvel Classics)

64-100x(1973)-Dracula-Redondo art, 64-131x-The Invisible Man-Nino art, 64-0968-Dr. Jekyll and Mr. Hyde-Redondo art, 64-1005-Black Beauty, 64-1010-Call of the Wild, 64-1020-Frankenstein, 64-1025-Hucklebury Finn, 64-1030-Moby Dick-Nino-a, 64-1040-Red Badge of Courage, 64-1045-The Time Machine-Nino-a, 64-1050-Tom Sawyer, 64-1055-Twenty Thousand Leagues Under the Sea, 64-1069-Treasure Island, 64-1328(1974)-Kidnapped, 64-1336-Three Musketeers-Nino art, 64-1344-A Tale of Two Cities, 64-1352-Journey to the Center of the Earth, 64-1360-The War of the Worlds-Nino-a, 64-1379-The Greatest Advs. of Sherlock Holmes-Redondo art, 64-1387-Mysterious Island, 64-1395-Hunchback of Notre Dame, 64-1409-Helen Keller-story of my life, 64-1417-Scarlet Letter, 64-1425-Gulliver's Travels, 64-2618(1977)-Around the World in Eighty Days, 64-2626-Captains Courageous, 64-2634-Connecticut Yankee, 64-2642-The Hound of the Baskervilles, 64-2650-The House of Seven Gables, 64-2669-Jane Eyre, 64-2677-The Last of the Mohicans, 64-2685-The Best of O'Henry, 64-2693-The Best of Poe-Redondo-a, 64-2707-Two Years Before the Mast, 64-2715-White Fang, 64-2723-Wuthering Heights, 64-3126(1978)-Ben Hur-Redondo art, 64-3134-A Christmas Carol, 64-3142-The Food of the Gods, 64-3150-Ivanhoe, 64-3169-The Man in the Iron Mask, 64-3177-The Prince and the Pauper, 64-3185-The Prisoner of Zenda, 64-3193-The Return of the Native, 64-3207-Robinson Crusoe, 64-3215-The Scarlet Pimpernel, 64-3223-The Sea Wolf, 64-3231-The Swiss Family Robinson, 64-3851-Billy Budd, 64-386x-Crime and Punishment, 64-3878-Don Quixote, 64-3886-Great Expectations, 64-3894-Heidi, 64-3908-The Iliad, 64-3916-Lord Jim, 64-3924-The Mutiny on Board H.M.S. Bounty, 64-3932-The Odyssey, 64-3940-Oliver Twist, 64-3959-Pride and Prejudice, 64-3967-The Turn of the Screw

	GD	VG	FN	VF	VF/NM	NM-
Softback						6.00
Hardback	1	2	3	5	6	8

NOTE: *All of the above books can be ordered from the publisher; some were reprinted as Marvel Classic Comics #1-12. In 1972 there was another brief series of 12 titles which contained Classics Ill. artwork. They were entitled **Now Age Books** Illustrated, but can be easily distinguished from later series by the small Classics Illustrated logo at the top of the front cover. The format is the same as the later series. The 48 pg. C.I. art was stretched out to make 62 pgs. After Twin Circle Publ. terminated the Classics Ill. series in 1971, they made a one year contract with Pendulum Press to print these twelve titles of C.I. art. Pendulum was unhappy with the contract, and at the end of 1972 began their own art series, utilizing the talents of the Filipino artist group. One detail which makes this rather confusing is that when they redid the art in 1973, they gave it the same identifying no. as the 1972 series. All 12 of the 1972 C.I. editions have new covers, taken from internal art panels. In spite of their recent age, all of the 1972 C.I. series are very rare. Mint copies would fetch at least $50. Here is a list of the 1972 series, with C.I. title no. counterpart:*

64-1005 (CI#60-A2) 64-1010 (CI#91) 64-1015 (CI-Jr #503) 64-1020 (CI#26)
64-1025 (CI#19-A2) 64-1030 (CI#5-A2) 64-1035 (CI#169) 64-1040 (CI#98)
64-1045 (CI#133) 64-1050 (CI#50-A2) 64-1055 (CI#47) 64-1060 (CI-Jr#535)

PENDULUM ILLUSTRATED ORIGINALS
Pendulum Press: 1979 (In color)

94-4254-Solarman: The Beginning (See Solarman) — 6.00

PENDULUM'S ILLUSTRATED STORIES
Pendulum Press: 1990 - No. 72, 1990? (No cover price ($4.95), squarebound, 68 pgs.)

1-72: Reprints Pendulum Ill. Classics series — 5.00

PENGUIN: PAIN & PREJUDICE (Batman)
DC Comics: Dec, 2011 - No. 5, Apr, 2012 ($2.99, limited series)

1-5-Hurwitz-s/Kudranski-a/c; Penguin's childhood and rise to power — 3.00

PENGUINS OF MADAGASCAR (Based on the DreamWorks movie and TV series)
Ape Entertainment: 2010 - No. 4, 2011 ($3.95, limited series)

1-4-Skipper, Kowalski, Private and Rico app. — 4.00

PENGUINS OF MADAGASCAR (Based on the DreamWorks movie and TV series)
Titan Comics: Dec, 2014 - No. 4, Mar, 2015 ($3.99, limited series)

1-4-Skipper, Kowalski, Private and Rico app. — 4.00

PENNY
Avon Comics: 1947 - No. 6, Sept-Oct, 1949 (Newspaper reprints)

	GD	VG	FN	VF	VF/NM	NM-
1-Photo & biography of creator	39	78	117	240	395	550
2-5	19	38	57	111	176	240
6-Perry Como photo on-c	20	40	60	114	182	250

PENNY CENTURY (See Love and Rockets)
Fantagraphics Books: Dec, 1997 - No. 7, Jul, 2000 ($2.95, B&W, mini-series)

1-7-Jaime Hernandez-s/a — 3.00

PENNY DORA AND THE WISHING BOX
Image Comics: Nov, 2014 - No. 5, Jun, 2015 ($2.99)

1-5-Michael Stock-s/Sina Grace-a — 3.00

PENNY DREADFUL (Based on the Showtime TV series)
Titan Comics: Jun, 2016 - No. 5, Nov, 2016 ($3.99)

1-5: 1-Wilson-Cairns-s/De Martinis-a; multiple covers — 4.00

PENNYWORTH (Alfred from Batman)
DC Comics: Oct, 2021 - No. 7, Apr, 2022 ($3.99)

1-7-Alfred's past in British Intelligence; Scott Bryan Wilson-s/Juan Gedeon-a — 4.00

PENULTIMAN (See Steel Cage #1 for debut)
AHOY Comics: 2020 - No. 5, 2021 ($3.99)

1-5-Tom Peyer-s/Alan Robinson-a — 4.00

PEP COMICS (See Archie Giant Series #576, 589, 601, 614, 624)
MLJ Magazines/Archie Publications No. 56 (3/46) on: Jan, 1940 - No. 411, Mar, 1987

	GD	VG	FN	VF	VF/NM	NM-
1-Intro. The Shield (1st patriotic hero) by Irving Novick; origin & 1st app. The Comet by Jack Cole, The Queen of Diamonds & Kayo Ward; The Rocket, The Press Guardian (The Falcon #1 only), Sergeant Boyle, Fu Chang, & Bentley of of Scotland Yard; Robot-c; Shield-c begin	1500	3000	4500	11,400	20,700	30,000
2-Origin The Rocket	371	742	1113	2600	4550	6500
3-Nazi WWII-c	300	600	900	2010	3505	5000
4-WWII brought to U.S. Capitol building; Wizard cameo; early robot-s						

	GD 2.0	VG 4.0	FN 6.0	VF 8.0	VF/NM 9.0	NM- 9.2
	371	742	1113	2600	4550	6500
5-Wizard cameo in Shield story	290	580	870	1856	3178	4500
6,7,9,10: 7-Bondage-c	226	452	678	1446	2473	3500
8-Last Jack Cole Comet; no Cole-a in #6,7; torture by branding-c	343	686	1029	2400	4200	6000
11-Dusty, Shield's sidekick begins (1st app.); last Press Guardian, Fu Chang	258	516	774	1651	2826	4000
12-Origin & 1st app. Fireball (2/41); last Rocket & Queen of Diamonds; Danny in Wonderland begins; bondage-c	271	542	813	1734	2967	4200
13-15: All bondage/torture covers	206	412	618	1318	2259	3200
16-Origin Madam Satan; blood drainage-c	465	930	1395	3395	5998	8600
17-Origin/1st app. The Hangman (7/41); death of The Comet; Comet is revealed as Hangman's brother	919	1838	2757	6709	11,855	17,000
18,19,21: 18,21-Bondage/torture-c. 19-WWII Nazi-c. 21-Last Madam Satan	219	438	657	1402	2401	3400
20-Classic Nazi swastika-c; last Fireball	1500	3000	4500	11,400	20,700	30,000
22-Intro. & 1st app. Archie, Betty, & Jughead (12/41); (on sale 10/41)(also see Jackpot)	33,800	67,600	101,400	225,500	332,750	440,000
23-Statue of Liberty-c & Nazi-c (1/42; on sale 11/41)	2900	5800	8700	17,400	24,700	32,000
24-Coach Kleats app. (unnamed until Archie #94); bondage/torture-c	975	1950	2919	7100	12,550	18,000
25-1st app. Archie's jalopy; 1st skinny Mr. Weatherbee prototype	649	1298	1947	4738	8369	12,000
26-1st app. Veronica Lodge (4/42); "Remember Pearl Harbor!" cover caption	1850	3700	5550	14,000	24,500	35,000
27-Bill of Rights & sunburst swastika-c	622	1244	1866	4541	8021	11,500
28-Classic swastika/Hangman-c	476	952	1428	3475	6138	8800
29,30: 29-Origin Shield retold; 30-Capt. Commando begins; bondage/torture-c; 1st Miss Grundy (definitive version); see Jackpot #4	459	918	1377	3350	5925	8500
31-MLJ offices & artists are visited in Sgt. Boyle story; 1st app. Mr. Lodge; cover has woman steam-broiled alive, Nazi bondage-c	595	1190	1785	4350	7675	11,000
32,33,35: 32-Shield dons new costume; bondage/brain drilling/Nazi-c. 33-Pre-Moose tryout (see Jughead #1); Nazi Viking-c. 35-WWII nurse bondage/torture-c	354	708	1062	2478	4339	6200
34-Classic Bondage/Hypo-c	2925	5850	8775	18,300	28,150	38,000
36-1st full Archie-c in Pep (2/43) w/Shield & Hangman (see Jackpot #4 where Archie's face appears in a small circle)	2100	4200	6300	14,700	24,600	34,500
37-40: 37-WWII Japanese firing squad-c. 38-Nazi WWII-c. 39-Bondage-c. 40-Bondage/Japanese WWII-c	300	600	900	1950	3375	4800
41-Archie-c begin	366	732	1098	2562	4487	6400
42-45	232	464	696	1485	2543	3600
46,47,49,50: 47-Last Hangman issue; infinity-c	200	400	600	1280	2190	3100
48-Black Hood begins (5/44); ends #51,59,60; Archie fish-c	265	530	795	1694	2897	4100
51-60: 52-Suzie begins; 1st Mr Weatherbee-c. 56-Last Capt. Commando. 59-Black Hood not in costume; lingerie panels; Archie dresses as his aunt; Suzie ends. 60-Katy Keene begins(3/47), ends #154	100	200	300	635	1093	1550
61-65-Last Shield. 62-1st app. Li'l Jinx (7/47)	81	162	243	518	884	1250
66-80: 66-G-Man Club becomes Archie Club (2/48); Nevada Jones by Bill Woggon. 76-Katy Keene story. 78-1st app. Dilton	43	86	129	271	461	650
81-99	29	58	87	172	281	390
100	35	70	105	208	339	470
101-130	20	40	60	115	185	255
131(2/59)-137	8	16	24	56	108	160
138-140-Neal Adams-a (1 pg.) in each	9	18	27	57	111	165
141-149(9/61)	7	14	21	48	89	130
150-160-Super-heroes app. in each (see note). 150 (10/61?)-2nd or 3rd app. The Jaguar? 151-154,156-158-Horror/Sci/Fi-c. 157-Li'l Jinx. 159-Both 12¢ and 15¢ covers exist	9	18	27	61	123	185
161(3/63) 3rd Josie app.; early Josie stories w/DeCarlo-a begin (see Note for others)	8	16	24	54	102	150
162-167,169-180	5	10	15	33	57	80
168,200: 168-(1/64)-Jaguar app. 200-(12/66)	5	10	15	34	60	85
181(5/65)-199: 187-Pureheart try-out story. 192-UFO-c. 198-Giantman-c(only)	4	8	12	27	44	60
201-217,219-226,228-240(4/70): 224-(12/68) 1st app. Archie's pet, Hot Dog (later becomes Jughead's pet)	3	6	9	17	25	34
218,227-Archies Band-c only	3	6	9	18	28	38
241-270(10/72)	3	6	9	14	19	24
271-297,299	2	4	6	10	14	18
298, 300: 298-Josie and the Pussycats-c. 300(4/75)	3	6	9	14	19	24
301-340(8/78)	2	4	6	8	10	12
341-382	1	2	3	5	6	8
383(4/82),393(3/84): 383-Marvelous Maureen begins (Sci/fi). 393-Thunderbunny begins	1	3	4	6	8	10
384-392,394,395,397-399,401-410						6.00
396-Early Cheryl Blossom-c	2	4	6	10	14	18
400(5/85),411: 400-Story featuring Archie staff (DeCarlo-a)	1	2	3	5	6	8

NOTE: ***Biro** a-2, 4, 5. **Jack Cole** a-1-5, 8. **Al Fagaly** c-55-72. **Fuje** a-39, 45, 47; c-34. **Meskin** a-2, 4, 5, 11(2). **Montana** c-30, 32, 33, 36, 73-87(most). **Novick** c-1-28, 29(w/**Schomburg**), 31i. **Harry Sahle** c-35, 39-50. **Schomburg** c-38. **Bob Wood** a-2, 4-6, 11. The Fly app. in 151, 154, 160. Flygirl app. in 153, 155, 156, 158. Jaguar app. in 150, 152, 157, 159, 168. Josie by **DeCarlo** in 161-166, 168-171, 173, 175-177, 179, 181. Katy Keene by **Bill Woggon** in 73-126. Bondage c-7, 12, 13, 15, 18, 21, 31, 32. Cover features: Shield #1-16; Shield/Hangman #17-27, 29-41; Hangman #28. Archie #36, 41-on.*

PEP COMICS FEATURING BETTY AND VERONICA
Archie Comic Publications: May, 2011 (Giveaway)

Free Comic Book Day Edition - Little Archie flashback — 5.00

PEPE
Dell Publishing Co.: No. 1194, Apr, 1961

	GD	VG	FN	VF	VF/NM	NM-
Four Color 1194-Movie, photo-c	5	10	15	33	57	80

PERFECT CRIME, THE
Cross Publications: Oct, 1949 - No. 33, May, 1953 (#2-14, 52 pgs.)

	GD	VG	FN	VF	VF/NM	NM-
1-Powell-a(2)	57	114	171	362	619	875
2 (4/50)	32	64	96	188	307	425
3-10: 7-Steve Duncan begins, ends #30. 10-Flag-c	26	52	78	154	252	350
11-Used in **SOTI**, pg. 159	28	56	84	168	274	380
12-14	24	48	72	142	234	325
15- "The Most Terrible Menace" 2 pg. drug editorial (8/51)	27	54	81	158	259	360
16,17,19-25,27-29,31-33	21	42	63	122	199	275
18-Drug cover, heroin drug propaganda story, plus 2 pg. anti-drug editorial (11/51)	45	90	135	284	480	675
26-Drug-c with hypodermic needle; drug propaganda story (7/52)	47	94	141	296	498	700
30-Strangulation cover (11/52)	53	106	159	334	567	800

NOTE: ***Powell** a-No. 1, 2, 4. **Wildey** a-1, 5. Bondage c-11.*

PERFECT LOVE
Ziff-Davis(Approved Comics)/St. John No. 9 on: #10, 8-9/51 (cover date; 5-6/51 indicia date); #2, 10-11/51 - #10, 12/53

	GD	VG	FN	VF	VF/NM	NM-
10(#1)(8-9/51)-Painted-c	34	68	102	199	325	450
2(10-11/51)	21	42	63	124	202	280
3,5-7: 3-Painted-c. 5-Photo-c	18	36	54	105	165	225
4,8 (Fall, 1952)-Kinstler-a; last Z-D issue	18	36	54	105	165	225
9,10 (10/53, 12/53, St. John): 9-Painted-c. 10-Photo-c	17	34	51	100	158	215

PERHAPANAUTS, THE
Dark Horse Comics: Nov, 2005 - No. 4, Feb, 2006 ($2.99, limited series)

1-4-Todd Dezago-s/Craig Rousseau-a/c — 3.00
... Annual #1 (2/08, $3.50) Two covers by Rousseau and Allred — 3.50
...: Danger Down Under! 1-5 (11/12 - No. 5, 6/13, $3.50) Two covers on each — 3.50
... Halloween Spooktacular 1 (10/09, $3.50) Hembeck, Rousseau and others-a — 3.50
,,, - Molly's Story (2/10, $3.50) Copland-a — 3.50
(2nd series) (4/08 - No. 6, $3.50) 1-6: 1-Two covers by Art Adams and Rousseau — 3.50

PERHAPANAUTS: SECOND CHANCES, THE
Dark Horse Comics: Oct, 2006 - No. 4, Jan, 2007 ($2.99, limited series)

1-4-Todd Dezago-s/Craig Rousseau-a/c — 3.00

PERRI (Disney)
Dell Publishing Co.: No. 847, Jan, 1958

	GD	VG	FN	VF	VF/NM	NM-
Four Color 847-Movie, w/2 diff-c publ.	6	12	18	38	69	100

PERRY MASON
David McKay Publications: No. 49, 1946 - No. 50, 1946

	GD	VG	FN	VF	VF/NM	NM-
Feature Books 49, 50-Based on Gardner novels	41	82	123	256	428	600

PERRY MASON MYSTERY MAGAZINE (TV)
Dell Publishing Co.: June-Aug, 1964 - No. 2, Oct-Dec, 1964

	GD	VG	FN	VF	VF/NM	NM-
1-Raymond Burr painted-c	9	18	27	61	123	185
2-Raymond Burr photo-c	6	12	18	41	76	110

PERSONAL LOVE (Also see Movie Love)
Famous Funnies: Jan, 1950 - No. 33, June, 1955

	GD	VG	FN	VF	VF/NM	NM-
1-Photo-c	29	58	87	172	281	390
2-Kathryn Grayson & Mario Lanza photo-c	17	34	51	98	154	210
3-7,10: 7-Robert Walker & Joanne Dru photo-c. 10-Loretta Young & Joseph Cotton photo-c	15	30	45	90	140	190
8,9: 8-Esther Williams & Howard Keel photo-c. 9-Debra Paget & Louis Jourdan photo-c	16	32	48	92	144	195
11-Toth-a; Glenn Ford & Gene Tierney photo-c	18	36	54	107	169	230
12,16,17-One pg. Frazetta each. 17-Rock Hudson & Yvonne DeCarlo photo-c	16	32	48	92	144	195
13-15,18-23: 12-Jane Greer & William Lundigan photo-c. 14-Kirk Douglas photo-c. 15-Dale Robertson & Joanne Dru photo-c. 18-Gregory Peck & Susan Hayworth photo-c. 19-Anthony Quinn & Suzan Ball photo-c. 20-Robert Wagner & Kathleen Crowley photo-c. 21-Roberta Peters & Byron Palmer photo-c. 22-Dale Robertson photo-c. 23-Rhonda Fleming-c	15	30	45	86	133	180
24,27,28-Frazetta-a in each (8,8&6 pgs.). 27-Rhonda Fleming & Fernando Lamas photo-c. 28-Mitzi Gaynor photo-c	57	114	171	362	619	875
25-Frazetta-a (tribute to Bettie Page, 7 pg. story); Tyrone Power/Terry Moore photo-c from "King of the Khyber Rifles"	93	186	279	591	1021	1450
26,29,30,33: 26-Constance Smith & Byron Palmer photo-c. 29-Charlton Heston & Nicol Morey photo-c. 30-Johnny Ray & Mitzi Gaynor photo-c. 33-Dana Andrews & Piper Laurie photo-c	15	30	45	84	127	170
31-Marlon Brando & Jean Simmons photo-c; last pre-code (2/55)	19	38	57	109	172	235
32-Classic Frazetta-a (8 pgs.); Kirk Douglas & Bella Darvi photo-c	90	180	270	576	988	1400

NOTE: *All have photo-c. Many feature movie stars. **Everett** a-5, 9, 10, 24.*

PERSONAL LOVE (Going Steady V3#3 on)
Prize Publ. (Headline): V1#1, Sept, 1957 - V3#2, Nov-Dec, 1959

	GD	VG	FN	VF	VF/NM	NM-
V1#1	15	30	45	88	137	185
2	10	20	30	58	79	100
3-6(7-8/58)	9	18	27	47	61	75
V2#1(9-10/58)-V2#6(7-8/59)	8	16	24	40	50	60
V3#1-Wood?/Orlando-a	8	16	24	42	54	65
2	7	14	21	37	46	55

PESTILENCE
AfterShock Comics: May, 2017 - No. 6, Jan, 2018 ($3.99)

1-6-Tieri-s/Okunev-a/Bradstreet-c; Crusaders and zombies in the year 1347 — 4.00

PESTILENCE: A STORY OF SATAN
AfterShock Comics: May, 2018 - No. 5, Nov, 2018 ($3.99)

1-5-Tieri-s/Okunev-a/Bradstreet-c — 4.00

PETER CANNON - THUNDERBOLT (See Crisis on Infinite Earths)(Also see Thunderbolt)
DC Comics: Sept, 1992 - No. 12, Aug, 1993 ($1.25)

1-12 — 3.00

PETER CANNON: THUNDERBOLT
Dynamite Entertainment: 2012 - No. 13, 2013 ($3.99)

Pep Comics #36 © ACP

Personal Love #9 © EAS

Peter Parker (2010) #3 © MAR

GD VG FN VF VF/NM NM-
2.0 4.0 6.0 8.0 9.0 9.2

1-10: 1-Darnell & Ross-s/Lau-a; back-up unpublished '80s Thunderbolt story; Pete Morisi-s/a. 1-3-Four covers on each. 4-7-Covers by Ross & Segovia 4.00

PETER CANNON: THUNDERBOLT, VOLUME 1
Dynamite Entertainment: 2019 - No. 5, 2019 ($3.99)
1-5-Gillen-s/Wijngaard-a 4.00

PETER COTTONTAIL
Key Publications: Jan, 1954; Feb, 1954 - No. 2, Mar, 1954 (Says 3/53 in error)
1(1/54)-Not 3-D 12 24 36 69 97 125
1(2/54)-(3-D, 25¢)-Came w/glasses; written by Bruce Hamilton 24 48 72 144 237 330
2-Reprints 3-D #1 but not in 3-D 7 14 21 37 46 55

PETER GUNN (TV)
Dell Publishing Co.: No. 1087, Apr-June, 1960
Four Color 1087-Photo-c 8 16 24 52 99 145

PETE ROSE: HIS INCREDIBLE BASEBALL CAREER
Masstar Creations Inc.: 1995
1-John Tartaglione-a 4.00

PETER PAN (Disney) (See Hook, Movie Classics & Comics, New Adventures of... & Walt Disney Showcase #36)
Dell Publishing Co.: No. 442, Dec, 1952 - No. 926, Aug, 1958
Four Color 442 (#1)-Movie 12 24 36 79 170 260
Four Color 926-Reprint of 442 6 12 18 40 73 105

PETER PAN
Disney Comics: 1991 ($5.95, graphic novel, 68 pgs.)(Celebrates video release)
nn-r/Peter Pan Treasure Chest from 1953 7.00

PETER PANDA
National Periodical Publications: Aug-Sept, 1953 - No. 31, Aug-Sept, 1958
1-Grossman-c/a in all 77 154 231 493 847 1200
2 36 72 108 214 347 480
3,4,6-8,10 29 58 87 172 281 390
5-Classic-c (scarce) 119 238 357 762 1306 1850
9-Robot-c 41 82 123 256 428 600
11-31 22 44 66 128 209 290

PETER PAN RECORDS (See Power Records)

PETER PAN TREASURE CHEST (See Dell Giants)

PETER PANZERFAUST
Image Comics (Shadowline): Feb, 2012 - No. 25, Dec, 2016 ($3.50/$3.99)
1-Kurtis Wiebe-s/Tyler Jenkins-a/c; Peter Pan-type character in WWII Europe 3 6 9 17 26 35
1-Second printing 1 3 4 6 8 10
2,3 1 2 3 5 6 8
4-8 5.00
9-1st full app. Kapitan Haken 6.00
10-24 4.00
25-Last issue; bonus preview of Rat Queens v2 5.00

PETER PARKER (See The Spectacular Spider-Man)

PETER PARKER
Marvel Comics: May, 2010 - No. 5, Sept, 2010 ($3.99/$2.99)
1-($3.99) Prints material from Marvel Digital Comics; Olliffe-a; back-up w/Hembeck-s/a 4.00
2-5-($2.99): 2-4-Olliffe-a. 3-Braithwaite-c. 5-Nauck-a; Thing app. 3.00

PETER PARKER & MILES MORALES: SPIDER-MEN DOUBLE TROUBLE (All ages)
Marvel Comics: Jan, 2023 - No. 4, Apr, 2023 ($3.99, limited series)
1-4-Tamaki & Ayala-s/Gurihiru-a; Mysterio & Thanos app. 4.00

PETER PARKER: SPIDER-MAN
Marvel Comics: Jan, 1999 - No. 57, Aug, 2003 ($2.99/$1.99/$2.25)
1-Mackie-s/Romita Jr.-a; wraparound-c 2 4 6 8 10 12
1-($6.95) DF Edition w/variant-c by the Romitas 2 4 6 11 16 20
2,3,5-11,13-17-($1.99): 2-Two covers; Thor app. 3-Iceman-c/app. 5-Spider-Woman app. 7,8-Blade app. 9,10-Venom app. 11-Iron Man & Thor-c/app. 4.00
4-1st Hunger; Marrow-c/app. 2 4 6 9 11 14
12-($2.99) Sinister Six and Venom app. 5.00
18-24,26-43: 18-Begin $2.25-c. 20-Jenkins-s/Buckingham-a start. 23-Intro Typeface. 24-Maximum Security x-over. 29-Rescue of MJ. 30-Ramos-c. 42,43-Mahfood-a 4.00
25-($2.99) Two covers; Spider-Man & Green Goblin 5.00
44-47-Humberto Ramos-c/a; Green Goblin-c/app. 4.00
48,49,51-57: 48,49-Buckingham-c/a. 51,52-Herrera-a. 56,57-Kieth-a; Sandman returns 4.00
50-($3.50) Buckingham-c/a 5.00
#156.1 (10/12, $2.99, 50th Anniversary one-shot) Stern-s/De La Torre-a/Romita Jr.-c 4.00
...'99 Annual (8/99, $3.50) Man-Thing app. 5.00
...'00 Annual ($3.50) Bounty app.; Joe Bennett-a; Black Cat back-up story 5.00
...'01 Annual ($2.99) Avery-s 5.00
...: A Day in the Life TPB (5/01, $14.95) r/#20-22,26; Webspinners #10-12 15.00
...: One Small Break TPB (2002, $16.95) r/#27,28,30-34; Andrews-c 17.00
Spider-Man: Return of the Goblin TPB (2002, $8.99) r/#44-47; Ramos-c 9.00
...Vol. 4: Trials & Tribulations TPB (2003, $11.99) r/#35,37,48-50; Cho-c 12.00

PETER PARKER: THE SPECTACULAR SPIDER-MAN
Marvel Comics: Aug, 2017 - No. 6, Jan, 2018; No. 297, Feb, 2018 - No. 313, Feb, 2019 ($4.99/$3.99)
1-($4.99) Zdarsky-s/Adam Kubert-a; Johnny Storm app.; back-up w/Black Widow app. 5.00
2-6-($3.99) 3,4-Kingpin app. 6-Walsh-a 4.00
[Title switches to legacy numbering after #6 (1/18)]
297-299-Kubert-a. 298,299-Black Panther app. 4.00
300-($5.99) Black Panther, Human Torch, Ironheart app.; bonus cover gallery 6.00
301-313: 301-303-Spider-Man teams with younger version; Quinones-a. 310-Zdarsky-a. 311-313-Spider-Geddon tie-in; Morlun app. 4.00
Annual 1 (8/18, $4.99) Zdarsky-s/Allred-a/c; spotlight on J. Jonah Jameson; Bachalo-a 5.00

PETER PAT
United Features Syndicate: No. 8, 1939
Single Series 8 40 80 120 246 411 575

PETER PAUL'S 4 IN 1 JUMBO COMIC BOOK
Capitol Stories (Charlton): No date (1953)
1-Contains 4 comics bound; Space Adventures, Space Western, Crime & Justice, Racket Squad in Action 47 94 141 296 498 700

PETER PIG
Standard Comics: No. 5, May, 1953 - No. 6, Aug, 1953
5,6 8 16 24 44 57 70

PETER PORKCHOPS (See Leading Comics #23) (Also see Capt. Carrot)
National Periodical Publications: 11-12/49 - No. 61, 9-11/59; No. 62, 10-12/60 (1-11: 52 pgs.)
1 39 78 117 240 395 550
2 18 36 54 107 169 230
3-10: 6- "Peter Rockets to Mars!" c/story 14 28 42 78 112 145
11-30 10 20 30 58 79 100
31-62 9 18 27 50 65 80
NOTE: ***Otto Feuer** a-all.* ***Rube Grossman**-a most issues.* ***Sheldon Mayer** a-30-38, 40-44, 46-52, 61.*

PETER PORKER, THE SPECTACULAR SPIDER-HAM
Star Comics (Marvel): May, 1985 - No. 17, Sept, 1987 (Also see Marvel Tails)
1-Michael Golden-c 3 6 9 16 23 30
2-17: 12-Origin/1st app. Bizarro Phil. 13-Halloween issue 5.00
NOTE: *Back-up features: 2-X-Bugs. 3-Iron Mouse. 4-Croctor Strange. 5-Thrr, Dog of Thunder.*

PETER POTAMUS (TV)
Gold Key: Jan, 1965 (Hanna-Barbera)
1-1st app. Peter Potamus & So-So, Breezly & Sneezly 9 18 27 63 129 195

PETER RABBIT (See New Funnies #65 & Space Comics)
Dell Publishing Co.: No. 1, 1942
Large Feature Comic 1 87 174 261 553 952 1350

PETER RABBIT (Adventures of...; New Advs. of... #9 on)(Also see Funny Tunes & Space Comics)
Avon Periodicals: 1947 - No. 34, Aug-Sept, 1956
1(1947)-Reprints 1943-44 Sunday strips; contains a biography & drawing of Cady 42 84 126 265 445 625
2 (4/48) 27 54 81 162 266 370
3 ('48) - 6(7/49)-Last Cady issue 24 48 72 142 234 325
7-10(1950-8/51): 9-New logo 13 26 39 72 101 130
11(11/51)-34('56)-Avon's character 10 20 30 58 79 100
...Easter Parade (1952, 25¢, 132 pgs.) 24 48 72 140 230 320
...Jumbo Book (1954-Giant Size, 25¢)-Jesse James by Kinstler (6 pgs.); space ship-c 28 56 84 165 270 375

PETER RABBIT 3-D
Eternity Comics: April, 1990 ($2.95, with glasses; sealed in plastic bag)
1-By Harrison Cady (reprints) 4.00

PETER, THE LITTLE PEST (#4 titled Petey)
Marvel Comics Group: Nov, 1969 - No. 4, May, 1970
1 9 18 27 57 111 165
2-4-r-Dexter the Demon & Melvin the Monster 5 10 15 33 57 80

GD 2.0 | VG 4.0 | FN 6.0 | VF 8.0 | VF/NM 9.0 | NM- 9.2

PETE'S DRAGON (See Walt Disney Showcase #43)

PETE THE PANIC
Stanmor Publications: November, 1955

nn-Code approved 10 20 30 54 72 90

PETEY (See Peter, the Little Pest)

PETTICOAT JUNCTION (TV, inspired Green Acres)
Dell Publ. Co.: Oct-Dec, 1964 - No. 5, Oct-Dec, 1965 (#1-3, 5 have photo-c)

1 7 14 21 44 82 120
2-5 5 10 15 33 57 80

PETUNIA (Also see Looney Tunes and Porky Pig)
Dell Publishing Co.: No. 463, Apr, 1953

Four Color 463 5 10 15 35 63 90

PHAGE (See Neil Gaiman's Teknophage & Neil Gaiman's Phage-Shadowdeath)

PHALANX, THE
Image Comics: Jun, 2022 ($3.99, one-shot)

1-Jonathan Luna-s/a 4.00

PHANTACEA
McPherson Publishing Co.: Sept, 1977 - No. 6, Summer, 1980 (B&W)

1-Early Dave Sim-a (32 pgs.) 4 8 12 28 47 65
2-Dave Sim-a(10 pgs.) 3 6 9 14 19 24
3-6: 3-Flip-c w/Damnation Bridge. 4-Gene Day-a 2 4 6 10 14 18

PHANTASMO (See The Funnies #45)
Dell Publishing Co.: No. 18, 1941

Large Feature Comic 18 48 96 144 302 514 725

PHANTOM, THE
David McKay Publishing Co.: 1939 - 1949

Feature Books 20 300 600 900 2010 3505 5000
Feature Books 22 103 206 309 659 1130 1600
Feature Books 39 77 154 231 493 847 1200
Feature Books 53,56,57 58 116 174 371 636 900

PHANTOM, THE (See Ace Comics, Defenders Of The Earth, Eat Right to Work and Win, Future Comics, Harvey Comics Hits #51,56, Harvey Hits #1, 6, 12, 15, 26, 36, 44, 48, & King Comics)

PHANTOM, THE (nn (#29)-Published overseas only) (Also see Comics Reading Libraries in the Promotional Comics section)
Gold Key(#1-17)/King(#18-28)/Charlton(#30 on): Nov, 1962 - No. 17, Jul, 1966; No. 18, Sept, 1966 - No. 28, Dec, 1967; No. 30, Feb, 1969 - No. 74, Jan, 1977

1-Origin revealed on inside-c & back-c 31 62 93 223 499 775
2-King, Queen & Jack begins, ends #11 11 22 33 72 154 235
3-5 9 18 27 58 114 170
6-10 7 14 21 46 86 125
11-17: 12-Track Hunter begins 6 12 18 38 69 100
18-Flash Gordon begins; Wood-a 5 10 15 31 53 75
19-24: 20-Flash Gordon ends (both by Gil Kane). 21-Mandrake begins. 20,24-Girl Phantom app. 4 8 12 28 47 65
25-28: 25-Jeff Jones-a(4 pgs.); 1 pg. Williamson ad. 26-Brick Bradford app. 28-Brick Bradford app. 4 8 12 23 37 50
30-33: 33-Last 12¢ issue 3 6 9 17 25
34
34-40: 36,39-Ditko-a 3 6 9 16 24 32
41-66,72: 46-Intro. The Piranha. 51-Grey tone-c. 62-Bolle-c 3 6 9 14 20 26
67-Origin retold; Newton-c/a; Humphrey Bogart, Lauren Bacall & Peter Lorre app. 3 6 9 17 25 34
68,70,71,73-Newton-c/a 3 6 9 14 19 24
69-Newton-c only 3 6 9 14 19 24
74-Classic flag-c by Newton; Newton-a; 3 6 9 18 28 38
NOTE: *Aparo a-31-34, 36-38; c-31-38, 60, 61. Painted c-1-17.*

PHANTOM, THE
DC Comics: May, 1988 - No. 4, Aug, 1988 ($1.25, mini-series)

1-4: Orlando-c/a in all 4.00

PHANTOM, THE
DC Comics: Mar, 1989 - No. 13, Mar, 1990 ($1.50)

1-13: 1-Brief origin 4.00

PHANTOM, THE
Wolf Publishing: 1992 - No. 8, 1993 ($2.25)

1-8 4.00

PHANTOM, THE
Moonstone: 2003 - No. 26, Dec, 2008 ($3.50/$3.99)

1-26: 1-Cassaday-c/Raab-s/Quinn-a 4.00
... Annual #1 (2007, $6.50) Blevins-c; stroy and art by various incl. Nolan 6.50
... - Captain Action 1 (2010, $3.99) covers by Thibert, Sparacio, and Gilbert 4.00

PHANTOM, THE
Hermes Press: 2014 - No. 6, 2016 ($3.99)

1-6: 1-Peter David-s/Sal Velluto-a; four covers 4.00

PHANTOM BLOT, THE (#1 titled New Adventures of...)
Gold Key: Oct, 1964 - No. 7, Nov, 1966 (Disney)

1 (Meets The Mysterious Mr. X) 8 16 24 55 105 155
2-1st Super Goof 6 12 18 37 66 95
3-7 3 6 9 21 33 45

PHANTOM EAGLE (See Mighty Midget, Marvel Super Heroes #16 & Wow #6)

PHANTOM FORCE
Image Comics/Genesis West #0, 3-7: 12/93 - #2, 1994; #0, 3/94; #3, 5/94 - #8, 10/94 ($2.50/$3.50, limited series)

0 (3/94, $2.50)-Kirby/Jim Lee-c; Kirby-p pgs. 1,5,24-29. 4.00
1 (12/93, $2.50)-Polybagged w/trading card; Kirby/Liefeld-c; Kirby plots/pencils w/inks by Liefeld, McFarlane, Jim Lee, Silvestri, Larsen, Williams, Ordway & Miki 4.00
2 ($3.50)-Kirby-a(p); Kirby/Larson-c 5.00
3-8: 3-(5/94, $2.50)-Kirby/McFarlane-c 4-(5/94)-Kirby-c(p). 5-(6/94) 4.00

PHANTOM GUARD
Image Comics (WildStorm Productions): Oct, 1997 - No. 6, Mar, 1998 ($2.50)

1-6: 1-Two covers 3.00
1-($3.50)-Voyager Pack w/Wildcore preview 4.00

PHANTOM JACK
Image Comics: Mar, 2004 - No. 5, July, 2004 ($2.95)

1-5-Mike San Giacomo-s/Mitchell Breitweiser-a. 4-Initial printings with errors exist 3.00
The Collected Edition (Speakeasy Comics, 2005, $17.99) r/series; Bendis intro 18.00

PHANTOM LADY (1st Series) (My Love Secret #24 on) (Also see All Top, Daring Adventures, Freedom Fighters, Jungle Thrills, & Wonder Boy)
Fox Feature Syndicate: No. 13, Aug, 1947 - No. 23, Apr, 1949

13(#1)-Phantom Lady by Matt Baker begins (see Police Comics #1 for 1st app.); Blue Beetle story 551 1102 1653 4022 7111 10,200
14-16: 14(#2)-Not Baker-c. 15-P.L. injected with experimental drug. 16-Negligee-c, panels; true crime stories begin 320 640 960 2240 3920 5600
17-Classic bondage cover; used in **SOTI**, illo "Sexual stimulation by combining 'headlights' with the sadist's dream of tying up a woman" 2725 5450 8175 20,900 38,450 56,000
18,19 308 616 924 2156 3778 5400
20-22 275 550 825 1746 3028 4300
23-Classic bondage-c 1200 2400 3600 9100 16,550 24,000
NOTE: ***Matt Baker** a-in all; c-13, 15-21. **Kamen** a-22, 23.*

PHANTOM LADY (2nd Series) (See Terrific Comics) (Formerly Linda)
Ajax/Farrell Publ.: V1#5, Dec-Jan, 1954/1955 - No. 4, June, 1955

V1#5(#1)-By Matt Baker 194 388 582 1242 2121 3000
V1#2-Last pre-code 129 258 387 826 1413 2000
3,4-Red Rocket. 3-Heroin story 106 212 318 673 1162 1650

PHANTOM LADY
Verotik Publications: 1994 ($9.95)

1-Reprints G. A. stories from Phantom Lady and All Top Comics; Adam Hughes-c 3 6 9 21 33 45

PHANTOM LADY
DC Comics: Oct, 2012 - No. 4, Jan, 2013 ($2.99, limited series)

1-4-Gray and Palmiotti-s/Staggs-a. 1-Re-intro with Doll Man; Conner-c 3.00

PHANTOM ON THE SCAN
AfterShock Comics: Apr, 2021 - No. 5, Sept, 2021 ($4.99/$3.99, limited series)

1-($4.99) Cullen Bunn-s/Mark Torres-a 5.00
2-5-($3.99) 4.00

PHANTOM PLANET, THE
Dell Publishing Co.: No. 1234, 1961

Four Color 1234-Movie 8 16 24 54 102 150

PHANTOM ROAD
Image Comics: Mar, 2023 - Present ($3.99)

1-Lemire-s/Walta-a 4.00

PHANTOM STRANGER, THE (1st Series)(See Saga of Swamp Thing)
National Periodical Publications: Aug-Sept, 1952 - No. 6, June-July, 1953

1(Scarce)-1st app. 514 1028 1542 3750 6625 9500
2 (Scarce) 300 600 900 1920 3310 4700
3-6 (Scarce) 284 568 852 1818 3109 4400
Ashcan (8,9/52) Not distributed to newsstands, only for in house use (no known sales)

PHANTOM STRANGER, THE (2nd Series) (See Showcase #80) (See Showcase Presents for B&W reprints)
National Periodical Publs.: May-June, 1969 - No. 41, Feb-Mar, 1976; No. 42, Mar, 2010

1-2nd S.A. app. P. Stranger; only 12¢ issue 12 24 36 79 170 260
2,3 6 12 18 38 69 100
4-1st new look Phantom Stranger; N. Adams-a 6 12 18 41 76 110
5-7 5 10 15 31 53 75
8-14: 14-Last 15¢ issue 4 8 12 23 37 50
15-19: All 25¢ giants (52 pgs.) 4 8 12 25 40 55
20-Dark Circle begins, ends #24. 3 6 9 16 24 32
21,22 3 6 9 14 20 25
23-Spawn of Frankenstein begins by Kaluta 4 8 12 25 40 55
24,25,27-30-Last Spawn of Frankenstein 3 6 9 19 30 40
26- Book-length story featuring Phantom Stranger, Dr. 13 & Spawn of Frankenstein 3 6 9 21 33 45
31-The Black Orchid begins (6-7/74). 3 6 9 18 28 38
32,34-38: 34-Last 20¢ issue (#35 on are 25¢) 2 4 6 13 18 22
33,39-41: 33-Deadman-c/story. 39-41-Deadman app. 3 6 9 14 20 25
42-(3/10, $2.99) Blackest Night one-shot; Syaf-a; Spectre, Deadman and Blue Devil app. 3.00
NOTE: ***N. Adams** a-4; c-3-19. **Anderson** a-4, 5i. **Aparo** a-7-17, 19-26; c-20-24, 33-41. **B. Bailey** a-27-30. **DeZuniga** a-12-16, 18, 19, 21, 22, 31, 34. **Grell** a-33. **Kaluta** a-23-25; c-26. **Meskin** r-15, 16, 18, 19. **Redondo** a-32, 35, 36. **Sparling** a-20. **Starr** a-17r. **Toth** a-15r. Black Orchid by **Carrilo**-38-41. Dr. 13 solo in-13, 18, 19, 20, 21, 34. Frankenstein by **Kaluta**-23-25; by **Baily**-27-30. No Black Orchid-33, 34, 37.*

PHANTOM STRANGER (See Justice League of America #103)
DC Comics: Oct, 1987 - No. 4, Jan, 1988 (75¢, limited series)

1-4-Mignola/Russell-c/a & Eclipso app. in all. 3,4-Eclipso-c 5.00

PHANTOM STRANGER (See intro. in DC Comics - The New 52 FCBD Special Edition) (Title changes to Trinity of Sin: The Phantom Stranger with #9 (Aug, 2013))
DC Comics: No. 0, Nov, 2012 - No. 22, Oct, 2015 ($2.99)

0-22: 0-Origin retold; Spectre app.; DiDio-s/Anderson-a. 2-Pandora app. 4,5-Jae Lee-c; Justice League Dark app. 6,7-Gene Ha-a/c; The Question app. 11-Trinity War. 12-17-Forever Evil tie-in. 18-Superman app. 20-The Spectre app. 3.00
...: Future's End (11/14, $3.99) 3-D lenticular cover; five years later; Winslade-a 4.00
...: Future's End (11/14, $2.99) regular cover; five years later 3.00

PHANTOM STRANGER (See Vertigo Visions-The Phantom Stranger)

PHANTOM: THE GHOST WHO WALKS
Marvel Comics: Feb, 1995 - No. 3, Apr, 1995 ($2.95, limited series)

Phantom Lady (2012) #1 © DC

Phenomx #1 © John Leguizamo

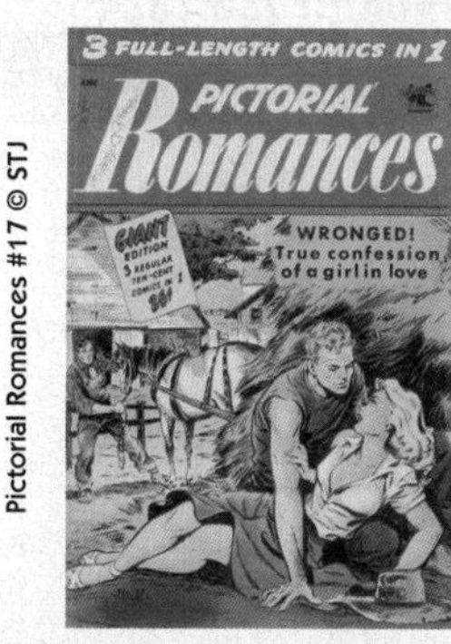

Pictorial Romances #17 © STJ

	GD 2.0	VG 4.0	FN 6.0	VF 8.0	VF/NM 9.0	NM- 9.2

1-3 4.00

PHANTOM: THE GHOST WHO WALKS
Moonstone: 2003 ($16.95, TPB)

nn-Three new stories by Raab, Goulart, Collins, Blanco and others; Klauba painted-c 17.00

PHANTOM 2040 (TV cartoon)
Marvel Comics: May, 1995 - No. 4, Aug, 1995 ($1.50)

1-4-Based on animated series; Ditko-a(p) in all 4.00

PHANTOM WITCH DOCTOR (Also see Durango Kid #8 & Eerie #8)
Avon Periodicals: 1952

1-Kinstler-c/a (7 pgs.) 113 226 339 718 1234 1750

PHANTOM ZONE, THE (See Adventure #283 & Superboy #100, 104)
DC Comics: January, 1982 - No. 4, April, 1982

1-4-Superman app. in all. 2-4: Batman, Green Lantern, Supergirl, Wonder Woman app. 4.00
NOTE: ***Colan** a-1-4p; c-1-4p. **Giordano** c-1-4i.*

PHAZE
Eclipse Comics: Apr, 1988 - No. 2, Oct, 1988 ($2.25)

1,2: 1-Sienkiewicz-c. 2-Gulacy painted-c 3.00

PHENOMX
Image Comics: Oct, 2021 - No. 4, Jan, 2022 ($6.99/$3.99)

1-($6.99) John Leguizamo co-plotter/Batista-a 7.00
2-4-($3.99) 4.00

PHIL RIZZUTO (Baseball Hero)(See Sport Thrills, Accepted reprint)
Fawcett Publications: 1951 (New York Yankees)

nn-Photo-c 74 148 222 470 810 1150

PHOENIX
Atlas/Seaboard Publ.: Jan, 1975 - No. 4, Oct, 1975

1-Origin; Rovin-s/Amendola-a 3 6 9 14 19 24
2-4: 3-Origin & only app. The Dark Avenger. 4-New origin/costume The Protector (formerly Phoenix) 2 4 6 9 13 16
NOTE: ***Infantino** appears in #1, 2. **Austin** a-3i. **Thorne** c-3.*

PHOENIX
Ardden Entertainment (Atlas Comics): Mar, 2011 - No. 6, May, 2012 ($2.99)

1-6-Krueger & Deneen-s/Zachary-a; origin re-told 3.00
... Issue Zero - NY Comicon Edtion (10/10, $2.99) Dorien-a; origin prequel to #1 3.00

PHOENIX (...The Untold Story)
Marvel Comics Group: April, 1984 ($2.00, one-shot)

1-Byrne/Austin-r/X-Men #137 with original unpublished ending 2 4 6 11 16 20

PHOENIX RESURRECTION, THE
Malibu Comics (Ultraverse): 1995 - 1996 ($3.95)

Genesis #1 (12/95)-X-Men app; wraparound-c, Revelations #1 (12/95)-X-Men app; wraparound-c, Aftermath #1 (1/96)-X-Men app. 5.00
0-($1.95)-r/series 4.00
0-American Entertainment Ed. 5.00

PHOENIX RESURRECTION: THE RETURN OF JEAN GREY
Marvel Comics: Feb, 2018 - No. 5 ($4.99/$3.99, limited series)

1,5-($4.99) Yu-a. 5-Leads into Jean Grey #11 and X-Men Red #1 5.00
2-4-($3.99) 2-Pacheco-a. 3-Bennett-a. 4-Rosanas-a 4.00

PHOENIX SONG: ECHO
Marvel Comics: Dec, 2021 - No. 5, Apr, 2022 ($4.99/$3.99, limited series)

1-($4.99) Maya Lopez gets the Phoenix Force; Roanhorse-s/Maresca-a 5.00
2-5-($3.99) 4.00

PHOENIX WITHOUT ASHES
IDW Publishing: Aug, 2010 - No. 4, Nov, 2010 ($3.99, limited series)

1-4-Harlan Ellison-s/Alan Robinson-a 4.00

PHONOGRAM
Image Comics: Aug, 2006 - No. 6, May, 2007 ($3.50, limited series)

1-Gillen-s/McKelvie-a 15.00
2-6 5.00

PHONOGRAM: THE SINGLES CLUB (Volume 2)
Image Comics: Dec, 2008 - No. 7, Feb, 2010 ($3.50, limited series)

1-7-Gillen-s/McKelvie-a. 5-Recalled for bar-code error 4.00

PHONOGRAM (Volume 3)(The Immaterial Girl)
Image Comics: Aug, 2015 - No. 6, Jan, 2016 ($3.99, limited series)

1-6-Gillen-s/McKelvie-a 4.00

PICNIC PARTY (See Dell Giants)

PICTORIAL CONFESSIONS (Pictorial Romances #4 on)
St. John Publishing Co.: Sept, 1949 - No. 3, Dec, 1949

1-Baker-c/a(3) 116 232 346 742 1271 1800
2-Baker-a; photo-c 43 86 129 271 461 650
3-Kubert, Baker-a; part Kubert-c 47 94 141 296 498 700

PICTORIAL LOVE STORIES (Formerly Tim McCoy)
Charlton Comics: No. 22, Oct, 1949 - No. 26, July, 1950 (all photo-c)

22-26: All have "Me-Dan Cupid". 25-Fred Astaire-c 24 48 72 142 234 325

PICTORIAL LOVE STORIES
St. John Publishing Co.: October, 1952

1-Baker-c 65 130 195 416 708 1000

PICTORIAL ROMANCES (Formerly Pictorial Confessions)
St. John Publ. Co.: No. 4, Jan, 1950; No. 5, Jan, 1951 - No. 24, Mar, 1954

4-Baker-a; photo-c 58 116 174 371 636 900
5,10-All Matt Baker issues. 5-Reprints all stories from #4 w/new Baker-c 68 136 204 435 743 1050
6-9,12,13,15,16-Baker-c, 2-3 stories 61 122 183 390 670 950
11-Baker-c/a(3); Kubert-r/Hollywood Confessions #1 68 136 204 435 743 1050
14,21-24: Baker-c/a each. 21,24-Each has signed story by Estrada 71 142 213 454 777 1100
17-20(7/53, 25¢, 100 pgs.): Baker-c/a; each has two signed stories by Estrada 126 252 378 806 1378 1950
NOTE: ***Matt Baker** art in most issues. **Estrada** a-17-20(2), 21, 24.*

PICTURE CRIMES
David McKay Publ.: June, 1937

1-Story in photo panels (a GD+ copy sold in 2012 for $478 and a certified 5.5 copy sold for $2051 in 2017)

PICTURE NEWS
Lafayette Street Corp.: Jan, 1946 - No. 10, Jan-Feb, 1947

1-Milt Gross begins, ends No. 6; 4 pg. Kirby-a; A-Bomb-c/story 52 104 156 328 552 775
2-Atomic explosion panels; Frank Sinatra/Perry Como story 27 54 81 158 259 360
3-Atomic explosion panels; Frank Sinatra, June Allyson, Benny Goodman stories 23 46 69 136 223 310
4-Atomic explosion panels; "Caesar and Cleopatra" movie adapt. w/Claude Raines & Vivian Leigh; Jackie Robinson story 27 54 81 158 259 360
5-7: 5-Hank Greenberg story; Atomic explosion panel. 6-Joe Louis-c/story 20 40 60 117 189 260
8,10: 8-Monte Hale story (9-10/46; 1st?). 10-Dick Quick; A-Bomb story; Krigstein, Gross-a 20 40 60 120 195 270
9-A-Bomb story; "Crooked Mile" movie adaptation; Joe DiMaggio story. 25 50 75 147 241 340

PICTURE PARADE (Picture Progress #5 on)
Gilberton Company (Also see A Christmas Adventure): Sept, 1953 - V1#4, Dec, 1953 (28 pgs.)

V1#1-Andy's Atomic Adventures; A-bomb blast-c; (Teachers version distributed to schools exists) 43 86 129 271 461 650
2-Around the World with the United Nations 15 30 45 85 130 175
3-Adventures of the Lost One(The American Indian), 4-A Christmas Adventure (r-under same title in 1969) 15 30 45 85 130 175

PICTURE PROGRESS (Formerly Picture Parade)
Gilberton Corp.: V1#5, Jan, 1954 - V3#2, Oct, 1955 (28-36 pgs.)

V1#5-9,V2#1-9: 5-News in Review 1953. 6-The Birth of America. 7-The Four Seasons. 8-Paul Revere's Ride. 9-The Hawaiian Islands(5/54). V2#1-The Story of Flight(9/54). 2-Vote for Crazy River (The Meaning of Elections). 3-Louis Pasteur. 4-The Star Spangled Banner. 5-News in Review 1954. 6-Alaska: The Great Land. 7-Life in the Circus. 8-The Time of the Cave Man. 9-Summer Fun(5/55) 9 18 27 50 65 80
V3#1,2: 1-The Man Who Discovered America. 2-The Lewis & Clark Expedition 9 18 27 47 61 75

PICTURE SCOPE JUNGLE ADVENTURES (See Jungle Thrills)

PICTURE STORIES FROM AMERICAN HISTORY
National/All-American/E. C. Comics: 1945 - No. 4, Sum, 1947 (#1,2: 10¢, 56 pgs.; #3,4: 15¢, 52 pgs.)

1 30 60 90 177 289 400

GD VG FN VF VF/NM NM-
2.0 4.0 6.0 8.0 9.0 9.2

2-4 24 48 72 140 230 320

PICTURE STORIES FROM SCIENCE
E.C. Comics: Spring, 1947 - No. 2, Fall, 1947
1-(15¢) 33 66 99 194 317 440
2-(10¢) 26 52 78 156 256 350

PICTURE STORIES FROM THE BIBLE (See Narrative Illustration, the Story of the Comics by M.C. Gaines)
National/All-American/E.C. Comics: 1942 - No. 4, Fall, 1943; 1944-46
1-4('42-Fall, '43)-Old Testament (DC) 27 54 81 158 259 360
Complete Old Testament Edition, (12/43-DC, 50¢, 232 pgs.);-1st printing; contains #1-4; 2nd - 8th (1/47) printings exist; later printings by E.C. some with 65¢-c
36 72 108 211 343 475
Complete Old Testament Edition (1945-publ. by Bible Pictures Ltd.)-232 pgs., hardbound, in color with dust jacket 36 72 108 211 343 475
NOTE: *Both Old and New Testaments published in England by Bible Pictures Ltd. in hardback, 1943, in color, 376 pgs. (2 vols.: O.T. 232 pgs. & N.T. 144 pgs.), and were also published by Scarf Press in 1979 (Old Test., $9.95) and in 1980 (New Test., $7.95)*
1-3(New Test.; 1944-46, DC)-52 pgs. ea. 21 42 63 122 199 275
The Complete Life of Christ Edition (1945, 25¢, 96 pgs.)-Contains #1&2 of the New Testament Edition 36 72 108 211 343 475
1,2(Old Testament-r in comic book form)(E.C., 1946; 52 pgs.)
21 42 63 122 199 275
1(DC),2(AA),3(EC)(New Testament-r in comic book form)(E.C., 1946; 52 pgs.)
21 42 63 122 199 275
Complete New Testament Edition (1945-E.C., 40¢, 144 pgs.)-Contains #1-3
1946 printing has 50¢-c 36 72 108 211 343 475
NOTE: *Another British series entitled* ***The Bible Illustrated*** *from 1947 has recently been discovered, with the same internal artwork. This eight edition series (5-OT, 3-NT) is of particular interest to Classics Ill. collectors because it exactly copied the C.I. logo format. The British publisher was Thorpe & Porter, who in 1951 began publishing the British Classics Ill. series. All editions of The Bible Ill. have new British painted covers. While this market is still new, and not all editions have as yet been found, current market value is about the same as the first U.S. editions of Picture Stories From The Bible.*

PICTURE STORIES FROM WORLD HISTORY
E.C. Comics: Spring, 1947 - No. 2, Summer, 1947 (52, 48 pgs.)
1-(15¢) 31 62 93 186 303 420
2-(10¢) 24 48 72 140 230 320

PIECEMEAL
AfterShock Comics: Dec, 2020 ($6.99, oversized 8-1/2" x 10-7/8", one shot)
1-Cullen Bunn-s/Szymon Kudranski-a 7.00

PIGS
Image Comics: Sept, 2011 - No. 8, Aug, 2012 ($2.99)
1-8: 1-Cosby & McCool-s/Tamura-a/Jock-c. 3-Conner-c. 5-Gibbons-c. 7-Ramos-c 3.00

PILGRIM, THE
IDW Publishing: Apr, 2010 - No. 2, Jun, 2010 ($3.99, limited series)
1,2-Mike Grell-a/c; Mark Ryan-s 4.00

PILOT SEASON...
Image Comics (Top Cow): 2008 - 2011 ($1.00/$2.99/$3.99, one-shots)
...: Asset (9/10, $3.99) Sablik-s/Marquez-a/Frison-c 4.00
...: City of Refuge (10/11, $3.99) Foehl-s/Calero-a/c 4.00
...: Crosshair (10/10, $3.99) Katz-s/Jefferson-a/Silvestri-c 4.00
...: Declassified (10/09, $1.00) Preview of one-shots with covers, script and sketch pgs. 3.00
...: Demonic (1/10, $2.99) Kirkman-s/Benitez-a; two covers by Silvestri 3.00
...: Fleshdigger (10/11, $3.99) Denton & Keene-s; Sanchez-a; Francavilla-c 4.00
...: Forever (10/10, $3.99) Inglesby-s/Nachlik-a/Hutomo-c 4.00
...: Murdered (11/09, $2.99) Kirkman-s/Blake-a; two covers by Silvestri 3.00
...: 7 Days From Hell (10/10, $3.99) Noto-a/Hill & Levin-s/Stelfreeze-c 4.00
...: Stellar (7/10, $2.99) Kirkman-s/Chang-a/Silvestri-c 3.00
...: The Beauty (10/11, $3.99) Haun & Hurley-s/Haun-a/c (becomes a 2015 series) 10.00
...: The Test (10/10, $3.99) Fialkov-s/Ekedal-a/Hutomo-c 4.00
...: 39 Minutes (9/10, $3.99) Harms-s/Lando-a/Albuquerque-c 4.00
...: Twilight Guardian (5/08, $3.99) Hickman-s 4.00

PINHEAD
Marvel Comics (Epic Comics): Dec, 1993 - No. 6, May, 1994 ($2.50)
1-($2.95)-Embossed foil-c by Kelley Jones; Intro Pinhead & Disciples (Snakeoil, Hangman, Fan Dancer & Dixie) 4.00
2-6 3.00

PINHEAD & FOODINI (TV)(Also see Foodini & Jingle Dingle Christmas...)
Fawcett Publications: July, 1951 - No. 4, Jan, 1952 (Early TV comic)
1-(52 pgs.)-Photo-c; based on TV puppet show 35 70 105 208 339 470
2,3-Photo-c 19 38 57 111 176 240
4 15 30 45 88 137 185

PINHEAD VS. MARSHALL LAW (Law in Hell)
Marvel Comics (Epic): Nov, 1993 - No. 2, Dec, 1993 ($2.95, lim. series)
1,2: 1-Embossed red foil-c. 2-Embossed silver foil-c 4.00

PINK DUST
Kitchen Sink Press: 1998 ($3.50, B&W, mature)
1-J. O'Barr-s/a 3.50

PINK PANTHER, THE (TV)(See The Inspector & Kite Fun Book)
Gold Key #1-70/Whitman #71-87: April, 1971 - No. 87, Mar, 1984
1-The Inspector begins 8 16 24 51 96 140
2-5 3 6 9 17 26 35
6-10 3 6 9 14 19 24
11-30: Warren Tufts-a #16-on 2 4 6 9 13 16
31-60 2 4 6 8 11 14
61-70 1 2 3 5 7 9
71-74,81-83: 81(2/82), 82(3/82), 83(4/82) 2 4 6 8 10 12
75(8/80)-77 (Whitman pre-pack) (scarce) 4 8 12 27 44 60
78(1/80)-80 (Whitman pre-pack) (not as scarce) 2 4 6 11 16 20
78 (1/81, 40¢-c) Cover price error variant 3 6 9 15 22 28
84-87(All #90266 on-c, no date or date code): 84(6/83), 85(8/83), 87(3/84)
3 6 9 14 20 26
Mini-comic No. 1(1976)(3-1/4x6-1/2") 2 4 6 8 10 12
NOTE: *Pink Panther began as a movie cartoon. (See Golden Comics Digest #38, 45 and March of Comics #376, 384, 390, 409, 418, 429, 441, 449, 461, 473, 486); #37, 72, 80-85 contain reprints.*

PINK PANTHER SUPER SPECIAL (TV)
Harvey Comics: Oct, 1993 ($2.25, 68 pgs.)
V2#1-The Inspector & Wendy Witch stories also 5.00

PINK PANTHER, THE
Harvey Comics: Nov, 1993 - No. 9, July, 1994 ($1.50)
V2#1-9 4.00

PINK PANTHER, THE (Volume 3)
American Mythology Productions: 2016 - Present ($3.99)
1-4-New and classic short stories by various; multiple covers on each. 4-Trick or Pink 4.00
... Anniversary Special 1 (2017, $3.99) New short stories and reprints; 3 covers 4.00
...: Cartoon Hour Special 1,2 (2017, $4.99) Short stories by various; 3 covers 5.00
...: Classic Christmas 1 (2018, $3.99) Reprint from Pink Panther #60 (1979) 4.00
... 55th Anniversary Special 1 (2019, $3.99) New short stories and reprints; 3 covers 4.00
... Presents the Ant & the Aardvark 1 (2018, $3.99) New short stories and reprints 4.00
...: Snow Day (2017, $3.99) New short stories by S.A. Check and reprint; 3 covers 4.00
... Super-Pink Special 1 (2017, $3.99) New short stories and reprint; 3 covers 4.00
... Surfside Special 1 (2018, $3.99) New short stories and reprints; 2 covers 4.00
... Vs. The Inspector 1 (2018, $3.99) New short stories and reprints; 2 covers 4.00
... Winter Special 1 (2018, $3.99) New short stories and reprints; 2 covers 4.00

PINKY & THE BRAIN (See Animaniacs)
DC Comics: July, 1996 - No. 27, Nov, 1998 ($1.75/$1.95/$1.99)
1-27, ...Christmas Special (1/96, $1.50) 4.00

PINKY LEE (See Adventures of...)

PINKY THE EGGHEAD
I.W./Super Comics: 1963 (Reprints from Noodnik)
I.W. Reprint #1,2(nd) 2 4 6 8 11 14
Super Reprint #14-r/Noodnik Comics #4 2 4 6 8 11 14

PINOCCHIO (See 4-Color #92, 252, 545, 1203, Mickey Mouse Mag. V5#3, Movie Comics under Wonderful Advs. of..., New Advs. of..., Thrilling Comics #2, Walt Disney Showcase, Walt Disney's..., Wonderful Advs. of..., & World's Greatest Stories #2)
Dell Publishing Co.: No. 92, 1945 - No. 1203, Mar, 1962 (Disney)
Four Color 92-The Wonderful Adventures of...; 16 pg. Donald Duck story ; entire book by Kelly 52 104 156 416 933 1450
Four Color 252 (10/49)-Origin, not by Kelly 13 26 39 87 195 300
Four Color 545 (3/54)-The Wonderful Advs. of...; part-r of 4-Color #92; Disney-movie
9 18 27 61 123 185
Four Color 1203 (3/62) 7 14 21 49 92 135

PINOCCHIO AND THE EMPEROR OF THE NIGHT
Marvel Comics: Mar, 1988 ($1.25, 52 pgs.)
1-Adapts film 4.00

PINOCCHIO LEARNS ABOUT KITES (See Kite Fun Book)

PIN-UP PETE (Also see Great Lover Romances & Monty Hall...)
Toby Press: 1952
1-Jack Sparling pin-ups 30 60 90 177 289 400

PIONEER MARSHAL (See Fawcett Movie Comics)

PIONEER PICTURE STORIES
Street & Smith Publications: Dec, 1941 - No. 9, Dec, 1943
1-The Legless Air Ace begins; WWII-c 53 106 159 334 567 800
2 -True life story of Errol Flynn 27 54 81 160 263 365
3-5,7-9 22 44 66 132 216 300
6-Classic Japanese WWII "Remember Pearl Harbor"-c
174 348 522 1114 1907 2700

PIONEER WEST ROMANCES (Firehair #1,2,7-11)
Fiction House Magazines: No. 3, Spring, 1950 - No. 6, Winter, 1950-51
3-(52 pgs.)-Firehair continues 22 44 66 126 209 290
4-6 22 44 66 132 216 300

PIPSQUEAK (See The Adventures of...)

PIRACY
E. C. Comics: Oct-Nov, 1954 - No. 7, Oct-Nov, 1955
1-Williamson/Torres-a; has full page subscription ad for unpublished Crypt of Terror #1
40 80 120 320 510 700
2-Williamson/Torres-a 23 46 69 184 292 400
3-7: 5-7-Comics Code symbol on cover 18 36 54 144 227 310
NOTE: ***Crandall*** *a-in all; c-2-4.* ***Davis*** *a-1, 2, 6.* ***Evans*** *a-3-7; c-7.* ***Ingels*** *a-3-7.* ***Krigstein*** *a-3-5, 7; c-5, 6.* ***Wood*** *a-1, 2; c-1.*

PIRACY
Gemstone Publishing: March, 1998 - No. 7, Sept, 1998 ($2.50)
1-7: E.C. reprints 4.00
Annual 1 ($10.95) Collects #1-4 11.00
Annual 2 ($7.95) Collects #5-7 8.00

PIRANA (See The Phantom #46 & Thrill-O-Rama #2, 3)

PIRATE CORP$, THE (See Hectic Planet)
Eternity Comics/Slave Labor Graphics: 1987 - No. 4, 1988 ($1.95)
1-4: 1,2-Color. 3,4-B&W 3.00
Special 1 ('89, B&W)-Slave Labor Publ. 3.00

PIRATE CORP$, THE (Volume 2)
Slave Labor Graphics: 1989 - No. 6, 1992 ($1.95)
1-6-Dorkin-s/a 3.00

PIRATE OF THE GULF, THE (See Superior Stories #2)

PIRATES COMICS
Hillman Periodicals: Feb-Mar, 1950 - No. 4, Aug-Sept, 1950 (All 52 pgs.)
1 36 72 108 211 343 475

Pink Panther Classic Christmas #1 © MGM

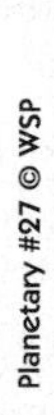

Planetary #27 © WSP

Planet Hulk: Worldbreaker #1 © MAR

	GD	VG	FN	VF	VF/NM	NM-
	2.0	4.0	6.0	8.0	9.0	9.2
2-Dave Berg-a	20	40	60	117	189	260
3,4-Berg-a	19	38	57	109	172	235

PIRATES OF CONEY ISLAND, THE
Image Comics: Oct, 2006 - No. 8 ($2.99)

1-6-Rick Spears-s/Vasilis Lolos-a; two covers. 2-Cloonan var-c 3.00

PIRATES OF DARK WATER, THE (Hanna Barbera)
Marvel Comics: Nov, 1991 - No. 9, Aug, 1992 ($1.95)

1-9: 9-Vess-c 3.00

PISCES
Image Comics: Apr, 2015 - No. 3, Jul, 2015 ($3.50/$3.99, unfinished series)

1-3-Kurtis Wiebe-s/Johnnie Christmas-a 4.00

P.I.'S: MICHAEL MAUSER AND MS. TREE, THE
First Comics: Jan, 1985 - No. 3, May, 1985 ($1.25, limited series)

1-3: Staton-c/a(p) 3.00

PITT, THE (Also see The Draft & The War)
Marvel Comics: Mar, 1988 ($3.25, 52 pgs., one-shot)

1-Ties into Starbrand, D.P.7 4.00

PITT (See Youngblood #4 & Gen 13 #3,#4)
Image Comics #1-9/Full Bleed #1/2,10-on: Jan, 1993 - No. 20 ($1.95, intended as a four part limited series)

1/2-(12/95)-1st Full Bleed issue 4.00
1-Dale Keown-c/a. 1-1st app. The Pitt 5.00
2-13: All Dale Keown-c/a. 3 (Low distribution). 10 (1/96)-Indicia reads "January 1995" 3.00
14-20: 14-Begin $2.50-c, pullout poster 3.00
TPB-(1997, $9.95) r/#1/2, 1-4 12.00
TPB 2-(1999, $11.95) r/#5-9 12.00

PITT CREW
Full Bleed Studios: Aug, 1998 - No. 5, Dec, 1999 ($2.50)

1-5: 1-Richard Pace-s/Ken Lashley-a. 2-4-Scott Lee-a 3.00

PITT IN THE BLOOD
Full Bleed Studios: Aug, 1996 ($2.50, one-shot)

nn-Richard Pace-a/script 3.00

PIXIE & DIXIE & MR. JINKS (TV)(See Jinks, Pixie, and Dixie & Whitman Comic Books)
Dell Publishing Co./Gold Key: July-Sept, 1960 - Feb, 1963 (Hanna-Barbera)

	GD	VG	FN	VF	VF/NM	NM-
Four Color 1112	8	16	24	54	102	150
Four Color 1196,1264, 01-631-207 (Dell, 7/62)	5	10	15	35	63	90
1(2/63-Gold Key)	6	12	18	37	66	95

PIXIE PUZZLE ROCKET TO ADVENTURELAND
Avon Periodicals: Nov, 1952

	GD	VG	FN	VF	VF/NM	NM-
1	25	50	75	150	245	340

PIXIES, THE (Advs. of...)(The Mighty Atom and ...#6 on)(See A-1 Comics #16)
Magazine Enterprises: Winter, 1946 - No. 4, Fall?, 1947; No. 5, 1948

	GD	VG	FN	VF	VF/NM	NM-
1-Mighty Atom	15	30	45	84	127	170
2-5-Mighty Atom	9	18	27	50	65	80
I.W. Reprint #1(1958), 8-(Pee-Wee Pixies), 10-I.W. on cover, Super on inside	3	6	9	14	19	24

PIZZAZZ
Marvel Comics: Oct, 1977 - No. 16, Jan, 1979 (slick-color kids mag. w/puzzles, games, comics)

	GD	VG	FN	VF	VF/NM	NM-
1-Star Wars photo-c/article; origin Tarzan; KISS photos/article; Iron-On bonus; 2 pg. pin-up calendars thru #8	5	10	15	31	53	75
2-Spider-Man-c; Beatles pin-up calendar	2	4	6	13	18	22
3-8: 3-Close Encounters-s; Bradbury-s. 4-Alice Cooper, Travolta; Charlie's Angels/Fonz/Hulk/Spider-Man-c. 5-Star Trek quiz. 6-Asimov-s. 7-James Bond; Spock/Darth Vader-c. 8-TV Spider-Man photo-c/article	2	4	6	11	16	20
9-14: 9-Shaun Cassidy-c. 10-Sgt. Pepper-c/s. 12-Battlestar Galactica-s; Spider-Man app. 13-TV Hulk-c/s. 14-Meatloaf-c/s	2	4	6	10	14	18
15,16: 15-Battlestar Galactica-s. 16-Movie Superman photo-c/s, Hulk.	2	4	6	11	16	20

NOTE: ***Star Wars** comics in all (1-6:Chaykin-a, 7-9: DeZuniga-a, 10-13:Simonson/Janson-a. 14-16:Cockrum-a). **Tarzan** comics, 1pg.-#1-8. 1pg. "Hey Look" by Kurtzman #12-16.*

PLANETARY (See Preview in flip book Gen13 #33)
DC Comics (WildStorm Prod.): Apr, 1999 - No. 27, Dec, 2009 ($2.50/$2.95/$2.99)

	GD	VG	FN	VF	VF/NM	NM-
1-Ellis-s/Cassaday-a/c	2	4	6	10	14	18

1-Special Edition (6/09, $1.00) r/#1 with "After Watchmen" cover frame 3.00
2-5 6.00
6-10 5.00
11-15: 12-Fourth Man revealed 4.00
16-26: 16-Begin $2.95-c. 23-Origin of The Drummer 3.00
27-($3.99) Wraparound gatefold-c 4.00
...: All Over the World and Other Stories (2000, $14.95) r/#1-6 & Preview 15.00
...: All Over the World and Other Stories-Hardcover (2000, $24.95) r/#1-6 & Preview; with dustjacket 25.00
.../Batman: Night on Earth 1 (8/03, $5.95) Ellis-s/Cassaday-a 6.00
...: Crossing Worlds (2004, $14.95) r/Batman, JLA, and The Authority x-overs 15.00
.../JLA: Terra Occulta (11/02, $5.95) Elseworlds; Ellis-s/Ordway-a 6.00
...: Leaving the 20th Century -HC (2004, $24.95) r/#13-18 25.00
...: Leaving the 20th Century -SC (2004, $14.99) r/#13-18 15.00
...: Spacetime Archaeology -HC (2010, $24.99) r/#19-27 25.00
...: Spacetime Archaeology -SC (2010, $17.99) r/#19-27 18.00
.../The Authority: Ruling the World (8/00, $5.95) Ellis-s/Phil Jimenez-a 6.00
...: The Fourth Man -Hardcover (2001, $24.95) r/#7-12 25.00
...: The Planetary Reader (8/03, $5.95) r/#13-15 6.00

PLANETARY BRIGADE (Also see Hero Squared)
BOOM! Studios: Feb, 2006 - No. 2, Mar, 2006 ($2.99)

1-3-Giffen & DeMatteis-s/art by various; Haley-c 3.00
... Origins 1-3 (10/06-4/07, $3.99) Giffen & DeMatteis-s/Julia Bax-a 4.00

PLANET COMICS
Fiction House Magazines: 1/40 - No. 62, 9/49; No. 63, Wint, 1949-50; No. 64, Spring, 1950; No. 65, 1951(nd); No. 66-68, 1952(nd); No. 69, Wint, 1952-53; No. 70-72, 1953(nd); No. 73, Winter, 1953-54

	GD	VG	FN	VF	VF/NM	NM-
1-Origin Auro, Lord of Jupiter by Briefer (ends #61); Flint Baker & The Red Comet begin; Eisner/Fine-c	1900	3800	5700	14,250	27,125	40,000
2-Lou Fine-c (Scarce)	975	1950	2919	7100	12,550	18,000
3-Eisner-c	423	846	1269	3088	5444	7800
4-Gale Allen and the Girl Squadron begins	377	754	1131	2639	4620	6600
5,6-(Scarce): 5-Eisner/Fine-c	411	822	1233	2877	5039	7200
7-12: 8-Robot-c. 12-The Star Pirate begins	308	616	924	2156	3778	5400
13,14: 13-Reff Ryan begins	300	600	900	1950	3375	4800
15-(Scarce)-Mars, God of War begins (11/41); see Jumbo Comics #31 for 1st app.	1400	2800	4200	10,600	19,300	28,000
16-20,22	219	438	657	1402	2401	3400
21-The Lost World & Hunt Bowman begin	245	490	735	1568	2684	3800
23-26: 26-Space Rangers begin (9/43), end #71	194	388	582	1242	2121	3000
27-30	155	310	465	992	1696	2400
31-35: 33-Origin Star Pirates Wonder Boots, reprinted in #52. 35-Mysta of the Moon begins, ends #62	142	284	426	909	1555	2200
36-45: 38-1st Mysta of the Moon-c. 41-New origin of "Auro, Lord of Jupiter". 42-Last Gale Allen. 43-Futura begins	119	238	357	762	1306	1850
46-60: 48-Robot-c. 53-Used in **SOTI**, pg. 32	100	200	300	635	1093	1550
61-68,70: 64,70-Robot-c. 65-70-All partial-r of earlier issues. 70-r/stories from #41	81	162	243	518	884	1250
69-Used in **POP**, pgs. 101,102	90	180	270	576	988	1400
71-73-No series stories. 71-Space Rangers strip	74	148	222	470	810	1150
I.W. Reprint 1,8,9: 1(nd)-r/#70; cover-r from Attack on Planet Mars. 8 (r/#72), 9-r/#73	10	20	30	64	132	200

NOTE: ***Anderson** a-33-38, 40-51 (Star Pirate), 58. **Matt Baker** a-53-59 (Mysta of the Moon). **Celardo** c-12. **Bill Discount** a-71 (Space Rangers). **Elias** c-70. **Evans** a-46-49 (Auro, Lord of Jupiter), 50-64 (Lost World). **Fine** c-2, 5. **Hopper** a-31, 35 (Gale Allen), 41, 42, 48, 49 (Mysta of the Moon). **Ingels** a-24-31 (Lost World), 56-61 (Auro, Lord of Jupiter). **Lubbers** a-44-47 (Space Rangers); c-40, 41. **Moreira** a-43, 44 (Mysta of the Moon). **Renee** a-40-49 (Lost World); c-33, 35, 39. **Tuska** a-30 (Star Pirate). **M. Whitman** a-50-52 (Mysta of the Moon), 53-58 (Star Pirate); c-71-73. **Starr** a-59. **Zolnerwich** c-10. 13-25. Bondage c-53.*

PLANET COMICS
Pacific Comics: 1984 ($5.95)

	GD	VG	FN	VF	VF/NM	NM-
1-Reprints Planet Comics #1(1940)	1	2	3	5	6	8

PLANET COMICS
Blackthorne Publishing: Apr, 1988 - No. 3 ($2.00, color/B&W #3)

	GD	VG	FN	VF	VF/NM	NM-
1-New stories; Dave Stevens-c	8	16	24	51	96	140
2,3: New stories	1	2	3	5	6	8

PLANET HULK (See Incredible Hulk and Giant-Size Hulk #1 (2006))

PLANET HULK (Secret Wars tie-in)
Marvel Comics: Jul, 2015 - No. 5, Nov, 2015 ($4.99/$3.99, limited series)

1-($4.99) Humphries-s/Laming-a; Steve Rogers app.; back-up Pak-s//Miyazawa-a 5.00
2-5-($3.99) Doc Green & Devil Dinosaur app. 4.00

PLANET HULK: WORLDBREAKER
Marvel Comics: Jan, 2023 - No. 5, May, 2023 ($4.99/$3.99, limited series)

1-($4.99) Pak-s/Garcia-a; a thousand years later on Sakaar; back-up story with Skaar 5.00
2-5-($3.99) 4.00

	GD 2.0	VG 4.0	FN 6.0	VF 8.0	VF/NM 9.0	NM- 9.2

PLANET OF THE APES (Magazine) (Also see Adventures on the... & Power Record Comics)
Marvel Comics Group: Aug, 1974 - No. 29, Feb, 1977 (B&W) (Based on movies)

Issue	GD	VG	FN	VF	VF/NM	NM-
1-Ploog-a	5	10	15	35	63	90
2-Ploog-a	3	6	9	16	24	32
3-10	3	6	9	14	20	26
11-20	3	6	9	15	22	28
21-28 (low distribution)	3	6	9	21	33	45
29 (low distribution)	6	12	18	37	66	95

NOTE: ***Alcala** a-7-11, 17-22, 24. **Ploog** a-1-4, 6, 8, 11, 13, 14, 19. **Sutton** a-11, 12, 15, 17, 19, 20, 23, 24, 29. **Tuska** a-1-6.*

PLANET OF THE APES
Adventure Comics: Apr, 1990 - No. 24, 1992 ($2.50, B&W)

Issue	GD	VG	FN	VF	VF/NM	NM-
1-New movie tie-in; comes w/outer-c (3 colors)						4.00
1-Limited serial numbered edition ($5.00)	1	2	3	5	6	8
1-2nd printing (no outer-c, $2.50)						3.00
2-24						3.00
Annual 1 ($3.50)						4.00
...Urchak's Folly 1-4 ($2.50, mini-series)						3.00

PLANET OF THE APES (The Human War)
Dark Horse Comics: Jun, 2001 - No. 3, Aug, 2001 ($2.99, limited series)

Issue	GD	VG	FN	VF	VF/NM	NM-
1-3-Follows the 2001 movie; Edginton-s						3.00

PLANET OF THE APES
Dark Horse Comics: Sept, 2001 - No. 6, Feb, 2002 ($2.99, ongoing series)

Issue	GD	VG	FN	VF	VF/NM	NM-
1-6: 1-3-Edginton-s. 1-Photo & Wagner covers. 2-Plunkett & photo-c						3.00

PLANET OF THE APES
BOOM! Studios: Apr, 2011 - No. 15, Jun, 2012 ($3.99)

Issue	GD	VG	FN	VF	VF/NM	NM-
1-4,6-15-Takes place 1200 years before Taylor's arrival; Magno-a; three covers						4.00
5-($1.00) Three covers						3.00
Annual 1 (8/12, $4.99) Short stories by various; six covers						5.00
Giant 1 (9/13, $4.99) Gregory-s/Barreto-a						5.00
Special 1 (2/13, $4.99) Continued from #15; Diego Barreto-a						5.00
Spectacular 1 (7/13, $4.99) Gregory-s/Barreto-a						5.00
...: The Simian Age 1 (12/18, $7.99) Short stories by various; 2 covers						8.00
...: The Time of Man 1 (10/18, $7.99) Short stories by various incl. Magno; 2 covers						8.00

PLANET OF THE APES: CATACLYSM
BOOM! Studios: Sept, 2012 - No. 12, Aug, 2013 ($3.99)

Issue	GD	VG	FN	VF	VF/NM	NM-
1-12-Takes place 8 years before Taylor's arrival; Couceiro-a. 1-Multiple covers						4.00

PLANET OF THE APES/ GREEN LANTERN
BOOM! Studios: Feb, 2017 - No. 6, Jul, 2017 ($3.99, limited series)

Issue	GD	VG	FN	VF	VF/NM	NM-
1-6-Bagenda-a; Hal Jordan & Sinestro on the POTA; Cornelius app.; multiple covers						4.00

PLANET OF THE APES: URSUS
BOOM! Studios: Jan, 2018 - No. 6, Jun, 2018 ($3.99, limited series)

Issue	GD	VG	FN	VF	VF/NM	NM-
1-6-Spotlight on General Ursus; Walker-s/Mooneyham-a						4.00

PLANET OF THE APES VISIONARIES
BOOM! Studios: Aug, 2018 ($19.99, hardcover graphic novel)

Issue	GD	VG	FN	VF	VF/NM	NM-
HC-Alternate version in an adaptation of Rod Serling's original screenplay; Dana Gould-s/ Chad Lewis-a/Paolo Rivera-c; bonus character design art						20.00

PLANET OF THE NERDS
AHOY Comics: 2019 - No. 5, 2019 ($3.99, limited series)

Issue	GD	VG	FN	VF	VF/NM	NM-
1-5-Paul Constant-s/Alan Robinson-a. 1,2-Nakayama-c						4.00

PLANET OF VAMPIRES
Seaboard Publications (Atlas): Feb, 1975 - No. 3, July, 1975

Issue	GD	VG	FN	VF	VF/NM	NM-
1-Neal Adams-c(i); 1st Broderick-c/a(p); Hama-s	3	6	9	19	30	40
2,3: 2-Neal Adams-c. 3-Heath-c/a	3	6	9	14	19	24

PLANET-SIZE X-MEN
Marvel Comics: Aug, 2021 ($4.99, one-shot)

Issue	GD	VG	FN	VF	VF/NM	NM-
1-X-Men terraform Mars to create the Planet Arakko for mutants; Duggan-s/Larraz-a						5.00

PLANET TERRY
Marvel Comics (Star Comics)/Marvel: April, 1985 - No. 12, March, 1986 (Children's comic)

Issue	GD	VG	FN	VF	VF/NM	NM-
1-12						5.00
1-Variant with "Star Chase" game on last page & inside back-c						15.00

PLANTS VS. ZOMBIES (Based on the Electronic Arts game)
Dark Horse Comics: Jun, 2015 - No. 12, Jun, 2016 ($2.99)

Issue	GD	VG	FN	VF	VF/NM	NM-
1-12: 1-3-Bully For You; Tobin-s/Chan-a. 4-6-Grown Sweet Home. 7-9-Petal to the Metal						3.00
...: Garden Warfare 1-3 (10/15 - No. 3, 12/15, $2.99) Tobin-s/Chabot-a						3.00

PLASM (See Warriors of Plasm)
Defiant: June, 1993

Issue	GD	VG	FN	VF	VF/NM	NM-
0-Came bound into Diamond Previews V3#6 (6/93); price is for complete Previews with comic still attached	3	6	9	17	26	35
0-Comic only removed from Previews	3	6	9	14	20	25
0-One staple variant	10	20	30	68	144	220

PLASMER
Marvel Comics UK: Nov, 1993 - No. 4, Feb, 1994 ($1.95, limited series)

Issue	GD	VG	FN	VF	VF/NM	NM-
1-($2.50)-Polybagged w/4 trading cards						4.00
2-4: Capt. America & Silver Surfer app.						3.00

PLASTIC FORKS
Marvel Comis (Epic Comics): 1990 - No. 5, 1990 ($4.95, 68 pgs., limited series, mature)

Issue	GD	VG	FN	VF	VF/NM	NM-
Book 1-5: Squarebound						5.00

PLASTIC MAN (Also see Police Comics & Smash Comics #17)
Vital Publ. No. 1,2/Quality Comics No. 3 on: Sum, 1943 - No. 64, Nov, 1956

Issue	GD	VG	FN	VF	VF/NM	NM-
nn(#1)- "In The Game of Death"; Skull-c; Jack Cole-c/a begins; ends-#64?	541	1082	1623	3950	6975	10,000
nn(#2, 2/44)- "The Gay Nineties Nightmare"	181	362	543	1158	1979	2800
3 (Spr, '46)	118	236	354	749	1287	1825
4 (Sum, '46)	89	178	267	565	970	1375
5 (Aut, '46)	73	146	219	467	796	1125
6-10	60	120	180	381	653	925
11-15,17-20	53	106	159	334	567	800
16-Classic-c	61	122	183	390	670	950
21-30: 26-Last non-r issue?	41	82	123	256	428	600
31-40: 40-Used in POP, pg. 91	34	68	102	199	325	450
41-64: 53-Last precode issue. 54-Robot-c. 64-Sci-fi-c	28	56	84	165	270	375
Super Reprint 11,16,18: 11('63)-r/#16. 16-r/#18 & #21; Cole-a. 18('64)-Spirit-r by Eisner from Police #95	4	8	12	24	37	50

NOTE: ***Cole** r-44, 49, 56, 58, 59 at least. **Cuidera** c-32-64i.*

PLASTIC MAN (See DC Special #15 & House of Mystery #160)
National Periodical Publications/DC Comics: 11-12/66 - No. 10, 5-6/68; V4#11, 2-3/76 - No. 20, 10-11/77

Issue	GD	VG	FN	VF	VF/NM	NM-
1-Real 1st app. Silver Age Plastic Man (House of Mystery #160 is actually tryout); Gil Kane-c/a; 12¢ issues begin	14	28	42	96	211	325
2-5: 4-Infantino-c; Mortimer-a	5	10	15	33	57	80
6-10('68): 7-G.A. Plastic Man & Woozy Winks (1st S.A. app.) app.; origin retold. 10-Sparling-a; last 12¢ issue	4	8	12	27	44	60
V4#11('76)-20: 11-20-Fradon-p. 17-Origin retold	2	4	6	8	11	14
...80-Page Giant (2003, $6.95) reprints origin and other stories in 80-Pg. Giant format						7.00
...Special 1 (8/99, $3.95)						4.00

PLASTIC MAN
DC Comics: Nov, 1988 - No. 4, Feb, 1989 ($1.00, mini-series)

Issue	GD	VG	FN	VF	VF/NM	NM-
1-4: 1-Origin; Woozy Winks app.						4.00

PLASTIC MAN
DC Comics: Feb, 2004 - No. 20, Mar, 2006 ($2.95/$2.99)

Issue	GD	VG	FN	VF	VF/NM	NM-
1-20-Kyle Baker-s/a in most. 1-Retells origin. 7,12-Scott Morse-s/a. 8-JLA cameo						3.00
...: On the Lam TPB (2004, $14.95) r/#1-6						15.00
...: Rubber Bandits TPB (2005, $14.99) r/#8-11,13,14						15.00

PLASTIC MAN
DC Comics: Aug, 2018 - No. 6, Jan, 2019 ($3.99, limited series)

Issue	GD	VG	FN	VF	VF/NM	NM-
1-6-Gail Simone-s/Adriana Melo-a. 1-Origin re-told. 2,3-Man-Bat app. 3-Ross-c						4.00

PLASTRON CAFE
Mirage Studios: Dec, 1992 - No. 4, July, 1993 ($2.25, B&W)

Issue	GD	VG	FN	VF	VF/NM	NM-
1-4: 1-Teenage Mutant Ninja Turtles app.; Kelly Freas-c. 2-Hildebrandt painted-c. 4-Spaced & Alien Fire stories						3.00

PLAYFUL LITTLE AUDREY (TV)(Also see Little Audrey #25)
Harvey Publications: 6/57 - No. 110, 11/73; No. 111, 8/74 - No. 121, 4/76

Issue	GD	VG	FN	VF	VF/NM	NM-
1	35	70	105	252	564	875
2	13	26	39	89	195	300
3-5	8	16	24	58	108	160
6-10	6	12	18	40	73	105
11-20	5	10	15	31	53	75
21-40	4	8	12	25	40	55
41-60	3	6	9	19	30	40
61-84: 84-Last 12¢ issue	3	6	9	15	22	28
85-99	2	4	6	11	16	20
100-52 pg. Giant	3	6	9	16	23	30
101-103: 52 pg. Giants	3	6	9	14	20	25
104-121	1	3	4	6	8	10
...In 3-D (Spring, 1988, $2.25, Blackthorne #66)						4.00

PLOP! (Also see The Best of DC #60,63 digests)
National Periodical Publications: Sept-Oct, 1973 - No. 24, Nov-Dec, 1976

Issue	GD	VG	FN	VF	VF/NM	NM-
1-Sergio Aragonés-a begins; Wrightson-a	4	8	12	27	44	60
2-4,6-20	3	6	9	14	20	26
5-Wrightson-a	3	6	9	15	22	28
21-24 (52 pgs.). 23-No Aragonés-a; Lord of the Rings parody with Wally Wood-s/a	3	6	9	16	23	30

NOTE: ***Alcala** a-1-3. **Anderson** a-5. **Aragonés** a-1-22, 24. **Ditko** a-16p. **Evans** a-1. **Mayer** a-1. **Orlando** a-21, 22; c-21. **Sekowsky** a-5, 6p. **Toth** a-11. **Wolverton** r-4, 22-24(1 pg.ea.); c-1-12, 14, 17, 18. **Wood** a-14, 16i, 18-24; c-13, 15, 16, 19.*

PLUNGE
DC Comics (Black Label/Hill House Comics): Apr, 2020 - No. 6, Oct, 2020 ($3.99)

Issue	GD	VG	FN	VF	VF/NM	NM-
1-6-Joe Hill-s/Stuart Immonen-a; back-up Sea Dogs serial in #1-5						4.00

PLUTO (See Cheerios Premiums, Four Color #537, Mickey Mouse Magazine, Walt Disney Showcase #4, 7, 13, 20, 23, 33 & Wheaties)
Dell Publ. Co.: No. 7, 1942; No. 429, 10/52 - No. 1248, 11-1/61-62 (Disney)

Issue	GD	VG	FN	VF	VF/NM	NM-
Large Feature Comic 7(1942)-Written by Carl Barks, Jack Hannah, & Nick George (Barks' 1st comic book work)	252	504	756	1613	2757	3900
Four Color 429 (#1)	12	24	36	80	173	265
Four Color 509	8	16	24	52	99	145
Four Color 595,654,736,853	7	14	21	46	86	125
Four Color 941,1039,1143,1248	5	10	15	35	63	90

PLUTONA
Image Comics: Sept, 2015 - No. 5, Jun, 2016 ($2.99)

Issue	GD	VG	FN	VF	VF/NM	NM-
1-5-Lemire-s/Lenox-a						3.00

POCKET CLASSICS
Academic Inc. Publications: 1984 (B&W, 4 1/4" x 6 3/4", 68 pages)

C1(Black Beauty). C2(The Call of the Wild). C3(Dr. Jekyll and Mr. Hyde). C4(Dracula). C5(Frankenstein). C6(Huckleberry Finn). C7(Moby Dick). C8(The Red Badge of Courage). C9(The Time Machine). C10(Tom Sawyer). C11(Treasure Island). C12(20,000 Leagues Under the Sea). C13(The Great Adventures of Sherlock Holmes). C14(Gulliver's Travels). C15(The Hunchback of Notre Dame). C16(The Invisible Man). C17(Journey to the Center of the Earth). C18(Kidnapped). C19(The Mysterious Island). C20(The Scarlet Letter). C21(The Story of My Life). C22(A Tale of Two Cities). C23(The Three Musketeers). C24(The War of the Worlds). C25(Around the World in Eighty Days). C26(Captains Courageous). C27 (A Connecticut Yankee in King Arthur's Court). C28(Sherlock Holmes - The Hound of the Baskervilles). C29(The House of the Seven Gables). C30(Jane Eyre). C31(The Last of the Mohicans). C32(The Best of O. Henry). C33(The Best of Poe). C34(Two Years Before the Mast). C35(White Fang). C36(Wuthering Heights). C37(Ben Hur). C38(A Christmas Carol). C39(The

Planet of th Apes (2011) #2 © 20-FOX

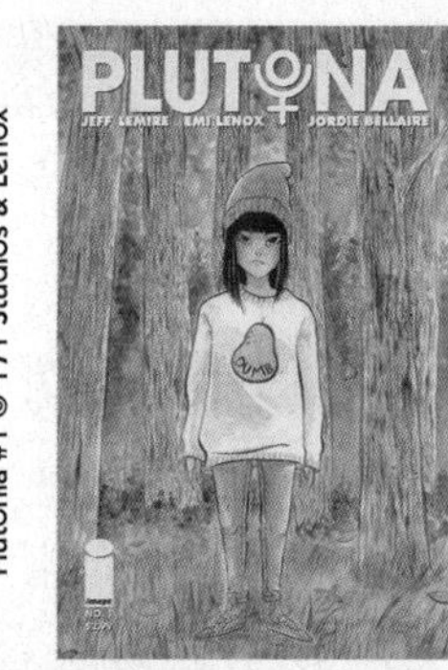

Plutonia #1 © 171 Studios & Lenox

Poison Ivy #1 © DC

GD VG FN VF VF/NM NM-
2.0 4.0 6.0 8.0 9.0 9.2

Food of the Gods). C40(Ivanhoe). C41(The Man in the Iron Mask). C42(The Prince and the Pauper). C43(The Prisoner of Zenda). C44(The Return of the Native). C45(Robinson Crusoe). C46(The Scarlet Pimpernel). C47(The Sea Wolf). C48(The Swiss Family Robinson). C49(Billy Budd). C50(Crime and Punishment). C51(Don Quixote). C52(Great Expectations). C53(Heidi). C54(The Illiad). C55(Lord Jim). C56(The Mutiny on Board H.M.S. Bounty). C57(The Odyssey). C58(Oliver Twist). C59(Pride and Prejudice). C60(The Turn of the Screw) each... 8.00

Shakespeare Series:
S1(As You Like It). S2(Hamlet). S3(Julius Caesar). S4(King Lear). S5(Macbeth). S6(The Merchant of Venice). S7(A Midsummer Night's Dream). S8(Othello). S9(Romeo and Juliet). S10(The Taming of the Shrew). S11(The Tempest). S12(Twelfth Night) each... 9.00

POCKET COMICS (Also see Double Up)
Harvey Publications: Aug, 1941 - No. 4, Jan, 1942 (Pocket size; 100 pgs.)
(Tied with Spitfire Comics #1 for earliest Harvey comic)

1-Origin & 1st app. The Black Cat, Cadet Blakey the Spirit of '76, The Red Blazer, The Phantom, Sphinx, & The Zebra; Phantom Ranger, British Agent #99, Spin Hawkins, Satan, Lord of Evil begin (1st app. of each); classic Simon horror cover showing an army battling a gigantic monster with the Statue of Liberty in its claws; Simon-c/a in #1-3 371 742 1113 2600 4550 6500
2 (9/41)-Black Cat & Nazi WWII-c by Simon 258 516 774 1651 2826 4000
3,4-Black Cat & Nazi WWII-c. 3-Simon-c 232 464 696 1485 2548 3600

POE DAMERON (Star Wars) (Title changes to Star Wars: Poe Dameron with #13)
Marvel Comics: Jun, 2016 - No. 12, May, 2017 ($4.99/$3.99)

1-($4.99) Soule-s/Noto-a/c; prelude to The Force Awakens; back-up w/Eliopoulos-a 5.00
2-6,8-12-($3.99) Black Squadron app. 4.00
7-($4.99) Anzueta-a; Leia cameo 5.00

POGO PARADE (See Dell Giants)

POGO POSSUM (Also see Animal Comics & Special Delivery)
Dell Publishing Co.: No. 105, 4/46 - No. 148, 5/47; 10-12/49 - No. 16, 4-6/54

Four Color 105(1946)-Kelly-c/a 64 128 192 512 1156 1800
Four Color 148-Kelly-c/a 44 88 132 326 738 1150
1-(10-12/49)-Kelly-c/a in all 38 76 114 281 628 975
2 23 46 69 161 356 550
3-5 15 30 45 105 233 360
6-10: 10-Infinity-c 13 26 39 91 201 310
11-16: 11-X-Mas-c 10 20 30 69 147 225
NOTE: *#1-4, 9-13: 52 pgs.; #5-8, 14-16: 36 pgs.*

POINT BLANK (See Wildcats)
DC Comics (WildStorm): Oct, 2002 - No. 5, Feb, 2003 ($2.95, limited series)

1-5-Brubaker-s/Wilson-a/Bisley-c. 1-Variant-c by Wilson; Grifter and John Lynch app. 3.00
TPB (2003, $14.95), (2009, $14.99) r/#1-5; afterword by Brubaker 15.00

POINT ONE
Marvel Comics: Jan, 2012 ($5.99, one-shot)

1-Short story preludes to Marvel's event storylines for 2012; s/a by various 6.00

POISON ELVES (Formerly I, Lusiphur)
Mulehide Graphics: No. 8, 1993- No. 20, 1995 (B&W, magazine/comic size, mature readers)

8-Drew Hayes-c/a/scripts. 2 4 6 8 10 12
9-11: 11-1st comic size issue 2 4 6 8 10 12
12,14,16 1 2 3 5 6 8
13,15-(low print) 2 4 6 8 11 14
15-2nd print 4.00
17-20 1 2 3 5 6 8
...Desert of the Third Sin-(1997, $14.95, TPB)-r/#13-18 15.00
...Patrons-($4.95, TPB)-r/#19,20 5.00
...Traumatic Dogs-(1996, $14.95,TPB)-Reprints I, Lusiphur #7, Poison Elves #8-12 15.00

POISON ELVES (See I, Lusiphur)
Sirius Entertainment: June, 1995 - No. 79, Sept, 2004 ; No. 80, Nov, 2007 ($2.50/$2.95, B&W, mature readers)

1-Linsner-c; Drew Hayes-a/scripts in all. 6.00
1-2nd print 3.00
2-25: 12-Purple Marauder-c/app. 3.00
26-45, 47-49 3.00
46,50-79: 61-Fillbäch Brothers-s/a. 74-Art by Crilley (3 pgs.) 3.00
80-($3.50) Tribute issue to Drew Hayes; sketchbook and notebook art with commentary 3.50
... Baptism By Fire-(2003, $19.95, TPB)-r/#48-59 20.00
... Color Special #1 (12/98, $2.95) 5.00
... Companion (12/02, $3.50) Back-story and character bios 3.50
... : Dark Wars TPB Vol. 1 (2005, $15.95) r/#60,62-68 16.00
... FAN Edition #1 mail-in offer; Drew Hayes-c/s/a 1 2 3 5 6 8
... Rogues-(2002, $15.95, TPB)-r/#40-47 16.00
...Salvation-(2001, $19.95, TPB)-r/#26-39 20.00
...Sanctuary-(1999, $14.95, TPB)-r/#1-12 15.00

POISON ELVES
Ape Entertainment: 2013 - No. 3 ($2.99, B&W)

1-3: 1-Horan-s/Montos-a; Davidsen-s/Ritchie-a; 3 covers by Robertson, Montos & Moore 3.00

POISON ELVES: DOMINION
Sirius Entertainment: Sept, 2005 - No. 6, Sept, 2006 ($3.50, B&W, limited series)

1-6-Keith Davidsen-s/Scott Lewis-a 3.50

POISON ELVES: HYENA
Sirius Entertainment: Sept, 2004 - No. 4, Feb, 2005 ($2.95, B&W, limited series)

1-4-Keith Davidsen-s/Scott Lewis-a 3.00
Ventures TPB Vol. 1: The Hyena Collection (2006, $14.95) r/#1-4 & 2 short stories 15.00

POISON ELVES: LOST TALES
Sirius Entertainment: Jan, 2006 - No. 11 ($2.95, B&W, limited series)

1-11-Aaron Bordner-a; Bordner & Davidsen-s 3.00

POISON ELVES: LUSIPHUR & LIRILITH
Sirius Entertainment: 2001 - No. 4, 2001 ($2.95, B&W, limited series)

1-4-Drew Hayes-s/Jason Alexander-a 3.00
TPB (2002, $11.95) r/#1-4 12.00

POISON ELVES: PARINTACHIN
Sirius Entertainment: 2001 - No. 3, 2002 ($2.95, B&W, limited series)

1-3-Drew Hayes-c/Fillbäch Brothers-s/a 3.00
TPB (2003, $8.95) r/#1-3 9.00

POISON ELVES VENTURES
Sirius Entertainment: May, 2005 - No. 4, Apr, 2006 ($3.50, B&W, limited series)

... #1: Cassanova; ...#2: Lynn; ...#3: The Purple Marauder; #4: Jace - Bordner-a 3.50

POISON IVY
DC Comics: Aug, 2022 - Present ($3.99)

1-10: 1-G. Willow Wilson-s/Marcio Takara-a. 5,6-Jason Woodrue app. 9-Harley Quinn app. 4.00

POISON IVY: CYCLE OF LIFE AND DEATH
DC Comics: Mar, 2016 - No. 6 ($2.99, limited series)

1-6: 1-Amy Chu-s/Clay Mann-a; covers by Mann & Dodson; Harley Quinn app. 3.00

POKÉMON (TV) (Also see Magical Pokémon Journey)
Viz Comics: Nov, 1998 - 2000 ($3.25/$3.50, B&W)

...Part 1: The Electric Tale of Pikachu
1-Toshiro Ono-s/a 3 6 9 16 23 30
1-4 (2nd through current printings) 4.00
2 2 4 6 8 10 12
3,4 1 3 4 6 8 10
TPB ($12.95) 2 4 6 9 13 16

...Part 2: Pikachu Strikes Back
1 2 4 6 8 11 14
2-4 5.00
TPB 13.00

...Part 3: Electric Pikachu Boogaloo
1 2 4 6 8 11 14
2-4 ($2.95-c) 5.00
TPB 13.00

...Part 4: Surf's Up Pikachu
1,3,4 5.00
2 ($2.95-c) 5.00
TPB 13.00
NOTE: Multiple printings exist for most issues

POKÉMON ADVENTURES
Viz Comics: Sept, 1999 - No. 4 ($5.95, B&W, magazine-size)

1-4-Includes stickers bound in 6.00

POKÉMON ADVENTURES
Viz Comics: 2000 - 2002 ($2.95/$4.95, B&W)

Part 2 (2/00-7/00) 1-6-Includes stickers bound in 5.00
Part 3 (8/00-2/01) 1-7 5.00
Part 4 (3/00-6/01) 1-4 5.00
Part 5 (7/01-10/01) 1-4 5.00
Part 6: 1-4, Part 7 1-5 5.00

POKÉMON: THE FIRST MOVIE
Viz Comics: 1999 ($3.95)

Mewtwo Strikes Back 1-4 5.00
Pikachu's Vacation 5.00

GD VG FN VF VF/NM NM-
2.0 4.0 6.0 8.0 9.0 9.2

POKÉMON: THE MOVIE 2000
Viz Comics: 2000 ($3.95)
1-Official movie adaption 5.00
Pikachu's Rescue Adventure 5.00
...:The Power of One (mini-series) 1-3 5.00

POLARITY
BOOM! Studios: Apr, 2013 - No. 4 ($3.99, limited series)
1-4: 1-Bemis-s/Coelho-a; 3 covers 4.00

POLICE ACADEMY (TV)
Marvel Comics: Nov, 1989 - No. 6, Feb, 1990 ($1.00)
1-6: Based on TV cartoon; Post-c/a(p) in all 4.00

POLICE ACTION
Atlas News Co.: Jan, 1954 - No. 7, Nov, 1954
1-Violent-a by Robert Q. Sale 37 74 111 222 361 500
2 19 38 57 111 176 240
3-7: 7-Powell-a 17 34 51 100 158 215
NOTE: ***Ayers** a-4, 5. **Colan** a-1. **Forte** a-1, 2. **Mort Lawrence** a-5. **Maneely** a-3; c-1, 5. **Reinman** a-6, 7.*

POLICE ACTION
Atlas/Seaboard Publ.: Feb, 1975 - No. 3, June, 1975
1-3: 1-Lomax, N.Y.P.D., Luke Malone begin; McWilliams-a. 2-Origin Luke Malone, Manhunter; Ploog-a 2 4 6 10 14 18
NOTE: ***Ploog** art in all. **Sekowsky/McWilliams** a-1-3. **Thorne** c-3.*

POLICE AGAINST CRIME
Premiere Magazines: April, 1954 - No. 9, Aug, 1955
1-Disbrow-a; extreme violence (man's face slashed with knife); Hollingsworth-a
50 100 150 315 533 750
2-Hollingsworth-a 28 56 84 165 270 375
3-9 23 46 69 136 223 310

POLICE BADGE #479 (Formerly Spy Thrillers #1-4)
Atlas Comics (PrPl): No. 5, Sept, 1955
5-Maneely-c/a (6 pgs.); Heck-a 16 32 48 94 147 200

POLICE CASE BOOK (See Giant Comics Editions)

POLICE CASES (See Authentic... & Record Book of...)

POLICE COMICS
Quality Comics Group (Comic Magazines): Aug, 1941 - No. 127, Oct, 1953
1-Origin/1st app. Plastic Man by Jack Cole (r-in DC Special #15), The Human Bomb by Gustavson, & No. 711; intro. The Firebrand by Reed Crandall, The Mouthpiece by Guardineer, Phantom Lady, & The Sword; Chic Carter by Eisner app.; Firebrand-c 1-4
1600 3200 4800 12,200 22,100 32,000
2-Plastic Man smuggles opium 326 652 978 2282 3991 5700
3 337 674 1011 2339 3130 3900
4 213 426 639 1363 2332 3300
5-Plastic Man covers begin, end #102; Plastic Man forced to smoke marijuana
377 754 1131 2639 4620 6600
6,7 181 362 543 1158 1979 2800
8-Manhunter begins (origin/1st app.) (3/42) 206 412 618 1318 2259 3200
9,10 142 284 426 909 1555 2200
11-The Spirit strip reprints begin by Eisner (origin-strip #1); 1st comic book app. The Spirit & 1st cover app. (9/42) 415 830 1245 2905 5103 7300
12-Intro. Ebony 194 388 582 1242 2121 3000
13-Intro. Woozy Winks; last Firebrand 194 388 582 1242 2121 3000
14-19: 15-Last No. 711; Destiny begins 81 162 243 518 884 1250
20-The Raven x-over in Phantom Lady; features Jack Cole himself
84 168 252 538 919 1300
21,22: 21-Raven & Spider Widow x-over in Phantom Lady (cameo in #22)
68 136 204 435 743 1050
23-30: 23-Last Phantom Lady. 24-26-Flatfoot Burns by Kurtzman in all
60 120 180 381 653 925
31-41: 37-1st app. Candy by Sahle & begins (12/44). 41-Last Spirit-r by Eisner
52 104 156 328 552 775
42,43-Spirit-r by Eisner/Fine 55 110 165 352 601 650
44-Fine Spirit-r begin, end #88,90,92 55 110 165 352 601 650
45-50: 50-(#50 on-c, #49 on inside, 1/46) 37 74 111 222 361 500
51-60: 58-Last Human Bomb 31 62 93 186 303 420
61-88,90,92: 63-(Some issues have #65 printed on cover, but #63 on inside) Kurtzman-a, 6 pgs. 90,92-Spirit by Fine 27 54 81 158 259 360
89,91,93-No Spirit stories 24 48 72 142 234 325
94-99,101,102: Spirit by Eisner in all; 101-Last Manhunter. 102-Last Spirit & Plastic Man by Jack Cole 34 68 102 199 325 450
100 39 78 117 240 395 550
103-Content change to crime; Ken Shannon & T-Man begin (1st app. of each, 12/50) 39 78 117 240 395 550
104-112,114-127: Crandall-a most issues (not in 104,105,122,125-127). 109-Atomic bomb story. 112-Crandall-a 25 50 75 150 245 340
113-Crandall-c/a(2), 9 pgs. each 27 54 81 162 266 370
NOTE: *Most Spirit stories signed by Eisner are not by him; all are reprints. **Crandall** Firebrand-1-8. Spirit by **Eisner** 1-41, 94-102; by **Eisner/Fine**-42, 43; by **Fine**-44-88, 90, 92. 103, 109. **Al Bryant** c-33, 34. **Cole** c-17-32, 35-102(most). **Crandall** c-13, 14. **Crandall/Cuidera** c-105-127. **Eisner** c-4i. **Gill Fox** c-1-3, 4p, 5-12, 15. Bondage c-103, 109, 125.*

POLICE LINE-UP
Avon Periodicals/Realistic Comics #3,4: Aug, 1951 - No. 4, July, 1952 (Painted-c #1-3)
1-Wood-a, 1 pg. plus part-c; spanking panel-r/Saint #5
54 108 162 343 574 825
2-Classic story "The Religious Murder Cult", drugs, perversion; r/Saint #5; c-r/Avon paperback #329 41 82 123 256 428 600
3,4: 3-Kubert-a(r?)/part-c; Kinstler-a (inside-c only) 32 64 96 188 307 425

POLICE TRAP (Public Defender In Action #7 on)
Mainline #1-4/Charlton #5,6: 8-9/54 - No. 4, 2-3/55; No. 5, 7/55 - No. 6, 9/55
1-S&K covers-all issues; Meskin-a; Kirby scripts 43 86 129 271 461 650
2-4 27 54 81 158 259 360
5,6-S&K-c/a 34 68 102 199 325 450

POLICE TRAP
Super Comics: No. 11, 1963; No. 16-18, 1964
Reprint #11,16-18: 11-r/Police Trap #3. 16-r/Justice Traps the Guilty #? 17-r/Inside Crime #3 & r/Justice Traps The Guilty #83; 18-r/Inside Crime #3
2 4 6 11 16 20

POLLY & HER PALS (See Comic Monthly #1)

POLLY & THE PIRATES
Oni Press: Sept, 2005 - No. 6, June, 2006 ($2.99, B&W, limited series)
1-6-Ted Naifeh-s/a; Polly is shanghaied by the pirate ship Titania 3.00
TPB (7/06, $11.95, digest) r/#1-6 12.00

POLLYANNA (Disney)
Dell Publishing Co.: No. 1129, Aug-Oct, 1960
Four Color 1129-Movie, Hayley Mills photo-c 8 16 24 52 99 145

POLLY PIGTAILS (Girls' Fun & Fashion Magazine #44 on)
Parents' Magazine Institute/Polly Pigtails: Jan, 1946 - V4#43, Oct-Nov, 1949
1-Infinity-c; photo-c 25 50 75 150 245 340
2-Photo-c 15 30 45 85 130 175
3-5: 3,4-Photo-c 12 24 36 69 97 125
6-10: 7-Photo-c 10 20 30 56 76 95
11-30: 22-Photo-c 9 18 27 50 65 80
31-43: 38-Natalie Wood photo-c 8 16 24 42 54 65

PONY EXPRESS (See Tales of the...)

PONYTAIL (Teen-age)
Dell Publishing Co./Charlton No. 13 on: 7-9/62 - No. 12, 10-12/65; No. 13, 11/69 - No. 20, 1/71
12-641-209(#1) 4 8 12 23 37 50
2-12 3 6 9 17 26 35
13-20 3 6 9 14 19 24

POP
Dark Horse Comics: Aug, 2014 - No. 4, Nov, 2014 ($3.99, limited series)
1-4-Curt Pires-s/Jason Copland-a 4.00

POP COMICS
Modern Store Publ.: 1955 (36 pgs.; 5x7"; in color) (7¢)
1-Funny animal 9 18 27 50 65 80

POPEYE (See Comic Album #7, 11, 15, Comics Reading Libraries *in the Promotional Comics section*, Eat Right to Work and Win, Giant Comic Album, King Comics, Kite Fun Book, Magic Comics, March of Comics #37,52, 66, 80, 96, 117, 134, 148, 157, 169, 194, 246, 264, 274, 294, 453, 465, 477 & Wow Comics, 1st series)

POPEYE
David McKay Publications: 1937 - 1939 (All by Segar)
Feature Books nn (100 pgs.) (Very Rare) 1225 2450 3675 9300 16,900 24,500
Feature Books 2 (52 pgs.) 161 322 483 1030 1765 2500
Feature Books 3 (100 pgs.)-r/nn issue with new-c 116 232 346 742 1271 1800
Feature Books 5,10 (76 pgs.) 106 212 318 673 1162 1650
Feature Books 14 (76 pgs.) (Scarce) 123 246 369 787 1344 1900

POPEYE (Strip reprints through 4-Color #70)
Dell #1-65/Gold Key #66-80/King #81-92/Charlton #94-138/Gold Key #139-155/Whitman #156 on: 1941 - 1947; #1, 2-4/48 - #65, 7-9/62; #66, 10/62 - #80, 5/66; #81, 8/66 - #92, 12/67; #94, 2/69 - #138, 1/77; #139, 5/78 - #171, 6/84 (no #93,160,161)
Large Feature Comic 24('41)-Half by Segar 106 212 318 673 1162 1650
Four Color 25('41)-by Segar 119 238 357 762 1306 1850
Large Feature Comic 10('43) 77 154 231 493 847 1200
Four Color 17('43),26('43)-by Segar 52 104 156 416 933 1450
Four Color 43('44) 30 60 90 216 483 750
Four Color 70('45)-Title: ...& Wimpy 24 48 72 168 372 575
Four Color 113('46-original strips begin),127,145('47),168
15 30 45 100 220 340
1(2-4/48)(Dell)-All new stories continue 38 76 114 285 641 1000
2 17 34 51 117 259 400
3-10: 5-Popeye on moon w/rocket-c 13 26 39 86 188 290
11-20 9 18 27 62 126 190
21-40,46: 46-Origin Swee' Pee 8 16 24 51 96 140
41-45,47-50 6 12 18 40 73 105
51-60 5 10 15 35 63 90
61-65 (Last Dell issue) 5 10 15 31 53 75
66(10/62),67-Both 84 pgs. (Gold Key) 6 12 18 40 73 105
68-80 4 8 12 25 40 55
81-92,94-97 (no #93): 97-Last 12¢ issue 3 6 9 20 31 42
98,99,101-107,109-138: 123-Wimpy beats Neil Armstrong to the moon. 130-1st app. Superstuff 3 6 9 14 19 24
100 3 6 9 17 26 35
108-Traces Popeye's origin from 1929 3 6 9 15 22 28
139-155: 144-50th Anniversary issue 2 4 6 8 10 12
156,157,162-167(Whitman)(no #160,161).167(3/82) 2 4 6 10 14 18
158(9/80),159(11/80)-pre-pack only 5 10 15 34 60 85
168-171:(All #90069 on-c; pre-pack) 168(6/83). 169(#168 on-c)(8/83). 170(3/84). 171(6/84) 3 6 9 17 26 35
NOTE: *Reprints-#145, 147, 149, 151, 153, 155, 157, 163-168(1/3), 170.*

POPEYE
Harvey Comics: Nov, 1993 - No. 7, Aug, 1994 ($1.50)
V2#1-7 3.00
...Summer Special V2#1-(10/93, $2.25, 68 pgs.)-Sagendorf-r & others 4.00

POPEYE
IDW Publishing: Apr, 2012 - No. 12, Apr, 2013 ($3.99)
1-12-New stories in classic style; Langridge-s. 1-Action #1 cover swipe. 12-Barney Google and Spark Plug app. 4.00

POPEYE (CLASSIC...)
IDW Publishing: Aug, 2012 - No. 65, Dec, 2017 ($3.99/$4.99)

Polarity #3 © BOOM!

Popeye (2012) #5 © KFS

Porky Pig #42 © WB

	GD 2.0	VG 4.0	FN 6.0	VF 8.0	VF/NM 9.0	NM- 9.2
1-43-Reprints of Bud Sagendorf's classic stories						4.00
44-65-($4.99)						5.00

POPEYE SPECIAL
Ocean Comics: Summer, 1987 - No. 2, Sept, 1988 ($1.75/$2.00)

	GD 2.0	VG 4.0	FN 6.0	VF 8.0	VF/NM 9.0	NM- 9.2
1,2: 1-Origin						4.00

POPPLES (TV, movie)
Star Comics (Marvel): Dec, 1986 - No. 4, Jun, 1987

	GD 2.0	VG 4.0	FN 6.0	VF 8.0	VF/NM 9.0	NM- 9.2
1-4-Based on toys						5.00

POPPO OF THE POPCORN THEATRE
Fuller Publishing Co. (Publishers Weekly): 10/29/55 - No. 13, 1956 (weekly)

	GD 2.0	VG 4.0	FN 6.0	VF 8.0	VF/NM 9.0	NM- 9.2
1	10	20	30	58	79	100
2-5	7	14	21	37	46	55
6-13	6	12	18	31	38	45

NOTE: *By **Charles Biro.** 10¢ cover, given away by supermarkets such as IGA.*

POP-POP COMICS
R. B. Leffingwell Co.: No date (Circa 1945) (52 pgs.)

	GD 2.0	VG 4.0	FN 6.0	VF 8.0	VF/NM 9.0	NM- 9.2
1-Funny animal	19	38	57	111	176	240

POPULAR COMICS
Dell Publishing Co.: Feb, 1936 - No. 145, July-Sept, 1948

	GD 2.0	VG 4.0	FN 6.0	VF 8.0	VF/NM 9.0	NM- 9.2
1-Dick Tracy (1st comic book app.), Little Orphan Annie, Terry & the Pirates, Gasoline Alley, Don Winslow (1st app.), Harold Teen, Little Joe, Skippy, Moon Mullins, Mutt & Jeff, Tailspin Tommy, Smitty, Smokey Stover, Winnie Winkle & The Gumps begin (all strip-r)	1071	2142	3213	7500	--	--
2	329	658	987	2300	--	--
3	243	486	729	1700	--	--
4-6(7/36): 5-Tom Mix begins. 6-1st app. Scribbly	186	372	558	1300	--	--
7-10: 8,9-Scribbly & Reglar Fellers app.	150	300	450	1050	--	--
11-20: 12-X-Mas-c	88	176	308	506	803	1100
21-27: 27-Last Terry & the Pirates, Little Orphan Annie, & Dick Tracy	64	128	224	368	584	800
28-37: 28-Gene Autry app. 31,32-Tim McCoy app. 35-Christmas-c; Tex Ritter app.	50	100	175	288	457	625
38-43: Tarzan in text only. 38-(4/39)-Gang Busters (Radio, 2nd app.) & Zane Grey's Tex Thorne begins? 43-The Masked Pilot app.; 1st non-funny-c?	46	92	161	265	423	580
44,45: 45-Hurricane Kid-c	42	84	149	242	384	525
46-Origin/1st app. Martan, the Marvel Man(12/39)	58	116	203	290	457	725
47-49-Martan, the Marvel Man-c	46	92	161	265	420	575
50-Gang Busters-c	39	78	137	224	355	485
51-Origin The Voice (The Invisible Detective) strip begins (5/40)	42	84	147	242	384	525
52-Classic Martan blasting robots-c/sty	76	152	266	437	694	950
53-56: 55-End of World story	37	74	130	213	337	460
57-59-Martan, the Marvel Man-c	46	92	161	265	420	575
60-Origin/1st app. Professor Supermind and Son (2/41)	43	86	151	247	394	540
61-64,66-Professor Supermind-c. 63-Smilin' Jack begins	35	70	123	201	318	435
65-Classic Professor Supermind WWII-c	50	100	175	288	457	625
67-71	23	46	69	136	223	310
72-The Owl & Terry & the Pirates begin (2/42); Smokey Stover reprints begin	42	84	126	242	371	500
73-75	29	58	87	167	259	350
76-78-Capt. Midnight in all (see The Funnies #57)	40	80	120	230	358	485
79-85-Last Owl	27	54	81	155	238	320
86-99: 86-Japanese WWII-c. 98-Felix the Cat, Smokey Stover-r begin	18	36	54	104	157	210
100	20	40	60	115	175	235
101-130	10	20	30	58	89	120
131-145: 142-Last Terry & the Pirates	9	18	27	52	79	105

NOTE: *Martan, the Marvel Man c-47-49, 52, 57-59. Professor Supermind c-60-63, 64(1/2), 65, 66. The Voice c-53.*

POPULAR FAIRY TALES (See March of Comics #6, 18)

POPULAR ROMANCE
Better-Standard Publications: No. 5, Dec, 1949 - No. 29, July, 1954

	GD 2.0	VG 4.0	FN 6.0	VF 8.0	VF/NM 9.0	NM- 9.2
5	22	44	66	128	209	290
6-9: 7-Palais-a; lingerie panels	15	30	45	90	140	190
10-Wood-a (2 pgs.)	18	36	54	103	162	220
11,12,14-16,18-21,28,29	14	28	42	82	121	160
13,17-Severin/Elder-a (3&8 pgs.)	15	30	45	84	127	170
22-27-Toth-a	15	30	45	88	137	185

NOTE: *All have photo-c. **Tuska** art in most issues.*

POPULAR TEEN-AGERS (Secrets of Love) (School Day Romances #1-4)
Star Publications: No. 5, Sept, 1950 - No. 23, Nov, 1954

	GD 2.0	VG 4.0	FN 6.0	VF 8.0	VF/NM 9.0	NM- 9.2
5-Toni Gay, Midge Martin & Eve Adams continue from School Day Romances; Ginger Bunn (formerly Ginger Snapp & becomes Honey Bunn #6 on) begins; all features end #8	54	108	162	343	574	825
6-8 (7/51)-Honey Bunn begins; all have L. B. Cole-c; 6-Negligee panels	43	86	129	271	461	650
9-(...Romances; 1st romance issue, 10/51)	71	142	2513	454	777	1100
10-(...Secrets of Love thru #23)	71	142	2513	454	777	1100
11,16,18,19,22,23	39	78	117	240	395	550
12,13,17,20,21-Disbrow-a	41	82	123	256	428	600
14-Harrison/Wood-a	52	104	156	328	552	775
15-Wood?, Disbrow-a	43	86	129	271	461	650
Accepted Reprint 5,6 (nd); L.B. Cole-c	12	24	36	69	97	125

NOTE: *All have **L. B. Cole** covers.*

PORCELAIN
Ablaze Publishing: 2021 - No. 5, 2021 ($3.99, limited series)

	GD 2.0	VG 4.0	FN 6.0	VF 8.0	VF/NM 9.0	NM- 9.2
1-5-Maria Llovet-s/a; multiple covers on each						4.00

PORKY PIG (See Bugs Bunny &..., Kite Fun Book, Looney Tunes, March of Comics #42, 57, 71, 89, 99, 113, 130, 143, 164, 175, 192, 209, 218, 367, and Super Book #6, 18, 30)

PORKY PIG (...& Bugs Bunny #40-69)
Dell Publishing Co./Gold Key No. 1-93/Whitman No. 94 on: No. 16, 1942 - No. 81, Mar-Apr, 1962; Jan, 1965 - No. 109, June, 1984

	GD 2.0	VG 4.0	FN 6.0	VF 8.0	VF/NM 9.0	NM- 9.2
Four Color 16(#1, 1942)	104	208	312	832	1866	2900
Four Color 48(1944)-Carl Barks-a	102	204	306	826	1838	2850
Four Color 78(1945)	30	60	90	216	483	750
Four Color 112(7/46)	18	36	54	124	275	425
Four Color 156,182,191('49)	12	24	36	79	170	260
Four Color 226,241('49),260,271,277,284,295	9	18	27	61	123	185
Four Color 303,311,322,330: 322-Sci/fi-c/story	8	16	24	51	96	140
Four Color 342,351,360,370,385,399,410,426	6	12	18	40	73	105
25 (11-12/52)-30	5	10	15	33	57	80
31-40	5	10	15	30	50	70
41-60	4	8	12	25	40	55
61-81(3-4/62)	3	6	9	21	33	45
1(1/65-Gold Key)(2nd Series)	5	10	15	31	53	75
2,4,5-r/4-Color 226,284 & 271 in that order	3	6	9	19	30	40
3,6-10: 3-r/Four Color #342	3	6	9	16	24	32
11-30	3	6	9	14	19	24
31-54	2	4	6	10	14	18
55-70	2	4	6	8	11	14
71-93(Gold Key)	2	3	4	6	8	10
94-96	2	4	6	8	10	12
97(9/80),98-pre-pack only (99 known not to exist)	4	8	12	27	44	60
100	2	4	6	10	14	18
101-105: 104(2/82). 105(4/82)	2	4	6	8	11	14
106-109 (All #90140 on-c, no date or date code): 106(7/83), 107(8/83), 108(2/84), 109(6/84) low print run	3	6	9	14	20	26

NOTE: *Reprints-#1-8, 9-35(2/3); 36-46(1/4-1/2), 58, 67, 69-74, 76, 78, 102-109(1/3-1/2).*

PORKY PIG'S DUCK HUNT
Saalfield Publishing Co.: 1938 (12pgs.)(large size)(heavy linen-like paper)

	GD 2.0	VG 4.0	FN 6.0	VF 8.0	VF/NM 9.0	NM- 9.2
2178-1st app. Porky Pig & Daffy Duck by Leon Schlesinger. Illustrated text story book written in verse. 1st book ever devoted to these characters. (see Looney Tunes #1 for their 1st comic book app.)	87	174	261	553	952	1350

PORTAL BOUND
Aspen MLT: No. 0, Feb, 2018 - No. 5, Aug, 2018 ($1.50/$3.99)

	GD 2.0	VG 4.0	FN 6.0	VF 8.0	VF/NM 9.0	NM- 9.2
0-($1.50) Roslan & Carrasco-s/Arizmendi-a; 2 covers; bonus character sketches						3.00
1-5-($3.99) Roslan & Carrasco-s/Arizmendi-a						4.00

PORTENT, THE
Image Comics: Feb, 2006 - No. 4, Aug, 2006 ($2.99)

	GD 2.0	VG 4.0	FN 6.0	VF 8.0	VF/NM 9.0	NM- 9.2
1-4-Peter Bergting-s/a						3.00
Vol. 1: Duende TPB (2006, 12.99) r/#1-4; pin-up art; intro. by Kaluta						13.00

PORTIA PRINZ OF THE GLAMAZONS
Eclipse Comics: Dec, 1986 - No. 6, Oct, 1987 ($2.00, B&W, Baxter paper)

	GD 2.0	VG 4.0	FN 6.0	VF 8.0	VF/NM 9.0	NM- 9.2
1-6						3.00

POSEIDON IX (Also see Aphrodite IX and (Ninth) IX Generation)
Image Comics (Top Cow): Sept, 2015 ($3.99, one-shot)

	GD 2.0	VG 4.0	FN 6.0	VF 8.0	VF/NM 9.0	NM- 9.2
1-Howard-s/Sevy-a; story continues in IX Generation #5						4.00

POSSESSED, THE
DC Comics (Cliffhanger): Sept, 2003 - No. 6, March, 2004 ($2.95, limited series)

GD 2.0 | VG 4.0 | FN 6.0 | VF 8.0 | VF/NM 9.0 | NM- 9.2

1-6-Johns & Grimminger-s/Sharp-a 3.00
TPB (2004, $14.95) r/#1-6; promo art and sketch pages 15.00

POSTAL (Also see Eden's Fall)
Image Comics (Top Cow): Feb, 2015 - Present ($3.99)

1-24: 1-Matt Hawkins & Bryan Hill-s/Issac Goodheart-a 4.00
25-($5.99) Matt Hawkins & Bryan Hill-s/Issac Goodheart-a 6.00
...: Dossier 1 (11/15, $3.99) Ryan Cady-a; background on Eden and character profiles 4.00
...: Mark 1 (2/18, $3.99) Spotlight on Mark; Ienco-a 4.00
...: Night Shift 1 (12/20, $3.99) Spotlights on Roy Magnus & Molly; Goodheart-c 4.00

POSTAL: DELIVERANCE
Image Comics (Top Cow): Jul, 2019 - Present ($3.99)

1-8-Bryan Hill-s/Raffaele Ienco-a 4.00

POST AMERICANA
Image Comics: Dec, 2020 - No. 7, Dec, 2021 ($3.99)

1-7-Steve Skroce-s/a 4.00

POST GAZETTE (See Meet the New... in the Promotional Comics section)

POWDER RIVER RUSTLERS (See Fawcett Movie Comics)

POWER & GLORY (See American Flagg! & Howard Chaykin's American Flagg!
Malibu Comics (Bravura): Feb, 1994 - No. 4, May, 1994 ($2.50, limited series, mature)

1A, 1B-By Howard Chaykin; w/Bravura stamp 3.00
1-Newsstand ed. (polybagged w/children's warning on bag), Gold ed., Silver-foil ed., Blue-foil ed.(print run of 10,000), Serigraph ed. (print run of 3,000)($2.95)-Howard Chaykin-c/a begin 4.00
2-4-Contains Bravura stamp 3.00
Holiday Special (Win '94, $2.95) 3.00

POWER COMICS
Holyoke Publ. Co./Narrative Publ.: 1944 - No. 4, 1945

1-L. B. Cole-c 258 516 774 1651 2826 4000
2-Hitler, Hirohito-c (scarce) 975 1950 2919 7100 12,550 18,000
3-Classic L.B. Cole-c; Dr. Mephisto begins? 975 1950 2919 7100 12,550 18,000
4-L.B. Cole-c; Miss Espionage app. #3,4; Leav-a 459 918 1377 3350 5925 8500

POWER COMICS
Power Comics Co.: 1977 - No. 5, Dec, 1977 (B&W)

1- "A Boy And His Aardvark" by Dave Sim; first Dave Sim aardvark (not Cerebus) 3 6 9 19 30 40
1-Reprint (3/77, black-c) 1 2 3 5 6 8
2-Cobalt Blue by Gustovich 1 3 4 6 8 10
3-5: 3-Nightwitch. 4-Northern Light. 5-Bluebird 1 3 4 6 8 10

POWER COMICS
Eclipse Comics (Acme Press): Mar, 1988 - No. 4, Sept, 1988 ($2.00, B&W, mini-series)

1-4: Bolland, Gibbons-r in all 3.00

POWER COMPANY, THE
DC Comics: Apr, 2002 - No. 18, Sep, 2003 ($2.50/$2.75)

1-6-Busiek-s/Grummett-a. 6-Green Arrow & Black Canary-c/app. 3.00
7-18: 7:Begin $2.75-c. 8,9-Green Arrow app. 11-Firestorm joins. 15-Batman app. 3.00
...Bork (3/02) Busiek-s/Dwyer-a; Batman & Flash (Barry Allen) app. 3.00
...Josiah Power (3/02) Busiek-s/Giffen-a; Superman app. 3.00
...Manhunter (3/02) Busiek-s/Jurgens-a; Nightwing app. 3.00
...Sapphire (3/02) Busiek-s/Bagley-a; JLA & Kobra app. 3.00
...Skyrocket (3/02) Busiek-s/Staton-a; Green Lantern (Hal Jordan) app. 3.00
...Striker Z (3/02) Busiek-s/Bachs-a; Superboy app. 3.00
...Witchfire (3/02) Busiek-s/Haley-a; Wonder Woman app. 3.00

POWER CUBED
Dark Horse Comics: Sept, 2015 - No. 4, Jan, 2016 ($3.99, limited series)

1-4-Aaron Lopresti-s/a 4.00

POWER FACTOR
Wonder Color Comics #1/Pied Piper #2: May, 1987 - No. 2, 1987 ($1.95)

1,2: Super team. 2-Infantino-c 3.00

POWER FACTOR
Innovation Publishing: Oct, 1990 - No. 3, 1991 ($1.95/$2.25)

1-3: 1-R-/1st story + new-a, 2-r/2nd story + new-a. 3-Infantino-a 3.00

POWER GIRL (See All-Star #58, Infinity, Inc., JSA Classified, Showcase #97-99)
DC Comics: June, 1988 - No. 4, Sept, 1988 ($1.00, color, limited series)

1 3 6 9 16 23 30
2-4 1 2 3 5 6 8
TPB (2006, $14.99) r/Showcase #97-99; Secret Origins #11; JSA Classified #1-4 and pages from JSA #32,39; cover gallery 15.00

POWER GIRL
DC Comics: Jul, 2009 - No. 27, Oct, 2011 ($2.99)

1-Amanda Conner-a; covers by Conner and Hughes; Ultra-Humanite app. 3 6 9 19 30 40
2-Conner-a; covers by Conner and Hughes 3 6 9 14 20 26
3-10: 3-6-Covers by Conner and March 5.00
11-26: 13-23-Winick-s/Basri-a. 20,21-Crossover with Justice League: Generation Lost #18-22 23-Zatanna app. 24,25-Batman app.; Prasetya-a 4.00
27-Ample cleavage cover; Cyclone app. 6 12 18 41 76 110
...: Aliens and Apes SC (2010, $17.99) r/#7-12 18.00
...: A New Beginning SC (2010, $17.99) r/#1-6; gallery of variant covers 18.00
...: Bomb Squad SC (2011, $14.99) r/#13-18 15.00

POWERHOUSE PEPPER COMICS (See Gay Comics, Joker Comics & Tessie the Typist)
Marvel Comics (20CC): No. 1, 1943; No. 2, May, 1948 - No. 5, Nov, 1948

1-(60 pgs.)-Wolverton-a in all; c-2,3 245 490 735 1568 2684 3800
2 116 232 348 742 1271 1800
3,4 100 200 300 640 1095 1550
5-(Scarce) 123 246 369 787 1344 1900

POWERLESS
Marvel Comics: Aug, 2004 - No. 6, Jan, 2005 ($2.99, limited series)

1-6-Peter Parker, Matt Murdock and Logan without powers; Gaydos-a 3.00
TPB (2005, $14.99) r/series; sketch page by Gaydos 15.00

POWER LINE
Marvel Comics (Epic Comics): May, 1988 - No. 8, Sept, 1989 ($1.25/$1.50)

1-8: 2-Williamson-i. 3-Dr. Zero app. 4-7-Morrow-a. 8-Williamson-i 3.00

POWER LINES
Image Comics: Mar, 2016 - No. 3 ($3.50/$3.99)

1-3-Jimmie Robinson-s/a. 1-($3.50-c). 2-Begin $3.99-c 4.00

POWER LORDS
DC Comics: Dec, 1983 - No. 3, Feb, 1984 (Limited series, Mando paper)

1-3: Based on Revell toys 4.00

POWER MAN (Formerly Hero for Hire; ...& Iron Fist #50 on; see Cage & Giant-Size...)
Marvel Comics Group: No. 17, Feb, 1974 - No. 125, Sept, 1986

17-Luke Cage continues; Iron Man app. 5 10 15 34 60 85
18,20: 18-Last 20¢ issue; intro. Wrecking Crew 3 6 9 16 23 30
19-1st app. Cottonmouth 5 10 15 30 50 70
21-23,25-30 2 4 6 9 12 15
24-Intro. Black Goliath 9 18 27 57 111 165
30-(30¢-c variant, limited distribution)(4/76) 5 10 15 30 50 70
31-46: 31-Part Neal Adams-i. 34-Last 25¢ issue. 36-r/Hero For Hire #12. 41-1st app. Thunderbolt. 45-Starlin-c. 2 4 6 8 10 12
31-34-(30¢-c variants, limited distribution)(5-8/76) 5 10 15 30 50 70
44-46-(35¢-c variants, limited distribution)(6-8/77) 10 20 30 64 132 200
47-Barry Smith-a 2 4 6 8 11 14
47-(35¢-c variant, limited distribution)(10/77) 9 18 27 58 114 170
48-Power Man/Iron Fist 1st meet; Byrne-a(p) 6 12 18 37 66 95
49-Byrne-a(p) 3 6 9 16 23 30
50-Iron Fist joins Cage; Byrne-a(p) 5 10 15 34 60 85
51-56,58-65,67-77: 58-Intro El Aguila. 75-Double size. 77-Daredevil app. 1 3 4 6 8 10
57-New X-Men app. (6/79) 4 8 12 25 40 55
66-2nd app. Sabretooth (see Iron Fist #14) 6 12 18 37 66 95
78,84: 78-3rd app. Sabretooth (cameo under cloak). 84-4th app. Sabretooth 4 8 12 25 40 55
79-83,85-99,101-124: 87-Moon Knight app. 109-The Reaper app. 6.00
100-Double size; Origin K'un L'un 2 4 6 8 10 12
125-Double size; Death of Iron Fist 2 4 6 9 12 15
Annual 1(1976)-Punisher cameo in flashback 3 6 9 18 28 38

NOTE: ***Austin*** *c-102i.* ***Byrne*** *a-48-50; c-102, 104, 106, 107, 112-116.* ***Kane*** *c(p)-24, 25, 28, 48.* ***Miller*** *a-68, 76(2 pgs.); c-66-68, 70-74, 80i.* ***Mooney*** *a-38i, 53i, 55i.* ***Nebres*** *a-76p.* ***Nino*** *a-42i, 43i.* ***Perez*** *a-27.* ***B. Smith*** *a-47i.* ***Tuska*** *a(p)-17, 20, 24, 26, 28, 29, 36, 47. Painted c-75, 100.*

POWER MAN AND IRON FIST
Marvel Comics: Apr, 2011 - No. 5, Jul, 2011 ($2.99, limited series)

1-5-Van Lente-s/Alves-a; Victor Alvarez as Power Man 3.00

POWER MAN AND IRON FIST
Marvel Comics: Apr, 2016 - No. 15, Jun, 2017 ($3.99)

1-15: 1-Luke Cage and Danny Rand; David Walker-s/Sanford Greene-a; Tombstone app. 6-9-Civil War II tie-in 4.00
...: Sweet Christmas Annual 1 (2/17, $4.99) Walker-s/Hepburn-a; Daimon Hellstrom app. 5.00

POWER OF PRIME
Malibu Comics (Ultraverse): July, 1995 - No. 4, Nov, 1995 ($2.50, lim. series)

1-4 3.00

POWER OF SHAZAM!, THE (See SHAZAM!)
DC Comics: 1994 (Painted graphic novel) (Prequel to new series)

Hardcover-($19.95)-New origin of Shazam!; Ordway painted-c/a & script 3 6 9 14 20 25
Softcover-($7.50), Softcover-($9.95)-New-c. 2 4 6 8 10 12

POWER OF SHAZAM!, THE
DC Comics: Mar, 1995 - No. 47, Mar, 1999; No. 48, Mar, 2010 ($1.50/$1.75/$1.95/$2.50)

1-Jerry Ordway scripts begin 2 4 6 8 10 12
2-20: 4-Begin $1.75-c. 6:Re-intro of Capt. Nazi. 8-Re-intro of Spy Smasher, Bulletman & Minuteman; Swan-a (7 pgs.). 11-Re-intro of Ibis, Swan-a(2 pgs.). 14-Gil Kane-a(p). 20-Superman-c/app.; "Final Night" 3.00
21-45,47: 21-Plastic Man-c/app. 22-Batman-c/app. 24-Spy Smasher WWII story. 35,36-X-over w/Starman #39,40. 38-41-Mr. Mind. 43-Bulletman app. 45-JLA-c/app. 3.00
46-Superman vs. Shazam 1 3 4 6 8 10
48-(3/10, $2.99) Blackest Night one-shot; Osiris rises as a Black Lantern; Kramer-a 3.00
#1,000,000 (11/98) 853rd Century x-over; Ordway-c/s/a 3.00
Annual 1 (1996, $2.95)-Legends of the Dead Earth story; Jerry Ordway-c; Mike Manley-a 4.00

POWER OF STRONGMAN, THE (Also see Strongman)
AC Comics: 1989 ($2.95)

1-Powell G.A.-r 3.00

POWER OF THE ATOM (See Secret Origins #29)
DC Comics: Aug, 1988 - No. 18, Nov, 1989 ($1.00)

1-18: 6-Chronos returns; Byrne-p. 9-JLI app. 3.00

POWER OF THE DARK CRYSTAL (Jim Henson)
BOOM! Studios (Archaia): Feb, 2017 - No. 12, Mar, 2018 ($3.99)

1-12-Simon Spurrier-s/Kelly & Nichole Matthews-a; multiple covers 4.00

POWER PACHYDERMS
Marvel Comics: Sept, 1989 ($1.25, one-shot)

1-Elephant super-heroes; parody of X-Men, Elektra, & 3 Stooges 3.00

POWER PACK
Marvel Comics Group: Aug, 1984 - No. 62, Feb, 1991

1-($1.00, 52 pgs.)-Origin & 1st app. Power Pack 3 6 9 16 23 30
2-18,20-26,28,30-45,47-62 3.00
19-(52 pgs.)-Cloak & Dagger, Wolverine app. 4.00
27-Mutant massacre; Wolverine & Sabretooth app. 5.00
29,46: 29-Spider-Man & Hobgoblin app. 46-Punisher app. 4.00

Power Girl (2009) #10 © DC

Powerpuff Girls (2014) #8 © CN

Powers V2 #17 © Jinxworld

	GD 2.0	VG 4.0	FN 6.0	VF 8.0	VF/NM 9.0	NM- 9.2

Graphic Novel: Power Pack & Cloak & Dagger: Shelter From the Storm ('89, SC, $7.95) Velluto/Farmer-a 10.00
...Holiday Special 1 (2/92, $2.25, 68 pgs.) 4.00
NOTE: *Austin scripts-53.* ***Mignola*** *c-20.* ***Morrow*** *a-51.* ***Spiegle*** *a-55i.* ***Williamson*** *a(i)-43, 50, 52.*

POWER PACK (Volume 2)
Marvel Comics: Aug, 2000 - No. 4, Nov, 2000 ($2.99, limited series)

1-4-Doran & Austin-c/a 3.00

POWER PACK
Marvel Comics: June, 2005 - No. 4, Aug, 2005 ($2.99, limited series)

1-4-Sumerak-s/Gurihiru-a; back-up Franklin Richards story. 3-Fantastic Four app. 3.00
... Digest (2006, $6.99) r/#1-4 7.00

POWER PACK (Marvel Legacy)
Marvel Comics: No. 63, Jan, 2018 ($3.99, one-shot)

63-Devin Grayson-s/Marika Cresta-a 4.00

POWER PACK (Also see Outlawed #1 and Champions)
Marvel Comics: Jun, 2020 - No. 5, Jun, 2021 ($3.99, limited series)

1-5-Ryan North-s/Nico Leon-a. 1-Origin retold. 2-The Wizard app. 3-Taskmaster app. 4.00

POWER PACK: DAY ONE
Marvel Comics: May, 2008 - No. 4, Aug, 2008($2.99, limited series)

1-4-Van Lente-s/Gurihiru-a; origin retold; Coover-a back-ups. 1-Fantastic Four cameo 3.00

POWER PACK: GROW-UP
Marvel Comics: Oct, 2019 ($4.99, one-shot)

1-Louise Simonson-s/June Brigman-a; back-up w/art by Gurihiru; Kofi & Wolverine app. 5.00

POWERPUFF GIRLS, THE (Also see Cartoon Network Starring... #1)
DC Comics: May, 2000 - No. 70, Mar, 2006 ($1.99/$2.25)

1 3 6 9 14 20 25
2-10 6.00
11-55,57-70: 25-Pin-ups by Allred, Byrne, Baker, Mignola, Hernandez, Warren 4.00
56-($2.95) Bonus pages; Mojo Jojo-c 5.00
...Double Whammy (12/00, $3.95) r/#1,2 & a Dexter's Lab story 2 4 6 9 12 15
...Movie: The Comic (9/02, $2.95) Movie adaptation; Phil Moy & Chris Cook-a 2 4 6 9 12 15

POWERPUFF GIRLS
IDW Publishing: Sept, 2013 - No. 10, Jun, 2014 ($3.99)

1-Five covers; Troy Little-s/a; Mojo Jojo app. 1 3 4 6 8 10
2-10-Multiple covers on each 4.00

POWERPUFF GIRLS (Based on the 2016 TV reboot)
IDW Publishing: Jul, 2016 - No. 6, Dec, 2016 ($3.99)

1-6: 1-4-Derek Charm-a; multiple covers on each. 1-Mojo Jojo app. 4.00

POWERPUFF GIRLS: BUREAU OF BAD
IDW Publishing: Nov, 2017 - No. 3, Jan, 2018 ($3.99, limited series)

1-3-Mancini & Goldman-s/Murphy-a; multiple covers on each 4.00

POWERPUFF GIRLS: SUPER SMASH-UP!
IDW Publishing: Jan, 2015 - No. 5, May, 2015 ($3.99, limited series)

1-5-Dexter's Laboratory's Dexter & Dee-Dee app.; multiple covers on each 4.00

POWERPUFF GIRLS: THE TIME TIE
IDW Publishing: May, 2017 - No. 3, Jul, 2017 ($3.99, limited series)

1-3-Mancini & Goldman-s/Murphy-a; multiple covers on each 4.00

POWER RANGERS (Mighty Morphin Power Rangers)
BOOM! Studios: Nov, 2020 - Present ($4.99/$3.99)

1-($4.99) Parrott-s/Mortarino-a; multiple covers; Omega Rangers app. 5.00
2-22-($3.99): 13-16-The Eltarian War 4.00
... Unlimited: Countdown to Ruin 1 (6/22, $7.99) Silver Ranger app. 8.00
... Unlimited: Edge of Darkness 1 (6/21, $7.99) Phantom Ranger app. 8.00
... Unlimited: Heir to Darkness 1 (3/21, $7.99) Origin of Astronema 8.00
... Unlimited: The Death Ranger 1 (8/22, $7.99) Sister Supernova app. 8.00

POWER RANGERS: DRAKKON NEW DAWN (Mighty Morphin Power Rangers)
BOOM! Studios: Aug, 2020 - No. 3, Oct, 2020 ($4.99, limited series)

1-3-Burch-s/Ragazzoni-a; multiple covers 5.00

POWER RANGERS: RANGER SLAYER (Mighty Morphin Power Rangers)
BOOM! Studios: Jul, 2020 ($7.99, one-shot)

1-Parrott-s/Mora-a; multiple covers 8.00

POWER RANGERS UNIVERSE (Mighty Morphin Power Rangers)
BOOM! Studios: Dec, 2021 - No. 6, May, 2022 ($4.99)

1-6-($4.99) Andelfinger-s/Ragazzoni-a; multiple covers 5.00

POWER RANGERS ZEO (TV)(Saban's...)(Also see Saban's Mighty Morphin Power Rangers)
Image Comics (Extreme Studios): Aug, 1996 ($2.50)

1-Based on TV show 2 4 6 11 16 20

POWER RECORD COMICS (Named Peter Pan Record Comics for #33-47)
Marvel Comics/Power Records: 1974 - 1978 ($1.49, 7x10" comics, 20 pgs. with 45 R.P.M. record) (Clipped corners - reduce value 20%) (Comic alone - 50%; record alone - 50%) (Some copies significantly warped by shrinkwrapping - reduce value 20%) (PR22, PR23, PR38, PR43, PR44 do not exist)

PR10-Spider-Man-r/from #124,125; Man-Wolf app. PR18-Planet of the Apes-r. PR19-Escape From the Planet of the Apes-r. PR20-Beneath the Planet of the Apes-r. PR21-Battle for the Planet of the Apes-r. PR24-Spider-Man II-New-a begins. PR27-Batman "Stacked Cards"; N. Adams-a(p). PR30-Batman "Robin Meets Man-Bat"; N. Adams-r/Det.(7 pgs.).
With record; each... 5 10 15 35 63 90

PR11-Incredible Hulk-r/#171. PR12-Captain America-r/#168. PR13-Fantastic Four-r/#126. PR14-Frankenstein-Ploog-r/#1. PR15-Tomb of Dracula-Colan-r/#2. PR16-Man-Thing-Ploog-r/#5. PR17-Werewolf By Night-Ploog-r/Marvel Spotlight #2. PR28-Superman "Alien Creatures". PR29-Space: 1999 "Breakaway". PR31-Conan-N. Adams-a; reprinted in Conan #116. PR32-Space: 1999 "Return to the Beginning". PR33-Superman-G.A. origin, Buckler-a(p). PR34-Superman. PR35-Wonder Woman-Buckler-a(p)
With record; each... 5 10 15 31 53 75

PR11, PR24-(1981 Peter Pan records re-issues) PR11-New Abomination & Rhino-c
With record; each... 5 10 15 33 57 80

PR25-Star Trek "Passage to Moauv". PR26-Star Trek "Crier in Emptiness." PR36-Holo-Man. PR37-Robin Hood. PR39-Huckleberry Finn. PR40-Davy Crockett. PR41-Robinson Crusoe. PR42-20,000 Leagues Under the Sea. PR47-Little Women
With record; each... 4 8 12 28 47 65

PR25, PR26 (Peter Pan records re-issues with photo covers). PR45-Star Trek "Dinosaur Planet". PR46-Star Trek "The Robot Masters" 4 8 12 28 47 65
NOTE: *Peter Pan re-issues exist for #25-32 and are valued the same.*

POWERS
Image Comics: 2000 - No. 37, Feb, 2004 ($2.95)

1-Bendis-s/Oeming-a; murder of Retro Girl 2 4 6 9 11 14
2-6: 6-End of Retro Girl arc. 6.00
7-14: 7-Warren Ellis app. 12-14-Death of Olympia 4.00
15-37: 31-36-Origin of the Powers 3.00
Annual 1 (2001, $3.95) 4.00
...: Anarchy TPB (11/03, $14.95) r/#21-24; interviews, sketchbook, cover gallery 15.00
...Coloring/Activity Book (2001, $1.50, B&W, 8 x 10.5") Oeming-a 3.00
... Firsts 1 (6/15, $1.00) r/#1 3.00
...: Forever TPB (2005, $19.95) r/#31-37; script for #31, sketchbook, cover gallery 20.00
...: Little Deaths TPB (2002, $19.95) r/#7,12-14, Ann. #1, Coloring/Activity Book; sketch pages, cover gallery 20.00
...: Roleplay TPB (2001, $13.95) r/#8-11; sketchbook, cover gallery 14.00
... Scriptbook (2001, $19.95) scripts for #1-11; Oeming sketches 20.00
...: Supergroup TPB (2003, $19.95) r/#15-20; sketchbook, cover gallery 20.00
...: The Definitive Collection Vol. 1 HC (2006, $29.99, dust jacket) r/#1-11 & Coloring/Activity Book, script for #1, sketch pages and covers, interviews, letter column highlights 30.00
...: The Definitive Collection Vol. 2 HC (2009, $29.99, dust jacket) r/#12-24 & Annual #1; cover gallery; 1st Bendis/Oeming Jinx story; interviews, letter column highlights 30.00
...: Who Killed Retro Girl TPB (2000, $21.95) r/#1-6; sketchbook, cover gallery, and promotional strips from Comic Shop News 22.00

POWERS
Marvel Comics (Icon): Jul, 2004 - No. 30, Sept, 2008 ($2.95/$3.95)

1-11,13-24-Bendis-s/Oeming-a. 14-Cover price error 3.00
12-($3.95, 64 pages) 2 covers; Bendis & Oeming interview 4.00
25-30-($3.95, 40 pages) 25-Two covers; Bendis interview 4.00
Annual 2008 (5/08, $4.95) Bendis-s/Oeming-a; interview with Brubaker, Simone, others 5.00
...: Legends TPB (2005, $17.95) r/#1-6; sketchbook, cover gallery 18.00
...: Psychotic TPB (1/06, $19.95) r/#7-12; Bendis & Oeming interview, cover gallery 20.00
...: Cosmic TPB (10/07, $19.95) r/#13-18; script and sketch pages 20.00
...: Secret Identity TPB (12/07, $19.95) r/#19-24; script pages 20.00

POWERS (Volume 3)
Marvel Comics (Icon): Nov, 2009 - No. 11, Jul, 2012 ($3.95)

1-11-Bendis-s/Oeming-a 4.00

POWERS (Volume 5)
Marvel Comics (Icon): Jan, 2015 - No. 8, Apr, 2017 ($3.99)

1-8-Bendis-s/Oeming-a. 1-Bonus photo spread of TV show cast 4.00

POWERS: BUREAU (Follows Volume 3)

GD VG FN VF VF/NM NM-
2.0 4.0 6.0 8.0 9.0 9.2

Marvel Comics (Icon): Feb, 2013 - No. 12, Nov, 2014 ($3.95)
1-12-Bendis-s/Oeming-a 4.00

POWERS OF X (Weekly series alternating with House of X #1-6)
Marvel Comics: Sept, 2019 - No. 6, Dec, 2019 ($5.99/$4.99)
1-($5.99) Hickman-s/Silva-a 6.00
2-6-($4.99) 4-Mr. Sinister app. 5.00

POWERS THAT BE (Becomes Star Seed No.7 on)
Broadway Comics: Nov, 1995 - No. 6, June, 1996 ($2.50)
1-6: 1-Intro of Fatale & Star Seed. 6-Begin $2.95-c. 3.00
Preview Editions 1-3 (9/95 - 11/95, B&W) 3.00

POWER UP
BOOM! Studios: Jul, 2015 - No. 6, Dec, 2015 ($3.99)
1-6-Katie Leth-s/Matt Cummings-a. 1-Multiple covers 4.00

POW MAGAZINE (Bob Sproul's) (Satire Magazine)
Humor-Vision: Aug, 1966 - No. 3, Feb, 1967 (30¢)
1,2: 2-Jones-a 4 8 12 28 47 65
3-Wrightson-a 5 10 15 34 60 85

PREACHER
DC Comics (Vertigo): Apr, 1995 - No. 66, Oct, 2000 ($2.50, mature)
nn-Preview 6 12 18 38 69 100
1 ($2.95)-Ennis scripts, Dillon-a & Fabry-c in all; 1st app. Jesse, Tulip, & Cassidy
6 12 18 42 79 115
1-Retailer Incentive Edition (5/16, $3.99) r/#1 with new cover by Steve Dillon 4.00
1-Special Edition (6/09, $1.00) r/#1 with "After Watchmen" cover frame 4.00
2-1st app. Saint of Killers. 3 6 9 19 30 40
3 3 6 9 16 23 30
4,5 3 6 9 14 20 25
6-10 2 4 6 10 14 18
11,12,14,15: 12-Polybagged w/videogame w/Ennis text
1 3 4 6 8 10
13-Hunters storyline begins; ends #17; 1st app. Herr Starr
3 6 9 21 33 45
16-20: 19-Saint of Killers app.; begin "Crusaders", ends #24 6.00
21-25: 21-24-Saint of Killers app. 25-Origin of Cassidy. 4.00
26-49,52-64: 52-Tulip origin 3.00
50-($3.75) Pin-ups by Jim Lee, Bradstreet, Quesada and Palmiotti 4.00
51-Includes preview of 100 Bullets; Tulip origin 2 4 6 8 10 12
65,66-($3.75) 65-Almost everyone dies. 66-Final issue
1 3 4 6 8 10
Alamo (2001, $17.95, TPB) r/#59-66; Fabry-c 18.00
All Hell's a-Coming (2000, $17.95, TPB)-r/#51-58, ...:Tall in the Saddle 18.00
... Book One HC (2009, $39.99, d.j.) r/#1-12; new Ennis intro.; pin-ups from #50,66 40.00
... Book Two HC (2010, $39.99, d.j.) r/#13-26; new Stuart Moore intro. 40.00
... Book Three HC (2010, $39.99, d.j.) r/#27-33, ...Special: Saint of Killers #1-4 & ...Special: Cassidy: Blood & Whiskey #1; new Ennis intro. 40.00
... Book Four HC (2011, $39.99, d.j.) r/#34-40, ...Special: One Man's War, ...Special: The Story of You-Know-Who, & ...Special: The Good Old Boys; new Dillon intro. 40.00
...: Dead or Alive HC (2000, $29.95) Gallery of Glenn Fabry's cover paintings for every Preacher issue; commentary by Fabry & Ennis 30.00
...: Dead or Alive SC (2003, $19.95) 20.00
Dixie Fried (1998, $14.95, TPB)-r/#27-33, Special: Cassidy 15.00
Gone To Texas (1996, $14.95, TPB)-r/#1-7; Fabry-c 15.00
Proud Americans (1997, $14.95, TPB)-r/#18-26; Fabry-c 15.00
Salvation (1999, $14.95, TPB)-r/#41-50; Fabry-c 15.00
Until the End of the World (1996, $14.95, TPB)-r/#8-17; Fabry-c 15.00
War in the Sun (1999, $14.95, TPB)-r/#34-40 15.00

PREACHER SPECIAL: CASSIDY: BLOOD & WHISKEY
DC Comics (Vertigo): 1998 ($5.95, one-shot)
1-Ennis-scripts/Fabry-c/Dillon-a 6.00

PREACHER SPECIAL: ONE MAN'S WAR
DC Comics (Vertigo): Mar, 1998 ($4.95, one-shot)
1-Ennis-scripts/Fabry-c /Snejbjerg-a 5.00

PREACHER SPECIAL: SAINT OF KILLERS
DC Comics (Vertigo): Aug, 1996 - No. 4, Nov, 1996 ($2.50, lim. series, mature)
1-4: Ennis-scripts/Fabry-c. 1,2-Pugh-a. 3,4-Ezquerra-a 4.00
1-Signed & numbered 20.00

PREACHER SPECIAL: THE GOOD OLD BOYS
DC Comics (Vertigo): Aug, 1997 ($4.95, one-shot, mature)
1-Ennis-scripts/Fabry-c /Esquerra-a 5.00

PREACHER SPECIAL: THE STORY OF YOU-KNOW-WHO
DC Comics (Vertigo): Dec, 1996 ($4.95, one-shot, mature)
1-Ennis-scripts/Fabry-c/Case-a 5.00

PREACHER: TALL IN THE SADDLE
DC Comics (Vertigo): 2000 ($5.95, one-shot)
1-Ennis-scripts/Fabry-c/Dillon-a; early romance of Tulip and Jesse 6.00

PRECINCT, THE
Dynamite Entertainment: 2015 - No. 5, 2016 ($3.99)
1-5-Barbarie-s/Zamora-a. 1-Covers by Benitez & Robertson 4.00

PREDATOR (Also see Aliens Vs. ..., Batman vs. ..., Dark Horse Comics, & Dark Horse Presents)
Dark Horse Comics: June, 1989 - No. 4, Mar, 1990 ($2.25, limited series)
1-Based on movie; 1st app. Predator 6 12 18 37 66 95
1-2nd printing 3 6 9 16 23 30
2 3 6 9 15 33 28
3,4 2 4 6 9 12 15
Trade paperback (1990, $12.95)-r/#1-4 15.00
... Omnibus Volume 1 (8/07, $24.95, 6" x 9") r/#1-4, ... Cold War, ... Dark River, ...Bloody Sands of Time mini-series and stories from Dark Horse Comics #1,2,4-7,10-12 50.00
... Omnibus Volume 2 (2/08, $24.95, 6" x 9") r/ ... Big Game, ... Race War, ...Invaders From The, Fourth Dimension mini-series and stories from Dark Horse Comics #16-18,20,21; Dark Horse Presents #46 and A Decade of Dark Horse 50.00
... Omnibus Volume 3 (6/08, $24.95, 6" x 9") r/ ... Bad Blood, ... Kindred, ...Hell and Hot Water, ... Strange Roux mini-series and stories from Dark Horse Comics #12-14 and Dark Horse Presents #119 & 124 50.00

PREDATOR
Dark Horse Comics: June, 2009 - No. 4, Jan, 2010 ($3.50, limited series)
1-4-Arcudi-s/Saltares-a/Swanland-c; variant-c by Warner 5.00

PREDATOR
Marvel Comics: Oct, 2022 - No. 6, Mar,2023 ($4.99/$3.99, limited series)
1-($4.99) Set in 2056; Ed Brisson-s/Kev Walker-a 5.00
2-6-($3.99) 4.00

PREDATOR: (title series) **Dark Horse Comics**
--BAD BLOOD, 12/93 - No. 4, 1994 ($2.50) 1-4 5.00
--BIG GAME, 3/91 - No. 4, 6/91 ($2.50) 1-4: 1-3-Contain 2 Dark Horse trading cards 5.00
--BLOODY SANDS OF TIME, 2/92 - No. 2, 2/92 ($2.50) 1,2-Dan Barry-c/a(p)/scripts 5.00
--CAPTIVE, 4/98 ($2.95, one-shot) 1 1 3 4 6 8 10
--COLD WAR, 9/91 - No. 4, 12/91 ($2.50) 1-4: All have painted-c 5.00
--DARK RIVER, 7/96 - No. 4, 10/96 ($2.95) 1-Miran Kim-c
2 4 6 8 10 12
2-4-Miran Kim-c 6.00
--HELL & HOT WATER, 4/97 - No. 3, 6/97 ($2.95) 1-3 5.00
--HELL COME A WALKIN', 2/98 - No. 2, 3/98 ($2.95) 1,2-In the Civil War
2 4 6 8 12 15
--HOMEWORLD, 3/99 - No. 4, 6/99 ($2.95) 1-4 5.00
--HUNTERS, 5/17 - No. 5, 8/17 ($3.99) 1-5-Warner-s/Velasco-a/Doug Wheatley-c 5.00
--HUNTERS II, 8/18 - No. 4, 1/19 ($3.99) 1-4-Warner-s/Padilla-a 4.00
--HUNTERS III, 2/20 - No. 4, ($3.99) 1,2-Warner-s/Thies-a 4.00
--INVADERS FROM THE FOURTH DIMENSION, 7/94 ($3.95, one-shot, 52 pgs.) 1 5.00
--JUNGLE TALES. 3/95 ($2.95) 1-r/Dark Horse Comics 5.00
--KINDRED, 12/96 - No. 4, 3/97 ($2.50) 1 2 4 6 9 12 15
2-4 5.00
--NEMESIS, 12/97 - No. 2, 1/98 ($2.95) 1,2-Predator in Victorian England; Taggart-c 5.00
--PRIMAL, 7/97 - No. 2, 8/97 ($2.95) 1,2 5.00
--RACE WAR (See Dark Horse Presents #67), 2/93 - No. 4,10/93 ($2.50, color)
1-4,0: 1-4-Dorman painted-c #1-4, 0(4/93) 5.00
--STRANGE ROUX, 11/96 ($2.95, one-shot) 1 5.00
--XENOGENESIS (Also see Aliens Xenogenesis), 8/99 - No. 4, 11/99 ($2.95)
1,2-Edginton-s 5.00

PREDATOR: FIRE AND STONE (Crossover with Aliens, AvP, and Prometheus)
Dark Horse Comics: Oct, 2014 - No. 4, Jan, 2015 ($3.50, limited series)
1-4-Williamson-s/Mooneyham-a 3.50

PREDATOR: LIFE AND DEATH (Continues in Prometheus: Life and Death)
Dark Horse Comics: Mar, 2016 - No. 4, Jun, 2016 ($3.99, limited series)
1-4-Abnett-s/Thies-a 4.00

PREDATORS (Based on the 2010 movie)
Dark Horse Comics: Jun, 2010 - No. 4, Jun, 2010 ($2.99, weekly limited series)
1-4-Prequel to the 2010 movie; stories by Andreyko and Lapham; Paul Lee-c 3.00
... Film Adaptation (7/10, $6.99) Tobin-s/Drujiniu-s/photo-c 7.00
...: Preserve the Game (7/10, $3.50) Sequel to the movie; Lapham-s/Jefferson-a 3.50

PREDATOR 2
Dark Horse Comics: Feb, 1991 - No. 2, June, 1991 ($2.50, limited series)
1,2: 1-Adapts movie; both w/trading cards & photo-c 5.00

PREDATOR VS. JUDGE DREDD
Dark Horse Comics: Oct, 1997 - No. 3 ($2.50, limited series)
1-Wagner-s/Alcatena-a/Bolland-c 2 4 6 9 12 15
2,3 5.00

PREDATOR VS. JUDGE DREDD VS. ALIENS
Dark Horse Comics/IDW: Jul, 2016 - No. 4, Jun, 2017 ($3.99, limited series)
1-4-Layman-s/Mooneyham-a/Fabry-c 2 4 6 9 12 15

PREDATOR VS. MAGNUS ROBOT FIGHTER
Dark Horse/Valiant: Oct, 1992 - No. 2, 1993 ($2.95, limited series)
(1st Dark Horse/Valiant x-over)
1,2: (Reg.)-Barry Smith-c; Lee Weeks-a. 2-w/trading cards 5.00
1 (Platinum edition, 11/92)-Barry Smith-c 10.00

PREHISTORIC WORLD (See Classics Illustrated Special Issue)

PRELUDE TO DEADPOOL CORPS (Leads into Deadpool Corps #1)
Marvel Comics: May, 2010 - No. 5, May, 2010 ($3.99/$2.99, weekly limited series)
1-($3.99) Deadpool & Lady Deadpool vs. alternate dimension Capt. America; Liefeld-a 4.00
2-5-($2.99) Alternate reality Deadpools team-up; Dave Johnson interlocking covers 3.00

PRELUDE TO INFINITE CRISIS
DC Comics: 2005 ($5.99, squarebound)
nn-Reprints stories and panels with commentary leading into Infinite Crisis series 6.00

PREMIERE (See Charlton Premiere)

PRESIDENTIAL MATERIAL
IDW Publishing: Oct, 2008 ($3.99/$7.99)
...: Barack Obama - Biography of the candidate; Mariotte-s/Morgan-a/Campbell-c 4.00
...: John McCain - Biography of the candidate; Helfer-s/Thompson-a/Campbell-c 4.00
Flipbook ($7.99) Both issues in flipbook format 8.00

PRESTO KID, THE (See Red Mask)

PRETTY BOY FLOYD (See On the Spot)

Preacher #54 © Ennis & Dillon

Predator (2022) #6 © 20th Cent. Studios

Princess Leia #4 © Lucasfilm

	GD 2.0	VG 4.0	FN 6.0	VF 8.0	VF/NM 9.0	NM- 9.2

PRETTY DEADLY
Image Comics: Oct, 2013 - No. 10, Jun, 2016 ($3.50)

1-10-DeConnick-s/Rios-a/c 3.50

PRETTY DEADLY: THE RAT
Image Comics: Sept, 2019 - No. 5, Jan, 2020 ($3.99, limited series)

1-5-DeConnick-s/Rios-a/c 4.00

PRETTY VIOLENT
Image Comics: Aug, 2019 - No. 11, Nov, 2020 ($3.99)

1-11-Derek Hunter-a; Hunter & Jason Young-s 4.00

PREZ (See Cancelled Comic Cavalcade, Sandman #54 & Supergirl #10)
National Periodical Publications: Aug-Sept, 1973 - No. 4, Feb-Mar, 1974

	GD	VG	FN	VF	VF/NM	NM-
1-Origin; Joe Simon scripts	3	6	9	17	26	35
2-4	2	4	6	13	18	22

PREZ
DC Comics: Aug, 2015 - No. 6, Feb, 2016 ($2.99)

1-6: 1-Intro. Beth Ross; Mark Russell-s/Ben Caldwell-a 3.00

PRICE, THE (See Eclipse Graphic Album Series)

PRIDE & JOY
DC Comics (Vertigo): July, 1997 - No. 4, Oct, 1997 ($2.50, limited series)

1-4-Ennis-s 3.00
TPB (2004, $14.95) r/#1-4 15.00

PRIDE & PREJUDICE
Marvel Comics: June, 2009 - No. 5, Oct, 2009 ($3.99, limited series)

1-5-Adaptation of the Jane Austen novel; Nancy Butler-s/Hugo Petrus-a 4.00

PRIDE AND THE PASSION, THE
Dell Publishing Co.: No. 824, Aug, 1957

	GD	VG	FN	VF	VF/NM	NM-
Four Color 824-Movie, Frank Sinatra & Cary Grant photo-c	10	20	30	66	138	210

PRIDE OF BAGHDAD
DC Comics (Vertigo): 2006 ($19.99, hardcover with dustjacket)

HC-A pride of lions escaping from the Baghdad zoo in 2003; Vaughan-s/Henrichon-a 20.00
SC-(2007, $12.99) 13.00

PRIDE OF THE YANKEES, THE (See Real Heroes & Sport Comics)
Magazine Enterprises: 1949 (The Life of Lou Gehrig)

	GD	VG	FN	VF	VF/NM	NM-
nn-Photo-c; Ogden Whitney-a	93	186	279	599	1025	1450

PRIEST (Also see Asylum)
Maximum Press: Aug, 1996 - No. 2, Oct, 1996 ($2.99)

1,2 3.00

PRIMAL FORCE
DC Comics: No. 0, Oct, 1994 - No. 14, Dec, 1995 ($1.95/$2.25)

0-14: 0- Teams Red Tornado, Golem, Jack O'Lantern, Meridian & Silver Dragon. 9-begin $2.25-c 3.00

PRIMAL MAN (See The Crusaders)

PRIMAL RAGE
Sirius Entertainment: 1996 ($2.95)

1-Dark One-c; based of video game 3.00

PRIME (See Break-Thru, Flood Relief & Ultraforce)
Malibu Comics (Ultraverse): June, 1993 - No. 26, Aug, 1995 ($1.95/$2.50)

1-1st app. Prime; has coupon for Ultraverse Premiere #0 4.00
1-With coupon missing 2.00
1-Full cover holographic edition; 1st of kind w/Hardcase #1 & Strangers #1 10.00
1-Ultra 5,000 edition w/silver ink-c 6.00
2-4,6-11,14-26: 2-Polybagged w/card & coupon for U. Premiere #0. 3,4-Prototype app. 4-Direct sale w/o card.4-($2.50)-Newsstand ed. polybagged w/card. 6-Bill & Chelsea Clinton app.115-Intro Papa Verite; Pérez-c/a. 16-Intro Turbo Charge 3.00
5-($2.50, 48 pgs.)-Rune flip-c/story part B by Barry Smith; see Sludge #1 for 1st app. Rune; 3-pg. Night Man preview 4.00
12-($3.50, 68 pgs.)-Flip book w/Ultraverse Premiere #3; silver foil logo 4.00
13-($2.95, 52 pgs.)-Variant covers 4.00
...: Gross and Disgusting 1 (10/94, $3.95)-Boris-c; "Annual" on cover, published monthly in indicia 4.00
...Month "Ashcan" (8/94, 75¢)-Boris-c 3.00
... Time: A Prime Collection (1994, $9.95)-r/1-4 10.00
...Vs. The Incredible Hulk (1995)-mail away limited edition 10.00
...Vs. The Incredible Hulk Premium edition 10.00
...Vs. The Incredible Hulk Super Premium edition 15.00

NOTE: *Perez a-15; c-15, 16.*

PRIME (Also see Black September)
Malibu Comics (Ultraverse): Infinity, Sept, 1995 - V2#15, Dec, 1996 ($1.50)

Infinity, V2#1-15: Post Black September storyline. 6-8-Solitaire app. 9-Breyfogle-c/a. 10-12-Ramos-c. 15-Lord Pumpkin app. 3.00

	GD	VG	FN	VF	VF/NM	NM-
Infinity Signed Edition (2,000 printed)	1	2	3	5	6	8

PRIME/CAPTAIN AMERICA
Malibu Comics: Mar, 1996 ($3.95, one-shot)

1-Norm Breyfogle-a 5.00

PRIME8: CREATION
Two Morrows Publishing: July, 2001 ($3.95, B&W)

1-Neal Adams-c 4.00

PRIMER (Comico...)
Comico: Oct (no month), 1982 - No. 6, Feb, 1984 (B&W)

	GD	VG	FN	VF	VF/NM	NM-
1 (52 pgs.)	3	6	9	17	26	35
2-1st app. Grendel & Argent by Wagner	46	92	138	340	770	1200
3,4	2	4	6	10	14	18
5-1st Sam Kieth art in comics ('83) & 1st The Maxx	7	14	21	46	86	125
6-Intro & 1st app. Evangeline	3	6	9	14	19	24

PRIMORDIAL
Image Comics: Sept, 2021 - No. 6, Feb, 2022 ($3.99)

1-6-Jeff Lemire-s/Andrea Sorrentino-a 4.00

PRIMORTALS (Leonard Nimoy's...)

PRIMOS
AWA Studios: Feb, 2022 - No. 4, Jun, 2022 ($3.99, limited series)

1-4-Al Madrigal-s/Carlo Barberi-a 4.00

PRIMUS (TV)
Charlton Comics: Feb, 1972 - No. 7, Oct, 1972

	GD	VG	FN	VF	VF/NM	NM-
1-Staton-a in all	2	4	6	11	16	20
2-7: 6-Drug propaganda story	2	4	6	8	11	14

PRINCE NAMOR, THE SUB-MARINER (Also see Namor ...)
Marvel Comics Group: Sept, 1984 - No. 4, Dec, 1984 (Limited-series)

1-4 5.00

PRINCE OF PERSIA: BEFORE THE SANDSTORM (Based on the 2010 movie)
Dynamite Entertainment: 2010 - No. 4, 2010 ($3.99, limited series)

1-4-Art by Fowler and various. 1-Chang-a. 2-Lopez-a. 3-Edwards-a 5.00

PRINCESS LEIA (Star Wars)
Marvel Comics: May, 2015 - No. 5, Sept, 2015 ($3.99)

1-5-Mark Waid-s/Terry Dodson-a; story follows the ending of Episode IV 4.00

PRINCESS SALLY (Video game)
Archie Publications: Apr, 1995 - No. 3, June, 1995 ($1.50, limited series)

1-3: Spin-off from Sonic the Hedgehog 4.00

PRINCESS UGG
Oni Press: Jun, 2014 - No. 8, Mar, 2015 ($3.99)

1-8-Ted Naifeh-s/a 4.00

PRINCE VALIANT (See Ace Comics, Comics Reading Libraries *in the Promotional Comics section*, & King Comics #146, 147)
David McKay Publ./Dell: No. 26, 1941; No. 67, June, 1954 - No. 900, May, 1958

	GD	VG	FN	VF	VF/NM	NM-
Feature Books 26 ('41)-Harold Foster-c/a; newspaper strips reprinted, pgs. 1-28,30-63; color & 68 pgs; Foster cover is only original comic book artwork by him	174	348	522	1114	1907	2700
Four Color 567 (6/54)(#1)-By Bob Fuje-Movie, photo-c	10	20	30	69	147	225
Four Color 650 (9/55), 699 (4/56), 719 (8/56),-Fuje-a	8	16	24	55	105	155
Four Color 788 (4/57), 849 (1/58), 900-Fuje-a	7	14	21	44	82	120

PRINCE VALIANT
Marvel Comics: Dec, 1994 - No. 4, Mar, 1995 ($3.95, limited series)

1-4: Kaluta-c in all 4.00

PRINCE VANDAL
Triumphant Comics: Nov, 1993 - Apr?, 1994 ($2.50)

1-6: 1,2-Triumphant Unleashed x-over 3.00

PRIORITY: WHITE HEAT
AC Comics: 1986 - No. 2, 1986 ($1.75, mini-series)

GD 2.0 | VG 4.0 | FN 6.0 | VF 8.0 | VF/NM 9.0 | NM- 9.2

1,2-Bill Black-a 3.00

PRISCILLA'S POP
Dell Publishing Co.: No. 569, June, 1954 - No. 799, May, 1957

Four Color 569 (#1), 630 (5/55), 704 (5/56),799 6 12 18 42 79 115

PRISON BARS (See Behind...)

PRISON BREAK!
Avon Per./Realistic No. 3 on: Sept, 1951 - No. 5, Sept, 1952 (Painted c-3)

1-Wood-c & 1 pg.; has-r/Saint #7 retitled Michael Strong Private Eye
171 348 522 1114 1907 2700
2-Wood-c; Kubert-a; Kinstler inside front-c 60 120 180 381 653 925
3-Orlando, Check-a; c-/Avon paperback #179 43 86 129 271 461 650
4,5: 4-Kinstler-c & inside f/c; Lawrence, Lazarus-a. 5-Kinstler-c; Infantino-a
41 82 123 256 428 600

PRISONER, THE (TV)
DC Comics: 1988 - No. 4, 1989 ($3.50, squarebound, mini-series)

1-4 (Books a-d) 5.00

PRISONER, THE: THE UNCERTAINTY MACHINE (TV)
Titan Comics: Jun, 2018 - No. 4, Sept, 2018 ($3.99, limited series)

1-4-Milligan-s/Lorimer-a 4.00

PRISON RIOT
Avon Periodicals: 1952

1-Marijuana Murders-1 pg. text; Kinstler-c; 2 Kubert illos on text pages
53 106 159 334 567 800

PRISON TO PRAISE
Logos International: 1974 (35¢) (Religious, Christian)

nn-True Story of Merlin R. Carothers 3 6 9 14 20 25

PRIVATE BUCK
Dell Publishing Co./Rand McNally: No. 21, 1941 - No. 12, 1942 (4-1/2" x 5-1/2", 1942)

Large Feature Comic 21 (#1)(1941)(Series I), 22 (1941)(Series I), 12 (1942)(Series II)
23 46 69 136 223 310
382-Rand McNally, one panel per page; small size 14 28 42 76 108 140

PRIVATE EYE (Cover title: Rocky Jorden...#6-8)
Atlas Comics (MCI): Jan, 1951 - No. 8, March, 1952

1-Cover title: Crime Cases... #1-5 34 68 102 199 325 450
2,3-Tuska c/a(3) 18 36 54 105 165 225
4-8 15 30 45 85 130 175

NOTE: *Henkel a-6(3), 7; c-7. Sinnott a-6.*

PRIVATE EYE (See Mike Shayne...)

PRIVATE SECRETARY
Dell Publishing Co.: Dec-Feb, 1962-63 - No. 2, Mar-May, 1963

1 5 10 15 31 53 75
2 4 8 12 23 37 50

PRIVATE STRONG (See The Double Life of...)

PRIZE COMICS (...Western #69 on) (Also see Treasure Comics)
Prize Publications: March, 1940 - No. 68, Feb-Mar, 1948

1-Origin Power Nelson, The Futureman & Jupiter, Master Magician; Ted O'Neil, Secret Agent M-11, Jaxon of the Jungle, Bucky Brady & Storm Curtis begin (1st app. of each)
423 846 1269 3000 5250 7500
2-The Black Owl begins (1st app.) 271 542 813 1734 2967 4200
3-Classic sci-fi-c 290 580 870 1856 3178 4500
4-Classic robot-c 314 628 942 2198 3849 5500
5-Dr. Dekkar, Master of Monsters app. 219 438 657 1402 2401 3400
6-Classic sci-fi-c; Dr. Dekkar app. 245 490 735 1568 2684 3800
7-(Scarce)-1st app. The Green Lama (12/40); Black Owl by S&K; origin/1st app. Dr. Frost & Frankenstein; Capt. Gallant, The Great Voodini & Twist Turner begin;
1100 2200 3300 8400 15,200 22,000
8,9-Black Owl & Ted O'Neil by S&K 219 438 657 1402 2401 3400
10-12,14,15: 11-Origin Bulldog Denny. 14-War-c 161 322 483 1030 1765 2500
13-Yank & Doodle begin (8/41, origin/1st app.) 200 400 600 1280 2190 3100
16-19: 16-Spike Mason begins 145 290 435 921 1586 2250
20-(Rare) Frankenstein, Black Owl, Green Lama, Yank and Doodle WWII parade-c
541 1082 1623 3950 6975 10,000
21,25,27,28,31-All WWII covers 142 284 426 909 1555 2200
22-24,26: 22-Statue of Liberty Japanese attack war-c. 23-Uncle Sam patriotic war-c.
24-Lincoln statue patriotic-c. 26-Liberty Bell-c 161 322 483 1030 1765 2500
29,30,32 116 232 348 742 1271 1800
33-Classic bondage/torture-c 258 516 774 1651 2826 4000
34-Origin Airmale, Yank & Doodle; The Black Owl joins army, Yank & Doodle's father assumes Black Owl's role 110 220 330 704 1202 1700
35-36,38-39: 35-Flying Fist & Bingo begin 71 142 213 454 777 1100
37-Intro. Stampy, Airmale's sidekick; Hitler-c 975 1950 2919 7100 12,550 18,000
40-Nazi WWII-c 168 336 504 1075 1838 2600
41-45,47-50: 45-Yank & Doodle learn Black Owl's I.D. (their father). 48-Prince Ra begins
57 114 171 362 619 875
46-Classic Zombie Horror-c/story 168 336 504 1075 1838 2600
51-62,64,67,68: 53-Transvestism story. 55-No Frankenstein. 57-X-Mas-c.
64-Black Owl retires 40 80 120 246 411 575
63-Simon & Kirby c/a 50 100 150 315 533 750
65,66-Frankenstein-c by Briefer 68 136 204 435 743 1050

NOTE: *Briefer a 7-on; c-65, 66. J. Binder a-16; c-21-29. Guardineer a-62. Kiefer c-62. Palais c-68. Simon & Kirby c-63, 75, 83.*

PRIZE COMICS WESTERN (Formerly Prize Comics #1-68)
Prize Publications (Feature): No. 69(V7#2), Apr-May, 1948 - No. 119, Nov-Dec, 1956 (No. 69-84: 52 pgs.)

69(V7#2) 24 48 72 142 234 325
70-75: 74-Kurtzman-a (8 pgs.) 18 36 54 105 165 225
76-Randolph Scott photo-c; "Canadian Pacific" movie adaptation
16 32 48 96 151 205
77-Photo-c; Severin/Elder, Mart Bailey-a; "Streets of Laredo" movie adaptation
15 30 45 90 140 190
78-Photo-c; S&K-a, 10 pgs.; Severin, Mart Bailey-a; "Bullet Code", & "Roughshod" movie adaptations 18 36 54 107 169 230
79-Photo-c; Kurtzman-a, 8 pgs.; Severin/Elder, Severin, Mart Bailey-a; "Stage To Chino" movie adaptation w/George O'Brien 18 36 54 103 169 230
80-82-Photo-c; 80,81-Severin/Elder-a(2). 82-1st app. The Preacher by Mart Bailey; Severin/Elder-a(3) 15 30 45 84 127 170
83,84 13 26 39 74 105 135
85-1st app. American Eagle by John Severin & begins (V9#6, 1-2/51)
24 48 72 142 234 325
86,101-105, 109-Severin/Williamson-a 14 28 42 78 112 145
87-99,110,111-Severin/Elder-a(2-3) each 14 28 42 81 110 155
100 15 30 45 85 124 165
106-108,112 10 20 30 56 76 95
113-Williamson/Severin-a(2)/Frazetta? 14 28 42 81 118 155
114-119: Drifter series in all; by Mort Meskin #114-118
9 18 27 52 69 85

NOTE: *Fass a-81. Severin & Elder c-84-99. Severin a-72, 75, 77-79, 83-86, 96, 97, 100-105; c-92,100-109(most), 110-119. Simon & Kirby c-75, 83.*

PRIZE MYSTERY
Key Publications: May, 1955 - No. 3, Sept, 1955

1 39 78 117 240 395 550
2,3 14 28 42 76 108 140

PRO, THE
Image Comics: July, 2002 ($5.95, squarebound, one-shot)

1-Ennis-s/Conner & Palmiotti-a; prostitute gets super-powers 8.00
1-Second printing with different cover 6.00
Hardcover Edition (10/04, $14.95) oversized reprint plus new 8 pg. story; sketch pages 15.00

PROCTOR VALLEY ROAD
BOOM! Studios: Mar, 2021 - No. 5, Jul, 2021 ($3.99, limited series)

1-5-Grant Morrison & Alex Child-s/Naomi Franquiz-a 4.00

PRODIGY
Image Comics: Dec, 2018 - No. 6, Jun, 2019 ($3.99)

1-6-Mark Millar-s/Rafael Albuquerque-a 4.00

PRODIGY: THE ICARUS SOCIETY
Image Comics: Jul, 2022 - No. 5, Nov, 2022 ($3.99, limited series)

1-5-Mark Millar-s/Matteo Buffagni-a 4.00

PROFESSIONAL FOOTBALL (See Charlton Sport Library)

PROFESSOR COFFIN
Charlton Comics: No. 19, Oct, 1985 - No. 21, Feb, 1986

19-21: Wayne Howard-a(r); low print run 1 2 3 5 6 8

PROFESSOR OM
Innovation Publishing: May, 1990 - No. 2, 1990 ($2.50, limited series)

1,2-East Meets West spin-off 3.00

PROFESSOR XAVIER AND THE X-MEN (Also see X-Men, 1st series)
Marvel Comics: Nov, 1995 - No. 18 (99¢)

1-18: Stories featuring the Original X-Men. 2-vs. The Blob. 5-Vs. the Original Brotherhood of Evil Mutants. 10-Vs. The Avengers 4.00

PROGRAMME, THE
DC Comics (WildStorm): Sept, 2007 - No. 12, Aug, 2008 ($2.99, limited series)

1-12: 1-Milligan-s/C.P. Smith-a; covers by Smith & Van Sciver 3.00
Book One TPB (2008, $17.99) r/#1-6; cover sketches 18.00
Book Two TPB (2008, $17.99) r/#7-12; cover sketches 18.00

PROJECT A-KO (Manga)
Malibu Comics: Mar, 1994 - No. 4, June, 1994 ($2.95)

1-4-Based on anime film 3.00

PROJECT A-KO 2 (Manga)
CPM Comics: May, 1995 - No. 3, Aug, 1995 ($2.95, limited series)

1-3 3.00

PROJECT A-KO VERSUS THE UNIVERSE (Manga)
CPM Comics: Oct, 1995 - No. 5, June, 1996 ($2.95, limited series, bi-monthly)

1-5 3.00

PROJECT BLACK SKY
Dark Horse Comics

... Sampler (10/14, $4.99) 1-Reprints The Occultist (2013) #1, Brain Boy (2013) #0, Ghost (2013) #1, Blackout #1 5.00
Free Comic Book Day: Project Black Sky (5/14, giveaway) Capt. Midnight & Brain Boy app. 3.00

PROJECT: PATRON
AfterShock Comics: Apr, 2021 - No. 5, Aug, 2021 ($4.99/$3.99, limited series)

1-($4.99) Steve Orlando-s/Patrick Piazzalunga-a 5.00
2-5-($3.99) 4.00

PROJECT SUPERPOWERS
Dynamite Entertainment: 2008 - No. 7, 2008 ($1.00/$3.50/$2.99)

0-($1.00) Two connecting covers by Alex Ross; re-intro of Golden Age heroes 3.00
0-($1.00) Variant cover by Michael Turner 5.00
1-($3.50) Covers by Ross and Turner; Jim Krueger-s/Carlos Paul-a 3.50
2-7-($2.99) 3.00
... Chapter One HC (2008, $29.99, dustjacket) r/#0-7; Ross sketch pages; layout art 30.00

PROJECT SUPERPOWERS: BLACKCROSS
Dynamite Entertainment: 2015 - No. 6, 2015 ($3.99)

1-6-Warren Ellis-s/Colton Worley-a; multiple covers on each 4.00

PROJECT SUPERPOWERS: CHAPTER TWO
Dynamite Entertainment: 2009 - No. 12, 2010 ($1.00/$2.99)

... Chapter Two Prelude (2008, $1.00) Ross sketch pages and mini-series previews 3.00
0-($1.00) Three connecting covers by Alex Ross; The Inheritors assemble 3.00
1-12-($2.99) 1-Krueger & Ross-s/Salazar-a; Ross sketch pages; 2 Ross covers 3.00

Prodigy #6 © Netflix

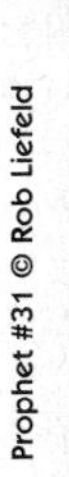

Prophet #31 © Rob Liefeld

Prowler #1 © MAR

GD 2.0 | VG 4.0 | FN 6.0 | VF 8.0 | VF/NM 9.0 | NM- 9.2

... X-Mas Carol (2010, $5.99) Berkenkotter-a/Ross-c 6.00

PROJECT SUPERPOWERS: CHAPTER THREE
Dynamite Entertainment: 2018 - No. 6, 2018 ($1.00/$2.99)

0-(10¢) Six covers; Rob Williams-s/Sergio Davila-a 3.00
1-6-($3.99)-Rob Williams-s/Sergio Davila-a; multiple covers on each 4.00

PROJECT SUPERPOWERS: FRACTURED STATES
Dynamite Entertainment: 2022 - No. 5, 2022 ($3.99, limited series)

1-5-Marz & Lanning-s/Utrera-a 4.00

PROJECT SUPERPOWERS: HERO KILLERS
Dynamite Entertainment: 2017 - No. 5, 2017 ($3.99)

1-5-Browne-s/Woods-a. 1-Black Terror killed 4.00

PROJECT SUPERPOWERS: MEET THE BAD GUYS
Dynamite Entertainment: 2009 - No. 4, 2009 ($2.99)

1-4: Ross & Casey-s. 1-Bloodlust. 2-The Revolutionary. 3-Dagon. 4-Supremacy 3.00

PROMETHEA
America's Best Comics: Aug, 1999 - No. 32, Apr, 2005 ($3.50/$2.95)

1-Alan Moore-s/Williams III & Gray-a; Alex Ross painted-c
1 3 4 6 8 10
1-Variant-c by Williams III & Gray 2 4 6 8 10 12
2-31-($2.95): 7-Villarrubia photo-a. 10-"Sex, Stars & Serpents". 26-28-Tom Strong app. 27-Cover swipe of Superman vs. Spider-Man treasury ed. 4.00
32-($3.95) Final issue; pages can be cut & assembled into a 2-sided poster
3 6 9 14 20 25
32-Limited edition of 1000; variant issue printed as 2-sided poster, signed by Moore and Williams; each came with a 48 page book of Promethea covers 120.00
Book 1 Hardcover ($24.95, dust jacket) r/#1-6 25.00
Book 1 TPB ($14.95) r/#1-6 15.00
Book 2 Hardcover ($24.95, dust jacket) r/#7-12 25.00
Book 2 TPB ($14.95) r/#7-12 15.00
Book 3 Hardcover ($24.95, dust jacket) r/#13-18 25.00
Book 3 TPB ($14.95) r/#13-18 15.00
Book 4 Hardcover ($24.95, dust jacket) r/#19-25 25.00
Book 4 TPB ($14.99) r/#19-25 15.00
Book 5 Hardcover ($24.95, d.j.) r/#26-32; includes 2-sided poster image from #32 25.00
Book 5 TPB ($14.99) r/#26-32; includes 2-sided poster image from #32 15.00

PROMETHEE 13:13
Ablaze Publishing: 2022 - No. 4, 2022 ($3.99, limited series)

1-4-Andy Diggle-s/Shawn Martinbrough-a 4.00

PROMETHEUS: FIRE AND STONE (Crossover with Aliens, AvP, and Predator)
Dark Horse Comics: Sept, 2014 - No. 4, Dec, 2014 ($3.50, limited series)

1-4-Tobin-s/Ferreyra-a 3.50
... – Omega (2/15, $4.99) DeConnick-s/Alessio-a; finale to the crossover 4.00

PROMETHEUS: LIFE AND DEATH (Continues in Aliens: Life and Death)
Dark Horse Comics: Jun, 2016 - No. 4, Sept, 2016 ($3.99, limited series)

1-4-Abnett-s/Mutti-a 4.00
... – Final Conflict (4/17, $5.99) Abnett-s/Thies-a; finale of Life and Death x-over 6.00

PROMETHEUS (VILLAINS) (Leads into JLA #16,17)
DC Comics: Feb, 1998 ($1.95, one-shot)

1-Origin & 1st app.; Morrison-s/Pearson-c 3.00

PROPELLERMAN
Dark Horse Comics: Jan, 1993 - No. 8, Mar, 1994 ($2.95, limited series)

1-8: 2,4,8-Contain 2 trading cards 3.00

PROPHECY
Dynamite Entertainment: 2012 - No. 7, 2013 ($3.99, limited series)

1-7: 1-Marz-s/Geovani-a; Vampirella,Red Sonja, Dracula & Pantha app. 4-Ash app. 4.00

PROPHET (See Youngblood #2)
Image Comics (Extreme Studios): Oct, 1993 - No. 10, 1995 ($1.95)

1-($2.50)-Liefeld/Panosian-c/a; 1st app. Mary McCormick; Liefeld scripts in 1-4; #1-3 contain coupons for Prophet #0 4.00
1-Gold foil embossed-c edition rationed to dealers 6.00
2-10: 2-Liefeld-c(p). 3-1st app. Judas. 4-1st app. Omen; Black and White Pt. 3 by Thibert. 4-Alternate-c by Stephen Platt. 5,6-Platt-c/a. 7-(9/94, $2.50)-Platt-c/a. 8-Bloodstrike app. 10-Polybagged w/trading card; Platt-c. 3.00
0-(7/94, $2.50)-San Diego Comic Con ed. (2200 copies) 4.00
... Facsimile Edition #1 (2/22, $3.99) Reprint of #1 4.00
... Remastered Edition #1 (7/22, $3.99) Issue #1 with pages re-drawn by modern artists 4.00

PROPHET
Image Comics (Extreme Studios): V2#1, Aug, 1995 - No. 8 ($3.50)

V2#1-8: Dixon scripts in all. 1-4-Platt-a. 1-Boris-c; F. Miller variant-c. 4-Newmen app. 5,6-Wraparound-c 3.50
Annual 1 (9/95, $2.50)-Bagged w/Youngblood gaming card; Quesada-c 3.00
Babewatch Special 1 (12/95, $2.50)-Babewatch tie-in 3.00
1995 San Diego Edition-B&W preview of V2#1. 3.00
TPB-(1996, $12.95) r/#1-7 13.00

PROPHET (Volume 3)
Awesome Comics: Mar, 2000 ($2.99)

1-Flip-c by Jim Lee and Liefeld 3.00

PROPHET
Image Comics: No. 21, Jan, 2012 - No. 45, Jul, 2014 ($2.99/$3.99)

21-27-($2.99): 21-Two covers; Graham-s 3.00
28-45-($3.99): 29-Dalrymple-a 4.00

PROPHET/CABLE
Image Comics (Extreme): Jan, 1997 - No. 2, Mar, 1997 ($3.50, limited series)

1,2-Liefeld-c/a: 2-#1 listed on cover 4.00

PROPHET/CHAPEL: SUPER SOLDIERS
Image Comics (Extreme): May, 1996 - No. 2, June, 1996 ($2.50, limited series)

1,2: 1-Two covers exist 3.00
1-San Diego Edition; B&W-c 3.00

PROPHET EARTHWAR
Image Comics: Jan, 2016 - No. 6, Nov, 2016 ($3.99)

1-6: 1-Graham & Roy-s/Milonogiannis & Roy-a 4.00

PROPHET: STRIKEFILE
Image Comics: Sept, 2014 - No. 2, Nov, 2015 ($3.99)

1,2-Short stories and profile pages by various 4.00

PROPOSITION PLAYER
DC Comics (Vertigo): Dec, 1999 - No. 6, May, 2000 ($2.50, limited series)

1-6-Willingham-s/Guinan-a/Bolton-c 3.00
TPB (2003, $14.95) r/#1-6; intro. by James McManus 15.00

PROTECTORS (Also see The Ferret)
Malibu Comics: Sept, 1992 - No. 20, May, 1994 ($1.95-$2.95)

1-20 ($2.50, direct sale)-With poster & diff-c: 1-Origin; has 3/4 outer-c. 3-Polybagged w/Skycap 3.50
1-12 ($1.95, newsstand)-Without poster 3.00

PROTECTORS, INC.
Image Comics: Nov, 2013 - No. 10, Nov, 2014 ($2.99)

1-10-Straczynski-s/Purcell-a; multiple covers on #1-7 3.00

PROTOTYPE (Also see Flood Relief & Ultraforce)
Malibu Comics (Ultraverse): Aug, 1993 - No. 18, Feb, 1995 ($1.95/$2.50)

1-Holo-c 1 2 3 5 6 8
1-Ultra Limited silver foil-c 6.00
1,3: 3-($2.50, 48 pgs.)-Rune flip-c/story by B. Smith (3 pgs.) 4.00
2,4-12,14-18: 4-Intro Wrath. 5-Break-Thru & Strangers x-over. 6-Arena cameo. 7,8-Arena-c/story. 12-(7/94). 14 (10/94) 3.00
13 (8/94, $3.50)-Flip book (Ultraverse Premiere #6) 4.00
#0-(8/94, $2.50, 44 pgs.) 4.00
Giant Size 1 (10/94, $2.50, 44 pgs.) 4.00

PROTOTYPE (Based on the Activision video game)
DC Comics (WildStorm): Jun, 2009 - No. 6, Nov, 2009 ($3.99, limited series)

1-6-Darick Robertson-c/a 4.00
TPB (2010, $19.99) r/#1-6 20.00

PROWLER (Also see Clone Conspiracy and Amazing Spider-Man)
Marvel Comics: Dec, 2016 - May, 2017 ($3.99)

1-6-Sean Ryan-s/Javier Saltares-a. 6-Spider-Man app. 4.00

PRUDENCE & CAUTION (Also see Dogs of War & Warriors of Plasm)
Defiant: May, 1994 - No. 2, June, 1994 ($3.50/$2.50)(Spanish versions exist)

1-($3.50, 52 pgs.)-Chris Claremont scripts in all 4.00
2-($2.50) 3.00

PRYDE AND WISDOM (Also see Excalibur)
Marvel Comics: Sept, 1996 - No. 3, Nov, 1996 ($1.95, limited series)

1-3: Warren Ellis scripts; Terry Dodson & Karl Story-c/a 3.00

PSI-FORCE
Marvel Comics Group: Nov, 1986 - No. 32, June, 1989 (75¢/$1.50)

1-25: 11-13-Williamson-i 3.00
26-32 3.00
Annual 1 (10/87) 4.00
... Classic Vol. 1 TPB (2008, $24.99) r/#1-9 25.00

PSI-JUDGE ANDERSON
Fleetway Publications (Quality): 1989 - No. 15, 1990 ($1.95, B&W)
1-15 4.00

PSI-LORDS
Valiant: Sept, 1994 - No. 10, June, 1995 ($2.25)
1-($3.50)-Chromium wraparound-c 5.00
1-Gold 8.00
2-10: 3-Chaos Effect Epsilon Pt. 2 3.00

PSI-LORDS
Valiant Entertainment: Jun, 2019 - No. 8, Jan, 2020 ($3.99)
1-8-Fred Van Lente-s/Renato Guedes-a. 7-X-O Manowar app. 4.00

PSYBA-RATS (Also see Showcase '94 #3,4)
DC Comics: Apr, 1995-No. 3, June, 1995 ($2.50, limited series)
1-3 3.00

PSYCHO (Magazine) (Also see Nightmare)
Skywald Publ. Corp.: Jan, 1971 - No. 24, Mar, 1975 (68 pgs.; B&W)
1-All reprints 9 18 27 58 114 170
2-Origin & 1st app. The Heap, series begins 6 12 18 41 76 110
3-Frankenstein series by Adkins begins 6 12 18 38 69 100
4-7,9,10: 4-7-Squarebound. 4-1st Out of Chaos/Satan-c/s
5 10 15 34 60 85
8-(Squarebound)1st app. Edward & Mina Sartyros, the Human Gargoyles
6 12 18 37 66 95
11-17: 13-Cannabalism; 3 pgs of Christopher Lee as Dracula photos
4 8 12 27 44 60
18-Injury to eye-c 5 10 15 34 60 85
19-Origin Dracula. 4 8 12 28 47 65
20-Severed Head-c 5 10 15 34 60 85
21-24: 22-1974 Fall Special; Reese, Wildey-a(r). 24-1975 Winter Special;
Dave Sim scripts (1st pro work) 5 10 15 30 50 70
Annual 1 (1972)(68 pgs.) Dracula & the Heap app. 5 10 15 30 50 70
Yearbook (1974-nn)-Everett, Reese-a 4 8 12 27 44 60
NOTE: *Boris* c-3, 5. *Buckler* a-2, 4, 5. *Gene Day* a-21, 23, 24. *Everett* a-3-6. *B. Jones* a-4. *Jeff Jones* a-6, 7, 9; c-12. *Kaluta* a-13. *Katz/Buckler* a-3. *Kim* a-24. *Morrow* a-1. *Reese* a-5. *Dave Sim* s-24. *Sutton* a-3. *Wildey* a-5.

PSYCHO, THE
DC Comics: 1991 - No. 3, 1991 ($4.95, squarebound, limited series)
1-3-Hudnall-s/Brereton painted-a/c 5.00
TPB (Image Comics, 2006, $17.99) r/series; Brereton sketch pages; Hudnall afterword 18.00

PSYCHOANALYSIS
E. C. Comics: Mar-Apr, 1955 - No. 4, Sept-Oct, 1955
1-All Kamen-c/a; not approved by code 30 60 90 240 383 525
2-4-Kamen-c/a in all 19 38 57 152 239 325

PSYCHOANALYSIS
Gemstone Publishing: Oct, 1999 - No. 4, Jan, 2000 ($2.50)
1-4-Reprints E.C. series 4.00
Annual 1 (2000, $10.95) r/#1-4 11.00

PSYCHO BONKERS
Aspen MLT: May, 2015 - No. 4, Sept, 2015 ($3.99)
1-4-Vince Hernandez-s/Adam Archer-a 4.00

PSYCHONAUTS
Marvel Comics (Epic Comics): Oct, 1993 - No. 4, Jan, 1994 ($4.95, lim. series)
1-4: American/Japanese co-produced comic 5.00

PSYLOCKE
Marvel Comics: Jan, 2010 - No. 4, Apr, 2010 ($3.99, limited series)
1-Finch-c/Yost-s/Tolibao-a in all 5 10 15 33 57 80
2 3 6 9 16 23 30
3,4-Wolverine app. 2 4 6 9 13 16

PSYLOCKE & ARCHANGEL CRIMSON DAWN
Marvel Comics: Aug, 1997 - No. 4, Nov, 1997 ($2.50, limited series)
1-4-Raab-s/Larroca-a(p) 4.00

PTOLUS: CITY BY THE SPIRE
Dabel Brothers Productions/Marvel Comics (Dabel Brothers) #2 on: June, 2006 - No. 6, Mar, 2007 ($2.99)
1-(1st printing, Dabel) Adaptation of the Monte Cook novel; Cook-s 4.00
1-(2nd printing, Marvel), 2-6 3.00
Monte Cooke's Ptolus: City By the Spire TPB (2007, $14.99) r/#1-6 15.00

P.T. 109 (See Movie Comics)

PUBLIC DEFENDER IN ACTION (Formerly Police Trap)
Charlton Comics: No. 7, Mar, 1956 - No. 12, Oct, 1957
7 15 30 45 88 137 185
8-12 10 20 30 58 79 100

PUBLIC DOMAIN
Image Comics: Jun, 2022 - No. 5, Oct, 2022 ($3.99, limited series)
1-5-Chip Zdarsky-s/a 4.00

PUBLIC ENEMIES
D. S. Publishing Co.: 1948 - No. 9, June-July, 1949
1-True Crime Stories 50 100 150 315 533 750
2-Used in **SOTI**, pg. 95 39 78 117 231 378 525
3-5: 5-Arrival date of 10/1/48 22 44 66 132 216 300
6,8,9 21 42 63 126 206 285
7-McWilliams-a; injury to eye panel 22 44 66 128 209 290

PUBLIC RELATIONS

Devil's Due/1First Comics: 2015 - No. 13, Nov, 2016 ($3.99)
1-13: 1-3-Sturges & Justus-s/Hahn-a; Annie Wu-c 4.00

PUBO
Dark Horse Comics: Dec, 2002 - No. 3, Mar, 2003 ($3.50, B&W, limited series)
1-3-Leland Purvis-s/a 3.50

PUDGY PIG
Charlton Comics: Sept, 1958 - No. 2, Nov, 1958
1,2 4 8 12 27 44 60

PUFFED
Image Comics: Jul, 2003 - No. 3, Sept, 2003 ($2.95, B&W)
1-3-Layman-s/Crosland-a. 1-Two covers by Crosland & Quitely 3.00

PULP
Image Comics: Jul, 2020 ($16.95, HC graphic novel)
HC - Ed Brubaker-s/Sean Phillips-a/c 17.00

PULP FANTASTIC (Vertigo V2K)
DC Comics (Vertigo): Feb, 2000 - No. 3, Apr, 2000 ($2.50, limited series)
1-3-Chaykin & Tischman-s/Burchett-a 3.00

PULP FICTION LIBRARY: MYSTERY IN SPACE
DC Comics: 1999 ($19.95, TPB)
nn-Reprints classic sci-fi stories from Mystery in Space, Strange Adventures, Real Fact Comics and My Greatest Adventure 20.00

PULSE, THE (Also see Alias and Deadline)
Marvel Comics: Apr, 2004 - No. 14, May, 2006 ($2.99)
1-Jessica Jones, Ben Urich, Kat Farrell app.; Bendis-s/Bagley-a 5.00
2-14: 2-5-Bendis-s/Bagley-a. 3-5-Green Goblin app. 6,7-Brent Anderson-a 9-Wolverine app. 10-House of M. 11-14-Gaydos-a 3.00
...: House of M Special (9/05, 50¢) tabloid newspaper format; Mayhew- "photos" 3.00
Vol. 1: Thin Air (2004, $13.99) r/#1-5, gallery of cover layouts and sketches 14.00
Vol. 2: Secret War (2005, $11.99) r/#6-9 12.00
Vol. 3: Fear (2006, $14.99) r/#11-14 and New Avengers Annual #1 15.00

PUMA BLUES
Aardvark One International/Mirage Studios #21 on: 1986 - No. 26, 1990 ($1.70-$1.75, B&W)
1-19, 21-26: 1-1st & 2nd printings. 25,26-$1.75-c 3.00
20 ($2.25)-By Alan Moore, Miller, Grell, others 5.00
Trade Paperback (12/88, $14.95) 15.00

PUMPKINHEAD (Movie)
Dynamite Entertainment: 2018 - No. 5, 2018 ($3.99, limited series)
1-5-Cullen Bunn-s/Blacky Shepherd-a. 1-Three covers. 2-5-Two covers 4.00

PUMPKINHEAD: THE RITES OF EXORCISM (Movie)
Dark Horse Comics: 1993 - No. 2, 1993 ($2.50, limited series)
1,2: Based on movie; painted-c by McManus 4.00

PUNCH & JUDY COMICS
Hillman Per.: 1944; No. 2, Fall, 1944 - V3#2, 12/47; V3#3, 6/51 - V3#9, 12/51
V1#1-(60 pgs.) 36 72 108 211 343 475
2 18 36 54 105 165 225
3-12(7/46) 15 30 45 86 133 180
V2#1(8/49),3-9 14 28 42 76 108 140
V2#2,10-12, V3#1-Kirby-a(2) each 25 50 75 150 245 340
V3#2-Kirby-a 22 44 66 132 216 300
3-9 11 22 33 62 86 110

PUNCH COMICS
Harry 'A' Chesler: 12/41; #2, 2/42; #9, 7/44 - #19, 10/46; #20, 7/47 - #23, 1/48
1-Mr. E, The Sky Chief, Hale the Magician, Kitty Kelly begin
308 616 924 2156 3778 5400
2-Captain Glory app. 155 310 465 992 1696 2400
9-Rocketman & Rocket Girl & The Master Key begin; classic-c
865 1730 2595 6315 11,158 16,000
10-Sky Chief app.; J. Cole-a; Master Key-r/Scoop #3
155 310 465 992 1696 2400
11-Origin Master Key-r/Scoop #1; Sky Chief, Little Nemo app.; Jack Cole-a; Fine-*ish* art by Sultan 258 516 774 1651 2826 4000
12-Rocket Boy & Capt. Glory app; classic Skull-c 5450 10,900 16,350 30,000 45,000 60,000
13-Cover has list of 4 Chesler artists' names on tombstone
161 322 483 1030 1765 2500
14,15,21: 21-Hypo needle story 103 206 309 659 1130 1600
16,17-Gag-c 50 100 150 315 533 750
18-Bondage-c; hypodermic panels 110 220 330 704 1202 1700
19-Giant bloody hands-c 206 412 618 1318 2259 3200
20-Unique cover with bare-breasted women. Rocket Girl-c
290 580 870 1856 3178 4500
22,23-Little Nemo-not by McCay. 22-Intro Baxter (teenage)(68 pgs.)
35 70 105 208 339 470

PUNCHLINE
DC Comics: Jan, 2021 ($4.99, one-shot)
1-Origin revealed; Tynion IV & Sam Johns-s/Mirka Andolfo-a 5.00

PUNCHLINE: THE GOTHAM GAME
DC Comics: Dec, 2022 - No. 6 ($3.99, limited series)
1-5: Tini & Blake Howard-s/Gleb Melnikov-a; Batman app. 4.00

PUNCHY AND THE BLACK CROW
Charlton Comics: No. 10, Oct, 1985 - No. 12, Feb, 1986
10-12: Al Fago funny animal-r; low print run 6.00

PUNISHER (See Amazing Spider-Man #129, Blood and Glory, Born, Captain America #241, Classic Punisher, Daredevil #182-184, 257, Daredevil and the..., Ghost Rider V2#5, 6, Marc Spector #8 & 9, Marvel Preview #2, Marvel Super Action, Marvel Tales, Power Pack #46, Spectacular Spider-Man #81-83, 140, 141, 143 & new Strange Tales #13 & 14)

PUNISHER (The...)

Public Domain #1 © Zdarsco Inc.

Punchline: The Gotham Game #1 © DC

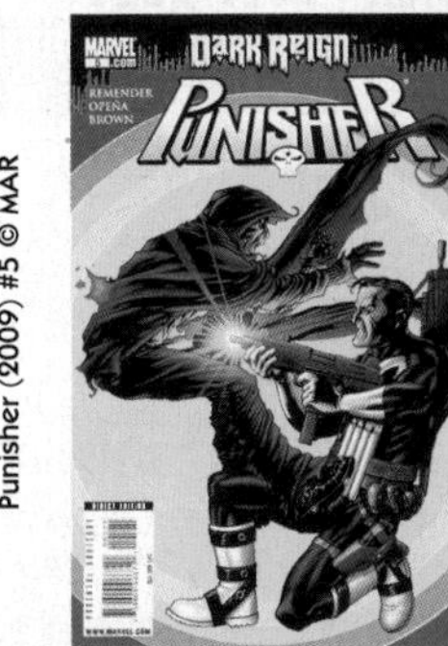

Punisher (2009) #5 © MAR

	GD	VG	FN	VF	VF/NM	NM-
	2.0	4.0	6.0	8.0	9.0	9.2

Marvel Comics Group: Jan, 1986 - No. 5, May, 1986 (Limited series)

	GD	VG	FN	VF	VF/NM	NM-
1-Double size; Grant-s/Zeck-a; Jigsaw app.	6	12	18	37	66	95
2	3	6	9	17	26	35
3-5	2	4	6	13	18	22

Trade Paperback (1988)-r/#1-5 16.00
Circle of Blood TPB (8/01, $15.95) Zeck-c 16.00
Circle of Blood HC (2008, $19.99) two covers 20.00
NOTE: ***Zeck** a-1-4; c-1-5.*

PUNISHER (The…) (Volume 2)
Marvel Comics: July, 1987 - No. 104, July, 1995

	GD	VG	FN	VF	VF/NM	NM-
1	4	8	12	27	44	60

2-9: 8-Portacio/Williams-c/a begins, ends #18. 9-Scarcer, low dist. 6.00

	GD	VG	FN	VF	VF/NM	NM-
10-Daredevil app; ties in w/Daredevil #257	3	6	9	16	23	30

11-25,50: 13-18-Kingpin app. 19-Stroman-c/a. 20-Portacio-c(p). 24-1st app. Shadowmasters. 25,50:($1.50,52 pgs.). 25-Shadowmasters app. 4.00
26-49,51-74,76-85,87-89: 57-Photo-c; came w/outer-c (newsstand ed. w/o outer-c). 59-Punisher is severely cut & has skin grafts (has black skin). 60-62-Luke Cage app. 62-Punisher back to white skin. 68-Tarantula-c/story. 85-Prequel to Suicide Run Pt. 0. 87,88-Suicide Run Pt. 6 & 9 3.00
75-($2.75, 52 pgs.)-Embossed silver foil-c 4.00
86-($2.95, 52 pgs.)-Embossed & foil stamped-c; Suicide Run part 3 4.00
90-99: 90-bound-in cards. 99-Cringe app. 3.00
100,104: 100-($2.95, 68 pgs.). 104-Last issue 4.00
100-($3.95, 68 pgs.)-Foil cover 5.00
101-103: 102-Bullseye 3.50
"Ashcan" edition (75¢)-Joe Kubert-c 3.00
Annual 1-7 ('88-'94, 68 pgs.) 1-Evolutionary War x-over. 2-Atlantis Attacks x-over; Jim Lee-a(p) (back-up story, 6 pgs.); Moon Knight app. 4-Golden-c(p). 6-Bagged w/card. 4.00
...: A Man Named Frank (1994, $6.95, TPB) 7.00
...and Wolverine in African Saga nn (1989, $5.95, 52 pgs.)-Reprints Punisher War Journal #6 & 7; Jim Lee-c/a(r) 6.00
... Assassin Guild ('88, $6.95, graphic novel) 10.00
Back to School Special 1-3 (11/92-10/94, $2.95, 68 pgs.) 4.00
.../Batman: Deadly Knights (10/94, $4.95) 6.00
.../Black Widow: Spinning Doomsday's Web (1992, $9.95, graphic novel) 12.00
...Bloodlines nn (1991, $5.95, 68 pgs.) 6.00
...: Die Hard in the Big Easy nn ('92, $4.95, 52 pgs.) 6.00
...: Empty Quarter nn ('94, $6.95) 7.00
...G-Force nn (1992, $4.95, 52 pgs.)-Painted-c 6.00
...Holiday Special 1-3 (1/93-1/95,, 52 pgs.,68pgs.)-1-Foil-c 4.00
...Intruder Graphic Novel (1989, $14.95, hardcover) 20.00
...Intruder Graphic Novel (1991, $9.95, softcover) 12.00
...Invades the 'Nam: Final Invasion nn (2/94, $6.95)-J. Kubert-c & chapter break art; reprints The 'Nam #84 & unpublished #85,86 10.00
...Kingdom Gone Graphic Novel (1990, $16.95, hardcover) 20.00
...Meets Archie (8/94, $3.95, 52 pgs.)-Die cut-c; no ads; same contents as Archie Meets The Punisher 6.00
...Movie Special 1 (6/90, $5.95, squarebound, 68 pgs.) painted-c; Brent Anderson-a; contents intended for a 3 issue series which was advertised but not published 6.00
...: No Escape nn (1990, $4.95, 52 pgs.)-New-a 6.00
...Return to Big Nothing Graphic Novel (Epic, 1989, $16.95, hardcover) 25.00
...Return to Big Nothing Graphic Novel (Marvel, 1989, $12.95, softcover) 15.00
...The Prize nn (1990, $4.95, 68 pgs.)-New-a 6.00
Summer Special 1-4(8/91-7/94, 52 pgs.):1-No ads. 2-Bisley-c; Austin-a(i). 3-No ads 4.00
NOTE: ***Austin** c(i)-47, 48. **Cowan** c-39. **Golden** c-50, 85, 86, 100. **Heath** a-26, 27, 89, 90, 91; c-26, 27. **Quesada** c-56p, 62p. **Sienkiewicz** c-Back to School 1.**Stroman** a-76p(9 pgs.). **Williamson** a(i)-25, 60-62i, 64-70, 74, Annual 5; c(i)-62, 65-68.*

PUNISHER (Also see Double Edge)
Marvel Comics: Nov, 1995 - No. 18, Apr, 1997 ($2.95/$1.95/$1.50)

1 ($2.95)-Ostrander scripts begin; foil-c. 5.00
2-18: 7-Vs. S.H.I.E.L.D. 11-"Onslaught." 12-17-X-Cutioner-c/app. 17-Daredevil, Spider-Man-c/app. 4.00

PUNISHER (Marvel Knights)
Marvel Comics: Nov, 1998 - No. 4, Feb, 1999 ($2.99, limited series)

1-4: 1-Wrightson-a; Wrightson & Jusko-c 4.00
1-($6.95) DF Edition; Jae Lee variant-c 7.00

PUNISHER (Marvel Knights) (Volume 3)
Marvel Comics: Apr, 2000 - No. 12, Mar, 2001 ($2.99, limited series)

	GD	VG	FN	VF	VF/NM	NM-
1-Ennis-s/Dillon & Palmiotti-a/Bradstreet-c	2	4	6	9	12	15
1-Bradstreet white variant-c	2	4	6	9	12	15
1-($6.95) DF Edition; Jurgens & Ordway variant-c	2	4	6	10	14	18

2-Two covers by Bradstreet & Dillon 3.00
3-($3.99) Bagged with Marvel Knights Genesis Edition; Daredevil app. 4.00
4-12: 9-11-The Russian app. 3.00
HC (6/02, $34.95) r/#1-12, Punisher Kills the Marvel Universe, and Marvel Knights Double Shot #1 35.00
... By Garth Ennis Omnibus (2008, $99.99) oversized r/#1-12, #1-7 & #13-37 of 2001 series, Punisher Kills the Marvel Universe, and Marvel Knights Double Shot #1; extras 100.00
.../Painkiller Jane (1/01, $3.50) Jusko-c; Ennis-s/Jusko and Dave Ross-a(p) 3.50
...: Welcome Back Frank TPB (4/01, $19.95) r/#1-12 20.00

PUNISHER (Marvel Knights) (Volume 4)
Marvel Comics: Aug, 2001 - No. 37, Feb, 2004 ($2.99)

1-Ennis-s/Dillon & Palmiotti-a/Bradstreet-c; The Russian app. 4.00
2-Two covers (Dillon & Bradstreet) Spider-Man-c/app. 3.00
3-37: 3-7-Ennis-s/Dillon-a. 9-12-Peyer-s/Gutierrez-a. 13,14-Ennis-s/Dilllon-a. 16,17-Wolverine app.; Robertson-a. 18-23,32-Dillon-a. 24-27-Mandrake-a. 27-Elektra app. 33-37-Spider-Man, Daredevil, & Wolverine app. 36,37-Hulk app. 3.00
...Army of One TPB (2/02, $15.95) r/#1-7; Bradstreet-c 16.00
Vol. 2 HC (2003, $29.95) r/#1-7,13-18; intro. by Mike Millar 30.00
Vol. 3 HC (2004, $29.95) r/#19-27; script pages for #19 30.00
Vol. 3: Business as Usual TPB (2003, $14.99) r/#13-18; Bradstreet-c 15.00
Vol. 4: Full Auto TPB (2003, $17.99) r/#20-26; Bradstreet-c 18.00
Vol. 5: Streets of Laredo TPB (2003, $17.99) r/#19,27-32 18.00
Vol. 6: Confederacy of Dunces TPB (2004, $13.99) r/#33-37 14.00

PUNISHER (Marvel MAX)(Title becomes "Punisher: Frank Castle MAX" with #66)
Marvel Comics: Mar, 2004 - No. 75, Dec, 2009 ($2.99/$3.99)

1-49,51-60: 1-Ennis-s/LaRosa-a/Bradstreet-c; flashback to his family's murder; Micro app. 6-Micro killed. 7-12,19-25-Fernandez-a. 13-18-Braithwaite-a. 31-36-Barracuda. 43-49-Medina-a. 51-54-Barracuda app. 60-Last Ennis-s/Bradstreet-c 3.00
50-($3.99) Barracuda returns; Chaykin-a 4.00
61-65-Gregg Hurwitz-s/Dave Johnson-c/Laurence Campbell-a 3.00
66-73-($3.99) 66-70-Six Hours to Kill; Swierczynski-s. 71-73-Parlov-a 4.00
74,75-($4.99) 74-Parlov-a. 75-Short stories; art by Lashley, Coker, Parlov & others 5.00
Annual (11/07, $3.99) Mike Benson-s/Laurence Campbell-a 4.00
...: Bloody Valentine (4/06, $3.99) Palmiotti & Gray-s/Gulacy & Palmiotti-a; Gulacy-c 4.00
...: Force of Nature (4/08, $4.99) Swierczynski-s/Lacombe-a/Deodato-c 5.00
...: MAX MGC #1 (5/10, $1.00) reprints #1 with "Marvel's Greatest Comics" cover logo 3.00
...: MAX: Naked Kill (8/09, $3.99) Campbell-a/Bradstreet-c 4.00
...: MAX Special: Little Black Book (8/08, $3.99) Gischler-s/Palo-a/Johnson-c 4.00
...: MAX X-Mas Special (2/09, $3.99) Aaron-s/Boschi-a/Bachalo-c 4.00
...: Red X-Mas (2/05, $3.99) Palmiotti & Gray-s/Texeira & Palmiotti-a; Texeira-c 4.00
...: Silent Night (2/06, $3.99) Diggle-s/Hotz-a/Deodato-c 4.00
...: The Cell (7/05, $4.99) Ennis-s/LaRosa-a/Bradstreet-c 5.00
...: The Tyger (2/06, $4.99) Ennis-s/Severin-a/Bradstreet-c; Castle's childhood 5.00
...: Very Special Holidays TPB ('06, $12.99) r/Red X-Mas, Bloody Valentine and Silent Night 13.00
...: X-Mas Special (1/07, $3.99) Stuart Moore-s/CP Smith-a 4.00
... MAX: From First to Last HC (2006, $19.99) r/The Tyger, The Cell and The End 1-shots 20.00
... MAX Vol. 1 (2005, $29.99) oversized r/#1-12; gallery of Fernandez art from #7 shown from layout to colored pages 30.00
... MAX Vol. 2 (2006, $29.99) oversized r/#13-24; gallery of Fernandez pencil art 30.00
... MAX Vol. 3 (2007, $29.99) oversized r/#25-36; gallery of Fernandez & Parlov art 30.00
... MAX Vol. 4 (2008, $29.99) oversized r/#37-49; gallery of Fernandez & Medina art 30.00
Vol. 1: In the Beginning TPB (2004, $14.99) r/#1-6 15.00
Vol. 2: Kitchen Irish TPB (2004, $14.99) r/#7-12 15.00
Vol. 3: Mother Russia TPB (2005, $14.99) r/#13-18 15.00
Vol. 4: Up is Down and Black is White TPB (2005, $14.99) r/#19-24 15.00
Vol. 5: The Slavers TPB (2006, $15.99) r/#25-30; Fernandez pencil pages 16.00
Vol. 6: Barracuda TPB (2006, $15.99) r/#31-36; Parlov sketch page 16.00
Vol. 7: Man of Stone TPB (2007, $15.99) r/#37-42 16.00
Vol. 8: Widowmaker TPB (2007, $17.99) r/#43-49 18.00
Vol. 9: Long Cold Dark TPB (2008, $15.99) r/#50-54 16.00

PUNISHER (Frank Castle in the Marvel Universe after Secret Invasion)
(Title changes to Franken-Castle for #17-21)
Marvel Comics: Mar, 2009 - No. 21, Nov, 2010 ($3.99/$2.99)

1-($3.99) Dark Reign; Sentry app.; Remender-s/Opena-a; character history; 2 covers 4.00
2-5,710($2.99) 2-7-The Hood app. 4-Microchip returns. 5-Daredevil #183 cover swipe 3.00
6-($3.99) Huat-a/McKone-c; profile pages of resurrected villains 4.00
11-Follows Dark Reign: The List - Punisher; Franken-Castle begins; Tony Moore-a 4.00
12-16-Franken-Castle continues; Legion of Monsters app. 14-Brereton & Moore-a 3.00
Franken-Castle 17-20: 19, 20-Wolverine & Daken app. 3.00
Franken-Castle 21-($3.99) Brereton-a/c; Legion of Monsters app.; Frank gets body back 4.00
Annual 1 (11/09, $3.99) Pearson-a/c; Spider-Man app. 4.00
...: Franken-Castle - The Birth of the Monster 1 (7/10, $4.99) r/#11 & Dark Reign: The List 5.00

PUNISHER (Frank Castle in the Marvel Universe)(Continues in Punisher: War Zone [2012])
Marvel Comics: Oct, 2011 - No. 16, Nov, 2012 ($3.99/$2.99)

1-($3.99) Rucka-s/Checchetto-a/Hitch-c 4.00
1-Variant-c by Sal Buscema 6.00
1-Variant-c by Neal Adams 10.00
2-16-($2.99): 2,3-Vulture app. 10-Spider-Man & Daredevil app. 3.00
..., Moon Knight & Daredevil: The Big Shots (10/11, $3.99) Previews new series for Punisher, Moon Knight & Daredevil; creator interviews and production art 4.00

PUNISHER, THE
Marvel Comics: Apr, 2014 - No. 20, Sept, 2015 ($3.99)

1-20: 1-Edmonson-s/Gerads-a; Howling Commandos app. 2-6-Electro app. 16,17-Captain America (Falcon) app. 19,20-Secret Wars tie-ins 4.00

PUNISHER, THE
Marvel Comics: Jul, 2016 - No. 17, Dec, 2017; No. 218, Jan, 2018 - No. 228, Sept, 2018 ($3.99)

1-17: 1-Becky Cloonan-s/Steve Dillon-a. 7-Steve Dillon's last work. 8-12-Horak-a. 13-Anka-a 14-17-Horak-a 4.00
[Title switches to legacy numbering after #11 (11/17)]
218-228-Castle gets the War Machine armor. 218-223-Vilanova-a 4.00
Annual 1 (12/16, $4.99) Gerry Conway-s/Felix Ruiz-a 5.00

PUNISHER, THE
Marvel Comics: Oct, 2018 - No. 16, Dec, 2019 ($4.99/$3.99)

1-($4.99) Rosenberg-s/Kudranski-a; Baron Zemo & The Mandarin app. 5.00
2-16-($3.99) 2-Luke Cage, Iron Fist & Daredevil app. 3-Daredevil app. 13-Thunderbolts 4.00
Annual 1 (9/19, $4.99) Acts of Evil; Karla Pacheco-s/Gorham-a; J. Jonah Jameson app. 5.00

PUNISHER
Marvel Comics: May, 2022 - Present ($5.99/$4.99)

1-($5.99) Aaron-s/Saiz-a; Frank Castle joins The Hand 6.00
2-9-($4.99) 2-Maria Castle returns; Ares app. 6,7-Daredevil app. 5.00
... War Journal: Base 1 (4/23, $4.99) Castle before becoming the Punisher 5.00

PUNISHER AND WOLVERINE: DAMAGING EVIDENCE (See Wolverine and...)

PUNISHER ARMORY, THE
Marvel Comics: 7/90 ($1.50); No. 2, 6/91; No. 3, 4/92 - 10/94($1.75/$2.00)

1-10: 1-r/weapons pgs. from War Journal. 1,2-Jim Lee-c. 3-10-All new material. 3-Jusko painted-c 4.00

PUNISHER: IN THE BLOOD (Marvel Universe Frank Castle)
Marvel Comics: Jan, 2011 - No. 5, May, 2011 ($3.99, limited series)

1-5-Remender-s/Boschi-a; Jigsaw & Microchip app. 4.00

PUNISHER KILL KREW (Follows War of the Realms series)
Marvel Comics: Oct, 2019 - No. 5, Jan, 2020 ($3.99, limited series)

1-5-Duggan-s/Ferreyra-a; Juggernaut & The Black Knight app. 4.00

PUNISHER KILLS THE MARVEL UNIVERSE
Marvel Comics: Nov, 1995 ($5.95, one-shot)

1-Garth Ennis script/Doug Braithwaite-a 4 8 12 23 37 50
1-2nd printing (3/00) Steve Dillon-c 6.00
1-3rd printing (2008, $4.99) original 1995 cover 5.00

PUNISHER MAGAZINE, THE
Marvel Comics: Oct, 1989 - No. 16, Nov, 1990 ($2.25, B&W, Magazine, 52 pgs.)

1-16: 1-r/Punisher #1('86). 2,3-r/Punisher 2-5. 4-16: 4-7-r/Punisher V2#1-8. 4-Chiodo-c. 8-r/Punisher #10 & Daredevil #257; Portacio & Lee-r. 14-r/Punisher War Journal #1,2 w/new Lee-c. 16-r/Punisher W. J. #3,8 4.00
NOTE: ***Chiodo*** *painted c-4, 7, 16.* ***Jusko*** *painted c-6, 8.* ***Jim Lee*** *r-8, 14-16; c-14.* ***Portacio/Williams*** *r-7-12.*

PUNISHERMAX
Marvel Comics (MAX): Jan, 2010 - No. 22, Apr, 2012 ($3.99)

1-22-Aaron-s/Dillon-a/Johnson-c. 1-5-Rise of the Kingpin. 6-11-Bullseye. 17-20-Elektra app. 21-Castle dies. 22-Afterword by Aaron 4.00
...: Butterfly (5/10, $4.99) Valerie D'Orazio-s/Laurence Campbell-a/c 5.00
...: Get Castle (3/10, $4.99) Rob Williams-s/Laurence Campbell-a/Bradstreet-c 5.00
...: Happy Ending (10/10, $3.99) Milligan-s/Ryp-a/c 4.00
...: Hot Rods of Death (11/10, $4.99) Huston-s/Martinbrough-a/Bradstreet-c 5.00
...: Tiny Ugly World (12/10, $4.99) Lapham-s/Talajic-a/Bradstreet-c 5.00

PUNISHER MAX: THE PLATOON (Titled Punisher: The Platoon for #3-6)
Marvel Comics: Dec, 2017 - No. 6, Apr, 2018 ($3.99, limited series)

1-6-Ennis-s/Parlov-a; Castle's first tour of Vietnam 4.00

PUNISHER: NIGHTMARE
Marvel Comics: Mar, 2013 - No. 5, Mar, 2013 ($3.99, weekly limited series)

1-5-Texeira-a/c; Gimple-s 4.00

PUNISHER NOIR
Marvel Comics: Oct, 2009 - No. 4, Jan, 2010 ($3.99, limited series)

1-4-Pulp-style set in 1935; Tieri-s/Azaceta-a 4.00

PUNISHER: OFFICIAL MOVIE ADAPTATION
Marvel Comics: May, 2004 - No. 3, May, 2004 ($2.99, limited series)

1-3-Photo-c of Thomas Jane; Milligan-s/Olliffe-a 3.00

PUNISHER: ORIGIN OF MICRO CHIP, THE
Marvel Comics: July, 1993 - No. 2, Aug, 1993 ($1.75, limited series)

1,2 4.00

PUNISHER: P.O.V.
Marvel Comics: 1991 - No. 4, 1991 ($4.95, painted, limited series, 52 pgs.)

1-4: Starlin scripts & Wrightson painted-c/a in all. 2-Nick Fury app. 6.00

PUNISHER PRESENTS: BARRACUDA MAX
Marvel Comics (MAX): Apr, 2007 - No. 5, Aug, 2007 ($3.99, limited series)

1-5-Ennis-s/Parlov-a/c 4.00
SC (2007, $17.99) r/series; sketch pages 18.00

PUNISHER: SOVIET
Marvel Comics (MAX): Jan, 2020 - No. 6, May, 2020 ($3.99, limited series)

1-6-Ennis-s/Burrows-a 4.00

PUNISHER: THE END
Marvel Comics: June, 2004 ($4.50, one-shot)

1-Ennis-s/Corben-a/c 4.50

PUNISHER: THE GHOSTS OF INNOCENTS
Marvel Comics: Jan, 1993 - No. 2, Jan, 1993 ($5.95, 52 pgs.)

1,2-Starlin scripts 6.00

PUNISHER: THE MOVIE
Marvel Comics: 2004 ($12.99,TPB)

nn-Reprints Amazing Spider-Man #129; Official Movie Adaptation and Punisher V3 #1 13.00

PUNISHER: THE PLATOON (See Punisher MAX: The Platoon)

PUNISHER: THE TRIAL OF THE PUNISHER
Marvel Comics: Nov, 2013 - No. 2, Dec, 2013 ($3.99, limited series)

1-Guggenheim-s/Yu-a/c. 2-Suayan-a; Matt Murdock app. 4.00

PUNISHER 2099 (See Punisher War Journal #50)
Marvel Comics: Feb, 1993 - No. 34, Nov, 1995 ($1.25/$1.50/$1.95)

1-Foil stamped-c 6.00
1-(Second printing) 4.00
2-24,26-34: 13-Spider-Man 2099 x-over; Ron Lim-c(p). 16-bound-in card sheet 4.00
25-($2.95, 52 pgs.)-Deluxe edition; embossed foil-cover 6.00
25-($2.25, 52 pgs.) 5.00
(Marvel Knights) #1 (11/04, $2.99) Kirkman-s/Mhan-a/Pat Lee-c 4.00
... No. 1 (1/20, $4.99) Matt Horak-a 5.00

PUNISHER VS. BULLSEYE
Marvel Comics: Jan, 2006 - No. 5, May, 2006 ($2.99, limited series)

1-5-Daniel Way-s/Steve Dillon-a 3.00
TPB (2006, $13.99) r/#1-5; cover sketch pages 14.00

PUNISHER VS. DAREDEVIL
Marvel Comics: Jun, 2000 ($3.50, one-shot)

1-Reprints Daredevil #183,#184 & #257 4.00

PUNISHER WAR JOURNAL, THE
Marvel Comics: Nov, 1988 - No. 80, July, 1995 ($1.50/$1.75/$1.95)

1-Origin The Punisher; Matt Murdock cameo; Jim Lee inks begin 3 6 9 18 27 36
2-7: 2,3-Daredevil x-over; Jim Lee-c(i). 4-Jim Lee c/a begins. 6-Two part Wolverine story begins. 7-Wolverine-c, story ends 5.00
8-49,51-60,62,63,65: 13-16,20-22: No Jim Lee-a. 13-Lee-c only. 13-15-Heath-i. 14,15-Spider-Man x-over. 19-Last Jim Lee-c/a.29,30-Ghost Rider app. 31-Andy & Joe Kubert art. 36-Photo-c. 47,48-Nomad/Daredevil-c/stories; see Nomad. 57,58-Daredevil & Ghost Rider-c/stories. 62,63-Suicide Run Pt. 4 & 7 4.00
50,61,64($2.95, 52 pgs.): 50-Preview of Punisher 2099 (1st app.); embossed-c. 61-Embossed foil cover; Suicide Run Pt. 1. 64-Die-cut-c; Suicide Run Pt. 10 5.00
64-($2.25, 52 pgs.)-Regular cover edition 5.00
66-74,76-80: 66-Bound-in card sheet 4.00
75 ($2.50, 52 pgs.) 5.00
NOTE: ***Golden*** *c-25-30, 40, 61, 62.* ***Jusko*** *painted c-31, 32.* ***Jim Lee*** *a-1i-3i, 4p-13p, 17p-19p; c-2i, 3i, 4p-15p, 17p, 18p, 19p. Painted c-40.*

PUNISHER WAR JOURNAL (Frank Castle back in the regular Marvel Universe)
Marvel Comics: Jan, 2007 - No. 26, Feb, 2009 ($2.99)

1-Civil War tie-in; Spider-Man app; Fraction-s/Olivetti-a 5.00
1-B&W edition (11/06) 5.00
2-5: 2,3-Civil War tie-in. 4-Deodato-a 4.00
6-11,13-24,26: 6-10-Punisher dons Captain America-*esque* outfit. 7-Two covers. 11-Winter Soldier app. 16-23-Chaykin-a. 18-23-Jigsaw app. 24-Secret Invasion 3.00
12,25-($3.99) 12-World War Hulk x-over; Fraction-s/Olivetti-a. 25-Secret Invasion 4.00
... Annual 1 (1/09, $3.99) Spurrier-s/Dell'edera-a 4.00
... Vol. 1: Civil War HC (2007, $19.99) r/#1-4 and #1 B&W edition; Olivetti sketch pages 20.00
... Vol. 1: Civil War SC (2007, $14.99) r/#1-4 and #1 B&W edition; Olivetti sketch pages 15.00
... Vol. 2: Goin' Out West HC (2007, $24.99) r/#5-11; Olivetti sketch page 25.00
... Vol. 2: Goin' Out West SC (2008, $17.99) r/#5-11; Olivetti sketch page 18.00
... Vol. 3: Hunter Hunted HC (2008, $19.99) r/#12-17 20.00

PUNISHER WAR JOURNAL
Marvel Comics: Aug, 2022 - Present ($4.99, series of one-shots)

...: Blitz 1 (8/22, $4.99) Frank Castle with the Hand; Gronbekk-s/Medina-a 5.00
...: Brother 1 (12/22, $4.99) Jigsaw app.; Gronbekk-s/Pimentel-a 5.00

PUNISHER: WAR ZONE, THE
Marvel Comics: Mar, 1992 - No. 41, July, 1995 ($1.75/$1.95)

1-($2.25, 40 pgs.)-Die cut-c; Romita, Jr.-c/a begins 6.00
2-22,24,26,27-41: 8-Last Romita, Jr.-c/a. 19-Wolverine app. 24-Suicide Run Pt. 5. 27-Bound-in card sheet. 31-36-Joe Kubert-a 4.00
23-($2.95, 52 pgs.)-Embossed foil-c; Suicide Run part 2; Buscema-a(part) 5.00
25-($2.25, 52 pgs.)-Suicide Run part 8; painted-c 5.00
Annual 1,2 ('93, 94, $2.95, 68 pgs.)-1-Bagged w/card; John Buscema-a 5.00
...: River Of Blood TPB (2006, $15.99) r/#31-36; Joe Kubert-a 16.00
NOTE: ***Golden*** *c-23.* ***Romita, Jr.*** *c/a-1-8.*

PUNISHER: WAR ZONE
Marvel Comics: Feb, 2009 - No. 6, Mar, 2009 ($3.99, weekly limited series)

1-6-Ennis-s/Dillon-a/c; return of Ma Gnucci 4.00
1-Variant cover by John Romita, Jr. 6.00

PUNISHER: WAR ZONE (Follows Punisher 2011-2012 series)
Marvel Comics: Dec, 2012 - No. 5, Apr, 2013 ($3.99, limited series)

1-5: Rucka-s; Spider-Man and The Avengers app. 4.00

PUNISHER: YEAR ONE
Marvel Comics: Dec, 1994 - No. 4, Apr, 1995 ($2.50, limited series)

1-4 4.00

PUNK MAMBO
Valiant Entertainment: No. 0, Nov, 2014; Apr, 2019 - No. 5, Aug, 2019 ($3.99, limited series)

0-(11/14) Milligan-s/Gill-a; bonus preview of The Valiant #1 4.00
1-5-Cullen Bunn-s/Adam Gorham-a/ Dan Brereton-c 4.00

Punisher (2022) #1 © MAR

Purgatori (2014) #1 © DYN

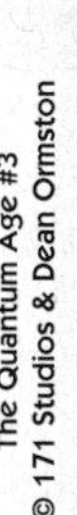

The Quantum Age #3
© 171 Studios & Dean Ormston

	GD 2.0	VG 4.0	FN 6.0	VF 8.0	VF/NM 9.0	NM- 9.2

PUNK ROCK JESUS
DC Comics (Vertigo): Sept, 2012 - No. 6, Feb, 2013 ($2.99, B&W, limited series)

1-6-Sean Murphy-s/a/c; cloning of Jesus 3.00

PUNKS NOT DEAD
IDW Publishing (Black Crown): Feb, 2018 - No. 6, Jul, 2018 ($3.99)

1-6-Barnett-s/Simmonds-a; 3 covers 4.00

PUNKS NOT DEAD: LONDON CALLING
IDW Publishing (Black Crown): Feb, 2019 - No. 5, Jun, 2019 ($3.99)

1-5-Barnett-s/Simmonds-a 4.00

PUNX
Acclaim (Valiant): Nov, 1995 - No. 3, Jan, 1996 ($2.50, unfinished lim. series)

1-3: Giffen story & art in all. 2-Satirizes Scott McCloud's Understanding Comics 3.00
(Manga) Special 1 (3/96, $2.50)-Giffen scripts 3.00

PUPPET COMICS
George W. Dougherty Co.: Spring, 1946 - No. 2, Summer, 1946

	GD	VG	FN	VF	VF/NM	NM-
1-Funny animal in both	28	56	84	165	270	375
2	16	32	48	94	147	200

PUPPETOONS (See George Pal's...)

PUREHEART (See Archie as...)

PURGATORI
Chaos! Comics: Prelude #-1, 5/96 ($1.50, 16 pgs.); 1996 - No. 3 Dec, 1996 (limited series)

Prelude #-1-Pulido story; Balent-c/a; contains sketches & interviews 3.00
0-(2/01, $2.99) Prelude to "Love Bites"; Rio-c/a 3.00
1/2 (12/00, $2.95) Al Rio-c/a 3.00
1-($3.50)-Wraparound cover; red foil embossed-c; Jim Balent-a 5.00
1-($19.95)-Premium Edition (1000 print run) 20.00
2-($3.00)-Wraparound-c 3.00
2-Variant-c 5.00
...: Heartbreaker 1 (3/02, $2.99) Jolley-s 3.00
...: Love Bites 1 (3/01, $2.99) Turnbull-a/Kaminski-s 3.00
...: Mischief Night 1 (11/01, $2.99) 3.00
...: Re-Imagined 1 (7/02, $2.99) Jolley-s/Neves-a 3.00
...The Dracula Gambit-($2.95) 3.00
...The Dracula Gambit Sketchbook-($2.95) 3.00
...The Vampire's Myth 1-($19.95) Premium Ed. (10,000) 20.00
...Vs. Chastity (7/00, $2.95) Two versions (Alpha and Omega) with different endings; Rio-a 3.00
...Vs. Lady Death (1/01, $2.95) Kaminski-s 3.00
...Vs. Vampirella (4/00, $2.95) Zanier-a; Chastity app. 3.00

PURGATORI
Chaos! Comics: Oct, 1998 - No. 7, Apr, 1999 ($2.95)

1-7-Quinn-s/Rio-c/a. 2-Lady Death-c 3.00

PURGATORI
Dynamite Entertainment: 2014 - No. 5, 2015 ($3.99)

1-5: 1-Gillespie-s; multiple covers. 2-4-Jade app. 4.00

PURGATORI: DARKEST HOUR
Chaos! Comics: Sept, 2001 - No. 2, Oct, 2001 ($2.99, limited series)

1,2 3.00

PURGATORI: EMPIRE
Chaos! Comics: May, 2000 - No. 3, July, 2000 ($2.95, limited series)

1-3-Cleavenger-c 3.00

PURGATORI: GODDESS RISING
Chaos! Comics: July, 1999 - No. 4, Oct, 1999 ($2.95, limited series)

1-4-Deodato-c/a 3.00

PURGATORI: GOD HUNTER
Chaos! Comics: Apr, 2002 - No. 2, May, 2002 ($2.99, limited series)

1,2-Molenaar-a/Jolley-s 3.00

PURGATORI: GOD KILLER
Chaos! Comics: Jun, 2002 - No. 2, July, 2002 ($2.99, limited series)

1,2-Molenaar-a/Jolley-s 3.00

PURGATORI MUST DIE
Dynamite Entertainment: 2022 - Present ($3.99, limited series)

1-3-Ray Fawkes-s/Salvatore Aiala-a 4.00

PURGATORI: THE HUNTED
Chaos! Comics: Jun, 2001 - No. 2, Aug, 2001 ($2.99, limited series)

1,2 3.00

PURGATORI, VOLUME 2
Dynamite Entertainment: 2021 - No. 5, 2021 ($3.99)

1-5-Ray Fawkes-s/Alvaro Sarraseca-a; multiple covers on all 4.00

PURPLE CLAW, THE (Also see Tales of Horror)
Minoan Publishing Co./Toby Press: Jan, 1953 - No. 3, May, 1953

	GD	VG	FN	VF	VF/NM	NM-
1-Origin; horror/weird stories in all	55	110	165	352	601	850
2,3: 1-3 r-in Tales of Horror #9-11	41	82	123	256	428	600
I.W. Reprint #8-Reprints #1	4	8	12	27	44	60

PUSH (Based on the 2009 movie)
DC Comics (WildStorm): Early Jan, 2009 - No. 6, Apr, 2009 ($3.50, limited series)

1-6-Movie prequel; Bruno Redondo-a. 1-Jock-c 3.50
TPB (2009, $19.99) r/#1-6 20.00

PUSSYCAT (Magazine)
Marvel Comics Group: Oct, 1968 (B&W reprints from Men's magazines)

	GD	VG	FN	VF	VF/NM	NM-
1-(Scarce)-Ward, Everett, Wood-a; Everett-c	81	162	243	518	884	1250

PUZZLE FUN COMICS (Also see Jingle Jangle)
George W. Dougherty Co.: Spring, 1946 - No. 2, Summer, 1946 (52 pgs.)

	GD	VG	FN	VF	VF/NM	NM-
1-Gustavson-a	32	64	96	188	307	425
2	20	40	60	117	189	260

NOTE: *#1 & 2('46) each contain a* ***George Carlson*** *cover plus a 6 pg. story "Alec in Fumbleland"; also many puzzles in each.*

PvP (Player vs. Player)
Image Comics: Mar, 2003 - No. 45, Mar, 2010 ($2.95/$2.99/$3.50, B&W, reads sideways)

1-34,36-Scott Kurtz-s/a in all. 1,16-Frank Cho-c. 11-Savage Dragon-c/app. 14-Invincible app. 19-Jonathan Luna-c. 25-Cho-a (2 pgs.) 3.00
35,37-45 ($3.50): 45-Brandy from Liberty Meadows app. 3.50
#0 (7/05, 50¢) Secret Origin of Skull 3.00
...: At Large TPB (7/04, $11.95) r/#1-6 12.00
... Vol. 2: Reloaded TPB (12/04, $11.95) r/#7-12 12.00
... Vol. 3: Rides Again TPB (2005, $11.99) r/#13-18 12.00
... Vol. 4: PVP Goes Bananas TPB (2007, $12.99) r/#19-24 13.00
... Vol. 5: PVP Treks On TPB (2008, $14.99) r/#25-31 15.00
...: The Dork Ages TPB (2/04, $11.95) r/#1-6 from Dork Storm Press 12.00

PYRATE QUEEN
Bad Idea: Sept, 2021 - No. 4, Dec, 2021 ($7.99, limited series)

1-4-Lead story with Peter Milligan-s/Adam Pollina-a; back-ups by Kindt-s/Foreman-a 8.00

Q2: THE RETURN OF QUANTUM & WOODY
Valiant Entertainment: Oct, 2014 - No. 5, Feb, 2015 ($3.99, limited series)

1-5: 1-Priest-s/Bright-a; multiple covers 4.00

QUACK!
Star Reach Productions: July, 1976 - No. 6, 1977? ($1.25, B&W)

	GD	VG	FN	VF	VF/NM	NM-
1-Brunner-c/a on Duckaneer (Howard the Duck clone); Dave Stevens, Gilbert, Shaw-a	2	4	6	11	16	20
1-2nd printing (10/76)						5.00
2-6: 2-Newton the Rabbit Wonder by Aragonés/Leialoha; Gilbert, Shaw-a; Leialoha-c. 3-The Beavers by Dave Sim begin, end #5; Gilbert, Shaw-a; Sim/Leialoha-c. 6-Brunner-a (Duckeneer); Gilbert-a	2	4	6	8	10	12

QUADRANT
Quadrant Publications: 1983 - No. 8, 1986 (B&W, nudity, adults)

	GD	VG	FN	VF	VF/NM	NM-
1-Peter Hsu-c/a in all	3	6	9	17	25	34
2-8	2	4	6	8	10	12

QUAKE: S.H.I.E.L.D. 50TH ANNIVERSARY
Marvel Comics: Nov, 2015 ($3.99, one-shot)

1-Spotlight on Daisy Johnson; Daniel Johnson-a/Nakayama-c; Avengers app. 4.00

QUANTUM AGE, THE (Also see Black Hammer)
Dark Horse Comics: Jul, 2018 - No. 6, Jan, 2019 ($3.99, limited series)

1-6-Lemire-s/Torres-a. 4-6-Colonel Weird app. 4.00

QUANTUM & WOODY
Acclaim Comics: June, 1997 - No. 17, No. 32 (9/99), No. 18 - No. 21, Feb, 2000 ($2.50)

	GD	VG	FN	VF	VF/NM	NM-
1-1st app.; drawn cover	1	2	3	5	6	8
1-Painted cover	2	4	6	9	12	15
2,4-17: 6-Copycat-c. 9-Troublemakers app.						3.00
3-1st Vincent Van Goat	2	4	6	11	16	20
32-(9/99); 18-(10/99),19-21						3.00
The Director's Cut TPB ('97, $7.95) r/#1-4 plus extra pages						12.00

QUANTUM & WOODY
Valiant Entertainment: Jul, 2013 - No. 12, Jul, 2014 ($3.99)

GD VG FN VF VF/NM NM-
2.0 4.0 6.0 8.0 9.0 9.2

1-12: 1-Asmus-s/Fowler-a; covers by Ryan Sook & Marcos Martin; origin re-told 4.00
#0 -(3/14, $3.99) Story of the goat; Asmus-s/Fowler-a/c 4.00
... Valiant-Sized #1 (12/14, $4.99) Thomas Edison app. 5.00

QUANTUM AND WOODY!
Valiant Entertainment: Dec, 2017 - No. 12, Nov, 2018 ($3.99)

1-3: 1-Daniel Kibblesmith-s/Kano-a. 3,6,7,12-Portela-a. 8-11-Eisma-a 4.00

QUANTUM AND WOODY
Valiant Entertainment: Jan, 2020 - Present ($3.99)

1-4-Hastings-s/Browne-a 4.00

QUANTUM & WOODY MUST DIE
Valiant Entertainment: Jan, 2015 - No. 4, Apr, 2015 ($3.99, limited series)

1-4: 1-James Asmus-s/Steve Lieber-a; multiple covers on each 4.00

QUANTUM LEAP (TV) (See A Nightmare on Elm Street)
Innovation Publishing: Sept, 1991 - No. 12, Jun, 1993 ($2.50, painted-c)

1-Based on TV show; all have painted-c 2 4 6 11 16 20
2-12: 8-Has photo gallery 4.00
Special Edition 1 (10/92)-r/#1 w/8 extra pgs. of photos & articles
1 3 4 6 8 10
Time and Space Special 1 (#13) ($2.95)-Foil logo 1 3 4 6 8 10

QUANTUM TUNNELER, THE
Revolution Studio: Oct, 2001 (no cover price, one-shot)

1-Prequel to "The One" movie; Clayton Henry-a 3.00

QUARANTINE ZONE
DC Comics: Apr, 2016 ($22.99, HC graphic novel)

HC - Daniel Wilson-s/Fernando Pasarin-a 23.00

QUASAR (See Avengers #302, Captain America #217, Incredible Hulk #234, Marvel Team-Up #113 & Marvel Two-in-One #53)
Marvel Comics: Oct, 1989 - No. 60, Jul, 1994 ($1.00/$1.25, Direct sales #17 on)

1-Gruenwald-s/Paul Ryan-c/a begin; Origin of Wendell Vaughn from Marvel Man to Quasar; Marvel Boy & Fantastic Four app. 6.00
2-6: 2-Origin of the Quantum-Bands; Deathurge & Eon app; Quasar becomes 'Protector of the Universe'. 3-Human Torch app. 4-Aquarian app. 5,6-Acts of Vengeance tie-in. 5-Absorbing Man & Loki app. 6-Red Ghost, Living Laser, Uatu the Watcher app; Venom cameo (2pgs); last Ryan-a(p) 3.00
7-Spider-Man & Quasar vs. Terminus 5.00
8-14,18: 8-Secret Wars x-over; Mike Manley-a begins. 9-Modam (female Modok) app. 10-Dr. Minerva app. 11-Excalibur & Mordred app; first Moondragon as 'H.D Steckley'. 12-Eternals app.; death of Quasar's father (Gilbert). 13-Squadron Supreme & Overmind app. 14-McFarlane-c; Squadron Supreme, Overmind app. 18-1st app. Origin & Unbeing; new Quasar costume; 1st Greg Capullo-a 3.00
15,16: 15-Mignola-c; Squadron Supreme, Overmind, the Stranger & the Watchers app. 16-($1.50, 52 pgs.) Squadron Supreme, Overmind, Stranger & the Watchers app. 4.00
17-Features Marvel's speedsters: Quicksilver, Makkari, Captain Marvel (Monica Rambeau), Speed Demon, Black Racer, Super Sabre & the Runner; Flash parody 'Buried Alien' 5.00
19-(2/91)-Re-intro Jack of Hearts & Maelstrom (neither one seen since 1984); Dr. Strange app. 6.00
20,21: 20-Fantastic Four & the Presence app. 21-Maelstrom revealed as the 'Cosmic Assassin' 5.00
22,23,27,29: 22-Quasar dies; Deathurge app. 'H.D Steckley' revealed to be Moondragon. 23-Ghost Rider app. 27-Original Marvel Boy app. 29-Kismet (Her) app; Vanity Fair Demi Moore pregnancy parody-c 3.00
24-Brief Infinity Gauntlet reference; Thanos & Mephisto app.; vs. Maelstrom; 1st app. Infinity (the female aspect of Eternity) 2 4 6 9 12 15
25-($1.50)-New costume Quasar (returns to life); Eternity, Infinity, Oblivion, Death, Celestials, Galactus, Watchers app.; 'death' of Maelstrom 4.00
26-Infinity Gauntlet tie-in; Thanos & Moondragon app. 5.00
28,30-33: 28-Kismet (Her) app.; Avengers; Warlock, Moondragon, Jack of Hearts app. 30-What If..? issue; Watcher, Thanos, Maelstrom app. 31-Quasar in the New Universe; gains the power of the Starbrand. 32-Operation Galactic Storm Pt. 3; continued from Avengers West Coast #80; Shi'ar Imperial Guard app.; 1st app. Korath the Pursuer. 33-Operation Galactic Storm Pt.10; continued from Avengers West Coast #81; story continues in Wonder Man #8 (#32-34 same as Special #1-3) 4.00
34-39,41-49,51-53: 34-Opertation Galactic Storm Pt. 17; continued from Captain America #400; continued in Avengers West Coast #82. 35-Operation Galactic Storm aftermath; Quasar quits the Avengers. 38-Infinity War x-over; Quasar & the Avengers vs. Warlock, Thanos & the Infinity Watch; last Capullo-a. 39-Infinity War x-over; Thanos & Deathurge app. 41-Avengers app. 42-Punisher app. 43-Quasar returns to life. 47,48-Thunderstrike app. 49-Kismet app. 51,52: 52-Squadron Supreme app. 53-Warlock & the Infinity Watch app. 3.00
40,50: 40-Infinity War x-over; Quasar uses the Ultimate Nullifier and dies; Thanos app. 50-($2.95, 52 pgs.)-Holo-grafix foil-c Silver Surfer, Man-Thing, Ren & Stimpy app. 4.00
54,55: 53-Warlock & the Infinity Watch app. 54-Starblast tie-in; continued from Starblast #1; Hyperion vs. Gladiator. 55-Starblast tie-in; continued from Starblast #2; Black Bolt app; continued in Starblast #3 4.00
56-57: 56-Starblast tie-in; continued from Starblast #4; New Universe app.; continued in Starblast #5. 57-Living Tribunal & the New Universe app. 5.00
58,59: 58-w/bound-in card sheet; Makkari wins the Galactic Race; DC Comics Flash (as Fastforward) app. 59-Thanos & Starfox app. 6.00
60-Last issue; Avengers, New Warriors & Fantastic Four app; Quasar leaves Earth
1 2 3 5 6 8
Special #1-3 ($1.25, newsstand)-Same as #32-34 3.00

QUEEN & COUNTRY (See Whiteout)
Oni Press: Mar, 2001 - No. 32, Aug, 2007 ($2.95/$2.99, B&W)

1-Rucka-s in all. Rolston-a/Sale-c 1 2 3 4 5 7
2-5: 2-4-Rolston-a/Sale-c. 5-Snyder-c/Hurtt-a 4.00
6-24,26-32: 6,7-Snyder-c/Hurtt-a. 13-15-Alexander-a. 16-20-McNeil-a. 21-24-Hawthorne-a 26-28-Norton-a 3.00
25-($5.99) Rolston-a 6.00
Free Comic Book Day giveaway (5/02) r/#1 with "Free Comic Book Day" banner on-c 3.00
Operation: Blackwall (10/03, $8.95, TPB) r/#13-15; John Rogers intro. 9.00
Operation: Broken Ground (2002, $11.95, TPB) r/#1-4; Ellis intro. 12.00
Operation: Crystal Ball (1/03, $14.95, TPB) r/#8-12; Judd Winick intro. 15.00
Operation: Dandelion HC (8/04, $25.00) r/#21-24; Jamie S. Rich intro. 25.00
Operation: Dandelion (8/04, $11.95, TPB) r/#21-24; Jamie S. Rich intro. 12.00
Operation: Morningstar (9/02, $8.95, TPB) r/#5-7; Stuart Moore intro. 9.00
Operation: Storm Front (3/04, $14.95, TPB) r/#16-20; Geoff Johns intro. 15.00

QUEEN & COUNTRY: DECLASSIFIED
Oni Press: Nov, 2002 - No. 3, Jan, 2003 ($2.95, B&W, limited series)

1-3-Rucka-s/Hurtt-a/Morse-c 3.00
TPB (7/03, $8.95) r/#1-3; intro. by Micah Wright 9.00

QUEEN & COUNTRY: DECLASSIFIED (Volume 2)
Oni Press: Jan, 2005 - No. 3, Feb, 2006 ($2.95/$2.99, B&W, limited series)

1-3-Rucka-s/Burchett-a/c 3.00
TPB (3/06, $8.95) r/#1-3 9.00

QUEEN & COUNTRY: DECLASSIFIED (Volume 3)
Oni Press: Jun, 2005 - No. 3, Aug, 2005 ($2.95, B&W, limited series)

1-3- "Sons & Daughters;" Johnston-s/Mitten-a/c 3.00
TPB (3/06, $8.95) r/#1-3 9.00

QUEEN OF THE WEST, DALE EVANS (TV)(See Dale Evans Comics, Roy Rogers & Western Roundup under Dell Giants)
Dell Publ. Co.: No. 479, 7/53 - No. 22, 1-3/59 (All photo-c; photo back c-4-8,15)

Four Color 479(#1, '53) 17 34 51 114 252 390
Four Color 528(#2, '54) 9 18 27 62 126 190
3,4: 3(4-6/54)-Toth-a. 4-Toth, Manning-a 7 14 21 46 86 125
5-10-Manning-a. 5-Marsh-a 6 12 18 40 73 105
11,19,21-No Manning 21-Tufts-a 5 10 15 31 53 75
12-18,20,22-Manning-a 5 10 15 34 60 85

QUEEN SONJA (See Red Sonja)
Dynamite Entertainment: 2009 - No. 35, 2013 ($2.99/$3.99)

1-10: 1-Rubi-a/Ortega-s; 3 covers; back-up r/Marvel Feature #1 4.00
11-35-($3.99) 16-Thulsa Doom returns 4.00

QUENTIN DURWARD
Dell Publishing Co.: No. 672, Jan, 1956

Four Color 672-Movie, photo-c 6 12 18 42 79 115

QUESTAR ILLUSTRATED SCIENCE FICTION CLASSICS
Golden Press: 1977 (224 pgs.) ($1.95)

11197-Stories by Asimov, Sturgeon, Silverberg & Niven; Starstream-r
3 6 9 20 30 40

QUEST FOR CAMELOT
DC Comics: July, 1998 ($4.95)

1-Movie adaption 5.00

QUEST FOR DREAMS LOST (Also see Word Warriors)
Literacy Volunteers of Chicago: July 4, 1987 ($2.00, B&W, 52 pgs.)(Proceeds donated to help fight illiteracy)

1-Teenage Mutant Ninja Turtles by Eastman/Laird, Trollords, Silent Invasion, The Realm, Wordsmith, Reacto Man, Eb'nn, Aniverse 4.00

QUESTION, THE (See Americomics, Blue Beetle (1967), Charlton Bullseye & Mysterious Suspense)

QUESTION, THE (Also see Showcase '95 #3)
DC Comics: Feb, 1987 - No. 36, Mar, 1990; No. 37, Mar, 2010 ($1.50)

1-36: Denny O'Neil scripts in all. 17-Rorshach app. 3.00
37-(3/10, $2.99) Blackest Night one-shot; Victor Sage rises; Shiva app.; Cowan-a 3.00
Annual 1 (1988, $2.50) 4.00
Annual 2 (1989, $3.50) 4.00
...: Epitaph For a Hero TPB (2008, $19.99) r/#13-18 20.00
...: Peacemaker TPB (2010, $19.99) r/#31-36 20.00
...: Pipeline TPB (2011, $14.99) r/stories from Detective Comics #854-865; sketch-a 15.00
...: Poisoned Ground TPB (2008, $19.99) r/#7-12 20.00
...: Riddles TPB (2009, $19.99) r/#25-30 20.00
...: Welcome to Oz TPB (2009, $19.99) r/#19-24 20.00
...: Zen and Violence TPB (2007, $19.99) r/#1-6 20.00

QUESTION, THE (Also see Crime Bible and 52)
DC Comics: Jan, 2005 - No. 6, Jun, 2005 ($2.95, limited series)

1-6-Rick Veitch-s/Tommy Lee Edwards-a. 4,6-Superman app. 3.00

QUESTION QUARTERLY, THE
DC Comics: Summer, 1990 - No. 5, Spring, 1992 ($2.50/$2.95, 52pgs.)

1-5 4.00
NOTE: *Cowan a-1, 2, 4, 5; c-1-3, 5.* ***Mignola*** *a-5i.* ***Quesada*** *a-3-5.*

QUESTION RETURNS, THE
DC Comics: Feb, 1997 ($3.50, one-shot)

1-Brereton-c 4.00

QUESTION, THE : THE DEATHS OF VIC SAGE
DC Comics (Black Label): Jan, 2020 - No. 4, Oct, 2020 ($6.99, over-sized 10-7/8" x 8-1/2", limited series)

1-4-Jeff Lemire-s/Denys Cowan & Bill Sienkiewicz-a; two covers on each 7.00

QUESTPROBE
Marvel Comics: 8/84; No. 2, 1/85; No. 3, 11/85 (lim. series)

1-3: 1-The Hulk app. by Romita. 2-Spider-Man; Mooney-a(i). 3-Human Torch & Thing 4.00

QUICK DRAW McGRAW (TV) (Hanna-Barbera)(See Whitman Comic Books)
Dell Publishing Co./Gold Key No. 12 on: No. 1040, 12-2/59-60 - No. 11, 7-9/62; No. 12, 11/62; No. 13, 2/63; No. 14, 4/63; No. 15, 6/69 (1st show aired 9/29/59)

Four Color 1040(#1) 1st app. Quick Draw & Baba Looey, Augie Doggie & Doggie Daddy and Snooper & Blabber 14 28 42 96 211 325
2(4-6/60)-4,6: 2-Augie Doggie & Snooper & Blabber stories (8 pgs. each); pre-dates both of their #1 issues. 4-Augie Doggie & Snooper & Blabber stories.
6 12 18 37 66 95
5-1st Snagglepuss app.; last 10¢ issue 6 12 18 42 79 115
7-11 5 10 15 30 50 70
12,13-Title change to ...Fun-Type Roundup (84pgs.) 6 12 18 38 69 100

Quantum & Woody Must Die #4 © VAL

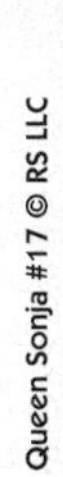

Queen Sonja #17 © RS LLC

Rachel Rising #7 © Terry Moore

	GD 2.0	VG 4.0	FN 6.0	VF 8.0	VF/NM 9.0	NM- 9.2

14,15: 15-Reprints 4 8 12 27 44 60

QUICK DRAW McGRAW (TV)(See Spotlight #2)
Charlton Comics: Nov, 1970 - No. 8, Jan, 1972 (Hanna-Barbera)

1 5 10 15 30 50 70
2-8 3 6 9 18 28 38

QUICKSILVER (See Avengers)
Marvel Comics: Nov, 1997 - No. 13, Nov, 1998 ($2.99/$1.99)

1-($2.99)-Peyer-s/Casey Jones-a; wraparound-c 4.00
2-11: 2-Two covers-variant by Golden. 4-6-Inhumans app. 3.00
12-($2.99) Siege of Wundagore pt. 4 4.00
13-Magneto-c/app.; last issue 3.00

QUICKSILVER: NO SURRENDER (Avengers)
Marvel Comics: Jul, 2018 - No. 5, Nov, 2018 ($3.99, limited series)

1-5-Saladin Ahmed-s/Eric Nguyen-a; Scarlet Witch app. 4.00

QUICK STOP (Set in the universe of Kevin Smith's Jay and Silent Bob)
Dark Horse Comics: Nov, 2022 - No. 4, Feb, 2023 ($3.99, B&W, limited series)

1-4-Kevin Smith-s. 2-Phil Hester-a 4.00

QUICK-TRIGGER WESTERN (...Action #12; Cowboy Action #5-11)
Atlas Comics (ACI #12/WPI #13-19): No. 12, May, 1956 - No. 19, Sept, 1957

12-Baker-a 23 46 69 136 223 310
13-Williamson-a, 5 pgs. 18 36 54 107 169 230
14-Everett, Crandall, Torres-a; Heath-c 16 32 48 94 147 200
15,16: 15-Torres, Crandall-a. 16-Orlando, Kirby-a 15 30 45 84 127 170
17,18: 18-Baker-a 15 30 45 83 124 165
19 13 26 39 74 105 135

NOTE: ***Ayers** a-17. **Colan** a-16. **Maneely** a-15, 17; c-15, 18. **Morrow** a-18. **Powell** a-14. **Severin** a-19; c-12, 13, 16, 17, 19. **Shores** a-16. **Tuska** a-17.*

QUINCY (See Comics Reading Libraries in the Promotional Comics section)

QUITTER, THE
DC Comics (Vertigo): 2005 ($19.99, B&W graphic novel)

HC ($19.99) Autobiography of Harvey Pekar; Pekar-s/Daen Haspiel-a 20.00
SC (2006, $12.99) 13.00

RACCOON KIDS, THE (Formerly Movietown Animal Antics)
National Periodical Publications (Arleigh No. 63,64): No. 52, Sept-Oct, 1954 - No. 62, Oct-Nov, 1956; No. 63, Sept, 1957; No. 64, Nov, 1957

52-Doodles Duck by Mayer 15 30 45 85 130 175
53-64: 53-62-Doodles Duck by Mayer 11 22 33 62 86 110

NOTE: ***Otto Feuer**-a most issues. **Rube Grossman**-a most issues.*

RACE FOR THE MOON
Harvey Publications: Mar, 1958 - No. 3, Nov, 1958

1-Powell-a(5); 1/2-pg. S&K-a; cover redrawn from Galaxy Science Fiction pulp (5/53)
24 48 72 142 234 325
2-Kirby/Williamson-c(r)/a(3); Kirby-p 7 more stys 32 64 96 188 307 425
3-Kirby/Williamson-c/a(4); Kirby-p 6 more stys 35 70 105 208 339 470

RACER-X
Now Comics: 8/88 - No. 11, 8/89; V2#1, 9/89 - V2#10, 1990 ($1.75)

0-Deluxe ($3.50) 5.00
1 (9/88) - 11, V2#1-10 4.00

RACER X (See Speed Racer)
DC Comics (WildStorm): Oct, 2000 - No. 3, Dec, 2000 ($2.95, limited series)

1-3: 1-Tommy Yune-s/Jo Chen-a; 2 covers by Yune. 2,3-Kabala app. 4.00

RACHEL RISING
Abstract Studio: 2011 - No. 42, 2016 ($3.99, B&W)

1-Terry Moore-s/a/c; back cover by Fabio Moon; green background on cover 50.00
1-(2nd printing) Red background on cover 35.00
1-(3rd printing) Red background on cover 35.00
2 35.00
3-6 10.00
7-42: 42-Final issue 4.00
Halloween ComicFest Edition (2014, giveaway) Reprints #1 with orange bkgd on cover 5.00

RACING PETTYS
STP Corp.: 1980 ($2.50, 68 pgs., 10 1/8" x 13 1/4")

1-Bob Kane-a. Kane bio on inside back-c. 2 4 6 9 13 16

RACK & PAIN
Dark Horse Comics: Mar, 1994 - No. 4, June, 1994 ($2.50, limited series)

1-4: Brian Pulido scripts in all. 1-Greg Capullo-c 3.00

RACK & PAIN: KILLERS
Chaos! Comics: Sept, 1996 - No. 4, Jan, 1997 ($2.95, limited series)

1-4: Reprints Dark Horse series; Jae Lee-c 3.00

RACKET SQUAD IN ACTION
Capitol Stories/Charlton Comics: May-June, 1952 - No. 29, Mar, 1958

1 39 78 117 240 395 550
2-4,6: 3,4,6-Dr. Neff, Ghost Breaker app. 20 40 60 118 192 265
5-Dr. Neff, Ghost Breaker app; headlights-c 58 116 174 371 636 900
7-10: 10-Explosion-c 18 36 54 105 165 225
11-Ditko-c/a 40 80 120 246 411 575
12-Ditko explosion-c (classic); Shuster-a(2) 77 154 231 493 847 1200
13-Shuster-c(p)/a; "Acid in Face story" titled "Your Money or Your Face"
16 32 48 92 144 195
14-Marijuana story "Shakedown"; Giordano-c 22 44 66 132 216 300
15-28: 15,20,22,23-Giordano-c 15 30 45 85 130 175
29-(15¢, 68 pgs.) 18 36 54 105 165 225

RADIANT BLACK
Image Comics: Feb, 2021 - Present ($3.99)

1-22: 1-5-Kyle Higgins-s/Marcelo Costa-a. 6-Lafuente-a 4.00

RADIANT LOVE (Formerly Daring Love #1)
Gilmor Magazines: No. 2, Dec, 1953 - No. 6, Aug, 1954

2 26 52 78 154 252 350
3-6 17 34 51 105 165 225

RADIANT PINK
Image Comics: Dec, 2022 - No. 5 ($3.99)

1-3-Meghan Camarena & Melissa Flores-s/Emma Kubert-a 4.00

RADIANT RED
Image Comics: Mar, 2022 - No. 5, Jul, 2022 ($3.99)

1-5-Cherish Chen-s/David Lafuente-a 4.00

RADICAL DREAMER
Blackball Comics: No. 0, May, 1994 - No. 4, Nov, 1994 ($1.99, bi-monthly)
(1st poster format comic)

0-4: 0-2-($1.99, poster format): 0-1st app. Max Wrighter. 3,4-($2.50-c) 3.00

RADICAL DREAMER
Mark's Giant Economy Size Comics: V2#1, June, 1995 - V2#6, Feb, 1996 ($2.95, B&W, limited series)

V2#1-6 3.00
Prime (5/96, $2.95) 3.00
Dreams Cannot Die!-(1996, $20.00, softcover)-Collects V1#0-4 & V2#1-6; intro by Kurt Busiek; afterward by Mark Waid 20.00
Dreams Cannot Die!-(1996, $60.00, hardcover)-Signed & limited edition; collects V1#0-4 & V2#1-6; intro by Kurt Busiek; afterward by Mark Waid 60.00

RADICALLY REARRANGED RONIN RAGDOLLS
Kevin Eastman Studios, Inc.: 2019 ($3.99)

1-TMNT pastiche with cats; Kevin Eastman & Troy Little-a; David Avallone-s 4.00

RADIOACTIVE MAN (Simpsons TV show)
Bongo Comics: 1993 - No. 6, 1994 ($1.95/$2.25, limited series)

1-($2.95)-Glow-in-the-dark-c; bound-in jumbo poster; origin Radioactive Man; (cover dated Nov. 1952) 4 8 12 23 37 50
2-6: 2-Says #88 on-c & inside & dated May 1962; cover parody of Atlas Kirby monster-c; Superior Squad app.; origin Fallout Boy. 3-($1.95)-Cover "dated" Aug 1972 #216. 4-($2.25)-Cover "dated" Oct 1980 #412; w/trading card. 5-Cover "dated" Jan 1986 #679; w/trading card. 6-(Jan 1995 #1000) 4.00
Colossal #1-($4.95) 2 4 6 8 10 12
#4 (2001, $2.50) Faux 1953 issue; Murphy Anderson-i (6 pgs.) 5.00
#100 (2000, $2.50) Comic Book Guy-c/app.; faux 1963 issue inside 5.00
#136 (2001, $2.50) Dan DeCarlo-c/a 5.00
#222 (2001, $2.50) Batton Lash-s; Radioactive Man in 1972-style 5.00
#575 (2002, $2.50) Chaykin-c; Radioactive Man in 1984-style 5.00
1963-106 (2002, $2.50) Radioactive Man in 1960s Gold Key-style; Groening-c 5.00
#7 Bongo Super Heroes Starring... (2003, $2.50) Marvel Silver Age-style Superior Squad 5.00
#8 Official Movie Adaptation (2004, $2.99) starring Rainier Wolfcastle and Milhouse 5.00
#9 (#197 on-c) (2004, $2.50) Kirby-esque New Gods spoof; Golden Age Radio Man app. 5.00

RADIO FUNNIES
DC Comics: Mar. 1939; undated variant

nn-(3/39) Ashcan comic, not distributed to newsstands, only for in-house use. Cover art is Adventure Comics #39 with interior being Detective Comics #19 (no known sales)
nn - Ashcan comic. No date. Cover art is Detective #26 with interior from Detective #17;

GD VG FN VF VF/NM NM-
2.0 4.0 6.0 8.0 9.0 9.2

one copy, graded at GD/VG, sold at auction for $4481.25 in Nov, 2009. Another copy graded at GD/VG sold at auction for $3346 in Feb, 2010.

RADIO SPACEMAN
Dark Horse Comics: Mar, 2022 - No. 2, Apr, 2022 ($3.99, limited series)
1,2-Mike Mignola-s/Greg Hinkle-a 4.00

RAGAMUFFINS
Eclipse Comics: Jan, 1985 ($1.75, one shot)
1-Eclipse Magazine-r, w/color; Colan-a 3.00

RAGE (Based on the id video game)
Dark Horse Comics: Jun, 2011 - No. 3, Aug, 2011 ($3.50, limited series)
1-3-Nelson-s/Mutti-a/Fabry-c. 1-Variant-c by Martiniere 3.50

RAGEMOOR
Dark Horse Comics: Mar, 2012 - No. 4, Jun, 2012 ($3.50, B&W, limited series)
1-4-Richard Corben-a/c; Jan Strnad-s 3.50

RAGGEDY ANN AND ANDY (See Dell Giants, March of Comics #23 & New Funnies)
Dell Publishing Co.: No. 5, 1942 - No. 533, 2/54; 10-12/64 - No. 4, 3/66
Four Color 5(1942) 50 100 150 400 900 1400
Four Color 23(1943) 35 70 105 252 564 875
Four Color 45(1943) 26 52 78 182 404 625
Four Color 72(1945) 21 42 63 147 324 500
1(6/46)-Billy & Bonnie Bee by Frank Thomas 29 58 87 209 467 725
2,3: 3-Egbert Elephant by Dan Noonan begins 15 30 45 100 220 340
4-Kelly-a, 16 pgs. 15 30 45 105 233 360
5,6,8-10 12 24 36 80 173 265
7-Little Black Sambo, Black Mumbo & Black Jumbo only app; Christmas-c
14 28 42 97 214 330
11-20 10 20 30 64 132 200
21-Alice In Wonderland cover/story 12 24 36 80 173 265
22-27,29-39(8/49), Four Color 262 (1/50): 34-"...In Candyland"
9 18 27 57 111 165
28-Kelly-c 9 18 27 59 117 175
Four Color 306,354,380,452,533 7 14 21 46 86 125
1(10-12/64-Dell) 4 8 12 23 37 50
2,3(10-12/65), 4(3/66) 3 6 9 16 23 30
NOTE: *Kelly art ("Animal Mother Goose")-#1-34, 36, 37; c-28. Peterkin Pottle by* ***John Stanley*** *in 32-38.*

RAGGEDY ANN AND ANDY
Gold Key: Dec, 1971 - No. 6, Sept, 1973
1 3 6 9 18 28 38
2-6 3 6 9 15 21 26

RAGGEDY ANN & THE CAMEL WITH THE WRINKLED KNEES (See Dell Jr. Treasury #8)

RAGMAN (See Batman Family #20, The Brave & The Bold #196 & Cancelled Comic Cavalcade)
National Per. Publ./DC Comics No. 5: Aug-Sept, 1976 - No. 5, Jun-Jul, 1977
1-Origin & 1st app. 4 8 12 25 40 55
2-5: 2-Origin ends; Kubert-c. 4-Drug use story 2 4 6 8 11 14
NOTE: ***Kubert*** *a-4, 5; c-1-5.* ***Redondo*** *studios a-1-4.*

RAGMAN (2nd Series)
DC Comics: Oct, 1991 - No. 8, May, 1992 ($1.50, limited series)
1-8: 1-Giffen plots/breakdowns. 3-Origin. 8-Batman-c/story 3.00

RAGMAN (3rd Series)
DC Comics: Dec, 2017 - No. 6, May, 2018 ($2.99, limited series)
1-6-Ray Fawkes-s/Inaki Miranda-a/Guillem March-c; new origin. 3-6-Etrigan app. 3.00

RAGMAN: CRY OF THE DEAD
DC Comics: Aug, 1993 - No. 6, Jan, 1994 ($1.75, limited series)
1-6: Joe Kubert-c 3.00

RAGMAN: SUIT OF SOULS
DC Comics: Dec, 2010 ($3.99, one-shot)
1-Gage-s/Segovia-a/Saiz-c; origin retold 4.00

RAGNAROK
IDW Publishing: Jul, 2014 - No. 12, Feb, 2017 ($3.99/$4.99)
1-7-Walt Simonson-s/a; two covers on each 4.00
8-12-($4.99) 5.00

RAGNAROK: THE BREAKING OF HELHEIM
IDW Publishing: Jul, 2019 - Present ($4.99)
1-4-Walt Simonson-s/a; multiple covers on each 4.00

RAGS RABBIT (Formerly Babe Ruth Sports #10 or Little Max #10?; also see Harvey Hits #2, Harvey Wiseguys & Tastee Freez)
Harvey Publications: No. 11, June, 1951 - No. 18, March, 1954 (Written & drawn for little folks)
11-(See Nutty Comics #5 for 1st app.) 9 18 27 47 61 75
12-18 6 12 18 31 38 45

RAI (Rai and the Future Force #9-23) (See Magnus #5-8)
Valiant: Mar, 1992 - No. 0, Oct, 1992; No. 9, May, 1993 - No. 33, Jun, 1995 ($1.95/$2.25)
1-Valiant's 1st original character 3 6 9 14 19 24
2-5: 4-Low print run 2 4 6 11 16 20
6-10: 6,7-Unity x-overs. 7-Death of Rai. 9-($2.50)-Gatefold-c; story cont'd from Magnus #24; Magnus, Eternal Warrior & X-O app. 6.00
11-33: 15-Manowar Armor app. 17-19-Magnus x-over. 21-1st app. The Starwatchers (cameo); trading card. 22-Death of Rai. 26-Chaos Effect Epsilon Pt. 3 4.00
#0-(11/92)-Origin/1st app. new Rai (Rising Spirit) & 1st full app. & partial origin Bloodshot; also see Eternal Warrior #4; tells future of all characters
3 6 9 14 20 25
NOTE: ***Layton*** *c-2i, 9i.* ***Miller*** *c-6.* ***Simonson*** *c-7.*

RAI
Valiant Entertainment: May, 2014 - No. 16, Aug, 2016 ($3.99)
1-16: 1-Kindt-s/Crain-a; Rai in Japan in the year 4001. 15,16-4001 AD tie-ins 4.00
...: The History of the Valiant Universe 1 (6/17, $3.99) Roberts-s/Portela-a; 2 covers 4.00

RAI
Valiant Entertainment: Nov, 2019 - Present ($3.99)
1-10: 1-Abnett-s/Ryp-a 4.00

RAIDERS OF THE LOST ARK (Movie)
Marvel Comics Group: Sept, 1981 - No. 3, Nov, 1981 (Movie adaptation)
1-r/Marvel Comics Super Special #18 3 6 9 16 23 30
2,3 2 4 6 8 10 12
NOTE: ***Buscema*** *a(p)-1-3; c(p)-1.* ***Simonson*** *a-3i; scripts-1-3.*

RAINBOW BRITE
Dynamite Entertainment: 2018 - No. 5, 2019 ($3.99, limited series)
1-5-Origin story; Jeremy Whitley-s/Brittney Williams-a; multiple covers on each 4.00

RAINBOW BRITE AND THE STAR STEALER
DC Comics: 1985
nn-Movie adaptation 3 6 9 14 20 25

RAISE THE DEAD
Dynamite Entertainment: 2007 - No. 4, Aug, 2007 ($3.50)
1-4-Arthur Suydam-c/Leah Moore & John Reppion-s/Petrus-a; Phillips var-c on all 4.00
... Vol. 1 HC (2007, $19.99) r/#1-4; script, interview & sketch pages; cover gallery 20.00

RAISE THE DEAD 2
Dynamite Entertainment: 2010 - No. 4, 2011 ($3.99)
1-4-Leah Moore & John Reppion-s/Vilanova-a 4.00

RALPH KINER, HOME RUN KING
Fawcett Publications: 1950 (Pittsburgh Pirates)
nn-Photo-c; life story 60 120 180 381 658 935

RALPH SNART ADVENTURES
Now Comics: June, 1986 - V2#9, 1987; V3#1 - #26, Feb, 1991; V4#1, 1992 - #4, 1992
1-3, V2#1-7,V3#1-23,25,26:1-($1.00, B&W)-1(B&W),V2#1(11/86), B&W), 8,9-color. V3#1(9/88)-Color begins 3.00
V3#24-($2.50)-3-D issue, V4#1-3-Direct sale versions w/cards 3.00
V4#1-3-Newsstand versions w/random cards 3.00
Book 1 1 2 3 5 6 8
3-D Special (11/92, $3.50)-Complete 12-card set w/3-D glasses 4.00

RAMAR OF THE JUNGLE (TV)
Toby Press No. 1/Charlton No. 2 on: 1954 (no month); No. 2, Sept, 1955 - No. 5, Sept, 1956
1-Jon Hall photo-c; last pre-code issue 28 56 84 168 274 380
2-5: 2-Jon Hall photo-c 19 38 57 112 179 245

RAMAYAN 3392 A.D.
Virgin Comics: Sept, 2006 - No. 8, Aug, 2008 ($2.99)
1-8: 1-Alex Ross-c; re-imagining of the Indian myth of Ramayana; poster of cover inside 3.00
... Reloaded (8/07 - No. 7, 7/08, $2.99) 1-7: 1-Two covers by Kang and Oeming 3.00
... Reloaded Guidebook (4/08, $2.99) Profiles of characters and weapons 3.00

RAMM
Megaton Comics: May, 1987 - No. 2, Sept, 1987 ($1.50, B&W)
1,2-Both have 1 pg. Youngblood ad by Liefeld 3.00

RAMPAGING HULK (The Hulk #10 on; also see Marvel Treasury Edition)
Marvel Comics Group: Jan, 1977 - No. 9, June, 1978 ($1.00, B&W magazine)
1-Bloodstone story w/Buscema & Nebres-a. Origin re-cap w/Simonson-a; Gargoyle, UFO story; Ken Barr-c 4 8 12 28 47 65
2-Old X-Men app; origin old w/Simonson-a & new X-Men in text w/Cockrum illos; Bloodstone story w/Brown & Nebres-a 3 6 9 19 30 40
3-9: 3-Iron Man app.; Norem-c. 4-Gallery of villains w/Giffen-a. 5,6-Hulk vs. Sub-Mariner. 7-Man-Thing story. 8-Original Avengers app. 9-Thor vs. Hulk battle; Shanna the She-Devil story w/DeZuniga-a 3 6 9 15 22 28
NOTE: ***Alcala*** *a-1-3i, 5i, 8i.* ***Buscema*** *a-1.* ***Giffen*** *a-4.* ***Nino*** *a-4i.* ***Simonson*** *a-1-3p.* ***Starlin*** *a-4(w/****Nino****), 7; c-4, 5, 7.*

RAMPAGING HULK
Marvel Comics: Aug, 1998 - No. 6, Jan, 1999 ($2.99/$1.99)
1-($2.99) Flashback stories of Savage Hulk; Leonardi-a 5.00
2-6-($1.99): 2-Two covers 4.00

RAMPAGING WOLVERINE
Marvel Comics: June, 2009 ($3.99, B&W, one-shot)
1-Short stories by Fialkov, Luque, Ted McKeever, Yost, Santolouco, Firth, Nelson 4.00

RANDOLPH SCOTT (Movie star)(See Crack Western #67, Prize Comics Western #76, Western Hearts #8, Western Love #1 & Western Winners #7)

RANGE BUSTERS
Fox Feature Syndicate: Sept, 1950 (10¢, one shot)
1-Saga of John Wesley Hardin 23 46 69 138 227 315

RANGE BUSTERS (Formerly Cowboy Love?; Wyatt Earp, Frontier Marshall #11 on)
Charlton Comics: No. 8, May, 1955 - No. 10, Sept, 1955
8 9 18 27 52 69 85
9,10 7 14 21 35 43 50

RANGELAND LOVE
Atlas Comics (CDS): Dec, 1949 - No. 2, Mar, 1950 (52 pgs.)
1-Robert Taylor & Arlene Dahl photo-c 28 56 84 165 270 375
2-Photo-c 20 40 60 114 182 250

RANGER, THE (See Zane Grey, Four Color #255)

RANGE RIDER, THE (TV)(See Flying A's...)

RANGE ROMANCES
Comic Magazines (Quality Comics): Dec, 1949 - No. 5, Aug, 1950 (#5: 52 pg)
1-Gustavson-c/a 32 64 96 188 307 425
2-Crandall-c/a 31 62 93 182 296 410
3-Crandall, Gustavson-a; photo-c 25 50 75 150 245 340
4-Crandall-a; photo-c 22 44 66 132 216 300
5-Gustavson-a; Crandall-a(p); photo-c 22 44 66 132 216 300

Ragnarok #1 © Walt Simonson

Rangers Comics #8 © FH

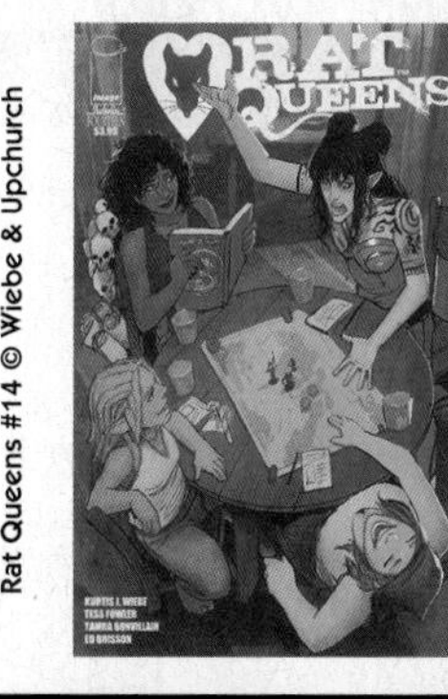

Rat Queens #14 © Wiebe & Upchurch

RANGERS COMICS (...of Freedom #1-7)
Fiction House Magazines: 10/41 - No. 67, 10/52; No. 68, Fall, 1952; No. 69, Winter, 1952-53 (Flying stories)

	GD 2.0	VG 4.0	FN 6.0	VF 8.0	VF/NM 9.0	NM- 9.2
1-Intro. Ranger Girl & The Rangers of Freedom; ends #7, cover app. only #5	595	1190	1785	4350	7675	11,000
2-WWII-c	295	590	885	1888	3244	4600
3-Good Girl bondage/torture-c	258	516	774	1651	2826	4000
4,5	135	270	405	864	1482	2100
6-10-All Japanese war covers. 8-U.S. Rangers begin	100	200	300	635	1093	1550
11,12-Commando Rangers app.	90	180	270	576	988	1400
13-Commando Ranger begins-not same as Commando Rangers; Nazi war-c	103	206	309	659	1130	1600
14-Classic Japanese bondage/torture WWII-c	194	388	582	1242	2121	3000
15-20: 15,17,19-Japanese war-c. 18-Nazi war-c	77	154	231	493	847	1200
21-Intro/origin Firehair (begins, 2/45)	354	708	1062	2478	4339	6200
22-25,27,29-Japanese war-c. 23-Kazanda begins, ends #28	61	122	183	390	670	950
26-Classic Japanese WWII good girl-c	354	708	1062	2478	4339	6200
28,30: 28-Tiger Man begins (origin/1st app., 4/46), ends #46. 30-Crusoe Island begins, ends #40	48	96	144	302	514	725
31-40: 33-Hypodermic panels	39	78	117	240	395	550
41-46: 41-Last Werewolf Hunter	31	62	93	182	296	410
47-56- "Eisnerish" Dr. Drew by Grandenetti. 48-Last Glory Forbes. 53-Last 52 pg. issue. 55-Last Sky Rangers	28	56	84	168	274	380
57-60-Straight run of Dr. Drew by Grandenetti	21	42	63	122	199	275
61-69: 64-Suicide Smith begins. 63-Used in **POP**, pgs. 85, 99. 67-Space Rangers begin, end #69	19	38	57	112	179	245

NOTE: Bondage, discipline covers, lingerie panels are common. Crusoe Island by ***Larsen****-#30-36. Firehair by* ***Lubbers****-#30-49. Glory Forbes by* ***Baker****-#36-45, 47; by* ***Whitman****-#34, 35. I Confess in #41-53. Jan of the Jungle in #42-58. King of the Congo in #49-53. Tiger Man by* ***Celardo****-#30-39.* ***M. Anderson*** *a-30?* ***Baker*** *a-36-38, 42, 44.* ***John Celardo*** *a-34, 36-39.* ***Lee Elias*** *a-21-28.* ***Evans*** *a-19, 38-46, 48-52.* ***Hopper*** *a-25, 26.* ***Ingels*** *a-13-16.* ***Larsen*** *a-34.* ***Bob Lubbers*** *a-30-38, 40-44; c-40-45.* ***Moreira*** *a-41-47.* ***Tuska*** *a-16, 17, 19, 22.* ***M. Whitman*** *c-61-66.* ***Zolnerwich*** *c-1-17.*

RANGERS OF THE DIVIDE
Dark Horse Comics: May, 2021 - No. 4, Aug, 2021 ($3.99, limited series)

1-4-Megan Huang-s/a/c 4.00

RANGO (TV)
Dell Publishing Co.: Aug, 1967

	GD	VG	FN	VF	VF/NM	NM-
1-Photo-c of comedian Tim Conway	4	8	12	28	47	65

RANN-THANAGAR HOLY WAR (Also see Hawkman Special #1)
DC Comics: July, 2008 - No. 8, Feb, 2009 ($3.50, limited series)

1-8-Adam Strange & Hawkman app.; Starlin-s/Lim-a. 1-Two covers by Starlin & Lim 3.50
Volume One TPB (2009, $19.99) r/#1-4 & Hawkman Special #1 20.00
Volume Two TPB (2009, $19.99) r/#5-8 & Adam Strange Special #1 20.00

RANN-THANAGAR WAR (See Adam Strange 2004 mini-series)(Prelude to Infinite Crisis)
DC Comics: July, 2005 - No. 6, Dec, 2005 ($2.50, limited series)

1-6-Adam Strange, Hawkman and Green Lantern (Kyle Rayner) app.; Gibbons-s/Reis-a 3.00
...: Infinite Crisis Special (4/06, $4.99) Kyle Rayner becomes Ion again; Jade dies 5.00
TPB (2005, $12.99) r/#1-6; cover gallery; new Bolland-c 13.00

RAPHAEL (See Teenage Mutant Ninja Turtles)
Mirage Studios: 1985 ($1.50, 7-1/2x11", B&W w/2 color cover, one-shot)

	GD	VG	FN	VF	VF/NM	NM-
1-1st Turtles one-shot spin-off; contains 1st drawing of the Turtles as a group from 1983; 1st app. Casey Jones	25	50	75	175	388	600
1-2nd printing (11/87); new-c & 8 pgs. art	5	10	15	31	53	75

RAPHAEL BAD MOON RISING (See Teenage Mutant Ninja Turtles)
Mirage Publishing: July, 2007 - No. 4, Oct, 2007 ($3.25, B&W, limited series)

	GD	VG	FN	VF	VF/NM	NM-
1-Continued from Tales of the TMNT #7; Lawson-a	3	6	9	19	30	40
2-4	2	4	6	11	16	20

RAPTURE
Dark Horse Comics: May, 2009 - No. 6, Jan, 2010 ($2.99, limited series)

1-6-Taki Soma & Michael Avon Oeming-s/a/c. 1-Maleev var-c. 2-Mack var-c 3.00

RAPTURE
Valiant Entertainment: May, 2017 - No. 4, Aug, 2017 ($3.99)

1-4-Kindt-s/Cafu-a; Ninjak, Shadowman & Punk Mambo app. 4-Ryp-a; preview of Eternity 4.00

RASCALS IN PARADISE
Dark Horse Comics: Aug, 1994 - No. 3, Dec, 1994 ($3.95, magazine size)

1-3-Jim Silke-a/story 4.00
Trade paperback-($16.95)-r/#1-3 17.00

RASL
Cartoon Books: Mar, 2008 - No. 15, Jul, 2012 ($3.50/$4.99, B&W)

1-14-Jeff Smith-s/a/c 3.50
15-($4.99) Conclusion 5.00

RASPUTIN: VOICE OF THE DRAGON
Dark Horse Comics: Nov, 2017 - No. 5, Mar, 2018 ($3.99, limited series)

1-5-Mignola & Roberson-s/Mittens-a; Rasputin in 1941 Nazi Germany 4.00

RATCHET & CLANK (Based on the Sony videogame)
DC Comics (WildStorm thru #4): Nov, 2010 - No. 6, Apr, 2011 ($3.99/$2.99, limited series)

1-4-Fixman-s/Archer-a 4.00
5,6-($2.99) 3.00
TPB (2011, $17.99) r/#1-6 18.00

RATFINK (See Frantic and Zany)
Canrom, Inc.: Oct, 1964

	GD	VG	FN	VF	VF/NM	NM-
1-Woodbridge-a	10	20	30	64	132	200

RAT GOD
Dark Horse Comics: Feb, 2015 - No. 5, Jun, 2015 ($3.99, limited series)

1-5-Richard Corben-s/a/c 5.00

RAT PATROL, THE (TV) (Also see Wild!)
Dell Publishing Co.: Mar, 1967 - No. 5, Nov, 1967; No. 6, Oct, 1969

	GD	VG	FN	VF	VF/NM	NM-
1-Christopher George photo-c	6	12	18	41	76	110
2-6: 3-6-Photo-c	4	8	12	28	47	65

RAT QUEENS
Image Comics (Shadowline): Sept, 2013 - No. 16, May, 2016 ($3.50/$3.99)

	GD	VG	FN	VF	VF/NM	NM-
1-Kurtis Wiebe-s/Roc Upchurch-a/c	1	3	4	6	8	10

1-Variant-c by Fiona Staples 40.00
2-10: 2-8-Two covers on each. 9,10-Sejic-a. 9-Frison-c 3.50
11-16-($3.99) Fowler-a 4.00
... Special: Braga #1 (1/15, $3.50) Wiebe-s/Tess Fowler-a; origin of Braga the Orc 3.50

RAT QUEENS (Volume 2)
Image Comics (Shadowline): Mar, 2017 - No. 25, Mar, 2021 ($3.99)

1-25: 1-15-Kurtis Wiebe-s/Owen Gieni-a/c. 16-19-Ferrier-s/Petraites-a. 22-25-Moritat-a 4.00
... Special: Neon Static 1 (7/18, $3.99) Wiebe-s/Kirkby-a/c; set in future city 4.00
... Special: Orc Dave 1 (9/17, $3.99) Staples-c; Dave's 1st meeting with the Queens 4.00
... Special: Swamp Romp 1 (4/19, $3.99) Ferrier-s/Petraites-a 4.00

RAVAGERS, THE (See Teen Titans and Superboy New 52 series)
DC Comics: Jul, 2012 - No. 12, Jul, 2013 ($2.99)

1-12: 1-Fairchild, Beast Boy, Terra, Thunder, Lightning, Ridge team; Churchill-a 3.00
#0 (11/12, $2.99) Churchill-a; origin of Beast Boy & Terra 3.00

RAVAGE 2099 (See Marvel Comics Presents #117)
Marvel Comics: Dec, 1992 - No. 33, Aug, 1995 ($1.25/$1.50)

1-($1.75)-Gold foil stamped-c; Stan Lee scripts 4.00
1-($1.75)-2nd printing 3.00
2-24,26-33: 5-Last Ryan-c. 6-Last Ryan-a. 14-Punisher 2099 x-over. 15-Ron Lim-c(p). 18-Bound-in card sheet 3.00
25 ($2.25, 52 pgs.) 4.00
25 ($2.95, 52 pgs.)-Silver foil embossed-c 5.00

RAVEN (See DC Special: Raven and Teen Titans titles)

RAVEN (From Teen Titans)
DC Comics: Nov, 2016 - No. 6, Apr, 2017 ($2.99, limited series)

1-6: 1-3-Wolfman-s/Borges-a. 4-6-Neves-a 3.00

RAVEN, THE (See Movie Classics)

RAVEN CHRONICLES
Caliber (New Worlds): 1995 - No. 16 ($2.95, B&W)

1-16: 10-Flip book w/Wordsmith #6. 15-Flip book w/High Caliber #4 3.00

RAVENCROFT (Also see Ruins of Ravencroft)(Leads into King in Black series)
Marvel Comics: Mar, 2020 - No. 5, Nov, 2020 ($3.99, limited series)

1-5-Tieri-s/Unzueta-a; Misty Knight app. 4.00

RAVEN: DAUGHTER OF DARKNESS (From Teen Titans)
DC Comics: Mar, 2018 - No. 12, Mar, 2019 ($3.99, limited series)

1-12-Wolfman-s/Mhan-a; Baron Winters app. 4.00

RAVENS AND RAINBOWS
Pacific Comics: Dec, 1983 (Baxter paper)(Reprints fanzine work in color)

1-Jeff Jones-c/a(r); nudity scenes 3.00

RAWHIDE (TV)
Dell Publishing Co./Gold Key: Sept-Nov, 1959 - June-Aug, 1962; July, 1963 - No. 2, Jan, 1964

	GD 2.0	VG 4.0	FN 6.0	VF 8.0	VF/NM 9.0	NM- 9.2
Four Color 1028 (#1)	25	50	75	175	388	600
Four Color 1097,1160,1202,1261,1269	13	26	39	91	201	310
01-684-208 (8/62, Dell)	11	22	33	73	157	240
1(10071-307) (7/63, Gold Key)	11	22	33	73	157	240
2-(12¢)	10	20	30	66	138	210

NOTE: *All have Clint Eastwood photo-c.* ***Tufts*** *a-1028.*

RAWHIDE KID
Atlas/Marvel Comics (CnPC No. 1-16/AMI No. 17-30): Mar, 1955 - No. 16, Sept, 1957; No. 17, Aug, 1960 - No. 151, May, 1979

	GD 2.0	VG 4.0	FN 6.0	VF 8.0	VF/NM 9.0	NM- 9.2
1-Rawhide Kid, his horse Apache & sidekick Randy begin; Wyatt Earp app.; #1 was not code approved; Maneely splash pg.	290	580	870	1856	3178	4500
2	68	136	204	435	743	1050
3-5	45	90	135	284	480	675
6-10: 7-Williamson-a (4 pgs.)	36	72	108	214	347	480
11-16: 16-Torres-a	31	62	93	182	296	410
17-Origin by Jack Kirby; Kirby-a begins	360	720	1080	2520	4410	6300
18-21,24-30	27	54	81	189	420	650
22-Monster-c/story by Kirby/Ayers	38	76	114	281	628	975
23-Origin retold by Jack Kirby	54	108	162	432	966	1500
31-35,40: 31,32-Kirby-a. 33-35-Davis-a. 34-Kirby-a. 35-Intro & death of The Raven. 40-Two-Gun Kid x-over.	14	28	42	98	217	335
36,37,39,41,42-No Kirby. 42-1st Larry Lieber issue	11	22	33	76	163	250
38-Red Raven-c/story; Kirby-c (2/64); Colan-a	17	34	51	119	265	410
43-Kirby-a (beware: pin-up often missing)	14	28	42	94	207	320
44,46: 44-Toth-a. 46-Doc Holliday-c/s	10	20	30	66	138	210
45-Origin retold, 17 pgs.	13	26	39	91	201	310
47-49,51-60	7	14	21	46	86	125
50-Kid Colt x-over; vs. Rawhide Kid	7	14	21	49	92	135
61-70: 64-Kid Colt story. 66-Two-Gun Kid story. 67-Kid Colt story. 70-Last 12¢ issue	5	10	15	34	60	85
71-78,80-83,85	3	6	9	20	31	42
79,84,86,95: 79-Williamson-a(r). 84,86: Kirby-a. 86-Origin-r; Williamson-r/Ringo Kid #13 (4 pgs.)	3	6	9	21	33	45
87-91: 90-Kid Colt app. 91-Last 15¢ issue	3	6	9	18	28	38
92,93 (52 pg.Giants). 92-Kirby-a	4	8	12	25	40	55
94,96-99	3	6	9	16	24	32
100 (6/72)-Origin retold & expanded	3	6	9	21	33	45
101-120: 115-Last new story	3	6	9	14	19	24
121-151	2	4	6	10	14	18
133,134-(30¢-c variants, limited distribution)(5,7/76)	9	18	27	63	129	185
140,141-(35¢-c variants, limited distribution)(7,9/77)	18	36	54	122	271	420
Special 1(9/71, 25¢, 68 pgs.)-All Kirby/Ayers-r	5	10	15	34	60	85

NOTE: ***Ayers*** *a-13, 14, 16, 29, 37-39, 61.* ***Colan*** *a-5, 35, 37, 38; c-145p, 148p, 149p.* ***Davis*** *a-125r.* ***Everett*** *a-54i, 65, 66, 88, 96i, 148i(r).* ***Gulacy*** *c-147.* ***Heath*** *c-4.* ***G. Kane*** *c-101, 144.* ***Keller*** *a-5, 39, 41, 144r.* ***Kirby*** *a-17-32, 34, 42, 43, 84, 86, 92, 109r, 112r, 116r, 117r, 137r, Spec. 1; c-17-35, 37, 38, 40, 41, 43-47, 137r.* ***Maneely*** *c-1-3, 5, 6, 14.* ***Morisi*** *a-13.* ***Morrow/Williamson*** *r-111.* ***Roussos*** *r-146i, 147i, 149-151i.* ***Severin*** *a-16; c-8, 13.* ***Sutton*** *a-61, 93.* ***Torres*** *a-99r.* ***Tuska*** *a-14.* ***Wildey*** *r-146-151(Outlaw Kid).* ***Williamson*** *r-79, 86, 95.*

RAWHIDE KID
Marvel Comics Group: Aug, 1985 - No. 4, Nov, 1985 (Mini-series)

	GD 2.0	VG 4.0	FN 6.0	VF 8.0	VF/NM 9.0	NM- 9.2
1-4						5.00

RAWHIDE KID
Marvel Comics (MAX): Apr, 2003 - No. 5, June, 2003 ($2.99, limited series)

	GD 2.0	VG 4.0	FN 6.0	VF 8.0	VF/NM 9.0	NM- 9.2
1-John Severin-a/Ron Zimmerman-s; Dave Johnson-c						3.00
2-5: 3-Dodson-c. 4-Darwyn Cooke-c. 5-J. Scott Campbell-c						3.00
Vol. 1: Slap Leather TPB (2003, $12.99) r/#1-5						13.00

RAWHIDE KID (The Sensational Seven)
Marvel Comics: Aug, 2010 - No. 4, Nov, 2010 ($3.99, limited series)

	GD 2.0	VG 4.0	FN 6.0	VF 8.0	VF/NM 9.0	NM- 9.2
1-4-Chaykin-a/Zimmerman-s. 1-Cassaday-c. 2-Dave Johnson-c. 4-Suydam-c						4.00

RAY, THE (See Freedom Fighters & Smash Comics #14)
DC Comics: Feb, 1992 - No. 6, July, 1992 ($1.00, mini-series)

	GD 2.0	VG 4.0	FN 6.0	VF 8.0	VF/NM 9.0	NM- 9.2
1-Sienkiewicz-c; Joe Quesada-a(p) in 1-5						5.00
2-6: 3-6-Quesada-c(p). 6-Quesada layouts only						3.00
...In a Blaze of Power (1994, $12.95)-r/#1-6 w/new Quesada-c						13.00

RAY, THE
DC Comics: May, 1994 - No. 28, Oct, 1996 ($1.75/$1.95/$2.25)

	GD 2.0	VG 4.0	FN 6.0	VF 8.0	VF/NM 9.0	NM- 9.2
1-Quesada-c(p); Superboy app.						3.00
1-($2.95)-Collectors Edition w/diff. Quesada-c; embossed foil-c						4.00
2-24,26-28: 2-Quesada-c(p); Superboy app. 5-(9/94); leads into issue #0						3.00
25-($3.50)-Future Flash (Bart Allen)-c/app; double size						4.00
#0-(10/94) Zero Hour; published between #5 & #6						3.00
Annual 1 ($3.95, 68 pgs.)-Superman app.						4.00

RAY, THE
DC Comics: Feb, 2012 - No. 4, May, 2012 ($2.99, limited series)

	GD 2.0	VG 4.0	FN 6.0	VF 8.0	VF/NM 9.0	NM- 9.2
1-4: 1-Igle-a/Palmiotti & Gray-s; origin of the new Ray; intro. Lucien Gates						3.00

RAY BRADBURY COMICS
Topps Comics: Feb, 1993 - V4#1, June, 1994 ($2.95)

	GD 2.0	VG 4.0	FN 6.0	VF 8.0	VF/NM 9.0	NM- 9.2
1-5-Polybagged w/3 trading cards each. 1-All dinosaur issue; Corben-a; Williamson/Torres/Krenkel-r/Weird Science-Fantasy #25. 3-All dinosaur issue; Steacy painted-c; Stout-a						3.00
Special Edition 1 (1994, $2.95)-The Illustrated Man						3.00
...Special: Tales of Horror #1 ($2.50), ...Trilogy of Terror V3#1 (5/94, $2.50), ...Martian Chronicles V4#1 (6/94, $2.50)-Steranko-c						3.00

NOTE: ***Kelley Jones*** *a-Trilogy of Terror V3#1.* ***Kaluta*** *a-Martian Chronicles V4#1.* ***Kurtzman/Matt Wagner*** *c-2.* ***McKean*** *c-4.* ***Mignola*** *a-4.* ***Wood*** *a-Trilogy of Terror V3#1r.*

RAZORLINE
Marvel Comics: Sept, 1993 (75¢, one-shot)

	GD 2.0	VG 4.0	FN 6.0	VF 8.0	VF/NM 9.0	NM- 9.2
1-Clive Barker super-heroes: Ectokid, Hokum & Hex, Hyperkind & Saint Sinner						3.00

RAZOR'S EDGE, THE
DC Comics (WildStorm): Dec, 2004 - No. 5, Apr, 2005 ($2.95)

	GD 2.0	VG 4.0	FN 6.0	VF 8.0	VF/NM 9.0	NM- 9.2
1-5-Warblade; Bisley-c/a; Ridley-s						3.00

REAL ADVENTURE COMICS (Action Adventure #2 on)
Gillmor Magazines: Apr, 1955

	GD 2.0	VG 4.0	FN 6.0	VF 8.0	VF/NM 9.0	NM- 9.2
1	14	28	42	81	118	155

REAL ADVENTURES OF JONNY QUEST, THE
Dark Horse Comics: Sept, 1996 - No. 12, Sept, 1997 ($2.95)

	GD 2.0	VG 4.0	FN 6.0	VF 8.0	VF/NM 9.0	NM- 9.2
1-12						3.00

REAL CLUE CRIME STORIES (Formerly Clue Comics)
Hillman Periodicals: V2#4, June, 1947 - V8#3, May, 1953

	GD 2.0	VG 4.0	FN 6.0	VF 8.0	VF/NM 9.0	NM- 9.2
V2#4(#1)-S&K c/a(3); Dan Barry-a	54	108	162	343	574	825
5-7-S&K c/a(3-4). 7-Iron Lady app.	41	82	123	256	428	600
8-12	15	30	45	90	140	190
V3#1-8,10-12, V4#1-3,5-8,11,12	14	28	42	82	121	160
V3#9-Used in **SOTI**, pg. 102	16	32	48	92	144	195
V4#4-S&K-a	16	32	48	94	147	200
V4#9,10-Krigstein-a	15	30	45	83	124	165
V5#1-5,7,8,10,12	12	24	36	67	94	120
6,9,11(1/54)-Krigstein-a	13	26	39	72	101	130
V6#1-5,8,9,11	10	20	30	58	79	100
6,7,10,12-Krigstein-a. 10-Bondage-c	13	26	39	72	101	130
V7#1-3,5-11, V8#1-3: V7#6-1 pg. Frazetta ad "Prayer" - 1st app.?	12	24	36	67	94	120
4,12-Krigstein-a	13	26	39	72	101	130

NOTE: ***Barry*** *a-9, 10; c-V2#8.* ***Briefer*** *a-V6#6.* ***Fuje*** *a- V2#7(2), 8, 11.* ***Infantino*** *a-V2#8; c-V2#11.* ***Lawrence*** *a-V3#8, V5#7.* ***Powell*** *a-V4#11, 12. V5#4, 5, 7 are 68 pgs.*

REAL EXPERIENCES (Formerly Tiny Tessie)
Atlas Comics (20CC): No. 25, Jan, 1950

	GD 2.0	VG 4.0	FN 6.0	VF 8.0	VF/NM 9.0	NM- 9.2
25-Virginia Mayo photo-c from movie "Red Light"	18	36	54	103	162	220

REAL FACT COMICS
National Periodical Publications: Mar-Apr, 1946 - No. 21, July-Aug, 1949

	GD 2.0	VG 4.0	FN 6.0	VF 8.0	VF/NM 9.0	NM- 9.2
1-S&K-c/a; Harry Houdini story; Just Imagine begins (not by Finlay); Fred Ray-a	52	104	156	328	552	775
2-S&K-a; Rin-Tin-Tin & P. T. Barnum stories	15	30	45	94	147	200
3-H.G. Wells, Lon Chaney stories; early DC letter column (New Fun Comics #3 from 1935 may be the 1st)	26	52	78	154	252	350
4-Virgil Finlay-a on 'Just Imagine' begins, ends #12 (2 pgs. each); Jimmy Stewart & Jack London stories; Joe DiMaggio 1 pg. biography	29	58	87	172	281	390
5-Batman/Robin-c taken from cover of Batman #9; 5 pg. story about creation of Batman & Robin; Tom Mix story	158	316	474	1011	1731	2450
6-Origin & 1st app. Tommy Tomorrow by Weisinger and Sherman (1-2/47); Flag-c; 1st writing by Harlan Ellison (letter column, non-professional); "First Man to Reach Mars" epic-c/story	84	168	252	538	919	1300
7-(No. 6 on inside)-Roussos-a; D. Fairbanks sty.	15	30	45	94	147	200
8-2nd app. Tommy Tomorrow by Finlay (5-6/47)	48	96	144	302	514	725
9-S&K-a; Glenn Miller, Indianapolis 500 stories	21	42	63	122	199	275
10-Vigilante by Meskin (based on movie serial); 4 pg. Finlay s/f story	21	42	63	122	199	275
11,12: 11-Annie Oakley, G-Men stories; Kinstler-a	14	28	42	82	121	160
13-Dale Evans and Tommy Tomorrow-c/stories	37	74	111	222	361	500
14,17,18: 14-Will Rogers story	14	28	42	80	115	150
15-Nuclear explosion part-c ("Last War on Earth" story); Clyde Beatty story	17	34	51	100	158	215
16-Tommy Tomorrow app.; 1st Planeteers?	36	72	108	211	343	475
19-Sir Arthur Conan Doyle story	15	30	45	85	130	175
20-Kubert-a, 4 pgs; Daniel Boone story	15	30	45	88	137	185
21-Kubert-a, 2 pgs; Kit Carson story	14	28	42	80	115	150

Ashcan (2/46) nn-Not distributed to newsstands, only for in house use. Covers were produced, but not the rest of the book. A copy sold in 2008 for $500.
NOTE: ***Barry*** *c-16.* ***Virgil Finlay*** *c-6, 8.* ***Meskin*** *c-10.* ***Roussos*** *a-1-4, 6.*

REAL FUNNIES
Nedor Publishing Co.: Jan, 1943 - No. 3, June, 1943

	GD 2.0	VG 4.0	FN 6.0	VF 8.0	VF/NM 9.0	NM- 9.2
1-Funny animal, humor; Black Terrier app. (clone of The Black Terror)	37	74	111	222	361	500
2,3	19	38	57	111	176	240

REAL GHOSTBUSTERS, THE (Also see Slimer)
Now Comics: Aug, 1988 - No. 28, Feb, 1991 ($1.75/$1.95)

	GD 2.0	VG 4.0	FN 6.0	VF 8.0	VF/NM 9.0	NM- 9.2
1-Based on Ghostbusters movie	4	8	12	23	37	50
2	2	4	6	9	12	15
3-28						5.00

REAL HEROES
Image Comics: Mar, 2014 - No. 4, Nov, 2014 ($3.99)

	GD 2.0	VG 4.0	FN 6.0	VF 8.0	VF/NM 9.0	NM- 9.2
1-3-Bryan Hitch-s/a						4.00
4-($4.99)						5.00

REAL HEROES COMICS
Parents' Magazine Institute: Sept, 1941 - No. 16, Oct, 1946

	GD 2.0	VG 4.0	FN 6.0	VF 8.0	VF/NM 9.0	NM- 9.2
1-Roosevelt-c/story	36	72	108	211	343	475
2-J. Edgar Hoover-c/story	15	30	45	83	124	185
3-5,7-10: 4-Churchill, Roosevelt stories	14	28	42	78	112	145
6-Lou Gehrig-c/story	20	40	60	115	190	260
11-16: 13-Kiefer-a	10	20	30	54	72	90

REALISTIC ROMANCES
Realistic Comics/Avon Periodicals: July-Aug, 1951 - No. 17, Aug-Sept, 1954 (No #9-14)

	GD 2.0	VG 4.0	FN 6.0	VF 8.0	VF/NM 9.0	NM- 9.2
1-Kinstler-a; c-/Avon paperback #211	47	94	141	296	498	700
2	25	50	75	150	245	340
3,4	24	48	72	140	230	320
5,8-Kinstler-a	24	48	72	142	234	325
6-c-/Diversey Prize Novels #6; Kinstler-a	24	48	72	144	237	330
7-Evans-a?; c-/Avon paperback #360	26	52	78	154	252	350
15,17: 17-Kinstler-c	22	44	66	132	216	300
16-Kinstler marijuana story-r/Romantic Love #6	24	48	72	142	234	325
I.W. Reprint #1,8,9: #1-r/Realistic Romances #4; Astarita-a. 9-r/Women To Love #1	3	6	9	17	26	35

Rawhide Kid (2010) #4 © MAR

Real Heroes #1 © Bryan Hitch

The Realm #12 © Peck & Haun

NOTE: *Astarita a-2-4, 7, 8, 17. Photo c-1, 2. Painted c-3, 4.*

REALITY CHECK
Image Comics: Sept, 2013 - No. 4, Dec, 2013 ($2.99)

	GD 2.0	VG 4.0	FN 6.0	VF 8.0	VF/NM 9.0	NM- 9.2
1-4-Brunswick-s/Bogdanovic-a						3.00

REAL LIFE COMICS
Nedor/Better/Standard Publ./Pictorial Magazine No. 13: Sept, 1941 - No. 59, Sept, 1952

	GD 2.0	VG 4.0	FN 6.0	VF 8.0	VF/NM 9.0	NM- 9.2
1-Uncle Sam-c/story; Daniel Boone story	84	168	252	538	919	1300
2-Woodrow Wilson-c/story	41	82	123	256	428	600
3-Classic Schomburg Hitler-c with "Emperor of Hate" emblazoned in blood behind him. Cover shows world at war, concentration camps and Nazis killing civilians; Hitler 10 pg. bio	1500	300	4500	11,400	20,700	30,000
4,5: 4-Story of American flag "Old Glory"	37	74	111	218	354	490
6-10: 6-Wild Bill Hickok story	30	60	90	177	289	400
11-14,16-20: 17-Albert Einstein story	24	48	72	144	237	330
15-Japanese WWII-c by Schomburg	34	68	102	199	325	450
21-23,25,26,29,30: 29-A-Bomb story. 28-Japanese WWII-c	21	42	63	126	206	285
24-Story of Baseball (Babe Ruth); Japanese WWII-c	32	64	96	188	307	425
27,28: 27-Schomburg A-Bomb-c; story of A-Bomb	29	58	87	172	281	390
31-33,35,36,42-44,48,49: 32-Frank Sinatra story. 49-Baseball issue	18	36	54	105	165	225
34,37-41,45-47: 34-Jimmy Stewart story. 37-Story of motion pictures; Bing Crosby story. 38-Jane Froman story. 39- "1,000,000 A.D." story. 40-Bob Feller. 41-Jimmie Foxx story ("Jimmy" on-c); "Home Run" Baker story. 45-Story of Olympic games; Burl Ives & Kit Carson story. 46-Douglas Fairbanks Jr. & Sr. story. 47-George Gershwin story	19	38	57	111	176	240
50-Frazetta-a (5 pgs.)	33	66	99	194	317	440
51-Jules Verne "Journey to the Moon" by Evans; Severin/Elder-a	23	46	69	138	227	315
52-Frazetta-a (4 pgs.); Severin/Elder-a(2); Evans-a	36	72	108	214	347	480
53-57-Severin/Elder-a. 54-Bat Masterson-c/story	19	38	57	111	176	240
58-Severin/Elder-a(2)	19	38	57	112	179	245
59-1 pg. Frazetta; Severin/Elder-a	19	38	57	112	179	245

NOTE: ***Guardineer** a-40(2), 44. **Meskin** a-52. **Roussos** a-50. **Schomburg** c-1-5, 7, 11, 13-21, 23, 24, 26-28, 30-32-40, 42, 44-50, 54, 55. **Tuska** a-53. Photo-c 5, 6.*

REAL LIFE SECRETS (Real Secrets #2 on)
Ace Periodicals: Sept, 1949 (one-shot)

	GD 2.0	VG 4.0	FN 6.0	VF 8.0	VF/NM 9.0	NM- 9.2
1-Painted-c	21	42	63	122	199	275

REAL LIFE STORY OF FESS PARKER (Magazine)
Dell Publishing Co.: 1955

	GD 2.0	VG 4.0	FN 6.0	VF 8.0	VF/NM 9.0	NM- 9.2
1	9	18	27	59	117	175

REAL LIFE TALES OF SUSPENSE (See Suspense)

REAL LOVE (Formerly Hap Hazard)
Ace Periodicals (A. A. Wyn): No. 25, April, 1949 - No. 76, Nov, 1956

	GD 2.0	VG 4.0	FN 6.0	VF 8.0	VF/NM 9.0	NM- 9.2
25	22	44	66	132	216	300
26	17	34	51	98	154	210
27-L. B. Cole-a	16	32	48	92	144	195
28-35	15	30	45	86	133	180
36-66: 66-Last pre-code (2/55)	14	28	42	84	127	170
67-76	14	28	42	80	115	150

NOTE: *Photo c-50-76. Painted c-46.*

REALM, THE
Arrow Comics/WeeBee Comics #13/Caliber Press #14 on: Feb, 1986 - No. 21, 1991 (B&W)

	GD 2.0	VG 4.0	FN 6.0	VF 8.0	VF/NM 9.0	NM- 9.2
1-3,5-21						3.00
4-1st app. Deadworld (9/86)						4.00
Book 1 ($4.95, B&W)						5.00

REALM, THE
Image Comics: Sept, 2017 - Present ($3.99)

	GD 2.0	VG 4.0	FN 6.0	VF 8.0	VF/NM 9.0	NM- 9.2
1-15-Seth Peck & Jeremy Haun-s/a. 1-Covers by Haun & Tony Moore						4.00

REAL McCOYS, THE (TV)
Dell Publ. Co.: No. 1071, 1-3/60 - 5-7/1962 (All have Walter Brennan photo-c)

	GD 2.0	VG 4.0	FN 6.0	VF 8.0	VF/NM 9.0	NM- 9.2
Four Color 1071,1134-Toth-a in both	9	18	27	62	126	190
Four Color 1193,1265	7	14	21	48	89	130
01-689-207 (5-7/62)	6	12	18	42	79	115

REALM OF KINGS (Also see Guardians of the Galaxy and Nova)
Marvel Comics: Jan, 2010 ($3.99, one-shot)

	GD 2.0	VG 4.0	FN 6.0	VF 8.0	VF/NM 9.0	NM- 9.2
1-Abnett & Lanning-s/Manco & Asrar-a; Guardians of the Galaxy app.	1	3	4	6	8	10

REALM OF KINGS: IMPERIAL GUARD
Marvel Comics: Jan, 2010 - No. 5, May, 2010 ($3.99, limited series)

	GD 2.0	VG 4.0	FN 6.0	VF 8.0	VF/NM 9.0	NM- 9.2
1-5-Abnett & Lanning-s/Walker-a; Starjammers app.						4.00

REALM OF KINGS: INHUMANS
Marvel Comics: Jan, 2010 - No. 5, May, 2010 ($3.99, limited series)

	GD 2.0	VG 4.0	FN 6.0	VF 8.0	VF/NM 9.0	NM- 9.2
1-5-Abnett & Lanning-s/Raimondi-a; Mighty Avengers app.						4.00

REALM OF KINGS: SON OF HULK
Marvel Comics: Apr, 2010 - No. 4, July, 2010 ($3.99, limited series)

	GD 2.0	VG 4.0	FN 6.0	VF 8.0	VF/NM 9.0	NM- 9.2
1-4-Reed-s/Munera-a; leads into Incredible Hulk #609	1	3	4	6	8	10

REALM OF THE CLAW (Also see Mutant Earth as part of a flipbook)
Image Comics: Oct, 2003 - No. 2 ($2.95)

	GD 2.0	VG 4.0	FN 6.0	VF 8.0	VF/NM 9.0	NM- 9.2
0-(7/03, $5.95) Convention Special; cover has gold-foil title logo						6.00
1,2-Two covers by Yardin						3.00
Vol. 1 TPB (2006, $16.99) r/series; concept art & sketch pages						17.00

REAL SCREEN COMICS (#1 titled Real Screen Funnies; TV Screen Cartoons #129-138)
National Periodical Publications: Spring, 1945 - No. 128, May-June, 1959 (#1-40: 52 pgs.)

	GD 2.0	VG 4.0	FN 6.0	VF 8.0	VF/NM 9.0	NM- 9.2
1-The Fox & the Crow, Flippity & Flop, Tito & His Burrito begin	123	246	369	787	1344	1900
2	50	100	150	315	533	750
3-5	32	64	96	188	307	425
6-10 (2-3/47)	21	42	63	122	199	275
11-20 (10-11/48): 13-The Crow x-over in Flippity & Flop	16	32	48	94	147	200
21-30 (6-7/50)	14	28	42	76	108	140
31-50	11	22	33	60	83	105
51-99	10	20	30	54	72	90
100	10	20	30	56	76	95
101-128	8	16	24	44	57	70

REAL SCREEN FUNNIES
DC Comics: Spring 1945

1-Ashcan comic, not distributed to newsstands, only for in-house use. Cover art is Real Screen Funnies #1 with interior being Detective Comics #92. Only ashcan cover to be produced using the regular production first issue art and only using the color yellow. A copy sold in 2008 for $3,000. A FN/VF copy sold for $1314.50 in 2012. A CGC 6.5 copy sold for $1050 in 2018.

REAL SECRETS (Formerly Real Life Secrets)
Ace Periodicals: No. 2, Nov, 1950 - No. 5, May, 1950

	GD 2.0	VG 4.0	FN 6.0	VF 8.0	VF/NM 9.0	NM- 9.2
2-Painted-c	18	36	54	105	165	225
3-5: 3-Photo-c	14	28	42	81	118	155

REAL SPORTS COMICS (All Sports Comics #2 on)
Hillman Periodicals: Oct-Nov, 1948 (52 pgs.)

	GD 2.0	VG 4.0	FN 6.0	VF 8.0	VF/NM 9.0	NM- 9.2
1-Powell-a (12 pgs.)	45	90	135	284	480	675

REAL WAR STORIES
Eclipse Comics: July, 1987; No. 2, Jan, 1991 ($2.00, 52 pgs.)

	GD 2.0	VG 4.0	FN 6.0	VF 8.0	VF/NM 9.0	NM- 9.2
1-Bolland-a(p), Bissette-a, Totleben-a(i); Alan Moore scripts (2nd printing exists, 2/88)						5.00
2-($4.95)						5.00

REAL WESTERN HERO (Formerly Wow #1-69; Western Hero #76 on)
Fawcett Publications: No. 70, Sept, 1948 - No. 75, Feb, 1949 (All 52 pgs.)

	GD 2.0	VG 4.0	FN 6.0	VF 8.0	VF/NM 9.0	NM- 9.2
70(#1)-Tom Mix, Monte Hale, Hopalong Cassidy, Young Falcon begin	22	44	66	132	216	300
71-75: 71-Gabby Hayes begins. 71,72-Captain Tootsie by Beck. 75-Big Bow and Little Arrow app.	15	30	45	85	130	175

NOTE: *Painted/photo c-70-73; painted c-74, 75.*

REAL WEST ROMANCES
Crestwood Publishing Co./Prize Publ.: 4-5/49 - V1#6, 3/50; V2#1, Apr-May, 1950 (All 52 pgs. & photo-c)

	GD 2.0	VG 4.0	FN 6.0	VF 8.0	VF/NM 9.0	NM- 9.2
V1#1-S&K-a(p)	32	64	96	188	307	425
2-Gail Davis and Rocky Shahan photo-c	16	32	48	94	147	200
3-Kirby-a(p) only	17	34	51	98	154	210
4-S&K-a; Whip Wilson, Reno Browne photo-c	21	42	63	122	199	275
5-Audie Murphy, Gale Storm photo-c; S&K-a	20	40	60	114	182	250
6-Produced by S&K, no S&K-a; Robert Preston & Cathy Downs photo-c	14	28	42	81	118	155
V2#1-Kirby-a(p)	14	28	42	81	118	155

NOTE: ***Meskin** a-V1#5, 6. **Severin/Elder** a-V1#3-6, V2#1. **Meskin** a-V1#6. **Leonard Starr** a-1-3. Photo-c V1#1-6, V2#1.*

REALWORLDS :...

GD VG FN VF VF/NM NM-
2.0 4.0 6.0 8.0 9.0 9.2

GD VG FN VF VF/NM NM-
2.0 4.0 6.0 8.0 9.0 9.2

DC Comics: 2000 ($5.95, one-shots, prestige format)

Batman - Marshall Rogers-a/Golden & Sniegoski-s; Justice League of America -Dematteis-s/ Barr-painted art; Superman - Vance-s/García-López & Rubenstein-a; Wonder Woman - Hanson & Neuwirth-s/Sam-a 6.00

REANIMATOR (Based on the 1985 horror movie)
Dynamite Entertainment: 2015 - No. 4, 2015 ($3.99, mini-series)

1-4-Further exploits of Herbert West; Davidsen-s/Valiente-a; four covers on each 4.00

RE-ANIMATOR IN FULL COLOR
Adventure Comics: Oct, 1991 - No. 3, 1992 ($2.95, mini-series)

1-3: Adapts horror movie. 1-Dorman painted-c 3.00

REAP THE WILD WIND (See Cinema Comics Herald)

REAVER
Image Comics (Skybound): Jul, 2019 - No. 11, Sept, 2020 ($3.99)

1-11: 1-Justin Jordan-s/Rebekah Isaacs-a. 7-11-Henrichon-a 4.00

REBEL, THE (TV)(Nick Adams as Johnny Yuma)
Dell Publishing Co.: No. 1076, Feb-Apr, 1960 - No. 1262, Dec-Feb, 1961-62

Four Color 1076 (#1)-Sekowsky-a, photo-c 10 20 30 68 144 220
Four Color 1138 (9-11/60), 1207 (9-11/61), 1262-Photo-c
8 16 24 55 105 155

REBELS (Also see Rebels: These Free And Independent States)
Dark Horse Comics: Apr, 2015 - No. 10, Jan, 2016 ($3.99)

1-Set in Revolutionary War 1775 Vermont; Brian Wood-s/Andrea Mutti-a/Tula Lotay-c 5.00
2-10: 4-General Washington app. 4.00

R.E.B.E.L.S.
DC Comics: Apr, 2009 - No. 28, Jul, 2011 ($2.99)

1-9,12-28: 1-Bedard-s/Clarke-a; Vril Dox returns; Supergirl app.; 2 covers. 15-Starfire app. 19-28-Lobo app. 3.00
10,11-($3.99) Blackest Night x-over; Vril Dox joins the Sinestro Corps 4.00
Annual 1 (12/09, $4.99) Origin of Starro the Conqueror; Despero app. 5.00
...: Sons of Brainiac TPB (2011, $14.99) r/#15-20 15.00
...: Strange Companions TPB (2010, $14.99) r/#7-9 & Annual #1 15.00
...: The Coming of Starro TPB (2010, $17.99) r/#1-6 18.00
...: The Son and the Stars TPB (2010, $17.99) r/#10-14 18.00

R.E.B.E.L.S. '94 (Becomes R.E.B.E.L.S. '95 & R.E.B.E.L.S. '96)
DC Comics: No. 0, Oct, 1994 - No. 17, Mar, 1996 ($1.95/$2.25)

0-17: 8-$2.25-c begins. 15-R.E.B.E.L.S '96 begins. 3.00

REBELS: THESE FREE AND INDEPENDENT STATES
Dark Horse Comics: Mar, 2017 - No. 8, Oct, 2017 ($3.99)

1-8: 1-5-Birth of the U.S. Navy in 1794; Brian Wood-s/Andrea Mutti-a 4.00

REBORN
Image Comics: Oct, 2016 - No. 6, Jun, 2017 ($3.99)

1-Mark Millar-s/Greg Capullo-a 5.00
2-5 4.00
6-($5.99) Bonus sketch pages and creator interview 6.00

RECKLESS (Also see Destroy All Monsters, Follow Me Down, Friend of the Devil & The Ghost in You)
Image Comics: Dec, 2020 ($24.99, HC graphic novel)

HC - Ed Brubaker-s/Sean Phillips-a; 1st book in the Reckless series 25.00

RECKONING WAR: TRIAL OF THE WATCHER
Marvel Comics: May, 2022 ($4.99, one-shot)

1-What if the Watcher never interfered in Fantastic Four #48-50; Slott-s/Rodríguez-a 5.00

RECORD BOOK OF FAMOUS POLICE CASES
St. John Publishing Co.: 1949 (25¢, 132 pgs.)

nn-Kubert-a(3); r/Son of Sinbad; Baker-c 84 168 252 538 919 1300

RED (Inspired the 2010 Bruce Willis movie)
DC Comics (Homage): Sept, 2003 - No. 3, Feb, 2004 ($2.95, limited series)

1-3-Warren Ellis-s/Cully Hamner-a/c 5.00
Red/Tokyo Storm Warning TPB (2004, $14.95) Flip book r/both series 15.00
Red: Eyes Only (2/11, $4.99) comic prequel; Hamner-s/a/c 5.00
Red: Frank (11/10, $3.99) movie prequel; Noveck-s/Masters-a/Hamner & photo-c 4.00
Red: Joe (11/10, $3.99) movie prequel; Wagner-s/Redondo-a/Hamner & photo-c 4.00
Red: Marvin (11/10, $3.99) movie prequel; Hoeber-s/Olmos-a/Hamner & photo-c 4.00
Red: Victoria (11/10, $3.99) movie prequel; Hoeber-s/Hahn-a/Hamner & photo-c 4.00
...: Better R.E.D. Than Dead TPB (2011, $14.99) r/movie prequel issues; sketch-a 15.00

RED ARROW
P. L. Publishing Co.: May-June, 1951 - No. 3, Oct, 1951

1-Bondage-c 19 38 57 111 176 240
2,3 14 28 42 76 108 140

RED ATLANTIS
AfterShock Comics: Nov, 2020 - No. 5, Mar, 2021 ($4.99, limited series)

1-5-Stephanie Phillips-s/Robert Carey-a 5.00

RED BAND COMICS
Enwil Associates: Nov, 1944, No. 2, Jan, 1945 - No. 4, May, 1945

1-Bogeyman-c/intro. (The Spirit swipe) 57 114 171 362 619 875
2-Origin Bogeyman & Santanas; c-reprint/#1 39 78 117 231 378 525
3,4-Captain Wizard app. in both (1st app.); each has identical contents/cover
37 74 111 218 354 490

REDBLADE
Dark Horse Comics: Apr, 1993 - No. 3, July, 1993 ($2.50, mini-series)

1-3: 1-Double gatefold-c 3.00

RED BORDER
AWA Studios: Mar, 2020 - No. 4, Aug, 2020 ($3.99, limited series)

1-4-Jason Starr-s/Will Conrad-a 4.00

RED CIRCLE, THE (Re-introduction of characters from MLJ/Archie publications)
DC Comics: Oct, 2009 ($2.99, series of one-shots)

...Inferno 1 - Hangman app.; Straczynski-s/Greg Scott-a 5.00
...The Hangman 1 - Origin retold; Straczynski-s/Derenick & Sienkiewicz-a 5.00
...The Shield 1 - Origin retold; Straczynski-s/McDaniel-a 5.00
...The Web 1 - Straczynski-s/Robinson-a 5.00

RED CIRCLE COMICS (Also see Blazing Comics & Blue Circle Comics)
Rural Home Publications (Enwil): Jan, 1945 - No. 4, April, 1945

1-The Prankster & Red Riot begin 87 174 261 553 952 1350
2-Starr-a; The Judge (costumed hero) app. 40 80 120 246 411 575
3,4-Starr-c/a. 3-The Prankster not in costume 34 68 102 204 332 460
4-(Dated 4/45)-Leftover covers to #4 were later restapled over early 1950s coverless comics; variations in the coverless comics used are endless; Woman Outlaws, Dorothy Lamour, Crime Does Not Pay, Sabu, Diary Loves, Love Confessions & Young Love V3#3 known
24 48 72 144 237 330

RED CIRCLE SORCERY (Chilling Adventures in Sorcery #1-5)
Red Circle Prod. (Archie): No. 6, Apr, 1974 - No. 11, Feb, 1975 (All 25¢ iss.)

6,8,9,11: 6-Early Chaykin-a. 7-Pino-a. 8-Only app. The Cobra
2 4 6 9 13 16
7-Bruce Jones-a with Wrightson, Kaluta, Jeff Jones 3 6 9 14 19 24
10-Wood-a(i) 2 4 6 10 14 18
NOTE: ***Chaykin** a-6, 10. **McWilliams** a-10(2 & 3 pgs.). **Mooney** a-11p. **Morrow** a-6-8, 9(text illos), 10, 11i; c-6-11. **Thorne** a-8, 10. **Toth** a-8, 9.*

RED DOG (See Night Music #7)

RED DRAGON
Comico: June, 1996 ($2.95)

1-Bisley-c 3.00

RED DRAGON COMICS (1st Series) (Formerly Trail Blazers; see Super Magician V5#7, 8)
Street & Smith Publications: No. 5, Jan, 1943 - No. 9, Jan, 1944

5-Origin Red Rover, the Crimson Crimebuster; Rex King, Man of Adventure, Captain Jack Commando, & The Minute Man begin; text origin Red Dragon; Binder-c
126 252 378 806 1378 1950
6-Origin The Black Crusader & Red Dragon (3/43); 1st story app. Red Dragon & 1st cover (classic-c) 265 530 795 1694 2897 4100
7-Classic Japanese exploding soldier WWII-c 432 864 1296 3154 5577 8000
8-The Red Knight app. 81 162 243 518 884 1250
9-Origin Chuck Magnon, Immortal Man 84 168 252 538 919 1300

RED DRAGON COMICS (2nd Series)(See Super Magician V2#8)
Street & Smith Publications: Nov, 1947 - No. 6, Jan, 1949; No. 7, July, 1949

1-Red Dragon begins; Elliman, Nigel app.; Edd Cartier-c/a
135 270 405 864 1482 2100
2-Cartier-c 68 136 204 435 743 1050
3-1st app. Dr. Neff Ghost Breaker by Powell; Elliman, Nigel app.
58 116 174 371 636 900
4-Cartier c/a 71 142 213 454 777 1100
5-7 41 82 123 256 428 600
NOTE: ***Maneely** a-5, 7. **Powell** a-2-7; c-3, 5, 7.*

RED EAGLE
David McKay Publications: No. 16, Aug, 1938

Feature Books 16 39 78 117 240 395 550

REDEMPTION
AWA Studios: Feb, 2021 - No. 5, Jun, 2021 ($3.99, limited series)

1-5-Christa Faust-s/Mike Deodato Jr.-a; 1-Bonus afterwords from the creators 4.00

REDEYE (See Comics Reading Libraries in the Promotional Comics section)

RED FOX (Formerly Manhunt! #1-14; also see Extra Comics)
Magazine Enterprises: No. 15, 1954

15(A-1 #108)-Undercover Girl story; L.B. Cole-c/a (Red Fox); r-from Manhunt; Powell-a
22 44 66 128 209 290

RED GOBLIN
Marvel Comics: Apr, 2023 - Present ($4.99/$3.99)

1-($4.99) Paknadel-s/Bazaldua-a Norman Osborn app. 5.00
2-($3.99) 4.00

RED GOBLIN: RED DEATH (See Absolute Carnage series)
Marvel Comics: Dec, 2019 ($4.99)

1-Norman Osborn and the Carnage symbiote 5.00

RED GOOSE COMIC SELECTIONS (See Comic Selections)

RED HAWK (See A-1 Comics, Bobby Benson's ..#14-16 & Straight Arrow #2)
Magazine Enterprises: No. 90, 1953

11-(A-1 Comics #90)-Powell-c/a 15 30 45 83 124 165

RED HERRING
DC Comics (WildStorm): Oct, 2009 - No. 6, Mar, 2010 ($2.99, limited series)

1-6-Tischman-s/Bond-a 3.00

RED HOOD (Title changed from Red Hood: Outlaw #50)
DC Comics: No. 51, Jan, 2021 - Present ($3.99)

51,52-Shawn Martinbrough-s/Tony Akins-a 4.00

RED HOOD AND THE OUTLAWS (DC New 52)
DC Comics: Nov, 2011 - No. 40, May, 2015 ($2.99)

1-Jason Todd, Starfire, Roy Harper team; Lobdell-s/Rocafort-a/c
2 4 6 9 13 16
2-4 6.00
5-8 4.00
9-Night of the Owls tie-in; Mr. Freeze vs. Talon 5.00
10-14 3.00
15-(2/13) Death of the Family tie-in; die-cut cover; Joker app. 5.00
16-18: 16,17-Death of the Family tie-in 4.00
19-24,26-40: 24,26,27-Ra's al Ghul app. 30,31-Lobo app. 37-Arsenal's origin 3.00
25-($3.99) Zero Year tie-in; Talia and the Red Hood Gang app.; Haun-a 4.00
#0-(11/12, $2.99) Jason Todd's origin re-told; Joker app. 6.00

Red Circle: The Shield #1 © DC

Red Hood: Outlaw #29 © DC

Red Robin #4 © DC

	GD 2.0	VG 4.0	FN 6.0	VF 8.0	VF/NM 9.0	NM- 9.2

Annual 1 (7/13, $4.99) Takes place between #20 & 21; Green Arrow app.; Barrionuevo-a 5.00
Annual 2 (2/15, $4.99) Christmas-themed; Derenick-a 5.00
...: Futures End 1 (11/14, $2.99, regular-c) Five years later; Lobdell-s/Kolins-a 3.00
...: Futures End 1 (11/14, $3.99, 3-D cover) 4.00

RED HOOD AND THE OUTLAWS (DC Rebirth)(Title changes to Red Hood: Outlaw with #27)
DC Comics: Oct, 2016 - No. 26, Nov, 2018 ($2.99/$3.99)

1-8: 1-Jason Todd, Artemis & Bizarro team; Lobdell-s/Soy-a; Blask Mask app. 3.00
9-24,26-($3.99) 12-Solomon Grundy app. 13-Lex Luthor app. 16,17-Harley Quinn app. 18-The Creeper app. 4.00
25-($4.99) Art by Soy & Hairsine; back-up with Hester-a; leads into Annual 2 5.00
Annual 1 (10/17, $4.99) Nightwing & KGBeast app.; Kirkham-a/c 5.00
Annual 2 (10/18, $4.99) Arsenal app.; Lobdell-s/Henry-a/Rocafort-c 5.00
Annual 3 (9/19, $4.99) Lobdell-s/Pollina-a/Soy-c; leads into Red Hood: Outlaw #37 5.00
...: Rebirth (9/16, $2.99) Jason Todd origin re-told; Batman app. 3.00

RED HOOD / ARSENAL
DC Comics: Aug, 2015 - No. 13, Aug, 2016 ($2.99)

1-13: 1-Jason Todd & Roy Harper team; Lobdell-s/Medri. 3-5-Batman (Gordon) app. 6-13-Joker's Daughter app. 7-"Robin War" tie-in. 13-Bonus flashback 1st meeting 3.00

RED HOOD: OUTLAW (Title changed from Red Hood and the Outlaws)(Becomes Red Hood #51)
DC Comics: No. 27, Dec, 2018 - No. 50, Dec, 2020 ($3.99)

27-49: 27-31,33,34-Lobdell-s/Woods-a. 28,29-Batwoman app. 32-Segovia-a. 48-Joker War tie-in; Punchline app. 4.00
50-($5.99) Duela Dent (Joker's Daughter) app.; Pantalena-a 6.00

RED HOOD: THE LOST DAYS
DC Comics: Aug, 2010 - No. 6, Jan, 2011 ($2.99, limited series)

1-6-The Return of Jason Todd; Winick-s/Raimondi-a/Tucci-c. 6-Joker & Hush app. 4.00
TPB (2011, $14.99) r/#1-6 15.00

RED LANTERNS (DC New 52)
DC Comics: Nov, 2011 - No. 40, May, 2015 ($2.99)

1-34: 1-Milligan-s/Benes-a/c; Atrocitus, Dex-Starr & Bleez app. 6-8,11-Guy Gardner app. 10-Stormwatch app. 13-15-Rise of the Third Army. 17-First Lantern app. 24-Lights Out pt. 4. 28-Flipbook with Green Lantern #28; Supergirl app. 29-Superman app. 3.00
35-40: 35-37-Godhead x-over; Simon Baz app. 3.00
#0-(11/12, $2.99) Origin of Atrocitus, the 1st Red Lantern; Syaf-a 3.00
Annual 1 (9/14, $4.99) Story occurs between #33 & 34; Batman cameo 5.00
...: Futures End 1 (11/14, $2.99, regular-c) Five years later; Soule-s/Calafiore-a 3.00
...: Futures End 1 (11/14, $3.99, 3-D cover) 4.00

RED MASK (Formerly Tim Holt; see Best Comics, Blazing Six-Guns)
Magazine Enterprises No. 42-53/Sussex No. 54 (M.E. on-c): No. 42, June-July, 1954 - No. 53, May, 1956; No. 54, Sept, 1957

	GD	VG	FN	VF	VF/NM	NM-
42-Ghost Rider by Ayers continues, ends #50; Black Phantom continues; 3-D effect c/stories begin	22	44	66	128	209	290
43- 3-D effect-c/stories	20	40	60	114	182	250
44-52: 3-D effect stories only. 47-Last pre-code issue. 50-Last Ghost Rider. 51-The Presto Kid begins by Ayers (1st app.); Presto Kid-c begins; last 3-D effect story. 52-Origin The Presto Kid	18	36	54	105	165	225
53,54-Last Black Phantom; last Presto Kid-c	15	30	45	85	130	175
I.W. Reprint #1 (r-/#52). 2 (nd, r/#51 w/diff.-c). 3, 8 (nd; Kinstler-c); 8-r/Red Mask #52	3	6	9	16	23	30

NOTE: *Ayers art on Ghost Rider & Presto Kid.* ***Bolle*** *art in all (Red Mask); c-43, 44, 49.* ***Guardineer*** *a-52. Black Phantom in #42-44, 47-50, 53, 54.*

REDMASK OF THE RIO GRANDE
AC Comics: 1990 ($2.50, 28 pgs.)(Has photos of movie posters)

1-Bolle-c/a(r); photo inside-c 3.00

RED MENACE
DC Comics (WildStorm): Jan, 2007 - No. 6, Jun, 2007 ($2.99, limited series)

1-6-Ordway-a/c; Bilson, DeMeo & Brody-s 3.00
TPB (2007, $17.99) r/series, sketch pages & variant covers 18.00

RED MOTHER, THE
BOOM! Studios: Dec, 2019 - No. 12, Jan, 2021 ($3.99)

1-12-Jeremy Haun-s/Danny Luckert-a 4.00

RED MOUNTAIN FEATURING QUANTRELL'S RAIDERS (Movie)(Also see Jesse James #28)
Avon Periodicals: 1952

	GD	VG	FN	VF	VF/NM	NM-
nn-Alan Ladd; Kinstler-c	36	72	108	211	343	475

REDNECK
Image Comics (Skybound): Apr, 2017 - Present ($3.99)

1-Donny Cates-s/Lisandro Estherren-a 5.00
2-32 4.00

	GD 2.0	VG 4.0	FN 6.0	VF 8.0	VF/NM 9.0	NM- 9.2

RED ONE
Image Comics: Mar, 2015 - No. 4, Oct, 2016 ($2.99)

1-4-Xavier Dorison-s/Terry Dodson-a/c 3.00

RED PROPHET: THE TALES OF ALVIN MAKER
Dabel Brothers Prods./Marvel Comics (Dabel Brothers): Mar, 2006 - No. 12, Mar, 2008 ($2.99)

1-12-Adaptation of Orson Scott Card novel. 1-Miguel Montenegro-a 3.00
... Vol. 1 HC (2007, $19.99, dustjacket) r/#1-6 20.00
... Vol. 1 SC (2007, $15.99) r/#1-6 16.00
... Vol. 2 HC (2008, $19.99, dustjacket) r/#7-12 20.00

"RED" RABBIT COMICS
Dearfield Comic/J. Charles Laue Publ. Co.: Jan, 1947 - No. 22, Aug-Sep, 1951

	GD	VG	FN	VF	VF/NM	NM-
1	18	36	54	107	169	230
2	13	26	39	72	101	130
3-10	10	20	30	58	79	100
11-17,19-22	9	18	27	52	69	85
18-Flying Saucer-c (1/51)	12	24	36	67	94	120

RED RAVEN COMICS (Human Torch #2 on)(See X-Men #44 & Sub-Mariner #26, 2nd series)
Timely Comics: August, 1940

	GD	VG	FN	VF	VF/NM	NM-
1-Jack Kirby-c (his 1st signed work); origin & 1st app. Red Raven; Comet Pierce & Mercury by Kirby, The Human Top & The Eternal Brain; intro. Magar, the Mystic & only app.	2750	5500	8250	20,900	37,950	55,000

RED ROBIN (Batman: Reborn)
DC Comics: Aug, 2009 - No. 26, Oct, 2011 ($2.99)

1-26-Tim (Drake) Wayne in the Kingdom Come costume; Bachs-a. 1-Two covers 3.00

RED ROCKET 7
Dark Horse Comics: Aug, 1997 - No. 7, June, 1998 ($3.95, square format, limited series)

1-7-Mike Allred-c/s/a 4.00

RED RYDER COMICS (Hi Spot #2)(Movies, radio)(See Crackajack Funnies & Super Book of Comics)
Hawley Publ. No. 1/Dell Publishing Co.(K.K.) No. 3 on: 9/40; No. 3, 8/41 - No. 5, 12/41; No. 6, 4/42 - No. 151, 4-6/57 (Beware of almost identical reprints of #1 made in the late 1980s)

	GD	VG	FN	VF	VF/NM	NM-
1-Red Ryder, his horse Thunder, Little Beaver & his horse Papoose strip reprints begin by Fred Harman; 1st meeting of Red & Little Beaver; Harman line-drawn-c #1-85	265	530	795	1694	2897	4100
3-(Scarce)-Alley Oop, Capt. Easy, Dan Dunn, Freckles & His Friends, King of the Royal Mtd., Myra North strip-r begin	57	114	171	456	1028	1600
4-6: 6-1st Dell issue (4/42)	27	54	81	194	435	675
7-10	23	46	69	161	356	550
11-20	16	32	48	108	239	370
21-32-Last Alley Oop, Dan Dunn, Capt. Easy, Freckles	10	20	30	69	147	225
33-40 (52 pgs.): 40-Photo back-c begin, end #57	9	18	27	58	114	170
41 (52 pgs.)-Rocky Lane photo back-c	9	18	27	60	120	180
42-46 (52 pgs.): 46-Last Red Ryder strip-r	7	14	21	49	92	135
47-53 (52 pgs.): 47-New stories on Red Ryder begin. 49,52-Harmon photo back-c	6	12	18	41	76	110
54-92: 54-73 (36 pgs.). 59-Harmon photo back-c. 73-Last King of the Royal Mtd; strip-r by Jim Gary. 74-85 (52 pgs.)-Harman line-drawn-c. 86-92 (52 pgs.)-Harman painted-c	6	12	18	37	66	95
93-99,101-106: 94-96 (36 pgs.)-Harman painted-c. 97,98,(36 pgs.)-Harman line-drawn-c. 99,101-106 (36 pgs.)-Jim Bannon Photo-c	5	10	15	33	57	80
100 (36 pgs.)-Bannon photo-c	5	10	15	34	60	85
107-118 (52 pgs.)-Harman line-drawn-c	5	10	15	31	53	75
119-129 (52 pgs.): 119-Painted-c begin, not by Harman, end #151	5	10	15	30	50	70
130-151 (36 pgs.): 145-Title change to Red Ryder Ranch Magazine 149-Title change to Red Ryder Ranch Comics	4	8	12	28	47	65
Four Color 916 (7/58)	4	8	12	28	47	65

NOTE: ***Fred Harman*** *a-1-99; c-1-98, 107-118. Don Red Barry, Allan Rocky Lane, Wild Bill Elliott & Jim Bannon starred as Red Ryder in the movies. Robert Blake starred as Little Beaver.*

RED RYDER PAINT BOOK
Whitman Publishing Co.: 1941 (8-1/2x11-1/2", 148 pgs.)

	GD	VG	FN	VF	VF/NM	NM-
nn-Reprints 1940 daily strips	77	154	231	493	847	1200

RED SEAL COMICS (Formerly Carnival Comics, and/or Spotlight Comics?)
Harry 'A' Chesler/Superior Publ. No. 19 on: No. 14, 10/45 - No. 18, 10/46; No. 19, 6/47 - No. 22, 12/47

	GD	VG	FN	VF	VF/NM	NM-
14-The Black Dwarf begins (continued from Spotlight?); Little Nemo app; bondage/hypo-c; Tuska-a	142	284	426	909	1555	2200

	GD 2.0	VG 4.0	FN 6.0	VF 8.0	VF/NM 9.0	NM- 9.2
15-Torture story; funny-c	48	96	144	302	514	725
16-Used in **SOTI**, pg. 181, illo "Outside the forbidden pages of de Sade, you find draining a girl's blood only in children's comics;" drug club story r-later in Crime Reporter #1; Veiled Avenger & Barry Kuda app; Tuska-a; funny-c	74	148	222	470	810	1150
17,18,20: Lady Satan, Yankee Girl & Sky Chief app; 17-Tuska-a	74	148	222	470	810	1150
19-No Black Dwarf (on-c only); Zor, El Tigre app.	74	148	222	470	810	1150
21-Lady Satan & Black Dwarf app.	42	84	126	265	445	625
22-Zor, Rocketman app. (68 pgs.)	42	84	126	265	445	625

RED SHE-HULK (Title continues from Hulk (2008 series) #57)
Marvel Comics: No. 58, Dec, 2012 - No. 67, Sept, 2013 ($2.99)

58-67-Betty Ross character; Pagulayan-a/c. 59,60-Avengers app. 66-Man-Thing app. 3.00

RED SITHA (From Red Sonja)
Dynamite Entertainment: 2022 - No. 4, 2022 ($3.99)

1-4-Andolfo & Blengino-s/Pinti-a; multiple covers 4.00

REDSKIN (Thrilling Indian Stories)(Famous Western Badmen #13 on)
Youthful Magazines: Sept, 1950 - No. 12, Oct, 1952

	GD 2.0	VG 4.0	FN 6.0	VF 8.0	VF/NM 9.0	NM- 9.2
1-Walter Johnson-a (7 pgs.)	26	52	78	154	252	330
2	15	30	45	90	140	190
3-12: 3-Daniel Boone story. 6-Geronimo story	14	28	42	81	118	155

NOTE: ***Walter Johnson** c-3, 4. **Palais** a-11. **Wildey** a-5, 11. Bondage c-6, 12.*

RED SKULL
Marvel Comics: Sept, 2011 - No. 5, Jan, 2012 ($2.99, limited series)

1-5-Pak-s/Colak-a/Aja-c; Red Skull's childhood and origin 5.00

RED SKULL (Secret Wars Battleworld tie-in)
Marvel Comics: Sept, 2015 - No. 3, Nov, 2015 ($3.99, limited series)

1-3-Joshua Williamson-s/Luca Pizzari-a; Crossbones, Magneto & Bucky app. 4.00

RED SONJA (Also see Conan #23, Kull & The Barbarians, Marvel Feature & Savage Sword Of Conan #1)
Marvel Comics Group: 1/77 - No. 15, 5/79; V1#1, 2/83 - V2#2, 3/83; V3#1, 8/83 - V3#4, 2/84; V3#5, 1/85 - V3#13, 5/86

	GD 2.0	VG 4.0	FN 6.0	VF 8.0	VF/NM 9.0	NM- 9.2
1-Created by Robert E. Howard	5	10	15	31	53	75
2-10: 5-Last 30¢ issue	2	4	6	8	11	14
4,5-(35¢-c variants, limited distribution)(7,9/77)	10	20	30	67	141	215
11-15, V2#1,V2#2: 14-Last 35¢ issue	1	3	4	6	8	10
V3#1 ($1.00, 52 pgs.)	1	3	4	6	8	10
V3#2-13: #2-4 ($1.00, 52 pgs.)						5.00
...Special Edition (2021, $3.99) Facsimile reprinting of #1						4.00

NOTE: ***Brunner** c-12-14. **J. Buscema** a(p)-12, 13, 15; c-V#1. **Nebres** a-V3#3i(part). **N. Redondo** a-8i, V3#2i, 3i. **Simonson** a-V3#1. **Thorne** c/a-1-11.*

RED SONJA (Continues in Queen Sonja) (Also see Classic Red Sonja)
Dynamite Entertainment: No. 0, Apr, 2005 - No. 80, 2013 (25¢/$2.99/$3.99)

0-(4/05, 25¢) Greg Land-c/Mel Rubi-a/Oeming & Carey-s 4.00
1-(6/05, $2.99) Five covers by Ross, Linsner, Cassaday, Turner, Rivera; Rubi-a 10.00
2-46-Multiple covers on all. 29-Sonja dies. 34-Sonja reborn 3.00
5-RRP Edition with Red Foil logo and Isanove-a 15.00
50-('10, $4.99) new stories and reprints; Marcos, Chin, Desjardins-a; 4 covers 5.00
51-79-($3.99): 51-56-Geovani-a; multiple covers on each 4.00
80-($4.99) Red Sonja vs. Dracula; bonus interview with Gail Simone 5.00
Annual #1 (2007, $3.50) Oeming-s/Sadowski-a; Red Sonja Comics Chronology 4.00
Annual #2 (2009, $3.99) Gage-s/Marcos-a; wraparound Prado-c & Marcos-c 4.00
Annual #3 (2010, $5.99) Brereton-s/c/a; Batista-a 6.00
Annual #4 (2013, $4.99) Beatty-s/Mena-a 5.00
... Blue (2011, $4.99) Brett-s/Geovani-a; covers by Geovani & Rubi 5.00
... Break the Skin (2011, $4.99) Winslade-c/Van Meter-s/Salazar-a 5.00
... Cover Showcase Vol. 1 (2007, $5.99) gallery of variant covers; Cho sketches 6.00
... Deluge (2011, $4.99) Brereton-s/c; Bolson-a/var-c; reprint from Conan #48 ('74) 5.00
Giant Size Red Sonja #1 (2007, $4.99) Chaykin-c; new story and reprints and pin-ups 5.00
Giant Size Red Sonja #2 (2008, $4.99) Segovia-c; new story and reprints and pin-ups 5.00
... Goes East ($4.99) three covers; Joe Ng-a 5.00
...: Monster Isle ($4.99) two covers; Pablo Marcos-a/Roy Thomas-s 5.00
... One More Day ($4.99) two covers; Liam Sharp-a 5.00
... Raven ('12, $4.99) Antonio-a/Martin-c; bonus pin-up gallery 5.00
...: Revenge of the Gods 1-5 (2011 - No. 5, 2011, $3.99) Sampare-a/Lieberman-s 4.00
... Vacant Shell ($4.99) two covers; Remender-s/Renaud-a 5.00
...: Wrath of the Gods 1-5 (2010 - No. 5, 2010, $3.99) Geovani-a 4.00
The Adventures of Red Sonja TPB (2005, $19.99) r/Marvel Feature #1-7 20.00
The Adventures of Red Sonja Vol. 2 TPB (2007, $19.99) r/#1-7 of '77 Marvel series 20.00
... Vol. 1 TPB (2006, $19.99) r/#0-6; gallery of covers and variants; creators interview 20.00
... Vol. 2 Arrowsmith TPB (2007, $19.99) r/#7-12; gallery of covers and variants 20.00
... Vol. 3 The Rise of Gath TPB (2007, $19.99) r/#13-18; gallery of covers and variants 20.00
... Vol. 4 Animals & More TPB (2007, $24.99) r/#19-24; gallery of covers and variants 25.00

RED SONJA (Volume 2)
Dynamite Entertainment: 2013 - No. 18, 2015 ($3.99)

1-18: 1-Gail Simone-s/Walter Geovani-a; six covers. 2-18-Multiple covers 4.00
#0 (2014, $3.99) Simone-s/Salonga-a/Hardman-c 4.00
#100 (2015, $7.99) Five short stories by various incl. Simone, Oeming, Marcos; 5 covers 8.00
#1973 (2015, $7.99) Five short stories by various incl. Simone, Bunn, Thomas & others 8.00
...: and Cub (2014, $4.99) Nancy Collins-s/Fritz Casas-a/J.M. Linsner-c 5.00
...: Berserker (2014, $4.99) Jim Zub-s/Jonathan Lau-a/Jeffrey Cruz-c 5.00
...: Dynamite Edition (2022, $3.99) Reprints #1 (2013) 4.00
...: Sanctuary (2014, $4.99) Mason-s/Salonga-a/Davila-c; includes full script 5.00

RED SONJA (Volume 3)
Dynamite Entertainment: 2016 - No. 6, 2016 ($3.99)

1-6: 1-Marguerite Bennett-s/Aneke-a; multiple covers 4.00

RED SONJA (Volume 4)
Dynamite Entertainment: No. 0, 2016 - No. 25, 2019 ($3.99)

0-(25¢) Sonja transported to present day New York City; Amy Chu-s/Carlos Gomez-a 3.00
1-25-($3.99) Chu-s/Gomez-a in most; multiple covers. 17-HDR-a. 23-Castro-a 4.00
... Halloween Special One-Shot (2018, $4.99) Burnham-s/Garcia-a; Reilly Brown-c 5.00
... Holiday Special One-Shot (2018, $4.99) Chu & Burnham-s/Jamie-a; Romero-c 5.00

RED SONJA (Volume 5) (Also see Killing Red Sonja)
Dynamite Entertainment: 2019 - No. 28, 2021 ($3.99)

1-28: 1-6-Mark Russell-s/Mirko Colak-a; multiple covers. 7-9,13-Bob Q-a. 10-12-Colak-a 4.00
..., Lord of Fools One-Shot (2019, $4.99) Russell-s/Bob Q-a; takes place around #6 5.00
... 1982 (2021, $4.99) Amy Chu-s/Eric Blake-a 5.00
... Valentine's Special (2021, $4.99) Willingham-s/Cafaro-a 5.00

RED SONJA
Dynamite Entertainment: 2021 - No. 12, 2022 ($3.99)

1-12-Andolfo & Blengino-s/Cafaro-a; multiple covers 4.00
..., Fairy Tales ($4.99) Sonja climbs Jack's beanstalk 5.00
... Holiday Special 2021 ($3.99) Andolfo & Blengino-s 4.00
... Valentine's Day Special (2022, $4.99) Chuck Brown-s; Sozomaika main-c 5.00

RED SONJA: AGE OF CHAOS
Dynamite Entertainment: 2020 - No. 6, 2020 ($3.99, limited series)

1-6-Erik Burnham-s/Jonathan Lau-a; Evil Ernie, Purgatori app.; multiple covers 4.00

RED SONJA AND VAMPIRELLA MEET BETTY AND VERONICA
Dynamite Entertainment: 2019 - No. 12, 2020 ($3.99)

1-12: 1-8,10,11-Amy Chu-s/Maria Sanapo-a; multiple covers. 6-11-Draculina app. 9-Parent-a 4.00

RED SONJA: ATLANTIS RISES
Dynamite Entertainment: 2012 - No. 4, 2012 ($3.99, limited series)

1-4-Lieberman-s/Dunbar-a/Parrillo-c 4.00

RED SONJA: BIRTH OF THE SHE-DEVIL
Dynamite Entertainment: 2019 - No. 4, 2019 ($3.99, limited series)

1-4-Luke Lieberman-s/Sergio Davila-a 4.00

RED SONJA BLACK WHITE RED
Dynamite Entertainment: 2021 - No. 8, 2022 ($3.99, B&W&Red)

1-8-Short story anthology by various; multiple covers 4.00

RED SONJA/CLAW: THE DEVIL'S HANDS (See Claw the Unconquered)
DC Comics (WildStorm)/Dynamite Ent.: May, 2006 - No. 4, Aug, 2006 ($2.99, limited series)

1-4-Covers by Jim Lee & Dell'Otto; Andy Smith-a 1-Alex Ross var-c. 2-Dell'Otto var-c. 3-Bermejo var-c. 4-Andy Smith var-c 3.00
TPB (2007, $12.99) r/#1-4; cover gallery 13.00

RED SONJA/ CONAN
Dynamite Entertainment: 2015 - No. 4, 2015 ($3.99, limited series)

1-4-Gischler-s/Castro-a; multiple covers 4.00

RED SONJA HELL SONJA
Dynamite Entertainment: 2022 - Present ($3.99, limited series)

1-3-Jordan Clark-s/Miriana Piglia-a; multiple covers 4.00

RED SONJA: SCAVENGER HUNT
Marvel Comics: Dec, 1995 ($2.95, one-shot)

1 4.00

RED SONJA/ TARZAN
Dynamite Entertainment: 2018 - No. 6, 2018 ($3.99, limited series)

1-6-Simone-s/Geovani-a; multiple covers 4.00

RED SONJA: THE BLACK TOWER
Dynamite Entertainment: 2014 - No. 4, 2015 ($3.99, limited series)

1-4-Tieri-s/Razek-a/Conner-c 4.00

RED SONJA: THE MOVIE
Marvel Comics Group: Nov, 1985 - No. 2, Dec, 1985 (Limited series)

1,2-Movie adapt-r/Marvel Super Spec. #38 4.00

RED SONJA: THE PRICE OF BLOOD
Dynamite Entertainment: 2020 - No. 3, 2021 ($3.99, limited series)

1-3-Lieberman-s/Geovani-a; multiple covers 4.00

RED SONJA: THE SUPERPOWERS
Dynamite Entertainment: 2020 - No. 5, 2021 ($3.99, limited series)

1-5-Abnett-s/Lau-a; multiple covers; Captain Future, Vana, Mr. Raven & The Sword app. 4.00

RED SONJA: UNCHAINED
Dynamite Entertainment: 2013 - No. 4, 2013 ($3.99, limited series)

1-4-Follows the Red Sonja: Blue one-shot; Jadsen-a 4.00

RED SONJA: VULTURE'S CIRCLE
Dynamite Entertainment: 2015 - No. 5, 2015 ($3.99, limited series)

1-5-Collins & Lieberman-s/Casas-a; three covers on each 4.00

RED SONJA VS. THULSA DOOM
Dynamite Entertainment: 2005 - No. 4, 2006 ($3.50)

1-4-Conrad-a; Conrad & Dell'Otto covers 3.50
..., Volume 1 TPB (2006, $14.99) r/series; cover gallery 15.00

RED STAR, THE
Image Comics/Archangel Studios: June, 2000 - No. 9, June, 2002 ($2.95)

1-Christian Gossett-s/a(p) 4.00
2-9: 9-Beck-c 3.00
#(7.5) Reprints Wizard #1/2 story with new pages 3.00
Annual 1 (Archangel Studios, 11/02, $3.50) "Run Makita Run" 4.00
TPB (4/01, $24.95, 9x12") oversized r/#1-4; intro. by Bendis 25.00
Nokgorka TPB (8/02, $24.95, 9x12") oversized r/#6-9; w/sketch pages 25.00
Wizard 1/2 (mail order) 10.00

RED STAR, THE (Volume 2)
CrossGen #1,2/Archangel Studios #3 on: Feb, 2003 - No. 5, July, 2004 ($2.95/$2.99)

1-5-Christian Gossett-s/a(p) 3.00
Prison of Souls TPB (8/04, $24.95, 9x12") oversized r/#1-5; w/sketch pages 25.00

RED STAR, THE: SWORD OF LIES
Archangel Studios: Aug, 2006 ($4.50)

1-Christian Gossett-s/a(p); origin of the Red Star team 4.50

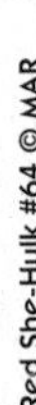
Red She-Hulk #64 © MAR

Red Sonja V2 #14 © RS LLC

Reggie and Me V2 #3 © ACP

GD 2.0 | VG 4.0 | FN 6.0 | VF 8.0 | VF/NM 9.0 | NM- 9.2

RED TEAM
Dynamite Entertainment: 2013 - No. 7, 2014 ($3.99)

1-7: 1-Ennis-s/Cermak-a; covers by Chaykin & Sook 4.00

RED TEAM, VOLUME 2: DOUBLE TAP, CENTER MASS
Dynamite Entertainment: 2016 - No. 9, 2017 ($3.99)

1-8: 1-Ennis-s/Cermak-a/Panosian-c 4.00
9-($4.99) 5.00

RED THORN
DC Comics (Vertigo): Jan, 2016 - No. 13, Feb, 2017 ($3.99)

1-13: 1-6-David Baillie-s/Meghan Hetrick-a. 7-Steve Pugh-a 4.00

RED TORNADO (See All-American #20 & Justice League of America #64)
DC Comics: July, 1985 - No. 4, Oct, 1985 (Limited series)

1-4: Kurt Busiek scripts in all. 1-3-Superman & Batman cameos 4.00

RED TORNADO
DC Comics: Nov, 2009 - No. 6, Apr, 2010 ($2.99, limited series)

1-6: 1-3-Benes-c. 5,6-Vixen app. 3.00
...: Family Reunion TPB (2010, $17.99) r/#1-6 18.00

RED WARRIOR
Marvel/Atlas Comics (TCI): Jan, 1951 - No. 6, Dec, 1951

	GD	VG	FN	VF	VF/NM	NM-
1-Red Warrior & his horse White Wing; Tuska-a	22	44	66	132	216	300
2-Tuska-c	13	26	39	74	105	135
3-6: 4-Origin White Wing. 6-Maneely-c	11	22	33	62	86	110

RED, WHITE & BLUE COMICS
DC Comics: 1941

nn - Ashcan comic, not distributed to newsstands, only for in-house use. Cover art is All-American Comics #20 with interior being Flash Comics #17 (no known sales)

RED WING
Image Comics: Jul, 2011 - No. 4, Oct, 2011 ($3.50, limited series)

1-4-Hickman-s/Pitarra-a 3.50

RED WOLF (See Avengers #80 & Marvel Spotlight #1)
Marvel Comics Group: May, 1972 - No. 9, Sept, 1973

	GD	VG	FN	VF	VF/NM	NM-
1-(Western hero); Gil Kane/Severin-c; Shores-a	5	10	15	33	57	80
2-9: 2-Kane-c; Shores-a. 6-Tuska-r in back-up. 7-Red Wolf as super hero begins. 9-Origin sidekick, Lobo (wolf)	3	6	9	16	23	30

RED WOLF (From the Secret Wars tie-in series 1872)
Marvel Comics: Feb, 2016 - No. 6, Jul, 2016 ($3.99)

1-6: 1-Edmondson-s/Talajic-a. 2-Red Wolf in the present 4.00

RED ZONE
Artists, Writers & Artisans: Mar, 2023 - No. 4 ($3.99, limited series)

1-Cullen Bunn-s/Mike Deodato Jr.-a 4.00

REESE'S PIECES
Eclipse Comics: Oct, 1985 - No.2, Oct, 1985 ($1.75, Baxter paper)

1,2-B&W-r in color 3.00

REFORM SCHOOL GIRL!
Realistic Comics: 1951

	GD	VG	FN	VF	VF/NM	NM-
nn-Used in **SOTI**, pg. 358, & cover ill. with caption "Comic books are supposed to be like fairy tales"; classic photo-c	1500	3000	4500	11,400	20,700	30,000

(Prices vary widely on this book)

NOTE: *The cover and title originated from a digest-sized book published by Diversey Publishing Co. of Chicago in 1948. The original book "House of Fury", Doubleday, came out in 1941. The girl's real name which appears on the cover of the digest and comic is Marty Collins, Canadian model and ice skating star who posed for this special color photograph for the Diversey novel.*

REFRIGERATOR FULL OF HEADS (Also see Basketful of Heads)
DC Comics (Black Label)(Hill House Comics): Dec, 2021 - No. 6, Jun, 2022 ($3.99)

1-6-Rio Youers-s/Tow Fowler-a 4.00

REFUSE X LAST RESORTS
Bad Idea: Nov, 2021 ($9.99, one-shot)

	GD	VG	FN	VF	VF/NM	NM-
1-Kindt-s/Sauvage-a; Russell-s/Pollina-a	1	3	4	6	8	10

REGARDING THE MATTER OF OSWALD'S BODY
BOOM! Studios: Nov, 2021 - No. 5, Mar, 2022 ($3.99, limited series)

1-5-Cantwell-s/Casalanguida-a 4.00

REGENTS ILLUSTRATED CLASSICS
Prentice Hall Regents, Englewood Cliffs, NJ 07632: 1981 (Plus more recent reprintings) (48 pgs., B&W-a with 14 pgs. of teaching helps)

NOTE: *This series contains Classics Ill. art, and was produced from the same illegal source as* ***Cassette Books.*** *But when Twin Circle sued to stop the sale of the Cassette Books, they decided to permit this series to continue. This series was produced as a teaching aid. The 20 title series is divided into four levels based upon number of basic words used therein. There is also a teacher's manual for each level. All of the titles are still available from the publisher for about $5 each retail. The number to call for mail order purchases is (201)767-5937. Almost all of the issues have new covers taken from some interior art panel. Here is a list of the series by Regents ident. no. and the Classics Ill. counterpart.*

16770(Cl#24-A2)18333(Cl#3-A2)21668(Cl#13-A2)32224(Cl#21)33051(Cl#26)35788(Cl#84)37153(Cl#16)44460(Cl#19-A2)44808(Cl#18-A2)52395(Cl#4-A2)58627(Cl#5-A2)60067(Cl#30)68405(Cl#23A1)70302(Cl#29)78192(Cl#7-A2)78193(Cl#10-A2)79679(Cl#85)92046(Cl#1-A2)93062(Cl#64)93512(Cl#25)

RE: GEX
Awesome-Hyperwerks: Jul, 1998 - No. 0, Dec, 1998; ($2.50)

Preview (7/98) Wizard Con Edition 3.00
0-(12/98) Loeb-s/Liefeld-a/Pat Lee-c, 1-(9/98) Loeb-s/Liefeld-a/c 3.00

REGGIE (Formerly Archie's Rival...; Reggie & Me #19 on)
Archie Publications: No. 15, Sept, 1963 - No. 18, Nov, 1965

	GD	VG	FN	VF	VF/NM	NM-
15(9/63), 16(10/64), 17(8/65), 18(11/65)	6	12	18	37	66	95

NOTE: *Cover title No. 15 & 16 is Archie's Rival Reggie.*

REGGIE AND ME (Formerly Reggie)
Archie Publ.: No. 19, Aug, 1966 - No. 126, Sept, 1980 (No. 50-68: 52 pgs.)

	GD	VG	FN	VF	VF/NM	NM-
19-Evilheart app.	4	8	12	28	47	65
20-23-Evilheart app.; with Pureheart #22	3	6	9	21	33	45
24-40(3/70)	3	6	9	16	23	30
41-49(7/71)	2	4	6	13	18	22
50(9/71)-68 (1/74, 52 pgs.)	3	6	9	14	20	26
69-99	2	4	6	8	10	12
100(10/77)	2	4	6	9	12	15
101-126	1	2	3	5	7	9

REGGIE AND ME (Volume 2)
Archie Comic Publications: Jan, 2017 - No. 5, ($3.99)

1-5-Multiple covers and classic back-up reprints in#1,2. Tom DeFalco-s/Sandy Jarrell-a 4.00

REGGIE'S JOKES (See Reggie's Wise Guy Jokes)

REGGIE'S REVENGE!
Archie Comic Publications, Inc.: Spring, 1994 - No. 3 ($2.00, 52 pgs.) (Published semi-annually)

	GD	VG	FN	VF	VF/NM	NM-
1-Bound-in pull-out poster	2	4	6	8	10	12
2,3						5.00

REGGIE'S WISE GUY JOKES
Archie Publications: Aug, 1968 - No. 55, 1980 (#5-28 are Giants)

	GD	VG	FN	VF	VF/NM	NM-
1	5	10	15	35	63	90
2-4	3	6	9	15	22	28
5-16 (1/71)(68 pg. Giants)	3	6	9	17	26	35
17-28 (52 pg. Giants)	2	4	6	13	18	22
29-40(1/77)	1	3	4	6	8	10
41-55	1	2	3	5	6	8

REGISTERED NURSE
Charlton Comics: Summer, 1963

	GD	VG	FN	VF	VF/NM	NM-
1-r/Nurse Betsy Crane & Cynthia Doyle	5	10	15	30	50	70

REG'LAR FELLERS
Visual Editions (Standard): No. 5, Nov, 1947 - No. 6, Mar, 1948

	GD	VG	FN	VF	VF/NM	NM-
5,6	11	22	33	64	90	115

REG'LAR FELLERS HEROIC (See Heroic Comics)

REGRESSION
Image Comics: May, 2017 - No. 15, Jan, 2019 ($3.99)

1-15-Bunn-s/Luckert-a 4.00

REGULAR SHOW (Based on Cartoon Network series)
Boom Entertainment (kaBOOM!): Apr, 2013 - No. 40, Oct, 2016 ($3.99)

1-40-Multiple covers on all 4.00
2014 Annual 1 (6/14, $4.99) Four short stories by various; three covers 5.00
2015 Special 1 (3/15, $4.99) Four short stories by various; two covers 5.00
2017 Special 1 (4/17, $7.99) Six short stories by various; two covers 8.00
2018 Special 1 (2/18, $7.99) Four short stories; McCreery-s; art by various 8.00

REGULAR SHOW: SKIPS (Based on Cartoon Network series)
Boom Entertainment (kaBOOM!): Nov, 2013 - No. 6, Apr, 2014 ($3.99)

1-6-Mad Rupert-s/a; multiple covers on all 4.00

REGULAR SHOW: 25 YEARS LATER (Based on Cartoon Network series)
Boom Entertainment (kaBOOM!): Jun, 2018 - No. 6, Nov, 2018 ($3.99)

1-6-Christopher Hastings-s/Anna Johnstone-a; multiple covers on all 4.00

REID FLEMING, WORLD'S TOUGHEST MILKMAN

GD 2.0 | VG 4.0 | FN 6.0 | VF 8.0 | VF/NM 9.0 | NM- 9.2

Eclipse Comics/ Deep Sea Comics: 1980; 8/86; V2#1, 12/86 - V2#3, 12/88; V2#4, 11/89; V2#5, 11/90 - V2#9, 4/98 (B&W)
1-(1980, self-published) David Boswell-s/a 5.00
1-2nd, 4th & 5th printings ($2.50); (3rd print, large size, 8/86, $2.50) 3.00
V2#1 (10/86, regular size, $2.00), 1-2nd print, 3rd print ($2.00, 2/89) 3.00
2-9 , V2#2-2nd & 3rd printings, V2#4-2nd printing, V2#5 ($2.00), V2#6 (Deep Sea, r/V2#5)
7-9-New stories 3.00

REIGN IN HELL
DC Comics: Sept, 2008 - No. 8, Apr, 2009 ($3.50, limited series)
1-8-Neron, Shadowpact app.; Giffen-s; Dr. Occult back-up w/Segovia-a. 1-Two covers 3.50
TPB (2009, $19.99) r/#1-8 20.00

REIGN OF THE ZODIAC
DC Comics: Oct, 2003 - No. 8, May, 2004 ($2.75)
1-8: 1-6,8-Giffen-s/Doran-a/Harris-c. 7-Byrd-a 3.00

RELATIVE HEROES
DC Comics: Mar, 2000 - No. 6, Aug, 2000 ($2.50, limited series)
1-6-Grayson-s/Guichet & Sowd-a. 6-Superman-c/app. 3.00

RELAY
AfterShock Comics: Jul, 2018 - No. 5, Apr, 2019 ($3.99, limited series)
1-5-Zac Thompson-s/Andy Clarke-a 4.00
#0 (Free Comic Book Day, 5/18, giveaway) Thompson-s/Clarke-a 3.00

RELOAD
DC Comics (Homage): May, 2003 - No. 3, Sept, 2003 ($2.95, limited series)
1-3-Warren Ellis-s/Paul Gulacy & Jimmy Palmiotti-a 3.00
.../Mek TPB (2004, $14.95, flip book) r/Reload #1-3 & Mek #1-3 15.00

RELUCTANT DRAGON, THE (Walt Disney's...)
Dell Publishing Co.: No. 13, 1940
Four Color 13-Contains 2 pgs. of photos from film; 2 pg. foreword to Fantasia by Leopold Stokowski; Donald Duck, Goofy, Baby Weems & Mickey Mouse (as the Sorcerer's Apprentice) app. 232 464 696 1485 2543 3600

REMAINS
IDW Publishing: May, 2004 - No. 5, Sept, 2004 ($3.99)
1-5-Steve Niles-s/Kieron Dwyer-a 4.00

REMARKABLE WORLDS OF PROFESSOR PHINEAS B. FUDDLE, THE
DC Comics (Paradox Press): 2000 - No. 4, 2000 ($5.95, limited series)
1-4-Boaz Yakin-s/Erez Yakin-a 6.00
TPB (2001, $19.95) r/series 20.00

REMEMBER PEARL HARBOR
Street & Smith Publications: 1942 (68 pgs.) (Illustrated story of the battle)
nn-Uncle Sam-c; Jack Binder-a 113 226 339 718 1234 1750

REN & STIMPY SHOW, THE (TV) (Nickelodeon cartoon characters)
Marvel Comics: Dec, 1992 - No. 44, July, 1996 ($1.75/$1.95)
1-($2.25)-Polybagged w/scratch & sniff Ren or Stimpy air fowler (equal numbers of each were made) 2 4 6 11 16 20
1-2nd & 3rd printing; different dialogue on-c 4.00
2-6: 4-Muddy Mudskipper back-up. 5-Bill Wray painted-c. 6-Spider-Man vs. Powdered Toast Man 5.00
7-17: 12-1st solo back-up story w/Tank & Brenner 4.00
18-44: 18-Powered Toast Man app. 4.00
25 ($2.95) Deluxe edition w/die cut cover 5.00
...Don't Try This at Home (3/94, $12.95, TPB)-r/#9-12 13.00
...Eenteractive Special ('95, $2.95) 6.00
...Holiday Special 1994 (2/95, $2.95, 52 pgs.) 1 2 3 5 6 8
...Mini Comic (1995) 1 2 3 5 6 8
...Pick of the Litter nn (1993, $12.95, TPB)-r/#1-4 13.00
...Radio Daze (11/95, $1.95) 6.00
...Running Joke nn (1993, $12.95, TPB)-r/#1-4 plus new-a 13.00
...Seeck Little Monkeys (1/95, $12.95)-r/#17-20 13.00
...Special 2 (7/94, $2.95, 52 pgs.), ...Special 3 (10/94, $2.95, 52 pgs.)-Choose adventure, ...Special: Around the World in a Daze ($2.95), ...Special: Four Swerks (1/95, $2.95, 52 pgs.)-FF #1 cover swipe; cover reads "Four Swerks w/5 pg. coloring book.", ...Special: Powdered Toast Man 1 (4/94, $2.95, 52 pgs.), ...Special: Powdered Toast Man's Cereal Serial (4/95, $2.95), ...Special: Sports (10/95, $2.95) 6.00
...Tastes Like Chicken nn (11/93,$12.95,TPB)-r/#5-8 13.00
...Your Pals (1994, $12.95, TPB)-r/#13-16 13.00

RENATO JONES: THE ONE %
Image Comics: May, 2016 - No. 5, Oct, 2016 ($3.99)
1-5-Kaare Andrews-s/a/c 4.00
Renato Jones, Season 2: Freelancer (5/17 - No. 5, 11/17, $3.99) 1-5-Andrews-s/a/c 4.00

RENFIELD
Caliber Press: 1994 - No. 3, 1995 ($2.95, B&W, limited series)
1-3 3.00

RENO BROWNE, HOLLYWOOD'S GREATEST COWGIRL (Formerly Margie Comics; Apache Kid #53 on; also see Western Hearts, Western Life Romances & Western Love)
Marvel Comics (MPC): No. 50, April, 1950 - No. 52, Sept, 1950 (52 pgs.)
50-Reno Browne photo-c on all 36 72 108 211 343 475
51,52 31 62 93 182 296 410

REPLACER, THE
AfterShock Comics: Apr, 2019 ($7.99, one-shot)
1-Zac Thompson-s/Arjuna Susini-a 8.00

REPLICA
AfterShock Comics: Dec, 2015 - No. 5, Apr, 2016 ($3.99)
1-5-Paul Jenkins-s/Andy Clarke-a 4.00

REPRESENT!
DC Comics: Aug, 2021 ($9.99, squarebound, one-shot, printing of digital first stories)
1-Short stories of social change and personal histories; Christian Cooper-s 10.00

REPTIL
Marvel Comics: Jul, 2021 - No. 4, Nov, 2021 ($3.99)
1-4-Terry Blas-s/Enid Balám-a/Paco Medina-c; variant-c on each 4.00

REPTILICUS (Becomes Reptisaurus #3 on)
Charlton Comics: Aug, 1961 - No. 2, Oct, 1961
1 (Movie) 23 46 69 161 356 550
2 11 22 33 77 166 255

REPTISAURUS (Reptilicus #1,2)
Charlton Comics: V2#3, Jan, 1962 - No. 8, Dec, 1962; Summer, 1963
V2#3-8: 3-Flying saucer-c/s. 8-Montes/Bache-c/a 6 12 18 38 69 100
Special Edition 1 (Summer, 1963) 6 12 18 37 66 95

REQUIEM FOR DRACULA
Marvel Comics: Feb, 1993 ($2.00, 52 pgs.)
nn-r/Tomb of Dracula #69,70 by Gene Colan 4.00

RESCUE (Pepper Potts in Iron Man armor)
Marvel Comics: July, 2010 ($3.99, one-shot)
1-DeConnick-s/Mutti-a/Foreman-c 4.00

RESCUERS, THE (See Walt Disney Showcase #40)

RESIDENT ALIEN
Dark Horse Comics: No. 0, Apr, 2012 - No. 3, Jul, 2012 ($3.50, limited series)
0-3-Hogan-s/Parkhouse-a: 0-Reprints chapters from Dark Horse Presents #4-6 3.50

RESIDENT ALIEN: AN ALIEN IN NEW YORK
Dark Horse Comics: Apr, 2018 - No. 4, Jul, 2018 ($3.99, limited series)
1-4-Hogan-s/Parkhouse-a 4.00

RESIDENT ALIEN: THE BOOK OF LOVE
Dark Horse Comics: Nov, 2022 - No. 4, Feb, 2023 ($3.99, limited series)
1-4-Hogan-s/Parkhouse-a 4.00

RESIDENT ALIEN: THE MAN WITH NO NAME
Dark Horse Comics: Sept, 2016 - No. 4, Dec, 2016 ($3.99, limited series)
1-4-Hogan-s/Parkhouse-a 4.00

RESIDENT ALIEN: THE SAM HAIN MYSTERY
Dark Horse Comics: No. 0, Apr, 2015 - No. 3, Jul, 2015 ($3.99, limited series)
0-3-Hogan-s/Parkhouse-a: 0-Reprints chapters from Dark Horse Presents V3 #1-3 4.00

RESIDENT ALIEN: THE SUICIDE BLONDE
Dark Horse Comics: No. 0, Aug, 2013 - No. 3, Nov, 2013 ($3.99, limited series)
0-3-Hogan-s/Parkhouse-a: 0-Reprints chapters from Dark Horse Presents #18-20 4.00

RESIDENT ALIEN: YOUR RIDE'S HERE
Dark Horse Comics: Nov, 2020 - No. 6, May, 2021 ($3.99, limited series)
1-6-Hogan-s/Parkhouse-a 4.00

RESIDENT EVIL (Based on video game)
Image Comics (WildStorm): Mar, 1998 - No. 5 ($4.95, quarterly magazine)
1 6 12 18 37 66 95
2-5 3 6 9 21 33 45
...Code: Veronica 1-4 (2002, $14.95) English reprint of Japanese comics 3 6 9 19 30 40
...Collection One ('99, $14.95, TPB) r/#1-4 5 10 15 31 53 75

RESIDENT EVIL (Volume 2)
DC Comics (WildStorm): May, 2009 - No. 6, Feb, 2011 ($3.99)
1-6: 1,2-Liam Sharpe-a. 1-Two covers 1 3 4 6 8 10
...: Volume 2 TPB (2011, $19.99) r/#1-6 3 6 9 19 30 40

RESIDENT EVIL: FIRE AND ICE
DC Comics (WildStorm): Dec, 2000 - No. 4, May, 2001 ($2.50, limited series)
1-Bermejo-c 2 4 6 8 10 12
2-4-Bermejo-c 6.00
TPB (2009, $24.99) r/#1-4 plus short stories from Resident Evil magazine 3 6 9 19 30 40

RESISTANCE (Based on the video game)
DC Comics (WildStorm): Early Mar, 2009 - No. 6, Jul, 2009 ($3.99, limited series)
1-6-Ramón Pérez-a/C.P. Smith-c 4.00
TPB (2010, $19.99) r/#1-6 20.00

RESISTANCE, THE
DC Comics (WildStorm): Nov, 2002 - No. 8, June, 2003 ($2.95)
1-8-Palmiotti & Gray-s/Santacruz-a 3.00

RESISTANCE, THE
AWA Studios: Mar, 2020 - No. 6, Sept, 2020 ($3.99, limited series)
1-6-Straczynski-s/Deodato Jr.-a 4.00
...: Reborns (1/21, $3.99) Straczynski-s/C.P. Smith-a 4.00

RESISTANCE, THE: UPRISING (Also see Moths)
AWA Studios: Apr, 2021 - No. 6, Sept, 2021 ($3.99, limited series)
1-6-Straczynski-s/C.P. Smith-a 4.00

REST (Milo Ventimiglia Presents...)
Devil's Due Publ.: No. 0, Aug, 2008 - No. 2 (99¢/$3.50)
0-(99¢) Prelude to series; Powers-s/McManus-a 3.00
1,2-($3.50) 1-Two covers (Tim Sale art & Milo Ventimiglia photo) 3.50

RESTAURANT AT THE END OF THE UNIVERSE, THE (See Hitchhiker's Guide to the Galaxy & Life, the Universe & Everything)
DC Comics: 1994 - No. 3, 1994 ($6.95, limited series)
1-3 7.00

RESTLESS GUN (TV)
Dell Publishing Co.: No. 934, Sept, 1958 - No. 1146, Nov-Jan, 1960-61
Four Color 934 (#1)-Photo-c 10 20 30 64 132 200
Four Color 986 (5/59), 1045 (11-1/60), 1089 (3/60), 1146-Wildey-a; all photo-c

Resident Alien #1 © Hogan & Parkhouse

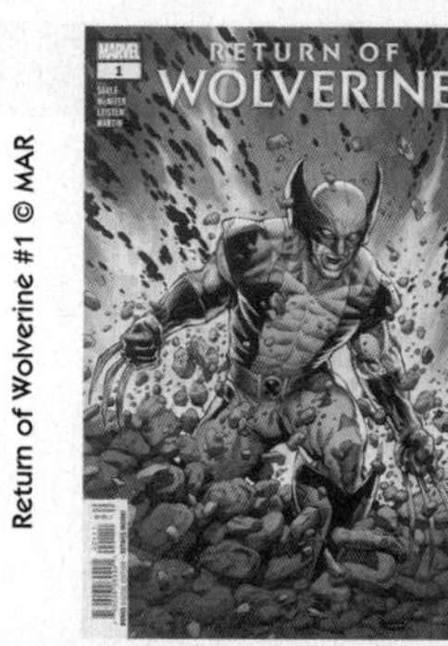

Return of Wolverine #1 © MAR

Revival #20 © Seeley & Norton

GD VG FN VF VF/NM NM-
2.0 4.0 6.0 8.0 9.0 9.2

7 14 21 49 92 135

RESURRECTIONISTS
Dark Horse Comics: Nov, 2014 - No. 4, Feb, 2015 ($3.50)
1-4-Van Lente-s/Rosenzweig-a 3.50

RESURRECTION MAN
DC Comics: May, 1997 - No. 27, Aug, 1999 ($2.50)
1-Lenticular disc on cover 5.00
2-5: 2-JLA app. 4.00
6-27: 6-Genesis-x-over. 7-Batman app. 10-Hitman-c/app. 16,17-Supergirl x-over. 18-Deadman & Phantom Stranger-c/app. 21-JLA-c/app. 3.00
#1,000,000 (11/98) 853rd Century x-over 3.00

RESURRECTION MAN (DC New 52)
DC Comics: Nov, 2011 - No. 12, Oct, 2012; No. 0, Nov, 2012 ($2.99)
1-12: 1-Abnett & Lanning-s/Dagnino-a/Reis-c; Body Doubles app. 9-Suicide Squad app. 3.00
#0 (11/12) Origin of Mitch Shelley and the Body Doubles; Bachs-a/Francavilla-c 3.00

RETIEF (Keith Laumer's)
Adventure Comics (Malibu): Dec, 1989 - Vol. 2, No.6, ($2.25, B&W)
1-6,Vol. 2, #1-6,Vol. 3 (...of The CDT) #1-6 3.00
...and The Warlords #1-6, ...: Diplomatic Immunity #1 (4/91), ...: Giant Killer #1 (9/91), ...: Crime & Punishment #1 (11/91) 3.00

RETROVIRUS
Image Comics: Nov, 2012 ($12.99, hardcover GN)
HC-Gray & Palmiotti-s/Fernandez-a/Conner-c 13.00

RETURN FROM WITCH MOUNTAIN (See Walt Disney Showcase #44)

RETURNING, THE
BOOM! Studios: Mar, 2014 - No. 4, Jun, 2014 ($3.99, limited series)
1-4-Jason Starr-s/Andrea Mutti-a/Frazer Irving-c 4.00

RETURN OF ALISON DARE: LITTLE MISS ADVENTURES, THE (Also see Alison Dare: Little Miss Adventures)
Oni Press: Apr, 2001 - No. 3, Sept, 2001 ($2.95, B&W, limited series)
1-3-J. Torres-s/J.Bone-c/a 3.00

RETURN OF CHILLING ADVENTURES IN SORCERY, THE
Archie Comic Publications: Dec, 2022 ($3.99)
1-Short horror stories, Madam Satan, Sabrina & Veronica app.; art by various 4.00

RETURN OF GORGO, THE (Formerly Gorgo's Revenge)
Charlton Comics: No. 2, Aug, 1963; No. 3, Fall, 1964 (12¢)
2,3-Ditko-c/a; based on M.G.M. movie 8 16 24 52 99 145

RETURN OF KONGA, THE (Konga's Revenge #2 on)
Charlton Comics: 1962
nn 8 16 24 54 102 150

RETURN OF MEGATON MAN
Kitchen Sink Press: July, 1988 - No. 3, 1988 ($2.00, limited series)
1-3: Simpson-c/a 4.00

RETURN OF THE GREMLINS (The Roald Dahl characters)
Dark Horse Comics: Mar, 2008 - No. 3, May, 2008 ($2.99, limited series)
1-3-Richardson-s/Yeagle-a. 1-Back-up reprint of intro. from 1943. 2-Back-up reprints of three Gremlin Gus 2-pagers from 1943. 3-Back-up reprints 3.00

RETURN OF THE LIVING DEADPOOL
Marvel Comics: Apr, 2015 - No. 4, Jul, 2015 ($3.99, limited series)
1-4-Cullen Bunn-s/Nik Virella-a 6.00

RETURN OF THE OUTLAW
Toby Press (Minoan): Feb, 1953 - No. 11, 1955
1-Billy the Kid 14 28 42 48 112 145
2 8 16 24 44 57 70
3-11 8 16 24 42 54 65

RETURN OF WOLVERINE (Continued in Wolverine: Infinity Watch)
Marvel Comics: Nov, 2018 - No. 5, Apr, 2019 ($4.99/$3.99, limited series)
1,5-($4.99) Soule-s/McNiven-a 5.00
2-4-($3.99) Shalvey-a 4.00

RETURN TO JURASSIC PARK
Topps Comics: Apr, 1995 - No. 9, Feb, 1996 ($2.50/$2.95)
1 2 4 6 9 12 15
2-9: 3-Begin $2.95-c. 9-Artists' Jam issue 5.00

RETURN TO THE AMALGAM AGE OF COMICS: THE MARVEL COMICS COLLECTION
Marvel Comics: 1997 ($12.95, TPB)
nn-Reprints Amalgam one-shots: Challengers of the Fantastic #1, The Exciting X-Patrol #1, Iron Lantern #1, The Magnetic Men Featuring Magneto #1, Spider-Boy Team-Up #1 & Thorion of the New Asgods #1 13.00

REVEAL
Dark Horse Comics: Nov, 2002 ($6.95, squarebound)
1-Short stories of Dark Horse characters by various; Lone Wolf 2100, Buffy, Spyboy app. 7.00

REVEALING LOVE STORIES (See Fox Giants)

REVEALING ROMANCES
Ace Magazines: Sept, 1949 - No. 6, Aug, 1950
1 28 56 84 165 270 375
2 15 30 45 84 127 170
3-6 14 28 42 78 112 145

REVELATIONS
Dark Horse Comics: Aug, 2005 - No. 6, Jan, 2006 ($2.99, limited series)
1-6-Paul Jenkins-s/Humberto Ramos-a/c 3.00
1-6-(BOOM! Studios, 1/14 - No. 6, 6/14, $3.99) reprints original series 4.00

REVENGE
Image Comics: Feb, 2014 - No. 4, Jun, 2014 ($2.99)
1-4-Jonathan Ross-s/Ian Churchill-a 3.00

REVENGE OF THE COSMIC GHOST RIDER (Also see Cosmic Ghost Rider)
Marvel Comics: Feb, 2020 - No. 5, Oct, 2020 ($4.99/$3.99, limited series)
1-($4.99) Hallum-s/Hepburn-a; back-up w/Gates-s/Shaw-a; present-day Frank Castle app. 5.00
2-5-($3.99) 3-5-Mephisto app. 4.00

REVENGE OF THE PROWLER (Also see The Prowler)
Eclipse Comics: Feb, 1988 - No. 4, June, 1988 ($1.75/$1.95)
1,3,4: 1-$1.75. 3,4-$1.95-c; Snyder III-a(p) 3.00
2 ($2.50)-Contains flexi-disc 4.00

REVISIONIST, THE
AfterShock Comics: Jun, 2016 - No. 6, Nov, 2016 ($3.99)
1-6: 1-Frank Barbiere-s/Garry Brown-a 4.00

REVIVAL
Image Comics: Jul, 2012 - No. 47, Feb, 2017 ($2.99/$3.99)
1-Tim Seeley-s/Mike Norton-a/Jenny Frison-c 12.00
1-Variant-c by Craig Thompson 18.00
1-Second-fourth printings 4.00
2-26 3.00
27-47-($3.99) 4.00

REVOLUTION
IDW Publishing: Sept, 2016 - No. 5, Nov, 2016 ($3.99, limited series)
1-5-Barber & Bunn-s/Ossio-a; multiple covers on each; G.I. Joe, Transformers, Rom, Micronauts, and M.A.S.K. app. 2-5-Bonus character profile pages 4.00

REVOLUTIONARIES (Follows the Revolution x-over)
IDW Publishing: Dec, 2016 - No. 8, Jul, 2017 ($3.99)
1-7: 1,2-Barber-s/Ossio-a; multiple covers on each; G.I. Joe, Transformers, Rom app. 4.00
8-($4.99) Barber-s/Ossio & Joseph-a 5.00

REVOLUTIONARY WAR
Marvel Comics: Mar, 2014 - May, 2014 ($3.99)
...: Alpha 1 (3/14) Part 1; Lanning & Cowsill-s/Elson-a; Capt. Britain & Pete Wisdom app. 4.00
...: Dark Angel 1 (3/14) Part 2; Gillen-s/Dietrich Smith-a; Mephisto app. 4.00
...: Death's Head II 1 (4/14) Part 4; Lanning & Cowsill-s/Roche-a 4.00
...: Knights of Pendragon 1 (3/14) Part 3; Williams-s/Sliney-a; Union Jack app. 4.00
...: Motormouth 1 (5/14) Part 6; Dakin-s/Cliquet-a; Killpower app. 4.00
...: Omega 1 (5/14) Part 8; conclusion; Lanning & Cowsill-s/Elson-a 4.00
...: Supersoldiers 1 (4/14) Part 5; Williams-s/Brent Anderson-a 4.00
...: Warheads 1 (5/14) Part 7; Lanning & Cowsill-s/Erskine-a 4.00

REVOLUTION: AW YEAH!
IDW Publishing: Feb, 2017 - No. 3, Jul, 2017 ($3.99, limited series)
1-3-All ages x-over of Rom, Transformers, G.I. Joe, Micronauts; Art Baltazar-s/a 4.00

REVOLUTION ON THE PLANET OF THE APES
Mr. Comics: Dec, 2005 - No. 6, Aug, 2006 ($3.95)
1-6: 1,2-Salgood Sam-a 4.00

REX ALLEN COMICS (Movie star)(Also see Four Color #877 & Western Roundup under Dell Giants)
Dell Publ. Co.: No. 316, Feb, 1951 - No. 31, Dec-Feb, 1958-59 (All-photo-c)

Four Color 316(#1)(52 pgs.)-Rex Allen & his horse Koko begin; Marsh-a
14 28 42 94 207 320
2 (9-11/51, 36 pgs.) 8 16 24 55 105 150
3-10 6 12 18 38 69 100
11-20 5 10 15 34 60 85
21-23,25-31 5 10 15 31 53 75
24-Toth-a 5 10 15 34 60 85
NOTE: *Manning a-20, 27-30. Photo back-c F.C. #316, 2-12, 20, 21.*

REX DEXTER OF MARS (See Mystery Men Comics)
Fox Feature Syndicate: Fall, 1940 (68 pgs.)
1-Rex Dexter, Patty O'Day, & Zanzibar (Tuska-a) app.; Briefer-c/a
300 600 900 1950 3375 4800

REX HART (Formerly Blaze Carson; Whip Wilson #9 on)
Timely/Marvel Comics (USA): No. 6, Aug, 1949 - No. 8, Feb, 1950 (All photo-c)
6-Rex Hart & his horse Warrior begin; Black Rider app; Captain Tootsie by Beck; Heath-a
29 58 87 172 281 390
7,8: 18 pg. Thriller in each. 7-Heath-a. 8-Blaze the Wonder Collie app. in text
20 40 60 1148 192 265

REX MORGAN, M.D. (Also see Harvey Comics Library)
Argo Publ.: Dec, 1955 - No. 3, Apr?, 1956
1-r/Rex Morgan daily newspaper strips & daily panel-r of "These Women" by D'Alessio & "Timeout" by Jeff Keate 17 34 51 100 158 215
2,3 14 28 42 76 108 140

REX MUNDI (Latin for "King of the World")
Image Comics: No. 0, Aug, 2002 - No. 18, Apr, 2006 ($2.95/$2.99)
0-18-Arvid Nelson-s. 0-13-Eric Johnson-a. 14,15-Jim DiBartolo-a. 18-Ramos-c 3.00
Vol. 1: The Guardian of the Temple TPB (1/04, $14.95) r/#0-5 15.00
Book 1: The Guardian of the Temple TPB (Dark Horse, 11/06, $16.95) r/#0-5 & Brother Matthew web comic; Dysart intro. 17.00
Vol. 2: The River Underground TPB (4/05, $14.95) r/#6-11 15.00
Book 2: The River Underground (Dark Horse, 2006, $16.95) r/#6-11 17.00
Vol. 3: The Lost Kings TPB (Dark Horse, 9/06, $16.95) r/#12-17 17.00
Book Four: Crowd and Sword TPB (Dark Horse, 12/07, $16.95) r/#18 plus V2 #1-5 and story from Dark Horse Book of Monsters 17.00

REX MUNDI (Volume 2)
Dark Horse Comics: July, 2006 - No. 19, Aug, 2009 ($2.99)
1-19-Arvid Nelson-s. 1-JH Williams-c. 16-Chen-c. 18-Linsner-c 3.00
Book Five: The Valley at the End of the World TPB (11/08, $17.95) r/#6-12 18.00

REX THE WONDER DOG (See The Adventures of...)

REYN
Image Comics: Jan, 2015 - No. 10, Nov, 2015 ($2.99)
1-10-Symons-s/Stockman-a 3.00

RHUBARB, THE MILLIONAIRE CAT
Dell Publishing Co.: No. 423, Sept-Oct, 1952 - No. 563, June, 1954
Four Color 423 (#1) 7 14 21 49 92 135
Four Color 466(5/53),563 6 12 18 38 69 100

RIB
Dilemma Productions: Oct, 1995 - April, 1996 ($1.95, B&W)
Ashcan, 1 3.00

RIB
Bookmark Productions: 1996 ($2.95, B&W)
1-Sakai-c; Andrew Ford-s/a 3.00

RIB
Caliber Comics: May, 1997 - No. 5, 1998 ($2.95, B&W)
1-5: 1-"Beginnings" pts. 1 & 2 3.00

RIBIT! (Red Sonja imitation)
Comico: Jan, 1989 - No. 4, Apr, 1989 ($1.95, limited series)
1-4: Frank Thorne-c/a/scripts 3.00

RIBTICKLER (Also see Fox Giants)
Fox Feature Synd./Green Publ. (1957)/Norlen (1959): 1945, No. 2, 1946, No. 3, Jul-Aug, 1946 - No. 9, Jul-Aug, 1947; 1957; 1959
1-Funny animal 27 54 81 162 266 370
2-(1946) 15 30 45 83 124 165
3-9: 3,5,7-Cosmo Cat app. 13 26 39 72 101 130
3,7,8 (Green Publ.-1957), 3,7,8 (Norlen Mag.-1959) 3 6 9 18 28 38

RICHARD DRAGON
DC Comics: July, 2004 - No. 12, Jun, 2005 ($2.50)
1-12: 1-Dixon-s/McDaniel-a/c; Ben Turner app. 2,3-Nightwing app. 4-6,11,12-Lady Shiva 3.00

RICHARD DRAGON, KUNG-FU FIGHTER (See The Batman Chronicles #5, Brave & the Bold, & The Question)
National Periodical Publ./DC Comics: Apr-May, 1975 - No. 18, Nov-Dec, 1977
1-Intro Richard Dragon, Ben Stanley (later Ben Turner) & O-Sensei; 1st app. Barney Ling; adaptation of Jim Dennis (Denny O'Neil) novel "Dragon's Fists" begins, ends #4
5 10 15 33 57 80
2,3: 2-Intro Carolyn Woosan; Starlin/Weiss-c/a; bondage-c. 3-Kirby-a(p); Giordano bondage-c 2 4 6 10 14 18
4,6-8-Wood inks. 4-Carolyn Woosan dies 2 4 6 8 11 14
5-1st app. Lady Shiva; Wood inks 8 16 24 54 102 150
9-13,15-17: 9-Ben Stanley becomes Ben Turner; intro Preying Mantis. 16-1st app. Prof Ojo.
1 3 4 6 8 12
14-"Spirit of Bruce Lee" 3 6 9 16 24 32
18-1st app. Ben Turner as The Bronze Tiger 2 4 6 10 14 20
NOTE: ***Buckler** a-14. c-15, 18. **Chua** c-13. **Estrada** a-9, 13-18. **Estrada/Abel** a-10-12. **Estrada/Wood** a-4-8. **Giordano** c-1, 3-11. **Weiss** a-2(partial) c-2i.*

RICHARD THE LION-HEARTED (See Ideal a Classical Comic)

RICHIE RICH (See Harvey Collectors Comics, Harvey Hits, Little Dot, Little Lotta, Little Sad Sack, Million Dollar Digest, Mutt & Jeff, Super Richie & 3-D Dolly; also Tastee-Freez Comics in the Promotional Comics section)

RICHIE RICH (...the Poor Little Rich Boy) (See Harvey Hits #3, 9)
Harvey Publ.: Nov, 1960 - #218, Oct, 1982; #219, Oct, 1986 - #254, Jan, 1991
1-(See Little Dot #1 for 1st app.) 400 800 1200 3400 7700 12,000
2 93 186 279 744 1672 2600
3-5 46 92 138 368 834 1300
6-10: 8-Christmas-c 27 54 81 189 420 650
11-20 16 32 48 112 249 385
21-30 11 22 33 76 163 250
31-40 9 18 27 61 123 185
41-50: 42(2/66)-X-mas-c 7 14 21 49 92 135
51-55,57-60: 59-Buck, prototype of Dollar the Dog 5 10 15 35 63 90
56-1st app. Super Richie 6 12 18 41 76 110
61-64,66-80: 71-Nixon & Robert Kennedy caricatures; outer space-c
4 8 12 28 47 65
65-Buck the Dog (Dollar prototype) on cover 6 12 18 40 73 105
81-99 3 6 9 21 33 45
100(12/70)-1st app. Irona the robot maid 4 8 12 25 40 55
101-111,117-120 3 6 9 14 20 26
112-116: All 52 pg. Giants 3 6 9 16 24 32
121-140: 137-1st app. Mr. Cheepers and Professor Keenbean
2 4 6 9 13 16
141-160: 145-Infinity-c. 155-3rd app. The Money Monster
2 4 6 8 10 12
161-180 1 3 4 6 8 10
181-199 1 2 3 5 6 8
200 1 3 4 6 8 10
201-218: 210-Stone-Age Riches app 1 2 3 4 5 7
219-254: 237-Last original material 6.00
Harvey Comics Classics Vol. 2 TPB (Dark Horse Books, 10/07, $19.95) Reprints Richie Rich's early appearances in this title, Little Dot and Richie Rich Success Stories, mostly B&W with some color stories; history and interview with Ernie Colón 20.00

RICHIE RICH
Harvey Comics: Mar, 1991 - No. 28, Nov, 1994 ($1.00, bi-monthly)
1-28: Reprints best of Richie Rich 3.00
Giant Size 1-4 (10/91-10/93, $2.25, 68 pgs.) 4.00

RICHIE RICH ADVENTURE DIGEST MAGAZINE
Harvey Comics: 1992 - No. 7, Sept, 1994 ($1.25, quarterly, digest-size)
1-7 4.00

RICHIE RICH AND...
Harvey Comics: Oct, 1987 - No. 11, May, 1990 ($1.00)
1-Professor Keenbean 4.00
2-11: 2-Casper. 3-Dollar the Dog. 4-Cadbury. 5 Mayda Munny. 6-Irona. 7-Little Dot. 8-Professor Keenbean. 9-Little Audrey. 10-Mayda Munny. 11-Cadbury 3.00

RICHIE RICH AND BILLY BELLHOPS
Harvey Publications: Oct, 1977 (52 pgs., one-shot)
1 2 4 6 11 16 20

RICHIE RICH AND CADBURY
Harvey Publ.: 10/77; #2, 9/78 - #23, 7/82; #24, 7/90 - #29, 1/91 (1-10: 52pgs.)
1-(52 pg. Giant) 2 4 6 11 16 20
2-10-(52 pg. Giant) 2 4 6 8 10 12
11-23 6.00
24-29: 24-Begin $1.00-c 4.00

RICHIE RICH AND CASPER
Harvey Publications: Aug, 1974 - No. 45, Sept, 1982
1 3 6 9 19 30 40
2-5 2 4 6 13 18 22
6-10: 10-Xmas-c 2 4 6 9 13 16
11-20 1 3 4 6 8 10
21-45: 22-Xmas-c 6.00

RICHIE RICH AND DOLLAR THE DOG (See Richie Rich #65)
Harvey Publications: Sept, 1977 - No. 24, Aug, 1982 (#1-10: 52 pgs.)
1-(52 pg. Giant) 2 4 6 11 16 20
2-10-(52 pg. Giant) 2 4 6 8 10 12
11-24 6.00

RICHIE RICH AND DOT
Harvey Publications: Oct, 1974 (one-shot)
1 3 6 9 15 22 28

RICHIE RICH AND GLORIA
Harvey Publications: Sept, 1977 - No. 25, Sept, 1982 (#1-11: 52 pgs.)
1-(52 pg. Giant) 2 4 6 11 16 20
2-11-(52 pg. Giant) 2 4 6 8 10 12
12-25 6.00

RICHIE RICH AND HIS GIRLFRIENDS
Harvey Publications: April, 1979 - No. 16, Dec, 1982
1-(52 pg. Giant) 2 4 6 9 13 16
2-(52 pg. Giant) 1 3 4 6 8 10
3-10 1 2 3 5 6 8
11-16 6.00

RICHIE RICH AND HIS MEAN COUSIN REGGIE
Harvey Publications: April, 1979 - No. 3, 1980 (50¢) (#1,2: 52 pgs.)
1 2 4 6 9 13 16
2-3: 1 3 4 6 8 10
NOTE: *No. 4 was advertised, but never released.*

RICHIE RICH AND JACKIE JOKERS (Also see Jackie Jokers)
Harvey Publications: Nov, 1973 - No. 48, Dec, 1982
1: 52 pg. Giant; contains material from unpublished Jackie Jokers #5
4 8 12 23 37 50
2,3-(52 pg. Giants). 2-R.R. & Jackie 1st meet 3 6 9 15 22 28
4,5 2 4 6 13 18 22

Reyn #1 © Symons & Stockman

Richie Rich #14 © HARV

Richie Rich Diamonds #2 © HARV

	GD 2.0	VG 4.0	FN 6.0	VF 8.0	VF/NM 9.0	NM- 9.2
6-10	2	4	6	9	13	16
11-20,26: 11-1st app. Kool Katz. 26-Star Wars parody	1	3	4	6	8	10
21-25,27-40	1	2	3	4	5	7
41-48						6.00
RICHIE RICH AND PROFESSOR KEENBEAN						
Harvey Comics: Sept, 1990 - No. 2, Nov, 1990 ($1.00)						
1,2						3.00
RICHIE RICH AND THE NEW KIDS ON THE BLOCK						
Harvey Publications: Feb, 1991 - No. 3, June, 1991 ($1.25, bi-monthly)						
1-3: 1,2-New Richie Rich stories						4.00
RICHIE RICH AND TIMMY TIME						
Harvey Publications: Sept, 1977 (50¢, 52 pgs, one-shot)						
1	2	4	6	11	16	20
RICHIE RICH BANK BOOK						
Harvey Publications: Oct, 1972 - No. 59, Sept, 1982						
1	5	10	15	31	53	75
2-5: 2-2nd app. The Money Monster	3	6	9	16	23	30
6-10	2	4	6	11	16	20
11-20: 18-Super Richie app.	2	4	6	8	10	12
21-30	1	2	3	5	7	9
31-40	1	2	3	4	5	7
41-59						6.00
RICHIE RICH BEST OF THE YEARS						
Harvey Publications: Oct, 1977 - No. 6, June, 1980 (128 pgs., digest-size)						
1(10/77)-Reprints	2	4	6	9	12	15
2-6(11/79-6/80, 95¢). #2(10/78)-Rep.. #3(6/79, 75¢)	1	2	3	5	7	9
RICHIE RICH BIG BOOK						
Harvey Publications: Nov, 1992 - No. 2, May, 1993 ($1.50, 52 pgs.)						
1,2						4.00
RICHIE RICH BIG BUCKS						
Harvey Publications: Apr, 1991 - No. 8, July, 1992 ($1.00, bi-monthly)						
1-8						3.00
RICHIE RICH BILLIONS						
Harvey Publications: Oct, 1974 - No. 48, Oct, 1982 (#1-33: 52 pgs.)						
1	3	6	9	21	33	45
2-5: 2-Christmas issue	3	6	9	14	20	25
6-10	2	4	6	10	14	18
11-20	2	4	6	8	10	12
21-33	1	2	3	5	6	8
34-48: 35-Onion app.						6.00
RICHIE RICH CASH						
Harvey Publications: Sept, 1974 - No. 47, Aug, 1982						
1-1st app. Dr. N-R-Gee	3	6	9	19	30	40
2-5	2	4	6	13	18	22
6-10	2	4	6	9	13	16
11-20	1	3	4	6	8	10
21-30	1	2	3	4	5	7
31-47: 33-Dr. Blemish app.						6.00
RICHIE RICH CASH MONEY						
Harvey Comics: May, 1992 - No. 2, Aug, 1992 ($1.25)						
1,2						3.00
RICHIE RICH, CASPER AND WENDY - NATIONAL LEAGUE						
Harvey Comics: June, 1976 (50¢)						
1-Newsstand version of the baseball giveaway	2	4	6	13	18	22
RICHIE RICH COLLECTORS COMICS (See Harvey Collectors Comics)						
RICHIE RICH DIAMONDS						
Harvey Publications: Aug, 1972 - No. 59, Aug, 1982 (#1, 23-45: 52 pgs.)						
1-(52 pg. Giant)	5	10	15	31	53	75
2-5	3	6	9	16	23	30
6-10	2	4	6	11	16	20
11-22	2	4	6	8	10	12
23-30-(52 pg. Giants)	2	4	6	8	11	14
31-45: 39-r/Origin Little Dot	1	2	3	5	7	9
46-50	1	2	3	4	5	7
51-59						6.00
RICHIE RICH DIGEST MAGAZINE						

	GD 2.0	VG 4.0	FN 6.0	VF 8.0	VF/NM 9.0	NM- 9.2
Harvey Publications: Oct, 1986 - No. 42, Oct, 1994 ($1.25/$1.75, digest-size)						
1	1	2	3	5	6	8
2-10						5.00
11-20						4.00
21-42						4.00
RICHIE RICH DIGEST STORIES (...Magazine #?-on)						
Harvey Publications: Oct, 1977 - No., 17, Oct, 1982 (75¢/95¢, digest-size)						
1-Reprints	2	4	6	9	12	15
2-10: Reprints	1	2	3	5	7	9
11-17: Reprints						6.00
RICHIE RICH DIGEST WINNERS						
Harvey Publications: Dec, 1977 - No. 16, Sept, 1982 (75¢/95¢, 132 pgs., digest-size)						
1	2	4	6	9	12	15
2-5	1	2	3	5	7	9
6-16						6.00
RICHIE RICH DOLLARS & CENTS						
Harvey Publications: Aug, 1963 - No. 109, Aug, 1982 (#1-43: 68 pgs.; 44-60, 71-94: 52 pgs.)						
1: (#1-64 are all reprint issues)	21	42	63	147	324	500
2	11	22	33	73	157	240
3-5: 5-r/1st app. of R.R. from Little Dot #1	8	16	24	54	102	150
6-10	6	12	18	40	73	105
11-20	4	8	12	28	47	65
21-30: 25-r/1st app. Nurse Jenny (Little Lotta #62)	3	6	9	21	33	45
31-43: 43-Last 68 pg. issue	3	6	9	17	26	35
44-60: All 52 pgs.	3	6	9	14	19	25
61-71	1	3	4	6	8	10
72-94: All 52 pgs.	2	4	6	8	10	12
95-99,101-109						6.00
100-Anniversary issue	1	2	3	5	7	9
RICHIE RICH FORTUNES						
Harvey Publications: Sept, 1971 - No. 63, July, 1982 (#1-15: 52 pgs.)						
1	5	10	15	34	60	85
2-5	3	6	9	19	30	40
6-10	2	4	6	13	18	22
11-15: 11-r/1st app. The Onion	2	4	6	9	12	15
16-30	1	2	3	5	7	9
31-40	1	2	3	4	5	7
41-63: 62-Onion app.						6.00
RICHIE RICH GEMS						
Harvey Publications: Sept, 1974 - No. 43, Sept, 1982						
1	3	6	9	19	30	40
2-5	2	4	6	13	18	22
6-10	2	4	6	9	13	16
11-20	1	3	4	6	8	10
21-30	1	2	3	4	5	7
31-43: 36-Dr. Blemish, Onion app. 38-1st app. Stone-Age Riches						6.00
44-48 (Ape Entertainment, 2011-2012, $3.99) new stories w/Colon-a & reprints						4.00
... Special Collection (Ape Entertainment, 2012, $6.99) r/Valentine & Winter Specials						7.00
... Valentines Special (Ape Entertainment, 2012, $3.99) new story w/Colon-a & reprints						4.00
... Winter Special (Ape Entertainment, 2011, $3.99) new story w/Colon-a & reprints						4.00
RICHIE RICH GOLD AND SILVER						
Harvey Publications: Sept, 1975 - No. 42, Oct, 1982 (#1-27: 52 pgs.)						
1	3	6	9	19	30	40
2-5	2	4	6	11	16	20
6-10	2	4	6	8	11	14
11-27	1	2	3	5	7	9
28-42: 34-Stone-Age Riches app.						6.00
RICHIE RICH GOLD NUGGETS DIGEST						
Harvey Publications: Dec., 1990 - No. 4, June, 1991 ($1.75, digest-size)						
1-4						4.00
RICHIE RICH HOLIDAY DIGEST MAGAZINE (...Digest #4)						
Harvey Publications: Jan, 1980 - #3, Jan, 1982; #4, 3/88; #5, 2/89 (annual)						
1-X-Mas-c	1	3	4	6	8	10
2-5: 2,3: All X-Mas-c. 4-(3/88, $1.25), 5-(2/89, $1.75)	1	2	3	4	5	7
RICHIE RICH INVENTIONS						
Harvey Publications: Oct, 1977 - No. 26, Oct, 1982 (#1-11: 52 pgs.)						
1	2	4	6	11	16	20
2-5	2	4	6	8	10	12
6-11	1	2	3	5	6	8

	GD 2.0	VG 4.0	FN 6.0	VF 8.0	VF/NM 9.0	NM- 9.2
12-26						6.00

RICHIE RICH JACKPOTS
Harvey Publications: Oct, 1972 - No. 58, Aug, 1982 (#41-43: 52 pgs.)

	GD 2.0	VG 4.0	FN 6.0	VF 8.0	VF/NM 9.0	NM- 9.2
1-Debut of Cousin Jackpots	4	8	12	28	47	65
2-5	3	6	9	16	23	30
6-10	2	4	6	11	16	20
11-15,17-20	2	4	6	8	10	12
16-Super Richie app.	2	4	6	9	12	15
21-30	1	2	3	5	7	9
31-40,44-50: 37-Caricatures of Frank Sinatra, Dean Martin, Sammy Davis, Jr. 45-Dr. Blemish app.	1	2	3	4	5	7
41-43 (52 pgs.)	1	3	4	6	8	10
51-58						6.00

RICHIE RICH MILLION DOLLAR DIGEST (...Magazine #?-on)(See Million Dollar Digest)
Harvey Publications: Oct, 1980 - No. 10, Oct, 1982 ($1.50)

	GD 2.0	VG 4.0	FN 6.0	VF 8.0	VF/NM 9.0	NM- 9.2
1	1	3	4	6	8	10
2-10						7.00

RICHIE RICH MILLIONS
Harvey Publ.: 9/61; #2, 9/62 - #113, 10/82 (#1-48: 68 pgs.; 49-64, 85-97: 52 pgs.)

	GD 2.0	VG 4.0	FN 6.0	VF 8.0	VF/NM 9.0	NM- 9.2
1: (#1-3 are all reprint issues)	26	52	78	182	404	625
2	12	24	36	80	173	265
3-5: All other giants are new & reprints. 5-1st 15 pg. Richie Rich story	9	18	27	59	117	175
6-10	7	14	21	49	92	135
11-20	5	10	15	35	63	90
21-30	4	8	12	27	44	60
31-48: 31-1st app. The Onion. 48-Last 68 pg. Giant	3	6	9	19	30	40
49-64: 52 pg. Giants	3	6	9	14	20	25
65-67,69-73,75-84	2	4	6	8	10	12
68-1st Super Richie-c (11/74)	2	4	6	13	18	22
74-1st app. Mr. Woody; Super Richie app.	2	4	6	8	11	14
85-97: 52 pg. Giants	2	4	6	8	11	14
98,99	1	2	3	4	5	7
100	1	2	3	5	7	9
101-113						6.00

RICHIE RICH MONEY WORLD
Harvey Publications: Sept, 1972 - No. 59, Sept, 1982

	GD 2.0	VG 4.0	FN 6.0	VF 8.0	VF/NM 9.0	NM- 9.2
1-(52 pg. Giant)-1st app. Mayda Munny	5	10	15	33	57	80
2-Super Richie app.	3	6	9	17	26	35
3-5	3	6	9	16	23	30
6-10: 9,10-Richie Rich mistakenly named Little Lotta on covers	2	4	6	11	16	20
11-20: 16,20-Dr. N-R-Gee	2	4	6	8	10	12
21-30	1	2	3	5	7	9
31-50	1	2	3	4	5	7
51-59						6.00
Digest 1 (2/91, $1.75)						5.00
2-8 (12/93, $1.75)						3.00

RICHIE RICH PROFITS
Harvey Publications: Oct, 1974 - No. 47, Sept, 1982

	GD 2.0	VG 4.0	FN 6.0	VF 8.0	VF/NM 9.0	NM- 9.2
1	3	6	9	19	30	40
2-5	2	4	6	13	18	22
6-10: 10-Origin of Dr. N-R-Gee	2	4	6	9	13	16
11-20: 15-Christmas-c	1	3	4	6	8	10
21-30	1	2	3	4	5	7
31-47						6.00

RICHIE RICH RELICS
Harvey Comics: Jan, 1988 - No.4, Feb, 1989 (75¢/$1.00, reprints)

	GD 2.0	VG 4.0	FN 6.0	VF 8.0	VF/NM 9.0	NM- 9.2
1-4						3.00

RICHIE RICH RICHES
Harvey Publications: July, 1972 - No. 59, Aug, 1982 (#1, 2, 41-45: 52 pgs.)

	GD 2.0	VG 4.0	FN 6.0	VF 8.0	VF/NM 9.0	NM- 9.2
1-(52 pg. Giant)-1st app. The Money Monster	5	10	15	33	57	80
2-(52 pg. Giant)	3	6	9	19	30	40
3-5	3	6	9	16	23	30
6-10: 7-1st app. Aunt Novo	2	4	6	11	16	20
11-20: 17-Super Richie app. (3/75)	2	4	6	8	10	12
21-40	1	2	3	5	6	8
41-45: 52 pg. Giants	1	3	4	6	8	10
46-59: 56-Dr. Blemish app.						6.00

RICHIE RICH: RICH RESCUE
Ape Entertainment: 2011 - No. 4, 2011 ($3.95, limited series)

	GD 2.0	VG 4.0	FN 6.0	VF 8.0	VF/NM 9.0	NM- 9.2
1-6-New short stories by various incl. Ernie Colon; Jack Lawrence-c						4.00
FCBD Edition (2011, giveaway) Flip book with Kung Fu Panda						3.00

RICHIE RICH SUCCESS STORIES
Harvey Publications: Nov, 1964 - No. 105, Sept, 1982 (#1-38: 68 pgs., 39-55, 67-90: 52 pgs.)

	GD 2.0	VG 4.0	FN 6.0	VF 8.0	VF/NM 9.0	NM- 9.2
1	21	42	63	147	324	500
2	9	18	27	58	114	170
3-5	8	16	24	51	96	140
6-10	5	10	15	35	63	90
11-20	5	10	15	31	53	75
21-30: 27-1st Penny Van Dough (8/69)	4	8	12	23	37	50
31-38: 38-Last 68 pg. Giant	3	6	9	19	30	40
39-55-(52 pgs.): 44-Super Richie app.	3	6	9	14	20	25
56-66	2	4	6	8	10	12
67-90: 52 pgs.	2	4	6	8	11	14
91-99,101-105: 91-Onion app. 101-Dr. Blemish app.						6.00
100	1	2	3	5	7	9

RICHIE RICH SUMMER BONANZA
Harvey Comics: Oct, 1991 ($1.95, one-shot, 68 pgs.)

	GD 2.0	VG 4.0	FN 6.0	VF 8.0	VF/NM 9.0	NM- 9.2
1-Richie Rich, Little Dot, Little Lotta						4.00

RICHIE RICH TREASURE CHEST DIGEST (...Magazine #3)
Harvey Publications: Apr, 1982 - No. 3, Aug, 1982 (95¢, Digest Mag.)
(#4 advertised but not publ.)

	GD 2.0	VG 4.0	FN 6.0	VF 8.0	VF/NM 9.0	NM- 9.2
1	1	3	4	6	8	10
2,3	1	2	3	4	5	7

RICHIE RICH VACATION DIGEST
Harvey Comics: Oct, 1991; Oct, 1992; Oct, 1993 ($1.75, digest-size)

	GD 2.0	VG 4.0	FN 6.0	VF 8.0	VF/NM 9.0	NM- 9.2
1-(10/91), 1-(10/92), 1-(10/93)						4.00

RICHIE RICH VACATIONS DIGEST
Harvey Publ.: 11/77; No. 2, 10/78 - No. 7, 10/81; No. 8, 8/82; No. 9, 10/82 (Digest, 132 pgs.)

	GD 2.0	VG 4.0	FN 6.0	VF 8.0	VF/NM 9.0	NM- 9.2
1-Reprints	2	4	6	9	12	15
2-6	1	2	3	5	7	9
7-9						6.00

RICHIE RICH VAULT OF MYSTERY
Harvey Publications: Nov, 1974 - No. 47, Sept, 1982

	GD 2.0	VG 4.0	FN 6.0	VF 8.0	VF/NM 9.0	NM- 9.2
1	4	8	12	23	37	50
2-5: 5-The Condor app.	2	4	6	13	18	22
6-10	2	4	6	9	13	16
11-20	1	3	4	6	8	10
21-30	1	2	3	4	5	7
31-47						6.00

RICHIE RICH ZILLIONZ
Harvey Publ.: Oct, 1976 - No. 33, Sept, 1982 (#1-4: 68 pgs.; #5-18: 52 pgs.)

	GD 2.0	VG 4.0	FN 6.0	VF 8.0	VF/NM 9.0	NM- 9.2
1	3	6	9	17	26	35
2-4: 4-Last 68 pg. Giant	2	4	6	11	16	20
5-10	2	4	6	8	10	12
11-18: 18-Last 52 pg. Giant	1	2	3	5	6	8
19-33						6.00

RICH JOHNSTON'S... (Parody of the Avengers movie characters)
BOOM! Studios: Apr, 2012 ($3.99, series of one-shots)

	GD 2.0	VG 4.0	FN 6.0	VF 8.0	VF/NM 9.0	NM- 9.2
... Captain American Idol 1 - Rich Johnston-s/Chris Haley-a						4.00
... Iron Muslim 1 - Rich Johnston-s/Bryan Turner-a; Demon in a Bottle cover swipe						4.00
... Scienthorlogy 1 - Rich Johnston-s/Michael Netzer-a						4.00
... The Avengefuls 1 - Rich Johnston-s/Joshua Covey; two printings						4.00

RICK AND MORTY (Based on the Adult Swim animated series)
Oni Press: Apr, 2015 - No. 60, Mar, 2020 ($3.99)

	GD 2.0	VG 4.0	FN 6.0	VF 8.0	VF/NM 9.0	NM- 9.2
1-Zac Gorman-s/CJ Cannon-a; multiple covers	10	20	30	68	144	220
2,3	3	6	9	19	30	40
4-49,51-60: 44-The Vindicators app.						4.00
50-($6.99) Morty's Mind Blowers						7.00
...#1 50th Issue Celebration Reprint (5/19, $3.99) r/#1						4.00
...#100 (10/22, $4.99) Reprints issues from various mini-series						5.00
... Free Comic Book Day 2017 (5/17, giveaway) r/#1; preview of Pocket Like You Stole It						3.00
... : Mr. Nimbus 1 (10/21, $4.99) Retells 1st meeting with Rick; Time Lord Jessica app.						5.00
Oni 25th Anniversary: Rick and Morty #1 (8/22, $9.99) Reprints #1; silver foil trade logo						10.00
... Presents: Big, Dumb, Summer Vacation 1 (7/22, $4.99) Griggs-s						5.00
... Presents: Birdperson 1 (7/20, $4.99) Origin & 1st meeting with Rick						5.00
... Presents: Council of Ricks 1 (6/20, $4.99) Goldman-s/Ellerby & Murphy-a						5.00
... Presents: Death Stalkers 1 (1/21, $4.99) Phillips-s/Ryan Lee-a; Hemorrhage app.						5.00
... Presents: HeRicktics of Rick 1 (1/22, $4.99) Homage to Dune						5.00
... Presents: Jaguar 1 (11/20, $4.99) Ellerby-s/a						5.00
... Presents: Jerry 1 (3/19, $4.99) Ferrier-s/Cannon-a						5.00
... Presents: Jerryboree 1 (3/21, $4.99) Grace Thomas-s/Gina Allnatt-a						5.00
... Presents: Krombopulos Michael 1 (6/18, $4.99) Ortberg-s/Cannon-a						5.00
... Presents: Morty's Run 1 (3/22, $4.99)						5.00
... Presents: Mr. Meeseeks 1 (6/19, $4.99) Asmus & Festante-s/Cannon-a						5.00
... Presents: Pickle Rick 1 (11/18, $4.99) Delilah S. Dawson-s/CJ Cannon-a; Jaguar app.						5.00
... Presents: Sleepy Gary 1 (9/18, $4.99) Visaggio-s/Cannon-a						5.00
... Presents: Snuffles Goes to War 1 (10/21, $4.99) Snowball app.						5.00
... Presents: The Flesh Curtains 1 (9/19, $4.99) Sturges-s/Cannon-a; Birdman app.						5.00
... Presents: The Hotel Immortal 1 (7/21, $4.99) Arbony-s/Ellerby-a						5.00
... Presents: The Vindicators 1 (3/18, $4.99) Cannon-a; Pickle Rick app.						5.00
... Presents: Time Zoo 1 (2/23, $4.99) Goldman-s/Murphy-a						5.00
... Presents: Unity 1 (11/19, $4.99) Tini Howard-s/Marco Mazzarello-a						5.00

RICK AND MORTY (Volume 2)
Oni Press: Jan, 2023 - Present ($3.99)

	GD 2.0	VG 4.0	FN 6.0	VF 8.0	VF/NM 9.0	NM- 9.2
1,2-The Multiverse of Goldenfolds app.; multiple covers						4.00

RICK AND MORTY: CORPORATE ASSETS (Adult Swim)
Oni Press: Nov, 2021 - No. 4, Feb, 2022 ($3.99, limited series)

	GD 2.0	VG 4.0	FN 6.0	VF 8.0	VF/NM 9.0	NM- 9.2
1-4-James Asmus-s/Jarrett Williams-a; multiple covers						4.00

RICK AND MORTY: CRISIS ON EARTH C-137 (Adult Swim)
Oni Press: Aug, 2022 - No. 4, Feb, 2023 ($3.99, limited series)

	GD 2.0	VG 4.0	FN 6.0	VF 8.0	VF/NM 9.0	NM- 9.2
1-4-Supernova & Noob Noob app.; multiple covers						4.00

RICK AND MORTY EVER AFTER (Adult Swim)
Oni Press: Oct, 2020 - No. 4, Jan, 2021 ($3.99, limited series)

	GD 2.0	VG 4.0	FN 6.0	VF 8.0	VF/NM 9.0	NM- 9.2
1-4-Sam Maggs-s/Sarah Stern-a; multiple covers						4.00

RICK AND MORTY GO TO HELL (Adult Swim)
Oni Press: Jun, 2020 - No. 5, Oct, 2020 ($3.99, limited series)

	GD 2.0	VG 4.0	FN 6.0	VF 8.0	VF/NM 9.0	NM- 9.2
1-5-Ferrier-s/Oroza-a; multiple covers						4.00

RICK AND MORTY INFINITY HOUR (Adult Swim)
Oni Press: Mar, 2022 - No. 4, Jul, 2022 ($3.99, limited series)

	GD 2.0	VG 4.0	FN 6.0	VF 8.0	VF/NM 9.0	NM- 9.2
1-4-Visaggio-s/Ellerby-a; multiple covers						4.00

RICK AND MORTY: LIL' POOPY SUPERSTAR (Adult Swim)
Oni Press: Jul, 2016 - No. 5, Nov, 2016 ($3.99, limited series)

	GD 2.0	VG 4.0	FN 6.0	VF 8.0	VF/NM 9.0	NM- 9.2
1-5-Sarah Graley-s/a; multiple covers						4.00

RICK AND MORTY: POCKET LIKE YOU STOLE IT (Adult Swim)
Oni Press: Jul, 2017 - No. 5, Nov, 2017 ($3.99, limited series)

Richie Rich Millions #10 © HARV

Rick and Morty #16 © Cartoon Network

Riddler: Year One #1 © DC

GD VG FN VF VF/NM NM-
2.0 4.0 6.0 8.0 9.0 9.2

1-5-Tim Howard-s/Marc Ellerby-a; multiple covers 4.00

RICK AND MORTY: RICK'S NEW HAT (Adult Swim)
Oni Press: Jun, 2021 - No. 5, Dec, 2021 ($3.99, limited series)
1-5-Alex Firer-s/Fred C. Stresing-a 4.00

RICK AND MORTY VS. CTHULHU (Adult Swim)
Oni Press: Dec, 2022 - No. 4, Mar, 2023 ($3.99, limited series)
1-4-Jim Zub-s/Troy Little-a 4.00

RICK AND MORTY VS. DUNGEONS & DRAGONS (Adult Swim)
Oni Press/IDW Publishing: Aug, 2018 - No. 4, Dec, 2018 ($3.99, limited series)
1-4-Patrick Rothfuss & Jim Zub-s/Troy Little-a 4.00
1: Director's Cut Edition (2/19, $4.99) r/#1 with some script pages and B&W art 5.00
...: The Meeseeks Adventure 1 (2/22, $5.99) Jim Zub-s/Troy Little-a 6.00

RICK AND MORTY VS. DUNGEONS & DRAGONS II: PAINSCAPE (Adult Swim)
Oni Press/IDW Publishing: Aug, 2019 - No. 4, Dec, 2019 ($3.99, limited series)
1-4-Jim Zub-s/Troy Little-a 4.00

RICK AND MORTY WORLDS APART (Adult Swim)
Oni Press: Feb, 2021 - No. 4, May, 2021 ($3.99, limited series)
1-4-Trujillo-s/Fleecs-a; the dragon Balthrowmaw app. 4.00

RICKY
Standard Comics (Visual Editions): No. 5, Sept, 1953
5-Teenage humor 11 22 33 64 90 115

RICKY NELSON (TV)(See Sweethearts V2#42)
Dell Publishing Co.: No. 956, Dec, 1958 - No. 1192, June, 1961 (All photo-c)
Four Color 956,998 17 34 51 114 252 390
Four Color 1115,1192: 1192-Manning-a 12 24 36 82 179 275

RIDDLER, THE : YEAR OF THE VILLAIN
DC Comics: 2019 ($4.99, one-shot)
1-King Tut and Apex Lex app.; origin re-told; Russell-s/Godlewski-a/Janin-c 4.00

RIDDLER, THE : YEAR ONE (Based on the 2022 Batman movie)
DC Comics (Black Label): Dec, 2022 - No. 6 ($4.99, limited series)
1-3-Origin of the Riddler from the 2022 Batman movie; Paul Dano-s/Stevan Subic-a 5.00

RIDE, THE (Also see Gun Candy flip-book)
Image Comics: June, 2004 - No. 2, July, 2004 ($2.95, B&W, anthology)
1,2: Hughes-c/Wagner-s. 1-Hamner & Stelfreeze-a. 2-Jeanty & Pearson-a 3.00
... Burning Desire 1-5 (6/19 - No. 5, 10/19, $3.99) 1-Hughes-c/a(6 pgs.) 4-Coker-a 4.00
... Die Valkyrie 1-3 (6/07 - No. 3, 2/08, $2.99) Stelfreeze-a/Wagner-s/Pearson-c 3.00
... Foreign Parts 1 (1/05, $2.95) Dixon-s/Haynes-a; Marz-s/Brunner-a; Pearson-c 3.00
... Halloween Special: The Key to Survival (10/07, $3.50) Tomm Coker-s/a 3.50
... Savannah 1 (4/07, $4.99) s/a by students of Savannah College of Art 5.00
... 2 For the Road 1 (10/04, $2.95) Dixon-s/Hamner & Gregory-a/Johnson-c 3.00
Vol. 1 TPB (2005, $9.99) r/#1,2, Foreign Parts, 2 For the Road; Chaykin intro. 10.00
Vol. 2 TPB (2005, $15.99) r/Gun Candy #1,2 & Die Valkyrie #1-3; sketch pages 16.00

RIDER, THE (Frontier Trail #6; also see Blazing Sixguns I.W. Reprint #10, 11)
Ajax/Farrell Publ. (Four Star Comic Corp.): Mar, 1957 - No. 5, 1958
1-Swift Arrow, Lone Rider begin 14 28 42 80 115 150
2-5 8 16 24 44 57 70

RIDERS OF THE PURPLE SAGE (See Zane Grey & Four Color #372)

RIFLEMAN, THE (TV)
Dell Publ. Co./Gold Key No. 13 on: No. 1009, 7-9/59 - No. 12, 7-9/62; No. 13, 11/62 - No. 20, 10/64
Four Color 1009 (#1) 23 46 69 161 358 550
2 (1-3/60) 10 20 30 67 141 215
3-Toth-a (4 pgs.); variant edition has back-c with "Something Special" comic strip
10 20 30 65 135 205
4-9: 6-Toth-a (4 pgs.) 9 18 27 59 117 175
10-Classic-c 46 92 138 368 834 1300
11-20 7 14 21 46 86 125
NOTE: ***Warren Tufts** a-2-9. All have Chuck Connors & Johnny Crawford photo-c. Photo back c-13-15.*

RIFTWAR
Marvel Comics: July, 2009 - No. 5, Dec, 2009 ($3.99, limited series)
1-5-Adaptation of Raymond E. Feist novel; Glass-s/Stegman-a 4.00

RIGHTEOUS THIRST FOR VENGEANCE, A
Image Comics: Oct, 2021 - Present ($3.99, limited series)
1-11-Remender-s/Araújo-a 4.00

RIMA, THE JUNGLE GIRL
National Periodical Publications: Apr-May, 1974 - No. 7, Apr-May, 1975
1-Origin, part 1 (#1-5: 20¢; 6,7: 25¢) 3 6 9 17 26 35
2-7: 2-4-Origin, parts 2-4. 7-Origin & only app. Space Marshal
2 3 4 6 8 10
NOTE: ***Kubert** c-1-7. **Nino** a-1-7. **Redondo** a-1-7.*

RING OF BRIGHT WATER (See Movie Classics)

RING OF THE NIBELUNG, THE
DC Comics: 1989 - No. 4, 1990 ($4.95, squarebound, 52 pgs., mature readers)
1-4: Adapts Wagner cycle of operas, Gil Kane-c/a 5.00

RING OF THE NIBELUNG, THE
Dark Horse Comics: Feb, 2000 - Sept, 2001 ($2.95/$2.99/$5.99, limited series)
Vol. 1 (The Rhinegold) 1-4: Adapts Wagner; P. Craig Russell-s/a 3.00
Vol. 2,3: Vol. 2 (The Valkyrie) 1-3: 1-(8/00). Vol. 3 (Siegfried) 1-3: 1-(12/00) 3.00
Vol. 4 (The Twilight of the Gods) 1-3: 1-(6/01) 3.00
4-(9/01, $5.99, 64 pgs.) Conclusion with sketch pages 6.00

RINGO KID, THE (2nd Series)
Marvel Comics Group: Jan, 1970 - No. 23, Nov, 1973; No. 24, Nov, 1975 - No. 30, Nov, 1976
1-Williamson-a r-from #10, 1956. 5 10 15 31 53 75
2-11: 2-Severin-c. 11-Last 15¢ issue 2 4 6 11 16 20
12 (52 pg. Giant) 3 6 9 16 24 32
13-20: 13-Wildey-r. 20-Williamson-r/#1 2 4 6 9 13 16
21-30 2 4 6 8 10 12
27,28-(30¢-c variant, limited distribution)(5,7/76) 14 28 42 96 211 325

RINGO KID WESTERN, THE (1st Series) (See Wild Western & Western Trails)
Atlas Comics (HPC)/Marvel Comics: Aug, 1954 - No. 21, Sept, 1957
1-Origin; The Ringo Kid begins 41 82 123 256 428 600
2-Black Rider app.; origin/1st app. Ringo's Horse Arab
22 44 66 132 216 300
3-5 15 30 45 86 133 180
6-8-Severin-a(3) each 15 30 45 90 140 190
9,11,12,14-21: 12-Orlando-a (4 pgs.) 14 28 42 78 112 145
10,13-Williamson-a (4 pgs.) 14 28 42 81 118 155
NOTE: ***Berg** a-8. **Maneely** a-1-5, 15, 16(text illos only), 17(4), 18, 20, 21; c-1-6, 8, 13, 15-18, 20. **J. Severin** c-10, 11. **Sinnott** a-1. **Wildey** a-16-18.*

RINGSIDE
Image Comics: Nov, 2015 - No. 15, Apr, 2018 ($3.99)
1-15-Keatinge-s/Barber-a 4.00

RINSE, THE
BOOM! Studios: Sept, 2011 - No. 4, Dec, 2011 ($1.00/$3.99)
1-($1.00)-Phillips-s/Laming-a 3.00
2-4-($3.99) 4.00

RIN TIN TIN (See March of Comics #163,180,195)

RIN TIN TIN (TV) (...& Rusty #21 on; see Western Roundup under Dell Giants)
Dell Publishing Co./Gold Key: Nov, 1952 - No. 38, May-July, 1961; Nov, 1963 (All Photo-c)
Four Color 434 (#1) 16 32 48 111 246 380
Four Color 476,523 9 18 27 62 126 190
4(3-5/54)-10 6 12 18 40 73 105
11-17,19,20 6 12 18 37 66 95
18-(4-5/57) 1st app. of Rusty and the Cavalry of Fort Apache; photo-c
7 14 21 46 86 125
21-38: 36-Toth-a (4 pgs.) 5 10 15 31 53 75
... & Rusty 1 (11/63-Gold Key) 5 10 15 33 57 80

RIO (Also see Eclipse Monthly)
Comico: June, 1987 ($8.95, 64 pgs.)
1-Wildey-c/a 9.00

RIO AT BAY
Dark Horse Comics: July, 1992 - No. 2, Aug, 1992 ($2.95, limited series)
1,2-Wildey-c/a 3.00

RIO BRAVO (Movie) (See 4-Color #1018)
Dell Publishing Co.: June, 1959
Four Color 1018-Toth-a; John Wayne, Dean Martin, & Ricky Nelson photo-c.
28 53 84 202 451 700

RIO CONCHOS (See Movie Comics)

RIOT (Satire)
Atlas Comics (ACI No. 1-5/WPI No. 6): Apr, 1954 - No. 3, Aug, 1954; No. 4, Feb, 1956 - No. 6, June, 1956
1-Russ Heath-a 53 106 159 334 567 800

	GD 2.0	VG 4.0	FN 6.0	VF 8.0	VF/NM 9.0	NM- 9.2
2-Li'l Abner satire by Post	33	66	99	194	317	440
3-Last precode (8/54)	29	58	87	172	281	390
4-Infinity-c; Marilyn Monroe "7 Year Itch" movie satire; Mad Rip-off ads	37	74	111	218	354	490
5-Marilyn Monroe, John Wayne parody; part photo-c	37	74	111	222	361	500
6-Lorna of the Jungle satire by Everett; Dennis the Menace satire-c/story; part photo-c	29	58	87	172	281	390

NOTE: ***Berg** a-3. **Burgos** c-1, 2. **Colan** a-1. **Everett** a-4, 6. **Heath** a-1. **Maneely** a-1, 2, 4-6; c-3, 4, 6. **Post** a-1-4. **Reinman** a-2. **Severin** a-4-6.*

RIOT GEAR
Triumphant Comics: Sept, 1993 - No. 11, July, 1994 ($2.50, serially numbered)

	GD	VG	FN	VF	VF/NM	NM-
1-8: 1-2nd app. Riot Gear. 2-1st app. Rabin. 3,4-Triumphant Unleashed x-over. 3-1st app. Surzar. 4-Death of Captain Tich						3.00
9-11 (May not exist)	1	3	4	6	8	10
Violent Past 1,2: 1-(2/94, $2.50)						3.00

R.I.P.
TSR, Inc.:1990 - No. 8, 1991 ($2.95, 44 pgs.)

	GD	VG	FN	VF	VF/NM	NM-
1-8-Based on TSR game						4.00

RIPCLAW (See Cyberforce)
Image Comics (Top Cow Prod.): Apr, 1995 - No. 3, June, 1995 (Limited series)

	GD	VG	FN	VF	VF/NM	NM-
1/2-Gold, 1/2-San Diego ed., 1/2-Chicago ed.	1	3	4	6	8	10
1-3: Brandon Peterson-a(p)						3.00
Special 1 (10/95, $2.50)						3.00

RIPCLAW
Image Comics (Top Cow Prod.): V2#1, Dec, 1995 - No. 6, June, 1996 ($2.50)

	GD	VG	FN	VF	VF/NM	NM-
V2#1-6: 5-Medieval Spawn/Witchblade Preview						3.00
...: Pilot Season 1 (2007, $2.99) Jason Aaron-s/Jorge Lucas-a/Tony Moore-c						3.00

RIPCORD (TV)
Dell Publishing Co.: Mar-May, 1962

	GD	VG	FN	VF	VF/NM	NM-
Four Color 1294	7	14	21	46	86	125

R.I.P.D.
Dark Horse Comics: Oct, 1999 - No. 4, Jan, 2000 ($2.95, limited series)

	GD	VG	FN	VF	VF/NM	NM-
1-4						3.00
TPB (2003, $12.95) r/#1-4						13.00

R.I.P.D.: CITY OF THE DAMNED
Dark Horse Comics: Nov, 2012 - No. 4, Mar, 2013 ($3.50, limited series)

	GD	VG	FN	VF	VF/NM	NM-
1-4-Barlow-s/Parker-a/Wilkins-c						3.50

RIP HUNTER TIME MASTER (See Showcase #20, 21, 25, 26 & Time Masters)
National Periodical Publications: Mar-Apr, 1961 - No. 29, Nov-Dec, 1965

	GD	VG	FN	VF	VF/NM	NM-
1-(3-4/61)	71	142	213	568	1284	2000
2	25	50	75	175	388	600
3-5: 5-Last 10¢ issue	15	30	45	105	232	360
6,7-Toth-a in each	11	22	33	73	157	240
8-15	8	16	24	54	102	150
16-19	6	12	18	41	76	110
20-Hitler-c/s	10	20	30	64	132	200
21-28	6	12	18	37	66	95
29-Gil Kane-c	7	14	21	49	92	135

RIP IN TIME (Also see Teenage Mutant Ninja Turtles #5-7)
Fantagor Press: Aug, 1986 - No.5, 1987 ($1.50, B&W)

	GD	VG	FN	VF	VF/NM	NM-
1-5: Corben-c/a in all						4.00

RIP KIRBY (Also see Harvey Comics Hits #57, & Street Comix)
David McKay Publications: 1948

	GD	VG	FN	VF	VF/NM	NM-
Feature Books 51,54: Raymond-c; 51-Origin	41	82	123	256	428	600

RIPLEY'S BELIEVE IT OR NOT! (See Ace Comics, All-American Comics, Mystery Comics Digest #1, 4, 7, 10, 13, 16, 19, 22, 25)

RIPLEY'S BELIEVE IT OR NOT!
Harvey Publications: Sept, 1953 - No. 4, March, 1954

	GD	VG	FN	VF	VF/NM	NM-
1-Powell-a	21	42	63	122	199	275
2-4	11	22	33	62	86	110

RIPLEY'S BELIEVE IT OR NOT! (Continuation of Ripleys'...True Ghost Stories & Ripley's...True War Stories)
Gold Key: No. 4, April, 1967 - No. 94, Feb, 1980

	GD	VG	FN	VF	VF/NM	NM-
4-Shrunken head photo-c; McWilliams-a	4	8	12	28	47	65
5-Subtitled "True War Stories"; Evans-a; 1st Jeff Jones-a in comics? (2 pgs.)	4	8	12	27	44	60
6-10: 6-McWilliams-a. 10-Evans-a(2)	3	6	9	19	30	40
11-20: 15-Evans-a	3	6	9	16	23	30
21-30	2	4	6	13	18	22
31-38,40-60	2	4	6	9	13	16
39-Crandall-a	2	4	6	10	14	18
61-73	1	3	4	6	8	10
74,77-83-(52 pgs.)	2	4	6	9	13	16
75,76,84-94	1	2	3	5	6	8
Story Digest Mag. 1(6/70)-4-3/4x6-1/2", 148pp.	5	10	15	31	53	75

NOTE: ***Evanish** art by **Luiz Dominguez** #22-25, 27, 30, 31, 40. **Jeff Jones** a-5(2 pgs.). **McWilliams** a-65, 66, 70, 89. **Orlando** a-8. **Sparling** c-68. Reprints-74, 77-84, 87 (part); 91, 93 (all). **Williamson, Wood** a-80r/#1.*

RIPLEY'S BELIEVE IT OR NOT!
Dark Horse Comics: May, 2002 - No. 3, Oct, 2002 ($2.99, B&W, unfinished limited series)

	GD	VG	FN	VF	VF/NM	NM-
1-3-Nord-c/a. 1-Stories of Amelia Earhart & D.B. Cooper						3.00

RIPLEY'S BELIEVE IT OR NOT! TRUE GHOST STORIES (Along with Ripley's...True War Stories, the three issues together precede the 1967 series that starts its numbering with #4) (Also see Dan Curtis)
Gold Key: June, 1965 - No. 2, Oct, 1966

	GD	VG	FN	VF	VF/NM	NM-
1-Williamson, Wood & Evans-a; photo-c	9	18	27	57	111	165
2-Orlando, McWilliams-a; photo-c	5	10	15	33	57	80
Mini-Comic 1(1976-3-1/4x6-1/2")	2	4	6	8	11	14
11186(1977)-Golden Press; ($1.95, 224 pgs.)-All-r	4	8	12	28	47	65
11401(3/79)-Golden Press; ($1.00, 96 pgs.)-All-r	3	6	9	16	23	30

RIPLEY'S BELIEVE IT OR NOT! TRUE WAR STORIES (Along with Ripley's...True Ghost Stories, the three issues together precede the 1967 series that starts its numbering with #4)
Gold Key: Nov, 1965 (Aug, 1965 in indicia)

	GD	VG	FN	VF	VF/NM	NM-
1-No Williamson-a	5	10	15	31	53	75

RIPLEY'S BELIEVE IT OR NOT! TRUE WEIRD
Ripley Enterprises: June, 1966 - No. 2, Aug, 1966 (B&W Magazine)

	GD	VG	FN	VF	VF/NM	NM-
1,2-Comic stories & text	4	8	12	25	40	55

RISE OF APOCALYPSE
Marvel Comics: Oct, 1996 - No. 4, Jan, 1997 ($1.95, limited series)

	GD	VG	FN	VF	VF/NM	NM-
1-Adam Pollina-c/a in all	1	3	4	6	8	10
2-4						5.00

RISE OF THE BLACK FLAME
Dark Horse Comics: Sept, 2016 - No. 5, Jan, 2017 ($3.99, limited series)

	GD	VG	FN	VF	VF/NM	NM-
1-5-Mignola & Roberson-s/Mitten-a/Laurence Campbell-c						4.00

RISE OF THE BLACK PANTHER
Marvel Comics: Mar, 2018 - No. 6, Aug, 2018 ($3.99, limited series)

	GD	VG	FN	VF	VF/NM	NM-
1-6: 1-Origin of T'Challa; Narcisse-s/Renaud-a/Stelfreeze-c; Klaw app. 2-Namor app.						4.00

RISE OF THE MAGI
Image Comics (Top Cow): No. 0, May, 2014 - No. 5 ($3.50)

	GD	VG	FN	VF	VF/NM	NM-
0 (5/14, Free Comic Book Day giveaway) Silvestri-s/c; bonus character & concept art						3.00
1-5: 1-(6/14) Silvestri-s/Kesgin-a; four covers						3.50

RISE OF THE TEENAGE MUTANT NINJA TURTLES
Image Comics (Top Cow): No. 0, Jul, 2018 - No. 5, Jan, 2019 ($3.99)

	GD	VG	FN	VF	VF/NM	NM-
0-5-Based on the Nickelodeon animated series; Matthew K. Manning-s/Chad Thomas-a						4.00

RISE OF THE TEENAGE MUTANT NINJA TURTLES: SOUND OFF!
Image Comics (Top Cow): Jul, 2019 - No. 3, Sept, 2019 ($3.99)

	GD	VG	FN	VF	VF/NM	NM-
1-3-Matthew K. Manning-s/Chad Thomas-a						4.00

RISE OF ULTRAMAN, THE (Also see The Trials of Ultraman)
Marvel Comics: Nov, 2020 - No. 5, Mar, 2021 ($5.99/$3.99, limited series)

	GD	VG	FN	VF	VF/NM	NM-
1-($5.99) Intro. Shin Hayata; Higgins & Groom-s/Manna-a; main cover by Alex Ross						6.00
2-5-($3.99) Origin of Ultraman						4.00

RISING STARS
Image Comics (Top Cow): Mar, 1999 - No. 24, Mar, 2005 ($2.50/$2.99)

	GD	VG	FN	VF	VF/NM	NM-
Preview-(3/99, $5.00) Straczynski-s						6.00
0-(6/00, $2.50) Gary Frank-a/c						3.00
1/2-(8/01, $2.95) Anderson-c; art & sketch pages by Zanier						3.00
1-Four covers; Keu Cha-c/a						5.00
1-($10.00) Gold Editions-four covers						10.00
1-($50.00) Holofoil-c						50.00
2-7: 5-7-Zanier & Lashley-a(p)						4.00
8-23: 8-13-Zanier & Lashley-a(p). 14-Immonen-a. 15-Flip book B&W preview of Universe. 15-23-Brent Anderson-a						3.00
24-($3.99) Series finale; Anderson-a/c						4.00
Born In Fire TPB (11/00, $19.95) r/#1-8; foreword by Neil Gaiman						20.00
Power TPB (2002, $19.95) r/#9-16						20.00
Prelude-(10/00, $2.95) Cha-a/Lashley-c						3.00
...: Visitations (2002, $8.99) r/#0, 1/2, Preview; new Anderson-c; cover gallery						9.00
Vol. 3: Fire and Ash TPB (2005, $19.99) r/#17-24; design pages & cover gallery						20.00
Vol. 4 TPB (2006, $19.99) r/Rising Stars Bright #1-3 and Voices of the Dead #1-6						20.00
Vol. 5 TPB (2007, $16.99) r/Rising Stars: Untouchable #1-5 and ...: Visitations						17.00
Wizard #0-(3/99) Wizard supplement; Straczynski-s						3.00
Wizard #1/2						5.00

RISING STARS BRIGHT
Image Comics (Top Cow): Mar, 2003 - No. 3, May, 2003 ($2.99, limited series)

	GD	VG	FN	VF	VF/NM	NM-
1-3-Avery-s/Jurgens & Gorder-a/Beck-c						3.00

RISING STARS: UNTOUCHABLE
Image Comics (Top Cow): Mar, 2006 - No. 5, July, 2006 ($2.99, limited series)

	GD	VG	FN	VF	VF/NM	NM-
1-5-Avery-s/Anderson-a						3.00

RISING STARS: VOICES OF THE DEAD
Image Comics (Top Cow): June, 2005 - No. 6, Dec, 2005 ($2.99, limited series)

	GD	VG	FN	VF	VF/NM	NM-
1-6-Avery-s/Staz Johnson-a						3.00

RISING SUN (Based on the CMON board game)
IDW Publishing: Nov, 2019 - Present ($4.99)

	GD	VG	FN	VF	VF/NM	NM-
1,2-Ron Marz & David Rodriguez-s/Martin Coccolo-a						5.00

RIVERDALE (Based on the 2017 TV series)
Archie Comic Publications: Apr, 2017; May, 2017 - No. 12, Jul, 2018 ($3.99)

	GD	VG	FN	VF	VF/NM	NM-
1-12: 1-4-Eisma-a. 5-12-Pitilli-a. 6-History of Pop's						4.00
... FCBD Edition (5/18, giveaway) r/#6						3.00
... One-Shot (4/17, $4.99) Short story prologues to the TV series; multiple covers						4.00

RIVERDALE (Volume 2)(Season 3 on cover)
Archie Comic Publications: May, 2019 - No. 5, Sept, 2019 ($3.99)

	GD	VG	FN	VF	VF/NM	NM-
1-5-Short stories; Ostow-s; art by Pitilli & Eisma						4.00
... FCBD Edition (5/19, giveaway) new story; Ostow-s/Pitilli-a						3.00

RIVERDALE DIGEST (Tie-in to 2017 TV series)
Archie Comic Publications: Jun, 2017 - No. 7, May, 2018 ($5.99/$6.99)

	GD	VG	FN	VF	VF/NM	NM-
1,2-($5.99): 1-Reprints of first issues of recent 2015-2017 Archie series; Francavilla TV cast-c. 2-Reprints of early 2015-2017 issues and classic reprints						6.00
3-7-($6.99)-Reprints of early 2015-2017 issues and classic reprints						7.00

RIVERDALE HIGH (Archie's... #7,8)
Archie Comics: Aug, 1990 - No. 8, Oct, 1991 ($1.00, bi-monthly)

	GD	VG	FN	VF	VF/NM	NM-
1						4.00
2-8						3.00

RIVER FEUD (See Zane Grey & Four Color #484)

Rise of the Black Panther #1 © MAR

Riverdale (2017) #6 © ACP

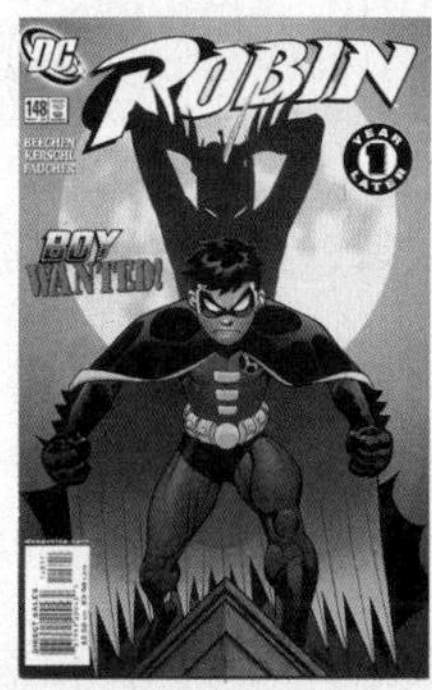

Robin #148 © DC

	GD 2.0	VG 4.0	FN 6.0	VF 8.0	VF/NM 9.0	NM- 9.2

RIVETS
Dell Publishing Co.: No. 518, Nov, 1953

Four Color 518	5	10	15	34	60	85

RIVETS (A dog)
Argo Publ.: Jan, 1956 - No. 3, May, 1956

1-Reprints Sunday & daily newspaper strips	7	14	21	37	46	55
2,3	5	10	15	22	26	30

ROACHMILL
Blackthorne Publ.: Dec, 1986 - No. 6, Oct, 1987 ($1.75, B&W)

1-6 3.00

ROACHMILL
Dark Horse Comics: May, 1988 - No. 10, Dec, 1990 ($1.75, B&W)

1-10: 10-Contains trading cards 3.00

ROADIE, THE
Dark Horse Comics: Sept, 2022 - No. 4, Dec, 2022 ($3.99, limited series)

1-4-Tim Seeley-s/Fran Galán-a 4.00

ROAD OF THE DEAD: HIGHWAY TO HELL
IDW Publishing: Oct, 2018 - No. 3, Dec, 2018 ($4.99, limited series)

1-3-Jonathan Maberry-s/Drew Moss-a 5.00

ROAD RUNNER (See Beep Beep, the...)

ROAD TO EMPYRE: THE KREE/SKRULL WAR (Leads into Empyre series)
Marvel Comics: May, 2020 ($4.99, one-shot)

1-Thompson-s/De Iulis & Rodríguez-a; origin of Hulkling & Kree/Skrull history re-told 4.00

ROAD TO OZ (Adaptation of the L. Frank Baum book)
Marvel Comics: Nov, 2012 - No. 6, May, 2013 ($3.99, limited series)

1-6-Eric Shanower-s/Skottie Young-a/c 4.00

ROAD TO PERDITION (Inspired the 2002 Tom Hanks/Paul Newman movie)
(Also see On the Road to Perdition)
DC Comics/Paradox Press: 1998, 2002 ($13.95, B&W paperback graphic novel)

nn-(1st printing) Max Allan Collins-s/Richard Piers Rayner-a 30.00
2nd & 3rd printings (2002, $13.95) 14.00
Movie photo cover edition (2002) 14.00

ROADTRIP
Oni Press: Aug, 2000 ($2.95, B&W, one-shot)

1-Reprints Judd Winick's back-up stories from Oni Double Feature #9,10 3.00

ROADWAYS
Cult Press: May, 1994 ($2.75, B&W, limited series)

1 3.00

ROARIN' RICK'S RARE BIT FIENDS
King Hell Press: July, 1994 - No. 21, Aug, 1996 ($2.95, B&W, mature)

1-21: Rick Veitch-c/a/scripts in all. 20-(5/96). 21-(8/96)-Reads Subtleman #1 on cover 3.00
Rabid Eye: The Dream Art of Rick Veitch ($14.95, B&W, TPB)-r/#1-8 & the appendix from #12 15.00
Pocket Universe (6/96, $14.95, B&W, TPB)-Reprints 15.00

ROBERT E. HOWARD'S CONAN THE BARBARIAN
Marvel Comics: 1983 ($2.50, 68 pgs., Baxter paper)

1-r/Savage Tales #2,3 by Smith, c-r/Conan #21 by Smith. 5.00

ROBERT LOUIS STEVENSON'S KIDNAPPED (See Kidnapped)

ROBIN (See Aurora, Birds of Prey, Detective Comics #38, New Teen Titans, Robin II, Robin III, Robin 3000, Star Spangled Comics #65, Teen Titans & Young Justice)

ROBIN (See Batman #457)
DC Comics: Jan, 1991 - No. 5, May, 1991 ($1.00, limited series)

1-Free poster by N. Adams; Bolland-c on all 6.00
1-2nd & 3rd printings (without poster) 3.00
2-5 4.00
2-2nd printing 3.00
Annual 1,2 (1992-93, $2.50, 68 pgs.): 1-Grant/Wagner scripts; Sam Kieth-c. 2-Intro Razorsharp; Jim Balent-c(p) 4.00

ROBIN (See Detective #668) (Also see Red Robin and Tim Drake: Robin)
DC Comics: Nov, 1993 - No. 183, Apr, 2009 ($1.50/$1.95/$1.99/$2.25/$2.50/$2.99)

1-($2.95)-Collector's edition w/foil embossed-c; 1st app. Robin's car, The Redbird; Azrael as Batman app. 6.00
1-Newsstand ed. 3.00
2-49,51-66-Regular editions: 3-5-The Spoiler app. 6-The Huntress-c/story cont'd from Showcase '94 #5. 7-Knightquest: The Conclusion w/new Batman (Azrael) vs. Bruce Wayne. 8-KnightsEnd Pt. 5. 9-KnightsEnd Aftermath; Batman-c & app. 10-(9/94)-Zero Hour. 11-(11/94). 25-Green Arrow-c/app. 26-Batman app. 27-Contagion Pt. 3; Catwoman-c/app.; Penguin & Azrael app. 28-Contagion Pt. 11. 29-Penguin app. 31-Wildcat-c/app. 32-Legacy Pt. 3. 33-Legacy Pt. 7. 35-Final Night. 46-Genesis. 52,53-Cataclysm pt. 7, conclusion. 55-Green Arrow app. 62-64-Flash-c/app. 3.50
14 ($2.50)-Embossed-c; Troika Pt. 4 4.00
50-($2.95)-Lady Shiva & King Snake app. 4.00
67-74,76-97: 67-72-No Man's Land. 79-Green Arrow app. 86-Pander Bros.-a 3.00
75-($2.95) 4.00
98,99-Bruce Wayne: Murderer x-over pt. 6, 11 3.00
100-($3.50) Last Dixon-s 4.00
101-174: 101-Young Justice x-over. 106-Kevin Lau-c. 121,122-Willingham-s/Mays-a. 125-Tim Drake quits. 126-Spoiler becomes the new Robin. 129-131-War Games. 132-Robin moves to Bludhaven, Batgirl app. 138-Begin $2.50-c. 139-McDaniel-a begins. 146-147-Teen Titans app. 148-One Year Later; new costume. 150-Begin $2.99-c. 152,153-Boomerang app. 168,169-Resurrection of Ra's al Ghul x-over. 174 Spoiler unmasked 3.00
175-183: 175,176-Batman R.I.P. x-over. 180-Robin vs. Red Robin 3.00
#0-(10/94) Zero Hour; released betwen #10 & #11 3.50
#1,000,000 (11/98) 853rd Century x-over 3.00
Annual 3-5: 3-(1994, $2.95)-Elseworlds story. 4-(1995, $2.95)-Year One story. 5-(1996, $2.95)-Legends of the Dead Earth story 4.00
Annual 6 (1997, $3.95)-Pulp Heroes story 4.00
Annual 7 (12/07, $3.99)-Pearson-c/a; prelude to Resurrection of Ra's al Ghul x-over 4.00
.../Argent 1 (2/98, $1.95) Argent (Teen Titans) app. 3.00
.../Batgirl: Fresh Blood TPB (2005, $12.99) r/#132,133 & Batgirl #58,59 13.00
...: Days of Fire and Madness (2006, $12.99, TPB) r/#140-145 13.00
...Eighty-Page Giant 1 (9/00, $5.95) Chuck Dixon-s/Diego Barreto-a 6.00
...: Flying Solo (2000, $12.95, TPB) r/#1-6, Showcase '94 #5,6 13.00
...Plus 1 (12/96, $2.95) Impulse-c/app.; Waid-s 4.00
...Plus 2 (12/97, $2.95) Fang (Scare Tactics) app. 4.00
...: Search For a Hero (2009, $19.99, TPB) r/#175-183; cover gallery 20.00
.../Spoiler Special 1 (8/08, $3.99) Follows Spoiler's return in Robin #174; Dixon-s 4.00
...: Teenage Wasteland (2007, $17.99, TPB) r/#154-162 18.00
...: The Big Leagues (2008, $12.99, TPB) r/#163-167 13.00
...: Unmasked (2004, $12.95, TPB) r/#121-125; Pearson-c 13.00
...: Violent Tendencies (2008, $17.99, TPB) r/#170-174 & Robin/Spoiler Special 1 18.00
...: Wanted (2007, $12.99, TPB) r/#148-153 13.00

ROBIN (Damian Wayne)
DC Comics: Jun, 2021 - No. 17, Oct, 2022 ($3.99)

1-17: 1-Williamson-s/Melnikov-a; intro Flatline; Connor Hawke app. 13,14-Shadow War. 16,17-Lord Death Man app. 4.00
... 2021 Annual 1 (1/22, $5.99) Takes place before Robin #6; origin of Flatline 6.00

ROBIN: A HERO REBORN
DC Comics: 1991 ($4.95, squarebound, trade paperback)

nn-r/Batman #455-457 & Robin #1-5; Bolland-c	2	4	6	8	10	12

ROBIN & BATMAN (Dick Grayson)
DC Comics: Jan, 2022 - No. 3, Mar, 2022 ($5.99, squarebound limited series)

1-3-Dick Grayson's early days as Robin; Lemire-s/Nguyen-a. 2-Teen Titans app. 6.00

ROBIN 80TH ANNIVERSARY 100-PAGE SUPER SPECTACULAR
DC Comics: May, 2020 ($9.99, squarebound, one-shot)

1-Short stories and pin-ups of the various Robins; s/a by various; multiple covers 10.00

ROBIN HOOD (See The Advs. of..., Brave and the Bold, Classic Comics #7, Classics Giveaways (12/44), Four Color #413, 669, King Classics, Movie Comics & Power Record Comics) (...& His Merry Men, The Illustrated Story of...)

ROBIN HOOD (Disney)
Dell Publishing Co.: No. 413, Aug, 1952; No. 669, Dec, 1955

Four Color 413-(1st Disney movie Four Color book)(8/52)-Photo-c	9	18	27	62	126	190
Four Color 669 (12/55)-Reprints #413 plus photo-c	6	12	18	38	69	100

ROBIN HOOD (Adventures of... #6-8)
Magazine Enterprises (Sussex Pub. Co.): No. 52, Nov, 1955 - No. 5, Mar, 1957

52 (#1)-Origin Robin Hood & Sir Gallant of the Round Table	18	36	54	105	165	225
53 (#2), 3-5	12	24	36	69	97	125
I.W. Reprint #1,2,9: 1-r/#3. 2-r/#4. 9-r/#52 (1963)	2	4	6	9	13	16
Super Reprint #10,15: 10-r/#53. 15-r/#5	2	4	6	9	13	16

NOTE: *Bolle a-in all; c-52.*

ROBIN HOOD (Not Disney)
Dell Publishing Co.: May-July, 1963 (one-shot)

1	3	6	9	16	23	30

	GD 2.0	VG 4.0	FN 6.0	VF 8.0	VF/NM 9.0	NM- 9.2

ROBIN HOOD (Disney) (Also see Best of Walt Disney)
Western Publishing Co.: 1973 ($1.50, 8-1/2x11", 52 pgs., cardboard-c)

	GD	VG	FN	VF	VF/NM	NM-
96151- "Robin Hood", based on movie, 96152- "The Mystery of Sherwood Forest", 96153- "In King Richard's Service", 96154- "The Wizard's Ring" each....	3	6	9	15	22	28

ROBIN HOOD
Eclipse Comics: July, 1991 - No. 3, Dec, 1991 ($2.50, limited series)

1-3: Timothy Truman layouts 3.00

ROBIN HOOD AND HIS MERRY MEN (Formerly Danger & Adventure)
Charlton Comics: No. 28, Apr, 1956 - No. 38, Aug, 1958

	GD	VG	FN	VF	VF/NM	NM-
28	11	22	33	60	83	105
29-37	8	16	24	44	57	70
38-Ditko-a (5 pgs.); Rocke-c	15	30	45	83	124	165

ROBIN HOOD TALES (Published by National Periodical #7 on)
Quality Comics Group (Comic Magazines): Feb, 1956 - No. 6, Nov-Dec, 1956

	GD	VG	FN	VF	VF/NM	NM-
1-All have Baker/Cuidera-c	37	74	111	218	354	490
2-6-Matt Baker-a	35	70	105	208	339	470

ROBIN HOOD TALES (Cont'd from Quality series)(See Brave & the Bold #5)
National Periodical Publ.: No. 7, Jan-Feb, 1957 - No. 14, Mar-Apr, 1958

	GD	VG	FN	VF	VF/NM	NM-
7-All have Andru/Esposito-c	37	74	111	218	354	490
8-14	31	62	93	186	303	420

ROBIN RISES: OMEGA (See Batman & Robin #33-37)
DC Comics: Sept, 2014; Feb, 2015 ($4.99, one-shots)

Alpha 1 (2/15)-Tomasi-s/Andy Kubert-a/c; Damien returns; Talia app. 5.00
Omega 1 (9/14)-Tomasi-s/Andy Kubert-a/c; Ra's al Ghul and Justice League app. 5.00

ROBINS
DC Comics: Jan, 2022 - No. 6, Jun, 2022 ($3.99, limited series)

1-6-Nightwing, Red Hood and the Robins app.; Seeley-s/Rivas-a 4.00

ROBINSON CRUSOE (See King Classics & Power Record Comics)
Dell Publishing Co.: Nov-Jan, 1963-64

	GD	VG	FN	VF	VF/NM	NM-
1	3	6	9	15	21	26

ROBIN: SON OF BATMAN (Damian Wayne)
DC Comics: Aug, 2015 - No. 13, Aug, 2016 ($3.99)

1-13: 1-Gleason-s/a. 4-Deathstroke app. 5-Damian vs. Talia. 7-"Robin War" tie-in 4.00

ROBIN II (The Joker's Wild)
DC Comics: Oct, 1991 - No. 4, Dec, 1991 ($1.50, mini-series)

1-(Direct sales, $1.50)-With 4 diff.-c; same hologram on each 6.00
1-(Newsstand, $1.00)-No hologram; 1 version 4.00
1-Collector's set ($10.00)-Contains all 5 versions bagged with hologram trading card inside 18.00
2-(Direct sales, $1.50)-With 3 different-c 5.00
2-4-(Newsstand, $1.00)-1 version of each 4.00
2-Collector's set ($8.00)-Contains all 4 versions bagged with hologram trading card inside 12.00
3-(Direct sale, $1.50)-With 2 different-c 4.00
3-Collector's set ($6.00)-Contains all 3 versions bagged with hologram trading card inside 10.00
4-(Direct sales, $1.50)-Only one version 4.00
4-Collector's set ($4.00)-Contains both versions bagged with Bat-Signal hologram trading card 6.00
Multi-pack (All four issues w/hologram sticker) 14.00
Deluxe Complete Set ($30.00)-Contains all 14 versions of #1-4 plus a new hologram trading card; numbered & limited to 25,000; comes with slipcase & 2 acid free backing boards 45.00

ROBIN III: CRY OF THE HUNTRESS
DC Comics: Dec, 1992 - No. 6, Mar, 1993 (Limited series)

1-6 ($2.50, collector's ed.)-Polybagged w/movement enhanced-c plus mini-poster of newsstand-c by Zeck 5.00
1-6 ($1.25, newsstand ed.): All have Zeck-c 4.00

ROBIN 3000
DC Comics (Elseworlds): 1992 - No. 2, 1992 ($4.95, mini-series, 52 pgs.)

1,2-Foil logo; Russell-c/a 6.00

ROBIN WAR (Crossover with Grayson, Robin: Son of Batman, and We Are Robin)
DC Comics: Feb, 2016 - No. 2, Mar, 2016 ($4.99)

1,2-Tom King-s; art by various; The Court of Owls app. 5.00

ROBIN: YEAR ONE
DC Comics: 2000 - No. 4, 2001 ($4.95, square-bound, limited series)

1-4: Earliest days of Robin's career; Javier Pulido-c/a. 2,4-Two-Face app. 6.00
TPB (2002, 2008, $14.95/$14.99, 2 printings) r/#1-4 15.00

ROBOCOP
Marvel Comics: Oct, 1987 ($2.00, B&W, magazine, one-shot)

	GD	VG	FN	VF	VF/NM	NM-
1-Movie adaptation	11	22	33	76	163	250

ROBOCOP (Also see Dark Horse Comics)
Marvel Comics: Mar, 1990 - No. 23, Jan, 1992 ($1.50)

	GD	VG	FN	VF	VF/NM	NM-
1-Based on movie	2	4	6	9	12	15

2-23 4.00
nn (7/90, $4.95, 52 pgs.)-r/B&W magazine in color; adapts 1st movie 5.00

ROBOCOP
Dynamite Entertainment: 2010 - No. 6, 2010 ($3.50, limited series)

1-6-Follows the events of the first film; Neves-a 4.00

ROBOCOP
BOOM! Studios: Jul, 2014 - No. 12, Jun, 2015 ($3.99)

1-12: 1-8-Williamson-s/Magno-a. 1-Multiple covers. 9,10-Aragon-a 4.00

ROBOCOP (FRANK MILLER'S...)
Avatar Press: July, 2003 - No. 9, Jan, 2006 ($3.50/$3.99, limited series)

1-9-Frank Miller-s/Juan Ryp-a. 1-Three covers by Miller, Ryp, and Barrows. 2-Two covers 4.00
Free Comic Book Day Edition (4/03) Previews Robocop & Stargate SG•1; Busch-c 3.00

ROBOCOP (Tie-ins to the 2014 movie)
BOOM! Studios: Feb, 2014 ($3.99)

...: Beta (2/14) Brisson-s/Laiso-a 4.00
...: Hominem Ex Machina (2/14) Moreci-s/Copland-a 4.00
...: Memento Mori (2/14) Barbiere-s/Vieira-a 4.00
...: To Live and Die in Detroit (2/14) Joe Harris-s/Piotr Kowalski-a 4.00

ROBOCOP: CITIZENS ARREST
BOOM! Studios: Apr, 2018 - No. 5, Aug, 2018 ($3.99, limited series)

1-5-Brian Wood-s/Jorge Coelho-a 4.00

ROBOCOP: LAST STAND
BOOM! Studios: Aug, 2013 - No. 8, Mar, 2014 ($3.99, limited series)

1-8: 1-Miller & Grant-s/Oztekin-a 4.00

ROBOCOP: MORTAL COILS
Dark Horse Comics: Sept, 1993 - No. 4, Dec, 1993 ($2.50, limited series)

1-4: 1,2-Cago painted-c 4.00

ROBOCOP: PRIME SUSPECT
Dark Horse Comics: Oct, 1992 - No. 4, Jan, 1993 ($2.50, limited series)

1-4: 1,3-Nelson painted-c. 2,4-Bolton painted-c 4.00

ROBOCOP: ROAD TRIP
Dynamite Entertainment: 2012 - No. 4, 2012 ($3.99, limited series)

1-4-De Zarate-a 4.00

ROBOCOP: ROULETTE
Dark Horse Comics: Dec, 1993 - No. 4, 1994 ($2.50, limited series)

1-4: 1,3-Nelson painted-c. 2,4-Bolton painted-c 4.00

ROBOCOP 2
Marvel Comics: Aug, 1990 ($2.25, B&W, magazine, 68 pgs.)

1-Adapts movie sequel scripted by Frank Miller; Bagley-a 5.00

ROBOCOP 2
Marvel Comics: Aug, 1990; Late Aug, 1990 - #3, Late Sept, 1990 ($1.00, limited series)

nn-(8/90, $4.95, 68 pgs., color)-Same contents as B&W magazine 5.00
1: #1-3 reprint no number issue 3.00
2,3: 2-Guice-c(i) 3.00

ROBOCOP 3
Dark Horse Comics: July, 1993 - No. 3, Nov, 1993 ($2.50, limited series)

1-3: Nelson painted-c; Nguyen-a(p) 4.00

ROBOCOP VERSUS THE TERMINATOR
Dark Horse Comics: Sept, 1992 - No. 4, 1992 (Dec.) ($2.50, limited series)

1-4: Miller scripts & Simonson-c/a in all 5.00
1-Platinum Edition 10.00
NOTE: *All contain a different Robocop cardboard cut-out stand-up.*

ROBO DOJO
DC Comics (WildStorm): Apr, 2002 - No. 6, Sept, 2002 ($2.95, limited series)

1-6-Wolfman-s 3.00

ROBO-HUNTER (Also see Sam Slade...)
Eagle Comics: Apr, 1984 - No. 5, 1984 ($1.00)

1-5-2000 A.D. 4.00

ROBONIC STOOGES (Three Stooges)
American Mythology: 2021 - No. 3, 2021 ($3.99)

1-3-The Stooges as robot heroes. 2-Fantastic Four #1 cover swipe. 3-X-Men #141 swipe 4.00

R.O.B.O.T. BATTALION 2050
Eclipse Comics: Mar, 1988 ($2.00, B&W, one-shot)

1 3.00

ROBOT COMICS
Renegade Press: No. 0, June, 1987 ($2.00, B&W, one-shot)

0-Bob Burden story & art 3.00

ROBOTECH
Antarctic Press: Mar, 1997 - No. 11, Nov, 1998 ($2.95)

1-11, Annual 1 (4/98, $2.95) 4.00
...Class Reunion (12/98, $3.95, B&W) 4.00
...Escape (5/98, $2.95, B&W), ...Final Fire (12/98, $2.95, B&W) 4.00

ROBOTECH
DC Comics (WildStorm): No. 0, Feb, 2003 - No. 6, Jul, 2003 ($2.50/$2.95, limited series)

0-Tommy Yune-s; art by Jim Lee, Garza, Bermejo and others; pin-up pages by various 3.00
1-6 ($2.95)-Long Vo-a 3.00
...: From the Stars (2003, $9.95, digest-size) r/#0-6 & Sourcebook 10.00
... Sourcebook (3/03, $2.95) pin-ups and info on characters and mecha; art by various 3.00

ROBOTECH
Titan Comics: Aug, 2017 - No. 24, Oct, 2019 ($3.99)

1-24: 1-11-Brian Wood-s/Marco Turini-a; multiple covers on each. 12-14-Prasetya-a 4.00
... Free Comic Book Day 2019 - Furman-s/Prasetya-a 3.00

ROBOTECH: COVERT-OPS
Antarctic Press: Aug, 1998 - No. 2, Sept, 1998 ($2.95, B&W, limited series)

1,2-Gregory Lane-s/a 4.00

ROBOTECH DEFENDERS
DC Comics: Mar, 1985 - No. 2, Apr, 1985 (Mini-series)

1,2 4.00

ROBOTECH IN 3-D (TV)
Comico: Aug, 1987 ($2.50)

1-Steacy painted-c 5.00

ROBOTECH: INVASION

Robin: Son of Batman #1 © DC

Robocop (2010) #2 © Orion

Rocket #4 © MAR

	GD	VG	FN	VF	VF/NM	NM-
	2.0	4.0	6.0	8.0	9.0	9.2

DC Comics (WildStorm): Feb, 2004 - No. 5, July, 2004 ($2.95, limited series)
1-5-Faerber & Yune-s/Miyazawa & Dogan-a — 3.00

ROBOTECH: LOVE AND WAR
DC Comics (WildStorm): Aug, 2003 - No. 6, Jan, 2004 ($2.95, limited series)
1-6-Long Vo & Charles Park-a/Faerber & Yune-s. 2-Variant-c by Warren — 3.00

ROBOTECH MASTERS (TV)
Comico: July, 1985 - No. 23, Apr, 1988 ($1.50)
1 — 6.00
2-23 — 4.00

ROBOTECH: PRELUDE TO THE SHADOW CHRONICLES
DC Comics (WildStorm): Dec, 2005 - No. 5, Mar, 2006 ($3.50, limited series)
1-5-Yune-s/Dogan & Udon Studios-a — 3.50
TPB (2010, $17.99) r/#1-5; production art — 18.00

ROBOTECH: REMIX
Titan Comics: Nov, 2019 - Present ($3.99)
1-4-Continues from Robotech 2017-19 series; Fletcher-s/Damaso-a — 4.00

ROBOTECH: SENTINELS - RUBICON
Antarctic Press: July, 1998 ($2.95, B&W)
1 — 4.00

ROBOTECH SPECIAL
Comico: May, 1988 ($2.50, one-shot, 44 pgs.)
1-Steacy wraparound-c; partial photo-c — 5.00

ROBOTECH THE GRAPHIC NOVEL
Comico: Aug, 1986 ($5.95, 8-1/2x11", 52 pgs.)
1-Origin SDF-1; intro T.R. Edwards, Steacy-c/a — 15.00
1-Second printing (12/86) — 10.00

ROBOTECH: THE MACROSS SAGA (TV)(Formerly Macross)
Comico: No. 2, Feb, 1985 - No. 36, Feb, 1989 ($1.50)

	GD	VG	FN	VF	VF/NM	NM-
2	1	2	3	5	6	8
3-10						5.00
11-36: 12,17-Ken Steacy painted-c. 26-Begin $1.75-c. 35,36-($1.95)						4.00
Volume 1-4 TPB (WildStorm, 2003, $14.95, 5-3/4" x 8-1/4")1-Reprints #2-6 & Macross #1. 2- r/#7-12. 3-r/#13-18. 4-r/#19-24						15.00

ROBOTECH: THE NEW GENERATION
Comico: July, 1985 - No. 25, July, 1988
1 — 6.00
2-25 — 4.00

ROBOTECH: VERMILION
Antarctic Press: Mar, 1997 - No. 4, ($2.95, B&W, limited series)
1-4 — 4.00

ROBOTECH / VOLTRON
Dynamite Entertainment: 2013 - No. 5, 2014 ($3.99, limited series)
1-5-Tommy Yune-s — 4.00

ROBOTECH: WINGS OF GIBRALTAR
Antarctic Press: Aug, 1998 - No. 2, Sept, 1998 ($2.95, B&W, limited series)
1,2-Lee Duhig-s/a — 4.00

ROBOTIX
Marvel Comics: Feb, 1986 (75¢, one-shot)
1-Based on toy — 4.00

ROBOTMEN OF THE LOST PLANET (Also see Space Thrillers)
Avon Periodicals: 1952 (Also see Strange Worlds #19)

	GD	VG	FN	VF	VF/NM	NM-
1-McCann-a (3 pgs.); Fawcette-a	206	412	618	1318	2259	3200

ROB ROY
Dell Publishing Co.: 1954 (Disney-Movie)

	GD	VG	FN	VF	VF/NM	NM-
Four Color 544-Manning-a, photo-c	9	18	27	57	111	165

ROCK, THE (WWF Wrestling)
Chaos! Comics: June, 2001 ($2.99, one-shot)
1-Photo-c; Grant-s/Neves-a — 4.00

ROCK & ROLL HIGH SCHOOL
Roger Corman's Cosmic Comics: Oct, 1995 ($2.50)
1-Bob Fingerman scripts — 3.00

ROCK AND ROLLO (Formerly TV Teens)
Charlton Comics: V2#14, Oct, 1957 - No. 19, Sept, 1958

	GD	VG	FN	VF	VF/NM	NM-
V2#14-19	7	14	21	37	46	55

ROCK COMICS
Landgraphic Publ.: Jul/Aug, 1979 ($1.25, tabloid size, 28 pgs.)

	GD	VG	FN	VF	VF/NM	NM-
1-N. Adams-c; Thor (not Marvel's) story by Adams	3	6	9	14	20	25

ROCKET (Rocket Raccoon from Guardians of the Galaxy)
Marvel Comics: Jul, 2017 - No. 6, Dec, 2017 ($3.99, limited series)
1-6: 1-Ewing-s/Gorham-a/Mayhew-c. 4-Deadpool app. — 4.00

ROCKET COMICS
Hillman Periodicals: Mar, 1940 - No. 3, May, 1940

	GD	VG	FN	VF	VF/NM	NM-
1-Rocket Riley, Red Roberts the Electro Man (origin), The Phantom Ranger, The Steel Shark, The Defender, Buzzard Barnes and his Sky Devils, Lefty Larson, & The Defender, the Man with a Thousand Faces begin (1st app. of each); all have Rocket Riley-c	343	686	1029	2400	4200	6000
2,3: 2-Jack Cole-a	258	316	774	1651	2826	4000

ROCKET COMICS: IGNITE
Dark Horse Comics: Apr, 2003 (Free Comic Book Day giveaway)
1-Previews Dark Horse series Syn, Lone, and Go Boy 7 — 3.00

ROCKETEER, THE (See Eclipse Graphic Album Series, Pacific Presents & Starslayer)

ROCKETEER ADVENTURE MAGAZINE, THE
Comico/Dark Horse Comics No. 3: July, 1988 ($2.00); No. 2, July, 1989 ($2.75); No. 3, Jan, 1995 ($2.95)

	GD	VG	FN	VF	VF/NM	NM-
1-(7/88, $2.00)-Dave Stevens-c/a in all; Kaluta back-up-a; 1st app. Jonas (character based on The Shadow)	2	4	6	11	16	20
2-(7/89, $2.75)-Stevens/Dorman painted-c	1	3	4	6	8	10
3-(1/95, $2.95)-Includes pinups by Stevens, Gulacy, Plunkett, & Mignola						5.00
Volume 2-(9/96, $9.95, magazine size TPB)-Reprints #1-3						10.00

ROCKETEER ADVENTURES
IDW Publishing: May, 2011 - No. 4, Aug, 2011 ($3.99, limited series)
1-4-Anthology of new stories by various; covers by Alex Ross and Dave Stevens — 4.00
The Rocketeer: The Best of Rocketeer Adventures: Funko Edition 1 (1/18, $4.99) r/stories from series; art by Cassaday, Ha, Kaluta, Sakai, & Weston; Funko fig cover — 5.00

ROCKETEER ADVENTURES VOLUME 2
IDW Publishing: Mar, 2012 - No. 4, Jun, 2012 ($3.99, limited series)
1-4-Anthology by various; covers by Darwyn Cooke and Stevens. 1-Sakai-a. 4-Simonson & Byrne-a — 4.00

ROCKETEER AT WAR, THE
IDW Publishing: Dec, 2015 - No. 4, Apr, 2016 ($4.99, limited series)
1-4-Guggenheim-s; covers by Bullock & Bradshaw. 1,2-Bullock-a. 3,4-J. Bone-a — 5.00

ROCKETEER: CARGO OF DOOM
IDW Publishing: Aug, 2012 - No. 4, Nov, 2012 ($3.99, limited series)
1-4-Waid-s/Samnee-a/c; variant-c by Stevens on all — 4.00

ROCKETEER: HOLLYWOOD HORROR
IDW Publishing: Feb, 2013 - No. 4, May, 2013 ($3.99, limited series)
1-4-Langridge-s/Bone-a/Simonson-c; variant-c on all — 4.00

ROCKETEER JETPACK TREASURY EDITION
IDW Publishing: Nov, 2011 ($9.99, oversized 13" x 9-3/4" format)
1-Recolored r/Starslayer #1-3, Pacific Presents #1,2 & Rocketeer Special Edition — 10.00

ROCKETEER SPECIAL EDITION, THE
Eclipse Comics: Nov, 1984 ($1.50, Baxter paper)(Chapter 5 of Rocketeer serial)

	GD	VG	FN	VF	VF/NM	NM-
1-Stevens-c/a; Kaluta back-c; pin-ups inside	3	6	9	14	20	25

NOTE: *Originally intended to be published in Pacific Presents.*

ROCKETEER, THE: THE COMPLETE ADVENTURES
IDW Publishing: Oct, 2009 ($29.99/$75.00, hardcover)
HC-Reprints of Dave Stevens' Rocketeer stories in Starslayer #1-3, Pacific Presents #1,2, Rocketeer Special Edition and Rocketeer Adventure Magazine #1-3; all re-colored — 30.00
... Deluxe Edition ($75.00, 8"x12" slipcased HC) larger size reprints of HC content plus 100 bonus pages of sketch art, layouts, design work; intro. by Thomas Jane — 110.00
... Deluxe Edition 2nd printing ($75.00, oversized slipcased HC) — 75.00

ROCKETEER, THE: THE OFFICIAL MOVIE ADAPTATION
W. D. Publications (Disney): 1991
nn-($5.95, 68 pgs.)-Squarebound deluxe edition — 6.00
nn-($2.95, 68 pgs.)-Stapled regular edition — 4.00
3-D Comic Book (1991, $7.98, 52 pgs.) — 8.00

ROCKETEER: THE GREAT RACE
IDW Publishing: Apr, 2022 - No. 4, Jul, 2022 ($3.99, limited series)

GD 2.0 | VG 4.0 | FN 6.0 | VF 8.0 | VF/NM 9.0 | NM- 9.2

1-4-Stephen Mooney-s/a; back-up history of Dave Stevens and the Rocketeer 5.00

ROCKETEER/THE SPIRIT: PULP FRICTION
IDW Publishing: Jul, 2013 - No. 4, Dec, 2013 ($3.99, limited series)

1-4: 1-Waid-s/Paul Smith-a; covers by Smith & Darwyn Cooke. 2-Wallace-a. 3,4-Bone-a 4.00

ROCKET GIRL
Image Comics: Oct, 2013 - No. 10, Oct, 2017 ($3.50/$3.99)

1-10-Brandon Montclare-a/Amy Reeder-a/c. 6-Begin $3.99-c 4.00

ROCKET KELLY (See The Bouncer, Green Mask #10); becomes Li'l Pan #6)
Fox Feature Syndicate: 1944; Fall, 1945 - No. 5, Oct-Nov, 1946

nn (1944), 1 (Fall, 1945) 48 96 144 302 514 725
2-The Puppeteer app. (costumed hero) 37 74 111 218 354 490
3-5: 5-(#5 on cover, #4 inside) 31 62 93 186 303 420

ROCKETMAN (Strange Fantasy #2 on) (See Hello Pal & Scoop Comics)
Ajax/Farrell Publications: June, 1952 (Strange Stories of the Future)

1-Rocketman & Cosmo 68 136 204 435 743 1050

ROCKET RACCOON (Also see Marvel Preview #7 and Incredible Hulk #271)
Marvel Comics: May, 1985 - No. 4, Aug, 1985 (color, limited series)

1-Mignola-a/Mantlo-s in all 4 8 12 28 47 65
2-4 2 4 6 11 16 20
...: Tales From Half-World 1 (10/13, $7.99) r/#1-4; new cover by McNiven 8.00

ROCKET RACCOON (Guardians of the Galaxy)
Marvel Comics: Sept, 2014 - No. 11, Jul, 2015 ($3.99)

1-Skottie Young-s/a; Groot app. 5.00
2-11-Skottie Young-s. 7,8-Andrade-a 4.00
Free Comic Book Day 2014 (5/14, giveaway) Archer-a; Groot and Wal-rus app. 3.00

ROCKET RACCOON (Guardians of the Galaxy)
Marvel Comics: Feb, 2017 - No. 5, Jun, 2017 ($3.99)

1-5-Rosenberg-s/Coelho-a. 1-Johnny Storm app. 2-5-Kraven app. 4.00

ROCKET RACCOON & GROOT (Guardians of the Galaxy)
Marvel Comics: Mar, 2016 - No. 10, Nov, 2016 ($3.99)

1-10: 1-6-Skottie Young-s. 1-3-Filipe Andrade-a. 8-10-Gwenpool app. 4.00

ROCKET SHIP X
Fox Feature Syndicate: September, 1951; 1952

1 87 174 261 553 952 1350
1952 (nn, nd, no publ.)-Edited 1951-c (exist?) 47 94 141 296 498 700

ROCKET TO ADVENTURE LAND (See Pixie Puzzle...)

ROCKET TO THE MOON
Avon Periodicals: 1951

nn-Orlando-c/a; adapts Otis Adelbert Kline's "Maza of the Moon"
206 412 618 1318 2259 3200

ROCK FANTASY COMICS
Rock Fantasy Comics: Dec, 1989 - No. 16?, 1991 ($2.25/$3.00, B&W)(No cover price)

1-Pink Floyd part 1 5.00
1-2nd printing ($3.00-c) 3.00
2,3: 2-Rolling Stones #1. 3-Led Zeppelin #1 4.00
2,3: 2nd printings ($3.00-c, 1/90 & 2/90) 3.00
4-Stevie Nicks Not published
5-Monstrosities of Rock #1; photo back-c 4.00
5-2nd printing ($3.00, 3/90 indicia, 2/90-c) 3.00
6-9,11-15,17,18: 6-Guns n' Roses #1 (1st & 2nd printings, 3/90)-Begin $3.00-c.
7-Sex Pistols #1. 8-Alice Cooper; not published. 9-Van Halen #1; photo back-c.
11-Jimi Hendrix #1; wraparound-c 3.00
10-Kiss #1; photo back-c 2 4 6 8 10 12
16-($5.00, 68 pgs.)-The Great Gig in the Sky(Floyd) 5.00

ROCK HAPPENING (See Bunny and Harvey Pop Comics:...)

ROCK N' ROLL COMICS
DC Comics: Dec./Jan 1956 (ashcan)

nn-Ashcan comic, not distributed to newsstands, only for in house use (no known sales)

ROCK N' ROLL COMICS
Revolutionary Comics: Jun, 1989 - No. 65 ($1.50/$1.95/$2.50, B&W/col. #15 on)

1-Guns N' Roses 1 3 4 6 8 10
1-2nd thru 7th printings. 7th printing (full color w/new-c/a) 3.00
2-Metallica 1 3 4 6 8 10
2-2nd thru 6th printings (6th in color) 3.00
3-Bon Jovi (no reprints) 1 2 3 5 6 8
4-8,10-20,22-29,31-65: 4-Motley Crue(2nd printing only, 1st destroyed). 5-Def Leppard (2 printings). 6-Rolling Stones(4 printings). 7-The Who (3 printings). 8-Skid Row; not publ'd. 10-Warrant/Whitesnake (2 printings; 1st has 2 diff.-c). 11-Aerosmith (2 printings?). 12-New Kids on the Block(2 printings). 12-3rd printing; rewritten & titled NKOTB Hate Book. 13-Led Zeppelin. 14-Sex Pistols. 15-Poison; 1st color issue. 16-Van Halen. 17-Madonna. 18-Alice Cooper. 19-Public Enemy/2 Live Crew. 20-Queensryche/Tesla. 22-AC/DC; begin $2.50-c. 23-Living Colour. 26-Michael Jackson. 29-Ozzy. 45,46-Grateful Dead. 49-Rush. 50,51-Bob Dylan. 56-David Bowie 6.00
9-Kiss 2 4 6 8 10 12
9-2nd & 3rd printings 3.00
21,30: 21-Prince. 30-The Cure 2 4 6 9 12 15

NOTE: *Most issues were reprinted except #3. Later reprints are in color. #8 was not released.*

ROCKO'S MODERN AFTERLIFE (TV)
BOOM! Studios (kaboom!): Apr, 2019 - No. 4, Jul, 2019 ($3.99, limited series)

1-4-Burch-s/Di Meo-a; multiple covers; the undead attach O-Town 4.00

ROCKO'S MODERN LIFE (TV) (Nickelodeon cartoon)
Marvel Comics: June, 1994 - No. 7, Dec, 1994 ($1.95)

1-7 3.00

ROCKO'S MODERN LIFE (TV) (Nickelodeon cartoon)
BOOM! Studios (kaboom!): Dec, 2017 - No. 8, Sept, 2018 ($3.99)

1-8-Ferrier-s/McGinty-a; multiple covers 4.00

ROCKSTARS
Image Comics: Dec, 2016 - No. 8 ($3.99)

1-8-Joe Harris-s/Megan Hutchison-a 4.00

ROCKY AND BULLWINKLE (TV)
IDW Publishing: Mar, 2014 - No. 4, Jun, 2014 ($3.99)

1-4-Evanier-s/Langridge-a; bonus Dudley Do-Right short story in each; two covers 4.00

ROCKY AND BULLWINKLE SHOW, THE (TV)
American Mythology: 2017 - No. 3, 2018 ($3.99, limited series)

1-3: 1-New short stories and reprints from Bullwinkle #1&2; three covers 4.00

ROCKY AND BULLWINKLE (TV)
American Mythology: 2019 - 2020 ($3.99, one-shots)

... As Seen on TV 1-3 (2019-2020, $3.99) new story & reprints; Peabody & Sherman app. 4.00
... Present: The Best of Boris & Natasha 1 (2019, $3.99) reprints from 1973-1976 4.00
... Present: The Best of Dudley Do-Right of the Mounties 1 (2019, $3.99) reps. from 1973 4.00
... Present: The Best of Mr. Peaboy & Sherman 1 (2019, $3.99) reprints from 1963-1974 4.00

ROCKY AND HIS FIENDISH FRIENDS (TV)(Bullwinkle)
Gold Key: Oct, 1962 - No. 5, Sept, 1963 (Jay Ward)

1 (25¢, 80 pgs.) 14 28 42 97 214 330
2,3 (25¢, 80 pgs.) 10 20 30 64 132 200
4,5 (Regular size, 12¢) 7 14 21 49 92 135

ROCKY AND HIS FRIENDS (See Kite Fun Book & March of Comics #216 in the Promotional Comics section)

ROCKY AND HIS FRIENDS (TV)
Dell Publishing Co.: No. 1128, 8-10/60 - No.1311,1962 (Jay Ward)

Four Color 1128 (#1) (8-10/60) 27 54 81 194 435 675
Four Color 1152 (12-2/61), 1166, 1208, 1275, 1311('62)
17 34 51 114 252 390

ROCKY HORROR PICTURE SHOW THE COMIC BOOK, THE
Caliber Press: Jul, 1990 - No. 3, Jan, 1991 ($2.95, mini-series, 52 pgs.)

1-Adapts cult film plus photos, etc. 3 6 9 14 20 25
1-2nd printing, 2,3 2 4 6 9 13 16
...Collection ($4.95) 2 4 6 10 14 18

ROCKY JONES SPACE RANGER (See Space Adventures #15-18)

ROCKY JORDEN PRIVATE EYE (See Private Eye)

ROCKY LANE WESTERN (Allan Rocky Lane starred in Republic movies & TV for a short time as Allan Lane, Red Ryder & Rocky Lane) (See Black Jack Fawcett Movie Comics, Motion Picture Comics & Six-Gun Heroes)
Fawcett Publications/Charlton No. 56 on: May, 1949 - No. 87, Nov, 1959

1 (36 pgs.)-Rocky, his stallion Black Jack, & Slim Pickens begin; photo-c
begin, end #57; photo back-c 55 110 165 352 601 850
2 (36 pgs.)-Last photo back-c 22 44 66 132 216 300
3-5 (52 pgs.): 4-Captain Tootsie by Beck 17 34 51 98 154 210
6,10 (36 pgs.): 10-Complete western novelette "Badman's Reward"
14 28 42 76 108 140
7-9 (52 pgs.) 14 28 42 82 121 160
11-13,15-17,19,20 (52 pgs.): 15-Black Jack's Hitching Post begins, ends #25.
20-Last Slim Pickens 12 24 36 67 94 120
14,18 (36 pgs.) 10 20 30 58 79 100
21,23,24 (52 pgs.): 21-Dee Dickens begins, ends #55,57,65-68
10 20 30 58 79 100
22,25-28,30 (36 pgs. begin) 10 20 30 54 72 90
29-Classic complete novel "The Land of Missing Men" with hidden land of ancient temple
ruins (r-in #65) 14 28 42 76 108 140
31-40 9 18 27 52 69 85
41-54 9 18 27 47 61 75
55-Last Fawcett issue (1/54) 9 18 27 52 69 85
56-1st Charlton issue (2/54)-Photo-c 14 28 42 82 121 160
57,60-Photo-c 10 20 30 54 72 90
58,59,61-64,66-78,80-86: 59-61-Young Falcon app. 64-Slim Pickens app.
66-68: Reprints #30,31,32 8 16 24 44 57 70
65-r/#29, "The Land of Missing Men" 9 18 27 50 65 80
79-Giant Edition (68 pgs.) 10 20 30 58 79 100
87-Last issue 9 18 27 52 69 85

NOTE: *Complete novels in #10, 14, 18, 22, 25, 30-32, 36, 38, 39, 49. Captain Tootsie in #4, 12, 20. Big Bow and Little Arrow in #11, 28, 63. Black Jack's Hitching Post in #15-25, 64, 73.*

ROCKY LANE WESTERN
AC Comics: 1989 ($2.50, B&W, one-shot?)

1-Photo-c; Giordano reprints 4.00
Annual 1 (1991, $2.95, B&W, 44 pgs.)-photo front/back & inside-c; reprints 4.00

ROD CAMERON WESTERN (Movie star)
Fawcett Publications: Feb, 1950 - No. 20, Apr, 1953

1-Rod Cameron, his horse War Paint, & Sam The Sheriff begin; photo front/back-c begin
31 62 93 182 296 410
2 15 30 45 90 140 190
3-Novel length story "The Mystery of the Seven Cities of Cibola"
14 28 42 82 121 160
4-10: 9-Last photo back-c 12 24 36 69 97 125
11-19 10 20 30 58 79 100
20-Last issue & photo-c 11 22 33 62 86 110

NOTE: *Novel length stories in No. 1-8, 12-14.*

RODEO RYAN (See A-1 Comics #8)

ROGAN GOSH
DC Comics (Vertigo): 1994 ($6.95, one-shot)

nn-Peter Milligan scripts 7.00

ROGER DODGER (Also in Exciting Comics #57 on)
Standard Comics: No. 5, Aug, 1952

5-Teen-age 22 44 66 132 216 300

ROGER RABBIT (Also see Marvel Graphic Novel)
Disney Comics: June, 1990 - No. 18, Nov, 1991 ($1.50)

Rocket Girl #5 © Montclare & Reeder

Rogues #1 © DC

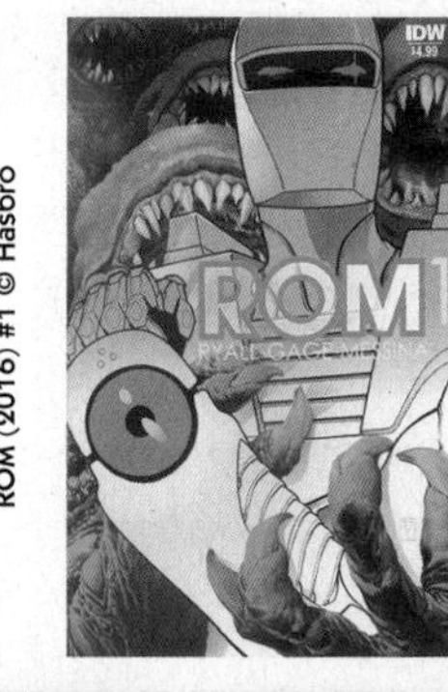

ROM (2016) #1 © Hasbro

GD VG FN VF VF/NM NM-
2.0 4.0 6.0 8.0 9.0 9.2

1-All new stories 3 6 9 14 20 25
2-5-All new stories 1 2 3 5 6 7
6-18-All new stories 4.00
In 3-D 1 (1992, $2.50)-Sold at Wal-Mart?; w/glasses 1 3 4 6 8 10

ROGER RABBIT'S TOONTOWN
Disney Comics: Aug, 1991 - No. 5, Dec, 1991 ($1.50)

1 2 4 6 8 10 12
2-5 6.00

ROGER ZELAZNY'S AMBER: THE GUNS OF AVALON
DC Comics: 1996 - No. 3, 1996 ($6.95, limited series)

1-3: Based on novel 7.00

ROG 2000
Pacific Comics: June, 1982 ($2.95, 44 pgs., B&W, one-shot, magazine)

nn-Byrne-c/a (r) 2 4 6 8 11 14
2nd printing (7/82) 1 2 3 4 5 7

ROGUE (From X-Men)
Marvel Comics: Jan, 1995 - No. 4, Apr, 1995 ($2.95, limited series)

1-4: 1-Gold foil logo 4.00
TPB-($12.95) r/#1-4 13.00

ROGUE (Volume 2)
Marvel Comics: Sept, 2001 - No. 4, Dec, 2001 ($2.50, limited series)

1-4-Julie Bell painted-c/Lopresti-a; Rogue's early days with X-Men 3.00

ROGUE (From X-Men)
Marvel Comics: Sept, 2004 - No. 12, Aug, 2005 ($2.99)

1-12: 1-Richards-a. 4-Gambit app. 11-Sunfire dies, Rogue absorbs his powers 3.00
...: Going Rogue TPB (2005, $14.99) r/#1-6 15.00
...: Forget-Me-Not TPB (2006, $14.99) r/#7-12 15.00

ROGUE & GAMBIT
Marvel Comics: Mar, 2018 - No. 5, Jul, 2018 ($3.99, limited series)

1-5-Kelly Thompson-s/Pere Pérez-a 4.00

ROGUE & GAMBIT
Marvel Comics: May, 2023 - Present ($3.99, limited series)

1-Phillips-s/Gómez-a; Destiny app. 4.00

ROGUE ANGEL: TELLER OF TALL TALES (Based on the Alex Archer novels)
IDW Publishing: Feb, 2008 - No. 5, Jun, 2008 ($3.99)

1-5-Annja Creed adventures; Barbara-Kesel-s/Renae De Liz-a 4.00

ROGUES
DC Comics (Black Label): May, 2022 - No. 4, Dec, 2022 ($6.99, oversized 8-1/2" x 10-3/4", lim. series)

1-4-Captain Cold reunites the Rogues after 10 years; Williamson-s/Leomacs-a 7.00

ROGUES GALLERY
DC Comics: 1996 ($3.50, one-shot)

1-Pinups of DC villains by various artists 4.00

ROGUES' GALLERY
Image Comics: Jul, 2022 - No. 4, Oct, 2022 ($3.99, limited series)

1-4-Hannah Rose May-s/Justin Mason-a 4.00

ROGUE SUN
Image Comics: Mar, 2022 - Present ($3.99)

1-10: 1-Ryan Parrott-s/Abel-a 4.00

ROGUE TROOPER
IDW Publishing: Feb, 2014 - No. 4, May, 2014 ($3.99)

1-4-Ruckley-s/Ponticelli-a/Fabry-c 4.00

ROGUE TROOPER CLASSICS
IDW Publishing: May, 2014 - No. 8, Dec, 2014 ($3.99)

1-8-Newly colored reprints of strips from 2000 AD magazine. 1-4-Gibbons-a 4.00

ROGUES, THE (VILLAINS) (See The Flash)
DC Comics: Feb, 1998 ($1.95, one-shot)

1-Augustyn-s/Pearson-c 3.00

ROKKIN
DC Comics (WildStorm): Sept, 2006 - No. 6, Feb, 2007 ($2.99, limited series)

1-6-Hartnell-s/Bradshaw-a 3.00

ROKU
Valiant Entertainment: Oct, 2019 - No. 4, Jan, 2020 ($3.99, limited series)

1-4-Cullen Bunn-s/Ramón Bachs-a; multiple covers on each 4.00

ROLLING STONES: VOODOO LOUNGE
Marvel Comics: 1995 ($6.95, Prestige format, one-shot)

nn-Dave McKean-script/design/art 7.00

ROLY POLY COMIC BOOK
Green Publishing Co.: 1945 - No. 15, 1946 (MLJ reprints)

1-(No number on cover or indicia, "1945 issue" on cover) Red Rube & Steel Sterling begin; Sahle-c 39 78 117 240 395 550
6-The Blue Circle & The Steel Fist app. 27 54 81 158 259 360
10-Origin Red Rube retold; Steel Sterling story (Zip #41) 31 62 93 186 303 420
11,12: The Black Hood app. in both 36 72 108 211 343 475
14-Classic decapitation-c; the Black Hood app. 371 742 1113 2600 4550 6500
15-The Blue Circle & The Steel Fist app.; cover exact swipe from Fox Blue Beetle #1 40 80 120 246 411 575

ROM (Based on the Parker Brothers toy)
Marvel Comics Group: Dec, 1979 - No. 75, Feb, 1986

1-Origin/1st app. 4 8 12 25 40 55
2-16,19-23,28-30: 5-Dr. Strange. 13-Saga of the Space Knights begins. 19-X-Men cameo. 23-Powerman & Iron Fist app. 1 2 3 5 6 8
17,18-X-Men app. 2 4 6 10 14 18
24-27: 24-F.F. cameo; Skrulls, Nova & The New Champions app. 25-Double size. 26,27-Galactus app. 1 2 3 5 7 9
31-49,51-60: 31,32-Brotherhood of Evil Mutants app. 32-X-Men cameo. 34,35-Sub-Mariner app. 41,42-Dr. Strange app. 56,57-Alpha Flight app. 58,59-Ant-Man app. 6.00
50-Skrulls app. (52 pgs.) Pin-ups by Konkle, Austin 1 2 3 4 5 7
61-74: 65-West Coast Avengers & Beta Ray Bill app. 65,66-X-Men app. 6.00
75-Last issue 2 4 6 9 12 15
Annual 1-4: (1982-85, 52 pgs.) 6.00
NOTE: ***Austin*** *c-3i, 18i, 61i.* ***Byrne*** *a-74i; c-56, 57, 74.* ***Ditko*** *a-59-75p, Annual 4.* ***Golden*** *c-7-12, 19.* ***Guice*** *a-61i; c-55, 58, 60p, 70p.* ***Layton*** *a-59i, 72i; c-15, 59i, 69.* ***Miller*** *c-2p?, 3p, 17p, 18p.* ***Russell*** *a(i)-64, 65, 67, 69, 71, 75; c-64, 65i, 66, 71i, 75.* ***Severin*** *c-41p.* ***Sienkiewicz*** *a-53i; c-46, 47, 52-54, 68, 71p, Annual 2.* ***Simonson*** *c-18.* ***P. Smith*** *c-59p.* ***Starlin*** *c-67.* ***Zeck*** *c-50.*

ROM (Based on the Parker Brothers toy) (Also see Rom & The Micronauts)
IDW Publishing: Jul, 2016 - No. 14, Aug, 2017 ($4.99/$3.99)

1-($4.99) Ryall & Gage-s/Messina-a 5.00
2-14-($3.99) 2-4-Revolution tie-in. 2-G.I. Joe app. 5-Transformers app. 4.00
Annual 2017 (1/17, $7.99) Origin of Rom; Ryall & Gage-s/Messina-a 8.00
... First Strike 1 (10/17, $3.99) Part of the Hasbro character x-over; Gage-s/Panda-a 4.00
FCBD 2016 Edition #0 - (5/16, giveaway) Prelude to series; Action Man flip book 3.00
...: Revolution (9/16, $3.99) Revolution x-over; Ryall-s/Gage-a; multiple covers 4.00
...: Tales of the Solstar Order (3/18, $4.99) Ryall & Gage-s/Dorian-a 5.00

ROMANCE (See True Stories of...)

ROMANCE AND CONFESSION STORIES (See Giant Comics Edition)
St. John Publishing Co.: No date (1949) (25¢, 100 pgs.)

1-Baker-c/a; remaindered St. John love comics 135 270 405 864 1482 2100

ROMANCE DIARY
Marvel Comics (CDS)(CLDS): Dec, 1949 - No. 2, Mar, 1950

1,2-Photo-c 24 48 72 142 234 325

ROMANCE OF FLYING, THE
David McKay Publications: 1942

Feature Books 33 (nn)-WW II photos 21 42 63 122 199 275

ROMANCES OF MOLLY MANTON (See Molly Manton)

ROMANCES OF NURSE HELEN GRANT, THE
Atlas Comics (VPI): Aug, 1957

1 32 64 96 188 307 425

ROMANCES OF THE WEST (Becomes Romantic Affairs #3?)
Marvel Comics (SPC): Nov, 1949 - No. 2, Mar, 1950 (52 pgs.)

1-Movie photo-c of Yvonne DeCarlo & Howard Duff (Calamity Jane & Sam Bass) 32 64 96 188 307 425
2-Photo-c 19 38 57 112 179 245

ROMANCE STORIES OF TRUE LOVE (Formerly True Love Problems & Advice Illustrated)
Harvey Publications: No. 45, 5/57 - No. 50, 3/58; No. 51, 9/58 - No. 52, 11/58

45-51: 45,46,48-50-Powell-a 8 16 24 40 50 60
52-Matt Baker-a 10 20 30 58 79 100

ROMANCE TALES (Formerly Western Winners #6?)
Marvel Comics (CDS): No. 7, Oct, 1949 - No. 9, April, 1950 (7-9: photo-c)

7 21 42 63 122 199 275

	GD 2.0	VG 4.0	FN 6.0	VF 8.0	VF/NM 9.0	NM- 9.2
8,9: 8-Everett-a	15	30	45	84	127	170

ROMANCE TRAIL
National Periodical Publications: July-Aug, 1949 - No. 6, May-June, 1950 (All photo-c & 52 pgs.)

	GD 2.0	VG 4.0	FN 6.0	VF 8.0	VF/NM 9.0	NM- 9.2
1-Kinstler, Toth-a; Jimmy Wakely photo-c	63	126	189	403	689	975
2-Kinstler-a; Jim Bannon photo-c	34	68	102	204	332	460
3-Tex Williams photo-c; Kinstler, Toth-a	37	74	111	218	354	490
4-Jim Bannon as Red Ryder photo-c; Toth-a	27	54	81	180	263	365
5,6: Photo-c on both. 5-Kinstler-a	25	50	75	150	245	340

ROM & THE MICRONAUTS (Based on the Parker Brothers toys)
IDW Publishing: Dec, 2017 - No. 5, Apr, 2018 ($3.99, limited series)

	GD 2.0	VG 4.0	FN 6.0	VF 8.0	VF/NM 9.0	NM- 9.2
1-5-Gage-s/Villanelli-a; multiple covers; Baron Karza app.						4.00

ROMAN HOLIDAYS, THE (TV)
Gold Key: Feb, 1973 - No. 4, Nov, 1973 (Hanna-Barbera)

	GD 2.0	VG 4.0	FN 6.0	VF 8.0	VF/NM 9.0	NM- 9.2
1	4	8	12	27	44	60
2-4	3	6	9	17	26	35

ROMANTIC ADVENTURES (My... #49-67, covers only)
American Comics Group (B&I Publ. Co.): Mar-Apr, 1949 - No. 71, Nov, 1956 (Becomes My... #72 on)

	GD 2.0	VG 4.0	FN 6.0	VF 8.0	VF/NM 9.0	NM- 9.2
1	27	54	81	158	259	360
2	15	30	45	90	140	190
3-10	13	26	39	74	105	135
11-20 (4/52)	11	22	33	64	90	115
21-45,51,52: 52-Last Pre-code (2/55)	10	20	30	58	79	100
46-49-3-D effect-c/stories (TrueVision)	16	32	48	94	147	200
50-Classic cover/story "Love of A Lunatic"	142	284	426	909	1555	2200
53-71	10	20	30	56	76	95

NOTE: *#1-23, 52 pgs.* ***Shelly*** *a-40. Whitney c/art in many issues.*

ROMANTIC AFFAIRS (Formerly Molly Manton's Romances #2 and/or Romances of the West #2 and/or Our Love #2?)
Marvel Comics (SPC): No. 3, Mar, 1950

	GD 2.0	VG 4.0	FN 6.0	VF 8.0	VF/NM 9.0	NM- 9.2
3-Photo-c from Molly Manton's Romances #2	18	36	54	105	165	225

ROMANTIC CONFESSIONS
Hillman Periodicals: Oct, 1949 - V3#1, Apr-May, 1953

	GD 2.0	VG 4.0	FN 6.0	VF 8.0	VF/NM 9.0	NM- 9.2
V1#1-McWilliams-a	27	54	81	158	259	360
2-Briefer-a; negligee panels	16	32	48	94	147	200
3-12	14	28	42	81	118	155
V2#1,2,4-8,10-12: 2-McWilliams-a	14	28	42	76	108	140
3-Krigstein-a	14	28	42	81	118	155
9-One pg. Frazetta ad	14	28	42	76	108	140
V3#1	13	26	39	74	105	135

ROMANTIC HEARTS
Story Comics/Master/Merit Pubs.: Mar, 1951 - No. 10, Oct, 1952; July, 1953 - No. 12, July, 1955

	GD 2.0	VG 4.0	FN 6.0	VF 8.0	VF/NM 9.0	NM- 9.2
1(3/51) (1st Series)	22	44	66	132	216	300
2	15	30	45	83	124	165
3-10: Cameron-a	14	28	42	81	118	155
1(7/53) (2nd Series)-Some say #11 on-c	16	32	48	94	147	200
2	14	28	42	80	115	150
3-12	13	26	39	74	105	135

ROMANTIC LOVE
Avon Periodicals/Realistic (No #14-19): 9-10/49 - #3, 1-2/50; #4, 2-3/51 - #13, 10/52; #20, 3-4/54 - #23, 9-10/54

	GD 2.0	VG 4.0	FN 6.0	VF 8.0	VF/NM 9.0	NM- 9.2
1-c-/Avon paperback #252	50	100	150	315	533	750
2-5: 3-c-/paperback Novel Library #12. 4-c-/paperback Diversey Prize Novel #5. 5-c-/paperback Novel Library #34	32	64	96	188	307	425
6- "Thrill Crazy" marijuana story; c-/Avon paperback #207; Kinstler-a	41	82	123	256	428	600
7,8: 8-Astarita-a(2)	30	60	90	177	289	400
9-c-/paperback Novel Library #41; Kinstler-a; headlights-c	41	82	123	256	428	600
10-12: 10-c-/Avon paperback #212. 11-c-/paperback Novel Library #17; Kinstler-a. 12-c-/paperback Novel Library #13	33	66	99	194	317	440
13,21-23: 22,23-Kinstler-c	30	60	90	177	289	400
20-Kinstler-c/a	31	62	93	182	296	410
nn(1-3/53)(Realistic-r)	20	40	60	115	185	255

NOTE: ***Astarita*** *a-7, 10, 11, 21. Painted c-1-3, 5, 7-11, 13. Photo c-4, 6.*

ROMANTIC LOVE
Quality Comics Group: 1963-1964

	GD 2.0	VG 4.0	FN 6.0	VF 8.0	VF/NM 9.0	NM- 9.2
I.W. Reprint #2,3,8,11: 2-r/Romantic Love #2	3	6	9	16	23	30

ROMANTIC MARRIAGE (Cinderella Love #25 on)
Ziff-Davis/St. John No. 18 on (#1-8: 52 pgs.): #1-3 (1950, no months); #4, 5-6/51 - #17, 9/52; #18, 9/53 - #24, 9/54

	GD 2.0	VG 4.0	FN 6.0	VF 8.0	VF/NM 9.0	NM- 9.2
1-Photo-c; Cary Grant/Betsy Drake photo back-c.	34	68	102	199	325	450
2-Painted-c; Anderson-a (also #15)	22	44	66	128	209	290
3-9: 3,4,8,9-Painted-c; 5-7-Photo-c	20	40	60	117	189	260
10-Unusual format; front-c is a painted-c; back-c is a photo-c complete with logo, price, etc.	33	66	99	194	317	440
11-17 13-Photo-c. 15-Signed story by Anderson. 17-(9/52)-Last Z-D issue	19	38	57	111	176	240
18-22: 20-Photo-c	19	38	57	111	176	240
23-Baker-c; all stories are reprinted from #15	58	116	174	371	636	900
24-Baker-c	106	212	318	673	1162	1650

ROMANTIC PICTURE NOVELETTES
Magazine Enterprises: 1946

	GD 2.0	VG 4.0	FN 6.0	VF 8.0	VF/NM 9.0	NM- 9.2
1-Mary Worth-r; Creig Flessel-c	24	48	72	142	234	325

ROMANTIC SECRETS (Becomes Time For Love)
Fawcett/Charlton Comics No. 5 (10/55) on: Sept, 1949 - No. 39, 4/53; No. 5, 10/55 - No. 52, 11/64 (#1-39: photo-c)

	GD 2.0	VG 4.0	FN 6.0	VF 8.0	VF/NM 9.0	NM- 9.2
1-(52 pg. issues begin, end #?)	21	42	63	126	206	285
2,3	14	28	42	78	112	145
4,9-Evans-a	14	28	42	81	118	155
5-8,10(9/50)	10	20	30	58	79	100
11-23	9	18	27	52	69	85
24-Evans-a	10	20	30	56	76	95
25-39('53)	9	18	27	50	65	80
5 (Charlton, 2nd Series)(10/55, formerly Negro Romances #4)	12	24	36	69	97	125
6-10	9	18	27	50	65	80
11-20	4	8	12	25	40	55
21-35	3	6	9	21	33	45
36-52('64)	3	6	9	18	27	36

NOTE: ***Bailey*** *a-20.* ***Powell*** *a(1st series)-5, 7, 10, 12, 16, 17, 20, 26, 29, 33, 34, 36, 37.* ***Sekowsky*** *a-26.* ***Swayze*** *a(1st series)-16, 18, 19, 23, 26-28, 31, 32, 39.*

ROMANTIC STORY (Cowboy Love #28 on)
Fawcett/Charlton Comics No. 23 on: 11/49 - #22, Sum, 1953; #23, 5/54 - #27, 12/54; #28, 8/55 - #130, 11/73

	GD 2.0	VG 4.0	FN 6.0	VF 8.0	VF/NM 9.0	NM- 9.2
1-Photo-c begin, end #24; 52 pgs. begins	21	42	63	126	206	285
2	14	28	42	80	115	150
3-5	11	22	33	62	86	110
6-14	10	20	30	56	76	95
15-Evans-a	11	22	33	62	86	110
16-22(Sum, '53; last Fawcett issue). 21-Toth-a?	9	18	27	47	61	75
23-39: 26,29-Wood swipes	8	16	24	42	54	65
40-(100 pgs.)	13	26	39	74	105	135
41-50	4	8	12	23	37	50
51-80: 57-Hypo needle story	3	6	9	17	26	35
81-99	3	6	9	14	19	24
100	3	6	9	14	20	26
101-130: 120-Bobby Sherman pin-up	2	4	6	11	16	20

NOTE: ***Jim Aparo*** *a-94.* ***Powell*** *a-7, 8, 16, 20, 30.* ***Marcus Swayze*** *a-2, 12, 20, 32.*

ROMANTIC THRILLS (See Fox Giants)

ROMANTIC WESTERN
Fawcett Publications: Winter, 1949 - No. 3, June, 1950 (All Photo-c)

	GD 2.0	VG 4.0	FN 6.0	VF 8.0	VF/NM 9.0	NM- 9.2
1	25	50	75	147	241	335
2-(Spr/50)-Williamson, McWilliams-a	21	42	63	126	206	285
3	16	32	48	98	154	210

ROM: DIRE WRAITHS
IDW Publishing: Oct, 2019 - No. 3, Oct, 2020 ($4.99, limited series)

	GD 2.0	VG 4.0	FN 6.0	VF 8.0	VF/NM 9.0	NM- 9.2
1-3: 1-Ryall-s/Pizzari & Dorian Sr.-a						5.00

ROMEO TUBBS (...That Lovable Teenager; formerly My Secret Life)
Fox Features Syndicate/Green Publ. Co. No. 27: No. 26, 5/50 - No. 28, 7/50; No. 1, 1950; No. 27, 12/52

	GD 2.0	VG 4.0	FN 6.0	VF 8.0	VF/NM 9.0	NM- 9.2
26-Teen-age	18	36	54	105	165	225
28 (7/50)	16	32	48	94	147	200
27 (12/52)-Contains Pedro on inside; Wood-a	19	38	57	111	176	240

ROMULUS
Image Comics: Oct, 2016 - No. 4, May, 2017 ($3.99)

	GD 2.0	VG 4.0	FN 6.0	VF 8.0	VF/NM 9.0	NM- 9.2
1-4-Bryan Hill-s/Nelson Blake II-a						4.00

ROM VS. TRANSFORMERS: SHINING ARMOR
IDW Publishing: Jul, 2017 - No. 5, Nov, 2017 ($3.99, limited series)

	GD 2.0	VG 4.0	FN 6.0	VF 8.0	VF/NM 9.0	NM- 9.2
1-5-Barber & Gage-s/Milne-a						4.00

RONALD McDONALD (TV)
Charlton Press: Sept, 1970 - No. 4, March, 1971

	GD 2.0	VG 4.0	FN 6.0	VF 8.0	VF/NM 9.0	NM- 9.2
1-Bill Yates-a in all	9	18	27	60	120	180
2-4: 2 & 3 both dated Jan, 1971	5	10	15	34	60	85
V2#1-4-Special reprint for McDonald systems; new cover art on each; "Not for resale" on cover	7	14	21	44	82	120

RONIN
DC Comics: July, 1983 - No. 6, Aug, 1984 ($2.50, limited series, 52 pgs.)

	GD 2.0	VG 4.0	FN 6.0	VF 8.0	VF/NM 9.0	NM- 9.2
1-Frank Miller-c/a/scripts in all	2	4	6	11	16	20
2-5	2	4	6	8	11	14
6-Scarcer; has fold-out poster.	3	6	9	14	19	24
Trade paperback (1987, $12.95)-Reprints #1-6						18.00

RONIN BOOK II
Frank Miller Presents: 2022 - Present ($7.99, B&W, limited series)

	GD 2.0	VG 4.0	FN 6.0	VF 8.0	VF/NM 9.0	NM- 9.2
1,2-Frank Miller-s/Philip Tan-a						8.00

RONIN ISLAND
BOOM! Studios: Mar, 2019 - No. 12, Jul, 2020 ($3.99, limited series)

	GD 2.0	VG 4.0	FN 6.0	VF 8.0	VF/NM 9.0	NM- 9.2
1-12-Greg Pak-s/Giannis Milonogiannis-a						4.00

RONNA
Knight Press: Apr, 1997 ($2.95, B&W, one-shot)

	GD 2.0	VG 4.0	FN 6.0	VF 8.0	VF/NM 9.0	NM- 9.2
1-Beau Smith-s						3.00

ROOK (See Eerie Magazine & Warren Presents: The Rook)
Warren Publications: Oct, 1979 - No. 14, April, 1982 (B&W magazine)

	GD 2.0	VG 4.0	FN 6.0	VF 8.0	VF/NM 9.0	NM- 9.2
1-Nino-a/Corben-c; with 8 pg. color insert	3	6	9	16	23	30
2-4,6,7: 2-Voltar by Alcala begins. 3,4-Toth-a	2	4	6	9	13	16
5,8-14: 11-Zorro-s. 12-14-Eagle by Severin	2	4	6	9	13	16

ROOK
Harris Comics: No. 0, Jun, 1995 - No. 4, 1995 ($2.95)

	GD 2.0	VG 4.0	FN 6.0	VF 8.0	VF/NM 9.0	NM- 9.2
0-4: 0-short stories (3) w/preview. 4-Brereton-c.						3.00

ROOK, THE
Dark Horse Comics: Oct, 2015 - No. 4, Jan, 2016 ($3.99)

	GD 2.0	VG 4.0	FN 6.0	VF 8.0	VF/NM 9.0	NM- 9.2
1-4-Steven Grant-s/Paul Gulacy-a/c						4.00

ROOKIE COP (Formerly Crime and Justice?)
Charlton Comics: No. 27, Nov, 1955 - No. 33, Aug, 1957

	GD 2.0	VG 4.0	FN 6.0	VF 8.0	VF/NM 9.0	NM- 9.2
27	14	28	42	76	108	140

Romantic Love #11 © AVON

Ronin Book II #2 © Frank Miller Ink

Roy Rogers Comics #15 © Roy Rogers

	GD 2.0	VG 4.0	FN 6.0	VF 8.0	VF/NM 9.0	NM- 9.2

28-33 9 18 27 47 61 75

ROOM 222 (TV)
Dell Publishing Co.: Jan, 1970; No. 2, May, 1970 - No. 4, Jan, 1971

1 6 12 18 37 66 95
2-4-Photo-c. 3-Marijuana story. 4 r/#1 4 8 12 25 40 55

ROOTIE KAZOOTIE (TV)(See 3-D-ell)
Dell Publishing Co.: No. 415, Aug, 1952 - No. 6, Oct-Dec, 1954

Four Color 415 (#1) 10 20 30 69 147 225
Four Color 459,502(#2,3), 4(4-6/54)-6 6 12 18 41 76 110

ROOTS OF THE SWAMP THING
DC Comics: July, 1986 - No.5, Nov, 1986 ($2.00, Baxter paper, 52 pgs.)

1-5: r/Swamp Thing #1-10 by Wrightson & House of Mystery-r. 1-new Wrightson-c (2-5 reprinted covers). 5.00

RORSCHACH
DC Comics (Black Label): Dec, 2020 - No. 12, Nov, 2021 ($4.99, limited series)

1-12-Tom King-s/Jorge Fornés-a 5.00

ROSE (See Bone)
Cartoon Books: Nov, 2000 - No. 3, Feb, 2002 ($5.95, lim. series, square-bound)

1-3-Prequel to Bone; Jeff Smith-s/Charles Vess painted-a/c 6.00
HC (2001, $29.95) r/#1-3; new Vess cover painting 30.00
SC (2002, $19.95) r/#1-3; new Vess cover painting 20.00
1-($6.00)-Blood & Glory Edition 6.00

ROSE
Image Comics: Apr, 2017 - No. 17, Feb, 2019 ($3.99)

1-17-Meredith Finch-s/Ig Guara-a 4.00

ROSE AND THORN
DC Comics: Feb, 2004 - No. 6, July, 2004 ($2.95, limited series)

1-6-Simone-s/Melo-a/Hughes-c 3.00

ROSWELL: LITTLE GREEN MAN (See Simpsons Comics #19-22)
Bongo Comics: 1996 - No. 6 ($2.95, quarterly)

1-6 4.00
...Walks Among Us ('97, $12.95, TPB) r/ #1-3 & Simpsons flip books 13.00

ROUGH RIDERS
AfterShock Comics: Apr, 2016 - No. 7, Nov, 2016 ($3.99)

1-7: 1-Teddy Roosevelt, Annie Oakley, Houdini, Jack Johnson, Thomas Edison team 4.00
... Nation 1 (11/16, $3.99) Dossier of other Rough Rider teams; art by various 4.00

ROUGH RIDERS: RIDE OR DIE
AfterShock Comics: Feb, 2018 - No. 4, May, 2018 ($3.99)

1-4-Glass-s/Olliffe-a; H.P. Lovecraft app. 4.00

ROUGH RIDERS: RIDERS ON THE STORM
AfterShock Comics: Feb, 2017 - No. 6, Sept, 2017 ($3.99)

1-6-Glass-s/Olliffe-a; Monk Eastman joins team 4.00

ROUND TABLE OF AMERICA: PERSONALITY CRISIS (See Big Bang Comics)
Image Comics: Aug, 2005 ($3.50, one-shot)

1-Carlos Rodriguez-a/Pedro Angosto-s 3.50

ROUNDUP (...Western Crime Stories)
D. S. Publishing Co.: July-Aug, 1948 - No. 5, Mar-Apr, 1949 (All 52 pgs.)

1-Kiefer-a 22 44 66 132 216 300
2-5: 2-Marijuana drug mention story 16 32 48 92 144 195

ROUTE 666
CrossGeneration Comics: July, 2002 - No. 22, Jun, 2004 ($2.95)

1-22-Bedard-s/Moline-a in most. 5-Richards-a. 15-McCrea-a 3.00

ROWANS RUIN
BOOM! Studios: Oct, 2015 - No. 4, Jan, 2016 ($3.99, limited series)

1-4-Mike Carey-s/Mike Perkins-a. 1-Multiple covers 4.00

ROYAL CITY
Image Comics: Mar, 2017 - No. 14, Aug, 2018 ($4.99/$3.99)

1-($4.99) Jeff Lemire-s/a 5.00
2-14-($3.99) 4.00

ROYAL ROY
Marvel Comics (Star Comics): May, 1985 - No. 6, Mar, 1986 (Children's book)

1-6 4.00

ROYALS (The Inhumans) (Leads into Inhumans: Judgment Day)
Marvel Comics: Jun, 2017 - No. 12, Feb, 2018 ($3.99)

1-12: 1-Ewing-s/Meyers-a; Marvel Boy app. 2-Maximus returns. 4,5-Ronan app. 4.00

ROYALS, THE: MASTERS OF WAR
DC Comics (Vertigo): Apr, 2014 - No. 6, Sept, 2014 ($2.99, limited series)

1-6-Rob Williams-s/Simon Coleby-a/c; super-powered Royal families during WWII 3.00

ROY CAMPANELLA, BASEBALL HERO
Fawcett Publications: 1950 (Brooklyn Dodgers)

nn-Photo-c; life story 65 130 195 416 708 1000

ROY ROGERS (See March of Comics #17, 35, 47, 62, 68, 73, 77, 86, 91, 100, 105, 116, 121, 131, 136, 146, 151, 161, 167, 176, 191, 206, 221, 236, 250)

ROY ROGERS AND TRIGGER
Gold Key: Apr, 1967

1-Photo-c; reprints 5 10 15 30 50 70

ROY ROGERS ANNUAL
Wilson Publ. Co., Toronto/Dell: 1947 ("Giant Edition" on-c)(132 pgs., 50¢)

nn-Seven known copies. Front and back cover art are from Roy Rogers #2. Stories reprinted from Roy Rogers #2, Four Color #137 and Four Color #153. (A copy in VG/FN was sold in 1986 for $400, in 1996 for $1200 & in 2000 for $1500; a FN+ sold for $1,650; a GD sold for $448 in 2008, a FN sold for $717 in 2009 and a FR sold for $156 in 2015.)

ROY ROGERS COMICS (See Western Roundup under Dell Giants)
Dell Publishing Co.: No. 38, 4/44 - No. 177, 12/47 (#38-166: 52 pgs.)

Four Color 38 (1944)-49 pg. story; photo front/back-c on all 4-Color issues (1st western comic with photo-c) 155 310 465 1279 2890 4500
Four Color 63 (1945)-Color photos on all four-c 40 80 120 296 673 1050
Four Color 86,95 (1945) 29 58 87 209 467 725
Four Color 109 (1946) 22 44 66 154 340 525
Four Color 117,124,137,144 17 34 51 119 265 410
Four Color 153,160,166: 166-48 pg. story 15 30 45 105 233 360
Four Color 177 (36 pgs.)-32 pg. story 15 30 45 100 220 340
HC (Dark Horse Books, 8/08, $49.95) r/Four Color #38,63,86,95,109; Roy Rogers Jr intro. 50.00

ROY ROGERS COMICS (...& Trigger #92(8/55)-on)(Roy starred in Republic movies, radio & TV) (Singing cowboy) (Also see Dale Evans, It Really Happened #8, Queen of the West Dale Evans, & Roy Rogers' Trigger)
Dell Publishing Co.: Jan, 1948 - No. 145, Sept-Oct, 1961 (#1-19: 36 pgs.)

1-Roy, his horse Trigger, & Chuck Wagon Charley's Tales begin; photo-c begin, end #145 64 128 192 512 1156 1800
2 21 42 63 147 324 500
3-5 14 28 42 96 211 325
6-10 12 24 36 80 173 265
11-19: 19-Chuckwagon Charley's Tales ends 10 20 30 68 144 220
20 (52 pgs.)-Trigger feature begins, ends #46 10 20 30 69 147 225
21-30 (52 pgs.) 9 18 27 60 120 180
31-46 (52 pgs.): 37-X-Mas-c 8 16 24 51 96 140
47-56 (36 pgs.): 47-Chuck Wagon Charley's Tales returns, ends #133. 49-X-mas-c. 55-Last photo back-c 6 12 18 40 73 105
57 (52 pgs.)-Heroin drug propaganda story 6 12 18 41 76 110
58-70 (52 pgs.): 58-Heroin drug use/dealing story. 61-X-Mas-c 6 12 18 40 73 105
71-80 (52 pgs.): 73-X-Mas-c 5 10 15 35 63 90
81-91 (36 pgs. #81-on): 85-X-Mas-c 5 10 15 34 60 85
92-99,101-110,112-118: 92-Title changed to Roy Rogers and Trigger (8/55) 5 10 15 33 57 80
100-Trigger feature returns, ends #131 6 12 18 37 66 95
111,119-124-Toth-a 6 12 18 38 69 100
125-131: 125-Toth-a (1 pg.) 5 10 15 31 53 75
132-144-Manning-a. 132-1st Dale Evans-sty by Russ Manning. 138,144-Dale Evans featured 5 10 15 34 60 85
145-Last issue 6 12 18 40 73 105

NOTE: *Buscema a-74-108(2 stories each). Manning a-123, 124, 132-144. Marsh a-110. Photo back-c No. 1-9, 11-35, 38-55.*

ROY ROGERS' TRIGGER
Dell Publishing Co.: No. 329, May, 1951 - No. 17, June-Aug, 1955

Four Color 329 (#1)-Painted-c 14 28 42 97 214 330
2 (9-11/51)-Photo-c 10 20 30 64 132 200
3-5: 3-Painted-c begin, end #17, most by S. Savitt 6 12 18 38 69 100
6-17: Title merges with Roy Rogers after #17 5 10 15 31 53 75

ROY ROGERS WESTERN CLASSICS
AC Comics: 1989 -No. 4 ($2.95/$3.95, 44pgs.) (24 pgs. color, 16 pgs. B&W)

1-4: 1-Dale Evans-r by Manning, Trigger-r by Buscema; photo covers & interior photos by Roy & Dale. 2-Buscema-r (3); photo-c & B&W photos inside. 3-Dale Evans-r by Manning;

GD VG FN VF VF/NM NM-
2.0 4.0 6.0 8.0 9.0 9.2

Trigger-r by Buscema plus other Buscema-r; photo-c 4.00

RUBY FALLS
Dark Horse Comics (Berger Books): Oct, 2019 - No. 4, Jan, 2020 ($3.99, limited series)
1-4-Ann Nocenti-s/Flavia Biondi-a 4.00

RUDOLPH, THE RED-NOSED REINDEER
National Per. Publ.: 1950 - No. 13, Winter, 1962-63 (Issues are not numbered)
1950 issue (#1); Grossman-c/a in all 45 90 135 284 480 675
1951-53 issues (3 total) 27 54 81 158 259 360
1954/55, 55/56, 56/57 22 44 66 128 209 290
1957/58, 58/59, 59/60, 60/61, 61/62 11 22 33 75 160 245
1962/63 (rare)(84 pgs.)(shows "Annual" in indicia) 21 42 63 147 324 500
NOTE: *13 total issues published. Has games & puzzles also.*

RUDOLPH, THE RED-NOSED REINDEER (Also see Limited Collectors' Edition C-20, C-24, C-33, C-42, C-50; and All-New Collectors' Edition C-53 & C-60)
National Per. Publ.: Christmas 1972 (Treasury-size)
nn-Precursor to Limited Collectors' Edition title (scarce)
(implied to be Lim. Coll .Ed. C-20) 19 38 57 133 297 460

RUFF AND REDDY (TV)
Dell Publ. Co.: No. 937, 9/58 - No. 12, 1-3/62 (Hanna-Barbera)(#9 on: 15¢)
Four Color 937(#1)(1st Hanna-Barbera comic book) 12 24 36 79 170 260
Four Color 981,1038 8 16 24 52 99 145
4(1-3/60)-12: 8-Last 10¢ issue 6 12 18 41 76 110

RUFF & REDDY SHOW, THE
DC Comics: Dec, 2017 - No. 6, May, 2018 ($3.99, limited series)
1-6-Ruff & Ready in the real world; Chaykin-s/Mac Rey-a; 2 covers (Chaykin & Rey) 4.00

RUGGED ACTION (Strange Stories of Suspense #5 on)
Atlas Comics (CSI): Dec, 1954 - No. 4, June, 1955
1-Brodsky-c 20 40 60 118 192 265
2-4: 2-Last precode (2/55) 15 30 45 84 127 170
NOTE: ***Ayers** a-2, 3. **Maneely** c-2, 3. **Severin** a-2.*

RUGRATS (TV) (Nickelodeon cartoon)
BOOM! Studios (kaboom!): Oct, 2017 - No. 8, May, 2018 ($3.99)
1-8: 1-3,5-Box Brown-s/Lisa DuBois-a; multiple covers 4.00
...: C Is For Chanukah 2018 Special 1 (11/18, $7.99) Kibblesmith & Crawford-s/Sherron-a 8.00
...: R Is For Reptar 2018 Special 1 (4/18, $7.99) Short stories by various 8.00

RUINS
Marvel Comics (Alterniverse): July, 1995 - No. 2, Sept, 1995 ($5.00, painted, limited series)
1,2: Phil Sheldon from Marvels; Warren Ellis scripts; acetate-c 6.00
Reprint (2009, $4.99) r/#1,2; cover gallery 5.00

RUINS OF RAVENCROFT
Marvel Comics: Mar, 2020 ($4.99, series of one-shots)
...: Carnage - Tieri-s/Unzueta-a; Set in the early 1400s New York 5.00
...: Dracula - Tieri-s/Unzueta-a; Dracula vs. Golden Age Captain America 5.00
...: Sabretooth - Tieri-s/Unzueta-a; Wolverine vs. Sabretooth in 1909 5.00

RULAH JUNGLE GODDESS (Formerly Zoot; I Loved #28 on) (Also see All Top Comics & Terrors of the Jungle)
Fox Feature Syndicate: No. 17, Aug, 1948 - No. 27, June, 1949
17 161 322 483 1030 1765 2500
18-Classic girl-fight interior splash 103 206 309 659 1130 1600
19,20 100 200 300 635 1093 1550
21-Used in **SOTI**, pg. 388,389 142 284 426 909 1555 2200
22-Used in **SOTI**, pg. 22,23 106 212 318 673 1162 1650
23-27 74 148 222 470 810 1150
NOTE: ***Kamen** c-17-19, 21, 22.*

RUNAWAY, THE (See Movie Classics)

RUNAWAYS
Marvel Comics: July, 2003 - No. 18, Nov, 2004 ($2.95/$2.25/$2.99)
1-($2.95) Vaughan-s/Alphona-a/Jo Chen-c 4.00
2-9-($2.50) 3.00
10-18-($2.99) 11,12-Miyazawa-a; Cloak and Dagger app. 16-The mole revealed 3.00
Hardcover (2005, $34.99) oversized r/#1-18; proposal & sketch pages; Vaughan intro. 35.00
Marvel Age Runaways Vol. 1: Pride and Joy (2004, $7.99, digest size) r/#1-6 8.00
...Vol. 2: Teenage Wasteland (2004, $7.99, digest size) r/#7-12 8.00
...Vol. 3: The Good Die Young (2004, $7.99, digest size) r/#13-18 8.00

RUNAWAYS (Also see X-Men/Runaways 2006 FCBD Edition)
Marvel Comics: Apr, 2005 - No. 30, Aug, 2008 ($2.99)
1-24: 1-6-Vaughan-s/Alphona-a/Jo Chen-c. 7,8-Miyazawa-a/Bachalo-c. 11-Spider-Man app. 12-New Avengers app. 18-Gert killed 3.00
25-30-Joss Whedon-s/Michael Ryan-a. 25-Punisher app. 3.00
...: Dead End Kids HC (2008, $19.99) r/#25-30 20.00
... Saga (2007, $3.99) re-caps the 2 series thru #24; 4 new pages w/Ramos-a; Ramos-c 4.00
Hardcover (2006, $24.99) oversized r/#1-12 & X-Men/Runaways; script & sketch pages 25.00
Hardcover Vol. 3 (2007, $24.99) oversized r/#13-24; sketch pages 25.00
...Vol. 4: True Believers (2006, $7.99, digest size) r/#1-6 8.00
...Vol. 5: Escape To New York (2006, $7.99, digest size) r/#7-12 8.00
...Vol. 6: Parental Guidance (2006, $7.99, digest size) r/#13-18 8.00

RUNAWAYS (3rd series)
Marvel Comics: Oct, 2008 - No. 14, Nov, 2009 ($2.99/$3.99)
1-9,11-14: 1-6-Terry Moore-s/Humberto Ramos-a/c. 7-9-Miyazawa-a 3.00
10-($3.99) Wolverine & the X-Men app.; Yost & Asmus-s; Pichelli & Rios-a; Lafuente-c 4.00

RUNAWAYS (Secret Wars Battleworld tie-in)
Marvel Comics: Aug, 2015 - No. 4, Nov, 2015 ($3.99, limited series)
1-4-Noelle Stevenson-s/Sanford Greene-a 4.00

RUNAWAYS
Marvel Comics: Nov, 2017 - No. 38 Oct, 2021 ($3.99)
1-37: 1-Gert revived; Rowell-s/Anka-a. 8-Julie Power app. 33-35-Wolverine app. 4.00
38-($4.99) Legacy issue #100 5.00

GD VG FN VF VF/NM NM-
2.0 4.0 6.0 8.0 9.0 9.2

... Halloween Comic Fest 2017 1 (12/17, giveaway) r/#1 (2003) first app. 3.00

RUN BABY RUN
Logos International: 1974 (39¢, Christian religious)
nn-By Tony Tallarico from Nicky Cruz's book 2 4 6 11 16 20

RUN, BUDDY, RUN (TV)
Gold Key: June, 1967 (Photo-c)
1 (10204-706) 3 6 9 17 26 35

RUNE (See Curse of Rune, Sludge & all other Ultraverse titles for previews)
Malibu Comics (Ultraverse): 1994 - No. 9, Apr, 1995 ($1.95)
0-Obtained by sending coupons from 11 comics; came w/Solution #0, poster, temporary tattoo, card 1 3 4 6 8 10
1,2,4-9: 1-Barry Windsor-Smith-c/a/stories begin, ends #6. 5-1st app. of Gemini. 6-Prime & Mantra app. 3.00
1-(1/94)-"Ashcan" edition flip book w/Wrath #1 3.00
1-Ultra 5000 Limited silver foil edition 6.00
3-(3/94, $3.50, 68 pgs.)-Flip book w/Ultraverse Premiere #1 4.00
Giant Size 1 ($2.50, 44 pgs.)-B.Smith story & art. 4.00

RUNE (2nd Series)(Formerly Curse of Rune)(See Ultraverse Unlimited #1)
Malibu Comics (Ultraverse): Infinity, Sept, 1995 - V2#7, Apr, 1996 ($1.50)
Infinity, V2#1-7: Infinity-Black September tie-in; black-c & painted-c exist. 1,3-7-Marvel's Adam Warlock app; regular & painted-c exist. 2-Flip book w/ "Phoenix Resurrection" Pt. 6 3.00
...Vs. Venom 1 (12/95, $3.95) 4.00

RUNE: HEARTS OF DARKNESS
Malibu Comics (Ultraverse): Sept, 1996 - No. 3, Nov, 1996 ($1.50, lim. series)
1-3: Moench scripts & Kyle Hotz-c/a; flip books w/6 pg. Rune story by the Pander Bros. 3.00

RUNE/SILVER SURFER
Marvel Comics/Malibu Comics (Ultraverse): Apr, 1995 ($5.95/$2.95, one-shot)
1 ($5.95, direct market)-BWS-c 6.00
1 ($2.95, newstand)-BWS-c 3.00
1-Collector's limited edition 6.00

RUNLOVEKILL
Image Comics: Apr, 2015 - No. 8 ($2.99, limited series)
1-4: 1-Tsuei-s/Canete-a 3.00

RUSE (Also see Archard's Agents)
CrossGeneration Comics: Nov, 2001 - No. 26, Jan, 2004 ($2.95)
1-Waid-s/Guice & Perkins-a 5.00
2-26: 6-Jeff Johnson-a. 11,15-Paul Ryan-a. 12-Last Waid-s 3.00
Enter the Detective Vol. 1 TPB (2002, $15.95) r/#1-6; Guice-c 16.00
...: The Silent Partner Vol. 2 (3/03, $15.95, TPB) r/#7-12 16.00
...: Criminal Intent Vol. 3 ('03, $15.95, TPB) r/#13-18 16.00
Traveler 1,2 ($9.95): Digest-size editions of the TPBs 10.00

RUSE
Marvel Comics: May, 2011 - No. 4 ($2.99, limited series)
1-4-Waid-s/Guice-c. 1,3,4-Pierfederici-a 3.00

RUSH CITY
DC Comics: Sept, 2006 - No. 6, May, 2007 ($2.99, limited series)
1-6: 1-Dixon-s/Green-a/Jock-c. 2,3-Black Canary app. 3.00

RUSTLERS, THE (See Zane Grey Four Color 532)

RUSTY, BOY DETECTIVE
Good Comics/Lev Gleason: Mar-April, 1955 - No. 5, Nov, 1955
1-Bob Wood, Carl Hubbell-a begins 13 26 39 74 105 135
2-5 9 18 27 52 69 85

RUSTY COMICS (Formerly Kid Movie Comics; Rusty and Her Family #21, 22; The Kelleys #23 on; see Millie The Model)
Marvel Comics (HPC): No. 12, Apr, 1947 - No. 22, Sept, 1949
12-Mitzi app. 36 72 108 211 343 475
13 22 44 66 128 209 290
14-Wolverton's Powerhouse Pepper (4 pgs.) plus Kurtzman's "Hey Look" 40 80 120 246 411 575
15-17-Kurtzman's "Hey Look" 24 48 72 142 234 325
18,19 20 40 60 117 189 260
20-Kurtzman-a (5 pgs.) 25 50 75 150 245 340
21,22-Kurtzman-a (17 & 22 pgs.) 32 64 96 188 307 425

RUSTY DUGAN (See Holyoke One-Shot #2)

RUSTY RILEY
Dell Publishing Co.: No. 418, Aug, 1952 - No. 554, April, 1954 (Frank Godwin strip reprints)
Four Color 418 (...a Boy, a Horse, and a Dog #1) 8 16 24 54 102 150
Four Color 451(2/53), 486 ('53), 554 5 10 15 33 57 80

RUULE
Beckett Comics: Dec, 2003 - No. 5, Apr, 2004 ($2.99)
1-5-David Mack-c/Mike Hawthorne-a 3.00

RUULE: KISS & TELL
Beckett Comics: Jun, 2004 - No. 8 ($1.99)
1-8: 1-Amano-s/c; Rousseau-a. 4-Maleev-c 3.00
TPB (2005, $19.99) r/#1-8 20.00

RWBY (Based on the online series from Rooster Teeth)(Issue #7 printing cancelled, digital only)
DC Comics: Dec, 2019 - No. 6, May, 2020 ($3.99)
1-6-Marguerite Bennett-s; two covers on each. 1-3,6-Mirka Andolfo-a. 4,5-Hetrick-a 4.00

RWBY / JUSTICE LEAGUE
DC Comics: Jun, 2021 - No. 7, Dec, 2021 ($3.99, limited series)
1-7-Marguerite Bennett-s; two covers on each. 1,4-Aneke-a. 2,5-Pepper-a 4.00

RYDER OF THE STORM
Radical Comics: Oct, 2010 - No. 3, Apr, 2011 ($4.99, limited series)
1-3-David Hine-s/Wayne Nichols-a 5.00

Rugrats (2017) #1 © Viacom

RWBY #1 © Rooster Teeth

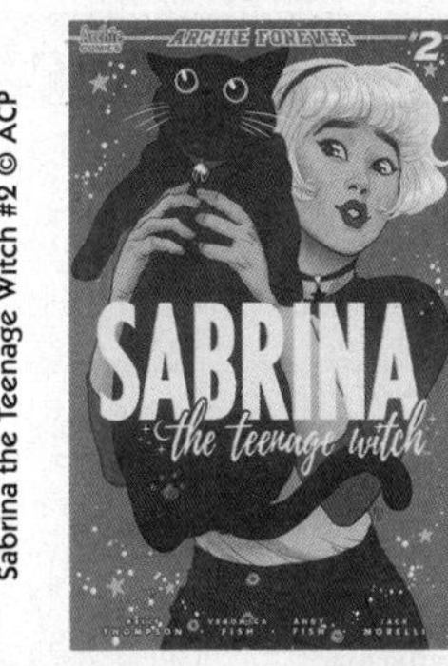

Sabrina the Teenage Witch #2 © ACP

	GD 2.0	VG 4.0	FN 6.0	VF 8.0	VF/NM 9.0	NM- 9.2

SAARI ("The Jungle Goddess")
P. L. Publishing Co.: November, 1951
1 65 130 195 416 708 1000

SABAN POWERHOUSE (TV)
Acclaim Books: 1997 ($4.50, digest size)
1,2-Power Rangers, BeetleBorgs, and others 2 4 6 11 16 20

SABAN PRESENTS POWER RANGERS TURBO VS. BEETLEBORGS METALLIX (TV)
Acclaim Books: 1997 ($4.50, digest size, one-shot)
nn 3 6 9 14 20 25

SABAN'S GO GO POWER RANGERS
BOOM! Studios: Jul, 2017 - No. 32, Jun, 2020 ($3.99)
1-32: 1-Parrott-s/Mora-a; multiple covers; retells 1st meeting with Rita Repulsa 4.00
...: Back To School 1 (9/18, $7.99) Rangers separately on Spring Break; art by various 8.00
...: Forever Rangers 1 (6/19, $7.99) Parrott-s/Carlini & Mortarino-a; origin of Zordon 8.00

SABAN'S MIGHTY MORPHIN POWER RANGERS
Hamilton Comics: Dec, 1994 - No. 6, May, 1995 ($1.95, limited series)
1-w/bound-in Power Ranger Barcode Card 3 6 9 16 23 30
2-6 6.00

SABAN'S MIGHTY MORPHIN POWER RANGERS (TV)
Marvel Comics: 1995 - No. 8, 1996 ($1.75)
1 2 4 6 11 16 20
2-8 5.00

SABAN'S POWER RANGERS: AFTERSHOCK
BOOM! Studios: Mar, 2017 ($14.99, SC)
SC - Sequel to the 2017 movie; Parrott-s/Werneck-a; movie photo-c 15.00

SABLE (Formerly Jon Sable, Freelance; also see Mike Grell's...)
First Comics: Mar, 1988 - No. 27, May, 1990 ($1.75/$1.95)
1-27: 10-Begin $1.95-c 3.00

SABLE & FORTUNE (Also see Silver Sable and the Wild Pack)
Marvel Comics: Mar, 2006 - No. 4, June, 2006 ($2.99, limited series)
1-4-John Burns-a/Brendan Cahill-s 3.00

SABRE (See Eclipse Graphic Album Series)
Eclipse Comics: Aug, 1982 - No. 14, Aug, 1985 (Baxter paper #4 on)
1-14: 1-Sabre & Morrigan Tales begin. 4-6-Incredible Seven origin 3.00

SABRETOOTH (See Iron Fist, Power Man, X-Factor #10 & X-Men)
Marvel Comics: Aug, 1993 - No. 4, Nov, 1993 ($2.95, lim. series, coated paper)
1-4: 1-Die-cut-c. 3-Wolverine app. 5.00
...Special 1 "In the Red Zone" (1995, $4.95) Chromium wraparound-c 6.00
V2 #1 (1/98, $5.95, one-shot) Wildchild app. 6.00
Trade paperback (12/94, $12.95) r/#1-4 13.00

SABRETOOTH
Marvel Comics: Dec, 2004 - No. 4, Feb, 2005 ($2.99, limited series)
1-4-Sears-a. 3,4-Wendigo app. 3.00
...: Open Season TPB (2005, $9.99) r/#1-4 10.00

SABRETOOTH
Marvel Comics: Apr, 2022 - No. 5, Sept, 2022 ($3.99, limited series)
1-($4.99)-LaValle-s/Kirk-a 5.00
2-5-($3.99) 4.00

SABRETOOTH AND MYSTIQUE (See Mystique and Sabretooth)

SABRETOOTH & THE EXILES
Marvel Comics: Jan, 2023 - Present ($4.99/$3.99, limited series)
1-($4.99)-LaValle-s/Kirk-a; Toad app. 5.00
2-4-($3.99) 4.00

SABRETOOTH CLASSIC
Marvel Comics: May, 1994 - No. 15, July, 1995 ($1.50)
1-15: 1-3-r/Power Man & Iron Fist #66,78,84. 4-r/Spec. S-M #116. 9-Uncanny X-Men #212, 10-r/Uncanny X-Men #213. 11-r/ Daredevil #238. 12-r/Classic X-Men #10 3.00

SABRETOOTH: MARY SHELLEY OVERDRIVE
Marvel Comics: Aug, 2002 - No. 4, Nov, 2002 ($2.99, limited series)
1-4-Jolley-s; Harris-c 3.00

SABRINA (Volume 2) (Based on animated series)
Archie Publications: Jan, 2000 - No. 104, Sept, 2009 ($1.79/$1.99/$2.19/$2.25/$2.50)
1-Teen-age Witch magically reverted to 12 years old 2 4 6 8 10 12
2-10: 4-Begin $1.99-c 4.00

	GD 2.0	VG 4.0	FN 6.0	VF 8.0	VF/NM 9.0	NM- 9.2

11-104: 38-Sabrina aged back to 16 years old. 39-Begin $2.19-c. 58-Manga-style begins; Tania Del Rio-a. 67-Josie and the Pussycats app. 101-Young Salem; begin $2.50-c 3.00
... And The Archies (2004, 8 1/2"x 5 1/2", Diamond Comic Dist. Halloween giveaway) - Tania Del Rio-s/a; manga-style; Josie and the Pussycats app. 3.00

SABRINA ANNIVERSARY SPECIAL
Archie Comic Publications: Oct, 2022 ($2.99, one-shot)
1-Intro. Amber Nightstone in new story; Dan Parent-s/a; bonus reprints 3.00

SABRINA'S CHRISTMAS MAGIC (See Archie Giant Series Magazine #196, 207, 220, 231, 243, 455, 467, 479, 491, 503, 515)

SABRINA'S HALLOWEEN SPOOOKTACULAR
Archie Publications: 1993 - 1995 ($2.00, 52 pgs.)
1-Neon orange ink-c; bound-in poster 2 4 6 8 10 12
2,3-Titled "Sabrina's Holiday Spectacular" 6.00

SABRINA, THE TEEN-AGE WITCH (TV)(See Archie Giant Series, Archie's Madhouse 22, Archie's TV..., Chilling Advs. In Sorcery, Little Archie #59)
Archie Publications: April, 1971 - No. 77, Jan, 1983 (52 pg.Giants No. 1-17)
1-52 pgs. begin, end #17 27 54 81 189 420 650
2-Archie's group x-over 9 18 27 61 123 185
3-5: 3,4-Archie's Group x-over 6 12 18 42 79 115
6-10 6 12 18 37 66 95
11-17(2/74) 4 8 12 27 44 60
18-30 3 6 9 19 30 40
31-40(8/77) 3 6 9 14 20 26
41-60(6/80) 2 4 6 10 14 18
61-70 2 4 6 8 11 14
71-76-low print run 2 4 6 11 16 20
77-Last issue; low print run 3 6 9 15 22 28

SABRINA, THE TEEN-AGE WITCH
Archie Publications: 1996 ($1.50, 32 pgs., one-shot)
1-Updated origin 2 4 6 8 10 12

SABRINA, THE TEEN-AGE WITCH (Continues in Sabrina, Vol. 2)
Archie Publications: May, 1997 - No. 32, Dec, 1999 ($1.50/$1.75/$1.79)
1-Photo-c with Melissa Joan Hart 2 4 6 8 10 12
2-10: 9-Begin $1.75-c 6.00
11-20 5.00
21-32: 24-Begin $1.79-c. 28-Sonic the Hedgehog-c/app. 4.00

SABRINA THE TEEN-AGE WITCH (Volume 3)
Archie Comic Publications: May, 2019 - No. 5, Nov, 2019 ($3.99)
1-5-Kelly Thompson-s/Veronica & Andy Fish-a; multiple covers 4.00

SABRINA THE TEEN-AGE WITCH (Volume 4)
Archie Comic Publications: May, 2020 - No. 5, Apr, 2021 ($3.99)
1-5-Kelly Thompson-s/Veronica & Andy Fish-a; multiple covers 4.00

SABU, "ELEPHANT BOY" (Movie; formerly My Secret Story)
Fox Feature Syndicate: No. 30, June, 1950 - No. 2, Aug, 1950
30(#1)-Wood-a; photo-c from movie 27 54 81 158 259 360
2-Photo-c from movie; Kamen-a 20 40 60 114 182 250

SACHS & VIOLENS
Marvel Comics (Epic Comics): Nov, 1993 - No. 4, July, 1994 ($2.25, limited series, mature)
1-($2.75)-Embossed-c w/bound-in trading card 3.00
1-($3.50)-Platinum edition (1 for each 10 ordered) 4.00
2-4: Perez-c/a; bound-in trading card: 2-(5/94) 3.00
TPB (DC, 2006, $14.99) r/series; intro. by Peter David; creator bios. 15.00

SACRAMENT
AWA Inc.: Aug, 2022 - No. 5, Dec, 2022 ($3.99, limited series)
1-5-Milligan-s/Frusin-a 4.00

SACRAMENTS, THE
Catechetical Guild Educational Society: Oct, 1955 (35¢)
30304 8 16 24 44 57 70

SACRED AND THE PROFANE, THE (See Eclipse Graphic Album Series #9 & Epic Illustrated #20)

SACRED CREATURES
Image Comics: Jul, 2017 - No. 6, May, 2018 ($4.99/$3.99)
1,4-6-($4.99) Pablo Raimondi & Klaus Janson-s/Raimondi-a. 4-6-Janson partial-a 5.00
2,3-($3.99) 4.00

SACRED SIX
Dynamite Entertainment: 2020 - No. 12, 2021 ($3.99)
1-12-Vampirella, Draculina, Pantha, Nyx, Chastity & Lilith app. 1-Jae Lee & Gabriel Ibarra-a 4.00

SADDLE JUSTICE (Happy Houlihans #1,2) (Saddle Romances #9 on)
E. C. Comics: No. 3, Spring, 1948 - No. 8, Sept-Oct, 1949

Issue	GD 2.0	VG 4.0	FN 6.0	VF 8.0	VF/NM 9.0	NM- 9.2
3-The 1st E.C. by Bill Gaines to break away from M. C. Gaines' old Educational Comics format. Craig, Feldstein, H. C. Kiefer, & Stan Asch-a; mentioned in Love and Death	87	174	261	553	952	1350
4-1st Graham Ingels-a for E.C.	65	130	195	416	708	1000
5-8-Ingels-a in all	57	114	171	362	619	875

NOTE: *Craig and Feldstein art in most issues. Canadian reprints known; see Table of Contents.* ***Craig*** *c-3, 4.* ***Ingels*** *c-5-8. #4 contains a biography of* ***Craig.***

SADDLE ROMANCES (Saddle Justice #3-8; Weird Science #12 on)
E. C. Comics: No. 9, Nov-Dec, 1949 - No. 11, Mar-Apr, 1950

Issue	GD 2.0	VG 4.0	FN 6.0	VF 8.0	VF/NM 9.0	NM- 9.2
9,11: 9-Ingels-c/a. 11-Ingels-a; Feldstein-c	65	130	195	416	708	1000
10-Wally Wood's 1st work at E. C.; Ingels-a; Feldstein-c	97	194	291	621	1061	1500

NOTE: *Canadian reprints known; see Table of Contents.* ***Wood/Harrison*** *a-10, 11.*

SADIE SACK (See Harvey Hits #93)

SAD SACK AND THE SARGE
Harvey Publications: Sept, 1957 - No. 155, June, 1982

Issue	GD 2.0	VG 4.0	FN 6.0	VF 8.0	VF/NM 9.0	NM- 9.2
1	12	24	36	82	179	275
2	7	14	21	46	86	125
3-10	5	10	15	35	63	90
11-20	5	10	15	30	50	70
21-30	3	6	9	19	30	40
31-50	3	6	9	14	20	25
51-70	2	4	6	9	13	16
71-90,97-99	1	3	4	6	8	10
91-96: All 52 pg. Giants	2	4	6	9	13	16
100	2	4	6	8	10	12
101-120	1	2	3	4	5	7
121-155						5.00

NOTE: ***George Baker*** *covers on numerous issues.*

SAD SACK COMICS (See Harvey Collector's Comics #16, Little Sad Sack, Tastee Freez Comics #4 & True Comics #55 for 1st app.)
Harvey Publications/Lorne-Harvey Publications (Recollections) #288 On: Sept, 1949 - No. 287, Oct, 1982; No. 288, 1992 - No. 291, 1993

Issue	GD 2.0	VG 4.0	FN 6.0	VF 8.0	VF/NM 9.0	NM- 9.2
1-Infinity-c; Little Dot begins (1st app.); civilian issues begin, end #21; based on comic strip (first app. in True Comics #55)	139	278	417	1112	2506	3900
2-Flying Fool by Powell	31	62	93	223	499	775
3	17	34	51	117	259	400
4-10	12	24	36	79	170	260
11-21	8	16	24	54	102	150
22-("Back In The Army Again" on covers #22-36); "The Specialist" story about Sad Sack's return to Army	9	18	27	59	117	175
23-30	5	10	15	34	60	85
31-50	4	8	12	28	47	65
51-80,100: 62-"The Specialist" reprinted	3	6	9	21	33	45
81-99	3	6	9	16	23	30
101-140	3	6	9	14	19	24
141-170,200	2	4	6	11	16	20
171-199	2	4	6	9	13	16
201-207: 207-Last 12¢ issue	2	4	6	8	11	14
208-222	1	3	4	6	8	10
223-228 (25¢ Giants, 52 pgs.)	2	4	6	8	11	14
229-250	1	3	4	6	8	10
251-285						6.00
286,287-Limited distribution	1	2	3	5	7	9
288,289 ($2.75, 1992): 289-50th anniversary issue						6.00
290,291 ($1.00, 1993, B&W)						3.00
3-D 1 (1/54, 25¢)-Came with 2 pairs of glasses; titled "Harvey 3-D Hits"	14	28	42	93	204	315
...At Home for the Holidays 1 (1993, no-c price)-Publ. by Lorne-Harvey' X-Mas issue						4.00

NOTE: *The Sad Sack Comics comic book was a spin-off from a Sunday Newspaper strip launched through John Wheeler's Bell Syndicate. The previous Sunday page and the first 21 comics depicted the Sad Sack in civvies. Unpopularity caused the Sunday page to be discontinued in the early '50s. Meanwhile Sad Sack returned to the Army, by popular demand, in issue No. 22, remaining there ever since. Incidentally, relatively few of the first 21 issues were ever collected and remain scarce due to this.* ***George Baker*** *covers on numerous issues.*

SAD SACK FUN AROUND THE WORLD
Harvey Publications: 1974 (no month)

Issue	GD 2.0	VG 4.0	FN 6.0	VF 8.0	VF/NM 9.0	NM- 9.2
1-About Great Britain	2	4	6	11	16	20

SAD SACK GOES HOME
Harvey Publications: 1951 (16 pgs. in color, no cover price)

Issue	GD 2.0	VG 4.0	FN 6.0	VF 8.0	VF/NM 9.0	NM- 9.2
nn-By George Baker	5	10	15	33	57	80

SAD SACK LAUGH SPECIAL
Harvey Publications: Winter, 1958-59 - No. 93, Feb, 1977 (#1-9: 84 pgs.; #10-60: 68 pgs.; #61-76: 52 pgs.)

Issue	GD 2.0	VG 4.0	FN 6.0	VF 8.0	VF/NM 9.0	NM- 9.2
1-Giant 25¢ issues begin	9	18	27	60	120	180
2	5	10	15	35	63	90
3-10	5	10	15	30	50	70
11-30	4	8	12	25	40	55
31-60: 31-Hi-Fi Tweeter app. 60-Last 68 pg. Giant	3	6	9	16	23	30
61-76-(All 52 pg. issues)	2	4	6	10	14	18
77-93	1	2	3	5	6	8

SAD SACK NAVY, GOBS 'N' GALS
Harvey Publications: Aug, 1972 - No. 8, Oct, 1973

Issue	GD 2.0	VG 4.0	FN 6.0	VF 8.0	VF/NM 9.0	NM- 9.2
1: 52 pg. Giant	3	6	9	16	23	30
2-8	2	4	6	9	12	15

SAD SACK'S ARMY LIFE (See Harvey Hits #8, 17, 22, 28, 32, 39, 43, 47, 51, 55, 58, 61, 64, 67, 70)

SAD SACK'S ARMY LIFE (...Parade #1-57, ...Today #58 on)
Harvey Publications: Oct, 1963 - No. 60, Nov, 1975; No. 61, May, 1976

Issue	GD 2.0	VG 4.0	FN 6.0	VF 8.0	VF/NM 9.0	NM- 9.2
1-(68 pg. issues begin)	7	14	21	44	82	120
2-10	4	8	12	27	44	60
11-20	3	6	9	19	30	40
21-34: Last 68 pg. issue	3	6	9	16	23	30
35-51: All 52 pgs.	2	4	6	10	14	18
52-61	1	3	4	6	8	10

SAD SACK'S FUNNY FRIENDS (See Harvey Hits #75)
Harvey Publications: Dec, 1955 - No. 75, Oct, 1969

Issue	GD 2.0	VG 4.0	FN 6.0	VF 8.0	VF/NM 9.0	NM- 9.2
1	9	18	27	60	120	180
2-10	5	10	15	35	63	90
11-20	4	8	12	23	37	50
21-30	3	6	9	17	26	35
31-50	3	6	9	14	20	25
51-75	2	4	6	9	13	16

SAD SACK'S MUTTSY (See Harvey Hits #74, 77, 80, 82, 84, 87, 89, 92, 96, 99, 102, 105, 108, 111, 113, 115, 117, 119, 121)

SAD SACK USA (...Vacation #8)
Harvey Publications: Nov, 1972 - No. 7, Nov, 1973; No. 8, Oct, 1974

Issue	GD 2.0	VG 4.0	FN 6.0	VF 8.0	VF/NM 9.0	NM- 9.2
1	3	6	9	14	20	25
2-8	2	4	6	8	10	12

SAD SACK WITH SARGE & SADIE
Harvey Publications: Sept, 1972 - No. 8, Nov, 1973

Issue	GD 2.0	VG 4.0	FN 6.0	VF 8.0	VF/NM 9.0	NM- 9.2
1-(52 pg. Giant)	3	6	9	14	20	25
2-8	2	4	6	8	10	12

SAD SAD SACK WORLD
Harvey Publ.: Oct, 1964 - No. 46, Dec, 1973 (#1-31: 68 pgs.; #32-38: 52 pgs.)

Issue	GD 2.0	VG 4.0	FN 6.0	VF 8.0	VF/NM 9.0	NM- 9.2
1	6	12	18	41	76	110
2-10	4	8	12	25	40	55
11-20	3	6	9	19	30	40
21-31: 31-Last 68 pg. issue	3	6	9	16	23	30
32-39-(All 52 pgs)	2	4	6	10	14	18
40-46	1	3	4	6	8	10

SAFEST PLACE IN THE WORLD, THE
Dark Horse Comics: 1993 ($2.50, one-shot)

Issue	GD 2.0	VG 4.0	FN 6.0	VF 8.0	VF/NM 9.0	NM- 9.2
1-Steve Ditko-c/a/scripts						4.00

SAFETY-BELT MAN
Sirius Entertainment: June, 1994 - No. 6, 1995 ($2.50, B&W)

Issue	GD 2.0	VG 4.0	FN 6.0	VF 8.0	VF/NM 9.0	NM- 9.2
1-6: 1-Horan-s/Dark One-a/Sprouse-c. 2,3-Warren-c. 4-Linsner back-up story. 5,6-Crilley-a						3.00

SAFETY-BELT MAN ALL HELL
Sirius Entertainment: June, 1996 - No. 6, Mar, 1997 ($2.95, color)

Issue	GD 2.0	VG 4.0	FN 6.0	VF 8.0	VF/NM 9.0	NM- 9.2
1-6-Horan-s/Fillbach Bros.-a						3.00

SAGA
Image Comics: Mar, 2012 - Present ($2.99)

Issue	GD 2.0	VG 4.0	FN 6.0	VF 8.0	VF/NM 9.0	NM- 9.2
1-Brian K. Vaughan-s/Fiona Staples-a/c; 1st app. Alana, Marko, Hazel, The Will, and Lying Cat	9	18	27	59	117	175
1-Second printing	3	6	9	15	22	28
2-1st app. The Stalk	3	6	9	17	26	35
3-5: 3-1st app. Izabel	3	6	9	14	20	25
6,7,9-12						6.00
8-1st app. Gwendolyn	3	6	9	14	19	24
13-53: 19-Intro. Ginny. 24-Lying Cat returns. 25,37-Wraparound-c. 43-(25¢-c). 51-Doff killed. 53-Prince Robot killed						4.00
54-(7/18) Marko dies						4.00
55-60: 55-(1/22) Jumps to 3 years later; intro Bombazine						3.00
61-62-($3.99)						4.00

SAGA OF BIG RED, THE
Omaha World-Herald: Sept, 1976 ($1.25) (In color)

Issue	GD 2.0	VG 4.0	FN 6.0	VF 8.0	VF/NM 9.0	NM- 9.2
nn-by Win Mumma; story of the Nebraska Cornhuskers (sports)						6.00

SAGA OF CRYSTAR, CRYSTAL WARRIOR, THE
Marvel Comics: May, 1983 - No. 11, Feb, 1985 (Remco toy tie-in)

Issue	GD 2.0	VG 4.0	FN 6.0	VF 8.0	VF/NM 9.0	NM- 9.2
1,6: 1-(Baxter paper). 6-Nightcrawler app; Golden-c						5.00
2-5,7-11: 3-Dr. Strange app. 3-11-Golden-c (painted-4,5). 11-Alpha Flight app.						4.00

SAGA OF RA'S AL GHUL, THE
DC Comics: Jan, 1988 - No. 4, Apr, 1988 ($2.50, limited series)

Issue	GD 2.0	VG 4.0	FN 6.0	VF 8.0	VF/NM 9.0	NM- 9.2
1-4-r/N. Adams Batman						6.00

SAGA OF SABAN'S MIGHTY MORPHIN POWER RANGERS (Also see Saban's Mighty Morphin Power Rangers)
Hamilton Comics: 1995 - No. 4, 1995 ($1.95, limited series)

Issue	GD 2.0	VG 4.0	FN 6.0	VF 8.0	VF/NM 9.0	NM- 9.2
1-4						6.00

SAGA OF SEVEN SUNS, THE : VEILED ALLIANCES
DC Comics (WildStorm): 2004 ($24.95, hardcover graphic novel with dustjacket)

Issue	GD 2.0	VG 4.0	FN 6.0	VF 8.0	VF/NM 9.0	NM- 9.2
HC-Kevin J. Anderson-s/Robert Teranishi-a						25.00
SC-(2004, $17.95)						18.00

SAGA OF THE ORIGINAL HUMAN TORCH
Marvel Comics: Apr, 1990 - No. 4, July, 1990 ($1.50, limited series)

Issue	GD 2.0	VG 4.0	FN 6.0	VF 8.0	VF/NM 9.0	NM- 9.2
1-4: 1-Origin; Buckler-c/a(p). 3-Hitler-c						4.00

SAGA OF THE SUB-MARINER, THE
Marvel Comics: Nov, 1988 - No. 12, Oct, 1989 ($1.25/$1.50 #5 on, maxi-series)

Issue	GD 2.0	VG 4.0	FN 6.0	VF 8.0	VF/NM 9.0	NM- 9.2
1-12: 9-Original X-Men app.						4.00

SAGA OF THE SWAMP THING, THE (See Swamp Thing)

SAILOR MOON (Manga)
Mixx Entertainment Inc.: 1998 - No. 25 ($2.95)

Issue	GD 2.0	VG 4.0	FN 6.0	VF 8.0	VF/NM 9.0	NM- 9.2
1	4	8	12	28	47	65
1-(San Diego edition)	11	22	33	76	163	250
2-5	2	4	6	11	16	20
6-10	1	3	4	6	8	10
11-25	1	2	3	4	5	7
26-35						5.00

Sacred Six #6 © DYN

Saga #60 © Vaughan & Staples

Samson #13 © AJAX

	GD 2.0	VG 4.0	FN 6.0	VF 8.0	VF/NM 9.0	NM- 9.2

... Rini's Moon Stick 1 15.00

SAILOR ON THE SEA OF FATE (See First Comics Graphic Novel #11)

SAILOR SWEENEY (Navy Action #1-11, 15 on)
Atlas Comics (CDS): No. 12, July, 1956 - No. 14, Nov, 1956

12-14: 12-Shores-a. 13,14-Severin-c 39 78 117 231 378 525

SAINT, THE (Also see Movie Comics(DC) #2 & Silver Streak #18)
Avon Periodicals: Aug, 1947 - No. 12, Mar, 1952

1-Kamen bondage-c/a 181 362 543 1158 1979 2800
2 68 136 204 435 743 1050
3,5 55 110 165 352 601 850
4-Lingerie panels, black background, Good Girl art-c
81 162 243 518 884 1250
6-Miss Fury app. by Tarpe Mills (14 pgs.) 87 174 261 553 952 1350
7-c-/Avon paperback #118 48 96 144 302 514 725
8,9(12/50): Saint strip-r in #8-12; 9-Kinstler-c 42 84 126 265 445 625
10-Wood-a, 1 pg; c-/Avon paperback #289 42 84 126 265 445 625
11 39 78 117 231 378 525
12-c-/Avon paperback #123 39 78 117 240 395 550

NOTE: *Lucky Dale, Girl Detective in #1,2,4,6.* **Hollingsworth** *a-4, 6. Painted-c 7, 8, 10-12.*

SAINT ANGEL
Image Comics: Mar, 2000 - No. 4, Mar, 2001 ($2.95/$3.95)

0-Altstaetter & Napton-s/Altstaetter-a 3.00
1-4-($3.95) Flip book w/Deity. 1-(6/00). 2-(10/00) 4.00

ST. GEORGE
Marvel Comics (Epic Comics): June, 1988 - No.8, Oct, 1989 ($1.25,/$1.50)

1-8: Sienkiewicz-c. 3-begin $1.50-c 3.00

SAINT GERMAINE
Caliber Comics: 1997 - No. 8, 1998 ($2.95)

1-8: 1,5-Alternate covers 3.00

ST. MERCY
Image Comics (Top Cow): Aug, 2021 - No. 4, Nov, 2021 ($3.99, limited series)

1-4-Platten-s/Rojo-a 4.00

ST. SWITHIN'S DAY
Trident Comics: Apr, 1990 ($2.50, one-shot)

1-Grant Morrison scripts 3.00

ST. SWITHIN'S DAY
Oni Press: Mar, 1998 ($2.95, B&W, one-shot)

1-Grant Morrison-s/Paul Grist-a 3.00

SALOMÉ (See Night Music #6)

SALVATION RUN
DC Comics: Jan, 2008 - No. 7, Jul, 2008 ($2.99/$3.50, limited series)

1-6-DC villains banished to an alien planet; Willingham-s/Chen-a/c. 1-Var-c by Corroney 3.00
7-($3.50) Luthor cover by Chen 3.50
7-($3.50) Variant Joker cover by Neal Adams 4 8 12 25 40 55

SAM AND MAX, FREELANCE POLICE SPECIAL
Fishwrap Prod./Comico: 1987 ($1.75, B&W); Jan, 1989 ($2.75, 44 pgs.)

1 ($1.75, B&W, Fishwrap) 4.00
2 ($2.75, color, Comico) 4.00

SAM AND TWITCH (See Spawn and Case Files:...)
Image Comics (Todd McFarlane Prod.): Aug, 1999 - No. 26, Feb, 2004 ($2.50)

1-26: 1-19-Bendis-s. 1-14-Medina-a. 15-19-Maleev-a. 20-24-McFarlane-s/Maleev-a 3.00
Book One: Udaku (2000, $21.95, TPB) B&W reprint of #1-8 22.00
...: The Brian Michael Bendis Collection Vol. 1 (2/06, $24.95) r/#1-9 in color; sketch pages 25.00
...: The Brian Michael Bendis Collection Vol. 2 (6/07, $24.95) r/#10-19; cover gallery 25.00

SAM AND TWITCH: THE WRITER
Image Comics (Todd McFarlane Prod.): May, 2010 - No. 4, Jun, 2010 ($2.99)

1-4-Blengino-s/Erbetta-a/c 3.00

SAMARITAN VERITAS
Image Comics: May, 2017 - No. 3, Jul, 2017 ($3.99)

1-3-Hawkins-s/Rojo-a 4.00

SAM HILL PRIVATE EYE
Close-Up (Archie): 1950 - No. 7, 1951

1 25 50 75 150 245 340
2 15 30 45 84 127 170
3-7 12 24 36 67 94 120

SAMSON (1st Series) (Captain Aero #7 on; see Big 3 Comics)
Fox Feature Syndicate: Fall, 1940 - No. 6, Sept, 1941 (See Fantastic Comics)

1-Samson begins, ends #6; Powell-a, signed 'Rensie;' Wing Turner by Tuska app; Fine-c?
232 464 696 1485 2543 3600
2-Dr. Fung by Powell; Fine-c? 110 220 330 704 1202 1700
3-Navy Jones app.; Joe Simon-c 81 162 243 518 884 1250
4-Yarko the Great, Master Magician begins 81 162 243 518 884 1250
5,6: 5-WWII Nazi-c. 6-Origin The Topper 65 130 195 416 708 1000

SAMSON (2nd Series) (Formerly Fantastic Comics #10, 11)
Ajax/Farrell Publications (Four Star): No. 12, April, 1955 - No. 14, Aug, 1955

12-Wonder Boy 39 78 117 240 395 550
13,14: 13-Wonder Boy, Rocket Man 34 68 102 204 332 460

SAMSON (See Mighty Samson)

SAMSON & DELILAH (See A Spectacular Feature Magazine)

SAMUEL BRONSTON'S CIRCUS WORLD (See Circus World under Movie Classics)

SAMURAI (Also see Eclipse Graphic Album Series #14)
Aircel Publications: 1985 - No. 23, 1987 ($1.70, B&W)

1, 14-16-Dale Keown-a 4.00
1-(reprinted),2-12,17-23: 2 (reprinted issue exists) 3.00
13-Dale Keown's 1st published artwork (1987) 6.00

SAMURAI
Warp Graphics: May, 1997 ($2.95, B&W)

1 3.00

SAMURAI: BROTHERS IN ARMS
Titan Comics: Oct, 2016 - No. 6 ($3.99)

1-6-Genet-a/DiGiorgio-s; English version of French comic 4.00

SAMURAI CAT
Marvel Comics (Epic Comics): June, 1991 - No. 3, Sept, 1991 ($2.25, limited series)

1-3: 3-Darth Vader-c/story parody 3.00

SAMURAI: HEAVEN & EARTH
Dark Horse Comics: Dec, 2004 - No. 5, Dec, 2005 ($2.99)

1-5-Luke Ross-a/Ron Marz-s 3.00
TPB (4/06, $14.95) r/#1-5; sketch pages and cover and pin-up gallery 15.00

SAMURAI: HEAVEN & EARTH (Volume 2)
Dark Horse Comics: Nov, 2006 - No. 5, June, 2007 ($2.99)

1-5-Luke Ross-a/Ron Marz-s 3.00
TPB (10/07, $14.95) r/#1-5; sketch pages and cover and pin-up gallery 15.00

SAMURAI JACK (TV)
IDW Publishing: Oct, 2013 - No. 20, May, 2015 ($3.99)

1-20: 1-5-Jim Zub-s/Andy Suriano-a; multiple covers on each 4.00
... Special - Director's Cut (2/14, $7.99) Reprints '02 DC issue; commentary by Bill Wray 8.00

SAMURAI JACK: LOST WORLDS (TV)
IDW Publishing: Apr, 2019 - No. 4, Jul, 2019 ($3.99, limited series)

1-4-Paul Allor-s/Adam Bryce Thomas-a; multiple covers on each 4.00

SAMURAI JACK: QUANTUM JACK (TV)
IDW Publishing: Sept, 2017 - No. 5, Jan, 2018 ($3.99, limited series)

1-5-Rangel, Jr.-s/Johnson-Cadwell-a; multiple covers 4.00

SAMURAI JACK SPECIAL (TV)
DC Comics: Sept, 2002 ($3.95, one-shot)

1-Adaptation of pilot episode with origin story; Tartakovsky-s/Naylor & Wray-a 4.00

SAMURAI: LEGEND
Marvel Comics (Soleil): 2008 - No. 4, 2009 ($5.99)

1-4-Genet-a/DiGiorgio-s; English version of French comic; preview of other titles 6.00

SAMURAI SONJA
Dynamite Entertainment: 2022 - No. 5, 2022 ($3.99, limited series)

1-5-Red Sonja-like warrior in ancient Japan 4.00

SAMUREE
Continuity Comics: May, 1987 - No. 9, Jan, 1991

1 6.00
2-9 4.00

SAMUREE
Continuity Comics: V2#1, May, 1993 - V2#4, Jan,1994 ($2.50)

V2#1-4-Embossed-c: 2,4-Adams plot, Nebres-i. 3-Nino-c(i) 4.00

GD VG FN VF VF/NM NM-
2.0 4.0 6.0 8.0 9.0 9.2

GD VG FN VF VF/NM NM-
2.0 4.0 6.0 8.0 9.0 9.2

SAMUREE
Acclaim Comics (Windjammer): Oct, 1995 - No. 2, Nov,1995 ($2.50, lim. series)
1,2 3.00

SAN DIEGO COMIC CON COMICS
Dark Horse Comics: 1992 - No.4, 1995 (B&W, promo comic for the San Diego Comic Con)
1-(1992)-Includes various characters published from Dark Horse including Concrete, The Mask, RoboCop and others; 1st app. of Sprint from John Byrne's Next Men; art by Quesada, Byrne, Rude, Burden, Moebius & others; pin-ups by Rude, Dorkin, Allred & others; Chadwick-c 2 4 6 9 13 16
2-(1993)-Intro of Legend imprint; 1st app. of John Byrne's Danger Unlimited, Mike Mignola's Hellboy (also see John Byrne's Next Men #21), Art Adams' Monkeyman & O'Brien; contains stories featuring Concrete, Sin City, Martha Washington & others; Grendel, Madman, & Big Guy pin-ups; Don Martin-c 9 18 27 61 123 185
3-(1994)-Contains stories featuring Barb Wire, The Mask, The Dirty Pair, & Grendel by Matt Wagner; contains pin-ups of Ghost, Predator & Rascals In Paradise; The Mask-c
1 2 3 5 6 8
4-(1995)-Contains Sin City story by Miller (3pg.), Star Wars, The Mask, Tarzan, Foot Soldiers; Sin City & Star Wars flip-c 1 3 4 6 8 10

SANDMAN, THE (1st Series) (Also see Adventure Comics #40, New York World's Fair, Sandman Special (2017) and World's Finest #3)
National Periodical Publ.: Winter, 1974; No. 2, Apr-May, 1975 - No. 6, Dec-Jan, 1975-76
1-1st app. Bronze Age Sandman by Simon & Kirby (last S&K collaboration)
6 12 18 41 76 110
2-6: 6-Kirby/Wood-c/a 3 6 9 21 33 45
The Sandman By Joe Simon & Jack Kirby HC (2009, $39.99, d.j.) r/Sandman app. from World's Finest #6,7, Adventure Comics #72-102 and Sandman #1; Morrow intro. 40.00
NOTE: *Kirby a-1p, 4-6p; c-1-5, 6p.*

SANDMAN (2nd Series) (See Books of Magic, Vertigo Jam & Vertigo Preview)
DC Comics (Vertigo imprint #47 on): Jan, 1989 - No. 75, Mar, 1996 ($1.50-$2.50, mature)
1 ($2.00, 52 pgs.)-1st app. Modern Age Sandman (Morpheus); Neil Gaiman scripts begin; Sam Kieth-a(p) in #1-5; Wesley Dodds (G.A. Sandman) cameo.
10 20 30 61 132 200
1 (Facsimile Edition) (2022, $3.99) r/1 with original 1989 ads 4.00
2-Cain & Abel app. (from HOM & HOS) 3 6 9 19 30 40
3,5: 3-John Constantine app. 3 6 9 16 23 30
4-1st app. Lucifer Morningstar; The Demon app. 5 10 15 35 63 90
6,7 2 4 6 10 14 18
8-Death-c/story (1st app.)-Regular ed. has Jeanette Kahn publishorial & American Cancer Society ad w/no indicia on inside front-c 8 16 24 54 102 150
8-Limited ed. (600+ copies?); has Karen Berger editorial and next issue teaser on inside covers (has indicia) 27 54 81 189 420 650
9-14: 10-Has explaination about #8 mixup; has bound-in Shocker movie poster.
14-(52 pgs.)-Bound-in Nightbreed fold-out 2 4 6 8 11 14
15-20: 16-Photo-c. 17,18-Kelley Jones-a. 19-Vess-a 1 3 4 6 8 10
18-Error version w/1st 3 panels on pg. 1 in blue ink 17 34 51 117 259 400
19-Error version w/pages 18 & 20 facing each other 3 6 9 14 19 24
21,23-27: Seasons of Mist storyline. 22-World Without End preview. 24-Kelley Jones/Russell-a 6.00
22-1st Daniel (Later becomes new Sandman) 3 6 9 16 23 30
28-30 5.00
31-49,51-74: 36-(52 pgs.). 41,44-48-Metallic ink on-c. 48-Cerebus appears as a doll. 54-Re-intro Prez; Death app.; Belushi, Nixon & Wildcat cameos. 57-Metallic ink on c. 65-w/bound-in trading card. 69-Death of Sandman. 70-73-Zulli-a. 74-Jon J. Muth-a. 4.00
50-($2.95, 52 pgs.)-Black-c w/metallic ink by McKean; Russell-a; McFarlane pin-up
1 2 3 5 6 8
50-($2.95)-Signed & limited (5,000) Treasury Edition with sketch of Neil Gaiman
3 6 9 14 20 26
50-Platinum 3 6 9 18 28 38
75-($3.95)-Vess-a. 5.00
Special 1 (1991, $3.50, 68 pgs.)-Glow-in-the-dark-c 5.00
Absolute Sandman Special Edition #1 (2006, 50¢) sampling from HC; recolored r/#1 3.00
Absolute Sandman Volume One (2006, $99.00, slipcased hardcover) recolored r/#1-20; Gaiman's original proposal; script and pencils from #19; character sketch gallery 100.00
Absolute Sandman Volume Two (2007, $99.00, slipcased hardcover) recolored r/#21-39; r/A Gallery of Dreams one-shot; bonus stories, scripts and pencil art 100.00
Absolute Sandman Volume Three (2008, $99.00, slipcased hardcover) recolored r/#40-56; & Special #1; bonus galleries, scripts and pencil art; Jill Thompson intro. 100.00
Absolute Sandman Volume Four (2008, $99.00, slipcased hardcover) recolored r/#57-75; scripts & sketch pages for #57 & 75; gallery of Dreaming memorabilia; Berger intro. 100.00
...: A Gallery of Dreams ($2.95)-Intro by N. Gaiman 4.00
...: Preludes & Nocturnes ($29.95, HC)-r/#1-8. 30.00
...: The Doll's House (1990, $29.95, HC)-r/#8-16. 30.00
...: Dream Country ($29.95, HC)-r/#17-20. 30.00
...: Season of Mists ($29.95, Leatherbound HC)-r/#21-28. 50.00
...: A Game of You ($29.95, HC)-r/32-37, ...: Fables and Reflections ($29.95, HC)-r/Vertigo Preview #1, Sandman Special #1, #29-31, #38-40 & #50. ...: Brief Lives ($29.95, HC)-r/#41-49. ...: World's End ($29.95, HC)-r/#51-56 30.00
...: The Kindly Ones (1996, $34.95, HC)-r/#57-69 & Vertigo Jam #1 35.00
...: The Wake ($29.95, HC)-r/#70-75. 30.00
NOTE: *A new set of hardcover printings with new covers was introduced in 1998-99. Multiple printings exist of softcover collections. Recolored (from the Absolute HC) softcover editions were released in 2010.* ***Bachalo*** *a-12;* ***Kelley Jones*** *a-17, 18, 22, 23, 26, 27.* ***Vess*** *a-19, 75.*

SANDMAN: ENDLESS NIGHTS
DC Comics (Vertigo): 2003 ($24.95, hardcover, with dust jacket)
HC-Neil Gaiman stories of Morpheus and the Endless illustrated by Fabry, Manara, Prado, Quitely, Russell, Sienkiewicz, and Storey; McKean-c 25.00
...Special (11/03, $2.95) Previews hardcover; Dream story w/Prado-a; McKean-c 4.00
SC (2004, $17.95) 18.00

SANDMAN MIDNIGHT THEATRE
DC Comics (Vertigo): Sept, 1995 ($6.95, squarebound, one-shot)
nn-Modern Age Sandman (Morpheus) meets G.A. Sandman; Gaiman & Wagner story; McKean-c; Kristiansen-a 7.00

SANDMAN MYSTERY THEATRE (Also see Sandman (2nd Series) #1)
DC Comics (Vertigo): Apr, 1993 - No. 70, Feb, 1999 ($1.95/$2.25/$2.50)
1-G.A. Sandman advs. begin; Matt Wagner scripts begin 5.00
2-49,51-70: 5-Neon ink logo. 29-32-Hourman app. 38-Ted Knight (G.A. Starman) app. 42-Jim Corrigan (Spectre) app. 45-48-Blackhawk app. 3.00
50-($3.50, 48 pgs.) w/bonus story of S.A. Sandman, Torres-a 4.00
Annual 1 (10/94, $3.95, 68 pgs.)-Alex Ross, Bolton & others-a 5.00
...: Dr. Death and the Night of the Butcher (2007, $19.99) r/#21-28 20.00
...: The Blackhawk and The Return of the Scarlet Ghost (2010, $19.99) r/#45-52 20.00
...: The Face and the Brute (2004, $19.95) r/#5-12 20.00
...: The Hourman and The Python (2008, $19.99) r/#29-36 20.00
...: The Mist and The Phantom of the Fair (2009, $19.99) r/#37-44 20.00
...: The Scorpion (2006, $12.99) r/#17-20 13.00
...: The Tarantula (1995, $14.95) r/#1-4 15.00
...: The Vamp (2005, $12.99) r/#13-16 13.00

SANDMAN MYSTERY THEATRE (2nd Series)
DC Comics (Vertigo): Feb, 2007 - No. 5, Jun, 2007 ($2.99, limited series)
1-5-Wesley Dodds and Dian in 1997; Rieber-s/Nguyen-a 3.00

SANDMAN: OVERTURE
DC Comics (Vertigo): Dec, 2013 - No. 6, Nov, 2015 ($4.99/$3.99, limited series)
1-($4.99) Prelude to Sandman #1 ('89); Gaiman-s/JH Williams III-a/c; var-c by McKean 5.00
2-6-($3.99) Gaiman-s/JH Williams III-a/c 4.00
... Special Edition 1 (1/14, $5.99) B&W version of #1 with creator interviews; bonus info 6.00
... Special Edition 2-6 ($4.99) B&W versions with creator interviews; bonus info. 6-(12/15) 5.00

SANDMAN PRESENTS...
DC Comics (Vertigo)
Taller Tales TPB (2003, $19.95) r/S.P: The Thessaliad #1-4; Merv Pumpkinhead, Agent...; The Dreaming #55; S.P. Everything You Always...; new McKean-c; intro by Willingham 20.00

SANDMAN PRESENTS: BAST
DC Comics (Vertigo): Mar, 2003 - No. 3, May, 2003 ($2.95, limited series)
1-3-Kiernan-s/Bennett-a/McKean-c 3.00

SANDMAN PRESENTS: DEADBOY DETECTIVES (See Sandman #21-28)
DC Comics (Vertigo): Aug, 2001 - No. 4, Nov, 2001 ($2.50, limited series)
1-4:Talbot-a/McKean-c/Brubaker-s 3.00
TPB (2008, $12.99) r/#1-4 13.00

SANDMAN PRESENTS: EVERYTHING YOU ALWAYS WANTED TO KNOW ABOUT DREAMS...BUT WERE AFRAID TO ASK
DC Comics (Vertigo): Jul, 2001 ($3.95, one-shot)
1-Short stories by Willingham; art by various; McKean-c 4.00

SANDMAN PRESENTS: LOVE STREET
DC Comics (Vertigo): Jul, 1999 - No. 3, Sept, 1999 ($2.95, limited series)
1-3: Teenage Hellblazer in 1968 London; Zulli-a 3.00

SANDMAN PRESENTS: LUCIFER
DC Comics (Vertigo): Mar, 1999 - No. 3, May, 1999 ($2.95, limited series)
1-Scott Hampton painted-c/a in all 1 2 3 5 6 8
2,3 4.00

SANDMAN PRESENTS: PETREFAX
DC Comics (Vertigo): Mar, 2000 - No. 4, Jun, 2000 ($2.95, limited series)
1-4-Carey-s/Leialoha-a 3.00

SANDMAN PRESENTS: THE CORINTHIAN
DC Comics (Vertigo): Dec, 2001 - No. 3, Feb, 2002 ($2.95, limited series)
1-3-Macan-s/Zezelj-a/McKean-c 3.00

SANDMAN PRESENTS, THE: THE FURIES
DC Comics (Vertigo): 2002 ($24.95, one-shot)
Hardcover-Mike Carey-s/John Bolton-painted art; Lyta Hall's reunion with Daniel 30.00
Softcover-(2003, $17.95) 18.00

SANDMAN PRESENTS, THE: THESSALY: WITCH FOR HIRE
DC Comics (Vertigo): Apr, 2004 - No. 4, July, 2004 ($2.95, limited series)
1-4-Willingham-s/McManus-a/McPherson-c 3.00
TPB-(2005, $12.99) r/#1-4 13.00

SANDMAN PRESENTS, THE: THE THESSALIAD
DC Comics (Vertigo): Mar, 2002 - No. 4, Jun, 2002 ($2.95, limited series)
1-4-Willingham-s/McManus-a/McKean-c 3.00

SANDMAN SPECIAL, THE (Jack Kirby 100th Birthday tribute)
DC Comics: Oct, 2017 ($4.99, one-shot)
1-Jurgens-s/Bogdanove-a and Orlando-s/Leonardi-a; Brute & Glob app.; Paul Pope-c 5.00

SANDMAN, THE: THE DREAM HUNTERS
DC Comics (Vertigo): Oct, 1999 ($29.95/$19.95, one-shot graphic novel)
Hardcover-Neil Gaiman-s/Yoshitaka Amano-painted art 30.00
Softcover-(2000, $19.95) new Amano-c 20.00

SANDMAN, THE: THE DREAM HUNTERS
DC Comics (Vertigo): Jan, 2009 - No. 4, Apr, 2009 ($2.99, limited series)
1-4-Adaptation of the Gaiman/Amano GN by P. Craig Russell-s/a; 2 covers on each 3.00
HC (2009, $24.99) afterwords by Gaiman, Russell, Berger; cover gallery & sketch art 25.00
SC (2010, $19.99) afterwords by Gaiman, Russell, Berger; cover gallery & sketch art 20.00

SANDMAN UNIVERSE, THE
DC Comics: Oct, 2018 ($4.99, one-shot)
1-Intro to 4 new related series (The Dreaming, Books of Magic, House of Whispers & Lucifer); stories by Gaiman & others; Jae Lee-c; Cain, Abel & Lucien app. 5.00

SANDMAN UNIVERSE: DEAD BOY DETECTIVES
DC Comics (Black Label): Feb, 2023 - Present ($3.99)
1-3-Pichetshote-s/Stokely-a; Thessaly app. 4.00

SANDMAN UNIVERSE: NIGHTMARE COUNTRY, THE
DC Comics (Black Label): Jun, 2022 - No. 6, Nov, 2022 ($3.99)
1-6: 1-Tynion IV-s/Estherren-a; The Corinthian app. 6-Llovet-a 4.00

SANDMAN UNIVERSE PRESENTS HELLBLAZER, THE

Sandman #50 © DC

Saucer Country #12 © Cornell & Kelly

Savage Avengers #2 © MAR

	GD 2.0	VG 4.0	FN 6.0	VF 8.0	VF/NM 9.0	NM- 9.2

DC Comics (Black Label): 2019 ($4.99)

1-Spurrier-s/Takara-a; two covers						5.00

SANDS OF THE SOUTH PACIFIC
Toby Press: Jan, 1953

1-Good Girl Art-c	65	130	195	416	708	1000

SANTA AND HIS REINDEER (See March of Comics #166)

SANTA AND THE ANGEL (See Dell Junior Treasury #7)
Dell Publishing Co.: Dec, 1949 (Combined w/Santa at the Zoo) (Gollub-a condensed from FC#128)

Four Color 259	9	18	27	59	117	175

SANTA AT THE ZOO (See Santa And The Angel)

SANTA CLAUS AROUND THE WORLD (See March of Comics #241 in Promotional Comics section)

SANTA CLAUS CONQUERS THE MARTIANS (See Movie Classics)

SANTA CLAUS FUNNIES (Also see Dell Giants)
Dell Publishing Co.: Dec?, 1942 - No. 1274, Dec, 1961

nn(#1)(1942)-Kelly-a	38	76	114	281	628	975
2(12/43)-Kelly-a	27	54	81	189	420	650
Four Color 61(1944)-Kelly-a	25	50	75	175	388	600
Four Color 91(1945)-Kelly-a	18	36	54	124	275	425
Four Color 128('46),175('47)-Kelly-a	15	30	45	103	227	350
Four Color 205,254-Kelly-a	12	24	36	84	185	285
Four Color 302,361,525,607,666,756,867	8	16	24	51	96	140
Four Color 958,1063,1154,1274	6	12	18	41	76	110

NOTE: *Most issues contain only one Kelly story.*

SANTA CLAUS PARADE
Ziff-Davis (Approved Comics)/St. John Publishing Co.: 1951; No. 2, Dec, 1952; No. 3, Jan, 1955 (25¢)

nn(1951-Ziff-Davis)-116 pgs. (Xmas Special 1,2)	39	78	117	231	378	525
2(12/52-Ziff-Davis)-100 pgs.; Dave Berg-a	31	62	93	186	303	420
V1#3(1/55-St. John)-100 pgs.; reprints-c/#1	24	48	72	142	234	325

SANTA CLAUS' WORKSHOP (See March of Comics #50,168 in Promotional Comics section)

SANTA IS COMING (See March of Comics #197 in Promotional Comics section)

SANTA IS HERE (See March of Comics #49 in Promotional Comics section)

SANTA'S BUSY CORNER (See March of Comics #31 in Promotional Comics section)

SANTA'S CANDY KITCHEN (See March of Comics #14 in Promotional Comics section)

SANTA'S CHRISTMAS BOOK (See March of Comics #123 in Promotional Comics section)

SANTA'S CHRISTMAS COMICS
Standard Comics (Best Books): Dec, 1952 (100 pgs.)

nn-Supermouse, Dizzy Duck, Happy Rabbit, etc.	25	50	75	150	245	340

SANTA'S CHRISTMAS LIST (See March of Comics #255 in Promotional Comics section)

SANTA'S HELPERS (See March of Comics #64, 106, 198 in Promotional Comics section)

SANTA'S LITTLE HELPERS (See March of Comics #270 in Promotional Comics section)

SANTA'S SHOW (See March of Comics #311 in Promotional Comics section)

SANTA'S SLEIGH (See March of Comics #298 in Promotional Comics section)

SANTA'S SURPRISE (See March of Comics #13 in Promotional Comics section)

SANTA'S TINKER TOTS
Charlton Comics: 1958

1-Based on "The Tinker Tots Keep Christmas"	6	12	18	42	79	115

SANTA'S TOYLAND (See March of Comics #242 in Promotional Comics section)

SANTA'S TOYS (See March of Comics #12 in Promotional Comics section)

SANTA'S VISIT (See March of Comics #283 in Promotional Comics section)

SANTA THE BARBARIAN
Maximum Press: Dec, 1996 ($2.99, one-shot)

1-Fraga/Mhan-s/a						3.00

SANTERIA: THE GODDESS KISS
Aspen MLT: Mar, 2016 - No. 5, Nov, 2017 ($3.99, limited series)

1-5-Wohl-s/Cafaro-a						4.00

SANTIAGO (Movie)
Dell Publishing Co.: Sept, 1956 (Alan Ladd photo-c)

Four Color 723-Kinstler-a	10	20	30	64	132	200

SARGE SNORKEL (Beetle Bailey)
Charlton Comics: Oct, 1973 - No. 17, Dec, 1976

1	2	4	6	11	16	20
2-10	2	4	6	8	10	12
11-17	1	2	3	5	7	9

SARGE STEEL (Becomes Secret Agent #9 on; also see Judomaster)
Charlton Comics: Dec, 1964 - No. 8, Mar-Apr, 1966 (All 12¢ issues)

1-Origin & 1st app.	4	8	12	28	47	65
2-5,7,8	3	6	9	16	23	30
6-2nd app. Judomaster	4	8	12	23	37	50

SASQUATCH DETECTIVE SPECIAL
DC Comics: Feb, 2019 ($7.99, one-shot)

1-New origin story; Stilwell-s/Randall-a; also reprints back-ups from Exit Stage Left: The Snagglepus Chronicles; bonus sketch art						8.00

SATAN'S SIX
Topps Comics (Kirbyverse): Apr, 1993 - No. 4, July, 1993 ($2.95, lim. series)

1-3: 1-Polybagged w/Kirbychrome trading card; Kirby/McFarlane-c plus 8 pgs. Kirby-a(p); has coupon for Kirbychrome ed. of Secret City Saga #0. 2,3-Polybagged w/3 cards.						4.00
4-Teenagents preview; polybagged w/3 cards	2	4	6	8	10	12

NOTE: *Ditko a-1. Miller a-1.*

SATAN'S SIX: HELLSPAWN
Topps Comics (Kirbyverse): June, 1994 - No. 3, July, 1994 ($2.50, limited series)

1-3: 1-(6/94)-Indicia incorrectly shows "Vol 1 #2". 2-(6/94)						3.00

SATELLITE FALLING
IDW Publishing: May, 2016 - No. 5, May, 2017 ($3.99)

1-5-Steve Horton-s/Stephen Thompson-a						4.00

SATELLITE SAM
Image Comics: Jul, 2013 - No. 15, Jul, 2015 ($3.50, B&W, mature)

1-15-Matt Fraction-s/Howard Chaykin-a/c						3.50

SAUCER COUNTRY
DC Comics (Vertigo): May, 2012 - No. 14, Jun, 2013 ($2.99)

1-14: 1-Cornell-s/Kelly-a. 6-Broxton-a. 11-Colak-a						3.00

SAUCER STATE (Sequel to Saucer Country)
IDW Publishing: May, 2017 - No. 6, Oct, 2017 ($3.99)

1-6-Cornell-s/Kelly-a						4.00

SAURIANS: UNNATURAL SELECTION (See Sigil)
CrossGeneration Comics: Feb, 2002 - No. 2, Mar, 2002 ($2.95, limited series)

1,2-Waid-s/DiVito-a						3.00

SAVAGE
Image Comics (Shadowline): Oct, 2008 - No. 4, Jan, 2009 ($3.50, limited series)

1-4-Mayhew-c/a; Niles and Frank-s						3.50

SAVAGE
Valiant Entertainment: Nov, 2016 - No. 4, Feb, 2017 ($3.99, limited series)

1-4-B. Clay Moore-s/Larosa & Henry-a						4.00

SAVAGE
Valiant Entertainment: Feb, 2021 - No. 4, May, 2021 ($3.99, limited series)

1-4-Max Bemis-s/Nathan Stockman-a						4.00

SAVAGE AVENGERS
Marvel Comics: Jul, 2019 - No. 28, Mar, 2022 ($4.99/$3.99)

1-($4.99) Team of Conan, Wolverine, Punisher, Doctor Voodoo; Duggan-s/Deodato-a						5.00
2-28-($3.99) 2-5-Kulan Gath & Venom app. 6-Jacinto-a. 13-16-Zircher-a. 14,16-Juggernaut & Black Knight app. 17-19-King In Black tie-in; Deadpool app. 25,26,28-Kang app.						4.00
#0 (4/20, $4.99) Reprints Uncanny X-Men #190 & 191 with Kulan Gath, new framing story						5.00
Annual 1 (12/19, $4.99) Garney-a; Conan, Black Widow & Hellstrom app.						5.00

SAVAGE AVENGERS
Marvel Comics: Jul, 2022 - No. 10, Apr, 2023 ($3.99)

1-10: 1-Team of Conan, Deathlok, Black Knight, Elektra, Anti-Venom, Cloak & Dagger						4.00

SAVAGE AXE OF ARES
Marvel Comics: June, 2010 ($3.99, B&W, one-shot)

1-B&W short stories by Hurwitz, Palo, McKeever, Swierczynski, Manco and others						4.00

SAVAGE COMBAT TALES
Atlas/Seaboard Publ.: Feb, 1975 - No. 3, July, 1975

1,3: 1-Sgt. Stryker's Death Squad begins (origin); Goodwin-s	2	4	6	11	16	20
2-Toth-a; only app. War Hawk; Goodwin-s	2	4	6	13	18	22

NOTE: *Buckler c-3. McWilliams a-1-3; c-1. Sparling a-1, 3.*

SAVAGE DRAGON, THE (See Megaton #3 & 4)

Image Comics (Highbrow Entertainment): July, 1992 - No. 3, Dec, 1992 ($1.95, lim. series)

1-Erik Larsen-c/a/scripts & bound-in poster in all; 4 cover color variations w/4 different posters; 1st Highbrow Entertainment title 1 3 4 6 8 10
2-Intro SuperPatriot-c/story (10/92) 5.00
3-Contains coupon for Image Comics #0 4.00
3-With coupon missing 2.00
...Vs. Savage Megaton Man 1 (3/93, $1.95)-Larsen & Simpson-c/a. 4.00
TPB-('93, $9.95) r/#1-3 10.00

SAVAGE DRAGON, THE
Image Comics (Highbrow Entertainment): June, 1993 - Present ($1.95/$2.50/$2.99/$3.50)

1-Erik Larsen-c/a/scripts 1 2 3 5 6 8
2-($2.95, 52 pgs.)-Teenage Mutant Ninja Turtles-c/story; flip book features Vanguard #0 (See Megaton for 1st app.); 1st app. Supreme 5.00
3-30: 3-7: Erik Larsen-c/a/scripts. 3-Mighty Man back-up story w/Austin-a(i). 4-Flip book w/Ricochet. 5-Mighty Man flip-c & back-up plus poster. 6-Jae Lee poster. 7-Vanguard poster. 8-Deadly Duo poster by Larsen. 13A (10/94)-Jim Lee-c/a; 1st app. Max Cash (Condition Red). 13B (6/95)-Larsen story. 15-Dragon poster by Larsen. 22-TMNT-c/a; Bisley pin-up. 27-"Wondercon Exclusive" new-c. 28-Maxx-c/app. 29-Wildstar-c/app. 30-Spawn app. 4.00
25 ($3.95)-variant-c exists. 5.00
31-49,51-71: 31-God vs. The Devil; alternate version exists w/o expletives (has "God Is Good" inside Image logo) 33-Birth of Dragon/Rapture's baby. 34,35-Hellboy-c/app. 51-Origin of She-Dragon. 70-Ann Stevens killed 4.00
50-($5.95, 100 pgs.) Kaboom and Mighty Man app.; Matsuda back-c; pin-ups by McFarlane, Simonson, Capullo and others 6.00
72-74: 72-Begin $2.95-c 4.00
75-($5.95) 6.00
76-99,101-106,108-114,116-124,126-127,129-131,133-136,138: 76-New direction starts. 83,84-Madman-c/app. 84-Atomics app. 97-Dragon returns home; Mighty Man app. 134-Bomb Queen app. 3.50
100-($8.95) Larsen-s/a; inked by various incl. Sienkiewicz, Timm, Austin, Simonson, Royer; plus pin-ups by Timm, Silvestri, Miller, Cho, Art Adams, Pacheco 9.00
107-($3.95) Firebreather, Invincible, Major Damage-c/app.; flip book w/Major Damage 4.00
115-($7.95, 100 pgs.) Wraparound-c; Freak Force app.; Larsen & Englert-a 8.00
125-($4.99, 64 pgs.) new story, The Fly, & various Mr. Glum reprints 5.00
128-Wesley and the villains from Wanted app.; J.G. Jones-c 4.00
132-($6.99, 80 pgs.) new story with Larsen-a; back-up story with Fosco-a 7.00
137-(8/08) Madman & Amazing Joy Buzzards-c/app. 1 2 3 5 6 8
137-(8/08) Variant cover with Barack Obama endorsed by Savage Dragon; yellow bkgrd 7 14 21 48 89 130
137-(8/08) 2nd printing of variant cover with Barack Obama and red background 1 3 4 6 8 10
137-3rd & 4th printings: 3rd-Blue background. 4th-Purple background 6.00
139-144,146-149,151-174,176-183: 139-Start $3.50-c; Invincible app. 140,141-Witchblade, Spawn app. 148-Also a FCBD edition.155-160-Dragon War. 160-163-Flip book 3.50
145-Obama-c/app. 1 2 3 5 6 8
150-($5.99, 100 pgs.) back up r/Daredevil's origin from Daredevil #18 (1943) 6.00
175-($3.99, 48 pgs.) Darklord app.; Vanguard back-c and back-up story 4.00
184-199,201-224 ($3.99) 184,186-188-The Claw app. 190-Regular & digest-size versions. 209-Malcolm's wedding. 217-Spawn app. 4.00
200-(12/14, $8.99, 100 pgs., squarebound) Back-up story w/Trimpe-a; Burnhum-a 9.00
225-(7/17, $9.99, 100 pgs., squarebound) Death of Savage Dragon; back-up by various 10.00
226-249,251-264: 226-Donald Trump on cover. 227-Malcolm & family move to Toronto. 252-Salutes the Funnies; newspaper comics homages. 259-North Force app. 4.00
250-(7/20, $9.99, 100 pgs., squarebound) Savage Dragon returns; back-up by various 10.00
#0-(7/06, $1.95) reprints origin story from 2005 Image Comics Hardcover 3.50
...Archives Vol. 1 (12/06, $19.99) B&W rep. 1st mini-series #1-3 & #1-21 20.00
...Archives Vol. 2 (2007, $19.99) B&W rep. #22-50; roster pages of Dragon's fellow cops 20.00
...Companion (7/02, $2.95) guide to issues #1-100, character backgrounds 3.50
...Endgame (2/04, $15.95, TPB) r/#47-52 16.00
The Fallen (11/97, $12.95, TPB) r/#7-11, ...Possessed (9/98, $12.95, TPB) r/#12-16, ...Revenge (1998, $12.95, TPB) r/#17-21 13.00
...Gang War (4/00, $16.95, TPB) r/#22-26 17.00
.../Hellboy (10/02, $5.95) r/#34 & #35; Mignola-c 6.00
Image Firsts: Savage Dragon #1 (4/10, $1.00) reprints #1 3.00
... Legacy FCBD 1 (5/15, giveaway) Story later re-worked for issue #211 3.00
...Team-Ups (10/98, $19.95, TPB) r/team-ups 20.00
...: Terminated HC (2/03, $28.95) r/#34-40 & #1/2 29.00
...: This Savage World HC (2002, $24.95) r/#76-81; intro. by Larsen 25.00
...: This Savage World SC (2003, $15.95) r/#76-81; intro. by Larsen 16.00
...: Worlds at War SC (2004, $16.95) r/#41-46; intro. by Larsen; sketch pages 17.00

SAVAGE DRAGON ARCHIVES (Also see Dragon Archives, The)

SAVAGE DRAGONBERT: FULL FRONTAL NERDITY
Image Comics: Oct, 2002 ($5.95, B&W, one-shot)

1-Reprints of the Savage Dragon/Dilbert spoof strips 6.00

SAVAGE DRAGON/DESTROYER DUCK, THE
Image Comics/ Highbrow Entertainment: Nov, 1996 ($3.95, one-shot)

1 4.00

SAVAGE DRAGON: GOD WAR
Image Comics: July, 2004 - No. 4, Oct, 2005 ($2.95, limited series)

1-4-Kirkman-s/Englert-a 3.50

SAVAGE DRAGON/MARSHALL LAW
Image Comics: July, 1997 - No. 2, Aug, 1997 ($2.95, B&W, limited series)

1,2-Pat Mills-s, Kevin O'Neill-a 4.00

SAVAGE DRAGON: SEX & VIOLENCE
Image Comics: Aug, 1997 - No. 2, Sept, 1997 ($2.50, limited series)

1,2-T&M Bierbaum-s, Mays, Lupka, Adam Hughes-a 4.00

SAVAGE DRAGON/TEENAGE MUTANT NINJA TURTLES CROSSOVER
Mirage Studios: Sept, 1993 ($2.75, one-shot)

1-Erik Larsen-c(i) only 5.00

SAVAGE DRAGON: THE RED HORIZON
Image Comics/ Highbrow Entertainment: Feb, 1997 - No. 3 ($2.50, lim. series)

1-3 4.00

SAVAGE FISTS OF KUNG FU
Marvel Comics Group: 1975 (Marvel Treasury)

1-Iron Fist, Shang Chi, Sons of Tiger; Adams, Starlin-a 4 8 12 25 40 55

SAVAGE HAWKMAN, THE (DC New 52)
DC Comics: Nov, 2011 - No. 20, Jun, 2013 ($2.99)

1-20: 1-Tony Daniel-s/Philip Tan-a/c; Carter Hall bonds with the Nth metal 3.00
#0-(11/12, $2.99) Origin story of Katar Hol on Thanagar; Bennett-a/c 3.00

SAVAGE HEARTS
Dark Horse Comics: Jul, 2021 - No. 5, Nov, 2021 ($3.99, limited series)

1-5-Sitterson-s/Dougherty-a 4.00

SAVAGE HULK, THE (Also see Incredible Hulk)
Marvel Comics: Jan, 1996 ($6.95, one-shot)

1-Bisley-c; David, Lobdell, Wagner, Loeb, Gibbons, Messner-Loebs scripts; McKone, Kieth, Ramos & Sale-a 7.00

SAVAGE HULK
Marvel Comics: Aug, 2014 - No. 6, Jan, 2015 ($3.99, limited series)

1-6: 1-4-Alan Davis-s/a; follows story from X-Men #66 ('70) Silver Age X-Men & The Leader app. 2-Abomination app. 5,6-Bechko-s/Hardman-a; Dr. Strange app. 4.00

SAVAGE RAIDS OF GERONIMO (See Geronimo #4)

SAVAGE RANGE (See Luke Short, Four Color 807)

SAVAGE RED SONJA: QUEEN OF THE FROZEN WASTES
Dynamite Entertainment: 2006 - No. 4, 2006 ($3.50, limited series)

1-4: 1-Three covers by Cho, Texeira & Homs; Cho & Murray-s/Homs-a 3.50
TPB (2007, $14.99) r/series; cover gallery and sketch pages 15.00

SAVAGE RETURN OF DRACULA
Marvel Comics: 1992 ($2.00, 52 pgs.)

1-r/Tomb of Dracula #1,2 by Gene Colan 4.00

SAVAGE SHE-HULK, THE (See The Avengers, Marvel Graphic Novel #18 & The Sensational She-Hulk)
Marvel Comics Group: Feb, 1980 - No. 25, Feb, 1982

	GD 2.0	VG 4.0	FN 6.0	VF 8.0	VF/NM 9.0	NM- 9.2
1-Origin & 1st app. She-Hulk	10	20	30	64	132	200
2	3	6	9	21	33	45
3-5,25: 25-(52 pgs.)	2	4	6	8	11	14
6,7,10-24: 6-She-Hulk vs. Iron Man.	1	3	4	6	8	10
8-Vs. Man-Thing	2	4	6	10	14	18
9-1st Ultiman	3	6	9	14	19	24

NOTE: ***Austin** a-25i; c-23i-25i. **J. Buscema** a-1p; c-1, 2p. **Golden** c-8-11.*

SAVAGE SHE-HULK (Titled All New Savage She Hulk for #3,4)
Marvel Comics: Jun, 2009 - No. 4, Sept, 2009 ($3.99, limited series)

1-4-Lyra, daughter of the Hulk; She-Hulk & Dark Avengers app. 2-Campbell-c 4.00

SAVAGE SKULLKICKERS (See Skullkickers #20)

SAVAGE SPIDER-MAN (Story continues from Non-Stop Spider-Man series)
Marvel Comics: Apr, 2022 - No. 5, Sept. 2022 ($3.99, limited series)

1-5-Joe Kelly-s/Gerardo Sandoval-a; Baron Zemo app. 4.00

SAVAGE SWORD (ROBERT E. HOWARD'S...)
Dark Horse Comics: Dec, 2010 - No. 9 ($7.99, squarebound)

1-9-Short stories by various incl. Roy Thomas, Barry-Windsor-Smith; Conan app. 8.00

SAVAGE SWORD OF CONAN (The... #41 on; ...The Barbarian #175 on)
Marvel Comics Group: Aug, 1974 - No. 235, July, 1995 ($1.00/$1.25/$2.25, B&W magazine, mature)

1-Smith-r; J. Buscema/N. Adams/Krenkel-a; origin Blackmark by Gil Kane (part 1, ends #3); Blackmark's 1st app. in magazine form-r/from paperback) & Red Sonja (3rd app.) 10 20 30 69 147 225
2-Neal Adams-c; Chaykin/N. Adams-a 5 10 15 35 63 90
3-Severin/B. Smith-a; N. Adams-a 4 8 12 28 47 65
4-Neal Adams/Kane-a(r) 3 6 9 21 33 45
5-10: 5-Jeff Jones frontispiece (r) 3 6 9 17 26 35
11-20 2 4 6 13 18 22
21-30 2 4 6 10 14 18
31-50: 34-3 pg. preview of Conan newspaper strip. 35-Cover similar to Savage Tales #1. 45-Red Sonja returns; begin $1.25-c 2 4 6 8 11 14
51-99: 63-Toth frontispiece. 65-Kane-a w/Chaykin/Miller/Simonson/Sherman finishes. 70-Article on movie. 83-Red Sonja-r by Neal Adams from #1 1 2 3 5 7 9
100 1 3 4 6 8 10
101-176: 163-Begin $2.25-c. 169-King Kull story. 171-Soloman Kane by Williamson (i). 172-Red Sonja story 6.00
177-199: 179,187,192-Red Sonja app. 190-193-4 part King Kull story. 196-King Kull story 5.00
200-220: 200-New Buscema-a; Robert E. Howard app. with Conan in story. 202-King Kull story. 204-60th anniversary (1932-92). 211-Rafael Kayanan's 1st Conan-a. 214-Sequel to Red Nails by Howard 6.00
221-230 2 4 6 8 10 12
231-234 2 4 6 11 16 20
235-Last issue 4 8 12 27 44 60
Special 1(1975, B&W)-B. Smith-r/Conan #10,13 3 6 9 18 27 36
Volume 1 TPB (Dark Horse Books, 12/07, $17.95, B&W) r/#1-10 and selected stories from Savage Tales #1-5 with covers 18.00
Volume 2 TPB (Dark Horse Books, 3/08, $17.95, B&W) r/#11-24 18.00
Volume 3 TPB (Dark Horse Books, 5/08, $19.95, B&W) r/#25-36 and selected pin-ups 20.00
Volume 4 TPB (Dark Horse Books, 9/08, $19.95, B&W) r/#37-48 and selected pin-ups 20.00
Volume 5 TPB (Dark Horse Books, 2/09, $19.95, B&W) r/#49-60 and selected pin-ups 20.00

NOTE: ***N. Adams** a-14p, 60, 83p(r). **Alcala** a-2 ,4, 7, 12, 15-20, 23, 24, 28, 59, 67, 69, 75, 76i, 80i, 82i, 83i, 89, 180i, 184i, 187i, 189i, 216p. **Austin** a-78i. **Boris** painted c-1, 4, 5, 7, 9, 10, 12, 15. **Brunner** a-30; c-8, 30. **Buscema** a-1-5, 7, 10-12, 15-24, 26-28, 31, 32, 36-43, 45, 47-58p, 60-67p, 70, 71-74p, 76-81p, 87-96p, 98, 99-101p, 190-204p; painted c-40. **Chaykin** c-31. **Chiodo** painted c-71, 76, 79, 81, 84, 85, 178. **Conrad** c-215, 217. **Corben** a-4, 16, 29. **Finlay** a-16. **Golden** a-98, 101; c-98, 101, 105, 106, 117, 124, 150. **Kaluta** a-11, 18; c-3, 91,*

Savage Dragon #136 © Larsen

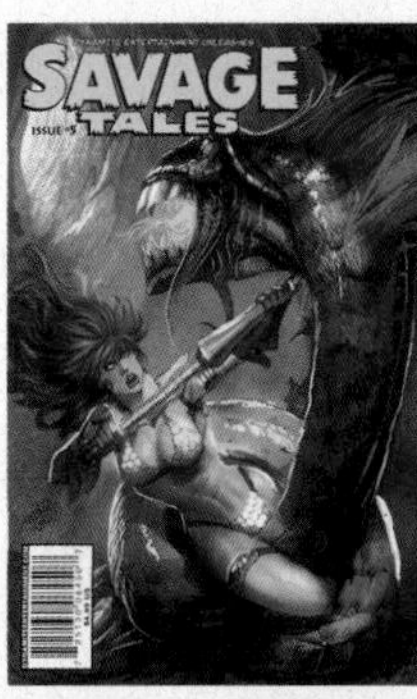

Savage Tales (2008) #5 © DFI

Scarlet Spider (2012) #1 © MAR

GD VG FN VF VF/NM NM-
2.0 4.0 6.0 8.0 9.0 9.2

GD VG FN VF VF/NM NM-
2.0 4.0 6.0 8.0 9.0 9.2

*93. **Gil Kane** a-2, 3, 8, 13r, 29, 47, 64, 65, 67, 85p, 86p. **Rafael Kayanan** a-211-213, 215, 217. **Krenkel** a-9, 11, 14, 16, 24. **Morrow** a-7. **Nebres** a-93i, 101i, 107, 114. **Newton** a-6. **Nino** c/a-6. **Redondo** painted c-48-50, 52, 56, 57, 85i, 90, 96i. **Marie & John Severin** a-Special 1. **Simonson** a-7, 8, 12, 15-17. **Barry Smith** a-7, 16, 24, 82r, Special 1r. **Starlin** c-26. **Toth** a-64. **Williamson** a(i)-162, 171, 186. No. 8 , 10 & 16 contain a Robert E. Howard Conan adaptation.*

SAVAGE SWORD OF CONAN
Marvel Comics: Apr, 2019 - No. 12, Feb, 2020 ($4.99/$3.99)

1-($4.99) Duggan-s/Garney-a; main cover by Alex Ross; bonus text story 5.00
2-5-($3.99) Duggan-s/Garney-a; main cover by Alex Ross; bonus text story 4.00
6-12: 6-Meredith Finch-s/Luke Ross-a; main cover by David Finch. 10,11-Alan Davis-a 4.00

SAVAGE TALES (...Featuring Conan #4 on)(Magazine)
Marvel Comics Group: May, 1971; No. 2, 10/73; No. 3, 2/74 - No. 12, Summer, 1975 (B&W)

1-Origin/1st app. The Man-Thing by Morrow; Conan the Barbarian by Barry Smith (1st Conan x-over outside his own title); Femizons by Romita-r/in #3; Ka-Zar story by Buscema 57 114 171 456 1028 1600
2-B. Smith, Brunner, Morrow, Williamson-a; Wrightson King Kull reprint/ Creatures on the Loose #10 6 12 18 37 66 95
3-B. Smith, Brunner, Steranko, Williamson-a 5 10 15 31 53 75
4,5-N. Adams-c; last Conan (Smith-r/#4) plus Kane/N. Adams-a. 5-Brak the Barbarian begins, ends #8 4 8 12 28 47 65
6-Ka-Zar begins; Williamson-r; N. Adams-c 3 6 9 21 33 45
7-N. Adams-i 3 6 9 16 23 30
8,9,11: 8-Shanna, the She-Devil app. thru #10; Williamson-r 3 6 9 15 22 28
10-Neal Adams-a(i), Williamson-r 3 6 9 17 26 35
...Featuring Ka-Zar Annual 1 (Summer, '75, B&W)(#12 on inside)-Ka-Zar origin by Gil Kane; B. Smith-r/Astonishing Tales 3 6 9 18 28 38

NOTE: ***Boris** c-7, 10. **Buscema** a-5r, 6p, 8p; c-2. **Colan** a-1p. **Fabian** c-8. **Golden** a-1, 4; c-1. **Heath** a-10p, 11p. **Kaluta** c-9. **Maneely** r-2, 4(The Crusader in both). **Morrow** a-1, 2, Annual 1. **Reese** a-2. **Severin** a-1-7. **Starlin** a-5. Robert E. Howard adaptations-1-4.*

SAVAGE TALES (Volume 2)
Marvel Comics Group: Oct, 1985 - No. 8, Dec, 1986 ($1.50, B&W, magazine, mature)

1-1st app. The Nam; Golden, Morrow-a (indicia incorrectly lists this as Volume 1) 6.00
2-8: 2,7-Morrow-a. 4-2nd Nam story; Golden-a 4.00

SAVAGE TALES
Dynamite Entertainment: 2007 - No. 10, 2008 ($4.99)

1-10: 1-Anthology; Red Sonja app.; three covers 5.00
... One-Shot (2022, $4.99) Short stories with Vampirella, Red Sonja, Allan Quartermane 5.00
... Red Sonja One-Shot (2019, $4.99) Russell-s; Sorcerers of Wigur-Nomadene app. 5.00
... Vampirella One-Shot (2018, $4.99) Burnham-s; back-up Valaka story; Robert Hack-c 5.00
... Winter Special One-Shot (2022, $4.99) Short stories with Vampirella, Draculina, John Carter & Dejah Thoris, Captain Gullivar Jones 5.00

SAVAGE THINGS
DC Comics (Vertigo): May, 2017 - No. 8, Dec, 2018 ($3.99)

1-8-Justin Jordan-s/Ibrahim Moustafa-a/J.P. Leon-c 4.00

SAVAGE WOLVERINE
Marvel Comics: Mar, 2013 - No. 23, Nov, 2014 ($3.99)

1-5-Frank Cho-s/a/c; Shanna & Amadeus Cho app. 4.00
1-Variant-c by Skottie Young 8.00
6-23: 6-8-Wells-s/Madureira-a/c; Elektra, Kingpin & Spider-Man app. 9-11-Jock-s/a. 14-17-Isanove-s/a. 19-Simone-s. 21,22-WWI; Quinones-a/Nowlan-c 4.00

SAVANT GARDE (Also see WildC.A.T.S...)
Image Comics/WildStorm Productions: Mar, 1997 - No. 7, Sept, 1997 ($2.50)

1-7 3.00

SAVED BY THE BELL (TV)
Harvey Comics: Mar, 1992 - No. 5, May, 1993 ($1.25, limited series)

1 2 4 6 9 12 15
2-5, Holiday Special (3/92), Special 1 (9/92, $1.50)-photo-c, Summer Break 1 (10/92) 6.00

SAVE YOURSELF
BOOM! Studios (BOOM! Box): Jun, 2021 - No. 4, Sept, 2021 ($4.99, limited series)

1-4-Bones Leopard-s/Kelly & Nichole Matthews-a 5.00

SAVIOR
Image Comics/Todd McFarlane Productions: Apr, 2015 - No. 8, Nov, 2015 ($2.99)

1-8-Todd McFarlane & Brian Holguin-s/Clayton Crain-a/c 3.00

SAW: REBIRTH (Based on 2004 movie Saw)
IDW Publ.: Oct, 2005 ($3.99, one-shot)

1-Guedes-a 4.00

SCALPED
DC Comics (Vertigo): Mar, 2007 - No. 60, Oct, 2012 ($2.99, limited series)

1-Aaron-s/Guera-a/Jock-c 5 10 15 30 50 70
1-Special Edition (7/10, $1.00) r/#1 with "What's Next?" cover frame 3.00
2-5 1 2 3 5 6 8
6-20: 12-Leon-a 4.00
21-60: 50-Bonus pin-ups by various 3.00
...: Casino Blood TPB (2008, $14.99) r/#6-11; intro. by Garth Ennis 15.00
...: Dead Mothers TPB (2008, $17.99) r/#12-18 18.00
...: High Lonesome TPB (2009, $14.99) r/#25-29; intro. by Jason Starr 15.00
...: Indian Country TPB (2007, $9.99) r/#1-5; intro. by Brian K. Vaughan 10.00
...: Rez Blues (2011, $17.99) r/#35-42 18.00
...: The Gnawing (2010, $14.99) r/#30-34; intro. by Matt Fraction 15.00
...: The Gravel in Your Guts (2009, $14.99) r/#19-24; intro. by Ed Brubaker 15.00

SCAMP (Walt Disney)(See Walt Disney's Comics & Stories #204)
Dell Publ. Co./Gold Key: No. 703, 5/56 - No. 1204, 8-10/61; 11/67 - No. 45, 1/79

Four Color 703(#1) 10 20 30 64 132 200
Four Color 777,806('57),833 6 12 18 42 79 115
5(3-5/58)-10(6-8/59) 5 10 15 31 53 75
11-16(12-2/60-61), Four Color 1204(1961) 4 8 12 27 44 60
1(12/67-Gold Key)-Reprints begin 4 8 12 25 40 55
2(3/69)-10 2 4 6 13 18 22
11-20 2 4 6 8 11 14
21-45 1 2 3 4 5 7

NOTE: *New stories-#20(in part), 22-25, 27, 29-31, 34, 36-40, 42-45. New covers-#11, 12, 14, 15, 17-25, 27, 29-31, 34, 36-38.*

SCARAB
DC Comics (Vertigo): Nov, 1993 - No. 8, June, 1994 ($1.95, limited series)

1-8-Glenn Fabry painted-c: 1-Silver ink-c. 2-Phantom Stranger app. 3.00

SCARECROW OF ROMNEY MARSH, THE (See W. Disney Showcase #53)
Gold Key: April, 1964 - No. 3, Oct, 1965 (Disney TV Show)

10112-404 (#1) 8 16 24 56 108 160
2,3 5 10 15 34 60 85

SCARECROW (VILLAINS) (See Batman)
DC Comics: Feb, 1998 ($1.95, one-shot)

1-Fegredo-a/Milligan-s/Pearson-c 3.00

SCARE TACTICS
DC Comics: Dec, 1996 - No. 12, Mar, 1998 ($2.25)

1-12: 1-1st app. 3.00

SCAR FACE (See The Crusaders)

SCARFACE: SCARRED FOR LIFE (Based on the 1983 movie)
IDW Publishing: Dec, 2006 - No. 5, Apr, 2007 ($3.99, limited series)

1-5-Tony Montana survives his shooting; Layman-s/Crosland-a 4.00
Scarface: Devil in Disguise (7/07 - No. 4, 10/07, $3.99) Alberto Dose-a 4.00

SCARLET
Marvel Comics (ICON): July, 2010 - No. 10, Aug, 2016 ($3.95)

1-10-Bendis-s/Maleev-a. 1-Second printing exists. 8-(5/16) 4.00
1-5-Variant covers. 1-Deodato & Lafuente. 2-Oeming & Mack. 3,4-Oeming. 5-Bendis 6.00

SCARLET
DC Comics (Jinxworld): Oct, 2018 - No. 5, Mar, 2019 ($3.99)

1-5-Bendis-s/Maleev-a 4.00

SCARLET O'NEIL (See Harvey Comics Hits #59 & Invisible...)

SCARLET SISTERS (From Project Superpowers)
Dynamite Entertainment: 2022 ($4.99, one-shot)

1-Alex Segura-s/Emiliana Pinna-a 5.00

SCARLET SPIDER
Marvel Comics: Nov, 1995 - No. 2, Jan, 1996 ($1.95, limited series)

1,2: Replaces Spider-Man title 4.00

SCARLET SPIDER
Marvel Comics: Mar, 2012 - No. 25, Feb, 2014 ($3.99/$2.99)

1-Kaine following "Spider Island"; Yost-s/Stegman-a; 2 covers by Stegman 4.00
2-12, 12.1, 13-24-($2.99) 10,11-Carnage & Venom app. 17-19-Wolverine app. 3.00
25-($3.99) Last issue; Yost-s/Baldeon-a 4.00

SCARLET SPIDERS (Tie-in for Spider-Verse in Amazing Spider-Man [2014] #9-15)
Marvel Comics: Jan, 2015 - No. 3, Mar, 2015 ($3.99, limited series)

1-3-Kaine, Ben Reilly and Jessica Drew app.; Costa-s/Diaz-a 4.00

SCARLET SPIDER UNLIMITED
Marvel Comics: Nov, 1995 ($3.95, one-shot)

	GD 2.0	VG 4.0	FN 6.0	VF 8.0	VF/NM 9.0	NM- 9.2
1-Replaces Spider-Man Unlimited title						4.00

SCARLETT COUTURE
Titan Comics: May, 2015 - No. 4, Aug, 2015 ($3.99)

	GD 2.0	VG 4.0	FN 6.0	VF 8.0	VF/NM 9.0	NM- 9.2
1-4-Des Taylor-s/a						4.00

SCARLETT'S STRIKE FORCE (G.I. Joe)
IDW Publishing: Dec, 2017 - No. 3, Feb, 2018 ($3.99, limited series)

	GD 2.0	VG 4.0	FN 6.0	VF 8.0	VF/NM 9.0	NM- 9.2
1-3-Sitterson-s/Daniel-a; Cobra Commander app.						4.00

SCARLET WITCH (See Avengers #16, Vision &... & X-Men #4)
Marvel Comics: Jan, 1994 - No. 4, Apr, 1994 ($1.75, limited series)

	GD 2.0	VG 4.0	FN 6.0	VF 8.0	VF/NM 9.0	NM- 9.2
1-Abnett & Lanning-s; Agatha Harkness app.	2	4	6	9	13	16
2-1st Lore	3	6	9	14	20	26
3,4						5.00

SCARLET WITCH
Marvel Comics: Feb, 2016 - No. 15, Apr, 2017 ($3.99)

	GD 2.0	VG 4.0	FN 6.0	VF 8.0	VF/NM 9.0	NM- 9.2
1-15: 1-3: 1-Robinson-s/Del Rey-a; Agatha Harkness app. 3-Dillon-a. 7-Wu-a. 9-Civil War II tie-in; Quicksilver app.; Joelle Jones-a						4.00

SCARLET WITCH
Marvel Comics: Mar, 2023 - Present ($4.99)

	GD 2.0	VG 4.0	FN 6.0	VF 8.0	VF/NM 9.0	NM- 9.2
1,2-Orlando-s/Pichelli-a; Viv Vision & Darcy app.						5.00

SCARY GODMOTHER (Hardcover story books)
Sirius: 1997 - 2002 ($19.95, HC with dust jackets, one-shots)

	GD 2.0	VG 4.0	FN 6.0	VF 8.0	VF/NM 9.0	NM- 9.2
Volume 1 (9/97) Jill Thompson-s/a; first app. of Scary Godmother						20.00
Vol. 2 - The Revenge of Jimmy (9/98, $19.95)						20.00
Vol. 3 - The Mystery Date (10/99, $19.95)						20.00
Vol. 4 - The Boo Flu (9/02, $19.95)						20.00

SCARY GODMOTHER
Sirius: 2001 - No. 6, 2002 ($2.95, B&W, limited series)

	GD 2.0	VG 4.0	FN 6.0	VF 8.0	VF/NM 9.0	NM- 9.2
1-6-Jill Thompson-s/a						3.00
...: Activity Book (12/00, $2.95, B&W) Jill Thompson-s/a						3.00
...: Bloody Valentine Special (2/98, $3.95, B&W) Jill Thompson-s/a; pin-ups by Ross, Mignola, Russell						4.00
...: Ghoul's Out For Summer (2002,$14.95, B&W) r/#1-6						15.00
...: Holiday Spooktakular (11/98, $2.95, B&W) Jill Thompson-s/a; pin-ups by Brereton, LaBan, Dorkin, Fingerman						3.00

SCARY GODMOTHER: WILD ABOUT HARRY
Sirius: 2000 - No. 3 ($2.95, B&W, limited series)

	GD 2.0	VG 4.0	FN 6.0	VF 8.0	VF/NM 9.0	NM- 9.2
1-3-Jill Thompson-s/a						3.00
TPB (2001, $9.95) r/series						10.00

SCARY TALES
Charlton Comics: 8/75 - #9, 1/77; #10, 9/77 - #20, 6/79; #21, 8/80 - #46, 10/84

	GD 2.0	VG 4.0	FN 6.0	VF 8.0	VF/NM 9.0	NM- 9.2
1-Origin/1st app. Countess Von Bludd, not in #2	4	8	12	27	44	60
2,4,6,9,10: 4,9-Sutton-c/a. 4-Man-Thing copy	2	4	6	11	16	20
3-Sutton painted-c; Ditko-a	3	6	9	14	20	25
5,11-Ditko-c/a.	3	6	9	16	23	30
7,8-Ditko-a	2	4	6	13	18	22
12,15,16,19,21,39-Ditko-a	2	4	6	11	16	20
13,17,20	2	4	6	9	12	15
14,18,30,32-Ditko-c/a	3	6	9	14	20	25
22-29,33-37,39,40: 37,38,40-New-a. 39-All Ditko reprints and cover	2	4	6	8	10	12
31,38: 31-Newton-c/a. 38-Mr. Jigsaw app.	2	4	6	8	10	12
41-45-New-a. 41-Ditko-a(3). 42-45-(Low print)	2	4	6	9	12	15
46-Reprints (Low print)	2	4	6	11	16	20
1(Modern Comics reprint, 1977)	1	3	4	6	8	10

NOTE: ***Adkins** a-31i; c-31i. **Ditko** a-3, 5, 7, 8(2), 11, 12, 14-16r, 18(3)r, 19r, 21r, 30r, 32, 39r, 41(3); c-5, 11, 14, 18, 30, 32. **Newton** a-31p; c-31p. **Powell** a-18r. **Staton** a-1(2 pgs.), 4, 20r; c-1, 20. **Sutton** a-4, 9; c-4, 9. **Zeck** a-9.*

SCATTERBRAIN
Dark Horse Comics: Jun, 1998 - No. 4, Sept, 1998 ($2.95, limited series)

	GD 2.0	VG 4.0	FN 6.0	VF 8.0	VF/NM 9.0	NM- 9.2
1-4-Humor anthology by Aragonés, Dorkin, Stevens and others						3.00

SCAVENGERS
Triumphant Comics: 1993(nd, July) - No. 11, May, 1994 ($2.50, serially numbered)

	GD 2.0	VG 4.0	FN 6.0	VF 8.0	VF/NM 9.0	NM- 9.2
1-9,0,10,11: 5,6-Triumphant Unleashed x-over. 9-(3/94). 0-Retail ed. (3/94, $2.50, 36 pgs.). 0-Giveaway edition (3/94, 20 pgs.). 0-Coupon redemption edition. 10-(4/94)						3.00

SCENE OF THE CRIME (Also see Vertigo: Winter's Edge #2)
DC Comics (Vertigo): May, 1999 - No. 4, Aug, 1999 ($2.50, limited series)

	GD 2.0	VG 4.0	FN 6.0	VF 8.0	VF/NM 9.0	NM- 9.2
1-4-Brubaker-s/Lark-a						3.00
...: A Little Piece of Goodnight TPB ('00, $12.95) r/#1-4; Winter's Edge #2						13.00

SCHOOL DAY ROMANCES (...of Teen-Agers #4; Popular Teen-Agers #5 on)
Star Publications: Nov-Dec, 1949 - No. 4, May-June, 1950 (Teenage)

	GD 2.0	VG 4.0	FN 6.0	VF 8.0	VF/NM 9.0	NM- 9.2
1-Toni Gayle (later Toni Gay), Ginger Snapp, Midge Martin & Eve Adams begin	4	86	129	271	461	650
2,3: 3-Jane Powell photo on-c & true life story	36	72	108	214	347	480
4-Ronald Reagan photo on-c; L.B. Cole-c	50	100	150	315	533	750

NOTE: *All have **L. B. Cole** covers.*

SCHWINN BICYCLE BOOK (...Bike Thrills, 1959)
Schwinn Bicycle Co.: 1949; 1952; 1959 (10¢)

	GD 2.0	VG 4.0	FN 6.0	VF 8.0	VF/NM 9.0	NM- 9.2
1949	8	16	24	42	54	65
1952-Believe It or Not facts; comic format; 36 pgs.	6	12	18	27	33	38
1959	4	9	13	18	22	26

SCIENCE COMICS (1st Series)
Fox Feature Syndicate: Feb, 1940 - No. 8, Sept, 1940

	GD 2.0	VG 4.0	FN 6.0	VF 8.0	VF/NM 9.0	NM- 9.2
1-Origin Dynamo (1st app., called Electro in #1), The Eagle (1st app.), & Navy Jones; Marga, The Panther Woman (1st app.), Cosmic Carson & Perisphere Payne, Dr. Doom begin; bondage/hypo-c; Electro-c	1200	2400	3600	9100	16,550	24,000
2-Classic Lou Fine Dynamo-c	1200	2400	3600	9100	16,550	24,000
3-Classic Lou Fine Dynamo-c	459	918	1377	3350	5925	8500
4-Kirby-a; Cosmic Carson-c by Joe Simon	811	1622	2433	5920	10,460	15,000
5-8: 5,8-Eagle-c. 6,7-Dynamo-c	308	616	924	2156	3778	5400

NOTE: *Cosmic Carson by **Tuska**-#1-3; by **Kirby**-#4. **Lou Fine** c-1-3 only.*

SCIENCE COMICS (2nd Series)
Humor Publications (Ace Magazines?): Jan, 1946 - No. 5, 1946

	GD 2.0	VG 4.0	FN 6.0	VF 8.0	VF/NM 9.0	NM- 9.2
1-Palais-c/a in #1-3; A-Bomb-c	32	64	96	188	307	425
2	18	36	54	103	162	220
3-Feldstein-a (6 pgs.); Palais-c	22	44	66	132	216	300
4,5: 4-Palais-c	15	30	45	83	124	165

SCIENCE COMICS
Ziff-Davis Publ. Co.: May, 1947 (8 pgs. in color)

	GD 2.0	VG 4.0	FN 6.0	VF 8.0	VF/NM 9.0	NM- 9.2
nn-Could be ordered by mail for 10¢; like the nn Amazing Adventures (1950) & Boy Cowboy (1950); used to test the market	57	114	171	362	619	875

SCIENCE COMICS (True Science Illustrated)
Export Publication Ent., Toronto, Canada: Mar, 1951 (Distr. in U.S. by Kable News Co.)

	GD 2.0	VG 4.0	FN 6.0	VF 8.0	VF/NM 9.0	NM- 9.2
1-Science Adventure stories plus some true science features; man on moon story	24	48	72	142	234	325

SCIENCE DOG SPECIAL (Also see Invincible)
Image Comics: Aug, 2010; No. 2, May, 2011 ($3.50)

	GD 2.0	VG 4.0	FN 6.0	VF 8.0	VF/NM 9.0	NM- 9.2
1,2: 1-Kirkman-s/Walker-a/c; leads into Invincible #75						3.50

SCIENCE FICTION SPACE ADVENTURES (See Space Adventures)

SCION (Also see CrossGen Chronicles)
CrossGeneration Comics: July, 2000 - No. 43, Apr, 2004 ($2.95)

	GD 2.0	VG 4.0	FN 6.0	VF 8.0	VF/NM 9.0	NM- 9.2
1-43: 1-Marz-s/Cheung-a						3.00

SCI-SPY
DC Comics (Vertigo): Apr, 2002 - No. 6, Sept, 2002 ($2.50, limited series)

	GD 2.0	VG 4.0	FN 6.0	VF 8.0	VF/NM 9.0	NM- 9.2
1-6-Moench-s/Gulacy-c/a						3.00

SCI-TECH
DC Comics (WildStorm): Sept, 1999 - No. 4, Dec, 1999 ($2.50, limited series)

	GD 2.0	VG 4.0	FN 6.0	VF 8.0	VF/NM 9.0	NM- 9.2
1-4-Benes-a/Choi & Peterson-s						3.00

SCOOBY APOCALYPSE (Scooby Doo)
DC Comics: Jul, 2016 - No. 36, Jun, 2019 ($3.99)

	GD 2.0	VG 4.0	FN 6.0	VF 8.0	VF/NM 9.0	NM- 9.2
1-36: 1-Giffen & DeMatteis-s/Porter-a; covers by Jim Lee and various; team's 1st meeting 4-Intro. Scrappy-Doo. 6-Velma's origin. 7-Eaglesham-a. 9-18-Scrappy-Doo app. 16-29-Secret Squirrel back-up. 25-Fred killed. 30-36-Atom Ant back-up; JLA app.						4.00
.../Hanna-Barbera Halloween Comics Fest Special Edition 1 (12/16, giveaway) previews Scooby Apocalypse, Future Quest, The Flintstones, and Wacky Races						3.00

SCOOBY DOO (TV)(...Where are you? #1-16,26; ...Mystery Comics #17-25, 27 on)
(See March Of Comics #356, 368, 382, 391 in the Promotional Comics section)
Gold Key: Mar, 1970 - No. 30, Feb, 1975 (Hanna-Barbera)

	GD 2.0	VG 4.0	FN 6.0	VF 8.0	VF/NM 9.0	NM- 9.2
1-First comic book app.	318	636	954	2226	3813	5400
2	22	44	66	154	340	525
3-5	19	38	57	131	291	450
6-10	13	26	39	86	188	290
11-20: 11-Tufts-a	10	20	30	64	132	200
21-30: 28-Whitman edition	9	18	27	57	111	165

SCOOBY DOO (TV)
Charlton Comics: Apr, 1975 - No. 11, Dec, 1976 (Hanna-Barbera)

	GD 2.0	VG 4.0	FN 6.0	VF 8.0	VF/NM 9.0	NM- 9.2
1	12	24	36	80	173	265
2-5	8	16	24	55	105	155
6-11	6	12	18	38	69	100
nn-(1976, digest, 68 pgs., B&W)	5	10	15	34	60	85

SCOOBY-DOO (TV) (Newsstand sales only) (See Dynamutt & Laff-A-Lympics)
Marvel Comics Group: Oct, 1977 - No. 9, Feb, 1979 (Hanna-Barbera)

	GD 2.0	VG 4.0	FN 6.0	VF 8.0	VF/NM 9.0	NM- 9.2
1-Dyno-Mutt begins	7	14	21	46	86	125
1-(35¢-c variant, limited distribution)(10/77)	14	28	42	96	211	325
2-5	4	8	12	22	35	48
6-9	4	8	12	25	40	55

SCOOBY-DOO (TV)
Harvey Comics: Sept, 1992 - No. 3, May, 1993 ($1.25)

	GD 2.0	VG 4.0	FN 6.0	VF 8.0	VF/NM 9.0	NM- 9.2
V2#1-3: 3-(Low print and scarce)	2	4	6	11	16	20
Big Book 1,2 (11/92, 4/93, $1.95, 52 pgs.)	2	4	6	9	11	14
Giant Size 1,2 (10/92, 3/93, $2.25, 68 pgs.)	2	4	6	9	11	14

SCOOBY DOO (TV)
Archie Comics: Oct, 1995 -No. 21, June, 1997 ($1.50)

	GD 2.0	VG 4.0	FN 6.0	VF 8.0	VF/NM 9.0	NM- 9.2
1	3	6	9	15	22	28
2	1	3	4	6	8	10
3-21: 12-Cover by Scooby Doo creative designer Iwao Takamoto						6.00

SCOOBY DOO (TV)
DC Comics: Aug, 1997 - No. 159, Oct, 2010 ($1.75/$1.95/$1.99/$2.25/$2.50/$2.99)

	GD 2.0	VG 4.0	FN 6.0	VF 8.0	VF/NM 9.0	NM- 9.2
1	2	4	6	9	12	15
2-10: 5-Begin-$1.95-c						5.00
11-45: 14-Begin $1.99-c						4.00
46-89,91-157: 63-Begin $2.25-c. 75-With 2 Garbage Pail Kids stickers. 100-Wray-c						3.00
90,158,159: 90-($2.95) Bonus stories. 158,159-($2.99-c)						4.00
...Spooky Spectacular 1 (10/99, $3.95) Comic Convention story						4.00
...Spooky Spectacular 2000 (10/00, $3.95)						4.00
...Spooky Summer Special 2001 (8/01, $3.95) Staton-a						4.00
...Super Scarefest (8/02, $3.95) r/#20,25,30-32						4.00

SCOOBY-DOO 50TH ANNIVERSARY GIANT (TV)
DC Comics: 2019 ($4.99, squarebound one-shot)

	GD 2.0	VG 4.0	FN 6.0	VF 8.0	VF/NM 9.0	NM- 9.2
1-Three new stories plus reprints from Scooby-Doo: Where Are You?; Brizuela-a						5.00

SCOOBY-DOO TEAM-UP (TV)
DC Comics: Jan, 2014 - No. 50, Nov, 2019 ($2.99)

1-11,13-20,22-50: 1-Batman & Robin app.; Man-Bat app. 2-Ace the Bat-Hound app. 3-Bat-Mite app. 4-Teen Titans Go! 6-Super Friends & Legion of Doom app. 7-Flintstones. 8-Jetsons. 10-Jonny Quest. 13-Spectre, Deadman & Phantom Stranger. 27-Plastic Man.

Scarlet Witch (2023) #1 © MAR

Scooby-Doo Team-Up #20 © H-B

Scorched #14 © TMP

GD 2.0 | VG 4.0 | FN 6.0 | VF 8.0 | VF/NM 9.0 | NM- 9.2

28-Jonah Hex app. 31-The Atom. 33-Legion of Super-Heroes. 34-Birds of Prey. 43-Doom Patrol. 45-Mr. Miracle & Big Barda. 46-Black Lightning. 50-Bat-Mite, Scooby-Mite, cartoon & movie versions and Scooby Apocalypse versions app. 3.00
12-Harley Quinn, Poison Ivy, Catwoman & Batgirl app. 2 4 6 8 10 12
21-Harley Quinn, Joker, Batman, Robin & Batgirl app. 6.00
... FCBD Special Edition 1 (6/15, giveaway) flipbook with Teen Titans Go! 4.00
... Halloween Special Edition (12/14, giveaway) r/#1 4.00

SCOOBY-DOO: WHERE ARE YOU? (TV)
DC Comics: Nov, 2010 - Present ($2.99)
1 3 6 9 14 20 25
2-5 1 3 4 6 8 10
6-20 6.00
21-31,33-50 4.00
32-KISS spoof 3 6 9 14 20 25
51-120 3.00

SCOOP COMICS (Becomes Yankee Comics #4-7, a digest sized cartoon book; then after #8 it becomes Snap #9)
Harry 'A' Chesler (Holyoke): November, 1941 - No. 3, Mar, 1943; No. 8, 1944
1-Intro. Rocketman & Rocketgirl & begins; origin The Master Key & begins; Dan Hastings begins; Charles Sultan-c/a 155 310 465 992 1696 2400
2-Rocket Boy begins; injury to eye story (reprinted in Spotlight #3); classic-c 476 952 1428 3475 6138 8800
3-Injury to eye story-r from #2; Rocket Boy 123 246 369 787 1344 1900
8-Formerly Yankee Comics; becomes Snap 161 322 483 1030 1765 2500

SCOOTER (See Swing With...)

SCOOTER COMICS
Rucker Publ. Ltd. (Canadian): Apr, 1946
1-Teen-age/funny animal 24 48 72 144 237 330

SCOOTER GIRL
Oni Press: May, 2003 - No. 6, Feb, 2004 ($2.99, B&W, limited series)
1-6-Chynna Clugston-Major-s/a 3.00
TPB (5/04, $14.95, digest size) r/series; sketch pages 15.00

SCORCHED, THE
Image Comics (Todd McFarlane Prods.): Jan, 2022 - Present ($5.99/$2.99)
1-Spawn, Medieval Spawn, She-Spawn, Gunslinger Spawn app.; Segovia-a 6.00
2-15-($2.99) 3.00

SCORPION
Atlas/Seaboard Publ.: Feb, 1975 - No. 3, July, 1975
1-Intro.; bondage-c by Chaykin 3 6 9 18 27 36
2-Chaykin-a w/Wrightson, Kaluta, Simonson assists(p) 3 6 9 15 22 28
3-Jim Craig-c/a 2 4 6 11 16 20
NOTE: ***Chaykin** a-1, 2; c-1. **Colon** c-2. **Craig** c/a-3.*

SCORPION KING, THE (Movie)
Dark Horse Comics: March, 2002 - No. 2, Apr, 2002 ($2.99, limited series)
1,2-Photo-c of the Rock; Richards-a 3.00

SCORPIO ROSE
Eclipse Comics: Jan, 1983 - No. 2, Oct, 1983 ($1.25, Baxter paper)
1,2: Dr. Orient back-up story begins. 2-origin. 4.00

SCOTLAND YARD (Inspector Farnsworth of)(Texas Rangers in Action #5 on?)
Charlton Comics Group: June, 1955 - No. 4, Mar, 1956
1-Tothish-a 16 32 48 92 144 195
2-4: 2-Tothish-a 10 20 30 56 76 95

SCOTT PILGRIM, ... (Inspired the 2010 movie)
Oni Press: Jul, 2004 - Vol. 6, Jul, 2010 ($11.99, B&W, 7-1/2" x 5", multiple printings exist)
Scott Pilgrim's Precious Little Life (Vol. 1) Bryan Lee O'Malley-s/a in all 12.00
Scott Pilgrim Vs. The World (Vol. 2), S.P. & The Infinite Sadness (Vol. 3), S.P. Gets it Together (Vol. 4), S.P. Vs. The Universe (Vol. 5), Scott Pilgrim's Finest Hour (Vol. 6) each 12.00
Free Scott Pilgrim #1 (Free Comic Book Day Edition, 2006) 15.00
Full-Colour Odds & Ends 2008 12.00

SCOURGE, THE
Aspen MLT: No. 0, Aug, 2010 - No. 6, Dec, 2011 ($2.50/$2.99)
0-($2.50) Lobdell-s/Battle-a; multiple covers 3.00
1-6-($2.99) Lobdell-s/Battle-a; multiple covers 3.00

SCOURGE OF THE GODS
Marvel Comics (Soleil): 2009 - No. 3, 2009 ($5.99, limited series)
1-3-Mangin-s/Gajic-a; English version of French comic 6.00
...: The Fall 1-3 (2009 - No. 3, 2009) 6.00

GD 2.0 | VG 4.0 | FN 6.0 | VF 8.0 | VF/NM 9.0 | NM- 9.2

SCOUT (See Eclipse Graphic Album #16, New America & Swords of Texas)
(Becomes Scout: War Shaman)
Eclipse Comics: Dec, 1985 - No. 24, Oct, 1987($1.75/$1.25, Baxter paper)
1-15,17,18,20-24: 19-Airboy preview. 10-Bissette-a. 11-Monday, the Eliminator begins. 15-Swords of Texas 3.00
16,19: 16-Scout 3-D Special ($2.50), 16-Scout 2-D Limited Edition, 19-contains flexidisk ($2.50) 4.00
...Handbook 1 (8/87, $1.75, B&W) 3.00
Mount Fire (1989, $14.95, TPB) r/#8-14 15.00

SCOUT'S HONOR
AfterShock Comics: Jan, 2021 - No. 5, May, 2021 ($4.99/$3.99)
1-($4.99) David Pepose-s/Luca Casalanguida-a 5.00
2-5-($3.99) 4.00

SCOUT: WAR SHAMAN (Formerly Scout)
Eclipse Comics: Mar, 1988 - No. 16, Dec, 1989 ($1.95)
1-16 3.00

SCRATCH
DC Comics: Aug, 2004 - No. 5, Dec, 2004 ($2.50, limited series)
1-5-Sam Kieth-s/a/c; Batman app. 3.00

SCREAM (...Comics) (Andy Comics #20 on)
Humor Publications/Current Books(Ace Magazines): Autumn, 1944 - No. 19, Apr, 1948
1-Teenage humor 23 46 69 136 223 310
2 15 30 45 85 130 175
3-16: 11-Racist humor (Indians). 16-Intro. Lily-Belle 13 26 39 74 105 135
17,19 12 24 36 67 94 120
18-Hypo needle story 13 26 39 74 105 135

SCREAM (Magazine)
Skywald Publ. Corp.: Aug, 1973 - No. 11, Feb, 1975 (68 pgs., B&W) (Painted-c on all)
1-Nosferatu-c/1st app. (series thru #11); Morrow-a. Cthulhu/Necronomicon-s 9 18 27 62 126 190
2,3: 2-(10/73) Lady Satan 1st app. & series begins; Edgar Allan Poe adaptations begin (thru #11); Phantom of the Opera-s. 3-(12/73) Origin Lady Satan 5 10 15 33 57 80
4-1st Cannibal Werewolf and 1st Lunatic Mummy 5 10 15 34 60 85
5,7,8: 5,7-Frankenstein app. 8-Buckler-a; Werewolf-s; Slither-Slime Man-s 4 8 12 28 50 70
6, 9,10: 6-(6/74) Saga of The Victims/ I Am Horror, classic GGA Hewetson series begins (thru #11); Frankenstein 2073-s. 9-Severed head-c; Marcos-a. 9,10-Werewolf-s. 10-Dracula-c/s 5 10 15 31 53 75
11- (1975 Winter Special) "Mr. Poe and the Raven" story 5 10 15 33 57 80
NOTE: ***Buckler** a-8. **Hewetson** s-1-11. **Marcos** a-9. **Miralles** c-2. **Morrow** a-1. **Poe** s-2-11. **Segrelles** a-7; c-1.*

SCREAM: CURSE OF CARNAGE (Follows the Absolute Carnage series)
Marvel Comics: Jan, 2020 - Present ($4.99/$3.99, limited series)
1-($4.99) Andi Benton with the Scream symbiote; Chapman-s/Mooneyham-a 5.00
2-5-($3.99) Brown & Mooneyham-a. 4,5-Thor app. 4.00

SCREEN CARTOONS
DC Comics: Dec, 1944 (cover only ashcan)
nn-Ashcan comic, not distributed to newsstands, only for in house use. Covers were produced, but not the rest of the book. A copy sold in 2006 for $400 and in 2008 for $500.

SCREEN COMICS
DC Comics: Dec, 1944 (cover only ashcan)
nn-Ashcan comic, not distributed to newsstands, only for in house use. Covers were produced, but not the rest of the book. A copy sold in 2006 for $400, in 2008 for $500 and in 2013 for $500.

SCREEN FABLES
DC Comics: Dec, 1944 (cover only ashcan)
nn-Ashcan comic, not distributed to newsstands, only for in house use. Covers were produced, but not the rest of the book. A copy sold in 2006 for $400 and in 2008 for $500.

SCREEN FUNNIES
DC Comics: Dec, 1944 (cover only ashcan)
nn-Ashcan comic, not distributed to newsstands, only for in house use. Covers were produced, but not the rest of the book. A copy sold in 2006 for $400 and in 2008 for $500.

SCREEN GEMS
DC Comics: Dec, 1944 (cover only ashcan)
nn-Ashcan comic, not distributed to newsstands, only for in house use. Covers were produced, but not the rest of the book. A copy sold in 2010 for $891 and a VF copy sold for $775.

	GD 2.0	VG 4.0	FN 6.0	VF 8.0	VF/NM 9.0	NM- 9.2

SCREWBALL SQUIRREL
Dark Horse Comics: July, 1995 - No. 3, Sept, 1995 ($2.50, limited series)

Issue	GD	VG	FN	VF	VF/NM	NM-
1-3: Characters created by Tex Avery						3.00

SCRIBBLENAUTS UNMASKED: A CRISIS OF IMAGINATION (Based on the video game)
DC Comics: Mar, 2014 - No. 7, Sept, 2014 ($2.99)

Issue	GD	VG	FN	VF	VF/NM	NM-
1-7: 1-The Bat Family, the Joker and Phantom Stranger app. 3-The Anti-Monitor app.						3.00

SCRIBBLY (See All-American Comics, Buzzy, The Funnies, Leave It To Binky & Popular Comics)
National Periodical Publ.: 8-9/48 - No. 13, 8-9/50; No. 14, 10-11/51 - No. 15, 12-1/51-52

Issue	GD	VG	FN	VF	VF/NM	NM-
1-Sheldon Mayer-c/a in all; 52 pgs. begin	110	220	330	704	1202	1700
2	65	130	195	416	708	1000
3-5	54	108	162	343	574	825
6-10	41	82	123	256	428	600
11-15: 13-Last 52 pgs.	36	72	108	214	347	480

SCUD: TALES FROM THE VENDING MACHINE
Fireman Press: 1998 - No. 5 ($2.50, B&W)

Issue	GD	VG	FN	VF	VF/NM	NM-
1-5: 1-Kaniuga-a. 2-Ruben Martinez-a						3.00

SCUD: THE DISPOSABLE ASSASSIN
Fireman Press: Feb, 1994 - No. 20, 1997 ($2.95, B&W)
Image Comics: No. 21, Feb, 2008 - No. 24, May, 2008 ($3.50, B&W)

Issue	GD	VG	FN	VF	VF/NM	NM-
1	7	14	21	46	86	125
1-2nd printing in color	1	3	4	6	8	10
2	2	4	6	10	14	18
3						6.00
4-20						3.00
21-24: 21-(2/08, $3.50) Ashley Wood-c. 22-Mahfood-c						3.50
Heavy 3PO ($12.95, TPB) r/#1-4						13.00
Programmed For Damage ($14.95, TPB) r/#5-9						15.00
Solid Gold Bomb ($17.95, TPB) r/#10-15						18.00

SCUMBAG, THE
Image Comics: Oct, 2020 - No. 14, Aug, 2022 ($3.99)

Issue	GD	VG	FN	VF	VF/NM	NM-
1-14: 1-Remender-s/Larosa-a; intro. Ernie Ray Clementine. 2-Robinson-a. 3-Powell-a						4.00

SEA DEVILS (See Showcase #27-29)
National Periodical Publications: Sept-Oct, 1961 - No. 35, May-June, 1967

Issue	GD	VG	FN	VF	VF/NM	NM-
1-(9-10/61)	59	118	177	472	1061	1650
2-Last 10¢ issue; grey-tone-c	27	54	81	194	435	675
3-Begin 12¢ issues thru #35; grey-tone-c	18	36	54	128	284	440
4,5-Grey-tone-c	16	32	48	110	243	375
6-10	10	20	30	69	147	225
11,12,14-20: 12-Grey-tone-c	8	16	24	54	102	150
13-Kubert, Colan-a; Joe Kubert app. in story	8	16	24	55	105	155
21-35: 22-Intro. International Sea Devils; origin & 1st app. Capt. X & Man Fish. 33,35-Grey-tone-c	6	12	18	40	73	105

NOTE: *Heath a-Showcase 27-29, 1-10; c-Showcase 27-29, 1-10, 14-16.* ***Moldoff*** *a-16i.*

SEA DEVILS (See Tangent Comics/ Sea Devils)

SEADRAGON (Also see the Epsilion Wave)
Elite Comics: May, 1986 - No. 8, 1987 ($1.75)

Issue	GD	VG	FN	VF	VF/NM	NM-
1-8: 1-1st & 2nd printings exist						3.00

SEAGUY
DC Comics (Vertigo): July, 2004 - No. 3, Sept, 2004 ($2.95, limited series)

Issue	GD	VG	FN	VF	VF/NM	NM-
1-3-Grant Morrison-s/Cameron Stewart-a/c						3.00
TPB (2005, $9.95) r/#1-3						10.00

SEAGUY: THE SLAVES OF MICKEY EYE
DC Comics (Vertigo): Jun, 2009 - No. 3, Aug, 2009 ($3.99, limited series)

Issue	GD	VG	FN	VF	VF/NM	NM-
1-3-Grant Morrison-s/Cameron Stewart-a/c						4.00

SEA HOUND, THE (Captain Silver's Log Of The...)
Avon Periodicals: 1945 (no month) - No. 2, Sept-Oct, 1945

Issue	GD	VG	FN	VF	VF/NM	NM-
nn (#1)-29 pg. novel length sty-"The Esmeralda's Treasure"	20	40	60	117	189	260
2	14	28	42	81	118	155

SEA HOUND, THE (Radio)
Capt. Silver Syndicate: No. 3, July, 1949 - No. 4, Sept, 1949

Issue	GD	VG	FN	VF	VF/NM	NM-
3,4	11	22	33	62	86	110

SEA HUNT (TV)
Dell Publishing Co.: No. 928, 8/58 - No. 1041, 10-12/59; No. 4, 1-3/60 - No. 13, 4-6/62 (All have Lloyd Bridges photo-c)

Issue	GD	VG	FN	VF	VF/NM	NM-
Four Color 928(#1)	12	24	36	80	173	265
Four Color 994(#2), 4-13: Manning-a #4-6,8-11,13	9	18	27	57	111	165
Four Color 1041(#3)-Toth-a	9	18	27	57	111	165

SEA OF RED
Image Comics: Mar, 2005 - No. 13, Nov, 2006 ($2.95/$2.99/$3.50)

Issue	GD	VG	FN	VF	VF/NM	NM-
1-12-Vampirates at sea; Remender & Dwyer-s/Dwyer & Sam-a						3.00
13-($3.50)						3.50
Vol. 1: No Grave But The Sea (9/05, $8.95) r/#1-4						9.00
Vol. 2: No Quarter (2006, $11.99) r/#5-8						12.00
Vol. 3: The Deadlights (2006, $14.99) r/#9-13						15.00

SEA OF STARS
Image Comics: Jul, 2019 - No. 11, Nov, 2021 ($3.99, limited series)

Issue	GD	VG	FN	VF	VF/NM	NM-
1-11-Jason Aaron & Dennis Hallum-s/Stephen Green-a						4.00

SEA OF THIEVES (Based on the Microsoft computer game)
Titan Comics: Apr, 2018 - No. 4, Jul, 2018 ($3.99)

Issue	GD	VG	FN	VF	VF/NM	NM-
1-4-Jeremy Whitley-s/Rhoald Marcellius-a; multiple covers; bonus character profiles						4.00

SEAQUEST (TV)
Nemesis Comics: Mar, 1994 ($2.25)

Issue	GD	VG	FN	VF	VF/NM	NM-
1-Has 2 diff-c stocks (slick & cardboard); Alcala-i						3.00

SEARCHERS, THE (Movie)
Dell Publishing Co.: No. 709, 1956

Issue	GD	VG	FN	VF	VF/NM	NM-
Four Color 709-John Wayne photo-c	27	54	81	194	435	675

SEARCHERS, THE
Caliber Comics: 1996 - No. 4, 1996 ($2.95, B&W)

Issue	GD	VG	FN	VF	VF/NM	NM-
1-4						3.00

SEARCHERS, THE : APOSTLE OF MERCY
Caliber Comics: 1997 - No. 2, 1997 ($2.95/$3.95, B&W)

Issue	GD	VG	FN	VF	VF/NM	NM-
1-($2.95)						3.00
2-($3.95)						4.00

SEARCH FOR HU
AfterShock Comics: Sept, 2021 - No. 5, Jan, 2022 ($4.99/$3.99, limited series)

Issue	GD	VG	FN	VF	VF/NM	NM-
1-($4.99) Tsuei & Orlando-s/Rubine-a						5.00
2-4-($3.99)						4.00

SEARCH FOR LOVE
American Comics Group: Feb-Mar, 1950 - No. 2, Apr-May, 1950 (52 pgs.)

Issue	GD	VG	FN	VF	VF/NM	NM-
1-Ken Bald-c	20	40	60	117	189	260
2	15	30	45	86	133	180

SEARS (See Merry Christmas From...)

SEASON'S BEATINGS
Marvel Comics: Feb, 2019 ($4.99, one-shot)

Issue	GD	VG	FN	VF	VF/NM	NM-
1-Christmas-themed short stories; Deadpool, X-Force, Spider-Man, Squirrel Girl app.						5.00

SEASON'S GREETINGS
Hallmark (King Features): 1935 (6-1/4x5-1/4", 24 pgs. in color)

Issue	GD	VG	FN	VF	VF/NM	NM-
nn-Cover features Mickey Mouse, Popeye, Jiggs & Skippy. "The Night Before Christmas" told one panel per page, each panel by a famous artist featuring their character. Art by Alex Raymond, Gottfredson, Swinnerton, Segar, Chic Young, Milt Gross, Sullivan (Messmer), Herriman, McManus, Percy Crosby & others (22 artists in all) Estimated value...						1000.00

SEBASTIAN O
DC Comics (Vertigo): May, 1993 - No. 3, July, 1993 ($1.95, limited series)

Issue	GD	VG	FN	VF	VF/NM	NM-
1-3-Grant Morrison scripts; Steve Yeowell-a						3.00
TPB (2004, $9.95) r/#1-3; intro. chronology by Morrison						10.00

SECOND CHANCES
Image Comics: Aug, 2021 - Present ($3.99, B&W)

Issue	GD	VG	FN	VF	VF/NM	NM-
1-3-Mammone-s/Bertolini-a						4.00

SECOND COMING
AHOY Comics: 2019 - No. 6, 2020 ($3.99, limited series)

Issue	GD	VG	FN	VF	VF/NM	NM-
1-6-Russell-s/Pace & Kirk-a/Conner-c; Jesus meets Sunstar. 1-3-Variant-c by Pace						4.00

SECOND COMING: ONLY BEGOTTEN SON
AHOY Comics: 2020 - No. 6, 2021 ($3.99, limited series)

Issue	GD	VG	FN	VF	VF/NM	NM-
1-6-Russell-s/Pace & Kirk-a/Pace-c. 1-Origin of Sunstar						4.00

SECOND LIFE OF DOCTOR MIRAGE, THE (See Shadowman #16)
Valiant: Nov, 1993 - No. 18, May, 1995 ($2.50)

Issue	GD	VG	FN	VF	VF/NM	NM-
1-18: 1-With bound-in poster. 5-Shadowman x-over. 7-Bound-in trading card						3.00
1-Gold ink logo edition; no price on-c	2	4	6	9	12	15

SECOND SIGHT
AfterShock Comics: Feb, 2016 - No. 6, Jul, 2016 ($3.99)

Issue	GD	VG	FN	VF	VF/NM	NM-
1-6-David Hine-s/Alberto Ponticelli-a						4.00

SECRET AGENT (Formerly Sarge Steel)
Charlton Comics: V2#9, Oct, 1966; V2#10, Oct, 1967

Issue	GD	VG	FN	VF	VF/NM	NM-
V2#9-Sarge Steel part-r begins	3	6	9	17	26	35
10-Tiffany Sinn, CIA app. (from Career Girl Romances #39); Aparo-a	3	6	9	14	20	26

SECRET AGENT (TV) (See Four Color #1231)
Gold Key: Nov, 1966; No. 2, Jan, 1968

Issue	GD	VG	FN	VF	VF/NM	NM-
1-John Drake photo-c	9	18	27	57	111	165
2-Photo-c	6	12	18	37	66	95

SECRET AGENT X-9 (See Flash Gordon #4 by King)
David McKay Publ.: 1934 (Book 1: 84 pgs.; Book 2: 124 pgs.) (8x7-1/2")

Issue	GD	VG	FN	VF	VF/NM	NM-
Book 1-Contains reprints of the first 13 weeks of the strip by Alex Raymond; complete except for 2 dailies	54	108	162	343	574	825
Book 2-Contains reprints immediately following contents of Book 1, for 20 weeks by Alex Raymond; complete except for two dailies. Note: Raymond mis-dated the last five strips from 6/34, and while the dating sequence is confusing, the continuity is correct	45	90	135	284	480	675

SECRET AGENT X-9 (See Magic Comics)
Dell Publishing Co.: Dec, 1937 (Not by Raymond)

Issue	GD	VG	FN	VF	VF/NM	NM-
Feature Books 8	61	122	183	390	670	950

SECRET AGENT Z-2 (See Holyoke One-Shot No. 7)

SECRET AVENGERS (The Heroic Age)
Marvel Comics: Jul, 2010 - No. 37, Mar, 2013 ($3.99)

Issue	GD	VG	FN	VF	VF/NM	NM-
1-Bendis-s/Deodato-a/Djurdjevic-c; Steve Rogers assembles covert squad	2	4	6	8	10	12
1-Variant-c by Yardin	2	4	6	9	12	15
2-12: 2-Two covers. 2-4-Deodato-a. 5-Nick Fury app.; Aja-a						4.00
12.1 ($2.99) Spencer-s/Eaton-a/Deodato-c						3.00
13-18,20, 21: 13-15-Fear Itself tie-in; Granov-c. 15-Aftermath of Bucky's demise. 16-21-Warren Ellis-s						4.00
19-1st Mr. Knight	3	6	9	14	19	24
21.2-($2.99) Remender-s/Zircher-a; intro. new Masters of Evil						3.00
22,24-37: 22-25-Remender-s/Hardman-a/Art Adams-c. 26-28-A vs. X						4.00
23-1st Agent Venom, joins team	3	6	9	17	26	35

SECRET AVENGERS (Marvel NOW!)
Marvel Comics: Apr, 2013 - No. 16, Apr, 2014 ($3.99)

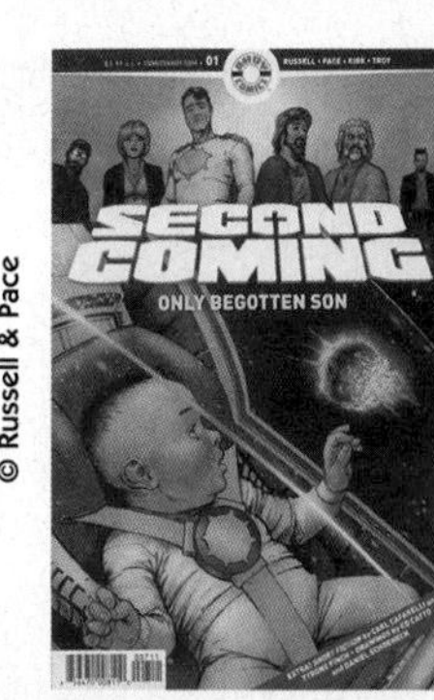

Second Coming: Only Begotten Son #1 © Russell & Pace

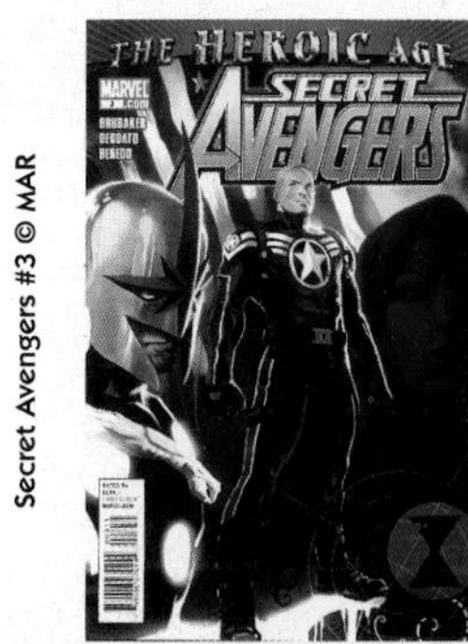

Secret Avengers #3 © MAR

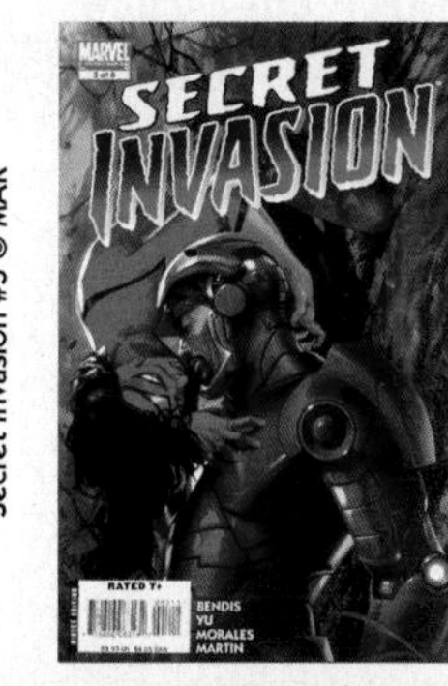

Secret Invasion #3 © MAR

	GD 2.0	VG 4.0	FN 6.0	VF 8.0	VF/NM 9.0	NM- 9.2

1-16: 1-5-Spencer-s/Luke Ross-a/Coker-c; Agent Coulson app. 5,7-Hulk app. 7,9-Guice-a 9,16-Winter Soldier app. 4.00

SECRET AVENGERS (All-New Marvel NOW!)
Marvel Comics: May, 2014 - No. 15, Jun, 2015 ($3.99)

1-15: 1-Ales Kot-s/Michael Walsh-a; M.O.D.O.K. app. 7-Deadpool app. 4.00

SECRET CITY SAGA (See Jack Kirby's Secret City Saga)

SECRET DEFENDERS (Also see The Defenders & Fantastic Four #374)
Marvel Comics: Mar, 1993 - No. 25, Mar, 1995 ($1.75/$1.95)

1-($2.50)-Red foil stamped-c; Dr. Strange, Nomad, Wolverine, Spider Woman & Darkhawk begin 4.00
2-11,13-24: 9-New team w/Silver Surfer, Thunderstrike, Dr. Strange & War Machine. 13-Thanos replaces Dr. Strange as leader; leads into Cosmic Powers limited series; 14-Dr. Druid. 15-Bound in card sheet. 15-17-Deadpool app. 18-Giant Man & Iron Fist app. 3.00
12,25: 12-($2.50)-Prismatic foil-c. 25 ($2.50, 52 pgs.) 4.00

SECRET DIARY OF EERIE ADVENTURES
Avon Periodicals: 1953 (25¢ giant, 100 pgs., one-shot)

	GD 2.0	VG 4.0	FN 6.0	VF 8.0	VF/NM 9.0	NM- 9.2
nn-(Rare)-Kubert-a; Hollingsworth-c; Sid Check back-c	459	918	1377	3350	5925	8500

SECRET EMPIRE (Also see Free Comic Book Day 2017 Secret Empire)
Marvel Comics: No. 0, Jun, 2017 - No. 10, Oct, 2017 ($4.99/$3.99, limited series)

0-2-($4.99): 0-Spencer-s/Acuña-a; Steve Rogers and Hydra take over. 1-McNiven-a 5.00
3-5,7-($3.99) 3,5-Sorrentino-a. 4-Yu-a. 5-Bruce Banner returns 4.00
6,8-10-($4.99): 6,9-Yu-a. 7-Black Widow killed. 8-Acuña-a. 10-McNiven-a 5.00
... Omega 1 (11/17, $4.99) Epilogue to series; Sorrentino & Bennett-a 5.00
...: Underground 1 (8/17, $4.99) Whitley-s/Koda-a; takes place after #4; Sauron app. 5.00
...: United 1 (8/17, $4.99) X-Men & Deadpool app.; Anindito-a 5.00
...: Uprising 1 (7/17, $4.99) The Champions & Black Widow app.; Landy-s/Cassara-a 5.00

SECRET EMPIRE: BRAVE NEW WORLD
Marvel Comics: Aug, 2017 - No. 5, Oct, 2017 ($3.99, limited series)

1-5: Namor/Invaders and back-up short stories of various heroes under Hydra rule 5.00

SECRET FILES & ORIGINS GUIDE TO THE DC UNIVERSE
DC Comics: Mar, 2000; Feb, 2002 ($6.95/$4.95)

2000 (3/00, $6.95)-Overview of DC characters; profile pages by various 7.00
2001-2002 (2/02, $4.95) Olivetti-c 5.00

SECRET FILES PRESIDENT LUTHOR
DC Comics: Mar, 2001 ($4.95, one-shot)

1-Short stories & profile pages by various; Harris-c 5.00

SECRET HEARTS
National Periodical Publications (Beverly)(Arleigh No. 50-113):
9-10/49 - No. 6, 7-8/50; No. 7, 12-1/51-52 - No. 153, 7/71

	GD 2.0	VG 4.0	FN 6.0	VF 8.0	VF/NM 9.0	NM- 9.2
1-Kinstler-a; photo-c begin, end #6	81	162	243	518	884	1250
2-Toth-a (1 pg.); Kinstler-a	39	78	117	240	395	550
3,6 (1950)	34	68	102	204	332	460
4,5-Toth-a	35	70	105	208	339	470
7(12-1/51-52) (Rare)	48	96	144	302	514	725
8-10 (1952)	27	54	81	158	259	360
11-20	20	40	60	114	182	250
21-26: 26-Last precode (2-3/55)	16	32	48	98	154	210
27-40	8	16	24	54	102	150
41-50	6	12	18	42	79	115
51-60	6	12	18	37	66	95
61-75,100: 75-Last 10¢ issue	5	10	15	33	57	80
76-99,101-109: 83,88-Each has panel which inspired a famous Roy Lichtenstein painting	4	8	12	25	40	55
110- "Reach for Happiness" serial begins, ends #138	4	8	12	27	44	60
111-119,121-126: 114-Colan-a/c	3	6	9	18	28	38
120,134-Neal Adams-c	4	8	12	27	44	60
127 (4/68)-Beatles cameo	4	8	12	28	47	65
128-133,135-142: 141,142- "20 Miles to Heartbreak", Chapter 2 & 3 (see Young Love for Chapters 1 & 4); Toth, Colletta-a	3	6	9	17	25	34
143-148,150-152: 144-Morrow-a	3	6	9	15	22	28
149,153: 149-Toth-a. 153-Kirby-i	3	6	9	16	23	30

SECRET HISTORY OF THE AUTHORITY: HAWKSMOOR
DC Comics (WildStorm): May, 2008 - No. 6, Oct, 2008 ($2.99, limited series)

1-6-Costa-s/Staples-a/Hamner-c 3.00
TPB (2009, $19.99) r/#1-6 20.00

SECRET HISTORY OF THE WAR ON WEED
Image Comics: Apr, 2022 ($4.99, one-shot)

1-Scotch McTiernan vs. marijuana; Duggan & Posehn-s/Koblish-a 5.00

SECRET IDENTITIES
Image Comics: Feb, 2015 - No. 7, Sept, 2015 ($3.50/$3.99)

1-6-Faerber & Joines-s/Kyriazis-a 3.50
7-($3.99) 4.00

SECRET INVASION (Also see Mighty Avengers, New Avengers, and Skrulls!)
Marvel Comics: June, 2008 - No. 8, Jan, 2009 ($3.99, limited series)

	GD 2.0	VG 4.0	FN 6.0	VF 8.0	VF/NM 9.0	NM- 9.2
1-Skrull invasion; Bendis-s/Yu-a/Dell'Otto-c	2	4	6	10	14	18
1-Variant cover with blank area for sketches	1	3	4	6	8	10

1-McNiven variant-c 12.00
1-Yu variant-c 30.00
1-2nd printing with old Avengers variant-c by Yu 4.00
1 Director's Cut (2008, $4.99) r/#1 with script; concept and promo art; cover gallery 5.00
2-8-Dell'Otto-c. 8-Wasp killed 4.00
2-4-McNiven variant-c. 2-Avengers. 3-Nick Fury. 4-Tony Stark, Spider-Woman, Black Widow 6.00
2-8-Yu variant-c. 2-Hawkeye & Mockingbird. 3-Spider-Woman. 4-Nick Fury 10.00
5-Rubi variant-c 5.00
6-Cho Spider-Woman variant-c 8.00
...:Aftermath: Beta Ray Bill - The Green of Eden (6/09, $3.99) Brereton-a 4.00
...: Chronicles 1,2 (4/09,6/09, $5.99) reprints from New Avengers & Illuminati issues 6.00
... Dark Reign (2/09, $3.99) villain meeting after #8; previews new series; Maleev-a/c 4.00
... Dark Reign (2/09, $3.99) Variant Green Goblin cover by Bryan Hitch 8.00
... Requiem (2009, $3.99) Hank Pym becomes The Wasp; r/TTA #44 & Avengers #215 4.00
... Saga (2008, giveaway) history of the Skrulls told through reprint panels and text 3.00
...: The Infiltration TPB (2008, $19.99) r/FF #2; New Avengers #31,32,38,39; New Avengers: Illuminati #1,5; Mighty Avengers #7; and Avengers: The Initiative Annual #1 20.00
...: War of Kings (2/09, $3.99) Black Bolt and the Inhumans; Pelletier & Dazo-a 4.00
...: Who Do You Trust? (8/08, $3.99) short tie-in stories by various; Jimenez-c 4.00

SECRET INVASION
Marvel Comics: Jan, 2023 - Present ($4.99/$3.99, limited series)

1-($4.99) North-s/Mobili-a; Nick Fury & Maria Hill app. 5.00
2-4-($3.99) 2-Avengers app. 4.00

SECRET INVASION: AMAZING SPIDER-MAN
Marvel Comics: Oct, 2008 - No. 3, Dec, 2008 ($2.99, limited series)

1-3-Jackpot battles a Super-Skrull; Santucci-a. 2-Menace app. 3.00

SECRET INVASION: FANTASTIC FOUR
Marvel Comics: July, 2008 - No. 3, Sept, 2008 ($2.99, limited series)

1-3-Skrulls and Lyja invade; Kitson-a/Davis-c 3.00
1-Variant Skrull cover by McKone 5.00

SECRET INVASION: FRONT LINE
Marvel Comics: Sept, 2008 - No. 5, Jan, 2009 ($2.99, limited series)

1-5-Ben Urich covering the Skrull invasion; Reed-s/Castiello-a 3.00

SECRET INVASION: INHUMANS
Marvel Comics: Oct, 2008 - No. 4, Jan, 2009 ($2.99, limited series)

1-4-Raney-a/Sejic-c/Pokasky-s; search for Black Bolt 3.00

SECRET INVASION: RUNAWAYS/YOUNG AVENGERS (Follows Runaways #30)
Marvel Comics: Aug, 2008 - No. 3, Nov, 2008 ($2.99, limited series)

1-3-Miyazawa-a/Ryan-c 3.00

SECRET INVASION: THOR
Marvel Comics: Oct, 2008 - No. 3, Dec, 2008 ($2.99, limited series)

1-3-Fraction-s/Braithwaite-a; Skrulls invade Asgard; Beta Ray Bill app. 3.00
1-2nd printing with Beta Ray Bill cover 3.00

SECRET INVASION: X-MEN
Marvel Comics: Oct, 2008 - No. 4, Jan, 2009 ($2.99, limited series)

1-4-Carey-s/Nord-a/Dodson-c; Skrulls invade San Francisco 3.00
1-2nd printing with variant Nord-c 3.00

SECRET ISLAND OF OZ, THE (See First Comics Graphic Novel)

SECRET LAND, THE
Dark Horse Comics: Jun, 2021 - No. 4, Oct, 2021 ($3.99, limited series)

1-4-Christofer Emgård-s/Tomás Aira-a 4.00

SECRET LIFE OF PETS, THE (Based on the 2016 animated movie)
Titan Comics: Jun, 2019 - Dec, 2019 ($3.99)

1,2-Lapuss-s/Goum-a 4.00
...Volume 2 (11/19 - No. 2, 12/19) 1,2-Lapuss-s/Goum-a 4.00

SECRET LOVE (See Fox Giants & Sinister House of...)

SECRET LOVE
Ajax-Farrell/Four Star Comic Corp. No. 2 on: 12/55 - No. 3, 8/56; 4/57 - No. 5, 2/58; No. 6, 6/58

	GD 2.0	VG 4.0	FN 6.0	VF 8.0	VF/NM 9.0	NM- 9.2
1(12/55-Ajax, 1st series)	16	32	48	94	147	200
2,3	12	24	36	69	97	125
1(4/57-Ajax, 2nd series)	14	28	42	80	115	150
2-6: 5-Bakerish-a	10	20	30	58	79	100

SECRET LOVES
Comic Magazines/Quality Comics Group: Nov, 1949 - No. 6, Sept, 1950

	GD 2.0	VG 4.0	FN 6.0	VF 8.0	VF/NM 9.0	NM- 9.2
1-Ward-c	39	78	117	231	378	525
2-Ward-c	32	64	96	188	307	425
3-Crandall-a	20	40	60	118	192	265
4,6	17	34	51	100	158	215
5-Suggestive art "Boom Town Babe"; photo-c	24	48	72	142	234	325

SECRET LOVE STORIES (See Fox Giants)

SECRET MISSIONS (Admiral Zacharia's...)
St. John Publishing Co.: February, 1950

	GD 2.0	VG 4.0	FN 6.0	VF 8.0	VF/NM 9.0	NM- 9.2
1-Joe Kubert-c; stories of U.S. foreign agents	36	72	108	214	347	480

SECRET MYSTERIES (Formerly Crime Mysteries & Crime Smashers)
Ribage/Merit Publications No. 17 on: No. 16, Nov, 1954 - No. 19, July, 1955

	GD 2.0	VG 4.0	FN 6.0	VF 8.0	VF/NM 9.0	NM- 9.2
16-Horror, Palais-a; Myron Fass-c	47	94	141	296	498	700
17-19-Horror. 17-Fass-c; mis-dated 3/54?	36	72	108	211	343	475

SECRET ORIGINS (1st Series) (See 80 Page Giant #8)
National Periodical Publications: Aug-Oct, 1961 (Annual) (Reprints)

	GD 2.0	VG 4.0	FN 6.0	VF 8.0	VF/NM 9.0	NM- 9.2
1-Origin Adam Strange (Showcase #17), Green Lantern (Green Lantern #1), Challengers (partial-r/Showcase #6, 6 pgs. Kirby-a), J'onn J'onzz (Det. #225), The Flash (Showcase #4), Green Arrow (1 pg. text), Superman-Batman team (World's Finest #94), Wonder Woman (Wonder Woman #105)	46	92	138	359	805	1250
Replica Edition (1998, $4.95) r/entire book and house ads						5.00
Even More Secret Origins (2003, $6.95) reprints origins of Hawkman, Eclipso, Kid Flash, Blackhawks, Green Lantern's oath, and Jimmy Olsen-Robin team in 80 pg. Giant style						7.00

SECRET ORIGINS (2nd Series)
National Periodical Publications: Feb-Mar, 1973 - No. 6, Jan-Feb, 1974; No. 7, Oct-Nov, 1974 (All 20¢ issues) (All origin reprints)

	GD 2.0	VG 4.0	FN 6.0	VF 8.0	VF/NM 9.0	NM- 9.2
1-Superman(r/1 pg. origin/Action #1, 1st time since G.A.), Batman(Detective #33), Ghost(Flash #88), The Flash(Showcase #4)	5	10	15	35	63	90
2-7: 2-Green Lantern & The Atom(Showcase #22 & 34), Supergirl(Action #252). 3-Wonder Woman (W.W. #1), Wildcat (Sensation #1). 4-Vigilante (Action #42) by Meskin, Kid Eternity(Hit #25). 5-The Spectre by Baily (More Fun #52,53). 6-Blackhawk(Military #1) & Legion of Super-Heroes(Superboy #147). 7-Robin (Detective #38), Aquaman (More Fun #73)	3	6	9	19	30	40

NOTE: *Infantino a-1. Kane a-2. Kubert a-1.*

SECRET ORIGINS (3rd Series)
DC Comics: Apr, 1986 - No. 50, Aug, 1990 (All origins)(52 pgs. #6 on)(#27 on: $1.50)

	GD 2.0	VG 4.0	FN 6.0	VF 8.0	VF/NM 9.0	NM- 9.2
1,3: 1-Origin Superman. 3-Shazam	1	3	4	6	8	10
2,4-6: 2-Blue Beetle. 4-Firestorm. 5-Crimson Avenger. 6-Halo/G.A. Batman						5.00
7-9,11,12,15-20,22-26: 7-Green Lantern (Guy Gardner)/G.A. Sandman. 8-Shadow Lass/Doll Man. 9-G.A. Flash/Skyman.11-G.A. Hawkman/Power Girl. 12-Challengers of Unknown/G.A. Fury (2nd modern app.). 15-Spectre/Deadman. 16-G.A. Hourman/Warlord. 17-Adam Strange story by Carmine Infantino; Dr. Occult. 18-G.A. Gr. Lantern/The Creeper. 19-Uncle Sam/The Guardian. 20-Batgirl/G.A. Dr. Mid-Nite. 22-Manhunters. 23-Floronic Man/Guardians of the Universe. 24-Blue Devil/Dr. Fate. 25-LSH/Atom. 26-Black Lightning/Miss America						5.00
10-Phantom Stranger w/Alan Moore scripts; Legends spin-off						5.00
13-Origin Nightwing; Johnny Thunder app.						5.00
14-Suicide Squad; Legends spin-off	1	3	4	6	8	10
21-Jonah Hex/Black Condor						5.00
27-30,36-38,40-49: 27-Zatara/Zatanna. 28-Midnight/Nightshade. 29-Power of the Atom/Mr. America; new 3 pg. Red Tornado story by Mayer (last app. of Scribbly, 8/88). 30-Plastic Man/Elongated Man. 36-Poison Ivy by Neil Gaiman & Mark Buckingham/Green Lantern. 37-Legion Of Substitute Heroes/Doctor Light. 38-Green Arrow/Speedy; Grell scripts. 40-All Ape issue. 41-Rogues Gallery of Flash. 42-Phantom Girl/GrimGhost. 43-Original Hawk & Dove/Cave Carson/Chris KL-99. 44-Batman app.; story based on Det. #40. 45-Blackhawk/El Diablo. 46-JLA/LSH/New Titans. 47-LSH. 48-Ambush Bug/Stanley & His Monster/Rex the Wonder Dog/Trigger Twins. 49-Newsboy Legion/Silent Knight/Bouncing Boy						4.00
31-35,39: 31-JSA. 32-JLA. 33-35-JLI. 39-Animal Man-c/story continued in Animal Man #10; Grant Morrison scripts; Batman app.						4.00
50-($3.95, 100 pgs.)-Batman & Robin in text, Flash of Two Worlds, Johnny Thunder, Dolphin, Black Canary & Space Museum						5.00
Annual 1 (8/87)-Capt. Comet/Doom Patrol						5.00
Annual 2 ('88, $2.00)-Origin Flash II & Flash III						5.00
Annual 3 ('89, $2.95, 84 pgs.)-Teen Titans; 1st app. new Flamebird who replaces original Bat-Girl						5.00
Special 1 (10/89, $2.00)-Batman villains: Penguin, Riddler, & Two-Face; Bolland-c; Sam Kieth-a; Neil Gaiman scripts(2)						5.00

NOTE: *Art Adams a-33i(part).* ***M. Anderson*** *8, 19, 21, 25i; c-19(part).* ***Aparo*** *c/a-10.* ***Bissette*** *c-23.* ***Bolland*** *c-7.* ***Byrne*** *c/a-Annual 1.* ***Colan*** *c/a-5p.* ***Forte*** *a-37.* ***Giffen*** *a-18p, 44p, 48.* ***Infantino*** *a-17, 50p.* ***Kaluta*** *c-39.* ***Gil Kane*** *a-2, 28; c-2p.* ***Kirby*** *c-19(part).* ***Erik Larsen*** *a-13.* ***Mayer*** *a-29.* ***Morrow*** *a-21.* ***Orlando*** *a-10.* ***Perez*** *a-50i, Annual 3i; c- Annual 3.* ***Rogers*** *a-6p.* ***Russell*** *a-27i.* ***Simonson*** *c-22.* ***Staton*** *a-36, 50p.* ***Steacy*** *a-35.* ***Tuska*** *a-4p, 9p.*

SECRET ORIGINS (4th Series)(DC New 52)
DC Comics: Jun, 2014 - No. 11, May, 2015 ($4.99)

	GD 2.0	VG 4.0	FN 6.0	VF 8.0	VF/NM 9.0	NM- 9.2
1-3,5-9,11: 1-Origin Superman, Robin. 2-Batman. 6-Wonder Woman						5.00
4-Harley Quinn	2	4	6	8	10	12
10-Batgirl; Stewart & Fletcher-s/Koh-a; Firestorm & Poison Ivy						6.00

SECRET ORIGINS 80 PAGE GIANT (Young Justice)
DC Comics: Dec, 1998 ($4.95, one-shot)

	GD 2.0	VG 4.0	FN 6.0	VF 8.0	VF/NM 9.0	NM- 9.2
1-Origin-s of Young Justice members; Ramos-a (Impulse)						5.00

SECRET ORIGINS FEATURING THE JLA
DC Comics: 1999 ($14.95, TPB)

	GD 2.0	VG 4.0	FN 6.0	VF 8.0	VF/NM 9.0	NM- 9.2
1-Reprints recent origin-s of JLA members; Cassaday-c						15.00

SECRET ORIGINS OF SUPER-HEROES (See DC Special Series #10, 19)

SECRET ORIGINS OF SUPER-VILLAINS 80 PAGE GIANT
DC Comics: Dec, 1999 ($4.95, one-shot)

	GD 2.0	VG 4.0	FN 6.0	VF 8.0	VF/NM 9.0	NM- 9.2
1-Origin-s of Sinestro, Amazo and others; Gibbons-c						5.00

SECRET ORIGINS OF THE WORLD'S GREATEST SUPER-HEROES
DC Comics: 1989 ($4.95, 148 pgs.)

	GD 2.0	VG 4.0	FN 6.0	VF 8.0	VF/NM 9.0	NM- 9.2
nn-Reprints Superman, JLA origins; new Batman origin-s; Bolland-c	1	3	4	6	8	10

SECRET ROMANCE
Charlton Comics: Oct, 1968 - No. 41, Nov, 1976; No. 42, Mar, 1979 - No. 48, Feb, 1980

	GD 2.0	VG 4.0	FN 6.0	VF 8.0	VF/NM 9.0	NM- 9.2
1-Begin 12¢ issues, ends #?	3	6	9	20	31	42
2-10: 9-Reese-a	2	4	6	11	16	20
11-16,18,19,21-30	2	4	6	9	13	16
17,20: 17-Susan Dey poster. 20-David Cassidy pin-up2	4	6	11	16	20	
31-48	2	4	6	8	10	12

NOTE: *Beyond the Stars app.-No. 9, 11, 12, 14.*

SECRET ROMANCES (Exciting Love Stories)
Superior Publications Ltd.: Apr, 1951 - No. 27, July, 1955

	GD 2.0	VG 4.0	FN 6.0	VF 8.0	VF/NM 9.0	NM- 9.2
1	26	52	78	154	252	350
2	18	36	54	105	165	225
3-10	15	30	45	86	133	180
11-13,15-18,20-27	14	28	42	81	118	155
14,19-Lingerie panels	14	28	42	82	121	160

SECRET SERVICE (See Kent Blake of the...)

SECRET SERVICE (Inspired the 2015 movie Kingsmen: The Secret Service)(Also see Kingsmen: The Red Diamond)
Marvel Comics (Icon): Jun, 2012 - No. 6, Jun, 2013 ($2.99/$4.99, limited series)

	GD 2.0	VG 4.0	FN 6.0	VF 8.0	VF/NM 9.0	NM- 9.2
1-5-Mark Millar-s/Dave Gibbons-a/c						3.00
6-($4.99)						5.00

SECRET SIX (See Action Comics Weekly)
National Periodical Publications: Apr-May, 1968 - No. 7, Apr-May, 1969 (12¢)

	GD 2.0	VG 4.0	FN 6.0	VF 8.0	VF/NM 9.0	NM- 9.2
1-Origin/1st app.	9	18	27	61	123	185
2-7	4	8	12	28	47	65

SECRET SIX (See Tangent Comics/ Secret Six)

SECRET SIX (See Villains United)
DC Comics: Jul, 2006 - No. 6, Jan, 2007 ($2.99, limited series)

	GD 2.0	VG 4.0	FN 6.0	VF 8.0	VF/NM 9.0	NM- 9.2
1-6-Gail Simone-s/Brad Walker-a. 4-Doom Patrol app.						3.00
...: Six Degrees of Devastation TPB (2007, $14.99) r/#1-6						15.00

SECRET SIX
DC Comics: Nov, 2008 - No. 36, Oct, 2011 ($2.99)

	GD 2.0	VG 4.0	FN 6.0	VF 8.0	VF/NM 9.0	NM- 9.2
1-36: 1-Gail Simone-s/Nicola Scott-a. 2-Batman app. 8-Rodriguez-a. 11-13-Wonder Woman & Artemis app. 16-Black Alice app. 17,18-Blackest Night						3.00
...: Cats in the Cradle TPB (2011, $14.99) r/#19-24						15.00
...: Danse Macabre TPB (2010, $14.99) r/#15-18 & Suicide Squad #67 (Blackest Night)						15.00
...: Depths TPB (2010, $14.99) r/#8-14						15.00
...: The Reptile Brain TPB (2011, $14.99) r/#25-29						15.00
...: Unhinged TPB (2009, $14.99) r/#1-7; intro. by Paul Cornell						15.00

SECRET SIX
DC Comics: Feb, 2015 - No. 14, Jul, 2016 ($2.99)

	GD 2.0	VG 4.0	FN 6.0	VF 8.0	VF/NM 9.0	NM- 9.2
1-14: 1,2-Simone-s/Lashley-a; Catman & Black Alice app. 10-Superman app. 12-14-Shiva app.; Elongated Man returns						3.00

SECRET SOCIETY OF SUPER-VILLAINS
National Per. Publ./DC Comics: May-June, 1976 - No. 15, June-July, 1978

	GD 2.0	VG 4.0	FN 6.0	VF 8.0	VF/NM 9.0	NM- 9.2
1-Origin; JLA cameo & Capt. Cold app.	3	6	9	21	33	45
2-5,15: 2-Re-intro/origin Capt. Comet; Green Lantern x-over. 5-Green Lantern, Hawkman x-over; Darkseid app. 15-G.A. Atom, Dr. Midnite, & JSA app.	2	4	6	8	11	14
6-14: 9,10-Creeper x-over. 11-Capt. Comet; Orlando-i2	3	4	6	8	10	

SECRET SOCIETY OF SUPER-VILLAINS SPECIAL (See DC Special Series #6)

SECRETS OF HAUNTED HOUSE
National Periodical Publications/DC Comics: 4-5/75 - #5, 12-1/75-76; #6, 6-7/77 - #14, 10-11/78; #15, 8/79 - #46, 3/82

	GD 2.0	VG 4.0	FN 6.0	VF 8.0	VF/NM 9.0	NM- 9.2
1	5	10	15	34	60	85
2-4	3	6	9	19	30	40
5-Wrightson-c	4	8	12	23	37	50
6-14	2	4	6	11	16	20
15-30	2	4	6	8	11	14
31,44: 31-(12/80) Mr. E series begins (1st app.), ends #41. 44-Wrightson-c	2	4	6	9	13	16
32-(1/81) Origin of Mr. E	2	4	6	8	11	14
33-43,45,46: 34,35-Frankenstein Monster app.	1	3	4	6	8	10

NOTE: ***Aparo*** *c-7.* ***Aragones*** *a-1.* ***B. Bailey*** *a-8.* ***Bissette*** *a-46.* ***Buckler*** *c-32-40p.* ***Ditko*** *a-9, 12, 41, 45.* ***Golden*** *a-10.* ***Howard*** *a-13i.* ***Kaluta*** *c-8, 10, 11, 14, 16, 29.* ***Kubert*** *c-41, 42.* ***Sheldon Mayer*** *a-43p.* ***McWilliams*** *a-35.* ***Nasser*** *a-24.* ***Newton*** *a-30p.* ***Nino*** *a-1, 13, 19.* ***Orlando*** *c-13, 30, 43, 45i.* ***N. Redondo*** *a-4, 5, 29.* ***Rogers*** *c-26.* ***Spiegle*** *a-31-41.* ***Wrightson*** *c-5, 44.*

SECRETS OF HAUNTED HOUSE SPECIAL (See DC Special Series #12)

SECRETS OF LIFE (Movie)
Dell Publishing Co.: 1956 (Disney)

	GD 2.0	VG 4.0	FN 6.0	VF 8.0	VF/NM 9.0	NM- 9.2
Four Color 749-Photo-c	5	10	15	31	53	75

SECRETS OF LOVE (See Popular Teen-Agers...)

SECRETS OF LOVE AND MARRIAGE
Charlton Comics: V2#1, Aug, 1956 - V2#25, June, 1961

	GD 2.0	VG 4.0	FN 6.0	VF 8.0	VF/NM 9.0	NM- 9.2
V2#1-Matt Baker-c?	13	26	39	89	195	300
V2#2-6	5	10	15	31	53	75
V2#7-9-(All 68 pgs.)	7	14	21	46	86	125
10-25	4	8	12	28	47	65

SECRETS OF MAGIC (See Wisco)

Secret Origins #2 © DC

Secret Six #19 © DC

Secret X-Men #1 © MAR

	GD 2.0	VG 4.0	FN 6.0	VF 8.0	VF/NM 9.0	NM- 9.2

SECRETS OF SINISTER HOUSE (Sinister House of Secret Love #1-4)
National Periodical Publ.: No. 5, June-July, 1972 - No. 18, June-July, 1974

	GD	VG	FN	VF	VF/NM	NM-
5-(52 pgs.).	8	16	24	54	102	150
6-9: 7-Redondo-a	4	8	12	23	37	50
10-Neal Adams-a(i)	4	8	12	25	40	55
11-18: 15-Redondo-a. 17-Barry-a; early Chaykin 1 pg. strip	3	6	9	16	23	30

NOTE: ***Alcala** a-6, 13, 14. **Glanzman** a-7. **Kaluta** c-6, 7. **Nino** a-8, 11-13. Ambrose Bierce adapt.-#14.*

SECRETS OF SINISTER HOUSE
DC Comics: Dec, 2019 ($9.99, square-bound oneshot, 80 pgs.)

1-Short stories of horror by various incl. Dini, Hester, Layman, Raney; Romita Jr.-c 10.00

SECRETS OF THE LEGION OF SUPER-HEROES
DC Comics: Jan, 1981 - No. 3, Mar, 1981 (Limited series)

1-3: 1-Origin of the Legion. 2-Retells origins of Brainiac 5, Shrinking Violet, Sun-Boy, Bouncing Boy, Ultra-Boy, Matter-Eater Lad, Mon-El, Karate Kid & Dream Girl 5.00

SECRETS OF TRUE LOVE
St. John Publishing Co.: Feb, 1958

	GD	VG	FN	VF	VF/NM	NM-
1-Matt Baker-c	34	68	102	199	325	450

SECRETS OF YOUNG BRIDES
Charlton Comics: No. 5, Sept, 1957 - No. 44, Oct, 1964; July, 1975 - No. 9, Nov, 1976

	GD	VG	FN	VF	VF/NM	NM-
5	5	10	15	35	63	90
6-10: 8-Negligee panel	4	8	12	27	44	60
11-20	4	8	12	23	37	50
21-30: Last 10¢ issue?	3	6	9	21	33	45
31-44(10/64)	3	6	9	16	23	30
1-(2nd series) (7/75)	3	6	9	19	30	40
2-9	2	4	6	9	12	15

SECRET SQUIRREL (TV)(See Kite Fun Book)
Gold Key: Oct, 1966 (12¢) (Hanna-Barbera)

	GD	VG	FN	VF	VF/NM	NM-
1-1st Secret Squirrel and Morocco Mole, Squiddly Diddly, Winsome Witch	12	24	36	79	170	260

SECRET STORY ROMANCES (Becomes True Tales of Love)
Atlas Comics (TCI): Nov, 1953 - No. 21, Mar, 1956

	GD	VG	FN	VF	VF/NM	NM-
1-Everett-a; Jay Scott Pike-c	30	60	90	177	289	400
2	18	36	54	105	165	225
3-11: 11-Last pre-code (2/55)	15	30	45	88	137	185
12-21	14	28	42	80	115	150

NOTE: ***Colletta** a-10, 14, 15, 17, 21; c-10, 14, 17.*

SECRET VOICE, THE (See Great American Comics Presents...)

SECRET WAR
Marvel Comics: Apr, 2004 - No. 5, Dec, 2005 ($3.99, limited series)

1-Bendis-s/Dell'Otto painted-a/c; 6.00
1-2nd printing with gold logo on white cover and full-color Spider-Man 4.00
1-3rd printing with white cover and B&W sketched Spider-Man 4.00
2-Wolverine-c; intro. Daisy Johnson (Quake) 14.00
2-2nd printing with white cover and B&W sketched Wolverine 12.00
3-5: 3-Capt. America-c. 4-Black Widow-c. 5-Daredevil-c 4.00
... : From the Files of Nick Fury (2005, $3.99) Fury's journal entries; profiles of characters 4.00
HC (2005, $29.99, dust jacket) r/#1-5 & ...From the Files of Nick Fury; additional art 30.00
SC (2006, $24.99) r/#1-5 & ...From the Files of Nick Fury; additional art 25.00

SECRET WARPS (Characters merging within the Soul Stone)
Marvel Comics: Sept, 2019 ($4.99, weekly series of one-shots)

...: Arachknight Annual 1 - Part 4; Spider-Man/Moon Knight vs Supreme Seven 5.00
...: Ghost Panther Annual 1 - Part 3; Ghost Rider/Black Panther 5.00
...: Iron Hammer Annual 1 - Part 5; Iron Man/Thor 5.00
...: Soldier Supreme Annual 1 - Part 1; Captain America/Doctor Strange vs. Madame Hel 5.00
...: Weapon Hex Annual 1 - Part 2; X-23/Scarlet Witch 5.00

SECRET WARRIORS (Also see 2009 Dark Reign titles)
Marvel Comics: Apr, 2009 - No. 28, Sept, 2011 ($3.99/$2.99)

1-Bendis & Hickman-s/Caselli-a/Cheung-c; Nick Fury app.; Hydra dossier; sketch pages 4.00
2-24,26-28-($2.99) 8-Dark Avengers app. 17-19-Howling Commandos return 3.00
25-($3.99) Baron Strucker app.; Vitti-a 4.00

SECRET WARRIORS (Tie-in to Secret Empire)
Marvel Comics: Jul, 2017 - No. 12, Mar, 2018 ($3.99)

1-12: 1-Rosenberg-s/Garrón-a; Ms. Marvel, Moon Girl, Karnak app. 7-Deadpool app. 4.00

SECRET WARS
Marvel Comics: 2014 (Giveaway)

... No. 1 Halloween Comic Fest 2014 - Reprints Marvel Super Heroes Secret Wars #1 3.00

SECRET WARS (See Free Comic Book Day 2015 for prelude)
Marvel Comics: Jul, 2015 - No. 9, Mar, 2016 ($4.99/$3.99, limited series, originally planned as 8 issues)

1,2-($4.99) Hickman-s/Ribic-a; end of the Marvel 616 and Ultimate universes 5.00
3-8-($3.99): 3-Miles Morales app. 4.00
9-($4.99) End of Battleworld, beginning of the Prime Earth 5.00
...: Agents of Atlas (12/15, $4.99) Taylor-s/Pugh-a/Kirk-c; Baron Zemo app. 5.00
...: Official Guide to the Marvel Multiverse 1 (12/15, $4.99) Handbook-style info on characters, events and realities tied-in with the Secret Wars series 5.00
...: Secret Love 1 (10/15, $4.99) Romance stories by various; Ms. Marvel, Squirrel Girl, Daredevil, Ghost Rider, Iron Fist & Misty Knight app.; 2 covers 5.00
..., Too 1 (1/16, $4.99) Humor short stories by various incl. Powell, Guillory, Leth 5.00

SECRET WARS: BATTLEWORLD
Marvel Comics: Jul, 2015 - No. 4, Oct, 2015 ($3.99, limited series)

1-4-Short stories by various. 2-Howard the Duck app. 4-Silver Surfer app.; Francavilla-c 4.00

SECRET WARS: JOURNAL
Marvel Comics: Jul, 2015 - No. 5, Nov, 2015 ($3.99, limited series)

1-5-Short stories by various. 1-Leads into Siege #1. 3-Isanove-a. 4-Lashley-a 4.00

SECRET WARS 2099
Marvel Comics: Jul, 2015 - No. 5, Nov, 2015 ($3.99, limited series)

1-5-Peter David-s/Will Sliney-a; Avengers vs. Defenders; Baron Mordo app. 4.00

SECRET WARS II (Also see Marvel Super Heroes...)
Marvel Comics Group: July, 1985 - No. 9, Mar, 1986 (Maxi-series)

1,9: 9-(52 pgs.) X-Men app., Spider-Man app. 6.00
2-8: 2,8-X-Men app. 5-1st app. Boom Boom. 5,8-Spider-Man app. 4.00

SECRET WEAPONS
Valiant: Sept, 1993 - No. 21, May, 1995 ($2.25)

1-10,12-21: 3-Reese-a(i). 5-Ninjak app. 9-Bound-in trading card. 12-Bloodshot app. 4.00
11-(Sept. on envelope, Aug on-c, $2.50)-Enclosed in manilla envelope; Bloodshot app; intro new team. 5.00

SECRET WEAPONS
Valiant Entertainment: Jun, 2017 - No. 4, Sept, 2017 ($3.99)

1-4-Heisserer-s/Allén-a 4.00
#0-(1/18, $3.99) Heisserer-s/Pollina-a; origin of Nikki Finch 4.00
...: Owen's Story #0 (3/18, $3.99) Heisserer-s/Allén-a 4.00

SECRET X-MEN, THE
Marvel Comics: Apr, 2022 ($4.99, one-shot)

1-Howard-s/Mobili-a 5.00

SECTAURS
Marvel Comics: June, 1985 - No. 8, Sept, 1986 (75¢) (Based on Coleco Toys)

1-8, 1-Giveaway; same-c with "Coleco 1985 Toy Fair Collectors' Edition" 4.00

SECTION ZERO
Image Comics (Gorilla): June, 2000 - No. 3, Sept, 2000 ($2.50)

1-3-Kesel-s/Grummett-a 3.00

SECTION ZERO
Image Comics (Gorilla): Apr, 2019 - No. 6, Sept, 2019 ($3.99)

1-6-Kesel-s/Grummett-a; 3 covers on each 4.00

SEDUCTION OF THE INNOCENT (Also see New York State Joint Legislative Committee to Study...)
Rinehart & Co., Inc., N. Y.: 1953, 1954 (400 pgs.) (Hardback, $4.00)(Written by Fredric Wertham, M.D.)(Also printed in Canada by Clarke, Irwin & Co. Ltd.)

	GD	VG	FN	VF	VF/NM	NM-
(1st Version)-with bibliographical note intact (pages 399 & 400)(several copies got out before the comic publishers forced the removal of this page)	283	566	849	1217	1459	1700
Dust jacket only	45	90	135	284	467	675
(1st Version)-without bibliographical note	129	258	387	555	665	775
Dust jacket only	26	52	78	151	251	350
(2nd Version)-Published in England by Rinehart, 1954, 399 pgs. has bibliographical page; "Second print" listed on inside flap of the dust jacket; publication page has no "R" colophon; unlike 1st version	20	40	60	117	189	260
1972 r-/of 2nd version; 400 pgs. w/bibliography page; Kennikat Press	7	14	21	48	89	130
2004 r/with new intro. by Wertham scholar James E. Reibman, 424 pgs; 6" x 9"; limited to 220 copies	7	14	21	46	86	125

NOTE: *Material from this book appeared in the November, 1953 (Vol.70, pp50-53,214) issue of the **Ladies' Home Journal** under the title "What Parents Don't Know About Comic Books". With the release of this book, Dr. Wertham reveals seven years of research attempting to link juvenile delinquency to comic books. Many illustrations showing*

GD VG FN VF VF/NM NM-
2.0 4.0 6.0 8.0 9.0 9.2

*excessive violence, sex, sadism, and torture are shown. This book was used at the Kefauver Senate hearings which led to the Comics Code Authority. Because of the influence this book had on the comic industry and the collector's interest in it, we feel this listing is justified. Modern printings exist in limited editions. Also see **Parade of Pleasure.***

SEDUCTION OF THE INNOCENT! (Also see Halloween Horror)
Eclipse Comics: Nov, 1985 - 3-D#2, Apr, 1986 ($1.75)

1-6: Double listed under cover title from #7 on 1 2 3 5 6 8
3-D 1 (10/85, $2.25, 36 pgs.)-contains unpublished Advs. Into Darkness #15 (pre-code); Dave Stevens-c 2 4 6 11 16 20
2-D 1 (100 copy limited signed & #ed edition)(B&W) 4 8 12 27 44 60
3-D 2 (4/86)-Baker, Toth, Wrightson-c 1 2 3 5 6 8
2-D 2 (100 copy limited signed & #ed edition)(B&W) 3 6 9 19 30 40
NOTE: **Anderson** r-2, 3. **Crandall** c/a(r)-1. **Meskin** c/a(r)-3, 3-D 1. **Moreira** r-2. **Toth** a-1-6r; c-4r. **Tuska** r-6.

SEDUCTION OF THE INNOCENT
Dynamite Entertainment: 2015 - No. 4, 2016 ($3.99, limited series)

1-4-Ande Parks-s/Esteve Polls-a/Francesco Francavilla-c 4.00

SEEDS, THE
Dark Horse Comics (Berger Books): Aug, 2018 - No. 4 ($3.99, limited series)

1,2-Ann Nocenti-s/David Aja-a 4.00

SEEKERS INTO THE MYSTERY
DC Comics (Vertigo): Jan, 1996 - No. 15, Apr, 1997 ($2.50)

1-14: J.M. DeMatteis scripts in all. 1-4-Glenn Barr-a. 5,10-Muth-c/a. 6-9-Zulli-c/a. 11-14-Bolton-c; Jill Thompson-a 3.00
15-($2.95)-Muth-c/a 3.00

SEEKER 3000 (See Marvel Premiere #41)
Marvel Comics: Jun, 1998 - No. 4, Sept, 1998 ($2.99/$2.50, limited series)

1-($2.99)-Set 25 years after 1st app.; wraparound-c 4.00
2-4-($2.50) 3.00
...Premiere 1 (6/98, $1.50) Reprints 1st app. from Marvel Premiere #41; wraparound-c 3.00

SELECT DETECTIVE (Exciting New Mystery Cases)
D. S. Publishing Co.: Aug-Sept, 1948 - No. 3, Dec-Jan, 1948-49

1-Matt Baker-a 45 90 135 284 480 675
2-Baker, McWilliams-a 37 74 111 222 361 500
3 23 46 69 136 223 310

SELF / MADE
Image Comics: Dec, 2018 - No. 6, May, 2019 ($3.99)

1-6-Mat Groom-s/Eduardo Ferigato-a 4.00

SEMPER FI (Tales of the Marine Corp)
Marvel Comics: Dec, 1988- No. 9, Aug, 1989 (75¢)

1-9: Severin-c/a 4.00

SENSATIONAL POLICE CASES (Becomes Captain Steve Savage, 2nd Series)
Avon Periodicals: 1952; No. 2, 1954 - No. 4, July-Aug, 1954

nn-(1952, 25¢, 100 pgs.)-Kubert-a?; Check, Larsen, Lawrence & McCann-a; Kinstler-c 65 130 195 416 708 1000
2-4: 2-Kirbyish-a (3-4/54). 4-Reprint/Saint #5 24 48 72 144 237 330
I.W. Reprint #5-(1963?, nd)-Reprints Prison Break #5(1952-Realistic); Infantino-a 3 6 9 21 33 45

SENSATIONAL SHE-HULK, THE (She-Hulk #21-23) (See Savage She-Hulk)
Marvel Comics: V2#1, 5/89 - No. 60, Feb, 1994 ($1.50/$1.75, deluxe format)

V2#1-Byrne-c/a(p)/scripts begin, end #8 3 6 9 19 30 40
2,3: 3-Spider-Man app. 2 4 6 8 10 12
4-8,14-17,21-23: 4-Reintro G.A. Blonde Phantom. 14-17-Howard the Duck app. 21-23-Return of the Blonde Phantom. 22-All Winners Squad app. 6.00
9-13,18-20,24-33,35-38,41,42,44-49,55-60: 25-Thor app. 26-Excalibur app.; Guice-c. 29-Wolverine app. (3 pgs.). 30-Hobgoblin-c & cameo. 31-Byrne-c/a/scripts begin again. 35-Last $1.50-c. 37-Wolverine/Punisher/Spidey-c, but no app. 39-Thing app. 56-War Zone app.; Hulk cameo. 57-Vs. Hulk-c/story. 58-Electro-c/story. 59-Jack O'Lantern app. 5.00
34-Classic swimsuit/beachball-c by Byrne 5 10 15 31 53 75
39-Swimsuit-c 3 6 9 21 33 45
40-Classic CCA logo/jump rope-c by Byrne 10 20 30 69 147 225
43-Byrne Good Girl/purple bra-c 3 6 9 17 26 35
50-($2.95, 52 pgs.)-Embossed green foil-c; Byrne app.; last Byrne-c/a; Austin, Chaykin, Simonson-a; Miller-a(2 pgs.) 2 4 6 9 12 15
51-Pink elephants, cat fight-c 2 4 6 10 14 18
52-Death-c by Adam Hughes 3 6 9 16 23 30
53-Cover swipe of Amazing Spider-Man #39 2 4 6 11 16 20
54-Headlights-c 3 6 9 14 20 25
60-Last issue 5 10 15 30 50 70
NOTE: **Dale Keown** a(p)-13, 15-22.

SENSATIONAL SHE-HULK IN CEREMONY, THE
Marvel Comics: 1989 - No. 2, 1989 ($3.95, squarebound, 52 pgs.)

nn-Part 1, nn-Part 2 6.00

SENSATIONAL SPIDER-MAN
Marvel Comics: Apr, 1989 ($5.95, squarebound, 80 pgs.)

1-r/Amazing Spider-Man Annual #14,15 by Miller & Annual #8 by Kirby & Ditko 6.00

SENSATIONAL SPIDER-MAN, THE
Marvel Comics: Jan, 1996 - No. 33, Nov, 1998 ($1.95/$1.99)

0 ($4.95)-Lenticular-c; Jurgens-a/scripts 2 4 6 9 12 15
1 1 2 3 5 6 8
1-($2.95) variant-c; polybagged w/cassette 4 8 12 25 40 55
2-5: 2-Kaine & Rhino app. 3-Giant-Man app. 5.00
6-18: 9-Onslaught tie-in; revealed that Peter & Mary Jane's unborn baby is a girl. 11-Revelations. 13-15-Ka-Zar app. 14,15-Hulk app. 4.00
19-24: Living Pharoah app. 22,23-Dr. Strange app. 4.00
25-($2.99) Spiderhunt pt. 1; Normie Osborne kidnapped 5.00
25-Variant-c 1 2 3 5 6 8
26-33: 26-Nauck-a. 27-Double-c with "The Sensational Hornet #1"; Vulture app. 28-Hornet vs. Vulture. 29,30-Black Cat-c/app. 33-Last issue; Gathering of Five concludes 4.00
33.1, 33.2 (10/12, $2.99) DeFalco-s/Barberi-a/Bianchi-c 4.00
#(-1) Flashback(7/97) Dezago-s/Wieringo-a 4.00
'96 Annual ($2.95) 5.00

SENSATIONAL SPIDER-MAN, THE (Previously Marvel Knights Spider-Man #1-22)
Marvel Comics: No. 23, Apr, 2006 - No. 41, Dec, 2007 ($2.99)

23-40: 23-25-Aguirre-Sacasa-s/Medina-a. 23-Wraparound-c. 24,34,37-Black Cat app. 26-New costume. 28-Unmasked; Dr. Octopus app.; Crain-a. 35-Black costume resumes 3.00
41-($3.99) One More Day pt. 3; Straczynski-s/Quesada-a/c 4.00
... Annual 1 (2007, $3.99) Flashbacks of Peter & MJ's relationship; Larroca-a/Fraction-s 4.00
... Feral HC (2006, $19.99, dustjacket) r/#23-27; sketch pages 20.00
Civil War: Peter Parker, Spider-Man TPB (2007, $17.99) r/#28-34; Crain cover concepts 18.00
...: Self Improvement 1(10/19, $4.99) Unpublished story of Spidey's 1st black costume 5.00

SENSATIONAL WONDER WOMAN (Printing of a digital first series)
DC Comics: May, 2021 - No. 7, Nov, 2021 ($3.99, limited series)

1-7: 1-Doctor Psycho & Hawkgirl app. 3-Colleen Doran-s/a 4.00
... Special 1 (5/22, $9.99) Short stories by various 10.00

SENSATION COMICS (Sensation Mystery #110 on)
National Per. Publ./All-American: Jan, 1942 - No. 109, May-June, 1952

1-Origin Mr. Terrific (1st app.), Wildcat (1st app.), The Gay Ghost, & Little Boy Blue; Wonder Woman (cont'd from All Star #8), The Black Pirate begin; intro. Justice & Fair Play Club 14,400 28,800 43,200 96,000 168,000 240,000
1-Reprint, Oversize 13-1/2x10". WARNING: This comic is an exact duplicate reprint of the original except for its size. DC published it in 1974 with a second cover titling it as a Famous First Edition. There have been many reported cases of the outer cover being removed and the interior sold as the original edition. The reprint with the new outer cover removed is practically worthless. See Famous First Edition for value.
2-Etta Candy begins 946 1892 2838 6906 12,203 17,500
3-W. Woman gets secretary's job 508 1016 1524 3708 6554 9400
4-1st app. Stretch Skinner in Wildcat 326 652 978 2282 3991 5700
5-Intro. Justin, Black Pirate's son 300 600 900 1950 3375 4800
6-Origin/1st app. Wonder Woman's magic lasso 757 1514 2271 5526 9763 14,000
7-10 252 504 756 1613 2757 3900
11,12,14-20 174 348 522 1114 1907 2700
13-Hitler, Tojo, Mussolini-c (as bowling pins) 459 918 1377 3350 5925 8500
21-30: 22-Cheetah app. (2nd cover) 135 270 405 864 1482 2100
31-33 113 226 339 718 1234 1750
34-Sargon, the Sorcerer begins (10/44), ends #36; begins again #52 123 246 369 787 1344 1900
35-40: 36-2nd app. Giganta/1st cover; Cheetah app. 38-Christmas-c 110 220 330 704 1202 1700
41-50: 43-The Whip app. 100 200 300 635 1093 1550
51-60: 51-Last Black Pirate. 56,57-Sargon by Kubert 97 194 291 621 1061 1500
61-67,70-80: 63-Last Mr. Terrific. 66-Wildcat by Kubert 87 174 261 553 952 1350
68-Origin & 1st app. Huntress (8/47) 300 600 900 1950 3375 4800
69-2nd app. Huntress 97 194 291 621 1061 1500
81-Used in **SOTI**, pg. 33,34; Krigstein-a 100 200 300 635 1093 1550
82-93: 83-Last Sargon. 86-The Atom app. 90-Last Wildcat. 91-Streak begins by Alex Toth. 92-Toth-a (2 pgs.) 87 174 261 553 952 1350
94-1st all girl issue 148 296 444 947 1624 2300
95-99,101-106: 95-Unmasking of Wonder Woman-c/story. 99-1st app. Astra, Girl of the Future, ends #106. 103-Robot-c. 105-Last 52 pgs. 106-Wonder Woman ends 116 232 348 742 1271 1800
100-(11-12/50) 158 316 474 1003 1727 2450
107-(Scarce, 1-2/52)-1st mystery issue; Johnny Peril by Toth(p), 8 pgs. & begins; continues from Danger Trail #5 (3-4/51)(see Comic Cavalcade #15 for 1st app.) 123 246 369 787 1344 1900
108-(Scarce)-Johnny Peril by Toth(p) 110 220 330 704 1202 1700
109-(Scarce)-Johnny Peril by Toth(p) 116 232 348 742 1271 1800
NOTE: **Krigstein** a-(Wildcat)-81, 83, 84. **Moldoff** Black Pirate-1-25; Black Pirate not in 34-36, 43-48. **Oskner** c(i)-89-91, 94-106. Wonder Woman by **H. G. Peter**, all issues except #8, 17-19, 21; c-4-7, 9-18, 20-88, 92, 93. **Toth** a-91, 98; c-107. Wonder Woman c-1-106.

SENSATION COMICS (Also see All Star Comics 1999 crossover titles)
DC Comics: May, 1999 ($1.99, one-shot)

1-Golden Age Wonder Woman and Hawkgirl; Robinson-s 4.00

SENSATION COMICS FEATURING WONDER WOMAN
DC Comics: Oct, 2014 - No. 17, Feb, 2016 ($3.99, printing of digital-first comics)

1-17-Short story anthology. 1-Simone-s/Van Sciver-a. 2-Gene Ha-c. 5-Darkseid app. 8-Noelle Stevenson-a; Jae Lee-c. 10-Francavilla-c. 12-Poison Ivy app. 13-Superwoman app. 15-Garcia-López-a; Cheetah app.; McNeil-s/a. 16-Scott Hampton-a; Harley Quinn app. 4.00

SENSATION MYSTERY (Formerly Sensation Comics #1-109)
National Periodical Publ.: No. 110, July-Aug, 1952 - No. 116, July-Aug, 1953

110-Johnny Peril continues 77 154 231 493 847 1200
111-116-Johnny Peril in all. 116-M. Anderson-a 77 154 231 493 847 1200
NOTE: **M. Anderson** c-110. **Colan** a-114p. **Giunta** a-112. **G. Kane** c(p)-108, 109, 111-115.

SENSE & SENSABILITY
Marvel Comics: July, 2010 - No. 5, Nov, 2010 ($3.99, limited series)

1-5-Adaptation of the Jane Austen novel; Nancy Butler-s/Sonny Liew-a/c 4.00

SENTENCES: THE LIFE OF M.F. GRIMM
DC Comics (Vertigo): 2007 ($19.99, B&W graphic novel)

HC-Autobiography of Percy Carey (M.F. Grimm); Ronald Wimberly-a 20.00
SC (2008, $14.99) 15.00

SENTINEL
Marvel Comics: June, 2003 - No. 12, April, 2004 ($2.99/$2.50)

1-Sean McKeever-s/Udon Studios-a 3.00
2-12 3.00
Marvel Age Sentinel Vol. 1: Salvage (2004, $7.99, digest size) r/#1-6 8.00
Vol. 2: No Hero (2004, $7.99, digest size) r/#7-12; sketch pages 8.00

SENTINEL (2nd series)
Marvel Comics: Jan, 2006 - No. 5, May, 2006 ($2.99, limited series)

1-5-Sean McKeever-s/Joe Vriens-a 3.00
Vol. 3: Past Imperfect (2006, $7.99, digest size) r/#1-5 8.00

Sensational Spider-Man #8 © MAR

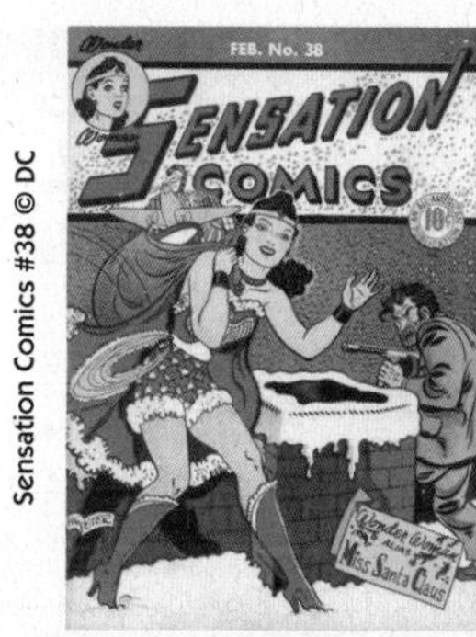

Sensation Comics #38 © DC

Serenity Better Days #1 © Universal

GD 2.0 | VG 4.0 | FN 6.0 | VF 8.0 | VF/NM 9.0 | NM- 9.2

SENTINELS OF JUSTICE, THE (See Americomics & Captain Paragon &...)

SENTINEL SQUAD O*N*E
Marvel Comics: Mar, 2006 - No. 5, July, 2006 ($2.99, limited series)
1-5-Lopresti-a/Layman-s 3.00
Decimation: Sentinel Squad O*N*E (2006, $13.99, TPB) r/series; sketch pg. by Caliafore 14.00

SENTRY (Also see New Avengers and Siege)
Marvel Comics: Sept, 2000 - No. 5, Jan, 2001 ($2.99, limited series)
1-5-Paul Jenkins-s/Jae Lee-a. 3-Spider-Man-c/app. 4-X-Men, FF app. 3.00
.../Fantastic Four (2/01, $2.99) Continues story from #5; Winslade-a 3.00
.../Hulk (2/01, $2.99) Sienkiewicz-c/a 3.00
.../Spider-Man (2/01, $2.99) back story of the Sentry; Leonardi-a 3.00
.../The Void (2/01, $2.99) Conclusion of story; Jae Lee-a 3.00
.../X-Men (2/01, $2.99) Sentry and Archangel; Texeira-a 3.00
TPB (10/01, $24.95) r/#1-5 & all one-shots; Stan Lee interview 25.00
TPB (2nd edition, 2005, $24.99) 25.00

SENTRY (Follows return in New Avengers #10)
Marvel Comics: Nov, 2005 - No. 8, Jun, 2006 ($2.99, limited series)
1-8-Paul Jenkins-s/John Romita Jr.-a. 1-New Avengers app. 3-Hulk app. 3.00
1-(Rough Cut) (12/05, $3.99) Romita sketch art and Jenkins script; cover sketches 4.00
...: Fallen Sun (7/10, $3.99) Siege epilogue; Jenkins-s/Raney-a/Yu-c 4.00
...: Reborn TPB (2006, $21.99) r/#1-8 22.00

SENTRY
Marvel Comics: Aug, 2018 - No. 5, Dec, 2018 ($3.99, limited series)
1-5: 1-Lemire-s/Jacinto-a/Hitch-c; Misty Knight app. 4.00

SEPTEMBER MOURNING
Image Comics (Top Cow): Feb, 2017 ($4.99)
1-Marc Silvestri-c; Lazar & McCourt-s 5.00

SERENITY (Based on 2005 movie Serenity and 2003 TV series Firefly)
Dark Horse Comics: July, 2005 - No. 3, Sept, 2005 ($2.99, limited series)
1-3: Whedon & Matthews-s/Conrad-a. Three covers for each issue by various 4.00
...: Float Out (6/10, $3.50) Story of Wash; Patton Oswalt-s; covers by Jo Chen & Stockton 3.50
...: One For One (9/10, $1.00) reprints #1, Cassaday-c with red cover frame 3.00
...: Those Left Behind HC (11/07, $19.95, dustjacket) r/series; intro. by Nathan Fillion; pre-production art for the movie; Hughes-c 20.00
...: Those Left Behind TPB (1/06, $9.95) r/series; intro. by Nathan Fillion; Hughes-c 10.00

SERENITY BETTER DAYS (Firefly)
Dark Horse Comics: Mar, 2008 - No. 3, May, 2008 ($2.99, limited series)
1-3: Whedon & Matthews-s/Conrad-a; Adam Hughes-c 3.00

SERENITY: FIREFLY CLASS 03-K64 - LEAVES ON THE WIND (Follows movie)
Dark Horse Comics: Jan, 2014 - No. 6, Jun, 2014 ($3.50, limited series)
1-6: Zack Whedon-s/Georges Jeanty-a; covers by Dos Santos & Jeanty 3.50

SERENITY: FIREFLY CLASS 03-K64 - NO POWER IN THE 'VERSE (Follows movie)
Dark Horse Comics: Oct, 2016 - No. 6, Mar, 2017 ($3.99, limited series)
1-6: Chris Roberson-s/Georges Jeanty-a; covers by Dos Santos & Jeanty 4.00

SERGEANT BARNEY BARKER (Becomes G. I. Tales #4 on)
Atlas Comics (MCI): Aug, 1956 - No. 3, Dec, 1956

	GD 2.0	VG 4.0	FN 6.0	VF 8.0	VF/NM 9.0	NM- 9.2
1-Severin-c/a(4)	32	46	69	188	307	425
2,3: 2-Severin-c/a(4). 3-Severin-c/a(5)	20	40	60	114	182	250

SERGEANT BILKO (Phil Silvers Starring as...) (TV)
National Periodical Publications: May-June, 1957 - No. 18, Mar-Apr, 1960

	GD 2.0	VG 4.0	FN 6.0	VF 8.0	VF/NM 9.0	NM- 9.2
1-All have Bob Oskner-c	65	130	195	416	708	1000
2	35	70	105	208	339	470
3-5	29	58	87	172	281	390
6-18: 11,12,15-17-Photo-c	22	44	66	132	216	300

SGT. BILKO'S PVT. DOBERMAN (TV)
National Periodical Publications: June-July, 1958 - No. 11, Feb-Mar, 1960

	GD 2.0	VG 4.0	FN 6.0	VF 8.0	VF/NM 9.0	NM- 9.2
1-Bob Oskner c-1-4,7,11	27	54	81	189	420	650
2	13	26	39	86	188	290
3-5: 5-Photo-c	19	18	27	60	120	180
6-11: 6,9-Photo-c	7	14	21	44	82	120

SGT. DICK CARTER OF THE U.S. BORDER PATROL (See Holyoke One-Shot)

SGT. FURY (& His Howling Commandos)(See Fury & Special Marvel Edition)
Marvel Comics Group (BPC earlier issues): May, 1963 - No. 167, Dec, 1981

	GD 2.0	VG 4.0	FN 6.0	VF 8.0	VF/NM 9.0	NM- 9.2
1-1st app. Sgt. Nick Fury (becomes agent of Shield in Strange Tales #135); Kirby/Ayers-c/a; 1st Dum-Dum Dugan & the Howlers	1025	2050	3075	8700	19,850	31,000
2-Kirby-a	68	136	204	544	1222	1900
3-5: 3-Reed Richards x-over. 4-Death of Junior Juniper. 5-1st Baron Strucker app.; Kirby-a	32	64	96	230	515	800
6-10: 8-Baron Zemo, 1st Percival Pinkerton app. 9-Hitler-c & app. 10-1st app. Capt. Savage (the Skipper)(9/64)	17	34	51	117	259	400
11,12,14-20: 14-1st Blitz Squad. 18-Death of Pamela Hawley	9	18	27	63	129	195
13-Captain America & Bucky app.(12/64); 2nd solo Capt. America x-over outside The Avengers; Kirby-a	54	108	162	432	966	1500
13-2nd printing (1994)	3	6	9	17	26	35
21-24,26,28-30	6	12	18	40	73	105
25,27: 25-Red Skull app. 27-1st app. Eric Koenig; origin Fury's eye patch	7	14	21	49	92	135
31-33,35-50: 35-Eric Koenig joins Howlers. 43-Bob Hope, Glen Miller app. 44-Flashback on Howlers' 1st mission	4	8	12	27	44	60
34-Origin Howling Commandos	6	12	18	37	66	95
51-60	4	8	12	23	37	50
61-67: 64-Capt. Savage & Raiders x-over; peace symbol-c. 67-Last 12¢ issue; flag-c	3	6	9	19	30	40
68-80: 76-Fury's Father app. in WWI story	3	6	9	16	24	32
81-91: 91-Last 15¢ issue	3	6	9	14	20	26
92-(52 pgs.)	3	6	9	16	24	32
93-99: 98-Deadly Dozen x-over	3	6	9	14	19	24
100-Capt. America, Fantastic 4 cameos; Stan Lee, Martin Goodman & others app.	3	6	9	21	33	45
101-120: 101-Origin retold	2	4	6	10	14	18
121-130: 121-123-r/#19-21	2	4	6	8	11	14
131-167: 167-Reprints (from 1963)	2	4	6	8	10	12
133,134-(30¢-c variants, limited dist.)(5,7/76)	9	18	27	62	126	190
141,142-(35¢-c variants, limited dist.)(7,9/77)	23	46	69	161	356	550
Annual 1(1965, 25¢, 72 pgs.)-r/#4,5 & new-a	14	28	42	93	204	315
Special 2(1966)	7	14	21	46	86	125
Special 3(1967) All new material	5	10	15	30	50	70
Special 4(1968)	3	6	9	21	33	45
Special 5-7(1969-11/71)	3	6	9	17	26	35

NOTE: ***Ayers** a-8, Annual 1. **Ditko** a-15i. **Gil Kane** c-37, 96. **Kirby** a-1-7, 13p, 167p(r). Special 5; c-1-8, 10-20, 25, 167p. **Severin** a-44-46, 48, 162, 164; inks-49-79, Special 4, 6; c-4i, 5, 6, 44, 46, 110, 149i, 155i, 162-166. **Sutton** a-57p. Reprints in #80, 82, 85, 87, 89, 91, 93, 95, 99, 101, 103, 105, 107, 109, 111, 121-123, 145-155, 167.*

SGT. FURY AND HIS HOWLING COMMANDOS
Marvel Comics: July, 2009 ($3.99, one-shot)
1-John Paul Leon-a/c; WWII tale set in 1942; Baron Strucker app. 4.00

SGT. FURY AND HIS HOWLING DEFENDERS (See The Defenders #147)

SERGEANT PRESTON OF THE YUKON (TV)
Dell Publishing Co.: No. 344, Aug, 1951 - No. 29, Nov-Jan, 1958-59

	GD 2.0	VG 4.0	FN 6.0	VF 8.0	VF/NM 9.0	NM- 9.2
Four Color 344(#1)-Sergeant Preston & his dog Yukon King begin; painted-c begin, end #18	14	28	42	94	207	320
Four Color 373,397,419('52)	9	18	27	58	114	170
5(11-1/52-53)-10(2-4/54): 6-Bondage-c.	6	12	18	38	69	100
11,12,14-17	5	10	15	34	60	85
13-Origin Sgt. Preston	6	12	18	37	66	95
18-Origin Yukon King; last painted-c	6	12	18	37	66	95
19-29: All photo-c	6	12	18	41	76	110

SGT. ROCK (Formerly Our Army at War; see Brave & the Bold #52 & Showcase #45)
National Periodical Publications/DC Comics: No. 302, Mar, 1977 - No. 422, July, 1988

	GD 2.0	VG 4.0	FN 6.0	VF 8.0	VF/NM 9.0	NM- 9.2
302	5	10	15	31	53	75
303-310	3	6	9	17	25	34
311-320: 318-Reprints	2	4	6	10	16	20
321-350	2	4	6	8	11	14
329-Whitman variant	3	6	9	14	19	24
351-399,401-421: 412-Mlle Marie & Haunted Tank	1	2	3	5	7	9
400-(6/85) Anniversary issue	2	4	6	8	11	14
422-1st Joe, Adam, Andy Kubert-a team; last issue	2	4	6	11	16	20
Annual 2-4: 2(1982)-Formerly Sgt. Rock's Prize Battle Tales #1. 3(1983). 4(1984)	2	4	6	8	11	14

NOTE: ***Estrada** a-322, 327, 331, 336, 337, 341, 342i. **Glanzman** a-384, 421. **Kubert** a-302, 303, 305r, 306, 328, 351, 356, 368, 373, 422; c-317, 318r, 319-323, 325-333-on, Annual 2, 3. **Severin** a-347. **Spiegle** a-382, Annual 2, 3. **Thorne** a-384. **Toth** a-385r. **Wildey** a-307, 311, 313, 314.*

SGT. ROCK: BETWEEN HELL AND A HARD PLACE
DC Comics (Vertigo): 2003 ($24.95, hardcover one-shot)
HC-Joe Kubert-a/c; Brian Azzarello-s 25.00
SC (2004, $17.95) 18.00

SGT. ROCK'S COMBAT TALES
DC Comics: 2005 ($9.99, digest)

	GD 2.0	VG 4.0	FN 6.0	VF 8.0	VF/NM 9.0	NM- 9.2

Vol. 1-Reprints early app. in Our Army at War, G.I. Combat, Star Spangled War Stories 10.00

SGT. ROCK SPECIAL (Sgt. Rock #14 on; see DC Special Series #3)
DC Comics: Oct, 1988 - No. 21, Feb, 1992; No. 1, 1992; No. 2, 1994 ($2.00, quarterly/monthly, 52 pgs)

1-Reprint begin 2 4 6 8 11 14
2-21: All-r; 5-r/early Sgt. Rock/Our Army at War #81. 7-Tomahawk-r by Thorne. 9-Enemy Ace-r by Kubert. 10-All Rock issue. 11-r/1st Haunted Tank story. 12-All Kubert issue; begins monthly. 13-Dinosaur story by Heath(r). 14-Enemy Ace-r (22 pgs.) by Adams/Kubert. 15-Enemy Ace (22 pgs.) by Kubert. 16-Iron Major-c/story. 16,17-Enemy Ace-r. 19-r/Batman/Sgt. Rock team-up/B&B #108 by Aparo 1 2 3 5 6 8
1 (1992, $2.95, 68 pgs.)-Simonson-c; unpubbed Kubert-a; Glanzman, Russell, Pratt, & Wagner-a 6.00
2 (1994, $2.95) Brereton painted-c 4.00
NOTE: ***Neal Adams*** *r-1, 8, 14p.* ***Chaykin*** *a-2; r-3, 9(2pgs.); c-3.* ***Drucker*** *r-6.* ***Glanzman*** *r-20.* ***Golden*** *a-1.* ***Heath*** *a-2; r-5, 9-13, 16, 19, 21.* ***Krigstein*** *r-4, 8.* ***Kubert*** *r-1-17, 20, 21; c-1p, 2, 8, 14-21.* ***Miller*** *r-6p.* ***Severin*** *r-3, 6, 10.* ***Simonson*** *r-2, 4; c-4.* ***Thorne*** *r-7.* ***Toth*** *r-2, 8, 11.* ***Wood*** *r-4.*

SGT. ROCK SPECTACULAR (See DC Special Series #13)

SGT. ROCK'S PRIZE BATTLE TALES (Becomes Sgt. Rock Annual #2 on; see DC Special Series #18 & 80 Page Giant #7)
National Periodical Publications: Winter, 1964 (Giant - 80 pgs., one-shot)

1-Kubert, Heath-r; new Kubert-c 36 72 108 259 580 900
... Replica Edition (2000, $5.95) Reprints entire issue 6.00

SGT. ROCK: THE LOST BATTALION
DC Comics: Jan, 2009 - No. 6, Jun, 2009 ($2.99, limited series)

1-6-Billy Tucci-s/a. 1-Tucci & Sparacio-c 3.00
HC (2009, $24.99, d.j.) r/#1-6; production art; cover art gallery 25.00
SC (2010, $17.99) r/#1-6; production art; cover art gallery 18.00

SGT. ROCK: THE PROPHECY
DC Comics: Mar, 2006 - No. 6, Aug, 2006 ($2.99, limited series)

1-6-Joe Kubert-s/a/c. 1-Variant covers by Andy and Adam Kubert 3.00
TPB (2007, $17.99) r/#1-6 18.00

SGT. ROCK VS. THE ARMY OF THE DEAD (See DC Horror Presents:...)

SGT. STRYKER'S DEATH SQUAD (See Savage Combat Tales)

SERGIO ARAGONÉS' ACTIONS SPEAK
Dark Horse Comics: Jan, 2001 - No. 6, Jun, 2001 ($2.99, B&W, limited series)

1-6-Aragonés-c/a; wordless one-page cartoons 3.00

SERGIO ARAGONÉS' BLAIR WHICH?
Dark Horse Comics: Dec, 1999 ($2.95, B&W, one-shot)

nn-Aragonés-c/a; Evanier-s. Parody of "Blair Witch Project" movie 4.00

SERGIO ARAGONÉS' BOOGEYMAN
Dark Horse Comics: June, 1998 - No. 4, Sept, 1998 ($2.95, B&W, lim. series)

1-4-Aragonés-c/a 4.00

SERGIO ARAGONÉS DESTROYS DC
DC Comics: June, 1996 ($3.50, one-shot)

1-DC Superhero parody book; Aragonés-c/a; Evanier scripts 4.00

SERGIO ARAGONÉS' DIA DE LOS MUERTOS
Dark Horse Comics: Oct, 1998 ($2.95, one-shot)

1-Aragonés-c/a; Evanier scripts 4.00

SERGIO ARAGONÉS FUNNIES
Bongo Comics: 2011 - No. 12, 2014 ($3.50)

1-12-Color and B&W humor strips by Aragonés 3.50

SERGIO ARAGONÉS' GROO & RUFFERTO
Dark Horse Comics: Dec, 1998 - No. 4, Mar, 1999 ($2.95, lim. series)

1-3-Aragonés-c/a 4.00

SERGIO ARAGONÉS' GROO: DEATH AND TAXES
Dark Horse Comics: Dec, 2001 - No. 4, Apr, 2002 ($2.99, lim. series)

1-4-Aragonés-c/a; Evanier-s 3.00

SERGIO ARAGONÉS' GROO: HELL ON EARTH
Dark Horse Comics: Nov, 2007 - No. 4, Apr, 2008 ($2.99, lim. series)

1-4-Aragonés-c/a; Evanier-s 3.00

SERGIO ARAGONÉS' GROO: MIGHTIER THAN THE SWORD
Dark Horse Comics: Jan, 2000 - No. 4, Apr, 2000 ($2.95, lim. series)

1-4-Aragonés-c/a; Evanier-s 3.00

SERGIO ARAGONÉS' GROO: THE HOGS OF HORDER
Dark Horse Comics: Oct, 2009 - No. 4, Mar, 2010 ($3.99, lim. series)

1-4-Aragonés-c/a; Evanier-s 4.00

SERGIO ARAGONÉS' GROO THE WANDERER (See Groo...)

SERGIO ARAGONÉS' GROO: 25TH ANNIVERSARY SPECIAL
Dark Horse Comics: Aug, 2007 ($5.99, one-shot)

nn-Aragonés-c/a; Evanier scripts; wraparound cover 6.00

SERGIO ARAGONÉS' LOUDER THAN WORDS
Dark Horse Comics: July, 1997 - No. 6, Dec, 1997 ($2.95, B&W, limited series)

1-6-Aragonés-c/a 4.00

SERGIO ARAGONÉS MASSACRES MARVEL
Marvel Comics: June, 1996 ($3.50, one-shot)

1-Marvel Superhero parody book; Aragonés-c/a; Evanier scripts 4.00

SERGIO ARAGONÉS STOMPS STAR WARS
Marvel Comics: Jan, 2000 ($2.95, one-shot)

1-Star Wars parody; Aragonés-c/a; Evanier scripts 4.00

SERIAL (See Rachel Rising and Five Years)
Abstract Studios: 2021 - No. 10, 2021 ($3.99)

1-10-Zoe from Rachel Rising app.; Terry Moore-s/a/c 4.00

SESAME STREET
Ape Entertainment: 2013 ($3.99)

1-Short stories by various; multiple covers 4.00
Free Comic Book Day edition (2013) Flip book with Strawberry Shortcake 3.00

SEVEN
Intrinsic Comics: July, 2007 ($3.00)

1-Jim Shooter-s/Paul Creddick-a 3.00

SEVEN BLOCK
Marvel Comics (Epic Comics): 1990 ($4.50, one-shot, 52 pgs.)

1-Dixon-s/Zaffino-a 6.00
nn-(IDW Publ., 2004, $5.99) reprints #1 6.00

SEVEN BROTHERS (John Woo's...)
Virgin Comics: Oct, 2006 - No. 5, Feb, 2007 ($2.99)

1-5-Garth Ennis-s/Jeevan Kang-a. 1-Two covers by Amano & Horn. 2-Kang var-c 3.00
TPB (6/07, $14.99) r/#1-5; cover gallery, deleted scenes and concept art 15.00
Volume 2 (9/07 - No. 5, 2/08) 1-Edison George-a. 4,5-David Mack-c 3.00

SEVEN DEAD MEN (See Complete Mystery #1)

SEVEN DWARFS (Also see Snow White)
Dell Publishing Co.: No. 227, 1949 (Disney-Movie)

Four Color 227 13 26 39 89 195 300

SEVEN MILES A SECOND
DC Comics (Vertigo Verité): 1996 ($7.95, one-shot)

nn-Wojnarowicz-s/Romberg-a 8.00

SEVEN-PER-CENT SOLUTION
IDW Publishing: Aug, 2015 - No. 5 ($3.99)

1-4-Sherlock Holmes/Sigmund Freud team-up; David & Scott Tipton-s/Joseph-a/Jones-c 4.00

SEVEN SAMUROID, THE (See Image Graphic Novel)

SEVEN SEAS COMICS
Universal Phoenix Features/Leader No. 6: Apr, 1946 - No. 6, 1947(no month)

1-South Sea Girl by Matt Baker, Capt. Cutlass begin; Tugboat Tessie by Baker app. 103 206 309 659 1130 1600
2-Swashbuckler-c 74 148 222 470 810 1150
3-Six pg. Feldstein-a 400 800 1200 2800 4900 7000
4-Classic Baker-c 975 1950 2919 7100 12,550 18,000
5-Baker Headlights Good Girl-c 290 580 870 1856 3178 4500
6-Baker Good Girl-c 649 1298 1947 4738 8369 12,000
NOTE: ***Baker*** *a-1-6; c-3-6.*

SEVEN SECRETS
BOOM! Studios: Aug, 2020 - No. 18, Jun, 2022 ($3.99)

1-18-Tom Taylor-s/Danielle Di Nicuolo-a 4.00

SEVEN SOLDIERS OF VICTORY (Book-ends for seven related mini-series)
DC Comics: No. 0, Apr, 2005; No. 1; Dec, 2006 ($2.95/$3.99)

0-Grant Morrison-s/J.H. Williams-a 3.00
1-($3.99) Series conclusion; Grant Morrison-s/J.H. Williams-a 4.00
... Volume One (2006, $14.99) r/#0, Shining Knight #1,2; Zatanna #1,2; Guardian #1,2; and Klarion the Witch Boy #1; intro. by Morrison; character design sketches 15.00
... Volume Two (2006, $14.99) r/Shining Knight #3,4; Zatanna #3; Guardian #3,4; and Klarion the Witch Boy #2,3 15.00
... Volume Three ('06, $14.99) r/Zatanna #4; Mister Miracle #1,2; Bulleteer #1,2; Frankenstein #1 and Klarion the Witch Boy #4; 15.00
... Volume Four ('07, $14.99) r/Mister Miracle #3,4; Bulleteer #3,4; Frankenstein #2-4 and Seven Soldiers of Victory #1; script pages 15.00

SEVEN SOLDIERS: BULLETEER
DC Comics: Jan, 2006 - No. 4, May, 2006 ($2.99, limited series)

1-4-Grant Morrison-s/Yanick Paquette-a/c 3.00

SEVEN SOLDIERS: FRANKENSTEIN
DC Comics: Jan, 2006 - No. 4, May, 2006 ($2.99, limited series)

1-4-Grant Morrison-s/Doug Mahnke-a/c 3.00

SEVEN SOLDIERS: GUARDIAN
DC Comics: May, 2005 - No. 4, Nov, 2005 ($2.99, limited series)

1-4-Grant Morrison-s/Cameron Stewart-a; Newsboy Army app. 3.00

SEVEN SOLDIERS: KLARION THE WITCH BOY
DC Comics: Jun, 2005 - No. 4, Dec, 2005 ($2.99, limited series)

1-4-Grant Morrison-s/Frazer Irving-a 3.00

SEVEN SOLDIERS: MISTER MIRACLE
DC Comics: Nov, 2005 - No. 4, May, 2006 ($2.99, limited series)

1-4: 1-Grant Morrison-s/Pasqual Ferry-a/c. 3,4-Freddie Williams II-a/c 3.00

SEVEN SOLDIERS: SHINING KNIGHT
DC Comics: May, 2005 - No. 4, Oct, 2005 ($2.99, limited series)

1-4-Grant Morrison-s/Simone Bianchi-a 3.00

SEVEN SOLDIERS: ZATANNA
DC Comics: Jun, 2005 - No. 4, Dec, 2005 ($2.99, limited series)

1-4-Grant Morrison-s/Ryan Sook-a 3.00

SEVEN SONS
Image Comics: Jun, 2022 - No. 7, Dec, 2022 ($3.99, limited series)

1-7-Robert Windom & Kelvin Mao-s/Jae Lee-a/c 4.00

SEVEN SWORDS
AfterShock Comics: Jun, 2021 - No. 5, Jan, 2022 ($4.99/$3.99, limited series)

1-($4.99) Evan Daugherty-s/Riccardo Latina-a; D'Artagnan & Cardinal Richelieu app. 5.00
2-5-($3.99) 4.00

1776 (See Charlton Classic Library)

7TH SWORD, THE
IDW Publishing (Darby Pop): Apr, 2014 - No. 6 ($3.99)

Sergio Aragonés Funnies #1 © Sergio Aragonés

Sex Criminals #30 © Milkfed & Zdarsco

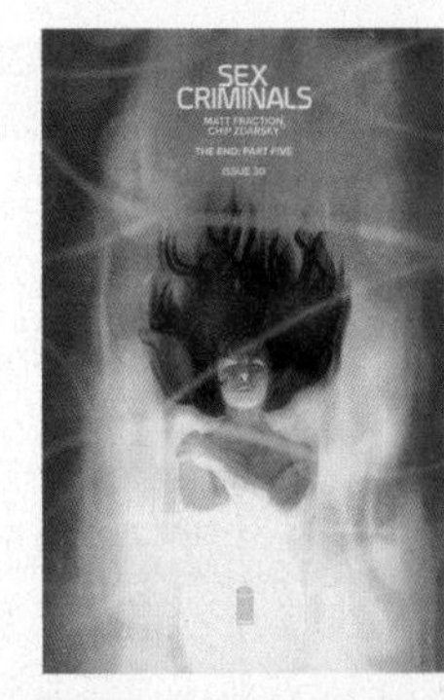

The Shadow (2013) #9 © AMP

	GD 2.0	VG 4.0	FN 6.0	VF 8.0	VF/NM 9.0	NM- 9.2
1-6: 1-John Raffo-s/Nelson Blake II-a. 3-6-Nur Iman-a						4.00

7TH VOYAGE OF SINBAD, THE (Movie)
Dell Publishing Co.: Sept, 1958 (photo-c)

Four Color 944-Buscema-a 12 24 36 81 176 270

SEVEN TO ETERNITY
Image Comics: Sept, 2016 - No. 17, Aug, 2021 ($3.99)

1-Rick Remender-s/Jerome Opeña-a 3 6 9 14 20 25
2 1 3 4 6 8 10
3-17: 7,8-James Harren-a 4.00

77 SUNSET STRIP (TV)
Dell Publ. Co./Gold Key: No. 1066, Jan-Mar, 1960 - No. 2, Feb, 1963
(All photo-c)

Four Color 1066-Toth-a 9 18 27 63 129 195
Four Color 1106,1159-Toth-a 7 14 21 49 92 135
Four Color 1211,1263,1291, 01-742-209(7-9/62)-Manning-a in all
7 14 21 46 86 125
1,2: Manning-a. 1(11/62-G.K.) 7 14 21 46 86 125

77TH BENGAL LANCERS, THE (TV)
Dell Publishing Co.: May, 1957

Four Color 791-Photo-c 7 14 21 44 82 120

SEVERED
Image Comics: Aug, 2011 - No. 7, Feb, 2012 ($2.99)

1-7-Scott Snyder & Scott Tuft-s/Attila Futaki-a/c 3.00

SEX
Image Comics: Mar, 2013 - No. 34, Dec, 2016 ($2.99/$3.99)

1-26-Joe Casey-s/Piotr Kowalski-a/c 3.00
27-34-($3.99) 4.00

SEX CRIMINALS
Image Comics: Sept, 2013 - No. 30, Aug, 2020; No. 69, Oct, 2020 ($3.50/$3.99)

1-Matt Fraction-s/Chip Zdarsky-a/c 3 6 9 16 24 32
1-Variant-c by Shimizu 3 6 9 14 20 25
2 1 3 4 6 8 10
3-10 5.00
11-24,26-30 4.00
11-24,26-30,69-($4.69) Variant cover in pink polybag 5.00
25-($4.99) 5.00
25-($5.69) Variant cover by Skottie Young, in pink polybag 6.00
69-($3.99) Final issue; numbering skips from 30 to 69 4.00
...: Sexual Gary Special (9/20, $4.99) Matt Fraction-s/Rachael Stott-a 5.00

SEYMOUR, MY SON (See More Seymour)
Archie Publications (Radio Comics): Sept, 1963

1-DeCarlo-c/a 5 10 15 33 57 80

SFSX
Image Comics: Sept, 2019 - Present ($3.99)

1-7-Tina Horn-s. 1,2,4-Michael Dowling-a. 6,7-Jen Hickman-a 4.00

SHADE, THE (See Starman)
DC Comics: Apr, 1997 - No. 4, July, 1997 ($2.25, limited series)

1-4-Robinson-s/Harris-c: 1-Gene Ha-a. 2-Williams/Gray-a 3-Blevins-a. 4-Zulli-a 3.00

SHADE, THE (From Starman)
DC Comics: Dec, 2011 - No. 12, Nov, 2012 ($2.99, limited series)

1-12: 1-Robinson-s/Hamner-a/Harris-c; Deathstroke app. 4-Cooke-a. 8-Thompson-a
12-Origin of the Shade; Gene Ha-a 3.00
1-12-Variant covers. 1-3-Hamner. 4-Darwyn Cooke. 5-7-Pulido. 11-Irving 4.00

SHADECRAFT
Image Comics: Mar, 2021 - Present ($3.99)

1-5-Joe Henderson-s/Lee Garbett-a 4.00

SHADE, THE CHANGING GIRL (Continues as Shade, The Changing Woman)
DC Comics (Young Animal): Dec, 2016 - No. 12, Nov, 2017 ($3.99)

1-12: 1-Castellucci-s/Zarcone-a; intro. Megan Boyer/Loma Shade. 4-Element Girl back-up.
7-Sauvage-a 4.00
.../ Wonder Woman Special 1 (4/18, $4.99) Part 3 of Milk Wars crossover; Quitely-c 5.00

SHADE, THE CHANGING MAN (See Cancelled Comic Cavalcade)
National Per. Publ./DC Comics: June-July, 1977 - No. 8, Aug-Sept, 1978

1-1st app. Shade; Ditko-c/a in all 3 6 9 17 25 34
2-8 2 3 4 6 8 10

	GD 2.0	VG 4.0	FN 6.0	VF 8.0	VF/NM 9.0	NM- 9.2

SHADE, THE CHANGING MAN (2nd series) (Also see Suicide Squad #16)
DC Comics (Vertigo imprint #33 on): July, 1990 - No. 70, Apr, 1996 ($1.50-$2.25, mature)

1-($2.50, 52 pgs.)-Peter Milligan scripts in all 4.00
2-41,45-49,51-59: 6-Preview of World Without End. 17-Begin $1.75-c. 33-Metallic ink on-c.
41-Begin $1.95-c 3.00
42-44-John Constantine app. 3.50
50-($2.95, 52 pgs.) 4.00
60-70: 60-begin $2.25-c 3.00
...: Edge of Vision TPB (2009, $19.99) r/#7-13 20.00
...: Scream Time TPB (2010, $19.99) r/#14-19 20.00
...: The American Scream TPB (2003, 2009, $17.95/$17.99) r/#1-6 18.00
NOTE: *Bachalo a-1-9, 11-13, 15-21, 23-26, 33-39, 42-45, 47, 49, 50; c-30, 33-41.*

SHADE, THE CHANGING WOMAN (Continues from Shade, The Changing Girl)
DC Comics (Young Animal): May, 2018 - No. 6, Oct, 2018 ($3.99)

1-6-Castellucci-s/Zarcone-a 4.00

SHADO: SONG OF THE DRAGON (See Green Arrow #63-66)
DC Comics: 1992 - No. 4, 1992 ($4.95, limited series, 52 pgs.)

Book One - Four: Grell scripts; Morrow-a(i) 6.00

SHADOW, THE (See Batman #253, 259 & Marvel Graphic Novel #35)

SHADOW, THE (Pulp, radio)
Archie Comics (Radio Comics): Aug, 1964 - No. 8, Sept, 1965 (All 12¢)

1-Jerry Siegel scripts in all; Shadow-c. 9 18 27 61 123 185
2-8: 2-App. in super-hero costume on-c only; Reinman-a(backup). 3-Superhero begins;
Reinman-a (book-length novel). 3,4,6,7-The Fly 1 pg. strips. 4-8-Reinman-a. 5-8-Siegel
scripts. 7-Shield app. 5 10 15 34 60 85

SHADOW, THE
National Periodical Publications: Oct-Nov, 1973 - No. 12, Aug-Sept, 1975

1-Kaluta-a begins 6 12 18 38 69 100
2 3 6 9 21 33 45
3-Kaluta/Wrightson-a 4 8 12 23 37 50
4,6-Kaluta-a ends. 4-Chaykin, Wrightson part-i 3 6 9 18 28 38
5,7-12: 11-The Avenger (pulp character) x-over 2 4 6 13 18 22
NOTE: *Craig a-10. Cruz a-10-12. Kaluta a-1, 2, 3p, 4, 6; c-1-4, 6, 10-12. Kubert c-9. Robbins a-5, 7-9; c-5, 7, 8.*

SHADOW, THE
DC Comics: May, 1986 - No. 4, Aug, 1986 (limited series)

1-4: Howard Chaykin art in all 4.00
Blood & Judgement ($12.95)-r/1-4 13.00

SHADOW, THE
DC Comics: Aug, 1987 - No. 19, Jan, 1989 ($1.50)

1-19: Andrew Helfer scripts in all. 4.00
Annual 1,2 (12/87, '88,)-2-The Shadow dies; origin retold (story inspired by the movie
"Citizen Kane"). 5.00
NOTE: *Kyle Baker a-7i, 8-19, Annual 2. Chaykin c-Annual 1. Helfer scripts in all. Orlando a-Annual 1. Rogers c/a-7. Sienkiewicz c/a-1-6.*

SHADOW, THE (Movie)
Dark Horse Comics: June, 1994 - No. 2, July, 1994 ($2.50, limited series)

1,2-Adaptation from Universal Pictures film 4.00
NOTE: *Kaluta c/a-1, 2.*

SHADOW, THE
Dynamite Entertainment: 2012 - No. 25, 2014 ($3.99)

1-25: 1-Ennis-s/Campbell-a; multiple covers on all. 7-10-Gischler-s 4.00
#0-(2014, $3.99) Cullen Bunn-s/Colton Worley-a/Gabriel Hardman-c 4.00
#100-(2014, $7.99, squarebound) Short stories by various incl. Francavilla, Chaykin, Wagner,
Uslan; 2 covers by Wagner & Hack 8.00
Annual 1 (2012, $4.99) Sniegoski-s/Calero-a/Alex Ross-c 5.00
Annual 2013 ($4.99) Parks-s/Evely-a/Worley-c 5.00
One Shot 2014: Agents of the Shadow ($7.99, squarebound) Robert Hack-c 8.00
... Over Innsmouth (2014, $4.99) Ron Marz-s/Ivan Rodriguez-a 5.00
Special 1 (2012, $4.99) Beatty-s/Cliquet-a/Alex Ross-c 5.00
Special 2014: Death Factory ($7.99, squarebound) Phil Hester-s/c; Ivan Rodriguez-a 8.00

SHADOW, THE (Volume 2)
Dynamite Entertainment: 2014 - No. 5, 2015 ($1.00/$3.99, limited series)

1-($1.00) Bunn-s/Timpano-a/Guice-c 3.00
2-5-($3.99) Bunn-s/Timpano-a/Guice-c 4.00

SHADOW, THE (Volume 3)
Dynamite Entertainment: 2017 - No. 6, 2018 ($3.99, limited series)

1-6: 1-Spurrier & Watters-s/Daniel HDR-a; multiple covers on all. 4-Jaime-a 4.00

SHADOW AND DOC SAVAGE, THE

GD VG FN VF VF/NM NM-
2.0 4.0 6.0 8.0 9.0 9.2

Dark Horse Comics: July, 1995 - No. 2, Aug, 1995 ($2.95, limited series)
1,2 4.00

SHADOW AND THE MYSTERIOUS 3, THE
Dark Horse Comics: Sept, 1994 ($2.95, one-shot)
1-Kaluta co-scripts. 4.00
NOTE: *Stevens c-1.*

SHADOW, THE / BATMAN
Dynamite Entertainment: 2017 - No. 6, 2018 ($3.99, limited series)
1-6-Orlando-s/Timpano-a; multiple covers on each; Ra's al Ghul & Shiwan Khan app. 4.00

SHADOW CABINET (See Heroes)
DC Comics (Milestone): No. 0, Jan, 1994 - No. 17, Oct, 1995 ($1.75/$2.50)
0-(1/94, $2.50, 52 pgs.)-Silver ink-c; Simonson-c 1 2 3 5 6 8
1-(6/94) Byrne-c 5.00
2-17 3.00

SHADOW COMICS (Pulp, radio)
Street & Smith Publications: Mar, 1940 - V9#5, Aug-Sept, 1949
NOTE: *The Shadow first appeared on radio in 1929 and was featured in pulps beginning in April, 1931, written by Walter Gibson. The early covers of this series were reprinted from the pulp covers.*
V1#1-Shadow, Doc Savage, Bill Barnes, Nick Carter (radio), Frank Merriwell, Iron Munro, the Astonishing Man begin 1000 2000 3000 7400 13,200 19,000
2-The Avenger begins, ends #6; Capt. Fury only app. 265 530 795 1694 2897 4100
3(nn-5/40)-Norgil the Magician app.; cover is exact swipe of Shadow pulp from 1/33 200 400 600 1280 2190 3100
4-The Three Musketeers begins, ends #8; classic painted decapitation-c 371 742 1113 2600 4550 6500
5-Doc Savage ends 142 284 426 909 1555 2200
6,8,9: 9-Norgil the Magician app. 116 232 348 742 1271 1800
7-Origin/1st app. The Hooded Wasp & Wasplet (11/40); series ends V3#8; Hooded Wasp/Wasplet app. on-c thru #9 126 252 378 806 1378 1950
10-Origin The Iron Ghost, ends #11; The Dead End Kids begins, ends #14 110 220 330 704 1202 1700
11-Origin Hooded Wasp & Wasplet retold 110 220 330 704 1202 1700
12-Dead End Kids app. 100 200 300 635 1093 1550
V2#1(11/41, Vol. II#2 in indicia) Dead End Kids -s 100 200 300 635 1093 1550
2-(Rare, 1/42, Vol. II#3 in indicia) Giant ant-c 194 388 582 1242 2121 3000
3-Origin & 1st app. Supersnipe (3/42); series begins; Little Nemo story (Vol.II#4 in indicia) 161 322 483 1030 1765 2500
4,5: 4,8-Little Nemo story 90 180 270 576 988 1400
6-9: 6-Blackstone the Magician story 87 174 261 553 952 1350
10,12: 10-Supersnipe app.' Skull-c 84 168 252 538 919 1300
11-Classic Devil Kyoti World War 2 sunburst-c 110 220 330 704 1202 1700
V3#1,2,5,7-12: 10-Doc Savage begins, not in V5#5, V6#10-12, V8#4 84 168 252 538 919 1300
3-1st Monstrodamus-c/sty 119 238 357 762 1306 1850
4-2nd Monstrodamus; classic-c of giant salamander getting shot in the head 119 238 357 762 1306 1850
6-Classic underwater-c 129 258 387 826 1413 2000
V4#1,3-12 55 110 165 352 601 850
2-Classic severed head-c 174 348 522 1114 1907 2700
V5#1-12: 1-(4/45). 12-(3/46) 53 106 159 334 567 800
V6#1-11: 9-Intro. Shadow, Jr. (12/46) 50 100 150 315 533 750
12-Powell-c/a; atom bomb panels 53 106 159 334 567 800
V7#1,2,5,7-9,12: 2,5-Shadow, Jr. app.; Powell-a 47 94 141 296 498 700
3,6,11-Powell-c/a 53 106 159 334 567 800
4-Powell-c/a; Atom bomb panels 54 108 162 343 574 825
10(1/48)-Flying Saucer-c/story (2nd of this theme; see The Spirit 9/28/47); Powell-c/a 87 174 261 553 952 1350
V8#1,2,4-12-Powell-a. 53 106 159 334 567 800
3-Powell Spider-c/a 55 110 165 352 601 850
V9#1,5-Powell-a 53 106 159 334 567 800
2-4-Powell-c/a 52 104 156 328 552 775
NOTE: *Binder c-V3#1.* ***Powell*** *art in most issues beginning V6#12. Painted c-1-6.*

SHADOW DOCTOR
AfterShock Comics: Feb, 2021 - No. 5, Jul, 2021 ($3.99, limited series)
1-5-Peter Calloway-s/Georges Jeanty-a; covers by Chiarello & Jeanty 4.00

SHADOWDRAGON
DC Comics: 1995 ($3.50, annual)
Annual 1-Year One story 4.00

SHADOW EMPIRES: FAITH CONQUERS
Dark Horse Comics: Aug, 1994 - No. 4, Nov, 1994 ($2.95, limited series)
1-4 3.00

SHADOW/GREEN HORNET: DARK NIGHTS (Pulp characters)
Dynamite Entertainment: 2013 - No. 5, 2013 ($3.99)
1-5-Lamont Cranston & Britt Reid team-up in 1939; Uslan-s; multiple covers on each 4.00

SHADOWHAWK (See Images of Shadowhawk, New Shadowhawk, Shadowhawk II, Shadowhawk III & Youngblood #2)
Image Comics (Shadowline Ink): Aug, 1992 - No. 4, Mar, 1993; No. 12, Aug, 1994 - No. 18, May, 1995 ($1.95/$2.50)
1-($2.50)-Embossed silver foil stamped-c; Valentino/Liefeld-c; Valentino-c/a/ scripts in all; has coupon for Image #0; 1st Shadowline Ink title 5.00
1-With coupon missing 2.00
1-($1.95)-Newsstand version w/o foil stamp 3.00
2-13,0,1418: 2-Shadowhawk poster w/McFarlane-i; brief Spawn app.; wraparound-c w/silver ink highlights. 3-($2.50)-Glow-in-the-dark-c. 4-Savage Dragon-c/story; Valentino/Larsen-c. 5-11-(See Shadowhawk II and III). 12-Cont'd from Shadowhawk III; pull-out poster by Texeira.13-w/ShadowBone poster; WildC.A.T.s app. 0 (10/94)-Liefeld c/a/story; ShadowBart poster. 14-(10/94, $2.50)-The Others app. 16-Supreme app. 17-Spawn app.; story cont'd from Badrock & Co. #6. 18-Shadowhawk dies; Savage Dragon & Brigade app. 3.00
Special 1(12/94, $3.50, 52 pgs.)-Silver Age Shadowhawk flip book 4.00
Gallery (4/94, $1.95) 3.00

GD VG FN VF VF/NM NM-
2.0 4.0 6.0 8.0 9.0 9.2

Out of the Shadows ($19.95)-r/Youngblood #2, Shadowhawk #1-4, Image Zero #0, Operation: Urban Storm (Never published) 20.00
.../Vampirella (2/95, $4.95)-Pt.2 of x-over (See Vampirella/Shadowhawk for Pt. 1) 5.00
NOTE: *Shadowhawk was originally a four issue limited series. The story continued in Shadowhawk II, Shadowhawk III & then became Shadowhawk again with issue #12.*

SHADOWHAWK II (Follows Shadowhawk #4)
Image Comics (Shadowline Ink): V2#1, May, 1993 - V2#3, Aug, 1993 ($3.50/$1.95/$2.95, limited series)
V2#1 ($3.50)-Cont'd from Shadowhawk #4; die-cut mirricard-c 4.00
2 ($1.95)-Foil embossed logo; reveals identity; gold-c variant exists 4.00
3 ($2.95)-Pop-up-c w/Pact ashcan insert 4.00

SHADOWHAWK III (Follows Shadowhawk II #3)
Image Comics (Shadowline Ink): V3#1, Nov, 1993 - V3#4, Mar, 1994 ($1.95, limited series);
V3#1-4: 1-Cont'd from Shadowhawk II; intro Valentine; gold foil & red foil stamped-c variations. 2-(52 pgs.)-Shadowhawk contracts HIV virus; U.S. Male by M. Anderson (p) in free 16 pg.insert. 4-Continues in Shadowhawk #12 4.00

SHADOWHAWK (Volume 2) (Also see New Man #4)
Image Comics: May, 2005 - No. 15, Sept, 2006 ($2.99/$3.50)
1-4-Eddie Collins as Shadowhawk; Rodríguez-a; Valentino-co-plotter 3.50
5-15-($3.50) 5-Cover swipe of Superman Vs. Spider-Man treasury edition 3.50
...One Shot #1 (7/06, $1.99) r/Return of Shadowhawk 3.00
Return of Shadowhawk (12/04, $2.99) Valentino-s/a/c; Eddie Collins origin retold 3.00

SHADOWHAWK (Volume 3)
Image Comics: May, 2010 - No. 5, Dec, 2010 ($3.50)
1-5-Rodríguez-a. 1-Back-up with Valentino-a/Niles-s 3.50

SHADOWHAWKS OF LEGEND
Image Comics (Shadowline Ink): Nov, 1995 ($4.95, one-shot)
nn-Stories of past Shadowhawks by Kurt Busiek, Beau Smith & Alan Moore 5.00

SHADOW, THE: HELL'S HEAT WAVE (Movie, pulp, radio)
Dark Horse Comics: Apr, 1995 - No. 3, June, 1995 ($2.95, limited series)
1-3: Kaluta story 4.00

SHADOW HUNTER (Jenna Jameson's...)
Virgin Comics: No. 0, Dec, 2007 - No. 3 ($2.99)
0-Preview issue; creator interviews; gallery of covers for upcoming issues; Greg Horn-c 3.00
1-3: 1-Two covers by Horn & Land; Jameson & Christina Z-s/Singh-a. 2-Three covers 3.00

SHADOWHUNT SPECIAL
Image Comics (Extreme Studios): Apr, 1996 ($2.50)
1-Retells origin of past Shadowhawks; Valentino script; Chapel app. 3.00

SHADOW, THE: IN THE COILS OF THE LEVIATHAN (Movie, pulp, radio)
Dark Horse Comics: Oct, 1993 - No. 4, Apr, 1994 ($2.95, limited series)
1-4-Kaluta-c & co-scripter 4.00
Trade paperback (10/94, $13.95)-r/1-4 14.00

SHADOWLAND (Also see Daredevil #508-512 & Black Panther: The Man Without Fear #513)
Marvel Comics: Sept, 2010 - No. 5, Jan, 2011 ($3.99, limited series)
1-5: 1-Diggle-s/Tan-a; Bullseye killed; Cassaday-c. 2-Ghost Rider app. 4.00
1-Variant-c by Tan 6.00
...: After the Fall 1 (2/11, $3.99) Finch-c; Black Panther app. 4.00
...: Bullseye 1 (10/10, $3.99) Chen-a; Bullseye's funeral 4.00
...: Elektra 1 (11/10, $3.99) Wells-s/Rios-a/Takeda-c 4.00
...: Ghost Rider 1 (11/10, $3.99) Williams-s/Crain-a/c 4.00
...: Spider-Man 1 (12/10, $3.99) Shang-Chi & Mr. Negative app.; Siqueira-a 4.00

SHADOWLAND: BLOOD IN THE STREETS (Leads into Heroes For Hire)
Marvel Comics: Oct, 2010 - No. 4, Jan, 2011 ($3.99, limited series)
1-4-Johnston-s/Alves-a; Misty Knight, Silver Sable, Paladin, Shroud app. 4.00

SHADOWLAND: DAUGHTERS OF THE SHADOW
Marvel Comics: Oct, 2010 - No. 3, Dec, 2010 ($3.99, limited series)
1-3-Henderson-s/Rodriguez-a; Colleen Wing app. 3-Preview of Black Panther #513 4.00

SHADOWLAND: MOON KNIGHT
Marvel Comics: Oct, 2010 - No. 3, Dec, 2010 ($3.99, limited series)
1-3-Hurwitz-s/Dazo-a 4.00

SHADOWLAND: POWER MAN
Marvel Comics: Oct, 2010 - No. 4, Jan, 2011 ($3.99, limited series)
1-4-Van Lente-s/Asrar-a. 1-New Power Man debut; Iron Fist app. 4.00

SHADOWLINE SAGA: CRITICAL MASS, A
Marvel Comics (Epic): Jan, 1990 - No. 7, July, 1990 ($4.95, lim. series, 68 pgs)
1-6: Dr. Zero, Powerline, St. George 5.00
7 ($5.95, 84 pgs.)-Morrow-a, Williamson-c(i) 6.00

SHADOWMAN (See X-O Manowar #4)
Valiant/Acclaim Comics (Valiant): May, 1992 - No. 43, Dec, 1995 ($2.50)
1-Partial origin 3 6 9 16 23 30
2-5: 3-1st app. Sousa the Soul Eater 5.00
6,7,9-42: 15-Minor Turok app. 16-1st app. Dr. Mirage (8/93). 17,18-Archer & Armstrong x-over. 19-Aerosmith-c/story. 23-Dr. Mirage x-over. 24-(4/94). 25-Bound-in trading card. 29-Chaos Effect. 4.00
8-1st app. Master Darque 2 4 6 8 11 14
43-Shadowman jumps to his death 1 3 4 6 8 10
0-($2.50, 4/94)-Regular edition 6.00
0-($3.50)-Wraparound chromium-c edition 1 2 3 5 6 8
0-Gold 20.00
Yearbook 1 (12/94, $3.95) 5.00

SHADOWMAN (Volume 2)
Acclaim Comics (Valiant Heroes): Mar, 1997 - No. 20, Jun, 1998 ($2.50, mature)
1-1st app. Zero; Garth Ennis scripts begin, end #4 1 2 3 5 6 8
2-20: 2-Zero becomes new Shadowman. 4-Origin; Jack Boniface (original Shadowman) rises from the grave. 5-Jamie Delano scripts begin. 9-Copycat-c 3.00
1-Variant painted cover 1 2 3 5 6 8

Shadow Comics #10 © Conde Nast

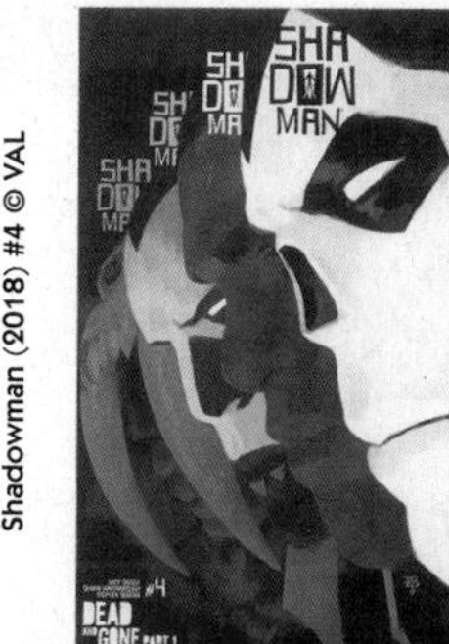

Shadowman (2018) #4 © VAL

Shadow War Zone #1 © DC

GD VG FN VF VF/NM NM-
2.0 4.0 6.0 8.0 9.0 9.2

SHADOWMAN (Volume 3)
Acclaim Comics: July, 1999 - No. 5, Nov, 1999 ($3.95/$2.50)
1-($3.95)-Abnett & Lanning-s/Broome & Benjamin-a 2 4 6 8 10 12
2-5-($2.50): 3,4-Flip book with Unity 2000 3.00

SHADOWMAN
Valiant Entertainment: Nov, 2012 - No. 16, Mar, 2014 ($3.99)
1-Jordan-s/Zircher-a; two covers by Zircher (regular & pullbox) 5.00
1-Variant-c by Dave Johnson 8.00
1-Variant-c by Bill Sienkiewicz 20.00
2-16: 2-6-Jordan-s/Zircher-a 4.00
2-4-Pullbox variants 6.00
5-16-Pullbox variants 4.00
11-Variant-c with detachable Halloween mask 4.00
13X-(10/13, bagged with Bleeding Cool Magazine #7) prelude to #13; Milligan-s 3.00
#0-(5/13, $3.99) Origin of Master Darque 4.00

SHADOWMAN
Valiant Entertainment: Mar, 2018 - No. 11, Jan, 2019 ($3.99)
1-11: 1-Diggle-s/Segovia-a. 4-Martinbrough & Segovia-a. 6-11-Guedes-a 4.00

SHADOWMAN
Valiant Entertainment: Apr, 2021 - No. 8, Apr, 2022 ($3.99)
1-8: 1-Cullen Bunn-s/Jon Davis-Hunt-a. 5-8-Pedro Andreo-a 4.00

SHADOWMAN END TIMES
Valiant Entertainment: Apr, 2014 - No. 3, Jun, 2014 ($3.99, limited series)
1-3-Milligan-s/De Landro-a 4.00

SHADOWMAN / RAE SREMMURD
Valiant Entertainment: Oct, 2017 ($3.99, one-shot)
1-Rahal-s/Guedes-a; bonus preview of Ninja•K #1 4.00

SHADOWMASTERS
Marvel Comics: Oct, 1989 - No.4, Jan, 1990 ($3.95, squarebound, 52 pgs.)
1-4: Heath-a(i). 1-Jim Lee-c; story cont'd from Punisher 4.00

SHADOW, THE: MIDNIGHT IN MOSCOW (Pulp character)
Dynamite Entertainment: 2014 - No. 6, 2014 ($3.99, limited series)
1-6:-Howard Chaykin-s/a/c 4.00

SHADOW NOW, THE (Pulp character)
Dynamite Entertainment: 2013 - No. 6, 2014 ($3.99, limited series)
1-6: 1-David Liss-s/ColtonWorley-a; The Shadow in present day New York 4.00

SHADOW OF THE BATMAN
DC Comics: Dec, 1985 - No. 5, Apr, 1986 ($1.75, limited series)
1-Detective-r (all have wraparound-c) 2 4 6 8 10 12
2,3,5: 3-Penguin-c & cameo. 5-Clayface app. 6.00
4-Joker-c/story 1 2 3 4 6 8
NOTE: ***Austin** a(new)-2i, 3i; r-2-4i. **Rogers** a(new)-1, 2p, 3p, 4, 5; r-1-5p; c-1-5. **Simonson** a-1r.*

SHADOW ON THE TRAIL (See Zane Grey & Four Color #604)

SHADOWPACT (See Day of Vengeance)
DC Comics: Jul, 2006 - No. 25, Jul, 2008 ($2.99)
1-25: 1-Bill Willingham-s; Detective Chimp, Ragman, Blue Devil, Nightshade, Enchantress and Nightmaster app. 1-Superman app. 13-Zauriel app.; S. Hampton-a 3.00
...: Cursed TPB (2007, $14.99) r/#4,9-13 15.00
...: Darkness and Light TPB (2008, $14.99) r/#14-19 15.00
...: The Burning Age TPB (2008, $17.99) r/#20-25 18.00
...: The Pentacle Plot TPB (2007, $14.99) r/#1-3,5-8 15.00

SHADOW PLAY (Tales of the Supernatural)
Whitman Publications: June, 1982
1-Painted-c 1 2 3 5 6 8

SHADOWPLAY
IDW Publ.: Sept, 2005 - No. 4, Dec, 2005 ($3.99)
1-4-Benson-s/Templesmith-a; Christina Z-s/Wood-a; 2 covers by Templesmith & Wood 6.00
TPB (3/06, $17.99) r/series; flip book format 18.00

SHADOW REAVERS
Black Bull Ent.: Oct, 2001 - No. 5, Mar, 2002 ($2.99)
1-5-Nelson-a; two covers for each issue 3.00
Limited Preview Edition (5/01, no cover price) 3.00

SHADOW RIDERS
Marvel Comics UK, Ltd.: June, 1993 - No. 4, Sept, 1993 ($1.75, limited series)
1-($2.50)-Embossed-c; Cable-c/story 4.00
2-4-Cable app. 2-Ghost Rider app. 3.00

GD VG FN VF VF/NM NM-
2.0 4.0 6.0 8.0 9.0 9.2

SHADOWS
Image Comics: Feb, 2003 - No. 4, Nov, 2003 ($2.95)
1-4-Jade Dodge-s/Matt Camp-a/c 3.00

SHADOWS & LIGHT
Marvel Comics: Feb, 1998 - No. 3, July, 1998 ($2.99, B&W, quarterly)
1-3: 1-B&W anthology of Marvel characters; Black Widow art by Gene Ha, Hulk by Wrightson, Iron Man by Ditko & Daredevil by Stelfreeze; Stelfreeze painted-c. 2-Weeks, Sharp, Starlin, Thompson-a. 3-Buscema, Grindberg, Giffen, Layton-a 3.00

SHADOW'S FALL
DC Comics (Vertigo): Nov, 1994 - No. 6, Apr, 1995 ($2.95, limited series)
1-6: Van Fleet-c/a in all. 3.00

SHADOWS FROM BEYOND (Formerly Unusual Tales)
Charlton Comics: V2#50, October, 1966
V2#50-Ditko-c 5 10 15 30 50 70

SHADOWS ON THE GRAVE
Dark Horse Comics: Dec, 2016 - No. 8, Sept, 2017 ($3.99, B&W, limited series)
1-8-Horror story anthology; Richard Corben-s/a/c 4.00

SHADOW STATE
Broadway Comics: Dec, 1995 - No. 5, Apr, 1996 ($2.50)
1-5: 1,2-Fatale back-up story; Cockrum-a(p) 3.00
Preview Edition 1,2 (10-11/95, $2.50, B&W) 3.00

SHADOW STRIKES!, THE (Pulp, radio)
DC Comics: Sept, 1989 - No.31, May, 1992 ($1.75)
1-4,7-31: 31-Mignola-c 4.00
5,6-Doc Savage x-over 5.00
Annual 1 (1989, $3.50, 68 pgs.)-Spiegle a; Kaluta-c 5.00

SHADOW, THE : THE DEATH OF MARGO LANE (Pulp characters)
Dynamite Entertainment: 2016 - No. 5, 2016 ($3.99, limited series)
1-5-Matt Wagner-s/a/c. 4-The Red Empress app. 4.00

SHADOW WALK
Legendary Comics: Nov, 2013 ($24.99, graphic novel)
HC - Mark Waid-s/Shane Davis-a 25.00

SHADOW WAR
DC Comics: May, 2022 - Jul, 2022 (limited series)
... Alpha (5/22, $5.99) Assassination of Ra's al Ghul; Deathstroke app. 6.00
... Omega (7/22, $5.99) Conclusion of x-over; Geo-Force app.; leads into Dark Crisis #1 6.00
Shadow War Zone (7/22, $5.99) Tales from the War Zone 6.00

SHADOW WAR OF HAWKMAN
DC Comics: May, 1985 - No. 4, Aug, 1985 (limited series)
1-4 4.00

SHADOW, THE: YEAR ONE
Dynamite Entertainment: 2012 - No. 10, 2014 ($3.99)
1-9: 1-Matt Wagner-s/Wilfredo Torres-a; multiple covers 4.00
10-($4.99) 5.00

SHAFT (Based on the movie character)
Dynamite Entertainment: 2014 - No. 6, 2015 ($3.99, limited series)
1-6-David F. Walker-s/Bilquis Evely-a; multiple covers on each 4.00

SHAFT: IMITATION OF LIFE (Based on the movie character)
Dynamite Entertainment: 2016 - No. 4, 2016 ($3.99, limited series)
1-4-David F. Walker-s/Dietrich Smith-a/Matthew Clark-c 4.00

SHAGGY DOG & THE ABSENT-MINDED PROFESSOR (See Movie Comics & Walt Disney Showcase #46)(Disney-Movie)
Dell Publ. Co.: No. 985, Apr-Jun, 1959; No. 1199, Apr, 1961; Aug, 1967
Four Color 985 8 16 24 54 102 150
Four Color 1199 (4/61) Movie, photo-c; variant "Double Feature" edition; has a "Fabulous Formula" strip on back-c 7 14 21 49 92 135
Four Color 1199-(8/67) Movie, photo-c 7 14 21 49 92 135

SHAHRAZAD
Big Dog Ink: No. 0, Apr, 2013 - No. 5, Apr, 2014 ($1.99/$3.99)
0-($1.99) Hutchison-s/Krome-a; multiple covers 3.00
1-3 ($3.99) Hutchison & Castor-s/Krome-a; multiple covers on each 4.00

SHAHRAZAD
Aspen MLT: Apr, 2015 - No. 5, Aug, 2015 ($2.99/$3.99)
1,2-($2.99) Remastered reprints of 2013 series; multiple covers on each 3.00

	GD 2.0	VG 4.0	FN 6.0	VF 8.0	VF/NM 9.0	NM- 9.2

3-5-($3.99) Hutchison & Castor-s/Krome-a; multiple covers on each 4.00

SHALOMAN (Jewish-themed stories and history)
Al Wiesner/ Mark 1 Comics: 1988 - 2012 (B&W)

V1#1-Al Wiesner-s/a in all 5.00
2-9 3.00
V2 #1(The New Adventures)-4,6-10, V3 (The Legend of...) #1-12 3.00
V2 #5 (Color)-Shows Vol 2, No. 4 in indicia 3.00
V4 (The Saga of ...) #1(2004), 2-8: 8-Chanukah & The Holocaust 3.00
...: The Sequel (2010) "11-9" , ...: The Sequel 2 (2011) Genesis #2 Jews in Space 3.00
...: The Sequel 3 (2012) Purim and the X-Suit 3.00
The Saga of Shaloman (20th Anniversary Edition) TPB (10/08, $15.99) r/V4 #1-8 16.00

SHAMAN'S TEARS (Also see Maggie the Cat)
Image Comics (Creative Fire Studio): 5/93 - No. 2, 8/93; No. 3, 11/94 - No. 0, 1/96 ($2.50/$1.95)

0-2: 0-(DEC-c, 1/96)-Last Issue. 1-(5/93)-Embossed red foil-c; Grell-c/a & scripts in all. 2-Cover unfolds into poster (8/93-c, 7/93 inside) 4.00
3-12: 3-Begin $1.95-c. 5-Re-intro Jon Sable. 12-Re-intro Maggie the Cat (1 pg.) 3.00

SHAME ITSELF
Marvel Comics: Jan, 2012 ($3.99, one-shot)

1-Spoof of "Fear Itself" x-over event; short stories by various incl. Cenac & Kupperman 4.00

SHANG-CHI
Marvel Comics: Nov, 2020 - No. 5, Mar, 2021 ($3.99)

1-5-Gene Luen Yang-s/Dike Ruan & Philip Tan-a. 1-Fin Fang Foom cameo 4.00

SHANG-CHI
Marvel Comics: Jul, 2021 - No. 12, Jul, 2022 ($3.99)

1-12: 1-8-Gene Luen Yang-s/Dike Ruan-a. 1-Spider-Man app. 9-12-Marcus To-a 4.00
...: Master of the Ten Rings 1 (3/23, $4.99) Gene Luen Yang-s/Michael Yg-a 5.00

SHANG-CHI AND THE TEN RINGS
Marvel Comics: Sept, 2022 - No. 6, Feb, 2023 ($3.99)

1-6-Gene Luen Yang-s/Marcus To-a 4.00

SHANG-CHI: MASTER OF KUNG-FU ("Master of Kung Fu" on cover for #1&2)
Marvel Comics: Nov, 2002 - No. 6, Apr, 2003 ($2.99, limited series)

1-6-Moench-s/Gulacy-c/a 3.00
...One-Shot 1 (11/09, $3.99, B&W) Deadpool app. 4.00
... Vol. 1: The Hellfire Apocalypse TPB (2003, $14.99) r/#1-6 15.00

SHANNA, THE SHE-DEVIL (See Savage Tales #8)
Marvel Comics Group: Dec, 1972 - No. 5, Aug, 1973 (All are 20¢ issues)

1-1st app. Shanna; Steranko-c; Tuska-a(p) 11 22 33 76 163 250
2-Steranko-c; heroin drug story 5 10 15 30 50 70
3-5 3 6 9 15 22 28

SHANNA, THE SHE-DEVIL
Marvel Comics: Apr, 2005 - No. 7, Oct, 2005 ($3.50, limited series)

1-7-Reintro of Shanna; Frank Cho-s/a/c in all 3.50
HC (2005, $24.99, dust jacket) r/#1-7 25.00
SC (2006, $16.99) r/#1-7 17.00

SHANNA, THE SHE-DEVIL: SURVIVAL OF THE FITTEST
Marvel Comics: Oct, 2007 - No. 4, Jan, 2008 ($2.99, limited series)

1-4-Khari Evans-a/c; Gray & Palmiotti-s 3.00
SC (2008, $10.99) r/#1-4 11.00

SHAOLIN COWBOY
Burlyman Entertainment: Dec, 2004 - No. 7, May, 2007 ($3.50)

1-7-Geof Darrow-s/a. 3-Moebius-c 3.50

SHAOLIN COWBOY
Dark Horse Comics: Oct, 2013 - No. 4, Feb, 2014 ($3.99)

1-4-Geof Darrow-s/a. 1-Variant-c by Simonson 4.00

SHAOLIN COWBOY: CRUEL TO BE KIN
Dark Horse Comics: May, 2022 - No. 7, Nov, 2022 ($4.99)

1-7-Geof Darrow-s/a. 1-Variant-c by Mignola 5.00

SHAOLIN COWBOY: WHO'LL STOP THE REIGN?
Dark Horse Comics: Apr, 2017 - No. 4, Jul, 2017 ($3.99)

1-4-Geof Darrow-s/a. 1-Variant-c by Frank Miller 4.00

SHAPER
Dark Horse Comics: Mar, 2015 - No. 5, Jul, 2015 ($3.99)

1-5: 1-Heisserer-s/Massafera-a. 2-5-Continuado-a 4.00

SHARKEY THE BOUNTY HUNTER
Image Comics: Feb, 2019 - No. 6, Oct, 2019 ($3.99, limited series)

1-6-Mark Millar-s/Simone Bianchi-a/c 4.00

SHARK FIGHTERS, THE (Movie)
Dell Publishing Co.: Jan, 1957

Four Color 762 - Buscema-a; photo-c 9 18 27 59 117 175

SHARK-MAN
Thrill House/Image Comics: Jul, 2006; Jul, 2007; Jan, 2008 - No. 3, Jun, 2008 ($3.99/$3.50)

1,2: 1-(Thrill House, 7/06, $3.99)-Steve Pugh-s/a. 2-(Image Comics, 7/07) 4.00
1-3: 1-(Image, 1/08, $3.50) reprints Thrill House #1 3.50

SHARKY
Image Comics: Feb, 1998 - No. 4, 1998 ($2.50, bi-monthly)

1-4: 1-Mask app.; Elliot-s/a. Horley painted-c. 3-Three covers by Horley, Bisley, & Horley/Elliot. 4-Two covers (swipe of Avengers #4 and wraparound) 3.00
1-($2.95) "$1,000,000" variant 3.00
2-($2.50) Savage Dragon variant-c 3.00

SHARP COMICS (Slightly large size)
H. C. Blackerby: Winter, 1945-46 - V1#2, Spring, 1946 (52 pgs.)

V1#1-Origin Dick Royce Planetarian 61 122 183 390 670 950
2-Origin The Pioneer; Michael Morgan, Dick Royce, Sir Gallagher, Planetarian, Steve Hagen, Weeny and Pop app. 61 122 183 390 670 950

SHARPY FOX (See Comic Capers & Funny Frolics)
I. W. Enterprises/Super Comics: 1958; 1963

1,2-I.W. Reprint (1958): 2-r/Kiddie Kapers #1 2 4 6 10 14 18
14-Super Reprint (1963) 2 4 6 9 13 16

SHATTER (See Jon Sable #25-30)
First Comics: June, 1985; Dec, 1985 - No. 14, Apr, 1988 ($1.75, Baxter paper/deluxe paper)

1 (6/85)-1st computer generated-a in a comic book (1st printing) 4.00
1-(2nd print.); 1(12/85)-14: computer generated-a & lettering in all 3.00
Special 1 (1988) 3.00

SHATTERED IMAGE
Image Comics (WildStorm Productions): Aug, 1996 - No. 4, Dec, 1996 ($2.50, lim. series)

1-4: 1st Image company-wide x-over; Kurt Busiek scripts in all. 1-Tony Daniel-c/a(p). 2-Alex Ross-c/swipe (Kingdom Come) by Ryan Benjamin & Travis Charest 3.00

SHATTERSTAR (From X-Force)
Marvel Comics: Dec, 2018 - No. 5, Apr, 2019 ($3.99, limited series)

1-Tim Seeley-s/Carlos Villa-a; Grandmaster app. 4.00

SHAUN OF THE DEAD (Movie)
IDW Publishing: June, 2005 - No. 4, Sept, 2005 ($3.99, limited series)

1-4-Adaptation of 2004 movie; Zach Howard-a 4.00
TPB (12/05, $17.99) r/series; sketch pages and cover gallery 18.00

SHAZAM (See Billy Batson and the Magic of Shazam!, Giant Comics to Color, Limited Collectors' Edition, Power Of Shazam! and Trials of Shazam!)

SHAZAM! (TV)(See World's Finest #253 for story from unpublished #36)
National Periodical Publ./DC Comics: Feb, 1973 - No. 35, May-June, 1978

1-1st revival of original Captain Marvel since G.A. (origin retold), by C.C. Beck; Mary Marvel & Captain Marvel Jr. app.; Superman-c 8 16 24 52 99 145
2-5: 2-Infinity photo-c.; re-intro Mr. Mind & Tawny. 3-Capt. Marvel-r. (10/46). 4-Origin retold; Capt. Marvel-r. (1949). 5-Capt. Marvel Jr. origin retold; Capt. Marvel-r. (1948, 7 pgs.) 3 6 9 19 30 40
6,7,9-11: 6-photo-c; Capt. Marvel-r (1950, 6 pgs.). 9-Mr. Mind app. 10-Last C.C. Beck issue. 11-Schaffenberger-a begins. 3 6 9 16 23 30
8-(100 pgs.) 8-r/1st Black Adam app. from Marvel Family #1; r/Capt. Marvel Jr. by Raboy; origin/C.M. #80; origin Mary Marvel/C.M.A. #18; origin Mr. Tawny/C.M.A. #79 10 20 30 64 132 200
12-17-(All 100 pgs.). 15-vs. Lex Luthor & Mr. Mind 5 10 15 33 57 80
18-24,26,27,29,30: 21-24-All reprints. 26-Sivana app. (10/76). 27-Kid Eternity teams up w/Capt. Marvel. 30-1st DC app. 3 Lt. Marvels 3 6 9 14 20 25
25-1st app. Isis 9 18 27 57 111 165
28-(3-4/77) 1st Bronze Age app. of Black Adam 21 42 63 147 324 500
31-35: 31-1st DC app. Minuteman. 34-Origin Capt. Nazi & Capt. Marvel Jr. retold 3 6 9 16 23 30
...: The Greatest Stories Ever Told TPB (2008, $24.99) reprints; Alex Ross-c 25.00
NOTE: *Reprints in #1-8, 10, 12-17, 21-24.* **Beck** *a-1-10, 12-17r, 21-24r; c-1, 3-9.* **Nasser** *c-35p.* **Newton** *a-35p.* **Raboy** *a-5r, 8r, 17r.* **Schaffenberger** *a-11, 14-20, 25, 26, 27p, 28, 29-31p, 33i, 35i; c-20, 22, 23, 25, 26i, 27i, 28-33.*

SHAZAM!
DC Comics: March, 2011 ($2.99, one-shot)

1-Richards-a/Chiang-c; Blaze app.; story continues in Titans #32 3.00

SHAZAM! (See back-up stories in Justice League [2011 series] #0,7-11,14-16,18-21)
DC Comics: Feb, 2019 - No. 15, Nov, 2020 ($4.99/$3.99)

1-($4.99) Johns-s/Eaglesham-a; back-up origin of Hoppy w/Naito-a 5.00
2-13,15-($3.99): 2-Johns-s/Santucci-a; Sivana & Mr. Mind app.; intro. King Kid. 4-6,8-11-Black Adam app. 8-Billy's father gains the power. 11,13-Monster Society app. 12-Batman & Scarecrow app.; Loveness-s/Peterson-a. 13-Eaglesham-a. 15-Peterson-a 4.00
14-($4.99) Superboy Prime app.; Eaglesham-a 5.00

SHAZAM!
DC Comics: Sept, 2021 - No. 4, Dec, 2021 ($3.99, limited series)

1-4-Sheridan-s/Henry-a. 1-Teen Titans app. 3,4-Black Adam app. 4.00

SHAZAM! AND THE SHAZAM FAMILY! ANNUAL
DC Comics: 2002 ($5.95, squarebound, one-shot)

1-Reprints Golden Age stories including 1st Mary Marvel and 1st Black Adam 1 3 4 6 8 10

SHAZAM! FURY OF THE GODS SPECIAL: SHAZAMILY MATTERS
DC Comics: Apr, 2023 ($9.99, one-shot)

1-Short stories of the Shazam Family characters, some written by their movie actors 10.00

SHAZAM!: POWER OF HOPE
DC Comics: Nov, 2000 ($9.95, treasury size, one-shot)

nn-Painted art by Alex Ross; story by Alex Ross and Paul Dini 10.00

SHAZAM!: THE MONSTER SOCIETY OF EVIL
DC Comics: 2007 - No. 4, 2007 ($5.99, square-bound, limited series)

1-4: Jeff Smith-s/a/c in all. 1-Retelling of origin. 2-Mary Marvel & Dr. Sivana app. 6.00
HC (2007, $29.99, over-sized with dust jacket that unfolds to a poster) r/#1-4; Alex Ross intro.; Smith afterword; sketch pages, script pages and production notes 30.00
SC (2009, $19.99) r/#1-4; Alex Ross intro. 20.00

SHAZAM: THE NEW BEGINNING
DC Comics: Apr, 1987 - No. 4, July, 1987 (Legends spin-off) (Limited series)

1-4: 1-New origin & 1st modern app. Captain Marvel; Marvel Family cameo. 2-4-Sivana & Black Adam app. 4.00

SHEA THEATRE COMICS
Shea Theatre: No date (1940's) (32 pgs.)

nn-Contains Rocket Comics; MLJ cover in one color 32 64 96 188 307 425

SHE-BAT (See Murcielaga, She-Bat & Valeria the She-Bat)

SHE COULD FLY
Dark Horse Comics (Berger Books): Jul, 2018 - No. 4, Oct, 2018 ($4.99, limited series)

1-4-Christopher Cantwell-s/Martín Morazzo-a 5.00

SHE COULD FLY: THE LOST PILOT

Shang-Chi (2020) #2 © MAR

Shazam! (2019) #1 © DC

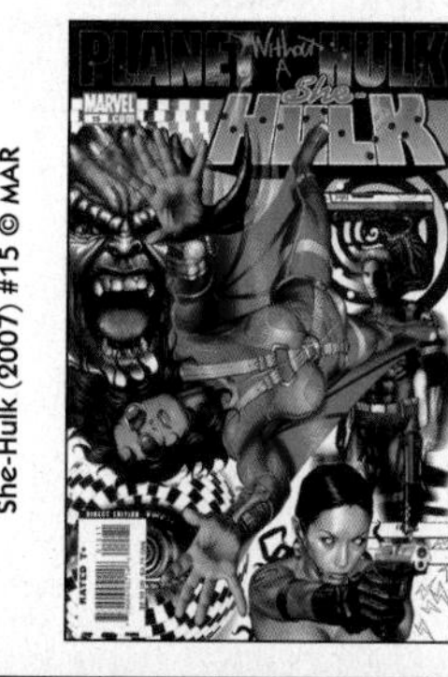

She-Hulk (2007) #15 © MAR

	GD 2.0	VG 4.0	FN 6.0	VF 8.0	VF/NM 9.0	NM- 9.2

Dark Horse Comics (Berger Books): Apr, 2019 - No. 5, Aug, 2019 ($3.99, limited series)

1-5-Christopher Cantwell-s/Martín Morazzo-a 4.00

SHE-DRAGON (See Savage Dragon #117)
Image Comics: July, 2006 ($5.99, one-shot)

nn- She-Dragon in Dimension-X; origin retold; Franchesco-a/Larsen-s; sketch pages 6.00

SHEENA (Movie)
Marvel Comics: Dec, 1984 - No. 2, Feb, 1985 (limited series)

1,2-r/Marvel Comics Super Special #34; Tanya Roberts movie 5.00

SHEENA, QUEEN OF THE JUNGLE (See Jerry Iger's Classic..., Jumbo Comics, & 3-D Sheena)
Fiction House Magazines: Spr, 1942; No. 2, Wint, 1942-43; No. 3, Spr, 1943; No. 4, Fall, 1948; No. 5, Sum, 1949; No. 6, Spr, 1950; No. 7-10, 1950(nd); No. 11, Spr, 1951 - No. 18, Wint, 1952-53 (#1-3: 68 pgs.; #4-7: 52 pgs.)

	GD	VG	FN	VF	VF/NM	NM-
1-Sheena begins	300	600	900	2040	3570	5100
2 (Winter, 1942-43)	168	336	504	1075	1838	2600
3 (Spring, 1943) Classic Giant Ape-c	187	374	561	1197	2049	2900
4,5 (Fall, 1948, Sum, 1949): 4-New logo; cover swipe from Jumbo #20	65	130	195	416	708	1000
6,7 (Spring, 1950, 1950)	53	106	159	334	567	800
8-10(1950 - Win/50, 36 pgs.)	47	94	141	296	498	700
11-17: 15-Cover swipe from Jumbo #43	42	84	126	265	445	625
18-Used in **POP**, pg. 98	45	90	135	284	480	675
I.W. Reprint #9-r/#18; c-r/White Princess #3	5	10	15	30	50	70

NOTE: *Baker c-5-10? Whitman c-11-18(most). Zolnerowich c-1-3.*

SHEENA, QUEEN OF THE JUNGLE
Devil's Due Publishing: Mar, 2007; Jun, 2007 - No. 5, Jan, 2008 (99¢/$3.50)

1-5: 1-Rodi-s/Merhoff-a; 5 covers 3.50
... 99¢ Special (3/07) Revival of the character; Rodi-s/Cummings-a; sketch pages; history 3.00
...: Dark Rising (10/08 - No. 3, 12/08) 1-3 3.50
... Trail of the Mapinguari (4/08, $5.50) Two covers 5.50

SHEENA, QUEEN OF THE JUNGLE
Dynamite Entertainment: No. 0, 2017 - No. 10, 2018 (25¢/$3.99)

0-(25¢) Marguerite Bennett & Christina Trujillo-s/Moritat-a; multiple covers 3.00
1-10-($3.99) 1-Bennett & Trujillo-s/Moritat-a. 4-10-Sanapo-a 4.00

SHEENA, QUEEN OF THE JUNGLE, VOLUME 2
Dynamite Entertainment: 2021 - No. 10, 2022 ($3.99)

1-10: 1-5-Stephen Mooney-s/Jethro Morales-a; multiple covers. 6-10-Steven E. de Souza-s 4.00

SHEENA 3-D SPECIAL (Also see Blackthorne 3-D Series #1)
Eclipse Comics: Jan, 1985 ($2.00)

	GD	VG	FN	VF	VF/NM	NM-
1-Dave Stevens-c	2	4	6	13	18	22

SHE-HULK (Also see The Savage She-Hulk & The Sensational She-Hulk)
Marvel Comics: May, 2004 - No. 12, Apr, 2005 ($2.99)

	GD	VG	FN	VF	VF/NM	NM-
1-Bobillo-a/Slott-s/Granov-c; Avengers app.	2	4	6	9	12	15
2-4-Bobillo-a/Slott-s/Granov-c. 4-Spider-Man-c/app.						5.00
5-12: Mayhew-c. 9-12-Pelletier-a. 10-Origin of Titania						5.00
Vol. 1: Single Green Female TPB (2004, $14.99) r/#1-6						15.00
Vol. 2: Superhuman Law TPB (2005, $14.99) r/#7-12						15.00

SHE-HULK (2nd series)
Marvel Comics: Dec, 2005 - No. 38, Apr, 2009 ($2.99)

	GD	VG	FN	VF	VF/NM	NM-
1-Bobillo-a/Slott-s/Horn-c; New Avengers app.	2	4	6	10	14	18
2,4,5,7,9,11-21,24: 2-Hawkeye-c/app. 9-Jen marries John Jameson. 12-Thanos app. 16-Wolverine app.						5.00
3-($3.99) 100th She-Hulk issue; new story w/art by various incl. Bobillo, Conner, Mayhew & Powell; r/Savage She-Hulk #1 and r/Sensational She-Hulk #1	3	6	9	14	20	25
6-Starfox sexual assault trial	3	6	9	16	23	30
8-Civil War	2	4	6	9	12	15
8-2nd printing with variant Bobillo-c	1	3	4	6	8	10
10- "I Married a Man-Wolf!!"-c	2	4	6	10	14	18
22-1st Jazinda	2	4	6	10	14	18
23-1st full app. Jazinda	2	4	6	13	18	22
25-($3.99) Intro. the Behemoth; Juggernaut cameo; Handbook bio pages of She-Hulk						5.00
26-28,30-37: 27-Iron Man app. 30-Hercules app. 31-X-Factor app. 32,33-Secret Invasion						4.00
29-Sexy-c by Deodato	2	4	6	11	16	20
38-($3.99) Thundra, Valkyrie & Invisible Woman app.	2	4	6	9	12	15
...: Cosmic Collision 1 (2/09, $3.99) Lady Liberators app.; David-s/Asrar-a/Sejic-c	1	3	4	6	8	10
... Sensational 1 (5/10, $4.99) 30th Anniversary celebration; Stan Lee app.; Frank-c	3	6	9	17	26	35
Vol. 3: Time Trials (2006, $14.99) r/#1-5; Bobillo sketch page						15.00
Vol. 4: Laws of Attraction (2007, $19.99) r/#6-12; Paul Smith sketch page						30.00
Vol. 5: Planet Without a Hulk (2007, $19.99) r/#14-21; Slott's original series pitch						20.00
...: Jaded HC (2008, $19.99) r/#22-27; cover gallery						20.00

SHE-HULK (3rd series)
Marvel Comics: Apr, 2014 - No. 12, Apr, 2015 ($2.99)

	GD	VG	FN	VF	VF/NM	NM-
1-Soule-s/Pulido-a/Wada-c; Tony Stark app.	2	4	6	11	16	20
2-12: 2-Hellcat app.						4.00

SHE-HULK (Marvel Legacy)
Marvel Comics: No. 159, Jan, 2018 - No. 163, May, 2018 ($3.99)

159-163: 159-Tamaki-s/Lindsay-a. 159-161-The Leader app. 4.00
Annual 1(10/19, $4.99) Acts of Evil; Bullseye-c/app.; Andolfo-c 5.00

SHE-HULK (5th series)
Marvel Comics: Mar, 2022 - Present ($3.99)

1-10: 1-Rowell-s/Antonio-a; multiple covers; Titania app.; Jack of Hearts returns 4.00

SHE-HULKS
Marvel Comics: Jan, 2011 - No. 4, Apr, 2011 ($3.99/$2.99, limited series)

1-($3.99) She-Hulk & Lyra team-up; Stegman-a/McGuinness-c; character profile pages 6.00
2-4-($2.99) McGuinness-c 4.00

SHELTERED
Image Comics: Jul, 2013 - No. 15, Mar, 2015 ($2.99)

1-15-Brisson-s/Christmas-a 3.00

SHERIFF BOB DIXON'S CHUCK WAGON (TV) (See Wild Bill Hickok #22)
Avon Periodicals: Nov, 1950

	GD	VG	FN	VF	VF/NM	NM-
1-Kinstler-c/a(3)	16	32	48	98	154	210

SHERIFF OF BABYLON, THE
DC Comics (Vertigo): Feb, 2016 - No. 12, Jan, 2017 ($3.99)

1-12-Tom King-s/Mitch Gerads-a/John Paul Leon-c 4.00

SHERIFF OF TOMBSTONE
Charlton Comics: Nov, 1958 - No. 17, Sept, 1961

	GD	VG	FN	VF	VF/NM	NM-
V1#1-Giordano-c; Severin-a	6	12	18	38	69	100
2	4	8	12	22	35	48
3-10	3	6	9	17	25	32
11-17	3	6	9	14	20	25

SHERLOCK: A SCANDAL IN BELGRAVIA (Adaptation of episode from the BBC TV series)
Titan Comics: Jan, 2020 - No. 5, May, 2020 ($4.99/$3.99, B&W, reads back to front, right to left)

1-5-($4.99) English version of original Japanese manga; art by Jay.; multiple covers 5.00
... Part 2 1-4 (9/22 - No. 4, 12/22) Art by Jay.; multiple covers 5.00

SHERLOCK: A STUDY IN PINK (Adaptation of episode from the BBC TV series)
Titan Comics: Jul, 2016 - No. 6, Dec, 2016 ($4.99/$3.99, B&W, reads back to front, right to left)

1-($4.99) English version of original Japanese manga; art by Jay.; multiple covers 5.00
2-6-($3.99) 4.00

SHERLOCK FRANKENSTEIN AND THE LEGION OF EVIL (Also see Black Hammer)
Dark Horse Comics: Oct, 2017 - No. 4, Jan, 2018 ($3.99, limited series)

1-4-Lemire-s/Rubín-a 4.00

SHERLOCK HOLMES (See Classic Comics #33, Marvel Preview, New Adventures of..., & Spectacular Stories)

SHERLOCK HOLMES (All New Baffling Adventures of...)(Young Eagle #3 on?)
Charlton Comics: Oct, 1955 - No. 2, Mar, 1956

	GD	VG	FN	VF	VF/NM	NM-
1-Dr. Neff, Ghost Breaker app.	47	94	141	296	498	700
2	40	80	120	246	411	575

SHERLOCK HOLMES (Also see The Joker)
National Periodical Publications: Sept-Oct, 1975

	GD	VG	FN	VF	VF/NM	NM-
1-Cruz-a; Simonson-c	3	6	9	17	26	35

SHERLOCK HOLMES
Dynamite Entertainment: 2009 - No. 5, 2009 ($3.50, limited series)

1-5-Cassaday-c/Moore & Reppion-s/Aaron Campbell-a 3.50

SHERLOCK HOLMES: MORIARTY LIVES
Dynamite Entertainment: 2014 - No. 5, 2014 ($3.99, limited series)

1-5-Liss-s/Indro-a/Francavilla-c 4.00

SHERLOCK HOLMES: THE LIVERPOOL DEMON
Dynamite Entertainment: 2012 - No. 5, 2013 ($3.99, limited series)

1-5-Moore & Reppion-s/Triano-a/Francavilla-c 4.00

SHERLOCK HOLMES: THE VANISHING MAN
Dynamite Entertainment: 2018 - No. 4, 2018 ($3.99, limited series)
1-4-Moore & Reppion-s/Ohta-a/Cassaday-c 4.00

SHERLOCK HOLMES VS. HARRY HOUDINI
Dynamite Entertainment: 2014 - No. 5, 2015 ($3.99, limited series)
1-5-Del Col & McCreery-s/Furuzono-a; multiple covers on each 4.00

SHERLOCK HOLMES: YEAR ONE
Dynamite Entertainment: 2011 - No. 6, 2011 ($3.99, limited series)
1-6-Beatty-s; multiple covers on each 4.00

SHERLOCK: THE BLIND BANKER (Adaptation of episode from the BBC TV series)
Titan Comics: Feb, 2017 - No. 6, Jul, 2017 ($4.99/$3.99, B&W, reads back to front, right to left)
1-6-English version of original Japanese manga; art by Jay.; multiple covers 5.00

SHERLOCK: THE GREAT GAME (Adaptation of episode from the BBC TV series)
Titan Comics: Sept, 2017 - No. 6, Feb, 2018 ($4.99, B&W, reads back to front, right to left)
1-6-English version of original Japanese manga; art by Jay.; multiple covers 5.00

SHERRY THE SHOWGIRL (Showgirls #4)
Atlas Comics: July, 1956 - No. 3, Dec, 1956; No. 5, Apr, 1957 - No. 7, Aug, 1957
1-Dan DeCarlo-c/a in all 314 628 942 2198 3849 5500
2 142 284 426 909 1555 2200
3,5-7 77 154 231 493 847 1200

SHE'S JOSIE (See Josie)

SHEVA'S WAR
DC Comics (Helix): Oct, 1998 - No. 5, Feb, 1999 ($2.95, mini-series)
1-5-Christopher Moeller-s/painted-a/c 3.00

SHI (one-shots and TPBs)
Crusade Comics
...: Akai (2001, $2.99)-Intro. Victoria Cross; Tucci-a/c; J.C. Vaughn-s 3.00
...: Akai Victoria Cross Ed. ($5.95, edition of 2000) variant Tucci-c 6.00
...: C.G.I. (2001, $4.99) preview of unpublished series 5.00
.../ Cyblade: The Battle for the Independents (9/95, $2.95) Tucci-c; Hellboy, Bone app. 3.00
.../ Cyblade: The Battle for the Independents (9/95, $2.95) Silvestri variant-c 3.00
.../ Daredevil: Honor Thy Mother (1/97, $2.95) Flip book 3.00
...: Judgment Night (200, $3.99) Wolverine app.; Battlebook card and pages; Tucci-a 4.00
...: Kaidan (10/96, $2.95) Two covers; Tucci-c; Jae Lee wraparound-c 3.00
...: Masquerade (3/98, $3.50) Painted art by Lago, Texeira, and others 3.50
...: Nightstalkers (9/97, $3.50) Painted art by Val Mayerik 3.50
...: Rekishi (1/97, $2.95) Character bios and story summaries of Shi: The Way of the Warrior told in Detective Joe Labianca's point of view; Christopher Golden script; Tucci-c; J.G. Jones-a; flip book w/Shi: East Wind Rain preview 3.00
...: The Art of War Tourbook (1998, $4.95) Blank cover for sketches; early Tucci-a inside 5.00
.../ Vampirella (10/97, $2.95) Ellis-s/Lau-a 3.00
... Vs. Tomoe (8/96, $3.95) Tucci-a/scripts; wraparound foil-c 4.00
... Vs. Tomoe (6/96, $5.00. B&W)-Preview Ed.; sold at San Diego Comic Con 5.00
The Definitive Shi Vol. 1 (2006-2007, $24.99, TPB) B&W r/Way of the Warrior, Tomoe, Rekishi, and Senryaku series; cover gallery with sketches; Tucci & Sparacio-c 25.00

SHI: BLACK, WHITE AND RED
Crusade Comics: Mar, 1998 - No. 2, May, 1998 ($2.95, B&W&Red, mini-series)
1,2-J.G. Jones-painted art 3.00
...- Year of the Dragon Collected Edition (2000, $5.95) r/#1&2 6.00

SHIDIMA
Image Comics: Jan, 2001 - No. 7, Nov, 2002 ($2.95, limited series)
1-7-Prequel to Warlands 3.00
#0-(10/01, $2.25) Short story and sketch pages 3.00

SHI: EAST WIND RAIN
Crusade Comics: Nov, 1997 - No. 2, Feb, 1998 ($3.50, limited series)
1,2-Shi at WW2 Pearl Harbor 3.50

S.H.I.E.L.D. (Nick Fury & His Agents of...) (Also see Nick Fury)
Marvel Comics Group: Feb, 1973 - No. 5, Oct, 1973 (All 20¢ issues)
1-All contain reprint stories from Strange Tales #146-155; new Steranko-c 5 10 15 31 53 75
2-New Steranko flag-c 3 6 9 17 26 35
3-5: 3-Kirby/Steranko-c(r). 4-Steranko-c(r) 2 4 6 10 14 18
NOTE: *Buscema a-3p(r). Kirby layouts 1-5; c-3 (w/Steranko). Steranko a-3r, 4r(2).*

S.H.I.E.L.D.
Marvel Comics: Jun, 2010 - No. 6, Apr, 2011 ($3.99/$2.99)
1-($3.99) Leonardo DaVinci app.; Weaver-a/Hickman-s/Parel-c; 4 printings 4.00
1-Variant-c by Weaver 6.00
1-Director's Cut (9/10, $4.99) r/#1 with character sketch-a and bios; design-a 5.00
2-6-($2.99) 2-Three printings. 3-Galactus app. 3.00
Infinity (6/11, $4.99) DaVinci, Nostradamus, Newton & Tesla app.; Parel-c 5.00
... Origins (1/14, $7.99) r/Battle Scars #6, Secret Avengers #1, Strange Tales #135 8.00

S.H.I.E.L.D. (2nd series; title becomes S.H.I.E.L.D. by Hickman & Weaver with #5)
Marvel Comics: Aug, 2011 - No. 4, Feb, 2012; No. 5, Jul, 2018 - No. 6, Aug, 2018 ($3.99/$2.99)
1-($3.99) Weaver-a/Hickman-s/Parel-c; profile pgs of main characters 4.00
2-4-($2.99) 3.00
5,6: 5-(7/18, $3.99) Continuation after 6-year hiatus 4.00
... By Hickman & Weaver: The Rebirth 1 (7/18, $5.99) r/#1-4; Parel-c 6.00

S.H.I.E.L.D. (Based on the TV series)
Marvel Comics: Feb, 2015 - No. 12, Jan, 2016 ($4.99/$3.99)
1-($4.99) Waid-s/Pacheco-a/Tedesco-c; Avengers app. 5.00
2-8-($3.99) 2-Ms. Marvel (Kamala Khan) app.; Ramos-a. 3-Spider-Man app.; Davis-a 4.00
9-($5.99) 50th Anniversary issue; Howling Commandos app.; r/Strange Tales #135 6.00
10-12: 10-Howard the Duck app. 11-Dominic Fortune app.; Chaykin-a 4.00

SHIELD, THE (Becomes Shield-Steel Sterling #3; #1 titled Lancelot Strong; also see Advs. of the Fly, Double Life of Private Strong, Fly Man, Mighty Comics, The Mighty Crusaders, The Original... & Pep Comics #1)
Archie Enterprises, Inc.: June, 1983 - No. 2, Aug, 1983
1,2: Steel Sterling app. 1-Weiss-c/a. 2-Kanigher-s/Buckler-c/Nebres-a 5.00
America's 1st Patriotic Comic Book Hero, The Shield (2002, $12.95, TPB) r/Pep Comics #1-5, Shield-Wizard Comics #1; foreward by Robert M. Overstreet 13.00

SHIELD, THE (Archie Ent. character) (Continued from The Red Circle)
DC Comics: Nov, 2009 - No. 10, Aug, 2010 ($3.99)
1-10: 1-Magog app.; Inferno back-up feature thru #6; Green Arrow app. 2,3-Grodd app. 4,5-The Great Ten app. 7-10-The Fox back-up feature; Oeming-a 4.00
...: Kicking Down the Door TPB ('10, $19.99) r/#1-6, Red Circle: The Web & RC: The Shield 20.00

SHIELD, THE
Archie Comic Publications: Dec, 2015 - No. 4, Jan, 2017 ($3.99)
1-4-Christopher & Wendig-s/Drew Johnson-a; a new Shield recruited; multiple covers 4.00

SHIELD, THE: SPOTLIGHT (TV)
IDW Publishing: Jan, 2004 - No. 5, May, 2004 ($3.99)
1-5-Jeff Marriote-s/Jean Diaz-a/Tommy Lee Edwards-c 4.00
TPB (7/04, $19.99) r/#1-5; Michael Chiklis photo-c 20.00

SHIELD-STEEL STERLING (Formerly The Shield)
Archie Enterprises, Inc.: No. 3, Dec, 1983 (Becomes Steel Sterling No. 4)
3-Nino-a; Steel Sterling by Kanigher & Barreto 5.00

SHIELD WIZARD COMICS (Also see Pep Comics & Top-Notch Comics)
MLJ Magazines: Summer, 1940 - No. 13, Spring, 1944
1-(V1#5 on inside)-Origin The Shield by Irving Novick & The Wizard by Ed Ashe, Jr; Flag-c 520 1040 1560 3800 7650 11,500
2-(Winter/40)-Origin The Shield retold; Wizard's sidekick, Roy the Super Boy begins (see Top-Notch #8 for 1st app.) 300 600 900 1920 3310 4700
3,4 226 452 678 1446 2473 3500
5-Dusty, the Boy Detective begins; Nazi bondage-c 194 388 582 1242 2121 3000
6,7: 6-Roy the Super Boy app. 7-Shield dons new costume (Summer, 1942); S & K-c? 174 348 522 1114 1907 2700
8-Nazi bondage-c; Hitler photo on-c 371 742 1113 2600 4550 6500
9-Japanese WWII bondage-c 232 464 696 1485 2543 3600
10-Nazi swastica-c 290 580 870 1856 3178 4500
11 155 310 465 992 1696 2400
12-Nazi bondage-c 371 742 1113 2600 4550 6500
13-Japanese WWII bondage/torture-c (scarce) 290 580 870 1856 3178 4500
NOTE: *Bob Montana c-13. Novick c-1,3-6,8-11. Harry Sahle c-12.*

SHI: FAN EDITIONS
Crusade Comics: 1997
1-3-Two covers polybagged in FAN #19-21 3.00
1-3-Gold editions 4.00

SHI: HEAVEN AND EARTH
Crusade Comics: June, 1997 - No. 4, Apr, 1998 ($2.95)
1-4 3.00
4-($4.95) Pencil-c variant 5.00
Rising Sun Edition-signed by Tucci in FanClub Starter Pack 4.00
"Tora No Shi" variant-c 3.00

SHI: JU-NEN
Dark Horse Comics: July, 2004 - No. 4, May, 2005 ($2.99, mini-series)
1-4-Tucci-a/Tucci & Vaughn-s; origin retold 3.00
TPB (2/06, $12.95) r/#1-4; Tucci and Sparacio-c 13.00

SHINING KNIGHT (See Adventure Comics #66)

SHINKU
Image Comics: Jun, 2011 - No. 5, Oct, 2012 ($2.99)
1-5-Marz-s/Moder-a 3.00

SHINOBI (Based on Sega video game)
Dark Horse Comics: Aug, 2002 ($2.99, one-shot)
1-Medina-a/c 3.00

SHIP AHOY
Spotlight Publishers: Nov, 1944 (52 pgs.)
1-L. B. Cole-c 30 60 90 177 289 400

SHIP OF FOOLS
Image Comics: Aug, 1997 - No. 3 ($2.95, B&W)
0-3-Glass-s/Oeming-a 3.00

SHI: POISONED PARADISE
Avatar Press: July, 2002 - No. 2, Aug, 2002 ($3.50, limited series)
1,2-Vaughn and Tucci-s/Waller-a; 1-Four covers 3.50

SHIPWRECK
AfterShock Comics: Oct, 2016 - No. 6, Jun, 2018 ($3.99)
1-6-Warren Ellis-s/Phil Hester-a 3.00

SHIPWRECKED! (Disney-Movie)
Disney Comics: 1990 ($5.95, graphic novel, 68 pgs.)
nn-adaptation; Spiegle-a 6.00

SHIRTLESS BEAR FIGHTER
Image Comics: Jun, 2017 - No. 5, Oct, 2017 ($3.99, limited series)
1-5-Leheup & Girner-s/Vendrell-a; multiple covers on each 4.00

SHIRTLESS BEAR FIGHTER 2
Image Comics: Aug, 2022 - No. 7, Feb, 2023 ($3.99, limited series)
1-7-Leheup-s/Vendrell-a; multiple covers on each 4.00

SHI: SEMPO
Avatar Press: Aug, 2003 - No. 2, ($3.50, B&W, limited series)
1,2-Vaughn and Tucci-s/Alves-a; 1-Four covers 3.50

SHI: SENRYAKU
Crusade Comics: Aug, 1995 - No. 3, Nov, 1995 ($2.95, limited series)
1-3: 1-Tucci-c; Quesada, Darrow, Sim, Lee, Smith-a. 2-Tucci-c; Silvestri, Balent, Perez,

S.H.I.E.L.D. (2010) #3 © MAR

Shi: Ju-Nen #3 © William Tucci

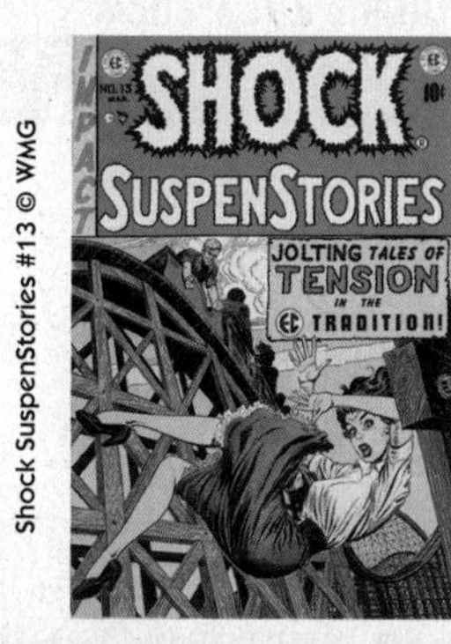

Shock SuspenStories #13 © WMG

GD 2.0 | VG 4.0 | FN 6.0 | VF 8.0 | VF/NM 9.0 | NM- 9.2

Mack-a. 3-Jusko-c; Hughes, Ramos, Bell, Moore-a 3.00
1-variant-c (no logo) 4.00
Hardcover ($24.95)-r/#1-3; Frazetta-c. 25.00
Trade Paperback ($13.95)-r/#1-3; Frazetta-c. 14.00

SHI: THE ILLUSTRATED WARRIOR
Crusade Comics: 2002 - No. 7, 2003 ($2.99, B&W)
1-7-Story text with Tucci full page art 3.00

SHI: THE SERIES
Crusade Comics: Aug, 1997 - No. 13 ($2.95, color #1-10, B&W #11)
1-10 3.00
11-13: 11-B&W. 12-Color; Lau-a 3.00
#0 Convention Edition 5.00

SHI: THE WAY OF THE WARRIOR
Crusade Comics: Mar, 1994 - No. 12, Apr, 1997 ($2.50/$2.95)
1/2 4.00
1 2 4 6 9 12 15
1-Commemorative ed., B&W, new-c; given out at 1994 San Diego Comic Con
2 4 6 11 16 20
1-Fan appreciation edition -r/#1 1 3 4 6 8 10
1-Fan appreciation edition (variant) 1 3 4 6 8 10
1- 10th Anniversary Edition (2004, $2.99) 3.00
2 5.00
2-Commemorative edition (3,000) 2 4 6 9 13 16
2-Fan appreciation edition -r/#2 6.00
3 4.00
4-7: 4-Silvestri poster. 7-Tomoe app. 3.00
5,6: 5-Silvestri variant-c. 6-Tomoe #1 variant-c 3.50
5-Gold edition 12.00
6,8-12: 6-Fan appreciation edition 3.00
8-Combo Gold edition 6.00
8-Signed Edition-(5000) 4.00
Trade paperback (1995, $12.95)-r/#1-4 15.00
Trade paperback (1995, $14.95)-r/#1-4 revised; Julie Bell-c 15.00

SHI: YEAR OF THE DRAGON
Crusade Comics: 2000 - No. 3, 2000 ($2.99, limited series)
1-3: 1-Two covers; Tucci-a/c; flashback to teen-aged Ana 3.00

SHMOO (See Al Capp's... & Washable Jones &...)

SHOCK (Magazine)
Stanley Publ.: May, 1969 - V3#4, Sept, 1971 (B&W reprints from horror comics, including some pre-code) (No V2#1,3)
V1#1-Cover-r/Weird Tales of the Future #7 by Bernard Baily; r/Weird Chills #1
8 16 24 51 96 140
2-Wolverton-r/Weird Mysteries 5; r-Weird Mysteries #7 used in **SOTI**; cover reprints cover to Weird Chills #1 6 12 18 38 69 100
3,5,6 4 8 12 28 47 65
4-Harrison/Williamson-r/Forbid. Worlds #6 5 10 15 30 50 70
V2#2(5/70), V1#8(7/70), V2#4(9/70)-6(1/71), V3#1-4: V2#4-Cover swipe from Weird Mysteries #6 4 8 12 27 44 60
NOTE: ***Disbrow** r-V2#4; Bondage c-V1#4, V2#6, V3#1.*

SHOCK DETECTIVE CASES (Formerly Crime Fighting Detective)
(Becomes Spook Detective Cases No. 22)
Star Publications: No. 20, Sept, 1952 - No. 21, Nov, 1952
20,21-L.B. Cole-c; based on true crime cases 142 284 426 909 1555 2200
NOTE: ***Palais** a-20. No. 21-Fox-r.*

SHOCK ILLUSTRATED (...Adult Crime Stories; Magazine format)
E. C. Comics: Sept-Oct, 1955 - No. 3, Spring, 1956 (Adult Entertainment on-c #1,2)(All 25¢)
1-All by Kamen; drugs, prostitution, wife swapping 30 60 90 177 289 400
2-Williamson-a redrawn from Crime SuspenStories #13 plus Ingels, Crandall, Evans & part Torres-i; painted-c 27 54 81 160 263 365
3-Only 100 known copies bound & given away at E.C. office; Crandall, Evans-a; painted-c; shows May, 1956 on-c 300 600 900 1920 3310 4700

SHOCKING MYSTERY CASES (Formerly Thrilling Crime Cases)
Star Publications: No. 50, Sept, 1952 - No. 60, Oct, 1954 (All crime reprints?)
50-Disbrow "Frankenstein" story 226 452 678 1446 2473 3500
51-Disbrow-a 155 310 465 992 1696 2400
52-60: 56-Drug use story 103 206 309 659 1130 1600
NOTE: ***L. B. Cole** covers on all; a-60(2 pgs.). **Hollingsworth** a-52. **Morisi** a-55.*

SHOCKING TALES DIGEST MAGAZINE
Harvey Publications: Oct, 1981 (95¢)

GD 2.0 | VG 4.0 | FN 6.0 | VF 8.0 | VF/NM 9.0 | NM- 9.2

1-1957-58-r; Powell, Kirby, Nostrand-a 2 4 6 9 13 16

SHOCK ROCKETS
Image Comics (Gorilla): Apr, 2000 - No. 6, Oct, 2000 ($2.50)
1-6-Busiek-s/Immonen & Grawbadger-a. 6-Flip book w/Superstar preview 3.00
...: We Have Ignition TPB (Dark Horse, 8/04, $14.95, 6" x 9") r/#1-6 15.00

SHOCK SHOP
Dark Horse Comics: Sept, 2022 - No. 4, Dec, 2022 ($3.99)
1-4-Cullen Bunn-s/Leila Leiz & Danny Luckert-a; flip cover on each 4.00

SHOCK SUSPENSTORIES (Also see EC Archives • Shock SuspenStories)
E. C. Comics: Feb-Mar, 1952 - No. 18, Dec-Jan, 1954-55
1-Classic Feldstein electrocution-c 143 286 429 1144 1822 2500
2 71 142 213 568 909 1250
3,4: 3-Classic decapitation splash. 4-Used in **SOTI**, pg. 387,388
57 114 171 456 728 1000
5-Hanging-c 120 240 360 960 1530 2100
6-Classic hooded vigilante bondage-c 240 480 720 1920 3060 4200
7-Classic face melting-c 97 194 291 776 1238 1700
8-Williamson-a 69 138 207 552 876 1200
9-11: 9-Injury to eye panel. 10-Junkie story 44 88 132 352 564 775
12- "The Monkey" classic junkie cover/story; anti-drug propaganda issue
143 284 429 1144 1822 2500
13-Frazetta's only solo story for E.C., 7 pgs, draws himself as main male character
74 148 222 592 946 1300
14-Used in Senate Investigation hearings 149 298 447 1192 1896 2600
15-Used in 1954 Reader's Digest article, "For the Kiddies to Read"
91 182 273 728 1164 1600
16-18: 16- "Red Dupe" editorial; rape story 40 80 120 320 510 700
NOTE: ***Ray Bradbury** adaptations-1, 7, 9. **Craig** a-11; c-11. **Crandall** a-9-13, 15-18. **Davis** a-1-5. **Evans** a-7, 8, 14-18; c-16-18. **Feldstein** c-1, 7-9, 12. **Ingels** a-1, 2, 6. **Kamen** a-in all; c-10, 13, 15. **Krigstein** a-14, 18. **Orlando** a-1, 3-7, 9, 10, 12, 16, 17. **Wood** a-2-15; c-2-6, 14.*

SHOCK SUSPENSTORIES (Also see EC Archives • Shock SuspenStories)
Russ Cochran/Gemstone Publishing: Sept, 1992 - No. 18, Dec, 1996 ($1.50/$2.00/$2.50, quarterly)
1-18: 1-3: Reprints with original-c. 17-r/HOF #17 4.00

SHOGUN WARRIORS
Marvel Comics Group: Feb, 1979 - No. 20, Sept, 1980 (Based on Mattel toys of the classic Japanese animation characters) (1-3: 35¢; 4-19: 40¢; 20: 50¢)
1-Raydeen, Combatra, & Dangard Ace begin; Trimpe-a
3 6 9 19 30 40
2-20: 2-Lord Maurkon & Elementals of Evil app.; Rok-Korr app. 6-Shogun vs. Shogun. 7,8-Cerberus. 9-Starchild. 11-Austin-c. 12-Simonson-c. 14-16-Doctor Demonicus. 17-Juggernaut. 19,20-FF x-over 2 4 6 8 10 12

SHOOK UP (Magazine) (Satire)
Dodsworth Publ. Co.: Nov, 1958
V1#1 5 10 15 30 50 70

SHOPLIFTERS WILL BE LIQUIDATED
AfterShock Comics: Oct, 2019 - No. 5, Mar, 2020 ($3.99, limited series)
1-5-Patrick Kindlon-s/Stefano Simeone-a 4.00

SHORT RIBS
Dell Publishing Co.: No. 1333, Apr - June, 1962
Four Color 1333 6 12 18 38 69 100

SHORTSTOP SQUAD (Baseball)
Ultimate Sports Ent. Inc.: 1999 ($3.95, one-shot)
1-Ripken Jr., Larkin, Jeter, Rodriguez app.; Edwards-c/a 4.00

SHORT STORY COMICS (See Hello Pal,...)

SHORTY SHINER (The Five-Foot Fighter in the Ten Gallon Hat)
Dandy Magazine (Charles Biro): June, 1956 - No. 3, Oct, 1956
1 9 18 27 50 65 80
2,3 7 14 21 37 46 55

SHOTGUN SLADE (TV)
Dell Publishing Co.: No. 1111, July-Sept, 1960
Four Color 1111-Photo-c 6 12 18 37 66 95

SHOWCASE (See Cancelled Comic Cavalcade & New Talent...)
National Per. Publ./DC Comics: 3-4/56 - No. 93, 9/70; No. 94, 8-9/77 - No. 104, 9/78
1-Fire Fighters; w/Fireman Farrell 327 654 981 2780 6290 9800
2-Kings of the Wild; Kubert-a (animal stories) 141 282 423 1142 2571 4000
3-The Frogmen by Russ Heath; Heath greytone-c (early DC example, 7-8/56)

	GD	VG	FN	VF	VF/NM	NM-
	2.0	4.0	6.0	8.0	9.0	9.2

125 250 375 1000 2250 3500
4-Origin/1st app. The Flash (1st DC Silver Age hero, Sept-Oct, 1956); Kanigher-s; Infantino & Kubert-c/a; 1st app. Iris West and The Turtle; r/in Secret Origins #1 ('61 & '73); Flash shown reading G.A. Flash Comics #13; back-up story w/Broome-s/Infantino & Kubert-a
7900 15,800 31,600 71,100 126,550 182,000
5-Manhunters; Meskin-a 107 214 321 856 1928 3000
6-Origin/1st app. Challengers of the Unknown by Kirby, partly r/in Secret Origins #1 & Challengers #64,65 (1st S.A. hero team & 1st original concept S.A. series)(1-2/57)
450 900 1350 3820 8660 13,500
7-Challengers of the Unknown by Kirby (2nd app.) reprinted in Challengers of the Unknown #75 172 344 516 1419 3210 5000
8-The Flash (5-6/57, 2nd app.); origin & 1st app. Captain Cold
1040 2080 3120 9360 17,680 26,000
9-Lois Lane (Pre-#1, 7-8/57) (1st Showcase character to win own series)
Superman app. on-c 715 1430 2145 5700 10,350 15,000
10-Lois Lane; Jor-El cameo; Superman app. on-c 220 440 660 1815 4108 6400
11-Challengers of the Unknown by Kirby (3rd) 141 282 429 1163 2632 4100
12-Challengers of the Unknown by Kirby (4th) 141 282 429 1163 2632 4100
13-The Flash (3rd app.); origin Mr. Element 430 860 1290 3650 8325 13,000
14-The Flash (4th app.); origin Dr. Alchemy, former Mr. Element (rare in NM)
430 860 1290 3650 8325 13,000
15-Space Ranger (7-8/58, 1st app., also see My Greatest Aventure #22)
179 358 537 1477 3339 5200
16-Space Ranger (9-10/58, 2nd app.) 100 200 300 800 1800 2800
17-(11-12/58)-Adventures on Other Worlds; origin/1st app. Adam Strange by Gardner Fox & Mike Sekowsky 567 1134 1700 4820 10,910 17,000
18-Adventures on Other Worlds (2nd A. Strange) 100 200 300 800 1800 2800
19-Adam Strange; 1st Adam Strange logo 104 208 312 832 1866 2900
20-Rip Hunter; origin & 1st app. (5-6/59); Moreira-a 152 304 456 1254 2827 4400
21-Rip Hunter (7-8/59, 2nd app.); Sekowsky-c/a 64 128 192 512 1156 1800
22-Origin & 1st app. Silver Age Green Lantern by Gil Kane and John Broome (9-10/59); reprinted in Secret Origins #2 1625 3250 6500 19,900 42,450 65,000
23-Green Lantern (11-12/59, 2nd app.); nuclear explosion-c
214 428 642 1766 3983 6200
24-Green Lantern (1-2/60, 3rd app.) 179 358 537 1477 3339 5200
25,26-Rip Hunter by Kubert. 25-Grey tone-c 49 98 147 382 866 1350
27-Sea Devils (7-8/60, 1st app.); Heath-c/a; Grey tone-c
82 164 246 656 1478 2300
28-Sea Devils (9-10/60, 2nd app.); Heath-c/a; Grey tone-c
42 84 126 311 706 1100
29-Sea Devils; Heath-c/a; grey tone c-27-29 44 88 132 326 738 1150
30-Origin Silver Age Aquaman (1-2/61) (see Adventure #260 for 1st S.A. origin)
282 564 846 2327 5264 8200
31-Aquaman 57 114 171 456 1028 1600
32,33-Aquaman 42 84 126 311 706 1100
34-Origin & 1st app. Silver Age Atom by Gil Kane & Murphy Anderson (9-10/61); reprinted in Secret Origins #2 190 380 570 15468 3534 5500
35-The Atom by Gil Kane (2nd); last 10¢ issue 52 104 156 413 932 1450
36-The Atom by Gil Kane (1-2/62, 3rd app.) 40 80 120 296 673 1050
37-Metal Men (3-4/62, 1st app.) 207 414 621 1708 3854 6000
38-Metal Men (5-6/62, 2nd app.) 33 66 99 238 532 825
39-Metal Men (7-8/62, 3rd app.) 25 50 75 175 388 600
40-Metal Men (9-10/62, 4th app.) 25 50 75 175 388 600
41,42-Tommy Tomorrow (parts 1 & 2). 42-Origin 13 26 39 91 201 310
43-Dr. No (James Bond); Nodel-a; originally published as British Classics Illustrated #158A & as #6 in a European Detective series, all with diff. painted-c. This Showcase #43 version is actually censored, deleting all racial skin color and dialogue thought to be racially demeaning (1st DC S.A. movie adaptation)(based on Ian Fleming novel & movie)
61 122 183 488 1094 1700
44-Tommy Tomorrow 10 20 30 68 144 220
45-Sgt. Rock (7-8/63); pre-dates B&B #52; origin retold; Heath-c
35 70 105 252 564 875
46,47-Tommy Tomorrow 9 18 27 61 123 185
48,49-Cave Carson (3rd tryout series; see B&B) 8 16 24 56 108 160
50,51-I Spy (Danger Trail-r by Infantino), King Farady story (#50 has new 4 pg. story)
7 14 21 48 89 130
52-Cave Carson 8 16 24 52 99 145
53,54-G.I. Joe (11-12/64, 1-2/65); Heath-a 12 24 36 81 176 270
55-Dr. Fate & Hourman (3-4/65); origin of each in text; 1st solo app. G.A. Green Lantern in Silver Age (pre-dates Gr. Lantern #40); 1st S.A. app. Solomon Grundy
54 108 162 432 966 1500
56-Dr. Fate & Hourman 14 28 42 96 211 325
57-Enemy Ace by Kubert (7-8/65, 4th app. after Our Army at War #155)
20 40 60 136 303 470
58-Enemy Ace by Kubert (5th app.) 16 32 48 107 236 365
59-Teen Titans (11-12/65, 3rd app.) 19 38 57 133 297 460
60-1st S. A. app. The Spectre; Anderson-a (1-2/66); origin in text
29 58 87 209 467 725
61-The Spectre by Anderson (2nd app.) 13 26 39 89 195 300
62-Origin & 1st app. Inferior Five (5-6/66) 10 20 30 66 138 210
63,65-Inferior Five. 63-Hulk parody. 65-X-Men parody (11-12/66)
6 12 18 38 69 100
64-The Spectre by Anderson (5th app.) 12 24 36 82 179 275
66,67-B'wana Beast 6 12 18 58 69 100
68-Maniaks (1st app., spoof of The Monkees) 5 10 15 35 63 90
69,71-Maniaks. 71-Woody Allen-c/app. 5 10 15 34 60 85
70-Binky (9-10/67)-Tryout issue; 1950's Leave It To Binky reprints with art changes
6 12 18 38 69 100
72-Top Gun (Johnny Thunder-r)-Toth-a 5 10 15 31 53 75
73-Origin/1st app. Creeper; Ditko-c/a (3-4/68) 14 28 42 96 211 325
74-Intro/1st app. Anthro; Post-c/a (5/68) 7 14 21 49 92 135
75-Origin/1st app. Hawk & the Dove; Ditko-c/a 14 28 42 96 211 325
76-1st app. Bat Lash (8/68) 8 16 24 55 105 155
77-1st app. Angel & The Ape (9/68) 7 14 21 48 89 130
78-1st app. Jonny Double (11/68) 5 10 15 30 50 70
79-1st app. Dolphin (12/68); Aqualad origin-r 33 66 99 238 532 825
80-1st S.A. app. Phantom Stranger (1/69); Neal Adams-c
16 32 48 110 243 375
81-Windy & Willy; r/Many Loves of Dobie Gillis #26 with art changes
5 10 15 34 60 85
82-1st app. Nightmaster (5/69) by Grandenetti & Giordano; Kubert-c
7 14 21 44 82 120
83,84-Nightmaster by Wrightson w/Jones/Kaluta ink assist in each; Kubert-c.
83-Last 12¢ issue 84-Origin retold; begin 15¢ 6 12 18 41 76 110
85-87-Firehair; Kubert-a 3 6 9 16 23 30
88-90-Jason's Quest: 90-Manhunter 2070 app. 3 6 9 14 20 25
91-93-Manhunter 2070: 92-Origin. 93-(9/70) Last 15¢ issue
3 6 9 14 20 25
94-Intro/origin new Doom Patrol & Robotman(8-9/77) 3 6 9 14 20 25
95,96-The Doom Patrol. 95-Origin Celsius 2 3 4 6 8 10
97-Power Girl; origin; JSA cameos 4 8 12 25 40 55
98,99-Power Girl; origin in #98; JSA cameos 2 4 6 11 16 20
100-(52 pgs.)-Most Showcase characters featured 2 4 6 11 16 20
101-103-Hawkman; Adam Strange x-over 2 4 6 8 10 12
104-(52 pgs.)-O.S.S. Spies at War 2 4 6 8 10 12

NOTE: ***Anderson** a-22-24i, 34-36i, 55, 56, 60, 61, 64, 101-103i; c-50i, 51i, 55, 56, 60, 61, 64. **Aparo** c-94-96. **Boring** c-10. **Estrada** a-104. **Fraden** c(p)-30, 31, 33. **Heath** c-3, 27-29. **Infantino** c/a(p)-4, 8, 13, 14; c-50p, 51p. **Gil Kane** a-22-24p, 34-36p; c-17-19, 22-24p(w/**Giella**), 31. **Kane/Anderson** c-34-36. **Kirby** c-11, 12. **Kirby/Stein** c-6, 7. **Kubert** a-2, 4i, 25, 26, 45, 53, 54, 72; c-25, 26, 53, 54, 57, 58, 82-87, 101-104; c-2, 4i. **Moreira** c-5. **Orlando** a-62p, 63p, 97i; c-62, 63, 97i. **Sekowsky** a-65p. **Sparling** a-78. **Staton** a-94, 95-99p, 100; c-97-100p.*

SHOWCASE '93
DC Comics: Jan, 1993 - No. 12, Dec, 1993 ($1.95, limited series, 52 pgs.)

1-12: 1-Begin 4 part Catwoman story & 6 part Blue Devil story; begin Cyborg story; Art Adams/Austin-c. 3-Flash by Charest (p). 6-Azrael in Bat-costume (2 pgs.). 7,8-Knightfall parts 13 & 14. 6-10-Deathstroke app. (6,10-cameo). 9,10-Austin-i. 10-Azrael as Batman in new costume app.; Gulacy-c. 11-Perez-c. 12-Creeper app.; Alan Grant scripts 4.00

NOTE: ***Chaykin** c-9. **Fabry** c-8. **Giffen** a-12. **Golden** c-3. **Zeck** c-6.*

SHOWCASE '94
DC Comics: Jan, 1994 - No. 12, Dec, 1994 ($1.95, limited series, 52 pgs.)

1-12: 1,2-Joker & Gunfire stories. 1-New Gods. 4-Riddler story. 5-Huntress-c/story w/app. new Batman. 6-Huntress-c/story w/app. Robin; Atom story. 7-Penguin story by Peter David, P. Craig Russell, & Michael T. Gilbert; Penguin-c by Jae Lee. 8,9-Scarface origin story by Alan Grant, John Wagner,& Teddy Kristiansen; Prelude to Zero Hour. 10-Zero Hour tie-in story. 11-Man-Bat. 4.00

NOTE: ***Alan Grant** scripts-3, 4. **Kelley Jones** c-12. **Mignola** c-3. **Nebres** a(i)-2. **Quesada** c-10. **Russell** a-7p. **Simonson** c-5.*

SHOWCASE '95
DC Comics: Jan, 1995 - No. 12, Dec, 1995 ($2.50/$2.95, limited series)

1-4-Supergirl story. 3-Eradicator-c.; The Question story. 4-Thorn c/story 4.00
5-12: 5-Thorn-c/story; begin $2.95-c. 8-Spectre story. 12-The Shade story by James Robinson & Wade Von Grawbadger; Maitresse story by Claremont & Alan Davis 4.00

SHOWCASE '96
DC Comics: Jan, 1996 - No. 12, Dec, 1996 ($2.95, limited series)

1-12: 1-Steve Geppi cameo. 3-Black Canary & Lois Lane-c/story; Deadman story by Jamie Delano & Wade Von Grawbadger, Gary Frank-c. 4-Firebrand & Guardian-c/story; The Shade & Dr. Fate "Times Past" story by James Robinson & Matt Smith begins, ends #5. 6-Superboy-c/app.; Atom app.; Capt. Marvel (Mary Marvel)-c/app. 8-Supergirl by David & Dodson. 11-Scare Tactics app. 11,12-Legion of Super-Heroes vs. Brainiac. 12-Jesse Quick app. 4.00

SHOWCASE PRESENTS... (B&W archive reprints of DC Silver Age stories)
DC Comics: 2005 - 2011 ($9.99/$16.99/$17.99/$19.99, B&W, over 500 pgs., squarebound)

Adam Strange Vol. 1 (2007, $16.99) r/Showcase #17-19 & Mystery in Space #53-84 17.00
Ambush Bug (2009, $16.99) r/first app. in DC Comics Presents #52 other early app. 17.00
Aquaman Vol. 1 (2007, $16.99) r/Aquaman #1-6 & other early app. 17.00
Aquaman Vol. 2 (2008, $16.99) r/Aquaman #7-23 & other early app. 17.00
Aquaman Vol. 3 (2009, $16.99) r/Aquaman #24-39 & other early app. 17.00
The Atom Vol. 1 (2007, $16.99) r/Showcase #34-36 & The Atom #1-17 17.00
The Atom Vol. 2 (2008, $16.99) r/The Atom #18-38 17.00
Batgirl Vol. 1 (2007, $16.99) r/early apps. from Detective #359 (1967) thru 1975 17.00
Bat Lash Vol. 1 (2009, $9.99) r/#1-7, Showcase #76, DC Special Series #16, and Jonah Hex #49,51,52 10.00
Batman Vol. 1 (2006, $16.99) r/"new look" from Detective #327-342, Batman #164-174 17.00
Batman Vol. 2 (2007, $16.99) r/"new look" from Detective #343-358, Batman #175-188 17.00
Batman Vol. 3 (2008, $16.99) r/"new look" from Detective #359-375, Batman #189, 190-192,194-197,199-202 17.00
Batman and the Outsiders Vol. 1 (2007, $16.99) r/#1-19, Annual #1; Brave and the Bold #200; and New Teen Titans #37 17.00
Blackhawk Vol. 1 (2008, $16.99) r/#108-127 17.00
Booster Gold Vol. 1 (2008, $16.99) r/#1-25 & Action Comics #594 17.00
The Brave and the Bold Batman Team-ups Vol. 1 (2007, $16.99) r/#59,64,67-71,74-87 17.00
The Brave and the Bold Batman Team-ups Vol. 2 (2007, $16.99) r/#88-108 17.00
The Brave and the Bold Batman Team-ups Vol. 3 (2008, $16.99) r/#109-134 17.00
Challengers of the Unknown Vol. 1 (2006, $16.99) r/#1-17 & Showcase #6,7,11,12 17.00
Challengers of the Unknown Vol. 2 (2008, $16.99) r/#18-37 17.00
DC Comics Presents: The Superman Team-ups Vol. 1 (2009, $17.99) r/#1-26 18.00
Dial H For Hero ('10, $9.99) r/early apps. in House of Mystery #156-173 10.00
Doc Savage ('11, $19.99) r/Doc Savage #1-8 (1975-77 Marvel B&W magazine) 20.00
The Doom Patrol Vol. 1 (2009, $16.99) r/#86-101 and My Greatest Adventure #80-85 17.00
The Doom Patrol Vol. 2 (2010, $19.99) r/#102-121 20.00
The Elongated Man Vol. 1 ('06, $16.99) r/early apps. in Flash & Detective ('60-'68) 17.00
Eclipso Vol. 1 (2009, $9.99) r/stories from House of Secrets #61-80 10.00
Enemy Ace Vol. 1 (2008, $16.99) r/Our Army at War #151 & other early app. 17.00
The Flash Vol. 1 (2007, $16.99) r/Flash Comics #104 (last G.A. issue), Showcase #4,8,13,14 & The Flash #105-119 17.00
The Flash Vol. 2 (2008, $16.99) r/The Flash #120-140 17.00
The Flash Vol. 3 (2009, $16.99) r/The Flash #141-161 17.00
The Flash, The Trial of ... (2011, $19.99) r/The Flash #323-327,329-336,340-350 20.00
The Great Disaster Featuring The Atomic Knights and Hercules Vol. 1 (2007, $16.99) 17.00
Green Arrow Vol. 1 (2006, $16.99) r/Adventure #250-269, Brave and the Bold #50,71,85; Justice League of America #4; World's Finest #95-134,136,138,140 17.00
Green Lantern Vol. 1 (2005, $9.99) r/Showcase #22-24 & Green Lantern #1-17 20.00
Green Lantern Vol. 1 (2010, $19.99) r/Showcase #22-24 & Green Lantern #1-17 20.00

Showcase #54 © DC

Shrek #2 © DreamWorks

Shuri #3 © MAR

	GD	VG	FN	VF	VF/NM	NM-
	2.0	4.0	6.0	8.0	9.0	9.2

Green Lantern Vol. 2 (2007, $16.99) r/Green Lantern #18-38 17.00
Green Lantern Vol. 3 (2008, $16.99) r/Green Lantern #39-59 17.00
Green Lantern Vol. 4 (2009, $16.99) r/Green Lantern #60-75 17.00
Green Lantern Vol. 5 (2011, $19.99) r/Green Lantern #76-87,89 and back up stories from Flash #217-246 20.00
Haunted Tank Vol. 1 ('06, $16.99) r/G.I. Combat #87-119, Brave & The Bold #52 and Our Army at War #155; Russ Heath-c 17.00
Haunted Tank Vol. 2 ('08, $16.99) r/G.I. Combat #120-156 17.00
Hawkman Vol. 1 ('07, $16.99) r/Brave & The Bold #34-36,42-44, Mystery in Space #87-90, Hawkman #1-11, and The Atom #7 17.00
Hawkman Vol. 2 ('08, $16.99) r/Brave & The Bold #70, Hawkman #12-27, The Atom #31, & The Atom and Hawkman #39-45 17.00
The House of Mystery Vol. 1 ('06, $16.99) r/House of Mystery #174-194 ('68-'71) 17.00
The House of Mystery Vol. 2 ('07, $16.99) r/House of Mystery #195-211 ('71-'73) 17.00
The House of Mystery Vol. 3 ('09, $16.99) r/House of Mystery #212-226 ('73-'74) 17.00
The House of Secrets Vol. 1 ('08, $16.99) r/House of Secrets #81-98 ('69-'72) 17.00
The House of Secrets Vol. 2 ('09, $17.99) r/House of Secrets #99-119 ('72-'74) 18.00
Jonah Hex Vol. 1 (2005, $16.99) r/All Star Western #10-12, Weird Western Tales #13,14, 16-33; plus the complete adventures of Outlaw from All Star Western #2-8 17.00
Justice League of America Vol. 1 ('05, $16.99) r/Brave & the Bold #28-30, J.L. of A. #1-16 and Mystery in Space #75 17.00
Justice League of America Vol. 2 ('07, $16.99) r/Justice League of America #17-36 17.00
Justice League of America Vol. 3 ('07, $16.99) r/Justice League of America #37-60 17.00
Justice League of America Vol. 4 ('09, $16.99) r/Justice League of America #61-83 17.00
Justice League of America Vol. 5 ('11, $19.99) r/Justice League of America #84-106 20.00
Legion of Super-Heroes Vol. 1 ('07, $16.99) r/Adventure #247 & early app. thru 1964 17.00
Legion of Super-Heroes Vol. 2 ('08, $16.99) r/app. in Adventure & Superboy 1964-66 17.00
Legion of Super-Heroes Vol. 3 ('09, $16.99) r/Adventure #349-368 & S.P. Jimmy Olsen #106 17.00
Legion of Super-Heroes Vol. 4 ('10, $19.99) r/app. in Adv., Action & Superboy 1968-72 20.00
Martian Manhunter Vol. 1 (2007, $16.99) r/Detective #225-304 & Batman #78 (prototype) 17.00
Martian Manhunter Vol. 2 ('09, $16.99) r/Detective #305-326 & House of Myst. #143-173 17.00
Metal Men Vol. 1 (2007, $16.99) r/#1-16; Brave & Bold #55, Showcase #37-40 17.00
Metamorpho Vol. 1 ('05, $16.99) r/Brave&Bold #57,58,66,68; Metamorpho #1-17;JLA #42 17.00
Our Army at War Vol. 1 ('10, $19.99) r/#1-20 20.00
Phantom Stranger Vol. 1 (2006, $16.99) r/#1-21 (2nd series) & Showcase #80 17.00
Phantom Stranger Vol. 2 (2008, $16.99) r/#22-41 and various 1970-1978 appearances 17.00
Robin The Boy Wonder Vol. 1 (2007, $16.99) r/back-ups from Batman, Detective, WF 17.00
Secrets of Sinister House ('10, $17.99) r/#5-18 and Sinister House of Secret Love #1-4 18.00
Sgt. Rock Vol. 1 ('07, $16.99) r/G.I. Combat #68, Our Army at War #81-117 17.00
Sgt. Rock Vol. 2 ('08, $16.99) r/Our Army at War #118-148 17.00
Sgt. Rock Vol. 3 ('10, $19.99) r/Our Army at War #149-163,165-172,174-176,178-180 20.00
Shazam! Vol. 1 ('06, $16.99) r/#1-33 17.00
Strange Adventures Vol. 1 ('08, $16.99) r/#54-73 17.00
Supergirl Vol. 1 ('07, $16.99) r/prototype from Superman #123 (8/58); 1st app. Action #252 (5/59) and early appearances thru Nov. 1961 17.00
Supergirl Vol. 2 ('08, $16.99) r/appearances in Action Comics #283-321 (1961-1965) 17.00
Superman Vol. 1 ('05, $9.99) r/Action #241-257 & Superman #122-134 (1958-59) 20.00
Superman Vol. 1 ('10, $19.99) r/Action #241-257 & Superman #122-134 (1958-59) 20.00
Superman Vol. 2 ('06, $16.99) r/Action #258-275 & Superman #134-145 (1959-61) 17.00
Superman Vol. 3 ('07, $16.99) r/Action #279-292 & Superman #146-156 & Annual #3,4 17.00
Superman Vol. 4 ('08, $16.99) r/Action #293-309 & Superman #157-166 (1962-64) 17.00
Superman Family Vol. 1 ('06, $16.99) Superman's Pal, Jimmy Olsen #1-22; Showcase #9 and Superman #22 17.00
Superman Family Vol. 2 ('08, $16.99) Superman's Pal, Jimmy Olsen #23-34; Showcase #10 and Superman's Girl Friend, Lois Lane #1-7 17.00
Superman Family Vol. 3 ('09, $16.99) Superman's Pal, Jimmy Olsen #35-44 and Superman's Girl Friend, Lois Lane #8-16 17.00
Teen Titans Vol. 1 ('06, $16.99) r/#1-18; Brave & the Bold #54,60; Showcase #59 17.00
Teen Titans Vol. 2 ('07, $16.99) r/#19-37, World's Finest #205 and Brave & Bold #83,94 17.00
The Unknown Soldier Vol. 1 ('06, $16.99) r/Star Spangled War Stories #158-188 17.00
The War That Time Forgot Vol. 1 ('07, $16.99) r/S.S.W.S. #90,92,94-125,127,128 17.00
Warlord Vol. 1 ('09, $16.99) r/#1-28 and debut in 1st Issue Special #1 17.00
The Witching Hour Vol. 1 ('11, $19.99) r/#1-19 20.00
Wonder Woman Vol. 1 ('07, $16.99) r/#98-117 17.00
Wonder Woman Vol. 2 ('08, $16.99) r/#118-137 17.00
World's Finest Vol. 1 ('07, $16.99) r/#71-111 & Superman #76 17.00
World's Finest Vol. 2 ('08, $16.99) r/#112-145 17.00
World's Finest Vol. 3 ('10, $17.99) r/#146-160,162-169,171-173 ('64-'68) 18.00

SHOWGIRLS (Formerly Sherry the Showgirl #3)
Atlas Comics (MPC No. 2): No. 4, 2/57; June, 1957 - No. 2, Aug, 1957

	GD	VG	FN	VF	VF/NM	NM-
4-(2/57) Dan DeCarlo-c/a begins	174	348	522	1114	1907	2700
1-(6/57) Millie, Sherry, Chili, Pearl & Hazel begin	219	438	657	1402	2401	3400
2	65	130	195	416	708	1000

	GD	VG	FN	VF	VF/NM	NM-
	2.0	4.0	6.0	8.0	9.0	9.2

SHREK (Movie)
Dark Horse Comics: Sept, 2003 - No. 3, Dec, 2003 ($2.99, limited series)
1-3-Takes place after 1st movie; Evanier-s/Bachs-a; CGI cover 4.00

SHREK (Movie)
Ape Entertainment: 2010 - No. 4, 2011 ($3.95, limited series)
1-3-Short stories by various 4.00

SHROUD, THE (See Super-Villain Team-Up #5)
Marvel Comics: Mar, 1994 - No. 4, June, 1994 ($1.75, mini-series)
1-4: 1,2,4-Spider-Man & Scorpion app. 4.00

SHROUD OF MYSTERY
Whitman Publications: June, 1982

	GD	VG	FN	VF	VF/NM	NM-
1	1	2	3	4	5	7

SHRUGGED
Aspen MLT, Inc.: No. 0, June, 2006 - No. 8, Feb, 2009 ($2.50/$2.99)
0-($2.50) Turner & Mastromauro-s/Gunnell-a; intro. story and character profiles 3.00
1-8-($2.99) 1-Six covers. 2-Three covers 3.00
... : Beginnings (5/06, $1.99) Prequel intro. to Ange and Dev; Gunnell-a; development art 3.00
Volume 2 (3/13, $1.00) 1-Marks & Gunnell-a; multiple covers 3.00
V2 #2-6-($3.99) Mastromauro-s/Marks-a. 6-(2/18) 4.00
Volume 3 (2/18, $3.99) 1-4-Mastromauro-s/André Risso-a; multiple covers 4.00

SHURI (From Black Panther)
Marvel Comics: Dec, 2018 - No. 10, Sept, 2019 ($3.99)

	GD	VG	FN	VF	VF/NM	NM-
1-Nnedi Okorafor-s/Leonardo Romero-a	3	6	9	14	19	24
2-Rocket & Groot app.; Okorafor-s/Romero-a	2	4	6	9	12	15

3-10: 3-5-Okorafor-s/Romero-a. 3-Rocket & Groot app. 6,7-Miles Morales app.; Ayala-s/Davidson-a. 8-10-Shuri in the Black Panther costume 6.00

SHUTTER
Image Comics: Apr, 2014 - No. 30, Jul, 2017 ($3.50/$3.99)
1-11-Keatinge-s/Del Duca-a 3.50
12-30-($3.99) 4.00

SHUT UP AND DIE
Image Comics/Halloween: 1998 - No. 3, 1998 ($2.95,B&W, bi-monthly)
1-3: Hudnall-s 3.00

SICK (Sick Special #131) (Magazine) (Satire)
Feature Publ./Headline Publ./Crestwood Publ. Co./Hewfred Publ./ Pyramid Comm./ Charlton Publ. No. 109 (4/76) on: Aug, 1960 - No. 134, Fall, 1980

	GD	VG	FN	VF	VF/NM	NM-
V1#1-Jack Paar photo on-c; Torres-a; Untouchables-s; Ben Hur movie photo-s	16	32	48	110	243	375
2-Torres-a; Elvis app.; Lenny Bruce app.	10	20	30	64	132	200
3-5-Torres-a in all. 3-Khruschev-c; Hitler-s. 4-Newhart-s; Castro-s; John Wayne. 5-JFK/Castro-c; Elvis pin-up; Hitler.	8	16	24	55	105	155
6-Photo-s of Ricky Nelson & Marilyn Monroe; JFK	9	18	27	57	111	165
V2#1,2,4-8 (#7,8,10-14): 1-(#7) Hitler-s; Brando photo-s. 2-(#8) Dick Clark-s. 4-(#10) Untouchables-c; Candid Camera-s. 5-(#11) Nixon-c; Lone Ranger-s; JFK-s. 6-(#12) Beatnik-c/s. 8-(#14) Liz Taylor pin-up, JFK-s; Dobie Gillis-s; Sinatra & Dean Martin photo-s	8	16	24	51	96	140
3-(#9) Marilyn Monroe/JFK-c; Kingston Trio-s	8	16	24	55	105	155
V3#1-7(#15-21): 1-(#15) JFK app.; Liz Tayor/Richard Burton-s. 2-(#16) Ben Casey/ Frankenstein-c/s; Hitler photo-s. 5-(#19) Nixon back-c/s; Sinatra photo-s. 6-(#20) 1st Huckleberry Fink-c	5	10	15	33	57	80
8-(#22) Cassius Clay vs. Liston-s; 1st Civil War Blackouts-/Pvt. Bo Reargard w/ Jack Davis-a	5	10	15	35	63	90
V4#1-5 (#23-27): Civil War Blackouts-/Pvt. Bo Reargard w/ Jack Davis-a in all. 1-(#23) Smokey Bear-c; Tarzan-s. 2-(#24) Goldwater & Paar-s; Castro-s. 3-(#25) Frankenstein-c; Cleopatra/Liz Taylor-s; Steve Reeves photo-s. 4-(#26) James Bond-s; Hitler-s. 5-(#27) Taylor/Burton pin-up; Sinatra, Martin, Andress, Ekberg photo-s	4	8	12	27	44	60
28,31,36,39: 31-Pink Panther movie photo-s; Burke's Law-s. 39-Westerns; Elizabeth Montgomery photo-s; Beat mag-s	4	8	12	23	37	50
29,34,37,38: 29-Beatles-c by Jack Davis. 34-Two pg. Beatles-s & photo pin-up. 37-Playboy parody issue. 38-Addams Family-s	4	8	12	27	44	60
30,32,35,40: 30-Beatles photo pin-up; James Bond photo-s. 32-Ian Fleming-s; LBJ-s; Tarzan-s. 35-Beatles cameo; Three Stooges parody. 40-Tarzan-s; Crosby/Hope-s; Beatles parody	4	8	12	28	47	65
33-Ringo Starr photo-c & spoof on "A Hard Day's Night"; inside-c has Beatles photos	5	10	15	35	63	90

41,50,51,53,54,60: 41-Sports Illustrated parody-c/s. 50-Mod issue; flip-c w/1967 calendar w/Bob Taylor-a. 51-Get Smart-s. 53-Beatles cameo; nudity panels. 54-Monkees-c.

60-TV Daniel Boone-s 3 6 9 19 30 40
42-Fighting American-c revised from Simon/Kirby-c; "Good girl" art by Sparling; profile on Bob Powell; superhero parodies 5 10 15 33 57 80
43-49,52,55-59: 43-Sneaker set begins by Sparling. 45-Has #44 on-c & #45 on inside; TV Westerns-s; Beatles cameo. 46-Hell's Angels-s; NY Mets-s. 47-UFO/Space-c. 49-Men's Adventure mag. parody issue; nudity. 52-LBJ-s. 55-Underground culture special. 56-Alfred E. Neuman-c; inventors issue. 58-Hippie issue-c/s. 59-Hippie-s 3 6 9 16 24 32
61-64,66-69,71,73,75-80: 63-Tiny Tim-c & poster; Monkees-s. 64-Flip-c. 66-Flip-c; Mod Squad-s. 69-Beatles cameo; Peter Sellers photo-s. 71-Flip-c; Clint Eastwood-s. 76-Nixon-s; Marcus Welby-s. 78-Ma Barker-s; Courtship of Eddie's Father-s; Abbie Hoffman-s 3 6 9 15 22 28
65,70,74: 65-Cassius Clay/Brando/J. Wayne-c; Johnny Carson-s. 70-(9/69) John & Yoko-c, 1/2 pg. story. 74-Clay, Agnew, Namath & others as superheroes-c/s; Easy Rider-s; Ghost and Mrs. Muir-s 3 6 9 16 24 32
72-(84 pgs.) Xmas issue w/2 pg. slick color poster; Tarzan-s; 2 pg. Superman & superheroes-s 3 6 9 21 33 45
81-85,87-95,98,99: 81-(2/71) Woody Allen photo-s. 85 Monster Mag. parody-s; Nixon-s w/Ringo & John cameo. 88-Klute photo-s; Nixon paper dolls page. 92-Lily Tomlin; Archie Bunker pin-up. 93-Woody Allen 2 4 6 13 18 22
86,96,97,100: 86-John & Yoko, Tiny Tim-c; Love Story movie photo-s. 96-Kung Fu-c; Mummy-s, Dracula & Frankenstein app. 97-Superman-s; 1974 Calendar; Charlie Brown & Snoopy pin-up. 100-Serpico-s; Cosell-s; Jacques Cousteau-s 3 6 9 14 19 24
101-103,105-114,116,119,120: 101-Three Musketeers-s; Dick Tracy-s. 102-Young Frankenstein-s. 103-Kojak-s; Evel Knievel-s. 105-Towering Inferno-s; Peanuts/Snoopy-s. 106-Cher-c/s. 10 7-Jaws-c/s. 108-Pink Panther-c/s; Archie-s. 109-Adam & Eve-s(nudity). 110-Welcome Back Kotter-s. 111-Sonny & Cher-s. 112-King Kong-c/s. 120-Star Trek-s 2 4 6 9 13 16
104,115,117,118: 104-Muhammad Ali-c/s. 115-Charlie's Angels-s. 117-Bionic Woman & Six Million $ Man-c/s; Cher D'Flower begins by Sparling (nudity). 118-Star Wars-s; Popeye-s 2 4 6 11 16 20
121-125,128-130: 122-Darth Vader-s. 123-Jaws II-s. 128-Superman-c/movie parody. 130-Alien movie-s 2 4 6 10 14 18
126,127: 126-(68 pgs.) Battlestar Galactica-c/s; Star Wars-s; Wonder Woman-s. 127-Mork & Mindy-s; Lord of the Rings-s 2 4 6 13 18 22
131-(1980 Special) Star Wars/Star Trek/Flash Gordon wraparound-c/s; Superman parody; Battlestar Galactica-s 3 6 9 14 19 24
132,133: 132-1980 Election-c/s; Apocalypse Now-s. 133-Star Trek-s; Chips-s; Superheroes page 2 4 6 13 18 22
134 (scarce)(68 pg. Giant)-Star Wars-c; Alien-s; WKRP-s; Mork & Mindy-s; Taxi-s; MASH-s 4 8 12 19 30 40
Annual 1- Birthday Annual (1966)-3 pg. Huckleberry Fink fold out 4 8 12 23 37 50
Annual 2- 7th Annual Yearbook (1967)-Davis-c, 2 pg. glossy poster insert 4 8 12 23 37 50
Annual 3 (1968) "Big Sick Laff-in" on-c (84 pgs.)-w/psychedelic posters; Frankenstein poster 3 6 9 17 26 35
Annual 1969 "Great Big Fat Annual Sick", 1969 "9th Year Annual Sick", 1970, 1971 3 6 9 16 24 32
Annual 12,13-(1972,1973, 84 pgs.) 13-Monster-c 3 6 9 16 24 32
Annual 14,15-(1974,1975, 84 pgs.) 14-Hitler photo-s 3 6 9 16 24 32
Annual 2-4 (1980) 2 4 6 9 13 16
Special 1 (1980) Buck Rogers-c/s; MASH-s 3 6 9 14 19 24
Special 2 (1980) Wraparound Star Wars: Empire Strikes Back-c; Charlie's Angels/Farrah-s; Rocky-s; plus reprints 3 6 9 14 19 24
Yearbook 15(1975, 84 pgs.) Paul Revere-c 3 6 9 16 23 30
NOTE: *Davis a-42, 87; c-22, 23, 25, 29, 31, 32.* **Powell** *a-7, 31, 57.* **Simon** *a-1-3, 10, 41, 42, 87, 99; c-1, 47, 57, 59, 69, 91, 95-97, 99, 100, 102, 107, 112.* **Torres** *a-1-3, 29, 31, 47, 49.* **Tuska** *a-14, 41-43. Civil War Blackouts-23, 24. #42 has biography of Bob Powell.*

SIDEKICK (Paul Jenkins'...)
Image Comics (Desperado): June, 2006 - No. 5, May, 2007 ($3.50, limited series)
1-5-Paul Jenkins-s/Chris Moreno-a 3.50
... Super Summer Sidekick Spectacular 1 (7/07, $2.99) 3.50
... Super Summer Sidekick Spectacular 2 (9/07, $3.50) 3.50

SIDEKICK
Image Comics (Joe's Comics): Aug, 2013 - No. 12, Dec, 2015 ($2.99)
1-7,9-12: 1-Straczynski-a/Mandrake-a; intro. The Cowl and Flyboy; 6 covers. 4-6-Two covers 3.00
8-($3.99) Chrome-c 4.00

SIDEKICKS
Fanboy Ent., Inc.: Jun, 2000 - No. 3, Apr, 2001 ($2.75, B&W, lim. series)
1-3-J.Torres-s/Takesi Miyazawa-a. 3-Variant-c by Wieringo 3.00
...: Super Fun Summer Special (Oni Press, 7/03, $2.99) art by various incl. Wieringo 3.00
...: The Substitute (Oni Press, 7/02, $2.95) 3.00
...: The Transfer Student TPB (Oni Press, 6/02, $8.95, 9" x 6") r/#1-3 9.00
...: The Transfer Student TPB 2nd Ed. (10/03, $11.95, 9" x 6") r/#1-3; The Substitute 12.00

SIDESHOW
Avon Periodicals: 1949 (one-shot)
1-(Rare)-Similar to Bachelor's Diary 168 336 504 1075 1838 2600

SIDEWAYS (Follows events from Dark Nights: Metal)
DC Comics: Apr, 2018 - No. 13, Apr, 2019 ($2.99)
1-13: 1-Didio-s/Rocafort-a; intro Derek James 4.00
Annual 1 (1/19, $4.99) Takes place after #9; New 52 Superman & Seven Soldiers app. 5.00

SIEGE
Marvel Comics: Mar, 2010 - No. 4, Jun, 2010 ($3.99, limited series)
1-4-Asgard is invaded; Bendis-s/Coipel-a. 4-End of The Sentry 4.00
1-4-Variant covers by Dell'Otto 8.00
...: Captain America (6/10, $2.99) Gage-s/Dallocchio-a/Djurdjevic-c; both Caps app. 4.00
...: Loki (6/10, $2.99) Gillen-s/McKelvie-a/Djurdjevic-c; Hela & Mephisto app. 4.00
...: Secret Warriors (6/10, $2.99) Hickman-s/Vitti-a/Djurdjevic-c; Phobos attacks 4.00
...: Spider-Man (6/10, $2.99) Reed-s/Santucci-a/Djurdjevic-c; Venom & Ms. Marvel app. 4.00
...: Storming Asgard - Heroes & Villains (3/10, $3.99) Dossiers on participants; Land-c 4.00
...: The Cabal (2/10, $3.99) series prelude; Bendis-s/Lark-a; covers by Finch & Davis 4.00
...: Young Avengers (6/10, $2.99) McKeever-s/Asrar-a/Djurdjevic-c; Wrecking Crew app. 4.00

SIEGE (Secret Wars tie-in) (Continued from Secret Wars: Journal #1)
Marvel Comics: Sept, 2015 - No. 4, Dec, 2015 ($3.99, limited series)
1-4-Gillen-s/Andrade-a; Abigail Brand, Kate Bishop & Ms. America app. 4.00

SIEGE: EMBEDDED
Marvel Comics: Mar, 2010 - No. 4, Jul, 2010 ($3.99, limited series)
1-4-Reed-s/Samnee-a/Granov-c; Ben Urich & Volstagg cover the invasion 4.00

SIEGEL AND SHUSTER: DATELINE 1930s
Eclipse Comics: Nov, 1984 - No. 2, Sept, 1985 ($1.50/$1.75, Baxter paper #1)
1,2: 1-Unpublished samples of strips from the '30s; includes 'Interplanetary Police'; Shuster-c. 2 ($1.75, B&W)-unpublished strips; Shuster-c 4.00

SIF (See Thor titles)
Marvel Comics: Jun, 2010 ($3.99, one shot)
1-Deconnick-s/Stegman-a/Foreman-c; Beta Ray Bill app. 4.00

SIGIL (Also see CrossGen Chronicles)
CrossGeneration Comics: Jul, 2000 - No. 42, Dec, 2003 ($2.95)
1-42: 1-Barbara Kesel-s/Ben & Ray Lai-a. 12-Waid-s begin. 21-Chuck Dixon-s begin 3.00

SIGIL
Marvel Comics: May, 2011 - No. 4, Aug, 2011 ($2.99)
1-4-Carey-s/Kirk-a 3.00
1-Variant-c by McGuinness 5.00

SIGMA
Image Comics (WildStorm): March, 1996 - No. 3, June, 1996 ($2.50, limited series)
1-3: 1-"Fire From Heaven" prelude #2; Coker-a. 2-"Fire From Heaven" pt. 6. 3-"Fire From Heaven" pt. 14. 3.00

SILENCER, THE
DC Comics: Mar, 2018 - No. 18, Aug, 2019 ($2.99/$3.99)
1-12: 1-Abnett-s/Romita Jr.-a; intro. Honor Guest; Talia al Ghul app. 3-6-Deathstroke app. 4-8-Bogdanovic-a 3.00
13-18-($3.99): 13-Origin of Silencer; Talia al Ghul app.; Marion-a/Kirkham-c 4.00

SILENT DRAGON
DC Comics (WildStorm): Sept, 2005 - No. 6, Feb, 2006 ($2.99, limited series)
1-6-Tokyo 2066 A.D.; Leinil Yu-a/c; Andy Diggle-s 3.00
TPB (2006, $19.99) r/series; sketch page 20.00

SILENT HILL: DEAD/ALIVE
IDW Publishing: Dec, 2005 - No. 5, Apr, 2006 ($3.99, limited series)
1-5-Stakal-a/Ciencin-s. 1-Four covers. 2-5-Two covers 4.00

SILENT HILL DOWNPOUR: ANNE'S STORY
IDW Publishing: Aug, 2014 - No. 4, Nov, 2014 ($3.99, limited series)
1-4-Tom Waltz-s/Tristan Jones-a; two covers on each 4.00

SILENT HILL: DYING INSIDE
IDW Publishing: Feb, 2004 - No. 5, June, 2004 ($3.99, limited series)
1-5-Based on the Konami computer game. 1-Templesmith-a; Ashley Wood-c 4.00
...: Paint It Black (2/05, $7.49) Ciencin-s/Thomas-a 7.50
...: The Grinning Man 5/05, $7.49) Ciencin-s/Stakal-a 7.50
TPB (8/04, $19.99) r/#1-5; Ashley Wood-c 20.00

SILENT HILL: PAST LIFE
IDW Publishing: Oct, 2010 - No. 4, Jan, 2011 ($3.99, limited series)
1-4-Waltz-s; two covers on each 4.00

SILENT HILL: SINNER'S REWARD
IDW Publishing: Feb, 2008 - No. 4, Apr, 2008 ($3.99, limited series)
1-4-Waltz-s/Stamb-a 4.00

SILENT INVASION, THE
Rengade Press: Apr, 1986 - No.12, Mar, 1988 ($1.70/$2.00, B&W)
1-12-UFO sightings of the '50's 3.00
Book 1- reprints ($7.95) 8.00

SILENT MOBIUS
Viz Select Comics: 1991 - No. 5, 1992 ($4.95, color, squarebound, 44 pgs.)
1-5: Japanese stories translated to English 5.00

SILENT NIGHT DEADLY NIGHT
American Mythology Productions: 2022 ($3.99)
1-Kuhoric & Check-s/Calzada-a 4.00

SILENT SCREAMERS (Based on the Aztech Toys figures)
Image Comics: Oct, 2000 ($4.95)
Nosferatu Issue - Alex Ross front & back-c 5.00

SILENT WAR
Marvel Comics: Mar, 2007 - No. 6, Aug, 2007 ($2.99, limited series)
1-6-Inhumans, Black Bolt and Fantastic Four app.; Hine-s/Irving-a/Watson-c 3.00
TPB (2007, $14.99) r/series 15.00

SILK (See Amazing Spider-Man 2014 series #1 & #4 for debut)
Marvel Comics: Apr, 2015 - No. 7, Nov, 2015 ($3.99)
1-Robbie Thompson-s/Stacey Lee-a/Dave Johnson-c; Spider-Man app. 2 4 6 11 16 20
2-7: 3-6-Black Cat app. 4-Fantastic Four app. 7-Secret Wars tie-in 4.00

SILK (Spider-Man)
Marvel Comics: Jan, 2016 - No. 19, Jun, 2017 ($3.99)
1-Robbie Thompson-s/Stacey Lee-a; Black Cat & Mockingbird app. 1 2 3 5 6 8
2-19: 4,5-Fish-a. 7,8-"Spider-Women" tie-in; Spider-Woman & Spider-Gwen app. 14-17-Clone Conspiracy 4.00

SILK (Spider-Man)
Marvel Comics: May, 2021 - No. 5, Oct, 2021 ($3.99)

Sideways #1 © DC

Silk (2022) #1 © MAR

Silver Streak Comics #14 © LEV

	GD	VG	FN	VF	VF/NM	NM-
	2.0	4.0	6.0	8.0	9.0	9.2

1-5: 1-Maurene Goo-s/Takeshi Miyazawa-a. 3-Silvermane app. 4.00

SILK (Spider-Man)
Marvel Comics: Mar, 2022 - No. 5, Jul, 2022 ($3.99, limited series)

1-5-Emily Kim-s/Takeshi Miyazawa-a 4.00

SILKE
Dark Horse Comics: Jan, 2001 - No. 4, Sept, 2001 ($2.95)

1-4-Tony Daniel-s/a 3.00

SILKEN GHOST
CrossGen Comics: June, 2003 - No. 5, Oct, 2003 ($2.95, limited series)

1-5-Dixon-s/Rosado-a 3.00
Traveler Vol. 1 (2003, $9.95) digest-sized reprint #1-5 10.00

SILLY PILLY (See Frank Luther's...)

SILLY SYMPHONIES (See Dell Giants)

SILLY TUNES
Timely Comics: Fall, 1945 - No. 7, June, 1947

	GD	VG	FN	VF	VF/NM	NM-
1-Silly Seal, Ziggy Pig begin	34	68	102	199	325	450
2-(2/46)	19	38	57	112	179	245
3-7: 6-New logo	15	30	45	92	144	195

SILVER (See Lone Ranger's Famous Horse...)

SILVER AGE
DC Comics: July, 2000 ($3.95, limited series)

1-Waid-s/Dodson-a; "Silver Age" style x-over; JLA & villains switch bodies 4.00
...: Challengers of the Unknown ($2.50) Joe Kubert-c; vs. Chronos 3.00
...: Dial H For Hero ($2.50) Jim Mooney-c; Waid-s/Kitson-a; vs. Martian Manhunter 3.00
...: Doom Patrol ($2.50) Ramona Fradon-c/Peyer-s 3.00
...: Flash ($2.50) Carmine Infantino-c; Kid Flash and Elongated Man app. 3.00
...: Green Lantern ($2.50) Gil Kane-c/Busiek-s/Anderson-a; vs. Sinestro 3.00
...: Justice League of America ($2.50) Ty Templeton-c; Millar-s/Kolins-a 3.00
...: Showcase ($2.50) Dick Giordano-c/a; Johns-s; Batgirl, Adam Strange app. 3.00
... Secret Files ($4.95) Intro. Agamemno; short stories & profile pages 5.00
...: Teen Titans ($2.50) Nick Cardy-c; vs. Penguin, Mr. Element, Black Manta 3.00
...: The Brave and the Bold ($2.50) Jim Aparo-c; Batman & Metal Men 3.00
... 80-Page Giant ($5.95) Conclusion of x-over; "lost" Silver Age stories 6.00

SILVERBACK
Comico: 1989 - No. 3, 1990 ($2.50, color, limited series, mature readers)

1-3: Character from Grendel: Matt Wagner-a 3.00

SILVERBLADE
DC Comics: Sept, 1987 - No. 12, Sept, 1988

1-12: Colan-c/a in all 4.00

SILVER CEREBUS
Aardvark-Vanaheim: Feb, 2020 ($4.00, B&W, one-shot)

1-Cerebus figures placed over outer space backgrounds; Silver Surfer #1-c swipe 4.00

SILVER CITY
AfterShock Comics: May, 2021 - No. 5, Sept, 2021 ($4.99/$3.99, limited series)

1-($4.99)-Olivia Cuartero-Briggs-s/Luca Merli-a 5.00
2-5-($3.99) 4.00

SILVER COIN, THE
Image Comics: May, 2021 - Present ($3.99, anthology)

1-15: 1-Zdarsky-s/Walsh-a. 2-Kelly Thompson-s. 3-Ed Brisson-s. 4-Jeff Lemire-s 4.00

SILVERHAWKS
Star Comics/Marvel Comics #6: Aug, 1987 - No. 6, June, 1988 ($1.00)

1-6 4.00

SILVERHEELS
Pacific Comics: Dec, 1983 - No. 3, May, 1984 ($1.50)

1-3-Bruce Jones-s, Scott Hampton-c/a; Steacy-a in back-up stories 4.00

SILVER KID WESTERN
Key/Stanmor Publications: Oct, 1954 - No. 5, July, 1955

	GD	VG	FN	VF	VF/NM	NM-
1	12	24	36	67	94	120
2	7	14	21	35	43	50
3-5	6	12	18	29	36	42
I.W. Reprint #1,2-Severin-c: 1-r/#? 2-r/#1	2	4	6	8	11	14

SILVER SABLE AND THE WILD PACK (See Amazing Spider-Man #265 and Sable & Fortune)
Marvel Comics: June, 1992 - No. 35, Apr, 1995; No. 36, Jan, 2018 ($1.25/$1.50)

1-($2.00)-Embossed & foil stamped-c; Spider-Man app. 4.00
2-24,26-35: 4,5-Dr. Doom-c/story. 6,7-Deathlok-c/story. 9-Origin Silver Sable. 10-Punisher-c/s. 15-Capt. America-c/s. 16,17-Intruders app. 18,19-Venom-c/s. 19-Siege of Darkness x-over. 23-Daredevil (in new costume) & Deadpool app. 24-Bound-in card sheet. Li'l Sylvie backup story 3.00
25-($2.00, 52 pgs.)-Li'l Sylvie backup story 4.00
36-(1/18, $3.99) Marvel Legacy one-shot; Faust-s/Siqueira-a 4.00

SILVER STAR (Also see Jack Kirby's...)
Pacific Comics: Feb, 1983 - No. 6, Jan, 1984 ($1.00)

1-6: 1-1st app. Last of the Viking Heroes. 1-5-Kirby-c/a. 2-Ditko-a 5.00
...: Graphite Edition TPB (TwoMorrows Publ., 3/06, $19.95) r/series in B&W including Kirby's original pencils; sketch pages; original screenplay 20.00
Jack Kirby's Silver Star, Volume 1 HC (Image Comics, 2007, $34.99) r/series in color; sketch pages; original screenplay 35.00

SILVER STREAK COMICS (Crime Does Not Pay #22 on)
Your Guide Publs. No. 1-7/New Friday Publs. No. 8-17/Comic House Publ./ Newsbook Publ.: Dec, 1939 - No. 21, May, 1942; No. 23, 1946; nn, Feb, 1946
(Silver logo-#1-5)

	GD	VG	FN	VF	VF/NM	NM-
1-(Scarce)-Intro the Claw by Cole (r-in Daredevil #21), Red Reeves Boy Magician (ends #2), Captain Fearless (ends #2), The Wasp (ends #2), Mister Midnight (ends #2) begin; Spirit Man only app. Calling The Duke begins (ends #2). Barry Lane only app. Silver Metallic-c begin, end #5; Claw-c 1,2,6-8	1200	2400	3600	9100	17,550	26,000
2-The Claw ends (by Cole); makes pact w/Hitler; Simon-c/a (The Claw); ad for Marvel Mystery Comics #2 (12/39). Lance Hale begins (receives super powers). Solar Patrol app.	476	952	1428	3475	6138	8800
3-1st app. & origin Silver Streak (2nd with Lightning speed); Dickie Dean the Boy Inventor, Lance Hale, Ace Powers (ends #6), Bill Wayne The Texas Terror (ends #6) & The Planet Patrol (ends #6) begin. Detective Snoop, Sergeant Drake only app.	423	846	1269	3088	5444	7800
4-Sky Wolf begins (ends #6); Silver Streak by Jack Cole (new costume); 1st app. Jackie, Lance Hale's sidekick. Lance Hale gains immortality	213	426	639	1363	2332	3300
5-Cole c/a(2); back-c ad for Claw app. in #6	245	490	735	1568	2684	3800
6-(Scarce, 9/40)-Origin & 1st app. Daredevil (blue & yellow costume) by Jack Binder; The Claw returns as the Green Claw; classic Cole Claw-c	3225	6450	9675	22,600	40,300	58,000
7-Claw vs. Daredevil serial begins c/sty, ends #11. Daredevil new costume-blue & red by Jack Cole & 3 other Cole stories (38 pgs.). Origin Whiz, S. S.'s Falcon 2nd app. Daredevil & 1st Daredevil-c (by Cole). Cloud Curtis, Presto Martin begins. Dynamo Hill & Zongar The Miracleman only app.	1100	2200	3300	8360	15,180	22,000
8-Classic Claw vs. Daredevil by Cole c/sty; last Cole Silver streak. Dan Dearborn begins (ends #12). Secret Agent X-101 begins, (ends #9)	975	1950	2919	7100	12,550	18,000
9-Claw vs. Daredevil by Cole. Silver Streak-c by Bob Wood	284	568	852	1818	3109	4400
10-Origin & 1st app. Captain Battle (5/41) by Binder; Claw vs. Daredevil by Cole; Silver Streak/robot-c by Bob Wood	258	516	774	1651	2826	4000
11-Intro./origin Mercury by Bob Wood, Silver Streak's sidekick; conclusion Claw vs. Daredevil by Rico; in 'Presto Martin,' 2nd pg., newspaper says 'Roussos does it again'	194	388	582	1242	2121	3000
12-Daredevil-c by Rico; Lance Hale finds lost valley w/cave men, battles dinosaurs, sabre-toothed cats; his last app.	174	348	522	1114	1907	2700
13-Origin Thun-Dohr; Scarlet Skull (a Red Skull swipe) vs. Daredevil; Bingham Boys app.	174	348	522	1114	1907	2700
14-Classic Nazi skull men-c/sty	271	542	813	1734	2967	4200
15-Classic Mummy horror-c	300	600	900	1980	3440	4900
16-(11/41) Hitler-c; Silver Streak battles Hitler sty w/classic splash page. Capt. Battle fights walking corpses	541	1082	1623	3950	6975	10,000
17-Last Daredevil issue.	187	374	561	1197	2049	2900
18-The Saint begins (2/42, 1st app.) by Leslie Charteris (see Movie Comics #2 by DC); The Saint-c	168	336	504	1075	1838	2600
19,20 (1942)-Ned of the Navy app. 19-Silver Streak ends. 20-Japanese WWII-c/sty; last Captain Battle, Dickie Dean, Cloud Curtis; Red Reed, Alonzo Appleseed only app.; Wolverton's Scoop Scuttle app.	84	168	252	538	919	1300
21-(5/42)-Hitler app. in strip on cover; Wolverton's Scoop Scuttle app.	116	232	348	742	1271	1800
nn(#22, 2/46, 60 pgs.)(Newsbook Publ.)-R-/S.S. story from #4-7 by Jack Cole plus 2 Captain Fearless stories-r from #1&2, all in color; bondage/torture-c by Dick Briefer w/torture meter	423	846	1269	3000	5250	7500
23 (nd, 11/1946?, 52 pgs.)(An Atomic Comic) bondage-c, Silver Streak c/sty	123	246	369	787	1344	1900

NOTE: **Jack Binder** *a-8-12, 15; c-3, 4, 13-15, 17.* **Dick Briefer** *a-9-20; c-nn(#22).* **Jack Cole** *a-(Claw)-#2, 3, 6-10, nn(#22). (Daredevil)-#6-10, (Dickie Dean)-#3-10, (Pirate Prince)-#7, (Silver Streak)-#4-8, nn; c-5 (Silver Streak), 6 (Claw), 7, 8 (Daredevil).* **Bill Everett** *Red Reed begins #20.* **Fred Guardineer** *a-#8-12.* **Don Rico** *a-11-17 (Daredevil), 15, 19 (Silver Streak); c-11, 12, 16.* **Joe Simon** *a-2 (Solar Patrol), 3 (Silver Streak); c-2.* **Basil Wolverton** *a-20, 21.* **Bob Wood** *a-8-15 (Presto Martin), 9 (Silver Streak); c-9, 10. Captain Battle c-11, 13-15, 17. Claw c-#1, 2, 6-8. Daredevil c-7, 8, 12. Dickie Dean c-19. Ned of the Navy c-20 (war). The Saint c-18. Silver Streak*

GD VG FN VF VF/NM NM- 2.0 4.0 6.0 8.0 9.0 9.2

GD VG FN VF VF/NM NM- 2.0 4.0 6.0 8.0 9.0 9.2

c-5, 10, 16, nn(#22), 23.

SILVER STREAK COMICS (Homage with Golden Age size and Golden Age art styles)
Image Comics: No. 24, Dec, 2009 ($3.99, one-shot)

24-New Daredevil, Claw, Silver Streak & Captain Battle stories; Larsen, Grist, Gilbert-a 5.00

SILVER SURFER (See Fantastic Four, Fantasy Masterpieces V2#1, Fireside Book Series, Marvel Graphic Novel, Marvel Presents #8, Marvel's Greatest Comics & Tales To Astonish #92)

SILVER SURFER, THE (Also see Essential Silver Surfer)
Marvel Comics Group: Aug, 1968 - No. 18, Sept, 1970; June, 1982

1-More detailed origin by John Buscema (p); The Watcher back-up stories begin (origin), end #7; (No. 1-7: 25¢, 68 pgs.) 221 442 663 1823 4112 6400
2-1st app. Badoon 21 42 63 147 324 500
3-1st app. Mephisto 111 222 333 888 1994 3100
4-Lower distribution; Thor & Loki app. 172 344 516 1419 3210 5000
5-7-Last giant size. 5-The Stranger app.; Fantastic Four app. 6-Brunner inks. 7-(8/69)-Early cameo Frankenstein's monster (see X-Men #40) 15 30 45 103 227 350
8-10: 8-18-(15¢ issues) 12 24 36 79 170 260
11-13,15-18: 15-Silver Surfer vs. Human Torch; Fantastic Four app. 17-Nick Fury app. 18-Vs. The Inhumans; Kirby-a; Trimpe-c 10 20 30 70 150 230
14-Spider-Man x-over 23 46 69 161 356 550
14 Facsimile Edition (3/2019, $3.99) reprints #14 with original ads and letter column 2 4 6 9 12 15
... Omnibus Vol. 1 Hardcover (2007, $74.99, dustjacket) r/#1-18 re-colored with original letter pages, Fantastic Four Annual #5 & Not Brand Echh #13; Lee and Buscema bios 80.00
V2#1 (6/82, 52 pgs.)-Byrne-c/a 2 4 6 9 13 16

NOTE: ***Adkins** a-8-15i. **Brunner** a-6i. **J. Buscema** a-1-17p. **Colan** a-1-3p. **Reinman** a-1-4i. #1-14 were reprinted in Fantasy Masterpieces V2#1-14.*

SILVER SURFER (Volume 3) (See Marvel Graphic Novel #38)
Marvel Comics Group: V3#1, July, 1987 - No. 146, Nov, 1998

1-Double-size ($1.25)-Englehart & Rogers-s/a begins; vs. the Champion; Fantastic Four app. w/She-Hulk; Nova (Frankie Raye) & Galactus app; Surfers exile on Earth ends 3 6 9 17 26 35
2-9: 2-Surfer returns to Zenn-La; Shalla-Bal app. as Empress of Zenn-La; Skrulls app.; Surfer story next in West Coat Avengers Annual #2 and Avengers Annual #16. 3-Collector & Champion app.; Surfer vs. the Runner; re-intro Mantis (not seen since 1975). 4-Elders of the Universe app.; Collector, Champion, Runner, Gardener, Contemplator, Grandmaster & Possessor; 1st app. of Astronomer, Obliterator & Trader; Ego revealed as an Elder; origin Mantis. 5-vs. the Obliterator. 6-Origin of the Obliterator. 7-Supreme Intelligence & the Elders app. 8-Supreme Intelligence app.; Surfer gains the Soul Gem. 9-Elders vs. Galactus; six Soul Gems app. 1 2 3 5 6 8
10-Galactus absorbs the Elders; Eternity app. 2 4 6 9 12 15
11-14: 11-1st app. Reptyl, Clumsy Foulup & the fake Surfer; Nova (Frankie Raye) app. 12-Death of fake Contemplator; Reptyl & Nova (Frankie Raye) app. 13-Ronan the Accuser vs. Surfer and Nova (Frankie Raye); fake Surfer app.; last Rogers-a. 14-Origin & death of the fake Surfer; Ronan app.; Nova (Frankie Raye) app.; story continues in Surfer Ann. #1 6.00
15,16: 15-Ron Lim-c/a begin (9/88); Soul Gems app.; Reed, Sue and Franklin of the Fantastic Four app.; Galactus & Nova (Frankie Raye), Elders of the Universe app.: Astronomer, Possessor & Trader. 16-Astromoner, Trader & In-Betweener app.; brief x-over w/Fantastic Four #319 1 2 3 5 6 8
17,18: 17-Elders of the Universe, In-Betweener, Death & Galactus app. 18-Galactus vs. the In-Betweener; Elders of the Universe, the Soul Gems & Lord Order & Master Chaos app. 1 2 3 5 6 8
19,20-Firelord & Starfox app. 6.00
21-24,26-30,32,33,39-43: 21-vs. the Obliterator. 22-Ego the Living Planet app. 26-Super-Skrull app. 27-Stranger & Super-Skrull app. 28-Death of Super-Skrull; Reptyl app. 29-Midnight Sun app; death of Reptyl. 30-Midnight Sun & the Stranger app. 32,33-Jim Valentino-s; 33-Impossible Man app. 39-Alan Grant scripts. 40-43-Surfer in Dynamo City 5.00
25,31-($1.50, 52 pgs.) 25-New Kree/Skrull war; Badoon app; Skrulls regain their shape-shifting ability. 31-Conclusion of Kree/Skrull war; Stranger & the Living Tribunal app. 6.00
34-Thanos returns (cameo); Starlin scripts begin; Death app. 3 6 9 19 30 40
35-38: 35-1st full Thanos in Silver Surfer (3/90); reintro Drax the Destroyer on last pg. (cameo). 36-Recaps history of Thanos, Captain Marvel & Warlock app. in recap. 37-Full reintro Drax the Destroyer; Drax-c. 38-Silver Surfer battles Thanos; Nebula app; Thanos story continues in Thanos Quest #1-2 1 3 4 6 8 10
44-Classic Thanos-c; 1st app. of the Infinity Gauntlet; Thanos defeats the Surfer & Drax; Mephisto cameo 5 10 15 35 63 90
45-Thanos-c; Mephisto app.; origin of the Infinity Gems 3 6 9 15 23 30
46-Return of Adam Warlock (2/91); reintro Gamora & Pip the Troll (within Soul World) 3 6 9 16 23 30
47-49: 47-Warlock vs. Drax. 48-Galactus app; last Starlin scripts (also #50). 49-Thanos & Mephisto app.; Ron Marz scripts begin 1 3 4 6 8 10
50-($1.50, 52 pgs.)-Embossed & silver foil-c; Silver Surfer has brief battle w/Thanos; story cont'd in Infinity Gauntlet #1; extended origin flashback to the Silver Surfer's life on Zenn-La 3 6 9 15 22 28
50-2nd & 3rd printings 5.00
51-59-Infinity Gauntlet x-overs; 51-Galactus and Nova (Frankie Raye) app. 52-Firelord vs. Drax; continued in Infinity Gauntlet #2. 53-Death of Clumsy Foulup. 54-vs the Rhino; Hulk cameo. 55,56-Thanos kills everyone (Surfer dream sequence); Warlock app; continued in Infinity Gauntlet #4. 57-x-over w/Infinity Gauntlet #4. 58-Defenders app. (dream sequence); Warlock app. 59-Warlock, Dr. Strange, Dr. Doom, Thor, Firelord, Drax & Thanos app; concluded in Infinity Gauntlet #6 6.00
60-69,71-73: 60-vs. Midnight Sun; Warlock & Dr. Strange cameo; Black Bolt, Gorgon & Karnak of the Inhumans app. 61-Collector app. 63-Captain Marvel app. 64-Collector app. 65-Reptyl returns. 66-Mistress Love & Master Hate app. 67-69-Infinity War x-overs. 67-Continued from Infinity War #1; x-over w/Dr. Strange #42; Nebula, Galactus, Nova (Frankie Raye) & Dr. Strange app; Magus cameo; continued in Infinity War #2. 68,69-Galactus, Nova & Dr. Strange app. 69-Magus cameo; continues in Infinity War #3. 71-Herald Ordeal Pt. 2; Nebula, Firelord & Galactus app; Surfer vs. Morg. 72-Herald Ordeal Pt. 3; 1st app. Cyborg Nebula (as seen in the GOTG movie); Firelord, Nova, Galactus & Morg app. 73-Herald Ordeal Pt. 4; reintro Gabriel the Airwalker; Firelord, Galactus, Nova, Morg app; Terrax cameo 4.00
70,74: Herald Ordeal Pts.1,5. 70-1st app. Morg (becomes the new Herald of Galactus), Nova released of her duties; Nebula app. 74-Terrax, Firelord, Airwalker, Nova, Nebula app. 5.00
75-($2.50, 52 pgs.)-Embossed foil-c; Lim-c/a; Herald Ordeal Pt. 6; Surfer, Firelord, Airwalker, Terrax & Nova vs. Morg; death of Nova; Morg stripped of the power cosmic; Firelord & Airwalker resume Herald duties 5.00
76-81,83-87,90-97: 76-Origin Jack of Hearts retold; Galactus, Airwalker, Firelord & Nebula app.; Morg cameo. 77-Jack of Hearts & Nebula app; return of Morg. 78-New Jack of Hearts costume; Nebula, Morg & Galactus app. 79-Captain Atlas & Dr. Minerva app.; Morg vs. Terrax; Gladiator & Beta Ray Bill cameo. 80-1st app. Ganymede (named in issue #81); Morg vs. Terrax. 81-1st cameo app. Tyrant; Morg, Terrax, Gladiator, Beta Ray Bill cameos. 83-85-Infinity Crusade x-overs. 83-Surfer vs. Firelord; x-over w/Infinity Crusade #3; Thanos cameo; cont'd in Infinity Crusade #4. 84-Thanos app. 85-Wonder Man & Storm vs. Surfer; concluded in Infinity Crusade #6. 86-Blood & Thunder Pt. 2; cont'd from Thor #468; Surfer & Beta Ray Bill vs. insane Thor; Pip the Troll & Warlock cameo; cont'd in Warlock Chronicles #6. 87-Blood & Thunder Pt. 6; cont'd from Thor #469; Dr. Strange, Warlock & the Infinity Watch app; cont'd in Warlock Chronicles #7. 89-Colleen Doran-a(p). 90-Legacy (son of Capt. Marvel) app. 92-Marvel Masterprints card insert; last Lim-a. 93-Fantastic Four app; Thing, Human Torch & Ant-Man (Scott Lang); Spider-Man cameo. 94-Fantastic Four & Warlock and the Infinity Watch app. 95-Fantastic Four app.; Hulk cameo. 97-Terrax app; Champion cameo 4.00
82-($1.75. 52 pgs.)-Surfer, Morg, Terrax, Gladiator, Beta Ray Bill, Jack of Hearts & Ganymede vs. Tyrant; Galactus app. 5.00
88,99: 88-Blood & Thunder Pt. 10-cont'd from Thor #470; Thanos vs. insane Thor; Dr. Strange, Warlock & the Infinity Watch app; cont'd in Warlock Chronicles #8; 'Kay-bee Toys' coupon insert for Ghost Rider 'Hot Pursuit' comic; 7-pg. Punisher 'Suicide Run' advertisement; 7-pg. 'Juice' magazine insert featuring interviews with the New Warriors. 99-Mephisto cameo 5.00
98-vs. Champion; Drax & Thanos app. 5.00
100-($2.25, 52 pgs.)-Wraparound-c; vs. Mephisto 6.00
100-($3.95, 52 pgs.)-Enhanced-silver holofoil-c 5.00
101-108,110: 101-Tyrant cameo; Surfer returns to Zenn-La; Shalla-Bal app. 102-Galactus & Morg app; Tyrant cameo; last Marz script. 104-Morg app. Galactus, Morg & Legacy app; Surfer vs. Super-Skrull; 4-pg Rune/Silver Surfer preview. 106-Galactus, Morg & Tyrant app. 108-Tyrant vs. Galactus; Morg & Legacy app. 110-Legacy & Nebula app; John Buscema-a. 4.00
109-Tyrant vs. Galactus; Legacy app.; Morg no longer Herald. 5.00
111-121: 111-New direction; Pérez scripts begin. 112-1st app. Uni-Lord. 114-Watcher app. 120-vs. Uni-Lord. 121-End of the Uni-Lord saga; Beta Ray Bill & Quasar cameo 4.00
122-Legacy & Beta Ray Bill app. 5.00
123-124,126-127,129-130: 123-1st Dematteis script; Surfer returns to Earth; Alicia Masters app. 124-Kymaera (Namorita) app. 126-Dr. Strange app. 127-Alicia Masters & the Puppet Master app. 130-Surfer learns that Zenn-La has been destroyed; Galactus app. 4.00
125 ($2.95)-Wraparound-c; vs. Hulk-c/app. 5.00
128-Spider-Man & Daredevil-c/app. 1 3 4 6 8 10
131-134: 131-Galactus app. 133-Puppet Master app. 134-Scrier & The Other app. 4.00
135-140: 135-Agatha Harkness, Scrier & the Thing app. 136,137-Scrier & Mephisto app. 138-Thing app. 140-Jon J. Muth-a begins 6.00
141-144: 143,144-Psycho-Man app. 1 2 3 4 6 7
145-Alicia Masters; Surfer returns to Earth 2 4 6 9 12 15
146-Firelord app; last issue. 3 6 9 19 30 40
#(-1) Flashback (7/97)-Stan Lee app; 1st app. The Other; Galactus app. 4.00
Annual 1 (1988, $1.75)-Evolutionary War Pt. 3; continued from Punisher Annual #1; 1st Ron Lim-a on Silver Surfer (20 pg. back-up story & pin-ups); Eternals app. Surfer & Super-Skrull team-up; Mantis app.; story continues in West Coast Avengers #37; Evolutionary War continues in New Mutants Annual #4 6.00
Annual 2 (1989, $2.00)-Atlantis Attacks Pt. 1; Ghaur the Deviant app; Dr. Strange cameo; story continues in Iron Man Annual #10 5.00
Annual 3-6: 3-(1990, $2.00)-Lifeform Pt. 4; continued from Punisher Annual #3. 4-(1991, $2.00)-The Korvac Quest Pt. 3; continued from Thor Annual #16; 3-pg. origin story; Silver Surfer battles the Guardians of the Galaxy (30th Century version); continued in Guardians of the Galaxy Annual #1. 5-(1992, $2.25)- Return of the Defenders Pt. 3; continued from Namor the Sub-Mariner Annual #2; Hulk & Dr. Strange app.; continued in Dr. Strange Annual #2; Nebula app. in Firelord & Starfox back-up story. 6-(1993, $2.95)-Polybagged w/trading card; 1st app. Legacy; card is by Lim/Austin; Surfer & Legacy vs. Ronan the Accuser; Terrax, Jack of Hearts & Ganymede back up features 5.00
Annual 7-(1994, $2.95)-Morg resumes being Herald to Galactus; Firelord leaves; Legacy app. in back-up 5.00
Annual '97-($2.99)-Scrier app. Annual '98-($2.99)..& Thor; vs. Millennius; Avengers app. 5.00
...Dangerous Artifacts-(1996, 48 pgs.)-Marz scripts w/Claudio Castellini-a; Galactus & Thanos app; 1st app. White Raven 1 3 4 6 8 10
Graphic Novel (1988, HC, $14.95)-Judgment Day; Lee-s/Buscema-a; Galactus vs. Mephisto 30.00
Graphic Novel (1988, SC, $10.95)-Judgment Day; Jusko-c 20.00
Graphic Novel (1990, HC, $16.95)-The Enslavers; Stan Lee-s & Pollard-a; non-canon Marvel universe story 25.00
Graphic Novel (1991, SC, $12.95)-Homecoming; Starlin-a; death of Shalla-Bal 15.00
Inner Demons TPB (4/98, $3.50)r/#123,125,126 5.00
...: Rebirth of Thanos TPB (2006, $24.99) r/#34-38, Thanos Quest #1,2; Logan's Run #6 25.00
...: The First Coming of Galactus nn (11/92, $5.95, 68 pgs.)-Reprints Fantastic Four #48-50 with new Lim-c 6.00
Wizard 1/2 2 4 6 9 12 15

NOTE: ***Austin** c(i)-7, 8, 71, 73, 74, 76, 79. **Cowan** a-143,146. **Cully Hamner** a-83p. **Ron Lim** a(p)-15-31, 33-38, 40-55, (56, 57-part-p), 60-65, 73-82, Annual 2, 4; c(p)-15-31, 32-38, 40-84, 86-92, Annual 2, 4-6. **Muth** c/a-140-142,144,145. **M. Rogers** a-1-10, 12, 19, 21; c-1-9, 11, 12, 21.*

SILVER SURFER (Volume 4)
Marvel Comics: Sept, 2003 - No. 14, Dec, 2004 ($2.25/$2.99)

1-6: 1-Milx-a; Jusko-c. 2-Jae Lee-c 4.00
7-14-($2.99) 4.00
...Vol. 1: Communion (2004, $14.99) r/#1-6 15.00

SILVER SURFER (Volume 5)
Marvel Comics: Apr, 2011 - No. 5, Aug, 2011 ($2.99, limited series)

1-5-Pagulayan-c. 1-Segovia-a. 4,5-Fantastic Four app. 4.00

SILVER SURFER (6th series)
Marvel Comics: May, 2014 - No. 15, Jan, 2016 ($3.99)

1-10: 1-Dan Slott-s/Michael Allred-a/c. 3-Guardians of the Galaxy app. 8-10-Galactus app. 4.00

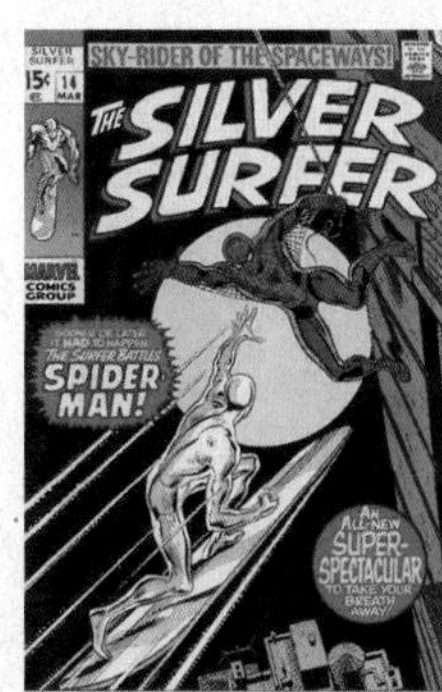

Silver Surfer #14 © MAR

Silver Surfer (2016) #1 © MAR

Simpsons Comics #124 © Bongo

GD 2.0 | VG 4.0 | FN 6.0 | VF 8.0 | VF/NM 9.0 | NM- 9.2

11-($4.99) Story runs upside down on top or bottom halves of the pages 5.00
12-15: 13-15-Secret Wars tie-in 4.00

SILVER SURFER (7th series)
Marvel Comics: Mar, 2016 - No. 14, Dec, 2017 ($3.99)

1-5,7-14-Slott-s/Allred-a. 1-4-The Thing app. 3-50th Anniversary issue; Shalla Bal app. 4.00
6-(10/16, $4.99) 200th issue; Spider-Man app.; cover gallery 5.00
Annual 1 (11/18, $4.99) Ethan Sacks-s/André Lima Araujo-a; Galactus app. 5.00
...: The Prodigal Sun 1 (10/19, $4.99) Peter David-s/Francesco Manna-a; Prah'd'gul app. 5.00

SILVER SURFER, THE
Marvel Comics (Epic): Dec, 1988 - No. 2, Jan, 1989 ($1.00, lim. series)

1-By Stan Lee scripts & Moebius-c/a 2 4 6 11 16 20
2 2 4 6 8 10 12
HC (1988, $19.95, dust jacket) r/#1,2; "Making Of" text section and sketch pages 30.00
... By Stan Lee & Moebius (3/13, $7.99) r/#1&2; bonus production diary from Moebius 3 6 9 19 30 40
...: Parable ('98, $5.99) r/#1&2 3 6 9 16 23 30

SILVER SURFER: BLACK
Marvel Comics: Aug, 2019 - No. 5, Dec, 2019 ($3.99, limited series)

1-5-Donny Cates-s/Tradd Moore-a; Ego & Knull app. 4.00

SILVER SURFER: IN THY NAME
Marvel Comics: Jan, 2008 - No. 4, Apr, 2008 ($2.99, limited series)

1-4-Spurrier-s/Huat-a. 1-Turner-c. 2-Dell'Otto-c. 3-Paul Pope-c. 4-Galactus app. 4.00

SILVER SURFER: LOFTIER THAN MORTALS
Marvel Comics: Oct, 1999 - No. 2, Oct, 1999 ($2.50, limited series)

1,2-Remix of Fantastic Four #57-60; Velluto-a 5.00

SILVER SURFER REBIRTH
Marvel Comics: Mar, 2022 - No. 5, Jul, 2022 ($3.99, limited series)

1-5-Ron Marz-s/Ron Lim-a; Mar-Vell and Thanos app. 4.00

SILVER SURFER: REQUIEM
Marvel Comics: July, 2007 - No. 4, Oct, 2007 ($3.99, limited series)

1-4-Straczynski-s/Ribic-a. 1-Origin retold; Fantastic Four app. 4.00
HC (2007, $19.99) r/#1-4, Ribic cover sketches 20.00

SILVER SURFER/SUPERMAN
Marvel Comics: 1996 ($5.95,one-shot)

1-Perez-s/Lim-c/a(p) 2 4 6 8 11 14

SILVER SURFER: THE BEST DEFENSE (Also see Immortal Hulk, Doctor Strange, Namor)
Marvel Comics: Feb, 2019 ($4.99, one-shot)

1-Jason Latour-s/a; Ron Garney-c; Galactus app. 5.00

SILVER SURFER VS. DRACULA
Marvel Comics: Feb, 1994 ($1.75, one-shot)

1-r/Tomb of Dracula #50; Everett Vampire-r/Venus #19; Howard the Duck back-up by Brunner; Lim-c(p) 1 3 4 6 8 10

SILVER SURFER/WARLOCK: RESURRECTION
Marvel Comics: Mar, 1993 - No. 4, June, 1993 ($2.50, limited series)

1-4-Starlin-c/a & scripts. 1-Surfer joins Warlock & the Infinity Watch to rescue Shalla-Bal; story continued from the 'Homecoming' GN. 2-Death app.; Mephisto cameo. 3-Surfer vs. Mephisto. 4-Warlock vs. Mephisto; Shalla-Bal revived. 4.00

SILVER SURFER/WEAPON ZERO
Marvel Comics: Apr, 1997 ($2.95, one-shot)

1-"Devil's Reign" pt. 8 3.00

SILVERTIP (Max Brand)
Dell Publishing Co.: No. 491, Aug, 1953 - No. 898, May, 1958

Four Color 491 (#1); all painted-c 8 16 24 56 108 160
Four Color 572,608,637,667,731,789,898-Kinstler-a 5 10 15 34 60 85
Four Color 835 5 10 15 34 60 85

SIM CITY
Aardvark-Vanaheim: ($4.00, B&W, with cover swipes from Sin City)

...: A Dave To Kill For 1 (2/19) Cerebus figures in Frank Miller style backgrounds 4.00
... - That Issue After 1 (3/19) Cerebus figures with Gustave Doré artwork of Hell 4.00

SIMON DARK
DC Comics: Dec, 2007 - No. 18, May, 2009 ($2.99)

1-Intro. Simon Dark; Steve Niles-s/Scott Hampton-a/c 4.00
1-Second printing with full face variant cover 3.00
2-18 3.00
...: Ashes TPB (2009, $17.99) r/#7-12 18.00

GD 2.0 | VG 4.0 | FN 6.0 | VF 8.0 | VF/NM 9.0 | NM- 9.2

...: The Game of Life TPB (2009, $17.99) r/#13-18 18.00
...: What Simon Does TPB (2008, $14.99) r/#1-6 18.00

SIMPSONS COMICS (See Bartman, Futurama, Itchy & Scratchy & Radioactive Man)
Bongo Comics Group: 1993 - No. 245, 2018 ($1.95/$2.50/$2.99/$3.99)

1-($2.25)-FF#1-c swipe; pull-out poster; flip book 4 8 12 23 37 50
2-5: 2-Patty & Selma flip-c/sty. 3-Krusty, Agent of K.L.O.W.N. flip-c/story. 4-Infinity-c; flip-c of Busman #1; w/trading card. 5-Wraparound-c w/trading card 1 3 4 6 8 10
6-40: All Flip books. 6-w/Chief Wiggum's "Crime Comics". 7-w/"McBain Comics". 8-w/"Edna, Queen of the Congo". 9-w/"Barney Gumble". 10-w/"Apu". 11-w/"Homer". 12-w/"White Knuckled War Stories". 13-w/"Jimbo Jones' Wedgie Comics". 14-w/"Grampa". 15-w/"Itchy & Scratchy". 16-w/"Bongo Grab Bag". 17-w/"Headlight Comics". 18-w/"Milhouse". 19,20-w/"Roswell." 21,22-w/"Roswell". 23-w/"Hellfire Comics". 24-w/"Lil' Homey". 36-39-Flip book w/Radioactive Man 6.00
41-49,51-99: 43-Flip book w/Poochie. 52-Dini-s. 77-Dixon-s. 85-Begin $2.99-c 5.00
50-($5.95) Wraparound-c; 80 pgs.; square-bound 1 2 3 5 6 8
100-($6.99) 100 pgs.; square-bound; clip issue of past highlights 1 3 4 6 8 10
101-182,184-199,201-224: 102-Barks Ducks homage. 117-Hank Scorpio app. 122-Archie spoof. 132-Movie poster enclosed. 132-133-Two-parter. 144-Flying Hellfish flashback. 150-w/Poster. 163-Aragonés-s/a. 218-Guardians of the Galaxy spoof 3.00
183-Archie Comics #1 cover swipe; Archie homage with Stan Goldberg-a 3.00
200-(2013, $4.99) Wraparound-c; short stories incl. Dorkin-s/a; Matt Groening cameo 5.00
225-244-($3.99) 225-Bonus back-up 1970s Eddie & Lou story. 237-Bartman app. 4.00
245-($3.99) Last issue; Bongo the rabbit app.; bonus cover gallery of #1-245 4.00
... A Go-Go (1999, $11.95)-r/#32-35; ...Big Bonanza (1998, $11.95)-r/#28-31, ...Extravaganza (1994, $10.00)-r/#1-4; infinity-c, ...On Parade (1998, $11.95)-r/#24-27, ...Simpsorama (1996, $10.95)-r/#11-14 12.00
Simpsons Classics 1-30 (2004 - 2011, $3.99, magazine-size, quarterly) reprints 4.00
Simpsons Comics Barn Burner ('04, $14.95) r/#57-61,63 15.00
Simpsons Comics Beach Blanket Bongo ('07, $14.95) r/#71-75,77 15.00
Simpsons Comics Belly Buster ('04, $14.95) r/#49,51,53-56 15.00
Simpsons Comics Hit the Road! ('08, $15.95) r/#85,86,88,89,90 16.00
Simpsons Comics Jam-Packed Jamboree ('06, $14.95) r/#64-69 15.00
Simpsons Comics Madness ('03, $14.95) r/#43-48 15.00
Simpsons Comics Royale ('01, $14.95) r/various Bongo issues 15.00
Simpsons Comics Treasure Trove 1-4 ('08-'09, $3.99, 6" x 8") r/various Bongo issues 4.00
Simpsons Summer Shindig ('07-'15, $4.99) 1-9-Anthology. 1-Batman/Ripken insert 5.00
Simpsons Winter Wing Ding ('06-'14, $4.99) 1-10-Holiday anthology. 1-Dini-s 5.00

SIMPSONS COMICS AND STORIES
Welsh Publishing Group: 1993 ($2.95, one-shot)

1-(Direct Sale)-Polybagged w/Bartman poster 3 6 9 21 33 45
1-(Newsstand Edition)-Without poster 4 8 12 27 44 60

SIMPSONS COMICS PRESENTS BART SIMPSON
Bongo Comics Group: 2000 - No. 100, 2016 ($2.50/$2.99)

1-Bill Morrison-c 2 4 6 8 10 12
2-40: 7-9-Dan DeCarlo-layouts. 13-Begin $2.99-c. 17,37-Bartman app. 5.00
41-99: 50-Aragonés-s/a 3.00
100-($4.99) 100-year old Bart, Mrs. Krabappel, Fruit Bat Man app. 5.00
The Big Book of Bart Simpson TPB (2002, $12.95) r/#1-4 15.00
The Big Bad Book of Bart Simpson TPB (2003, $12.95) r/#5-8 15.00
The Big Bratty Book of Bart Simpson TPB (2004, $12.95) r/#9-12 15.00
The Big Beefy Book of Bart Simpson TPB (2005, $13.95) r/#13-16 15.00
The Big Bouncy Book of Bart Simpson TPB (2006, $13.95) r/#17-20 15.00
The Big Beastly Book of Bart Simpson TPB (2007, $14.95) r/#21-24 15.00
The Big Brilliant Book of Bart Simpson TPB (2008, $14.95) r/#25-28 15.00

SIMPSONS FUTURAMA CROSSOVER CRISIS II (TV) (Also see Futurama/Simpsons Infinitely Secret Crossover Crisis)
Bongo Comics: 2005 - No. 2, 2005 ($3.00, limited series)

1,2-The Professor brings the Simpsons' Springfield crew to the 31st century 2 4 6 9 12 15

SIMPSONS ILLUSTRATED (TV)
Bongo Comics: 2012 - No. 27, 2017 ($3.99, quarterly)

1-Reprints in all 2 4 6 8 10 12
2-20 4.00
21-27-($4.99) 25-All-monster issue 5.00

SIMPSONS ONE-SHOT WONDERS (TV)
Bongo Comics: 2012 - 2018 ($2.99/$3.99)

...: Bart Simpson's Pal Milhouse 1 - Short stories; centerfold with decal 1 3 4 6 8 10
...: Chief Wiggum's Felonius Funnies 1 ($3.99) - Future Cop app.

1 2 3 5 6 8
...: Duffman 1 ($3.99) - Green Lantern spoof; centerfold with die-cut Duffman mask
2 4 6 9 12 15
...: Grampa 1 ($3.99) - "Choose Your Adventure" format; wraparound-c
1 3 4 6 8 10
...: Jimbo 1 ($3.99) - Short stories; centerfold with die-cut skull sticker 4.00
...: Kang & Kodos 1 ($3.99) - Short stories; centerfold with bumper stickers
1 3 4 6 8 10
...: Krusty 1 ($3.99) - Krusty's backstory; back-c swipe of Uncanny X-Men #141 6.00
...: Li'l Homer 1 - Short stories of Homer's childhood; centerfold with cut-outs
1 2 3 5 6 8
...: Lisa 1 ($3.99) - Short stories by Matsumoto and others; sticker page centerfold 6.00
...: Maggie 1 - Short stories by Aragonés and others; paperdoll centerfold; Aragonés-c 6.00
...: McBain 1 ($3.99) - Entire issue unfolds for a poster on the back
1 3 4 6 8 10
...: Mr. Burns 1 ($3.99) - Short stories incl. Richie Rich spoof; Fruit Bat Man mask
1 2 3 5 6 8
...: Professor Frink 1 ($3.99) - Short stories; 3-D glasses insert; 3-D story and back-c
1 3 4 6 8 10
...: Ralph Wiggums Comics 1 - Short stories by Aragonés and others
3 6 9 14 20 25
...: The Mighty Moe Szyslak 1 - Short stories by various; Flintstones homage back-c
2 4 6 9 12 15

SIMPSONS SUPER SPECTACULAR (TV)
Bongo Comics: 2006 - No. 16, 2013 ($2.99)

1-16: 2-Bartman, Stretch Dude and The Cupcake Kid team up; back-up story Brereton-a. 5-Fradon-a on Metamorpho spoof. 8-Spirit spoof. 9,10,14-16-Radioactive Man app. 4.00

SINBAD, JR (TV Cartoon)
Dell Publishing Co.: Sept-Nov, 1965 - No. 3, May, 1966

1 4 8 12 23 37 50
2,3 3 6 9 17 26 35

SIN BOLDLY
Image Comics: Dec, 2013 ($3.50, B&W, one-shot)

1-J.M. Linsner-s/a/c; short stories with Sinful Suzi and Obsidian Stone 3.50

SIN CITY (See Dark Horse Presents, A Decade of Dark Horse, & San Diego Comic Con Comics #2,4)
Dark Horse Comics (Legend)
TPB ($15.00) Reprints early DHP stories 15.00
Booze, Broads & Bullets TPB ($15.00) 15.00
Frank Miller's Sin City: One For One (8/10, $1.00) reprints debut story from DHP #51 3.00

SIN CITY (FRANK MILLER'S...) (Reissued TPBs to coincide with the April 2005 movie)
Dark Horse Books: Feb, 2005 ($17.00/$19.00, 6" x 9" format with new Miller covers)

Volume 1: The Hard Goodbye ($17.00) reprints stories from Dark Horse Presents #51-62 and DHP Fifth Anniv. Special; covers and publicity pieces 17.00
Volume 2: A Dame to Kill For ($17.00) r/Sin City: A Dame to Kill For #1-6 17.00
Volume 3: The Big Fat Kill ($17.00) r/Sin City: The Big Fat Kill #1-5; pin-up gallery 17.00
Volume 4: That Yellow Bastard ($19.00) r/Sin City: That Yellow Bastard #1-6; pin-up gallery by Mike Allred, Kyle Baker, Jeff Smith and Bruce Timm; cover gallery 19.00
Volume 5: Family Values ($12.00) r/Sin City: Family Values GN 12.00
Volume 6: Booze, Broads & Bullets ($15.00) r/Sin City: The Babe Wore Red and Other Stories; Silent Night; story from A Decade of Dark Horse; Lost Lonely & Lethal; Sex & Violence; and Just Another Saturday Night 15.00
Volume 7: Hell and Back ($28.00) r/Sin City: Hell and Back #1-9; pin-up gallery 28.00

SIN CITY: A DAME TO KILL FOR
Dark Horse Comics (Legend): Nov, 1993 - No. 6, May, 1994 ($2.95, B&W, limited series)

1-6: Frank Miller-c/a & story in all. 1-1st app. Dwight. 6.00
1-3-Second printing 3.00
Limited Edition Hardcover 85.00
Hardcover 25.00
TPB ($15.00) 15.00

SIN CITY: FAMILY VALUES
Dark Horse Comics (Legend): Oct, 1997 ($10.00, B&W, squarebound, one-shot)

nn-Miller-c/a & story 10.00
Limited Edition Hardcover 75.00

SIN CITY: HELL AND BACK
Dark Horse (Maverick): Jul, 1999 - No. 9 ($2.95/$4.95, B&W, limited series)

1-8-Miller-c/a & story. 7-Color 5.00
9-($4.95) 6.00

SIN CITY: JUST ANOTHER SATURDAY NIGHT
Dark Horse Comics (Legend): Aug, 1997 (Wizard 1/2 offer, B&W, one-shot)

1/2-Miller-c/a & story 1 2 3 5 6 8
nn (10/98, $2.50) r/#1/2 4.00

SIN CITY: LOST, LONELY & LETHAL
Dark Horse Comics (Legend): Dec, 1996 ($2.95, B&W and blue, one-shot)

nn-Miller-c/s/a; w/pin-ups 5.00

SIN CITY: SEX AND VIOLENCE
Dark Horse Comics (Legend): Mar, 1997 ($2.95, B&W and blue, one-shot)

nn-Miller-c/a & story 5.00

SIN CITY: SILENT NIGHT
Dark Horse Comics (Legend): Dec, 1995 ($2.95, B&W, one-shot)

1-Miller-c/a & story; Marv app. 6.00

SIN CITY: THAT YELLOW BASTARD (Second Ed. TPB listed under Sin City (Frank Miller's...)
Dark Horse Comics (Legend): Feb, 1996 - No. 6, July, 1996 ($2.95/$3.50, B&W and yellow, limited series)

1-5: Miller-c/a & story in all. 1-1st app. Hartigan. 6.00
6-($3.50) Error & corrected 6.00
Limited Edition Hardcover 25.00
TPB ($15.00) 15.00

SIN CITY: THE BABE WORE RED AND OTHER STORIES
Dark Horse Comics (Legend): Nov, 1994 ($2.95, B&W and red, one-shot)

1-r/serial run in Previews as well as other stories; Miller-c/a & scripts; Dwight app. 6.00

SIN CITY: THE BIG FAT KILL (Second Edition TPB listed under Sin City (Frank Miller's...)
Dark Horse Comics (Legend): Nov, 1994 - No. 5, Mar, 1995 ($2.95, B&W, limited series)

1-5-Miller story & art in all; Dwight app. 6.00
Hardcover 25.00
TPB ($15.00) 15.00

SIN CITY: THE FRANK MILLER LIBRARY
Dark Horse Books: Set 1, Nov, 2005; Set 2, Mar, 2006 ($150, slipcased hardcover, 8" x 12")

Set 1 - Individual hardcovers for Volume 1: The Hard Goodbye, Volume 2: A Dame to Kill For, Volume 3: The Big Fat Kill, Volume 4: That Yellow Bastard; new red foil stamped covers; slipcase box is black with red foil graphics 150.00
Set 2 - Individual hardcovers for Volume 5: Family Values, Volume 6: Booze, Broads & Bullets, Volume 7: Hell and Back, new red foil stamped covers; The Art of Sin City red hardcover; slipcase box is black with red foil graphics 150.00

SINDBAD (See Capt. Sindbad under Movie Comics, and Fantastic Voyages of Sindbad)

SINERGY
Image Comics (Shadowline): Nov, 2014 - No. 5, Mar, 2015 ($3.50)

1-5: 1-Oeming & Soma-s/Oeming-a/c 3.50

SINESTRO
DC Comics: Jun, 2014 - No. 23, Jul, 2016 ($2.99)

1-23: 1-Bunn-s/Eaglesham-a; Lyssa Drak & Arkillo app. 6-8-Godhead x-over; New Gods app. 7-Van Sciver-a. 9-11-Mongul app. 15-Lobo app. 16-20-Black Adam app. 17-20-Wonder Woman app. 19,20-Harley Quinn & Superman app. 3.00
Annual 1 (6/15, $4.99) Bunn-s/Eaglesham-c; art by various 5.00
...: Futures End 1 (11/14, $2.99, regular-c) Five years later; Bunn-s/Lima-a/Nowlan-c 3.00
...: Futures End 1 (11/14, $3.99, 3-D cover) 4.00
...: Year of the Villain 1 (10/19, $4.99) Russell-s/Cinar-a; Apex Lex Luthor app. 5.00

SINGING GUNS (See Fawcett Movie Comics)

SINGLE SERIES (Comics on Parade #30 on)(Also see John Hix...)
United Features Syndicate: 1938 - No. 28, 1942 (All 68 pgs.)

Note: See Individual Alphabetical Listings for prices

1-Captain and the Kids (#1)
2-Broncho Bill (1939) (#1)
3-Ella Cinders (1939)
4-Li'l Abner (1939) (#1)
5-Fritzi Ritz (#1)
6-Jim Hardy by Dick Moores (#1)
7-Frankie Doodle
8-Peter Pat (On sale 7/14/39)
9-Strange As It Seems
10-Little Mary Mixup
11-Mr. and Mrs. Beans
12-Joe Jinks
13-Looy Dot Dope
14-Billy Make Believe
15-How It Began (1939)
16-Illustrated Gags (1940)-Has ad for Captain and the Kids #1 reprint listed below
17-Danny Dingle
18-Li'l Abner (#2 on-c)
19-Broncho Bill (#2 on-c)
20-Tarzan by Hal Foster
21-Ella Cinders (#2 on-c; on sale 3/19/40)
22-Iron Vic
23-Tailspin Tommy by Hal Forrest (#1)
24-Alice in Wonderland (#1)
25-Abbie and Slats
26-Little Mary Mixup (#2 on-c, 1940)
27-Jim Hardy by Dick Moores (1942)
28-Ella Cinders & Abbie and Slats (1942)
1-Captain and the Kids (1939 reprint)-2nd Edition
1-Fritzi Ritz (1939 reprint)-2nd ed.

NOTE: *Some issues given away at the 1939-40 New York World's Fair (#6).*

SINISTER DEXTER
IDW Publishing: Dec, 2013 - No. 7, Jun, 2014 ($3.99)

1-7: 1-Dan Abnett-s/Andy Clarke-a; two covers by Clarke and Fuso 4.00

SINISTER HOUSE OF SECRET LOVE, THE (Becomes Secrets of Sinister House No. 5 on)
National Periodical Publ.: Oct-Nov, 1971 - No. 4, Apr-May, 1972

1 (All 52 pgs.) -Grey-tone-c 13 26 39 91 201 310
2,4 7 14 21 48 89 130
3-Toth-a; Grey-tone-c 8 16 24 51 96 140

SINISTER WAR
Marvel Comics: Sept, 2021 - No. 4, Nov, 2021 ($4.99, limited series)

1-4-Spider-Man vs. Sinister Six & others; Doctor Strange & Mephisto app.; Bagley-a 5.00

SINS OF SINISTER
Marvel Comics: Mar, 2023 ($5.99, one-shot)

1-Mister Sinister from X-Men; Gillen-s/Werneck-a; part 1 of crossover saga 6.00

SINS OF THE BLACK FLAMINGO
Image Comics: Jun, 2022 - No. 5, Oct, 2022 ($3.99, limited series)

1-5-Andrew Wheeler-s/Travis Moore-a 4.00

SINS OF YOUTH... (Also see Young Justice: Sins of Youth)
DC Comics: May 2000 ($4.95/$2.50, limited crossover series)

Secret Files 1 ($4.95) Short stories and profile pages; Nauck-c 5.00
...Aquaboy/Lagoon Man; Batboy and Robin; JLA Jr.; Kid Flash/Impulse; Starwoman and the JSA, Superman, Jr./Superboy, Sr.; The Secret/ Deadboy, Wonder Girls ($2.50-c) Old and young heroes switch ages 3.00

SIP KIDS (Strangers in Paradise)
Abstract Studio: 2014 - No. 4, 2015 ($4.99, color)

1-4-Strangers in Paradise characters as young kids; Terry Moore-s/a/c 5.00

SIR CHARLES BARKLEY AND THE REFEREE MURDERS
Hamilton Comics: 1993 ($9.95, 8-1/2" x 11", 52 pgs.)

nn-Photo-c; Sports fantasy comic book fiction (uses real names of NBA superstars). Script by Alan Dean Foster, art by Joe Staton. Comes with bound-in sheet of 35 gummed "Moods of Charles Barkley" stamps. Photo/story on Barkley 2 4 6 9 12 15
Special Edition of 100 copies for charity signed on an affixed book plate by Barkley, Foster & Staton 175.00
Ashcan edition given away to dealers, distributors & promoters (low distribution). Four pages in color, balance of story in b&w 2 4 6 9 12 15

SIR EDWARD GREY: ACHERON (From Hellboy)

Sinestro #8 © DC

Six-Gun Gorilla #1 © BOOM!

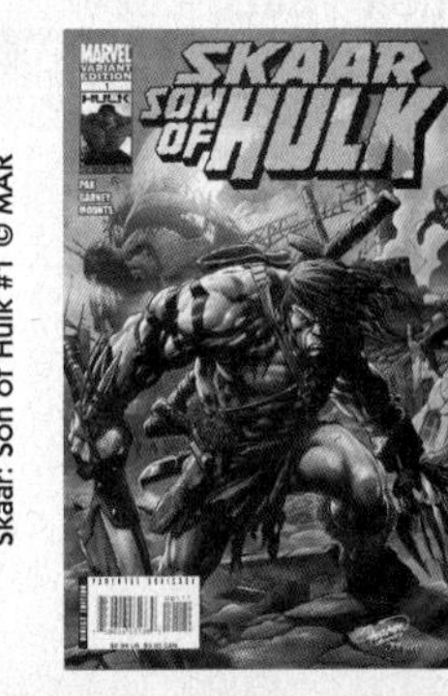

Skaar: Son of Hulk #1 © MAR

	GD 2.0	VG 4.0	FN 6.0	VF 8.0	VF/NM 9.0	NM- 9.2

Dark Horse Comics: Dec, 2021 ($3.99, one-shot)
1-Mike Mignola-s/a 4.00

SIR EDWARD GREY, WITCHFINDER: IN THE SERVICE OF ANGELS (From Hellboy)
Dark Horse Comics: July, 2009 - No. 5, Nov, 2009 ($2.99, limited series)
1-5-Mignola-s/c; Stenbeck-a 3.00

SIR EDWARD GREY, WITCHFINDER: THE MYSTERIES OF UNLAND (From Hellboy)
Dark Horse Comics: Jun, 2014 - No. 5, Oct, 2014 ($3.50, limited series)
1-5-Newman & McHugh-s/Crook-a/Tedesco-c 3.50

SIREN (Also see Eliminator & Ultraforce)
Malibu Comics (Ultraverse): Sept, 1995 - No. 3, Dec, 1995 ($1.50)
Infinity, 1-3: Infinity-Black-c & painted-c exists. 1-Regular-c & painted-c; War Machine app. 2-Flip book w/Phoenix Resurrection Pt. 3 3.00
Special 1-(2/96, $1.95, 28 pgs.)-Origin Siren; Marvel Comic's Juggernaut-c/app. 3.00

SIRENS (See George Pérez's Sirens)

SIRENS GATE
Dynamite Entertainment: 2022 - Present ($3.99, limited series)
1-3-Shannon Maer-s/a 4.00

SIR LANCELOT (TV)
Dell Publishing Co.: No. 606, Dec, 1954 - No. 775, Mar, 1957

	GD	VG	FN	VF	VF/NM	NM-
Four Color 606 (not TV)	7	14	21	46	86	125
Four Color 775(...and Brian)-Buscema-a; photo-c	9	18	27	59	117	175

SIR WALTER RALEIGH (Movie)
Dell Publishing Co.: May, 1955 (Based on movie "The Virgin Queen")

	GD	VG	FN	VF	VF/NM	NM-
Four Color 644-Photo-c	6	12	18	42	79	115

SISTERHOOD OF STEEL (See Eclipse Graphic Adventure Novel #13)
Marvel Comics (Epic Comics): Dec, 1984 - No. 8, Feb, 1986 ($1.50, Baxter paper, mature)
1-8 4.00

SISTERS OF SORROW
BOOM! Studios: Jul, 2017 - No. 4, Oct, 2017 ($3.99, limited series)
1-4-Kurt Sutter & Courtney Alameda-s/Hyeonjin Kim-a. 1-Jae Lee-c 4.00

SITUATION, THE (TV's Jersey Shore)
Wizard World: July, 2012 (no cover price)
1-Jenkins-s/Caldwell-a; two covers by Horn & Caldwell 3.00

6 BLACK HORSES (See Movie Classics)

SIX FROM SIRIUS
Marvel Comics (Epic Comics): July, 1984 - No. 4, Oct, 1984 ($1.50, limited series, mature)
1-4: Moench scripts; Gulacy-c/a in all 4.00

SIX FROM SIRIUS II
Marvel Comics (Epic Comics): Feb, 1986 - No. 4, May, 1986 ($1.50, limited series, mature)
1-4: Moench scripts; Gulacy-c/a in all 4.00

SIX-GUN GORILLA
BOOM! Studios: Jun, 2013 - No. 6, Nov, 2013 ($3.99, limited series)
1-6: 1-Spurrier-s/Stokely-a 4.00

SIX-GUN HEROES
Fawcett Publications: March, 1950 - No. 23, Nov, 1953 (Photo-c #1-23)

	GD	VG	FN	VF	VF/NM	NM-
1-Rocky Lane, Hopalong Cassidy, Smiley Burnette begin (same date as Smiley Burnette #1)	31	62	93	186	303	420
2	16	32	48	94	147	200
3-5: 5-Lash LaRue begins	14	28	42	76	108	140
6-15	11	22	33	62	86	110
16-22: 17-Last Smiley Burnette. 18-Monte Hale begins	10	20	30	54	72	90
23-Last Fawcett issue	10	20	30	58	79	100

NOTE: *Hopalong Cassidy photo c-1-3. Monte Hale photo c-18. Rocky Lane photo c-4, 5, 7, 9, 11, 13, 15, 17, 20, 21, 23. Lash LaRue photo c-6, 8, 10, 12, 14, 16, 19, 22.*

SIX-GUN HEROES (Cont'd from Fawcett; Gunmasters #84 on) (See Blue Bird)
Charlton Comics: No. 24, Jan, 1954 - No. 83, Mar-Apr, 1965 (All Vol. 4)

	GD	VG	FN	VF	VF/NM	NM-
24-Lash LaRue, Hopalong Cassidy, Rocky Lane & Tex Ritter begin; photo-c	14	28	42	80	115	150
25	10	20	30	54	72	90
26-30: 26-Rod Cameron story. 28-Tom Mix begins?	9	18	27	47	61	75
31-40: 38-40-Jingles & Wild Bill Hickok (TV)	8	16	24	42	54	65
41-46,48,50: 41-43-Wild Bill Hickok (TV)	8	16	24	40	50	60
47-Williamson-a, 2 pgs; Torres-a	8	16	24	42	54	65
49-Williamson-a (5 pgs.)	9	18	27	50	65	80
51-56,58-60: 58-Gunmaster app.	3	6	9	19	30	40
57-Origin & 1st app. Gunmaster	4	8	12	25	40	55
61-70	3	6	9	16	23	30
71-75,77,78,80-83	2	4	6	13	18	22
76,79: 76-Gunmaster begins. 79-1st app. & origin of Bullet, the Gun-Boy	3	6	9	14	19	24

SIXGUN RANCH (See Luke Short & Four Color #580)

SIX GUNS
Marvel Comics: Jan, 2012 - No. 5, Apr, 2012 ($2.99, limited series)
1-5-Diggle-s/Gianfelice-a; Tarantula and Tex Dawson app. 3.00

SIX-GUN WESTERN
Atlas Comics (CDS): Jan, 1957 - No. 4, July, 1957

	GD	VG	FN	VF	VF/NM	NM-
1-Crandall-a; two Williamson text illos	24	48	72	142	234	325
2,3-Williamson-a in both	16	32	48	94	147	200
4-Woodbridge-a	14	28	42	80	115	150

NOTE: ***Ayers** a-2, 3. **Maneely** a-1; c-2, 3. **Orlando** a-2. **Pakula** a-2. **Powell** a-3. **Romita** a-1, 4. **Severin** c-1, 4. **Shores** a-2.*

SIX MILLION DOLLAR MAN, THE (TV) (Also see The Bionic Man)
Charlton Comics: 6/76 - No. 4, 12/76; No. 5, 10/77; No. 6, 2/78 - No. 9, 6/78

	GD	VG	FN	VF	VF/NM	NM-
1-Staton-c/a; Lee Majors photo on-c	6	12	18	37	66	95
2-Neal Adams-c; Staton-a	4	8	12	27	44	60
3-9	3	6	9	14	19	24

SIX MILLION DOLLAR MAN, THE (TV)(Magazine)
Charlton Comics: July, 1976 - No. 7, Nov, 1977 (B&W)

	GD	VG	FN	VF	VF/NM	NM-
1-Neal Adams-c/a	5	10	15	33	57	80
2-Neal Adams-c	3	6	9	17	25	34
3-N. Adams part inks; Chaykin-a	3	6	9	14	19	24
4-7	2	4	6	11	16	20

SIX MILLION DOLLAR MAN, THE: FALL OF MAN (TV)
Dynamite Entertainment: 2016 - No. 5, 2016 ($3.99)
1-5: 1-Van Jensen-s/Ron Salas-a; three covers 4.00

SIX MILLION DOLLAR MAN, THE: SEASON 6 (TV)
Dynamite Entertainment: 2014 - No. 6, 2014 ($3.99)
1-Jim Kuhoric-s/Juan Antonio Ramirez-a; covers by Alex Ross & Ken Haeser & photo-c 4.00
2-6-Two covers by Ross & Haeser on each. 2-Maskatron returns 4.00

SIX MILLION DOLLAR MAN, THE: VOLUME 1 (TV)
Dynamite Entertainment: 2019 - No. 5, 2019 ($3.99, limited series)
1-5-Christopher Hastings-s/David Hahn-a; set in 1974 4.00

SIXPACK AND DOGWELDER: HARD TRAVELIN' HEROZ (See All-Star Section Eight)
DC Comics: Oct, 2016 - No. 6, Mar, 2017 ($3.99, limited series)
1-6-Ennis-s/Braun-a/Dillon-c. 1-Power Girl, Catwoman, & Starfire app. 2-6-Constantine app. 2-The Spectre app. 4.00

SIX STRING SAMURAI
Awesome-Hyperwerks: Sept, 1998 ($2.95)
1-Stinsman & Fraga-a; Liefeld-c 3.00

1602 WITCH HUNTER ANGELA (Secret Wars tie-in)
Marvel Comics: Aug, 2015 - No. 4, Dec, 2015 ($3.99, limited series)
1-4-Marguerite Bennett-s; Hans & Sauvage-a; The Enchantress app. 4.00

67 SECONDS
Marvel Comics (Epic Comics): 1992 ($15.95, 54 pgs., graphic novel)

	GD	VG	FN	VF	VF/NM	NM-
nn-James Robinson scripts; Steve Yeowell-c/a	2	4	6	11	14	18

SKAAR: KING OF THE SAVAGE LAND
Marvel Comics: Jun, 2011 - No. 5 ($2.99, limited series)
1-5-Shanna & Ka-Zar app.; Ching-a. 1-Komarck-c. 2-McGuinness-c 3.00

SKAAR: SON OF HULK (Title continues in Son of Hulk #13)(Also see World War Hulk x-over)
Marvel Comics: Aug, 2008 - No. 12, Aug, 2009 ($2.99)
1-Garney-a/Pak-s; 2 covers by Pagulayan and Julie Bell; origin 4.00
1-Second printing - 2 covers by Garney and Hulk movie image 3.00
1-Third printing - Garney sketch variant-c 3.00
2-12: 2-6-Back-up story with Guice-a. 7-12-Silver Surfer app. 3.00
Planet Skaar Prologue 1 (7/09, $3.99) Panosian-a; Fantastic Four & She-Hulk app. 4.00
... Presents - Savage World of Sakaar (11/08, $3.99) Pak-s/art by various; Garney-c 4.00

SKATEMAN
Pacific Comics: Nov, 1983 (Baxter paper, one-shot)
1-Adams-c/a 4.00

GD 2.0 VG 4.0 FN 6.0 VF 8.0 VF/NM 9.0 NM- 9.2

SKELETON HAND (...In Secrets of the Supernatural)
American Comics Gr. (B&M Dist. Co.): Sept-Oct, 1952 - No. 6, Jul-Aug, 1953

1 93 186 279 591 1021 1450
2 50 100 150 315 533 750
3-6 41 82 123 256 428 600

SKELETON KEY
Amaze Ink: July, 1995 - No. 30, Jan, 1998 ($1.25/$1.50/$1.75, B&W)

1-30 3.00
Special #1 (2/98, $4.95) Unpublished short stories 5.00
Sugar Kat Special (10/98, $2.95) Halloween stories 3.00
Beyond The Threshold TPB (6/96. $11.95)-r/#1-6 12.00
Cats and Dogs TPB ($12.95)-r/#25-30 13.00
The Celestial Calendar TPB ($19.95)-r/#7-18 20.00
Telling Tales TPB ($12.95)-r/#19-24 13.00

SKELETON KEY (Volume 2)
Amaze Ink: 1999 - No. 4, 1999 ($2.95, B&W)

1-4-Andrew Watson-s/a 3.00

SKELETON WARRIORS
Marvel Comics: Apr, 1995 - No. 4, July, 1995 ($1.50)

1-4: Based on animated series. 3.00

SKIN GRAFT: THE ADVENTURES OF A TATTOOED MAN
DC Comics (Vertigo): July, 1993 - No. 4, Oct, 1993 ($2.50, lim. series, mature)

1-4 3.00

SKINWALKER
Oni Press: May, 2002 - No. 4, Sept, 2002 ($2.95, limited series)

1-4-Hurtt & Dela Cruz-a; Talon-c 3.00
1-(5/05) Free Comic Book Day Edition 3.00

SKI PARTY (See Movie Classics)

SKREEMER
DC Comics: May, 1989 - No. 6, Oct, 1989 ($2.00, limited series, mature)

1-6: Contains graphic violence; Milligan-s 3.00
TPB (2002, $19.95) r/#1-6 20.00

SKRULL KILL KREW
Marvel Comics: Sept, 1995 - No. 5, Dec, 1995 ($2.95, limited series)

1-5: Grant Morrison & Mark Millar scripts; Steve Yeowell-a. 2,3-Cap America app. 5.00
TPB (2006, $16.99) r/#1-5 17.00

SKRULL KILL KREW
Marvel Comics: Jun, 2009 - No. 5, Dec, 2009 ($3.99, limited series)

1-5-Felber-s/Robinson-a 4.00

SKRULLS! (Tie-in to Secret Invasion crossover)
Marvel Comics: 2008 ($4.99, one-shot)

1-Skrull history, profiles of Skrulls, their allies & foes; checklist of appearances; Horn-c 5.00

SKRULLS VS. POWER PACK (Tie-in to Secret Invasion crossover)
Marvel Comics: Sept, 2008 - No. 4 ($2.99, limited series)

1-4-Van Lente-s/Hamscher-a; Franklin Richards app. 3.00

SKUL, THE
Virtual Comics (Byron Preiss Multimedia): Oct, 1996 - No. 3, Dec, 1996 ($2.50, lim. series)

1-3: Ron Lim & Jimmy Palmiotti-a 3.00

SKULL & BONES
DC Comics: 1992 - No. 3, 1992 ($4.95, limited series, 52 pgs.)

Book 1-3: 1-1st app. 5.00

SKULLDIGGER AND SKELETON BOY (From Black Hammer)
Dark Horse Comics: Dec, 2019 - No. 6, Feb, 2021 ($3.99)

1-6-Lemire-s/Zonjic-a; origin of Skeleton Boy 5.00

SKULLKICKERS
Image Comics: Sept, 2010 - No. 33, Jul, 2015; No. 100, Aug, 2015 ($2.99/$3.50)

1-Jim Zubkavich-s/Edwin Huang-a; two covers 4.00
1-(2nd & 3rd printings), 2-18 3.00
24-29,31-33: 24-($3.50) "Before Watchmen" cover swipe (no issues #34-99) 3.50
30-($3.99) Multi-dimensional variant Skullkickers 4.00
#100 ($3.99, 8/15) Last issue; conclusion of Infinite Icons of the Endless Epic 4.00
All-New Secret Skullkickers 1 (6/13, $3.50) issue #22; cover swipe of X-Men #125 ('79) 3.50
Dark Skullkickers Dark 1 (7/13, $3.50) issue #23; cover swipe of Green Lantern #85 ('71) 3.50
Savage Skullkickers 1 (3/13, $3.50) issue #20; cover swipe of Savage Wolverine #1 3.50
The Mighty Skullkickers 1 (4/13, $3.50) issue #21; cover swipe of Thor #337 3.50
... Super Special 1 (11/22, $3.99) 10th Anniversary Special 4.00
Uncanny Skullkickers 1 (2/13, $3.50) issue #19 3.50

SKULL, THE SLAYER
Marvel Comics Group: Aug, 1975 - No. 8, Nov, 1976 (20¢/25¢)

1-Origin & 1st app.; Gil Kane-c 3 6 9 18 27 36
2-8: 2-Gil Kane-c. 5,6-(Regular 25¢-c). 8-Kirby-c 2 4 6 8 10 12
5,6-(30¢-c variants, limited distribution)(5,7/76) 4 8 12 27 44 60

SKY BLAZERS (CBS Radio)
Hawley Publications: Sept, 1940 - No. 2, Nov, 1940

1-Sky Pirates, Ace Archer, Flying Aces begin 87 174 261 553 952 1350
2-WWII air battle grey-tone-c 43 86 129 271 461 650

SKYBOUND PRESENTS AFTERSCHOOL
Image Comics (Skybound): Jun, 2022 - No. 4, Nov, 2022 ($4.99, horror anthology series)

1-4: 1-Hinkle-a. 2-Leila Leiz-a. 3-Zarcone & Sterle-a. 4-Zadwadzki-a 5.00

SKYBOUND X
Image Comics (Skybound): Jul, 2021 - No. 5, Aug, 2021 ($4.99, square-bound, weekly limited anthology series)(Issues #6-24 don't exist)

1-5-Rick Grimes 2000 (Walking Dead) w/Kirkman-s/Ottley-a in all. 1-1st comic app. of Clementine. 2-Stillwater & Birthright. 3-5-Negan app. 4-Excellence & Redneck 5.00
25-(7/22, $4.99) Battle Beast, Dark Ride, Kroma & Scurry 5.00

SKYBOURNE
BOOM! Studios: Sept, 2016 - No. 5, Feb, 2018 ($3.99)

1-5-Frank Cho-s/a 4.00

SKY DOLL
Marvel Comics (Soleil): 2008 - No. 3, 2008 ($5.99, mature)

1-3-Barbucci & Canepa-s/a; English version of French comic; preview of other titles 6.00
...: Doll's Factory 1,2 (2009 - No. 2, 2009, $5.99) Barbucci & Canepa-s/a 6.00
...: Lacrima Christi 1,2 (9/10 - No. 2, 10/10, $5.99) Barbucci & Canepa and others-s/a 6.00
...: Space Ship 1,2 (7/10 - No. 2, 8/10, $5.99) Barbucci & Canepa and others-s/a 6.00

SKY DOLL: SUDRA
Titan Comics: Apr, 2017 - No. 2, May, 2017 ($3.99, mature)

1,2-Barbucci & Canepa-s/a; English version of French comic 4.00

SKYE RUNNER
DC Comics (WildStorm): June, 2006 - No. 6, Mar, 2007 ($2.99)

1-6: 1-Three covers; Warner-s/Garza-a. 2-Three covers, incl. Campbell 3.00

SKYLANDERS (Based on the Activision video game)
IDW Publishing: No. 0, Jul, 2014 - No. 12, Aug, 2015 ($3.99)

0-(no cover price) Lord Kaos app.; Bowden-a; character bios 3.00
1-12: 1-Marz & Rodriguez-s/Baldeón-a 4.00
... Quarterly - Spyro & Friends: Biting Back (3/18, $4.99) Marz & Rodriguez-s 5.00
... Quarterly - Spyro & Friends: Full Blast (7/17, $4.99) Marz & Rodriguez-s 5.00
... Quarterly - Spyro & Friends: Goldslinger (11/17, $4.99) Marz & Rodriguez-s 5.00
... Superchargers 1-6 (10/15 - No. 6, 3/16, $3.99) Marz & Rodriguez-s 4.00

SKYMAN (See Big Shot Comics & Sparky Watts)
Columbia Comics Gr.: Fall?, 1941 - No. 2, Fall?, 1942; No. 3, 1948 - No. 4, 1948

1-Origin Skyman, The Face, Sparky Watts app.; Whitney-c/a; 3rd story-r from Big Shot #1; Whitney c-1-4 135 270 409 864 1482 2100
2 (1942)-Yankee Doodle 77 154 231 493 847 1200
3,4 (1948) 45 90 135 284 480 675

SKYMAN (Also see Captain Midnight 2013 series #4)
Dark Horse Comics: Jan, 2014 - No. 4, Apr, 2014 ($2.99)

1-4: 1-Fialkov-s/Garcia-a; origin of a new Skyman. 3,4-Captain Midnight app. 3.00
... One-Shot (11/14, $2.99) Garcia-a 3.00

SKYPILOT
Ziff-Davis Publ. Co.: No. 10, 1950(nd) - No. 11, Apr-May, 1951

10,11-Frank Borth-a; Saunders painted-c 21 42 63 122 199 275

SKY RANGER (See Johnny Law...)

SKYROCKET
Harry 'A' Chesler: 1944

nn-Alias the Dragon, Dr. Vampire, Skyrocket & The Desperado app.; WWII Japan zero-c 65 130 195 416 708 1000

SKY SHERIFF (Breeze Lawson...) (Also see Exposed & Outlaws)
D. S. Publishing Co.: Summer, 1948

1-Edmond Good-c/a 21 42 63 126 206 285

SKYWARD
Image Comics: Apr, 2018 - No. 15, Jul, 2019 ($3.99)

1-15: 1-Joe Henderson-s/Lee Garbett-a 4.00

SKY WOLF (Also see Airboy)
Eclipse Comics: Mar, 1988 - No. 3, Oct, 1988 ($1.25/$1.50/$1.95, lim. series)

1-3 3.00

SLAINE, THE BERSERKER (Slaine the King #21 on)
Quality: July, 1987 - No. 28, 1989 ($1.25/$1.50)

1-28 3.00

SLAINE, THE HORNED GOD
Fleetway: 1998 - No. 3 ($6.99)

1-3-Reprints series from 2000 A.D.; Bisley-a 7.00

SLAM!
BOOM! Studios (Boom! Box): Nov, 2016 - No. 4, Feb, 2017 ($3.99)

1-4-Roller derby; Pamela Ribon-s/Veronica Fish-a 4.00

SLAM BANG COMICS (Western Desperado #8)
Fawcett Publications: Mar, 1940 - No. 7, Sept, 1940 (Combined with Master Comics #7)

1-Diamond Jack, Mark Swift & The Time Retarder, Lee Granger, Jungle King begin & continue in Master 290 580 870 1856 3178 4500
2 129 258 387 826 1413 2000
3-Classic monster-c (scarce) 337 674 1011 2359 4130 5900
4,6,7: 6-Intro Zoro, the Mystery Man (also in #7) 110 220 330 704 1202 1700
5-Classic Dragon-c 123 246 369 787 1344 1900
Ashcan (1940) Not distributed to newsstands, only for in house use. A copy sold in 2006 for $4,500.

SLAM! THE NEXT JAM
BOOM! Studios (Boom! Box): Sept, 2017 - No. 4, Dec, 2017 ($3.99)

1-4-Roller derby; Pamela Ribon-s/Marina Julia-a 4.00

SLAPSTICK
Marvel Comics: Nov, 1992 - No. 4, Feb, 1993 ($1.25, limited series)

1-4: Fry/Austin-c/a. 4-Ghost Rider, D.D., F.F. app. 3.00

SLAPSTICK
Marvel Comics: Feb, 2017 - No. 6, Jul, 2017 ($3.99, limited series)

1-6-Brown & Van Lente-s/Olortegui-a 4.00

SLAPSTICK COMICS
Comic Magazines Distributors: nd (1946?) (36 pgs.)

nn-Firetop feature; Post-a(2); Munson Paddock-c 42 84 126 265 445 625

SLASH & BURN

Skybourne #2 © Frank Cho

Slapstick (2017) #1 © MAR

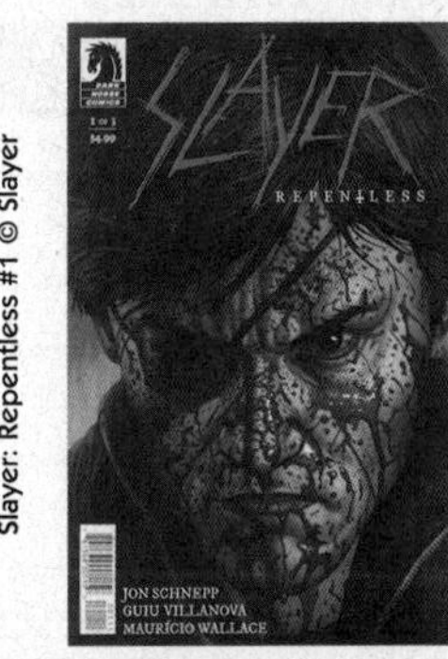

Slayer: Repentless #1 © Slayer

	GD 2.0	VG 4.0	FN 6.0	VF 8.0	VF/NM 9.0	NM- 9.2

DC Comics (Vertigo): Jan, 2016 - No. 6, Jun, 2016 ($3.99/$4.99)

1-5-Si Spencer-s/Max Dunbar-a 4.00
6-($4.99) 5.00

SLASH-D DOUBLECROSS
St. John Publishing Co.: 1950 (Pocket-size, 132 pgs.)

nn-Western comics 26 52 78 154 252 350

SLASH MARAUD
DC Comics: Nov, 1987 - No. 6, Apr, 1988 ($1.75, limited series)

1-6-Moench-s/Gulacy-a/c 3.00

SLAVE GIRL COMICS (See Malu... & White Princess of the Jungle #2)
Avon Periodicals/Eternity Comics (1989): Feb, 1949 - No. 2, 1949 (52 pgs.); Mar, 1989 (B&W, 44 pgs)

1-Larsen-c/a 187 374 561 1197 2049 2900
2-Larsen-a (no month listed) 148 296 444 947 1624 2300
1-(3/89, $2.25, B&W, 44 pgs.)-r/#1 2 4 6 9 12 15

SLAVE LABOR STORIES
SLG Publishing: May, 2003 (Giveaway, B&W)

1-Free Comic Book Day Edition; short stories by various; Dorkin Milk & Cheese-c 3.00

SLAY BELLS
Bad Idea: Jul, 2021 ($7.99, one-shot)

1-Wells-s/Lafuente-a; Rahal-s/Pollina-a 1 2 3 5 6 8

SLAYER: REPENTLESS (Based on the band Slayer)
Dark Horse Comics: Jan, 2017 - No. 3, Jun, 2017 ($4.99, limited series)

1-3-Jon Schnepp-s/Guiu Villanova-a/Glenn Fabry-c; Slayer app. 5.00

SLEDGE HAMMER (TV)
Marvel Comics: Feb, 1988 - No. 2, Mar,1988 ($1.00, limited series)

1,2 3.00

SLEDGEHAMMER 44
Dark Horse Comics: Mar, 2013 - No. 2, Apr, 2013 ($3.50, limited series)

1,2-Mignola & Arcudi-s/Latour-a; Mignola-c 3.50

SLEDGEHAMMER 44: THE LIGHTNING WAR
Dark Horse Comics: Nov, 2013 - No. 3, Jan, 2014 ($3.50, limited series)

1-3-Mignola & Arcudi-s/Laurence Campbell-a. 1-Mignola-c. 2,3-Campbell-c 3.50

SLEEPER
DC Comics (WildStorm): Mar, 2003 - No. 12, Mar, 2004 ($2.95)

1-12-Brubaker-s/Phillips-c/a. 3-Back-up preview of The Authority: High Stakes pt. 2 3.00
...: All False Moves TPB (2004, $17.95) r/#7-12 18.00
...: Out in the Cold TPB (2004, $17.95) r/#1-6 18.00

SLEEPER: SEASON TWO
DC Comics (WildStorm): Aug, 2004 - No. 12, July, 2005 ($2.95/$2.99)

1-12-Brubaker-s/Phillips-c/a. 3.00
TPB (2009, $24.99) r/#1-12 25.00
...: A Crooked Line TPB (2005, $17.99) r/#1-6 18.00
...: The Long Way Home TPB (2005, $14.99) r/#7-12 15.00

SLEEPING BEAUTY (See Dell Giants & Movie Comics)
Dell Publishing Co.: No. 973, May, 1959 - No. 984, June, 1959 (Disney)

Four Color 973 (...and the Prince) 12 24 36 82 179 275
Four Color 984 (...Fairy Godmother's) 10 20 30 67 141 215

SLEEPLESS
Image Comics: Dec, 2017 - No. 11, Jan, 2019 ($3.99)

1-11-Sarah Vaughn-s/Leila Del Duca-a 4.00

SLEEPWALKER (Also see Infinity Wars: Sleepwalker)
Marvel Comics: June, 1991 - No. 33, Feb, 1994 ($1.00/$1.25)

1-1st app. Sleepwalker 4.00
2-33: 4-Williamson-i. 5-Spider-Man-c/story. 7-Infinity Gauntlet x-over. 8-Vs. Deathlok-c/story. 11-Ghost Rider-c/story. 12-Quesada-c/a(p) 14-Intro Spectra. 15-F.F.-c/story. 17-Darkhawk & Spider-Man x-over. 18-Infinity War x-over; Quesada/Williamson-c. 21,22-Hobgoblin app. 19-($2.00)-Die-cut Sleepwalker mask-c 3.00
25-($2.95, 52 pgs.)-Holo-grafx foil-c; origin 4.00
Holiday Special 1 (1/93, $2.00, 52 pgs.)-Quesada-c(p) 4.00

SLEEPWALKING
Hall of Heroes: Jan, 1996 ($2.50, B&W)

1-Kelley Jones-c 3.00

SLEEPY HOLLOW (Movie Adaption)
DC Comics (Vertigo): 2000 ($7.95, one-shot)

1-Kelley Jones-a/Seagle-s 8.00

SLEEPY HOLLOW (Based on the Fox TV show)
BOOM! Studios: Oct, 2014 - No. 4, Jan, 2015 ($3.99, limited series)

1-4-Marguerite Bennett-s/Jorge Coelho-a/Phil Noto-c 4.00
...: Origins 1 (4/15, $4.99) Mike Johnson-s/Matias Bergara-a; Quinones-c 5.00
...: Providence 1-4 (8/15 - No. 4 11/15, $3.99) Carrasco-s/Santos-a 4.00

SLEEZE BROTHERS, THE
Marvel Comics (Epic Comics): Aug, 1989 - No. 6, Jan, 1990 ($1.75, mature)

1-6: 4-6 (9/89 - 11/89 indicia dates) 3.00
nn-(1991, $3.95, 52 pgs.) 4.00

SLICK CHICK COMICS
Leader Enterprises: 1947(nd) - No. 3, 1947(nd)

1-Teenage humor 45 90 135 284 480 675
2,3 30 60 90 177 289 400

SLIDERS (TV)
Acclaim Comics (Armada): June, 1996 - No. 2, July, 1996 ($2.50, lim. series)

1,2: D.G. Chichester scripts; Dick Giordano-a. 3.00

SLIDERS: DARKEST HOUR (TV)
Acclaim Comics (Armada): Oct, 1996 - No. 3, Dec, 1996 ($2.50, limited series)

1-3 3.00

SLIDERS SPECIAL
Acclaim Comics (Armada): Nov, 1996 - No 3, Mar, 1997 ($3.95, limited series)

1-3: 1-Narcotica-Jerry O'Connell-s. 2-Blood and Splendor. 3-Deadly Secrets 4.00

SLIDERS: ULTIMATUM (TV)
Acclaim Comics (Armada): Sept, 1996 - No. 2, Sept, 1996 ($2.50, lim. series)

1,2 3.00

SLIMER! (TV cartoon) (Also see the Real Ghostbusters)
Now Comics: 1989 - No. 19, Nov, 1990 ($1.75)

1-19: Based on animated cartoon 4.00

SLIM MORGAN (See Wisco)

SLINGERS (See Spider-Man: Identity Crisis issues)
Marvel Comics: Dec, 1998 - No. 12, Nov, 1999 ($2.99/$1.99)

0-(Wizard #88 supplement) Prelude story 3.00
1-($2.99) Four editions w/different covers for each hero, 16 pages common to all, the other pages from each hero's perspective 4.00
2-12: 2-Two-c. 12-Saltares-a 3.00

SLITHISS ATTACKS! (Also see Very Weird Tales)
Oceanspray Comics Group: Dec, 2001 – No. 4, Aug, 2004 ($3.00/$4.00)

1-($3.00) Origin and 1st app. of the monster Slithiss; 1st app. Overconfident Man 15.00
2-($4.00) 2nd app. Overconfident Man; "Chris Lamo" Newport, OR murder parody 12.00
3-($3.00) Rutland Vermont Halloween x-over; 3rd app. Overconfident Man 12.00
4-($3.00) 4th app. Overconfident Man 10.00
Special Edition 1($20.00) reprints #1-2 without letter column 20.00
Special Edition 1($20.00) second printing 20.00

NOTE: *Created in prevention classes taught by Jon McClure at the Oceanspray Family Center in Newport, OR and paid for by the Housing Authority of Lincoln County, all books are b&w with color covers. Bob Overstreet and other comics' professionals wrote letters of encouragement that were published in issues #2-4. Issues #1-2 penciled and inked by various artists; #3-4 penciled by James Gilmer. All comics feature characters created by students, signed and numbered by Jon McClure. Issue #1 had a 200 issue print run, while issues #2-4 have print runs of 100 each. Special Edition #1 had a print run of 26 issues, while the second printing had a 10 issue print run. Ties in with live action movie Face Eater released in 2007 and card game FaceEater released in 2010.*

SLOTS
Image Comics: Oct, 2017 - No. 6, Mar, 2018 ($3.99)

1-6-Dan Panosian-s/a/c 4.00

SLUDGE
Malibu Comics (Ultraverse): Oct, 1993 - No. 12, Dec, 1994 ($2.50/$1.95)

1-($2.50, 48 pgs.)-Intro/1st app. Sludge; Rune flip-c/story Pt. 1 (1st app., 3 pgs.) by Barry Smith; The Night Man app. (3 pg. preview); The Mighty Magnor 1 pg strip begins by Aragonés (cont. in other titles) 4.00
1-Ultra 5000 Limited silver foil 8.00
2-11: 3-Break-Thru x-over. 4-2 pg. Mantra origin. 8-Bloodstorm app. 3.00
12 ($3.50)-Ultraverse Premiere #8 flip book; Alex Ross poster 4.00
...:Red Xmas (12/94, $2.50, 44 pgs.) 4.00

SLUGGER (Little Wise Guys Starring...)(Also see Daredevil Comics)
Lev Gleason Publications: April, 1956

1-Biro-c 10 20 30 58 79 100

GD VG FN VF VF/NM NM-
2.0 4.0 6.0 8.0 9.0 9.2

SMALLVILLE (Based on TV series)
DC Comics: May, 2003 - No. 11, Jan, 2005 ($3.50/$3.95, bi-monthly)
1-6-Photo-c. 1-Plunkett-a; interviews with cast; season 1 episode guide begins 4.00
7-11-($3.95) 7-Chloe Chronicles begin; season 2 episode guide begins 4.00
Vol. 1 TPB (2004, $9.95) r/#1-4 & Smallville: The Comic; photo-c 10.00

SMALLVILLE: ALIEN (Based on TV series)
DC Comics: Feb, 2014 - No. 4, May, 2014 ($3.99, printings of previously released digital comics)
1-4: 1-The Monitor lands on Earth; Staggs-a. 2-4-Batman app. 4.00

SMALLVILLE: CHAOS (Based on TV series)(Season 11)
DC Comics: Oct, 2014 - No. 4, Jan, 2015 ($3.99, printings of previously released digital comics)
1-4: 1-Eclipso app.; Padilla-a. 3-Darkseid app. 3,4-Supergirl & Superboy app. 4.00

SMALLVILLE: LANTERN (Based on TV series)
DC Comics: Jun, 2014 - No. 4, Sept, 2014 ($3.99, printings of previously released digital comics)
1-4: 1-Kal-El joins the Green Lantern Corps; Takara-a. 2-4-Parallax app. 4.00

SMALLVILLE SEASON 11 (Based on TV series)
DC Comics: Jul, 2012 - No. 19, Jan, 2014 ($3.99, printings of previously released digital comics)
1-19: 1-Two covers by Gary Frank & Cat Staggs; Pere Perez-a. 5-8-Batman app.
13-15-Legion app. 15-Doomsday app. 16-19-Diana of Themyscira app. 4.00
... Special 1 (7/13, $4.99) Batman, Nightwing and Martian Manhunter app. 5.00
... Special 2 (9/13, $4.99) Lana Lang and John Corben app. 5.00
... Special 3 (12/13, $4.99) Spotlight on Luthor and Tess; Lobel-a 5.00
... Special 4 (3/14, $4.99) Superboy, Jay Garrick, Blue Beetle, Wonder Twins app. 5.00
... Special 5 (9/14, $4.99) Zatanna and John Constantine app. 5.00

SMALLVILLE SEASON 11: CONTINUITY (Based on TV series)
DC Comics: Feb, 2015 - No. 4, May, 2015 ($3.99, printings of previously released digital comics)
1-4-The Crisis vs. the Monitors; Legion of Super-Heroes app.; Guara-a 4.00

SMALLVILLE: THE COMIC (Based on TV series)
DC Comics: Nov, 2002 ($3.95, 64 pages, one-shot)
1-Photo-c; art by Martinez and Leon; interviews with cast; season 2 preview 5.00

SMASH COMICS (Becomes Lady Luck #86 on)
Quality Comics Group: Aug, 1939 - No. 85, Oct, 1949
1-Origin Hugh Hazard & His Iron Man, Bozo the Robot, Espionage, Starring Black X by Eisner, & Hooded Justice (Invisible Justice #2 on); Chic Carter & Wings Wendall begin; 1st Robot on the cover of a comic book (Bozo) 377 754 1131 2639 4620 6600
2-The Lone Star Rider app; Invisible Hood gains power of invisibility; bondage/torture-c 174 348 522 1114 1907 2700
3-Captain Cook & Eisner's John Law begin 103 206 309 659 1130 1600
4,5: 4-Flash Fulton begins 100 200 300 635 1093 1550
6-12: 12-One pg. Fine-a 93 186 279 599 1025 1450
13-Magno begins (8/40); last Eisner issue; The Ray app. in full page ad; The Purple Trio begins 93 186 279 599 1025 1450
14-Intro. The Ray (9/40) by Lou Fine & others 371 373 1113 2600 4550 6500
15-1st Ray-c, 2nd app. 181 362 543 1158 1979 2800
16-The Scarlet Seal begins 142 284 426 909 1555 2200
17-Wun Cloo becomes plastic super-hero by Jack Cole (9-months before Plastic Man); Ray-c 155 310 465 992 1696 2400
18-Midnight by Jack Cole begins (origin & 1st app., 1/41) 194 388 582 1242 2121 3000
19-22: Last Ray by Fine; The Jester begins-#22. 19,21-Ray-c 100 200 300 635 1093 1550
23,24: 23-Ray-c. 24-The Sword app.; last Chic Carter; Wings Wendall dons new costume #24,25 84 168 252 538 919 1300
25-Origin/1st app. Wildfire; Rookie Rankin begins; Ray-c 90 180 270 576 988 1400
26-30: 28-Midnight-c begin, end #85 71 142 213 454 777 1100
31,32,34: The Ray by Rudy Palais; also #33 65 130 195 416 708 1000
33-Origin The Marksman 68 136 204 435 743 1050
35-37 53 106 159 334 567 800
38-The Yankee Eagle begins; last Midnight by Jack Cole; classic-c by Cole 103 206 309 621 1061 1600
39,40-Last Ray issue 52 104 156 328 552 775
41,44-50 42 84 126 265 445 625
42-Lady Luck begins by Klaus Nordling 142 284 426 909 1555 2200
43-Lady Luck-c (1st & only in Smash) 94 188 282 597 1025 1450
51-60 33 66 99 194 317 440
61-70 25 50 75 150 245 340
71-85: 79-Midnight battles the Men from Mars-c/s 21 42 63 126 206 285
NOTE: ***Al Bryant*** *c-54, 63-68.* ***Cole*** *a-17-38, 68, 69, 72, 73, 78, 80, 83, 85; c-38, 60-62, 69-84.* ***Crandall*** *a-(Ray)-23-29, 35-38; c-36, 39, 40, 42-44, 46.* ***Fine*** *a(Ray)-14, 15, 16(w/****Tuska****), 17-22.* ***Fox*** *c-24-35.* ***Fuje*** *Ray-30.* ***Gil Fox*** *a-6-7, 9, 11-13.* ***Guardineer*** *a-(The Marksman)-39-?, 49, 52.* ***Gustavson*** *a-4-7, 9, 11-13 (The Jester)-22-46; (Magno)-13-21; (Midnight)-39(Cole inks), 49, 52, 63-65.* ***Kotzky*** *a-(Espionage)-33-38; c-45, 47-53.* ***Nordling*** *a-49, 52, 63-65.* ***Powell*** *a-11, 12, (Abdul the Arab)-13-24.Black X c-2, 6, 9, 11, 13, 16. Bozo the Robot c-1, 3, 5, 8, 10, 12, 14, 18, 20, 22, 24, 26. Midnight c-28-85. The Ray c-15, 17, 19, 21, 23, 25, 27. Wings Wendall c-4, 7.*

SMASH COMICS (Also see All Star Comics 1999 crossover titles)
DC Comics: May, 1999 ($1.99, one-shot)
1-Golden Age Doctor Mid-nite and Hourman 4.00

SMASH HIT SPORTS COMICS
Essankay Publications: V2#1, Jan, 1949
V2#1-L.B. Cole-c/a 39 78 117 240 395 550

SMAX (Also see Top Ten)
America's Best Comics: Oct, 2003 - No. 5, May, 2004 ($2.95, limited series)
1-5-Alan Moore-s/Zander Cannon-a 3.00
... Collected Edition (2004, $19.95, HC with dustjacket) r/#1-5 20.00
... Collected Edition SC (2005, $12.99) r/#1-5 13.00

SMILE COMICS (Also see Gay Comics, Tickle, & Whee)
Modern Store Publ.: 1955 (52 pgs.; 5x7-1/4") (7¢)
1 10 20 30 58 79 100

SMILEY BURNETTE WESTERN (Also see Patches #8 & Six-Gun Heroes)
Fawcett Publ.: March, 1950 - No. 4, Oct, 1950 (All photo front & back-c)
1-Red Eagle begins 26 52 78 154 252 350
2-4 17 34 51 98 154 210

SMILEY (THE PSYCHOTIC BUTTON) (See Evil Ernie)
Chaos! Comics: July, 1998 - May, 1999 ($2.95, one-shots)
1-Ivan Reis-a 3.00
... Holiday Special (1/99), ...'s Spring Break (4/99), ...Wrestling Special (5/99) 3.00

SMILIN' JACK (See Famous Feature Stories and Popular Comics) (Also see Super Book of Comics #1&2 and Super-Book of Comics #7&19 in the Promotional Comics section)
Dell Publishing Co.: No. 5, 1940 - No. 8, Oct-Dec, 1949
Four Color 5 (1940) 100 200 300 635 1093 1550
Four Color 10 (1940) 84 168 252 538 919 1300
Large Feature Comic 12,14,25 (1941) 77 154 231 493 847 1200
Four Color 4 (1942) 77 154 231 493 847 1200
Four Color 14 (1943) 34 68 102 245 548 850
Four Color 36,58 (1943-44) 23 46 69 164 362 560
Four Color 80 (1945) 14 28 42 93 204 315
Four Color 149 (1947) 10 20 30 66 138 210
1 (1-3/48) 12 24 36 80 173 265
2 6 12 18 41 76 110
3-8 (10-12/49) 5 10 15 34 60 85

SMILING SPOOK SPUNKY (See Spunky)

SMITTY (See Popular Comics, Super Book #2, 4 & Super Comics)
Dell Publishing Co.: No. 11, 1940 - No. 7, Aug-Oct, 1949; No. 909, Apr, 1958
Four Color 11 (1940) 61 122 183 390 670 950
Large Feature Comic 26 (1941) 47 94 141 296 498 700
Four Color 6 (1942) 34 68 102 245 548 850
Four Color 32 (1943) 18 36 54 124 275 425
Four Color 65 (1945) 14 28 42 96 211 325
Four Color 99 (1946) 11 22 33 73 157 240
Four Color 138 (1947) 10 20 30 64 132 200
1 (2-4/48) 9 18 27 61 123 185
2-(5-7/48) 5 10 15 33 57 80
3,4: 3-(8-10/48), 4-(11-1/48-49) 4 8 12 28 47 65
5-7, Four Color 909 (4/58) 4 8 12 25 40 55

SMOKEY BEAR (TV) (See March Of Comics #234, 362, 372, 383, 407)
Gold Key: Feb, 1970 - No. 13, Mar, 1973
1 3 6 9 18 28 38
2-5 2 4 6 10 14 18
6-13 2 4 6 8 10 12

SMOKEY STOVER (See Popular Comics, Super Book #5,17,29 & Super Comics)
Dell Publishing Co.: No. 7, 1942 - No. 827, Aug, 1957
Four Color 7 (1942)-Reprints 27 54 81 189 420 650
Four Color 35 (1943) 17 34 51 114 252 390
Four Color 64 (1944) 12 24 36 84 185 285
Four Color 229 (1949) 6 12 18 42 79 115
Four Color 730,827 5 10 15 34 60 85

SMOKEY THE BEAR (See Forest Fire for 1st app.)
Dell Publ. Co.: No. 653, 10/55 - No. 1214, 8/61 (See March of Comics #234)
Four Color 653 (#1) 10 20 30 67 141 215
Four Color 708,754,818,932 6 12 18 40 73 105
Four Color 1016,1119,1214 5 10 15 31 53 75

SMOKY (See Movie Classics)

SMOOTH CRIMINALS
BOOM! Studios (BOOM! Box): Nov, 2018 - No. 8, Aug, 2019 ($3.99)
1-8-Kurt Lustgarten & Kirsten Smith-s/Leisha Riddel-a 4.00

SMOSH
Dynamite Entertainment: 2016 - No. 6, 2016 ($3.99)
1-6: 1-3-McDermott-s/Viglino-a; back-up with Yale Stewart-s/a. 4-Boxman origin 4.00

SMURFS (TV)
Marvel Comics: 1982 (Dec) - No. 3, 1983
1-3 3 6 9 16 23 30
...Treasury Edition 1 (64 pgs.)-r/#1-3 3 6 9 21 33 45

SNAFU (Magazine)
Atlas Comics (RCM): Nov, 1955 - V2#2, Mar, 1956 (B&W)
V1#1-Heath/Severin-a; Everett, Maneely-a 19 38 57 111 176 240
V2#1,2-Severin-a 15 30 45 83 124 165

SNAGGLEPUSS (TV)(See Hanna-Barbera Band Wagon, Quick Draw McGraw #5 & Spotlight #4)
Gold Key: Oct, 1962 - No. 4, Sept, 1963 (Hanna-Barbera)
1 9 18 27 59 117 175
2-4 6 12 18 38 69 100

SNAGGLEPUSS CHRONICLES (See Exit Stage Left: The Snagglepuss Chronicles)

SNAKE EYES (G.I. Joe)
Devil's Due Publ.: Aug, 2005 - No. 6, Jan, 2006 ($2.95)
1-6-Santalucia-a 5.00
...: Declassified TPB (4/06, $18.95) r/series; source guide 19.00

SNAKE EYES (... and Storm Shadow #13-on)(Cont. from G.I. Joe: Snake Eyes, Volume 2 #7)
IDW Publishing: No. 8, Dec, 2011 - No. 21, Nov, 2011 ($3.99)
8-21: 13-Title change to Snake Eyes and Storm Shadow 4.00

SNAKE EYES: DEADGAME
IDW Publishing: Jul, 2020 - No. 5, Jul, 2021 ($4.99, limited series)
1-5-Rob Liefeld-s/a; multiple covers; Joseph Colton app. 5.00
... - Declassified 1 (10/21, $6.99) B&W artwork inked by various w/commentary by Liefeld 7.00

SNAKE PLISSKEN CHRONICLES, (John Carpenter's...)
Hurricane Entertainment: June, 2003 - No. 4, Feb, 2004 ($2.99)
Preview Issue (8/02, no cover price) B&W preview; John Carpenter interview 3.00

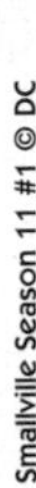
Smallville Season 11 #1 © DC

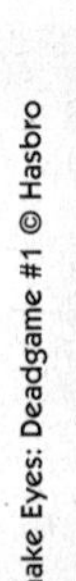
Snake Eyes: Deadgame #1 © Hasbro

Snow Fall #5 © Harris & Morazzo

GD VG FN VF VF/NM NM-
2.0 4.0 6.0 8.0 9.0 9.2

1-4: 1-Three covers; Rodriguez-a 3.00

SNAKES AND LADDERS
Eddie Campbell Comics: 2001 ($5.95, B&W, one-shot)
nn-Alan Moore-s/Eddie Campbell-a 6.00

SNAKES ON A PLANE (Adaptation of the 2006 movie)
Virgin Comics: Oct, 2006 - No. 2, Nov, 2006 ($2.99, limited series)
1,2: 1-Dixon-s/Purcell-a. JG Jones and photo-c. 2-Klebs, Jr.-a; Moore & photo-c 3.00

SNAKE WOMAN (Shekhar Kapur's...)
Virgin Comics: July, 2006 - No. 10, Apr, 2007 ($2.99)
1-10: 1-6-Michael Gaydos-a/Zeb Wells-s. 1-Two covers by Gaydos & Singh 3.00
#0 (5/07, 99¢) origin of the Snake Goddess; background info; Gaydos-a/c 3.00
... Curse of the 68 (3/08 - No. 4, 5/08, $2.99) 1-4: 1-Ingale-a. 2-Manu-a 3.00
... Tale of the Snake Charmer 1-6 (6/07-12/07, $2.99) Vivek Shinde-a 3.00
... Vol. 1 TPB (6/07, $14.99) r/#1-5; Gaydos sketch pages; creator commentary 15.00
... Vol. 2 TPB (9/07, $14.99) r/#6-10; Cebulski intro. 15.00

SNAP (Formerly Scoop #8; becomes Jest #10,11 & Komik Pages #10)
Harry 'A' Chesler: No. 9, 1944
9-Manhunter, The Voice; WWII gag-c 39 78 117 231 378 525

SNAPPY COMICS
Cima Publ. Co. (Prize Publ.): 1945
1-Airmale app.; 9 pg. Sorcerer's Apprentice adapt; Kiefer-a
41 82 123 256 428 600

SNAPSHOT
Image Comics: Feb, 2013 - No. 4, May, 2013 ($2.99, B&W, limited series)
1-4-Andy Diggle-s/Jock-a/c 3.00

SNARKED
Boom Entertainment (Kaboom!): No. 0, Aug, 2011 - No. 12, Sept, 2012 ($1.00/$3.99)
0-($1.00) Roger Langridge-s/a; sketch gallery, bonus content and games 3.00
1-12: 1-($3.99) Covers by Langridge & Samnee 4.00

SNARKY PARKER (See Life With...)

SNELSON: COMEDY IS DYING
Image Comics: 2021 - No. 5, 2021 ($3.99, limited series)
1-5-Paul Constant-s/Fred Harper-a; back-up prose stories by various 4.00

SNIFFY THE PUP
Standard Publ. (Animated Cartoons): No. 5, Nov, 1949 - No. 18, Sept, 1953
5-Two Frazetta text illos 15 30 45 88 137 185
6-10 10 20 30 54 72 90
11-18 8 16 24 44 57 70

SNOOPER AND BLABBER DETECTIVES (TV) (See Whitman Comic Books)
Gold Key: Nov, 1962 - No. 3, May, 1963 (Hanna-Barbera)
1 7 14 21 46 86 125
2,3 5 10 15 34 60 85

SNOTGIRL
Image Comics: Jul, 2016 - Present ($2.99/$3.99)
1-10-Bryan O'Malley-s/Leslie Hung-a; two covers by O'Malley & Hung on each 3.00
11-15-($3.99) 4.00

SNOW BLIND
BOOM! Studios: Dec, 2015 - No. 4, Mar, 2016 ($3.99)
1-4-Ollie Masters-s/Tyler Jenkins-a 4.00

SNOWFALL
Image Comics: Feb, 2016 - No. 9, Jun, 2017 ($3.99)
1-9-Joe Harris-s/Martin Morazzo-a 4.00

SNOW WHITE (See Christmas With... (in Promotional Comics section), Mickey Mouse Magazine, Movie Comics & Seven Dwarfs)
Dell Publishing Co.: No. 49, July, 1944 - No. 382, Mar, 1952 (Disney-Movie)
Four Color 49 (...& the Seven Dwarfs) 52 104 156 413 932 1450
Four Color 382 (1952)-origin; partial reprint of Four Color 49
12 24 36 82 179 275

SNOW WHITE
Marvel Comics: Jan, 1995 ($1.95, one-shot)
1-r/1937 Sunday newspaper pages 4.00

SNOW WHITE AND THE SEVEN DWARFS
Whitman Publications: April, 1982 (60¢)
nn-r/Four Color 49 2 4 6 8 10 12

SNOW WHITE AND THE SEVEN DWARFS
Dark Horse Comics: Jun, 2019 - No. 3, Aug, 2019 ($3.99, limited series)
1-3-Cecil Castellucci-s/Gabriele Bagnoli-a 4.00

SNOW WHITE AND THE SEVEN DWARFS GOLDEN ANNIVERSARY
Gladstone: Fall, 1987 ($2.95, magazine size, 52 pgs.)
1-Contains poster 2 4 6 9 13 16

SOAP OPERA LOVE
Charlton Comics: Feb, 1983 - No. 3, June, 1983
1-3-Low print run 3 6 9 19 30 40

SOAP OPERA ROMANCES
Charlton Comics: July, 1982 - No. 5, March, 1983
1-5-Nurse Betsy Crane-r; low print run 3 6 9 19 30 40

SOCK MONKEY
Dark Horse Comics: Sept, 1998 - No. 2, Oct, 1998 ($2.95/$2.99, B&W)
1,2-Tony Millionaire-s/a 1 2 3 5 6 8
Vol. 2 -(Tony Millionaire's Sock Monkey) July, 1999 - No. 2, Aug, 1999
1,2 3.00
Vol. 3 -(Tony Millionaire's Sock Monkey) Nov, 2000 - No. 2, Dec, 2000
1,2 3.00
Vol. 4 -(Tony Millionaire's Sock Monkey) May, 2003 - No. 2, Aug, 2003
1,2 3.00
...The Inches Incident (Sept, 2006 - No. 4, Apr, 2007) 1-4-Tony Millionaire-s/a 3.00

SOJOURN
White Cliffs Publ. Co.: Sept, 1977 - No. 2, 1978 ($1.50, B&W & color, tabloid size)
1,2: 1-Tor by Kubert, Eagle by Severin, E. V. Race, Private Investigator by Doug Wildey, T. C. Mars by Aragonés begin plus other strips 2 4 6 8 10 12
NOTE: Most copies came folded. Unfolded copies are worth 50% more.

SOJOURN
CrossGeneration Comics: July, 2001 - No. 34, May, 2004 ($2.95)
Prequel -Ron Marz-s/Greg Land-c/a; preview pages 3.00
1-Ron Marz-s/Greg Land-c/a in most 6.00
2,3 5.00
4-24: 7-Immonen-a. 12-Brigman-a. 17-Lopresti-a. 21-Luke Ross-a 3.00
25-34: 25-$1.00-c. 34-Cariello-a 3.00
...: From the Ashes TPB (2001, $19.95) r/#1-6; Land painted-c 20.00
...: The Dragon's Tale TPB (2002, $15.95) r/#7-12; Jusko painted-c 16.00
...: The Warrior's Tale TPB (2003, $15.95) r/#13-18 16.00
Vol. 4: The Thief's Tale (2003, $15.95) r/#19-24 16.00
Vol. 5: The Sorcerer's Tale (Checker Book Publ.,2007, $17.95) r/#25-30 18.00
Vol. 6: The Berzerker's Tale (Checker Book Publ.,2007, $17.95) r/#31-34, Prequel 18.00
Traveler Vol.1,2 ($9.95) digest-sized reprints of TPBs 10.00

SOLAR (...Man of the Atom) (Also see Doctor Solar)
Valiant/Acclaim Comics (Valiant): Sept, 1991 - No. 60, Apr, 1996 ($1.75-$2.50, 44 pgs.)
1-Layton-a(i) on Solar; Barry Windsor-Smith-c/a 3 6 9 14 20 25
2,4-9: 2-Layton-a(i) on Solar, B. Smith-a. 7-vs. X-O Armor
1 3 4 6 8 10
3-1st app. Harada (11/91); intro. Harbinger 4 8 12 23 37 50
10-(6/92, $3.95)-1st app. Eternal Warrior (6 pgs.); black embossed-c; origin & 1st app. Geoff McHenry (Geomancer) 4 8 12 25 40 55
10-($3.95)-2nd printing 6.00
11-15: 11-1st full app. Eternal Warrior. 12,13-Unity x-overs. 14-1st app. Fred Bender (becomes Dr. Eclipse). 15-2nd Dr. Eclipse 5.00
16-60: 17-X-O Manowar app. 23-Solar splits. 29-1st Valiant Vision book. 33-Valiant Vision; bound-in trading card. 38-Chaos Effect Epsilon Pt.1. 46-52-Dan Jurgens-a(p)/scripts w/Giordano-i. 53,54-Jurgens scripts only. 60-Giffen scripts; Jeff Johnson-a(p) 4.00
0-($9.95, trade paperback)-r/Alpha and Omega origin story; polybagged w/poster 15.00
...: Second Death (1994, $9.95)-r/issues #1-4. 20.00
NOTE: #1-10 all have free 8 pg. insert "Alpha and Omega" which is a 10 chapter Solar origin story. All 10 centerfolds can pieced together to show climax of story. ***Ditko*** *a-11p, 14p.* ***Giordano*** *a-46, 47, 48, 49, 50, 51, 52i.* ***Johnson*** *a-60p.* ***Jurgens*** *a-46, 47, 48, 49, 50 , 51, 52p.* ***Layton*** *a-1-3i; c-2i, 11i, 17i, 25i.* ***Miller*** *c-12.* ***Quesada*** *c-17p, 20-23p, 29p.* ***Simonson*** *c-13.* ***B. Smith*** *a-1-10; c-1, 3, 5, 7, 19i.* ***Thibert*** *c-22i, 23i.*

SOLARMAN (See Pendulum Ill. Originals)
Marvel Comics: Jan, 1989 - No. 2, May, 1990 ($1.00, limited series)
1,2 3.00

SOLAR, MAN OF THE ATOM (Man of the Atom on cover)
Acclaim Comics (Valiant Heroes): Vol. 2, May, 1997 ($3.95, one-shot, 46 pgs)
(1st Valiant Heroes Special Event)
Vol. 2-Reintro Solar; Ninjak cameo; Warren Ellis scripts; Darick Robertson-a 4.00

SOLAR: MAN OF THE ATOM

	GD 2.0	VG 4.0	FN 6.0	VF 8.0	VF/NM 9.0	NM- 9.2

Dynamite Entertainment: 2014 - No. 12, 2015 ($3.99)

	GD	VG	FN	VF	VF/NM	NM-
1-12: 1-Barbiere-s/Bennett-a; 5 covers. 3-Female Solar in costume. 5-White costume						4.00

SOLAR, MAN OF THE ATOM: HELL ON EARTH
Acclaim Comics (Valiant Heroes): Jan, 1998 - No. 4 ($2.50, limited series)

	GD	VG	FN	VF	VF/NM	NM-
1-4-Priest-s/ Zircher-a(p)						3.00

SOLAR, MAN OF THE ATOM: REVELATIONS
Acclaim Comics (Valiant Heroes): Nov, 1997 ($3.95, one-shot, 46 pgs.)

	GD	VG	FN	VF	VF/NM	NM-
1-Krueger-s/ Zircher-a(p)						5.00

SOLDIER & MARINE COMICS (Fightin' Army #16 on)
Charlton Comics (Toby Press of Conn. V1#11): No. 11, Dec, 1954 - No. 15, Aug, 1955; V2#9, Dec, 1956

	GD	VG	FN	VF	VF/NM	NM-
V1#11 (12/54)-Bob Powell-a	14	28	42	80	115	150
V1#12(2/55)-15: 12-Photo-c. 14-Photo-c; Colan-a	10	20	30	58	79	100
V2#9(Formerly Never Again; Jerry Drummer V2#10 on)	10	20	30	54	72	90

SOLDIER COMICS
Fawcett Publications: Jan, 1952 - No. 11, Sept, 1953

	GD	VG	FN	VF	VF/NM	NM-
1	18	36	54	103	162	220
2	10	20	30	58	79	100
3-5: 4-What Happened in Taewah	10	20	30	54	72	90
6-11: 8-Illo. in **POP**	9	18	27	50	65	80

SOLDIERS OF FORTUNE
American Comics Group (Creston Publ. Corp.): Mar-Apr, 1951 - No. 13, Feb-Mar, 1953

	GD	VG	FN	VF	VF/NM	NM-
1-Capt. Crossbones by Shelly, Ace Carter, Lance Larson begin	30	60	90	177	289	400
2-(52 pgs.)	15	30	45	94	147	200
3-10: 6-Bondage-c	15	30	45	83	124	165
11-13 (War format)	10	20	30	58	79	100

NOTE: *Shelly a-1-3, 5. Whitney a-6, 8-11, 13; c-1-3, 5, 6.*

SOLDIERS OF FREEDOM
Americomics: 1987 - No. 2, 1987 ($1.75)

	GD	VG	FN	VF	VF/NM	NM-
1,2						3.00

SOLDIER STORIES
Image Comics: Nov, 2022 ($5.99, one-shot)

	GD	VG	FN	VF	VF/NM	NM-
1-Military-themed stories by various; Tucci-c						6.00

SOLDIER X (Continued from Cable)
Marvel Comics: Sept, 2002 - No. 12, Aug, 2003 ($2.99/$2.25)

	GD	VG	FN	VF	VF/NM	NM-
1,10,11,12-($2.99) 1-Kordey-a/Macan-s. 10-Bollers-s/Ranson-a						3.00
2-9-($2.25)						3.00

SOLDIER ZERO (From Stan Lee)
BOOM! Studios: Oct, 2010 - No. 12, Sept, 2011 ($3.99)

	GD	VG	FN	VF	VF/NM	NM-
1-12: 1-4-Cornell-s/Pina-a						4.00

SOLID BLOOD
Image Comics: No. 17, Dec, 2020 ($3.99, one-shot, newsprint paper)

	GD	VG	FN	VF	VF/NM	NM-
17-Robert Kirkman-s/Ryan Ottley-a; homage to 1990s Image comics; Michonne cameo						4.00

SOLITAIRE (Also See Prime V2#6-8)
Malibu Comics (Ultraverse): Nov, 1993 - No. 12, Dec, 1994 ($1.95)

	GD	VG	FN	VF	VF/NM	NM-
1-($2.50)-Collector's edition bagged w/playing card						4.00
1-12: 1-Regular edition w/o playing card. 2,4-Break-Thru x-over. 3-2 pg. origin The Night Man. 4-Gatefold-c. 5-Two pg. origin the Strangers						3.00

SOLO
Marvel Comics: Sept, 1994 - No. 4, Dec, 1994 ($1.75, limited series)

	GD	VG	FN	VF	VF/NM	NM-
1-4: Spider-Man app.						4.00

SOLO (Movie)
Dark Horse Comics: July, 1996 - No. 2, Aug, 1996 ($2.50, limited series)

	GD	VG	FN	VF	VF/NM	NM-
1,2: Adaptation of film; photo-c						3.00

SOLO (Anthology showcasing individual artists)
DC Comics: Dec, 2004 - No. 12, Oct, 2006 ($4.95/$4.99)

	GD	VG	FN	VF	VF/NM	NM-
1-12: 1-Tim Sale-a; stories by Sale and various. 2-Richard Corben-a; stories by Corben and Arcudi. 3-Paul Pope. 4-Howard Chaykin. 5-Darwyn Cooke. 6-Jordi Bernet. 7-Michael Allred; Teen Titans & Doom Patrol app. 8-Teddy Kristiansen. 9-Scott Hampton. 10-Damion Scott. 11-Sergio Aragonés. 12-Brendan McCarthy	1	2	3	5	6	8

SOLO
Marvel Comics: Dec, 2016 - No. 5, Apr, 2017 ($3.99)

	GD	VG	FN	VF	VF/NM	NM-
1-5: 1-Thorne & Duggan-s/Diaz-a; Dum Dum Dugan app.						4.00

SOLO: A STAR WARS STORY ADAPTATION (Titled Star Wars: Solo Adaptation for #1)
Marvel Comics: Dec, 2018 - No. 7, Jun, 2019 ($4.99/$3.99, limited series)

	GD	VG	FN	VF	VF/NM	NM-
1-($4.99) Thompson-s/Sliney-a; 1st Qi'ra	3	6	9	19	30	40
2-5,7-($3.99) Noto-c						4.00
6-1st Darth Maul Crime Syndicate	2	4	6	9	12	15

SOLO AVENGERS (Becomes Avenger Spotlight #21 on)
Marvel Comics: Dec, 1987 - No. 20, July, 1989 (75¢/$1.00)

	GD	VG	FN	VF	VF/NM	NM-
1-Jim Lee-a on back-up story	1	3	4	6	8	10
2-20: 11-Intro Bobcat						4.00

SOLOMON AND SHEBA (Movie)
Dell Publishing Co.: No. 1070, Jan-Mar, 1960

	GD	VG	FN	VF	VF/NM	NM-
Four Color 1070-Sekowsky-a; photo-c	10	20	30	64	132	200

SOLOMON GRUNDY
DC Comics: May, 2009 - No. 7, Nov, 2009 ($2.99)

	GD	VG	FN	VF	VF/NM	NM-
1-7-Scott Kolins-s/a. 2-Bizarro app. 7-Blackest Night prelude						3.00
TPB (2010, $19.99) r/#1-7						20.00

SOLOMON KANE (Based on the Robert E. Howard character. Also see Blackthorne 3-D Series #60 & Marvel Premiere)
Marvel Comics: Sept, 1985 - No. 6, July, 1986 (Limited series)

	GD	VG	FN	VF	VF/NM	NM-
1-Double size						5.00
2-6: 3-6-Williamson-a(i)						4.00

SOLOMON KANE
Dark Horse Comics: Sept, 2008 - No. 5, Feb, 2009 ($2.99)

	GD	VG	FN	VF	VF/NM	NM-
1-5: 1-Two covers by Cassaday and Joe Kubert; Guevara-a						3.00
...: Death's Black Riders 1-4 (1/10 - No. 4, 6/10, $3.50) Robertson-c						3.50
...: Red Shadows 1-4 (4/11 - No. 4, 7/11, $3.50) Bruce Jones-s/Rahsan Ekedal-a; two covers by Davis & Manchess on each						3.50

SOLUS
CG Entertainment, Inc.: Apr, 2003 - No. 8, Jan, 2004 ($2.95)

	GD	VG	FN	VF	VF/NM	NM-
1-8: 1-4,6,7-George Pérez-a/c; Barbara Kesel-s. 5-Ryan-a. 8-Kirk-a						3.00

SOLUTION, THE
Malibu Comics (Ultraverse): Sept, 1993 - No. 17, Feb, 1995 ($1.95)

	GD	VG	FN	VF	VF/NM	NM-
1,3-15: 1-Intro Meathook, Deathdance, Black Tiger, Tech. 4-Break-Thru x-over; gatefold-c. 5-2 pg. origin The Strangers. 11-Brereton-c						3.00
1-($2.50)-Newsstand ed. polybagged w/trading card						4.00
1-Ultra 5000 Limited silver foil						8.00
0-Obtained w/Rune #0 by sending coupons from 11 comics						5.00
2-($2.50, 48 pgs.)-Rune flip-c/story by B. Smith; The Mighty Magnor 1 pg. strip by Aragonés						4.00
16 ($3.50)-Flip-c Ultraverse Premiere #10						4.00
17 ($2.50)						3.00

SOMERSET HOLMES (See Eclipse Graphic Novel Series)
Pacific Comics/ Eclipse Comics No. 5, 6: Sept, 1983 - No. 6, Dec, 1984 ($1.50, Baxter paper)

	GD	VG	FN	VF	VF/NM	NM-
1-6: 1-Brent Anderson-c/a. Cliff Hanger by Williamson in all						4.00

SOMETHING IS KILLING THE CHILDREN (Also see Enter the House of Slaughter)
BOOM! Studios: Sept, 2019 - Present ($3.99)

	GD	VG	FN	VF	VF/NM	NM-
1-Tynion IV-s/Dell'edera-a	11	22	33	76	163	250
2	3	6	9	21	33	45
3	3	6	9	17	26	35
4-8	2	4	6	9	12	15
9-1st Jessica (cameo)	3	6	9	14	20	25
10-20: 16-19-Origin of Erica						6.00
21-24,26-29						4.00
25-($4.99)						5.00

SONATA
Image Comics: Jun, 2019 - Present ($3.99)

	GD	VG	FN	VF	VF/NM	NM-
1-12-David Hine-s/Brian Haberlin-s/a. 12-Flashback to the 1st meeting of Sonata and Treen						4.00
12-(3D Edition, $7.99) Polybagged with 3D glasses; bonus cover gallery in 3D						8.00

SONG OF THE SOUTH (See Brer Rabbit)

SONIC & KNUCKLES
Archie Comics: Aug, 1995 ($2.00)

	GD	VG	FN	VF	VF/NM	NM-
1	2	4	6	9	13	16

SONIC BOOM
Archie Comic Publications: Dec, 2014 - No. 11, Oct, 2015 ($3.99)

	GD	VG	FN	VF	VF/NM	NM-
1-11: 1-Regular-c and 4 interlocking variant covers. 2-7,11-Two covers on each. 8-10-"Worlds Unite" Sonic/Mega Man x-over; 3 covers						4.00

SONIC COMIC ORIGINS AND MEGA MAN X
Archie Comic Publications: Jun/Jul 2014 (giveaway)

	GD	VG	FN	VF	VF/NM	NM-
... Free Comic Book Day Edition - Flipbook; Freedom Fighters app.						3.00

SONIC DISRUPTORS
DC Comics: Dec, 1987 - No. 7, July, 1988 ($1.75, unfinished limited series)

	GD	VG	FN	VF	VF/NM	NM-
1-7	1	3	4	6	8	10

SONIC MEGA DRIVE
Archie Comic Publications: Aug, 2016 ($3.99, limited series)

	GD	VG	FN	VF	VF/NM	NM-
1-25th Anniversary celebration; Flynn-s/Hesse-a						4.00
... - The Next Level (12/16, $4.99) Flynn-s/Hesse-a; Metal Sonic app.						5.00

SONIC'S FRIENDLY NEMESIS KNUCKLES
Archie Publications: July, 1996 - No. 3, Sept, 1996 ($1.50, limited series)

	GD	VG	FN	VF	VF/NM	NM-
1-3	1	2	3	5	6	8

SONIC SUPER DIGEST
Archie Publications: Dec, 2012 - No. 17 ($3.99/$4.99)

	GD	VG	FN	VF	VF/NM	NM-
1-7-($3.99)						4.00
8-17-($4.99)						5.00

SONIC SUPER SPECIAL
Archie Publications: 1997 - No. 15, Feb, 2001 ($2.00/$2.25/$2.29, 48 pgs)

	GD	VG	FN	VF	VF/NM	NM-
1	2	4	6	11	16	20
2,3						5.00
4-6,8-12: 10-Sabrina-c/app.						4.00
7-(w/Image) Spawn, Maxx, Savage Dragon-c/app.; Valentino-a	2	4	6	11	16	20
13-Epic story conclusion	3	6	9	16	23	30
14,15-Low print run. 15-Sin City spoof	2	4	6	11	16	20

SONIC THE HEDGEHOG (TV, video game)
Archie Comics: No. 0, Feb, 1993 - No. 3, May, 1993 ($1.25, mini-series)

	GD	VG	FN	VF	VF/NM	NM-
0(2/93),1: Shaw-a(p) & covers on all	4	8	12	28	47	65
2,3	3	6	9	16	23	30
Beginnings TPB (2003, $10.95) r/#0-3						11.00
...: The Beginning TPB (2006, $10.95) r/#0-3						11.00

SONIC THE HEDGEHOG (TV, video game)
Archie Comics: July, 1993 - No. 290, Feb, 2017 ($1.25-$2.99)

	GD	VG	FN	VF	VF/NM	NM-
1	6	12	18	38	69	100
2	4	8	12	23	37	50
3	3	6	9	16	23	30
4-10: 8-Neon ink-c.	2	4	6	11	16	20

Soldier Zero #1 © BOOM!

Sonic the Hedgehog #288 © Sega

Sonjaversal #1 © RS LLC

	GD 2.0	VG 4.0	FN 6.0	VF 8.0	VF/NM 9.0	NM- 9.2
11-20	2	4	6	9	13	16
21-30 ($1.50): 25-Silver ink-c	2	4	6	8	10	12
31-50	1	2	3	5	6	8
51-55,57-93						4.00
56-Super Sonic and Hyper Knuckles app.	2	4	6	9	12	15
94-97,99-212: 117-Begin $2.19-c. 152-Begin $2.25-c. 157-Shadow app. 198-Begin $2.50						3.00
98-1st Shadow the Hedgehog	8	16	24	56	108	160
213-249,251-263: 213-Begin $2.99-c. 248-263-Two covers						3.00
250-($3.99) Wraparound-c; part 9 of Worlds Collide x-over with Mega Man						4.00
264-274,276-290-($3.99) Two covers on most. 273,274-"Worlds Unite" Sonic/Mega Man x-over; 3 covers on each. 288-290-Genesis of a Hero						4.00
275-($4.99) "Worlds Unite" Sonic/Mega Man x-over; six covers						5.00
Free Comic Book Day Edition 1 (2007)- Leads into Sonic the Hedgehog #175	2	4	6	9	12	15
Free Comic Book Day Edition 2009 - Reprints Sonic the Hedgehog #1 from July 1993	2	4	6	9	12	15
Free Comic Book Day Edition 2010 - 2012: 2010-New story						4.00
Free Comic Book Day Edition 2021-Previews "Battle For the Empire" story						3.00
Sonic and Mega Man: World's Collide Prelude, FCBD Edition (6-7/13)	1	3	4	6	8	10
Sonic and Mega Man: Worlds Unite FCBD Edition (6-7/15) Prelude to crossover						4.00
Sonic Sampler: Free Comic Book Day Edition (5/16) Sonic & Sonic Universe stories	1	2	3	5	6	8
Sonic: Worlds Unite Battles (9/15, $3.99) Sonic/Mega Man x-over; 3 wraparound covers						4.00
Triple Trouble Special (10/95, $2.00, 48 pgs.)	1	3	4	6	8	10

SONIC THE HEDGEHOG (TV, video game)
IDW Publishing: Apr, 2018 - Present ($3.99, #1-4 weekly, #5-on monthly)

1-12,14-24,26-49,51-58: 1-Flynn-s/Yardley-a. 3-Knuckles app. 4-Intro. Tangle the Lemur 4.00
13,25-($4.99) 13-Tails, Rough & Tumble app.; four covers. 25-The Deadly Six app. 5.00
50-($7.99) Sonic vs. Surge the Tenrec 8.00
Annual 2022 (8/22, $7.99) Short stories by various 8.00
... Halloween Comicfest 1 (10/19, free giveaway) r/#1 3.00
... 30th Anniversary Special (6/21, $8.99) Five covers; Knuckles app. 9.00
... 2: The Official Movie Pre-Quill (3/22, $6.99) Short stories; Knuckles app. 7.00

SONIC THE HEDGEHOG: IMPOSTER SYNDROME
IDW Publishing: Nov, 2020 - No. 4, May, 2022 ($3.99, limited series)

1-4-Ian Flynn-s/Thomas Rothlisberger-a. 1,4-Four covers. 2,3-Three covers 4.00

SONIC THE HEDGEHOG: BAD GUYS
IDW Publishing: Sept, 2020 - No. 4, Dec, 2020 ($3.99, limited series)

1-4-Ian Flynn-s/Jack Lawrence-a. 1-Five covers. 2-4-Three covers 4.00

SONIC THE HEDGEHOG: SCRAPNIK ISLAND
IDW Publishing: Oct, 2022 - No. 4, Jan, 2023 ($3.99, limited series)

1-4-Daniel Barnes-s/Jack Lawrence-a 4.00

SONIC THE HEDGEHOG: TANGLE & WHISPER
IDW Publishing: No. 0, Apr, 2019 - No. 4, Oct, 2019 ($3.99, limited series)

0-(4/19, no price) Ian Flynn-s/Evan Stanley-a; previews series and Sonic storyline 3.00
1-4-($3.99) Ian Flynn-s/Evan Stanley-a; Mimic app.; multiple covers on each 4.00

SONIC UNIVERSE (Sonic the Hedgehog)
Archie Publications: Apr, 2009 - No. 94, Mar, 2017 ($2.50/$2.99/$3.99)

1-15 3.00
16-66: 16-Begin $2.99-c. 51-66-Two covers. 51-54-Worlds Collide 3.00
67-94-($3.99) Two covers on most. 75-"Worlds Unite" Sonic/Mega Man x-over prelude with nine covers. 76-78-"Worlds Unite" x-over; 3 covers on each. 87-90-Shattered 4.00

SONIC VS. KNUCKLES "BATTLE ROYAL" SPECIAL
Archie Publications: 1997 ($2.00, one-shot)

	GD	VG	FN	VF	VF/NM	NM-
1	2	4	6	9	12	15

SONIC X (Sonic the Hedgehog)
Archie Publications: Nov, 2005 - No. 40, Feb, 2009 ($2.25)

1-Sam Speed app. 4.00
2-40 3.00

SONJAVERSAL (Red Sonja) (Leads into Hell Sonja #1)
Dynamite Entertainment: 2021 - No. 10, 2021 ($3.99)

1-10: 1-Hastings-s/Qualano & Perez-a; alternate Sonjas meet 4.00

SON OF AMBUSH BUG (See Ambush Bug)
DC Comics: July, 1986 - No. 6, Dec, 1986 (75¢)

1-6: Giffen-c/a in all. 5-Bissette-a. 4.00

SON OF BLACK BEAUTY (Also see Black Beauty)
Dell Publishing Co.: No. 510, Oct, 1953 - No. 566, June, 1954

	GD	VG	FN	VF	VF/NM	NM-
Four Color 510,566	5	10	15	31	53	75

SON OF FLUBBER (See Movie Comics)

SON OF HULK (Continues from Skaar: Son of Hulk #12) (See Realm of Kings)
Marvel Comics: No. 13, Sept, 2009 - No. 17, Jan, 2010 ($2.99)

13-17: 13,15-17-Galactus app. 3.00

SON OF M (Also see House of M series)
Marvel Comics: Feb, 2006 - No. 6, July, 2006 ($2.99, limited series)

1-6: 1-Powerless Quicksilver; Martinez-a. 2-Quicksilver regains powers; Inhumans app. 3.00
Decimation: Son of M (2006, $13.99, TPB) r/series; Martinez sketch pages 14.00

SON OF MERLIN
Image Comics (Top Cow): Feb, 2013 - No. 5, Jun, 2013 ($1.00/$2.99, limited series)

1-5: 1-($1.00-c); Napton-s/Zid-a; covers by Zid & Sejic. 2-($2.99) 3.00

SON OF MUTANT WORLD
Fantagor Press: 1990 - No. 5, 1990? ($2.00, bi-monthly)

1-5: 1-3: Corben-c/a. 4,5 ($1.75, B&W) 3.00

SON OF ORIGINS OF MARVEL COMICS (See Fireside Book Series)

SON OF SATAN (Also see Ghost Rider #1 & Marvel Spotlight #12)
Marvel Comics Group: Dec, 1975 - No. 8, Feb, 1977 (25¢)

	GD	VG	FN	VF	VF/NM	NM-
1-Mooney-a; Kane-c(p), Starlin splash(p)	5	10	15	33	57	80
2,6-8: 2-Origin The Possessor. 8-Heath-a	3	6	9	14	19	24
3-5-(Regular 25¢ editions)(4-8/76): 5-Russell-p	3	6	9	14	19	24
3-5-(30¢-c variants, limited distribution)	4	8	12	28	47	65
...: Marvel Spotlight #12 Facsimile Edition (11/19, $3.99) r/issue with original 1973 ads						4.00

SON OF SINBAD (Also see Abbott & Costello & Daring Adventures)
St. John Publishing Co.: Feb, 1950

	GD	VG	FN	VF	VF/NM	NM-
1-Kubert-c/a	61	122	183	390	670	950

SON OF SUPERMAN (Elseworlds)
DC Comics: 1999 ($14.95, prestige format, one-shot)

nn-Chaykin & Tischman-s/Williams III & Gray-a 15.00

SON OF TOMAHAWK (See Tomahawk)

SON OF VULCAN (Formerly Mysteries of Unexplored Worlds #1-48; Thunderbolt V3#51 on)
Charlton Comics: V2#49, Nov, 1965 - V2#50, Jan, 1966

	GD	VG	FN	VF	VF/NM	NM-
V2#49,50: 50-Roy Thomas scripts (1st pro work)	3	6	9	17	26	35

SONS OF ANARCHY (Based on the TV series)
BOOM! Studios: Sept, 2013 - No. 25, Sept, 2015 ($3.99, originally a 6-issue limited series)

1-24: 1-6-Christopher Golden-s/Damian Couceiro-a; multiple covers on each 4.00
25-($4.99) Last issue; Ferrier-s/Bergara-a; three covers 5.00

SONS OF ANARCHY REDWOOD ORIGINAL (TV series)
BOOM! Studios: Aug, 2016 - No. 12, Jul, 2017 ($3.99)

1-12: 1-Prequel with 18-year-old Jax Teller. 1-4-Masters-s/Pizzari-a; multiple covers 4.00

SONS OF KATIE ELDER (See Movie Classics)

SONS OF THE DEVIL
Image Comics: May, 2015 - No. 14, Jul, 2017 ($2.99/$3.99)

1-5: 1-Brian Buccellato-s/Toni Infante-a 3.00
6-14-($3.99) 4.00

SORCERY (See Chilling Adventures in... & Red Circle...)

SORORITY SECRETS
Toby Press: July, 1954

	GD	VG	FN	VF	VF/NM	NM-
1	43	86	129	271	461	650

SOULFIRE (MICHAEL TURNER PRESENTS:...) (Also see Eternal Soulfire)
Aspen MLT, Inc.: No. 0, 2004 - No. 10, Jul, 2009 ($2.50/$2.99)

0-($2.50) Turner-a/c; Loeb-s; intro. to characters & development sketches 3.00
1-($2.99) Two covers 3.00
1-Diamond Previews Exclusive 5.00
1 Special Edition (4/22, $1.99) R/#1; preview of Soulfire: The Core 3.00
2-9: 2,3-Two covers. 4-Four covers 3.00
10-($3.99) Benitez-a 4.00
... Sourcebook 1 (3/15, $4.99) Character profiles; two covers by Turner 5.00
...: The Collected Edition Vol. 1 (5/05, $6.99) r/#1,2; cover gallery 7.00
Hardcover Volume 1 (12/05, $24.99) r/#0-5 & preview from Wizard Mag.; Johns intro. 25.00

SOULFIRE (MICHAEL TURNER PRESENTS:...) (Volume 2)
Aspen MLT, Inc.: No. 0, Oct, 2009 - No. 9, Jan, 2011 ($2.50/$2.99)

0-($2.50) Marcus To-a 3.00

GD VG FN VF VF/NM NM-
2.0 4.0 6.0 8.0 9.0 9.2

1-9-($2.99) 1-Five covers. 9-Covers by To and Linsner 3.00

SOULFIRE (MICHAEL TURNER'S...) (Volume 3)
Aspen MLT, Inc.: No. 0, Apr, 2011 - No. 8, May, 2012 ($1.99/$2.99)
0-($1.99) Krul-s/Fabok-a; 4 covers 3.00
1-8-($2.99) 1-Four covers 3.00
... Despair (7/12, $3.99) Schwartz-s/Marks-a; 3 covers 4.00
... Faith (7/12, $3.99) McMurray-s/Oum-a; 3 covers 4.00
... Hope (7/12, $3.99) Krul-s/Varese-a; 3 covers 4.00
... Power (7/12, $3.99) Wohl-s/Randolph-a; 3 covers 4.00
... Primer (6/12, $1.00) Reprints and story summaries 3.00

SOULFIRE (MICHAEL TURNER'S...) (Volume 4)
Aspen MLT, Inc.: Aug, 2012 - No. 8, Oct, 2013 ($3.99)
1-8-Krul-s/DeBalfo-a; multiple covers on each 4.00

SOULFIRE (MICHAEL TURNER'S...) (Volume 5)
Aspen MLT, Inc.: Nov, 2013 - No. 8, Oct, 2014 ($1.00/$3.99)
1-($1.00) Krul-s/Marion-a; multiple covers 3.00
2-8-($3.99) Multiple covers on each 4.00
Annual 1 2014 (7/14, $5.99) Art by Garbowska, Hanson, Turner, Cafaro 6.00

SOULFIRE (ALL NEW MICHAEL TURNER'S...) (Volume 6)
Aspen MLT, Inc.: Mar, 2017 - No. 8, Oct, 2017 ($3.99)
1-8-($3.99) Multiple covers on each. 1-Krul-s/Cafaro-a 4.00

SOULFIRE (MICHAEL TURNER'S...) (Volume 7)
Aspen MLT, Inc.: Jul, 2018 - No. 8, Feb, 2019 ($3.99)
1-8: 1-Krul-s/Ladjouze-a; multiple covers 4.00
... Primer 1 (7/18, 25¢) Series intro. and bonus text recaps of previous volumes 3.00

SOULFIRE (MICHAEL TURNER'S...) (Volume 8)
Aspen MLT, Inc.: Jun, 2019 - No. 6, Nov, 2019 ($3.99)
1-6: 1-Krul-s/Forté-a; multiple covers 4.00

SOULFIRE: CHAOS REIGN
Aspen MLT, Inc.: No. 0, June, 2006 - No. 3, Jan, 2007 ($2.50/$2.99)
0-($2.50) Three covers; Marcus To-a; J.T. Krul-s 3.00
1-3-($2.99) 1-Three covers 3.00
...: Beginnings (7/06, $1.99) Marcus To-a; J.T. Krul-s 3.00
...: Beginnings 1 (7/07, $1.99) Francisco Herrera-a; J.T. Krul-s 3.00

SOULFIRE: DYING OF THE LIGHT
Aspen MLT, Inc.: No. 0, 2004 - No. 5, Feb, 2006 ($2.50/$2.99)
0-($2.50) Three covers; Gunnell-a; Krul-s; back-story to the Soulfire universe 3.00
1-5-($2.99) 1-Five covers 3.00
... Vol. 1 TPB (2007, $14.99) r/#0-5; Gunnell sketch pages, cover gallery 15.00

SOULFIRE: NEW WORLD ORDER
Aspen MLT, Inc.: No. 0, Jul, 2007; May, 2009 - No. 5, Dec, 2009 ($2.50/$2.99)
0 (7/07, $2.50) Two covers; Herrera-a/Krul-s 3.00
1-5-($2.99) 1-Four covers 3.00

SOULFIRE: SHADOW MAGIC
Aspen MLT, Inc.: No. 0, Nov, 2008 - No. 5, May, 2009 ($2.50/$2.99)
0-($2.50) Two covers; Sana Takeda-a 3.00
1-5-($2.99) 1-Two covers 3.00

SOULFIRE: THE CORE
Aspen MLT, Inc.: Oct, 2022 - Present ($3.99)
1,2-Krul-s/Konat-a; multiple covers on each 4.00

SOUL SAGA
Image Comics (Top Cow): Feb, 2000 - No. 5, Apr, 2001 ($2.50)
1-5: 1-Madureira-c; Platt & Batt-a 3.00

SOULSEARCHERS AND COMPANY
Claypool Comics: June, 1995 - No. 82, Jan, 2007 ($2.50, B&W)
1-10: Peter David scripts 5.00
11-82 3.00

SOULWIND
Image Comics: Mar, 1997 - No. 8 ($2.95, B&W, limited series)
1-8: 5-"The Day I Tried To Live" pt. 1 3.00
Book Five; The August Ones (Oni Press, 3/01, $8.50) 8.50
...The Kid From Planet Earth (1997, $9.95, TPB) 10.00
...The Kid From Planet Earth (Oni Press, 1/00, $8.50, TPB) 8.50
...The Day I Tried to Live (Oni Press, 4/00, $8.50, TPB) 8.50
The Complete Soulwind TPB ($29.95, 11/03, 8" x 5 1/2") r/Oni Books #1-5 30.00

SOUPY SALES COMIC BOOK (TV)(The Official...)
Archie Publications: 1965
1-(Teen-age) 8 16 24 56 108 160

SOUTHERN BASTARDS
Image Comics: Apr, 2014 - No. 20, May, 2018 ($3.50/$3.99)
1-Jason Aaron-s/Jason Latour-a 8.00
2-20: 18-Chris Brunner-a 4.00

SOUTHERN CROSS
Image Comics: Mar, 2014 - No. 14, Mar, 2018 ($2.99/$3.99)
1-6-Becky Cloonan-s/c; Andy Belanger-a 3.00
7-14-($3.99) Cloonan-s/c; Belanger-a 4.00

SOUTHERN KNIGHTS, THE (See Crusaders #1)
Guild Publ/Fictioneer Books: No. 2, 1983 - No. 41, 1993 (B&W)
2-Magazine size 1 2 3 5 6 8
3-35, 37-41 3.00
36-($3.50-c) 4.00
Dread Halloween Special 1, Primer Special 1 (Spring, 1989, $2.25) 3.00
Graphic Novels #1-4 4.00

SOUTH SIDE SERPENTS (Based on the Riverdale TV series)
Archie Comic Publications: Mar, 2021 ($3.99, one-shot)
1-Jughead, FP Jones & Toni Topaz app.; David Barnett-s/Richard Ortiz-a 4.00

SOVEREIGNS
Dynamite Entertainment: No. 0, 2017 - No. 5, 2017 ($1.00/$3.99)
0-($1.00) Short stories of Magnus, Turok, Solar and Doctor Spektor 3.00
1-5-($3.99) Fawkes-s/Desjardins-a; back-up stories on each 4.00

SOVEREIGN SEVEN (Also see Showcase '95 #12)
DC Comics: July, 1995 - No. 36, July, 1998 ($1.95) (1st creator-owned mainstream DC comic)
1-1st app. Sovereign Seven (Reflex, Indigo, Cascade, Finale, Cruiser, Network & Rampart); 1st app. Maitresse; Darkseid app.; Chris Claremont-s & Dwayne Turner-c/a begins 4.00
1-Gold 8.00
1-Platinum 40.00
2-36: 2-Wolverine cameo. 4-Neil Gaiman cameo. 5,8-Batman app. 7-Ramirez cameo (from the movie Highlander). 9-Humphrey Bogart cameo from Casablanca. 10-Impulse app; Manoli Wetherell & Neal Conan cameo from Uncanny X-Men #226. 11-Robin app. 16-Final Night. 24-Superman app. 25-Power Girl app. 28-Impulse-c/app. 3.00
Annual 1 (1995, $3.95)-Year One story; Big Barda & Lobo app.; Jeff Johnson-c/a 4.00
Annual 2 (1996, $2.95)-Legends of the Dead Earth; Leonardi-c/a 4.00
...Plus 1(2/97, $2.95)-Legion-c/app. 4.00
TPB-($12.95) r/#1-5, Annual #1 & Showcase '95 #12 13.00

SPACE: ABOVE AND BEYOND (TV)
Topps Comics: Jan, 1996 - No. 3, Mar, 1996 ($2.95, limited series)
1-3: Adaptation of pilot episode; Steacy-c. 3.00

SPACE: ABOVE AND BEYOND--THE GAUNTLET (TV)
Topps Comics: May, 1996 -No. 2, June, 1996 ($2.95, limited series)
1,2 3.00

SPACE ACE (Also see Manhunt!)
Magazine Enterprises: No. 5, 1952
5(A-1 #61)-Guardineer-a 81 162 243 518 884 1250

SPACE ACE: DEFENDER OF THE UNIVERSE (Based on the Don Bluth video game)
CrossGen Comics: Oct, 2003 - No. 6 ($2.95, limited series)
1,2-Kirkman-s/Borges-a 3.00

SPACE ACTION
Ace Magazines (Junior Books): June, 1952 - No. 3, Oct, 1952
1-Cameron-a in all (1 story) 110 220 330 704 1202 1700
2,3 68 136 204 435 743 1050

SPACE ADVENTURES (War At Sea #22 on)
Capitol Stories/Charlton Comics: 7/52 - No. 21, 8/56; No. 23, 5/58 - No. 59, 11/64; V3#60, 10/67; V1#2, 7/68 - V1#8, 7/69; No. 9, 5/78 - No. 13, 3/79
1-Fago/Morales world on fire-c 90 180 270 576 988 1400
2 37 74 111 222 361 500
3-5: 4,6-Flying saucer-c/stories 31 62 93 186 303 420
6,8,9: 8-Robot-c. 9-A-Bomb panel 27 54 81 162 266 370
7-Sex change story "Transformation" 116 232 348 742 1271 1800
10,11-Ditko-c/a. 10-Robot-c. 11-Two Ditko stories 84 168 252 538 919 1300
12-Ditko-c (classic) 423 846 1269 3000 5250 7500
13-(Fox-r, 10-11/54); Blue Beetle-c/story 20 40 60 118 192 265
14,15,17,18: 14-Blue Beetle-c/story; Fox-r (12-1/54-55, last pre-code). 15,17,18-Rocky Jones-c/s.(TV); 15-Part photo-c 24 48 72 140 230 320
16-Krigstein-a; Rocky Jones-c/story (TV) 27 54 81 158 259 360
19-Robot-c by Giordano 30 60 90 177 289 400
20-Reprints Fawcett's "Destination Moon" 27 54 81 158 259 360
21-(8/56) (no #22)(Becomes War At Sea) 19 38 57 111 176 240
23-(5/58; formerly Nyoka, The Jungle Girl)-Reprints Fawcett's "Destination Moon" 24 48 72 142 234 325
24,25,31,32-Ditko-a. 24-Severin-a(signed "LePoer") 24 48 72 142 234 325
26,27-Ditko-a(4) each. 26,28-Flying saucer-c 25 50 75 150 245 340
28-30 14 28 42 80 115 150
33-Origin/1st app. Capt. Atom by Ditko (3/60) 271 542 813 1734 2967 4200
34-40,42-All Captain Atom by Ditko 31 62 93 186 303 420
41,43,45-59: 43-Alan Shephard strory, 2nd man in space. 45-Mercury Man app. 5 10 15 35 63 90
44-1st app. Mercury Man 6 12 18 42 79 115
V3#60(#1, 10/67)-Presents UFO origin & 1st app. Paul Mann & The Saucers From the Future 5 10 15 35 63 90
2,5,6,8 (1968-69)-Ditko-a: 2-Aparo-c/a 4 8 12 23 37 50
3,4,7: 4-Aparo-c/a 3 6 9 19 30 40
9-13(1978-79)-Capt. Atom-r/Space Adventures by Ditko; 9-Reprints origin/1st app. Capt. Atom from #33 6.00
NOTE: *Aparo a-V3#60. c-V3#8. Ditko c-12, 31-42. Giordano c-3, 4, 7-9, 18p, 19 Krigstein c-15. Shuster a-11.* *Issues 13 & 14 have Blue Beetle logos; #15-18 have Rocky Jones logos.*

SPACE BANDITS
Image Comics: Jul, 2019 - No. 5, Nov, 2019 ($3.99/$5.99, limited series)
1-4-($3.99) Mark Millar-s/Matteo Scalera-a 4.00
5-($5.99) 6.00

SPACE BASTARDS
Humanoids Inc.: 2021 - Present ($5.99/$4.99)
1-($5.99) Darick Robertson-a/Eric Peterson & Joe Aubrey-s 6.00
2-6,8,9-($4.99) 5.00
7-($5.99) "Giant-Size Manny issue"; Bisley-a; back-up w/Langley-a 6.00
... Special Delivery (2022, $7.99) Short stories; art by Bisley, Gabo & Boo Cook 8.00

SPACE BUSTERS
Ziff-Davis Publ. Co.: Spring, 1952 - No. 2, Fall, 1952
1-Krigstein-a(3); Painted-c by Norman Saunders 100 200 300 635 1093 1550
2-Kinstler-a(2 pgs.); Saunders painted-c 84 168 252 538 919 1300
NOTE: *Anderson a-2. Bondage c-2.*

SPACE CADET (See Tom Corbett,...)

SPACE CIRCUS
Dark Horse Comics: July, 2000 - No. 4, Oct, 2000 ($2.95, limited series)
1-4-Aragonés-a/Evanier-s 3.00

Soulfire V2 #9 © Aspen MLT

Space Adventures #2 © CC

Spaceknights #1 © MAR

GD VG FN VF VF/NM NM-
2.0 4.0 6.0 8.0 9.0 9.2

GD VG FN VF VF/NM NM-
2.0 4.0 6.0 8.0 9.0 9.2

SPACE COMICS (Formerly Funny Tunes)
Avon Periodicals: No. 4, Mar-Apr, 1954 - No. 5, May-June, 1954

4,5-Space Mouse, Peter Rabbit, Super Pup (formerly Spotty the Pup), & Merry Mouse continue from Funny Tunes 12 24 36 69 97 125
I.W. Reprint #8 (nd)-Space Mouse-r 2 4 6 11 16 20

SPACE DETECTIVE
Avon Periodicals: July, 1951 - No. 4, July, 1952

1-Rod Hathway, Space Detective begins, ends #4; Wood-c/a(3)-23 pgs.; "Opium Smugglers of Venus" drug story; Lucky Dale-r/Saint #4 181 362 543 1158 1979 2800
2-Tales from the Shadow Squad story; Wood/Orlando-c; Wood inside layouts; "Slave Ship of Saturn" story 129 258 387 826 1413 2000
3-Classic Kinstler-c 129 258 387 826 1413 2000
4-Kinstlerish-a by McCann 63 126 189 403 689 975
I.W. Reprint #1(Reprints #2), 8(Reprints cover #1 & part Famous Funnies #191) 4 8 12 28 47 65

SPACE EXPLORER (See March of Comics #202)

SPACE FAMILY ROBINSON (TV)(...Lost in Space #15-37, ...Lost in Space On Space Station One #38 on)(See Gold Key Champion)
Gold Key: Dec, 1962 - No. 36, Oct, 1969; No. 37, 10/73 - No. 54, 11/78; No. 55, 3/81 - No. 59, 5/82 (All painted covers)

1-(Low distribution); Spiegle-a in all 38 76 114 281 628 975
2(3/63)-Family becomes lost in space 12 24 36 84 185 285
3-5 8 16 24 54 102 150
6-10: 6-Captain Venture back-up stories begin 6 12 18 41 76 110
11-20: 14-(10/65). 15-Title change (1/66) 5 10 15 31 53 75
21-36: 28-Last 12¢ issue. 36-Captain Venture ends 4 8 12 25 40 55
37-48: 37-Origin retold 3 6 9 14 19 24
49-59: Reprints #49,50,55-59 2 4 6 8 11 14
NOTE: *The TV show first aired on 9/15/65. Title changed after TV show debuted.*

SPACE FAMILY ROBINSON (See March of Comics #320, 328, 352, 404, 414)

SPACE GHOST (TV) (Also see Golden Comics Digest #2 & Hanna-Barbera Super TV Heroes #3-7)
Gold Key: March, 1967 (Hanna-Barbera) (TV debut was 9/10/66)

1 (10199-703)-Spiegle-a 35 70 105 252 564 875

SPACE GHOST (TV cartoon)
Comico: Mar, 1987 ($3.50, deluxe format, one-shot) (Hanna-Barbera)

1-Steve Rude-c/a; Evanier-s; Steacy painted-a 3 6 9 16 23 30

SPACE GHOST (TV cartoon)
DC Comics: Jan, 2005 - No. 6, June, 2005 ($2.95/$2.99, limited series)

1-6-Alex Ross-c/Ariel Olivetti-a/Joe Kelly-s; origin of Space Ghost 3.00
TPB (2005, $14.99) r/series; cover gallery 15.00

SPACE GIANTS, THE (TV cartoon)
FBN Publications: 1979 ($1.00, B&W, one-shots)

1-Based on Japanese TV series 3 6 9 15 22 28

SPACEHAWK
Dark Horse Comics: 1989 - No. 3, 1990 ($2.00, B&W)

1-3-Wolverton-c/a(r) plus new stories by others. 5.00

SPACE JAM
DC Comics: 1996 ($5.95, one-shot, movie adaption)

1-Wraparound photo cover of Michael Jordan 3 6 9 17 26 35

SPACE JOB
Dark Horse Comics: Feb, 2023 - No. 4 ($3.99, limited series)

1-Goodman-s/Sarraseca-a 4.00

SPACE KAT-ETS (...in 3-D)
Power Publishing Co.: Dec, 1953 (25¢, came w/glasses)

1 39 78 117 231 378 525

SPACEKNIGHTS
Marvel Comics: Oct, 2000 - No. 5, Feb, 2001 ($2.99, limited series)

1-5-Starlin-s/Batista-a 3.00

SPACEKNIGHTS
Marvel Comics: Dec, 2012 - No. 3, Feb, 2013 ($3.99, limited series)

1-3-Reprints the 2000-2001 series & Annihilation: Conquest Prologue 4.00

SPACEMAN (Speed Carter...)
Atlas Comics (CnPC): Sept, 1953 - No. 6, July, 1954

1-Grey tone-c 126 252 378 806 1378 1950
2 63 126 189 403 689 975
3-6: 4-A-Bomb explosion-c 57 114 171 362 619 875

NOTE: ***Everett** c-1, 3. **Heath** a-1. **Maneely** a-1(3), 2(4), 3(3), 4-6; c-5, 6. **Romita** a-1. **Sekowsky** c-4. **Sekowsky/Abel** a-4(3). **Tuska** a-5(3).*

SPACE MAN
Dell Publ. Co.: No. 1253, 1-3/62 - No. 8, 3-5/64; No. 9, 7/72 - No. 10, 10/72

Four Color 1253 (#1)(1-3/62)(15¢-c) 9 18 27 59 117 175
2,3: 2-(15¢-c). 3-(12¢-c) 5 10 15 30 50 70
4-8-(12¢-c) 3 6 9 21 33 45
9,10-(15¢-c): 9-Reprints #1253. 10-Reprints #2 2 4 6 9 12 15

SPACEMAN (From the Atomics)
Oni Press: July, 2002 ($2.95, one-shot)

1-Mike Allred-s/a; Lawrence Marvit additional art 3.00

SPACEMAN
DC Comics (Vertigo): Dec, 2011 - No. 9, Oct, 2012 ($1.00/$2.99, limited series)

1-($1.00) Azzarello-s/Risso-a/Johnson-c 4.00
2-9-($2.99) 3.00

SPACE MOUSE (Also see Funny Tunes & Space Comics)
Avon Periodicals: April, 1953 - No. 5, Apr-May, 1954

1 16 32 48 94 147 200
2 10 20 30 54 72 90
3-5 8 16 24 42 54 65

SPACE MOUSE (Walter Lantz...#1; see Comic Album #17)
Dell Publishing Co./Gold Key: No. 1132, Aug-Oct, 1960 - No. 5, Nov, 1963 (Walter Lantz)

Four Color 1132,1244, 1(11/62)(G.K.) 6 12 18 37 66 95
2-5 4 8 12 27 44 60

SPACE MYSTERIES
I.W. Enterprises: 1964 (Reprints)

1-r/Journey Into Unknown Worlds #4 w/new-c 3 6 9 18 28 38
8,9: 9-r/Planet Comics #73 3 6 9 18 28 38

SPACE: 1999 (TV) (Also see Power Record Comics)
Charlton Comics: Nov, 1975 - No. 7, Nov, 1976

1-Origin Moonbase Alpha; Staton-c/a 4 8 12 23 37 50
2,7: 2-Staton-a 3 6 9 17 26 35
3-6: All Byrne-a; c-3,5,6 3 6 9 16 23 30
nn (Charlton Press, digest, 100 pgs., B&W, no cover price) new stories & art 4 8 12 28 47 65

SPACE: 1999 (TV)(Magazine)
Charlton Comics: Nov, 1975 - No. 8, Nov, 1976 (B&W) (#7 shows #6 inside)

1-Origin Moonbase Alpha; Morrow-c/a 3 6 9 18 28 38
2-8: 2,3-Morrow-c/a. 4-6-Morrow-c. 5,8-Morrow-a 2 4 6 11 16 20

SPACE PATROL (TV)
Ziff-Davis Publishing Co. (Approved Comics): Summer, 1952 - No. 2, Oct-Nov, 1952 (Painted-c by Norman Saunders)

1-Krigstein-a 103 206 309 659 1130 1600
2-Krigstein-a(3) 74 148 222 470 810 1150

SPACE PIRATES (See Archie Giant Series #533)

SPACE: PUNISHER
Marvel Comics: Sept, 2012 - No. 4, Dec, 2012 ($3.99, limited series)

1-4-Outer space sci-fi pulp version of the Punisher; Tieri-s/Texeira-a/c 4.00

SPACE RANGER (See Mystery in Space #92, Showcase #15 & Tales of the Unexpected)

SPACE SQUADRON (In the Days of the Rockets)(Becomes Space Worlds #6)
Marvel/Atlas Comics (ACI): June, 1951 - No. 5, Feb, 1952

1-Space team; Brodsky c-1,5 110 220 330 704 1202 1700
2: Tuska c-2-4 81 162 243 518 884 1250
3-5: 3-Capt. Jet Dixon by Tuska(3); Maneely-a. 4-Weird advs. begin 71 142 213 454 777 1100

SPACE THRILLERS
Avon Periodicals: 1954 (25¢ Giant)

nn-(Scarce)-Robotmen of the Lost Planet; contains 3 rebound comics of The Saint & Strange Worlds. Contents could vary 168 336 504 1075 1838 2600

SPACE TRIP TO THE MOON (See Space Adventures #23)

SPACE USAGI
Mirage Studios: June, 1992 - No. 3, 1992 ($2.00, B&W, mini-series)
V2#1, Nov, 1993 - V2#3, Jan, 1994 ($2.75)

1-Stan Sakai-c/a/scripts 3 6 9 21 33 45
2,3, V2#1-3 2 4 6 9 12 15

SPACE USAGI
Dark Horse Comics: Jan, 1996 - No. 3, Mar, 1996 ($2.95, B&W, limited series)

	GD 2.0	VG 4.0	FN 6.0	VF 8.0	VF/NM 9.0	NM- 9.2
1-Stan Sakai-c/a/scripts	2	4	6	9	12	15
2,3						6.00

SPACE WAR (Fightin' Five #28 on)
Charlton Comics: Oct, 1959 - No. 27, Mar, 1964; No. 28, Mar, 1978 - No. 34, 3/79

	GD 2.0	VG 4.0	FN 6.0	VF 8.0	VF/NM 9.0	NM- 9.2
V1#1-Giordano-c begin, end #3	15	30	45	103	227	350
2,3	9	18	27	59	117	175
4-6,8,10-Ditko-c/a	13	26	39	91	201	310
7,9,11-15 (3/62): Last 10¢ issue	7	14	21	44	82	120
16 (6/62)-27 (3/64): 18,19-Robot-c	5	10	15	35	63	90
28 (3/78),29-31,33,34-Ditko-c/a(r): 30-Staton, Sutton/Wood-a. 31-Ditko-c/a(3); same-c as Strange Suspense Stories #2 (1968); atom blast-c	2	4	6	8	11	14
32-r/Charlton Premiere V2#2; Sutton-a	1	3	4	6	8	10

SPACE WARPED
Boom Entertainment (Kaboom!): Jun, 2011 - No. 6, Dec, 2011 ($3.99, limited series)

	GD 2.0	VG 4.0	FN 6.0	VF 8.0	VF/NM 9.0	NM- 9.2
1-6-Star Wars spoof; Bourhis-s/Spiessert-a						4.00

SPACE WESTERN (Formerly Cowboy Western Comics; becomes Cowboy Western Comics #46 on)
Charlton Comics (Capitol Stories): No. 40, Oct, 1952 - No. 45, Aug, 1953

	GD 2.0	VG 4.0	FN 6.0	VF 8.0	VF/NM 9.0	NM- 9.2
40-Intro Spurs Jackson & His Space Vigilantes; flying saucer story	142	284	426	909	1555	2200
41,43: 41-Flying saucer-c	65	130	195	416	708	1000
42-Atom bomb explosion-c	77	154	231	493	847	1200
44-Cowboys battle Nazis on Mars	123	246	369	787	1344	1900
45-"The Valley That Time Forgot", a pre-Turok story with dinosaurs & a bow-hunting Indian; Hitler app.	77	154	231	493	847	1200

SPACE WORLDS (Formerly Space Squadron #1-5)
Atlas Comics (Male): No. 6, April, 1952

	GD 2.0	VG 4.0	FN 6.0	VF 8.0	VF/NM 9.0	NM- 9.2
6-Sol Brodsky-c	60	120	180	381	653	925

SPANKY & ALFALFA & THE LITTLE RASCALS (See The Little Rascals)

SPARKIE, RADIO PIXIE (Radio)(Becomes Big Jon & Sparkie #4)
Ziff-Davis Publ. Co.: Winter, 1951 - No. 3, July-Aug, 1952 (Painted-c)(Sparkie #2,3; #1?)

	GD 2.0	VG 4.0	FN 6.0	VF 8.0	VF/NM 9.0	NM- 9.2
1-Based on children's radio program	32	64	96	188	307	425
2,3: 3-Big Jon and Sparkie on-c only	20	40	60	120	195	270

SPARKLE COMICS
United Features Synd.: Oct-Nov, 1948 - No. 33, Dec-Jan, 1953-54

	GD 2.0	VG 4.0	FN 6.0	VF 8.0	VF/NM 9.0	NM- 9.2
1-Li'l Abner, Nancy, Captain & the Kids, Ella Cinders (#1-3: 52 pgs.)	20	40	60	114	182	250
2	12	24	36	67	94	120
3-10	9	18	27	50	65	80
11-20	8	16	24	44	57	70
21-32	8	16	24	40	50	60
33-(2-3/54) 2 pgs. early Peanuts by Schulz	15	30	45	90	140	190

SPARKLE PLENTY (See Harvey Comics Library #2 & Dick Tracy)
Dell Publishing Co.: 1949

	GD 2.0	VG 4.0	FN 6.0	VF 8.0	VF/NM 9.0	NM- 9.2
Four Color 215 - Dick Tracy reprint by Gould	12	24	36	82	179	275

SPARKLER COMICS (1st series)
United Feature Comic Group: July, 1940 - No. 2, 1940

	GD 2.0	VG 4.0	FN 6.0	VF 8.0	VF/NM 9.0	NM- 9.2
1-Jim Hardy	45	90	135	284	480	675
2-Frankie Doodle	37	74	111	222	361	500

SPARKLER COMICS (2nd series)(Nancy & Sluggo #121 on)(Cover title becomes Nancy and Sluggo #101? on)
United Features Syndicate: July, 1941 - No. 120, Jan, 1955

	GD 2.0	VG 4.0	FN 6.0	VF 8.0	VF/NM 9.0	NM- 9.2
1-Origin 1st app. Sparkman; Tarzan (by Hogarth in all issues), Captain & the Kids, Ella Cinders, Danny Dingle, Dynamite Dunn, Nancy, Abbie & Slats, Broncho Bill, Frankie Doodle, begin; Spark Man c-1-9,11,12; Hap Hopper c-10,13	194	388	582	1242	2121	3000
2	71	142	213	454	777	1100
3,4	53	106	159	334	567	800
5-9: 9-Spark Man's new costume	45	90	135	284	480	675
10-Spark Man's secret ID revealed	48	96	144	302	514	725
11,12-Spark Man war-c. 12-Spark Man's new costume (color change)	42	84	126	265	445	625
13-Hap Hopper war-c	34	68	102	204	332	460
14-Tarzan-c by Hogarth	71	142	213	454	777	1100
15,17: 15-Capt & Kids-c. 17-Nancy & Sluggo-c	27	54	81	162	266	370
16,18-Spark Man-c. 16-Japanese WWII-c. 18-Nazi WWII-c	43	86	129	271	461	650
19-1st Race Riley and the Commandos-c/s	40	80	120	246	411	575
20-Nancy war-c	31	62	93	186	303	420
21,25,28,31,34,37-Tarzan-c by Hogarth	53	106	159	334	567	800
22-24,26,27,29,30: 22-Race Riley & the Commandos strips begin, ends #44	24	48	72	144	232	330
32,33,35,36,38,40	15	30	45	84	127	170
39-Classic Tarzan shooting an arrow into a dinosaur's eye on cover by Hogarth	90	180	270	576	988	1400
41,43,45,46,48,49	12	24	36	69	97	125
42,44,47,50-Tarzan-c (42,47,50 by Hogarth)	30	60	90	177	289	400
51,52,54-68,70: 57-Li'l Abner begins (not in #58); Fearless Fosdick app. in #58	12	24	36	67	94	120
53-Tarzan-c by Hogarth	29	58	87	174	285	375
69-Wolverton-*esque* Horror-c	14	28	42	76	108	140
71-80	9	18	27	52	69	85
81,82,84-86: 86 Last Tarzan; lingerie panels	8	16	24	44	57	70
83-Tarzan-c; Li'l Abner ends	14	28	42	80	115	150
87-96,98-99	8	16	24	42	54	65
97-Origin Casey Ruggles by Warren Tufts	9	18	27	47	61	75
100	9	18	27	47	61	75
101-107,109-112,114-119	7	14	21	37	46	55
108,113-Toth-a	8	16	24	42	54	65
120-(10-11/54) 2 pgs. early Peanuts by Schulz	15	30	45	85	130	175

SPARKLING LOVE
Avon Periodicals/Realistic (1953): June, 1950; 1953

	GD 2.0	VG 4.0	FN 6.0	VF 8.0	VF/NM 9.0	NM- 9.2
1(Avon)-Kubert-a; photo-c	39	78	117	231	378	525
nn(1953)-Reprint; Kubert-a	15	30	45	90	140	190

SPARKLING STARS
Holyoke Publishing Co.: June, 1944 - No. 33, March, 1948

	GD 2.0	VG 4.0	FN 6.0	VF 8.0	VF/NM 9.0	NM- 9.2
1-Hell's Angels, FBI, Boxie Weaver, Petey & Pop, & Ali Baba begin	28	56	84	168	274	380
2-Speed Spaulding story	16	32	48	94	147	200
3-Actual FBI case photos & war photos	14	28	42	76	108	140
4-10: 7-X-Mas-c	12	24	36	67	94	120
11-19: 13-Origin/1st app. Jungo the Man-Beast-c/s	10	20	30	58	79	100
20-Intro Fangs the Wolf Boy	12	24	36	67	94	120
21-33: 29-Bondage-c. 31-Sid Greene-a	10	20	30	56	76	95

SPARK MAN (See Sparkler Comics)
Frances M. McQueeny: 1945 (36 pgs., one-shot)

	GD 2.0	VG 4.0	FN 6.0	VF 8.0	VF/NM 9.0	NM- 9.2
1-Origin Spark Man r/Sparkler #1-3; female torture story; cover redrawn from Sparkler #1	53	106	159	334	567	800

SPARKY WATTS (Also see Big Shot Comics & Columbia Comics)
Columbia Comic Corp.: Nov?, 1942 - No. 10, 1949

	GD 2.0	VG 4.0	FN 6.0	VF 8.0	VF/NM 9.0	NM- 9.2
1(1942)-Skyman & The Face app; Hitler/Goering story/c	148	296	444	947	1624	2300
2(1943)	40	80	120	246	411	575
3(1944) "6000 Lbs. Block Buster to Bust Adolf"-c	30	60	90	177	289	400
4(1944)-Origin	21	42	63	124	202	280
5(1947)-Skyman app.; Boody Rogers-c/a	18	36	54	107	169	230
6,7,9,10: 6(1947). 9-Haunted House-c. 10(1949)	14	28	42	78	112	145
8(1948)-Surrealistic-c	15	30	45	85	130	175

NOTE: ***Boody Rogers** c-1-8.*

SPARROWHAWK
BOOM! Studios: Oct, 2018 - No. 5, Mar, 2019 ($3.99, limited series)

	GD 2.0	VG 4.0	FN 6.0	VF 8.0	VF/NM 9.0	NM- 9.2
1-5-Delilah S. Dawson-s/Matias Basla-a						4.00

SPARTACUS (Movie)
Dell Publishing Co.: No. 1139, Nov, 1960 (Kirk Douglas photo-c)

	GD 2.0	VG 4.0	FN 6.0	VF 8.0	VF/NM 9.0	NM- 9.2
Four Color 1139-Buscema-a	11	22	33	77	166	255

SPARTACUS (Television series)
Devil's Due Publishing: Oct, 2009 - No. 2 ($3.99)

	GD 2.0	VG 4.0	FN 6.0	VF 8.0	VF/NM 9.0	NM- 9.2
1,2: 1-DeKnight-s. 2-Palmiotti-s						4.00

SPARTAN: WARRIOR SPIRIT (Also see WildC.A.T.S: Covert Action Teams)
Image Comics (WildStorm Productions): July, 1995 - No. 4, Nov, 1995 ($2.50, lim. series)

	GD 2.0	VG 4.0	FN 6.0	VF 8.0	VF/NM 9.0	NM- 9.2
1-4: Kurt Busiek scripts; Mike McKone-c/a						3.00

SPARTA: USA
DC Comics (WildStorm): May, 2010 - No. 6, Oct, 2010 ($2.99, limited series)

	GD 2.0	VG 4.0	FN 6.0	VF 8.0	VF/NM 9.0	NM- 9.2
1-6: 1-Lapham-s/Timmons-a; covers by Timmons and Lapham						3.00

SPAWN (Also see Curse of the Spawn and Sam & Twitch)
Image Comics (Todd McFarlane Prods.): May, 1992 - Present ($1.95/$2.50/$2.99)

	GD 2.0	VG 4.0	FN 6.0	VF 8.0	VF/NM 9.0	NM- 9.2
1-1st app. Spawn; McFarlane-c/a begins; McFarlane/Steacy-c; 1st Todd McFarlane Productions title.	5	10	15	30	50	70
1-Newsstand edition	7	14	21	46	86	125
1-Black & white edition	25	50	75	175	388	600
2,3: 2-1st app. Violator; McFarlane/Steacy-c	3	6	9	19	30	40
4-Contains coupon for Image Comics #0	3	6	9	14	19	24
4-With coupon missing						3.00
4-Newsstand edition w/o poster or coupon	2	4	6	9	12	15
5-Cerebus cameo (1 pg.) as stuffed animal; Spawn mobile poster #1	3	6	9	14	20	25
6-8,10: 7-Spawn Mobile poster #2. 8-Alan Moore scripts; Miller poster. 10-Cerebus app.; Dave Sim scripts; 1 pg. cameo app. by Superman	2	4	6	9	12	15
9-Neil Gaiman scripts; Jim Lee poster; 1st Angela.	3	6	9	19	30	40
11-17,19,20,22-30: 11-Miller script; Darrow poster. 12-Bloodwulf poster by Liefeld. 14,15-Violator app. 16,17-Grant Morrison scripts; Capullo-c/a(p). 23,24-McFarlane-a/stories. 25-(10/94). 19-(10/94). 20-(11/94)	1	2	3	5	6	8
18-Grant Morrison script, Capullo-c/a(p); low distr.	2	4	6	8	10	12
21-low distribution	2	4	6	8	10	12
31-49: 31-1st app. The Redeemer; new costume (brief). 32-1st full app. new costume. 38-40,42,44,46,48-Tony Daniel-c/a(p). 38-1st app. Cy-Gor. 40,41-Cy-Gor & Curse app.	1	2	3	5	6	8
50-($3.95, 48 pgs.)	2	4	6	9	12	15
51-87,89,90,92,93,95,96: 52-Savage Dragon app. 56-w/ Darkchylde preview. 57-Cy-Gor-c/app. 64-Polybagged w/McFarlane Toys catalog. 65-Photo-c of movie Spawn and McFarlane. 81-Billy Kincaid returns	1	2	3	5	6	8
88-Halloween-c	3	6	9	14	20	25
91,94-Low print run	2	4	6	9	12	15
97-Angela-c/app.	3	6	9	19	30	40
98,99-Angela app.	3	6	9	14	19	24
100-($4.95) Angela dies; 6 total covers; the 3 variants by McFarlane, Miller, and Mignola	3	6	9	16	24	32
100-($4.95) 3 variant covers by Ross, Capullo, and Wood	3	6	9	14	20	25
101-111,114,116,118,123,124,134,152,158,159,164,169,170,172,173,176,177,201-208,210, 212-219-Low print run: 101-Begin $2.50-c. 210-215-Michael Golden-c	2	4	6	8	10	12
112,113,115,117,120,121,125-130,132,136-138,144,146,148,155,157,161,163,166-168,171,178, 180-182,186-188,190-192,198-Lower print run: 167-Clown app.	2	4	6	11	16	20
119-Gunslinger Spawn cameo	7	14	21	46	86	125
122-1st Nyx She-Spawn	6	12	18	38	69	100

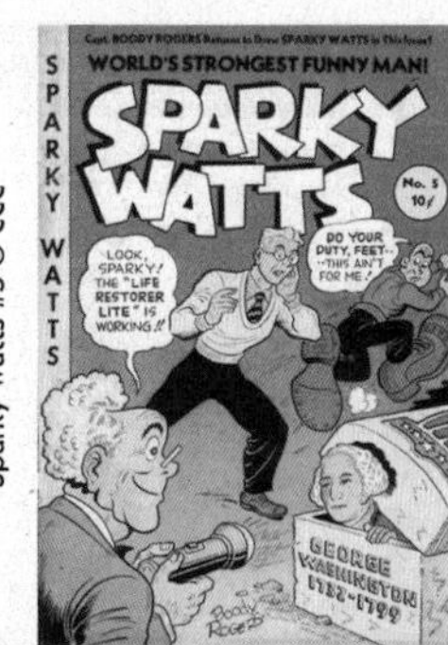

Sparky Watts #5 © CCC

Spawn #250 © TMP

Spawn Unwanted Violence #1 © TMP

	GD 2.0	VG 4.0	FN 6.0	VF 8.0	VF/NM 9.0	NM- 9.2
131,199,209-Low print run	4	8	12	25	40	55
133,135,140,142,145,147,149,153,156,160,162,184,189,194-197,211-Low print run: 184-2nd app. Morana. 211-Michael Golden-c	3	6	9	16	23	30
139-Nyx She-Spawn app.	5	10	15	35	63	90
141-She-Spawn-c	8	16	24	54	102	150
143,151,193-Low print run: 151-Begin $2.95-c; wraparound-c by Tan	3	6	9	21	33	45
150-($4.95) 4 covers by McFarlane, Capullo, Tan, Jim Lee	4	8	12	23	37	50
154-1st app. Zera	3	6	9	16	23	30
165-1st Mandarin Spawn	6	12	18	42	79	115
174-Origin/1st full app. of Gunslinger Spawn	16	32	48	107	236	365
175-Origin of Gunslinger Spawn continues	11	22	33	76	163	250
179-1st War Spawn; Mayhew-a	5	10	15	31	53	75
183-1st Morena Daughter of Spawn	5	10	15	31	53	75
185-1st Jim Downing and death of Al Simmons; McFarlane & Holguin-s; Portacio-a begins	6	12	18	38	69	100
200-(1/11, $3.99) 7 covers by McFarlane, Capullo, Finch, Jim Lee, Liefeld, Silvestri, Wood	3	6	9	14	20	25
220-(6/12, $3.99) 20th Anniversary issue; McFarlane-s/Kudranski-a; bonus interview, timeline and cover gallery	2	4	6	11	16	20
220: 20th Anniversary Collector's Special-(6/12, $4.99) B&W version of #220 w/bonuses	4	8	12	23	37	50
221-Cover swipe of Amazing Fantasy #15	7	14	21	46	86	125
222-226,229,231-241,244-249,251-299: 222-231-Cover swipes of classic covers. 225-Election special with 2 covers (Obama & Romney). 231-Spider-Man #1 ('90) c-swipe. 234-Haunt app. 251-Follows Spawn Resurrection #1. 258-Erik Larsen & McFarlane-a begin. 265-Ant app. 266-Savage Dragon app. 267-275,291,292-Kudranski-a. 276-282-Darragh Savage-s/Alexander-a	1	3	4	6	8	10
227-Cover swipe of Amazing Spider-Man #300	5	10	15	35	63	90
228-Cover swipe of Action Comics #1	5	10	15	31	53	75
230-Cover swipe of Batman #423	7	14	21	46	86	125
242,243-Low print run	5	10	15	30	50	70
250-($5.99) McFarlane-s/Kudranski-a; Al Simmons returns; multiple covers	2	4	6	11	16	20
300-(9/19, $7.99) McFarlane-s; art by Capullo, McFarlane, JS Campbell, Alexander & Opeña; intro. She-Spawn, bonus cover gallery; multiple covers	2	4	6	8	10	12
301-($4.99) McFarlane-s; art by Capullo, McFarlane, Crain, Alexander & Opeña	3	6	9	14	20	25
302-326: 302-305-Alexander-a; She-Spawn app. 306-Tan-a; intro. Raptor. 309,311-313-Gunslinger Spawn returns	1	2	3	5	6	8
309-Gunslinger Spawn variant-c by McFarlane						10.00
327-338						3.00
Annual 1-Blood & Shadows ('99, $4.95) Ashley Wood-c/a; Jenkins-s						6.00
... #1 Director's Cut (5/17, $4.99) 25th Anniversary edition; r/#1 B&W inked art with McFarlane commentary; bonus promotional art; 3 covers (McFarlane, Crain, Ashley Wood)	3	6	9	14	19	24
... #1 Free Comic Book Day 2019 (giveaway) r/#1; new cover by Francesco Mattina						3.00
...: Architects of Fear (2/11, $6.99, squarebound GN) Briclot-a	2	4	6	11	16	20
...: Armegeddon Complete Collection TPB ('07, $29.95) r/#150-163	7	14	21	46	86	125
...: Armegeddon, Part 1 TPB (10/06, $14.99) r/#150-155	5	10	15	31	53	75
...: Armegeddon, Part 2 TPB (2/07, $15.95) r/#156-164	5	10	15	31	53	75
...Bible-(8/96, $1.95)-Character bios	2	4	6	10	14	18
Book 1 TPB($9.95) r/#1-5; Book 2-r/#6-9,11; Book 3 -r/#12-15, Book 4- r/#16-20; Book 5-r/#21-25; Book 6- r/#26-30; Book 7-r/#31-34; Book 8-r/#35-38; Book 9-r/#39-42; Book 10-r/#43-47						11.00
Book 11 TPB ($10.95) r/#48-50; Book 12-r/#51-54						11.00
... Collection Vol. 1 (10/05, $19.95) r/#1-8,11,12; intro. by Frank Miller						20.00
... Collection Vol. 2 HC (7/07, $49.95) r/#13-33						50.00
... Collection Vol. 2 SC (9/06, $29.95) r/#13-33						30.00
... Collection Vol. 3 (3/07, $29.95) r/#34-54						30.00
... Collection Vol. 4 (9/07, $29.95) r/#55-75						30.00
... Collection Vol. 5 ('08, $29.95) r/#76-95						30.00
... Collection Vol. 6 (8/08, $29.95) r/#96-116; cover gallery						30.00
Image Firsts: Spawn #1 (4/10, $1.00) reprints #1	1	3	4	6	8	10
... Godslayer Vol. 1 (9/06, $6.99) Anacleto-c/a; Holguin-s; sketch pages	1	3	4	6	8	10
... Kills Everyone! 1 (8/16, $2.99) McFarlane-s/JJ Kirby-a; mini Spawn vs. cosplayers	1	3	4	6	8	10
...: Neonoir TPB (11/08, $14.95) r/#170-175						15.00
...: New Flesh TPB ('07, $14.95) r/#166-169						15.00
... Resurrection 1 (3/15, $2.99) Follows issue #250; Jenkins-s/Jonboy-a	2	4	6	8	10	12
...Simony (5/04, $7.95) English translation of French Spawn story; Briclot-a	2	4	6	8	10	12

NOTE: ***Capullo*** *a-16p-18p; c-16p-18p.* ***Daniel*** *a-38-40, 42, 44, 46.* ***McFarlane*** *a-1-15; c-1-15p.* ***Thibert*** *a-16i(part). Posters come with issues 1, 4, 7-9, 11, 12. #25 was released before #19 & 20.*

SPAWN-BATMAN (Also see Batman/Spawn: War Devil under Batman: One-Shots)
Image Comics (Todd McFarlane Productions): 1994 ($3.95, one-shot)

	GD 2.0	VG 4.0	FN 6.0	VF 8.0	VF/NM 9.0	NM- 9.2
1-Miller scripts; McFarlane-c/a	3	6	9	16	23	30

SPAWN: BLOOD FEUD
Image Comics (Todd McFarlane Prods.): June, 1995 - No. 4, Sept, 1995 ($2.25, lim. series)

	GD 2.0	VG 4.0	FN 6.0	VF 8.0	VF/NM 9.0	NM- 9.2
1-4-Alan Moore scripts, Tony Daniel-a						6.00

SPAWN FAN EDITION
Image Comics (Todd McFarlane Productions): Aug, 1996 - No. 3, Oct, 1996 (Giveaway, 12 pgs.) (Polybagged w/Overstreet's FAN)

	GD 2.0	VG 4.0	FN 6.0	VF 8.0	VF/NM 9.0	NM- 9.2
1-3: Beau Smith scripts; Brad Gorby-a(p). 1-1st app. Nordik, the Norse Hellspawn. 2-1st app. McFallon. 3-1st app. Mercy	1	2	3	5	6	8
1-3-(Gold): All retailer incentives						16.00
1-3-Variant-c	1	2	3	5	6	8
2-(Platinum)-Retailer incentive						25.00

SPAWN GODSLAYER
Image Comics (Todd McFarlane Prods.): May, 2007 - No. 8, Apr, 2008 ($2.99)

	GD 2.0	VG 4.0	FN 6.0	VF 8.0	VF/NM 9.0	NM- 9.2
1-8: 1-Holguin-s/Tan-a/Anacleto-c	1	2	3	5	6	8

SPAWN KILLS EVERYONE TOO (Also titled Spawn Kills Everyone 2)
Image Comics (Todd McFarlane Prod.): Dec, 2018 - No. 4, Mar, 2019 ($3.99, limited series)

	GD 2.0	VG 4.0	FN 6.0	VF 8.0	VF/NM 9.0	NM- 9.2
1-4-McFarlane-s/Robson-a; Baby Spawn having babies. 3,4-Infinity Gauntlet spoof						4.00

SPAWN'S UNIVERSE (Leads into King Spawn #1, Gunslinger Spawn #1 & The Scorched #1)
Image Comics (Todd McFarlane Productions): Jun, 2021 ($5.99, one-shot)

	GD 2.0	VG 4.0	FN 6.0	VF 8.0	VF/NM 9.0	NM- 9.2
1-Gunslinger Spawn, Medieval Spawn, She-Spawn & Cy-Gor app.; Cheung-a						6.00

SPAWN: THE DARK AGES
Image Comics (Todd McFarlane Productions): Mar, 1999 - No. 28, Oct, 2001 ($2.50)

	GD 2.0	VG 4.0	FN 6.0	VF 8.0	VF/NM 9.0	NM- 9.2
1-Fabry-c; Holguin-s/Sharp-a; variant-c by McFarlane	1	3	4	6	8	10
2-28						4.00

SPAWN THE IMPALER
Image Comics (Todd McFarlane Prods.): Oct, 1996 - No. 3, Dec, 1996 ($2.95, limited series)

	GD 2.0	VG 4.0	FN 6.0	VF 8.0	VF/NM 9.0	NM- 9.2
1-3-Mike Grell scripts, painted-a						5.00

SPAWN: THE UNDEAD
Image Comics (Todd McFarlane Prod.): Jun, 1999 - No. 9, Feb, 2000 ($1.95/$2.25)

	GD 2.0	VG 4.0	FN 6.0	VF 8.0	VF/NM 9.0	NM- 9.2
1-9-Dwayne Turner-c/a; Jenkins-s. 7-9-($2.25-c)						5.00
TPB (6/08, $24.99) r/#1-9						25.00

SPAWN: UNWANTED VIOLENCE
Image Comics (Todd McFarlane Prod): Jan, 2023 - No. 2, Feb, 2023 ($4.99, limited series)

	GD 2.0	VG 4.0	FN 6.0	VF 8.0	VF/NM 9.0	NM- 9.2
1,2-McFarlane-s/Del Mundo-a						5.00

SPAWN/WILDC.A.T.S
Image Comics (WildStorm): Jan, 1996 - No. 4, Apr, 1996 ($2.50, lim. series)

	GD 2.0	VG 4.0	FN 6.0	VF 8.0	VF/NM 9.0	NM- 9.2
1-4: Alan Moore scripts in all.						4.00

SPEAKER FOR THE DEAD (ORSON SCOTT CARD'S...) (Ender's Game)
Marvel Comics: Mar, 2011 - No. 5, Jul, 2011 ($3.99, limited series)

	GD 2.0	VG 4.0	FN 6.0	VF 8.0	VF/NM 9.0	NM- 9.2
1-3-Johnston-s/Mhan-a/Camuncoli-c						4.00

SPECIAL AGENT (Steve Saunders...)(Also see True Comics #68)
Parents' Magazine Institute (Commended Comics No. 2): Dec, 1947 - No. 8, Sept, 1949 (Based on true FBI cases)

	GD 2.0	VG 4.0	FN 6.0	VF 8.0	VF/NM 9.0	NM- 9.2
1-J. Edgar Hoover photo on-c	18	36	54	105	165	225
2	12	24	36	69	97	125
3-8	10	20	30	56	76	95

SPECIAL COLLECTORS' EDITION (See Savage Fists of Kung-Fu)

SPECIAL COMICS (Becomes Hangman #2 on)
MLJ Magazines: Winter, 1941-42

	GD 2.0	VG 4.0	FN 6.0	VF 8.0	VF/NM 9.0	NM- 9.2
1-Origin The Boy Buddies (Shield & Wizard x-over); death of The Comet retold (see Pep #17); origin The Hangman retold; Hangman-c	423	846	1269	3088	5444	7800

SPECIAL EDITION (See Gorgo and Reptisaurus)

SPECIAL EDITION COMICS (See Promotional Section)

SPECIAL EDITION COMICS
Fawcett Publications: 1940 (August) (68 pgs., one-shot)

GD VG FN VF VF/NM NM-
2.0 4.0 6.0 8.0 9.0 9.2

1-1st book devoted entirely to Captain Marvel; C.C. Beck-c/a; only app. of Captain Marvel with belt buckle; Capt. Marvel appears with button-down flap; 1st story (came out before Captain Marvel #1) 1000 2000 3000 7400 13,200 19,000

NOTE: *Prices vary widely on this book. Since this book is all Captain Marvel stories, it is actually a pre-Captain Marvel #1. There is speculation that this book almost became **Captain Marvel #1**. After **Special Edition** was published, there was an editor change at Fawcett. The new editor commissioned Kirby to do a nn **Captain Marvel** book early in 1941. This book was followed by a 2nd book several months later. This 2nd book was advertised as a #3 (making Special Edition the #1, & the nn issue the #2). However, the 2nd book did come out as a #2.*

SPECIAL EDITION: SPIDER-MAN VS. THE HULK (See listing under The Amazing Spider-Man)

SPECIAL EDITION X-MEN
Marvel Comics Group: Feb, 1983 ($2.00, one-shot, Baxter paper)
1-r/Giant-Size X-Men #1 plus one new story 3 6 9 16 23 30

SPECIAL FORCES
Image Comics: Oct, 2007 - No. 4, Mar, 2009 ($2.99)
1-4-Iraq war combat; Kyle Baker-s/a/c 3.00

SPECIAL MARVEL EDITION (Master of Kung Fu #17 on)
Marvel Comics Group: Jan, 1971 - No. 16, Feb, 1974 (#1-3: 25¢, 68 pgs.; #4: 52 pgs.; #5-16: 20¢, regular ed.)
1-Thor-r by Kirby; 68 pgs. 5 10 15 31 53 75
2-4: Thor-r by Kirby; 2,3-68 pg. Giant. 4-(52 pgs.) 3 6 9 17 26 35
5-14: Sgt. Fury-r; 11-r/Sgt. Fury #13 (Capt. America) 2 4 6 10 14 18
15-Master of Kung Fu (Shang-Chi) begins (1st app., 12/73); Starlin-a; origin/1st app. Nayland Smith & Dr. Petrie 37 74 111 274 612 950
16-1st app. Midnight; Starlin-a (2nd Shang-Chi) 9 18 27 59 117 175
NOTE: ***Kirby** c-10-14.*

SPECIAL MISSIONS (See G.I. Joe...)

SPECIAL WAR SERIES (Attack V4#3 on?)
Charlton Comics: Aug, 1965 - No. 4, Nov, 1965
V4#1-D-Day (also see D-Day listing) 5 10 15 30 50 70
2-Attack! 3 6 9 16 23 30
3-War & Attack (also see War & Attack) 3 6 9 14 20 25
4-Judomaster (intro/1st app.; see Sarge Steel) 13 26 39 89 195 300

SPECIES (Movie)
Dark Horse Comics: June, 1995 - No. 4, Sept, 1995 ($2.50, limited series)
1-4: Adaptation of film 3.00

SPECIES: HUMAN RACE (Movie)
Dark Horse Comics: Nov, 1996 - No. 4, Feb, 1997 ($2.95, limited series)
1-4 3.00

SPECS
BOOM! Studios: Nov, 2022 - No. 4, Feb, 2023 ($3.99, limited series)
1-4-Booher-s/Shehan-a 4.00

SPECTACULAR ADVENTURES (See Adventures)

SPECTACULAR FEATURE MAGAZINE, A (Formerly My Confession)
(Spectacular Features Magazine #12)
Fox Feature Syndicate: No. 11, April, 1950
11 (#1)-Samson and Delilah 33 66 99 194 317 440

SPECTACULAR FEATURES MAGAZINE (Formerly A Spectacular Feature Magazine)
Fox Feature Syndicate: No. 12, June, 1950 - No. 3, Aug, 1950
12 (#2)-Iwo Jima; photo flag-c 31 62 93 182 296 410
3-True Crime Cases From Police Files 24 48 72 144 237 330

SPECTACULAR SCARLET SPIDER
Marvel Comics: Nov, 1995 - No. 2, Dec, 1995 ($1.95, limited series)
1,2: Replaces Spectacular Spider-Man 3.00

SPECTACULAR SPIDER-GIRL
Marvel Comics: Jul, 2010 - No. 4, Oct, 2010 ($3.99, limited series)
1-4-Frenz-a; Frank Castle and the Hobgoblin app. 4.00

SPECTACULAR SPIDER-MAN, THE (See Marvel Special Edition and Marvel Treasury Edition)

SPECTACULAR SPIDER-MAN, THE (Magazine)
Marvel Comics Group: July, 1968 - No. 2, Nov, 1968 (35¢)
1-(B&W)-Romita/Mooney 52 pg. story plus updated origin story with Everett-a(i) 12 24 36 83 182 280
1-Variation w/single c-price of 40¢ 12 24 36 82 179 275
2-(Color)-Green Goblin-c & 58 pg. story; Romita painted-c (story reprinted in King Size Spider-Man #9); Romita/Mooney-a 11 22 33 76 163 250

SPECTACULAR SPIDER-MAN, THE (Peter Parker...#54-132, 134)
Marvel Comics Group: Dec, 1976 - No. 263, Nov, 1998
1-Origin recap in text; return of Tarantula 6 12 18 37 66 95
2-Kraven the Hunter app. 4 8 12 23 37 50
3-5: 3-Intro Lightmaster. 4-Vulture app. 3 6 9 15 22 28
6-8-Morbius app.; 6-r/Marvel Team-Up #3 w/Morbius 3 6 9 16 24 32
7,8-(35¢-c variants, limited distribution)(6,7/77) 9 18 27 61 123 185
9-20: 9,10-White Tiger app. 11-Last 30¢-c. 17,18-Angel & Iceman app. (from Champions); Ghost Rider cameo. 18-Gil Kane-c 2 4 6 9 13 16
9-11-(35¢-c variants, limited distribution)(8-10/77) 9 18 27 61 123 185
21,24-26: 21-Scorpion app. 26-Daredevil app. 2 3 4 6 10 12
22-Moon Knight app. 4 8 12 28 47 65
23-Moon Knight app. 3 6 9 21 33 45
27-Miller's 1st art on Daredevil (2/79); also see Captain America #235 5 10 15 35 63 90
28-Miller Daredevil (p) 3 6 9 19 30 40
29-55,57,59: 33-Origin Iguana. 38-Morbius app. 1 2 3 5 6 8
56-2nd app. Jack O'Lantern (Macendale) & 1st Spidey/Jack O'Lantern battle (7/81) 2 4 6 11 16 20
58-Byrne-a(p) 1 3 4 6 8 10
60-Double size; origin retold with new facts revealed 2 4 6 8 10 12
61-63,65-68,71-74: 65-Kraven the Hunter app. 1 2 3 5 6 8
64-1st app. Cloak & Dagger (3/82) 7 14 21 46 86 125
69,70-Cloak & Dagger app. (origin retold in #69). 70-1st app. of Silvermane in cyborg form 2 4 6 9 12 15
75-Double size 1 2 3 5 6 8
76-80: 78,79-Punisher cameo 6.00
81,82-Punisher, Cloak & Dagger app. 1 3 4 6 8 10
83-Origin Punisher retold (10/83) 2 4 6 10 14 18
84,86-89,91-99: 94-96-Cloak & Dagger app. 98-Intro The Spot 6.00
85-Hobgoblin (Ned Leeds) app. (12/83); gains powers of original Green Goblin (see Amazing Spider-Man #238) 2 4 6 9 13 16
90-Spider-Man's new black costume, last panel (ties w/Amazing Spider-Man #252 & Marvel Team-Up #141 for 1st app.) 5 10 15 30 50 70
100-(3/85)-Double size 1 3 4 6 8 10
101-115,117,118,120-129: 107-110-Death of Jean DeWolff. 111-Secret Wars II tie-in. 128-Black Cat new costume 5.00
116,119-Sabretooth-c/story 2 4 6 9 12 15
130-132: 130-Hobgoblin app. 131-Six part Kraven tie-in. 132-Kraven tie-in 2 3 4 6 8 10
133-137,139,140: 140-Punisher cameo 5.00
138-1st full app. Tombstone (origin #139) 2 4 6 8 10 12
141-143-Punisher app. 1 2 3 4 5 7
144-146,148-157: 151-Tombstone returns 4.00
147-1st brief app. new Hobgoblin (Macendale), 1 page; continued in Web of Spider-Man #48 2 4 6 11 16 20
158-Spider-Man gets new powers (1st Cosmic Spidey, cont'd in Web of Spider-Man #59) 3 6 9 16 23 30
159-Cosmic Spider-Man app. 1 2 3 4 5 7
160-175,177-188,190-199: 161-163-Hobgoblin app. 168-170-Avengers x-over. 169-1st app. The Outlaws. 180-184-Green Goblin app. 197-199-Original X-Men-c/story 4.00
176-1st Corona (Dagny Forrester) 2 4 6 10 14 18
189-($2.95, 52 pgs.)-Silver hologram on-c; battles Green Goblin; origin Spidey retold; Vess poster w/Spidey & Hobgoblin 6.00
189-(2nd printing)-Gold hologram on-c 4.00
195-(Deluxe ed.)-Polybagged w/"Dirt" magazine #2 & Beastie Boys/Smithereens music cassette 2 4 6 8 10 12
200-($2.95)-Holo-grafx foil-c; Green Goblin-c/story 6.00
201-219,221,222,224,226-228,230-247: 212-w/card sheet. 203-Maximum Carnage x-over. 204-Begin 4 part death of Tombstone story. 207,208-The Shroud-c/story. 208-Siege of Darkness x-over (#207 is a tie-in). 209-Black Cat back-up. 215,216-Scorpion app. 217-Power & Responsibility Pt. 4. 231-Return of Kaine; Spider-Man corpse discovered. 232-New Doc Octopus app. 233-Carnage-c/app. 235-Dragon Man cameo. 236-Dragon Man-c/app; Lizard app.; Peter Parker regains powers. 238,239-Lizard app. 239-w/card insert. 240-Revelations storyline begins. 241-Flashback 5.00
213-Collectors ed. polybagged w/16 pg. preview & animation cel; foil-c; 1st meeting Spidey & Typhoid Mary 5.00
213-Version polybagged w/Gamepro #7; no-c date, price 4.00
217,219 ($2.95)-Deluxe edition foil-c: flip book 5.00
220 ($2.25, 52 pgs.)-Flip book, Mary Jane reveals pregnancy 5.00
223,229: ($2.50) 229-Spidey quits 5.00
223,225: ($2.95)-223-Die Cut-c. 225-Newsstand ed. 5.00
225,229: ($3.95) 225-Direct Market Holodisk-c (Green Goblin). 229-Acetate-c, Spidey quits 5.00
240-Variant-c 5.00
248,249,251-254,256: 249-Return of Norman Osborn 256-1st app. Prodigy 4.00
250-($3.25) Double gatefold-c 5.00
255-($2.99) Spiderhunt pt. 4 5.00
257-262: 257-Double cover with "Spectacular Prodigy #1"; battles Jack O'Lantern. 258-Spidey is cleared. 259,260-Green Goblin & Hobgoblin app. 262-Byrne-s 4.00
263-Final issue; Byrne-c; Aunt May returns 5.00
#(-1) Flashback (7/97) 4.00
#1000 (6/11, $4.99) Punisher app.; Nauck & Ryan-a/Rivera-c; r/ASM #129 5.00
Annual 1 (1979)-Doc Octopus-c & 46 pg. story 2 4 6 11 16 20
Annual 2 (1980)-Origin/1st app. Rapier 1 3 4 6 8 10
Annual 3-5: ('81-'83) 3-Last Man-Wolf 6.00
Annual 6-14: 8 ('88,$ 1.75)-Evolutionary War x-over; Daydreamer returns Gwen Stacy "clone" back to real self (not Gwen Stacy). 9 ('89, $2.00, 68 pgs.)-Atlantis Attacks. 10 ('90, $2.00, 68 pgs.)-McFarlane-a. 11 ('91, $2.00, 68 pgs.)-Iron Man app. 12 ('92, $2.25, 68 pgs.)-Venom solo story cont'd from Amazing Spider-Man Annual #26. 13 ('93, $2.95, 68 pgs.)-Polybagged w/trading card; John Romita, Sr. back-up-a 6.00
... No. 1 Facsimile Edition (6/22, $3.99) Reprints #1 with original 1976 ads 4.00
Special 1 (1995, $3.95)-Flip book 1 2 3 5 6 8
NOTE: ***Austin** c-21i, Annual 11i. **Buckler** a-103, 107-111, 116, 117, 119, 122, Annual 1, Annual 10; c-103, 107-111, 113, 116-119, 122, Annual 1. **Buscema** a-121. **Byrne** c(p)-17, 43, 58, 101, 102. **Giffen** a-120p. **Hembeck** c/a-86p. **Larsen** c-Annual 11p. **Miller** c-46p, 48p, 50, 51p, 52p, 54p, 55, 56p, 57, 60. **Mooney** a-7i, 11i, 21p, 23p, 25p, 26p, 29-34p, 36p, 37p, 39i, 41, 42i, 49p, 50i, 51i, 53p, 54-57i, 59-66i, 68i, 71i, 73-79i, 81-83i, 85i, 87-99i, 102i, 125p, Annual 1i, 2p. **Nasser** c-37p. **Perez** c-10. **Simonson** c-54i. **Zeck** a-22, 118, 131, 132; c-131, 132.*

SPECTACULAR SPIDER-MAN (2nd series)
Marvel Comics: Sept, 2003 - No. 27, June, 2005 ($2.25/$2.99)
1-Jenkins-s/Ramos-a/c; Venom-c/app. 4.00
2-26: 2-5-Venom app. 6-9-Dr. Octopus app. 11-13-The Lizard app. 14-Rivera painted-a. 15,16-Capt. America app. 17,18-Ramos-a. 20-Spider-Man gets organic webshooters 21,22-Caldwell-a. 23-26-Sarah & Gabriel app.; Land-c 3.00
27-($2.99) Last issue; Uncle Ben app. in flashback; Buckingham-a 4.00
... Vol. 1: The Hunger TPB (2003, $11.99) r/#1-5 12.00
... Vol. 2: Countdown TPB (2004, $11.99) r/#6-10 12.00
... Vol. 3: Here There Be Monsters TPB (2004, $9.99) r/#11-14 10.00
... Vol. 4: Disassembled TPB (2004, $14.99) r/#15-20 15.00
... Vol. 5: Sins Remembered (2005, $9.99) r/#23-26 10.00
... Vol. 6: The Final Curtain (2005, $14.99) r/#21,22,27 & Peter Parker: Spider-Man #39-4115.00

SPECTACULAR STORIES MAGAZINE (Formerly A Star Presentation)
Fox Feature Syndicate (Hero Books): No. 4, July, 1950; No. 3, Sept, 1950
4-Sherlock Holmes (true crime stories) 41 82 123 256 428 600
3-The St. Valentine's Day Massacre (true crime) 29 58 87 172 281 390

SPECTER INSPECTORS
BOOM! Studios (BOOM! Box): Feb, 2021 - No. 5, Jun, 2021 ($4.99)
1-5-Bowen McCurdy & Kaityn Musto-s/Musto-a 5.00

SPECTRE, THE (1st Series) (See Adventure Comics #431-440, More Fun & Showcase)

Specs #1 © David M Booher

Spectacular Spider-Girl #1 © MAR

Speed Racer: Chronicles of the Racer #1 © Speed Racer Enterprises

GD VG FN VF VF/NM NM-
2.0 4.0 6.0 8.0 9.0 9.2

National Periodical Publ.: Nov-Dec, 1967 - No. 10, May-June, 1969 (All 12¢)

1-(11-12/67)-Anderson-c/a 17 34 51 114 252 390
2-5-Neal Adams-c/a; 3-Wildcat x-over 9 18 27 61 123 185
6-8,10: 6-8-Anderson inks. 7-Hourman app. 7 14 21 48 89 130
9-Wrightson-a 8 16 24 52 99 145

SPECTRE, THE (2nd Series) (See Saga of the Swamp Thing #58, Showcase '95 #8 & Wrath of the...)
DC Comics: Apr, 1987 - No. 31, Oct, 1989 ($1.00, new format)

1-Colan-a begins 1 2 3 5 6 8
2-32: 9-Nudity panels. 10-Batman cameo. 10,11-Millennium tie-ins 4.00
Annual 1 (1988, $2.00)-Deadman app. 5.00
NOTE: ***Art Adams*** *c-Annual 1.* ***Colan*** *a-1-6.* ***Kaluta*** *c-1-3.* ***Mignola*** *c-7-9.* ***Morrow*** *a-9-15.* ***Sears*** *c/a-22.* ***Vess*** *c-13-15.*

SPECTRE, THE (3rd Series) (Also see Brave and the Bold #72, 75, 116, 180, 199 & Showcase '95 #8)
DC Comics: Dec, 1992 - No. 62, Feb, 1998 ($1.75/$1.95/$2.25/$2.50)

1-($1.95)-Glow-in-the-dark-c; Mandrake-a begins 1 3 4 6 8 10
2,3 5.00
4-7,9-12,14-20: 10-Kaluta-c. 11-Hildebrandt painted-c. 16-Aparo/K. Jones-a. 19-Snyder III-c. 20-Sienkiewicz-c 4.00
8,13-($2.50)-Glow-in-the-dark-c 6.00
21-62: 22-(9/94)-Superman-c & app. 23-(11/94). 43-Kent Williams-c. 44-Kaluta-c. 47-Final Night x-over. 49-Begin Bolton-c. 51-Batman-c/app. 52-Gianni-c. 54-1st app. Michael Holt (Mr. Terrific); Corben-c. 60-Harris-c 3.00
#0 (10/94) Released between #22 & #23 3.00
Annual 1 (1995, $3.95)-Year One story 5.00
NOTE: ***Bisley*** *c-27.* ***Fabry*** *c-2.* ***Kelley Jones*** *c-31.* ***Vess*** *c-5.*

SPECTRE, THE (4th Series) (Hal Jordan; also see Day of Judgment #5 and Legends of the DC Universe #33-36)
DC Comics: Mar, 2001 - No. 27, May, 2003 ($2.50/$2.75)

1-DeMatteis-s/Ryan Sook-c/a 4.00
2-27: 3,4-Superman & Batman-c/app. 5-Two-Face-c/app. 20-Begin $2.75-c. 21-Sinestro returns. 24-JLA app. 3.00

SPECTRE, THE (See Crisis Aftermath: The Spectre)

SPECTRO
AfterShock Comics: May, 2022 ($7.99, oversized 8-1/2" x 10-7/8", one shot)

1-Juan Doe-s/a 8.00

SPEEDBALL (See Amazing Spider-Man Annual #12, Marvel Super-Heroes & The New Warriors)
Marvel Comics: Sept, 1988(10/88-inside) - No. 10, Jun, 1989 (75¢)

1-Ditko/Guice-a/c 2 4 6 10 14 18
2-10: Ditko/Guice-a-2-4; Ditko a-2-10; c-2-10p 4.00

SPEED BUGGY (TV)(Also see Fun-In #12, 15)
Charlton Comics: July, 1975 - No. 9, Nov, 1976 (Hanna-Barbera)

1 3 6 9 16 23 30
2-9 2 4 6 11 16 20

SPEED CARTER SPACEMAN (See Spaceman)

SPEED COMICS (New Speed)(Also see Double Up)
Brookwood Publ./Speed Publ./Harvey Publications No. 14 on:
10/39 - #11, 8/40; #12, 3/41 - #44, 1-2/47 (#14-16: pocket size, 100 pgs.)

1-Origin & 1st app. Shock Gibson; Ted Parrish, the Man with 1000 Faces begins; Powell-a; becomes Champion #2 on?; has earliest? full page panel in comics; classic war-c 486 972 1458 3550 6275 9000
2-Powell-a 232 464 696 1485 2543 3600
3-War-c 174 348 522 1114 1907 2700
4,5: 4-Powell-a. 5-Dinosaur-c 155 310 405 992 1696 2400
6-9,11: 7-Mars Mason begins, ends #11. 9,11-War-c 142 284 426 909 1555 2200
10-Classsic Giant Moth Monster-c 206 412 618 1318 2259 3200
12 (3/41; shows #11 in indicia)-The Wasp begins; Major Colt app. (Capt. Colt #12) 174 348 522 1114 1907 2700
13-Intro. Captain Freedom & Young Defenders; Girl Commandos, Pat Parker (costumed heroine), War Nurse begins; Major Colt app. 271 542 813 1734 2967 4200
14,15-(100 pg. pocket size, 1941): 14-2nd Harvey comic (See Pocket); Shock Gibson dons new costume; Nazi war-c. 15-Pat Parker dons costume, last in costume #23; no Girl Commandos; Nazi monsters war-c. 331 662 993 2317 4059 5800
16-(100 pg. pocket size, 1941) Cover with Hitler leading an army of Nazi ghouls to the White House 371 742 1113 2600 4550 6500
17-Classic Simon & Kirby WWII Nazi bondage/torture-c; Black Cat begins (4/42, early app.; see Pocket #1); origin Black Cat-r/Pocket #1; not in #40,41 371 742 1113 2600 4550 6500
18-20-S&K-c. 18-Bondage/torture-c. 19,20-Japanese war-c 284 568 852 1818 3109 4400
21-Hitler, Tojo-c; Kirby-c 371 742 1113 2600 4550 6500
22-Nazi WWII-c by Kirby 271 542 813 1734 2967 4200
23-Origin Girl Commandos; war-c by Kirby 271 542 813 1734 2967 4200
24-Pat Parker team-up with Girl Commandos; Hitler, Tojo, & Mussolini-c 314 628 942 2198 3849 5500
25,27,29: 25-War-c. 27 Nazi WWII-c. 29-Nazi WWII bondage-c 213 426 639 1363 2332 3300
26-Flag-c 290 580 870 1856 3178 4500
28-Classic Nazi monster WWII-c 649 1298 1947 4738 8369 12,000
30-Nazi WWII Death Chamber bondage-c 290 580 870 1856 3178 4500
31-Classic Schomburg Hitler & Tojo-c 459 918 1377 3350 5925 8500
32-35-Schomburg-c. 32,34-Nazi war-c. 33,35-Japanese war-c 213 426 639 1363 2332 3300
36-Schomburg Japanese war-c 142 284 426 909 1555 2200
37,39-42,44: 37-Japanese war-c. 41-War-c 53 106 159 334 567 800
38-Iwo-Jima Flag-c 66 132 198 419 722 1025
43-Robot-c 61 122 183 390 670 950
NOTE: ***Al Avison*** *c-14-16, 30, 43.* ***Briefer*** *a-6, 7.* ***Jon Henri*** *(Kirbyesque) c-17-20.* ***Kubert*** *a-37, 38, 42-44.* ***Kirby/Caseneuve*** *c-21-23.* ***Cecelia Munson*** *a-7-11(Mars Mason).* ***Palais*** *c-37, 39-42.* ***Powell*** *a-1, 2, 4-7, 28, 31, 44.* ***Schomburg*** *c-31-36.* ***Tuska*** *a-3, 6, 7. Bondage c-18, 35. Captain Freedom c-16-24, 25(part), 26-44(w/Black Cat #27, 29, 31, 32-40). Shock Gibson c-1-15.*

SPEED DEMON (Also see Marvel Versus DC #3 & DC Versus Marvel #4)
Marvel Comics (Amalgam): Apr, 1996 ($1.95, one-shot)

1 3.00

SPEED DEMONS (Formerly Frank Merriwell at Yale #1-4?; Submarine Attack #11 on)
Charlton Comics: No. 5, Feb, 1957 - No. 10, 1958

5-10 8 16 24 40 50 60

SPEED FORCE (See The Flash 2nd Series #143-Cobalt Blue)
DC Comics: Nov, 1997 ($3.95, one-shot)

1-Flash & Kid Flash vs. Cobalt Blue; Waid-s/Aparo & Sienkiewicz-a; Flash family stories and pin-ups by various 4.00

SPEED RACER (Also see The New Adventures of...)
Now Comics: July, 1987 - No. 38, Nov, 1990 ($1.75)

1 4.00
2-38, 1-2nd printing 3.00
Special 1 (1988, $2.00), Special 2 (1988, $3.50) 4.00

SPEED RACER (Also see Racer X)
DC Comics (WildStorm): Oct, 1999 - No. 3, Dec, 1999 ($2.50, limited series)

1-3-Tommy Yune-s/a; origin of Racer X; debut of the Mach 5 3.00
...: Born To Race (2000, $9.95, TPB) r/series & conceptual art 10.00
...: The Original Manga Vol. 1 ('00, $9.95, TPB) r/1950s B&W manga 10.00

SPEED RACER: CHRONICLES OF THE RACER
IDW Publishing: 2007 - No. 4, Apr, 2008 ($3.99)

1-4-Multiple covers for each 4.00

SPEED RACER FEATURING NINJA HIGH SCHOOL
Now Comics: Aug, 1993 - No. 2, 1993 ($2.50, mini-series)

1,2: 1-Polybagged w/card. 2-Exists? 3.00

SPEED RACER: RETURN OF THE GRX
Now Comics: Mar, 1994 - No. 2, Apr, 1994 ($1.95, limited series)

1,2 3.00

SPEED SMITH-THE HOT ROD KING (Also see Hot Rod King)
Ziff-Davis Publishing Co.: Spring, 1952

1-Saunders painted-c 29 58 87 172 281 390

SPEEDY GONZALES
Dell Publishing Co.: No. 1084, Mar, 1960

Four Color 1084 7 14 21 46 86 125

SPEEDY RABBIT (See Television Puppet Show)
Realistic/I. W. Enterprises/Super Comics: nd (1953); 1963

nn (1953)-Realistic Reprint? 3 6 9 16 23 30
I.W. Reprint #1 (2 versions w/diff. c/stories exist)-Peter Cottontail #?
Super Reprint #14(1963) 2 4 6 11 16 20

SPELLBINDERS
Quality: Dec, 1986 - No. 12, Jan, 1988 ($1.25)

1-12: Nemesis the Warlock, Amadeus Wolf 3.00

SPELLBINDERS
Marvel Comics: May, 2005 - No. 6, Oct, 2005 ($2.99, limited series)
1-6-Carey-s/Perkins-a 3.00
...: Signs and Wonders TPB (2006, $7.99, digest) r/#1-6 8.00

SPELLBOUND (See The Crusaders)

SPELLBOUND (Tales to Hold You... #1, Stories to Hold You...)
Atlas Comics (ACI 1-15/Male 16-23/BPC 24-34): Mar, 1952 - #23, June, 1954; #24, Oct, 1955 - #34, June, 1957

	GD 2.0	VG 4.0	FN 6.0	VF 8.0	VF/NM 9.0	NM- 9.2
1-Horror/weird stories in all	142	284	426	909	1555	2200
2-Edgar A. Poe app.	116	232	348	742	1271	1800
3-Whitney-a; cannibalism story; classic Heath-c	181	362	543	1158	1979	2800
4,5	65	130	195	416	708	1000
6-Krigstein-a	68	136	204	435	743	1050
7-10: 7,8-Ayers-a	57	114	171	362	619	875
11-13,15,16,18-20	53	106	159	334	567	800
14-Ed Win-a; classic Everett-c	271	542	813	1734	2967	4200
17-Krigstein-a; classic Everett skeleton-c	168	336	504	1075	1838	2600
21-23: 23-Last precode (6/54)	45	90	135	284	480	675
24-28,30,31,34: 25-Orlando-a	37	74	111	222	361	500
29-Ditko-a (4 pgs.)	39	78	117	240	395	550
32,33-Torres-a	37	74	111	222	361	500

NOTE: ***Brodsky*** *a-5; c-1, 5-7, 10, 11, 13, 15, 25-27, 32.* ***Colan*** *a-17.* ***Everett*** *a-2, 5, 7, 10, 16, 28, 31; c-2, 8, 9, 14, 17-19, 28, 30.* ***Forgione/Abel*** *a-29.* ***Forte/Fox*** *a-16.* ***Al Hartley*** *a-2.* ***Heath*** *a-2, 4, 8, 9, 12, 14, 16; c-3, 4, 12, 16, 20, 21.* ***Infantino*** *a-15.* ***Keller*** *a-5.* ***Kida*** *a-2, 14.* ***Maneely*** *a-7, 14, 27; c-24, 29, 31.* ***Mooney*** *a-5, 13, 18.* ***Mac Pakula*** *a-22, 32.* ***Post*** *a-8.* ***Powell*** *a-19, 20, 32.* ***Robinson*** *a-1.* ***Romita*** *a-24, 26, 27.* ***R.Q. Sale*** *a-29.* ***Sekowsky*** *a-5.* ***Severin*** *c-29.* ***Sinnott*** *a-8, 16, 17.*

SPELLBOUND
Marvel Comics: Jan, 1988 - Apr, 1988 ($1.50, bi-weekly, Baxter paper)
1-5 4.00
6 ($2.25, 52 pgs.) 5.00

SPELLJAMMER (Also see TSR Worlds Comics Annual)
DC Comics: Sept, 1990 - No. 15, Nov, 1991 ($1.75)
1-15: Based on TSR game. 11-Heck-a. 3.00

SPELL ON WHEELS
Dark Horse Comics: Oct, 2016 - No. 5, Feb, 2017 ($3.99)
1-5-Kate Leth-s/Megan Levens-a. 1-Ming Doyle-c 4.00

SPENCER SPOOK (Formerly Giggle Comics)
American Comics Group: No. 100, Mar-Apr, 1955 - No. 101, May-June, 1955
100,101 9 18 27 50 65 80

SPIDER, THE
Eclipse Books: 1991 - Book 3, 1991 ($4.95, 52 pgs., limited series)
Book 1-3-Truman-c/a 5.00

SPIDER, THE
Dynamite Entertainment: 2012 - No. 18, 2014 ($3.99)
1-18: 1-Revival of the pulp character; Liss-s/Worley-a; 4 covers. 2-18-Multiple covers 4.00
Annual 1 (2013, $4.99) Denton-s/Vitorino-a/c 5.00

SPIDER-BOY (Also see Marvel Versus DC #3)
Marvel Comics (Amalgam): Apr, 1996 ($1.95)
1-Mike Wieringo-c/a; Karl Kesel story; 1st app. of Bizarnage, Insect Queen, Challengers of the Fantastic, Sue Storm: Agent of S.H.I.E.L.D., & King Lizard 3.00

SPIDER-BOY TEAM-UP
Marvel Comics (Amalgam): June, 1997 ($1.95, one-shot)
1-Karl Kesel & Roger Stern-s/Jo Ladronn-a(p) 3.00

SPIDER-FORCE (Tie-in to Spider-Geddon)
Marvel Comics: Dec, 2018 - No. 3, Feb, 2019 ($3.99, limited series)
1-3: 1-Priest-s/Siqueira-a; Spider-Woman, Spider-Kid, Scarlet Spider app. 4.00

SPIDER-GEDDON (Also see Edge of Spider-Geddon, Spider-Girls and Superior Octopus)
Marvel Comics: No. 0, Nov, 2018 - No. 5, Feb, 2019 ($4.99/$3.99)
0,5-($4.99) 0-Clayton Crain-a; 1st app. Spider-Man from PS4 videogame 5.00
1-4-($3.99) 1-Gage-s/Molina-a; multiverse of Spider-Mans app.; Morlun returns 4.00
... Handbook 1 (2/19, $4.99) Profiles of various Spider-Men of the Multiverse 5.00

SPIDER-GIRL (See What If... #105)
Marvel Comics: Oct, 1998 - No. 100, Sept, 2006 ($1.99/$2.25/$2.99)
0-($2.99)-r/1st app. Peter Parker's daughter from What If #105; previews regular series, Avengers-Next and J2 2 4 6 8 11 14
1-DeFalco-s/Olliffe & Williamson-s 2 4 6 10 14 18
2-Two covers 4.00
3-16,18-20: 3-Fantastic Five-c/app. 10,11-Spider-Girl time-travels to meet teenaged Spider-Man 3.00
17-($2.99) Peter Parker suits up 4.00
21-24,26-49,51-59: 21-Begin $2.25-c. 31-Avengers app. 3.00
25-($2.99) Spider-Girl vs. the Savage Six 4.00
50-($3.50) 4.00
59-99-($2.99) 59-Avengers app.; Ben Parker born. 75-May in Black costume. 82-84-Venom bonds with Normie Osborn. 93-Venom-c. 95-Tony Stark app. 3.00
100-($3.99) Last issue; story plus Rogues Gallery, profile pages; r/#27,53 4.00
1999 Annual ($3.99) 4.00
...: The End! (10/10, $3.99) Frenz & Buscema-a; Mayhem app. 4.00
Wizard #1/2 (1999) 3.00
... A Fresh Start (1/99,$5.99, TPB) r/#1&2 6.00
... Presents The Buzz and Darkdevil (2007, $7.99, digest) r/mini-series 8.00

SPIDER-GIRL (Araña Corazon from Arana Heart of the Spider)
Marvel Comics: Jan, 2011 - No. 8, Sept, 2011 ($3.99/$2.99)
1-($3.99) Tobin-s/Henry-a/Kitson-c; back-up w/Haspiel-a; Fantastic Four app. 4.00
1-Variant-c by Del Mundo 5.00
2-8-($2.99) 2,3-Red Hulk app. 4,5-Ana Kravenoff app. 6-Hobgoblin app. 8-Powers return 3.00

SPIDER-GIRLS (Spider-Geddon tie-in)
Marvel Comics: Dec, 2018 - No. 3, Feb, 2019 ($3.99, limited series)
1-3-Houser-s/Genolet-a; Mayday Parker, Anya Corazon & Annie Parker app. 4.00

SPIDER-GWEN (See debut in Edge of Spider-Verse #2)
Marvel Comics: Apr, 2015 - No. 5, Aug, 2015 ($3.99)
1-Latour-s/Robbi Rodriguez-a/c; The Vulture app. 3 6 9 14 20 25
2-5: 2-Spider-Ham app. 3-The Vulture & The Punisher app. 5.00

SPIDER-GWEN
Marvel Comics: Dec, 2015 - No. 34, Sept, 2018 ($3.99)
1-Latour-s/Robbi Rodriguez-a; The Lizard & female Capt. America app. 1 2 3 5 6 8
2-23,25-34: 7,8-"Spider-Women" tie-in; Silk & Spider-Woman app. 10-Kraven app. 1 6-18-Miles app.; x-over with Spider-Man #12-14. 25-32-Gwenom app. 4.00
24-1st app. Gwenom 6 12 18 38 69 100
#0 (1/16, $4.99) Reprints #1 (4/15) plus script of Edge of Spider-Verse #2 5.00
Annual 1 (8/16, $4.99) Short stories; Latour-s; art by various 5.00

SPIDER-GWEN: GHOST-SPIDER (Spider-Geddon tie-in)(Also see Ghost-Spider series)
Marvel Comics: Dec, 2018 - No. 10, Sept, 2019 ($3.99)
1-Spider-Ham app. 1 3 4 6 8 10
2-10: 4-10-Miyazawa-a. 10-Adapts Ghost-Spider name 4.00

SPIDER-GWEN: GWENVERSE
Marvel Comics: May, 2022 - No. 5, Oct, 2022 ($4.99/$3.99, limited series)
1-($4.99) Seeley-s/Nishijima-a; Multiverse Gwens app.; ThorGwen & Nightbird app. 5.00
2-5-($3.99) Iron Gwen and Gwen versions of Capt. America, Wolverine, Capt Marvel app. 4.00

SPIDER-HAM (Peter Porker, The Spectacular...)(See Marvel Tails & Spider-Geddon)
Marvel Comics: Feb, 2020 - No. 5, Jun, 2020 ($3.99)
1-5: 1-Origin re-told; Sca-vengers and the Unhumanati app. 2-5-Spider-Man app. 4.00

SPIDER-HAM 25TH ANNIVERSARY SPECIAL
Marvel Comics: Aug, 2010 ($3.99, one-shot)
1-Jusko-c/DeFalco-s/Chabot-a; Peter Porker vs. the Swinester Six 4.00

SPIDER ISLAND... (one-shots) (See Amazing Spider-Man #666-673)
Marvel Comics
...: Deadly Foes 1 (10/11, $4.99) Hobgoblin & Jackal stories; Caselli-c 5.00
...: Emergence of Evil - Jackal & Hobgoblin 1 (10/11, $4.99) Hobgoblin & Jackal reprints 5.00
...: Heroes For Hire 1 (12/11, $2.99) Misty Knight & Paladin; Hotz-a/Yardin-c 3.00
...: I Love New York City 1 (11/11, $3.99) Short stories by various; Punisher app. 4.00
...: Spider-Woman 1 (11/11, $2.99) Van Lente-s/Camuncoli-a; Alicia Masters app. 3.00
... Spotlight 1 ('11, $3.99) Creator interviews and story previews 4.00
...: The Avengers 1 (11/11, $2.99) McKone-a/Yu-c; Frog-Man app. 3.00

SPIDER-ISLAND (Secret Wars tie-in)(Back-up MC2 Spider-Girl story in each issue)
Marvel Comics: Sept, 2015 - No. 5, Dec, 2015 ($4.99/$3.99, limited series)
1-($4.99) Gage-s/Diaz-a/Ramos-c; Venom and Werewolf By Night app. 5.00
2-5-($3.99) Tony Stark as the Green Goblin. 3-5-Peter Parker returns 4.00

SPIDER ISLAND: CLOAK & DAGGER (See Amazing Spider-Man #666-673)
Marvel Comics: Oct, 2011 - No. 3, Dec, 2011 ($2.99, limited series)
1-3-Spencer-s/Rios-a/Choi-c; Mr. Negative app. 3.00

SPIDER ISLAND: DEADLY HANDS OF KUNG FU (See Amazing Spider-Man #666-673)
Marvel Comics: Oct, 2011 - No. 3, Dec, 2011 ($2.99, limited series)
1-3-Johnston-s/Fiumara-a; Madame Web & Iron Fist app. 3.00

SPIDER ISLAND: THE AMAZING SPIDER-GIRL (Continued from Spider-Girl #8)
Marvel Comics: Oct, 2011 - No. 3, Dec, 2011 ($2.99, limited series)
1-3-Hobgoblin & Kingpin app.; Tobin-s/Larraz-a 3.00

SPIDER-MAN (See Amazing..., Friendly Neighborhood..., Giant-Size..., Marvel Age..., Marvel Knights..., Marvel Tales, Marvel Team-Up, Spectacular..., Spidey Super Stories, Ultimate Marvel Team-Up, Ultimate..., Venom, & Web Of...)

SPIDER-MAN (Peter Parker Spider-Man on cover but not indicia #75-on)
Marvel Comics: Aug, 1990 - No. 98, Nov, 1998 ($1.75/$1.95/ $1.99)
1-Silver edition, direct sale only (unbagged) 2 4 6 11 16 20
1-Silver bagged edition; direct sale, no price on comic, but $2.00 on plastic bag (125,000 print run) 3 6 9 17 26 35
1-Regular edition w/Spidey face in UPC area (unbagged); green-c 2 4 6 13 18 22
1-Regular bagged edition w/Spidey face in UPC area; green cover (125,000) 14.00
1-Newsstand bagged w/UPC code 3 6 9 16 23 30
1-Gold edition, 2nd printing (unbagged) with Spider-Man in box (400,000-450,000) 3 6 9 20 31 42
1-Gold 2nd printing w/UPC code; (less than 10,000 print run) intended for Wal-Mart; much scarcer than originally believed 13 26 39 86 188 290
1-Platinum ed. mailed to retailers only (10,000 print run); has new McFarlane-a & editorial material instead of ads; stiff-c, no cover price 17 34 51 114 252 390
1-Facsimile Edition (10/20, $3.99) reprints #1 with original ads and letter page 1 3 4 6 8 10
2-10: 2-McFarlane-c/a/scripts cont.; Lizard origin retold in brief. 3-Spider-Man origin retold in brief. 6,7-Ghost Rider & Hobgoblin app. 8-Wolverine cameo; Wolverine storyline begins 1 2 3 5 6 8
11-25: 12-Wolverine storyline ends. 13-Spidey's black costume returns; Morbius app. 14-Morbius app. 15-Erik Larsen-c/a; Beast c/s. 16-X-Force-c/story w/Liefeld assists; continues in X-Force #4; reads sideways; last McFarlane issue. 17-Thanos-c/story; Leonardi/Williamson-c/a. 18-Ghost Rider-c/story. 18-23-Sinister Six storyline w/Erik Larsen-c/a/scripts. 19-Hulk & Hobgoblin-c & app. 20-22-Deathlok app. 22,23-Ghost Rider, Hulk, Hobgoblin app. 23-Wrap-around gatefold-c. 24-Infinity War x-over w/Demogoblin & Hobgoblin-c/story. 24-Demogoblin dons new costume & battles Hobgoblin-c/story 5.00
26-($3.50, 52 pgs.)-Silver hologram on-c w/gatefold poster by Ron Lim; origin retold 6.00
26-2nd printing; gold hologram on-c 4.00
27-45: 32-34-Punisher-c/story. 37-Maximum Carnage x-over. 39,40-Electro-c/s (cameo #38). 41-43-Iron Fist-c/stories w/Jae Lee-c/a. 42-Intro Platoon. 44-Hobgoblin app. 3.50
46-49,51-53, 55, 56,58-74,76-81: 46-Begin $1.95-c; bound-in card sheet. 51-Power & Responsibility Pt. 3. 52,53-Venom app. 60-Kaine revealed. 61-Origin Kaine. 65-Mysterio app. 66-Kaine-c/app.; Peter Parker app. 67-Carnage-c/app. 68,69-Hobgoblin-c/app. 72-Onslaught x-over; Spidey vs. Sentinels. 74-Daredevil-c/app. 77-80-Morbius-c/app. 3.00
46-($2.95)-Polybagged; silver ink-c w/16 pg. preview of cartoon series & animation style

The Spider #12 © Argosy

Spider-Gwen #5 © MAR

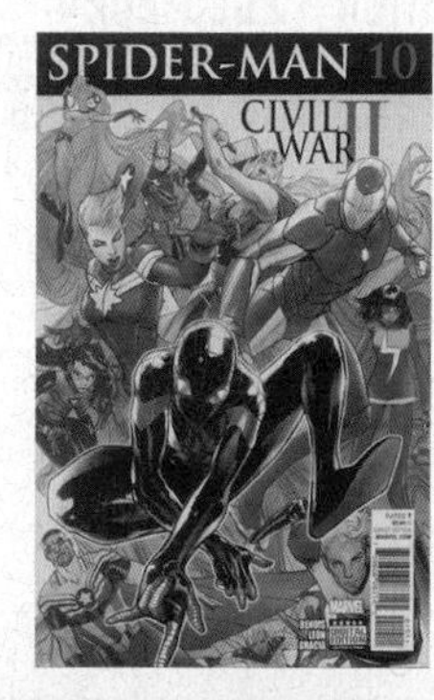

Spider-Man (2016) #10 © MAR

GD VG FN VF VF/NM NM-
2.0 4.0 6.0 8.0 9.0 9.2

print; bound-in trading card sheet 4.00
50-($2.50)-Newsstand edition 4.00
50-($3.95)-Collectors edition w/holographic-c 5.00
51-($2.95)-Deluxe edition foil-c; flip book 4.00
54-($2.75, 52 pgs.)-Flip book 4.00
57-($2.50) 4.00
57-($2.95)-Die cut-c 5.00
65-($2.95)-Variant-c; polybagged w/cassette 4.00
75-($2.95)-Wraparound-c; Green Goblin returns; death of Ben Reilly (who was the clone) 4.00
82-97: 84-Juggernaut app. 91-Double cover with "Dusk #1"; battles the Shocker.
93-Ghost Rider app. 3.00
98-Double cover; final issue 4.00
#(-1) Flashback (7/97) 3.00
Annual '97 ($2.99), '98 ($2.99)-Devil Dinosaur-c/app. 5.00
NOTE: ***Erik Larsen** c/a-15, 18-23. **M. Rogers/Keith Williams** c/a-27, 28.*

SPIDER-MAN (Miles Morales in regular Marvel Universe)
Marvel Comics: Apr, 2016 - No. 21, Dec, 2017; No. 234, Jan, 2018 - No. 240, Jul, 2018 ($3.99)
1-19,21: 1,2-Bendis-s/Pichelli-a; Avengers & Peter Parker app. 3-Ms. Marvel app.
6-10-Civil War II tie-ins. 12,13-Crossover with Spider-Gwen #16-18. 16,18-Black Cat app.
21-Nico Leon-a 4.00
20-Miles Morales pinned down by police officer-c; Nico Leon-a
2 4 6 11 16 20
[Title switches to legacy numbering after #21 (12/17)]
234-240: 234-239-Hobgoblin, Sandman, Electro, The Spot, Bombshell, Iron Spider app. 4.00
Annual 1 (10/18, $4.99) Morbius app. 5.00

SPIDER-MAN
Marvel Comics: Nov, 2019 - No. 5, Feb, 2021 ($3.99)
1-($4.99) J.J. & Henry Abrams-s/Pichelli-a; intro Cadaverous and future Ben Parker 5.00
2-5-($3.99) Ben becomes the new Spider-Man. 3-5-Tony Stark and Riri Williams app. 4.00

SPIDER-MAN (Peter Parker)
Marvel Comics: Dec, 2022 - Present ($4.99/$3.99)
1-($4.99) Slott-s/Bagley-a; Morlun returns; multiverse Spiders app. 5.00
2-4,6-($3.99) 4.00
5-($4.99) Back-up story with Monica Rambeau 4.00

SPIDER-MAN (one-shots, hardcovers and TPBs)
...& Arana Special: The Hunter Revealed (5/06, $3.99) Del Rio-s; art by Del Rio & various 4.00
...and Batman ('95, $5.95) DeMatteis-s; Joker, Carnage app.
3 6 9 14 20 26
...and Daredevil ('84, $2.00) 1-r/Spectacular Spider-Man #26-28 by Miller
1 2 3 5 6 8
...and The Human Torch in...Bahia de Los Muertos! 1 (5/09, $3.99) Beland-s/Juan Doe-a;
Diablo app.; printed in two versions (English and Spanish language)
2 4 6 11 16 20
... Annual 1 (8/19, $4.99) Spider-Ham spotlight; back-up by Phil Lord & Christopher Miller
1 3 4 6 8 10
...: Back in Black HC (2007, $34.99, dustjacket) oversized r/Amaz. S-M #539-543, Friendly
Neighborhood S-M #17-23 & Annual #1; cover pencils and sketch pages 50.00
...: Back in Black SC (2008, $24.99) same contents as HC 25.00
...: Back in Black Handbook (2007, $3.99) Official Handbook format; Lopresti-c 10.00
...: Back in Quack (11/10, $3.99) Howard the Duck, Beverly and Man-Thing app.
1 2 3 5 6 8
...: Birth of Venom TPB (2007, $29.99) r/Secret Wars #8, AS-M #252-259,298-300,315-317,
AS-M Annual #25, Fantastic Four #274 and Web of Spider-Man #1 30.00
...: Brand New Day HC (2008, $24.99, dustjacket) r/Amaz. S-M #546-551, Spider-Man: Swing
Shift and story from Venom Super-Special 25.00
...: Carnage nn (6/93, $6.95, TPB)-r/Amazing S-M #344,345,359-363; spot varnish-c 10.00
...: Curse of the Man-Thing 1 (6/21, $4.99) Orlando-s/Failla-a (Also see Avengers: Curse
of the Man-Thing and X-Men: Curse of the Man-Thing) 5.00
.../Daredevil (10/02, $2.99) Vatche Mavlian-c/a; Brett Matthews-s 3.00
...: Dead Man's Hand 1 (4/97, $2.99) 3.00
...: Death of the Stacys HC (2007, $19.99, dustjacket) r/Amazing Spider-Man #88-92 and
#121,122; intro. by Gerry Conway; afterword by Romita; cover gallery incl. reprints 20.00
.../Dr. Strange: "The Way to Dusty Death" nn (1992, $6.95, 68 pgs.) 8.00
...: Election Day HC (2009, $29.99) r/#584-588; includes Barack Obama app from #583 30.00
.../Elektra '98-($2.99) vs. The Silencer 3.00
... Family (2005, $4.99, 100 pgs.) new story and reprints; Spider-Ham app. 5.00
... Fear Itself (3/09, $3.99) Spider-Man and Man-Thing; Stuart Moore-s/Joe Suitor-a
1 3 4 6 8 10
... Fear Itself Graphic Novel (2/92, $12.95) 20.00
Free Comic Book Day 2012 (Spider-Man: Season One) #1 (Giveaway) Previews the GN 3.00
Giant-Sized Spider-Man (12/98, $3.99) r/team-ups 4.00
...: Grim Hunt - The Kraven Saga (5/10, free) prelude to Grim Hunt arc; Kraven history 3.00
Holiday Special 1995 ($2.95) 6.00

GD VG FN VF VF/NM NM-
2.0 4.0 6.0 8.0 9.0 9.2

...: Hot Shots nn (1/96, $2.95) fold out posters by various, inc. Vess and Ross 4.00
Identity Crisis (9/98, $19.95, TPB) 20.00
...: Kraven's Last Hunt HC (2006, $19.99) r/Amaz. S-M #293,294; Web of S-M #31,32 and
Spect. S-M #131-132; intro. by DeMatteis; Zeck-a; cover pencils and interior pencils 20.00
...: Legacy of Evil 1 (6/96, $3.95) Kurt Busiek script & Mark Texeira-c/a 6.00
...Legends Vol. 1: Todd McFarlane ('03, $19.95, TPB)-r/Amaz. S-M #298-305 20.00
...Legends Vol. 2: Todd McFarlane ('03, $19.99, TPB)-r/Amaz. S-M #306-314, &
Spec. Spider-Man Annual #10 20.00
...Legends Vol. 3: Todd McFarlane ('04, $24.99, TPB)-r/Amaz. S-M #315-323,325,328 25.00
...Legends Vol. 4: Spider-Man & Wolverine ('03, $13.95, TPB) r/Spider-Man & Wolverine #1-4
and Spider-Man/Daredevil #1 14.00
.../Marrow (2/01, $2.99) Garza-a 5.00
...: Marvels Snapshots 1 (12/20, $4.99) Howard Chaykin-s/a; Alex Ross-c 5.00
.../Mary Jane: ... You Just Hit the Jackpot TPB (2009, $24.99) early apps. & key stories 25.00
...: Master Plan 1 (9/17, $3.99) Thompson-s/Stockman-a; bonus r/ASM #2 4.00
100th Anniversary Special: Spider-Man 1 (9/14, $3.99) In-Hyk Lee-a/c; Venom app. 4.00
...: One More Day HC (2008. $24.99, dustjacket) r/Amaz. S-M #544-545, Friendly N.S-M #24,
Sensational S-M #41 and Marvel Spotlight: Spider-Man-One More Day 25.00
...: Origin of the Hunter (6/10, $3.99) r/Kraven apps. in ASM #15 & 34; new Mayhew-a
1 3 4 6 8 10
..., Peter Parker: Back in Black HC (2007, $34.99) oversized r/Sensational Spider-Man #35-40
& Annual #1, Spider-Man Family #1,2; Marvel Spotlight: Spider-Man and Spider-Man Back
in Black Handbook; cover sketches 35.00
..., Punisher, Sabretooth: Designer Genes (1993, $8.95) 10.00
...: Reptilian Rage 1 (8/19, $3.99) Macchio-s/Chris Allen-a; The Lizard app. 4.00
...Return of the Goblin TPB (See Peter Parker: Spider-Man)
...Revelations ('97, $14.99, TPB) r/end of Clone Saga plus 14 new pages by Romita Jr. 15.00
...: Saga of the Sandman TPB (2007, $19.99) r/1st app. Amazing S-M #4 and other app. 20.00
...: Season One HC (2012, $24.99) Origin and early days; Bunn-s/Neil Edwards-a 25.00
...: Son of the Goblin (2004, $15.99, TPB) r/AS-M#136-137,312 & Spec. S-M #189,200 16.00
... Special: Black and Blue and Read All Over 1 (11/06, $3.99) new story and r/ASM #12 4.00
Special Edition 1 (12/92-c, 11/92 inside)-The Trial of Venom; ordered thru mail with $5.00
donation or more to UNICEF; embossed metallic ink; came bagged w/bound-in poster;
Daredevil app. 3 6 9 14 20 25
... Spectacular 1 (8/14, $4.99) Reprints all-ages tales; Green Goblin, Kraven app. 5.00
Super Special (7/95, $3.95)-Planet of the Symbiotes 2 4 6 11 16 20
The Best of Spider-Man Vol. 2 (2003, $29.99, HC with dust jacket) r/AS-M V2 #37-45,
Peter Parker: S-M #44-47, and S-M's Tangled Web #10,11; Pearson-c 30.00
The Best of Spider-Man Vol. 3 (2004, $29.99, HC with d.j.) r/AS-M V2 #46-58, 500 30.00
The Best of Spider-Man Vol. 4 (2005, $29.99, HC with d.j.) r/#501-514; sketch pages 30.00
The Best of Spider-Man Vol. 5 (2006, $29.99, HC with d.j.) r/#515-524; sketch pages 30.00
The Complete Frank Miller Spider-Man (2002, $29.95, HC) r/Miller-s/a 30.00
The Death of Captain Stacy (2000, $3.50) r/AS-M#88-90 5.00
The Death of Gwen Stacy ($14.95) r/AS-M#96-98,121,122 15.00
...: The Movie ($12.95) adaptation by Stan Lee-s/Alan Davis-a; plus r/Ultimate
Spider-Man #8, Peter Parker #35, Tangled Web #10; photo-c 13.00
...: The Official Movie Adaptation (2002, $5.95) Stan Lee-s/Alan Davis-a 6.00
...: The Other HC (2006, $29.99, dust jacket) r/Amazing S-M #525-528, Friendly Neighborhood
S-M #1-4 and Marvel Knights S-M #19-22; gallery of variant covers 30.00
...: The Other SC (2006, $24.99) r/crossover; gallery of variant covers 25.00
...: The Other Sketchbook (2005, $2.99) sketch page preview of 2005-6 x-over 3.00
Torment TPB (5/01$15.95) r/#1-5, Spec. S-M #10 16.00
...: Unforgiven (5/23, $4.99) Seeley-s/Kotian-a; leads into X-Men: Unforgiven 5.00
... Vs. Doctor Octopus ($17.95) reprints early battles; Sean Chen-c 18.00
... Vs. Punisher (7/00, $2.99) Michael Lopez-c/a 5.00
...Vs. Silver Sable (2006, $15.99, TPB)-r/Amazing Spider-Man #265,279-281 & Peter Parker,
The Spectacular Spider-Man #128,129 16.00
...Vs. The Black Cat (2005, $14.99, TPB)-r/Amaz. S-M #194,195,204,205,226,227 15.00
...Vs. Vampires (12/10, $3.99) Blade app.; Castro-a/Grevioux-s 4.00
...Vs. Venom (1990, $8.95, TPB)-r/Amaz. S-M #300,315-317 w/new McFarlane-c 15.00
...Visionaries (10/01, $19.95, TPB)-r/Amaz. S-M #298-305; McFarlane-a 20.00
...Visionaries: John Romita (8/01, $19.95, TPB)-r/Amaz. S-M #39-42, 50,68,69,108,109;
new Romita-c 20.00
...Visionaries: Kurt Busiek (2006, $19.99, TPB)-r/Untold Tales of Spider-Man #1-8 20.00
...Visionaries: Roger Stern (2007, $24.99, TPB)-r/Amazing Spider-Man #206 & Spectacular
Spider-Man #43-52,54; Stern interview 25.00
Wizard 1/2 ($10.00) Leonardi-a; Green Goblin app. 10.00

SPIDER-MAN ADVENTURES
Marvel Comics: Dec, 1994 - No. 15, Mar, 1996 ($1.50)
1-15 ($1.50)-Based on animated series 4.00
1-($2.95)-Foil embossed-c 5.00

SPIDER-MAN AND HIS AMAZING FRIENDS (See Marvel Action Universe)
Marvel Comics Group: Dec, 1981 (one-shot)
1-Adapted from NBC TV cartoon show; Green Goblin-c/story; 1st Spidey, Firestar, Iceman

GD VG FN VF VF/NM NM-
2.0 4.0 6.0 8.0 9.0 9.2

team-up; Spiegle-p 6 12 18 37 66 95

SPIDER-MAN AND POWER PACK
Marvel Comics: Jan, 2007 - No. 4, Apr, 2007 ($2.99, limited series)

1-4-Sumerak-s/Gurihiru-a; Sandman app. 3,4-Venom app. 3.00
...: Big City Heroes (2007, $6.99, digest) r/#1-4 7.00

SPIDER-MAN AND THE FANTASTIC FOUR
Marvel Comics: Jun, 2007 - No. 4, Sept, 2007 ($2.99, limited series)

1-4-Mike Wieringo-a/c; Jeff Parker-s. 1,4-Impossible Man app. 3.00
...: Silver Rage TPB (2007, $10.99) r/#1-4; series outline and cover sketches 11.00

SPIDER-MAN AND THE LEAGUE OF REALMS (War of the Realms tie-in)
Marvel Comics: Jul, 2019 - No. 3, Aug, 2019 ($3.99, limited series)

1-3-Sean Ryan-s/Nico Leon-a 4.00

SPIDER-MAN AND THE SECRET WARS
Marvel Comics: Feb, 2010 - No. 4, May, 2010 ($2.99, limited series)

1-4-Tobin-s/Scherberger-a. 3-Black costume app. 3.00

SPIDER-MAN AND THE INCREDIBLE HULK (See listing under Amazing...)

SPIDER-MAN AND THE UNCANNY X-MEN
Marvel Comics: Mar, 1996 ($16.95, trade paperback)

nn-r/Uncanny X-Men #27, Uncanny X-men #35, Amazing Spider-Man #92, Marvel Team-Up Annual #1, Marvel Team-Up #150, & Spectacular Spider-Man #197-199 17.00

SPIDER-MAN & THE X-MEN
Marvel Comics: Feb, 2015 - No. 6, Jub, 2015 ($3.99)

1-3: Spider-Man teaching at the Jean Grey School; Kalan-s/Failla-a. 2,3-Mojo app. 4.00

SPIDER-MAN & VENOM: DOUBLE TROUBLE (All-ages)
Marvel Comics: Jan, 2020 - No. 4, Apr, 2020 ($3.99, limited series)

1-4-Spider-Man & Venom as roommates; Tamaki-s/Gurihiru-a; Ghost-Spider app. 4.00

SPIDER-MAN & WOLVERINE (See Spider-Man Legends Vol. 4 for TPB reprint)
Marvel Comics: Aug, 2003 - No. 4, Nov, 2003 ($2.99, limited series)

1-4-Matthews-s/Mavlian-a 3.00

SPIDER-MAN AND X-FACTOR
Marvel Comics: May, 1994 - No. 3, July, 1994 ($1.95, limited series)

1-3 4.00

SPIDER-MAN /BADROCK
Maximum Press: Mar, 1997 ($2.99, mini-series)

1A, 1B(#2)-Jurgens-s 5.00

SPIDER-MAN/BLACK CAT: THE EVIL THAT MEN DO (Also see Marvel Must Haves)
Marvel Comics: Aug, 2002 - No. 6, Mar, 2006 ($2.99, limited series)

1-6-Kevin Smith-s/Terry Dodson-c/a 3.00
HC (2006, $19.99, dust jacket) r/#1-6; script to #6 with sketches 20.00

SPIDER-MAN: BLUE
Marvel Comics: July, 2002 - No. 6, Apr, 2003 ($3.50, limited series)

1-6: Jeph Loeb-s/Tim Sale-a/c; flashback to early MJ and Gwen Stacy 3.50
HC (2003, $21.99, with dust jacket) over-sized r/#1-6; intro. by John Romita 22.00
SC (2004, $14.99) r/#1-6; cover gallery 15.00

SPIDER-MAN: BRAND NEW DAY (See Amazing Spider-Man Vol. 2)

SPIDER-MAN: BREAKOUT (See New Avengers #1)
Marvel Comics: June, 2005 - No. 5, Oct, 2005 ($2.99, limited series)

1-5-Bedard-s/Garcia-a. 1-U-Foes app. 5-New Avengers app. 3.00
TPB (2006, $13.99) r/#1-5 14.00

SPIDER-MAN: CHAPTER ONE
Marvel Comics: Dec, 1998 - No. 12, Oct, 1999 ($2.50, limited series)

1-Retelling/updating of origin; John Byrne-s/c/a 4.00
1-($6.95) DF Edition w/variant-c by Jae Lee 7.00
2-11: 2-Two covers (one is swipe of ASM #1); Fantastic Four app. 9-Daredevil. 11-Giant-Man-c/app. 4.00
12-($3.50) Battles the Sandman 5.00
0-(5/99) Origins of Vulture, Lizard and Sandman 4.00

SPIDER-MAN CLASSICS
Marvel Comics: Apr, 1993 - No. 16, July, 1994 ($1.25)

1-14,16: 1-r/Amaz. Fantasy #15 & Strange Tales #115. 2-16-r/Amaz. Spider-Man #1-15. 6-Austin-c(i) 4.00
15-($2.95)-Polybagged w/16 pg. insert & animation style print; r/Amazing Spider-Man #14 (1st Green Goblin) 5.00

SPIDER-MAN COLLECTOR'S PREVIEW
Marvel Comics: Dec, 1994 ($1.50, 100 pgs., one-shot)

1-wraparound-c; no comics 4.00

SPIDER-MAN COMICS MAGAZINE
Marvel Comics Group: Jan, 1987 - No. 13, 1988 ($1.50, digest-size)

1-13-Reprints 1 3 4 6 8 10

SPIDER-MAN/DEADPOOL
Marvel Comics: Mar, 2016 - No. 50, Jul, 2019 ($3.99)

1-49: 1-Joe Kelly-s/Ed McGuinness-a; back-up reprint of Vision #1. 6-Aukerman-s. 7-Art in 1968 Ditko-style by Koblish. 8-New black Spidey suit. 11-Penn Jillette-s. 16-Dracula app. 17,18-McGuinness-a. 19,20-Slapstick app. 23-25,27,28-Bachalo-a. 48,49-Gwenpool app. 4.00
50-($4.99) Last issue; Gwenpool app. 5.00
#1.MU (3/17, $4.99) Corin-s/Walker-a/Dave Johnson-c 5.00

SPIDER-MAN: DEATH AND DESTINY
Marvel Comics: Aug, 2000 - No. 3, Oct, 2000 ($2.99, limited series)

1-3-Aftermath of the death of Capt. Stacy 3.00

SPIDER-MAN/ DOCTOR OCTOPUS: OUT OF REACH
Marvel Comics: Jan, 2004 - No. 5, May, 2004 ($2.99, limited series)

1-5: 1-Keron Grant-a/Colin Mitchell-s 3.00
Marvel Age... TPB (2004, $5.99, digest size) r/#1-5 6.00

SPIDER-MAN/ DOCTOR OCTOPUS: YEAR ONE
Marvel Comics: Aug, 2004 - No. 5, Dec, 2004 ($2.99, limited series)

1-5-Kaare Andrews-a/Zeb Wells-s 3.00

SPIDER-MAN: ENTER THE SPIDER-VERSE
Marvel Comics: Jan, 2019 ($4.99, one-shot)

1-Web-Warriors and Sinister Six app.; Macchio-s/Flaviano-a; r/Spider-Man #1 (2016) 5.00

SPIDER-MAN FAIRY TALES
Marvel Comics: July, 2007 - No. 4, Oct, 2007 ($2.99, limited series)

1-4: 1-Cebulski-s/Tercio-a. 2-Henrichon-a. 3-Kobayashi-a. 4-Dragotta-p/Allred-i 3.00
TPB (2007, $10.99) r/#1-4 11.00

SPIDER-MAN FAMILY (Also see Amazing Spider-Man Family)
Marvel Comics: Apr, 2007 - No. 9, Aug, 2008 ($4.99, anthology)

1-9-New tales and reprints. 1-Black costume, Sandman, Black Cat app. 4-Agents of Atlas app., Kirk-a; Puppet Master by Eliopoulos. 8-Iron Man app. 9-Hulk app. 5.00
... Featuring Spider-Clan 1 (1/07, $4.99) new Spider-Clan story; reprints w/Spider-Man 2099 and Amazing Spider-Man #252 (black costume) 5.00
... Featuring Spider-Man's Amazing Friends 1 (10/06, $4.99) new story with Iceman and Firestar; Mini Marvels w/Giarrusso-a; reprints w/Spider-Man 2099 5.00
...: Back In Black (2007, $7.99, digest) r/new content from #1-3 8.00
...: Untold Team-Ups (2008, $9.99, digest) r/new content from #4-6 10.00

SPIDER-MAN/FANTASTIC FOUR (Spider-Man and the Fantastic Four on cover)
Marvel Comics: Sept, 2010 - No. 4, Dec, 2010 ($3.99, limited series)

1-4-Gage-s/Alberti-a; Dr. Doom app. 4.00

SPIDER-MAN: FAR FROM HOME PRELUDE
Marvel Comics: May, 2019 - No. 2, Jun, 2019 ($3.99, limited series)

1,2-Adaptation of Spider-Man: Homecoming movie; Pilgrim-s/Maresca-a; photo-c 4.00

SPIDER-MAN: FEVER
Marvel Comics: Jun, 2010 - No. 3, Aug, 2010 ($3.99, limited series)

1-3-Brendan McCarthy-s/a; Dr. Strange app. 4.00

SPIDER-MAN: FRIENDS AND ENEMIES
Marvel Comics: Jan, 1995 - No. 4, Apr, 1995 ($1.95, limited series)

1-4-Darkhawk, Nova & Speedball app. 4.00

SPIDER-MAN: FUNERAL FOR AN OCTOPUS
Marvel Comics: Mar, 1995 - No. 3, May, 1995 ($1.50, limited series)

1-3 4.00

SPIDER-MAN/ GEN 13
Marvel Comics: Nov, 1996 ($4.95, one-shot)

nn-Peter David-s/Stuart Immonen-a 5.00

SPIDER-MAN: GET KRAVEN
Marvel Comics: Aug, 2002 - No. 6, Jan, 2003 ($2.99/$2.25, limited series)

1-($2.99) McCrea-a/Quesada-c; back-up story w/Rio-a 4.00
2-6-($2.25) 2-Sub-Mariner app. 3.00

SPIDER-MAN: HOBGOBLIN LIVES
Marvel Comics: Jan, 1997 - No. 3, Mar, 1997 ($2.50, limited series)

1-3-Wraparound-c 4.00
TPB (1/98, $14.99) r/#1-3 plus timeline 15.00

SPIDER-MAN: HOUSE OF M (Also see House of M and related x-overs)
Marvel Comics: Aug, 2005 - No. 5, Dec, 2005 ($2.99, limited series)

1-5-Waid & Peyer-s/Larroca-a; rich and famous Peter Parker in mutant-ruled world 3.00
House of M: Spider-Man TPB (2006, $13.99) r/series 14.00

SPIDER-MAN/ HUMAN TORCH
Marvel Comics: Mar, 2005 - No. 5, July, 2005 ($2.99, limited series)

1-5-Ty Templeton-a/Dan Slott-s; team-ups from early days to the present 3.00
...: I'm With Stupid (2006, $7.99, digest) r/#1-5 8.00

SPIDER-MAN: INDIA
Marvel Comics: Jan, 2005 - No. 4, Apr, 2005 ($2.99, limited series)

1-4-Pavitr Prabhakar gains spider powers; Kang-a/Seetharaman-s 3.00

SPIDER-MAN: LEGEND OF THE SPIDER-CLAN (See Marvel Mangaverse for TPB)
Marvel Comics: Dec, 2002 - No. 5, Apr, 2003 ($2.25, limited series)

1-5-Marvel Mangaverse Spider-Man; Kaare Andrews-s/Skottie Young-c/a 3.00

SPIDER-MAN: LIFELINE
Marvel Comics: Apr, 2001 - No. 3, June, 2001 ($2.99, limited series)

1-3-Nicieza-s/Rude-c/a; The Lizard app. 3.00

SPIDER-MAN: LIFE STORY
Marvel Comics: May, 2019 - No. 6, Oct, 2019 ($4.99, limited series)

1-6-The 1962 Spider-Man ages in real time; Zdarsky-s/Bagley-a. 2-The '70s. 3-The '80s; Venom app. 5-Morlun app.; Civil War. 6-The 2010s; Venom/Kraven & Miles app. 5.00
Annual 1 (10/21, $4.99) Zdarsky-s/Bagley-a; spotlght on Jameson; Scorpion app. 5.00

SPIDER-MAN LOVES MARY JANE (Also see Mary Jane limited series)
Marvel Comics: Feb, 2006 - No. 20, Sept, 2007 ($2.99)

1-20-Mary Jane & Peter in high school; McKeever-s/Miyazawa-a/c. 5-Gwen Stacy app. 16-18,20-Firestar app. 17-Felicia Hardy app. 3.00
... Vol. 1: Super Crush (2006, $7.99, digest) r/#1-5; cover concepts page 8.00
... Vol. 2: The New Girl (2006, $7.99, digest) r/#6-10; sketch pages 8.00
... Vol. 3: My Secret Life (2007, $7.99, digest) r/#11-15; sketch pages 8.00
... Vol. 4: Still Friends (2007, $7.99, digest) r/#16-20 8.00
Hardcover Vol. 1 (2007, $24.99) oversized reprints of #1-5, Mary Jane #1-4 and Mary Jane: Homecoming #1-4; series proposals, sketch pages and covers; coloring process 25.00
Hardcover Vol. 2 (2008, $39.99) oversized reprints of #6-20, sketch & layout pages 40.00

SPIDER-MAN LOVES MARY JANE SEASON 2
Marvel Comics: Oct, 2008 - No. 5, Feb, 2009 ($2.99, limited series)

1-5-Terry Moore-s/c; Craig Rousseau-a 3.00
1-Variant-c by Alphona 8.00

Spider-Man / Deadpool #8 © MAR

Spider-Man Loves Mary Jane #10 © MAR

Spider-Man / Red Sonja #5 © MAR & RS LLC

	GD 2.0	VG 4.0	FN 6.0	VF 8.0	VF/NM 9.0	NM- 9.2

SPIDER-MAN: MADE MEN
Marvel Comics: Aug, 1998 ($5.99, one-shot)
1-Spider-Man & Daredevil vs. Kingpin 6.00

SPIDER-MAN MAGAZINE
Marvel Comics: 1994 - No. 3, 1994 ($1.95, magazine)
1-3: 1-Contains 4 S-M promo cards & 4 X-Men Ultra Fleer cards; Spider-Man story by Romita, Sr.; X-Men story; puzzles & games. 2-Doc Octopus & X-Men stories 4.00

SPIDER-MAN: MAXIMUM CLONAGE
Marvel Comics: 1995 ($4.95)
Alpha #1-Acetate-c, Omega #1-Chromium-c. 6.00

SPIDER-MAN MEGAZINE
Marvel Comics: Oct, 1994 - No. 6, Mar, 1995 ($2.95, 100 pgs.)
1-6: 1-r/ASM #16,224,225, Marvel Team-Up #1 5.00

SPIDER-MAN NOIR
Marvel Comics: Dec, 2008 - No. 4, May, 2009 ($3.99, limited series)
1-4-Pulp-style Spider-Man in 1933; DiGiandomenico-a; covers by Zircher & Calero 4.00
...: Eyes Without a Face 1-4 (2/10 - No. 4, 5/10) DiGiandomenico-a; Zircher & Calero-c 4.00

SPIDER-MAN NOIR
Marvel Comics: May, 2020 - No. 5, Dec, 2020 ($3.99, limited series)
1-5-Pulp-style Spider-Man in 1939; Stohl-s/Ferreyra-a 4.00

SPIDER-MAN: POWER OF TERROR
Marvel Comics: Jan, 1995 - No. 4, Apr, 1995 ($1.95, limited series)
1-4-Silvermane & Deathlok app. 4.00

SPIDER-MAN/PUNISHER: FAMILY PLOT
Marvel Comics: Feb, 1996 - No. 2, Mar, 1996 ($2.95, limited series)
1,2 4.00

SPIDER-MAN: QUALITY OF LIFE
Marvel Comics: Jul, 2002 - No. 4, Oct, 2002 ($2.99, limited series)
1-4-All CGI art by Scott Sava; Rucka-s; Lizard app. 3.00
TPB (2002, $12.99) r/#1-4; a "Making of..." section detailing the CGI process 13.00

SPIDER-MAN: REDEMPTION
Marvel Comics: Sept, 1996 - No. 4, Dec, 1996 ($1.50, limited series)
1-4: DeMatteis scripts; Zeck-a 4.00

SPIDER-MAN/ RED SONJA
Marvel Comics: Oct, 2007 - No. 5, Feb, 2008 ($2.99, limited series)
1-5-Rubi-a/Oeming-s/Turner-c; Venom & Kulan Gath app. 3.00
HC (2008, $19.99, dustjacket) r/#1-5 and Marvel Team-Up #79; sketch pages 20.00

SPIDER-MAN: REIGN
Marvel Comics: Feb, 2007 - No. 4, May, 2007 ($3.99, limited series)
1-Kaare Andrews-s/a; red costume on cover 4.00
1-Variant cover with black costume 10.00
2-4 4.00
HC (2007, $19.99, dustjacket) r/#1-4; sketch pages and cover variant gallery 20.00
HC 2nd printing (2007, $19.99, dustjacket) with variant black cover 20.00
SC (2008, $14.99) r/#1-4; sketch pages and cover variant gallery 15.00

SPIDER-MAN: REVENGE OF THE GREEN GOBLIN
Marvel Comics: Oct, 2000 - No. 3, Dec, 2000 ($2.99, limited series)
1-3-Frenz & Olliffe-a; continues in AS-M #25 & PP:S-M #25 3.00

SPIDER-MAN SAGA
Marvel Comics: Nov, 1991 - No. 4, Feb, 1992 ($2.95, limited series)
1-4: Gives history of Spider-Man: text & illustrations 4.00

SPIDER-MAN 1602
Marvel Comics: Dec, 2009 - No. 5, Apr, 2010 ($3.99, limited series)
1-5- Peter Parquagh from Marvel 1602; Parker-s/Rosanas-a 4.00

SPIDER-MAN: SPIDER'S SHADOW (See Spider-Man: The Spider's Shadow)

SPIDER-MAN: SWEET CHARITY
Marvel Comics: Aug, 2002 ($4.95, one-shot)
1-The Scorpion-c/app.; Campbell-c/Zimmerman-s/Robertson-a 5.00

SPIDER-MAN'S TANGLED WEB (Titled **"Tangled Web"** in indicia for #1-4)
Marvel Comics: Jun, 2001 - No. 22, Mar, 2003 ($2.99)
1-3: "The Thousand" on-c; Ennis-s/McCrea-a/Fabry-c 4.00
4-"Severance Package" on-c; Rucka-s/Risso-a; Kingpin-c/app. 5.00
5,6-Flowers for Rhino; Milligan-s/Fegredo-a 3.00
7-10,12,15-20,22: 7-9-Gentlemen's Agreement; Bruce Jones-s/Lee Weeks-a. 10-Andrews-s/a. 12-Fegredo-a. 15-Paul Pope-s/a. 18-Ted McKeever-s/a. 19-Mahfood-a. 20-Haspiel-a 3.00
11,13,21-($3.50) 11-Darwyn Cooke-s/a. 13-Phillips-a. 21-Christmas-s by Cooke & Bone 4.00
14-Azzarello & Scott Levy (WWE's Raven)-s about Crusher Hogan 4.00
TPB (10/01, $15.95) r/#1-6 16.00
Volume 2 TPB (4/02, $14.95) r/#7-11 15.00
Volume 3 TPB (2002, $15.99) r/#12-17; Jason Pearson-c 16.00
Volume 4 TPB (2003, $15.99) r/#18-22; Frank Cho-c 16.00

SPIDER-MAN TEAM-UP
Marvel Comics: Dec, 1995 - No. 7, June, 1996 ($2.95)
1-7: 1-w/ X-Men. 2-w/Silver Surfer. 3-w/Fantastic Four. 4-w/Avengers. 5-Gambit & Howard the Duck-c/app. 7-Thunderbolts-c/app. 4.00
... Special 1 (5/05, $2.99) Fantastic Four app.; Todd Dezago-s/Shane Davis-a 4.00

SPIDER-MAN: THE ARACHNIS PROJECT
Marvel Comics: Aug, 1994 - No. 6, Jan, 1995 ($1.75, limited series)
1-6-Venom, Styx, Stone & Jury app. 4.00

SPIDER-MAN: THE CLONE JOURNAL
Marvel Comics: Mar, 1995 ($2.95, one-shot)
1 4.00

SPIDER-MAN: THE CLONE SAGA
Marvel Comics: Nov, 2009 - No. 6, Apr, 2010 ($3.99, limited series)
1-6-Retelling of the saga with different ending; DeFalco & Mackie-s/Nauck-a 4.00

SPIDER-MAN: THE FINAL ADVENTURE
Marvel Comics: Nov, 1995 - No. 4, Feb, 1996 ($2.95, limited series)
1-4: 1-Nicieza scripts; foil-c 4.00

SPIDER-MAN: THE JACKAL FILES
Marvel Comics: Aug, 1995 ($1.95, one-shot)
1 4.00

SPIDER-MAN: THE LOST HUNT
Marvel Comics: Jan, 2023 - Present ($4.99/$3.99)
1-($4.99) DeMatteis-s/Messias-a 5.00
2-4-($3.99) 4-Origin of Gregor the Hunter 4.00

SPIDER-MAN: THE LOST YEARS
Marvel Comics: Aug, 1995-No. 3, Oct, 1995; No. 0, 1996 ($2.95/$3.95,lim. series)
0-(1/96, $3.95)-Reprints. 5.00
1-3-DeMatteis scripts, Romita, Jr.-c/a 4.00
NOTE: ***Romita** c-0i. **Romita, Jr.** a-0r, 1-3p. c-0-3p. **Sharp** a-0r.*

SPIDER-MAN: THE MANGA
Marvel Comics: Dec, 1997 - No. 31, June, 1999 ($3.99/$2.99, B&W, bi-weekly)
1-($3.99)-English translation of Japanese Spider-Man 5.00
2-31-($2.99) 4.00

SPIDER-MAN: THE MUTANT AGENDA
Marvel Comics: No. 0, Feb, 1994; No. 1, Mar, 1994 - No. 3, May, 1994 ($1.75, limited series)
0-(2/94, $1.25, 52 pgs.)-Crosses over w/newspaper strip; has empty pages to paste in newspaper strips; gives origin of Spidey 5.00
1-3: Beast & Hobgoblin app. 1-X-Men app. 4.00

SPIDER-MAN: THE MYSTERIO MANIFESTO (Listed as "Spider-Man and Mysterio" in indicia)
Marvel Comics: Jan, 2001 - No. 3, Mar, 2001 ($2.99, limited series)
1-3-Daredevil-c/app.; Weeks & McLeod-a 3.00

SPIDER-MAN: THE PARKER YEARS
Marvel Comics: Nov, 1995 ($2.50, one-shot)
1 4.00

SPIDER-MAN: THE SPIDER'S SHADOW
Marvel Comics: Jun, 2021 - No. 5, Oct, 2021 ($4.99/$3.99, limited series)
1-($4.99) What If..Spider-Man kept the Venom suit; Zdarsky-s/Ferry-a 5.00
2-5-($3.99) 2-Sinister Six & Eddie Brock app. 4,5-Avengers & FF app. 4.00

SPIDER-MAN 2: THE MOVIE
Marvel Comics: Aug, 2004 ($3.50/$12.99, one-shot)
1-($3.50) Movie adaptation; Johnson, Lim & Olliffe-a 4.00
TPB-($12.99) Movie adaptation; r/Amazing Spider-Man #50, Ultimate Spider-Man #14,15 13.00

SPIDER-MAN 2099 (See Amazing Spider-Man #365)
Marvel Comics: Nov, 1992 - No. 46, Aug, 1996 ($1.25/$1.50/$1.95)
1-(stiff-c)-Red foil stamped-c; begins origin of Miguel O'Hara (Spider-Man 2099); Leonardi/Williamson-c/a begins 1 3 4 6 8 10
1-2nd printing, 2-12,14-24,26-34,39,40: 2-Origin continued, ends #3. 4-Doom 2099 app.

19-Bound-in trading cards. 3.00
13-Extra 16 pg. insert on Midnight Sons 4.00
25-($2.25, 52 pgs.)-Newsstand edition 4.00
25-($2.95, 52 pgs.)-Deluxe edition w/embossed foil-c 5.00
35-38-Venom app. 35-Variant-c. 36-Two-c; Jae Lee-a. 37,38-Two-c 5.00
41-46: 46-The Vulture app; Mike McKone-a(p) 3.00
Annual 1 (1994, $2.95, 68 pgs.) 5.00
Special 1 (1995, $3.95) 5.00
NOTE: ***Chaykin*** *c-37.* ***Ron Lim*** *a(p)-18; c(p)-13, 16, 18.* ***Kelley Jones*** *c/a-9.* ***Leonardi/Williamson*** *a-1-8, 10-13, 15-17, 19, 20, 22-25; c-1-13, 15, 17-19, 20, 22-25, 35.*

SPIDER-MAN 2099
Marvel Comics: Sept, 2014 - No. 12, Jul, 2015 ($3.99)
1-12: 1-Miguel O'Hara in 2014; Peter David-s/Will Sliney-a. 5-8-Spider-Verse tie-in 4.00

SPIDER-MAN 2099
Marvel Comics: Dec, 2015 - No. 25, Sept, 2017 ($3.99)
1-24: 1-Miguel O'Hara still in the present; David-s/Sliney-a. 2-New costume. 13-16-Civil War II tie-ins. 14-16-Power Pack app. 17-19-Elektra app. 4.00
25-($4.99) David-s/Sliney-a 5.00

SPIDER-MAN 2099 (Tie-in to 2099 Alpha & 2099 Omega crossover)
Marvel Comics: Feb, 2020 ($4.99)
1-Spencer-s/Carlos-a 5.00

SPIDER-MAN 2099: EXODUS
Marvel Comics: Jul, 2022 - Oct, 2022 ($4.99/$3.99, limited series)
Alpha 1-($4.99) Ghost Rider 2099 app. 5.00
1-5-($3.99) 1-Winter Soldier 2099 app. 2-Loki 2099 app. 4-Black Widow 2099 app. 4.00
Omega 1-($4.99) Conclusion to series; Avengers app. 5.00

SPIDER-MAN 2099 MEETS SPIDER-MAN
Marvel Comics: 1995 ($5.95, one-shot)
nn-Peter David script; Leonardi/Williamson-c/a. 6.00

SPIDER-MAN UNIVERSE
Marvel Comics: Mar, 2000 - No. 7, Oct, 2000 ($4.95/$3.99, reprints)
1-5-Reprints recent issues from the various Spider-Man titles 5.00
6,7-($3.99) 4.00

SPIDER-MAN UNLIMITED
Marvel Comics: May, 1993 - No. 22, Nov, 1998 ($3.95, #1-12 were quarterly, 68 pgs.)
1-Begin Maximum Carnage storyline, ends; Carnage-c/story 2 4 6 9 12 15
2-12: 2-Venom & Carnage-c/story; Lim-c/a(p) in #2-6. 10-Vulture app. 4.00
13-22: 13-Begin $2.99-c; Scorpion-c/app. 15-Daniel-c; Puma-c/app. 19-Lizard-c/app. 20-Hannibal King and Lilith app. 21,22-Deodato-a 4.00

SPIDER-MAN UNLIMITED (Based on the TV animated series)
Marvel Comics: Dec, 1999 - No. 5, Apr, 2000 ($2.99/$1.99)
1-($2.99) Venom and Carnage app. 5.00
2-5: 2-($1.99) Green Goblin app. 4.00

SPIDER-MAN UNLIMITED (3rd series)
Marvel Comics: Mar, 2004 - No. 15, July, 2006 ($2.99)
1-16: 1-Short stories by various incl. Miyazawa & Chen-a. 2-Mays-a. 6-Allred-c. 14-Finch-c/a; Black Cat app. 3.00

SPIDER-MAN UNMASKED
Marvel Comics: Nov, 1996 ($5.95, one-shot)
nn-Art w/text 6.00

SPIDER-MAN: VENOM AGENDA
Marvel Comics: Jan, 1998 ($2.99, one-shot)
1-Hama-s/Lyle-c/a 5.00

SPIDER-MAN VS. DRACULA
Marvel Comics: Jan, 1994 ($1.75, 52 pgs., one-shot)
1-r/Giant-Size Spider-Man #1 plus new Matt Fox-a 4.00

SPIDER-MAN VS. WOLVERINE
Marvel Comics Group: Feb, 1987; V2#1, 1990 (68 pgs.)
1-Williamson-c/a(i); intro Charlemagne; death of Ned Leeds (old Hobgoblin) 3 6 9 21 33 45
V2#1 (1990, $4.95)-Reprints #1 (2/87) 6.00

SPIDER-MAN: WEB OF DOOM
Marvel Comics: Aug, 1994 - No. 3, Oct, 1994 ($1.75, limited series)
1-3 4.00

SPIDER-MAN: WITH GREAT POWER...
Marvel Comics: Mar, 2008 - No. 5, Sept, 2008 ($3.99, limited series)
1-5-Origin and early days re-told; Lapham-s/Harris-a/c 4.00

SPIDER-MAN: WITH GREAT POWER COMES GREAT RESPONSIBILITY
Marvel Comics: Jun, 2011 - No. 7, Dec, 2011 ($3.99, limited series)
1-7: Reprints of noteworthy Spider-Man stories. 1-R/Ultimate Spider-Man #33,97, and Ultimate Comics Spider-Man #1. 4-R/ Amazing Spider-Man #1,11,20 4.00

SPIDER-MAN: YEAR IN REVIEW
Marvel Comics: Feb, 2000 ($2.99)
1-Text recaps of 1999 issues 3.00

SPIDER-MEN
Marvel Comics: Aug, 2012 - No. 5, Nov, 2012 ($3.99, limited series)
1-5-Peter Parker goes to Ultimate Universe; teams with Miles Morales; Pichelli-a 4.00

SPIDER-MEN II
Marvel Comics: Sept, 2017 - No. 5, Feb, 2018 ($3.99, limited series)
1-5-Peter Parker teams with Miles Morales; Bendis-s/Pichelli-a 4.00

SPIDER-PUNK (Hobie Brown)
Marvel Comics: Jun, 2022 - No. 5, Nov, 2022 ($3.99, limited series)
1-5-Cody Ziglar-s/Justin Mason-a 4.00

SPIDER REIGN OF THE VAMPIRE KING, THE (Also see The Spider)
Eclipse Books: 1992 - No. 3, 1992 ($4.95, limited series, coated stock, 52 pgs.)
Book One - Three: Truman scripts & painted-c 5.00

SPIDER'S WEB, THE (See G-8 and His Battle Aces)

SPIDER-VARK
Aardvark-Vanaheim: Aug, 2020 ($8.00, B&W, one-shot)
1-Cerebus figures w/Doré artwork of Hell; cover swipe of Amazing Spider-Man Annual #21 8.00

SPIDER-VERSE (See Amazing Spider-Man 2014 series #7-14)
Marvel Comics: Jan, 2015 - No. 2, Mar, 2015 ($4.99, limited series)
1,2-Short stories of alternate Spider-Men; s/a by various. 2-Anarchic Spider-Man 5.00

SPIDER-VERSE (Secret Wars tie-in)
Marvel Comics: Jul, 2015 - No. 5, Nov, 2015 ($4.99/$3.99, limited series)
1-($4.99) Costa-s/Araujo-a; Spider-Gwen, Spider-Ham & Norman Osborn app. 5.00
2-5-($3.99) Alternate Spider-Men vs. Sinister Six 4.00

SPIDER-VERSE (Secret Wars tie-in)
Marvel Comics: Dec, 2019 - No. 6, May, 2020 ($3.99, limited series)
1-6: Miles teams up with Spider-heroes. 4-Killam-s/Gedeon-a. 5-Spider-Man Noir app. 4.00

SPIDER-VERSE TEAM-UP (See Amazing Spider-Man 2014 series #7-14)
Marvel Comics: Jan, 2015 - No. 3, Mar, 2015 ($3.99, limited series)
1-3-Short stories of alternate Spider-Men team-ups; s/a by various. 2-Spider-Gwen, Miles Morales and '67 animated Spider-Man app. 4.00

SPIDER-WHORE
Aardvark-Vanaheim: Nov, 2020 ($4.00, B&W, one-shot)
1-Cerebus figures with Gustave Doré artwork of Hell; cover swipe of What If #105 1 3 4 6 8 10

SPIDER-WOMAN (Also see The Avengers #240, Marvel Spotlight #32, Marvel Super Heroes Secret Wars #7, Marvel Two-In-One #29 and New Avengers)
Marvel Comics Group: April, 1978 - No. 50, June, 1983 (New logo #47 on)
1-New complete origin & mask added 5 10 15 34 60 85
2-5,7-18: 2-Excalibur app. 3,11,12-Brother Grimm app. 13,15-The Shroud-c/s. 16-Sienkiewicz-c 1 2 3 5 6 8
6,19,20,28,29,32: 6-Morgan LeFay app. 6,19,32-Werewolf by Night-c/s. 20,28,29-Spider-Man app. 32-Universal Monsters photo/Miller-c 1 3 4 6 8 10
21-27,30,31,33-36 1 2 3 5 6 8
37-1st app. Siryn of X-Force; X-Men x-over; origin retold 4 8 12 25 40 55
38-X-Men x-over 2 4 6 11 16 20
39-49: 46-Kingpin app. 49-Tigra-c/story 6.00
50-(52 pgs.)-Death of Spider-Woman; photo-c 2 4 6 11 16 20
... No. 1 Facsimile Edition (11/19, $3.99) Reprints #1 with original 1978 ads
NOTE: ***Austin*** *a-37i.* ***Byrne*** *c-26p.* ***Infantino*** *a-1-19.* ***Layton*** *c-19.* ***Miller*** *c-32p.*

SPIDER-WOMAN
Marvel Comics: Nov, 1993 - No. 4, Feb, 1994 ($1.75, mini-series)
V2#1-Origin; U.S. Agent app. 2 4 6 8 10 12
V2#2-4: 2-Origin continues; U.S. Agent app. 4.00

SPIDER-WOMAN
Marvel Comics: July, 1999 - No. 18, Dec, 2000 ($2.99/$1.99/$2.25)
1-($2.99) Byrne-s/Sears-a 2 4 6 11 16 20
2-18: 2-11-($1.99). 2-Two covers. 12-Begin $2.25-c. 15-Capt. America-c/app. 4.00

SPIDER-WOMAN (Printed version of the motion comic for computers)
Marvel Comics: Nov, 2009 - No. 7, May, 2010 ($3.99/$2.99)
1-($3.99) Bendis-s/Maleev-a; covers by Maleev & Alex Ross; Jessica joins S.W.O.R.D. 1 3 4 6 8 10
2-6-($2.99) 2-4-Madame Hydra app. 6-Thunderbolts app. 3.00
7-($3.99) New Avengers app. 4.00

SPIDER-WOMAN (Also see Spider-Verse event in Amazing Spider-Man 2014 series #7-14)
Marvel Comics: Jan, 2015 - No. 10, Oct, 2015 ($3.99)
1-4-Spider-Verse tie-ins; Silk app.; Hopeless-s/Land-a/c. 4-Avengers app. 4.00
5-10: 5-New costume; Javier Rodriguez-a/c. 10-Black Widow app. 4.00

SPIDER-WOMAN
Marvel Comics: Jan, 2016 - No. 17, May, 2017 ($3.99)
1-17: 1-5-Hopeless-s/Javier Rodriguez-a. 4-Jessica's baby is born. 6,7-"Spider-Women x-over; Spider-Gwen & Silk app.; Joelle Jones-a. 9-11-Civil War II tie-in. 13-16-Hobgoblin app. 4.00

SPIDER-WOMAN
Marvel Comics: May, 2020 - No. 21, May, 2022 ($4.99/$3.99)
1-($4.99) Karla Pacheco-s/Pere Pérez-a; new costume debuts; Siqueira-a 5.00
2-4,6-21-($3.99) 2-Night Nurse & Rhino app. 6-Capt. Marvel app. 7,8-King in Black tie-in. 11-Back to classic costume. 18,19-Devil's Reign 4.00
5-($4.99) Legacy issue #100; back-up story with Captain Marvel app. 5.00

SPIDER-WOMAN: ORIGIN (Also see New Avengers)
Marvel Comics: Feb, 2006 - No. 5, June, 2006 ($2.99, limited series)
1-5-Bendis & Reed-s/Jonathan & Joshua Luna-a/c 3.00
1-Variant cover by Olivier Coipel 3.00
HC (2006, $19.99) r/series 20.00
SC (2007, $13.99) r/series 14.00

SPIDER-WOMEN (Crossover with Silk, Spider-Gwen and Spider-Woman)
Marvel Comics: Alpha, Jun, 2016 - Omega, Aug, 2016 ($4.99, limited series)
... Alpha 1 - Thompson-s/Del Rey-a/Putri-c; part 1 of x-over; intro. Earth-65 Cindy Moon 5.00
... Omega 1 - Hopeless-s/Leon-a/Putri-c; part 8 conclusion of x-over 5.00

SPIDEY (Spider-Man)
Marvel Comics: Feb, 2016 - No. 12, Jan, 2017 ($3.99)
1-12-High school-era Spider-Man. 1-3-Bradshaw-a. 1-Doc Ock app. 7-Black Panther app. 4.00
... No. 1 Halloween Comic Fest 2016 (12/16, giveaway) r/#1 3.00

SPIDEY SUPER STORIES (Spider-Man) (Also see Fireside Books)
Marvel/Children's TV Workshop: Oct, 1974 - No. 57, Mar, 1982 (35¢, no ads)

Spider-Man 2099 (2014) #1 © MAR

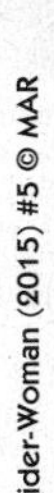
Spider-Woman (2015) #5 © MAR

The Spirit (2007) #4 © Will Eisner Studios

	GD 2.0	VG 4.0	FN 6.0	VF 8.0	VF/NM 9.0	NM- 9.2
1-Origin (stories simplified for younger readers)	7	14	21	49	92	135
2-Kraven	3	6	9	21	33	45
3-10,15: 6-Iceman. 15-Storm-c/sty	3	6	9	14	20	26
11-14,16-20: 19,20-Kirby-c	3	6	9	14	19	24
21-30: 22-Early Ms. Marvel app.	2	4	6	13	18	22
31-53: 31-Moondragon-c/app.; Dr. Doom app. 33-Hulk. 34-Sub-Mariner. 38-F.F. 39-Thanos-c/story. 44-Vision. 45-Silver Surfer & Dr. Doom app.	2	4	6	11	16	20
54-57: 56-Battles Jack O'Lantern-c/sty (exactly one year after 1st app. in Machine Man #19)	3	6	9	14	20	26

SPIKE AND TYKE (See M.G.M.'s...)

SPIKE... (Also see Buffy the Vampire Slayer and related titles)
IDW Publ.: Aug, 2005; Jan, 2006; Apr, 2006 ($7.49, squarebound, one-shots)

...: Lost & Found (4/06, $7.49) Scott Tipton-s/Fernando Goni-a 8.00
...: Old Times (8/05, $7.49) Peter David-s/Fernando Goni-a; Cecily/Halfrek app. 8.00
...: Old Wounds (1/06, $7.49) Tipton-s/Goni-a; flashback to Black Dahlia murder case 8.00
TPB (7/06, $19.99) r/one-shots 20.00

SPIKE (Buffy the Vampire Slayer)
IDW Publ.: Oct, 2010 - No. 8, May, 2011 ($3.99, limited series)

1-8-Lynch-s; multiple covers on each. 1,2-Urru-a. 5-7-Willow app. 4.00
... 100 Page Spectacular (6/11, $7.99) reprints of four IDW Spike stories; Frison-c 8.00

SPIKE (A Dark Place) (From Buffy the Vampire Slayer)
Dark Horse Comics: Aug, 2012 - No. 5, Dec, 2012 ($2.99, limited series)

1-5-Paul Lee-a; 2 covers by Frison & Morris on each 3.00

SPIKE: AFTER THE FALL (Also see Angel: After the Fall) (Follows the last Angel TV episode)
IDW Publ.: July, 2008 - No. 4, Oct, 2008 ($3.99, limited series)

1-4-Lynch-s/Urru-a; multiple covers on each 4.00

SPIKE: ASYLUM (Buffy the Vampire Slayer)
IDW Publ.: Sept, 2006 - No. 5, Jan, 2007 ($3.99, limited series)

1-5-Lynch-s/Urru-a; multiple covers on each 4.00

SPIKE: SHADOW PUPPETS (Buffy the Vampire Slayer)
IDW Publ.: June, 2007 - No. 4, Sept, 2007 ($3.99, limited series)

1-4-Lynch-s/Urru-a; multiple covers on each 4.00

SPIKE: THE DEVIL YOU KNOW (Buffy the Vampire Slayer)
IDW Publ.: Jun, 2010 - No. 4, Sept, 2010 ($3.99, limited series)

1-4-Bill Williams-s/Chris Cross-a/Urru-c 4.00

SPIKE VS. DRACULA (Buffy the Vampire Slayer)
IDW Publ.: Feb, 2006 - No. 5, Mar, 2006 ($3.99, limited series)

1-5: 1-Peter David-s/Joe Corroney-a; Dru and Bela Lugosi app. 4.00

SPIN & MARTY (TV) (Walt Disney's)(See Walt Disney Showcase #32)
Dell Publishing Co. (Mickey Mouse Club): No. 714, June, 1956 - No. 1082, Mar-May, 1960 (All photo-c)

	GD 2.0	VG 4.0	FN 6.0	VF 8.0	VF/NM 9.0	NM- 9.2
Four Color 714 (#1)	11	22	33	75	160	245
Four Color 767,808 (#2,3)	9	18	27	58	114	170
Four Color 826 (#4)-Annette Funicello photo-c	18	36	54	126	281	435
5(3-5/58) - 9(6-8/59)	7	14	21	44	82	120
Four Color 1026,1082	7	14	21	44	82	120

SPIN ANGELS
Marvel Comics (Soleil): 2009 - No. 4, 2009 ($5.99)

1-4-English version of French comics; Jean-Luc Sala-s/Pierre-Mony Chan-a 6.00

SPINE-TINGLING TALES (Doctor Spektor Presents...)
Gold Key: May, 1975 - No. 4, Jan, 1976 (All 25¢ issues)

	GD 2.0	VG 4.0	FN 6.0	VF 8.0	VF/NM 9.0	NM- 9.2
1-1st Tragg-r/Mystery Comics Digest #3	3	6	9	14	19	24
2-4: 2-Origin Ra-Ka-Tep-r/Mystery Comics Digest #1; Dr. Spektor #12. 3-All Durak-r issue; 4-Baron Tibor's 1st app.-r/Mystery Comics Digest #4; painted-c	1	2	3	5	7	9

SPINWORLD
Amaze Ink (Slave Labor Graphics): July, 1997 - No. 4, Jan, 1998 ($2.95/$3.95, B&W, mini-series)

1-3-Brent Anderson-a(p) 3.00
4-($3.95) 4.00

SPIRAL ZONE
DC Comics: Feb, 1988 - No. 4, May, 1988 ($1.00, mini-series)

1-4-Based on Tonka toys 3.00

SPIRIT, THE (Newspaper comics - see Promotional Comics section)

SPIRIT, THE (1st Series)(Also see Police Comics #11 and The Best of the Spirit TPB)
Quality Comics Group (Vital): 1944 - No. 22, Aug, 1950

	GD 2.0	VG 4.0	FN 6.0	VF 8.0	VF/NM 9.0	NM- 9.2
nn(#1)- "Wanted Dead or Alive"	161	322	483	1030	1765	2500
nn(#2)- "Crime Doesn't Pay"	58	116	174	371	636	900
nn(#3)- "Murder Runs Wild"	54	108	162	343	574	825
4,5: 4-Flatfoot Burns begins, ends #22. 5-Wertham app.	45	90	135	284	480	675
6-10	39	78	117	231	378	525
11-Crandall-c	39	78	117	231	378	525
12-17-Eisner-c. 19-Honeybun app.	52	104	156	328	552	775
18,19-Strip-r by Eisner; Eisner-c	71	142	213	454	777	1100
20,21-Eisner good girl covers; strip-r by Eisner	129	258	387	826	1413	2000
22-Used by N.Y. Legis. Comm; classic Eisner-c	919	1838	2757	6709	11,855	17,000
Super Reprint #11-r/Quality Spirit #19 by Eisner	3	6	9	19	30	40
Super Reprint #12-r/Spirit #17 by Fine; Sol Brodsky-c	3	6	9	19	30	40

SPIRIT, THE (2nd Series)
Fiction House Magazines: Spring, 1952 - No. 5, 1954

	GD 2.0	VG 4.0	FN 6.0	VF 8.0	VF/NM 9.0	NM- 9.2
1-Not Eisner	65	130	195	416	708	1000
2-Eisner-c/a(2)	60	120	180	381	653	925
3-Eisner/Grandenetti-c	61	122	183	390	670	950
4-Eisner/Grandenetti-c; Eisner-a	63	126	189	403	689	975
5-Eisner-c/a(4)	65	130	195	416	708	1000

SPIRIT, THE
Harvey Publications: Oct, 1966 - No. 2, Mar, 1967 (Giant Size, 25¢, 68 pgs.)

	GD 2.0	VG 4.0	FN 6.0	VF 8.0	VF/NM 9.0	NM- 9.2
1-Eisner-r plus 9 new pgs.(origin Denny Colt, Take 3, plus 2 filler pgs.) (#3 was advertised, but never published)	8	16	24	56	108	160
2-Eisner-r plus 9 new pgs.(origin of the Octopus)	7	14	21	44	82	120

SPIRIT, THE (Underground)
Kitchen Sink Enterprises (Krupp Comics): Jan, 1973 - No. 2, Sept, 1973 (Black & White)

	GD 2.0	VG 4.0	FN 6.0	VF 8.0	VF/NM 9.0	NM- 9.2
1-New Eisner-c & 4 pgs. new Eisner-a plus-r (titled Crime Convention)	4	8	12	23	37	50
2-New Eisner-c & 4 pgs. new Eisner-a plus-r (titled Meets P'Gell)	4	8	12	25	40	55

SPIRIT, THE (Magazine)
Warren Publ. Co./Krupp Comic Works No. 17 on: 4/74 - No. 16, 10/76; No. 17, Winter, 1977 - No. 41, 6/83 (B&W w/color) (#6-14,16 are squarebound)

	GD 2.0	VG 4.0	FN 6.0	VF 8.0	VF/NM 9.0	NM- 9.2
1-Eisner-r begin; 8 pg. color insert	6	12	18	41	76	110
2-5: 2-Powder Pouf-s; UFO-s. 4-Silk Satin-s	4	8	12	27	44	60
6-9,11-15: 7-All Ebony issue. 8-Female Foes issue. 8,12-Sand Seref-s. 9-P'Gell & Octopus-s. 12-X-Mas issue	4	8	12	25	40	55
10-Giant Summer Special ($1.50)-Origin	4	8	12	27	44	60
16-Giant Summer Special ($1.50)-Olga Bustle-c/s	4	8	12	25	40	55
17,18(8/78): 17-Lady Luck-r	3	6	9	17	26	35
19-21-New Eisner-a. 20,21-Wood-r (#21-r/A DP on the Moon by Wood). 20-Outer Space-r	3	6	9	17	26	35
22-41: 22,23-Wood-r (#22-r/Mission the Moon by Wood). 28-r/last story (10/5/52). 30-(7/81)-Special Spirit Jam issue w/Caniff, Corben, Bolland, Byrne, Miller, Kurtzman, Rogers, Sienkiewicz-a & 40 others. 36-Begin Spirit Section-r; r/1st story (6/2/40) in color; new Eisner-c/a(18 pgs.)($2.95). 37-r/2nd story in color plus 18 pgs. new Eisner-a. 38-41: r/3rd - 6th stories in color. 41-Lady Luck Mr. Mystic in color	3	6	9	15	22	28
Special 1(1975)-All Eisner-a (mail only, 1500 printed, full color)	13	26	39	89	195	300

NOTE: *Covers pencilled/inked by* ***Eisner*** *only #1-9,12-16; painted by Eisner & Ken Kelly #10 & 11; painted by Eisner #17-up; one color story reprinted in #1-10.* ***Austin*** *a-30i.* ***Byrne*** *a-30p.* ***Miller*** *a-30p.*

SPIRIT, THE
Kitchen Sink Enterprises: Oct, 1983 - No. 87, Jan, 1992 ($2.00, Baxter paper)

1-60: 1-Origin-r/12/23/45 Spirit Section. 2-r/ 1/20/46-2/10/46. 3-r/2/17/46-3/10/46. 4-r/3/17/46-4/7/46. 11-Last color issue. 54-r/section 2/19/50 4.00
61-87: 85-87-Reprint the Outer Space Spirit stories by Wood. 86-r/A DP on the Moon by Wood from 1952 4.00

SPIRIT, THE (Also see Batman/The Spirit in Batman one-shots)
DC Comics: Feb, 2007 - No. 32, Oct, 2009 ($2.99)

1-32: 1-6,8-12-Darwyn Cooke-s/a/c. 2-P'Gell app. 3-Origin re-told. 7-Short stories by Baker, Bernet, Palmiotti, Simonson & Sprouse; Cooke-c. 13-Short stories by various 3.00
... Femme Fatales TPB (2008, $19.99) r/1940s stories focusing on the Spirit's female adversaries like Silk Satin, P'gell, Powder Pouf and Silken Floss; Michael Uslan intro. 20.00
... Special 1 (2008, $2.99) r/stories from '47, '49, '50 newspaper strips; the Octopus app. 3.00

SPIRIT, THE (First Wave)
DC Comics: Jun, 2010 - No. 17, Oct, 2011 ($3.99/$2.99)(B&W back-up stories by various)

1-10: 1-Schultz-s/Moritat-a; covers by Ladronn and Schultz; back-up by O'Neil & Sienkiewicz. 2-Back-up by Ellison & Baker. 7-Corben-a back-up. 8-Ploog-a back-up 4.00
11-17-($2.99) 11-16-Hine-s/Moritat-a; no back-up story. 17-B&W; Bolland, Russell-a 3.00

GD VG FN VF VF/NM NM-
2.0 4.0 6.0 8.0 9.0 9.2

...: Angel Smerti TPB (2011, $17.99) r/#1-7 18.00

SPIRIT, (WILL EISNER'S THE...)
Dynamite Entertainment: 2015 - No. 12, 2016 ($3.99)

1-12: 1-Wagner-s/Schkade-a; multiple covers. 2-12-Powell-c 4.00

SPIRIT, (WILL EISNER'S THE...): CORPSE MAKERS (Volume 2)
Dynamite Entertainment: 2017 - No. 5, 2018 ($3.99)

1-5-Francesco Francavilla-s/a/c 4.00

SPIRIT JAM
Kitchen Sink Press: Aug, 1998 ($5.95, B&W, oversized, square-bound)

nn-Reprints Spirit (Magazine) #30 by Eisner & 50 others; and "Cerebus Vs. The Spirit" from Cerebus Jam #1 6.00

SPIRITMAN (Also see Three Comics)
No publisher listed: No date (1944) (10¢)(Triangle Sales Co. ad on back cover)

1-Three 16pg. Spirit sections bound together, (1944, 10¢, 52 pgs.)
37 74 111 222 361 500
2-Two Spirit sections (3/26/44, 4/2/44) bound together; by Lou Fine
32 64 96 188 307 425

SPIRIT OF THE BORDER (See Zane Grey & Four Color #197)

SPIRIT OF THE TAO
Image Comics (Top Cow): Jun, 1998 - No. 15, May, 2000 ($2.50)

Preview 5.00
1-14: 1-D-Tron-s/Tan & D-Tron-a 3.00
15-($4.95) 5.00

SPIRIT, THE: THE NEW ADVENTURES
Kitchen Sink Press: 1997 - No. 8, Nov, 1998 ($3.50, anthology)

1-Moore-s/Gibbons-c/a 4.00
2-8: 2-Gaiman-s/Eisner-c. 3-Moore-s/Bolland-c/Moebius back-c. 4-Allred-s/a; Busiek-s/Anderson-a. 5-Chadwick-s/c/a(p); Nyberg-i. 6-S.Hampton & Mandrake-a 3.50
Will Eisner's The Spirit Archives Volume 27 (Dark Horse, 2009, $49.95) r/#1-8 50.00

SPIRIT: THE ORIGIN YEARS
Kitchen Sink Press: May, 1992 - No. 10, Dec, 1993 ($2.95, B&W)

1-10: 1-r/sections 6/2/40(origin)-6/23/40 (all 1940s) 3.00

SPIRITS OF GHOST RIDER: MOTHER OF DEMONS (Story continues in Ghost Rider #5)
Marvel Comics: Apr, 2020 ($3.99, one-shot)

1-Story of Lilith; Jack O'Lantern app.; Brisson-s/Boschi-a 4.00

SPIRITS OF VENGEANCE (Marvel Legacy)
Marvel Comics: Dec, 2017 - No. 5, Apr, 2018 ($3.99)

1-5-Gischler-s/Baldeón-a; Blade, Ghost Rider, Daimon Hellstrom, Satana app. 4.00
...: Spirit Rider 1 (10/21, $4.99) Kushala and Johnny Blaze app.; Davidson-a 5.00

SPIRIT WORLD (Magazine)
Hampshire Distributors Ltd.: Fall, 1971 (B&W)

1-New Kirby-a; Neal Adams-c; poster inside 7 14 21 46 86 125
(1/2 price without poster)

SPITFIRE (Female undercover agent)
Malverne Herald (Elliot)(J. R. Mahon): No. 132, 1944 (Aug) - No. 133, 1945
Both have Classics Gift Box ads on back-c with checklist to #20

132-British spitfire WWII-c. 47 94 141 296 488 700
133-Female agent/Nazi WWII-c 314 628 942 2198 3849 5500

SPITFIRE (WW2 speedster from MI:13)
Marvel Comics: Oct, 2010 ($3.99, one-shot)

1-Cornell-s/Casagrande-a; Blade app. 4.00

SPITFIRE AND THE TROUBLESHOOTERS
Marvel Comics: Oct, 1986 - No. 9, June, 1987 (Codename: Spitfire #10 on)

1-3,5-9 3.00
4-McFarlane-a 6.00

SPITFIRE COMICS (Also see Double Up) (Tied with Pocket Comics #1 for earliest Harvey)
Harvey Publications: Aug, 1941 - No. 2, Oct, 1941 (Pocket size; 100 pgs.)

1-Origin The Clown, The Fly-Man, The Spitfire & The Magician From Bagdad; British spitfire, Nazi bomber WWII-c 123 246 369 787 1344 1900
2-(Rare) Fly-Man-c 110 220 330 704 1202 1700

SPLITTING IMAGE
Image Comics: Mar, 1993 - No. 2, 1993 ($1.95)

1,2-Simpson-c/a; parody comic 3.00
...80-Page Giant 1 (4/17, $7.99) r/#1,2 plus Normalman - Megaton Man Special 8.00

SPONGEBOB COMICS (TV's Spongebob Squarepants)
United Plankton Pictures: 2011 - No. 85, 2018 ($2.99/$3.99)

1-51-Short stories by various. 1-Kochalka back-c. 3-Aquaman homage w/Fradon-a. 32-36-Showdown at the Shady Shoals; Mermaid Man app; Ordway-a 3.00
52-85-($3.99) 53,59,60,68-Chuck Dixon-s. 63,64-Mermaid Girl spotlight. 66-70-Ordway-a 4.00
Annual-Size Super-Giant Swimtacular 1 (2013, $4.99) art by Fradon, Ordway, Kochalka 5.00
Annual-Size Super-Giant Swimtacular 2 (2014, $4.99) Mermaid Man app. 5.00
Annual-Size Super-Giant Swimtacular 3 (2015, $4.99) art by Barta, Kochalka, Chabot 5.00
Annual-Size Super-Giant Swimtacular 4 (2016, $4.99) Neal Adams & others-a; Ordway-c 5.00
Annual-Size Super-Giant Swimtacular 2017 (2017, $4.99) Mayerik & others-a; Chabot-c 5.00
Annual-Size Super-Giant Swimtacular 2018 (2018, $4.99) Ordway & others-a; Gianni-c 5.00
SpongeBob Freestyle Funnies 1 (2013, Free Comic Book Day giveaway) Short stories 3.00
SpongeBob Freestyle Funnies 2014 (Free Comic Book Day giveaway) Short stories 3.00
SpongeBob Freestyle Funnies 2015 (Free Comic Book Day giveaway) Short stories 3.00
SpongeBob Freestyle Funnies 2016 (FCBD giveaway) Short stories; Fradon-a 3.00
SpongeBob Freestyle Funnies 2017 (FCBD giveaway) Short stories; Kochalka-a 3.00
SpongeBob Freestyle Funnies 2018 (FCBD giveaway) Short stories; Mermaid Man app. 3.00

SPOOF
Marvel Comics Group: Oct, 1970; No. 2, Nov, 1972 - No. 5, May, 1973

1-Infinity-c; Dark Shadows-c & parody 4 8 12 25 40 55
2-5: 2-All in the Family. 3-Beatles, Osmonds, Jackson 5, David Cassidy, Nixon & Agnew-c.
5-Rod Serling, Woody Allen, Ted Kennedy-c 3 6 9 16 24 32

SPOOK (Formerly Shock Detective Cases)
Star Publications: No. 22, Jan, 1953 - No. 30, Oct, 1954

22-Sgt. Spook-r; acid in face story; hanging-c 284 568 852 1818 3109 4400
23,25,27: 25-Jungle Lil-r. 27-Two Sgt. Spook-r 71 142 213 454 777 1100
24-Used in **SOTI**, pgs. 182,183-r/Inside Crime #2; Transvestism story
97 194 291 621 1061 1500
26,28-30: 26-Disbrow-a. 28,29-Rulah app. 29-Jo-Jo app. 30-Disbrow-c/a(2); only Star-c 77 154 231 493 847 1200

*NOTE: **L. B. Cole** covers-all issues except #30; a-28(1 pg.). **Disbrow** a-26(2), 28, 29(2), 30(2); No. 30 r/Blue Bolt Weird Tales #114.*

SPOOK COMICS
Baily Publications/Star: 1946

1-Mr. Lucifer story 77 154 231 493 847 1200

SPOOK HOUSE
Albatross Funnybooks: 2016 - No. 5, 2017 ($3.99)

1-5-Horror anthology by Eric Powell and others; Powell-c 4.00
... 2019 Halloween Special (2019, $3.99) Short stories by Eric Powell & others; Powell-c 4.00

SPOOK HOUSE 2
Albatross Funnybooks: 2018 - No. 4, 2018 ($3.99)

1-4-Horror anthology by Eric Powell and others; Powell-c. 2-Lula app. 4.00

SPOOKY (The Tuff Little Ghost; see Casper The Friendly Ghost)
Harvey Publications: 11/55 - 139, 11/73; No. 140, 7/74 - No. 155, 3/77; No. 156, 12/77 - No. 158, 4/78; No. 159, 9/78; No. 160, 10/79; No. 161, 9/80

1-Nightmare begins (see Casper #19) 86 172 258 688 1544 2400
2 24 48 72 168 372 575
3-10(1956-57) 12 24 36 82 179 275
11-20(1957-58) 7 14 21 44 82 120
21-40(1958-59) 5 10 15 33 57 80
41-60 4 8 12 27 44 60
61-80,100 3 6 9 19 30 40
81-99 3 6 9 16 24 32
101-120 2 4 6 11 16 20
121-126,133-140 2 4 6 8 11 14
127-132: All 52 pg. Giants 2 4 6 11 16 20
141-161 1 2 3 5 7 9

SPOOKY
Harvey Comics: Nov, 1991 - No. 4, Sept, 1992 ($1.00/$1.25)

1 4.00
2-4: 3-Begin $1.25-c 3.00
...Digest 1-3 (10/92, 6/93, 10/93, $1.75, 100 pgs.)-Casper, Wendy, etc. 4.00

SPOOKY HAUNTED HOUSE
Harvey Publications: Oct, 1972 - No. 15, Feb, 1975

1 3 6 9 19 30 40
2-5 2 4 6 10 14 18
6-10 2 4 6 8 10 12
11-15 1 2 3 5 7 9

SPOOKY MYSTERIES
Your Guide Publ. Co.: No date (1946) (10¢)

1-Mr. Spooky, Super Snooper, Pinky, Girl Detective app.
34 68 102 204 332 460

SPOOKY SPOOKTOWN
Harvey Publ.: 9/61; No. 2, 9/62 - No. 52, 12/73; No. 53, 10/74 - No. 66, 12/76

1-Casper, Spooky; 68 pgs. begin 14 28 42 94 207 320
2 8 16 24 54 102 150
3-5 6 12 18 38 69 100
6-10 5 10 15 31 53 75
11-20 4 8 12 23 37 50
21-39: 39-Last 68 pg. issue 3 6 9 19 30 40
40-45: All 52 pgs. 2 4 6 11 16 20
46-66: 61-Hot Stuff/Spooky team-up story 1 2 3 5 7 9

SPORT COMICS (Becomes True Sport Picture Stories #5 on)
Street & Smith Publications: Oct, 1940 (No mo.) - No. 4, Nov, 1941

1-Life story of Lou Gehrig 65 130 195 416 708 1000
2 35 70 105 208 339 470
3,4: 4-Story of Notre Dame coach Frank Leahy 30 60 90 177 289 400

SPORT LIBRARY (See Charlton Sport Library)

SPORTS ACTION (Formerly Sport Stars)
Marvel/Atlas Comics (ACI No. 2,3/SAI No. 4-14): No. 2, Feb, 1950 - No. 14, Sept, 1952

2-Powell-a; George Gipp life story 43 86 129 269 455 640
1-(nd,no price, no publ., 52pgs, #1 on-c; has same-c as #2; blank inside-c (giveaway?) 22 44 66 132 216 300
3-Everett-a 24 48 72 142 234 325
4-11,14: Weiss-a 22 44 66 128 209 290
12,13: 12-Everett-c. 13-Krigstein-a 23 46 69 136 223 310

*NOTE: Title may have changed after No. 3, to Crime Must Lose No. 4 on, due to publisher change. **Sol Brodsky** c-4-7, 13, 14. **Maneely** c-3, 8-11.*

SPORT STARS
Parents' Magazine Institute (Sport Stars): Feb-Mar, 1946 - No. 4, Aug-Sept, 1946 (Half comic, half photo magazine)

1- "How Tarzan Got That Way" story of Johnny Weissmuller
40 80 120 243 402 560
2-Baseball greats 26 52 78 154 252 350
3,4 23 46 69 136 223 310

SPORT STARS (Becomes Sports Action #2 on)
Marvel Comics (ACI): Nov, 1949 (52 pgs.)

1-Knute Rockne; painted-c 47 94 141 296 498 700

SPORT THRILLS (Formerly Dick Cole; becomes Jungle Thrills #16)

Spongebob Comics #12 © UPP

Spook House #3 © Eric Powell

Spy Smasher #9 © FAW

Star Publications: No. 11, Nov, 1950 - No. 15, Nov, 1951

	GD 2.0	VG 4.0	FN 6.0	VF 8.0	VF/NM 9.0	NM- 9.2
11-Dick Cole begins; Ted Williams & Ty Cobb life stories	36	72	108	211	343	475
12-Joe DiMaggio, Phil Rizzuto stories & photos on-c; L.B. Cole-c/a	26	52	78	154	252	350
13-15-All L. B. Cole-c. 13-Jackie Robinson, Pee Wee Reese stories & photo on-c. 14-Johnny Weissmuler life story	26	52	78	154	252	350
Accepted Reprint #11 (#15 on-c, nd); L.B. Cole-c	10	20	30	54	72	90
Accepted Reprint #12 (nd); L.B. Cole-c; Joe DiMaggio & Phil Rizzuto life stories-r/#12	10	20	30	54	72	90

SPOTLIGHT (TV) (newsstand sales only)
Marvel Comics Group: Sept, 1978 - No. 4, Mar, 1979 (Hanna-Barbera)

	GD 2.0	VG 4.0	FN 6.0	VF 8.0	VF/NM 9.0	NM- 9.2
1-Huckleberry Hound, Yogi Bear; Shaw-a	3	6	9	21	33	45
2,4: 2-Quick Draw McGraw, Augie Doggie, Snooper & Blabber. 4-Magilla Gorilla, Snagglepuss	3	6	9	16	23	30
3-The Jetsons; Yakky Doodle	3	6	9	19	30	40

SPOTLIGHT COMICS
Country Press Inc.: Sept, 1940

nn-Ashcan, not distributed to newsstands, only for in house use. A NM copy sold in 2009 for $1015.

SPOTLIGHT COMICS (Becomes Red Seal Comics #14 on?)
Harry 'A' Chesler (Our Army, Inc.): Nov, 1944, No. 2, Jan, 1945 - No. 3, 1945

	GD 2.0	VG 4.0	FN 6.0	VF 8.0	VF/NM 9.0	NM- 9.2
1-The Black Dwarf (cont'd in Red Seal?), The Veiled Avenger, & Barry Kuda begin; Tuska-c	148	296	444	947	1624	2300
2	93	186	279	391	1021	1450
3-Injury to eye story (reprinted from Scoop #3)	93	186	279	391	1021	1450

SPOTTY THE PUP (Becomes Super Pup #4, see Television Puppet Show)
Avon Periodicals/Realistic Comics: No. 2, Oct-Nov, 1953 - No. 3, Dec-Jan, 1953-54
(Also see Funny Tunes)

	GD 2.0	VG 4.0	FN 6.0	VF 8.0	VF/NM 9.0	NM- 9.2
2,3	9	18	27	52	69	85
nn (1953, Realistic-r)	6	12	18	32	39	45

SPUNKY (...Junior Cowboy)(...Comics #2 on)
Standard Comics: April, 1949 - No. 7, Nov, 1951

	GD 2.0	VG 4.0	FN 6.0	VF 8.0	VF/NM 9.0	NM- 9.2
1-Text illos by Frazetta	18	36	54	105	165	225
2-Text illos by Frazetta	14	28	42	76	108	140
3-7	10	20	30	56	76	95

SPUNKY THE SMILING SPOOK
Ajax/Farrell (World Famous Comics/Four Star Comic Corp.): Aug, 1957 - No. 4, May, 1958

	GD 2.0	VG 4.0	FN 6.0	VF 8.0	VF/NM 9.0	NM- 9.2
1-Reprints from Frisky Fables	14	28	42	76	108	140
2-4	8	16	24	42	54	65

SPY AND COUNTERSPY (Becomes Spy Hunters #3 on)
American Comics Group: Aug-Sept, 1949 - No. 2, Oct-Nov, 1949 (52 pgs.)

	GD 2.0	VG 4.0	FN 6.0	VF 8.0	VF/NM 9.0	NM- 9.2
1-Origin, 1st app. Jonathan Kent, Counterspy	35	70	105	208	339	470
2	20	40	60	120	195	270

SPYBOY
Dark Horse Comics: Oct, 1999 - No. 17, May, 2001 ($2.50/$2.95/$2.99)

	GD 2.0	VG 4.0	FN 6.0	VF 8.0	VF/NM 9.0	NM- 9.2
1-17: 1-6-Peter David-s/Pop Mhan-a. 7,8-Meglia-a. 9-17-Mhan-a						3.00
13.1-13.3 (4/03-8/03, $2.99), 13.2,13.3-Mhan-a						3.00
... Special (5/02, $4.99) David-s/Mhan-a						5.00

SPYBOY: FINAL EXAM
Dark Horse Comics: May, 2004 - No. 4, Aug, 2004 ($2.99, limited series)

	GD 2.0	VG 4.0	FN 6.0	VF 8.0	VF/NM 9.0	NM- 9.2
1-4-Peter David-s/Pop Mhan-a/c						3.00
TPB (2005, $12.95) r/series						13.00

SPYBOY/ YOUNG JUSTICE
Dark Horse Comics: Feb, 2002 - No. 3, Apr, 2002 ($2.99, limited series)

	GD 2.0	VG 4.0	FN 6.0	VF 8.0	VF/NM 9.0	NM- 9.2
1-3: 1-Peter David-s/Todd Nauck-a/Pop Mhan-c. 2-Mhan-a						3.00

SPY CASES (Formerly The Kellys)
Marvel/Atlas Comics (Hercules Publ.): No. 26, Sept, 1950 - No. 19, Oct, 1953

	GD 2.0	VG 4.0	FN 6.0	VF 8.0	VF/NM 9.0	NM- 9.2
26 (#1)	37	74	111	222	361	500
27(#2),28(#3, 2/51): 27-Everett-a; bondage-c	21	42	63	122	199	275
4(4/51) - 7,9,10: 4-Heath-a	19	38	57	112	179	245
8-A-Bomb-c/story	20	40	60	118	192	265
11-19: 10-14-War format	18	36	54	105	165	225

NOTE: *Sol Brodsky c-1-5, 8, 9, 11-14, 17, 18. **Maneely** a-8; c-7, 10. **Tuska** a-7.*

SPY FIGHTERS
Marvel/Atlas Comics (CSI): March, 1951 - No. 15, July, 1953
(Cases from official records)

	GD 2.0	VG 4.0	FN 6.0	VF 8.0	VF/NM 9.0	NM- 9.2
1-Clark Mason begins; Tuska-a; Brodsky-c	37	74	111	222	361	500
2-Tuska-a	21	42	63	122	199	275
3-13: 3-5-Brodsky-c. 7-Heath-c	19	38	57	105	165	225
14,15-Pakula-a(3), Ed Win-a. 15-Brodsky-c	19	38	57	109	172	235

SPY-HUNTERS (Formerly Spy & Counterspy)
American Comics Group: No. 3, Dec-Jan, 1949-50 - No. 24, June-July, 1953 (#3-14: 52 pgs.)

	GD 2.0	VG 4.0	FN 6.0	VF 8.0	VF/NM 9.0	NM- 9.2
3-Jonathan Kent continues, ends #10	28	56	84	165	270	375
4-10: 4,8,10-Starr-a	15	30	45	86	133	180
11-15,17-22,24: 18-War-c begin. 21-War-c/stories begin	12	24	36	67	94	120
16-Williamson-a (9 pgs.)	17	34	51	100	158	215
23-Graphic torture, injury to eye panel	22	44	66	130	213	295

NOTE: ***Drucker** a-12. **Whitney** a-many issues; c-7, 8, 10-12, 15, 16.*

SPY ISLAND
Dark Horse Comics: Apr, 2020 - No. 4, Dec, 2020 ($3.99, limited series)

	GD 2.0	VG 4.0	FN 6.0	VF 8.0	VF/NM 9.0	NM- 9.2
1-4-Chelsea Cain-s/Elise McCall-a						4.00

SPYMAN (Top Secret Adventures on cover)
Harvey Publications (Illustrated Humor): Sept, 1966 - No. 3, Feb, 1967 (12¢)

	GD 2.0	VG 4.0	FN 6.0	VF 8.0	VF/NM 9.0	NM- 9.2
1-Origin and 1st app. of Spyman. Steranko-a(p)-1st pro work; 1 pg. Neal Adams ad; Tuska-c/a, Crandall-a(i)	13	26	39	89	195	300
2-Simon-c; Steranko-a(p)	5	10	15	34	60	85
3-Simon-c	5	10	15	30	50	70

SPY SMASHER (See Mighty Midget, Whiz & Xmas Comics) (Also see Crime Smasher)
Fawcett Publications: Fall, 1941 - No. 11, Feb, 1943

	GD 2.0	VG 4.0	FN 6.0	VF 8.0	VF/NM 9.0	NM- 9.2
1-Spy Smasher begins; silver metallic-c	349	698	1047	2443	4272	6100
2-Raboy-c	168	336	504	1075	1838	2600
3,4: 3-Bondage-c. 4-Irvin Steinberg-c	123	246	369	787	1344	1900
5-7: Raboy-a; 6-Raboy-c/a. 7-Part photo-c (movie) Japanese dragon-c	100	200	300	635	1093	1550
8,11: War-c	87	174	261	553	952	1350
9-Hitler, Tojo, Mussolini-c.	174	348	522	1114	1907	2700
10-Hitler-c	168	336	504	1075	1838	2600

SPY THRILLERS (Police Badge No. 479 #5)
Atlas Comics (PrPl): Nov, 1954 - No. 4, May, 1955

	GD 2.0	VG 4.0	FN 6.0	VF 8.0	VF/NM 9.0	NM- 9.2
1-Brodsky c-1,2	32	64	96	188	307	425
2-Last precode (1/55)	19	38	57	111	176	240
3,4	16	32	48	92	144	195

SQUADRON SINISTER (Secret Wars tie-in)
Marvel Comics: Aug, 2015 - No. 4, Jan, 2016 ($3.99, limited series)

	GD 2.0	VG 4.0	FN 6.0	VF 8.0	VF/NM 9.0	NM- 9.2
1-4-Guggenheim-s/Pacheco-a/c. 1-Squadron Supreme app. 2-Frightful Four app.						4.00

SQUADRON SUPREME (Also see Marvel Graphic Novel - ...: Death of a Universe)
Marvel Comics Group: Aug, 1985 - No. 12, Aug, 1986 (Maxi-series)

	GD 2.0	VG 4.0	FN 6.0	VF 8.0	VF/NM 9.0	NM- 9.2
1-Double size						5.00
2-12						4.00
TPB ($24.99) r/#1-12; Alex Ross painted-c; printing inks contain some of the cremated remains of late writer Mark Gruenwald						50.00
TPB-2nd printing ($24.99): Inks contain no ashes						25.00
...Death of a Universe TPB (2006, $24.99) r/Marvel Graphic Novel, Thor #280, Avengers #5,6; Avengers/Squadron Supreme Annual and Squadron Supreme: New World Order						25.00

SQUADRON SUPREME (Also see Supreme Power)
Marvel Comics: May, 2006 - No. 7, Nov, 2006 ($2.99)

	GD 2.0	VG 4.0	FN 6.0	VF 8.0	VF/NM 9.0	NM- 9.2
1-7-Straczynski-s/Frank-a/c						3.00
Saga of Squadron Supreme (2006, $3.99) summary of Supreme Power #1-18; plus Hyperion and Nighthawk limited series; wraparound-c; preview of Squadron Supreme #1						4.00
... Vol. 1: The Pre-War Years (2006, $20.99, dustjacket) r/#1-5 & Saga of S.S.						21.00

SQUADRON SUPREME
Marvel Comics: Sept, 2008 - No. 12, Aug, 2009 ($2.99)

	GD 2.0	VG 4.0	FN 6.0	VF 8.0	VF/NM 9.0	NM- 9.2
1-12: 1-Set 5 years after Ultimate Power; Nick Fury app.; Chaykin-s/Turini-a/Land-c						3.00

SQUADRON SUPREME
Marvel Comics: Feb, 2016 - No. 15, Mar, 2017 ($3.99)

	GD 2.0	VG 4.0	FN 6.0	VF 8.0	VF/NM 9.0	NM- 9.2
1-15-Robinson-s; main covers by Alex Ross thru #4. 1-Kirk-a; Namor killed. 3-Avengers app. 9-12-Civil War II tie-in. 10-Thundra & Blue Marvel app. 11,12-Spider-Man app.						4.00

SQUADRON SUPREME: HYPERION VS. NIGHTHAWK
Marvel Comics: Mar, 2007 - No. 4, June, 2007 ($2.99, limited series)

	GD 2.0	VG 4.0	FN 6.0	VF 8.0	VF/NM 9.0	NM- 9.2
1-4-Hyperion and Nighthawk in Darfur; Gulacy-a/c; Guggenheim-s						3.00
TPB (2007, $10.99) r/#1-4						11.00

SQUADRON SUPREME: MARVEL TALES
Marvel Comics: June, 2021 ($7.99, one-shot)

1-Reprints Avengers #69,70,85,86; foreward by Ralph Macchio 8.00

SQUADRON SUPREME: NEW WORLD ORDER
Marvel Comics: Sept, 1998 ($5.99, one-shot)
1-Wraparound-c; Kaminski-s 6.00

SQUALOR
First Comics: Dec, 1989 - Aug, 1990 ($2.75, limited series)
1-4: Sutton-a 3.00

SQUEE (Also see Johnny The Homicidal Maniac)
Slave Labor Graphics: Apr, 1997 - No. 4, May, 1998 ($2.95, B&W)
1-4: Jhonen Vasquez-s/a in all 3.00

SQUEEKS (Also see Boy Comics)
Lev Gleason Publications: Oct, 1953 - No. 5, June, 1954
1-Funny animal; Biro-c; Crimebuster's pet monkey "Squeeks" begins
14 28 42 76 108 140
2-Biro-c 9 18 27 47 61 75
3-5: 3-Biro-c 8 16 24 42 54 65

S.R. BISSETTE'S SPIDERBABY COMIX
SpiderBaby Grafix: Aug, 1996 - No. 2 ($3.95, B&W, magazine size)
Preview-(8/96, $3.95)-Graphic violence & nudity; Laurel & Hardy app. 4.00
1,2 4.00

S.R. BISSETTE'S TYRANT
SpiderBaby Grafix: Sept, 1994 - No. 4 ($2.95, B&W)
1-4 4.00

STALKER (Also see All Star Comics 1999 and crossover issues)
National Periodical Publications: June-July, 1975 - No. 4, Dec-Jan, 1975-76
1-Origin & 1st app; Ditko/Wood-c/a 3 6 9 14 19 24
2-4-Ditko/Wood-c/a 2 3 4 6 8 10

STALKERS
Marvel Comics (Epic Comics): Apr, 1990 - No. 12, Mar, 1991 ($1.50)
1-12: 1-Chadwick-c 3.00

STAMP COMICS (Stamps... on-c; Thrilling Adventures In...#8)
Youthful Magazines/Stamp Comics, Inc.: Oct, 1951 - No. 7, Oct, 1952
1-(15¢) ('Stamps' on indicia No. 1-3,5,7) 29 58 87 172 281 390
2 15 30 45 94 147 200
3-6: 3,4-Kiefer, Wildey-a 15 30 45 85 130 175
7-Roy Krenkel (4 pgs.) 19 38 57 111 176 240
NOTE: *Promotes stamp collecting; gives stories behind various commemorative stamps. No. 2, 10¢ printed over 15¢ c-price.* ***Kiefer*** *a-1-7.* ***Kirkel*** *a-1-6.* ***Napoli*** *a-2-7.* ***Palais*** *a-2-4, 7.*

STAND, THE ... (Based on the Stephen King novel)
Marvel Comics: 2008 - 2012 ($3.99, limited series)
...: American Nightmares 1-5 (5/09 - No. 5, 10/09, $3.99) Aguirre-Sacasa-s/Perkins-a 4.00
...: Captain Trips 1-5 (12/08 - No. 5, 3/09, $3.99) Aguirre-Sacasa-s/Perkins-a 4.00
...: Hardcases 1-5 (8/10 - No. 5, 1/11, $3.99) Aguirre-Sacasa-s/Perkins-a 4.00
...: No Man's Land 1-5 (4/11 - No. 5, 8/11, $3.99) Aguirre-Sacasa-s/Perkins-a 4.00
...: Soul Survivors 1-5 (12/09 - No. 5, 5/10, $3.99) Aguirre-Sacasa-s/Perkins-a 4.00
...: The Night Has Come 1-6 (10/11 - No. 6, 3/12, $3.99) Aguirre-Sacasa-s/Perkins-a 4.00

STAN LEE MEETS...
Marvel Comics: Nov, 2006 - Jan, 2007 ($3.99, series of one-shots)
Doctor Doom 1 (12/06) Lee-s/Larroca-a/c; Loeb-s/McGuinness-a; r/Fantastic Four #87 4.00
Doctor Strange 1 (11/06) Lee-s/Davis-a/c; Bendis-s/Bagley-a; r/Marvel Premiere #3 4.00
Silver Surfer 1 (1/07) Lee-s/Wieringo-a/c; Jenkins-s/Buckingham-a; r/S.S. #14 4.00
Spider-Man 1 (11/06) Lee-s/Coipel-a/c; Whedon-s/Gaydos-a; Hembeck-s/a; r/AS-M #87 4.00
The Thing 1 (12/06) Lee-s/Weeks-a/c; Thomas-s/Kolins-a; r/FF #79; FF #51 cover swipe 4.00
HC (2007, $24.99, dustjacket) r/one-shots; interviews and features 25.00

STAN LEE'S MIGHTY 7
Archie Comics (Stan Lee Comics): May, 2012 - No. 3, Sept, 2012 ($2.99, limited series)
1-3-Co-written by Stan Lee; Alex Saviuk-a; multiple covers on each 3.00

STANLEY & HIS MONSTER (Formerly The Fox & the Crow)
National Periodical Publ.: No. 109, Apr-May, 1968 - No. 112, Oct-Nov, 1968
109-112 3 6 9 21 33 45

STANLEY & HIS MONSTER
DC Comics: Feb, 1993 - No. 4, May, 1993 ($1.50, limited series)
1-4 3.00

STAN SHAW'S BEAUTY & THE BEAST
Dark Horse Comics: Nov, 1993 ($4.95, one-shot)
1 5.00

STAR (See Captain Marvel 2019 series #8)
Marvel Comics: Mar, 2020 - No. 5, Nov, 2020 ($3,99)
1-5: 1-Loki, Jessica Jones and Scarlet Witch app. 2-5-The Black Order app.
3-5-Captain Marvel. 3,5-Scarlet Witch app. 4.00

STARBLAST
Marvel Comics: Jan, 1994 - No. 4, Apr, 1994 ($1.75, limited series)
1-($2.00, 52 pgs.)-Nova, Quasar, Black Bolt; painted-c 4.00
2-4 3.00

STAR BLAZERS
Comico: Apr, 1987 - No. 4, July, 1987 ($1.75, limited series)
1-4 3.00

STAR BLAZERS
Comico: 1989 ($1.95/$2.50, limited series)
1-5- Steacy wraparound painted-c on all 3.00

STAR BLAZERS (The Magazine of Space Battleship Yamato)
Argo Press: No. 0, Aug, 1995 - No. 3, Dec, 1995 ($2.95)
0-3 3.00

STARBORN (From Stan Lee)
BOOM! Studios: Dec, 2010 - No. 12, Nov, 2011 ($3.99)
1-12: 1-9,11-Roberson-s/Randolph-a. 1-7-Three covers on each. 10-Scalera-a 4.00

STAR BRAND
Marvel Comics (New Universe): Oct, 1986 - No. 19, May, 1989 (75¢/$1.25)
1-15: 14-begin $1.25-c 3.00
16-19-Byrne story & art; low print run 5.00
Annual 1 (10/87) 4.00
... Classic Vol. 1 TPB (2006, $19.99) r/#1-7 20.00

STARBRAND & NIGHTMASK
Marvel Comics: Feb, 2016 - No. 6, Jul, 2016 ($3.99)
1-6: 1-Weisman-s/Stanton-a; Kevin and Adam go to college; Nitro & Graviton app. 4.00

STARCADIA QUEST (Based on the tabletop game)
IDW Publishing: Aug, 2019 - No. 3, Oct, 2019 ($4.99, limited series)
1-3-James Roberts-s/Aurelio Mazzara-a 5.00

STARCHILD
Tailspin Press: 1992 - No. 12 ($2.25/$2.50, B&W)
1,2-('92),0(4/93),3-12: 0-Illos by Chadwick, Eisner, Sim, M. Wagner. 3-(7/93). 4-(11/93).
6-(2/94) 3.00

STARCHILD: MYTHOPOLIS
Image Comics: No. 0, July, 1997 - No. 4, Apr, 1998 ($2.95, B&W, limited series)
0-4-James Owen-s/a 3.00

STAR COMICS
Ultem Publ. (Harry 'A' Chesler)/Centaur Publications: Feb, 1937 - V2#7 (No. 23), Aug, 1939 (#1-6: large size)
V1#1-Dan Hastings (s/f) begins 454 908 1362 3314 5857 8400
2-(4/37) 271 542 813 1734 2967 4200
3-Classic Black Americana cover (rare) 454 908 1362 3314 5857 8400
4,5-Classic Winsor McCay Little Nemo-c/stories (rare)
300 600 900 1950 3375 4800
6-(9/37) 258 516 774 1651 2826 4000
7-9: 8-Severed head centerspread; Impy & Little Nemo by Winsor McCay Jr, Popeye app. by Bob Wood; Mickey Mouse & Popeye app. as toys in Santa's bag on-c;
X-Mas-c 181 362 543 1158 1979 2800
10 (1st Centaur; 3/38)-Impy by Winsor McCay Jr; Don Marlow by Guardineer begins
213 426 639 1363 2332 3300
11-1st Jack Cole comic-a, 1 pg. (4/38) 271 542 813 1734 2967 4200
12-15: 12-Riders of the Golden West begins; Little Nemo app. 15-Speed Silvers by
Gustavson & The Last Pirate by Burgos begins 129 258 387 826 1413 2000
16 (12/38)-The Phantom Rider & his horse Thunder begins, ends V2#6
155 310 465 992 1696 2400
V2#1(#17, 2/39)-Phantom Rider-c (only non-funny-c)
187 374 561 1197 2049 2900
2-7(#18-23): 2-Diana Deane by Tarpe Mills app. 3-Drama of Hollywood by Mills begins.
106 212 318 673 1162 1650
NOTE: ***Biro*** *c-6, 9, 10.* ***Burgos*** *a-15, 16, V2#1-7.* ***Ken Ernst*** *a-10, 12, 14.* ***Filchock*** *c-15, 18, 22.* ***Gill Fox*** *c-14, 19.* ***Guardineer*** *a-6, 8-14.* ***Gustavson*** *a-13-16, V2#1-7.* ***Winsor McCay*** *c-4, 5.* ***Tarpe Mills*** *a-15, V2#1-7.* ***Schwab*** *c-20, 23.* ***Bob Wood*** *a-10, 12, 13; c-7, 8.*

STAR COMICS MAGAZINE
Marvel Comics (Star Comics): Dec, 1986 - No. 13, 1988 ($1.50, digest-size)
1,9-Spider-Man-c/s 2 4 6 8 11 14
2-8-Heathcliff, Ewoks, Top Dog, Madballs-r in #1-13 1 2 3 5 7 9
10-13 2 4 6 8 10 12

S.T.A.R. CORPS
DC Comics: Nov, 1993 - No. 6, Apr, 1994 ($1.50, limited series)
1-6: 1,2-Austin-c(i). 1-Superman app. 3.00

STARCRAFT (Based on the video game)
DC Comics (WildStorm): Jul, 2009 - No. 7, Jan, 2010 ($2.99)
1-7-Furman-s; two covers on each 3.00
HC (2010, $19.99, dustjacket) r/#1-7 20.00
SC (2011, $14.99) r/#1-7 15.00

STARCRAFT: SCAVENGERS (Based on the Blizzard Ent. video game)
Dark Horse Comics: Jul, 2018 - No. 4, Oct, 2018 ($3.99, limited series)
1-4-Jody Houser-s/Gabriel Guzmán-a 4.00

STARCRAFT: SOLDIERS (Based on the Blizzard Ent. video game)
Dark Horse Comics: Jan, 2019 - No. 4, Apr, 2019 ($3.99, limited series)
1-4-Jody Houser & Andrew Robinson-s/Miguel Sepulveda-a 4.00

STARCRAFT: SURVIVORS (Based on the Blizzard Ent. video game)
Dark Horse Comics: Jul, 2019 - No. 4, Apr, 2019 ($3.99, limited series)
1-4-Jody Houser-s/Gabriel Guzmán-a 4.00

STAR CROSSED
DC Comics (Helix): June, 1997 - No. 3, Aug, 1997 ($2.50, limited series)
1-3-Matt Howarth-s/a 3.00

STARDUST (See Neil Gaiman and Charles Vess' Stardust)

STARDUST KID, THE
Image Comics/Boom! Studios #4-on: May, 2005 - No. 4 ($3.50)
1-4-J.M. DeMatteis-s/Mike Ploog-a 3.50

STAR FEATURE COMICS
I. W. Enterprises: 1963
Reprint #9-Stunt-Man Stetson-r/Feat. Comics #141 3 6 9 14 19 24

STARFIRE (Not the Teen Titans character)
National Periodical Publ./DC Comics: Aug-Sept, 1976 - No. 8, Oct-Nov, 1977
1-Origin (CCA stamp fell off cover art; so it was approved by code)
3 6 9 14 20 25
2-8 1 3 4 6 8 10

STARFIRE (Teen Titans character)(Also see Red Hood and the Outlaws)
DC Comics: Aug, 2015 - No. 12, Jul, 2016 ($2.99)

Stalker #3 © DC

Stargate Atlantis #1 © MGM

Star-Lord (2017) #1 © MAR

GD 2.0 | VG 4.0 | FN 6.0 | VF 8.0 | VF/NM 9.0 | NM- 9.2

1-12: 1-Conner & Palmiotti-s/Lupacchino-a; Conner-c. 3-Intro. Atlee. 7,8-Grayson app. 9-Charretier-a begins; intro. Syl'khee 3.00

STARGATE
Dynamite Entertainment
...: Daniel Jackson 1-4 (2010 - No. 4, 2010, $3.99) Watson-a/Murray-s 4.00
...: Vala Mal Doran 1-5 (2010 - No. 5, 2010, $3.99) Razek-a/Jerwa-s 4.00

STARGATE ATLANTIS (Based on the TV series)
American Mythology Prods.: 2016 - No. 6 ($3.99)
1-6: 1-Haynes & Vaughn-s/LaRocque-a; covers by Wheatley & LaRocque. 4-6-Gateways #1-3 on cover; Watson-a 4.00

STARGATE ATLANTIS HEARTS & MINDS
American Mythology Prods.: 2017 - No. 3, 2017 ($3.99)
1-3-Haynes & Vaughn-s/LaRocque-a 4.00

STARGATE ATLANTIS SINGULARITY
American Mythology Prods.: 2018 - No. 3, 2018 ($3.99)
1-3: 1-Haynes & Vaughn-s/Purcell & LaRocque-a. 2,3-Purcell-a 4.00

STARGATE ATLANTIS / STARGATE UNIVERSE ANTHOLOGY
American Mythology Prods.: 2018 ($3.99)
1-Haynes & Vaughn-s/LaRocque & Purcell-a; 3 covers 4.00

STARGATE ATLANTIS / STARGATE UNIVERSE ANTHOLOGY ONGOING
American Mythology Prods.: 2018 - No. 3, 2018 ($3.99)
1-3: 1-Haynes & Vaughn-s/Hilinski-a; Check-s/Gouveia-a; 3 covers. 3-Purcell-a 4.00

STARGATE UNIVERSE (Based on the TV series)
American Mythology Prods.: 2017 - No. 6, 2018 ($3.99)
1-6: 1-Haynes & Vaughn-s/Caracuzzo-a. 2,3-Gouveia-a. 4-6-Hilinski-a 4.00

STARGIRL SPRING BREAK SPECIAL
DC Comics: Jul, 2021 ($5.99, one-shot)
1-Seven Soldiers of Victory & Clock King app.; Johns-s/Nauck-a; Hitch-a 6.00

STARGIRL: THE LOST CHILDREN (See Flashpoint Beyond)
DC Comics: Jan, 2023 - No. 6 ($3.99, limited series)
1-4-The search for the forgotten Golden Age sidekicks; Johns-s/Nauck-a 4.00

STARHENGE, BOOK ONE: THE DRAGON & THE BOAR
Image Comics: Jul, 2022 - No. 6, Dec, 2022 ($3.99, limited series)
1-6-Liam Sharp-s/a 4.00

STAR HUNTERS (See DC Super Stars #16)
National Periodical Publ./DC Comics: Oct-Nov, 1977 - No. 7, Oct-Nov, 1978
1,7: 1-Newton-a(p). 7-44 pgs. 2 4 6 8 10 12
2-6 1 2 3 4 5 7
NOTE: ***Buckler** a-4-7p; c-1-7p. **Layton** a-1-5i; c-1-6i. **Nasser** a-3p. **Sutton** a-6i.*

STARJAMMERS (See X-Men Spotlight on Starjammers)

STARJAMMERS (Also see Uncanny X-Men)
Marvel Comics: Oct, 1995 - No. 4, Jan, 1996 ($2.95, limited series)
1-4: Foil-c; Ellis scripts 4.00

STARJAMMERS
Marvel Comics: Sept, 2004 - No. 6, Jan, 2005 ($2.99, limited series)
1-6-Kevin J. Anderson-s. 1-Garza-a. 2-6-Lucas-a 3.00

STARK TERROR
Stanley Publications: Dec, 1970 - No. 5, Aug, 1971 (B&W, magazine, 52 pgs.) (1950s Horror reprints, including pre-code)
1-Bondage, torture-c 9 18 27 62 126 190
2-4 (Gillmor/Aragon-r) 5 10 15 34 60 85
5 (ACG-r) 5 10 15 30 50 70

STARLET O'HARA IN HOLLYWOOD (Teen-age) (Also see Cookie)
Standard Comics: Dec, 1948 - No. 4, Sept, 1949
1-Owen Fitzgerald-a in all 57 114 171 362 619 875
2 42 84 126 265 445 625
3,4 37 74 111 222 361 500

STARLIGHT
Image Comics: Mar, 2014 - No. 6, Oct, 2014 ($2.99)
1-5-Mark Millar-s/Goran Parlov-a. 1-Covers by Cassaday & Parlov. 2-Sienkiewicz var-c 3.00
6-($4.99) Two covers by Cassaday and Chiang 5.00

STARLORD
Marvel Comics: Dec, 1996 - No. 3, Feb, 1997 ($2.50, limited series)
1-3-Timothy Zahn-s 4.00

STAR-LORD (Guardians of the Galaxy)
Marvel Comics: Aug, 2013; 2014 ($7.99, series of reprints)
...: Annihilation - Conquest 1 (2014) r/Annihilation: Conquest - Starlord #1-4; design art 8.00
...: Tears For Heaven 1 (2014) r/Marvel Preview #18, Marvel Spotlight #6,7, and Marvel Premiere #61; bonus art; new cover by Pichelli 8.00
...: The Hollow Crown 1 (8/13) r/Marvel Preview #4,11 and Star-Lord Special Edition 8.00

STAR-LORD
Marvel Comics: Jan, 2016 - No. 8, Aug, 2016 ($3.99)
1-8: 1-Humphries-s/Garron-a; 18-year-old Peter Quill's 1st meeting with Yondu 4.00

STAR-LORD
Marvel Comics: Feb, 2017 - No. 6, Jun, 2017 ($3.99)
1-6-Zdarsky-s/Anka-a. 1,5,6-Old Man Logan app. 3-5-Daredevil app. 4.00
Annual 1 (7/17, $4.99) Zdarsky-s/Morissette-a/Anka-c 5.00

STAR-LORD & KITTY PRYDE (Secret Wars tie-in)
Marvel Comics: Sept, 2015 - No. 3, Nov, 2015 ($3.99, limited series)
1-3-Humphries-s/Firmansyah-a; Gambit app. 4.00

STARLORD MEGAZINE
Marvel Comics: Nov, 1996 ($2.95, one-shot)
1-Reprints w/preview of new series 4.00

STAR-LORD THE SPECIAL EDITION (Also see Marvel Comics Super Special #10, Marvel Premiere & Preview & Marvel Spotlight V2#6,7)
Marvel Comics Group: Feb, 1982 (one-shot, direct sales) (1st Baxter paper comic)
1-Byrne/Austin-a; Austin-c; 8 pgs. of new-a by Golden (p); Dr. Who story by Dave Gibbons; 1st deluxe format comic 3 6 9 16 23 30

STAR MAGE
IDW Publishing: Apr, 2014 - No. 6, Sept, 2014 ($3.99, limited series)
1-6: 1-JC De La Torre-s/Ray Dillon-a. 2-6-Franco Cespedes-a 4.00

STARMAN (1st Series) (Also see Justice League & War of the Gods)
DC Comics: Oct, 1988 - No. 45, Apr, 1992 ($1.00)
1-Origin 1 2 3 5 6 8
2-25,29-45: 4-Intro The Power Elite. 9,10,34-Batman app. 14-Superman app. 17-Power Girl app. 38-War of the Gods x-over. 42-45-Eclipso-c/stories 3.00
26-1st app. David Knight (G.A.Starman's son). 5.00
27,28: 27-Starman (David Knight) app. 28-Starman disguised as Superman; leads into Superman #50 4.00

STARMAN (2nd Series) (Also see The Golden Age, Showcase 95 #12, Showcase 96 #4,5)
DC Comics: No. 0, Oct, 1994 - No. 80, Aug, 2001; No. 81, Mar, 2010 ($1.95/$2.25/$2.50)
0,1: 0-James Robinson scripts, Tony Harris-c/a(p) & Wade Von Grawbadger-a(i) begins; Sins of the Father storyline begins, ends #3; 1st app. new Starman (Jack Knight); reintro of the G.A. Mist & G.A. Shade; 1st app. Nash; David Knight dies 2 4 6 8 10 12
2-7: 2-Reintro Charity from Forbidden Tales of Dark Mansion. 3-Reintro/2nd app. "Blue" Starman (1st app. in 1st Issue Special #12); Will Payton app. (both cameos). 5-David Knight app. 6-The Shade "Times Past" story; Kristiansen-a. 7-The Black Pirate cameo 5.00
8-17: 8-Begin $2.25-c. 10-1st app. new Mist (Nash). 11-JSA "Times Past" story; Matt Smith-a. 12-16-Sins of the Child. 17-The Black Pirate app. 4.00
18-37: 18-G.A. Starman "Times Past" story; Watkiss-a. 19-David Knight app. 20-23-G.A. Sandman app. 24-26-Demon Quest; all 3 covers make-up triptych. 33-36-Batman-c/app. 37-David Knight and deceased JSA members app. 3.00
38-49,51-56: 38-Nash vs. Justice League Europe. 39,40-Crossover w/ Power of Shazam! #35,36; Bulletman app. 42-Demon-c/app. 43-JLA-c/app. 44-Phantom Lady-c/app. 46-Gene Ha-a. 51-Jor-El app. 52,53-Adam Strange-c/app. 3.00
50-($3.95) Gold foil logo on-c; Star Boy (LSH) app. 4.00
57-79: 57-62-Painted covers by Harris and Alex Ross. 72-Death of Ted Knight 3.00
80-($3.95) Final issue; cover by Harris & Robinson 4.00
81-(3/10, $2.99) Blackest Night one-shot; The Shade vs. David Knight; Harris-c 3.00
#1,000,000 (11/98) 853rd Century x-over; Snejbjerg-a 3.00
Annual 1 (1996, $3.50)-Legends of the Dead Earth story; Prince Gavyn & G.A. Starman stories; J.H. Williams III, Bret Blevins, Craig Hamilton-c/a(p) 4.00
Annual 2 (1997, $3.95)-Pulp Heroes story; 4.00
...80 Page Giant (1/99, $4.95) Harris-c 5.00
...Secret Files 1 (4/98, $4.95)-Origin stories and profile pages 5.00
...The Mist (6/98, $1.95) Girlfrenzy; Mary Marvel app. 3.00
A Starry Knight-($17.95, TPB) r/#47-53 18.00
Grand Guignol-(2004, $19.95, TPB)-r/#61-73 20.00
Infernal Devices-($17.95, TPB) r/#29-35,37,38 18.00
Night and Day-($14.95, TPB)-r/#7-10,12-16 15.00
Sins of the Father-($12.95, TPB)-r/#0-5 13.00
Sons of the Father-($14.99, TPB)-r/#75-80 15.00

GD 2.0 | VG 4.0 | FN 6.0 | VF 8.0 | VF/NM 9.0 | NM- 9.2

Stars My Destination-(2003, $14.95, TPB)-r/#55-60 15.00
Times Past-($17.95, TPB)-r/stories of other Starmen 18.00
The Starman Omnibus Vol. One (2008, $49.99, HC with dj) r/#0,1-16; James Robinson intro. 50.00
The Starman Omnibus Vol. Two (2009, $49.99, HC with dj) r/#17-29, Annual #1, Showcase '95 #12, Showcase '96 #4,5; Harris intro.; merchandise gallery 50.00
The Starman Omnibus Vol. Three (2009, $49.99, HC with dj) r/#30-38, Annual #2, Starman Secret Files #1 and The Shade #1-4 50.00
The Starman Omnibus Vol. Four (2010, $49.99, HC with dj) r/#39-46, 80 Page Giant #1, Power of Shazam! #35,36; Starman: The Mist #1 and Batman/Hellboy/Starman #1,2 50.00
The Starman Omnibus Vol. Five (2010, $49.99, HC with dj) r/#47-60, #1,000,000; Stars and S.T.R.I.P.E. #0; All Star Comics 80 Page Giant #1; JSA: All Stars #4 50.00
The Starman Omnibus Vol. Six (2011, $49.99, HC with dj) r/#61-81, Johns intro. 50.00

STARMAN/CONGORILLA (See Justice League: Cry For Justice)
DC Comics: Mar, 2011 ($2.99, one-shot)

1-Animal Man and Rex the Wonder Dog app.; Robinson-s/Booth-a/Ha-c 3.00

STARMASTERS
Marvel Comics: Dec, 1995 - No. 3, Feb, 1996 ($1.95, limited series)

1-3-Continues in Cosmic Powers Unlimited #4 3.00

STAR PIG
IDW Publishing: Jul, 2019 - No. 4, Oct, 2019 ($3.99, limited series)

1-4-Delilah S. Dawson-s/Francesco Gaston-a; two covers on each 4.00

STAR PRESENTATION, A (Formerly My Secret Romance #1,2; Spectacular Stories #4 on) (Also see This Is Suspense)
Fox Feature Syndicate (Hero Books): No. 3, May, 1950

3-Dr. Jekyll & Mr. Hyde by Wood & Harrison (reprinted in Startling Terror Tales #10); "The Repulsing Dwarf" by Wood; Wood-c 77 154 231 493 847 1200

STAR QUEST COMIX (Warren Presents... on cover)
Warren Publications: Oct, 1978 ($1.50, B&W magazine, 84 pgs., square-bound)

1-Corben, Maroto, Neary-a; Ken Kelly-c; Star Wars 2 4 6 9 12 15

STAR RAIDERS (See DC Graphic Novel #1)

STAR RANGER (Cowboy Comics #13 on)
Chesler Publ./Centaur Publ.: Feb, 1937 - No. 12, May, 1938 (Large size: No. 1-6)

1-(1st Western comic)-Ace & Deuce, Air Plunder; Creig Flessel-a 331 662 993 2317 4059 5800
2 181 362 543 1158 1979 2800
3-6 168 336 504 1075 1838 2600
7-9: 8(12/37)-Christmas-c; Air Patrol, Gold coast app.; Guardineer centerfold 135 270 405 864 1482 2100
V2#10 (1st Centaur; 3/38) 148 296 444 947 1624 2300
11,12 129 258 387 826 1413 2000

NOTE: ***J. Cole** a-10, 12; c-12. **Ken Ernst** a-11. **Gill Fox** a-8(illo), 9, 10. **Guardineer** a-1-3, 5-7, 8(illos), 9, 10, 12. **Gustavson** a-8-10, 12. **Fred Schwab** c-2-11. **Bob Wood** a-8-10.*

STAR RANGER FUNNIES (Formerly Cowboy Comics)
Centaur Publications: V1#15, Oct, 1938 - V2#5, Oct, 1939

V1#15-Lyin Lou, Ermine, Wild West Junior, The Law of Caribou County by Eisner, Cowboy Jake, The Plugged Dummy, Spurs by Gustavson, Red Coat, Two Buckaroos & Trouble Hunters begin 148 296 444 947 1624 2300
V2#1 (1/39) 123 246 369 787 1344 1900
2-5: 2-Night Hawk by Gustavson. 4-Kit Carson app. 103 206 309 659 1130 1600

NOTE: ***Jack Cole** a-V2#1, 3; c-V2#1. **Filchock** c-V2#2, 3. **Guardineer** a-V2#3. **Gustavson** a-V2#2. **Pinajian** c/a-V2#5.*

STAR REACH (Mature content)
Star Reach Publ.: Apr, 1974 - No. 18, Oct, 1979 (B&W, #12-15 w/color)

1-(75¢, 52 pgs.) Art by Starlin, Simonson. Chaykin-c/a; origin Death. Cody Starbuck-sty 3 6 9 17 26 35
1-2nd, 3th, and 4th printings ($1.00-$1.50-c) 6.00
2-11: 2-Adams, Giordano-a; 1st Stephanie Starr-c/s. 3-1st Linda Lovecraft. 4-1st Sherlock Duck. 5-1st Gideon Faust by Chaykin. 6-Elric-c. 7-BWS-c. 9-14-Sacred & Profane-c/s by Steacy. 11-Samurai 2 4 6 8 11 14
2-2nd printing 4.00
12-15 (44 pgs.): 12-Zelazny-s. Nasser-a, Brunner-c 2 4 6 9 13 16
16-18-Magazine size: 17-Poe's Raven-c/s 2 4 6 9 13 16

NOTE: ***Adams** c-2. **Bonivert** a-17. **Brunner** a-3,5; c-3,10,12. **Chaykin** a-1,4,5; c-1(1st ed),4,5; back-c-1(2nd,3rd,4th ed). **Gene Day** a-6,8,9,11,15. **Friedrich** s-2,3,8,10. **Gasbarri** a-7. **Gilbert** a-9,12. **Giordano** a-2. **Gould** a-6. **Hirota/Mukaide** s/a-7. **Jones** c-6. **Konz** a-17. **Leialoha** a-3,4,6-i, 13,15; c-13,15. **Lyda** a-6,12-15. **Marrs** a-2-5,7,10,14,15,16,18; c-18; back-c-2. **Mukaide** a-18. **Nasser** a-12. **Nino** a-6; **Russell** a-8,10; c-8. **Dave Sim** s-7; lettering-9. **Simonson** a-1. **Skeates** a-1,2. **Starlin** a-1(x2), 2(x2); back-c-1(1st ed); c-1(2nd,3rd,4th ed). **Barry Smith** c-7. **Staton** a-5,6,7. **Steacy** a-8-14; c-9,11,14,16. **Vosburg** a-2-5,7,10. **Workman** a-2-5,8. Nudity panels in most. Wraparound-c: 3-5,7-11,13-16,18.*

STAR REACH CLASSICS
Eclipse Comics: Mar, 1984 - No. 6, Aug, 1984 ($1.50, Baxter paper)

1-6: 1-Neal Adams-r/Star Reach #1; Sim & Starlin-a 3.00

STARR FLAGG, UNDERCOVER GIRL (See Undercover...)

STARRIORS
Marvel Comics: Aug, 1984 - Feb, 1985 (Limited series) (Based on Tomy toys)

1-4 4.00

STARR THE SLAYER
Marvel Comics (MAX): Nov, 2009 - No. 4, Feb, 2010 ($3.99, limited series)

1-4- Richard Corben-c/a; Daniel Way-s 4.00

STARS AND S.T.R.I.P.E. (Also see JSA)
DC Comics: July, 1999 - No. 14, Sept, 2000 ($2.95/$2.50)

0-($2.95) 1st app. Courtney Whitmore; Moder and Weston-a; Starman app. 3.00
1-Johns and Robinson-s/Moder-a; origin new Star Spangled Kid 3.00
2-14: 4-Marvel Family app. 9-Seven Soldiers of Victory-c/app. 3.00
JSA Presents: Stars and S.T.R.I.P.E. Vol. 1 TPB (2007, $17.99) r/#1-8; Johns intro. 18.00
JSA Presents: Stars and S.T.R.I.P.E. Vol. 2 TPB (2008, $17.99) r/#0,9-14 18.00

STARS AND STRIPES COMICS
Centaur Publications: No. 2, May, 1941 - No. 6, Dec, 1941

2(#1)-The Shark, The Iron Skull, A-Man, The Amazing Man, Mighty Man, Minimidget begin; The Voice & Dash Dartwell, the Human Meteor, Reef Kinkaid app.; Gustavson Flag-c 300 600 900 1950 3375 4800
3-Origin Dr. Synthe; The Black Panther app. 271 542 813 1734 2967 4200
4-Origin/1st app. The Stars and Stripes; injury to eye-c 174 348 522 1114 1907 2700
5(#5 on cover & inside) 135 270 405 864 1482 2100
5(#6)-(#5 on cover, #6 on inside) 135 270 405 864 1482 2100

NOTE: ***Gustavson** c/a-3. **Myron Strauss** c-4, 5(#5), 5(#6).*

STAR SEED (Formerly Powers That Be)
Broadway Comics: No. 7, 1996 - No. 9 ($2.95)

7-9 3.00

STARSHIP DOWN
Dark Horse Comics: Mar, 2020 - Present ($3.99)

1-Justin Giampaoli-s/Andrea Mutti-a 4.00

STARSHIP TROOPERS
Dark Horse Comics: 1997 - No. 2, 1997 ($2.95, limited series)

1,2-Movie adaptation 1 2 3 5 6 8

STARSHIP TROOPERS: BRUTE CREATIONS
Dark Horse Comics: 1997 ($2.95, one-shot)

1 5.00

STARSHIP TROOPERS: DOMINANT SPECIES
Dark Horse Comics: Aug, 1998 - No. 4, Nov, 1998 ($2.95, limited series)

1-4-Strnad-s/Bolton-c 4.00

STARSHIP TROOPERS: INSECT TOUCH
Dark Horse Comics: 1997 - No. 3, 1997 ($2.95, limited series)

1-3 4.00

STAR SLAMMERS (See Marvel Graphic Novel #6)
Malibu Comics (Bravura): May, 1994 - No. 4, Aug, 1994 ($2.50, unfinished limited series)

1-4: W. Simonson-a/stories; contain Bravura stamps 3.00

STAR SLAMMERS
IDW Publishing: Mar, 2014 - No. 8, Oct, 2014 ($3.99)

1-8-Recolored reprint of 1994 series; Walt Simonson-s/a. 1-4-Two covers by Simonson 4.00

STAR SLAMMERS SPECIAL
Dark Horse Comics (Legend): June, 1996 ($2.95, one-shot)

nn-Simonson-c/a/scripts; concludes Bravura limited series. 3.00

STARSLAYER
Pacific Comics/First Comics No. 7 on: Feb, 1982 - No. 6, Apr, 1983; No. 7, Aug, 1983 - No. 34, Nov, 1985

1-Origin & 1st app.; 1 pg. Rocketeer brief app. which continues in #2 3 6 9 14 19 24
2-Origin/1st full app. the Rocketeer (4/82) by Dave Stevens (Chapter 1 of Rocketeer saga; see Pacific Presents #1,2) 3 6 9 19 30 40
3-Chapter 2 of Rocketeer saga by Stevens 2 4 6 13 18 22
4,6,7: 7-Grell-a ends 5.00
5-2nd app. Groo the Wanderer by Aragonés 2 4 6 9 13 16
8,9,11-34: 18-Starslayer meets Grimjack. 20-The Black Flame begins (9/84, 1st app.), ends #33. 27-Book length Black Flame story 5.00
10-1st app. Grimjack (11/83, ends #17) 2 4 6 9 12 15

NOTE: ***Grell** a-1-7; c-1-8. **Stevens** back c-2, 3. **Sutton** a-17p, 20-22p, 24-27p, 29-33p.*

STARSLAYER (The Director's Cut)
Acclaim Comics (Windjammer): June, 1994 - No. 8, Dec, 1995 ($2.50)

1-8: Mike Grell-c/a/scripts 4.00

STAR SPANGLED COMICS (Star Spangled War Stories #131 on)
National Periodical Publications: Oct, 1941 - No. 130, July, 1952

1-Origin/1st app. Tarantula; Captain X of the R.A.F., Star Spangled Kid (see Action #40), Armstrong of the Army begin; Robot-c 595 1190 1785 4350 7675 11,000
2 194 388 582 1242 2121 3000
3-5 119 238 357 762 1306 1850
6-Last Armstrong/Army; Penniless Palmer begins 77 154 231 493 847 1200
7-(4/42)-Origin/1st app. The Guardian by S&K, & Robotman (by Paul Cassidy & created by Siegel);The Newsboy Legion (1st app.), Robotman & TNT begin; last Captain X 865 1730 2595 6315 11,158 16,000
8-Origin TNT & Dan the Dyna-Mite 258 516 774 1651 2826 4000
9,10 168 336 504 1075 1838 2600
11-17 123 246 369 787 1344 1900
18-Origin Star Spangled Kid 155 310 465 992 1696 2400
19-Last Tarantula 123 246 369 787 1344 1900
20-Liberty Belle begins (5/43) 155 310 465 992 1696 2400
21-29-Last S&K issue; 23-Last TNT. 25-Robotman by Jimmy Thompson begins. 29-Intro Robbie the Robotdog 103 206 309 659 1130 1600
30-40: 31-S&K-c 63 126 189 403 689 975
41-51: 41,49-Kirby-c. 51-Robot-c by Kirby 57 114 171 362 619 875
52-64: 53 by S&K. 64-Last Newsboy Legion & The Guardian 52 104 156 328 552 775
65-Robin begins with c/app. (2/47); Batman cameo in 1 panel; Robin-c begins, end #95 219 438 657 1402 2401 3400
66-Batman cameo in Robin story 100 200 300 635 1093 1550
67,68,70-80: 68-Last Liberty Belle? 72-Burnley Robin-c 74 148 222 470 810 1150
69-Origin/1st app. Tomahawk by F. Ray; atom bomb story & splash (6/47); black-c (rare in high grade) 265 530 795 1694 2897 4100
81-Origin Merry, Girl of 1000 Gimmicks in Star Spangled Kid story 65 130 195 416 708 1000
82,85: 82-Last Robotman? 85-Last Star Spangled Kid? 57 114 171 362 619 875
83-Tomahawk enters the lost valley, a land of dinosaurs; Capt. Compass begins, ends #130 60 120 180 381 653 925
84,87 (Rare): 87-Batman cameo in Robin 90 180 270 576 988 1400

Starslayer #16 © FC

Star Spangled Comics #50 © DC

Star Spangled War Stories #45 © DC

	GD 2.0	VG 4.0	FN 6.0	VF 8.0	VF/NM 9.0	NM- 9.2
86-Batman cameo in Robin story	65	130	195	416	708	1000
88(1/49)-94: Batman-c/stories in all. 91-Federal Men begin, end #93. 94-Manhunters Around						
the World begin, end #121	81	162	243	518	884	1250
95-Batman story; last Robin-c	63	126	189	403	689	975
96,98-Batman cameo in Robin stories. 96-1st Tomahawk-c (also #97-121)						
	43	86	129	271	461	650
97,99	39	78	117	231	378	525
100 (1/50)-Pre-Bat-Hound tryout in Robin story (pre-dates Batman #92).						
	47	94	141	296	498	700
101-109,118,119,121: 121-Last Tomahawk-c	35	70	105	208	339	470
110,111,120-Batman cameo in Robin stories. 120-Last 52 pg. issue						
	37	74	111	222	361	500
112-Batman & Robin story	39	78	117	240	395	550
113-Frazetta-a (10 pgs.)	43	86	129	271	461	650
114-Retells Robin's origin (3/51); Batman & Robin story						
	47	94	141	296	498	700
115,117-Batman app. in Robin stories	39	78	117	240	395	550
116-Flag-c	40	80	120	246	411	575
122-(11/51)-Ghost Breaker-c/stories begin (origin/1st app.), ends #130 (Ghost Breaker						
covers #122-130)	63	126	189	403	689	975
123-126,128,129	40	80	120	246	411	575
127-Batman app.	43	86	129	271	461	650
130-Batman cameo in Robin story	47	94	141	296	498	700

NOTE: *Most all issues after #29 signed by Simon & Kirby are not by them.* ***Bill Ely*** *c-122-130.* ***Mortimer*** *c-65-74(most), 76-95(most).* ***Fred Ray*** *c-96-106, 109, 110, 112, 113, 115-120.* ***S&K*** *c-7-31, 33, 34, 36, 37, 39, 40, 48, 49, 50-54, 56-58.* ***Hal Sherman*** *c-1-6.* ***Dick Sprang*** *c-75.*

STAR SPANGLED COMICS (Also see All Star Comics 1999 crossover titles)
DC Comics: May, 1999 ($1.99, one-shot)

1-Golden Age Sandman and the Star Spangled Kid 3.00

STAR SPANGLED KID (See Action #40, Leading Comics & Star Spangled Comics)

STAR SPANGLED WAR STORIES
DC Comics: Aug/Sept 1952

nn - Ashcan comic, not distributed to newsstands, only for in-house use. Cover art is Western Comics #28 with interior being Western Comics #13 (a VG- copy sold for $2151 in 2012)

STAR SPANGLED WAR STORIES (Formerly Star Spangled Comics #1-130; Becomes The Unknown Soldier #205 on) (See Showcase)
National Periodical Publ.: No. 131, 8/52 - No. 133, 10/52; No. 3, 11/52 - No. 204, 2-3/77

	GD 2.0	VG 4.0	FN 6.0	VF 8.0	VF/NM 9.0	NM- 9.2
131(#1)	219	438	657	1402	2401	3400
132	129	258	387	826	1413	2000
133-Used in **POP**, pg. 94	106	212	318	673	1162	1650
3,5,6: 6-Evans-a	71	142	213	454	777	1100
4-Devil Dog Dugan app.	74	148	222	470	810	1150
7-10	33	66	99	238	532	825
11-20	27	54	81	194	435	675
21-30: 30-Last precode (2/55)	24	48	72	168	372	575
31-33,35-40	20	40	60	138	307	475
34-Krigstein-a	21	42	63	147	324	500
41-44,46-50: 50-1st S.A. issue	18	36	54	125	276	430
45-1st DC grey tone war-c (5/56)	50	100	150	400	900	1400
51,52,54-63,65,66, 68-83	16	32	48	108	239	370
53-"Rock Sergeant," 3rd Sgt. Rock prototype; inspired "P.I. & The Sand Fleas"						
in G.I. Combat #56 (1/57)	29	58	87	209	467	725
64-Pre-Sgt. Rock Easy Co. story (12/57)	21	42	63	147	324	500
67-Two Easy Co. stories without Sgt. Rock	22	44	66	154	340	525
84-Origin Mlle. Marie	141	282	423	1163	2632	4100
85-89-Mlle. Marie in all	34	68	102	245	540	850
90-1st app. "War That Time Forgot" series; dinosaur issue-c/story (4-5/60)						
(also see Weird War Tales #94 & #99)	107	214	321	856	1928	3000
91,93-No dinosaur stories	17	34	51	119	265	410
92-2nd dinosaur-c/s	33	66	99	238	532	825
94 (12/60)- "Ghost Ace" story; Baron Von Richter as The Enemy Ace (predates						
Our Army at War #151)	36	72	108	266	596	925
95-99: Dinosaur-c/s	24	48	72	168	372	575
100-Dinosaur-c/story.	25	50	75	175	388	600
101-115: All dinosaur issues. 102-Panel inspired a famous Roy Lichtenstein painting						
	17	34	51	119	265	410
116-125,127-133,135-137: 120-1st app. Caveboy and Dino. 137-Last dinosaur story;						
Heath Birdman-#129,131	14	28	42	94	207	320
126-No dinosaur story	11	22	33	73	157	240
134-Dinosaur story; Neal Adams-a	17	34	51	114	252	390
138-New Enemy Ace-c/stories begin by Joe Kubert (4-5/68), end #150 (also see Our Army						
at War #151 and Showcase #57)	18	36	54	122	271	420
139-Origin Enemy Ace (7/68)	10	20	30	69	147	225
140-143,145: 145-Last 12¢ issue (6-7/69)	8	16	24	54	102	150
144-Neal Adams/Kubert-a	9	18	27	58	114	170
146-Enemy Ace-c/app.	6	12	18	41	76	110
147,148-New Enemy Ace stories	7	14	21	48	89	130
149,150-Last new Enemy Ace by Kubert. Viking Prince by Kubert						
	7	14	21	44	82	120
151-1st solo app. Unknown Soldier (6-7/70); Enemy Ace-r begin (from Our Army at War,						
Showcase & SSWS); end #161	18	36	54	128	284	440
152-Reprints 2nd Enemy Ace app.	6	12	18	38	69	100
153,155-Enemy Ace reprints; early Unknown Soldier stories						
	5	10	15	34	60	85
154-Origin Unknown Soldier	13	26	39	87	191	295
156-1st Battle Album; Unknown Soldier story; Kubert-c/a						
	5	10	15	31	53	75
157-Sgt. Rock x-over in Unknown Soldier story.	4	8	12	28	47	65
158-163-(52 pgs.): New Unknown Soldier stories; Kubert-c/a. 161-Last Enemy Ace-r						
	4	8	12	25	40	55
164-183,200: 181-183-Enemy Ace vs. Balloon Buster serial app; Frank Thorne-a.						
200-Enemy Ace back-up	3	6	9	15	22	28
184-199,201-204	2	4	6	13	18	22

NOTE: ***Anderson*** *a-28.* ***Chaykin*** *a-167.* ***Drucker*** *a-59, 61, 64, 66, 67, 73-84.* ***Estrada*** *a-149.* ***John Giunta*** *a-72.* ***Glanzman*** *a-167, 171, 172, 174.* ***Heath*** *a-42,122, 132, 133; c-67, 122, 132-134.* ***Kaluta*** *a-197i; c-167.* ***G. Kane*** *a-169.* ***Kubert*** *a-6-163(most later issues), 200.* ***Maurer*** *a-160, 165.* ***Severin*** *a-65, 162.* ***S&K*** *c-7-31, 33, 34, 37, 40.* ***Simonson*** *a-170, 172, 174, 180.* ***Sutton*** *a-168.* ***Thorne*** *a-183.* ***Toth*** *a-164.* ***Wildey*** *a-161. Suicide Squad in 110, 116-118, 120, 121, 127.*

STAR SPANGLED WAR STORIES (Featuring Mademoiselle Marie)
DC Comics: Nov, 2010 ($3.99, one-shot)

1-Mademoiselle Marie in 1944 France; Tucci-s/Justiniano-a/Bolland-c 4.00

STAR SPANGLED WAR STORIES (Featuring G.I. Zombie)
DC Comics: Sept, 2014 - No. 8, May, 2015 ($2.99)

1-8-Palmiotti & Gray-s/Scott Hampton-a. 1-6-Darwyn Cooke-c. 7-Dave Johnson-c 3.00
...: Futures End 1 (11/14, $2.99, regular-c) Five years later; Dave Johnson-c 3.00
...: Futures End 1 (11/14, $3.99, 3-D cover) 4.00

STARSTREAM (Adventures in Science Fiction)(See Questar illustrated)
Whitman/Western Publishing Co.: 1976 (79¢, 68 pgs, cardboard-c)

	GD 2.0	VG 4.0	FN 6.0	VF 8.0	VF/NM 9.0	NM- 9.2
1-4: 1-Bolle-a. 2-4-McWilliams & Bolle-a	2	4	6	10	14	18

STARSTRUCK
Marvel Comics (Epic Comics): Feb, 1985 - No. 6, Feb, 1986 ($1.50, mature)

1-6: Kaluta-a 6.00

STARSTRUCK
Dark Horse Comics: Aug, 1990 - No. 4, Nov?, 1990 ($2.95, B&W, 52pgs.)

1-3: Kaluta-r/Epic series plus new-c/a in all 4.00
4 (68 pgs.)-contains 2 trading cards 5.00
Reprint 1-13 (IDW, 8/09 - No. 13, Sept, 2010, $3.99) newly colored; Galactic Girl Guides 4.00

STARSTRUCK: OLD PROLDIERS NEVER DIE
IDW Publishing: Feb, 2017 - No. 6, Jul, 2017 ($4.99)

1-Expanded version of old stories with new art; Elaine Lee-s/Michael Kaluta-a 5.00

STAR STUDDED
Cambridge House/Superior Publishers: 1945 (25¢, 132 pgs.); 1945 (196 pgs.)

	GD 2.0	VG 4.0	FN 6.0	VF 8.0	VF/NM 9.0	NM- 9.2
nn-Captain Combat by Giunta, Ghost Woman, Commandette, & Red Rogue app.; Infantino-a						
	52	104	156	328	552	775
nn-The Cadet, Edison Bell, Hoot Gibson, Jungle Lil (196 pgs.); copies vary; Blue Beetle						
in some	54	108	162	343	574	825

STARTLING COMICS
Better Publications (Nedor): June, 1940 - No. 53, Sept, 1948

	GD 2.0	VG 4.0	FN 6.0	VF 8.0	VF/NM 9.0	NM- 9.2
1-Origin Captain Future-Man Of Tomorrow, Mystico (By Sansone), The Wonder Man;						
The Masked Rider & his horse Pinto begins; Masked Rider formerly in pulps;						
drug use story	383	766	1149	2681	4691	6700
2 -Don Davis, Espionage Ace begins	200	400	600	1280	2190	3100
3	164	328	492	1041	1796	2550
4	135	270	405	864	1482	2100
5,6,9	116	232	348	742	1271	1800
7,8-Nazi WWII-c	155	310	465	992	1696	2400
10-The Fighting Yank begins (9/41, origin/1st app.); Nazi WWII-c						
	1100	2200	3300	8400	15,200	22,000
11-2nd app. Fighting Yank; Nazi WWII-c	300	600	900	1950	3375	4800
12-Hitler, Tojo, Mussolini-c	371	742	1113	2600	4550	6500
13-15	135	270	405	864	1482	2100
16-Origin The Four Comrades; not in #32,35	155	310	465	992	1696	2400
17-Last Masked Rider & Mystico	142	284	426	909	1555	2200
18-Pyroman begins (12/42, origin)(also see America's Best Comics #3 for 1st app., 11/42)						

GD VG FN VF VF/NM NM-
2.0 4.0 6.0 8.0 9.0 9.2

206 412 618 1318 2259 3200
19-Nazi WWII-c 290 580 870 1856 3178 4500
20-Classic hooded Nazi giant snake bondage/torture-c (scarce); The Oracle begins (3/43); not in issues 26,28,33,34 486 972 1458 3550 6275 9000
21-Origin The Ape, Oracle's enemy; Schomburg hypo-c 219 438 657 1402 2401 3400
22-34: All have Schomburg WWII-c. 34-Origin The Scarab & only app. 161 322 483 1030 1765 2500
35-Hypodermic syringe attacks Fighting Yank in drug story; Schomburg WWII-c 174 348 522 1114 1907 2700
36-43: 36-Last Four Comrades. 38-Bondage/torture-c. 40-Last Capt. Future & Oracle. 41-Front Page Peggy begins; A-Bomb-c. 43-Last Pyroman 77 154 231 493 847 1200
44,45: 44-Lance Lewis, Space Detective begins; Ingels-c; sci/fi-c begin. 45-Tygra begins (intro/origin, 5/47); Ingels-c/a (splash pg. & inside f/c B&W ad) 129 258 387 826 1413 2000
46-Classic Ingels-c; Ingels-a 275 550 825 1746 3023 4300
47,48,50-53: 50,51-Sea-Eagle app. 142 284 426 909 1555 2200
49-Classic Schomburg Robot-c; last Fighting Yank 1575 3150 4725 11,800 20,900 30,000
NOTE: ***Ingels** a-44, 45; c-44, 45, 46(wash). **Schomburg (Xela)** c-21-43; 47-53 (airbrush). **Tuska** c-45? Bondage c-16, 21, 37, 46-49. Captain Future c-1-9, 13, 14. Fighting Yank c-10-12, 15-17, 21, 22, 24, 26, 28, 30, 32, 34, 36, 38, 40, 42. Pyroman c-18-20, 23, 25, 27, 29, 31, 33, 35, 37, 39, 41, 43.*

STARTLING STORIES: BANNER
Marvel Comics: July, 2001 - No. 4, Oct, 2001 ($2.99, limited series)
1-4-Hulk story by Azzarello; Corben-c/a 3.00
TPB (11/01, $12.95) r/1-4 13.00

STARTLING STORIES: FANTASTIC FOUR - UNSTABLE MOLECULES (See Fantastic Four - ...)

STARTLING STORIES: THE MEGALOMANIACAL SPIDER-MAN
Marvel Comics: Jun, 2002 ($2.99, one-shot)
1-Spider-Man spoof; Peter Bagge-s/a 3 4 6 9 12 15

STARTLING STORIES: THE THING
Marvel Comics: 2003 ($3.50, one-shot)
1-Zimmerman-s/Kramer-a; Inhumans and the Hulk app. 3.50

STARTLING STORIES: THE THING - NIGHT FALLS ON YANCY STREET
Marvel Comics: Jun, 2003 - No. 4, Sept, 2003 ($3.50, limited series)
1-4-Dorkin-s/Haspiel-a. 2,3-Frightful Four app. 3.50

STARTLING TERROR TALES
Star Publications: No. 10, May, 1952 - No. 14, Feb, 1953; No. 4, Apr, 1953 - No. 11, 1954
10-(1st Series)-Wood/Harrison-a (r/A Star Presentation #3) Disbrow/Cole-c; becomes 4 different titles after #10; becomes Confessions of Love #11 on, The Horrors #11 on, Terrifying Tales #11 on, Terrors of the Jungle #11 on & continues w/Startling Terror #11 135 270 405 864 1482 2100
11-(8/52)-L. B. Cole Spider-c; r-Fox's "A Feature Presentation" #5 (blue-c) 541 1082 1623 3950 6975 10,000
11-Black-c (variant; believed to be a pressrun change) (Unique) 595 1190 1785 4350 7675 11,000
12,14 65 130 195 416 708 1000
13-Jo-Jo-r; Disbrow-a 68 136 204 435 743 1050
4-9,11(1953-54) (2nd Series): 11-New logo 47 94 141 296 498 700
10-Disbrow-a 53 106 159 334 567 800
NOTE: ***L. B. Cole** covers-all issues. **Palais** a-V2#8r, V2#11r.*

STAR TREK (TV) (See Dan Curtis Giveaways, Dynabrite Comics & Power Record Comics)
Gold Key: 7/67; No. 2, 6/68; No. 3, 12/68; No. 4, 6/69 - No. 61, 3/79
1-Photo-c begin, end #9; photo back-c is on all copies, no variant exists with an ad on the back-c 145 290 435 1196 2698 4200
2-Regular version has an ad on back-c 28 56 84 202 451 700
2 (rare variation w/photo back-c) 57 114 171 456 1028 1600
3-5-All have back-c ads 18 36 54 124 275 425
3 (rare variation w/photo back-c) 34 68 102 245 548 850
6-9 12 24 36 79 170 260
10-20 6 12 18 37 66 95
21-30 5 10 15 31 53 80
31-40 4 8 12 27 44 60
41-61: 52-Drug propaganda story 3 6 9 21 33 45
... Gold Key 100-Page Spectacular (IDW, 2/17, $7.99) r/#1,8,14; cover & pin-up gallery8.00
...the Enterprise Logs nn (8/76)-Golden Press, ($1.95, 224 pgs.)-r/#1-8 plus 7 pgs. by McWilliams (#11185)-Photo-c 7 14 21 48 89 130
...the Enterprise Logs Vol. 2 ('76)-r/#9-17 (#11187)-Photo-c 5 10 15 34 60 85
...the Enterprise Logs Vol. 3 ('77)-r/#18-26 (#11188); McWilliams-a (4 pgs.)-Photo-c 5 10 15 33 57 80
Star Trek Vol. 4 (Winter '77)-Reprints #27,28,30-34,36,38 (#11189) plus 3 pgs. new art 5 10 15 31 53 75
... : The Key Collection (Checker Book Publ. Group, 2004, $22.95) r/#1-8 23.00
... : The Key Collection Volume 2 (Checker, 2004, $22.95) r/#9-16 23.00
... : The Key Collection Volume 3 (Checker, 2005, $22.95) r/#17-24 23.00
... : The Key Collection Volume 4 (Checker, 2005, $22.95) r/#25-33 23.00
... : The Key Collection Volume 5 (Checker, 2006, $22.95) r/#34,36,38,39,40-43 23.00
NOTE: ***McWilliams** a-38, 40-44, 46-61. #29 reprints #1; #35 reprints #4; #37 reprints #5; #45 reprints #7. The tabloids all have photo covers and blank inside covers. Painted covers #10-44, 46-59.*

STAR TREK
Marvel Comics Group: April, 1980 - No. 18, Feb, 1982
1: 1-3-r/Marvel Super Special; movie adapt. 3 6 9 16 23 30
2-16: 5-Miller-c 2 4 6 8 10 12
17-Low print run 2 4 6 10 14 18
18-Last issue; low print run 2 4 6 11 16 20
NOTE: ***Austin** c-18i. **Buscema** a-13. **Gil Kane** a-15. **Nasser** c/a-7. **Simonson** c-17.*

STAR TREK (Also see Who's Who In Star Trek)
DC Comics: Feb, 1984 - No. 56, Nov, 1988 (75¢, Mando paper)
1-Sutton-a(p) begins 2 4 6 13 18 22
2-5 6.00
6-10: 7-Origin Saavik 5.00
11-32,34-49,51-56: 19-Walter Koenig story. 37-Painted-c 4.00
33-($1.25, 52 pgs.)-20th anniversary issue 5.00
50-($1.50, 52 pgs.) 5.00
Annual 1-3: 1(1985). 2(1986). 3(1988, $1.50) 5.00
...: To Boldly Go TPB (Titan Books, 7/05, $19.95) r/#1-6; Koenig foreward; cast interviews 20.00
...: The Trial of James T. Kirk TPB (Titan Books, 6/06, $19.95) r/#7-12; cast interviews 20.00
...: The Return of the Worthy TPB (Titan Books, 12/06, $19.95) r/#13-18; cast interviews 20.00
NOTE: ***Morrow** a-28, 35, 36, 56. **Orlando** c-8i. **Perez** c-1-3. **Spiegle** a-19. **Starlin** c-24, 25. **Sutton** a-1-6p, 8-18p, 20-27p, 29p, 31-34p, 39-52p, 55p; c-4-6p, 8-22p, 46p.*

STAR TREK
DC Comics: Oct, 1989 - No. 80, Jan, 1996 ($1.50/$1.75/$1.95/$2.50)
1-Capt. Kirk and crew 2 4 6 8 10 12
2,3 5.00
4-23,25-30: 10-12-The Trial of James T. Kirk. 21-Begin $1.75-c 3.00
24-($2.95, 68 pgs.)-40 pg. epic w/pin-ups 4.00
31-49,51-74,76-80 3.00
50-($3.50, 68 pgs.)-Painted-c 4.00
75 ($3.95) 4.00
Annual 1-6('90-'95, 68 pgs.): 1-Morrow-a. 3-Painted-c 4.00
Special 1-3 ('9-'95, 68 pgs.)-1-Sutton-a. 4.00
...: The Ashes of Eden (1995, $14.95, 100 pgs.)-Shatner story 18.00
...Generations (1994, $3.95, 68 pgs.)-Movie adaptation 1 3 4 6 8 10
...Generations (1994, $5.95, 68 pgs.)-Squarebound 1 3 4 6 8 10

STAR TREK...(TV)
DC Comics (WildStorm): one-shots
All of Me (4/00, $5.95, prestige format) Lopresti-a 6.00
Enemy Unseen TPB (2001, $17.95) r/Perchance to Dream, Embrace the Wolf, The Killing Shadows; Struzan-c 18.00
Enter the Wolves (2001, $5.95) Crispin & Weinstein-s; Mota-a/c 6.00
New Frontier - Double Time (11/00, $5.95)-Captain Calhoun's USS Excalibur; Peter David-s; Stelfreeze-c 6.00
Other Realities TPB (2001, $14.95) r/All of Me, New Frontier - Double Time, and DS9-N-Vector; Van Fleet-c 15.00
Special (2001, $6.95) Stories from all 4 series by various; Van Fleet-c 7.00

STAR TREK (Further adventures of the crew from the 2009 movie)
IDW Publishing: Sept, 2011 - No. 60, Aug, 2016 ($3.99)
1-49: 1,2-Gary Mitchell app.; Molnar-a. 11,12-Tribbles. 15,16-Mirror Universe. 21-Follows the 2013 movie; Klingons & Section 31 app. 35-40-The Q Gambit; DS9 crew app. 4.00
50-($4.99) Mirror Universe; Khan app.; bonus history of Star Trek comics, aliens 5.00
51-60: 51,52-Mirror Universe. 52-Variant Archie Comics cover. 55-58-Legacy of Spock 4.00
Annual (12/13, $7.99) "Strange New Worlds" on cover; photonovel by John Byrne 8.00
... #1: Greatest Hits (3/16, $1.00) reprints #1 3.00
... #1: Hundred Penny Press (8/13, $1.00) reprints #1 3.00
...: Deviations 1 (3/17, $4.99) Timeline where Romulans, not Vulcans made 1st Contact 5.00
...: Ferengi 1 (4/22, $7.99) Quark, Rom and Moogie app; Christina Rice-s/Andy Price-a 8.00
...: 50th Anniversary Cover Celebration (8/16, $7.99) Gallery of IDW Star Trek covers 8.00
...: Flesh and Stone (7/14, $3.99) Doctors Bashir, Crusher, Pulaski, McCoy app. 4.00
...: IDW 20/20 (1/19, $4.99) Picard on the Stargazer 20 years before TNG; Woodward-a 5.00
...: Klingons 1 (2/22, $7.99) Story of Kahless; Timothy Green II-a 8.00
... Space Spanning Treasury Edition (4/13, $9.99, 13" x 8.5") Reprints #9,10,13 10.00

STAR TREK (400th issue published by IDW)
IDW Publishing: No. 400, Sept, 2022 ($7.99, one-shot)
400-IDW Legacy issue; short story anthology spanning all the crews by various 8.00

STAR TREK
IDW Publishing: Oct, 2022 - Present ($4.99)
1-4-Crew of Sisko, Data, Dr. Crusher, Tom Paris and Worf 5.00
...: Trill 1 (11/22, $7.99) Houser-s/Prasetya-a 8.00

STAR TREK: ALIEN SPOTLIGHT
IDW Publishing: Sept, 2007 - Feb, 2008 ($3.99, series of one-shots)
... Andorians (11/07) Storrie-s/O'Grady-a; Counselor Troi app.; two art & one photo-c 4.00
... Borg (1/08) Harris-s/Murphy-a; Janeway & Next Gen crew app.; two art & one photo-c 4.00
... Cardassians (12/09) Padilla-a; Garak & Kira app. 4.00
... The Gorn (9/07) Messina-a; Chekov app.; two art & one photo-c 4.00
... Orions (12/07) Casagrande-a; Capt. Pike app.; two art & one photo-c 4.00
... Q (8/09) Casagrande-a; takes place after Star Trek 8 movie; two art & one photo-c 4.00
... Romulans (2/08) John Byrne-s/a; Kirk era; two art & one photo-c 4.00
... Romulans (5/09) Wagner Reis-a; David Williams-c 4.00
... Tribbles (3/09) Hawthorne-a; first encounter with Klingons; one art & one photo-c 4.00
... Vulcans (10/07) Spock's early Enterprise days with Capt. Pike; two art & one photo-c 4.00

STAR TREK: ASSIGNMENT EARTH
IDW Publishing: May, 2008 - No. 5, Sept, 2008 ($3.99, limited series)
1-5-Further adventures of Gary Seven and Roberta; John Byrne-s/a/c. 5-Nixon app. 4.00

STAR TREK: BOLDLY GO (Takes place after the 2016 movie Star Trek Beyond)
IDW Publishing: Oct, 2016 - No. 18, Mar, 2018 ($3.99)
1-18-The 2009 movie crew; Mike Johnson-s/Shasteen-a; The Borg app.; multiple covers 4.00

STAR TREK: BURDEN OF KNOWLEDGE
IDW Publishing: Jun, 2010 - No. 4, Sept, 2010 ($3.99, limited series)
1-4-Original series Kirk and crew; Manfredi-a 4.00

STAR TREK: CAPTAIN'S LOG
IDW Publishing: one-shots
...: Harriman (4/10, $3.99) Captain of the Enterprise-B following Kirk's "demise"; Currie-a 4.00
...: Jellico (10/10, $3.99) Woodward-a 4.00
...: Pike (9/10, $3.99) Events that put Pike in the chair; Woodward-a 4.00
...: Sulu (1/10, $3.99) Manfredi-a 4.00

STAR TREK: COUNTDOWN (Prequel to the 2009 movie)
IDW Publishing: Jan, 2009 - No. 4, Apr, 2009 ($3.99, limited series)
1-4: 1-Ambassador Spock on Romulus; intro. Nero; Messina-a 4.00
Hundred Penny Press: Star Trek: Countdown #1 (4/11, $1.00) r/#1 w/new cover frame 3.00

STAR TREK: COUNTDOWN TO DARKNESS (Prequel to the 2013 movie)

Startling Terror Tales #8 © STAR

Star Trek (2011) #1 © CBS

Star Trek: Lower Decks #1 © CBS

	GD 2.0	VG 4.0	FN 6.0	VF 8.0	VF/NM 9.0	NM- 9.2

IDW Publishing: Jan, 2013 - No. 4, Apr, 2013 ($3.99, limited series)
1-4-Captain April app.; Messina-a; regular & photo covers on each 4.00

STAR TREK: CREW
IDW Publishing: Mar, 2009 - No. 5, Jul, 2009 ($3.99, limited series)
1-5: John Byrne-s/a; Captain Pike era 4.00

STAR TREK: DEBT OF HONOR
DC Comics: 1992 ($24.95/$14.95, graphic novel)
Hardcover ($24.95) Claremont-s/Hughes-a(p) 25.00
Softcover ($14.95) 15.00

STAR TREK: DEEP SPACE NINE (TV)
Malibu Comics: Aug, 1993 - No. 32, Jan, 1996 ($2.50)
1-Direct Sale Edition w/line drawn-c 1 2 3 5 6 8
1-Newsstand Edition with photo-c 6.00
0-(1/95, $2.95)-Terok Nor 4.00
2-30: 2-Polybagged w/trading card. 9-4 pg. prelude to Hearts & Minds 4.00
31-($3.95) 5.00
32-($3.50) 5.00
Annual 1 (1/95, $3.95, 68 pgs.) 5.00
Special 1 (1995, $3.50) 5.00
Ultimate Annual 1 (12/95, $5.95) 6.00
...:Lightstorm (12/94, $3.50) 5.00

STAR TREK: DEEP SPACE NINE (TV)
Marvel Comics (Paramount Comics): Nov, 1996 - No. 15, Mar, 1998 ($1.95/$1.99)
1-15: 12,13-"Telepathy War" pt. 2,3 4.00

STAR TREK: DEEP SPACE NINE: FOOL'S GOLD
IDW Publishing: Dec, 2009 - No. 4, Mar, 2010 ($3.99)
1-4-Mantovani-a 4.00

STAR TREK: DEEP SPACE NINE -- N-VECTOR (TV)
DC Comics (WildStorm): Aug, 2000 - No. 4, Nov, 2000 ($2.50, limited series)
1-4-Cypress-a 3.00

STAR TREK DEEP SPACE NINE-THE CELEBRITY SERIES
Malibu Comics: May, 1995 ($2.95)
1-Blood and Honor; Mark Lenard script 4.00
1-Rules of Diplomacy; Aron Eisenberg script 4.00

STAR TREK: DEEP SPACE NINE HEARTS AND MINDS
Malibu Comics: June, 1994 - No. 4, Sept, 1994 ($2.50, limited series)
1-4 4.00
1-Holographic-c 5.00

STAR TREK: DEEP SPACE NINE, THE MAQUIS
Malibu Comics: Feb, 1995 - No. 3, Apr, 1995 ($2.50, limited series)
1-3-Newsstand-c, 1-Photo-c 4.00

STAR TREK: DEEP SPACE NINE/THE NEXT GENERATION
Malibu Comics: Oct, 1994 - No. 2, Nov, 1994 ($2.50, limited series)
1,2: Parts 2 & 4 of x-over with Star Trek: TNG/DS9 from DC Comics 4.00

STAR TREK: DEEP SPACE NINE – TOO LONG A SACRIFICE
IDW Publishing: Apr, 2020 - No. 4, Oct, 2020 ($3.99, limited series)
1-4-Steve & David Tipton-s/Greg Scott-a 4.00

STAR TREK: DEEP SPACE NINE WORF SPECIAL
Malibu Comics: Dec, 1995 ($3.95, one-shot)
1-Includes pinups 6.00

STAR TREK: DISCOVERY (Based on the 2017 TV series)
IDW Publishing: Mar, 2018 ($7.99)
Annual 2018 (3/18, $7.99)-Beyer & Johnson-s/Hernandez-a; spotlight on Lt. Stamets 8.00
...: Captain Saru (2/19, $7.99) Beyer & Johnson-s/Hernandez-a; two covers 8.00

STAR TREK: DISCOVERY: ADVENTURES IN THE 32ND CENTURY (2017 TV series)
IDW Publishing: Mar, 2022 - No. 4, Jun, 2022 ($3.99, limited series)
1-4-Johnson-s/Hernandez-a 4.00

STAR TREK: DISCOVERY – AFTERMATH (Based on the 2017 TV series)
IDW Publishing: Aug, 2019 - No. 3, Oct, 2019 ($3.99, limited series)
1-3-Beyer & Johnson-s/Shasteen-a; takes place before Spock joins the Enterprise 4.00

STAR TREK: DISCOVERY: SUCCESSION (Based on the 2017 TV series)
IDW Publishing: Apr, 2018 - No. 4, Jul, 2018 ($3.99, limited series)
1-4-Beyer & Johnson-s/Hernandez-a; takes place in the Mirror Universe 4.00

STAR TREK: DISCOVERY: THE LIGHT OF KAHLESS (Based on the 2017 TV series)
IDW Publishing: Oct, 2017 - No. 4, Jan, 2018 ($3.99, limited series)
1-4-Beyer & Johnson-s/Shasteen-a 4.00

STAR TREK: DIVIDED WE FALL
DC Comics (WildStorm): July, 2001 - No. 4, Oct, 2001 ($2.95, limited series)
1-4: Ordover & Mack-s; Lenara Kahn, Verad and Odan app. 3.00

STAR TREK EARLY VOYAGES (TV)
Marvel Comics (Paramount Comics): Feb, 1997 - No. 17, Jun, 1998 ($2.95/$1.95/$1.99)
1-($2.95) 6.00
2-17 4.00

STAR TREK: ENTERPRISE EXPERIMENT
IDW Publishing: Apr, 2008 - No. 5, Aug, 2008 ($3.99, limited series)
1-5-Year Four story; D.C. Fontana & Derek Chester-s; Purcell-a 4.00

STAR TREK: FIRST CONTACT (Movie)
Marvel Comics (Paramount Comics): Nov, 1996 ($5.95, one-shot)
nn-Movie adaption 6.00

STAR TREK/ GREEN LANTERN (The Spectrum War)
IDW Publishing: Jul, 2015 - No. 6, Dec, 2015 ($3.99, limited series)
1-6-Crew from 2009 movie and Hal Jordan; Sinestro & Nekron app.; multiple covers 4.00

STAR TREK/ GREEN LANTERN (Stranger Worlds)
IDW Publishing: Dec, 2016 - No. 6, May, 2017 ($3.99, limited series)
1-6-Sinestro & The Manhunters app.; multiple covers. 2-6-Khan app. 4.00

STAR TREK: HARLAN ELLISON'S ORIGINAL CITY ON THE EDGE OF FOREVER TELEPLAY
IDW Publishing: Jun, 2014 - No. 5, Oct, 2014 ($3.99, limited series)
1-5-Adaptation of Ellison's teleplay; J.K. Woodward-a; two covers on each 4.00

STAR TREK: INFESTATION (Crossover with G.I. Joe, Transformers & Ghostbusters)
IDW Publishing: Feb, 2011 - No. 2, Feb, 2011 ($3.99, limited series)
1,2-Zombies in the Kirk era; Maloney & Erskine-a; two covers on each 4.00

STAR TREK: KHAN
IDW Publishing: Oct, 2013 - No. 5, Feb, 2014 ($3.99, limited series)
1-5-Follows the 2013 movie; Khan's origin; Messina & Balboni-a 4.00

STAR TREK: KHAN RULING IN HELL
IDW Publishing: Oct, 2010 - No. 4, Jan, 2011 ($3.99, limited series)
1-4-Khan and the Botany Bay crew after banishment on Ceti Alpha V; Mantovani-a 4.00

STAR TREK: KLINGONS: BLOOD WILL TELL
IDW Publishing: Apr, 2007 - No. 5 ($3.99, limited series)
1-5-Star Trek TOS episodes from the Klingon viewpoint; Messina-a. 2-Tribbles 4.00
1-($4.99) Klingon Language Variant; comic with Kliingon text; English script 5.00

STAR TREK/ LEGION OF SUPER-HEROES
IDW Publishing: Oct, 2011 - No. 6, Mar, 2012 ($3.99, limited series)
1-6-Jeff Moy-a/Jimenez-c 1-Giffen var-c. 2-Lightle var-c. 3-Grell var-c. 5-Allred var-c 4.00

STAR TREK: LEONARD McCOY, FRONTIER DOCTOR
IDW Publishing: Apr, 2010 - No. 4, Jul, 2010 ($3.99, limited series)
1-4-Dr. McCoy right before Star Trek: TMP; John Byrne-s/a 4.00

STAR TREK: LOWER DECKS (Based on the animated TV series)
IDW Publishing: Sept, 2022 - No. 3, Nov, 2022 ($6.99, limited series)
1-3-Ryan North-s/Chris Fenoglio-a 7.00

STAR TREK: MANIFEST DESTINY
IDW Publishing: Apr, 2016 - No. 4, May, 2016 ($4.99/$3.99, limited series)
1-The 2009 movie crew vs. Klingons; Angel Hernandez-a 5.00
2-4-($3.99) 4.00

STAR TREK: MIRROR BROKEN (Series previewed in Star Trek: The Next Generation: Mirror Broken #0 FCBD giveaway)
IDW Publishing: May, 2017 - No. 5, Oct, 2017 ($3.99, limited series)
1-5-The Mirror Universe Next Generation crew; David & Scott Tipton-s/Woodward-a 4.00

STAR TREK: MIRROR IMAGES
IDW Publishing: June, 2008 - No. 5, Nov, 2008 ($3.99, limited series)
1-5-Further adventures in the Mirror Universe. 3-Mirror-Picard app. 4.00

STAR TREK: MIRROR MIRROR
Marvel Comics (Paramount Comics): Feb, 1997 ($3.95, one-shot)
1-DeFalco-s 4.00

STAR TREK: MISSION'S END

	GD 2.0	VG 4.0	FN 6.0	VF 8.0	VF/NM 9.0	NM- 9.2

IDW Publishing: Mar, 2009 - No. 5, July, 2009 ($3.99, limited series)
1-5-Kirk, Spock, Bones crew, their last mission on the pre-movie Enterprise 4.00

STAR TREK MOVIE ADAPTATION
IDW Publishing: Feb, 2010 - No. 6, Aug, 2010 ($3.99, limited series)
1-6-Adaptation of 2009 movie; Messina-a; regular & photo-c on each 4.00

STAR TREK MOVIE SPECIAL
DC Comics: 1984 (June) - No. 2, 1987 ($1.50); No. 1, 1989 ($2.00, 52 pgs)
nn-(#1)-Adapts Star Trek III; Sutton-p (68 pgs.) 5.00
2-Adapts Star Trek IV; Sutton-a; Chaykin-c. (68 pgs.) 5.00
1 (1989)-Adapts Star Trek V; painted-c 5.00

STAR TREK: NERO
IDW Publishing: Aug, 2009 - No. 4, Nov, 2009 ($3.99, limited series)
1-4-Nero's ship after the attack on the Kelvin to the arrival of Spock 4.00

STAR TREK: NEW FRONTIER
IDW Publishing: Mar, 2008 - No. 5, July, 2008 ($3.99, limited series)
1-5-Capt. Calhoun & Adm. Shelby app.; Peter David-s 4.00

STAR TREK: NEW VISIONS
IDW Publishing: May, 2014 - No. 22, Jun, 2018 ($7.99, squarebound)
1-22-Photonovels of original crew by John Byrne. 1-Mirror Universe 8.00
... Special: More Of The Serpent Than The Dove (9/16, Humble Bundle) Gorn app. 20.00
... Special: The Cage (7/16, $7.99) 8.00

STAR TREK 100 PAGE...
IDW Publishing: Nov, 2011 - 2012 ($7.99)
...Spectacular #1 (11/11) Reprints stories of the original crew; s/a by Byrne and others 8.00
...Spectacular 2012 (2/12) Reprints; Khan, Q, Capt. Pike, the Gorn app. 8.00
...Spectacular Summer 2012 (8/12) Reprints of TNG and Voyager stories 8.00
...Spectacular Winter 2012 - Reprints; Capt. Harriman, Mirror Universe 8.00

STAR TREK: OPERATION ASSIMILATION
Marvel Comics (Paramount Comics): Dec, 1996 ($2.95, one-shot)
1 4.00

STAR TREK: PICARD COUNTDOWN (Prelude to the 2020 TV series)
IDW Publishing: Nov, 2019 - No. 3, Jan, 2020 ($3.99, limited series)
1-3-Beyer & Johnson-s/Hernandez-a; intro. Raffi Musiker, Laris & Zhaban 4.00

STAR TREK: PICARD STARGAZER (Follows season 2 of the TV series)
IDW Publishing: Aug, 2022 - No. 3, Nov, 2022 ($4.99, limited series)
1-3-Beyer & Johnson-s/Hernandez-a; Seven app. 5.00

STAR TREK/PLANET OF THE APES: THE PRIMATE DIRECTIVE
IDW Publishing: Dec, 2014 - No. 5, Apr, 2015 ($3.99, limited series)
1-5-Classic crew on the Planet of the Apes; Klingons app. 2-Kirk meets Taylor 8.00

STAR TREK: RESURGENCE (Prequel to the video game)
IDW Publishing: Nov, 2022 - Present ($3.99, limited series)
1-4-Leah Brahms app.; Josh Hood-a 4.00

STAR TREK: ROMULANS SCHISMS
IDW Publishing: Sept, 2009 - No. 3, Nov, 2009 ($3.99, limited series)
1-3-John Byrne-s/a/c 4.00

STAR TREK: ROMULANS THE HOLLOW CROWN
IDW Publishing: Sept, 2008 - No. 2, Oct, 2008 ($3.99, limited series)
1,2-John Byrne-s/a/c 4.00

STAR TREK VI: THE UNDISCOVERED COUNTRY (Movie)
DC Comics: 1992
1-($2.95, regular edition, 68 pgs.)-Adaptation of film 1 2 3 5 6 8
nn-($5.95, prestige edition)-Has photos of movie not included in regular edition; painted-c by Palmer; photo back-c 1 3 4 6 8 10

STAR TREK: SPOCK: REFLECTIONS
IDW Publishing: July, 2009 - No. 4, Oct, 2009 ($3.99, limited series)
1-4-Flashbacks of Spock's childhood and career; Messina & Manfredi-a 4.00

STAR TREK: STARFLEET ACADEMY
Marvel Comics (Paramount Comics): Dec, 1996 - No. 19, Jun, 1998 ($1.95/$1.99)
1-19: Begin new series. 12-"Telepathy War" pt. 1. 18-English & Klingon editions 4.00

STAR TREK: STARFLEET ACADEMY
IDW Publishing: Dec, 2015 - No. 5, Apr, 2016 ($3.99, limited series)
1-5-Crew of the 2009 movie at the academy; Charm-a 4.00

STAR TREK: STRANGE NEW WORLDS - THE ILLYRIAN ENIGMA
IDW Publishing: Dec, 2022 - Present ($3.99, limited series)
1-Beyer & Johnson-s/Levens-a 4.00

STAR TREK: TELEPATHY WAR
Marvel Comics (Paramount Comics): Nov, 1997 ($2.99, 48 pgs., one-shot)
1-"Telepathy War" x-over pt. 6 4.00

STAR TREK: THE MIRROR WAR
IDW Publishing: No. 0, Aug, 2021 - No. 8, Aug, 2022 ($3.99)
0-8-Mirror Universe Enterprise crew. 1-5-Scott & David Tipton-s/Gavin Smith-a 4.00
...: Data 1 (12/21, $3.99) Bronfman-s/Ingranata-a; Barclay app. 4.00
...: La Forge 1 (3/22, $3.99) Holtham-s/Rodriguez-a 4.00
...: Sisko 1 (6/22, $3.99) Lore-s/Prasetya-a 4.00
...: Troi 1 (9/22, $3.99) Nijkamp-s/Levens-a 4.00

STAR TREK - THE MODALA IMPERATIVE
DC Comics: Late July, 1991 - No. 4, Late Sept, 1991 ($1.75, limited series)
1-4 4.00
TPB ($19.95) r/series and ST:TNG - The Modala Imperative 20.00

STAR TREK: THE NEXT GENERATION (TV)
DC Comics: Feb, 1988 - No. 6, July, 1988 (limited series)
1 ($1.50, 52 pgs.)-Sienkiewicz painted-c 2 4 6 9 13 16
2-6 ($1.00) 5.00

STAR TREK: THE NEXT GENERATION (TV)
DC Comics: Oct, 1989 -No. 80, 1995 ($1.50/$1.75/$1.95)
1-Capt. Picard and crew from TV show 2 4 6 9 13 16
2,3 6.00
4-10 5.00
11-23,25-49,51-60 4.00
24,50: 24-($2.50, 52 pgs.). 50-($3.50, 68 pgs.)-Painted-c 6.00
61-74,76-80 4.00
75-($3.95, 50 pgs.) 5.00
Annual 1-6 ('90-'95, 68 pgs.) 5.00
Special 1 -3('93-'95, 68 pgs.)-1-Contains 3 stories 5.00
...-The Series Finale (1994, $3.95, 68 pgs.) 5.00

STAR TREK: THE NEXT GENERATION (TV)
DC Comics (WildStorm): one-shots
Embrace the Wolf (6/00, $5.95, prestige format) Golden & Sniegoski-s 6.00
Forgiveness (2001, $24.95, HC) David Brin-s/Scott Hampton painted-a; dust jacket-c 30.00
Forgiveness (2002, $17.95, SC) 18.00
The Gorn Crisis (1/01, $29.95, HC) Kordey painted-a/dust jacket-c 30.00
The Gorn Crisis (1/01, $17.95, SC) Kordey painted-a 18.00

STAR TREK: THE NEXT GENERATION – BEST OF PICARD
IDW Publishing: Jan, 2022 ($6.99, one-shot)
1-Reprints ST:TNG #1 (1989) and 3 recent stories; Mirror Universe Picard & Q app. 7.00

STAR TREK: THE NEXT GENERATION/DEEP SPACE NINE (TV)
DC Comics: Dec, 1994 - No. 2, Jan, 1995 ($2.50, limited series)
1,2-Parts 1 & 3 of x-over with Star Trek: DS9/TNG from Malibu Comics 4.00

STAR TREK: THE NEXT GENERATION / DOCTOR WHO: ASSIMILATION²
IDW Publishing: May, 2012 - No. 8, Dec, 2012 ($3.99, limited series)
1-8-The Borg and Cybermen team-up; Tipton-s/Woodward-a; multiple covers on each 4.00

STAR TREK: THE NEXT GENERATION: GHOSTS
IDW Publishing: Nov, 2009 - No. 5, Mar, 2010 ($3.99)
1-5-Cannon-s/Aranda-a 4.00

STAR TREK: THE NEXT GENERATION - ILL WIND
DC Comics: Nov, 1995 - No. 4, Feb, 1996 ($2.50, limited series)
1-4: Hugh Fleming painted-c on all 4.00

STAR TREK: THE NEXT GENERATION: INTELLIGENCE GATHERING
IDW Publishing: Jan, 2008 - No. 5, May, 2008 ($3.99)
1-5-Messina-a/Scott & David Tipton-s; two covers on each 4.00

STAR TREK: THE NEXT GENERATION: MIRROR BROKEN (See Star Trek: Mirror Broken)
IDW Publishing: May, 2017 (free giveaway)
0-(5/17, FCBD giveaway) Mirror Universe crew, prelude to series; J.K. Woodward-a/c; bonus design art 3.00

STAR TREK: THE NEXT GENERATION - PERCHANCE TO DREAM
DC Comics/WildStorm: Feb, 2000 - No. 4, May, 2000 ($2.50, limited series)
1-4-Bradstreet-c 3.00

STAR TREK: THE NEXT GENERATION - RIKER
Marvel Comics (Paramount Comics): July, 1998 ($3.50, one-shot)
1-Riker joins the Maquis 4.00

STAR TREK: THE NEXT GENERATION - SHADOWHEART
DC Comics: Dec, 1994 - No. 4, Mar, 1995 ($1.95, limited series)
1-4 4.00

STAR TREK: THE NEXT GENERATION: TERRA INCOGNITA
IDW Publishing: Jul, 2018 - No. 6, Dec, 2018 ($3.99)
1-6: 1-Shasteen-a; Mirror Universe Barclay app. 4.00

STAR TREK: THE NEXT GENERATION: THE GIFT FACSIMILE EDITION
IDW Publishing: Feb, 2021 ($5.99, one-shot)
1-Reprints ST:TNG Annual #1 (1990); John de Lancie-s/Gordon Purcell-a; Q app. 6.00

STAR TREK: THE NEXT GENERATION - THE KILLING SHADOWS
DC Comics/WildStorm: Nov, 2000 - No. 4, Feb, 2001 ($2.50, limited series)
1-4-Scott Ciencin-s; Sela app. 3.00

STAR TREK: THE NEXT GENERATION: THE LAST GENERATION
IDW Publishing: Nov, 2008 - No. 5, Mar, 2009 ($3.99, limited series)
1-5-Purcell-a; alternate timeline with Klingon war; Sulu app. 4.00

STAR TREK: THE NEXT GENERATION - THE MODALA IMPERATIVE
DC Comics: Early Sept, 1991 - No. 4, Late Oct, 1991 ($1.75, limited series)
1-4 4.00

STAR TREK: THE NEXT GENERATION: THE SPACE BETWEEN
IDW Publishing: Jan, 2007 - No. 6, June, 2007 ($3.99)
1-6-Single issue stories from various seasons; photo & art covers 4.00

STAR TREK: THE NEXT GENERATION: THROUGH THE MIRROR
IDW Publishing: May, 2018 - No. 5, May, 2018 ($3.99, weekly limited series)
1-5-David & Scott Tipton-s; Mirror Universe crew crosses over 4.00

STAR TREK: THE Q CONFLICT
IDW Publishing: Jan, 2019 - No. 6, Jun, 2019 ($3.99, limited series)
1-6-Crews of Kirk, Picard, Sisko, Janeway vs. Q, Metron, Ayelborne & Trelane; Messina-a 4.00

STAR TREK: THE WRATH OF KHAN
IDW Publishing: Jun, 2009 - No. 3, Jul, 2009 ($3.99, limited series)
1-3-Movie adaptation; Chee Yang Ong-a 4.00

STAR TREK: TNG: HIVE
IDW Publishing: Sept, 2012 - No. 4, Feb, 2013 ($3.99, limited series)
1-4-Brannon Braga-s/Joe Corroney-a; Next Generation crew vs. the Borg 4.00

STAR TREK UNLIMITED

Star Trek: The Mirror War #4 © CBS

Star Trek: Waypoint #1 © CBS

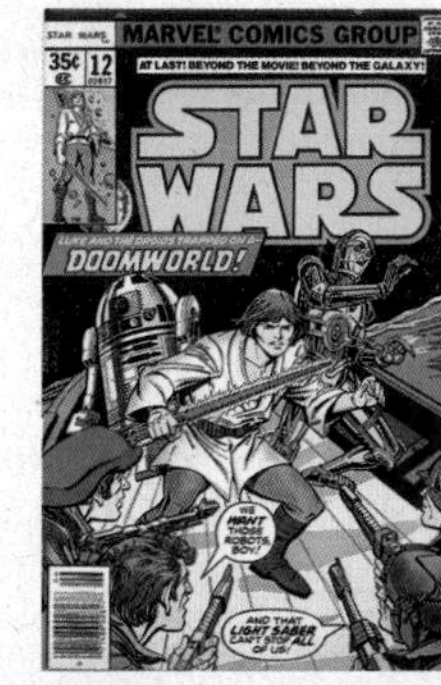

Star Wars #12 © Lucasfilm

	GD 2.0	VG 4.0	FN 6.0	VF 8.0	VF/NM 9.0	NM- 9.2

Marvel Comics (Paramount Comics): Nov, 1996 - No. 10, July, 1998 ($2.95/$2.99)

1,2-Stories from original series and Next Generation 5.00
3-10: 3-Begin $2.99-c. 6-"Telepathy War" pt. 4. 7-Q & Trelane swap Kirk & Picard 4.00

STAR TREK UNTOLD VOYAGES
Marvel Comics (Paramount Comics): May, 1998 - No. 5, July, 1998 ($2.50)

1-5-Kirk's crew after the 1st movie 4.00

STAR TREK: VOYAGER
Marvel Comics (Paramount Comics): Nov, 1996 - No. 15, Mar, 1998 ($1.95/$1.99)

1-15: 13-"Telepathy War" pt. 5. 14-Seven of Nine joins crew 4.00

STAR TREK: VOYAGER
DC Comics/WildStorm/IDW: one-shots and trade paperbacks

- Elite Force (7/00, $5.95) The Borg app.; Abnett & Lanning-s 6.00
... Encounters With the Unknown TPB (2001, $19.95) reprints 20.00
- False Colors (1/00, $5.95) Photo-c and Jim Lee-c; Jeff Moy-a 6.00
...: Mirrors and Smoke (IDW, 10/19, $4.99) Mirror Universe Janeway's crew; Woodward-a 5.00

STAR TREK: VOYAGER – SEVEN'S RECKONING
IDW Publishing: Nov, 2020 - No. 4, Feb, 2021 ($3.99, limited series)

1-4-Dave Baker-s/Angel Hernandez-a 4.00

STAR TREK: VOYAGER-- THE PLANET KILLER
DC Comics/WildStorm: Mar, 2001 - No. 3, May, 2001 ($2.95, limited series)

1-3-Voyager vs. the Planet Killer from the ST:TOS episode; Teranishi-a 3.00

STAR TREK: VOYAGER SPLASHDOWN
Marvel Comics (Paramount Comics): Apr, 1998 - No. 4, July, 1998 ($2.50, limited series)

1-4-Voyager crashes on a water planet 4.00

STAR TREK VS. TRANSFORMERS
IDW Publishing: Sept, 2018 - No. 5, Jan, 2019 ($3.99, limited series)

1-5-Crew from Star Trek animated series meets Transformers; multiple covers 4.00

STAR TREK: WAYPOINT
IDW Publishing: Sept, 2016 - No. 6, Jul, 2017 ($4.99/$3.99)

1-($4.99) Short story anthology; future Next Gen Data & Geordi; multiple covers 5.00
2-6-($3.99) 2-Gold Key style story. 3-Voyager & DS9 crews 4.00
... Special 1 (11/18, $7.99) Ezri Dax, Q, Will Decker & Ilia app.; Sonny Liew-a 8.00
... Special 2019 (3/19, $7.99) Short stories by various; Mooney-c 8.00

STAR TREK/ X-MEN
Marvel Comics (Paramount Comics): Dec, 1996 ($4.99, one-shot)

1-Kirk's crew & X-Men; art by Silvestri, Tan, Winn & Finch; Lobdell-s 6.00

STAR TREK/ X-MEN: 2ND CONTACT
Marvel Comics (Paramount Comics): May, 1998 ($4.99, 64 pgs., one-shot)

1-Next Gen. crew & X-Men battle Kang, Sentinels & Borg following First Contact movie 6.00
1-Painted wraparound variant cover 6.00

STAR TREK: YEAR FIVE
IDW Publishing: Apr, 2019 - No. 25, Jul, 2021 ($3.99)

1-24-Original series crew; multiple covers on each. 7-Intro. Ayal. 10-Lt. Arex app. 17-Origin of Gary Seven & Isis; Woodward painted-a 4.00
25-($4.99) Epilogue to the Five Year Mission; leads into the 1979 movie 5.00
...: Valentine's Day Special (2/20, $3.99) Paul Cornell-s/Christopher Jones-a; 3 covers 4.00

STAR TREK: YEAR FOUR (Also see Star Trek: Enterprise Experiment)
IDW Publishing: July, 2007 - No. 5, Nov, 2007 ($3.99, limited series)

1-5: 1-Original series crew; Tischman-s/Conley-a; three covers on each 4.00

STARVE
Image Comics: Jun, 2015 - No. 10, Jun, 2016 ($3.99)

1-10-Brian Wood-s/Danijel Zezelj-a 4.00

STAR WARS (Movie) (See Classic..., Contemporary Motivators, Dark Horse Comics, The Droids, The Ewoks, Marvel Movie Showcase, Marvel Special Ed.)
Marvel Comics Group: July, 1977 - No. 107, Sept, 1986

1-(Regular 30¢ edition)-Price in square w/UPC code; #1-6 adapt first movie; first issue on sale before movie debuted 21 42 63 147 324 500
1-(35¢-c; limited distribution - 1500 copies?)- Price in square w/UPC code (Prices vary widely on this book. In 2005 a CGC certified 9.4 sold for $6,500, a CGC certified 9.2 sold for $3,403, and a CGC certified 6.0 sold for $610)
500 1000 1500 4250 9625 15,000

NOTE: *The rare 35¢ edition has the cover price in a square box, and the UPC box in the lower left hand corner has the UPC code lines running through it.*

1-Reprint; has "reprint" in upper lefthand corner of cover or on inside or price and number inside a diamond with no date or UPC on cover; 30¢ and 35¢ issues published
7 14 21 46 86 125

2-9: Reprints; has "reprint" in upper lefthand corner of cover or on inside or price and number inside a diamond with no date or UPC on cover; 30¢ and 35¢ issues published
2 4 6 8 10 12

	GD	VG	FN	VF	VF/NM	NM-
2-(30¢ cover)	11	22	33	76	163	250
2-(35¢ with UPC code; not reprint)	79	158	237	632	1416	2200
3,4-(30¢ issues). 4-Battle with Darth Vader	6	12	18	38	69	100
3,4-(35¢ with UPC code; not reprints)	75	150	225	600	1350	2100
5,6: 5-Begin 35¢-c on all editions. 6-Stevens-a(i)	4	8	12	27	44	60
7-20	3	6	9	15	22	28
21-38,45-67,69,70: 50-Giant	2	4	6	11	16	20
39-41,43,44-The Empire Strikes Back-r by Al Williamson in all	2	4	6	10	14	18
42-Reprints 1st Boba Fett app. in comics	13	26	39	89	195	300
68-Reintro Boba Fett	12	24	36	82	179	275
71-80	2	4	6	8	11	14
81-Boba Fett app.	7	14	21	46	86	125
82-90	2	4	6	10	14	18
91,93-99: 98-Williamson-a	3	6	9	14	19	24
92,100-106: 92,100-($1.00, 52 pgs.)	3	6	9	15	22	28
107 (low dist.); Portacio-a(i)	7	14	21	44	82	120
Annual 1 (12/79, 52 pgs.)-Simonson-c	3	6	9	17	26	35
Annual 2 (11/82, 52 pgs.), 3(12/83, 52 pgs.)	2	4	6	11	16	20

... A Long Time Ago...Vol. 1 TPB (Dark Horse Comics, 6/02, $29.95) r/#1-14 30.00
... A Long Time Ago...Vol. 2 TPB (Dark Horse Comics, 7/02, $29.95) r/#15-28 30.00
... A Long Time Ago...Vol. 3 TPB (Dark Horse Comics, 11/02, $29.95) r/#39-53 30.00
... A Long Time Ago...Vol. 4 TPB (Dark Horse Comics, 1/03, $29.95) r/#54-67 & Ann. 2 30.00
... A Long Time Ago...Vol. 5 TPB (Dark Horse Comics, 3/03, $29.95) r/#68-81 & Ann. 3 30.00
... A Long Time Ago...Vol. 6 TPB (Dark Horse Comics, 5/03, $29.95) r/#82-93 30.00
... A Long Time Ago...Vol. 7 TPB (Dark Horse Comics, 6/03, $29.95) r/#96-107 30.00
... No. 1 Facsimile Edition (2/20, $3.99) Reprints #1 with original 1977 ads 4.00

__Austin__ a-11-15i, 21i, 38; c-12-15i, 21i. __Byrne__ c-13p. __Chaykin__ a-1-10p; c-1. __Golden__ c/a-38. __Miller__ c-47p; pin-up-43. __Nebres__ c/a-Annual 2i. __Portacio__ a-107i. __Sienkiewicz__ c-92i, 98. __Simonson__ a-16p, 49p, 51-63p, 65p, 66p; c-16, 49-51, 52p, 53-62, Annual 1. __Steacy__ painted a-105i, 106i; c-105. __Williamson__ a-39-44p, 50p, 98; c-39, 40, 41-44p. Painted c-81, 87, 92, 95, 98, 100, 105.

STAR WARS (Modern continuation from 1986's Star Wars #107)
Marvel Comics: No. 108, Jul, 2019 ($5.99, one-shot)

108-Valence the Hunter, Jaxon & Amaiza app.; Rosenberg-s; art by various; Simonson-c 6.00

STAR WARS (Monthly series) (Becomes Star Wars Republic #46-on)
Dark Horse Comics: Dec, 1998 - No. 45, Aug, 2005 ($2.50/$2.95/$2.99)

1-Prelude To Rebellion; Strnad-s 1 3 4 6 8 10
2-6,8,9,11-45: 2-6-Prelude To Rebellion; Strnad-s. 4-Brereton-c. 8-12-Outlander. 13,17-18-($2.95). 13-18-Emissaries to Malastare; Truman-s. 14-16-($2.50) Schultz-c. 19-22-Twilight; Duursema-a. 23-26-Infinity's End. 42-45-Rite of Passage 5.00
5,6 (Holochrome-c variants) 1 2 3 5 6 8
7-1st app. Aurra Sing; Outlander story arc begins 4 8 12 27 44 60
10-1st A'shared Hett (later becomes Darth Krayt) 6 12 18 38 69 100
#0 Another Universe.com Ed.($10.00) r/serialized pages from Pizzazz Magazine; new Dorman painted-c 12.00
... A Valentine Story (2/03, $3.50) Leia & Han Solo on Hoth; Winick-s/Chadwick-a/c 3.50
...: Rite of Passage (2004, $12.95) r/#42-45 13.00
...: The Stark Hyperspace War (903, $12.95) r/#36-39 13.00

STAR WARS (Monthly series)
Dark Horse Comics: Jan, 2013 - No. 20, Aug, 2014 ($2.99)

1-Takes place after Episode IV; Brian Wood-s/Carlos D'Anda-a/Alex Ross-c 8.00
2-Ross-c 5.00
3-20: 3,4-Ross-c. 5-7-Migliari-c 3.00

STAR WARS
Dark Horse Comics (Free Comic Book Day giveaways)

...: and Captain Midnight (5/13) flip book with new Captain Midnight story & Avatar 3.00
...: Clone Wars #0 (5/09) flip book with short stories of Usagi Yojimbo, Emily the Strange 3.00
...: Clone Wars Adventures (7/04) based on Cartoon Network series; Fillbach Bros. -a
1 3 4 6 8 10
...: FCBD 2005 Special (5/05) Anakin & Obi-Wan during Clone Wars 3.00
...: FCBD 2006 Special (5/06) Clone Wars story; flip book with Conan FCBD Special 3.00
...: Tales - A Jedi's Weapon (5/02, 16 pgs.) Anakin Skywalker Episode 2 photo-c 3.00
Free Comic Book Day and Star Wars: The Clone Wars (5/11) flip book with Avatar: The Last Airbender 3.00

STAR WARS (Also see Darth Vader and Star Wars: Vader Down)
Marvel Comics: Mar, 2015 - No. 75, Jan, 2020 ($4.99/$3.99)

1-($4.99) Takes place after Episode IV; Aaron-s/Cassaday-a; multiple covers
1 3 4 6 8 10
2-6-($3.99) Darth Vader app.; Cassaday-a. 4-6-Boba Fett app. 6-Intro Sana Solo 4.00

GD VG FN VF VF/NM NM-
2.0 4.0 6.0 8.0 9.0 9.2

7-24,26-36: 7-Bianchi-a; Obi-Wan flashback. 8-12-Immonen-a. 13,14-Vader Down pts. 3,5; Deodato-a. 15,20-Obi-Wan flashback; Mayhew-a. 16-19-Yu-a. 26-30-Yoda app. 31,32-Doctor Aphra app. 4.00
25-($4.99) Darth Vader app.; Molina-a; back-up Droids story by Eliopoulos 5.00
37-($4.99) SCAR Squadron app.; back-up Tusken Raiders story; Sorrentino-a 5.00
38-49,51-55-Larroca-a. 45-Wedge app. 55-Leia promoted to General 4.00
50-(9/18, $5.99) Larroca-a; back-up with Camuncoli-a; bonus cover gallery 6.00
56-74: 56,61,62-Broccardo-a. 57-60,63-67-Unzueta-a. 57-Intro Thane Markona & Tula 4.00
75-($4.99) Luke & Chewbacca vs. Vader; Noto-a 5.00
Annual 1 (2/16, $4.99) Gillen-s/Unzueta-a/Cassaday-c; Emperor Palpatine app. 5.00
Annual 2 (1/17, $4.99) Kelly Thompson-s/Emilio Laiso-a; intro. Pash Davane 5.00
Annual 3 (11/17, $4.99) Latour-s/Walsh-a 5.00
Annual 4 (7/18, $4.99) Bunn-s/Anindito, Boschi & Laming-a; Sana Starros app. 5.00
...: Empire Ascendant 1 (2/20, $5.99) Short stories following #75; the Rebels reach Hoth; Beilert Valance app.; leads into events of Empire Strikes Back 6.00
... Saga 1 (2/20, $3.99) Synopsis of the 2015-2020 series; panels and summaries 4.00
... Special: C-3PO 1 (6/16, $4.99) Robinson-s/Harris-a/c; story of C-3PO's red arm 5.00

STAR WARS (Also see Star Wars: Darth Vader 2020 series)
Marvel Comics: Mar, 2020 - Present ($4.99/$3.99)

1-($4.99) Takes place after Empire Strikes Back; Soule-s/Saiz-a; multiple covers 5.00
2-32-($3.99): 2-Jabba the Hutt app. 3,4-Return to Cloud City; Lobot app. 13-18-Tie in to "War of the Bounty Hunters." 22-24-Crimson Reign 4.00
...: Revelations 1 (1/23, $5.99) Short stories with framing scenes of Vader; Noto-c 6.00

STAR WARS, THE
Dark Horse Comics: Sept, 2013 - No. 8, May, 2014 ($3.99)

1-Adaptation of George Lucas' original rough-draft screenplay; Mayhew-a/Runge-c
1 2 3 5 6 8
2-8 4.00
#0-(1/14, $3.99) Design work of characters, settings, vehicles
1 2 3 5 6 8

STAR WARS ADVENTURES (Anthology of All-ages stories)
IDW Publishing: Sept, 2017 - No. 32, Mar, 2020 ($3.99)

1 1 3 4 6 8 10
2-5,8-13,15,17-32: 2-Charretier-a. 3-Tudyk-s. 5-Porgs app. 10,11-Lando app. 30-Kylo Ren-c 4.00
6-1st Rose Tico 2 4 6 9 12 15
7-Hondo Ohnaka-c 3 6 9 17 26 35
14-Full app. Fulcrum Agent Kallus 3 6 9 16 23 30
16-Embo & Kaz Xiono 2 4 6 9 12 15
Annual 2018 (4/18, $7.99) John Jackson Miller-s; Jaxxon app.; Sommariva-c 8.00
Annual 2019 (5/19, $7.99) Lando & Jaxxon app.; Stan Sakai-c
2 4 6 9 12 15
...: Flight of the Falcon (1/19, $4.99) Moreci-s/Florean-a; Chewbacca app. 5.00
... Free Comic Book Day 2018 (5/18, giveaway) Derek Charm-a/c; Han & Chewie app. 6.00
... Free Comic Book Day 2019 (5/19, giveaway) Derek Charm-a/c; Han & Chewie app. 6.00
... Greatest Hits (12/19, $1.00) Reprints #1; Scott-s/Charm-a; Rey on Jakku 3.00

STAR WARS ADVENTURES (Anthology of All-ages stories)
IDW Publishing: Sept, 2020 - No. 14, Jan, 2022 ($3.99)

1-14-Francavilla-c. 3-Darth Maul app. 4.00
Annual 2020 (8/20, $5.99) Jaxxon app.; Scott-s/Gaston-a; IG-88 app.; Brokenshire-s/a 6.00
Annual 2021 (11/21, $7.99) Jaxxon app.; Scott-s/Florean-a; Lando app.; Zdarsky & Loo-s 8.00

STAR WARS ADVENTURES: DESTROYER DOWN (All-ages stories)
IDW Publishing: Nov, 2018 - No. 3, Jan, 2019 ($3.99, limited series)

1-3: Rey app.; Beatty-s/Charm-a; back-up with Beatty-s/Sommariva-a 5.00

STAR WARS ADVENTURES: GHOSTS OF VADER'S CASTLE (All-ages stories)
IDW Publishing: Sept, 2021 - No. 5, Oct, 2021 ($3.99, weekly limited series)

1-5-Francavilla-c on all. 2-5-Jaxxon app. 3-Robert Hack-a. 5-Francavilla-a 4.00

STAR WARS ADVENTURES: RETURN TO VADER'S CASTLE (All-ages stories)
IDW Publishing: Oct, 2019 - No. 5, Oct, 2019 ($3.99, weekly limited series)

1-5-Francavilla-c on all. 1-Darth Maul app. 2-Kelley Jones-a. 5-Darth Vader spotlight 5.00

STAR WARS ADVENTURES: SMUGGLER'S RUN (All-ages stories)
IDW Publishing: Dec, 2020 - No. 2, Jan, 2021 ($5.99, limited series)

1,2-Adaptation of the Greg Rucka novel; Han Solo & Chewbacca app.; Römling-a 6.00

STAR WARS ADVENTURES: TALES FROM VADER'S CASTLE (All-ages stories)
IDW Publishing: Oct, 2018 - No. 5, Oct, 2018 ($3.99, weekly limited series)

1-5-Francavilla-c on all. 2-Count Dooku app.; Kelley Jones-a. 4-Hack-a 5.00

STAR WARS ADVENTURES: THE WEAPON OF A JEDI (Based on the novel by Jason Fry)
IDW Publishing: May, 2021 - No. 2, Jun, 2021 ($5.99, limited series)

1,2-Luke Skywalker during the original trilogy; Worley-s/Coleman-a 6.00

STAR WARS: AGENT OF THE EMPIRE - HARD TARGETS
Dark Horse Comics: Oct, 2012 - No. 5, Feb, 2013 ($2.99, limited series)

1-5: 1-Ostrander-s/Fabbri-a; Boba Fett app. 5.00

STAR WARS: AGENT OF THE EMPIRE - IRON ECLIPSE
Dark Horse Comics: Dec, 2011 - No. 5, Apr, 2012 ($3.50, limited series)

1-5: 1-Ostrander-s/Roux-a; Han Solo & Chewbacca app. 4.00

STAR WARS: AGE OF REBELLION ...
Marvel Comics: Jun, 2019 - Aug, 2019 ($3.99, series of one-shots)

... - Boba Fett 1 (7/19) Pak-s/Laming-a/Dodson-c 2 4 6 8 10 12
... - Darth Vader 1 (8/19) Greg Pak-s/Ramon Bachs-a 1 3 4 6 8 10
... - Grand Moff Tarkin 1 (6/19) Pak-s/Laming-a/Dodson-c; Princess Leia app. 4.00
... - Han Solo 1 (7/19) Pak-s/Sprouse-a/Dodson-c; Luke and Chewbacca app. 4.00
... - Jabba The Hutt 1 (7/19) Pak-s/Laiso, Boschi & Turini-a/Dodson-c 4.00
... - Lando Calrissian 1 (7/19) Pak-s/Buffagni-a/Dodson-c; Lobot app. 4.00
... - Luke Skywalker 1 (8/19) Pak-s/Sprouse-a/Dodson-c; Vader & The Emperor app. 4.00
... - Princess Leia 1 (6/19) Pak-s/Sprouse-a/Dodson-c; Lando & Chewbacca app. 4.00
... Special 1 (6/19, $4.99) Short stories of Yoda, IG-88, Biggs and Porkins 5.00

STAR WARS: AGE OF REPUBLIC ...
Marvel Comics: Feb, 2019 - Aug, 2019 ($3.99, series of one-shots)

... - Anakin Skywalker 1 (4/19) Houser-s/Smith & Santos-a; Obi-Wan Kenobi app. 4.00
... - Count Dooku 1 (4/19) Houser-s/Luke Ross-a 4.00
... - Darth Maul 1 (2/19) Houser-s/Smith & Santos-a; Darth Sidious app.
2 4 6 9 12 15
... - General Grievous 1 (5/19) Houser-s/Luke Ross-a 4.00
... - Jango Fett 1 (3/19) Houser-s/Luke Ross-a; young Boba Fett app. 6.00
... - Obi-Wan Kenobi 1 (3/19) Houser-s/Smith & Santos-a; early days of Anakin's training
1 3 4 6 8 10
... - Padmé Amidala 1 (5/19) Houser-s/Smith & Santos-a; takes place during Clone Wars 4.00
... - Qui-Gon Jinn 1 (2/19) Houser-s/Cory Smith-a; Yoda app. 4.00
... Special 1 (3/19, $4.99) Short stories of Mace Windu, Asajj Ventress, Jar Jar Binks
2 4 6 9 12 15

STAR WARS: AGE OF RESISTANCE ... (Each has a bonus character essay)
Marvel Comics: Sept, 2019 - Nov, 2019 ($3.99, series of one-shots)

... - Captain Phasma 1 (9/19) Taylor-s/Kirk-a/Noto-c 4.00
... - Finn 1 (9/19) Taylor-s/Rosanas/Noto-c; FN-2187's custodian days 4.00
... - General Hux 1 (109/19) Taylor-s/Kirk-a/Noto-c; Kylo Ren app. 4.00
... - Kylo Ren 1 (11/19) Taylor-s/Kirk-a/Noto-c 4.00
... - Poe Dameron 1 (10/19) Taylor-s/Rosanas/Noto-c 4.00
... - Rey 1 (9/19) Taylor-s/Rosanas/Noto-c; takes place after Han Solo's death; Leia app. 4.00
... - Rose Tico 1 (11/19) Taylor-s/Rosanas/Noto-c; Paige and Leia app. 4.00
... Special 1 (9/19, $4.99) Short stories of Maz Kanata, Adm. Holdo, BB-8 by various 5.00
... - Supreme Leader Snoke 1 (11/19) Taylor-s/Rosanas/Noto-c; training Kylo Ren 4.00

STAR WARS: A NEW HOPE - THE SPECIAL EDITION
Dark Horse Comics: Jan, 1997 - No. 4, Apr, 1997 ($2.95, limited series)

1-4-Dorman-c 5.00

STAR WARS BECKETT (From Solo: A Star Wars Story movie)
Marvel Comics: Oct, 2018 ($4.99, one-shot)

1-Prelude to Star Wars: Solo Adaptation; Duggan-s; art by Salazar, Laming, Sliney 5.00

STAR WARS: BLOOD TIES - BOBA FETT IS DEAD
Dark Horse Comics: Apr, 2012 - No. 4, Jul, 2012 ($3.50, limited series)

1-Scalf painted-a/c on all 3 6 9 14 20 25
2-4 1 3 4 6 8 10

STAR WARS: BLOOD TIES: JANGO AND BOBA FETT
Dark Horse Comics: Aug, 2010 - No. 4, Nov, 2010 ($3.50, limited series)

1,4-Scalf painted-a/c on all 2 4 6 11 16 20
2,3 1 2 3 5 6 8

STAR WARS: BOBA FETT
Dark Horse Comics: Dec, 1995 - No. 3, Aug, 1997 ($3.95) (Originally intended as a one-shot)

1-Kennedy-c/a 2 4 6 9 12 15
2,3 5.00
Death, Lies, & Treachery TPB (1/98, $12.95) r/#1-3 13.00
... - Agent of Doom (11/00, $2.99) Ostrander-s/Cam Kennedy-a
2 4 6 9 12 15
... - Overkill (3/06, $2.99) Hughes-c/Velasco-a 2 4 6 9 12 15
Twin Engines of Destruction (1/97, $2.95) 2 4 6 8 10 12

STAR WARS: BOBA FETT: ENEMY OF THE EMPIRE
Dark Horse Comics: Jan, 1999 - No. 4, Apr, 1999 ($2.95, limited series)

1-Recalls 1st meeting of Fett and Vader 3 6 9 16 23 30
2-4 1 3 4 6 8 10

STAR WARS: BOUNTY HUNTERS
Marvel Comics: May, 2020 - Present ($3.99)

1-31: 1-Valance, Bossk, Boba Fett, Doctor Aphra app.; Sacks-s/Villanelli-a 4.00

STAR WARS: CHEWBACCA
Dark Horse Comics: Jan, 2000 - No. 4, Apr, 2000 ($2.95, limited series)

1-4-Macan-s/art by various incl. Anderson, Kordey, Gibbons; Phillips-c 5.00

STAR WARS: CLONE WARS ADVENTURES
Dark Horse Comics: 2004 - No. 10, 2007 ($6.95, digest-sized)

1-10-Short stories inspired by Clone Wars animated series 7.00

STAR WARS: CRIMSON EMPIRE
Dark Horse Comics: Dec, 1997 - No. 6, May, 1998 ($2.95, limited series)

1-Richardson-s/Gulacy-a 3 6 9 19 30 40
2-6 1 2 3 5 6 8

STAR WARS: CRIMSON EMPIRE II: COUNCIL OF BLOOD
Dark Horse Comics: Nov, 1998 - No. 6, Apr, 1999 ($2.95, limited series)

1-Richardson & Stradley-s/Gulacy-a in all 1 2 3 5 6 8
2-6 5.00

STAR WARS: CRIMSON EMPIRE III: EMPIRE LOST
Dark Horse Comics: Oct, 2011 - No. 6, Apr, 2012 ($3.50, limited series)

1-6: 1-Richardson-s/Gulacy-a/Dorman-c 6.00

STAR WARS: CRIMSON REIGN
Marvel Comics: Feb, 2022 - No. 5. Aug, 2022 ($4.99/$3.99)

1-($4.99) Soule-s/Cummings-a; Qi'ra, Deathstick, The Knights of Ren app. 5.00
2-5-($3.99) 4,5-Darth Vader app. 4.00

STAR WARS: DARK EMPIRE
Dark Horse Comics: Dec, 1991 - No. 6, Oct, 1992 ($2.95, limited series)

Preview-(99¢) 6.00
1-All have Dorman painted-c 2 4 6 10 14 18
1-3-2nd printing 4.00
2-Low print run 2 4 6 9 12 15
3 1 3 4 6 8 10
4-6 5.00
Gold Embossed Set (#1-6)-With gold embossed foil logo (price is for set) 150.00
Platinum Embossed Set (#1-6) 175.00
Trade paperback (4/93, $16.95) 24.00
Dark Empire 1 - TPB 3rd printing (2003, $16.95) 17.00
Ltd. Ed. Hardcover ($99.95) Signed & numbered 100.00

Star Wars (2020) #28 © Lucasfilm

Star Wars: Dark Times #2 © Lucasfilm

Star Wars: Doctor Aphra (2020) #3 © Lucasfilm

GD 2.0 | VG 4.0 | FN 6.0 | VF 8.0 | VF/NM 9.0 | NM- 9.2

STAR WARS: DARK EMPIRE II
Dark Horse Comics: Dec, 1994 - No. 6, May, 1995 ($2.95, limited series)
1-Dave Dorman painted-c 2 4 6 9 12 15
2-6: Dorman-c in all. 4.00
Platinum Embossed Set (#1-6) 45.00
Trade paperback ($17.95) 18.00
TPB Second Edition (9/06, $19.95) r/#1-6 and Star Wars: Empire's End #1,2 20.00

STAR WARS: DARK FORCE RISING
Dark Horse Comics: May, 1997 - No. 6, Oct, 1997 ($2.95, limited series)
1-6 1 3 4 6 8 10
TPB (2/98, $17.95) r/#1-6 25.00

STAR WARS: DARK TIMES (Continued from Star Wars Republic #83)(Storyline continues in Star Wars: Rebellion #15)
Dark Horse Comics: Oct, 2006 - No. 17, Jun, 2010 ($2.99)
1-17-Nineteen years before Episode IV; Doug Wheatley-a. 11-Celeste Morne awakens 13-17-Blue Harvest 4.00
#0-(7/09, $2.99) Prologue to Blue Harvest 5.00

STAR WARS: DARK TIMES - A SPARK REMAINS
Dark Horse Comics: Jul, 2013 - No. 5, Dec, 2013 ($3.50, limited series)
1-5-Stradley-s/Wheatley-a; Darth Vader app. 4.00

STAR WARS: DARK TIMES - FIRE CARRIER
Dark Horse Comics: Feb, 2013 - No. 5, Jun, 2013 ($2.99, limited series)
1-5-Stradley-s/Guzman-a; Darth Vader app. 4.00

STAR WARS: DARK TIMES - OUT OF THE WILDERNESS
Dark Horse Comics: Aug, 2011 - No. 5, Apr, 2012 ($2.99, limited series)
1-5-Doug Wheatley-a 4.00

STAR WARS: DARTH MAUL
Dark Horse Comics: Sept, 2000 - No. 4, Dec, 2000 ($2.95, limited series)
1-Photo-c and Struzan painted-c; takes place 6 months before Ep. 1 2 4 6 11 16 20
2-4-Photo-c and Struzan painted-c 1 3 4 6 8 10

STAR WARS: DARTH MAUL (Issue #1 titled Darth Maul)
Marvel Comics: Apr, 2017 - No. 5, Sept, 2017 ($4.99, limited series)
1-($4.99) Cullen Bunn-s/Luke Ross-a; back-up by Eliopoulos-s/a 2 4 6 9 12 15
2-1st Cad Bane 3 6 9 16 23 30
3-5-($3.99) Aurra Sing & Cad Bane app. 4.00
... Halloween Comic Fest 2017 1 (12/17, giveaway) r/#1 without Eliopoulos back-up 5.00

STAR WARS: DARTH MAUL - DEATH SENTENCE
Dark Horse Comics: Jul, 2012 - No. 4, Oct, 2012 ($2.99, limited series)
1-Tom Taylor-s/Bruno Redondo-a/Dave Dorman-c 2 4 6 9 12 15
2-4 1 3 4 6 8 10

STAR WARS: DARTH MAUL - SON OF DATHOMIR
Dark Horse Comics: May, 2014 - No. 4, Aug, 2014 ($3.50, limited series)
1-Barlow-s/Frigeri-a/Scalf-c 6 12 18 41 76 110
2-4 3 6 9 16 23 30

STAR WARS: DARTH VADER (Also see Star Wars 2020 series)
Marvel Comics: Apr, 2020 - Present ($4.99/$3.99)
1-($4.99) Takes place after Empire Strikes Back; Pak-s/Ienco-a; multiple covers 3 6 9 17 26 35
2-5,7-31-($3.99) 2-Intro. Sabé. 12-17-War of the Bounty Hunters tie-ins 4.00
6-1st Ochi 2 4 6 9 12 15

STAR WARS: DARTH VADER AND THE CRY OF SHADOWS
Dark Horse Comics: Dec, 2013 - No. 5, Apr, 2014 ($3.50, limited series)
1-5-Siedell-s/Guzman-a/Massaferra-c 5.00

STAR WARS: DARTH VADER AND THE GHOST PRISON
Dark Horse Comics: May, 2012 - No. 5, Sept, 2012 ($3.50, limited series)
1-Blackman-s/Alessio-a/Wilkins-c; variant-c by Sanda 1 2 3 5 6 8
2-5-Blackman-s/Alessio-a/Wilkins-c 4.00

STAR WARS: DARTH VADER AND THE LOST COMMAND
Dark Horse Comics: Jan, 2011 - No. 5, May, 2011 ($3.50, limited series)
1-Blackman-s/Leonardi-a/Sanda-c; variant-c by Wheatley 1 3 4 6 8 10
2-5-Blackman-s/Leonardi-a/Sanda-c 4.00

STAR WARS: DARTH VADER AND THE NINTH ASSASSIN
Dark Horse Comics: Apr, 2013 - No. 5, Aug, 2013 ($3.50, limited series)
1-5-Siedell-s. 1,2,4-Thompson-a. 3,5-Fernandez-a 4.00

STAR WARS: DAWN OF THE JEDI
Dark Horse Comics: No. 0, Feb, 2012 ($3.50, one-shot)
0-Guide to the worlds, characters, sites, vehicles; Migliari-c 3 6 9 14 19 24

STAR WARS: DAWN OF THE JEDI - FORCE STORM
Dark Horse Comics: Feb, 2012 - No. 5, Jun, 2012 ($3.50, limted series)
1-Ostrander-s/Duursema-a/c 4 8 12 23 37 60
2-5 1 3 4 6 8 10

STAR WARS: DAWN OF THE JEDI - FORCE WAR
Dark Horse Comics: Nov, 2013 - No. 5, Mar, 2014 ($3.50, limted series)
1-Ostrander-s/Duursema-a/c 2 4 6 11 16 20
2-5 1 3 4 6 8 10

STAR WARS: DAWN OF THE JEDI - PRISONER OF BOGAN
Dark Horse Comics: Nov, 2012 - No. 5, May, 2013 ($2.99, limted series)
1-5-Ostrander-s/Duursema-a/c 1 3 4 6 8 10

STAR WARS: DOCTOR APHRA (See Doctor Aphra for #1-6)(See Darth Vader #3 for debut)
Marvel Comics: No. 7, Jul, 2017 - No. 40, Feb, 2020 ($3.99)
7-24: 7,8-Luke, Han, Leia & Sana app. 12,13-Darth Vader app. 20-24-Sana Starros app. 4.00
25-($4.99) Darth Vader & Sana Starros app. 5.00
26-40: 26-31-Laiso-a. 40-Darth Vader app. 4.00
Annual 1 (10/17, $4.99) Gillen-s/Laming & Sliney-a 1 3 4 6 8 10
Annual 2 (11/18, $4.99) Spurrier-s/Wijngaard-a 2 4 6 9 12 15
Annual 3 (12/19, $4.99) Spurrier-s/Charretier-a 5.00

STAR WARS: DOCTOR APHRA (Star Wars)(2nd series)(First issue titled Doctor Aphra)
Marvel Comics: Jun, 2020 - Present ($3.99)
1-Alyssa Wong-s/Marika Cresta-a 2 4 6 9 12 15
2-29: 2-5-Alyssa Wong-s/Marika Cresta-a. 5-Lady Domina app. 7-18-Sana Starros app. 12-15-War of the Bounty Hunters tie-ins. 19-21-Crimson Reign 4.00

STAR WARS: DROIDS (See Dark Horse Comics #17-19)
Dark Horse Comics: Apr, 1994 - #6, Sept, 1994; V2#1, Apr, 1995 - V2#8, Dec, 1995 ($2.50, limited series)
1-($2.95)-Embossed-c 1 3 4 6 8 10
2-6, Special 1 (1/95, $2.50), V2#1-8 4.00
Star Wars Omnibus: Droids One TPB (6/08, $24.95) r/#1-6, Special 1, V2#1-8, Star Wars: The Protocol Offensive and "Artoo's Day Out" story from Star Wars Galaxy Magazine #1 25.00

STAR WARS: DROIDS UNPLUGGED
Marvel Comics: Aug, 2017 ($4.99, one-shot)
1-Chris Eliopoulos-s/a; short stories with R2-D2, BB-8 and a probe droid 5.00

STAR WARS: EMPIRE
Dark Horse Comics: Sept, 2002 - No. 40, Feb, 2006 ($2.99)
1-Benjamin-a; takes place weeks before SW: A New Hope 1 3 4 6 8 10
2-40: 7,28-Boba Fett-c. 14-Vader after the destruction of the Death Star. 15-Death of Biggs; Wheatley-a 4.00
... Volume 1 (2003, $12.95, TPB) r/#1-4 13.00
... Volume 2 (2004, $17.95, TPB) r/#8-12,15 18.00
... Volume 3: The Imperial Perspective (2004, $17.95, TPB) r/#13,14,16-19 18.00
... Volume 4: The Heart of the Rebellion (2005, $17.95, TPB) r/#5,6,20-22 & Star Wars: A Valentine Story 18.00
... Volume 5 (2006, $14.95, TPB) r/#23-27 15.00
... Volume 6: In the Shadows of Their Fathers (10/06, $17.95, TPB) r/#29-34 18.00
... Volume 7: The Wrong Side of the War (1/07, $17.95, TPB) r/#34-40 18.00

STAR WARS: EMPIRE'S END
Dark Horse Comics: Oct, 1995 - No. 2, Nov, 1995 ($2.95, limited series)
1,2-Dorman-c 1 3 4 6 8 10

STAR WARS: EPISODE 1 THE PHANTOM MENACE
Dark Horse Comics: May, 1999 - No. 4, May, 1999 ($2.95, movie adaptation)
1-Damaggio & Williamson-a; full cast painted-c 2 4 6 11 16 20
1-Qui-Gon & Obi-Wan photo variant-c 2 4 6 8 10 12
2-Darth Maul app.; painted pod race-c 3 6 9 21 33 45
2-Anakin photo variant-c 3 6 9 14 20 25
3-Painted Darth Maul-c by Fleming 5 10 15 33 57 80
3-Darth Maul photo variant-c 3 6 9 14 20 25
4-Fleming painted lightsaber battle-c 6.00
4-Padmé photo variant-c 1 2 3 5 6 8

GD 2.0 | VG 4.0 | FN 6.0 | VF 8.0 | VF/NM 9.0 | NM- 9.2

TPB ($12.95) r/#1-4 13.00
...Anakin Skywalker-Photo-c & Bradstreet-c, ...Obi-Wan Kenobi-Photo-c & Egeland-c,
...Queen Amidala-Photo-c & Bradstreet-c, ...Qui-Gon Jinn-Photo-c & Bradstreet-c
1 3 4 6 8 10
Wizard 1/2 3 6 9 17 26 35
Gold Wizard 1/2 5 10 15 35 63 90

STAR WARS: EPISODE II - ATTACK OF THE CLONES
Dark Horse Comics: Apr, 2002 - No. 4, May, 2002 ($3.99, movie adaptation)
1-4-Regular and photo-c; Duursema-a 1 3 4 6 8 10
TPB ($17.95) r/#1-4; Struzan-c 18.00

STAR WARS: EPISODE III - REVENGE OF THE SITH
Dark Horse Comics: May, 2005 - No. 4, May, 2005 ($2.99, movie adaptation)
1-4-Wheatley-a/Dorman-c 6.00
TPB ($12.95) r/#1-4; Dorman-c 13.00

STAR WARS FORCES OF DESTINY (All-ages anthology spotlighting female characters)
IDW Publishing: Jan, 2018 ($3.99, series of one-shots)
... – Ahsoka & Padme - Revis-s/Pinto-a 2 4 6 11 16 20
... – Hera - Grayson-s/Widermann-a 1 2 3 5 6 8
... – Leia - Charretier-a; Leia on planet Hoth before the events of Empire
1 2 3 5 6 8
... – Rey - Houser-s/Florean-a; Rey meets BB-8 on Jakku
1 2 3 5 6 8
... – Rose & Paige - Dawson-s/Baldari-a; the sisters before the events of The Last Jedi
1 2 3 5 6 8

STAR WARS: GALAXY'S EDGE
Marvel Comics: Jun, 2019 - No. 5, Oct, 2019 ($3.99, limited series)
1-5: 1-Han Solo & Chewbacca app.; Sacks-s/Sliney-a. 2-Greedo app. 4-Dr. Aphra app. 4.00

STAR WARS: GENERAL GRIEVOUS
Dark Horse Comics: Mar, 2005 - No. 4, June, 2005 ($2.99, limited series)
1-4-Leonardi-a/Dixon-s 5.00
TPB (2005, $12.95) r/#1-4 13.00

STAR WARS HANDBOOK
Dark Horse Comics: July, 1998 - Mar, 2000 ($2.95, one-shots)
... X-Wing Rogue Squadron (7/98)-Guidebook to characters and spacecraft
1 3 4 6 8 10
... Crimson Empire (7/99) Dorman-c 1 3 4 6 8 10
... Dark Empire (3/00) Dorman-c 1 3 4 6 8 10

STAR WARS: HAN SOLO & CHEWBACCA
Marvel Comics: May, 2022 - No. 10, May, 2023 ($4.99/$3.99)
1-($4.99) Guggenheim-s/Messina-a; takes place before Episode 4; Greedo app. 5.00
2-10-($3.99) 3,4-Krrsantan app. 4.00

STAR WARS: HAN SOLO - IMPERIAL CADET
Marvel Comics: Jan, 2019 - No. 5, May, 2019 ($3.99)
1-5-Robbie Thompson-s/Leonard Kirk-a; Han's early days in Imperial Navy; Qi'Ra app. 4.00

STAR WARS: HEIR TO THE EMPIRE (Adaptation of Timothy Zahn novel)
Dark Horse Comics: Oct, 1995 - No. 6, Apr, 1996 ($2.95, limited series)
1-1st app. Grand Admiral Thrawn & Mara Jade 10 20 30 64 132 200
2-2nd app. of Admiral Thrawn 3 6 9 17 25 34
3,5,6 1 3 4 6 8 10
4-1st cover app. of Mara Jade 3 6 9 21 33 45

STAR WARS: HIDDEN EMPIRE
Marvel Comics: Jan, 2023 - Present ($4.99/$3.99)
1-($4.99) Soule-s/Cummings-a; Lady Qi'ra app. 5.00
2-4-($3.99) Darth Vader app. 4.00

STAR WARS HYPERSPACE STORIES
Dark Horse Comics: Aug, 2022 - Present ($3.99, anthology, limited series)
1-3: 1-Set after Episode 2; General Grievous app. 4.00

STAR WARS: INFINITIES - A NEW HOPE
Dark Horse Comics: May, 2001 - No. 4, Oct, 2001 ($2.99, limited series)
1- "What If..." the Death Star wasn't destroyed in Episode 4
1 3 4 6 8 10
2-4 5.00
TPB (2002, $12.95) r/ #1-4 13.00

STAR WARS: INFINITIES - THE EMPIRE STRIKES BACK
Dark Horse Comics: July, 2002 - No. 4, Oct, 2002 ($2.99, limited series)
1-4: "What If..." Luke died on the ice planet Hoth; Bachalo-c
1 2 3 5 6 8
TPB (2/03, $12.95) r/ #1-4 13.00

STAR WARS: INFINITIES - RETURN OF THE JEDI
Dark Horse Comics: Nov, 2003 - No. 4, Mar, 2004 ($2.99, limited series)
1-4:"What If..." ; Benjamin-a 1 3 4 6 8 10

STAR WARS: INVASION
Dark Horse Comics: July, 2009 - No. 5, Nov, 2009 ($2.99)
1-5-Jo Chen-c 5.00
#0-(10/09, $3.50) Dorman-c; Han Solo and Chewbacca app.
1 2 3 5 6 8
... - Rescues 1-6 (5/10 - No. 6, 12/10) Chen-c 5.00
... - Revelations 1-5 (7/11 - No. 5, 11/11, $3.50) Luke Skywalker app.; Scalf-c 5.00

STAR WARS: JABBA THE HUTT
Dark Horse Comics: Apr, 1995 ($2.50, one-shots)
nn, ...The Betrayal, ...The Dynasty Trap, ...The Hunger of Princess Nampi
1 3 4 6 8 10

STAR WARS: JANGO FETT - OPEN SEASONS
Dark Horse Comics: Apr, 2002 - No. 4, July, 2002 ($2.99, limited series)
1-Bachs & Fernandez-a 4 8 12 23 37 50
2 3 6 9 14 20 25
3,4 2 4 6 9 12 15

STAR WARS: JEDI
Dark Horse Comics: Feb, 2003 - Jun, 2004 ($4.99, one-shots)
... - Aayla Secura (8/03) Ostrander-s/Duursema-a 2 4 6 11 16 20
... - Count Dooku (11/03) Duursema-a 2 4 6 8 10 12
... - Mace Windu (2/03) Duursema-a; 1st app. Asajj Ventress
10 20 30 64 132 200
... - Shaak Ti (5/03) Ostrander-s/Duursema-a 2 4 6 11 16 20
... - Yoda (6/04) Barlow-s/Hoon-a; 1st app. Cal Kestis 4 8 12 23 37 50

STAR WARS: JEDI ACADEMY - LEVIATHAN
Dark Horse Comics: Oct, 1998 - No. 4, Jan, 1999 ($2.95, limited series)
1-1st app. Kyp Durron; Lago-c 3 6 9 16 23 30
2-4-Chadwick-c 5.00

STAR WARS: JEDI COUNCIL: ACTS OF WAR
Dark Horse Comics: Jun, 2000 - No. 4, Sept, 2000 ($2.95, limited series)
1-4-Stradley-s; set one year before Episode 1 1 2 3 5 6 8

STAR WARS: JEDI FALLEN ORDER – DARK TEMPLE (Based on video game)
Marvel Comics: Nov, 2019 - No. 5, Feb, 2020 ($3.99, limited series)
1-Rosenburg-s/Villanelli-a/Checchetto-c; Trilla Suduri app. (see Darth Vader #19 [10/18] for debut) 3 6 9 16 23 30
2-4 5.00
5-Cal Kestis app. (see Star Wars: Jedi - Yoda for debut)
2 4 6 9 12 15

STAR WARS: JEDI QUEST
Dark Horse Comics: Sept, 2001 - No. 4, Dec, 2001 ($2.99, limited series)
1-4-Anakin's Jedi training; Windham-s/Mhan-a 5.00

STAR WARS: JEDI - THE DARK SIDE
Dark Horse Comics: May, 2011 - No. 5, Sept, 2011 ($2.99, limited series)
1-5: 1-Qui-Gon Jinn 21 years befor Episode 1; Asrar-a 5.00

STAR WARS: JEDI VS. SITH
Dark Horse Comics: Apr, 2001 - No. 6, Sept, 2001 ($2.99, limited series)
1-Macan-s/Bachs-a/Robinson-c 6 12 18 38 69 100
2,4-6 1 2 3 5 6 8
3-Darth Bane-c 3 6 9 21 33 45

STAR WARS: KNIGHT ERRANT
Dark Horse Comics: Oct, 2010 - No. 5, Feb, 2011 ($2.99)
1-5: 1-John Jackson Miller-s/Federico Dallocchio-a 5.00
... - Deluge 1-5 (8/11 - No. 5 12/11, $3.50) 1-Miller-s/Rodriguez-a/Quinones-c 5.00
... - Escape 1-5 (6/12 - No. 5 10/12, $3.50) 1-Miller-s/Castiello-a/Carré-c 5.00

STAR WARS: KNIGHTS OF THE OLD REPUBLIC
Dark Horse Comics: Jan, 2006 - No. 50, Feb, 2010 ($2.99)
1-Takes place 3,964 years before Episode IV, Brian Ching-a/Charest-c in #1-6
3 6 9 19 30 40
2,4,5,10-15 1 2 3 5 6 8
3-1st Jarael 2 4 6 14 20 25
6-Cameo Rohlan Dyre 2 4 6 11 16 20
7-1st full app. Rohlan Dyre 3 6 9 17 25 34
8-1st Carth Onasi 2 4 6 11 16 20
9-1st full app. of Revan 12 24 36 82 179 275
16-41,43-50 4.00
42-Origin Darth Malak 8 16 24 54 102 150
... Handbook (11/07, $2.99) profiles of characters, ships, locales
1 2 3 5 6 8
.../Rebellion #0 (3/06, 25¢) flip book preview of both series
1 3 4 6 8 10
... - War 1-5 (1/12 - No. 5, 5/12, $3.50) J.J. Miller-s/Mutti-a 5.00
... Vol. 1 Commencement TPB (11/06, $18.95) r/#0-6 19.00
... Vol. 2 Flashpoint TPB (5/07, $18.95) r/#17-12 19.00
... Vol. 3 Days of Fear, Nights of Anger TPB (1/08, $18.95) r/#13-18 19.00

STAR WARS: LANDO - DOUBLE OR NOTHING
Marvel Comics: Jul, 2018 - No. 5, Nov, 2018 ($3.99, limited series)
1-5: 1-Barnes-s/Villanelli-a; young Lando & L3-37 before Solo movie 4.00

STAR WARS: LEGACY
Dark Horse Comics: No. 0, June, 2006 - No. 50, Aug, 2010 ($2.99)
Volume 2, Mar, 2013 - No. 18, Aug, 2014 ($2.99)
0-(25¢) Dossier of characters, settings, ships and weapons; 1st app. Cade Skywalker and Darth Talon; Duursema-c 3 6 9 14 20 25
0 1/2-(1/08, $2.99) Updated dossier of characters, settings, ships, and history 4.00
1-Takes place 130 years after Episode IV; Darth Krayt app.; see Star Wars #7 (6/99) for debut; Hughes-c/Duursema-a 4 8 12 23 37 50
2-1st Darth Ruyn 3 6 9 21 33 45
3-Hughes-c 2 4 6 11 16 20
4-50: 4-Duursema-c. 7,39-Luke Skywalker on-c. 16-Obi-Wan Kenobi app. 50-Wraparound-c
4.00
...: Broken Vol. 1 TPB (4/07, $17.95) r/#1-3,5,6 18.00
...: One for One (9/10, $1.00) reprints #1 with red cover frame
2 4 6 11 16 20
... Volume Two 1 (3/13 - No. 18, 8/14, $2.99) 1-18: 1-Bechko-s/Hardman-a/Wilkins-c 4.00
... War 1-6 (12/10 - No. 6, 5/11, $3.50) 1-Ostrander-s/Duursema-a; Darth Krayt app. 4.00

STAR WARS: LIFE DAY
Marvel Comics: Jan, 2022 ($4.99, one-shot)
1-Three short stories from the Wookiee holiday; Han Solo and Chewbacca app. 5.00

STAR WARS: LOST TRIBE OF THE SITH - SPIRAL
Dark Horse Comics: Aug, 2012 - No. 5, Dec, 2012 ($2.99, limited series)
1-J.J. Miller-s/Mutti-a/Renaud-c 2 4 6 9 12 15
2-5 6.00

STAR WARS: MACE WINDU

Star Wars: Galaxy's Edge #1 © Lucasfilm

Star Wars: Knight Errant #1 © Lucasfilm

Star Wars: Sana Starros #1 © Lucasfilm

	GD	VG	FN	VF	VF/NM	NM-
	2.0	4.0	6.0	8.0	9.0	9.2

Marvel Comics: Oct, 2017 - No. 5, Feb, 2018 ($3.99, limited series)

1-Matt Owens-s/Denys Cowan-a; follows after the Battle of Geonosis 1 3 4 6 8 10
2-4 4.00
5-Ahsoka Tano app. 3 6 9 14 20 25

STAR WARS: MARA JADE
Dark Horse Comics: Aug, 1998 - No. 6, Jan, 1999 ($2.95, limited series)

1-Ezquerra-a in all 3 6 9 16 23 30
2-6 6.00

STAR WARS: OBI-WAN (Titled STAR WARS: OBI-WAN KENOBI in Indicia for issue #1)
Marvel Comics: Jul, 2022 - No. 5, Nov, 2022 ($3.99, limited series)

1-5-Flashback stories from various times before Episode 4 4.00

STAR WARS: OBSESSION (Clone Wars)
Dark Horse Comics: Nov, 2004 - No. 5, Apr, 2005 ($2.99, limited series)

1-Blackman-s/Ching-a/c; Anakin & Obi-Wan 5 months before Episode III 2 4 6 11 16 20
2-5 5.00
...: Clone Wars Vol. 7 (2005, $17.95) r/#1-5 and 2005 Free Comic Book Day edition 18.00

STAR WARS: POE DAMERON (Titled Poe Dameron for #1-12)
Marvel Comics: No. 13, Jun, 2017 - No. 31, Nov, 2018 ($3.99)

13-31: 13-Soule-s/Noto-a. 14-22-Unzueta-a. 20-25-Lor San Tekka app. 26-28-Recounts events from Episode VII & VIII 4.00
Annual 1 (8/17, $4.99) Thompson-s/Virella-a; General Organa app. 5.00
Annual 2 (10/18, $4.99) Houser-s/Broccardo-a; Leia, Han Solo & Chewbacca app. 5.00

STAR WARS: PURGE
Dark Horse Comics: Dec, 2005 ($2.99, one-shot)

nn-Vader vs. remaining Jedi one month after Episode III; Hughes-c/Wheatley-a 1 3 4 6 8 10
... - Seconds To Die (11/09, $3.50) Vader app.; Charest-c/Ostrander-s 1 3 4 6 8 10
... - The Hidden Blade (4/10, $3.50) Vader app.; Scalf-c/a; Blackman-s 1 3 4 6 8 10
... - The Tyrant's Fist 1,2 (12/12 - No, 2, 1/13, $3.50) Vader app.; Freed-s/Dan Scott-c 5.00

STAR WARS: QUI-GON & OBI-WAN - LAST STAND ON ORD MANTELL
Dark Horse Comics: Dec, 2000 - No. 3, Mar, 2001 ($2.99, limited series)

1-3: 1-Three covers (photo, Tony Daniel, Bachs) Windham-s 3.00

STAR WARS: QUI-GON & OBI-WAN - THE AURORIENT EXPRESS
Dark Horse Comics: Feb, 2002 - No. 2, Mar, 2002 ($2.99, limited series)

1,2-Six years prior to Phantom Menace; Marangon-a 3.00

STAR WARS: REBEL HEIST
Dark Horse Comics: Apr, 2014 - No. 4, Jul, 2014 ($3.50)

1-4-Kindt-s/Castiello-a; two covers by Kindt and Adam Hughes on each 5.00

STAR WARS: REBELLION (Also see Star Wars: Knights of the Old Republic flip book)
Dark Horse Comics: Apr, 2006 - No. 16, Aug, 2008 ($2.99)

1-16-Takes place 9 months after Episode IV; Luke Skywalker app. 1-Badeaux-a/c 3.00
Vol. 1 TPB (2/07, $14.95) r/#0 (flip book) & #1-5 15.00

STAR WARS: REPUBLIC (Formerly Star Wars monthly series)
Dark Horse Comics: No. 46, Sept, 2002 - No. 83, Feb, 2006 ($2.99)

46-83-Events of the Clone Wars 3.00
...: Clone Wars Vol. 1 (2003, $14.95) r/#46-50 15.00
...: Clone Wars Vol. 2 (2003, $14.95) r/#51-53 & Star Wars: Jedi - Shaak Ti 15.00
...: Clone Wars Vol. 3 (2004, $14.95) r/#55-59 15.00
...: Clone Wars Vol. 4 (2004, $16.95) r/#54, 63 & Star Wars: Jedi - Aayla Secura & Dooku 17.00
...: Clone Wars Vol. 5 (2004, $17.95) r/#60-62, 64 & Star Wars: Jedi - Yoda 18.00
...: Clone Wars Vol. 6 (2005, $17.95) r/#65-71 18.00
(Clone Wars Vol. 7 - see Star Wars: Obsession)
...: Clone Wars Vol. 8 (2006, $17.95) r/#72-78 18.00
...: Clone Wars Vol. 9 (2006, $17.95) r/#79-83 & Star Wars: Purge 18.00
...: Honor and Duty TPB (5/06, $12.95) r/#46-48,78 13.00

STAR WARS: RETURN OF THE JEDI (Movie)
Marvel Comics Group: Oct, 1983 - No. 4, Jan, 1984 (limited series)

1-Williamson-p in all; r/Marvel Super Special #27 3 6 9 14 20 25
2-4-Continues r/Marvel Super Special #27 2 4 6 9 12 15
Oversized issue (1983, $2.95, 10-3/4x8-1/4", 68 pgs., cardboard-c)-r/#1-4 2 4 6 10 13 16

STAR WARS: RIVER OF CHAOS
Dark Horse Comics: June, 1995 - No. 4, Sept, 1995 ($2.95, limited series)

1-4: Louise Simonson scripts 4.00

STAR WARS: ROGUE ONE ADAPTATION
Marvel Comics: Jun, 2017 - No. 6, Nov, 2017 ($4.99/$3.99, limited series)

1-($4.99) Houser-s/Laiso & Bazaldua-a; Noto-c; afterword by director Gareth Edwards 3 6 9 14 20 25
2-6-($3.99) 3-Villanelli-a. 4-6-Laiso-a 4.00
Star Wars: Rogue One - Cassian & K2-SO Special 1 (10/17, $4.99) Swierczynski-s 1 3 4 6 8 10

STAR WARS: SANA STARROS
Marvel Comics: Apr, 2023 - Present ($4.99/$3.99)

1-($4.99) Justina Ireland-s/Pere Pérez-a 5.00
2-($3.99) 4.00

STAR WARS: SHADOWS OF THE EMPIRE
Dark Horse Comics: May, 1996 - No. 6, Oct, 1996 ($2.95, limited series)

1-Story details events between The Empire Strikes Back & Return of the Jedi; Russell-a(i) 3 6 9 17 26 35
2,3 2 4 6 11 16 20
4-6 5.00

STAR WARS: SHADOWS OF THE EMPIRE - EVOLUTION
Dark Horse Comics: Feb, 1998 - No. 5, June, 1998 ($2.95, limited series)

1-5: Perry-s/Fegredo-c. 5.00

STAR WARS: SHADOW STALKER
Dark Horse Comics: Sept, 1997 ($2.95, one-shot)

nn-Windham-a. 4.00

STAR WARS: SOLO ADAPTATION (See Solo: A Star Wars Story Adaptation)

STAR WARS: SPLINTER OF THE MIND'S EYE
Dark Horse Comics: Dec, 1995 - No. 4, June, 1996 ($2.50, limited series)

1-4: Adaption of Alan Dean Foster novel 5.00

STAR WARS: STARFIGHTER
Dark Horse Comics: Jan, 2002 - No. 3, March, 2002 ($2.99, limited series)

1-3-Williams & Gray-c 4.00

STAR WARS: TAG & BINK ARE DEAD
Dark Horse Comics: Oct, 2001 - No. 2, Nov, 2001($2.99, limited series)

1,2-Rubio-s 5.00
Star Wars: Tag & Bink Were Here TPB (11/06, $14.95) r/both SW: Tag & Bink series 15.00
Star Wars: Tag & Bink Were Here (Marvel, 7/18, $7.99) r/both SW: Tag & Bink series 8.00

STAR WARS: TAG & BINK II
Dark Horse Comics: Mar, 2006 - No. 2, Apr, 2006($2.99, limited series)

1-Tag & Bink invade Return of the Jedi; Rubio-s 5.00
2-1st app. Darth Plagueis; Tag & Bink as Jedi younglings during Ep II 2 4 6 9 12 15

STAR WARS TALES
Dark Horse Comics: Sept, 1999 - No. 24, Jun, 2005 ($4.95/$5.95/$5.99, anthology)

1-Short stories by various in all 2 4 6 9 12 15
2,3,5,8,11,12,14-17,20,23: 5-Begin art and photo-c on all thru #24 6.00
4-1st Dark Troopers 2 4 6 9 12 15
6-Darth Vader, Boba Fett, Yoda app. 3 6 9 16 23 30
7-1st Ailyn Vel (daughter of Boba Fett) 3 6 9 21 33 45
9-Darth Vader vs. Darth Maul 3 6 9 19 30 40
10-A'Sharad Hett app. (becomes Darth Krayt) 6 12 18 38 69 100
13-1st app. Yoda-like infant (similar to Grogu) 3 6 9 17 26 35
18-Boba Fett-c 3 6 9 14 20 25
19-1st Ben Skywalker 4 8 12 23 37 50
24-1st Darth Nihilus & Darth Traya 6 12 18 38 69 100
Volume 1-6 ($19.95) 1-(1/02) r/#1-4. 2-('02) r/#5-8. 3-(1/03) r/#9-12. 4-(1/04) r/#13-16 5-(1/05) r/#17-20; introduction pages from #1-20. 6-(1/06) r/#21-24 20.00

STAR WARS: TALES FROM MOS EISLEY
Dark Horse Comics: Mar, 1996 ($2.95, one-shot)

nn-Bret Blevins-a. 4.00

STAR WARS: TALES OF THE JEDI (See Dark Horse Comics #7)
Dark Horse Comics: Oct, 1993 - No. 5, Feb, 1994 ($2.50, limited series)

1-Dave Dorman painted-c 2 4 6 11 16 20
1-5-Gold foil embossed logo; limited # printed-7500 (set) 10 20 30 64 132 200
2-5: All have Dave Dorman painted-c. 3-r/Dark Horse Comics #7-9 w/new coloring & some panels redrawn 5.00
Star Wars Omnibus: Tales of the Jedi Volume One TPB (11/07, $24.95) r/#1-5, ... - The Golden

GD VG FN VF VF/NM NM-
2.0 4.0 6.0 8.0 9.0 9.2

Age of the Sith #0-5 and ... - The Fall of the Sith Empire #1-5 4 8 12 23 37 50

STAR WARS: TALES OF THE JEDI-DARK LORDS OF THE SITH
Dark Horse Comics: Oct, 1994 - No. 6, Mar, 1995 ($2.50, limited series)
1-6: 1-Polybagged w/trading card 1 2 3 5 6 8

STAR WARS: TALES OF THE JEDI-REDEMPTION
Dark Horse Comics: July, 1998 - No. 5, Nov, 1998 ($2.95, limited series)
1-5: 1-Kevin J. Anderson-s/Kordey-c 1 3 4 6 8 10

STAR WARS: TALES OF THE JEDI-THE FALL OF THE SITH EMPIRE
Dark Horse Comics: June, 1997 - No. 5, Oct, 1997 ($2.95, limited series)
1-5 5.00

STAR WARS: TALES OF THE JEDI-THE FREEDON NADD UPRISING
Dark Horse Comics: Aug, 1994 - No. 2, Nov, 1994 ($2.50, limited series)
1,2 1 3 4 6 8 10

STAR WARS: TALES OF THE JEDI-THE GOLDEN AGE OF THE SITH
Dark Horse Comics: July, 1996 - No. 5, Feb, 1997 (99¢/$2.95, limited series)
0-(99¢)-Anderson-s 5.00
1-5-Anderson-s 1 2 3 5 6 8

STAR WARS: TALES OF THE JEDI-THE SITH WAR
Dark Horse Comics: Aug, 1995 - No. 6, Jan, 1996 ($2.50, limited series)
1-6: Anderson scripts 1 3 4 6 8 10

STAR WARS: TARGET VADER
Marvel Comics: Sept, 2019 - No. 6, Feb, 2020 ($3.99, limited series)
1-6-Robbie Thompson-s; Valance app. 5.00

STAR WARS: THE BOUNTY HUNTERS
Dark Horse Comics: July, 1999 - Oct, 1999 ($2.95, one-shots)
...Aurra Sing (7/99), ...Kenix Kil (10/99), ...Scoundrel's Wages (8/99) Lando Calrissian app. 5.00

STAR WARS: THE CLONE WARS (Based on the Cartoon Network series)
Dark Horse Comics: Sept, 2008 - No. 12, Jan, 2010 ($2.99)
1-1st comic app. of Ahsoka Tano 32 64 96 230 515 800
2-Gilroy-s/Hepburn-a/Filoni-c 5 10 15 34 60 85
3,4-Gilroy-s/Hepburn-a/Filoni-c 3 6 9 16 23 30
5,8-12: 5-Gilroy-s/Hepburn-a/Filoni-c 2 4 6 10 14 18
6-Ahsoka Tano-c by Filoni 4 8 12 28 47 65
7-Cameo of Clone Commander 3 6 9 17 26 35

STAR WARS: THE FORCE AWAKENS ADAPTATION (Episode VII movie)
Marvel Comics: Aug, 2016 - No. 6, Jan, 2017 ($4.99, limited series)
1-Chuck Wendig-s/Luke Ross-a/Esad Ribic-c 1 3 4 6 8 10
2,3,5,6: 3-Marc Laming-a 5.00
4-1st Knights of Ren 2 4 6 8 10 12

STAR WARS: THE FORCE UNLEASHED (Based on the LucasArts video game)
Dark Horse Comics: Aug, 2008 ($15.95, one-shot graphic novel)
GN-Intro. Starkiller, Vader's apprentice; takes place 2 years before Battle of Yavin 3 6 9 14 20 25

STAR WARS: THE HALCYON LEGACY
Marvel Comics: Apr, 2022 - No. 5, Oct, 2022 ($4.99/$3.99)
1-($4.99) Sacks-s/Sliney-a 5.00
2-5-($3.99) 2-Aurra Sing app. 3-Anakin, Padmé & Asajj Ventress app. 4-Lando app. 4.00

STAR WARS: THE HIGH REPUBLIC (Takes place before Phantom Menace)
Marvel Comics: Mar, 2021 - No. 15, May, 2022 ($3.99)
1-15: 1-Cavan Scott-s/Ario Anindito-a; intro Keeve Trennis; Yoda app. 4.00

STAR WARS: THE HIGH REPUBLIC
Marvel Comics: Dec, 2022 - No. 10 ($4.99/$3.99)
1-($4.99) Cavan Scott-s/Ario Anindito-a 5.00
2-5-($3.99) 4.00

STAR WARS: THE HIGH REPUBLIC ADVENTURES (Takes place before Phantom Menace)
IDW Publishing: Feb, 2021 - No. 13, Feb, 2022 ($3.99)
1-13: 1-7,11,12-Older-s/Talibao-a. 8-10-Bruno-a 4.00
Annual 2021 (12/21, $7.99) Five short stories by various incl. Soule, Gray & Scott 8.00
... Free Comic Book Day 2021 (8/21, giveaway) Art by Tolibao & Brokenshire 3.00
... Galactic Bake-Off Special (1/22, $5.99) Older & Ayala-s/Geyong & Bruno-a 6.00

STAR WARS: THE HIGH REPUBLIC ADVENTURES
IDW Publishing: Nov, 2022 - Present ($3.99)
1,2 4.00

STAR WARS: THE HIGH REPUBLIC – EYE OF THE STORM
Marvel Comics: Mar, 2022 - No. 2, May, 2022 ($4.99, limited series)
1,2-Charles Soule-s/Guillermo Sanna-a 5.00

STAR WARS: THE HIGH REPUBLIC – THE BLADE
Marvel Comics: Feb, 2023 - No. 4, ($4.99, limited series)
1-3-Charles Soule-s/Marco Castiello-a 5.00

STAR WARS: THE HIGH REPUBLIC – THE MONSTER OF TEMPLE PEAK
IDW Publishing: Aug, 2021 - No. 4, Nov, 2021 ($4.99, limited series)
1-4-Cavan Scott-s/Rachael Stott-a 5.00

STAR WARS: THE HIGH REPUBLIC – THE NAMELESS TERROR
IDW Publishing: Feb, 2023 - No. 4, ($4.99, limited series)
1-George Mann-s/Eduardo Mello-a 5.00

STAR WARS: THE HIGH REPUBLIC – TRAIL OF SHADOWS
Marvel Comics: Dec, 2021 - No. 5, Apr, 2022 ($3.99, limited series)
1-5-Older-s/Wachter-a 4.00

STAR WARS: THE JABBA TAPE
Dark Horse Comics: Dec, 1998 ($2.95, one-shot)
nn-Wagner-s/Plunkett-a 6.00

STAR WARS: THE LAST COMMAND
Dark Horse Comics: Nov, 1997 - No. 6, July, 1998 ($2.95, limited series)
1-6: Based on the Timothy Zaun novel 6.00

STAR WARS: THE LAST JEDI ADAPTATION
Marvel Comics: Jul, 2018 - No. 6, Nov, 2018 ($4.99/$3.99, limited series)
1,6-($4.99) Whitta-s/Walsh-a. 1-Del Mundo-c 5.00
2-5-($3.99) 2-Shirahama-c. 3-Noto-c. 4-Rahzzah-c. 5-Rivera-c 4.00

STAR WARS: THE LAST JEDI - DJ - MOST WANTED
Marvel Comics: Mar, 2018 ($4.99, one-shot)
1-Acker & Blacker-s/Walker-a 5.00

STAR WARS: THE MANDALORIAN
Marvel Comics: Sept, 2022 - No. 8, May, 2023 ($4.99)
1-8-Adaptation of the TV series 1st season; Barnes-s/Jeanty-a 5.00

STAR WARS: THE OLD REPUBLIC (Based on the video game)
Dark Horse Comics: July, 2010 - No. 6, Dec, 2010 ($2.99, limited series)
1-(Threat of Peace)-Sanchez-a; two covers 3 6 9 14 20 25
2-3 (Threat of Peace)-Chestny-s/Sanchez-a 5.00
4-(Blood of the Empire) 1st Darth Marr 3 6 9 16 23 30
5,6 (Blood of the Empire)-Freed-s/Dave Ross-a 5.00

STAR WARS: THE OLD REPUBLIC - THE LOST SUNS (Based on the video game)
Dark Horse Comics: Jun, 2011 - No. 5, Oct, 2011 ($3.50, limited series)
1-5-Freed-s/Carré-c/Freeman-a 3.50

STAR WARS: THE PROTOCOL OFFENSIVE
Dark Horse Comics: Sept, 1997 ($4.95, one-shot)
nn-Anthony Daniels & Ryder Windham-s 5.00

STAR WARS: THE RISE OF KYLO REN
Marvel Comics: Feb, 2020 - No. 4, May, 2020 ($4.99/$3.99, limited series)
1-($4.99)-Soule-s/Sliney-a; Ben Solo after the burning of the temple 5.00
2-4-($3.99) 2-Young Ben meets the Knights of Ren; Snoke app. 4.00

STAR WARS: THRAWN
Marvel Comics: Apr, 2018 - No. 6, Sept, 2018 ($3.99, limited series)
1-6-Houser-s/Luke Ross-a; Thrawn's intro to the Empire; Palpatine app. 4.00

STAR WARS: TIE FIGHTER (Tie-in to Alphabet Squadron novel)
Marvel Comics: Jun, 2019 - No. 5, Oct, 2019 ($3.99, limited series)
1-5-Houser-s/Antonio-a; spotlight on Shadow Wing squad 4.00

STAR WARS: UNDERWORLD - THE YAVIN VASSILIKA
Dark Horse Comics: Dec, 2000 - No. 5, June, 2001 ($2.99, limited series)
1-5-(Photo and Robinson covers) 1 3 4 6 8 10

STAR WARS: UNION
Dark Horse Comics: Nov, 1999 - No. 4, Feb, 2000 ($2.95, limited series)
1-4-Wedding of Luke and Mara Jade; Teranishi-a/Stackpole-s 6.00

STAR WARS: VADER – DARK VISIONS
Marvel Comics: May, 2019 - No. 5, Aug, 2019 ($4.99/$3.99, limited series)
1-($4.99)-Hallum-s/Villanelli-a/Smallwood-c 1 3 4 6 8 10
2-5-($3.99)-Hallum-s/Smallwood-c. 2-Level-a. 3-David Lopez-a. 4-Mooney-a. 5-Borges-a 4.00

STAR WARS: VADER DOWN
Marvel Comics: Jan, 2016 ($4.99, one-shot)
1-Part 1 of x-over with Star Wars (2015) #13,14 and Darth Vader #13-15; Deodato-a 1 3 4 6 8 10

STAR WARS: VADER'S QUEST
Dark Horse Comics: Feb, 1999 - No. 4, May, 1999 ($2.95, limited series)
1-Follows destruction of 1st Death Star; Gibbons-a 1 3 4 6 8 10
2-4 4.00

STAR WARS: VISIONS
Marvel Comics: Dec, 2022 ($4.99, one-shot)
1-Samurai version of Mace Windu in manga-style; Takashi Okazaki-s/a 5.00

STAR WARS: VISIONARIES
Dark Horse Comics: Apr, 2005 ($17.95, TPB)
nn-Short stories from the concept artists for Revenge of the Sith movie 18.00

STAR WARS: WAR OF THE BOUNTY HUNTERS
Marvel Comics: Jul, 2021 - No. 5, Dec, 2021 ($3.99/$4.99)
... Alpha (7/21, $3.99) Boba Fett with Han Solo frozen in carbonite; Soule-s/McNiven-a 4.00
... Alpha Director's Cut (7/21, $5.99) Reprints #1 with bonus B&W art and cover gallery 6.00
1-(8/21, $4.99) Part 2; Luke Ross-a; Qi'ra app. 5.00
2-4-($3.99) 2-Boba Fett, Bossk, Aphra, Sana & Darth Vader app. 4.00
5-($4.99) Conclusion; leads into Star Wars: Crimson Reign series 5.00
... – Boussh 1 (11/21, $4.99) Alyssa Wong-s/David Baldeón-a 5.00
... – 4-Lom & Zuckuss 1 (10/21, $4.99) Daniel José Older-s/Kei Zama-a 5.00
... – IG-88 1 (12/21, $4.99) Rodney Barnes/Guiu Vilanova-a; Boba Fett-a 5.00
... – Jabba the Hutt 1 (9/21, $4.99) Ireland-s/Roberson & Pizzari-a; Boba Fett-a 5.00

STAR WARS: X-WING ROGUE SQUADRON (Star Wars: X-Wing Rogue Squadron-The Phantom Affair #5-8 appears on cover only)
Dark Horse Comics: July, 1995 - No. 35, Nov, 1998 ($2.95)
1/2 8.00
1-Baron script 2 4 6 8 10 12
2-24,26-35: 2-4-Baron scripts. 5-20-Stackpole scripts 4.00
25-($3.95) 5.00
The Phantom Affair TPB ($12.95) r/#5-8 13.00

STAR WARS: X-WING ROGUE SQUADRON: ROGUE LEADER
Dark Horse Comics: Sept, 2005 - No. 3, Nov, 2005 ($2.99)
1-3-Takes place one week after the Batttle of Endor 3.00

STAR WARS: YODA
Marvel Comics: Jan, 2023 - Present ($4.99/$3.99)

Star Wars: The Mandalorian #5 © Lucasfilm

Static: Season One #4 © DC

Stellar #3 © Skybound

	GD 2.0	VG 4.0	FN 6.0	VF 8.0	VF/NM 9.0	NM- 9.2
1-($4.99) Cavan Scott-s/Nico Leon-a						5.00
2-($3.99) 4-Dooku app.						4.00

STATIC (See Charlton Action: Featuring "Static")

STATIC (See Heroes)
DC Comics (Milestone): June, 1993 - No. 45, Mar, 1997 ($1.50/$1.75/$2.50)

	GD	VG	FN	VF	VF/NM	NM-
1-($2.95)-Collector's Edition; Static on red background; polybagged w/poster & trading card & backing board (direct sales only)	3	6	9	21	33	45
1-Platinum Edition with red background cover	10	20	30	64	132	200
1-Intro. Virgil Hawkins; blue background cover	4	8	12	25	40	55
1-Facsimile Edition (2023, $9.99) reprints Collector's Edition with polybag & extras						10
2-13,15-24,26-44: 2-Origin. 8-Shadow War; Simonson silver ink-c. 27-Kent Williams-c						4.00
14-($2.50, 52 pgs.)-Worlds Collide Pt. 14						6.00
25 ($3.95)						5.00
45-Last issue; cover by Moebius	13	26	39	89	195	300
...: Trial by Fire (2000, $9.95) r/#1-4; Leon-c	2	4	6	11	16	20

STATIC: SEASON ONE (Milestone Returns)
DC Comics: Aug, 2021 - No. 6, May, 2022 ($3.99, limited series)

1-6: 1-Vita Ayala-s/ChrisCross-a — 4.00

STATIC: SHADOWS OF DAKOTA (Season Two)
DC Comics: Apr, 2023 - No. 6 ($3.99, limited series)

1,2-Nikolas Draper-Ivey & Vita Ayala-s/Draper-Ivey-a — 4.00

STATIC SHOCK (DC New 52)
DC Comics: Nov, 2011 - No. 8, Jun, 2012 ($2.99)

	GD	VG	FN	VF	VF/NM	NM-
1-McDaniel & Rozum-s/McDaniel-a/c	2	4	6	11	16	20
1-2nd printing	1	3	4	6	8	10
2-8: 6-Hardware & Technique app. 8-Origin retold						4.00

STATIC SHOCK!: REBIRTH OF THE COOL (TV)
DC Comics: Jan, 2001 - No. 4, Sept, 2001 ($2.50, limited series)

	GD	VG	FN	VF	VF/NM	NM-
1-McDuffie-s/Leon-c/a	5	10	15	34	60	85
2	4	8	12	27	44	60
3,4	3	6	9	19	30	40

STATIC SHOCK SPECIAL
DC Comics: Aug, 2011 ($2.99, one-shot)

	GD	VG	FN	VF	VF/NM	NM-
1-Cowan-a/Williams III-c; pin-ups by various; tribute to Dwayne McDuffie	2	4	6	9	13	16

STATIC-X
Chaos! Comics: Aug, 2002 ($5.99)

	GD	VG	FN	VF	VF/NM	NM-
1-Polybagged with music CD; metal band as super-heroes; Pulido-s	2	4	6	11	16	20

STEALTH (Pilot Season: ...)
Image Comics (Top Cow): May, 2010; Mar, 2020 - No. 6, Oct, 2020 ($2.99/$3.99)

1-(5/10) Kirkman-s/Mitchell-a/Silvestri-c — 3.00
1-6: 1-(3/20, $3.99) Costa-s/Bellegarde-a — 4.00

STEAM MAN, THE
Dark Horse Comics: Oct, 2015 - No. 5, Feb, 2016 ($3.99)

1-5-Kowalski-a; Steam robot and crew in 1899 — 4.00

STEAMPUNK
DC/WildStorm (Cliffhanger): Apr, 2000 - No. 12, Aug, 2002 ($2.50/$3.50)

Catechism (1/00) Prologue -Kelly-s/Bachalo-a — 3.00
1-4,6-11: 4-Four covers by Bachalo, Madureira, Ramos, Campbell — 3.00
5,12-($3.50) — 4.00
...: Drama Obscura ('03, $14.95) r/#6-12 — 15.00
...: Manimatron ('01, $14.95) r/#1-5, Catechism, Idiosincratica — 15.00

STEAMPUNK BATTLESTAR GALACTICA 1880 (See Battlestar Galactica 1880)

STEED AND MRS. PEEL (TV)(Also see The Avengers)
Eclipse Books/ ACME Press: 1990 - No. 3, 1991 ($4.95, limited series)

Books One - Three: Grant Morrison scripts/Ian Gibson-a — 5.00
1-6: 1-(BOOM! Studios, 1/12 - No. 6, 6/12, $3.99) r/Books One - Three — 4.00

STEED AND MRS. PEEL (TV)(The Avengers)
BOOM! Studios: No. 0, Aug, 2012 - No. 11, Jul, 2013 ($3.99)

0-11: 0-Mark Waid-s/Steve Bryant-a; eight covers. 1-3-Sliney-a; five covers — 4.00

STEED AND MRS. PEEL: WE'RE NEEDED (TV)(The Avengers)
BOOM! Studios: Jul, 2014 - No. 3, Sept, 2014 ($3.99)(Issue #1 says "1 of 6")

1-3-Edginton-s/Cosentino-a. 1-Two covers — 4.00

STEEL (Also see JLA)
DC Comics: Feb, 1994 - No. 52, July, 1998 ($1.50/$1.95/$2.50)

1-8,0,9-52: 1-From Reign of the Supermen storyline. 6,7-Worlds Collide Pt. 5 &12. 8-(9/94). 0-(10/94). 9-(11/94). 46-Superboy-c/app. 50-Millennium Giants x-over — 3.00
1-(3/11, $2.99, one-shot) Benes-a/Garner-c; Reign of Doomsday x-over — 4.00
Annual 1 (1994, $2.95)-Elseworlds story — 4.00
Annual 2 (1995, $3.95)-Year One story — 4.00
...Forging of a Hero TPB (1997, $19.95) reprints early app. — 20.00

STEEL: THE OFFICIAL COMIC ADAPTATION OF THE WARNER BROS. MOTION PICTURE
DC Comics: 1997 ($4.95, Prestige format, one-shot)

nn-Adaptation of the Shaquille O'Neal movie; Bogdanove & Giordano-a — 5.00

STEEL CAGE (Also see Penultiman)
AHOY Comics: 2019 ($3.99)

1-Series try-outs for Bright Boy, Noah Zark and Penultiman; Elsa Charretier-c — 4.00

STEELGRIP STARKEY
Marvel Comics (Epic): June, 1986 - No. 6, July, 1987 ($1.50, lim. series, Baxter paper)

1-6 — 3.00

STEEL STERLING (Formerly Shield-Steel Sterling; see Blue Ribbon, Jackpot, Mighty Comics, Mighty Crusaders, Roly Poly & Zip Comics)
Archie Enterprises, Inc.: No. 4, Jan, 1984 - No. 7, July, 1984

4-7: 4-6-Kanigher-s; Barreto-a. 5,6-Infantino-a. 6-McWilliams-a — 5.00

STEEL, THE INDESTRUCTIBLE MAN (See All-Star Squadron #8 and J.L. of A. Annual #2)
DC Comics: Mar, 1978 - No. 5, Oct-Nov, 1978

	GD	VG	FN	VF	VF/NM	NM-
1	3	6	9	17	26	35
2-5: 5-44 pgs.	1	3	4	6	8	10

STEELTOWN ROCKERS
Marvel Comics: Apr, 1990 - No. 6, Sept, 1990 ($1.00, limited series)

1-6: Small town teens form rock band — 3.00

STEEPLE
Dark Horse Comics: Sept, 2019 - No. 5, Jan, 2020 ($3.99, limited series)

1-5-John Allison-s/a/c; variant-c for each by various — 4.00

STELLAR
Image Comics (Skybound): Jun, 2018 - No. 6, Nov, 2018 ($3.99, limited series)

1-6-Joseph Keatinge-s/Bret Blevins-a — 4.00

STEPHEN COLBERT'S TEK JANSEN (From the animated shorts on The Colbert Report)
Oni Press: July, 2007 - No. 5, Jan, 2009 ($3.99, limited series)

1-Chantier-a/Layman & Peyer-s; back-up story by Massey-s/Rodriguez-a; Chantier-c — 4.00
1-Variant-c by John Cassaday — 6.00
1-Second printing with flip book of Cassaday & Chantier covers — 4.00
2-5: 2-(6/08) Flip book with covers by Rodriguez & Wagner. 3-Flip-c by Darwyn Cooke — 4.00

STEPHEN KING'S N. THE COMIC SERIES
Marvel Comics: May, 2010 - No. 4, Aug, 2010 ($3.99, limited series)

1-4-Guggenheim-s/Maleev-a/c — 4.00

STEVE AUSTIN (See Stone Cold Steve Austin)

STEVE CANYON (See Harvey Comics Hits #52)
Dell Publishing Co.: No. 519, 11/53 - No. No. 1033, 9/59 (All Milton Caniff-a except #519, 939, 1033)

	GD	VG	FN	VF	VF/NM	NM-
Four Color 519 (1, 1953)	9	18	27	59	117	175
Four Color 578 (8/54), 641 (7/55), 737 (10/56), 804 (5/57), 939 (10/58), 1033 (9/59) (photo-c)	5	10	15	35	63	90

STEVE CANYON
Grosset & Dunlap: 1959 (6-3/4x9", 96 pgs., B&W, no text, hardcover)

	GD	VG	FN	VF	VF/NM	NM-
100100-Reprints 2 stories from strip (1953, 1957)	6	12	18	31	38	45
100100 (softcover edition)	5	10	15	24	30	35

STEVE CANYON COMICS
Harvey Publ.: Feb, 1948 - No. 6, Dec, 1948 (Strip reprints, No. 4,5: 52pgs.)

	GD	VG	FN	VF	VF/NM	NM-
1-Origin; has biography of Milton Caniff; Powell-a, 2 pgs.; Caniff-a	20	40	60	120	195	270
2-Caniff, Powell-a in #2-6	14	28	42	80	115	150
3-6: 6-Intro Madame Lynx-c/story	14	28	42	76	108	140

STEVE CANYON IN 3-D
Kitchen Sink Press: June, 1986 ($2.25, one-shot)

1-Contains unpublished story from 1954 — 5.00

STEVE DITKO'S STRANGE AVENGING TALES
Fantagraphics Books: Feb, 1997 ($2.95, B&W)

	GD	VG	FN	VF	VF/NM	NM-
	2.0	4.0	6.0	8.0	9.0	9.2

1-Ditko-c/s/a 5.00

STEVE DONOVAN, WESTERN MARSHAL (TV)
Dell Publishing Co.: No. 675, Feb, 1956 - No. 880, Feb, 1958 (All photo-c)

Four Color 675-Kinstler-a	8	16	24	51	96	140
Four Color 768-Kinstler-a	6	12	18	38	69	100
Four Color 880	5	10	15	31	53	75

STEVEN UNIVERSE (TV)
BOOM! Studios (kaBOOM): Aug, 2014 - No. 8, Mar, 2015 ($3.99)

1-8: 1-Four covers; Uncle Grandpa preview. 2-8-Three covers 4.00
...: Anti-Gravity OGN (11/17, $14.99, 9" x 6") Perper-s/Chan & Ayoub-a 15.00
...: Greg Universe Special 1 (4/15, $4.99) Short stories by various; two covers 5.00
...: 2016 Special 1 (12/16, $7.99) Short donut-themed stories by various; two covers 8.00

STEVEN UNIVERSE (Ongoing)(TV)
BOOM! Studios (kaBOOM): Feb, 2017 - No. 36, Jan, 2020 ($3.99)

1-24,26-36: 1-Four covers; Lapis & Peridot app. 19-Sugilite app. 4.00
25-($4.99) Captain Lars and his crew vs. Emerald 5.00
...: Fusion Frenzy 1 (3/19, $7.99) Short stories by various; 3 covers 8.00

STEVEN UNIVERSE AND THE CRYSTAL GEMS (TV)
BOOM! Studios (kaBOOM): Mar, 2016 - No. 4, Jun, 2016 ($3.99)

1-4-Fenton-s/Garland-a; multiple covers on each. 1-Preview of Over the Garden Wall 4.00

STEVEN UNIVERSE: HARMONY (TV)
BOOM! Studios (kaBOOM): Aug, 2018 - No. 5, Dec, 2018 ($3.99, 8" x 8" square size)

1-5-S.M. Vidaurri-s/Mollie Rose-a; Aquamarine, Topaz & Sugilite app. 4.00

STEVE ROGERS: SUPER-SOLDIER (Captain America - The Heroic Age)
Marvel Comics: Sept, 2010 - No. 4, Dec, 2010 ($3.99, limited series)

1-4-Brubaker-s/Eaglesham-a/Pacheco-c. 1-Back-up rep. of origin from CA #1 ('41) 4.00
Annual 1 (6/11, $3.99) Continued from Uncanny X-Men Annual #3; Roberson-a 4.00

STEVE ROPER
Famous Funnies: Apr, 1948 - No. 5, Dec, 1948

1-Contains 1944 daily newspaper-r	15	30	45	85	130	175
2	10	20	30	56	76	95
3-5	9	18	27	47	61	75

STEVE SAUNDERS SPECIAL AGENT (See Special Agent)

STEVE SAVAGE (See Captain...)

STEVE ZODIAC & THE FIRE BALL XL-5 (TV)
Gold Key: Jan, 1964

10108-401 (#1)	8	16	24	56	108	160

STEVIE (Mazie's boy friend)(Also see Flat-Top, Mazie & Mortie)
Mazie (Magazine Publ.): Nov, 1952 - No. 6, Apr, 1954

1-Teenage humor; Stevie, Mortie & Mazie begin	17	34	51	100	158	215
2-6	10	20	30	54	72	90

STEVIE MAZIE'S BOY FRIEND (See Harvey Hits #5)

STEWART THE RAT (See Eclipse Graphic Album Series)

ST. GEORGE (See listing under Saint...)

STIG'S INFERNO
Vortex/Eclipse: 1985 - No. 7, Mar, 1987 ($1.95, B&W)

1-7 ($1.95) 3.00
Graphic Album (1988, $6.95, B&W, 100 pgs.) 7.00

STILLWATER
Image Comics (Skybound): Sept, 2020 - Present ($3.99)

1-17-Chip Zdarsky-s/Ramón Perez-a 4.00
... The Escape (3/22, $4.99) Four short stories by Zdarsky-s/Perez-a and others 5.00

STING OF THE GREEN HORNET (See The Green Hornet)
Now Comics: June, 1992 - No. 4, 1992 ($2.50, limited series)

1-4: Butler-c/a 3.00
1-4 ($2.75)-Collectors Ed.; polybagged w/poster 4.00

STOKER'S DRACULA (Reprints unfinished Dracula story from 1974-75 with new ending)
Marvel Comics: 2004 - No. 4, May, 2005 ($3.99, B&W)

1-4: 1-Reprints from Dracula Lives! #5-8; Roy Thomas-s/Dick Giordano-a. 2-R/#10,11 & Legion of Monsters #1. 3,4-New story/artwork to finish story. 4-Giordano afterword 4.00
HC (2005, $24.99) r/#1-4; foreward by Thomas; Giordano afterword; bonus art & covers 25.00

STONE
Avalon Studios: Aug, 1998 - No. 4, Apr, 1999 ($2.50, limited series)

1-4-Portacio-a/Haberlin-s 3.00
1-Alternate-c 5.00
2-($14.95) DF Stonechrome Edition 15.00

STONE (Volume 2)
Avalon Studios: Aug, 1999 - No. 4, May, 2000 ($2.50)

1-4-Portacio-a/Haberlin-s 3.00
1-Chrome-c 5.00

STONE COLD STEVE AUSTIN (WWF Wrestling)
Chaos! Comics: Oct, 1999 - No. 4, Feb, 2000 ($2.95)

1-Reg. & photo-c; Steven Grant-s	1	3	4	6	8	10
1-Premium Ed. ($10.00)	2	4	6	9	12	15
2-4-Reg. & photo-c						4.00
Preview ($5.00)						5.00

STONE PROTECTORS
Harvey Pubications: May, 1994 - No. 3, Sept, 1994

nn (1993, giveaway)(limited distribution, scarce) 6.00
1-3-Ace Novelty action figures 4.00

STONEY BURKE (TV Western)
Dell Publishing Co.: June-Aug, 1963 - No. 2, Sept-Nov, 1963

1,2-Jack Lord photo-c on both	3	6	9	16	24	32

STONY CRAIG
Pentagon Publishing Co.: 1946 (No #)

nn-Reprints Bell Syndicate's "Sgt. Stony Craig" newspaper strips; story of the Japanese soldier who wouldn't surrender	14	28	42	76	108	140

STORIES BY FAMOUS AUTHORS ILLUSTRATED (Fast Fiction #1-5)
Seaboard Publ./Famous Authors Ill.: No. 6, Aug, 1950 - No. 13, Mar, 1951

1-Scarlet Pimpernel-Baroness Orczy	27	54	81	160	263	365
2-Capt. Blood-Raphael Sabatini	26	52	78	154	252	350
3-She, by Haggard	30	60	90	177	289	400
4-The 39 Steps-John Buchan	18	36	54	107	169	230
5-Beau Geste-P. C. Wren	18	36	54	107	169	230

NOTE: *The above five issues are exact reprints of Fast Fiction #1-5 except for the title change and new Kiefer covers on #1 and 2. Kiefer c(r)-3-5. The above 5 issues were released before Famous Authors #6.*

6-Macbeth, by Shakespeare; Kiefer art (8/50); used in **SOTI**, pg. 22,143; Kiefer-c; 36 pgs.	24	48	72	142	234	325
7-The Window; Kiefer-c/a; 52 pgs.	18	36	54	107	169	230
8-Hamlet, by Shakespeare; Kiefer-c/a; 36 pgs.	21	42	63	126	206	285
9,10: 9-Nicholas Nickleby, by Dickens; G. Schrotter-a; 52 pgs. 10-Romeo & Juliet, by Shakespeare; Kiefer-c/a; 36 pgs.	18	36	54	107	169	230
11-13: 11-Ben-Hur; Schrotter-a; 52 pgs. 12-La Svengali; Schrotter-a; 36 pgs. 13-Scaramouche; Kiefer-c/a; 36 pgs.	18	36	54	103	162	220

NOTE: *Artwork was prepared/advertised for #14, The Red Badge Of Courage. Gilberton bought out Famous Authors, Ltd. and used that story as C.I. #98. Famous Authors, Ltd. then published the Classics Junior series. The Famous Authors titles were published as part of the regular Classics Ill. Series in Brazil starting in 1952.*

STORIES FROM THE TWILIGHT ZONE
Skylark Pub: Mar, 1979, 68 pgs. (B&W comic digest, 5-1/4x7-5/8")

15405-2: Pfevfer-a, 56 pgs, new comics	3	6	9	17	26	35

STORIES OF ROMANCE (Formerly Meet Miss Bliss)
Atlas Comics (LMC): No. 5, Mar, 1956 - No. 13, Aug, 1957

5-Baker-a?	21	42	63	124	202	280
6-10,12,13	15	30	45	85	130	175
11-Baker, Romita-a; Colletta-c/a	21	42	63	124	202	280

NOTE: ***Ann Brewster** a-13. **Colletta** a-9(2), 11; c-5, 11.*

STORM (X-Men)
Marvel Comics: Feb, 1996 - No. 4, May, 1996 ($2.95, limited series)

1-Foil-c on all; Dodson-a(p)/Ellis-s	2	4	6	10	14	18
2-4-Callisto app.						4.00

STORM (X-Men)
Marvel Comics: Apr, 2006 - No. 6, Sept, 2006 ($2.99, limited series)

1-6: Ororo and T'Challa meet as teens; Eric Jerome Dickey-s 3.00
HC (2007, $19.99, dustjacket) r/#1-6 20.00
SC (2008, $14.99) r/#1-6 15.00

STORM (X-Men)
Marvel Comics: Sept, 2014 - No. 11, Jul, 2015 ($3.99)

1-11: 1-Greg Pak-s/Victor Ibañez-a. 9-Gambit app. 4.00

STORMBREAKER: THE SAGA OF BETA RAY BILL (Also see Thor)
Marvel Comics: Mar, 2005 - No. 6, Aug, 2005 ($2.99, limited series)

1-6-Oeming & Berman-s/DiVito-a; Galactus app. 6-Spider-Man app. 3.00
TPB (2006, $16.99) r/#1-6 17.00

STORMING PARADISE
DC Comics (WildStorm): Sept, 2008 - No. 6, Aug, 2009 ($2.99, limited series)

1-6-WWII invasion of Japan; Dixon-s/Guice-a/c 3.00
TPB (2009, $19.99) r/#1-6 20.00

STORM SHADOW (G.I. Joe character)
Devil's Due Publishing: May, 2007 - No. 7, Nov, 2007 ($3.50)

1-7-Larry Hama-s 3.50

STORMWATCH (Also see The Authority)
Image Comics (WildStorm Prod.): May, 1993 - No. 50, Jul, 1997 ($1.95/$2.50)

1-8,0,9-36: 1-Intro StormWatch (Battalion, Diva, Winter, Fuji, & Hellstrike); 1st app. Weatherman; Jim Lee-c & part scripts; Lee plots in all. 1-Gold edition.1-3-Includes coupon for limited edition StormWatch trading card #00 by Lee. 3-1st brief app. Backlash. 0-($2.50)-Polybagged w/card; 1st full app. Backlash. 9-(4/94, $2.50)-Intro Defile. 10-(6/94),11,12-Both (8/94). 13,14-(9/94). 15-(10/94). 21-Reads #1 on-c. 22-Direct Market; Wildstorm Rising Pt. 9, bound-in card. 23-Spartan joins team. 25-(6/94, June 1995 on-c, $2.50). 35-Fire From Heaven Pt. 5. 36-Fire From Heaven Pt. 12 3.00
10-Alternate Portacio-c, see Deathblow #5 3.00
22-($1.95)-Newsstand, Wildstorm Rising Pt. 9 3.00
37-(7/96, $3.50, 38 pgs.)-Weatherman forms new team; 1st app. Jenny Sparks, Jack Hawksmoor & Rose Tattoo; Warren Ellis scripts begin; Justice League #1-c/swipe 4.00
38-49: 44-Three covers. 3.00
50-($4.50) 4.50
Special 1 ,2(1/94, 5/95, $3.50, 52 pgs.) 4.00
Sourcebook 1 (1/94, $2.50) 3.00

STORMWATCH (Also see The Authority)
Image Comics (WildStorm): Oct, 1997 - No. 11, Sept, 1998 ($2.50)

1-Ellis-s/Jimenez-a(p); two covers by Bennett 3.00
1-($3.50)-Voyager Pack bagged w/Gen 13 preview 4.00
2-11: 4-1st app. Midnighter and Apollo. 7,8-Freefall app. 9-Gen13 & DV8 app. 3.00
A Finer World ('99, $14.95, TPB) r/V2 #4-9 15.00
Change or Die ('99, $14.95, TPB) r/V1 #48-50 & V2 #1-3 15.00
Final Orbit ('01, $9.95, TPB) r/V2 #10,11 & WildC.A.T.S./Aliens; Hitch-c 10.00

STORMWATCH (DC New 52)
DC Comics: Nov, 2011 - No. 30, Jun, 2014 ($2.99)

1-Cornell-s/Sepulveda-a; Martian Manhunter app.; blue bkgrd cover 4.00
1-(2nd printing, cover has red bkgrd), 2-8: 7,8-Jenkins-s. 12-Martian Manhunter leaves 3.00
13-30: 13,14-Etrigan returns. 18-Team re-booted; Starlin-s/c. 20-Lobo origin 3.00
#0-(11/12, $2.99) Flashback to Demon Knights; Milligan-s/Conrad-a 3.00

STORMWATCH: P.H.D. (Post Human Division)
DC Comics (WildStorm): Jan, 2007 - No. 24, Jan, 2010 ($2.99)

Steven Universe #1 © CN

Stillwater #15 © Skybound

Strange (2022) #1 © MAR

	GD 2.0	VG 4.0	FN 6.0	VF 8.0	VF/NM 9.0	NM- 9.2

1-24: 1-Two covers by Mahnke & Hairsine; Gage-s/Mahnke-a. 2-Var-c by Dell'Otto 3.00
...: Armageddon 1 (2/08, $2.99) Gage-s/Fernández-a/McKone-c 3.00
TPB (2007, $17.99) r/#1-4,6,7 & story from Worldstorm #1 18.00
... Book Two TPB (2008, $17.99) r/#5,8-12; sketch pages and concept art 18.00
... Book Three TPB (2009, $17.99) r/#13-19 18.00

STORMWATCH: TEAM ACHILLES
DC Comics (WildStorm): Sept, 2002 - No. 23, Aug, 2004 ($2.95)

1-8: 1-Two covers by Portacio; Portacio-a/Wright-s. 5,6-The Authority app. 3.00
9-23: 9-Back-up preview of The Authority: High Stakes pt. 1 3.00
TPB (2003, $14.95) r/Wizard Preview and #1-6; Portacio art pages 15.00
Book 2 (2004, $14.95) r/#7-11 & short story from Eye of the Storm Annual 15.00

STORMY (Disney) (Movie)
Dell Publishing Co.: No. 537, Feb, 1954

Four Color 537 (...the Thoroughbred)-on top 2/3 of each page; Pluto story on bottom 1/3 6 12 18 40 73 105

STORY OF JESUS (See Classics Illustrated Special Issue)

STORY OF MANKIND, THE (Movie)
Dell Publishing Co.: No. 851, Jan, 1958

Four Color 851-Vincent Price/Hedy Lamarr photo-c 8 16 24 51 96 140

STORY OF MARTHA WAYNE, THE
Argo Publ.: April, 1956

1-Newspaper strip-r 7 14 21 37 46 55

STORY OF RUTH, THE
Dell Publishing Co.: No. 1144, Nov-Jan, 1961 (Movie)

Four Color 1144-Photo-c 9 18 27 57 111 165

STORY OF THE COMMANDOS, THE (Combined Operations)
Long Island Independent: 1943 (15¢, B&W, 68 pgs.) (Distr. by Gilberton)

nn-All text (no comics); photos & illustrations; ad for Classic Comics on back cover (Rare) 50 100 150 315 533 750

STORY OF THE GLOOMY BUNNY, THE (See March of Comics #9)

STORYTELLER, THE: FAIRIES (Jim Henson's)
BOOM! Studios (Archaia): Dec, 2017 - No. 4, Mar, 2018 ($3.99, limited series)

1-4: 1-Matt Smith-s/a. 2-Benjamin Schipper-s/a. 3-Tyler Jenkins-s/a. 4-Celia Lowenthal-s/a 4.00

STORYTELLER, THE: GIANTS (Also see Jim Henson's The Storyteller)
BOOM! Studios (Archaia): Dec, 2016 - No. 4, Mar, 2017 ($3.99, limited series)

1-4: 1-Conor Nolan-s/a. 2-Brandon Dayton-s/a. 3-Jared Cullum-s/a. 4-Feifei Ruan-s/a 4.00

STORYTELLER, THE: SIRENS (Jim Henson's)
BOOM! Studios (Archaia): Apr, 2019 - No. 4 ($3.99, limited series)

1-4: 1-Rebelka-a. 2-Chan Chau-s/a. 3-Sarah Webb-s/a. 4-Aud Koch-s/a 4.00

STRAIGHT ARROW (Radio)(See Best of the West & Great Western)
Magazine Enterprises: Feb-Mar, 1950 - No. 55, Mar, 1956 (All 36 pgs.)

1-Straight Arrow (alias Steve Adams) & his palomino Fury begin; 1st mention of Sundown Valley & the Secret Cave 47 94 141 296 498 700
2-Red Hawk begins (1st app?) by Powell (origin), ends #55 24 48 72 140 230 320
3-Frazetta-c 60 120 180 381 653 925
4,5: 4-Secret Cave-c 22 44 66 132 216 300
6-10 17 34 51 100 158 215
11-Classic story "The Valley of Time", with an ancient civilization made of gold 24 48 72 142 234 325
12-19 14 28 42 82 121 160
20-Origin Straight Arrow's Shield 16 32 48 92 144 195
21-Origin Fury 19 38 57 109 172 235
22-Frazetta-c 37 74 111 222 361 500
23,25-30: 25-Secret Cave-c. 28-Red Hawk meets The Vikings 11 22 33 62 86 110
24-Classic story "The Dragons of Doom!" with prehistoric pteradactyls 15 30 45 84 127 170
31-38: 36-Red Hawk drug story by Powell 10 20 30 54 72 90
39-Classic story "The Canyon Beast", with a dinosaur egg hatching a Tyranosaurus Rex 14 28 42 76 108 140
40-Classic story "Secret of The Spanish Specters", with Conquistadors' lost treasure 11 22 33 64 90 115
41,42,44-54: 45-Secret Cave-c 9 18 27 50 65 80
43-Intro & 1st app. Blaze, S. Arrow's Warrior dog 10 20 30 58 79 100
55-Last issue 11 22 33 62 86 110

NOTE: *Fred Meagher a 1-55; c-1, 2, 4-21, 23-55.* ***Powell*** *a 2-55.* ***Whitney*** *a-1. Many issues advertise the radio premiums associated with Straight Arrow.*

STRAIGHT ARROW'S FURY (Also see A-1 Comics)
Magazine Enterprises: No. 119, 1954 (one-shot)

A-1 119-Origin; Fred Meagher-c/a 19 38 57 111 176 240

STRAIN, THE (Adaptation of novels by Guillermo del Toro and Chuck Hogan)
Dark Horse Comics: Dec, 2011 - No. 11, Feb, 2013 ($1.00/$3.50)

1-($1.00) Lapham, Hogan & del Toro-s/Huddleston-a/c; variant-c by Morris 3.50
2-11-($3.50) Lapham-s/Huddleston-a/c 3.50

STRAIN, THE: MISTER QUINLAN - VAMPIRE HUNTER
Dark Horse Comics: Sept, 2016 - No. 5 ($3.99)

1-5: 1-Lapham, Hogan & del Toro-s/Salazar-a; origin of Mister Quinlan in ancient Rome 4.00

STRAIN, THE: THE FALL (Guillermo del Toro and Chuck Hogan)
Dark Horse Comics: Jul, 2013 - No. 9, Mar, 2014 ($3.99)

1-9-Lapham, Hogan & del Toro-s/Huddleston-a/Gist-c 4.00

STRAIN, THE: THE NIGHT ETERNAL (Guillermo del Toro and Chuck Hogan)
Dark Horse Comics: Aug, 2014 - No. 12, Aug, 2015 ($3.99)

1-12-Lapham, Hogan & del Toro-s/Huddleston-a/Gist-c 4.00

STRANGE (Tales You'll Never Forget)
Ajax-Farrell Publ. (Four Star Comic Corp.): March, 1957 - No. 6, May, 1958

1 32 64 96 188 307 425
2-Censored r/Haunted Thrills 18 36 54 105 165 225
3-6 15 30 45 86 133 180

STRANGE (Dr. Strange)
Marvel Comics (Marvel Knghts): Nov, 2004 - No. 6, July, 2005 ($3.50)

1-6-Straczynski & Barnes-s/Peterson-a; Dr. Strange's origin retold 3.50
...: Beginnings and Endings TPB (2006, $17.99) r/#1-6 18.00

STRANGE (Dr. Strange)
Marvel Comics: Jan, 2010 - No. 4, Apr, 2010 ($3.99, limited series)

1-4-Waid-s/Rios-a/Coker-c 4.00

STRANGE (Clea as the Sorceror Supreme)
Marvel Comics: May, 2022 - No. 10, Mar, 2023 ($4.99/$3.99, limited series)

1-($4.99) MacKay-s/Ferreira-a; Doctor Doom app. 5.00
2-10-($3.99) 2-Clea vs. The Harvestman. 5-Moon Knight app. 4.00

STRANGE ACADEMY
Marvel Comics: May, 2020 - No. 18, Jun, 2022 ($4.99/$3.99)

1-($4.99) Skottie Young-s/Humberto Ramos-a; Dr. Strange, Doctor Voodoo, Loki app. 6 12 18 41 76 110
2-($3.99) Ancient One, Man-Thing app. 4 8 12 25 40 55
3-18: 10-Field trip to Asgard; The Enchantress app. 11-Howard the Duck app. 4.00
... Presents: The Death of Doctor Strange 1 (12/21, $4.99) Young-s/Del Mundo-a 5.00

STRANGE ACADEMY: FINALS
Marvel Comics: Dec, 2022 - Present ($3.99)

1-4-Skottie Young-s/Humberto Ramos-a 4.00

STRANGE ADVENTURE MAGAZINE
CJH Publications: Dec, 1936 (10¢)

1-Flash Gordon, The Master of Mars, text stories w/some full pg. panels of art by Fred Meagher (a FN+ copy sold for $1075 in 2012)

STRANGE ADVENTURES
DC Comics: July/Aug 1950

nn - Ashcan comic, not distributed to newsstands, only for in-house use. Cover art is All Star Comics #47 with interior being Detective Comics #140. A second example has the interior of Detective Comics #146. A third example has an unidentified issue of Detective Comics as the interior. This is the only ashcan with multiple interiors. A FN+ copy sold for $1,000 in 2007.

STRANGE ADVENTURES
National Periodical Publ.: Aug-Sept, 1950 - No. 244, Oct-Nov, 1973 (No. 1-12: 52 pgs.)

1-Adaptation of "Destination Moon"; preview of movie w/photo-c from movie (also see Fawcett Movie Comic #2); adapt. of Edmond Hamilton's "Chris KL-99" in #1-3; Darwin Jones begins 183 366 549 1510 3405 5300
2 84 168 252 672 1511 2350
3,4 61 122 183 488 1094 1700
5-8,10: 7-Origin Kris KL-99 48 96 144 374 862 1350
9-(6/51)-Origin/1st app. Captain Comet (c/story) 118 236 354 944 2122 3300
11-20: 12,13,17,18-Toth-a. 14-Robot-c 34 68 102 245 548 850
21-30: 28-Atomic explosion panel. 30-Robot-c 32 64 96 230 515 800
31,34-38 29 58 87 209 467 725
32,33-Krigstein-a 30 60 90 216 483 750
39-Ill. in **SOTI** "Treating police contemptuously" (top right)

GD	VG	FN	VF	VF/NM	NM-
2.0	4.0	6.0	8.0	9.0	9.2

38 76 114 281 628 975
40-49-Last Capt. Comet; not in 45,47,48 28 56 84 202 451 700
50-53-Last precode issue (2/55) 25 50 75 175 388 600
54-70 20 40 60 144 317 490
71-79,81-99 17 34 51 114 252 390
80-Grey-tone-c 30 60 90 216 483 750
100 19 38 57 131 291 450
101-110: 104-Space Museum begins by Sekowsky 13 26 39 89 195 300
111-116,118,119: 114-Star Hawkins begins, ends #185; Heath-a in Wood E.C. style
13 26 39 86 188 290
117-(6/60)-Origin/1st app. Atomic Knights. 50 100 150 400 900 1400
120-2nd app. Atomic Knights 22 44 66 154 340 525
121,122,125,127,128,130,131,133,134: 134-Last 10¢ issue
11 22 33 76 163 250
123,126-3rd & 4th app. Atomic Knights 15 30 45 100 220 340
124-Intro/origin Faceless Creature 17 34 51 114 252 390
129,132,135,138,141,147-Atomic Knights app. 12 24 36 82 179 275
136,137,139,140,143,145,146,148,149,151,152,154,155,157-159: 136-Robot cover.
159-Star Rovers app.; Gil Kane/Anderson-a. 9 18 27 63 129 195
142-2nd app. Faceless Creature 11 22 33 76 163 250
144-Only Atomic Knights-c (by M. Anderson) 15 30 45 100 220 340
150,153,156,160: Atomic Knights in each. 150-Greytone-c. 153-(6/63)-3rd app. Faceless Creature; atomic explosion-c. 160-Last Atomic Knights
11 22 33 73 157 240
161-179: 161-Last Space Museum. 163-Star Rovers app. 170-Infinity-c.
177-Intro/origin Immortal Man 8 16 24 52 99 145
180-Origin/1st app. Animal Man 68 136 204 544 1222 1900
181-183,185,186,188,189 6 12 18 41 76 110
184-2nd app. Animal Man by Gil Kane 12 24 36 80 173 265
187-Intro/origin The Enchantress 38 76 114 285 641 1000
190-1st app. Animal Man in costume 15 30 45 105 233 360
191-194,196-200,202-204 6 12 18 37 66 95
195-1st full app. Animal Man 9 18 27 59 117 175
201-Last Animal Man; 2nd full app. 7 14 21 46 86 125
205-(10/67)-Intro/origin Deadman by Infantino & begin series, ends #216
86 172 258 688 1544 2400
206-Neal Adams-a begins 16 32 48 110 243 375
207-210 10 20 30 69 147 225
211-216: 211-Space Museum-r. 215-1st app. League of Assassins. 216-(1-2/69)-Deadman story finally concludes in Brave & the Bold #86 (10-11/69); secret message panel by Neal Adams (pg. 13); tribute to Steranko 9 18 27 62 126 190
217-r/origin & 1st app. Adam Strange from Showcase #17, begin-r; Atomic Knights-r begin
3 6 9 21 33 45
218-221,223-225: 218-Last 12¢ issue. 225-Last 15¢ issue
3 6 9 16 23 30
222-New Adam Strange story; Kane/Anderson-a 4 8 12 23 37 50
226,227,230-236-(68-52 pgs.): 226, 227-New Adam Strange text story w/illos by Anderson (8,6 pgs.) 231-Last Atomic Knights-r. 235-JLA-c/s 3 6 9 16 23 30
228,229 (68 pgs.) 3 6 9 17 26 35
237-243 2 4 6 11 16 20
244-Last issue 3 6 9 14 20 25

NOTE: ***Neal Adams** a-206-216; c-207-218, 228, 235. **Anderson** a-8-52, 94, 96, 99, 115, 117, 119-163, 217r, 218r, 222, 223-225r, 226, 229r, 242i(r); c-18, 19, 21, 23, 24, 27, 30, 32-44(most); c/r-157i, 190i, 217-224, 228-231, 233, 235-239, 241-243. **Ditko** a-188, 189. **Drucker** a-42, 43, 45. **Elias** a-212. **Finlay** a-2, 3, 6, 7, 210r, 229r. **Giunta** a-237r. **Heath** a-116. **Infantino** a-10-101, 106-151, 154, 157-163, 180, 190, 218-221r, 223-244p(r); c-50; c(r)-190p, 197, 199-211, 218-221, 223-244. **Kaluta** c-238, 240. **Gil Kane** a-8-116, 124, 125, 130, 138, 146-157, 173-186, 204r, 222r, 227-231r; c(p)-11-17, 25, 154, 157. **Kubert** a-55(2 pgs.), 226; c-219, 220, 225-227, 232, 234. **Moreira** c-26, 28, 29, 71. **Morrow** c-230. **Mortimer** c-8. **Powell** a-4. **Sekowsky** a-71p, 97-162p, 217p(r), 218p(r); c-206, 217-219r. **Simon & Kirby** a-2r (2 pgs) **Sparling** a-201. **Toth** a-8, 12, 13, 17-19. **Wood** a-154i. Atomic Knights in #117, 120, 123, 126, 129, 132, 135, 138, 141, 144, 147, 150, 153, 156, 160. Atomic Knights reprints by **Anderson** in 217-221, 223-231. Chris KL99 in 1-3, 5, 7, 9, 11, 15. Capt. Comet covers-9-14, 17-19, 24, 26, 27, 32-44.*

STRANGE ADVENTURES
DC Comics (Vertigo): Nov, 1999 - No. 4, Feb, 2000 ($2.50, limited series)
1-4: 1-Bolland-c; art by Bolland, Gibbons, Quitely 3.00

STRANGE ADVENTURES
DC Comics: May, 2009 - No. 8, Dec, 2009 ($3.99, limited series)
1-8: 1-Starlin-s in all; Adam Strange, Capt. Comet, Bizarro & Prince Gavyn app. 4.00
TPB (2010, $19.99) r/#1-8; cover gallery 20.00

STRANGE ADVENTURES
DC Comics (Vertigo): Jul, 2011 ($7.99, one-shot)
1-Short story anthology; s/a by Azzarello, Risso, Milligan and others; Paul Pope-c 8.00

STRANGE ADVENTURES
DC Comics (Black Label): May, 2020 - No. 12, Dec, 2021 ($4.99, limited series)
1-12-Adam Strange's book tour; Tom King-s/Mitch Gerads & Evan Shaner-a; 2 covers on each. 2-12-Mister Terrific & Batman app. in most 5.00
1-Director's Cut (1/21, $5.99) Original script with black & white art 6.00

STRANGE AS IT SEEMS (See Famous Funnies-A Carnival of Comics, Feature Funnies #1, The John Hix Scrap Book & Peanuts)

STRANGE AS IT SEEMS
United Features Syndicate: 1939
Single Series 9, 1, 2 41 82 123 256 428 600

STRANGE CEREBUS (Reprints from Cerebus in Hell)
Aardvark-Vanaheim: Oct, 2017 ($4.00, B&W)
1-Cerebus figures placed over original Doré artwork of Hell; Dr. Strange #180-c swipe 4.00

STRANGE COMBAT TALES
Marvel Comics (Epic Comics): Oct, 1993 - No. 4, Jan, 1994 ($2.50, limited series)
1-4 3.00

STRANGE CONFESSIONS
Ziff-Davis Publ. Co.: Jan-Mar (Spring on-c), 1952 - No. 4, Fall, 1952 (All have photo-c)
1(Scarce)-Kinstler-a 93 186 279 591 1021 1450
2(Scarce, 7-8/52) 60 120 180 381 653 925
3(Scarce, 9-10/52)-#3 on-c, #2 on inside; Reformatory girl story; photo-c
57 114 171 362 619 875
4(Scarce) 54 108 162 343 574 825

STRANGE DAYS
Eclipse Comics: Oct, 1984 - No. 3, Apr, 1985 ($1.75, Baxter paper)
1-3: Freakwave, Johnny Nemo, & Paradax from Vanguard Illustrated; nudity, violence & strong language 6.00

STRANGE DAYS (Movie)
Marvel Comics: Dec, 1995 ($5.95, squarebound, one-shot)
1-Adaptation of film 6.00

STRANGE FANTASY (Eerie Tales of Suspense!)(Formerly Rocketman #1)
Ajax-Farrell: Aug, 1952 - No. 14, Oct-Nov, 1954
2(#1, 8/52)-Jungle Princess story; Kamenish-a; reprinted from Ellery Queen #1
92 184 276 584 1005 1425
2(10/52)-No Black Cat or Rulah; Bakerish, Kamenish-a; hypo/meathook-c
81 162 243 518 884 1250
3-Rulah story, called Pulah 57 114 171 362 619 875
4-Rocket Man app. (2/53) 54 108 162 343 574 825
5,6,8,10,12,14 47 94 141 296 498 700
7-Madam Satan/Slave story 97 194 291 621 1061 1500
9(w/Black Cat), 9(w/Boy's Ranch; S&K-a), 9(w/War)(A rebinding of Harvey interiors; not publ. by Ajax) 110 220 330 704 1202 1700
9-Regular issue; Steve Ditko's 3rd published work (tied with Captain 3D)
97 194 291 621 1061 1500
11-Jungle story 54 108 162 343 574 825
13-Bondage-c; Rulah (Kolah) story 60 120 180 381 653 925

STRANGE FRUIT
BOOM! Studios: Jul, 2015 - No. 4, Nov, 2016 ($3.99, limited series)
1-4-J.G. Jones-a; Jones & Mark Waid-s 4.00

STRANGE GALAXY
Eerie Publications: V1#8, Feb, 1971 - No. 11, Aug, 1971 (B&W, magazine)
V1#8-Reprints-c/Fantastic V19#3 (2/70) (a pulp) 4 8 12 23 37 50
9-11 3 6 9 19 30 40

STRANGE GIRL
Image Comics: June, 2005 - No. 18, Sept, 2007 ($2.95/$2.99/$3.50)
1-18: 1-Rick Remender-s/Eric Nguyen-a. 13-18-($3.50) 3.50
... Vol. 1: Girl Afraid TPB (2005, $12.99) r/#1-4; sketch pages and pin-ups 13.00

STRANGE JOURNEY
America's Best (Steinway Publ.) (Ajax/Farrell): Sept, 1957 - No. 4, Jun, 1958 (Farrell reprints)
1-The Phantom Express 27 54 81 158 259 360
2-4: 2-Flying saucer-c. 3-Titanic-c 20 40 60 114 182 250

STRANGE LOVE (See Fox Giants)

STRANGE LOVE ADVENTURES
DC Comics: Apr, 2022 ($9.99, squarebound, one-shot)
1-Short story romance anthology; Harley Quinn, Sgt. Rock, Peacemaker app.; Paquette-c 10.00

STRANGE MYSTERIES
Superior/Dynamic Publications: Sept, 1951 - No. 21, Jan, 1955
1-Kamenish-a & horror stories begin 110 220 330 704 1202 1700
2 61 122 183 390 670 950
3-5 54 108 162 343 574 825
6-8 48 96 144 302 514 725
9-Bondage 3-D effect-c 129 258 387 826 1413 2000
10-Used in **SOTI**, pg. 181 90 180 270 576 988 1400
11-18: 13-Eyeball-c 53 106 159 334 567 800
19-r/Journey Into Fear #1; cover is a splash from one story; Baker-r(2)
48 96 144 302 514 725
20,21-Reprints; 20-r/#1 with new-c (The Devil) 36 72 108 211 343 475

STRANGE MYSTERIES
I. W. Enterprises/Super Comics: 1963 - 1964
I.W. Reprint #9; Rulah-r/Spook #28; Disbrow-a 3 6 9 21 33 45
Super Reprint #10-12,15-17(1963-64): 10,11-r/Strange #2,1. 12-r/Tales of Horror #5 (3/53) less-c. 15-r/Dark Mysteries #23. 16-r/The Dead Who Walk. 17-r/Dark Mysteries #22
3 6 9 21 33 45
Super Reprint #18-r/Witchcraft #1; Kubert-a 3 6 9 21 33 45

STRANGE PLANETS
I. W. Enterprises/Super Comics: 1958; 1963-64
I.W. Reprint #1(nd)-Reprints E. C. Incredible S/F #30 plus-c/Strange Worlds #3
6 12 18 41 76 110
I.W. Reprint #9-Orlando/Wood-r/Strange Worlds #4; cover-r from Flying Saucers #1
8 16 24 51 96 140
Super Reprint #10-Wood-r (22 pg.) from Space Detective #1; cover-r/Attack on Planet Mars
8 16 24 51 96 140
Super Reprint #11-Wood-r (25 pg.) from An Earthman on Venus
8 16 24 52 99 145
Super Reprint #12-Orlando-r/Rocket to the Moon 8 16 24 54 102 150
Super Reprint #15-Reprints Journey Into Unknown Worlds #8; Heath, Colan-r
5 10 15 31 53 75
Super Reprint #16-Reprints Avon's Strange Worlds #6; Kinstler, Check-a
5 10 15 33 57 80
Super Reprint #18-r/Great Exploits #1 (Daring Adventures #6); Space Busters, Explorer Joe, The Son of Robin Hood; Krigstein-a 4 8 12 28 47 65

STRANGERS
Image Comics: Mar, 2003 - No. 6, Sept, 2003 ($2.95)
1-6-Randy & Jean-Marc Lofficier-s; two covers. 2-Nexus back-up story 3.00

STRANGERS, THE
Malibu Comics (Ultraverse): June, 1993 - No. 24, May, 1995 ($1.95/$2.50)
1-4,6-12,14-20: 1-1st app. The Strangers; has coupon for Ultraverse Premiere #0; 1st app. the Night Man (not in costume). 2-Polybagged w/trading card. 7-Break-Thru x-over. 8-2 pg. origin Solution. 12-Silver foil logo; wraparound-c. 17-Rafferty app. 3.00
1-With coupon missing 2.00

Strange Adventures #28 © DC

Strangers in Paradise #90 © Terry Moore

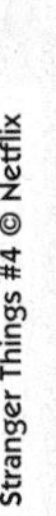
Stranger Things #4 © Netflix

	GD 2.0	VG 4.0	FN 6.0	VF 8.0	VF/NM 9.0	NM- 9.2
1-Full cover holographic edition, 1st of kind w/Hardcase #1 & Prime #1	1	3	4	6	8	10
1-Ultra 5000 limited silver foil						6.00
4-($2.50)-Variant Newsstand edition bagged w/card						4.00
5-($2.50, 52 pgs.)-Rune flip-c/story by B. Smith (3 pgs.); The Mighty Magnor 1 pg. strip by Aragones; 3-pg. Night Man preview						4.00
13-($3.50, 68 pgs.)-Mantra app.; flip book w/Ultraverse Premiere #4						4.00
21-24 ($2.50)						3.00
...:The Pilgrim Conundrum Saga (1/95, $3.95, 68pgs.)						4.00

STRANGERS IN CEREBUS (Strangers in Paradise: I Dream of You cover parody)
Aardvark-Vanaheim: June, 2021 ($4.00, B&W)

	GD	VG	FN	VF	VF/NM	NM-
1-Cerebus figures placed over original Gustave Doré artwork of Hell						4.00

STRANGERS IN PARADISE (Also see SIP Kids)
Antarctic Press: Nov, 1993 - No. 3, Feb, 1994 ($2.75, B&W, limited series)

	GD	VG	FN	VF	VF/NM	NM-
1	14	28	42	96	211	325
1-2nd/3rd prints	2	4	6	11	16	20
2 (2300 printed)	5	10	15	34	60	85
3	3	6	9	21	33	45
Trade paperback (Antarctic Press, $6.95)-Red -c (5000 print run)						10.00
Trade paperback (Abstract Studios, $6.95)-Red-c (2000 print run)						15.00
Trade paperback (Abstract Studios, $6.95, 1st-4th printing)-Blue-c						7.00
Hardcover ('98, $29.95) includes first draft pages						30.00
Gold Reprint Series ($2.75) 1-3-r/#1-3						3.00

STRANGERS IN PARADISE
Abstract Studios: Sept, 1994 - No. 14, July, 1996 ($2.75, B&W)

	GD	VG	FN	VF	VF/NM	NM-
1	2	4	6	11	16	20
1,3- 2nd printings						4.00
2,3: 2-Color dream sequence	1	3	4	6	8	10
4-10						5.00
4-6-2nd printings						4.00
11-14: 14-The Letters of Molly & Poo						4.00
Gold Reprint Series ($2.75) 1-13-r/#1-13						4.00
I Dream Of You ($16.95, TPB) r/#1-9						17.00
It's a Good Life ($8.95, TPB) r/#10-13						9.00

STRANGERS IN PARADISE (Volume Three)
Homage Comics #1-8/Abstract Studios #9-on: Oct, 1996 - No. 90, May, 2007 ($2.75-$2.99, color #1-5, B&W #6-on)

	GD	VG	FN	VF	VF/NM	NM-
1-Terry Moore-c/s/a in all; dream seq. by Jim Lee-a	1	2	3	5	6	8
1-Jim Lee variant-c	2	4	6	8	10	12
2-5						5.00
6-16: 6-Return to B&W. 13-15-High school flashback. 16-Xena Warrior Princess parody; two covers						4.00
17-89: 33-Color issue. 46-Molly Lane. 49-Molly & Poo. 86-David dies						4.00
90-Last issue; 3 covers of Katchoo, Francine and David forming a triptych						5.00
...Lyrics and Poems (2/99)						4.00
...Source Book (2003, $2.95) Background on characters & story arcs, checklists						4.00
Brave New World ('02, $8.95, TPB) r/#44,45,47,48						9.00
Child of Rage ($15.95, TPB) r/#31-38						16.00
David's Story (6/04, $8.95, TPB) r/#61-63						9.00
Ever After ('07, $15.95, TPB) r/#83-90						16.00
Flower to Flame ('03, $15.95, TPB) r/#55-60						16.00
Heart in Hand ('03, $12.95, TPB) r/#50-54						13.00
High School ('98, $8.95, TPB) r/#13-16						9.00
Immortal Enemies ('98, $14.95, TPB) r/#6-12						15.00
Love & Lies (2006, $14.95, TPB)r/#77-82						15.00
Love Me Tender ($12.95, TPB) r/#1-5 in B&W w/ color Lee seq.						13.00
Molly & Poo (2005, $8.95, TPB)r/#46,49,73						9.00
My Other Life ($14.95, TPB) r/#25-30						15.00
Pocket Book 1-5 ($17.95, 5 1/2" x 8", TPB) 1-r/Vol.1 & 2. 2-r/#1-17 in B&W. 3-r/#18-24,26-32,34-38. 4-r/#41-45,47,48,50-60. 5-r/#46,49,61-76						18.00
Sanctuary ($15.95, TPB) r/#17-24						16.00
Tattoo ($14.95, TPB) r/#70-76; sketch pages and fan tattoo photos						15.00
Tomorrow Now (11/04, $14.95, TPB) r/#64-69						15.00
Tropic of Desire ($12.95, TPB) r/#39-43						13.00
The Complete... : Volume 3 Part 1 HC ($49.95) r/#1-12						50.00
The Complete... : Volume 3 Part 2 HC ($49.95) r/#13-15,17-25						50.00
The Complete... : Volume 3 Part 3 HC ('01, $49.95) r/#26-38						50.00
The Complete... : Volume 3 Part 4 HC ('02, $39.95) r/#39-46,49						40.00
The Complete... : Volume 3 Part 5 HC ('03, $49.95) r/#47,48,50-57						50.00
The Complete... : Volume 3 Part 6 HC ('04, $49.95) r/#58-69						50.00
The Complete... : Volume 3 Part 7 HC ('06, $49.95) r/#70-80						50.00

STRANGERS IN PARADISE XXV
Abstract Studio: 2018 - No. 10, 2019 ($3.99, B&W)

	GD	VG	FN	VF	VF/NM	NM-
1-10-Terry Moore-c/s/a; Rachel, Zoe & Lilith app.						4.00
1-Free Comic Book Day edition (2018, giveaway) r/#1						3.00

STRANGER THINGS (Based on the Netflix TV series)
Dark Horse Comics: Sept, 2018 - No. 4, Jan 2019 ($3.99, limited series)

	GD	VG	FN	VF	VF/NM	NM-
1-4-Will Byers time in the Upside Down; Houser-s/Martino-a; multiple covers						4.00
...: Halloween Special One Shot (10/20, $3.99) Moreci-s/Hristov-a/Francavilla-c						4.00
...: Summer Special One Shot (7/22, $3.99) Officers Powell & Callahan during season 3						6.00
...: Winter Special One Shot (11/21, $6.99) Roberson-s/ABEL-a; 2 covers						7.00

STRANGER THINGS / D&D CROSSOVER (Based on the Netflix TV series)
Dark Horse Comics: Nov, 2020 - No. 4 Feb, 2021 ($3.99, limited series)

	GD	VG	FN	VF	VF/NM	NM-
1-4-Houser & Zub-s/Galindo-a/multiple covers						4.00

STRANGER THINGS: INTO THE FIRE (Based on the Netflix TV series)
Dark Horse Comics: Jan, 2020 - No. 4, Jul, 2020 ($3.99, limited series)

	GD	VG	FN	VF	VF/NM	NM-
1-4-The search for subject Eight; Houser-s/Kelly-a/Kalvachev-c						4.00

STRANGER THINGS: KAMCHATKA (Based on the Netflix TV series)
Dark Horse Comics: Mar, 2022 - No. 4, Aug, 2022 ($3.99, limited series)

	GD	VG	FN	VF	VF/NM	NM-
1-4-The demogorgon in Russia; Moreci-s/Hristov-a						4.00

STRANGER THINGS: SCIENCE CAMP (Based on the Netflix TV series)
Dark Horse Comics: Sept, 2020 - No. 4, Dec, 2020 ($3.99, limited series)

	GD	VG	FN	VF	VF/NM	NM-
1-4-Houser-s/Salazar-a/Kalvachev-c						4.00

STRANGER THINGS SIX (Based on the Netflix TV series)
Dark Horse Comics: May, 2019 - No. 4, Aug, 2019 ($3.99, limited series)

	GD	VG	FN	VF	VF/NM	NM-
1-4-Prequel focusing on subject Six, Francine; Houser-s/Salazar-a						4.00

STRANGER THINGS: TALES FROM HAWKINS (Based on the Netflix TV series)
Dark Horse Comics: Feb, 2023 - No. 4, ($3.99, limited series)

	GD	VG	FN	VF	VF/NM	NM-
1-Houser-s/Filipe-a						4.00

STRANGER THINGS TOMB OF YBWEN (Based on the Netflix TV series)
Dark Horse Comics: Sept, 2021 - No. 4, Dec, 2021 ($3.99, limited series)

	GD	VG	FN	VF	VF/NM	NM-
1-4-Bob Newby's treasure map to the Tomb of Ybwen; Pak-s/Galindo-a						4.00

STRANGE SKIES OVER EAST BERLIN
BOOM! Studios: Oct, 2019 - No. 4, Jan, 2020 ($3.99, limited series)

	GD	VG	FN	VF	VF/NM	NM-
1-4-Jeff Loveness-s/Lisandro Estherren-a						4.00

STRANGE SPORTS STORIES (See Brave & the Bold #45-49, DC Special, and DC Super Stars #10)
National Periodical Publications: Sept-Oct, 1973 - No. 6, July-Aug, 1974

	GD	VG	FN	VF	VF/NM	NM-
1-Devil-c	3	6	9	18	27	36
2-6: 2-Swan/Anderson-a	2	4	6	10	14	18

STRANGE SPORTS STORIES
DC Comics (Vertigo): May, 2015 - No. 4, Aug, 2015 ($4.99, limited series)

	GD	VG	FN	VF	VF/NM	NM-
1-4-Anthology of short stories by various. 1-Paul Pope-c. 4-Pope-s/a						5.00

STRANGE STORIES FROM ANOTHER WORLD (Unknown World #1)
Fawcett Publications: No. 2, Aug, 1952 - No. 5, Feb, 1953

	GD	VG	FN	VF	VF/NM	NM-
2-Saunders painted-c	63	126	189	403	689	975
3-5-Saunders painted-c	52	104	156	328	552	775

STRANGE STORIES OF SUSPENSE (Rugged Action #1-4)
Atlas Comics (CSI): No. 5, Oct, 1955 - No. 16, Aug, 1957

	GD	VG	FN	VF	VF/NM	NM-
5(#1)	57	114	171	362	619	875
6,7,9	40	80	120	246	411	575
8-Morrow/Williamson-a; Pakula-a	41	82	123	256	428	600
10-Crandall, Torres, Meskin-a	39	78	117	231	378	525
11-13: 12-Torres, Pakula-a. 13-E.C. art swipes	34	68	102	199	325	450
14-16: 14-Williamson/Mayo-a. 15-Krigstein-a. 16-Fox, Powell-a	36	72	108	211	343	475

NOTE: ***Everett*** *a-6, 7, 13; c-8, 9, 11-14.* ***Forte*** *a-12, 16.* ***Heath*** *a-5.* ***Maneely*** *c-5.* ***Morisi*** *a-11.* ***Morrow*** *a-13.* ***Powell*** *a-8.* ***Sale*** *a-11.* ***Severin*** *c-7.* ***Wildey*** *a-14.*

STRANGE STORY (Also see Front Page)
Harvey Publications: June-July, 1946 (52 pgs.)

	GD	VG	FN	VF	VF/NM	NM-
1-The Man in Black Called Fate by Powell	45	90	135	284	480	675

STRANGE SUSPENSE STORIES (Lawbreakers Suspense Stories #10-15; This Is Suspense #23-26; Captain Atom V1#78 on)
Fawcett Publications/Charlton Comics No. 16 on: 6/52 - No. 5, 2/53; No. 16, 1/54 - No. 22, 11/54; No. 27, 10/55 - No. 77, 10/65; V3#1, 10/67 - V1#9, 9/69

	GD	VG	FN	VF	VF/NM	NM-
1-(Fawcett)-Powell, Sekowsky-a	100	200	300	635	1093	1550
2-George Evans horror story	55	110	165	352	601	850

GD 2.0 | VG 4.0 | FN 6.0 | VF 8.0 | VF/NM 9.0 | NM- 9.2

3-5 (2/53)-George Evans horror stories 47 94 141 296 498 700
16(1-2/54)-Formerly Lawbreakers S.S. 40 80 120 246 411 575
17 32 64 96 188 307 425
18-E.C. swipe/HOF 7; Ditko-c/a(2) 58 116 174 371 636 900
19-Ditko electric chair-c; Ditko-a 676 1352 2028 4935 8718 12,500
20-Ditko-c/a(2) 53 106 159 334 567 800
21-Shuster-a; a woman dangling over an alligator pit while a madman smashes her fingers with a hammer 53 106 159 334 567 800
22(11/54)-Ditko-c, Shuster-a; last pre-code issue; becomes This Is Suspense 52 104 156 328 552 775
27(10/55)-(Formerly This Is Suspense #26) 20 40 60 114 182 250
28-30,38 15 30 45 84 122 170
31-33,35,37,40-Ditko-c/a(2-3 each) 24 48 72 142 234 325
34-Story of ruthless business man, Wm. B. Gaines; Ditko-c/a 61 122 183 390 670 950
36-(15¢, 68 pgs.); Ditko-a(4) 29 58 87 172 281 390
39,41,52,53-Ditko-a 21 42 63 122 199 275
42-44,46,49,54-60 6 12 18 37 66 95
45,47,48,50,51-Ditko-c/a 13 26 39 89 195 300
61-74: 72-Has panel which inspired a famous Roy Lichtenstein painting 5 10 15 33 57 80
75(6/65)-Reprints origin/1st app. Captain Atom by Ditko from Space Advs. #33; r/Severin-a/Space Advs. #24 (75-77: 12¢ issues) 10 20 30 70 150 230
76,77-Captain Atom-r by Ditko/Space Advs. 7 14 21 46 86 125
V3#1(10/67): 12¢ issues begin 3 6 9 20 31 42
V1#2-Ditko-c/a; atom bomb-c 3 6 9 20 31 42
V1#3-9: 3-8-All 12¢ issues. 9-15¢ issue 3 6 9 14 19 24

NOTE: ***Alascia** a-19. **Aparo** a-60, V3#1, 2, 4; c-V1#4, 8, 9. **Baily** a-1-3; c-2, 5. **Evans** c-3, 4. **Giordano** c-16, 17p, 24p, 25p. **Montes/Bache** c-66. **Powell** a-4. **Shuster** a-19, 21. **Marcus Swayze** a-27.*

STRANGE TALENT OF LUTHER STRODE, THE (Also see The Legend of Luther Strode)
Image Comics: Oct, 2011 - No. 6, Mar, 2012 ($2.99, limited series)

1-6: Justin Jordan-s/Tradd Moore-a 3.00

STRANGE TALES (...Featuring Warlock #178-181; Doctor Strange #169 on)
Atlas (CCPC #1-67/ZPC #68-79/VPI #80-85)/Marvel #86(7/61) on:
June, 1951 - No. 168, May, 1968; No. 169, Sept, 1973 - No. 188, Nov, 1976

1-Horror/weird stories begin 919 1838 2757 6709 11,855 17,000
2 226 452 678 1446 2473 3500
3,5: 3-Atom bomb panels 174 348 522 1114 1907 2700
4-Cosmic eyeball story "The Evil Eye" 181 362 543 1158 1979 2800
6-9: 6-Heath-c/a. 7-Colan-a 135 270 405 864 1482 2100
10-Krigstein-a 142 284 426 909 1555 2200
11-14,16-20 110 220 330 704 1202 1700
15-Krigstein-a; detached head-c 116 232 348 742 1271 1800
21,23-27,29-34: 27-Atom bomb panels. 33-Davis-a. 34-Last pre-code issue (2/55) 97 194 291 621 1061 1500
22-Krigstein, Forte/Fox-a 103 206 309 659 1130 1600
28-Jack Katz story used in Senate Investigation report, pgs. 7 & 169; classic skull-c 595 1190 1785 4350 7675 11,000
35-41,43,44: 37-Vampire story by Colan 48 96 144 374 862 1350
42,45,59,61-Krigstein-a; #61 (2/58) 50 100 150 400 900 1400
46-57,60: 51-(10/56) 1st S.A. issue. 53,56-Crandall-a. 60-(8/57) 46 92 138 340 770 1200
58,64-Williamson-a in each, with Mayo-#58 46 92 138 359 805 1250
62,63,65,66: 62-Torres-a. 66-Crandall-a 46 92 138 340 770 1200
67-Prototype ish. (Quicksilver) 54 108 162 432 966 1500
68,71,72,74,77,80: Ditko/Kirby-a in #67-80 46 92 138 340 770 1200
69,70,73,75,76,78,79: 69-Prototype ish. (Prof. X). 70-Prototype ish. (Giant Man). 73-Prototype ish. (Ant-Man). 75-Prototype ish. (Iron Man). 76-Prototype ish. (Human Torch). 78-Prototype ish. (Ant-Man). 79-Prototype ish. (Dr. Strange) (12/60) 50 100 150 400 900 1400
81-83,85-88,90,91-Ditko/Kirby-a in all: 86-Robot-c. 90-(11/61)-Atom bomb blast panel 44 88 132 326 738 1150
84-Prototype ish. (Magneto)(5/61); has powers like Magneto of X-Men, but two years earlier; Ditko/Kirby-a 61 122 183 488 1094 1700
89-1st app. Fin Fang Foom (10/61) by Kirby 333 666 1000 2831 6416 10,000
92-Prototype ish. (Ancient One & Ant-Man); last 10¢ issue 46 92 138 359 805 1250
93,95,96,98-100: Kirby-a 38 76 114 281 628 975
94-Creature similar to The Thing; Kirby-a 46 92 138 340 470 1200
97-1st app. of an Aunt May & Uncle Ben by Ditko (6/62), before Amazing Fantasy #15; (see Tales Of Suspense #7); Kirby-a 136 272 408 1088 2444 3800
101-Human Torch begins by Kirby (10/62); origin recap Fantastic Four & Human Torch; Human Torch-c begin 179 358 537 1477 3339 5200
102-1st app. Wizard; robot-c 52 104 156 416 933 1450
103-105: 104-1st app. Trapster (as Paste-Pot Pete). 105-2nd Wizard 44 88 132 326 738 1150
106,108,109: 106-Fantastic Four guests (3/63) 36 72 108 259 580 900
107-(4/63)-Human Torch/Sub-Mariner battle; 4th S.A. Sub-Mariner app. & 1st x-over outside of Fantastic Four 79 158 237 632 1416 2200
110-(7/63)-Intro Doctor Strange, Ancient One & Wong by Ditko 1500 3000 6000 11,400 21,200 31,000
111-2nd Dr. Strange; intro. Baron Mordo 114 228 342 912 2056 3200
112-1st Eel 34 68 102 245 548 850
113-Origin/1st app. Plantman 30 60 90 216 483 750
114-Acrobat disguised as Captain America, 1st app. since the G.A.; intro. & 1st app. Victoria Bentley; 3rd Dr. Strange app. & begin series (11/63) 61 122 183 488 1094 1700
115-Origin Dr. Strange; Human Torch vs. Sandman (Spidey villain; 2nd app. & brief origin); early Spider-Man x-over, 12/63 129 258 387 1032 2316 3600
116-(1/64)-Human Torch battles The Thing; 1st Thing x-over 27 54 81 194 435 675
117,118,120: 118-1st cover app. of Dr. Strange. 120-1st Iceman x-over (from X-Men) 17 34 51 117 259 400
119-Spider-Man x-over (2 panel cameo) 20 40 60 138 307 475
121,122,124,127-134: Thing/Torch team-up in 121-134. 128-Quicksilver & Scarlet Witch app. (1/65). 130-The Beatles cameo. 134-Last Human Torch; The Watcher-c/story; Wood-a(i) 13 26 39 91 201 310
123-1st app. The Beetle (see Amazing Spider-Man #21 for next app.); 1st Thor x-over (8/64); Loki app. 23 46 69 161 356 550
125-Torch & Thing battle Sub-Mariner (10/64) 21 42 63 147 324 500
126-Intro Clea and Dormammu (cont'd in #127) 89 178 267 712 1606 2500
135-Col. (formerly Sgt.) Nick Fury becomes Nick Fury Agent of Shield (origin/1st app.) by Kirby (8/65); series begins 75 150 225 600 1350 2100
136,137,139,140 9 18 27 57 111 165
138-Intro Eternity 29 58 87 209 467 725
141-147,149: 145-Begins alternating-c features w/Nick Fury (odd #'s) & Dr. Strange (even #'s). 146-Last Ditko Dr. Strange who is in consecutive stories since #113; only full Ditko Dr. Strange-c this title. 147-Dr. Strange (by Everett #147-152) continues thru #168, then Dr. Strange #169 7 14 21 46 86 125
148-Origin Ancient One 9 18 27 59 117 175
150(11/66)-John Buscema's 1st work at Marvel 12 24 36 82 179 275
151-Kirby/Steranko-c/a; 1st Marvel work by Steranko 11 22 33 73 157 240
152,153-Kirby/Steranko-a 7 14 21 49 92 135
154-158-Steranko-a/script. 157,158-Debut of The Living Tribunal 7 14 21 49 92 135
159-Origin Nick Fury retold; Intro Val; Captain America-c/story; Steranko-a 33 66 99 238 532 825
160-162-Steranko-a/scripts; Capt. America app. 7 14 21 49 92 135
163-166,168-Steranko-a(p). 168-Last Nick Fury (gets own book next month) & last Dr. Strange who also gets own book 7 14 21 46 86 125
167-Steranko pen/script; classic flag-c 12 24 36 79 170 260
169-1st app. Brother Voodoo(origin in #169,170) & begin series, ends #173 54 108 162 432 966 1500
170-174: 174-Origin Golem 6 12 18 38 69 100
175-177: 177-Brunner-c 3 6 9 15 22 28
178-(2/75)-Warlock by Starlin begins; origin Warlock & Him retold; 1st app. Magus; Starlin-c/a/scripts in #178-181 (all before Warlock #9) 12 24 36 82 179 275
179-Intro/1st app. Pip the Troll; Warlock app. 10 20 30 69 147 225
180-(6/75) Intro. Gamora (Guardians of the Galaxy) (5 panels); Warlock by Starlin 13 26 39 89 195 300
181-(8/75)-Warlock story continued in Warlock #9; 1st full app. of Gamora 6 12 18 42 79 115
182-188: 185,186-(Regular 25¢ editions) 2 4 6 10 14 18
185,186-(30¢-c variants, limited distribution)(5,7/76) 6 12 18 38 69 100
Annual 1(1962)-Reprints from Strange Tales #73,76,78, Tales of Suspense #7,9, Tales to Astonish #1,6,7, & Journey Into Mystery #53,55,59; (1st Marvel annual) 93 186 279 744 1672 2600
Annual 2(7/63)-New Human Torch vs. Spider-Man story by Kirby/Ditko (1st Spidey x-over; 4th app.); reprints from Strange Tales #67, Strange Worlds (Atlas) #1-3, World of Fantasy #16; Kirby-c 145 290 435 1196 2698 4200

NOTE: ***Briefer** a-17. **Burgos** a-123p. **J. Buscema** a-174p. **Colan** a-7, 11, 20, 37, 53, 169-173p, 188p. **Davis** c-71. **Ditko** a-46, 50, 67-122, 123-125p, 126-146, 175r, 182-188r; c-51, 93, 115, 121, 146. **Everett** a-4, 21, 40-42, 73, 147-152, 164i; c-8, 10, 11, 13, 15, 24, 45, 49-54, 56, 58, 60, 61, 63, 148, 150, 152, 158i. **Forte** a-27, 43, 50, 53, 54, 60. **Heath** a-2, 6; c-6, 18-20. **Kamen** a-45. **G. Kane** c-170-173, 182p. **Kirby** Human Torch-101-105, 108, 109, 114, 120; Nick Fury-135p, 141-143p; (Layouts)-135-153; other **Kirby** a-67-100p; c-68-70, 72-74, 76-92, 94, 95, 101-114, 116-123, 125-130, 132-135, 136p, 138-145, 147, 149, 151p. **Kirby/Ayers** c-101-106, 108-110. **Kirby/Ditko** a-80, 88, 121; c-75, 93, 97, 100, 139. **Lawrence** a-29. **Leiber/ Fox** a-110-113. **Maneely** a-3, 7, 37, 42; c-33, 40. **Moldoff** a-20. **Mooney** a-174i. **Morisi** a-53, 56. **Morrow** a-54. **Orlando** a-41, 44, 46, 49, 52. **Powell** a-42, 44, 49, 54, 130-134p; c-131p. **Reinman** a-11, 50, 74, 80, 88, 91, 95, 104, 106, 112i, 124-127i. **Robinson** a-17. **Romita** c-169. **Roussos** c-201i. **R.Q. Sale** a-56; c-16. **Sekowski** a-3, 11. **Severin** a(i)-136-138; c-137. **Starlin** a-178, 179, 180p, 181p; c-178-180, 181p. **Steranko** a-151-161, 162-168p; c-151i, 153, 155, 157, 159, 161, 163, 165, 167. **Torres** a-53, 62. **Tuska** a-14, 166p. **Whitney** a-149. **Wildey** a-42, 56. **Woodbridge** a-59. Fantastic Four cameos #101-134. Jack Katz app.-26.*

STRANGE TALES
Marvel Comics Group: Apr, 1987 - No. 19, Oct, 1988

V2#1-19 5.00

STRANGE TALES
Marvel Comics: Nov, 1994 ($6.95, one-shot)

V3#1-acetate-c 1 2 3 5 6 8

STRANGE TALES (Anthology; continues stories from Man-Thing #8 and Werewolf By Night #6)
Marvel Comics: Sept, 1998 - No. 2, Oct, 1998 ($4.99)

1,2: 1-Silver Surfer app. 2-Two covers 5.00

STRANGE TALES (Humor anthology)
Marvel Comics: Nov, 2009 - No. 3, Jan, 2010 ($4.99, limited series)

1-3: 1-Paul Pope, Kochalka, Bagge and others-s/a. 2-Bagge-c/a. 3-Sakai-c/a 5.00

STRANGE TALES II (Humor anthology)
Marvel Comics: Dec, 2010 - No. 3, Feb, 2011 ($4.99, limited series)

1-3: 2-Jaime Hernandez-c. 3-Terry Moore-s/a; Pekar-s/Templeton-a 5.00

STRANGE TALES: DARK CORNERS
Marvel Comics: May, 1998 ($3.99, one-shot)

1-Anthology; stories by Baron & Maleev, McGregor & Dringenberg, DeMatteis & Badger; Estes painted-c 4.00

STRANGE TALES OF THE UNUSUAL
Atlas Comics (ACI No. 1-4/WPI No. 5-11): Dec, 1955 - No. 11, Aug, 1957

1-Powell-a 65 130 195 416 708 1000
2 40 80 120 246 411 575
3-Williamson-a (4 pgs.) 41 82 123 256 428 600
4,6,8,11: 4-UFO-c 33 66 99 194 317 440
5-Crandall, Ditko-a 37 74 111 222 361 500
7,9: 7-Kirby, Orlando-a. 9-Krigstein-a 37 74 111 218 354 490
10-Torres, Morrow-a 33 66 99 194 317 440

NOTE: ***Baily** a-6. **Brodsky** c-2-4. **Everett** a-2, 6; c-6, 9, 11. **Heck** a-1. **Maneely** c-1. **Orlando** a-7. **Pakula** a-10. **Romita** a-1. **R.Q. Sale** a-3. **Wildey** a-3.*

STRANGE TERRORS
St. John Publishing Co.: June, 1952 - No. 7, Mar, 1953

1-Bondage-c; Zombies spelled Zoombies on-c; Fine-*esque* -a 97 194 291 621 1061 1500
2 47 94 141 296 498 700
3-Kubert-a; painted-c 57 114 171 362 619 875

Strange Tales #148 © MAR

Strawberry Shortcake #4 © Shortcake I.P.

Stray Bullets: Killers #5 © David Lapham

GD VG FN VF VF/NM NM-
2.0 4.0 6.0 8.0 9.0 9.2

4-Kubert-a (reprinted in Mystery Tales #18); Ekgren painted-c; Fine-*esque* -a;
Jerry Iger caricature 113 226 339 718 1234 1750
5-Kubert-a; painted-c 55 110 165 352 601 850
6-Giant (25¢, 100 pgs.)(1/53); Tyler classic bondage/skull-c
90 180 270 576 988 1400
7-Giant (25¢, 100 pgs.); Kubert-c/a 81 162 243 518 884 1250
NOTE: ***Cameron** a-6, 7. **Morisi** a-6.*

STRANGE WORLD OF YOUR DREAMS
Prize Publications: Aug, 1952 - No. 4, Jan-Feb, 1953
1-Simon & Kirby-a 87 174 261 553 952 1350
2,3-Simon & Kirby-c/a. 2-Meskin-a 61 122 183 390 670 950
4-S&K-c; Meskin-a 52 104 156 328 552 775

STRANGE WORLDS (#18 continued from Avon's Eerie #1-17)
Avon Periodicals: 11/50 - No. 9, 11/52; No. 18, 10-11/54 - No. 22, 9-10/55
(No #11-17)
1-Kenton of the Star Patrol by Kubert (r/Eerie #1 from 1947); Crom the Barbarian by
John Giunta 187 374 561 1197 2049 2900
2-Wood-a; Crom the Barbarian by Giunta; Dara of the Vikings app.; used in **SOTI**,
pg. 112; injury to eye panel 181 362 543 1158 1979 2800
3-Wood/Orlando-a (Kenton), Wood/Williamson/Frazetta/Krenkel/Orlando-a (7 pgs.);
Malu Slave Girl Princess app.; Kinstler-c 271 542 613 1734 2967 4200
4-Wood-c/a (Kenton); Orlando-a; origin The Enchanted Daggar; Sultan-a; classic cover
271 542 813 1734 2967 4200
5-Orlando/Wood-a (Kenton); Wood-c 200 400 600 1280 2190 3100
6-Kinstler-a(2); Orlando/Wood-c; Check-a 168 336 504 1075 1838 2600
7-Fawcette & Becker/Alascia-a 77 154 231 493 847 1200
8-Kubert, Kinstler, Hollingsworth & Lazarus-a; Lazarus Robot-c
81 162 243 518 884 1250
9-Kinstler, Fawcette, Alascia, Kubert-a 74 148 222 470 810 1150
18-(Formerly Eerie #17)-Reprints "Attack on Planet Mars" by Kubert
54 108 162 343 574 825
19-r/Avon's "Robotmen of the Lost Planet"; last pre-code issue; Robot-c
55 110 165 352 601 850
20-War-c/story; Wood-c(r)/U.S. Paratroops #1 19 38 57 111 176 240
21,22-War-c/stories. 22-New logo 15 30 45 84 127 170
I.W. Reprint #5-Kinstler-a(r)/Avon's #9 5 10 15 33 57 80

STRANGE WORLDS
Marvel Comics (MPI No. 1,2/Male No. 3,5): Dec, 1958 - No. 5, Aug, 1959
1-Kirby & Ditko-a; flying saucer issue 126 252 378 806 1378 1950
2-Ditko-c/a 71 142 213 454 777 1100
3-Kirby-a(2) 63 126 189 403 689 975
4-Williamson-a 57 114 171 362 619 875
5-Ditko-a 54 108 162 343 574 825
NOTE: ***Buscema** a-3, 4. **Ditko** a-1-5; c-2.. **Heck** a-2. **Kirby** a-1, 3. **Kirby/Brodsky** c-1, 3-5.*

STRAWBERRY SHORTCAKE
Marvel Comics (Star Comics): Jun, 1985 - No. 6, Feb, 1986 (Children's comic)
1-Howie Post-a in all 3 6 9 14 19 24
2-6 2 4 6 8 10 12

STRAWBERRY SHORTCAKE
Ape Entertainment: 2011 - No. 4, 2011 ($3.95, limited series)
1-4: 1-Scratch 'n' sniff cover 5.00
Volume 2 (2012, $3.99) 1,2 5.00

STRAWBERRY SHORTCAKE
IDW Publishing: Apr, 2016 - No. 8, Nov, 2016 ($3.99)
1-8: Multiple covers on each. 1-Georgia Ball-s/Amy Mebberson-a 4.00
... Funko Universe One-Shot (5/17, $4.99) Ball-s; art in Funko Pop! style 5.00

STRAY
DC Comics (Homage Comics): 2001 ($5.95, prestige format, one-shot)
1-Pollina-c/a; Lobdell & Palmiotti-s 6.00

STRAY
Dark Horse Comics: 2004 (8 1/2"x 5 1/2", Diamond Comic Dist. Halloween giveaway)
nn-Reprint from The Dark Horse Book of Hauntings; Evan Dorkin-s/Jill Thompson-a 3.00

STRAY BULLETS
El Capitan Books/Image Comics: 1995 - No. 41, Mar, 2014 ($2.95/$3.50, B&W, mature)
1-David Lapham-c/a/scripts 2 4 6 11 16 20
2,3 6.00
4-8 4.00
9-21,31,32-($2.95) 3.50
22-30,33-41-($3.50) 22-Includes preview to Murder Me Dead. 40-(10/05). 41-(3/14) 3.50
Free Comic Book Day giveaway (5/02) Reprints #2 with "Free Comic Book Day" banner on-c;
flip book with The Matrix (printing of internet comic) 3.00
Innocence of Nihilism Volume 1 HC ($29.95, hardcover) r/#1-7 30.00
Somewhere Out West Volume 2 HC ($34.95, hardcover) r/#8-14 35.00
Other People Volume 3 HC ($34.95, hardcover) r/#15-22 35.00
Volume 1-3 TPB ($11.95, softcover) 1-r/#1-4. 2-r/#5-8. 3-r/ #9-12 12.00
Volume 4-7 TPB ($14.95) 4- r/#13-16. 5- r/#17-20. 6- r/#21-24. 7-r/#25-28 15.00
NOTE: *Multiple printings of most issues exist & are worth cover price.*

STRAY BULLETS: KILLERS
Image Comics (El Capitan Books): Mar, 2014 - No. 8, Oct, 2014 ($3.50, B&W)
1-8-David Lapham-c/a/scripts; set in 1978 3.50

STRAY BULLETS: SUNSHINE AND ROSES
Image Comics (El Capitan Books): Feb, 2015 - No. 41, Jun, 2019 ($3.50/$3.99, B&W)
1-10-David Lapham-c/a/scripts; set in 1979 Baltimore 3.50
11-36,41-($3.99) 20-Amy Racecar app. 4.00
37-40-($4.99) 5.00

STRAY DOGS
Image Comics: Feb, 2021 - No. 5, Jun, 2021 ($3.99, limited series)
1-Tony Fleecs-s/Trish Forstner-a; two covers 3 6 9 19 30 40
2-4-Two covers on each 1 3 4 6 8 10
5-Two covers 4.00

STRAY DOGS: DOG DAYS
Image Comics: Dec, 2021 - Present ($4.99, limited series)
1,2-Tony Fleecs-s/Trish Forstner-a 6.00
1-Creepshow homage variant-c 5.00

STRAYER
AfterShock Comics: Jan, 2016 - No. 5 ($3.99)
1-5-Justin Jordan-s/Juan Gedeon-a 4.00

STRAY TOASTERS
Marvel Comics (Epic Comics): Jan, 1988 - No. 4, April, 1989 ($3.50, squarebound, limited series)
1-4: Sienkiewicz-c/a/scripts 4.00

STREET COMIX
Street Enterprises/King Features: 1973 (50¢, B&W, 36 pgs.)(20,000 print run)
1-Rip Kirby 2 4 6 8 11 14
2-Flash Gordon 2 4 6 10 14 18

STREETFIGHTER
Ocean Comics: Aug, 1986 - No. 4, Spr, 1987 ($1.75, limited series)
1-4: 2-Origin begins 5.00

STREET FIGHTER
Malibu Comics: Sept, 1993 - No. 3, Nov, 1993 ($2.95)
1 1 3 4 6 8 10
2,3: 3-Includes poster; Ferret x-over 4.00

STREET FIGHTER
Image Comics: Sept, 2003 - No. 14, Feb, 2005 ($2.95)
1-Back-up story w/Madureira-a; covers by Madureira and Tsang
1 2 3 5 6 8
2-6,8-14: 2-Two covers by Campbell and Warren; back-up story w/Warren-a 3.00
7-($4.50) Larocca-c 4.50
... Vol. 1 (3/04, $9.99, digest-size) r/main stories from #1-6 10.00

STREET FIGHTER: THE BATTLE FOR SHADALOO
DC Comics/CAP Co. Ltd.: 1995 ($3.95, one-shot)
1-Polybagged w/trading card & Tattoo 1 3 4 6 8 10

STREET FIGHTER II
Tokuma Comics (Viz): Apr, 1994 - No. 8, Nov, 1994 ($2.95, limited series)
1-8 3.00

STREET FIGHTER II
UDON Comics: No. 0, Oct, 2005 - No. 6, Nov, 2006 ($1.99/$3.95/$2.95)
0-(10/05, $1.99) prelude to series; Alvin Lee-a 3.00
1-($3.95) Two covers by Alvin Lee & Ed McGuinness 4.00
2-6-($2.95) 3.00
... Legends 1 (8/06, $3.95) Spotlight on Sakura; two covers 4.00

STREET FIGHTER X G.I. JOE
IDW Publishing: Feb, 2016 - No. 6, Jul, 2016 ($4.99)
1-Sitterson-s/Laiso-a; multiple covers; Destro, Snake Eyes, Baroness, Ryu app. 5.00
2-6-($3.99) Multiple covers on each 4.00

	GD 2.0	VG 4.0	FN 6.0	VF 8.0	VF/NM 9.0	NM- 9.2

STREET SHARKS
Archie Publications: Jan, 1996 - No. 3, Mar, 1996 ($1.50, limited series)

	GD	VG	FN	VF	VF/NM	NM-
1	3	6	9	14	20	25
2,3	1	3	4	6	8	10

STREET SHARKS
Archie Publications: May, 1996 - No. 6 ($1.50)

	GD	VG	FN	VF	VF/NM	NM-
1	2	4	6	11	16	20
2-6						6.00

STRETCH ARMSTRONG AND THE FLEX FIGHTERS (Based on the Netfix animated series)
IDW Publishing: Jan, 2018 - No. 3, Mar, 2018 ($3.99, limited series)

1-3-Burke & Wyatt-s/Koutsis-a; 3 covers 4.00

STRICTLY PRIVATE (You're in the Army Now)
Eastern Color Printing Co.: July, 1942 (#1 on sale 6/15/42)

	GD	VG	FN	VF	VF/NM	NM-
1,2: Private Peter Plink. 2-Says 128 pgs. on-c	39	78	117	231	378	525

STRIKE!
Eclipse Comics: Aug, 1987 - No. 6, Jan, 1988 ($1.75)

1-6, ...Vs. Sgt. Strike Special 1 (5/88, $1.95) 3.00

STRIKEBACK! (The Hunt For Nikita)
Malibu Comics (Bravura): Oct, 1994 - No. 3, Jan, 1995 ($2.95, unfinished limited series)

1-3: Jonathon Peterson script, Kevin Maguire-c/a 3.00
1-Gold foil embossed-c 5.00

STRIKEBACK!
Image Comics (WildStorm Productions): Jan, 1996 - No. 5, May, 1996 ($2.50, lim. series)

1-5: Reprints original Bravura series w/additional story & art by Kevin Maguire & Jonathon Peterson; new Maguire-c in all. 4,5-New story & art 3.00

STRIKEFORCE
Marvel Comics: Nov, 2019 - No. 9, Oct, 2020 ($3.99)

1-9: 1-Team of Blade, Angela, Spectrum, Winter Soldier, Spider-Woman, Wiccan and Hellstrom; Howard-s/Peralta-a. 7-9-Deadpool app. 4.00

STRIKEFORCE: AMERICA
Comico: Dec, 1995 ($2.95)

V2#1-Polybagged w/gaming card; S. Clark-a(p) 5.00

STRIKEFORCE: MORITURI
Marvel Comics Group: Dec, 1986 - No. 31, July, 1989

1,13: 13-Double size 4.00
2-12,14-31: 14-Williamson-i. 25-Heath-c 3.00
... – We Who Are About To Die 1 (3/12, $0.99) r/#1 with profile pages and cover gallery 3.00

STRIKEFORCE MORITURI: ELECTRIC UNDERTOW
Marvel Comics: Dec, 1989 - No. 5, Mar, 1990 ($3.95, 52 pgs., limited series)

1-5 Squarebound 4.00

STRONG GUY REBORN (See X-Factor)
Marvel Comics: Sept, 1997 ($2.99, one-shot)

1-Dezago-s/Andy Smith, Art Thibert-a 3.00

STRONGHOLD
AfterShock Comics: Feb, 2019 - No. 5, Aug, 2019 ($3.99)

1-5-Phil Hester-s/Ryan Kelly-a 4.00

STRONG MAN (Also see Complimentary Comics & Power of...)
Magazine Enterprises: Mar-Apr, 1955 - No. 4, Sept-Oct, 1955

	GD	VG	FN	VF	VF/NM	NM-
1(A-1 #130)-Powell-c/a	27	54	81	158	259	360
2-4: (A-1 #132,134,139)-Powell-a. 2-Powell-c	20	40	60	117	189	260

STRONTIUM DOG
Eagle Comics: Dec, 1985 - No. 4, Mar, 1986 ($1.25, limited series)

1-4, Special 1: 4-Moore script. Special 1 (1986)-Moore script 4.00

STRYFE'S STRIKE FILE
Marvel Comics: Jan, 1993 ($1.75, one-shot, no ads)

1-Stroman, Capullo, Andy Kubert, Brandon Peterson-a; silver metallic ink-c; X-Men tie-in to X-Cutioner's Song 4.00
1-Gold metallic ink 2nd printing 3.00

STRYKEFORCE
Image Comics (Top Cow): May, 2004 - No. 5, Oct, 2004 ($2.99)

1-5-Faerber-s/Kirkham-a. 4,5-Preview of HumanKind 3.00
Vol. 1 TPB (2005, $16.99) r/#1-5 & Codename: Strykeforce #0-3; sketch pages 17.00

STUFF OF NIGHTMARES
BOOM! Studios: Sept, 2022 - No. 4, Dec, 2022 ($4.99, limited series)

1-4-R.L. Stine-s/A.L. Kaplan-a 5.00

STUMBO THE GIANT (See Harvey Hits #49,54,57,60,63,66,69,72,78,88 & Hot Stuff #2)

STUMBO TINYTOWN
Harvey Publications: Oct, 1963 - No. 13, Nov, 1966 (All 25¢ giants)

	GD	VG	FN	VF	VF/NM	NM-
1-Stumbo, Hot Stuff & others begin	14	28	42	98	217	335
2	8	16	24	54	102	150
3-5	6	12	18	38	69	100
6-13	5	10	15	33	57	80

STUNTMAN COMICS (Also see Thrills Of Tomorrow)
Harvey Publ.: Apr-May, 1946 - No. 2, June-July, 1946; No. 3, Oct-Nov, 1946

	GD	VG	FN	VF	VF/NM	NM-
1-Origin Stuntman by S&K reprinted in Black Cat #9; S&K-c	123	246	369	787	1344	1900
2-S&K-c/a; The Duke of Broadway story	71	142	213	454	777	1100
3-Small size (5-1/2x8-1/2"; B&W; 32 pgs.); distributed to mail subscribers only; S&K-a; Kid Adonis by S&K reprinted in Green Hornet #37	123	246	369	787	1344	1900

(Also see All-New #15, Boy Explorers #2, Flash Gordon #5 & Thrills of Tomorrow)

STUPID COMICS (Also see 40 oz. Collected)
Oni Press/Image Comics: July, 2000; Sept, 2002 - No. 3, Aug, 2005 ($2.95, B&W)

1-(Oni Press, 7/00) Jim Mahfood 1 page satire strips reprinted from JAVA magazine 3.00
1-3-(Image Comics, 9/02; 10/03) Jim Mahfood 1 page and 2 page satire strips 3.00
TPB (4/06, $12.99) r/#1(Oni) and #1-3(Image); Phoenix New Times strips 13.00

STUPID HEROES
Mirage Studios: Sept, 1993 - No. 3, Dec, 1994 ($2.75, unfinished limited series)

1-3-Laird-c/a & scripts; 2 trading cards bound in 3.00

STUPID, STUPID RAT TAILS (See Bone)
Cartoon Books: Dec, 1999 - No. 3, Feb, 2000 ($2.95, limited series)

1-3-Jeff Smith-a/Tom Sniegoski-s 4.00

SUBMARINE ATTACK (Formerly Speed Demons)
Charlton Comics: No. 11, May, 1958 - No. 54, Feb-Mar, 1966

	GD	VG	FN	VF	VF/NM	NM-
11	5	10	15	30	50	70
12-20: 16-Atomic bomb panels	3	6	9	21	33	45
21-30	3	6	9	18	28	38
31-54: 43-Cuban missile crisis story. 47-Atomic bomb panels	3	6	9	18	23	30

NOTE: ***Glanzman** c/a-25. **Montes/Bache** a-38, 40, 41.*

SUB-MARINER (See All-Select, All-Winners, Blonde Phantom, Daring, The Defenders, Fantastic Four #4, Human Torch, The Invaders, Iron Man &..., Marvel Mystery, Marvel Spotlight #27, Men's Adventures, Motion Picture Funnies Weekly, Namora, Namor, The..., Prince Namor, The Sub-Mariner, Saga Of The..., Tales to Astonish #70 & 2nd series, USA & Young Men)

SUB-MARINER, THE (2nd Series)(Sub-Mariner #31 on)
Marvel Comics Group: May, 1968 - No. 72, Sept, 1974 (No. 43: 52 pgs.)

	GD	VG	FN	VF	VF/NM	NM-
1-Origin Sub-Mariner; story continued from Iron Man & Sub-Mariner #1	61	122	183	488	1094	1700
2-Triton app.	11	22	33	73	157	240
3,4	8	16	24	55	105	155
5-1st Tiger Shark (9/68)	27	54	81	189	420	650
6,7,9,10: 6-Tiger Shark-c & 2nd app., cont'd from #5. 7-Photo-c. (1968). 9-1st app. Serpent Crown (origin in #10 & 12)	6	12	18	38	69	100
8-Sub-Mariner vs. Thing	27	54	81	194	435	675
8-2nd printing (1994)	2	4	6	11	16	20
11-13,15: 15-Last 12¢ issue	5	10	15	33	57	80
14-Sub-Mariner vs. G.A. Toro, who assumes identity of G. A. Human Torch; death of Toro (1st modern app. & only app. Toro, 6/69)	7	14	21	46	86	125
16-20: 19-1st Sting Ray (11/69); Stan Lee, Romita, Heck, Thomas, Everett & Kirby cameos. 20-Dr. Doom app.	4	8	12	23	37	50
21,23-33,37-42: 25-Origin Atlantis. 30-Capt. Marvel x-over. 37-Death of Lady Dorma. 38-Origin retold. 40-Spider-Man x-over. 42-Last 15¢ issue	3	6	9	17	26	35
22-Dr. Strange x-over	7	14	21	44	82	120
34-Prelude (w/#35) to 1st Defenders story; Hulk & Silver Surfer x-over	13	26	39	86	188	290
35-Namor/Hulk/Silver Surfer team-up to battle The Avengers-c/story (3/71); hints at teaming up again	10	20	30	66	138	210
36-Wrightson-a(i)	3	6	9	20	31	42
43-King Size Special (52 pgs.)	4	8	12	23	37	50
44,45-Sub-Mariner vs. Human Torch	3	6	9	21	33	45
46-49,56,62,64-72: 47,48-Dr. Doom app. 49-Cosmic Cube story. 52-1st app. Dragon-Lord. 52,53-Sunfire app. 62-1st Tales of Atlantis, Chaykin-s/a; ends #66. 64-Hitler cameo. 67-New costume; F.F. x-over. 69-Spider-Man x-over (6 panels)	2	4	6	10	14	18
50-1st app. Nita, Namor's niece (later Namorita in New Warriors)	13	26	39	89	195	300
51-55,57,58,60,61,63-Everett issues: 57-Venus app. (1st since 4/52); anti-Vietnam War panels. 61-Last artwork by Everett; 1st 4 pgs. completed by Mortimer; pgs. 5-20 by Mooney	2	4	6	11	16	20
59-1st battle with Thor; Everett-a	8	16	24	51	96	140
Special 1 (1/71)-r/Tales to Astonish #70-73	5	10	15	34	60	85
Special 2 (1/72)-(52 pgs.)-r/T.T.A. #74-76; Everett-a	4	8	12	23	37	50

NOTE: ***Bolle** a-67i. **Buscema** a(p)-1-8, 20, 24. **Colan** a(p)-10, 11, 40, 43, 46-49, Special 1, 2; c(p)-10, 11, 40. **Craig** a-17i, 19-23i. **Everett** a-45r, 50-55, 57, 58, 59-61(plot), 63(plot); c-47, 48i, 55, 57, 58-59i, 61, Spec. 2. **G. Kane** c(p)-42-52, 58, 66, 70, 71. **Mooney** a-24i, 25i, 32-35i, 39i, 42i, 44i, 45i, 60i, 61i, 65p, 66p, 68i. **John Severin** c/a-38i. **Marie Severin** c-a 14p. **Starlin** c-59p. **Tuska** a-41p, 42p, 69-71p. **Wrightson** a-36i. #53, 54-r/stories Sub-Mariner Comics #41 & 39.*

SUB-MARINER (The Initiative, follows Civil War series)
Marvel Comics: Aug, 2007 - No. 6, Jan, 2008 ($2.99, limited series)

1-6: 1-Turner-c/Briones-a/Cherniss & Johnson-s; Iron Man app. 3-Yu-c; Venom app. 4.00
...: Revolution TPB (2008, $14.99) r/#1-6 15.00

SUB-MARINER COMICS (1st Series) (The Sub-Mariner #1, 2, 33-42)(Official True Crime Cases #24 on; Amazing Mysteries #32 on; Best Love #33 on)
Timely/Marvel Comics (TCI 1-7/SePI 8/MPI 9-32/Atlas Comics (CCC 33-42)):
Spring, 1941 - No. 23, Sum, 1947; No. 24, Wint, 1947 - No. 31, 4/49; No. 32, 7/49; No. 33, 4/54 - No. 42, 10/55

	GD	VG	FN	VF	VF/NM	NM-
1-The Sub-Mariner by Everett & The Angel begin: Nazi WWII-c	7000	14,000	24,500	52,500	113,750	175,000
2-Everett-a; Nazi WWII-c	975	1950	2010	7100	12,550	18,000
3-Churchill assassination-c; 40 pg. S-M story	838	1676	2514	6117	10,809	15,500
4-Everett-a, 40 pgs.; 1 pg. Wolverton-a; Nazi WWII-c	757	1514	2271	5526	9763	14,000
5-Gabrielle/Klein-c; Japanese WWII-c	443	886	1329	3234	5717	8200
6-8,10-Japanese WWII-c	420	840	1260	2940	5170	7400
9-Classic Japanese WWII flag-c (Spr. 1943); Wolverton-a, 3 pgs.	486	972	1458	3550	6275	9000
11-Classic Schomburg-c	757	1514	2271	5526	9763	14,000
12,14-Nazi WWII-c	371	742	1113	2600	4550	6500
13-Classic Schomburg hooded Japanese WWII bondage-c	541	1082	1623	3950	6975	10,000
15-Schomburg Japanese WWII-c	365	730	1095	2555	4478	6400
16,17-Japanese WWII-c	314	628	942	2198	3849	5500
18-20	290	580	870	1856	3178	4500
21-Last Angel; Everett-a	206	412	618	1318	2259	3200
22-Young Allies app.	219	438	657	1402	2401	3400

23-The Human Torch, Namora x-over (Sum/47); 2nd app. Namora after

Sub-Mariner Comics #32 © MAR

Sugar and Spike #26 © DC

Suicide Squad (2016) #11 © DC

	GD 2.0	VG 4.0	FN 6.0	VF 8.0	VF/NM 9.0	NM- 9.2
Marvel Mystery #82	226	452	678	1446	2473	3500
24-Namora x-over (3rd app.)	239	478	717	1530	2615	3700
25-The Blonde Phantom begins (Spr/48), ends No. 31; Kurtzman-a; Namora x-over; last quarterly issue	226	452	678	1446	2473	3500
26,27: 26-Namora c/app.	194	388	582	1242	2121	3000
28-Namora cover; Everett-a	239	478	717	1530	2615	3700
29-31 (4/49): 29-The Human Torch app. 31-Capt. America app.	213	426	639	1363	2332	3300
32 (7/49, Scarce)-Origin Sub-Mariner	459	918	1377	3350	5925	8500
33 (4/54)-Origin Sub-Mariner; The Human Torch app.; Namora x-over in Sub-Mariner #33-42	194	388	582	1242	2121	3000
34,35-Human Torch in ea. 34-Namora bondage-c	142	284	426	909	1555	2200
36,37,39-41: 36,39-41-Namora app.	129	258	387	826	1413	2000
38-Origin Sub-Mariner's wings; Namora app.; last pre-code (2/55)	155	310	465	992	1696	2400
42-Last issue	161	322	483	1030	1765	2500

NOTE: *Angel by **Gustavson**-#1, 8. **Brodsky** c-34-36, 42. **Everett** a-1-4, 22-24, 26-42; c-32, 33, 40. **Maneely** a-38; c-37, 39-41. **Rico** c-27-31. **Schomburg** c-1-4, 6, 8-18, 20. **Sekowsky** c-24. 25, 26(w/**Rico**). **Shores** c-21-23, 38. Bondage c-13, 22, 24, 25, 34.*

SUB-MARINER COMICS 70th ANNIVERSARY SPECIAL
Marvel Comics: June, 2009 ($3.99, one-shot)

1-New WWII story, Breitweiser-a; Williamson-a; r/debut app. from Marvel Comics #1 5.00

SUB-MARINER: MARVELS SNAPSHOTS
Marvel Comics: May, 2020 ($4.99, one-shot)

1-Alan Brennert-s/Jerry Ordway-a; set in Spring 1946; All-Winners Squad app. 5.00

SUB-MARINER: THE DEPTHS
Marvel Comics: Nov, 2008 - No. 5, May, 2009 ($3.99, limited series)

1-5-Peter Milligan-s/Esad Ribic-a/c 4.00

SUBSPECIES
Eternity Comics: May, 1991 - No. 4, Aug, 1991 ($2.50, limited series)

1-4: New stories based on horror movie 4.00

SUBTLE VIOLENTS
CFD Productions: 1991 ($2.50, B&W, mature)

	GD	VG	FN	VF	VF/NM	NM-
1-Linsner-c & story	1	3	4	8	10	12
San Diego Limited Edition	4	8	12	28	47	65

SUE & SALLY SMITH (Formerly My Secret Life)
Charlton Comics: V2#48, Nov, 1962 - No. 54, Nov, 1963 (Flying Nurses)

	GD	VG	FN	VF	VF/NM	NM-
V2#48-2nd app.	3	6	9	19	30	40
49-54	3	6	9	14	20	26

SUGAR & SPIKE (Also see The Best of DC, DC Silver Age Classics and Legends of Tomorrow)
National Periodical Publications: Apr-May, 1956 - No. 98, Oct-Nov, 1971

	GD	VG	FN	VF	VF/NM	NM-
1 (Scarce)	508	1016	1524	3708	6554	9400
2	174	348	522	1114	1907	2700
3-5: 3-Letter column begins	97	194	291	621	1061	1500
6-10	55	110	165	352	601	850
11-20	41	82	123	256	428	600
21-29: 26-Christmas-c	28	56	84	168	274	380
30-Scribbly & Scribbly, Jr. x-over	29	58	87	172	281	390
31-40	22	44	66	128	209	290
41-60	9	18	27	60	120	180
61-80: 69-1st app. Tornado-Tot-c/story. 72-Origin & 1st app. Bernie the Brain	8	16	24	52	99	140
81-84,86-93,95: 84-Bernie the Brain apps. as Superman in 1 panel (9/69)	6	12	18	38	69	100
85 (68 pgs.)-r/#72	7	14	21	44	82	120
94-1st app. Raymond, African-American child	7	14	21	44	82	120
96 (68 pgs.)	7	14	21	48	89	130
97,98 (52 pgs.)	7	14	21	44	82	120
No. 1 Replica Edition (2002, $2.95) reprint of #1						4.00

NOTE: *All written and drawn by **Sheldon Mayer.** Issues with Paper Doll pages cut or missing are common.*

SUGAR BOWL COMICS (Teen-age)
Famous Funnies: May, 1948 - No. 5, Jan, 1949

	GD	VG	FN	VF	VF/NM	NM-
1-Toth-c/a	19	38	57	111	176	240
2,4,5	12	24	36	67	94	120
3-Toth-a	13	26	39	74	105	135

SUGARFOOT (TV)
Dell Publishing Co.: No. 907, May, 1958 - No. 1209, Oct-Dec, 1961

	GD	VG	FN	VF	VF/NM	NM-
Four Color 907 (#1)-Toth-a, photo-c	11	22	33	73	157	240
Four Color 992 (5-7/59), Toth-a, photo-c	10	20	30	66	138	210
Four Color 1059 (11-1/60), 1098 (5-7/60), 1147 (11-1/61), 1209-all photo-c. 1059,1098,1147-all have variant edition, back-c comic strip	7	14	21	49	92	135

SUGARSHOCK (Also see MySpace Dark Horse Presents)
Dark Horse Comics: Oct, 2009 ($3.50, one-shot)

1-Joss Whedon-s/Fabio Moon-a/c; story from online comic; Moon sketch pgs. 3.50

SUICIDE RISK
BOOM! Studios: May, 2013 - No. 25, May, 2015 ($3.99)

1-25: 1-Carey-s/Casagrande-a. 5-Joëlle Jones-a. 10-Coelho-a 4.00

SUICIDERS
DC Comics (Vertigo): Apr, 2015 - No. 6, Nov, 2015 ($3.99)

1-6-Lee Bermejo-s/a/c 4.00

SUICIDERS: KINGS OF HELL.A.
DC Comics (Vertigo): May, 2016 - No. 6 ($3.99)

1-6-Lee Bermejo-s/c. 1-5-Alessandro Vitti-a. 6-Gerardo Zaffino-a; Bermejo-a (2 pgs.) 4.00

SUICIDE SQUAD (See Brave & the Bold, Doom Patrol & Suicide Squad Spec., Legends #3 & note under Star Spangled War stories)
DC Comics: May, 1987 - No. 66, June, 1992; No. 67, Mar, 2010 (Direct sales only #32 on)

	GD	VG	FN	VF	VF/NM	NM-
1-Chaykin-c	5	10	15	30	50	70
2-10: 9-Millennium x-over. 10-Batman-c/story						6.00
11-22,24-47,50-66: 13-JLI app. (Batman). 16-Re-intro Shade The Changing Man. 27-34,36,37-Snyder-a. 38-Origin Bronze Tiger. 40-43-"The Phoenix Gambit" Batman storyline. 40-Free Batman/Suicide Squad poster						4.00
23-1st Oracle	4	8	12	23	37	50
48-Joker/Batgirl-c/s	3	6	9	20	31	42
49-Joker/Batgirl-c/s	2	4	6	11	16	20
67-(3/10, $2.99) Blackest Night one-shot; Fiddler rises as a Black Lantern; Califiore-a						4.00
Annual 1 (1988, $1.50)-Manhunter x-over						5.00
...: Trial By Fire TPB (2011, $19.99) r/#1-8 & Secret Origins #14						20.00

SUICIDE SQUAD (2nd series)
DC Comics: Nov, 2001 - No. 12, Oct, 2002 ($2.50)

	GD	VG	FN	VF	VF/NM	NM-
1-Giffen-s/Medina-a; Sgt. Rock app.						5.00
2-9: 4-Heath-a						4.00
10-12-Suicide Squad vs. Antiphon: 10-J. Severin-a. 12-JSA app.	1	3	4	6	8	10

SUICIDE SQUAD (3rd series)
DC Comics: Nov, 2007 - No. 8, Jun, 2008 ($2.99, limited series)

1-8-Ostrander-s/Pina-a/Snyder III-c 4.00
...: From the Ashes TPB (2008, $19.99) r/#1-8 20.00

SUICIDE SQUAD (DC New 52)(Also see New Suicide Squad)
DC Comics: Nov, 2011 - No. 30, Jul, 2014 ($2.99)

	GD	VG	FN	VF	VF/NM	NM-
1-Harley Quinn, Deadshot, King Shark, El Diablo, Voltaic, Black Spider team up	4	8	12	23	37	50
1-(2nd printing)	2	4	6	13	28	22
1 Special Edition (5/16, FCBD giveaway)						3.00
2-5	1	2	3	5	6	8
6-Origin Harley Quinn part 1	2	4	6	11	16	20
6,7-(2nd printing)	1	2	3	5	6	8
7-Origin Harley Quinn part 2	2	4	6	9	12	15
8-13,16-20,22-30: 19-Unknown Soldier joins. 24-29-Forever Evil tie-in. 24-Omac returns						4.00
14,15-Death of the Family tie-in; Joker app.						5.00
14-Variant die-cut Joker mask-c; Death of the Family tie-in						6.00
21-Harley Quinn-c/s	1	3	4	6	8	10
30-($3.99) Forever Evil tie-in; Coelho-a/Mahnke-c						4.00
#0 (11/12, $2.99) Amanda Waller pre-Suicide Squad; Dagnino-a						5.00
...: Amanda Waller (5/14, $4.99) Jim Zub-s/Coelho-a						5.00

SUICIDE SQUAD (DC Rebirth)
DC Comics: Oct, 2016 - No. 50, Mar, 2019 ($2.99)

1-Harley Quinn, Deadshot, Killer Croc, Katana, Boomerang team up; Jim Lee-a; back-up origin of Deadshot retold; Fabok-a 3.00
1-Director's Cut (5/17, $5.99) r/#1,2 with pencil-a; bonus original script for #1 6.00
2-7: 2,3-Zod app. 2-Back-up Boomerang origin w/Reis-a. 3-Back-up Katana origin 3.00
8-24: 8-Killer Frost joins; Justice League vs. Suicide Squad prelude; Lee-a. 9,10-JL vs. SS tie-ins. 11-15-Romita Jr.-a. 16-18-Daniel-a. 20-Sejic-a. 23,24-Batman app. 3.00
25-($3.99) Batman app.; Cafaro-a; cameo app. Rick Flag & Karin Grace 4.00
26-49: 26-Dark Nights: Metal tie-in. 27-32-Secret History of Task Force X. 41-44-Batman app. 3.00
50-($4.99) Williams-s/Peralta, Schoonover & Conrad-a 5.00
Annual 1 (10/18, $4.99) New team with Merlyn vs. Swamp Thing; Cliquet-a 5.00
.../Banana Splits Special 1 (5/17, $4.99) Caldwell-a; Snagglepuss back-up; Porter-a 5.00

	GD 2.0	VG 4.0	FN 6.0	VF 8.0	VF/NM 9.0	NM- 9.2
...: Rebirth (10/16, $2.99) Rick Flag joins; Harley Quinn, Deadshot, Boomerang app.						3.00
... Special: War Crimes 1 (10/16, $4.99) Ostrander-s/Gus Vazquez-a; Shado app.						5.00

SUICIDE SQUAD
DC Comics: Feb, 2020 - No. 11, Jan, 2021 ($4.99/$3.99)

	GD 2.0	VG 4.0	FN 6.0	VF 8.0	VF/NM 9.0	NM- 9.2
1-($4.99) Harley Quinn, Deadshot, The Shark, Zebra-Man; intro The Revolutionaries						5.00
2-11-($3.99) 6-Batman app.						4.00

SUICIDE SQUAD
DC Comics: May, 2021 - No. 15, Jul, 2022 ($3.99)

	GD 2.0	VG 4.0	FN 6.0	VF 8.0	VF/NM 9.0	NM- 9.2
1-15: 1-Rick Flag, Peacemaker, Shrike, Talon team. 5,6-Crime Syndicate app. 7-Ambush Bug joins. 13-War for Earth-3 tie-in						4.00
2021 Annual 1 (11/21, $5.99) Superboy app.; follows Suicide Squad #6						6.00
... Special Edition (FCBD) 1 (10/21, giveaway) Previews Suicide Squad: King Shark & Suicide Squad: Get Joker series						3.00

SUICIDE SQUAD BLACK FILES
DC Comics: Jan, 2019 - No. 6, Jun, 2019 ($4.99, limited series)

	GD 2.0	VG 4.0	FN 6.0	VF 8.0	VF/NM 9.0	NM- 9.2
1-6-New squad incl. Gentleman Ghost, El Diablo, Klarion, Enchantress; Eaton-a						5.00

SUICIDE SQUAD: BLAZE
DC Comics (Black Label): Apr, 2022 - No. 3 ($6.99, oversized 8-1/2" x 10-3/4", lim. series)

	GD 2.0	VG 4.0	FN 6.0	VF 8.0	VF/NM 9.0	NM- 9.2
1,2-Simon Spurrier-s/Aaron Campbell-a; Harley Quinn & Peacemaker app.						7.00

SUICIDE SQUAD: GET JOKER
DC Comics (Black Label): Oct, 2021 - No. 3, Jul, 2022 ($6.99, over-sized squarebound, limited series)

	GD 2.0	VG 4.0	FN 6.0	VF 8.0	VF/NM 9.0	NM- 9.2
1-3-Azzarello-s/Maleev-a; Jason Todd & Harley Quinn app.						7.00

SUICIDE SQUAD: KING SHARK (Printing of a digital first series)
DC Comics: Nov, 2021 - No. 6, Apr, 2022 ($3.99, limited series)

	GD 2.0	VG 4.0	FN 6.0	VF 8.0	VF/NM 9.0	NM- 9.2
1-6-Seeley-s/Kolins-a; Defacer & B'Wana Beast app. 3,4-The Demon app.						4.00

SUICIDE SQUAD MOST WANTED: DEADSHOT & KATANA
DC Comics: Mar, 2016 - No. 6, Aug, 2016 ($4.99, limited series)

	GD 2.0	VG 4.0	FN 6.0	VF 8.0	VF/NM 9.0	NM- 9.2
1-6-Deadshot by Buccellato-s/Bogdanovic-a; Katana by Barr-s/Neves-a; Nord-c						5.00

SUICIDE SQUAD MOST WANTED: EL DIABLO & BOOMERANG (Title changes to Suicide Squad Most Wanted: El Diablo & Amanda Waller for #5,6)
DC Comics: Oct, 2016 - No. 6, Mar, 2017 ($4.99, limited series)

	GD 2.0	VG 4.0	FN 6.0	VF 8.0	VF/NM 9.0	NM- 9.2
1-4-El Diablo by Nitz-s/Richards-a; Boomerang by Moreci-s/Bazaldua-a; Huddleston-c						5.00
5,6-Amanda Waller by Ayala-s/Merhoff-a; El Diablo by Nitz-s/Richards-a						5.00

SUMMER FUN (See Dell Giants)

SUMMER FUN (Formerly Li'l Genius; Holiday Surprise #55)
Charlton Comics: No. 54, Oct, 1966 (Giant)

	GD 2.0	VG 4.0	FN 6.0	VF 8.0	VF/NM 9.0	NM- 9.2
54	3	6	9	21	33	45

SUMMER FUN (Walt Disney's...)
Disney Comics: Summer, 1991 ($2.95, annual, 68 pgs.)

	GD 2.0	VG 4.0	FN 6.0	VF 8.0	VF/NM 9.0	NM- 9.2
1-D. Duck, M. Mouse, Brer Rabbit, Chip 'n' Dale & Pluto, Li'l Bad Wolf, Super Goof, Scamp stories						5.00

SUMMER LOVE (Formerly Brides in Love?)
Charlton Comics: V2#46, Oct, 1965; V2#47, Oct, 1966; V2#48, Nov, 1968

	GD 2.0	VG 4.0	FN 6.0	VF 8.0	VF/NM 9.0	NM- 9.2
V2#46-Beatles-c & 8 pg. story	14	28	42	96	211	325
47-(68 pgs.) Beatles-c & 12 pg. story	11	22	33	73	157	240
48	3	6	9	21	33	45

SUMMER MAGIC (See Movie Comics)

SUMMONER'S WAR: LEGACY (Based on the online mobile game)
Image Comics (Skybound): Apr, 2021 - No. 6, Sept, 2021 ($3.99)

	GD 2.0	VG 4.0	FN 6.0	VF 8.0	VF/NM 9.0	NM- 9.2
1-6-Justin Jordan-s/Luca Claretti-a						4.00

SUNDANCE (See Hotel Deparee...)

SUNDANCE KID (Also see Blazing Six-Guns)
Skywald Publications: June, 1971 - No. 3, Sept, 1971 (52 pgs.)(Pre-code reprints & new-s)

	GD 2.0	VG 4.0	FN 6.0	VF 8.0	VF/NM 9.0	NM- 9.2
1-Durango Kid; Two Kirby Bullseye-r	3	6	9	16	23	30
2,3: 2-Swift Arrow, Durango Kid, Bullseye by S&K; Meskin plus 1 pg. origin. 3-Durango Kid, Billy the Kid, Red Hawk-r	2	4	6	11	16	20

SUNDAY PIX (Christian religious)
David C. Cook Pub/USA Weekly Newsprint Color Comics: V1#1, Mar,1949 - V16#26, July 19, 1964 (7x10", 12 pgs., mail subscription only)

	GD 2.0	VG 4.0	FN 6.0	VF 8.0	VF/NM 9.0	NM- 9.2
V1#1	9	18	27	52	69	85
V1#2-35	6	12	18	31	38	45
V2#1-52 (1950)	5	10	15	23	28	32
V3-V6 (1951-1953)	4	9	13	18	22	26
V7-V11#1-7,23-52 (1954-1959)	2	4	6	13	18	22
V11#8-22 (2/22-5/31/59) H.G. Wells First Men in the Moon serial	3	6	9	14	19	24
V12#1-19,21-52; V13-V15#1,2,9-52; V16#1-26(7/19/64)	2	4	6	10	14	18
V12#20 (5/15/60) 2 page interview with Peanuts' Charles Schulz	4	8	12	25	40	55
V15#3-8 (2/24/63) John Glenn, Christian astronaut	3	6	9	16	23	30

SUN DEVILS
DC Comics: July, 1984 - No. 12, June, 1985 ($1.25, maxi series)

	GD 2.0	VG 4.0	FN 6.0	VF 8.0	VF/NM 9.0	NM- 9.2
1-12: 6-Death of Sun Devil						4.00

SUNDIATA: A LEGEND OF AFRICA
NBM Publishing Inc.: 2002 ($15.95, hardcover with dustjacket)

	GD 2.0	VG 4.0	FN 6.0	VF 8.0	VF/NM 9.0	NM- 9.2
nn-Will Eisner-s/a; adaptation of an African folk tale						16.00

SUNDOWNERS
Dark Horse Comics: Aug, 2014 - No. 6, Jan, 2015 ($3.50)

	GD 2.0	VG 4.0	FN 6.0	VF 8.0	VF/NM 9.0	NM- 9.2
1-6: 1-Tim Seeley-s/Jim Terry-a						3.50

SUN FUN KOMIKS
Sun Publications: 1939 (15¢, B&W & red)

	GD 2.0	VG 4.0	FN 6.0	VF 8.0	VF/NM 9.0	NM- 9.2
1-Satire on comics (rare); 1st Hitler app. in comics?	811	1622	2433	5920	10,460	15,000

NOTE: *Hitler, Stalin and Mussolini featured gag in 1-page story written in Hebrew and English. Nazi swastika and Nazi flag app. in a different 1-page "Gussie the Gob" story.*

SUNFIRE & BIG HERO SIX (See Alpha Flight)
Marvel Comics: Sept, 1998 - No. 3, Nov, 1998 ($2.50, limited series)

	GD 2.0	VG 4.0	FN 6.0	VF 8.0	VF/NM 9.0	NM- 9.2
1-Lobdell-s	5	10	15	31	63	75
2,3	3	6	9	14	19	24

SUN GIRL (See The Human Torch & Marvel Mystery Comics #88)
Marvel Comics (CCC): Aug, 1948 - No. 3, Dec, 1948

	GD 2.0	VG 4.0	FN 6.0	VF 8.0	VF/NM 9.0	NM- 9.2
1-1st app. Sun Girl; Miss America app.	366	732	1098	2562	4481	6400
2,3: 2-The Blonde Phantom begins	271	542	813	1734	2967	4200

SUNNY, AMERICA'S SWEETHEART (Formerly Cosmo Cat #1-10)
Fox Feature Syndicate: No. 11, Dec, 1947 - No. 14, June, 1948

	GD 2.0	VG 4.0	FN 6.0	VF 8.0	VF/NM 9.0	NM- 9.2
11-Feldstein-c/a	206	412	618	1318	2259	3200
12-14: 12,13-Feldstein-a; 13,14-Lingerie panels. 13-L.B. Cole-a	129	258	387	826	1413	2000
I.W. Reprint #8-Feldstein-a; r/Fox issue	11	22	33	73	157	240

SUN-RUNNERS (Also see Tales of the...)
Pacific Comics/Eclipse Comics/Amazing Comics: 2/84 - No. 3, 5/84; No. 4, 11/84 - No. 7, 1986 (Baxter paper)

	GD 2.0	VG 4.0	FN 6.0	VF 8.0	VF/NM 9.0	NM- 9.2
1-7: P. Smith-a in #2-4						4.00
Christmas Special 1 (1987, $1.95)-By Amazing						4.00

SUNSET CARSON (Also see Cowboy Western)
Charlton Comics: Feb, 1951 - No. 4, 1951 (No month) (Photo-c on each)

	GD 2.0	VG 4.0	FN 6.0	VF 8.0	VF/NM 9.0	NM- 9.2
1-Photo/retouched-c (Scarce, all issues)	65	130	195	416	708	1000
2-Kit Carson story; adapts "Kansas Raiders" w/Brian Donlevy, Audie Murphy & Margaret Chapman	45	90	135	284	480	675
3,4	37	74	111	218	354	490

SUNSET PASS (See Zane Grey & 4-Color #230)

SUPER ANGRY BIRDS (Based on Rovio videogame Angry Birds)
IDW Publishing: Sept, 2015 - No. 4, Dec, 2015 ($3.99, limited series)

	GD 2.0	VG 4.0	FN 6.0	VF 8.0	VF/NM 9.0	NM- 9.2
1-4: 1-The Eagle's Eye - Jeff Parker-s/Ron Randall-a; two covers						4.00

SUPER ANIMALS PRESENTS PIDGY & THE MAGIC GLASSES
Star Publications: Dec, 1953 (25¢, came w/glasses)

	GD 2.0	VG 4.0	FN 6.0	VF 8.0	VF/NM 9.0	NM- 9.2
1-(3-D Comics)-L. B. Cole-c	45	90	135	284	480	675

SUPER BAD JAMES DYNOMITE
5-D Comics: Dec, 2005 - No. 5, Feb, 2007 ($3.99)

	GD 2.0	VG 4.0	FN 6.0	VF 8.0	VF/NM 9.0	NM- 9.2
1-5-Created by the Wayans brothers						4.00

SUPERBOY
DC Comics: Jan, 1942

nn-Ashcan comic, not distributed to newsstands, only for in house use. Covers were produced, but not the rest of the book. A CGC certified 9.2 copy sold in 2003 for $6,600.

SUPERBOY (See Adventure, Aurora, DC Comics Presents, DC 100 Page Super Spectacular #15, DC Super Stars, 80 Page Giant #10, More Fun Comics, The New Advs. of... & Superman Family #191, Young Justice)

SUPERBOY (1st Series)(...& the Legion of Super-Heroes with #231)
(Becomes The Legion of Super-Heroes No. 259 on)
National Periodical Publ./DC Comics: Mar-Apr, 1949 - No. 258, Dec, 1979 (#1-16: 52 pgs.)

	GD 2.0	VG 4.0	FN 6.0	VF 8.0	VF/NM 9.0	NM- 9.2
1-Superman cover; intro in More Fun #101 (1-2/45)	1250	2500	3750	9500	17,250	25,000
2-Used in **SOTI**, pg. 35-36,226	290	580	870	1856	3178	4500
3	206	412	618	1318	2259	3200
4	155	310	465	992	1696	2400
5-1st pre-Supergirl tryout (c/story, 11-12/49)	177	354	531	1124	1937	2750
6-9: 8-1st Superbaby	129	258	387	826	1413	2000
10-1st app. Lana Lang	181	362	543	1158	1979	2800
11-15: 11-2nd Lana Lang app.; 1st Lana cover	97	194	291	621	1061	1500
16-20: 20-2nd Jor-El cover	68	136	204	435	743	1050
21-26,28-30: 21-Lana Lang app.	57	114	171	362	619	875
27-Low distribution	68	136	204	435	743	1050
31-38: 38-Last pre-code issue (1/55)	50	100	150	315	533	750
39-48,50 (7/56)	45	90	135	284	480	675
49 (6/56)-1st app. Metallo (this one's Jor-El's robot)	93	186	279	591	1021	1450
51-60: 51-Krypto app. 52-1st S.A. issue. 56-Krypto-c	37	74	111	218	354	490
61-67	31	62	93	182	296	410
68-Origin/1st app. original Bizarro (10-11/58)	460	920	1380	3500	7250	11,000
69-77,79: 76-1st Supermonkey	27	54	81	158	259	360
78-Origin Mr. Mxyzptlk & Superboy's costume	37	74	111	222	361	500
80-1st meeting Superboy/Supergirl (4/60)	43	86	129	271	461	650
81,83-85,87,88: 83-Origin/1st app. Kryptonite Kid	14	58	42	94	207	320
82-1st Bizarro Krypto	18	36	54	124	275	425
86-(1/61)-4th Legion app; Intro Pete Ross	29	58	87	209	467	725
89-(6/61)-1st app. Mon -El; 2nd Phantom Zone	44	88	132	326	738	1150
90-92: 90-Pete Ross learns Superboy's I.D. 92-Last 10¢ issue	12	24	36	82	179	275
93-10th Legion app.(12/61); Chameleon Boy app.	13	26	39	87	191	295
94-97,99: 94-1st app. Superboy Revenge Squad	11	22	33	72	154	235
98-(7/62) Legion app; origin & 1st app. Ultra Boy; Pete Ross joins Legion	17	34	51	117	259	400
100-(10/62)-Ultra Boy app; 1st app. Phantom Zone villains, Dr. Xadu & Erndine. 2 pg. map of Krypton; origin Superboy retold; r-cover of Superman #1	18	36	54	121	268	415
101-120: 104-Origin Phantom Zone. 115-Atomic bomb-c. 117-Legion app.	9	18	27	59	117	175
121-128: 124-(10/65)-1st app. Insect Queen (Lana Lang). 125-Legion cameo. 126-Origin Krypto the Super Dog retold with new facts	8	16	24	52	99	145
129-(80-pg. Giant G-22)-Reprints origin Mon-El	9	18	27	59	117	175
130-137,139,140: 131-Legion statues cameo in Dog Legionnaires story. 132-1st app. Supremo. 133-Superboy meets Robin	7	14	21	44	82	120
138 (80-pg. Giant G-35)	7	14	21	49	92	135

141-146,148-155,157: 145-Superboy's parents regain their youth. 148-Legion app.

Sundowners #2 © Seeley & Terry

Superboy #10 © DC

Superboy (2010) #5 © DC

	GD 2.0	VG 4.0	FN 6.0	VF 8.0	VF/NM 9.0	NM- 9.2
157-Last 12¢ issue	6	12	18	37	66	95
147(6/68)-Giant G-47; 1st origin of L.S.H. (Saturn Girl, Lightning Lad, Cosmic Boy); origin Legion of Super-Pets-r/Adv. #293	8	16	24	56	108	160
147 Replica Edition (2003, $6.95) reprints entire issue; cover recreation by Ordway						7.00
156-(Giant G-59)	6	12	18	38	69	100
158-164,166-171,175: 171-1st app. Aquaboy	3	6	9	19	30	40
165,174 (Giant G-71,G-83): 165-r/1st app. Krypto the Superdog from Adventure Comics #210	5	10	15	35	63	90
172,173,176-Legion app.: 172-1st app. & origin Yango (The Super Ape). 176-Partial photo-c; last 15¢ issue	3	6	9	20	31	42
177-184,186,187 (All 52 pgs.): 182-All new origin of the classic World's Finest team (Superman & Batman) as teenagers (2/72, 22pgs). 184-Origin Dial H for Hero-r	3	6	9	21	33	45
185-Also listed as DC 100 Pg. Super Spectacular #12; Legion-c/story; Teen Titans, Kid Eternity(r/Hit #46), Star Spangled Kid-r(S.S. #55)	8	16	24	56	108	160
188-190,192,194,196: 188-Origin Karkan. 196-Last Superboy solo story	3	6	9	14	20	26
191,193,195: 191-Origin Sunboy retold; Legion app. 193-Chameleon Boy & Shrinking Violet get new costumes. 195-1st app. Erg-1/Wildfire; Phantom Girl gets new costume	3	6	9	15	22	28
197-Legion series begins; Lightning Lad's new costume	5	10	15	31	53	75
198,199: 198-Element Lad & Princess Projectra get new costumes	3	6	9	15	22	28
200-Bouncing Boy & Duo Damsel marry; J'onn J'onzz cameo	3	6	9	18	28	38
201,204,206,207,209: 201-Re-intro Erg-1 as Wildfire. 204-Supergirl resigns from Legion. 206-Ferro Lad & Invisible Kid app. 209-Karate Kid gets new costume	3	6	9	14	19	24
202,205-(100 pgs.): 202-Light Lass gets new costume; Mike Grell's 1st comic work-i (5-6/74)	5	10	15	33	57	80
203-Invisible Kid killed by Validus	3	6	9	19	30	40
208,210: 208-(68 pgs.). 208-Legion of Super-Villains app. 210-Origin Karate Kid	3	6	9	15	22	28
211-220: 212-Matter-Eater Lad resigns. 216-1st app. Tyroc, who joins the Legion in #218	2	4	6	10	14	18
221-230,246-249: 226-Intro. Dawnstar. 228-Death of Chemical King	2	4	6	8	11	14
231-245: (Giants). 240-Origin Dawnstar; Chaykin-a. 242-(52 pgs.). 243-Legion of Substitute Heroes app. 243-245-(44 pgs.).	2	4	6	10	14	18
244,245-(Whitman variants; low print run, no issue# shown on cover)	3	6	9	16	23	30
246-248-(Whitman variants; low ...)	3	6	9	14	19	24
250-258: 253-Intro Blok. 257-Return of Bouncing Boy & Duo Damsel by Ditko	2	4	6	8	10	12
251-258-(Whitman variants; low print run)	2	4	6	11	16	20
Annual 1 (Sum/64, 84 pgs.)-Origin Krypto-r	17	34	51	117	259	400
Spectacular 1 (1980, Giant)-1st comic distributed only through comic stores; mostly-r	2	4	6	9	13	16
...: The Greatest Team-Up Stories Ever Told TPB (2010, $19.99) r/team-ups with Robin, Supergirl, young versions of Aquaman, Green Arrow, Bruce Wayne; Davis-c						20.00

NOTE: ***Neal Adams*** *c-143, 145, 146, 148-155, 157-161, 163, 164, 166-168, 172, 173, 175, 176, 178.* ***M. Anderson*** *a-178,179, 245i.* ***Ditko*** *a-257p.* ***Grell*** *a-202i, 203-219, 220-224p, 235p; c-207-232, 235, 236p, 237, 239p, 240p, 243p, 246, 258.* ***Nasser*** *a(p)-222, 225, 226, 230, 231, 233, 236.* ***Simonson*** *a-237p.* ***Starlin*** *a(p)-239, 250, 251; c-238.* ***Staton*** *a-227p, 243-249p, 252-258p; c-247-251p.* ***Swan/Moldoff*** *c-109.* ***Tuska*** *a-172, 173, 176, 183, 235p.* ***Wood*** *inks-153-155, 157-161. Legion app.-172, 173, 176, 177, 183, 184, 188, 190, 191, 193, 195, 197-258.*

SUPERBOY (TV)(2nd Series)(The Adventures of...#19 on)
DC Comics: Feb, 1990 - No. 22, Dec, 1991 ($1.00/$1.25)

1-Photo-c from TV show; Mooney-a(p) 6.00
2-22: Mooney-a in 2-8,18-20; 8-Bizarro-c/story; Arthur Adams-a(i). 9-12,14-17-Swan-a 4.00
...Special 1 (1992, $1.75) Swan-a 5.00

SUPERBOY (3rd Series)
DC Comics: Feb, 1994 - No. 100, Jul, 2002 ($1.50/$1.95/$1.99/$2.25)

	GD	VG	FN	VF	VF/NM	NM-
1-Metropolis Kid from Reign of the Supermen	2	4	6	8	10	12
2-8,10-24,26-76: 6,7-Worlds Collide Pts. 3 & 8. 8-(9/94)-Zero Hour x-over. 21-Legion app. 28-Supergirl-c/app. 33-Final Night. 38-41-"Meltdown". 45-Legion-c/app. 47-Green Lantern app. 50-Last Boy on Earth begins. 60-Crosses Hypertime. 68-Demon-c/app.						4.00
9-(11/94)-1st full app. King Shark	5	10	15	30	50	70
25-($2.95)-New Gods & Female Furies app.; w/pin-ups						5.00
77-99: 77-Begin $2.25-c. 79-Superboy's powers return. 80,81-Titans app. 83-New costume. 85-Batgirl app. 90,91-Our Worlds at War x-over						4.00
100-($3.50) Sienkiewicz-c; Grummett & McCrea-a; Superman cameo						5.00
#0-(10/94) Zero Hour issue released between #8 & #9; cameo of King Shark	2	4	6	9	12	15
#1,000,000 (11/98) 853rd Century x-over						4.00
Annual 1 (1994, $2.95, 68 pgs.)-Elseworlds story, Pt. 2 of The Super Seven (see Adventures Of Superman Annual #6)						6.00
Annual 2 (1995, $3.95)-Year One story						5.00
Annual 3 (1996, $2.95)-Legends of the Dead Earth						5.00
Annual 4 (1997, $3.95)-Pulp Heroes story						5.00
...Plus 1 (Jan, 1997, $2.95) w/Capt. Marvel Jr.						4.00
...Plus 2 (Fall, 1997, $2.95) w/Slither (Scare Tactics)						4.00
.../Risk Double-Shot 1 (Feb, 1998, $1.95) w/Risk (Teen Titans)						4.00

SUPERBOY (4th Series)
DC Comics: Jan, 2011 - No. 11, Early Oct, 2011 ($2.99)

1-11: 1-Lemire-s/Gallo-a/Albuquerque-c; Parasite & Poison Ivy app. 2,3-Noto-c 3.00
1-5: 1-Variant-c by Cassaday. 2-March-var-c. 3-Nguyen var-c. 4-Lau var-c. 5-Manapul 4.00

SUPERBOY (DC New 52)
DC Comics: Nov, 2011 - No. 34, Oct, 2014 ($2.99)

1-34: 1-New origin; Lobdell-s/Silva-a/Canete-c; Caitlin Fairchild app. 6-Supergirl app. 8-Grunge, Beast Boy & Terra app. 9-"The Culling" x-over cont. from Teen Titans Annual #1; Teen Titans and the Legion app. 14-17-H'El on Earth tie-in; Batman app. 3.00
#0-(11/12, $2.99) Origin of Kryptonian clones; Silva-a 3.00
Annual 1 (3/13, $4.99) H'El on Earth tie-in between Superboy #16 & Superman #16 5.00
...: Futures End 1 (11/14, $2.99, regular-c) Five years later, Freefall app.; Caldwell-a 3.00
...: Futures End 1 (11/14, $3.99, 3-D cover) 4.00

SUPERBOY AND THE LEGION OF SUPER-HEROES
DC Comics: 2011 ($14.99, TPB)

SC-Reprints stories from Adventure Comics #515-520 15.00

SUPERBOY & THE RAVERS
DC Comics: Sept, 1996 - No. 19, March, 1998 ($1.95)

1-19: 4-Adam Strange app. 7-Impulse-c/app. 9-Superman-c/app. 3.00

SUPERBOY COMICS
DC Comics: Jan. 1942

nn - Ashcan comic, not distributed to newsstands, only for in-house use. Cover art is Detective Comics #57 with interior being Action Comics #38. A CGC certified 9.2 copy sold for $6,600 in 2003 and for $15,750 in 2008.

SUPERBOY/ROBIN: WORLD'S FINEST THREE
DC Comics: 1996 - No. 2, 1996 ($4.95, squarebound, limited series)

1,2: Superboy & Robin vs. Metallo & Poison Ivy; Karl Kesel & Chuck Dixon scripts; Tom Grummett-c(p)/a(p) 5.00

SUPERBOY'S LEGION (Elseworlds)
DC Comics: 2001 - No. 2, 2001 ($5.95, squarebound, limited series)

1,2- 31st century Superboy forms Legion; Farmer-s/i; Davis-a(p)/c 6.00

SUPERBOY: THE BOY OF STEEL
DC Comics: 2010 ($19.99, hardcover with dustjacket)

HC-Reprints stories from Adventure Comics #0-3,5,6 & Superman Secret Files 2009 20.00
SC-(2011, $14,99) Same contents as HC 15.00

SUPER BRAT (Li'l Genius #6 on)
Toby Press: Jan, 1954 - No. 4, July, 1954

	GD	VG	FN	VF	VF/NM	NM-
1	14	28	42	78	112	145
2-4: 4-Li'l Teevy by Mel Lazarus	8	16	24	40	50	60
I.W. Reprint #1,2,3,7,8('58): 1-r/#1	2	4	6	9	13	16
I.W. (Super) Reprint #10('63)	2	4	6	8	11	14

SUPERCAR (TV)
Gold Key: Nov, 1962 - No. 4, Aug, 1963 (All painted-c)

	GD	VG	FN	VF	VF/NM	NM-
1	12	24	36	80	173	265
2,3	7	14	21	48	89	130
4-Last issue	8	16	24	55	105	155

SUPER CAT (Formerly Frisky Animals; also see Animal Crackers)
Star Publications #56-58/Ajax/Farrell Publ. (Four Star Comic Corp.):
No. 56, Nov, 1953 - No. 58, May, 1954; Aug, 1957 - No. 4, May, 1958

	GD	VG	FN	VF	VF/NM	NM-
56-58-L.B. Cole-c on all	22	44	66	132	216	300
1(1957-Ajax)- "The Adventures of..." c-only	11	22	33	64	90	115
2-4	8	16	24	42	54	65

SUPER CEREBUS ANNUAL
Aardvark-Vanaheim: Apr, 2019 ($8.00, B&W)

1-Cerebus figures with original Gustave Doré artwork; Superman Annual #1-c swipe 8.00

SUPER CEREBUS VS. COVID-19
Aardvark-Vanaheim: Oct, 2021 ($4.00, B&W)

	GD 2.0	VG 4.0	FN 6.0	VF 8.0	VF/NM 9.0	NM- 9.2
1-Cerebus figures with Doré artwork; Superman vs. Muhammad Ali-c swipe						4.00

SUPER CIRCUS (TV)
Cross Publishing Co.: Jan, 1951 - No. 5, Sept, 1951 (Mary Hartline)

	GD 2.0	VG 4.0	FN 6.0	VF 8.0	VF/NM 9.0	NM- 9.2
1-(52 pgs.)-Cast photos on-c	21	42	63	122	199	275
2-Cast photos on-c	14	28	42	80	115	150
3-5	12	24	36	69	97	120

SUPER CIRCUS (TV)
Dell Publ. Co.: No. 542, Mar, 1954 - No. 694, Mar, 1956 (Mary Hartline)

	GD 2.0	VG 4.0	FN 6.0	VF 8.0	VF/NM 9.0	NM- 9.2
Four Color 542: Mary Hartline photo-c	8	16	24	56	108	160
Four Color 592,694: Mary Hartline photo-c	6	12	18	41	76	110

SUPER COMICS
Dell Publishing Co.: May, 1938 - No. 121, Feb-Mar, 1949

	GD 2.0	VG 4.0	FN 6.0	VF 8.0	VF/NM 9.0	NM- 9.2
1-Terry & The Pirates, The Gumps, Dick Tracy, Little Orphan Annie, Little Joe, Gasoline Alley, Smilin' Jack, Smokey Stover, Smitty, Tiny Tim, Moon Mullins, Harold Teen, Winnie Winkle begin	252	504	756	1613	2757	3900
2	100	200	300	635	1093	1550
3	84	168	252	538	919	1300
4,5: 4-Dick Tracy-c; also #8-10,17,26(part),31	63	126	189	403	689	975
6-10	52	104	156	328	552	775
11-20: 20-Smilin' Jack-c (also #29,32)	41	82	123	256	428	600
21-29: 21-Magic Morro begins (origin & 1st app., 2/40). 22,27-Ken Ernst-c (also #25?); Magic Morro c-22,25,27,34	36	72	108	211	343	475
30- "Sea Hawk" movie adaptation-c/story with Errol Flynn	36	72	108	214	347	480
31-40: 34-Ken Ernst-c	29	58	87	170	278	385
41-50: 41-Intro Lightning Jim. 43-Terry & The Pirates ends	24	48	72	142	234	325
51-60	19	38	57	112	179	245
61-70: 62-Flag-c. 65-Brenda Starr-r begin? 67-X-Mas-c	17	34	51	103	162	220
71-80	14	28	42	82	121	160
81-99	14	28	42	78	112	145
100	14	28	42	81	118	155
101-115-Last Dick Tracy (moves to own title)	10	20	30	58	79	100
116-121: 116,118-All Smokey Stover. 117-All Gasoline Alley. 119-121-Terry & The Pirates app. in all	9	18	27	52	69	85

SUPER COPS, THE
Red Circle Productions (Archie): July, 1974 (one-shot)

	GD 2.0	VG 4.0	FN 6.0	VF 8.0	VF/NM 9.0	NM- 9.2
1-Morrow-c/a; art by Pino, Hack, Thorne	2	4	6	8	11	14

SUPER COPS
Now Comics: Sept, 1990 - No. 4, Dec?, 1990 ($1.75)

	GD 2.0	VG 4.0	FN 6.0	VF 8.0	VF/NM 9.0	NM- 9.2
1-($2.75, 52 pgs.)-Dave Dorman painted-c (both printings)						4.00
2-4						3.00

SUPER CRACKED (See Cracked)

SUPERCROOKS
Marvel Comics (Icon): May, 2012 - No. 4, Aug, 2012 ($2.99/$4.99)

	GD 2.0	VG 4.0	FN 6.0	VF 8.0	VF/NM 9.0	NM- 9.2
1-3-($2.99) Millar-s/Yu-a. 1-Covers by Yu & Gibbons. 2-Covers by Yu & Hitch						3.00
4-($4.99) Bonus preview of Jupiter's Children (later re-titled Jupiter's Legacy)						5.00

SUPER DC GIANT (25-50¢, all 68-52 pg. Giants)
National Per. Publ.: No. 13, 9-10/70 - No. 26, 7-8/71; V3#27, Summer, 1976 (No #1-12)

	GD 2.0	VG 4.0	FN 6.0	VF 8.0	VF/NM 9.0	NM- 9.2
S-13-Binky	10	20	30	69	147	225
S-14-Top Guns of the West; Kubert-c; Trigger Twins, Johnny Thunder, Wyoming Kid-r; Moreira-r (9-10/70)	5	10	15	33	57	80
S-15-Western Comics; Kubert-c; Pow Wow Smith, Vigilante, Buffalo Bill-r; new Gil Kane-a (9-10/70)	5	10	15	33	57	80
S-16-Best of the Brave & the Bold; Batman-r & Metamorpho origin-r from Brave & the Bold; Spectre pin-up.	4	8	12	27	44	60
S-17-Love 1970 (scarce)	27	54	81	189	420	650
S-18-Three Mouseketeers; Dizzy Dog, Doodles Duck, Bo Bunny-r; Sheldon Mayer-a	9	18	27	57	111	165
S-19-Jerry Lewis; Neal Adams pin-up	9	18	27	59	117	175
S-20-House of Mystery; N. Adams-c; Kirby-r(3)	7	14	21	48	89	130
S-21-Love 1971 (scarce)	29	58	87	209	467	725
S-22-Top Guns of the West; Kubert-c	4	8	12	25	40	55
S-23-The Unexpected	4	8	12	28	47	65
S-24-Supergirl	4	8	12	27	44	60
S-25-Challengers of the Unknown; all Kirby/Wood-r	4	8	12	22	35	48
S-26-Aquaman (1971)-r/S.A. Aquaman origin story from Showcase #30	4	8	12	27	44	60
27-Strange Flying Saucers Adventures (Sum, 1976)	3	6	9	18	28	38

NOTE: *Sid Greene r-27p(2), Heath r-27. G. Kane a-14r(2), 15, 27r(p). Kubert r-16.*

SUPER DINOSAUR
Image Comics: Apr, 2011 - No. 23, Dec, 2014 ($2.99)

	GD 2.0	VG 4.0	FN 6.0	VF 8.0	VF/NM 9.0	NM- 9.2
1-23: 1-Robert Kirkman-s/Jason Howard-a; origin story and character profiles						3.00
... Origin Special #1 FCBD Edition (5/11, giveaway) r/#1						3.00

SUPER-DOOPER COMICS
Able Mfg. Co./Harvey: 1946 - No. 7, May, 1946; No. 8, 1946 (10¢, 32 pgs., paper-c)

	GD 2.0	VG 4.0	FN 6.0	VF 8.0	VF/NM 9.0	NM- 9.2
1-The Clock, Gangbuster app. (scarce)	103	206	309	659	1130	1600
2	20	40	60	120	195	270
3-6	18	36	54	111	176	240
7,8-Shock Gibson. 7-Where's Theres A Will by Ed Wheelan, Steve Case Crime Rover, Penny & Ullysses Jr. 8-Sam Hill app.	24	48	72	140	230	320

SUPER DUCK
Archie Comics Publications: May, 2020 - No. 4 ($3.99, limited series)

	GD 2.0	VG 4.0	FN 6.0	VF 8.0	VF/NM 9.0	NM- 9.2
1-Frank Tieri & Ian Flynn-s/Ryan Jampole-a; revival of Golden Age character						4.00

SUPER DUCK COMICS (The Cockeyed Wonder) (See Jolly Jingles)
MLJ Mag. No. 1-4(9/45)/Close-Up No. 5 on (Archie): Fall, 1944 - No. 94, Dec, 1960 (Also see Laugh #24)(#1-5 are quarterly)

	GD 2.0	VG 4.0	FN 6.0	VF 8.0	VF/NM 9.0	NM- 9.2
1-Origin; Hitler & Hirohito-c	187	374	561	1197	2049	2900
2-Bill Vigoda-c	39	78	117	240	395	550
3-5: 4-20-Al Fagaly-c (most)	27	54	81	162	266	370
6-10	15	30	45	90	140	190
11-20(6/48)	13	26	39	72	101	130
21,23-40 (10/51)	11	22	33	62	86	110
22-Used in **SOTI**, pg. 35,307,308	15	30	45	85	130	175
41-60 (2/55)	10	20	30	54	72	90
61-94	8	16	24	44	57	70

SUPER DUPER (Formerly Pocket Comics #1-4?)
Harvey Publications: No. 5, 1941 - No. 11, 1941

	GD 2.0	VG 4.0	FN 6.0	VF 8.0	VF/NM 9.0	NM- 9.2
5-Captain Freedom & Shock Gibson app.	81	162	243	518	884	1250
8,11	55	110	165	352	601	850

SUPER DUPER COMICS (Formerly Latest Comics?)
F. E. Howard Publ.: No. 3, May-June, 1947

	GD 2.0	VG 4.0	FN 6.0	VF 8.0	VF/NM 9.0	NM- 9.2
3-1st app. Mr. Monster	290	580	870	1856	3178	4500

SUPER FREAKS (See Savage Dragon titles)
Image Comics: Jun, 2022 ($4.99, one-shot)

	GD 2.0	VG 4.0	FN 6.0	VF 8.0	VF/NM 9.0	NM- 9.2
1-Fan-made tribute comic to the Savage Dragon; s/a by various; Larsen-c						5.00

SUPER FRIENDS (TV) (Also see Best of DC & Limited Collectors' Edition)
National Periodical Publications/DC Comics: Nov, 1976 - No. 47, Aug, 1981 (#14 is 44 pgs.)

	GD 2.0	VG 4.0	FN 6.0	VF 8.0	VF/NM 9.0	NM- 9.2
1-Superman, Batman, Robin, Wonder Woman, Aquaman, Atom, Wendy, Marvin & Wonder Dog begin (1st Super Friends)	7	14	21	46	86	125
2-Penquin-c/sty	3	6	9	16	23	30
3-5	3	6	9	14	20	26
6,8-10,14: 8-1st app. Jack O'Lantern. 9-1st app. Icemaiden. 14-Origin Wonder Twins	2	4	6	13	18	22
7-1st app. Wonder Twins & The Seraph	11	22	33	73	157	240
11-13,15-30: 13-1st app. Dr. Mist. 25-1st app. Fire as Green Fury. 28-Bizarro app.	2	4	6	9	13	16
13-16,20-23,25,32-(Whitman variants; low print run, no issue# on cover)	2	4	6	11	16	20
31,47: 31-Black Orchid app. 47-Origin Fire & Green Fury	2	4	6	10	14	18
32-46: 36,43-Plastic Man app.	2	4	6	8	11	14
TBP (2001, $14.95) r/#1,6-9,14,21,27 & Limited Collectors' Edition C-41; Alex Ross-c						15.00
...: Truth, Justice and Peace TPB (2003, $14.95) r/#10,12,13,25,28,29,31,36,37						15.00

NOTE: *Estrada a-1p, 2p. Orlando a-1p. Staton a-43, 45.*

SUPER FRIENDS (All ages stories with puzzles and games)(Based on Mattel toy line)
DC Comics: May, 2008 - No. 29, Sept, 2010 ($2.25/$2.99)

	GD 2.0	VG 4.0	FN 6.0	VF 8.0	VF/NM 9.0	NM- 9.2
1-29-Superman, Batman, Wonder Woman, Aquaman, Flash & Green Lantern. 29-Begin $2.99-c; Bat-Mite & Mr. Mxyzptlk app.						3.00
...: Calling All Super Friends TPB (2009, $12.99) r/#8-14; puzzles and games						13.00
...: For Justice TPB (2009, $12.99) r/#1-7; puzzles and games						13.00
...: Head of the Class TPB (2010, $12.99) r/#15-21; puzzles and games						13.00
...: Mystery in Space TPB (2011, $12.99) r/#22-28; puzzles and games						13.00

SUPER FUN
Gillmor Magazines: Jan, 1956 (By A.W. Nugent)

	GD 2.0	VG 4.0	FN 6.0	VF 8.0	VF/NM 9.0	NM- 9.2
1-Comics, puzzles, cut-outs by A.W. Nugent	10	20	30	58	79	100

SUPER FUNNIES (...Western Funnies #3,4)
Superior Comics Publishers Ltd. (Canada): Dec, 1953 - No. 4, Sept, 1954

	GD 2.0	VG 4.0	FN 6.0	VF 8.0	VF/NM 9.0	NM- 9.2
1-(3-D, 10¢)-...Presents Dopey Duck; make your own 3-D glasses cut-out inside front-c; did not come w/glasses	41	82	123	256	428	600
2-Horror & crime satire	18	36	54	105	165	225
3-Phantom Ranger-c/s; Geronimo, Billy the Kid app.	12	24	36	67	94	120
4-Phantom Ranger-c/story	12	24	36	67	94	120

SUPERGIRL
DC Comics: Feb. 1944

nn - Ashcan comic, not distributed to newsstands, only for in-house use. Cover art is Boy Commandos #1 with interior being Action Comics #80. A copy sold for $15,750 in 2008.

SUPERGIRL (See Action, Adventure #281, Brave & the Bold, Crisis on Infinite Earths #7, Daring New Advs. of..., Super DC Giant, Superman Family, & Super-Team Family)

SUPERGIRL
National Periodical Publ.: Nov, 1972 - No. 9, Dec-Jan, 1973-74; No. 10, Sept-Oct, 1974 (1st solo title)(20¢)

	GD 2.0	VG 4.0	FN 6.0	VF 8.0	VF/NM 9.0	NM- 9.2
1-Zatanna back-up stories begin, end #5	12	24	36	81	176	270
2-4,6,7,9: 7-Zatanna battles Supergirl	4	8	12	27	44	60
5,8,10: 5-Zatanna origin-r. 8-JLA x-over; Batman cameo. 10-Prez app.	4	8	12	28	47	65

NOTE: *Zatanna in #1-5, 7(Guest); Prez app. in #10. #1-10 are 20¢ issues.*

SUPERGIRL (Formerly Daring New Adventures of...)
DC Comics: No. 14, Dec, 1983 - No. 23, Sept, 1984

	GD 2.0	VG 4.0	FN 6.0	VF 8.0	VF/NM 9.0	NM- 9.2
14-23: 16-Ambush Bug app. 20-JLA & New Teen Titans app.						5.00
...Movie Special (1985)-Adapts movie; Morrow-a; photo back-c						5.00

SUPERGIRL
DC Comics: Feb, 1994 - No. 4, May, 1994 ($1.50, limited series)

	GD 2.0	VG 4.0	FN 6.0	VF 8.0	VF/NM 9.0	NM- 9.2
1-Matrix clone Supergirl; Stern-s/Brigman-a	2	4	6	8	10	12
2-4: Guice-a(i)						5.00

SUPERGIRL (See Showcase '96 #8)
DC Comics: Sept, 1996 - No. 80, May, 2003 ($1.95/$1.99/$2.25/$2.50)

	GD 2.0	VG 4.0	FN 6.0	VF 8.0	VF/NM 9.0	NM- 9.2
1-Peter David scripts & Gary Frank-c/a	2	4	6	11	16	20
1-2nd printing						4.00
2,4-9: 4-Gorilla Grodd-c/app. 6-Superman-c/app. 9-Last Frank-a						5.00
3-Final Night, Gorilla Grodd app.						6.00
10-19: 14-Genesis x-over. 16-Power Girl app.						4.00
20-35: 20-Millennium Giants x-over; Superman app. 23-Steel-c/app. 24-Resurrection Man x-over. 25-Comet ID revealed; begin $1.99-c						4.00
36-46: 36,37-Young Justice x-over						4.00
47-49,51-74: 47-Begin $2.25-c. 51-Adopts costume from animated series. 54-Green Lantern app. 59-61-Our Worlds at War x-over. 62-Two-Face-c/app. 66,67-Demon-c/app.						

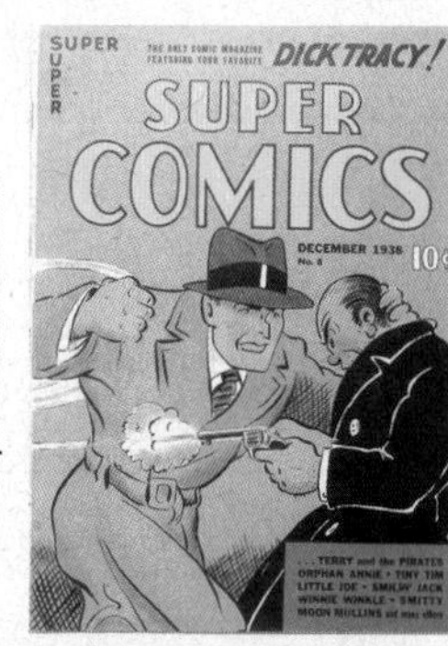

Super Comics #8 © DELL

Supergirl: Woman of Tomorrow #6 © DC

Super Goof #60 © DIS

GD VG FN VF VF/NM NM-
2.0 4.0 6.0 8.0 9.0 9.2

68-74-Mary Marvel app. 70-Nauck-a. 73-Begin $2.50-c 4.00
50-($3.95) Supergirl's final battle with the Carnivore 5.00
75-80: 75-Re-intro. Kara Zor-El; cover swipe of Action Comics #252 by Haynes; Benes-a. 78-Spectre app. 80-Last issue; Romita-c 4.00
#1,000,000 (11/98) 853rd Century x-over 4.00
Annual 1 (1996, $2.95)-Legends of the Dead Earth 6.00
Annual 2 (1997, $3.95)-Pulp Heroes; LSH app.; Chiodo-c 5.00
...: Many Happy Returns TPB (2003, $14.95) r/#75-80; intro. by Peter David 15.00
...Plus (2/97, $2.95) Capt.(Mary) Marvel-c/app.; David-s/Frank-a 4.00
.../Prysm Double-Shot 1 (Feb, 1998, $1.95) w/Prysm (Teen Titans) 4.00
...: Wings (2001, $5.95) Elseworlds; DeMatteis-s/Tolagson-a 6.00
TPB-('98, $14.95) r/Showcase '96 #8 & Supergirl #1-9 15.00

SUPERGIRL (See Superman/Batman #8 & #19)
DC Comics: No. 0, Oct, 2005 - No. 67, Oct, 2011 ($2.99)

0-Reprints Superman/Batman #19 with white variant of that cover 4.00
1-Loeb-s/Churchill-a; two covers by Churchill & Turner; Power Girl app.
1 3 4 6 8 10
1-2nd printing with B&W sketch variant of Turner-c 3.00
1-3rd printing with variant-c homage to Action Comics #252 by Churchill 3.00
2-4: 2-Teen Titans app. 3-Outsiders app.; covers by Turner & Churchill 3.00
5-($3.99) Supergirl vs. Supergirl; Churchill & Turner-c 4.00
6-49: 6-9-One Year Later; Power Girl app. 11-Intro. Powerboy. 12-Terra debut; Conner-a 20-Amazons Attack x-over. 21,22-Karate Kid app. 28-31-Resurrection Man app. 35,36-New Krypton x-over; Argo City story re-told; Superwoman app. 35-Ross-c. 36-Zor-El dies 3.00
50-($4.99) Lana Lang Insect Queen app.; Superwoman returns; back-up story co-written by Helen Slater with Chiang-a; Turner-c 5.00
50-Variant cover by Middleton 6.00
51-67: 51-52-New Krypton. 52-Brainiac 5 app. 53-57-Bizarro-Girl app. 55-63-Reeder-c 3.00
58-DC 75th Anniversary variant cover by Conner 6.00
Annual 1 (11/09, $3.99) Origin of Superwoman 4.00
Annual 2 (12/10, $4.99) Silver Age Legion of Super-Heroes app.; Reeder-c 5.00
...: Beyond Good and Evil TPB (2008, $17.99) r/#23-27 and Action Comics #850 18.00
...: Bizarrogirl TPB (2011, $19.99) r/#53-59 & Annual #2 20.00
...: Candor TPB (2007, $14.99) r/#6-9; and pages from JSA Classified #2, Superman #223, Superman/Batman #27 and JLA #122,123 15.00
...: Death & The Family TPB (2010, $17.99) r/#48-50 & Annual #1 18.00
...: Friends & Fugitives TPB (2010, $17.99) r/#43,45-47; Action Comics #881,882 18.00
...: Identity TPB (2007, $19.99) r/#10-16 and story from DCU Infinite Holiday Special 20.00
...: Power TPB (2006, $14.99) r/#1-5 and Superman/Batman #19; variant-c gallery 15.00
...: Way of the World TPB (2009, $17.99) r/#28-33 18.00
...: Who is Superwoman TPB (2009, $17.99) r/#34,37-42 18.00

SUPERGIRL (DC New 52)
DC Comics: Nov, 2011 - No. 40, May, 2015 ($2.99)

1-New origin; Green & Johnson-s/Asrar-a/c; Superman app.
1 3 4 6 8 10
2-40: 2,3-Superman app. 8-Pérez-a. 14-17-H'El on Earth tie-in. 17-Wonder Woman app. 19,20-Power Girl app. 19-Power Girl gets classic costume. 23,24-Cyborg Superman app. 26-28-Lobo app. 28-33-Kara joins Red Lanterns. 33-Gen13 app. 36-40-Maxima app. 3.00
#0-(11/12, $2.99) Kara's escape from Krypton 3.00
...: Futures End 1 (11/14, $2.99, regular-c) Five years later; Cyborg Superman app. 3.00
...: Futures End 1 (11/14, $3.99, 3-D cover) 4.00
... Special Edition 1 (12/15, $1.00) reprints #1 with Supergirl TV banner at top of cover 3.00

SUPERGIRL (DC Rebirth)(Issues #41 & #42 were only released digitally)
DC Comics: Nov, 2016 - No. 40, May, 2020 ($2.99/$3.99)

1-Orlando-s/Ching-a; Cyborg Superman app. 1 2 3 5 6 8
2-7 3.00
8-24,26-40-($3.99) 8-Superman & Emerald Empress app. 9-11-Batgirl app. 12-Fatal Five. 12-20-Variant covers by Stanley "Artgerm" Lau. 20-The Unexpected app. 26-Omega Men app. 31-33-Maguire-a. 33-Legion of Super-Heroes app. 36-40-The Infected 4.00
25-($4.99) Lupacchino-a 5.00
Annual 1 (10/17, $4.99) The new Fatal Five app.; takes place between #11,12 5.00
Annual 2 (1/20, $4.99) Venditti-s/Braga-a; follows #36; The Batman Who Laughs app. 5.00
...: Rebirth 1 (10/16, $2.99) Orlando-s/Lupacchino-a; gets the Kara Danvers identity 3.00

SUPERGIRL AND THE LEGION OF SUPER-HEROES (Continues from Legion of Super-Heroes #15, Apr, 2006)(Continues as Legion of Super-Heroes #37)
DC Comics: No. 16, May, 2006 - No. 36, Jan, 2008 ($2.99)

16-Supergirl appears in the 31st century 4.00
16-2nd printing 3.00
17-36: 23-Mon-El cameo. 24,25-Mon-El returns 3.00
23-Variant-c by Adam Hughes 8 16 24 54 102 150
...: Adult Education TPB (2007, $14.99) r/#20-25 & LSH #6,9,13-15 15.00
...: Dominator War TPB (2007, $14.99) r/#26-30 15.00
...: Strange Visitor From Another Century TPB (2006, $14.99) r/#16-19 & LSH #11,12,15 15.00
...: The Quest For Cosmic Boy TPB (2008, $14.99) r/#31-36 15.00

SUPERGIRL: BEING SUPER
DC Comics: Feb, 2017 - No. 4, Aug, 2017 ($5.99, limited series)

1-4-Mariko Tamaki-s/Joëlle Jones-a 6.00

SUPERGIRL: COSMIC ADVENTURES IN THE 8TH GRADE (Cartoony all-ages title)
DC Comics: Feb, 2008 - No. 6, Jul, 2009 ($2.50, limited series)

1-6: 1-Supergirl lands on Earth; Eric Jones-a. 5,6-Comet & Streaky app. 3.00

SUPERGIRL/LEX LUTHOR SPECIAL (Supergirl and Team Luthor on-c)
DC Comics: 1993 ($2.50, 68 pgs., one-shot)

1-Pin-ups by Byrne & Thibert 6.00

SUPERGIRL: WOMAN OF TOMORROW
DC Comics: Aug, 2021 - No. 8, Apr, 2022 ($4.99, limited series)

1-8-Tom King-s/Bilquis Evely-a 5.00

SUPERGOD (Warren Ellis'...)
Avatar Press: Oct, 2009 - No. 5, Nov, 2010 ($3.99, limited series)

1-5-Warren Ellis-s/Garrie Gastony-a; multiple covers on each 4.00

SUPER GOOF (Walt Disney) (See Dynabrite & The Phantom Blot)
Gold Key No. 1-57/Whitman No. 58 on: Oct, 1965 - No. 74, July, 1984

	GD 2.0	VG 4.0	FN 6.0	VF 8.0	VF/NM 9.0	NM- 9.2
1	5	10	15	35	63	90
2-5	3	6	9	17	26	35
6-10	3	6	9	14	19	24
11-20	2	4	6	8	11	14
21-30	1	3	4	6	8	10
31-50	1	2	3	4	5	7
51-57						6.00
58,59 (Whitman)	1	2	3	5	6	8
60(8/80), 62(11/80) 3-pack only (scarce)	6	12	18	41	76	110
61(9-10/80) 3-pack only (rare)	9	18	27	63	129	195
63-66('81)	1	2	3	5	6	8
63 (1/81, 40¢-c) Cover price error variant (scarce)	3	6	9	14	19	24
67-69: 67(2/82), 68(2-3/82), 69(3/82)						6.00
70-74 (#90180 on-c; pre-pack, nd, nd code): 70(5/83), 71(8/83), 72(5/84), 73(6/84), 74(7/84)	3	6	9	15	22	28

NOTE: *Reprints in #16, 24, 28, 29, 37, 38, 43, 45, 46, 54(1/2), 56-58, 65(1/2), 72(r-#2).*

SUPER GREEN BERET (Tod Holton...)
Lightning Comics (Milson Publ. Co.): Apr, 1967 - No. 2, Jun, 1967

1-(25¢, 68 pgs) 5 10 15 30 50 70
2-(25¢, 68 pgs) 3 6 9 21 33 45

SUPER HEROES (See Giant-Size... & Marvel...)

SUPER HEROES
Dell Publishing Co.: Jan, 1967 - No. 4, June, 1967

1-Origin & 1st app. Fab 4 5 10 15 34 60 85
2-4 3 6 9 16 24 32

SUPER-HEROES BATTLE SUPER-GORILLAS (See DC Special #16)
National Periodical Publications: Winter, 1976 (52 pgs., all reprints, one-shot)

1-Superman, Batman, Flash stories; Infantino-a(p) 2 4 6 11 16 20

SUPER HEROES VERSUS SUPER VILLAINS
Archie Publications (Radio Comics): July, 1966 (no month given)(68 pgs.)

1-Flyman, Black Hood, Web, Shield-r; Reinman-a 6 12 18 37 66 95

SUPER HERO SQUAD (See Marvel Super Hero Squad)

SUPERHERO WOMEN, THE - FEATURING THE FABULOUS FEMALES OF MARVEL COMICS (See Fireside Book Series)

SUPERICHIE (Formerly Super Richie)
Harvey Publications: No. 5, Oct, 1976 - No. 18, Jan, 1979 (52 pgs. giants)

5-Origin/1st app. new costumes for Rippy & Crashman 2 4 6 9 13 16
6-18 2 4 6 8 10 12

SUPERIOR
Marvel Comics (ICON): Dec, 2010 - No. 7, Mar, 2012 ($2.99/$4.99)

1-6-Mark Millar-s/Leinil Yu-a. 1-1st & 2nd printings 3.00
7-($4.99) Bonus preview of Supercrooks #1 5.00
... World Record Special 1 (12/11, $2.99, B&W) Comic created in less than 12 hours 3.00

SUPERIOR CARNAGE
Marvel Comics: Sept, 2013 - No. 5, Jan, 2014 ($3.99)

1-5: 1-Shinick-s/Segovia-a; covers by Crain & Checchetto. 2-5-Superior Spider-Man app. 4.00
Annual 1 (4/14, $4.99) Bunn-s/Jacinto & Henderson-a; follows #5; Kasady in prison 5.00

GD VG FN VF VF/NM NM-
2.0 4.0 6.0 8.0 9.0 9.2

SUPERIOR FOES OF SPIDER-MAN (Superior Spider-Man)
Marvel Comics: Sept, 2013 - No. 17, Jan, 2015 ($3.99)

1-17: 1-Boomerang, Shocker, Overdrive, Speed Demon & Beetle team; Spencer-s 4.00

SUPERIOR IRON MAN (Follows events of the Avengers & X-Men: Axis series)
Marvel Comics: Jan, 2015 - No. 9, Aug, 2015 ($3.99)

1-9: 1-Tom Taylor-s/Yildiray Cinar-a. 1-4-Daredevil app. 4.00

SUPERIOR OCTOPUS (Tie-in to Spider-Geddon event)
Marvel Comics: Dec, 2018 ($3.99)

1-Cloned Otto Octavius; Arnim Zola & The Gorgon app.; Gage-s/Hawthorne-a 4.00

SUPERIOR SPIDER-MAN (Follows Amazing Spider-Man #700)
Marvel Comics: Mar, 2013 - No. 31, Jun, 2014; No. 32, Oct, 2014 - No. 33, Nov, 2014 ($3.99)

1-Doc Ock as Spider-Man; new Sinister Six app.; Slott-s/Stegman-a 8.00
1-Variant baby-c by Skottie Young 10.00
2-6: 4,5-Camuncoli-a. 4-Green Goblin cameo. 6-Ramos-a 5.00
6AU (5/13, $3.99) Alternate timeline Age of Ultron tie-in; Gage-s/Soy-a 4.00
7-24: 7,8-Ramos-a; Avengers app. 9-Peter's memories removed. 14-New costume. 17-19-Spider-Man 2099 app. 20-Black Cat app. 22-24-Venom app. 4.00
25-($4.99) Superior Venom vs. the Avengers; Ramos-a 5.00
26-30: 27-Goblin Nation begins. 29-Spider-Man 2099 app. 4.00
31-($5.99) Goblin Nation finale; covers by Camuncoli & Campbell; Silver Surfer bonus 6.00
32,33-($4.99) Edge of Spider-Verse tie-ins; takes place during issue #19 5.00
Annual 1 (1/14, $4.99) Blackout app.; Gage-s/Rodriguez-a 5.00
Annual 2 (5/14, $4.99) Leads into Superior Spider-Man #30; Gage-s/Rodriguez-a 5.00

SUPERIOR SPIDER-MAN (Otto Octavius)(See Spider-Geddon)
Marvel Comics: Feb, 2019 - No. 12, Dec, 2019 ($3.99)

1-6-Gage-s/Hawthorne-a. 1-Stilt-Man app. 1-3-Terrax app. 5,6-Doctor Strange app. 4.00
7-12: 7,8-War of the Realms tie-ins. 11-Doctor Octopus returns; Mephisto app. 4.00

SUPERIOR SPIDER-MAN TEAM UP
Marvel Comics: Sept, 2013 - No. 12, Jun, 2014 ($3.99)

1-10: 1-Avengers app. 8-Namor app. 9,10-Daredevil & The Punisher app. 4.00
... Special 1 (12/13, $4.99) Hulk & the original X-Men app.; Dialynas-a/Lozano-c 5.00

SUPERIOR STORIES
Nesbit Publishers, Inc.: May-June, 1955 - No. 4, Nov-Dec, 1955

1-The Invisible Man by H.G. Wells 30 60 90 177 289 400
2-4: 2-The Pirate of the Gulf by J.H. Ingrahams. 3-Wreck of the Grosvenor by William Clark Russell. 4-The Texas Rangers by O'Henry 14 28 42 80 115 150
NOTE: *Morisi c/a in all. Kiwanis stories in #3 & 4. #4 has photo of Gene Autry on-c.*

SUPER MAGIC (Super Magician Comics #2 on)
Street & Smith Publications: May, 1941

V1#1-Blackstone the Magician-c/story; origin/1st app. Rex King (Black Fury); Charles Sultan-c; Blackstone-c begin 213 426 639 1363 2332 3300

SUPER MAGICIAN COMICS (Super Magic #1)
Street & Smith Publications: No. 2, Sept, 1941 - V5#8, Feb-Mar, 1947

V1#2-Blackstone the Magician continues; Rex King, Man of Adventure app.
93 186 279 591 1021 1450
3-Tao-Anwar, Boy Magician begins 57 114 171 362 619 875
4-7,9-12: 4-Origin Transo. 11-Supersnipe app. 53 106 159 334 567 800
8-Abbott & Costello story (1st app?, 11/42) 55 110 165 352 601 850
V2#1-The Shadow app. 52 104 156 328 552 775
2-12: 5-Origin Tigerman. 8-Red Dragon begins 32 64 96 188 307 425
V3#1-12: 5-Origin Mr. Twilight 30 60 90 177 289 400
V4#1-4,6-12: 11-Nigel Elliman Ace of Magic begins (3/46)
25 50 75 150 245 340
5-KKK-c/sty 55 110 165 352 601 850
V5#1-6 24 48 72 142 234 325
7,8-Red Dragon by Edd Cartier-c/a 47 94 141 296 498 700
NOTE: *Jack Binder c-1-14(most). Red Dragon c-V5#7, 8.*

SUPERMAN (See Action Comics, Advs. of..., All-New Coll. Ed., All-Star Comics, Best of DC, Brave & the Bold, Cosmic Odyssey, DC Comics Presents, Heroes Against Hunger, JLA, The Kents, Krypton Chronicles, Limited Coll. Ed., Man of Steel, Phantom Zone, Power Record Comics, Special Edition, Steel, Super Friends, Superman: The Man of Steel, Superman: The Man of Tomorrow, Taylor's Christmas Tabloid, Three-Dimension Advs., World Of Krypton, World Of Metropolis, World Of Smallville & World's Finest)

SUPERMAN (Becomes Adventures of...#424 on)
National Periodical Publ./DC Comics: Summer, 1939 - No. 423, Sept, 1986
(#1-5 are quarterly)

1(nn)-1st four Action stories reprinted; origin Superman by Siegel & Shuster; has a new 2 pg. origin plus 4 pgs. omitted in Action story; see The Comics Magazine #1 & More Fun #14-17 for Superman prototype app.; cover r/splash page from Action #10; 1st pin-up Superman on back-c - 1st pin-up in comics 180,000 360,000 720,000 1,350,000 2,025,000 2,700,000

1-Reprint, Oversize 13-1/2x10". **WARNING**: This comic is an exact duplicate reprint of the original except for its size. DC published it in 1978 with a second cover titling it as a Famous First Edition. There have been many reported cases of the outer cover being removed and the interior sold as the original edition. The reprint with the new outer cover removed is practically worthless. See Famous First Edition for value.

2-All daily strip-r; full pg. ad for N.Y. World's Fair 4000 8000 12,000 30,000 63,000 96,000
3-2nd story-r from Action #5; 3rd story-r from Action #6
2020 4040 6060 14,700 30,000 48,000
4-2nd mention of Daily Planet (Spr/40); also see Action #23; 2nd & 3rd app. Luthor (red-headed; also see Action #23); first issue of title to feature original stories
1250 2500 3750 9500 17,250 25,000
5-4th Luthor app. (grey hair) 919 1838 2757 6709 11,855 17,000
6,7: 6-1st splash pg. in a Superman comic. 7-1st Perry White? (11-12/40)
541 1082 1623 3950 6975 10,000
8-10: 10-5th app. Luthor (1st bald Luthor, 5-6/41) 476 952 1428 3475 6138 8800
11-13,15: 13-Jimmy Olsen & Luthor app. 394 788 1182 2758 4829 6900
14-Patriotic Shield-c classic by Fred Ray 1500 3000 4500 11,400 20,700 30,000
16,19,20: 16-1st Lois Lane-c this title (5-6/42); 2nd Lois-c after Action #29
331 663 993 2317 4059 5800
17-Hitler, Hirohito-c 1400 2800 4200 10,600 19,300 28,000
18-Classic WWII-c 423 846 1269 3000 5250 7500
21,22,25: 25-Clark Kent's only military service; Fred Ray's only super-hero story
271 542 813 1734 2967 4200
23-Classic periscope-c 423 846 1269 3000 5250 7500
24-Classic Jack Burnley flag-c 865 1730 2595 6315 11,158 16,000
26-Classic war-c 432 864 1296 3154 5577 8000
27-29: 27,29-Lois Lane-c. 28-Lois Lane Girl Reporter series begins, ends #40,42 219 438 657 1402 2401 3400
28-Overseas edition for Armed Forces; same as reg. #28
219 438 657 1402 2401 3400
30-Origin & 1st app. Mr. Mxyztplk (9-10/44)(pronounced "Mix-it-plk") in comic books; name later became Mxyzptlk ("Mix-yez-pit-l-ick"); the character was inspired by a combination of the name of Al Capp's Joe Blyfstyk (the little man with the black cloud over his head) & the devilish antics of Bugs Bunny; he first app. in newspapers 3/7/44; Superman flies for the first time 443 886 1329 3234 5717 8200
31-40: 33-(3-4/45)-3rd app. Mxyztplk. 35,36-Lois Lane-c. 38-Atomic bomb story (1-2/46); delayed because of gov't censorship; Superman shown reading Batman #32 on cover. 40-Mxyztplk-c 174 348 522 1114 1907 2700
41-50: 42-Lois Lane-c. 45-Lois Lane as Superwoman (see Action #60 for 1st app.). 46-(5-6/47)-1st app. Superboy this title? 48-1st time Superman travels thru time
148 296 444 947 1624 2300
51,52: 51-Lois Lane-c 135 270 405 864 1482 2100
53-Third telling of Superman origin; 10th anniversary issue ('48); classic origin-c by Boring
443 886 1329 3234 5717 8200
54,56-60: 57-Lois Lane as Superwoman-c. 58-Intro Tiny Trix. 59-Early use of heat vision (possibly first time) 129 258 387 826 1413 2000
55-Used in **SOTI**, pg. 33 135 270 405 864 1482 2100
61-Origin Superman retold; origin Green Kryptonite (1st Kryptonite story); Superman returns to Krypton for 1st time & sees his parents for 1st time since infancy, discovers he's not an Earth man 271 542 813 1734 2967 4200
62-70: 62-Orson Welles-c/story. 65-1st Krypton Foes: Mala, Kizo, & U-Ban. 66-2nd Superbaby story. 67-Perry Como-c/story. 68-1st Luthor-c this title (see Action Comics)
129 258 387 826 1413 2000
71-75: 74-2nd Luthor-c this title. 75-Some have #74 on-c
123 246 369 787 1344 1900
76-Batman x-over; Superman & Batman learn each other's I.D. for the 1st time (5-6/52) (also see World's Finest #71) 423 846 1269 3000 5250 7500
77-81: 78-Last 52 pg. issue; 1st meeting of Lois Lane & Lana Lang. 81-Used in **POP**, pg. 88. 81-"Superwoman From Space" story 110 220 330 704 1202 1700
82-87,89,90: 89-1st Curt Swan-c in title 97 194 291 621 1061 1500
88-Prankster, Toyman & Luthor team-up 110 220 330 704 1200 1700
91-95: 95-Last precode issue (2/55) 90 180 270 576 988 1400
96-99: 96-Mr. Mxyztplk-c/story 84 168 252 538 919 1300
100 (9-10/55)-Shows cover to #1 on-c 284 568 852 1818 3109 4400
101-105,107-110: 109-1st S.A. issue 61 122 183 384 817 1250
106 (7/56)-Retells origin 66 132 198 416 883 1350
111-120 54 108 162 340 720 1100
121,122,124-127,129: 127-Origin/1st app. Titano. 129-Intro/origin Lori Lemaris, The Mermaid
48 96 144 302 639 975
123-Pre-Supergirl tryout-c/story (8/58). 180 360 720 1680 3840 6000
128-(4/59)-Red Kryptonite used. Bruce Wayne x-over who protects Superman's i.d. (3rd story)
49 98 147 308 654 1000
130-(7/59)-2nd app, Krypto, the Superdog with Superman (see Sup.'s Pal Jimmy Olsen #29) (all other previous app. w/Superboy) 51 102 153 320 675 1050
131-139: 135-2nd Lori Lemaris app. 139-Lori Lemaris app.;
39 78 117 234 492 750
140-1st Blue Kryptonite & Bizarro Supergirl; origin Bizarro Jr. #1
41 82 123 246 511 775
141-145,148: 142-2nd Batman x-over 34 68 102 204 427 650
146-(7/61)-Superman's life story; back-up hints at Earth II. Classic-c
53 106 159 318 659 1000
147(8/61)-7th Legion app; 1st app. Legion of Super-Villains; 1st app. Adult Legion; swipes-c to Adv. #247 45 90 135 270 560 850
149(11/61)-8th Legion app. (cameo); "The Death of Superman" imaginary story; last 10¢ issue 43 86 129 258 542 825
150,151,153,154,157,159,160: 157-Gold Kryptonite used (see Adv. #299); Mon -El app.; Lightning Lad cameo (11/62) 15 30 45 105 233 360
152,155,156,158,162: 152(4/62)-15th Legion app. 155-(8/62)-Legion app; Lightning Man & Cosmic Man, & Adult Legion app. 156,162-Legion app. 158-1st app. Superman as Nightwing & Jimmy Olsen as Flamebird & Nor-Kann of Kandor (12/62)
16 32 48 108 239 370
161-1st told death of Ma and Pa Kent 16 32 48 110 243 375
161-2nd printing (1987, $1.25)-New DC logo; sold thru So Much Fun Toy Stores (cover title: Superman Classic) 5.00
163-166,168-180: 166-XMas-c. 168-All Luthor issue; JFK tribute/memorial. 169-Bizarro Invasion of Earth-c/story; last Sally Selwyn. 170-Pres. Kennedy story is finally published after delay from #168 due to assassination. 172,173-Legion cameos. 174-Super-Mxyzptlk; Bizarro app. 176-Legion of Super-Pets 12 24 36 82 179 275
167-New origin Brainiac, text reference of Brainiac 5 descending from adopted human son Brainiac II; intro Tharla (later Luthor's wife) 18 36 54 124 275 425
181,182,184-186,188-192,194-196,198,200: 181-1st 2965 story/series. 182-1st S.A. app. of The Toyman (1/66). 189-Origin/destruction of Krypton II.
10 20 30 64 132 200
183 (Giant G-18) 12 24 36 82 179 275
187,193,197 (Giants G-23,G-31,G-36) 10 20 30 65 135 205
199-1st Superman/Flash race (8/67): also see Flash #175 & World's Finest #198,199 (r-in Limited Coll. Ed. C-48) 52 104 156 416 933 1450
201,203-206,208-211,213-216: 213-Brainiac-5 app. 216-Last 12¢ issue
6 12 18 41 76 110
202 (80-pg. Giant G-42)-All Bizarro issue 8 16 24 51 96 140
207,212,217 (Giants G-48,G-54,G-60): 207-30th anniversary Superman (6/68)
7 14 21 46 86 125
218-221,223-226,228-231 6 12 18 37 66 95
222,239(Giants, G-66,G-84) 7 14 21 44 82 120
227,232(Giants, G-72,G-78): 232-All Krypton issue 7 14 21 44 82 120
233-2nd app. Morgan Edge; Clark Kent switches from newspaper reporter to TV newscaster; all Kryptonite on Earth destroyed; classic Neal Adams-c; 1st Fabulous World of Krypton story; Superman pin-up by Swan 33 66 99 238 532 825
234-238 5 10 15 34 60 85
240-Kaluta-a; last 15¢ issue 5 10 15 33 57 80

Superior Spider-Man (2019) #6 © MAR

Superman #2 © DC

Superman #233 © DC

GD VG FN VF VF/NM NM-
2.0 4.0 6.0 8.0 9.0 9.2

241-244 (All 52 pgs.): 241-New Wonder Woman app. 243-G.A.-r/#38
5 10 15 31 53 75
245-Also listed as DC 100 Pg. Super Spectacular #7; Air Wave, Kid Eternity, Hawkman-r; Atom-r/Atom #3 10 20 30 68 144 220
246-248,250,251,253 (All 52 pgs.): 246-G.A.-r/#40. 248-World of Krypton story. 251-G.A.-r/#45. 253-Finlay-a, 2 pgs., G.A.-r/#1 5 10 15 31 53 75
249,254-Neal Adams-a. 249-(52 pgs.); 1st app. Terra-Man (Swan-a) & origin-s by Dick Dillin (p) & Neal Adams (inks) 6 12 18 40 73 105
252-Also listed as DC 100 Pg. Super Spectacular #13; Ray(r/Smash #17), Black Condor, (r/Crack #18), Hawkman(r/Flash #24); Starman-r/Adv. #67; Dr. Fate & Spectre-r/More Fun #57; N. Adams-c 10 20 30 70 150 230
255-271,273-277,279-283: 263-Photo-c. 264-1st app. Steve Lombard. 276-Intro Capt. Thunder. 279-Batman, Batgirl app. 282-Luthor battlesuit 3 6 9 15 22 28
272,278,284-All 100 pgs. G.A.-r in all. 272-r/2nd app. Mr. Mxyztplk from Action #80
5 10 15 31 53 75
285-299: 289-Partial photo-c. 292-Origin Lex Luthor retold
2 4 6 13 19 24
300-(6/76) Superman in the year 2001 4 8 12 28 47 65
301-316,318-350: 301,320-Solomon Grundy app. 323-Intro. Atomic Skull. 327-329-(44 pgs.). 327-Kobra app. 330-More facts revealed about I.D. 331,332-1st/2nd app. Master Jailer. 335-Mxyzptlk marries Ms. Bgbznz. 336-Rose & Thorn app. 338-(8/79) 40th Anniv. issue; the bottled city of Kandor enlarged. 344-Frankenstein & Dracula app.
2 4 6 8 11 14
317-Classic Neal Adams kryptonite cover 5 10 15 30 50 70
321-323,325-327,329-332,335-345,348,350 (Whitman variants; low print run; no issue # on cover) 2 4 6 11 16 20
351-399: 353-Brief origin. 354,355,357-Superman 2020 stories (354-Debut of Superman III). 356-World of Krypton story (also #360,367,375). 366-Fan letter by Todd McFarlane. 369-Christmas-c. 372-Superman 2021 story. 376-Free 6 pg. preview Daring New Advs. of Supergirl. 377-Terra-Man-c/app.; free 16 pg. preview Masters of the Universe. 378-Origin & 1st app. Colonel Future. 379-Bizarro World app. 2 4 6 8 10 12
400 (10/84, $1.50, 68 pgs.)-Many top artists featured; Chaykin painted cover, Miller back-c; Steranko-s/a (10 pages) 2 4 6 9 13 16
401-422: 405-Super-Batman story. 408-Nuclear Holocaust-c/story. 411-Special Julius Schwartz tribute issue. 414,415-Crisis x-over. 422-Horror-c by Bolland
1 3 4 6 8 10
409-(7/85) Var-c with Superman/Superhombre logo 17 34 51 114 252 390
423-Alan Moore scripts; Curt Swan-a/George Pérez-a(i); "Whatever Happened to the Man of Tomorrow?" story, cont'd in Action #583 4 6 13 18 22
Annual 1 (10/60, 84 pgs.)-Reprints 1st Supergirl story/Action #252; r/Lois Lane #1; Krypto-r (1st Silver Age DC annual) 96 192 288 768 1734 2700
Annual 2 (Win, 1960-61)-Super-villain issue; Brainiac, Titano, Metallo, Bizarro origin-r
37 74 111 274 612 950
Annual 3 (Sum, 1961)-Strange Lives of Superman 27 54 81 189 420 650
Annual 4(Win, 1961-62)-11th Legion app; 1st Legion origins (text & pictures); advs. in time, space & on alien worlds 21 42 63 147 324 500
Annual 5 (Sum, 1962)-All Krypton issue 17 34 51 117 259 400
Annual 6 (Win, 1962-63)-Legion-r/Adv. #247; Superman Family portrait on back-c
16 32 48 107 236 365
Annual 7 (Sum, 1963)-Silver Anniversary Issue; origin-r/Superman-Batman team/Adv. #275; cover gallery of famous issues 12 24 36 82 179 275
Annual 8 (Win, 1963-64)-All origins issue 12 24 36 80 173 265
Annual 9 (8/64)-Was advertised but came out as 80 Page Giant #1 instead
Annual 9 (1983)-Toth/Austin-a 2 4 6 8 10 12
Annuals 10,12: 10(1984, $1.25)-M. Anderson-i. 12(1986)-Bolland-c
1 2 3 5 6 8
Annual 11 (1985) "For the Man Who Has Everything" story; Alan Moore-s/Dave Gibbons-a; Mongul and the Black Mercy app.; Wonder Woman, Batman & Robin app. (adapted for a Justice League Unlimited animated episode) 5 10 15 30 50 70
... 1 (Facsimile Edition) (2022, $6.99) Reprints #1 with original 1939 ads 7.00
Special 1-3 ('83-'85): 1-G. Kane-c/a; contains German-r 6.00
The Amazing World of Superman "Official Metropolis Edition" (1973, $2.00, treasury-size)-Origin retold; Wood-r(i) from Superboy #153,161; poster incl. (half price if poster missing)
4 8 12 27 44 60
11195 (2/79, $1.95, 224 pgs.)-Golden Press 4 8 12 23 37 50

NOTE: ***N. Adams** a-249i, 254p; c-204-206, 210, 212-215, 219, 231i, 233-237, 240-243, 249-252, 254, 263, 307, 308, 313, 314, 317. **Adkins** a-323i. **Austin** c-368i. **Wayne Boring** art-late 1940's to early 1960's. **Buckler** a(p)-352, 363, 364, 369; c(p)-324-327, 356, 363, 368, 369, 373, 376, 378. **Burnley** a-252r; c-19-25, 30, 33, 34, 35p, 38p, 39p, 45p. **Fine** a-252r. **Kaluta** a-400. **Gil Kane** a-272r, 367, 372, 375, Special 2; c-374p, 375p, 377, 381, 382, 384-390, 392, Annual 9, Special 2. **Joe Kubert** c-216. **Morrow** a-238. **Mortimer** a-250r. **Perez** c-364p. **Fred Ray** a-25; c-6, 8-18. **Starlin** c-355. **Staton** a-354i, 355i. **Swan/Moldoff** c-149. **Williamson** a(i)-408-410, 412-416; c-408i, 409i. **Wrightson** a-400, 416.*

SUPERMAN (2nd Series) (Title continues numbering from Adventures of Superman #649)
DC Comics: Jan, 1987 - No. 226, Apr, 2006; No. 650, May, 2006 - No. 714, Oct, 2011

0-(10/94) Zero Hour; released between #93 & #94 1 3 4 6 8 10
1-Byrne-c/a begins; intro new Metallo 2 4 6 11 16 20

GD VG FN VF VF/NM NM-
2.0 4.0 6.0 8.0 9.0 9.2

2,3,5,6,8,10: 3-Legends x-over; Darkseid-c & app. 8-Legion app. 6.00
4-1st Bloodsport 3 6 9 14 20 25
7-Origin/1st app. Rampage 1 3 4 6 8 10
9-Joker-c 1 2 3 5 6 8
11-15,17-20,22-49,51,52,54-56,58-67: 11-1st new Mr. Mxyzptlk. 12-Lori Lemaris revived. 13-1st app. new Toyman. 13,14-Millennium x-over. 20-Doom Patrol app.; Supergirl cameo. 31-Mr. Mxyzptlk app. 37-Newsboy Legion app. 41-Lobo app. 44-Batman storyline, part 1. 45-Free extra 8 pgs. 54-Newsboy Legion story. 63-Aquaman x-over. 67-Last $1.00-c 5.00
16,21: 16-1st app. new Supergirl (4/88). 21-Supergirl-c/story; 1st app. Matrix who becomes new Supergirl 6.00
50-($1.50, 52 pgs.)-Clark Kent proposes to Lois 6.00
50-2nd printing 4.00
53-Clark reveals i.d. to Lois (Cont'd from Action #662) 5.00
53-2nd printing 4.00
57-($1.75, 52 pgs.) 5.00
68-72: 65,66,68-Deathstroke-c/stories. 70-Superman & Robin team-up 5.00
73-Doomsday cameo 1 3 4 6 8 10
74-Doomsday Pt. 2 (Cont'd from Justice League #69); Superman battles Doomsday
2 4 6 9 12 15
73,74-2nd printings 4.00
75-(1/93, $2.50)-Collector's Ed.; Doomsday Pt. 6; Superman dies; polybagged w/poster of funeral, obituary from Daily Planet, postage stamp & armband premiums (direct sales only)
3 6 9 19 30 40
75-Direct sales copy (no upc code, 1st print) 2 4 6 9 12 15
75-Direct sales copy (no upc code, 2nd-4th prints) 4.00
75-Newsstand copy w/upc code 3 6 9 21 33 45
75-Platinum Edition; given away to retailers 8 16 24 54 102 150
75-Special Edition (2022, $3.99) 30th Anniversary reprint; creators interview 4.00
76,77-Funeral For a Friend parts 4 & 8 6.00
78-($1.95)-Collector's Edition with die-cut outer-c & mini poster; Doomsday cameo 6.00
78-($1.50)-Newsstand Edition w/poster and different-c; Doomsday-c & cameo 5.00
79-81,83-89: 83-Funeral for a Friend epilogue; new Batman (Azrael) cameo. 87,88-Bizarro-c/story 4.00
82-($3.50)-Collector's Edition w/all chromium-c; real Superman revealed; Green Lantern x-over from G.L. #46; no ads 1 2 3 5 6 8
82-($2.00, 44 pgs.)-Regular Edition w/different-c 5.00
90-99: 93-(9/94)-Zero Hour. 94-(11/94). 95-Atom app. 96-Brainiac returns 4.00
100-Death of Clark Kent foil-c 6.00
100-Newsstand 4.00
101-122: 101-Begin $1.95-c; Black Adam app. 105-Green Lantern app. 110-Plastic Man-c/app. 114-Brainiac app; Dwyer-c. 115-Lois leaves Metropolis. 116-(10/96)-1st app. Teen Titans by Jurgens & Perez in 8 pg. preview. 117-Final Night. 118-Wonder Woman app. 119-Legion app. 122-New powers 4.00
123-Collector's Edition w/glow in the dark-c, new costume
1 3 4 6 8 10
123-Standard ed., new costume 5.00
124-149: 128-Cyborg-c/app. 131-Birth of Lena Luthor. 132-Superman Red/Superman Blue. 134-Millennium Giants. 136,137-Superman 2999. 139-Starlin-a. 140-Grindberg-a 4.00
150-($2.95) Standard Ed.; Brainiac 2.0 app.; Jurgens-s 5.00
150-($3.95) Collector's Ed. w/holo-foil enhanced variant-c 5.00
151-158: 151-Loeb-s begins; Daily Planet reopens 4.00
159-174: 159-$2.25-c begin. 161-Joker-c/app. 162-Aquaman-c/app. 163-Young Justice app. 165-JLA app.; Ramos; Madureira, Liefeld, A. Adams, Wieringo, Churchill-a. 166-Collector's and reg. editions. 167-Return to Krypton. 168-Batman-c/app.(cont'd in Detective #756). 171-173-Our Worlds at War. 173-Sienkiewicz-a (2 pgs.). 174-Adopts black & red "S" logo 3.00
175-($3.50) Joker: Last Laugh x-over; Doomsday-c/app. 4.00
176-189,191-199: 176,180-Churchill-a. 180-Dracula app. 181-Bizarro-c/app. 184-Return to Krypton II. 189-Van Fleet-c. 192,193,195,197-199-New Supergirl app. 3.00
190-($2.25) Regular edition 3.00
190-($3.95) Double-Feature Issue; included reprint of Superman: The 10¢ Adventure 4.00
200-($3.50) Gene Ha-c/art by various; preview art by Yu & Bermejo 4.00
201-Mr Majestic-c/app.; cover swipe of Action #1 3.00
202,203-Godfall parts 3,6; Turner-c; Caldwell-a(p). 203-Jim Lee sketch pages 3.00
204-Jim Lee-c/a begins; Azzarello-s 2 4 6 11 16 20
204-Diamond Retailer Summit edition with sketch-c 6 12 18 41 76 110
205-214: 205-Two covers by Jim Lee and Michael Turner. 208-JLA app. 211-Battles Wonder Woman 3.00
215-($2.99) Conclusion to Azzarello/Lee arc 4.00
216-218,220-226: 216-Captain Marvel app. 221-Bizarro & Zoom app. 226-Earth-2 Superman story; Chaykin,Sale, Benes, Ordway-a 3.00
219-Omac/Sacrifice pt. 1; JLA app. 4.00
219-2nd printing with red background variant-c 3.00
(Title continues numbering from Adventures of Superman #649)
650-(5/06) One Year Later; Clark powerless after Infinite Crisis 4.00

651-665,667-669,671-674.676-680: 652-Begin $2.99-c. 654-658,662-664,667-Pacheco-a. 665-Origin of Jimmy Olsen. 671-673-Insect Queen. 676-680-Ross-c 3.00
666, 670,675-($3.99) 666-Simonson-a. 670-The Third Kryptonian. 675-Ross-c 4.00
681-699: 681-683-New Krypton x-over; Ross-c. 685-Mon-El freed from Phantom Zone. 694-Mon-El new costume. 698,699-Last Stand of New Krypton x-over 3.00
700-(8/10, $4.99) Cover by Gary Frank; Robinson-s; Straczynski-s begin 5.00
700-Variant-c by Risso 8.00
701-714: 701-"Grounded" begins; Straczynski-s/Cassaday-c. 704,706-Wilson-s 3.00
701-DC 75th Variant-c by Cassaday (Superman #1 swipe) 8.00
#1,000,000 (11/98) 853rd Century x-over; Gene Ha-c 4.00
Annual 1,2: 1 (1987)-No Byrne-a. 2 (1988)-Byrne-a; Newsboy Legion; Guardian returns 5.00
Annual 3-6 ('91-'94 68 pgs.): 1-Armageddon 2001 x-over; Batman app.; Austin-c(i) & part inks. 4-Eclipso app. 6-Elseworlds sty 5.00
Annual 3-2nd & 3rd printings; 3rd has silver ink 5.00
Annual 7 (1995, $3.95, 69 pgs.)-Year One story 5.00
Annual 8 (1996, $2.95)-Legends of the Dead Earth story 5.00
Annual 9 (1997, $3.95)-Pulp Heroes story 5.00
Annual 10 (1998, $2.95)-Ghosts; Wrightson-c 5.00
Annual 11 (1999, $2.95)-JLApe; Art Adams-c 5.00
Annual 12 (2000, $3.50)-Planet DC 4.00
Annual 13 (1/08, $3.99) Finale of Camelot Falls 4.00
Annual 14 (10/09, $3.99) Origin of Mon-El re-told; Pina-a/Guedes-c 4.00
...: 80 Page Giant (2/99, $4.95) Jurgens-c 6.00
...: 80 Page Giant 1 (5/10, $5.99) Lopresti-c; short stories by various 6.00
...: 80 Page Giant 2 (6/99, $4.95) Harris-c 6.00
...: 80 Page Giant 3 (11/00, $5.95) Nowlan-c; art by various 6.00
...: 80 Page Giant 2011 (4/11, $5.99) Nguyen-c; art by various; Bizarros app. 6.00
Special 1 (1992, $3.50, 68 pgs.)-Simonson-c/a 6.00

SUPERMAN (DC New 52)
DC Comics: Nov, 2011 - No. 52, Jul, 2016 ($2.99/$3.99)

1-Pérez-s/c; Merino-a 2 4 6 11 16 20
1-Variant-c by Jim Lee 2 4 6 11 16 20
2-23: 3-6-Nicola Scott-a. 6-Supergirl app. 13-Clark quits job. 14-17-H'El on Earth x-over with Superboy & Supergirl. 17-H'El on Earth conclusion. 19,20-Orion app. 3.00
23.1, 23.2, 23.3, 23.4 (11/13, $2.99, regular covers) 3.00
23.1 (11/13, $3.99, 3-D cover) "Bizarro #1" on cover; Fisch-s/Kuder-c/Jeff Johnson-a 5.00
23.2 (11/13, $3.99, 3-D cover) "Brainiac #1" on cover; origin; Bedard-s/Alixe-a 5.00
23.3 (11/13, $3.99, 3-D cover) "H'El #1" on cover; Jor-El app.; Lobdell-s/Jurgens-a 5.00
23.4 (11/13, $3.99, 3-D cover) "Parasite #1" on cover; origin; Kuder-s/a 5.00
24-31: 25-Krypton Returns pt. 4. 26,27-Parasite app. 28,29-Starfire app. 3.00
32-($3.99) Romita Jr.-a/Johns-s begin; intro. Ulysses; wraparound-c by Romita Jr. 4.00
33-49: 33-39-Romita Jr.-a/Johns-s. 41-Yang-s begin. 45-48-Porter-a. 49-Vandal Savage 4.00
50-($4.99) Conclusion vs. Vandal Savage; Romita Jr. -c 5.00
51,52-Final Days of Superman x-over. 52-Superman dies; pre-Flashpoint Superman app. 4.00
#0-(11/12, $2.99) Jor-El & Lara flashback on Krypton; Rocafort-a/c 3.00
Annual 1 (10/12, $4.99) Alixe-a/Rocafort-c; Helspont app. 5.00
Annual 2 (9/13, $4.99) Jurgens-a/Andy Kubert-c; Brainiac app. 5.00
Annual 3 (2/16, $4.99) Origin/history of Vandal Savage; art by Sienkiewicz & others 5.00
... By Geoff Johns and John Romita Jr. Director's Cut 1 (11/14, $4.99) r/#32 B&W pencil art and full script 5.00
...: Futures End 1 (11/14, $2.99, regular-c) Five years later; Jurgens-s/Weeks-a 3.00
...: Futures End 1 (11/14, $3.99, 3-D cover) 4.00

SUPERMAN (DC Rebirth)
DC Comics: Aug, 2016 - No. 45, Jun, 2018 ($2.99)

1-24-Tomasi & Gleason-s. 2-The Eradicator returns. 8,9-Dinosaur Island. 10,11-Batman & Robin (Damian) app. 14-16-Multiplicity; alternate Earth Supermans & Capt. Carrot app. 18,19-Superman Reborn. 23,24-Manchester Black app. 3.00
25-($3.99) Manchester Black & Batman app.; Mahnke & Gleason-a 4.00
26-45: 29,30-Parallax & Sinestro app. 31,32-Deathstroke app. 38-Teen Titans app. 3.00
Annual 1 (1/17, $4.99) Swamp Thing app.; Tomasi & Gleason-s/Jimenez-a 5.00
...: Rebirth (8/16, $2.99) Pre-52 Superman and Lana Lang app.; Tomasi-s/Mahnke-a 3.00
... Special 1 (7/18, $4.99) Dinosaur Island; Capt. Storm app.; bonus short stories 5.00

SUPERMAN
DC Comics: Sept, 2018 - No. 32, Aug, 2021 ($3.99/$4.99)

1-17: 1-Bendis-s/Reis-a; Martian Manhunter app. 2-6,12-Rogol Zaar app. 7-Lobo app. 8-10-Crime Syndicate app. 14,15-Legion of Super-Heroes app. 4.00
13-($4.99) Variant "Year of the Villain" Lois Lane-c by Adam Hughes 5.00
18-24,26-28: 18-Superman reveals his Clark Kent ID to the world. 19-22-Mongul app. 22-24-Maguire-a. 23,24-Dr. Fate app. 4.00
25-($5.99) Intro. Synmar 6.00
29-32-($4.99) Tales of Metropolis back-up stories is all. 30-32-Godlewski-a 5.00

SUPERMAN
DC Comics: Apr, 2023 - Present ($4.99)

1-Williamson-s/Campbell-a; LexCorp becomes SuperCorp; Livewire app. 5.00

SUPERMAN (Hardcovers and Trade Paperbacks)
... and the Legion of Super-Heroes HC (2008, $24.99) r/Action Comics #858-863, covers and variants; intro. by Giffen; Gary Frank design sketch pages 25.00
... and the Legion of Super-Heroes SC (2009, $14.99) same contents as HC 15.00
...: Back in Action TPB (2007, $14.99) r/Action Comics #841-843 and DC Comics Presents #4,17,24; commentary by Busiek 15.00
.../Batman: Saga of the Super Sons TPB (2007, $19.99) r/Super Sons stories from '70s World's Finest #215,216,221,222,224,228,230,231,233,242,263 & Elseworlds 80-Page Giant 20.00
...: Brainiac HC (2009, $19.99, dustjacket) r/Action Comics #866-870 & Superman: New Krypton Special #1 20.00
...: Brainiac SC (2010, $12.99) r/Action #866-870 & Superman: New Krypton Spec. #1 13.00
...: Camelot Falls HC (2007, $19.99, dustjacket) r/Superman #654-658 20.00
...: Camelot Falls SC (2008, $12.99) r/Superman #654-658 13.00
...: Camelot Falls Vol. 2 HC (2008, $19.99, dj) r/Superman #662-664,667 & Ann. #13 20.00
...: Camelot Falls Vol. 2 The Weight of the World SC (2008, $12.99) r/Superman #662-664,667 & Ann. #13 13.00
...: Chronicles Vol. 1 ('06, $14.99, TPB) r/early Superman app. in Action Comics #1-13, New York World's Fair 1939 and Superman #1 15.00
...: Chronicles Vol. 2 ('07, $14.99, TPB) r/early Superman app. in Action Comics #14-20 and Superman #2,3 15.00
...: Chronicles Vol. 3 ('07, $14.99, TPB) r/early Superman app. in Action Comics #21-25, Superman #3,4 and New York World's Fair 1940 15.00
...: Chronicles Vol. 4 ('08, $14.99, TPB) r/early Superman app. in Action Comics #26-31, Superman #6,7 15.00
...: Chronicles Vol. 5 ('08, $14.99, TPB) r/early Superman app. in Action Comics #32-36, Superman #8,9 and World's Best Comics #1 15.00
...: Chronicles Vol. 6 ('09, $14.99, TPB) r/early Superman app. in Action Comics #37-40, Superman #10,11 and World's Finest Comics #2,3 15.00
...: Chronicles Vol. 7 ('09, $14.99, TPB) r/early Superman app. in Action Comics #41-43, Superman #12,13 and World's Finest Comics #4 15.00
...: Chronicles Vol. 8 ('10, $14.99, TPB) r/early Superman app. in Action Comics #44-47, and Superman #14,15 15.00
...: Chronicles Vol. 9 ('11, $17.99, TPB) r/early Superman app. in Action Comics #48-52, and Superman #16,17 and World's Finest Comics #6 18.00
...: Codename: Patriot HC ('10, $24.99, d.j.) r/partial New Krypton storyline 25.00
...: Codename: Patriot SC ('11, $14.99) r/partial New Krypton storyline 15.00
...: Critical Condition ('03, $14.95, TPB) r/2000 Kryptonite poisoning storyline 15.00
.../ Doomsday: The Collection Edition (2006, $19.99) r/Superman/Doomsday: Hunter/Prey #1-3, Doomsday Ann. #1, Superman: The Doomsday Wars #1-3, Advs. of Superman #594 and Superman #175; intro. by Dan Jurgens 20.00
...: Daily Planet (2006, $19.99, TPB)-Reprints stories of Daily Planet staff 20.00
... Earth One HC (2010, $19.99)-Updated re-imagining of Superman's debut in Metropolis; Straczynski-s/Shane Davis-a; sketch pages by Davis 20.00
... Earth One Volume Two HC (2012, $22.99)-Straczynski-s/Davis-a; sketch pages 23.00
... Earth One Volume Three HC (2014, $22.99)-Straczynski-s/Syaf-a; sketch pages 23.00
...: Emperor Joker TPB (2007, $14.99) reprints 2000 x-over from Superman titles 15.00
...: Endgame (2000, $14.95, TPB)-Reprints Y2K and Brainiac story line 15.00
...: Ending Battle (2009, $14.99, TPB) r/crossover of Superman titles from 2002 15.00
...: Eradication! The Origin of the Eradicator (1996, $12.95, TPB) 13.00
...: Escape From Bizarro World HC (2008, $24.99, dustjacket) r/Action #855-857; early apps. in Superman #140, DC Comics Presents #71 and Man of Steel #5; Vaughan intro. 25.00
...: Escape From Bizarro World SC (2009, $14.99) same contents as hardcover 15.00
...: Exile (1998, $14.95, TPB)-Reprints space exile following execution of Kryptonian criminals; 1st Eradicator 15.00
...: For Tomorrow Volume 1 HC (2005, $24.99, dustjacket) r/#204-209; intro by Azzarello; new cover and sketch section by Lee 25.00
...: For Tomorrow Volume 1 SC (2005, $14.99) r/#204-209; foil-stamped S emblem-c 15.00
...: For Tomorrow Volume 2 HC (2005, $24.99, dustjacket) r/#210-215; afterword and sketch section by Lee; new Lee-c with foil-stamped S emblem 25.00
...: For Tomorrow Volume 2 SC (2005, $14.99) r/#210-215; foil-stamped S emblem-c 15.00
...: Godfall HC (2004, $19.95, dustjacket) r/Action #812-813, Advs. of Superman #625-626, Superman #202-203; Caldwell sketch pages; Turner cover gallery; new Turner-c 20.00
...: Godfall SC (2004, $9.99) r/Action #812-813, Advs. of Superman #625-626, Superman #202-203; Caldwell sketch pages; Turner cover gallery; new Turner-c 10.00
...: Infinite Crisis TPB (2006, $12.99) r/Infinite Crisis #5, I.C. Secret Files and Origins 2006, Action Comics #836, Superman #226 and Advs. of Superman #649 13.00
... In the Forties ('05, $19.99, TPB) Intro. by Bob Hughes 20.00
... In the Fifties ('02, $19.95, TPB) Intro. by Mark Waid 20.00
... In the Sixties ('01, $19.95, TPB) Intro. by Mark Waid 20.00
... In the Seventies ('00, $19.95, TPB) Intro. by Christopher Reeve 20.00
... In the Eighties ('06, $19.99, TPB) Intro. by Jerry Ordway 20.00
... In the Name of Gog ('05, $17.99, TPB) r/Action Comics #820-825 18.00
... Kryptonite HC ('08, $24.99) r/Superman Confidential #1-5,11; Darwyn Cooke intro. 25.00
...: Last Son HC (2008, $19.99) r/Action Comics #844-846,851 and Annual #11; sketch pages and variant covers; Marc McClure intro. 20.00
... Mon-El HC ('10, $24.99) r/Superman #684-690, Action #874 & Annual #1, Superman: Secret Files 2009 #1 25.00
... Mon-El SC ('11, $17.99) r/Superman #684-690, Action #874 & Annual #1, Superman: Secret Files 2009 #1 18.00
... Mon-El - Man of Valor HC ('10, $24.99) r/Superman #692-697 & Annual #14, Adventure #11, Superman: Secret Files 2009 #1 25.00
... : New Krypton Vol. 1 HC ('09, $24.99, d.j.) r/Superman #681, Action #871 & one-shots 25.00
... : New Krypton Vol. 1 SC ('10, $17.99) r/Superman #681, Action #871 & one-shots 18.00
... : New Krypton Vol. 2 HC ('09, $24.99, d.j.) r/Superman #682,683, Action #872,873 & Supergirl #35,36; gallery of covers and variants 25.00
... : New Krypton Vol. 2 SC ('10, $17.99) same contents as HC 18.00
... : New Krypton Vol. 3 HC ('10, $24.99, d.j.) r/Superman: World of New Krypton #1-5 & Action Comics Annual #10; gallery of covers and variants 25.00
... : New Krypton Vol. 3 SC ('11, $17.99) same contents as HC 18.00
... : New Krypton Vol. 4 HC ('10, $24.99, d.j.) r/Superman: World of New Krypton #6-12; gallery of covers and variants; sketch and design art 25.00
... : New Krypton Vol. 4 SC ('11, $17.99) same contents as HC 18.00
... : Nightwing and Flamebird HC ('10, $24.99, d.j.) r/Action #875-879 & Annual #12 25.00
... : Nightwing and Flamebird SC ('10, $17.99) r/Action #875-879 & Annual #12 18.00
... : Nightwing and Flamebird Vol. 2 HC ('10, $24.99, d.j.) r/Action #883-889, Superman #696 & Adventure Comics #8-10 25.00
... No Limits ('00, $14.95, TPB) Reprints early 2000 stories 15.00
...: Our Worlds at War Book 1 ('02, $19.95, TPB) r/1st half of x-over 20.00
...: Our Worlds at War Book 2 ('02, $19.95, TPB) r/2nd half of x-over 20.00
...: Our Worlds at War - The Complete Collection ('06, $24.99, TPB) r/entire x-over 25.00
...: Past and Future (2008, $19.99, TPB) r/time travel stories 1947-1983 20.00
...: President Lex TPB (2003, $17.95) r/Luthor's run for the White House; Harris-c 18.00
...: Redemption TPB (2007, $12.99) r/Superman #659,666 & Action Comics #848,849 13.00
...: Return to Krypton (2004, $17.95, TPB) r/2001-2002 x-over 18.00
...: Sacrifice (2005, $14.99, TPB) prelude x-over to Infinite Crisis; r/Superman #218-220, Advs. of Superman #642,643; Action #829, Wonder Woman #219,220 15.00
...: Shadows Linger (2008, $14.99, TPB) r/Superman #671-675 15.00
... : Strange Attractors (2006, $14.99, TPB) r/Action Comics #827,828,830-835 15.00
... : Tales From the Phantom Zone ('09, $19.99, TPB) r/Phantom Zone stories 1961-68 20.00
...: That Healing Touch TPB (2005, $14.99) r/Advs. of Superman #633-638 & Superman Secret Files 2004 15.00
...: The Adventures of Nightwing and Flamebird TPB (2009, $19.99)-reprints appearances in Superman Family #173,183-194 20.00
...: The Black Ring Volume One HC (2011, $19.99, d.j.) r/Action Comics #890-895 20.00
The Bottle City of Kandor TPB (2007, $14.99)-Reprints 1st app. in Action #242 and other stories; Nightwing and Flamebird app. 15.00
The Coming of Atlas HC (2009, $19.99, dustjacket)-r/Superman #677-680 & Atlas' debut from

Superman (2018) #13 © DC

Superman Earth One HC © DC

Superman Adventures #18 © DC

	GD	VG	FN	VF	VF/NM	NM-
	2.0	4.0	6.0	8.0	9.0	9.2

First Issue Special #1 (1975); intro by James Robinson 20.00
The Coming of Atlas SC (2010, $14.99) same contents as HC 15.00
The Death of Clark Kent (1997, $19.95, TPB)-Reprints Man of Steel #43 (1 page), Superman #99 (1 page),#100-102, Action #709 (1 page), #710,711, Advs. of Superman #523-525, Superman:The Man of Tomorrow #1 20.00
The Death of Superman (1993, $4.95, TPB)-Reprints Man of Steel #17-19, Superman #73-75, Advs. of Superman #496,497, Action #683,684, & Justice League #69 2 4 6 9 12 15
The Death of Superman, 2nd & 3rd printings 1 3 4 6 8 10
The Death of Superman Platinum Edition 3 6 9 14 20 25
...: The Greatest Stories Ever Told ('04, $19.95, TPB) Ross-c, Uslan intro. 20.00
...: The Greatest Stories Ever Told Vol. 2 ('06, $19.99, TPB) Ross-c, Greenberger intro. 20.00
...: The Journey ('06, $14.99, TPB) r/Action Comics #831 & Superman #217,221-225 15.00
...: The Man of Steel Vol. 2 ('03, $19.95, TPB) r/Superman #1-3, Action #584-586, Advs. of Superman #424-426 & Who's Who Update '87 20.00
...: The Man of Steel Vol. 3 ('04, $19.95, TPB) r/Superman #4-6, Action #587-589, Advs. of Superman #427-429; intro. by Ordway; new Ordway-c 20.00
...: The Man of Steel Vol. 4 ('05, $19.99, TPB) r/Superman #7,8; Action #590,591; Advs. of Superman #430,431; Legion of Super-Heroes #37,38; new Ordway-c 20.00
...: The Man of Steel Vol. 5 ('06, $19.99, TPB) r/Superman #9-11, Action #592-593, Advs. of Superman #432-435; intro. by Mike Carlin; new Ordway-c 20.00
...: The Man of Steel Vol. 6 ('08, $19.99, TPB) r/Superman #12 & Ann. #1, Action #594-595 & Ann. #1, Advs. of Superman Ann.#1; Booster Gold #23; new Ordway-c 20.00
The Third Kryptonian ('08, $14.99, TPB) r/Action #847, Superman #668-670 & Ann. #13 15.00
The Trial of Superman ('97, $14.95, TPB) reprints story arc 15.00
The World of Krypton ('08, $14.99, TPB) r/World of Krypton Vol. 2 #1-4 and various tales of Krypton and its history; Kupperberg intro. 15.00
The Wrath of Gog ('05, $14.99, TPB) reprints Action Comics #812-819 15.00
...: They Saved Luthor's Brain ('00, $14.95) r/ "death" and return of Luthor 15.00
...: 3-2-1 Action! ('08, $14.99) Jimmy Olsen super-powered stories; Steve Rude-c 15.00
...: 'Til Death Do Us Part ('01, $17.95) reprints; Mahnke-c 18.00
...: Time and Time Again (1994, $7.50, TPB)-Reprints 10.00
...: Transformed ('98, $12.95, TPB) r/post Final Night powerless Superman to Electric Superman 13.00
...: Unconventional Warfare (2005, $14.95, TPB) r/Adventures of Superman #625-632 and pages from Superman Secret Files 2004 15.00
...: Up, Up and Away! (2006, $14.99, TPB) r/Superman #650-653 and Action #837-840 15.00
... Vs. Brainiac (2008, $19.99, TPB) reprints 1st meeting in Action #242 and other duels 20.00
... Vs. Lex Luthor (2006, $19.99, TPB) reprints 1st meeting in Action #23 and 11 other classic duels 1940-2001 20.00
... Vs. The Flash (2005, $19.99, TPB) reprints their races from Superman #199, Flash #175, World's Finest #198, DC Comics Presents #1&2, Advs. of Superman #463 & DC First: Flash/Superman; new Alex Ross-c 20.00
... Vs. The Revenge Squad (1999, $12.95, TPB) 13.00
...: Whatever Happened to the Man of Tomorrow? TPB (1/97, $5.99) r/Superman #423 & Action Comics #583, intro. by Paul Kupperberg 8.00
...: Whatever Happened to the Man of Tomorrow? Deluxe Edition HC (2009, $24.99, d.j.) r/Superman #423, Action #583, DC Comics Presents #85, Superman Ann #11 25.00
...: Whatever Happened to the Man of Tomorrow? SC (2010, $14.99) r/same as HC 15.00

NOTE: ***Austin*** *a(i)-1-3.* ***Byrne*** *a-1-16p, 17, 19-21p, 22; c-1-17, 20-22; scripts-1-22.* ***Guice*** *c/a-64.* ***Kirby*** *c-37p.* ***Joe Quesada*** *c-Annual 4.* ***Russell*** *c/a-23i.* ***Simonson*** *c-69i. #19-21 2nd printings sold in multi-packs.*

SUPERMAN (one-shots)
Daily News Magazine Presents DC Comics' Superman nn-(1987, 8 pgs.)-Supplement to New York Daily News; Perez-c/a 5.00
...: A Nation Divided (1999, $4.95)-Elseworlds Civil War story 5.00
... & Robin Special (2022, $5.99) Jon Kent & Damian Wayne; Bogdanovic-a 6.00
... & Savage Dragon: Chicago (2002, $5.95) Larsen-a; Ross-c 6.00
... & Savage Dragon: Metropolis (11/99, $4.95) Bogdanove-a 5.00
...: At Earth's End (1995, $4.95)-Elseworlds story 5.00
...Beyond #0 (10/11, $3.99) The Batman Beyond future; Frenz-a/Nguyen-c 4.00
...: Blood of My Ancestors (2003, $6.95)-Gil Kane & John Buscema-a 7.00
...: Distant Fires (1998, $5.95)-Elseworlds; Chaykin-s 6.00
...: Emperor Joker (10/00, $3.50)-Follows Action #769 4.00
... : Endless Winter Special 1 (2/21, $3.99) Part 3 of crossover event; Hester-a 5.00
...: End of the Century (2/00, $24.95, HC)-Immonen-s/a 25.00
...: End of the Century (2003, $17.95, SC)-Immonen-s/a 18.00
... For Earth (1991, $4.95, 52 pgs, printed on recycled paper)-Ordway wraparound-c 6.00
...IV Movie Special (1987, $2.00)-Movie adaptation; Heck-a 4.00
...Gallery, The 1 (1993, $2.95)-Poster-a 3.00
...: Heroes 1 (4/20, $5.99) Aftermath of revealing Clark Kent ID to world; art by various 6.00
..., Inc. (1999, $6.95)-Elseworlds Clark as a sports hero; Garcia-Lopez-a 7.00
...: Infinite City HC (2005, $24.99, dustjacket) Mike Kennedy-s/Carlos Meglia-a 25.00
...: Infinite City SC (2006, $17.99) Mike Kennedy-s/Carlos Meglia-a 18.00
...: Kal (1995, $5.95)-Elseworlds story 6.00
...: Kal-El Returns Special 1 (1/23, $5.99) Short stories from after Superman's return from Warworld; s/a by Waid, Grace, Wolfman, Segura, Henry, Haspiel, Herbert & others 6.00
...: Leviathan Rising Special 1 (7/19, $9.99) Leads into Event Leviathan series 10.00
...: Lex 2000 (1/01, $3.50) Election night for the Luthor Presidency 4.00
...: Lois Lane 1 (4/14, $4.99) Marguerite Bennett-s; Rocafort-c 5.00
...: Monster (1999, $5.95)-Elseworlds story; Anthony Williams-a 6.00
... Movie Special-(9/83)-Adaptation of Superman III; other versions exist with store logos on bottom 1/3 of-c 4.00
...: New Krypton Special 1 (12/08, $3.99) Funeral of Pa Kent; newly enlarged Kandor 4.00
...: Our Worlds at War Secret Files 1-(8/01, $5.95)-Stories & profile pages 6.00
... Plus 1(2/97, $2.95)-Legion of Super-Heroes-c/app. 4.00
...'s Metropolis-(1996, $5.95, prestige format)-Elseworlds; McKeever-c/a 6.00
...: Speeding Bullets-(1993, $4.95, 52 pgs.)-Elseworlds 6.00
.../Spider-Man-(1995, $3.95)-r/DC and Marvel Presents... 4.00
... 10-Cent Adventure 1 (3/02, 10¢) McDaniel-a; intro. Cir-El Supergirl 3.00
...: The Earth Stealers 1-(1988, $2.95, 52 pgs, prestige format) Byrne script; painted-c 6.00
...: The Earth Stealers 1-2nd printing 4.00
...: The Legacy of Superman #1 (3/93, $2.50, 68 pgs.)-Art Adams-c; Simonson-a 6.00
...: The Last God of Krypton ('99,$4.95) Hildebrandt Bros.-a/Simonson-s 5.00
...: The Last Son of Krypton FCBD Special Edition (7/13) r/Action #844; Jim Lee-c 3.00
...: The Odyssey ('99, $4.95) Clark Kent's post-Smallville journey 5.00
...: 3-D (12/98, $3.95)-with glasses 4.00
.../Thundercats (1/04, $5.95) Winick-s/Garza-a; two covers by Garza & McGuinness 6.00
.../Through the Ages (2006, $3.99) r/Action #1, Superman ('87) #7; origins and pin-ups 4.00
.../Top Cat Special 1 (12/18, $4.99) Amazo app.; Shane Davis-a; Secret Squirrel back-up 5.00
.../Toyman-(1996, $1.95) 3.00
...: True Brit (2004, $24.95, HC w/dust jacket) Elseworlds; Kal-El's rocket lands in England; co-written by John Cleese and Kim Howard Johnson; John Byrne-a 25.00
...: True Brit (2005, $17.99, TPB) Elseworlds; Kal-El's rocket lands in England 18.00
...: Under A Yellow Sun (1994, $5.95, 68 pgs.)-A Novel by Clark Kent; embossed-c 6.00
... Vs. Darkseid: Apokolips Now! 1 (3/03, $2.95) McKone-a; Kara (Supergirl #75) app. 4.00
...: Villains 1 (5/20, $5.99) Aftermath of revealing Clark Kent ID to world; art by various 6.00
...: War of the Worlds (1999, $5.95)-Battles Martians 6.00
...: Warworld Apocalypse 1 (10/22, $6.99) Conclusion of Warworld Saga 7.00
...: Where is thy Sting? (2001, $6.95)-McCormack-Sharp-c/a 7.00
...: Y2K (2/00, $4.95)-1st Brainiac 13 app.; Guice-c/a 5.00

SUPERMAN ADVENTURES, THE (Based on animated series)
DC Comics: Oct, 1996 - No. 66, Apr, 2002 ($1.75/$1.95/$1.99)
1-Rick Burchett-c/a begins; Paul Dini script; Lex Luthor app.; 1st app. Mercy Graves in comics; silver ink, wraparound-c 5.00
2-20,22: 2-McCloud scripts begin; Metallo-c/app. 3-Brainiac-c/app. 5-1st app. Livewire in comics. 6-Mxyzptlk-c/app. 3.00
21-($3.95) 1st animated Supergirl 5.00
23-66: 23-Begin $1.99-c; Livewire app. 25-Batgirl-c/app. 28-Manley-a. 54-Retells Superman #233 "Kryptonite Nevermore" 58-Ross-c 3.00
Annual 1 (1997, $3.95)-Zatanna and Bruce Wayne app. 4.00
Special 1 (2/98, $2.95) Superman vs. Lobo 4.00
TPB (1998, $7.95) r/#1-6 8.00
... Vol 1: Up, Up and Away (2004, $6.95, digest) r/#16,19,22-24; Amancio-a 7.00
... Vol 2: The Never-Ending Battle (2004, $6.95) r/#25-29 7.00
... Vol 3: Last Son of Krypton (2006, $6.99) r/#30-34 7.00
... Vol 4: The Man of Steel (2006, $6.99) r/#35-39 7.00

SUPERMAN ALIENS 2: GOD WAR (Also see Superman Vs. Aliens)
DC Comics/Dark Horse Comics: May, 2002 - No. 4, Nov, 2002 ($2.99, limited series)
1-4-Bogdanove & Nowlan-a; Darkseid & New Gods app. 3.00
TPB (6/03, $12.95) r/#1-4 13.00

SUPERMAN: AMERICAN ALIEN
DC Comics: Jan, 2016 - No. 7, Jul, 2016 ($3.99, limited series)
1-7-Flashbacks to Clark Kent's upbringing; Max Landis-s in all. 1-Dragotta-a. 4-Jae Lee-a; Batman app. 7-Lobo app.; Jock-a 4.00

SUPERMAN & BATMAN: GENERATIONS (Elseworlds)
DC Comics: 1999 - No. 4, 1999 ($4.95, limited series)
1-4-Superman & Batman team-up from 1939 to the future; Byrne-c/s/a 5.00
TPB (2000, $14.95) r/series 15.00

SUPERMAN & BATMAN: GENERATIONS II (Elseworlds)
DC Comics: 2001 - No. 4, 2001 ($5.95, limited series)
1-4-Superman, Batman & others team-up from 1942-future; Byrne-c/s/a 6.00
TPB (2003, $19.95) r/series 20.00

SUPERMAN & BATMAN: GENERATIONS III (Elseworlds)
DC Comics: Mar, 2003 - No. 12, Feb, 2004 ($2.95, limited series)
1-12-Superman & Batman through the centuries; Byrne-c/s/a 3.00

SUPERMAN AND BATMAN VS. ALIENS AND PREDATOR

DC Comics: 2007 - No. 2, 2007 ($5.99, squarebound, limited series)

1,2-Schultz-s/Olivetti-a 1 3 4 6 8 10
TPB (2007, $12.99) r/#1,2; pencil breakdown pages 13.00

SUPERMAN AND BATMAN VS. VAMPIRES AND WEREWOLVES
DC Comics: Early Dec, 2008 - No. 6, Late Feb, 2009 ($2.99, limited series)

1-6-Van Hook-s/Mandrake-a/c. 1-Wonder Woman app. 5-Demon-c/app. 3.00
TPB (2009, $14.99) r/#1-6; intro. by John Landis 15.00

SUPERMAN & BATMAN: WORLD'S FUNNEST (Elseworlds)
DC Comics: 2000 ($6.95, square-bound, one-shot)

nn-Mr. Mxyzptlk and Bat-Mite destroy each DC Universe; Dorkin-s; art by various incl. Ross, Timm, Miller, Allred, Moldoff, Gibbons, Cho, Jimenez 7.00

SUPERMAN & BUGS BUNNY
DC Comics: Jul, 2000 - No. 4, Oct, 2000 ($2.50, limited series)

1-4-JLA & Looney Tunes characters meet 5.00

SUPERMAN/BATMAN
DC Comics: Oct, 2003 - No. 87, Oct, 2011 ($2.95/$2.99)

1-Two covers (Superman or Batman in foreground) Loeb-s/McGuinness-a; Metallo app.
1 2 3 6 8 10
1-2nd printing (Batman cover) 3.00
1-3rd printing; new McGuinness cover 3.00
1-Diamond/Alliance Retailer Summit Edition-variant 7 14 21 46 86 125
1-(6/06, Free Comic Book Day giveaway) reprints #1 3.00
2-6: 2,5-Future Superman app. 6-Luthor in battlesuit 3.00
7-Pat Lee-c/a; Superboy & Robin app. 3.00
8-Michael Turner-c/a; intro. new Kara Zor-El 5.00
8-Second printing with sketch cover 3.00
8-Third printing with new Turner cover 3.00
9-13-Michael Turner-c/a; Wonder Woman app. 10,13-Variant-c by Jim Lee 3.00
14-25: 14-18-Pacheco-a; Lightning Lord, Saturn Queen & Cosmic King app. 19-Supergirl app.; leads into Supergirl #1. 21-25-Bizarro app. 25-Superman & Batman covers; 2nd printing with white bkgrd cover 3.00
26-($3.99) Sam Loeb tribute issue; 2 covers by Turner; story & art by 26 various; back-up by Loeb & Sale 5.00
27-49: 27-Flashback to Earth-2 Power Girl & Huntress; Maguire-a. 34-36-Metal Men app. 3.00
50-($3.99) Thomas Wayne meets Jor-El; Justice League app. 4.00
51-74: 51,52-Mr. Mxyzptlk app. 66,67-Blackest Night; Man-Bat and Bizarro app. 3.00
75-($4.99) Quitely-c; Legion of Super-Heroes app.; Ordway-a; 2-pg. features by various 5.00
76-87: 76-Aftermath of Batman's "death". 77-Supergirl/Damian team-up 3.00
Annual #1 (12/06, $3.99) Re-imaging of 1st meeting from World's Finest #71 4.00
Annual #2 (5/08, $3.99) Kolins-a; re-imaging of Superman as Supernova story 4.00
Annual #3 (3/09, $3.99) Composite Superman-c by Wrightson; Batista-a 4.00
Annual #4 (8/10, $4.99) Batman Beyond; Levitz-s/Guedes-a/Lau-c 8.00
Annual #5 (6/11, $4.99) Reign of Doomsday x-over, Cyborg Superman app.; Sepulveda-a 5.00
...Absolute Power HC (2005, $19.99) r/#14-18 20.00
...Absolute Power SC (2006, $12.99) r/#14-18 13.00
..."Batman V Superman: Dawn of Justice Day" Special Edition 1 (4/16, free) r/#1 3.00
...Big Noise SC (2010, $14.99) r/#64,68-71 15.00
...Enemies Among Us SC (2009, $12.99) r/#28-33 13.00
...Finest Worlds SC (2010, $14.99) r/#50-56 15.00
...Night and Day HC (2010, $19.99) r/#60-63,65-67 20.00
...Public Enemies HC (2004, $19.95) r/#1-6 & Secret Files 2003; sketch art pages 20.00
...Public Enemies SC (2005, $12.99) r/#1-6 & Secret Files 2003; sketch art pages 15.00
...Public Enemies SC (2009, $14.99) r/#1-6 & Secret Files 2003; sketch art pages 15.00
...Secret Files 2003 (11/03, $4.95) Reis-a; pin-ups by various; Loeb/Sale short-s 5.00
... : Supergirl HC (2004, $19.95) r/#8-13; intro by Loeb, cover gallery, sketch pages 20.00
... : Supergirl SC (2005, $12.99) r/#8-13; intro by Loeb, cover gallery, sketch pages 13.00
... : The Search For Kryptonite HC (2008, $19.99) r/#44-49; Davis sketch pages 20.00
... : The Search For Kryptonite SC (2009, $12.99) r/#44-49; Davis sketch pages 13.00
... : Torment HC (2008, $19.99) r/#37-42; cover gallery, Nguyen sketch pages 20.00
... : Vengeance HC (2006, $19.99) r/#20-25; sketch pages 20.00
... : Vengeance SC (2008, $12.99) r/#20-25; sketch pages 13.00
... : Worship SC (2011, $17.99) r/#72-75 & Annual #4 18.00

SUPERMAN/BATMAN: ALTERNATE HISTORIES
DC Comics: 1996 ($14.95, trade paperback)

nn-Reprints Detective Comics Annual #7, Action Comics Annual #6, Steel Annual #1, Legends of the Dark Knight Annual #4 15.00

SUPERMAN: BIRTHRIGHT
DC Comics: Sept, 2003 - No. 12, Sept, 2004 ($2.95, limited series)

1-12-Waid-s/Leinil Yu-a; retelling of origin and early Superman years 3.00
HC (2004, $29.95, dustjacket) r/series; cover gallery; Waid proposal with Yu concept art 30.00
SC (2005, $19.99) r/series; cover gallery; Waid proposal with Yu concept art 20.00

SUPERMAN COMICS
DC Comics: 1939

nn - Ashcan comic, not distributed to newsstands, only for in-house use. Cover art is Action Comics #7 with interior being Action Comics #8. A CGC certified 9.0 copy sold for $90,000 in 2007 and for $83,000 in Sept. 2018. A CGC 8.5 sold for $288,000 in Apr. 2022.

SUPERMAN CONFIDENTIAL (See Superman Hardcovers and TPBs listings for reprint)
DC Comics: Jan, 2007 - No. 14, Jun, 2008 ($2.99)

1-14: 1-5,9-Darwyn Cooke-s/Tim Sale-a/c; origin of Kryptonite re-told. 8-10-New Gods and Darkside app. 3.00
...: Kryptonite TPB (2009, $14.99) r/#1-5,11; intro. by Darwyn Cooke; Tim Sale sketch-a 15.00

SUPERMAN: DAY OF DOOM
DC Comics: Jan, 2003 - No. 4, Feb, 2003 ($2.95, weekly limited series)

1-4-Jurgens-s/Jurgens & Sienkiewicz-a 3.00
TPB (2003, $9.95) r/#1-4 10.00

SUPERMAN DOOMED (DC New 52) (See Action Comics #31-34 and Superman/Wonder Woman)
DC Comics: Jul, 2014 - No. 2, Nov, 2014 ($4.99, bookends for crossover)

1,2: 1-Lashley-a; Wonder Woman & Steel app. 2-Superman vs. Brainiac 6.00

SUPERMAN/DOOMSDAY: HUNTER/PREY
DC Comics: 1994 - No. 3, 1994 ($4.95, limited series, 52 pgs.)

1-3 6.00

SUPERMAN FAMILY, THE (Formerly Superman's Pal Jimmy Olsen)
National Per. Publ./DC Comics: No. 164, Apr-May, 1974 - No. 222, Sept, 1982

164-(100 pgs.) Jimmy Olsen, Supergirl, Lois Lane begin
4 8 12 28 47 65
165-169 (100 pgs.) 3 6 9 18 28 38
170-176 (68 pgs.) 3 6 9 14 19 24
177-190 (52 pgs.): 177-181-52 pgs. 182-Marshall Rogers-a; $1.00 issues begin; Krypto begins, ends #192. 183-Nightwing-Flamebird begins, ends #194. 189-Brainiac 5, Mon -El app. 2 4 6 9 13 16
191-193,195-199: 191-Superboy begins, ends #198 2 3 4 6 8 10
194,200: 194-Rogers-a. 200-Book length sty 2 4 6 8 10 12
201-210,212-222 1 2 3 5 6 8
211-Earth II Batman & Catwoman marry 2 4 6 8 11 14

*NOTE: **N. Adams** c-182-185. **Anderson** a-186i. **Buckler** c(p)-190, 191, 209, 210, 215, 217, 220. **Jones** a-191-193. **Gil Kane** c(p)-221, 222. **Mortimer** a(p)-191-193, 199, 201-222. **Orlando** a(i)-186, 187. **Rogers** a-182, 194. **Staton** a-191-194, 196p. **Tuska** a(p)-203, 207-209.*

SUPERMAN FAMILY ADVENTURES
DC Comics: Jul, 2012 - No. 12, Jun, 2013 ($2.99)

1-12-Young-reader stories, games and DC Nation character profiles; Baltazar-a 3.00

SUPERMAN/FANTASTIC FOUR
DC Comics/Marvel Comics: 1999 ($9.95, tabloid size, one-shot)

1-Battle Galactus and the Cyborg Superman; wraparound-c by Alex Ross and Dan Jurgens; Jurgens-s/a; Thibert-a 10.00

SUPERMAN FOR ALL SEASONS
DC Comics: 1998 - No, 4, 1998 ($4.95, limited series, prestige format)

1-Loeb-s/Sale-a/c; Superman's first year in Metropolis 6.00
2-4 5.00
Hardcover (1999, $24.95) r/#1-4 25.00

SUPERMAN FOR EARTH (See Superman one-shots)

SUPERMAN FOREVER
DC Comics: Jun, 1998 ($5.95, one-shot)

1-($5.95)-Collector's Edition with a 7-image lenticular-c by Alex Ross; Superman returns to normal; s/a by various 1 3 4 6 8 10
1-($4.95) Standard Edition with single image Ross-c 5.00

SUPERMAN/GEN13
DC Comics (WildStorm): Jun, 2000 - No. 3, Aug, 2000 ($2.50, limited series)

1-3-Hughes-s/ Bermejo-a; Campbell variant-c for each 3.00
TPB (2001, $9.95) new Bermejo-c; cover gallery 10.00

SUPERMAN GIANT (See reprint of new stories in Superman: Up In The Sky)
DC Comics: 2018 - No. 16, 2019 ($4.99, 100 pgs., squarebound, Walmart exclusive)

1-New story Palmiotti-s/Derenick-a; reprints from Superman/Batman, Green Lantern ('05), and The Terrifics in all 8.00
2-6,8-16: 2-Palmiotti-s/Derenick-a. 3-Tom King-s/Andy Kubert-a begins plus reprints 5.00
7-Many deaths of Lois Lane 10.00

SUPERMAN GIANT
DC Comics: Dec, 2019 - No. 3, 2020 ($4.99, 100 pgs., squarebound, Mass Market & Direct Market editions exist for each issue, with different covers)

1-3: 1-New story w/Parasite; plus reprints. 2,3-New story w/Pelletier-a 5.00

SUPERMAN: KING OF THE WORLD
DC Comics: June, 1999 ($3.95/$4.95, one-shot)

1-($3.95) Regular Ed. 4.00
1-($4.95) Collectors' Ed. with gold foil enhanced-c 5.00

SUPERMAN: LAST SON OF EARTH
DC Comics: 2000 - No. 2, 2000 ($5.95, limited series, prestige format)

1,2-Elseworlds; baby Clark rockets to Krypton; Gerber-s/Wheatley-a 6.00

SUPERMAN: LAST STAND OF NEW KRYPTON
DC Comics: May, 2010 - No. 3, Late June, 2010 ($3.99, limited series)

1-3-Robinson & Gates-s/Woods-a. 2-Pérez-c. 3-Sook-c 4.00
HC (2010, $24.99, DJ) r/#1,2, Adventure Comics #8,9, Supergirl #51 & Superman #698 25.00
Vol. 2 HC (2010, $19.99, DJ) r/#3, Adventure #10,11, Supergirl #52 & Superman #699 20.00

SUPERMAN: LAST STAND ON KRYPTON
DC Comics: 2003 ($6.95, one-shot, prestige format)

1-Sequel to Superman: Last Son of Earth; Gerber-s/Wheatley-a 7.00

SUPERMAN: LOIS & CLARK (See Convergence Superman #1 & 2)
DC Comics: Dec, 2015 - No. 8, Jul, 2016 ($3.99)

1-8: 1-Pre-Flashpoint Superman & Lois on New 52 Earth; Jurgens-s/Weeks-a 4.00

SUPERMAN: LOIS LANE (Girlfrenzy)
DC Comics: Jun, 1998 ($1.95, one shot)

1-Connor & Palmiotti-a 4.00

SUPERMAN: LOST
DC Comics: May, 2023 - No. 10 ($4.99, limited series)

1-Priest-s/Pagulayan-a; Justice League app. 5.00

SUPERMAN/MADMAN HULLABALOO!
Dark Horse Comics: June, 1997 - No. 3, Aug, 1997 ($2.95, limited series)

1-3-Mike Allred-c/s/a 4.00
TPB (1997, $8.95) 9.00

SUPERMAN: METROPOLIS
DC Comics: Apr, 2003 - No. 12, Mar, 2004 ($2.95, limited series)

1-12-Focus on Jimmy Olsen; Austen-s. 1-6-Zezelj-a. 7-12-Kristiansen-a. 8,9-Creeper app. 3.00

SUPERMAN METROPOLIS SECRET FILES
DC Comics: Jun, 2000 ($4.95, one shot)

1-Short stories, pin-ups and profile pages; Hitch and Neary-c 5.00

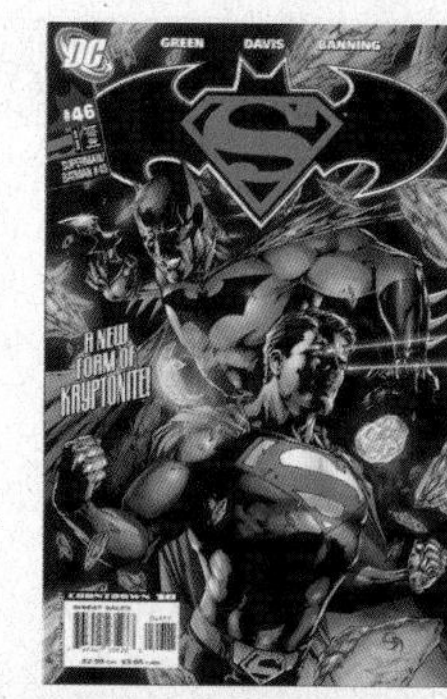

Superman / Batman #46 © DC

Superman: Son of Kal-El #1 © DC

Superman: Space Age #1 © DC

GD VG FN VF VF/NM NM-
2.0 4.0 6.0 8.0 9.0 9.2

SUPERMAN: PEACE ON EARTH
DC Comics: Jan, 1999 ($9.95, Treasury-sized, one-shot)
1-Alex Ross painted-c/a; Paul Dini-s 3 6 9 16 23 30

SUPERMAN RED AND BLUE
DC Comics: May, 2021 - No. 6, Oct, 2021 ($5.95, limited series, squarebound)
1-6-Short story anthology; art in B&W with red & blue coloring; three covers on each 6.00

SUPERMAN: RED SON
DC Comics: 2003 - No. 3, 2003 ($5.95, limited series, prestige format)
1-Elseworlds; Superman's rocket lands in Russia; Mark Millar-s/Dave Johnson-c/a 28.00
2,3 15.00
TPB (2004, $17.95) r/#1-3; intro. by Tom DeSanto; sketch pages 18.00
... - The Deluxe Edition HC (2009, $24.99, d.j.) r/#1-3; sketch art by various 45.00

SUPERMAN RED/ SUPERMAN BLUE
DC Comics: Feb, 1998 ($4.95, one shot)
1-Polybagged w/3-D glasses and reprint of Superman 3-D (1955); Jurgens-plot/3-D cover; script and art by various 5.00
1-($3.95)-Standard Ed.; comic only, non 3-D cover 4.00

SUPERMAN RETURNS... (2006 movie)
DC Comics: Aug, 2006 ($3.99, movie tie-in stories by Singer, Dougherty and Harris)
Prequel 1 - Krypton to Earth; Olivetti-a/Hughes-c; retells Jor-El's story 6.00
Prequel 2 - Ma Kent; Kerschl-a/Hughes-c; Ma Kent during Clark childhood and absence 4.00
Prequel 3 - Lex Luthor; Leonardi-a/Hughes-c; Luthor's 5 years in prison 4.00
Prequel 4 - Lois Lane; Dias-a/Hughes-c; Lois during Superman's absence 4.00
The Movie and Other Tales of the Man of Steel (2006, $12.99, TPB) adaptation; origin from Amazing World of Superman; Action #810, Superman #185; Advs. of Superman #575 13.00
The Official Movie Adaptation (2006, $6.99) Pasko-s/Haley-a; photo-c 7.00
...: The Prequels TPB (2006, $12.99) r/the 4 prequels 13.00

SUPERMAN: SAVE THE PLANET
DC Comics: Oct, 1998 ($2.95, one-shot)
1-($2.95) Regular Ed.; Luthor buys the Daily Planet 4.00
1-($3.95) Collector's Ed. with acetate cover 5.00

SUPERMAN SCRAPBOOK (Has blank pages; contains no comics)

SUPERMAN: SECRET FILES
DC Comics: Jan, 1998; May 1999 ($4.95)
1,2: 1-Retold origin story, "lost" pages & pin-ups 5.00
... & Origins 2004 (8/04) pin-ups by Lee, Turner and others 5.00
... & Origins 2005 (1/06) short stories and pin-ups by various 5.00
... 2009 (10/09, $4.99) short stories and pin-ups about New Krypton x-over 5.00

SUPERMAN: SECRET IDENTITY
DC Comics: 2004 - No. 4, 2004 ($5.95, squarebound, limited series)
1-4-Busiek-s/Immonen-a/c 6.00

SUPERMAN: SECRET ORIGIN
DC Comics: Nov, 2009 - No. 6, Oct, 2010 ($3.99, limited series)
1-6-Geoff Johns-s/Gary Frank-a/c; origin mythos re-told. 2-Legion app. 5-Metallo app. 4.00
1-6-Variant covers by Frank 6.00
HC (2011, $29.99) r/#1-6; intro. by David Goyer; variant covers 30.00

SUPERMAN '78 (Based on the Christopher Reeve movie version)
DC Comics: Oct, 2021 - No. 6, Mar, 2022 ($3.99, limited series)
1-6-Venditti-s/Torres-a; Brainiac app. 4.00
1-6-($4.99) Cardstock variant covers 5.00

SUPERMAN'S GIRLFRIEND LOIS LANE (See Action Comics #1, 80 Page Giant #3, 14, Lois Lane, Showcase #9, 10, Superman #28 & Superman Family)

SUPERMAN'S GIRLFRIEND LOIS LANE (See Showcase #9,10)
National Periodical Publ.: Mar-Apr, 1958 - No. 136, Jan-Feb, 1974; No. 137, Sept-Oct, 1974
1-(3-4/58) 400 800 1600 4400 10,200 16,000
2 111 222 333 888 1994 3100
3 71 142 213 568 1284 2000
4,5 50 100 150 400 900 1400
6,7 40 80 120 296 673 1050
8-10: 9-Pat Boone-c/story 34 68 102 245 548 850
11-13,15-19: 12-(10/59)-Aquaman app. 17-(5/60) 2nd app. Brainiac.
21 42 63 147 324 500
14-Supergirl x-over; Batman app. on-c only 25 50 75 175 388 600
20-Supergirl-c/sty 24 48 72 168 372 575
21-28: 23-1st app. Lena Thorul, Lex Luthor's sister; 1st Lois as Elastic Lass. 27-Bizarro-c/story 15 30 45 100 220 340
29-Aquaman, Batman, Green Arrow cover app. and cameo; last 10¢ issue
17 34 51 119 265 410

GD VG FN VF VF/NM NM-
2.0 4.0 6.0 8.0 9.0 9.2

30-32,34-46,48,49 9 18 27 61 123 185
33(5/62)-Mon -El app. 10 20 30 68 144 220
47-Legion app. 10 20 30 66 138 210
50(7/64)-Triplicate Girl, Phantom Girl & Shrinking Violet app.
9 18 27 63 129 195
51-55,57-67,69: 59-Jor -El app.; Batman back-up sty 7 14 21 44 82 120
56-Saturn Girl app. 8 16 24 52 99 145
68-(Giant G-26) 8 16 24 56 108 160
70-Penguin & Catwoman app. (1st S.A. Catwoman, 11/66; also see Detective #369 for 3rd app.); Batman & Robin cameo 61 122 183 488 1094 1700
71-Batman & Robin cameo (3 panels); Catwoman story cont'd from #70 (2nd app.); see Detective #369 for 3rd app 12 24 36 79 170 260
72,73,75,76,78 5 10 15 34 60 85
74-1st Bizarro Flash (5/67); JLA cameo 7 14 21 44 82 120
77-(Giant G-39) 7 14 21 48 89 130
79-Neal Adams-c or c(i) begin, end #95,108 7 14 21 44 82 120
80-85,87,88,90-92: 92-Last 12¢ issue 4 8 12 28 47 65
86,95 (Giants G-51,G-63)-Both have Neal Adams-c 7 14 21 44 82 120
89,93: 89-Batman x-over; all N. Adams-c. 93-Wonder Woman-c/story
5 10 15 33 57 80
94,96-99,101-103,107-110 4 8 12 23 37 50
100 4 8 12 25 40 55
104-(Giant G-75) 5 10 15 34 60 85
105-Origin/1st app. The Rose & the Thorn. 10 20 30 69 147 225
106-"I Am Curious (Black)" story; Lois changes her skin color to black (11/70)
42 84 126 311 706 1100
111-Justice League-c/s; Morrow-a; last 15¢ issue 6 12 18 37 66 95
112,114-123 (52 pgs.): 115-Black Racer app. 116,119-Darkseid app. 122-G.A. Lois Lane-r/ Superman #30. 123-G.A.Batman-r/Batman #35 (w/Catwoman)
4 8 12 23 37 50
113-(Giant G-87) Kubert-a (previously unpublished G.A. story)(scarce in NM)
6 12 18 41 76 110
124-135: 130-Last Rose & the Thorn. 132-New Zatanna story
3 6 9 16 23 30
136,137: 136-Wonder Woman x-over 3 6 9 21 33 45
Annual 1(Sum, 1962)-r/L. Lane #12; Aquaman app. 21 42 63 147 324 500
Annual 2(Sum, 1963) 15 30 45 100 220 340
NOTE: *Buckler a-117-121p. Curt Swan or Kurt Schaffenberger a-1-81(most); c(p)-1-15.*

SUPERMAN/SHAZAM: FIRST THUNDER
DC Comics: Nov, 2005 - No. 4, Feb, 2006 ($3.50, limited series)
1-4-Retells first meeting; Winick-s/Middleton-a. Dr. Sivana app. 6.00

SUPERMAN: SILVER BANSHEE
DC Comics: Dec, 1998 - No. 2, Jan, 1999 ($2.25, mini-series)
1,2-Brereton-s/c; Chin-a 4.00

SUPERMANSION (Based on the animated series)
Titan Comics: May, 2018 - No. 2, Jun, 2018 ($5.99, limited series)
1,2-Hutchinson-s/Elphick-a; multiple covers 6.00

SUPERMAN SMASHES THE KLAN (Inspired by the 1940s Superman radio show)
DC Comics: Oct, 2019 - No. 3, Feb, 2020 ($7.99, 6" x 9" squarebound, limited series)
1-3-Gene Luen Yang-s/Gurihiru-a/c; set in 1946. 1-Variant-c by Kyle Baker 8.00

SUPERMAN'S NEMESIS: LEX LUTHOR
DC Comics: Mar, 1999 - No. 4, Jun, 1999 ($2.50, mini-series)
1-4-Semeiks-a 4.00

SUPERMAN: SON OF KAL-EL (Leads into Adventures of Superman: Jon Kent series)
DC Comics: Sept, 2021 - No. 18, Feb, 2023 ($3.99)
1-Jon Kent as Superman; Taylor-s/Timms-a; birth re-told; Damian app. 4.00
2-18: 2-Intro. Jay Nakamura; Henry Bendix app. 9-Nightwing app. 4.00
... 2021 Annual 1 (2/22, $5.99) Lex Luthor app.; Pugh & Henry-a 6.00

SUPERMAN: SPACE AGE
DC Comics: Sept, 2022 - No. 3, ($9.99, limited series)
1-3-Mark Russell-s/Mike Allred-a. 1-Set in the 1960s. 3-Events of Crisis on Infinite Earths 10.00

SUPERMAN'S PAL JIMMY OLSEN (Superman Family #164 on)
(See Action Comics #6 for 1st app. & 80 Page Giant)
National Periodical Publ.: Sept-Oct, 1954 - No. 163, Feb-Mar, 1974 (Fourth World #133-148)
1 540 1080 1890 5400 12,450 19,500
2 186 372 558 1535 3468 5400
3-Last pre-code issue 121 242 363 968 2184 3400
4,5 75 150 225 600 1350 2100
6-10 46 92 138 368 834 1300
11-20: 15-1st S.A. issue 35 70 105 252 564 875

GD VG FN VF VF/NM NM-
2.0 4.0 6.0 8.0 9.0 9.2

21-28,30 24 48 72 168 372 575
29-(6/58) 1st app. Krypto with Superman 27 54 81 194 435 675
31-Origin & 1st app. Elastic Lad (Jimmy Olsen) 26 52 78 182 404 625
32-40: 33-One pg. biography of Jack Larson (TV Jimmy Olsen). 36-Intro Lucy Lane.
37-2nd app. Elastic Lad & 1st cover app. 15 30 45 100 220 340
41-50: 41-1st J.O. Robot. 48-Intro/origin Superman Emergency Squad
11 22 33 76 163 250
51-56: 56-Last 10¢ issue 9 18 27 58 114 170
57-62,64-70: 57-Olsen marries Supergirl. 62-Mon-El & Elastic Lad app. but not as Legionnaires. 70-Element Boy (Lad) app. 7 14 21 44 82 120
63 (9/62)-Legion of Super-Villains app. 8 16 24 54 102 150
71,74,75,78,80-84,86,89,90: 86-Jimmy Olsen Robot becomes Congorilla
5 10 15 35 63 90
72,73,76,77,79,85,87,88: 72(10/63)-Legion app; Elastic Lad (Olsen) joins. 73-Ultra Boy app. 76,85-Legion app. 76-Legion app. 77-Olsen with Colossal Boy's powers & costume; origin Titano retold. 79-(9/64)-Titled The Red-headed Beatle of 1000 B.C. 85-Legion app. 87-Legion of Super-Villains app. 88-Star Boy app. 6 12 18 37 66 95
91-94,96-98 5 10 15 31 53 75
95 (Giant G-25) 8 16 24 52 99 145
99-Olsen w/powers & costumes of Lightning Lad, Sun Boy & Element Lad
5 10 15 34 60 85
100-Legion cameo 5 10 15 34 60 85
101-103,105-112,114-120: 106-Legion app. 110-Infinity-c. 117-Batman & Legion cameo. 120-Last 12¢ issue 4 8 12 27 44 60
104 (Giant G-38) 6 12 18 37 66 95
113,122,131,140 (Giants G-50,G-62,G-74,G-86) 5 10 15 34 60 85
121,123-130,132 4 8 12 25 40 55
133-(10/70)-Jack Kirby story & art begins; re-intro Newsboy Legion; 1st app. Morgan Edge
8 16 24 56 108 160
134-1st app. Darkseid (1 panel, 12/70) 62 124 186 434 742 1050
135-2nd app. Darkseid (1 pg. cameo; see New Gods & Forever People); G.A. Guardian app. 10 20 30 66 138 210
136-139: 136-Origin new Guardian. 138-Partial photo-c. 139-Last 15¢ issue
4 8 12 27 44 60
141-150: (25¢,52 pgs.). 141-Photo-c with Don Rickles; Newsboy Legion-r by S&K begin; full pg. self-portrait of Jack Kirby; Don Rickles cameo. 149,150-G.A. Plastic Man-r in both; 150-Newsboy Legion app. 4 8 12 25 40 55
151-163 3 6 9 16 24 34
... Special 1 (12/08, $4.99) New Krypton tie-in; The Guardian and Dubbilex app. 5.00
... Special 2 (10/09, $4.99) New Krypton tie-in; Mon-El app.; Chang-a 5.00
Superman: The Amazing Transformations of Jimmy Olsen TPB (2007, $14.99) reprints Olsen's transformations into Wolf-Man, Elastic Lad, Turtle Boy and others; new Bolland-c 15.00
*NOTE: Issues #141-148 contain **Simon & Kirby** Newsboy Legion reprints from Star Spangled #7, 8, 9, 10, 11, 12, 13, 14 in that order. **N. Adams** c-109-112, 115, 117, 118, 120, 121, 132, 134-136, 147, 148. **Kirby** a-133-139p, 141-148p; c-133, 137, 139, 142, 145p. **Kirby/N. Adams** c-137, 138, 141-144, 146. **Curt Swan** c-1-14(most)., 140.*

SUPERMAN'S PAL JIMMY OLSEN
DC Comics: Sept, 2019 - No. 12, Sept, 2020 ($3.99)
1-12-Matt Fraction-s/Steve Lieber-a. 5,6-Batman app. 4.00

SUPERMAN'S PAL JIMMY OLSEN'S BOSS PERRY WHITE
DC Comics: Aug, 2022 ($4.99, one-shot)
1-New story with Matt Fraction-s/Steve Lieber-a; 5 reprint stories; Lieber-c 5.00

SUPERMAN SPECTACULAR (Also see DC Special Series #5)
DC Comics: 1982 (Magazine size, 52 pgs., square binding)
1-Saga of Superman Red/ Superman Blue; Luthor and Terra-Man app.; Gonzales & Colletta-a 2 4 6 9 13 16

SUPERMAN: STRENGTH
DC Comics: 2005 - No. 3, 2005 ($5.95, limited series)
1-3: Alex Ross-c/Scott McCloud-s/Aluir Amancio-a 6.00

SUPERMAN / SUPERGIRL: MAELSTROM
DC Comics: Early Jan, 2009 - No. 5, Mar, 2009 ($2.99, limited series)
1-5: Palmiotti & Gray-s/Noto-c/a; Darkseid app. 3.00
TPB (2009, $12.99) r/#1-5 13.00

SUPERMAN / SUPERHOMBRE
DC Comics: Apr, 1945
nn - Ashcan comic, not distributed to newsstands, only for in-house use (no known sales)

SUPERMAN / TARZAN: SONS OF THE JUNGLE
Dark Horse Comics: Oct, 2001 - No. 3, May, 2002 ($2.99, limited series)
1-3-Elseworlds; Kal-El lands in the jungle; Dixon-s/Meglia-a/Ramos-c 3.00

SUPERMAN: THE COMING OF THE SUPERMEN
DC Comics: Apr, 2016 - No. 6, Sept, 2016 ($3.99, limited series)
1-6: 1-Neal Adams-s/a/c in all; Kalibak app. 3,4-Orion app. 3-6-Darkseid app. 4.00

SUPERMAN: THE DARK SIDE
DC Comics: 1998 - No. 3, 1998 ($4.95, squarebound, mini-series)
1-3: Elseworlds; Kal-El lands on Apokolips 1 2 3 5 6 8

SUPERMAN: THE DOOMSDAY WARS
DC Comics: 1998 - No. 3, 1999 ($4.95, squarebound, mini-series)
1-3: Superman & JLA vs. Doomsday; Jurgens-s/a(p) 5.00

SUPERMAN: THE KANSAS SIGHTING
DC Comics: 2003 - No. 2, 2003 ($6.95, squarebound, mini-series)
1,2-DeMatteis-s/Tolagson-a 7.00

SUPERMAN: THE LAST FAMILY OF KRYPTON
DC Comics: Oct, 2010 - No. 3, Dec, 2010 ($4.99, limited series)
1-3-Elseworlds; the El family lands on Earth; Bates-s/Arlem-a/Massafera-c 5.00

SUPERMAN: THE MAN OF STEEL (Also see Man of Steel, The)
DC Comics: July, 1991 - No. 134, Mar, 2003 ($1.00/$1.25/$1.50/$1.95/$2.25)
0-(10/94) Zero Hour; released between #37 & #38 1 3 4 6 8 10
1-($1.75, 52 pgs.)-Painted-c 1 3 4 6 8 10
2-16: 3-War of the Gods x-over. 5-Reads sideways. 10-Last $1.00-c. 14-Superman & Robin team-up 4.00
17-1st brief app. Doomsday 3 6 9 16 23 30
17-(2nd printing) 3 6 9 15 22 28
18-1st full app. Doomsday 3 6 9 19 30 40
18-(2nd-4th printings) 2 4 6 11 16 20
18-(5th printing) 4 8 12 28 47 65
19-Doomsday battle issue (c/story) 2 4 6 8 11 14
19-(2nd & 3rd printings) 3 6 9 16 23 30
20-22: 20,21-Funeral for a Friend. 22-($1.95)-Collector's Edition w/die-cut outer-c & bound-in poster; Steel-c/story 5.00
22-($1.50)-Newsstand Ed. w/poster & different-c 5.00
23-49,51-99: 30-Regular edition. 32-Bizarro-c/story. 35,36-Worlds Collide Pt. 1 & 10. 37-(9/94)-Zero Hour x-over. 38-(11/94). 48-Aquaman app. 54-Spectre-c/app; Lex Luthor app. 56-Mxyzptlk-c/app. 57-G.A. Flash app. 58-Supergirl app. 59-Parasite-c/app.; Steel app. 60-Reintro Bottled City of Kandor. 62-Final Night. 64-New Gods app. 67-New powers. 75-"Death" of Mxyzptlk. 78,79-Millennium Giants. 80-Golden Age style. 92-JLA app. 98-Metal Men app. 4.00
30-($2.50)-Collector's Edition; polybagged with Superman & Lobo vinyl clings that stick to wraparound-c; Lobo-c/story 5.00
50 ($2.95)-The Trial of Superman 4.00
100-($2.99) New Fortress of Solitude revealed 3.00
100-($3.99) Special edition with fold out cardboard-c 4.00
101,102-101-Batman app. 3.00
103-133: 103-Begin $2.25. 105-Batman-c/app. 111-Return to Krypton. 115-117-Our Worlds at War. 117-Maxima killed. 121-Royal Flush Gang app. 128-Return to Krypton II. 3.00
134-($2.75) Last issue; Steel app.; Bogdanove-c 3.00
#1,000,000 (11/98) 853rd Century x-over; Gene Ha-c 4.00
Annual 1-5 ('92-'96,68 pgs.): 1-Eclipso app.; Joe Quesada-c(p). 2-Intro Edge. 3 -Elseworlds; Mignola-c; Batman app. 4-Year One story. 5-Legends of the Dead Earth story 5.00
Annual 6 (1997, $3.95)-Pulp Heroes story 5.00
...Gallery (1995, $3.50) Pin-ups by various 4.00

SUPERMAN: THE MAN OF TOMORROW
DC Comics: 1995 - No. 15, Fall, 1999 ($1.95-$2.95, quarterly)
1-15: 1-Lex Luthor app. 3-Lex Luthor-c/app; Joker app. 4-Shazam! app. 5-Wedding of Lex Luthor. 10-Maxima-c/app. 13-JLA-c/app. 4.00
#1,000,000 (11/98) 853rd Century x-over; Gene Ha-c 4.00

SUPERMAN: THE SECRET YEARS
DC Comics: Feb, 1985 - No. 4, May, 1985 (limited series)
1-4-Miller-c on all 5.00

SUPERMAN: THE WEDDING ALBUM
DC Comics: Dec, 1996 ($4.95, 96 pgs, one-shot)
1-Standard Edition-Story & art by past and present Superman creators; gatefold back-c. Byrne-c 5.00
1-Collector's Edition-Embossed cardstock variant-c w/ metallic silver ink and matte and gloss varnishes 8.00
Retailer Rep. Program Edition (#'d to 250, signed by Bob Rozakis on back-c) 55.00
TPB ('97, $14.95) r/Wedding and honeymoon stories 15.00

SUPERMAN 3-D (See Three-Dimension Adventures)

SUPERMAN-TIM (See Promotional Comics section)

SUPERMAN UNCHAINED (DC New 52)
DC Comics: Aug, 2013 - No. 9, Jan, 2015 ($4.99/$3.99)
1-($4.99) Snyder-s/Jim Lee-a/c; back-up with Nguyen-a; bonus creator interviews 5.00
1-Director's Cut (9/13, $5.99) Lee's pencil art and Scott Snyder's scripts; cover gallery 6.00
2-8-($3.99) 2,6,7-Batman app. 4.00
9-($4.99) Wraparound-c by Jim Lee 5.00

SUPERMAN: UP IN THE SKY (Reprints serialized story in Walmart exclusive Superman Giant)
DC Comics: Sept, 2019 - No. 6, Feb, 2020 ($4.99, limited series)
1-6:1-Reprints Superman Giant #3,4; Andy Kubert-a. 2-R/#5,6. 3-R/#7,8; Sgt. Rock app. 4-R/#9,10; Flash app. 5-R/#12,13; Darkseid app. 6-R/#15,16 5.00

SUPERMAN VILLAINS SECRET FILES
DC Comics: Jun, 1998 ($4.95, one shot)
1-Origin stories, "lost" pages & pin-ups 5.00

SUPERMAN VS. ALIENS (Also see Superman Aliens 2: God War)
DC Comics/Dark Horse Comics: July, 1995 - No. 3, Sept, 1995 ($4.95, limited series)
1-3: Jurgens/Nowlan-a 5.00

SUPERMAN VS. LOBO
DC Comics (Black Label): Oct, 2021 - No. 3, May, 2022 ($6.99, oversized 8-1/2" x 10-3/4", lim. series)
1-3-Seeley & Beattie-s/Andolfo-a. 2-Lobo goes to Krypton, Superman to Czarnia 7.00

SUPERMAN VS. MUHAMMAD ALI (See All-New Collectors' Edition C-56 for original 1978 printing)
DC Comics: 2010
... Deluxe Edition (2010, $19.99, HC w/dustjacket) recolored reprint in comic size; new intro. by Neal Adams; afterword by Jenette Kahn; sketch pages, key to cover celebs 20.00
... Facsimile Edition (2010, $39.99, HC no dustjacket) recolored reprint in original Treasury size; new intro. by Neal Adams; key to cover celebs 40.00

SUPERMAN VS. PREDATOR
DC Comics/Dark Horse Comics: 2000 - No. 3, 2000 ($4.95, limited series)
1-3-Micheline-s/Maleev-a 5.00
TPB (2001, $14.95) r/series 15.00

SUPERMAN VS. THE AMAZING SPIDER-MAN (Also see Marvel Treasury Edition No. 28)
National Periodical Publications/Marvel Comics Group: 1976
($2.00, Treasury sized, 100 pgs.)
1-Superman and Spider-Man battle Lex Luthor and Dr. Octopus; Andru/Giordano-a; 1st Marvel/DC x-over. 10 20 30 64 132 200
1-2nd printing; 2000 numbered copies signed by Stan Lee on front cover & sold through mail
18 36 54 122 271 420
nn-(1995, $5.95)-r/#1 3 6 9 19 30 40

SUPERMAN VS. THE TERMINATOR: DEATH TO THE FUTURE
Dark Horse/DC Comics: Dec, 1999 - No. 4, Mar, 2000 ($2.95, limited series)

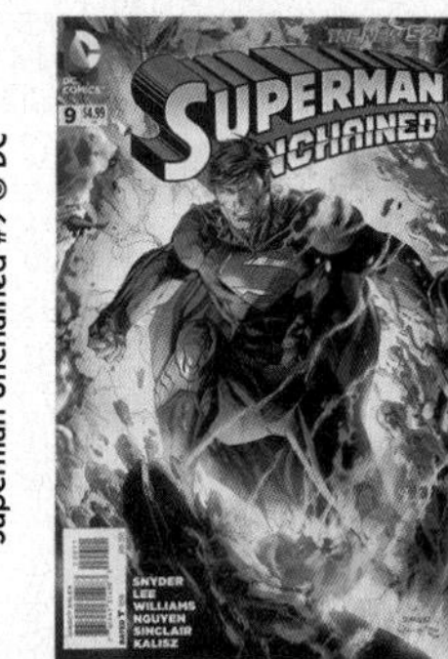
Superman Unchained #9 © DC

Superman / Wonder Woman #4 © DC

Supernatural: Origins #6 © WB

	GD	VG	FN	VF	VF/NM	NM-
	2.0	4.0	6.0	8.0	9.0	9.2

1-4-Grant-s/Pugh-a/c: Steel and Supergirl app. 5.00

SUPERMAN: WAR OF THE SUPERMEN
DC Comics: No. 0, Jun, 2010 - No. 4, Jul, 2010 ($2.99, limited series)

0-Free Comic Book Day issue; Barrows-c 3.00
1-4: 1-New Krypton destroyed 3.00
HC (2011, $19.99) r/#0-4 & Superman #700 20.00

SUPERMAN/WONDER WOMAN (DC New 52)
DC Comics: Dec, 2013 - No. 29, Jul, 2016 ($3.99)

1-Soule-s/Daniel-a; wraparound gatefold-c; Doomsday app. 5.00
2-29: 2-6-Zod app. 4-6-Faora app. 7-Doomsday app. 8-12-Doomed x-over. 14-17-Magog app. 18,19-Suicide Squad app. 26,27-Vandal Savage app. 28,29-Supergirl app. 4.00
Annual 1 (9/14, $4.99) Doomsday Superman vs. Cyborg Superman 5.00
Annual 2 (2/16, $4.99) Short stories by various; Paquette-c 5.00
...: Futures End 1 (11/14, $2.99, regular-c) Cont'd from Wonder Woman: FE #1 3.00
...: Futures End 1 (11/14, $3.99, 3-D cover) 4.00

SUPERMAN/WONDER WOMAN: WHOM GODS DESTROY
DC Comics: 1997 ($4.95, prestige format, limited series)

1-4-Elseworlds; Claremont-s 5.00

SUPERMAN WORKBOOK
National Periodical Publ./Juvenile Group Foundation: 1945 (B&W, reprints, 68 pgs)

nn-Cover-r/Superman #14 300 600 900 2010 3505 5000

SUPERMAN: WORLD OF NEW KRYPTON
DC Comics: May, 2009 - No. 12,Apr, 2010 ($2.99, limited series)

1-12: Robinson & Rucka-s/Woods-a; Frank-c and variant for each. 4-Green Lantern app. 3.00

SUPERMAN YEAR ONE
DC Comics (Black Label): Aug, 2019 - No. 3, Dec, 2019 ($7.99, 10-7/8" x 8-1/2", lim. series)

1-3-Frank Miller-s/John Romita Jr.-a; two covers on each; origin re-told 8.00

SUPER MARIO BROS. (Also see Adventures of the..., Blip, Gameboy, and Nintendo Comics System)
Valiant Comics: 1990 - No. 6, 1991 ($1.95, slick-c) V2#1, 1991 - No. 5, 1991

1-Wildman-a 13 26 39 89 195 300
2 5 10 15 31 53 75
3-6, V2#1-5-($1.50) 2 4 6 10 14 18
Special Edition 1 (1990, $1.95)-Wildman-a; 1st Valiant comic
8 16 24 54 102 150

SUPER MARKET COMICS
Fawcett Publications: No date (1950s)

nn - Ashcan comic, not distributed to newsstands, only for in-house use (no known sales)

SUPER MARKET VARIETIES
Fawcett Publications: No date (1950s)

nn - Ashcan comic, not distributed to newsstands, only for in-house use (no known sales)

SUPERMASSIVE
Image Comics: Feb, 2022 ($5.99, one-shot)

1-Crossover of Radiant Black, Radiant Red, Rogue Sun & Inferno Girl Red 6.00

SUPERMEN OF AMERICA
DC Comics: Mar, 1999 ($3.95/$4.95, one-shot)

1-($3.95) Regular Ed.; Immonen-s/art by various 4.00
1-($4.95) Collectors' Ed. with membership kit 5.00

SUPERMEN OF AMERICA (Mini-series)
DC Comics: Mar, 2000 - No. 6, Aug, 2000 ($2.50)

1-6-Nicieza-s/Braithwaite-a 3.00

SUPERMOUSE (...the Big Cheese; see Coo Coo Comics)
Standard Comics/Pines No. 35 on (Literary Ent.): Dec, 1948 - No. 34, Sept, 1955; No. 35, Apr, 1956 - No. 45, Fall, 1958

1-Frazetta text illos (3) 42 84 126 265 445 625
2-Frazetta text illos 20 40 60 120 195 270
3,5,6-Text illos by Frazetta in all 15 30 45 88 137 185
4-Two pg. text illos by Frazetta 16 32 48 92 144 195
7-10 10 20 30 56 76 95
11-20: 13-Racist humor (Indians) 9 18 27 47 61 75
21-45 8 16 24 40 50 60
1-Summer Holiday issue (Summer, 1957, 25¢, 100 pgs.)-Pines
15 30 45 90 140 190
2-Giant Summer issue (Summer, 1958, 25¢, 100 pgs.)-Pines; has games, puzzles & stories 12 24 36 69 97 125

SUPER-MYSTERY COMICS

	GD	VG	FN	VF	VF/NM	NM-
	2.0	4.0	6.0	8.0	9.0	9.2

Ace Magazines (Periodical House): July, 1940 - V8#6, July, 1949

V1#1-Magno, the Magnetic Man & Vulcan begins (1st app.); Q-13, Corp. Flint, & Sky Smith begin 514 1028 1542 3750 6625 9500
2 245 490 735 1568 2684 3800
3-The Black Spider begins (1st app.) 258 516 774 1651 2826 4000
4-Origin Davy 135 270 405 864 1482 2100
5-Intro. The Clown & begin series (12/40) 142 284 426 909 1555 2200
6(2/41) 119 238 357 762 1306 1850
V2#1(4/41)-Origin Buckskin 116 232 348 742 1271 1800
2-6(2/42): 3-Hitler & Mussolini app. 4-WWII Nazi-c. 6-Vulcan begins again; bondage/torture-c 116 232 348 742 1271 1800
V3#1(4/42),2: 1-Black Ace begins 129 258 387 826 1413 2000
3-Classic Kurtzman Japanese WWII giant robot bondage-c; intro. The Lancer; Dr. Nemesis & The Sword begin; Kurtzman-a(2)(Mr. Risk & Paul Revere Jr.)
181 362 543 1158 1979 2800
4-Kurtzman-c/a; classic-c 271 542 813 1734 2967 4200
5-Kurtzman-a(2); L.B. Cole-a; Mr. Risk app. 168 336 504 1075 1838 2600
6(10/43)-Mr. Risk app.; Kurtzman's Paul Revere Jr.; L.B. Cole-a
116 232 348 742 1271 1800
V4#1(1/44)-L.B. Cole-a; Hitler app. 84 168 252 538 919 1300
2-6(4/45): 2,5,6-Mr. Risk app. 63 126 189 403 689 975
V5#1(7/45)-6 60 120 180 381 653 925
V6#1,2,4,5,6: 4-Last Magno. Mr. Risk app. in #2,4-6. 6-New logo
57 114 171 362 619 875
3-Classic torture c/story 1250 2500 3750 9500 17,250 25,000
V7#1-6, V8#1-4,6 54 108 162 343 574 825
V8#5-Meskin, Tuska, Sid Greene-a 55 110 165 352 601 850

NOTE: ***Sid Greene*** *a-V7#4.* ***Mooney*** *c-V1#5, 6, V2#1-6.* ***Palais*** *a-V5#3, 4; c-V4#6-V5#4, V6#2, V8#4. Bondage c-V2#5, 6, V3#2, 5. Magno c-V1#1-V3#6, V4#2-V5#5, V6#2. The Sword c-V4#1, 6(w/Magno).*

SUPERNATURAL (Volume 4) (Based on the CW television series)
DC Comics: Dec, 2011 - No. 6, May, 2012 ($2.99, limited series)

1-6: 1-Sam in Scotland; Brian Wood-s/Grant Bond-a 3.00

SUPERNATURAL: BEGINNING'S END (Based on the CW television series)
DC Comics (WildStorm): Mar, 2010 - No. 6, Aug, 2010 ($2.99, limited series)

1-6-Prequel to the series; Dabb & Loflin-s/Olmos-a. 1-Olmos and photo-c 3.00
TPB (2010, $14.99) r/#1-6; character sketch pages 15.00

SUPERNATURAL FREAK MACHINE: A CAL MCDONALD MYSTERY
IDW Publishing: Mar, 2005 - No. 3 ($3.99)

1-3-Steve Niles-s/Kelley Jones-a 4.00

SUPERNATURAL LAW (Formerly Wolff & Byrd, Counselors of the Macabre)
Exhibit A Press: No. 24, Oct, 1999 - No. 45, 2008 ($2.50/$2.95/$3.50, B&W)

24-35-Batton Lash-s/a. 29-Marie Severin-c. 33-Cerebus spoof 3.00
36-40-($2.95). 37-Frank Cho pin-up and story panels 3.00
(#41) ...First Amendment Issue (2005, $3.50) anti-censorship story; CBLDF info 3.50
(#42) With a Silver Bullet (2006, $3.50) new stories and pin-ups 3.50
(#43) At the Box Office (2006, $3.50) new stories and pin-ups 3.50
(#44) Wolff & Byrd: The Movie (2007, $3.50) new stories and pin-ups 3.50
45-($3.50) Toxic Avenger and Lloyd Kaufman app. 3.50
#1 (2005, $2.95) r/Wolff & Byrd with redrawn and re-toned art; relettered 3.00

SUPERNATURAL LAW SECRETARY MAVIS
Exhibit A Press: 2001 - No. 5, 2008 ($2.95/$3.50, B&W)

1-3: 3-DeCarlo-c 3.00
4,5-($3.50) Jaime Hernandez-c 3.50

SUPERNATURAL: ORIGINS (Based on the CW television series)
DC Comics (WildStorm): July, 2007 - No. 6, Dec, 2007 ($2.99, limited series)

1-6: 1-Bradstreet-c; Johnson-s/Smith-a; back-up w/Johns-s/Hester-a 3.00
TPB (2008, $14.99) r/#1-6; sketch pages 15.00

SUPERNATURAL: RISING SON (Based on the CW television series)
DC Comics (WildStorm): Jun, 2008 - No. 6, Nov, 2008 ($2.99, limited series)

1-6-Johnson & Dessertine-s/Olmos-a. 1-Oliver-c 3.00
1-Variant-c by Nguyen 6.00
TPB (2009, $14.99) r/#1-6 15.00

SUPERNATURALS
Marvel Comics: Dec, 1998 - No. 4, Dec, 1998 ($3.99, weekly limited series)

1-4-Pulido-s/Balent-c; bound-in Halloween masks 4.00
1-4-With bound-in Ghost Rider mask (1 in 10) 4.00
... Preview Tour Book (10/98, $2.99) Reis-c 4.00

SUPERNATURAL THRILLERS
Marvel Comics Group: Dec, 1972 - No. 6, Nov, 1973; No. 7, Jun, 1974 - No. 15, Oct, 1975

GD 2.0 | VG 4.0 | FN 6.0 | VF 8.0 | VF/NM 9.0 | NM- 9.2

1-It!; Sturgeon adap. (see Astonishing Tales #21) 5 10 15 34 60 85
2-4,6: 2-The Invisible Man; H.G. Wells adapt. 3-The Valley of the Worm; R.E. Howard adapt. 4-Dr. Jekyll & Mr. Hyde; R.L. Stevenson adapt.. 6-The Headless Horseman; last 20¢ issue 3 6 9 14 20 25
5-1st app. The Living Mummy 9 18 27 61 123 185
7-15: 7-The Living Mummy begins. 8-1st app. The Elementals 3 6 9 17 26 35
NOTE: ***Brunner** c-11. **Buckler** a-5p. **Ditko** a-8r, 9r. **G. Kane** a-3p; c-3, 9p, 15p. **Mayerik** a-2p, 7, 8, 9p, 10p, 11. **McWilliams** a-14i. **Mortimer** a-4. **Steranko** c-1, 2. **Sutton** a-15. **Tuska** a-6p.*

SUPERPATRIOT (Also see Freak Force & Savage Dragon #2)
Image Comics (Highbrow Entertainment): July, 1993 - No. 4, Dec, 1993 ($1.95, lim. series)
1-4: Dave Johnson-c/a; Larsen scripts; Giffen plots 3.00

SUPERPATRIOT: AMERICA'S FIGHTING FORCE
Image Comics: July, 2002 - No. 4, Oct, 2002 ($2.95, limited series)
1-4-Cory Walker-a/c; Savage Dragon app. 3.00

SUPERPATRIOT: LIBERTY & JUSTICE
Image Comics (Highbrow Entertainment): July, 1995 - No. 4, Oct, 1995 ($2.50, lim. series)
1-4: Dave Johnson-c/a. 1-1st app. Liberty & Justice 3.00
TPB (2002, $12.95) r/#1-4; new cover by Dave Johnson; sketch pages 13.00

SUPERPATRIOT: WAR ON TERROR
Image Comics: July, 2004 - No. 4, May, 2007 ($2.95/$2.99, limited series)
1-4-Kirkman-s/Su-a 3.00

SUPER POWERS (1st Series)
DC Comics: July, 1984 - No. 5, Nov, 1984
1-5: 1-Joker/Penguin-c/story; Batman app.; all Kirby-c. 5-Kirby c/a 6.00

SUPER POWERS (2nd Series)
DC Comics: Sept, 1985 - No. 6, Feb, 1986
1-6: Kirby-c/a; Capt. Marvel & Firestorm join; Batman cameo; Darkseid storyline in all. 4-Batman cameo. 5,6-Batman app. 5.00

SUPER POWERS (3rd Series)
DC Comics: Sept, 1986 - No. 4, Dec, 1986
1-4: 1-Cyborg joins; 1st app. Samurai from Super Friends TV show. 1-4-Batman cameos; Darkseid storyline in #1-4 4.00

SUPER POWERS (All ages series)
DC Comics: Jan, 2017 - No. 6, Jun, 2017 ($2.99, limited series)
1-6-Franco & Baltazar-s/Baltazar-a/c; Superman, Batman & Wonder Woman vs. Brainiac 3.00

SUPER PUP (Formerly Spotty The Pup) (See Space Comics)
Avon Periodicals: No. 4, Mar-Apr, 1954 - No. 5, 1954
4,5: 4-Atom bomb-c. 5-Robot-c 10 20 30 58 79 100

SUPER RABBIT (See All Surprise, Animated Movie Tunes, Comedy Comics, Comic Capers, Ideal Comics, It's A Duck's Life, Li'l Pals, Movie Tunes & Wisco)
Timely Comics (CmPI): Fall, 1944 - No. 14, Nov, 1948
1-Hitler & Hirohito-c; war effort paper recycling PSA by S&K; Ziggy Pig & Silly Seal begin 300 600 900 2010 3505 5000
2 57 114 171 362 619 875
3-5 37 74 111 218 354 490
6-Origin 39 78 117 231 378 525
7-10: 9-Infinity-c 25 50 75 150 245 340
11-Kurtzman's "Hey Look" 28 56 84 168 274 380
12-14 25 50 75 150 245 340
I.W. Reprint #1,2('58),7,10('63): 1-r/#13. 2-r/#10. 3 6 9 18 27 36

SUPER RICHIE (Superichie #5 on) (See Richie Rich Millions #68)
Harvey Publications: Sept, 1975 - No. 4, Mar, 1976 (All 52 pg. Giants)
1 3 6 9 16 23 30
2-4 2 4 6 11 16 20

SUPER SECRET CRISIS WAR! (Crossover of Cartoon Network characters)
IDW Publishing: Jun, 2014 - No. 6, Nov, 2014 ($3.99, limited series)
1-6-Powerpuff Girls, Samurai Jack, Dexter, Ben 10 vs. Aku, Mojo Jojo, Mandark 4.00
... Codename: Kids Next Door One-Shot (11/14 $3.99) 3 covers; Jampole-a 4.00
... Cow and Chicken One-Shot (10/14 $3.99) 3 covers; Jim Zub-s 4.00
... Foster's Home For Imaginary Friends One-Shot (9/14 $3.99) 3 covers; Ganucheau-a 4.00
... Johnny Bravo One-Shot (7/14 $3.99) 3 covers; Erica Henderson-a 4.00
... The Grimm Adventures of Billy and Mandy One-Shot (7/14 $3.99) 3 covers; Leth-s 4.00

SUPER SLUGGERS (Baseball)
Ultimate Sports Ent. Inc.: 1999 ($3.95, one-shot)
1-Bonds, Piazza, Caminiti, Griffey Jr. app.; Martinbrough-c/a 4.00

SUPERSNIPE COMICS (Formerly Army & Navy #1-5)
Street & Smith Publications: V1#6, Oct, 1942 - V5#1, Aug-Sept, 1949
(See Shadow Comics V2#3)
V1#6-Rex King - Man of Adventure (costumed hero, see Super Magic/Magician) by Jack Binder begins; Supersnipe by George Marcoux continues from Army & Navy #5; Bill Ward-a 97 194 291 621 1061 1500
7,10-12: 10,11-Little Nemo app. 54 108 162 343 574 825
8-Hitler, Tojo, Mussolini in Hell with Devil-c 459 918 1377 3350 5925 8500
9-Doc Savage x-over in Supersnipe; Hitler-c 423 846 1269 3000 5250 7500
V2 #1: Both V2#1(2/44) & V2#2(4/44) have V2#1 on outside-c; Huck Finn by Clare Dwiggins begins, ends V3#5 (rare) 61 122 183 390 670 950
V2#2 (4/44) has V2#1 on outside-c; classic shark-c 48 96 144 302 514 725
3-12: 12-Statue of Liberty-c 25 50 75 150 245 340
V3#1-12: 8-Bobby Crusoe by Dwiggins begins, ends V3#12. 9-X-Mas-c 22 44 66 128 209 290
V4#1-12, V5#1: V4#10-X-Mas-c 19 38 57 111 176 240
NOTE: ***George Marcoux** c-V1#6-V3#4. Doc Savage app. in some issues.*

SUPER SOLDIER (See Marvel Versus DC #3)
DC Comics (Amalgam): Apr, 1996 ($1.95, one-shot)
1-Mark Waid script & Dave Gibbons-c/a. 4.00

SUPER SOLDIER: MAN OF WAR
DC Comics (Amalgam): June, 1997 ($1.95, one-shot)
1-Waid & Gibbons-s/Gibbons & Palmiotti-c/a. 4.00

SUPER SOLDIERS
Marvel Comics UK: Apr, 1993 - No. 8, Nov, 1993 ($1.75)
1-($2.50)-Embossed silver foil logo 5.00
2-8: 5-Capt. America app. 6-Origin; Nick Fury app.; neon ink-c 4.00

SUPER SONS
DC Comics: Apr, 2017 - No. 16, Jul, 2018 ($2.99/$3.99)
1,2: 1-Damian Wayne (Robin) & Jon Kent (Superboy) team-up; Tomasi-s/Jimenez-a 3.00
3-16-($3.99) 3,4-Battle Kid Amazo. 6,7-Teen Titans app. 11,12-Future adult Superboy (Conner), Wonder Girl (Cassie) and Kid Flash (Bart) app. 13,14-Talia app. 4.00
Annual 1 (1/18, $4.99) Tomasi-s/Pelletier-a; Krypto, Titus & the Super-Pets app. 5.00
... / Dynomutt Special 1 (7/18, $4.99) Blue Falcon and Red Vulture app.; Pasarin-a 5.00

SUPERSPOOK (Formerly Frisky Animals on Parade)
Ajax/Farrell Publications: No. 4, June, 1958
4 10 20 30 54 72 90

SUPER SPY (See Wham Comics)
Centaur Publications: Oct, 1940 - No. 2, Nov, 1940 (Reprints)
1-Origin The Sparkler 119 238 357 762 1306 1850
2-The Inner Circle, Dean Denton, Tim Blain, The Drew Ghost, The Night Hawk by Gustavson, & S.S. Swanson by Glanz app. 258 516 774 1651 2826 4000

SUPERSTAR: AS SEEN ON TV
Image Comics (Gorilla): 2001 ($5.95)
1-Busiek-s/Immonen-a 6.00

SUPER STAR HOLIDAY SPECIAL (See DC Special Series #21)

SUPER-TEAM FAMILY
National Periodical Publ./DC Comics: Oct-Nov, 1975 - No. 15, Mar-Apr, 1978
1-Reprints by Neal Adams & Kane/Wood; 68 pgs. begin, ends #4. New Gods app. 4 8 12 25 40 55
2,3: New stories 3 6 9 15 22 28
4-7: Reprints. 4-G.A. JSA-r & Superman/Batman/Robin-r from World's Finest. 5-52 pgs. begin 2 4 6 10 14 18
8-14: 8-10-New Challengers of the Unknown stories. 9-Kirby-a. 11-14: New stories 3 6 9 14 19 24
15-New Gods app. New stories 3 6 9 14 20 26
NOTE: ***Neal Adams** r-1-3. **Brunner** c-3. **Buckler** c-8p. **Tuska** a-7r. **Wood** a-1i(r), 3.*

SUPER TV HEROES (See Hanna-Barbera...)

SUPER-VILLAIN CLASSICS
Marvel Comics Group: May, 1983
1-Galactus -The Origin; Kirby-a 3 6 9 21 33 45

SUPER-VILLAIN TEAM-UP (See Fantastic Four #6 & Giant-Size...)
Marvel Comics Group: 8/75 - No. 14, 10/77; No. 15, 11/78; No. 16, 5/79; No. 17, 6/80
1-Continued from Giant-Size Super-Villain Team-Up #2; Sub-Mariner & Dr. Doom begin, end #10 6 12 18 38 69 100
2-5: 5-1st app. The Shroud 3 6 9 16 23 30
5-(30¢-c variant, limited distribution)(4/76) 6 12 18 41 76 110
6,7-(25¢ editions) 6-(6/76)-F.F., Shroud app. 7-Origin Shroud 2 4 6 10 14 18
6,7-(30¢-c, limited distribution)(6,8/76) 5 10 15 35 63 90
8,9,11-17: 9-Avengers app. 11-15-Dr. Doom & Red Skull app. 2 4 6 9 13 16
10-Classic Dr. Doom, Red Skull, Captain America battle-c 3 6 9 16 24 32
12-14-(35¢-c variants, limited distribution)(6,8,10/77) 12 24 36 83 182 280
NOTE: ***Buckler** c-4p, 5p, 7p. **Buscema** c-1. **Byrne/Austin** c-14. **Evans** a-1p, 3p. **Everett** a-1p. **Giffen** a-8p, 13p; c-13p. **Kane** c-2p, 9p. **Mooney** a-4i. **Starlin** c-6. **Tuska** r-1p, 15p. **Wood** r-15p.*

SUPER-VILLAIN TEAM-UP/ MODOK'S 11
Marvel Comics: Sept, 2007 - No. 5, Jan, 2008 ($2.99, limited series)
1-5: 1-MODOK's origin re-told; Portela-a/Powell-c; Purple Man & Mentallo app. 3.00
... TPB (2008, $13.99) r/#1-5 14.00

SUPER WESTERN COMICS (Also see Buffalo Bill)
Youthful Magazines: Aug, 1950 (One shot)
1-Buffalo Bill begins; Wyatt Earp, Calamity Jane & Sam Slade app; Powell-c/a 20 40 60 117 189 260

SUPER WESTERN FUNNIES (See Super Funnies)

SUPERWOMAN
DC Comics: Jan 1942
nn - Ashcan comic, not distributed to newsstands, only for in-house use. Cover art is More Fun Comics #73 with interior being Action Comics #38 (no known sales)

SUPERWOMAN (DC Rebirth)
DC Comics: Oct, 2016 - No. 18, Mar, 2018 ($2.99/$3.99)
1-8: 1-Phil Jimenez-s/a; Lois and Lana with powers. 2-8-Lena Luthor app. 3.00
9-18-($3.99): 9,10-Segovia-a. 13-15-Supergirl app. 14-18-Maxima app. 4.00

SUPERWORLD COMICS
Hugo Gernsback (Komos Publ.): Apr, 1940 - No. 3, Aug, 1940 (68 pgs.)
1-Origin & 1st app. Hip Knox, Super Hypnotist; Mitey Powers & Buzz Allen, the Invisible Avenger, Little Nemo begin; cover by Frank R. Paul (all have sci/fi-c) (Scarce) 1050 2100 3150 7700 16,350 25,000
2-Marvo 1-2 Go+, the Super Boy of the Year 2680 (1st app.); Paul-c (Scarce) 865 1730 2595 6315 11,158 16,000
3 (Scarce) 530 1060 1590 3869 6835 9800

SUPERZERO
AfterShock Comics: Dec, 2015 - No. 6, Jun, 2016 ($3.99)
1-6-Conner & Palmiotti-s/De Latorre-a. 1-Covers by Conner, Cooke & Hester 4.00

SUPER ZOMBIES

Super Powers (2017) #2 © DC

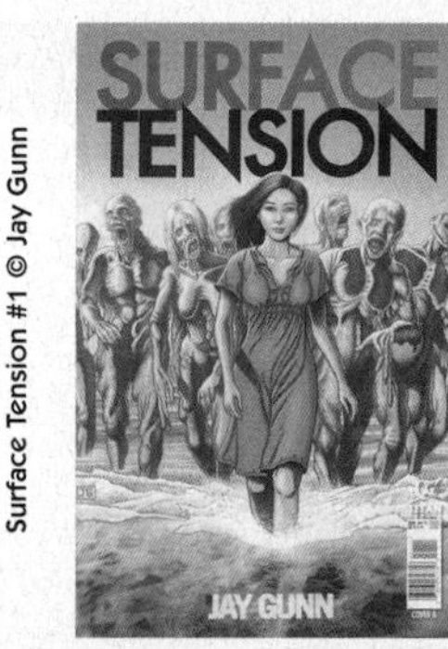

Surface Tension #1 © Jay Gunn

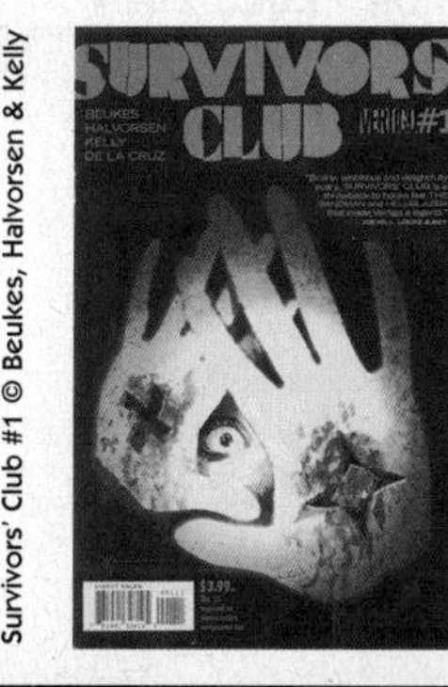

Survivors' Club #1 © Beukes, Halvorsen & Kelly

	GD 2.0	VG 4.0	FN 6.0	VF 8.0	VF/NM 9.0	NM- 9.2

Dynamite Entertainment: 2009 - No. 5, 2009 ($3.50)

1-5-Mel Rubi-a; Guggenheim & Gonzales-s; two covers for each by Rubi & Neves 3.50

SUPREME (Becomes ...The New Adventures #43-48)(See Youngblood #3)
(Also see Bloodwulf Special, Legend of Supreme, & Trencher #3)
Image Comics (Extreme Studios)/ Awesome Entertainment #49 on:
V2#1, Nov, 1992 - V2#42, Sept, 1996; V3#49 - No. 56, Feb, 1998

V2#1-Liefeld-a(i) & scripts; embossed foil logo 4.00
1-Gold Edition 1 2 3 5 6 8
2-(3/93)-Liefeld co-plots & inks; 1st app. Grizlock 3.00
3-42: 3-Intro Bloodstrike; 1st app. Khrome. 5-1st app. Thor. 6-1st brief app. The Starguard. 7-1st full app. The Starguard. 10-Black and White Pt 1 (1st app.) by Art Thibert (2 pgs. ea. installment). 25-(5/94)-Platt-c. 11-Coupon #4 for Extreme Prejudice #0; Black and White Pt. 7 by Thibert. 12-(4/94)-Platt-c. 13,14-(6/94). 15 (7/94). 16 (7/94)-Stormwatch app. 18-Kid Supreme Sneak Preview; Pitt app.19,20-Polybagged w/trading card. 20-1st app. Woden & Loki (as a dog); Overtkill app. 21-1st app. Loki (in true form). 21-23-Poly-bagged trading card. 32-Lady Supreme cameo. 33-Origin & 1st full app. of Lady Supreme (Probe from the Starguard); Babewatch! tie-in. 37-Intro Loki; Fraga-c. 40-Retells Supreme's past advs. 41-Alan Moore scripts begin; Supreme revised; intro The Supremacy; Jerry Ordway-c (Joe Bennett variant-c exists). 42-New origin w/Rick Veitch-a; intro Radar, The Hound Supreme & The League of Infinity 3.00
28-Variant-c by Quesada & Palmiotti 3.00
(#43-48-**See Supreme: The New Adventures**)
V3#49,51: 49-Begin $2.99-c 3.00
50-($3.95)-Double sized, 2 covers, pin-up gallery 4.00
52a,52b-($3.50) 4.00
53-56: 53-Sprouse-a begins. 56-McGuinness-c 3.00
Annual 1-(1995, $2.95) 4.00
...: Supreme Sacrifice (3/06, $3.99) Flip book with Suprema; Kirkman-s/Malin-a 4.00
...: The Return TPB (Checker Book Publ., 2003, $24.95) r/#53-56 & Supreme; The Return #1-6; Ross-c; additional sketch pages by Ross 25.00
...: The Story of the Year TPB (Checker Book Publ., 2002, $26.95) r/#41-52; Ross-c 27.00
NOTE: ***Rob Liefeld** a(i)-1, 2; co-plots-2-4; scripts-1, 5, 6. **Ordway** c-41. **Platt** c-12, 25. **Thibert** c(i)-7-9.*

SUPREME
Image Comics: No. 63, Apr, 2012 - No. 68, Jan, 2013 ($2.99)

63-66: 63-Moore-s; two covers by Larsen & Hamscher; Larsen-a in all 3.00
67,68-($3.99) 67-Omni-Man (from Invincible) app.; Larsen-a 4.00

SUPREME BLUE ROSE
Image Comics: Jul, 2014 - No. 7, Mar, 2015 ($2.99)

1-7-Warren Ellis-s/Tula Lotay-a 3.00

SUPREME: GLORY DAYS
Image Comics (Extreme Studios): Oct, 1994 - No. 2, Dec, 1994 ($2.95/$2.50, limited series)

1,2: 2-Diehard, Roman, Superpatriot, & Glory app. 3.00

SUPREME POWER (Also see Squadron Supreme 2006 series)
Marvel Comics (MAX): Oct, 2003 - No. 18, Oct, 2005 ($2.99)

1-($2.99) Straczynski-s/Frank-a; Frank-c 3.00
1-($4.99) Special Edition with variant Quesada-c; includes r/early Squadron Supreme apps. 5.00
2-18: 4-Intro. Nighthawk. 6-The Blur debuts. 10-Princess Zarda returns. 17-Hyperion revealed as alien. 18-Continues in mini-series 3.00
... MGC #1 (7/11, $1.00) r/#1 with "Marvel's Greatest Comics" banner on cover 3.00
Vol. 1: Contact TPB (2004, $14.99) r/#1-6 15.00
Vol. 2: Powers & Principalities TPB (2004, $14.99) r/#7-12 15.00
Vol. 3: High Command TPB (2005, $14.99) r/#13-18 15.00
Vol. 1 HC (2005, $29.99, 7 1/2" x 11" with dustjacket) r/#1-12; Avengers #85 & 86, Straczynski intro., Frank cover sketches and character design pages 30.00
Vol. 2 HC (2006, $29.99, 7 1/2" x 11" with dustjacket) r/#13-18; ...: Hyperion #1-5; character design pages 30.00

SUPREME POWER
Marvel Comics (MAX): Aug, 2011 - No. 4, Nov, 2011 ($3.99, limited series)

1-4-Higgins-s/Garcia-a/Fiumara-c; Doctor Spectrum app. 4.00

SUPREME POWER: HYPERION
Marvel Comics (MAX): Nov, 2005 - No. 5, Mar, 2006 ($2.99, limited series)

1-5: 1-Straczynski-s/Jurgens-a/Dodson-c 3.00
TPB (2006, $14.99) r/#1-5 15.00

SUPREME POWER: NIGHTHAWK
Marvel Comics (MAX): Nov, 2005 - No. 6, Apr, 2006 ($2.99, limited series)

1-6-Daniel Way-s/Steve Dillon-a; origin of Whiteface 3.00
TPB (2006, $16.99) r/#1-6; cover concept art 17.00

SUPREME: THE NEW ADVENTURES (Formerly Supreme)
Maximum Press: V3#43, Oct, 1996 - V3#48, May, 1997 ($2.50)

V3#43-48: 43-Alan Moore scripts in all; Joe Bennett-a; Rick Veitch-a (8 pgs.); Dan Jurgens-a (1 pg.); intro Citadel Supreme & Suprematons; 1st Allied Supermen of America 4.00

SUPREME: THE RETURN
Awesome Entertainment: May, 1999 - No. 6, June, 2000 ($2.99)

1-6: Alan Moore-s. 1,2-Sprouse & Gordon-a/c. 2,4-Liefeld-c. 6-Kirby app. 4.00

SUPURBIA (GRACE RANDOLPH'S...)
BOOM! Studios: Mar, 2012 - No. 4, Jun, 2012 ($3.99, limited series)

1-4-Grace Randolph-s/Dauterman-a. 1-Garza-c 4.00

SUPURBIA (GRACE RANDOLPH'S...)(Volume 2)
BOOM! Studios: Nov, 2012 - No. 12, Oct, 2013 ($3.99, limited series)

1-12-Grace Randolph-s/Dauterman-a; multiple covers on #1-5 4.00

SURE-FIRE COMICS (Lightning Comics #4 on)
Ace Magazines: June, 1940 - No. 4, Oct, 1940 (Two No. 3's)

	GD	VG	FN	VF	VF/NM	NM-
V1#1-Origin Flash Lightning & begins; X-The Phantom Fed, Ace McCoy, Buck Steele, Marvo the Magician, The Raven, Whiz Wilson (Time Traveler) begin (all 1st app.); Flash Lightning c-1-4	300	600	900	1980	3440	4900
2	194	388	582	1242	2121	3000
3(9/40), 3(#4)(10/40)-nn on-c, #3 on inside	142	284	426	909	1555	2200

SURFACE TENSION
Titan Comics: Jun, 2015 - No. 5, Oct, 2015 ($3.99, limited series)

1-5-Jay Gunn-s/a. 1,2-Two covers 4.00

SURF 'N' WHEELS
Charlton Comics: Nov, 1969 - No. 6, Sept, 1970

	GD	VG	FN	VF	VF/NM	NM-
1	3	6	9	19	30	40
2-6	3	6	9	14	19	24

SURGE
Eclipse Comics: July, 1984 - No. 4, Jan, 1985 ($1.50, lim. series, Baxter paper)

1-4-Ties into DNAgents series 3.00

SURGEON X
Image Comics: Sept, 2016 - No. 6, Feb, 2017 ($3.99)

1-6: 1-Sara Kenney-s/John Watkiss-a/c. 6-Watkiss & Pleece-a 4.00

SURPRISE ADVENTURES (Formerly Tormented)
Sterling Comic Group: No. 3, Mar, 1955 - No. 5, July, 1955

	GD	VG	FN	VF	VF/NM	NM-
3-5: 3,5-Sekowsky-a	14	28	42	78	112	145

SURVIVAL STREET
Dark Horse Comics: Aug, 2022 - No. 4, Nov, 2022 ($3.99, limited series)

1-4-Asmus & Festante-s/Kussainov-a 4.00

SURVIVE (Follows Cataclysm: The Ultimates Last Stand)
Marvel Comics: May, 2014 ($3.99, one-shot)

1-Bendis-s/Quinones-a; the new Ultimates team is formed 4.00

SURVIVORS' CLUB
DC Comics (Vertigo): Dec, 2015 - No. 9, Aug, 2016 ($3.99)

1-9-Beukes & Halvorsen-s/Ryan Kelly-a/Sienkiewicz-c 4.00

SUSIE Q. SMITH
Dell Publishing Co.: No. 323, Mar, 1951 - No. 553, Apr, 1954

	GD	VG	FN	VF	VF/NM	NM-
Four Color 323 (#1)	8	16	24	51	96	140
Four Color 377, 453 (2/53), 553	5	10	15	35	63	90

SUSPENSE (Radio/TV issues #1-11; Real Life Tales of... #1-4) (Amazing Detective Cases #3 on?)
Marvel/Atlas Comics (CnPC No. 1-10/BFP No. 11-29): Dec, 1949 - No. 29, Apr, 1953 (#1-8, 17-23: 52 pgs.)

	GD	VG	FN	VF	VF/NM	NM-
1-Powell-a; Peter Lorre, Sidney Greenstreet photo-c from Hammett's "The Verdict"	116	232	348	742	1271	1800
2-Crime stories; Dennis O'Keefe & Gale Storm photo-c from Universal movie "Abandoned"	52	104	156	328	552	775
3-Change to horror	65	130	195	416	708	1000
4,7-10: 7-Dracula-sty	53	106	159	334	567	800
5-Krigstein, Tuska, Everett-a	55	110	165	352	601	850
6-Tuska, Everett, Morisi-a	50	100	150	315	533	750
11-13,15-17,19,20	45	90	135	284	480	675
14-Classic Heath Hypo-c; A-Bomb panels	129	258	387	826	1413	2000
18,22-Krigstein-a	45	90	135	284	480	675
21,23,24,26-29: 24-Tuska-a	41	82	123	256	428	600
25-Electric chair-c/story	57	114	171	362	619	875

NOTE: ***Ayers** a-20. **Briefer** a-5, 7, 27. **Brodsky** c-4, 6-9, 11, 16, 17, 25. **Colan** a-8(2), 9. **Everett** a-5, 6(2), 19, 23, 28; c-21-23, 26. **Fuje** a-29. **Heath** a-5, 6, 8, 10, 12, 14; c-14, 19, 24. **Maneely** a-11, 12, 23, 24, 28, 29; c-5, 6p, 10, 13, 15, 18. **Mooney** a-24, 28. **Morisi** a-6, 12. **Palais** a-10. **Rico** a-7-9. **Robinson** a-29. **Romita** a-20(2), 25.*

	GD 2.0	VG 4.0	FN 6.0	VF 8.0	VF/NM 9.0	NM- 9.2

Sekowsky a-11, 13, 14. Sinnott a-23, 25. Tuska a-5, 6(2), 12; c-12. Whitney a-15, 16, 22. Ed Win a-27.

SUSPENSE COMICS
Continental Magazines: Dec, 1943 - No. 12, Sept, 1946

	GD	VG	FN	VF	VF/NM	NM-
1-The Grey Mask begins; bondage/torture-c; L. B. Cole-a (7 pgs.)	975	1950	2919	7100	12,550	18,000
2-Intro. The Mask; Rico, Giunta, L. B. Cole-a (7 pgs.)	411	822	1233	2877	5039	7200
3-L.B. Cole-a; classic Schomburg-c (Scarce)	11,900	23,800	35,700	71,400	123,200	175,000
4-L. B. Cole-c begin	326	652	978	2282	3991	5700
5,6	290	580	870	1856	3178	4500
7,9,10,12: 9-L.B. Cole eyeball-c	232	464	696	1485	2543	3600
8-Classic L. B. Cole spider-c	865	1730	2595	6315	11,158	16,000
11-Classic Devil-c	459	918	1377	3350	5925	8500

NOTE: *L. B. Cole c-4-12. Fuje a-8. Larsen a-11. Palais a-10, 11. Bondage c-1, 3, 4.*

SUSPENSE DETECTIVE
Fawcett Publications: June, 1952 - No. 5, Mar, 1953

	GD	VG	FN	VF	VF/NM	NM-
1-Evans-a (11 pgs); Baily-c/a	61	122	183	390	670	950
2-Evans-a (10 pgs.)	33	66	99	194	317	440
3-5	29	58	87	172	281	390

NOTE: *Baily a-4, 5; c-1-3. Sekowsky a-2, 4, 5; c-5.*

SUSPENSE STORIES (See Strange Suspense Stories)

SUSSEX VAMPIRE, THE (Sherlock Holmes)
Caliber Comics: 1996 ($2.95, 32 pgs., B&W, one-shot)

nn-Adapts Sir Arthur Conan Doyle's story; Warren Ellis scripts 3.00

SUZIE COMICS (Formerly Laugh Comix; see Laugh Comics, Liberty Comics #10, Pep Comics & Top-Notch Comics #28)
Close-Up No. 49,50/MLJ Mag./Archie No. 51 on: No. 49, Spring, 1945 - No. 100, Aug, 1954

	GD	VG	FN	VF	VF/NM	NM-
49-Ginger begins	66	132	198	419	722	1025
50-55: 54-Transvestism story. 55-Woggon-a	41	82	123	256	428	600
56-Katy Keene begins by Woggon	65	130	195	416	708	1000
57-65	25	50	75	150	245	340
66-80	20	40	60	120	195	270
81-87,89-99	19	38	57	111	176	240
88,100: 88-Used in **POP**, pgs. 76,77; Bill Woggon draws himself in story. 100-Last Katy Keene	20	40	60	120	195	270

NOTE: *Al Fagaly c-49-67. Katy Keene app. in 53-82, 85-100.*

SWAMP FOX, THE (TV, Disney)(See Walt Disney Presents #2)
Dell Publishing Co.: No. 1179, Dec, 1960

	GD	VG	FN	VF	VF/NM	NM-
Four Color 1179-Leslie Nielsen photo-c	9	18	27	62	126	190

SWAMP THING (See Brave & the Bold, Challengers of the Unknown #82, DC Comics Presents #8 & 85, DC Special Series #2, 14, 17, 20, House of Secrets #92, Limited Collectors' Edition C-59, & Roots of the...)

SWAMP THING
National Per. Publ./DC Comics: Oct-Nov, 1972 - No. 24, Aug-Sept, 1976

	GD	VG	FN	VF	VF/NM	NM-
1-Wrightson-c/a begins; origin	21	42	63	147	324	500
2-1st brief app. Patchwork Man (1 panel)	8	16	24	56	108	160
3-1st full app. Patchwork Man (see House of Secrets #140)	8	16	24	54	102	150
4-6,	5	10	15	35	63	90
7-Batman-c/story	8	16	24	54	102	150
8-10: 10-Last Wrightson issue	5	10	15	33	57	80
11-20: 11-19-Redondo-a. 13-Origin retold (1 pg.)	3	6	9	19	30	40
21-24: 22,23-Redondo-a. 23,24-Swamp Thing reverts back to Dr. Holland. 23-New logo	3	6	9	19	30	40
Secret of the Swamp Thing (2005, $9.99, digest) r/#1-10						10.00

NOTE: *J. Jones a-9i(assist). Kaluta a-9i. Redondo c-11-19, 21. Wrightson issues (#1-10) reprinted in DC Special Series #2, 14, 17, 20 & Roots of the Swamp Thing.*

SWAMP THING (Saga Of The... #1-38,42-45) (See Essential Vertigo:...)
DC Comics (Vertigo imprint #129 on): May, 1982 - No. 171, Oct, 1996 (Direct sales #65 on)

	GD	VG	FN	VF	VF/NM	NM-
1-Origin retold; Phantom Stranger series begins; ends #13; Yeates-c/a begins	3	6	9	16	23	30
2-15: 2-Photo-c from movie. 13-Last Yeates-a						5.00
16-19: Bissette-a.						6.00
20-1st Alan Moore issue	5	10	15	30	50	70
21-New origin	4	8	12	28	47	65
21 Special Editon (5/09, $1.00) reprint with "After Watchmen" cover frame						5.00
22,23	2	4	6	9	13	16
24-JLA x-over; last Yeates-c.	2	4	6	11	16	20
25-John Constantine 1-panel cameo	4	8	12	28	47	65
26-30	1	3	4	6	8	10
31-33,35,36: 33-r/1st app. from House of Secrets #92						6.00
34-Classic-c	2	4	6	13	18	22
37-1st app. John Constantine (Hellblazer) (6/85)	17	34	51	117	259	400
38-40: John Constantine app.	2	4	6	8	11	14
41-52,54-64: 44-Batman cameo. 44-51-John Constantine app. 46-Crisis x-over; Batman cameo. 49-Spectre app. 50-($1.25, 52 pgs.)-Deadman, Dr. Fate, Demon. 52-Arkham Asylum-c/story; Joker-c/cameo. 58-Spectre preview. 64-Last Moore issue						4.00
53-($1.25, 52 pgs.)-Arkham Asylum; Batman-c/story						5.00
65-83,85-99,101-124,126-149,151-153: 65-Direct sales only begins. 66-Batman & Arkham Asylum story. 70,76-John Constantine x-over; 76-X-over w/Hellblazer #9. 79-Superman-c/story. 85-Jonah Hex app. 102-Preview of World Without End. 116-Photo-c. 129-Metallic ink on-c. 140-Millar scripts begin, end #171						4.00
84-Sandman (Morpheus) cameo.						5.00
100,125,150: 100 ($2.50, 52 pgs.). 125-($2.95, 52 pgs.)-20th anniversary issue. 150 (52 pgs.)-Anniversary issue						5.00
154-171: 154-$2.25-c begins. 165-Curt Swan-a(p). 166,169,171-John Constantine & Phantom Stranger app. 168-Arcane returns						4.00
Annual 1,3-6('82-91): 1-Movie Adaptation; painted-c. 3-New format; Bolland-c. 4-Batman-c/story. 5-Batman cameo; re-intro Brother Power (Geek),1st app. since 1968						6.00
Annual 2 (1985)-Moore scripts; Bissette-a(p); Deadman, Spectre app.	1	2	3	5	6	8
Annual 7(1993, $3.95)-Children's Crusade						5.00
...A Murder of Crows (2001, $19.95)-r/#43-50; Moore-s						20.00
...: Earth To Earth (2002, $17.95)-r/#51-56; Batman app.						18.00
...: Infernal Triangles (2006, $19.99, TPB) r/#77-81 & Annual #3; cover gallery						20.00
...Love and Death (1990, $17.95)-r/#28-34 & Annual #2; Totleben painted-c						18.00
...: Regenesis (2004, $17.95, TPB) r/#65-70; Veitch-s						18.00
...: Reunion (2003, $19.95, TPB) r/#57-64; Moore-s						20.00
...: Roots (1998, $7.95) Jon J Muth-s/painted-a/c						8.00
Saga of the Swamp Thing ('87, '89)-r/#21-27 (1st & 2nd print)						15.00
Saga of the Swamp Thing Book One HC (2009, $24.99, d.j.) r/#20-27; Wein intro.						25.00
Saga of the Swamp Thing Book Two HC (2009, $24.99, d.j.) r/#28-34 & Annual #2						25.00
Saga of the Swamp Thing Book Three HC (2010, $24.99, d.j.) r/#35-42; Bissette intro.						25.00
Saga of the Swamp Thing Book Four HC (2010, $24.99, d.j.) r/#43-50; Gaiman foreword						25.00
Saga of the Swamp Thing Book Five HC (2011, $24.99, d.j.) r/#51-56; Bissette intro.						25.00
...: Spontaneous Generation (2005, $19.99) r/#71-76						20.00
...: The Curse (2000, $19.95, TPB) r/#35-42; Bisley-c						20.00

NOTE: *Bissette a(p)-16-19, 21-27, 29, 30, 34-36, 39-42, 44, 46, 50, 64; c-17i, 24-32p, 35-37p, 40p, 44p, 46-50p, 51-58, 61, 62, 63p. Kaluta c/a-74. Spiegle a-1-3, 6. Sutton a-98p. Totleben a(i)-10, 16-27, 29, 31, 34-40, 42, 44, 46, 48, 50, 53, 55i; c-25-32i, 33, 35-40i, 42i, 44i, 46-50i, 53, 55i, 59p, 64, 65, 68, 73, 76, 80, 82, 84, 89, 91-100, Annual 4, 5. Vess painted c-121, 129-139, Annual 7. Williamson 86i. Wrightson a-18i(r), 33r. John Constantine appears in #37-40, 44-51, 65-67, 70-77, 80-90, 99, 114, 115, 130, 134-138.*

SWAMP THING
DC Comics (Vertigo): May, 2000 - No. 20, Dec, 2001 ($2.50)

1-3-Tefé Holland's return; Vaughan-s/Petersen-a; Hale painted-c. 4.00
4-20: 7-9-Bisley-c. 10-John Constantine-c/app. 10-12-Fabry-c. 13-15-Mack-c 18-Swamp Thing app. 3.00
Preview-16 pg. flip book w/Lucifer Preview 3.00

SWAMP THING
DC Comics (Vertigo): May, 2004 - No. 29, Sept, 2006 ($2.95/$2.99)

1-29: 1-Diggle-s/Breccia-a; Constantine app. 2-6-Sargon app. 7,8,20-Corben-c/a. 21-29-Eric Powell-c 3.00
...: Bad Seed (2004, $9.95) r/#1-6 10.00
...: Healing the Breach (2006, $17.99) r/#15-20 18.00
...: Love in Vain (2005, $14.99) r/#9-14 15.00

SWAMP THING (DC New 52)
DC Comics: Nov, 2011 - No. 40, May, 2015 ($2.99)

1-Snyder-s/Paquette-a; Superman app. 8.00
1-(2nd & 3rd printing) 3.00
2-18: 2-Abigail Arcane returns. 7-Holland transforms. 10-Francavilla-a; Anton Arcane returns. 12-X-over with Animal Man #12. 13-Poison Ivy & Deadman app.; leads into Annual #1 3.00
19-23: 19-Soule-s/Kano-a begin. 19,20-Superman app. 22,23-Constantine app. 3.00
23.1 (11/13, $2.99, regular cover) 3.00
23.1 (11/13, $3.99, 3-D cover) "Arcane #1" on cover; Soule-s/Saiz-a/c; origin of Arcane 5.00
24-39: 24-Leads into Annual #2. 26-Woodrue's origin; Animal Man app. 32-Aquaman app. 39-Constantine app. 3.00
40-($3.99) 4.00
#0-(11/12, $2.99) Kano-a; Arcane app.; Swamp Thing origin re-told 3.00
Annual #1 (12/12, $4.99) Flashback to 1st meeting of Alec & Abby; Cloonan-a 5.00
Annual #2 (12/13, $4.99) Soule-s/Pina-a 5.00
Annual #3 (12/14, $4.99) Soule-s/Pina-a: Etrigan app. 5.00
...: Futures End 1 (11/14, $2.99, regular-c) Five years later; Soule-s/Saiz-a; Arcane app. 3.00
...: Futures End 1 (11/14, $3.99, 3-D cover) 4.00

SWAMP THING
DC Comics: Mar, 2016 - No. 6, Aug, 2016 ($2.99)

1-6-Len Wein-s/Kelley Jones-a. 1,2-Phantom Stranger app. 2-Matt Cable returns. 3,4,6-Zatanna app. 3.00
... Winter Special 1 (3/18, $7.99) Wein-s/Jones-a; King-s/Fabok-a; Wein script & tribute 8.00

SWAMP THING, THE
DC Comics: May, 2021 - No. 16, Oct, 2022 ($3.99, originally a 10-issue series)

1-16: 1-Ram V-s/Mike Perkins-a; intro Levi Kamei. 3,4-Poison Ivy & Alec Holland app. 5-John Constantine app.; McCrea-a. 6-8-Peacemaker & Suicide Squad app. 4.00

SWAMP THING GIANT
DC Comics: 2019 - No. 5, 2019 ($4.99, 100 pgs., squarebound, Walmart exclusive)

1-5: 1-New story Seeley-s/Perkins-a; reprints from Animal Man ('11), Swamp Thing ('11), and Shadowpact ('06). 2-New story with Joëlle Jones-a plus reprints continue 5.00
Halloween Horror Giant ('18, $4.99) Intro. Briar in new story; Capullo-a; plus reprints 5.00

SWAMP THING GIANT
DC Comics: 2019 - No. 5, 2020 ($4.99, 100 pgs., squarebound, Mass Market & Direct Market editions exist for each issue, with different covers)

1-5-New stories Russell-s/Santucci-a & Hester-s/Mandrake-a; plus reprints 5.00

SWAMP THING: GREEN HELL
DC Comics (Black Label): Feb, 2022 - No. 3, May, 2023 ($6.99, oversized 8-1/2" x 10-3/4", lim. series)

1-3-Jeff Lemire-s/Doug Mahnke-a; John Constantine app. 7.00
1-Second printing (3/22, $6.99) 7.00

SWASHBUCKLERS: THE SAGA CONTINUES (See Marvel Graphic Novel #14 and Swords of The Swashbucklers)
Dynamite Entertainment: 2018 - No. 5, 2018 ($3.99, limited series)

1-5-Marc Guggenheim-s/Andrea Mutti-a 4.00

SWAT MALONE (America's Home Run King)
Swat Malone Enterprises: Sept, 1955

	GD	VG	FN	VF	VF/NM	NM-
V1#1-Hy Fleishman-a	13	26	39	72	101	130

SWEATSHOP
DC Comics: Jun, 2003 - No. 6, Nov, 2003 ($2.95)

1-6-Peter Bagge-s/a; Destefano-a 3.00

SWEENEY (Formerly Buz Sawyer)
Standard Comics: No. 4, June, 1949 - No. 5, Sept, 1949

	GD	VG	FN	VF	VF/NM	NM-
4,5: 5-Crane-a	10	20	30	54	72	90

SWEE'PEA (Also see Popeye #46)
Dell Publishing Co.: No. 219, Mar, 1949

	GD	VG	FN	VF	VF/NM	NM-
Four Color 219	10	20	30	64	132	200

Swamp Thing (2006) #25 © DC

Sweet Tooth #10 © Jeff Lemire

Switch #1 © TCOW

SWEET CHILDE
Advantage Graphics Press: 1995 - No. 2, 1995 ($2.95, B&W, mature)

	GD 2.0	VG 4.0	FN 6.0	VF 8.0	VF/NM 9.0	NM- 9.2
1,2						3.00

SWEETHEART DIARY (Cynthia Doyle #66-on)
Fawcett Publications/Charlton Comics No. 32 on: Wint, 1949; #2, Spr, 1950; #3, 6/50 - #5, 10/50; #6, 1951(nd); #7, 9/51 - #14, 1/53; #32, 10/55; #33, 4/56 - #65, 8/62 (#1-14: photo-c)

	GD 2.0	VG 4.0	FN 6.0	VF 8.0	VF/NM 9.0	NM- 9.2
1	23	46	69	136	223	310
2	15	30	45	83	124	165
3,4-Wood-a	17	34	51	98	154	210
5-10: 8-Bailey-a	10	20	30	56	76	95
11-14: 13-Swayze-a. 14-Last Fawcett issue	9	18	27	47	61	75
32 (10/55; 1st Charlton issue)(Formerly Cowboy Love #31)	9	18	27	52	69	85
33-40: 34-Swayze-a	7	14	21	35	43	50
41-(68 pgs.)	8	16	24	40	50	60
42-60	3	6	9	19	30	40
61-65	3	6	9	17	26	35

SWEETHEARTS (Formerly Captain Midnight)
Fawcett Publications/Charlton No. 122 on: #68, 10/48 - #121, 5/53; #122, 3/54; V2#23, 5/54 - #137, 12/73

	GD 2.0	VG 4.0	FN 6.0	VF 8.0	VF/NM 9.0	NM- 9.2
68-Photo-c begin	21	42	63	122	199	275
69,70	13	26	39	72	101	130
71-80	9	18	27	52	69	85
81-84,86-93,95-99,105	9	18	27	47	61	75
85,94,103,110,117-George Evans-a	10	20	30	54	72	90
100	9	18	27	52	69	85
101,107-Powell-a	9	18	27	50	65	80
102,104,106,108,109,112-116,118	8	16	24	44	57	70
111-1 pg. Ronald Reagan biography	11	22	33	62	86	110
119-Marilyn Monroe & Richard Widmark photo-c (1/53); also appears in story; part Wood-a	148	296	444	947	1624	2300
120-Atom Bomb story	12	24	36	67	94	120
121-Liz Taylor/Fernanado Lamas photo-c	41	82	123	256	428	600
122-(1st Charlton? 3/54)-Marijuana story	14	28	42	76	108	140
V2#23 (5/54)-28: 28-Last precode issue (2/55)	8	16	24	42	54	65
29-39,41,43,45,47-50	4	8	12	25	40	55
40-Photo-c; Tommy Sands story	4	8	12	27	44	60
42-Ricky Nelson photo-c/story	7	14	21	49	92	135
44-Pat Boone photo-c/story	4	8	12	27	44	60
46-Jimmy Rodgers photo-c/story	4	8	12	27	44	60
51-60	3	6	9	21	33	45
61-80,100	3	6	9	18	28	38
81-99	3	6	9	16	24	32
101-110	2	4	6	13	18	22
111-120,122-124,126-137	2	4	6	10	14	18
121,125-David Cassidy pin-ups	2	4	6	13	18	22

NOTE: *Photo c-68-121(Fawcett), 40, 42, 46(Charlton).* **Swayze** *a(Fawcett)-70-118(most).*

SWEETHEART SCANDALS (See Fox Giants)

SWEETIE PIE
Dell Publishing Co.: No. 1185, May-July, 1961 - No. 1241, Nov-Jan, 1961/62

	GD 2.0	VG 4.0	FN 6.0	VF 8.0	VF/NM 9.0	NM- 9.2
Four Color 1185 (#1)	6	12	18	38	69	100
Four Color 1241	5	10	15	31	53	75

SWEETIE PIE
Ajax-Farrell/Pines (Literary Ent.): Dec, 1955 - No. 15, Fall, 1957

	GD 2.0	VG 4.0	FN 6.0	VF 8.0	VF/NM 9.0	NM- 9.2
1-By Nadine Seltzer	14	28	42	76	108	140
2 (5/56; last Ajax?)	8	16	24	42	54	65
3-15	7	14	21	37	46	55

SWEET LOVE
Home Comics (Harvey): Sept, 1949 - No. 5, May, 1950 (All photo-c)

	GD 2.0	VG 4.0	FN 6.0	VF 8.0	VF/NM 9.0	NM- 9.2
1	14	28	42	80	115	150
2	8	16	24	42	54	65
3,4: 3-Powell-a	7	14	21	37	46	55
5-Kamen, Powell-a	9	18	27	52	69	85

SWEET ROMANCE
Charlton Comics: Oct, 1968

	GD 2.0	VG 4.0	FN 6.0	VF 8.0	VF/NM 9.0	NM- 9.2
1	3	6	9	14	20	25

SWEET SIXTEEN (...Comics and Stories for Girls)
Parents' Magazine Institute: Aug-Sept, 1946 - No. 13, Jan, 1948 (All have movie stars photos on covers)

	GD 2.0	VG 4.0	FN 6.0	VF 8.0	VF/NM 9.0	NM- 9.2
1-Van Johnson's life story; Dorothy Dare, Queen of Hollywood Stunt Artists begins (in all issues); part photo-c	34	68	102	199	325	450
2-Jane Powell, Roddy McDowall "Holiday in Mexico" photo on-c; Alan Ladd story	22	44	66	128	209	290
3,5,6,8-11: 5-Ann Francis photo on-c; Gregory Peck story. 6-Dick Haymes story. 8-Shirley Jones photo on-c. 10-Jean Simmons photo on-c; James Stewart story	17	34	51	100	158	215
4-Elizabeth Taylor photo on-c	39	78	117	231	378	525
7-Ronald Reagan's life story	33	66	99	194	317	440
12-Bob Cummings, Vic Damone story	18	36	54	105	165	225
13-Robert Mitchum's life story	18	36	54	105	165	225

SWEET XVI
Marvel Comics: May, 1991 - No. 5, Sept, 1991 ($1.00)

	GD 2.0	VG 4.0	FN 6.0	VF 8.0	VF/NM 9.0	NM- 9.2
1-5: Barbara Slate story & art						4.00

SWEET TOOTH
DC Comics (Vertigo): Nov, 2009 - No. 40, Feb, 2013 ($1.00/$2.99)

	GD 2.0	VG 4.0	FN 6.0	VF 8.0	VF/NM 9.0	NM- 9.2
1-($1.00) Jeff Lemire-s/a	6	12	18	38	69	100
2	1	2	3	6	8	10
3-39-($2.99) 18,33-Printed sideways. 26-28-Kindt-a						3.00
40-($4.99) Final issue; two covers by Lemire and Truman						5.00
...: Animal Armies TPB (2011, $14.99) r/#12-17						15.00
...: In Captivity TPB (2010, $12.99) r/#6-11						13.00
...: Out of the Deep Woods TPB (2010, $9.99) r/#1-5						10.00

SWEET TOOTH: THE RETURN
DC Comics (Black Label): Jan, 2021 - No. 6, Jun, 2021 ($3.99, limited series)

	GD 2.0	VG 4.0	FN 6.0	VF 8.0	VF/NM 9.0	NM- 9.2
1-6-Jeff Lemire-s/a						4.00

SWIFT ARROW (Also see Lone Rider & The Rider)
Ajax/Farrell Publications: Feb-Mar, 1954 - No. 5, Oct-Nov, 1954; Apr, 1957 - No. 3, Sept, 1957

	GD 2.0	VG 4.0	FN 6.0	VF 8.0	VF/NM 9.0	NM- 9.2
1(1954) (1st Series)	19	38	57	111	176	240
2	12	24	36	67	94	120
3-5: 5-Lone Rider story	9	18	27	50	65	80
1 (2nd Series) (Swift Arrow's Gunfighters #4)	9	18	27	50	65	80
2,3: 2-Lone Rider begins	8	16	24	40	50	60

SWIFT ARROW'S GUNFIGHTERS (Formerly Swift Arrow)
Ajax/Farrell Publ. (Four Star Comic Corp.): No. 4, Nov, 1957

	GD 2.0	VG 4.0	FN 6.0	VF 8.0	VF/NM 9.0	NM- 9.2
4	8	16	24	40	50	60

SWING WITH SCOOTER
National Periodical Publ.: June-July, 1966 - No. 35, Aug-Sept, 1971; No. 36, Oct-Nov, 1972

	GD 2.0	VG 4.0	FN 6.0	VF 8.0	VF/NM 9.0	NM- 9.2
1	9	18	27	62	126	190
2,6-10: 9-Alfred E. Newman swipe in last panel	5	10	15	33	57	80
3-5: 3-Batman cameo on-c. 4-Batman cameo inside. 5-JLA cameo	5	10	15	34	60	85
11-13,15-19: 18-Wildcat of JSA 1pg. text. 19-Last 12¢-c	3	6	9	20	31	42
14-Alfred E. Neuman cameo	4	8	12	23	37	50
20 (68 pgs.)	5	10	15	30	50	70
21-23,25-31	3	6	9	17	26	35
24-Frankenstein-c.	4	8	12	23	37	50
32-34 (68 pgs.). 32-Batman cameo. 33-Interview with David Cassidy. 34-Interview with Rick Ely (The Rebels)	4	8	12	28	47	65
35-(52 pgs.). 1 pg. app. Clark Kent and 4 full pgs. of Superman	7	14	21	49	92	135
36-Bat-signal refererence to Batman	3	6	9	21	33	45

NOTE: **Aragonés** *a-13 (1pg.), 18(1pg.), 30(2pgs.)* **Orlando** *a-1-11; c-1-11, 13. #20, 33, 34: 68 pgs.; #35: 52 pgs.*

SWISS FAMILY ROBINSON (Walt Disney's..; see King Classics & Movie Comics)
Dell Publishing Co.: No. 1156, Dec, 1960

	GD 2.0	VG 4.0	FN 6.0	VF 8.0	VF/NM 9.0	NM- 9.2
Four Color 1156-Movie-photo-c	9	18	27	59	117	175

SWITCH (Also see Witchblade titles)
Image Comics: Oct, 2015 - No. 4, Jul, 2016 ($3.99)

	GD 2.0	VG 4.0	FN 6.0	VF 8.0	VF/NM 9.0	NM- 9.2
1-4-Stjepan Sejic-s/a; 3 covers on each						4.00

S.W.O.R.D. (Sentient World Observation and Response Department)
Marvel Comics: Jan, 2010 - No. 5, May, 2010 ($3.99/$2.99)

	GD 2.0	VG 4.0	FN 6.0	VF 8.0	VF/NM 9.0	NM- 9.2
1-($3.99) Cassaday-c/Gillen-s/Sanders-a; Commander Brand & Henry Gyrich app.						4.00
2-5-($2.99): 2,3-Cassaday-c. 4,5-Del Mundo-c						3.00

S.W.O.R.D. (Sentient World Observation and Response Department)
Marvel Comics: Feb, 2021 - No. 11, Feb, 2022 ($4.99/$3.99)

	GD 2.0	VG 4.0	FN 6.0	VF 8.0	VF/NM 9.0	NM- 9.2
1-($4.99) Al Ewing-s/Valerio Schiti-a; Abigail Brand & Magneto app.						5.00
2-11-($3.99) 2-4- "King in Black" tie-ins. 6-Hellfire Gala tie-in						4.00

SWORD, THE

GD	VG	FN	VF	VF/NM	NM-
2.0	4.0	6.0	8.0	9.0	9.2

Image Comics: Oct, 2007 - No. 24, May, 2010 ($2.99/$4.99)

1-Luna Brothers-s/a 4.00
1-(2nd printing), 2-23: 12-Zakros killed 3.00
24-($4.99) Final issue 5.00

SWORD & THE DRAGON, THE
Dell Publishing Co.: No. 1118, June, 1960

Four Color 1118-Movie, photo-c 8 16 24 54 102 150

SWORD & THE ROSE, THE (Disney)
Dell Publishing Co.: No. 505, Oct, 1953 - No. 682, Feb, 1956

Four Color 505-Movie, photo-c 9 18 27 58 114 170
Four Color 682-When Knighthood Was in Flower-Movie, reprint of #505; Renamed the Sword & the Rose for the novel; photo-c 6 12 18 42 79 115

SWORD DAUGHTER
Dark Horse Publishing: Jun, 2018 - No. 9, Jan, 2020 ($4.99)

1-9-Brian Wood-s/Mack Chater-a/Greg Smallwood-c 5.00

SWORD IN THE STONE, THE (See March of Comics #258 & Movie Comics & Wart and the Wizard)

SWORD MASTER
Marvel Comics: Sept, 2019 - No. 12, Jan, 2021 ($3.99)

1-12: 1-Shang-Chi & Ares app.; Shuizhu-s/Gunji-a. 5,6-Doctor Strange app. 4.00

SWORD OF AGES
IDW Publishing: Nov, 2017 - No. 4 ($3.99)

1-4-Gabriel Rodríguez-s/a 4.00
1 Special Edition (6/18, $6.99) bonus interview with Gabriel Rodríguez; uncolored art 7.00

SWORD OF AZRAEL
DC Comics: Oct, 2022 - No. 6, Mar, 2023 ($3.99, limited series)

1-6-Watters-s/Cizmesija-a; Bane's daughter Vengeance app. 4.00
...: Dark Knight of the Soul 1(10/22, $3.99) Prelude to the series 4.00

SWORD OF DAMOCLES
Image Comics (WildStorm Productions): Mar, 1996 - No. 2, Apr, 1996 ($2.50, limited series)

1,2: Warren Ellis scripts. 1-Prelude to "Fire From Heaven" x-over; 1st app. Sword 3.00

SWORD OF DRACULA
Image Comics: Oct, 2003 - No. 6, Sept, 2004 ($2.95, B&W, limited series)

1-6-Tony Harris-c. 1,2-Greg Scott-a 3.00
TPB (IDW, 2/05, $14.99) r/series 15.00

SWORD OF HYPERBOREA, THE
Dark Horse Comics: Jan, 2022 - No. 4, Apr, 2022 ($3.99, limited series)

1-Mike Mignola & Rob Williams-s/Laurence Campbell-a 4.00

SWORD OF RED SONJA: DOOM OF THE GODS
Dynamite Entertainment: 2007 - No. 4, 2007 ($3.50, limited series)

1-4-Lui Antonio-a; multiple covers on each 3.50

SWORD OF SORCERY
National Periodical Publications: Feb-Mar, 1973 - No. 5, Nov-Dec, 1973 (20¢)

1-Leiber Fafhrd & The Grey Mouser; Chaykin/Neal Adams (Crusty Bunkers) art; Kaluta-c 3 6 9 19 30 40
2,3: 2-Wrightson-c(i); Adams-a(i). 3-Wrightson-i(5 pgs.) 2 4 6 9 13 16
4,5: 5-Starlin-a(p); Conan cameo 2 4 6 8 10 12

NOTE: ***Chaykin** a-1-4p; c-2p, 3-5. **Kaluta** a-3i. **Simonson** a-3i, 4i, 5p; c-5.*

SWORD OF SORCERY (DC New 52)
DC Comics: No. 0, Nov, 2012 - No. 8, Jun, 2013 ($3.99)

0-8: 0-Origin of Amethyst retold; Lopresti-a; Beowulf back-up; Saiz-a. 4-Stalker back-up 4.00

SWORD OF THE ATOM
DC Comics: Sept, 1983 - No. 4, Dec, 1983 (Limited series)

1-4: Gil Kane-c/a in all 4.00
Special 1-3('84, '85, '88): 1,2-Kane-c/a each 4.00
TPB (2007, $19.99) r/#1-4 and Special #1-3 20.00

SWORDQUEST (Based on the Atari game)
Dynamite Entertainment: No. 0, 2017 - No. 5, 2017 (25¢/$3.99)

0-(25¢) Bowers & Sims-s/Ghostwriter X-a; bonus game history and character art 3.00
1-5-($3.99) Multiple covers on each; George Peréz & others 4.00

SWORDS OF SORROW
Dynamite Entertainment: 2015 - No. 6, 2015 ($3.99, limited series with tie-in series)

1-6-Simone-s/Davila-a; crossover of Vampirella, Red Sonja, Dejah Thoris, Lady Zorro and other female Dynamite characters; multiple covers on each 4.00
...: Black Sparrow & Lady Zorro Special 1 ($3.99, one-shot) Schultz-s/Zamora-a 4.00
...: Chaos! Prequel 1 ($3.99, one-shot) Mairghread Scott-s/Mirka Andolfo-a 4.00
...: Dejah Thoris & Irene Adler 1-3 ($3.99, lim. series) Leah Moore-s/Francesco Manna-a 4.00
...: Masquerade & Kato 1 ($3.99, one-shot) G. Willow Wilson & Erica Schultz-s 4.00
...: Miss Fury & Lady Rawhide 1 ($3.99, one-shot) Mikki Kendall-s/Ronilson Freire-a 4.00
...: Pantha & Jane Porter ($3.99, one-shot) Emma Beeby-s/Rod Rodolfo-a 4.00
...: Red Sonja & Jungle Girl 1-3 ($3.99, lim. series) Bennett-s/Andolfo-a/Anacleto-c 4.00
...: Vampirella & Jennifer Blood 1-4 ($3.99, lim. series) Nancy Collins-s/Dave Acosta-a 4.00

SWORDS OF TEXAS (See Scout #15)
Eclipse Comics: Oct, 1987 - No. 4, Jan, 1988 ($1.75, color, Baxter paper)

1-4: Scout app. 3.00

SWORDS OF THE SWASHBUCKLERS (See Marvel Graphic Novel #14)
Marvel Comics (Epic Comics): May, 1985 - No. 12, Jun, 1987 ($1.50; mature)

1-12-Butch Guice-c/a (cont'd from Marvel G.N. #14) 3.00

SWORN TO PROTECT
Marvel Comics: Sept, 1995 ($1.95) (Based on card game)

nn-Overpower Game Guide; Jubilee story 4.00

SYMBIOTE SPIDER-MAN (Takes place right after acquiring black costume in Secret Wars)
Marvel Comics: Jun, 2019 - No. 5, Oct, 2019 ($4.99/$3.99, limited series)

1-($4.99) Peter David-s/Greg Land-a; Mysterio and Felicia Hardy app. in all 5.00
2-5-($3.99) 3-Kingpin & Electro app. 4.00
...: Marvel Tales 1 (3/21, $7.99) Reprints of notable early Symbiote apps.; Macchio intro. 8.00

SYMBIOTE SPIDER-MAN: ALIEN REALITY
Marvel Comics: Feb, 2020 - No. 5, Sept, 2020 ($4.99/$3.99, limited series)

1-($4.99) Peter David-s/Greg Land-a; Hobgoblin, Doctor Strange & Black Widow app. 5.00
2-5-($3.99) 2-Uncle Ben app. 3-5-Baron Mordo app. 4.00

SYMBIOTE SPIDER-MAN: CROSSROADS
Marvel Comics: Sept, 2021 - No. 5, Jan, 2022 ($4.99/$3.99, limited series)

1-($4.99) Peter David-s/Greg Land-a; Black Cat and Moondark app. 5.00
2-5-($3.99) 2-4-Hulk & Devil Dinosaur app. 4-Eternals app. 4.00

SYMBIOTE SPIDER-MAN: KING IN BLACK (Tie-in to King in Black crossover)
Marvel Comics: Jan, 2021 - No. 5, May, 2021 ($4.99/$3.99, limited series)

1-($4.99) Peter David-s/Greg Land-a; The Watcher and Kang app. 5.00
2-5-($3.99) 2-Black Knight app. 3,4-Captain Marvel (Monica Rambeau) app. 4.00

SYMMETRY
Image Comics (Top Cow): Dec, 2015 - No. 8, Oct, 2016 ($3.99)

1-8-Hawkins-s/Ienco-a 4.00

SYMPATHY FOR NO DEVILS
AfterShock Comics: Oct, 2020 - No. 5, Feb, 2021 ($3.99)

1-5-Brandon Thomas-s/Lee Ferguson-a 4.00

SYN
Dark Horse Comics: Aug, 2003 - No. 5, Feb, 2004 ($2.99, limited series)

1-5-Giffen-s/Titus-a 3.00

SYNERGY: A HASBRO CREATORS SHOWCASE
IDW Publishing: Mar, 2019 ($7.99, one-shot)

1-Short stories and pin-ups of My Little Pony, Jem, Transformers by women creators 8.00

SYPHON
Image Comics (Top Cow): Jul, 2021 - No. 3, Sept, 2021 ($3.99, limited series)

1-3-Meaney & Ashraf-s/Edwards-a 4.00

SYPHONS
Now Comics: V2#1, May, 1994 - V2#3, 1994 ($2.50, limited series)

V2#1-3: 1-Stardancer, Knightfire, Raze & Brigade begin 3.00
TPB (9/04, $15.95) B&W reprints #1-3; intro. by Tony Caputo 16.00

SYSTEM, THE
DC Comics (Vertigo Verite): May, 1996 - No. 3, July, 1996 ($2.95, lim. series)

1-3: Kuper-c/a 3.00

TAFFY COMICS (Also see Dotty Dripple)
Rural Home/Orbit Publ.: Mar-Apr, 1945 - No. 12, 1948

1-L.B. Cole-c; origin & 1st app. of Wiggles The Wonderworm plus 7 chapter WWII funny animal adventures 74 148 222 470 810 1150
2-L.B. Cole-c with funny animal Hitler; Wiggles-c/stories in #1-4 65 130 195 416 708 1000
3,4,6-12: 6-Perry Como-c/story. 7-Duke Ellington, 2 pgs. 8-Glenn Ford-c/story. 9-Lon McCallister part photo-c & story. 10-Mort Leav-c. 11-Mickey Rooney-c/story 19 38 57 111 176 240
5-L.B. Cole-c; Van Johnson-c/story 27 54 81 162 266 370

TAILGUNNER JO
DC Comics: Sept, 1988 - No. 6, Jan, 1989 ($1.25)

1-6 3.00

TAILS
Archie Publications: Dec, 1995 - No. 3, Feb, 1996 ($1.50, limited series)

1-3: Based on Sonic, the Hedgehog video game 6.00

TAILS OF THE PET AVENGERS (Also see Lockjaw and the Pet Avengers)
Marvel Comics: Apr, 2010 ($3.99, one-shot)

1-Lockjaw, Frog Thor, Zabu, Lockheed and Redwing in short solo stories by various 4.00
...: The Dogs of Summer (9/10, $3.99) Eliopolous-s; see Avengers vs. the Pet Avengers 4.00

TAILSPIN
Spotlight Publishers: November, 1944

nn-Firebird app.; L.B. Cole-c 43 86 129 271 461 650

TAILSPIN TOMMY (Also see Popular Comics)
United Features Syndicate/Service Publ. Co.: 1940; 1946

Single Series 23(1940) 50 100 150 315 533 750
1-Best Seller (nd, 1946)-Service Publ. Co. 24 48 72 142 234 325

TAKIO
Marvel Comics (Icon): 2011; May, 2012 - No. 4 ($3.95/$9.95)

HC (2011, $9.95) Bendis-s/Oeming-a/c; Oeming sketch pages 10.00
1-4: 1-(5/12, $3.95) Bendis-s/Oeming-a/c 4.00

TAKION
DC Comics: June, 1996 - No. 7, Dec, 1996 ($1.75)

1-7: Lopresti-c/a(p). 1-Origin; Green Lantern app. 6-Final Night x-over 3.00

TALENT SHOWCASE (See New Talent Showcase)

TALE OF ONE BAD RAT, THE
Dark Horse Comics: Oct, 1994 - No. 4, Jan, 1995 ($2.95, limited series)

1-4: Bryan Talbot-c/a/scripts 3.00
HC ($69.95, signed and numbered) R/#1-4 70.00

TALES CALCULATED TO DRIVE YOU BATS
Archie Publications: Nov, 1961 - No. 7, Nov, 1962; 1966 (Satire)

1-Only 10¢ issue; has cut-out Werewolf mask (price includes mask) 16 32 48 110 243 375
2-Begin 12¢ issues 9 18 27 60 120 180
3-6: 3-UFO cover 7 14 21 49 92 135
7-Storyline change 7 14 21 46 86 125
1(1966, 25¢, 44 pg. Giant)-r/#1; UFO cover 8 16 24 51 96 140

Symbiote Spider-Man #2 © MAR

Takio #2 © Jinxworld

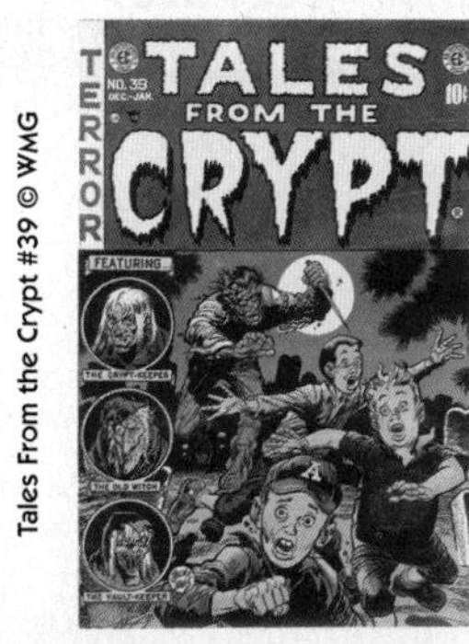

Tales From the Crypt #39 © WMG

	GD 2.0	VG 4.0	FN 6.0	VF 8.0	VF/NM 9.0	NM- 9.2

TALES CALCULATED TO DRIVE YOU MAD
E.C. Publications: Summer, 1997 - No. 8, Winter, 1999 ($3.99/$4.99, satire)

1-6-Full color reprints of Mad: 1-(#1-3), 2-(#4-6), 3-(#7-9), 4-(#10-12) 5-(#13-15), 6-(#16-18) 6.00
7,8-($4.99-c): 7-(#19-21), 8-(#22,23) 6.00

TALES FROM EARTH-6: A CELEBRATION OF STAN LEE (Characters from "Just Imagine Stan Lee With..." series of one-shots)
DC Comics: Feb, 2023 ($9.99, squarebound one-shot)

1-Short stories by Waid, Ordway, Maguire, Uslan, Weeks, Cloonan & others; Cheung-c 10.00

TALES FROM HARROW COUNTY (Also see Harrow County)
Dark Horse Comics: Dec, 2019 - No. 4, Mar, 2020 ($3.99, limited series)

1-4-Cullen Bunn-s/Naomi Franquiz-a; set 10 years after the events of Harrow County 4.00

TALES FROM HARROW COUNTY: FAIR FOLK
Dark Horse Comics: Jul, 2021 - No. 4, Oct, 2021 ($3.99, limited series)

1-4-Cullen Bunn-s/Emily Schnall-a 4.00

TALES FROM HARROW COUNTY: LOST ONES
Dark Horse Comics: May, 2022 - No. 4, Aug, 2022 ($3.99, limited series)

1-4-Cullen Bunn-s/Emily Schnall-a 4.00

TALES FROM RIVERDALE DIGEST
Archie Publ.: June, 2005 - No. 39, Oct, 2010 ($2.39/$2.49/$2.69, digest-size)

1-39: 1-Sabrina and Josie & the Pussycats app. 11-Begin $2.49-c. 34-Begin $2.69 3.00

TALES FROM THE AGE OF APOCALYPSE
Marvel Comics: 1996 ($5.95, prestige format, one-shots)

1, ...: Sinister Bloodlines (1997, $5.95) 6.00

TALES FROM THE BOG
Aberration Press: Nov, 1995 - No. 7, Nov, 1997 ($2.95/$3.95, B&W)

1-7 4.00
Alternate #1 (Director's Cut) (1998, $2.95) 3.00

TALES FROM THE BULLY PULPIT
Image Comics: Aug, 2004 ($6.95, square-bound)

1-Teddy Roosevelt and Edison's ghost with a time machine; Cereno-s/MacDonald-a 7.00

TALES FROM THE CLERKS (See Jay and Silent Bob, Clerks and Oni Double Feature)
Graphitti Designs, Inc.: 2006 ($29.95, TPB)

nn-Reprints all the Kevin Smith Clerks and Jay and Silent Bob stories; new Clerks II story with Mahfood-a; cover gallery, sketch pages, Mallrats credits covers; Smith intro. 30.00

TALES FROM THE CON
Image Comics: May, 2014 ($3.50, one-shot)

...: Year 1 - Brad Guigar-s/Chris Giarrusso-a/c; comic convention humor strips 3.50

TALES FROM THE CRYPT (Formerly The Crypt Of Terror; see Three Dimensional...) (Also see EC Archives • Tales From the Crypt)
E.C. Comics: No. 20, Oct-Nov, 1950 - No. 46, Feb-Mar, 1955

	GD	VG	FN	VF	VF/NM	NM-
20-See Crime Patrol #15 for 1st Crypt Keeper	257	514	771	2056	3278	4500
21-Kurtzman-r/Haunt of Fear #15(#1)	123	246	369	984	1567	2150
22-Moon Girl costume at costume party, one panel	120	240	360	960	1530	2100
23-25: 23-"Reflection of Death" adapted for 1972 TFTC film. 24-E. A. Poe adaptation	91	182	273	728	1164	1600
26-30: 26-Wood's 2nd EC-c	74	148	222	592	946	1300
31-Williamson-a(1st at E.C.); B&W and color illos. in **POP**; Kamen draws himself, Gaines & Feldstein; Ingels, Craig & Davis draw themselves in his story	80	160	240	640	1020	1400
32,35-39: 38-Censored-c	66	132	198	528	839	1150
33-Origin The Crypt Keeper	97	194	291	776	1238	1700
34-Used in **POP**, pg. 83; classic Frankenstein Monster, Jack the Ripper-c by Davis; lingerie panels	91	182	273	728	1164	1600
40-Used in Senate hearings & in Hartford Courant anti-comics editorials-1954	91	182	273	728	1164	1600
41-45: 45-2 pgs. showing E.C. staff; anti-censorship editorial of upcoming Senate hearings	69	138	207	552	876	1200
46-Low distribution; pre-advertised cover for unpublished 4th horror title "Crypt of Terror" used on this book; "Blind Alleys" adapted for 1972 TFTC film; classic werewolf-c by Davis	137	274	411	1096	1748	2400

NOTE: ***Ray Bradbury** adaptations-34, 36. **Craig** a-20, 22-24; c-20. **Crandall** a-38, 44. **Davis** a-24-46; c-29-46. **Elder** a-37, 38. **Evans** a-32-34, 36, 40, 41, 43, 46. **Feldstein** a-20-23; c-21-25, 28. Ingels a-in all. **Kamen** a-20, 22, 25, 27-31, 33-36, 39, 41-45. **Krigstein** a-40, 42, 45. **Kurtzman** a-21. **Orlando** a-27-30, 35, 37, 39, 41-45. **Wood** a-21, 24, 25; c-26, 27. Canadian reprints known; see Table of Contents.*

TALES FROM THE CRYPT (Magazine)
Eerie Publications: No. 10, July, 1968 (35¢, B&W)

	GD	VG	FN	VF	VF/NM	NM-
10-Contains Farrell reprints from 1950s	7	14	21	48	89	130

TALES FROM THE CRYPT
Gladstone Publishing: July, 1990 - No. 6, May, 1991 ($1.95/$2.00, 68 pgs.)

1-r/TFTC #33 & Crime S.S. #17; Davis-c(r) 5.00
2-6: 2,3,5,6-Davis-c(r). 4-Begin $2.00-c; Craig-c(r) 5.00

TALES FROM THE CRYPT
Extra-Large Comics (Russ Cochran)/Gemstone Publishing: Jul, 1991 - No. 6 ($3.95, 10 1/4 x13 1/4", 68 pgs.)

1-6: 1-Davis-c(r); Craig back-c(r); E.C. reprints. 2-6 ($2.00, comic sized) 5.00

TALES FROM THE CRYPT
Russ Cochran: Sept, 1991 - No. 7, July, 1992 ($2.00, 64 pgs.)

1-7 5.00

TALES FROM THE CRYPT (Also see EC Archives • Tales From the Crypt)
Russ Cochran/Gemstone: Sept, 1992 - No. 30, Dec, 1999 ($1.50, quarterly)

1-4-r/Crypt of Terror #17-19, TFTC #20 w/original-c 4.00
5-30: 5-15 ($2.00)-r/TFTC #21-23 w/original-c. 16-30 ($2.50) 4.00
Annual 1-6('93-'99) 1-r/#1-5. 2- r/#6-10. 3- r/#11-15. 4- r/#16-20. 5-r/#21-25. 6- r/#26-30 14.00

TALES FROM THE DARK MULTIVERSE
DC Comics: Dec, 2019 - Feb, 2021 ($5.99, series of one-shots)

...: Batman: Hush 1 (1/21) - Tommy Elliot and Batman The Silenced app.; Soy-a 6.00
...: Batman: Knightfall 1 - What if Jean-Paul Valley remained as Batman; Fernandez-a 6.00
...: Blackest Night 1 - What if Sinestro kept the White Lantern power; Lobo app.; Hotz-a 6.00
...: Crisis on Infinite Earths 1 (2/21) - Justice Society app.; Orlando-s/Perkins-a 6.00
...: Dark Nights Metal 1 (2/21) - What if Barbatos had won; Duke Thomas app. 6.00
...: Flashpoint 1 (2/21) - What if the Flashpoint reality was never undone; Currie-a 6.00
...: Infinite Crisis 1 - What if Blue Beetle killed Max Lord; Tynion IV-s/Lopresti-a 6.00
...: The Death of Superman 1 - What if Lois gained the Eradicator's powers; Brad Walker-a 8.00
...: Teen Titans: The Judas Contract 1 - What if Terra didn't die; Raney-a 6.00
...: Wonder Woman War of the Gods 1 (2/21) - Evil Wonder Woman; Olivetti-a 6.00

TALES FROM THE DARKSIDE
IDW Publishing: Jun, 2016 - No. 4, Sept, 2016 ($3.99, limited series)

1-4-Joe Hill-s/Gabriel Rodriguez-a. 1-Five covers. 2-4-Two covers 4.00

TALES FROM THE GREAT BOOK
Famous Funnies: Feb, 1955 - No. 4, Jan, 1956 (Religious themes)

	GD	VG	FN	VF	VF/NM	NM-
1-Story of Samson; John Lehti-a in all	13	26	39	74	105	135
2-4: 2-Joshua. 3-Joash the Boy King. 4-David	9	18	27	50	65	80

TALES FROM THE HEART OF AFRICA (The Temporary Natives)
Marvel Comics (Epic Comics): Aug, 1990 ($3.95, 52 pgs.)

1 4.00

TALES FROM THE TOMB (Also see Dell Giants)
Dell Publishing Co.: Oct, 1962 (25¢ giant)

	GD	VG	FN	VF	VF/NM	NM-
1(02-810-210)-All stories written by John Stanley	20	40	60	138	307	475

TALES FROM THE TOMB (Magazine)
Eerie Publications: V1#6, July, 1969 - V7#3, 1975 (52 pgs.)

	GD	VG	FN	VF	VF/NM	NM-
V1#6	10	20	30	65	135	205
V1#7,8	7	14	21	49	92	135
V2#1-6: 4-LSD story-r/Weird V3#5. 6-Rulah-r	6	12	18	38	69	100
V3#1-Rulah-r	7	14	21	44	82	120
2-6('71),V4#1-5('72),V5#1-6('73),V6#1-6('74),V7#1-3('75)	5	10	15	35	63	90

TALES OF ASGARD
Marvel Comics Group: Oct, 1968 (25¢, 68 pgs.); Feb, 1984 ($1.25, 52 pgs.)

	GD	VG	FN	VF	VF/NM	NM-
1-Reprints Tales of Asgard (Thor) back-up stories from Journey into Mystery #97-106; new Kirby-c; Kirby-a	9	18	27	62	126	190

V2#1 (2/84)-Thor-r; Simonson-c 5.00

TALES OF ARMY OF DARKNESS
Dynamite Entertainment: 2006 ($5.95, one-shot)

1-Short stories by Kuhoric, Kirkman, Bradshaw, Sablik, Ottley, Acs, O'Hare and others 6.00

TALES OF EVIL
Atlas/Seaboard Publ.: Feb, 1975 - No. 3, July, 1975 (All 25¢ issues)

	GD	VG	FN	VF	VF/NM	NM-
1-3: 1-Werewolf w/Sekowsky-a. 2-Intro. The Bog Beast; Sparling-a. 3-Origin The Man-Monster; Buckler-a(p)	2	4	6	13	18	22

NOTE: ***Grandenetti** a-1, 2. **Lieber** c-1. **Sekowsky** a-1. **Sutton** a-2. **Thorne** c-2.*

TALES OF GHOST CASTLE
National Periodical Publications: May-June, 1975 - No. 3, Sept-Oct, 1975 (All 25¢ issues)

1-Redondo-a; 1st app. Lucien the Librarian from Sandman (1989 series)

GD 2.0 · VG 4.0 · FN 6.0 · VF 8.0 · VF/NM 9.0 · NM- 9.2

3 6 9 18 28 38
2,3: 2-Nino-a. 3-Redondo-a. 2 4 6 10 14 18

TALES OF G.I. JOE
Marvel Comics: Jan, 1988 - No. 15, Mar, 1989

1 ($2.25, 52 pgs.) 5.00
2-15 ($1.50): 1-15-r/G.I. Joe #1-15 4.00

TALES OF HONOR (Based on the David Weber novels)
Image Comics (Top Cow): Mar, 2014 - No. 5, Oct, 2015 ($2.99)

1-5: 1-Matt Hawkins-s/Jung-Geun Yoon-a. 2-5-Sang-il Jeong-a 3.00

TALES OF HONOR VOLUME 2 (Bred to Kill on cover)
Image Comics (Top Cow): No. 0, May, 2015 - No. 4, Dec, 2015 ($3.99)

0-Free Comic Book Day giveaway; Hawkins-s/Linda Sejic-a 3.00
1-4-Hawkins-s/Linda Sejic-a 4.00

TALES OF HORROR
Toby Press/Minoan Publ. Corp.: June, 1952 - No. 13, Oct, 1954

1-"This is Terror-Man" 77 154 231 493 847 1200
2-Torture scenes 54 108 162 343 574 825
3-11,13: 9-11-Reprints Purple Claw #1-3 37 74 111 222 361 500
12-Myron Fass-c/a; torture scenes 40 80 120 246 411 575
NOTE: *Andru a-5. Baily a-5. Myron Fass a-2, 3, 12; c-1-3, 12. Hollingsworth a-2. Sparling a-6, 9; c-9.*

TALES OF JUSTICE
Atlas Comics(MjMC No. 53-66/Male No. 67): No. 53, May, 1955 - No. 67, Aug, 1957

53 22 44 66 132 216 300
54-57: 54-Powell-a 15 30 45 90 140 190
58,59-Krigstein-a 17 34 51 98 154 210
60-63,65: 60-Powell-a 15 30 45 84 127 170
64,66,67: 64,67-Crandall-a. 66-Torres, Orlando-a 15 30 45 85 130 175
NOTE: *Everett a-53, 60. Orlando a-65, 66. Severin a-64; c-58, 60, 65. Wildey a-64, 67.*

TALES OF LEONARDO BLIND SIGHT (See Tales of the TMNT Vol. 2 #5)
Mirage Publishing: June, 2006 - No. 4, Sept, 2006 ($3.25, B&W, limited series)

1-Jim Lawson-s/a in all 3 6 9 21 33 45
2-4 2 4 6 10 14 18

TALES OF MOTHER F. GOOSE
AfterShock Comics: Dec, 2021 ($6.99, one-shot, oversized 8-1/2" x 10-7/8")

1-Frank Tieri-s/Joe Eisma-a 7.00

TALES OF SOPHISTICATION (Cerebus)
Aardvark-Vanaheim: Aug, 2019 ($4.00, B&W)

1-Cerebus figures with Doré artwork of Hell; cover swipe of Tales of Suspense #39 4.00

TALES OF SUSPENSE (Becomes Captain America #100 on)
Atlas (WPI No. 1,2/Male No. 3-12/VPI No. 13-18)/Marvel No. 19 on:
Jan, 1959 - No. 99, Mar, 1968

1-Williamson-a (5 pgs.); Heck-c; #1-4 have sci/fi-c 600 1200 1800 5100 11,550 18,000
2-Ditko robot-c 162 324 486 1337 3019 4700
3-Flying saucer-c/story 121 242 363 968 2184 3400
4-Williamson-a (4 pgs.); Kirby/Everett-c/a 114 228 342 912 2056 3200
5-Kirby monster-c begin 93 186 279 744 1672 2600
6,8,10 71 142 213 568 1284 2000
7-Prototype ish. (Lava Man); 1 panel app. Aunt May (see Str. Tales #97)
79 158 237 632 1416 2200
9-Prototype ish. (Iron Man) 68 136 204 544 1222 1900
11,12,15,17-19: 12-Crandall-a. 54 108 162 432 966 1500
13-Elektro-c/story 64 128 192 512 1156 1800
14-Intro/1st app. Colossus-c/sty 69 138 207 552 1101 1950
16-1st Metallo-c/story (4/61, Iron Man prototype) 79 158 237 632 1416 2200
20-Colossus-c/story (2nd app.) 57 114 171 456 1028 1600
21-25: 25-Last 10¢ issue 46 92 138 359 805 1250
26,27,29,30,31,33,34,36-38: 33-(9/62)-Hulk 1st x-over cameo (picture on wall)
42 84 126 311 706 1100
28-Prototype ish. (Stone Men) 46 92 138 340 770 1200
31-Prototype ish. (Doctor Doom) 96 192 288 768 1734 2700
32-Prototype ish. (Dr. Strange)(8/62)-Sazzik The Sorcerer app.; "The Man and the Beehive" story, 1 month before TTA #35 (2nd Antman), came out after "The Man in the Ant Hill" in TTA #27 (1/62) (1st Antman)-Characters from both stories were tested to see which got best fan response 114 228 342 912 2056 3200
35-Prototype issue (The Watcher) 46 92 138 368 834 1300
39 (3/63)-Origin/1st app. Iron Man & begin series; 1st Iron Man story has Kirby layouts
3520 7040 12,320 24,600 56,300 88,000
40-2nd app. Iron Man (in new armor) 231 462 693 1906 4303 6700
41-3rd app. Iron Man; Dr. Strange (villain) app. 166 332 498 1370 3085 4800
42-45: 45-Intro. & 1st app. Happy & Pepper 94 188 282 756 1753 2750
46,47: 46-1st app. Crimson Dynamo 69 138 207 552 1251 1950
48-New Iron Man red & gold armor by Ditko 79 158 237 632 1416 2200
49-1st X-Men x-over (same date as X-Men #3, 1/64); also 1st Avengers x-over (w/o Captain America); 1st Tales of the Watcher back-up story & begins (2nd app. Watcher; see F.F. #13) 89 178 267 712 1606 2500
50-1st app. Mandarin 107 214 321 856 1928 3000
51-1st Scarecrow 38 76 114 285 641 1000
52-1st app. The Black Widow (4/64) 383 766 1149 3256 7378 11,500
53-Origin The Watcher; 2nd Black Widow app. 58 116 174 464 1057 1650
54,55-2nd & 3rd Mandarin app. 34 68 102 245 548 850
56-1st app. Unicorn 28 56 84 202 451 700
57-Origin/1st app. Hawkeye (9/64) 283 566 849 2335 5268 8200
58-Captain America battles Iron Man (10/64)-Classic-c; 2nd Kraven app. (Cap's 1st app. in this title) 66 132 198 528 1189 1850
59-Iron Man plus Captain America double feature begins (11/64); 1st S.A. Captain America solo story; intro Jarvis, Avenger's butler; classic-c 57 114 171 456 1028 1600
60-2nd app. Hawkeye (#64 is 3rd app.) 28 56 84 202 451 700
61,62,64: 62-Origin Mandarin (2/65). 64-1st Black Widow in costume
17 34 51 117 259 400
63-1st Silver Age origin Captain America (3/65) 33 66 99 238 532 825
65-G.A. Red Skull in WWII stories (also in #66-68);-1st Silver-Age Red Skull (5/65); Iron Man wears old yellow armor 38 76 114 285 641 1000
66-Origin Red Skull 26 52 78 182 404 625
67,68,70: 70-Begin alternating-c features w/Capt. America (even #'s) & Iron Man (odd #'s) 10 20 30 67 141 215
69-1st app. Titanium Man 13 26 39 91 201 310
71-74,78: 78-Col. Nick Fury app. 8 16 24 54 102 150
75-1st app. Agent 13 later named Sharon Carter; intro Batroc
25 50 75 175 388 600
76-2nd app. Batroc & 1st cover app. 9 18 27 63 129 195
77-1st app. Peggy Carter (unnamed) in WW2 flashback (see Captain America #161 & 162)
25 50 75 175 388 600
79-Begin 3 part Iron Man Sub-Mariner battle story; Sub-Mariner-c & cameo; 1st app. Cosmic Cube; 1st modern Red Skull 17 34 51 117 259 400
80-Iron Man battles Sub-Mariner story cont'd in Tales to Astonish #82; classic Red Skull-c
13 26 39 86 188 290
81-93,95,96: 82-Intro the Adaptoid by Kirby (also in #83,84). 88-Mole Man app. in Iron Man story. 92-1st Nick Fury x-over (cameo, as Agent of S.H.I.E.L.D., 8/67). 95-Capt. America's i.d. revealed 7 14 21 48 89 130
94-Intro Modok 40 80 120 296 673 1050
97-1st Whiplash 14 28 42 93 204 315
98-Black Panther-c/s; 1st brief app. new Zemo (son?); #99 is 1st full app.
14 28 42 96 211 325
99-Captain America story cont'd in Captain America #100; Iron Man story cont'd in Iron Man & Sub-Mariner #1 9 18 27 61 123 185
... No. 39 Facsimile Edition (11/20, $3.99) Reprints #39 with original ads
2 4 6 9 13 16
... No. 57 Facsimile Edition (8/22, $3.99) Reprints #57 (1st Hawkeye) with original ads
1 3 4 6 8 10
Omnibus (See Iron Man Omnibus for reprints of #39-83)
NOTE: *Abel a-73-81i(as Gary Michaels), J. Buscema a-1; c-3. Colan a-39, 73-99p; c(p)-73, 75, 77, 79, 81, 83, 85-87, 89, 91, 93, 95, 97, 99. Crandall a-12. Davis a-38. Ditko a-1-15, 17-44, 46, 47-49p; c-2, 10i, 13i, 23i. Kirby/Ditko a-7; c-10, 13, 22, 28, 34. Everett a-8. Forte a-5, 9. Giacoia a-82. Heath a-2, 10. Gil Kane a-88p, 89-91; c-88, 89-91p. Kirby a(p)-2-4, 6-35, 40, 41, 43, 59-75, 77-86, 92-99; layouts-69-75. 77: c(p)4-28(most), 29-56, 58-72, 74, 76, 78, 80, 82, 84, 86, 92, 94, 96, 98. Leiber/Fox a-42, 43, 45, 51. Reinman a-13, 25, 26, 44i, 49i, 52i, 53i. Tuska a-58, 70-74. Wood c/a-71i.*

TALES OF SUSPENSE
Marvel Comics: V2#1, Jan, 1995 ($6.95, one-shot)

V2#1-James Robinson script; acetate-c. 1 3 4 6 8 10

TALES OF SUSPENSE (Marvel Legacy)
Marvel Comics: No. 100, Feb, 2018 - No. 104, Jun, 2018 ($3.99)

100-104-Hawkeye & Winter Soldier team-up; Black Widow app.; Foreman-a 4.00

TALES OF SUSPENSE: CAPTAIN AMERICA & IRON MAN #1 COMMEMORATIVE EDITION
Marvel Comics: 2004 ($3.99, one-shot)

nn-Reprints Captain America (2004) #1 and Iron Man (2004) #1 5.00

TALES OF SWORD & SORCERY (See Dagar)

TALES OF TELLOS (See Tellos)
Image Comics: Oct, 2004 - No. 3, ($3.50, anthology)

1-3: 1-Dezago-s; art by Yates & Rousseau; Wieringo-c. 3-Porter-a 3.50

TALES OF TERROR
Toby Press Publications: 1952 (no month)

1-Fawcette-c; Ravielli-a 65 130 195 416 708 1000
NOTE: *This title was cancelled due to similarity to the E.C. title.*

TALES OF TERROR (See Movie Classics)

TALES OF TERROR (Magazine)
Eerie Publications: Summer, 1964

1 7 14 21 49 92 135

TALES OF TERROR
Eclipse Comics: July, 1985 - No. 13, July, 1987 ($2.00, Baxter paper, mature)

1 1 3 4 6 8 10
2-13: 5-1st Lee Weeks-a. 7-Sam Kieth-a. 10-Snyder-a. 12-Vampire story 4.00

TALES OF TERROR (IDW's...)
IDW Publishing: Sept, 2004 ($16.99, hardcover)

1-Anthology of short graphic stories and text stories; incl. 30 Days of Night 17.00

TALES OF TERROR ANNUAL
E.C. Comics: 1951 - No. 3, 1953 (25¢, 132 pgs., 16 stories each)

nn(1951)(Scarce)-Feldstein infinity-c 2500 5000 7500 17,500 -- --
2(1952)-Feldstein-c 331 663 993 2317 4059 5800
3(1953)-Feldstein bondage/torture-c 300 600 900 1920 3310 4700
NOTE: *No. 1 contains three horror and one science fiction comic which came out in 1950. No. 2 contains a horror, crime, and science fiction book which generally had cover dates in 1951, and No. 3 had horror, crime, and shock books that generally appeared in 1952. All E.C. annuals contain four complete books that did not sell on the stands which were rebound in the annual format, minus the covers, and sold from the E.C. office and on the stands in key cities. The contents of each annual may vary in the same year. Crypt Keeper, Vault Keeper, Old Witch app. on all-c.*

TALES OF TERROR ILLUSTRATED (See Terror Illustrated)

TALES OF TEXAS JOHN SLAUGHTER (See Walt Disney Presents, 4-Color #997)

TALES OF THE BEANWORLD
Beanworld Press/Eclipse Comics: Feb, 1985 - No. 19, 1991; No. 20, 1993 - No. 21, 1993 ($1.50/$2.00, B&W)

1-21 3.00

TALES OF THE BIZARRO WORLD
DC Comics: 2000 ($14.95, TPB)

nn-Reprints early Bizarro stories; new Jaime Hernandez-c 15.00

TALES OF THE DARKNESS
Image Comics (Top Cow): Apr, 1998 - No. 4, Dec, 1998 ($2.95)

1-4: 1,2-Portacio-c/a(p). 3,4-Lansing & Nocon-a(p) 3.00
1-American Entertainment Ed. 3.00
#1/2 (1/01, $2.95) 3.00

TALES OF THE DRAGON GUARD (English version of French comic title)
Marvel Comics (Soleil): Apr, 2010 - No. 3, Jun, 2010 ($5.99, limited series)

Tales of Suspense #59 © MAR

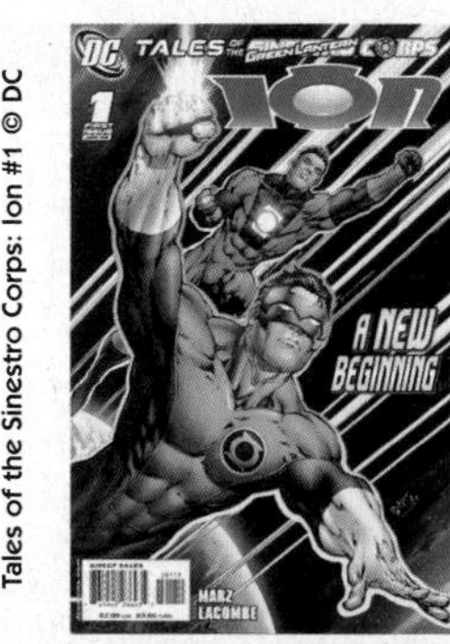

Tales of the Sinestro Corps: Ion #1 © DC

Tales of the Unexpected #13 © DC

	GD 2.0	VG 4.0	FN 6.0	VF 8.0	VF/NM 9.0	NM- 9.2

1-3: 1-Ange-s/Varanda-a. 2-Briones-a. 3-Guinebaud-a 6.00
...: Into the Veil 1-3 (11/10 - No. 3, 1/11) 1-Briones-a. 2-Paty-a. 3-Sieurac-a 6.00

TALES OF THE GREEN BERET
Dell Publishing Co.: Jan, 1967 - No. 5, Oct, 1969

1-Glanzman-a in 1-4 & 5r 4 8 12 25 40 55
2-5: 5-Reprints #1 3 6 9 17 26 35

TALES OF THE GREEN HORNET
Now Comics: Sept, 1990 - No. 2, 1990; V2#1, Jan, 1992 - No.4, Apr, 1992; V3#1, Sept, 1992 - No. 3, Nov, 1992

1,2 4.00
V2#1-4 ($1.95) 3.00
V3#1 ($2.75)-Polybagged w/hologram trading card 4.00
V3#2,3 ($2.50) 3.00

TALES OF THE GREEN LANTERN CORPS (See Green Lantern #107)
DC Comics: May, 1981 - No. 3, July, 1981 (Limited series)

1-Origin of G.L. & the Guardians 2 4 6 11 16 20
2-1st app. Nekron 3 6 9 14 20 25
3 2 4 6 8 10 12
Annual 1 (1/85)-Gil Kane-c/a 1 2 3 5 6 8
TPB (2009, $19.99) r/#1-3 & stories from G.L. #148-151-154,161,162,164-167 ('82-'83)20.00
Volume 2 TPB (2010, $19.99) r/Annual #1 and stories from G.L. ('83-'85) 20.00
Volume 3 TPB (2010, $19.99) r/Green Lantern #201-206 ('86) 20.00

TALES OF THE HUMAN TARGET (Leads into 2022's Human Target #7)
DC Comics (Black Label): Oct, 2022 ($5.99, one-shot)

1-Past cases; King-s; art by Maguire, Janin, Albuquerque & Smallwood 6.00

TALES OF THE INVISIBLE SCARLET O'NEIL (See Harvey Comics Hits #59)

TALES OF THE KILLERS (Magazine)
World Famous Periodicals: V1#10, Dec, 1970 - V1#11, Feb, 1971 (B&W, 52 pg)

V1#10-One pg. Frazetta; r/Crime Does Not Pay 5 10 15 33 57 80
11-similar-c to Crime Does Not Pay #47; contains r/Crime Does Not Pay 5 10 15 30 50 70

TALES OF THE LEGION (Formerly Legion of Super-Heroes)
DC Comics: No. 314, Aug, 1984 - No. 354, Dec, 1987

314-354: 326-r-begin 4.00
Annual 4,5 (1986, 1987)-Formerly LSH Annual 5.00

TALES OF THE MARINES (Formerly Devil-Dog Dugan #1-3)
Atlas Comics (OPI): No. 4, Feb, 1957 (Marines At War #5 on)

4-Powell-a; grey tone-c by Severin 18 36 54 105 165 225

TALES OF THE MARVELS
Marvel Comics: 1995/1996 (all acetate, painted-c)

...Blockbuster 1 (1995, $5.95, one-shot), ...Inner Demons 1 (1996, $5.95, one shot), ...Wonder Years 1,2 (1995, $4.95, limited series) 6.00

TALES OF THE MARVEL UNIVERSE
Marvel Comics: Feb, 1997 ($2.95, one-shot)

1-Anthology; wraparound-c; Thunderbolts, Ka-Zar app. 4.00

TALES OF THE MYSTERIOUS TRAVELER (See Mysterious...)
Charlton Comics: Aug, 1956 - No. 13, June, 1959; V2#14, Oct, 1985 - No. 15, Dec, 1985

1-No Ditko-a; Giordano/Alascia-c 54 108 162 343 574 825
2-Ditko-a(1) 42 84 126 265 445 625
3-Ditko-c/a(1) 43 86 129 271 461 650
4-7-Ditko-c/a(3-4 stories each) 50 100 150 315 533 750
8,9-Ditko-a(1-3 each). 8-Rocke-c 41 82 123 256 428 600
10,11-Ditko-c/a(3-4 each) 47 94 141 296 498 700
12 19 38 57 111 176 240
13-Baker-a (r?) 20 40 60 115 185 255
V2#14,15 (1985)-Ditko-c/a-low print run 2 3 4 6 8 10

TALES OF THE NEW GODS
DC Comics: 2008 ($19.99, TPB)

SC-Reprints from Jack Kirby's Fourth World, Orion and Mister Miracle Special; includes previously unpublished story by Millar-s/Ditko-a 20.00

TALES OF THE NEW TEEN TITANS
DC Comics: June, 1982 - No. 4, Sept, 1982 (Limited series)

1 3 6 9 16 23 30
2-4 2 4 6 8 10 12

TALES OF THE PONY EXPRESS (TV)
Dell Publishing Co.: No. 829, Aug, 1957 - No. 942, Oct, 1958

Four Color 829 (#1) -Painted-c 6 12 18 42 79 115
Four Color 942-Title -Pony Express 5 10 15 34 60 85

TALES OF THE REALM
CrossGen Comics/MVCreations #4-on: Oct, 2003 - No. 5, May, 2004 ($2.95, limited series)

1-5-Robert Kirkman-s/Matt Tyree-a 3.00
Volume 1 HC (8/04, $39.95, dust jacket) r/#1-5; sketch pages and concept art 40.00

TALES OF THE SINESTRO CORPS (See Green Lantern and Green Lantern Corps x-over)
DC Comics: Nov, 2007 - Jan, 2008 ($2.99/$3.99, one-shots)

...: Cyborg-Superman (12/07, $2.99) Burnett-s/Blaine-a/VanSciver-c; JLA app. 3.00
...: Ion (1/08, $2.99) Marz-s/Lacombe-a/Benes-c; Sodam Yat app. 3.00
...: Parallax (11/07, $2.99) Marz-s/Melo-a; Kyle Rayner vs. Parallax 3.00
...: Superman-Prime (12/07, $3.99) Johns-s/VanSciver-c; origin re-told w/Ordway-a 4.00

TALES OF THE TEENAGE MUTANT NINJA TURTLES (See Teenage Mutant...)
Mirage Studios: May, 1987 - No. 7, Aug (Apr-c), 1989 (B&W, $1.50)

1 4 8 12 25 40 55
2-Title merges w/Teenage Mutant Ninja... 3 6 9 14 20 25
3-7 2 4 6 8 11 14

TALES OF THE TEEN TITANS (Formerly The New Teen Titans)
DC Comics: No. 41, Apr, 1984 - No. 91, July, 1988 (75¢)

41,45-49: 46-Aqualad & Aquagirl join 5.00
42,43: The Judas Contract parts 1&2 with Deathstroke the Terminator; concludes with part 4 in Annual #3. 1 2 3 5 6 8
44-Dick Grayson becomes Nightwing (3rd to be Nightwing) & joins Titans; Judas Contract part 3; Jericho (Deathstroke's son) joins; origin Deathstroke 6 12 18 37 66 110
50-Double size; app. Betty Kane (Bat-Girl) out of costume 1 3 4 6 8 10
51,52,56-91: 52-1st brief app. Azrael (not same as newer character). 56-Intro Jinx. 57-Neutron app. 59-r/DC Comics Presents #26. 60-91-r/New Teen Titans Baxter series. 68-B. Smith-c. 70-Origin Kole 3.00
53-55: 53-1st full app. Azrael; Deathstroke cameo. 54,55-Deathstroke-c/stories 4.00
Annual 3(1984, $1.25)-Part 4 of The Judas Contract; Deathstroke-c/story; Death of Terra; indicia says Teen Titans Annual; previous annuals listed as New Teen Titans Annual #1,2 1 3 4 6 8 10
Annual 4-(1986, $1.25) 4.00

TALES OF THE TEXAS RANGERS (See Jace Pearson...)

TALES OF THE THING (Fantastic Four)
Marvel Comics: May, 2005 - No. 3, July, 2005 ($2.50, limited series)

1-3-Dr. Strange app; Randy Green-c 3.00

TALES OF THE TMNT (Also see Teenage Mutant Ninja Turtles)
Mirage Studios: Jan, 2004 - No. 70, May, 2010 ($2.95/$3.25, B&W)

1-7: 1-Brizuela-a 5.00
8-70: 8-Begin $3.25-c. 47-Origin of the Super Turtles 4.00

TALES OF THE UNEXPECTED (Becomes The Unexpected #105 on)(See Adventure #75, Super DC Giant)
National Periodical Publications: Feb-Mar, 1956 - No. 104, Dec-Jan, 1967-68

1 159 318 477 1312 2956 4600
2 61 122 183 488 1094 1700
3-5 40 80 120 296 673 1050
6-10: 6-1st Silver Age issue 32 64 96 230 515 800
11,14,19,20 24 48 72 168 372 575
12,13,16,18,21-24: All have Kirby-a. 16-Characters named 'Thor' (with a magic hammer) and Loki by Kirby (8/57, characters do not look like Marvel's Thor & Loki) 28 56 84 202 451 700
15,17-Grey tone-c; Kirby-a 32 64 96 230 515 800
25-30 19 38 57 133 297 460
31-39 17 34 51 117 259 400
40-Space Ranger begins (8/59, 3rd ap.), ends #82 107 214 321 856 1928 3000
41,42-Space Ranger stories 44 88 132 326 738 1150
43-1st Space Ranger-c this title; grey tone-c 75 150 225 600 1350 2100
44-46 31 62 93 223 499 775
47-50 26 52 78 182 404 625
51-60: 54-Dinosaur-c/story 21 42 63 147 324 500
61-67: 67-Last 10¢ issue 17 34 51 117 259 400
68-82: 82-Last Space Ranger 10 20 30 66 138 210
83-90,92-99 6 12 18 40 73 105
91,100: 91-1st Automan (also in #94,97) 6 12 18 41 76 110
101-104 6 12 18 37 66 95

NOTE: ***Neal Adams** c-104. **Anderson** a-50. **Brown** a-50-82(Space Ranger); c-19, 40, & many Space Ranger-c. **Cameron** a-24, 27, 29; c-24. **Heath** a-49. **Bob Kane** a-24, 48. **Kirby** a-12, 13, 15-18, 21-24; c-13, 18, 22. **Meskin** a-15, 18, 26, 27, 35, 66. **Moreira** a-16, 20, 29, 38, 44, 62, 71; c-38. **Roussos** c-10. **Wildey** a-31.*

TALES OF THE UNEXPECTED (See Crisis Aftermath: The Spectre)
DC Comics: Dec, 2006 - No. 8, Jul, 2007 ($3.99, limited series)

	GD 2.0	VG 4.0	FN 6.0	VF 8.0	VF/NM 9.0	NM- 9.2
1-8-The Spectre, Lapham-s/Battle-a; Dr. 13, Azzarello-s/Chiang-a. 4-Wrightson-c						4.00
1-Variant Spectre cover by Neal Adams						5.00
The Spectre: Tales of the Unexpected TPB (2007, $14.99) r/#4-8						15.00

TALES OF THE VAMPIRES (Also see Buffy the Vampire Slayer and related titles)
Dark Horse Comics: 2003 - No. 5, Apr, 2004 ($2.99, limited series)

	GD 2.0	VG 4.0	FN 6.0	VF 8.0	VF/NM 9.0	NM- 9.2
1-Short stories by Joss Whedon and others. 1-Totleben-c. 3-Powell-c. 4-Edlund-c						3.00
TPB (11/04, $15.95) r/#1-5; afterword by Marv Wolfman						16.00

TALES OF THE WEST (See 3-D...)

TALES OF THE WITCHBLADE
Image Comics (Top Cow Productions): Nov, 1996 - No. 9 ($2.95)

	GD 2.0	VG 4.0	FN 6.0	VF 8.0	VF/NM 9.0	NM- 9.2
1/2	2	4	6	9	12	15
1/2 Gold	2	4	6	9	12	15
1-Daniel-c/a(p)	1	3	4	6	8	10
1-Variant-c by Turner	2	4	6	9	12	15
1-Platinum Edition	3	6	9	16	23	30
2,3						6.00
4-6: 6-Green-c						5.00
7-9: 9-Lara Croft-c						4.00
7-Variant-c by Turner	1	2	3	5	6	8
Witchblade: Distinctions (4/01, $14.95, TPB) r/#1-6; Green-c						15.00

TALES OF THE WITCHBLADE COLLECTED EDITION
Image Comics (Top Cow): May, 1998 - No. 2 ($4.95/$5.95, square-bound)

	GD 2.0	VG 4.0	FN 6.0	VF 8.0	VF/NM 9.0	NM- 9.2
1,2: 1-r/#1,2. 2-($5.95) r/#3,4						6.00

TALES OF THE WIZARD OF OZ (See Wizard of OZ, 4-Color #1308)

TALES OF THE ZOMBIE (Magazine)
Marvel Comics Group: Aug, 1973 - No. 10, Mar, 1975 (75¢, B&W)

	GD 2.0	VG 4.0	FN 6.0	VF 8.0	VF/NM 9.0	NM- 9.2
V1#1-Reprint/Menace #5; origin Simon Garth	8	16	24	54	102	150
2,3: 2-2nd app. of Brother Voodoo; Everett biog. & memorial	5	10	15	31	53	75
V2#1(#4)-Photos & text of James Bond movie "Live & Let Die"	4	8	12	25	40	55
5-10: 8-Kaluta-a	3	6	9	18	28	38
Annual 1(Summer,'75)(#11)-B&W; Everett, Buscema-a	3	6	9	20	31	42

NOTE: *Brother Voodoo app. 2, 5, 6, 10.* ***Alcala*** *a-7-9.* ***Boris*** *c-1-4.* ***Colan*** *a-2r, 6.* ***Heath*** *a-5r.* ***Reese*** *a-2.* ***Tuska*** *a-2r.*

TALES OF VOODOO
Eerie Publications: V1#11, Nov, 1968 - V7#6, Nov, 1974 (Magazine)

	GD 2.0	VG 4.0	FN 6.0	VF 8.0	VF/NM 9.0	NM- 9.2
V1#11	9	18	27	59	117	175
V2#1(3/69)-V2#4(9/69)	9	12	18	38	69	100
V3#1-6('70): 4- "Claws of the Cat" redrawn from Climax #1	5	10	15	31	53	75
V4#1-6('71), V5#1-7('72), V6#1-6('73), V7#1-6('74)	5	10	15	31	53	75
Annual 1	5	10	15	33	57	80

NOTE: *Bondage-c-V1#10, V2#4, V3#4.*

TALES OF WELLS FARGO (TV)(See Western Roundup under Dell Giants)
Dell Publishing Co.: No. 876, Feb, 1958 - No. 1215, Oct-Dec, 1961

	GD 2.0	VG 4.0	FN 6.0	VF 8.0	VF/NM 9.0	NM- 9.2
Four Color 876 (#1)-Photo-c	9	18	27	59	117	175
Four Color 968 (2/59), 1023, 1075 (3/60), 1113 (7-9/60)-All photo-c. 1075,1113-Both have variant edition, back-c comic strip	8	16	24	54	102	150
Four Color 1167 (3-5/61), 1215-Photo-c	7	14	21	48	89	130

TALESPIN (Also see Cartoon Tales & Disney's Talespin Limited Series)
Disney Comics: June, 1991 - No. 7, Dec, 1991 ($1.50)

	GD 2.0	VG 4.0	FN 6.0	VF 8.0	VF/NM 9.0	NM- 9.2
1-7						3.00

TALES TO ASTONISH (Becomes The Incredible Hulk #102 on)
Atlas (MAP No. 1/ZPC No. 2-14/VPI No. 15-21/Marvel No. 22 on: Jan, 1959 - No. 101, Mar, 1968

	GD 2.0	VG 4.0	FN 6.0	VF 8.0	VF/NM 9.0	NM- 9.2
1-Jack Davis-a; monster-c.	633	1266	1900	5400	12,200	19,000
2-Ditko flying saucer-c (Martians); #2-4 have sci/fi-c.	152	304	456	1254	2827	4400
3,4	129	258	387	1032	2316	3600
5-Prototype issue (Stone Men); Williamson-a (4 pgs.); Kirby monster-c begin	96	192	288	768	1734	2700
6-Prototype issue (Stone Men)	100	200	300	800	1800	2800
7-Prototype issue (Toad Men)	71	142	213	568	1284	2000
8-10	68	136	204	544	1222	1900
11,12,14,17-20	54	108	162	432	966	1500
13-(11/60) 1st app. Groot (Guardians of the Galaxy) by Kirby-cvr/sty; swipes story from Menace #8	1530	3060	4590	11,100	19,550	28,000
15-Prototype issue (Electro)	61	122	183	488	1094	1700
16-Prototype issue (Stone Men) named "Thorr"	62	124	186	496	1123	1750
21-(7/61)-Hulk prototype	68	136	204	544	1222	1900
22-26,28-31,33,34	42	84	126	311	706	1100
27-1st Ant-Man app. (1/62); last 10¢ issue (see Strange Tales #73,78 & Tales of Suspense #32)	1200	2400	4800	14,700	37,350	60,000
32-Sandman prototype	48	96	144	374	862	1350
35-(9/62)-2nd app. Ant-Man, 1st in costume; begin series & Ant-Man-c	500	1000	1500	4300	11,150	18,000
36-3rd app. Ant-Man	107	214	321	856	1928	3000
37,39,40	54	108	162	432	966	1500
38-1st app. Egghead	58	116	174	464	1057	1650
41-43	46	92	138	364	820	1275
44-Origin & 1st app. The Wasp (6/63)	443	886	1329	3234	5717	8200
45-47	31	62	93	223	499	775
48-Origin & 1st app. The Porcupine	35	70	105	252	564	875
49-Ant-Man becomes Giant Man (11/63)	61	122	183	488	1094	1700
50,51,53-56,58: 50-Origin/1st app. Human Top (alias Whirlwind). 58-Origin Colossus	20	40	60	143	317	490
52-Origin/1st app. Black Knight (2/64)	42	84	126	311	706	1100
57-Early Spider-Man app. (7/64)	40	80	120	296	673	1050
59-Giant Man vs. Hulk feature story (9/64); Hulk's 1st app. this title; 1st mention that anger triggers his transformation	39	78	117	289	657	1025
60-Giant Man & Hulk double feature begins	36	72	108	259	580	900
61,64-69: 61-All Ditko issue; 1st app. of Glenn Talbot; 1st mailbag. 65-New Giant Man costume. 68-New Human Top costume. 69-Last Giant Man	15	30	45	100	220	340
62-1st app./origin The Leader; new Wasp costume; Hulk pin-up page missing from many copies	42	84	126	311	706	1100
63-Origin Leader continues	36	72	108	259	580	900
70-Sub-Mariner & Incredible Hulk begins (8/65)	28	56	84	202	451	700
71-81: 72-Begin alternating-c features w/Sub-Mariner (even #'s) & Hulk (odd #'s). 79-Hulk vs. Hercules-c/story. 81-1st app. Boomerang	8	16	24	52	79	145
82-Iron Man battles Sub-Mariner (1st Iron Man x-over outside The Avengers & TOS); story cont'd from Tales of Suspense #80	9	18	27	62	126	190
83-89,94-99: 97-X-Men cameo (brief)	6	12	18	41	76	110
90-1st app. The Abomination	38	76	114	285	641	1000
91-The Abomination debut continues & 1st cover	19	38	57	133	297	460
92-1st Silver Surfer x-over (outside of Fantastic Four, 6/67); 1 panel cameo only	9	18	27	62	126	190
93-Hulk battles Silver Surfer-c/story (1st full x-over)	50	100	150	400	900	1400
100-Hulk battles Sub-Mariner full-length story	10	20	30	68	144	220
101-Hulk story cont'd in Incredible Hulk #102; Sub-Mariner story continued in Iron Man & Sub-Mariner #1	10	20	30	67	141	215

NOTE: ***Ayers*** *c(i)-9-12, 16, 18, 19.* ***Berg*** *a-1.* ***Burgos*** *a-62-64p.* ***Buscema*** *a-85-87p.* ***Colan*** *a(p)-70-76, 78-82, 84, 85, 101; c(p)-71-76, 78, 80, 82, 84, 86, 88, 90.* ***Ditko*** *a-1, 3-48, 50i, 60-67p; c-2, 7i, 8i, 14i, 17i.* ***Everett*** *a-78, 79i, 80-84, 85-90i, 94i, 95, 96; c(i)-79-81, 83, 86, 88.* ***Forte*** *a-6.* ***Kane*** *a-76, 88-91; c-89, 91.* ***Kirby*** *a(p)-1, 5-34-40, 44, 49-51, 68-70, 82, 83; layouts-71-84; c(p)-1, 3-48, 50-70, 72, 73, 75, 77, 78, 79, 81, 85, 90.* ***Kirby/Ditko*** *a-7, 8, 12, 13, 50; c-7, 8, 10, 13.* ***Leiber/Fox*** *a-47, 48, 50, 51.* ***Powell*** *a-65-69p, 73, 74.* ***Reinman*** *a-6, 36, 45, 46, 54i, 56-60i.*

TALES TO ASTONISH (2nd Series)
Marvel Comics Group: Dec, 1979 - No. 14, Jan, 1981

	GD 2.0	VG 4.0	FN 6.0	VF 8.0	VF/NM 9.0	NM- 9.2
V1#1-Reprints Sub-Mariner #1 by Buscema	3	6	9	16	23	32
2-14: Reprints Sub-Mariner #2-14	1	3	4	6	8	10

TALES TO ASTONISH
Marvel Comics: V3#1, Oct, 1994 ($6.95, one-shot)

	GD 2.0	VG 4.0	FN 6.0	VF 8.0	VF/NM 9.0	NM- 9.2
V3#1-Peter David scripts; acetate, painted-c						7.00

TALES TO HOLD YOU SPELLBOUND (See Spellbound)

TALES TO OFFEND
Dark Horse Comics: July, 1997 ($2.95, one-shot)

	GD 2.0	VG 4.0	FN 6.0	VF 8.0	VF/NM 9.0	NM- 9.2
1-Frank Miller-s/a, EC-style cover						4.00

TALES TOO TERRIBLE TO TELL (Becomes Terrology #10, 11)
New England Comics: Wint, 1989-90 - No. 11, Nov-Dec.1993 ($2.95/$3.50, B&W with cardstock covers)

	GD 2.0	VG 4.0	FN 6.0	VF 8.0	VF/NM 9.0	NM- 9.2
1-($2.95) Reprints of non-EC pre-code horror; EC-style cover by Bissette						5.00
1-($3.50, 5-6/93) Second printing with alternate cover not by Bissette						4.00
2-8-($3.50) Story reprints, history of the pre-code titles and creators; cover galleries (B&W) inside & on back-c (color)						4.00
9-11-($2.95) 10,11-"Terrology" on cover						4.00

TALKING KOMICS
Belda Record & Publ. Co.: 1947 (20 pgs, slick-c)

	GD 2.0	VG 4.0	FN 6.0	VF 8.0	VF/NM 9.0	NM- 9.2
Each comic contained a record that followed the story - much like the Golden Record sets. Known titles: Chirpy Cricket, Lonesome Octopus, Sleepy Santa, Grumpy Shark, Flying Turtle, Happy Grasshopper with records...	4	8	12	28	47	65

TALLY-HO COMICS
Swappers Quarterly (Baily Publ. Co.): Dec, 1944

	GD 2.0	VG 4.0	FN 6.0	VF 8.0	VF/NM 9.0	NM- 9.2
nn-Frazetta's 1st work as Giunta's assistant; Man in Black horror story; violence; Giunta-c	81	162	243	518	884	1250

TALULLAH (See Comic Books Series I)

TALON (From Batman Court of Owls crossover)
DC Comics: No. 0, Nov, 2012 - No. 17, May, 2014 ($2.99)

	GD 2.0	VG 4.0	FN 6.0	VF 8.0	VF/NM 9.0	NM- 9.2
0-17: 0-Origin of Calvin Rose; March-a. 7-11-Bane app.						3.00

TAMMY, TELL ME TRUE
Dell Publishing Co.: No. 1233, 1961

	GD 2.0	VG 4.0	FN 6.0	VF 8.0	VF/NM 9.0	NM- 9.2
Four Color 1233-Movie	8	16	24	52	99	145

TANGENT COMICS

.../ THE ATOM, DC Comics: Dec, 1997 ($2.95, one-shot)

1-Dan Jurgens-s/Jurgens & Paul Ryan-a — 4.00

.../ THE BATMAN, DC Comics: Sept, 1998 ($1.95, one-shot)

1-Dan Jurgens-s/Klaus Janson-a — 4.00

.../ DOOM PATROL, DC Comics: Dec, 1997 ($2.95, one-shot)

1- Dan Jurgens-s/Sean Chen & Kevin Conrad-a — 4.00

.../ THE FLASH, DC Comics: Dec, 1997 ($2.95, one-shot)

1-Todd Dezago-s/Gary Frank & Cam Smith-a — 4.00

.../ GREEN LANTERN, DC Comics: Dec, '97 ($2.95, one-shot)

1-James Robinson-s/J.H. Williams III & Mick Gray-a — 4.00

.../ JLA, DC Comics: Sept, 1998 ($1.95, one-shot)

1-Dan Jurgens-s/Banks & Rapmund-a — 4.00

.../ THE JOKER, DC Comics: Dec, 1997 ($2.95, one-shot)

1-Karl Kesel-s/Matt Haley & Tom Simmons-a — 4.00

.../ THE JOKER'S WILD, DC Comics: Sept, 1998 ($1.95, one-shot)

1-Kesel & Simmons-s/Phillips & Rodriguez-a — 4.00

.../ METAL MEN, DC Comics: Dec, 1997 ($2.95, one-shot)

1-Ron Marz-s/Mike McKone & Mark McKenna-a — 4.00

.../ NIGHTWING, DC Comics: Dec, 1997 ($2.95, one-shot)

1-John Ostrander-s/Jan Duursema-a — 4.00

.../ NIGHTWING: NIGHTFORCE, DC Comics: Sept, 1998 ($1.95, one-shot)

1-John Ostrander-s/Jan Duursema-a — 4.00

.../ POWERGIRL, DC Comics: Sept, 1998 ($1.95, one-shot)

Tales of Wells Fargo FC #968 © DELL

Tangled #1 © DIS

Tank Girl All Stars #3 © Hewlett & Martin

GD VG FN VF VF/NM NM-
2.0 4.0 6.0 8.0 9.0 9.2

1-Marz-s/Abell & Vines-a 4.00

.../ SEA DEVILS, DC Comics: Dec, 1997 ($2.95, one-shot)
1-Kurt Busiek-s/Vince Giarrano & Tom Palmer-a 4.00

.../ SECRET SIX, DC Comics: Dec, 1997 ($2.95, one-shot)
1-Chuck Dixon-s/Tom Grummett & Lary Stucker-a 4.00

.../ THE SUPERMAN, DC Comics: Sept, 1998 ($1.95, one-shot)
1-Millar-s/Guice-a 4.00

.../ TALES OF THE GREEN LANTERN, DC Comics: Sept, 1998 ($1.95, one-shot)
1-Story & art by various 4.00

.../ THE TRIALS OF THE FLASH, DC Comics: Sept, 1998 ($1.95, one-shot)
1-Dezago-s/Pelletier & Lanning-a 4.00

.../ WONDER WOMAN DC Comics: Sept, 1998 ($1.95, one-shot),
1-Peter David-s/Unzueta & Mendoza-a 4.00
... Volume One TPB (2007, $19.99) r/The Atom, Metal Men, Green Lantern, The Flash, Sea Devils one-shots; intro and new cover by Jurgens 20.00
... Volume Two TPB (2008, $19.99) r/Batman, Doom Patrol, Joker, Nightwing and Secret Six one-shots; new cover by Jurgens 20.00
... Volume Three TPB (2008, $19.99) r/The Superman, Wonder Woman, Nightwing: Nightforce, The Joker's Wild, The Trials of the Flash, Tales of the Green Lantern, Powergirl, and JLA one-shots; new cover by Jurgens 20.00

TANGENT: SUPERMAN'S REIGN
DC Comics: May, 2008 - No. 12, Apr, 2009 ($2.99, limited series)
1-12-Jurgens-s; Flash & Green Lantern app.; back-up histories of Tangent heroes 3.00
Volume 1 TPB (2009, $19.99) r/#1-6 & Justice League of America #16 20.00
Volume 2 TPB (2009, $19.99) r/#7-12 20.00

TANGLED (Disney movie)
IDW Publishing: Jan, 2018 - No. 3, Mar, 2018 ($3.99)
1-3: 1-Three covers. 2,3-Two covers 4.00
...: The Series: Hair and Now 1-3 (3/19 - 5/19, $3.99) Katie Cook-s 4.00
...: The Series: Hair It Is (8/19, $4.99, one-shot) Short stories by various 5.00
...: The Series: Hair-Raising Adventures 1-3 (9/18 - 11/18, $3.99) 1-Katie Cook-s 4.00

TANGLED WEB (See Spider-Man's Tangled Web)

TANKERS
Bad Idea: May, 2021 - No. 3, Aug, 2021 ($5.99, limited series)
1-3-Venditti-s/Ryp-a; back-ups by various. 3-Hank Howard, Pizza Detective app. 6.00

TANK GIRL
Dark Horse Comics: May, 1991 - No. 4, Aug, 1991 ($2.25, B&W, mini-series)

	GD	VG	FN	VF	VF/NM	NM-
1-Contains Dark Horse trading cards	8	16	24	53	108	160
2,3	2	4	6	11	16	20
4	3	6	9	19	30	40

...: Dark Nuggets (Image Comics, 12/09, $3.99) Martin-s/Dayglo-a 8.00
...: Dirty Helmets (Image Comics, 4/10, $3.99) Martin-s/Dayglo-a 8.00
...: Hairy Heroes (Image Comics, 8/10, $3.99) Martin-s/Dayglo-a 8.00

TANK GIRL ALL STARS
Titan Comics: Jul, 2018 - No. 4, Oct, 2018 ($3.99, limited series)
1-4: Alan Martin-s; art by Hewlett, Bond, Mahfood, Parson & others; bonus pin-ups 4.00

TANK GIRL: APOCALYPSE
DC Comics: Nov, 1995 - No. 4, Feb, 1996 ($2.25, limited series)
1-4 6.00

TANK GIRL FULL COLOUR CLASSICS
Titan Comics: Jun, 2018 - Present ($6.99, limited series)
1-3.1-Newly colored reprints of original stories from Deadline Magazine; bonus photos 7.00

TANK GIRL: MOVIE ADAPTATION
DC Comics: 1995 ($5.95, 68 pgs., one-shot)
nn-Peter Milligan scripts 2 4 6 8 10 12

TANK GIRL ONGOING
Titan Comics: Jan, 2019 - No. 8, Dec, 2019 ($3.99, limited series)
1-4-Action Alley - Martin-s/Parson-a; multiple covers and centerfold poster on each 4.00
5-8-Forever - Martin-s/Parson-a; multiple covers and centerfold poster on each 4.00

TANK GIRL: TANK GIRL GOLD
Titan Comics: Sept, 2016 - No. 4, Mar, 2017 ($3.99, limited series)
1-4: Alan Martin-s/Brett Parson-a. 2-MAD spoof 4.00

TANK GIRL: THE GIFTING
IDW Publishing: May, 2007 - No. 4, Aug, 2007 ($3.99, limited series)
1-4: 1-Ashley Wood-a/c; Alan Martin-s; 3 covers 6.00

GD VG FN VF VF/NM NM-
2.0 4.0 6.0 8.0 9.0 9.2

TANK GIRL: THE ODYSSEY
DC Comics: May, 1995 - No.4, Oct, 1995 ($2.25, limited series)
1-4: Peter Milligan scripts; Hewlett-a 1 3 4 6 8 10

TANK GIRL: THE ROYAL ESCAPE
IDW Publishing: Mar, 2010 - No. 4, Jun, 2010 ($3.99, limited series)
1-4: Alan Martin-s/Rufus Dayglo-a/c 4.00

TANK GIRL: 21ST CENTURY TANK GIRL
Titan Comics: Jul, 2015 - No. 3, Sept, 2015 ($3.99, limited series)
1-3: Alan Martin-s; art by Hewlett, Bond, Mahfood, Parson & others 4.00

TANK GIRL 2
Dark Horse Comics: June, 1993 - No. 4, Sept, 1993 ($2.50, lim. series, mature)
1-4: Jamie Hewlett & Alan Martin-s/a 1 3 4 6 8 10
TPB (2/95, $17.95) r/#1-4 18.00

TANK GIRL: TWO GIRLS, ONE TANK
Titan Comics: Jun, 2016 - No. 4, Sept, 2016 ($3.99, limited series)
1-4: Alan Martin-s/Brett Parson-a 4.00

TAPPAN'S BURRO (See Zane Grey & 4-Color #449)

TAPPING THE VEIN (Clive Barker's...)
Eclipse Comics: 1989 - No. 5, 1992 ($6.95, squarebound, mature, 68 pgs.)
Book 1-5: 1-Russell-a, Bolton-c. 2-Bolton-a. 4-Die-cut-c 7.00
TPB (2002, $24.95, Checker Book Publ. Group) r/#1-5 25.00

TARANTULA (See Weird Suspense)

TARGET: AIRBOY
Eclipse Comics: Mar, 1988 ($1.95)
1 4.00

TARGET COMICS (...Western Romances #106 on)
Funnies, Inc./Novelty Publications/Star Publ.: Feb, 1940 - V10#3 (#105), Aug-Sept, 1949

	GD	VG	FN	VF	VF/NM	NM-
V1#1-Origin & 1st app. Manowar, The White Streak by Burgos, & Bulls-Eye Bill by Everett; City Editor (ends #5), High Grass Twins by Jack Cole (ends #4), T-Men by Joe Simon (ends #9), Rip Rory (ends #4), Fantastic Feature Films by Tarpe Mills (ends #39), & Calling 2-R (ends #14) begin; marijuana use story	470	940	1410	3431	6066	8700
2-Everett-c/a	276	552	828	1766	3033	4300
3,4-Everett, Jack Cole-a	187	374	561	1197	2049	2900
5-Origin The White Streak in text; Space Hawk by Wolverton begins (6/40) (see Blue Bolt & Circus)	476	952	1428	3475	6138	8800
6-The Chameleon by Everett begins (7/40, 1st app.); White Streak origin cont'd. in text; early mention of comic collecting in letter column; 1st letter column in comics? (7/40)	284	568	852	1818	3109	4400
7-Wolverton Spacehawk-c/story (scarce)	1400	2800	4200	10,300	19,650	29,000
8-Classic sci-fi cover (scarce)	400	800	1200	2800	4900	7000
9-White Streak-c	232	464	696	1485	2543	3600
10-Intro/1st app. The Target (11/40); Simon-c; Spacehawk-s; text piece by Wolverton	308	616	924	2156	3778	5400
11-Origin The Target & The Targeteers	206	412	618	1318	2254	3200
12-(1/41) Target & The Targeteers-c	155	310	465	992	1696	2400
V2#1-Target by Bob Wood; Uncle Sam flag-c	116	232	348	742	1271	1800
2-Ten part Treasure Island serial begins; Harold Delay-a; reprinted in Catholic Comics V3#1-10 (see Key Comics #5)	81	162	243	518	884	1250
3-5: 4-Kit Carter, The Cadet begins	74	148	222	470	810	1150
6-9: Red Seal with White Streak in #6-10	68	136	204	435	743	1050
10-Classic-c	148	296	444	947	1624	2300
11,12: 12-10-part Last of the Mohicans serial begins; Delay-a	63	126	189	403	689	975
V3#1-3,5-7,9,10: 10-Last Wolverton issue	52	104	156	328	552	775
4-V for Victory-c	90	180	270	576	988	1400
8-Hitler, Tojo, Flag-c; 6-part Gulliver Travels serial begins; Delay-a.	129	258	387	826	1413	2000
11,12	22	44	66	132	216	300
V4#1-4,7-12: 8-X-Mas-c	16	32	48	94	147	200
5-Classic Statue of Liberty-c	36	72	108	211	343	475
6-Targetoons by Wolverton	20	40	60	120	195	270
V5#1-8	15	30	45	85	130	175
V6#1-4,6-10	14	28	42	82	121	160
5-Classic Tojo hanging/Buy War Bonds WWII-c	93	186	279	591	1021	1450
V7#1-12	14	28	42	76	108	140
V8#1,3-5,8,9,11,12	12	24	36	69	97	125
2,6,7-Krigstein-a	14	28	42	76	108	140
10-L.B. Cole-c	28	56	84	168	274	380

GD VG FN VF VF/NM NM-
2.0 4.0 6.0 8.0 9.0 9.2

V9#1,4,6,8,10-L.B. Cole-c 28 56 84 168 274 380
2,3,5,7,9,11, V10#1 12 24 36 69 97 125
12-Classic L.B. Cole-c 331 662 993 2317 4059 5800
V10#2,3-L.B. Cole-c 30 60 90 177 289 400
NOTE: *Certa c-V8#9, 11, 12, V9#5, 9, 11, V10#1.* ***Jack Cole*** *a-1-8.* ***Everett*** *a-1-9; c(signed Blake)-1, 2.* ***Al Fago*** *c-V6#8.* ***Sid Greene*** *c-V2#9, 12, V3#3.* ***Walter Johnson*** *c-V5#6, V6#4.* ***Tarpe Mills*** *a-1-4, 6, 8, 11, V3#1.* ***Rico*** *a-V7#4, 10, V8#5, 6, V9#3; c-V7#6, 8, 10, V8#2, 4, 6, 7.* ***Simon*** *a-1, 2.* ***Bob Wood*** *c-V2#2, 3, 5, 6.*

TARGET: THE CORRUPTORS (TV)
Dell Publishing Co.: No. 1306, Mar-May, 1962 - No. 3, Oct-Dec, 1962 (All have photo-c)
Four Color 1306(#1), #2,3 5 10 15 35 63 90

TARGET WESTERN ROMANCES (Formerly Target Comics; becomes Flaming Western Romances #3)
Star Publications: No. 106, Oct-Nov, 1949 - No. 107, Dec-Jan, 1949-50
106(#1)-Silhouette nudity panel; L.B. Cole-c 34 68 102 204 332 460
107(#2)-L.B. Cole-c; lingerie panels 28 56 84 165 270 375

TARGITT
Atlas/Seaboard Publ.: March, 1975 - No. 3, July, 1975
1-3: 1-Origin; Nostrand-a in all. 2-1st in costume. 3-Becomes Man-Stalker
2 4 6 10 14 18

TAROT
Marvel Comics: Mar, 2020 - No. 4, May, 2020 ($4.99, limited series)
1-4-Alan Davis-s/Paul Renaud-a; Defenders & Avengers vs. Diablo 5.00

TAROT: WITCH OF THE BLACK ROSE
Broadsword Comics: Mar, 2000 - Present ($2.95, mature)
1-Jim Balent-s/c/a; at least two covers on all issues 4 8 12 27 44 60
1-Second printing (10/00) 1 2 3 5 6 8
2 2 4 6 13 18 22
3-20 1 2 3 5 6 8
21-40 5.00
41-121: 84,113-The Krampus app. 90-Crossover with School Bites characters 3.00
122/Alternate Paths: Raven Hex #1 - Raven Hex as the Swordmaiden 3.00
123/Alternate Paths: Raven Hex #2 ($12.50, sold online) 12.50
123/Alternate Paths: Raven Hex #2 (7/21, $3.99) 4.00
124,125/Alternate Paths: Boo-Cat #1,2 ($3.99)1- Boo-Cat on vacation. 2-Krampus app. 4.00
126-138 ($3.99) 4.00

TARZAN (See Aurora, Comics on Parade, Crackajack, DC 100-Page Super Spec., Edgar Rice Burroughs'..., Famous Feature Stories #1, Golden Comics Digest #4, 9, Jeep Comics, Jungle Tales of..., Limited Collectors' Edition, Popular, Sparkler, Sport Stars #1, Tip Top & Top Comics)

TARZAN
Dell Publishing Co./United Features Synd.: No. 5, 1939 - No. 161, Aug, 1947
Large Feature Comic 5 ('39)-(Scarce)-By Hal Foster; reprints 1st dailies from 1929
265 530 795 1694 2897 4100
Single Series 20 ('40)-By Hal Foster 206 412 618 1318 2259 3200
Four Color 134 (2/47)-Marsh-c/a 59 118 177 472 1061 1650
Four Color 161 (8/47)-Marsh-c/a 46 92 138 368 834 1300

TARZAN (...of the Apes #138 on)
Dell Publishing Co./Gold Key No. 132 on: 1-2/48 - No. 131, 7-8/62; No. 132, 11/62 - No. 206, 2/72
1-Jesse Marsh-a begins 107 214 321 856 1928 3000
2 44 88 132 326 738 1150
3-5 32 64 96 230 515 800
6-10: 6-1st Tantor the Elephant. 7-1st Valley of the Monsters
26 52 78 182 404 625
11-15: 11-Two Against the Jungle begins, ends #24. 13-Lex Barker photo-c begin
19 38 57 131 291 450
16-20 15 30 45 105 233 360
21-24,26-30 13 26 39 86 188 290
25-1st "Brothers of the Spear" episode; series ends #156,160,161,196-206
14 28 42 98 217 335
31-40 10 20 30 66 138 210
41-54: Last Barker photo-c 8 16 24 56 108 160
55-60: 56-Eight pg. Boy story 7 14 21 49 92 135
61,62,64-70 6 12 18 41 76 110
63-Two Tarzan stories, 1 by Manning 6 12 18 42 79 115
71-79 6 12 18 37 66 95
80-99: 80-Gordon Scott photo-c begin 5 10 15 34 60 85
100 6 12 18 37 66 95
101-109 5 10 15 33 57 80
110 (Scarce)-Last photo-c 6 12 18 37 66 95
111-120 5 10 15 31 53 75
121-131: Last Dell issue 5 10 15 30 50 70
132-1st Gold Key issue 5 10 15 31 53 75
133-138,140-154 4 8 12 25 40 55
139-(12/63)-1st app. Korak (Boy); leaves Tarzan & gets own book (1/64)
6 12 18 40 73 105
155-Origin Tarzan; text article on Tarzana, CA 5 10 15 30 50 70
156-161: 157-Banlu, Dog of the Arande begins, ends #159, 195. 169-Leopard Girl app.
3 6 9 21 33 45
162,165,168,171 (TV)-Ron Ely photo covers 4 8 12 22 35 48
163,164,166,167,169,170: 169-Leopard Girl app. 3 6 9 20 31 42
172-199,201-206: 178-Tarzan origin-r/#155; Leopard Girl app., also in #179, 190-193
3 6 9 18 28 38
200 3 6 9 21 33 45
Story Digest 1-(6/70, G.K., 148pp.)(scarce) 6 12 18 41 76 110
NOTE: *#162, 165, 168, 171 are TV issues. #1-153 all have* ***Marsh*** *art on Tarzan. #154-161, 163, 164, 166, 167, 172-177 all have* ***Manning*** *art on Tarzan. #178, 202 have* ***Manning*** *Tarzan reprints. No "Brothers of the Spear" in #1-24, 157-159, 162-195. #39-126, 128-156 all have* ***Russ Manning*** *art on "Brothers of the Spear". #196-201, 203-205 all have* ***Manning*** *B.O.T.S. reprints; #25-38, 127 all have Jesse* ***Marsh*** *art on B.O.T.S. #206 has a Marsh B.O.T.S. reprint.* ***Gollub*** *c-8-12.* ***Marsh*** *c-1-7.* ***Doug Wildey*** *a-162, 179-187. Many issues have front and back photo covers.*

TARZAN (Continuation of Gold Key series)
National Periodical Publications: No. 207, Apr, 1972 - No. 258, Feb, 1977
207-Origin Tarzan by Joe Kubert, part 1; John Carter begins (origin); 52 pg. issues thru #209 5 10 15 35 63 90
208,209-(52 pgs.): 208-210-Parts 2-4 of origin. 209-Last John Carter
3 6 9 21 33 45
210-220: 210-Kubert-a. 211-Hogarth, Kubert-a. 212-214: Adaptations from "Jungle Tales of Tarzan". 213-Beyond the Farthest Star begins, ends #218. 215-218,224,225-All by Kubert. 215-part Foster-r. 219-223: Adapts "The Return of Tarzan" by Kubert
3 6 9 14 20 25
221-229: 221-223-Continues adaptation of "The Return of Tarzan". 226-Manning-a
2 4 6 10 14 18
230-DC 100 Page Super Spectacular; Kubert, Kaluta-a(p); Korak begins, ends #234; Carson of Venus app. 4 8 12 25 40 55
231-235-New Kubert-a.: 231-234-(All 100 pgs.)-Adapts "Tarzan and the Lion Man"; Rex, the Wonder Dog r-#232, 233. 235-(100 pgs.)-Last Kubert issue.
4 8 12 23 37 50
236,237,239-258: 240-243 adapts "Tarzan & the Castaways". 250-256 adapts "Tarzan the Untamed." 252,253-r/#213 2 4 6 8 10 12
238-(68 pgs.) 2 4 6 13 18 22
Digest 1-(Fall, 1972, 50¢, 164 pgs.)(DC)-Digest size; Kubert-c; Manning-a
4 8 12 25 40 55
Edgar Rice Burroughs' Tarzan The Joe Kubert Years - Volume One HC (Dark Horse Books, 10/05, $49.95, dust jacket) recolored r/#207-214; intro. by Joe Kubert 50.00
Edgar Rice Burroughs' Tarzan The Joe Kubert Years - Volume Two HC (Dark Horse Books, 2/06, $49.95, dust jacket) recolored r/#215-224; intro. by Joe Kubert 50.00
Edgar Rice Burroughs' Tarzan The Joe Kubert Years - Volume Three HC (Dark Horse Books, 6/06, $49.95, dust jacket) recolored r/#225,227-235; Kubert intro. and sketch pages 50.00
NOTE: ***Anderson*** *a-207, 209, 217, 218.* ***Chaykin*** *a-216.* ***Finlay*** *a(r)-212.* ***Foster*** *strip-r #207-209, 211, 212, 221.* ***Heath*** *a-230i.* ***G. Kane*** *a(r)-232p, 233p.* ***Kubert*** *a-207-225, 227-235, 257r, 258r; c-207-249, 253.* ***Lopez*** *a-250-255p; c-250p, 251, 252, 254.* ***Manning*** *strip-r 230-235, 238.* ***Morrow*** *a-208.* ***Nino*** *a-231-234.* ***Sparling*** *a-230, 231.* ***Starr*** *a-233r.*

TARZAN (Lord of the Jungle)
Marvel Comics Group: June, 1977 - No. 29, Oct, 1979
1-New adaptions of Burroughs stories; Buscema-a 3 6 9 16 23 30
1-(35¢-c variant, limited distribution)(6/77) 7 14 21 49 92 135
2-29: 2-Origin by John Buscema. 9-Young Tarzan. 12-14-Jungle Tales of Tarzan. 25-29-New stories 1 3 4 6 8 10
2-5-(35¢-c variants, limited distribution)(7-10/77) 5 10 15 33 57 80
Annual 1-3: 1-(1977). 2-(1978). 3-(1979) 1 3 4 6 8 10
NOTE: ***N. Adams*** *c-11i, 12i.* ***Alcala*** *a-9i, 10i; c-8i, 9i.* ***Buckler*** *c-25-27p, Annual 3p.* ***John Buscema*** *a-1-3, 4-18p, Annual 1; c-1-7, 8p, 9p, 10, 11p, 12p, 13, 14-19p, 21p, 22, 23p, 24p, 28p, Annual 1.* ***Mooney*** *a-22i.* ***Nebres*** *a-22i.* ***Russell*** *a-29i.*

TARZAN
Dark Horse Comics: July, 1996 - No. 20, Mar, 1998 ($2.95)
1-20: 1-6-Suydam-c 4.00

TARZAN / CARSON OF VENUS
Dark Horse Comics: May, 1998 - No. 4, Aug, 1998 ($2.95, limited series)
1-4-Darko Macan-s/Igor Korday-a 4.00

TARZAN FAMILY, THE (Formerly Korak, Son of Tarzan)
National Periodical Publications: No. 60, Nov-Dec, 1975 - No. 66, Nov-Dec, 1976
60-62-(68 pgs.): 60-Korak begins; Kaluta-r 2 4 6 11 16 20
63-66 (52 pgs.) 2 4 6 9 12 15
NOTE: *Carson of Venus-r 60-65. New John Carter-62-64, 65r, 66r. New Korak-60-66. Pellucidar feature-66. Foster strip r-60(9/4/32-10/16/32), 62(6/29/32-7/31/32), 63(10/11/31-12/13/31).* ***Kaluta*** *Carson of Venus-60-65.* ***Kubert*** *a-61, 64; c-60-64.* ***Manning*** *strip-r 60-62, 64.* ***Morrow*** *a-66r.*

TARZAN/JOHN CARTER: WARLORDS OF MARS
Dark Horse Comics: Jan, 1996 - No. 4, June, 1996 ($2.50, limited series)
1-4: Bruce Jones scripts in all. 1,2,4-Bret Blevins-c/a. 2-(4/96)-Indicia reads #3 4.00

TARZAN KING OF THE JUNGLE (See Dell Giant #37, 51)

TARZAN, LORD OF THE JUNGLE
Gold Key: Sept, 1965 (Giant) (25¢, soft paper-c)
1-Marsh-r 7 14 21 48 89 130

TARZAN: LOVE, LIES AND THE LOST CITY (See Tarzan the Warrior)
Malibu Comics: Aug. 10, 1992 - No. 3, Sept, 1992 ($2.50, limited series)
1-($3.95, 68 pgs.)-Flip book format; Simonson & Wagner scripts 5.00
2,3-No Simonson or Wagner scripts 4.00

TARZAN MARCH OF COMICS (See March of Comics #82, 98, 114, 125, 144, 155, 172, 185, 204, 223, 240, 252, 262, 272, 286, 300, 332, 342, 354, 366)

TARZAN OF THE APES
Metropolitan Newspaper Service: 1934? (Hardcover, 4x12", 68 pgs.)
1-Strip reprints 29 58 87 172 281 390

TARZAN OF THE APES
Marvel Comics Group: July, 1984 - No. 2, Aug, 1984 (Movie adaptation)
1,2: Origin-r/Marvel Super Spec. 4.00

TARZAN ON THE PLANET OF THE APES
Dark Horse Comics: Sept, 2016 - No. 5, Jan, 2017 ($3.99, limited series)
1-5-Seeley & Walker-s/Dagnino-a. 1-Cornelius & Zira adopt young Tarzan on Earth 4.00

TARZAN'S JUNGLE ANNUAL (See Dell Giants)

TARZAN'S JUNGLE WORLD (See Dell Giant #25)

TARZAN: THE BECKONING
Malibu Comics: 1992 - No. 7, 1993 ($2.50, limited series)
1-7 4.00

TARZAN: THE LOST ADVENTURE (See Edgar Rice Burroughs' ...)

TARZAN-THE RIVERS OF BLOOD
Dark Horse Comics: Nov, 1999 - No. 8 ($2.95, limited series)
1-4: Korday-c/a 4.00

TARZAN THE SAVAGE HEART
Dark Horse Comics: Apr, 1999 - No. 4, July, 1999 ($2.95, limited series)
1-4: Grell-c/a 4.00

TARZAN THE WARRIOR (Also see Tarzan: Love, Lies and the Lost City)
Malibu Comics: Mar, 19, 1992 - No. 5, 1992 ($2.50, limited series)

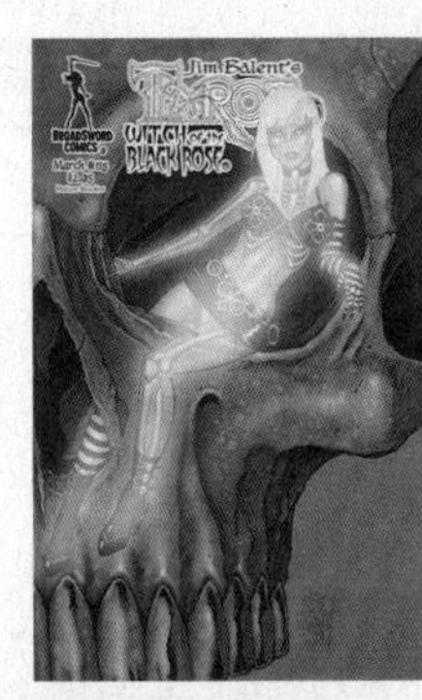

Tarot: Witch of the Black Rose #115 © Jim Balent

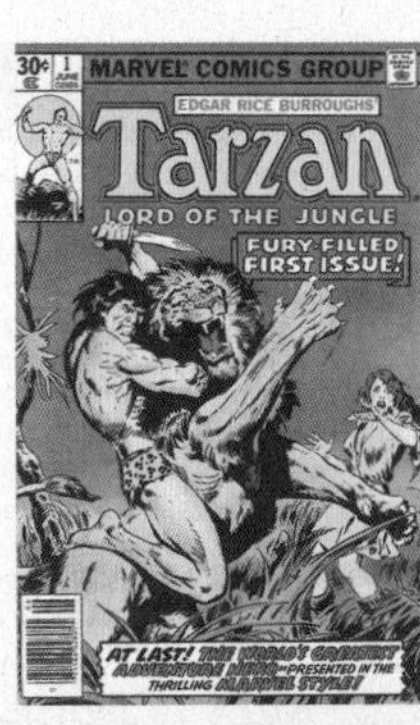

Tarzan (1977) #1 © ERB

Tech Jacket #1 © Kirkman & Su

GD 2.0 | VG 4.0 | FN 6.0 | VF 8.0 | VF/NM 9.0 | NM- 9.2

1-5: 1-Bisley painted pack-c (flip book format-c) 4.00
1-2nd printing w/o flip-c by Bisley 4.00

TARZAN VS. PREDATOR AT THE EARTH'S CORE
Dark Horse Comics: Jan, 1996 - No. 4, June, 1996 ($2.50, limited series)
1-4: Lee Weeks-c/a; Walt Simonson scripts 4.00

TASK FORCE Z
DC Comics: Dec, 2021 - No. 12, Nov, 2022 ($3.99)
1-12-Red Hood leads a team of zombies; Bane, Man-Bat, Mr. Bloom, Deadshot app. 4.00

TASKMASTER
Marvel Comics: Apr, 2002 - No. 4, July, 2002 ($2.99, limited series)
1-4-Udon Studio-s/a. 1-Iron Man app. 3.00

TASKMASTER
Marvel Comics: Nov, 2010 - No. 4, Feb, 2011 ($3.99, limited series)
1-4-Van Lente-s/Palo-a; Hydra & A.I.M. app. 4.00

TASKMASTER
Marvel Comics: Jan, 2021 - No. 5, May, 2021 ($3.99, limited series)
1-5-MacKay-s/Vitti-a; Nick Fury and Black Widow app. 2-Hyperion app. 3-White Fox app. 4.00

TASMANIAN DEVIL & HIS TASTY FRIENDS
Gold Key: Nov, 1962 (12¢)
1-Bugs Bunny, Elmer Fudd, Sylvester, Yosemite Sam, Road Runner & Wile E. Coyote x-over
18 36 54 124 275 425

TATTERED BANNERS
DC Comics (Vertigo): Nov, 1998 - No. 4, Feb, 1999 ($2.95, limited series)
1-4-Grant & Giffen-s/McMahon-a 3.00

TATTERED MAN
Image Comics: May 2011 ($4.99, one-shot)
1-Justin Gray & Jimmy Palmiotti-s/Norberto Fernandez-a; covers by Fernandez & Conner 5.00

TEAM AMERICA (See Captain America #269)
Marvel Comics Group: June, 1982 - No. 12, May, 1983
1,12: 1-Origin; Ideal Toy motorcycle characters. 12-Double size 5.00
2-11: 9-Iron Man app. 11-Ghost Rider app. 4.00
NOTE: *There are 16 pg. variants known for most issues, possibly all. The only ad is on the inside front cover.*

TEAM HELIX
Marvel Comics: Jan, 1993 - No. 4, Apr, 1993 ($1.75, limited series)
1-4: Teen Super Group. 1,2-Wolverine app. 3.00

TEAM ONE: STORMWATCH (Also see StormWatch)
Image Comics (WildStorm Productions): June, 1995 - No. 2, Aug, 1995 ($2.50, lim. series)
1,2: Steven T. Seagle scripts 3.00

TEAM ONE: WILDC.A.T.S (Also see WildC.A.T.S)
Image Comics (WildStorm Productions): July, 1995 - No. 2, Aug, 1995 ($2.50, lim. series)
1,2: James Robinson scripts 3.00

TEAM 7
Image Comics (WildStorm): Oct, 1994 - No.4, Feb, 1995 ($2.50, limited series)
1-4: Dixon scripts in all, 1-Portacio variant-c 3.00

TEAM 7 (DC New 52)
DC Comics: No. 0, Nov, 2012 - No. 8, Jul, 2013 ($2.99)
0-8: 0-Merino-a/Lashley-c; Slade Wilson, John Lynch, Grifter and others assemble team. 3,4-Eclipso returns. 7-Pandora & Majestic app. 3.00

TEAM 7-DEAD RECKONING
Image Comics (WildStorm): Jan, 1996 - No. 4, Apr, 1996 ($2.50, limited series)
1-4: Dixon scripts in all 3.00

TEAM 7-OBJECTIVE HELL
Image Comics (WildStorm): May, 1995 - No. 3, July, 1995 ($1.95/$2.50, limited series)
1-($1.95)-Newstand; Dixon scripts in all; Barry Smith-c 3.00
1-3: 1-($2.50)-Direct Market; Barry Smith-c, bound-in card 3.00

TEAM SONIC RACING
IDW Publishing: Oct, 2018; May, 2019 ($4.99/$5.99, one-shots)
1-Caleb Goellner-s/Adam Bryce Thomas-a; videogame tie-in 5.00
... Deluxe Turbo Championship Edition (5/19, $5.99) Goellner-s/Thomas-a 6.00

TEAM SUPERMAN
DC Comics: July, 1999 ($2.95, one-shot)
1-Jeanty-a/Stelfreeze-c 4.00
...Secret Files 1 (5/98, $4.95)Origin-s and pin-ups of Superboy, Supergirl and Steel 5.00

GD 2.0 | VG 4.0 | FN 6.0 | VF 8.0 | VF/NM 9.0 | NM- 9.2

TEAM TITANS (See Deathstroke & New Titans Annual #7)
DC Comics: Sept, 1992 - No. 24, Sept, 1994 ($1.75/$1.95)
1-Five different #1s exist w/origins in 1st half & the same 2nd story in each: Kilowat, Mirage, Nightrider w/Netzer/Pérez-a, Redwing, & Terra w/part Pérez-p; Total Chaos Pt. 3 5.00
2-24: 2-Total Chaos Pt 6. 11-Metallik app. 24-Zero Hour x-over 4.00
Annual 1,2 ('93, '94, $3.50, 68 pgs.): 2-Elseworlds tory 5.00

TEAM X/TEAM 7
Marvel Comics: Nov, 1996 ($4.95, one-shot)
1 5.00

TEAM X 2000
Marvel Comics: Feb, 1999 ($3.50, one-shot)
1-Kevin Lau-a; Bishop vs. Shi'ar Empire 4.00

TEAM YOUNGBLOOD (Also see Youngblood)
Image Comics (Extreme Studios): Sept, 1993 - No. 22, Sept, 1995 ($1.95/$2.50)
1-22: 1-9-Liefeld scripts in all: 1,2,4-6,8-Thibert-c(i). 1-1st app. Dutch & Masada. 3-Spawn cameo. 5-1st app. Lynx. 7,8-Coupons 1 & 4 for Extreme Prejudice #0; Black and White Pt. 4 & 8 by Thibert. 8-Coupon #4 for E. P. #0. 9-Liefeld wraparound-c &(p)/a(p) on Pt. I. 16,17-Bagged w/trading card. 21-Angela & Glory-app. 3.00

TEAM ZERO
DC Comics (WildStorm Productions): Feb, 2006 - No. 6, Jul, 2006 ($2.99, limited series)
1-6-Dixon-s/Mahnke-a 3.00
TPB (2008, $17.99) r/#1-6 18.00

TECH JACKET
Image Comics: Nov, 2002 - No. 6, Apr, 2003 ($2.95)
1-6-Kirkman-s/Su-a 3.00
Vol. 1: Lost and Found TPB (7/03, $12.95, 7-3/4" x 5-1/4") B&W r/#1-6; Valentino intro. 13.00

TECH JACKET (2nd series)
Image Comics: Jul, 2014 - No. 12, Dec, 2015 ($2.99)
1-12-Keatinge-s/Randolph-a 3.00

TEDDY ROOSEVELT & HIS ROUGH RIDERS (See Real Heroes #1)
Avon Periodicals: 1950
1-Kinstler-c; Palais-a; Flag-c 22 44 66 132 216 300

TEDDY ROOSEVELT ROUGH RIDER (See Battlefield #22 & Classics Illustrated Special Issue)

TED MCKEEVER'S METROPOL (See Transit)
Marvel Comics (Epic Comics): Mar, 1991 - No. 12, Mar, 1992 ($2.95, limited series)
V1#1-12: Ted McKeever-c/a/scripts 4.00

TED MCKEEVER'S METROPOL A.D.
Marvel Comics (Epic Comics): Oct, 1992 - No. 3, Dec, 1992 ($3.50, limited series)
V2#1-3: Ted McKeever-c/a/scripts 4.00

TEENA
Magazine Enterprises/Standard Comics No. 20 on: No. 11, 1948 - No. 15, 1948; No. 20, Aug, 1949 - No. 22, Oct, 1950
A-1 #11-Teen-age; Ogden Whitney-c 17 34 51 100 158 215
A-1 #12, 15 15 30 45 85 130 175
20-22 (Standard) 13 26 39 72 101 130

TEEN-AGE BRIDES (True Bride's Experiences #8 on)
Harvey/Home Comics: Aug, 1953 - No. 7, Aug, 1954
1-Powell-a 14 28 42 81 118 155
2-Powell-a 10 20 30 54 72 90
3-7: 3,6-Powell-a 9 18 27 50 65 80

TEEN-AGE CONFESSIONS (See Teen Confessions)

TEEN-AGE CONFIDENTIAL CONFESSIONS
Charlton Comics: July, 1960 - No. 22, 1964
1 5 10 15 33 57 80
2-10 3 6 9 20 31 42
11-22 3 6 9 15 22 28

TEEN-AGE DIARY SECRETS (Formerly Blue Ribbon Comics; becomes Diary Secrets #10 on)
St. John Publishing Co.: No. 4, 9/49; nn (#5), 9/49 - No. 7, 11/49; No. 8, 2/50; No. 9, 8/50
4(9/49)-Oversized; part mag., part comic 63 126 189 403 689 975
nn(#5)(no indicia)-Oversized, all comics; contains sty "I Gave Boys the Green Light."
61 122 183 390 670 950
6-(Reg. size) pre-fame Marilyn Monroe photo-c; Baker-a(2-3)
110 220 330 704 1202 1700
7-Digest size (Pocket Comics); Baker-a(5); same contents as #9; diff.-c
100 200 300 635 1093 1550

	GD 2.0	VG 4.0	FN 6.0	VF 8.0	VF/NM 9.0	NM- 9.2
8-(Reg. size) Photo-c; Baker-a(2-3)	71	142	213	454	777	1100
9-Digest size (Pocket Comics); Baker-a(5); same contents as #7; diff.-c by Baker	148	296	444	947	1624	2300

TEEN-AGE DOPE SLAVES (See Harvey Comics Library #1)

TEENAGE HOTRODDERS (Top Eliminator #25 on; see Blue Bird)
Charlton Comics: Apr, 1963 - No. 24, July, 1967

	GD	VG	FN	VF	VF/NM	NM-
1	6	12	18	42	79	115
2-10	4	8	12	22	35	48
11-24	3	6	9	17	26	35

TEEN-AGE LOVE (See Fox Giants)

TEEN-AGE LOVE (Formerly Intimate)
Charlton Comics: V2#4, July, 1958 - No. 96, Dec, 1973

	GD	VG	FN	VF	VF/NM	NM-
V2#4	5	10	15	33	57	80
5-9	4	8	12	27	44	60
10(9/59)-20	3	6	9	19	30	40
21-35	3	6	9	16	24	32
36-70	3	6	9	14	20	26
71-79,81,82,85-87,90-96: 61&62-Jonnie Love begins (origin)	2	4	6	10	16	20
80,84,88-David Cassidy pin-ups	3	6	9	15	22	28
83,89: 83-Bobby Sherman pin-up. 89-Danny Bonaduce pin-up	3	6	9	15	22	28

TEENAGE MUTANT NINJA CEREBI (Reprints from Cerebus in Hell)
Aardvark-Vanaheim: 2018 ($4.00, B&W)

	GD	VG	FN	VF	VF/NM	NM-
1-Cerebus figures placed over original Gustave Doré artwork of Hell; TMNT #1-c swipe						4.00

TEENAGE MUTANT NINJA TURTLES (Also see Anything Goes, Donatello, First Comics Graphic Novel, Gobbledygook, Grimjack #26, Leonardo, Michaelangelo, Raphael & Tales Of The...)
Mirage Studios: 1984 - No. 62, Aug, 1993 ($1.50/$1.75, B&W; all 44-52 pgs.)

	GD	VG	FN	VF	VF/NM	NM-
1-1st printing (3000 copies)-Origin and 1st app. of the Turtles and Splinter. Only printing to have ad for Gobbledygook #1 & 2; Shredder app. (#1-4: 7-1/2x11")	2200	4400	6600	11,000	16,500	22,000
1-2nd printing (6/84)(6,000 copies)	93	186	279	744	1672	2600
1-3rd printing (2/85)(36,000 copies)	40	80	120	296	673	1050
1-4th printing, new-c (50,000 copies)	8	16	24	54	102	150
1-5th printing, new-c (8/88-c, 11/88 inside)	8	16	24	51	96	140
1-Counterfeit. **Note**: Most counterfeit copies have a half inch wide white streak or scratch marks across the center of back cover. Black part of cover is a bluish black instead of a deep black. Inside paper is very white & inside cover is bright white (no value)						
2-1st printing (1984; 15,000 copies)	25	50	75	175	388	600
2-2nd printing	8	16	24	55	105	155
2-3rd printing; new Corben-c/a (2/85)	4	8	12	28	47	65
2-Counterfeit with glossy cover stock (no value).						
3-1st printing (1985, 44 pgs.)	10	20	30	69	147	225
3-Variant, 500 copies, cover printed at different plant, has 'Laird's Photo' in white rather than light blue	68	136	204	544	1222	1900
3-2nd printing; contains new back-up story	5	10	15	33	57	80
4-1st printing (1985, 44 pgs.)	10	20	30	69	147	225
4-2nd printing (5/87) all have manufacturing error	16	32	48	110	243	375
5-Fugitoid begins, ends #7; 1st full color-c (1985)	6	12	18	38	69	100
5-2nd printing (11/87)	3	6	9	19	30	40
6-1st printing (1986)	5	10	15	30	50	70
6-2nd printing (4/88-c, 5/88 inside)	2	4	6	11	16	20
7-Four pg. Eastman/Corben color insert; 1st color TMNT (1986, $1.75-c); Bade Biker back-up story	4	8	12	28	47	65
7-2nd printing (1/89) w/o color insert	6	12	18	38	69	100
8-Cerebus-c/story with Dave Sim-a (1986)	4	8	12	25	40	55
9-(9/86)-Rip In Time by Corben	3	6	9	17	26	35
10-Shredder-c	4	8	12	23	37	50
11,12,14,15	3	6	9	14	20	25
13-1st Jhanna	3	6	9	19	30	40
16-18: 18-Mark Bodé-a	2	4	6	11	16	20
18-2nd printing ($2.25, color, 44 pgs.)-New-c	1	3	4	6	8	10
19-31,33,34: 19-Begin $1.75-c. 24-26-Veitch-c/a.	2	4	6	8	10	12
32-Good Girl art-c	2	4	6	11	16	20
32-2nd printing ($2.75, 52 pgs., full color)						6.00
35-46,48,49,51: 35-Begin $2.00-c.	2	4	6	8	10	12
47-1st Space Usagi	7	14	21	48	89	130
50-Features pin-ups by Larsen, McFarlane, Simonson, etc.	2	4	6	9	12	15
52-62: 52-Begin $2.25-c	1	3	4	6	8	10
nn (1990, $5.95, B&W)-Movie adaptation	2	4	6	11	16	20
Book 1,2($1.50, B&W): 2-Corben-c	2	4	6	9	12	15
...Christmas Special 1 (12/90, $1.75, B&W, 52 pgs.)-Cover title: Michaelangelo Christmas Special; r/Michaelangelo one-shot plus new Raphael story	3	6	9	14	19	24
... Color Special (11/09, $3.25) full color reprint of issue #1	3	6	9	14	20	26
...Special: The Haunted Pizza nn (10/92, $2.25, B&W, 32 pgs.) Howarth-s/a	2	4	6	9	12	15
...Special (The Maltese Turtle) nn (1/93, $2.95, color, 44 pgs.)	2	4	6	9	12	15
...Special: "Times" Pipeline nn (9/92, $2.95, color, 44 pgs.)-Mark Bodé-c/a	2	4	6	9	12	15
Hardcover ($100)-r/#1-10 plus one-shots w/dust jackets - limited to 1000 w/letter of authenticity (1988)						300.00
Softcover ($40)-r/#1-10						45.00

TEENAGE MUTANT NINJA TURTLES
Mirage Studios: V2#1, Oct, 1993 - V2#13, Oct, 1995 ($2.75)

	GD	VG	FN	VF	VF/NM	NM-
V2#1-Wraparound-c	3	6	9	15	22	28
2-13						6.00

TEENAGE MUTANT NINJA TURTLES (Volume 3)
Image Comics (Highbrow Ent.): June, 1996 - No. 23, Oct, 1999 ($1.95-$2.95)

	GD	VG	FN	VF	VF/NM	NM-
1-Erik Larsen-c(i)	3	6	9	15	22	28
2-23: 2-8-Erik Larsen-c(i) on all. 10-Savage Dragon-c/app.						6.00

TEENAGE MUTANT NINJA TURTLES
Mirage Publishing: V4#1, Dec, 2001 - No. 28, Jun, 2006 ($2.95, B&W)

	GD	VG	FN	VF	VF/NM	NM-
V4#1-Laird-s/a(i)/Lawson-a(p)	2	4	6	11	16	20
V4#2-9,11-28-Laird-s/a(i)/Lawson-a(p).						6.00
10-($3.95) Splinter dies	1	3	4	6	8	10

TEENAGE MUTANT NINJA TURTLES
Dreamwave Productions: June 2003 - No. 7 ($2.95, color)

	GD	VG	FN	VF	VF/NM	NM-
1-Animated style; Peter David-s/Lesean-a	2	4	6	9	12	15
2-7						6.00

TEENAGE MUTANT NINJA TURTLES
IDW Publishing: Aug, 2011 - Present ($3.99)

	GD	VG	FN	VF	VF/NM	NM-
1-Kevin Eastman-s & layouts; four covers by Duncan (each turtle); origin flashback	4	8	12	27	44	60
1-Variant-c by Eastman	6	12	18	38	69	100
1-Halloween Edition (10/12, no cover price) Reprints #1	1	3	4	6	8	10
2-43,45-49,52-74,76-92-Multiple variant covers on each						6.00
44-Donatello killed						20.00
50-(9/15, $7.99) Multiple variant covers; Turtles & Splinter vs. Shredder; Santolouco-a	1	3	4	6	8	10
51-First appearance of Jennika (mutated into Ninja Turtle in #95)	4	8	12	23	37	50
75-(10/17, $7.99) Multiple variant covers; Trial of Krang pt. 3; Santolouco-a	1	3	4	6	8	10
93,94,96-98-City at War. 97-Jennika dons the yellow mask						6.00
95-Jennika mutated into a Ninja Turtle	3	6	9	19	30	40
99,100-($7.99) Conclusion to City at War. 100-Splinter killed	1	3	4	6	8	10
101-114: 101-105-Mutanimals app.						6.00
115-137						4.00
Annual 2012 (10/12, $8.99) Eastman-s/a; wraparound-c	1	3	4	6	8	10
Annual 2014 (8/14, $7.99) Eastman-s/a; Renet app.						8.00
Annual 2021 (6/21, $6.99) Waltz-s/Maloney-a; spotlight on The Rat King						7.00
Annual 2022 (3/22, $6.99) Juni Ba-s/a						7.00
...: Deviations (3/16, $4.99) What If... the Turtles joined Shredder; Waltz-s/Howard-a						5.00
... FCBD (3/15, giveaway) Santolouco-a						3.00
...: Free Comic Book Day 2019 (5/19, giveaway) Wachter-a; prelude to #94; Jennika app.						3.00
... Funko Universe One Shot (5/17, $4.99) Character rendered in Funko Pop figure style						5.00
Greatest Hits - Teenage Mutant Ninja Turtles #1 (2/16, $1.00) r/#1						3.00
... Kevin Eastman Cover Gallery (12/13, $3.99) Collection of recent Eastman covers						4.00
... Microseries 1-8 (11/11 - No. 8, 9/12) 1-Raphael. 2-Michelangelo. 3-Donatello. 4-Leonardo. 5-Splinter. 6-Casey Jones. 7-April. 8-Fugitoid						4.00
...100 Page Spectacular (4/12, $7.99) r/TMNT Adventures (1988) mini-series #1-3						8.00
...: Road to 100 (11/19, free) Story summary leading to issue #100						3.00
... Samurai Special (7/17, no price, B&W) Stan Sakai-s/a; reprints Usagi Yojimbo x-overs						3.00
... 30th Anniversary Special (5/14, $7.99) History and reprints from all eras; pin-ups by various; multiple covers						8.00
... 20/20 1 (1/19, $4.99) Takes place 20 years in the future; Paul Allor-s/Nelson Daniel-a						5.00
.../ Usagi Yojimbo (7/17, $7.99) Stan Sakai-s/a; multiple covers						8.00
... Villains Microseries 1-8 (4/13 - No. 8, 11/13, $3.99) 1-Krang. 2-Baxter. 8-Shredder						4.00

TEENAGE MUTANT NINJA TURTLES (Adventures)
Archie Publications: Jan, 1996 - No. 3, Mar, 1996 ($1.50, limited series)

	GD	VG	FN	VF	VF/NM	NM-
1	3	6	9	14	20	26
2,3	1	3	4	6	8	10

TEENAGE MUTANT NINJA TURTLES ADVENTURES (TV)
Archie Comics: Oct, 1988 - No. 3, Dec, 1988; Mar, 1989 - No. 72, Oct, 1995 ($1.00-$1.75)

	GD	VG	FN	VF	VF/NM	NM-
1-Adapts TV cartoon; not by Eastman/Laird	7	14	21	44	82	120
2,3 (Mini-series)	3	6	9	16	23	30
1 (2nd on-going series)	5	10	15	30	50	70
1-2nd printing	2	4	6	8	10	12
2	3	6	9	14	19	24
2-11: 2nd printings						4.00
3-5: 5-Begins original stories not based on TV	2	4	6	10	14	18
6-18,20-22,25-30: 14-Simpson-a(p). 22-Colan-c/a	1	2	3	5	6	8
19-1st Mighty Mutanimals (also in #20, 51-54)	3	6	9	14	20	25
20,51-54	2	4	6	10	14	18
23-1st Slash	3	6	9	19	30	40
24-2nd Slash	2	4	6	11	16	20
31-48	1	2	3	5	6	8
49-Alien Abduction-c	2	4	6	11	16	20
50-Poster by Eastman/Laird	1	3	4	6	8	10
55-60	1	2	3	5	6	8
61-70: 62-w/poster	2	4	6	8	10	12
71-Turtles origin	5	10	15	35	63	90
72- Last issue	6	12	18	38	69	100
nn (1990, $2.50)-Movie adaptation	2	4	6	11	16	20
nn (Spring, 1991, $2.50, 68 pgs.)-(Meet Archie)	1	3	4	6	8	10
nn (Sum, 1991, $2.50, 68 pgs.)-(Movie II)-Adapts movie sequel	2	4	6	9	12	15
...Meet the Conservation Corps 1 (1992, $2.50, 68 pgs.)	1	3	4	6	8	10
...III The Movie: The Turtles are Back...In Time (1993, $2.50, 68 pgs.)	2	4	6	9	12	15
Special 1,4,5 (Sum/92, Spr/93, Sum/93, 68 pgs.)-1-Bill Wray-c	1	2	3	5	6	8
Giant Size Special 6 (Fall/93, $1.95, 52 pgs.)						6.00
Special 7-10 (Win/93-Fall//94, 52 pgs.): 9-Jeff Smith-c						5.00

NOTE: *There are 2nd printings of #1-11 w/B&W inside covers. Originals are color.*

TEENAGE MUTANT NINJA TURTLES AMAZING ADVENTURES
IDW Publishing: Aug, 2015 - No. 14, Sept, 2016 ($3.99)

	GD	VG	FN	VF	VF/NM	NM-
1-14-All-ages animated-style stories; two covers						5.00

Teenage Mutant Ninja Turtles #24 © Mirage

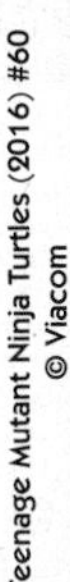
Teenage Mutant Ninja Turtles (2016) #60 © Viacom

Teen-Age Romances #9 © STJ

	GD 2.0	VG 4.0	FN 6.0	VF 8.0	VF/NM 9.0	NM- 9.2
... Carmelo Anthony Special One-Shot (5/16, $5.99) Turtles meet the NBA player						6.00

TEENAGE MUTANT NINJA TURTLES AMAZING ADVENTURES: ROBOTANIMALS
IDW Publishing: Jun, 2017 - No. 3, Sept, 2017 ($3.99, limited series)

1-3-All-ages animated-style stories; three covers on each; Goellner-s/Thomas-a						4.00

TEENAGE MUTANT NINJA TURTLES BEBOP & ROCKSTEADY DESTROY EVERYTHING
IDW Publishing: Jun, 2016 - No. 5, Jun, 2016 ($3.99, weekly limited series)

1-5-Dustin Weaver-s; art by various; interlocking covers						4.00

TEENAGE MUTANT NINJA TURTLES BEBOP & ROCKSTEADY HIT THE ROAD
IDW Publishing: Aug, 2018 - No. 5, Aug, 2018 ($3.99, weekly limited series)

1-5-Dustin Weaver & Ben Bates-s/a; interlocking covers						4.00

TEENAGE MUTANT NINJA TURTLES: CASEY AND APRIL
IDW Publishing: Jun, 2015 - No. 4, Sept, 2015 ($3.99, limited series)

1-4-Mariko Tamaki-s/Irene Koh-a; two covers on each						4.00

TEENAGE MUTANT NINJA TURTLES CLASSICS DIGEST (TV)
Archie Comics: Aug, 1993 - No. 8, Mar, 1995? ($1.75)

1-8: Reprints TMNT Advs.	1	3	4	6	8	10

TEENAGE MUTANT NINJA TURTLES COLOR CLASSICS
IDW Publishing: May, 2012 - Mar, 2016 ($3.99)

1-11-Colored reprints of the original 1984 B&W series	1	2	3	5	6	8
...: Donatello Micro-Series One-Shot (3/13, $3.99) r/Donatello, TMNT #1 (1986)						5.00
...: Leonardo Micro-Series One-Shot (4/13, $3.99) r/Leonardo, TMNT #1						5.00
...: Michaelangelo Micro-Series One-Shot (12/12, $3.99) r/Michaelangelo, TMNT #1						5.00
...: Raphael Micro-Series One-Shot (8/12, $3.99) r/Raphael #1 (1985)						5.00
... Volume 2 (11/13 - No. 7, 5/14, $3.99) 1-7: 1-Reprints TMNT #12 (1987)						4.00
... Volume 3 (1/15 - No. 15, 3/16, $3.99) 1-15: 1-Reprints TMNT #48 (1992)						4.00

TEENAGE MUTANT NINJA TURTLES: DIMENSION X
IDW Publishing: Aug, 2017 - No. 5, Aug, 2017 ($3.99, weekly limited series)

1-5-Takes place during the Trial of Krang (between TMNT #73 & 74); multiple-c on each						4.00

TEENAGE MUTANT NINJA TURTLES/FLAMING CARROT CROSSOVER
Mirage Publishing: Nov, 1993 - No. 4, Feb, 1994 ($2.75, limited series)

1-4: Bob Burden story	1	3	4	6	8	10

TEENAGE MUTANT NINJA TURTLES / GHOSTBUSTERS
IDW Publishing: Oct, 2014 - No. 4, Jan, 2015 ($3.99, limited series)

1-4-Burnham & Waltz-s/Schoening-a; multiple covers on each						4.00
... #1 Director's Cut (5/15, $5.99) r/#1 with creator commentary; bonus script pages						6.00

TEENAGE MUTANT NINJA TURTLES / GHOSTBUSTERS 2
IDW Publishing: Nov, 2017 - No. 5, Nov, 2017 ($3.99, limited series)

1-5-Burnham & Waltz-s/Schoening-a; multiple covers on each						4.00

TEENAGE MUTANT NINJA TURTLES MACRO-SERIES
IDW Publishing: Sept, 2018 - Dec, 2018 ($7.99, limited series)

... #1 Donatello; Paul Allor-s/Brahm Revel-a; four covers; Metalhead app.						8.00
... #2 Michelangelo; Ian Flynn-s/Michael Dialynas-a; four covers						8.00
... #3 Leonardo; Sophie Campbell-s/a; four covers						8.00
... #4 Raphael; Kevin Eastman-s/Eastman and Ben Bishop-a; four covers						8.00

TEENAGE MUTANT NINJA TURTLES: MUTANIMALS
IDW Publishing: Feb, 2015 - No. 4, May, 2015 ($3.99, limited series)

1-4-Paul Allor-s/Andy Kuhn-a; two covers						4.00

TEENAGE MUTANT NINJA TURTLES NEW ANIMATED ADVENTURES
IDW Publishing: Jul, 2013 - No. 24, Jun, 2015 ($3.99)

1-24-Multiple covers on each						4.00
... Free Comic Book Day (5/13) Burnham-s/Brizuela-a						3.00

TEENAGE MUTANT NINJA TURTLES PRESENTS: APRIL O'NEIL
Archie Comics: Mar, 1993 - No. 3, June, 1993 ($1.25, limited series)

1-3						6.00

TEENAGE MUTANT NINJA TURTLES PRESENTS: DONATELLO AND LEATHERHEAD
Archie Comics: July, 1993 - No. 3, Sept, 1993 ($1.25, limited series)

1-3						6.00

TEENAGE MUTANT NINJA TURTLES PRESENTS: MERDUDE
Archie Comics: Oct, 1993 - No. 3, Dec, 1993 ($1.25, limited series)

1-3-See Mighty Mutanimals #7 for 1st app. Merdude						6.00

TEENAGE MUTANT NINJA TURTLES: SATURDAY MORNING ADVENTURES
IDW Publishing: Oct, 2022 - No. 4, Jan, 2023 ($3.99, limited series)

1-4-Burnham-s/Lattie-a						4.00

TEENAGE MUTANT NINJA TURTLES/SAVAGE DRAGON CROSSOVER
Mirage Studios: Aug, 1995 ($2.75, one-shot)

1						6.00

TEENAGE MUTANT NINJA TURTLES: SHREDDER IN HELL
IDW Publishing: Jan, 2019 - No. 5, Jun, 2019 ($3.99, limited series)

1-5-Mateus Santolouco-s/a; 3 covers						4.00
1-Director's Cut (4/19, $4.99) Reprints #1 with uncolored art and commentary						5.00

TEENAGE MUTANT NINJA TURTLES: THE ARMAGEDDON GAME
IDW Publishing: Sept, 2022 - Present ($5.99/$4.99, limited series)

1-($5.99) Waltz-s/Federici-a						6.00
2-5-($4.99)						5.00
... – Alliance 1-4 (11/22 - Present, $3.99) Spotlight on Oroku Karai						4.00
... – Opening Moves 1,2 (7/22, 8/22, $5.99) Prelude to the series						6.00

TEENAGE MUTANT NINJA TURTLES: THE LAST RONIN – LOST YEARS
IDW Publishing: Jan, 2023 - Present ($4.99, limited series)

1-Waltz & Eastman-s/Gallant-a						5.00

TEENAGE MUTANT NINJA TURTLES: THE SECRET HISTORY OF THE FOOT CLAN
IDW Publishing: Dec, 2012 - No. 4, Mar, 2013 ($3.99, limited series)

1-4-Santolouco-a/Santolouco & Burnham-s						4.00

TEENAGE MUTANT NINJA TURTLES: TURTLES IN TIME
IDW Publishing: Jun, 2014 - No. 4, Sept, 2014 ($3.99, limited series)

1-4: 1-Paul Allor-s/Ross Campbell-a; Renet app.; three covers. 2-4-Two covers each						4.00

TEENAGE MUTANT NINJA TURTLES UNIVERSE
IDW Publishing: Aug, 2016 - No. 25, Aug, 2018($4.99)

1-25: 1-Allor-s/Couceiro-a; Eastman & Sienkiewicz-a; multiple covers on each						4.00

TEENAGE MUTANT NINJA TURTLES: URBAN LEGENDS
IDW Publishing: May, 2018 - Present ($3.99)

1-22-Reprints the 1996 B&W series in color; multiple covers on each						4.00

TEENAGE MUTANT NINJA TURTLES UTROM EMPIRE
IDW Publishing: Jan, 2014 - No. 3, Mar, 2014 ($3.99, limited series)

1-3-Paul Allor-s/Andy Kuhn-a; two covers on each						4.00

TEEN-AGE ROMANCE (Formerly My Own Romance)
Marvel Comics (ZPC): No. 77, Sept, 1960 - No. 86, Mar, 1962

77-83	8	16	24	52	99	145
84-86-Kirby-c. 84-Kirby-a(2 pgs.). 85,86-(3 pgs.)	8	16	24	56	108	160

TEEN-AGE ROMANCES
St. John Publ. Co. (Approved Comics): Jan, 1949 - No. 45, Dec, 1955 (#3,7,10-18,21 are 1/2 inch taller than other issues)

1-Baker-c/a(1)	194	388	582	1242	2121	3000
2,3: 2-Baker-c/a. 3-Baker-c/a(3)	129	258	387	826	1413	2000
4,5,7,8-Photo-c; Baker-a(2-3) each	50	100	150	315	533	750
6-Photo-c; part magazine; Baker-a (10/49)	53	106	159	334	567	800
9-Baker-c/a; Kubert-a	308	616	924	2156	3778	5400
10-12,20-Baker-c/a(2-3) each	206	412	618	1318	2259	3200
13-19,21,22-Complete issues by Baker	219	438	657	1402	2401	3400
23-25-Baker-c/a(2-3) each	194	388	582	1242	2121	3000
26,27,33,34,36,37,39,40,42: Baker-c/a. 33,40-Signed story by Estrada. 42-r/Cinderella Love #9; last pre-code (3/55)	74	148	222	470	810	1150
28-30-No Baker-a. 28-Estrada-a; painted-c	21	42	63	122	199	275
31,32-Baker-c. 31-Estrada-s	90	180	270	576	988	1400
35-Baker-c/a (16 pgs.)	103	206	309	659	1130	1600
38-Baker-c/a; suggestive-c	161	322	483	1030	1765	2500
41-Baker-c; Infantino-a(r); all stories are Ziff-Davis-r	90	180	270	576	988	1400
43-45-Baker-c/a	97	194	291	621	1061	1500

TEEN-AGE TALK
I.W. Enterprises: 1964

Reprint #1	2	4	6	11	16	20
Reprint #5,8,9: 5-r/Hector #? 9-Punch Comics #?; L.B. Cole-c reprint from School Day Romances #1	2	4	6	10	14	18

TEEN-AGE TEMPTATIONS (Going Steady #10 on)(See True Love Pictorial)
St. John Publishing Co.: Oct, 1952 - No. 9, Aug, 1954

1-Baker-c/a; has story "Reform School Girl" by Estrada	239	478	717	1530	2615	3700
2,4-Baker-c	181	362	543	1158	1979	2800
3,5-7,9-Baker-c/a	181	362	543	1158	1979	2800
8-Teenagers smoke reefer; Baker-c/a	206	412	618	1318	2259	3200

NOTE: *Estrada a-1, 3-5.*

GD VG FN VF VF/NM NM-
2.0 4.0 6.0 8.0 9.0 9.2

TEEN BEAM (Formerly Teen Beat #1)
National Periodical Publications: No. 2, Jan-Feb, 1968

2-Superman cameo; Herman's Hermits, Yardbirds, Simon & Garfunkel, Lovin Spoonful, Young Rascals app.; Orlando, Drucker-a(r); Monkees photo-c; 16 32 48 112 249 385

TEEN BEAT (Becomes Teen Beam #2)
National Periodical Publications: Nov-Dec, 1967

1-Photos & text only; Monkees photo-c; Beatles, Herman's Hermits, Animals, Supremes, Byrds app. 19 38 57 131 291 450

TEEN COMICS (Formerly All Teen; Journey Into Unknown Worlds #36 on)
Marvel Comics (WFP): No. 21, Apr, 1947 - No. 35, May, 1950

21-Kurtzman's "Hey Look"; Patsy Walker, Cindy (1st app.?), Georgie, Margie app.; Syd Shores-a begins, end #23 37 74 111 222 361 500
22,23,25,27,29,31-35: 22-(6/47)-Becomes Hedy Devine #22 (8/47) on? 27 54 81 160 263 365
24,26,28,30-Kurtzman's "Hey Look". 30-Has anti-Wertham editorial 27 54 81 162 266 370

TEEN CONFESSIONS
Charlton Comics: Aug, 1959 - No. 97, Nov, 1976

1 9 18 27 61 123 185
2 5 10 15 35 63 90
3-10 4 8 12 25 40 55
11-30 3 6 9 20 31 42
31-Beatles-c 12 24 36 83 182 280
32-36,38-55 3 6 9 15 22 29
37 (1/66)-Beatles Fan Club story; Beatles-c 11 22 33 76 163 250
56-58,60-76,78-97: 89,90-Newton-c 2 4 6 11 16 20
59-Kaluta's 1st pro work? (12/69) 3 6 9 20 31 42
77-Partridge Family poster 3 6 9 14 20 26

TEENIE WEENIES, THE (America's Favorite Kiddie Comic)
Ziff-Davis Publishing Co.: No. 10, 1950 - No. 11, Apr-May, 1951 (Newspaper reprints)

10,11-Painted-c 23 46 69 138 227 315

TEEN-IN (Tippy Teen)
Tower Comics: Summer, 1968 - No. 4, Fall, 1969

nn(#1, Summer, 1968)(25¢) Has 3 full pg. B&W photos of Sonny & Cher, Donovan and Herman's Hermits; interviews and photos of Eric Clapton, Jim Morrison and others 9 18 27 62 126 190
nn(#2, Spring, 1969),3,4 6 12 18 37 66 95

TEEN LIFE (Formerly Young Life)
New Age/Quality Comics Group: No. 3, Winter, 1945 - No. 5, Fall, 1945 (Teenage magazine)

3-June Allyson photo on-c & story 16 32 48 92 144 195
4-Duke Ellington photo on-c & story 15 30 45 83 124 165
5-Van Johnson, Woody Herman & Jackie Robinson articles; Van Johnson & Woody Herman photos on-c 16 32 48 92 144 195

TEEN LOVE STORIES (Magazine)
Warren Publ. Co.: Sept, 1969 - No. 3, Jan, 1970 (68 pgs., photo covers, B&W)

1-Photos & articles plus 36-42 pgs. new comic stories in all; Frazetta-a 8 16 24 52 99 145
2,3: 2-Anti-marijuana story 5 10 15 35 63 90

TEEN ROMANCES
Super Comics: 1964

10,11,15-17-Reprints 2 4 6 8 11 14

TEEN SECRET DIARY (Nurse Betsy Crane #12 on)
Charlton Comics: Oct, 1959 - No. 11, June, 1961

1 6 12 18 37 66 95
2 4 8 12 23 37 50
3-11 3 6 9 18 28 38

TEEN TALK (See Teen)

TEEN TITANS (See Brave & the Bold #54,60, DC Super-Stars #1, Marvel & DC Present, New Teen Titans, New Titans, Official...Index and Showcase #59)
National Periodical Publ./DC Comics: 1-2/66 - No. 43, 1-2/73; No. 44, 11/76 - No. 53, 2/78

1-(1-2/66)-Titans join Peace Corps; Batman, Flash, Aquaman, Wonder Woman cameos 44 88 132 326 738 1150
2 14 28 42 96 211 325
3-5: 4-Speedy app. 9 18 27 62 126 190
6-10: 6-Doom Patrol app.; Beast Boy x-over; readers polled on him joining Titans 7 14 21 49 92 135
11-18: 11-Speedy app. 13-X-Mas-c 6 12 18 40 73 105
19-Wood-i; Speedy begins as regular 7 14 21 46 86 125
20-22: All Neal Adams-a. 21-Hawk & Dove app.; last 12¢ issue. 22-Origin Wonder Girl 9 18 27 61 123 185
23-Wonder Girl dons new costume 9 18 27 59 117 175
24-31: 25-Flash, Aquaman, Batman, Green Arrow, Green Lantern, Superman, & Hawk & Dove guests; 1st app. Lilith who joins T.T. West in #50. 29-Hawk & Dove & Ocean Master app. 30-Aquagirl app. 31-Hawk & Dove app. 5 10 15 30 50 70
32-34,40-43: 34-Last 15¢ issue 3 6 9 19 30 40
35-39-(52 pgs.): 36,37-Superboy-r. 38-Green Arrow/Speedy-r; Aquaman/Aqualad story. 39-Hawk & Dove-r. 4 8 12 22 35 48
44-(11/76) Dr. Light app.; Mal becomes the Guardian 3 6 9 16 23 30
45,47,49,51,52 3 6 9 14 19 24
46-Joker's daughter begins (see Batman Family) 4 8 12 23 37 50
48-Intro Bumblebee; Joker's daughter becomes Harlequin 4 8 12 28 47 65
50-1st revival original Bat-Girl; intro. Teen Titans West (Bat-Girl, Golden Eagle, Hawk & Dove, Lilith and Beast Boy) 4 8 12 25 40 55
53-Origin retold 3 6 9 17 26 35
... Lost Annual 1 (3/08, $4.99) Sixties-era story by Bob Haney; Jay Stephens & Mike Allred-a; President Kennedy app.; Nick Cardy-c and sketch pages 5.00

NOTE: Aparo a-36. Buckler c-46-53. Cardy a(p)-1-5, 7, 13, 14, 16, 17, 25, 26, 28-30, 32, c-1-43. Kane a(p)-19, 22-24, 39r. Tuska a(p)-31, 36, 38, 39. DC Super-Stars #1 (3/76) was released before #44.

TEEN TITANS (Also see Titans Beat for series preview)
DC Comics: Oct, 1996 - No. 24, Sept, 1998 ($1.95)

1-Dan Jurgens-c/a(p)/scripts & George Pérez-c/a(i) begin; Atom forms new team (Risk, Argent, Prysm, & Joto); 1st app. Loren Jupiter & Omen; no indicia. 1-3-Origin. 5.00
2-24: 4,5-Robin, Nightwing, Supergirl, Capt. Marvel Jr. app. 12-"Then and Now" begins w/original Teen Titans-c/app. 15-Death of Joto. 17-Capt. Marvel Jr. and Fringe join. 19-Millennium Giants x-over. 23,24-Superman app. 4.00
Annual 1 (1997, $3.95)-Pulp Heroes story 5.00

TEEN TITANS (Also see Titans/Young Justice: Graduation Day)
DC Comics: Sept, 2003 - No. 100, Late Oct, 2011 ($2.50/$2.99/$3.99)

1-McKone-c/a;Johns-s 5.00
1-Variant-c by Michael Turner 2 4 6 9 12 15
1-2nd and 3rd printings 3.00
2-Deathstroke app. 5.00
2-2nd printing 3.00
3-15: 4-Impulse becomes Kid Flash. 5-Raven returns. 6-JLA app. 4.00
16-33: 16-Titans go to 31st Century; Legion and Fatal Five app. 17-19-Future Titans app. 21-23-Dr. Light. 24,25-Outsiders #24,25 x-over. 27,28-Liefeld-a. 32,33-Infinite Crisis 3.00
34-49,51-71: 34-One Year Later begins; two covers by Daniel and Benes. 36-Begin $2.99-c. 40-Jericho returns. 42-Kid Devil origin; Snejbjerg-a. 43-Titans East. 48,49-Amazons Attack x-over; Supergirl app. 51-54-Future Titans app. 3.00
50-($3.99) Art by Pérez (4 pgs.), McKone (6 pgs.), Nauck and Green; future Titans app. 4.00
72-88: 72-Begin $3.99-c; Ravager back-up features. 77,78-Blackest Night. 83-87-Coven of Three back-up; Naifeh-a. 88-Nicola Scott-a begins 4.00
89-99-($2.99) 89-Robin (Damian) joins. 93-Solstice app. 98 Superboy-Prime returns 3.00
100-($4.99) Nicola Scott-a; pin-ups by various 5.00
Annual 1 (4/06, $4.99) Infinite Crisis x-over; Benes-c 5.00
Annual 2009 (6/09, $4.99) Deathtrap x-over prelude; McKeever-s 5.00
... And Outsiders Secret Files and Origins 2005 (10/05, $4.99) Daniel-c 5.00
...: Cold Case (2/11, $4.99) Captain Cold and the Rogues app.; Sean Murphy-a 6.00
.../Legion Special (11/04, $3.50) (cont'd from #16) Reis-a; leads into 2005 Legion of Super-Heroes series; LSH preview by Waid & Kitson 4.00
#1/2 (Wizard mail offer) origin of Ravager; Reis-a 8.00
.../Outsiders Secret Files 2003 (12/03, $5.95) Reis & Jimenez-a; pin-ups by various 6.00
...: A Kid's Game TPB (2004, $9.95) r/#1-7; Turner-c from #1; McKone sketch pages 10.00
...: Beast Boys and Girls TPB (2005, $9.99) r/#13-15 and Beast Boy #1-4 10.00
....: Changing of the Guard TPB (2009, $14.99) r/#62-69 15.00
....: Child's Play TPB (2010, $14.99) r/#71-78 15.00
....: Deathtrap TPB (2009, $14.99) r/#70, Annual #1, Titans #12,13, Vigilante #4-6 15.00
....: Family Lost TPB (2004, $9.95) r/#8-12 & #1/2 10.00
....: Life and Death TPB (2006, $14.99) r/#29-33 and pages from Infinite Crisis x-over 15.00
...: On the Clock TPB (2008, $14.99) r/#55-61 15.00
.../ Outsiders: The Death and Return of Donna Troy (2006, $14.99) r/Titans/Young Justice: Graduation Day #1-3, Teen Titans/Outsiders Secret Files 2003 and DC Special: The Return of Donna Troy #1-4; cover gallery 15.00
.../ Outsiders: The Insiders (2006, $14.99) r/Teen Titans/ #24-26 & Outsiders #24,25,28 15.00
...: Ravager - Fresh Hell TPB (2010, $14.99) r/#71-76,79-82 & Faces of Evil: Deathstroke 15.00
... Spotlight: Cyborg TPB (2009, $19.99) r/DC Special: Cyborg #1-6 20.00
... Spotlight: Raven TPB (2008, $14.99) r/DC Special: Raven #1-5 15.00
...: The Future is Now (2005, $9.99) r/#15-23 & Teen Titans/Legion Special 10.00
...: The Hunt For Raven (2011, $17.99) r/#79-87 18.00
...: Titans Around the World TPB (2007, $14.99) r/#34-41 15.00
...: Titans of Tomorrow TPB (2008, $14.99) r/#50-54 15.00

TEEN TITANS (DC New 52)
DC Comics: Nov, 2011 - No. 30, Jun, 2014 ($2.99)

1-14,17-23: 1-Lobdell-s/Booth-a/c; Red Robin assembles a team; Kid Flash, Wonder Girl app. 5-Superboy app. 9-The Culling conclusion. 13,14-Wonder Girl origin; Garza-a 3.00
15,16-"Death of the Family" tie-in. 15-Die-cut Joker mask cover. 16-Red Hood app. 5.00
23.1, 23.2 (11/13, $2.99, regular covers) 3.00
23.1 (11/13, $3.99, 3-D cover) "Trigon #1" on cover; origin; Wolfman-s/Cafu-a 5.00
23.2 (11/13, $3.99, 3-D cover) "Deathstroke #1" on cover; flashback; Deathblow app. 1 2 3 5 6 8
24-29: 24-Leads into Annual #2. 25,26-Origin of Kid Flash 3.00
30-($3.99) Last issue; origin of Skitter; Kirkham-a 4.00
#0 (11/12, $2.99) Origin of Red Robin; Kirkham-a 3.00
Annual 1 (7/12, $4.99) The Culling x-over part 1; Legion Lost members app. 5.00
Annual 2 (12/13, $4.99) Future Teen Titans; Lobdell-s/Kitson-a 5.00
Annual 3 (7/14, $4.99) Follows #30; Harvest app. 5.00
... Earth One Volume One HC (2014, $22.99) Lemire-s/Dodson-a/c; new origin story 23.00

TEEN TITANS (DC New 52)
DC Comics: Sept, 2014 - No. 24, Nov, 2016 ($2.99)

1-24: 1-Pfeifer-s/Rocafort-a/c; Manchester Black app. 5-Hepburn-a; new Power Girl app. 15-Robin War tie-in; Professor Pyg app. 18,19-Wonder Woman app. 3.00
Annual 1 (6/15, $4.99) Superboy returns; Borges & St. Claire-a; March-c 5.00
Annual 2 (8/16, $4.99) Lobdell-s/Cory Smith-a/Jonboy Meyers-c; Sister Blood app. 5.00
...: Futures End 1 (11/14, $2.99, regular-c) Five years later; Andy Smith-a 3.00
...: Futures End 1 (11/14, $3.99, 3-D cover) 4.00

TEEN TITANS (DC Rebirth)
DC Comics: Nov, 2016 - No. 47, Jan, 2021 ($2.99/$3.99)

1-6: 1-Percy-s/Meyers-a; Ra's al Ghul app. 3-6-Pham-a. 6-Intro. Aqualad (Jackson Hyde) 3.00
7-11,13-24-($3.99) 7-Aqualad joins; Black Manta cameo. 8-Lazarus Contact x-over; Titans & Deathstroke app. 9-11-Black Manta app. 15-Future adult Superboy (Conner), Wonder Girl (Cassie) and Kid Flash (Bart) app. 20-New team with Crush, Roundhouse, Djinn 4.00
12-Dark Nights: Metal tie-in; 1st full app. The Batman Who Laughs, Harley Quinn app. 50.00
25-($4.99) Origin of Crush; Rocha-a; Roundhouse back-up story 5.00
26-47: 26-32-Chang-a. 28-30-Crossover with Deathstroke #42-44. 31-33,35-37-Lobo app. 4.00
Annual 1 (7/17, $4.99) Conclusion of Lazarus Contact x-over; Titans & Deathstroke app. 5.00
Annual 1 (3/19, $4.99) Red Hood app.; intro. Joystick 5.00
Annual 2 (10/20, $4.99) Batman app.; leads into #45; Crush becomes leader; Fernandez-a 5.00
... : Endless Winter Special 1 (2/21, $3.99) Part 6 of crossover event; Merino-a 5.00
...: Rebirth 1 (11/16, $2.99) Meyers-a; Robin, Raven, Starfire, Beast Boy, Kid Flash app. 3.00
...: Special 1 (8/18, $4.99) Glass-s/Rocha-a; Harley Quinn & Black Mask app. 5.00

TEEN TITANS ACADEMY
DC Comics: May, 2021 - No. 15, Jul, 2022 ($3.99)

Teen Titans (2009) #75 © DC

Teen Titans Go (2014) #5 © DC

Ten Grand #1 © Studio JMS

GD 2.0 VG 4.0 FN 6.0 VF 8.0 VF/NM 9.0 NM- 9.2

1-15: 1-Sheridan-s/Sandoval-a; original Titans mentoring the next gen of heroes. 2,3-Peacemaker app. 7-Grodd app. 8-Roy Harper returns. 13-War For Earth-3 4.00

TEEN TITANS GIANT (Continues in Titans Giant #1)
DC Comics: 2018 - No. 7, 2019 ($4.99, 100 pgs., squarebound, Walmart exclusive)

1-New story Jurgens-s/Eaton-a; reprints from Teen Titans ('03), Super Sons #1 ('17), and Sideways ('18) 8.00
2-7-New story Jurgens-s/Eaton-a plus reprints continue 5.00

TEEN TITANS GO! (Based on Cartoon Network series)
DC Comics: Jan, 2004 - No. 55, Jul, 2008 ($2.25)

1-12,14-55: 1,2-Nauck-a/Bullock-c/J. Torres-s. 8-Mad Mod app. 14-Speedy-c. 28-Doom Patrol app. 31-Nightwing app. 36-Wonder Girl. 38-Mad Mod app.; Clugston-a 3.00
1-(9/04, Free Comic Book Day giveaway) r/#1; 2 bound-in Wacky Packages stickers 4.00
13-($2.95) Bonus pages with Shazam! reprint 4.00
Jam Packed Action (2005, $7.99, digest) adaptations of two TV episodes 8.00
... Vol 1: Truth, Justice, Pizza! (2004, $6.95, digest-size) r/#1-5 7.00
... Vol 2: Heroes on Patrol (2005, $6.99, digest-size) r/#6-10 7.00
... Vol 3: Bring It On! (2005, $6.99, digest-size) r/#11-15 7.00
... Vol 4: Ready For Action! (2006, $6.99, digest-size) r/#16-20 7.00
... Vol 5: On The Move! (2006, $6.99, digest-size) r/#21-25 7.00
... Titans Together TPB (2007, $12.99) r/#26-32 13.00

TEEN TITANS GO! (Based on the 2013 Cartoon Network series)
DC Comics: Feb, 2014 - Present ($2.99)

1-36: 1-Fisch-s. 2-Brotherhood of Evil app. 4-HIVE Five app. 13-Aqualad app. 3.00
... FCBD Special Edition 1 (6/14, giveaway) r/#1 3.00
... FCBD Special Edition 1 (6/15, giveaway) flipbook with Scooby-Doo! Team Up 3.00
... Giant 1 (2019, $4.99) Two new stories plus reprints 5.00

TEEN TITANS SPOTLIGHT
DC Comics: Aug, 1986 - No. 21, Apr, 1988

1-21: 7-Guice's 1st work at DC. 14-Nightwing; Batman app. 15-Austin-c(i). 18,19-Millennium x-over. 21-($1.00-c)-Original Teen Titans; Spiegle-a 4.00
Note: ***Guice*** *a-7p, 8p; c-7,8.* ***Orlando*** *c/a-11p.* ***Perez*** *c-1, 17i, 19.* ***Sienkiewicz*** *c-10*

TEEN TITANS YEAR ONE
DC Comics: Mar, 2008 - No. 6, Aug, 2008 ($2.99, limited series)

1-6-The original five form a team; Wolfram-s/Kerschl-a 3.00
TPB (2008, $14.99) r/#1-6; bonus pin-up 15.00

TEEN WOLF: BITE ME (Based on the MTV series)
Image Comics (Top Cow): Sept, 2011 - No. 3, Nov, 2011 ($3.99, limited series)

1-3: 1-Tischman-s/Mooney-a/c 4.00

TEEPEE TIM (...Heap Funny Indian Boy)(Formerly Ha Ha Comics)(Also see "Cookie")
American Comics Group: No. 100, Feb-Mar, 1955 - No. 102, June-July, 1955

100-102 8 16 24 44 57 70

TEGRA JUNGLE EMPRESS (Zegra Jungle Empress #2 on)
Fox Feature Syndicate: August, 1948

1-Blue Beetle, Rocket Kelly app.; used in **SOTI**, pg. 31 103 206 309 659 1130 1600

TEK JANSEN (See Stephen Colbert's...)

TEKKEN: BLOOD FEUD (Based on the Bandai Namco video game)
Titan Comics: Jun, 2017 - No. 4, Sept, 2017 ($3.99, limited series)

1-4-Cavan Scott-s/Andie Tong-a; multiple covers on each 4.00

TEKNO COMIX HANDBOOK
Tekno Comix: May, 1996 ($3.95, one-shot)

1-Guide to the Tekno Universe 4.00

TEKNOPHAGE (See Neil Gaiman's...)

TEKNOPHAGE VERSUS ZEERUS
BIG Entertainment: July, 1996 ($3.25, one-shot)

1-Paul Jenkins script 3.25

TEKWORLD (William Shatner's... on-c only)
Epic Comics (Marvel): Sept, 1992 - Aug, 1994 ($1.75)

1-Based on Shatner's novel, TekWar, set in L.A. in the year 2120 4.00
2-24 3.00

TELARA CHRONICLES (Based on the videogame Rift: Planes of Telara)
DC Comics (WildStorm): Jan, 2010; Nov, 2010 - No. 4, Feb, 2011 ($3.99, limited series)

0-(1/10, free) Preview of series 3.00
1-4-Pop Mhan-a/Drew Johnson-c 4.00
TPB (2011, $17.99) r/#0-4; background info on Telara 18.00

TELEPATHS
Artists, Writers & Artisans, Inc.: Sept, 2021 - No. 6, Feb, 2022 ($3.99, limited series)

1-6-Straczynski-s/Epting-a 4.00

TELEVISION (See TV)

TELEVISION COMICS (Early TV comic)
Standard Comics (Animated Cartoons): No. 5, Feb, 1950 - No. 8, Nov, 1950

5-1st app. Willy Nilly 14 28 42 80 115 150
6-8: #6 on inside has #2 on cover 10 20 30 58 79 100

TELEVISION PUPPET SHOW (Early TV comic) (See Spotty the Pup)
Avon Periodicals: 1950 - No. 2, Nov, 1950

1-1st app. Speedy Rabbit, Spotty The Pup 29 58 87 172 281 390
2 20 40 60 115 185 255

TELEVISION TEENS MOPSY (See TV Teens)

TELL IT TO THE MARINES
Toby Press Publications: Mar, 1952 - No. 15, July, 1955

1-Lover O'Leary and His Liberty Belles (with pin-ups), ends #6; Spike & Bat begin, end #6 39 78 117 240 395 550
2-Madame Cobra-c/story; headlights-c 39 78 117 240 395 550
3,5 22 44 66 128 209 290
4-Headlights-c 55 110 165 352 601 850
6-12,14,15: 7-9,14,15-Photo-c 18 36 54 105 165 225
13-John Wayne photo-c 25 50 75 150 245 340
I.W. Reprint #9-r/#1 above 3 6 9 16 23 30
Super Reprint #16(1964)-r/#4 above 2 4 6 10 14 18

TELLOS
Image Comics: May, 1999 - No. 10, Nov, 2000 ($2.50)

1-Dezago-s/Wieringo-a 3.00
1-Variant-c ($7.95) 8.00
2-10: 4-Four covers 3.00
...: Maiden Voyage (3/01, $5.95) Didier Crispeels-a/c 6.00
...: Sons & Moons (2002, $5.95) Nick Cardy-c 6.00
...: The Last Heist (2001, $5.95) Rousseau-a/c 6.00
Prelude ($5.00, AnotherUniverse.com) 5.00
Prologue ($3.95, Dynamic Forces) 4.00
...Collected Edition 1 (12/99, $8.95) r/#1-3 9.00
... Colossal, Vol. 1 TPB (2008, $17.99) r/#1-10, Prelude, Prologue, Scatterjack-s from Section Zero #1, cover gallery, Wieringo sketch pages; Dezago afterword 18.00
...: Kindred Spirits (2/01, $17.95) r/#6-10, Section Zero #1 (Scatterjack-s) 18.00
...: Reluctant Heroes (2/01, $17.95) r/#1-5, Prelude, Prologue; sketchbook 18.00

TELOS (See Convergence)
DC Comics: Dec, 2015 - No. 6, May, 2016 ($2.99)

1-6: 1,2-King-s/Pagulayan-a. 1-Brainiac app. 2-Arak, Son of Thunder and Validus app. 3-6-Hal Jordan Parallax app. 3.00

TEMPEST (See Aquaman, 3rd Series)
DC Comics: Nov, 1996 - No. 4, Feb, 1997 ($1.75, limited series)

1-4: Formerly Aqualad; Phil Jimenez-c/a/scripts in all 4.00

TEMPLARS (Assassin's Creed)
Titan Comics: Apr, 2016 - No. 9, Feb, 2017 ($3.99)

1-9-Black Cross; set in 1927; Van Lente-s/Calero-a 4.00

TEMPUS FUGITIVE
DC Comics: 1990 - No. 4, 1991 ($4.95, squarebound, 52 pgs.)

Book 1,2: Ken Steacy painted-c/a & scripts 6.00
Book 3,4-($5.95-c) 6.00
TPB (Dark Horse Comics, 1/97, $17.95) 18.00

TEN COMMANDMENTS (See Moses & the... and Classics Illustrated Special)

TENDER LOVE STORIES
Skywald Publ. Corp.: Feb, 1971 - No. 4, July, 1971 (Pre-code reprints and new stories)

1 (All 25¢, 52 pgs.) 9 18 27 60 120 180
2-4 6 12 18 37 66 95

TENDER ROMANCE (Ideal Romance #3 on)
Key Publications (Gilmour Magazines): Dec, 1953 - No. 2, Feb, 1954

1-Headlight & lingerie panels; B. Baily-c 36 72 108 211 343 475
2-Bernard Baily-c 20 40 60 115 185 255

TEN GRAND
Image Comics (Joe's Comics): May, 2013 - No. 12, Jan, 2015 ($2.99)

1-12: 1-4-Straczynski-s/Templesmith-a. 1-Multiple variant covers. 2-Two covers 3.00

TENSE SUSPENSE

	GD	VG	FN	VF	VF/NM	NM-
	2.0	4.0	6.0	8.0	9.0	9.2

Fago Publications: Dec, 1958 - No. 2, Feb, 1959

1	15	30	45	85	130	175
2	11	22	33	64	90	115

TEN STORY LOVE (Formerly a pulp magazine with same title)
Ace Periodicals: V29#3, June-July, 1951 - V36#5(#209), Sept, 1956 (#3-6: 52 pgs.)

V29#3(#177)-Part comic, part text; painted-c	22	44	66	132	216	300
4-6(1/52)	15	30	45	85	130	175
V30#1(3/52)-6(1/53)	14	28	42	82	121	160
V31#1(2/53),V32#2(4/53)-6(12/53)	14	28	42	81	118	155
V33#1(1/54)-3(5#54, #195), V34#4(7/54, #196)-6(10/54, #198)	14	28	42	80	115	150
V35#1(12/54, #199)-3(4/55, #201)-Last precode	14	28	42	78	112	145
V35#4-6(9/55, #201-204), V36#1(11/55, #205)-3, 5(9/56, #210)	14	28	42	76	108	140
V36#4-L.B. Cole-a	15	30	45	83	124	165

TENTH, THE
Image Comics: Jan, 1997 - No. 4, June, 1997 ($2.50, limited series)

1-4-Tony Daniel-c/a, Beau Smith-s 5.00
Abuse of Humanity TPB ($10.95) r/#1-4 12.00
Abuse of Humanity TPB (10/98, $11.95) r/#1-4 & 0(8/97) 12.00

TENTH, THE
Image Comics: Sept, 1997 - No. 14, Jan, 1999 ($2.50)

0-(8/97, $5.00) American Ent. Ed. 6.00
1-Tony Daniel-c/a, Beau Smith-s 6.00
2-9: 3,7-Variant-c 4.00
10-14 3.00
...Configuration (8/98) Re-cap and pin-ups 3.00
...Collected Edition 1 ('98, $4.95, square-bound) r/#1,2 5.00
...Special (4/00, $2.95) r/#0 and Wizard #1/2 3.00
Wizard #1/2-Daniel-s/Steve Scott-a 10.00

TENTH, THE (Volume 3) (The Black Embrace)
Image Comics: Mar, 1999 - No. 4, June, 1999 ($2.95)

1-4-Daniel-c/a 3.00
TPB (1/00, $12.95) r/#1-4 13.00

TENTH, THE (Volume 4) (Evil's Child)
Image Comics: Sept, 1999 - No. 4, Mar, 2000 ($2.95, limited series)

1-4-Daniel-c/a 3.00

TENTH, THE (Darkk Dawn)
Image Comics: July, 2005 ($4.99, one-shot)

1-Kirkham-a/Bonny-s 5.00

TENTH, THE : RESURRECTED
Dark Horse Comics: July, 2001 - No. 4, Feb, 2002 ($2.99, limited series)

1-4: 1-Two covers; Daniel-s/c; Romano-a 3.00

10th MUSE
Image Comics (TidalWave Studios): Nov, 2000 - No. 9, Jan, 2002 ($2.95)

1-Character based on wrestling's Rena Mero; regular & photo covers 3.00
2-9: 2-Photo and 2 Lashley covers; flip book Dollz preview. 5-Savage Dragon app.; 2 covers by Lashley and Larsen. 6-Tellos x-over 3.00

TEN WHO DARED (Disney)
Dell Publishing Co.: No. 1178, Dec, 1960

Four Color 1178-Movie, painted-c; cast member photo on back-c	7	14	21	46	86	125

10 YEARS TO DEATH
AfterShock Comics: Sept, 2021 ($6.99, oversized 8-1/2" x 10-7/8", one shot)

1-Aaron Douglas-s/Cliff Richards-a 7.00

TERMINAL CITY
DC Comics (Vertigo): July, 1996 - No. 9, Mar, 1997 ($2.50, limited series)

1-9: Dean Motter scripts, 7,8-Matt Wagner-c 3.00
TPB ('97, $19.95) r/series 20.00

TERMINAL CITY: AERIAL GRAFFITI
DC Comics (Vertigo): Nov, 1997 - No. 5, Mar, 1998 ($2.50, limited series)

1-5: Dean Motter-s/Lark-a/Chiarello-c 3.00

TERMINAL HERO
Dynamite Entertainment: 2014 - No. 6, 2015 ($2.99, limited series)

1-6-Milligan-s/Kowalski-a/Jae Lee-c 3.00

TERMINATOR, THE (See Robocop vs. ... & Rust #12 for 1st app.)
Now Comics: Sept, 1988 - No. 17, 1989 ($1.75, Baxter paper)

1-Based on movie	2	4	6	10	14	18
2-5						6.00
6-11,13-17						4.00
12-($2.95, 52 pgs.)-Intro. John Connor						5.00
Trade paperback (1989, $9.95)						15.00

TERMINATOR, THE
Dark Horse Comics: Aug, 1990 - No. 4, Nov, 1990 ($2.50, limited series)

1-Set 39 years later than the movie	1	2	3	5	6	8
2-4						4.00

TERMINATOR, THE
Dark Horse Comics: 1998 - No. 4, Dec, 1998 ($2.95, limited series)

1-4-Alan Grant-s/Steve Pugh-a/c 4.00
...Special (1998, $2.95) Darrow-c/Grant-s 4.00

TERMINATOR, THE: ALL MY FUTURES PAST
Now Comics: V3#1, Aug, 1990 - V3#2, Sept, 1990 ($1.75, limited series)

V3#1,2 4.00

TERMINATOR, THE: ENDGAME
Dark Horse Comics: Sept, 1992 - No. 3, Nov, 1992 ($2.50, limited series)

1-3: Guice-a(p); painted-c 4.00

TERMINATOR, THE: ENEMY OF MY ENEMY
Dark Horse Comics: Feb, 2014 - No. 6, Oct, 2014 ($3.99, limited series)

1-6-Jolley-s/Igle-a; set in 1985 4.00

TERMINATOR, THE: HUNTERS AND KILLERS
Dark Horse Comics: Mar, 1992 - No. 3, May, 1992 ($2.50, limited series)

1-3 4.00

TERMINATOR, THE: 1984
Dark Horse Comics: Sept, 2010 - No. 3, Nov, 2010 ($3.50, limited series)

1-3: Takes place during and after the 1st movie; Zack Whedon-s/Andy MacDonald-a 3.50

TERMINATOR, THE: ONE SHOT
Dark Horse Comics: July, 1991 ($5.95, 56 pgs.)

nn-Matt Wagner-a; contains stiff pop-up inside 6.00

TERMINATOR: REVOLUTION (Follows Terminator 2: Infinity series)
Dynamite Entertainment: 2008 - No. 5, 2009 ($3.50, limited series)

1-5-Furman-s/Antonio-a. 1-3-Two covers 3.50

TERMINATOR / ROBOCOP: KILL HUMAN
Dynamite Entertainment: 2011 - No. 4, 2011 ($3.99, limited series)

1-4: 1-Covers by Simonson, Lau & Feister. 2-4-Three covers on each 4.00

TERMINATOR: SALVATION MOVIE PREQUEL
IDW Publishing: Jan, 2009 - No. 4, Apr, 2009 ($3.99, limited series)

1-4: Alan Robinson-a/Dara Naraghi-s 4.00
0-Salvation Movie Preview (4/09) Mariotte-s/Figueroa-a 4.00

TERMINATOR SALVATION: THE FINAL BATTLE
Dark Horse Comics: Dec, 2013 - No. 12, Dec, 2014 ($3.99, limited series)

1-12-Straczynski-s/Woods-a 4.00

TERMINATOR, THE: SECONDARY OBJECTIVES
Dark Horse Comics: July, 1991 - No. 4, Oct, 1991 ($2.50, limited series)

1-4: Gulacy-c/a(p) in all 4.00

TERMINATOR SECTOR WAR
Dark Horse Comics: Aug, 2018 - No. 4 ($3.99, limited series)

1-3-Brian Wood-s/Jeff Stokely-a; a different Terminator in 1984 New York City 4.00

TERMINATOR, THE: THE BURNING EARTH
Now Comics: V2#1, Mar, 1990 - V2#5, July, 1990 ($1.75, limited series)

V2#1: Alex Ross painted art (1st published work)	3	6	9	14	19	24
2-5: Ross-c/a in all	1	3	4	6	8	10
Trade paperback (1990, $9.95)-Reprints V2#1-5						18.00
Trade paperback (ibooks, 2003, $17.95)-Digitally remastered reprint						18.00

TERMINATOR, THE: THE DARK YEARS
Dark Horse Comics: Aug, 1999 - No. 4, Dec, 1999 ($2.95, limited series)

1-4-Alan Grant-s/Mel Rubi-a; Jae Lee-c 4.00

TERMINATOR, THE: THE ENEMY WITHIN
Dark Horse Comics: Nov, 1991 - No. 4, Feb, 1992 ($2.50, limited series)

1-4: All have Simon Bisley painted-c 4.00

TERMINATOR, THE: 2029
Dark Horse Comics: Mar, 2010 - No. 3, May, 2010 ($3.50, limited series)

1-3: Kyle Reese before his time-jump to 1984; Zack Whedon-s/Andy MacDonald-a 3.50

TERMINATOR 2: CYBERNETIC DAWN
Malibu: Nov, 1995 - No.4, Feb, 1996; No. 0. Apr, 1996 ($2.50, lim. series)

0 (4/96, $2.95)-Erskine-c/a; flip book w/Terminator 2: Nuclear Twilight 4.00
1-4: Continuation of film. 4.00

TERMINATOR 2: INFINITY
Dynamite Entertainment: 2007 - No. 7 ($3.50)

1-7: 1-Furman-s/Raynor-a; 3 covers. 6,7-Painkiller Jane x-over 3.50

TERMINATOR 2: JUDGEMENT DAY
Marvel Comics: Early Sept, 1991 - No. 3, Early Oct, 1991 ($1.00, lim. series)

1-3: Based on movie sequel; 1-3-Same as nn issues 4.00
nn (1991, $4.95, squarebound, 68 pgs.)-Photo-c 6.00
nn (1991, $2.25, B&W, magazine, 68 pgs.) 4.00

TERMINATOR 2: NUCLEAR TWILIGHT
Malibu: Nov, 1995 - No.4, Feb, 1996; No. 0, Apr, 1996 ($2.50, lim. series)

0 (4/96, $2.95)-Erskine-c/a; flip book w/Terminator 2: Cybernetic Dawn 4.00
1-4:Continuation of film. 4.00

TERMINATOR 3: RISE OF THE MACHINES (... BEFORE THE RISE on cover)
Beckett Comics: July, 2003 - No. 6, Jan, 2004 ($5.95, limited series)

1-6: 1,2-Leads into movie; 2 covers on each. 3-6-Movie adaptation 6.00

TERM LIFE
Image Comics (Shadowline): Jan, 2011 ($16.99, graphic novel)

SC-Lieberman-s/Thornborrow-a/DeStefano-l 17.00

TERRA (See Supergirl {2005 series} #12)
DC Comics: Jan, 2009 - No. 4, Feb, 2009 ($2.99, limited series)

1-4-Conner-a/c. 1,2,4-Power Girl app. 2-4-Geo-Force app. 4.00
TPB (2009, $14.99) r/#1-4 & Supergirl #12 15.00

TERRAFORMERS
Wonder Color Comics: April, 1987 - No. 2, 1987 ($1.95, limited series)

1,2-Kelley Jones-a 3.00

TERRA OBSCURA (See Tom Strong)
America's Best Comics: Aug, 2003 - No. 6, Feb, 2004 ($2.95)

1-6-Alan Moore & Peter Hogan-s/Paquette-a 3.00
TPB (2004, $14.95) r/#1-6 15.00

TERRA OBSCURA VOLUME 2 (See Tom Strong)

Terminal Hero #1 © DYN

The Terrifics #1 © DC

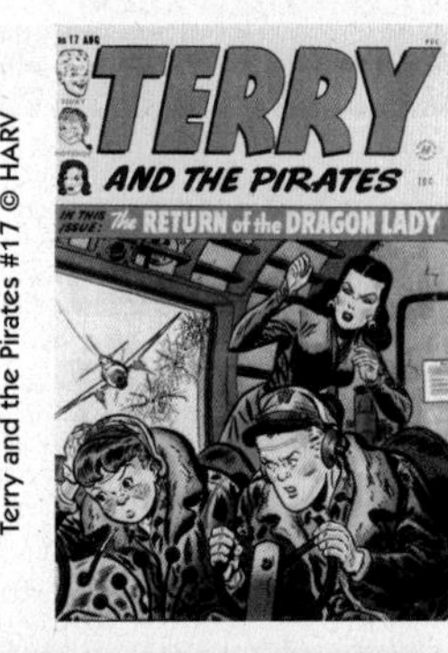

Terry and the Pirates #17 © HARV

	GD 2.0	VG 4.0	FN 6.0	VF 8.0	VF/NM 9.0	NM- 9.2

America's Best Comics: Oct, 2004 - No. 6, May, 2005 ($2.95)

1-6-Alan Moore & Peter Hogan-s/Paquette-a; Tom Strange app.						3.00
TPB (2005, $14.99) r/#1-6						15.00

TERRARISTS
Marvel Comics (Epic): Nov, 1993 - No. 4, Feb, 1994 ($2.50, limited series)

1-4-Bound-in trading cards in all						3.00

TERRIFIC COMICS (Also see Suspense Comics)
Continental Magazines: Jan, 1944 - No. 6, Nov, 1944

1-Kid Terrific; opium story	383	766	1149	2681	4691	6700
2-1st app. The Boomerang by L.B. Cole & Ed Wheelan's "Comics" McCormick, called the world's #1 comic book fan begins	314	628	942	2198	3849	5500
3-Diana becomes Boomerang's costumed aide; L.B. Cole-c	277	554	831	1759	3030	4300
4-Classic war-c (Scarce)	649	1298	1947	4738	8369	12,000
5-The Reckoner begins; Boomerang & Diana by L.B. Cole; Classic Schomburg bondage & hooded vigilante-c (Scarce)	2925	5850	8775	17,600	34,640	60,000
6-L.B. Cole-c/a	265	530	795	1694	2897	4100

NOTE: ***L.B. Cole** a-1, 2(2), 3-6. **Fuje** a-5, 6. **Rico** a-2; c-1. **Schomburg** c-2, 5.*

TERRIFIC COMICS (Formerly Horrific; Wonder Boy #17 on)
Mystery Publ.(Comic Media)/(Ajax/Farrell): No. 14, Dec, 1954; No. 16, Mar, 1955 (No #15)

14-Art swipe/Advs. into the Unknown #37; injury-to-eye-c; pg. 2, panel 5 swiped from Phantom Stranger #4; surrealistic Palais-a; Human Cross story; classic-c	116	232	348	742	1271	1800
16-Wonder Boy-c/story (last pre-code)	37	74	111	222	361	500

TERRIFICS, THE
DC Comics: Apr, 2018 - No. 27, Jun, 2020 ($2.99/$3.99)

1-13: 1-Mr. Terrific, Metamorpho, Phantom Girl & Plastic Man team; Lemire-s/Reis-a. 7-10-Tom Strong app. 8,9-Swamp Thing app.						3.00
14-24,26-29-($3.99) 18-23-Bizarro & The Terribles app. 27-Simon Stagg dies						4.00
25-($4.99) Choose Your Adventure; Harley Quinn & Poison Ivy cameo; Yang-s/Mora-a						5.00
Annual 1 (12/18, $4.99) Yang-s/Bennett-a; Tom Strong back-up story						5.00

TERRIFYING TALES (Formerly Startling Terror Tales #10)
Star Publications: No. 11, Jan, 1953 - No. 15, Apr, 1954

11-Used in **POP**, pgs. 99,100; all Jo-Jo-r	97	194	291	621	1061	1500
12-Reprints Jo-Jo #19 entirely; L.B. Cole splash	84	168	252	538	919	1300
13-All Rulah-r; classic devil-c	206	412	618	1318	2259	3200
14-All Rulah reprints	66	132	198	419	722	1025
15-Rulah, Zago-r; used in **SOTI**-r/Rulah #22	63	126	189	403	689	975

NOTE: *All issues have **L.B. Cole** covers; bondage covers-No. 12-14.*

TERROR ILLUSTRATED (Adult Tales of...)
E.C. Comics: Nov-Dec, 1955 - No. 2, Spring (April on-c), 1956 (Magazine, 25¢)

1-Adult Entertainment on-c	39	78	117	240	395	550
2-Charles Sultan-a	24	48	72	142	234	325

NOTE: ***Craig, Evans, Ingels, Orlando** art in each. **Crandall** c-1, 2.*

TERROR INC. (See A Shadowline Saga #3)
Marvel Comics: July, 1992 - No. 13, July, 1993 ($1.75)

1-8,11-13: 6,7-Punisher-c/story. 13-Ghost Rider app.						3.00
9,10-Wolverine-c/story						4.00

TERROR INC.
Marvel Comics (MAX): Oct, 2007 - No. 5, Apr, 2008 ($3.99, limited series)

1-5: 1-Lapham-s/Zircher-a; origin of Mr. Terror retold						4.00

TERROR INC. - APOCALYPSE SOON
Marvel Comics (MAX): July, 2009 - No. 4, Sept, 2009 ($3.99, limited series)

1-4: 1-Lapham-s/Turnbull-a						4.00

TERRORS OF DRACULA (Magazine)
Modern Day Periodical/Eerie Publ.: Vol. 1 #3, May, 1979 - Vol. 3 #2, Sept, 1981 (B&W)

Vol. 1 #3 (5/79, 1st issue)	4	8	12	27	44	60
#4(8/79), #5(11/79)	3	6	9	20	31	42
Vol. 2 #1-3: 1-(2/80). 2-(5/80). 3-(8/80)	3	6	9	17	25	34
Vol. 3 #1 (5/81), #2 (9/81)	3	6	9	19	30	40

TERRORS OF THE JUNGLE (Formerly Jungle Thrills)
Star Publications: No. 17, 5/52 - No. 21, 2/53; No. 4, 4/53 - No. 10, 9/54

17-Reprints Rulah #21, used in **SOTI**; L.B. Cole bondage-c	161	322	483	1030	1765	2500
18-Jo-Jo-r	129	258	387	826	1413	2000
19,20(1952)-Jo-Jo-r; Disbrow-a	65	130	195	416	708	1000
21-Jungle Jo, Tangi-r; used in **POP**, pg. 100 & color illos.	68	136	204	435	743	1050
4-10: All Disbrow-a. 5-Jo-Jo-r. 8-Rulah, Jo-Jo-r. 9-Jo-Jo-r; Disbrow-a; Tangi by Orlando10-Rulah-r	65	130	195	416	708	1000

NOTE: ***L.B. Cole** c-all; bondage c-17, 19, 21, 5, 7.*

TERROR TALES (See Beware Terror Tales)

TERROR TALES (Magazine)
Eerie Publications: V1#7, 1969 - V6#6, Dec, 1974; V7#1, Apr, 1976 - V10, 1979? (V1-V6: 52 pgs.; V7 on: 68 pgs.)

V1#7	9	18	27	59	117	175
V1#8-11('69): 9-Bondage-c	6	12	18	41	76	110
V2#1-6('70), V3#1-6('71), V4#1-7('72), V5#1-6('73), V6#1-6('74), V7#1,4('76) (no V7#2), V8#1-3('77)	5	10	15	34	60	85
V7#3-(7/76) LSD story-r/Weird V3#5	5	10	15	34	60	85
V9#2-4, V10#1(1/79)	5	10	15	35	63	90

TERROR TITANS
DC Comics: Dec, 2008 - No. 6, May, 2009 ($2.99, limited series)

1-6: 1-Ravager and Clock King at the Dark Side Club; Bennett-a. 3-Static app.						3.00
TPB (2009, $17.99) r/#1-6						18.00

TERRY AND THE PIRATES (See Famous Feature Stories, Merry Christmas From Sears Toyland, Popular Comics, Super Book #3,5,9,16,28, & Super Comics)

TERRY AND THE PIRATES
Dell Publishing Co.: 1939 - 1953 (By Milton Caniff)

Large Feature Comic 2(1939)	119	238	357	762	1306	1850
Large Feature Comic 6(1938)-r/1936 dailies	93	186	279	591	1021	1450
Four Color 9(1940)	84	168	252	538	919	1300
Large Feature Comic 27('41), 6('42)	74	148	222	470	810	1150
Four Color 44('43)	32	64	96	230	515	800
Four Color 101('45)	20	40	60	135	300	465
Family Album(1942)	21	42	63	122	199	275

TERRY AND THE PIRATES (Formerly Boy Explorers; Long John Silver & the Pirates #30 on) (Daily strip-r) (Two #26's)
Harvey Publications/Charlton No. 26-28: No. 3, 4/47 - No. 26, 4/51; No. 26, 6/55 - No. 28, 10/55

3(#1)-Boy Explorers by S&K; Terry & the Pirates begin by Caniff; 1st app. The Dragon Lady	40	80	120	246	411	575
4-S&K Boy Explorers	22	44	66	132	216	300
5-11: 11-Man in Black app. by Powell	13	26	39	72	101	130
12-20: 16-Girl threatened with red hot poker	10	20	30	56	76	95
21-26(4/51)-Last Caniff issue & last pre-code issue	10	20	30	54	72	90
26-28('55)(Formerly This Is Suspense)-No Caniff-a	9	18	27	47	61	75

NOTE: ***Powell** a (Tommy Tween)-5-10, 12, 14; 15-17(1/2 to 2 pgs. each).*

TERRY BEARS COMICS (TerryToons, The... #4)
St. John Publishing Co.: June, 1952 - No. 3, Mar, 1953

1-By Paul Terry	15	30	45	84	127	170
2,3	10	20	30	54	72	90

TERRY-TOONS ALBUM (See Giant Comics Edition)

TERRY-TOONS COMICS (1st Series) (Becomes Paul Terry's Comics #85 on; later issues titled "Paul Terry's...")
Timely/Marvel No. 1-59 (8/47)(Becomes Best Western No. 58 on?, Marvel)/ St. John No. 60 (9/47) on: Oct, 1942 - No. 86, May, 1951

1 (Scarce)-Features characters that 1st app. on movie screen; Gandy Goose & Sourpuss begin; war-c; Gandy Goose c-1-37	275	550	825	1746	3023	4300
2	97	194	291	621	1061	1500
3-5	63	126	189	403	689	975
6,8-10: 9,10-World War II gag-c	48	96	144	302	514	725
7-Hitler, Hirohito, Mussolini-c	275	550	825	1746	3023	4300
11-20	34	68	102	196	321	445
21-37	24	48	72	140	230	320
38-Mighty Mouse begins (1st app., 11/45); Mighty Mouse-c begin, end #86; Gandy, Sourpuss welcome Mighty Mouse on-c	258	516	774	1651	2826	4000
39-2nd app. Mighty Mouse	74	148	222	470	810	1150
40-49: 43-Infinity-c	37	74	111	222	361	500
50-1st app. Heckle & Jeckle (11/46)	74	148	222	470	810	1150
51-60: 55-Infinity-c. 60-(9/47)-Atomic explosion panel; 1st St. John issue	20	40	60	114	182	250
61-86: 85,86-Same book as Paul Terry's Comics #85,86 with only a title change; published at same time?	15	30	45	88	137	185

TERRY-TOONS COMICS (2nd Series)
St. John Publishing Co./Pines: June, 1952 - No. 9, Nov, 1953; 1957; 1958

1-Gandy Goose & Sourpuss begin by Paul Terry	20	40	60	117	189	260
2	11	22	33	62	86	110

GD VG FN VF VF/NM NM-
2.0 4.0 6.0 8.0 9.0 9.2

3-9 9 18 27 52 69 85
Giant Summer Fun Book 101,102-(Sum, 1957, Sum, 1958, 25¢, Pines)(TV)
CBS Television Presents...; Tom Terrific, Mighty Mouse, Heckle & Jeckle
Gandy Goose app. 14 28 42 82 121 160

TERRYTOONS, THE TERRY BEARS (Formerly Terry Bears Comics)
Pines Comics: No. 4, Summer, 1958 (CBS Television Presents...)

4 9 18 27 47 61 75

TESSIE THE TYPIST (Tiny Tessie #24; see Comedy Comics, Gay Comics & Joker Comics)
Timely/Marvel Comics (20CC): Summer, 1944 - No. 23, Aug, 1949

1-Doc Rockblock & others by Wolverton 284 568 852 1818 3109 4400
2-Wolverton's Powerhouse Pepper 97 194 291 621 1061 1500
3-(3/45)-No Wolverton 47 94 141 296 498 700
4,5,7,8-Wolverton-a, 4-(Fall/45) 53 106 159 334 567 800
6-Kurtzman's "Hey Look", 2 pgs. Wolverton-a 54 108 162 343 574 825
9-Wolverton's Powerhouse Pepper (8 pgs.) & 1 pg. Kurtzman's "Hey Look"
55 110 165 352 601 850
10-Wolverton's Powerhouse Pepper (4 pgs.) 57 114 171 362 619 875
11-Wolverton's Powerhouse Pepper (8 pgs.) 60 120 180 381 653 925
12-Wolverton's Powerhouse Pepper (4 pgs.) & 1 pg. Kurtzman's "Hey Look"
55 110 165 352 601 850
13-Wolverton's Powerhouse Pepper (4 pgs.) 55 110 165 352 601 850
14,15: 14-Wolverton's Dr. Whackyhack (1 pg.); 1-1/2 pgs. Kurtzman's "Hey Look".
15-Kurtzman's "Hey Look" (3 pgs.) & 3 pgs. Giggles 'n' Grins
39 78 117 240 395 550
16-18-Kurtzman's "Hey Look" (?, 2 & 1 pg.) 36 72 108 211 343 475
19-Annie Oakley story (8 pgs.) 29 58 87 172 281 390
20-23: 20-Anti-Wertham editorial (2/49) 27 54 81 162 266 370
NOTE: *Lana app.-21. Millie The Model app.-13, 15, 17, 21. Rusty app.-10, 11, 13, 15, 17.*

TESTAMENT
DC Comics (Vertigo): Feb, 2006 - No. 22, Mar, 2008 ($2.99)

1-22: 1-5-Rushkoff-s/Sharp-a. 6,7-Gross & Erskine-a 3.00

TEXAN, THE (Fightin' Marines #15 on; Fightin' Texan #16 on)
St. John Publishing Co.: Aug, 1948 - No. 15, Oct, 1951

1-Buckskin Belle 30 60 90 177 289 400
2 15 30 45 88 137 185
3,10: 10-Oversized issue 15 30 45 90 140 190
4,5,7,15-Baker-c/a 155 310 465 992 1696 2400
6,9-Baker-c 41 82 123 256 428 600
8,11,13,14-Baker-c/a(2-3) each 48 96 144 302 514 725
12-All Matt Baker-c/a; Peyote story 52 104 156 328 552 775
NOTE: ***Matt Baker** c-4-9, 11-15. **Larsen** a-4-6, 8-10, 15. **Tuska** a-1, 2, 7-9.*

TEXAN, THE (TV)
Dell Publishing Co.: No. 1027, Sept-Nov, 1959 - No. 1096, May-July, 1960

Four Color 1027 (#1)-Photo-c 9 18 27 57 111 165
Four Color 1096-Rory Calhoun photo-c 7 14 21 46 86 125

TEXAS CHAINSAW MASSACRE
DC Comics (WildStorm): Jan, 2007 - No. 6, Jun, 2007 ($2.99, limited series)

1-6: 1-Two covers by Bermejo & Bradstreet; Abnett & Lanning-s 3.00
...: About a Boy #1 (9/07, $2.99) Abnett & Lanning-s/Gomez-a/Robertson-c 3.00
...: Book Two TPB (2009, $14.99) r/one shots & New Line Cinema's Tales of Horror story 15.00
...: By Himself #1 (10/07, $2.99) Abnett & Lanning-s/Craig-a/Robertson-c 3.00
...: Cut! #1 (8/07, $2.99) Pfeiffer-s/Raffaele-a/Robertson-c 3.00
...: Raising Cain 1-3 (7/08 - No. 3, 9/08, $3.50) Bruce Jones-s/Chris Gugliotti-a 3.50

TEXAS JOHN SLAUGHTER (See Walt Disney Presents, 4-Color #997, 1181 & #2)

TEXAS KID (See Two-Gun Western, Wild Western)
Marvel/Atlas Comics (LMC): Jan, 1951 - No. 10, July, 1952

1-Origin; Texas Kid (alias Lance Temple) & his horse Thunder begin;
Tuska-a 33 66 99 194 317 440
2 16 32 48 98 154 210
3-10 14 28 42 81 118 155
NOTE: ***Maneely** a-1-4; c-1, 3, 5-10.*

TEXAS RANGERS, THE (See Jace Pearson of... and Superior Stories #4)

TEXAS RANGERS IN ACTION (Formerly Captain Gallant or Scotland Yard?)
Charlton Comics: No. 5, Jul, 1956 - No. 79, Aug, 1970 (See Blue Bird Comics)

5 9 18 27 47 61 75
6,7,9,10 6 12 18 31 38 45
8-Ditko-a (signed) 10 20 30 54 72 90
11-(68 pg. Giant) Williamson-a (5&8 pgs.); Torres/Williamson-a (5 pgs.)
10 20 30 54 72 90
12-(68 pg. Giant, 6/58) 6 12 18 28 34 40
13-Williamson-a (5 pgs); Torres, Morisi-a 8 16 24 42 54 65
14-20 5 10 15 23 28 32
21-30 3 6 9 15 22 28
31-59: 32-Both 10¢-c & 15¢-c exist 2 4 6 13 18 22
60-Riley's Rangers begin 3 6 9 14 19 24
61-65,68-70 2 4 6 8 11 14
66,67: 66-1st app. The Man Called Loco. 67-Origin 2 4 6 9 13 16
71-79: 77-(4/70) Ditko-c & a (8 pgs.) 1 3 4 6 8 10
76 (Modern Comics-r, 1977) 6.00

TEXAS SLIM (See A-1 Comics)

TEX DAWSON, GUN-SLINGER (Gunslinger #2 on)
Marvel Comics Group: Jan, 1973 (20¢)(Also see Western Kid, 1st series)

1-Steranko-c; Williamson-r (4 pgs.); Tex Dawson-r by Romita(3) from 1955;
Tuska-r 4 8 12 23 37 50

TEX FARNUM (See Wisco)

TEX FARRELL (...Pride of the Wild West)
D. S. Publishing Co.: Mar-Apr, 1948

1-Tex Farrell & his horse Lightning; Shelly-c 19 38 57 111 176 240

TEX GRANGER (Formerly Calling All Boys; see True Comics)
Parents' Magazine Inst./Commended: No. 18, Jun, 1948 - No. 24, Sept, 1949

18-Tex Granger & his horse Bullet begin 14 28 42 80 115 150
19 11 22 33 62 86 110
20-24: 22-Wild Bill Hickok story. 23-Vs. Billy the Kid; Tim Holt app.
9 18 27 50 65 80

TEX MORGAN (See Blaze Carson and Wild Western)
Marvel Comics (CCC): Aug, 1948 - No. 9, Feb, 1950

1-Tex Morgan, his horse Lightning & sidekick Lobo begin
34 68 102 204 332 460
2 21 42 63 124 202 280
3-6: 3,4-Arizona Annie app. 5-Blaze Carson app. 14 28 42 80 115 150
7-9: All photo-c. 7-Captain Tootsie by Beck. 8-18 pg. story "The Terror of Rimrock Valley";
Diablo app. 19 38 57 111 176 240
NOTE: *Tex Taylor app. 2-6, 7, 9. **Brodsky** c-6. **Syd Shores** c-2, 5.*

TEX RITTER WESTERN (Movie star; singing cowboy; see Six-Gun Heroes and Western Hero)
Fawcett No. 1-20 (1/54)/Charlton No. 21 on: Oct, 1950 - No. 46, May, 1959 (Photo-c: 1-21)

1-Tex Ritter, his stallion White Flash & dog Fury begin; photo front/back-c begin
43 86 129 271 461 650
2 21 42 63 124 202 280
3-5: 5-Last photo back-c 16 32 48 94 147 200
6-10 14 28 42 80 115 150
11-19 10 20 30 58 79 100
20-Last Fawcett issue (1/54) 11 22 33 62 86 110
21-1st Charlton issue; photo-c (3/54) 14 28 42 80 115 150
22-B&W photo back-c begin, end #32 9 18 27 52 69 85
23-30: 23-25-Young Falcon app. 9 18 27 47 61 75
31-38,40-45 8 16 24 42 54 65
39-Williamson-a; Whitman-c (1/58) 9 18 27 47 61 75
46-Last issue 8 16 24 44 57 70

TEX TAYLOR (...The Fighting Cowboy on-c #1, 2)(See Blaze Carson, Kid Colt, Tex Morgan, Wild West, Wild Western, & Wisco)
Marvel Comics (HPC): Sept, 1948 - No. 9, March, 1950

1-Tex Taylor & his horse Fury begin; Blaze Carson app.
35 70 105 208 339 470
2-Blaze Carson app. 18 36 54 107 169 230
3-Arizona Annie app. 16 32 48 94 147 200
4-6: All photo-c; Blaze Carson app. 4-Anti-Wertham editorial
19 38 57 111 176 240
7-9: 7-Photo-c;18 pg. Movie-Length Thriller "Trapped in Time's Lost Land!" with sabretoothed tigers, dinosaurs; Diablo app. 8-Photo-c; 18 pg. Movie-Length Thriller "The Mystery of Devil-Tree Plateau!" with dwarf horses, dwarf people & a lost miniature Inca type village; Diablo app. 9-Photo-c; 18 pg. Movie-Length Thriller "Guns Along the Border!" Captain Tootsie by Schreiber; Nimo the Mountain Lion app.; Heth-a
21 42 63 122 199 275
NOTE: ***Syd Shores** c-1-3.*

THANE OF BAGARTH (Also see Hercules, 1967 series)
Charlton Comics: No. 24, Oct, 1985 - No. 25, Dec, 1985

24,25-Low print run 6.00

THANOS
Marvel Comics: Dec, 2003 - No. 12, Sept, 2004 ($2.99)

1-12: 1-6-Starlin-s/a(p)/Milgrom-i; Galactus app. 7-12-Giffen-s/Lim-a 5.00
Annual 1 (7/14, $4.99) Starlin-s/Lim-a/Keown-c 5.00
...: The Final Threat (11/12, $4.99) r/Avengers Ann. #7 & Marvel Two-In-One Ann. #2 5.00
Vol. 4: Epiphany TPB (2004, $14.99) r/#1-6 15.00
Vol. 5: Samaritan TPB (2004, $14.99) r/#7-12 15.00

THANOS (Also see Cosmic Ghost Rider series)
Marvel Comics: Jan, 2017 - No. 18, Jun, 2018 ($3.99)

1-Lemire-s/Deodato-a; Starfox & Thane app. 2 4 6 8 10 12
2-12: 2-6-Lemire-s/Deodato-a. 2-Nebula app. 3-Imperial Guard app. 7-12-Peralta-a 4.00
13-1st app. Cosmic Ghost Rider 5 10 15 33 57 80
14-Cosmic Ghost Rider app. 2 4 6 9 12 15
15-Cosmic Ghost Rider revealed as Frank Castle 3 6 9 17 25 34
16-18: 16-Origin Cosmic Ghost Rider. 17,18-Death app. 5.00
Annual 1 (6/18, $4.99) Short stories by various; hosted by Cosmic Ghost Rider 5.00
... Legacy 1 (11/18, $4.99) Cates & Duggan-s; Cosmic Ghost Rider app. 5.00

THANOS
Marvel Comics: Jun, 2019 - No. 6, Nov, 2019 ($3.99, limited series)

1-($4.99) Tini Howard-s/Ariel Olivetti-a; retells Thanos' first meeting with Gamora 5.00
2-6-($3.99) 4.00
...: Death Notes 1 (1/23, $4.99) Backstory on Thanos; art by various incl. Lim 5.00

THANOS: A GOD UP THERE LISTENING
Marvel Comics: Dec, 2014 - No. 4, Dec, 2014 ($3.99, weekly limited series)

1-4-Thane and Ego The Living Planet app. 4.00

THANOS IMPERATIVE, THE
Marvel Comics: Aug, 2010 - No. 6, Jan, 2011 ($3.99, limited series)

1-6-Abnett & Lanning-s/Sepulveda-a; Vision and Silver Surfer app. 4.00
...: Devastation (3/11, $3.99) Sepulveda-a; leads into The Annihilators #1 4.00
...: Ignition (7/10, $3.99) Walker-a; prequel to series 4.00
Thanos Sourcebook (8/10, $3.99) profiles/history of Thanos and Nova Corps members 4.00

THANOS QUEST, THE (See Capt. Marvel #25, Infinity Gauntlet, Iron Man #55, Logan's Run, Marvel Feature #12, Marvel Universe: The End, Silver Surfer #34 & Warlock #9)
Marvel Comics: 1990 - No. 2, 1990 ($4.95, squarebound, 52 pgs.)

1,2-Both have Starlin scripts & covers (both printings) 3 6 9 17 25 34
1-(3/2000, $3.99) r/material from #1&2 5.00
1-(11/12, $7.99) r/#1&2, new cover by Andy Park 8.00
...: Marvel Tales 1 (7/21, $7.99) r/#1 & 2; intro. by Ralph Macchio 8.00

THANOS: THE INFINITY FINALE (Conclusion to The Infinity Entity series)
Marvel Comics: 2016 ($24.99, HC original graphic novel)

HC - Jim Starlin-s/Ron Lim-a; Adam Warlock & Annihilus app. 25.00

Testament #7 © Rushkoff & Sharp

Thanos (2016) #4 © MAR

That Texas Blood #7 © Condon & Phillips

	GD 2.0	VG 4.0	FN 6.0	VF 8.0	VF/NM 9.0	NM- 9.2

THANOS: THE INFINITY REVELATION (Prelude to The Infinity Entity series)
Marvel Comics: 2014 ($24.99, HC original graphic novel)
HC - Jim Starlin-s/a; Adam Warlock & Silver Surfer app. 25.00

THANOS VS. HULK
Marvel Comics: Feb, 2015 - No. 4, May, 2015 ($3.99, limited series)
1-Jim Starlin-s/a/c; Annihilus, Pip the Troll and Iron Man app.
2 4 6 9 12 15
2-4 4.00

THAT DARN CAT (See Movie Comics & Walt Disney Showcase #19)

THAT'S MY POP! GOES NUTS FOR FAIR
Bystander Press: 1939 (76 pgs., B&W)
nn-by Milt Gross (Rare) 41 82 123 256 428 600

THAT TEXAS BLOOD
Image Comics: Jun, 2020 - Present ($3.99)
1-20-Chris Condon-s/Jacob Phillips-a 4.00

THAT WILKIN BOY (Meet Bingo...)
Archie Publications: Jan, 1969 - No. 52, Oct, 1982
1-1st app. Bingo's Band, Samantha & Tough Teddy 5 10 15 33 57 80
2-5 3 6 9 16 23 30
6-11 2 4 6 13 18 22
12-26-Giants. 12-No # on-c 3 6 9 14 20 26
27-40(1/77) 2 4 6 8 10 12
41-49 1 2 3 4 5 7
50-52 (low print) 2 4 6 8 10 12

THB
Horse Press: Oct, 1994 - 2002 ($5.50/$2.50/$2.95, B&W)
1 ($5.50) Paul Pope-s/a in all 4 8 12 23 37 50
1 (2nd Printing)-r/#1 w/new material 6.00
2 ($2.50) 3 6 9 15 22 28
3-5 2 4 6 8 10 12
69 (1995, no price, low distribution, 12 pgs.)-story reprinted in #1 (2nd Printing) 4.00
Giant THB-($4.95) 5.00
Giant THB 1 V2-(2003, $6.95) 7.00
...M3/THB: Mars' Mightiest Mek #1 (2000, $3.95) 4.00
...6A: Mek-Power #1, 6B: Mek-Power #2, 6C: Mek-Power #3 (2000, $3.95) 4.00
... 6D: Mek-Power #4 (2002, $4.95) 5.00

T.H.E. CAT (TV)
Dell Publishing Co.: Mar, 1967 - No. 4, Oct, 1967 (All have photo-c)
1 4 8 12 22 35 48
2-4 3 6 9 16 24 32

THERE'S A NEW WORLD COMING
Spire Christian Comics/Fleming H. Revell Co.: 1973 (35/49¢)
nn 2 4 6 10 14 18

THEY ALL KISSED THE BRIDE (See Cinema Comics Herald)

THEY'RE NOT LIKE US
Image Comics: Dec, 2014 - No. 16, Oct, 2017 ($2.99)
1-16-Stephenson-s/Gane-a/c 3.00

THIEF OF BAGHDAD
Dell Publishing Co.: No. 1229, Oct-Dec, 1961 (one-shot)
Four Color 1229-Movie, Crandall/Evans-a, photo-c 6 12 18 41 76 110

THIEF OF THIEVES
Image Comics: Feb, 2012 - No. 43, Jul, 2019 ($2.99/$3.99)
1-Kirkman & Spencer-s/Martinbrough-a/c 3 6 9 16 23 30
1-Second printing 1 2 3 5 6 8
2 1 3 4 6 8 10
3,4 1 2 3 5 6 8
5-37: 8-13-Asmus-s 3.00
38-43-($3.99) 4.00

THIMK (Magazine) (Satire)
Counterpoint: May, 1958 - No. 6, May, 1959
1 14 28 42 78 112 145
2-6 9 18 27 52 69 85

THING!, THE (Blue Beetle #18 on)
Song Hits No. 1,2/Capitol Stories/Charlton: Feb, 1952 - No. 17, Nov, 1954
1-Weird/horror stories in all; shrunken head-c 142 284 426 909 1555 2200
2,3 90 180 270 576 988 1400
4,6,8,10: 6-Classic decapitation story 84 168 252 538 919 1300
5-Severed head-c; headlights 155 310 465 992 1696 2400
7-Injury to eye-c & inside panel 123 246 369 787 1344 1900
9-Used in **SOTI**, pg. 388 & illo "Stomping on the face is a form of brutality which modern children learn early" 142 284 426 909 1555 2200
11-Necronomicon story; Hansel & Gretel parody; Injury-to-eye panel; Check-a
174 348 522 1114 1907 2700
12-1st published Ditko-c; "Cinderella" parody; lingerie panels. Ditko-a
258 516 774 1651 2826 4000
13,15-Ditko-c/a(3 & 5) 155 310 465 992 1696 2400
14-Extreme violence/torture; Rumpelstiltskin story; Ditko-c/a(4)
168 336 504 1075 1838 2600
16-Injury to eye panel 39 78 117 231 378 525
17-Ditko-c; classic parody "Through the Looking Glass"; Powell-r/Beware Terror Tales #1 & recolored 116 232 348 742 1271 1800
NOTE: *Excessive violence, severed heads, injury to eye are common No. 5 on.* ***Al Fago*** *c-4.* ***Forgione*** *c-1i, 2, 6, 8, 9. All* ***Ditko*** *issues #14, 15.* ***Giordano*** *a-6.*

THING, THE (See Fantastic Four, Marvel Fanfare, Marvel Feature #11,12, Marvel Two-In-One and Startling Stories:...- Night Falls on Yancy Street)
Marvel Comics Group: July, 1983 - No. 36, June, 1986
1-Life story of Ben Grimm; Byrne scripts begin 3 6 9 16 24 32
2-5: 5-Spider-Man, She-Hulk and Wonder-Man app. 6.00
6-10: 7-1st app. Goody Two-Shoes. 8-She-Hulk app. 10-Secret Wars tie-in 5.00
11-36 4.00
NOTE: ***Byrne*** *a-2i, 7; c-1, 7, 36i; scripts-1-13, 19-22.* ***Sienkiewicz*** *c-13i.*

THING, THE (Fantastic Four)
Marvel Comics: Jan, 2006 - No. 8, Aug, 2006 ($2.99)
1-8: 1-DiVito-a/Slott-s. 4-Lockjaw app. 6-Spider-Man app. 8-Super-Hero poker game 3.00
...: Idol of Millions TPB (2006, $20.99) r/#1-8; Divito sketch page 21.00

THING, THE (Fantastic Four)
Marvel Comics: Jan, 2022 - No. 6, Jun, 2022 ($4.99/$3.99)
1-($4.99) Walter Mosley-s/Tom Reilly-a; set in the classic era; Hercules cameo 5.00
2-6-($3.99) 4-Silver Surfer app. 5,6-Doctor Doom app. 4.00

THING & SHE-HULK: THE LONG NIGHT (Fantastic Four)
Marvel Comics: May, 2002 ($2.99, one-shot)
1-Hitch-c/a(pg. 1-25); Reis-a(pg. 26-39); Dezago-s 3.00

THING, THE (From Another World)
Dark Horse Comics: 1991 - No. 2, 1992 ($2.95, mini-series, stiff-c)
1,2-Based on Universal movie; painted-c/a 5.00

THING CALLED TRUTH, A
Image Comics: Nov, 2021 - No. 5, Mar, 2022 ($3.99)
1-5-Iolanda Zanfardino-s/Elisa Romboli-a 4.00

THING, THE: FREAKSHOW (Fantastic Four)
Marvel Comics: Aug, 2002 - No. 4, Nov, 2002 ($2.99, limited series)
1-4-Geoff Johns-s/Scott Kolins-a 3.00
TPB (2005, $17.99) r/#1-4 & Thing & She-Hulk: The Long Night one-shot 18.00

THING FROM ANOTHER WORLD: CLIMATE OF FEAR, THE
Dark Horse Comics: July, 1992 - No. 4, Dec, 1992 ($2.50, mini-series)
1-4: Painted-c 4.00

THING FROM ANOTHER WORLD: ETERNAL VOWS
Dark Horse Comics: Dec, 1993 - No. 4, 1994 ($2.50, mini-series)
1-4-Gulacy-c/a 4.00

THINK TANK (Also see Eden's Fall)
Image Comics (Top Cow): Aug, 2012 - No. 12, Feb, 2014 ($3.99)
1-12-Hawkins-s/Ekedal-a 4.00

THINK TANK: ANIMAL
Image Comics (Top Cow): Mar, 2017 - No. 3 ($3.99)
1-3-Hawkins-s/Ekedal-a 4.00

THINK TANK: CREATIVE DESTRUCTION
Image Comics (Top Cow): Apr, 2016 - No. 4, Jul, 2016 ($3.99, limited series)
1-4-Hawkins-s/Ekedal-a 4.00

THIRTEEN (...Going on 18)
Dell Publishing Co.: 11-1/61-62 - No. 25, 12/67; No. 26, 7/69 - No. 29, 1/71
1 6 12 18 40 73 105
2-10 4 8 12 28 47 65
11-25 4 8 12 23 37 50
26-29-r 3 6 9 17 26 35

NOTE: *John Stanley script-No. 3-29; art?*

13: ASSASSIN
TSR, Inc.: 1990 - No. 8, 1991 ($2.95, 44 pgs.)

1-8: Agent 13; Alcala-a(i); Springer back-up-a 4.00

13th ARTIFACT, THE
Image Comics (Top Cow): Mar, 2016 ($3.99, one-shot)

1-Amit Chauhan-s/Eli Powell-a 4.00

13th SON, THE
Dark Horse Comics: Nov, 2005 - No. 4, Feb, 2006 ($2.99, limited series)

1-4-Kelley Jones-s/a/c 3.00

30 DAYS OF NIGHT
Idea + Design Works: June, 2002 - No. 3, Oct, 2002 ($3.99, limited series)

1-Vampires in Alaska; Steve Niles-s/Ben Templesmith-a/Ashley Wood-c 95.00
1-2nd printing 10.00
2 26.00
3 12.00
Annual 2004 (1/04, $4.99) Niles-s/art by Templesmith and others 5.00
Annual 2005 (12/05, $7.49) Niles-s/art by Nat Jones 7.50
... 5th Anniversary (10/07 - No. 3, $2.99) reprints original series 3.00
... Sourcebook (10/07, $7.49) Illustrated guide to the 30 Days world 7.50
... Three Tales TPB (7/06, $19.99) r/Annual 2005, ...: Dead Space #1-3, and short story from Tales of Terror (IDW's...) 20.00
Hundred Penny Press: 30 Days of Night #1 (5/11, $1.00) r/#1 3.00
... 100-Page Giant (3/19, $4.99) r/30 Days of Night: Eben & Stella #1-3 5.00
TPB (2003, $17.99) r/#1-3, foreward by Clive Barker; script for #1 18.00
The Complete 30 Days of Night (2004, $75.00, oversized hardcover with slipcase) r/#1-3; prequel; script pages for #1-3; original cover and promotional materials 75.00

30 DAYS OF NIGHT
IDW Publishing: July, 2004 (Free Comic Book Day edition)

Previews CSI: Bad Rap; The Shield: Spotlight; 24: One Shot; and 30 Days of Night 3.00

30 DAYS OF NIGHT (Ongoing series)
IDW Publishing: Oct, 2011 - No. 12, Nov, 2012 ($3.99)

1-12: 1-4-Niles-s/Kieth-a; covers by Kieth and Furno. 5-12-Niles-s 4.00

30 DAYS OF NIGHT (2017 reimagining of original series)
IDW Publishing: Dec, 2017 - No. 6, May, 2018 ($3.99, limited series)

1-6-Niles-s/Kowalski-a; covers by Kowalski, Wood and Templesmith 4.00

30 DAYS OF NIGHT: BEYOND BARROW
IDW Publishing: Sept, 2007 - No. 3, Dec, 2007 ($3.99, limited series)

1-3-Niles-s/Sienkiewicz-a/c 4.00

30 DAYS OF NIGHT: BLOODSUCKER TALES
IDW Publishing: Oct, 2004 - No. 8, May, 2005 ($3.99, limited series)

1-8-Niles-s/Chamberlain-a; Fraction-s/Templesmith-a/c 4.00
HC (8/05, $49.99) r/#1-8; cover gallery 50.00
SC (8/05, $24.99) r/#1-8; cover gallery 25.00

30 DAYS OF NIGHT: DEAD SPACE
IDW Publishing: Jan, 2006 - No. 3, Mar, 2006 ($3.99, limited series)

1-3-Niles and Wickline-s/Milx-a/c 4.00

30 DAYS OF NIGHT: EBEN & STELLA
IDW Publishing: May, 2007 - No. 3, July, 2007 ($3.99, limited series)

1-3-Niles and DeConnick-s/Randall-a/c 4.00

30 DAYS OF NIGHT: NIGHT, AGAIN
IDW Publishing: May, 2011 - No. 4, Aug, 2011 ($3.99, limited series)

1-4-Lansdale-s/Kieth-a/c 4.00

30 DAYS OF NIGHT: RED SNOW
IDW Publishing: Aug, 2007 - No. 3, Oct, 2007 ($3.99, limited series)

1-3-Ben Templesmith-s/a/c 4.00

30 DAYS OF NIGHT: RETURN TO BARROW
IDW Publishing: Mar, 2004 - No. 6, Aug, 2004 ($3.99, limited series)

1-6-Steve Niles-s/Ben Templesmith-a/c 4.00
TPB (2004, $19.99) r/#1-6; cover gallery 20.00

30 DAYS OF NIGHT: SPREADING THE DISEASE
IDW Publishing: Dec, 2006 - No. 5, Apr, 2007 ($3.99, limited series)

1-5: 1-Wickline-s/Sanchez-a. 3-5-Sandoval-a 4.00

30 DAYS OF NIGHT: 30 DAYS 'TIL DEATH
IDW Publishing: Dec, 2008 - No. 4, Mar, 2009 ($3.99, limited series)

1-4-David Lapham-s/a; covers by Lapham and Templesmith 4.00

THIRTY SECONDS OVER TOKYO (See American Library)

THIS DAMNED BAND
Dark Horse Comics: Aug, 2016 - No. 6, Jan, 2016 ($3.99, limited series)

1-6-Paul Cornell-s/Tony Parker-a 4.00

THIS IS SUSPENSE! (Formerly Strange Suspense Stories; Strange Suspense Stories #27 on)
Charlton Comics: No. 23, Feb, 1955 - No. 26, Aug, 1955

23-Wood-a(r)/A Star Presentation #3 "Dr. Jekyll & Mr. Hyde"; last pre-code issue 30 60 90 177 289 400
24-Censored Fawcett-r; Evans-a (r/Suspense Detective #1) 17 34 51 98 154 210
25,26: 26-Marcus Swayze-a 14 28 42 80 115 150

THIS IS THE PAYOFF (See Pay-Off)

THIS IS WAR
Standard Comics: No. 5, July, 1952 - No. 9, May, 1953

5-Toth-a 22 44 66 128 209 290
6,9-Toth-a 16 32 48 94 147 200
7,8: 8-Ross Andru-c 14 28 42 80 115 150

THIS IS YOUR LIFE, DONALD DUCK (See Donald Duck..., Four Color #1109)

THIS MAGAZINE IS CRAZY (Crazy #? on)
Charlton Publ. (Humor Magazines): V3#2, July, 1957 - V4#8, Feb, 1959 (25¢, magazine, 68 pgs.)

V3#2-V4#7: V4#5-Russian Sputnik-c parody 14 28 42 78 112 145
V4#8-Davis-a (8 pgs.) 14 28 42 81 118 155

THIS MAGAZINE IS HAUNTED (Danger and Adventure #22 on)
Fawcett Publications/Charlton No. 15(2/54) on: Oct, 1951 - No. 14, 12/53; No. 15, 2/54 - V3#21, Nov, 1954

1-Evans-a; Dr. Death as host begins 110 220 330 704 1202 1700
2,5-Evans-a 61 122 183 390 670 950
3,4: 3-Vampire-c/story 60 120 180 381 653 925
6-9,12 43 86 129 271 461 650
10-Severed head-c 135 270 405 864 1482 2100
11-Classic skeleton-c 103 206 309 659 1130 1600
13-Severed head-c/story 90 180 270 576 988 1400
14-Classic burning skull-c 258 516 774 1651 2826 4000
15,20: 15-Dick Giordano-c. 20-Cover is swiped from panel in The Thing #16 58 116 174 371 636 900
16,19-Ditko-c. 19-Injury-to-eye panel; story-r/#1 290 580 870 1856 3178 4500
17-Ditko-c/a(4); blood drainage story 90 180 270 576 988 1400
18-Ditko-c/a(1 story); E.C. swipe/Haunt of Fear #5; injury-to-eye panel; reprints "Caretaker of the Dead" from Beware Terror Tales & recolored 77 154 231 493 847 1200
21-Ditko-c, Evans-r/This Magazine Is Haunted #1 65 130 195 416 708 1000

NOTE: *Baily a-1, 3, 4, 21r/#1. Moldoff c/a-1-13. Powell a-3-5, 11, 12, 17. Shuster a-18-20. Issues 19-21 have reprints which have been recolored from This Magazine is Haunted #1.*

THIS MAGAZINE IS HAUNTED (2nd Series) (Formerly Zaza the Mystic; Outer Space #17 on)
Charlton Comics: V2#12, July, 1957 - V2#16, May, 1958

V2#12-14-Ditko-c/a in all 60 120 180 381 653 925
15-No Ditko-c/a 25 50 75 150 245 340
16-Ditko-a(4). 41 82 123 256 428 600

THIS MAGAZINE IS WILD (See Wild)

THIS WAS YOUR LIFE (Religious)
Jack T. Chick Publ.: 1964 (3 1/2 x 5 1/2", 40 pgs., B&W and red)

nn, Another version (5x2 3/4", 26 pgs.) 2 4 6 10 14 18

THOR (See Avengers #1, Giant-Size..., Marvel Collectors Item Classics, Marvel Graphic Novel #33, Marvel Preview, Marvel Spectacular, Marvel Treasury Edition, Special Marvel Edition & Tales of Asgard)

THOR (Journey Into Mystery #1-125, 503-on)(The Mighty Thor #413-490)
Marvel Comics Group: No. 126, Mar, 1966 - No. 502, Sept, 1996

126-Thor continues (#125-130 Thor vs. Hercules); Tales of Asgard back-up stories continue through issue #145 46 92 138 359 805 1250
127-130: 127-1st app. Pluto. 129-1st Ares Olympian God of War & Tana Nile of the Rigillian Colonizers 12 24 36 79 170 260
131,135,137-140: 135-Origin of the High Evolutionary. 137-1st Ulik the Troll. 138-139-Thor vs. Ulik. 140-Kang app; 1st Growing Man 9 18 27 63 129 195
132-1st app. Ego the Living Planet 10 20 30 66 138 210
133-Thor vs. Ego 14 28 42 97 214 330
134-Intro High Evolutionary and Man-Beast 46 92 138 340 770 1200
136-(1/67) Re-intro. Sif 12 24 36 82 179 275
141-145: 142-Thor vs. Super-Skrull. 143,144-Thor vs. the Enchanters 8 16 24 52 99 145
146,147: 146-Inhumans origin; begin (early app.) in back-up stories, end #152 (see Fantastic Four #45 for 1st app.). 147-Origin continues 9 18 27 59 117 175
148-Origin Black Bolt; 1st app. Wrecker 17 34 51 117 259 400
149-Origin Black Bolt continues. 149-Origin Medusa, Crystal, Maximus, Gorgon, Karnak 10 20 30 64 132 200
150-152: Inhumans app. 150-Hela app. 151,152-Destroyer and Ulik app. 8 16 24 55 105 155
153-157,159: 154-1st Mangog. 155-157-Thor vs Mangog. 159-Origin Dr. Blake (Thor) concl. 7 14 21 46 86 125
158-Origin-r/#83; origin Dr. Blake 9 18 27 62 126 190
160-162-Galactus app. 8 16 24 52 99 145
163,164-2nd & 3th brief app. Warlock (Him) 6 12 18 38 69 100
165-1st full app. Warlock (Him) (6/69, see Fantastic Four #67); last 12¢ issue; Kirby-a 107 214 321 856 1928 3000
166-2nd full app. Warlock (Him); battles Thor; see Marvel Premiere #1 16 32 48 110 243 375
167,170-179: 170-1st Thermal Man. 171-Thor vs. the Wrecker. 173-Circus of Crime app. 174-1st Crypto-Man. 176-177-Surtur app. 178-1st Buscema-a on Thor; vs the Abomination. 179-Last Kirby issue 6 12 18 38 69 100
168-Origin Galactus; Kirby-a 36 72 108 259 580 900
169-Origin Galactus continues; Kirby-a 21 42 63 147 324 500
180,181-Neal Adams-a; Mephisto & Loki app. 6 12 18 37 66 95
182,183-Thor vs. Doctor Doom. 182-Buscema-a begins (11/70) 5 10 15 35 63 90
184-192: 184-1st Infinity & the Silent One. 187-Thor vs Odin. 188-Origin of Infinity. 189,190-Thor vs. Hela. 191-1st Durok the Demolisher. 192-Last 15¢ issue; Thor vs. Durok 5 10 15 30 50 70
193-(25¢, 52 pgs.); Silver Surfer x-over; Thor vs. Durok; last Stan Lee story as regular writer 12 24 36 80 173 265
194-199: 194-Gerry Conway stories begin (ends #238). 195-Mangog returns. 196-198-Thor vs. Mangog. 199-1st Ego-Prime; Pluto app. 4 8 12 25 40 55
200-Special Ragnarok issue by Stan Lee 5 10 15 34 60 85
201-206,208-220,222-224: 201-Pluto & Hela app; origin of Ego-Prime. 202-vs Ego-Prime. 203-1st Young Gods. 204-Thor exiled on Earth; Mephisto app. 205-vs Mephisto; Hitler app. 206-vs. the Absorbing Man. 208-1st Mercurio the 4th Dimensional Man. 210-211-vs. Ulik. 214-Mercurio the 4-D Man app; 1st Xorr the God-Jewel. 215-Origin of Xorr; Mecurio the 4-D Man app. 216-Xorr & Mecurio app. 217-Thor vs Odin-c. 218-220-Saga of the Black Stars. 222,223-vs Pluto. 224-The Destroyer app. 3 6 9 16 23 30
207-Rutland, Vermont Halloween x-over; leads into Avengers/Defenders war 4 8 12 22 35 48
221-Thor vs. Hercules; Hercules guest stars through issue #232,234-239

30 Days of Night (2017) #5 © Niles & IDW

Thor #175 © MAR

Thor #494 © MAR

	GD 2.0	VG 4.0	FN 6.0	VF 8.0	VF/NM 9.0	NM- 9.2

3 6 9 18 28 38
225-Intro. Firelord 16 32 48 111 246 380
226-Galactus and Firelord app. 3 6 9 17 26 35
227-231: 227-228-Thor, Firelord & Galactus vs Ego the Living Planet. 228-Origin of Ego
2 4 6 11 16 20
229 Facsimile Edition (5/20, $3.99) Reprints 1974 issue with original ads & letter column 4.00
232,233: 232-Firelord app. 233-Numerous guest stars; Asgard invades Earth
3 6 9 14 20 25
234-245: 234-Iron Man & Firelord app. 235-1st Kamo Tharnn, Elder of the Universe. 236-Thor vs. Absorbing Man. 237-239-Thor vs. Ulik. 240-1st Egyptian Gods; Osiris & Horus; 1st Seth-Egyptian God of Death. 241-Thor vs. Seth. 242-Len Wein scripts begin; ends #271. 242-245-Thor vs. Time-Twisters; Zarko the Tomorrow Man app.
2 4 6 11 16 20
246-250-(Regular 25¢ editions)(4-8/76): 246-247-Firelord app. 249-250-Thor vs. Mangog
2 4 6 11 16 20
246-250-(30¢-c variants, limited distribution) 5 10 15 34 60 85
251-280: 251-Thor vs. Hela. 252,253-Thor vs. Ulik. 255-Re-intro Stone Men of Saturn. 257-259-Thor vs. Grey Gargoyle. 260-Thor vs. Enchantress & Executioner. 261-272-Simonson-a. 264-266-Thor vs. Loki. 265,266-The Destroyer app. 269-Thor vs. Stilt-Man. 270-Thor vs. Blastaar. 271-Iron Man x-over. 272-Roy Thomas scripts begin. 274-Death of Balder the Brave. 276-Thor vs. Red Norvell Thor. 280-Thor vs. Hyperion
2 4 6 8 10 12
260-264-(35¢-c variants, limited distribution)(6-10/77) 9 18 27 62 126 190
281-299: 281-Space Phantom app. 282-Immortus app. 283,284-Celestials app. 284-286-Eternals app. 287-288-Thor vs. the Forgotten one. 291,292-Asgard vs Olympus. 292-1st Eye of Odin (as sentient being). 294-Origin Asgard & Odin
2 4 6 8 10 12
300-(12/80)-End of Asgard; origin of Odin & The Destroyer; double-size
3 6 9 14 20 25
301-Numerous pantheons (skyfathers) app. 1 3 4 6 8 10
302-304 1 2 3 5 6 8
305-306: 305-Airwalker app. 306-Firelord 1 3 4 6 8 10
307-331,334-336: 310-Thor vs. Mephisto. 314-Moondragon and Drax app. 315,316-Bi-Beast & Man-Beast app. 316-Iron Man x-over. 325-Mephisto app. 331-1st Crusader 6.00
332,333-Dracula app. 1 2 3 5 6 8
337-Simonson-c/a begins, ends #382; 1st app. of Beta Ray Bill who becomes the new Thor; intro Lorelei 10 20 30 64 132 200
338-Beta Ray Bill vs. Thor; origin Beta Ray Bill 3 6 9 19 30 40
339,340: 339-Beta Ray Bill gains Thor's powers. 340-Donald Blake returns as Thor; Beta Ray Bill app.; more facts revealed about origin 2 4 6 8 10 12
341-343,345-371,373,375-381,383,386: 341-Clark Kent & Lois Lane cameo. 345-349-Malekith the Accursed app. 350-352-Avengers app. 353-'Death' of Odin. 356-Hercules app. 363-Secret Wars II crossover. 364-366-Thor as a frog. 367-Malekith app. 373-X-Factor tie-in. 383-Secret Wars flashback 6.00
344-(6/84) 1st app. of Malekith the Accursed (Ruler of the Dark Elves)(villain in the 2013 movie Thor: The Dark World); Simonson-c/a 3 6 9 15 22 28
372-1st Time Variance Authority (Loki TV) 3 6 9 16 23 30
374-Mutant Massacre; X-Factor app. 1 2 3 5 6 8
382-($1.25)-Anniversary issue; last Simonson-a 1 2 3 5 6 8
384-Intro. Thor of the 26th century (Dargo Ktor) 1 2 3 5 6 8
385-Thor vs. Hulk by Stan Lee and Erik Larsen 2 4 6 8 10 12
387-399: Thor vs. the Celestials. 389- 'Alone against the Celestials' climax. 390-Avengers app.; Captain America lifts Mjolnir. 391-Spider-Man x-over; 1st Eric Masterson. 393-395-Daredevil app. 395-Intro. Earth Force. 396-399-Black Knight app. 6.00
400-($1.75, 68 pgs.)-Origin Loki 1 2 3 5 6 8
401-410: 404,405-Annihilus app. 409-410-Dr. Doom app. 5.00
411-Intro New Warriors (appear in costume in last panel); Juggernaut-c/story
3 6 9 21 33 45
412-1st full app. New Warriors (Marvel Boy, Kid Nova, Namorita, Night Thrasher, Firestar & Speedball) 3 6 9 21 33 45
413-428: 413-Dr. Strange app. 419-425-Black Galaxy saga; origin Celestials 427-428-Excalibur app. 428-Ghost Rider app. 5.00
429-431: 429-Thor vs Juggernaut; Ghost Rider app. 430-Ghost Rider app. 4.00
432-(52 pgs.) Thor's 350th issue (vs. Loki) reprints origin and 1st app. from Journey into Mystery #83 5.00
433-449,451-467: 433-Intro. Eric Masterson as Thor. 434,435-Annihilus app. 437-Quasar app.; Tales of Asgard back-up stories begin. 438-441-Thor War; Beta Ray Bill app. 443-Dr. Strange & Silver Surfer x-over; last $1.00-c. 445,446-Operation Galactic Storm. 445-Thor vs. Gladiator. 448-Spider-Man app. 451,452-Bloodaxe app. 457-Original Thor returns. 458-Thor vs. Thor. 459-Intro Thunderstrike. 460-Starlin scripts begin. 461-Thor vs. Beta Ray Bill. 463-467-Infinity Crusade x-over. 466-Drax app. 4.00
450-($2.50, 68 pgs.)-Flip-book format; r/story JIM #85 (1st Loki) plus-c plus a gallery of past-c; gatefold-c 5.00
468,469-Blood and Thunder x-over. 468-Thor vs. Silver Surfer. 469-Infinity Watch app. 6.00
470,471-Blood and Thunder x-over. 470-Thanos and the Infinity Watch app. 471-Blood and Thunder story conclusion; Infinity Watch and Silver Surfer app. 6.00
472-474: 472-Intro the Godlings. 474-Begin $1.50-c; bound-in trading cards 4.00
475 ($2.00, 52 pgs.)-Regular edition; High Evolutionary and Man-Beast app. 5.00
475 ($2.50, 52 pgs.)-Collectors edition w/foil embossed-c 6.00
476-481, 483,486,487,488: 476-Destroyer app. 477-Thunderstrike app. 478-Return of Red Norvell Thor. 479-Detailed Origin of Thor. 486-Kurse app. 4.00
482 ($2.95, 84 pgs.)-400th Thor issue 5.00
484,485,490: 484-War Machine app. 485-Thing app. 490-Absorbing Man app.; Buscema-a 5.00
489-Hulk app. 6.00
491-Warren Ellis scripts begins, ends #494; Worldengine pt.1; Deodato-c/a begins 6.00
492-494: Worldengine pt. 2-4. 492-Reintro The Enchantress; Beta Ray Bill dies 5.00
495-499: 495-Messner-Loebs scripts begin; Isherwood-c/a. 496-Captain America app. 4.00
500 ($2.50)-Double-size; wraparound-c; Deodato-c/a; Dr. Strange app. 5.00
501-Reintro Red Norvell 4.00
502-(9/96) Onslaught tie-in; Red Norvell, Jane Foster & Hela app. 5.00
NOTE: *Numbering continues with Journey Into Mystery #503 (11/96)*
600-up (See Thor 2007 series)
Special 2(9/66)-(See Journey Into Mystery for 1st annual) Destroyer app.
15 30 45 103 227 350
Special 2 (2nd printing, 1994) 2 4 6 8 10 12
King Size Special 3 (1/71) 5 10 15 35 63 90
Special 4 (12/71)-r/Thor #131,132 & JIM #113 3 6 9 21 33 45
Annual 5 (11/76)-Asgard vs Olympus; Hercules app. 3 6 9 14 19 24
Annual 6 (10/77)-Guardians of the Galaxy app. 5 10 15 30 50 70
Annual 7,8: 7 (1978)-Eternals app. 8 (1979)-Thor vs. Zeus-c/story
2 4 6 9 13 16
Annual 9-13: 9 ('81)-Dormammu app. 10 ('82)-1st Demogorge-the God Eater. 11 ('83)-Origin of Thor expanded. 12 ('84)-Intro Vidar (Thor's brother). 13 ('85)-Mephisto app. 6.00
Annual 14-19 ('86-'94, 68 pgs.): 14-Atlantis Attacks. 15 ('90)-Terminus factor Pt. 3. 16-3 pg. origin; Guardians of the Galaxy x-over. 17 ('92)-Citizen Kang Pt. 2. 18-Polybagged w/card; intro the Flame. 19 ('94) vs. Pluto 5.00
...Alone Against the Celestials nn (6/92, $5.95)-r/Thor #387-389 6.00
...Legends Vol. 2: Walter Simonson Book 2 TPB (2003, $24.99) r/#349-355,357-359 25.00
...Legends Vol. 3: Walter Simonson Book 3 TPB (2004, $24.99) r/#360-369 25.00
...: The Eternals Saga TPB (2006, $24.99) r/#283-291 & Annual #7; profile pages 25.00
...: The Eternals Saga Vol. 2 TPB ('07, $24.99) r/#292-301; Thomas & Gruenwald essays 25.00
... Visionaries: Mike Deodato Jr. TPB (2004, $19.99) r/#491-494,498-500 20.00
... Visionaries: Walter Simonson (Vol. 1) TPB (5/01, $24.95) r/#337-348 25.00
... Visionaries: Walter Simonson Vol. 4 TPB (2007, $24.99) r/#371-373 & Balder the Brave #1-4 25.00
... Visionaries: Walter Simonson Vol. 5 TPB (2008, $24.95) r/#375-382 25.00
...: Worldengine (8/96, $9.95)-r/#491-494; Deodato-c/a; story & new intermission by Warren Ellis 10.00
NOTE: ***Neal Adams** a-180,181; c-179-181. **Austin** a-342i, 346i; c-312i. **Buscema** a(p)-178, 182-213, 215-226, 231-238, 241-253, 254r, 256-259, 272-278, 283-285, 370, Annual 6, 8, 11i; c(p)-175, 178, 182-196, 198-200, 202-204, 206, 211, 212, 215, 219, 221, 226, 256, 259, 261, 262, 272-278, 283, 289, 370, Annual 6. **Everett** a(i)-143, 170-175; c(i)-171, 172, 174, 176, 241. **Gil Kane** a-318p; c(p)-201, 205, 207-210, 216, 220, 222, 223, 231, 233-240, 242, 243, 318. **Kirby** a(p)-126-177, 179, 194r, 254r; c(p)-126-169, 171-174, 176, 177, 249-253, 255, 257, 258, Annual 5, Special 2-4. **Mooney** a(i)-201, 204, 214-216, 218, 322i, 324i, 325i, 327i. **Sienkiewicz** c-332, 333, 335. **Simonson** a-260-271p, 337-354, 357-367, 380, Annual 7p; c-260, 263-271, 337-355, 357-369, 371, 373-382, Annual 7. **Starlin** c-213.*

THOR (Volume 2)
Marvel Comics: July, 1998 - No. 85, Dec, 2004 ($2.99/$1.99/$2.25)

1-($2.99)-Follows Heroes Return; Jurgens-s/Romita Jr. & Janson-a; wraparound-c; battles the Destroyer 1 2 3 5 6 8
1-Variant-c 2 4 6 8 10 12
1-Rough Cut-($2.99) Features original script and pencil pages 4.00
1-Sketch cover 35.00
2-($1.99) Two covers; Avengers app. 5.00
3-11,13-23: 3-Assumes Jake Olson ID. 4-Namor-c/app. 8-Spider-Man-c/app. 14-Iron Man c/app. 17-Juggernaut-c 4.00
12-($2.99) Wraparound-c; Hercules appears 5.00
12-($10.00) Variant-c by Jusko 10.00
24,26-31,33,34: 24-Begin $2.25-c. 26-Mignola-c/Larsen-a. 29-Andy Kubert-a. 30-Maximum Security x-over; Beta Ray Bill-c/app. 33-Intro. Thor Girl 4.00
25-($2.99) Regular edition 5.00
25-($3.99) Gold foil enhanced cover 6.00
32-($3.50, 100 pgs.) new story plus reprints w/Kirby-a; Simonson-a 6.00
35-($2.99) Thor battles The Gladiator; Andy Kubert-a 5.00
36-49,51-61: 37-Starlin-a. 38,39-BWS-c. 38-42-Immonen-a. 40-Odin killed. 41-Orbik-c. 44-'Nuff Said silent issue. 51-Spider-Man app. 57-Art by various. 58-Davis-a; x-over with Iron Man #64. 60-Brereton-c 4.00
50-($4.95) Raney-c/a; back-ups w/Nuckols-a & Armenta-s/Bennett-a 5.00
62-84: 62-Begin $2.99-c. 64-Loki-c/app. 80-Oeming-s begins; Avengers app. 4.00
85-Last issue; Thor dies; Oeming-s/DiVito-a/Epting-c 5.00
...1999 Annual ($3.50) Jurgens-s/a(p) 5.00

GD	VG	FN	VF	VF/NM	NM-
2.0	4.0	6.0	8.0	9.0	9.2

...2000 Annual ($3.50) Jurgens-s/Ordway-a(p); back-up stories 5.00
...2001 Annual ($3.50) Jurgens-s/Grummett-a(p); Lightle-c 5.00
...Across All Worlds (9/01, $19.95, TPB) r/#28-35 20.00
Avengers Disassembled: Thor TPB (2004, $16.99) r/#80-85; afterword by Oeming 17.00
...Resurrection ($5.99, TPB) r/#1,2 6.00
...: The Dark Gods (7/00, $15.95, TPB) r/#9-13 16.00
...Vol. 1: The Death of Odin (7/02, $12.99, TPB) r/#39-44 13.00
...Vol. 2: Lord of Asgard (9/02, $15.99, TPB) r/#45-50 16.00
...Vol. 3: Gods on Earth (2003, $21.99, TPB) r/#51-58, Avengers #63, Iron Man #64, Marvel Double-Shot #1; Beck-c 22.00
...Vol. 4: Spiral (2003, $19.99, TPB) r/#59-67; Brereton-c 20.00
...Vol. 5: The Reigning (2004, $17.99, TPB) r/#68-74 18.00
...Vol. 6: Gods and Men (2004, $13.99, TPB) r/#75-79 14.00

THOR (Also see Fantastic Four #538)(Resumes original numbering with #600)
Marvel Comics: Sept, 2007 - No. 12, Mar, 2009; No. 600, Apr, 2009 - No. 621, May, 2011 ($2.99/$3.99) (Continues numbering as Journey Into Mystery #622) (Also see Mighty Thor #1)

1-Straczynski-s/Coipel-a/c 4.00
1-Variant-c by Michael Turner 5.00
1-Zombie variant-c by Suydam 5.00
1-Non-zombie variant-c by Suydam 5.00
1-"Marvel's Greatest Comics" edition (5/10, $1.00) r/#1 3.00
2-12: 2-Two covers by Dell'Otto and Coipel. 3-Iron Man app.; McGuinness var-c. 4-Bermejo var-c. 5-Campbell var-c. 6-Art Adams var-c. 7,8-Djurdjevic-a/c; Coipel var-c 3.00
2-Second printing with wraparound-c 3.00
7-"Marvel's Greatest Comics" edition (6/11, $1.00) r/#7 3.00

(After #12 [Mar, 2009] numbering reverted back to original Journey Into Mystery/Thor numbering with #600, Apr, 2009)

600 (4/09, $4.99) Two wraparound-c by Coipel & Djurdjevic; Coipel, Djurdjevic & Aja-a; r/Tales of Asgard from Journey Into Mystery #106,107,112,113,115; Kirby-a 5.00
601-603,611-621-($3.99) 601-603-Djurdjevic-a. 602-Sif returns. 617-Loki returns 4.00
604-610-($2.99) Tan-a. 607-609-Siege x-over. 610-Braithwaite-a; Ragnarok app. 3.00
620.1 (5/11, $2.99) Brooks-a; Grey Gargoyle app. 3.00
Annual 1 (11/09, $3.99) Suayan, Grindberg, Gaudiano-a; Djurdjevic-c 4.00
...: Ages of Thunder (6/08, $3.99) Fraction-s/Zircher-a/Djurdjevic-c 4.00
... & Hercules: Encyclopaedia Mythologica (2009, $4.99) profile pages of the Pantheons 5.00
... Asgard's Avenger 1 (6/11, $4.99) profile pages of Thor characters 5.00
... By Simonson Halloween Comic Fest 2017 1 (12/17, giveaway) r/#354 & JIM #102 3.00
... Crown of Fools 1 (12/13, $3.99) Di Vito & Simonson-a 4.00
... Giant-Size Finale 1 (1/01, $3.99) Dr. Doom app.; r/origin from JIM #83 4.00
... God-Size Special (2/09, $3.99) story of Skurge the Executioner re-told; art by Brereton, Braithwaite, Allred and Sepulveda; plus reprint of Thor #362 (1985) 4.00
... Goes Hollywood 1 ('11, $3.99) Collection of movie-themed variant Thor covers 4.00
...: Man of War (1/09, $3.99) Fraction-s/Mann & Zircher-a/Djurdjevic-c 4.00
...: Reign of Blood (8/08, $3.99) Fraction-s/Evans & Zircher-a/Djurdjevic-c 4.00
...: Spotlight (5/11, $3.99) movie photo-c; movie preview; creator interviews 4.00
...: The Rage of Thor (10/10, $3.99) Milligan-s/Suayan-c/a 4.00
...: The Trial of Thor (8/09, $3.99) Milligan-s/Nord-c/a 4.00
...: Truth of History (12/08, $3.99) Thor and crew in ancient Egypt; Alan Davis-s/a/c 4.00
...: Where Walk the Frost Giants 1 (12/17, $3.99) Macchio-s/Nauck-a; plus r/JIM #112 4.00
...: Whosoever Wields This Hammer 1 (6/11, $4.99) recolored r/J.I.M. #83,84,88 5.00
...: Wolves of the North (2/11, $3.99) Carey-s/Perkins-a 4.00
... By J. Michael Straczynski Vol. 1 HC (2008, $19.99) r/#1-6; variant cover gallery 20.00

THOR (Female Thor)
Marvel Comics: Dec, 2014 - No. 8, Jul, 2015 ($3.99)

1-Aaron-s/Dauterman-a/c; Thor, Odin and Malekith app. 10.00
2-8 2-4-Malekith app. 4-Thor vs. Thor. 5-Molina-a. 8-Identity revealed 4.00
Annual 1 (4/15, $4.99) Female Thor, King Thor stories; Young Thor by CM Punk-s 5.00

THOR (Odinson back as Thor)(Leads into King Thor series)
Marvel Comics: Aug, 2018 - No. 16, Oct, 2019 ($5.99/$3.99)

1-($5.99) Aaron-s/Del Mundo-a/c; Juggernaut and Loki app. 6.00
2-16-($3.99) 2-4-Skurge & Hela app. 5,6-Ward-a; future Doctor Doom app. 7-Tony Moore-a. 8-10,12,13,15,16-Del Mundo-a. 12-14-War of the Realms tie-ins. 16-Wraparound-c 4.00

THOR (Odinson as King Thor)
Marvel Comics: Mar, 2020 - Present ($4.99/$3.99)

1-($4.99) Cates-s/Klein-a; Galactus, Silver Surfer and Loki app. 5.00
2-8: 2-6-($3.99) Thor as the Herald to Galactus; Beta Ray Bill app. 4,5-Sif app. 7,8-Kuder-a; intro. Adam Aziz 4.00
9-Donald Blake returns 4.00
10-23,26-30: 10-14-Beta Ray Bill & Sif app. 15-Capt. America app. 17-Angela app. 4.00
24-($8.99) Legacy issue #750; funeral for Odin; art by Klein, Simonson, Coipel, Garbett 9.00
25-($5.99) Hulk vs. Thor; Banner of War; Avengers app. 6.00
31-($4.99) Bonus story with Black Panther 5.00
Annual 1 (9/21, $4.99) Infinite Destinies; Aaron Kuder-s/a 5.00
...: Lightning and Lament 1 (8/22, $3.99) Nauck-a 4.00
...: The Worthy 1 (2/20, $4.99) Short stories with Beta Ray Bill, Thunderstrike, Sif 5.00

THOR ADAPTATION (MARVEL'S...)
Marvel Comics: Mar, 2012 - No. 2, Apr, 2012 ($2.99, limited series)

1,2-Adaptation of 2012 movie; Gage-s/Medina-a; photo-c 3.00

THOR AND THE WARRIORS FOUR
Marvel Comics: Jun, 2010 - No. 4, Sept, 2010 ($2.99, limited series)

1-4-Thor and Power Pack team-up; Gurihiru-a; back-up with Coover-s/a 3.00

THOR: BLOOD OATH
Marvel Comics: Nov, 2005 - No. 6, Feb, 2006 ($2.99, limited series)

1-6-Oeming-s/Kolins-a/c 3.00
HC (2006, $19.99, dust jacket) r/series; afterword by Oeming 20.00
SC (2006, $14.99) r/series; afterword by Oeming 15.00

THOR CORPS
Marvel Comics: Sept, 1993 - No. 4, Jan, 1994 ($1.75, limited series)

1-4: 1-Invaders cameo. 2-Invaders app. 3-Spider-Man 2099, Rawhide Kid, Two-Gun Kid & Kid Colt app. 4-Painted-c 4.00

THOR: DOUBLE TROUBLE (All ages)
Marvel Comics: May, 2021 - No. 4, Sept, 2021 ($3.99, limited series)

1-4-Tamaki-s/Gurihiru-a; Thor, Loki, Jane Thor and Lady Loki app. 4.00

THOR: FIRST THUNDER
Marvel Comics: Nov, 2010 - No. 5, Mar, 2011 ($3.99, limited series)

1-5: 1-Huat-a; new retelling of origin; reprint of debut in JIM #83 4.00

THOR: FOR ASGARD
Marvel Comics: Nov, 2010 - No. 6, Apr, 2011 ($3.99, limited series)

1-6-Bianchi-a/c. 1-Frost Giants app. 4.00

THOR: GOD OF THUNDER (Marvel NOW!)
Marvel Comics: Jan, 2013 - No. 25, Nov, 2014 ($3.99)

	GD 2.0	VG 4.0	FN 6.0	VF 8.0	VF/NM 9.0	NM- 9.2
1-Aaron-s/Ribic-a thru #5	2	4	6	11	16	20
2-1st Gorr the God Butcher	5	10	15	34	60	85
3-2nd app. Gorr	2	4	6	9	12	15
4-Gorr app.	2	4	6	11	16	20
5-Origin Gorr	4	8	12	23	37	50
6-(3/13) 1st Knull app. in cameo (unnamed)(see Venom #3 [6/18] for 1st full app.)	6	12	18	37	69	100

7,9-24: 6-Guice-a. 13-17-Malekith app. 19-23-Galactus app. 21-1st app. S.H.I.E.L.D. Agent Roz Solomon 4.00

	GD 2.0	VG 4.0	FN 6.0	VF 8.0	VF/NM 9.0	NM- 9.2
8-1st Goddesses of Thunder	3	6	9	16	23	30

25-($4.99) Art by Guera, Bisley, and Ribic; Malekith app.; new female Thor cameo 5.00

THOR: GODSTORM
Marvel Comics: Nov, 2001 - No. 3, Jan, 2002 ($3.50, limited series)

1-3-Steve Rude-c/a; Busiek-s. 1-Avengers app. 4.00

THOR: HEAVEN & EARTH
Marvel Comics: Sept, 2011 - No. 4, Nov, 2011 ($2.99, limited series)

1-4: 1-Jenkins-s/Olivetti-a/c; Loki app. 2-Texeira-a/c. 3-Alixe-a. 4-Medina-a 3.00

THORION OF THE NEW ASGODS
Marvel Comics (Amalgam): June, 1997 ($1.95, one-shot)

1-Keith Giffen-s/John Romita Jr.-c/a 4.00

THORS (Secret Wars Battleworld tie-in)
Marvel Comics: Aug, 2015 - No. 4, Jan, 2016 ($3.99, limited series)

1-4: Police squad of Thors on Doomworld; Aaron-s/Sprouse-a. 2,3-Sudzuka-a 4.00

THOR: SON OF ASGARD
Marvel Comics: May, 2004 - No. 12, Mar, 2005 ($2.99, limited series)

1-12: Teenaged Thor, Sif, and Balder; Tocchini-a. 1-6-Granov-c. 7-12-Jo Chen-c 3.00
... Vol. 1: The Warriors Teen (2004, $7.99, digest) r/#1-6 8.00
... Vol. 2: Worthy (2005, $7.99, digest) r/#7-12 8.00

THOR: TALES OF ASGARD BY STAN LEE & JACK KIRBY
Marvel Comics: 2009 - No. 6, 2009 ($3.99, limited series)

1-6-Reprints back-up stories from Journey Into Mystery #97-120; new covers by Coipel 4.00

THOR: THE DEVIANTS SAGA
Marvel Comics: Jan, 2012 - No. 5, May, 2012 ($3.99, limited series)

1-5-Rodi-s/Segovia-a; Ereshkigal app. 4.00

THOR: THE DARK WORLD PRELUDE (MARVEL'S...)
Marvel Comics: Aug, 2013 - No. 2, Aug, 2013 ($2.99, limited series)

1,2-Prelude to 2013 movie; Eaton-a; photo-c 3.00

THOR: THE LEGEND
Marvel Comics: Sept, 1996 ($3.95, one-shot)

nn-Tribute issue 4.00

THOR THE MIGHTY AVENGER
Marvel Comics: Sept, 2010 - No. 8, Mar, 2011 ($2.99, limited series)

1-8-Re-imagining of Thor's origin; Langridge-s/Samnee-a. 1-Mr. Hyde app. 3.00
Free Comic Book Day 2011 (giveaway) Captain America app. 3.00

THOR: VIKINGS
Marvel Comics (MAX): Sept, 2003 - No. 5, Jan, 2004 ($3.50, limited series)

1-5-Garth Ennis-s/Glenn Fabry-a/c 3.50
TPB (2004, $13.99) r/series 14.00

THOSE MAGNIFICENT MEN IN THEIR FLYING MACHINES (See Movie Comics)

THREE
Image Comics: Oct, 2013 - No. 5, Feb, 2014 ($2.99)

1-5-Spartans 100 years after the Battle of Thermopylae; Ryan Kelly-a/Kieron Gillen-s 3.00

THREE CABALLEROS (Walt Disney's...)
Dell Publishing Co.: No. 71, 1945

	GD 2.0	VG 4.0	FN 6.0	VF 8.0	VF/NM 9.0	NM- 9.2
Four Color 71-by Walt Kelly, c/a	69	138	207	552	1251	1950

THREE CHIPMUNKS, THE (TV) (Also see Alvin)
Dell Publishing Co.: No. 1042, Oct-Dec, 1959

	GD 2.0	VG 4.0	FN 6.0	VF 8.0	VF/NM 9.0	NM- 9.2
Four Color 1042 (#1)-(Alvin, Simon & Theodore)	10	20	30	66	138	210

THREE COMICS (Also see Spiritman)
The Penny King Co.: 1944 (10¢, 52 pgs.) (2 different covers exist)

	GD 2.0	VG 4.0	FN 6.0	VF 8.0	VF/NM 9.0	NM- 9.2
1,3,4-Lady Luck, Mr. Mystic, The Spirit app. (3 Spirit sections bound together); Lou Fine-a (Rare)	39	78	117	231	378	525

NOTE: *No. 1 contains Spirit Sections 4/9/44 - 4/23/44, and No. 4 is also from 4/44.*

3-D (NOTE: The prices of all the 3-D comics listed include glasses. Deduct 40-50 percent if glasses are missing, and reduce slightly if glasses are loose.)

3-D ACTION
Atlas Comics (ACI): Jan, 1954 (Oversized, 15¢)(2 pairs of glasses included)

	GD 2.0	VG 4.0	FN 6.0	VF 8.0	VF/NM 9.0	NM- 9.2
1-Battle Brady; Sol Brodsky-c	61	122	183	390	670	950

3-D ALIEN TERROR
Eclipse Comics: June, 1986 ($2.50)

	GD 2.0	VG 4.0	FN 6.0	VF 8.0	VF/NM 9.0	NM- 9.2
1-Old Witch, Crypt-Keeper, Vault Keeper cameo; Morrow, John Pound-a, Yeates-c	1	2	3	5	6	8
...in 2-D: 100 copies signed, numbered(B&W)	3	6	9	15	22	28

Thor: God of Thunder #5 © MAR

3 Geeks: Slab Madness #1 © Rich Koslowski

300 #1 © Miller & Varley

GD VG FN VF VF/NM NM-
2.0 4.0 6.0 8.0 9.0 9.2

3-D ANIMAL FUN (See Animal Fun)

3-D BATMAN (Also see Batman 3-D)
National Periodical Publications: 1953 (Reprinted in 1966)
1953-(25¢)-Reprints Batman #42 & 48 (Penguin-c/story); Tommy Tomorrow story; came with pair of 3-D Bat glasses 119 238 357 762 1306 1850
1966-Reprints 1953 issue; new cover by Infantino/Anderson; has inside-c photos of Batman & Robin from TV show (50¢) 22 44 66 154 340 525

3-D CIRCUS
Fiction House Magazines (Real Adventures Publ.): 1953 (25¢, w/glasses)
1 31 62 93 184 300 415

3-D COMICS (See Mighty Mouse, Tor and Western Fighters)

3-D DOLLY
Harvey Publications: December, 1953 (25¢, came with 2 pairs of glasses)
1-Richie Rich story redrawn from his 1st app. in Little Dot #1; shows cover in 3-D on inside 27 54 81 158 259 360

3-D-ELL
Dell Publishing Co.: No. 1, 1953; No. 3, 1953 (3-D comics) (25¢, came w/glasses)
1-Rootie Kazootie (#2 does not exist) 26 52 78 154 252 350
3-Flukey Luke 24 48 72 142 234 325

3 DEVILS
IDW Publishing: Mar, 2016 - No. 4, Jun, 2016 ($3.99, limited series)
1-4-Bo Hampton-s/a/c 4.00

3-D EXOTIC BEAUTIES
The 3-D Zone: Nov, 1990 ($2.95, 28 pgs.)
1-L.B. Cole-c 3 6 9 14 19 24

3-D FEATURES PRESENTS JET PUP
Dimensions Publications: Oct-Dec (Winter on-c), 1953 (25¢, came w/glasses)
1-Irving Spector-a(2) 32 64 96 188 307 425

3-D FUNNY MOVIES
Comic Media: 1953 (25¢, came w/glasses)
1-Bugsey Bear & Paddy Pelican 36 72 108 211 343 475

THREE-DIMENSION ADVENTURES (Superman)
National Periodical Publications: 1953 (25¢, large size, came w/glasses)
nn-Origin Superman (new art) 110 220 330 704 1202 1700
Reprint (1997) Regular size, bagged with glasses 1 2 3 5 6 8

THREE DIMENSIONAL ALIEN WORLDS (See Alien Worlds)
Pacific Comics: July, 1984 (1st Ray Zone 3-D book)(one-shot)
1-Bolton-a(p); Stevens-a(i); Art Adams 1st published-a(p) 1 3 4 6 8 10

THREE DIMENSIONAL DNAGENTS (See New DNAgents)

THREE DIMENSIONAL E. C. CLASSICS (Three Dimensional Tales From the Crypt No. 2)
E. C. Comics: Spring, 1954 (Prices include glasses; came with 2 pair)
1-Stories by Wood (Mad #3), Krigstein (W.S. #7), Evans (F.C. #13), & Ingels (CSS #5); Kurtzman-c (rare in high grade due to unstable paper) 129 258 387 826 1413 2000
NOTE: *Stories redrawn to 3-D format. Original stories not necessarily by artists listed. CSS: Crime SuspenStories; F.C.: Frontline Combat; W.S.: Weird Science.*

THREE DIMENSIONAL TALES FROM THE CRYPT (Formerly Three Dimensional E. C. Classics)(Cover title: ...From the Crypt of Terror)
E. C. Comics: No. 2, Spring, 1954 (Prices include glasses; came with 2 pair)
2-Davis (TFTC #25), Elder (VOH #14), Craig (TFTC #24), & Orlando (TFTC #22) stories; Feldstein-c (rare in high grade) 119 238 357 762 1306 1850
NOTE: *Stories redrawn to 3-D format. Original stories not necessarily by artists listed. TFTC: Tales From the Crypt; VOH: Vault of Horror.*

3-D LOVE
Steriographic Publ. (Mikeross Publ.): Dec, 1953 (25¢, came w/glasses)
1 40 80 120 246 411 575

3-D NOODNICK (See Noodnick)

3-D ROMANCE
Steriographic Publ. (Mikeross Publ.): Jan, 1954 (25¢, came w/glasses)
1 37 74 111 222 361 500

3-D SHEENA, JUNGLE QUEEN (Also see Sheena 3-D)
Fiction House Magazines: 1953 (25¢, came w/glasses)
1-Maurice Whitman-c 77 154 231 493 847 1200

GD VG FN VF VF/NM NM-
2.0 4.0 6.0 8.0 9.0 9.2

3-D SUBSTANCE
The 3-D Zone: July, 1990 ($2.95, 28 pgs.)
1-Ditko-c/a(r) 5.00

3-D TALES OF THE WEST
Atlas Comics (CPS): Jan, 1954 (Oversized) (15¢, came with 2 pair of glasses)
1 (3-D)-Sol Brodsky-c 52 104 156 328 552 775

3-D THREE STOOGES (Also see Three Stooges)
Eclipse Comics: Sept, 1986 - No. 2, Nov, 1986; No. 3, Oct, 1987; No. 4, 1989 ($2.50)
1-4: 3-Maurer-r. 4-r-/"Three Missing Links" 5.00
1-3 (2-D) 5.00

3-D WHACK (See Whack)

3-D ZONE, THE
The 3-D Zone (Renegade Press)/Ray Zone: Feb, 1987 - No. 20, 1989 ($2.50)
1,3,4,7-9,11,12,14,15,17,19,20: 1-r/A Star Presentation. 3-Picture Scope Jungle Advs. 4-Electric Fear. 7-Hollywood 3-D Jayne Mansfield photo-c. 8-High Seas 3-D, 9-Redmask-r. 11-Danse Macabre; Matt Fox c/a(r). 12-3-D Presidents. 14-Tyranostar. 15-3-Dementia Comics; Kurtzman-c, Kubert, Maurer-a. 17-Thrilling Love. 19-Cracked Classics. 20-Commander Battle and His Atomic Submarine 1 3 4 6 8 10
2,5,6,10,13,18: 2-Wolverton-r. 5-Krazy Kat-r. 6-Ratfink. 10-Jet 3-D; Powell & Williamson-r. 13-Flash Gordon. 18-Spacehawk; Wolverton-r 2 4 6 8 10 12
16-Space Vixens; Dave Stevens-c/a 5 10 15 34 60 85
NOTE: ***Davis*** *r-19.* ***Ditko*** *r-19.* ***Elder*** *r-19.* ***Everett*** *r-19.* ***Feldstein*** *r-17.* ***Frazetta*** *r-17.* ***Heath*** *r-19.* ***Kamen*** *r-17.* ***Severin*** *r-19.* ***Ward*** *r-17,19.* ***Wolverton*** *r-2,18,19.* ***Wood*** *r-1,17. Photo c-12*

3 GEEKS, THE (Also see Geeksville)
3 Finger Prints: 1996 - No. 11, Jun, 1999 (B&W)
1,2 -Rich Koslowski-s/a in all 1 2 3 5 6 8
1-(2nd printing) 3.00
3-7, 9-11 3.00
8-(48 pgs.) 4.00
10-Variant-c 3.50
...48 Page Super-Sized Summer Spectacular (7/04, $4.95) 5.00
...Full Circle (7/03, $4.95) Origin story of the 3 Geeks; "Buck Rodinski" app. 5.00
How to Pick Up Girls If You're a Comic Book Geek (color)(7/97) 4.00
When the Hammer Fallls TPB (2001, $14.95) r/#8-11 15.00

3 GEEKS: SLAB MADNESS!
3 Finger Prints: Sept, 2008 - No. 3, Mar, 2009 ($2.99, B&W, limited series)
1-3-Rich Koslowski-s/a; intro. The Cee-Gee-Cee 3.00

3 GUNS
BOOM! Studios: Aug, 2013 - No. 6, Jan, 2014 ($3.99)
1-6-Steven Grant-s/Emilio Laiso-a 4.00

300 (Adapted for 2007 movie)
Dark Horse Comics: May, 1998 - No. 5, Sept, 1998 ($2.95/$3.95, limited series)
1-Frank Miller-s/c/a; Spartans vs. Persians war 3 6 9 18 28 38
1-Second printing 5.00
2-4 2 4 6 8 10 12
5-($3.95-c) 2 4 6 8 10 12
HC ($30.00) -oversized reprint of series 30.00

3 LITTLE KITTENS
BroadSword Comics: Aug, 2002 - No. 3, Dec, 2002 ($2.95, limited series)
1-3-Jim Balent-s/a; two covers 3.00

3 LITTLE PIGS (Disney)(...and the Wonderful Magic Lamp)
Dell Publishing Co.: No. 218, Mar, 1949
Four Color 218 (#1) 11 22 33 78 163 250

3 LITTLE PIGS, THE (See Walt Disney Showcase #15 & 21)
Gold Key: May, 1964; No. 2, Sept, 1968 (Walt Disney)
1-Reprints Four Color #218 3 6 9 19 30 40
2 3 6 9 15 21 26

THREE MOUSEKETEERS, THE (1st Series)(See Funny Stuff #1)
National Per. Publ.: 3-4/56 - No. 24, 9-10/59; No. 25, 8-9/60 - No. 26, 10-12/60
1 24 48 72 168 372 575
2 11 22 33 73 157 240
3-5,7,9,10 8 16 24 56 108 160
6,8-Grey tone-c 10 20 30 66 138 210
11-26: 24-Cover says 11/59, inside says 9-10/59 7 14 21 49 92 135
NOTE: ***Rube Grossman*** *a-1-26.* ***Sheldon Mayer*** *a-1-8; c-1-7.*

THREE MOUSEKETEERS, THE (2nd Series) (See Super DC Giant)
National Periodical Publications: May-June, 1970 - No. 7, May-June, 1971 (#5-7: 68 pgs.)

GD VG FN VF VF/NM NM-
2.0 4.0 6.0 8.0 9.0 9.2

1-Mayer-r in all 6 12 18 40 73 105
2-4: 4-Doodles Duck begins (1st app.) 4 8 12 25 40 55
5-7:(68 pgs.). 5-Dodo & the Frog, Bo Bunny begin 5 10 15 31 53 75

THREE MUSKETEERS, THE (Also see Disney's The Three Musketeers)
Gemstone Publishing: 2004 ($3.95, squarebound, one-shot)

nn-Adaptation of the 2004 DVD movie; Petrossi-c/a 4.00

THREE NURSES (Confidential Diary #12-17; Career Girl Romances #24 on)
Charlton Comics: V3#18, May, 1963 - V3#23, Mar, 1964

V3#18-23 4 8 12 28 47 65

THREE RASCALS
I. W. Enterprises: 1958; 1963

I.W. Reprint #1,2,10: 1-(Says Super Comics on inside)-(M.E.'s Clubhouse Rascals) DeCarlo-a.
#2-(1958). 10-(1963)-r/#1 2 4 6 10 14 18

THREE RING COMICS
Spotlight Publishers: March, 1945

1-Funny animal 22 44 66 132 216 300

THREE RING COMICS (Also see Captain Wizard & Meteor Comics)
Century Publications: April, 1946

1-Prankster-c; Captain Wizard, Impossible Man, Race Wilkins, King O'Leary, & Dr. Mercy app.
43 86 129 271 461 650

THREE ROCKETEERS (See Blast-Off)

THREE STOOGES (See Comic Album #18, Top Comics, The Little Stooges, March of Comics #232, 248, 268, 280, 292, 304, 316, 336, 373, Movie Classics & Comics & 3-D Three Stooges)

THREE STOOGES
Jubilee No. 1/St. John No. 1 (9/53) on: Feb, 1949 - No. 2, May, 1949; Sept, 1953 - No. 7, Oct, 1954

1-(Scarce, 1949)-Kubert-a; infinity-c 194 388 582 1242 2121 3000
2-(Scarce)-Kubert, Maurer-a 113 226 339 718 1234 1750
1(9/53)-Hollywood Stunt Girl by Kubert (7 pgs.) 97 194 291 621 1061 1500
2(3-D, 10/53, 25¢)-Came w/glasses; Stunt Girl story by Kubert
48 96 144 302 514 725
3(3-D, 10/53, 25¢)-Came w/glasses; has 3-D-c 43 86 129 271 461 650
4(3/54)-7(10/54): 4-1st app. Li'l Stooge? 43 86 129 271 461 650
NOTE: *All issues have **Kubert-Maurer** art & **Maurer** covers. 6, 7-Partial photo-c.*

THREE STOOGES
Dell Publishing Co./Gold Key No. 10 (10/62) on: No. 1043, Oct-Dec, 1959 - No. 55, June, 1972

Four Color 1043 (#1) 23 46 69 161 356 550
Four Color 1078,1127,1170,1187 11 22 33 76 163 250
6(9-11/61) - 10: 6-Professor Putter begins; ends #16
9 18 27 58 114 170
11-14,16,18-20 7 14 21 48 89 130
15-Go Around the World in a Daze (movie scenes) 8 16 24 51 96 140
17-The Little Monsters begin (5/64)(1st app.?) 8 16 24 51 96 140
21,23-30 6 12 18 38 69 100
22-Movie scenes from "The Outlaws Is Coming" 6 12 18 41 76 110
31-55 5 10 15 31 53 75
NOTE: *All Four Colors, 6-50, 52-55 have photo-c.*

THREE STOOGES IN 3-D, THE
Eternity Comics: 1991 ($3.95, high quality paper, w/glasses)

1-Reprints Three Stooges by Gold Key; photo-c 5.00

THREE STOOGES
American Mythology Prods.: 2016 - Present (series of one-shots)

...: April Fools' Day Special (2017, $3.99) Check-s/Fraim brothers-a; 5 covers 4.00
...: Astro-Nuts 1 (2019, $3.99, B&W) Check-s/Fraim brothers-a; reprint from FC #1078 4.00
...: Curly Celebration 1 (2022, $3.99) Check-s/Fraim brothers-a; Kuhoric-s 4.00
...: Curse of the Frankenstooge (2016, $4.99) New stories and reprint from #24; 5 covers 5.00
...: Dell 1959 Edition 1 (2019, $3.99) Reprints Four Color #1043 from 1959 4.00
...: Halloween Hullabaloo (2016, giveaway) New stories by various; Ropp-c 3.00
...: Halloween Stoogetacular (2017, $3.99) Check-s/Fraim brothers-a; 4 covers 4.00
...: Jubilee Reprint (2022, $3.99) Reprints #1 from 1949; Mauer-s/a 4.00
...: Matinee Madness (2018, $3.99, B&W) New stories; Wolfer-s/Shanover-a 4.00
...: Merry Stoogemas (2016, $3.99) New stories and reprint from #7; 5 covers 4.00
...: Monsters & Mayhem (2018, $3.99, B&W) Check-s/Fraim brothers-a; reprint from #2 4.00
...: Red, White, & Stooge (2016, $3.99) New story and reprint from #44; 4 covers 4.00
...: Shemptastic Shemptacular (2018, $3.99) New story and reprint from #1; 4 covers 4.00
...: Slaptastic Special (2018, $3.99) Check-s/Fraim brothers-a; reprint from #7 4.00
...: Stooge-A-Palooza 1 (2016, $4.99) New stories and reprint from FC #1170; 3 covers 5.00
...: The Boys are Back (2016, $3.99) New stories and reprint from FC #1170; 4 covers 4.00
...: Thru the Ages (2021, $3.99) Check-s/Fraim brothers-a; 2 covers 4.00
...: TV Time Special (2017, $3.99) Check-s/Fraim brothers-a; 4 covers 4.00

3 WORLDS OF GULLIVER
Dell Publishing Co.: No. 1158, July, 1961 (2 issues exist with diff. covers)

Four Color 1158-Movie, photo-c 6 12 18 42 79 115

THRESHOLD
DC Comics: Mar, 2013 - No. 8 ($3.99)

1-8-Anthology. 1-5-Back-up Larfleeze stories. 5,6-Brainiac app. 4.00

THRILL COMICS (See Flash Comics, Fawcett)

THRILLER
DC Comics: Nov, 1983 - No. 12, Nov, 1984 ($1.25, Baxter paper)

1-12: 1-Intro Seven Seconds; Von Eeden-c/a begins. 2-Origin. 5,6-Elvis satire 4.00

THRILLING ADVENTURE HOUR, THE
BOOM! Studios: Jul, 2018 - No. 4, Oct, 2018 ($3.99, limited series)

1-4-Acker & Blacker-s/Erickson-a/Case-c 4.00

THRILLING ADVENTURE HOUR PRESENTS:...
Image Comics: ($3.50)

... Beyond Belief 1-3 (4/15 - No. 3, 3/16) Acker & Blacker-s/Hester-a 3.50
... Sparks Nevada: Marshal on Mars 1-4 (2/15 - No. 4, 7/15) Acker & Blacker-s/Bone-a 3.50

THRILLING ADVENTURES IN STAMPS COMICS (Formerly Stamp Comics)
Stamp Comics, Inc. (Very Rare): V1#8, Jan, 1953 (25¢, 100 pgs.)

V1#8-Harrison, Wildey, Kiefer, Napoli-a 90 180 270 576 988 1400

THRILLING ADVENTURE STORIES (See Tigerman)
Atlas/Seaboard Publ.: Feb, 1975 - No. 2, Aug, 1975 (B&W, 68 pgs.)

1-Tigerman, Kromag the Killer begin; Heath, Thorne-a; Doc Savage movie photos of Ron Ely 3 6 9 21 33 45
2-Heath, Toth, Severin, Simonson-a; Adams-c 4 8 12 25 40 55

THRILLING COMICS
Better Publ./Nedor/Standard Comics: Feb, 1940 - No. 80, April, 1951

1-Origin & 1st app. Dr. Strange (37 pgs.), ends #?; Nickie Norton of the Secret Service begins 423 846 1269 3046 5323 7600
2-The Rio Kid, The Woman in Red, Pinocchio begins
258 516 774 1651 2826 4000
3-The Ghost & Lone Eagle begin 206 412 618 1318 2259 3200
4-6,8,9: 5-Dr. Strange changed to Doc Strange 181 362 543 1158 1979 2800
7-Classic-c 454 908 1362 3314 5857 8400
10-1st WWII-c (Nazi)(11/40) 194 388 582 1242 2121 3000
11-18,20: 17-WWII-Nazi-c 181 362 543 1158 1979 2800
19-Origin & 1st app. The American Crusader (8/41), ends #39,41; Schomburg Nazi WWII-c
239 478 717 1530 2615 3700
21-26,28-30: 24-Intro. Mike, Doc Strange's sidekick (1/42). 29-Last Rio Kid
135 270 405 864 1482 2100
27-Robot-c 168 336 504 1075 1838 2600
31-35,37,39,40: 39-Nazi WWII-c. 40-Japan WWII-c 119 238 357 762 1306 1850
36-Commando Cubs begin (7/43, 1st app.) 129 285 387 826 1413 2000
38-Classic Nazi bondage-c 300 600 900 1920 3310 4700
41-Classic Hitler & Mussolini WWII-c 649 1298 1947 4738 8369 12,000
42-Classic Schomburg Japanese WWII-c 174 348 522 1114 1907 2700
43,46-51: 51(12/45)-Last WWII-c (Japanese) 103 206 309 659 1130 1600
44-Hitler WWII-c by Schomburg 420 840 1260 2940 5170 7400
45-Hitler pict. on-c 142 284 426 909 1555 2200
52-Classic Schomburg hooded bondage-c; the Ghost ends
113 226 339 718 1234 1750
53,54: 53-The Phantom Detective begins. The Cavalier app. in both; no Commando Cubs in either 71 142 213 454 777 1100
55-The Lone Eagle ends 54 108 162 343 574 825
56 (10/46)-Princess Pantha begins (not on-c), 1st app.
74 148 222 470 810 1150
57-Doc Strange-c; 2nd Princess Pantha 60 120 180 381 653 925
58-66: All Princess Pantha jungle-c, w/Doc Strange #59, his last-c. 61-Ingels-a; The Lone Eagle app. 65-Last Phantom Detective & Commando Cubs. 66-Frazetta text illo
58 116 174 371 636 900
67,70,71-Last jungle-c; Frazetta-a(5-7 pgs.) in each 65 130 195 416 708 1000
68,69-Frazetta-a(2), 8 & 6 pgs.; 9 & 7 pgs. 71 142 213 454 777 1100
72,73: 72-Buck Ranger, Cowboy Detective c/stys begin (western theme), end #80; Frazetta-a(5-7 ps.) in each 47 94 141 296 498 700
74-Last Princess Pantha; Tara app. 35 70 105 208 339 470
75-78: 75-All western format begins 20 40 60 117 189 260
79-Krigstein-a 20 40 60 120 195 270
80-Severin & Elder, Celardo, Moreira-a 20 40 60 120 195 270
NOTE: *Bondage c-5, 9, 13, 20, 22, 27-30, 38, 41, 52, 54, 70. **Kinstler** a-45. **Leo Morey** a-7. **Schomburg** (sometimes signed as **Xela**) c-7, 9-19, 36-80 (airbrush 62-71). **Tuska** a-62, 63. Woman in Red not in #19, 23, 31-33, 39-45. No. 45 exists as a Canadian reprint but numbered #48. No. 72 exists as a Canadian reprint with no **Frazetta** story. American Crusader c-20-24. Buck Ranger c-72-80. Commando Cubs c-37, 39, 41, 43, 45, 47, 49, 51. Doc Strange c-1-19, 25-36, 38, 40, 42, 44, 46, 48, 50, 52-57, 59. Princess Pantha c-58, 60-71.*

THRILLING COMICS (Also see All Star Comics 1999 crossover titles)
DC Comics: May, 1999 ($1.99, one-shot)

1-Golden Age Hawkman and Wildcat; Russ Heath-a 3.00

THRILLING CRIME CASES (Formerly 4Most; becomes Shocking Mystery Cases #50 on)
Star Publications: No. 41, June-July, 1950 - No. 49, July, 1952

41 43 86 129 271 461 650
42-45: 42-L. B. Cole-c/a (1); Chameleon story (Fox-r)
39 78 117 231 378 525
46-48: 47-Used in **POP**, pg. 84 37 74 111 222 361 500
49-(7/52)-Classic L. B. Cole-c 365 730 1095 2555 4478 6400
NOTE: ***L. B. Cole** c-all; a-43p, 45p, 46p, 49(2 pgs.). **Disbrow** a-48. **Hollingsworth** a-48.*

THRILLING ROMANCES
Standard Comics: No. 5, Dec, 1949 - No. 26, June, 1954

5 27 54 81 158 259 360
6,8 16 32 48 94 147 200
7-Severin/Elder-a (7 pgs.) 18 36 54 105 165 225
9,10-Severin/Elder-a; photo-c 17 34 51 100 158 215
11,14-21,26: 14-Gene Tierney & Danny Kaye photo-c from movie "On the Riviera". 15-Tony Martin/Janet Leigh photo-c 15 30 45 86 133 180
12-Wood-a (2 pgs.); Tyrone Power/ Susan Hayward photo-c
19 38 57 111 176 240
13-Severin-a 15 30 45 90 140 190
22-25-Toth-a 17 34 51 98 154 210
NOTE: *All photo-c. **Celardo** a-9, 16. **Colletta** a-23, 24(2). **Toth** text illos-19. **Tuska** a-9.*

THRILLING SCIENCE TALES
AC Comics: 1989 - No. 2 ($3.50, 2/3 color, 52 pgs.)

1,2: 1-r/Bob Colt #6(saucer); Frazetta, Guardineer (Space Ace), Wood, Krenkel, Orlando, Williamson-r; Kaluta-c. 2-Capt. Video-r by Evans, Capt. Science-r by Wood, Star Pirate-r by Whitman & Mysta of the Moon-r by Moreira 4.00

THRILLING TRUE STORY OF THE BASEBALL...
Fawcett Publications: 1952 (Photo-c, each)

...Giants-photo-c; has Willie Mays rookie photo-biography; Willie Mays, Eddie Stanky & others photos on-c 69 138 207 442 759 1075
...Yankees-photo-c; Yogi Berra, Joe DiMaggio, Mickey Mantle & others photos on-c
71 142 213 454 777 1100

THRILLING WONDER TALES
AC Comics : 1991 ($2.95, B&W)

Threshold #1 © DC

T.H.U.N.D.E.R. Agents (2013) #2 © Radiant

Thunderbolts #119 © MAR

GD 2.0 | VG 4.0 | FN 6.0 | VF 8.0 | VF/NM 9.0 | NM- 9.2

1-Includes a Bob Powell Thun'da story 4.00

THRILLKILLER
DC Comics : Jan, 1997 - No. 3, Mar, 1997($2.50, limited series)

1-3-Elseworlds Robin & Batgirl; Chaykin-s/Brereton-c/a 4.00
...'**62** ('98, $4.95, one-shot) Sequel; Chaykin-s/Brereton-c/a 5.00
TPB-(See Batman: Thrillkiller)

THRILLOGY
Pacific Comics: Jan, 1984 (One-shot, color)

1-Conrad-c/a 4.00

THRILL-O-RAMA
Harvey Publications (Fun Films): Oct, 1965 - No. 3, Dec, 1966

1-Fate (Man in Black) by Powell app.; Doug Wildey-a(2); Simon-c
5 10 15 31 53 75
2-Pirana begins (see Phantom #46); Williamson 2 pgs.; Fate (Man in Black) app.; Tuska/Simon-c 3 6 9 21 33 45
3-Fate (Man in Black) app.; Sparling-c 3 6 9 18 28 38

THRILLS OF TOMORROW (Formerly Tomb of Terror)
Harvey Publications: No. 17, Oct, 1954 - No. 20, April, 1955

17-Powell-a (horror); r/Witches Tales #7 32 64 96 188 307 425
18-Powell-a (horror); r/Tomb of Terror #1 17 34 51 98 154 210
19,20-Stuntman-c/stories by S&K (r/from Stuntman #1 & 2); 19 has origin & is last pre-code (2/55) 36 72 108 211 343 475
NOTE: *Kirby c-19, 20. Palais a-17. Simon c-18?*

THROBBING LOVE (See Fox Giants)

THROUGH GATES OF SPLENDOR
Spire Christian Comics (Flemming H. Revell Co.): 1973, 1974 (36 pages) (39-49 cents)

nn-1973 Edition 3 6 9 14 19 24
nn-1974 Edition 2 4 6 9 13 16

THULSA DOOM (Robert E. Howard character)
Dynamite Entertainment: 2009 - No. 4, 2009 ($3.50, limited series)

1-4-Alex Ross-c/Lui Antonio-a 3.50

THUMPER (Disney)
Dell Publishing Co.: No, 19, 1942 - No. 243, Sept, 1949

Four Color 19-Walt Disney's...Meets the Seven Dwarfs; reprinted in Silly Symphonies
50 100 150 400 900 1400
Four Color 243-...Follows His Nose 13 26 39 89 195 300

THUN'DA (...King of the Congo)
Magazine Enterprises: 1952 - No. 6, 1953

1(A-1 #47)-Origin; Frazetta c/a; only comic done entirely by Frazetta; all Thun'da stories, no Cave Girl 295 590 885 1888 3244 4600
2(A-1 #56)-Powell-c/a begins, ends #6; Intro/1st app. Cave Girl in filler strip (also app. in 3-6)
37 74 111 222 361 500
3(A-1 #73), 4(A-1 #78) 27 54 81 158 254 360
5(A-1 #83), 6(A-1 #86) 27 54 81 162 266 370

THUN'DA
Dynamite Entertainment: 2012 - No. 5, 2012 ($3.99, limited series)

1-5-Napton-s/Richards-a/Jae Lee-c. 1-4-Bonus reprints of Thun'da #1 (1952) Frazetta-a 4.00

THUN'DA TALES (See Frank Frazetta's...)

THUNDER AGENTS (See Dynamo, Noman & Tales Of Thunder)
Tower Comics: 11/65 - No. 17, 12/67; No. 18, 9/68, No. 19, 11/68, No. 20, 11/69 (No. 1-16: 68 pgs.; No. 17 on: 52 pgs.)(All are 25¢)

1-Origin & 1st app. Dynamo, Noman, Menthor, & The Thunder Squad; 1st app. The Iron Maiden 19 38 57 133 297 460
2-Death of Egghead; A-bomb blast panel 9 18 27 63 129 195
3-5: 4-Guy Gilbert becomes Lightning who joins Thunder Squad; Iron Maiden app.
7 14 21 49 92 135
6-10: 7-Death of Menthor. 8-Origin & 1st app. The Raven
6 12 18 38 69 100
11-15: 13-Undersea Agent app.; no Raven story 5 10 15 35 63 90
16-19 5 10 15 34 60 85
20-Special Collectors Edition; all reprints 4 8 12 27 44 60
...Archives Vol. 1 (DC Comics, 2003, $49.95, HC) r/#1-4, restored and recolored 50.00
...Archives Vol. 2 (DC Comics, 2003, $49.95, HC) r/#5-7, Dynamo #1 50.00
...Archives Vol. 3 (DC Comics, 2003, $49.95, HC) r/#8-10, Dynamo #2 50.00
...Archives Vol. 4 (DC Comics, 2004, $49.95, HC) r/#11, Noman #1,2 & Dynamo #3 50.00
NOTE: *Crandall a-1, 4p, 5p, 18, 20r; c-18. Ditko a-6, 7p, 12p, 13?, 14p, 16, 18. Giunta a-6. Kane a-1, 5p, 6p?, 14, 16p; c-14, 15. Reinman a-13. Sekowsky a-6. Tuska a-1p, 7, 8, 10, 13-17, 19. Whitney a-9p, 10, 13, 15, 17, 18; c-17. Wood a-1-11, 15(w/Ditko-12, 18), (inks-#9, 13, 14, 16, 17), 19i, 20r; c-1-8, 9i, 10-13(#10 w/ Williamson(p)), 16.*

T.H.U.N.D.E.R. AGENTS (See Blue Ribbon Comics, Hall of Fame Featuring the..., JCP Features & Wally Wood's...)
JC Comics (Archie Publications): May, 1983 - No. 2, Jan, 1984

1,2: 1-New Manna/Blyberg-c/a. 2-Blyberg-c 6.00

T.H.U.N.D.E.R. AGENTS
DC Comics: Jan, 2011 - No. 10, Oct, 2011 ($3.99/$2.99)

1-3-($3.99): 1-Spencer-s/Cafu-a/Quitely-c. 3-Chaykin-a (5 pgs.) 4.00
4-10-($2.99): 4-Pérez-a (5 pgs.). 7-10-Grell & Dragotta-a 3.00
1-Variant-c by Darwyn Cooke 8.00

T.H.U.N.D.E.R. AGENTS
DC Comics: Jan, 2012 - No. 6, Jun, 2012 ($2.99, limited series)

1-6-Spencer-s/Craig-a. 1-Andy Kubert-c. 3-Craig & Simonson-a 3.00

T.H.U.N.D.E.R. AGENTS
IDW Publishing: Aug, 2013 - No. 8, Apr, 2014 ($3.99)

1-8: 1-4-Hester-s/Di Vito-a. 1-Four interlocking covers by Di Vito. 5-8-Roger Robinson-a 4.00

THUNDER BIRDS (See Cinema Comics Herald)

THUNDERBOLT (See The Atomic...)

THUNDERBOLT (Peter Cannon...; see Crisis on Infinite Earths, Peter Cannon, Captain Atom and Judomaster)
Charlton Comics: Jan, 1966; No. 51, Mar-Apr, 1966 - No. 60, Nov, 1967

1-Origin & 1st app. Thunderbolt 6 12 18 42 79 115
51-(Formerly Son of Vulcan #50) 3 6 9 21 33 45
52-Judomaster story 3 6 9 16 23 30
53-Captain Atom story, 2 pgs. 3 6 9 16 23 30
54-59: 54-Sentinels begin. 59-Last Thunderbolt & Sentinels (back-up story)
3 6 9 14 19 24
60-Prankster only app. 3 6 9 15 21 26
57,58 ('77)-Modern Comics-r 1 3 4 6 8 10
NOTE: *Aparo a-60. Morisi a-1, 51-56, 58; c-1, 51-56, 58, 59.*

THUNDERBOLT JAXON (Revival of 1940s British comics character)
DC Comics (WildStorm): Apr, 2006 - No. 5, Sept, 2006 ($2.99, limited series)

1-5-Dave Gibbons-s/John Higgins-a 3.00
TPB (2007, $19.99) r/#1-5; intro. by Gibbons; cover gallery 20.00

THUNDERBOLTS (Title re-named Dark Avengers with #175)(Also see New Thunderbolts and Incredible Hulk #449)
Marvel Comics: Apr, 1997 - No. 81, Sept, 2003; No. 100, May, 2006 - No. 174, Jul, 2012 ($1.95-$2.99)

1-($2.99)-Busiek-s/Bagley-c/a 2 4 6 10 14 18
1-2nd printing; new cover colors 3.00
2-4: 2-Two covers. 4-Intro. Jolt 6.00
5-11: 9-Avengers app. 3.50
12-($2.99)-Avengers and Fantastic Four-c/app. 4.00
13-24: 14-Thunderbolts return to Earth. 21-Hawkeye app. 3.00
25-($2.99) Wraparound-c 4.00
26-38: 26-Manco-a 3.00
39-($2.99) 100 Page Monster; Iron Man reprints 4.00
40-49: 40-Begin $2.25-c; Sandman-c/app. 44-Avengers app. 47-Captain Marvel app. 49-Zircher-a 3.00
50-($2.99) Last Bagley-a; Captain America becomes leader 4.00
51-74,76,77,80,81: 51,52-Zircher-a; Dr. Doom app. 80,81-Spider-Man app. 3.00
75-($3.50) Hawkeye leaves the team; Garcia-a 4.00
78,79-($2.99-c) Velasco-a begins 3.00
(See New Thunderbolts for #82-99)
100 (5/06, $3.99) resumes from New Thunderbolts #18; back-up origin stories 4.00
101-109: 103-105-Civil War x-over 3.00
110-New team begins including Bullseye, Venom and Norman Osborn; Ellis-s/Deodato-a 5.00
111-136,138-149: 111-121-Ellis-s/Deodato-a. 112-Stan Lee cameo. 123-125-Secret Invasion x-over. 128-Dark Reign begins. 130,131-X-over with Deadpool #8,9. 141-143-Siege 3.00
137-(12/09, $3.99) Iron Fist and Luke Cage app. 4.00
150-(1/11, $4.99) Thunderbolts vs. Avengers; r/#1; storyline synopses of #1-150 5.00
151-158,160-163, 163.1, 164-174-($2.99) 151-153-Land-c. 155-Satana joins. 158-162-Fear Itself tie-in. 163-165-Thunderbolts in WWII; Invaders app. 3.00
159-($4.99) Fear Itelf tie-in; Juggernaut app.; short stories of escape from The Raft 5.00
Annual '97 ($2.99)-Wraparound-c 4.00
Annual 2000 ($3.50) Breyfogle-a 4.00
...: Breaking Point (1/08, $2.99, one-shot) Gage-s/Denham-a/Djurdjevic-c 3.00
... By Warren Ellis Vol. 1 HC (2007, $24.99, dustjacket) r/#150-154, ...: Desperate Measures and stories from Civil War: Choosing Sides and The Initiative 25.00
... By Warren Ellis Vol. 1: Faith in Monsters SC (2008, $19.99) same contents as HC 20.00
Civil War: Thunderbolts TPB (2007, $13.99) r/#101-105 14.00

GD VG FN VF VF/NM NM-
2.0 4.0 6.0 8.0 9.0 9.2

...: Desperate Measures (9/07, $2.99, one-shot) Jenkins-s/Steve Lieber-a 3.00
...: Distant Rumblings (#-1) (7/97, $1.95) Busiek-s 5.00
First Strikes (1997, $4.99,TPB) r/#1,2 5.00
...: From the Marvel Vault (6/11, $3.99) Jack Monroe app.; Nicieza-s/Aucoin-a 4.00
...: Guardian Protocols (2007, $10.99) r/#106-109 11.00
...: International Incident (4/08, $2.99, one-shot) Gage-s/Oliver-a/Djurdjevic-c 3.00
...: Life Sentences (7/01, $3.50) Adlard-a 4.00
...: Marvel's Most Wanted TPB ('98, $16.99) r/origin stories of original Masters of Evil 17.00
...: Reason in Madness (7/08, $2.99, one-shot) Gage-s/Oliver-a/Djurdjevic-c 3.00
Wizard #0 (bagged with Wizard #89) 3.00

THUNDERBOLTS (Marvel NOW!)
Marvel Comics: Feb, 2013 - No. 32, Dec, 2014 ($2.99)

1-32: 1-Punisher, Red Hulk, Elektra, Venom & Deadpool team; Dillon-a. 7-11-Noto-a. 14-18-Infinity tie-ins; Soule-s/Palo-a. 20-Ghost Rider joins 3.00
Annual 1 (2/14, $4.99) Dr. Strange & Elsa Bloodstone app.; Lolli-a 5.00

THUNDERBOLTS
Marvel Comics: Jul, 2016 - No. 12, Jun, 2017 ($3.99)

1-9,11,12: 1-Bucky Barnes leads the team of Kobik, Atlas, Fixer, Moonstone, & Mach-X. 4-Squadron Supreme app. 5-Spider-Man (Miles) app. 11,12-Secret Empire tie-ins 4.00
10-($4.99) 20th Anniversary Special; prologue by Busiek-s/Bagley-a; Jolt returns 5.00

THUNDERBOLTS
Marvel Comics: Oct, 2022 - No. 5, Feb, 2023 ($4.99/$3.99)

1-($4.99) Jim Zub-s/Sean Izaaksa-a; Hawkeye, America Chavez, John Walker app. 5.00
2-5-($3.99) 2-Eegro the Unbreakable app. 4.00
...: Marvel Tales 1 (10/22, $7.99) r/Thunderbolts (1997) #1,2, Inc. Hulk #449 8.00

THUNDERBOLTS PRESENTS: ZEMO - BORN BETTER
Marvel Comics: Apr, 2007 - No. 4, July, 2007 ($2.99, limited series)

1-4-History of Baron Zemo; Nicieza-s/Grummett-a/c 3.00
TPB (2007, $10.99) r/#1-4 11.00

THUNDERBUNNY (See Blue Ribbon Comics #13, Charlton Bullseye & Pep Comics #393)
Red Circle Comics: Jan, 1984 (Direct sale only)
WaRP Graphics: Second series No. 1, 1985 - No. 6, 1985
Apple Comics: No. 7, 1986 - No. 12, 1987

1-Humor/parody; origin Thunderbunny; 2 page pin-up by Anderson 5.00
(2nd series) 1,2-Magazine size 4.00
3-12-Comic size 4.00

THUNDERCATS (TV)
Marvel Comics (Star Comics)/Marvel #22 on: Dec, 1985 - No. 24, June, 1988 (75¢)

1-Mooney-c/a begins 8 16 24 51 96 140
2-(65¢ & 75¢ cover exists) 2 4 6 11 16 20
3-20: 12-Begin $1.00-c. 18-20-Williamson-i 2 4 6 8 10 12
21-24: 23-Williamson-c(i) 2 4 6 8 11 14

THUNDERCATS (TV)
DC Comics (WildStorm): No. 0, Oct, 2002 - No. 5, Feb, 2003 ($2.50/$2.95, limited series)

0-($2.50) J. Scott Campbell-c/a 4.00
1-5-($2.95) 1-McGuinness-a/c; variant cover by Art Adams; rebirth of Mumm-Ra 4.00
.../ Battle of the Planets (7/03, $4.95) Kaare Andrews-s/a; 2 covers by Campbell & Ross 5.00
...: Origins-Heroes & Villains (2/04, $3.50) short stories by various 3.50
...Reclaiming Thundera TPB (2003, $12.95) r/#0-5 13.00
... Sourcebook (1/03, $2.95) pin-ups and info on characters; art by various; A. Adams-c 4.00

THUNDERCATS: DOGS OF WAR
DC Comics (WildStorm): Aug, 2003 - No. 5, Dec, 2003 ($2.95, limited series)

1-5: 1-Two covers by Booth & Pearson; Booth-a/Layman-s. 2-4-Two covers 3.00
TPB (2004, $14.95) r/#1-5 15.00

THUNDERCATS: ENEMY'S PRIDE
DC Comics (WildStorm): Aug, 2004 - No. 5 ($2.95, limited series)

1-5-Vriens-a/Layman-s 3.00
TPB (2005, $14.99) r/#1-5 15.00

THUNDERCATS: HAMMERHAND'S REVENGE
DC Comics (WildStorm): Dec, 2003 - No. 5, Apr, 2004 ($2.95, limited series)

1-5-Avery-s/D'Anda-a. 2-Variant-c by Warren 3.00
TPB (2004, $14.95) r/#1-5 15.00

THUNDERCATS: THE RETURN
DC Comics (WildStorm): Apr, 2003 - No. 5, Aug, 2003 ($2.95, limited series)

1-5: 1-Two covers by Benes & Cassaday; Gilmore-s 3.00
TPB (2004, $12.95) r/series 13.00

THUNDER MOUNTAIN (See Zane Grey, Four Color #246)

THUNDERSTRIKE (See Thor #459)
Marvel Comics: June, 1993 - No. 24, July, 1995 ($1.25)

1-($2.95, 52 pgs.)-Holo-grafx lightning patterned foil-c; Bloodaxe returns 4.00
2-24: 2-Juggernaut-c/s. 4-Capt. America app. 4-6-Spider-Man app. 8-bound-in trading card sheet. 18-Bloodaxe app. 24-Death of Thunderstrike 3.00
Marvel Double Feature...Thunderstrike/Code Blue #13 ($2.50)-Same as Thunderstrike #13 w/Code Blue flip book 4.00

THUNDERSTRIKE
Marvel Comics: Jan, 2011 - No. 5, Jun, 2011 ($3.99, limited series)

1-5-DeFalco-s/Frenz-a. 1-Back-up origin retold; Nauck-a 4.00

TICK, THE (Also see The Chroma-Tick)
New England Comics Press: Jun, 1988 - No. 12, May, 1993 ($1.75/$1.95/$2.25; B&W, over-sized)

Special Edition 1-1st comic book app. serially numbered & limited to 5,000 copies
12 24 36 80 173 265
Special Edition 1-(5/96, $5.95)-Double-c; foil-c; serially numbered (5,001 thru 14,000) & limited to 9,000 copies 3 6 9 16 23 30
Special Edition 2-Serially numbered and limited to 3000 copies
5 10 15 35 63 90
Special Edition 2-(8/96, $5.95)-Double-c; foil-c; serially numbered (5,001 thru 14,000) & limited to 9,000 copies 1 2 3 5 6 8
1-Regular Edition 1st printing; reprints Special Ed. 1 w/minor changes
6 12 18 42 79 115
1-2nd printing 6.00
1-3rd-5th printing 4.00
2-Reprints Special Ed. 2 w/minor changes 3 6 9 16 23 30
2-8-All reprints 4.00
3-5: 4-1st app. Paul the Samurai 2 4 6 8 10 12
6,8 ($2.25) 6.00
7-1st app. Man-Eating Cow 1 3 4 6 8 10
8-Variant with no logo, price, issue number or company logos.
3 6 9 16 24 32
9-12 ($2.75) 5.00
12-Special Edition; card-stock, virgin foil-c; numbered edition
3 6 9 14 19 24
100: The Tick Meets Invincible (6/12, $6.99) Invincible travels to Tick's universe 7.00
101: The Tick Meets Madman (11/12, $6.99) Bonus publishing history of the Tick 7.00
Pseudo-Tick #13 (11/00, $3.50) Continues story from #12 (1993) 5.00
Promo Sampler-(1990)-Tick-c/story 1 2 3 5 6 8

TICK, THE (One shots)

... Big Back to School Special 1-(10/98, $3.50, B&W) Tick & Arthur undercover in H.S. 4.00
... Big Cruise Ship Vacation Special 1-(9/00, $3.50, B&W) 4.00
... Big Father's Day Special 1-(6/00, $3.50, B&W) 4.00
... Big Halloween Special 1-(10/99, $3.50, B&W) 4.00
... Big Halloween Special 2000 (10/00, $3.50) 4.00
... Big Halloween Special 2001 (9/01, $3.95) 4.00
... Big Mother's Day Special 1-(4/00, $3.50, B&W) 4.00
... Big Red-N-Green Christmas Spectacle 1-(12/01, $3.95) 4.00
... Big Romantic Adventure 1-(2/98, $2.95, B&W) Candy box-c with candy map on back 4.00
... Big Summer Annual 1-(7/99, $3.50, B&W) Chainsaw Vigilante vs. Barry 4.00
... Big Summer Fun Special 1-(8/98, $3.50, B&W) Tick and Arthur at summer camp 4.00
... Big Tax Time Terror 1-(4/00, $3.50, B&W) 4.00
... Big Year 2000 Spectacle 1-(3/00, $3.50, B&W) 4.00
FCBD Special Edition (5/10) - reprints debut from 1988; Ben Edlund-s/a 3.00
Free Comic Book Day 2013 (6/13) - New stories; McClelland-s/Redhead-a 3.00
Free Comic Book Day 2014 (6/14) - New stories; McClelland-s/Redhead-a 3.00
Free Comic Book Day 2015 (6/15) - New stories; McClelland-s/Redhead-a 3.00
Free Comic Book Day 2016 (6/16) - New stories; McClelland-s/Redhead-a; Nichols-a 3.00
Free Comic Book Day 2017 (6/17) - New stories; McClelland-s/Redhead-a 3.00
Free Comic Book Day 2018 (6/18) - New stories; McClelland-s/Nichols-a 3.00
Free Comic Book Day 2019 (6/19) - New stories; Nichols-s/a 3.00
...: Halloween Comicfest 2017 (11/17, giveaway) r/#1 (1988) in color 3.00
... Incredible Internet Comic 1-(7/01, $3.95, color) r/New England Comics website story 4.00
Introducing the Tick 1-(4/02, $3.95, color) summary of Tick's life and adventures 4.00
The Tick's Back #0 -(8/97, $2.95, B&W) 4.00
The Tick's Comic Con Extravaganza -(6/07, $3.95, color) Wang-c 4.00
The Tick's 20th Anniversary Special Edition #1 (5/07, $5.95) short stories by various; history of the character; creator profiles; 2 covers by Suydam & Bisley 6.00

--MASSIVE SUMMER DOUBLE SPECTACLE
1,2-(7,8/00, $3.50, B&W) 5.00

TICK & ARTIE
1-(6/02, $3.50, color) prints strips from Internet comic 4.00
2-(10/02, $3.95) 4.00

TICK AND ARTHUR, THE
New England Comics: Feb, 1999 - No. 6 ($3.50, B&W)

1-6-Sean Wang-s/a 4.00

TICK BIG BLUE DESTINY, THE
New England Comics: Oct, 1997 - No. 9 ($2.95)

1-4: 1-"Keen" Ed. 2-Two covers 4.00
1-($4.95) "Wicked Keen" Ed. w/die cut-c 5.00
5-($3.50) 4.00
6-Luny Bin Trilogy Preview #0 (7/98, $1.50) 4.00
7-9: 7-Luny Bin Trilogy begins 4.00

TICK BIG BLUE YULE LOG SPECIAL, THE
New England Comics: Dec, 1997; 1999 ($2.95, B&W)

1-"Jolly" and "Traditional" covers; flip book w/"Arthur Teaches the Tick About Hanukkah" 4.00
...1999 ($3.50) 4.00
Tick Big Yule Log Special 2001-(12/00, $3.50, B&W) 4.00

TICK, THE : CIRCUS MAXIMUS
New England Comics: Mar, 2000 - No. 4, Jun, 2000 ($3.50, B&W)

1-4-Encyclopedia of characters from Tick comics 4.00
Giant No. 1 (8/03, $14.95) r/#1-4, Redux 15.00
Redux No. 1 (4/01, $3.50) 4.00

TICK, THE - COLOR
New England Comics: Jan, 2001 - No. 6 ($3.95)

1-6: 1-Marc Sandroni-a 4.00

TICK, THE : DAYS OF DRAMA
New England Comics: July, 2005 - No. 6, June, 2006 ($4.95/$3.95, limited series)

1-($4.95) Dave Garcia-a; has a mini-comic attached to cover 5.00
2-6-($3.95) 4.00

TICK, THE - HEROES OF THE CITY
New England Comics: Feb, 1999 - No. 6 ($3.50, B&W)

1-6-Short stories by various 4.00

TICK KARMA TORNADO (The...)
New England Comics Press: Oct, 1993 - No. 9, Mar, 1995 ($2.75, B&W)

1-($3.25) 5.00
2-9: 2-$2.75-c begins 4.00

TICK NEW SERIES (The...)
New England Comics: Dec, 2009 - No. 8 ($4.95)

1-8 5.00

Thunderstrike (2011) #2 © MAR

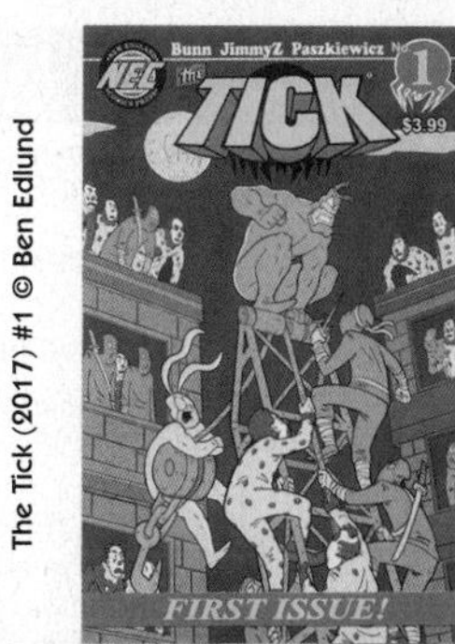

The Tick (2017) #1 © Ben Edlund

Tim Drake: Robin #1 © DC

	GD 2.0	VG 4.0	FN 6.0	VF 8.0	VF/NM 9.0	NM- 9.2

TICK'S BIG XMAS TRILOGY, THE
New England Comics: Dec, 2002 - No. 3, Dec, 2002 ($3.95, limited series)
1-3 4.00

TICK'S GOLDEN AGE COMIC, THE
New England Comics: May, 2002 - No. 3, Feb, 2003 ($4.95, Golden Age size)
1-3-Facsimile 1940s-style Tick issue; 2 covers 5.00
Giant Edition TPB (9/03, $12.95) r/#1-3 13.00

TICK'S GIANT CIRCUS OF THE MIGHTY, THE
New England Comics: Summer, 1992 - No. 3, Fall, 1993 ($2.75, B&W, magazine size)
1-(A-O). 2-(P-Z). 3-1993 Update 5.00

TICK 2017, THE
New England Comics: Sept, 2017 - No. 4, Jun, 2018 ($3.99)
1-4: 1-Bunn & JimmyZ-s/Paszkiewicz-a 4.00

TICKLE COMICS (Also see Gay, Smile, & Whee Comics)
Modern Store Publ.: 1955 (7¢, 5x7-1/4", 52 pgs)
1 10 20 30 58 79 100

TICK TOCK TALES
Magazine Enterprises: Jan, 1946 - V3#33, Jan-Feb, 1951
1-Koko & Kola begin 27 54 81 158 259 360
2 14 28 42 82 121 160
3-10 13 26 39 72 101 130
11-33: 19-Flag-c. 23-Muggsy Mouse, The Pixies & Tom-Tom the Jungle Boy app. 24-X-mas-c. 25-The Pixies & Tom-Tom app. 11 22 33 64 90 115

TIGER (Also see Comics Reading Libraries in the Promotional Comics section)
Charlton Press (King Features): Mar, 1970 - No. 6, Jan, 1971 (15¢)
1 3 6 9 14 20 26
2-6: 3-Ad for life-size inflatable doll 2 4 6 8 11 14

TIGER BOY (See Unearthly Spectaculars)

TIGER DIVISION
Marvel Comics: Jan, 2023 - Present ($3.99)
1-4-Emily Kim-s/Creees Lee-a 4.00

TIGER GIRL
Gold Key: Sept, 1968 (15¢)
1(10227-809)-Sparling-c/a; Jerry Siegel scripts; advertising on back-c 5 10 15 33 57 80
1-Variant edition with pin-up on back cover 6 12 18 38 69 100

TIGERMAN (Also see Thrilling Adventure Stories)
Seaboard Periodicals (Atlas): Apr, 1975 - No. 3, Sept, 1975 (All 25¢ issues)
1-3: 1-Origin; Colan-c. 2,3-Ditko-p in each 2 4 6 11 16 20

TIGER WALKS, A (See Movie Comics)

TIGRA (The Avengers)
Marvel Comics: May, 2002 - No. 4, Aug, 2002 ($2.99, limited series)
1-4-Christina Z-s/Deodato-c/a 3.00

TIGRESS, THE
Hero Graphics: Aug, 1992 - No. 6?, June, 1993 ($3.95/$2.95, B&W)
1,6: 1-Tigress vs. Flare. 6-44 pgs. 4.00
2-5: 2-$2.95-c begins 3.00

TILLIE THE TOILER (See Comic Monthly)
Dell Publishing Co.: No. 15, 1941 - No. 237, July, 1949
Four Color 15(1941) 71 142 213 454 777 1100
Large Feature Comic 30(1941) 43 86 129 271 461 650
Four Color 8(1942) 28 56 84 202 451 700
Four Color 22(1943) 19 38 57 131 291 450
Four Color 55(1944), 89(1945) 14 28 42 96 211 325
Four Color 106('45),132('46): 132-New stories begin 10 20 30 70 150 230
Four Color 150,176,184 10 20 30 66 138 210
Four Color 195,213,237 9 18 27 57 111 165

TIMBER WOLF (See Action Comics #372, & Legion of Super-Heroes)
DC Comics: Nov, 1992 - No. 5, Mar, 1993 ($1.25, limited series)
1-5 3.00

TIM DRAKE: ROBIN (Also see DC Pride: Tim Drake Special)
DC Comics: Nov, 2022 - Present ($3.99)
1-6-Fitzmartin-s/Rossmo-a; Darcy Thomas app. 4.00

TIME BANDITS
Marvel Comics Group: Feb, 1982 (one-shot, Giant)
1-Movie adaptation 4.00

TIME BEAVERS (See First Comics Graphic Novel #2)

TIME BEFORE TIME
Image Comics: May, 2021 - Present ($3.99)
1-20-Declan Shalvey & Rory McConville-s/Joe Palmer-a. 6-Shalvey-a 4.00

TIME BOMB
Radical Comics: Jul, 2010 - No. 3, Dec, 2010 ($4.99, limited series)
1-3-Palmiotti & Gray-s/Gulacy-a/c 5.00

TIMECOP (Movie)
Dark Horse Comics: Sept, 1994 - No. 2, Nov, 1994 ($2.50, limited series)
1,2-Adaptation of film 3.00

TIME FOR LOVE (Formerly Romantic Secrets)
Charlton Comics: V2#53, Oct, 1966; Oct, 1967 - No. 47, May, 1976
V2#53(10/66) Herman-s Hermits app. 4 8 12 23 37 50
1-(10/67) 4 8 12 25 40 55
2-(12/67) -10 3 6 9 15 21 26
11,12,14-20 2 4 6 11 16 20
13-(11/69) Ditko-a (7 pgs.) 3 6 9 16 23 30
21-27 2 4 6 9 13 16
28,29,31: 28-Shirley Jones poster. 29-Bobby Sherman pin-up. 31-Bobby Sherman pin-up 2 4 6 11 16 20
30-(10/72)-David Cassidy full page poster 3 6 9 16 24 32
32-47 2 4 6 8 11 14

TIMELESS
Marvel Comics: Feb, 2022 ($5.99, one-shot)
1-Spotlight on Kang the Conqueror; MacKay-s/Walker, Land & Bagley-a 6.00

TIMELESS
Marvel Comics: Feb, 2023 ($5.99, one-shot)
1-Kang in search of the Missing Moment; MacKay-s/Land, Zircher & Larroca-a 6.00

TIMELESS TOPIX (See Topix)

TIMELY COMICS... (Reprints of recent Marvel issues)
Marvel Comics: Aug, 2016 ($3.00)
...: All-New, All-Different Avengers (8/16) r/#1-3; Alex Ross-c 3.00
...: All-New Inhumans (8/16) r/#1-3; Caselli-c 3.00
...: Carnage (8/16) r/#1-3; Del Mundo-c 3.00
...: Daredevil (8/16) r/#1-3; Garney-c 3.00
...: Doctor Strange (8/16) r/#1-3; Bachalo-c 3.00
...: Drax (8/16) r/#1-3; Hepburn-c 3.00
...: Invincible Iron Man (8/16) r/#1-3; Marquez-c 3.00
...: Moon Girl and Devil Dinosaur (8/16) r/#1-3; Reeder-c 3.00
...: New Avengers (8/16) r/#1-3; Sandoval-c 3.00
...: Scarlet Witch (8/16) r/#1-3; Aja-c 3.00
...: Squadron Supreme (8/16) r/#1-3; Alex Ross-c 3.00
...: The Totally Awesome Hulk (8/16) r/#1-3; Cho-c 3.00
...: Ultimates (8/16) r/#1-3; Rocafort-c 3.00
...: Uncanny Inhumans (8/16) r/#1-3; McNiven-c 3.00
...: Venom: Space Knight (8/16) r/#1-3; Olivetti-c 3.00
...: Web Warriors (8/16) r/#1-3; Tedesco-c 3.00

TIMELY PRESENTS: ALL WINNERS
Marvel Comics: Dec, 1999 ($3.99)
1-Reprints All Winners Comics #19 (Fall 1946); new Lago-c 5.00

TIMELY PRESENTS: HUMAN TORCH
Marvel Comics: Feb, 1999 ($3.99)
1-Reprints Human Torch Comics #5 (Fall 1941); new Lago-c 5.00

TIME MACHINE, THE
Dell Publishing Co.: No. 1085, Mar, 1960 (H.G. Wells)
Four Color 1085-Movie, Alex Toth-a; Rod Taylor photo-c 16 32 48 110 243 375

TIME MASTERS
DC Comics: Feb, 1990 - No. 8, Sept, 1990 ($1.75, mini-series)
1-8: New Rip Hunter series. 5-Cave Carson, Viking Prince app. 6-Dr. Fate app. 3.00
TPB (2008, $19.99) r/#1-8 and Secret Origins #43; intro. by Geoff Johns 20.00

TIME MASTERS: VANISHING POINT (Tie-in to Batman: The Return of Bruce Wayne)
DC Comics: Sept, 2010 - No. 6, Feb, 2011 ($3.99, limited series)
1-6-Jurgens-s/a/c; Rip Hunter, Superman, Green Lantern & Booster Gold app. 4.00

GD 2.0 | VG 4.0 | FN 6.0 | VF 8.0 | VF/NM 9.0 | NM- 9.2

TPB (2011, $14.99) r/#1-6 15.00

TIMESLIP COLLECTION
Marvel Comics: Nov, 1998 ($2.99, one-shot)

1-Pin-ups reprinted from Marvel Vision magazine 3.00

TIMESLIP SPECIAL (The Coming of the Avengers)
Marvel Comics: Oct, 1998 ($5.99, one-shot)

1-Alternate world Avengers vs. Odin 6.00

TIMESTORM 2009/2099
Marvel Comics: June, 2009 - No. 4, Oct, 2009 ($3.99, limited series)

1-4-Punisher 2099 transports Spider-Man to 2099; Wolverine app.; Battle-a 4.00
...: Spider-Man One Shot (8/09, $3.99) Reed-s/Craig-a/Renaud-c 4.00
...: X-Men One Shot (8/09, $3.99) Reed-s/Irving-a/Renaud-c 4.00

TIME TO RUN (Based on 1973 Billy Graham movie)
Spire Christian Comics (Fleming H. Revell Co.): 1975 (39¢)

nn-By Al Hartley 2 4 6 13 18 22

TIME TUNNEL, THE (TV)
Gold Key: Feb, 1967 - No. 2, July, 1967 (12¢)

1-Photo back-c on both issues 7 14 21 49 92 135
2 5 10 15 33 57 80

TIME TWISTERS
Quality Comics: Sept, 1987 - No. 21, 1989 ($1.25/$1.50)

1-21: Alan Moore scripts in 1-4, 6-9, 14 (2 pg.). 14-Bolland-a (2 pg.). 15,16-Guice-c 4.00

TIME 2: THE EPIPHANY (See First Comics Graphic Novel #9)

TIMEWALKER (Also see Archer & Armstrong)
Valiant: Jan, 1994 - No. 15, Oct, 1995 ($2.50)

1-15,0(3/96): 2-"JAN" on-c, February, 1995 in indicia. 3.00
Yearbook 1 (5/95, $2.95) 3.00

TIME WARP (See The Unexpected #210)
DC Comics, Inc.: Oct-Nov, 1979 - No. 5, June-July, 1980 ($1.00, 68 pgs.)

1 2 4 6 13 18 22
2-5 2 4 6 8 11 14

NOTE: ***Aparo** a-1. **Buckler** a-1p. **Chaykin** a-2. **Ditko** a-1-4. **Kaluta** c-1-5. **G. Kane** a-2. **Nasser** a-4. **Newton** a-1-5p. **Orlando** a-2. **Sutton** a-1-3.*

TIME WARP
DC Comics (Vertigo): May, 2013 ($7.99, one-shot)

1-Short story anthology by various incl. Lindelof, Simone; covers by Risso & Jae Lee 8.00

TIME WARRIORS: THE BEGINNING
Fantasy General Comics: 1986 (Aug) - No. 2, 1986? ($1.50)

1,2-Alpha Track/Skellon Empire 3.00

TIM HOLT (Movie star) (Becomes Red Mask #42 on; also see Crack Western #72, & Great Western)
Magazine Enterprises: 1948 - No. 41, April-May, 1954 (All 36 pgs.)

1-(A-1 #14)-Line drawn-c w/Tim Holt photo on-c; Tim Holt, His horse Lightning & sidekick Chito begin 55 110 165 352 601 850
2-(A-1 #17)(9-10/48)-Photo-c begin, end #18 27 54 81 158 259 360
3-(A-1 #19)-Photo back-c 20 40 60 117 189 260
4(1-2/49),5: 5-Photo front/back-c 15 30 45 85 130 175
6-(5/49)-1st app. The Calico Kid (alias Rex Fury), his horse Ebony & Sidekick Sing-Song (begin series); photo back-c 26 52 78 154 252 350
7-10: 7-Calico Kid by Ayers. 8-Calico Kid by Guardineer (r-in/Great Western #10). 9-Map of Tim's Home Range 15 30 45 83 124 165
11-The Calico Kid becomes The Ghost Rider (origin & 1st app.) by Dick Ayers (r-in/Great Western I.W. #8); his horse Spectre & sidekick Sing-Song begin series 235 470 705 1492 1946 2400
12-16,18-Last photo-c 14 28 42 78 112 145
17-Frazetta Ghost Rider-c 235 470 705 1492 1946 2400
19,22,24: 19-Last Tim Holt-c; Bolle line-drawn-c begin; Tim Holt photo on covers #19-28, 30-41. 22-interior photo-c 12 24 36 67 94 120
20-Tim Holt becomes Redmask (origin); begin series; Redmask-c #20-on 18 36 54 103 162 220
21-Frazetta Ghost Rider/Redmask-c 47 94 141 296 498 700
23-Frazetta Redmask-c 37 74 111 218 354 490
25-1st app. Black Phantom 22 44 66 132 216 300
26-30: 28-Wild Bill Hickok, Bat Masterson team up with Redmask. 29-B&W photo-c 12 24 36 67 94 120
31-33-Ghost Rider ends 10 20 30 58 79 100
34-Tales of the Ghost Rider begins (horror)-Classic "The Flower Women" & "Hard Boiled Harry!" 16 32 48 94 147 200
35-Last Tales of the Ghost Rider 13 26 39 72 101 130
36-The Ghost Rider returns, ends #41; liquid hallucinogenic drug story 15 30 45 88 137 185
37-Ghost Rider classic "To Touch Is to Die!", about Inca treasure 15 30 45 88 137 185
38-The Black Phantom begins (not in #39); classic Ghost Rider "The Phantom Guns of Feather Gap!" 15 30 45 88 137 185
39-41: All 3-D effect c/stories 17 34 51 98 154 210

NOTE: ***Dick Ayers** a-7, 9-41. **Bolle** a-1-41; c-19, 20, 22, 24-28, 30-41.*

TIM McCOY (Formerly Zoo Funnies; Pictorial Love Stories #22 on)
Charlton Comics: No. 16, Oct, 1948 - No. 21, Aug, 1949 (Western Movie Stories)

16-John Wayne, Montgomery Clift app. in "Red River"; photo back-c 37 74 111 222 361 500
17-21: 17-Allan "Rocky" Lane guest stars. 18-Rod Cameron guest stars. 19-Whip Wilson, Andy Clyde guest star; Jesse James story. 20-Jimmy Wakely guest stars. 21-Johnny Mack Brown guest stars 29 58 87 170 278 385

TIMMY
Dell Publishing Co.: No. 715, Aug, 1956 - No. 1022, Aug-Oct, 1959

Four Color 715 (#1) 6 12 18 41 76 110
Four Color 823 (8/57), 923 (8/58), 1022 5 10 15 34 60 85

TIMMY THE TIMID GHOST (Formerly Win-A-Prize?; see Blue Bird)
Charlton Comics: No. 3, 2/56 - No. 44, 10/64; No. 45, 9/66; 10/67 - No. 23, 7/71; V4#24, 9/85 - No. 26, 1/86

3(1956) (1st Series) 15 30 45 85 130 175
4,5 9 18 27 50 65 80
6-10 3 6 9 19 30 40
11,12(4/58,10/58)-(100 pgs.) 6 12 18 37 66 95
13-20 3 6 9 17 26 35
21-45(1966): 27-Nazi story 3 6 9 14 19 24
1(10/67, 2nd series) 3 6 9 15 22 28
2-10 2 4 6 10 14 18
11-23: 23 (7/71) 1 3 4 8 10 12
24-26 (1985-86): Fago-r (low print run) 6.00

TIM TYLER (See Harvey Comics Hits #54)

TIM TYLER (Also see Comics Reading Libraries in the Promotional Comics section)
Better Publications: 1942

1 19 38 57 111 176 240

TIM TYLER COWBOY
Standard Comics (King Features Synd.): No. 11, Nov, 1948 - No. 18, Aug, 1950

11-By Lyman Young 12 24 36 69 97 125
12-18: 13-15-Full length western adventures 9 18 27 47 61 75

TINKER BELL (Disney, TV)(See Walt Disney Showcase #37)
Dell Publishing Co.: No. 896, Mar, 1958 - No. 982, Apr-June, 1959

Four Color 896 (#1)-The Adventures of... 12 24 36 82 179 275
Four Color 982-The New Advs. of... 10 20 30 66 138 210

TINY FOLKS FUNNIES
Dell Publishing Co.: No. 60, 1944

Four Color 60 17 34 51 117 259 400

TINY TESSIE (Tessie #1-23; Real Experiences #25)
Marvel Comics (20CC): No. 24, Oct, 1949 (52 pgs.)

24 21 42 63 122 199 275

TINY TIM (Also see Super Comics)
Dell Publishing Co.: No. 4, 1941 - No. 235, July, 1949

Large Feature Comic 4('41) 53 106 159 334 567 800
Four Color 20(1941) 47 94 141 296 498 700
Four Color 42(1943) 18 36 54 128 284 440
Four Color 235 7 14 21 48 89 130

TINY TITANS (Teen Titans)
DC Comics: Apr, 2008 - No. 50, May, 2012 ($2.25/$2.50/$2.99)

1-29-All ages stories of Teen Titans in Elementary school; Baltazar & Franco-s/a 3.00
1-(6/08, Free Comic Book Day giveaway) r/#1; Baltazar & Franco-s/a 3.00
30-50: 30-Begin $2.99-c. 37-Marvel Family app. 44-Doom Patrol app. 3.00

TINY TITANS / LITTLE ARCHIE (Teen Titans) (Digest-size reprint in World of Archie Double Digest Magazine #5)
DC Comics: Dec, 2010 - No. 3, Feb, 2011 ($2.99, limited series)

1-3-Character crossover; Baltazar & Franco-s/a. 2-Josie and the Pussycats app. 3.00

TINY TITANS: RETURN TO THE TREEHOUSE
DC Comics: Aug, 2014 - No. 6, Jan, 2015 ($2.99, limited series)

1-Baltazar & Franco-s/a in all; Brainiac app. 6.00
2-6: 3-Marvel Family app. 4.00

TINY TOT COMICS
E. C. Comics: Mar, 1946 - No. 10, Nov-Dec, 1947 (For younger readers)

1(nn)-52 pg. issues begin, end #4 68 136 204 435 743 1050
2 (5/46) 36 72 108 211 343 475
3-10: 10-Christmas-c 30 60 90 177 289 400

TINY TOT FUNNIES (Formerly Family Funnies; becomes Junior Funnies)
Harvey Publ. (King Features Synd.): No. 9, June, 1951

9-Flash Gordon, Mandrake, Dagwood, Daisy, etc. 10 20 30 54 72 90

TINY TOTS COMICS
Dell Publishing Co.: 1943 (Not reprints)

1-Kelly-a(2); fairy tales 43 86 129 271 461 650

TIPPY & CAP STUBBS (See Popular Comics)
Dell Publishing Co.: No. 210, Jan, 1949 - No. 242, Aug, 1949

Four Color 210 (#1) 9 18 27 57 111 165
Four Color 242 6 12 18 41 76 110

TIPPY'S FRIENDS GO-GO & ANIMAL
Tower Comics: July, 1966 - No. 15, Oct, 1969 (25¢)

1 10 20 30 68 138 210
2-5,7,9-15: 12-15 titled "Tippy's Friend Go-Go" 6 12 18 41 76 110
6-The Monkees photo-c 9 18 27 59 117 175
8-Beatles app. on front/back-c 11 22 33 76 163 250

TIPPY TEEN (See Vicki)
Tower Comics: Nov, 1965 - No. 25, Oct, 1969 (25¢)

1 12 24 36 82 179 275
2-4,6-10 6 12 18 40 73 105
5-1 pg. Beatles pin-up 8 16 24 51 96 140
11-20: 16-Twiggy photo-c 6 12 18 37 66 95
21-25 5 10 15 34 60 85
Special Collectors' Editions nn-(1969, 25¢) 6 12 18 37 66 95

TIPPY TERRY
Super/I. W. Enterprises: 1963

Super Reprint #14('63)-r/Little Groucho #1 2 4 6 8 10 16
I.W. Reprint #1 (nd)-r/Little Groucho #1 2 4 6 8 10 16

TIP TOP COMICS
United Features #1-188/St. John #189-210/Dell Publishing Co. #211 on:

Time Warp (2013) #1 © DC

Tip Top Comics #203 © STJ

Titans Hunt #4 © DC

	GD 2.0	VG 4.0	FN 6.0	VF 8.0	VF/NM 9.0	NM- 9.2
4/36 - No. 210, 1957; No. 211, 11-1/57-58 - No. 225, 5-7/61						
1-Tarzan by Hal Foster, Li'l Abner, Broncho Bill, Fritzi Ritz, Ella Cinders, Capt. & The Kids begin; strip-r (1st comic book app. of each)	1050	2100	3150	6400	11,950	17,500
2-Tarzan-c (6/36)	219	438	657	1402	2401	3400
3-Tarzan-c (7/36)	213	426	639	1363	2332	3300
4-(8/36)	113	226	339	718	1234	1750
5-8,10: 7-Photo & biography of Edgar Rice Burroughs. 8-Christmas-c	84	168	252	538	919	1300
9-Tarzan-c (1/37)	116	232	348	742	1271	1800
11,13,16,18-Tarzan-c: 11-Has Tarzan pin-up	84	168	252	538	919	1300
12,14,15,17,19,20: 20-Christmas-c	58	116	174	371	636	900
21,24,27,30-(10/38)-Tarzan-c	65	130	195	416	708	1000
22,23,25,26,28,29	41	82	123	256	428	600
31,35,38,40	40	80	120	246	411	525
32,36-Tarzan-c: 32-1st published Jack Davis-a (cartoon). 36-Kurtzman panel (1st published comic work)	65	130	195	416	708	1000
33,34,37,39-Tarzan-c	58	116	174	371	636	900
41-Reprints 1st Tarzan Sunday; Tarzan-c	65	130	195	416	708	1000
42,44,46,48,49	35	70	105	208	339	470
43,45,47,50,52-Tarzan-c. 43-Mort Walker panel	45	90	135	284	480	675
51,53	33	66	99	194	317	440
54-Origin Mirror Man & Triple Terror, also featured on cover	42	84	126	265	445	625
55,56,58: Last Tarzan by Foster	28	56	84	168	274	380
57,59-62-Tarzan by Hogarth	35	70	105	208	339	470
63-80: 65,67-70,72-74,77,78-No Tarzan	19	38	57	111	176	240
81-90	15	30	45	90	140	190
91-99	15	30	45	83	124	165
100	15	30	45	85	130	175
101-140: 110-Gordo story. 111-Li'l Abner app. 118, 132-No Tarzan. 137-Sadie Hawkins Day story	12	24	36	67	94	120
141-170: 145,151-Gordo stories. 153-Fritzi Ritz lingerie panels. 157-Last Li'l Abner; lingerie panels	10	20	30	54	72	90
171,172,174-183: 171-Tarzan reprints by B. Lubbers begin; end #188	10	20	30	56	76	95
173-(3/52) Ties with United Comics #21 for first app. of Peanuts in comics; reprints Peanuts dailies 2/06/51 & 3/05/51 (also see Tip Topper Comics)	423	846	1269	3000	5250	7500
184-Peanuts app. (1-2/54)	28	56	84	165	270	375
185-188-Peanuts stories with Charlie Brown & Snoopy on the covers. 185-(3-4/54)	300	600	900	1800	2250	2700
189,191-225-Peanuts apps.(4 pg. to 8 pg stories) in most						
Issues with Peanuts	16	32	48	94	147	200
Issues without Peanuts	9	18	27	47	61	75
190-Peanuts with Charlie Brown & Snoopy partial-c (comic strip at bottom of cover)	40	80	120	246	411	575
Bound Volumes (Very Rare) sold at 1939 World's Fair; bound by publisher in pictorial comic boards (also see Comics on Parade)						
Bound issues 1-12 (Rare)	394	788	1182	2758	4829	6900
Bound issues 13-24	184	368	552	1178	2014	2850
Bound issues 25-36	158	316	474	1011	1731	2450

NOTE: *Tarzan by* ***Foster****-#1-40, 44-50; by* ***Rex Maxon****-#41-43; by* ***Burne Hogarth****-#57, 59, 62.*

TIP TOPPER COMICS
United Features Syndicate: Oct-Nov, 1949 - No. 28, 1954

	GD 2.0	VG 4.0	FN 6.0	VF 8.0	VF/NM 9.0	NM- 9.2
1-Li'l Abner, Abbie & Slats	32	64	96	188	307	425
2	13	26	39	74	105	135
3-5: 5-Fearless Fosdick app.	11	22	33	60	83	105
6-10: 6-Fearless Fosdick app.	10	20	30	54	72	90
11-15	9	18	27	50	65	80
16(4-5/52)-2nd app. of Peanuts (2 pgs.) by Schulz in comics (See United Comics #21 for 1st app. & #22 for 5-6/52 app.)(Also see Tip Top Comics #173)	123	246	369	787	1344	1900
17(6-7/52)-4th app. of Peanuts by Schulz, 2 pgs.	54	108	162	343	574	825
18-28: 18-24,26-28-Early Peanuts (2 pgs.). 25-Early Peanuts (3 pgs.) 26-28-Twin Earths	20	40	60	115	190	260

NOTE: *Many lingerie panels in Fritzi Ritz stories.*

'TIS THE SEASON TO BE FREEZIN'
DC Comics: Feb, 2022 ($9.99, 80 pages, one-shot)
1-Winter-themed short story anthology by various incl. Dini, Franklin, Hetrick, Mhan 10.00

TITAN A.E.
Dark Horse Comics: May, 2000 - No. 3, July, 2000 ($2.95, limited series)
1-3-Movie prequel; Al Rio-a 3.00

TITANS (Also see Teen Titans, New Teen Titans and New Titans)
DC Comics: Mar, 1999 - No. 50, Apr, 2003 ($2.50/$2.75)
1-Titans re-form; Grayson-s; 2 covers 4.00
2-11,13-24,26-50: 2-Superman-c/app. 9,10,21,22-Deathstroke app. 24-Titans from "Kingdom Come" app. 32-36-Asamiya-c. 44-Begin $2.75-c 3.00
12-($3.50, 48 pages) 4.00
25-($3.95) Titans from "Kingdom Come" app.; Wolfman & Faerber-s; art by Pérez, Cardy, Grummett, Jimenez, Dodson, Pelletier 4.00
Annual 1 ('00, $3.50) Planet DC; intro Bushido 4.00
... East Special 1 (1/08, $3.99) Winick-s/Churchill-a; continues in Titans #1 (2008) 4.00
...Secret Files 1,2 (3/99, 10/00; $4.95) Profile pages & short stories 5.00

TITANS (Also see Teen Titans)
DC Comics: Jun, 2008 - No. 38, Oct, 2011 ($3.50/$2.99)
1-($3.50) Titans re-form again; Winick-s/Churchill-a; covers by Churchill & Van Sciver 4.00
2-38: 2-4-Trigon returns. 6-10-Jericho app. 24-Deathstroke & Luthor app. 3.00
Annual 1 (9/11, $4.99) Justice League app.; Jericho returns; Richards-a 5.00
...: Villains For Hire Special 1 (7/10, $4.99) Deathstroke's team; Atom (Ryan Choi) killed 5.00
...: Fractured TPB (2010, $17.99) r/#14,16-22 18.00
...: Lockdown TPB (2009, $14.99) r/#7-11 15.00
...: Old Friends HC (2008, $24.99) r/#1-6 & Titans East Special 25.00
...: Villains For Hire TPB (2011, $14.99) r/#24-27 & Villains For Hire Special 1 15.00

TITANS (DC Rebirth)(Follows Titans Hunt series)
DC Comics: Aug, 2016 - No. 36, Jun, 2019 ($2.99/$3.99)
1-9: 1-Abnett-s/Booth-a; Abra Kadabra returns. 7-Superman app. 3.00
10-24,26-36-($3.99) 10-Fearsome Five app. 11-Lazarus Contract x-over; Teen Titans & Deathstroke app. 12-Rocafort-a. 28-"Drowned Earth" tie-in. 30-34-Kyle Rayner app. 4.00
25-($4.99) Peterson, March & Medri-a 5.00
Annual 1 (5/17, $4.99) Justice League and The Key app.; Abnett-s/Jung-a 5.00
Annual 2 (6/18, $4.99) Abnett-s/Grummett & Derenick-a; Monsieur Mallah & the Brain app. 5.00
...: Rebirth 1 (8/16, $2.99) Abnett-s/Booth-a; Wally West reunites with the Titans 3.00
...: Special 1 (8/18, $4.99) Abnett-s/art by various; Justice League app. 5.00

TITANS BEAT (Teen Titans)
DC Comics: Aug, 1996 (16 pgs., paper-c)
1-Intro./preview new Teen Titans members; Pérez-a 4.00

TITANS: BURNING RAGE (Teen Titans)(Reprints new story from Walmart exclusive)
DC Comics: Oct, 2019 - No. 7, Apr, 2020 ($4.99, limited series)
1-7-Jurgens-s/Eaton-a. 6-Mento app. 7-Blackfire and Mongul app. 4.00

TITANS GIANT (Continued from Teen Titans Giant #7)
DC Comics: 2019 - No. 7, 2019 ($4.99, 100 pgs., squarebound, Walmart exclusive)
1-7: 1-New story Jurgens-s/Eaton-a; reprints from Teen Titans ('03), Super Sons #1 ('17), and Sideways ('18) continue (Issues #8-on) 8.00

TITANS GIANT
DC Comics: 2020 - No. 2, 2020 ($4.99, 100 pgs., squarebound, Mass Market & Direct Market editions exist for each issue, with different covers)
1,2-New stories plus 1st series Teen Titans, Starfire & Super Sons reprints 5.00

TITANS HUNT (Also see DC Universe: Rebirth)
DC Comics: Dec, 2015 - No. 8, Jun, 2016 ($3.99, limited series)
1-7: 1-Abnett-s/Siqueira-a; 1970s-era Titans app. incl. Lilith & Gnarrk. 2,4-Segovia-a 4.00
8-Titans vs. Mr. Twister 4.00

TITANS/ LEGION OF SUPER-HEROES: UNIVERSE ABLAZE
DC Comics: 2000 - No. 4, 2000 ($4.95, prestige format, limited series)
1-4-Jurgens-s/a; P. Jimenez-a; teams battle Universo 5.00

TITAN SPECIAL
Dark Horse Comics: June, 1994 ($3.95, one-shot)
1-($3.95, 52 pgs.) 4.00

TITANS: SCISSORS, PAPER, STONE
DC Comics: 1997 ($4.95, one-shot)
1-Manga style Elseworlds; Adam Warren-s/a(p) 5.00

TITANS SELL-OUT SPECIAL
DC Comics: Nov, 1992 ($3.50, 52 pgs., one-shot)
1-Fold-out Nightwing poster; 1st Teeny Titans 4.00

TITANS UNITED (Teen Titans)
DC Comics: Nov, 2021 - No. 7, May, 2022 ($3.99, limited series)
1-7: 1-Cavan Scott-s/Jose Luis-a. 3,4-Blackfire app. 5-Black Zero returns 4.00

TITANS UNITED: BLOODPACT (Teen Titans)
DC Comics: Nov, 2022 - No. 6, Apr, 2023 ($3.99, limited series)
1-6-Cavan Scott-s/Lucas Meyer-a; Brother Blood & Mother Mayhem app. 4.00

	GD 2.0	VG 4.0	FN 6.0	VF 8.0	VF/NM 9.0	NM- 9.2

TITANS/ YOUNG JUSTICE: GRADUATION DAY
DC Comics: Early July, 2003 - No. 3, Aug, 2003 ($2.50, limited series)

1,2-Winick-s/Garza-a; leads into Teen Titans and The Outsiders series. 2-Lilith dies 3.00
3-Death of Donna Troy (Wonder Girl) 3.00
TPB (2003, $6.95) r/#1-3; plus previews of Teen Titans and The Outsiders series 7.00

TITHE, THE (Also see Eden's Fall)
Image Comics (Top Cow): Apr, 2015 - No. 8 ($3.99, limited series)

1-7-Hawkins-s/Ekedal-a; multiple covers on each. 5-7-Sevy-a 4.00

T-MAN (Also see Police Comics #103)
Quality Comics Group: Sept, 1951 - No. 38, Dec, 1956

	GD	VG	FN	VF	VF/NM	NM-
1-Pete Trask, T-Man begins; Jack Cole-a	60	120	180	381	653	925
2-Crandall-c	35	70	105	208	339	470
3,7,8: All Crandall-c	30	60	90	177	289	400
4,5-Crandall-c/a each	31	62	93	186	303	420
6-"The Man Who Could Be Hitler" c/story; Crandall-c.	50	100	150	315	533	750
9,10-Crandall-c	27	54	81	158	259	360
11-Used in **POP**, pg. 95 & color illo.	24	48	72	142	234	325
12,13,15-19,22-26: 23-H-Bomb panel. 24-Last pre-code issue (4/55). 25-Not Crandall-a	17	34	51	105	165	225
14-Hitler-c	36	72	108	211	343	475
20-H-Bomb explosion-c/story	24	48	72	140	230	320
21- "The Return of Mussolini" c/story	24	48	72	140	230	320
27-33,35-38	17	34	51	100	158	215
34-Hitler-c	43	86	129	271	461	650

NOTE: *Anti-communist stories common.* ***Crandall*** *c-2-10p.* ***Cuidera*** *c(i)-1-38. Bondage c-15.*

TMNT... (Also see Teenage Mutant Ninja Turtles and related titles)
Mirage Publishing: March 2007 ($3.25/$4.95, B&W, one-shots)

...: Raphael Movie Prequel 1; ...: Michelangelo Movie Prequel 2; ...: Donatello Movie Prequel 3; ...: April Movie Prequel 4; ...: Leonardo Movie Prequel 5; back-story for movie 5.00
...: The Official Movie Adaptation ($4.95) adapts 2007 movie; Munroe-c 5.00

TMNT: BEST OF...
IDW Publishing: Sept, 2020 - Nov, 2022 ($5.99)

... April O'Neil (10/21) Reprints TMNT #2 (1984), Micro-Series #7 ('11) TMNT #118 6.00
... Baxter Stockman (8/22) Reprints TMNT #2 (1984) & #2 (2003), Micro-Series 6.00
... Casey Jones (7/21) Reprints TMNT #14 & #48 (1984), Micro-Series #6 ('11) 6.00
... Donatello (11/20) Reprints Donatello #1 (1986), Micro-Series #3 ('11) Macro-Series #1 6.00
... Jennika (2/22) Reprints TMNT #52 (2011) and early apps. 6.00
... Leatherhead (11/22) Reprints Tales of the TMNT #6, TMNT #45 ('84) & TMNT #56 ('11) 6.00
... Leonardo (1/21) Reprints Leonardo #1 (1986), Micro-Series #4 ('11) Macro-Series #3 6.00
... Michelangelo (3/21) Reprints Michelangelo #1 (1986), Micro-Series #2 ('11) Macro-Series #2 6.00
... Raphael (9/20) Reprints Raphael #1 (1985), Micro-Series #1 ('11) Macro-Series #4 6.00
... Rat King (5/22) Reprints Tales of the TMNT #4, TMNT Advs. #11 and TMNT #36 ('11) 6.00
... Shredder (12/21) Reprints TMNT #1 (1984), Villain Micro-Series #8 ('13), TMNT: Shredder In Hell #1 ('19) 6.00
... Splinter (5/21) Reprints TMNT Advs #45, Tales of TMNT V2 #2, TMNT #5 ('11), and Micro-Series #5 ('11) 6.00

TMNT: JENNIKA
IDW Publishing: Feb, 2020 - No. 3, Apr, 2020 ($4.99, limited series)

1-3-Brahm Revel-s/a 5.00

TMNT: JENNIKA II
IDW Publishing: Nov, 2020 - No. 6, Apr, 2021 ($4.99)

1-6: 1-3-Brahm Revel-s/a. 4-Ronda Pattison-s/Jodi Nishijima-a 5.00

TMNT MUTANT UNIVERSE SOURCEBOOK
Archie Comics: 1992 - No. 3, 1992? ($1.95, 52 pgs.)(Lists characters from A-Z)

	GD	VG	FN	VF	VF/NM	NM-
1-3: 3-New characters; fold-out poster	1	3	4	6	8	10

TMNT: THE LAST RONIN
IDW Publishing: Oct, 2020 - No. 5, Feb, 2022 ($8.99, oversized 7" x 10-7/8", squarebound)

	GD	VG	FN	VF	VF/NM	NM-
1-One Turtle in the future; Waltz & Eastman-s/Eastman & Esau-a; Oroku Hiroto app.	4	8	12	27	44	60
1-Director's Cut (3/21, $10.99) r/#1 with layout pages, characters designs, story outline	2	4	6	11	16	20
2-April O'Neil app.; intro. Casey Marie Jones	2	4	6	11	16	20
3-5	1	3	4	6	8	10

...: Design Archive (11/21, $8.99) Eastman sketch art for characters, settings, vehicles 9.00

TNT COMICS
Charles Publishing Co.: Feb, 1946 (36 pgs.)

	GD	VG	FN	VF	VF/NM	NM-
1-Yellowjacket app.	43	86	129	271	461	650

TOBY TYLER (Disney, see Movie Comics)
Dell Publishing Co.: No. 1092, Apr-June, 1960

	GD	VG	FN	VF	VF/NM	NM-
Four Color 1092-Movie, photo-c	6	12	18	41	76	110

TODAY'S BRIDES
Ajax/Farrell Publishing Co.: Nov, 1955; No. 2, Feb, 1956; No. 3, Sept, 1956; No. 4, Nov, 1956

	GD	VG	FN	VF	VF/NM	NM-
1	15	30	45	83	124	165
2-4	11	22	33	60	83	105

TODAY'S ROMANCE
Standard Comics: No. 5, March, 1952 - No. 8, Sept, 1952 (All photo-c?)

	GD	VG	FN	VF	VF/NM	NM-
5-Photo-c	16	32	48	92	144	195
6-Photo-c; Toth-a	16	32	48	94	147	200
7,8	14	28	42	82	121	160

TODD, THE UGLIEST KID ON EARTH
Image Comics: Jan, 2013 - No. 8, Jan, 2014 ($2.99)

1-8-Perker-a/Kristensen-s 3.00

TOE TAGS FEATURING GEORGE A. ROMERO
DC Comics: Dec, 2004 - No. 6, May, 2005 ($2.95/$2.99)

1-6-Zombie story by George Romero; Wrightson-c/Castillo-a 3.00

TOIL AND TROUBLE
BOOM! Studios (Archaia): Sept, 2015 - No. 6 ($3.99)

1-6-Mairghread Scott-s/Kelly & Nicole Matthews-a 4.00

TOKA (Jungle King)
Dell Publishing Co.: Aug-Oct, 1964 - No. 10, Jan, 1967 (Painted-c #1,2)

	GD	VG	FN	VF	VF/NM	NM-
1	4	8	12	28	47	65
2	3	6	9	17	26	35
3-10	3	6	9	15	22	28

TOKYO GHOST
Image Comics: Sept, 2015 - No. 10, Aug, 2016 ($3.99)

1-10-Rick Remender-s/Sean Murphy-a 4.00

TOKYO STORM WARNING (See Red/Tokyo Storm Warning for TPB)
DC Comics (Cliffhanger): Aug, 2003 - No. 3, Dec, 2003 ($2.95, limited series)

1-3-Warren Ellis-s/James Raiz-a 3.00

TOMAHAWK (Son of... on-c of #131-140; see Star Spangled Comics #69 & World's Finest Comics #65)
National Periodical Publications: Sept-Oct, 1950 - No. 140, May-June, 1972

	GD	VG	FN	VF	VF/NM	NM-
1-Tomahawk & boy sidekick Dan Hunter begin by Fred Ray	187	374	561	1197	2049	2900
2-Frazetta/Williamson-a (4 pgs.)	74	148	222	470	810	1150
3-5	41	82	123	256	428	600
6-10: 7-Last 52 pg. issue	36	72	108	211	343	475
11-20	24	48	72	142	234	325
21-27,30: 30-Last precode (2/55)	21	42	63	126	206	285
28-1st app. Lord Shilling (arch-foe)	22	44	66	132	216	300
29-Frazetta-r/Jimmy Wakely #3 (3 pgs.)	26	52	78	154	252	350
31-40	18	36	54	107	169	230
41-50	10	20	30	64	132	200
51-56,58-60	9	18	27	58	114	170
57-Frazetta-r/Jimmy Wakely #6 (3 pgs.)	10	20	30	64	132	200
61-77: 77-Last 10¢ issue	8	16	24	54	102	150
78-85: 81-1st app. Miss Liberty. 83-Origin Tomahawk's Rangers	7	14	21	46	86	125
86-99: 96-Origin/1st app. The Hood, alias Lady Shilling	5	10	15	35	63	90
100	6	12	18	37	66	95
101-110: 107-Origin/1st app. Thunder-Man	5	10	15	30	50	70
111-115,120,122: 122-Last 12¢ issue	4	8	12	28	47	65
116-1st Neal Adams cover on title (5/68)	24	48	72	168	372	575
117-119,121,123-130-Neal Adams-c. 118-Origin of the Rangers	6	12	18	41	76	110
131-Frazetta-r/Jimmy Wakely #7 (3 pgs.); origin Firehair retold	3	6	9	21	33	45
132-135: 135-Last 15¢ issue	3	6	9	16	24	32
136-138,140 (52 pg. Giants)	3	6	9	19	30	40
139-Frazetta-r/Star Spangled #113	3	6	9	21	33	45

NOTE: ***Fred Ray*** *c-1, 2, 8, 11, 30, 34, 35, 40-43, 45, 46, 82. Firehair by* ***Kubert****-131-134, 136.* ***Maurer*** *a-138.* ***Severin*** *a-135.* ***Starr*** *a-5.* ***Thorne*** *a-137, 140.*

TOM AND JERRY (See Comic Album #4, 8, 12, Dell Giant #21, Dell Giants, Golden Comics Digest #1, 5, 8, 13, 15, 18, 22, 25, 28, 35, Kite fun Book & March of Comics #21, 46, 61, 70, 88, 103, 119, 128, 145, 154, 173, 190, 207, 224, 281, 295, 305, 321,333, 345, 361, 365, 388, 400, 444, 451, 463, 480)

TOM AND JERRY (...Comics, early issues) (M.G.M.)
(Formerly Our Gang No. 1-59) (See Dell Giants for annuals)
Dell Publishing Co./Gold Key No. 213-327/Whitman No. 328 on: No. 193, 6/48; No. 60, 7/49 - No. 212, 7-9/62; No. 213, 11/62 - No. 291, 2/75; No. 292, 3/77 - No. 342, 5/82 - No. 344, 6/84

	GD	VG	FN	VF	VF/NM	NM-
Four Color 193 (#1)-Titled "M.G.M. Presents..."	34	68	102	245	548	850
60-Barney Bear, Benny Burro cont. from Our Gang; Droopy begins	12	24	36	84	185	285
61	9	18	27	61	123	185
62-70: 66-X-Mas-c	7	14	21	49	92	135
71-80: 77,90-X-Mas-c. 79-Spike & Tyke begin	6	12	18	40	73	105
81-99	5	10	15	35	63	90
100	6	12	18	37	66	95
101-120	5	10	15	31	53	75
121-140: 126-X-Mas-c	4	8	12	28	47	65
141-160	4	8	12	25	40	55
161-200	4	8	12	23	37	50
201-212(7-9/62)(Last Dell issue)	3	6	9	21	33	45
213,214-(84 pgs.)-Titled "...Funhouse"	5	10	15	35	63	90
215-240: 215-Titled "...Funhouse"	3	6	9	16	24	32
241-270	2	4	6	11	16	20
271-300: 286- "Tom & Jerry"	2	4	6	8	11	14
301-327 (Gold Key)	1	3	4	6	8	10
328,329 (Whitman)	2	4	6	8	11	14
330(8/80),331(10/80), 332-(3-pack only)	4	8	12	27	44	60
333-341: 339(2/82), 340(2-3/82), 341(4/82)	2	4	6	8	10	12
342-344 (All #90058, no date, date code, 3-pack): 342(6/83), 343(8/83), 344(6/84)	3	6	9	16	24	32
Mouse From T.R.A.P. 1(7/66)-Giant, G. K.	4	8	12	28	47	65
Summer Fun 1(7/67, 68 pgs.)(Gold Key)-Reprints Barks' Droopy from Summer Fun #1	4	8	12	28	47	65

NOTE: *#60-87, 98-121, 268, 277, 289, 302 are 52 pgs.. Reprints-#225, 241, 245, 247, 252, 254, 266, 268, 270, 292-327, 329-342, 344.*

TOM & JERRY
Harvey Comics: Sept, 1991 - No. 18, Aug, 1994 ($1.25)

1-18: 1-Tom & Jerry, Barney Bear-r by Carl Barks 4.00
50th Anniversary Special 1 (10/91, $2.50, 68 pgs.)-Benny the Lonesome Burro-r by Barks (story/a)/Our Gang #9 5.00

TOMB OF DARKNESS (Formerly Beware)
Marvel Comics Group: No. 9, July, 1974 - No. 23, Nov, 1976

	GD	VG	FN	VF	VF/NM	NM-
9	4	8	12	27	44	60

10-23: 11,16,18-21-Kirby-a. 15,19-Ditko-r. 17-Woodbridge-r/Astonishing #62; Powell-r.

Tokyo Ghost #8 © Remender & Murphy

Tomb of Dracula #12 © MAR

Tomb Raider (2014) #2 © Square Enix

	GD 2.0	VG 4.0	FN 6.0	VF 8.0	VF/NM 9.0	NM- 9.2
20-Everett Venus-r/Venus #19. 23-Everett-r	3	6	9	16	23	30
20,21-(30¢-c variants, limited distribution)(5,7/76)	10	20	30	58	144	220

TOMB OF DRACULA (See Giant-Size Dracula, Dracula Lives, Nightstalkers, Power Record Comics & Requiem for Dracula)
Marvel Comics Group: Apr, 1972 - No. 70, Aug, 1979

	GD 2.0	VG 4.0	FN 6.0	VF 8.0	VF/NM 9.0	NM- 9.2
1-1st app. Dracula & Frank Drake; Colan-p in all; Neal Adams-c	42	84	126	311	706	1100
1-Facsimile Edition (12/22, $3.99) Reprints #1 with original ads	1	3	4	6	8	10
2	10	20	30	64	132	200
3-6: 3-Intro. Dr. Rachel Van Helsing & Inspector Chelm. 6-Neal Adams-c	7	14	21	46	86	125
7-9	6	12	18	38	69	100
10-1st app. Blade the Vampire Slayer (who app. in 1998, 2002 and 2004 movies)	141	282	423	1142	2571	4000
10-Facsimile Edition (1/20, $3.99) Reprints #10 with original ads	2	4	6	9	13	16
11,14-16,20:	5	10	15	31	53	75
12-2nd app. Blade; Brunner-c(p)	13	26	39	89	195	300
13-Origin Blade	21	42	63	147	324	500
17,19: 17-Blade bitten by Dracula. 19-Blade discovers he is immune to vampire's bite. 1st mention of Blade having vampire blood in him	7	14	21	44	82	120
18-Two-part x-over cont'd in Werewolf by Night #15	10	20	30	70	150	230
21,24-Blade app.	5	10	15	34	60	85
22,23,26,27,29	3	6	9	21	33	45
25-1st app. & origin Hannibal King	14	28	42	96	211	325
25-2nd printing (1994)	2	4	6	9	12	15
28-Blade app. on-c & inside as an illusion	5	10	15	33	57	80
30,41,42,44,45-Blade app. 45-Intro. Deacon Frost, the vampire who bit Blade's mother	4	8	12	27	44	60
31-40	3	6	9	18	28	38
43-Blade-c by Wrightson	5	10	15	34	60	85
43-45-(30¢-c variants, limited distribution)	9	18	27	59	117	175
46,47-(Regular 25¢ editions)(4-8/76)	3	6	9	16	23	30
46,47-(30¢-c variants, limited distribution)	9	18	27	59	117	175
48,49,51-57,59,60: 57,59,60-(30¢-c)	3	6	9	15	22	28
50-Silver Surfer app.	7	14	21	44	82	120
57,59,60-(35¢-c variants)(6-9/77)	12	24	36	80	173	265
58-All Blade issue (Regular 30¢ edition)	6	12	18	38	69	100
58-(35¢-c variant)(7/77)	13	26	39	86	188	290
61-69	3	6	9	15	22	28
70-Double size	4	8	12	28	47	65

NOTE: ***N. Adams*** *c-1, 6.* ***Colan*** *a-1-70p; c(p)-8, 38-42, 44-56, 58-70.* ***Wrightson*** *c-43.*

TOMB OF DRACULA, THE (Magazine)
Marvel Comics Group: Oct, 1979 - No. 6, Aug, 1980 (B&W)

	GD 2.0	VG 4.0	FN 6.0	VF 8.0	VF/NM 9.0	NM- 9.2
1,3: 1-Colan-a; features on movies "Dracula" and "Love at First Bite" w/photos. 3-Good girl cover-a; Miller-a (2 pg. sketch)	2	4	6	11	16	20
2,6: 2-Ditko-a (36 pgs.); Nosferatu movie feature. 6-Lilith story w/Sienkiewicz-a	2	4	6	8	11	14
4,5: Stephen King interview	2	4	6	13	18	22

NOTE: ***Buscema*** *a-4p, 5p.* ***Chaykin*** *c-5, 6.* ***Colan*** *a(p)-1, 3-6.* ***Miller*** *a-3.* ***Romita*** *a-2p.*

TOMB OF DRACULA
Marvel Comics (Epic Comics): 1991 - No. 4, 1992 ($4.95, 52 pgs., squarebound, mini-series)

Book 1-4: Colan/Williamson-a; Colan painted-c 5.00

TOMB OF DRACULA
Marvel Comics: Dec, 2004 - No. 4, Mar, 2005 ($2.99, limited series)

1-4-Blade app.; Tolagson-a/Sienkiewicz-c 3.00

TOMB OF DRACULA PRESENTS: THRONE OF BLOOD
Marvel Comics: Jun, 2011 ($3.99, one-shot)

1-Story of Raizo Kodo in 1585 Japan; Parlov-a; Hitch-c 4.00

TOMB OF LEGEIA (See Movie Classics)

TOMB OF TERROR (Thrills of Tomorrow #17 on)
Harvey Publications: June, 1952 - No. 16, July, 1954

	GD 2.0	VG 4.0	FN 6.0	VF 8.0	VF/NM 9.0	NM- 9.2
1	77	154	231	493	847	1200
2	50	100	150	315	533	750
3-Bondage-c; atomic disaster story	58	116	174	371	636	900
4-12: 4-Heart ripped out. 8-12-Nostrand-a	43	86	129	271	461	650
13-Special S/F issue (1/54) White letter shadow-c	84	168	252	538	919	1300
13-Logo variant-c (striped letter shadow)	93	186	279	591	1021	1450
14-Classic S/F-c; Check-a	103	206	309	659	1130	1600
15-S/F issue; c-shows face exploding	703	1406	2109	5732	9066	13,000
16-Special S/F issue; horror-c; Nostrand-a	90	180	270	576	988	1400

NOTE: ***Edd Cartier*** *a-13?* ***Elias*** *c-2, 5-16.* ***Kremer*** *a-1, 7; c-1.* ***Nostrand*** *a-8-12, 15r 16.* ***Palais*** *a-2, 3, 5-7.* ***Powell*** *a-1, 3, 5, 9-16.* ***Sparling*** *a-12, 13, 15.*

TOMB OF TERROR
Marvel Comics: Dec, 2010 ($3.99, B&W, one-shot)

1-Short stories of Man-Thing, Son of Satan, Werewolf By Night & The Living Mummy 4.00

TOMB RAIDER (Also see Lara Croft And The Frozen Omen)
Dark Horse Comics: Feb, 2014 - No. 18, Jul, 2015 ($3.50/$3.99)

1-18: 1-6-Gail Simone-s/Nicolás Daniel Selma-a. 13-Begin $3.99-c 4.00

TOMB RAIDER
Dark Horse Comics: Feb, 2016 - No. 12, Jan, 2017 ($3.99)

1-12-Mariko Tamaki-s/Phillip Sevy-a 4.00

TOMB RAIDER (one-shots)
Image Comics (Top Cow Prod.)

...: Arabian Nights (8/04, $5.99) Avery-s/Tan-a/c 6.00
... Cover Gallery 2006 (4/06, $2.99) artist galleries and series gallery; pin-ups 3.00
.../The Darkness Special 1 (2001, TopCowStore.com)-Wohl-s/Tan-a 3.00
Epiphany 1 (8/03, $4.99)-Jurgens-s/Banks-a/Haley-c; preview of Witchblade Animated 5.00
Takeover 1 (1/04, $2.99)-Benefiel-a/Daniel-c 3.00
... Vs. The Wolf-Men: Monster War 2005 (7/05, $2.99) 2nd part of Monster War x-over 3.00
.../Witchblade/Magdalena/Vampirella #1 (8/05, $2.99, B&W) three covers; Chin-a 3.00

TOMB RAIDER: INFERNO
Dark Horse Comics: Jun, 2018 - No. 4, Oct, 2018 ($3.99, limited series)

1-4-Lanzing & Kelly-s/Sevy-a 4.00

TOMB RAIDER: JOURNEYS
Image Comics (Top Cow Prod.): Jan, 2002 - No. 12, May, 2003 ($2.50/$2.99)

1-12: 1-Avery-s/Drew Johnson-a. 1-Two covers by Johnson & Hughes 3.00

TOMB RAIDER: SURVIVOR'S CRUSADE
Dark Horse Comics: Nov, 2017 - No. 4, Apr, 2018 ($3.99, limited series)

1-4-Lanzing & Kelly-s/Ashley Woods-a 4.00

TOMB RAIDER: THE GREATEST TREASURE OF ALL
Image Comics (Top Cow Prod.): 2002; Oct, 2005 ($6.99)

Prelude (2002, 16 pgs., no cover price) Jusko-c/a 3.00
1-(10/05, $6.99) Jusko-a/Jurgens-s; sketch pages, reference photos, art in progress 7.00

TOMB RAIDER: THE SERIES (Also see Witchblade/Tomb Raider)
Image Comics (Top Cow Prod.): Dec, 1999 - No. 50, Mar, 2005 ($2.50/$2.99)

1-Jurgens-s/Park-a; 3 covers by Park, Finch, Turner 5.00
2-24,26-29,31-50: 21-Black-c w/foil. 31-Mhan-a. 37-Flip book preview of Stryke Force 3.00
25-Michael Turner-c/a; Witchblade app.; Endgame x-over with Witchblade #60 & Evo #1 4.00
30-($4.99) Tony Daniel-a 5.00
#0 (6/01, $2.50) Avery-s/Ching-a/c 3.00
#1/2 (10/01, $2.95) Early days of Lara Croft; Jurgens-s/Lopez-a 3.00
...: Chasing Shangri-La (2002, $12.95, TPB) r/#11-15 13.00
Free Comic Book Day giveaway - (5/02) r/#1 with "Free Comic Book Day" banner on-c 3.00
... Gallery (12/00, $2.95) Pin-ups & previous covers by various 3.00
... Magazine (6/01, $4.95) Hughes-c; r/#1,2; Jurgens interview 5.00
...: Mystic Artifacts (2001, $14.95, TPB) r/#5-10 15.00
...: Saga of the Medusa Mask (9/00, $9.95, TPB) r/#1-4; new Park-c 10.00
... Vol. 1 Compendium (11/06, $59.99) r/#1-50; variant covers and pin-up art 60.00

TOMB RAIDER/WITCHBLADE SPECIAL (Also see Witchblade/Tomb Raider)
Top Cow Prod.: Dec, 1997 (mail-in offer, one-shot)

	GD 2.0	VG 4.0	FN 6.0	VF 8.0	VF/NM 9.0	NM- 9.2
1-Turner-s/a(p); green background cover	2	4	6	11	16	20
1-Variant-c with orange sun background	2	4	6	10	14	18
1-Variant-c with black sides	2	4	6	11	16	20
1-Revisited (12/98, $2.95) reprints #1, Turner-c						3.00
...: Trouble Seekers TPB (2002, $7.95) rep. T.R./W & W/T.R. & W/T.R. 1/2; new Turner-c						8.00

TOMBSTONE TERRITORY
Dell Publishing Co.: No. 1123, Aug, 1960

	GD 2.0	VG 4.0	FN 6.0	VF 8.0	VF/NM 9.0	NM- 9.2
Four Color 1123	7	14	21	49	92	135

TOM CAT (Formerly Bo; Atom The Cat #9 on)
Charlton Comics: No. 4, Apr, 1956 - No. 8, July, 1957

	GD 2.0	VG 4.0	FN 6.0	VF 8.0	VF/NM 9.0	NM- 9.2
4-Al Fago-c/a	8	16	24	44	57	70
5-8	6	12	18	31	38	45

TOM CLANCY'S SPLINTER CELL: ECHOES
Dynamite Entertainment: 2014 - No. 4, 2014 ($3.99)

1-4-Nathan Edmonson-s/Marc Laming-a 4.00

	GD 2.0	VG 4.0	FN 6.0	VF 8.0	VF/NM 9.0	NM- 9.2

TOM CLANCY'S THE DIVISION: EXTREMIS MALIS
Dark Horse Comics: Jan, 2019 - No. 3, Apr, 2019 ($3.99, limited series)
1-3-Christofer Emgard-s/Fernando Baldó-a 4.00

TOM CORBETT, SPACE CADET (TV)
Dell Publishing Co.: No. 378, Jan-Feb, 1952 - No. 11, Sept-Nov, 1954 (All painted covers)

	GD	VG	FN	VF	VF/NM	NM-
Four Color 378 (#1)-McWilliams-a	19	38	57	133	297	460
Four Color 400,421-McWilliams-a	11	22	33	73	157	240
4(11-1/53) - 11	8	16	24	52	99	145

TOM CORBETT SPACE CADET (See March of Comics #102)

TOM CORBETT SPACE CADET (TV)
Prize Publications: V2#1, May-June, 1955 - V2#3, Sept-Oct, 1955

	GD	VG	FN	VF	VF/NM	NM-
V2#1-Robot-c	39	78	117	240	395	550
2,3-Meskin-c	30	60	90	177	289	400

TOM, DICK & HARRIET (See Gold Key Spotlight)

TOM LANDRY AND THE DALLAS COWBOYS
Spire Christian Comics/Fleming H. Revell Co.: 1973 (35/49¢)

	GD	VG	FN	VF	VF/NM	NM-
nn-35¢ edition	3	6	9	17	26	35
nn-49¢ edition	3	6	9	14	19	24

TOM MIX WESTERN (Movie, radio star) (Also see The Comics, Crackajack Funnies, Master Comics, 100 Pages Of Comics, Popular Comics, Real Western Hero, Six Gun Heroes, Western Hero & XMas Comics)
Fawcett Publications: Jan, 1948 - No. 61, May, 1953 (1-17: 52 pgs.)

	GD	VG	FN	VF	VF/NM	NM-
1 (Photo-c, 52 pgs.)-Tom Mix & his horse Tony begin; Tumbleweed Jr. begins, ends #52,54,55	54	108	162	343	574	825
2 (Photo-c)	25	50	75	150	245	340
3-5 (Painted/photo-c): 5-Billy the Kid & Oscar app.	19	38	57	111	176	240
6-8: 6,7 (Painted/photo-c). 8-Kinstler tempera-c	16	32	48	94	147	200
9,10 (Paint/photo-c) 9-Used in **SOTI**, pgs. 323-325	15	30	45	90	140	190
11-Kinstler oil-c	14	28	42	82	121	160
12 (Painted/photo-c)	14	28	42	78	112	145
13-17 (Painted-c, 52 pgs.)	14	28	42	78	112	145
18,22 (Painted-c, 36 pgs.)	12	24	36	69	97	125
19 (Photo-c, 52 pgs.)	13	26	39	74	105	135
20,21,23 (Painted-c, 52 pgs.)	12	24	36	69	97	125
24,25,27-29 (52 pgs.): 24-Photo-c begin, end #61. 29-Slim Pickens app.	11	22	33	60	83	105
26,30 (36 pgs.)	10	20	30	56	76	95
31-33,35-37,39,40,42 (52 pgs.): 39-Red Eagle app.	10	20	30	56	76	95
34,38 (36 pgs. begin)	9	18	27	52	69	85
41,43-60: 57-(9/52)-Dope smuggling story	8	16	24	40	50	60
61-Last issue	9	18	27	47	61	75

NOTE: *Photo-c from 1930s Tom Mix movies (he died in 1940). Many issues contain ads for Tom Mix, Rocky Lane, Space Patrol and other premiums. Captain Tootsie by* ***C.C. Beck*** *in #6-11, 20.*

TOM MIX WESTERN
AC Comics: 1988 - No. 2, 1989? ($2.95, B&W w/16 pgs. color, 44 pgs.)
1-Tom Mix-r/Master #124,128,131,102 plus Billy the Kid-r by Severin; photo front/back/inside-c 4.00
2-($2.50, B&W)-Gabby Hayes-r; photo covers 4.00
...Holiday Album 1 (1990, $3.50, B&W, one-shot, 44 pgs.)-Contains photos & 1950s Tom Mix-r; photo inside-c 4.00

TOMMY GUN WIZARDS (Titled Machine Gun Wizards for #4)
Dark Horse Comics: Aug, 2019 - No. 4, Nov, 2019 ($3.99, limited series)
1-4-Christian Ward-s/Sami Kivelä-a; Prohibition era magicians in 1931 Chicago 4.00

TOMMY OF THE BIG TOP (Thrilling Circus Adventures)
King Features Synd./Standard Comics: No. 10, Sep, 1948 - No. 12, Mar, 1949

	GD	VG	FN	VF	VF/NM	NM-
10-By John Lehti	15	30	45	83	124	165
11,12	10	20	30	56	76	95

TOMMY TOMORROW (See Action Comics #127, Real Fact #6, Showcase #41,42,44,46,47 & World's Finest #102)

TOMOE (Also see Shi: The Way Of the Warrior #6)
Crusade Comics: July, 1995 - No. 3, June, 1996($2.95)

	GD	VG	FN	VF	VF/NM	NM-
0-3: 2-B&W Dogs o' War preview. 3-B&W Demon Gun preview						3.00
0 (3/96, $2.95)-variant-c.						3.00
0-Commemorative edition (5,000)	2	4	6	8	10	12
1-Commemorative edition (5,000)	2	4	6	9	12	15
1-($2.95)-FAN Appreciation edition						3.00
TPB (1997, $14.95) r/#0-3						15.00

TOMOE: UNFORGETTABLE FIRE
Crusade Comics: June, 1997 ($2.95, one-shot)
1-Prequel to Shi: The Series 3.00

TOMOE-WITCHBLADE/FIRE SERMON
Crusade Comics: Sept, 1996 ($3.95, one-shot)
1-Tucci-c 5.00
1-($9.95)-Avalon Ed. w/gold foil-c 10.00

TOMOE-WITCHBLADE/MANGA SHI PREVIEW EDITION
Crusade Comics: July, 1996 ($5.00, B&W)
nn-San Diego Preview Edition 5.00

TOMORROW
Dark Horse Comics (Berger Books): Feb, 2020 - No. 5 ($3.99, limited series)
1,2-Peter Milligan-s/Jesús Hervás-a 4.00

TOMORROW KNIGHTS
Marvel Comics (Epic Comics): June, 1990 - No. 6, Mar, 1991 ($1.50)
1-($1.95, 52 pgs.) 4.00
2-6 3.00

TOMORROW STORIES
America's Best Comics: Oct, 1999 - No. 12, Aug, 2002 ($3.50/$2.95)
1-Two covers by Ross and Nowlan; Moore-s 4.00
2-12-($2.95) 6-1st app. Splash Brannigan 3.00
... Special (1/06, $6.99) Nowlan-c; Moore-s; Greyshirt tribute to Will Eisner 7.00
... Special 2 (5/06, $6.99) Gene Ha-c; Moore-s; Promethea app. 7.00
Book 1 Hardcover (2002, $24.95) r/#1-6 25.00
Book 1 TPB (2003, $17.95) r/#1-6 18.00
Book 2 Hardcover (2004, $24.95) r/#7-12 25.00
Book 2 TPB (2005, $17.99) r/#7-12 18.00

TOM SAWYER (See Adventures of... & Famous Stories)

TOM SKINNER-UP FROM HARLEM (See Up From Harlem)

TOM STRONG (Also see Many Worlds of Tesla Strong)
America's Best Comics: June, 1999 - No. 36, May, 2006 ($3.50/$2.95/$2.99)
1-Two covers by Ross and Sprouse; Moore-s/Sprouse-a 4.00
1-Special Edition (9/09, $1.00) reprint with "After Watchmen" cover frame 3.00
2-36: 4-Art Adams-a (8 pgs.) 13-Fawcett homage w/art by Sprouse, Baker, Heath 20-Origin of Tom Stone. 22-Ordway-a. 31,32-Moorcock-s 3.00
...: Book One HC ('00, $24.95) r/#1-7, cover gallery and sketchbook 25.00
...: Book One TPB ('01, $14.95) r/#1-7, cover gallery and sketchbook 15.00
...: Book Two HC ('02, $24.95) r/#8-14, sketchbook 25.00
...: Book Two TPB ('03, $14.95) r/#8-14, sketchbook 15.00
...: Book Three HC ('04, $24.95) r/#15-19, sketchbook 25.00
...: Book Three TPB ('04, $17.95) r/#15-19, sketchbook 18.00
...: Book Four HC ('04, $24.95) r/#20-25, sketch pages 25.00
...: Book Four TPB ('05, $17.99) r/#20-25, sketch pages 18.00
...: Book Five HC ('05, $24.99) r/#26-30, sketch pages 25.00
...: Book Five TPB ('06, $17.99) r/#26-30, sketch pages 18.00
...: Book Six HC ('06, $24.99) r/#31-36 25.00
...: Book Six TPB ('08, $17.99) r/#31-36 18.00
...: The Deluxe Edition Book One (2009, $39.99, d.j.) r/#1-12; Moore intro.; sketch-a 40.00
...: The Deluxe Edition Book Two (2010, $39.99, d.j.) r/#13-24; sketch-a 40.00

TOM STRONG AND THE PLANET OF PERIL
DC Comics (Vertigo): Sept, 2013 - No. 6. Feb, 2014 ($2.99, limited series)
1-6-Hogan-s/Sprouse-a/c. 2-Travel to Terra Obscura 3.00

TOM STRONG AND THE ROBOTS OF DOOM
DC Comics (WildStorm): Aug, 2010 - No. 6, Jan, 2011 ($3.99, limited series)
1-6-Hogan-s/Sprouse-a. 1-Covers by Sprouse & Williams 4.00
TPB (2011, $17.99) r/#1-6 18.00

TOM STRONG'S TERRIFIC TALES
America's Best Comics: Jan, 2002 - No. 12 ($3.50/$2.95)
1-Short stories; Moore-s; art by Art Adams, Rivoche, Hernandez, Weiss 3.50
2-12-($2.95) 2-Adams, Ordway, Weiss-a; Adams-c. 4-Rivoche-a. 5-Pearson, Aragonés-a 11-Timm-a 3.00
...: Book One HC ('04, $24.95) r/#1-6, cover gallery and sketch pages 25.00
...: Book One SC ('05, $17.99) r/#1-6, cover gallery and sketch pages 18.00
...: Book Two HC ('05, $24.95) r/#7-12, covers 25.00

TOM TERRIFIC! (TV)(See Mighty Mouse Fun Club Magazine #1)
Pines Comics (Paul Terry): Summer, 1957 - No. 6, Fall, 1958
(See Terry Toons Giant Summer Fun Book)

	GD	VG	FN	VF	VF/NM	NM-
1-1st app.?; CBS Television Presents...	25	50	75	150	245	340
2-6-(scarce)	20	40	60	117	189	260

TOM THUMB
Dell Publishing Co.: No. 972, Jan, 1959

	GD	VG	FN	VF	VF/NM	NM-
Four Color 972-Movie, George Pal	8	16	24	52	99	145

TOM-TOM, THE JUNGLE BOY (See A-1 Comics & Tick Tock Tales)
Magazine Enterprises: 1947 - No. 3, 1947; Nov, 1957 - No. 3, Mar, 1958

	GD	VG	FN	VF	VF/NM	NM-
1-Funny animal	15	30	45	88	137	185
2,3(1947): 3-Christmas issue	12	24	36	67	94	120
Tom-Tom & Itchi the Monk 1(11/57) - 3(3/58)	7	14	21	35	43	50
I.W. Reprint No. 1,2,8,10: 1,2,8-r/Koko & Kola #?	2	4	6	10	14	18

TONGUE LASH
Dark Horse Comics: Aug, 1996 - No. 2, Sept, 1996 ($2.95, lim. series, mature)
1,2: Taylor-c/a 3.00

TONGUE LASH II
Dark Horse Comics: Feb, 1999 - No. 2, Mar, 1999 ($2.95, lim. series, mature)
1,2: Taylor-c/a 3.00

TONKA (Disney)
Dell Publishing Co.: No. 966, Jan, 1959

	GD	VG	FN	VF	VF/NM	NM-
Four Color 966-Movie (Starring Sal Mineo)-photo-c	8	16	24	56	108	160

TONTO (See The Lone Ranger's Companion...)

TONY STARK: IRON MAN (Leads into Iron Man 2020 #1)
Marvel Comics: Aug, 2018 - No. 19, Feb, 2020 ($4.99/$3.99)
1-($4.99) Slott-s/Schiti-a; Fin Fang Foom & The Controller app. 5.00
2-19-($3.99) 3-Machine Man app. 4,6-8-Janet Van Dyne app. 5-Arno Stark app. 12,13-War of the Realms tie-ins; Simone-s. 14-Capt. Marvel app. 16-19 Ultron app. 4.00

TONY TRENT (The Face #1,2)
Big Shot/Columbia Comics Group: No. 3, 1948 - No. 4, 1949

	GD	VG	FN	VF	VF/NM	NM-
3,4: 3-The Face app. by Mart Bailey	22	44	66	128	209	290

TOODLES, THE (The Toodle Twins with #1)
Ziff-Davis (Approved Comics)/Argo: No. 10, July-Aug, 1951; Mar, 1956 (Newspaper-r)

	GD	VG	FN	VF	VF/NM	NM-
10-Painted-c, some newspaper-r by The Baers	16	32	48	92	144	195
...Twins 1(Argo, 3/56)-Reprints by The Baers	9	18	27	50	65	80

TOO MUCH COFFEE MAN
Adhesive Comics: July, 1993 - No. 10, Dec, 2000 ($2.50, B&W)

	GD	VG	FN	VF	VF/NM	NM-
1-Shannon Wheeler story & art	2	4	6	9	12	15
2,3	1	2	3	5	7	9
4,5						6.00
6-10						4.00
Full Color Special-nn($2.95),2-(7/97, $3.95)						4.00

Tom Mix Western #3 © FAW

Tony Stark: Iron Man #4 © MAR

Top Dog #10 © MAR

	GD 2.0	VG 4.0	FN 6.0	VF 8.0	VF/NM 9.0	NM- 9.2

TOO MUCH COFFEE MAN SPECIAL
Dark Horse Comics: July, 1997 ($2.95, B&W)

nn-Reprints Dark Horse Presents #92-95						4.00

TOO MUCH HOPELESS SAVAGES
Oni Press: June, 2003 - No. 4, Apr, 2004 ($2.99, B&W, limited series)

1-4-Van Meter-s/Norrie-a						3.00
TPB (8/04, $11.95, digest-size) r/series						12.00

TOOTH & CLAW (See Autumnlands: Tooth & Claw)

TOOTS AND CASPER
Dell Publishing Co.: No. 5, 1942

Large Feature Comic 5	25	50	75	150	245	340

TOP ADVENTURE COMICS
I. W. Enterprises: 1964 (Reprints)

1-r/High Adv. (Explorer Joe #2); Krigstein-r	2	4	6	13	18	22
2-Black Dwarf-r/Red Seal #22; Kinstler-c	3	6	9	14	20	25

TOP CAT (TV) (Hanna-Barbera)(See Kite Fun Book)
Dell Publ.Co./Gold Key No. 4 on: 12-2/61-62 - No. 3, 6-8/62; No. 4, 10/62 - No. 31, 9/70

1 (TV show debuted 9/27/61)	15	30	45	105	233	360
2-Augie Doggie back-ups in #1-4	9	18	27	58	114	170
3-5: 3-Last 15¢ issue. 4-Begin 12¢ issues; Yakky Doodle app. in 1 pg. strip. 5-Touché Turtle app.	6	12	18	37	66	95
6-10	5	10	15	30	50	70
11-20	4	8	12	23	37	50
21-31-Reprints	3	6	9	18	28	38

TOP CAT (TV) (Hanna-Barbera)(See TV Stars #4)
Charlton Comics: Nov, 1970 - No. 20, Nov, 1973

1	7	14	21	54	82	120
2-10	3	6	9	19	30	40
11-20	3	6	9	16	24	32

NOTE: *#8 (1/72) went on sale late in 1972 between #14 and #15 with the 1/73 issues.*

TOP COMICS
K. K. Publications/Gold Key: July, 1967 (All reprints)

nn-The Gnome-Mobile (Disney-movie)	3	6	9	14	20	25
1-Beagle Boys (#7), Beep Beep the Road Runner (#5), Bugs Bunny, Chip 'n' Dale, Daffy Duck (#50), Flipper, Huey, Dewey & Louie, Junior Woodchucks, Lassie, The Little Monsters (#71), Moby Duck, Porky Pig (has Gold Key label - says Top Comics on inside), Scamp, Super Goof, Tom & Jerry, Top Cat (#21), Tweety & Sylvester (#7), Walt Disney C&S (#322), Woody Woodpecker known issues; each character given own book	2	4	6	9	13	16
1-Donald Duck (not Barks), Mickey Mouse	2	4	6	13	18	22
1-Flintstones	4	8	12	23	37	50
1-Huckleberry Hound, Yogi Bear (#30)	3	6	9	14	19	24
1-The Jetsons	5	10	15	30	50	70
1-Tarzan of the Apes (#169)	3	6	9	16	23	30
1-Three Stooges (#35)	3	6	9	19	30	40
1-Uncle Scrooge (#70)	3	6	9	16	23	30
1-Zorro (r/G.K. Zorro #7 w/Toth-a; says 2nd printing)	3	6	9	14	19	24
2-Bugs Bunny, Daffy Duck, Mickey Mouse (#114), Porky Pig, Super Goof, Tom & Jerry, Tweety & Sylvester, Walt Disney's C&S (r/#325), Woody Woodpecker	2	4	6	9	12	15
2-Donald Duck (not Barks), Three Stooges, Uncle Scrooge (#71)-Barks-c, Yogi Bear (#30), Zorro (r/#8; Toth-a)	2	4	6	11	16	20
2-Snow White & 7 Dwarfs(6/67)(1944-r)	2	4	6	11	16	20
3-Donald Duck	2	4	6	11	16	20
3-Uncle Scrooge (#72)	2	4	6	13	18	22
3,4-The Flintstones	3	6	9	21	33	45
3,4: 3-Mickey Mouse (r/#115), Tom & Jerry, Woody Woodpecker, Yogi Bear. 4-Mickey Mouse, Woody Woodpecker	2	4	6	9	12	15

NOTE: *Each book in this series is identical to its counterpart except for cover, and came out at same time. The number in parentheses is the original issue it contains.*

TOP COW (Company one-shots)
Image Comics (Top Cow Productions)

... Book of Revelations (7/03, $3.99)-Pin-ups and info; art by various; Gossett-c						4.00
... Convention Sketchbook 2004 (4/04, $3.00, B&W) art by various						3.00
... Holiday Special Vol. 1 (12/10, $12.99) Flip book with Jingle Belle						13.00
... Preview Book 2005 (3/05, 99¢) Preview pages of Tomb Raider, Darkness, Rising Stars						3.00
... Productions, Inc./Ballistic Studios Swimsuit Special (5/95, $2.95)						3.00
...'s Best of: Dave Finch Vol. 1 TPB (8/06, $19.99) r/issues of Cyberforce, Aphrodite IX, Ascension and The Darkness; art & cover gallery						20.00
...'s Best of: Michael Turner Vol. 1 TPB (12/05, $24.99) r/Witchblade #1,10,12,18,19,25 & Witchblade/Tomb Raider chapters 1&3; Tomb Raider #25; art & cover gallery						25.00
... Secrets: Special Winter Lingerie Edition 1 (1/96, $2.95) Pin-ups						3.00
... 2001 Preview (no cover price) Preview pages of Tomb Raider; Jusko-a; flip cover & pages of Inferno						3.00

TOP COW CLASSICS IN BLACK AND WHITE
Image Comics (Top Cow): Feb, 2000 - Jan, 2003 ($2.95, B&W reprints)

...: Aphrodite IX #1(9/00) B&W reprint						3.00
...: Ascension #1(4/00) B&W reprint plus time-line of series						3.00
...: Battle of the Planets #1(1/03) B&W reprint plus script and cover gallery						3.00
...: Darkness #1(3/00) B&W reprint plus time-line of series						3.00
...: Fathom #1(5/00) B&W reprint						3.00
...: Magdalena #1(10/02) B&W reprint plus time-line of series						3.00
...: Midnight Nation #1(9/00) B&W preview						3.00
...: Rising Stars #1(7/00) B&W reprint plus cover gallery						3.00
...: Tomb Raider #1(12/00) B&W reprint plus back-story						3.00
...: Witchblade #1(2/00) B&W reprint plus back-story						3.00
...: Witchblade #25(5/01) B&W reprint plus interview with Wohl & Haberlin						3.00

TOP DETECTIVE COMICS
I. W. Enterprises: 1964 (Reprints)

9-r/Young King Cole #14; Dr. Drew (not Grandenetti)	2	4	6	11	16	20

TOP DOG (See Star Comics Magazine, 75¢)
Star Comics (Marvel): Apr, 1985 - No. 14, June, 1987 (Children's book)

1-14: 10-Peter Parker & J. Jonah Jameson cameo						5.00

TOP ELIMINATOR (Teenage Hotrodders #1-24; Drag 'n' Wheels #30 on)
Charlton Comics: No. 25, Sept, 1967 - No. 29, July, 1968

25-29	3	6	9	16	23	30

TOP FLIGHT COMICS: Four Star Publ.: 1947 (Advertised, not published)

TOP FLIGHT COMICS
St. John Publishing Co.: July, 1949

1(7/49, St. John)-Hector the Inspector; funny animal	14	28	42	78	112	145

TOP GUN (See Luke Short, 4-Color #927 & Showcase #72)

TOP GUNS OF THE WEST (See Super DC Giant)

TOPIX (...Comics) (Timeless Topix-early issues) (Also see Men of Battle, Men of Courage & Treasure Chest)(V1-V5#1,V7 on-paper-c)
Catechetical Guild Educational Society: 11/42 - V10#15, 1/28/52 (Weekly - later issues)

V1#1(8 pgs.,8x11")	25	50	75	150	245	340
2,3(8 pgs.,8x11")	14	28	42	82	121	160
4-8(16 pgs.,8x11")	12	24	36	69	97	125
V2#1-10(16 pgs.,8x11"): V2#8-Pope Pius XII	10	20	30	58	79	100
V3#1-10(16 pgs.,8x11"): V3#1-(9/44)	10	20	30	56	76	95
V4#1-10: V4#1-(9/45)	9	18	27	50	65	80
V5#1(10/46,52 pgs.,2(11/46),no #3),4(1/47)-9(6/47),10(7/47), no #13,4(10/47), 14(11/47),15(12/47)	8	16	24	42	54	65
11(8/47),12(9/47)-Life of Christ editions	10	20	30	56	76	95
V6#4(1/48),5(2/48),7(3/48),8(4/48),9(5/48),10(6/48),11(7/48)-14 (no #1-3,6)	7	14	21	35	43	50
V7#1(9/1/48)-20(6/15/49), 36 pgs.	6	12	18	29	36	42
V8#1(9/19/49)-3,5-11,13-30(5/15/50) 30-Hitler app.	6	12	18	28	34	40
4-Dagwood Splits the Atom(10/10/49)-Magazine format	8	16	24	42	54	65
12-Ingels-a	10	20	30	56	76	95
V9#1(9/25/50)-11,13-30(5/14/51)	6	12	18	27	33	38
12-Special 36 pg. Xmas issue, text illos format	6	12	18	28	34	40
V10#1(10/1/51)-15: 14-Hollingsworth-a	6	12	18	27	33	38

TOP JUNGLE COMICS
I. W. Enterprises: 1964 (Reprint)

1(nd)-Reprints White Princess of the Jungle #3, minus cover; Kintsler-a	3	6	9	16	24	34

TOP LOVE STORIES (Formerly Gasoline Alley #2)
Star Publications: No. 3, 5/51 - No. 19, 3/54

3(#1)	36	72	108	211	343	475
4,5,7-9: 8-Wood story	27	54	81	158	259	360
6-Wood-a	32	64	96	188	307	425
10-16,18,19-Disbrow-a	25	50	75	150	245	340
17-Wood art (Fox-r)	26	52	78	154	252	350

NOTE: *All have* **L. B. Cole** *covers.*

TOP-NOTCH COMICS (...Laugh #28-45; Laugh Comix #46 on)
MLJ Magazines: Dec, 1939 - No. 45, June, 1944

1-Origin/1st app. The Wizard; Kardak the Mystic Magician, Swift of the Secret Service (ends #3), Air Patrol, The Westpointer, Manhunters (by J. Cole), Mystic (ends #2) & Scott Rand (ends #3) begin; Wizard covers begin, end #8 595 1190 1785 4350 7675 11,000
2-(1/40)-Dick Storm (ends #8), Stacy Knight M.D. (ends #4) begin; Jack Cole-a; 1st app. Nazis swastika on-c 300 600 900 1920 3310 4700
3-Bob Phantom, Scott Rand on Mars begin; J. Cole-a 219 438 657 1402 2401 3400
4-Origin/1st app. Streak Chandler on Mars; Moore of the Mounted only app.; J. Cole-a 194 388 582 1242 2121 3000
5-Flag-c; origin/1st app. Galahad; Shanghai Sheridan begins (ends #8); Shield cameo; Novick-a; classic-c 232 464 696 1485 2543 3600
6-Meskin-a 148 296 444 947 1624 2300
7-The Shield x-over in Wizard; The Wizard dons new costume 181 362 543 1158 1979 2800
8-Origin/1st app. The Firefly & Roy, the Super Boy (9/40, 2nd costumed boy hero after Robin?; also see Toro in Human Torch #1 (Fall/40) 194 388 582 1242 2121 3000
9-Origin & 1st app. The Black Hood; 1st Black Hood-c & logo (10/40); Fran Frazier begins (Scarce) 784 1568 2352 5723 10,112 14,500
10-2nd app. Black Hood 258 516 774 1651 2826 4000
11-3rd Black Hood 174 348 522 1114 1907 2700
12-15 142 284 426 509 1555 2200
16-18,20 129 258 387 826 1413 2000
19-Classic bondage-c 161 322 483 1030 1765 2500
21,23-30: 23-26-Roy app. 24-No Wizard. 25-Last Bob Phantom. 27-Last Firefly; Nazi war-c. 28-1st app. Suzie; Pokey Oakey begins. 29-Last Kardak 100 200 300 635 1093 1550
22-Archie cameo in ad (12/41) same date as Pep Comics #22 622 1244 1866 4541 8021 11,500
31-44: 33-Dotty & Ditto by Woggon begins (2/43, 1st app.). 44-Black Hood series ends 53 106 159 334 567 800
45-Last issue 65 130 195 416 708 1000

NOTE: *J. Binder a-1-3. **Meskin** a-2, 3, 6, 15. **Bob Montana** a-30; c-28-31. **Harry Sahle** c-42-45. **Woggon** a-33-40, 42. Bondage c-17, 19. Black Hood also appeared on radio in 1944. Black Hood app. on c-9-34, 41-44. Roy the Super Boy app. on c-8, 9, 11-27. The Wizard app. on c-1-8, 11-13, 15-22, 24, 25, 27. Pokey Oakey app. on c-28-43. Suzie app. on c-44-on.*

TOPPER & NEIL (TV)
Dell Publishing Co.: No. 859, Nov, 1957

Four Color 859 7 14 21 44 82 120

TOPPS COMICS: Four Star Publications: 1947 (Advertised, not published)

TOPS
July, 1949 - No. 2, Sept, 1949 (25¢, 10-1/4x13-1/4", 68 pgs.)
Tops Magazine, Inc. (Lev Gleason): (Large size-magazine format; for the adult reader)

1 (Rare)-Story by Dashiell Hammett; Crandall/Lubbers, Tuska, Dan Barry, Fuje-a; Biro painted-c 300 600 900 1980 3440 4900
2 (Rare)-Crandall/Lubbers, Biro, Kida, Fuje, Guardineer-a 271 542 813 1734 2967 4200

TOPS COMICS
Consolidated Book Publishers: 1944 (10¢, 132 pgs.)

2000-(Color-c, inside in red shade & some in full color)-Ace Kelly by Rick Yager, Black Orchid, Don on the Farm, Dinky Dinkerton (Rare) 57 114 171 362 619 875

NOTE: *This book is printed in such a way that when the staple is removed, the strips on the left side of the book correspond with the same strips on the right side. Therefore, if strips are removed from the book, each strip can be folded into a complete comic section of its own.*

TOPS COMICS
Consolidated Book Publs. (Lev Gleason): 1944 (7-1/4x5" digest-size, 32 pgs.)

2001-Origin The Jack of Spades (costumed hero) 36 72 108 211 343 475
2002-Rip Raider 22 44 66 132 216 300
2003-Red Birch (gag cartoons) 14 28 42 78 112 145
2004-"Don't Bother to Dry Off" (gag cartoons) 22 44 66 128 209 290

TOP SECRET
Hillman Publ.: Jan, 1952

1 28 56 84 165 270 375

TOP SECRET ADVENTURES (See Spyman)

TOP SECRETS (...of the F.B.I.)
Street & Smith Publications: Nov, 1947 - No. 10, July-Aug, 1949

1-Powell-c/a 43 86 129 271 461 650
2-Powell-c/a 30 60 90 177 289 400
3-6,8,10-Powell-a 26 52 78 154 252 350
9-Powell-c/a 27 54 81 158 259 360
7-Used in SOTI, pg. 90 & illo. "How to hurt people"; used by N.Y. Legis. Comm.; Powell-c/a 40 80 120 246 411 575

NOTE: ***Powell** c-1-3, 5-10.*

TOPS IN ADVENTURE
Ziff-Davis Publishing Co.: Fall, 1952 (25¢, 132 pgs.)

1-Crusader from Mars, The Hawk, Football Thrills, He-Man; Powell-a; painted-c 55 110 165 352 601 850

TOPS IN HUMOR
Remington Morse Publ. (Harry A. Chesler, Jr.): No date (1944) (7-1/4x5" digest size, 64 pgs., 10¢)

1-WWII serviceman humor (scarce) 30 60 90 177 289 400
2-(Wise Publ.) WWII serviceman humor 18 36 54 105 165 225

TOP SPOT COMICS
Top Spot Publ. Co.: 1945

1-The Menace, Duke of Darkness app. 55 110 165 352 601 850

TOPSY-TURVY (Teenage)
R. B. Leffingwell Publ.: Apr, 1945

1-1st app. Cookie 37 74 111 222 361 500

TOP TEN
America's Best Comics: Sept, 1999 - No. 12, Oct, 2001 ($3.50/$2.95)

1-Two covers by Ross and Ha/Cannon; Alan Moore-s/Gene Ha-a 3.50
2-11-($2.95) 3.00
12-($3.50) 3.50
Hardcover ('00, $24.95) Dust jacket with Gene Ha-a; r/#1-7 25.00
Softcover ('00, $14.95) new Gene Ha-c; r/#1-7 15.00
Book 2 HC ('02, $24.95) Dust jacket with Gene Ha-a; r/#8-12 25.00
Book 2 SC ('03, $14.95) new Gene Ha-c; r/#8-12 15.00
...: The Forty-Niners HC (2005, $24.99, dust jacket) prequel set in 1949; Moore-s/Ha-a 25.00

TOP TEN: BEYOND THE FARTHEST PRECINCT
America's Best Comics: Oct, 2005 - No. 5, Feb, 2006 ($2.99, limited series)

1-5-Jerry Ordway-a/Paul DiFilippo-s 3.00
TPB (2006, $14.99) r/series; cover sketch pages 15.00

TOP TEN SEASON TWO
America's Best Comics: Dec, 2008 - No. 4, Mar, 2009 ($2.99, limited series)

1-4-Cannon-s/Ha-a 3.00
... Special (5/09, $2.99) Cannon-s/Daxiong-a/Ha-c 3.00

TOR (Prehistoric Life on Earth) (Formerly One Million Years Ago)
St. John Publ. Co.: No. 2, Oct, 1953; No. 3, May, 1954 - No. 5, Oct, 1954

3-D 2(10/53)-Kubert-c/a 15 30 45 90 140 190
3-D 2(10/53)-Oversized, otherwise same contents 15 30 45 83 124 165
3-D 2(11/53)-Kubert-c/a; has 3-D cover 15 30 45 83 124 165
3-5-Kubert-c/a: 3-Danny Dreams by Toth; Kubert 1 pg. story (w/self portrait) 21 42 63 122 199 275

NOTE: *The two October 3-D's have same contents and **Powell** art; the October & November issues are titled 3-D Comics. All 3-D issues are 25¢ and came with 3-D glasses.*

TOR (See Sojourn)
National Periodical Publications: May-June, 1975 - No. 6, Mar-Apr, 1976

1-New origin by Kubert 2 4 6 11 16 20
2-6: 2-Origin-r/St. John #1 1 2 3 5 6 8

NOTE: ***Kubert** a-1, 2-6r; c-1-6. **Toth** a(p)-3r.*

TOR (3-D)
Eclipse Comics: July, 1986 - No. 2, Aug, 1987 ($2.50)

1,2: 1-r/One Million Years Ago. 2-r/Tor 3-D #2 5.00
...2-D: 1,2-Limited signed & numbered editions 2 4 6 11 16 20

TOR
Marvel Comics (Epic Comics/Heavy Hitters): June, 1993 - No. 4, 1993 ($5.95, lim. series)

1-4: Joe Kubert-c/a/scripts 6.00

TOR (Joe Kubert's...)
DC Comics: Jul, 2008 - No. 6, Dec, 2008 ($2.99, limited series)

1-6-New story; Joe Kubert-c/a/scripts 3.00
...: A Prehistoric Odyssey HC (2009, $24.99, DJ) r/#1-6; Roy Thomas intro.; sketch-a 25.00
...: A Prehistoric Odyssey SC (2010, $14.99) r/#1-6; Roy Thomas intro.; sketch-a 15.00

TOR BY JOE KUBERT
DC Comics: 2001 - 2003 ($49.95, hardcovers with dust jacket)

Volume 1 (2001) r/One Million Years Ago #1 & 3-D Comics #1&2 in flat color; script pages, sketch pages, proposals for TV and newspapers strips; intro. by Roy Thomas 50.00
Volume 2 (2002) r/Tor (St. John) #3-5; Danny Dreams; portfolio section 50.00
Volume 3 (2003) r/Tor (DC '75) #1; (Marvel '93) #1-4; portfolio section 50.00

TORCH, THE
Marvel Comics (with Dynamite Ent.): Nov, 2009 - No. 8, Jul, 2010 ($3.99, limited series)

1-8-Thinker resurrects the Golden Age Human Torch; Toro app; Alex Ross-c on all; Berkenkotter-a. 3-5-Namor app. 4.00

TORCH OF LIBERTY SPECIAL
Dark Horse Comics (Legend): Jan, 1995 ($2.50, one-shot)

1-Byrne scripts 3.00

TORCHWOOD (Based on the BBC TV series)
Titan Comics: Sept, 2010 - No. 6, Jan, 2011 ($3.99)

1-6: 1-Barrowman-s/Edwards-a; Churchill & photo-c. 2-Art by Yeowell & Grist 4.00

TORCHWOOD (Based on the BBC TV series)
Titan Comics: Aug, 2016 - No. 4, Jan, 2017; Vol. 2: Mar, 2017 - No. 4, Jun, 2017; Vol. 3: Nov, 2017 - No. 4, Mar, 2018 ($3.99)

1-4-John & Carole Barrowman-s/Fuso & Qualano-a; multiple covers 4.00
Vol. 2 1-4-John & Carole Barrowman-s/Edwards-a; multiple covers 4.00
Vol. 3 1-4-John & Carole Barrowman-s/Edwards-a; multiple covers; Capt. John Hart app. 4.00

TORCHY (...Blonde Bombshell) (See Dollman, Military, & Modern)
Quality Comics Group: Nov, 1949 - No. 6, Sept, 1950

1-Bill Ward-c, Gil Fox-a 252 504 756 1613 2757 3900
2,3-Fox-c/a 123 246 369 787 1344 1900
4-Fox-c/a(3), Ward-a (9 pgs.) 155 310 465 992 1696 2400
5,6-Ward-c/a, 9 pgs; Fox-a(3) each 161 322 483 1030 1765 2500
Super Reprint #16(1964)-r/#4 with new-c 9 18 27 59 117 175

TO RIVERDALE AND BACK AGAIN (Archie Comics Presents...)
Archie Comics: 1990 ($2.50, 68 pgs.)

nn-Byrne-c, Colan-a(p); adapts NBC TV movie 2 4 6 8 10 12

TORMENTED, THE (Becomes Surprise Adventures #3 on)
Sterling Comics: July, 1954 - No. 2, Sept, 1954

1-Good Girl torture-c 258 516 774 1651 2826 4000
2-Devil's circus-c 97 194 291 621 1061 1500

TORNADO TOM (See Mighty Midget Comics)

TORSO (See Jinx: Torso)

TOTAL ECLIPSE
Eclipse Comics: May, 1988 - No. 5, Apr, 1989 ($3.95, 52 pgs., deluxe size)

Book 1-5: 3-Intro/1st app. new Black Terror. 4-Many copies have upside down pages and are mis-cut 5.00

TOTAL ECLIPSE
Image Comics: July, 1998 (one-shot)

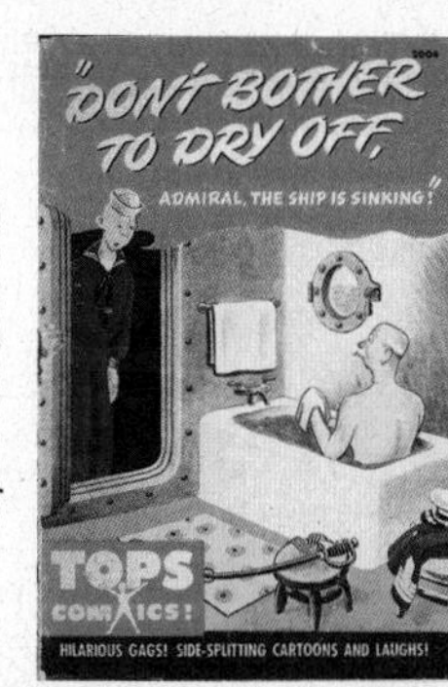

Tops Comics 2004 © LEV

Torchwood (2016) #1 © BBC

Toy Story #4 © DIS & Pixar

GD VG FN VF VF/NM NM-
2.0 4.0 6.0 8.0 9.0 9.2

1-McFarlane-c; Eclipse Comics character pin-ups by Image artists 3.00

TOTAL ECLIPSE: THE SERAPHIM OBJECTIVE
Eclipse Comics: Nov, 1988 ($1.95, one-shot, Baxter paper)
1-Airboy, Valkyrie, The Heap app. 3.00

TOTAL JUSTICE
DC Comics: Oct, 1996 - No. 3, Nov, 1996 ($2.25, bi-weekly limited series) (Based on toyline)
1-3 3.00

TOTALLY AWESOME HULK, THE (Amadeus Cho as The Hulk)(Continues in Inc. Hulk #709)
Marvel Comics: Feb, 2016 - No. 23, Nov, 2017 ($4.99/$3.99)
1-($4.99) Frank Cho-a/Greg Pak-s; She-Hulk and Spider-Man (Miles) app. 3 6 9 14 20 25
2,4-23-($3.99) 2-Fin Fang Foom and Lady Hellbender app. 5,6-Mike Choi-a. 7,8-Alan Davis-a. 9-11-Civil War II tie-in. 9-Del Mundo-a. 10-12-Black Panther app. 13-15-Jeremy Lin app. 19-22-Crossover with Weapon X #5,6 and Weapons of Mutant Destruction: Alpha #1; Old Man Logan & Sabretooth app. 23-Frank Cho-c 4.00
3-1st Kid Kaiju; Fin Fang Foom & Lady Hellbender app. 2 4 6 9 12 15
#1.MU (5/17, $4.99) Monsters Unleashed tie-in; art by Templeton, Ortiz, Lindsay 5.00

TOTAL RECALL (Movie)
DC Comics: 1990 ($2.95, 68 pgs., movie adaptation, one-shot)
1-Arnold Schwarzenegger photo-c 6.00

TOTAL RECALL (Continuation of movie)
Dynamite Entertainment: 2011 - No. 4, 2011 ($3.99, limited series)
1-4-Quaid and Melina on Mars following the movie; Razek-a/Robertson-c 4.00

TOTAL WAR (M.A.R.S. Patrol #3 on)
Gold Key: July, 1965 - No. 2, Oct, 1965 (Painted-c)
1-Wood-a in both issues 7 14 21 49 92 135
2 5 10 15 34 60 85

TOTEMS (Vertigo V2K)
DC Comics (Vertigo): Feb, 2000 ($5.95, one-shot)
1-Swamp Thing, Animal Man, Zatanna, Shade app.; Fegredo-c 6.00

TO THE HEART OF THE STORM
Kitchen Sink Press: 1991 (B&W, graphic novel)
Softcover-Will Eisner-s/a/c 20.00
Hardcover ($24.95) 30.00
TPB-(DC Comics, 9/00, $14.95) reprints 1991 edition 15.00

TO THE LAST MAN (See Zane Grey Four Color #616)

TOUCH OF SILVER, A
Image Comics: Jan, 1997 - No. 6, Nov, 1997 ($2.95, B&W, bi-monthly)
1-6-Valentino-s/a; photo-c: 5-color pgs. w/Round Table 3.00
TPB ($12.95) r/#1-6 13.00

TOUGH KID SQUAD COMICS
Timely Comics (TCI): Mar, 1942
1-(Scarce)-Origin & 1st app.The Human Top & The Tough Kid Squad; The Flying Flame app. 1000 2000 3000 7400 13,200 19,000

TOWER OF SHADOWS (Creatures on the Loose #10 on)
Marvel Comics Group: Sept, 1969 - No. 9, Jan, 1971
1-Romita-c, classic Steranko-a; Craig-a(p) 8 16 24 52 99 145
2,3: 2-Neal Adams-a. 3-Barry Smith, Tuska-a 5 10 15 31 53 75
4,6: 4-Marie Severin-c. 6-Wood-a 4 8 12 28 47 65
5-B. Smith-a(p), Wood-a; Wood draws himself (1st pg., 1st panel) 5 10 15 30 50 70
7-9: 7-B. Smith-a(p), Wood-a. 8-Wood-a; Wrightson-c. 9-Wrightson-c; Roy Thomas app. 5 10 15 31 53 75
Special 1(12/71, 52 pgs.)-Neal Adams-a; Romita-c 4 8 12 28 47 65
NOTE: ***J. Buscema** a-1p, 2p, Special 1r. **Colan** a-3p, 6p, Special 1. **J. Craig** a(r)-1p. **Ditko** a-6, 8, 9r, Special 1. **Everett** a-9(i)r; c-5i. **Kirby** a-9(p)r. **Severin** c-5p, 6. **Steranko** a-1p. **Tuska** a-3. **Wood** a-5-8. Issues 1-9 contain new stories with some pre-Marvel age reprints in 6-9. **H. P. Lovecraft** adaptation-9.*

TOWN CALLED TERROR, A
Image Comics: Apr, 2022 - Present ($3.99)
1-6-Steve Niles-s/Szymon Kudranski-a 4.00

TOXIC AVENGER (Movie)
Marvel Comics: Apr, 1991 - No. 11, Feb, 1992 ($1.50)
1-Based on movie character 3 6 9 21 33 45
2-11: 3,10-Photo-c 4.00

TOXIC CRUSADERS (TV)
Marvel Comics: May, 1992 - No. 8, Dec, 1992 ($1.25)
1-8: 1-3,8-Sam Kieth-c; based on USA Network cartoon 4.00

TOXIN (Son of Carnage)
Marvel Comics: June, 2005 - No. 6, Nov, 2005 ($2.99, limited series)
1-Milligan-s/Robertson-a in all; Spider-Man app. 3 6 9 14 20 25
2-6 1 3 4 6 8 10
...: The Devil You Know TPB (2006, $17.99) r/#1-6 18.00

TOYBOY
Continuity Comics: Oct, 1986 - No. 7, Mar, 1989 ($2.00, Baxter paper)
1-7 4.00
*NOTE: **N. Adams** a-1; c-1, 2,5. **Golden** a-7p; c-6,7. **Nebres** a(i)-1,2.*

TOYLAND COMICS
Fiction House Magazines: Jan, 1947 - No. 2, Mar, 1947; No. 3, July, 1947
1-Wizard of the Moon begins 34 68 102 204 332 460
2,3-Bob Lubbers-c. 3-Tuska-a 20 40 60 114 182 250
NOTE: *All above contain strips by **Al Walker.***

TOY STORY (Disney/Pixar movies)
BOOM! Entertainment (BOOM! KIDS): No. 0, Nov, 2009 - No. 7, Sept, 2010 ($2.99)
0-Three covers 1 3 4 6 8 10
1-Three covers 2 4 6 9 12 15
2-7-Two covers on each 4.00
Free Comic Book Day Edition (5/10, giveaway) r/#0 The Return of Buzz Lightyear 3.00
...: The Return of Buzz Lightyear (10/10, Halloween giveaway, 8-1/2" x 5-1/4") 3.00

TOY STORY (Disney/Pixar movies)
Marvel Comics: May, 2012 - No. 4, 2012 ($2.99, limited series)
1-Master Woody 1 3 4 6 8 10
2-4: 2-A Scary Night. 3-To The Attic. 4-Water Rescue 3.00

TOY STORY: MYSTERIOUS STRANGER (Disney/Pixar movies)
BOOM! Entertainment (BOOM! KIDS): May, 2009 - No. 4, July, 2009 ($2.99)
1-4-Jolley-s/Moreno-a. 1-Three covers. 2-4-Two covers 3.00

TOY STORY: TALES FROM THE TOY CHEST (Disney/Pixar movies)
BOOM! Entertainment (BOOM! KIDS): July, 2010 - No. 4, Oct, 2010 ($2.99)
1-4-Snider-s/Luthi-a. 1-Two covers. 2-4-One cover 3.00

TOY TOWN COMICS
Toytown/Orbit Publ./B. Antin/Swapper Quarterly: 1945 - No. 7, May, 1947
1-Mertie Mouse; L. B. Cole-c/a; funny animal 45 90 135 284 480 675
2-L. B. Cole-a 26 52 78 154 252 350
3-7-L. B. Cole-a. 5-Wiggles the Wonderworm-c 21 42 63 126 206 285

TRAGG AND THE SKY GODS (See Gold Key Spotlight, Mystery Comics Digest #3,9 & Spine Tingling Tales)
Gold Key/Whitman No. 9: June, 1975 - No. 8, Feb, 1977; No. 9, May, 1982 (Painted-c #3-8)
1-Origin 3 6 9 14 19 24
2-8: 4-Sabre-Fang app. 8-Ostellon app. 2 4 6 8 11 14
9-(Whitman, 5/82) r/#1 1 2 3 5 7 9
NOTE: ***Santos** a-1, 2, 9r; c-3-7. **Spiegel** a-3-8.*

TRAILBLAZER
Image Comics: June 2011 ($5.99, one shot, graphic novel)
nn-Gray & Palmiotti-s/Daly-a; covers by Johnson and Conner 6.00

TRAIL BLAZERS (Red Dragon #5 on)
Street & Smith Publications: 1941; No. 2, Apr, 1942 - No. 4, Oct, 1942
(True stories of American heroes)
1-Life story of Jack Dempsey & Wright Brothers 45 90 135 284 480 675
2-Brooklyn Dodgers-c/story; Ben Franklin story 28 56 84 165 270 375
3,4: 3-Fred Allen, Red Barber, Yankees stories 24 48 72 142 234 325

TRAIL COLT (Also see Extra Comics, Manhunt! & Undercover Girl)
Magazine Enterprises: 1949 - No. 2, 1949
nn(A-1 #24)-7 pg. Frazetta-a r-in Manhunt #13; Undercover Girl app.; The Red Fox by L. B. Cole; Ingels-c; Whitney-a (Scarce)(Republished as Manhunt #12 with a different-c) 43 86 129 271 461 650
2(A-1 #26)-Undercover Girl; Ingels-c; L. B. Cole-a (6 pgs.) 34 68 102 199 325 450

TRAILER PARK BOYS (Based on the TV show)
Devil's Due Comics: Jul, 2021; Jun, 2022 (series of one-shots)
... Get A F#c*!ng Comic Book 1-(7/21, $7.99) Short stories by various 8.00
... House of 1000 Conkys 1-(6/22, $4.99) Halloween-themed story; Molloy-s/Rogers-a 5.00

TRAIN CALLED LOVE, A
Dynamite Entertainment: 2015 - No. 10, 2016 ($3.99)

GD 2.0 | VG 4.0 | FN 6.0 | VF 8.0 | VF/NM 9.0 | NM- 9.2

1-9-Garth Ennis-s/Mark Dos Santos-a 4.00
10-($5.99) Last issue 6.00

TRANSFORMERS, THE (TV)(See G.I. Joe and...)
(Continues in Transformers: Regeneration)
Marvel Comics Group: Sept, 1984 - No. 80, July, 1991 (75¢/$1.00)

1-Based on Hasbro Toys 9 18 27 59 117 175
1-2nd & 3rd printing 3 6 9 14 20 26
2-5: 2-Golden-c. 3-(1/85) Spider-Man (black costume)-c/app. 4-Texeira-c; brief app. of Dinobots 3 6 9 19 30 40
2-10: 2nd & 3rd prints 4.00
6,7,9: 6-1st Josie Beller. 9-Circuit Breaker 1st full app. 2 4 6 9 13 16
8-Dinobots 1st full app. 5 10 15 30 50 70
10-Intro. Constructicons 3 6 9 17 26 35
11,14: 11-1st app. Jetfire. 14-Jetfire becomes an Autobot; 1st app. of Grapple, Hoist, Smokescreen, Skids, and Tracks 2 4 6 8 11 14
12,13,15,17,18,20-24,26-49: 17-1st app. of Blaster, Powerglide, Cosmos, Seaspray, Warpath, Beachcomber, Preceptor, Straxus, Kickback, Bombshell, Shrapnel, Dirge, and Ramjet. 21-1st app. of Aerialbots; 1st Slingshot; Circuit Breaker app. 22-Retells origin of Circuit Breaker, 1st Stunticons. 23-Battle at Statue of Liberty. 24-1st app. Protectobots, Combaticons; Optimus Prime killed. 26-Intro The Mechanic, Prime's Funeral. 27-Grimlock named new Autobot leader. 28-The Mechanic app. 29-Intro Scraplets, 1st app. of Triple Changers 1 2 3 5 6 8
16-Plight of the Bumblebee 3 6 9 14 20 26
19-1st Omega Supreme 2 4 6 11 16 20
25-1st Predacons 2 4 6 13 18 22
50-60: 53-Jim Lee-c. 54-Intro Micromasters. 60-Brief 1st app. of Primus 2 4 6 8 10 12
61-70: 61-Origin of Cybertron and the Transformers, Unicron app.; app. of Primus, creator of the Transformers. 62-66 Matrix Quest 5-part series. 67-Jim Lee-c 2 4 6 10 14 18
71-77: 75-($1.50, 52 pgs.) (Low print run) 3 6 9 19 30 40
78,79 (Low print run) 4 8 12 28 47 65
80-Last issue 6 12 18 37 66 95

NOTE: Second and third printings of most early issues (1-9?) exist and are worth less than originals. Was originally planned as a four issue mini-series. ***Wrightson** a-64i(4 pgs.).*

TRANSFORMERS
IDW Publishing: No. 0, Oct, 2005 (99¢, one-shot)

0-Prelude to Transformers: Infiltration series; Furman-s/Su-a; 4 covers 4.00

TRANSFORMERS
IDW Publishing: Nov, 2009 - No. 31, Dec, 2011 ($3.99)

1-Multple covers 1 3 4 6 8 10
2-31: Multple covers on each, 21-Chaos arc begins 4.00
...: Continuum (11/09, $3.99) Plot synopses of recent Transformers storylines 4.00
...: Death of Optimus Prime (12/11, $3.99) Roche-a 4.00
Hundred Penny Press: Transformers Classics #1 (6/11, $1.00) r/#1 (1984 Marvel series) 3.00
Hundred Penny Press (3/14, $1.00) r/#1 (1984 Marvel series) 3.00

TRANSFORMERS (See Transformers: Robots in Disguise for #1-34)
IDW Publishing: No. 34, Nov, 2014 - No. 57, Sept, 2016 ($3.99)

35-49: 39-42-Combiner Wars x-over 4.00
50-($7.99, squarebound) Barber-s/Griffith-a 8.00
51-57: 51-55-All Hail Optimus. 56-Revolution tie-in 4.00
Annual 2017 (2/17, $7.99) Barber-s/Tramontano-a; bonus character profile pages 8.00
...: Deviations (3/16, $4.99) What If... Optimus Prime never died; Easton-s; 2 covers 5.00
... First Strike 1 (10/17, $3.99) Part of Hasbro character crossover 4.00
... Historia (12/18, $5.99) Text history of the Transformers with comic panels 6.00
... Holiday Special (12/15, $5.99) Covers by Coller & Garbowska 6.00
...: Requiem of the Wreckers Annual (5/18, $7.99) Roche-s/a 8.00
...: Revolution 1 (10/16, $3.99) Revolution tie-in; Barber-s/Griffith-a; multiple covers 4.00
...: Salvation One Shot (6/17, $7.99) Barber-s/Ramondelli-a; 2 covers 8.00
...: Titans Return (7/16, $4.99) Road to Revolution; Ramondelli-a 5.00

TRANSFORMERS (Rise of the Decepticons on cover #19-24; War World on cover #25-30)
IDW Publishing: Mar, 2019 - Present ($3.99)

1-24,26-42: 1-Intro Rubble; Ruckley-s. 7,8-Polybagged w/Transformers card game pack 4.00
25-($7.99) Ruckley-s/Malkova-a; Orion Pax becomes Optimus Prime 8.00
43-($5.99) Story concludes in Transformers: Fate of Cybertron Special 6.00
Annual 2021 (5/21, $5.99) Ruckley-s/Milne-a 6.00
...: Best of Arcee One-Shot (10/22, $6.99) Reprints character highlights 7.00
...: Best of Bumblebee One-Shot (9/22, $6.99) Reprints character highlights 7.00
...: Best of Grimlock One-Shot (11/22, $6.99) Reprints character highlights 7.00
...: Best of Hot Rod One-Shot (5/22, $6.99) Reprints of 6 stories 7.00
...: Best of Megatron One-Shot (3/22, $6.99) Reprints Transformers #70 and other stories 7.00
...: Best of Optimus Prime One-Shot (1/22, $6.99) Reprints of 5 stories 7.00
...: Best of Shockwave One-Shot (11/22, $6.99) Reprints character highlights 7.00
...: Best of Starscream One-Shot (9/22, $6.99) Reprints character highlights 7.00
...: Best of The Beasts One-Shot (7/22, $6.99) Highlights of characters from Beast Wars 7.00
...: Best of The Rarities One-Shot (8/22, $6.99) Highlights of characters from Beast Wars 7.00
...: Best of Windblade One-Shot (12/22, $6.99) Reprints character highlights 7.00
...: Fate of Cybertron Special (6/22, $7.99) Conclusion of title's storyline; follows #43 8.00
...: Halloween Special 2021 (9/21, $5.99) Dan Watters-s/Beth McGuire-Smith-a 6.00
... 100-Page Giant: Power of the Predacons (1/20, $5.99) Reprints from UK & US comics 6.00
... Valentine's Day Special (2/20, $3.99) Story of Glyph & Tap-Out 4.00

TRANSFORMERS (Free Comic Book Day Editions)
Dreamwave Productions/IDW Publishing

... Animated (IDW, 5/08) Free Comic Book Day Edition; from the Cartoon Network series 3.00
... Armada (Dreamwave Prods., 5/03) Free Comic Book Day Edition 3.00
.../Beast Wars Special (IDW, 2006) Free Comic Book Day Edition; flip book 3.00
.../G.I. Joe (IDW, 2009) Free Comic Book Day Edition; flip book 3.00
... Movie Prequel (IDW, 5/07) Free Comic Book Day Edition; Figueroa-c 3.00

TRANSFORMERS: ALL HAIL MEGATRON
IDW Publishing: Jul, 2008 - No. 16, Oct, 2009 ($3.99, limited series)

1-McCarthy-s/Guidi-a; 2 covers 1 3 4 6 8 10
2-16: 2-8,10-12-McCarthy-s/Guidi-a; 2 covers 4.00

TRANSFORMERS: ALLIANCE (Prequel to 2009 Transformers 2 movie)
IDW Publishing: Dec, 2008 - No. 4, Mar, 2009 ($3.99, limited series)

1-4-Milne-a; 2 covers 5.00

TRANSFORMERS ANIMATED: THE ARRIVAL
IDW Publishing: Sept, 2008 - No. 5, Dec, 2008 ($3.99, limited series)

1-5-Brizuela-a; 2 covers 4.00

TRANSFORMERS ARMADA (Continues as Transformers Energon with #19)
Dreamwave Productions: July, 2002 - No. 18, Dec, 2003 ($2.95)

1-Sarracini-s/Raiz-a; wraparound gatefold-c 6.00
2-18 4.00
Vol. 1 TPB (2003, $13.95) r/#1-5 14.00
Vol. 2 TPB (2003, $15.95) r/#6-11 16.00

TRANSFORMERS ARMADA: MORE THAN MEETS THE EYE
Dreamwave Productions: Mar, 2004 - No. 3, May, 2004 ($4.95, limited series)

1-3-Pin-ups with tech info; art by Pat Lee & various 5.00

TRANSFORMERS / BACK TO THE FUTURE
IDW Publishing: Oct, 2020 - No. 4, Jan, 2021 ($3.99, limited series)

1-4-Cavan Scott-s/Juan Samu-a; multiple covers on all 4.00

TRANSFORMERS: BEAST WARS
IDW Publishing: Feb, 2021 - No. 17, Jun, 2022 ($5.99/$3.99, limited series)

1-($5.99) Maximals and Predacons app.; Erik Burnham-s/Josh Burcham-a 6.00
2-17 ($3.99) 4.00
Annual 2022 (4/22, $5.99) Three short stories by various 6.00

TRANSFORMERS, BEAST WARS: THE ASCENDING
IDW Publishing: Aug, 2007 - No. 4, Nov, 2007 ($3.99, limited series)

1-4-Furman-s/Figueroa-a; multiple covers on all 4.00

TRANSFORMERS, BEAST WARS: THE GATHERING
IDW Publishing: Feb, 2006 - No. 4, May, 2006 ($2.99, limited series)

1-4-Furman-s/Figueroa-a; multiple covers on all 4.00
TPB (8/06, $17.99) r/series; sketch pages & gallery of covers and variants 18.00

TRANSFORMERS: BUMBLEBEE
IDW Publishing: Dec, 2009 - No. 4, Mar, 2010 ($3.99, limited series)

1-Zander Cannon-s; multiple covers on all 1 3 4 6 8 10
2-4 4.00
... – Go For the Gold (12/18, $3.99) Asmus-s/Ferreira-a 4.00

TRANSFORMERS: BUMBLEBEE MOVIE PREQUEL
IDW Publishing: Jun, 2018 - No. 4, Sept, 2018 ($3.99, limited series)

1-4: Bumblebee assisting a British spy in 1964; Barber-s/Griffith-a; multiple covers 4.00

TRANSFORMERS COMICS MAGAZINE (Digest)
Marvel Comics: Jan, 1987 - No. 10, July, 1988

1,2-Spider-Man-c/s 2 4 6 11 16 20
3-10 2 4 6 8 11 14

TRANSFORMERS: DARK CYBERTRON
IDW Publishing: Nov, 2013 ($3.99)

1-Part 1 of a 12-part crossover with Transformers: More Than Meets the Eye #23-27 and Transformers: Robots in Disguise #23-27; multiple covers 4.00
1-Deluxe Edition ($7.99, squarebound) r/#1 with bonus script and B&W art pages 8.00
... Finale (3/14, $3.99) Three covers 4.00

TRANSFORMERS: DARK OF THE MOON MOVIE ADAPTATION (2011 movie)
IDW Publishing: Jun, 2011 - No. 4, Jun, 2011 ($3.99, weekly limited series)

1-4-Barber-s/Jimenez-a 4.00

TRANSFORMERS: DEFIANCE (Prequel to 2009 Transformers 2 movie)
IDW Publishing: Jan, 2009 - No. 4, Apr, 2009 ($3.99, limited series)

1-4-Mowry-s; 2 covers 4.00

TRANSFORMERS: DEVASTATION
IDW Publishing: Sept, 2007 - No. 6, Feb, 2008 ($3.99, limited series)

1-6-Furman-s/Su-a; multiple covers on all 4.00

TRANSFORMERS: DRIFT
IDW Publishing: Sept, 2010 - No. 4, Oct, 2010 ($3.99, limited series)

1-4-McCarthy-s/Milne-a; multiple covers on all 4.00

TRANSFORMERS: DRIFT – EMPIRE OF STONE
IDW Publishing: Nov, 2014 - No. 4, Feb, 2015 ($3.99, limited series)

1-4-McCarthy-s/Guidi & Ferreira-a; multiple covers on all 4.00

TRANSFORMERS '84
IDW Publishing: No. 0, Aug, 2019 - No. 4, Oct, 2021 ($3.99, limited series)

0 (8/19, $4.99) New story in art style of 1984 comics; Furman-s/Guidi-a 5.00
1-4-Furman-s/Guidi-a; multiple covers 4.00
...: Legends & Rumors (2/21, $7.99, 100 pgs) r/Transformers #1, ... UK #9-12 & ... '84 #0 8.00

TRANSFORMERS ENERGON (Continued from Transformers Armada #18)
Dreamwave Productions: No. 19, Jan, 2004 - No. 30, Dec, 2004 ($2.95)

19-30-Furman-s 4.00

TRANSFORMERS: ESCALATION
IDW Publishing: Nov, 2006 - No. 6, Apr, 2007 ($3.99, limited series)

1-6-Furman-s/Su-a; multiple covers 4.00

TRANSFORMERS ESCAPE
IDW Publishing: Dec, 2020 - No. 5, Apr, 2021 ($3.99, limited series)

1-5-Brian Ruckley-s/Beth McGuire-Smith; multiple covers on all 4.00

TRANSFORMERS: EVOLUTIONS - HEARTS OF STEEL
IDW Publishing: June, 2006 - No. 4, Sept, 2006 ($2.99, limited series)

1-4-Bumblebee meets John Henry in 1880s railroad times 4.00

TRANSFORMERS: FOUNDATION (Prequel to 2011 Transformers: Dark of the Moon movie)
IDW Publishing: Feb, 2011 - No. 4, May, 2011 ($3.99, limited series)

Transformers (2010) #5 © Hasbro

Transformers: Beast Wars #10 © Hasbro

Transformers: Lost Light #7 © Hasbro

GD VG FN VF VF/NM NM-
2.0 4.0 6.0 8.0 9.0 9.2

1-4-Barber-s/Griffith-a; 2 covers 4.00

TRANSFORMERS: GALAXIES
IDW Publishing: Sept, 2019 - No. 12, Oct, 2020 ($3.99)
1-12: 1-Tyler Bleszinski-s/Livio Ramondelli-a; Constructicons app. 4.00

TRANSFORMERS: GENERATION 1
Dreamwave Productions: Apr, 2002 - No. 6, Oct, 2002 ($2.95)
Preview- 6 pg. story; robot sketch pages; Pat Lee-a 3.00
1-Pat Lee-a; 2 wraparound covers by Lee 5.00
2-6: 2-Optimus Prime reactivated; 2 covers by Pat Lee 4.00
...Vol. 1 HC (2003, $49.95) r/#1-6; black hardcover with red foil lettering and art 50.00
...Vol. 1 TPB (2002, $17.95) r/#1-6 plus six page preview; 8 pg. preview of future issues 18.00

TRANSFORMERS: GENERATION 1 (Volume 2)
Dreamwave Productions: Apr, 2003 - No. 6, Sept, 2003 ($2.95)
1-6: 1-Pat Lee-a; 2 wraparound gatefold covers by Lee 4.00
1-($5.95) Chrome wraparound variant-c 6.00
...Vol. 2 TPB (IDW Publ., 3/06, $19.99) r/#1-6 plus cover gallery 20.00

TRANSFORMERS: GENERATION 1 (Volume 3)
Dreamwave Productions: No. 0, Dec, 2003 - No. 10, Nov, 2004 ($2.95)
0-10: 0-Pat Lee-a. 1-Figueroa-a; wrapaound-c 4.00

TRANSFORMERS: GENERATION 2
Marvel Comics: Nov, 1993 - No. 12, Oct, 1994 ($1.75)
1-($2.95, 68 pgs.)-Collector's ed. w/bi-fold metallic-c 2 4 6 8 11 14
1-11: 1-Newsstand edition (68 pgs.). 2-G.I. Joe app., Snake-Eyes, Scarlett, Cobra Commander app. 5-Red Alert killed, Optimus Prime gives Grimlock leadership of Autobots. 6-G.I. Joe app. 1 2 3 4 5 7
12-($2.25, 52 pgs.) 1 3 4 6 8 10

TRANSFORMERS: GENERATIONS
IDW Publishing: Mar, 2006 - No. 12, Mar, 2007 ($1.99/$2.49/$3.99)
1,2: 1-R/Transformers #7 (1985); preview of Transformers, Beast Wars. 2-R/#13 4.00
3-10-($2.49) 3-R/Transformers #14 (1986). 4-6-Reprint #16-18. 7-R/#24 4.00
11,12-($3.99) 4.00
Volume 1 (12/06, $19.99) r/#1-6; cover gallery 20.00

TRANSFORMERS / GHOSTBUSTERS
IDW Publishing: Jun, 2019 - No. 5, Oct, 2019 ($3.99, limited series)
1-5-Burnham-s/Schoening-a; Ghostbusters vs. ghost of Starscream 4.00

TRANSFORMERS/G.I. JOE
Dreamwave Productions: Aug, 2003 - No. 6, Mar, 2004 ($2.95/$5.25)
1-Art & gatefold wraparound-c by Jae Lee; Ney Rieber-s; variant-c by Pat Lee 1 2 3 5 6 8
1-($5.95) Holofoil wraparound-c by Norton 2 4 6 8 10 12
2-6-Jae Lee-a/c 4.00
TPB (8/04, $17.95) r/#1-6; cover gallery and sketch pages 18.00

TRANSFORMERS/G.I. JOE: DIVIDED FRONT
Dreamwave Productions: Oct, 2004 ($2.95)
1-Art & gatefold wraparound-c by Pat Lee 4.00

TRANSFORMERS: HEADMASTERS
Marvel Comics Group: July, 1987 - No. 4, Jan, 1988 ($1.00, limited series)
1-Springer, Akin, Garvey-a 2 4 6 9 12 15
2-4-Springer-c on all 6.00

TRANSFORMERS: HEART OF DARKNESS
IDW Publishing: Mar, 2011 - No. 4, Jun, 2011 ($3.99, limited series)
1-4-Abnett & Lanning-s/Farinas-a 4.00

TRANSFORMERS: INFESTATION (Crossover with Star Trek, Ghostbusters & G.I. Joe)
IDW Publishing: Feb, 2011 - No. 2, Feb, 2011 ($3.99, limited series)
1,2-Abnett & Lanning-s/Roche-a; covers by Roche & Snyder III 4.00

TRANSFORMERS: INFILTRATION
IDW Publishing: Jan, 2006 - No. 6, June, 2006 ($2.99, limited series)
1-6-Furman-s/Su-a; multiple covers on all 4.00
... Cover Gallery (8/06, $5.99) 6.00

TRANSFORMERS: IRONHIDE
IDW Publishing: May, 2010 - No. 4, Aug, 2010 ($3.99, limited series)
1-4: Mike Costa-s; multiple covers on all 4.00

TRANSFORMERS: KING GRIMLOCK
IDW Publishing: Aug, 2021 - No. 5, Feb, 2022 ($4.99, limited series)
1-5-Steve Orlando-s/Agustin Padilla-a; multiple covers on all 5.00

GD VG FN VF VF/NM NM-
2.0 4.0 6.0 8.0 9.0 9.2

TRANSFORMERS: LAST BOT STANDING
IDW Publishing: May, 2022 - No. 4, Aug, 2022 ($5.99, limited series)
1-4-Nick Roche-s/Roche & E.J. Su-a; multiple covers on each 6.00

TRANSFORMERS: LAST STAND OF THE WRECKERS
IDW Publishing: Jan, 2010 - No. 5, May, 2010 ($3.99, limited series)
1-5-Nick Roche-s/a; two covers 4.00

TRANSFORMERS: LOST LIGHT
IDW Publishing: Dec, 2016 - No. 25, Oct, 2018 ($3.99)
1-15: 1-7-Roberts-s/Lawrence-a; multiple covers on each. 8,9-Tramontano-a 4.00

TRANSFORMERS: MAXIMUM DINOBOTS
IDW Publishing: Dec, 2008 - No. 5, Apr, 2009 ($3.99, limited series)
1-5-Furman-s/Roche-a; 2 covers for each 4.00

TRANSFORMERS: MEGATRON ORIGIN
IDW Publishing: May, 2007 - No. 4, Sept, 2008 ($3.99, limited series)
1-4-Alex Milne-a; 2 covers 4.00

TRANSFORMERS: MICROMASTERS
Dreamwave Productions: June, 2004 - No. 4 ($2.95, limited series)
1-4-Ruffolo-a; Pat Lee-c 4.00

TRANSFORMERS: MONSTROSITY
IDW Publishing: Jun, 2013 - No. 4, Sept, 2013 ($3.99)
1-4: 1-Three covers; Ramondelli-a 4.00

TRANSFORMERS: MORE THAN MEETS THE EYE
Dreamwave Productions: Apr, 2003 - No. 8, Nov, 2003 ($5.25)
1-8-Pin-ups with tech info on Autobots and Decepticons; art by Pat Lee & various 5.25
Vol. 1,2 (2004, $24.95, TPB) 1-r/#1-4. 2-r/#5-8 25.00

TRANSFORMERS: MORE THAN MEETS THE EYE
IDW Publishing: Jan, 2012 - No. 57, Sept, 2016 ($3.99)
1-49: 1-Five covers; Roche-a. 2-Three covers; Milne-a. 23-27-Dark Cybertron x-over. 26-1st app. of Windblade 4.00
50-(2/16, $7.99) "The Dying of the Light" begins; five covers 8.00
51-57: 51-55-The Dying of the Light. 56,57-Titans Return 4.00
Annual 2012 (8/12, $7.99) Salgado & Cabaltierra-a; three covers 8.00
...: Revolution 1 (11/16, $3.99) Revolution tie-in; Roche-s/Roberts-a; multiple covers 4.00

TRANSFORMERS: MOVIE ADAPTATION (For the 2007 live action movie)
IDW Publishing: June, 2007 - No. 4, June, 2007 ($3.99, weekly limited series)
1-4: Wraparound covers on each; Milne-a 4.00

TRANSFORMERS: MOVIE PREQUEL (For the 2007 live action movie)
IDW Publishing: Feb, 2007 - No. 4, May, 2007 ($3.99, limited series)
1-4: 1-Origin of the Transformers on Cybertron; multiple covers on each 4.00
Special (6/08, $3.99) 2 covers 4.00
TPB (6/07, $19.99) r/series; gallery of covers and variants 20.00

TRANSFORMERS: NEFARIOUS (Sequel to Transformers: Revenge of the Fallen movie)
IDW Publishing: Mar, 2010 - No. 6, Aug, 2010 ($3.99, limited series)
1-6: Furman-s; multiple covers on all 4.00

TRANSFORMERS: PRIMACY
IDW Publishing: Aug, 2014 - No. 4, Nov, 2014 ($3.99, limited series)
1-4-Metzen & Dille-s/Ramondelli-a; Omega Supreme app.; multiple covers on each 4.00

TRANSFORMERS: PRIME
IDW Publishing: Jan, 2011 - No. 4, Jan, 2011 ($3.99, weekly limited series)
1-4: 1-Mike Johnson-s/E.J. Su-a 4.00

TRANSFORMERS PRIME: BEAST HUNTERS
IDW Publishing: May, 2013 - No. 8, Dec, 2013($3.99, limited series)
1-8-Agustin Padilla-a 4.00

TRANSFORMERS PRIME: RAGE OF THE DINOBOTS
IDW Publishing: Nov, 2012 - No. 4, Feb, 2013 ($3.99, limited series)
1-4: 1-Mike Johnson-s/Agustin Padilla-a 4.00

TRANSFORMERS: PUNISHMENT
IDW Publishing: Jan, 2015 ($5.99, squarebound, one-shot)
1-Windblade app.; Barber-s/Ramondelli-a 6.00

TRANSFORMERS: REDEMPTION
IDW Publishing: Oct, 2015 ($7.99, squarebound, one-shot)
1-Dinobots app.; John Barber-s/Livio Ramondelli-a 8.00

TRANSFORMERS: REGENERATION ONE (Continues story from Transformers #80 (1991))

	GD	VG	FN	VF	VF/NM	NM-
	2.0	4.0	6.0	8.0	9.0	9.2

IDW Publishing: No. 80.5, May, 2012 - No. 100, Mar, 2014 ($3.99)

80.5 (5/12, Free Comic Book Day giveaway) Furman-s/Wildman-a 3.00
81-99 ($3.99) 81-92-Furman-s/Wildman-a; multiple covers on all 4.00
100-($5.99) Six covers; Furman-s/Wildman, Senior & Guidi-a; bonus cover gallery 6.00
#0 (9/13, $3.99) Hot Rod in the timestream; various artists; 4 covers 4.00
... 100-Page Spectacular (7/12, $7.99) Reprints Transformers #76-80 (1991) 8.00

TRANSFORMERS: REVENGE OF THE FALLEN OFFICIAL MOVIE ADAPTATION
(For the 2009 live action movie sequel)
IDW Publishing: May, 2009 - No. 4, June, 2009 ($3.99, weekly limited series)

1-4: Furman-s; 2 covers on each 4.00

TRANSFORMERS: RISING STORM (Prequel to 2011 Transformers: Dark of the Moon movie)
IDW Publishing: Feb, 2011 - No. 4, May, 2011 ($3.99, limited series)

1-3-Barber-s/Magno-a; 2 covers 4.00

TRANSFORMERS: ROBOTS IN DISGUISE (Re-titled Transformers #35-on)
IDW Publishing: Jan, 2012 - No. 34, Oct, 2014 ($3.99)

1-34: 1-Five covers; Griffith-a. 2-27-Three covers. 23-27-Dark Cybertron x-over 4.00

TRANSFORMERS: ROBOTS IN DISGUISE (Based on the animated series)
IDW Publishing: No. 0, May, 2015 - No. 5, Dec, 2015 ($3.99)

0-Free Comic Book Day Edition; Barber-s/Tramontano-a; Bumblebee & Strongarm app. 3.00
1-5: 1-Georgia Ball-s/Priscilla Tramontano-a 4.00

TRANSFORMERS: SAGA OF THE ALLSPARK (From the 2007 live action movie)
IDW Publishing: Jul, 2008 - No. 4, Oct, 2008 ($3.99, limited series)

1-4-Launch of the Allspark into outer space; Furman-s/Roche-c 4.00

TRANSFORMERS: SECTOR 7 (From the 2007 live action movie)
IDW Publishing: Sept, 2010 - No. 5, Jan, 2011 ($3.99, limited series)

1-5-Barber-s 4.00

TRANSFORMERS: SHATTERED GLASS
IDW Publishing: Aug, 2021 - No. 5, Dec, 2021 ($3.99, limited series)

1-5-Danny Lore-s/Guido Guidi-a; multiple covers on all 4.00

TRANSFORMERS: SHATTERED GLASS II
IDW Publishing: Aug, 2022 - No. 5, Dec, 2022 ($3.99, limited series)

1-5-Danny Lore-s/Marcelo Matere-a; multiple covers on all 4.00

TRANSFORMERS: SINS OF THE WRECKERS
IDW Publishing: Nov, 2015 - No. 5, May, 2016 ($3.99, limited series)

1-5-Roche-s/Burcham-a 4.00

TRANSFORMERS: SPOTLIGHT
IDW Publishing: Sept, 2006 - May, 2013 ($3.99, multiple covers on each)

... Arcee (2/08); ... Blaster (1/08); ... Blurr (11/08); ... Bumblebee (3/13); ... Cliffjumper (6/09); ... Cyclonus (6/08); ...Doubledealer (8/08); ...Drift (4/09); ...Galvatron (7/07);...Grimlock (3/08); ...Hardhead (7/08); ... Hoist (5/13); ... Hot Rod (11/06); ... Jazz (3/09); ... Kup (4/07); ... Megatron (2/13); ... Metroplex (7/09); ... Mirage (3/08); ... Nightbeat (10/06); ... Orion Pax (12/12); ... Prowl (4/10);... Ramjet (11/07); ... Shockwave (9/06); ... Sideswipe (9/08); ... Sixshot (12/06); ... Soundwave (3/07); Thundercracker (1/13); ... Trailcutter (4/13); ... Ultra Magnus (1/07) 4.00
... Optimus Prime: 3-D (11/08, $5.99, with glasses) Furman-s/Figueroa-a 6.00

TRANSFORMERS: STORMBRINGER
IDW Publishing: Jul, 2006 - No. 4, Oct, 2006 ($2.99, limited series)

1-4-Furman-s/Figueroa-a; multiple covers on all 4.00
TPB (2/07, $17.99) r/series; cover gallery and sketch pages 18.00

TRANSFORMERS SUMMER SPECIAL
Dreamwave Productions: May, 2004 ($4.95)

	GD	VG	FN	VF	VF/NM	NM-
1-Pat Lee-a; Figueroa-a	1	2	3	5	6	8

TRANSFORMERS: TALES OF THE FALLEN
IDW Publishing: Aug, 2009 - No. 6 ($3.99, limited series)

1-6: 2,4-Furman-s mulitple covers on all 4.00

TRANSFORMERS: TARGET 2006
IDW Publishing: Apr, 2007 - No. 5, Aug, 2007 ($3.99, limited series)

1-5-Reprints from 1980s series; multiple covers on all 4.00

TRANSFORMERS: THE ANIMATED MOVIE
IDW Publishing: Oct, 2006 - No. 4, Jan, 2007 ($3.99, limited series)

1-4-Adapts animated movie; Don Figueroa-a 4.00

TRANSFORMERS, THE MOVIE
Marvel Comics Group: Dec, 1986 - No. 3, Feb, 1987 (75¢, limited series)

	GD	VG	FN	VF	VF/NM	NM-
1-3-Adapts animated movie	2	4	6	10	14	18

TRANSFORMERS: THE REIGN OF STARSCREAM
IDW Publishing: Apr, 2008 - No. 5, Aug, 2008 ($3.99, limited series)

1-5-Continuation of the 2007 movie; Milne-a; multiple covers 4.00

TRANSFORMERS: THE WAR WITHIN
Dreamwave Productions: Oct, 2002 - No. 6, Mar, 2003 ($2.95)

1-6-Furman-s/Figueroa-a. 1-Wraparound gatefold-c 4.00
TPB (2003, $15.95) r/#1-6; plus cover gallery 16.00

TRANSFORMERS: TILL ALL ARE ONE
IDW Publishing: Jun, 2016 - No. 12, Jul, 2017 ($3.99)

1-12-Road to Revolution; Mairghread Scott-s; multiple covers on all 4.00
Annual 2017 (12/17, $7.99) Mairghread Scott-s/Pitre-Durocher-a
...: Revolution 1 (10/16, $3.99) Revolution tie-in; Windblade app.; multiple covers 4.00

TRANSFORMERS: UNICRON (Crossover with Optimus Prime & Transformers: Lost Light)
IDW Publishing: Jul, 2018 - No. 6, Oct, 2018 ($4.99)

1-6-Barber-s/Milne-a; multiple covers on all; Rom app. 5.00
#0 (5/18, FCBD giveaway) Barber-s/Milne-a; Rom app. 3.00

TRANSFORMERS UNIVERSE
Marvel Comics Group: Dec, 1986 - No. 4, Mar, 1987 ($1.25, limited series)

	GD	VG	FN	VF	VF/NM	NM-
1-4-A guide to all characters	2	4	6	8	11	14

TPB-r/#1-4 15.00

TRANSFORMERS VS. G.I. JOE
IDW Publishing: No. 0, May, 2014 - No. 13, Jun, 2016 ($3.99)

Free Comic Book Day #0 (5/14, giveaway) Tom Scioli-a; Scioli & John Barber-s 3.00
1-12-Tom Scioli-a; Scioli & John Barber-s; multiple covers on each; creator commentary 4.00
13-($7.99, squarebound) Last issue; bonus commentary; 3 covers 8.00
...: The Movie Adaptation (3/17, $4.99) Tom Scioli-s/a; 4 covers; bonus sketch-a 5.00

TRANSFORMERS VS. VISIONARIES
IDW Publishing: Dec, 2017 - No. 5, Apr, 2018 ($3.99, limited series)

1-5-Vissagio-s/Ossio-a 4.00

TRANSFORMERS: WAR'S END
IDW Publishing: Feb, 2022 - No. 4, May, 2022 ($3.99/$5.99, limited series)

1-3-($3.99) Ruckley-s/Lawrence-a; multiple covers on all 4.00
4-($5.99) Concludes in Transformers: Fate of Cybertron #1; multiple covers 6.00

TRANSFORMERS WAR WITHIN: THE AGE OF WRATH
Dreamwave Productions: Sept, 2004 - No. 6 ($2.95, limited series)

1-3-Furman-s/Ng-a 4.00

TRANSFORMERS WAR WITHIN: THE DARK AGES
Dreamwave Productions: Oct, 2003 - No. 6 ($2.95)

1-6: 1-Furman-s/Wildman-a; two covers by Pat Lee & Figueroa 4.00
TPB (2004, $17.95) r/#1-6; plus cover gallery and design sketches 18.00

TRANSFORMERS: WINDBLADE (See Transformers More Than Meets the Eye #26)
IDW Publishing: Apr, 2014 - No. 4, Jul, 2014 ($3.99, limited series)

1-4-Mairghread Scott-s/Sarah Stone-a; three covers on each 4.00
Vol. 2 (3/15 - No. 7, 9/15, $3.99) 1-7-Scott-s; multiple covers on each. 1-Stone-a 4.00

TRANSFORMERS: WRECKERS – TREAD & CIRCUITS
IDW Publishing: Oct, 2021 - No. 4, Jan, 2022 ($3.99, limited series)

1-4-David Mariotte-s/Jack Lawrence-a; multiple covers on each 4.00

TRANSIT
Vortex Publ.: March, 1987 - No. 5, Nov, 1987 (B&W)

	GD	VG	FN	VF	VF/NM	NM-
1-5-Ted McKeever-s/a	1	2	3	5	6	8

TRANSLUCID
BOOM! Studios: Apr, 2014 - No. 6, Sept, 2014 ($3.99)

1-6-Sanchez & Echert-s/Bayliss-a; multiple covers on each 4.00

TRANSMETROPOLITAN
DC Comics (Helix/Vertigo): Sept, 1997 - No. 60, Nov, 2002 ($2.50)

	GD	VG	FN	VF	VF/NM	NM-
1-Warren Ellis-s/Darick Robertson-a(p)	5	10	15	35	63	90
1-Special Edition (5/09, $1.00) r/#1 with "After Watchmen" cover frame						5.00
2,3	2	4	6	8	10	12
4-8						5.00
9-60: 15-Jae Lee-c. 25-27-Jim Lee-c. 37-39-Bradstreet-c						3.00
Back on the Street ('97, $7.95) r/#1-3						10.00
Back on the Street ('09, $14.99) r/#1-6; intro. by Garth Ennis						15.00
Dirge ('03/'10, $14.95/$14.95) r/#43-48						15.00
Filth of the City ('01, $5.95) Spider's columns with pin-up art by various						6.00
Gouge Away ('02/'09, $14.95/$14.99) r/#31-36						15.00
I Hate It Here ('00, $5.95) Spider's columns with pin-up art by various						6.00
Lonely City ('01/'09, $14.95/$14.99) r/#25-30; intro. by Patrick Stewart						15.00
Lust For Life ('98, $14.95) r/#4-12						20.00
Lust For Life ('09, $14.99) r/#7-12						15.00
One More Time ('04, $14.95) r/#55-60						15.00
One More Time ('11, $19.99) r/#55-60 & Filth of the City & I Hate It Here one-shots						20.00
Spider's Thrash ('02/'10, $14.95/$14.99) r/#37-42; intro. by Darren Aronofsky						15.00
Tales of Human Waste ('04, $9.95) r/Filth of the City, I Hate It Here & story from Vertigo Winter's Edge 2						10.00
The Cure ('03/'11, $14.95/$14.99) r/#49-54						15.00
The New Scum ('00, $12.95) r/#19-24 & Vertigo: Winter's Edge #3						15.00
The New Scum ('09, $14.99) r/#19-24 & Vertigo: Winter's Edge #3						15.00
Year of the Bastard ('99, $12.95)('09, $12.99) r/#13-18						13.00

TRANSMUTATION OF IKE GARUDA, THE
Marvel Comics (Epic Comics): July, 1991 - No. 2, 1991 ($3.95, 52 pgs.)

1,2 4.00

TRAPPED!
Periodical House Magazines (Ace): Oct, 1954 - No. 4, April, 1955

	GD	VG	FN	VF	VF/NM	NM-
1 (All reprints)	13	26	39	74	105	135
2-4: 4-r/Men Against Crime #4 in its entirety	8	16	24	44	57	70

NOTE: *Colan a-1, 4. Sekowsky a-1.*

TRASH
Trash Publ. Co.: Mar, 1978 - No. 4, Oct, 1978 (B&W, magazine, 52 pgs.)

	GD	VG	FN	VF	VF/NM	NM-
1,2: 1-Star Wars parody. 2-UFO-c	3	6	9	16	24	32
3-Parodies of KISS, the Beatles, and monsters	3	6	9	17	25	34
4-(84 pgs.)-Parodies of Happy Days, Rocky movies	3	6	9	18	28	38

TRAVELER, THE (Developed by Stan Lee)
BOOM! Studios: Nov, 2010 - No. 12, Oct, 2011 ($3.99)

1-12-Waid-s/Hardin-a; three covers on each 4.00

TRAVELING TO MARS
Ablaze Publishing: 2022 - No. 8 ($3.99)

1-3-Mark Russell-s/Roberto Meli-a 4.00

TRAVELS OF JAIMIE McPHEETERS, THE (TV)
Gold Key: Dec, 1963

	GD	VG	FN	VF	VF/NM	NM-
1-Kurt Russell photo on-c plus photo back-c	4	8	12	27	44	60

TREASURE CHEST (Catholic Guild; also see Topix)
George A. Pflaum: 3/12/46 - V27#8, July, 1972 (Educational comics)
(Not published during Summer)

	GD	VG	FN	VF	VF/NM	NM-
V1#1	36	72	108	211	343	475
2-6 (5/21/46): 5-Dr. Styx app. by Baily	15	30	45	88	137	185

Transformers: Unicron #1 © Hasbro

Traveling to Mars #2 © Arancia Studios

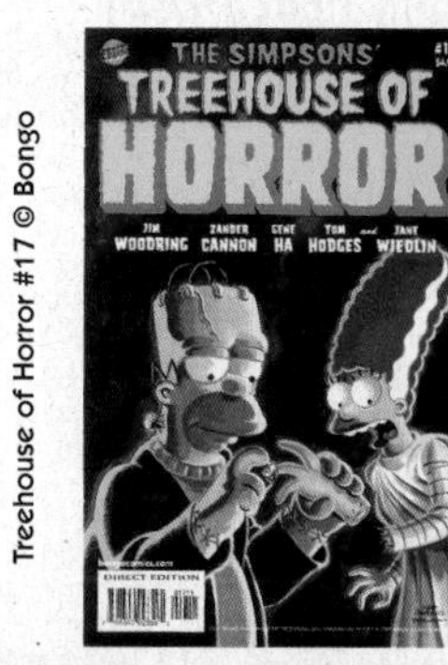

Treehouse of Horror #17 © Bongo

GD 2.0 | VG 4.0 | FN 6.0 | VF 8.0 | VF/NM 9.0 | NM- 9.2

V2#1-20 (9/3/46-5/27/47) 11 22 33 60 83 105
V3#1-5,7-20 (1st slick cover) 10 20 30 54 72 90
V3#6-Jules Verne's "Voyage to the Moon" 14 28 42 76 108 140
V4#1-20 (9/9/48-5/31/49) 9 18 27 47 61 75
V5#1-20 (9/6/49-5/31/50) 8 16 24 44 57 70
V6#1-20 (9/14/50-5/31/51) 8 16 24 42 54 65
V7#1-20 (9/13/51-6/5/52) 8 16 24 40 50 60
V8#1-20 (9/11/52-6/4/53) 7 14 21 37 46 55
V9#1-20 ('53-'54), V10#1-20 ('54-'55) 7 14 21 35 43 50
V11('55-'56), V12('56-'57) 6 12 18 29 36 42
V13#1,3-5,7,9-20-V17#1 ('57-'63) 6 12 18 27 33 38
V13#2,6,8-Ingels-a 5 10 15 35 63 90
V17#2- "This Godless Communism" series begins(not in odd #'d issues); cover shows hammer & sickle over Statue of Liberty; 8 pg. Crandall-a of family life under communism (9/28/61) 19 38 57 131 291 450
V17#3,5,7,9,11,13,15,17,19 3 6 9 16 24 32
V17#4,6,14- "This Godless Communism" stories 15 30 45 100 220 340
V17#8-Shows red octopus encompassing Earth, firing squad; 8 pgs. Crandall-a (12/21/61) 18 36 54 124 275 425
V17#10- "This Godless Communism" - how Stalin came to power, part I; Crandall-a 15 30 45 103 227 350
V17#12-Stalin in WWII, forced labor, death by exhaustion; Crandall-a 15 30 45 103 227 350
V17#16-Kruschev takes over; de-Stalinization 15 30 45 103 227 350
V17#18-Kruschev's control; murder of revolters, brainwash, space race by Crandall 15 30 45 103 227 350
V17#20-End of series; Kruschev-people are puppets, firing squads hammer & sickle over Statue of Liberty, snake around communist manifesto by Crandall 19 38 57 131 291 450
V18#1,3,4,6-10,12-20, V19#11-20, V20#1-20(1964-65): V20#6-JFK photo-c & story. V20#16-Babe Ruth-c & story by Sinnott 3 6 9 16 23 30
V18#2-Kruschev on-c (9/27/62) 3 6 9 19 30 40
V18#5- "What About Red China?" - describes how communists took over China 9 18 27 59 117 175
V18#11-Crandall draws himself & 13 other artists on cover (1/31/63) 3 6 9 21 33 45
V19#1-10- "Red Victim" anti-communist series in all 9 18 27 59 117 175
V21, V22 #1-16,18-20,V23-V25(1965-70)-(two V24#5's 11/7/68 & 11/21/68) (no V24#6): 3 6 9 14 19 24
V22#17-Flying saucer wraparound-c 3 6 9 17 26 35
V26, V27#1-8 (V26,27-68 pgs.) 3 6 9 15 22 28
Summer Edition V1#1-6('66), V2#1-6('67) 3 6 9 16 23 30

NOTE: **Anderson** *a-V18#13.* **Borth** *a-V7#10-19 (serial), V8#8-17 (serial), V9#1-10 (serial), V13#2, 6, 11, V14-V25 (except V22#1-3, 11-13), Summer Ed. V1#3-6.* **Crandall** *a-V16#7, 9, 12, 14, 16-18, 20; V17#1, 2, 4-6, 10, 12, 14, 16-18, 20; V18#1, 2, 3(2 pg.), 7, 9-20; V19#4, 11, 13, 16, 19, 20; V20#1, 2, 4, 6, 8-10, 12, 14-16, 18, 20; V21#1-5, 8-11, 13, 16-18; V22#3, 7, 9-11, 14; V23#3, 6, 9, 16, 18; V24#7, 8, 10, 13, 16; V25#8, 16; V27#1-7r, 8r(2 pg.), Summer Ed. V1#3-5, V2#3; c-V16#7, V18#2(part), 7, 11, V19#4, 19, 20, V20#15, V21#5, 9, V22#3, 7, 9, 11, V23#9, 16, V24#13, 16, V25#8, Summer Ed. V1#2 (back c-V1#2-5).* **Powell** *a-V10#11. V19#11, 15, V10#13, V13#6, 8 all have wraparound covers.*

TREASURE CHEST OF THE WORLD'S BEST COMICS
Superior, Toronto, Canada: 1945 (500 pgs., hard-c)

Contains Blue Beetle, Captain Combat, John Wayne, Dynamic Man, Nemo, Li'l Abner; contents can vary - represents random binding of extra books; Captain America on-c 168 336 504 1075 1838 2600

TREASURE COMICS
Prize Publications? (no publisher listed): No date (1943) (50¢, 324 pgs., cardboard-c)

1-(Rare)-Contains rebound Prize Comics #7-11 from 1942 (blank inside-c) 411 822 1233 2877 5039 7200

TREASURE COMICS
Prize Publ. (American Boys' Comics): June-July, 1945 - No. 12, Fall, 1947

1-Paul Bunyan & Marco Polo begin; Highwayman & Carrot Topp only app.; Kiefer-a 60 120 180 381 653 925
2-Arabian Knight, Gorilla King, Dr. Styx begin 37 74 111 222 361 500
3,4,9,12: 9-Kiefer-a 29 58 87 172 281 390
5-Marco Polo-c; Krigstein-a 36 72 108 214 347 480
6,11-Krigstein-a; 11-Krigstein-c 36 72 108 211 343 475
7,8-Frazetta-a (5 pgs. each). 7-Capt. Kidd Jr. app. 47 94 141 296 498 700
10-Simon & Kirby-c/a 47 94 141 296 498 700

NOTE: **Barry** *a-9-11; c-12.* **Kiefer** *a-3, 5, 7; c-2, 6, 7.* **Roussos** *a-11.*

TREASURE ISLAND (See Classics Illustrated #64, Doc Savage Comics #1, King Classics, Movie Classics & Movie Comics)
Dell Publishing Co.: No. 624, Apr, 1955 (Disney)

Four Color 624-Movie, photo-c 9 18 27 59 117 175

TREASURY OF COMICS
St. John Publishing Co.: 1947; No. 2, July, 1947 - No. 4, Sept, 1947; No. 5, Jan, 1948

nn(#1)-Abbie an' Slats (nn on-c, #1 on inside) 15 30 45 94 147 200
2-Jim Hardy Comics; featuring Windy & Paddles 13 26 39 74 105 135
3-Bill Bumlin 11 22 33 62 86 110
4-Abbie an' Slats 13 26 39 74 105 135
5-Jim Hardy Comics #1 13 26 39 74 105 135

TREASURY OF COMICS
St. John Publishing Co.: Mar, 1948 - No. 5, 1948 (Reg. size); 1948-1950 (Over 500 pgs., $1.00)

1 20 40 60 115 188 260
2(#2 on-c, #1 on inside) 13 26 39 74 105 135
3-5 11 22 33 62 86 110
1-(1948, 500 pgs., hard-c)-Abbie & Slats, Abbott & Costello, Casper, Little Annie Rooney, Little Audrey, Jim Hardy, Ella Cinders (16 books bound together) (Rare) 209 418 627 1338 2294 3250
1(1949, 500 pgs.)-Same format as above 164 328 492 1050 1800 2550
1(1950, 500 pgs.)-Same format as above; different-c; (also see Little Audrey Yearbook) (Rare) 164 328 492 1050 1800 2550

TREASURY OF DOGS, A (See Dell Giants)

TREASURY OF HORSES, A (See Dell Giants)

TREEHOUSE OF HORROR (Bart Simpson's...)
Bongo Comics: 1995 - 2017 ($2.95/$2.50/$3.50/$4.50/$4.99, annual)

1-(1995, $2.95)-Groening-c; Allred, Robinson & Smith stories 3 6 9 17 26 35
2-(1996, $2.50)-Stories by Dini & Bagge; infinity-c by Groening 2 4 6 10 14 18
3-(1997, $2.50)-Dorkin-s/Groening-c 2 4 6 8 10 12
4-(1998, $2.50)-Lash & Dixon-s/Groening-c 2 4 6 8 10 12
5-(1999, $3.50)-Thompson-s; Shaw & Aragonés-s/a; TenNapel-s/a 2 4 6 8 10 12
6-(2000, $4.50)-Mahfood-s/a; DeCarlo-a; Morse-s/a; Kuper-s/a 8.00
7-(2001, $4.50)-Hamill-s/Morrison-a; Ennis-s/McCrea-a; Sakai-s/a; Nixey-s/a; Brereton back-c 8.00
8-(2002, $3.50)-Templeton, Shaw, Barta, Simone, Thompson-s/a 8.00
9-(2003, $4.99)-Lord of the Rings-Brereton-a; Dini, Naifeh, Millidge, Boothby, Noto-s/a 8.00
10-(2004, $4.99)-Monsters of Rock w/Alice Cooper, Gene Simmons, Rob Zombie and Pat Boone; art by Rodriguez, Morrison, Morse, Templeton 15.00
11-(2005, $4.99)-EC style w/art by John Severin, Angelo Torres & Al Williamson and flip book with Dracula by Wolfman/Colan and Squish Thing by Wein/Wrightson 8.00
12-(2006, $4.99)-Terry Moore, Kyle Baker, Eric Powell-s/a 8.00
13-(2007, $4.99)-Oswalt, Posehn, Lennon-s; Guerra, Austin, Barta, Rodriguez-a 8.00
14-(2008, $4.99)-s/a by Niles & Fabry; Boothby & Matsumoto; Gilbert Hernandez 8.00
15-(2009, $4.99)-s/a by Jeffrey Brown, Tim Hensley, Ben Jones and others 8.00
16-(2010, $4.99)-s/a by Kelley Jones, Evan Dorkin and others; Mars Attacks homage 15.00
17-(2011, $4.99)-s/a by Gene Ha, Jane Wiedlin and others; Nosferatu homage 12.00
18-(2012, $4.99)-s/a by Jim Valentino, Phil Noto and others; Rosemary's Baby spoof 8.00
19-(2013, $4.99)-s/a by Len Wein, Dan Brereton and others; Cthulhu spoof 8.00
20-(2014, $4.99)-All Zombie issue, including The Walking Ned 8.00
21-(2015, $4.99)-Gremlins & Metropolis spoofs 8.00
22-(2016, $4.99)-Ghostbusters & Gossamer spoofs 8.00
23-(2017, $4.99)-Spoofs of Stephen King stories: It, Dreamcatcher and Thinner 12.00

TREES
Image Comics: May, 2014 - No. 14, Aug, 2016 ($2.99)

1-14-Warren Ellis-s/Jason Howard-a 3.00

TREES: THREE FATES
Image Comics: Sept, 2019 - No. 5, Jan, 2020 ($3.99, limited series)

1-5-Warren Ellis-s/Jason Howard-a 4.00

TREKKER (See Dark Horse Presents #6)
Dark Horse Comics: May, 1987 - No. 6, Mar, 1988 ($1.50, B&W)

1-6: Sci/Fi stories 3.00
Color Special 1 (1989, $2.95, 52 pgs.) 4.00
Collection ($5.95, B&W) 6.00
Special 1 (6/99, $2.95, color) 3.00

TRENCHCOAT BRIGADE, THE
DC Comics (Vertigo): Mar, 1999 - No. 4, Jun, 1999 ($2.50, limited series)

1-4: Hellblazer, Phantom Stranger, Mister E, Dr. Occult app. 3.00

TRENCHER (See Blackball Comics)
Image Comics: May, 1993 - No. 4, Oct, 1993 ($1.95, unfinished limited series)

1-4: Keith Giffen-c/a/scripts. 3-Supreme-c/story 3.00

	GD 2.0	VG 4.0	FN 6.0	VF 8.0	VF/NM 9.0	NM- 9.2

TRIAGE
Dark Horse Comics: Sept, 2019 - No. 5, Jan, 2020 ($3.99, limited series)
1-5-Phillip Sevy-s/a/c; variant covers for each 4.00

TRIAL OF THE AMAZONS (See Wonder Woman #785,786)
DC Comics: May, 2022 - No. 2, Jun, 2022 ($4.99, limited series)
1,2: 1-First part of 7-part storyline; death of Hippolyta. 2-Conclusion of story 5.00

TRIAL OF THE AMAZONS: WONDER GIRL (Yara Flor)
DC Comics: May, 2022 - No. 2, Jun, 2022 ($3.99, limited series)
1,2-Two covers form one image: 1-Part 4 of 7-part storyline. 2-Part 6 of 7 4.00

TRIALS OF SHAZAM!
DC Comics: Oct, 2006 - No. 12, May, 2008 ($2.99)
1-12: 1-8-Winick-s/Porter-a. 9-11-Cascioli-a. 10-Shadowpact app. 12-JLA app. 3.00
... Volume 1 TPB (2007, $14.99) r/#1-6 and story from DCU Brave New World #1 15.00
... Volume 2 TPB (2008, $14.99) r/#7-12 15.00

TRIALS OF ULTRAMAN, THE (Also see The Rise of Ultraman)
Marvel Comics: May, 2021 - No. 5, Oct, 2021 ($4.99/$3.99)
1-($4.99) Main story by Higgins & Groom-s/Manna-a; back-up w/Gurihiru-a 5.00
2-5-($3.99) 4.00

TRIB COMIC BOOK, THE
Winnipeg Tribune: Sept. 24, 1977 - Vol. 4, #36, 1980 (8-1/2"x11", 24 pgs., weekly) (155 total issues)
V1# 1-Color pages (Sunday strips)-Spiderman, Asterix, Disney's Scamp, Wizard of Id, Doonesbury, Inside Woody Allen, Mary Worth, & others (similar to Spirit sections) 2 4 6 10 14 18
V1#2-15, V2#1-52, V3#1-52, V4#1-33 1 3 4 6 8 10
V4#34-36 (not distributed) 2 4 6 11 16 20
NOTE: *All issues have Spider-Man. Later issues contain Star Trek and Star Wars. 20 strips in ea. The first newspaper to put Sunday pages into a comic book format.*

TRIBE (See WildC.A.T.S #4)
Image Comics/Axis Comics No. 2 on: Apr, 1993; No. 2, Sept, 1993 - No. 3, 1994 ($2.50/$1.95)
1-By Johnson & Stroman; gold foil & embossed on black-c 4.00
1-($2.50)-Ivory Edition; gold foil & embossed on white-c; available only through the creators 4.00
2,3: 2-1st Axis Comics issue. 3-Savage Dragon app. 3.00

TRIBUTE TO STEVEN HUGHES, A
Chaos! Comics: Sept, 2000 ($6.95)
1-Lady Death & Evil Ernie pin-ups by various artists; testimonials 7.00

TRICK 'R TREAT
DC Comics (WildStorm): 2009 ($19.95,SC)
nn-Short Halloween-themed story anthology; Andreyko-s; art by Huddleston & others 20.00

TRIGGER (See Roy Rogers'...)

TRIGGER
DC Comics (Vertigo): Feb, 2005 - No. 8, Sept, 2005 ($2.95/$2.99)
1-8-Jason Hall-s/John Watkiss-a/c 3.00

TRIGGER TWINS
National Periodical Publications: Mar-Apr, 1973 (20¢, one-shot)
1-Trigger Twins & Pow Wow Smith-r/All-Star Western #94,103 & Western Comics #81; Infantino-r(p) 2 4 6 13 18 22

TRILLIUM
DC Comics (Vertigo): Oct, 2013 - No. 8, Jun, 2014 ($2.99)
1-8-Jeff Lemire-s/a. 1-Flip-book 3.00

TRINITY (See DC Universe: Trinity)

TRINITY
DC Comics: Aug, 2008 - No. 52, July, 2009 ($2.99, weekly series)
1-52-Superman, Batman & Wonder Woman star; Busiek-s/Bagley-a. 52-Wraparound-c 3.00
Vol. 1 TPB (2009, $29.99) r/#1-17 30.00
Vol. 2 TPB (2009, $29.99) r/#18-35 30.00
Vol. 3 TPB (2009, $29.99) r/#36-52 30.00

TRINITY (DC Rebirth)
DC Comics: Nov, 2016 - No. 22, ($2.99/$3.99)
1-7: 1-Superman, Batman & Wonder Woman; Manapul-s/a. 3-Mann-a. 4-6-Mongul app. 3.00
8-22-($3.99): 9-11-Manapul-s/a; Justice League app. 12-15-Zatanna, Constantine & Deadman app.; Marion-a. 16-Deadshot app. 17-19,21,22-Warlord of Skartaris app. 4.00
Annual 1 (7/17, $4.99) Ra's al Ghul, Circe and Etrigan app.; Guillem March-a/c 5.00

TRINITY ANGELS
Acclaim Comics (Valiant Heroes): July, 1997 - No. 12, June, 1998 ($2.50)
1-12-Maguire-s/a(p). 4-Copycat-c 3.00

TRINITY: BLOOD ON THE SANDS
Image Comics (Top Cow): July, 2009 ($2.99, one-shot)
1-Witchblade, The Darkness and Angelus in the 14th century Arabian desert 3.00

TRINITY OF SIN (DC New 52)
DC Comics: Dec, 2014 - No. 6, May, 2015 ($2.99)
1-6-Pandora, The Question and Phantom Stranger; Guichet-a 3.00

TRINITY OF SIN: PANDORA (DC New 52)
DC Comics: Aug, 2013 - No. 14, Oct, 2014 ($2.99)
1-14: 1-Fawkes-s; origin re-told. 1-3-Trinity War tie-ins. 4-9-Forever Evil tie-ins 3.00
...: Futures End 1 (11/14, $2.99, regular-c) Five years later; Pandora vs. 7 Deadly Sins 3.00
...: Futures End 1 (11/14, $3.99, 3-D cover) 4.00

TRINITY OF SIN: THE PHANTOM STRANGER (See Phantom Stranger 2012 series)

TRIO (Continues in Triple Helix #1)
IDW Publishing: May, 2012 - No. 4, Aug, 2012 ($3.99, limited series)
1-4-John Byrne-s/a/c 4.00

TRIPLE GIANT COMICS (See Archie All-Star Specials under Archie Comics)

TRIPLE HELIX (Also see Trio)
IDW Publishing: Oct, 2013 - No. 4, Jan, 2014 ($3.99, limited series)
1-4-John Byrne-s/a/c; The Trio app. 4.00

TRIPLE THREAT
Special Action/Holyoke/Gerona Publ.: Winter, 1945
1-Duke of Darkness, King O'Leary 40 80 120 246 411 575

TRISH OUT OF WATER
Aspen MLT: Oct, 2013 - No. 5, Mar, 2014 ($1.00/$3.99)
1-($1.00) Vince Hernandez-s/Giuseppe Cafaro-a; multiple covers 3.00
2-5-($3.99) Multiple covers on each 4.00

TRIUMPH (Also see JLA #28-30, Justice League Task Force & Zero Hour)
DC Comics: June, 1995 - No. 4, Sept, 1995 ($1.75, limited series)
1-4: 3-Hourman, JLA app. 3.00

TRIUMPHANT UNLEASHED
Triumphant Comics: No. 0, Nov, 1993 - No. 1, Nov, 1993 ($2.50, lim. series)
0-Serially numbered, 0-Red logo, 0-White logo (no cover price; giveaway), 1-Cover is negative & reverse of #0-c 3.00

TROJAN
Artist, Writers & Artisans, Inc.: Jan, 2023 - No. 4 ($3.99, limited series)
1,2-Daniel Kraus-s/Laci-a 4.00

TROJAN WAR (Adaptation of Trojan war histories from ancient Greek and Roman sources)
Marvel Comics: July, 2009 - No. 5, Nov, 2009 ($3.99, limited series)
1-5-Roy Thomas-s/Miguel Sepulveda-a/Dennis Calero-c 4.00

TROLL (Also see Brigade)
Image Comics (Extreme Studios): Dec, 1993 ($2.50, one-shot, 44 pgs.)
1-1st app. Troll; Liefeld scripts; Matsuda-c/a(p) 4.00
Halloween Special (1994, $2.95)-Maxx app. 4.00
...Once A Hero (8/94, $2.50) 4.00

TROLLORDS
Tru Studios/Comico V2#1 on: 2/86 - No. 15, 1988; V2#1, 11/88 - V2#4, 1989 (1-15: $1.50, B&W)
1-First printing 5.00
1-Second printing, 2-15: 6-Christmas issue; silver logo 3.00
V2#1-4 ($1.75, color, Comico) 3.00
Special 1 ($1.75, 2/87, color)-Jerry's Big Fun Bk. 3.00

TROLLORDS
Apple Comics: July, 1989 - No. 6, 1990 ($2.25, B&W, limited series)
1-6: 1-"The Big Batman Movie Parody" 3.00

TROLL PATROL
Harvey Comics: Jan, 1993 ($1.95, 52 pgs.)
1 4.00

TROLL II (Also see Brigade)
Image Comics (Extreme Studios): July, 1994 ($3.95, one-shot)
1 4.00

TRON (Based on the video game and film)
Slave Labor Graphics: Apr, 2006 - No. 6 ($3.50/$3.95)
1-6: 1-DeMartinis-a/Walker & Jones-s. 5,6-($3.95) 5.00

TRON: BETRAYAL
Marvel Comics: Nov, 2010 - No. 2, Dec, 2010 ($3.99, limited series)
1,2-Prequel to Tron Legacy movie; Larroca-c 4.00

TRON: ORIGINAL MOVIE ADAPTATION
Marvel Comics: Jan, 2011 - No. 2, Feb, 2011 ($3.99, limited series)
1,2-Peter David-s/Mirco Pierfederici-a/Greg Land-c 1 3 4 6 8 10

TROUBLE
Marvel Comics (Epic): Sept, 2003 - No. 5, Jan, 2004 ($2.99, limited series)
1-5-Photo-c; Richard and Ben meet Mary and May; Millar-s/Dodson-a 3.00
1-2nd printing with variant Frank Cho-c 5.00

TROUBLED SOULS
Fleetway: 1990 ($9.95, trade paperback)
nn-Garth Ennis scripts & John McCrea painted-c/a. 10.00

TROUBLEMAKERS
Acclaim Comics (Valiant Heroes): Apr, 1997 - No. 19, June, 1998 ($2.50)
1-19: Fabian Nicieza scripts in all. 1-1st app. XL, Rebound & Blur; 2 covers. 8-Copycat-c. 12-Shooting of Parker 3.00

TROUBLE SHOOTERS, THE (TV)
Dell Publishing Co.: No. 1108, Jun-Aug, 1960
Four Color 1108-Keenan Wynn photo-c 6 12 18 42 79 115

TROUBLE WITH GIRLS, THE
Malibu Comics (Eternity Comics) #7-14/Comico V2#1-4/Eternity V2#5 on: 8/87 - #14, 1988; V2#1, 2/89 - V2#23, 1991? ($1.95, B&W/color)
1-14 ($1.95, B&W, Eternity)-Gerard Jones scripts & Tim Hamilton-c/a in all 3.00
V2#1-23-Jones scripts, Hamilton-c/a. 3.00
Annual 1 (1988, $2.95) 4.00
Christmas Special 1 (12/91, $2.95, B&W, Eternity)-Jones scripts, Hamilton-c/a 4.00
Graphic Novel 1,2 (7/88, B&W)-r/#1-3 & #4-6 8.00

TROUBLE WITH GIRLS, THE: NIGHT OF THE LIZARD
Marvel Comics (Epic Comics/Heavy Hitters): 1993 - No. 4, 1993 ($2.50/$1.95, lim. series)
1-Embossed-c; Gerard Jones scripts & Bret Blevins-c/a in all 4.00
2-4: 2-Begin $1.95-c. 3.00

TROVER SAVES THE UNIVERSE (Based on the video game by Justin Roiland)
Image Comics (Skybound): Aug, 2021 - No. 5, Dec, 2021 ($3.99, limited series)
1-5-Tess Stone-s/a 4.00

TRUE ADVENTURES (Formerly True Western)(Men's Adventures #4 on)

The Trials of Shazam #1 © DC

Trojan #2 © AWA

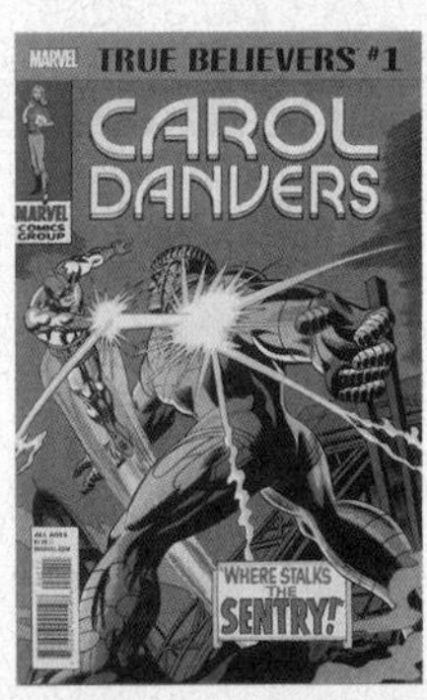

True Believers: Carol Danvers #1 © MAR

Marvel Comics (CCC): No. 3, May, 1950 (52 pgs.)

	GD 2.0	VG 4.0	FN 6.0	VF 8.0	VF/NM 9.0	NM- 9.2
3-Powell, Sekowsky, Maneely-a; Brodsky-c	28	56	84	165	270	375

TRUE ANIMAL PICTURE STORIES
True Comics Press: Winter, 1947 - No. 2, Spring-Summer, 1947

	GD 2.0	VG 4.0	FN 6.0	VF 8.0	VF/NM 9.0	NM- 9.2
1	15	30	45	88	137	185
2	14	28	42	76	112	145

TRUE AVIATION PICTURE STORIES (Becomes Aviation Adventures & Model Building #16 on)
Parents' Mag. Institute: 1942; No. 2, Jan-Feb, 1943 - No. 15, Sept-Oct, 1946

	GD 2.0	VG 4.0	FN 6.0	VF 8.0	VF/NM 9.0	NM- 9.2
1-(#1 & 2 titled ...Aviation Comics Digest)(not digest size)	20	40	60	115	185	255
2	12	24	36	69	97	125
3-14: 3-10-Plane photos on-c. 11,13-Photo-c	10	20	30	58	79	100
15-(Titled "True Aviation Adventures & Model Building")	10	20	30	54	72	90

TRUE BELIEVERS
Marvel Comics: Sept, 2008 - No. 5, Jan, 2009 ($2.99, limited series)

	GD 2.0	VG 4.0	FN 6.0	VF 8.0	VF/NM 9.0	NM- 9.2
1-5-Cary Bates-s/Paul Gulacy-a. 1,2-Reed Richards app. 3-Luke Cage app.						4.00

TRUE BELIEVERS...
Marvel Comics: Jun, 2015 - Present ($1.00, series of one-shot reprints)

	GD 2.0	VG 4.0	FN 6.0	VF 8.0	VF/NM 9.0	NM- 9.2
...: Absolute Carnage – Carnage 1 - Reprints Amazing Spider-Man #361; Bagley-a	1	2	3	5	6	8
...: Absolute Carnage – Carnage, U.S.A. 1 - Reprints Carnage, U.S.A. #1; Crain-a						6.00
...: Absolute Carnage – Mania 1 - Reprints Venom #1 (2003); Herrera-a						3.00
...: Absolute Carnage – Maximum Carnage 1 - Reprints Spider-Man Unlimited #1						6.00
...: Absolute Carnage – Mind Bomb 1 - Reprints Carnage: Mind Bomb #1; Hotz-a	1	3	4	6	8	10
...: Absolute Carnage – Planet of the Symbiotes 1 - R/ Amaz. Spider-Man Super Special						3.00
...: Absolute Carnage – Savage Rebirth 1 - Reprints Amazing Spider-Man #430						5.00
...: Absolute Carnage – Separation Anxiety 1 - Reprints Venom: Separation Anxiety #1	1	3	4	6	8	10
...: Absolute Carnage – She-Venom 1 - Reprints Venom: Sinner Takes All #3	1	3	4	6	8	10
...: Absolute Carnage – Venom vs. Carnage 1 - Reprints Venom vs. Carnage #1	3	6	9	16	23	30
...: Age of Apocalypse 1 - Reprints X-Men: Alpha #1; Cruz & Epting-a; wraparound-c						3.00
...: Age of Ultron 1 - Reprints Age of Ultron #1; Bendis-s/Hitch-a						3.00
...: All-New, All-Different Avengers - Cyclone 1 - Reprints issue #4; Waid-s/Asrar-a						3.00
...: All-New Wolverine 1 - Reprints issue #1; Taylor-s/Lopez-a						6.00
...: Amazing Spider-Man 1 - Reprints Amazing Spider-Man #1						5.00
...: Amazing Spider-Man - The Dark Kingdom 1 - Reprints Amazing Spider-Man #6						3.00
...: Annihilation – Annihilus 1 - Reprints Fantastic Four #140						3.00
...: Annihilation – Mantis 1 - Reprints Avengers #112; Heck-a						3.00
...: Annihilation – Man-Wolf in Space 1 - Reprints Marvel Premiere #45						3.00
...: Annihilation – Moondragon 1 - Reprints Iron Man #54; Sub-Mariner app.						3.00
...: Annihilation – Nova 1 - Reprints Nova #1; John Buscema-a						3.00
...: Annihilation – Odinpower 1 - Reprints Thor #349; Simonson-s/a						3.00
...: Annihilation – Omega the Unknown 1 - Reprints Omega the Unknown #1						3.00
...: Annihilation – Quasar 1 - Reprints Incredible Hulk #234; Sal Buscema-a						3.00
...: Annihilation – Super-Adaptoid 1 - Reprints Tales of Suspense #82 & 84; Kirby-a						3.00
...: Annihilation – Super-Skrull 1 - Reprints Thor #142; Kirby-a						3.00
...: Ant-Man and Hawkeye - Avengers Assemble 1 - Reprints Avengers #223						3.00
...: Ant-Man and the Wasp - On the Trail of Spider-Man 1 - Reprints Tales to Astonish #57						3.00
...: Ant-Man and the Wasp - The Birth of Giant-Man 1 - Rep. Tales to Astonish #35 & 49						3.00
...: Ant-Man and the Wasp - 'Til Death Do Us Part 1 - Reprints Avengers #60						3.00
...: Ant-Man Presents Iron Man - The Ghost and the Machine 1 - Reprints Iron Man #219	2	4	6	8	10	12
...: Ant-Man - The Incredible Shrinking Doom 1 - Reprints Marvel Feature #4						3.00
...: Armor Wars 1 - Reprints Iron Man #225; Michelinie-s/Bright & Layton-a						3.00
...: Astonishing X-Men 1 - Reprints Astonishing X-Men #1 (2004); Whedon-s/Cassaday-a						3.00
...: Avengers – Endgame 1 - Reprints Avengers #71; Sal Buscema-a						3.00
...: Avengers Forever 1 - Reprints Avengers Forever #1; Busiek-s/Pacheco-a						3.00
...: Avengers – Nebula 1 - Reprints Avengers #260; John Buscema-a						3.00
...: Avengers – Rocket Raccoon 1 - Reprints Rocket Raccoon #1; Mignola-a						3.00
...: Avengers – Ronin 1 - Reprints New Avengers #30; Bendis-s/Yu-a						3.00
...: Avengers – Stormbreaker 1 - Reprints Thor #339; Simonson-s/a						3.00
...: Avengers – Thanos & Gamora 1 - Reprints Warlock and the Infinity Watch #9						3.00
...: Avengers – Thanos: The Final Battle 1 - Reprints Infinity Gauntlet #6; Starlin-s/Lim-a						3.00
...: Avengers – Thanos vs. The Marvel Universe 1 - Reprints Infinity Gauntlet #4						3.00
...: Avengers – The Gatherers Saga 1 - Reprints Avengers #343; Epting-a						3.00
...: Avengers vs. Thanos 1 - Reprints Avengers #125; Buscema & Cockrum-a						3.00
...: Black Widow 1 - Reprints Black Widow #1 (2014); Edmondson-s/Noto-a						3.00
...: Black Widow – Amazing Adventures 1 - Reprints stories from Amazing Advs. #1,2						3.00
...: Black Widow & Daredevil 1 - Reprints Daredevil #81 (1971); Conway-s/Colan-a						3.00
...: Black Widow & The Avengers 1 - Reprints Avengers #111 (1973); Magneto app.						3.00
...: Black Widow & The Thing 1 - Reprints Marvel Two-In-One #10 (1975); Brown-a						3.00
...: Black Widow – Darkstar 1 - Reprints Champions #7 (1976); Tuska-a						3.00
...: Black Widow, Introducing The... 1 - Reprints Tales of Suspense #52-53 (1964)						3.00
...: Black Widow – Red Guardian 1 - Reprints Avengers #43 (1967); John Buscema-a						3.00
...: Black Widow – Taskmaster 1 - Reprints Avengers #196 (1980); origin; Pérez-a						3.00
...: Black Widow – Yelena Belova 1 - Reprints Black Widow #1 (1999); J.G. Jones-a						3.00
...: Cable & The New Mutants 1 - Reprints New Mutants #87; L. Simonson-s/Liefeld-a						3.00
...: Captain Marvel 1 - Reprints Captain Marvel #1 (2014); DeConnick-s/Lopez-a						3.00
...: Captain Marvel - Avenger 1 - Reprints Avengers #183; Michelinie-s/Byrne-a						3.00
...: Captain Marvel - Betrayed! 1 - Reprints Avengers Annual #10; Claremont-s/Golden-a						3.00
...: Captain Marvel - Binary 1 - Reprints (Uncanny) X-Men #164; Claremont-s/Cockrum-a						3.00
...: Captain Marvel - Earth's Mightiest Hero 1 - Reprints Captain Marvel #1 (2012)						3.00
...: Captain Mar-vell 1 - Reprints Marvel Super-Heroes #12 & Marvel Fanfare #24						3.00
...: Captain Marvel - Ms. Marvel 1 - Reprints Ms. Marvel #1 (1977); Buscema-a						3.00
...: Captain Marvel - Spider-Man and Ms. Marvel 1 - Reprints Marvel Team-Up #62						3.00
...: Captain Marvel - The Kree/Skrull War 1 - Reprints Avengers #89; Rick Jones app.						3.00
...: Captain Marvel - The New Ms. Marvel 1 - Reprints Ms. Marvel #20 (1978); Cockrum-a						3.00
...: Captain Marvel vs. Ronan 1 - Reprints Captain Marvel #41 (1975); Milgrom-a						3.00
...: Carol Danvers 1 - Reprints Marvel Super-Heroes #13; 1st app. Carol Danvers						3.00
...: Chewbacca 1 - Reprints Chewbacca #1; Duggan-s/Noto-a						3.00
...: Civil War 1 - Reprints Civil War #1; Millar-s/McNiven-a	1	3	4	6	8	10
...: Conan - Curse of the Golden Skull! 1 - Reps Conan the Barbarian #37; Neal Adams-a						3.00
...: Conan - Queen of the Black Coast! 1 - Reps Conan the Barbarian #58; Bêlit app.						3.00
...: Conan - Resurrection 1 - Reprints Conan the Barbarian #187; Buscema-a						3.00
...: Conan: Serpent War #0 – The Valley of the Worm - Reprints Supernatural Thrillers #3						3.00
...: Conan - Swords in the Night! 1 - Reprints Conan the Barbarian #23; Barry Smith-a						3.00
...: Conan the Barbarian 1 - Reprints Conan the Barbarian #1; Barry Smith-a						3.00
...: Conan - The Devil-God of Bal-Sagoth! 1 - Reprints Conan the Barbarian #17; Kane-a						3.00
...: Conan - The Secret of Skull River 1 - Reprints Savage Tales #5; Starlin-a						3.00
...: Conan - The Tower of the Elephant 1 - Reprints Conan the Barbarian #4; B. Smith-a						3.00
...: Daredevil - Practice to Deceive 1 - Reprints Daredevil #6 (2016); Soule-s/Buffagni-a						3.00
...: Darth Vader 1 - Reprints Darth Vader #1; Gillen-s/Larroca-a	1	3	4	6	8	10
...: Deadpool 1 - Reprints 1st app. from New Mutants #98 (1991); Liefeld-a	1	3	4	6	8	10
...: Deadpool - Deadpool vs. Sabretooth 1 - Reprints Deadpool #8 (2016)						3.00
...: Deadpool Origins 1 - Reprints Wolverine Origins #25; Dillon-a						3.00
...: Deadpool The Musical 1 - Reprints Deadpool #49.1; McCrea-a						3.00
...: Deadpool Variants 1 - Gallery of variant covers						3.00
...: Death of Phoenix 1 - Reprints New X-Men #150						3.00
...: Detective Deadpool 1 - Reprints Cable & Deadpool #13; Nicieza-s/Zircher-a						3.00
...: Doctor Strange - The Last Days of Magic 1 - Reprints Doctor Strange #6 (2015)						3.00
...: Droids 1 - Reprints Droids #1; Star Wars C-3PO & R2-D2 app.; John Romita-a						3.00
...: Empyre – Anelle 1 - Reprints Fantastic Four #37 (1965) intro Princess Anelle						3.00
...: Empyre – Galactus 1 - Reprints Fantastic Four #257 (1983) Byrne-s/a						3.00
...: Empyre – Hulkling 1 - Reprints Young Avengers #11 (2006) Cheung-a						3.00
...: Empyre – Lyja 1 - Reprints Fantastic Four #357 (1991) Paul Ryan-a						3.00
...: Empyre – Mantis 1 - Reprints Avengers #133 (1975) origin of Mantis; Sal Buscema-a						3.00
...: Empyre – Mar-Vell 1 - Reprints Avengers #89 (1971) Kree/Skrull war begins						3.00
...: Empyre – Quoi 1 - Reprints Avengers Celestial Quest #3 (12003) Englehart-s						3.00
...: Empyre – She-Hulk 1 - Reprints Savage She-Hulk #1 (1980) John Buscema-a						6.00
...: Empyre – Swordsman 1 - Reprints Avengers #19 (1965) Swordsman's debut; Heck-a						3.00
...: Empyre – Vision 1 - Reprints Giant-Size Avengers #4 (1974) Dormammu app.						3.00
...: Enter – The Phoenix 1 - Reprints X-Men #100-101 (1976) Cockrum-a						3.00
...: Evil Deadpool 1 - Reprints Deadpool #45; Espin-a						3.00
...: Exiles 1 - Reprints Exiles #1 (2001); Winick-s/McKone-a						3.00
...: Extraordinary X-Men - The Burning Man 1 - Reprints issue #6; Ibañez-a						3.00
...: Fantastic Four - Blastaar 1 - Reprints Fantastic Four #62; Kirby-a; Inhumans app.						3.00
...: Fantastic Four By John Byrne 1 - Reprints Fantastic Four #232; Diablo app.						3.00
...: Fantastic Four By Walter Simonson 1 - Reprints Fantastic Four #337						3.00
...: Fantastic Four - Dragon Man 1 - Reprints Fantastic Four #35; Kirby-a						3.00
...: Fantastic Four - Frightful Four 1 - Reprints Fantastic Four #36; Kirby-a						3.00
...: Fantastic Four - Galactus Hungers 1 - Reprints Fantastic Four #175; Buscema-a						3.00
...: Fantastic Four - Hulk vs. Thing 1 - Reprints Fantastic Four #112; Buscema-a						3.00
...: Fantastic Four - Klaw 1 - Reprints Fantastic Four #53; Kirby-a; Black Panther app.						3.00
...: Fantastic Four - Mad Thinker & Awesome Android 1 - Reprints Fantastic Four #15						3.00
...: Fantastic Four - Molecule Man 1 - Reprints Fantastic Four #20; Kirby-a; Watcher app.						3.00
...: Fantastic Four - Puppet Master 1 - Reprints Fantastic Four #8; Kirby-a; intro. Alicia						3.00
...: Fantastic Four - Ronan & The Kree 1 - Reprints Fantastic Four #65; Kirby-a						3.00
...: Fantastic Four - Skrulls 1 - Reprints Fantastic Four #2; Kirby-a						3.00
...: Fantastic Four - Super-Skrull 1 - Reprints Fantastic Four #18; Kirby-a						3.00
...: Fantastic Four - The Birth of Valeria 1 - Reprints Fantastic Four #54 (2002)						3.00

	GD	VG	FN	VF	VF/NM	NM-
	2.0	4.0	6.0	8.0	9.0	9.2

...: Fantastic Four - The Coming of Galactus 1 - Reprints Fantastic Four #48 3.00
...: Fantastic Four - The Coming of H.E.R.B.I.E. 1 - Reprints Fantastic Four #209 3.00
...: Fantastic Four - The Wedding of Reed & Sue 1 - Reprints Fantastic Four Annual #3 3.00
...: Fantastic Four vs. Doctor Doom 1 - Reprints 1st app. in Fantastic Four #5
1 3 4 6 8 10
...: Fantastic Four vs. The New Fantastic Four 1 - Reprints Fantastic Four #374 3.00
...: Generation X 1 - Reprints Generation X #1; Lobdell-s/Bachalo-a 3.00
...: Giant-Size X-Men 1 - Reprints Giant-Size X-Men #1; Wein-s/Cockrum-a
1 2 3 5 6 8
...: Guardians of the Galaxy - Galaxy's Most Wanted 1 - Reprints GOTG #6 (2015) 3.00
...: House of M 1 - Reprints House of M #1; Bendis-s/Coipel-a 3.00
...: Hulk - Devil Hulk 1 - Reprints Incredible Hulk #13 (2000); Jenkins-s/Garney-a
1 3 4 6 8 10
...: Hulk - Grey Hulk Returns 1 - Reprints Incredible Hulk #324; Milgrom-s/a
1 2 3 5 6 8
...: Hulk - Head of Banner 1 - Reprints Incredible Hulk #6; Stan Lee-s/Steve Ditko-a 3.00
...: Hulk - Intelligent 1 - Reprints Incredible Hulk #272; Mantlo-s/Sal Buscema-a 3.00
...: Hulk - Joe Fixit 1 - Reprints Incredible Hulk #347; David-s/Purves-a 3.00
...: Hulk - Mindless Hulk 1 - Reprints Incredible Hulk #299; Mantlo-s/Sal Buscema-a 3.00
...: Hulk - Professor Hulk 1 - Reprints Incredible Hulk #377; David-s/Keown-a 3.00
...: Hulk - Red Hulk 1 - Reprints Hulk #1 (2008); Loeb-s/McGuinness-a 3.00
...: Hulk - The Other Hulks 1 - r/Journey Into Mystery #62 (Xemnu) & Strange Tales #75 3.00
...: Infinity Gauntlet 1 - Reprints Infinity Gauntlet #1; Starlin-s/Pérez-a
1 3 4 6 8 10
...: Infinity Incoming! 1 - Reprints Avengers #1 (2013); Hickman-s/Opeña-a 3.00
...: Infinity War 1 - Reprints Infinity War #1; Starlin-s/Lim-a 3.00
...: Invincible Iron Man - The War Machines 1 - Reprints Invincible Iron Man #6 3.00
...: Iron Man 2020 - Albert & Elsie-Dee 1 - Reprints Wolverine #37 (1988); Silvestri-a 3.00
...: Iron Man 2020 - Arno Stark 1 - Reprints Machine Man #2 (1984); Trimpe-a 3.00
...: Iron Man 2020 - Jocasta 1 - Reprints Avengers #162; Ultron app.; Perez-a 3.00
...: Iron Man 2020 - Pepper Potts 1 - Reprints Tales of Suspense #45; Heck-a 3.00
...: Iron Man 2020 - War Machine 1 - Reprints Iron Man #118 (1979); Byrne-a 3.00
...: Kanan 1 - Reprints Kanan #1; Star Wars; Weisman-s/Larraz-a
2 4 6 11 16 20
...: King Conan 1 - Reprints King Conan #1; Buscema-a 3.00
...: King in Black – Beta Ray Bill 1 - Reprints Thor #337; 1st app. Bill; Simonson-s/a 3.00
...: King in Black – Black Cat 1 - Reprints 1st app. in Amazing Spider-Man #194 3.00
...: King in Black – Black Knight 1 - Reprints Avengers #48 (1968); 1st app.; Tuska-a 3.00
...: King in Black – Black Panther 1 - Reprints Fantastic Four #52 (1966); 1st app. 3.00
...: King in Black – Franklin Richards 1 - Reprints Fantastic Four #245; Byrne-s/a 3.00
...: King in Black – Gamma Flight's Doc Samson 1 - Reprints Incredible Hulk #141; origin 3.00
...: King in Black – Iron Man/Doctor Doom 1 - Reprints Iron Man #149; Romita Jr.-a 3.00
...: King in Black – Monsterworld 1 - Reprints Venom Super Special #1 (1995); Hotz-a 3.00
...: King in Black – Thunderbolts 1 - Reprints Incredible Hulk #449; Deodato Jr.-a 3.00
...: King in Black – Valkyrie 1 - Reprints Avengers #83 (1970); origin.; Buscema-a 3.00
...: Kitty Pryde and Wolverine 1 - Reprints Kitty Pryde and Wolverine #1; Milgrom-a 3.00
...: Lando 1 - Reprints Lando #1; Star Wars; Soule-s/Maleev-a 3.00
...: Marvel Knights 20th Anniversary – Black Widow By Grayson & Jones 1 - r/#1('99) 3.00
...: Marvel Knights 20th Anniversary – Daredevil and the Defenders 1 - r/Daredevil #80 3.00
...: Marvel Knights 20th Anniversary – Daredevil By Bendis & Maleev 1 - r/Daredevil #26 3.00
...: Marvel Knights 20th Anniversary – Daredevil By Lee & Everett 1 - r/Daredevil #1 ('64) 3.00
...: Marvel Knights 20th Anniversary – Daredevil By Smith, Quesada & Palmiotti 1 - r/#1 ('98) 3.00
...: Marvel Knights 20th Anniversary – Hellcat: The First Appearance 1 - r/Avengers #144 3.00
...: Marvel Knights 20th Anniversary – Iron Fist By Thomas & Kane 1 - r/Marvel Prem. #15 6.00
...: Marvel Knights 20th Anniversary – Jessica Jones: Alias By Bendis & Gaydos 1 - r/Alias #1 3.00
...: Marvel Knights 20th Anniversary – Luke Cage, Hero For Hire 1 - r/Hero For Hire #1 3.00
...: Marvel Knights 20th Anniversary – Power Man and Iron Fist 1 - r/Power Man #48 3.00
...: Marvel Knights 20th Anniversary – Punisher: The First Appearance 1 - r/AS-M #129
1 3 4 6 8 10
...: Marvel Knights 20th Anniversary – Punisher By Ennis, Dillon & Palmiotti 1 - r/#1 ('00) 3.00
...: Marvel Knights 20th Anniversary – Punisher By Grant & Zeck 1 - r/Punisher #1 ('86) 3.00
...: Marvel Knights 20th Anniversary – Punisher War Journal By Potts & Lee 1 - r/#1 ('88) 3.00
...: Marvel Tails Starring Peter Porker, The Spectacular Spider-Ham 1 - Reprints #1 3.00
...: Marvel Zombies 1 - Reprints Marvel Zombies #1; Bendis-s/Phillips-a
2 4 6 8 10 12
...: Mighty Thor - The Strongest Viking There Is 1 - Reprints Mighty Thor #6 3.00
...: Miles Morales 1 - Reprints Ultimate Comics Spider-Man #1; Bendis-s/Pichelli-a
1 3 4 6 8 10
...: Ms. Marvel 1 - Reprints Ms. Marvel #1 (2014); Wilson-s/Alphona-a 3.00
...: New Mutants 1 - Reprints New Mutants #1; Claremont-s/McLeod-a 3.00
...: Old Man Logan 1 - Reprints Wolverine #66 (2008); Millar-s/McNiven-a; wraparound-c 5.00
...: Phoenix – Bizarre Adventures 1 - Reprints Bizarre Adventures #27; Buscema-a 3.00
...: Phoenix Classic 1 - Reprints Classic X-Men #13 & 18; Bolton-a 3.00
...: Phoenix Origins 1 - Reprints X-Men Origins: Jean Grey; Mayhew-a 3.00
...: Phoenix Presents Cyclops & Marvel Girl 1 - Reprints X-Men #48 & 57 (1968,1969) 3.00
...: Phoenix Presents Jean Grey vs. Sabretooth 1 - Reprints X-Men #28 (1994) 3.00
...: Phoenix Presents The Wedding of Scott Summers & Jean Grey 1 - Reprints X-Men #30 3.00
...: Phoenix Returns 1 - Reprints Fantastic Four #286; Byrne-s/a 3.00
...: Phoenix – What If? 1 - Reprints What If? #27 (Phoenix Had Not Died?) 3.00
...: Planet Hulk 1 - Reprints Incredible Hulk #92 (2006); Pak-s/Pagulayan-a 3.00
...: Princess Leia 1 - Reprints Princess Leia #1; Waid-s/Dodson-a 6.00
...: Rebirth of Thanos 1 - Reprints Silver Surfer #34 (1990); Starlin-s/Lim-a 3.00
...: Scott Lang, The Astonishing Ant-Man 1 - Reprints Marvel Premiere #47; Byrne-a 3.00
...: Shattered Empire 1 - Reprints Journey to Star Wars: The Force Awakens – Shattered Empire #1; Rucka-s/Checchetto-a 3.00
...: She-Hulk 1 - Reprints She-Hulk #1 (2014); Soule-s/Pulido-a 6.00
...: Silk 1 - Reprints Silk #1 (2015); Thompson-a/Stacey Lee-a; Spider-Man app. 3.00
...: Spider-Gwen 1 - Reprints Spider-Gwen #1 (2015); Latour-s/Robbi Rodriguez-a
1 3 4 6 8 10
...: Spider-Man – Morbius 1 - Reprints Amazing Spider-Man #101; Gil Kane-a
1 3 4 6 8 10
...: Spider-Man – Spider-Armor 1 - Reprints Web of Spider-Man #100; Saviuk-a 3.00
...: Spider-Man – Spidey Fights in London 1 - Reprints Amazing Spider-Man #95 3.00
...: Spider-Man – The New Spider-Man 1 - Reprints Marvel Team-Up #141 3.00
...: Spider-Man – The Wedding of Aunt May & Doc Ock 1 - Reprints ASM #131 3.00
...: Spider-Man vs. Hulk 1 - Reprints Amazing Spider-Man #328; McFarlane-a 3.00
...: Spider-Man vs. Mysterio 1 - Reprints debut in Amazing Spider-Man #13 3.00
...: Spider-Woman 1 - Reprints Spider-Woman #5 (2015); Hopeless-s/Javier Rodriguez-a 3.00
...: Star Wars 1 - Reprints Star Wars #1 (2015); Aaron-s/Cassaday-a 6.00
...: Star Wars – According to the Droids 1 - Reprints Droids #6 3.00
...: Star Wars Classic 1 - Reprints Star Wars #1 (1977); Roy Thomas-s/Howard Chaykin-a 6.00
...: Star Wars Covers 1 - Gallery of variant covers for Star Wars #1 (2015) 3.00
...: Star Wars – Darth Maul 1 - Reprints Star Wars: Darth Maul – Son of Dathomir #1
1 3 4 6 8 10
...: Star Wars – Darth Vader 1 - Reprints Darth Vader #1 1 3 4 6 8 10
...: Star Wars – Dead Probe 1 - Reprints Star Wars #45 (1977); Infantino-a 6.00
...: Star Wars – Ewoks 1 - Reprints Ewoks #1; Kremer-a
1 3 4 6 8 10
...: Star Wars – Hutt Run 1 - Reprints Star Wars #35 (2015); Larroca-a 3.00
...: Star Wars – Rebel Jail 1 - Reprints Star Wars #16 (2015); Doctor Aphra app.; Yu-a 3.00
...: Star Wars – Skywalker Strikes - Reprints Star Wars #1 (2015); Aaron-s/Cassaday-a 3.00
...: Star Wars – The Ashes of Jedha 1 - Reprints Star Wars #38 (2015); Larroca-a 3.00
...: Star Wars – The Hunter 1 - Reprints Star Wars #16 (1977); Simonson-a 3.00
...: Star Wars – The Original Marvel Years No. 107 - Reprints Star Wars #107 (1986)
1 3 4 6 8 10
...: Star Wars – Thrawn 1 - Reprints Star Wars: Thrawn #1; Luke Ross-a
1 3 4 6 8 10
...: Star Wars – Vader vs. Leia 1 - Reprints Star Wars #48 (1977); Infantino-a
1 3 4 6 8 10
...: Thanos the First 1 - Reprints Iron Man #55 (1973); 1st app. Thanos & Drax 3.00
...: Thanos Rising 1 - Reprints Thanos Rising #1; Aaron-s/Bianchi-a 3.00
...: The Criminally Insane – Absorbing Man 1 - Reprints Journey Into Mystery #114 3.00
...: The Criminally Insane – Bullseye 1 - Reprints debut in Daredevil #131 3.00
...: The Criminally Insane – Bushman 1 - Reprints Moon Knight #1 (1980) 3.00
...: The Criminally Insane – Dracula 1 - Reprints Tomb of Dracula #24; Colan-a 3.00
...: The Criminally Insane – Green Goblin 1 - Reprints debut in Amazing Spider-Man #14 3.00
...: The Criminally Insane – Gypsy Moth 1 - Reprints Spider-Woman #10; Infantino-a 3.00
...: The Criminally Insane – Klaw 1 - Reprints Black Panther #14 (1977) 3.00
...: The Criminally Insane – Mandarin 1 - Reprints Tales of Suspense #50 & 55 3.00
...: The Criminally Insane – Masters of Evil 1 - Reprints Avengers #6 (1963) 3.00
...: The Criminally Insane – Purple Man 1 - Reprints Daredevil #4 (1964) 3.00
...: The Groovy Deadpool 1 - Reprints Deadpool #13 (2013) 1970s art style 3.00
...: The Meaty Deadpool 1 - Reprints Deadpool #11 (2008) Bullseye (as Hawkeye) app. 3.00
...: The Sinister Secret of Spider-Man's New Costume 1 - Rep. Amaz. Spider-Man #258 3.00
...: The Unbeatable Squirrel Girl 1 - Reprints The Unbeatable Squirrel Girl #1 (2015) 3.00
...: The Wedding of Deadpool 1 - Reprints Deadpool #27 (2013) wraparound-c 3.00
...: Thor 1 - Reprints Thor #1 (2014); debut of female Thor; Aaron-s/Dauterman-a 6.00
...: Uncanny Avengers - The Bagalia Job 1 - Reprints Uncanny Avengers #5 3.00
...: Uncanny Deadpool 1 - Reprints Cable & Deadpool #38; Nicieza-s/Brown-a 3.00
...: Vader Down 1 - Reprints Star Wars: Vader Down #1; Aaron-s/Deodato-a 3.00
...: Venom - Agent Venom 1 - Reprints Venom #1 (2011) Remender-s/Moore-a 3.00
...: Venom - Carnage 1 - Reprints Amazing Spider-Man #363 (1992) Bagley-a
1 3 4 6 8 10
...: Venom - Dark Origin 1 - Reprints Venom: Dark Origin #3 (2008) Wells-s/Medina-a 3.00
...: Venom - Flashpoint 1 - Reprints Amazing Spider-Man #654.1 (2011) Ramos-a 3.00
...: Venom - Homecoming 1 - Reprints Venom #6 (2017) Costa-s/Sandoval-a 3.00
...: Venom - Lethal Protector 1 - Reprints Venom: Lethal Protector #1; Bagley-a
1 3 4 6 8 10
...: Venom - Shiver 1 - Reprints Venom #1 (2003) Way-s/Herrera-a 3.00
...: Venom - Symbiosis 1 - Reprints Web of Spider-Man #1 (1985) Larocque-a 3.00
...: Venom - Toxin 1 - Reprints Venom #17 (2011) Remender & Bunn-s/Walker-a 3.00
...: Venom vs. Spider-Man 1 - Reprints Amazing Spider-Man #300 (1988) McFarlane-a
2 4 6 8 10 12
...: What If Conan the Barbarian Walked the Earth Today? 1 - Reprints What If? #13 3.00
...: What If Doctor Doom Had Become a Hero? 1 - Reprints What If? #22 3.00
...: What If Jane Foster Had Found the Hammer of Thor? 1 - Reprints What If? #10 3.00
...: What If Kraven the Hunter Had Killed Spider-Man? 1 - Reprints What If? #17 3.00
...: What If Legion Had Killed Magneto? 1 - Reprints What If? #77; Gomez-a 3.00
...: What If Spider-Man Had Rescued Gwen Stacy? 1 - Reprints What If? #24; Kane-a
2 4 6 8 10 12
...: What If Spider-Man Joined the Fantastic Four? 1 - Reprints What If? #1 3.00
...: What If The Alien Costume Had Possessed Spider-Man? 1 - Reprints What If? #4 3.00
...: What If The Avengers Had Fought Evil During the 1950s? 1 - Reprints What If? #9 3.00
...: What If The Fantastic Four Had Different Super-Powers? 1 - r/What If? #6 3.00
...: What If The Fantastic Four Had Not Gained Their Super-Powers? 1 - r/What If? #36 3.00
...: What If The Silver Surfer Possessed the Infinity Gauntlet? 1 - Reprints What If? #49 5.00
...: Wolverine 1 - Reprints #1 (1982) Claremont-s/Miller-a 3.00
...: Wolverine and the X-Men 1 - Reprints #1; Aaron-s/Bachalo-a 3.00
...: Wolverine – Blood Hungry 1 - Reprints Marvel Comics Presents #85-87; Kieth-a 3.00
...: Wolverine – Enemy of the State 1 - Reprints Wolverine #20 (2003); Millar-s/Romita Jr.-a 3.00
...: Wolverine – Evolution 1 - Reprints Wolverine #50 (2007); Loeb-s/Bianchi-a 3.00
...: Wolverine – Fatal Attractions 1 - Reprints X-Men #25 (1993); Nicieza-s/Andy Kubert-a 3.00
...: Wolverine – Old Man Logan 1 - Reprints Old Man Logan #1; Bendis-s/Sorrentino-a 3.00
...: Wolverine – Origin 1 - Reprints Wolverine: The Origin #1; Andy Kubert-a 3.00
...: Wolverine – Save the Tiger 1 - Reprints Marvel Comics Presents #1-3; Buscema-a 3.00
...: Wolverine – Sword Quest 1 - Reprints Wolverine #1 (1988); Claremont-s/Buscema-a 3.00
...: Wolverine – The Brothers 1 - Reprints Wolverine #1 (2003); Rucka-s/Robertson-a 3.00
...: Wolverine – The Dying Game 1 - Reprints Wolverine #90 (1995); Adam Kubert-a 3.00
...: Wolverine vs. Hulk 1 - Reprints Incredible Hulk #181; Wein-s/Trimpe-a 6.00
...: Wolverine vs. Sabretooth 1 - Reprints Wolverine #10 (1989); Buscema-a 3.00
...: Wolverine vs. Venom 1 - Reprints Venom: Tooth and Claw #1; Hama-s/St. Pierre-a 5.00
...: Wolverine – Weapon X 1 - Reprints Marvel Comics Presents #72-74 3.00
...: Wolverine – X-23 1 - Reprints X-23 #1; Craig Kyle-s/Billy Tan-a 3.00
...: X-Factor - Mutant Genesis 1 - Reprints X-Factor #71; David-s/Stroman-a 3.00
...: X-Force 1 – Reprints X-Force #1; Liefeld-s/a; Nicieza-s 3.00
...: X-Men 1 – Reprints X-Men #1 (1963); Stan Lee-s/Jack Kirby-a 3.00
...: X-Men – Apocalypse 1 - Reprints X-Factor #6; Louise Simonson-s/Jackson Guice-a 3.00
...: X-Men – Betsy Braddock 1 - Reprints from Captain Britain #8-10 3.00
...: X-Men – Bishop 1 - Reprints debut in Uncanny X-Men #282; Portacio-a 3.00
...: X-Men Blue 1 – Reprints X-Men #1 (1991); Chris Claremont-s/Jim Lee-a 3.00
...: X-Men – Cypher - Reprints New Mutants #13; Chris Claremont-s/Sal Buscema-a 3.00
...: X-Men – Empath - Reprints New Mutants #16; Chris Claremont-s/Sal Buscema-a 3.00
...: X-Men Gold 1 – Reprints Uncanny X-Men #281; Byrne-s/Portacio-a 3.00
...: X-Men – Greycrow - Reprints Uncanny X-Men #211; Claremont-s/Romita Jr.-a 3.00

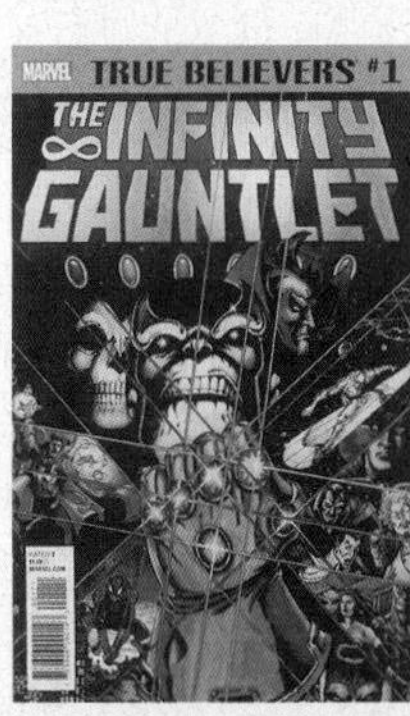

True Believers: Infinity Gauntlet #1 © MAR

True Blood #6 © HBO

True Comics #53 © PMI

GD VG FN VF VF/NM NM-
2.0 4.0 6.0 8.0 9.0 9.2

GD VG FN VF VF/NM NM-
2.0 4.0 6.0 8.0 9.0 9.2

...: X-Men – Havok - Reprints X-Men #58; Roy Thomas-s/Neal Adams-a 3.00
...: X-Men – Jubilee 1 - Reprints debut in Uncanny X-Men #244; Silvestri-a 3.00
...: X-Men – Karima Shapandar, Omega Sentinel 1 - Reprints X-Men Unlimited #27 3.00
...: X-Men – Kitty Pryde & Emma Frost 1 - Reprints debuts in X-Men #129; Byrne-a 3.00
...: X-Men – Kwannon 1 - Reprints debut in X-Men #17 (1992); Andy Kubert-a 3.00
...: X-Men – Magik - Reprints Magik #1; Chris Claremont-s/John Buscema-a 3.00
...: X-Men – Mister Sinister - Reprints Uncanny X-Men #221; Claremont-s/Silvestri-a 3.00
...: X-Men – Moira MacTaggert 1 - Reprints debut in X-Men #96 3.00
...: X-Men – Nanny & Orphan Maker - Reprints X-Factor #35; Louise Simonson-s 3.00
...: X-Men – Pyro 1 - Reprints debut in Uncanny X-Men #141; Byrne-a 3.00
...: X-Men – Rictor 1 - Reprints debut in X-Factor #17; Simonson-a 3.00
...: X-Men – Saturnyne - Reprints Marvel Super Heroes UK #380-383; Captain Britain 3.00
...: X-Men – Soulsword - Reprints Uncanny X-Men #171; Claremont-s/Simonson-a 3.00
...: X-Men – Wild Child - Reprints Alpha Flight #11 & Marvel Comics Presents #51 3.00

TRUE BELIEVERS: KIRBY 100TH
Marvel Comics: Oct, 2017 ($1.00, one-shot reprints celebrating Jack Kirby's 100th birthday)

... – Ant-Man and The Wasp #1 - Reprints Tales to Astonish #27 & #44 3.00
... – Avengers: Captain America Lives Again! #1 - Reprints Avengers #4; bonus pin-ups 3.00
... – Black Panther #1 - Reprints Black Panther #1 6.00
... – Captain America #1 - Reprints Captain America Comics #1 & Tales of Suspense #63 3.00
... – Devil Dinosaur #1 - Reprints Devil Dinosaur #1; cover gallery & letter columns 3.00
... – Eternals #1 - Reprints Eternals #1; pin-ups & letter columns 3.00
... – Groot #1 - Reprints Tales to Astonish #13 & Journey Into Mystery #62 (Hulk/Xemnu)
1 3 4 6 8 10
... – Inhumans #1 - Reprints Amazing Adventures #1,2; bonus pin-ups 3.00
... – Introducing... The Mighty Thor #1 - Reprints Journey Into Mystery #83,85 3.00
... – Iron Man #1 - Reprints Tales of Suspense #40,41 3.00
... – Nick Fury #1 - Reprints Strange Tales #135,141 3.00
... – Thor vs. Hulk #1 - Reprints Journey Into Mystery #112 6.00

TRUE BLOOD (Based on the HBO vampire series)
IDW Publishing: Aug, 2010 - No. 6, Dec, 2010 ($3.99)

1-Messina-a; 4 covers by Messina, Campbell, Currie and Corroney 5.00
2-6-Multiple covers on each 4.00
...: Legacy Edition (1/11, $4.99) r/#1, cover gallery; full script 5.00

TRUE BLOOD (2nd series)(Based on the HBO vampire series)
IDW Publishing: May, 2012 - No. 14, Jun, 2013 ($3.99)

1-14-Gaydos-a in most; 2 covers (photo & Bradstreet-c) on each. 5-Manfredi-a 4.00

TRUE BLOOD: TAINTED LOVE (Based on the HBO vampire series)
IDW Publishing: Feb, 2011 - No. 6, Jul, 2011 ($3.99, limited series)

1-4: 1,2,4,5-Corroney-a; multiple covers. 3-Molnar-a 4.00
... Legacy Edition 1 (7/11, $4.99) r/#1 with full script and cover gallery 5.00

TRUE BLOOD: THE FRENCH QUARTER (Based on the HBO vampire series)
IDW Publishing: Aug, 2011 - No. 6, Jan, 2012 ($3.99, limited series)

1-6-Huehner & Tischman-s; multiple covers. 3-Molnar-a 4.00

TRUE BLOOD: THE GREAT REVELATION (Prequel to the 2008 HBO vampire series)
HBO/Top Cow: July, 2008 (no cover price, one shot continued on HBO website)

1-David Wohl-s/Jason Badower-a/c 4.00

TRUE BRIDE'S EXPERIENCES (Formerly Teen-Age Brides)
(True Bride-To-Be Romances No. 17 on)
True Love (Harvey Publications): No. 8, Oct, 1954 - No. 16, Feb, 1956

8-"I Married a Farmer" 12 24 36 67 94 120
9,10: 10-Last pre-code (2/55) 8 16 24 44 57 70
11-15 7 14 21 37 46 55
16-Last issue 8 16 24 44 57 70
NOTE: ***Powell*** *a-8-10, 12, 13.*

TRUE BRIDE-TO-BE ROMANCES (Formerly True Bride's Experiences)
Home Comics/True Love (Harvey): No. 17, Apr, 1956 - No. 30, Nov, 1958

17-S&K-c, Powell-a 12 24 36 67 94 120
18-20,22,25-28,30 7 14 21 37 46 55
21,23,24,29-Powell-a. 29-Baker-a (1 pg.) 8 16 24 40 50 60

TRUE COMICS (Also see Outstanding American War Heroes)
True Comics/Parents' Magazine Press: April, 1941 - No. 84, Aug, 1950

1-Marathon run story; life story Winston Churchill 40 80 120 246 411 575
2-Red Cross story; Everett-a 20 40 60 114 182 250
3-Baseball Hall of Fame story; Chiang Kai-Shek-c/s 18 36 54 109 172 235
4,5: 4-Story of American flag "Old Glory". 5-Life story of Joe Louis
15 30 45 86 133 180
6-Baseball World Series story 16 32 48 98 154 210
7-10: 7-Buffalo Bill story. 10,11-Teddy Roosevelt 13 26 39 72 101 130
11-14,16,18-20: 11-Thomas Edison, Douglas MacArthur stories. 13-Harry Houdini story.
14-Charlie McCarthy story. 18-Story of America begins, ends #26. 19-Eisenhower-c/s
11 22 33 62 86 110
15-Flag-c; Bob Feller story 14 28 42 76 108 140
17-Brooklyn Dodgers story 14 28 42 81 118 155
21-30: 24-Marco Polo story. 28-Origin of Uncle Sam. 29-Beethoven story.
30-Cooper Brothers baseball story 9 18 27 52 69 85
31-Red Grange "Galloping Ghost" story 8 16 24 44 57 70
32-46: 33-Origin/1st app. Steve Saunders, Special Agent of the FBI, series begins.
35-Mark Twain story. 38-General Bradley-c/s. 39-FDR story. 44-Truman story.
46-George Gershwin story 8 16 24 42 54 65
47-Atomic bomb issue (c/story, 3/46) 14 28 42 82 121 160
48-(4/46) "Hero Without a Gun" Desmond Doss story; inspired 2016 movie Hacksaw Ridge
9 18 27 50 65 80
49-54,56-65: 49-1st app. Secret Warriors. 53-Bobby Riggs story. 58-Jim Jeffries (boxer) story; Harry Houdini story. 59-Bob Hope story; pirates-c/s. 60-Speedway Speed Demon-c/story.
8 16 24 40 50 60
55-(12/46)-1st app. Sad Sack by Baker (1/2 pg.) 58 116 174 371 636 900
66-Will Rogers-c/story 8 16 24 42 54 65
67-1st oversized issue (12/47); Steve Saunders, Special Agent begins
9 18 27 50 65 80
68-70,74-77,79: 68-70,74-77-Features Steve Sanders True FBI advs.
68-Oversized; Admiral Byrd-c/s. 69-Jack Benny story. 74-Amos 'n' Andy story
8 16 24 40 50 60
71-Joe DiMaggio-c/story. 10 20 30 54 72 90
72-Jackie Robinson story; True FBI advs. 9 18 27 50 65 80
73-Walt Disney's life story 10 20 30 54 72 90
78-Stan Musial-c/story; True FBI advs. 9 18 27 47 61 75
80-84 (Scarce)-All distr. to subscribers through mail only; paper-c. 80-Rocket trip to the moon story. 81-Red Grange story. 84-Wyatt Earp app. (1st app. in comics?); Rube Marquard story
21 42 63 122 199 275
(Prices vary widely on issues 80-84)
NOTE: ***Bob Kane*** *a-7.* ***Palais*** *a-80.* ***Powell*** *c/a-80. #80-84 have soft covers and combined with Tex Granger, Jack Armstrong, and Calling All Kids. #68-78 featured true FBI adventures.*

TRUE COMICS AND ADVENTURE STORIES
Parents' Magazine Institute: 1965 (Giant) (25¢)

1,2: 1-Fighting Hero of Viet Nam; LBJ on-c 3 6 9 21 33 45

TRUE COMPLETE MYSTERY (Formerly Complete Mystery)
Marvel Comics (PrPl): No. 5, Apr, 1949 - No. 8, Oct, 1949

5-Criminal career of Rico Mancini 37 74 111 222 361 500
6-8: 6-8-Photo-c 25 50 75 150 245 340

TRUE CONFIDENCES
Fawcett Publications: 1949 (Fall) - No. 4, June, 1950 (All photo-c)

1-Has ad for Fawcett Love Adventures #1, but publ. as Love Memoirs #1 as Marvel published the title first; Swayze-a 20 40 60 118 192 265
2-4: 3-Swayze-a. 4-Powell-a 14 28 42 81 118 155

TRUE CRIME CASES (...From Official Police Files)
St. John Publishing Co.: 1951 (25¢, 100 pg. Giant)

nn-Matt Baker-c 110 220 330 704 1202 1700

TRUE CRIME COMICS (Also see Complete Book of...)
Magazine Village: No. 2, May, 1947; No. 3, July-Aug, 1948 - No. 6, June-July, 1949; V2#1, Aug-Sept, 1949 (52 pgs.)

2-Jack Cole-c/a; used in **SOTI**, pgs. 81,82 plus illo. "A sample of the injury-to-eye motif" & illo. "Dragging living people to death"; used in **POP**, pg. 105; "Murder, Morphine and Me" classic drug propaganda story used by N.Y. Legis. Comm.
300 600 900 1920 3310 4700
3-Classic Cole-c/a; drug story with hypo, opium den & with drawing addict
258 516 774 1651 2826 4000
4-Jack Cole-c/a; c-taken from a story panel in #3 (r-(2) **SOTI** & **POP** stories/#2?) 135 270 405 864 1482 2100
5-Jack Cole-c, Marijuana racket story (Canadian ed. w/cover similar to #3 exists w/out drug story) 116 232 348 742 1271 1800
6-Not a reprint, original story (Canadian ed. reprints #4 w/different coloring on-c)
103 206 309 659 1130 1600
V2#1-Used in **SOTI**, pgs. 81,82 & illo. "Dragging living people to death"; Toth, Wood (3 pgs.), Roussos-a; Cole-r from #2 129 258 387 826 1413 2000
NOTE: *V2#1 was reprinted in Canada as V2#9 (12/49); same-c & contents minus Wood-a.*

TRUE FAITH
Fleetway: 1990 ($9.95, graphic novel)

nn-Garth Ennis scripts 2 4 6 12 16 20
Reprinted by DC/Vertigo ('97, $12.95) 13.00

TRUE GHOST STORIES (See Ripley's...)

TRUE LIFE ROMANCES (...Romance on cover)

Ajax/Farrell Publications: Dec, 1955 - No. 3, Aug, 1956

	GD 2.0	VG 4.0	FN 6.0	VF 8.0	VF/NM 9.0	NM- 9.2
1	17	34	51	100	158	215
2	13	26	39	72	101	130
3-Disbrow-a	14	28	42	78	112	145

TRUE LIFE SECRETS
Romantic Love Stories/Charlton: Mar-April, 1951 - No. 28, Sept, 1955; No. 29, Jan, 1956

	GD 2.0	VG 4.0	FN 6.0	VF 8.0	VF/NM 9.0	NM- 9.2
1-Photo-c begin, end #3?	24	48	72	142	234	325
2	15	30	45	85	130	175
3-11,13-19:	14	28	42	80	115	150
12-"I Was An Escort Girl" story	21	42	63	126	206	285
20-22,24-29: 25-Last precode (3/55)	14	28	42	76	108	140
23-Classic-c	47	94	141	296	498	700

TRUE LIFE TALES (Formerly Mitzi's Romances #8?)
Marvel Comics (CCC): No. 8, Oct, 1949 - No. 2, Jan, 1950 (52 pgs.)

	GD 2.0	VG 4.0	FN 6.0	VF 8.0	VF/NM 9.0	NM- 9.2
8(#1, 10/49), 2-Both have photo-c	18	36	54	107	169	230

TRUE LIVES OF THE FABULOUS KILLJOYS
Dark Horse Comics: Jun, 2013 - No. 6, Jan, 2014 ($3.99)

	GD 2.0	VG 4.0	FN 6.0	VF 8.0	VF/NM 9.0	NM- 9.2
1-6-Gerald Way & Shaun Simon-s/Becky Cloonan-a; covers by Cloonan & Bá						4.00

TRUE LIVES OF THE FABULOUS KILLJOYS: NATIONAL ANTHEM
Dark Horse Comics: Oct, 2020 - No. 6, Mar, 2021 ($3.99, limited series)

	GD 2.0	VG 4.0	FN 6.0	VF 8.0	VF/NM 9.0	NM- 9.2
1-6-Gerald Way & Shaun Simon-s/Leonardo Romero-a						4.00

TRUE LOVE
Eclipse Comics: Jan, 1986 - No. 2, Jan, 1986 ($2.00, Baxter paper)

	GD 2.0	VG 4.0	FN 6.0	VF 8.0	VF/NM 9.0	NM- 9.2
1-Love stories reprinted from pre-code Standard Comics; Toth-a(p); Dave Stevens-c	1	3	4	6	8	10
2-Toth-a; Mayo-a						4.00

TRUE LOVE CONFESSIONS
Premier Magazines: May, 1954 - No. 11, Jan, 1956

	GD 2.0	VG 4.0	FN 6.0	VF 8.0	VF/NM 9.0	NM- 9.2
1-Marijuana story	24	48	72	142	234	325
2	15	30	45	86	133	180
3-11	15	30	45	83	124	165

TRUE LOVE PICTORIAL
St. John Publishing Co.: Dec, 1952 - No. 11, Aug, 1954

	GD 2.0	VG 4.0	FN 6.0	VF 8.0	VF/NM 9.0	NM- 9.2
1-Only photo-c	40	80	120	246	411	575
2-Baker-c/a	181	362	543	1158	1979	2800
3-5(All 25¢, 100 pgs.): 4-Signed story by Estrada. 5-(4/53)-Formerly Teen-Age Temptations; Kubert-a in #3; Baker-c/a in #3-5	142	284	426	909	1555	2200
6,7: Baker-c/a; signed stories by Estrada	148	296	444	947	1624	2300
8,10,11-Baker-c/a	148	296	444	947	1624	2300
9-Baker-c	110	220	330	704	1202	1700

TRUE LOVE PROBLEMS AND ADVICE ILLUSTRATED (Becomes Romance Stories of True Love No. 45 on)
McCombs/Harvey Publ./Home Comics: June, 1949 - No. 6, Apr, 1950; No. 7, Jan, 1951 - No. 44, Mar, 1957

	GD 2.0	VG 4.0	FN 6.0	VF 8.0	VF/NM 9.0	NM- 9.2
V1#1	19	38	57	111	176	240
2-Elias-c	13	26	39	72	101	130
3-10: 3,4,7-9-Elias-c	9	18	27	50	65	80
11-13,15-23,25-31: 31-Last pre-code (1/55)	8	16	24	42	54	65
14,24-Rape scene	9	18	27	50	65	80
32-37,39-44	7	14	21	37	46	55
38-S&K-c	10	20	30	58	79	100

NOTE: ***Powell** a-1, 2, 7-14, 17-25, 28, 29, 33, 40, 41. #3 has True Love... on inside.*

TRUE MOVIE AND TELEVISION (Part teenage magazine)
Toby Press: Aug, 1950 - No. 3, Nov, 1950; No. 4, Mar, 1951 (52 pgs.)(1-3: 10¢)

	GD 2.0	VG 4.0	FN 6.0	VF 8.0	VF/NM 9.0	NM- 9.2
1-Elizabeth Taylor photo-c; Gene Autry, Shirley Temple app.	84	168	252	538	919	1300
2-(9/50)-Janet Leigh/Liz Taylor/Ava Gardner & others photo-c; Frazetta John Wayne illo from J.Wayne Adv. Comics #2 (4/50)	57	114	171	362	619	875
3-June Allyson photo-c; Montgomery Cliff, Esther Williams, Andrews Sisters app; Li'l Abner featured; Sadie Hawkins' Day	39	78	117	231	378	525
4-Jane Powell photo-c (15¢)	25	50	75	150	245	340

NOTE: *16 pgs. in color, rest movie material in black & white.*

TRUE SECRETS (Formerly Our Love?)
Marvel (IPS)/Atlas Comics (MPI) #4 on: No. 3, Mar, 1950; No. 4, Feb, 1951 - No. 40, Sept, 1956

	GD 2.0	VG 4.0	FN 6.0	VF 8.0	VF/NM 9.0	NM- 9.2
3 (52 pgs.)(IPS one-shot)`	25	50	75	150	245	340
4,5,7-10	17	34	51	98	154	210
6,22-Everett-a	19	38	57	111	176	240
11-20	15	30	45	88	137	185
21,23-28: 24-Colletta-c. 28-Last pre-code (2/55)	15	30	45	85	130	175
29-40: 34,36-Colletta-a	14	28	42	83	124	165

TRUE SPORT PICTURE STORIES (Formerly Sport Comics)
Street & Smith Publications: V1#5, Feb, 1942 - V5#2, July-Aug, 1949

	GD 2.0	VG 4.0	FN 6.0	VF 8.0	VF/NM 9.0	NM- 9.2
V1#5-Joe DiMaggio-c/story	39	78	117	231	378	525
6-12 (1942-43): 12-Jack Dempsey story	21	42	63	122	199	275
V2#1-12 (1943-45): 7-Stan Musial-c/story; photo story of the New York Yankees	20	40	60	115	185	255
V3#1-12 (1946-47): 7-Joe DiMaggio, Stan Musial, Bob Feller & others back from the armed service story. 8-Billy Conn vs. Joe Louis-c/story	19	38	57	111	176	240
V4#1-12 (1947-49), V5#1,2: v4#8-Joe Louis on-c	18	36	54	105	165	225

NOTE: ***Powell** a-V3#10, V4#1-4, 6-8, 10-12; V5#1, 2; c-V3#10-12, V4#2-7, 9-12. **Ravielli** c-V5#2.*

TRUE STORIES OF ROMANCE
Fawcett Publications: Jan, 1950 - No. 3, May, 1950 (All photo-c)

	GD 2.0	VG 4.0	FN 6.0	VF 8.0	VF/NM 9.0	NM- 9.2
1	18	36	54	105	165	225
2,3: 3-Marcus Swayze-a	14	28	42	80	115	150

TRUE STORY OF JESSE JAMES, THE (See Jesse James, Four Color 757)

TRUE SWEETHEART SECRETS
Fawcett Publs.: 5/50; No. 2, 7/50; No. 3, 1951(nd); No. 4, 9/51 - No. 11, 1/53 (All photo-c)

	GD 2.0	VG 4.0	FN 6.0	VF 8.0	VF/NM 9.0	NM- 9.2
1-Photo-c; Debbie Reynolds?	20	40	60	118	192	265
2-Wood-a (11 pgs.)	22	44	66	130	213	295
3-11: 4,5-Powell-a. 8-Marcus Swayze-a. 11-Evans-a	15	30	45	83	124	165

TRUE TALES OF LOVE (Formerly Secret Story Romances)
Atlas Comics (TCI): No. 22, April, 1956 - No. 31, Sept, 1957

	GD 2.0	VG 4.0	FN 6.0	VF 8.0	VF/NM 9.0	NM- 9.2
22	16	32	48	94	147	200
23-24,26-31-Colletta-a in most:	13	26	39	72	101	130
25-Everett-a; Colletta-a	14	28	42	76	108	140

TRUE TALES OF ROMANCE
Fawcett Publications: No. 4, June, 1950

	GD 2.0	VG 4.0	FN 6.0	VF 8.0	VF/NM 9.0	NM- 9.2
4-Photo-c	14	28	42	78	112	145

TRUE 3-D
Harvey Publications: Dec, 1953 - No. 2, Feb, 1954 (25¢)(Both came with 2 pair of glasses)

	GD 2.0	VG 4.0	FN 6.0	VF 8.0	VF/NM 9.0	NM- 9.2
1-Nostrand, Powell-a	5	10	15	35	63	90
2-Powell-a	6	12	18	37	66	95

NOTE: *Many copies of #1 surfaced in 1984.*

TRUE-TO-LIFE ROMANCES (Formerly Guns Against Gangsters)
Star Publ.: #8, 11-12/49; #9, 1-2/50; #3, 4/50 - #5, 9/50; #6, 1/51 - #23, 10/54

	GD 2.0	VG 4.0	FN 6.0	VF 8.0	VF/NM 9.0	NM- 9.2
8(#1, 1949)	39	78	117	231	378	525
9(#2),4-10	28	56	84	168	274	380
3-Janet Leigh/Glenn Ford photo on-c plus true life story of each	30	60	90	177	289	400
11,22,23	24	48	72	142	234	325
12-14,17-21-Disbrow-a	27	54	81	158	259	360
15,16-Wood & Disbrow-a in each	29	58	87	172	281	390

NOTE: ***Kamen** a-13. **Kamen/Feldstein** a-14. All have **L.B. Cole** covers.*

TRUE WAR EXPERIENCES
Harvey Publications: Aug, 1952 - No. 4, Dec, 1952

	GD 2.0	VG 4.0	FN 6.0	VF 8.0	VF/NM 9.0	NM- 9.2
1-Korean War	9	18	27	62	126	190
2-4	5	10	15	35	63	90

TRUE WAR ROMANCES (Becomes Exotic Romances #22 on)
Quality Comics Group: Sept, 1952 - No. 21, June, 1955

	GD 2.0	VG 4.0	FN 6.0	VF 8.0	VF/NM 9.0	NM- 9.2
1-Photo-c	22	44	66	132	216	300
2-(10/52)	15	30	45	83	124	165
3-10: 3-(12/52). 8,9-Whitney-a	13	26	39	74	105	135
11-21: 20-Last precode (4/55). 14-Whitney-a	12	24	36	67	94	120

TRUE WAR STORIES (See Ripley's...)

TRUE WESTERN (True Adventures #3)
Marvel Comics (MMC): Dec, 1949 - No. 2, March, 1950

	GD 2.0	VG 4.0	FN 6.0	VF 8.0	VF/NM 9.0	NM- 9.2
1-Photo-c; Billy The Kid story	21	42	63	126	206	285
2-Alan Ladd photo-c	24	48	72	142	234	325

TRUMP
HMH Publishing Co.: Jan, 1957 - No. 2, Mar, 1957 (50¢, magazine)

	GD 2.0	VG 4.0	FN 6.0	VF 8.0	VF/NM 9.0	NM- 9.2
1-Harvey Kurtzman satire	30	60	90	177	289	400
2-Harvey Kurtzman satire	23	46	69	136	223	310

NOTE: ***Davis, Elder, Heath, Jaffee** art-#1,2; **Wood** a-1. Article by Mel Brooks in #2.*

TRUMPETS WEST (See Luke Short, Four Color #875)

TRUTH ABOUT CRIME (See Fox Giants)

TRUTH ABOUT MOTHER GOOSE (See Mother Goose, Four Color #862)

TRUTH & JUSTICE
DC Comics: Apr, 2021 - No. 7, Oct, 2021 ($4.99, printing of digital first anthology series)

	GD 2.0	VG 4.0	FN 6.0	VF 8.0	VF/NM 9.0	NM- 9.2
1-7: 1-Vixen. 2-Superman. 3-Constantine. 4-Jason Todd. 5-Batwoman. 7-Zatanna						5.00

TRUTH BEHIND THE TRIAL OF CARDINAL MINDSZENTY, THE (See Cardinal Mindszenty in the Promotional Comics section)

TRUTHFUL LOVE (Formerly Youthful Love)
Youthful Magazines: No. 2, July, 1950

	GD 2.0	VG 4.0	FN 6.0	VF 8.0	VF/NM 9.0	NM- 9.2
2-Ingrid Bergman's true life story	19	38	57	111	176	240

TRUTH RED, WHITE & BLACK
Marvel Comics: Jan, 2003 - No. 7, Jul, 2003 ($3.50, limited series)

	GD 2.0	VG 4.0	FN 6.0	VF 8.0	VF/NM 9.0	NM- 9.2
1-Kyle Baker-a/Robert Morales-s; the testing of Captain America's super-soldier serum	3	6	9	19	30	40
2-7: 3-Isaiah Bradley 1st dons the Captain America costume	1	3	4	6	8	10
TPB (2004, $17.99) r/series						18.00

TRY-OUT WINNER BOOK
Marvel Comics: Mar, 1988

	GD 2.0	VG 4.0	FN 6.0	VF 8.0	VF/NM 9.0	NM- 9.2
1-Spider-Man vs. Doc Octopus	3	6	9	21	33	45

TSR WORLD (...Annual on cover only)
DC Comics: 1990 ($3.95, 84 pgs.)

	GD 2.0	VG 4.0	FN 6.0	VF 8.0	VF/NM 9.0	NM- 9.2
1-Advanced D&D, ForgottenRealms, Dragonlance & 1st app. Spelljammer						4.00

TSUNAMI GIRL
Image Comics: 1999 - No. 3, 1999 ($2.95)

	GD 2.0	VG 4.0	FN 6.0	VF 8.0	VF/NM 9.0	NM- 9.2
1-3-Sorayama-c/Paniccia-s/a						3.00

TUBBY (See Marge's...)

TUFF GHOSTS STARRING SPOOKY
Harvey Publications: July, 1962 - No. 39, Nov, 1970; No. 40, Sept, 1971 - No. 43, Oct, 1972

	GD 2.0	VG 4.0	FN 6.0	VF 8.0	VF/NM 9.0	NM- 9.2
1-12¢ issues begin	16	32	48	110	243	375
2-5	7	14	21	44	82	120
6-10	5	10	15	31	53	75
11-20	4	8	12	23	37	50
21-30: 29-Hot Stuff/Spooky team-up story	3	6	9	16	23	30
31-39,43	2	4	6	13	18	22
40-42: 52 pg. Giants	3	6	9	14	20	25

TUFFY
Standard Comics: No. 5, July, 1949 - No. 9, Oct, 1950

	GD 2.0	VG 4.0	FN 6.0	VF 8.0	VF/NM 9.0	NM- 9.2
5-All by Sid Hoff	11	22	33	64	90	115

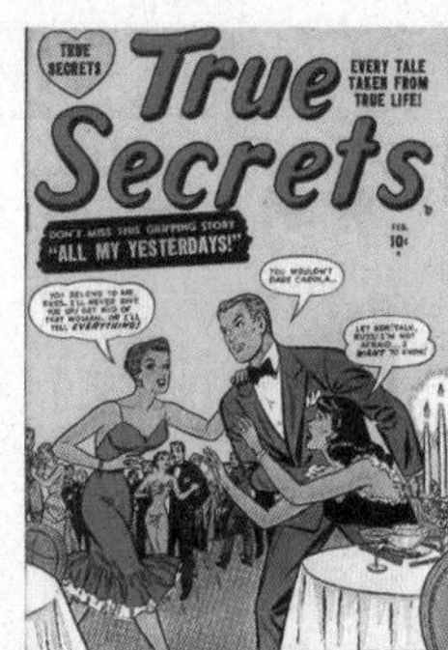

True Secrets #4 © MAR

Turok, Son of Stone #1 © RH

TV Stars #3 © H-B

	GD 2.0	VG 4.0	FN 6.0	VF 8.0	VF/NM 9.0	NM- 9.2
6-9	9	18	27	47	61	75

TUFFY TURTLE
I. W. Enterprises: No date

	GD 2.0	VG 4.0	FN 6.0	VF 8.0	VF/NM 9.0	NM- 9.2
1-Reprint	2	4	6	13	18	22

TUG & BUSTER
Art & Soul Comics: Nov, 1995 - No. 7, Feb, 1998 ($2.95, B&W, bi-monthly)

	GD 2.0	VG 4.0	FN 6.0	VF 8.0	VF/NM 9.0	NM- 9.2
1-7: Marc Hempel-c/a/scripts						3.00
1-(Image Comics, 8/98, $2.95, B&W)						3.00

TUKI
Cartoon Books: Jul, 2014 - No. 4, Jan, 2016 ($3.99)

	GD 2.0	VG 4.0	FN 6.0	VF 8.0	VF/NM 9.0	NM- 9.2
1-4-Jeff Smith-s/a/c; story reads sideways						4.00

TURF
Image Comics: Apr, 2010 - No. 2 ($2.99, limited series)

	GD 2.0	VG 4.0	FN 6.0	VF 8.0	VF/NM 9.0	NM- 9.2
1,2-Jonathan Ross-s/Tommy Lee Edwards-a						3.00

TUROK
Acclaim Comics: Mar, 1998 - No. 4, Jun, 1998 ($2.50)

	GD 2.0	VG 4.0	FN 6.0	VF 8.0	VF/NM 9.0	NM- 9.2
1-4-Nicieza-s/Kayanan-a						4.00
..., Child of Blood 1 (1/98, $3.95) Nicieza-s/Kayanan-a						6.00
... Evolution 1 (8/02, $2.50) Nicieza-s/Kayanan-a	3	6	9	14	19	24
..., Redpath 1 (10/97, $3.95) Nicieza-s/Kayanan-a						4.00
... / Shadowman 1 (2/99, $3.95) Priest-s/Broome & Jimenez-a	2	4	6	8	10	12
...: Spring Break in the Lost Land 1 (7/97, $3.95) Nicieza-s/Kayanan-a						4.00
...: Tales of the Lost Land 1 (4/98, $3.95)						4.00
...: The Empty Souls 1 (4/97, $3.95) Nicieza-s/Kayanan-a; variant-c						4.00

TUROK (Volume 1) (Also see Sovereigns and Magnus)
Dynamite Entertainment: 2017 - No. 5, 2017 ($3.99)

	GD 2.0	VG 4.0	FN 6.0	VF 8.0	VF/NM 9.0	NM- 9.2
1-5: 1-Wendig-s/Sarraseca-a; Doctor Spektor back-up serial with other Sovereigns titles						4.00

TUROK, DINOSAUR HUNTER (See Magnus Robot Fighter #12 & Archer & Armstrong #2)
Valiant/Acclaim Comics: June, 1993 - No. 47, Aug, 1996 ($2.50)

	GD 2.0	VG 4.0	FN 6.0	VF 8.0	VF/NM 9.0	NM- 9.2
1-($3.50)-Chromium & foil-c						4.00
1-Gold foil-c variant						20.00
0, 2-47: 4-Andar app. 5-Death of Andar. 7-9-Truman/Glanzman-a. 11-Bound-in trading card. 16-Chaos Effect						3.00
Yearbook 1 (1994, $3.95, 52 pgs.)						4.00

TUROK: DINOSAUR HUNTER
Dynamite Entertainment: 2014 - No. 12, 2015 ($3.99)

	GD 2.0	VG 4.0	FN 6.0	VF 8.0	VF/NM 9.0	NM- 9.2
1-12: 1-5-New version; Greg Pak-s/Mirko Colak-a; Sears-c. 6-8-Miyazawa-a						4.00
1-12-Variant-c by Jae Lee						4.00

TUROK, SON OF STONE (See Dan Curtis, Golden Comics Digest #31, Space Western #45 & March of Comics #378, 399, 408)
Dell Publ. Co. #1-29(9/62)/Gold Key #30(12/62)-85(7/73)/Gold Key or Whitman #86(9/73)-125(1/80)/Whitman #126(3/81) on: No. 596, 12/54 - No. 29, 9/62; No. 30, 12/62 - No. 91, 7/74; No. 92, 9/74 - No. 125, 1/80; No. 126, 3/81 - No. 130, 4/82

	GD 2.0	VG 4.0	FN 6.0	VF 8.0	VF/NM 9.0	NM- 9.2
Four Color 596 (12/54)(#1)-1st app./origin Turok & Andar; dinosaur-c. Created by Matthew H. Murphy; written by Alberto Giolitti	96	192	288	768	1734	2700
Four Color 656 (10/55)(#2)-1st mention of Lanok	42	84	126	311	706	1100
3(3-5/56)-5: 3-Cave men	22	44	66	154	340	525
6-10: 8-Dinosaur of the deep; Turok enters Lost Valley; series begins. 9-Paul S. Newman-s (most issues thru end)	15	30	45	103	227	350
11-20: 17-Prehistoric Pygmies	11	22	33	76	163	250
21-29	9	18	27	58	114	170
30-1st Gold Key. 30-33-Painted back-c.	9	18	27	60	120	180
31-Drug use story	9	18	27	58	114	170
32-40	7	14	21	46	86	125
41-50	6	12	18	37	66	95
51-57,59,60	5	10	15	34	60	85
58-Flying Saucer c/story	5	10	15	35	63	90
61-70: 62-12¢ & 15¢ covers. 63,68-Line drawn-c	5	10	15	30	50	70
71-84: 84-Origin & 1st app. Hutec	4	8	12	27	44	60
85-99: 93-r-c/#19 w/changes. 94-r-c/#28 w/changes. 97-r-c/#31 w/changes. 98-r/#58 w/o spaceship & spacemen on-c. 99-r-c/#52 w/changes.	4	8	12	23	37	50
100	4	8	12	28	47	65
101-129: 114,115-(52 pgs.). 129(2/82)	4	8	12	23	37	50
130(4/82)-Last issue	5	10	15	35	63	90
Giant 1(30031-611) (11/66)-Slick-c; r/#10-12 & 16 plus cover to #11	10	20	30	68	144	220
Giant 1-Same as above but with paper-c	11	22	33	73	157	240

NOTE: *Most painted-c; line-drawn #63 & 130.* ***Alberto Gioletti*** *a-24-27, 30-119, 123; painted-c No. 30-129.* ***Sparling*** *a-117, 120-130. Reprints-#36, 54, 57, 75, 112, 114(1/3), 115(1/3), 118, 121, 125, 127(1/3), 128, 129(1/3), 130(1/3), Giant 1. Cover r-93, 94, 97-99, 126(all different from original covers.*

TUROK, SON OF STONE
Dark Horse Comics: Oct, 2010 - No. 4, Oct, 2011 ($3.50)

	GD 2.0	VG 4.0	FN 6.0	VF 8.0	VF/NM 9.0	NM- 9.2
1-4: 1-Shooter-s/Francisco-a/Swanland-c; back-up reprint of debut in Four Color 596						3.50
1-Variant-c by Francisco						3.50

TUROK THE HUNTED
Acclaim Comics (Valiant): Mar, 1996 - No. 2, Mar, 1996 ($2.50, limited series)

	GD 2.0	VG 4.0	FN 6.0	VF 8.0	VF/NM 9.0	NM- 9.2
1,2-Mike Grell & Simon Furman-s/Mike Deodato & Mozart Couto-a						4.00

TUROK, TIMEWALKER
Acclaim Comics (Valiant): Aug, 1997 - No. 2, Sept, 1997 ($2.50, limited series)

	GD 2.0	VG 4.0	FN 6.0	VF 8.0	VF/NM 9.0	NM- 9.2
1,2-Nicieza story						5.00

TUROK 2 (Magazine)
Acclaim Comics: Oct, 1998 ($4.99, magazine size)

	GD 2.0	VG 4.0	FN 6.0	VF 8.0	VF/NM 9.0	NM- 9.2
...Seeds of Evil - Nicieza-s/Broome & Benjamin-a; origin back-up story						8.00
#2 Adon's Curse - Mack painted-c/Broome & Benjamin-a; origin pt. 2						8.00

TUROK 3: SHADOW OF OBLIVION
Acclaim Comics: Sept, 2000 ($4.95, one-shot)

	GD 2.0	VG 4.0	FN 6.0	VF 8.0	VF/NM 9.0	NM- 9.2
1-Includes pin-up gallery	1	3	4	6	8	10

TUROK VOLUME 4
Dynamite Entertainment: 2019 - No. 5, 2019 ($3.99)

	GD 2.0	VG 4.0	FN 6.0	VF 8.0	VF/NM 9.0	NM- 9.2
1-5-Ron Marz-s/Roberto Castro-a						4.00

TURTLE SOUP
Mirage Studios: Sept, 1987 ($2.00, 76 pgs., B&W, one-shot)

	GD 2.0	VG 4.0	FN 6.0	VF 8.0	VF/NM 9.0	NM- 9.2
1-Featuring Teenage Mutant Ninja Turtles	2	4	6	11	16	20

TURTLE SOUP
Mirage Studios: Nov, 1991 - No. 4, 1992 ($2.50, limited series, coated paper)

	GD 2.0	VG 4.0	FN 6.0	VF 8.0	VF/NM 9.0	NM- 9.2
1-4: Features the Teenage Mutant Ninja Turtles						6.00

TV CASPER & COMPANY
Harvey Publications: Aug, 1963 - No. 46, April, 1974 (25¢ Giants)

	GD 2.0	VG 4.0	FN 6.0	VF 8.0	VF/NM 9.0	NM- 9.2
1- 68 pg. Giants begin; Casper, Little Audrey, Baby Huey, Herman & Catnip, Buzzy the Crow begin	10	20	30	66	138	210
2-5	6	12	18	37	66	95
6-10	4	8	12	28	47	65
11-20	4	8	12	23	37	50
21-31: 31-Last 68 pg. issue	3	6	9	17	26	35
32-46: All 52 pgs.	3	6	9	16	23	30

NOTE: *Many issues contain reprints.*

TV FUNDAY FUNNIES (See Famous TV...)

TV FUNNIES (See New Funnies)

TV FUNTIME (See Little Audrey)

TV LAUGHOUT (See Archie's...)

TV SCREEN CARTOONS (Formerly Real Screen)
National Periodical Publ.: No. 129, July-Aug, 1959 - No. 138, Jan-Feb, 1961

	GD 2.0	VG 4.0	FN 6.0	VF 8.0	VF/NM 9.0	NM- 9.2
129-138 (Scarce) Fox and the Crow	6	12	18	40	73	105

TV STARS (TV) (Newsstand sales only)
Marvel Comics Group: Aug, 1978 - No. 4, Feb, 1979 (Hanna-Barbera)

	GD 2.0	VG 4.0	FN 6.0	VF 8.0	VF/NM 9.0	NM- 9.2
1-Great Grape Ape app.	4	8	12	22	35	48
2,4: 4-Top Cat app.	3	6	9	15	22	28
3-Toth-c/a; Dave Stevens inks	3	6	9	16	24	32

TV TEENS (Formerly Ozzie & Babs; Rock and Rollo #14 on)
Charlton Comics: V1#14, Feb, 1954 - V2#13, July, 1956

	GD 2.0	VG 4.0	FN 6.0	VF 8.0	VF/NM 9.0	NM- 9.2
V1#14 (#1)-Ozzie & Babs	15	30	45	83	124	165
15 (#2)	9	18	27	52	69	85
V2#3(6/54),4, 6-Don Winslow	9	18	27	50	65	80
5(10-11/54) Headlight/groping-c by Chic Stone	43	86	129	271	461	650
7-13-Mopsy. 8(7/55). 9-Paper dolls	9	18	27	47	61	75

TWEETY AND SYLVESTER (1st Series) (TV) (Also see Looney Tunes and Merrie Melodies)
Dell Publishing Co.: No. 406, June, 1952 - No. 37, June-Aug, 1962

	GD 2.0	VG 4.0	FN 6.0	VF 8.0	VF/NM 9.0	NM- 9.2
Four Color 406 (#1)	14	28	42	97	214	330
Four Color 489,524	9	18	27	59	117	175
4 (3-5/54) - 20	5	10	15	35	63	90
21-37	5	10	15	31	53	75

(See March of Comics #421, 433, 445, 457, 469, 481)

TWEETY AND SYLVESTER (2nd Series)(See Kite Fun Book)
Gold Key No. 1-102/Whitman No. 103 on: Nov, 1963; No. 2, Nov, 1965 - No. 121, Jun, 1984

	GD 2.0	VG 4.0	FN 6.0	VF 8.0	VF/NM 9.0	NM- 9.2
1	9	18	27	62	129	135
2-10	4	8	12	23	37	50

	GD 2.0	VG 4.0	FN 6.0	VF 8.0	VF/NM 9.0	NM- 9.2
11-30	3	6	9	14	20	25
31-50	2	4	6	9	12	15
51-70	1	3	4	6	8	10
71-102	1	2	3	5	6	8
103,104 (Whitman)	1	3	4	6	8	10
105(9/80),106(10/80),107(12/80) 3-pack only	4	8	12	28	47	65
108-116: 113(2/82),114(2-3/82),115(3/82),116(4/82)	2	4	6	8	10	12
117-121 (All # 90094 on-c; nd, nd code): 117(6/83). 118(7/83). 119(2/84)-r(1/3). 120(5/84). 121(6/84)	3	6	9	17	26	35
Digest nn (Charlton/Xerox Pub., 1974) (low print run)	3	6	9	16	23	30
Mini Comic No. 1(1976, 3-1/4x6-1/2")	1	3	4	6	8	10

TWELVE, THE (Golden Age Timely heroes)
Marvel Comics: No. 0; 2008; No. 1, Mar, 2008 - No. 12, Jun, 2012 ($2.99, limited series)

0-Rockman, Laughing Mask & Phantom Reporter intro. stories (1940s); series preview 4.00
1/2 (2008, $3.99) r/early app. of Fiery Mask, Mister E and Rockman; Weston-c 5.00
1-12-Straczynski-s/Weston-a; Timely heroes re-surface in the present 4.00
... Must Have 1 (4/12, $3.99) r/#7,8 4.00
...: Spearhead 1 (5/10, $3.99) Weston-s/a; Phantom Reporter in WW2; Invaders app. 5.00

12 O'CLOCK HIGH (TV)
Dell Publishing Co.: Jan-Mar, 1965 - No. 2, Apr-June, 1965 (Photo-c)

	GD 2.0	VG 4.0	FN 6.0	VF 8.0	VF/NM 9.0	NM- 9.2
1- Sinnott-a	5	10	15	35	63	90
2	4	8	12	28	47	65

TWELVE REASONS TO DIE
Black Mask Studios: 2013 - No. 6, 2014 ($3.50)

1-6: 1-Five covers; created by Ghostface Killah 3.50

2099
Marvel Comics: Jan, 2020 - Feb, 2020 ($4.99, bookends for series of one-shots)

... Alpha 1 (1/20) Spencer-s/Bogdanovic-a; Miguel O'Hara and Herbie app. 5.00
... Omega 1 (2/20) Spencer-s/Sandoval-a; Doom and the Watcher app. 5.00

2099 A.D.
Marvel Comics: May, 1995 ($3.95, one-shot)

1-Acetate-c by Quesada & Palmiotti 4.00

2099 APOCALYPSE
Marvel Comics: Dec, 1995 ($4.95, one-shot)

1-Chromium wraparound-c; Ellis script 5.00

2099 GENESIS
Marvel Comics: Jan, 1996 ($4.95, one-shot)

1-Chromium wraparound-c; Ellis script 5.00

2099 MANIFEST DESTINY
Marvel Comics: Mar, 1998 ($5.99, one-shot)

	GD 2.0	VG 4.0	FN 6.0	VF 8.0	VF/NM 9.0	NM- 9.2
1-Origin of Fantastic Four 2099; intro Moon Knight 2099	4	8	12	23	37	50

2099 UNLIMITED
Marvel Comics: Sept, 1993 - No. 10, 1996 ($3.95, 68 pgs.)

1-10: 1-1st app. Hulk 2099 & begins. 1-3-Spider-Man 2099 app. 9-Joe Kubert-c; Len Wein & Nancy Collins scripts 4.00

2099 WORLD OF DOOM SPECIAL
Marvel Comics: May, 1995 ($2.25, one-shot)

1-Doom's "Contract w/America" 4.00

2099 WORLD OF TOMORROW
Marvel Comics: Sept, 1996 - No. 8, Apr, 1997 ($2.50) (Replaces 2099 titles)

1-8: 1-Wraparound-c. 2-w/bound-in card. 4,5-Phalanx 3.00

20XX
Image Comics: Dec, 2019 - Present ($3.99, B&W)

1-6-Jonathan Luna-s/a; Lauren Keely-s 4.00
...: Transport 1 (8/22, $3.99, full color) Jonathan Luna-s/a 4.00

21
Image Comics (Top Cow Productions): Feb, 1996 - No. 3, Apr, 1996 ($2.50)

1-3: Len Wein scripts 3.00
1-Variant-c 3.00

21 DOWN
DC Comics (WildStorm): Nov, 2002 - No. 12, Nov, 2003 ($2.95)

1-12: 1-Palmiotti & Gray-s/Saiz-a/Jusko-c 3.00
...: The Conduit (2003, $19.95, TPB) r/#1-7; intro. by Garth Ennis 20.00

24 (Based on TV series)
IDW Publishing: Apr, 2014 - No. 5, Aug, 2014 ($3.99, limited series)

1-5-Brisson-s/Gaydos-a; multiple covers on each 4.00

24 (Based on TV series)
IDW Publishing: July, 2004 - July, 2005 ($6.99/$7.49, square-bound, one-shots)

...: Midnight Sun (7/05, $7.49) J.C. Vaughn & Mark Haynes-s; Renato Guedes-a 7.50
...: One Shot (7/04, $6.99)-Jack Bauer's first day on the job at CTU; Vaughn & Haynes-s; Guedes-a 7.50
...: Stories (1/05, $7.49) Manny Clark-a; Vaughn & Haynes-s 7.50

24: LEGACY – RULES OF ENGAGEMENT (Based on TV series)
IDW Publishing: Apr, 2017 - No. 5, Aug, 2017 ($3.99, limited series)

1-5-Early days of Eric Carter in DC & Iraq; Farnsworth-s/Fuso-a; art and photo-c 4.00

24: NIGHTFALL (Based on TV series)
IDW Publishing: Nov, 2006 - No. 5, Mar, 2007 ($3.99, limited series)

1-5-Two years before Season One; Vaughn & Haynes-s; Diaz-a; two covers 4.00

28 DAYS LATER (Based on the 2002 movie)
Boom! Studios: July, 2009 - No. 24, Jun, 2011 ($3.99)

1-Covers by Bradstreet and Phillips 6.00
2-24 4.00

2020 FORCE WORKS
Marvel Comics: Apr, 2020 - No. 3, Oct, 2020 ($3.99, limited series)

1-3-Rosenberg-s/Ramírez-a; War Machine and Mockingbird app. 4.00

2020 IRON AGE
Marvel Comics: May, 2020 ($4.99, one-shot)

1-Machine Man, Alkhema, & Doctor Shapiro in short stories by various 5.00

2020 iWOLVERINE
Marvel Comics: Sept, 2020 - No. 2, Oct, 2020 ($3.99, limited series)

1,2-Larry Hama-s/Roland Boschi-a; Wolverine android copy; Tyger Tiger app. 4.00

2020 MACHINE MAN
Marvel Comics: Apr, 2020 - No. 2, May, 2020 ($4.99, limited series)

1,2-Ties in with Iron Man 2020 series; Jocasta & X-52 app. 5.00

2020 RESCUE
Marvel Comics: Apr, 2020 - No. 2, Jun, 2020 ($3.99, limited series)

1,2-Schwartz-s/Burrows-a; Pepper Potts in the Rescue armor 4.00

2020 VISIONS
DC Comics (Vertigo): May, 1997 - No. 12, Apr, 1998 ($2.25, limited series)

1-12-Delano-s: 1-3-Quitely-a. 4-"la tormenta"-Pleece-a 3.00

20,000 LEAGUES UNDER THE SEA (Movie)(See King Classics, Movie Comics & Power Record Comics)
Dell Publishing Co.: No. 614, Feb, 1955 (Disney)

	GD 2.0	VG 4.0	FN 6.0	VF 8.0	VF/NM 9.0	NM- 9.2
Four Color 614-Movie, painted-c	10	20	30	64	132	200

TWICE TOLD TALES (See Movie Classics)

TWIG
Image Comics: May, 2022 - No. 5, Sept, 2022 ($3.99, limited series)

1-5-Skottie Young-s/Kyle Strahm-a 4.00

TWILIGHT
DC Comics: 1990 - No. 3, 1991 ($4.95, 52 pgs, lim. series, squarebound, mature)

1-3: Tommy Tomorrow app; Chaykin scripts, Garcia-Lopez-c/a 5.00

TWILIGHT CHILDREN, THE
DC Comics (Vertigo): Dec, 2015 - No. 4, Mar, 2016 ($4.99, limited series)

1-4-Gilbert Hernandez-s/Darwyn Cooke-a/c 5.00

TWILIGHT EXPERIMENT
DC Comics (WildStorm): Apr, 2004 - No. 6, Sept, 2005 ($2.95, limited series)

1-6-Gray & Palmiotti-s/Santacruz-a 3.00
TPB (2011, $17.99) r/#1-6 18.00

TWILIGHT GUARDIAN (Also see Pilot Season: Twilight Guardian)
Image Comics (Top Cow): Jan, 2011 - No. 4, Apr, 2011 ($3.99, limited series)

1-4-Hickman-s/Kotean-a 4.00

TWILIGHT MAN
First Publishing: June, 1989 - No. 4, Sept, 1989 ($2.75, limited series)

1-4 3.00

TWILIGHT ZONE, THE (TV) (See Dan Curtis & Stories From...)
Dell Publishing Co./Gold Key/Whitman No. 92: No. 1173, 3-5/61 - No. 91, 4/79; No. 92, 5/82

	GD 2.0	VG 4.0	FN 6.0	VF 8.0	VF/NM 9.0	NM- 9.2
Four Color 1173 (#1)-Crandall-c/a	23	46	69	161	356	550
Four Color 1288-Crandall/Evans-c/a	12	24	36	79	170	260
01-860-207 (5-7/62-Dell, 15¢)	9	18	27	63	129	195
12-860-210 on-c; 01-860-210 on inside(8-10/62-Dell)-Evans-c/a (3 stories); art by Frazetta & Crandall	9	18	27	62	126	190
1(11/62-Gold Key)-Crandall/Frazetta-a (10 & 11 pgs.); Evans-a	17	34	51	117	259	400
2	8	16	24	52	99	145
3-11: 3(11 pgs.),4(10 pgs.),9-Toth-a	6	12	18	37	66	95
12-15: 12-Williamson-a. 13,15-Crandall-a. 14-Orlando/Crandall/Torres-a	5	10	15	31	53	75
16-20	4	8	12	25	40	55
21-25: 21-Crandall-a(r). 25-Evans/Crandall-a(r); Toth-r/#4; last 12¢ issue	3	6	9	19	30	40
26,27: 26-Flying Saucer-c/story; Crandall, Evans-a(r). 27-Evans-r(2)	3	6	9	18	28	38
28-32: 32-Evans-a(r)	3	6	9	16	24	32
33-51: 43-Celardo-a. 51-Williamson-a	2	4	6	13	18	22
52-70	2	4	6	10	14	18
71-82,86-91: 71-Reprint	2	4	6	8	11	14
83-(52 pgs.)	3	6	9	14	20	25
84-(52 pgs.) Frank Miller's 1st comic book work	13	26	39	86	188	290
85-Frank Miller-a (2nd)	5	10	15	35	63	90
92-(Whitman, 5/82) Last issue; r/#1.	2	4	6	9	13	16
Mini Comic #1(1976, 3-1/4x6-1/2")	2	4	6	8	10	12

NOTE: ***Bolle** a-13(w/**McWilliams**), 50, 55, 57, 59, 77, 78, 80, 83, 84. **McWilliams** a-59, 78, 80, 82, 84. **Miller** a-84, 85. **Orlando** a-15, 19, 20, 22, 23. **Sekowsky** a-3. **Simonson** a-50, 54, 55, 83r. **Weiss** a-39, 79r(#39). (See Mystery Comics Digest 3, 6, 9, 12, 15, 18, 21, 24). Reprints-26(1/3), 71, 73, 79, 83, 84, 86, 92. Painted c-1-91.*

TWILIGHT ZONE, THE (TV)
Now Comics: Nov, 1990 ($2.95); Oct, 1991; V2#1, Nov, 1991 - No. 11, Oct, 1992 ($1.95); V3#1, 1993 - No. 4, 1993 ($2.50)

1-(11/90, $2.95, 52 pgs.)-Direct sale edition; Neal Adams-a, Sienkiewicz-c; Harlan Ellison scripts 6.00
1-(11/90, $1.75)-Newsstand ed. w/N. Adams-c 5.00
1-Prestige Format (10/91, $4.95)-Reprints above with extra Harlan Ellison short story 5.00
1-Collector's Edition (10/91, $2.50)-Non-code approved and polybagged; reprints 11/90 issue; gold logo, 1-Reprint ($2.50)-r/direct sale 11/90 version, 1-Reprint ($2.50)-r/newsstand 11/90 version each... 5.00
V2#1-Direct sale & newsstand ed. w/different-c 4.00
V2#2-8,10-11 4.00
V2#9-($2.95)-3-D Special; polybagged w/glasses & hologram on-c 5.00
V2#9-($4.95)-Prestige Edition; contains 2 extra stories & a different hologram on-c; polybagged w/glasses 5.00
V3#1-4, Anniversary Special 1 (1992, $2.50) 4.00

The Twelve #1 © MAR

Two-Fisted Tales #18 © WMG

Two-Gun Kid #37 © MAR

	GD 2.0	VG 4.0	FN 6.0	VF 8.0	VF/NM 9.0	NM- 9.2
Annual 1 (4/93, $2.50)-No ads						5.00
...Science Fiction Special (3/93, $3.50)						5.00

TWILIGHT ZONE, THE (TV)
Dynamite Entertainment: 2014 - No. 12, 2015 ($3.99)

	GD 2.0	VG 4.0	FN 6.0	VF 8.0	VF/NM 9.0	NM- 9.2
1-12-Straczynski-s/Vilanova-a/Francavilla-c						4.00
#1959 (2016, $5.99) Short stories set in 1959; Valiente & Worley-a; Lau-c						6.00
Annual 2014 ($7.99) Three short stories; Rahner-s/Valiente, Malaga, Menna-a						8.00

TWILIGHT ZONE THE SHADOW (TV)
Dynamite Entertainment: 2016 - No. 4, 2016 ($3.99, limited series)

	GD 2.0	VG 4.0	FN 6.0	VF 8.0	VF/NM 9.0	NM- 9.2
1-4-Avallone-s/Acosta-a/Francavilla-c; Shiwwan Khan app.						4.00

TWILIGHT ZONE, THE: SHADOW & SUBSTANCE (TV)
Dynamite Entertainment: 2015 - No. 4, 2015 ($3.99)

	GD 2.0	VG 4.0	FN 6.0	VF 8.0	VF/NM 9.0	NM- 9.2
1-4-Rahner-s/Menna-a; multiple covers on each						4.00

TWINKLE COMICS
Spotlight Publishers: May, 1945

	GD 2.0	VG 4.0	FN 6.0	VF 8.0	VF/NM 9.0	NM- 9.2
1	32	64	96	188	307	425

TWIST, THE
Dell Publishing Co.: July-Sept, 1962

	GD 2.0	VG 4.0	FN 6.0	VF 8.0	VF/NM 9.0	NM- 9.2
01-864-209-Painted-c	11	22	33	76	163	250

TWISTED TALES (See Eclipse Graphic Album Series #15)
Pacific Comics/Independent Comics Group (Eclipse) #9,10: 11/82 - No. 8, 5/84; No. 9, 11/84; No. 10, 12/84 (Baxter paper)

	GD 2.0	VG 4.0	FN 6.0	VF 8.0	VF/NM 9.0	NM- 9.2
1-9: 1-B. Jones/Corben-c; Alcala-a; nudity/violence in al. 2-Wrightson-c; Ploog-a						5.00
10-Wrightson painted art; Morrow-a	1	2	3	4	5	7

NOTE: *Bolton painted c-4, 6, 7; a-7.* ***Conrad*** *a-1, 3, 5; c-1i, 3, 5.* ***Guice*** *a-8.* ***Wildey*** *a-3.*

TWO BIT THE WACKY WOODPECKER (See Wacky...)
Toby Press: 1951 - No. 3, May, 1953

	GD 2.0	VG 4.0	FN 6.0	VF 8.0	VF/NM 9.0	NM- 9.2
1	15	30	45	84	127	170
2,3	9	18	27	50	65	80

TWO FACE: YEAR ONE
DC Comics: 2008 - No. 2, 2008 ($5.99, squarebound, limited series)

	GD 2.0	VG 4.0	FN 6.0	VF 8.0	VF/NM 9.0	NM- 9.2
1,2-Origin re-told; Sable-s/Saiz & Haun-a						6.00

TWO-FISTED TALES (Formerly Haunt of Fear #15-17)
(Also see EC Archives • Two-Fisted Tales)
E. C. Comics: No. 18, Nov-Dec, 1950 - No. 41, Feb-Mar, 1955

	GD 2.0	VG 4.0	FN 6.0	VF 8.0	VF/NM 9.0	NM- 9.2
18(#1)-Kurtzman-c	129	258	387	1032	1641	2250
19-Kurtzman-c	83	166	249	664	1057	1450
20-Kurtzman-c	56	112	168	448	712	975
21,22-Kurtzman-c	46	92	138	368	584	800
23-25-Kurtzman-c	36	72	108	288	457	625
26-29,31-Kurtzman-c. 31-Civil War issue	27	54	81	216	346	475
30-Classic Davis-c	36	72	108	288	457	625
32-34: 33- "Atom Bomb" by Wood	27	54	81	216	346	475
35-Classic Davis Civil War-c/s	37	74	111	256	473	650
36-41: 41-Contains "In Memoriam" editorial about the ending of EC War titles	22	44	66	176	285	390
Two-Fisted Annual (1952, 25¢, 132 pgs.)	144	288	432	1152	1726	2300
Two-Fisted Annual (1953, 25¢, 132 pgs.)	113	226	339	904	1352	1800

NOTE: ***Berg*** *a-29.* ***Colan*** *a-30,39p.* ***Craig*** *a-18, 19, 32.* ***Crandall*** *a-35, 36.* ***Davis*** *a-20-36, 40; c-30, 34, 35, 41, Annual 2.* ***Estrada*** *a-30.* ***Evans*** *a-34, 40, 41; c-40.* ***Feldstein*** *a-18.* ***Krigstein*** *a-41.* ***Kubert*** *a-32, 33.* ***Kurtzman*** *a-18-25; c-18-29, 31, Annual 1.* ***Severin*** *a-26, 28, 29, 31, 34-41 (No. 37-39 are all-**Severin** issues); c-36-39.* ***Severin/Elder*** *a-19-29, 31, 33, 36.* ***Wood*** *a-18-28, 30-35, 41; c-32, 33. Special issues: #26 (ChanJin Reservoir), 31 (Civil War), 35 (Civil War). Canadian reprints known; see Table of Contents. #25-Davis biog. #27-Wood biog. #28-Kurtzman biog.*

TWO-FISTED TALES
Russ Cochran/Gemstone Publishing: Oct, 1992 - No. 24, May, 1998 ($1.50/$2.00/$2.50)

	GD 2.0	VG 4.0	FN 6.0	VF 8.0	VF/NM 9.0	NM- 9.2
1-24: 1-4r/Two-Fisted Tales #18-21 w/original-c						4.00

TWO GRAVES
Image Comics: Nov, 2022 - Present ($3.99)

	GD 2.0	VG 4.0	FN 6.0	VF 8.0	VF/NM 9.0	NM- 9.2
1-4-Genevieve Valentine-s/Ming Doyle & Annie Wu-a						4.00

TWO-GUN KID (Also see All Western Winners, Best Western, Black Rider, Blaze Carson, Kid Colt, Western Winners, Wild West, & Wild Western)
Marvel/Atlas (MCI No. 1-10/HPC No. 11-59/Marvel No. 60 on): 3/48(No mo.) - No. 10, 11/49; No. 11, 12/53 - No. 59, 4/61; No. 60, 11/62 - No. 92, 3/68; No. 93, 7/70 - No. 136, 4/77

	GD 2.0	VG 4.0	FN 6.0	VF 8.0	VF/NM 9.0	NM- 9.2
1-Two-Gun Kid & his horse Cyclone begin; The Sheriff begins	174	348	522	1114	1907	2700
2	63	126	189	403	689	975
3,4: 3-Annie Oakley app.	47	94	141	296	498	700
5-Pre-Black Rider app. (Wint. 48/49); Anti-Wertham editorial (1st?)	50	100	150	315	533	750
6-10(11/49): 8-Blaze Carson app. 9-Black Rider app.	40	80	120	246	411	575
11(12/53)-Black Rider app.; 1st to have Atlas globe on-c; explains how Kid Colt became an outlaw	36	72	108	211	343	475
12-Black Rider app.	30	60	90	177	289	400
13-20: 14-Opium story	25	50	75	150	245	340
21-24,26-29	23	46	69	136	223	310
25,30: 25-Williamson-a (5 pgs.). 30-Williamson/Torres-a (4 pgs.)	24	48	72	144	237	330
31-33,35,37-40	12	24	36	84	185	285
34-Crandall-a	13	26	39	89	195	300
36,41,42,48-Origin in all	13	26	39	91	201	310
43,44,47	12	24	36	80	173	265
45,46-Davis-a	12	24	36	84	185	285
49,50,52,53-Severin-a(2/3) in each	11	22	33	77	166	255
51-Williamson-a (5 pgs.)	12	24	36	82	179	275
54,55,57,59-Severin-a(3) in each. 59-Kirby-a; last 10¢ issue (4/61)	12	24	36	80	173	265
56	12	24	36	79	170	260
58-New origin; Kirby/Ayers-c/a "The Monster of Hidden Valley" cover/story (Kirby monster-c)	34	68	102	245	548	850
60-New origin	79	158	237	632	1416	2200
60-Edition w/handwritten issue number on cover	86	172	258	688	1544	2400
61,62-Kirby-a	16	32	48	110	243	375
63-74: 64-Intro. Boom-Boom	9	18	27	59	117	175
75,76-Kirby-a (reprint)	9	18	27	61	123	185
77-Kirby-a (reprint); Black Panther-esque villain	27	54	81	189	420	650
78-89	5	10	15	35	63	90
90,95-Kirby-a	5	10	15	35	63	90
91,92: 92-Last new story; last 12¢ issue	5	10	15	31	53	75
93,94,96-99	3	6	9	18	28	38
100-Last 15¢-c	3	6	9	19	30	40
101-Origin retold/#58; Kirby-a	3	6	9	19	30	40
102-120-reprints	3	6	9	17	26	35
121-136-reprints. 129-131-(Regular 25¢ editions)	3	6	9	14	20	25
129-131-(30¢-c variants, limited distribution)(4-8/76)	9	18	27	57	111	165

NOTE: ***Ayers*** *a-13, 24, 26, 27, 63, 66.* ***Davis*** *c-45-47.* ***Drucker*** *a-23.* ***Everett*** *a-82, 91.* ***Fuje*** *a-13.* ***Heath*** *a-3(2), 4(3), 5(2), 7; c-13, 21, 23, 53.* ***Keller*** *a-16, 19, 28, 42.* ***Kirby*** *a-54, 55, 57-62, 75-77, 90, 95, 101, 119, 120, 129; c-10, 52, 54-65, 67-72, 74-76, 116.* ***Maneely*** *a-20; c-11, 12, 16, 19, 20, 24-28, 30, 35, 41, 42, 49.* ***Powell*** *a-38, 102, 104.* ***Severin*** *a-9, 29, 51, 55, 57, 99r(3); c-9, 39, 51.* ***Shores*** *c-1-8, 11.* ***Trimpe*** *c-99.* ***Tuska*** *a-11, 12.* ***Whitney*** *a-87, 89-92, 98-113, 124, 129; c-87, 89, 91, 113.* ***Wildey*** *a-21.* ***Williamson*** *a-110r. Kid Colt in #13, 14, 16-21.*

TWO GUN KID: SUNSET RIDERS
Marvel Comics: Nov, 1995 - No. 2, Dec, 1995 ($6.95, squarebound, lim. series)

	GD 2.0	VG 4.0	FN 6.0	VF 8.0	VF/NM 9.0	NM- 9.2
1,2: Fabian Nicieza scripts in all. 1-Painted-c.						7.00

TWO GUN WESTERN (1st Series) (Formerly Casey Crime Photographer #1-4? or My Love #1-4?)
Marvel/Atlas Comics (MPC): No. 5, Nov, 1950 - No. 14, June, 1952

	GD 2.0	VG 4.0	FN 6.0	VF 8.0	VF/NM 9.0	NM- 9.2
5-The Apache Kid (Intro & origin) & his horse Nightwind begin by Buscema	36	72	108	211	343	475
6-10: 8-Kid Colt, The Texas Kid & his horse Thunder begin?	24	48	72	142	234	325
11-14: 13-Black Rider app.	18	36	54	105	165	225

NOTE: ***Maneely*** *a-6, 7, 9; c-6, 11-13.* ***Morrow*** *a-9.* ***Romita*** *a-8.* ***Wildey*** *a-8.*

2-GUN WESTERN (2nd Series) (Formerly Billy Buckskin #1-3; Two-Gun Western #5 on)
Atlas Comics (MgPC): No. 4, May, 1956

	GD 2.0	VG 4.0	FN 6.0	VF 8.0	VF/NM 9.0	NM- 9.2
4-Colan, Ditko, Severin, Sinnott-a; Maneely-c	20	40	60	120	195	270

TWO-GUN WESTERN (Formerly 2-Gun Western)
Atlas Comics (MgPC): No. 5, July, 1956 - No. 12, Sept, 1957

	GD 2.0	VG 4.0	FN 6.0	VF 8.0	VF/NM 9.0	NM- 9.2
5-Return of the Gun-Hawk-c/story; Black Rider app.	21	42	63	122	199	275
6,7	15	30	45	94	147	200
8,10,12-Crandall-a	16	32	48	98	154	210
9,11-Williamson-a in both (5 pgs. each)	17	34	51	103	162	220

NOTE: ***Ayers*** *a-9.* ***Colan*** *a-5.* ***Everett*** *c-12.* ***Forgione*** *a-5, 6.* ***Kirby*** *a-12.* ***Maneely*** *a-6, 8, 12; c-5, 6, 8, 11.* ***Morrow*** *a-9, 10.* ***Powell*** *a-7, 11.* ***Severin*** *c-10.* ***Sinnott*** *a-5.* ***Wildey*** *a-9.*

TWO MINUTE WARNING
Ultimate Sports Ent.: 2000 - No. 2 ($3.95, cardstock covers)

	GD 2.0	VG 4.0	FN 6.0	VF 8.0	VF/NM 9.0	NM- 9.2
1,2-NFL players & Teddy Roosevelt battle evil						4.00

TWO MOONS
Image Comics: Feb, 2021 - Present ($3.99)

	GD 2.0	VG 4.0	FN 6.0	VF 8.0	VF/NM 9.0	NM- 9.2
1-10-Arcudi-s/Giangiordano-a; set during the Civil War						4.00

TWO MOUSEKETEERS, THE (See 4-Color #475, 603, 642 under M.G.M.'s...)

TWO ON A GUILLOTINE (See Movie Classics)

GD 2.0 | VG 4.0 | FN 6.0 | VF 8.0 | VF/NM 9.0 | NM- 9.2

TWO-STEP
DC Comics (Cliffhanger): Dec, 2003 - No. 3, Jul, 2004 ($2.95, limited series)
1-3-Warren Ellis-s/Amanda Conner-a 3.00
TPB (2010, $19.99) r/#1-3; sketch pages; script for #1 with B&W art 20.00

2000 A.D. MONTHLY/PRESENTS (Showcase #25 on)
Eagle Comics/Quality Comics No. 5 on: 4/85 - #6, 9/85; 4/86 - #54, 1991 ($1.25-$1.50, Mando paper)
1-6,1-25:1-4 r/British series featuring Judge Dredd; Alan Moore scripts begin.
1-25 ($1.25)-Reprints from British 2000 AD 4.00
26,27/28, 29/30, 31-54: 27/28, 29/30,31-Guice-c 3.00

2001, A SPACE ODYSSEY (Movie) (See adaptation in Treasury edition)
Marvel Comics Group: Dec, 1976 - No. 10, Sept, 1977 (30¢)
1-Kirby-c/a in all 4 8 12 23 37 50
2-7,9,10 2 4 6 9 12 15
7,9,10-(35¢-c variants, limited distribution)(6-9/77) 9 18 27 60 120 180
8-Origin/1st app. Machine Man (called Mr. Machine) 6 12 18 41 76 110
8-(35¢-c variant, limited distribution)(6,8/77) 19 38 57 133 297 460
...Treasury 1 ('76, 84 pgs.)-All new Kirby-a 3 6 9 16 23 30

2010 (Movie)
Marvel Comics Group: Apr, 1985 - No. 2, May, 1985
1,2-r/Marvel Super Special movie adaptation. 4.00

TYPHOID (Also see Daredevil)
Marvel Comics: Nov, 1995 - No. 4, Feb, 1996 ($3.95, squarebound, lim. series)
1-4: Typhoid Mary; Van Fleet-c/a 4.00

TYPHOID FEVER
Marvel Comics: Dec, 2018 - Feb, 2019 ($4.99, limited series)
...: Iron Fist 1 (2/19, $4.99) Typhoid Mary conclusion; Chapman-s/Villanelli-a 5.00
...: Spider-Man 1 (12/18, $4.99) Typhoid Mary returns; Chapman-s/Landini-a 5.00
...: X-Men 1 (1/19, $4.99) Spider-Man app.; Chapman-s/Robson & Beyruth-a 5.00

ÜBER
Avatar Press: No. 0, Mar, 2013 - No. 27, Jul, 2015 ($3.99)
0-27: 0-11-Kieron Gillen-s/Caanan White-a. 12-14-Andrade-a 4.00
... FCBD 2014 (2/14, Free Comic Book Day giveaway) Text synopsis of early storyline 3.00
... Special 1 (3/14, $5.99) Andrade-a 6.00

UFO & ALIEN COMIX
Warren Publishing Co.: Jan, 1978 (B&W magazine, 84 pgs., one-shot)
nn-Toth-a, J. Severin-a(r); Pie-s 3 6 9 14 20 25

UFO & OUTER SPACE (Formerly UFO Flying Saucers)
Gold Key: No. 14, June, 1978 - No. 25, Feb, 1980 (All painted covers)
14-Reprints UFO Flying Saucers #3 1 3 4 6 8 10
15,16-Reprints 1 3 4 6 8 10
17-25: 17-20-New material. 23-McWilliams-a. 24-(3 pg.-r). 25-Reprints UFO Flying Saucers #2 w/cover 1 3 4 6 8 10

UFO ENCOUNTERS
Western Publishing Co.: May, 1978 ($1.95, 228 pgs.)
11192-Reprints UFO Flying Saucers 5 10 15 31 53 75
11404-Vol.1 (128 pgs.)-See UFO Mysteries for Vol. 2 4 8 12 27 44 60

UFO FLYING SAUCERS (UFO & Outer Space #14 on)
Gold Key: Oct, 1968 - No. 13, Jan, 1977 (No. 2 on, 36 pgs.)
1(30035-810) (68 pgs.) 7 14 21 46 86 125
2(11/70), 3(11/72), 4(11/74) 3 6 9 19 30 40
5(2/75)-13: Bolle-a #4 on 3 6 9 14 20 25

UFOLOGY
BOOM! Studios: Apr, 2015 - No. 6, Nov, 2015 ($3.99, limited series)
1-6-James Tynion IV & Noah J. Yuenkel-s/Matthew Fox-a 4.00

UFO MYSTERIES
Western Publishing Co.: 1978 ($1.00, reprints, 96 pgs.)
11400-(Vol.2)-Cont'd from UFO Encounters, pgs. 129-224 5 10 15 33 57 80

ULTIMAN GIANT ANNUAL (See Big Bang Comics)
Image Comics: Nov, 2001 ($4.95, B&W, one-shot)
1-Homage to DC 1960's annuals 5.00

ULTIMATE... (Collects 4-issue alternate titles from X-Men Age of Apocalypse crossovers)
Marvel Comics: May, 1995 ($8.95, trade paperbacks, gold foil covers)
Amazing X-Men, Astonishing X-Men, Factor-X, Gambit & the X-Ternals, Generation Next, X-Calibre, X-Man 9.00
Weapon X 10.00

ULTIMATE ADVENTURES
Marvel Comics: Nov, 2002 - No. 6, Dec, 2003 ($2.25)
1-6: 1-Intro. Hawk-Owl; Zimmerman-s/Fegredo-a. 3-Ultimates app. 3.00
One Tin Soldier TPB (2005, $12.99) r/#1-6 13.00

ULTIMATE ANNUALS
Marvel Comics: 2006; 2007 ($13.99, SC)
Vol. 1 (2006, $13.99) r/Ult. FF Ann. #1, Ult. X-Men Ann. #1, Ult S-M #1, Ultimates Ann #1 14.00
Vol. 2 (2007, $13.99) r/Ult. FF Ann. #2, Ult. X-Men Ann. #2, Ult S-M #2, Ultimates Ann #2 14.00

ULTIMATE ARMOR WARS (Follows Ultimatum x-over)
Marvel Comics: Nov, 2009 - No. 4, Apr, 2010 ($3.99, limited series)
1-4-Warren Ellis-s/Steve Kurth-a/Brandon Peterson-c. 1-Variant-c by Kurth 4.00

ULTIMATE AVENGERS (Follows Ultimatum x-over)
Marvel Comics: Oct, 2009 - No. 18 ($3.99)
1-6-Mark Millar-s/Carlos Pacheco-a/c; Red Skull app. 4.00
1-Variant Red Skull-c by Leinil Yu 8.00
7-12-(Ultimate Avengers 2 #1-6 on cover) Yu-a; Punisher joins. 10-Origin Ghost Rider 4.00
7-Variant Ghost Rider-c by Silvestri 8.00
13-18-(Ultimate Avengers 3 #1-6 on cover) Dillon-a; Blade and a new Daredevil app. 4.00

ULTIMATE AVENGERS VS. NEW ULTIMATES (Death of Spider-Man tie-in)
Marvel Comics: Apr, 2011 - No. 6, Sept, 2011 ($3.99, limited series)
1-6: 1-Millar-s/Yu-a/c; variant covers by Cho & Hitch. 3-6-Punisher app. 4.00

ULTIMATE CAPTAIN AMERICA
Marvel Comics: Mar, 2011 - No. 4, Jun, 2011 ($3.99)
1-4: 1-Aaron-s/Garney-a; 2 covers by Garney & McGuinness 4.00
Annual 1 (12/08, $3.99, one-shot) Origin of the Black Panther; Djurdjevic-a 4.00

ULTIMATE CIVIL WAR: SPIDER-HAM (See Civil War and related titles)
Marvel Comics: March, 2007 ($2.99, one-shot)
1-Spoof of Civil War series featuring Spider-Ham; art by various incl. Olivetti, Severin 5.00

ULTIMATE COMICS IRON MAN
Marvel Comics: Dec, 2012 - No. 4, Mar, 2013 ($3.99, limited series)
1-4-Edmonson-s/Buffagni-a/Stockton-c 4.00

ULTIMATE COMICS SPIDER-MAN (See Ultimate Spider-Man 2011 series)

ULTIMATE COMICS ULTIMATES (See Ultimates 2011 series)

ULTIMATE COMICS WOLVERINE
Marvel Comics: May, 2013 - No. 4, Jul, 2013 ($3.99, limited series)
1-4: 1-Bunn-s/Messina-a/Art Adams-c; Wolverine app. in flashback 4.00

ULTIMATE COMICS X-MEN (See Ultimate X-Men 2011 series)

ULTIMATE DAREDEVIL AND ELEKTRA
Marvel Comics: Jan, 2003 - No. 4, Mar, 2003 ($2.25, limited series)
1-4-Rucka-s/Larroca-c/a; 1st meeting of Elektra and Matt Murdock 3.00
... Vol.1 TPB (2003, $11.99) r/#1-4, Daredevil Vol. 2 #9; Larroca sketch pages 12.00

ULTIMATE DOOM (Follows Ultimate Mystery mini-series)
Marvel Comics: Feb, 2011 - No. 4, May, 2011 ($3.99, limited series)
1-4-Bendis-s/Sandoval-a; Fantastic Four, Spider-Man, Jessica Drew & Nick Fury app. 4.00

ULTIMATE ELEKTRA
Marvel Comics: Oct, 2004 - No. 5, Feb, 2005 ($2.25, limited series)
1-5-Carey-s/Larroca-c/a. 2-Bullseye app. 3.00
... : Devil's Due TPB (2005, $11.99) r/#1-5 12.00

ULTIMATE END (Secret Wars Battleworld tie-in)
Marvel Comics: Jul, 2015 - No. 5, Feb, 2016 ($3.99, limited series)
1-5-Bendis-s/Bagley-a; Spider-Man & Earth-616 Avengers & Ultimate Universe app. 4.00

ULTIMATE ENEMY (Follows Ultimatum x-over)(Leads into Ultimate Mystery)
Marvel Comics: Mar, 2010 - No. 4, July, 2010 ($3.99, limited series)
1-4-Bendis-s/Sandoval-a 1-Covers by McGuinness and Pearson 4.00

ULTIMATE EXTINCTION (See Ultimate Nightmare and Ultimate Secret limited series)
Marvel Comics: Mar, 2006 - No. 5, July, 2006 ($2.99, limited series)
1-5-The coming of Gah Lak Tus; Ellis-s/Peterson-a 3.00
TPB (2006, $12.99) r/#1-5 13.00

ULTIMATE FALLOUT (Follows Death of Spider-Man in Ultimate Spider-Man #160)
Marvel Comics: Sept, 2011 - No. 6, Oct, 2011 ($3.99, weekly limited series)
1-Bendis-s/Bagley-a/c 3 6 9 16 23 30
2,5,6: 2,6-Hitch-c. 5-Andy Kubert-c 4.00
3-Ad for Miles Morales; Andy Kubert-c 4 8 12 27 44 60
4-Debut of Miles Morales as the new Spider-Man; polybagged 21 42 63 147 324 500
Ultimate Comics Fallout No. 4 Facsimile Edition (11/21, $3.99) reprint with original ads 4.00

ULTIMATE FANTASTIC FOUR (Continues in Ultimatum mini-series)
Marvel Comics: Feb, 2004 - No. 60, Apr, 2009 ($2.25/$2.50/$2.99)
1-Bendis & Millar-s/Adam Kubert-a/Hitch-c 5.00
2-20: 2-Adam Kubert-a/c; intro. Moleman 7-Ellis-s/Immonen-a begin; Dr. Doom app. 13-18-Kubert-a. 19,20-Jae Lee-a. 20-Begin $2.50-c 3.50
21-Marvel Zombies; begin Greg Land-c/a; Mark Millar-s; variant-c by Land 5.00
22-29,33-59: 24-26-Namor app. 28-President Thor. 33-38-Ferry-a. 42-46-Silver Surfer 3.00
30-32-Marvel Zombies; Millar-s/Land-a; Dr. Doom app. 5.00
30-32-Zombie variant-c by Suydam 6.00
50-White variant-c by Kirkham 5.00
60-($3.99) Ultimatum crossover; Kirkham-a 4.00
Annual 1 (10/05, $3.99) The Inhumans app.; Jae Lee-a/Mark Millar-s/Greg Land-c 4.00
Annual 2 (10/06, $3.99) Mole Man app.; Immonen & Irving-a/Carey-s 4.00
... MGC #1 (6/11, $1.00) r/#1 with "Marvel's Greatest Comics" logo on cover 3.00
.../Ult. X-Men Annual 1 (11/08, $3.99) Continued from Ult. X-Men/Ult. F.F. Annual #1 4.00
.../X-Men 1 (3/06, $2.99) Carey-s/Ferry-a; continued from Ult. X-Men/Fantastic Four #1 3.00
... Vol. 1: The Fantastic (2004, $12.99, TPB) r/#1-6; cover gallery 13.00
... Vol. 2: Doom (2004, $12.99, TPB) r/#7-12 13.00
... Vol. 3: N-Zone (2005, $12.99, TPB) r/#13-18 13.00
... Vol. 4: Inhuman (2005, $12.99, TPB) r/#19,20 & Annual #1 13.00
... Vol. 5: Crossover (2006, $12.99, TPB) r/#21-26 13.00
... Vol. 6: Frightful (2006, $14.99, TPB) r/#27-32; gallery of cover sketches & variants 15.00
... Vol. 7: God War (2007, $16.99, TPB) r/#33-38 17.00
... Vol. 8: Devils (2007, $12.99, TPB) r/#39-41 & Annual #2 13.00
... Vol. 9: Silver Surfer (2007, $13.99, TPB) r/#42-46 14.00
Volume 1 HC (2005, $29.99, 7x11", dust jacket) r/#1-12; introduction, proposals and scripts by Millar and Bendis; character design pages by Hitch 30.00
Volume 2 HC (2006, $29.99, 7x11", dust jacket) r/#13-20; Jae Lee sketch page 30.00
Volume 3 HC (2007, $29.99, 7x11", dust jacket) r/#21-32; Greg Land sketch pages 30.00
Volume 4 HC (2007, $29.99, 7x11", dust jacket) r/#33-41, Annual #2, Ultimate FF/X-Men and Ultimate X-Men/FF; character design pages 30.00
Volume 5 HC (2008, $34.99, 7x11", dust jacket) r/#42-53 35.00

ULTIMATE FF
Marvel Comics: Jun, 2014 - No. 6, Oct, 2014 ($3.99)
1-6: 1-Team of Sue Storm, Iron Man, Falcon, Machine Man. 4,5-Spider-Ham app. 4.00

ULTIMATE GALACTUS TRILOGY
Marvel Comics: 2007 ($34.99, hardcover, dustjacket)
HC-Oversized reprint of Ultimate Nightmare #1-5, Ultimate Secret #1-4, Ultimate Vision #0, and Ultimate Extinction #1-5; sketch pages and cover galery 35.00

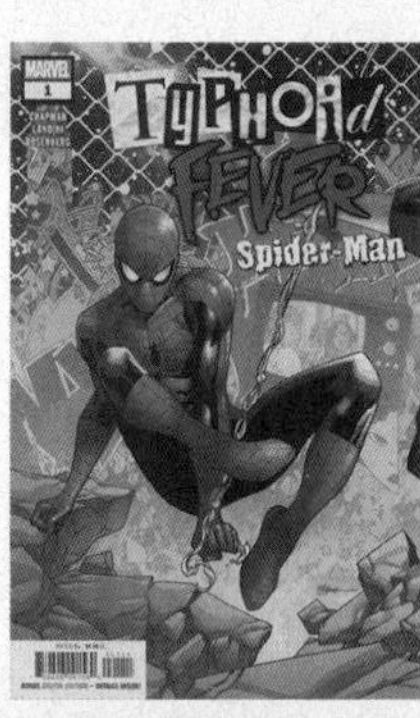

Typhoid Fever: Spider-Man #1 © MAR

Ultimate Comics Spider-Man #12 © MAR

Ultimates 2 #12 © MAR

GD 2.0 | VG 4.0 | FN 6.0 | VF 8.0 | VF/NM 9.0 | NM- 9.2

ULTIMATE HAWKEYE (Ultimate Comics)
Marvel Comics: Oct, 2011 - No. 4, Jan, 2012 ($3.99, limited series)
1-4: 1-Hickman-s/Sandoval-a/Andrews-c; polybagged. 2-4-Hulk app. 4.00
1-Variant-c by Neal Adams 6.00
1-Variant-c by Adam Kubert 8.00

ULTIMATE HULK
Marvel Comics: Dec, 2008 ($3.99, one-shot)
Annual 1 (12/08, $3.99) Zarda battles Hulk; McGuinness & Djurdjevic-a/Loeb-s 4.00

ULTIMATE HUMAN
Marvel Comics: Mar, 2008 - No. 4, Jun, 2008 ($2.99, limited series)
1-4-Iron Man vs. The Hulk; The Leader app.; Ellis-s/Nord-a 3.00
HC (2008, $19.99) r/#1-4 20.00

ULTIMATE IRON MAN
Marvel Comics: May, 2005 - No. 5, Feb, 2006 ($2.99, limited series)
1-Origin of Iron Man; Orson Scott Card-s/Andy Kubert-a; two covers 4.00
1-2nd & 3rd printings; each with B&W variant-c 3.00
2-5-Kubert-c 3.00
Volume 1 HC (2006, $19.99, dust jacket) r/#1-5; rough cut of script for #1, cover sketches 20.00
Volume 1 SC (2006, $14.99) r/#1-5; rough cut of script for #1, cover sketches 15.00

ULTIMATE IRON MAN II
Marvel Comics: Feb, 2008 - No. 5, July, 2008 ($2.99, limited series)
1-5-Early days of the Iron Man prototype; Orson Scott Card-s/Pasqual Ferry-a/c 3.00

ULTIMATE MARVEL FLIP MAGAZINE
Marvel Comics: July, 2005 - No. 26, Aug, 2007 ($3.99/$4.99)
1-11-Reprints Ultimate Fantastic Four and Ultimate X-Men in flip format 4.00
12-26-($4.99) 5.00

ULTIMATE MARVEL MAGAZINE
Marvel Comics: Feb, 2001 - No. 11, 2002 ($3.99, magazine size)
1-11: Reprints of recent stories from the Ultimate titles plus Marvel news and features. 1-Reprints Ultimate Spider-Man #1&2. 11-Lord of the Rings-c 4.00

ULTIMATE MARVEL SAMPLER
Marvel Comics: 2007 (no cover price, limited series)
1-Previews of 2008 Ultimate Marvel story arcs; Finch-c 3.00

ULTIMATE MARVEL TEAM-UP (Spider-Man Team-up)
Marvel Comics: Apr, 2001 - No. 16, July, 2002 ($2.99/$2.25)
1-Spider-Man & Wolverine; Bendis-s in all; Matt Wagner-a/c 5.00
2,3-Hulk; Hester-a 3.50
4,5,9-16: 4,5-Iron Man; Allred-a. 9-Fantastic Four; Mahfood-a. 10-Man-Thing; Totleben-a. 11-X-Men; Clugston-Major-a. 12,13-Dr. Strange; McKeever-a.14-Black Widow; Terry Moore-a. 15,16-Shang-Chi; Mays-a 3.00
6-8-Punisher; Sienkiewicz-a. 7,8-Daredevil app. 4.00
TPB (11/01, $14.95) r/#1-5 15.00
... Ultimate Collection TPB ('06, $29.99) r/#1-16 & Ult. Spider-Man Spec.; sketch pages 30.00
HC (8/02, $39.99) r/#1-16 & Ult. Spider-Man Special; Bendis afterword 40.00
...: Vol. 2 TPB (2003, $11.99) r/#9-13; Mahfood-c 12.00
...: Vol. 3 TPB (2003, $12.99) r/#14-16 & Ultimate Spider-Man Super Special; Moore-c 13.00

ULTIMATE MYSTERY (Follows Ultimate Enemy)(Leads into Ultimate Doom)
Marvel Comics: Sept, 2010 - No. 4, Dec, 2010 ($3.99, limited series)
1-4-Bendis-s/Sandoval-a; Rick Jones returns; Captain Marvel app. 1-3-Campbell-c 4.00

ULTIMATE NEW ULTIMATES (Follows Ultimatum x-over)
Marvel Comics: May, 2010 - No. 5, Mar, 2011 ($3.99)
1-5: 1-Jeph Loeb-s/Frank Cho-a; 6-page wraparound-c by Cho; Defenders app. 4.00
1-Villains variant-c by Yu 8.00

ULTIMATE NIGHTMARE (Leads into Ultimate Secret limited series)
Marvel Comics: Oct, 2004 - No. 5, Feb, 2005 ($2.25, limited series)
1-5: Ellis-s; Ultimates, X-Men, Nick Fury app. 1,2,4,5-Hairsine-a/c. 3-Epting-a 3.00
Ultimate Galactus Book 1: Nightmare TPB (2005, $12.99) r/Ultimate Nightmare #1-5 13.00

ULTIMATE ORIGINS
Marvel Comics: Aug, 2008 - No. 5, Dec, 2008 ($2.99, limited series)
1-5-Bendis-s/Guice-a. 1-Nick Fury origin in the 1940s. 2-Capt. America origin 3.00

ULTIMATE POWER
Marvel Comics: Dec, 2006 - No. 9, Feb, 2008 ($2.99, limited series)
1-9: 1-Ultimate FF meets the Squadron Supreme; Bendis-s; Land-a/c. 2-Spider-Man, X-Men and the Ultimates app. 6-Doom app. 3.00
1-Variant sketch-c 5.00
1-Director's Cut (2007, $3.99) r/#1 and B&W pencil and ink pages; covers to #2,3 4.00
HC (2008, $34.99) oversized r/series; profile pages; B&W sketch art 35.00

ULTIMATES, THE (Avengers of the Ultimate line)
Marvel Comics: Mar, 2002 - No. 13, Apr, 2004 ($2.25)
1-Intro. Capt. America; Millar-s/Hitch-a & wraparound-c 1 2 3 5 6 8
2-Intro. Giant-Man, the Wasp and 1st app. Nick Fury modeled after Samuel L. Jackson 2 4 6 8 10 12
3-12: 3-1st Capt. America in new costume. 4-Intro. Thor. 5-Ultimates vs. The Hulk. 8-Intro. Hawkeye 3.00
13-($3.50) 4.00
... MGC #1 (5/11, $1.00) r/#1 with "Marvel's Greatest Comics" logo on cover 3.00
... Saga (2007, $3.99) Re-caps 1st 2 Ultimates series; new framing art by Charest; prelude to Ultimates 3 series; Brooks-c 4.00
... Volume 1 HC (2004, $29.99) oversized r/series; commentary pages with Millar & Hitch; cover gallery and character design pages; intro. by Joss Whedon 30.00
... Volume 1: Super-Human TPB (8/02, $12.99) r/#1-6 13.00
... Volume 2: Homeland Security TPB (2004, $17.99) r/#7-13 18.00

ULTIMATES (Ultimate Comics) (Continues in Hunger)
Marvel Comics: Oct, 2011 - No. 30, Nov, 2013 ($3.99)
1-30: 1-Hickman-s/Ribic-a/Andrews-c; polybagged. 4-Reed Richards returns 4.00
1-Variant-c by Esad Ribic 6.00
#18.1 (2/13, $2.99) Eaglesham-a; Stark gets the Iron Patriot armor 3.00
Ultimate Comics Ultimates Must Have 1 (2/12, $4.99) r/#1-3 5.00

ULTIMATES (Follows Secret War event)
Marvel Comics: Jan, 2016 - No. 12, Dec, 2016 ($3.99)
1-12: 1-Ewing-s/Rocafort-a; team of Capt. Marvel, Blue Marvel, Black Panther, Spectrum, and Ms. America; Galactus app. 5,7-11-Thanos app. 6,12-Christian Ward-a. 8-12-Civil War II tie-ins 4.00

ULTIMATES 2
Marvel Comics: Feb, 2005 - No. 13, Feb, 2007 ($2.99/$3.99)
1-Millar-s/Hitch-a; Giant-Man becomes Ant-Man 4.00
2-11: 6-Intro. The Defenders. 7-Hawkeye shot. 8-Intro The Liberators 3.00
12,13-($3.99) Wraparound-c; X-Men, Fantastic Four, Spider-Man app. 4.00
13-Variant white cover featuring The Wasp 15.00
Annual 1 (10/05, $3.99) Millar-s/Dillon-a/Hitch-c; Defenders app. 4.00
Annual 2 (10/06, $3.99) Deodato-a; flashback to WWII with Sook-a; Falcon app. 4.00
HC (2007, $34.99) oversized r/series; commentary pages with Millar & Hitch; cover gallery, sketch and script pages; intro. by Jonathan Ross 35.00
... Volume 1: Gods & Monsters TPB (2005, $15.99) r/#1-6 16.00
... Volume 2: Grand Theft America TPB (2007, $19.99) r/#7-13; cover gallery w/sketches 20.00

ULTIMATES 2
Marvel Comics: Jan, 2017 - No. 9, Sept, 2017; No. 100, Oct, 2017 ($3.99)
1-9: 1-Ewing-s/Foreman-a; team of Capt. Marvel, Blue Marvel, Black Panther, Spectrum, and Ms. America. 7,8-Secret Empire tie-ins; Koch-a. 8,9-Ego the Living Planet app. 4.00
100-(10/17, $4.99) The original Ultimates app. 5.00

ULTIMATES 3
Marvel Comics: Feb, 2008 - No. 5, Nov, 2008 ($2.99)
1-Loeb-s/Madureira-a; two gatefold wraparound covers by Madureira; Scarlet Witch shot 4.00
1,2-Second printings: 1-Wraparound cover by Madureira. 2-Madureira-c 3.00
2-5: 2-Spider-Man app. 3-Wolverine app. 5-Two gatefold wraparound-c (Heroes & Ultron) 3.00
2-Variant Thor cover by Turner 8.00
3-Variant Scarlet Witch cover by Cho 8.00
4-Variant Valkyrie cover by Finch 4.00

ULTIMATE SECRET (See Ultimate Nightmare limited series)
Marvel Comics: May, 2005 - No. 4, Dec, 2005 ($2.99, limited series)
1-4-Ellis-s; Captain Marvel app. 1,2-McNiven-a. 2,3-Ultimates & FF app. 3.00
Ultimate Galactus Book 2: Secret TPB (2006, $12.99) r/#1-4 13.00

ULTIMATE SECRETS
Marvel Comics: 2008 ($3.99, one-shot)
1-Handbook-styled profiles of secondary teams and characters from Ultimate universe 4.00

ULTIMATE SIX (Reprinted in Ultimate Spider-Man Vol. 5 hardcover)
Marvel Comics: Nov, 2003 - No. 7, June, 2004 ($2.25) (See Ultimate Spider-Man for TPB)
1-The Ultimates & Spider-Man team-up; Bendis-s/Quesada & Hairsine-a; Cassaday-c 5.00
2-7-Hairsine-a; Cassaday-c 3.00

ULTIMATE SPIDER-MAN
Marvel Comics: Oct, 2000 - No. 133, June, 2009 ($2.99/$2.25/$2.99/$3.99)
1-Bendis-s/Bagley & Thibert-a; cardstock-c; introduces revised origin and cast separate from regular Spider-continuity 7 14 21 44 82 120
1-Variant white-c (Retailer incentive) 9 18 27 62 126 190
1-Dynamic Forces Edition 5 10 15 35 63 90
1-Kay Bee Toys variant edition 2 4 6 9 12 15

GD VG FN VF VF/NM NM-
2.0 4.0 6.0 8.0 9.0 9.2

2-Cover with Spider-Man on car 3 6 9 18 27 35
2-Cover with Spider-Man swinging past building 3 6 9 18 27 35
3,4: 4-Uncle Ben killed 2 4 6 10 14 18
5-7: 6,7-Green Goblin app. 2 4 6 9 12 15
8-13: 13-Reveals secret to MJ 1 3 4 6 8 10
14-21: 14-Intro. Gwen Stacy & Dr. Octopus 5.00
22-($3.50) Green Goblin returns 6.00
23-32 4.00
33-1st Ultimate Venom-c; intro. Eddie Brock 1 3 4 6 8 10
34-38-Ultimate Venom 6.00
39-49,51-59: 39-Nick Fury app. 43,44-X-Men app. 46-Prelude to Ultimate Six; Sandman app. 51-53-Elektra app. 54-59-Doctor Octopus app. 3.00
50-($2.99) Intro. Black Cat 4.00
60-Intro. Ultimate Carnage on cover 1 2 3 5 6 8
61-Intro Ben Reilly; Punisher app. 3.00
62-Gwen Stacy killed by Carnage 5.00
63-92: 63,64-Carnage app. 66,67-Wolverine app. 68,69-Johnny Storm app. 78-Begin $2.50-c. 79-Debut Moon Knight. 81-85-Black Cat app. 90-Vulture app. 91-94-Deadpool 3.00
93-99: 93-Begin $2.99-c. 95-Morbius & Blade app. 97-99-Clone Saga 3.00
100-($3.99) Wraparound-c; Clone Saga; re-cap of previous issues 4.00
101-103-Clone Saga continues; Fantastic Four app. 102-Spider-Woman origin 3.00
104-($3.99) Clone Saga concludes; Fantastic Four and Dr. Octopus app. 4.00
105-132: 106-110-Daredevil app. 111-Last Bagley art; Immonen-a (6 pgs.) 112-Immonen-a; Norman Osborn app. 118-Liz Allen ignites. 123,128-Venom app. 129-132-Ultimatum 3.00
133-($3.99) Ultimatum crossover; Spider-Woman app. 4.00
(Issues #150-up, see second series)
Annual 1 (10/05, $3.99) Kitty Pryde app.; Bendis-s/Brooks-a/Bagley-c 4.00
Annual 2 (10/06, $3.99) Punisher, Moon Knight and Daredevil app.; Bendis-s/Brooks-a 4.00
Annual 3 (12/08, $3.99) Mysterio app.; Bendis-s/Lafuente-a 4.00
Collected Edition (1/01, $3.99) r/#1-3 4.00
Free Comic Book Day giveaway (5/02) - r/#1 with "Free Comic Book Day" banner on-c 3.00
... MGC #1 (5/11, $1.00) r/#1 with "Marvel's Greatest Comics" logo on cover 3.00
...Special (7/02, $3.50) art by Bagley and various incl. Romita, Sr., Brereton, Cho, Mack, Sienkiewicz, Phillips, Pearson, Oeming, Mahfood, Russell 4.00
Ultimate Spider-Man 100 Project (2007, $10.00, SC, charity book for the HERO Initiative) collection of 100 variant covers by Romita Sr. & Jr., Cho, Bagley, Quesada and more 10.00
...: Venom HC (2007, $19.99) r/#33-39 20.00
...(Vol. 1): Power and Responsibility TPB (4/01, $14.95) r/#1-7 15.00
...(Vol. 2): Learning Curve TPB (12/01, $14.95) r/#8-13 15.00
...(Vol. 3): Double Trouble TPB (6/02, $17.95) r/#14-21 18.00
Vol. 4: Legacy TPB (2002, $14.99) r/#22-27 15.00
Vol. 5: Public Scrutiny TPB (2003, $11.99) r/#28-32 12.00
Vol. 6: Venom TPB (2003, $15.99) r/#33-39 16.00
Vol. 7: Irresponsible TPB (2003, $12.99) r/#40-45 13.00
Vol. 8: Cats & Kings TPB (2004, $17.99) r/#47-53 18.00
Vol. 9: Ultimate Six TPB (2004, $17.99) r/#46 & Ultimate Six #1-7 18.00
Vol. 10: Hollywood TPB (2004, $12.99) r/#54-59 13.00
Vol. 11: Carnage TPB (2004, $12.99) r/#60-65 13.00
Vol. 12: Superstars TPB (2005, $12.99) r/#66-71 13.00
Vol. 13: Hobgoblin TPB (2005, $15.99) r/#72-78 16.00
Vol. 14: Warriors TPB (2005, $17.99) r/#79-85 18.00
Vol. 15: Silver Sable TPB (2006, $15.99) r/#86-90 & Annual #1 16.00
Vol. 16: Deadpool TPB (2006, $19.99) r/#91-96 & Annual #2 20.00
Vol. 17: Clone Saga TPB (2007, $24.99) r/#97-105 25.00
Vol. 18: Ultimate Knights TPB (2007, $13.99) r/#106-111 14.00
Vol. 19: Death of a Goblin TPB (2008, $14.99) r/#112-117 15.00
Hardcover (3/02, $34.95, 7x11", dust jacket) r/#1-13 & Amazing Fantasy #15; sketch pages and Bill Jemas' initial plot and character outlines 35.00
Volume 2 HC (2003, $29.99, 7x11", dust jacket) r/#14-27; pin-ups & sketch pages 30.00
Volume 3 HC (2003, $29.99, 7x11", dust jacket) r/#28-39 & #1/2; script pages 30.00
Volume 4 HC (2004, $29.99, 7x11", dust jacket) r/#40-45, 47-53; sketch pages 30.00
Volume 5 HC (2004, $29.99, 7x11", dust jacket) r/#46,54-59, Ultimate Six #1-7 30.00
Volume 6 HC (2005, $29.99, 7x11", dust jacket) r/#60-71; sketch page 30.00
Volume 7 HC (2006, $29.99, 7x11", dust jacket) r/#72-85; sketch & profile pages 30.00
Volume 8 HC (2007, $29.99, 7x11", dust jacket) r/#86-96 & Annual #1&2; sketch page 30.00
Volume 9 HC (2008, $39.99, 7x11", dust jacket) r/#97-111; sketch pages 40.00
Volume 10 HC (2009, $39.99, 7x11", dust jacket) r/#112-122; sketch pages 40.00
Wizard #1/2 1 3 4 6 8 10

ULTIMATE SPIDER-MAN (2nd series)(Follows Ultimatum x-over)
Marvel Comics: Oct, 2009 - No. 15, Dec, 2010; No. 150, Jan, 2011 - No. 160, Aug, 2011 ($3.99)

1-15: 1-Bendis-s/Lafuente-a/c; new Mysterio. 1-Variant-c by Djurdjevic. 7,8-Miyazawa-a. 9-Spider-Woman app. 4.00
150-(1/11, $5.99) Resumes original numbering; wraparound-c by Lafuente; Bendis-s with art by Lafuente, Pichelli, Joëlle Jones, McKelvie & Young; r/Ult. S-M Special #1 6.00
150-Variant wraparound-c by Bagley 10.00
151-159: 151-154-Black Cat & Mysterio app. 157-Spider-Man shot by Punisher 4.00
153-159-Variant covers. 153-155-Pichelli. 157-McGuinness. 158-McNiven. 159-Cho 8.00
160-Black Polybagged; Bagley cover inside; Death of Spider-Man part 5 4.00
160-Red Polybagged variant; Kaluta cover inside; Death of Spider-Man part 5 20.00

ULTIMATE SPIDER-MAN (3rd series, with Miles Morales)(See Ultimate Fallout #4 for debut)
Marvel Comics: Nov, 2011 - No. 28, Dec, 2013 ($3.99)

1-Polybagged, with Kaare Andrews-c; Bendis-s/Pichelli-a; origin 10 20 30 64 132 200
1-Variant Pichelli-c with unmasked Spider-Man 17 34 51 117 259 400
1-Variant Pichelli-c with Spider-Man & city bkgrd 17 34 51 117 259 400
2 3 6 9 19 30 40
3-Spider-Woman app. 3 6 9 14 20 25
4-Spider-Woman app. 4 8 12 23 37 50
5-Origin of suit; Spider-Woman, Nick Fury & Ultimates app. 3 6 9 19 30 40
6-28: 6-Samnee-a. 19-22-Venom War; Pichelli-a. 23-Cloak and Dagger app. 28-Leads into Cataclysm 5.00
#16.1 (12/12, $2.99) Marquez-a; Venom returns 4.00
200-(6/14, $4.99) Art by Marquez and others; 2 interlocking covers by Bagley & Marquez 2 4 6 9 12 15
Ultimate Comics Spider-Man Must Have 1 (2/12, $4.99) r/#1-3 50.00

ULTIMATE SPIDER-MAN (Based on the animated series)(See Marvel Universe...)

ULTIMATE TALES FLIP MAGAZINE
Marvel Comics: July, 2005 - No. 26, Aug, 2007 ($3.99/$4.99)

1-11-Each reprints 2 issues of Ultimate Spider-Man in flip format 4.00
12-26-($4.99) 5.00

ULTIMATE THOR
Marvel Comics: Dec, 2010 - No. 4, Apr, 2011 ($3.99, limited series)

1-4: 1-Hickman-s/Pacheco-a; two covers by Pacheco & Choi; origin story 4.00

ULTIMATE VISION
Marvel Comics: No. 0, Jan, 2007 - No. 5, Jan, 2008 ($2.99, limited series)

0-Reprints back-up serial from Ultimate Extinction and related series; pin-ups 3.00
1-5: 1-(2/07) Carey-s/Peterson-a/c 3.00
TPB (2007, $14.99) r/#0-5; design pages and cover gallery 15.00

ULTIMATE WAR
Marvel Comics: Feb, 2003 - No. 4, Apr, 2003 ($2.25, limited series)

1-4-Millar-s/Bachalo-c/a; The Ultimates vs. Ultimate X-Men 3.00
Ultimate X-Men Vol. 5: Ultimate War TPB (2003, $10.99) r/#1-4 11.00

ULTIMATE WOLVERINE VS. HULK
Marvel Comics: Feb, 2006 - No. 6, July, 2009 ($2.99, limited series)

1,2-Leinil Yu-a/c; Damon Lindelof-s. 2-(4/06) 4.00
1,2-(2009) New printings 3.00
3-6: 3-(5/09) Intro. She-Hulk. 4-Origin She-Hulk 3.00

ULTIMATE X (Follows Ultimatum x-over)
Marvel Comics: Apr, 2010 - No. 5, Aug, 2011 ($3.99)

1-5: 1-Jeph Loeb-s/Art Adams-a; two covers by Adams. 5-Hulk app. 4.00

ULTIMATE X-MEN
Marvel Comics: Feb, 2001 - No. 100, Apr, 2009 ($2.99/$2.25/$2.50)

1-Millar-s/Adam Kubert & Thibert-a; cardstock-c; introduces revised origin and cast separate from regular X-Men continuity 3 6 9 14 19 24
1-DF Edition 3 6 9 15 22 28
1-DF Sketch Cover Edition 3 6 9 17 25 34
1-Free Comic Book Day Edition (7/03) r/#1 with "Free Comic Book Day" banner on-c 3.00
2 2 4 6 9 12 15
3-6 1 3 4 6 8 10
7-10 6.00
11-24,26-33: 13-Intro. Gambit. 18,19-Bachalo-a. 23,24-Andrews-a 4.00
25-($3.50) leads into the Ultimate War mini-series; Kubert-a 5.00
34-Spider-Man-c/app.; Bendis-s begin; Finch-a 5.00
35-74: 35-Spider-Man app. 36,37-Daredevil-c/app. 40-Intro. Angel. 42-Intro. Dazzler. 44-Beast dies. 46-Intro. Mr. Sinister. 50-53-Kubert-a; Gambit app. 54-57,59-63-Immonen-a. 60-Begin $2.50-c. 61-Variant Coipel-c. 66-Kirkman-s begin. 69-Begin $2.99-c 3.00
61-Retailer Edition with variant Coipel B&W sketch-c 10.00
75-($3.99) Turner-c; intro. Cable; back-up story with Emma Frost's students 4.00
76-99: 76-Intro. Bishop. 91-Fantastic Four app. 92-96-Phoenix app. 96-Spider-Man app. 99-Ultimatum x-over 3.00
100-($3.99) Ultimatum x-over; Brooks-a 4.00
Annual 1 (10/05, $3.99) Vaughan-s/Raney-a; Gambit & Rogue in Vegas 4.00
Annual 2 (10/06, $3.99) Kirkman-s/Larroca-a; Nightcrawler & Dazzler 4.00
.../Fantastic Four 1 (2/06, $2.99) Carey-s/Ferry-a; concluded in Ult. Fantastic Four/X-Men 3.00
... MGC #1 (6/11, $1.00) r/#1 with "Marvel's Greatest Comics" logo on cover 3.00
.../Ult. Fantastic Four Ann. 1 (11/08, $3.99) Continues in Ult. F.F./Ult. X-Men Annual #1 4.00
.../Fantastic Four TPB (2006, $12.99) reprints Ult X-Men/Ult. FF x-over and Official Handbook of the Ultimate Marvel Universe #1-2 13.00
... No. 1 Facsimile Edition (2/23, $3.99) r/#1 with original ads 4.00
... Ultimate Collection Vol. 1 (2006, $24.99) r/#1-12 & #1/2; unused Bendis script for #1 25.00
... Ultimate Collection Vol. 2 (2007, $24.99) r/#13-25; Kubert cover sketch pages 25.00
...: (Vol. 1) The Tomorrow People TPB (7/01, $14.95) r/#1-6 15.00
...: (Vol. 2) Return to Weapon X TPB (4/02, $14.95) r/#7-12 15.00
Vol. 3: World Tour TPB (2002, $17.99) r/#13-20 18.00
Vol. 4: Hellfire and Brimstone TPB (2003, $12.99) r/#21-25 13.00
Vol. 5 (See Ultimate War)
Vol. 6: Return of the King TPB (2003, $16.99) r/#26-33 17.00
Vol. 7: Blockbuster TPB (2004, $12.99) r/#34-39 13.00
Vol. 8: New Mutants TPB (2004, $12.99) r/#40-45 13.00
Vol. 9: The Tempest TPB (2004, $10.99) r/#46-49 11.00
Vol. 10: Cry Wolf TPB (2005, $8.99) r/#50-53 9.00
Vol. 11: The Most Dangerous Game TPB (2005, $9.99) r/#54-57 10.00
Vol. 12: Hard Lessons TPB (2005, $12.99) r/#58-60 & Annual #1 13.00
Vol. 13: Magnetic North TPB (2006, $12.99) r/#61-65 13.00
Vol. 14: Phoenix? TPB (2006, $14.99) r/#66-71 15.00
Vol. 15: Magical TPB (2007, $11.99) r/#72-74 & Annual #2 12.00
Vol. 16: Cable TPB (2007, $14.99) r/#75-80; sketch pages 15.00
Vol. 17: Sentinels TPB (2008, $17.99) r/#81-88 18.00
Volume 1 HC (8/02, $34.99, 7x11", dust jacket) r/#1-12 & Giant-Size X-Men #1; sketch pages and Millar and Bendis' initial plot and character outlines 35.00
Volume 2 HC (2003, $29.99, 7x11", dust jacket) r/#13-25; script for #20 30.00
Volume 3 HC (2003, $29.99, 7x11", dust jacket) r/#26-33 & Ultimate War #1-4 30.00
Volume 4 HC (2005, $29.99, 7x11", dust jacket) r/#34-45 30.00
Volume 5 HC (2006, $29.99, 7x11", dust jacket) r/#46-57; Vaughan intro.; sketch pages 30.00
Volume 6 HC (2006, $29.99, 7x11", dust jacket) r/#58-65, Annual #1 & Wizard #1/2 30.00
Volume 7 HC (2007, $29.99, 7x11", dust jacket) r/#66-74, Annual #2 30.00
Wizard #1/2 2 4 6 9 12 15

ULTIMATE X-MEN (Ultimate Comics X-Men) (See Cataclysm)
Marvel Comics: Nov, 2011 - No. 33, Dec, 2013 ($3.99)

1-Spencer-s/Medina-a/Andrews-c; polybagged 4.00
1-Variant-c by Mark Bagley 6.00
2-33: 2-Rogue returns. 6-Prof. X returns. 21-Iron Patriot app. 4.00
#18.1 (1/13, $2.99) Andrade-a/Pichelli-c 3.00
Ultimate Comics X-Men Must Have 1 (2/12, $4.99) r/#1-3 5.00

ULTIMATUM
Marvel Comics: Jan, 2009 - No. 5, July, 2009 ($3.99, limited series)

Ultimate Spider-Man V3 #1 © MAR

Ultimate X-Men #89 © MAR

Umbrella Academy: Dallas #6 © Gerald Way

	GD 2.0	VG 4.0	FN 6.0	VF 8.0	VF/NM 9.0	NM- 9.2

1-5-Loeb-s/Finch-a; cover by Finch & ; Ultimate heroes vs. Magneto 4.00
1-5-Variant covers by McGuinness 8.00
5-Double gatefold variant-c by Finch 4.00
March on Ultimatum Saga ('08, giveaway) text and art panel history of Ultimate universe 3.00
...: Fantastic Four Requiem 1 (9/09,$3.99) Pokaski-s/Atkins-a; Dr. Strange app. 4.00
...: Spider-Man Requiem 1,2 (8/09, 9/09,$3.99) Bendis-s/Bagley & Immonen-a 4.00
...: X-Men Requiem 1 (9/09,$3.99) Coleite-s/Oliver-a/Brooks-c 4.00
NOTE: *Numerous variant covers and 2nd & 3rd printings exist.*

ULTRA
Image Comics: Aug, 2004 - No. 8, Mar, 2005 ($2.95, limited series)
1-8: 1-Intro. Ultra/Pearl Penalosa; Luna Brothers-s/a 3.00
Vol. 1: Seven Days TPB (4/05, $17.95) r/#1-8; sketch pages 18.00

ULTRAFORCE (1st Series) (Also see Avengers/Ultraforce #1)
Malibu Comics (Ultraverse): Aug, 1994 - No. 10, Aug, 1995 ($1.95/$2.50)
0 (9/94, $2.50)-Perez-c/a. 4.00
1-($2.50, 44 pgs.)-Bound-in trading card; team consisting of Prime, Prototype, Hardcase, Pixx, Ghoul, Contrary & Topaz; Gerard Jones scripts begin, ends #6; Pérez-c/a begins 4.00
1-Ultra 5000 Limited Silver Foil Edition 1 2 3 5 6 8
1-Holographic-c, no price 1 2 3 6 8 10
2-5: Perez-c/a in all. 2 (10/94, $1.95)-Prime quits, Strangers cameo. 3-Origin of Topaz; Prime rejoins. 5-Pixx dies. 3.00
2 ($2.50)-Florescent logo; limited edition stamp on-c 4.00
6-10: 6-Begin $2.50-c, Perez-c/a. 7-Ghoul story, Steve Erwin-a. 8-Marvel's Black Knight enters the Ultraverse (last seen in Avengers #375); Perez-c/a. 9,10-Black Knight app.; Perez-c. 10-Leads into Ultraforce/Avengers Prelude 3.00
Malibu "Ashcan ": Ultraforce #0A (6/94) 3.00
.../Avengers Prelude 1 (8/95, $2.50)-Perez-c. 3.00
.../Avengers 1 (8/95, $3.95)-Warren Ellis script; Perez-c/a; foil-c 4.00

ULTRAFORCE (2nd Series)(Also see Black September)
Malibu Comics (Ultraverse): Infinity, Sept, 1995 - V2#15, Dec, 1996 ($1.50)
Infinity, V2#1-15: Infinity-Team consists of Marvel's Black Knight, Ghoul, Topaz, Prime & redesigned Prototype; Warren Ellis scripts begin, ends #3; variant-c exists. 1-1st app.Cromwell, Lament & Wreckage. 2-Contains free encore presentation of Ultraforce #1; flip book "Phoenix Resurrection" Pt. 7. 7-Darick Robertson, Jeff Johnson & others-a. 8,9-Intro. Future Ultraforce (Prime, Hellblade, Angel of Destruction, Painkiller & Whipslash); Gary Erskine-c/a. 9-Foxfire app. 10-Len Wein scripts & Deodato Studios-c/a begin. 10-Lament back-up story. 11-Ghoul back-up story by Pander Bros. 12-Ultraforce vs. Maxis (cont'd in Ultraverse Unlimited #2); Exiles & Iron Clad app. 13-Prime leaves; Hardcase returns 3.00
Infinity (2000 signed) 4.00
.../Spider-Man ($3.95)-Marv Wolfman script; Green Goblin app; 2 covers exist. 4.00

ULTRAGIRL
Marvel Comics: Nov, 1996 - No. 3 Mar, 1997 ($1.50, limited series)
1-1st app.; Barbara Kesel-s/Leonard Kirk-a 6.00
2,3-New Warriors app. 3.00

ULTRA KLUTZ
Onward Comics: 1981; 6/86 - #27, 1/89, #28, 4/90 - #31, 1990? ($1.50/$1.75/$2.00, B&W)
1 (1981)-Re-released after 2nd #1 3.00
1-30: 1-(6/86). 27-Photo back-c 3.00
31-($2.95, 52 pgs.) 4.00

ULTRAMAN (Also see The Rise of Ultraman and The Trials of Ultraman)
Nemesis Comics: Mar, 1994 - No. 4, Sept, 1994 ($1.75/$1.95)
1-($2.25)-Collector's edition; foil-c; special 3/4 wraparound-c 4.00
1-($1.75)-Newsstand edition 3.00
2-4: 3-$1.95-c begins 3.00
#(-1) (3/93) 3.00

ULTRAMAN: THE MYSTERY OF ULTRASEVEN
Marvel Comics: Oct, 2022 - No. 5, Mar, 2023 ($4.99/$3.99)
1-($4.99) Higgins & Groom-s; art by Tinto & Lopez; back-up with Gurihiru-a 5.00
2-5-($3.99): 3-Ultraman vs. Ultraseven 4.00

ULTRAMAN TIGA
Dark Horse Comics: Aug, 2003 - No. 10, June, 2004 ($3.99)
1-10-Khoo Fuk Lung-a/Tony Wong-s 4.00

ULTRAMEGA
Image Comics (Skybound): Mar, 2021 - Present ($7.99, squarebound)
1-4-James Harren-s/a 8.00

ULTRAVERSE DOUBLE FEATURE
Malibu Comics (Ultraverse): Jan, 1995 ($3.95, one-shot, 68 pgs.)
1-Flip-c featuring Prime & Solitaire. 4.00

ULTRAVERSE: FUTURE SHOCK
Malibu Comics (Ultraverse): Feb, 1997 ($2.50, one-shot)
1-Paniccia-s 3.00

ULTRAVERSE ORIGINS
Malibu Comics (Ultraverse): Jan, 1994 (99¢, one-shot)
1-Gatefold-c; 2 pg. origins all characters 3.00
1-Newsstand edition; different-c, no gatefold 3.00

ULTRAVERSE PREMIERE
Malibu Comics (Ultraverse): 1994 (one-shot)
0-Ordered thru mail w/coupons 5.00

ULTRAVERSE UNLIMITED
Malibu Comics (Ultraverse): June, 1996; No. 2, Sept, 1996 ($2.50)
1,2: 1-Adam Warlock returns to the Marvel Universe; Rune-c/app. 2-Black Knight, Reaper & Sierra Blaze return to the Marvel Universe 3.00

ULTRAVERSE YEAR ONE
Malibu Comics (Ultraverse): Sept, 1994 ($4.95, one-shot)
1-In-depth synopsis of the first year's titles & stories. 5.00

ULTRAVERSE YEAR TWO
Malibu Comics (Ultraverse): Aug, 1995 ($4.95, one-shot)
1-In-depth synopsis of second year's titles & stories 5.00

ULTRAVERSE YEAR ZERO: THE DEATH OF THE SQUAD
Malibu Comics (Ultraverse): Apr, 1995 - No. 4, July, 1995 ($2.95, lim. series)
1-4: 3-Codename: Firearm back-up story. 3.00

ULTRON (See Age of Ultron series)
Marvel Comics: Jun, 2013 ($3.99, one-shot)
1AU-Victor Mancha from the Runaways (son of Ultron); K. Immonen-s/Pinna-a 4.00

UMBRAL
Image Comics: Nov, 2013 - No. 12, Jan, 2015 ($2.99)
1-12-Johnston-s/Mitten-a 3.00

UMBRELLA ACADEMY (Also see Hazel & Cha Cha Save Christmas)
Dark Horse Comics: Apr, 2007
1-Free Comic Book Day Edition - previews of the upcoming series; James Jean-c; Zero Killer & Pantheon City on back-c 5 10 15 30 50 70

UMBRELLA ACADEMY: APOCALYPSE SUITE
Dark Horse Comics: Sept, 2007 - No. 6, Feb, 2008 ($2.99, limited series)
1-Origin of the Umbrella Academy; Gerald Way-s/Gabriel Bá-a/James Jean-c 4 8 12 27 44 60
1-White variant-c by Bá 5 10 15 34 60 85
1-Variant-c by Gerald Way 6 12 18 42 79 115
1-2nd printing with variant-c by Bá 1 3 4 6 8 10
2-6 2 4 6 8 10 12
...: One for One (9/10, $1.00) r/#1 with red cover frame 2 4 6 9 12 15
Vol.1: Apocalypse Suite TPB (7/08, $17.95) r/#1-6, FCBD story and web shorts; design art; Grant Morrison intro.; cover gallery 3 6 9 18 24 32

UMBRELLA ACADEMY: DALLAS
Dark Horse Comics: Nov, 2008 - No. 6, May, 2009 ($2.99, limited series)
1-6-Gerald Way-s/Gabriel Bá-a/c 2 4 6 8 10 12
1-Wraparound variant-c by Jim Lee 3 6 9 19 30 40

UMBRELLA ACADEMY: HOTEL OBLIVION
Dark Horse Comics: Oct, 2018 - No. 7, Jun, 2019 ($3.99, limited series)
1-Gerald Way-s/Gabriel Bá-a/c in all 1 3 4 6 8 10
2-7 4.00

UNBEATABLE SQUIRREL GIRL, THE
Marvel Comics: Mar, 2015 - No. 8, Oct, 2015 ($3.99)
1-Doreen Green and Tippy-Toe at college; North-s/Henderson-a; Kraven app. 2 4 6 9 12 15
2-8: 3,4-Galactus app. 7-Avengers cameo. 8-Lady Thor, Odinson & Loki app. 4.00

UNBEATABLE SQUIRREL GIRL, THE
Marvel Comics: Dec, 2015 - No. 50, Jan, 2020 ($3.99)
1-25,27-50: 1-North-s/Henderson-a. 2-Doreen goes to the 1960s; Doctor Doom app. 6-Crossover with Howard the Duck #6. 10-Mole Man app. 13,14-Scott Lang app. 16-25th Anniversary issue; origin re-told; Hulk app. 23-25-Dinosaur Ultron app. 43-46-War of the Realms tie-ins. 43-Intro. Ratatoskr. 48-50-Iron Man app. 4.00
26-"Zine" issue; includes Silver Surfer/Galactus by Garfield's Jim Davis (2 pgs.) 4.00
... Beats Up The Marvel Universe (2016, $24.99, HC) original graphic novel; North-s;

Henderson-a; Spider-Man & Avengers app.; bonus game pages and design art 25.00
...: You Choose the Story No. 1 Halloween Comic Fest 2016 (giveaway, 12/16) r/#7 3.00

UN-BEDABLE VARK, THE (Reprints from Cerebus in Hell)
Aardvark-Vanaheim: Jun, 2018 ($4.00, B&W)
1-Cerebus figures over original Gustave Doré artwork of Hell; Inc. Hulk #1-c swipe 4.00

UNBELIEVABLE GWENPOOL, THE (Also see Gwenpool Special)
Marvel Comics: Jun, 2016 - No. 25, Apr, 2018 ($3.99)
1-($4.99) Hastings-s/Gurihiru-a; MODOK app. 2 4 6 9 12 15
2-25-($3.99) 2-Thor (Jane) app. 3-Doctor Strange app. 5,6,19,20-Spider-Man (Miles) app. 13-Deadpool app. 14,15-Hawkeye & Ghost Rider app. 22,23-Doctor Doom app. 4.00
#0-(7/16, $4.99) Reprints apps. in Howard the Duck #1-3 & Gwenpool Special #1 2 4 6 9 12 15

UNBELIEVABLE UNTEENS, THE (From Black Hammer)
Dark Horse Comics: Aug, 2021 - No. 4, Nov, 2021 ($3.99)
1-4-Jeff Lemire-s/Tyler Crook-a; main cover by Crook; variant-c for each 4.00

UNBIRTHDAY PARTY WITH ALICE IN WONDERLAND (See Alice In Wonderland, Four Color #341)

UNBREAKABLE RED SONJA
Dynamite Entertainment: 2022 - Present ($3.99)
1-4: 1-Jim Zub-s/Giovanni Valletta-a 4.00

UNCANNY
Dynamite Entertainment: 2013 - No. 6, 2014 ($3.99)
1-6-Andy Diggle-s/Aaron Campbell-a 4.00

UNCANNY, (SEASON TWO)
Dynamite Entertainment: 2015 - No. 6, 2015 ($3.99)
1-6-Andy Diggle-s/Aaron Campbell-a 4.00

UNCANNY AVENGERS (Marvel NOW!)
Marvel Comics: Dec, 2012 - No. 25, Dec, 2014 ($3.99)
1-25: 1-Capt. America, Thor, Scarlet Witch, Wolverine, Havok & Rogue team; Remender-s/Cassaday-a; Red Skull app. 5-Coipel-a. 14-Rogue & Scarlet Witch die. 24,25-Axis 4.00
8AU-(7/13, $3.99) Age of Ultron tie-in; Adam Kubert-a 4.00
Annual 1 (6/14, $4.99) Remender-s/Renaud-a/Art Adams-c; Mojo app. 5.00

UNCANNY AVENGERS
Marvel Comics: Mar, 2015 - No. 5, Aug, 2015 ($3.99)
1-5: 1-Capt. America (Sam Wilson), Vision, Scarlet Witch, Quicksilver, Sabretooth, Rogue & Doctor Voodoo team; Remender-s/Acuna-a 4.00

UNCANNY AVENGERS
Marvel Comics: Dec, 2015 - No. 30, Feb, 2018 ($3.99)
1-($4.99) Steve Rogers, Spider-Man, Deadpool, Human Torch, Quicksilver, Rogue, Synapse & Doctor Voodoo team; Duggan-s/Stegman-a 5.00
2-20,26-30-($3.99) 2-5-Cable app. 5,6-Pacheco-a. 7,8-Pleasant Hill Standoff tie-ins. 13,14-Civil War II tie-in. 16,17-Hulk returns. 24-Secret Empire tie-in. 26-Scarlet Witch joins. 29-Juggernaut app. 4.00
25-($4.99) Secret Empire tie-in; Shocker & Scorpina app.; Zub-s/Jacinto-a 5.00
Annual 1 (1/16, $4.99) Robinson-s/Laming & Giles-a/Deodato-c; Emerald Warlock app. 5.00

UNCANNY AVENGERS: ULTRON FOREVER
Marvel Comics: Jul, 2015 ($4.99)(Continued from New Avengers: Ultron Forever)
1-Part 3 of 3-part crossover with Avengers and New Avengers; Ewing-s/Alan Davis-a; team-up of past, present and future Avengers vs. Ultron 5.00

UNCANNY INHUMANS
Marvel Comics: No. 0, Jun, 2015; No. 1, Dec, 2015 - No. 20, May, 2017 ($4.99/$3.99)
0-Soule-s/McNiven-a/c; Black Bolt, Medusa & Kang the Conqueror app. 5.00
1-($4.99) Johnny Storm, Beast & Kang the Conqueror app. 5.00
2-19-($3.99) 2-4-Kang app. 5-Mad Thinker and The Leader app. 11-14-Civil War II tie-in 4.00
20-($4.99) Leads into Inhumans Prime #1 5.00
#1.MU (4/17, $4.99) Monsters Unleashed tie-in; Allor-s/Level-a 5.00
Annual 1 (10/16, $4.99) Soule-s/Kev Walker-a 5.00

UNCANNY ORIGINS
Marvel Comics: Sept, 1996 - No. 14, Oct, 1997 (99¢)
1-14: 1-Cyclops. 2-Quicksilver. 3-Archangel. 4-Firelord. 5-Hulk. 6-Beast. 7-Venom. 8-Nightcrawler. 9-Storm. 10-Black Cat. 11-Black Knight. 12-Dr. Strange. 13-Daredevil. 14-Iron Fist 3.00

UNCANNY SKULLKICKERS (See Skullkickers #19)

UNCANNY TALES
Atlas Comics (PrPI/PPI): June, 1952 - No. 56, Sept, 1957
1-Heath-a; horror / weird stories begin 161 322 483 1030 1765 2500
2 77 154 231 493 847 1200
3-5 71 142 213 454 777 1100
6-Wolvertonish-a by Matt Fox 76 152 228 486 831 1175
7-10: 8-Atom bomb story; Tothish-a (by Sekowsky?). 9-Crandall-a 61 122 183 390 670 950
11-20: 17-Atom bomb panels; anti-communist story; Hitler story. 19-Krenkel-a. 20-Robert Q. Sale-c 53 106 159 334 567 800
21-25,27: 25-Nostrand-a? 47 94 141 296 498 700
26-Spider-Man prototype c/story 93 186 279 591 1021 1450
28-Last precode issue (1/55); Kubert-a; #1-28 contain 2-3 sci/fi stories each 47 94 141 296 498 700
29-41,43-49,51: 29-Variant-c exists with Feb. blanked out and Mar. printed on. Regular version just has Mar. 36 72 108 211 343 475
42,54,56-Krigstein-a 37 74 111 218 354 490
50,53,55-Torres-a 36 72 108 211 343 475
52-Oldest Iron Man prototype (2/57) 42 84 126 265 445 625
NOTE: ***Andru** a-15, 27. **Ayers** a-14, 22, 28, 37. **Bailey** a-51. **Briefer** a-19, 20. **Brodsky** c-1, 3, 4, 6, 8, 12-16, 19. **Brodsky/Everett** c-9. **Cameron** a-47. **Colan** a-11, 16, 17, 49, 52. **Drucker** a-37, 42, 45. **Everett** a-2, 9, 12, 32, 36, 39, 48; c-7, 11, 17, 39, 41, 50, 52, 53. **Fass** a-9, 10, 15, 24. **Forte** a-18, 27, 33-35, 52, 53. **Heath** a-13, 14; c-5, 10, 18. **Keller** a-3. **Lawrence** a-14, 17, 19, 23, 27, 28, 35. **Maneely** a-4, 8, 10, 16, 29, 35; c-2, 22, 26, 33, 38. **Moldoff** a-23. **Morisi** a-48, 52. **Morrow** a-46, 51. **Orlando** a-49, 50, 53. **Powell** a-12, 18, 34, 36, 38, 43, 50, 56. **Robinson** a-3, 13. **Reinman** a-12, 36. **Romita** a-10. **Roussos** a-8. **Sale** a-34, 47, 53; c-20. **Sekowsky** a-25. **Sinnott** a-14, 15, 38, 52. **Torres** a-53. **Tothish**-a by **Andru**-27. **Wildey** a-22, 48.*

UNCANNY TALES
Marvel Comics Group: Dec, 1973 - No. 12, Oct, 1975
1-Crandall-r/Uncanny Tales #9('50s) 5 10 15 30 50 70
2-12: 7,12-Kirby-a 3 6 9 18 28 38
NOTE: ***Ditko** reprints-#4, 6-8, 10-12.*

UNCANNY X-FORCE
Marvel Comics: Dec, 2010 - No. 35, Feb, 2013 ($3.99)
1-17: 1-Wolverine, Psylocke, Archangel, Fantomex & Deadpool team; Opeña-a; Ribic-c 4.00
1-Variant-c by Clayton Crain 10.00
5.1 (5/11, $2.99) Albuquerque-a/Bianchi-c; Lady Deathstrike app. 3.00
18-Polybagged; Dark Angel Saga conclusion 4.00
19-35: 19-Grampa-c. 20-Yu-c 4.00
19.1 (3/12, $2.99) Remender-s/Tan-a; other-dimension X-Men vs. Apocalypse 3.00
...: The Apocalypse Solution 1 (5/11, $4.99) r/#1-3 5.00

UNCANNY X-FORCE (Marvel NOW!)
Marvel Comics: Mar, 2013 - No. 17, Mar, 2014 ($3.99)
1-17: 1-Storm, Psylocke, Spiral, Fantomex & Puck team; Bishop app.; Garney-a 4.00

UNCANNY X-MEN, THE (See **X-Men, The**, 1st series, #142-on)

UNCANNY X-MEN (2nd series) (X-Men Regenesis)
Marvel Comics: Dec, 2010 - No. 20, Dec, 2012 ($3.99)
1-10: 1-3-Gillen-s/Pacheco-a/c; Mr. Sinister app. 4-Peterson-a. 5-8-Land-a 4.00
1-Variant-c by Keown 6.00
11-20: 11-19-Avengers vs. X-Men x-over 4.00

UNCANNY X-MEN (3rd series) (Marvel NOW!)
Marvel Comics: Apr, 2013 - No. 35, Sept, 2015 ($3.99)
1-24,26-35: 1-Cyclops, Emma Frost, Magneto, Magik team; Bendis-s/Bachalo-a. 2,3-Avengers app. 5-7,10,11-Irving-a. 8,9,12,13,16,17,19,20-22,25,27-32-Bachalo-a. 12,13-Battle of the Atom. 23,24-Original Sin tie-in 4.00
25-($4.99) Original Sin tie-in 5.00
#600-(1/16, $5.99) Stories by various incl. Bendis, Pichelli, Immonen; Bachalo-c 6.00
Annual 1 (2/15, $4.99) Story of Eva Bell; Bendis-s/Sorrentino-a 5.00
Special 1 (8/14, $4.99) Death's Head & Iron Man app.; Ackins-a 5.00

UNCANNY X-MEN (4th series) (After Secret Wars)
Marvel Comics: Mar, 2016 - No. 19, May, 2017 ($3.99)
1-5: 1-Bunn-s/Land-a; Magneto, Psylocke, Sabretooth, M, and Archangel team 4.00
6-($4.99) Apocalypse Wars x-over; Lashley-a 5.00
7-19: 7-10-Apocalypse Wars x-over; Lashley-a. 11-14-Land-a; Hellfire Club app. 4.00
Annual 1 (1/17, $4.99) Bunn-s/Lashley-a; Elixir returns 5.00

UNCANNY X-MEN (5th series)
Marvel Comics: Jan, 2019 - No. 22, Sept, 2019 ($7.99/$3.99)
1-($7.99) Asrar-a; Apocalypse app. 8.00
2-9,12-22-($3.99) 2-Silva-a; Legion returns. 4-Nate Grey returns. 12-16,20-22-Larroca-a 4.00
10-($4.99) Leads into Uncanny X-Men Annual #1 5.00
11-($7.99) Cyclops returns; Captain America app.; Wolverine returns; McCrea-a 8.00
22-($4.99) Leads into X-Men #1 (2019 series); Larrocca-a 5.00
Annual 1 (3/19, $4.99) Cyclops saved by Cable; leads into #11; Carlos Gomez-a 5.00
...: Winter's End 1 (5/19, $4.99) Grace-s/Stockman-a; future Iceman app. 5.00

UNCANNY X-MEN AND THE NEW TEEN TITANS (See Marvel and DC Present...)

UNCANNY X-MEN: FIRST CLASS
Marvel Comics: Sept, 2009 - No. 8, Apr, 2010 ($2.99)
1-8: 1-The X-Men #94 (1975) team; Cruz-a; Inhumans app. 3.00
... Giant-Size Special (8/09, $3.99) short stories by various; Scottie Young-c 4.00

UNCENSORED MOUSE, THE
Eternity Comics: Apr, 1989 - No. 2, Apr, 1989 ($1.95, B&W)(Came sealed in plastic bag) (Both contain racial stereotyping & violence)
1,2-Early Gottfredson strip-r in each 2 4 6 11 16 20
NOTE: *Both issues contain unauthorized reprints. Series was cancelled. **Win Smith** r-1, 2.*

UNCHARTED (Based on the video game)
DC Comics: Jan, 2012 - No. 6, Jun, 2012 ($2.99, limited series)
1-Williamson-s/Sandoval-a in all; Harris-c 4 8 12 25 40 55
2-6: 2,3-Harris-c 2 4 6 9 12 15

UNCLE CHARLIE'S FABLES (Also see Adventures in Wonderland)
Lev Gleason Publ.: Jan, 1952 - No. 5, Sept, 1952 (All have Biro painted-c)
1-Peter Pester by Hy Mankin begins, ends #5. Michael the Misfit by Kida, Janice & the Lazy Giant by Maurer, Lawrence the Fortune Teller app.; has photo of Biro 21 42 63 126 206 285
2-Fuje-a; Biro photo 14 28 42 76 108 140
3-5: 5-Two Who Built a Dream, The Blacksmith & The Gypsies by Maurer, The Sleepy King by Hubbel; has photo of Biro 11 22 33 64 90 115
NOTE: ***Kida** a-1. Hubbell a-5. **Hy Mankin** a-1-5. **Norman Maurer** a-1, 5. **Dick Rockwell** a-5.*

UNCLE DONALD & HIS NEPHEWS DUDE RANCH (See Dell Giant #52)

UNCLE DONALD & HIS NEPHEWS FAMILY FUN (See Dell Giant #38)

UNCLE GRANDPA (Based on the Cartoon Network series)
BOOM! Studios (kaboom!): Oct, 2014 - No. 4, Jan, 2015 ($3.99)
1-4-Short stories and gag pages; multiple covers on each 4.00
...: Good Morning Special 1 (4/16, $4.99) Short stories and gag pages; back-c mask 5.00
...: Pizza Steve Special 1 (6/15, $4.99) Short stories and gag pages 5.00

UNCLE JOE'S FUNNIES
Centaur Publications: 1938 (B&W)
1-Games, puzzles & magic tricks, some interior art; Bill Everett-c 258 516 774 1651 2826 4000

UNCLE MILTY (TV)
Victoria Publications/True Cross: Dec, 1950 - No. 4, July, 1951 (52 pgs.)(Early TV comic)
1-Milton Berle photo on-c of #1,2 58 116 174 371 636 900
2 39 78 117 231 378 525
3,4 32 64 96 188 307 425

UNCLE REMUS & HIS TALES OF BRER RABBIT (See Brer Rabbit, 4-Color #129, 208, 693)

Uncanny Avengers #13 © MAR

Uncharted #1 © Sony

Uncle Scrooge #391 © DIS

GD VG FN VF VF/NM NM-
2.0 4.0 6.0 8.0 9.0 9.2

GD VG FN VF VF/NM NM-
2.0 4.0 6.0 8.0 9.0 9.2

UNCLE SAM
DC Comics (Vertigo): 1997 - No. 2, 1997 ($4.95, limited series)
1,2-Alex Ross painted c/a. Story by Ross and Steve Darnell
1 2 3 5 6 8
Hardcover (1998, $17.95) 18.00
Softcover (2000, $9.95) 10.00

UNCLE SAM AND THE FREEDOM FIGHTERS
DC Comics: Sept, 2006 - No. 8, Apr, 2007 ($2.99, limited series)
1-8-Acuña-a/c; Gray & Palmiotti-s. 3-Intro. Black Condor 3.00
TPB (2007, $14.99) r/#1-8 and story from DCU Brave New World #1 15.00

UNCLE SAM AND THE FREEDOM FIGHTERS
DC Comics: Nov, 2007 - No. 8, Jun, 2008 ($2.99, limited series)
1-8-Gray & Palmiotti-s/Arlem-a/Johnson-c 3.00
...: Brave New World TPB (2008, $14.99) r/#1-8 15.00

UNCLE SAM QUARTERLY (Blackhawk #9 on)(See Freedom Fighters)
Quality Comics Group: Autumn, 1941 - No. 8, Autumn, 1943 (see National Comics)
1-Origin Uncle Sam; Fine/Eisner-c, chapter headings, 2 pgs. by Eisner;
(2 versions: dark cover, no price; light cover with price sticker); Jack Cole-a
377 754 1131 2639 4620 6600
2-Cameos by The Ray, Black Condor, Quicksilver, The Red Bee, Alias the Spider, Hercules
& Neon the Unknown; Eisner, Fine-c/a 164 328 492 1041 1796 2550
3-Tuska-c/a; Eisner-a(2) 129 258 387 826 1413 2000
4-Hitler app. 126 252 378 806 1378 1950
5,7-Hitler, Mussolini & Tojo-c 258 516 774 1651 2826 4000
6,8 84 168 252 538 919 1300
NOTE: *Kotzky (or Tuska) a-3-8.*

UNCLE SCROOGE (Disney) (Becomes Walt Disney's... #210 on) (See Cartoon Tales, Dell Giants #33, 55, Disney Comic Album, Donald and Scrooge, Dynabrite, Four Color #178, Gladstone Comic Album, Walt Disney's Comics & Stories #98, Walt Disney's ...)
Dell #1-39/Gold Key #40-173/Whitman #174-209: No. 386, 3/52 - No. 39, 8-10/62; No. 40, 12/62 - No. 209, 7/84
Four Color 386(#1)-in "Only a Poor Old Man" by Carl Barks; r-in Uncle Scrooge & Donald Duck #1('65) & The Best of Walt Disney Comics ('74). The 2nd cover app. of Uncle Scrooge (see Dell Giant Vacation Parade #2 (7/51) for 1st-c) 195 390 585 1600 4200 6800
1-(1986)-Reprints F.C. #386; given away with lithograph "Dam Disaster at Money Lake" & as a subscription offer giveaway to Gladstone subscribers
3 6 9 15 20 24
Four Color 456(#2)-in "Back to the Klondike" by Carl Barks; r-in Best of U.S. & D.D. #1('66)
& Gladstone C.A. #4 95 190 285 760 1955 3150
Four Color 495(#3)-r-in #105 60 120 180 480 1240 2000
4(12-2/53-54)-r-in Gladstone Comic Album #11 48 96 144 374 862 1350
5-r-in Gladstone Special #2 & Walt Disney Digest #1
38 76 114 285 641 1000
6-r-in U.S. #106,165,233 & Best of U.S. & D.D. #1('66)
36 72 108 259 580 900
7-The Seven Cities of Cibola by Barks; r-in #217 & Best of D.D. & U.S. #2 ('67)
32 64 96 230 515 800
8-10: 8-r-in #111,222. 9-r-in #104,214. 10-r-in #67 27 54 81 194 435 675
11-20: 11-r-in #237. 17-r-in #215. 19-r-in Gladstone C.A. #1. 20-r-in #213
23 46 69 161 356 550
21-30: 24-X-Mas-c. 26-r-in #211 16 32 48 112 249 385
31-35,37-40: 34-r-in #228. 40-X-Mas-c 13 26 39 91 201 310
36-1st app. Magica De Spell; Number one dime 1st identified by name
16 32 48 110 243 375
41-60: 48-Magica De Spell-c/story (3/64). 49-Sci/fi-c. 51-Beagle Boys-c/story
(8/64) 11 22 33 73 157 240
61-63,65,66,68-71:71-Last Barks issue w/original story (#71-he only storyboarded the script)
10 20 30 66 138 210
64-(7/66) Barks Vietnam War story "Treasure of Marco Polo" banned for reprints by Disney from 1977-1989 because of its Third World revolutionary war theme. It later appeared in the hardcover Carl Barks Library set (4/89) and Walt Disney's Uncle Scrooge Adventures #42
(1/97) 17 34 51 114 252 390
67,72,73: 67,72,73-Barks-r 9 18 27 60 120 180
74-84: 74-Barks-r(1pg.). 75-81,83-Not by Barks. 82,84-Barks-r begin
7 14 21 44 82 120
85-100 6 12 18 38 69 100
101-110 5 10 15 33 57 80
111-120 4 8 12 27 44 60
121-141,143-152,154-157 3 6 9 21 33 45
142-Reprints Four Color #456 with-c 4 8 12 22 35 48
153,158,162-164,166,168-170,178,180: No Barks 3 6 9 15 22 28
155-Whitman edition 3 6 9 17 26 35
159-160,165,167 3 6 9 16 23 30
161(r/#14), 171(r/#11), 177(r/#16),183(r/#6)-Barks-r 3 6 9 16 23 30
172(1/80),173(2/80)-Gold Key. Barks-a 3 6 9 17 26 35
174(3/80),175(4/80),176(5/80)-Whitman. Barks-a 4 8 12 22 35 48
177(6/80),178(7/80) 4 8 12 23 37 50
179(9/80)(r/#9)-(Very low distribution) 40 80 120 296 673 1050
180(11/80),181(12/80, r/4-Color #495), pre-pack? 8 16 24 51 96 140
182-195: 182-(50¢-c). 184,185,187,188-Barks-a. 182,186,191-194-No Barks. 189(r/#5),
190(r/#4), 195(r/4-Color #386) 3 6 9 16 23 30
182(1/81, 40¢-c) Cover price error variant 4 8 12 22 35 48
196(4/82),197(5/82): 196(r/#13) 3 6 9 17 26 35
198-209 (All #90038 on-c; pre-pack; no date or date code): 198(4/83), 199(5/83), 200(6/83), 201(6/83), 202(7/83), 203(7/83), 204(8/83), 205(8/83), 206(4/84), 207(5/83), 208(6/84), 209(7/84). 198-202,204-206: No Barks. 203(r/#12), 207(r/#93,92), 208(r/U.S. #18),
209(r/U.S. #21)-Barks-r 4 8 12 25 40 55
Uncle Scrooge & Money(G.K.)-Barks-r/from WDC&S #130 (3/67)
5 10 15 31 53 75
Mini Comic #1(1976)(3-1/4x6-1/2")-r/U.S. #115; Barks-c
2 4 6 8 10 12
NOTE: *Barks c-Four Color 386, 456, 495, #4-37, 39, 40, 43-71.*

UNCLE SCROOGE (See Walt Disney's Uncle Scrooge for previous issues)
Boom Entertainment (BOOM! Kids): No. 384, Oct, 2009 - No. 404, Jun, 2011 ($2.99/$3.99)
384-399: 384-Magica de Spell app.; 2 covers. 392-399-Duck Tales 3.00
400-(2/11, $3.99) "Carl Barks" apps. as Scrooge story-teller; Rosa wraparound-c 4.00
400-$6.99) Deluxe Edition with Barks painted cover of Four Color #386 cover image 7.00
401-404: 401-($3.99)-Rosa-s/a 4.00
...: The Mysterious Stone Ray and Cash Flow (5/11, $6.99) reprints; Barks-s/a; Rosa-s/a 7.00

UNCLE SCROOGE
IDW Publishing: Apr, 2015 - Present ($3.99/$4.99)
1-Legacy numbered #405; art by Scarpa and others; multiple covers 4.00
2-43-English translations of Dutch, Norwegian & Italian stories; multiple covers on each 4.00
44-49,51-54 ($4.99) 5.00
50-($5.99) Magica de Spell app. 6.00

UNCLE SCROOGE AND DONALD DUCK
Gold Key: June, 1965 (25¢, paper cover)
1-Reprint of Four Color #386(#1) & lead story from Four Color #29
9 18 27 57 111 165

UNCLE SCROOGE COMICS DIGEST
Gladstone Publishing: Dec, 1986 - No. 5, Aug, 1987 ($1.25, Digest-size)
1,3 1 2 3 5 6 8
2,4 6.00
5 (low print run) 1 2 3 5 7 9

UNCLE SCROOGE GOES TO DISNEYLAND (See Dell Giants)
Gladstone Publishing Ltd.: Aug, 1985 ($2.50)
1-Reprints Dell Giant w/new-c by Mel Crawford, based on old cover
2 4 6 8 10 12
...Comics Digest 1 ($1.50, digest size) 2 4 6 8 11 14

UNCLE SCROOGE IN COLOR
Gladstone Publishing: 1987 ($29.95, Hardcover, 9-1/4"X12-1/4", 96 pgs.)
nn-Reprints "Christmas on Bear Mountain" from Four Color 178 by Barks; Uncle Scrooge's Christmas Carol (published as Donald Duck & the Christmas Carol, A Little Golden Book), reproduced from the original art as adapted by Norman McGary from pencils by Barks; and Uncle Scrooge the Lemonade King, reproduced from the original art, plus Barks' original pencils 4 8 12 25 40 55
nn-Slipcase edition of 750, signed by Barks, issued at $79.95 350.00

UNCLE SCROOGE: MY FIRST MILLIONS
IDW Publishing: Sept, 2018 - No. 4, Dec, 2018 ($3.99, limited series)
1-4-English version of Italian comics; Vitaliano-s; multiple covers 4.00

UNCLE SCROOGE THE LEMONADE KING
Whitman Publishing Co.: 1960 (A Top Top Tales Book, 6-3/8"x7-5/8", 32 pgs.)
2465-Storybook pencilled by Carl Barks, finished art adapted by Norman McGary
33 66 99 238 532 825

UNCLE WIGGILY (See March of Comics #19) (Also see Animal Comics)
Dell Publishing Co.: No. 179, Dec, 1947 - No. 543, Mar, 1954
Four Color 179 (#1)-Walt Kelly-c 16 32 48 108 239 370
Four Color 221 (3/49)-Part Kelly-c 10 20 30 64 132 200
Four Color 276 (5/50), 320 (#1, 3/51) 7 14 21 49 92 135
Four Color 349 (9-10/51), 391 (4-5/52) 6 12 18 41 76 110
Four Color 428 (10/52), 503 (10/53), 543 5 10 15 34 63 90

UNDATEABLE VARK, THE (Reprints from Cerebus in Hell)
Aardvark-Vanaheim: May, 2018 ($4.00, B&W)

GD 2.0 | VG 4.0 | FN 6.0 | VF 8.0 | VF/NM 9.0 | NM- 9.2

1-Cerebus figures over Gustave Doré artwork of Hell; Uncanny X-Men #141-c swipe 4.00

UNDEAD, THE
Chaos! Comics (Black Label): Feb, 2002 ($4.99, B&W)

1-Pulido-s/Denham-a 5.00

UNDERCOVER GIRL (Starr Flagg) (See Extra Comics, Manhunt! & Trail Colt)
Magazine Enterprises: No. 5, 1952 - No. 7, 1954

5(#1)(A-1 #62)-Fallon of the F.B.I. in all 68 136 204 435 743 1050
6(A-1 #98), 7(A-1 #118)-All have Starr Flagg 60 120 180 381 653 925
NOTE: ***Powell*** *c-6, 7.* ***Whitney*** *a-5-7.*

UNDERDOG (TV)(See Kite Fun Book, March of Comics #426, 438, 467, 479)
Charlton Comics/Gold Key: July, 1970 - No. 10, Jan, 1972; Mar, 1975 - No. 23, Feb, 1979

1 (1st series, Charlton)-1st app. Underdog 21 42 63 147 324 500
2-10 6 12 18 38 69 100
1 (2nd series, Gold Key) 7 14 21 44 82 120
2-10 4 8 12 23 37 50
11-20: 13-1st app. Shack of Solitude 3 6 9 18 28 38
21-23 3 6 9 19 30 40

UNDERDOG
Spotlight Comics: 1987 - No. 3?, 1987 ($1.50)

1-3 4.00

UNDERDOG (Volume 2)
Harvey Comics: Nov, 1993 - No. 5, July, 1994 ($2.25)

1-5 4.00
Summer Special (10/93, $2.25, 68 pgs.) 4.00

UNDERDOG
American Mythology Productions: Apr, 2017 - No. 3, 2018 ($3.99)

1-3: 1-New stories and reprint #1 (1970); multiple covers incl. Action #1 swipe 4.00
...and Pals 1-3 (2019, $3.99) New stories and reprint; 2 covers on each 4.00
... 1975 #1 (2017, $3.99) Reprints stories from #23 (1979) and unpublished #24 4.00

UNDERSEA AGENT
Tower Comics: Jan, 1966 - No. 6, Mar, 1967 (25¢, 68 pgs.)

1-Davy Jones, Undersea Agent begins 8 16 24 56 108 160
2-6: 2-Jones gains magnetic powers. 5-Origin & 1st app. of Merman.
6-Kane/Wood-c(r) 5 10 15 35 63 90
NOTE: ***Gil Kane*** *a-3-6; c-4, 5.* ***Moldoff*** *a-2i.*

UNDERSEA FIGHTING COMMANDOS (See Fighting Undersea...)
I.W. Enterprises: 1964

I.W. Reprint #1,2('64): 1-r/#? 2-r/#1; Severin-c 2 4 6 11 16 20

UNDERTAKER (World Wrestling Federation)(Also see WWE Undertaker)
Chaos! Comics: Feb, 1999 - No. 10, Jan, 2000 ($2.50/$2.95)

Preview (2/99) 5.00
1-10: Reg. and photo covers for each. 1-(4/99) 4.00
1-($6.95) DF Ed.; Brereton painted-c 2 4 6 11 16 20
...Halloween Special (10/99, $2.95) Reg. & photo-c 1 3 4 6 8 10
Wizard #0 6.00

UNDERWATER CITY, THE
Dell Publishing Co.: No. 1328, 1961

Four Color 1328-Movie, Evans-a 7 14 21 49 92 135

UNDERWINTER
Image Comics: Mar, 2017 - No. 6, Aug, 2017 ($3.99)

1-6-Ray Fawkes-s/a/c. 1-Lemire var-c. 2-Nguyen var-c. 3-Zdarsky var-c 4.00

UNDERWINTER: A FIELD OF FEATHERS
Image Comics: Oct, 2017 - No. 5, Feb, 2018 ($3.99)

1-4-Ray Fawkes-s/a/c. 1-Fawkes var-c 4.00

UNDERWORLD (...True Crime Stories)
D. S. Publishing Co.: Feb-Mar, 1948 - No. 9, June-July, 1949 (52 pgs.)

1-Moldoff (Shelly)-c; excessive violence 60 120 180 381 653 925
2-Moldoff (Shelly)-c; Ma Barker story used in **SOTI**, pg. 95; female electrocution panel;
lingerie art 53 106 159 334 567 800
3-McWilliams-c/a; extreme violence, mutilation 47 94 141 296 498 700
4-Used in Love and Death by Legman; Ingels-a 52 104 156 328 552 775
5-Ingels-a 29 58 87 172 281 390
6-9: 8-Ravielli-a. 9-R.Q. Sale-a 22 44 66 132 216 300

UNDERWORLD
DC Comics: Dec, 1987 - No. 4, Mar, 1988 ($1.00, limited series, mature)

1-4 3.00

UNDERWORLD (Movie)
IDW Publishing: Sept, 2003; Dec, 2005 ($6.99)

1-Movie adaptation; photo-c 7.00
... Evolution (12/05, $7.49) adaptation of movie sequel; Vazquez-a 7.50
TPB (7/04, $19.99) r/#1 and Underworld:Red in Tooth and Claw #1-3 20.00

UNDERWORLD
Marvel Comics: Apr, 2006 - No. 5, Aug, 2006 ($2.99, limited series)

1-5: Staz Johnson-a. 2-Spider-Man app. 3,4-Punisher app. 3.00

UNDERWORLD CRIME
Fawcett Publications: June, 1952 - No. 7, Sept, 1953

1 39 78 117 240 395 550
2 24 48 72 142 234 325
3-6 21 42 63 126 206 285
7-(9/53)-Red hot poker/bondage/torture-c 649 1298 1947 4738 8369 12,000

UNDERWORLD: RED IN TOOTH AND CLAW (Movie)
IDW Publishing: Feb, 2004 - No. 3, Apr, 2004 ($3.99, limited series)

1-3-The early days of the Vampire and Lycan war; Postic & Marinkovich-a 5.00

UNDERWORLD: RISE OF THE LYCANS (Movie)
IDW Publishing: Nov, 2008 - No. 2, Nov, 2008 ($3.99, limited series)

1,2-Grevioux-s/Huerta-a 4.00

UNDERWORLD STORY, THE (Movie)
Avon Periodicals: 1950

nn-(Scarce)-Ravielli-c 39 78 117 240 395 550

UNDERWORLD UNLEASHED
DC Comics: Nov, 1995 - No. 3, Jan, 1996 ($2.95, limited series)

1-3: Mark Waid scripts & Howard Porter-c/a(p) 4.00
...: Abyss: Hell's Sentinel 1-($2.95)-Alan Scott, Phantom Stranger, Zatanna app. 3.00
...: Apokolips-Dark Uprising 1 ($1.95) 3.00
...: Batman-Devil's Asylum 1-($2.95)-Batman app. 3.00
...: Patterns of Fear-($2.95) 3.00
TPB (1998, $17.95) r/#1-3 & Abyss-Hell's Sentinel 18.00

UNDISCOVERED COUNTRY
Image Comics: Nov, 2019 - Present ($3.99)

1-23-Snyder & Soule-s/Camuncoli-a 4.00
...: Destiny Man 1 (6/22, $3.99) Snyder & Soule-s/Camuncoli-a 4.00

UNEARTH
Image Comics: Jul, 2019 - No. 10, Mar, 2021 ($3.99)

1-10-Bunn & Strahm-s/Rivas-a 4.00

UNEARTHLY SPECTACULARS
Harvey Publications: Oct, 1965 - No. 3, Mar, 1967

1-(12¢)-Tiger Boy; Simon-c 4 8 12 27 44 60
2-(25¢ giants)-Jack Q. Frost, Tiger Boy & Three Rocketeers app.; Williamson, Wood, Kane-a;
r-1 story/Thrill-O-Rama #2 5 10 15 30 50 70
3-(25¢ giants)-Jack Q. Frost app.; Williamson/Crandall-a; r-from Alarming Advs. #1,1962
5 10 15 30 50 70
NOTE: ***Crandall*** *a-3r.* ***G. Kane*** *a-2.* ***Orlando*** *a-3.* ***Simon, Sparling, Wood*** *c-2.* ***Simon/Kirby*** *a-3r.* ***Torres*** *a-1?.* ***Wildey*** *a-1(3).* ***Williamson*** *a-2, 3r.* ***Wood*** *a-2(2).*

UNETHICAL SPIDER-VARK, THE (Cerebus in Hell)
Aardvark-Vanaheim: Jul, 2021 ($4.00, B&W)

1-Cerebus figures placed over Gustave Doré artwork; Amaz. Spider-Man #129-c swipe 4.00

UNEXPECTED, THE (Formerly Tales of the...)
National Per. Publ./DC Comics: No. 105, Feb-Mar, 1968 - No. 222, May, 1982

105-Begin 12¢ cover price 6 12 18 41 76 110
106-113: 113-Last 12¢ issue (6-7/69) 5 10 15 31 53 75
114,115,117,118,120-125 4 8 12 22 35 48
116 (36 pgs.)-Wrightson-a 4 8 12 23 37 50
119-Wrightson-a, 8pgs.(36 pgs.) 5 10 15 31 53 75
126,127,129-136-(52 pgs.) 4 8 12 22 35 48
128(52 pgs.)-Wrightson-a 5 10 15 31 53 75
137-156 3 6 9 15 22 28
157-162-(100 pgs.) 4 8 12 28 47 65
163-188: 187,188-(44 pgs.) 2 4 6 11 16 20
189,190,192-195 ($1.00, 68 pgs.): 189 on are combined with House of Secrets
& The Witching Hour 2 4 6 13 18 22
191-Rogers-a(p) ($1.00, 68 pgs.) 3 6 9 14 19 24
196-222: 200-Return of Johhny Peril by Tuska. 205-213-Johnny Peril app.
210-Time Warp story. 222-Giffen-a 2 4 6 8 10 12
NOTE: ***Neal Adams*** *c-110, 112-115, 118, 121, 124.* ***J. Craig*** *a-195.* ***Ditko*** *a-189, 221p, 222p; c-222.* ***Drucker*** *a-107r, 132r.* ***Giffen*** *a-219, 222.* ***Kaluta*** *c-203, 212.* ***Kirby*** *a-127r, 162.* ***Kubert*** *c-204, 214-216, 219-221.* ***Mayer*** *a-217p, 220, 221p.* ***Moldoff*** *a-136r.* ***Moreira*** *a-133.* ***Mortimer*** *a-212p.* ***Newton*** *a-204p.* ***Orlando*** *a-202; c-191.* ***Perez*** *a-217p.* ***Redondo*** *a-155, 166, 195.* ***Reese*** *a-145.* ***Sparling*** *a-107, 205-209p, 212p.* ***Spiegle*** *a-217.* ***Starlin*** *c-198.* ***Toth*** *a-126r, 127r.* ***Tuska*** *a-127, 132, 134, 136, 139, 152, 180, 200p.* ***Wildey*** *a-128r, 193.* ***Wood*** *a-122i, 133i, 137i, 138i.* ***Wrightson*** *a-161r(2 pgs.). Johnny Peril in #106-114, 116, 117, 200, 205-213.*

UNEXPECTED, THE
DC Comics: Dec, 2011 ($7.99, one-shot)

1-Short horror stories by various incl. Gibbons, Thompson, Lapham, Fialkov; 2 covers 8.00

UNEXPECTED, THE (Follows events of Dark Nights: Metal)
DC Comics: Aug, 2018 - No. 8, Mar, 2019 ($2.99)

1-8: 1-Orlando-s/Sook & Nord-a; intro. Firebrand, Bad Samaritan & Neon the Unknown.
4-Huntress app. 4-8-Hawkman app. 3.00

UNEXPECTED ANNUAL, THE (See DC Special Series #4)

UNFOLLOW
DC Comics (Vertigo): Jan, 2016 - No 18, Jun, 2017 ($3.99)

1-18: 1-Rob Williams-s/Mike Dowling-a. 6-R.M. Guéra-a. 7-Marguerite Sauvage-a 4.00
... Special Edition 1 (3/16, $4.99) r/#1&2 5.00

UNHOLY BASTARDS (Characters from The Goon)
Albatross Funnybooks: 2020 ($3.99, one-shot)

1-Eric Powell-c/Sniegoski-s/Mannion & Brown-a; The Goon and Franky app. 4.00

UNHOLY GRAIL
AfterShock Comics: July, 2017 - No. 5, Dec, 2017 ($3.99)

1-5-Cullen Bunn-s/Mirko Colak-a. 1-Multiple covers. 2-Covers by Colak & Francavillla 4.00

UNHOLY UNION
Image Comics (Top Cow): July, 2007 ($3.99, one-shot)

1-Witchblade & The Darkness meet Hulk, Ghost Rider & Doctor Strange; Silvestri-c
1 3 4 6 8 10

UNIDENTIFIED FLYING ODDBALL (See Walt Disney Showcase #52)

UNION
Image Comics (WildStorm Productions): June, 1993 - No. 0, July, 1994 ($1.95, lim. series)

0-(7/94, $2.50) 3.00
0-Alternate Portacio-c (See Deathblow #5) 5.00
1-($2.50)-Embossed foil-c; Texeira-c/a in all 4.00
1-($1.95)-Newsstand edition w/o foil-c 3.00
2-4: 4-(7/94) 3.00

UNION
Image Comics (WildStorm Prod.): Feb, 1995 - No. 9, Dec, 1995 ($2.50)

1-3,5-9: 3-Savage Dragon app. 6-Fairchild from Gen 13 app. 3.00
4-($1.95, Newsstand)-WildStorm Rising Pt. 3 3.00

Underworld (2006) #2 © MAR

United States of Captain America #1 © MAR

Unknown Soldier #216 © DC

	GD 2.0	VG 4.0	FN 6.0	VF 8.0	VF/NM 9.0	NM- 9.2

4-($2.50, Direct Market)-WildStorm Rising Pt. 3, bound-in card 3.00

UNION, THE (Tie-in series to The King in Black crossover event)
Marvel Comics: Feb, 2021 - No. 5, Jul, 2021 ($3.99)
1-5-Grist-s/Di Vito-a; team of Britannia, Snakes, Kelpie and The Choir; Union Jack app. 4.00

UNION: FINAL VENGEANCE
Image Comics (WildStorm Productions): Oct, 1997 ($2.50)
1-Golden-c/Heisler-s 3.00

UNION JACK
Marvel Comics: Dec, 1998 - No. 3, Feb, 1999 ($2.99, limited series)
1-3-Raab-s/Cassaday-s/a 3.00

UNION JACK
Marvel Comics: Nov, 2006 - No. 4, Feb, 2007 ($2.99, limited series)
1-4-Gage-s/Perkins-c/a 3.00
...: London Falling TPB (2007, $10.99) r/#1-4; Perkins sketch page 11.00

UNITED COMICS (Formerly Fritzi Ritz #7; has Fritzi Ritz logo)
United Features Syndicate: Aug, 1940; No. 8, 1950 - No. 26, Jan-Feb, 1953

	GD 2.0	VG 4.0	FN 6.0	VF 8.0	VF/NM 9.0	NM- 9.2
1(68 pgs.)-Fritzi Ritz & Phil Fumble	34	68	102	204	332	460
8-Fritzi Ritz, Abbie & Slats	15	30	45	86	133	180
9-20: 20-Strange As It Seems; Russell Patterson Cheesecake-a	14	28	42	78	112	145
21-(3-4/52) 2 pg. early Peanuts by Schulz; ties with Tip Top Comics #173 for 1st app. of Peanuts in comics. (Also see Tip Topper Comics)	314	628	942	2198	3849	5500
22-(5-6/52) 2 pgs. early Peanuts by Schulz (3rd app.)	54	108	162	343	574	825
23-26: 23-(7-8/52). 24-(9-10/52). 25-(11-12/52). 26-(1-2/53). All have 2 pgs. early Peanuts by Schulz	32	64	96	188	307	425

NOTE: *Abbie & Slats reprinted from Tip Top.*

UNITED NATIONS, THE (See Classics Illustrated Special Issue)

UNITED STATES AIR FORCE PRESENTS: THE HIDDEN CREW
U.S. Air Force: 1964 (36 pgs.)

	GD 2.0	VG 4.0	FN 6.0	VF 8.0	VF/NM 9.0	NM- 9.2
nn-Schaffenberger-a	3	6	9	14	20	25

UNITED STATES FIGHTING AIR FORCE (Also see U.S. Fighting Air Force)
Superior Comics Ltd.: Sept, 1952 - No. 29, Oct, 1956

	GD 2.0	VG 4.0	FN 6.0	VF 8.0	VF/NM 9.0	NM- 9.2
1	20	40	60	115	185	255
2	13	26	39	72	101	130
3-10	10	20	30	56	76	95
11-29	9	18	27	52	69	85

UNITED STATES MARINES
William H. Wise/Life's Romances Publ. Co./Magazine Ent. #5-8/Toby Press #7-11: 1943 - No. 4, 1944; No. 5, 1952 - No. 8, 1952; No. 7 - No. 11, 1953

	GD 2.0	VG 4.0	FN 6.0	VF 8.0	VF/NM 9.0	NM- 9.2
nn-Mart Bailey-c/a; Marines in the Pacific theater	41	82	123	256	428	600
2-Bailey-a; Tojo classic-c	142	284	426	909	1555	2200
3-Classic WWII Tojo-c	135	270	405	864	1482	2100
4-WWII photos; Tony DiPreta-a; grey-tone-c	26	52	78	154	252	350
5(A-1 #55)-Bailey-a, 6(A-1 #60), 8(A-1 #72)	15	30	45	90	140	190
7(A-1 #68) Flamethrower with burning bodies-c	232	464	696	1485	2543	3600
7-11 (Toby)	15	30	45	85	130	175

NOTE: ***Powell** a-5-7.*

UNITED STATES OF CAPTAIN AMERICA, THE
Marvel Comics: Aug, 2021 - No. 5, Dec, 2021 ($4.99)
1-5: 1-1st app. Aaron Fischer. 2-Intro. Nichelle Wright. 3-Intro. Joe Gomez 5.00

UNITED STATES OF MURDER INC., THE
Marvel Comics (Icon): May, 2014 - No. 6, Feb, 2015 ($3.99)
1-6-Bendis-s/Oeming-a 4.00

UNITED STATES OF MURDER INC.
DC Comics (Jinxworld): Nov, 2018 - No. 6, Apr, 2019 ($3.99)
1-6-Bendis-s/Oeming-a; second story arc 4.00

UNITY
Valiant: No. 0, Aug, 1992 - No. 1, 1992 (Free comics w/limited dist., 20 pgs.)

	GD 2.0	VG 4.0	FN 6.0	VF 8.0	VF/NM 9.0	NM- 9.2
0 (Blue)-Prequel to Unity x-overs in all Valiant titles; B. Smith-c/a. (Free to everyone that bought all 8 titles that month.)	1	3	4	6	8	10
0 (Red)-Same as above, but w/red logo (5,000)	5	10	15	30	50	70
1-Epilogue to Unity x-overs; B. Smith-c/a. (1 copy available for every 8 Valiant books ordered by dealers.)						5.00
1 (Gold), 1-(Platinum)-Promotional copy.	2	4	6	9	12	15
... : The Lost Chapter 1 (Yearbook) (2/95, $3.95)-"1994" in indicia						6.00

UNITY
Valiant Entertainment: Nov, 2013 - No. 25, Dec, 2015 ($3.99)
1-24: Multiple covers on each. 1-Kindt-s/Braithwaite-a. 5,6-Cafu-a 4.00
25-($4.99) Short stories by various incl. Kindt, Asmus, Kano, Jordan, Schkade 5.00
#0 (10/14, $3.99) Kindt-s/Nord-a; the story of Unit Y in WW One 4.00

UNITY 2000 (See preludes in Shadowman #3,4 flipbooks)
Acclaim Comics: Nov, 1999 - No. 3, Jan, 2000 ($2.50, unfinished limited series planned for 6 issues)
Preview -B&W plot preview and cover art; paper cover 3.00
1-3-Starlin-a/Shooter-s 3.00

UNIVERSAL MONSTERS
Dark Horse Comics: 1993 ($4.95/$5.95, 52 pgs.)(All adapt original movies)

	GD 2.0	VG 4.0	FN 6.0	VF 8.0	VF/NM 9.0	NM- 9.2
Creature From the Black Lagoon nn-($4.95)-Art Adams/Austin-c/a	2	4	6	9	12	15
Dracula nn-($4.95), Frankenstein nn-($3.95)-Painted-c/a, The Mummy nn-($4.95)-Painted-c	1	2	3	4	5	7
...: Cavalcade of Horror TPB (1/06, $19.95) r/one-shots; Eric Powell intro. & cover						20.00

UNIVERSAL PICTURES PRESENTS DRACULA-THE MUMMY& OTHER STORIES
Dell Publishing Co.: Sept-Nov, 1963 (one-shot, 84 pgs.) (Also see Dell Giants)

	GD 2.0	VG 4.0	FN 6.0	VF 8.0	VF/NM 9.0	NM- 9.2
02-530-311-r/Dracula 12-231-212, The Mummy 12-437-211 & part of Ghost Stories No. 1	16	32	48	108	239	370

UNIVERSAL SOLDIER (Movie)
Now Comics: Sept, 1992 - No. 3, Nov, 1992 (Limited series, polybagged, mature)
1-3 ($2.50, Direct Sales) 1-Movie adapatation; hologram on-c (all direct sales editions have painted-c) 4.00
1-3 ($1.95, Newsstand)-Rewritten & redrawn code approved version; all newsstand editions have photo-c 3.00

UNIVERSE
Image Comics (Top Cow): Sept, 2001 - No. 8, July, 2002 ($2.50)
1-7-Jenkins-s 3.00
8-($4.95) extra short-s by Jenkins; pin-up pages 5.00

UNIVERSE X (See Earth X)
Marvel Comics: Sept, 2000 - No. 12, Sept, 2001 ($3.99/$3.50, limited series)
0-Ross-c/Braithwaite-a/Ross & Krueger-s 4.00
1-12: 5-Funeral of Captain America 4.00
... Beasts (6/00, $3.99) Yeates-a/Ross-c 4.00
... Cap (Capt. America) (2/01, $3.99) Yeates & Totleben-a/Ross-c; Cap dies 4.00
... 4 (Fantastic 4) (10/00, $3.99) Brent Anderson-a/Ross-c 4.00
... Iron Men (9/01, $3.99) Anderson-a/Ross-c; leads into #12 4.00
... Omnibus (6/01, $3.99) Ross B&W sketchbook and character bios 4.00
Sketchbook- Wizard supplement; B&W character sketches and bios 3.00
...Spidey (1/01, $3.99) Romita Sr. flashback-a/Guice-a/Ross-c 4.00
...X (11/01, $3.99) Series conclusion; Braithwaith-a/Ross wraparound-c 4.00
Volume 1 TPB (1/02, $24.95) r/#0-7 & Spidey, 4, & Cap; new Ross-c 25.00
Volume 2 TPB (6/02, $24.95) r/#8-12 &X, Beasts, Iron Men and Omnibus 25.00

UNKINDNESS OF RAVENS, AN
BOOM! Studios: Sept, 2020 - No. 5, Jan, 2021 ($3.99, limited series)
1-5-Dan Panosian-s/Marianna Ignazzi-a 4.00

UNKNOWN, THE
BOOM! Studios: May, 2009 - No. 4, Aug, 2009 ($3.99)
1-4-Mark Waid-s/Minck Oosterveer-a; two covers on each 4.00
...: The Devil Made Flesh 1-4 (9/09 - No. 4, 12/09, $3.99) Waid-s/Oosterveer-a 4.00

UNKNOWN MAN, THE (Movie)
Avon Periodicals: 1951

	GD 2.0	VG 4.0	FN 6.0	VF 8.0	VF/NM 9.0	NM- 9.2
nn-Kinstler-c	39	78	117	240	395	550

UNKNOWN SOLDIER (Formerly Star-Spangled War Stories)
National Periodical Publications/DC Comics: No. 205, Apr-May, 1977 - No. 268, Oct, 1982 (See Our Army at War #168 for 1st app.)

	GD 2.0	VG 4.0	FN 6.0	VF 8.0	VF/NM 9.0	NM- 9.2
205	3	6	9	17	26	35
206-210,220,221,251: 220,221 (44pgs.). 251-Enemy Ace begins	3	6	9	14	19	24
211-218,222-247,250,252-264	2	4	6	11	16	20
219-Miller-a (44 pgs.)	3	6	9	16	23	30
248,249,265-267: 248,249-Origin. 265-267-Enemy Ace vs. Balloon Buster.	2	4	6	11	16	20
268-Death of Unknown Soldier	3	6	9	19	30	40

NOTE: ***Chaykin** a-234. **Evans** a-265-267; c-235. **Kubert** c-Most. **Miller** a-219p. **Severin** a-251-253, 260, 261, 265-267. **Simonson** a-254-256. **Spiegle** a-258, 259, 262-264.*

UNKNOWN SOLDIER, THE (Also see Brave &the Bold #146)
DC Comics: Winter, 1988-'89 - No. 12, Dec, 1989 ($1.50, maxi-series, mature)
1-12: 8-Begin $1.75-c 5.00

UNKNOWN SOLDIER
DC Comics (Vertigo): Apr, 1997 - No 4, July, 1997 ($2.50, mini-series)

	GD 2.0	VG 4.0	FN 6.0	VF 8.0	VF/NM 9.0	NM- 9.2
1-Ennis-s/Plunkett-a/Bradstreet-c in all						6.00
2-4						4.00
TPB (1998, $12.95) r/#1-4						13.00

UNKNOWN SOLDIER
DC Comics (Vertigo): Dec, 2008 - No. 25, Dec, 2010 ($2.99)

	GD 2.0	VG 4.0	FN 6.0	VF 8.0	VF/NM 9.0	NM- 9.2
1-25: 1-Dysart-s/Ponticelli-a; intro. Lwanga Moses; two covers by Kordey and Corben. 2-20,22-25-Ponticelli-a. 21-Veitch-a						3.00
...: Beautiful World TPB (2011, $14.99) r/#21-25; Dysart afterword; sketch/design art						15.00
...: Dry Season TPB (2010, $14.99) r/#15-20; war history						15.00
...: Easy Kill TPB (2010, $17.99) r/#7-14; war history						18.00
...: Haunted House TPB (2009, $9.99) r/#1-6; glossary						10.00

UNKNOWN WORLD (Strange Stories From Another World #2 on)
Fawcett Publications: June, 1952

	GD 2.0	VG 4.0	FN 6.0	VF 8.0	VF/NM 9.0	NM- 9.2
1-Norman Saunders painted-c	135	270	405	864	1482	2100

UNKNOWN WORLDS (See Journey Into...)

UNKNOWN WORLDS
American Comics Group/Best Synd. Features: Aug, 1960 - No. 57, Aug, 1967

	GD 2.0	VG 4.0	FN 6.0	VF 8.0	VF/NM 9.0	NM- 9.2
1-Schaffenberger-c	26	52	78	182	404	625
2-Dinosaur-c/story	11	22	33	75	160	245
3-5	9	18	27	58	114	170
6-11: 9-Dinosaur-c/story. 11-Last 10¢ issue	7	14	21	49	92	135
12-19: 12-Begin 12¢ issues?; ends #57	6	12	18	38	69	100
20-Herbie cameo (12-1/62-63)	7	14	21	48	89	130
21-35: 27-Devil on-c. 31-Herbie one pagers thru #39	5	10	15	30	50	70
36- "The People vs. Hendricks" by Craig; most popular ACG story ever	5	10	15	35	63	90
37-46	4	8	12	28	47	65
47-Williamson-a r-from Adventures Into the Unknown #96, 3 pgs.; Craig-a	5	10	15	30	50	70
48-57: 53-Frankenstein app.	4	8	12	27	44	60

NOTE: ***Ditko** a-49, 50p, 54. **Forte** a-3, 6, 11. **Landau** a-56(2). **Reinman** a-3, 9, 13, 20, 22, 23, 36, 38, 54. **Whitney** c/a-most issues. John Force, Magic Agent app.-35, 36, 48, 50, 52, 54, 56.*

UNKNOWN WORLDS OF FRANK BRUNNER
Eclipse Comics: Aug, 1985 - No. 2, Aug, 1985 ($1.75)

	GD 2.0	VG 4.0	FN 6.0	VF 8.0	VF/NM 9.0	NM- 9.2
1,2-B&W-r in color						4.00

UNKNOWN WORLDS OF SCIENCE FICTION
Marvel Comics: Jan, 1975 - No. 6, Nov, 1975; 1976 ($1.00, B&W Magazine)

	GD 2.0	VG 4.0	FN 6.0	VF 8.0	VF/NM 9.0	NM- 9.2
1-Williamson/Krenkel/Torres/Frazetta-r/Witzend #1, Neal Adams-r/Phase 1; Brunner & Kaluta-r; Freas/Romita-c	3	6	9	19	30	40
2-6: 5-Kaluta text illos	3	6	9	14	20	26
Special 1(1976,100 pgs.)-Newton painted-c	3	6	9	17	25	34

NOTE: ***Brunner** a-2; c-4, 6. **Buscema** a-Special 1p. **Chaykin** a-5. **Colan** a(p)-1, 3, 5, 6. **Corben** a-4. **Kaluta** a-2, Special 1(ext illos); c-2. **Morrow** a-3, 5. **Nino** a-3, 6, Special 1. **Perez** a-2, 3. Ray Bradbury interview in #1.*

UNLIMITED ACCESS (Also see Marvel Vs. DC))
Marvel Comics: Dec, 1997 - No. 4, Mar, 1998 ($2.99/$1.99, limited series)

	GD 2.0	VG 4.0	FN 6.0	VF 8.0	VF/NM 9.0	NM- 9.2
1-Spider-Man, Wonder Woman, Green Lantern & Hulk app.						4.00
2,3-($1.99): 2-X-Men, Legion of Super-Heroes app. 3-Original Avengers vs. original Justice League						3.00
4-($2.99) Amalgam Legion vs. Darkseid & Magneto						4.00

UN-MEN, THE
DC Comics (Vertigo): Oct, 2007 - No. 13, Oct, 2008 ($2.99)

	GD 2.0	VG 4.0	FN 6.0	VF 8.0	VF/NM 9.0	NM- 9.2
1-13-Whalen-s/Hawthorne-a/Hanuka-c						3.00
...: Children of Paradox TPB (2008, $19.99) r/#6-13						20.00
...: Get Your Freak On! TPB (2008, $9.99) r/#1-5; cover gallery						10.00

UNNATURAL
Image Comics: Jul, 2018 - No. 12, Aug, 2019 ($3.99)

	GD 2.0	VG 4.0	FN 6.0	VF 8.0	VF/NM 9.0	NM- 9.2
1-12-Mirka Andolfo-s/a; English version of a 2016 Italian comic series						4.00

UNNATURAL: BLUE BLOOD
Image Comics: May, 2022 - Present ($3.99)

	GD 2.0	VG 4.0	FN 6.0	VF 8.0	VF/NM 9.0	NM- 9.2
1-5-Mirka Andolfo-s/a; Bidarella-a						4.00

UN/SACRED
Ablaze Publishing: 2019 - No. 7, 2020 ($3.99)

	GD 2.0	VG 4.0	FN 6.0	VF 8.0	VF/NM 9.0	NM- 9.2
1-7-Mirka Andolfo-s/a; multiple covers on each						4.00
Vol. 2 (2020 - No. 6, 2021) 1-6-Mirka Andolfo-s/a						4.00

UNSANE (Formerly Mighty Bear #13, 14? or The Outlaws #10-14?)(Satire)
Star Publications: No. 15, June, 1954

	GD 2.0	VG 4.0	FN 6.0	VF 8.0	VF/NM 9.0	NM- 9.2
15-Disbrow-a(2); L. B. Cole-c	40	80	120	246	411	575

UNSEEN, THE
Visual Editions/Standard Comics: No. 5, 1952 - No. 15, July, 1954

	GD 2.0	VG 4.0	FN 6.0	VF 8.0	VF/NM 9.0	NM- 9.2
5-Horror stories in all; Toth-a	71	142	213	454	777	1100
6,7,9,10-Jack Katz-a	50	100	150	315	533	750
8,11,13,14	43	86	129	271	461	650
12,15-Toth-a. 12-Tuska-a	54	108	162	343	574	825

NOTE: ***Nick Cardy** c-12. **Fawcette** a-13, 14. **Sekowsky** a-7, 8(2), 10, 13, 15.*

UNSTOPPABLE WASP, THE
Marvel Comics: Mar, 2017 - No. 8, Oct, 2017 ($3.99)

	GD 2.0	VG 4.0	FN 6.0	VF 8.0	VF/NM 9.0	NM- 9.2
1-8: 1-6-Whitley-s/Charretier-a. 1-Ms. Marvel & Mockingbird app. 2,3-Moon Girl app.						4.00

UNSTOPPABLE WASP, THE
Marvel Comics: Dec, 2018 - No. 10, Sept, 2019 ($3.99)

	GD 2.0	VG 4.0	FN 6.0	VF 8.0	VF/NM 9.0	NM- 9.2
1-10: Whitley-s. 1-5,8-10-Gurihiru-a. 7-Winter Soldier and Young Avengers app.						4.00

UNTAMED
Marvel Comics (Epic Comics/Heavy Hitters): June, 1993 - No. 3, Aug, 1993 ($1.95, lim. series)

	GD 2.0	VG 4.0	FN 6.0	VF 8.0	VF/NM 9.0	NM- 9.2
1-($2.50)-Embossed-c						4.00
2,3						3.00

UNTAMED LOVE (Also see Frank Frazetta's Untamed Love)
Quality Comics Group (Comic Magazines): Jan, 1950 - No. 5, Sept, 1950

	GD 2.0	VG 4.0	FN 6.0	VF 8.0	VF/NM 9.0	NM- 9.2
1-Ward-c, Gustavson-a	43	86	129	271	461	650
2,4: 2-5-Photo-c	26	52	78	154	252	350
3,5-Gustavson-a	36	72	108	214	347	480

UNTOLD LEGEND OF CAPTAIN MARVEL, THE
Marvel Comics: Apr, 1997 - No. 3, June, 1997 ($2.50, limited series)

	GD 2.0	VG 4.0	FN 6.0	VF 8.0	VF/NM 9.0	NM- 9.2
1-3						5.00

UNTOLD LEGEND OF THE BATMAN, THE (Also see Promotional section)
DC Comics: July, 1980 - No. 3, Sept, 1980 (Limited series)

	GD 2.0	VG 4.0	FN 6.0	VF 8.0	VF/NM 9.0	NM- 9.2
1-Origin; Joker-c; Byrne's 1st work at DC	3	6	9	14	20	25
2,3	2	4	6	8	10	12

NOTE: ***Aparo** a-1i, 2, 3. **Byrne** a-1p.*

UNTOLD ORIGIN OF THE FEMFORCE, THE (Also see Femforce)
AC Comics: 1989 ($4.95, 68 pgs.)

	GD 2.0	VG 4.0	FN 6.0	VF 8.0	VF/NM 9.0	NM- 9.2
1-Origin Femforce; Bill Black-a(i) & scripts						6.00

UNTOLD TALES OF BLACKEST NIGHT (Also see Blackest Night crossover titles)
DC Comics: Dec, 2010 ($4.99, one-shot)

	GD 2.0	VG 4.0	FN 6.0	VF 8.0	VF/NM 9.0	NM- 9.2
1-Short stories by various incl. Johns, Benes, Booth; 2 covers by Kirkham & Van Sciver						5.00

UNTOLD TALES OF CHASTITY
Chaos! Comics: Nov, 2000 ($2.95, one-shot)

	GD 2.0	VG 4.0	FN 6.0	VF 8.0	VF/NM 9.0	NM- 9.2
1-Origin; Steven Grant-s/Peter Vale-c/a						5.00
1-Premium Edition with glow in the dark cover						10.00

UNTOLD TALES OF LADY DEATH
Chaos! Comics: Nov, 2000 ($2.95, one-shot)

	GD 2.0	VG 4.0	FN 6.0	VF 8.0	VF/NM 9.0	NM- 9.2
1-Origin of Lady Death; Cremator app.; Kaminski-s	1	3	4	6	8	10
1-Premium Edition with glow in the dark cover by Steven Hughes						15.00

UNTOLD TALES OF PUNISHER MAX
Marvel Comics: Aug, 2012 - No. 5, Dec, 2012 ($4.99/$3.99, limited series)

	GD 2.0	VG 4.0	FN 6.0	VF 8.0	VF/NM 9.0	NM- 9.2
1-($4.99) Anthology; Starr-s/Boschi-a/c						5.00
2-5-($3.99) 2-Andrews-c. 3-Ribic-c. 5-Skottie Young-s/Del Mundo-c						4.00

UNTOLD TALES OF PURGATORI
Chaos! Comics: Nov, 2000 ($2.95, one-shot)

	GD 2.0	VG 4.0	FN 6.0	VF 8.0	VF/NM 9.0	NM- 9.2
1-Purgatori in 57 B.C.; Rio-a/Grant-s						3.00
1-Premium Edition with glow in the dark cover						10.00

UNTOLD TALES OF SPIDER-MAN (Also see Amazing Fantasy #16-18)
Marvel Comics: Sept, 1995 - No. 25, Sept, 1997 (99¢)

	GD 2.0	VG 4.0	FN 6.0	VF 8.0	VF/NM 9.0	NM- 9.2
1-Kurt Busiek scripts begin; Pat Olliffe-c/a in all (except #9).						4.00
2-22, -1(7/97), 23-25: 2-1st app. Batwing. 4-1st app. The Spacemen (Gantry, Orbit, Satellite & Vacuum). 8-1st app. The Headsman; The Enforcers (The Big Man, Montana, The Ox & Fancy Dan) app. 9-Ron Frenz-a. 10-1st app. Commanda. 16-Reintro Mary Jane Watson. 21-X-Men-c/app. 25-Green Goblin						3.00
...'96-(1996, $1.95, 46 pgs.)-Kurt Busiek scripts; Mike Allred-c/a; Kurt Busiek & Pat Olliffe app. in back-up story; contains pin-ups						4.00
...'97-(1997, $1.95)-Wraparound-c						4.00
...: Strange Encounters ('98, $5.99) Dr. Strange app.						6.00

UNTOLD TALES OF THE NEW UNIVERSE (Based on Marvel's 1986 New Universe titles)
Marvel Comics: May, 2006 ($2.99, series of one-shots)

	GD 2.0	VG 4.0	FN 6.0	VF 8.0	VF/NM 9.0	NM- 9.2
...: D. P. 7 - Takes place between issues #4 & 5 of D. P. 7 series; Bright-a/Cebulski-s						3.00
...: Justice - Peter David-s/Carmine Di Giandomenico-a						3.00
...: Nightmask - Takes place between issues #4 & 5 of Nightmask series; The Gnome app.						3.00
...: Psi-Force - Tony Bedard-s/Russ Braun-a						3.00
...: Star Brand - Romita & Romita Jr.-c/Pulido-a						3.00
TPB (2006, $15.99) r/one-shots & stories from Amaz. Fantasy #18,19 & New Avengers #16						16.00

UNTOUCHABLES, THE (TV)
Dell Publishing Co.: No. 1237, 10-12/61 - No. 4, 8-10/62 (All have Robert Stack photo-c)

	GD 2.0	VG 4.0	FN 6.0	VF 8.0	VF/NM 9.0	NM- 9.2
Four Color 1237(#1)	18	36	54	124	275	425
Four Color 1286	13	26	39	89	195	300
01-879-207, 12-879-210(01879-210 on inside)	9	18	27	59	117	175

UNTOUCHABLES
Caliber Comics: Aug, 1997 - No. 4 ($2.95, B&W)

	GD 2.0	VG 4.0	FN 6.0	VF 8.0	VF/NM 9.0	NM- 9.2
1-4: 1-Pruett-s; variant covers by Kaluta & Showman						3.00

UNUSUAL COMICS
Bell Features: No date (1940s)(10¢)

8-Zago Jungle Princess (a VG copy sold in 2018 for $185)

UNUSUAL TALES (Blue Beetle & Shadows From Beyond #50 on)
Charlton Comics: Nov, 1955 - No. 49, Mar-Apr, 1965

	GD 2.0	VG 4.0	FN 6.0	VF 8.0	VF/NM 9.0	NM- 9.2
1-Horror stories	39	78	117	240	395	550
2	21	42	63	122	199	275
3-5	16	32	48	94	147	200
6-Ditko-c only	24	48	72	142	234	325
7,8-Ditko-c/a. 8-Robot-c	36	72	108	211	343	475
9-Ditko-c/a (20 pgs.)	37	74	111	222	361	500
10-Ditko-c/a(4)	39	78	117	231	378	525
11-(3/58, 68 pgs.)-Ditko-a(4)	37	74	111	222	361	500
12,14-Ditko-a	22	44	66	132	216	300
13,16-20	8	16	24	54	102	150
15-Ditko-c/a	32	64	96	188	307	425
21,24,28	7	14	21	44	82	120
22,23,25-27,29-Ditko-a	10	20	30	69	147	225
30-49	5	10	15	35	63	90

NOTE: ***Colan** a-11. **Ditko** c-22, 23, 25-27, 31(part).*

UNWORTHY THOR, THE (See Original Sin)
Marvel Comics: Jan, 2017 - No. 5, May, 2017 ($3.99)

	GD 2.0	VG 4.0	FN 6.0	VF 8.0	VF/NM 9.0	NM- 9.2
1-5-Aaron-s/Coipel-a; multiple covers; Beta Ray Bill app. 2-Thanos app.						4.00

UNWRITTEN, THE
DC Comics (Vertigo): July, 2009 - No. 54, Dec, 2013 ($1.00/$2.99)

	GD 2.0	VG 4.0	FN 6.0	VF 8.0	VF/NM 9.0	NM- 9.2
1-($1.00) Intro. Tommy Taylor; Mike Carey-s/Peter Gross-a; two covers (white & black)						3.00

Unstoppable Wasp #3 © MAR

U.S.Agent (2020) #1 © MAR

Usagi Yojimbo #106 © Stan Sakai

	GD	VG	FN	VF	VF/NM	NM-
	2.0	4.0	6.0	8.0	9.0	9.2

2-16,18-31,(31.5), 32, (32.5), 33, (33.5), 34, (34.5), (35.5), 36-49-($2.99): 31.5-Art by Gross, Kaluta, Geary & Talbot. 37-Series re-cap 3.00
17-($3.99) Story printed sideways; Pick-a-Story format 4.00
35-($4.99) 5.00
50-(8/13, $4.99) Fables characters app.; Carey & Willingham-s; Gross & Buckingham-a 5.00
51-54-Fables characters app. 3.00
...: Dead Man's Knock TPB (2011, $14.99) r/#13-18; intro. by novelist Steven Hall 15.00
...: Inside Man TPB (2010, $12.99) r/#6-12; intro. by Paul Cornell 13.00
...: Tommy Taylor and the Bogus Identity TPB (2010, $9.99) r/#1-5; sketch art; prose 10.00

UNWRITTEN, THE: APOCALYPSE
DC Comics (Vertigo): Mar, 2014 - No. 12, Mar, 2015 ($3.99)

1-11-Mike Carey-s/Peter Gross-a 4.00
12-($4.99) Mike Carey-s/Peter Gross-a 5.00

UP FROM HARLEM (Tom Skinner...)
Spire Christian Comics (Fleming H. Revell Co.): 1973 (35/49¢)

nn-(35¢ cover) 3 6 9 15 22 28
nn-(49¢ cover) 2 4 6 10 14 18

UP-TO-DATE COMICS
King Features Syndicate: No date (1938) (36 pgs.; B&W cover) (10¢)

nn-Popeye & Henry cover; The Phantom, Jungle Jim & Flash Gordon by Raymond, The Katzenjammer Kids, Curley Harper & others. Note: Variations in content exist. 37 74 111 222 361 500

UP YOUR NOSE AND OUT YOUR EAR (Satire)
Klevart Enterprises: Apr, 1972 - No. 2, June, 1972 (52 pgs., magazine)

V1#1,2 3 6 9 14 19 24

URTH 4 (Also see Earth 4)
Continuity Comics: May, 1989 - No. 4, Dec, 1990 ($2.00, deluxe format)

1-4: Ms. Mystic characters. 2-Neal Adams-c(i) 4.00

URZA-MISHRA WAR ON THE WORLD OF MAGIC THE GATHERING
Acclaim Comics (Armada): 1996 - No. 2, 1996 ($5.95, limited series)

1,2 2 4 6 11 16 20

U.S. (See Uncle Sam)

USA COMICS
Timely Comics (USA): Aug, 1941 - No. 17, Fall, 1945

1-Origin Major Liberty (called Mr. Liberty #1), Rockman by Wolverton; 1st app. The Whizzer by Avison; The Defender with sidekick Rusty & Jack Frost begin; The Young Avenger only app.; S&K-c plus 1 pg. art 1170 2340 3510 8200 16,100 24,000
2-Origin Captain Terror & The Vagabond; last Wolverton Rockman; Hitler-c 541 1082 1623 3950 6975 10,000
3-No Whizzer 423 846 1269 3000 5250 7500
4-Last Rockman, Major Liberty, Defender, Jack Frost, & Capt. Terror; Corporal Dix app.; "Remember Pearl Harbor" small cover logo 394 788 1182 2758 4829 6900
5-Origin American Avenger & Roko the Amazing; The Blue Blade, The Black Widow & Victory Boys, Gypo the Gypsy Giant & Hills of Horror only app.; Sergeant Dix begins; no Whizzer; Hitler, Mussolini & Tojo-c 649 1298 1947 4738 8369 12,000
6-Captain America (ends #17), The Destroyer, Jap Buster Johnson, Jeep Jones begin; Terror Squad only app. 1250 2500 3750 9500 17,250 25,000
7-Captain Daring, Disk-Eyes the Detective by Wolverton app.; origin & only app. Marvel Boy (3/43); Secret Stamp begins; no Whizzer, Sergeant Dix; classic Schomburg-c 2000 4000 6000 15,200 27,600 40,000
8-Classic Japanese WWII bondage/torture-c 1200 2400 3600 9100 16,550 24,000
9-Last Secret Stamp; Hitler-c; classic-c 1250 2500 3750 9500 17,250 25,000
10-The Thunderbird only app.; Schomburg Japanese WWII-c 1000 2000 3000 7600 13,800 20,000
11-13: 11-No Jeep Jones. 13-No Whizzer; Jeep Jones ends; Schomburg Japanese WWII-c 508 1016 1524 3708 6554 9400
14-17: 15-No Destroyer; Jap Buster Johnson ends 271 542 813 1734 2967 4200

NOTE: ***Brodsky** c-14. **Gabrielle** c-4. **Schomburg** c-6, 7, 10, 12, 13, 15-17. **Shores** a-1, 4; c-9, 11. **Ed Win** a-4. Cover features: 1-The Defender; 2, 3-Captain Terror; 4-Major Liberty; 5-Victory Boys; 6-17-Captain America & Bucky.*

USA COMICS 70TH ANNIVERSARY SPECIAL
Marvel Comics: Sept, 2009 ($3.99, one-shot)

1-New story of The Destroyer; Arcudi-s/Ellis-a; r/All Winners #3; two covers 5.00

U.S. AGENT (See Jeff Jordan...)

U.S. AGENT (See Captain America #354)
Marvel Comics: June, 1993 - No. 4, Sept, 1993 ($1.75, limited series)

1-4 4.00

U.S. AGENT
Marvel Comics: Aug, 2001 - No. 3, Oct, 2001 ($2.99, limited series)

1-3: Ordway-s/a(p)/c. 2,3-Captain America app. 3.00

U.S.AGENT (John Walker)(See Captain America #354 for 1st app.)
Marvel Comics: Jan, 2021 - No. 5, Jun, 2021 ($3.99)

1-5-Priest-s/Jeanty-a 4.00

USAGI YOJIMBO (See Albedo, Doomsday Squad #3 & Space Usagi)
Fantagraphics Books: July, 1987 - No. 38 ($2.00/$2.25, B&W)

1 8 16 24 54 102 150
1,8,10-2nd printings 5.00
2 2 4 6 11 16 20
3-9 2 4 6 8 10 12
10-Leonardo app. (TMNT) 5 10 15 33 57 80
11-Aragonés-a 3 6 9 14 19 24
12-29 5.00
30-38: 30-Begin $2.25-c 6.00
Color Special 1 (11/89, $2.95, 68 pgs.)-new & r 3 6 9 14 20 25
Color Special 2 (10/91, $3.50) 2 4 6 8 10 12
Color Special #3 (10/92, $3.50)-Jeff Smith's Bone promo on inside-c 2 4 6 8 10 12
Summer Special 1 (1986, B&W, $2.75)-r/early Albedo issues 3 6 9 17 26 35

USAGI YOJIMBO (Volume 2)
Mirage Studios: V2#1, Mar, 1993 - No. 16, 1994 ($2.75)

V2#1-Teenage Mutant Ninja Turtles app. 3 6 9 14 19 24
2-16 5.00

USAGI YOJIMBO (Volume 3)
Dark Horse Comics: Apr, 1996 - No. 165, Jan, 2018 ($2.95/$2.99/$3.50, B&W)

V3#1-Stan Sakai-c/a in all 2 4 6 9 13 16
2-10 6.00
11-99,101-116: Stan Sakai-c/a 3.50
100-(1/07, $3.50) Stan Sakai roast by various incl. Aragonés, Wagner, Miller, Geary 1 3 4 6 8 10
117-150-($3.50) 136-Variant-c. 141-"200th issue" 3.50
151-165-($3.99) 152-The River Rising 4.00
...: One For One (8/10, $1.00) Reprints #1 4.00
Color Special #4 (7/97, $2.95) "Green Persimmon" 4.00
Color Special #5: The Artist (7/14, $3.99) Bonus preview of Usagi Yojimbo: Senso 4.00
Daisho TPB ('98, $14.95) r/Mirage series #7-14 15.00
Demon Mask TPB ('01, $15.95) 16.00
Glimpses of Death TPB (7/06, $15.95) r/#76-82 16.00
Grasscutter TPB ('99, $16.95) r/#13-22 17.00
Gray Shadows TPB ('00, $14.95) r/#23-30 15.00
Seasons TPB ('99, $14.95) r/#7-12 15.00
Shades of Death TPB ('97, $14.95) r/Mirage series #1-6 15.00
The Brink of Life and Death TPB ('98, $14.95) r/Mirage series #13,15,16 & Dark Horse series #1-6 15.00
The Shrouded Moon TPB (1/03, $15.95) r/#46-52 16.00

USAGI YOJIMBO (Volume 4)
IDW Publishing: Jun, 2019 - Present ($3.99, color)

1-31-Stan Sakai-c/a in all. 17-Cover swipe of Creepy #4 by Frazetta 4.00

USAGI YOJIMBO: COLOR CLASSICS
IDW Publishing: Jan, 2020 - No. 7, Sept, 2020 ($3.99, color)

1-7-Reprints early Fantagraphics B&W issues with added color; Stan Sakai-c/a in all 4.00

USAGI YOJIMBO: DRAGON BELLOW CONSPIRACY
IDW Publishing: Jun, 2021 - No. 6, Nov, 2021 ($3.99, color)

1-6-Reprints #13-18 (1989) with new color; Stan Sakai-c/a 4.00

USAGI YOJIMBO: LONE GOAT AND KID
IDW Publishing: Jan, 2022 - Present ($3.99, color)

1-6-Reprints #19-24 (1989) with new color; Stan Sakai-c/a 4.00

USAGI YOJIMBO: SENSO
Dark Horse Comics: Aug, 2014 - No. 6, Jan, 2015 ($3.99, B&W)

1-Stan Sakai-s/c/a; Martian invasion set 20 years later; wraparound-c on each 1 3 4 6 8 10
2-6 4.00

USAGI YOJIMBO: THE HIDDEN (Doubles as issues #166-172 for Volume 3)
Dark Horse Comics: Mar, 2018 - No. 7, Oct, 2018 ($3.99, B&W)

1-7-Stan Sakai-s/c/a 4.00

USAGI YOJIMBO: WANDERER'S ROAD
IDW Publishing: Nov, 2020 - No. 6, Apr, 2021 ($3.99, color)

1-6: 1-Reprints #7 (3/88) with new color; Stan Sakai-c/a. 2-6-Reprint #8-#12 4.00

GD VG FN VF VF/NM NM-
2.0 4.0 6.0 8.0 9.0 9.2

U.S. AIR FORCE COMICS (Army Attack #38 on)
Charlton Comics: Oct, 1958 - No. 37, Mar-Apr, 1965

	GD	VG	FN	VF	VF/NM	NM-
1	8	16	24	55	105	155
2	5	10	15	30	50	70
3-10	4	8	12	23	37	50
11-20	3	6	9	21	33	45
21-37	3	6	9	17	26	35

NOTE: *Glanzman c/a-9, 10, 12. Montes/Bache a-33.*

USA IS READY
Dell Publishing Co.: 1941 (68 pgs., one-shot)
1-War propaganda 97 194 291 621 1061 1500

U.S.AVENGERS (Also see Avengers #675 -678)
Marvel Comics: Mar, 2017 - No. 12, Jan, 2017 ($3.99)
1-3-Ewing-s/Medina-a; team of Squirrel Girl, Cannonball, Iron Patriot, Enigma, Red Hulk. 5-9-Secret Empire tie-ins. 11,12-Archie Riverdale spoof; Skrulls app. 4.00

U.S. BORDER PATROL COMICS (Sgt. Dick Carter of the...) (See Holyoke One Shot)

USER
DC Comics (Vertigo): 2001 - No. 3, 2001 ($5.95, limited series)
1-3-Devin Grayson-s; Sean Phillips & John Bolton-a 6.00

U.S. FIGHTING AIR FORCE (Also see United States Fighting Air Force)
I. W. Enterprises: No date (1960s?)
1,9(nd): 1-r/United States Fighting...#?. 9-r/#1 2 4 6 11 16 20

U.S. FIGHTING MEN
Super Comics: 1963 - 1964 (Reprints)
10-r/With the U.S. Paratroops #4(Avon) 2 4 6 9 13 16
11,12,15-18: 11-r/Monty Hall #10. 12,16,17,18-r/U.S. Fighting Air Force #10,3,?&?
15-r/Man Comics #11 2 4 6 9 13 16

U.S. JONES (Also see Wonderworld Comics #28)
Fox Feature Syndicate: Nov, 1941 - No. 2, Jan, 1942
1-U.S. Jones & The Topper begin; Nazi-c 300 600 900 2070 3635 5200
2-Nazi-c 314 628 942 2198 3849 5500

U.S. MARINES
Charlton Comics: Fall, 1964 (12¢, one-shot)
1-1st app. Capt. Dude; Glanzman-a 5 10 15 31 53 75

U.S. MARINES IN ACTION
Avon Periodicals: Aug, 1952 - No. 3, Dec, 1952
1-Louis Ravielli-c/a 18 36 54 105 165 225
2,3: 3-Kinstler-c 14 28 42 81 118 155

U.S. 1
Marvel Comics Group: May, 1983 - No. 12, Oct, 1984 (7,8: painted-c)
1-12: 2-Sienkiewicz-c. 3-12-Michael Golden-c 4.00

U.S. PARATROOPS (See With the...)

U.S. PARATROOPS
I. W. Enterprises: 1964?
1,8: 1-r/With the U.S. Paratroops #1; Wood-c. 8-r/With the U.S. Paratroops #6; Kinstler-c 3 6 9 14 20 25

U.S. TANK COMMANDOS
Avon Periodicals: June, 1952 - No. 4, Mar, 1953
1-Kinstler-c 18 36 54 105 165 225
2-4: Kinstler-c 14 28 42 82 121 160
I.W. Reprint #1,8: 1-r/#1. 8-r/#3 3 6 9 14 19 24
NOTE: *Kinstler a-I.W. #1; c-1-4, I.W. #1, 8.*

U.S. WAR MACHINE (Also see Iron Man and War Machine)
Marvel Comics (MAX): Nov, 2001 - No. 12, Jan, 2002 ($1.50, B&W, weekly limited series)
1-12-Chuck Austen-s/a/c 3.00
TPB (12/01, $14.95) r/#1-12 15.00

U.S. WAR MACHINE 2.0
Marvel Comics (MAX): Sept, 2003 - No. 3, Sept, 2003 ($2.99, weekly, limited series)
1-3-Austen-s/Christian Moore-CGI art 3.00

"V" (TV)
DC Comics: Feb, 1985 - No. 18, July, 1986
1-Based on TV movie & series (Sci/Fi) 5.00
2-18: 17,18-Denys Cowan-c/a 4.00

VACATION COMICS (Also see A-1 Comics)
Magazine Enterprises: No. 16, 1948 (one-shot)
A-1 16-The Pixies, Tom Tom, Flying Fredd & Koko & Kola 13 26 39 74 105 135

VACATION DIGEST
Harvey Comics: Sept, 1987 ($1.25, digest size)
1 1 2 3 5 6 8

VACATION IN DISNEYLAND (Also see Dell Giants)
Dell Publishing Co./Gold Key (1965): Aug-Oct, 1959; May, 1965 (Walt Disney)
Four Color 1025-Barks-a 15 30 45 103 227 350
1(30024-508)(G.K., 5/65, 25¢)-r/Dell Giant #30 & cover to #1 ('58); celebrates Disneyland's 10th anniversary 5 10 15 31 53 75

VACATION PARADE (See Dell Giants)

VALEN THE OUTCAST
BOOM! Studios: Dec, 2011 - No. 8, Jul, 2012 ($1.00/$3.99)
1-($1.00) Nelson-s/Scalera-a; eight covers 3.00
2-8-($3.99) 2-4-Six covers on each. 5-8-Five covers on each 4.00

VALERIA THE SHE BAT
Continuity Comics: May, 1993 - No. 5, Nov, 1993
1-Premium; acetate-c; N. Adams-a/scripts; given as gift to retailers 1 3 4 6 8 10
5 (11/93)-Embossed-c; N. Adams-a/scripts 5.00
NOTE: *Due to lack of continuity, #2-4 do not exist.*

VALERIA THE SHE BAT
Acclaim Comics (Windjammer): Sept, 1995 - No.2, Oct, 1995 ($2.50, limited series)
1,2 4.00

VALHALLA MAD
Image Comics: May, 2015 - No. 4, Aug, 2015 ($3.50, limited series)
1-4-Joe Casey-s/Paul Maybury-a 3.50

VALIANT, THE (Leads into Bloodshot Reborn series)
Valiant Entertainment: Dec, 2014 - No. 4, Mar, 2015 ($3.99, limited series)
1-4-Lemire & Kindt-s/Rivera-a; Eternal Warrior & Bloodshot app. 4.00

VALIANT...
Valiant Entertainment: May, 2012 - Present (giveaways)
... Bloodshot FCBD 2019 Special (5/19) Previews Bloodshot & Fallen World; Brereton-c 3.00
... Comics FCBD 2012 Special 1 (5/12) Previews X-O Manowar, Harbinger and other Valiant 2012 titles; creator interviews 3.00
... FCBD 2013 Special #1 (5/13) Previews Harbinger Wars, X-O Manowar and others 3.00
... FCBD 2014 Armor Hunters Special #1 (5/14) Previews Armor Hunters and others 3.00
... FCBD 2014 Valiant Universe Handbook #1 (5/14) Character profiles 3.00
... FCBD 2015 Valiant 25th Anniversary Special (5/15) Previews Bloodshot and Ninjak 3.00
... FCBD 2021 Special (8/21) Previews Ninjak, X-O Manowar, Shadowman & Harbinger 3.00
... : 4001 A.D. FCBD Special (5/16) Prelude to the 4001 A.D. series; Crain-c 3.00
... Masters: 2013 Showcase Edition #1 (5/13) Samples of hardcover volume offerings 3.00
... : Shadowman FCBD 2018 Special (5/18) Short stories of Shadowman, X-O Manowar, Harbinger Wars 3.00
... Universe Handbook 2015 Edition #1 (5/15, $2.99) Character profiles 3.00
... Universe Handbook 2016 Edition #1 (8/16, $2.99) Character profiles 3.00
... Universe Handbook 2019 Edition #1 (6/19, $3.99) Character profiles; Massafera-c 4.00
... : X-O Manowar 2017 FCBD Special (5/17) Short stories of X-O Manowar, Secret Weapons, Bloodshot Salvation 3.00

VALIANT HIGH
Valiant Entertainment: May, 2018 - No. 4, Aug, 2018 ($3.99, limited series)
1-4-Valiant heroes as high-schoolers; Kibblesmith-s/Charm-a 4.00

VALKYRIE (See Airboy)
Eclipse Comics: May, 1987 - No. 3, July, 1987 ($1.75, limited series)
1-3: 2-Holly becomes new Black Angel 5.00

VALKYRIE
Marvel Comics: Jan, 1997; Nov, 2010 ($2.95/$3.99, one-shots)
1-(1/97, $2.95) w/pin-ups 4.00
1-(11/10, $3.99) Origin re-told; Winslade-a/Glass-s; Anacleto-c 4.00

VALKYRIE!
Eclipse Comics: July, 1988 - No. 3, Sept, 1988 ($1.95, limited series)
1-3 4.00

VALKYRIE: JANE FOSTER (See the 2016 Mighty Thor series and War of the Realms Omega)
Marvel Comics: Sept, 2019 - No. 10, Oct, 2020 ($3.99)
1-10: 1,2-Aaron & Ewing-s/Cafu-a; Bullseye & Heimdall app. 4-7-Dr. Strange app. 4.00

VALLEY OF THE DINOSAURS (TV)
Charlton Comics: Apr, 1975 - No. 11, Dec, 1976 (Hanna-Barbara)
1-W. Howard-i 3 6 9 16 24 32
2,4-11: 2-W. Howard-i 2 4 6 8 11 14
3-Byrne text illos (early work, 7/75) 2 4 6 10 14 18

VALLEY OF THE DINOSAURS (Volume 2)
Harvey Comics: Oct, 1993 ($1.50, giant-sized)
1-Reprints 5.00

VALLEY OF GWANGI (See Movie Classics)

VALOR
E. C. Comics: Mar-Apr, 1955 - No. 5, Nov-Dec, 1955
1-Williamson/Torres-a; Wood-c/a 40 80 120 320 510 700
2-Williamson-c/a; Wood-a 29 58 87 232 366 500
3,4: 3-Williamson, Crandall-a. 4-Wood-c 23 46 69 184 292 400
5-Wood-c/a; Williamson/Evans-a 22 44 66 176 278 380
NOTE: *Crandall a-3, 4. Ingels a-1, 2, 4, 5. Krigstein a-1-5. Orlando a-3, 4; c-3. Wood a-1, 2, 5; c-1, 4, 5.*

VALOR
Gemstone Publishing: Oct, 1998 - No. 5, Feb, 1999 ($2.50)
1-5-Reprints 4.00

VALOR (Also see Legion of Super-Heroes & Legionnaires)
DC Comics: Nov, 1992 - No. 23, Sept, 1994 ($1.25/$1.50)
1-22: 1-Eclipso The Darkness Within aftermath. 2-Vs. Supergirl. 4-Vs. Lobo. 12-Lobo cameo. 14-Legionnaires, JLA app. 17-Austin-c(i); death of Valor. 18-22-Build-up to Zero Hour 3.00
23-Zero Hour tie-in 3.00

VAMPI (Vampirella's...)
Harris Publications (Anarchy Studios): Aug, 2000 - No. 25, Feb, 2003 ($2.95/$2.99)
Limited Edition Preview Book (5/00) Preview pages & sketchbook 4.00
1-(8/00, $2.95) Lau-a(p)/Conway-s 6.00
1-Platinum Edition 20.00
2-25: 17-Barberi-a 4.00
2-25-Deluxe Edition variants ($9.95): 4-Finch-c. 5-Wieringo-c. 6-Cha-c 10.00
...Digital 1 (11/01, $2.95) CGI art; Haberlin-s 4.00
...Digital Preview (Anarchy Studios, 7/01, $2.95) preview of CGI art 4.00
Switchblade Kiss HC (2001, $24.95) r/#1-6 25.00
Vicious Preview Ed. (Apr, 2003, $1.99) Flip book w/ Xin: Journey of the Monkey King Preview Ed. 4.00
Wizard #1/2 (mail order, $9.95) includes sketch pages 10.00

VAMPIRE BITES
Brainstorm Comics: May, 1995 - No. 2, Sept, 1996 ($2.95, B&W)
1,2:1-Color pin-up 4.00

U.S. Air Force Comics #1 © CC

Valiant High #1 © VAL

Vampirella (2010) #1 © DFI

GD VG FN VF VF/NM NM-
2.0 4.0 6.0 8.0 9.0 9.2

VAMPIRE DIARIES, THE (Based on the CW television series)
DC Comics: Mar, 2014 - No. 6, Aug, 2014 ($3.99, printings of online comics)

1-6: 1,3-Doran-s/Shasteen-a. 5-Calero-a. 6-Doran-s/a 4.00

VAMPIRE LESTAT, THE
Innovation Publishing: Jan, 1990 - No. 12, 1991 ($2.50, painted limited series)

1-Adapts novel; Bolton painted-c on all 2 4 6 10 14 18
1-2nd printing (has UPC code, 1st prints don't) 3.00
1-3rd & 4th printings 3.00
2-1st printing 1 2 3 5 6 8
2-2nd & 3rd printings 3.00
3-5 5.00
3-6,9-2nd printings 3.00
6-12 4.00

VAMPIRELLA (Magazine)(See Warren Presents)(Also see Heidi Saha)
Warren Publishing Co./Harris Publications #113: Sept, 1969 - No. 112, Feb, 1983; No. 113, Jan, 1988? (B&W)

1-Intro. Vampirella in original costume & wings; Frazetta-c/intro. page; Adams-a; Crandall-a 136 272 408 1088 2444 3800
2-1st app. Vampirella's cousin Evily-c/s; 1st/only app. Draculina, Vampirella's blonde twin sister 14 28 42 96 211 325
3 (Low distribution) 19 38 57 133 297 460
4,6 8 16 24 56 108 160
5,7,9: 5,7-Frazetta-c. 9-Barry Smith-a; Boris/Wood-c 9 18 27 57 111 165
8-Vampirella begins by Tom Sutton as serious strip (early issues-gag line) 9 18 27 63 129 195
10-No Vampi story; Brunner, Adams, Wood-a 6 12 18 40 73 105
11-Origin & 1st app. Pendragon; Frazetta-c 8 16 24 51 96 140
12-Vampi by Gonzales begins 8 16 24 51 96 140
13-15: 14-1st Maroto-a; Ploog-a 6 12 18 42 79 115
16,22,25: 16-1st full Dracula-c/app. 22-Color insert preview of Maroto's Dracula. 25-Vampi on cocaine-s 6 12 18 41 76 110
17,18,20,21,23,24: 17-Tomb of the Gods begins by Maroto, ends #22. 18-22-Dracula-s 6 12 18 38 69 100
19 (1973 Annual) Creation of Vampi text bio 7 14 21 48 89 130
26-35,38-40,45: 26,28,34,35,39,40-All have 8 pg. color inserts. 27-(1974 Annual) New color Vampi-s; mostly-r. 28-Board game inside covers. 30-Intro. Pantha; Corben-a(color). 31-Origin Luana, the Beast Girl. 32-Jones-a. 33-Wrightson-a; Pantha ends. 34,35-1st Fleur the Witch Woman. 38-2nd Vampi as Cleopatra/Blood Red Queen of Hearts; 1st Mayo-a. 39,40-Color Dracula-s. 40-Wrightson bio 5 10 15 31 53 75
36,37: 36-1st Vampi as Cleopatra/Blood Red Queen of Hearts; issue has 8 pg. color insert. 37-(1975 Annual) 6 12 18 37 66 95
41-44,47,48: 41-Dracula-s 4 8 12 28 47 65
46-(10/75) Origin-r from Annual 1 5 10 15 31 53 75
49-1st Blind Priestess; The Blood Red Queen of Hearts storyline begins; Poe-s 5 10 15 31 53 75
50-Spirit cameo by Eisner; 40 pg. Vampi-s; Pantha & Fleur app.; Jones-a 5 10 15 30 50 70
51-57,59-63,65,66,68,75,79-89: 54-Vampi-s (42 pgs.); 8 pg. color Corben-a. 55-All Gonzales-a(r). 60-62,65,66-The Blood Red Queen of Hearts app. 60-1st Blind Priestess-c. 63-10 pgs. Wrightson-a 4 8 12 23 37 50
58,70,72: 58-(92 pgs.) 70-Rook app. 4 8 12 27 44 60
64,73: 64-(100 pg. Giant) All Mayo-a; 70 pg. Vampi-s. 73-69 pg. Vampi-s; Mayo-a 4 8 12 28 47 65
67,69,71,74,76-78-All Barbara Leigh photo-c 4 8 12 27 44 60
90-99: 90-Toth-a. 91-All-r; Gonzales-a. 93-Cassandra St. Knight begins, ends #103; new Pantha series begins, ends #108 4 8 12 23 37 50
100 (96 pg. r-special)-Origin reprinted from Ann. 1; mostly reprints; Vampirella appears topless in new 21 pg. story 7 14 21 44 82 120
101-104,106,107: All lower print run. 101,102-The Blood Red Queen of Hearts app. 107-All Maroto reprint-a issue 5 10 15 34 60 85
105,108-110: 108-Torpedo series by Toth begins; Vampi nudity splash page. 110-(100 pg. Summer Spectacular) 5 10 15 34 60 85
111,112: Low print run. 111-Giant Collector's Edition ($2.50) 112-(84 pgs.) last Warren issue 8 16 24 52 99 145
113 (1988)-1st Harris Issue; very low print run 24 48 72 168 372 575
Annual 1(1972)-New definitive origin of Vampirella by Gonzales; reprints by Neal Adams (from #1), Wood (from #9) 21 42 63 147 324 500
Special 1 (1977) Softcover (color, large-square bound)-Only available thru mail order 15 30 45 100 220 340
Special 1 (1977) Hardcover (color, large-square bound)-Only available through mail order (scarce)(500 produced, signed & #'d) 30 60 90 216 483 750
#1 1969 Commemorative Edition (2001, $4.95) reprints entire #1 5.00
#30 (1974) Facsimile Edition (2020, $6.99) reprints entire #30 7.00
...Crimson Chronicles Vol. 1 (2004, $19.95, TPB) reprints stories from #1-10 20.00

GD VG FN VF VF/NM NM-
2.0 4.0 6.0 8.0 9.0 9.2

...Crimson Chronicles Vol. 2 (2005, $19.95, TPB) reprints stories from #11-18 20.00
...Crimson Chronicles Vol. 3 (2005, $19.95, TPB) reprints stories from #19-28 20.00
...Crimson Chronicles Vol. 4 (2006, $19.95, TPB) reprints stories from #29-41 20.00

NOTE: ***Ackerman** s-1-3. **Neal Adams** a-1, 10p, 19p(r/#10), 44(1 pg.), Annual 1. **Alcala** a-78, 90, 93i. **Bodé/Todd** c-3. **Bodé/Jones** c-4. **Boris/Wood** c-9. **Brunner** a-10, 12(1 pg.). **Corben** a-30, 31, 33, 36, 54; c-30, 31, 33, 54. **Crandall** a-1, 19(r/#1). **Frazetta** c-1, 5, 7, 11, 31. **Heath** a-58, 61, 67, 76-78, 83. **Infantino** a-57-62. **Jones** a-5, 9, 12, 27, 32 (color), 33(2 pg.), 34, 50i, 83r. **Ken Kelly** c-6, 38, 39, 40(back-c), 46, 70, 95. **Nebres** a-84, 88-90, 92-96. **Nino** a-59i, 61i, 67, 76, 85, 90. **Ploog** a-14. **Barry Smith** a-9. **Starlin** a-78. **Sutton** a-1-5, 7-11, Annual 1. **Toth** a-90i, 108, 110. **Wood** a-9, 10, 12, 19(r/#12), 27r, Annual 1; c-9(partial). **Wrightson** a-33(w/**Jones**), 40(Bio cameo) 63r. All reprint issues-19, 74, 83, 91, 105, 107, 109, 111. Annuals from 1973 on are included in regular numbering. Later annuals are same format as regular issues. Color inserts (8 pgs.) in 22, 25-28, 30-35, 39, 40, 45, 46, 49, 54, 55, 67, 72. 16 pg color insert in #36.*

VAMPIRELLA (Also see Cain/... & Vengeance of...)
Harris Publications: Nov, 1992 - No. 5, Nov, 1993 ($2.95)

0-Bagged 1 3 4 6 8 10
0-Gold 3 6 9 19 30 40
1-Jim Balent inks in #1-3; Adam Hughes c-1-3 3 6 9 17 26 35
1-2nd printing 5.00
1-(11/97) Commemorative Edition 4.00
2 2 4 6 10 14 18
3-5: 4-Snyder III-c. 5-Brereton painted-c 1 3 4 6 8 10
Trade paperback nn (10/93, $5.95)-r/#1-4; Jusko-c 1 3 4 6 8 10

NOTE: *Issues 1-5 contain certificates for free **Dave Stevens** Vampirella poster.*

VAMPIRELLA (THE NEW MONTHLY)
Harris Publications: Nov, 1997 - No. 26, Apr, 2000 ($2.95)

1-3-"Ascending Evil" -Morrison & Millar-s/Conner & Palmiotti-a. 1-Three covers by Quesada/Palmiotti, Conner, and Conner/Palmiotti 5.00
1-3-($9.95) Jae Lee variant covers 10.00
1-($24.95) Platinum Ed.w/Quesada-c 25.00
4-6-"Holy War"-Small & Stull-a, 4-Linsner variant-c 4.00
7-9-"Queen's Gambit"-Shi app. 7-Two covers. 8-Pantha-c/app. 4.00
7-($9.95) Conner variant-c 10.00
10-12-"Hell on Earth"; Small-a/Coney-s. 12-New costume 4.00
10-Jae Lee variant-c 1 3 4 6 8 10
13-15-"World's End" Zircher-p; Pantha back-up, Texeira-a 4.00
16,17: 16-Pantha-c;Texeira-a; Vampi back-up story. 17-(Pantha #2) 4.00
18-20-"Rebirth": Jae Lee-c on all. 18-Loeb-s/Sale-a. 19-Alan Davis-a. 20-Bruce Timm-a 4.00
18-20-($9.95) Variant covers: 18-Sale. 19-Davis. 20-Timm 12.00
21-26: 21,22-Dangerous Games; Small-a. 23-Lady Death-c/app.; Cleavenger-a. 24,25-Lau-a. 26-Lady Death & Pantha-c/app.; Cleavenger-a. 4.00
0-(1/99) also variant-c with Pantha #0; same contents 4.00
TPB ($7.50) r/#1-3 "Ascending Evil" 8.00
Ascending Evil Ashcan (8/97, $1.00) 3.00
...: Grant Morrison/Mark Millar Collection TPB (2006, $24.95) r/#1-6; interviews 25.00
Hell on Earth Ashcan (7/98, $1.00) 3.00
... Presents: Tales of Pantha TPB (2006, $19.95) r/stories from #13-17 & one-shots 20.00
The End Ashcan (3/00, $6.00) 6.00
...30th Anniversary Celebration Preview (7/99) B&W preview of #18-20 10.00

VAMPIRELLA
Harris Publications: June, 2001 - No. 22, Aug, 2003 ($2.95/$2.99)

1-Four covers (Mayhew w/foil logo, Campbell, Anacleto, Jae Lee) Mayhew-a; Mark Millar-s 5.00
2-22: 2-Two covers (Mayhew & Chiodo). 3-Timm var-c. 4-Horn var-c. 7-10-Dawn Brown-a; Pantha back-up w/Texeira-a. 15-22-Conner-c 4.00
Giant-Size Ashcan (5/01, $5.95) B&W preview art and Mayhew interview 6.00
...: Halloween Trick & Treat (10/04, $4.95) stories & art by various; three covers 5.00
... : Nowheresville Preview Edition (3/01, $2.95)- previews Mayhew art and photo models 4.00
...Nowheresville TPB (1/02, $12.95) r/#1-3 with cover gallery 13.00
... Summer Special #1 (2005, $5.95) Batman Begins photo-c and 2 variant-c 6.00
...: 2006 Halloween Special (2006, $2.95) Conner-c; Hester-s/Segovia-a; 4 covers 4.00

VAMPIRELLA
Dynamite Entertainment: 2010 - No. 38, 2014 ($3.99)

1-Four covers (Campbell, Madureira, J. Djurdjevic, Alex Ross swipe of Frazetta's #1) 4.00
1-Variant-c of blood-soaked Vampirella by Alex Ross 8.00
2-37: 2-6-Trautmann-s/Wagner Reis-a; four covers. 7-Geovani-a 4.00
38-($4.99, 40 pgs.) Pantha and Dracula app. 5.00
Annual 1 (2011, $4.99) Jerwa-s/Casalos-a; reprint with Alan Davis-a 5.00
Annual 2 (2012, $4.99) Rahner-s/Kyriazis-a; reprint with Pantha app.; Linsner-c 5.00
Annual 2013 ($4.99) Rahner-s/Valiente-a/Bolson-c 5.00
...: NuBlood (2013, $4.99) Spoof of True Blood; Rahner-s/Razek-a/c; back-up w/Timm-a 5.00
... Vs. Fluffy (2012, $4.99) Spoof of Buffy the Vampire Slayer; Bradshaw-c 5.00

VAMPIRELLA (Volume 2)
Dynamite Entertainment: 2014 - No. 13, 2015 ($3.99)

1-12: Multiple covers on each. 1-Nancy Collins-s/Berkenkotter-a 4.00

13-($4.99) Lord Drago app.; Collins-s/Berkenkotter-a; 3 covers 5.00
#100 (2015, $7.99) Short stories by various incl. Tim Seeley; multiple covers 8.00
#1969 (2015, $7.99) Short stories by various incl. Hester & Worley; 2 covers 8.00
Annual 2015 ($5.99) Collins-s/Aneke-a/Anacleto-c 6.00
...: Prelude to Shadows (2014, $7.99) Collins-s/Zamora-a; r/Vampirella #13 w/new color 8.00

VAMPIRELLA (Volume 3)
Dynamite Entertainment: 2016 - No. 6, 2016 ($3.99)

1-6: Multiple covers on each. 1-Kate Leth-s/Eman Casallos-a; new costume 4.00

VAMPIRELLA (Volume 4)
Dynamite Entertainment: 2017 - No. 11, 2018 ($3.99)

#0-(25¢) Multiple covers; Cornell-s/Broxton-a 3.00
1-11-($3.99) Vampirella in the far future. 1-5-Cornell-s/Broxton-a. 6-10-Belanger-a 4.00
... Halloween Special One-Shot (2018, $4.99) Reilly Brown-c 5.00
... Valentine's Day Special (2019, $4.99) Williams-s/Sanapo-a 5.00

VAMPIRELLA (Volume 5)
Dynamite Entertainment: 2019 - No. 25, 2021 ($3.99)

0-(2019 Free Comic Book Day giveaway) Priest-s/Gündüz-a; reprint with Art Adams-a 3.00
1-25-Vampirella's mother Lilith app.; Priest-s/Gündüz-a; multiple covers on each. 25-Vampirella marries Dracula 4.00
...: Fairy Tales (2022, $4.99) Soo Lee-s/Emiliana Pinna-a; Red Riding Hood homage 5.00
...: Holiday Special (2021, $4.99) Robson-s/a; Federici-s/a; Carratu-s/a; Krampus app. 5.00
... 1992 (2021, $4.99) Bemis-s/Castro & Ramos-a 5.00
...: Trial of the Soul (2020, $4.99) Intro. Prester John; Willingham-s/Cafaro-a 5.00
...: Valentine's Day Special (2021, $4.99) Marcos Ramos-a; Dracula app. 5.00
...: Valentine's Day Special (2022, $4.99) Sozomaika main-c 5.00

VAMPIRELLA / ALIENS
Dynamite Entertainment: 2015 - No. 6, 2016 ($3.99, limited series)

1-Corinna Bechko-s/Javier Garcia-Miranda-a; multiple covers on each 2 4 6 9 12 15
2-6 4.00

VAMPIRELLA & PANTHA SHOWCASE
Harris Publications: Jan, 1997 ($1.50, one-shot)

1-Millar-s/Texeira-c/a; flip book w/"Blood Lust"; Robinson-s/Jusko-c/a 4.00

VAMPIRELLA & THE BLOOD RED QUEEN OF HEARTS
Harris Publications: Sept, 1996 ($9.95, 96 pgs., B&W, squarebound, one-shot)

nn-r/Vampirella #49,60-62,65,66,101,102; John Bolton-c; Michael Bair back-c 1 3 4 6 8 10

VAMPIRELLA AND THE SCARLET LEGION
Dynamite Entertainment: 2011 - No. 5 ($3.99)

1-5: 1-Three covers (Campbell, Chen and Tucci); Malaga-a 4.00

VAMPIRELLA / ARMY OF DARKNESS
Dynamite Entertainment: 2015 - No. 4, 2015 ($3.99, limited series)

1-4-Ash meets Vampirella in 1300 AD; Mark Rahner-s/Jeff Morales-a 4.00

VAMPIRELLA: BLOODLUST
Harris Publications: July, 1997 - No. 2, Aug, 1997 ($4.95, limited series)

1,2-Robinson-s/Jusko-painted c/a 6.00
1-(2022, $4.99) Reprints 1997 issue 5.00

VAMPIRELLA CLASSIC
Harris Publications: Feb, 1995 - No. 5, Nov, 1995 ($2.95, limited series)

1-5: Reprints Archie Goodwin stories. 5.00

VAMPIRELLA COMICS MAGAZINE
Harris Publications: Oct, 2003 - No. 9 ($3.95/$9.95, magazine-sized)

1-9-($3.95) 1-Texiera-c; b&w and color stories, Alan Moore interview; reviews. 2-KISS interview. 4-Chiodo-c. 6-Brereton-c 4.00
1-9-($9.95) 1-Three covers (Model Photo cover, Palmiotti-c, Wheatley Frankenstein-c) 10.00

VAMPIRELLA: CROSSOVER GALLERY
Harris Publications: Sept, 1997 ($2.95, one-shot)

1-Wraparound-c by Campbell, pinups by Jae Lee, Mack, Allred, Art Adams, Quesada & Palmiotti and others 1 3 4 6 8 10

VAMPIRELLA: DEATH & DESTRUCTION
Harris Publications: July, 1996 - No. 3, Sept, 1996 ($2.95, limited series)

1-3: Amanda Conner-a(p) in all. 1-Tucci-c. 2-Hughes-c. 3-Jusko-c 4.00
1-($9.95)-Limited Edition; Beachum-c 10.00

VAMPIRELLA / DEJAH THORIS
Dynamite Entertainment: 2018 - No. 5, 2019 ($3.99, limited series)

1-5-Erik Burnham-s/Ediano Silva-a; multiple covers on each; Vampirella on Barsoom 4.00

VAMPIRELLA/DRACULA & PANTHA SHOWCASE
Harris Publications: Aug, 1997 ($1.50, one-shot)

1-Ellis, Robinson, and Moore-s; flip book w/"Pantha" 4.00

VAMPIRELLA/DRACULA: THE CENTENNIAL
Harris Publications: Oct, 1997 ($5.95, one-shot)

1-Ellis, Robinson, and Moore-s; Beachum, Frank/Smith, and Mack/Mays-a Bolton-painted-c 6.00

VAMPIRELLA DRACULA UNHOLY (Follows their wedding in Vampirella #25)
Dynamite Entertainment: 2021 ($3.99)

1-6: 1-Priest-s/Hadiwidjaja-a; main cover by Adam Hughes 4.00

VAMPIRELLA: FEARY TALES
Dynamite Entertainment: 2014 - No. 5, 2015 ($3.99, limited series)

1-5: Anthology of short stories by various; multiple covers on each 4.00

VAMPIRELLA: INTIMATE VISIONS
Harris Publications: 2006 ($3.95, one-shots)

..., Amanda Conner 1 - r/Vampirella Monthly #1 with commentary; interview; 2 covers 4.00
..., Joe Jusko 1 - r/Vampirella; Blood Lust #1 with commentary; interview; 2 covers 4.00

VAMPIRELLA: JULIE STRAIN SPECIAL
Harris Publications: Sept, 2000 ($3.95, one-shot)

1-Photo-c w/yellow background; interview and photo gallery 4.00
1-Limited Edition ($9.95); cover photo w/black background 10.00

VAMPIRELLA/LADY DEATH (Also see Lady Death/Vampirella)
Harris Publications: Feb, 1999 ($3.50, one-shot)

1-Small-a/Nelson painted-c 6.00
1-Valentine Edition ($9.95); pencil-c by Small 10.00

VAMPIRELLA: LEGENDARY TALES
Harris Publications: May, 2000 - No. 2, June, 2000 ($2.95, B&W)

1,2-Reprints from magazine; Cleavenger painted-c 4.00
1,2-($9.95) Variant painted-c by Mike Mayhew 10.00

VAMPIRELLA LIVES
Harris Publications: Dec, 1996 - No. 3, Feb, 1997 ($3.50/$2.95, limited series)

1-Die cut-c; Quesada & Palmiotti-c, Ellis-s/Conner-a 6.00
1-Deluxe Ed.-photo-c 6.00
2,3-($2.95)-Two editions (1 photo-c): 3-J. Scott Campbell-c 5.00

VAMPIRELLA: MINDWARP
Dynamite Entertainment: 2022 - No. 5, 2022 ($3.99, limited series)

1-5-Jeff Parker-s/Benjamin Dewey-a 4.00

VAMPIRELLA: MORNING IN AMERICA
Harris Publications/Dark Horse Comics: 1991 - No. 4, 1992 ($3.95, B&W, lim. series, 52 pgs.)

1,2-All have Kaluta painted-c 2 4 6 8 10 12
3,4 2 4 6 8 10 12

VAMPIRELLA OF DRAKULON
Harris Publications: Jan, 1996 - No. 5, Sept, 1996 ($2.95)

0-5: All reprints. 0-Jim Silke-c. 3-Polybagged w/card. 4-Texeira-c 4.00

VAMPIRELLA/PAINKILLER JANE
Harris Publications: May, 1998 ($3.50, one-shot)

1-Waid & Augustyn-s/Leonardi & Palmiotti-a 4.00
1-($9.95) Variant-c 10.00

VAMPIRELLA PIN-UP SPECIAL
Harris Publications: Oct, 1995 ($2.95, one-shot)

1-Hughes-c, pin-ups by various 5.00
1-Variant-c 5.00

VAMPIRELLA QUARTERLY
Harris Publications: Spring, 2007 - Summer, 2008 ($4.95/$4.99, quarterly)

Spring, 2007 - Summer, 2008-New stories and re-colored reprints; five or six covers 5.00

VAMPIRELLA / RED SONJA
Dynamite Entertainment: 2019 - No. 12, 2020 ($3.99, limited series)

1-12: 1-Set in 1969; Jordie Bellaire-s/Drew Moss-a; multiple-c on each. 7,8-1920s NY 4.00

VAMPIRELLA: RETRO
Harris Publications: Mar, 1998 - No. 3, May, 1998 ($2.50, B&W, limited series)

1-3: Reprints; Silke painted covers 4.00

VAMPIRELLA: REVELATIONS
Harris Publications: No. 0, Oct, 2005 - No. 3, Feb, 2006 ($2.99, limited series)

0-3-Vampirella's origin retold, Lilith app.; Carey-s/Lilly-a; two covers on each 4.00
... Book 1 TPB (2006, $12.95) r/series; Carey interview, script for #1, Lilly sketch pages 13.00

VAMPIRELLA: ROSES FOR THE DEAD
Dynamite Entertainment: 2018 - No. 4, 2019 ($3.99, limited series)

1-4-Kristina Deak-Linsner-s/Joseph Linsner-a; covers by Linsner & Tucci; Evily app. 4.00

VAMPIRELLA: SAD WINGS OF DESTINY
Harris Publications: Sept, 1996 ($3.95, one-shot)

1-Jusko-c 6.00

VAMPIRELLA: SECOND COMING
Harris Publications: 2009 - No. 4 ($1.99, limited series)

1-4: 1-Hester-s/Sampere-a; multiple covers on each. 3,4-Rio-a 4.00

VAMPIRELLA/SHADOWHAWK: CREATURES OF THE NIGHT (Also see Shadowhawk)
Harris Publications: 1995 ($4.95, one-shot)

1 5.00

VAMPIRELLA/SHI (See Shi/Vampirella)
Harris Publications: Oct, 1997 ($2.95, one-shot)

1-Ellis-s 6.00
1-Chromium-c 1 2 3 5 6 8

VAMPIRELLA: SILVER ANNIVERSARY COLLECTION
Harris Publications: Jan, 1997 - No. 4 Apr, 1997 ($2.50, limited series)

1-4: Two editions: Bad Girl by Beachum, Good Girl by Silke 5.00

VAMPIRELLA: SOUTHERN GOTHIC
Dynamite Entertainment: 2013 - No. 5, 2014 ($3.99)

1-5-Nate Cosby-s/José Luis-a; regular & photo-c on each 4.00

VAMPIRELLA'S SUMMER NIGHTS
Harris Publications: 1992 (one-shot)

1-Art Adams infinity cover; centerfold by Stelfreeze 2 4 6 10 14 18

VAMPIRELLA STRIKES
Harris Publications: Sept, 1995 - No. 8, Dec, 1996 ($2.95, limited series)

1-8: 1-Photo-c. 2-Deodato-c; polybagged w/card. 5-Eudaemon-c/app; wraparound-c; alternate-c exists. 6-(6/96)-Mark Millar script; Texeira-c; alternate-c exists. 7-Flip book 4.00
1-Newsstand Edition; diff. photo-c., 1-Limited Ed.; diff. photo-c 4.00
Annual 1-(12/96, $2.95) Delano-s; two covers 4.00

VAMPIRELLA STRIKES
Dynamite Entertainment: 2013 - No. 6, 2013 ($3.99)

1-6: 1-Five covers (Turner, Finch, Manara, Desjardins & photo); Desjardins-a 4.00

VAMPIRELLA STRIKES (Follows events of Vengeance of Vampirella #25)

Vampirella / Red Sonja #1 © DYN & RS LLC

The Vampire Slayer #2 © 20th TV

Vampironica #4 © ACP

	GD 2.0	VG 4.0	FN 6.0	VF 8.0	VF/NM 9.0	NM- 9.2

Dynamite Entertainment: 2022 - Present ($3.99)

1-10: 1-Sniegoski-s/Lau-a 4.00

VAMPIRELLA: THE DARK POWERS
Dynamite Entertainment: 2020 - No. 5, 2021 ($3.99)

1-5-Vampirella joins Project Superpowers team; Abnett-s/Davidson-a. 3-The Flame app. 4.00

VAMPIRELLA THE RED ROOM
Dynamite Entertainment: 2012 - No. 4, 2012 ($3.99)

1-4-Three covers on each; Brereton-s/Diaz-a 4.00

VAMPIRELLA: 25TH ANNIVERSARY SPECIAL
Harris Publications: Oct, 1996 ($5.95, squarebound, one-shot)

	GD	VG	FN	VF	VF/NM	NM-
nn-Reintro The Blood Red Queen of Hearts; James Robinson, Grant Morrison & Warren Ellis scripts; Mark Texeira, Michael Bair & Amanda Conner-a(p); Frank Frazetta-c	1	2	3	5	6	8
nn-($6.95)-Silver Edition	1	3	4	6	8	10

VAMPIRELLA VERSUS PURGATORI
Dynamite Entertainment: 2020 - No. 5, 2021 ($3.99, limited series)

1-5-Fawkes-s/Sarraseca-a; multiple covers on each; Lilith & Hel app. 4.00

VAMPIRELLA VERSUS RED SONJA
Dynamite Entertainment: 2022 - No. 5, 2022 ($3.99, limited series)

1-4-Abnett-s/Ranaldi-a; multiple covers on each 4.00

VAMPIRELLA VS. DRACULA
Dynamite Entertainment: 2012 - No. 6, 2012 ($3.99, limited series)

1-6-Harris-s/Rodriguez-a/Linsner-c 4.00

VAMPIRELLA VS. HEMORRHAGE
Harris Publications: Apr, 1997 ($3.50)

1 6.00

VAMPIRELLA VS. PANTHA
Harris Publications: Mar, 1997 ($3.50)

1-Two covers; Millar-s/Texeira-c/a 4.00

VAMPIRELLA VS. REANIMATOR
Dynamite Entertainment: 2018 - No. 4, 2019 ($3.99, limited series)

1-4-Herbert West app.; Cullen Bunn-s/Blacky Shepherd-a; multiple covers on each 4.00

VAMPIRELLA/WETWORKS (See Wetworks/Vampirella)
Harris Publications: June, 1997 ($2.95, one-shot)

1 4.00
1-($9.95) Alternate Edition; cardstock-c 10.00

VAMPIRELLA/WITCHBLADE
Harris Publications: 2003; Oct, 2004; Oct, 2005 ($2.99, one-shots)

1-Brian Wood-s/Steve Pugh-a; 3 covers by Texeira, Conner and Pugh 4.00
...: The Feast (10/05, $2.99) Joyce Chin-a; covers by Chin, Conner, Rodriguez 4.00
...: Union of the Damned (10/04, $2.99, one-shot) Sharp-a; three covers 4.00
Trilogy TPB (2006, $12.95) r/one-shots; art gallery and gallery of multiple covers 13.00

VAMPIRELLA YEAR ONE
Dynamite Entertainment: 2022 - Present ($3.99, limited series)

1-5-Priest-s/Gündüz-a 4.00

VAMPIRE, PA (Also see Al Capone, Vampire)
Moonstone: 2010 - No. 3, Oct, 2010 ($3.99)

1-3: 1-Intro. Vampire Hunter Dean; J.C. Vaughn-s/Brendon & Brian Fraim-a; three covers. 3-Zombie Proof back-up; Spencer-a 4.00
...: Bite Out of Crime (American Mythology, 7/19, $3.99) Vaughn-s/Fraims-a; six covers 4.00

VAMPIRE'S CHRISTMAS, THE (Also see Dark Ivory)
Image Comics: Oct, 2003 ($5.95, over-sized graphic novel)

nn-Linsner-s/a; Dubisch-painted-a 6.00

VAMPIRE SLAYER, THE (See the Buffy the Vampire Slayer titles)
BOOM! Studios: Apr, 2022 - Present ($4.99)

1-11: 1-Sarah Gailey-s/Michael Shelfer-a; alternate reality where Willow is the Slayer 5.00

VAMPIRE STATE BUILDING
Ablaze Publishing: 2019 - No. 4, 2020 ($3.99)

1-4-Charlie Adlard-a; Ange & Renault-s 4.00

VAMPIRES: THE MARVEL UNDEAD
Marvel Comics: Dec, 2011 ($3.99, one-shot)

1-Handbook-style profiles of vampire characters in the Marvel Universe; Seeley-c 4.00

VAMPIRE TALES
Marvel Comics Group: Aug, 1973 - No. 11, June, 1975 (75¢, B&W, magazine)

	GD 2.0	VG 4.0	FN 6.0	VF 8.0	VF/NM 9.0	NM- 9.2
1-Morbius, the Living Vampire begins by Pablo Marcos (1st solo Morbius series & 5th Morbius app.)	10	20	30	64	132	200
2-Intro. Satana; Steranko-r	19	38	57	133	297	460
3,5,6: 3-Satana app. 5-Origin Morbius. 6-1st full Lilith app. in this title (continued from Giant-Size Chillers #1)	5	10	15	33	57	80
4,7: 4-1st Lilith cameo app. on inside back-c	5	10	15	30	50	70
8-1st solo Blade story (see Tomb of Dracula)	8	16	24	52	99	145
9-Blade app.	5	10	15	33	57	80
10,11	4	8	12	23	37	50
Annual 1(10/75)-Heath-r/#9	4	8	12	25	40	55

NOTE: ***Alcala** a-6, 8, 9i. **Boris** c-4, 6. **Chaykin** a-7. **Everett** a-1r. **Gulacy** a-7p. **Heath** a-9. **Infantino** a-3r. **Gil Kane** a-4, 5r.*

VAMPIRE VERSES, THE
CFD Productions: Aug, 1995 - No. 4, 1995 ($2.95, B&W, mature)

1-4 3.00

VAMPIRONICA (Archie Comics' Veronica)(Continues in Jughead The Hunger vs Vampironica)
Archie Comic Publications: May, 2018 - No. 5, Feb, 2019 ($3.99, limited series)

1-5: 1-Veronica becomes a vampire; Greg & Meg Smallwood-s/Greg S.-a; multiple covers. 4,5-Greg Scott-a 4.00

VAMPIRONICA: NEW BLOOD (Archie Comics' Veronica)
Archie Comic Publications: Jan, 2020 - No. 4, Aug, 2020 ($3.99, limited series)

1-4: 1-Tieri & Moreci-s/Mok-a; multiple covers. 3-Story of Sir Francis Lodge 4.00

VAMPIVERSE (Vampirella)
Dynamite Entertainment: 2021 - No. 6, 2022 ($3.99, limited series)

1-6-Sniegoski & Acheson-s/Maine-a; multiple covers on each. 1-Main-c by Hughes 4.00
... Presents: The Vamp 1 (2022, $4.99) 5.00

VAMPI VICIOUS
Harris Publications (Anarchy Studios): Aug, 2003 - No. 3, Nov, 2003 ($2.99)

1-3: 1-McKeever-s/Dogan-a; 3 covers by Dogan, Lau & Noto. 3-Kau-a 4.00

VAMPI VICIOUS CIRCLE
Harris Publications (Anarchy Studios): Jun, 2004 - No. 3, Sept, 2004 ($2.99/$9.95)

1-3: B. Clay Moore-s 4.00
1-3-($9.95) Limited Edition w/variant-c. 1-Noto-c. 2-Norton-c. 3-Lucas-c 10.00

VAMPI VICIOUS RAMPAGE
Harris Publications (Anarchy Studios): Feb, 2005 - No. 2, Apr, 2005 ($2.99)

1,2: Raab-s/Lau-a; two covers on each 4.00

VAMPI VS. XIN
Harris Publications (Anarchy Studios): Oct, 2004 - No. 2, Jan, 2005 ($2.99)

1,2-Faerber-s/Lau-a; two covers 4.00

VAMPS
DC Comics (Vertigo): Aug, 1994 - No. 6, Jan, 1995 ($1.95, lim. series, mature)

1-6-Bolland-c 3.00
Trade paperback ($9.95)-r/#1-6 10.00

VAMPS: HOLLYWOOD & VEIN
DC Comics (Vertigo): Feb, 1996 - No. 6, July, 1996 ($2.25, lim. series, mature)

1-6: Winslade-c 3.00

VAMPS: PUMPKIN TIME
DC Comics (Vertigo): Dec, 1998 - No. 3, Feb, 1999 ($2.50, lim. series, mature)

1-3: Quitely-c 3.00

VANDROID
Dark Horse Comics: Feb, 2014 - No. 5, Jun, 2014 ($3.99, limited series)

1-5-Tommy Lee Edwards & Noah Smith-s/Dan McDaid-a/Edwards-c 4.00

VANGUARD (...Outpost: Earth) (See Megaton)
Megaton Comics: 1987 ($1.50)

1-Erik Larsen-c(p) 4.00

VANGUARD (See Savage Dragon #2)
Image Comics (Highbrow Entertainment): Oct, 1993 - No. 6, 1994 ($1.95)

1-6: 1-Wraparound gatefold-c; Erik Larsen back-up-a; Supreme x-over. 3-(12/93)-Indicia says December 1994. 4-Berzerker back-up. 5-Angel Medina-a(p) 3.00

VANGUARD (See Savage Dragon #2)
Image Comics: Aug, 1996 - No. 4, Feb, 1997 ($2.95, B&W, limited series)

1-4 3.00

VANGUARD: ETHEREAL WARRIORS
Image Comics: Aug, 2000 ($5.95, B&W)

1-Fosco & Larsen-a 6.00

GD VG FN VF VF/NM NM-
2.0 4.0 6.0 8.0 9.0 9.2

VANGUARD ILLUSTRATED
Pacific Comics: Nov, 1983 - No. 11, Oct, 1984 (Baxter paper)(Direct sales only)
1,3-6,8-11: 1-Nudity scenes 5.00
2-1st app. Stargrazers (see Legends of the Stargrazers; Dave Stevens-c
3 6 9 14 20 26
7-1st app. Mr. Monster (r-in Mr. Monster #1); nudity scenes 6.00
NOTE: ***Evans** a-7. **Kaluta** c-5, 7p. **Perez** a-6; c-6. **Rude** a-1-4; c-4. **Williamson** c-3.*

VANGUARD: STRANGE VISITORS
Image Comics: Oct, 1996 - No.4, Feb, 1997 ($2.95, B&W, limited series)
1-4: 3-Supreme-c/app. 3.00

VAN HELSING: FROM BENEATH THE RUE MORGUE (Based on the 2004 movie)
Dark Horse Comics: Apr, 2004 ($2.99, one-shot)
1-Hugh Jackman photo-c; Dysart-s/Alexander-a 3.00

VANISH
Image Comics: Sept, 2022 - Present ($3.99)
1-4-Cates-s/Stegman-a 4.00

VANITY (See Pacific Presents #3)
Pacific Comics: Jun, 1984 - No. 2, Aug, 1984 ($1.50, direct sales)
1,2: Origin 3.00

VARIANTS, THE
Marvel Comics: Aug, 2022 - No. 5 ($3.99)
1-5-A Jessica Jones mystery; Gail Simone-s/Phil Noto-a. 2,3-She-Hulk app. 4.00

VARIETY COMICS (The Spice of Comics)
Rural Home Publ./Croyden Publ. Co.: 1944 - No. 2, 1945; No. 3, 1946
1-Origin Captain Valiant 37 74 111 222 361 500
2-Captain Valiant 20 40 60 114 182 250
3(1946-Croyden)-Captain Valiant 17 34 51 98 154 210

VARIETY COMICS (See Fox Giants)

VARKING DEAD (Cerebus)
Aardvark-Vanaheim: Mar, 2020 ($4.00, B&W)
1-Walking Dead homage; Cerebus figures placed over original Doré artwork of Hell 4.00

VARK THING (Cerebus)
Aardvark-Vanaheim: Dec, 2019 ($4.00, B&W)
1-Swamp Thing homage figures placed over original Gustave Doré artwork of Hell 4.00

VARK WARS (Cerebus)
Aardvark-Vanaheim: Nov, 2019 ($4.00, B&W)
1-Cerebus figures placed over original Gustave Doré artwork of Hell 4.00

VARSITY
Parents' Magazine Institute: 1945
1 14 28 42 78 112 145

VAULT OF CEREBUS (Imagery from Glamourpuss & Cerebus in Hell)
Aardvark-Vanaheim: Oct, 2020 ($4.00, B&W)
1-Cerebus figures placed over Doré artwork and zombies; Vault of Horror #19-c swipe 4.00

VAULT OF EVIL
Marvel Comics Group: Feb, 1973 - No. 23, Nov, 1975
1 (1950s reprints begin) 6 12 18 38 69 100
2-23: 3,4-Brunner-c. 11-Kirby-a 3 6 9 19 30 40
NOTE: ***Ditko** a-14r, 15r, 20-22r. **Drucker** a-10r(Mystic #52), 13r(Uncanny Tales #42). **Everett** a-11r(Menace #2), 13r(Menace #4); c-10. **Heath** a-5r. **Gil Kane** c-1, 6. **Kirby** a-11. **Krigstein** a-20r(Uncanny Tales #54). **Reinman** r-1. **Tuska** a-6r.*

VAULT OF HORROR (Formerly War Against Crime #1-11) (Also see EC Archives)
E. C. Comics: No. 12, Apr-May, 1950 - No. 40, Dec-Jan, 1954-55
12 (Scarce)-ties w/Crypt Of Terror as 1st horror comic; classic horror story "Terror Train" reprinted by popular demand in Haunt of Fear #20
943 1886 2829 7544 12,022 16,500
13-Morphine story 166 332 498 1328 2114 2900
14-Classic horror story "The Strong Couple" redrawn in 3-D Tales of Terror #2
126 252 378 1008 1604 2200
15- "Terror in the Swamp" is same story w/minor changes as "The Thing in the Swamp" from Haunt of Fear #15 114 228 342 912 1456 2000
16 83 166 249 664 1057 1450
17-Classic werewolf-c 97 194 291 776 1238 1700
18,19 71 142 213 568 909 1250
20-25: 22-Frankenstein-c & adaptation. 23-Used in **POP**, pg. 84; Davis-a(2); Ingels bio. 24-Craig bio. 57 114 171 456 728 1000
26-B&W & color illos in **POP** 80 160 240 640 1020 1400
27-29,31,33,34,36: 31-Ray Bradbury bio. 36- "Pipe Dream" classic opium addict story by Krigstein; "Twin Bill" cited in articles by T.E. Murphy, Wertham
53 106 159 424 675 925
30-Classic severed arm-c 120 240 360 960 1530 2100
32-Censored-c 86 172 258 688 1094 1500
35-X-Mas-c; "And All Through the House" adapted for 1972 Tales From The Crypt film
251 502 753 2008 3204 4400
37-1st app. Drusilla, a Vampirella look alike; Williamson-a
74 148 222 592 946 1300
38 53 106 159 424 675 925
39-Classic Craig woman in bondage/torture-c 94 188 282 752 1201 1650
40-Low distribution 74 148 222 592 946 1300
NOTE: ***Craig** art in all but No. 13 & 33; c-12-40. **Crandall** a-33, 34, 39. **Davis** a-17-38. **Evans** a-27, 28, 30, 32, 33. **Feldstein** a-12-16. **Ingels** a-13-20, 22-40. **Kamen** a-15-22, 25, 29, 35. **Krigstein** a-36, 38-40. **Kurtzman** a-12, 13. **Orlando** a-24, 31, 40. **Wood** a-12-14. #22, 29 & 31 have Ray Bradbury adaptations. #16 & 17 have H. P. Lovecraft adaptations.*

VAULT OF HORROR, THE
Gladstone Publ.: Aug, 1990 - No. 6, June, 1991 ($1.95, 68 pgs.)(#4 on: $2.00)
1-Craig-c(r); all contain EC reprints 6.00
2-6: 2,4-6-Craig-c(r). 3-Ingels-c(r) 5.00

VAULT OF HORROR
Russ Cochran/Gemstone Publishing: Sept, 1991 - No. 5, May, 1992 ($2.00); Oct, 1992 - No. 29, Oct, 1999 ($1.50/$2.00/$2.50)
1-29: E.C reprints. 1-4r/VOH #12-15 w/original-c 4.00

VAULT OF SPIDERS (Tie-ins to the Spider-Geddon x-over)
Marvel Comics: Dec, 2018 - No. 2, Jan, 2019 ($4.99)
1,2-Short stories of alternate Spider-Verse Spider-heroes; s/a by various 5.00

V...-COMICS (Morse code for "V" - 3 dots, 1 dash)
Fox Feature Syndicate: Jan, 1942 - No. 2, Mar-Apr, 1942
1-Origin V-Man & the Boys; The Banshee & The Black Fury, The Queen of Evil, & V-Agents begin; Nazi-c 314 628 942 2198 3849 5500
2-Nazi bondage/torture-c 300 600 900 2040 3570 5100

VECTOR
Now Comics: 1986 - No. 4, 1986? ($1.50, 1st color comic by Now Comics)
1-4: Computer-generated art 3.00

VEIL
Dark Horse Comics: Mar, 2014 - No. 5, Oct, 2014 ($3.50)
1-5-Greg Rucka-s/Toni Fejzula-a/c 3.50

VEILS
DC Comics (Vertigo): 1999 ($24.95, one-shot)
Hardcover-($24.95) Painted art and photography; McGreal-s 25.00
Softcover ($14.95) 15.00

VELOCITY (Also see Cyberforce)
Image Comics (Top Cow Productions): Nov, 1995 - No. 3, Jan, 1996 ($2.50, limited series)
1-3: Kurt Busiek scripts in all. 2-Savage Dragon-c/app. 4.00
...: Pilot Season 1 (10/07, $2.99) Casey-s/Maguire-a 4.00
Vol. 2 #1-4 (6/10 - No. 4, 4/11, $3.99) Rocafort-a/Marz-s; multiple covers 4.00

VELVET
Image Comics: Oct, 2013 - No. 15, Jul, 2016 ($3.50/$3.99)
1-14-Brubaker-s/Epting-a/c. 5-$2.99-c 3.50
15-($3.99) 4.00

VENGEANCE
Marvel Comics: Sept, 2011 - No. 6, Feb, 2012 ($3.99, limited series)
1-6-Casey-s/Dragotta-a. 1-Magneto and Red Skull app. 4-Loki cover 4.00

VENGEANCE OF THE MOON KNIGHT
Marvel Comics: Nov, 2009 - No. 10, Sept, 2010 ($3.99/$2.99)
1,9: 1-($3.99) Hurwitz-s/Opeña-a; covers by Yu, Ross & Finch; back-up r/Moon Knight #1 ('80) 9-Spider-Man & Sandman app.; Campbell-c 2 4 6 8 10 12
2-8,10: 2-Sentry app. 5-Spider-Man app. 7,8-Deadpool app. 10-Secret Avengers app. 5.00

VENGEANCE OF VAMPIRELLA (Becomes Vampirella: Death & Destruction)
Harris Comics: Apr, 1994 - No. 25, Apr, 1996 ($2.95)
1-($3.50)-Quesada/Palmiotti "bloodfoil" wraparound-c 2 4 6 8 10 12
1-2nd printing; blue foil-c 4.00
1-Gold 24.00
2-8: 8-Polybagged w/trading card 5.00
9-25: 10-w/coupon for Hyde -25 poster. 11,19-Polybagged w/ trading card. 25-Quesada & Palmiotti red foil-c 4.00
...: Bloodshed (1995, $6.95) 7.00

VENGEANCE OF VAMPIRELLA (Volume 2)
Dynamite Entertainment: 2019 - No. 25, 2021 ($3.99)
1-25: 1-Set 25 years in the future; Sniegoski-s/Sta. Maria-a; multiple covers on each 4.00

VENGEANCE OF VAMPIRELLA: THE MYSTERY WALK
Harris Comics: Nov, 1995 ($2.95, one-shot)
0 1 2 3 5 6 8

VENGEANCE SQUAD
Charlton Comics: July, 1975 - No. 6, May, 1976 (#1-3 are 25¢ issues)
1-Mike Mauser, Private Eye begins by Staton 2 4 6 11 16 20
2-6: Morisi-a in all 1 3 4 6 8 10
5,6 (Modern Comics-r, 1977) 1 2 3 5 6 8

VENOM
Marvel Comics: June, 2003 - No. 18, Nov, 2004 ($2.25/$2.99)
1-Herrera-a/Way-s 2 4 6 9 12 15
2-15: 2-7-Herrera-a/Way-s. 6,7-Wolverine app. 8-10-Wolverine-c/app.; Kieth-c. 11-Fantastic Four app. 5.00
16-18 1 2 3 5 6 8
... Vol. 1: Shiver (2004, $13.99, TPB) r/#1-5 14.00
... Vol. 2: Run (2004, $19.99, TPB) r/#6-13 20.00
... Vol. 3: Twist (2004, $13.99, TPB) r/#14-18 14.00

VENOM (See Amazing Spider-Man #654 & 654.1)(Also see Secret Avengers)
Marvel Comics: May, 2011 - No. 42, Dec, 2013 ($3.99/$2.99)
1-Flash Thompson with the symbiote; Remender-s/Tony Moore-a/Quesada-c
3 6 9 15 22 28
2-Cover swipe of ASM #300; Kraven app. 3 6 9 17 25 34
3-12-($2.99) 3-Deodato-c. 6-8-Spider Island 4.00
13-($3.99) Circle of Four; Red Hulk, X-23, and Ghost Rider app. 4.00
13.1, 13.2, 13.3, 13.4, 14-($2.99) Circle of Four parts 2-6 3.00
15-27, 27.1, 28-42: 15-Secret Avengers app. 16,17-Toxin app. 26,27-Minimum Carnage. 38-1st app. Mania. 42-Mephisto app. 4.00
...: Flashpoint 1 (2011, $4.99) r/Amazing Spider-Man #654, 654.1 and Venom #1
3 6 9 14 20 25

VENOM (Also see Amazing Spider-Man: Venom Inc.)
Marvel Comics: Jan, 2017 - No. 6, Jun, 2017; No. 150, Jul, 2017 - No. 165, Jun, 2018 ($3.99)
1-Mike Costa-s/Gerardo Sandoval-a; intro. Lee Price; Mac Gargan app.
1 3 4 6 8 10
2-6 4.00
[Title switches to legacy numbering after #6 (6/17)]
150-($5.99) Eddie Brock as Venom; Spider-Man app.; Tradd Moore-a; cover gallery 6.00
151-165: 152,153-Moon Girl and Devil Dinosaur app. 155-158-Kraven app.; Bagley-a.

The Variants #1 © MAR

Venom #38 © MAR

Venus #19 © MAR

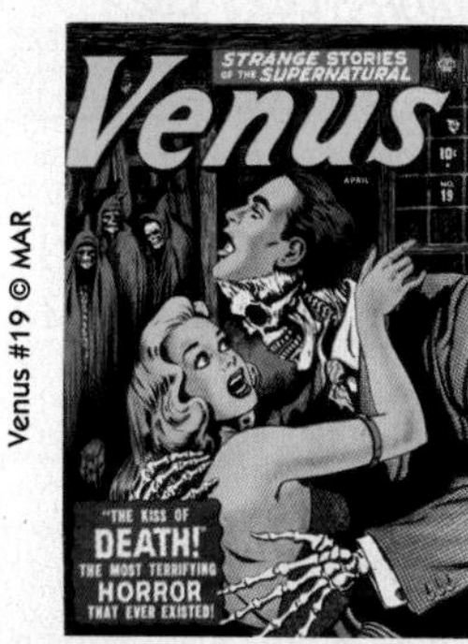

	GD	VG	FN	VF	VF/NM	NM-
	2.0	4.0	6.0	8.0	9.0	9.2

159-Venom Inc. part 3; Sandoval-a. 160-Venom Inc. part 5 4.00

VENOM (Follows Venomized series)
Marvel Comics: Jul, 2018 - No. 35, Aug, 2021 ($4.99/$3.99)
1-($4.99) Cates-s/Stegman-a; Eddie Brock with the symbiote; intro. Rex Strickland 2 4 6 8 10 12
2,4-24,26-34 ($3.99) 2-5-Spider-Man (Miles Morales) app. 4-Origin of Knull. 13-15-War of the Realms tie-ins. 17-20-Absolute Carnage tie-ins. 21-24-Venom Island; Bagley-a. 31-34-King In Black 4.00
3-1st full app. Knull (6/18) 7 14 21 46 86 125
25-($5.99) 1st app. Virus; Cates-s/Bagley-a; Carnage app.; back-up w/Michelinie-s/Lim-a 6.00
35-($9.99) 200th Legacy issue; Venom gets a new host; bonus cover gallery 10.00
Annual 1 (12/18, $4.99) Short stories by various incl. Cates, Michelinie, Lim, Stokoe 5.00
Annual 1 (9/19, $4.99) Cady-s/Di Meo-a; Lady Hellbender app.; back-up origin; Ibáñez-a 5.00
...: The End 1 (3/20, $4.99) Warren-s/Cruz-a; Venom's last story in the far future 5.00
... 2099 #1 (2/20, $4.99) Tie-in to 2099 x-over; Venom's new host; Houser-s 5.00

VENOM
Marvel Comics: Dec, 2021 - Present ($5.99/$3.99)
1-($5.99) Ewing & Ram V-s/Hitch-a; Dylan Brock with the symbiote 6.00
2-17-($3.99) 8,9-Kang app.; Ewing-s. 13-16-Dark Web tie-ins 4.00

VENOMIZED
Marvel Comics: Jun, 2018 - No. 5, Jul, 2018 ($4.99/$3.99, weekly limited series)
1-($4.99) Bunn-s/Coello-a; X-Men vs. The Poisons 5.00
2-5-($3.99) 2,3,5-Bunn-s/Coello-a. 4-Libranda-a 4.00

VENOM: LETHAL PROTECTOR
Marvel Comics: Feb, 1993 - No. 6, July, 1993 ($2.95, limited series)
1-Red holo-grafx foil-c; Bagley-c/a in all 4 8 12 25 40 55
1-Gold variant sold to retailers 16 32 48 111 246 380
1-Black-c 100 200 300 800 1800 2800
NOTE: Counterfeit copies of the black-c exist and are valueless
2,4-6: Spider-Man app. in all 2 4 6 10 14 18
5-1st app. Phage, Lasher, Riot & Agony 3 6 9 16 23 30

VENOM: LETHAL PROTECTOR
Marvel Comics: May, 2022 - No. 5, Oct, 2022 ($4.99/$3.99, limited series)
1-($4.99) Michelinie-s/Fiorelli-a; set in the early days with Eddie Brock 5.00
2-5-($3.99) 5-Taskmaster app. 4.00

VENOM: SPACE KNIGHT
Marvel Comics: Jan, 2016 - No. 13, Dec, 2016 ($3.99)
1-13: 1-Robbie Thompson-s/Ariel Olivetti-a. 8-10-Jacinto-a. 11,12-Civil War II tie-in 4.00

VENOM: Marvel Comics (Also see Amazing Spider-Man #298-300)
... ALONG CAME A SPIDER, 1/96 - No. 4, 4/96 ($2.95)-Spider-Man & Carnage app. 2 4 6 9 12 15
... CARNAGE UNLEASHED, 4/95 - No. 4, 7/95 ($2.95) 1 3 4 6 8 10
... DARK ORIGIN, 10/08 - No. 5, 2/09 ($2.99) 1-5-Medina-a 6.00
... /DEADPOOL: WHAT IF?, 4/11 ($2.99) Remender-s/Moll-a/Young-c; Galactus app. 13 26 39 89 195 300
... DEATHTRAP: THE VAULT, 3/93 ($6.95) r/Avengers: Deathtrap: The Vault 2 4 6 8 10 12
... FIRST HOST, 10/18 - No. 5, 11/18 ($3.99) 1-5-Costa-s/Bagley & Lim-a 4.00
... FUNERAL PYRE, 8/93- No. 3, 10/93 ($2.95)-#1-Holo-grafx foil-c; Punisher app. in all 1 3 4 6 8 10
... LICENSE TO KILL,6/97 - No. 3, 8/97 ($1.95) 1 3 4 6 8 10
... NIGHTS OF VENGEANCE, 8/94 - No. 4, 11/94 ($2.95), #1-Red foil-c 1 3 4 6 8 10
... ON TRIAL, 3/97 - No. 3, 5/97 ($1.95) 1 3 4 6 8 10
... SEED OF DARKNESS, 7/97 ($1.95) #(-1) Flashback 1 3 4 6 8 10
... SEPARATION ANXIETY,12/94- No. 4, 3/95 ($2.95) #1-Embossed-c 1 3 4 6 8 10
... SIGN OF THE BOSS,3/97 - No. 2, 10/97 ($1.99) 1 3 4 6 8 10
... SINNER TAKES ALL, 8/95 - No. 5, 10/95 ($2.95) 1,2,4,5 1 3 4 6 8 10
3-1st time Ann Weying app. as female Venom 6 12 18 38 69 100
... SUPER SPECIAL, 8/95($3.95) #1-Flip book 2 4 6 11 16 20
... THE ENEMY WITHIN, 2/94 - No. 3, 4/94 ($2.95)-Demogoblin & Morbius app.
1-Glow-in-the-dark-c 2 4 6 11 16 20
... THE FINALE, 11/97 - No. 3, 1/98 ($1.99) 1 3 4 6 8 10
... THE HUNGER, 8/96- No. 4, 11/96 ($1.95) 1 3 4 6 8 10
... THE HUNTED, 5/96-No. 3, 7/96 ($2.95) 1 3 4 6 8 10
... THE MACE, 5/94 - No. 3, 7/94 ($2.95)-#1-Embossed-c 1 3 4 6 8 10
... THE MADNESS, 11/93- No. 3, 1/94 ($2.95)-Kelley Jones-c/a(p).
1-Embossed-c; Juggernaut app. 1 3 4 6 8 10
... TOOTH AND CLAW, 12/96 - No. 3, 2/97 ($1.95)-Wolverine-c/app. 1 3 4 6 8 10
... VS. CARNAGE, 9/04 - No. 4, 12/04 ($2.99)-Milligan-s/Crain-a; Spider-Man app. 1 3 4 6 8 10
TPB (2004, $9.99) r/#1-4 10.00

VENOMVERSE
Marvel Comics: Nov, 2017 - No. 5, Dec, 2017 ($4.99/$3.99, weekly limited series)
1-($4.99) Bunn-s/Coello-a; Venoms vs. The Poisons 5.00
2-5-($3.99) Bunn-s/Coello-a 4.00
...: War Stories 1 (11/17, $4.99) Multiverse of Venoms; short stories by various 5.00

VENTURE
AC Comics (Americomics): Aug, 1986 - No. 3, 1986? ($1.75)
1-3: 1-3-Bolt. 1-Astron. 2-Femforce. 3-Fazers 3.00

VENTURE
Image Comics: Jan, 2003 - No. 4, Sept, 2003 ($2.95)
1-4-Faerber-s/Igle-a 3.00

VENUS (See Agents of Atlas, Marvel Spotlight #2 & Weird Wonder Tales)
Marvel/Atlas Comics (CMC 1-9/LCC 10-19): Aug, 1948 - No. 19, Apr, 1952 (Also see Marvel Mystery #91)
1-Venus & Hedy Devine begin; 1st app. Venus; Kurtzman's "Hey Look" 366 732 1098 2562 4481 6400
2 168 336 504 1075 1838 2600
3,5 106 212 318 673 1162 1650
4-Kurtzman's "Hey Look" 168 336 504 1075 1838 2600
6-9: 6-Loki app. 7,8-Painted-c. 9-Begin 52 pgs.; book-length feature "Whom the Gods Destroy!" 93 186 279 591 1021 1450
10-S/F-horror issues begin (7/50) 129 258 387 826 1413 2000
11-S/F end of the world (11/50) 142 284 426 909 1555 2200
12-Colan-a 93 186 279 591 1021 1450
13-16-Venus by Everett, 2-3 stories each; covers-#13,15,16; 14-Everett part cover (Venus). 161 322 483 1030 1765 2500
17-Classic Everett horror & skeleton/bondage-c (scarce) 524 1048 1572 3825 6763 9700
18-Classic Everett horror-c 423 846 1289 3000 5250 7500
19-Classic Everett skeleton Good Girl-c 1250 2500 3750 9500 17,250 25,000
*NOTE: **Berg** s/f story-13. **Everett** c-13, 14(part; Venus only), 15-19. **Heath** s/f story-11. **Maneely** s/f story 10(3pg.), 16. **Morisi** a-19. **Syd Shores** c-6.*

VENUS
BOOM! Studios: Dec, 2015 - No. 4, Mar, 2016 ($3.99)
1-4-Loverd-s/Danlan-a 4.00

VERI BEST SURE FIRE COMICS
Holyoke Publishing Co.: No date (circa 1945) (Reprints Holyoke one-shots)
1-Captain Aero, Alias X, Miss Victory, Commandos of the Devil Dogs, Red Cross, Hammerhead Hawley, Capt. Aero's Sky Scouts, Flagman app.; same-c as Veri Best Sure Shot #1 55 110 165 352 601 850

VERI BEST SURE SHOT COMICS
Holyoke Publishing Co.: No date (circa 1945) (Reprints Holyoke one-shots)
1-Capt. Aero, Miss Victory by Quinlan, Alias X, The Red Cross, Flagman, Commandos of the Devil Dogs, Hammerhead Hawley, Capt. Aero's Sky Scouts; same-c as Veri Best Sure Fire #1 57 114 171 362 619 875

VERMILLION
DC Comics (Helix): Oct, 1996 - No. 12, Sept, 1997 ($2.25/$2.50)
1-12: 1-4: Lucius Shepard scripts. 4,12-Kaluta-c 3.00

VERONICA (Also see Archie's Girls, Betty &...)
Archie Comics: Apr, 1989 - No. 210, Feb, 2012
1-(75¢-c) 2 4 6 11 16 20
2-10: 2-(75¢-c) 5.00
11-22,24-38 4.00
23-Pot of Gold bikini-c (9/92) 3 6 9 19 30 40
39-Love Showdown pt. 4, Cheryl Blossom 6.00
40-70: 34-Neon ink-c 3.00

71-201,203-206: 134-Begin $2.19-c. 152,155-Cheryl Blossom app. 163-Begin $2.25-c 3.00
202-Intro. Kevin Keller, 1st openly gay Archie character; cover has blue background
3 6 9 14 19 24
202-Second printing; cover has black background 1 3 4 6 8 10
207-210-Kevin Keller mini-series 3.00

VERONICA'S PASSPORT DIGEST MAGAZINE (Becomes Veronica's Digest Magazine #3 on)
Archie Comics: Nov, 1992 - No. 6 ($1.50/$1.79, digest size)

1 5.00
2-6 3.00

VERONICA'S SUMMER SPECIAL (See Archie Giant Series Magazine #615, 625)

VERTICAL
DC Comics (Vertigo): 2003 ($4.95, 3-1/4" wide pages, one-shot)

1-Seagle-s/Allred & Bond-a; odd format 1/2 width pages with some 20" long spreads 5.00

VERTIGO DOUBLE SHOT
DC Comics (Vertigo): 2008 ($2.99)

1-Reprints House of Mystery (2008) #1 and Young Liars #1 in flip-book format 3.00

VERTIGO ESSENTIALS
DC Comics (Vertigo): Dec, 2013 - Feb, 2014 ($1.00, Flip book reprints with DC & Vertigo Essential Graphics novels catalog)

...: American Vampire 1 (2/14) Reprints #1; flip-c by Ryan Sook 3.00
...: Fables 1 (1/14) Reprints #1; flip-c by Ryan Sook 3.00
...: 100 Bullets 1 (2/14) Reprints #1; flip-c by Ryan Sook 3.00
...: The Sandman #1 (12/13, $1.00) Reprints Sandman #1 (1989) with flipbook 3.00
...: V For Vendetta 1 (12/13) Reprints first chapter; flip-c by Ryan Sook 3.00
...: Y: The Last Man 1 (1/14) Reprints #1; flip-c by Ryan Sook 3.00

VERTIGO: FIRST BLOOD
DC Comics (Vertigo): Feb, 2012 ($7.99, squarebound)

TPB-Reprints first issues of American Vampire, I Zombie, The Unwritten & Sweet Tooth 8.00

VERTIGO: FIRST CUT
DC Comics (Vertigo): 2008 ($4.99, TPB)

TPB-Reprints first issues of DMZ, Army@Love, Jack of Fables, Exterminators, Scalped, Crossing Midnight, and Loveless; preview of Air 5.00

VERTIGO: FIRST OFFENSES
DC Comics (Vertigo): 2005 ($4.99, TPB)

TPB-Reprints first issues of The Invisibles, Preacher, Fables, Sandman Mystery Theater, and Lucifer 5.00

VERTIGO: FIRST TASTE
DC Comics (Vertigo): 2005 ($4.99, TPB)

TPB-Reprints first issues of Y: The Last Man, 100 Bullets, Transmetropolitan, Books of Magick: Life During Wartime, Death: The High Cost of Living, and Saga of the Swamp Thing #21 (Alan Moore's first story on that title) 5.00

VERTIGO GALLERY, THE: DREAMS AND NIGHTMARES
DC Comics (Vertigo): 1995 ($3.50, one-shot)

1-Pin-ups of Vertigo characters by Sienkiewicz, Toth, Van Fleet & others; McKean-c 4.00

VERTIGO JAM
DC Comics (Vertigo): Aug, 1993 ($3.95, one-shot, 68 pgs.)(Painted-c by Fabry)

1-Sandman by Neil Gaiman, Hellblazer, Animal Man, Doom Patrol, Swamp Thing, Kid Eternity & Shade the Changing Man 5.00

VERTIGO POP! BANGKOK
DC Comics (Vertigo): July, 2003 - No. 4, Oct, 2003 ($2.95, limited series)

1-4-Camuncoli-c/a; Jonathan Vankin-s 3.00

VERTIGO POP! LONDON
DC Comics (Vertigo): Jan, 2003 - No. 4, Apr, 2003 ($2.95, limited series)

1-4-Philip Bond-c/a; Peter Milligan-s 3.00

VERTIGO POP! TOKYO
DC Comics (Vertigo): Sept, 2002 - No. 4, Dec, 2002 ($2.95, limited series)

1-4-Seth Fisher-c/a; Jonathan Vankin-s 3.00
Tokyo Days, Bangkok Nights TPB (2009, $19.99) r/#1-4 & Vertogo Pop! Bangkok #1-4 20.00

VERTIGO PREVIEW
DC Comics (Vertigo): 1992 (75¢, one-shot, 36 pgs.)

1-Vertigo previews; Sandman story by Neil Gaiman 3.00

VERTIGO QUARTERLY CMYK
DC Comics (Vertigo): Jun, 2014 - No. 4, Mar, 2015 ($7.99, limited series)

1-4-Color themed short story anthology. 1-Cyan. 2-Magenta. 3-Yellow. 4-Black 8.00

VERTIGO QUARTERLY SFX
DC Comics (Vertigo): Jun, 2015 - No. 4, Mar, 2016 ($7.99, limited series)

1-4-Sound effect-themed short story anthology. 1-"Pop!". 2-"Slam!". 3-"Krak!". 4-"Bang" 8.00

VERTIGO RAVE
DC Comics (Vertigo): Fall, 1994 (99¢, one-shot)

1-Vertigo previews 3.00

VERTIGO RESURRECTED: ...
DC Comics (Vertigo): Dec, 2010 - Feb, 2012 ($7.99, squarebound, reprints)

The Extremist 1 (1/11, 12/13) r/The Extremist #1-4 8.00
Finals 1 (5/11) r/Finals #1-4; Jill Thompson-a 8.00
Hellblazer 1 (2/11) r/Hellblazer #57,58,245,246 8.00
Hellblazer - Bad Blood 1 (6/11) r/Hellblazer Special: Bad Blood #1-4 8.00
Jonny Double 1 (10/11) r/Jonny Double #1-4; Azzarello-s/Risso-a 8.00
My Faith in Frankie 1 (1/12) r/My Faith in Frankie #1-4; Carey-s 8.00
Sandman Presents - Petrefax 1 (8/11) r/Sandman Presents: Petrefax #1-4 8.00
Sgt. Rock: Between Hell and a Hard Place 1,2 (1/12, 2/12) r/the 2003 HC 8.00
Shoot 1 (12/10) r/short stories by various incl. Quitely, Sale, Bolland, Risso, Jim Lee 8.00
The Eaters 1 (12/11) r/Vertigo Visions - The Eaters and other short stories 8.00
Winter's Edge 1 (2/11) r/Vertigo's Winter Edge #1-3; Bermejo-c 8.00

VERTIGO SECRET FILES
DC Comics (Vertigo): Aug, 2000 ($4.95)

...: Hellblazer 1 (8/00, $4.95) Background info and story summaries 5.00
...: Swamp Thing 1 (11/00, $4.95) Backstories and origins; Hale-c 5.00

VERTIGO VERITE: THE UNSEEN HAND
DC Comics (Vertigo): Sept, 1996 - No. 4, Dec, 1996 ($2.50, limited series)

1-4: Terry LaBan scripts in all 3.00

VERTIGO VISIONS
DC Comics (Vertigo): June, 1993 - Sept, 1998 (one-shots)

Dr. Occult 1 (7/94, $3.95) 4.00
Dr. Thirteen 1 (9/98, $5.95) Howarth-s 6.00
Prez 1 (7/95, $3.95) 4.00
The Geek 1 (6/93, $3.95) 4.00
The Eaters ($4.95, 1995)-Milligan story. 5.00
The Phantom Stranger 1 (10/93, $3.50) 4.00
Tomahawk 1 (7/98, $4.95) Pollack-s 5.00

VERTIGO WINTER'S EDGE
DC Comics (Vertigo): 1998, 1999 ($7.95/$6.95, square-bound, annual)

1-Winter stories by Vertigo creators; Desire story by Gaiman/Bolton; Bolland wraparound-c 8.00
2,3-($6.95)-Winter stories: 2-Allred-c. 3-Bond-c; Desire by Gaiman/Zulli 7.00

VERTIGO X ANNIVERSARY PREVIEW
DC Comics (Vertigo): 2003 (99¢, one-shot, 48 pgs.)

1-Previews of upcoming titles and interviews; Endless Nights, Shade, The Originals 4.00

VERY BEST OF DENNIS THE MENACE, THE
Fawcett Publ.: July, 1979 - No. 2, Apr, 1980 (95¢/$1.00, digest-size, 132 pgs.)

1,2-Reprints 2 4 6 8 10 12

VERY BEST OF DENNIS THE MENACE, THE
Marvel Comics Group: Apr, 1982 - No. 3, Aug, 1982 ($1.25, digest-size)

1-3: Reprints 2 3 4 6 8 10
1,2-Mistakenly printed with DC logo on cover 2 4 6 9 12 15

NOTE: ***Hank Ketcham** c-all. A few thousand of #1 & 2 were printed with DC emblem.*

VERY VICKY
Meet Danny Ocean: 1993? - No. 8, 1995 ($2.50, B&W)

1-8, ...: Calling All Hillbillies (1995, $2.50) 4.00

VERY WEIRD TALES (Also see Slithiss Attacks!)
Oceanspray Comics Group: Aug, 2002 - No. 2, Oct, 2002 ($4.00)

1-Mutant revenge, methamphetamine, corporate greed horror stories
3 6 9 16 23 30
2-Weird fantasy and horror stories 2 4 6 9 12 15

NOTE: *Created in prevention classes taught by Jon McClure at the Oceanspray Family Center in Newport, Oregon, and paid for by the Housing Authority of Lincoln County. All books are b&w with color covers. Issues #1-2 penciled and inked by various artists. All comics feature characters created by students and are signed and numbered by Jon McClure. Issues #1-2 have print runs of 100 each.*

VEXT
DC Comics: Mar, 1999 - No. 6, Aug, 1999 ($2.50, limited series)

1-6-Giffen-s. 1-Superman app. 3.00

V FOR VENDETTA
DC Comics: Sept, 1988 - No. 10, May, 1989 ($2.00, maxi-series)

1-Alan Moore scripts in all; David Lloyd-a 4 8 12 28 47 65
2-10 2 4 6 8 10 12
HC (1990) Limited edition 60.00
HC (2005, $29.99, dustjacket) r/series; foreward by Lloyd; promo art and sketches 30.00
Trade paperback (1990, $14.95) 20.00

VICE
Image Comics (Top Cow): Nov, 2005 - No. 5 ($2.99)

1-5-Coleite-s/Kirkham-a. 1-Three covers 3.00
1-Code Red Edition; variant Benitez-c 3.00

VIC FLINT (Crime Buster...)(See Authentic Police Cases #10-14 & Fugitives From Justice #2)
St. John Publ. Co.: Aug, 1948 - No. 5, Apr, 1949 (Newspaper reprints; NEA Service)

1 34 68 102 199 325 450
2 16 32 48 94 147 200
3-5 15 30 45 83 124 165

VIC FLINT (Crime Buster...)
Argo Publ.: Feb, 1956 - No. 2, May, 1956 (Newspaper reprints)

1,2 10 20 30 58 79 100

VICIOUS CIRCLE, A
BOOM! Studios: Dec, 2022 - No. 3 ($9.99, oversized 10.875" x 8.5")

1-Tomilin-s/Bermejo-a 1 3 4 6 8 10

VIC JORDAN (Also see Big Shot Comics #32)
Civil Service Publ.: April, 1945

1-1944 daily newspaper-r; WWII-c 26 52 78 154 252 350

VICKI (Humor)
Atlas/Seaboard Publ.: Feb, 1975 - No. 4, Aug, 1975 (No. 1,2: 68 pgs.)

1,2-(68 pgs.)-Reprints Tippy Teen; Good Girl art 5 10 15 35 63 90
3,4 (Low print) 6 12 18 37 66 95

VICKI VALENTINE (...Summer Special #1)
Renegade Press: July, 1985 - No. 4, July, 1986 ($1.70, B&W)

1-4: Woggon, Rausch-a; all have paper dolls. 2-Christmas issue 4.00

VICKY
Ace Magazine: Oct, 1948 - No. 5, June, 1949

nn(10/48)-Teenage humor 16 32 48 92 144 195
4(12/48), nn(2/49), 4(4/49), 5(6/49): 5-Dotty app. 13 26 39 74 105 135

VICTOR CROWLEY'S HATCHET HALLOWEEN TALES (Based on the 2007 movie)
American Mythology Productions: 2019, 2020 ($3.99)

1-Short stories by Pell-s/Mesarcia-a, Check-s/Bonk-a, Kuhoric-s/Calzada-a; 4 covers 4.00
... II (2020) Short stories by Kuhoric-s/Cantada-a, Pell-s/Miracolo-a, Green-s/Hoey-a 4.00

Vic Flint #2 © STJ

The Victories #1 © Michael Oeming

Villains For Hire #1 © MAR

GD 2.0 | VG 4.0 | FN 6.0 | VF 8.0 | VF/NM 9.0 | NM- 9.2

VICTORIAN UNDEAD
DC Comics (WildStorm): Jan, 2010 - No. 6, Jun, 2010 ($2.99)

1-6-Sherlock Holmes vs. Zombies; Edginton-s/Fabbri-a. 1-Two covers (Moore, Coleby) 3.00
...: Sherlock Holmes vs. Jekyll and Hyde (12/10, $4.99) Domingues-a/Van Sciver-c 5.00
...: Sherlock Holmes vs. Zombies TPB (2010, $17.99) r/#1-6; character design sketch art 18.00
... Volume 2 (1/11 - No. 5, 5/11) 1-3-($3.99) "Sherlock Holmes vs. Dracula" on-c; Fabbri-a 4.00
... Volume 2 - 4,5-($2.99) "Sherlock Holmes vs. Dracula" on-c; Fabbri-a 3.00

VICTORIES, THE
Dark Horse Comics: Aug, 2012 - No. 5, Dec, 2012 ($3.99 limited series)

1-5-Michael Avon Oeming-s/a/c 4.00
...Volume 2: Transhuman 1-15 (6/13 - No. 15, 9/14) Oeming-s/a/c. 11-15 Metahuman 4.00

VIC TORRY & HIS FLYING SAUCER (Also see Mr. Monster's...#5)
Fawcett Publications: 1950 (one-shot)

nn-Book-length saucer story by Powell; photo/painted-c 74 148 222 470 810 1150

VICTORY
Topps Comics: June, 1994 ($2.50, unfinished limited series)

1-Kurt Busiek script; Giffen-c/a; Rob Liefeld variant-c exists 3.00

VICTORY COMICS
Hillman Periodicals: Aug, 1941 - No. 4, Dec, 1941 (#1 by Funnies, Inc.)

1-The Conqueror by Bill Everett, The Crusader, & Bomber Burns begin; Conqueror's origin in text; Everett-c 400 800 1200 2800 4900 7000
2-Everett-c/a 213 426 639 1363 2332 3300
3,4: 4-WWII Japanese-c 181 362 543 1158 1979 2800

VIC VERITY MAGAZINE
Vic Verity Publ: 1945; No. 2, Jan?, 1946 - No. 7, Sept, 1946 (A comic book)

1-C. C. Beck-c/a 48 96 144 302 514 725
2-Beck-c 34 68 102 199 325 450
3-7: 6-Beck-a. 7-Beck-c 32 64 96 188 307 425

VIDEO JACK
Marvel Comics (Epic Comics): Nov, 1987 - No. 6, Nov, 1988 ($1.25)

1-5 3.00
6-Neal Adams, Keith Giffen, Wrightson, others-a 5.00

VIETNAM JOURNAL
Apple Comics: Nov, 1987 - No. 16, Apr, 1991 ($1.75/$1.95, B&W)

1-16: Don Lomax-c/a/scripts in all, 1-2nd print 4.00
...: Indian Country Vol. 1 (1990, $12.95)-r/#1-4 plus one new story 13.00

VIETNAM JOURNAL: VALLEY OF DEATH
Apple Comics: June, 1994 - No. 2, Aug, 1994 ($2.75, B&W, limited series)

1,2: By Don Lomax 4.00

VIGILANTE, THE (Also see New Teen Titans #23 & Annual V2#2)
DC Comics: Oct, 1983 - No. 50, Feb, 1988 ($1.25, Baxter paper)

1-Origin 1 3 4 6 8 10
2-16,19-49: 3-Cyborg app. 4-1st app. The Exterminator; Newton-a(p). 6,7-Origin. 20,21-Nightwing app. 35-Origin Mad Bomber. 47-Batman-c/s 4.00
17,18-Alan Moore scripts 5.00
50-Ken Steacy painted-c 5.00
Annual nn, 2 ('85, '86) 5.00

VIGILANTE
DC Comics: Nov, 2005 - No. 6, Apr, 2006 ($2.99, limited series)

1-6-Bruce Jones-s. 1,2,4-6-Ben Oliver-a 3.00

VIGILANTE
DC Comics: Feb, 2009 - No. 12, Jan, 2010 ($2.99)

1-12: 1-Wolfman-s/Leonardi-a. 3-Nightwing app. 5-X-over with Titans and Teen Titans 3.00

VIGILANTE: CITY LIGHTS, PRAIRIE JUSTICE (Also see Action Comics #42, Justice League of America #78, Leading Comics & World's Finest #244)
DC Comics: Nov, 1995 - No. 4, Feb, 1996 ($2.50, limited series)

1-4: James Robinson scripts/Tony Salmons-a/Mark Chiarello-c 3.00
TPB (2009, $19.99) r/#1-4 20.00

VIGILANTE 8: SECOND OFFENSE
Chaos! Comics: Dec, 1999 ($2.95, one-shot)

1-Based on video game 5.00

VIGILANTES, THE
Dell Publishing Co.: No. 839, Sept, 1957

Four Color 839-Movie 8 16 24 54 102 150

VIGILANTE: SOUTHLAND
DC Comics: Dec, 2016 - No. 3, Feb, 2017 ($3.99, unfinished series originally set for 6 issues)

1-3-Phillips-s/Casagrande-a; intro. Donny Fairchild 4.00

VIKING PRINCE, THE
DC Comics: 2010 ($39.99, hardcover with dustjacket)

HC-Recolored reprints of apps. in Brave and the Bold #1-5, 7-24 & team-up with Sgt. Rock in Our Army at War #162,163; new intro. by Joe Kubert 40.00

VIKINGS, THE (Movie)
Dell Publishing Co.: No. 910, May, 1958

Four Color 910-Buscema-a, Kirk Douglas photo-c 9 18 27 59 117 175

VIKINGS: GODHEAD (Based on the History Channel series)
Titan Comics: May, 2016 - No. 4, Sept, 2016 ($3.99)

1-4: 1-Cavan Scott-s/Staz Johnson-a; 3 covers 4.00

VIKINGS: UPRISING (Based on the History Channel series)
Titan Comics: Oct, 2016 - No. 4, Jan, 2017 ($3.99)

1-4: 1-Cavan Scott-s/Daniel Indro-a. 1-Five covers. 2-4-Three covers 4.00

VILLAINS AND VIGILANTES
Eclipse Comics: Dec, 1986 - No. 4, May, 1987 ($1.50/$1.75, limited series, Baxter paper)

1-4: Based on role-playing game. 2-4 ($1.75-c) 3.00

VILLAINS FOR HIRE
Marvel Comics: No. 0.1, Jan, 2012; No. 1, Feb, 2012 - No. 4, May, 2012 ($2.99)

0.1-Misty Knight, Silver Sable, Black Panther app.; Arlem-a 3.00
1-4-Abnett & Lanning-s/Arlem-a; Misty Knight app. 3.00

VILLAINS GIANT
DC Comics: 2019 ($4.99, 100 pgs., square-bound)

1-Three new short stories and three reprints; Joker, Harley, Deathstroke, Darkseid app. 5.00

VILLAINS UNITED (Leads into Infinite Crisis)
DC Comics: July, 2005 - No. 6, Dec, 2005 ($2.95/$2.50, limited series)

1-6-Simone-s/JG Jones-c. 1-The Secret Six and the "Society" form 3.00
...: Infinite Crisis Special 1 (6/06, $4.99) Simone-s/Eaglesham-a 5.00

VILLAINY OF DOCTOR DOOM, THE
Marvel Comics: 1999 ($17.95, TPB)

nn-Reprints early battle with the Fantastic Four 18.00

VIMANARAMA
DC Comics (Vertigo): Apr, 2005 - No. 3, June, 2005 ($2.95, limited series)

1-3-Grant Morrison-s/Philip Bond-a 3.00
TPB (2005, $12.99) r/#1-3 13.00

VINDICATION
Image Comics: Feb, 2019 - No. 4, May, 2019 ($3.99, limited series)

1-4-MD Marie-s/Carlos Miko-a 4.00

VINTAGE MAGNUS (...Robot Fighter)
Valiant: Jan, 1992 - No. 4, Apr, 1992 ($2.25, limited series)

1-4: 1-Layton-c; r/origin from Magnus R.F. #22 3.00

VINYL
Image Comics: Jun, 2021 - No. 6, Nov, 2021 ($3.99, limited series)

1-6-Doug Wagner-s/Daniel Hillyard-a 4.00

VINYL UNDERGROUND
DC Comics (Vertigo): Dec, 2007 - No. 12, Nov, 2008 ($2.99)

1-12: 1-Spencer-s/Gane & Stewart-a/Phillips-c 3.00
...: Pretty Dead Things TPB ('08, $17.99) r/#6-12 18.00
...: Watching the Detectives TPB ('08, $9.99) r/#1-5; David Laphan intro. 10.00

VIOLATOR (Also see Spawn #2)
Image Comics (Todd McFarlane Prods.): May, 1994 - No. 3, Aug, 1994 ($1.95, lim. series)

1-Alan Moore scripts in all 5.00
2,3: Bart Sears-c(p)/a(p) 4.00

VIOLATOR VS. BADROCK
Image Comics (Extreme Studios): May, 1995 - No. 4, Aug, 1995 ($2.50, limited series)

1-4: Alan Moore scripts in all. 1-1st app Celestine; variant-c (3?) 3.00

VIOLENT, THE
Image Comics: Dec, 2015 - No. 5, Jul, 2016 ($2.99)

1-5-Brisson-s/Gorham-a 3.00

VIOLENT LOVE
Image Comics: Nov, 2016 - No. 10, Dec, 2017 ($3.99)

1-10-Frank Barbiere-s/Victor Santos-a/c 4.00

VIOLENT MESSIAHS (...: Lamenting Pain on cover for #9-12, numbered as #1-4)
Image Comics: June, 2000 - No. 12 ($2.95)

1-Two covers by Travis Smith and Medina 4.00
1-Tower Records variant edition 5.00
2-8: 5-Flip book sketchbook 3.00
9-12-Lamenting Pain; 2 covers on each 3.00
...: Genesis (12/01, $5.95) r/'97 B&W issue, Wizard 1/2 prologue 6.00
...: The Book of Job TPB (7/02, $24.95) r/#1-8; Foreward by Gossett 25.00

VIP (TV)
TV Comics: 2000 ($2.95, unfinished series)

1-Based on the Pamela Lee (Anderson) TV show; photo-c 3.00

VIPER (TV)
DC Comics: Aug, 1994 - No. 4, Nov, 1994 ($1.95, limited series)

1-4-Adaptation of television show 3.00

VIRGINIAN, THE (TV)
Gold Key: June, 1963

1(10060-306)-Part photo-c of James Drury plus photo back-c
4 8 12 27 44 60

VIRTUA FIGHTER (Video Game)
Marvel Comics: Aug, 1995 (2.95, one-shot)

1-Sega Saturn game 3.00

VIRUS
Dark Horse Comics: 1993 - No. 4, 1993 ($2.50, limited series)

1-4: Ploog-c 4.00

VISION, THE
Marvel Comics: Nov, 1994 - No. 4, Feb, 1995 ($1.75, limited series)

1-4 4.00

VISION, THE (AVENGERS ICONS: ...)
Marvel Comics: Oct, 2002 - No. 4, Jan, 2003 ($2.99, limited series)

1-4-Geoff Johns-s/Ivan Reis-a 4.00
...: Yesterday and Tomorrow TPB (2005, $14.99) r/#1-4 & Avengers #57 (1st app.) 15.00

VISION (From the Avengers)
Marvel Comics: Jan, 2016 - No. 12, Dec, 2016 ($3.99)

1-Tom King-s/Gabriel Walta-a; the Vison and his new synthezoid family
3 6 9 16 23 30
2-4,7-12 4.00
5-Low print run 2 4 6 9 12 15
6-1st Sparky the Dog 2 4 6 9 12 15
... Director's Cut 1-6 (8/17 - No. 6, 1/18, $6.99) r/2 issues each with script and bonus art 7.00

VISION AND THE SCARLET WITCH, THE (See Marvel Fanfare)
Marvel Comics Group: Nov, 1982 - No. 4, Feb, 1983 (Limited series)

1-Mantlo-s/Leonardi-a 2 4 6 11 16 20
2-4: 2-Nuklo & Future Man app. 5.00

VISION AND THE SCARLET WITCH, THE
Marvel Comics Group: Oct, 1985 - No. 12, Sept, 1986 (Maxi-series)

V2#1-Retells origin; 1st app. in Avengers #57 2 4 6 9 12 15
2-11: 2-West Coast Avengers x-over 5.00
12-Birth of Wiccan & Speed 3 6 9 14 20 25

VISIONS
Vision Publications: 1979 - No. 5, 1983 (B&W, fanzine)

1-Flaming Carrot begins (1st app?); N. Adams-c 22 44 66 154 340 525
2-N. Adams, Rogers-a; Gulacy back-c; signed & numbered to 2000
9 18 27 57 111 165
3-Williamson-c(p); Steranko back-c 4 8 12 23 37 50
4-Flaming Carrot-c & info. 4 8 12 25 40 55
5-1 pg. Flaming Carrot 3 6 9 19 30 40

NOTE: ***Eisner** a-4. **Miller** a-4. **Starlin** a-3. **Williamson** a-5. After #4, Visions became an annual publication of The Atlanta Fantasy Fair.*

VISITOR, THE
Valiant/Acclaim Comics (Valiant): Apr, 1995 - No. 13, Nov, 1995 ($2.50)

1-13: 8-Harbinger revealed. 13-Visitor revealed to be Sting from Harbinger 3.00

VISITOR, THE
Valiant Entertainment: Dec, 2019 - No. 6, Jul, 2021 ($3.99)

1-6-Paul Levitz-s. 1-4,6-MJ Kim-a. 5-Soo Lee-a 4.00

VISITOR: HOW AND WHY HE STAYED, THE (Character from Hellboy)
Dark Horse Comics: Feb, 2017 - No. 5, Jul, 2017 ($3.99, limited series)

1-5-Mignola & Roberson-s/Grist-a/c; Hellboy app. 4.00

VISITOR VS. THE VALIANT UNIVERSE, THE
Valiant: Feb, 1995 - No. 2, Mar, 1995 ($2.95, limited series)

1,2 3.00

VIXEN: RETURN OF THE LION (From Justice League of America)
DC Comics: Dec, 2008 - No. 5, Apr, 2009 ($2.99, limited series)

1-5-G. Willow Wilson-s/Cafu-a; Justice League app. 3.00
TPB (2009, $17.99) r/#1-5 18.00

VOGUE (Also see Youngblood)
Image Comics (Extreme Studios): Oct, 1995 - No.3, Jan, 1996 ($2.50, limited series)

1-3: 1-Liefeld-c, 1-Variant-c 3.00

VOID INDIGO (Also see Marvel Graphic Novel)
Marvel Comics (Epic Comics): 11/84 - No. 2, 3/85 ($1.50, direct sales, unfinished series, mature)

1,2: Cont'd from Marvel G.N.; graphic sex & violence 3.00

VOLCANIC REVOLVER
Oni Press: Dec, 1998 - No. 3, Mar, 1999 ($2.95, B&W, limited series)

1-3: Scott Morse-s/a 3.00
TPB (12/99, $9.95, digest size) r/#1-3 and Oni Double Feature #7 prologue 10.00

VOLITION
AfterShock Comics: Aug, 2018 - No. 6, Jun, 2019 ($3.99)

1-6: 1-Ryan Parrott-s/Omar Francia-a 4.00

VOLTRON (TV)
Modern Publishing: 1985 - No. 3, 1985 (75¢, limited series)

1-Ayers-a in all; Jim Fry-c 5 10 15 35 63 90
2,3 2 4 6 11 16 20

VOLTRON (Volume 1)
Dynamite Entertainment: 2011 - No. 12, 2013 ($3.99)

1-12: 1-Padilla-a; covers by Alex Ross, Sean Chen & Wagner Reis. 2-5-Two covers 4.00

VOLTRON: A LEGEND FORGED (TV)
Devils Due Publishing: Jul, 2008 - No. 5, Apr, 2009 ($3.50)

1-5-Blaylock-s/Bear-a; 4 covers 3.50

VOLTRON: DEFENDER OF THE UNIVERSE (TV)
Image Comics: No. 0, May, 2003 - No. 5, Sept, 2003 ($2.50)

0-Jolley-s/Brooks-a; character pin-ups with background info 3.00
1-5-($2.95) 1-Three covers by Norton, Brooks and Andrews; Norton-a 3.00
...: Revelations TPB (2004, $11.95, digest-sized) r/#1-5; cover gallery 12.00

VOLTRON: DEFENDER OF THE UNIVERSE (TV)
Image Comics: Jan, 2004 - No. 11, Dec, 2004 ($2.95)

1-11: 1-Jolley-s; wraparound-c 3.00

VOLTRON: FROM THE ASHES
Dynamite Entertainment: 2015 - No. 6, 2016 ($3.99)

1-6: 1-Cullen Bunn-s/Blacky Shepherd-a 4.00

VOLTRON: YEAR ONE
Dynamite Entertainment: 2012 - No. 6, 2012 ($3.99, limited series)

1-6: 1-Two covers; Brandon Thomas-s/Craig Cermak-a 4.00

VOODA (Jungle Princess) (Formerly Voodoo) (See Crown Comics)
Ajax-Farrell (Four Star Publications): No. 20, April, 1955 - No. 22, Aug, 1955

20-Baker-c/a (r/Seven Seas #6) 71 142 213 454 777 1100
21,22-Baker-a plus Kamen/Baker story, Kimbo Boy of Jungle, & Baker-c(p) in all.
22-Censored Jo-Jo-r (name Powaa) 65 130 195 416 708 1000

NOTE: *#20-22 each contain one heavily censored-r of South Sea Girl by **Baker** from Seven Seas Comics with name changed to Vooda. #20-r/Seven Seas #6; #21-r/#4; #22-r/#3.*

VOODOO (Weird Fantastic Tales) (Vooda #20 on)
Ajax-Farrell (Four Star Publ.): May, 1952 - No. 19, Jan-Feb, 1955

1-South Sea Girl-r by Baker 200 400 600 1280 2190 3100
2-Rulah story-r plus South Sea Girl from Seven Seas #2 by Baker (name changed from Alani to El'nee) 129 258 387 826 1413 2000
3-Bakerish-a; man stabbed in face 103 206 309 659 1130 1600
4,8-Baker-r. 8-Severed head panels 103 206 309 659 1130 1600
5-Nazi death camp story (flaying alive) 84 168 252 538 919 1300
6,7,9,10: 6-Severed head panels 68 136 204 435 743 1050
11-18: 14-Zombies take over America. 15-Opium drug story-r/Ellery Queen #3. 16-Post nuclear world story.17-Electric chair panels
65 130 195 416 708 1000
19-Bondage-c; Baker-r(2)/Seven Seas #5 w/minor changes & #1, heavily modified; last pre-code; contents & covers change to jungle theme
71 142 213 454 777 1100
Annual 1(1952, 25¢, 100 pgs.)-Baker-a (scarce) 649 1298 1947 4738 8369 12,000

VOODOO
Image Comics (WildStorm): Nov, 1997 - No. 4, Mar, 1998 ($2.50, lim. series)

1-4: Alan Moore-s in all; Hughes-c. 2-4-Rio-a 5.00
1-Platinum Ed 10.00
Dancing on the Dark TPB ('99, $9.95) r/#1-4 10.00
...-Zealot: Skin Trade (8/95, $4.95) 5.00

VOODOO (DC New 52) (Also see Grifter)
DC Comics: Nov, 2011 - No. 12, Oct, 2012; No. 0, Nov, 2012 ($2.99)

1-12: 1-Marz-s/Basri-a/c. 3-Green Lantern (Kyle) app. 3.00
#0 (11/12, $2.99) Origin of Voodoo; Basri-a/c 3.00

VOODOO (See Tales of...)

VOODOO CHILD (Weston Cage & Nicolas Cage's...)
Virgin Comics: July, 2007 - No. 6, Dec, 2007 ($2.99)

1-6: 1-Mike Carey-s/Dean Hyrapiet-a; covers by Hyrapiet & Templesmith 3.00
Vol. 1 TPB (1/08, $14.99) r/#1-6; variant covers; intro by Weston Cage & Nicolas Cage 15.00

VOODOOM
Oni Press: June, 2000 ($4.95, B&W)

1-Scott Morse-s/Jim Mahfood-a 5.00

VORTEX
Vortex Publs.: Nov, 1982 - No. 15, 1988 (No month) ($1.50/$1.75, B&W)

1 ($1.95)-Peter Hsu-a; Ken Steacy-c; nudity 1 3 4 6 8 10
2,12: 2-1st app. Mister X (on-c only). 12-Sam Kieth-a 6.00
3-11,13-15 4.00

VORTEX
Comico: 1991 - No. 2? ($2.50, limited series)

1,2: Heroes from The Elementals 4.00

VOTE LOKI
Marvel Comics: Aug, 2016 - No. 4, Nov, 2016 ($3.99, limited series)

1-Loki runs for President; Hastings-s/Foss-a 2 4 6 9 12 15
2-4: 2-McCaffrey-a 6.00

VOYAGE TO THE BOTTOM OF THE SEA (Movie, TV)
Dell Publishing Co./Gold Key: No. 1230, Sept-Nov, 1961; Dec, 1964 - #16, Apr, 1970 (Painted-c)

Four Color 1230 (1961) 12 24 36 79 170 260

The Vision (2016) #6 © MAR

Vote Loki #2 © MAR

Walking Dead #40 © Robert Kirkman

	GD 2.0	VG 4.0	FN 6.0	VF 8.0	VF/NM 9.0	NM- 9.2
10133-412(#1, 12/64)(Gold Key)	10	20	30	64	132	200
2(7/65) - 5: Photo back-c, 1-5	6	12	18	41	76	110
6-14	4	8	12	28	47	65
15,16-Reprints	3	6	9	18	27	36

VOYAGE TO THE DEEP
Dell Publishing Co.: Sept-Nov, 1962 - No. 4, Nov-Jan, 1964 (Painted-c)

	GD 2.0	VG 4.0	FN 6.0	VF 8.0	VF/NM 9.0	NM- 9.2
1	5	10	15	33	57	80
2-4	4	8	12	23	37	50

VOYAGIS
Image Comics: Nov, 2022 - No. 5, Apr, 2023 ($3.99, limited series)

	GD 2.0	VG 4.0	FN 6.0	VF 8.0	VF/NM 9.0	NM- 9.2
1-5-Sumeyye Kesgin-s/a						4.00

VS
Image Comics: Feb, 2018 - No. 5, Jul, 2018 ($3.99)

	GD 2.0	VG 4.0	FN 6.0	VF 8.0	VF/NM 9.0	NM- 9.2
1-5-Ivan Brandon-s/Esad Ribic-a						4.00

V-WARS
IDW Publishing: Apr, 2014 - No. 11, Mar, 2015 ($3.99)

	GD 2.0	VG 4.0	FN 6.0	VF 8.0	VF/NM 9.0	NM- 9.2
1-11: 1-Vampire epidemic; Jonathan Maberry-s/Alan Robinson-a						4.00
...: God of Death One-Shot (4/19, $4.99) Maberry-s/Milne-a						5.00

WACKO
Ideal Publ. Corp.: Sept, 1980 - No. 3, Oct, 1981 (84 pgs., B&W, magazine)

	GD 2.0	VG 4.0	FN 6.0	VF 8.0	VF/NM 9.0	NM- 9.2
1-3	2	4	6	9	13	16

WACKY ADVENTURES OF CRACKY (Also see Gold Key Spotlight)
Gold Key: Dec, 1972 - No. 12, Sept, 1975

	GD 2.0	VG 4.0	FN 6.0	VF 8.0	VF/NM 9.0	NM- 9.2
1	3	6	9	14	20	26
2	2	4	6	10	14	18
3-12	2	4	6	8	10	12

(See March of Comics #405, 424, 436, 448)

WACKY DUCK (...Comics #3-6; formerly Dopey Duck; Justice Comics #7 on)(See Film Funnies)
Marvel Comics (NPP): No. 3, Fall, 1946 - No. 6, Summer, 1947; Aug, 1948 - No. 2, Oct, 1948

	GD 2.0	VG 4.0	FN 6.0	VF 8.0	VF/NM 9.0	NM- 9.2
3	39	78	117	231	378	525
4-Infinity-c	29	58	87	172	281	390
5,6(1947)-Becomes Justice comics	25	50	75	150	245	370
1(1948)	28	56	84	165	270	375
2(1948)	20	40	60	117	189	260
I.W. Reprint #1,2,7('58): 1-r/Wacky Duck #6	3	6	9	14	19	24
Super Reprint #10(I.W. on-c, Super-inside)	2	4	6	11	16	20

WACKY QUACKY (See Wisco)

WACKY RACELAND (Update of Hanna-Barbera's Wacky Races)
DC Comics: Aug, 2016 - No. 6, Jan, 2017 ($3.99)

	GD 2.0	VG 4.0	FN 6.0	VF 8.0	VF/NM 9.0	NM- 9.2
1-6: 1-Pontac-s/Manco-a; multiple covers; Penelope Pitstop & Dick Dastardly app.						4.00

WACKY RACES (TV)
Gold Key: Aug, 1969 - No. 7, Apr, 1972 (Hanna-Barbera)

	GD 2.0	VG 4.0	FN 6.0	VF 8.0	VF/NM 9.0	NM- 9.2
1	5	10	15	35	63	90
2-7	3	6	9	21	33	45

WACKY SQUIRREL (Also see Dark Horse Presents)
Dark Horse Comics: Oct, 1987 - No. 4, 1988 ($1.75, B&W)

	GD 2.0	VG 4.0	FN 6.0	VF 8.0	VF/NM 9.0	NM- 9.2
1	1	3	4	6	8	10
2,3						4.00
4-Superman parody with Action #1 cover homage	2	4	6	9	12	15
Halloween Adventure Special 1 (1987, $2.00)	1	2	3	5	6	8
Summer Fun Special 1 (1988, $2.00)						4.00

WACKY WITCH (Also see Gold Key Spotlight)
Gold Key: March, 1971 - No. 21, Dec, 1975

	GD 2.0	VG 4.0	FN 6.0	VF 8.0	VF/NM 9.0	NM- 9.2
1	4	8	12	25	40	55
2	3	6	9	14	20	26
3-10	2	4	6	10	14	18
11-21	2	4	6	8	10	12

(See March of Comics #374, 398, 410, 422, 434, 446, 458, 470, 482)

WACKY WOODPECKER (See Two Bit the...)
I. W. Enterprises/Super Comics: 1958; 1963

	GD 2.0	VG 4.0	FN 6.0	VF 8.0	VF/NM 9.0	NM- 9.2
I.W. Reprint #1,2,7 (nd-reprints Two Bit...): 7-r/Two-Bit, the Wacky Woodpecker #1.	2	4	6	11	16	20
Super Reprint #10('63): 10-r/Two-Bit, The Wacky Woodpecker #?	2	4	6	10	14	18

WAGON TRAIN (1st Series) (TV) (See Western Roundup under Dell Giants)
Dell Publishing Co.: No. 895, Mar, 1958 - No. 13, Apr-June, 1962 (All photo-c)

	GD 2.0	VG 4.0	FN 6.0	VF 8.0	VF/NM 9.0	NM- 9.2
Four Color 895 (#1)	10	20	30	64	132	200
Four Color 971(#2),1019(#3)	6	12	18	41	76	110
4(1-3/60),6-13	5	10	15	34	60	85
5-Toth-a	6	12	18	37	66	95

WAGON TRAIN (2nd Series)(TV)
Gold Key: Jan, 1964 - No. 4, Oct, 1964 (All front & back photo-c)

	GD 2.0	VG 4.0	FN 6.0	VF 8.0	VF/NM 9.0	NM- 9.2
1-Tufts-a in all	5	10	15	30	50	70
2-4	4	8	12	23	37	50

WAITING PLACE, THE
Slave Labor Graphics: Apr, 1997 - No. 6, Sept, 1997 ($2.95)

	GD 2.0	VG 4.0	FN 6.0	VF 8.0	VF/NM 9.0	NM- 9.2
1-6-Sean McKeever-s						3.00
Vol. 2 - 1(11/99), 2-11						3.00
12-($4.95)						5.00

WAITING ROOM WILLIE (See Sad Case of...)

WAKANDA (Black Panther anthology)
Marvel Comics: Dec, 2022 - No. 5, Apr, 2023 ($4.99/$3.99)

	GD 2.0	VG 4.0	FN 6.0	VF 8.0	VF/NM 9.0	NM- 9.2
1-($4.99) Focus on Shuri; back-up story with history of the Black Panthers						5.00
2-5 ($3.99) 2-M'Baku. 3-Killmonger. 4-Tosin. 5-Okoye						4.00

WAKANDA FOREVER (See Amazing Spider-Man: Wakanda Forever for part 1)
Marvel Comics: Sept, 2018 - Oct, 2018 ($4.99, limited series)

	GD 2.0	VG 4.0	FN 6.0	VF 8.0	VF/NM 9.0	NM- 9.2
... Avengers (10/18) Part 3; Capt. America, She-Hulk, Black Panther, Storm, Rogue app.						5.00
... X-Men (9/18) Part 2; Storm, Rogue, Nightcrawler app.						5.00

WAKE, THE
DC Comics (Vertigo): Jul, 2013 - No. 10, Sept, 2014 ($2.99)

	GD 2.0	VG 4.0	FN 6.0	VF 8.0	VF/NM 9.0	NM- 9.2
1-Scott Snyder-s/Sean Murphy-a/c						5.00
1-Variant-c by Andy Kubert						8.00
1-Director's Cut (10/13, $4.99) B&W version, behind-the-scenes production content						5.00
2-10: 6-Story jumps 200 years ahead; Leeward app.						3.00
... Part One TPB (2/14, $9.99) r/#1-5						10.00

WAKE THE DEAD
IDW Publishing: Sept, 2003 - No. 5, Mar, 2004 ($3.99, limited series)

	GD 2.0	VG 4.0	FN 6.0	VF 8.0	VF/NM 9.0	NM- 9.2
1-5-Steve Niles-s/Chee-a						4.00
TPB (6/04, $19.99) r/series; intro. by Michael Dougherty; embossed die cut cover						20.00

WALK IN (Dave Stewart's ...)
Virgin Comics: Dec, 2006 - No. 6, May, 2007 ($2.99)

	GD 2.0	VG 4.0	FN 6.0	VF 8.0	VF/NM 9.0	NM- 9.2
1-6: 1-5-Parker-s/Padlekar-a. 6-Parker-a						3.00

WALKING DEAD, THE (Inspired the 2010 AMC television series)(Also see Negan Lives!)
Image Comics: Oct, 2003 - No. 193, Jul, 2019 ($2.95/$2.99, B&W)

	GD 2.0	VG 4.0	FN 6.0	VF 8.0	VF/NM 9.0	NM- 9.2
1-Robert Kirkman-s in all/Tony Moore-a; 1st app. Rick Grimes, Shane, Morgan & Duane	48	96	138	359	805	1250
1 Special Edition (5/08, $3.99) r/#1; Kirkman afterword; original script and proposal	3	6	9	16	23	30
2-Tony Moore-a through #6	16	32	48	111	246	380
3	9	18	27	61	123	185
4	8	16	24	52	99	145
5,6: 6-Shane killed	6	12	18	41	76	110
7-Charlie Adlard-a begins; 1st app. Tyreese	5	10	15	31	53	75
8-10	4	8	12	25	40	55
11-18,20: 13-Prison arc begins	3	6	9	16	23	30
19-1st app. Michonne	10	20	30	69	147	225
21-26,28-47,49,50: 25-Adlard covers begin. 28-Rick loses his hand. 46-Tyreese killed.	2	4	6	9	12	15
27-1st app of The Governor	7	14	21	46	86	125
48-Lori, Herschel, others killed	4	8	12	25	40	55
50-Variant wraparound superhero-style cover by Erik Larsen	5	10	15	34	60	85
51,52,54-60: 58-Morgan returns	2	4	6	8	10	12
53-1st app. Abraham & Rosita	5	10	15	33	57	80
61-Preview of Chew; 1st app. Gabriel	4	8	12	25	40	55
62,64-74: 66-Dale dies. 70-1st Douglas Monroe	1	3	4	6	8	10
63-Flip book with B&W reprint of Chew #1	3	6	9	16	24	32
75-(7/10, $3.99) Orange background-c; back-up alien/sci-fi "fantasy" in color; TV series preview with cast photos	2	4	6	9	12	15
75-Variant-c homage to issue #1	3	6	9	21	33	45
76-91: 85-Flip book w/Witch Doctor #0. 86-Flip book w/Elephantmen	1	3	4	6	8	10
92-Intro. Paul Monroe (Jesus)	3	6	9	17	26	35
93-96						6.00
97-99,101-114: 97-"Something to Fear" pt. 1. 98-Abraham killed. 107-Intro Ezekiel						5.00
100-(7/12, $3.99) 1st app. Negan; Glen killed; multiple covers by Adlard, Silvestri, Quitely, McFarlane, Phillips, Hitch, & Ottley	3	6	9	16	23	30

	GD	VG	FN	VF	VF/NM	NM-
	2.0	4.0	6.0	8.0	9.0	9.2

100-Wraparound-c by Adlard 2 4 6 9 12 15
106-Variant wraparound-c by Adlard for his 100th issue
2 4 6 10 16 20
115-"All Out War" begins; 10 connecting covers by Adlard
1 2 3 5 6 8
116-126-"All Out War" 4.00
127-(5/14) Intro. Magna; bonus preview of Outcast 2 4 6 8 10 12
128-174: 132-1st Whisperers attack. 135-Intro. Lydia. 138-Intro. Alpha. 139-Michonne returns 144-Death of Ezekiel and Rosita and others. 150-Six covers. 156-Death of Alpha. 157-162-Whisperer War; 2 covers (Adlard & Art Adams). 163-(25¢-c). 167-Death of Andrea. 171-Intro Princess 4.00
175-191-($3.99) 175-1st app. The Commonwealth. 185-Flip book with Outpost Zero #1 4.00
192-Death of Rick Grimes 5.00
193-($3.99, 84 pgs.) Final issue; afterword by Kirkman; fake cover art for #194-196 4.00
193-2nd printing ($3.99, 84 pgs.) 4.00
... FCBD 2013 Special (5/13, giveaway) reprints bonus stories from Michonne Special and The Governor Special; new Tyreese background story 3.00
Image Firsts: The Walking Dead #1 (3/10, $1.00) reprints #1
2 4 6 13 18 22
...: Michonne Special (10/12, $2.99) Reprints debut from #19 and story from Playboy
1 3 4 6 8 10
...: Michonne Special - 2nd printing (3/13, $2.99) 3.00
... #1 Tenth Anniversary Special (10/13, $5.99) reprints #1 with color; Kirkman's original series proposal; Kirkman interview 2 4 6 8 11 14
... "The Alien" (2020, $19.99, HC) New story taking place in Barcelona; Brian K. Vaughan-s/ Marcos Martin-a; bonus character sketches, page layouts and cover concepts 20.00
...: The Governor Special (2/13, $2.99) Reprints debut from #27 and story from CBLDF Liberty Annual 2012 6.00
...: Tyreese Special (10/13, $2.99) Reprints debut from #7 and story from FCBD 2013 4.00
... Book 1 HC (2006, $29.99) r/#1-12; sketch pages, cover gallery; Kirkman afterword 45.00
... Book 2 HC (2006, $29.99) r/#13-24; sketch pages, cover gallery 40.00
... Book 3 HC (2007, $29.99) r/#25-36; sketch pages, cover gallery 35.00
... Book 4 HC (2008, $29.99) r/#37-48; sketch pages, cover gallery 35.00
... Book 5 HC (2010, $29.99) r/#49-60; sketch pages, cover gallery 35.00
... Book 6 HC (2010, $34.99) r/#61-72; sketch pages, cover gallery 35.00
... Book 7 HC (2011, $34.99) r/#73-84; sketch pages, cover gallery 35.00
... Book 8 HC (2012, $34.99) r/#85-96; sketch pages, cover gallery 35.00
... Book 9 HC (2013, $34.99) r/#97-108; sketch pages, cover gallery 35.00
... Book 10 HC (2014, $34.99) r/#109-120; sketch pages, cover gallery 35.00
... Book 11 HC (2015, $34.99) r/#121-132; sketch pages, cover gallery 35.00
...Vol. 1: Days Gone Bye (5/04, $9.95, TPB) r/#1-4 20.00
...Vol. 2: Miles Behind Us (10/04, $12.95, TPB) r/#7-12 18.00
...Vol. 3: Safety Behind Bars (2005, $12.95, TPB) r/#13-18 18.00
...Vol. 4: The Heart's Desire (2005, $12.99, TPB) r/#19-24 18.00
...Vol. 5: The Best Defense (2006, $12.99, TPB) r/#25-30 18.00
...Vol. 6: This Sorrowful Life (2007, $12.99, TPB) r/#31-36 15.00
...Vol. 7: The Calm Before (2007, $12.99, TPB) r/#37-42 15.00
...Vol. 8: Made to Suffer (2008, $14.99, TPB) r/#43-48 15.00
...Vol. 9: Here We Remain (2009, $14.99, TPB) r/#49-54 15.00
...Vol. 10: The Road Ahead (2009, $14.99, TPB) r/#55-60 15.00
...Vol. 11: Fear the Hunters (2010, $14.99, TPB) r/#61-66 15.00
...Vol. 12: Life Among Them (2010, $14.99, TPB) r/#67-72 15.00
...Vol. 13: Too Far Gone (2010, $14.99, TPB) r/#73-78 15.00
...Vol. 14: No Way Out (2011, $14.99, TPB) r/#79-84 15.00
...Vol. 15: We Find Ourselves (2011, $14.99, TPB) r/#85-90 15.00
...Vol. 16: A Larger World (2012, $14.99, TPB) r/#91-96 15.00
...Vol. 17: Something to Fear (2012, $14.99, TPB) r/#97-102 15.00
...Vol. 18: What Comes After (2013, $14.99, TPB) r/#103-108 15.00
...Vol. 19: March To War (2013, $14.99, TPB) r/#109-114 15.00
...Vol. 20: All Out War Part 1 (2014, $14.99, TPB) r/#115-120 15.00
...Vol. 21: All Out War Part 2 (2014, $14.99, TPB) r/#121-126 15.00
...Vol. 22: A New Beginning (2014, $14.99, TPB) r/#127-132 15.00
...Vol. 23: Whispers Into Screams (2015, $14.99, TPB) r/#133-138 15.00
...Vol. 24: Life and Death (2015, $14.99, TPB) r/#139-144 15.00
...Vol. 25: No Turning Back (2016, $14.99, TPB) r/#145-150 15.00
...Vol. 26: Call to Arms (2016, $14.99, TPB) r/#151-156 15.00
...Vol. 27: The Whisperer War (2017, $14.99, TPB) r/#157-162 15.00
...Vol. 28: A Certain Doom (2017, $16.99, TPB) r/#163-168 17.00
...Vol. 29: Lines We Cross (2018, $16.99, TPB) r/#169-174 17.00
...Vol. 30: New World Order (2018, $16.99, TPB) r/#175-180 17.00
...Vol. 31: The Rotten Core (2018, $16.99, TPB) r/#181-186 17.00
...Vol. 32: Rest in Peace (2019, $16.99, TPB) r/#187-193 17.00

WALKING DEAD DELUXE, THE
Image Comics: Oct, 2020 - Present ($3.99)

1-58-Newly colored reprints of original issues with Kirkman commentary and bonus "cutting room floor" content; multiple variant covers on each 4.00

WALKING DEAD SURVIVORS' GUIDE, THE
Image Comics: Apr, 2011 - No. 4 ($2.99, B&W)

1,2-Alphabetical listings of character profiles, first (and last) apps. and current status
2 4 6 11 16 20
3,4 1 3 4 6 8 10

WALKING DEAD WEEKLY, THE (Reprints)
Image Comics: Jan, 2011 - No. 52, Dec, 2011 ($2.99, B&W, weekly)

1-Reprints issues with original letter columns; new Kirkman afterword
3 6 9 21 33 45
1-Arizona Comic Con variant-c 3 6 9 16 23 30
2-4,7 2 4 6 9 12 15
5-Death of Amy 4 8 12 27 44 60
6-Death of Shane 3 6 9 19 30 40
8-18,20-26,28-52 1 2 3 5 6 8
19-r/1st Michonne 6 12 18 38 69 100
27-r/1st app. The Governor 3 6 9 16 23 30

WALK THROUGH HELL, A
AfterShock Comics: May, 2018 - No. 12, Jul, 2019 ($3.99)

1-12-Garth Ennis-s/Goran Sudzuka-a 4.00

WALL·E (Based on the Disney/Pixar movie)
BOOM! Studios: No. 0, Nov, 2009 - No. 7, Jun, 2010 ($2.99)

0-7: 0-Prequel; J. Torres-s 4.00

WALLY (Teen-age)
Gold Key: Dec, 1962 - No. 4, Sept, 1963

1 4 8 12 22 35 48
2-4 3 6 9 16 24 32

WALLY THE WIZARD
Marvel Comics (Star Comics): Apr, 1985 - No. 12, Mar, 1986 (Children's comic)

1-12: Bob Bolling a-1,3; c-1,9,11,12 5.00
1-Variant with "Star Chase" game on last page and inside back-c
2 4 6 9 12 15

WALLY WOOD'S T.H.U.N.D.E.R. AGENTS (See Thunder Agents)
Deluxe Comics: Nov, 1984 - No. 5, Oct, 1986 ($2.00, 52 pgs.)

1-5: 5-Jerry Ordway-c/a in Wood style 6.00

NOTE: ***Anderson** a-2i, 3i. **Buckler** a-4. **Ditko** a-3, 4. **Giffen** a-1p-4p. **Perez** a-1p, 2, 4; c-1-4.*

WALT DISNEY CHRISTMAS PARADE (Also see Christmas Parade)
Whitman Publ. Co. (Golden Press): Wint, 1977 ($1.95, cardboard-c, 224 pgs.)

11191-Barks-r/Christmas in Disneyland #1, Dell Christmas Parade #9 & Dell Giant #53
4 8 12 27 44 60

WALT DISNEY COMICS DIGEST
Gold Key: June, 1968 - No. 57, Feb, 1976 (50¢, digest size)

1-Reprints Uncle Scrooge #5; 192 pgs. 7 14 21 46 86 125
2-4-Barks-r 5 10 15 31 53 75
5-Daisy Duck by Barks (8 pgs.); last published story by Barks (art only) plus 21 pg. Scrooge-r by Barks 7 14 21 48 89 130
6-13-All Barks-r 3 6 9 21 33 45
14,15 3 6 9 16 23 30
16-Reprints Donald Duck #26 by Barks 3 6 9 20 31 42
17-20-Barks-r 3 6 9 17 26 35
21-31,33,35-37-Barks-r; 24-Toth Zorro 3 6 9 16 23 30
32,41,45,47-49 2 4 6 11 16 20
34,38,39: 34-Reprints 4-Color #318. 38-Reprints Christmas in Disneyland #1. 39-Two Barks-r/WDC&S #272, 4-Color #1073 plus Toth Zorro-r
3 6 9 16 23 30
40-Mickey Mouse-r by Gottfredson 2 4 6 13 18 22
42,43-Barks-r 2 4 6 13 18 22
44-(Has Gold Key emblem, 50¢)-Reprints 1st story of 4-Color #29,256,275,282
5 10 15 30 50 70
44-Republished in 1976 by Whitman; not identical to original; a bit smaller, blank back-c, 69¢
3 6 9 16 23 30
46,50,52-Barks-r. 52-Barks-r/WDC&S #161,132 2 4 6 11 16 20
51-Reprints 4-Color #71 3 6 9 16 23 30
53-55: 53-Reprints Dell Giant #30. 54-Reprints Donald Duck Beach Party #2. 55-Reprints Dell Giant #49 2 4 6 10 14 18
56-r/Uncle Scrooge #32 (Barks) 2 4 6 13 18 22
57-r/Mickey Mouse Almanac('57) & two Barks stories 2 4 6 11 16 20

NOTE: ***Toth** a-52r. #1-10, 196 pgs.; #11-41, 164 pgs.; #42 on, 132 pgs. Old issues were being reprinted & distributed by Whitman in 1976.*

WALT DISNEY GIANT (Disney)
Bruce Hamilton Co. (Gladstone): Sept, 1995 - No. 7, Sept, 1996 ($2.25, bi-monthly, 48 pgs.)

1-7: 1-Scrooge McDuck in "Hearts of the Yukon"; Rosa-c/a/scripts plus r/F.C. #218; Scrooge & Glittering Goldie-c. 2-Uncle Scrooge-r by Barks plus 17 pg. text story. 3-Donald the Mighty Duck; Rosa-c; Barks & Rosa-r. 4-Mickey and Goofy; new-a (story actually stars Goofy. Mickey Mouse by Caesar Ferioli; Donald Duck by Giorgio Cavazzano (1st in U.S.). 6-Uncle Scrooge & the Jr. Woodchucks; new-a and Barks-r. 7-Uncle Scrooge-r by Barks plus new-a 4.00

NOTE: *Series was initially solicited as Uncle Walt's Collectory. Issue #8 was advertised, but later cancelled.*

WALT DISNEY PAINT BOOK SERIES
Whitman Publ. Co.: No dates; circa 1975 (Beware! Has 1930s copyright dates) (79¢-c, 52 pgs. B&W, treasury-sized) (Coloring books, text stories & comics-r)

#2052 (Whitman #886-r) Mickey Mouse & Donald Duck Gag Book
3 6 9 20 31 42
#2053 (Whitman #677-r) 3 6 9 20 31 42
#2054 (Whitman #670-r) Donald-c 4 8 12 22 35 48
#2055 (Whitman #627-r) Mickey-c 3 6 9 20 31 42
#2056 (Whitman #660-r) Buckey Bug-c 3 6 9 18 28 38
#2057 (Whitman #887-r) Mickey & Donald-c 3 6 9 20 31 42

WALT DISNEY PRESENTS (TV)(Disney)
Dell Publishing Co.: No. 997, 6-8/59 - No. 6, 12-2/1960-61; No. 1181, 4-5/61 (All photo-c)

Four Color 997 (#1) 7 14 21 46 86 125
2(12-2/60)-The Swamp Fox(origin), Elfego Baca, Texas John Slaughter (Disney TV show) begin 5 10 15 31 53 75
3-6: 5-Swamp Fox by Warren Tufts 4 8 12 28 47 65
Four Color 1181-Texas John Slaughter 6 12 18 38 69 100

WALT DISNEY'S CHRISTMAS PARADE (Also see Christmas Parade)
Gladstone: Winter, 1988; No. 2, Winter, 1989 ($2.95, 100 pgs.)

1-Barks-r/painted-c 2 4 6 8 10 12
2-Barks-r 1 2 3 5 7 9

WALT DISNEY'S CHRISTMAS PARADE
Gemstone Publishing: Dec, 2003; 2004, 2005, 2006, 2008 ($8.95/$9.50, prestige format)

1-4: 1-Reprints and 3 new European holiday stories. 2-All reprints. 3-Reprints and 2 new stories, 4-Reprints and 5 new stories 9.00
5-($9.50) R/Uncle Scrooge #47 and European stories 9.50

WALT DISNEY'S COMICS AND STORIES (Cont. of Mickey Mouse Magazine)
(#1-30 contain Donald Duck newspaper reprints) (Titled "Comics And Stories" #264 to #?; titled "Walt Disney's Comics And Stories" #511 on)
Dell Publishing Co./Gold Key #264-473/Whitman #474-510/Gladstone #511-547/ Disney Comics #548-585/Gladstone #586-633/Gemstone Publishing #634-698/ Boom! Kids #699-720/IDW Publishing #721-on: 10/40 - #263, 8/62; #264, 10/62 - #510, 7/84; #511, 10/86 - #633, 2/99; #634, 7/03 - #698, 11/08; #699, 10/09 - #720, 6/11;

Walking Dead Deluxe #19 © Robert Kirkman

Wall•E #4 © DIS & Pixar

Walt Disney's Comics and Stories #140 © DIS

	GD 2.0	VG 4.0	FN 6.0	VF 8.0	VF/NM 9.0	NM- 9.2
#721, 7/15 - No. 743, 7/18						
NOTE: The whole number can always be found at the bottom of the title page in the lower left-hand or right hand panel.						
1(V1#1-c; V2#1-indicia)-Donald Duck strip-r by Al Taliaferro & Gottfredson's Mickey Mouse begin	2430	4860	7290	17,000	36,500	56,000
2	870	1740	2610	6100	13,050	20,000
3	391	782	1173	2737	5869	9000
4-Christmas-c; 1st Huey, Dewey & Louie-c this title (See Mickey Mouse Magazine V4#2 for 1st-c ever)	339	678	1017	2373	5087	7800
4-Special promotional, complimentary issue; cover same except one corner was blanked out & boxed in to identify the giveaway (not a paste-over). This special pressing was probably sent out to former subscribers to Mickey Mouse Mag. whose subscriptions had expired. (Very rare-5 known copies)	585	1170	1755	4100	8800	13,500
5-Goofy-c	272	544	816	1741	3521	5300
6-10: 8-Only Clarabelle Cow-c. 9-Taliaferro-c (1st)	226	452	678	1446	2923	4400
11-14: 11-Huey, Dewey & Louie-c/app.	174	348	522	1114	2257	3400
15-17: 15-The 3 Little Kittens (17 pgs.). 16-The 3 Little Pigs (29 pgs.); Christmas-c. 17-The Ugly Duckling (4 pgs.)	144	288	432	922	1861	2800
18-21	133	266	399	851	1726	2600
22-30: 22-Flag-c. 24-The Flying Gauchito (1st original comic book story done for WDC&S). 27-Jose Carioca by Carl Buettner (2nd original story in WDC&S)	113	226	339	723	1472	2200
31-New Donald Duck stories by Carl Barks begin (See F.C. #9 for 1st Barks Donald Duck)	400	800	1200	2560	5180	7800
32-Barks-a	232	464	696	1485	2543	3600
33-Barks-a; Gremlins app. (Vivie Risto-s/a); infinity-c	181	362	543	1158	1979	2800
34-Gremlins by Walt Kelly begin, end #41; Barks-a	141	282	423	902	1576	2250
35,36-Barks-a	138	276	414	883	1542	2200
37-Donald Duck by Jack Hannah	81	162	243	518	909	1300
38-40-Barks-a. 39-X-Mas-c. 40,41-Gremlins by Kelly	88	176	264	563	982	1400
41-50-Barks-a. 43-Seven Dwarfs-c app. (4/44). 45-50-Nazis in Gottfredson's Mickey Mouse Stories. 46-War Bonds-c	78	156	234	499	875	1250
51-60-Barks-a. 51-X-Mas-c. 52-Li'l Bad Wolf begins, ends #203 (not in #55). 58-Kelly flag-c	32	64	96	230	515	800
61-70: Barks-a. 61-Dumbo story. 63,64-Pinocchio stories. 63-Cover swipe from New Funnies #94. 64-X-Mas-c. 65-Pluto story. 66-Infinity-c. 67,68-Mickey Mouse Sunday-r by Bill Wright	28	56	84	202	451	700
71-80: Barks-a. 75-77-Brer Rabbit stories, no Mickey Mouse. 76-X-Mas-c. 78-"Bark's" name on wooden box shown on cover	25	50	75	175	388	600
81-87,89,90: Barks-a. 82-Goofy-c. 82-84-Bongo stories. 86-90-Goofy & Agnes app. 89-Chip 'n' Dale story	20	40	60	138	307	475
88-1st app. Gladstone Gander by Barks (1/48)	26	52	78	182	404	625
91-97,99: Barks-a. 95-1st WDC&S Barks-c. 96-No Mickey Mouse; Little Toot begins, ends #97. 99-X-Mas-c	18	36	54	126	281	435
98-1st Uncle Scrooge app. in WDC&S (11/48)	32	64	96	230	515	800
100-(1/49)-Barks-a	22	44	66	154	340	525
101-110-Barks-a. 107-Taliaferro-c; Donald acquires super powers	16	32	48	107	236	365
111,114,117-All Barks-a	13	26	39	89	195	300
112-Drug (ether) issue (Donald Duck)	20	40	60	138	307	475
113,115,116,118-123: No Barks. 116-Dumbo x-over. 121-Grandma Duck begins, ends #168; not in #135,142,146,155	10	20	30	64	132	200
124,126-130-All Barks-a. 124-X-Mas-c	10	20	30	70	150	230
125-1st app. Junior Woodchucks (2/51); Barks-a	18	36	54	124	275	425
131,133,135-137,139-All Barks-a	10	20	30	67	141	215
132-Barks-a(2) (D. Duck & Grandma Duck)	10	20	30	69	147	225
134-Intro. & 1st app. The Beagle Boys (11/51)	25	50	75	175	388	600
138-Classic Scrooge money story	16	32	48	110	243	375
140-(5/52)-1st app. Gyro Gearloose by Barks; 2nd Barks Uncle Scrooge-c; 3rd Uncle Scrooge cover app.	22	44	66	154	340	525
141-150-All Barks-a. 143-Little Hiawatha begins, ends #151,159	9	18	27	58	114	170
151-170-All Barks-a	8	16	24	51	96	140
171-199-All Barks-a	7	14	21	46	86	125
200	7	14	21	49	92	135
201-240: All Barks-a. 204-Chip 'n' Dale & Scamp begin	6	12	18	40	73	105
241-283: Barks-a. 241-Dumbo x-over. 247-Gyro Gearloose begins, ends #274. 256-Ludwig Von Drake begins, ends #274	5	10	15	35	63	90
284,285,287,290,295,296,309-311-Not by Barks	3	6	9	19	30	40
286,288,291-294,297,298,308-All Barks stories; 293-Grandma Duck's Farm Friends. 297-Gyro Gearloose. 298-Daisy Duck's Diary-r	4	8	12	23	37	50
289-Annette-c & back-c & story; Barks-s	4	8	12	27	44	60

	GD 2.0	VG 4.0	FN 6.0	VF 8.0	VF/NM 9.0	NM- 9.2
299-307-All contain early Barks-r (#43-117). 305-Gyro Gearloose	4	8	12	25	40	55
312-Last Barks issue with original story	4	8	12	25	40	55
313-315,317-327,329-334,336-341	3	6	9	15	22	28
316-Last issue published during life of Walt Disney	3	6	9	15	22	28
328,335,342-350-Barks-r	3	6	9	15	22	28
351-360-With posters inside; Barks reprints (2 versions of each with & without posters)	4	8	12	25	40	55
351-360-Without posters...	3	6	9	14	19	24
361-400-Barks-r	3	6	9	14	20	26
401-429-Barks-r	3	6	9	14	19	24
430,433,437,438,441,444,445,466-No Barks	2	4	6	8	11	14
431,432,434-436,439,440,442,443-Barks-r	2	4	6	10	14	18
440-Whitman edition	3	6	9	14	19	24
446-465,467-473-Barks-r	2	4	6	9	13	16
474(3/80),475-478 (Whitman)	3	6	9	14	19	24
479(8/80),481(10/80)-484(1/81) pre-pack only	5	10	15	30	50	70
480 (8-12/80)-(Very low distribution)	13	26	39	89	195	300
484 (1/81, 40¢-c) Cover price error variant (scarce)	6	12	18	38	69	100
484 (1/81) Regular 50¢ cover price; not pre-pack	3	6	9	19	30	40
485-499: 494-r/WDC&S #98	2	4	6	11	16	20
500-510 (All #90011 on-c; pre-packs): 500(4/83), 501(5/83), 502&503(7/83), 504-506(all 8/83), 507(4/84), 508(5/84), 509(6/84), 510(7/84). 506-No Barks	2	4	6	13	18	22
511-Donald Duck by Daan Jippes (1st in U.S.; in all through #518); Gyro Gearloose Barks-r begins (in most through #547); Wuzzles by Disney Studio (1st by Gladstone)	3	6	9	16	24	32
512,513	2	4	6	10	14	18
514-516,520	2	4	6	8	10	12
517-519,521,522,525,527,529,530,532-546: 518-Infinity-c. 522-r/1st app. Huey, Dewey & Louie from D. Duck Sunday. 535-546-Barks-r. 537-1st Donald Duck by William Van Horn in WDC&S. 541-545-52 pgs. 546,547-68 pgs. 546-Kelly-r. 547-Rosa-a						6.00
523,524,526,528,531,547: Rosa-s/a in all. 523-1st Rosa 10 pager	2	4	6	9	12	15
548-($1.50, 6/90)-1st Disney issue; new-a; no M. Mouse	1	2	3	4	5	7
549,551-570,572,573,577-579,581,584 ($1.50): 549-Barks-r begin, ends #585, not in #555, 556, & 564. 551-r/1 story from F.C. #29. 556,578-r/Mickey Mouse Cheerios Premium by Dick Moores. 562,563,568-570, 572, 581-Gottfredson strip-r. 570-Valentine issue; has Mickey/Minnie centerfold. 584-Taliaferro strip-r						4.00
550 ($2.25, 52 pgs.)-Donald Duck by Barks; previously printed only in The Netherlands (1st time in U.S.); r/Chip 'n Dale & Scamp from #204						5.00
571-($2.95, 68 pgs)-r/Donald Duck's Atom Bomb by Barks from 1947 Cheerios premium						6.00
574-576,580,582,583 ($2.95, 68 pgs.): 574-r/1st Pinocchio Sunday strip (1939-40). 575-Gottfredson-r, Pinocchio-r/WDC&S #64. 580-r/Donald Duck's 1st app. from Silly Symphony strip 12/16/34 by Taliaferro; Gottfredson strip-r begin; not in #584 & 600. 582,583-r/Mickey Mouse on Sky Island from WDC&S #1,2						5.00
585 ($2.50, 52 pgs.)-r/#140; Barks-r/WDC&S #140						5.00
586,587: 586-Gladstone issues begin again; begin $1.50-c; Gottfredson-r begins (not in #600). 587-Donald Duck by William Van Horn begins						4.00
588-597: 588,591-599-Donald Duck by William Van Horn						3.00
598,599 ($1.95, 36 pgs.): 598-r/1st drawings of Mickey Mouse by Ub Iwerks						3.00
600 ($2.95, 48 pgs.)-L.B. Cole-c(r)/WDC&S #1; Barks-r/WDC&S #32 plus Rosa, Jippes, Van Horn-r and new Rosa centerspread						4.00
601-611 ($5.95, 64 pgs., squarebound, bi-monthly): 601-Barks-c, r/Mickey Mouse V1#1, Rosa-a/scripts. 602-Rosa-c. 604-Taliaferro strip-r/1st Silly Symphony Sundays from 1932. 604,605-Jippes-a. 605-Walt Kelly-c; Gottfredson "Mickey Mouse Outwits the Phantom Blot" r/F.C. #16						6.00
612-633 ($6.95): 633-(2/99) Last Gladstone issue						7.00
634-675: 634-(7/03) First Gemstone issue; William Van Horn-c. 666-Mickey's Inferno						7.00
676-681: 676-Begin $7.50-c. 677-Bucky Bug's 75th Anniversary						7.50
682-698-($7.99)						8.00
699-714: 699-(9/09, $2.99) First BOOM! Kids issue. 700-Back-up story w/Van Horn-a						3.00
715-720: 715-(1/11, $3.99) 70th Anniversary issue; cover swipe of #1 by Van Horn; Jippes, Rosa-a. 716-Barks reprints						4.00
721-738: 721-(7/15, $3.99) First IDW issue; Italian, Dutch & classic reprints						4.00
739-743-($5.99): 741-Eurasia Toft app. 743-(7/18)						6.00
... 75th Anniversary Special (10/15, $5.99) Classic short story reprints by various						6.00

NOTE: *(#1-38, 68 pgs.; #39-42, 60 pgs.; #43-57, 61-134, 143-168, 446, 447, 52 pgs.; #58-60, 135-142, 169-540, 36 pgs.)*

NOTE: **Barks** *art in all issues #31 on, except where noted; c-95, 96, 104, 108, 109, 130-172, 174-178, 183, 198-200, 204, 206-209, 212-216, 218, 220, 226, 228-233, 235-238, 240-243, 247, 250, 253, 256, 260, 261, 276-283, 288-292, 295-298, 301, 303, 304, 306, 307, 309, 310, 313-316, 319, 321, 322, 324, 326, 328, 329, 331, 332, 334, 341, 342, 350, 351, 527r, 530r, 540(never before published), 546r, 557-586r(most), 596p, 601p.* **Kelly** *a-24p, 34-41, 43; r-522-524, 546, 547, 582, 583; covers(most)-34-118, 531r, 537r, 541r-543r, 562r, 571r, 605r. Walt Disney's Comics & Stories featured Mickey Mouse serials which were in practically every issue from #1 through #394 and #511 to date. The titles of the serials, along with the issues they are in, are listed in previous editions*

	GD 2.0	VG 4.0	FN 6.0	VF 8.0	VF/NM 9.0	NM- 9.2

*of this price guide. **Floyd Gottfredson** Mickey Mouse serials in issues #1-14, 18-66, 69-74, 78-100, 128, 562, 563, 568-572, 582, 583, 586-599 , 601-603 , 605-present , plus "Service with a Smile" in #13; "Mickey Mouse in a Warplant" (3 pgs.), and "Pluto Catches a Nazi Spy" (4 pgs.) in #62; "Mystery Next Door", #93; "Sunken Treasure", #94; "Aunt Marissa", #95 (r in #575); "Gangland", #98 (r in #562); "Thanksgiving Dinner", #99 (r in #567); and "The Talking Dog", #100 (r in #563); "Morty's Escapade," #128. "The Brave Little Tailor", #580; "Introducing Mickey Mouse Movies ", #581; Circus Roustabout, #585; "Rumplewatt the Giant", #604. Mickey Mouse by **Paul Murry** #152-547 except 155-57 (**Dick Moore**), 327-29 (**Tony Strobl**), 348-50 (**Jack Manning**), 533 (**Bill Wright**). **Don Rosa** story/a-523, 524, 526, 528, 531, 547, 601-present. **Al Taliaferro** Silly Symphonies in #5-"Three Little Pigs"; #13-"Birds of a Feather"; #14-"The Boarding School Mystery"; #15-"Cookieland" and "Three Little Kittens"; #16-"The Practical Pig"; #17-"The Ugly Duckling"; "The Wise Little Hen" in #580; and "Ambrose the Robber Kitten"; #19-"Penguin Isle"; and "Bucky Bug" in #20-23, 25, 26, 28 (one continuous story from 1932-34; first 2 pgs. not Taliaferro). **Gottfredson** strip r-562, 563, 568-572, 581, 585, 586, 590. **Taliaferro** strip r-584, 580. **Van Horn** a-537, 545, 561, 574, 587, 588, 591-on.*

WALT DISNEY'S COMICS DIGEST
Gladstone: Dec, 1986 - No. 7, Sept, 1987

1 — 1 2 3 5 6 8
2-7 — 6.00

WALT DISNEY'S COMICS PENNY PINCHER
Gladstone: May, 1997 - No. 4, Aug, 1997 (99¢, limited series)

1-4 — 4.00

WALT DISNEY'S DONALD AND MICKEY (Formerly Walt Disney's Mickey and Donald)
Gladstone (Bruce Hamilton Co.): No. 19, Sept, 1993 - No. 30, 1995 ($1.50, 36 & 68 pgs.)

19,21-24,26-30: New & reprints. 19,21,23,24-Barks-r. 19,26-Murry-r. 22-Barks "Omelet" story r/WDC&S #146. 27-Mickey Mouse story by Caesar Ferioli (1st U.S work). 29-Rosa-c; Mickey Mouse story actually starring Goofy (does not include Mickey except on title page.) — 4.00
20,25-($2.95, 68 pgs.): 20-Barks, Gottfredson-r — 5.00
NOTE: *Donald Duck stories were all reprints.*

WALT DISNEY'S DONALD DUCK
Gemstone Publishing: 2006, 2008

... Free Comic Book Day (5/06) r/WDC&S #531; Rosa-s/a; P&S. Block-s/a; Van Horn-s/a — 3.00
nn-(8-1/2"x 5-1/2", Halloween giveaway) r/"A Prank Above" -Barks-s/a; Rosa-s/a — 3.00
nn-(2008, 8-1/2"x 5-1/2", Halloween giveaway) "The Halloween Huckster"; Rota-s/a — 3.00

WALT DISNEY'S DONALD DUCK ADVENTURES (D.D. Adv. #1-3)
Gladstone: 11/87-No. 20, 4/90 (1st Series); No. 21,8/93-No. 48, 2/98(3rd Series)

1 — 1 2 3 5 6 8
2-r/F.C. #308 — 4.00
3,4,6,7,9-11,13,15-18: 3-r/F.C. #223. 4-r/F.C. #62. 9-r/F.C. #159, "Ghost of the Grotto". 11-r/F.C. #159, "Adventure Down Under." 16-r/F.C. #291; Rosa-c. 18-r/FC #318; Rosa-c — 4.00
5,8: 5-Don Rosa-c/a. 8-Rosa-a — 5.00
12($1.50, 52pgs)-Rosa-c/s/a; "Return to Plain Awful" story; sequel to Four Color #223 (square egg story); Barks centerfold poster — 6.00
14-r/F.C. #29, "Mummy's Ring" — 4.00
19($1.95, 68 pgs.)-Barks-r/F.C. #199 (1 pg.) — 4.00
20($1.95, 68 pgs.)-Barks-r/F.C. #189 & cover-r; William Van Horn-a — 4.00
21,22: 21-r/D.D. #46. 22-r/F.C. #282 — 3.00
23-25,27,29,31,32-($1.50, 36 pgs.): 21,23,29-Rosa-c. 23-Intro/1st app. Andold Wild Duck by Marco Rota. 24-Van Horn-a. 27-1st Pat Block-a, "Mystery of Widow's Gap." 31,32-Block-c — 3.00
26,28($2.95, 68 pgs.): 26-Barks-r/F.C. #108, "Terror of the River". 28-Barks-r/F.C. #199, "Sheriff of Bullet Valley" — 4.00
30($2.95, 68 pgs.)-r/F.C. #367, Barks' "Christmas for Shacktown" — 4.00
33($1.95, 68 pgs.)-r/F.C. #408, Barks' "The Golden Helmet;"Van Horn-c — 4.00
34-43: 34-Resume $1.50-c. 34,35,37-Block-a/scripts. 38-Van Horn-c/a — 3.00
44-48-($1.95-c) — 3.00
NOTE: ***Barks** a-1-22r, 26r, 28r, 33r, 36r; c-3r, 8r, 10r, 14r, 20r. **Block** a-27, 30, 34, 35, 37; c-27, 30-32, 34, 35, 37; c-27, 30, 31, 32, 34, 35, 37. **Rosa** a-5, 8, 12, 43; c-13, 16, 18, 21, 23, 43.*

WALT DISNEY'S DONALD DUCK ADVENTURES (2nd Series)
Disney Comics: June, 1990 - No. 38, July, 1993 ($1.50)

1-Rosa-a & scripts — 5.00
2-21,23,25,27-33,35,36,38: 2-Barks-r/WDC&S #35; William Van Horn-a begins, ends #20. 9-Barks-r/F.C. #178. 9,11,14,17-No Van Horn-a. 11-Mad #1 cover parody. 14-Barks-r. 17-Barks-r. 21-r/FC #203 by Barks. 29-r/MOC #20 by Barks — 3.00
22,24,26,34,37: 22-Rosa-a (10 pgs.) & scripts. 24-Rosa-a & scripts. 26-r/March of Comics #41 by Barks. 34-Rosa-c/a. 37-Rosa-a; Barks-r — 4.00
NOTE: ***Barks** r-2, 4, 9(F.C. #178), 14(D.D. #45), 17, 21, 26, 27, 29 , 35, 36(D.D #60)-38. **Taliaferro** a-34r, 36r.*

WALT DISNEY'S DONALD DUCK ADVENTURES
Gemstone Publishing: May, 2003 (giveaway promoting 2003 return of Disney Comics)

...Free Comic Book Day Edition - cover logo on red background; reprints "Maharajah Donald" & "The Peaceful Hills" from March of Comics #4; Barks-s/a; Kelly original-c on back-c — 3.00
...San Diego Comic-Con 2003 Edition - cover logo on gold background — 3.00
...ANA World's Fair of Money Baltimore Edition - cover logo on green background — 3.00
...WizardWorld Chicago 2003 Edition - cover logo on blue background — 3.00

WALT DISNEY'S DONALD DUCK ADVENTURES (Take-Along Comic)
Gemstone Publishing: July, 2003 - No. 21, Nov, 2006 ($7.95, 5" x 7-1/2")

1-21-Mickey Mouse & Uncle Scrooge app. 9-Christmas-c — 8.00
..., The Barks/Rosa Collection Vol. 2 (3/08, $8.99) reprints Donald Duck's Atom Bomb, Super Snooper & The Trouble With Dimes by Barks; The Duck Who Fell to Earth, Super Snooper Strikes Again & The Money Pit by Rosa — 9.00
..., The Barks/Rosa Collection Vol. 3 (9/08, $8.99) r/FC #408 "The Golden Helmet" by Barks & DDA #43 "The Lost Charts of Columbus" by Rosa; cover gallery and bonus art — 9.00

WALT DISNEY'S DONALD DUCK AND FRIENDS (Continues as Donald Duck and Friends)
Gemstone Publishing: No. 308, Oct, 2003 - No. 346, Dec, 2006 ($2.95)

308-346: 308-Numbering resumes from Gladstone Donald Duck series; Halloween-c. 332-Halloween-c; r/#26 by Carl Barks — 3.00

WALT DISNEY'S DONALD DUCK AND MICKEY MOUSE (Formerly Walt Disney's Donald and Mickey)
Gladstone (Bruce Hamilton Company): Sept, 1995 - No. 7, Sept, 1996 ($1.50, 32 pgs.)

1-7: 1-Barks-r and new Mickey Mouse stories in all. 5,6-Mickey Mouse stories by Caesar Ferioli. 7-New Donald Duck and Mickey Mouse x-over story; Barks-r/WDC&S #51 — 3.00
NOTE: *Issue #8 was advertised, but cancelled.*

WALT DISNEY'S DONALD DUCK AND UNCLE SCROOGE
Gemstone Publishing: Nov, 2005 ($6.95, square-bound one-shot)

nn-New story by John Lustig and Pat Block and r/Uncle Scrooge #59 — 7.00

WALT DISNEY'S DONALD DUCK FAMILY
Gemstone Publishing: Jun, 2008 ($8.99, square-bound)

... The Daan Jippes Collection Vol. 1 - R/Barks-s re-drawn by Jippes for Dutch comics — 9.00

WALT DISNEY'S DONALD DUCK IN THE CASE OF THE MISSING MUMMY
Gemstone Publishing: Oct, 2007 ($8.99, square-bound one-shot)

nn-New story by Shelley and Pat Block and r/Donald Duck FC #29 — 9.00

WALT DISNEY'S GYRO GEARLOOSE
Gemstone Publishing: May, 2008

... Free Comic Book Day (5/08) short stories by Barks, Rosa, Van Horn, Gerstein — 3.00

WALT DISNEY SHOWCASE
Gold Key: Oct, 1970 - No. 54, Jan, 1980 (No. 44-48: 68pgs., 49-54: 52pgs.)

	GD 2.0	VG 4.0	FN 6.0	VF 8.0	VF/NM 9.0	NM- 9.2
1-Boatniks (Movie)-Photo-c	3	6	9	17	26	35
2-Moby Duck	3	6	9	14	19	24
3,4,7: 3-Bongo & Lumpjaw-r. 4,7-Pluto-r	2	4	6	10	14	18
5-$1,000,000 Duck (Movie)-Photo-c	3	6	9	15	22	28
6-Bedknobs & Broomsticks (Movie)	3	6	9	15	22	28
8-Daisy & Donald	2	4	6	11	16	20
9- 101 Dalmatians (cartoon feat.); r/F.C. #1183	3	6	9	16	24	32
10-Napoleon & Samantha (Movie)-Photo-c	3	6	9	15	22	28
11-Moby Duck-r	2	4	6	10	14	18
12-Dumbo-r/Four Color #668	2	4	6	11	16	20
13-Pluto-r	2	4	6	10	14	18
14-World's Greatest Athlete (Movie)-Photo-c	3	6	9	15	22	28
15- 3 Little Pigs-r	2	4	6	11	16	20
16-Aristocats (cartoon feature); r/Aristocats #1	3	6	9	15	22	28
17-Mary Poppins; r/M.P. #10136-501-Photo-c	3	6	9	15	22	28
18-Gyro Gearloose; Barks-r/F.C. #1047,1184	3	6	9	17	26	35
19-That Darn Cat; r/That Darn Cat #10171-602-Hayley Mills photo-c	3	6	9	15	22	28
20,23-Pluto-r	2	4	6	11	16	20
21-Li'l Bad Wolf & The Three Little Pigs	2	4	6	10	14	18
22-Unbirthday Party with Alice in Wonderland; r/Four Color #341	3	6	9	14	19	24
24-26: 24-Herbie Rides Again (Movie); sequel to "The Love Bug"; photo-c. 25-Old Yeller (Movie); r/F.C. #869; Photo-c. 26-Lt. Robin Crusoe USN (Movie); r/Lt. Robin Crusoe USN #10191-601; photo-c	2	4	6	11	16	20
27-Island at the Top of the World (Movie)-Photo-c	3	6	9	14	19	24
28-Brer Rabbit, Bucky Bug-r/WDC&S #58	2	4	6	11	16	20
29-Escape to Witch Mountain (Movie)-Photo-c	3	6	9	14	19	24
30-Magica De Spell; Barks-r/Uncle Scrooge #36 & WDC&S #258	3	6	9	20	31	42
31-Bambi (cartoon feature); r/Four Color #186	2	4	6	13	18	22
32-Spin & Marty-r/F.C. #1026; Mickey Mouse Club (TV)-Photo-c	3	6	9	14	19	24
33-40: 33-Pluto-r/F.C. #1143. 34-Paul Revere's Ride with Johnny Tremain (TV); r/F.C. #822. 35-Goofy-r/F.C. #952. 36-Peter Pan-r/F.C. #442. 37-Tinker Bell & Jiminy Cricket-r/F.C. #982,989. 38,39-Mickey & the Sleuth, Parts 1 & 2. 40-The Rescuers (cartoon feature)	2	4	6	9	13	16
41-Herbie Goes to Monte Carlo (Movie); sequel to "Herbie Rides Again"; photo-c	2	4	6	10	14	18
42-Mickey & the Sleuth	2	4	6	9	13	16
43-Pete's Dragon (Movie)-Photo-c	2	4	6	13	18	22
44-Return From Witch Mountain (new) & In Search of the Castaways-r (Movies)-Photo-c; 68 pg. giants begin	3	6	9	14	19	24
45-The Jungle Book (Movie); r/#30033-803	3	6	9	16	24	32
46-48: 46-The Cat From Outer Space (Movie)(new), & The Shaggy Dog (Movie)-r/F.C. #985; photo-c. 47-Mickey Mouse Surprise Party-r. 48-The Wonderful Advs. of Pinocchio-r/F.C. #1203; last 68 pg. issue	2	4	6	10	14	18
49-54: 49-North Avenue Irregulars (Movie); Zorro-r/Zorro #11; 52 pgs. begin; photo-c. 50-Bedknobs & Broomsticks-r/#6; Mooncussers-r/World of Adv. #1; photo-c. 51-101 Dalmatians-r. 52-Unidentified Flying Oddball (Movie); r/Picnic Party #8; photo-c. 53-The Scarecrow-r (TV). 54-The Black Hole (Movie)-Photo-c (predates Black Hole #1)	2	4	6	9	13	16

WALT DISNEY SHOWCASE
IDW Publishing: Jan, 2018 - No. 6, Jun, 2018 ($3.99)

1-6-English versions of Italian Disney stories; 3 covers — 4.00

WALT DISNEY'S MAGAZINE (TV)(Formerly Walt Disney's Mickey Mouse Club Magazine) (50¢, bi-monthly)
Western Publishing Co.: V2#4, June, 1957 - V4#6, Oct, 1959

	GD 2.0	VG 4.0	FN 6.0	VF 8.0	VF/NM 9.0	NM- 9.2
V2#4-Stories & articles on the Mouseketeers, Zorro, & Goofy and other Disney characters & people	6	12	18	41	76	110
V2#5, V2#6(10/57)	6	12	18	37	66	95
V3#1(12/57), V3#3-5	5	10	15	34	60	85
V3#2-Annette Funicello photo-c	11	22	33	73	157	240
V3#6(10/58)-TV Zorro photo-c	7	14	21	48	89	130
V4#1(12/58) - V4#2-4,6(10/59)	5	10	15	33	57	80
V4#5-Annette Funicello photo-c, w/ 2-photo articles	11	22	33	73	157	240

NOTE: *V2#4-V3#6 were 11-1/2x8-1/2", 48 pgs.; V4#1 on were 10x8", 52 pgs. (Peak circulation of 400,000).*

WALT DISNEY'S MERRY CHRISTMAS (See Dell Giant #39)

WALT DISNEY'S MICKEY AND DONALD (M & D #1,2)(Becomes Walt Disney's Donald & Mickey #19 on)
Gladstone: Mar, 1988 - No. 18, May, 1990 (95¢)

1-Don Rosa-a; r/1949 Firestone giveaway — 6.00
2-8: 3-Infinity-c. 4-8-Barks-r — 4.00
9-15: 9-r/1948 Firestone giveaway; X-Mas-c — 3.00
16($1.50, 52 pgs.)-r/FC #157 — 5.00
17-(68 pgs.) Barks M.M.-r/FC #79 plus Barks D.D.-r; Rosa-a; x-mas-c — 6.00
18($1.95, 68 pgs.)-Gottfredson-r/WDC&S #13,72-74; Kelly-c(r); Barks-r — 5.00
NOTE: ***Barks** reprints in 1-15, 17, 18. **Kelly** c-13r, 14 (r/Walt Disney's C&S #58), 18r.*

WALT DISNEY'S MICKEY MOUSE
Gemstone Publishing: May, 2007

Walt Disney's Donald Duck and Friends #338 © DIS

Walt Disney Showcase #16 © DIS

Walt Disney's Uncle Scrooge #219 © DIS

	GD	VG	FN	VF	VF/NM	NM-
	2.0	4.0	6.0	8.0	9.0	9.2

... Free Comic Book Day (5/07) Floyd Gottfredson-s/a 3.00

WALT DISNEY'S MICKEY MOUSE ADVENTURES (Take-Along Comic)
Gemstone Publishing: Aug, 2004 - No. 12 ($7.95, 5" x 7-1/2")

1-12-Goofy, Donald Duck & Uncle Scrooge app. 8.00

WALT DISNEY'S MICKEY MOUSE AND BLOTMAN IN BLOTMAN RETURNS
Gemstone Publishing: Dec, 2006 ($5.99, squarebound, one-shot)

nn-Wraparound-c by Noel Van Horn; Super Goof back-up story 6.00

WALT DISNEY'S MICKEY MOUSE AND FRIENDS (See Mickey Mouse and Friends for #296)
Gemstone Publishing: No. 257, Oct, 2003 - No. 295, Dec, 2006 ($2.95)

257-295: 257-Numbering resumes from Gladstone Mickey Mouse series; Halloween-c. 285-Return of the Phantom Blot 3.00

WALT DISNEY'S MICKEY MOUSE AND UNCLE SCROOGE
Gemstone Publishing: June, 2004 (Free Comic Book Day giveaway)

nn-Flip book with r/Uncle Scrooge #15 and r/Mickey Mouse Four Color #79 (only Barks drawn Mickey Mouse story) 3.00

WALT DISNEY'S MICKEY MOUSE CLUB MAGAZINE (TV)(Becomes Walt Disney's Magazine)
Western Publishing Co.: Winter, 1956 - V2#3, Apr, 1957 (11-1/2x8-1/2", quarterly, 48 pgs.)

	GD	VG	FN	VF	VF/NM	NM-
V1#1	15	30	45	100	220	340
2-4	9	18	27	58	114	170
V2#1,2	8	16	24	51	96	140
3-Annette photo-c	13	26	39	89	195	300
Annual(1956)-Two different issues; ($1.50-Whitman); 120 pgs., cardboard covers, 11-3/4x8-3/4"; reprints	14	28	42	96	211	325
Annual(1957)-Same as above	12	24	36	79	170	260

WALT DISNEY'S MICKEY MOUSE MEETS BLOTMAN
Gemstone Publishing: Aug, 2005 ($5.99, squarebound, one-shot)

nn-Wraparound-c by Noel Van Horn; Super Goof back-up story 6.00

WALT DISNEY'S PINOCCHIO SPECIAL
Gladstone: Spring, 1990 ($1.00)

1-50th anniversary edition; Kelly-r/F.C. #92 3.00

WALT DISNEY'S SEBASTIAN
Disney Comics, Inc.: 1992

1-(36 pgs.) 3.00

WALT DISNEY'S SPRING FEVER
Gemstone Publishing: Apr, 2007; Apr, 2008 ($9.50, squarebound)

1,2: 1-New stories and reprints incl. "Mystery of the Swamp" by Carl Barks 9.50

WALT DISNEY'S THE ADVENTUROUS UNCLE SCROOGE MCDUCK
Gladstone: Jan, 1998 - No. 2, Mar, 1998 ($1.95)

1,2: 1-Barks-a(r). 2-Rosa-a(r) 3.00

WALT DISNEY'S THE JUNGLE BOOK
W.D. Publications (Disney Comics): 1990 ($5.95, graphic novel, 68 pgs.)

nn-Movie adaptation; movie rereleased in 1990 6.00
nn-($2.95, 68 pgs.)-Comic edition; wraparound-c 4.00

WALT DISNEY'S UNCLE SCROOGE (Formerly Uncle Scrooge #1-209)
Gladstone #210-242/Disney Comics #243-280/Gladstone #281-318/Gemstone #319 on: No. 210, 10/86 - No. 242, 4/90; No. 243, 6/90 - No. 318, 2/99; No. 319, 7/03 - No. 383, 11/08

	GD	VG	FN	VF	VF/NM	NM-
210-1st Gladstone issue; r/WDC&S #134 (1st Beagle Boys)	2	4	6	9	13	16
211-218: 216-New story ("Go Slowly Sands of Time") plotted and partly scripted by Barks. 217-r/U.S. #7, "Seven Cities of Cibola"	2	4	6	9	12	15
219-"Son Of The Sun" by Rosa (his 1st pro work)	3	6	9	14	20	25
220-Don Rosa-a/scripts	1	2	3	5	6	8
221-223,225,228-234,236-240						4.00
224,226,227,235: 224-Rosa-c/a. 226,227-Rosa-a. 235-Rosa-a/scripts						5.00
241-($1.95, 68 pgs.)-Rosa finishes over Barks-r						6.00
242-($1.95, 68 pgs.)-Barks-r; Rosa-a(1 pg.)						6.00
243-249,251-260,264-275,277-280,282-284-($1.50): 243-1st by Disney Comics. 274-All Barks issue. 275-Contains centerspread by Rosa. 279-All Barks issue; Rosa-c. 283-r/WDC&S #98						3.00
250-($2.25, 52 pgs.)-Barks-r; wraparound-c						4.00
261-263,276-Don Rosa-c/a						5.00
281-Gladstone issues start again; Rosa-c						6.00
285-The Life and Times of Scrooge McDuck Pt. 1; Rosa-c/a/scripts	1	3	4	6	8	10
286-293: The Life and Times of Scrooge McDuck Pt. 2-9; Rosa-c/a/scripts. 292-Scrooge & Glittering Goldie & Goose Egg Nugget on-c						6.00
294-299, 301-308-($1.50, 32 pgs.): 294-296-The Life and Times of Scrooge McDuck Pt. 10-12. 295-Titanic on-c. 296-Beagle Boys & Christmas-c. 297-The Life and Times of Uncle Scrooge Pt. 0; Rosa-c/a/scripts						3.00
300-($2.25, 48 pgs.)-Rosa-c; Barks-r/WDC&S #104 and U.S. #216; r/U.S. #220; includes new centerfold.						4.00
309-($6.95) Low print run	3	6	9	14	20	25
310-($6.95) Low print run	4	8	12	27	44	60
311-320-($6.95) 318-(2/99) Last Gladstone issue. 319-(7/03) First Gemstone issue; The Dutchman's Secret by Don Rosa	2	4	6	8	10	12
321-360						7.00
361-366: 361-Begin $7.50-c						7.50
367-383-($7.99)						8.00
... Adventures, The Barks/Rosa Collection Vol. 1 (Gemstone, 7/07, $8.50) reprints Pygmy Indians appearances in U.S. #18 by Barks and WDC&S #633 by Rosa						8.50
Walt Disney's The Life and Times of Scrooge McDuck by Don Rosa TPB (Gemstone, 2005, $16.99) Reprints #285-296, with foreword, commentaries & sketch pages by Rosa						17.00
Walt Disney's The Life and Times of Scrooge McDuck Companion by Don Rosa TPB (Gemstone, 2006, $16.99) additional chapters, with foreword & commentaries						17.00

NOTE: ***Barks** r-210-218, 220-223, 224(2pg.), 225-234, 236-242, 245, 246, 250-253, 255, 256, 258, 261(2 pg.), 265, 267, 268, 270(2), 272-284, 299-present; c(r)-210, 212, 221, 228, 229, 232, 233, 284. scripts-287, 293. **Rosa** a-219, 220, 224, 226, 227, 235, 261-263, 268, 275-277, 285-297; c-219, 224, 231, 261-263, 276, 278-281, 285-296; scripts-219, 220, 224, 235, 261-263, 268, 276, 285-296.*

WALT DISNEY'S UNCLE SCROOGE
Gemstone Publishing

nn-(5/05, FCBD) Reprints Uncle Scrooge's debut in Four Color Comics #386; Barks-s/a 3.00
nn-(2007, 8-1/2"x 5-1/2", Halloween giveaway) Hound of the Whiskevilles; Barks-s/a 3.00

WALT DISNEY'S UNCLE SCROOGE ADVENTURES (U. Scrooge Advs. #1-3)
Gladstone Publishing: Nov, 1987 - No. 21, May, 1990; No. 22, Sept, 1993 - No. 54, Feb, 1998

	GD	VG	FN	VF	VF/NM	NM-
1-Barks-r begin, ends #26	2	4	6	8	10	12
2-4						4.00
5,9,14: 5-Rosa-c/a; no Barks-r. 9,14-Rosa-a						5.00
6-8,10-13,15-19: 10-r/U.S. #18(all Barks)						3.00
20,21 ($1.95, 68 pgs.) 20-Rosa-c/a. 21-Rosa-a						5.00
22 ($1.50)-Rosa-c; r/U.S. #26						5.00
23-($2.95, 68 pgs.)-Vs. The Phantom Blot-r/P.B. #3; Barks-r						4.00
24-26,29,31,32,34-36: 24,25,29,31,32-Rosa-c. 25-r/U.S. #21						3.00
27-Guardians of the Lost Library - Rosa-c/a/story; origin of Junior Woodchuck Guidebook						4.00
28-($2.95, 68 pgs.)-r/U.S. #13 w/restored missing panels						4.00
30-($2.95, 68 pgs.)-r/U.S. #12; Rosa-c						4.00
33-($2.95, 64 pgs.)-New Barks story						4.00
37-54						3.00

NOTE: ***Barks** r-1-4, 6-8, 10-13, 15-21, 23, 22, 24; c(r)-15, 16, 17, 21. **Rosa** a-5, 9, 14, 20, 21, 27, 51; c-5, 13, 14, 17(finishes), 20, 22, 24, 25, 27, 28, 51; scripts-5, 9, 14, 27.*

WALT DISNEY'S UNCLE SCROOGE AND DONALD DUCK
Gladstone: Jan, 1998 - No. 2, Mar, 1998 ($1.95)

1,2: 1-Rosa-a(r) 3.00

WALT DISNEY'S UNCLE SCROOGE ADVENTURES IN COLOR
Gladstone Publ.: Dec, 1995 - No. 56 ($8.95/$9.95, squarebound, 56 issue limited series) (Polybagged w/card) (Series chronologically reprints all the stories written & drawn by Carl Barks)

1-56: 1-(12/95)-r/FC #386. 15-(12/96)-r/US #15. 16-(12/96)-r/US #16. 18-(1/97)-r/US #18 10.00

WALT DISNEY'S VACATION PARADE
Gemstone Publishing: 2004 - No. 5, July, 2008 ($8.95/$9.95, squarebound, annual)

1-3: 1-Reprints stories from Dell Giant Comics Vacation Parade 1 (July 1950) 10.00
4,5-($9.95): 4-(5/07). 5-(7/08) 10.00

WALT DISNEY'S WHEATIES PREMIUMS (See Wheaties in the Promotional section)

WALT DISNEY'S WORLD OF THE DRAGONLORDS
Gemstone Publishing: 2005 ($12.99, squarebound, graphic novel)

SC-Uncle Scrooge, Donald & nephews app.; Byron Erickson-s/Giorgio Cavazzano-a 13.00

WALT DISNEY TREASURES - DISNEY COMICS: 75 YEARS OF INNOVATION
Gemstone Publishing: 2006 ($12.99, TPB)

SC-Reprints from 1930-2004, including debut of Mickey Mouse newspaper strip 13.00

WALT DISNEY TREASURES - UNCLE SCROOGE: A LITTLE SOMETHING SPECIAL
Gemstone Publishing: 2008 ($16.99, TPB)

SC-Uncle Scrooge classics from 1954-2006, including "The Seven Cities of Cibola" 17.00

WALT DISNEY UNCLE SCROOGE AND DONALD DUCK
Fantagraphic Books: 2014 (giveaway)

Free Comic Book Day - A Matter of Some Gravity; Don Rosa-s/a 3.00

WALTER LANTZ ANDY PANDA (Also see Andy Panda)
Gold Key: Aug, 1973 - No. 23, Jan, 1978 (Walter Lantz)

	GD 2.0	VG 4.0	FN 6.0	VF 8.0	VF/NM 9.0	NM- 9.2
1-Reprints	3	6	9	16	23	30
2-10-All reprints	2	4	6	9	12	15
11-23: 15,17-19,22-Reprints	1	2	3	5	7	9

WALT KELLY'S...
Eclipse Comics: Dec, 1987; Apr, 1988 ($1.75/$2.50, Baxter paper)

	GD	VG	FN	VF	VF/NM	NM-
...Christmas Classics 1 (12/87)-Kelly-r/Peter Wheat & Santa Claus Funnies, ...Springtime Tales 1 (4/88, $2.50)-Kelly-r						4.00

WALTONS, THE (See Kite Fun Book)

WALT SCOTT (See Little People)

WALT SCOTT'S CHRISTMAS STORIES (See Little People, 4-Color #959, 1062)

WAMBI, JUNGLE BOY (See Jungle Comics)
Fiction House Magazines: Spr, 1942; No. 2, Win, 1942-43; No. 3, Spr, 1943; No. 4, Fall, 1948; No. 5, Sum, 1949; No. 6, Spr, 1950; No. 7-10, 1950(nd); No. 11, Spr, 1951 - No. 18, Win, 1952-53 (#1-3: 68 pgs.)

	GD	VG	FN	VF	VF/NM	NM-
1-Wambi, the Jungle Boy begins	123	246	369	787	1344	1900
2 (1942)-Kiefer-c	48	96	144	302	514	725
3 (1943)-Kiefer-c/a	41	82	123	256	428	600
4 (1948)-Origin in text	32	64	96	192	314	435
5 (Fall, 1949, 36 pgs.)-Kiefer-c/a	21	42	63	126	206	285
6-10: 7-(52 pgs.)-New logo	17	34	51	100	158	215
11-18	15	30	45	83	124	165
I.W. Reprint #8('64)-r/#12 with new-c	3	6	9	14	20	25

NOTE: ***Alex Blum** c-8. **Kiefer** c-1-5. **Whitman** c-11-18.*

WANDERERS (See Adventure Comics #375, 376)
DC Comics: June, 1988 - No. 13, Apr, 1989 ($1.25) (Legion of Super-Heroes spin off)

	GD	VG	FN	VF	VF/NM	NM-
1-13: 1,2-Steacy-c. 3-Legion app.						4.00

WANDERING STAR
Pen & Ink Comics/Sirius Entertainment No. 12 on: 1993 - No. 21, Mar, 1997 ($2.50/$2.75, B&W)

	GD	VG	FN	VF	VF/NM	NM-
1-1st printing; Teri Sue Wood c/a/scripts in all	1	2	3	5	6	8
1-2nd and 3rd printings						3.00
2-1st printing.						4.00
2-21: 2-2nd printing. 12-(1/96)-1st Sirius issue						3.00
Trade paperback ($11.95)-r/1-7; 1st printing of 1000, signed and #'d						18.00
Trade paperback-2nd printing, 2000 signed						15.00
TPB Volume 2,3 (11/98, 12/98, $14.95) 2-r/#8-14, 3-r/#15-21						15.00

WANTED
Image Comics (Top Cow): Dec, 2003 - No. 6, Feb, 2004 ($2.99)

	GD	VG	FN	VF	VF/NM	NM-
1-Three covers; Mark Millar-s/J.G. Jones-a; intro Wesley Gibson						4.00
1-4-Death Row Edition; r/#1-4 with extra sketch pages and deleted panels						3.00
2-6: 2-Cameos of DC villains. 6-Giordano-a in flashback scenes						3.00
...Dossier (5/04, $2.99) Pin-ups and character info; art by Jones, Romita Jr. & others						3.00
Image Firsts: Wanted #1 (9/10, $1.00) reprints #1						3.00
... Movie Edition Vol. 1 TPB (2008, $19.99) r/#1-6 & Dossier; movie photo-c; sketch pages & cover gallery; interviews with movie cast and director						20.00
HC (2005, $29.99) r/#1-6 & Dossier; intro by Vaughan, sketch pages & cover gallery						30.00

WANTED COMICS
Toytown Publications/Patches/Orbit Publ.: No. 9, Sept-Oct, 1947 - No. 53, April, 1953 (#9-33: 52 pgs.)

	GD	VG	FN	VF	VF/NM	NM-
9-True crime cases; radio's Mr. D. A. app.	41	82	123	256	428	600
10,11: 10-Giunta-a; radio's Mr. D. A. app.	27	54	81	162	266	370
12-Used in **SOTI**, pg. 277	29	58	87	172	281	390
13-Heroin drug propaganda story	29	58	87	170	278	385
14-Marijuana drug mention story (2 pgs.)	25	50	75	150	245	340
15-17,19,20	21	42	63	124	202	280
18-Marijuana story, "Satan's Cigarettes"; r-in #45 & retitled	43	86	129	271	461	650
21,22: 21-Krigstein-a. 22-Extreme violence	22	44	66	128	209	290
23,25-32,34,36-38,40-44,46-48,53	20	40	60	114	182	250
24-Krigstein-a; "The Dope King", marijuana mention story	25	50	75	150	245	340
33-Spider web-c	47	94	141	296	498	700
35-Used in **SOTI**, pg. 160	25	50	75	150	245	340
39-Drug propaganda story "The Horror Weed"	37	74	111	222	361	500
45-Marijuana story from #18	23	46	69	136	223	310
49-Has unstable pink-c that fades easily; rare in mint condition	34	68	102	199	325	450
50-Has unstable pink-c like #49; surrealist-c by Buscema; horror stories	39	78	117	240	395	550
51- "Holiday of Horror" junkie story; drug-c	39	78	117	231	378	525
52-Classic "Cult of Killers" opium use story	258	516	774	1651	2826	4000

NOTE: ***Buscema** c-50, 51. **Lawrence** and **Leav** c/a most issues. **Syd Shores** c/a-48; c-37. Issues 9-46 have wanted criminals with their descriptions & drawn picture on cover.*

WANTED: DEAD OR ALIVE (TV)
Dell Publishing Co.: No. 1102, May-July, 1960 - No. 1164, Mar-May, 1961

	GD	VG	FN	VF	VF/NM	NM-
Four Color 1102 (#1)-Steve McQueen photo-c	14	28	42	96	211	325
Four Color 1164-Steve McQueen photo-c	10	20	30	64	132	200

WANTED, THE WORLD'S MOST DANGEROUS VILLAINS (See DC Special)
National Periodical Publ.: July-Aug, 1972 - No. 9, Aug-Sept, 1973 (All reprints & 20¢ issues)

	GD	VG	FN	VF	VF/NM	NM-
1-Batman, Green Lantern (story r-from G.L. #1), & Green Arrow	4	8	12	25	40	55
2-Batman/Joker/Penguin-c/story r-from Batman #25; plus Flash story (r-from Flash #121)	3	6	9	17	25	34
3-9: 3-Dr. Fate(r/More Fun #65), Hawkman(r/Flash #100), & Vigilante(r/Action #69). 4-Green Lantern(r/All-American #61) & Kid Eternity(r/Kid Eternity #15). 5-Dollman/Green Lantern. 6-Burnley Starman; Wildcat/Sargon. 7-Johnny Quick(r/More Fun #76), Hawkman(r/Flash #90), Hourman by Baily(r/Adv. #72). 8-Dr. Fate/Flash(r/Flash #114). 9-S&K Sandman/Superman	3	6	9	15	22	28

NOTE: ***B. Bailey** a-7r. **Infantino** a-2r. **Kane** r-1, 5. **Kubert** r-3i, 6, 7. **Meskin** r-3, 7. **Reinman** r-4, 6.*

WAR (See Fightin' Marines #122)
Charlton Comics: Jul, 1975 - No. 9, Nov, 1976; No. 10, Sept, 1978 - No. 47, 1984

	GD	VG	FN	VF	VF/NM	NM-
1-Boyette painted-c	3	6	9	14	20	26
2-10: 3-Sutton painted-c	2	4	6	8	11	14
11-20	1	2	3	5	6	8
21-40	1	2	3	4	5	7
41,42,44-47 (lower print run): 47-Reprints	1	2	3	5	6	8
43 (2/84) (lower print run) Ditko-a (7 pgs.)	2	4	6	8	10	12
7,9 (Modern Comics-r, 1977)						6.00

WAR, THE (See The Draft & The Pitt)
Marvel Comics: 1989 - No. 4, 1990 ($3.50, squarebound, 52 pgs.)

	GD	VG	FN	VF	VF/NM	NM-
1-4: Characters from New Universe						5.00

WAR ACTION (Korean War)
Atlas Comics (CPS): April, 1952 - No. 14, June, 1953

	GD	VG	FN	VF	VF/NM	NM-
1	43	86	129	271	461	650
2-Hartley-a	32	64	96	188	307	425
3-10,14: 7-Pakula-a/Heath-c. 14-Colan-a	24	48	72	140	230	320
11-13-Krigstein-a. 11-Romita-a	25	50	75	150	245	340

NOTE: ***Berg** c-11. **Brodsky** a-2; c-1-4. **Heath** a-1; c-7, 14. **Keller** a-6. **Maneely** a-1; c-12. **Sale** a-7. **Tuska** a-2, 8.*

WAR ADVENTURES (Korean War)
Atlas Comics (HPC): Jan, 1952 - No. 13, Feb, 1953

	GD	VG	FN	VF	VF/NM	NM-
1-Tuska-a	43	86	129	271	461	650
2	32	64	96	188	307	425
3-7,9-11,13: 3-Pakula-a. 7-Maneely-c. 9-Romita-a	24	48	72	140	230	320
8-Krigstein-a	25	50	75	150	245	340
12-Grey tone-c	47	174	141	296	498	700

NOTE: ***Brodsky** c-1-3, 6, 8, 11, 12. **Heath** a-2, 5, 7, 10; c-4, 5, 9, 13. **Reinman** a-13. **Robinson** a-3; c-10.*

WAR ADVENTURES ON THE BATTLEFIELD (See Battlefield)

WAR AGAINST CRIME! (Becomes Vault of Horror #12 on)
E. C. Comics: Spring, 1948 - No. 11, Feb-Mar, 1950

	GD	VG	FN	VF	VF/NM	NM-
1-Real Stories From Police Records on-c #1-9	206	412	618	1318	2259	3200
2,3	110	220	330	704	1202	1700
4-9	68	136	204	435	743	1050
10-1st Vault Keeper app. & 1st Vault of Horror	300	600	900	2010	3505	5000
11-2nd Vault Keeper app.; 1st EC horror-c	290	580	870	1856	3178	4500

NOTE: *All have **Johnny Craig** covers. **Feldstein** a-4, 7-9. **Harrison/Wood** a-11. **Ingels** a-1, 2, 8. **Palais** a-8. Changes to horror with #10.*

WAR AGAINST CRIME
Gemstone Publishing: Apr, 2000 - No. 11, Feb, 2001 ($2.50)

	GD	VG	FN	VF	VF/NM	NM-
1-11: E.C. reprints						4.00

WAR AND ATTACK (Also see Special War Series #3)
Charlton Comics: Fall, 1964; V2#54, June, 1966 - V2#63, Dec, 1967

	GD	VG	FN	VF	VF/NM	NM-
1-Wood-a (25 pgs.)	6	12	18	42	79	115
V2#54(6/66)-#63 (Formerly Fightin' Air Force)	3	6	9	16	23	30

NOTE: ***Montes/Bache** a-55, 56, 60, 63.*

WAR AT SEA (Formerly Space Adventures)
Charlton Comics: No. 22, Nov, 1957 - No. 42, June, 1961

	GD	VG	FN	VF	VF/NM	NM-
22	14	28	42	76	108	140
23-30: 26-Pearl Harbor, FDR app.	9	18	27	50	65	80
31-42: 42-Cuba's Fidel Castro story	4	8	12	28	47	65

WAR BATTLES
Harvey Publications: Feb, 1952 - No. 9, Dec, 1953

	GD	VG	FN	VF	VF/NM	NM-
1-Powell-a; Elias-c	12	24	36	82	179	275
2-Powell-a	7	14	21	44	82	120
3,4,7-9: 3,7-Powell-a	6	12	18	42	79	115
5-Flamethrower cover	25	50	75	175	388	600
6-Nostrand-a	14	28	42	96	211	325

WAR BEARS
Dark Horse Comics: Sept, 2018 - No. 3, Dec, 2018 ($4.99, limited series)

	GD	VG	FN	VF	VF/NM	NM-
1-3-Margaret Atwood-s/Ken Steacy-a; story about creators of Canadian Whites comics in 1943						5.00

WAR BIRDS
Fiction House Magazines: 1952(nd) - No. 3, Winter, 1952-53

	GD	VG	FN	VF	VF/NM	NM-
1	27	54	81	160	263	365
2,3	16	32	48	92	144	195

WARBLADE: ENDANGERED SPECIES (Also see WildC.A.T.S: Covert Action Teams)
Image Comics (WildStorm Productions): Jan, 1995 - No. 4, Apr, 1995 ($2.50, limited series)

	GD	VG	FN	VF	VF/NM	NM-
1-4: 1-Gatefold wraparound-c						3.00

WAR COMBAT (Becomes Combat Casey #6 on)
Atlas Comics (LBI No. 1/SAI No. 2-5): March, 1952 - No. 5, Nov, 1952

	GD	VG	FN	VF	VF/NM	NM-
1	40	80	120	244	402	550
2	21	42	63	122	199	275
3-5	20	40	60	114	182	250

NOTE: ***Berg** a-2, 4, 5. **Brodsky** c-1, 2, 4. **Henkel** a-5. **Maneely** a-1, 4; c-3. **Reinman** a-2. **Sale** a-5; c-5.*

WAR COMICS (War Stories #5 on)(See Key Ring Comics)
Dell Publishing Co.: May, 1940 (No month given) - No. 4, Sept, 1941

	GD	VG	FN	VF	VF/NM	NM-
1-Sikandur the Robot Master, Sky Hawk, Scoop Mason, War Correspondent begin; McWilliams-c; 1st war comic	129	258	387	826	1413	2000
2-Origin Greg Gilday (5/41)	53	106	159	334	567	800
3-Joan becomes Greg Gilday's aide	39	78	117	240	395	550
4-Origin Night Devils	40	80	120	246	411	575

WAR COMICS
Marvel/Atlas (USA No. 1-41/JPI No. 42-49): Dec, 1950 - No. 49, Sept, 1957

	GD	VG	FN	VF	VF/NM	NM-
1-1st Atlas War comic	65	130	195	416	708	1000
2	32	64	96	188	307	425
3-10	25	50	75	150	245	340
11-Flame thrower w/burning bodies on-c	168	336	504	1075	1838	2600
12-20: 16-Romita-a	22	44	66	132	216	300
21,23-32: 26-Valley Forge story. 32-Last pre-code issue (2/55)	21	42	63	126	206	285
22-Krigstein-a	22	44	66	130	213	295

War Adventures #12 © MAR

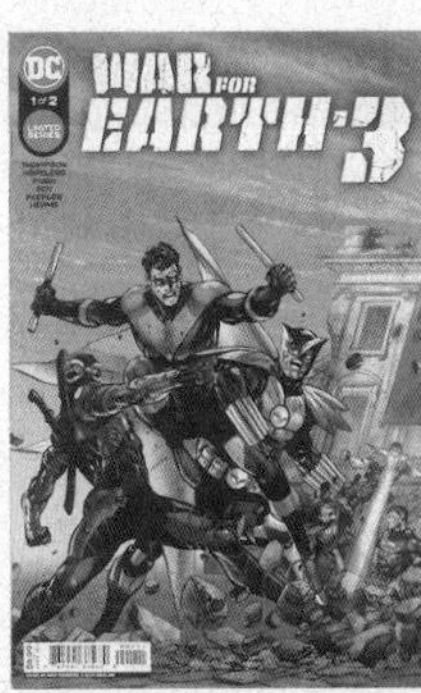

War For Earth-3 #1 © DC

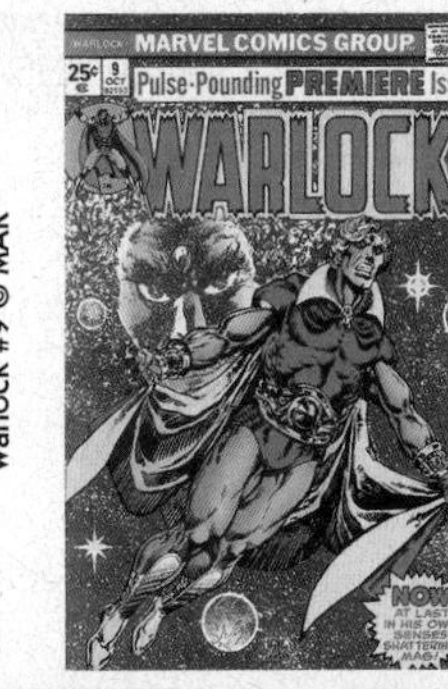

Warlock #9 © MAR

	GD 2.0	VG 4.0	FN 6.0	VF 8.0	VF/NM 9.0	NM- 9.2
33-37,39-42,44,45,47,48: 40-Romita-a	20	40	60	120	195	270
38-Kubert/Moskowitz-a	21	42	63	124	202	280
43,49-Torres-a. 43-Severin/Elder E.C. swipe from Two-Fisted Tales #31	21	42	63	124	202	280
46-Crandall-a	21	42	63	124	202	280

NOTE: ***Ayers** a-17, 32. **Berg** a-13. **Colan** a-4, 28, 34, 36, 48, 49; c-17. **Drucker** a-37, 43, 48. **Everett** a-17. **Heath** a-6-9, 16, 19, 25, 36; c-11, 16, 19, 23, 25, 26, 29-32, 36. **G. Kane** a-19. **Katz** a-34. **Lawrence** a-36. **Maneely** a-7, 9, 13, 14, 20, 23, 28; c-6, 27, 37. **Orlando** a-42, 48. **Pakula** a-26, 40. **Ravielli** a-27. **Reinman** a-11, 16, 26. **Robinson** a-15; c-13. **Sale** c-28. **Severin** a-26, 27; c-48. **Shores** a-13. **Sinnott** a-37.*

WARD, THE
Dark Horse Comics: Jun, 2022 - No. 4, Sept, 2022 ($3.99, limited series)

1-4-Cavan Scott-s/Andres Ponce-a — 4.00

WAR DANCER (Also see Charlemagne, Doctor Chaos #2 & Warriors of Plasm)
Defiant: Feb, 1994 - No. 6, July, 1994 ($2.50)

1-3,5,6: 1-Intro War Dancer; Weiss-c/a begins. 1-3-Weiss-a(p). 6-Pre-Schism issue — 3.00
4-($3.25, 52 pgs.)-Charlemagne app.; Billy Ballistic gains quantum powers — 4.00

WAR DOGS OF THE U.S. ARMY
Avon Periodicals: 1952

	GD	VG	FN	VF	VF/NM	NM-
1-Kinstler-c/a	22	44	66	132	216	300

WAREHOUSE 13 (Based on the Syfy TV series)
Dynamite Entertainment: 2011 - No. 5, 2012 ($3.99)

1-5: 1-Raab & Hughes-s/Morse-a — 4.00

WAR FOR EARTH-3
DC Comics: May, 2022 - No. 2, May, 2022 ($5.99, limited series)

1,2-Crime Syndicate, Suicide Squad & Titans app. — 6.00

WAR FOR THE PLANET OF THE APES (Prequel to the 2017 movie)
BOOM! Studios: Jul, 2017 - No. 4, Oct, 2017 ($3.99, limited series)

1-4-David F. Walker-s/Jonas Scharf-a — 4.00

WARFRAME: GHOULS (Based on the video game)
Image Comics (Top Cow): Oct, 2017 - No. 5, May, 2018 ($3.99)

1-5-Matt Hawkins & Ryan Cady-s/Studio Hive-a — 4.00

WARFRONT
Harvey Publications: 9/51 - #35, 11/58; #36, 10/65; #39, 2/67

	GD	VG	FN	VF	VF/NM	NM-
1-Korean War	34	68	102	199	325	450
2	7	14	21	49	92	135
3-10	5	10	15	35	63	90
11,12,14,16-20	5	10	15	31	53	75
13,15,22-Nostrand-a	6	12	18	38	69	100
21,23-27,31-33,35	5	10	15	31	53	75
28-30,34-Kirby-c	6	12	18	41	76	110
36-(12/66)-Dynamite Joe begins, ends #39; Williamson-a	5	10	15	34	60	85
37-Wood-a (17 pgs.)	5	10	15	34	60	85
38,39-Wood-a, 2-3 pgs.; Lone Tiger app.	5	10	15	31	53	75

NOTE: ***Powell** a-1-6, 9-11, 14, 17, 20, 23, 25-28, 30, 31, 34, 36. **Powell/Nostrand** a-12, 13, 15. **Simon** c-36?, 38.*

WAR FURY
Comic Media/Harwell (Allen Hardy Assoc.): Sept, 1952 - No. 4, Mar, 1953

	GD	VG	FN	VF	VF/NM	NM-
1-Heck-c/a in all; Palais-a; bullet hole in forehead-c; all issues are very violent; soldier using flame thrower on enemy	420	840	1260	2940	5170	7400
2-4: 4-Morisi-a	47	94	141	296	498	700

WAR GODS OF THE DEEP (See Movie Classics)

WARHAMMER 40,000: MARNEUS CALGAR (Based on the game)
Marvel Comics: Dec, 2020 - No. 5, Apr, 2021 ($4.99, limited series)

1-5-Kieron Gillen-s/Jacen Burrows-a — 5.00

WARHAMMER 40,000: SISTERS OF BATTLE (Based on the game)
Marvel Comics: Oct, 2021 - No. 5, Mar, 2022 ($4.99, limited series)

1-5-Torunn Gronbekk-s/Edgar Salazar-a — 5.00

WARHAWKS
TSR, Inc.: 1990 - No. 10, 1991 ($2.95, 44 pgs.)

1-10-Based on TSR game, Spiegle a-1-6 — 4.00

WARHEADS
Marvel Comics UK: June, 1992 - No. 14, Aug, 1993 ($1.75)

1-Wolverine-c/story; indicia says #2 by mistake — 4.00
2-14: 2-Nick Fury app. 3-Iron Man-c/story. 4,5-X-Force. 5-Liger vs. Cable. 6,7-Death's Head II app. (#6 is cameo) — 3.00

WAR HEROES (See Marine War Heroes)

WAR HEROES
Dell Publishing Co.: 7-9/42 (no month); No. 2, 10-12/42 - No. 10, 10-12/44 (Quarterly)

	GD	VG	FN	VF	VF/NM	NM-
1-General Douglas MacArthur-c	45	90	135	284	480	675
2-James Doolittle and other officers-c	20	40	60	118	192	265
3,5: 3-Pro-Russian back-c; grey-tone-c. 5-General Patton-c	17	34	51	100	158	215
4-Disney's Gremlins app.; grey-tone-c	28	56	84	165	270	375
6-10: 6-Tothish-a by Discount. 6,9-Grey-tone-c	15	30	45	84	127	170

NOTE: *No. 1 was to be released in July, but was delayed. Painted c-4, 6-9.*

WAR HEROES
Ace Magazines: May, 1952 - No. 8, Apr, 1953

	GD	VG	FN	VF	VF/NM	NM-
1	34	68	102	199	325	450
2-Lou Cameron-a	15	30	45	83	124	165
3-8: 6,7-Cameron-a	14	28	42	78	112	145

WAR HEROES (Also see Blue Bird Comics)
Charlton Comics: Feb, 1963 - No. 27, Nov, 1967

	GD	VG	FN	VF	VF/NM	NM-
1,2: 2-John F. Kennedy story	5	10	15	30	50	70
3-10	3	6	9	18	28	38
11-26: 22-True story about plot to kill Hitler	3	6	9	15	22	28
27-1st Devils Brigade by Glanzman	3	6	9	18	28	38

NOTE: ***Montes/Bache** a-3-7, 21, 25, 27; c-3-7.*

WAR HEROES
Image Comics: July, 2008 - No. 6 ($2.99, limited series)

1-3-Soldiers given super powers; Mark Millar-s/Tony Harris-a/c; four covers — 3.00

WAR IS HELL
Marvel Comics Group: Jan, 1973 - No. 15, Oct, 1975

	GD	VG	FN	VF	VF/NM	NM-
1-Williamson-a(r), 5 pgs.; Ayers-a	5	10	15	30	50	70
2-8-Reprints. 6-(11/73). 7-(6/74). 7,8-Kirby-a	3	6	9	14	20	25
9-Intro Death	9	18	27	60	120	180
10-15-Death app.	3	6	9	19	30	40

NOTE: ***Bolle** a-3r. **Powell** a-1. **Woodbridge** a-1. Sgt. Fury reprints-7, 8.*

WAR IS HELL (Marvel 80th Anniversary salute to War comics)
Marvel Comics: Mar, 2019 ($3.99, one-shot)

1-Howard Chaykin-s/a; P.K. Johnson-s/Alberto Alburquerque-a; Panosian-c — 4.00

WAR IS HELL: THE FIRST FLIGHT OF THE PHANTOM EAGLE
Marvel Comics (MAX): May, 2008 - No. 5, Sept, 2008 ($3.99, limited series)

1-5-World War I fighter pilots; Ennis-s/Chaykin-a/Cassaday-c — 4.00

WARLANDS
Image Comics: Aug, 1999 - No. 12, Feb, 2001 ($2.50)

1-9,11,12-Pat Lee-a(p)/Adrian Tsang-s — 3.00
10-($2.95) Flip book w/Shidima preview — 4.00
... Chronicles 1,2 (2/00, 7/00; $7.95) 1-r/#1-3. 2-r/#4-6 — 8.00
...Darklyte TPB (8/01, $14.95) r/#0,1/2,1-6 w/cover gallery; new Lee-c — 15.00
...Epilogue: Three Stories (3/01, $5.95) includes r/Wizard #1/2 & AE #0 — 6.00
Another Universe #0 — 3.00
Wizard #1/2 — 5.00

WARLANDS: THE AGE OF ICE (Volume 2)
Image Comics: July, 2001 - No. 9, Nov, 2002 ($2.95)

#0-(2/02, $2.25) — 3.00
#1/2 (4/02, $2.25) — 3.00
1-9: 2-Flip book preview of Banished Knights — 3.00
TPB (2003, $15.95) r/#1-9 — 16.00

WARLANDS: DARK TIDE RISING (Volume 3)
Image Comics: Dec, 2002 - No. 6, May, 2003 ($2.95)

1-6: 1-Wraparound gatefold-c — 3.00

WARLOCK (The Power of...)(Also see Avengers Annual #7, Fantastic Four #66, 67, Incredible Hulk #178, Infinity Crusade, Infinity Gauntlet, Infinity War, Marvel Premiere #1, Marvel Two-In-One Annual #2, Silver Surfer V3#46, Strange Tales #178-181 & Thor #165)
Marvel Comics Group: Aug, 1972 - No. 8, Oct, 1973; No. 9, Oct, 1975 - No. 15, Nov, 1976

	GD	VG	FN	VF	VF/NM	NM-
1-Origin by Gil Kane	10	20	30	67	141	215
2,3	5	10	15	31	53	75
4-8: 4-Death of Eddie Roberts	3	6	9	19	30	40
9-Starlin's 2nd Thanos saga begins, ends #15; new costume Warlock; Thanos cameo only; story cont'd from Strange Tales #178-181; Starlin-c/a in #9-15	5	10	15	35	63	90
10-Origin Thanos & Gamora; recaps events from Capt. Marvel #25-34. Thanos vs.The Magus-c/story	5	10	15	35	63	90
11-Thanos app.; Warlock dies	4	8	12	28	47	65
12-14: (Regular 25¢ edition) 14-Origin Star Thief; last 25¢ issue	3	6	9	18	28	38

	GD	VG	FN	VF	VF/NM	NM-
	2.0	4.0	6.0	8.0	9.0	9.2

12-14-(30¢-c, limited distribution) 5 10 15 35 63 90
15-Thanos-c/story 5 10 15 34 60 85
NOTE: *Buscema a-2p; c-8p. G. Kane a-1p, 3-5p; c-1p, 2, 3, 4p, 5p, 7p. Starlin a-9-14p, 15; c-9, 10, 11p, 12p, 13-15. Sutton a-1-8i.*

WARLOCK (...Special Edition on-c)
Marvel Comics Group: Dec, 1982 - No. 6, May, 1983 ($2.00, slick paper, 52 pgs.)
1-Warlock-r/Strange Tales #178-180. 1 3 4 6 8 10
2-6: 2-r/Str. Tales #180,181 & Warlock #9. 3-r/Warlock #10-12(Thanos origin recap). 4-r/Warlock #12-15. 5-r/Warlock #15, Marvel Team-Up #55 & Avengers Ann. #7. 6-r/2nd half Avengers Annual #7 & Marvel Two-in-One Annual #2 5.00
Special Edition #1(12/83) 5.00
NOTE: *Byrne a-5r. Starlin a-1-6r; c-1-6(new). Direct sale only.*

WARLOCK
Marvel Comics: V2#1, May, 1992 - No. 6, Oct, 1992 ($2.50, limited series)
V2#1-6: 1-Reprints 1982 reprint series w/Thanos 4.00

WARLOCK
Marvel Comics: Nov, 1998 - No. 4, Feb, 1999 ($2.99, limited series)
1-4-Warlock vs. Drax 4.00

WARLOCK (M-Tech)
Marvel Comics: Oct, 1999 - No. 9, June, 2000 ($1.99/$2.50)
1-5: 1-Quesada-c. 2-Two covers 4.00
6-9: 6-Begin $2.50-c. 8-Avengers app. 4.00

WARLOCK
Marvel Comics: Nov, 2004 - No. 4, Feb, 2005 ($2.99, limited series)
1-4-Adlard-a/Williams-c 4.00

WARLOCK AND THE INFINITY WATCH (Also see Infinity Gauntlet)
Marvel Comics: Feb, 1992 - No. 42, July, 1995 ($1.75) (Sequel to Infinity Gauntlet)
1-Starlin-s begin; continued from Infinity Gauntlet #6; brief origin recap; Living Tribunal app. 2 4 6 11 16 20
2-7: 2-1st app. Infinity Watch: Infinity Gauntlet broken up; Warlock (Soul gem), Gamora (Time gem), Drax (Power gem), Moondragon (Mind gem) & Pip (Space gem). 3,4-High Evolutionary app. 5,6-Man-Beast app. 7-Re-intro Magus (dream sequence); brief Thanos app; leads into Infinity War #1. Tom Raney-a begins 4.00
8-10: 8-Thanos teams up w/Infinity Watch; Magus app; X-Men, Avengers, Alpha Flight & Fantastic Four cameo; leads into Infinity War #4. 9-Origin Gamora; Galactus, Eternity, Thanos & Infinity app; leads into Infinity War #5. 10-Thanos vs. his doppelganger; Magus app.; continues in Infinity War #6 4.00
11-22: 11-Eternity & Living Tribunal app.; origins of the Watch. 12-1st app Maxam (brief cameo); Hulk cameo. 13-Drax vs Hulk; last Raney-a. 14-1st app. Count Abyss. 15-Eternity app. 16-1st full app. Maxam; Count Abyss app. 17-Maxam joins the Watch. 18-22-Infinity Crusade tie-ins; 18-Goddess & Reed Richards app; continued in Infinity Crusade #2. 19-X-Men, Avengers, Fantastic Four, Thanos app.; continued in Infinity Crusade #3. 20-Pip becomes master of reality; Goddess app; continued in Infinity Crusade #4. 21-Drax vs. Thor; continued in Infinity Crusade #5. 22-Goddess app; continued in Infinity Crusade #6 4.00
23,24-Blood and Thunder Pts. 4 & 8; continued from Warlock Chronicles #6; Silver Surfer & Warlock vs. Thor; continued in Thor #469. 24-Continued from Warlock Chronicles #7; Silver Surfer app.; continued in Thor #470 5.00
25-($2.95, 52 pgs.)-Die-cut & embossed double-c; Blood & Thunder Pt.12; continued from Warlock Chronicles #8; Thor, Dr. Strange, Beta Ray Bill & Silver Surfer app.; Thanos vs. Odin 2 4 6 9 12 15
26-32: 26-Avengers & Count Abyss app. 27-vs. the Avengers. 28-Avengers, Man-Beast & Count Abyss app. 29,30-Count Abyss app. 31-Origin Count Abyss; last Starlin-s. 32-Count Abyss defeats the Watch 4.00
33-35: 33-vs. Count Abyss. 34-Mole Man app.; Tyrannus cameo. 35-Mole Man & Tyrannus app. 4.00
36-Dr. Strange app; as 'Strange' 7.00
37-39: 37-1st app. Zakaius; Firelord app. 38-1st app. Domitan; Zakaius app. 39-Zakaius, Domitan & Firelord app. 6.00
40,41: 40-Thanos app.; Gamora leaves the Watch; Maxam receives the Time gem. 41-Origin Maxam; Gamora joins Thanos 1 2 3 5 6 8
42-Last issue; the Watch breaks up; the Infinity Gems disappear (see Rune/Silver Surfer #1); Thanos app. 2 4 6 10 14 18
NOTE: *Austin c/a-1-4i, 7i. Leonardi a(p)-3, 4. Medina c/a(p)-1, 2, 5; 6, 9, 10, 14, 15, 20. Williams a(i)-8, 12, 13, 16-19.*

WARLOCK CHRONICLES
Marvel Comics: June, 1993 - No. 8, Feb, 1994 ($2.00, limited series)
1-($2.95)-Holo-grafx foil & embossed-c; Starlin/Raney-s/a; Infinity Crusade tie-in; 1st app. Darklore; origin of Warlock & the Infinity Gems; cont'd in Warlock & the Infinity Watch #18 5.00
2-5-Infinity Crusade x-overs; 2-Cont'd from Infinity Crusade #2; Lord Order, Master Chaos, Eternity & Thanos app.; cont'd in Warlock & the Infinity Watch #19. 3-Cont'd from Infinity Crusade #3; Mephisto teams up w/Warlock & Thanos; cont'd in Warlock & the Infinity Watch #20. 4-Magus app.; cont'd in Warlock & the Infinity Watch #21. 5-Cont'd from Infinity Crusade #5; Goddess & Magus app.; cont'd in Warlock & the Infinity Watch #22 4.00
6-Blood & Thunder Pt. 3; cont'd from Silver Surfer #86; insane Thor cameo; brief Silver Surfer app.; cont'd in Warlock & the Infinity Watch #23 5.00
7-Blood & Thunder Pt. 7; cont'd from Silver Surfer #87; Dr. Strange, Beta Ray Bill & Silver Surfer app.; cont'd in Warlock & the Infinity Watch #24 6.00
8-Blood & Thunder Pt. 11; cont'd from Silver Surfer #88; Thanos, Silver Surfer, Dr. Strange app.; cont'd in Warlock & the Infinity Watch #25 1 2 3 5 6 8

WARLOCK 5
Aircel Pub.: 11/86 - No. 22, 5/89; V2#1, June, 1989 - V2#5, 1989 ($1.70, B&W)
1-5,7-11-Gordon Derry-s/Denis Beauvais-a thru #11. 5-Green Cyborg on-c. 5-Misnumbered as #6 (no #6); Blue Girl on-c. 4.00
12-22-Barry Blair-s/a. 18-$1.95-c begins 4.00
V2#1-5 ($2.00, B&W)-All issues by Barry Blair 4.00
Compilation 1,2: 1-r/#1-5 (1988, $5.95); 2-r/#6-9 6.00

WARLORD (See 1st Issue Special #8) (B&W reprints in Showcase Presents: Warlord)
National Periodical Publications/DC Comics #123 on: 1-2/76; No.2, 3-4/76; No.3, 10-11/76 - No. 133, Win, 1988-89
1-Story cont'd. from 1st Issue Special #8 4 8 12 27 44 60
2-Intro. Machiste 3 6 9 14 20 25
3-5 2 4 6 9 12 15
6-10: 6-Intro Mariah. 7-Origin Machiste. 9-Dons new costume 1 3 4 6 8 10
11-20: 11-Origin-r. 12-Intro Aton. 15-Tara returns; Warlord has son 6.00
21-36,40,41: 27-New facts about origin. 28-1st app. Wizard World. 32-Intro Shakira. 40-Warlord gets new costume 5.00
22-Whitman variant edition 3 6 9 16 24 32
37-39: 37,38-Origin Omac by Starlin; cont'd from Kamandi #59. 38-Intro Jennifer Morgan, Warlord's daughter. 39-Omac ends. 6.00
42-48: 42-47-Omac back-up series. 48-(52 pgs.)-1st app. Arak; contains free 14 pg. Arak Son of Thunder; Claw The Unconquered app. 5.00
49-62,64-99,101-132: 49-Claw The Unconquered app. 50-Death of Aton. 51-Reprints #1. 55-Arion Lord of Atlantis begins, ends #62. 91-Origin w/new facts. 114,115-Legends x-over. 125-Death of Tara. 131-1st DC work by Rob Liefeld (9/88) 4.00
63-The Barren Earth begins; free 16pg. Masters of the Universe preview 5.00
100-($1.25, 52 pgs.) 5.00
133-($1.50, 52 pgs.) 5.00
Annual 1-6 ('82-'87): 1-Grell-c,/a(p). 6-New Gods app. 5.00
The Savage Empire TPB (1991, $19.95) r/#1-10,12 & First Issue Special #8; Grell intro. 25.00
NOTE: *Grell a-1-15, 16-50p, 51r, 52p, 59p, Annual 1p; c-1-70, 100-104, 112, 116, 117, Annual 1, 5. Wayne Howard a-64i. Starlin a-37-39p.*

WARLORD
DC Comics: Jan, 1992 - No. 6, June, 1992 ($1.75, limited series)
1-6: Grell-c & scripts in all 3.00

WARLORD
DC Comics: Apr, 2006 - No. 10, Jan, 2007 ($2.99)
1-10: 1-Bruce Jones-s/Bart Sears-a. 10-Winslade-a 3.00

WARLORD
DC Comics: Jun, 2009 - No. 16, Sept, 2010 ($2.99)
1-16: 1-Grell-s/Prado-a/Grell-c. 7-9,11,12,15,16-Grell-s/a/c. 10-Hardin-a 3.00
...: The Saga SC (2010, $17.99) r/#1-6; cover gallery 18.00

WARLORD OF MARS
Dynamite Entertainment: 2010 - No. 35, 2014 ($1.00/$3.99)
1-($1.00) John Carter on Earth; Sadowski-a; covers by Ross, Campbell, Jusko. Parrillo 3.00
2-35-($3.99) Multiple covers on each. 3-Carter arrives on Mars. 4-Dejah Thoris intro. 4.00
100-($7.99, squarebound) Short stories; art by Antonio, Malaga, Luis; multiple covers 8.00
#0 (2014, $3.99) Brady-s/Jadson-a; John Carter back on Earth 4.00
... Annual 1 (2012, $4.99) Sadowski-a/Parrillo-c 5.00

WARLORD OF MARS ATTACKS
Dynamite Entertainment: 2019 - No. 5, 2019 ($3.99, limited series)
1-5-John Carter battles the Topps card Martians; Jeff Parker-s/Dean Kotz-a 4.00

WARLORD OF MARS: DEJAH THORIS
Dynamite Entertainment: 2011 - No. 37, 2014 ($3.99/$4.99)
1-36: 1-Five covers; Nelson-s/Rafael-a. 2-5-Four covers. 6-31-Multiple covers on all 4.00
37-($4.99) Napton-s/Carita-a; Neves & Anacleto-c 5.00

WARLORD OF MARS: FALL OF BARSOOM
Dynamite Entertainment: 2011 - No. 5, 2012 ($3.99, limited series)
1-5-Napton-s/Castro-a/Jusko-c 4.00

WARLORDS (See DC Graphic Novel #2)

WARLORDS OF APPALACHIA
BOOM! Studios: Oct, 2016 - No. 4 ($3.99)
1,2-Phillip Kennedy Johnson-s/Jonas Scharf-a 4.00

WAR MACHINE (Also see Iron Man #281,282 & Marvel Comics Presents #152)
Marvel Comics: Apr, 1994 - No. 25, Apr, 1996 ($1.50)
"Ashcan" edition (nd, 75¢, B&W, 16 pgs.) 5.00
1-($2.00, 52 pgs.)-Newsstand edition; Cable app. 5.00
1-($2.95, 52 pgs.)-Collectors ed.; embossed foil-c 1 3 4 6 8 10
2-14, 16-25: 2-Bound-in trading card sheet; Cable app. 2,3-Deathlok app. 8-red logo 3.00
8-($2.95)-Polybagged w/16 pg. Marvel Action Hour preview & acetate print; yellow logo 4.00
15 ($2.50)-Flip book 4.00

WAR MACHINE (Also see Dark Reign and Secret Invasion crossovers)
Marvel Comics: Feb, 2009 - No. 12, Feb, 2010 ($2.99)
1-12: 1-5-Pak-s/Manco-a/c; cyborg Jim Rhodes. 10-12-Dark Reign 3.00
1-Variant Titanium Man cover by Deodato 6.00

WAR MAN
Marvel Comics (Epic Comics): Nov, 1993 - No. 2, Dec, 1993 ($2.50, limited series)
1,2-Chuck Dixon-s 4.00

WAR MOTHER
Valiant Entertainment: Aug, 2017 - No. 4, Nov, 2017 ($3.99, limited series)
1-4-Van Lente-s/Segovia-a; multiple covers; Ana in 4001 AD 4.00

WAR OF KINGS
Marvel Comics: May, 2009 - No. 6, Oct, 2009 ($3.99, limited series)
1-6-Pelletier-a/Abnett & Lanning-s; Inhumans vs. the Shi'Ar 4.00
... Saga (2009, giveaway) synopsies of stories involving Kree, Shi'Ar, Inhumans, etc. 3.00
...: Savage World of Skaar 1 (8/09, $3.99) Gorgon & Starbolt land on Sakaar 4.00
...: Who Will Rule? 1 (11/09, $3.99) Pelletier-a; profile pages 4.00

WAR OF KINGS: ASCENSION
Marvel Comics: June, 2009 - No. 4, Sept, 2009 ($3.99, limited series)
1-4-Alves-a/Abnett & Lanning-s; Darkhawk app. 4.00

WAR OF KINGS: DARKHAWK (Leads into War Of Kings: Ascension limited series)
Marvel Comics: Apr, 2009 - No. 2, May, 2009 ($3.99, limited series)
1,2-Cebulski-s/Tolibao & Dazo-a/Peterson-c; r/Darkhawk #1,2 (1991) origin 4.00

WAR OF KINGS: WARRIORS
Marvel Comics: Sept, 2009 - No. 2, Oct, 2009 ($3.99, limited series)
1,2-Prequel to x-over; Gage-s/Asrar & Magno-a 4.00

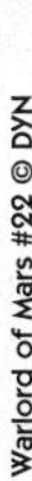

Warlord of Mars #22 © DYN

War of Kings #1 © MAR

War Stories #6 © Avatar

	GD 2.0	VG 4.0	FN 6.0	VF 8.0	VF/NM 9.0	NM- 9.2

WAR OF THE GODS
DC Comics: Sept, 1991 - No. 4, Dec, 1991 ($1.75, limited series)

1-4: Perez layouts, scripts & covers. 1-Contains free mini posters (Robin, Deathstroke). 2-4-Direct sale versions include 4 pin-ups printed on cover stock plus different-c 4.00

WAR OF THE GREEN LANTERNS: AFTERMATH
DC Comics: Sept, 2011 - No. 2, Oct, 2011 ($3.99, limited series)

1,2: 1-Bedard-s/Sepulveda & Kirkham-a. 2-Getty & Smith-a 4.00

WAR OF THE REALMS (Tie-in issues exist in many 2019 Marvel titles)
Marvel Comics: Jun, 2019 - No. 6, Aug, 2019 ($5.99/$4.99, limited series)

1-($5.99) Aaron-s/Dauterman-a; Malekith attacks Earth; Loki eaten
1 3 4 6 8 10
2-5-($4.99) 2-Avengers, Punisher, Jane Foster app. 4-Venom app. 5.00
6-($5.99) Jane Thor app. 6.00
... Omega 1 (9/19, $4.99) Short stories; Jane Foster becomes Valkyrie; Punisher app. 5.00

WAR OF THE REALMS: JOURNEY INTO MYSTERY
Marvel Comics: Jun, 2019 - No. 5, Aug, 2019 ($3.99, limited series)

1-5-Spider-Man (Miles), Hawkeye (Kate), Wonder Man, Ares app. 4.00

WAR OF THE REALMS: NEW AGENTS OF ATLAS
Marvel Comics: Jul, 2019 - No. 4, Aug, 2019 ($3.99, limited series)

1-Greg Pak-s/Gang Hyuk Lim-a; Ms. Marvel, Silk, Shang-Chi & Amedeus Cho app.
4 8 12 23 37 50
2-1st Swordmaster 4 8 12 28 47 65
3,4 4.00

WAR OF THE REALMS STRIKEFORCE:...
Marvel Comics: Jul, 2019 ($4.99, series of one-shots)

... The Dark Elf Realm 1 - Bryan Hill-s/Yu-a; Punisher, She-Hulk, Blade, Ghost Rider 5.00
... The Land of Giants 1 - Taylor-s/Molina-a; Wolverine, Capt. America, Luke Cage app. 5.00
... The War Avengers 1 - Anindito-a; Deadpool, Namor, Capt. Marvel, Sif, Venom app. 5.00

WAR OF THE REALMS: THE PUNISHER
Marvel Comics: Jun, 2019 - No. 3, Aug, 2019 ($3.99, limited series)

1-3-Duggan-s/Ferreira-a 4.00

WAR OF THE REALMS: UNCANNY X-MEN
Marvel Comics: Jun, 2019 - No. 3, Aug, 2019 ($3.99, limited series)

1-3-Rosenberg-s/Pere Pérez-a; Cyclops, Dani Moonstar app. 2-Sabretooth app. 4.00

WAR OF THE REALMS: WAR SCROLLS
Marvel Comics: Jun, 2019 - No. 3, Aug, 2019 ($4.99, limited series)

1-Short stories by various; Daredevil serial in all w/Sorrentino-a; Alan Davis-c
1 2 3 5 6 8
2,3-Alan Davis-c 5.00

WAR OF THE UNDEAD
IDW Publishing: Jan, 2007 - No. 3, Apr, 2007 ($3.99, limited series)

1-3-Bryan Johnson-s/Walter Flanagan-a 2 4 6 9 12 15

WAR OF THE WORLDS, THE
Caliber: 1996 - No. 5 ($2.95, B&W, 32 pgs.)(Based on H. G. Wells novel)

1-5: 1-Randy Zimmerman scripts begin 4.00

WARP
First Comics: Mar, 1983 - No. 19, Feb, 1985 ($1.00/$1.25, Mando paper)

1-Sargon-Mistress of War app.; Brunner-c/a thru #9 4.00
2-19: 2-Faceless Ones begin. 10-New Warp advs., & Outrider begin 3.00
Special 1-3: 1(7/83, 36 pgs.)-Origin Chaos-Prince of Madness; origin of Warp Universe begins, ends #3; Chaykin-c/a. 2,3-Silvestri-c/a. 2(1/84)-Lord Cumulus vs. Sargon Mistress of War ($1.00). 3(6/84)-Chaos-Prince of Madness 3.00

WARPATH (Indians on the...)
Key Publications/Stanmor: Nov, 1954 - No. 3, Apr, 1955

1 13 26 39 74 105 135
2,3 9 18 27 47 61 75

WARP GRAPHICS ANNUAL
WaRP Graphics: Dec, 1985; 1988 ($2.50)

1-Elfquest, Blood of the Innocent, Thunderbunny & Myth Adventures 5.00
1 (1988) 4.00

WARREN PRESENTS
Warren Publications: Jan, 1979 - No. 14, Nov, 1981(B&W magazine)

1-Eerie, Creepy, & Vampirella-r; Ring of the Warlords; Merlin-s; Dax-s; Sanjulian-c
3 6 9 18 27 36
2-6(10/79): 2-The Rook. 3-Alien Invasions Comix. 4-Movie Aliens. 5-Dracula '79. 6-Strange Stories of Vampires Comix 2 4 6 10 14 18
8(10/80)-r/1st app. Pantha from Vamp. #30 2 4 6 13 18 22
9(11/80) Empire Encounters Comix 2 4 6 11 16 20
13(10/81),14(11/81):13-Sword and Sorcery Comix 3 6 9 14 19 24
(#7,10,11,12 may not exist, or may be a Special below)
Special-Alien Collectors Edition (1979) 3 6 9 14 20 26
Special-Close Encounters of the Third Kind (1978) 2 4 6 10 14 18
Special-Lord of the Rings (6/79) 3 6 9 19 30 40
Special-Meteor (1/80) 2 4 6 10 14 18
Special-Moonraker/James Bond (10/79) 2 4 6 10 14 18
Special-Star Wars (1977) 3 6 9 21 33 45

WAR REPORT
Ajax/Farrell Publications (Excellent Publ.): Sept, 1952 - No. 5, May, 1953

1 26 52 78 154 252 350
2-Flame thrower w/burning bodies on-c 34 68 102 204 332 460
3,5 14 28 42 81 118 155
4-Used in **POP**, pg. 94 15 30 45 85 130 175

WARRIOR (Wrestling star)
Ultimate Creations: May, 1996 - No. 4, 1997 ($2.95)

1-4: Warrior scripts; Callahan-c/a. 3-Wraparound-c. 4-Warrior #3 in indicia; pin-ups 4.00
1-Variant-c 1 3 4 6 8 10
X-Mas (11/96, $3.50) listed as "No. 3" in indicia; pin-ups by various; Quesada-c 4.00

WARRIOR COMICS
H.C. Blackerby: 1945 (1930s DC reprints)

1-Wing Brady, The Iron Man, Mark Markon 29 58 87 172 281 390

WARRIOR OF WAVERLY STREET, THE
Dark Horse Comics: Nov, 1996 - No. 2, Dec, 1996 ($2.95, mini-series)

1,2-Darrow-c 4.00

WARRIORS
CFD Productions: 1993 (B&W, one-shot)

1-Linsner, Dark One-a 2 4 6 11 16 20

WARRIORS, THE: OFFICIAL MOVIE ADAPTATION (Based on the 1979 movie)
Dabel Brothers Publishing/Dynamite Ent.: Feb, 2009 - No. 5, 2010 ($3.99, limited series)

1-5: 1-Three covers plus wraparound photo-c; Dibari-a. 3-Eric Powell-c 4.00
...: Jailbreak 1 (7/09, $3.99) Apon & Herman-a 4.00

WARRIORS OF MARS (Also see Warlord of Mars titles)
Dynamite Entertainment: 2012 - No. 5, 2012 ($3.99, limited series)

1-5-Gullivar Jones visits Barsoom; Jusko-c 4.00

WARRIORS OF PLASM (Also see Plasm and Dogs of War #5)
Defiant: Aug, 1993 - No. 13, Aug, 1995 ($2.95/$2.50)

1-4: Shooter-scripts; Lapham-c/a: 1-1st app. Glory. 4-Bound-in fold-out poster 4.00
5-7,10-13: 5-Begin $2.50-c. 13-Schism issue; last Defiant comic published 3.00
8,9-($2.75, 44 pgs.) 4.00
...Graphic Novel #1 (Home for the Holidays)(11/93, $5.95) Len Wein story; Cockrum-a; Christmas issue; story takes place between Warriors of Plasm #4 and #5 6.00
The Collected Edition (2/94, $9.95)-r/Plasm #0, WOP #1-4 & Splatterball
2 4 6 8 11 14

WARRIORS THREE (Fandral, Volstagg, and Hogun from Thor)
Marvel Comics: Jan, 2011 - No. 4, Apr, 2011 ($3.99, limited series)

1-4-Bill Willingham-s/Neil Edwards-a. 2,4-Conner-c 4.00

WAR ROMANCES (See True...)

WAR SHIPS
Dell Publishing Co.: 1942 (36 pgs.)(Similar to Large Feature Comics)

nn-Cover by McWilliams; contains photos & drawings of U.S. war ships
24 48 72 142 234 325

WAR STORIES (Formerly War Comics)
Dell Publ. Co.: No. 5, 1942(nd); No. 6, Aug-Oct, 1942 - No. 8, Feb-Apr, 1943

5-Origin The Whistler 39 78 117 231 378 525
6-8: 6-8-Night Devils app. 8-Painted-c 30 60 90 177 289 400

WAR STORIES (Korea)
Ajax/Farrell Publications (Excellent Publ.): Sept, 1952 - No. 5, May, 1953

1 22 44 66 132 216 300
2 15 30 45 83 124 165
3-5 15 30 45 85 130 175

WAR STORIES
Avatar Press: Sept, 2014 - No. 26, Jan, 2018 ($3.99)

1-26: Garth Ennis-s in all; multiple covers on all. 1-Matt Martin-a 4.00

WAR STORIES (See Star Spangled...)

GD 2.0 · VG 4.0 · FN 6.0 · VF 8.0 · VF/NM 9.0 · NM- 9.2

GD 2.0 · VG 4.0 · FN 6.0 · VF 8.0 · VF/NM 9.0 · NM- 9.2

WAR STORY
DC Comics (Vertigo): Nov, 2001 - Apr, 2003 ($4.95, series of World War II one-shots)
...: Archangel (4/03) Ennis-s/Erskine-a 5.00
...: Condors (3/03) Ennis-s/Ezquerra-a 5.00
...: D-Day Dodgers (12/01) Ennis-s/Higgins-a 5.00
...: J For Jenny (2/03) Ennis-s/Lloyd-a 5.00
...: Johann's Tiger (11/01) Ennis-s/Weston-a 5.00
...: Nightingale (2/02) Ennis-s/Lloyd-a 5.00
...: Screaming Eagles (1/02) Ennis-s/Gibbons-a 5.00
...: The Reivers (1/03) Ennis-s/Kennedy-a 5.00
Vol. 1 (2004, $19.95) r/Johann's Tiger, D-Day Dodgers, Screaming Eagles, Nightingale 20.00
Vol. 2 (2006, $19.99) r/J For Jenny, The Reivers, Condors, Archangel; Ennis afterword 20.00

WARSTRIKE
Malibu Comics (Ultraverse): May, 1994 - No. 7, Nov, 1995 ($1.95)
1-7: 1-Simonson-c 3.00
1-Ultra 5000 Limited silver foil 6.00
Giant Size 1 (12/94, $2.50, 44pgs.)-Prelude to Godwheel 4.00

WART AND THE WIZARD (See The Sword & the Stone under Movie Comics)
Gold Key: Feb, 1964 (Walt Disney)(Characters from Sword in the Stone movie)
1 (10102-402) 4 8 12 28 47 65

WAR THAT TIME FORGOT, THE
DC Comics: Jul, 2008 - No. 12, Jun, 2009 ($2.99, limited series)
1-12: 1-Bruce Jones-s/Al Barrionuevo-a/Neal Adams-c; Enemy Ace app. 3.00

WARTIME ROMANCES
St. John Publishing Co.: July, 1951 - No. 18, Nov, 1953
1-All Baker-c/a 174 348 522 1114 1907 2700
2-All Baker-c/a 116 232 348 742 1271 1800
3,4-All Baker-c/a 123 246 369 787 1344 1900
5-8-Baker-c/a(2-3) each 103 206 309 659 1130 1600
9,11,12,16,18: Baker-c/a each. 9-Two signed stories by Estrada
71 142 213 454 777 1100
10,13-15,17-Baker-c only 65 130 195 416 708 1000

WAR VICTORY ADVENTURES (#1 titled War Victory Comics)
U.S. Treasury Dept./War Victory/Harvey Publ.: Sum, 1942 - No. 3, Wint, 1943-44 (5¢/10¢)
1-(5¢)(Promotion of Savings Bonds)-Featuring America's greatest comic art by top syndicated cartoonists; Blondie, Joe Palooka, Green Hornet, Dick Tracy, Superman, Gumps, etc.; (36 pgs.); all profits were contributed to U.S.O. & Army/Navy relief funds
84 168 252 538 919 1300
2-(10¢) Battle of Stalingrad story; Powell-a (8/43); flag & WWII Japanese-c
116 232 348 742 1271 1800
3-(10¢) Capt. Red Cross-c & text only; WWII Nazi-c; Powell-a
103 206 309 659 1130 1600

WAR WAGON, THE (See Movie Classics)

WAR WINGS
Charlton Comics: Oct, 1968
1 3 6 9 16 23 30

WARWORLD!
Dark Horse Comics: Feb, 1989 ($1.75, B&W, one-shot)
1-Gary Davis sci/fi art in Moebius style 4.00

WASHABLE JONES AND THE SHMOO (Also see Al Capp's Shmoo)
Toby Press: June, 1953
1- "Super-Shmoo" 22 44 66 128 209 290

WASH TUBBS (See The Comics, Crackajack Funnies)
Dell Publishing Co.: No. 11, 1942 - No. 53, 1944
Four Color 11 (#1) 27 54 81 194 435 675
Four Color 28 (1943) 19 38 57 131 291 450
Four Color 53 15 30 45 103 227 350

WASP (Also see Unstoppable Wasp)
Marvel Comics: Mar, 2023 - Present ($3.99, limited series)
1,2-Al Ewing-s/Kasia Nie-a; Janet Van Dyne & Nadia. 1-Whirlwind app. 4.00

WASTELAND
DC Comics: Dec, 1987 - No. 18, May, 1989 ($1.75-$2.00 #13 on, mature)
1-5(4/88), 5(5/88), 6(5/88)-18: 13,15-Orlando-a 4.00
NOTE: ***Orlando** a-12, 13, 15. **Truman** a-10; c-13.*

WASTELANDERS (The world of Old Man Logan; see Wolverine [2003] #66-72)
Marvel Comics: Feb, 2022 - Mar, 2022 ($3.99, series of one-shots)
...: Black Widow 1 (3/22) DeKnight-s/Well-Bee-a; Yelena Belova app. 4.00
...: Doom 1 (3/22) Gronbekk-s/Ohta-a; Baron Mordo app. 4.00
...: Hawkeye 1 (2/22) Sacks-s/Roberson-a; Matt Murdock & Elektra app. 4.00
...: Star-Lord 1 (2/22) Douek-s/Peeples-a; Shadow King app. 4.00
...: Wolverine 1 (2/22) DeKnight-s/Moustafa-a; Banner app. 4.00

WATCHMEN (Also see 2012-2013 Before Watchmen prequel titles)
DC Comics: Sept, 1986 - No. 12, Oct, 1987 (maxi-series)
1-Alan Moore scripts & Dave Gibbons-c/a in all 6 12 18 37 66 95
1-(2009, $1.50) Second printing 3.00
2-12 3 6 9 14 19 24
Hardcover Collection-Slip-cased-r/#1-12 w/new material; produced by Graphitti Designs 100.00
HC (2008, $39.99) recolored r/#1-12; design & promotional art; Moore & Gibbons intros 40.00
Trade paperback (1987, $14.95)-r/#1-12 25.00

WATCHVARK COMICS (Reprints from Cerebus in Hell)(Also see Aardvark Comics)
Aardvark-Vanaheim: Jan, 2018 ($4.00, B&W)
1-Cerebus figures placed over original Doré artwork of Hell; Watchmen #6-c swipe 4.00

WATER BIRDS AND THE OLYMPIC ELK (Disney)
Dell Publishing Co.: No. 700, Apr, 1956
Four Color 700-Movie 5 10 15 33 57 80

WATERWORLD: CHILDREN OF LEVIATHAN
Acclaim Comics: Aug, 1997 - No. 4, Nov, 1997 ($2.50, mini-series)
1-4 3.00

WAY OF THE RAT
CrossGeneration Comics: Jun, 2002 - No. 24, June, 2004 ($2.95)
1-24: 1-Dixon-s/ Jeff Johnson-a. 5-Whigham-a. 9,14-Luke Ross-a 3.00
Free Comic Book Day Special (6/03) reprints #1 w/features, interviews, CrossGen info 3.00
...: The Walls of Zhumar Vol. 1 (1/03, $15.95) r/#1-6 16.00
Vol. 2: The Dragon's Wake (2003, $15.95) r/#7-12 16.00

WAY OF X (X-Men)
Marvel Comics: Jun, 2021 - No. 5, Oct, 2021 ($4.99/$3.99, limited series)
1-($4.99) Spurrier-s/Quinn-a; Legion app. 5.00
2-5-($3.99) 3-Hellfire Gala 4.00

WAYWARD
Image Comics: Aug, 2014 - No. 30, Oct, 2018 ($3.50/$3.99)
1-29: 1-Jim Zub-s/Cummings-a; multiple covers. 16-Begin $3.99-c 4.00
30-($4.99) Last issue; bonus pin-up gallery 5.00

WEAPON H (See Weapon X [2017 series] #6 for debut)(See Hulkverines #1)
Marvel Comics: May, 2018 - No. 12, Mar, 2019 ($4.99/$3.99)
1-($4.99) Greg Pak-s/Cory Smith-a; Wendigo app. 5.00
2-12-($3.99) 2-Doctor Strange app. 3-7-Man-Thing app. 6,7-Captain America app. 4.00

WEAPON PLUS: WORLD WAR IV
Marvel Comics: Mar, 2020 ($4.99, one-shot)
1-Percy-s/Jeanty-a; Weapon IV app. (Man-Thing-like soldier) 5.00

WEAPONS OF MUTANT DESTRUCTION: ALPHA
Marvel Comics: Aug, 2017 ($4.99, one-shot)
1-Crossover with Weapon X #4-6 and Totally Awesome Hulk #19-22; Stryker app. 4.00

WEAPON X
Marvel Comics: Apr, 1994 ($12.95, one-shot)
nn-r/Marvel Comics Presents #72-84 3 6 9 14 20 25

WEAPON X
Marvel Comics: Mar, 1995 - No. 4, June, 1995 ($1.95)
1-Age of Apocalypse 4.00
2-4 3.00

WEAPON X
Marvel Comics: Nov, 2002 - No. 28, Nov, 2004 ($2.25/$2.99)
1-7: 1-Sabretooth-c/app.; Tieri-s/Jeanty-a 3.00
8-28: 8-Begin $2.99-c. 14-Invaders app. 15-Chamber joins. 16-18,21-25-Wolverine app. 3.00
Vol. 1: The Draft TPB (2003, $21.99) r/#1-5, #1/2 & The Draft one-shots 22.00
Vol. 2: The Underground TPB (2003, $19.99) r/#6-13 20.00
Wizard #1/2 (2002) 5.00

WEAPON X
Marvel Comics: Jun, 2017 - No. 27, Feb, 2019 ($3.99)
1-27: 1-Pak-s/Land-a; Old Man Logan & Sabretooth. 4-6-Crossover with Totally Awesome Hulk #19-22. 6-Intro. Weapon H. 17-19-Omega Red app. 23-27-Deadpool app. 4.00

WEAPON X: DAYS OF FUTURE NOW
Marvel Comics: Sept, 2005 - No. 5, Jan, 2006 ($2.99, limited series)
1-5-Tieri-s/Sears-a; Chamber, Sauron & Fantomex app. 3.00
TPB (2006, $13.99) r/#1-5 14.00

WEAPON X: FIRST CLASS
Marvel Comics: Jan, 2009 - No. 3, Mar, 2009 ($3.99, limited series)
1-3:1-Sabretooth-c/app. 2-Deadpool-c/app. 4.00

WEAPON X NOIR
Marvel Comics: May, 2010 ($3.99, one-shot)
1-Dennis Calero-s/a; C.P. Smith-c 4.00

WEAPON X: THE DRAFT (Leads into 2002 Weapon X series)
Marvel Comics: Oct, 2002 ($2.25, one-shots)
...Kane 1- JH Williams-c/Raimondi-a 3.00
...Marrow 1- JH Williams-c/Badeaux-a 3.00
...Sauron 1- JH Williams-c/Kerschl-a; Emma Frost app. 3.00
...Wild Child 1- JH Williams-c/Van Sciver-a; Aurora (Alpha Flight) app. 3.00
...Zero 1- JH Williams-c/Plunkett-a; Wolverine app. 3.00

WEAPON ZERO
Image Comics (Top Cow Productions): No. T-4(#1), June, 1995 - No. T-0(#5), Dec, 1995 ($2.50, limited series)
T-4(#1): Walt Simonson scripts in all. 5.00
T-3(#2) - T-1(#4) 4.00
T-0(#5) 3.00

WEAPON ZERO
Image Comics (Top Cow Productions): V2#1, Mar, 1996 - No. 15, Dec, 1997 ($2.50)
V2#1-Walt Simonson scripts. 4.00
2-14: 8-Begin Top Cow. 10-Devil's Reign 3.00
15-($3.50) Benitez-a 4.00

WEAPON ZERO/SILVER SURFER
Image Comics/Marvel Comics: Jan, 1997 ($2.95, one-shot)
1-Devil's Reign Pt. 1 3.00

WE ARE ROBIN (Also see Batman: Rebirth #1)
DC Comics: Aug, 2015 - No. 12, Jul, 2016 ($3.99)
1-12: 1-Bermejo-s/c; Corona-a. 3-Batman (Gordon) app. 4-Batgirl app.; Harvey-a 4.00

WEASELGUY: ROAD TRIP
Image Comics: Sept, 1999 - No. 2 ($3.50, limited series)
1,2-Steve Buccellato-s/a 3.50
1-Variant-c by Bachalo 5.00

WEASELGUY/WITCHBLADE
Hyperwerks: July, 1998 ($2.95, one-shot)
1-Steve Buccellato-s/a; covers by Matsuda and Altstaetter 4.00

The War That Time Forgot #1 © DC

We Are Robin #4 © DC

Web of Black Widow (2019) #1 © MAR

GD VG FN VF VF/NM NM-
2.0 4.0 6.0 8.0 9.0 9.2

WEASEL PATROL SPECIAL, THE (Also see Fusion #17)
Eclipse Comics: Apr, 1989 ($2.00, B&W, one-shot)
1-Funny animal 4.00

WEATHERMAN, THE
Image Comics: Jun, 2018 - No. 6, Nov, 2018 ($3.99)
1-6-Jody LeHeup-s/Nathan Fox-a 4.00

WEATHERMAN, THE (Volume 2)
Image Comics: Jun, 2019 - Present ($3.99)
1-6-Jody LeHeup-s/Nathan Fox-a 4.00

WEAVEWORLD
Marvel Comics (Epic): Dec, 1991 - No. 3, 1992 ($4.95, lim. series, 68 pgs.)
1-3: Clive Barker adaptation 5.00

WEB, THE (Also see Mighty Comics & Mighty Crusaders)
DC Comics (Impact Comics): Sept, 1991 - No. 14, Oct, 1992 ($1.00)
1-14: 5-The Fly x-over 9-Trading card inside 5.00
Annual 1 (1992, $2.50, 68 pgs.)-With Trading card 5.00
NOTE: ***Gil Kane** c-5, 9, 10, 12-14. **Bill Wray** a(i)-1-9, 10(part).*

WEB, THE (Continued from The Red Circle)
DC Comics: Nov, 2009 - No. 10, Aug, 2010 ($3.99)
1-10: 1-Roger Robinson-a; The Hangman back-up feature. 3-Batgirl app. 5-Caldwell-a 4.00

WEB OF BLACK WIDOW, THE
Marvel Comics: Nov, 2019 - No. 5, Mar, 2020 ($3.99, limited series)
1-5-Jody Houser-s/Stephen Mooney-a. 1,5-Iron Man app. 2-Winter Soldier app. 4.00

WEB OF EVIL
Comic Magazines/Quality Comics Group: Nov, 1952 - No. 21, Dec, 1954
1-Used in **SOTI**, pg. 388. Jack Cole-a; morphine use story
106 212 318 673 1162 1650
2-4,6,7: 2,3-Jack Cole-a. 4,6,7-Jack Cole-c/a 58 116 174 371 636 900
5-Electrocution-c/story; Jack Cole-c/a 371 742 1113 2600 4550 6500
8-11-Jack Cole-a 52 104 156 328 552 775
12,13,15,16,19-21 37 74 111 222 361 500
14-Part Crandall-c; Old Witch swipe 43 86 129 271 461 650
17-Opium drug propaganda story 41 82 123 256 428 600
18-Acid-in-face story 58 116 174 371 636 900
NOTE: ***Jack Cole** a(2 each)-2, 6, 8, 9. **Cuidera** c-1-21i. **Ravielli** a-13.*

WEB OF HORROR
Major Magazines: Dec, 1969 - No. 3, Apr, 1970 (Magazine)
1-Jeff Jones painted-c; Wrightson-a, Kaluta-a 12 24 36 83 182 280
2-Jones painted-c; Wrightson-a(2), Kaluta-a 9 18 27 62 126 190
3-Wrightson-c/a (1st published-c); Brunner, Kaluta, Bruce Jones-a
12 24 36 82 179 275

WEB OF MYSTERY
Ace Magazines (A. A. Wyn): Feb, 1951 - No. 29, Sept, 1955
1 119 238 357 762 1306 1850
2-Bakerish-a 50 100 150 315 533 750
3-10: 4-Colan-a 42 84 126 265 445 625
11-18,20-26: 12-John Chilly's 1st cover art. 13-Surrealistic-c. 20-r/The Beyond #1
40 80 120 246 411 575
19-Reprints Challenge of the Unknown #6 used in N.Y. Legislative Committee
42 84 126 265 445 625
27-Bakerish-a(r/The Beyond #2); last pre-code ish 40 80 120 246 411 575
28,29: 28-All-r 32 64 96 188 307 425
NOTE: *This series was to appear as "Creepy Stories", but title was changed before publication. **Cameron** a-6, 8, 11-13, 17-20, 22, 24, 25, 27; c-8, 13, 17. **Palais** a-28r. **Sekowsky** a-1-3, 7, 8, 11, 14, 21, 29. **Tothish** a-by **Bill Discount** #16. 29-all-r, 19-28-partial-r.*

WEB OF SCARLET SPIDER
Marvel Comics: Oct, 1995 - No. 4, Jan, 1996 ($1.95, limited series)
1-Replaces "Web of Spider-Man" 2 4 6 9 12 15
2-4 4.00

WEB OF SPIDER-MAN (Replaces Marvel Team-Up)
Marvel Comics Group: Apr, 1985 - No. 129, Sept, 1995
1-Painted-c by Charles Vess (black costume app.) 4 8 12 25 40 55
2,3 2 4 6 8 10 12
4-8: 7-Hulk x-over; Wolverine splash 6.00
9-13: 10-Dominic Fortune guest stars; painted-c 5.00
14-17,19-28: 19-Intro Humbug & Solo 5.00
18-1st app. Venom (behind the scenes, 9/86) 3 6 9 19 30 40
29-Wolverine, new Hobgoblin (Macendale) app. 2 4 6 9 13 16
30-Origin recap The Rose & Hobgoblin I (entire book is flashback story);
Punisher & Wolverine cameo 6.00
31,32-Six part Kraven storyline begins 2 4 6 9 12 15
33-35,37,39-47,49 4.00
36-1st app. Tombstone 3 6 9 19 30 40
38-Hobgoblin app.; begin $1.00-c 5.00
48-Origin Hobgoblin II(Demogoblin) cont'd from Spectacular Spider-Man #147;
Kingpin app. 2 4 6 8 10 12
50-($1.50, 52 pgs.) 5.00
51-58 4.00
59-Cosmic Spidey cont'd from Spect. Spider-Man 5.00
60-89,91-99,101-106: 66,67-Green Goblin (Norman Osborn) app. as a super-hero. 69,70-Hulk x-over. 74-76-Austin-c(i). 76-Fantastic Four x-over. 78-Cloak & Dagger app. 81-Origin/1st app. Bloodshed. 84-Begin 6 part Rose & Hobgoblin II storyline; last $1.00-c. 86-Demon leaves Hobgoblin; 1st Demogoblin. 93-Gives brief history of Hobgoblin. 93,94-Hobgoblin (Macendale) Reborn-c/story, parts 1,2; MoonKnight app. 94-Venom cameo. 95-Begin 4 part x-over w/Spirits of Venom w/Ghost Rider/Blaze/Spidey vs. Venom & Demogoblin (cont'd in Ghost Rider/Blaze #5,6). 96-Spirits of Venom part 3; painted-c. 101,103-Maximum Carnage x-over. 103-Venom & Carnage app. 104-Infinity Crusade tie-in. 104-106-Nightwatch back-up stories 4.00
90-(7/92, $2.95, 52 pgs.)-Polybagged w/silver hologram-c, gatefold poster showing Spider-Man & Spider-Man 2099 (1st image of the character; pre-dates Spider-Man 2099 story debut in ASM #365 by one month) 2 4 6 8 11 14
90-2nd printing; gold hologram-c 4.00
100-($2.95, 52 pgs.)-Holo-grafx foil-c; intro new Spider-Armor 5.00
107-111: 107-Intro Sandstorm; Sand & Quicksand app. 4.00
112-116,121-124, 126-128: 112-Begin $1.50-c; bound-in trading card sheet.
113-Regular Ed.; Gambit & Black Cat app. 4.00
113-($2.95)-Collector's ed. polybagged w/foil-c; 16 pg. preview of Spider-Man cartoon & animation cel 5.00
117-($1.50)-Flip book; Power & Responsibility Pt.1 4.00
117-($2.95)-Collector's edition; foil-c; flip book 5.00
118-1st solo Scarlet Spider story; Venom app. 6 12 18 41 76 110
119-Regular edition 6.00
119-($6.45)-Direct market edition; polybagged w/ Marvel Milestone Amazing Spider-Man #150 & coupon for Amazing Spider-Man #396, Spider-Man #53, & Spectacular Spider-Man #219.
3 6 9 14 19 24
120 ($2.25)-Flip book w/ preview of the Ultimate Spider-Man 4.00
125 ($3.95)-Holodisk-c; Gwen Stacy clone 5.00
125,129: 125 ($2.95)-Newsstand. 129-Last issue 5.00
#129.1, #129.2 (both 10/12, $2.99) Brooklyn Avengers app.; Damion Scott-a 4.00
Annual 1 (1985) 1 3 4 6 8 10
Annual 2 (1986)-New Mutants; Art Adams-a 2 4 6 8 10 12
Annual 3-10 ('87-'94, 68 pgs.): 4-Evolutionary War x-over. 5-Atlantis Attacks; Captain Universe by Ditko (p) & Silver Sable stories; F.F. app. 6-Punisher back-up plus Capt. Universe by Ditko; G. Kane-a. 7-Origins of Hobgoblin I, Hobgoblin II, Green Goblin I & II & Venom; Larsen/Austin-c. 9-Bagged w/card 5.00
Super Special 1 (1995, $3.95)-flip book 5.00
NOTE: ***Art Adams** a-Annual 2. **Byrne** c-3-6. **Chaykin** c-10. **Mignola** a-Annual 2. **Vess** c-1, 8, Annual 1, 2. **Zeck** a-6i, 31, 32; c-31, 32.*

WEB OF SPIDER-MAN (Anthology)
Marvel Comics: Dec, 2009 - No. 12, Nov, 2010 ($3.99)
1-12: 1-Spider-Girl app. thru #7; Ben Reilly app. 2-6-Origins of villains retold. 7-Kraven origin; Paper Doll app.; Mahfood-a. 9-11-Jackpot back-up; Takeda-a. 11,12-Black Cat app. 4.00

W.E.B. OF SPIDER-MAN (All ages stories)
Marvel Comics: Aug, 2021 - No. 5, Nov, 2021 ($3.99, limited series)
1-5-Teenage Spidey with Moon Girl, Onome, Harley Keener, Squirrel Girl 4.00

WEB OF VENOM...
Marvel Comics: Oct, 2018 - Jan, 2021 ($4.99, one-shots)
...: Carnage Born 1 (1/19) Story of Cletus Kasady; Cates-s/Beyruth-a
1 2 3 5 6 8
...: Cult of Carnage 1 (6/19) Misty Knight & John Jameson app.; Tieri-s/Beyruth-a 5.00
...: Empyre's End 1 (1/21) Knull app.; Chapman-s/Vilanova-a 5.00
...: Funeral Pyre 1 (9/19) Story of Andi Benton (Mania); Carnage app.
1 2 3 5 6 8
...: The Good Son 1 (3/20) Story of Eddie Brock's son Dylan and Normie Osborn 5.00
...: Ve'Nam 1 (10/18) The first symbiote & Rex Strickland app.; Cates-s/Ramírez-a
1 2 3 5 6 8
...: Venom Unleashed 1 (3/19) Venom Dog and Carnage app.; Cates-s/Hotz & Gedeon-a 5.00
...: Wraith 1 (11/20) Origin of Wraith re-told; Cates-s/Vilanova-a 5.00

WEBSPINNERS: TALES OF SPIDER-MAN
Marvel Comics: Jan, 1999 - No. 18, Jun, 2000 ($2.99/$2.50)
1-DeMatteis-s/Zulli-a; back-up story w/Romita Sr. art 6.00
1-($6.95) DF Edition 1 2 3 5 6 8
2,3: 2-Two covers 4.00

GD VG FN VF VF/NM NM-
2.0 4.0 6.0 8.0 9.0 9.2

4-11,13-18: 4,5-Giffen-a; Silver Surfer-c/app. 7-9-Kelly-s/Sears and Smith-a. 10,11-Jenkins-s/Sean Phillips-a 4.00
12-($3.50) J.G. Jones-c/a; Jenkins-s 5.00

WEB WARRIORS
Marvel Comics: Jan, 2016 - No. 11, Nov, 2016 ($4.99/$3.99)

1-($4.99) Spider-verse characters team-up; Mike Costa-s/David Baldeon-a; alternate Black Cat app. 5.00
2-11-($3.99) 2-5-Multiple Spider-Mans vs. multiple Electros 4.00

WEDDING BELLS
Quality Comics Group: Feb, 1954 - No. 19, Nov, 1956

1-Whitney-a 25 50 75 150 245 340
2 15 30 45 88 137 185
3-9: 8-Last precode (4/55) 14 28 42 78 112 145
10-Ward-a (9 pgs.) 19 38 57 112 179 245
11-14,17 13 26 39 74 105 135
15-Baker-c 34 68 102 199 325 450
16-Baker-c/a 32 64 96 188 307 425
18,19-Baker-a each 21 42 63 122 199 275

WEDDING OF DRACULA
Marvel Comics: Jan, 1993 ($2.00, 52 pgs.)

1-Reprints Tomb of Dracula #30,45,46 4.00

WEDNESDAY COMICS (Newspaper-style, twice folded pages on 20" x 14" newsprint)
DC Comics: Sept, 2009 - No. 12, Nov, 2009 ($3.99, weekly limited series)

1-12-Superman, Batman, Kamandi, Hawkman, Deadman, Green Lantern, Flash, Teen Titans, Metamorpho, Adam Strange, Supergirl, Metal Men, Wonder Woman, The Demon with Catwoman, Sgt. Rock; s-a/ by various incl. Ryan Sook, Joe Kubert, Gaiman, Allred, Risso, Kyle Baker, Paul Pope, Conner, Simonson, Garcia-Lopez, Stelfreeze, Bermejo 4.00
HC (2010, $49.99, 17-3/4"x11-1/4") r/#1-12 plus new 1 pg. stories of Plastic Man by Dorkin-s/ DeStefano-a and Beware the Creeper by Giffen-s/Canete-a; bonus sketch art 50.00

WEEKENDER, THE (Illustrated...)
Rucker Pub. Co.: V1#1, Sept, 1945? - V1#4, Nov, 1945; V2#1, Jan, 1946 - V2#3, Aug, 1946 (52 pgs.)

V#1-Same-c as Zip Comics #45 (nurse in peril), inside-c and back-c blank; Steel Sterling, Senor Banana, Red Rube and Ginger 58 116 174 371 636 900
V1#2-4: 2-Capt. Victory on-c. 3-Super hero-c; Mr. E, Dan Hastings, Sky Chief and the Echo. 4-Same-c as Punch Comics #10 (9/44); r/Hale the Magician (7 pgs.) & r/Mr. E (8 pgs.-Lou Fine? or Gustavson?) plus 3 humor strips & many B&W photos & r/newspaper articles plus cheesecake photos of Hollywood stars 50 100 150 315 533 750
V2#1-Same-c as Dynamic Comics #11; 36 pgs. comics, 16 in newspaper format with photos; partial Dynamic Comics reprints; 4 pgs. of cels from the Disney film Pinocchio; Little Nemo story by Winsor McCay, Jr.; Jack Cole-a 71 142 213 454 777 1100
V2#2,3: 2-Same-c as Dynamic Comics #9 by Raboy; Dan Hastings (Tuska), Rocket Boy, The Echo, Lucky Coyne. 3-Humor-c by Boddington?; Dynamic Man, Ima Slooth, Master Key, Dynamic Boy, Captain Glory 43 86 129 271 461 650

WEEKND PRESENTS, THE: STARBOY
Marvel Comics: Aug, 2018 ($3.99, one-shot)

1-Abel Tesfaye, La Mar Taylor & Christos Gage-s/Eric Nguyen-a/c 4.00

WE HAVE DEMONS
Dark Horse Comics: Mar, 2022 - No. 3, Jun, 2022 ($4.99, limited series)

1-3-Scott Snyder-s/Greg Capullo-a 5.00

WEIRD
Eerie Publications: V1#10, 1/66 - V8#6, 12/74; V9#1, 1/75 - V14#3, Nov, 1981 (Magazine) (V1-V8: 52 pgs.; V9 on: 68 pgs.)

V1#10(#1)-Intro. Morris the Caretaker of Weird (ends V2#10); Burgos-a 10 20 30 64 132 200
11,12 7 14 21 44 82 120
V2#1-4(10/67), V3#1(1/68), V2#6(4/68)-V2#7,9,10(12/68) 7 14 21 44 82 120
V2#8-r/Ditko's 1st story/Fantastic Fears #5 8 16 24 52 99 145
V3#1(2/69)-V3#4 6 12 18 38 69 100
V3#5(12/69)-Rulah reprint; "Rulah" changed to "Pulah", LSD story reprinted in Horror Tales V4#4, Tales From the Tomb V2#4, & 20 6 12 18 38 69 100
V4#1-6('70), V5#1-6('71), V6#1-7('72), V7#1-7('73), V8#1-3, V8#4(8/74), V8#4(10/74), (V8#5 does not exist), V8#6('74), V9#1-4(1/75-'76), V10#1-3('77), V11#1-4('78), V12#1(2/79)-V14#3(11/81) 6 12 18 37 66 95

NOTE: *There are two V8#4 issues (8/74 & 10/74). V9#4 (12/76) has a cover swipe from Horror Tales V5#1 (2/73). There are two V13#3 issues (6/80 & 9/80).*

WEIRD
DC Comics (Paradox Press): Sum, 1997 - No. 4 ($2.99, B&W, magazine)

1-4: 4-Mike Tyson-c 3.00

WEIRD, THE
DC Comics: Apr, 1988 - No. 4, July, 1988 ($1.50, limited series)

1-4: Wrightson-c/a in all 5.00

WEIRD ADVENTURES
P. L. Publishing Co. (Canada): May-June, 1951 - No. 3, Sept-Oct, 1951

1- "The She-Wolf Killer" by Matt Baker (6 pgs.) 81 162 243 518 884 1250
2-Bondage/hypodermic panel 60 120 180 381 653 925
3-Male bondage/torture-c; severed head story 54 108 162 343 574 825

WEIRD ADVENTURES
Ziff-Davis Publishing Co.: No. 10, July-Aug, 1951

10-Painted-c 53 106 159 334 567 800

WEIRD CHILLS
Key Publications: July, 1954 - No. 3, Nov, 1954

1-Wolverton-r/Weird Mysteries No. 4; blood transfusion-c by Baily 290 580 870 1856 3178 4500
2-Extremely violent injury to eye-c by Baily; Hitler story 290 580 870 1856 3178 4500
3-Bondage E.C. swipe-c by Baily 226 452 678 1446 2473 3500

WEIRD COMICS
Fox Feature Syndicate: Apr, 1940 - No. 20, Jan, 1942

1-The Birdman, Thor, God of Thunder (ends #5), The Sorceress of Zoom, Blast Bennett, Typhon, Voodoo Man, & Dr. Mortal begin; George Tuska bondage-c 1250 2500 3750 9500 17,250 25,000
2-Lou Fine-c 622 1244 1866 4541 8021 11,500
3,4: 3-Simon-c. 4-Torture-c 300 600 900 2070 3635 5200
5-Intro. Dart & sidekick Ace (8/40) (ends #20); bondage/hypo-c 314 628 942 2198 3849 5500
6-Dynamite Thor app.; super hero covers begin 187 374 561 1197 2049 2900
7-Dynamite Thor app. 258 516 774 1651 2826 4000
8-Dynamo, the Eagle (11/40, early app.; see Science #1) & sidekick Buddy & Marga, the Panther Woman begin 206 412 618 1318 2259 3200
9,10: 10-Navy Jones app. 161 322 483 1030 1765 2500
11-19: 16-The Eagle vs. Nazi battle-c/flag-c. 17-Origin The Black Rider; WWII Nazi-c 148 296 444 947 1624 2300
20-Origin The Rapier; Swoop Curtis app; Churchill & Hitler-c 1250 2500 3750 9500 17,250 25,000

NOTE *Cover features: Sorceress of Zoom-4; Dr. Mortal-5; Dart & Ace-6-13, 15; Eagle-14, 16-20.*

WEIRD DETECTIVE
Dark Horse Comics: Jun, 2016 - No. 5, Oct, 2016 ($3.99)

1-5-Van Lente-s/Vilanova-a 4.00

WEIRD FANTASY (Formerly A Moon, A Girl, Romance; becomes Weird Science-Fantasy #23 on)
E. C. Comics: No. 13, May-June, 1950 - No. 22, Nov-Dec, 1953

13(#1) (1950) 263 526 789 2104 3352 4600
14-Necronomicon story; Cosmic Ray Bomb explosion-c/story by Feldstein; Feldstein & Gaines star 129 258 387 1032 1641 2250
15,16: 16-Used in **SOTI**, pg. 144 100 200 300 800 1275 1750
17 (1951) 77 154 231 616 1183 1350
6-Robot-c 80 160 240 640 1020 1400
7-10 66 132 198 528 839 1150
11-13 (1952): 11-Cover inspired by Chesley Bonstell painting "The End of the World" from Coronet magazine (July 1947); Feldstein bio. 12-E.C. artists cameo; Orlando bio. 13-Anti-Wertham "Cosmic Correspondence" 51 102 153 408 654 900
14-Frazetta/Williamson(1st team-up at E.C.)/Krenkel-a (7 pgs.); Orlando draws E.C. staff 69 138 207 552 876 1200
15-Williamson/Evans-a(3), 4,3,&7 pgs. 57 114 171 456 728 1000
16-19-Williamson/Krenkel-a in all. 17-Feldstein dinosaur-c; classic sci-fi story "The Aliens". 18-Williamson/Feldstein-c; classic anti-prejudice story "Judgment Day". 19-Williamson bio. 49 98 147 392 621 850
20-Frazetta/Williamson-a (7 pgs.); contains house ad for original, uncensored cover to Vault of Horror #32 (meat cleaver in forehead) 63 126 189 504 802 1100
21-Frazetta/Williamson-c & Williamson/Krenkel-a 91 182 273 728 1164 1600
22-Bradbury adaptation 49 98 147 392 621 850

NOTE: ***Crandall** a-22. **Elder** a-17. **Feldstein** a-13(#1)-8; c-13(#1)-18 (#18 w/**Williamson**), 20. **Harrison/Wood** a-13. **Kamen** a-13(#1)-16, 18-22. **Krigstein** a-22. **Kurtzman** a-13(#1)-17(#5), 6. **Orlando** a-9-22 (2 stories in #16); c-19, 22. **Severin/Elder** a-18-21. **Wood** a-13(#1)-14, 17(2 stories ea. in #10-13). Ray Bradbury adaptations in #13,17-22. Canadian reprints exist; see Table of Contents.*

WEIRD FANTASY
Russ Cochran/Gemstone Publ.: Oct, 1992 - No. 22, Jan, 1998 ($1.50/$2.00/$2.50)

1-22: 1,2: 1,2-r/Weird Fantasy #13,14; Feldstein-c. 3-5-r/Weird Fantasy #15-17 4.00

WEIRD HORRORS (Nightmare #10 on)
St. John Publishing Co.: June, 1952 - No. 9, Oct, 1953

1-Tuska-a 93 186 279 591 1021 1450
2,3: 3-Hashish story 50 100 150 315 533 750
4,5 45 90 135 284 480 675
6-Ekgren-c; atomic bomb story 116 232 348 742 1271 1800
7-Ekgren-c; Kubert, Cameron-a 129 258 387 826 1413 2000
8,9-Kubert-c/a 58 116 174 371 636 900

NOTE: ***Cameron** a-7, 9. **Finesque** a-1-5. **Forgione** a-6. **Morisi** a-3. Bondage c-8.*

WEIRD MYSTERIES
Gillmor Publications: Oct, 1952 - No. 12, Sept, 1954

1-Partial Wolverton-c swiped from splash page "Flight to the Future" in Weird Tales of the Future #2; "Eternity" has an Ingels swipe 194 388 582 1242 2121 3000
2- "Robot Woman" by Wolverton; Bernard Baily-c reprinted in Mister Mystery #18; acid in face panel 271 542 813 1734 2967 4200
3,6: Both have decapitation-c 142 284 426 909 1555 2200
4- "The Man Who Never Smiled" (3 pgs.) by Wolverton; Classic B. Baily skull-c 1000 2000 3000 7600 13,800 20,000
5-Wolverton story "Swamp Monster" (6 pgs.). Classic exposed brain-c 1300 2600 3900 9900 17,950 26,000
7-Used in **SOTI**, illo "Indeed", illo "Sex and blood" 219 438 657 1402 2401 3400
8-Wolverton-c panel-r/#5; used in a '54 Readers Digest anti-comics article by T. E. Murphy entitled "For the Kiddies to Read" 123 246 369 787 1344 1900
9-Excessive violence, gore & torture 110 220 330 704 1202 1700
10-Silhouetted nudity panel 116 232 348 742 1271 1800
11,12: 12-r/Mr. Mystery #8(2), Weird Mysteries #3 & Weird Tales of the Future #6 97 194 291 621 1061 1500

NOTE: ***Baily** c-2-12. Anti-Wertham column in #5. #1-12 all have 'The Ghoul Teacher' (host).*

WEIRD MYSTERIES (Magazine)
Pastime Publications: Mar-Apr, 1959 (35¢, B&W, 68 pgs.)

1-Torres-a; E. C. swipe from Tales From the Crypt #46 by Tuska "The Ragman" 18 36 54 105 165 225

WEIRD MYSTERY TALES (See DC 100 Page Super Spectacular)

WEIRD MYSTERY TALES (See Cancelled Comic Cavalcade)
National Periodical Publications: July-Aug, 1972 - No. 24, Nov, 1975

1-Kirby-a; Wrightson splash pg. 6 12 18 38 69 100
2-Titanic-c/s 3 6 9 21 33 45
3,21: 21-Wrightson-c 3 6 9 17 26 35
4-10 3 6 9 14 19 24
11-20,22-24 2 4 6 11 16 20

NOTE: ***Alcala** a-5, 10, 13, 14. **Aparo** c-4. **Bailey** a-8. **Bolle** a-8?. **Howard** a-4. **Kaluta** a-4, 24; c-1. **G. Kane** a-10. **Kirby** a-1, 2p, 3p. **Nino** a-5, 6, 9, 13, 16, 21. **Redondo** a-9, 17. **Sparling** c-6. **Starlin** a-3?, 4. **Wood** a-23.*

WEIRD ROMANCE (Seduction of the Innocent #9)

Wednesday Comics #8 © DC

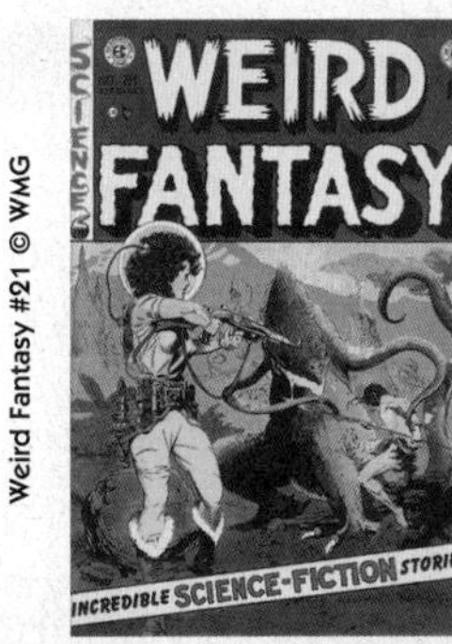

Weird Fantasy #21 © WMG

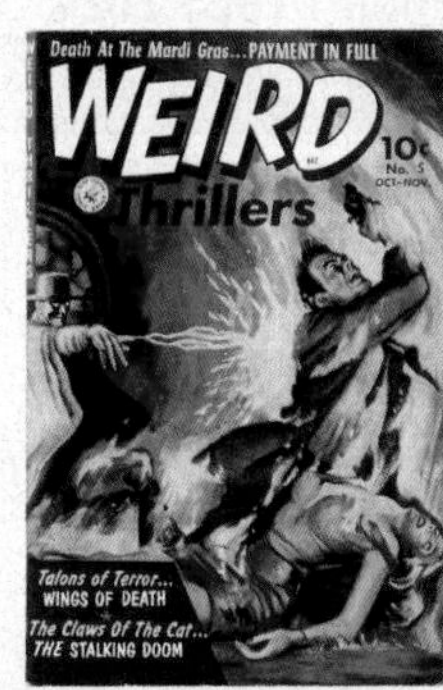

Weird Thrillers #5 © Z-D

Eclipse Comics: Feb, 1988 ($2.00, B&W)

	GD 2.0	VG 4.0	FN 6.0	VF 8.0	VF/NM 9.0	NM- 9.2
1-Pre-code horror-r; Lou Cameron-r(2)						4.00

WEIRD SCIENCE (Formerly Saddle Romances) (Becomes Weird Science-Fantasy #23 on) (Also see EC Archives • Weird Science)
E. C. Comics: No. 12, May-June, 1950 - No. 22, Nov-Dec, 1953

	GD 2.0	VG 4.0	FN 6.0	VF 8.0	VF/NM 9.0	NM- 9.2
12(#1) (1950)-"Lost in the Microcosm" classic-c/story by Kurtzman; "Dream of Doom" stars Gaines & E.C. artists	331	662	993	2648	4224	5800
13-Flying saucers over Washington-c/story, 2 years before supposed UFO sighting	143	286	429	1144	1822	2500
14-Robot, End of the World-c/story by Feldstein	126	252	378	1008	1604	2200
15-War of Worlds-c/story (1950)	106	212	318	848	1349	1850
5-Atomic explosion-c	86	172	258	688	1094	1500
6-8,10	69	138	207	552	876	1200
9-Wood's 1st EC-c	86	172	258	688	1094	1500
11-14 (1952) 11-Kamen bio. 12-Wood bio	57	114	171	456	728	1000
15-18-Williamson/Krenkel-a in each; 15-Williamson-a. 17-Used in **POP**, pgs. 81,82. 18-Bill Gaines doll app. in story	54	108	162	432	691	950
19,20-Williamson/Frazetta-a (7 pgs. each). 19-Used in **SOTI**, illo "A young girl on her wedding night stabs her sleeping husband to death with a hatpin..." 19-Bradbury bio.	86	172	258	688	1094	1500
21-Williamson/Frazetta-a (6 pgs.); Wood draws E.C. staff; Gaines & Feldstein app. in story	86	172	258	688	1094	1500
22-Williamson/Frazetta/Krenkel-a (8 pgs.); Wood draws himself in his story (last pg. & panel)	89	178	267	712	1131	1550

NOTE: ***Elder** a-14, 19. **Evans** a-22. **Feldstein** a-12(#1)-8; c-12(#1)-8, 11. **Ingels** a-15. **Kamen** a-12(#1)-13, 15-18, 20, 21. **Kurtzman** a-12(#1)-7. **Orlando** a-10-22. **Wood** a-12(#1), 13(#2), 5-22 (#9, 10, 12, 13 all have 2 **Wood** stories); c-9, 10, 12-22. Canadian reprints exist; see Table of Contents. Ray Bradbury adaptations in #17-22.*

WEIRD SCIENCE
Gladstone Publishing: Sept, 1990 - No. 4, Mar, 1991 ($1.95/$2.00, 68 pgs.)

	GD 2.0	VG 4.0	FN 6.0	VF 8.0	VF/NM 9.0	NM- 9.2
1-4: Wood-c(r); all reprints in each						5.00

WEIRD SCIENCE (Also see EC Archives • Weird Science)
Russ Cochran/Gemstone Publishing: Sept, 1992 - No. 22, Dec, 1997 ($1.50/$2.00/$2.50)

	GD 2.0	VG 4.0	FN 6.0	VF 8.0	VF/NM 9.0	NM- 9.2
1-22: 1,2: r/Weird Science #12,13 w/original-c. ,4-r/#14,15. 5-7-w/original-c						4.00

WEIRD SCIENCE-FANTASY (Formerly Weird Science & Weird Fantasy) (Becomes Incredible Science Fiction #30)
E. C. Comics: No. 23 Mar, 1954 - No. 29, May-June, 1955 (#23,24: 15¢)

	GD 2.0	VG 4.0	FN 6.0	VF 8.0	VF/NM 9.0	NM- 9.2
23-Williamson, Wood-a; Bradbury adaptation	54	108	162	432	691	950
24-Williamson & Wood-a; Harlan Ellison's 1st professional story, "Upheaval!", later adapted into a short story as "Mealtime", and then into a TV episode of Voyage to the Bottom of the Sea as "The Price of Doom"	54	108	162	432	691	950
25-Williamson dinosaur-c; Williamson/Torres/Krenkel-a plus Wood-a; Bradbury adaptation and fan letter; cover price back to 10¢	60	120	180	480	765	1050
26-Flying Saucer Report; Wood, Crandall-a; A-bomb panels	53	106	159	424	675	925
27-Adam Link/I Robot series begins	50	100	150	400	638	875
28-Williamson/Krenkel/Torres-a; Wood-a	50	100	150	400	638	875
29-Classic Frazetta-c; Williamson/Krenkel & Wood-a; Adam Link/I Robot series concludes; last pre-code issue; new logo	217	434	651	1736	2768	3800

NOTE: ***Crandall** a-26, 27, 29. **Evans** a-26. **Feldstein** c-24, 26, 28. **Kamen** a-27, 28. **Krigstein** a-23-25. **Orlando** a-in all. **Wood** a-in all; c-23, 27. The cover to #29 was originally intended for Famous Funnies #217 (Buck Rogers), but was rejected for being "too violent."*

WEIRD SCIENCE-FANTASY
Russ Cochran/Gemstone Publishing: Nov, 1992 - No. 7, May , 1994 ($1.50/$2.00/$2.50)

	GD 2.0	VG 4.0	FN 6.0	VF 8.0	VF/NM 9.0	NM- 9.2
1-7: 1,2: r/Weird Science-Fantasy #23,24. 3-7 r/#25-29						4.00

WEIRD SCIENCE-FANTASY ANNUAL
E. C. Comics: 1952, 1953 (Sold thru the E. C. office & on the stands in some major cities) (25¢, 132 pgs.)

	GD 2.0	VG 4.0	FN 6.0	VF 8.0	VF/NM 9.0	NM- 9.2
1952-Feldstein-c	400	800	1200	3200	5100	7000
1953-Feldstein-c	233	466	699	1864	3032	4200

NOTE: *The 1952 annual contains books cover-dated in 1951 & 1952, and the 1953 annual from 1952 & 1953. Contents of each annual may vary in same year.*

WEIRD SECRET ORIGINS
DC Comics: Oct, 2004 ($5.95, square-bound, one-shot)

	GD 2.0	VG 4.0	FN 6.0	VF 8.0	VF/NM 9.0	NM- 9.2
nn-Reprints origins of Dr. Fate, Spectre, Congorilla, Metamorpho, Animal Man & others						6.00

WEIRD SUSPENSE
Atlas/Seaboard Publ.: Feb, 1975 - No. 3, July, 1975

	GD 2.0	VG 4.0	FN 6.0	VF 8.0	VF/NM 9.0	NM- 9.2
1-3: 1-Tarantula begins. 3-Freidrich-s	2	4	6	11	16	20

NOTE: ***Boyette** a-1-3. **Buckler** c-1, 3.*

WEIRD SUSPENSTORIES
Superior Comics (Canada): Oct, 1951 - No. 3, Dec, 1951; No. 3, no date (EC reprints)

	GD 2.0	VG 4.0	FN 6.0	VF 8.0	VF/NM 9.0	NM- 9.2
1-3,3(no date)-(Rare): Reprints Crime SuspenStories #1-3, covers & contents w/Canadian ads replacing U.S. ads	1100	2200	3300	-	-	-

NOTE: *Canada passed a law against importing crime comic books between 1949-1953, thus Crime Suspenstories became Weird Suspenstories in Canada creating a new EC title. The word "crime" was not allowed on comic books in Canada during this time.*

WEIRD TALES ILLUSTRATED
Millennium Publications: 1992 - No. 2, 1992 ($2.95, high quality paper)

	GD 2.0	VG 4.0	FN 6.0	VF 8.0	VF/NM 9.0	NM- 9.2
1,2-Bolton painted-c. 1-Adapts E.A. Poe & Harlan Ellison stories. 2-E.A. Poe & H.P. Lovecraft adaptations						4.00
1-($4.95, 52 pgs.)-Deluxe edition w/Tim Vigil-a not in regular #1; stiff-c; Bolton painted-c						6.00

WEIRD TALES OF THE FUTURE
S.P.M. Publ. No. 1-4/Aragon Publ. No. 5-8: Mar, 1952 - No. 8, July-Aug, 1953

	GD 2.0	VG 4.0	FN 6.0	VF 8.0	VF/NM 9.0	NM- 9.2
1-Andru-a(2); Wolverton partial-c	290	580	870	1856	3178	4500
2,3-Wolverton-c/a(3) each. 2- "Jumpin Jupiter" satire by Wolverton begins, ends #5	432	864	1296	3154	5577	8000
4-(11/52) Wolverton-c from three panels of Wolverton's "Nightmare World" from issue #3 (9/52) and the girl on the cover from Mister Mystery #6 (7/52) "The Fatal Chord" by Ed Robbins, pg. 4, which was cut apart, pasted up to form the cover and partially redrawn by Harry Kantor, the editor; "Jumpin Jupiter" satire by Wolverton	187	374	561	1197	2049	2900
5-Wolverton-c/a(2); "Jumpin Jupiter" satire	486	972	1458	3550	6275	9000
6-Bernard Baily-c	168	336	504	1075	1838	2600
7- "The Mind Movers" from the art to Wolverton's "Brain Bats of Venus" from Mr. Mystery #7 which was cut apart, pasted up, partially redrawn, and rewritten by Harry Kantor, the editor; Baily-c	389	778	1167	2723	4762	6800
8-Reprints Weird Mysteries #1(10/52) minus cover; gory cover showing heart ripped out, by B. Baily	541	1082	1623	3950	6975	10,000

WEIRD TALES OF THE MACABRE (Magazine)
Atlas/Seaboard Publ.: Jan, 1975 - No. 2, Mar, 1975 (75¢, B&W)

	GD 2.0	VG 4.0	FN 6.0	VF 8.0	VF/NM 9.0	NM- 9.2
1-Jeff Jones painted-c; Boyette-a	5	10	15	35	63	90
2-Boris Vallejo painted-c; Severin-a	6	12	18	37	66	95

WEIRD TERROR (Also see Horrific)
Allen Hardy Associates (Comic Media): Sept, 1952 - No. 13, Sept, 1954

	GD 2.0	VG 4.0	FN 6.0	VF 8.0	VF/NM 9.0	NM- 9.2
1- "Portrait of Death", adapted from Lovecraft's "Pickman's Model"; lingerie panels, Hitler story	113	226	339	718	1234	1750
2-Text on Marquis DeSade, Torture, Demonology, & St. Elmo's Fire	90	180	270	576	988	1400
3-Extreme violence, whipping, torture; article on sin eating, dowsing	258	516	774	1651	2826	4000
4-Dismemberment, decapitation, article on human flesh for sale, Devil, whipping	194	388	582	1242	2121	3000
5-Article on body snatching, mutilation; cannibalism story	161	322	483	1030	1765	2500
6-Dismemberment, decapitation, man hit by lightning story	194	388	582	1242	2121	3000
7-Body burning in fireplace-c	226	452	678	1446	2473	3500
8,11: 8-Decapitation story; Ambrose Bierce adapt. 11-End of the world story w/atomic blast panels; Tothish-a by Bill Discount	71	142	213	454	777	1100
9,10,13: 13-Severed head panels	58	116	174	371	636	900
12-Discount-a	60	120	180	381	653	925

NOTE: ***Don Heck** a-most issues; c-1-13. **Landau** a-6. **Morisi** a-2-5, 7, 9, 12. **Palais** a-1, 5, 6, 8(2), 10, 12. **Powell** a-10. **Ravielli** a-11.*

WEIRD THRILLERS
Ziff-Davis Publ. Co. (Approved Comics): Sept-Oct, 1951 - No. 5, Oct-Nov, 1952 (#2-5: painted-c)

	GD 2.0	VG 4.0	FN 6.0	VF 8.0	VF/NM 9.0	NM- 9.2
1-Rondo Hatton photo-c	119	238	357	762	1306	1850
2-Toth, Anderson, Colan-a	84	168	252	538	919	1300
3-Two Powell, Tuska-a; classic-c; Everett-a	116	232	348	742	1271	1800
4-Kubert, Tuska-a	77	154	231	493	847	1200
5-Powell-a	74	148	222	470	810	1150

NOTE: ***M. Anderson** a-2, 3. **Roussos** a-4. #2, 3 reprinted in Nightmare #10 & 13; #4, 5 reprinted in Amazing Ghost Stories #16 & #15.*

WEIRD VAMPIRE TALES (Comic magazine)
Modern Day Periodical Pub.: V3 #1, Apr, 1979 - V5 #3, Mar, 1982 (B&W)

	GD 2.0	VG 4.0	FN 6.0	VF 8.0	VF/NM 9.0	NM- 9.2
V3 #1 (4/79) First issue, no V1 or V2	5	10	15	31	53	75
V3 #2-4	3	6	9	19	30	40
V4 #2 (4/80), V4 #3 (7/80) (no V4 #1)	3	6	9	17	26	35
V5 #1 (1/81), V5 #2 (two issues, 4/81 & 8/81)	3	6	9	17	26	35
V5 #3 (3/82) Last issue; low print	3	6	9	21	33	45

WEIRD WAR TALES
National Periodical Publ./DC Comics: Sept-Oct, 1971 - No. 124, June, 1983 (#1-5: 52 pgs.)

	GD 2.0	VG 4.0	FN 6.0	VF 8.0	VF/NM 9.0	NM- 9.2
1-Kubert-a in #1-4,7; c-1-7	21	42	63	147	324	500
2,3-Drucker-a: 2-Crandall-a. 3-Heath-a	10	20	30	64	132	200

	GD 2.0	VG 4.0	FN 6.0	VF 8.0	VF/NM 9.0	NM- 9.2
4,5: 5-Toth-a; Heath-a	8	16	24	54	102	150
6,7,9,10: 6,10-Toth-a. 7-Heath-a	6	12	18	37	66	95
8-Neal Adams-c/a(i)	6	12	18	41	76	110
11-20	4	8	12	22	35	48
21-35	3	6	9	16	24	32
36-(68 pgs.)-Crandall & Kubert-r/#2; Heath-r/#3; Kubert-c	3	6	9	18	28	38
37-50: 38,39-Kubert-c	2	4	6	10	14	18
51-63: 58-Hitler-c/app. 60-Hindenburg-c/s	2	4	6	9	13	16
64-Frank Miller-a (1st DC work)	6	12	18	41	76	110
65-67,69-89,91,92: 89-Nazi Apes-c/s.	2	4	6	8	10	12
68-Frank Miller-a (2nd DC work)	3	6	9	21	33	45
90-Hitler app.	2	4	6	10	14	18
93-Intro/origin Creature Commandos	3	6	9	16	23	30
94-Return of War that Time Forgot; dinosaur-c/s	2	4	6	11	16	20
95,96,98,102-123: 98-Sphinx-c. 102-Creature Commandos battle Hitler. 110-Origin/1st app. Medusa. 123-1st app. Captain Spaceman	2	4	6	8	10	12
97,99,100,101,124: 99-War that Time Forgot. 100-Creature Commandos in War that Time Forgot. 101-Intro/origin G.I. Robot	2	4	6	8	11	14

NOTE: ***Chaykin** a-76, 82. **Ditko** a-95, 99, 104-106. **Evans** c-73, 74, 83, 85. **Kane** c-116, 118. **Kubert** c-55, 58, 60, 62, 72, 75-81, 87, 88, 90-96, 100, 103, 104, 106, 107. **Newton** a-122. **Starlin** c-89. **Sutton** a-91, 92, 103. **Creature Commandos** -93, 97, 100, 102, 105, 108-112, 114, 116-119, 121, 124. **G.I. Robot** - 101, 108, 111, 113, 116-118, 120, 122. **War That Time Forgot** - 94, 99, 100, 103, 106, 109, 120.*

WEIRD WAR TALES
DC Comics (Vertigo): June, 1997 - No. 4, Sept, 1997 ($2.50)

1-4-Anthology by various 4.00

WEIRD WAR TALES
DC Comics (Vertigo): April, 2000 ($4.95, one-shot)

1-Anthology by various; last Biukovic-a 5.00

WEIRD WAR TALES
DC Comics: Nov, 2010 ($3.99, one-shot)

1-Anthology by various incl. Cooke, Strnad, Pugh; Cooke-c 4.00

WEIRD WESTERN TALES (Formerly All-Star Western)
National Per. Publ./DC Comics: No. 12, June-July, 1972 - No. 70, Aug, 1980

	GD 2.0	VG 4.0	FN 6.0	VF 8.0	VF/NM 9.0	NM- 9.2
12-(52 pgs.)-3rd app. Jonah Hex; Bat Lash, Pow Wow Smith reprints; El Diablo by Neal Adams/Wrightson	10	20	30	64	132	200
13-Jonah Hex-c & 4th app.; Neal Adams-a	7	14	21	48	89	130
14-Toth-a	5	10	15	35	63	90
15-Adams-c/a; no Jonah Hex	4	8	12	28	47	65
16,17,19,20	4	8	12	28	47	65
18,29: 18-1st all Jonah Hex issue (7-8/73) & begins. 29-Origin Jonah Hex; 1st full app. of Quentin Turnbull	6	12	18	37	66	95
21-28,30: Jonah Hex in all	4	8	12	23	37	50
31-38: Jonah Hex in all. 38-Last Jonah Hex	3	6	9	18	28	38
39-Origin/1st app. Scalphunter & begins	2	4	6	13	18	22
40-47,50-69: 64-Bat Lash-c/story	2	4	6	8	10	12
48,49: (44 pgs.)-1st & 2nd app. Cinnamon	2	4	6	8	11	14
70-Last issue	2	4	6	9	13	16

NOTE: ***Alcala** a-16, 17. **Evans** inks-39-48; c-39i, 40, 47. **G. Kane** a-15, 20. **Kubert** c-12, 33. **Starlin** c-44, 45. **Wildey** a-26. 48 & 49 are 44 pgs..*

WEIRD WESTERN TALES (Blackest Night crossover)
DC Comics: No. 71, March, 2010 ($2.99, one-shot)

71-Jonah Hex, Scalphunter, Super-Chief, Firehair and Bat Lash rise as Black Lanterns 3.00

WEIRD WESTERN TALES
DC Comics (Vertigo): Apr, 2001 - No. 4, Jul, 2001 ($2.50, limited series)

1-4-Anthology by various 3.00

WEIRD WONDER TALES
Marvel Comics Group: Dec, 1973 - No. 22, May, 1977

	GD 2.0	VG 4.0	FN 6.0	VF 8.0	VF/NM 9.0	NM- 9.2
1-Wolverton-r/Mystic #6 (Eye of Doom)	5	10	15	30	50	70
2-10	3	6	9	17	26	35
11-22: 16-18-Venus-r by Everett from Venus #19,18 & 17. 19-22-r/Dr. Droom (re-named Dr. Druid) by Kirby. 22-New art by Byrne	3	6	9	16	23	30
15-17-(30¢-c variants, limited distribution)(4-8/76)	6	12	18	38	69	100

NOTE: *All 1950s & early 1960s reprints. **Check** r-1. **Colan** r-17. **Ditko** r-4, 5, 10-13, 19-21. **Drucker** r-12, 20. **Everett** r-3(Spellbound #16), 6(Astonishing #10), 9(Adv. Into Mystery #5). **Heath** a-13r. **Heck** a-1or, 14r. **Gil Kane** c-1, 2, 10. **Kirby** r-4, 6, 10, 11, 13, 15-22; c-17, 19, 20. **Krigstein** r-19. **Kubert** r-22. **Maneely** r-8. **Mooney** r-7p. **Powell** r-3, 7. **Torres** r-7. **Wildey** r-2, 7.*

WEIRDWORLD (Secret Wars tie-in)
Marvel Comics: Aug, 2015 - No. 5, Dec, 2015 ($3.99, limited series)

1-5-Aaron-s/Del Mundo-a; Arkon, Morgan Le Fay, and Skull the Slayer app. 4.00

WEIRDWORLD (After Secret Wars)
Marvel Comics: Feb, 2016 - No. 6, Jul, 2016 ($3.99)

1-6-Humphries-s/Del Mundo-a; Goleta the Wizardslayer & Morgan Le Fay app. 4.00

WEIRD WORLD OF JACK STAFF (See Jack Staff)
Image Comics: Feb, 2010 - No. 6, Apr, 2011 ($3.50)

1-6-Paul Grist-s/a. 2-Ian Churchill-c 3.50

WEIRD WORLDS (See Adventures Into...)

WEIRD WORLDS (Magazine)
Eerie Publications: V1#10(12/70), V2#1(2/71) - No. 4, Aug, 1971 (52 pgs.)

	GD 2.0	VG 4.0	FN 6.0	VF 8.0	VF/NM 9.0	NM- 9.2
V1#10-Sci-fi/horror	6	12	18	40	73	105
V2#1-4	5	10	15	34	60	85

WEIRD WORLDS (Also see Ironwolf: Fires of the Revolution)
National Periodical Publications: Aug-Sept, 1972 - No. 9, Jan-Feb, 1974; No. 10, Oct-Nov, 1974 (All 20¢ issues)

	GD 2.0	VG 4.0	FN 6.0	VF 8.0	VF/NM 9.0	NM- 9.2
1-Edgar Rice Burrough's John Carter Warlord of Mars & David Innes begin (1st DC app.); Kubert-c	3	6	9	21	33	45
2-4: 2-Infantino/Orlando-c. 3-Murphy Anderson-c. 4-Kaluta-a	2	4	6	10	14	18
5-7: 5-Kaluta-c. 7-Last John Carter.	2	4	6	8	11	14
8-10: 8-Iron Wolf begins by Chaykin (1st app.)	2	4	6	8	11	14

NOTE: ***Neal Adams** a-2i, 3i. John Carter by **Andersonin** #1-3. **Chaykin** c-7, 8. **Kaluta** a-4; c-4-6, 10. **Orlando** a-4i; c-2, 3, 4i. **Wrightson** a-2i, 4i.*

WEIRD WORLDS
DC Comics: Mar, 2011 - No. 6, Aug, 2011 ($3.99, limited series)

1-6-Short stories of Lobo, Garbage Man and Tanga; Ordway-a; Maguire-s/a; Lopresti-s/a 4.00

WELCOME BACK, KOTTER (TV) (See Limited Collectors' Edition #57 for unpublished #11)
National Periodical Publ./DC Comics: Nov, 1976 - No. 10, Mar-Apr, 1978

	GD 2.0	VG 4.0	FN 6.0	VF 8.0	VF/NM 9.0	NM- 9.2
1-Sparling-a(p)	3	6	9	20	31	42
2-10: 3-Estrada-a	2	4	6	11	16	20

WELCOME SANTA (See March of Comics #63,183)

WELCOME TO THE LITTLE SHOP OF HORRORS
Roger Corman's Cosmic Comics: May, 1995 -No. 3, July, 1995 ($2.50, limited series)

	GD 2.0	VG 4.0	FN 6.0	VF 8.0	VF/NM 9.0	NM- 9.2
1-3	1	3	4	6	8	10

WELCOME TO TRANQUILITY
DC Comics (WildStorm): Feb, 2007 - No. 12, Jan, 2008 ($2.99)

1-12: 1-Simone-s/Googe-a; two covers by Googe and Campbell. 8-Pearson-a 3.00
...: Armageddon 1 (1/08, $2.99) Gage-s/Googe-a 3.00
...: One Foot in the Grave 1-6 (7/10 - No. 6, 2/11, $3.99) Simone-s/Domingues-a 4.00
...: One Foot in the Grave TPB (2011, $17.99) r/mini-series #1-6 18.00
... Book One TPB (2008, $19.99) r/#1-6 and variant cover gallery 20.00
... Book Two TPB (2008, $19.99) r/#7-12; sketch pages 20.00

WE LIVE
AfterShock Comics: Oct, 2020 - No. 5, Feb, 2021 ($4.99, limited series)

1-5-Inaki Miranda-s/a; Roy Miranda-s 5.00

WE LIVE VOL. 2 (Age of the Palladions on cover)
AfterShock Comics: Mar, 2022 - No. 5, Aug, 2022 ($4.99/$3.99, limited series)

1 Black -($4.99) Inaki Miranda-s/a; Roy Miranda-s 5.00
1 White -($4.99) Inaki Miranda-s/a; Roy Miranda-s 5.00
2-5-($3.99) Inaki Miranda-s/a; Roy Miranda-s 4.00

WELLS FARGO (See Tales of...)

WELLINGTON
IDW Publishing: Dec, 2019 - Present ($3.99)

1-3-Aaron Mahnke & Delilah S. Dawson-s/Piotr Kowalski-a; 2 covers on each 4.00

WENDY AND THE NEW KIDS ON THE BLOCK
Harvey Comics: Mar, 1991 - No. 3, July, 1991 ($1.25)

1-3 5.00

WENDY DIGEST
Harvey Comics: Oct, 1990 - No. 5, Mar, 1992 ($1.75, digest size)

1-5 4.00

WENDY PARKER COMICS
Atlas Comics (OMC): July, 1953 - No. 8, July, 1954

	GD 2.0	VG 4.0	FN 6.0	VF 8.0	VF/NM 9.0	NM- 9.2
1	40	80	120	246	411	575
2	31	62	93	182	296	410
3-8	24	48	72	142	234	325

WENDY, THE GOOD LITTLE WITCH (TV)
Harvey Publ.: 8/60 - #82, 11/73; #83, 8/74 - #93, 4/76; #94, 9/90 - #97, 12/90

	GD 2.0	VG 4.0	FN 6.0	VF 8.0	VF/NM 9.0	NM- 9.2
1-Wendy & Casper the Friendly Ghost begin	46	92	138	359	805	1250
2	12	24	36	84	185	285
3-5	9	18	27	62	126	190
6-10	7	14	21	44	82	120
11-20	5	10	15	34	60	85
21-30	4	8	12	27	44	60
31-50	3	6	9	17	26	35
51-64,66-69	2	4	6	13	18	22
65 (2/71)-Wendy origin.	3	6	9	16	24	32
70-74: All 52 pg. Giants	3	6	9	16	23	30
75-93	2	4	6	9	13	16

94-97 (1990, $1.00-c): 94-Has #194 on-c 5.00
(See Casper the Friendly Ghost #20 & Harvey Hits #7, 16, 21, 23, 27, 30, 33)

WENDY THE GOOD LITTLE WITCH (2nd Series)
Harvey Comics: Apr, 1991 - No. 15, Aug, 1994 ($1.00/$1.25 #7-11/$1.50 #12-15)

1-15-Reprints Wendy & Casper stories. 12-Bunny app. 3.00

WENDY WITCH WORLD
Harvey Publications: 10/61; No. 2, 9/62 - No. 52, 12/73; No. 53, 9/74

	GD 2.0	VG 4.0	FN 6.0	VF 8.0	VF/NM 9.0	NM- 9.2
1-(25¢, 68 pg. Giants begin)	13	26	39	89	195	300
2-5	7	14	21	44	82	120
6-10	5	10	15	33	57	80
11-20	4	8	12	27	44	60
21-30	3	6	9	21	33	45
31-39: 39-Last 68 pg. issue	3	6	9	16	24	32
40-45: 52 pg. issues	2	4	6	13	18	22
46-53	2	4	6	9	13	16

WE ONLY FIND THEM WHEN THEY'RE DEAD
BOOM! Studios: Sept, 2020 - No. 15, Dec, 2022 ($3.99)

1-15-Al Ewing-s/Simone Di Meo-a 4.00

WEREWOLF (Super Hero) (Also see Dracula & Frankenstein)
Dell Publishing Co.: Dec, 1966 - No. 3, April, 1967

	GD 2.0	VG 4.0	FN 6.0	VF 8.0	VF/NM 9.0	NM- 9.2
1-1st app.	4	8	12	25	40	55
2,3	3	6	9	16	23	30

WEREWOLF BY NIGHT (See Giant-Size..., Marvel Spotlight #2-4 & Power Record Comics)
Marvel Comics Group: Sept, 1972 - No. 43, Mar, 1977

	GD 2.0	VG 4.0	FN 6.0	VF 8.0	VF/NM 9.0	NM- 9.2
1-Ploog-a cont'd. from Marvel Spotlight #4	27	54	81	194	435	675
2	8	16	24	54	102	150
3-5	5	10	15	34	60	85
6-10	4	8	12	28	47	65
11-14,16-20	3	6	9	21	33	45

15-New origin Werewolf; Dracula-c/story cont'd from Tomb of Dracula #18;

Weird Western Tales #71 © DC

Werewolf By Night (2020) #1 © MAR

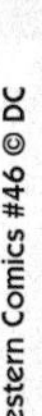
Western Comics #46 © DC

	GD 2.0	VG 4.0	FN 6.0	VF 8.0	VF/NM 9.0	NM- 9.2
classic Ploog-c	8	16	24	51	96	140
21-31	3	6	9	16	24	32
32-Origin & 1st app. Moon Knight (8/75)	370	740	1110	2220	3610	5000
33-2nd app. Moon Knight	21	42	63	147	324	500
34,36	5	10	15	35	63	90
38-43	3	6	9	14	20	26
35-Starlin/Wrightson-c	4	8	12	22	35	48
37-Moon Knight app; part Wrightson-c	10	20	30	67	141	215
38,39-(30¢-c variants, limited distribution)(5,7/76)	6	12	18	37	66	95
... No. 32 Facsimile Edition (9/21, $3.99) Reprints #32 with original ads & letter column	2	4	6	8	10	12

NOTE: *Bolle a-6i. G. Kane a-11p, 12p; c-21, 22, 24-30, 34p. Mooney a-7i. Ploog 1-4p, 5, 6p, 7p, 13-16p; c-5-8, 13-16. Reinman a-8i. Sutton a(i)-9, 11, 16, 35.*

WEREWOLF BY NIGHT (Vol. 2, continues in Strange Tales #1 (9/98))
Marvel Comics Group: Feb, 1998 - No. 6, July, 1998 ($2.99)

1-6-Manco-a: 2-Two covers. 6-Ghost Rider-c/app. 3.00

WEREWOLF BY NIGHT
Marvel Comics: Dec, 2020 - No. 4, Mar, 2021 ($3.99)

1-4: 1-Intro. Jake Gomez; Scot Eaton-a 4.00

WEREWOLVES & VAMPIRES (Magazine)
Charlton Comics: 1962 (One Shot)

1 9 18 27 63 129 195

WEREWOLVES ON THE MOON: VERSUS VAMPIRES
Dark Horse Comics: June, 2009 - No. 3 ($3.50, limited series)

1,2-Dave Land-s & Fillbach Brothers-s/a 3.50

WE STAND ON GUARD
Image Comics: Jul, 2015 - No. 6, Dec, 2015 ($2.99, limited series)

1-U.S. invasion of Canada; Vaughan-s/Skroce-a 5.00
2-6 3.00

WEST COAST AVENGERS
Marvel Comics Group: Sept, 1984 - No. 4, Dec, 1984 (lim. series, Mando paper)

1-Origin & 1st app. W.C. Avengers (Hawkeye, Iron Man, Mockingbird & Tigra) 3 6 9 19 30 40
2-4 6.00

WEST COAST AVENGERS (Becomes Avengers West Coast #48 on)
Marvel Comics Group: Oct, 1985 - No. 47, Aug, 1989

V2#1 3 6 9 15 22 28
2-41 5.00
42-44,46,47: 42-Byrne-a(p)/scripts begin. 46-Byrne-c; 1st app. Great Lakes Avengers 5.00
45-(6/89) 1st app. Vision in all-white exterior; cover swipe of Avengers #57 5 10 15 31 53 75
Annual 1 (1986) 1 3 4 6 8 10
Annual 2,3 (1987,1988): 3-Evolutionary War app. 6.00
Annual 4 (1989, $2.00)-Atlantis Attacks; Byrne/Austin-a 6.00

WEST COAST AVENGERS
Marvel Comics: Oct, 2018 - No. 10, Jun, 2019 ($4.99/$3.99)

1-($4.99) Hawkeye, Kate Bishop, Gwenpool, America, Kid Omega, Fuse team 5.00
2-10-($3.99) 2-4-Tigra app. 4-M.O.D.O.K. app. 6-Marvel Boy returns 4.00

WESTERN ACTION
I. W. Enterprises: No. 7, 1964

7-Reprints Cow Puncher #? by Avon 2 4 6 10 14 18

WESTERN ACTION
Atlas/Seaboard Publ.: Feb, 1975

1-Kid Cody by Wildey & The Comanche Kid stories; intro. The Renegade 3 6 9 14 20 25

WESTERN ACTION THRILLERS
Dell Publishers: Apr, 1937 (10¢, square binding; 100 pgs.)

1-Buffalo Bill, The Texas Kid, Laramie Joe, Two-Gun Thompson, & Wild West Bill app. 135 270 405 864 1482 2100

WESTERN ADVENTURES COMICS (Western Love Trails #7 on)
Ace Magazines: Oct, 1948 - No. 6, Aug, 1949

nn(#1)-Sheriff Sal, The Cross-Draw Kid, Sam Bass begin 24 48 72 142 234 325
nn(#2)(12/48) 14 28 42 82 121 160
nn(#3)(2/49)-Used in **SOTI**, pgs. 30,31 16 32 48 94 147 200
4-6 13 26 39 74 105 135

WESTERN BANDITS
Avon Periodicals: 1952 (Painted-c)

1-Butch Cassidy, The Daltons by Larsen; Kinstler-a; c-part-r/paperback Avon Western Novel #1 24 48 72 142 234 325

WESTERN BANDIT TRAILS (See Approved Comics)
St. John Publishing Co.: Jan, 1949 - No. 3, July, 1949

1-Tuska-a; Baker-c; Blue Monk, Ventrilo app. 47 94 141 296 498 700
2-Baker-c 39 78 117 231 378 525
3-Baker-c/a; Tuska-a 42 84 126 265 445 625

WESTERN COMICS (See Super DC Giant #15)
National Per. Publ: Jan-Feb, 1948 - No. 85, Jan-Feb, 1961 (1-27: 52pgs.)

1-Wyoming Kid & his horse Racer, The Vigilante in "Jesse James Rides Again" (Meskin-a), Cowboy Marshal, Rodeo Rick begin 90 180 270 576 988 1400
2 37 74 111 222 361 500
3,4-Last Vigilante 33 66 99 194 317 440
5-Nighthawk & his horse Nightwind begin (not in #6); Captain Tootsie by Beck 30 60 90 177 289 400
6,7,9,10 21 42 63 126 206 285
8-Origin Wyoming Kid; 2 pg. pin-ups of rodeo queens 34 68 102 204 332 460
11-20 18 36 54 107 169 230
21-40: 24-Starr-a. 27-Last 52 pgs. 28-Flag-c 15 30 45 84 127 170
41,42,44-49: 49-Last precode issue (2/55) 14 28 42 82 121 160
43-Pow Wow Smith begins, ends #85 15 30 45 83 124 165
50-60 13 26 39 72 101 130
61-85-Last Wyoming Kid. 77-Origin Matt Savage Trail Boss. 82-1st app. Fleetfoot, Pow Wow's girlfriend 10 20 30 58 79 100

NOTE: *G. Kane, Infantino art in most. Meskin a-1-4. Moreira a-28-39. Post a-3-5.*

WESTERN CRIME BUSTERS
Trojan Magazines: Sept, 1950 - No. 10, Mar-Apr, 1952

1-Six-Gun Smith, Wilma West, K-Bar-Kate, & Fighting Bob Dale begin; headlight-a 40 80 120 246 411 575
2 22 44 66 128 209 290
3-5: 3-Myron Fass-c 18 36 54 109 172 235
6-Wood-a 33 66 99 194 317 440
7-Six-Gun Smith by Wood 33 66 99 194 317 440
8 18 36 54 109 172 235
9-Tex Gordon & Wilma West by Wood; Lariat Lucy app. 33 66 99 194 317 440
10-Wood-a 30 60 90 177 289 400

WESTERN CRIME CASES (Formerly Indian Warriors #7,8; becomes The Outlaws #10 on)
Star Publications: No. 9, Dec, 1951

9-White Rider & Super Horse; L. B. Cole-c 27 54 81 158 259 360

WESTERNER, THE (Wild Bill Pecos)
"Wanted" Comic Group/Toytown/Patches: No. 14, June, 1948 - No. 41, Dec, 1951 (#14-31: 52 pgs.)

14 18 36 54 105 165 225
15-17,19-21: 19-Meskin-a 11 22 33 62 86 110
18,22-25-Krigstein-a 12 24 36 69 97 125
26(4/50)-Origin & 1st app. Calamity Kate, series ends #32; Krigstein-a 15 30 45 85 130 175
27-Krigstein-a(2) 14 28 42 82 121 160
28-41: 33-Quest app. 37-Lobo, the Wolf Boy begins 8 16 24 44 57 70

NOTE: *Mort Lawrence a-20-27, 29, 37, 39; c-19, 22-24, 26, 27. Leav c-14-18, 20, 31. Syd Shores a-39; c-34, 35, 37-41.*

WESTERNER, THE
Super Comics: 1964

Super Reprint 15-17: 15-r/Oklahoma Kid #? 16-r/Crack West. #65; Severin-c; Crandall-r. 17-r/Blazing Western #2; Severin-c 2 4 6 11 16 20

WESTERN FIGHTERS
Hillman Periodicals/Star Publ.: Apr-May, 1948 - V4#7, Mar-Apr, 1953 (#1-V3#2: 52 pgs.)

V1#1-Simon & Kirby-c 40 80 120 246 411 575
2-Not Kirby-a 15 30 45 90 140 190
3-Fuje-c 14 28 42 80 115 150
4-Krigstein, Ingels, Fuje-a 15 30 45 83 124 165
5,6,8,9,12 11 22 33 62 86 110
7,10-Krigstein-a 13 26 39 72 101 130
11-Williamson/Frazetta-a 36 72 108 211 343 475
V2#1-Krigstein-a 13 26 39 72 101 130
2-12: 4-Berg-a 9 18 27 50 65 80
V3#1-11,V4#1,4-7 9 18 27 47 61 75
12,V4#2,3-Krigstein-a 13 26 39 72 101 130
3-D 1(12/53, 25¢, Star Publ.)-Came w/glasses; L. B. Cole-c

GD 2.0 | VG 4.0 | FN 6.0 | VF 8.0 | VF/NM 9.0 | NM- 9.2

39 78 117 231 378 525
NOTE: *Kinstlerish a-V2#6, 8, 9, 12; V3#2, 5-7, 11, 12; V4#1(plus cover). McWilliams a-11. Powell a-V2#2. Reinman a-1-12, V4#3. Rowich c-5, 6i. Starr a-5.*

WESTERN FRONTIER
P. L. Publishers: Apr-May, 1951 - No. 7, 1952
1 18 36 54 105 165 225
2 10 20 30 58 79 100
3-7 9 18 27 52 69 85

WESTERN GUNFIGHTERS (1st Series) (Apache Kid #11-19)
Atlas Comics (CPS): No. 20, June, 1956 - No. 27, Aug, 1957
20 18 36 54 105 165 225
21-Crandall-a 18 36 54 105 165 225
22-Wood & Powell-a 24 48 72 140 230 320
23,24: 23-Williamson-a. 24-Toth-a 16 32 48 98 154 210
25-27 14 28 42 81 118 155
NOTE: *Berg a-20. Colan a-20, 26, 27. Crandall a-21. Heath a-25. Maneely a-24, 25; c-22, 23, 25. Morisi a-24. Morrow a-26. Pakula a-23. Severin c-20, 27. Torres a-26. Woodbridge a-27.*

WESTERN GUNFIGHTERS (2nd Series)
Marvel Comics Group: Aug, 1970 - No. 33, Nov, 1975 (#1-6: 25¢, 68 pgs.)
1-Ghost Rider begins; Fort Rango, Renegades & Gunhawk app.
6 12 18 41 76 110
2,3,5,6: 2-Origin Nightwind (Apache Kid's horse) 3 6 9 21 33 45
4-Barry Smith-a 4 8 12 23 37 50
7-(52 pgs) Origin Ghost Rider retold 3 6 9 19 30 40
8-13: 10-Origin Black Rider. 12-Origin Matt Slade 3 6 9 14 20 25
14-Steranko-c 3 6 9 16 24 32
15-20 2 4 6 10 14 18
21-33 2 4 6 9 13 16
NOTE: *Baker r-2, 3. Colan r-2. Drucker r-3. Everett a-6i. G. Kane c-29, 31. Kirby a-1p(r), 5, 10-12; c-19, 21. Kubert r-2. Maneely r-2, 10. Morrow r-29. Severin c-10. Shores a-3, 4. Barry Smith a-4. Steranko c-14. Sutton a-1, 2i, 5, 4. Torres r-26('57). Wildey r-8, 9. Williamson r-2, 18. Woodbridge r-27('57). Renegades in #4, 5; Ghost Rider in #1-7.*

WESTERN HEARTS
Standard Comics: Dec, 1949 - No. 10, Mar, 1952 (All photo-c)
1-Severin-a; Whip Wilson & Reno Browne photo-c 26 52 78 154 252 350
2-Beverly Tyler & Jerome Courtland photo-c from movie "Palomino"; Williamson/Frazetta-a (2 pgs.) 24 48 72 144 237 330
3-Rex Allen photo-c 15 30 45 84 127 170
4-7,10: 4-Severin & Elder, Al Carreno-a. 5-Ray Milland & Hedy Lamarr photo-c from movie "Copper Canyon". 6-Fred MacMurray & Irene Dunn photo-c from movie "Never a Dull Moment". 7-Jock Mahoney photo-c. 10-Bill Williams & Jane Nigh photo-c
14 28 42 81 118 155
8-Randolph Scott & Janis Carter photo-c from "Santa Fe"; Severin & Elder-a
14 28 42 82 121 160
9-Whip Wilson & Reno Browne photo-c; Severin & Elder-a
15 30 45 85 130 175

WESTERN HERO (Wow Comics #1-69; Real Western Hero #70-75)
Fawcett Publications: No. 76, Mar, 1949 - No. 112, Mar, 1952
76(#1, 52 pgs.)-Tom Mix, Hopalong Cassidy, Monte Hale, Gabby Hayes, Young Falcon (ends #78,80), & Big Bow and Little Arrow (ends #102,105) begin; painted-c begin
16 32 48 94 147 200
77 (52 pgs.) 11 22 33 64 90 115
78,80-82 (52 pgs.): 81-Capt. Tootsie by Beck 11 22 33 60 83 105
79,83 (36 pgs.): 83-Last painted-c 10 20 30 54 72 90
84-86,88-90 (52 pgs.): 84-Photo-c begin, end #112. 86-Last Hopalong Cassidy
10 20 30 53 76 95
87,91,95,99 (36 pgs.): 87-Bill Boyd begins, ends #95
9 18 27 50 65 80
92-94,96-98,101 (52 pgs.): 96-Tex Ritter begins. 101-Red Eagle app.
9 18 27 52 69 85
100 (52 pgs.) 10 20 30 56 76 95
102-111: 102-Begin 36 pg. issues 9 18 27 50 65 80
112-Last issue 9 18 27 52 69 85
NOTE: *1/2 to 1 pg. Rocky Lane (Carnation) in 80-83, 86, 88, 97. Photo covers feature Hopalong Cassidy #84, 86, 89; Tom Mix #85, 87, 90, 92, 94, 97; Monte Hale #88, 91, 93, 95, 98, 100, 104, 107, 110; Tex Ritter #96, 99, 101, 105, 108, 111; Gabby Hayes #103.*

WESTERN KID (1st Series)
Atlas Comics (CPC): Dec, 1954 - No. 17, Aug, 1957
1-Origin; The Western Kid (Tex Dawson), his stallion Whirlwind & dog Lightning begin
27 54 81 158 259 360
2 (2/55)-Last pre-code 15 30 45 90 140 190
3-8 14 48 42 80 115 150
9,10-Williamson-a in both (4 pgs. each) 14 28 42 81 118 155
11-17 13 26 39 74 105 130
NOTE: *Ayers a-6, 7. Heck a-3. Maneely c-2-7, 10, 13-15. Romita a-1-17; c-1, 12. Severin c-11, 16, 17.*

WESTERN KID, THE (2nd Series)
Marvel Comics Group: Dec, 1971 - No. 5, Aug, 1972 (All 20¢ issues)
1-Reprints; Romita-c/a(3) 3 6 9 19 30 40
2,4,5: 2-Romita-a; Severin-c. 4-Everett-r 3 6 9 14 20 25
3-Williamson-a 3 6 9 15 22 28

WESTERN KILLERS
Fox Feature Syndicate: nn, July?, 1948; No. 60, Sept, 1948 - No. 64, May, 1949; No. 6, July, 1949
nn(#59?)(nd, F&J Trading Co.)-Range Busters; formerly Blue Beetle #57?
30 60 90 177 289 400
60 (#1, 9/48)-Extreme violence; lingerie panel 34 68 102 199 325 450
61-Jack Cole, Starr-a 25 50 75 150 245 340
62-64, 6 (#6-exist?) 23 46 69 136 223 310

WESTERN LIFE ROMANCES (My Friend Irma #3 on?)
Marvel Comics (IPP): Dec, 1949 - No. 2, Mar, 1950 (52 pgs.)
1-Whip Wilson & Reno Browne photo-c 24 48 72 142 234 325
2-Audie Murphy & Gale Storm photo-c 20 40 60 117 189 260

WESTERN LOVE
Prize Publ.: July-Aug, 1949 - No. 5, Mar-Apr, 1950 (All photo-c & 52 pgs.)
1-S&K-a; Randolph Scott photo-c from movie "Canadian Pacific" (see Prize Comics #76)
34 68 102 199 325 450
2,5-S&K-a: 2-Whip Wilson & Reno Browne photo-c. 5-Dale Robertson photo-c 27 54 81 158 259 360
3,4: 3-Pat Williams photo-c 17 34 51 98 154 210
NOTE: *Meskin & Severin/Elder a-2-5.*

WESTERN LOVE TRAILS (Formerly Western Adventures)
Ace Magazines (A. A. Wyn): No. 7, Nov, 1949 - No. 9, Mar, 1950
7 14 28 42 76 108 140
8,9 10 20 30 56 76 95

WESTERN MARSHAL (See Steve Donovan...)
Dell Publishing Co.: No. 534, 2-4/54 - No. 640, 7/55 (Based on Ernest Haycox's "Trailtown")
Four Color 534 (#1)-Kinstler-a 7 14 21 44 82 120
Four Color 591 (10/54), 613 (2/55), 640-All Kinstler-a 5 10 15 35 63 90

WESTERN OUTLAWS (Junior Comics #9-16; My Secret Life #22 on)
Fox Feature Syndicate: No. 17, Sept, 1948 - No. 21, May, 1949
17-Kamen-a; Iger shop-a in all; 1 pg. "Death and the Devil Pills" r-in Ghostly Weird #122
37 74 111 222 361 500
18-21 21 42 63 122 199 275

WESTERN OUTLAWS
Atlas Comics (ACI No. 1-14/WPI No. 15-21): Feb, 1954 - No. 21, Aug, 1957
1-Heath, Powell-a; Maneely hanging-c 30 60 90 177 289 400
2 15 30 45 88 137 185
3-10: 7-Violent-a by R.Q. Sale 14 28 42 78 112 145
11,14-Williamson-a in both (6 pgs. each) 14 28 42 82 121 160
12,18,20,21: Severin covers 13 26 39 74 105 135
13,15: 13-Baker-a. 15-Torres-a 14 28 42 78 112 145
16-Williamson text illo 13 26 39 74 105 135
17,19-Crandall-a. 17-Williamson text illo 14 28 42 80 115 150
NOTE: *Ayers a-7, 10, 18, 20. Bolle a-21. Colan a-5, 10, 11, 17. Drucker a-11. Everett a-9, 10. Heath a-1; c-3, 4, 8, 16. Kubert a-9p. Maneely a-13, 16, 17, 19; c-1, 5, 7, 9, 10, 12, 13. Morisi a-18. Powell a-3, 16. Romita a-7, 13. Severin a-8, 16, 19; c-17, 18, 20, 21. Tuska a-6, 15.*

WESTERN OUTLAWS & SHERIFFS (Formerly Best Western)
Marvel/Atlas Comics (IPC): No. 60, Dec, 1949 - No. 73, June, 1952
60 (52 pgs.) Photo-c; first Maneely Atlas work 28 56 84 165 270 375
61-65: 61-Photo-c 20 40 60 120 195 270
66-Story contains 5 hangings 21 42 63 124 202 280
67-Cannibalism story 21 42 63 124 202 280
68-72 15 30 45 92 144 195
73-Black Rider story; Everett-c 18 36 54 107 169 230
NOTE: *Maneely a-60-62, 67; c-62, 69-73. Robinson a-68. Sinnott a-70. Tuska a-69-71.*

WESTERN PICTURE STORIES (1st Western comic)
Comics Magazine Company: Feb, 1937 - No. 4, June, 1937
1-Will Eisner-a 271 542 813 1734 2967 4200
2-Will Eisner-a 161 322 483 1030 1765 2500
3,4: 3-Eisner-a. 4-Caveman Cowboy story 135 270 405 864 1482 2100

WESTERN PICTURE STORIES (See Giant Comics Edition #6, 11)

WESTERN ROMANCES (See Target...)

WESTERN ROUGH RIDERS
Gillmor Magazines No. 1,4 (Stanmor Publ.): Nov, 1954 - No. 4, May, 1955
1 11 22 33 62 86 110
2-4 8 16 24 44 57 70

WESTERN ROUNDUP (See Dell Giants & Fox Giants)

WESTERN SERENADE
DC Comics: May/June, 1949
nn - Ashcan comic, not distributed to newsstands, only for in-house use (no known sales)

WESTERN TALES (Formerly Witches...)
Harvey Publications: No. 31, Oct, 1955 - No. 33, July-Sept, 1956
31,32-All S&K-a; Davy Crockett app. in each 17 34 51 100 158 215
33-S&K-a; Jim Bowie app. 16 32 48 94 147 200
NOTE: *#32 & 33 contain Boy's Ranch reprints. Kirby c-31.*

WESTERN TALES OF BLACK RIDER (Formerly Black Rider; Gunsmoke Western #32 on)
Atlas Comics (CPS): No. 28, May, 1955 - No. 31, Nov, 1955
28 (#1): The Spider (a villain) dies 27 54 81 158 259 360
29-31 18 36 54 107 169 230
NOTE: *Lawrence a-30. Maneely c-28-30. Severin a-28. Shores c-31.*

WESTERN TEAM-UP
Marvel Comics Group: Nov, 1973 (20¢)
1-Origin & 1st app. The Dakota Kid; Rawhide Kid-r; Gunsmoke Kid-r by Jack Davis
4 8 12 25 40 55

WESTERN THRILLERS (My Past Confessions #7 on)
Fox Feature Syndicate/M.S. Distr. No. 52: Aug, 1948 - No. 6, June, 1949; No. 52, 1954?
1- "Velvet Rose" (Kamenish-a); "Two-Gun Sal", "Striker Sisters" (all women outlaws issue); Brodsky-c 65 130 195 416 708 1000
2 32 64 96 188 307 425
3-6: 4,5-Bakerish-a; 5-Butch Cassidy app. 22 44 66 132 216 300
52-(Reprint, M.S. Dist.)-1954? No date given (becomes My Love Secret #53)
12 24 36 67 94 120

WESTERN THRILLERS (Cowboy Action #5 on)
Atlas Comics (ACI): Nov, 1954 - No. 4, Feb, 1955 (All-r/Western Outlaws & Sheriffs)
1 24 48 72 142 234 325
2-4 15 30 45 84 127 170
NOTE: *Heath c-3. Maneely a-1; c-2. Powell a-4. Robinson a-4. Romita c-4. Tuska a-2.*

WESTERN TRAILS (Ringo Kid Starring in...)
Atlas Comics (SAI): May, 1957 - No. 2, July, 1957
1-Ringo Kid app.; Severin-c 17 34 51 100 158 215
2-Severin-c 12 24 36 69 97 125
NOTE: *Bolle a-1, 2. Maneely a-1, 2. Severin c-1, 2.*

Western Hero #96 © FAW

Wet Hot American Summer GN © ETDW

What If? #8 © MAR

GD 2.0 | VG 4.0 | FN 6.0 | VF 8.0 | VF/NM 9.0 | NM- 9.2

WESTERN TRUE CRIME (Becomes My Confessions)
Fox Feature Syndicate: No. 15, Aug, 1948 - No. 6, June, 1949

15(#1)-Kamen-a; formerly Zoot #14 (5/48)? 39 78 117 231 378 525
16(#2)-Kamenish-a; headlight panels, violence 28 56 84 165 270 375
3-Kamen-a 29 58 87 172 281 390
4-6: 4-Johnny Craig-a 17 34 51 105 165 225

WESTERN WINNERS (Formerly All-Western Winners; becomes Black Rider #8 on & Romance Tales #7 on?)
Marvel Comics (CDS): No. 5, June, 1949 - No. 7, Dec, 1949

5-Two-Gun Kid, Kid Colt, Black Rider; Shores-c 37 74 111 222 361 500
6-Two-Gun Kid, Black Rider, Heath Kid Colt story; Captain Tootsie by C.C. Beck 31 62 93 182 296 410
7-Randolph Scott Photo-c w/true stories about the West 31 62 93 182 296 410

WEST OF THE PECOS (See Zane Grey, 4-Color #222)

WESTWARD HO, THE WAGONS (Disney)(Also see Classic Comics #14)
Dell Publishing Co.: No. 738, Sept, 1956 (Movie)

Four Color 738-Fess Parker photo-c 8 16 24 54 102 150

WET HOT AMERICAN SUMMER (Based on the 2001 movie and Netflix series)
BOOM! Studios: Nov, 2018 ($19.99, squarebound graphic novel)

nn-Christopher Hastings-s/Noah Hayes-a; takes place after the 1st week of camp 20.00

WE3
DC Comics (Vertigo): Oct, 2004 - No. 3, May, 2005 ($2.95, limited series)

1-3-Domestic animal cyborgs: Grant Morrison-s/Frank Quitely-a 3.00
TPB (2005, $12.99) r/series 13.00

WETWORKS (See WildC.A.T.S: Covert Action Teams #2)
Image Comics (WildStorm): June, 1994 - No. 43, Aug, 1998 ($1.95/$2.50)

1-"July" on-c; gatefold wraparound-c; Portacio/Williams-c/a 4.00
1-Chicago Comicon edition 6.00
1-(2/98, $4.95) "3-D Edition" w/glasses 5.00
2-4 3.00
2-Alternate Portacio-c, see Deathblow #5 6.00
5-7,9-24: 5-($2.50). 13-Portacio-c. 16,17-Fire From Heaven Pts. 4 & 11 3.00
8 ($1.95)-Newstand, Wildstorm Rising Pt. 7 3.00
8 ($2.50)-Direct Market, Wildstorm Rising Pt. 7 3.00
25-($3.95) 4.00
26-43: 32-Variant-c by Pat Lee & Charest. 39,40-Stormwatch app. 42-Gen 13 app. 3.00
Sourcebook 1 (10/94, $2.50)-Text & illustrations (no comics) 3.00
Voyager Pack (8/97, $3.50)- #32 w/Phantom Guard preview 4.00

WETWORKS
DC Comics (WildStorm): Nov, 2006 - No. 15, Jan, 2008 ($2.99)

1-15: 1-Carey-s/Portacio-a; two covers by Portacio and Van Sciver. 2-Golden var-c 3-Pearson var-c. 4-Powell var-c 3.00
...: Armageddon 1 (1/08, $2.99) Gage-s/Badeaux-a 3.00
... Book One (2007, $14.99) r/#1-5 and stories from Eye of the storm Annual and Coup D'Etat Afterword 15.00
... Book Two (2008, $14.99) r/#6-9,13-15 15.00
...: Mutations 1 (11/10, $3.99) Grevioux & Long-s/Gopez-a 4.00

WETWORKS/VAMPIRELLA (See Vampirella/Wetworks)
Image Comics (WildStorm Productions): July, 1997 ($2.95, one-shot)

1-Gil Kane-c 4.00

WHACK (Satire)
St. John Publishing Co. (Jubilee Publ.): Oct, 1953 - No. 3, May, 1954

1-(3-D, 25¢)-Kubert-a; Maurer-c; came w/glasses 32 64 96 188 307 425
2,3-Kubert-a in each. 2-Bing Crosby on-c; Mighty Mouse & Steve Canyon parodies. 3-Li'l Orphan Annie parody; Maurer-c 20 40 60 114 182 250

WHACKY (See Wacky)

WHA...HUH?
Marvel Comics: 2005 ($3.99, one-shot)

1-Humor spoofs of Marvel characters; Mahfood-a/c; Bendis, Stan Lee and others-s 4.00

WHALESVILLE X ROCKS AND MINERALS
Bad Idea: May, 2021 ($9.99, one-shot)

1-(First Printing) Kindt-s/Pollina-a; Millionaire-a 1 3 4 6 8 10
1-(Not First Printing, 8/21) 1 3 4 6 8 10

WHAM COMICS (See Super Spy)
Centaur Publications: Nov, 1940 - No. 2, Dec, 1940

1-The Sparkler, The Phantom Rider, Craig Carter and his Magic Ring, Detecto, Copper Slug, Speed Silvers by Gustavson, Speed Centaur & Jon Linton (s/f) begin

GD 2.0 | VG 4.0 | FN 6.0 | VF 8.0 | VF/NM 9.0 | NM- 9.2

226 452 678 1446 2473 3500
2-Origin Blue Fire & Solarman; The Buzzard app. 187 374 561 1197 2049 2900

WHAM-O GIANT COMICS
Wham-O Mfg. Co. : April, 1967 (98¢, newspaper size, one-shot)(Six issue subscription was advertised)

1-Radian & Goody Bumpkin by Wood; 1 pg. Stanley-a; Fine, Tufts-a; flying saucer reports; wraparound-c 10 20 30 66 138 210

WHATEVER HAPPENED TO BARON VON SHOCK?
Image Comics: May, 2010 - No. 4, Nov, 2010 ($3.99, unfinished limited series)

1-4-Rob Zombie-s/Donny Hadiwidjaja-a 4.00

WHAT IF? (1st Series) (What If? Featuring... #13 & #?-33) (Also see Hero Initiative)
Marvel Comics Group: Feb, 1977 - No. 47, Oct, 1984; June, 1988 (All 52 pgs.)

1-Brief origin Spider-Man, Fantastic Four 6 12 18 38 69 100
2-Origin The Hulk retold 3 6 9 21 33 45
3,4: 3-Avengers. 4-Invaders 3 6 9 21 33 45
5-Capt. America 2 4 6 11 16 20
6-9,13,17: 7-Betty Brant as Spider-Girl. 8-Daredevil; Spidey parody. 9-Origins Venus, Marvel Boy, Human Robot, 3-D Man. 13-Conan app.; John Buscema-c/a(p). 17-Ghost Rider & Son of Satan app. 2 4 6 8 11 14
10-(8/78) What if Jane Foster was Thor 9 18 27 62 126 190
11,12,14-16: 11-Marvel Bullpen as F.F. 2 4 6 8 10 12
18-26,29: 18-Dr. Strange. 19-Spider-Man. 22-Origin Dr. Doom retold 1 3 4 6 8 10
27-X-Men app.; Miller-c 3 6 9 16 23 30
28-Daredevil by Miller; Ghost Rider app. 3 6 9 14 19 24
30-"What If...Spider-Man's Clone Had Lived?" 2 4 6 10 14 18
31-Begin $1.00-c; featuring Wolverine & the Hulk; X-Men app.; death of Hulk, Wolverine & Magneto 5 10 15 31 53 75
32-34,36-47: 32,36-Byrne-a. 34-Marvel crew each draw themselves. 37-Old X-Men & Silver Surfer app. 39-Thor battles Conan 6.00
35-What if Elektra had lived?; Miller/Austin-a. 2 4 6 8 11 14
Special 1 ($1.50, 6/88)-Iron Man, F.F., Thor app. 6.00
... Classic Vol. 1 TPB (2004, $24.99) r/#1-6; checklist 25.00
... Classic Vol. 2 TPB (2005, $24.99) r/#7-12 25.00
... Classic Vol. 3 TPB (2006, $24.99) r/#14,15,17-20 25.00
... Classic Vol. 4 TPB (2007, $24.99) r/#21-26; checklist of all What If? series/issues 25.00

NOTE: ***Austin** a-27p, 32i, 34, 35i; c-35i, 36i. **J. Buscema** a-13p, 15p; c-10, 13p, 23p. **Byrne** a-32i, 36; c-36p. **Colan** a-21p; c-17p, 18p, 21p. **Ditko** a-35, Special 1. **Golden** c-29, 40-42. **Guice** a-40p. **Gil Kane** a-3p, 24p; c(p)-2-4, 7, 8. **Kirby** a-11p; c-9p, 11p. **Layton** a-32i, 33i; c-30, 32p, 33i, 34. **Mignola** c-39i. **Miller** a-28p, 32i, 34(1), 35p; c-27, 28p. **Mooney** a-8i, 30i. **Perez** a-15p. **Robbins** a-4p. **Sienkiewicz** c-43-46. **Simonson** a-15p, 32i. **Starlin** a-32i. **Stevens** a-8, 16i(part). **Sutton** a-2i, 18p, 28. **Tuska** a-5p. **Weiss** a-37p.*

WHAT IF...? (2nd Series)
Marvel Comics: V2#1, July, 1989 - No. 114, Nov, 1998 ($1.25/$1.50)

V2#1-...The Avengers Had Lost the Evolutionary War 1 2 3 5 6 8
2,3,5: 2-Daredevil, Punisher app. 5.00
4-Alien costume had possessed Spider-Man 3 6 9 14 20 25
6-X-Men app. 6.00
7-Wolverine app.; Liefeld-c/a(1st on Wolvie?) 1 3 4 6 8 10
8,10,11,13-15,17-30: 10-Punisher app. 11-Fantastic Four app.; McFarlane-c(i).13-Prof. X; Jim Lee-c. 14-Capt. Marvel; Lim/Austin-c.15-F.F.; Capullo-c/a(p). 17-Spider-Man/Kraven. 18-F.F. 19-Vision. 20,21-Spider-Man. 22-Silver Surfer by Lim/Austin-c/a 23-X-Men. 24-Wolverine; Punisher app. 25-(52 pgs.)-Wolverine app. 26-Punisher app. 27-Namor/F.F. 28,29-Capt. America. 29-Swipes cover to Avengers #4. 30-(52 pgs.)-F.F. 5.00
9,12-X-Men 6.00
16-Wolverine battles Conan; Red Sonja app.; X-Men cameo 6.00
31-40,42,43,45-48: 31-Cosmic Spider-Man & Venom app.; Hobgoblin cameo. 32,33-Phoenix; X-Men app. 35-Fantastic Five (w/Spidey). 36-Avengers vs. Guardians of the Galaxy. 37-Wolverine; Thibert-c(i). 38-Thor; Rogers-p(part). 40-Storm; X-Men app. 42-Spider-Man. 43-Wolverine. 45-Ghost Rider. 46-Cable. 47-Magneto 4.00
41,50: 41-(52 pgs.)-Avengers vs. Galactus. 50-(52 pgs.)-Foil embossed-c; "What If Hulk Had Killed Wolverine" 2 4 6 8 10 12
44-Venom had possessed the Punisher 2 4 6 11 16 20
49-Infinity Gauntlet w/Silver Surfer & Thanos 4 8 12 23 37 50
51-(7/93) "What If the Punisher Became Captain America" (see it happen in 2007's Punisher War Journal #6-10) 1 2 3 5 6 8
52-99,101-103: 52-Dr. Doom. 54-Death's Head. 57-Punisher as Shield. 58-"What if Punisher Had Killed Spider-Man" w/cover similar to Amazing S-M #129. 59-...Wolverine led Alpha Flight. 60-X-Men Wedding Album. 61-Bound-in card sheet. 61,86,88-Spider-Man. 74,77,81,84,85-X-Men. 76-Last app. Watcher in title. 78-Bisley-c. 80-Hulk. 87-Sabretooth. 89-Fantastic Four. 90-Cyclops & Havok. 91-The Hulk. 93-Wolverine. 94-Juggernaut. 95-Ghost Rider 4.00
100-($2.99, double-sized) Gambit and Rogue, Fantastic Four 1 3 4 6 8 10
104-Silver Surfer, Thanos vs. Impossible Man 1 3 4 6 8 10

105-Spider-Girl (Peter Parker's daughter) debut; Sienkiewicz-a; (Betty Brant also app. as a Spider-Girl in What If? (1st series) #7) 9 18 27 59 117 175
106,107,109-114: 106-Gambit. 111-Wolverine. 114-Secret Wars 4.00
108-Avengers vs. Carnage 2 4 6 9 14 18
#(-1) Flashback (7/97) 1 2 3 5 6 8

WHAT IF...? (one-shots)
Marvel Comics: Feb, 2005 ($2.99)

... Aunt May Had Died Instead of Uncle Ben? - Brubaker-s/DiVito-a/Brase-c 3.00
... Dr. Doom Had Become The Thing? - Karl Kesel-s/Paul Smith-a/c 3.00
... General Ross Had Become The Hulk? - Peter David-s/Pat Olliffe-a/Gary Frank-c 3.00
... Jessica Jones Had Joined The Avengers? - Bendis-s/Gaydos-a/McNiven-c 3.00
... Karen Page Had Lived? - Bendis-s/Lark-a/c 3.00
... Magneto and Professor X Had Formed The X-Men Together? - Claremont-s/Raney-a 3.00
What If...: Why Not? TPB (2005, $16.99) r/one-shots 17.00

WHAT IF... (one-shots)
Marvel Comics: Feb, 2006 ($2.99)

... : Captain America - Fought in the Civil War?; Bedard-s/Di Giandomenico-a 3.00
... : Daredevil - The Devil Who Dares; Daredevil in feudal Japan; Veitch-s/Edwards-a 3.00
... : Fantastic Four - Were Cosmonauts?; Marshall Rogers-a/c; Mike Carey-s 3.00
... : Submariner - Grew Up on Land?; Pak-s/Lopez-a 3.00
... : Thor - Was the Herald of Galactus?; Kirkman-s/Oeming-a/c 3.00
... : Wolverine - In the Prohibition Era; Way-s/Proctor-a/Harris-c 3.00
What If: Mirror Mirror TPB (2006, $16.99) r/one-shots; design pages and Rogers sketches 17.00

WHAT IF ?... (one-shots altering recent Marvel "event" series)
Marvel Comics: Jan, 2007 - Feb, 2007 ($3.99)

... Avengers Disassembled; Parker-s/Lopresti-a/c 4.00
... Spider-Man The Other; Peter David-s/Khoi Pham-a; Venom app. 4.00
... Wolverine Enemy of the State; Robinson-s/DiGiandomenico-a/Alexander-c 4.00
... X-Men Age of Apocalypse; Remender-s/Wilkins-a/Djurdjevic-c 4.00
... X-Men Deadly Genesis; Hine-s/Yardin-a/c 4.00
What If?: Event Horizon TPB (2007, $16.99) r/one-shots; design pages and cover sketches 17.00

WHAT IF ?... (one-shots altering recent Marvel "event" series)
Marvel Comics: Dec, 2007 - Feb, 2008 ($3.99)

... Annihilation; Nova, Iron Man, Captain America app. 2 4 6 9 12 15
... Civil War; 2 covers by Silvestri & Djurdjevic 1 3 4 6 8 10
... Planet Hulk; Pagulayan-c; Kirk, Sandoval & Hembeck-a; Skaar, son of Hulk app. 3 6 9 23 37 50
... Spider-Man vs. Wolverine; Romita Jr.-c; Henry-a; Nick Fury app. 2 4 6 9 12 15
... X-Men - Rise and Fall of the Shi'ar Empire; Coipel-c 4.00
What If?: Civil War TPB (2008, $16.99) r/one-shots; design pages and cover sketches 17.00

WHAT IF ?... (one-shots altering recent Marvel "event" series)
Marvel Comics: Feb, 2009 ($3.99) (Serialized back-up Runaways story in each issue)

... Fallen Son; if Iron Man had died instead of Capt. America; McGuinness-c 4.00
... House of M; if the Scarlet Witch had said "No more powers" instead; Cheung-c 4.00
... Newer Fantastic Four; team of Spider-Man, Hulk, Iron Man and Wolverine 4.00
... Secret Wars; if Doctor Doom had kept the Beyonder's power; origin re-told 4.00
... Spider-Man Back in Black; if Mary Jane had been shot instead of Aunt May 4.00

WHAT IF ?... (one-shots)
Marvel Comics: Feb, 2010 ($3.99)

... Astonishing X-Men; if Ord resurrected Jean Grey; Campbell-c 4.00
... Daredevil vs. Elektra; Kayanan-a; Klaus Janson-c swipe of Daredevil #168 4.00
... Secret Invasion; if the Skrulls succeeded; Yu-c 4.00
... Spider-Man: House of M; if Gwen Stacy survived the House of M; Dodson-c 4.00
... World War Hulk; if the heroes lost the war; Romita Jr.-c 4.00

WHAT IF ?... (one-shots) (4 part Deadpool back-up story in all but #200)
(Also see Venom/Deadpool: What If?)
Marvel Comics: Feb, 2011 ($3.99)

... #200 ($4.99) Siege on cover; if Osborn won the Siege of Asgard; Stan Lee back-up 5.00
... Dark Reign; if Norman Osborn was killed; Tanaka-a/Deodato-c 4.00
... Iron Man: Demon in an Armor; if Tony Stark became Dr. Doom; Nolan-a 4.00
... Spider-Man; if Spider-Man killed Kraven; Jimenez-c 4.00
... Wolverine: Father; if Wolverine raised Daken; Tocchini-a; Yu-a 4.00

WHAT IF ?... (one-shots)
Marvel Comics: Dec, 2018 ($3.99)

... Ghost Rider 1; Girner-s/Wijngaard-a; heavy metal band becomes the Ghost Rider 4.00
... Majik 1; if Majik became Sorceror Supreme; Belasco app.; Williams-s/Andrade-a 4.00
... Spider-Man 1; if Flash Thompson became Spider-Man; Conway-s/Olortegui-a 4.00
... The Punisher 1; if Peter Parker became The Punisher; Potts-s/Ramirez-a 4.00
... Thor 1; if Thor was raised by the Frost Giants; Sacks-s/Bandini-a 4.00
... X-Men 1; X-Men in cyberspace; Hill-s/Milonogiannis & Edwards-a 4.00

WHAT IF ? AGE OF ULTRON
Marvel Comics: Jun, 2014 - No. 5, Jun, 2014 ($3.99, weekly limited series)

1-5: 1-Hank Pym's story. 2-Wolverine, Hulk, Spider-Man, Ghost Rider app. 4.00

WHAT IF ? AVX (Avengers vs. X-Men)
Marvel Comics: Sept, 2013 - No. 4, Sept, 2013 ($3.99, weekly limited series)

1-4-Palmiotti-s/Molina-a; Hope merges with the Phoenix force 4.00

WHAT IF ? INFINITY - ... (one-shots)
Marvel Comics: Dec, 2015 ($3.99)

... Dark Reign; if The Green Goblin stole the Infinity Gauntlet; Williamson-s/Sudzuka-a 4.00
... Guardians of the Galaxy; if The Guardians tried to free Thanos; Copland-a 4.00
... Inhumans; if Black Bolt betrayed Earth; Rossmo-a 4.00
... Thanos; if Thanos joined the Avengers; Henderson-a 4.00
... X-Men; if the X-Men were the sole survivors of Infinity; Norton-a 4.00

WHAT IF...? MILES MORALES
Marvel Comics: May, 2022 - No. 5, Sept, 2022 ($4.99/$3.99, limited series)

1-($4.99) What if Miles became Captain America; Ziglar-s/Medina-a 5.00
2-5-($3.99) 2-Miles becomes Wolverine. 3-Hulk. 4-Thor. 5-All team-up with Spider-Miles 4.00

'WHAT'S NEW? - THE COLLECTED ADVENTURES OF PHIL & DIXIE'
Palliard Press: Oct, 1991 - No. 2, 1991 ($5.95, mostly color, sq.-bound, 52 pgs.)

1,2-By Phil Foglio 6.00

WHAT'S THE FURTHEST PLACE FROM HERE?
Image Comics: Nov, 2021 - No. 11, Present ($4.99/$3.99)

1-($4.99) Boss & Rosenberg-s&a 5.00
2-11-($3.99) 4.00

WHAT THE- -?!
Marvel Comics: Aug, 1988 - No. 26, 1993 ($1.25/$1.50/$2.50, semi-annual #5 on)

1-All contain parodies 6.00
2-24: 3-X-Men parody; Todd McFarlane-a. 5-Punisher/Wolverine parody; Jim Lee-a. 6-Punisher, Wolverine, Alpha Flight. 9-Wolverine. 16-EC back-c parody. 17-Wolverine/Punisher parody. 18-Star Trek parody w/Wolverine. 19-Punisher, Wolverine, Ghost Rider. 21-Weapon X parody. 22-Punisher/Wolverine parody 4.00
25-Summer Special 1 (1993, $2.50)-X-Men parody 5.00
26-Fall Special ($2.50, 68 pgs.)-Spider-Ham 2099-c/story; origin Silver Surfer; Hulk & Doomsday parody; indica reads "Winter Special." 5.00

NOTE: ***Austin** a-6i. **Byrne** a-2, 6, 10; c-2, 6-8, 10, 12, 13. **Golden** a-22. **Dale Keown** a-8p(8 pgs.). **McFarlane** a-3. **Rogers** c-15i, 16p. **Severin** a-2. **Staton** a-21p. **Williamson** a-2i.*

WHEDON THREE WAY, THE
Dark Horse Comics: Sept, 2014 ($1.00, one-shot)

1-Reprints Buffy Season 10 #1, Angel & Faith Season 10 #1, Serenity: Leaves #1 3.00

WHEE COMICS (Also see Gay, Smile & Tickle Comics)
Modern Store Publications: 1955 (7¢, 5x7-1/4", 52 pgs.)

1-Funny animal 10 20 30 56 76 95

WHEEDIES (See Panic #11 -EC Comics)

WHEELIE AND THE CHOPPER BUNCH (TV)
Charlton Comics: July, 1975 - No. 7, July, 1976 (Hanna-Barbera)

1-3: 1-Byrne text illo (see Nightmare for 1st art); Staton-a. 2-Byrne-a. 2,3-Mike Zeck text illos. 3-Staton-a; Byrne-c/a 3 6 9 17 26 35
4-7-Staton-a 2 4 6 12 16 20

WHEN KNIGHTHOOD WAS IN FLOWER (See The Sword & the Rose, 4-Color #505, 682)

WHEN SCHOOL IS OUT (See Wisco in Promotional Comics section)

WHERE CREATURES ROAM
Marvel Comics Group: July, 1970 - No. 8, Sept, 1971

1-Kirby/Ayers-c/a(r) 6 12 18 38 69 100
2-8: 2-5,7,8-Kirby-c/a(r). 6-Kirby-a(r) 4 8 12 23 37 50

NOTE: ***Ditko** r-1-6, 7. **Heck** r-2, 5. All contain pre super-hero reprints.*

WHERE IN THE WORLD IS CARMEN SANDIEGO (TV)
DC Comics: June, 1996 - No. 4, Dec, 1996 ($1.75)

1-4: Adaptation of TV show 4.00

WHERE MONSTERS DWELL
Marvel Comics Group: Jan, 1970 - No. 38, Oct, 1975

1-Kirby/Ditko-r; all contain pre super-hero-r 7 14 21 46 86 125
2-5,7-10: 4-Crandall-a(r) 4 8 12 23 37 50
6-(11/70) Reprints Groot's 1st app. in Tales to Astonish #13 8 16 24 54 102 150
11,13-20: 11-Last 15¢ issue. 16-Googam app. 18,20-Starlin-c 3 6 9 19 30 40
12-Giant issue (52 pgs.) 4 8 12 27 44 60
21-Reprints 1st Fin Fang Foom app. 4 8 12 23 37 50
22-37 3 6 9 16 24 32
38-Williamson-r/World of Suspense #3 3 6 9 17 26 35

NOTE: ***Colan** r-12. **Ditko** a(r)-4, 6, 8, 10, 12, 17-19, 23-25, 37. **Kirby** r-1-3, 5-16, 18-27, 30-32, 34-36, 38; c-12? **Reinman** a-3r, 4r, 12r. **Severin** c-15.*

WHERE MONSTERS DWELL (Secret Wars tie-in)
Marvel Comics: Jul, 2015 - No. 5, Dec, 2015 ($3.99, limited series)

1-5-Garth Ennis-s/Russ Braun-a/Frank Cho-c; The Phantom Eagle app. 4.00

WHERE'S HUDDLES? (TV) (See Fun-In #9)
Gold Key: Jan, 1971 - No. 3, Dec, 1971 (Hanna-Barbera)

1 3 6 9 18 28 38
2,3: 3-r/most #1 2 4 6 11 16 20

WHIP WILSON (Movie star) (Formerly Rex Hart; Gunhawk #12 on; see Western Hearts, Western Life Romances, Western Love)
Marvel Comics: No. 9, April, 1950 - No. 11, Sept, 1950 (#9,10: 52 pgs.)

9-Photo-c; Whip Wilson & his horse Bullet begin; origin Bullet; issue #23 listed on splash page; cover changed to #9; Maneely-a 53 106 159 334 567 800
10,11: Both have photo-c. 11-36 pgs.; Maneely-a 31 62 93 182 296 410
I.W. Reprint #1(1964)-Kinstler-c; r-Marvel #11 3 6 9 17 26 35

WHIRLWIND COMICS (Also see Cyclone Comics)
Nita Publication: June, 1940 - No. 3, Sept, 1940

1-Origin & 1st app. Cyclone; Cyclone-c 343 686 1029 2400 4200 6000
2,3: Cyclone-c 206 412 618 1318 2259 3200

WHIRLYBIRDS (TV)
Dell Publishing Co.: No. 1124, Aug, 1960 - No. 1216, Oct-Dec, 1961

Four Color 1124 (#1)-Photo-c 7 14 21 49 92 135
Four Color 1216-Photo-c 7 14 21 46 86 125

WHISKEY DICKEL, INTERNATIONAL COWGIRL
Image Comics: Aug, 2003 ($12.95, softcover, B&W)

nn-Mark Ricketts-s/Mike Hawthorne-a; pin-up by various incl. Oeming, Thompson, Mack 13.00

WHISPER (Female Ninja)
Capital Comics: Dec, 1983 - No. 2, 1984 ($1.75, Baxter paper)

1,2: 1-Origin; Golden-c, Special (11/85, $2.50) 4.00

WHISPER (Vol. 2)
First Comics: Jun, 1986 - No. 37, June, 1990 ($1.25/$1.75/$1.95)

1-37 3.00

WHISPER

What If...? Miles Morales #2 © MAR

White Savior #2 © Nguyen & Burman

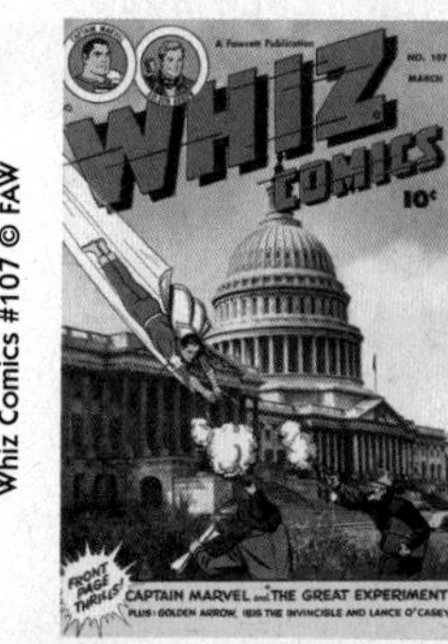

Whiz Comics #107 © FAW

GD 2.0 | VG 4.0 | FN 6.0 | VF 8.0 | VF/NM 9.0 | NM- 9.2

BOOM! Studios: Nov, 2006 ($3.99)
1-Grant-s/Dzialowski-a 4.00

WHISPERING DARK, THE
Dark Horse Comics: Oct, 2018 - No. 4, Feb, 2019 ($3.99)
1-4-Christopher Emgård-s/Tomás Aira-a 4.00

WHISPERS
Image Comics: Jan, 2012 - No. 6, Oct, 2013 ($2.99)
1-6-Joshua Luna-s/a 3.00

WHITE CHIEF OF THE PAWNEE INDIANS
Avon Periodicals: 1951
nn-Kit West app.; Kinstler-c 23 46 69 136 223 310

WHITE EAGLE INDIAN CHIEF (See Indian Chief)

WHITE FANG
Disney Comics: 1990 ($5.95, 68 pgs.)
nn-Graphic novel adapting new Disney movie 6.00

WHITE INDIAN
Magazine Enterprises: No. 11, July, 1953 - No. 15, 1954
11(A-1 94), 12(A-1 101), 13(A-1 104)-Frazetta-r(Dan Brand) in all from Durango Kid.
11-Powell-c 24 48 72 144 237 330
14(A-1 117), 15(A-1 135)-Check-a; Torres-a-#15 16 32 48 92 144 195
NOTE: *#11 contains reprints from Durango Kid #1-4; #12 from #5, 9, 10, 11; #13 from #7, 12, 13, 16. #14 & 15 contain all new stories.*

WHITEOUT (Also see Queen & Country)
Oni Press: July, 1998 - No. 4, Nov, 1998 ($2.95, B&W, limited series)
1-4: 1-Matt Wagner-c. 2-Mignola-c. 3-Gibbons-c 3.00
TPB (5/99, $10.95) r/#1-4; Miller-c 11.00

WHITEOUT: MELT
Oni Press: Sept, 1999 - No. 4, Feb, 2000 ($2.95, B&W, limited series)
1-4-Greg Rucka-s/Steve Lieber-a 3.00
Whiteout: Melt, The Definitive Edition TPB (9/07, $13.95) r/#1-4; Rucka afterword 14.00

WHITE PRINCESS OF THE JUNGLE (Also see Jungle Adventures & Top Jungle Comics)
Avon Periodicals: July, 1951 - No. 5, Nov, 1952
1-Origin of White Princess (Taanda) & Capt'n Courage (r); Kinstler-c
90 180 270 576 988 1400
2-Reprints origin of Malu, Slave Girl Princess from Avon's Slave Girl Comics #1 w/Malu changed to Zora; Kinstler-c/a(2) 55 110 165 352 601 850
3-Origin Blue Gorilla; Kinstler-c/a 50 100 150 315 533 750
4-Jack Barnum, White Hunter app.; r/Sheena #9 43 86 129 271 461 650
5-Blue Gorilla by McCann?; Kinstler inside-c; Fawcette/Alascia-a(3)
45 90 135 284 480 675

WHITE RIDER AND SUPER HORSE (Formerly Humdinger V2#2; Indian Warriors #7 on; also see Blue Bolt #1, 4Most & Western Crime Cases)
Novelty-Star Publications/Accepted Publ.: No. 4, 9/50 - No. 6, 3/51
4-6-Adapts "The Last of the Mohicans". 4(#1)-(9/50)-Says #11 on inside
20 40 60 117 189 260
Accepted Reprint #5(r/#5),6 (nd); L.B. Cole-c 10 20 30 56 76 95
NOTE: *All have* **L. B. Cole** *covers.*

WHITE SAVIOR
Dark Horse Comics: Jan, 2023 - No. 4 ($3.99, limited series)
1,2-Eric Nguyen & Scott Burman-s/Nguyen-a 4.00

WHITE TIGER
Marvel Comics: Jan, 2007 - No. 6, Nov, 2007 ($2.99, limited series)
1-David Mack-c; Pierce & Liebe-s/Briones-a; Spider-Man & Black Widow app.
1 3 4 6 8 10
2-6 4.00
...: A Hero's Compulsion SC (2007,$14.99) r/#1-6; re-cap art and profile page 15.00

WHITE TREES: A BLACKSAND TALE
Image Comics: Aug, 2019 - No. 2, Sept, 2019 ($4.99, limited series)
1,2-Chip Zdarsky-s/Kris Anka-a/c 5.00

WHITE WILDERNESS (Disney)
Dell Publishing Co.: No. 943, Oct, 1958
Four Color 943-Movie 6 12 18 37 66 95

WHITMAN COMIC BOOK, A
Whitman Publishing Co.: Sept., 1962 (136 pgs.; 7-3/4x5-3/4; hardcover) (B&W)
1-3,5,7: 1-Yogi Bear. 2-Huckleberry Hound. 3-Mr. Jinks and Pixie & Dixie. 5-Augie Doggie & Loopy de Loop. 7-Bugs Bunny-r from #47,51,53,54 & 55
6 12 18 41 76 110
4,6: 4-The Flintstones. 6-Snooper & Blabber Fearless Detectives/Quick Draw McGraw of the Wild West 7 14 21 44 82 120
8-Donald Duck-reprints most of WDC&S #209-213. Includes 5 Barks stories, 1 complete Mickey Mouse serial by Paul Murry & 1 Mickey Mouse serial missing the 1st episode
7 14 21 49 92 135
NOTE: *Hanna-Barbera #1-6(TV), reprints of British tabloid comics. Dell reprints-#7,8.*

GD 2.0 | VG 4.0 | FN 6.0 | VF 8.0 | VF/NM 9.0 | NM- 9.2

WHIZ COMICS (Formerly Flash & Thrill Comics #1)(See 5 Cent Comics)
Fawcett Publications: No. 2, Feb, 1940 - No. 155, June, 1953
1-(nn on cover, #2 inside)-Origin & 1st newsstand app. Captain Marvel (formerly Captain Thunder) by C. C. Beck (created by Bill Parker), Spy Smasher, Golden Arrow, Ibis the Invincible, Dan Dare, Scoop Smith, Sivana, & Lance O'Casey begin
37,500 75,000 112,500 225,000 337,500 450,000
(The only Mint copy sold in 1995 for $176,000 cash)
1-Reprint, oversize 13-1/2x10". **WARNING**: This comic is an exact duplicate reprint (except for dropping "Gangway for Captain Marvel" from-c) of the original except for its size. DC published it in 1974 with a second cover titling it as a Famous First Edition. There have been many reported cases of the outer cover being removed and the interior sold as the original edition. The reprint with the new outer cover removed is practically worthless. See Famous First Edition for value.
2-(3/40, nn on cover, #3 inside); cover to Flash #1 redrawn, pg. 12, panel 4; Spy Smasher reveals I.D. to Eve 1100 2200 3300 8400 15,200 22,000
3-(4/40, #3 on-c, #4 inside)-1st app. Beautia 514 1028 1542 3750 6625 9500
4-(5/40, #4 on cover, #5 inside)-Brief origin Capt. Marvel retold
423 846 1269 3000 5250 7500
5-Captain Marvel wears button-down flap on splash page only
377 754 1131 2639 4620 6600
6-10: 7-Dr. Voodoo begins (by Raboy-#9-22) 290 580 870 1856 3178 4500
11-14: 12-Capt. Marvel does not wear cape 213 426 639 1363 2332 3300
15-Origin Sivana; Dr. Voodoo by Raboy 213 426 639 1363 2332 3300
16-18-Spy Smasher battles Captain Marvel 239 478 717 1530 2615 3700
19-Classic shark-c 226 452 678 1446 2473 3500
20 135 270 405 864 1482 2100
21-(9/41)-Origin & 1st cover app. Lt. Marvels, the 1st team in Fawcett comics. In this issue, Capt. Death similar to Ditko's later Dr. Strange 142 284 426 909 1555 2200
22-24: 23-Only Dr. Voodoo by Tuska 110 220 330 704 1202 1700
25-(12/41)-Captain Nazi jumps from Master Comics #21 to take on Capt. Marvel solo after being beaten by Capt. Marvel/Bulletman team, causing the creation of Capt. Marvel Jr.; 1st app./origin of Capt. Marvel Jr. (part II of trilogy origin by CC. Beck & Mac Raboy); Captain Marvel sends Jr. back to Master #22 to aid Bulletman against Capt. Nazi; origin Old Shazam in text 919 1838 2757 6709 11,855 17,000
26-30 74 148 222 470 810 1150
31,32: 32-1st app. The Trolls; Hitler/Mussolini satire by Beck
63 126 189 403 689 975
33-Spy Smasher, Captain Marvel x-over on cover and inside
84 168 252 538 919 1300
34,36-40: 37-The Trolls app. by Swayze 50 100 150 315 533 750
35-Captain Marvel & Spy Smasher-c 74 148 222 470 810 1150
41-50: 42-Classic time travel-c. 43-Spy Smasher, Ibis, Golden Arrow x-over in Capt. Marvel. 44-Flag-c. 47-Origin recap (1 pg.) 42 84 126 265 445 625
51-60: 52-Capt. Marvel x-over in Ibis. 57-Spy Smasher, Golden Arrow, Ibis cameo
36 72 108 211 343 475
61-70 33 66 99 194 317 440
71,77-80 32 64 96 188 307 425
72-76-Two Captain Marvel stories in each; 76-Spy Smasher becomes Crime Smasher
33 66 99 194 317 440
81-85,87-99: 91-Infinity-c 32 64 96 188 307 425
86-Captain Marvel battles Sivana Family; robot-c 37 74 111 222 361 500
100-(8/48)-Anniversary issue 41 82 123 256 428 600
101-106: 102-Commando Yank app. 106-Bulletman app.
33 66 99 194 317 440
107-149: 107-Capitol Building photo-c. 108-Brooklyn Bridge photo-c. 112-Photo-c. 139-Infinity-c. 140-Flag-c. 142-Used in **POP**, pg. 89 34 68 102 199 325 450
150-152-(Low dist.) 41 82 123 256 428 600
153-155-(Scarce):154,155-1st/2nd Dr. Death stories 58 116 174 371 636 900
NOTE: **C.C. Beck** *Captain Marvel-No. 25(part).* **Krigstein** *Golden Arrow-No. 75, 78, 91, 95, 96, 98-100.* **Mac Raboy** *Dr. Voodoo-No. 9-22. Captain Marvel-No. 25(part).* **M.Swayze** *a-37, 38, 59; c-38.* **Schaffenberger** *c-138-155(most).* **Wolverton** *1/2 pg. "Culture Corner"-No. 65-67, 68(2 1/2 pgs), 70-85, 87-96, 98-100, 102-109, 112-121, 123, 125, 126, 128-131, 133, 134, 136, 142, 143, 146.*

WHIZ COMICS 2 (FACSIMILE EDITION)
DC Comics: 2023 ($6.99, one-shot)
2-Reprints all of Whiz Comics #1(#2) with original 1940 ads 7.00

WHIZ KIDS (Also see Big Bang Comics)
Image Comics: Apr, 2003 ($4.95, B&W, one-shot)
1-Galahad, Cyclone, Thunder Girl and Moray app.; Jeff Austin-a 5.00

	GD	VG	FN	VF	VF/NM	NM-
	2.0	4.0	6.0	8.0	9.0	9.2

WHOA, NELLIE (Also see Love & Rockets)
Fantagraphics Books: July, 1996 - No. 3, Sept, 1996 ($2.95, B&W, lim. series)
1-3: Jamie Hernandez-c/a/scripts 4.00

WHODUNIT
D.S. Publishing Co.: Aug-Sept, 1948 - No. 3, Dec-Jan, 1948-49 (#1,2: 52 pgs.)
1-Baker-a (7 pgs.) 39 78 117 231 378 525
2,3-Detective mysteries 18 36 54 107 169 230

WHODUNNIT?
Eclipse Comics: June, 1986 - No. 3, Apr, 1987 ($2.00, limited series)
1-3: Spiegle-a. 2-Gulacy-c 4.00

WHO FRAMED ROGER RABBIT (See Marvel Graphic Novel)

WHO IS NEXT?
Standard Comics: No. 5, Jan, 1953
5-Toth, Sekowsky, Andru-a; crime stories; Strangler on the Loose-c
258 516 774 1651 2826 4000

WHO'S MINDING THE MINT? (See Movie Classics)

WHO'S WHO IN STAR TREK
DC Comics: Mar, 1987 - #2, Apr, 1987 ($1.50, limited series)
1,2 1 2 3 5 6 8
NOTE: ***Byrne** a-1, 2. **Chaykin** c-1, 2. **Morrow** a-1, 2. **McFarlane** a-2. **Perez** a-1, 2. **Sutton** a-1, 2.*

WHO'S WHO IN THE LEGION OF SUPER-HEROES
DC Comics: Apr, 1987 - No. 7, Nov, 1988 ($1.25, limited series)
1-7 4.00

WHO'S WHO: THE DEFINITIVE DIRECTORY OF THE DC UNIVERSE
DC Comics: Mar, 1985 - No. 26, Apr, 1987 (Maxi-series, no ads)
1-DC heroes from A-Z 4.00
2-26: All have 1-2 pgs-a by most DC artists 4.00
NOTE: ***Art Adams** a-4, 11, 18, 20. **Anderson** a-1-5, 7-12, 14, 15, 19, 21, 23-25. **Aparo** a-2, 3, 9, 10, 12, 13, 14, 15, 17, 18, 21, 23. **Byrne** a-4, 7, 14, 16, 18i, 19, 22i, 24; c-22. **Cowan** a-3-5, 8, 10-13, 16-18, 22-25. **Ditko** a-19-22. **Evans** a-20. **Giffen** a-1, 3,-6, 8, 13, 15, 17, 18, 23. **Grell** a-6, 9, 14, 20, 23, 25, 26. **Infantino** a-1-10, 12, 15, 17-22, 24, 25. **Kaluta** a-14, 21. **Gil Kane** a-1-11, 13, 14, 16, 19, 21-23, 25. **Kirby** a-2-6, 8-18, 20, 22, 25. **Kubert** a-2, 3, 7-11, 19, 20, 25. **Erik Larsen** a-24. **McFarlane** a-10-12, 17, 19, 25, 26. **Morrow** a-4, 7, 25, 26. **Orlando** a-1, 4, 10, 11, 21i. **Perez** a-1-5, 8-19, 22-26; c-1-4, 13-18. **Rogers** a-1, 2, 5-7, 11, 12, 15, 24. **Starlin** a-13, 14, 16. **Stevens** a-4, 7, 18.*

WHO'S WHO UPDATE '87
DC Comics: Aug, 1987 - No. 5, Dec, 1987 ($1.25, limited series)
1-5: Contains art by most DC artists 4.00
NOTE: ***Giffen** a-1. **McFarlane** a-1-4; c-4. **Perez** a-1-4.*

WHO'S WHO UPDATE '88
DC Comics: Aug, 1988 - No. 4, Nov, 1988 ($1.25, limited series)
1-4: Contains art by most DC artists 4.00
NOTE: ***Giffen** a-1. **Erik Larsen** a-1.*

WICKED, THE
Avalon Studios: Dec, 1999 - No. 7, Aug, 2000 ($2.95)
Preview-(7/99, $5.00, B&W) 5.00
1-7-Anacleto-c/Martinez-a 4.00
...: Medusa's Tale (11/00, $3.95, one shot) story plus pin-up gallery 4.00
...: Vol. 1: Omnibus (2003, $19.95) r/#0-8; Drew-c 20.00

WICKED + THE DIVINE, THE
Image Comics: Jun, 2014 - No. 45, Sept, 2019 ($3.50/$3.99)
1-25: 1-Gillen-s/McKelvie-a. 12-Kate Brown-a. 13-Lotay-a. 15-Hans-a. 23-Wada-a 3.50
26-45-($3.99) 4.00
... Christmas Annual (12/17, $3.99) Art by Anka, Clugston, McNeil 4.00
455 One-Shot (5/17, $3.99) Set in 455 AD Rome; André Araújo-a 4.00
1373 One-Shot (9/18, $3.99) Set in 1373; Ryan Kelly-a; Lucifer during the Black Death 4.00
1831 One-Shot (9/16, $3.99) Set in 1831; Stephanie Hans-a 4.00
1923 One-Shot (2/18, $4.99) Set in 1923; Aud Koch-a 5.00
...: The Funnies 1 (11/18, $3.99) Short humor stories by various incl. Zdarsky 5.00

WICKED THINGS
BOOM! Studios: Mar, 2020 - Present ($3.99)
1-5-John Allison-s/Max Sarin-a; intro. Charlotte Grote 4.00

WIDOWMAKER
Marvel Comics: Feb, 2011 - No. 4, Apr, 2011 ($3.99, limited series)
1-4-Black Widow, Hawkeye & Mockingbird app. 1,2-Jae Lee-c. 3,4-Noto-c 4.00

WIDOWMAKERS: RED GUARDIAN AND YELENA BELOVA
Marvel Comics: Jan, 2021 ($3.99, one-shot)
1-Devin Grayson-s/Michele Bandini-a 4.00

WIDOW WARRIORS
Dynamite Entertainment: 2010 - No. 4, 2010 ($3.99, limited series)
1-4-Pat Lee-a/c 4.00

WILBUR COMICS (Teen-age) (Also see Laugh Comics, Laugh Comix, Liberty Comics #10 & Zip Comics)
MLJ Magazines/Archie Publ. No. 8, Spring, 1946 on: Sum', 1944 - No. 87, 11/59; No. 88, 9/63; No. 89, 10/64; No. 90, 10/65 (No. 1-46: 52 pgs.) (#1-11 are quarterly)
1 81 162 243 518 884 1250
2(Fall, 1944) 42 84 126 265 445 625
3,4(Wint, '44-45; Spr, '45) 32 64 96 188 307 425
5-1st app. Katy Keene (Sum, '45) & begin series; Wilbur story same as Archie story in Archie #1 except Wilbur replaces Archie 300 600 900 1950 3375 4800
6-10: 10-(Fall, 1946) 37 74 111 222 361 500
11-20 20 40 60 118 192 265
21-30: 30-(4/50) 15 30 45 83 124 165
31-50 13 26 39 72 101 130
51-70 10 20 30 58 79 100
71-90: 88-Last 10¢ issue (9/63) 5 10 15 34 60 85
NOTE: *Katy Keene in No. 5-56, 58-61, 63-69. **Al Fagaly** c-6-9, 12-24 at least. **Vigoda** c-2.*

WILD
Atlas Comics (IPC): Feb, 1954 - No. 5, Aug, 1954
1 41 82 123 256 428 600
2 25 50 75 150 245 340
3-5 22 44 66 132 216 300
NOTE: ***Berg** a-5; c-4. **Burgos** a-5, c-2,3. **Colan** a-4. **Everett** a-1-3. **Heath** a-2, 3, 5. **Maneely** a-1-3, 5; c-1, 5. **Post** a-2, 5. **Ed Win** a-1, 3.*

WILD! (This Magazine Is...) (Satire)
Dell Publishing Co.: Jan, 1968 - No. 3, 1968 (35¢, magazine, 52 pgs.)
1-3: Hogan's Heroes, The Rat Patrol & Mission Impossible TV spoofs
3 6 9 16 23 30

WILD ANIMALS
Pacific Comics: Dec, 1982 ($1.00, one-shot, direct sales)
1-Funny animal; Sergio Aragonés-a; Shaw-c/a 4.00

WILD BILL ELLIOTT (Also see Western Roundup under Dell Giants)
Dell Publishing Co.: No. 278, 5/50 - No. 643, 7/55 (No #11,12) (All photo-c)
Four Color 278 (#1, 52 pgs.)-Titled "Bill Elliott"; Bill & his horse Stormy begin; photo front/back-c begin 13 26 39 89 195 300
2 (11/50), 3 (52 pgs.) 7 14 21 44 82 120
4-10 (10-12/52) 5 10 15 35 63 90
Four Color 472 (6/53), 520(12/53)-Last photo back-c 5 10 15 35 63 90
13 (4-6/54) - 17 (4-6/55) 5 10 15 30 50 70
Four Color 643 (7/55) 5 10 15 33 57 80

WILD BILL HICKOK (Also see Blazing Sixguns)
Avon Periodicals: Sept-Oct, 1949 - No. 28, May-June, 1956
1-Ingels-c 36 72 108 211 343 475
2-Painted-c; Kit West app. 18 36 54 105 165 225
3-5-Painted-c (4-Cover by Howard Winfield) 14 28 42 78 112 145
6-10,12: 8-10-Painted-c. 12-Kinsler-c? 14 28 42 76 108 140
11,13,14-Kinstler-c/a (#11-c & inside-f/c art only) 14 28 42 80 115 150
15,17,18,20: 18-Kit West story. 20-Kit West by Larsen
12 24 36 69 97 125
16-Kamen-a; r-3 stories/King of the Badmen of Deadwood
13 26 39 72 101 130
19-Meskin-a 12 24 36 69 97 125
21-Reprints 2 stories/Chief Crazy Horse 11 22 33 62 86 110
22-McCann-a?; r/Sheriff Bob Dixon's... 11 22 33 62 86 110
23-27: 23-Kinstler-c. 24-27-Kinstler-c/a(r) (24,25-r?) 11 22 33 62 86 110
28-Kinstler-c/a (new); r-/Last of the Comanches 11 22 33 64 90 115
I.W. Reprint #1-r/#2; Kinstler-c 2 4 6 9 13 16
Super Reprint #10-12: 10-r/#18. 11-r/#?. 12-r/#8 2 4 6 9 13 16
NOTE: *#23, 25 contain numerous editing deletions in both art and script due to code. **Kinstler** c-6, 7, 11-14, 17, 18, 20-22, 24-28. **Howard Larsen** a-1, 2, 4, 5, 6(3), 7-9, 11, 12, 17, 18, 20-24, 26. **Meskin** a-7. **Reinman** a-6, 17.*

WILD BILL HICKOK AND JINGLES (TV)(Formerly Cowboy Western) (Also see Blue Bird)
Charlton Comics: No. 68, Aug, 1958 - No. 75, Dec, 1959
68,69-Williamson-a (all are 10¢ issues) 11 22 33 60 83 105
70-Two pgs. Williamson-a 8 16 24 42 54 65
71-75 (#76, exist?) 6 12 18 28 34 40

WILD BILL PECOS WESTERN (Also see The Westerner)
AC Comics: 1989 ($3.50, 1/2 color, 1/2 B&W, 52 pgs.)
1-Syd Shores-c/a(r)/Westerner; photo back-c 4.00

WILD BOY OF THE CONGO (Also see Approved Comics)
Ziff-Davis No. 10-12,4-8/St. John No. 9,11 on: No. 10, 2-3/51 - No. 12, 8-9/51; No. 4, 10-11/51 - No. 9, 10/53; No. 11-#15,6/55 (No #10, 1953)
10(#1)(2-3/51)-Origin; bondage-c by Saunders (painted); used in **SOTI**, pg. 189; painted-c begin thru #9 (except #7) 37 74 111 222 361 500
11(4-5/51),12(8-9/51)-Norman Saunders painted-c 20 40 60 118 192 265
4(10-11/51)-Saunders painted bondage-c 19 38 57 112 179 245
5(Winter,'51)-Saunders painted-c 15 30 45 94 147 200
6,8,9(10/53): Painted-c. 6-Saunders-c 15 30 45 94 147 200
7(8-9/52)-Kinstler-a 19 38 57 111 176 240
11-13-Baker-c. 11-r/#7 w/new Baker-c; Kinstler-a (2 pgs.)
97 194 291 621 1061 1500
14(4/55)-Baker-c; r-#12('51) 100 200 300 635 1093 1550
15(6/55)-Baker-c 58 116 174 371 636 900

WILD CARDS: THE DRAWING OF CARDS (George R. R. Martin)
Marvel Comics: Sept, 2022 - No. 4, Dec, 2022 ($4.99)
1-4: 1,2-Cornell-s/Hawthorne-a. 3-Balám-a 5.00

WILDCAT (See Sensation Comics #1)

WILDC.A.T.S ADVENTURES (TV cartoon)
Image Comics (WildStorm): Sept, 1994 - No. 10, June, 1995 ($1.95/$2.50)
1-10: 1,2-Templeton-c. 2,3-Templeton-a. 4,5-Joe Phillips-a. 7,9-Wieringo-c 4.00
Sourcebook 1 (1/95, $2.95) Jeff Smith-c; art by Hamner, Phillips, Staton, Stelfreeze 4.00

WILDC.A.T.S: COVERT ACTION TEAMS (Also see Alan Moore's... for TPB reprints)
Image Comics (WildStorm Productions): Aug, 1992 - No. 4, Mar, 1993; No. 5, Nov, 1993 - No. 50, June, 1998 ($1.95/$2.50)
1-1st app; Jim Lee/Williams-c/a & Lee scripts begin; contains 2 trading cards (Two diff versions of cards inside); 1st WildStorm Productions title
2 4 6 8 10 12
1-All gold foil signed edition 3 6 9 19 30 40
1-All gold foil unsigned edition 3 6 9 16 23 30
1-Newsstand edition w/o cards 4.00
1-"3-D Special"(8/97, $4.95) w/3-D glasses; variant-c by Jim Lee. 5.00
2-($2.50)-Prism foil stamped-c; contains coupon for Image Comics #0 & 4 pg. preview to Portacio's Wetworks (back-up) 5.00
2-With coupon missing 2.00
2-Direct sale misprint w/o foil-c 5.00
2-Newsstand ed., no prism or coupon 3.00
3-Lee/Liefeld-c (1/93-c, 12/92 inside) 4.00
4-($2.50)-Polybagged w/Topps trading card; 1st app. Tribe by Johnson & Stroman; Youngblood cameo 4.00
4-Variant w/red card 6.00
5-7-Jim Lee/Williams-c/a; Lee script 3.00

The Wicked + The Divine #28 © Gillen

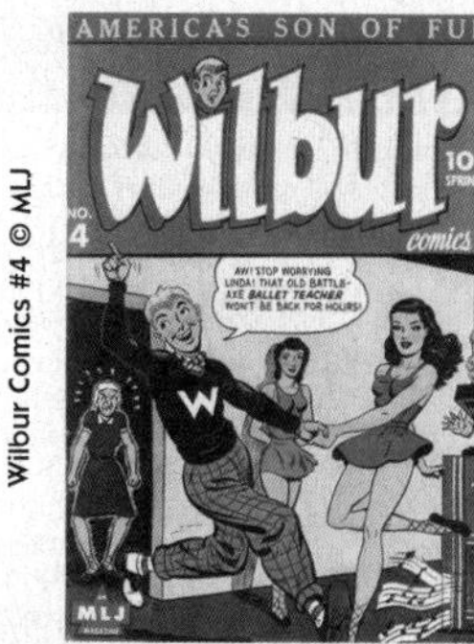

Wilbur Comics #4 © MLJ

Wildcats V4 #1 © WSP

GD 2.0 | VG 4.0 | FN 6.0 | VF 8.0 | VF/NM 9.0 | NM- 9.2

8-X-Men's Jean Grey & Scott Summers cameo 4.00
9-12: 10-1st app. Huntsman & Soldier; Claremont scripts begin, ends #13.
11-1st app. Savant, Tapestry & Mr. Majestic. 3.00
11-Alternate Portacio-c, see Deathblow #5 5.00
13-19,21-24: 15-James Robinson scripts begin, ends #20. 15,16-Black Razor story. 21-Alan Moore scripts begin, end #34; intro Tao & Ladytron; new WildC.A.T.S team forms (Mr. Majestic, Savant, Condition Red (Max Cash), Tao & Ladytron). 22-Maguire-a 3.00
20-($2.50)-Direct Market, WildStorm Rising Pt. 2 w/bound-in card 4.00
20-($1.95)-Newsstand, WildStorm Rising Part 2 3.00
25-($4.95)-Alan Moore script; wraparound foil-c. 5.00
26-49: 29-(5/96)-Fire From Heaven Pt 7; reads Apr on-c. 30-(6/96)-Fire From Heaven Pt. 13; Spartan revealed to have transplanted personality of John Colt (from Team One: WildC.A.T.S). 31-(9/96)-Grifter rejoins team; Ladytron dies 3.00
40-($3.50)Voyager Pack bagged w/Divine Right preview 5.00
50-($3.50) Stories by Robinson/Lee, Choi & Peterson/Benes, and Moore/Charest; Charest sketchbook; Lee wraparound-c 4.00
50-Chromium cover 6.00
Annual 1 (2/98, $2.95) Robinson-s 4.00
Compendium (1993, $9.95)-r/#1-4; bagged w/#0 15.00
Sourcebook 1 (9/93, $2.50)-Foil embossed-c 3.00
Sourcebook 1-($1.95)-Newsstand ed. w/o foil embossed-c 3.00
Sourcebook 2 (11/94, $2.50)-wraparound-c 3.00
Special 1 (11/93, $3.50, 52 pgs.)-1st Travis Charest WildC.A.T.S-a 4.00
...A Gathering of Eagles (5/97, $9.95, TPB) r/#10-12 10.00
.../ Cyberforce: Killer Instinct TPB (2004, $14.95) r/#5-7 & Cyberforce V2 #1-3 15.00
...Gang War ('98, $16.95, TPB) r/#28-34 17.00
...Homecoming (8/98, $19.95, TPB) r/#21-27 20.00
James Robinson's Complete Wildc.a.t.s TPB (2009, $24.99) r/#15-20,50; Annual 1, WildStorm Rising #1, Team One Wildc.a.t.s #1,2; cover and pin-up gallery 25.00

WILDCATS (3rd series)
DC Comics (WildStorm): Mar, 1999 - No. 28, Dec, 2001 ($2.50)

1-Charest-a; six covers by Lee, Adams, Bisley, Campbell, Madureira and Ramos; Lobdell-s 4.00
1-($6.95) DF Edition; variant cover by Ramos 7.00
2-28: 2-Voodoo cover. 3-Bachalo variant-c. 5-Hitch-a/variant-c. 7-Meglia-a. 8-Phillips-a begins. 17-J.G. Jones-c. 18,19-Jim Lee-c. 20,21-Dillon-a 3.00
Annual 2000 (12/00, $3.50) Bermejo-a; Devil's Night x-over 4.00
...: Battery Park ('03, $17.95, TPB) r/#20-28; Phillips-c 18.00
... Ladytron (10/00, $5.95) Origin; Casey-s/Canete-a 6.00
... Mosaic (2/00, $3.95) Tuska-a (10 pg. back-up story) 4.00
...: Serial Boxes ('01, $14.95, TPB) r/#14-19; Phillips-c 15.00
...: Street Smart ('00, $24.95, HC) r/#1-6; Charest-c 25.00
...: Street Smart ('02, $14.95, SC) r/#1-6; Charest-c 15.00
...: Vicious Circles ('00, $14.95, TPB) r/#8-13; Phillips-c 15.00

WILDCATS (Volume 4)
DC Comics (WildStorm): Dec, 2006 ($2.99)

1-Grant Morrison-s/Jim Lee-a; Jim Lee-c 3.00
1-Variant-c by Todd McFarlane/Jim Lee 6.00
...: Armageddon 1 (2/08, $2.99) Gage-s/Caldwell-a 3.00

WILDCATS (Volume 5) (World's End on cover for #1,2)
DC Comics (WildStorm): Sept, 2008 - No. 30, Feb, 2011 ($2.99)

1-30: 1-Christos Gage-s/Neil Googe-a. 5-Woods-a 3.00
...: Family Secrets TPB (2010, $17.99) r/#8-12 18.00
...: World's End TPB (2009, $17.99) r/#1-7 18.00

WILDC.A.T.S (Volume 6)
DC Comics: Jan, 2023 - Present ($3.99)

1-5: 1-Rosenberg-s/Segovia-a; Fairchild app. 5-Superman app. 4.00

WILDC.A.T.S/ ALIENS
Image Comics/Dark Horse: Aug, 1998 ($4.95, one-shot)

1-Ellis-s/Sprouse-a/c; Aliens invade Skywatch; Stormwatch app.; death of Winter; destruction of Skywatch 1 2 3 5 6 8
1-Variant-c by Gil Kane 1 3 4 6 8 10

WILDCATS: NEMESIS
DC Comics (WildStorm): Nov, 2005 - No. 9, July, 2006 ($2.99, limited series)

1-9: 1-Robbie Morrison-s/Talent Caldwell & Horacio Domingues-a/Caldwell-c 3.00
TPB (2006, $19.99) r/#1-9; cover gallery 20.00

WILDC.A.T.S: SAVANT GARDE FAN EDITION
Image Comics/WildStorm Productions: Feb, 1997 - No. 3, Apr, 1997 (Giveaway, 8 pgs.) (Polybagged w/Overstreet's FAN)

1-3: Barbara Kesel-s/Christian Uche-a(p) 4.00
1-3-(Gold): All retailer incentives 10.00

WILDC.A.T.S TRILOGY
Image Comics (WildStorm Productions): June, 1993 - No. 3, Dec, 1993 ($1.95, lim. series)

1-($2.50)-1st app. Gen 13 (Fairchild, Burnout, Grunge, Freefall) Multi-color foil-c; Jae Lee-c/a in all 6.00
1-($1.95)-Newsstand ed. w/o foil-c 4.00
2,3-($1.95)-Jae Lee-c/a 4.00

WILDCATS VERSION 3.0
DC Comics (WildStorm): Oct, 2002 - No. 24, Oct, 2004 ($2.95)

1-24: 1-Casey-s/Nguyen-a; two covers by Nguyen and Rian Hughes and Nguyen. 8-Back-up preview of The Authority: High Stakes pt. 3 3.00
...: Brand Building TPB (2003, $14.95) r/#1-6 15.00
...: Full Disclosure TPB (2004, $14.95) r/#7-12 15.00
...: Year One TPB (2010, $24.99) r/#1-12 25.00
...: Year Two TPB (2011, $24.99) r/#13-24 25.00

WILDC.A.T.S/ X-MEN: THE GOLDEN AGE (See also X-Men/WildC.A.T.S.: The Dark Age)
Image Comics (WildStorm Productions): Feb, 1997 ($4.50, one-shot)

1-Lobdell-s/Charest-a; Two covers (Charest, Jim Lee) 5.00
1-"3-D" Edition ($6.50) w/glasses 7.00

WILDC.A.T.S/ X-MEN: THE MODERN AGE
Image Comics (WildStorm Productions): Aug, 1997 ($4.50, one-shot)

1-Robinson-s/Hughes-a; Two covers (Hughes, Paul Smith) 5.00
1-"3-D" Edition ($6.50) w/glasses 7.00

WILDC.A.T.S/ X-MEN: THE SILVER AGE
Image Comics (WildStorm Productions): June, 1997 ($4.50, one-shot)

1-Lobdell-s/Jim Lee-a; Two covers(Neal Adams, Jim Lee) 5.00
1-"3-D" Edition ($6.50) w/glasses 7.00

WILDCORE
Image Comics (WildStorm Prods.): Nov, 1997 - No. 10, Dec, 1998 ($2.50)

1-10: 1-Two covers (Booth/McWeeney, Charest) 3.00
1-($3.50)-Voyager Pack w/DV8 preview 4.00
1-Chromium-c 5.00

WILD DOG
DC Comics: Sept, 1987 - No. 4, Dec, 1987 (75¢, limited series)

1-4 3.00
Special 1 (1989, $2.50, 52 pgs.) 4.00

WILDERNESS TREK (See Zane Grey, Four Color 333)

WILDFIRE (See Zane Grey, FourColor 433)

WILDFIRE
Image Comics (Top Cow): Jun, 2014 - No. 4, Oct, 2014 ($3.99, limited series)

1-4-Matt Hawkins-s/Linda Sejic-a 4.00

WILD FRONTIER (Cheyenne Kid #8 on)
Charlton Comics: Oct, 1955 - No. 7, Apr, 1957

1-Davy Crockett 12 24 36 67 94 120
2-6-Davy Crockett in all 8 16 24 42 54 65
7-Origin & 1st app. Cheyenne Kid 9 18 27 52 69 85

WILD GIRL
DC Comics (WildStorm): Jan, 2005 - No. 6, Jun, 2005 ($2.95/$2.99)

1-6-Leah Moore & John Reppion-s/Shawn McManus-a/c 3.00

WILDGUARD: CASTING CALL
Image Comics: Sept, 2003 - No. 6, Feb, 2004 ($2.95)

1-6: 1-Nauck-s/a; two covers by Nauck and McGuinness. 2-Wieringo var-c. 6-Noto var-c 3.00
... Vol. 1: Casting Call (1/05, $17.95, TPB) r/#1-6; cover gallery; Todd Nauck bio 18.00
Wildguard: Fire Power 1 (12/04, $3.50) Nauck-a; two covers 3.50
Wildguard: Fool's Gold (7/05 - No. 2, 7/05, $3.50) 1,2-Todd Nauck-s/a 3.50
Wildguard: Insider (5/08 - No. 3, 7/08, $3.50) 1-3-Todd Nauck-s/a 3.50

WILD'S END
BOOM! Studios: Sept, 2014 - No. 6, Feb, 2015 ($3.99, limited series)

1-6-Dan Abnett-s/I.N.J. Culbard-a/c 4.00

WILD'S END: THE ENEMY WITHIN
BOOM! Studios: Sept, 2015 - No. 6, Feb, 2016 ($3.99, limited series)

1-6-Dan Abnett-s/I.N.J. Culbard-a/c 4.00

WILDSIDERZ
DC Comics (WildStorm): No. 0, Aug, 2005 - No. 2, Jan, 2006 ($1.99/$3.50)

0-(8/05, $1.99) Series preview & character profiles; J. Scott Campbell-a 3.00
1,2: 1-(10/05, $3.50) J. Scott Campbell-s/a; Andy Hartnell-s 3.50

WILDSTAR (Also see The Dragon & The Savage Dragon)

Image Comics (Highbrow Entertainment): Sept, 1995 - No. 3, Jan, 1996 ($2.50, lim. series)
1-3: Al Gordon scripts; Jerry Ordway-c/a 3.00

WILDSTAR: SKY ZERO
Image Comics (Highbrow Entertainment): Mar, 1993 - No. 4, Nov, 1993 ($1.95, lim. series)
1-4: 1-($2.50)-Embossed-c w/silver ink; Ordway-c/a in all 3.00
1-($1.95)-Newsstand ed. w/silver ink-c, not embossed 3.00
1-Gold variant 6.00

WILD STARS
Collector's Edition/Little Rocket Productions: Summer, 1984 - Present (B&W)
Vol. 1 #1 (Summer 1984, $1.50) 5.00
Vol. 2 #1 (Winter 1988, $1.95) Foil-c; die-cut front & back-c 5.00
Vol. 3: #1-6-Brunner-c; Tierney-s. 1,2-Brewer-a. 3-6-Simons-a 3.00
7-($5.95) Simons-a 6.00
TPB (2004, $17.95) r/Vol. 1-3 18.00

WILDSTORM
Image Comics/DC Comics (WildStorm Publishing): 1994 - 2009 (one-shots, TPBs)
... After the Fall TPB (2009, $19.99) r/back-up stories from Wildcats V5 #1-11, The Authority V5 #1-11; Gen 13 V4 #21-28, and Stormwatch: PHD #13-20 20.00
...Annual 2000 (12/00, $3.50) Devil's Night x-over; Moy-a 4.00
...: Armageddon TPB (2008, $17.99) r/Armageddon one-shots in Midnighter, Welcome To Tranquility, Wetworks, Gen13, Stormwatch PHD, and Wildcats titles 18.00
...Chamber of Horrors (10/95, $3.50)-Bisley-c 4.00
...Fine Arts: Spotlight on Gen13 (2/08, $3.50) art and covers with commentary 3.50
...Fine Arts: Spotlight on Jim Lee (2/07, $3.50) art and covers by Lee with commentary 3.50
...Fine Arts: Spotlight on J. Scott Campbell (5/07, $3.50) art and covers with commentary 3.50
...Fine Arts: Spotlight on The Authority (1/08, $3.50) art and covers with commentary 3.50
...Fine Arts: Spotlight on WildCATs (3/08, $3.50) art and covers with commentary 3.50
...Fine Arts: The Gallery Collection (12/98, $19.95) Lee-c 20.00
...Halloween 1 (10/97, $2.50) Warner-c 3.00
...Rarities 1(12/94, $4.95, 52 pgs.)-r/Gen 13 1/2 & other stories 5.00
...Summer Special 1 (2001, $5.95) Short stories by various; Hughes-c 6.00
...Swimsuit Special 1 (12/94, $2.95), ...Swimsuit Special 2 (1995, $2.50) 3.00
...Swimsuit Special '97 #1 (7/97, $2.50) 3.00
... 30th Anniversary Special 1 (1/23, $7.99) Short stories & pin-ups by various; Jim Lee-c 8.00
...Thunderbook 1 (10/00, $6.95) Short stories by various incl. Hughes, Moy 7.00
...Ultimate Sports 1 (8/97, $2.50) 3.00
...Universe Sourcebook (5/95, $2.50) 3.00
...Universe 2008 Convention Exclusive ('08, no cover price) preview of World's End x-over 3.00

WILDSTORM!
Image Comics (WildStorm): Aug, 1995 - No. 4, Nov, 1995 ($2.50, B&W/color, anthology)
1-4: 1-Simonson-a 3.00

WILD STORM, THE
DC Comics (WildStorm): Apr, 2017 - No. 24, Sept, 2019 ($3.99)
1-24-Warren Ellis-s/Jon Davis-Hunt-a; Zealot and the Engineer app. 19-New Apollo & Midnighter 4.00

WILD STORM: MICHAEL CRAY, THE
DC Comics (WildStorm): Dec, 2017 - No. 12, Dec. 2018 ($3.99)
1-12: 1-Bryan Hill-s/N. Steven Harris-a; Oliver Queen app. 8-10,12-Constantine app. 4.00

WILDSTORM PRESENTS: ...
DC Comics (WildStorm): Jan, 2011 - Feb, 2011 ($7.99, squarebound, reprints)
1-(1/11) r/short stories by various incl. Pearson, Conner, Corben, Jeanty, Mahnke 8.00
Planetary: Lost Worlds (2/11) r/Planetary/Authority & Planetary/JLA: Terra Occulta 8.00

WILDSTORM REVELATIONS
DC Comics (WildStorm): Mar, 2008 - No. 6, May, 2008 ($2.99, limited series)
1-6-Beatty & Gage-s/Craig-a. 2-The Authority app. 3.00
TPB (2008, $17.99) r/#1-6; cover sketches 18.00

WILDSTORM RISING
Image Comics (WildStorm Publishing): May, 1995 - No.2, June, 1995 ($1.95/$2.50)
1-($2.50)-Direct Market, WildStorm Rising Pt. 1 w/bound-in card 3.00
1-($1.95)-Newstand, WildStorm Rising Pt. 1 3.00
2-($2.50)-Direct Market, WildStorm Rising Pt. 10 w/bound-in card; continues in WildC.A.T.S #21. 3.00
2-($1.95)-Newstand, WildStorm Rising Pt. 10 3.00
Trade paperback (1996, $19.95)-Collects x-over; B. Smith-c 20.00

WILDSTORM SPOTLIGHT
Image Comics (WildStorm Publishing): Feb, 1997 - No. 4 ($2.50)
1-4: 1-Alan Moore-s 3.00

WILDSTORM UNIVERSE '97
Image Comics (WildStorm Publishing): Dec, 1996 - No. 3 ($2.50, limited series)
1-3: 1-Wraparound-c. 3-Gary Frank-c 3.00

WILDTHING
Marvel Comics UK: Apr, 1993 - No. 7, Oct, 1993 ($1.75)
1-($2.50)-Embossed-c; Venom & Carnage cameo 5.00
2-7: 2-Spider-Man & Venom. 6-Mysterio app. 4.00

WILD THING (Wolverine's daughter in the M2 universe)
Marvel Comics: Oct, 1999 - No. 5, Feb, 2000 ($1.99)
1-5: 1-Lim-a in all. 2-Two covers 3.00
Wizard #0 supplement; battles the Hulk 3.00
Spider-Girl Presents Wild Thing. Crash Course (2007, $7.99, digest) r/#0-5 8.00

WILDTIMES
DC Comics (WildStorm Productions): Aug, 1999 ($2.50, one-shots)
...Deathblow #1 -set in 1899; Edwards-a; Jonah Hex app., ...DV8 #1 -set in 1944; Altieri-s/p; Sgt. Rock app., ...Gen13 #1 -set in 1969; Casey-s/Johnson-a; Teen Titans app., ...Grifter #1 -set in 1923; Paul Smith-a, ...Wetworks #1 -Waid-s/Lopresti-a; Superman app. 3.00
...WildC.A.T.s #0 -Wizard supplement; Charest-c 3.00

WILD WEST (Wild Western #3 on)
Marvel Comics (WFP): Spring, 1948 - No. 2, July, 1948
1-Two-Gun Kid, Arizona Annie, & Tex Taylor begin; Shores-c 41 82 123 256 428 600
2-Captain Tootsie by Beck; Shores-c 32 64 96 188 307 425

WILD WEST (Black Fury #1-57)
Charlton Comics: V2#58, Nov, 1966
V2#58 2 4 6 11 16 20

WILD WEST C.O.W.-BOYS OF MOO MESA (TV)
Archie Comics: Dec, 1992 - No. 3, Feb, 1993 (limited series)
V2#1, Mar, 1993 - No. 3, July, 1993 ($1.25)
1-3,V2#1-3 3.00

WILD WESTERN (Formerly Wild West #1,2)
Marvel/Atlas (WFP): No. 3, 9/48 - No. 57, 9/57 (3-11: 52 pgs, 12-on: 36 pgs)
3(#1)-Tex Morgan begins; Two-Gun Kid, Tex Taylor, & Arizona Annie continue from Wild West 34 68 102 204 332 460
4-Last Arizona Annie; Captain Tootsie by Beck; Kid Colt app. 25 50 75 150 245 340
5-2nd app. Black Rider (1/49); Blaze Carson, Captain Tootsie (by Beck) app. 29 58 87 172 281 390
6-8: 6-Blaze Carson app; anti-Wertham editorial 17 34 51 98 154 210
9-Photo-c; Black Rider app., also in #11-19 22 44 66 128 209 290
10-Charles Starrett photo-c 24 48 72 140 230 320
11-(Last 52 pg. issue) The Prairie Kid app. 19 38 57 111 176 240
12-14,16-19: All Black Rider-c/stories. 12-14-The Prairie Kid & his horse Fury app. 20 40 60 117 189 260
15-Red Larabee, Gunhawk (origin), his horse Blaze, & Apache Kid begin, end #22; Black Rider-c/story 21 42 63 126 206 285
20-30: 20-Kid Colt-c begin. 24-Has 2 Kid Colt stories. 26-1st app. The Ringo Kid? (2/53); 4 pg. story. 30-Katz-a 14 28 42 82 121 160
31-40 11 22 33 67 94 120
41-47,49-51,53,57 11 22 33 60 83 105
48-Williamson/Torres-a (4 pgs); Drucker-a 14 28 42 76 108 140
52-Crandall-a 13 26 39 72 101 130
54,55-Williamson-a in both (5 & 4 pgs.), #54 with Mayo plus 2 text illos 14 28 42 81 118 155
56-Baker-a? 14 28 42 80 115 150

NOTE: *Annie Oakley in #46, 47. Apache Kid in #15-22, 39. Arizona Kid in #21, 23. Arrowhead in #34-39. Black Rider in #5, 8-19, 33-44. Fighting Texan in #17. Kid Colt in #4-6, 8-11, 20-47, 51, 52, 54-56. Outlaw Kid in #43. Red Hawkins in #13, 14. Ringo Kid in #26, 39, 41, 43, 44, 46, 47, 50-56. Tex Morgan in #3, 4, 6, 9, 11. Tex Taylor in #3-6, 9, 11. Texas Kid in #23-25. Two-Gun Kid in #3-6, 8, 9, 11, 12, 33-39, 41. Wyatt Earp in #47.* ***Ayers*** *a-41, 42, 53, 54.* ***Berg*** *a-26; c-24.* ***Colan*** *a-49.* ***Forte*** *a-28, 30.* ***Al Hartley*** *a-16, 51.* ***Heath*** *a-4, 5, 8; c-34, 44.* ***Keller*** *a-24, 26(2), 29-40, 44-46, 48, 51, 52.* ***Maneely*** *a-10, 12, 15, 16, 28, 35, 38, 40-45; c-11, 18-22, 33, 35, 36, 38-42, 45, 51, 53, 54, 56, 57.* ***Morisi*** *a-23, 52.* ***Pakula*** *a-42, 52.* ***Powell*** *a-51.* ***Romita*** *a-24(2).* ***Severin*** *a-46, 47; c-48.* ***Shores*** *a-3, 5, 30, 31, 33, 35, 36, 38, 41; c-3-5.* ***Sinnott*** *a-34-39.* ***Wildey*** *a-43. Bondage c-19.*

WILD WESTERN ACTION (Also see The Bravados)
Skywald Publ. Corp.: Mar, 1971 - No. 3, June, 1971 (25¢, reprints, 52 pgs.)
1-Durango Kid, Straight Arrow-r; with all references to "Straight" in story relettered to "Swift"; Bravados begin; Shores-a (new) 3 6 9 16 24 32
2,3: 2-Billy Nevada, Durango Kid. 3-Red Mask, Durango Kid 2 4 6 13 18 22

WILD WESTERN ROUNDUP
Red Top/Decker Publications/I. W. Enterprises: Oct, 1957; 1960-'61
1(1957)-Kid Cowboy-r 5 10 15 24 29 34
I.W. Reprint #1('60-61)-r/#1 by Red Top 2 4 6 9 13 16

WILD WEST RODEO
Star Publications: 1953 (15¢)
1-A comic book coloring book with regular full color cover & B&W inside 12 24 36 67 94 120

WILD WILD WEST, THE (TV)
Gold Key: June, 1966 - No. 7, Oct, 1969 (All have Robert Conrad photo-c)
1-McWilliams-a 12 24 36 82 179 275
1-Variant edition with photo back-c (scarce) 13 26 39 86 188 290
2-Robert Conrad photo-c; McWilliams-a 8 16 24 52 99 145
2-Variant edition with Conrad photo back-c (scarce) 9 18 27 59 117 175
3-7 6 12 18 42 79 115
3-Variant edition with photo back-c (scarce) 8 16 24 56 108 160

WILD, WILD WEST, THE (TV)
Millennium Publications: Oct, 1990 - No. 4, Jan?, 1991 ($2.95, limited series)
1-4-Based on TV show 3.00

WILKIN BOY (See That...)

WILL EISNER READER
Kitchen Sink Press: 1991 ($9.95, B&W, 8 1/2" x 11", TPB)
nn-Reprints stories from Will Eisner's Quarterly; Eisner-s/a/c 15.00
nn-(DC Comics, 10/00, $9.95) 10.00

WILL EISNER'S JOHN LAW: ANGELS AND ASHES, DEVILS AND DUST
IDW Publ.: Apr, 2006 - No. 4 ($3.99, B&W, limited series)
1-New stories with Will Eisner's characters; Gary Chaloner-s/a 4.00

WILLIE COMICS (Formerly Ideal #1-4; Crime Cases #24 on; Li'l Willie #20 & 21)
(See Gay Comics, Laugh, Millie The Model & Wisco)
Marvel Comics (MgPC): #5, Fall, 1946 - #19, 4/49; #22, 1/50 - #23, 5/50 (No #20 & 21)
5(#1)-George, Margie, Nellie the Nurse & Willie begin 47 94 141 296 498 700
6,8,9 27 54 81 162 266 370
7(1),10,11-Kurtzman's "Hey Look" 28 56 84 168 274 380
12,14-18,22,23 25 50 75 150 245 340
13,19-Kurtzman's "Hey Look" (#19-last by Kurtzman?) 27 54 81 158 259 360

NOTE: *Cindy app. in #17. Jeanie app. in #17. Little Lizzie app. in #22.*

WILLIE MAYS (See The Amazing...)

WILLIE THE PENGUIN

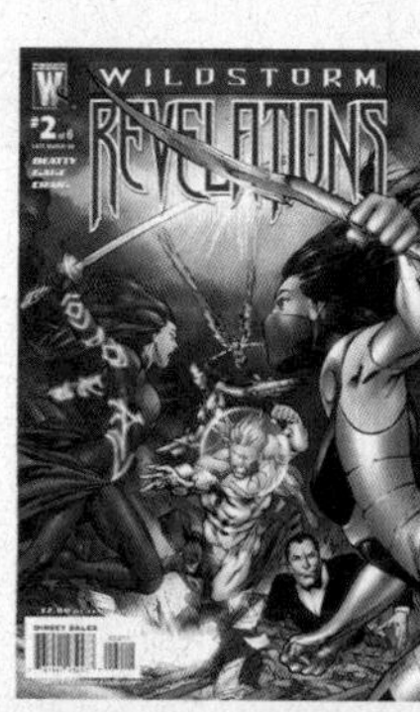

Wildstorm Revelations #2 © WSP

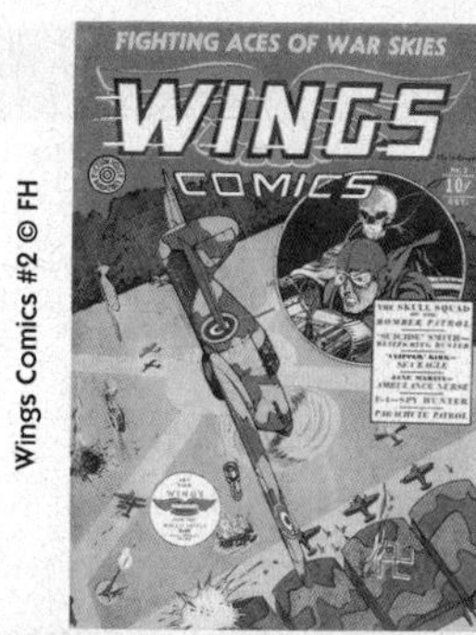

Wings Comics #2 © FH

Winter Soldier #4 © MAR

	GD 2.0	VG 4.0	FN 6.0	VF 8.0	VF/NM 9.0	NM- 9.2

Standard Comics: Apr, 1951 - No. 6, Apr, 1952

1-Funny animal	14	28	42	80	115	150
2-6	8	16	24	44	57	70

WILLIE THE WISE-GUY (Also see Cartoon Kids)
Atlas Comics (NPP): Sept, 1957

1-Kida, Maneely-a	20	40	60	117	189	260

WILLOW
Marvel Comics: Aug, 1988 - No. 3, Oct, 1988 ($1.00)

1-R/Marvel Graphic Novel #36 (movie adaptation)	2	4	6	10	14	18
2,3						6.00

WILLOW (From Buffy the Vampire Slayer)
Dark Horse Comics: Nov, 2012 - No. 5, Mar, 2013 ($2.99, limited series)

1-5-Jeff Parker-s/Brian Ching-a; covers by David Mack & Megan Lara; Aluwyn app.						3.00

WILL ROGERS WESTERN (Formerly My Great Love #1-4; see Blazing & True Comics #66)
Fox Feature Syndicate: No. 5, June, 1950 - No. 2, Aug, 1950

5(#1) Photo-c	31	62	93	186	303	420
2: Photo-c	26	52	78	154	252	350

WILL TO POWER (Also see Comic's Greatest World)
Dark Horse Comics: June, 1994 - No. 12, Aug, 1994 ($1.00, weekly limited series, 20 pgs.)

1-12: 12-Vortex kills Titan.						3.00

NOTE: *Mignola c-10-12. Sears c-1-3.*

WILL-YUM!
Dell Publishing Co.: No. 676, Feb, 1956 - No. 902, May, 1958

Four Color 676 (#1), 765 (1/57), 902	5	10	15	30	50	70

WIN A PRIZE COMICS (Timmy The Timid Ghost #3 on?)
Charlton Comics: Feb, 1955 - No. 2, Apr, 1955

V1#1-S&K-a; Poe adapt; E.C. War swipe	81	162	243	518	884	1250
2-S&K-a	57	114	171	362	619	875

WINDY & WILLY (Also see Showcase #81)
National Periodical Publications: May-June, 1969 - No. 4, Nov-Dec, 1969

1- r/Dobie Gillis with some art changes begin	6	12	18	38	69	100
2-4	4	8	12	23	37	50

WINGS COMICS
Fiction House Mag.: 9/40 - No. 109, 9/49; No. 110, Wint, 1949-50; No. 111, Spring, 1950; No. 112, 1950(nd); No. 113 - No. 115, 1950(nd); No. 116, 1952(nd); No. 117, Fall, 1952 - No. 122, Wint, 1953-54; No. 123 - No. 124, 1954(nd)

1-Skull Squad, Clipper Kirk, Suicide Smith, Jane Martin, War Nurse, Phantom Falcons, Greasemonkey Griffin, Parachute Patrol & Powder Burns begin; grey-tone-c	300	600	900	1980	3440	4900
2	138	276	414	887	1519	2150
3-5	90	180	270	576	988	1400
6-10: 8-Indicia shows #7 (#8 on cover)	69	138	207	442	759	1075
11-15	65	130	195	416	708	1000
16-Origin & 1st app. Captain Wings & begin series	74	148	222	470	810	1150
17-20: 20-(4/42) 1st Japanese WWII-c	55	110	165	352	601	850
21-25,27-30	50	100	150	315	533	750
26-1st Good Girl WWII-c for this title	97	194	291	621	1061	1500
31-34,36-40	41	82	123	256	428	600
35-Classic Nazi WWII-c	54	108	162	343	574	825
41-50	36	72	108	211	343	475
51-60: 60-Last Skull Squad	32	64	96	192	314	435
61-67: 66-Ghost Patrol begins (becomes Ghost Squadron #71 on), ends #112?	30	60	90	177	289	400
68,69: 68-Clipper Kirk becomes The Phantom Falcon-origin, Part 1; part 2 in #69	30	60	90	177	289	400
70-72: 70-1st app. The Phantom Falcon in costume, origin-Part 3; Capt. Wings battles Col. Kamikaze in all	29	58	87	170	278	385
73-85,87,88,92,93,95-99: 80-Phantom Falcon by Larsen. 99-King of the Congo begins?	29	58	87	170	278	385
86-Graphic decapitation panel	32	64	96	188	307	425
89-91,94-Classic Good Girl covers	97	194	291	621	1061	1500
100-(12/48)	32	64	96	188	307	425
101-124: 111-Last Jane Martin. 112-Flying Saucer-c (1950). 115-Used in **POP**, pg. 89. 121-Atomic Explosion-c. 122-Korean War	22	44	66	130	213	295

NOTE: *World War II covers (Nazi or Japanese) on #1-17, 19-67. Bondage covers are common. Captain Wings battles Sky Hag-#75, 76; ...Mr. Atlantis-#85-92; ...Mr. Pupin(Red Agent)-#98-103. Capt. Wings by* **Elias***-#52-64, 68, 69; by* **Lubbers***-#29-32, 70-111; by* **Renee***-#33-46.* **Evans** *a-85-106, 108-111(Jane Martin); text illos-72-84.* **Larsen** *a-52, 59, 64, 73-77. Jane Martin by* **Fran Hopper***-#68-84; Suicide Smith by* **John Celardo***-#72, 74, 76, 80-104; by* **Hollingsworth***-#68-70, 105-109, 111; Ghost Squadron by* **Astarita***-#67-79; by* **Maurice Whitman***-#80-111. King of the Congo by* **Moreira***-#99, 100. Skull Squad by* **M. Baker***-#52-60; Clipper Kirk by* **Baker***-#60, 61; by* **Colan***-#53; by* **Ingels***-(some issues?). Phantom Falcon by* **Larsen***-#73-84.* **Elias** *c-58-72.* **Fawcette** *c-3-12, 16, 17, 19, 22-33.* ***Lubbers*** *c-74-109.* ***Tuska*** *a-5.* ***Whitman*** *c-110-124.* ***Zolnerwich*** *c-15, 21.*

	GD 2.0	VG 4.0	FN 6.0	VF 8.0	VF/NM 9.0	NM- 9.2

WINGS OF THE EAGLES, THE
Dell Publishing Co.: No. 790, Apr, 1957 (10¢ & 15¢ editions exist)

Four Color 790-Movie; John Wayne photo-c; Toth-a	13	26	39	89	195	300

WINKY DINK (Adventures of...)
Pines Comics: No. 75, Mar, 1957 (one-shot)

75-Marv Levy-c/a	7	14	21	37	46	55

WINKY DINK (TV)
Dell Publishing Co.: No. 663, Nov, 1955

Four Color 663 (#1)	9	18	27	60	120	180

WINNEBAGO GRAVEYARD
Image Comics: Jun, 2017 - No. 4, Sept, 2017 ($3.99)

1-4-Steve Niles-s/Alison Sampson-a						4.00

WINNIE-THE-POOH (Also see Dynabrite Comics)
Gold Key No. 1-17/Whitman No. 18 on: January, 1977 - No. 33, July, 1984
(Walt Disney) (Winnie-The-Pooh began as Edward Bear in 1926 by Milne)

1-New art	11	22	33	76	163	250
2-5: 5-New material	3	6	9	14	20	26
6-17: 12-up-New material	2	4	6	9	13	16
18,19(Whitman)	2	4	6	13	18	22
20,21('80) pre-pack only	5	10	15	34	60	85
22('80) (scarcer) pre-pack only	9	18	27	61	123	185
23-28: 27(2/82), 28(4/82)	3	6	9	14	19	24
29-33 (#90299 on-c, no date or date code; pre-pack): 29(4/82), 30(5/83), 31(8/83), 32(4/84), 33(7/84)	3	6	9	21	33	45

WINNIE WINKLE (See Popular Comics & Super Comics)
Dell Publishing Co.: 1941 - No. 7, Sept-Nov, 1949

Large Feature Comic 2 (1941)	37	74	111	222	361	500
Four Color 94 (1945)	13	26	39	87	191	295
Four Color 174	9	18	27	60	120	180
1(3-5/48)-Contains daily & Sunday newspaper-r from 1939-1941	9	18	27	57	111	165
2 (6-8/48)	5	10	15	35	63	90
3-7	4	8	12	28	47	65

WINTER GUARD
Marvel Comics: Oct, 2021 - No. 4, Jan, 2022 ($4.99/$3.99)

1-($4.99) Cady-s/Bazaldua-a; Red Guardian & Yelena Belova app.						5.00
2-4-($3.99) 2,3-Dracula app.						4.00

WINTER MEN, THE
DC Comics (WildStorm): Oct, 2005 - No. 5, Nov, 2006 ($2.99, limited series)

1-5-Brett Lewis-s/John Paul Leon-a						3.00
... Winter Special (2/09, $3.99) Lewis-s/Leon-a						4.00

WINTER SOLDIER (See Captain America 2005 series)
Marvel Comics: Apr, 2012 - No. 19, Aug, 2013 ($2.99)

1-Black Widow app.; Brubaker-s/Guice-a/Bermejo-c	1	3	4	6	8	10
2						6.00
3-19: 3-5-Dr. Doom app.						4.00

WINTER SOLDIER (See Captain America 2005 series)
Marvel Comics: Feb, 2019 - No. 5, Jun, 2019 ($3.99)

1-5-Kyle Higgins-s/Rod Reis-a; origin re-cap; intro RJ. 3-New robot arm						4.00

WINTER SOLDIER: THE BITTER MARCH
Marvel Comics: Apr, 2014 - No. 5, Sept, 2014 ($3.99, limited series)

1-5: 1-Remender-s/Boschi-a/Robinson-c; set in 1966; Nick Fury app.						4.00

WINTER SOLDIER: WINTER KILLS
Marvel Comics: Feb, 2007 ($3.99, one-shot)

1-Flashback to Christmas Eve 1944; Toro & Sub-Mariner app.; Brubaker-s/Weeks-a						5.00

WINTERWORLD
Eclipse Comics: Sept, 1987 - No. 3, Mar, 1988 ($1.75, limited series)

1-3						3.00

WINTERWORLD
IDW Publishing: Jun, 2014 - No. 7, Jan, 2015 ($3.99)

1-7: 1-Chuck Dixon-s/Butch Guice-a; three covers. 5-7-Giorello-a						4.00
#0-(3/15, $3.99) Origin of Wynn; Dixon-s/Edwards-a; covers by Edwards & Guice						4.00

WINTERWORLD: FROZEN FLEET
IDW Publishing: May, 2015 - No. 3, Jul, 2015 ($3.99, limited series)

1-3: 1-Chuck Dixon-s/Esteve Polls-a; three covers. 2,3-Two covers						4.00

GD 2.0 · VG 4.0 · FN 6.0 · VF 8.0 · VF/NM 9.0 · NM- 9.2

WISDOM
Marvel Comics (MAX): Jan, 2007 - No. 6, July, 2007 ($3.99, limited series)
1-6: 1-Hairsine-a/c; Cornell-s. 3-6-Manuel Garcia-a 4.00
...: Rudiments of Wisdom TPB (2007, $21.99) r/#1-6; series pitch and sketch page 22.00

WISE GUYS (See Harvey...)

WISE LITTLE HEN, THE
David McKay Publ./Whitman: 1934 ,1935(48 pgs.); 1937 (Story book)
nn-(1934 edition w/dust jacket)(48 pgs. with color, 8-3/4x9-3/4") -Debut of Donald Duck (see Advs. of Mickey Mouse); Donald app. on cover with Wise Little Hen & Practical Pig; painted cover; same artist as the B&W's from Silly Symphony Cartoon, The Wise Little Hen (1934) (McKay)
Book w/dust jacket 265 530 795 1694 2897 4100
Dust jacket only 63 126 189 403 689 975
nn-(1935 edition w/dust jacket), same as 1934 ed. 152 304 456 965 1658 2350
888 (1937)(9-1/2x13", 12 pgs.)(Whitman) Donald Duck app. 39 78 117 231 378 525

WISE SON: THE WHITE WOLF
DC Comics (Milestone): Nov, 1996 - No. 4, Feb, 1997 ($2.50, limited series)
1-Ho Che Anderson-c/a 1 3 4 6 8 10
2-4 5.00

WIT AND WISDOM OF WATERGATE (Humor magazine)
Marvel Comics: 1973, 76 pgs., squarebound
1-Low print run 5 10 15 33 57 80

WITCHBLADE (Also see Cyblade/Shi, Tales Of The..., & Top Cow Classics)
Image Comics (Top Cow Productions): Nov, 1995 - No. 185, Nov, 2015 ($2.50/$2.99)
0 1 2 3 5 6 8
1/2-Mike Turner/Marc Silvestri-c. 3 6 9 19 30 40
1/2 Gold Ed., 1/2 Chromium-c 3 6 9 19 30 40
1/2-(Vol. 2, 11/02, $2.99) Wohl-s/Ching-a/c 3.00
1-Mike Turner-a(p) 4 8 12 19 30 45
1-Anniversary Edition (7/20, $4.99) r/#1 with creator interviews and character history 5.00
1,2-American Ent. Encore Ed. 1 2 3 4 5 7
2,3 2 4 6 11 16 20
4,5 2 4 6 8 10 12
6-9: 8-Wraparound-c. 9-Tony Daniel-a(p) 1 2 3 5 6 8
9-Sunset variant-c 2 4 6 8 10 12
9-DF variant-c 2 4 6 9 12 15
10-Flip book w/Darkness #0, 1st app. the Darkness 2 4 6 9 12 15
10-Variant-c 2 4 6 9 12 15
10-Gold logo 3 6 9 14 20 25
10-($3.95) Dynamic Forces alternate-c 1 2 3 5 6 8
11-15 5.00
16-19: 18,19-"Family Ties" Darkness x-over pt. 1,4 4.00
18-Face to face variant-c, 18-American Ent. Ed., 19-AE Gold Ed. 1 2 3 5 6 8
20-25: 24-Pearson, Green-a. 25-($2.95) Turner-a(p) 4.00
25 (Prism variant) 25.00
25 (Special) 10.00
26-39: 26-Green-a begins 3.00
27 (Variant) 6.00
40-49,51-53: 40-Begin Jenkins & Veitch-s/Keu Cha-a. 47-Zulli-c/a 3.00
40-Pittsburgh Convention Preview edition; B&W preview of #40 3.00
49-Gold logo 5.00
50-($4.95) Darkness app.; Ching-a; B&W preview of Universe 5.00
54-59: 54-Black outer-c with gold foil logo; Wohl-s/Manapul-a 3.00
60-74,76-91,93-99: 60-($2.99) Endgame x-over with Tomb Raider #25 & Evo #1. 64,65-Magdalena app. 71-Kirk-a. 77,81-85-Land-c. 80-Four covers. 87-Bachalo-a 3.00
75-($4.99) Manapul-a 5.00
92-($4.99) Origin of the Witchblade; art by various incl. Bachalo, Perez, Linsner, Cooke 5.00
100-($4.99) Five covers incl. Turner, Silvestri, Linsner; art by various; Jake dies 5.00
101-124,126-143: 103-Danielle Baptiste gets the Witchblade; Linsner variant-c. 116-124,140,141-Sejic-a. 126-128-War of the Witchblades. 134-136-Aphrodite IV app. 139-Gaydos-a. 143-Matt Dow Smith-a 3.00
125-($3.99) War of the Witchblades begins; 3 covers; Sejic-a 4.00
144-($4.99) Origin retold; wraparound-c; Sejic-a; back-up w/Sablik-s; pin-up gallery 5.00
145-149-($3.99) Sejic-a/c. 149-Angelus app. 4.00
150-($4.99) Four covers; last Marz-s; Sejic-a; cover gallery & series timeline 5.00
151-174-($2.99) Altered reality after Artifacts #13; Seeley-s; multiple covers 3.00
175-($5.99) Three covers; Marz-s; Laura Braga-a; Temple of Shadows back-up 6.00
176-184-($3.99) 180-Hine-s/Rearte-a 4.00
185-($5.99)-Last issue; Marz & Hawkins-s; art by various; bonus preview of Switch #1 6.00
... and Tomb Raider (4/05, $2.99) Jae Lee-c; art by Lee and Texiera 3.00
...: Animated (8/03, $2.99) Magdalena & Darkness app.; Dini-s/Bone, Bullock, Cooke-a/c 3.00
... Annual 2009 (4/09, $3.99) Basaldua-a 4.00
... Annual #1 (12/10, $4.99) the Witchblade in Stalingrad 1942, Shasteen-a; Haley-a 5.00
...: Art of the Witchblade (7/06, $2.99) pin-ups by various incl. Turner, Land, Linsner 3.00
...: Bearers of the Blade (7/06, $2.99) pin-up/profiles of bearers of the Witchblade 3.00
...: Blood Oath (8/04, $4.99) Sara teams with Phenix & Sibilla; Roux-a 5.00
...: Blood Relations TPB (2003, $12.99) r/#54-58 13.00
... Case Files 1 (10/14, $3.99) Character profiles and story summaries 4.00
... Compendium Vol. 1 (2006, $59.99) r/#1-50; gallery of variant covers and art 60.00
... Compendium Vol. 2 (2007, $59.99) r/#51-100; gallery of variant covers and art 60.00
... Cover Gallery Vol. 1 (12/05, $2.99) intro. by Stan Lee 3.00
.../Darkchylde (7/00, $2.50) Green-s/a(p) 3.00
.../Dark Minds (6/04, $9.99) new story plus r/Dark Minds/Witchblade #1 10.00
.../Darkness: Family Ties Collected Edition (10/98, $9.95) r/#18,19 and Darkness #9,10 10.00
.../Darkness Special (12/99, $3.95) Green-c/a 4.00
... Day of the Outlaws (4/13, $3.99) Fialkov-s/Blake-a; Witchblade in 1878 Colorado 4.00
...: Demon 1 (2003, $6.99) Mark Millar-s/Jae Lee-c/a 7.00
.../Devi (4/08, $3.99) Basaldua-a/Land-c; continues in Devi/Witchblade 4.00
...: Distinctions (See Tales of the Witchblade)
...: Due Process (8/10, $3.99) Alina Urusov-a/c; Phil Smith-s 4.00
.../Elektra (3/97, $2.95) Devil's Reign Pt. 6 4.00
... Gallery (11/00, $2.95) Profile pages and pin-ups by various; Turner-c 3.00
Image Firsts: Witchblade #1 (4/10, $1.00) reprints #1 3.00
Infinity (5/99, $3.50) Lobdell-s/Pollina-c/a 4.00
.../Lady Death (11/01, $4.95) Manapul-c/a 5.00
...: Prevailing TPB (2000, $14.95) r/#20-25; new Turner-c 15.00
...: Revelations TPB (2000, $24.95) r/#9-17; new Turner-c 25.00
.../The Punisher (6/07, $3.99) Marz-s/Melo-a/Linsner-c 4.00
.../Tomb Raider #1/2 (7/00, $2.95) Covers by Turner and Cha 4.00
... Unbalanced Pieces FCBD Edition (5/12, giveaway) Christopher-c 3.00
...: Vol. 1 TPB (1/08, $4.99) r/#80-85; Marz intro.; cover gallery 5.00
...: Vol. 2 TPB (2/08, $14.99) r/#86-92; cover gallery 15.00
...: Vol. 3 TPB (3/08, $14.99) r/#93-100; Edginton intro.; cover gallery 15.00
... vs. Frankenstein: Monster War 2005 (8/05, $2.99) pt. 3 of x-over 3.00
...: Witch Hunt Vol. 1 TPB (2/06, $14.99) r/#80-85; Marz intro.; Choi afterward; cover gallery 15.00
Wizard #500 10.00
.../Wolverine (6/04, $2.99) Basaldua-c/a; Claremont-s 3.00

WITCHBLADE
Image Comics (Top Cow): Dec, 2017 - Present ($3.99)
1-18: 1-Kittredge-s/Ingranata-a; intro. Alex Underwood 4.00

WITCHBLADE/ALIENS/THE DARKNESS/PREDATOR
Dark Horse Comics/Top Cow Productions: Nov, 2000 ($2.99)
1-3-Mel Rubi-a 4.00

WITCHBLADE COLLECTED EDITION
Image Comics (Top Cow Productions): July, 1996 - No. 8 ($4.95/$6.95, squarebound, limited series)
1-7-($4.95): Two issues reprinted in each 5.00
8-($6.95) r/#15-17 7.00
...Slipcase (10/96, $10.95)-Packaged w/ Coll. Ed. #1-4 11.00

WITCHBLADE: DEMON REBORN
Dynamite Entertainment: 2012 - No. 4, 2012 ($3.99, limited series)
1-4-Ande Parks-s/Jose Luis-a; covers by Calero & Jae Lee 4.00

WITCHBLADE: DESTINY'S CHILD
Image Comics (Top Cow): Jun, 2000 - No. 3, Sept, 2000 ($2.95, limited series)
1-3: 1-Boller-a/Keu Cha-c 3.00

WITCHBLADE: MANGA (Takeru Manga)
Image Comics (Top Cow): Feb, 2007 - No. 12, Mar, 2008 ($2.99/$3.99)
1-4-Colored reprints of Japanese Witchblade manga. 1-Three covers. 2-Two covers 3.00
5-12-($3.99) 4.00

WITCHBLADE: OBAKEMONO
Image Comics (Top Cow Productions): 2002 ($9.95, one-shot graphic novel)
1-Fiona Avery-s/Billy Tan-a; forward by Straczynski 10.00

WITCHBLADE/ RED SONJA
Dynamite Ent./Top Cow: 2012 - No. 5, 2012 ($3.99, limited series)
1-5-Doug Wagner-s/Cezar Razek-a/Alé Garza-c 4.00

WITCHBLADE: SHADES OF GRAY
Dynamite Ent./Top Cow: 2007 - No. 4, 2007 ($3.50, lim. series)
1,2: 1-Sara Pezzini meets Dorian Gray; Segovia-a; multiple covers 3.50

WITCHBLADE/ TOMB RAIDER SPECIAL (Also see Tomb Raider/...)
Image Comics (Top Cow Productions): Dec, 1998 ($2.95)
1-Based on video game character; Turner-a(p) 4.00
1-Silvestri variant-c 6.00
1-Turner bikini variant-c 10.00
1-Prism-c 12.00
Wizard 1/2 -Turner-s 10.00

WITCHCRAFT (See Strange Mysteries, Super Reprint #18)
Avon Periodicals: Mar-Apr, 1952 - No. 6, Mar, 1953
1-Kubert-a; 1 pg. Check-a 135 270 405 864 1482 2100
2-Kubert & Check-a; classic skull-c 226 452 678 1446 2473 3500
3,6: 3-Lawrence-a; Kinstler inside-c 69 138 207 442 759 1075
4-People cooked alive c/story 174 348 522 1114 1907 2700
5-Kelly Freas painted-c 181 362 543 1158 1979 2800
NOTE: *Hollingsworth a-4-6; c-4, 6.* ***McCann*** *a-3?*

WITCHCRAFT
DC Comics (Vertigo): June, 1994 - No. 3, Aug, 1994 ($2.95, limited series)
1-3: James Robinson scripts & Kaluta-c in all 4.00
1-Platinum Edition 15.00
Trade paperback-(1996, $14.95)-r/#1-3; Kaluta-c 15.00

WITCHCRAFT: LA TERREUR
DC Comics (Vertigo): Apr, 1998 - No. 3, Jun, 1998 ($2.50, limited series)
1-3: Robinson-s/Zulli & Locke-a; interlocking cover images 3.00

WITCH DOCTOR (See Walking Dead #85 flip book for preview)
Image Comics: Jun, 2011 - No. 4, Nov, 2011 ($2.99, limited series)
1-4-Seifert-s/Ketner-a/c 3.00
...: Mal Practice 1-6 (11/12 - No. 6, 4/13, $2.99) Seifert-s/Ketner-a/c 3.00
...: The Resuscitation (12/11, $2.99) Seifert-s/Ketner-a/c 3.00

WITCHER, THE
Dark Horse Comics: Mar, 2014 - No. 5, Jul, 2014 ($3.99, limited series)
1-5-Tobin-s/Querio-a 4.00

WITCHER, THE: FADING MEMORIES
Dark Horse Comics: Nov, 2020 - No. 4, Mar, 2021 ($3.99, limited series)
1-4-Bartosz Sztybor-s/Amad Mir-a 4.00

WITCHER, THE: FOX CHILDREN
Dark Horse Comics: Apr, 2015 - No. 5, Aug, 2015 ($3.99, limited series)
1-5-Tobin-s/Querio-a 4.00

WITCHER, THE: OF FLESH AND FLAME
Dark Horse Comics: Dec, 2018 - No. 4, Mar, 2019 ($3.99, limited series)
1-4-Motyka-s/Strychowska-a 4.00

Witchblade #134 © TCOW

The Witcher: Fading Memories #4 © CD Projekt Red

Wizards of Mickey #1 © DIS

WITCHER, THE: THE BALLAD OF TWO WOLVES
Dark Horse Comics: Dec, 2022 - No. 4, Mar, 2023 ($3.99, limited series)

	GD 2.0	VG 4.0	FN 6.0	VF 8.0	VF/NM 9.0	NM- 9.2
1-4-Bartosz Sztybor-s/Miki Montllo-a						4.00

WITCHER, THE: WITCH'S LAMENT
Dark Horse Comics: May, 2021 - No. 4, Sept, 2021 ($3.99, limited series)

	GD 2.0	VG 4.0	FN 6.0	VF 8.0	VF/NM 9.0	NM- 9.2
1-4-Bartosz Sztybor-s/Vanesa Del Rey-a						4.00

WITCHES
Marvel Comics: Aug, 2004 - No. 4, Sept, 2004 ($2.99, limited series)

	GD 2.0	VG 4.0	FN 6.0	VF 8.0	VF/NM 9.0	NM- 9.2
1-4: 1,2-Deodato, Jr-a; Dr. Strange app. 3,4-Conrad-a						3.00
... Vol. 1: The Gathering (2004, $9.99) r/series						10.00

WITCHES TALES (Witches Western Tales #29,30)
Witches Tales/Harvey Publications: Jan, 1951 - No. 28, Dec, 1954 (date misprinted as 4/55)

	GD 2.0	VG 4.0	FN 6.0	VF 8.0	VF/NM 9.0	NM- 9.2
1-Powell-a (1 pg.)	142	284	426	909	1555	2200
2-Eye injury panel	58	116	174	371	636	900
3-7,9,10	43	86	129	271	461	650
8-Eye injury panels	53	106	159	334	567	800
11-13,15,16: 12-Acid in face story	40	80	120	246	411	575
14,17-Powell/Nostrand-a. 17-Atomic disaster story	42	84	126	265	445	625
18-Nostrand-a; E.C. swipe/Shock S.S.	41	82	123	256	428	600
19-Nostrand-a; E.C. swipe/ "Glutton"; Devil-c	71	142	213	454	777	1100
20-24-Nostrand-a. 21-E.C. swipe; rape story. 23-Wood E.C. swipes/Two-Fisted Tales #34	42	84	126	265	445	625
25-Nostrand-a; E.C. swipe/Mad Barber; decapitation-c	541	1082	1623	3950	6975	10,000
26-28: 27-r/#6 with diff.-c. 28-r/#8 with diff.-c	37	74	111	222	361	500

NOTE: *Check a-24. **Elias** c-8, 10, 16-27. **Kremer** a-18; c-25. **Nostrand** a-17-25; 14, 17(w/**Powell**). **Palais** a-1, 2, 4(2), 5(2), 7-9, 12, 14, 15, 17. **Powell** a-3-7, 10, 11, 19-27. Bondage-c 1, 3, 5, 6, 8, 9.*

WITCHES TALES (Magazine)
Eerie Publications: V1#7, July, 1969 - V7#1, Feb, 1975 (B&W, 52 pgs.)

	GD 2.0	VG 4.0	FN 6.0	VF 8.0	VF/NM 9.0	NM- 9.2
V1#7(7/69)	9	18	27	60	120	180
V1#8(9/69), 9(11/69)	7	14	21	48	89	130
V2#1-6('70), V3#1-6('71)	6	12	18	37	66	95
V4#1-6('72), V5#1-6('73), V6#1-6('74), V7#1	5	10	15	34	60	85

NOTE: *Ajax/Farrell reprints in early issues.*

WITCHES' WESTERN TALES (Formerly Witches Tales)(Western Tales #31 on)
Harvey Publications: No. 29, Feb, 1955 - No. 30, Apr, 1955

	GD 2.0	VG 4.0	FN 6.0	VF 8.0	VF/NM 9.0	NM- 9.2
29,30-Featuring Clay Duncan & Boys' Ranch; S&K-r/from Boys' Ranch including-c. 29-Last pre-code	18	36	54	105	165	225

WITCHFINDER, THE
Image Comics (Liar): Sept, 1999 - No. 3, Jan, 2000 ($2.95)

	GD 2.0	VG 4.0	FN 6.0	VF 8.0	VF/NM 9.0	NM- 9.2
1-3-Romano-a/Sharon & Matthew Scott-plot						3.00

WITCHFINDER: CITY OF THE DEAD
Dark Horse Comics: Aug, 2016 - No. 5, Dec, 2016 ($3.99, limited series)

	GD 2.0	VG 4.0	FN 6.0	VF 8.0	VF/NM 9.0	NM- 9.2
1-5-Mignola & Roberson-s/Stenbeck-a/Tedesco-c						4.00

WITCHFINDER: LOST AND GONE FOREVER
Dark Horse Comics: Feb, 2011 - No. 5, Jun, 2011 ($3.50, limited series)

	GD 2.0	VG 4.0	FN 6.0	VF 8.0	VF/NM 9.0	NM- 9.2
1-5-John Severin-a; Mignola & Arcudi-s. 1-Two covers by Mignola & Severin						3.50

WITCHFINDER: THE GATES OF HEAVEN
Dark Horse Comics: May, 2018 - No. 5, Sept, 2018 ($3.99, limited series)

	GD 2.0	VG 4.0	FN 6.0	VF 8.0	VF/NM 9.0	NM- 9.2
1-5-Mignola & Roberson-s/D'Israeli-c/a						4.00

WITCHFINDER: THE REIGN OF DARKNESS
Dark Horse Comics: Nov, 2019 - No. 5, Mar, 2020 ($3.99, limited series)

	GD 2.0	VG 4.0	FN 6.0	VF 8.0	VF/NM 9.0	NM- 9.2
1-5-Mignola & Roberson-s/Mitten-a/c						4.00

WITCH HUNTER
Malibu Comics (Ultraverse): Apr, 1996 ($2.50, one-shot)

	GD 2.0	VG 4.0	FN 6.0	VF 8.0	VF/NM 9.0	NM- 9.2
1						3.00

WITCHING, THE
DC Comics (Vertigo): Aug, 2004 - No. 10, May, 2005 ($2.95/$2.99)

	GD 2.0	VG 4.0	FN 6.0	VF 8.0	VF/NM 9.0	NM- 9.2
1-10-Vankin-s/Gallagher-a/McPherson-c. 1,2-Lucifer app.						3.00

WITCHING HOUR ("The ..." in later issues)
National Periodical Publ./DC Comics: Feb-Mar, 1969 - No. 85, Oct, 1978

	GD 2.0	VG 4.0	FN 6.0	VF 8.0	VF/NM 9.0	NM- 9.2
1-Toth-a, plus Neal Adams-a (2 pgs.)	18	36	54	124	275	425
2,6: 6-Toth-a	8	16	24	51	96	140
3,5-Wrightson-a; Toth-p. 3-Last 12¢ issue	8	16	24	52	99	145
4,12-Toth-a	5	10	15	33	57	80
7-11-Adams-c; Toth-a in all. 8-Adams-a	6	12	18	41	76	110
13-Neal Adams-c/a, 2pgs.	7	14	21	48	89	130
14-Williamson/Garzon, Jones-a; N. Adams-c	7	14	21	44	82	120
15	3	6	9	19	30	40
16-21-(52 pg. Giants)	4	8	12	23	37	50
22-37,39,40	3	6	9	14	19	24
38-(100 pgs.)	5	10	15	31	53	75
41-60	2	4	6	10	14	18
61-83,85	2	4	6	8	11	14
84-(44 pgs.)	2	4	6	9	13	16

NOTE: *Combined with The Unexpected with #189. **Neal Adams** c-7-11, 13, 14. **Alcala** a-24, 27, 33, 41, 43. **Anderson** a-9, 38. **Cardy** c-4, 5. **Kaluta** a-7. **Kane** a-12p. **Morrow** a-10, 13, 15, 16. **Nino** a-31, 40, 45, 47. **Redondo** a-20, 23, 24, 34, 65; c-53. **Reese** a-23. **Sparling** a-1. **Toth** a-1, 3-12, 38r. **Tuska** a-11, 12. **Wood** a-15.*

WITCHING HOUR, THE
DC Comics (Vertigo): 1999 - No. 3, 2000 ($5.95, limited series)

	GD 2.0	VG 4.0	FN 6.0	VF 8.0	VF/NM 9.0	NM- 9.2
1-3-Bachalo & Thibert-c/a; Loeb & Bachalo-s						6.00
Hardcover (2000, $29.95) r/#1-3; embossed cover						30.00
Softcover (2003, $19.95), (2009, $19.99) r/#1-3						20.00

WITCHING HOUR, THE
DC Comics (Vertigo): Dec, 2013 ($7.99, one-shot)

	GD 2.0	VG 4.0	FN 6.0	VF 8.0	VF/NM 9.0	NM- 9.2
1-Short story anthology by various incl. DeConnick, Doyle, Buckingham; Frison-c						8.00

WITHIN OUR REACH
Star Reach Productions: 1991 ($7.95, 84 pgs.)

	GD 2.0	VG 4.0	FN 6.0	VF 8.0	VF/NM 9.0	NM- 9.2
nn-Spider-Man, Concrete by Chadwick, Gift of the Magi by Russell; Christmas stories; Chadwick-c; Spidey back-c						8.00

WITH THE MARINES ON THE BATTLEFRONTS OF THE WORLD
Toby Press: 1953 (no month) - No. 2, Mar, 1954 (Photo covers)

	GD 2.0	VG 4.0	FN 6.0	VF 8.0	VF/NM 9.0	NM- 9.2
1-John Wayne story	36	72	108	211	343	475
2-Monty Hall in #1,2	14	28	42	81	118	155

WITH THE U.S. PARATROOPS BEHIND ENEMY LINES (Also see U.S. Paratroops...; #2-6 titled U.S. Paratroops...)
Avon Periodicals: 1951 - No. 6, Dec, 1952

	GD 2.0	VG 4.0	FN 6.0	VF 8.0	VF/NM 9.0	NM- 9.2
1-Wood-c & inside f/c	24	48	72	142	234	325
2-Kinstler-c & inside f/c only	15	30	45	85	130	175
3-6: 5-Extreme violence. 6-Kinstler-c & inside f/c only	14	28	42	81	118	155

NOTE: ***Kinstler** c-2, 4-6.*

WITNESS, THE (Also see Amazing Mysteries, Captain America #71, Ideal #4, Marvel Mystery #92 & Mystic #7)
Marvel Comics (MjMe): Sept, 1948

	GD 2.0	VG 4.0	FN 6.0	VF 8.0	VF/NM 9.0	NM- 9.2
1(Scarce)-Rico-c?	343	686	1029	2400	4200	6000

WITTY COMICS
Irwin H. Rubin Publ./Chicago Nite Life News No. 2: 1945 - No. 2, 1945

	GD 2.0	VG 4.0	FN 6.0	VF 8.0	VF/NM 9.0	NM- 9.2
1-The Pioneer, Junior Patrol; Japanese war-c	41	82	123	256	428	600
2-The Pioneer, Junior Patrol	21	42	63	122	199	275

WIZARD BEACH
BOOM! Studios: Dec, 2018 - No. 5, Apr, 2019 ($3.99, limited series)

	GD 2.0	VG 4.0	FN 6.0	VF 8.0	VF/NM 9.0	NM- 9.2
1-5-Shaun Simon-s/Conor Nolan-a						4.00

WIZARD OF FOURTH STREET, THE
Dark Horse Comics: Dec, 1987 - No. 2, 1988 ($1.75, B&W, limited series)

	GD 2.0	VG 4.0	FN 6.0	VF 8.0	VF/NM 9.0	NM- 9.2
1,2: Adapts novel by S/F author Simon Hawke						3.00

WIZARD OF OZ (See Classics Illustrated Jr. 535, Dell Jr. Treasury No. 5, First Comics Graphic Novel, Marvel Treasury of Oz, and MGM's Marvelous...)
Dell Publishing Co.: No. 1308, Mar-May, 1962 (TV)

	GD 2.0	VG 4.0	FN 6.0	VF 8.0	VF/NM 9.0	NM- 9.2
Four Color 1308	14	28	42	97	214	325

WIZARDS OF MICKEY (Mickey Mouse)
BOOM! Studios: Jan, 2010 - No. 8, Aug, 2010 ($2.99)

	GD 2.0	VG 4.0	FN 6.0	VF 8.0	VF/NM 9.0	NM- 9.2
1-8: 1,2-Ambrosio-s; 3 covers on each. 3-8-Two covers						3.00

WIZARD'S TALE, THE
Image Comics (Homage Comics): 1997 ($19.95, squarebound, one-shot)

	GD 2.0	VG 4.0	FN 6.0	VF 8.0	VF/NM 9.0	NM- 9.2
nn-Kurt Busiek-s/David Wenzel-painted-a/c						20.00

WOLF & RED
Dark Horse Comics: Apr, 1995 - No. 3, June, 1995 ($2.50, limited series)

	GD 2.0	VG 4.0	FN 6.0	VF 8.0	VF/NM 9.0	NM- 9.2
1-Characters created by Tex Avery	2	4	6	11	16	20
2,3						6.00

WOLF COP
Dynamite Entertainment: 2016 - No. 3, 2016 ($3.99)

	GD 2.0	VG 4.0	FN 6.0	VF 8.0	VF/NM 9.0	NM- 9.2
1-3-Max Marks-s/Arcana Studios-a						4.00

WOLFF & BYRD, COUNSELORS OF THE MACABRE (Becomes Supernatural Law

GD VG FN VF VF/NM NM-
2.0 4.0 6.0 8.0 9.0 9.2

with issue #24)
Exhibit A Press: May, 1994 - No. 23, Aug, 1999 ($2.50, B&W)
1-23-Batton Lash-s/a 3.00

WOLF GAL (See Al Capp's...)

WOLFMAN, THE (See Movie Classics)

WOLF MOON
DC Comics (Vertigo): Feb, 2015 - No. 6, Jul, 2015 ($3.99, limited series)
1-6-Bunn-s/Haun-a. 1-Covers by Jae Lee and Jeremy Haun 4.00

WOLFPACK
Marvel Comics: Feb, 1988 ($7.95); Aug, 1988 - No. 12, July, 1989 (Lim. series)
1-(2/88) 1st app./origin (Marvel Graphic Novel #31) 2 4 6 8 10 12
1-12: 1-(8/88) Hama-s 4.00

WOLVERINE (See Alpha Flight, Daredevil #196, 249, Ghost Rider; Wolverine; Punisher, Havok &..., Incredible Hulk #180, Incredible Hulk &..., Kitty Pryde And..., Marvel Comics Presents, New Avengers, Power Pack, Punisher and..., Rampaging ..., Spider-Man vs... & X-Men #94)

WOLVERINE (See Incredible Hulk #180 for 1st app.)
Marvel Comics Group: Sept, 1982 - No. 4, Dec, 1982 (limited series)
1-Frank Miller-c/a(p) in all; Claremont-s 10 20 30 64 132 200
2-4 5 10 15 30 50 70
... By Claremont & Miller No. 1 Facsimile Edition (4/20, $3.99) r/#1 with original ads 4.00
... By Claremont & Miller HC (2006, $19.99) r/#1-4 & Uncanny X-Men #172-173 20.00
TPB 1(7/87, $4.95)-Reprints #1-4 with new Miller-c 2 4 6 11 16 20
TPB nn (2nd printing, $9.95)-r/#1-4 2 4 6 8 10 12

WOLVERINE
Marvel Comics: Nov, 1988 - No. 189, June, 2003 ($1.50/$1.75/$1.95/$1.99/$2.25)
1-Claremont-s/Buscema-a/c 6 12 18 38 69 100
2 3 6 9 17 25 34
3-5: 4-BWS back-c 2 4 6 13 18 22
6,7,9: 6-McFarlane back-c. 7-Hulk app. 2 4 6 8 10 12
8-Classic Grey Hulk-c; Hulk app. 6 12 18 38 69 100
10-1st battle with Sabretooth (before Wolverine had his claws)
4 8 12 25 40 55
11-16: 11-New costume 1 3 4 6 8 10
17-20: 17-Byrne-c/a(p) begins, ends #23 1 2 3 5 6 8
21-30: 24,25,27-Jim Lee-c. 26-Begin $1.75-c 6.00
31-40,44,47 5.00
41-Sabretooth claims to be Wolverine's father; Cable cameo
2 4 6 10 14 18
41-Gold 2nd printing ($1.75) 2 4 6 10 14 18
42-Sabretooth, Cable & Nick Fury app.; Sabretooth proven not to be Wolverine's father
2 4 6 8 10 12
42-Gold ink 2nd printing ($1.75) 2 4 6 8 10 12
43-Sabretooth cameo (2 panels); saga ends 6.00
45,46-Sabretooth-c/stories 6.00
48,49,51-Sabretooth app. 48-Begin 3 part Weapon X sequel. 51-Sabretooth-c & app. 6.00
50-(64 pgs.)-Die cut-c; Wolverine back to old yellow costume; Forge, Cyclops, Jubilee, Jean Grey & Nick Fury app. 2 4 6 10 14 18
52-74,76-80: 54-Shatterstar (from X-Force) app. 55-Gambit, Jubilee, Sunfire-c/story. 55-57,73-Gambit app. 57-Mariko Yashida dies (Late 7/92). 58,59-Terror, Inc. x-over. 60-64-Sabretooth storyline (60,62,64-c) 5.00
75-($3.95, 68 pgs.)-Wolverine hologram on-c 1 3 4 6 8 10
81-84,86: 81-bound-in card sheet 5.00
85-($2.50)-Newsstand edition 5.00
85-($3.50)-Collectors edition 6.00
87-90 ($1.95)-Deluxe edition 5.00
87-90 ($1.50)-Regular edition 4.00
91-99,101-114: 91-Return from "Age of Apocalypse," 93-Juggernaut app. 94-Gen X app. 101-104-Elektra app. 104-Origin of Onslaught. 105-Onslaught x-over. 110-Shaman-c/app. 114-Alternate-c 4.00
100 ($3.95)-Hologram-c; Wolverine loses humanity 2 4 6 9 13 16
100 ($2.95)-Regular-c. 1 3 4 6 8 10
102.5 (1996 Wizard mail-away)-Deadpool app.; Vallejo-c/Buckingham-a 110.00
115-124: 115- Operation Zero Tolerance 4.00
125-($2.99) Wraparound-c; Viper secret 5.00
125-($6.95) Jae Lee variant-c 8.00
126-144: 126,127-Sabretooth-c/app. 128-Sabretooth & Shadowcat app.; Platt-a. 129-Wendigo-c/app. 131-Initial printing contained lettering error. 133-Begin Larsen-s/Matsuda-a. 138-Galactus-c/app. 139-Cable app.; Yu-a. 142,143-Alpha Flight app. 4.00
145-($2.99) 25th Anniversary issue; Hulk and Sabretooth app.
1 3 4 6 8 10
145-($3.99) Foil enhanced cover (also see Promotional section for Nabisco mail-in ed.)
2 4 6 11 16 20
146,147-Apocalypse: The Twelve; Angel-c/app. 1 3 4 6 8 10
148,149: 149-Nova-c/app. 4.00
150-($2.99) Steve Skroce-s/a 5.00
151-153,156-174,176-182,184-189: 151-Begin $2.25-c. 156-Churchill-a. 159-Chen-a begins. 160-Sabretooth app. 163-Texeira-a(p). 167-BWS-c. 172,173-Alpha Flight app. 176-Colossus app. 185,186-Punisher app. 4.00
154,155-Deadpool app.; Liefeld-s/a. 3 6 9 14 20 26
175,183-($3.50) 175-Sabretooth app. 4.00
#(-1) Flashback (7/97) Logan meets Col. Fury; Nord-a 3.00
Annual nn (1990, $4.50, squarebound, 52 pgs.)-The Jungle Adventure; Simonson scripts; Mignola-c/a 1 2 3 5 6 8
Annual 2 (12/90, $4.95, squarebound, 52 pgs.)-Bloodlust 6.00
Annual nn (#3, 8/91, $5.95, 68 pgs.)-Rahne of Terror; Cable & The New Mutants app.; Andy Kubert-c/a (2nd print exists) 6.00
Annual '95 (1995, $3.95) 5.00
Annual '96 (1996, $2.95)- Wraparound-c; Silver Samurai, Yukio, and Red Ronin app. 5.00
Annual '97 ($2.99) - Wraparound-c 5.00
Annual 1999, 2000 ($3.50) : 1999-Deadpool app. 5.00
Annual 2001 ($2.99) - Tieri-s; JH Williams-c 5.00
...Battles The Incredible Hulk nn (1989, $4.95, squarebound, 52 pg.) r/Incr. Hulk #180,181
2 4 6 10 14 18
Best of Wolverine Vol. 1 HC (2004, $29.99) oversized reprints of Hulk #181, mini-series #1-4, Capt. America Ann, #8, Uncanny X-Men #205 & Marvel Comics Presents #72-84 30.00
...Black Rio (11/98, $5.99)-Casey-s/Oscar Jimenez-a 6.00
...Blood Debt TPB (7/01, $12.95)-r/#150-153; Skroce-c 13.00
...Blood Hungry nn (1993, $6.95, 68 pgs.)-Kieth-r/Marvel Comics Presents #85-92 w/ new Kieth-c 7.00
...: Bloody Choices nn (1993, $7.95, 68 pgs.)-r/Graphic Novel; Nick Fury app. 8.00
... By Claremont & Buscema No. 1 Facsimile Edition (4/20, $3.99) r/#1 with original ads 4.00
... Cable Guts and Glory (10/99, $5.99) Platt-a 6.00
... Classic Vol. 1 TPB (2005, $12.99) r/#1-5 15.00
... Classic Vol. 2 TPB (2005, $12.99) r/#6-10 15.00
... Classic Vol. 3 TPB (2006, $14.99) r/#11-16; The Gehenna Stone Affair 15.00
... Classic Vol. 4 TPB (2006, $14.99) r/#17-23 15.00
... Classic Vol. 5 TPB (2007, $14.99) r/#24-30 15.00
.../Deadpool: Weapon X TPB (7/02, $21.99)-r/#162-166 & Deadpool #57-60 22.00
... Doombringer (11/97, $5.99)-Silver Samurai-c/app. 6.00
... Evilution (9/94, $5.95) 6.00
... Exit Wounds 1 (8/19, $4.99) Short stories by Hama/Eaton; Claremont/Larroca; Kieth 5.00
...: Global Jeopardy 1 (12/93, $2.95, one-shot)-Embossed-c; Sub-Mariner, Zabu, Ka-Zar, Shanna & Wolverine app.; produced in cooperation with World Wildlife Fund 5.00
...:Inner Fury nn (1992, $5.95, 52 pgs.)-Sienkiewicz-c/a 6.00
...: Judgment Night (2000, $3.99) Shi app.; Battlebook 4.00
...: Killing (9/93)-Kent Williams-a 6.00
...: Knight of Terra (1995, $6.95)-Ostrander script 7.00
... Legends Vol. 2: Meltdown (2003, $19.99) r/Havok & Wolverine: Meltdown #1-4 20.00
... Legends Vol. 3 (2003, $12.99) r/#181-186 13.00
... Legends Vol. 4,5: 4-(See Wolverine: Xisle). 5-(See Wolverine: Snikt!)
... Legends Vol. 6: Marc Silvestri Book 1 (2004, $19.99) r/#31-34, 41-42, 48-50 20.00
.../ Nick Fury: The Scorpio Connection Hardcover (1989, $16.95) 25.00
.../ Nick Fury: The Scorpio Connection Softcover(1990, $12.95) 15.00
...: Not Dead Yet (12/98, $14.95, TPB)-r/#119-122 15.00
...: Save The Tiger 1 (7/92, $2.95, 84 pgs.)-Reprints Wolverine stories from Marvel Comics Presents #1-10 w/new Kieth-c 4.00
...Scorpio Rising ($5.95, prestige format, one-shot) 6.00
.../Shi: Dark Night of Judgment (Crusade Comics, 2000, $2.99) Tucci-a 4.00
...Triumphs And Tragedies-(1995, $16.95, trade paperback)-r/Uncanny X-Men #109,172,173, Wolverine limited series #4, & Wolverine #41,42,75 17.00
...Typhoid's Kiss (6/94, $6.95)-r/Wolverine stories from Marvel Comics Presents #109-116 7.00
...Vs. Sabretooth 3D 1 (3/20, $7.99) -r/Wolverine #10; bagged with 3D glasses 8.00
...Vs. Spider-Man 1 (3/95, $2.50) -r/Marvel Comics Presents #48-50 5.00
.../Witchblade 1 (3/97, $2.95) Devil's Reign Pt. 5 4.00
Wizard #1/2 (1997) Joe Phillips-a(p) 10.00
NOTE: ***Austin*** *c-3i.* ***Bolton*** *c(back)-5.* ***Buscema*** *a-1-16,25,27p; c-1-10.* ***Byrne*** *a-17-22p, 23; c-1(back), 17-22, 23p.* ***Colan*** *a-24.* ***Andy Kubert*** *c/a-51.* ***Jim Lee*** *c-24, 25, 27.* ***Silvestri*** *a(p)-31-43, 45, 46, 48-50, 52, 53, 55-57; c-31-42p, 43, 45p, 46p, 48, 49p, 50p, 52p, 53p, 55-57p.* ***Stroman*** *a-44p; c-60p.* ***Williamson*** *a-1i, 3-8i; c(i)-1, 3-6.*

WOLVERINE (Volume 3) (Titled Dark Wolverine from #75-90)(See Daken: Dark Wolverine)
Marvel Comics: July, 2003 - No. 90, Oct, 2010 ($2.25/$2.50/$2.99)
1-Rucka-s/Robertson-a 2 4 6 8 10 12
2-19: 6-Nightcrawler app. 13-16-Sabretooth app. 3.00
20-Millar-s/Romita, Jr.-a begin, Elektra app. 4.00
20-B&W variant-c 2 4 6 8 10 12
21-39: 21-Elektra-c/app. 23,24-Daredevil app. 26-28-Land-c. 29-Quesada-c; begin $2.50-c. 33-35-House of M. 36,37-Decimation. 36-Quesada-c. 39-Winter Soldier app. 3.00
40,43-48: 40-Begin $2.99-c; Winter Soldier app.; Texeira-a. 43-46-Civil War; Ramos-a. 45-Sub-Mariner app. 3.00
41,49-($3.99) 41-C.P. Smith-a/Stuart Moore-s 4.00
42-Civil War 5.00
50-($3.99) Sabretooth app.; Bianchi-a/c & Loeb-s begin; wraparound-c; McGuinness-a 4.00
50-($3.99) Variant Edition; uncolored art and cover; Bianchi pencil art page 4.00
51-55-(Regular and variant uncolored editions) Bianchi-a/Loeb-s; Sabretooth app. 3.00
55-EC-style variant-c by Greg Land 5.00
56-($3.99) Howard Chaykin-a/c 4.00
57-65: 57-61-Suydam Zombie-c; Chaykin-a. 62-65-Mystique app. 3.00
66-Old Man Logan begins; Millar-s/McNiven-a; McNiven wraparound-c
3 6 9 21 33 45
66-Variant-c by Michael Turner 6 12 18 38 69 100
66-Variant sketch-c by Michael Turner 140.00
66-2nd printing with McNiven variant-c of Logan and Hulk gang member
3 6 9 17 26 34
66-(5/10, $1.00) Reprint with "Marvel's Greatest Comics" on cover 3.00
67-70,72-Old Man Logan (concludes in Wolverine: Old Man Logan Giant-Sized Special). 67-Intro. Ashley, Spider-Man's granddaughter. 72-Red Skull app.
1 3 4 6 8 10
71-Old Man Logan; Venom-ized T-Rex app. 2 4 6 11 16 20
73,74-Andy Kubert-a 4.00
75-($3.99) Dark Reign, Daken as Wolverine on Osborn's team; Camuncoli-a 5.00
76-90: 76-86-Multiple covers for each. 76-Dark Reign; Yu-c. 82-84-Siege. 88,89-Franken-Castle x-over; Punisher app. 3.00
#900 (7/10, $4.99) Short stories by various incl. Finch, Rivera, Segovia, McGuinness 5.00
Annual 1 (12/07, $3.99) Hurwitz-s/Frusin-a 4.00
Annual 2 (11/08, $3.99) Swierczynski-s/Deodato-a/c 4.00
...: Blood & Sorrow TPB (2007, $13.99) r/#41,49, stories from Giant-Size Wolverine #1 and X-Men Unlimited #12 14.00
...: Chop Shop 1 (1/09, $2.99) Benson-s/Boschi-a/Hanuka-c 3.00
Civil War: Wolverine TPB (2007, $17.99) r/#42-48; gallery of B&W cover inks 18.00
... Dangerous Games 1 (8/08, $3.99) Spurrier-s/Oliver-a; Remender-s/Opena-a 4.00
...Enemy of the State HC Vol. 1 (2005, $19.99) r/#20-25; Ennis intro.; variant covers 20.00
...Enemy of the State HC Vol. 2 (2005, $19.99) r/#26-32 20.00
...Enemy of the State SC Vol. 1 (2005, $14.99) r/#20-25; Ennis intro.; variant covers 15.00
...Enemy of the State SC Vol. 2 (2006, $16.99) r/#26-32 17.00
...Enemy of the State - The Complete Edition (2006, $34.99) r/#20-32; Ennis intro.; sketch pages, variant covers and pin-up art 35.00
...: Evolution SC (2008, $14.99) r/#50-55 15.00
...: Flies to a Spider (2/09, $3.99) Bradstreet-c/Hurwitz-s/Opena-a 4.00
...: Killing Made Simple (10/08, $3.99) Yost-s/Turnbull-a 4.00
...: Enemy of the State MGC #20 (7/11, $1.00) r/#20 with "Marvel's Greatest Comics" logo 3.00
...: Japan's Most Wanted HC (2014, $34.99) printing of material that debuted online 35.00
...: Mr. X (5/10, $3.99) Tieri-s/Diaz-a/Mattina-c 4.00

Wolverine #30 © MAR

Wolverine (2013) #7 © MAR

Wolverine: Noir #3 © MAR

GD VG FN VF VF/NM NM-
2.0 4.0 6.0 8.0 9.0 9.2

...: Old Man Logan Giant-Sized Special (11/09, $4.99) Continued from #72; cover gallery 5.00
...Origins & Endings HC (2006, $19.99) r/#36-40 20.00
...Origins & Endings SC (2006, $13.99) r/#36-40 14.00
...: Origin of an X-Man Free Comic Book Day 2009 (5/09) Gurihiru-a/McGuinness-c 3.00
...: Revolver (8/09, $3.99) Gischler-s/Pastoras-a 4.00
... Saga (2009, giveaway) history of the character in text and comic panels 3.00
...: Saudade (2008, $4.99) English adaptation of Wolverine story from French comic 5.00
...: Savage (4/10, $3.99) J. Scott Campbell-c; The Lizard app. 4.00
...Special: Firebreak (2/08, $3.99) Carey-s/Kolins-a; Lolos-a 4.00
...: Switchback 1 (3/09, $3.99) short stories; art by Pastoras & Doe 4.00
...: The Amazing Immortal Man & Other Bloody Tales (7/08, $3.99) Lapham short stories 4.00
...: The Anniversary (6/09, $3.99) Mariko flashback short stories; art by various 4.00
...: The Death of Wolverine HC (2008, $19.99) r/#56-61 20.00
...: The Road to Hell (11/10, $3.99) Previews new Wolverine titles and Generation Hope 4.00
...: Under the Boardwalk (2/10, $3.99) Coker-a 4.00
...Vol. 1: The Brotherhood (2003, $12.99) r/#1-6 13.00
...Vol. 2: Coyote Crossing (2004, $11.99) r/#7-11 12.00
... Weapon X Files (2009, $4.99) Handbook-style pages of Wolverine characters 5.00
...: Wendigo! 1 (3/10, $3.99) Gulacy-a; back-up with Thor 4.00

WOLVERINE (Volume 4) (Also see Savage Wolverine)
Marvel Comics: Nov, 2010 - No. 20, Feb, 2012; No. 300, Mar, 2012 - No. 317, Feb, 2013 ($3.99/$4.99)

1-5-Jae Lee-c/Guedes-a; Wolverine Goes to Hell. 1-Back-up with Silver Samurai 4.00
5.1-(4/11, $2.99) Aaron-s/Palo-a/Rivera-c 3.00
6-20: 6-Jae Lee-c/Acuña-a; X-Men & Magneto app. 20-Kingpin & Sabretooth app. 4.00
300-(3/12, $4.99) Adam Kubert-c; Sabretooth & new Silver Samurai app. 5.00
301-308,310-317: 301-304-Aaron-s. 302-Art Adams-c. 310-313-Bianchi-a/c 4.00
309-($4.99) Elixir with X-Force; Albuquerque-a; Ribic-c 5.00
#1000 (4/11, $4.99) Short stories by various incl. Palmiotti, Green, Luke Ross; Segovia-c 5.00
Annual 1 (10/12, $4.99) Alan Davis-s/a/c; the Clan Destine app. (see Daredevil Ann. #1) 5.00
...: Debt of Death 1 (11/11, $3.99) Lapham-s/Aja-a/c; Nick Fury app. 4.00
.../Deadpool: The Decoy 1 (9/11, $3.99) prints online story from Marvel.com; Young-c 4.00

WOLVERINE (5th series)
Marvel Comics: May, 2013 - No. 13, Mar, 2014 ($3.99)

1-13: 1-4-Cornell-s/Alan Davis-a/c; Nick Fury II app. 5-7-Pierfederici-a. 8-13-Killable 4.00
... In the Flesh (9/13, $3.99) Cosentino-s/Talajic-a 4.00

WOLVERINE (6th series)
Marvel Comics: Apr, 2014 - No. 12, Oct, 2014 ($3.99)

1-11: 1-Cornell-s/Stegman-a. 2-Superior Spider-Man app. 8,9-Iron Fist app. 4.00
12-($5.99) "1 Month To Die"; Cornell-s/Woods-a; Thor & Sabretooth app. 6.00
Annual 1 (10/14, $4.99) Jubilee app; Nguyen-c/Kalan-s/Marks-a 5.00

WOLVERINE (7th series)
Marvel Comics: Apr, 2020 - Present ($7.99/$3.99)

1-($7.99) Percy-s/Adam Kubert-a; multiple covers; Dracula app. 8.00
2-7,9-24,26-30-($3.99) 2,3-Percy-s/Adam Kubert-a. 4-6-Bogdanovic-a. 6,7-"X of Swords" tie-in. 13-Hellfire Gala tie-in. 20-23-Deadpool app. 24-Judgment Day tie-in 4.00
8-($4.99) 350th Wolverine issue; short stories; Kubert, Bogdanovic-a; Patch returns 5.00
25-($4.99) Judgment Day tie-in 5.00
Annual 1 (11/19, $4.99) "Acts of Evil" tie-in; Houser-s/Borges-a; Morgan Le Fay app. 5.00
...: Through the Years Primer 1 (4/20, free) Previews #1; creator interviews; iconic covers 3.00
... vs. Blade Special (9/19, $5.99) Guggenheim-s/Wilkins-a/c; Doctor Strange app. 6.00

WOLVERINE & BLACK CAT: CLAWS 2 (See Claws for 1st series)
Marvel Comics: Aug, 2011 - No. 3, Nov, 2011 ($3.99, limited series)

1-3-Linsner-a/c; Palmiotti & Gray-s; Killraven app. 4.00

WOLVERINE & CAPTAIN AMERICA: WEAPON PLUS
Marvel Comics: Sept, 2019 ($4.99, one-shot)

1-Sacks-s/Neves-a 5.00

WOLVERINE AND JUBILEE
Marvel Comics: Mar, 2011 - No. 4, Jun, 2011 ($2.99, limited series)

1-4: 1-Vampire Jubilee; Kathryn Immonen-s/Phil Noto-a; Coipel-c
1 2 3 5 6 8

WOLVERINE AND POWER PACK
Marvel Comics: Jan, 2009 - No. 4, Apr, 2009 ($2.99, limited series)

1-4-Sumerak-s. 1,2-GuriHiru-a. 1-Sauron app. 3-Meet Wolverine as a child; Koblish-a 3.00

WOLVERINE AND THE PUNISHER: DAMAGING EVIDENCE
Marvel Comics: Oct, 1993 - No. 3, Dec, 1993 ($2.00, limited series)

1-3: 2,3-Indicia says "The Punisher and Wolverine..." 5.00

WOLVERINE & THE X-MEN (Regenesis)(See X-Men: Schism)
Marvel Comics: Dec, 2011 - No. 42, Apr, 2014 ($3.99)

GD VG FN VF VF/NM NM-
2.0 4.0 6.0 8.0 9.0 9.2

1-8: 1-3-Aaron-s/Bachalo-a/c. 3-Sabretooth app. 4-Bradshaw-a; Deathlok app. 4.00
9-27: 9-16,18-Avengers vs. X-Men tie-in. 17-Allred-a 4.00
27AU (6/13, $3.99) Age of Ultron tie-in; continues in Age of Ultron #6 4.00
28-41: 30-35-Hellfire Saga. 36,37-Battle of the Atom 4.00
42-($4.99) Cover swipe of X-Men #141 (1981) Graduation Day 5.00
Annual 1 (1/14, $4.99) Aaron-s/Bradshaw-a; Gladiator app. 5.00

WOLVERINE & THE X-MEN (2nd series)
Marvel Comics: May, 2014 - No. 12, Jan, 2015 ($3.99)

1-9,11,12: 1-Latour-s/Asrar-a; Fantomex app. 7-Daredevil app. 11-Spider-Man app. 4.00
10-($4.99) Follows Wolverine's death; art by various incl. Anka, Bertram, Rugg, Shalvey 5.00

WOLVERINE AND THE X-MEN: ALPHA & OMEGA
Marvel Comics: Dec, 2011 - No. 5, Jul, 2012 ($3.99, limited series)

1-5-Brooks-c/Boschi & Brooks-a; Quentin Quire vs. Wolverine 4.00

WOLVERINE: BLACK, WHITE & BLOOD
Marvel Comics: Jan, 2021 - No. 4, May, 2021 ($4.99, limited series, B&W&Red)

1-4-Short story anthology by various. 1-Duggan-s/Adam Kubert-a; Shalvey-s/a 5.00

WOLVERINE/CAPTAIN AMERICA
Marvel Comics: Apr, 2004 - No. 4, Apr, 2004 ($2.99, limited series)

1-4-Derenick-a/c 3.00

WOLVERINE: DAYS OF FUTURE PAST
Marvel Comics: Dec, 1997 - No. 3, Feb, 1998 ($2.50, limited series)

1-3: J.F. Moore-s/Bennett-a 4.00

WOLVERINE/DOOP (Also see X-Force and X-Statix)(Reprinted in X-Statix Vol. 2)
Marvel Comics: July, 2003 - No. 2, July, 2003 ($2.99, limited series)

1,2-Peter Milligan-s/Darwyn Cooke & J. Bone-a 3.00

WOLVERINE: FIRST CLASS
Marvel Comics: May, 2008 - No. 21, Jan, 2010 ($2.99)

1-21: 1-Wolverine and Kitty Pryde's first mission; DiVito-a. 2,9-Sabretooth app. 3.00

WOLVERINE/GAMBIT: VICTIMS
Marvel Comics: Sept, 1995 - No. 4, Dec, 1995 ($2.95, limited series)

1-4: Jeph Loeb scripts & Tim Sale-a; foil-c 5.00

WOLVERINE/HERCULES: MYTHS, MONSTERS & MUTANTS
Marvel Comics: May, 2011 - No. 4, Aug, 2011 ($2.99, limited series)

1-4-Tieri-s/Santacruz-a/Jusko-c 3.00

WOLVERINE/HULK
Marvel Comics: Apr, 2002 - No. 4, July, 2002 ($3.50, limited series)

1-4-Sam Kieth-s/a/c 4.00
Wolverine Legends Vol. 1: Wolverine/Hulk (2003, $9.99, TPB) r/#1-4 10.00

WOLVERINE: INFINITY WATCH
Marvel Comics: Apr, 2019 - No. 5, Aug, 2019 ($3.99, limited series)

1-5-Duggan-s/MacDonald-a; Loki app. 4.00

WOLVERINE: MANIFEST DESTINY
Marvel Comics: Dec, 2008 - No. 4, Mar, 2009 ($2.99, limited series)

1-4-Aaron-s/Segovia-a 3.00

WOLVERINE MAX
Marvel Comics: Dec, 2012 - No. 15, Mar, 2014 ($3.99)

1-15: 1-5-Starr-s/Boschi-a/Jock-c; Victor Creed app. 4.00

WOLVERINE: NETSUKE
Marvel Comics: Nov, 2002 - No. 4, Feb, 2003 ($3.99, limited series)

1-4-George Pratt-s/painted-a 4.00

WOLVERINE: NOIR (1930s Pulp-style)
Marvel Comics: Apr, 2009 - No. 4, Sept, 2009 ($3.99, limited series)

1-4-C.P. Smith-a/Stuart Moore; covers by Smith & Calero; alternate Logan as detective 4.00

WOLVERINE: ORIGINS
Marvel Comics: June, 2006 - No. 50, Sept, 2010 ($2.99)

1-15: 1-Daniel Way-s/Steve Dillon-a/Quesada-c 3.00
1-10-Variant covers. 1-Turner. 2-Quesada & Hitch. 3-Bianchi. 4-Dell'Otto. 7-Deodato 4.00
16-($3.99) Captain America WW2 app.; preview of Wolverine #56; r/X-Men #268 4.00
16-Variant-c by McGuinness 4.00
17-24: 17-20-Capt. America & Bucky app. 21-24-Deadpool app.; Bianchi-c 3.00
25-($3.99) Deadpool app.; Bianchi-c; r/Deadpool's 1st app. in New Mutants #98 5.00
26-49: 26-Origin of Dakan; Way-s/Segovia-a/Land-c. 28-Hulk & Wendigo app. 3.00
50-($3.99) Last issue; Nick Fury app. 4.00
Annual 1 (9/07, $3.99) Way-s/Andrews-a; flashback to 1932 4.00
... Vol. 1 - Born in Blood HC (2006, $19.99, dustjacket) r/#1-5; variant covers 20.00

GD VG FN VF VF/NM NM-
2.0 4.0 6.0 8.0 9.0 9.2

... Vol. 1 - Born in Blood SC (2007, $13.99) r/#1-5; variant covers 14.00
... Vol. 2 - Savior HC (2007, $19.99, dustjacket) r/#6-10; variant covers 20.00
... Vol. 2 - Savior SC (2007, $13.99) r/#6-10; variant covers 14.00
... Vol. 3 - Swift & Terrible HC (2007, $19.99, dustjacket) r/#11-15 20.00
... Vol. 3 - Swift & Terrible SC (2007, $13.99) r/#11-15 14.00
... Vol. 4 - Our War HC (2008, $19.99, dustjacket) r/#16-20 & Annual #1 20.00
... Vol. 4 - Our War SC (2008, $14.99) r/#16-20 & Annual #1 15.00

WOLVERINE: PATCH
Marvel Comics: May, 2022 - No. 5, Oct, 2022 ($3.99, limited series)
1-5-Larry Hama-s/Andrea Di Vito-a; Nick Fury app. 4.00

WOLVERINE/PUNISHER
Marvel Comics: May, 2004 - No. 5, Sept, 2004 ($2.99, limited series)
1-5: Milligan-s/Weeks-a 3.00
... Vol. 1 TPB (2004, $13.99) r/series 14.00

WOLVERINE, PUNISHER & GHOST RIDER: OFFICIAL INDEX TO THE MARVEL UNIVERSE
Marvel Comics: Oct, 2011 - No. 8, May, 2012 ($3.99)
1-8-Each issue has chronological synopsies, creator credits, character lists for 30-40 issues of their own titles and headlining mini-series 4.00

WOLVERINE/PUNISHER REVELATIONS (Marvel Knights)
Marvel Comics: Jun, 1999 - No. 4, Sept, 1999 ($2.95, limited series)
1-4: Pat Lee-a(p) 4.00
...: Revelation (4/00, $14.95, TPB) r/#1-4 15.00

WOLVERINES (Follows Death of Wolverine)
Marvel Comics: Mar, 2015 - No. 20, Aug, 2015 ($3.99, weekly series)
1-20: 1-Soule-s/Bradshaw-a; Sabretooth, Daken, Mystique, X-23 app. 13-Deadpool app. 4.00

WOLVERINE SAGA
Marvel Comics: Sept, 1989 - No. 4, Mid-Dec, 1989 ($3.95, lim. series, 52 pgs.)
1-Gives history; Liefeld/Austin-c (front & back) 6.00
2-4: 2-Romita, Jr./Austin-c. 4-Kaluta-c 6.00

WOLVERINE: SNIKT!
Marvel Comics: July, 2003 - No. 5, Nov, 2003 ($2.99, limited series)
1-5-Manga-style; Tsutomu Nihei-s/a 3.00
Wolverine Legends Vol. 5: Snikt! TPB (2003, $13.99) r/#1-5 14.00

WOLVERINE: SOULTAKER
Marvel Comics: May, 2005 - No. 5, Aug, 2005 ($2.99, limited series)
1-5-Yoshida-s/Nagasawa-a/Terada-c; Yukio app. 3.00
TPB (2005, $13.99) r/#1-5 14.00

WOLVERINE: THE BEST THERE IS
Marvel Comics: Feb, 2011 - No. 12, Jan, 2012 ($3.99)
1-12: 1,2-Huston-s/Ryp-a; covers by Hitch and Djurdjevic. 3-12-Hitch-c 4.00
... - Contagion 1 (6/11, $4.99) r/#1-3, cover gallery 5.00

WOLVERINE: THE END
Marvel Comics: Jan, 2004 - No. 6, Dec, 2004 ($2.99, limited series)
1-5-Jenkins-s/Castellini-a 3.00
1-Wizard World Texas variant-c 20.00
TPB (2005, $14.99) r/#1-5 15.00

WOLVERINE: THE LONG NIGHT ADAPTATION (Based on the 2018 10-part podcast)
Marvel Comics: Mar, 2019 - No. 5, Jul, 2019 ($4.99/$3.99, limited series)
1-($4.99) Benjamin Percy-s/Marcio Takara-a; Wolverine in Alaska 5.00
2-5-($3.99) 4.00

WOLVERINE: THE ORIGIN
Marvel Comics: Nov, 2001 - No. 6, July, 2002 ($3.50, limited series)
1-Origin of Logan; Jenkins-s/Andy Kubert-a; Quesada-c 35.00
1-DF edition 25.00
2 10.00
3-6 6.00
HC (3/02, $34.95, 11" x 7-1/2") r/#1-6; dust jacket; sketch pages and treatments 35.00
HC (2006, $19.99) r/#1-6; dust jacket; sketch pages and treatments 20.00
SC (2002, $14.95) r/#1-6; afterwords by Jemas and Quesada 15.00

WOLVERINE WEAPON X
Marvel Comics: June, 2009 - No. 16, Oct, 2010 ($3.99)
1-16: 1-5,11-Aaron-s/Garney-a. 1-Four covers. 2,3-Two covers. 11-15-Deathlok app. 4.00

WOLVERINE: XISLE
Marvel Comics: June, 2003 - No. 5, June, 2003 ($2.50, weekly limited series)
1-5-Bruce Jones-s/Jorge Lucas-a 3.00
Wolverine Legends Vol. 4 TPB (2003, $13.99) r/ #1-5 14.00

WOMANTHOLOGY: SPACE
IDW Publishing: Sept, 2012 - No. 5, Feb, 2013 ($3.99)
1-5-Anthology of short stories by women creators 4.00

WOMEN IN LOVE (A Feature Presentation #5)
Fox Feature Synd./Hero Books: Aug, 1949 - No. 4, Feb, 1950
1 53 106 159 334 567 800
2-Kamen/Feldstein-c 45 90 135 284 480 675
3 36 72 108 211 343 475
4-Wood-a 42 84 126 265 445 625

WOMEN IN LOVE (Thrilling Romances for Adults)
Ziff-Davis Publishing Co.: Winter, 1952 (25¢, 100 pgs.)
nn-(Scarce)-Kinstler-a; painted-c 103 206 309 659 1130 1600

WOMEN OF MARVEL
Marvel Comics: 2006, 2007 ($24.99, TPB)
SC-Reprints 1st apps. of Dazzler, Ms. Marvel, Shanna, The Cat plus notable stories of other female Marvel characters; Mayhew-c 25.00
Vol. 2 (2007) More stories of female Marvel characters; Mayhew-c; cover process art 25.00

WOMEN OF MARVEL
Marvel Comics: Jan, 2011 - No. 2, Feb, 2011 ($3.99, limited series)
1,2-Short stories of female Marvel characters. 1-Pichelli-c. 2-Land-c 4.00
1-(6/21, $5.99) Short stories by female creators; intro by Louise Simonson 6.00
1-(5/22, $5.99) Short stories by female creators; intro by Gail Simone 6.00

WOMEN OUTLAWS (My Love Memories #9 on)(Also see Red Circle)
Fox Feature Syndicate: July, 1948 - No. 8, Sept, 1949
1-Used in **SOTI**, illo "Giving children an image of American womanhood"; negligee panels
113 226 339 718 1234 1750
2,3: 3-Kamenish-a 77 154 231 493 847 1200
4-8 61 122 183 390 670 950
nn(nd)-Contains Cody of the Pony Express; same cover as #7
34 68 102 199 325 450

WOMEN TO LOVE
Realistic: No date (1953)
nn-(Scarce)-Reprints Complete Romance #1; c-/Avon paperback #165
60 120 180 381 653 925

WONDER BOY (Formerly Terrific Comics) (See Blue Bolt, Bomber Comics & Samson)
Ajax/Farrell Publ.: No. 17, May, 1955 - No. 18, July, 1955 (Code approved)
17-Phantom Lady app. Bakerish-c/a 60 120 180 381 653 925
18-Phantom Lady app. 52 104 156 328 552 775
NOTE: *Phantom Lady not by Matt Baker.*

WONDER COMICS (Wonderworld #3 on)
Fox Feature Syndicate: May, 1939 - No. 2, June, 1939 (68 pgs.)
1-(Scarce)-Wonder Man only app. by Will Eisner; Dr. Fung (by Powell), K-5 begins; Bob Kane-a; Eisner-c 3700 7400 11,100 25,900 45,450 65,000
2-(Scarce)-Yarko the Great, Master Magician (see Samson) by Eisner begins; 'Spark' Stevens by Bob Kane, Patty O'Day, Tex Mason app. Lou Fine's 1st-c; Fine-a (2 pgs.); Yarko-c (Wonder Man-c #1) 1100 2200 3300 8360 15,180 22,000

WONDER COMICS
Great/Nedor/Better Publications: May, 1944 - No. 20, Oct, 1948
1-The Grim Reaper & Spectro, the Mind Reader begin; Hitler/Hirohito bondage-c
423 846 1269 3046 5323 7600
2-Origin The Grim Reaper; Super Sleuths begin, end #8,17; Schomburg Nazi WWII-c
258 516 774 1651 2826 4000
3-5: All Schomburg Nazi WWII-c. 3-Indicia reads "Vol. 1, #2"
213 426 639 1363 2332 3300
6-Japanese WWII Flag-c 155 310 465 992 1696 2400
7-10: 8-Last Spectro. 9-Wonderman begins 106 212 318 673 1162 1650
11-13: 11-Dick Devens, King of Futuria begins, ends #14. 11,12-Ingels-c & splash pg.
12-Bondage/headlight-c by Ingels 126 252 378 806 1378 1950
14-Classic Schomburg sci-fi good girl bondage-c 194 388 582 1242 2121 3000
15-Tara begins (origin), ends #20; classic Schomburg bondage/torture-c
290 580 870 1856 3178 4500
16,18: 16-Spectro app.; last Grim Reaper. 18-The Silver Knight begins
100 200 300 635 1093 1550
17-Wonderman with Frazetta panels; Jill Trent with all Frazetta inks
119 238 357 762 1306 1850
19-Frazetta panels 110 220 330 704 1202 1700
20-Most of Silver Knight by Frazetta 129 258 387 826 1413 2000
NOTE: ***Ingels** c-11, 12. **Roussos** a-19. **Schomburg (Xela)** c-1-10; (airbrush)-13-20. Bondage c-12, 13, 15. Cover features: Grim Reaper #1-8; Wonder Man #9-15; Tara #16-20.*

WONDER DUCK (See Wisco)
Marvel Comics (CDS): Sept, 1949 - No. 3, Mar, 1950
1-Funny animal 28 56 84 165 270 375
2,3 19 38 57 111 176 240

WONDERFUL ADVENTURES OF PINOCCHIO, THE (See Movie Comics & Walt Disney Showcase #48)
Whitman Publishing Co.: April, 1982 (Walt Disney)
nn-(#3 Continuation of Movie Comics?); r/FC #92 6.00

WONDERFUL WIZARD OF OZ (Adaptation of the original 1900 L. Frank Baum book)
(Also see the sequels Marvelous Land of Oz, Ozma of Oz, and Dorothy & The Wizard in Oz)
Marvel Comics: Feb, 2009 - No. 8, Sept, 2009 ($3.99, limited series)
1-8-Eric Shanower-a/Skottie Young-a/c 4.00
1-Variant Good Witch & Dorothy wraparound cover by J. Scott Campbell 8.00
1-Variant Scarecrow & Dorothy cover by Eric Shanower 10.00
1-(4/10, $1.00) Reprint with "Marvel's Greatest Comics" on cover 3.00
... Sketchbook (2008, giveaway) Young character design sketches; Shanower intro. 3.00
HC (2009, $29.99, dustjacket) r/#1-8; Shanower intro.; cover gallery; sketch art 30.00

WONDERFUL WORLD FOR BOYS AND GIRLS
DC Comics: May, 1964
nn - Ashcan comic, not distributed to newsstands, only for in-house use (no known sales)

WONDERFUL WORLD OF DISNEY, THE (Walt Disney)
Whitman Publishing Co.: 1978 (Digest, 116 pgs.)
1-Barks-a (reprints) 3 6 9 16 23 30
2 (no date) 2 4 6 11 16 20

WONDERFUL WORLD OF TANK GIRL
Titan Comics: Nov, 2017 - No. 4, May, 2018 ($3.99, limited series)
1-4: 1-Tank Girl Strikes Again; Martin-s/Parson-a; multiple covers 4.00

WONDERFUL WORLD OF THE BROTHERS GRIMM (See Movie Comics)

WONDER GIRL (Cassandra Sandsmark from Teen Titans)
DC Comics: Nov, 2007 - No. 6, Apr, 2008 ($2.99, limited series)
1-6-Torres-s/Greene-a; Hercules app. 2-6-Female Furies app. 5,6-Wonder Woman app. 3.00
Teen Titans Spotlight: Wonder Girl TPB (2008, $17.99) r/#1-6 18.00
1-(3/11, $2.99, one-shot) Nicola Scott-c; intro. Solstice 3.00

WONDER GIRL (Yara Flor from Future State)
DC Comics: Jul, 2021 - No. 7, Mar, 2022 ($3.99, limited series)
1-7: 1-Joëlle Jones-s/a. 2-4-Jones & Melo-a. 5-7-Donna Troy app. 4.00
2022 Annual 1 (10/22, $5.99) Joëlle Jones-s; art by various 6.00

WONDERLAND (See Grimm Fairy Tales Presents Wonderland)

WONDERLAND COMICS

Women of Marvel #1 © MAR

Wonder Twins #7 © DC

Wonder Woman #177 © DC

	GD 2.0	VG 4.0	FN 6.0	VF 8.0	VF/NM 9.0	NM- 9.2
Feature Publications/Prize: Summer, 1945 - No. 9, Feb-Mar, 1947						
1-Alex in Wonderland begins; Howard Post-c	39	78	117	240	395	550
2-Howard Post-c/a(2)	21	42	63	122	199	275
3-9: 3,4-Post-c	19	38	57	111	176	240
WONDER MAN (See The Avengers #9, 151)						
Marvel Comics Group: Mar, 1986 ($1.25, one-shot, 52 pgs.)						
1						6.00
WONDER MAN						
Marvel Comics Group: Sept, 1991 - No. 29, Jan, 1994 ($1.00)						
1-29: 1-Free fold out poster by Johnson/Austin. 1-3-Johnson/Austin-c/a. 2-Avengers West Coast x-over. 4 Austin-c(i)						3.00
Annual 1 (1992, $2.25)-Immonen-a (10 pgs.)						4.00
Annual 2 (1993, $2.95)-Bagged w/trading card						4.00
WONDER MAN						
Marvel Comics: Feb, 2007 - No. 5, June, 2007 ($2.99, limited series)						
1-5: 1-Peter David-s/Andrew Currie-a; Beast app. 4-Nauck-a						3.00
...: My Fair Super Hero TPB (2007, $13.99) r/#1-5; Currie sketch page						14.00
WONDERS OF ALADDIN, THE						
Dell Publishing Co.: No. 1255, Feb-Apr, 1962						
Four Color 1255-Movie	6	12	18	42	79	115
WONDER TWINS (From Superfriends)						
DC Comics (Wonder Comics): Apr, 2019 - No. 12, Apr, 2020 ($3.99)						
1-12: 1-Mark Russell-s/Stephen Byrne-a; Justice League and Mr. Mxyzptlk app. 3-Intro Gleek						4.00
WONDER WOMAN (See Adventure Comics #459, All-Star Comics, Brave & the Bold, DC Comics Presents, JLA, Justice League of America, Legend of..., Power Record Comics, Sensation Comics, Super Friends and World's Finest Comics #244)						
WONDER WOMAN						
DC Comics: Jan 1942						
1-Ashcan comic, not distributed to newsstands, only for in-house use. Cover art is Sensation Comics #1 with interior being Sensation Comics #2. A CGC certified 8.5 copy sold for $17,250 in 2002. A CGC certified 8.5 copy sold for $57,668 in 2018.						
WONDER WOMAN						
National Periodical Publications/All-American Publ./DC Comics: Summer, 1942 - No. 329, Feb, 1986						
1-Origin Wonder Woman retold (more detailed than All Star #8); H. G. Peter-c/a begins	14,100	28,200	42,300	94,000	172,000	250,000
1-Reprint, Oversize 13-1/2x10". **WARNING:** This comic is an exact reprint of the original except for its size. DC published it in 1974 with a second cover titling it as a Famous First Edition. There have been many reported cases of the outer cover being removed and the interior sold as the original edition. The reprint with the new outer cover removed is practically worthless. See Famous First Edition for value.						
2-Origin/1st app. Mars; Duke of Deception app.	946	1892	2838	6909	12,203	17,500
3	400	800	1200	2800	4900	7000
4,5: 5-1st Dr. Psycho app.	314	628	942	2198	3849	5500
6-1st Cheetah app.	1100	2200	3300	8150	14,575	21,000
7-Wonder Woman for President-c/sty	1100	2200	3300	8150	14,575	21,000
8,9: 9-1st app. Giganta (Sum/44)	258	516	774	1651	2826	4000
10-Invasion from Saturn classic sci-fi-c/s	265	530	795	1694	2897	4100
11-20	158	316	474	1003	1727	2450
21-30: 23-Story from Wonder Woman's childhood. 28-Cheetah and Giganta-c/app.	135	2470	405	864	1482	2100
31-33,35-40: 37-1st app. Circe. 38-Last H.G. Peter-c	126	252	378	806	1378	1950
34-Robot-c	129	258	387	826	1413	2000
41-44,46-48	119	238	357	762	1306	1850
45-Origin retold	245	490	735	1568	2684	3800
49-Used in **SOTI**, pgs. 234,236; last 52 pg. issue	129	258	387	826	1413	2000
50-(44 pgs.)-Used in **POP**, pg. 97	123	246	369	787	1344	1900
51-60: 60-New logo	110	220	330	704	1202	1700
61-72: 62-Origin of W.W. i.d. 64-Story about 3-D movies. 70-1st Angle Man app. 72-Last pre-code (2/55)	103	206	309	659	1130	1600
73-90: 80-Origin The Invisible Plane. 89-Flying saucer-c/story	93	186	279	599	1025	1450
91-94,96,97: 97-Last H. G. Peter-a	77	154	231	493	847	1200
95-A-Bomb-c	90	180	270	576	988	1400
98-(5/58) 1st Silver Age Wonder Woman; new origin & new art team (Andru & Esposito) begin; Kanigher-s; 1st meets Steve Trevor	649	1298	1947	4738	8369	12,000
99-New origin continues; origin Diana Prince i.d.	103	206	309	659	1130	1600
100-(8/58)	100	200	300	635	1093	1550
101-104,106,108-110	57	114	171	362	619	875
105-(Scarce, 4/59)-Wonder Woman's origin (part 3); she appears as a girl (no costume yet) (called Wonder Girl - see DC Super-Stars #1)	295	590	885	1888	3244	4600
107-1st advs. of Wonder Girl; 1st Merboy; tells how Wonder Woman won her costume	68	136	204	435	743	1050
111-120	42	84	126	265	445	625
121-126: 121-1st app. Wonder Woman Family. 122-1st app. Wonder Tot. 124-Wonder Woman Family app. 126-Last 10¢ issue	36	72	108	214	347	480
127-130: 128-Origin The Invisible Plane retold. 129-3rd app. Wonder Woman Family (#133 is 4th app.)	16	32	48	112	249	380
131-150: 132-Flying saucer-c	13	26	39	89	195	300
151-155,157,158,161-170 (1967): 151-Wonder Girl solo issue.	10	20	30	67	141	215
156-(8/65)-Early mention of a comic book shop & comic collecting; mentions DCs selling for $100 a copy	10	20	30	69	147	225
159-Origin retold (1/66); 1st S.A. origin?	13	26	39	89	195	300
160-1st S.A. Cheetah app.	37	74	111	274	612	950
171-176	8	16	24	56	108	160
177-W. Woman/Supergirl battle	11	22	33	73	157	240
178-(10/68) 1st new Wonder Woman on-c only; appears in old costume w/powers inside	13	26	39	86	188	290
179-Classic-c; wears no costume to issue #203	13	26	39	86	188	290
180-195: 180-Death of Steve Trevor. 182-Last 12¢ issue. 195-Wood inks	6	12	18	42	79	115
196 (52 pgs.)-Origin-r/All Star #8 (6 out of 9 pgs.)	10	20	30	64	132	200
197,198 (52 pgs.)-Reprints	7	14	21	46	86	125
199-Jeff Jones painted-c; 52 pgs.	10	20	30	66	138	210
200 (5-6/72)-Jeff Jones-c; 52 pgs.	10	20	30	69	147	225
201,202-Catwoman app. 202-Fafhrd & The Grey Mouser debut.	5	10	15	35	63	90
203,205-210,212: 212-The Cavalier app.	4	8	12	23	37	50
204-(2/73) Return to old costume; death of I Ching; intro. Nubia	28	56	84	202	451	700
204 (Facsimile Edition) (1/23, $3.99) Reprints #204 with original 1973 ads						4.00
211,214-(100 pgs.)	8	16	24	54	102	150
213,215,216,218-220: 220-N. Adams assist	3	6	9	19	30	40
217: (68 pgs.)	4	8	12	27	44	60
221,222,224-227,229,230,233-236,238-240: 227-Judy Garland tribute	3	6	9	15	22	28
223,228,231,232,237,241,248: 223-Steve Trevor revived as Steve Howard & learns W.W.'s I.D. 228-Both Wonder Women team up & new World War II stories begin, end #243. 231,232: JSA app. 237-Origin retold. 240-G.A. Flash app. 241-Intro Bouncer; Spectre app. 248-Steve Trevor Howard dies (44 pgs.)	3	6	9	16	23	30
242-246,252-266,269,270: 243-Both W. Women team-up again. 269-Last Wood a(i) for DC? (7/80)	2	4	6	9	13	16
247,249,250,271: 247,249 (44 pgs.). 249-Hawkgirl app. 250-Origin/1st app. Orana, the new Wonder Woman. 271-Huntress & 3rd Life of Steve Trevor begin	2	4	6	10	14	18
250-252,255-262-264-(Whitman variants, low print run, no issue # on cover)	3	6	9	17	26	35
251-Orana dies	3	6	9	14	20	26
267,268-Re-intro Animal Man (5/80 & 6/80)	2	4	6	10	14	18
272-280,284-286,289,290,294-299,301-325	2	4	6	8	10	12
281-283: Joker-c/stories in Huntress back-ups	2	4	6	9	13	16
287,288,291-293: 287-New Teen Titans x-over. 288-New costume & logo. 291-293-Three part epic with Super-Heroines	1	3	4	6	8	10
300-($1.50, 76 pgs.)-Anniv. issue; Giffen-a; New Teen Titans, Bronze Age Sandman, JLA & G.A. Wonder Woman app.; 1st app. Lyta Trevor who becomes Fury in All-Star Squadron #25; G.A. Wonder Woman & Steve Trevor revealed as married	3	6	9	14	19	24
326-328	1	3	4	6	8	10
329 (Double size)-S.A. W.W. & Steve Trevor wed	3	6	9	15	20	26
...: Chronicles Vol. 1 TPB (2010, $17.99) reprints debut in All Star Comics #8, apps. in Sensation Comics #1-9 and Wonder Woman #1						18.00
Diana Prince: Wonder Woman Vol. 1 TPB (2008, $19.99) r/#178-183						20.00
Diana Prince: Wonder Woman Vol. 2 TPB (2008, $19.99) r/#185-189, Brave and the Bold #87, and Superman's Girl Friend, Lois Lane #93						20.00
Diana Prince: Wonder Woman Vol. 3 TPB ('08, $19.99) r/#190-198, World's Finest #204						20.00
Diana Prince: Wonder Woman Vol. 4 TPB ('09, $19.99) r/#199-204, Brave & Bold #105						20.00
...: The Greatest Stories Ever Told TPB (2007, $19.99) intro. by Lynda Carter; Ross-c						20.00

NOTE: ***Andru/Esposito*** *c-66-160(most).* ***Buckler*** *a-300.* ***Colan*** *a-288-305p; c-288-290p.* ***Giffen*** *a-300p.* ***Grell*** *c-217.* ***Kaluta*** *c-297.* ***Gil Kane*** *c-294p, 303-305, 307, 312, 314.* ***Miller*** *c-298p.* ***Morrow*** *c-233.* ***Nasser*** *a-232p; c-231p, 232p.* ***Bob Oskner*** *c(i)-39-65(most).* ***Perez*** *c-283p, 284p.* ***Spiegle*** *a-312.* ***Staton*** *a(p)-241, 271-287, 289, 290, 294-299; c(p)-241, 245, 246. Huntress back-up stories 271-287, 289, 290, 294-299, 301-321.*

	GD 2.0	VG 4.0	FN 6.0	VF 8.0	VF/NM 9.0	NM- 9.2
WONDER WOMAN						
DC Comics: Feb, 1987 - No. 226, Apr, 2006 (75¢/$1.00/$1.25/$1.95/$1.99/$2.25/$2.50)						
0-(10/94) Zero Hour; released between #90 & #91	2	4	6	10	14	18
1-New origin; Pérez-c/a begins	4	8	12	25	40	55

	GD 2.0	VG 4.0	FN 6.0	VF 8.0	VF/NM 9.0	NM- 9.2

1 (Facsimile Edition) (12/20, $3.99) Reprints #1 with original ads 4.00
2-5 1 3 4 6 8 10
6-20: 9-Origin Cheetah. 12,13-Millennium x-over. 18,26-Free 16 pg. story 5.00
21-49: 24-Last Pérez-a; scripts continue thru #62 4.00
50-($1.50, 52 pgs.)-New Titans, Justice League 5.00
51-62: Pérez scripts. 60-Vs. Lobo; last Pérez-c. 62-Last $1.00-c 4.00
63-New direction & Bolland-c begin; Deathstroke story continued from W. W. Special #1 5.00
64-84 4.00
85-1st Deodato-a; ends #100 2 4 6 9 13 16
86-88: 88-Superman-c & app. 6.00
89-97: 90-(9/94)-1st Artemis. 91-(11/94). 93-Hawkman app. 96-Joker-c 5.00
98,99 4.00
100 ($2.95, Newsstand)-Death of Artemis; Bolland-c ends. 5.00
100 ($3.95, Direct Market)-Death of Artemis; foil-c 1 2 3 5 6 8
101-119, 121-125: 101-Begin $1.95-c; Byrne-c/a/scripts begin. 101-104-Darkseid app. 105-Phantom Stranger cameo. 106-108-Phantom Stranger & Demon app. 107,108-Arion app. 111-1st app. new Wonder Girl. 111,112-Vs. Doomsday. 112-Superman app. 113-Wonder Girl-c/app; Sugar & Spike app. 3.00
120 ($2.95)-Perez-c 4.00
126-149: 128-Hippolyta becomes new W.W. 130-133-Flash (Jay Garrick) & JSA app. 136-Diana returns to W.W. role; last Byrne issue. 137-Priest-s. 139-Luke-s/Paquette-a begin; Hughes-c thru #146 3.00
150-($2.95) Hughes-c/Clark-a; Zauriel app. 4.00
151-158-Hughes-c. 153-Superboy app. 3.00
159-163: 159-Begin $2.25-c. 160,161-Clayface app. 162,163-Aquaman app. 3.00
164-171: Phil Jimenez-s/a begin; Hughes-c; Batman app. 168,169-Pérez co-plot 169-Wraparound-c.170-Lois Lane-c/app. 3.00
172-Our Worlds at War; Hippolyta killed 4.00
173,174: 173-Our Worlds at War; Darkseid app. 174-Every DC heroine app. 3.00
175-($3.50) Joker: Last Laugh; JLA app.; Jim Lee-c 4.00
176-199: 177-Paradise Island returns. 179-Jimenez-c. 184,185-Hippolyta-c/app.; Hughes-c 186-Cheetah app. 189-Simonson-s/Ordway-a begin. 190-Diana's new look. 195-Rucka-s/Drew Johnson-a begin. 197-Flash-c/app. 198,199-Noto-c 3.00
200-($3.95) back-up stories in 1940s and 1960s styles; pin-ups by various 4.00
201-218,220-225: 203,204-Batman-c/app. 204-Matt Wagner-c. 212-JLA app. 214-Flash app. 215-Morales-a begins. 218-Begin $2.50-c. 220-Batman app. 3.00
219-Omac tie-in/Sacrifice pt. 4; Wonder Woman kills Max Lord; Superman app. 4.00
219-(2nd printing) Altered cover with red background 3.00
226-Last issue; flashbacks to meetings with Superman; Rucka-s/Richards-a 4.00
#1,000,000 (11/98) 853rd Century x-over; Deodato-c 3.00
Annual 1,2: 1 ('88, $1.50)-Art Adams-a. 2 ('89, $2.00, 68 pgs.)-All women artists issue; Perez-c(i)/a. 5.00
Annual 3 (1992, $2.50, 68 pgs.)-Quesada-c(p) 4.00
Annual 4 (1995, $3.50)-Year One 4.00
Annual 5 (1996, $2.95)-Legends of the Dead Earth story; Byrne scripts; Cockrum-a 4.00
Annual 6 (1997, $3.95)-Pulp Heroes 4.00
Annual 7,8 ('98,'99, $2.95)-7-Ghosts; Wrightson-c. 8-JLApe, A.Adams-c 4.00
...: Beauty and the Beasts TPB (2005, $19.95) r/#15-19 & Action Comics #600 20.00
...: Bitter Rivals TPB (2004, $13.95) r/#200-205; Jones-c 14.00
...: Challenge of the Gods TPB ('04, $19.95) r/#8-14; Pérez-s/a 20.00
...: Destiny Calling TPB (2006, $19.99) r/#20-24 & Annual #1; Pérez-c & pin-up gallery 20.00
...Donna Troy (6/98, $1.95) Girlfrenzy; Jimenez-a 3.00
...: Down To Earth TPB (2004, $14.95) r/#195-200; Greg Land-c 15.00
... 80-Page Giant 1 (2002, $4.95) reprints in format of 1960s' 80-Page Giants 5.00
...: Eyes of the Gorgon TPB ('05, $19.99) r/#206-213 20.00
Gallery (1996, $3.50)-Bolland-c; pin-ups by various 4.00
...: Gods and Mortals TPB ('04, $19.95) r/#1-7; Pérez-a 20.00
...: Gods of Gotham TPB ('01, $5.95) r/#164-167; Jimenez-s/a 6.00
...: Land of the Dead TPB ('06, $12.99) r/#214-217 & Flash #219 13.00
Lifelines TPB ('98, $9.95) r/#106-112; Byrne-c/a 10.00
...: Mission's End TPB ('06, $19.99) r/#218-226; cover gallery 20.00
...: Our Worlds at War (10/01, $2.95) History of the Amazons; Jae Lee-c 3.00
...: Paradise Found TPB ('03, $14.95) r/#171-177, Secret Files #3; Jimenez-s/a 15.00
...: Paradise Lost TPB ('02, $14.95) r/#164-170; Jimenez-s/a 15.00
Plus 1 (1/97, $2.95)-Jesse Quick-c/app. 4.00
Second Genesis TPB (1997, $9.95)-r/#101-105 10.00
Secret Files 1-3 (3/98, 7/99, 5/02; $4.95) 5.00
Special 1 (1992, $1.75, 52 pgs.)-Deathstroke-c/story continued in Wonder Woman #63 5.00
...: The Blue Amazon (2003, $6.95) Elseworlds; McKeever-a 7.00
The Challenge Of Artemis TPB (1996, $9.95)-r/#94-100; Deodato-c/a 10.00
...: The Once and Future Story (1998, $4.95) Trina Robbins-s/Doran & Guice-a 5.00
NOTE: ***Art Adams** a-Annual 1. **Byrne** c/a 101-107. **Bolton** a-Annual 1. **Deodato** a-85-100. **Perez** a-Annual 1; c-Annual 1(i). **Quesada** c(p)-Annual 3.*

WONDER WOMAN (Also see Amazons Attack mini-series)
DC Comics: Aug, 2006 - No. 44, Jul, 2010; No. 600, Aug, 2010 - No. 614, Oct, 2011 ($2.99)

1-Donna Troy as Wonder Woman after Infinite Crisis; Heinberg-s/Dodson-a/c 5.00
1-Variant-c by Adam Kubert 6.00
2-44: 2-4-Giganta & Hercules app. 6-Jodi Picoult-s begins. 8-Hippolyta returns. 9-12-Amazons Attack tie-in; JLA app. 14-17-Simone-s/Dodson-a/c. 20-23-Stalker app. 26-33-Rise of the Olympian app. 40,41-Power Girl app. 3.00
14-DC Nation Convention giveaway edition 6.00
(Title re-numbered after #44, July 2010 to cumilative numbering of #600)
600-(8/10, $4.99) Short stories and pin-ups by various incl. Pérez, Conner, Kramer, Jim Lee; intro. by Lynda Carter; debut of new costume; cover by Pérez 5.00
600-Variant cover by Adam Hughes 8.00
600-2nd printing with new costume cover by Don Kramer 5.00
601-614: 601-606-Kramer-a; two covers by Kramer and Garner. 608-Borges-a 3.00
... Annual 1 (11/07, $3.99) Story cont'd from #4; Heinberg-s/Dodson-a/c; back-up Frank-a 4.00
...: Contagion SC (2010, $14.99) r/#40-44 15.00
...: Ends of the Earth HC (2009, $24.99) r/#20-25 25.00
...: Ends of the Earth SC (2010, $14.99) r/#20-25 15.00
...: Love and Murder HC (2007, $19.99) r/#6-10 20.00
...: Odyssey Volume One HC (2011, $22.99) r/#600-606; afterwords by Jim Lee & JMS 23.00
...: Rise of the Olympian HC (2009, $24.99) r/#26-33 & pages from DC Universe #0 25.00
...: Rise of the Olympian SC (2009, $14.99) r/#26-33 & pages from DC Universe #0 15.00
...: The Circle HC (2008, $24.99) r/#14-19; Mercedes Lackey intro.; Dodson sketch pages 25.00
...: The Circle SC (2009, $14.99) r/#14-19; Mercedes Lackey intro.; Dodson sketch pages 15.00
...: Warkiller SC (2010, $14.99) r/#34-39 15.00
...: Who is Wonder Woman? HC (2007, $19.99) r/#1-4 & Annual #1; Vaughan intro. 20.00
...: Who is Wonder Woman? SC (2009, $14.99) r/#1-4 & Annual #1; Vaughan intro. 15.00

WONDER WOMAN (DC New 52)
DC Comics: Nov, 2011 - No. 52, Jul, 2016 ($2.99/$3.99)

1-Azzarello-s/Chiang-a/c 2 4 6 11 16 20
2-23: 2-4-Azzarello-s/Chiang-a/c. 5,6,9,10,13,14,17-Akins-a. 14-19,21-23-Orion app. 3.00
23.1, 23.2 (11/13, $2.99, regular covers) 3.00
23.1 (11/13, $3.99, 3-D cover) "Cheetah #1" on cover; origin; Ostrander-s/Ibanez-a 5.00
23.2 (11/13, $3.99, 3-D cover) "First Born #1" on cover; origin; Azzarello-s/Aco-a 5.00
24-35: 25-Orion app. 29-Diana becomes God of War. 35-Last Azzarello-s/Chiang-a/c 3.00
36-40: 36-Meredith Finch-s/David Finch-a begins. 37-Donna Troy returns 3.00
41-49,51,52: 41-New costume; begin $3.99-c. 43-Churchill-a 4.00
50-($4.99) Finch & Desjardins-a; Ares app.; back-up Donna Troy story 5.00
#0 (11/12, $2.99) 12 year-old Princess Diana's training; Azzarello-s/Chiang-a/c 3.00
Annual 1 (8/15, $4.99) Concludes "War Torn" arc from #36-40; David Finch-a 5.00
...: Futures End 1 (11/14, $2.99, regular-c) Five years later; Soule-s/Morales-a 3.00
...: Futures End 1 (11/14, $3.99, 3-D cover) 4.00

WONDER WOMAN (DC Rebirth)(Reverts to legacy numbering with #750)
DC Comics: Aug, 2016 - No. 83, Late Feb, 2020; No. 750, Late March, 2020 - Present ($2.99/$3.99/4499)

1-24: 1,3,5,7-Rucka-s/Sharp-a; Cheetah app. 2,4,6,10,12,14-Year One; Nicola Scott-a 3.00
25-($3.99) Justice League and Shaggy Man app. 4.00
26-49: 26-Andolfo-a. 31,33-Grail & baby Darkseid app. 35-Intro. Jason. 37-Zeus vs. Darkseid. 38-40-Silver Swan app. 42-45-Darkseid app. 47-Supergirl app.; leads into Annual 2 3.00
50-74-($3.99): 50-Justice League app. 52,53-Aztek app. 56,57-The Witching Hour tie-in 4.00
75-($4.99) Amazons vs. Grail; Wilson-s/Xermanico & Merino-a 5.00
76-83-Cheetah app. (Year of the Villain) 4.00
750-($9.99, 96 pages) Conclusion vs. Cheetah; short stories and pin-ups by various incl. Simone-s/Doran-a, Rucka-s/Scott-a, Snyder-s/Hitch-a; multiple covers 10.00
751-769-($3.99) 751-Intro. Valda, The Iron Maiden. 758-Phantom Stranger app. 760-767-Max Lord app. 762-Intro. Liar Liar. 768-Deathstroke app. 4.00
770-796-($4.99) 770-Afterworlds begins. 777-Justice Guild of Earth-11 app. 780-Diana returns to the living world. 781-783-Dr. Cizko app. 791,792-Cheetah app. 5.00
Annual 1 (7/17, $4.99) Retells 1st meeting with Superman & Batman; Scott-a 5.00
Annual 2 (8/18, $4.99) The Star Sapphires app.; Putri-c/Laming, Calafiore, & Irving-a 5.00
Annual 3 (12/19, $4.99) Gorilla Grodd app.; Orlando-s/Marion-a 5.00
Annual 4 (10/20, $4.99) Orlando-s/Herbert-a 5.00
2021 Annual (1/22, $5.99) Cloonan & Conrad-s/MacDonald-s; intro. Altuum 6.00
... and Justice League Dark: The Witching Hour 1 (12/18, $4.99) Part 1 of x-over 5.00
... 1984 (11/20, $3.99) Movie tie-in; art by Blevins & Sauvage; Steve Trevor app. 4.00
... #1 FCBD 2017 Special Edition (5/17, giveaway) r/#2; Year One; Nicola Scott-a 3.00
... #1 Wonder Woman Day Special Edition (12/21, giveaway) r/#1 3.00
...: Rebirth 1 (8/16, $2.99) Rucka-s; multiples origins; new costume 3.00
... 75th Anniversary Special 1 (12/16, $7.99) short stories and pin-ups by various incl. Sharp, Moon, Bolland, DeLiz, Frison, Albuquerque, Larson, Jimenez, Sauvage; Jim Lee-c 8.00
...: Steve Trevor 1 (8/17, $3.99) Seeley-s/Duce-a 4.00
... / Tasmanian Devil Special 1 (8/17, $4.99) Bedard-s/Kitson-a; Circe app.; cartoon-style back-up with Caldwell-a; Daffy Duck & Wile E. Coyote app. 5.00
...: The Adventures of Young Diana Special 1 (12/21, $9.99) R/back-ups from #770-779 10.00

WONDER WOMAN: AMAZONIA
DC Comics: 1997 ($7.95, Graphic Album format, one shot)

1-Elseworlds; Messner-Loebs-s/Winslade-a 2 4 6 8 10 12

WONDER WOMAN BLACK & GOLD
DC Comics: Aug, 2021 - No. 6, Jan, 2022 ($5.99, B&W&shades of gold, limited series)

1-6-Anthology of short stories from all eras. 1-Art by Sook, Reeder, Cloonan 6.00

WONDER WOMAN: COME BACK TO ME
DC Comics: Sept, 2019 - No. 6, Feb, 2020 ($4.99, limited series)

1-6: 1-Reprints serialized story from Walmart exclusive Justice League Giant #3,4 5.00

WONDER WOMAN / CONAN
DC Comics: Nov, 2017 - No. 6, Apr, 2018 ($3.99, limited series)

1-6-Simone-s/Lopresti-a; meet-up in Conan's time; the Corvidae app. 4.00

WONDER WOMAN: DEAD EARTH
DC Comics (Black Label): Feb, 2020 - No. 4, Oct, 2020 ($6.99, 10-7/8" x 8-1/2", lim. series)

1-4-Wonder Woman in post-apocalyptic future; Daniel Warren Johnson-s/a; 2 covers 7.00

WONDER WOMAN: EARTH ONE
DC Comics: 2016; 2018 ($22.99/$24.99, HC Graphic Novel)

Volume 1 ($22.99) - Morrison-s/Paquette-a; alternate retelling of origin; bonus art 23.00
Volume 2 ($24.99) - Morrison-s/Paquette-a; Dr. Psycho app.; bonus art 25.00

WONDER WOMAN 80TH ANNIVERSARY 100-PAGE SUPER SPECTACULAR
DC Comics: Dec, 2021 ($9.99, squarebound, one-shot)

1-Short stories & pin-ups by various incl. García-López, Cheung, Reeder; multiple covers 10.00

WONDER WOMAN: EVOLUTION
DC Comics: Jan, 2022 - No. 8, Sept, 2022 ($3.99, limited series)

1-8: 1-Phillips-s/Hawthorne-a; Silver Swan app. 4.00

WONDER WOMAN GIANT (See reprint of new stories in Wonder Woman: Come Back to Me) (See Justice League Giant #1-7 for previous JL & Aquaman reprints)
DC Comics: 2019 - No. 7, 2019 ($4.99, 100 pgs., squarebound, Walmart exclusive)

1-7-New Wonder Woman story Conner & Palmiotti-s/Derenick-a; Jonah Hex app. plus reprints Justice League ('11), Wonder Woman ('06), and Aquaman ('11) in all 5.00

WONDER WOMAN GIANT
DC Comics: 2019 - No. 4, 2020 ($4.99, 100 pgs., squarebound, Mass Market & Direct Market editions exist for each issue, with different covers)

1-4: 1-New story with Harley Quinn and reprints. 2-4-New stories and reprints 5.00

WONDER WOMAN HISTORIA: THE AMAZONS
DC Comics (Black Label): Jan, 2022 - No. 3, Feb, 2023 ($7.99, oversized 8-1/2" x 10-3/4", lim. series)

1-3-Kelly Sue DeConnick-s. 1-Phil Jimenez-a. 2-Gene Ha-a. 3-Nicola Scott-a 8.00

Wonder Woman #780 © DC

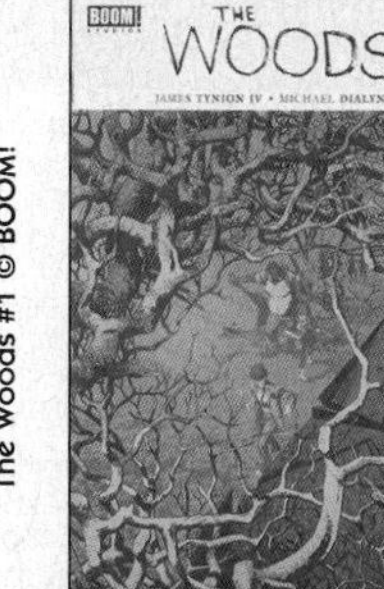

The Woods #1 © BOOM!

World Around Us #25 © GIL

	GD	VG	FN	VF	VF/NM	NM-
	2.0	4.0	6.0	8.0	9.0	9.2

WONDER WOMAN '77
DC Comics: Jun, 2015 - No. 4, Nov, 2016 ($7.99, square-bound, printing of digital-first stories)

1-4-Stories based on the Lynda Carter series. 1-Covers by Nicola Scott & Phil Jimenez; Dr. Psycho app.; bonus sketch design art; afterword by Mangels. 2-(11/15) Scott-c; The Cheetah, Celsia & Solomon Grundy app. 3-Clayface app. 8.00

WONDER WOMAN '77 MEETS THE BIONIC WOMAN (TV)
Dynamite Entertainment: 2016 - No. 6, 2017 ($3.99, limited series)

1-6-Andy Mangels-s/Judit Tondora-a; multiple covers 4.00

WONDER WOMAN SPECTACULAR (See DC Special Series #9)

WONDER WOMAN: SPIRIT OF TRUTH
DC Comics: Nov, 2001 ($9.95, treasury size, one-shot)

nn-Painted art by Alex Ross; story by Alex Ross and Paul Dini 10.00

WONDER WOMAN: THE HIKETEIA
DC Comics: 2002 ($24.95, hardcover, one-shot)

nn-Wonder Woman battles Batman; Greg Rucka-s/J.G. Jones-a 25.00
Softcover (2003, $17.95) 18.00

WONDER WOMAN: THE TRUE AMAZON
DC Comics: 2016 ($22.99, HC Graphic Novel)

HC-Retelling of childhood & origin; Jill Thompson-s/painted-a; bonus design pages 23.00

WONDERWORLD COMICS (Formerly Wonder Comics)
Fox Feature Syndicate: No. 3, July, 1939 - No. 33, Jan, 1942

	GD	VG	FN	VF	VF/NM	NM-
3-Intro The Flame by Fine; Dr. Fung (Powell-a), K-51 (Powell-a?), & Yarko the Great, Master Magician (Eisner-a) continues; Eisner/Fine-c	1350	2700	4050	10,300	18,650	27,000
4-Lou Fine-c	459	918	1377	3350	5925	8500
5,6,9,10: Lou Fine-c	314	628	942	2198	3849	5500
7-Classic Lou Fine-c	1500	3000	4500	11,400	20,700	30,000
8-Classic Lou Fine-c	975	1950	2919	7100	12,550	18,000
11-Origin The Flame	400	800	1200	2800	4900	7000
12-15: 13-Dr. Fung ends; last Fine-c(p)	245	490	735	1568	2684	3800
16-20	181	362	543	1158	1979	2800
21-Origin The Black Lion & Cub	187	374	561	1197	2049	2900
22-27: 22,25-Dr. Fung app.	148	296	444	947	1624	2300
28-Origin & 1st app. U.S. Jones (8/41); Lu-Nar, the Moon Man begins	371	742	1113	2600	4550	6500
29,31: 29-Torture-c	135	270	405	864	1482	2100
30-Intro & Origin Flame Girl	168	336	504	1075	1838	2600
32-Hitler-c	400	800	1200	2800	4900	7000
33-Last issue	371	742	1113	2600	4550	6500

NOTE: *Spies at War by* ***Eisner*** *in #13, 17. Yarko by* ***Eisner*** *in #3-11.* ***Eisner*** *text illos-3.* ***Lou Fine*** *a-3-11; c-3-13, 15(i); text illos-4.* ***Nordling*** *a-4-14.* ***Powell*** *a-3-12.* ***Tuska*** *a-5-9. Bondage-c 14, 15, 28, 31, 32. Cover features: The Flame-#3, 5-31; U.S. Jones-#32, 33.*

WONDERWORLDS
Innovation Publishing: 1992 ($3.50, squarebound, 100 pgs.)

1-Rebound super-hero comics, contents may vary; Hero Alliance, Terraformers, etc. 5.00

WOODS, THE
BOOM! Studios: May, 2014 - No. 36, Oct, 2017 ($3.99)

1-36: 1-Tynion-s/Dialynas-a; multiple covers 4.00

WOODSY OWL (See March of Comics #395)
Gold Key: Nov, 1973 - No. 10, Feb, 1976 (Some Whitman printings exist)

	GD	VG	FN	VF	VF/NM	NM-
1	2	4	6	13	18	22
1-Whitman variant	3	6	9	14	20	25
2-10	2	4	6	8	10	12

WOODY WOODPECKER (Walter Lantz... #73 on?)(See Dell Giants for annuals)
(Also see The Funnies, Jolly Jingles, Kite Fun Book, New Funnies)
Dell Publishing Co./Gold Key No. 73-187/Whitman No. 188 on:
No. 169, 10/47 - No. 72, 5-7/62; No. 73, 10/62 - No. 201, 3/84 (nn 192)

	GD	VG	FN	VF	VF/NM	NM-
Four Color 169(#1)-Drug turns Woody into a Mr. Hyde	21	42	63	147	324	500
Four Color 188	12	24	36	82	179	275
Four Color 202,249,264,288	9	18	27	59	117	175
Four Color 232-Classic-c	21	42	63	147	324	500
Four Color 305,336,350	9	18	27	59	117	175
Four Color 364,374,390,405,416,431('52)	6	12	18	37	66	95
16 (12-1/52-53) - 30('55)	4	8	12	27	44	60
31-50	3	6	9	21	33	45
51-72 (Last Dell)	3	6	9	17	26	35
73-75 (Giants, 84 pgs., Gold Key)	5	10	15	30	50	70
76-80	3	6	9	15	22	28
81-103: 103-Last 12¢ issue	3	6	9	14	19	24
104-120	2	4	6	11	16	20
121-140	2	4	6	9	12	15
141-160: 141-UFO-c	1	3	4	6	8	10
161-187	1	2	3	5	7	9
188,189 (Whitman)	2	4	6	9	13	16
190(9/80),191(11/80)-pre-pack only	6	12	18	38	69	100
(No #192)						
193-197: 196(2/82), 197(4/82)	2	4	6	11	16	20
198-201 (All #90062 on-c, no date or date code, pre-pack): 198(6/83), 199(7/83), 200(8/83), 201(3/84)	3	6	9	16	24	32
Christmas Parade 1(11/68-Giant)(G.K.)	4	8	12	25	40	55
Summer Fun 1(6/66-G.K.)(84 pgs.)	4	8	12	28	47	65
nn (1971, 60¢, 100 pgs. digest) B&W one page gags	3	6	9	16	24	32

NOTE: *15¢ Canadian editions of the 12¢ issues exist. Reprints-No. 92, 102, 103, 105, 106, 124, 125, 152, 153, 157, 162, 165, 194(1/3)-200(1/3).*

WOODY WOODPECKER (See Comic Album #5,9,13, Dell Giant #24, 40, 54, Dell Giants, The Funnies, Golden Comics Digest #1, 3, 5, 8, 15, 16, 20, 24, 32, 37, 44, March of Comics #16, 34, 85, 93, 109, 124, 139, 158, 177, 184, 203, 222, 239, 249, 261, 420, 454, 466, 478, New Funnies & Super Book #12, 24)

WOODY WOODPECKER
Harvey Comics: Sept, 1991 - No. 15, Aug, 1994 ($1.25)

1-15: 1-r/W.W. #53 4.00
50th Anniversary Special 1 (10/91, $2.50, 68 pgs.) 5.00

WOODY WOODPECKER AND FRIENDS
Harvey Comics: Dec, 1991 - No. 4, 1992 ($1.25)

1-4 4.00

WOOL (Hugh Howey's...)
Cryptozoic Entertainment: Jul, 2014 - No. 6, Nov, 2014 ($3.99)

1-6-Palmiotti & Gray-s/Broxton-a/Darwyn Cooke-c 4.00

WORD WARRIORS (Also see Quest for Dreams Lost)
Literacy Volunteers of Chicago: 1987 ($1.50, B&W)(Proceeds donated to help literacy)

1-Jon Sable by Grell, Ms. Tree, Streetwolf; Chaykin-c 3.00

WORLD AROUND US, THE (Illustrated Story of...)
Gilberton Publishers (Classics Illustrated): Sep, 1958 -No. 36, Oct, 1961 (25¢)

	GD	VG	FN	VF	VF/NM	NM-
1-Dogs; Evans-a	9	18	27	52	69	85
2-4: 2-Indians; Check-a. 3-Horses; L. B. Cole-c. 4-Railroads; L. B. Cole-a (5 pgs.)	9	18	27	47	61	75
5-Space; Ingels-a	10	20	30	56	76	95
6-The F.B.I.; Disbrow, Evans, Ingels-a	10	20	30	56	76	95
7-Pirates; Disbrow, Ingels, Kinstler-a	9	18	27	52	69	85
8-Flight; Evans, Ingels, Crandall-a	9	18	27	52	69	85
9-Army; Disbrow, Ingels, Orlando-a	9	18	27	47	61	75
10-13: 10-Navy; Disbrow, Kinstler-a. 11-Marine Corps. 12-Coast Guard; Ingels-a (9 pgs.). 13-Air Force; L.B. Cole-c	9	18	27	47	61	75
14-French Revolution; Crandall, Evans, Kinstler-a	10	20	30	56	76	95
15-Prehistoric Animals; Al Williamson-a, 6 & 10 pgs. plus Morrow-a	10	20	30	58	79	100
16-18: 16-Crusades; Kinstler-a. 17-Festivals; Evans, Crandall-a. 18-Great Scientists; Crandall, Evans, Torres, Williamson, Morrow-a	9	18	27	52	69	85
19-Jungle; Crandall, Williamson, Morrow-a	10	20	30	58	79	100
20-Communications; Crandall, Evans, Torres-a	10	20	30	56	76	95
21-American Presidents; Crandall/Evans, Morrow-a	10	20	30	56	76	95
22-Boating; Morrow-a	8	16	24	44	57	70
23-Great Explorers; Crandall, Evans-a	9	18	27	52	69	85
24-Ghosts; Morrow, Evans-a	10	20	30	56	76	95
25-Magic; Evans, Morrow-a	10	20	30	56	76	95
26-The Civil War	11	22	33	62	86	110
27-Mountains (High Advs.); Crandall/Evans, Morrow, Torres-a	9	18	27	52	69	85
28-Whaling; Crandall, Evans, Morrow, Torres, Wildey-a; L.B. Cole-c	9	18	27	52	69	85
29-Vikings; Crandall, Evans, Torres, Morrow-a	10	20	30	58	79	100
30-Undersea Adventure; Crandall/Evans, Kirby, Morrow, Torres-a	10	20	30	56	76	95
31-Hunting; Crandall/Evans, Ingels, Kinstler, Kirby-a	9	18	27	52	69	85
32,33: 32-For Gold & Glory; Morrow, Kirby, Crandall, Evans-a. 33-Famous Teens; Torres, Crandall, Evans-a	9	18	27	52	69	85
34-36: 34-Fishing; Crandall/Evans-a. 35-Spies; Kirby, Morrow?, Evans-a. 36-Fight for Life (Medicine); Kirby-a	9	18	27	52	69	85

NOTE: See Classics Illustrated Special Edition. Another *World Around Us* issue entitled *The Sea* had been prepared in 1962 but was never published in the U.S. It was published in the British/European *World Around Us* series. Those series then continued with seven additional WAU titles not in the U.S. series.

WORLD BELOW, THE
Dark Horse Comics: Mar, 1999 - No. 4, Jun, 1999 ($2.50, limited series)

GD VG FN VF VF/NM NM-
2.0 4.0 6.0 8.0 9.0 9.2

1-4-Paul Chadwick-s/c/a 3.00
TPB (1/07, $12.95) r/#1-4; intro. by Chadwick; gallery of sketches and covers 13.00

WORLD BELOW, THE: DEEPER AND STRANGER
Dark Horse Comics: Dec, 1999 - No. 4, Mar, 2000 ($2.95, B&W)

1-4-Paul Chadwick-s/c/a 3.00

WORLD FAMOUS HEROES MAGAZINE
Comic Corp. of America (Centaur): Oct, 1941 - No. 4, Apr, 1942 (comic book)

1-Gustavson-c; Lubbers, Glanzman-a; Davy Crockett, Paul Revere, Lewis & Clark, John Paul Jones stories; Flag-c 135 270 405 864 1482 2100
2-Lou Gehrig life story; Lubbers-a 68 136 204 435 743 1050
3,4-Lubbers-a. 4-Wild Bill Hickok story; 2 pg. Marlene Dietrich story 63 126 189 403 689 975

WORLD FAMOUS STORIES
Croyden Publishers: 1945

1-Ali Baba, Hansel & Gretel, Rip Van Winkle, Mid-Summer Night's Dream 15 30 45 90 140 190

WORLD IS HIS PARISH, THE
George A. Pflaum: 1953 (15¢)

nn-The story of Pope Pius XII 7 14 21 35 43 50

WORLD OF ADVENTURE (Walt Disney's...)(TV)
Gold Key: Apr, 1963 - No. 3, Oct, 1963 (12¢)

1-Disney TV characters; Savage Sam, Johnny Shiloh, Capt. Nemo, The Mooncussers 3 6 9 20 31 42
2,3 3 6 9 15 21 26

WORLD OF ANIMOSITY (See Animosity)
AfterShock Comics: Sept, 2017 ($3.99, one-shot)

nn-Character profiles and series summary 4.00

WORLD OF ARCHIE, THE (See Archie Giant Series Mag. #148, 151, 156, 160, 165, 171, 177, 182, 188, 193, 200, 208, 213, 225, 232, 237, 244, 249, 456, 461, 468, 473, 480, 485, 492, 497, 504, 509, 516, 521, 532, 543, 554, 565, 574, 587, 599, 612, 627)

WORLD OF ARCHIE
Archie Comics: Aug, 1992 - No. 22 ($1.25/$1.50)

1 1 2 3 5 6 8
2-15: 9-Neon ink-c 3.00
16-22 3.00

WORLD OF ARCHIE DOUBLE DIGEST MAGAZINE (World of Archie Comics Digest #41-on)
Archie Comics: Dec, 2010 - Present ($3.99/$4.99/$5.99/$6.99/$7.99/$8.99/$9.99)

1-29,31-37,39,40: 5-r/Tiny Titans/Little Archie #1-3 with sketch-a. 17-Archie babies 4.00
30-($5.99) Double Double Digest 6.00
38-$4.99-c 5.00
41,46,51,55,60,63,67,71,73,75-91-($6.99) 41-World of Archie Double Double Digest 7.00
42-45,47-50,52,54,57,58,61,64,65,68-($4.99) Titled World of Archie Comics Digest 5.00
53,56,59,62,66,70,72,74-($5.99): 56-Winter Annual. 59,70-Summer Annual 6.00
92-115-($7.99): 100-Time Police app. 103-Halloween-c. 104,105-Christmas-c 8.00
116-125-($8.99): 116-Valentine's Day cover. 125-Christmas-c 9.00
126-128-($9.99) 10.00
World of Archie Digest, Free Comic Book Day Edition (6-7/13, giveaway) Reprints 3.00

WORLD OF BETTY AND VERONICA JUMBO COMICS DIGEST
Archie Comics: Feb, 2021 - Present ($7.99/$8.99)

1-11-New story and reprints 8.00
12-21-($8.99) 20,21-Christmas cover 9.00
22-24-($9.99) 10.00

WORLD OF BLACK HAMMER ENCYCLOPEDIA, THE (See Black Hammer)
Dark Horse Comics: Jul, 2019 ($3.99, one-shot)

nn-Character profiles with art by various and series timeline; Sorrentino-c 4.00

WORLD OF FANTASY
Atlas Comics (CPC No. 1-15/ZPC No. 16-19): May, 1956 - No. 19, Aug, 1959

1 97 194 291 621 1061 1500
2-Williamson-a (4 pgs.) 50 100 150 315 533 750
3-Sid Check, Roussos-a 45 90 135 284 480 675
4-7 40 80 120 246 411 575
8-Matt Fox, Orlando, Berg-a 43 86 129 271 46 650
9-Krigstein-a 40 80 120 246 411 575
10-15: 10-Colan-a. 11-Torres-a 37 74 111 222 361 500
16-Williamson-a (4 pgs.); Ditko, Kirby-a 54 108 162 343 574 825
17-19-Ditko, Kirby-a 53 106 159 334 567 800

NOTE: ***Ayers** a-3. **B. Baily** a-4. **Berg** a-5, 6, 8. **Brodsky** c-3. **Check** a-3. **Ditko** a-17, 19. **Everett** a-2; c-4-7, 9, 12, 13. **Forte** a-4, 8, 18. **Heck** a-18. **Infantino** a-14. **Kirby** c-15, 17-19. **Krigstein** a-9. **Maneely** c-2, 14. **Mooney** a-14. **Morrow** a-7. **Orlando** a-8, 13, 14. **Pakula** a-9. **Powell** a-4, 6. **Reinman** a-8, 10. **R.Q. Sale** a-3, 7, 9, 10. **Severin** c-1. **Sinnott** a-16,18.*

WORLD OF GIANT COMICS, THE (See Archie All-Star Specials under Archie Comics)

WORLD OF GINGER FOX, THE (Also see Ginger Fox)
Comico: Nov, 1986 ($6.95, 8 1/2 x 11", 68 pgs., mature)

Graphic Novel ($6.95) 10.00
Hardcover ($27.95) 30.00

WORLD OF JUGHEAD, THE (See Archie Giant Series Mag. #9, 14, 19, 24, 30, 136, 143, 149, 152, 157, 161, 166, 172, 178, 183, 189, 194, 202, 209, 215, 227, 233, 239, 245, 251, 457, 463, 469, 475, 481, 487, 493, 499, 505, 511, 517, 523, 531, 542, 553, 564, 577, 590, 602)

WORLD OF KRYPTON, THE (World of...#3) (See Superman #248)
DC Comics, Inc.: 7/79 - No. 3, 9/79; 12/87 - No. 4, 3/88 (Both are lim. series)

1-3 (1979, 40¢; 1st comic book mini-series): 1-Jor-El marries Lara. 3-Baby Superman sent to Earth; Krypton explodes; Mon-El app. 1 3 4 6 8 10
1-4 (75¢)-Byrne scripts; Byrne/Simonson-c 4.00

WORLD OF KRYPTON
DC Comics: Feb, 2022 - No. 6, Jul, 2022 ($3.99, limited series)

1-6: 1-Venditti-s/Oeming-a; Jor-El, Lara, and baby Kara Zor-El app. 2-Trial of Kru-El 4.00

WORLD OF METROPOLIS, THE
DC Comics: Aug, 1988 - No. 4, July, 1988 ($1.00, limited series)

1-4: Byrne scripts 4.00

WORLD OF MYSTERY
Atlas Comics (GPI): June, 1956 - No. 7, July, 1957

1-Torres, Orlando-a; Powell-a? 74 148 222 470 810 1150
2-Woodish-a 32 64 96 188 307 425
3-Torres, Davis, Ditko-a 36 72 108 211 343 475
4-Pakula, Powell-a 36 72 108 211 343 475
5,7: 5-Orlando-a 32 64 96 188 307 425
6-Williamson/Mayo-a (4 pgs.); Ditko-a; Colan-a; Crandall text illo 36 72 108 211 343 475

NOTE: ***Ayers** a-4. **Brodsky** c-2, 5, 6. **Colan** a-6, 7. **Everett** c-1, 3. **Pakula** a-4, 6. **Romita** a-2. **Severin** c-7.*

WORLD OF SMALLVILLE
DC Comics: Apr, 1988 - No. 4, July, 1988 (75¢, limited series)

1-4: Byrne scripts. 3-Baby torture-c 5.00

WORLD OF SUSPENSE
Atlas News Co.: Apr, 1956 - No. 8, July, 1957

1 65 130 195 416 708 1000
2-Ditko-a (4 pgs.) 39 78 117 240 395 550
3,7-Williamson-a in both (4 pgs.); #7-with Mayo 36 72 108 211 343 475
4-6,8 29 58 87 172 281 390

NOTE: ***Berg** a-6. **Cameron** a-2. **Ditko** a-2. **Drucker** a-1. **Everett** a-1, 5; c-6. **Heck** a-5. **Maneely** a-1; c-1-3. **Orlando** a-5. **Powell** a-6. **Reinman** a-4. **Roussos** a-6. **Sale** a-4. **Shores** a-1.*

WORLD OF TANKS
Dark Horse Comics: Aug, 2016 - No. 5, Feb, 2017 ($3.99)

1-5-Ennis-s/Ezquerra-a; set in 1944 Normandy 4.00

WORLD OF TANKS II: CITADEL
Dark Horse Comics: May, 2018 - No. 5, Sept, 2018 ($3.99)

1-5-Ennis-s/Holden-a; set in 1943 Russia during the Battle of Kursk 4.00

WORLD OF WARCRAFT (Based on the Blizzard Entertainment video game)
DC Comics (WildStorm): Jan, 2008 - No. 25, Jan, 2010 ($2.99)

1-Walt Simonson-s/Lullabi-a; cover by Samwise Didier 8.00
1-Variant cover by Jim Lee 12.00
1,2-Second printing with Jim Lee sketch cover 5.00
2-Two covers by Jim Lee and Samwise Didier 5.00
3-24: 3-14-Two covers on each 3.00
25-($3.99) Walt & Louise Simonson-s 4.00
... Special 1 (2/10, $3.99) Costa-s/Mhan-a/c 4.00
... Book One HC (2008, $19.99, dustjacket) r/#1-7; intro. by Chris Metzen of Blizzard 20.00
... Book One SC (2009, $14.99) r/#1-7; intro. by Chris Metzen of Blizzard 15.00
... Book Two HC (2009, $19.99, dustjacket) r/#8-14 20.00
... Book Two SC (2010, $14.99) r/#8-14 15.00
... Book Three HC (2010, $19.99, dustjacket) r/#15-21 20.00
... Book Three SC (2011, $17.99) r/#15-21 18.00

WORLD OF WARCRAFT: ASHBRINGER
DC Comics (WildStorm): Nov, 2008 - No. 4, Feb, 2009 ($3.99)

1-4-Neilson-s/Lullabi & Washington-a; 2 covers by Robinson & Lullabi 4.00
TPB (2010, $14.99) r/#1-4 15.00

WORLD OF WARCRAFT: CURSE OF THE WORGEN
DC Comics (WildStorm #1,2): Jan, 2011 - No. 5, May, 2011 ($3.99/$2.99)

1,2-($3.99) Neilson & Waugh-s/Lullabi & Washington-a; Polidora-c 4.00
3-5-($2.99) 3.00

WORLD OF WHEELS (Formerly Dragstrip Hotrodders)
Charlton Comics: No. 17, Oct, 1967 - No. 32, June, 1970

17-20-Features Ken King 3 6 9 17 26 35
21-32-Features Ken King 3 6 9 15 22 28
Modern Comics Reprint 23(1978) 6.00

WORLD OF WOOD
Eclipse Comics: 1986 - No. 4, 1987; No. 5, 2/89 ($1.75, limited series)

1,2: 1-Dave Stevens-c. 2-Wood/Stevens-c 2 4 6 8 11 14
3-5: 5-($2.00, B&W)-r/Avon's Flying Saucers 5.00

WORLD OF ZORRO
American Mythology Productions: 2021 (Free Comic Book Day giveaway)

1-Sample stories from Zorro series Swords of Hell, Legendary Adventures & Flights 3.00

WORLD READER
AfterShock Comics: Apr, 2017 - No. 6, Sept, 2017 ($3.99, limited series)

1-6-Jeff Loveness-s/Juan Doe-a 4.00

WORLD'S BEST COMICS
DC Comics: Feb 1940

nn - Ashcan comic, not distributed to newsstands, only for in-house use. Cover art is Action Comics #29 with interior being Action Comics #24. One copy sold for $21,000 in 2000.

WORLD'S BEST COMICS (World's Finest Comics #2 on)
National Per. Publications (100 pgs.): Spring, 1941 (Cardboard-c)(DC's 6th annual format comic)

1-The Batman, Superman, Crimson Avenger, Johnny Thunder, The King, Young Dr. Davis, Zatara, Lando, Man of Magic, & Red, White & Blue begin; Superman, Batman & Robin covers begin (inside-c is blank); Fred Ray-c; 15¢ cover price 1775 3550 5325 13,700 23,850 34,000

WORLD'S BEST COMICS: GOLDEN AGE SAMPLER
DC Comics: 2003 (99¢, one-shot, samples from DC Archive editions)

1-Golden Age reprints from Superman #6, Batman #5, Sensation #11, Police #11 3.00

WORLD'S BEST COMICS: SILVER AGE SAMPLER
DC Comics: 2004 (99¢, one-shot, samples from DC Archive editions)

1-Silver Age reprints from Justice League #4, Adventure #247, Our Army at War #81 3.00

WORLDS BEYOND (Stories of Weird Adventure)(Worlds of Fear #2 on)
Fawcett Publications: Nov, 1951

1-Powell, Bailey-a; Moldoff-c 110 220 330 704 1202 1700

World of Archie Double Digest #73 © ACP

World of Warcraft #5 © Blizzard Ent.

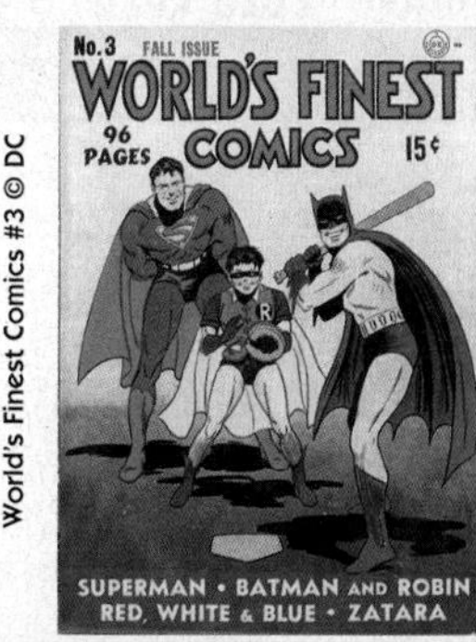

World's Finest Comics #3 © DC

GD VG FN VF VF/NM NM-
2.0 4.0 6.0 8.0 9.0 9.2

WORLDS COLLIDE
DC Comics: July, 1994 ($2.50, one-shot)

1-($2.50, 52 pgs.)-Milestone & Superman titles x-over 4.00
1-($3.95, 52 pgs.)-Polybagged w/vinyl clings 5.00
1-Platinum Edition 5 10 15 31 53 75

WORLD'S FAIR COMICS (See New York...)

WORLD'S FINEST (Also see Legends of The World's Finest)
DC Comics: 1990 - No. 3, 1990 ($3.95, squarebound, limited series, 52 pgs.)

1-3: Batman & Superman team-up against The Joker and Lex Luthor; Dave Gibbons scripts & Steve Rude-c/a. 2,3-Joker/Luthor painted-c by Steve Rude 5.00
TPB-(1992, $19.95) r/#1-3; Gibbons intro. 20.00
...: The Deluxe Edition HC (2008, $29.99) r/#1-3; Gibbons intro. from 1992; Gibbons story outline and sketches; Rude sketch pages and notes 30.00

WORLD'S FINEST
DC Comics: Dec, 2009 - No. 4, Mar, 2010 ($2.99, limited series)

1-4: Gates-s/two covers by Noto on each. 3-Supergirl/Batgirl team up. 4-Noto-a 3.00
TPB (2010, $14.99) r/#1-4, Action Comics #865 & DC Comics Presents #31 15.00

WORLDS' FINEST (Also see Earth 2 series)
DC Comics: Jul, 2012 - No. 32, May, 2015 ($2.99)

1-32: 1-Huntress and Power Girl; Levitz-s/art by Pérez & Maguire. 6,7-Damian app. 19-Huntress meets Batman. 20,21-X-over with Batman/Superman #8,9. 25-Return to Earth-2. 27-29-Secret History of Earth 2. 32-Death of Lois 3.00
1-Variant-c by Maguire 5.00
#0-(11/12, $2.99) Flashback to Robin's and Supergirl's training 3.00
Annual 1 (3/14, $4.99) Earth 2 flashback; Wonder Woman & Fury app. 5.00
...: Futures End 1 (11/14, $2.99, regular-c) Five years later; Cinar-a; Deathstroke app. 3.00
...: Futures End 1 (11/14, $3.99, 3-D cover) 4.00

WORLD'S FINEST COMICS (Formerly World's Best Comics #1)
National Periodical Publ./DC Comics: No. 2, Sum, 1941 - No. 323, Jan, 1986 (#1-17 have cardboard covers) (#2-9 have 100 pgs.)

2 (100 pgs.)-Superman, Batman & Robin covers continue from World's Best; (cover price 15¢ #2-70) 454 908 1362 3314 5857 8400
3-The Sandman begins; last Johnny Thunder; origin & 1st app. The Scarecrow 622 1244 1866 4541 8021 11,500
4-Hop Harrigan app.; last Young Dr. Davis 290 580 870 1856 3178 4500
5-Intro. TNT & Dan the Dyna-Mite; last King & Crimson Avenger 284 568 852 1818 3109 4400
6-Star Spangled Kid begins (Sum/42); Aquaman app.; S&K Sandman with Sandy in new costume begins, ends #7 226 452 678 1446 2473 3500
7-Green Arrow begins (Fall/42); last Lando & Red, White & Blue; S&K art 252 504 756 1613 2757 3900
8-Boy Commandos begin (by Simon(p) #12); last The King; includes "Minute Man Answers the Call" promo 219 438 657 1402 2401 3400
9-Batman cameo in Star Spangled Kid; S&K-a; last 100 pg. issue; Hitler, Mussolini, Tojo-c 314 628 942 2198 3849 5500
10-S&K-a; 76 pg. issues begin 187 374 561 1197 2049 2900
11-17: 17-Last cardboard cover issue 177 354 531 1124 1937 2750
18-20: 18-Paper covers begin; last Star Spangled Kid. 19-Joker story. 20-Last quarterly issue 168 336 504 1075 1838 2600
21-30: 21-Begin bi-monthly. 30-Johnny Everyman app. 116 232 348 742 1271 1800
31-40: 33-35-Tomahawk app. 35-Penguin app. 113 226 339 718 1234 1750
41-43,45-50: 41-Boy Commandos end. 42-The Wyoming Kid begins (9-10/49), ends #63. 43-Full Steam Foley begins, ends #48. 48-Last square binding. 49-Tom Sparks, Boy Inventor begins; robot-c 110 220 330 704 1202 1700
44-Used in SOTI, ref. to Batman & Robin being gay, and a cop being shot in the face 135 270 405 864 1482 2100
51-60: 51-Zatara ends. 54-Last 76 pg. issue. 59-Manhunters Around the World begins (7-8/52), ends #62 106 212 318 673 1162 1650
61-Joker story 135 270 405 864 1482 2100
62-64: 63-Capt. Compass app. 103 206 309 659 1130 1600
65-Origin Superman; Tomahawk begins (7-8/53), ends #101 161 322 483 1030 1765 2500
66-70-(15¢ issues, scarce)-Last 15¢, 68pg. issue 110 220 330 704 1200 1700
71-(10¢ issue, scarce)-Superman & Batman begin as team (7-8/54); were in separate stories until now; Superman & Batman exchange identities; 10¢ issues begin 320 640 960 2240 3920 5600
72,73-(10¢ issue, scarce) 142 284 426 909 1555 2200
74-Last pre-code issue 103 206 309 659 1130 1600
75-(1st code approved, 3-4/55) 100 200 300 635 1093 1550
76-80: 77-Superman loses powers & Batman obtains them 74 148 222 470 810 1150
81-87,89: 84-1st S.A. issue. 89-2nd Batmen of All Nations (aka Club of Heroes) 55 110 165 352 601 850
88-1st Joker/Luthor team-up 71 142 213 454 777 1100
90-Batwoman's 1st app. in World's Finest (10/57, 3rd app. anywhere) plus-c app. 90 180 270 576 988 1400
91-93,95-99: 96-99-Kirby Green Arrow. 99-Robot-c 27 54 81 189 420 650
94-New origin of Superman/Batman team 68 136 204 544 1222 1900
100 (3/59) 40 80 120 296 673 1050
101-110: 102-Tommy Tomorrow begins, ends #124 17 34 51 114 252 390
111-121: 111-1st app. The Clock King. 113-Intro. Miss Arrowette in Green Arrow; 1st Bat-Mite/Mr. Mxyzptlk team-up (11/60). 117-Batwoman-c. 121-Last 10¢ issue 13 26 39 86 188 290
122-128: 123-2nd Bat-Mite/Mr. Mxyzptlk team-up (2/62). 125-Aquaman begins (5/62), ends #139 (Aquaman #1 is dated 1-2/62) 10 20 30 68 144 220
129-Joker/Luthor team-up-c/story 13 26 39 89 195 300
130-142: 135-Last Dick Sprang story. 140-Last Green Arrow. 142-Origin The Composite Superman (villain); Legion app. 8 16 24 54 102 150
143-150: 143-1st Mailbag. 144-Clayface/Brainiac team-up. 148-Clayface/Luthor team-up; last Clayface until Action #443 7 14 21 46 86 125
151-153,155,157-160: 157-2nd Super Sons story; last app. Kathy Kane (Bat-Woman) until Batman Family #10; 1st Bat-Mite Jr. 6 12 18 37 66 95
154-1st Super Sons story; last Bat-Woman in costume until Batman Family #10. 8 16 24 52 99 145
156-1st Bizarro Batman; Joker-c/story 15 30 45 103 227 350
161,170 (80-Pg. Giants G-28,G-40) 6 12 18 42 79 115
162-165,167,168,171,172: 168,172-Adult Legion app. 5 10 15 33 57 80
166-Joker-c/story 8 16 24 54 102 150
169-3rd app. new Batgirl(9/67)(cover and 1 panel cameo); 3rd Bat-Mite/Mr. Mxyzptlk team-up 10 20 30 69 147 225
173-('68)-1st S.A. app. Two-Face as Batman becomes Two-Face in story 9 18 27 62 126 190
174-Adams-c 5 10 15 35 63 90
175,176-Neal Adams-c/a; both reprint J'onn J'onzz origin/Detective #225,226 7 14 21 44 82 120
177-Joker/Luthor team-up-c/story 7 14 21 49 92 135
178-(9/68) Intro. of Super Nova (revived in "52" weekly series); Adams-c 6 12 18 38 69 100
179-(80 Page Giant G-52) -Adams-c; r/#94 6 12 18 41 76 110
180,182,183,185,186: Adams-c on all. 182-Silent Knight-r/Brave & Bold #6. 185-Last 12¢ issue. 186-Johnny Quick-r 4 8 12 28 47 65
181,184,187: 187-Green Arrow origin-r by Kirby (Adv. #256) 4 8 12 25 40 55
188,197:(Giants G-64,G-76; 64 pages) 5 10 15 35 63 90
189-196: 190-193-Robin-r 3 6 9 21 33 45
198,199-3rd Superman/Flash race (see Flash #175 & Superman #199). 199-Adams-c 10 20 30 69 147 225
200-Adams-c 4 8 12 27 44 60
201-203: 203-Last 15¢ issue. 3 6 9 19 30 40
204,205-(52 pgs.) Adams-c: 204-Wonder Woman app. 205-Shining Knight-r (6 pgs.) by Frazetta/Adv. #153; Teen Titans x-over 4 8 12 23 37 50
206 (Giant G-88, 64 pgs.) 5 10 15 33 57 80
207,212-(52 pgs.) 3 6 9 21 33 45
208-211(25¢-c) Adams-c: 208-(52 pgs.) Origin Robotman-r/Det. #138. 209-211-(52 pgs.) 4 8 12 23 37 50
213,214,216-222,229: 217-Metamorpho begins, ends #220; Batman/Superman team-ups resume. 229-r/origin Superman-Batman team 3 6 9 14 20 25
215-(12/72-1/73) Intro. Batman Jr. & Superman Jr. (see Superman/Batman: Saga of the Super Sons TPB for all the Super Sons stories) 3 6 9 19 30 40
223-228-(100 pgs.). 223-N. Adams-r. 223-Deadman origin. 226-N. Adams, S&K, Toth-r; Manhunter part origin-r/Det. #225,226. 227-Deadman app. 5 10 15 31 53 75
230-(68 pgs.) 3 6 9 18 28 38
231-243: 231, 233, 238, 242-Super Sons 2 4 6 10 14 18
244-246-Adams-c: 244-$1.00, 84 pg. issues begin; Green Arrow, Black Canary, Wonder Woman, Vigilante begin; 246-Death of Stuff in Vigilante; origin Vigilante retold 3 6 9 16 23 30
247-252 (84 pgs.): 248-Last Vigilante. 249-The Creeper begins by Ditko, 84 pgs. 250-The Creeper origin retold by Ditko. 251-1st app. Count Vertigo. 252-Last 84 pg. issue 3 6 9 14 19 24
253-257,259-265: 253-Capt. Marvel begins; 68 pgs. begin, end #265. 255-Last Creeper. 256-Hawkman begins. 257-Black Lightning begins. 263-Super Sons. 264-Clay Face app. 2 4 6 9 13 16
258-Adams-c 2 4 6 13 18 22
266-270,272-282-(52 pgs.). 267-Challengers of the Unknown app.; 3 Lt. Marvels return. 268-Capt. Marvel Jr. origin retold. 274-Zatanna begins. 279, 280-Capt. Marvel Jr. & Kid Eternity learn they are brothers 2 4 6 8 10 12

GD VG FN VF VF/NM NM-
2.0 4.0 6.0 8.0 9.0 9.2

271-(52pgs.) Origin Superman/Batman team retold 2 4 6 8 11 14
283-299: 284-Legion app. 1 2 3 5 6 8
300-($1.25, 52pgs.)-Justice League of America, New Teen Titans & The Outsiders app.;
Perez-a (4 pgs.) 1 3 4 6 8 10
301-322: 304-Origin Null and Void. 309,319-Free 16 pg. story in each
(309-Flash Force 2000, 319-Mask preview) 6.00
323-Last issue 1 2 3 5 6 8
NOTE: ***Neal Adams** a-230ir; c-174-176, 178-180, 182, 183, 185, 186, 199-205, 208-211, 244-246, 258. **Austin** a-244-246i. **Burnley** a-8, 10; c-7-9, 11-14, 15p?, 16-18p, 20-31p. **Colan** a-274p, 297, 299. **Ditko** a-249-255. **Giffen** a-322; c-284p, 322. **G. Kane** a-38, 174r, 282, 283; c-281, 282, 289. **Kirby** a-187. **Kubert** Zatara-40-44. **Miller** c-285p. **Mooney** c-134. **Morrow** a-245-248. **Mortimer** c-16-21, 26-71. **Nasser** a(p)-244-246, 259, 260. **Newton** a-253-281p. **Orlando** a-224r. **Perez** a-300i; c-271, 276, 277p, 278p. **Fred Ray** c-1-5. **Fred Ray/Robinson** c-13-16. **Robinson** a-5, 6, 9-11, 13?, 14-16; c-6. **Rogers** a-259p. **Roussos** a-212r. **Simonson** c-291. **Spiegle** a-275-278, 284. **Staton** a-262p, 273p. **Swan/Moldoff** c-126. **Swan/Mortimer** c-79-82. **Toth** a-228r. **Tuska** a-230r, 250p, 252p, 254p, 257p, 283p, 284p, 308p. Boy Commandos by **Infantino** #39-41.*

WORLD'S FINEST COMICS DIGEST (See DC Special Series #23)

WORLD'S FINEST: OUR WORLDS AT WAR
DC Comics: Oct, 2001 ($2.95, one-shot)

1-Concludes the Our Worlds at War x-over; Jae Lee-c; art by various 3.00

WORLD'S FINITE CEREBUS(Reprints from Cerebus in Hell)
Aardvark-Vanaheim: Mar, 2018 ($4.00, B&W)

1-Cerebus figures with original Gustave Doré artwork of Hell; World's Finest #7-c swipe 4.00

WORLD'S GREATEST ATHLETE (See Walt Disney Showcase #14)

WORLD'S GREATEST SONGS
Atlas Comics (Male): Sept, 1954

1-(Scarce)-Heath & Harry Anderson-a; Eddie Fisher life story plus-c; gives lyrics to
Frank Sinatra song "Young at Heart" 58 116 174 371 636 900

WORLD'S GREATEST STORIES
Jubilee Publications: Jan, 1949 - No. 2, May, 1949

1-Alice in Wonderland; Lewis Carroll adapt. 43 86 129 271 461 650
2-Pinocchio 39 78 117 240 395 550

WORLD'S GREATEST SUPER-HEROES HOLIDAY SPECIAL
DC Comics: 2018 ($4.99, 100 pgs., squarebound, Walmart exclusive)

1-New Flash story Lobdell-s/Booth-a; plus holiday-themed reprints; Andy Kubert-c 5.00

WORLDS OF ASPEN
Aspen MLT, Inc.: 2006 - Present (Free Comic Book Day giveaways)

...: FCBD 2006, 2007, #3, #4 Editions; Fathom, Soulfire, Shrugged short stories; Turner-c 3.00
... 2010 (5/10) Previews Fathom, Mindfield, Soulfire, Executive Assistant: Iris and Dellec 3.00
... 2011 (5/11) Previews Fathom, Soulfire, Charismagic, Lady Mechanika & others 3.00
... 2012 (5/12) Previews Fathom, Homecoming, Idolized, Shrugged & others 3.00
... 2013 (5/13) Flip book; previews Fathom, Zoohunters & others 3.00
... 2014 (5/14) Flip book; previews Damsels in Excess & Zoohunters; pin-ups 3.00
... 2015 (5/15) Flip book; previews Eternal Soulfire & Fathom Blue; pin-ups 3.00
... 2016 (5/16) Prelude to Aspen Universe: Revelations; character profile pages 3.00
... 2018 (5/18) Dimension: War Eternal; Nu Way 3.00

WORLDS OF FEAR (Stories of Weird Adventure)(Formerly Worlds Beyond #1)
Fawcett Publications: V1#2, Jan, 1952 - V2#10, June, 1953

V1#2 68 136 204 435 743 1050
3-Evans-a 55 110 165 352 601 850
4-6(9/52) 48 96 114 302 514 725
V2#7,8 45 90 135 284 480 675
9-Classic drowning-c (4/53) 206 412 618 1318 2259 3200
10-Saunders painted-c; man with no eyes surrounded by eyeballs-c plus
eyes ripped out story 300 600 900 2010 3505 5000
NOTE: ***Moldoff** c-2-8. **Powell** a-2, 4, 5. **Sekowsky** a-4, 5.*

WORLDSTORM
DC Comics (WildStorm): Nov, 2006 (Dec on cover) - No. 2, May, 2007 ($2.99)

1,2-Previews and pin-ups for re-launched WildStorm titles.1-Art Adams-c 3.00

WORLDS UNKNOWN
Marvel Comics Group: May, 1973 - No. 8, Aug, 1974

1-r/from Astonishing #54; Torres, Reese-a 4 8 12 25 40 55
2-8 3 6 9 15 22 28
NOTE: ***Adkins/Mooney** a-5. **Buscema** c/a-4p. W. **Howard** c/a-3i. **Kane** a(p)-1,2; c(p)-5, 6, 8. **Sutton** a-2. **Tuska** a(p)-7, 8; c-7p. No. 7, 8 has Golden Voyage of Sinbad movie adaptation.*

WORLD WAR HULK (See Incredible Hulk #106)
Marvel Comics: Aug, 2007 - No. 5, Jan, 2008 ($3.99, limited series)

1-Hulk returns to Earth; Iron Man and Avengers app.; Romita Jr.-a/Pak-s/Finch-c
2 4 6 10 14 18
1-Variant cover by Romita Jr. 2 4 6 11 16 20
2-5: 2-Hulk battles The Avengers and FF; Finch-c. 3,4-Dr. Strange app. 5-Sentry app.
1 3 4 6 8 10
2-5-Variant cover by Romita Jr. 2 4 6 11 16 20
...: Aftersmash 1 (1/08, $3.99) Sandoval-a/Land-c; Hercules, Iron Man app. 4.00
...: Gamma Files (2007, $3.99) profile pages of Hulk characters 4.00
...Prologue: World Breaker 1 (7/07, one-shot) Rio, Weeks, Phillips, Miyazawa-a 4.00
TPB (2008, $19.99) r/#1-5 20.00

WORLD WAR HULK AFTERSMASH: DAMAGE CONTROL
Marvel Comics: Mar, 2008 - No. 3, May, 2008 ($2.99, limited series)

1-3-The clean-up; McDuffie-s. 2-Romita- Jr.-c. 3-Romita Sr.-c 3.00

WORLD WAR HULK AFTERSMASH: WARBOUND
Marvel Comics: Feb, 2008 - No. 5, Jun, 2008 ($2.99, limited series)

1-5-Kirk & Sandoval-a/Cheung-c 3.00

WORLD WAR HULK: FRONT LINE (See Incredible Hulk #106)
Marvel Comics: Aug, 2007 - No. 6, Dec, 2007 ($2.99, limited series)

1-6-Ben Urich & Sally Floyd report World War Hulk; Jenkins-s/Bachs-a 3.00
TPB (2008, $16.99) r/#1-5 & WWH Prologue: World Breaker 17.00

WORLD WAR HULK: GAMMA CORPS
Marvel Comics: Sept, 2007 - No. 4, Jan, 2008 ($2.99, limited series)

1-4-Tieri-s/Ferreira-a/Roux-c 3.00

TPB (2008, $10.99) r/#1-4 11.00

WORLD WAR HULKS
Marvel Comics: Jun, 2010; Sept, 2010 ($3.99, one-shot & limited series)

1-Short stories by various; Deadpool app.; Romita Jr.-c 4.00
...: Spider-Man vs. Thor 1,2 (9/10 - No. 2, 9/10) Gillen-s/Molina-a 4.00
...: Wolverine vs. Captain America 1,2 (9/10 - No. 2, 9/10) "Capt America vs Wolv." on-c 4.00

WORLD WAR HULK: X-MEN (See New Avengers: Illuminati and Incredible Hulk #92)
Marvel Comics: Aug, 2007 - No. 3, Oct, 2007 ($2.99, limited series)

1-3-Gage-s/DiVito-a/McGuinness-c; Hulk invades the Xavier Institute 3.00
TPB (2008, $24.99) r/#1-3, Avengers: The Initiative #4-5, Irredeemable Ant-Man #10,
Iron Man #19-20, and Ghost Rider #12-13 25.00

WORLD WAR STORIES
Dell Publishing Co.: Apr-June, 1965 - No. 3, Dec, 1965

1-Glanzman-a in all 4 8 12 28 47 65
2,3 3 6 9 17 25 34

WORLD WAR TANK GIRL
Titan Comics: May, 2017 - No. 4, Sept, 2017 ($3.99, limited series)

1-4-Tank Girl and crew in 1944 Germany; Alan Martin-s/Brett Parson-a; multiple covers 4.00

WORLD WAR II (See Classics Illustrated Special Issue)

WORLD WAR III
Ace Periodicals: Mar, 1953 - No. 2, May, 1953

1-(Scarce)-Atomic bomb blast-c; Cameron-a 226 452 678 1446 2473 3500
2-Used in **POP**, pg. 78 & B&W & color illos; Cameron-a
103 206 309 659 1130 1600

WORLD WAR X
Titan Comics: Jan, 2017 - No. 6, Jun, 2017 ($3.99, English version of French comic series)

1-6-Jerry Frissen-s/Peter Snejbjerg-a; multiple covers on each 4.00

WORLD WITHOUT END
DC Comics: 1990 - No. 6, 1991 ($2.50, limited series, mature, stiff-c)

1-6: Horror/fantasy; all painted-c/a 3.00

WORLD WRESTLING FEDERATION BATTLEMANIA
Valiant: 1991 - No. 5?, 1991 ($2.50, magazine size, 68 pgs.)

1-5: 5-Includes 2 free pull-out posters 4.00

WORST DUDES, THE
Dark Horse Comics: Jun, 2021 - No. 5, Oct, 2021 ($3.99, limited series)

1-5-Aubrey Sitterson-s/Tony Gregori-a 4.00

WORST FROM MAD, THE (Annual)
E. C. Comics: 1958 - No. 12, 1969 (Each annual cover is reprinted from the cover of the Mad issues being reprinted)(Value is 1/2 if bonus is missing)

nn(1958)-Bonus; record labels & travel stickers; 1st Mad annual; r/Mad #29-34
50 100 150 315 533 750
2(1959)-Bonus is small 33 1/3 rpm record entitled "Meet the Staff of Mad"; r/Mad #35-40
48 96 144 302 514 725
3(1960)-Has 20x30" campaign poster "Alfred E. Neuman for President"; r/Mad #41-46
16 32 48 110 243 375
4(1961)-Sunday comics section; r/Mad #47-54 14 28 42 97 214 330
5(1962)-Has 33-1/3 record; r/Mad #55-62 20 40 60 138 307 475
6(1963)-Has 33-1/3 record; r/Mad #63-70 20 40 60 138 307 475
7(1964)-Mad protest signs; r/Mad #71-76 9 18 27 61 123 185
8(1965)-Build a Mad Zeppelin 10 20 30 66 138 210
9(1966)-33-1/3 rpm record; Beatles on-c 14 28 42 97 214 330
10(1967)-Mad bumper sticker 6 12 18 40 73 105
11(1968)-Mad cover window stickers 6 12 18 37 66 95
12(1969)-Mad picture postcards; Orlando-a 6 12 18 37 66 95
NOTE: *Covers: **Bob Clarke**-#8. **Mingo**-#7, 9-12.*

WOTALIFE COMICS (Formerly Nutty Life #2; Phantom Lady #13 on)
Fox Feature Syndicate/Norlen Mag.: No. 3, Aug-Sept, 1946 - No. 12, July, 1947; 1959

3-Cosmo Cat, Li'l Pan, others begin 16 32 48 92 144 195
4-12-Cosmo Cat, Li'l Pan in all 13 26 39 74 105 135
1(1959-Norlen)-Atomic Rabbit, Atomic Mouse; reprints cover to #6; reprints entire book?
9 18 27 47 61 75

WOTALIFE COMICS
Green Publications: 1959 - No. 5, 1959

1-Funny animal; Li'l Pan & Tamale app. 8 16 24 40 50 60
2-5 5 10 15 24 29 34

WOW COMICS ("Wow, What A Magazine!" on cover of first issue)
Henle Publishing Co.: July, 1936 - No. 4, Nov, 1936 (52 pgs., magazine size)

1-Buck Jones in "The Phantom Rider" (1st app. in comics), Fu Manchu; Capt. Scott Dalton begins; Will Eisner-a (1st in comics); Baily-a(1); Briefer-c
432 864 1296 3154 5577 8000
2-Ken Maynard, Fu Manchu, Popeye by Segar plus article on Popeye; Eisner-a
300 600 900 2010 3505 5000
3-Eisner-c/a(3); Popeye by Segar, Fu Manchu, Hiram Hick by Bob Kane, Space Limited app.; Jimmy Dempsey talks about Popeye's punch; Bob Ripley Believe it or Not begins; Briefer-a
300 600 900 1950 3375 4800
4-Flash Gordon by Raymond, Mandrake, Popeye by Segar, Tillie The Toiler, Fu Manchu, Hiram Hick by Bob Kane; Eisner-a(3); Briefer-c/a
331 662 993 2317 4059 5800

WOW COMICS (Real Western Hero #70 on)(See XMas Comics)
Fawcett Publ.: Winter, 1940-41; No. 2, Summer, 1941 - No. 69, Fall, 1948

nn(#1)-Origin Mr. Scarlet by S&K; Atom Blake, Boy Wizard, Jim Dolan, & Rick O'Shay begin; Diamond Jack, The White Rajah, & Shipwreck Roberts, only app.; 1st mention of Gotham City in comics; the cover was printed on unstable paper stock and is rarely found in fine or mint condition; blank inside-c; bondage-c by Beck
1525 3050 4575 11,600 21,050 30,500
2 (Scarce)-The Hunchback begins 200 400 600 1280 2190 3100
3 (Fall, 1941) 116 232 348 742 1271 1800
4-Origin & 1st app. Pinky 123 246 369 787 1344 1900

World War Hulk #4 © MAR

Wow Comics #29 © FAW

WWE (2017) #1 © WWE

	GD 2.0	VG 4.0	FN 6.0	VF 8.0	VF/NM 9.0	NM- 9.2
5	74	148	222	470	810	1150
6-Origin & 1st app. The Phantom Eagle (7/15/42); Commando Yank begins	84	168	252	538	919	1300
7,8	63	126	189	403	689	975
9-(1/6/43)-Capt. Marvel, Capt. Marvel Jr., Shazam app.; Scarlet & Pinky x-over; Mary Marvel-c/stories begin	309	618	927	2163	3782	5400
10-Swayze-c/a on Mary Marvel	290	580	870	1856	3178	4500
11-17,19,20: 15-Flag-c	60	120	180	381	653	925
18-1st app. Uncle Marvel (10/43); infinity-c	74	148	222	470	810	1150
21-30: 23-Robot-c. 28-Pinky x-over in Mary Marvel	41	82	123	256	428	600
31-40: 32-68-Phantom Eagle by Swayze	32	64	96	188	307	425
41-50	29	58	87	172	281	390
51-58: Last Mary Marvel	25	50	75	150	245	340
59-69: 59-Ozzie (teenage) begins. 62-Flying Saucer gag-c (1/48). 65-69-Tom Mix stories (cont'd in Real Western Hero)	22	44	66	128	209	290

NOTE: *Cover features: Mr. Scarlet-#1-5; Commando Yank-#6, 7, (w/Mr. Scarlet #8); Mary Marvel-#9-56, (w/ Commando Yank-#46-50), (w/Mr. Scarlet & Commando Yank-#51), (w/Mr. Scarlet & Pinky #53), (w/Phantom Eagle #54, 56), (w/Commando Yank & Phantom Eagle #58); Ozzie-#59-69.*

WRAITH (Prequel to the novel NOS4A2)
IDW Publishing: Nov, 2013 (incorrect Nov, 2012 in indicia) - No. 7, May, 2014 ($3.99)

1-7: Joe Hill-s/C.P. Wilson III-a. 5-(incorrect #4 in indicia) 4.00
1-Director's Cut (7/14, $4.99) Includes full script 5.00

WRAITHBORN
DC Comics (WildStorm): Nov, 2005 - No. 6, July, 2006 ($2.99, limited series)

1-6-Marcia Chen & Joe Benitez-s/a 3.00
TPB (2007, $19.99) r/series; sketch pages and unused cover sketches 20.00

WRAITHBORN REDUX
Benitez Productions: Feb, 2016 - No. 6, Aug, 2016 ($3.99)

1-6-Remastered printing of the 2005 series; Chen & Benitez-s/a; multiple covers 4.00
... HCF 2016 #1 (10/16, Halloween giveaway) r/#1 3.00

WRATH (Also see Prototype #4)
Malibu Comics: Jan, 1994 - No. 9, Nov, 1995 ($1.95)

1-9: 2-Mantra x-over. 3-Intro/1st app. Slayer. 4,5-Freex app. 8-Mantra & Warstrike app. 9-Prime app. 3.00
1-Ultra 5000 Limited silver foil 6.00
Giant Size 1 (2.50, 44 pgs.) 4.00

WRATH OF THE ETERNAL WARRIOR
Valiant Entertainment: Nov, 2015 - No. 14, Dec, 2016 ($3.99)

1-14: 1-Venditti-s/Allén-a 4.00

WRATH OF THE SPECTRE, THE
DC Comics: May, 1988 - No. 4, Aug, 1988 ($2.50, limited series)

1-3: Aparo-r/Adventure #431-440 5.00
4-Three scripts intended for Adventure #441-on, but not drawn by Aparo until 1988 1 2 3 5 6 8
TPB (2005, $19.99) r/series; Peter Sanderson intro. 20.00

WRECK OF GROSVENOR (See Superior Stories #3)

WRETCH, THE
Caliber: 1996 ($2.95, B&W)

1-Phillip Hester-a/scripts 3.00

WRETCH, THE
Amaze Ink: 1997 - No. 4, 1998 ($2.95, B&W)

1-4-Phillip Hester-a/scripts 3.00
... Vol. 1: Everyday Doomsday (4/03, $13.95) 14.00

WRINGLE WRANGLE (Disney)
Dell Publishing Co.: No. 821, July, 1957

Four Color 821-Based on movie "Westward Ho, the Wagons"; Marsh-a; Fess Parker photo-c 7 14 21 46 86 125

WRONG EARTH, THE (Also see "Dragonfly & Dragonflyman")
AHOY Comics: 2018 - No. 6, 2019 ($3.99)

1-6-Tom Peyer-s/Jamal Igle-a; intro. Dragonfly & Dragonflyman 4.0
...: Confidence Men 1 (2022, $4.99) Mark Waid-s/Leonard Kirk-a 5.00
...: Fame & Fortune 1 (2022, $4.99) Mark Russell-s/Michael Montenat-a 5.00
...: Meat 1 (2022, $4.99) Tom Peyer-s/Greg Scott-a 5.00
...: Purple 1 (2022, $4.99) Stuart Moore-s/Fred Harper-a 5.00
...: Trapped on Teen Planet 1 (2022, $4.99) Gail Simone-s/Bill Morrison & Walter Geovani-a 5.00

WRONG EARTH, THE : NIGHT & DAY
AHOY Comics: 2020 - No. 6, 2021 ($3.99)

1-6-Dragonfly & Dragonflyman meet; Tom Peyer-s/Jamal Igle-a; Lady Dragonflyman app. 4.00

WULF
Ardden Entertainment: Mar, 2011 - No. 6, Sept, 2012 ($2.99)

1-6-Steve Niles-s/Nat Jones-a/c; Lomax app. 3-6-Iron Jaw app. 3.00

WULF THE BARBARIAN
Atlas/Seaboard Publ.: Feb, 1975 - No. 4, Sept, 1975

	GD 2.0	VG 4.0	FN 6.0	VF 8.0	VF/NM 9.0	NM- 9.2
1,2: 1-Origin; Janson-a. 2-Intro. Berithe the Swordswoman; Janson-a w/Neal Adams, Wood, Reese-a assists	3	6	9	14	19	24
3,4: 3-Skeates-s. 4-Friedrich-s	2	4	6	10	14	18

WWE (WWE Wrestling)
BOOM! Studios: Jan, 2017 - No. 25, Feb, 2019 ($3.99)

1-24: 1-4-Seth Rollins & Triple H app.; Serg Acuña-a; multiple covers. 1-Back-up w/Guillory-a. 13-Raw 25 Years. 14-17-Spotlight on the Four Horsewomen 4.00
25-($4.99) Hopeless-s/Serg Acuña-a; AJ Styles and Samoa Joe app. 5.00
... Attitude Era 2018 Special 1 (8/18, $7.99) Mick Foley & Steve Austin app. 8.00
...: Forever 1 (1/19, $7.99) Short stories by various; multiple covers 8.00
... Royal Rumble 2018 Special 1 (1/18, $7.99) Ric Flair & Randy Savage app. 8.00
...: SmackDown 1 (10/19, $4.99) Short stories by various; multiple covers 5.00
...: Summerslam 2017 Special 1 (8/17, $7.99) Art by Guillory and others 8.00
... Survivor Series 2017 Special 1 (11/17, $7.99) Shawn Michaels & Kurt Angle app. 8.00
...Then. Now. Forever. 1 (11/16, $3.99) Short stories by various; multiple covers 4.00
...: Wrestlemania 2017 Special 1 (8/17, $7.99) Art by Guillory, Corona, Mora and others 8.00
...: Wrestlemania 2018 Special 1 (4/18, $7.99) Art by Goode, Lorenzo and others 8.00
...: Wrestlemania 2019 Special 1 (3/19, $7.99) Art by Goode, Acuña and others 8.00

WWE HEROES (WWE Wrestling) (#7,8 titled WWE Undertaker)
Titan Comics: Apr, 2010 - No. 8 ($3.99)

1-6: 1-Two covers by Andy Smith and Liam Sharp. 5-Covers by Smith and Mayhew 4.00
7,8-"Undertaker" on cover; Rey Mysterio app. 4.00

WWE: NXT TAKEOVER (WWE Wrestling)
BOOM! Studios: Sept, 2018 ($3.99, weekly series of one-shots)

... – Into the Fire 1; Dennis Hopeless-s/Hyoenjin Kim-a; the rise of Asuka 4.00
... – Proving Ground 1; Dennis Hopeless-s/Kendall Goode-a; Finn Balor vs. Samoa Joe 4.00
... – Redemption 1; Hopeless-s/Lorenzo-a; Johnny Gargano & Shayna Baszler app. 4.00
... – The Blueprint 1; Hopeless-s/Elphick-a; Triple H & Dusty Rhodes app. 4.00

WWE SUPERSTARS (WWE Wrestling)
Papercutz (Super Genius): Dec, 2013 - No. 12, Feb, 2015 ($2.99/$3.99)

1-($2.99)-Mick Foley-s; John Cena, Randy Orton & CM Punk app. 3.00
2-12: 2-($3.99) Mick Foley-s. 9-Hulk Hogan cover by Jusko 4.00

WWE THE NEW DAY: POWER OF POSITIVITY (WWE Wrestling)
BOOM! Studios: Jul, 2021 - No. 2, Aug, 2021 ($7.99, limited series)

1,2-Spotlight on Kofi Kingston, Big E, and Xavier Woods; Bayliss-a 8.00

WYATT EARP
Atlas Comics/Marvel No. 23 on (IPC): Nov, 1955 - #29, Jun, 1960; #30, Oct, 1972 - #34, Jun, 1973

	GD 2.0	VG 4.0	FN 6.0	VF 8.0	VF/NM 9.0	NM- 9.2
1	30	60	90	177	289	400
2-Williamson-a (4 pgs.)	17	34	51	98	154	210
3-6,8-11: 3-Black Bart app. 8-Wild Bill Hickok app.	12	24	36	69	97	125
7,12-Williamson-a, 4 pgs. ea.; #12 with Mayo	13	26	39	74	105	135
13-20: 17-1st app. Wyatt's deputy, Grizzly Grant	11	22	33	62	86	110
21-Davis-c	10	20	30	58	79	100
22-24,26-29: 22-Ringo Kid app. 23-Kid From Texas app. 29-Last 10¢ issue	9	18	27	52	69	85
25-Davis-a	10	20	30	58	79	100
30-Williamson-r (1972)	2	4	6	13	18	22
31-34-Reprints. 32-Torres-a(r)	2	4	6	9	13	16

NOTE: ***Ayers** a-8, 10(2), 16(4), 17, 20(4), 26(5), 27(3), 29(3). **Berg** a-9. **Everett** c-6. **Kirby** c-22, 24-26, 29. **Maneely** a-1; c-1-4, 8, 12, 17, 20. **Maurer** a-2(2), 3(4), 4(4), 8(4). **Severin** a-4, 9(4), 10; c-2, 9, 10, 14. **Wildey** a-5, 17, 24, 27, 28.*

WYATT EARP (TV) (Hugh O'Brian Famous Marshal)
Dell Publishing Co.: No. 860, Nov, 1957 - No. 13, Dec-Feb, 1960-61 (Hugh O'Brian photo-c)

	GD 2.0	VG 4.0	FN 6.0	VF 8.0	VF/NM 9.0	NM- 9.2
Four Color 860 (#1)-Manning-a	11	22	33	72	154	235
Four Color 890,921(6/58)-All Manning-a	8	16	24	52	99	145
4 (9-11/58) - 12-Manning-a. 4-Variant edition exists with back-c comic strip; Russ Manning-a. 5-Photo back-c	5	10	15	34	60	85
13-Toth-a	5	10	15	35	63	90

WYATT EARP FRONTIER MARSHAL (Formerly Range Busters) (Also see Blue Bird)
Charlton Comics: No. 12, Jan, 1956 - No. 72, Dec, 1967

	GD 2.0	VG 4.0	FN 6.0	VF 8.0	VF/NM 9.0	NM- 9.2
12	9	18	27	50	65	80
13-19	6	12	18	31	38	45
20-(68 pgs.)-Williamson-a(4), 8,5,5,& 7 pgs.	10	20	30	56	76	95
21-(100 pgs.) Mastroserio, Maneely, Severin-a (signed LePoer)	5	10	15	31	53	75

GD VG FN VF VF/NM NM-
2.0 4.0 6.0 8.0 9.0 9.2

22-30 3 6 9 16 23 30
31-50 2 4 6 12 16 20
51-72 (1967) 2 4 6 9 11 14

WYNONNA EARP
Image Comics (WildStorm Productions): Dec, 1996 - No. 5, Apr, 1997 ($2.50)
1-5-Beau Smith-s/Joyce Chin-a/c 3.00

WYNONNA EARP
IDW Publishing: Feb, 2016 - No. 8, Sept, 2016 ($3.99)
1-8: 1-Beau Smith-s/Lora Innes-a; multiple covers; bonus look at the SyFy TV series 4.00
...: Greatest Hits 1 (7/18, $1.00) Reprints #1 3.00

WYNONNA EARP: HOME ON THE STRANGE
IDW Publishing: Dec, 2003 - No. 3, Feb, 2004 ($3.99)
1-3-Beau Smith-s/Ferreira-a 4.00

WYNONNA EARP LEGENDS: DOC HOLLIDAY
IDW Publishing: Nov, 2016 - No. 2, Dec, 2016 ($3.99)
1,2: 1-Beau Smith & Tim Rozon-s/Chris Evenhuis-a; multiple covers; 4.00

WYNONNA EARP LEGENDS: THE EARP SISTERS
IDW Publishing: No. 3, Jan, 2017 - No. 4, Feb, 2017 ($3.99)
3,4-Beau Smith & Melanie Scrofano-s/Chris Evenhuis-a; multiple covers; 4.00

WYNONNA EARP SEASON ZERO
IDW Publishing: Jun, 2017 - No. 5, Oct, 2017 ($3.99)
1-5-Beau Smith & Tim Rozon-s/Angel Hernandez-a; multiple covers; 4.00

WYNONNA EARP: THE YETI WARS
IDW Publishing: May, 2011 - No. 4, Aug, 2011 ($3.99)
1-4-Beau Smith-s/Enrique Villagran-a 4.00

WYRD
Dark Horse Comics: Jan, 2019 - No. 4, Sept, 2019 ($3.99, limited series)
1-4-Curt Pires-s/Antonio Fuso-a 4.00

WYRMS
Marvel Comics (Dabel Brothers): Feb, 2007 - No. 6, Jan, 2008 ($2.99)
1-6-Orson Scott Card & Jake Black-s. 1-3-Batista-a 3.00
TPB (2008, $14.99) r/#1-6 15.00

WYTCHES
Image Comics: Oct, 2014 - No. 6, May, 2015 ($2.99/$3.99)
1-Scott Snyder-s/Jock-a 5.00
2-5 3.00
6-($3.99) Bonus production art and Snyder afterword 4.00
...: Bad Egg Halloween Special 1 (10/18, $7.99) reprints serial from Image+ magazine 8.00
Image Firsts: Wytches (12/14, $1.00) r/#1 3.00

X (Comics' Greatest World: X #1 only) (Also see Comics' Greatest World & Dark Horse Comics #8)
Dark Horse Comics: Feb, 1994 - No. 25, Apr, 1996 ($2.00/$2.50)
1-25: 3-Pit Bulls x-over. 8-Ghost-c & app. 18-Miller-c.; Predator app. 19-22-Miller-c. 3.00
Hero Illustrated Special #1,2 (1994, $1.00, 20 pgs.) 3.00
One Shot to the Head (1994, $2.50, 36 pgs.)-Miller-c. 3.00
NOTE: ***Miller** c-18-22. **Quesada** c-6. **Russell** a-6.*

X (Comics' Greatest World)
Dark Horse Comics: No. 0, Apr, 2013 - No. 24, Apr, 2015 ($2.99)
0-24: 0-Swierczynski-s/Eric Nguyen-a. 13,14-Atkins-a 3.00
One For One (1/14, $1.00) r/#1 3.00

XANADU COLOR SPECIAL
Eclipse Comics: Dec, 1988 ($2.00, one-shot)
1-Continued from Thoughts & Images 4.00

XAVIER INSTITUTE ALUMNI YEARBOOK (See X-Men titles)
Marvel Comics: Dec, 1996 ($5.95, square-bound, one-shot)
1-Text w/art by various 6.00

X-BABIES
Marvel Comics: Dec, 2009 - No. 4, Mar, 2010 ($3.99, limited series)
1-4-Schigiel-s/Chabot-a; Skottie Young-c 4.00
...: Murderama (8/98, $2.95) J.J. Kirby-a 4.00
...: Reborn (1/00, $3.50) J.J. Kirby-a 4.00

X-CALIBRE
Marvel Comics: Mar, 1995 - No. 4, July, 1995 ($1.95, limited series)
1-4-Age of Apocalypse 4.00

X-CAMPUS
Marvel Comics: July, 2010 - No. 4, Nov, 2010 ($4.99, limited series)
1-4-Alternate version of X-Men; stories by European creators; Nauck-c 5.00

X-CELLENT (Characters from X-Statix)
Marvel Comics: Apr, 2022 - No. 5, Sept, 2022 ($3.99, limited series)
1-5-Milligan-s/Allred-a 4.00

X-CLUB
Marvel Comics: Feb, 2012 - No. 5, Jun, 2012 ($2.99, limited series)
1-5-X-Men scientist team; Dr. Nemesis & Danger app. 1-Bradshaw-c. 2-5-Esquejo-c 3.00

X-CORP
Marvel Comics: Jul, 2021 - No. 5, Nov, 2021 ($4.99/$3.99, limited series)
1-($4.99) X-Men pharmaceutical team; Angel and Monet app.; Howard-s/Foche-a 5.00
2-5-($3.99) 2-Hellfire Gala tie-in. 3-De Landro-a 4.00

X DEATHS OF WOLVERINE (Bi-weekly series alternating with X Lives of Wolverine)
Marvel Comics: Mar, 2022 - No. 5, May, 2022 ($5.99/$4.99, limited series)
1-($5.99) Percy-s/Vicenti-a; spotlight on Moira MacTaggert; Mystique app. 6.00
2-5-($4.99) 3-5-Daken & Laura app. 5.00

XENA (TV)
Dynamite Entertainment: 2006 - 2007 ($3.50)
1-4-Three covers on each; Neves-a/Layman-s 3.50
Vol. 2 #1-4-(Dark Xena) Four covers; Salonga-a/Layman-s 3.50
Annual 1 (2007, $4.95) Three covers; Salonga-a/Champagne-s 5.00
... Vol. 2: Dark Xena TPB (2007, $14.99) r/Vol. 2 #1-4; variant cover gallery 15.00

XENA (Volume 4) (TV)
Dynamite Entertainment: 2018 - No. 10, 2018 ($3.99)
1-10: 1-Meredith Finch-s/Vicente Cifuentes-a; main covers by Cifuentes & David Finch 4.00

XENA / ARMY OF DARKNESS: WHAT...AGAIN?!
Dynamite Entertainment: 2008 - No. 4, 2009 ($3.50, limited series)
1-4-Xena, Gabrielle, & Autolycus team up with Ash; Montenegro-a; two covers on each 3.50

XENA: WARRIOR PRINCESS (TV)
Topps Comics: Aug, 1997 - No. 0, Oct, 1997 ($2.95)
1-Two stories by various; J. Scott Campbell-c 1 3 4 6 8 10
1,2-Photo-c 1 3 4 6 8 10
2-Stevens-c 1 3 4 6 8 10
0-(10/97)-Lopresti-c, 0-(10/97)-Photo-c 1 2 3 5 6 8
...First Appearance Collection ('97, $9.95) r/Hercules the Legendary Journeys #3-5 and 5-page story from TV Guide 10.00

XENA: WARRIOR PRINCESS (TV)
Dark Horse Comics: Sept, 1999 - No. 14, Oct, 2000 ($2.95/$2.99)
1-14: 1-Mignola-c and photo-c. 2,3-Bradstreet-c & photo-c 4.00

XENA: WARRIOR PRINCESS (Volume 2) (TV)
Dynamite Entertainment: 2016 - No. 6, 2016 ($3.99)
1-6: 1-Valentine-s/Medel-a; main covers by Land & Frison 4.00

XENA: WARRIOR PRINCESS (Volume 3) (TV)
Dynamite Entertainment: 2018 - No. 6, 2019 ($3.99)
1-6: Vita Ayala-s; covers by David Mack and others. 1,2-Sweetman-a 4.00

XENA: WARRIOR PRINCESS AND THE ORIGINAL OLYMPICS (TV)
Topps Comics: Jun, 1998 - No. 3, Aug, 1998 ($2.95, limited series)
1-3-Regular and Photo-c; Lim-a/T&M Bierbaum-s 3.50

XENA: WARRIOR PRINCESS-BLOODLINES (TV)
Topps Comics: May, 1998 - No. 2, June, 1998 ($2.95, limited series)
1,2-Lopresti-s/c/a. 2-Reg. and photo-c 3.50
1-Bath photo-c, 1-American Ent. Ed. 4.50

XENA: WARRIOR PRINCESS / JOXER: WARRIOR PRINCE (TV)
Topps Comics: Nov, 1997 - No. 3, Jan, 1998 ($2.95, limited series)
1-3-Regular and Photo-c; Lim-a/T&M Bierbaum-s 3.50

XENA: WARRIOR PRINCESS-THE DRAGON'S TEETH (TV)
Topps Comics: Dec, 1997 - No. 3, Feb, 1998 ($2.95, limited series)
1-3-Regular and Photo-c; Teranishi-a/Thomas-s 3.50

XENA: WARRIOR PRINCESS-THE ORPHEUS TRILOGY (TV)
Topps Comics: Mar, 1998 - No. 3, May, 1998 ($2.95, limited series)
1-3-Regular and Photo-c; Teranishi-a/T&M Bierbaum-s 3.50

XENA: WARRIOR PRINCESS VS. CALLISTO (TV)
Topps Comics: Feb, 1998 - No. 3, Apr, 1998 ($2.95, limited series)
1-3-Regular and Photo-c; Morgan-a/Thomas-s 3.50

XENOBROOD
DC Comics: No. 0, Oct, 1994 - No. 6, Apr, 1995 ($1.50, limited series)
0-6: 0-Indicia says "Xenobroods" 3.00

XENOZOIC TALES (Also see Cadillacs & Dinosaurs, Death Rattle #8)
Kitchen Sink Press: Feb, 1986 - No. 14, Oct, 1996
1-Mark Schultz-s/a in all 2 4 6 9 12 15
1(2nd printing)(1/89) 4.00
2-14 6.00
Volume 1 ($14.95) r/#1-6 & Death Rattle #8 15.00
Volume 2 (5/03, $14.95, TPB) B&W r/#7-14; intro by Frank Cho 15.00

XENYA
Sanctuary Press: Apr, 1994 - No. 3 ($2.95)
1-3: 1-Hildebrandt-c; intro Xenya 3.00

XERO
DC Comics: May, 1997 - No. 12, Apr, 1998 ($1.75)
1-7 3.00
8-12 3.00

XERXES: THE FALL OF THE HOUSE OF DARIUS AND THE RISE OF ALEXANDER
Dark Horse Comics: Apr, 2018 - No. 5, Aug, 2018 ($4.99, limited series)
1-5-Prequel to 300; Frank Miller-s/a 5.00

X-FACTOR (Also see The Avengers #263, Fantastic Four #286 and Mutant X)
Marvel Comics Group: Feb, 1986 - No. 149, Sept, 1998
1-($1.25, 52 pgs)-Story recaps 1st app. from Avengers #263; story cont'd from F.F. #286; return of original X-Men (now X-Factor); Guice/Layton-a; Baby Nathan app. (2nd after X-Men #201) 3 6 9 17 26 35
2-4 1 3 4 6 8 10
5-1st brief app. Apocalypse (1 page) 3 6 9 18 27 36
6-1st full app. Apocalypse 8 16 24 38 69 100
7-10: 10-Sabretooth app. (11/86, 3 pgs.) cont'd in X-Men #212; 1st app. in an X-Men comic book 1 2 3 5 6 8
11-18,20-22: 13-Baby Nathan app. in flashback. 14-Cyclops vs. The Master Mold. 15-Intro wingless Angel 5.00
19-Apocalypse-c/app. 2 4 6 11 16 20
23-1st brief app. Archangel (2 pages) 2 4 6 9 13 16
24-1st full app. Archangel (now in Uncanny X-Men); Fall Of The Mutants begins; origin Apocalypse 4 8 12 28 47 65
25,26: Fall Of The Mutants; 26-New outfits 1 2 3 5 6 8
27-37,39,41-49,51-59,63-70,72-83,87-91,93-99,101: 35-Origin Cyclops. 51-53-Sabretooth app. 52-Liefeld-c(p). 54-Intro Crimson; Silvestri-c/a(p). 63-Portacio/Thibert-c/a(p) begins, ends #69. 65-68-Lee co-plots. 65-The Apocalypse Files begins, ends #68. 66,67-Baby

Wynonna Earp (2016) #7 © Beau Smith

X-Factor #212 © MAR

X-Files (2008) #5 © 20-FOX

GD 2.0 VG 4.0 FN 6.0 VF 8.0 VF/NM 9.0 NM- 9.2

Nathan app. 67-Inhumans app. 68-Baby Nathan is sent into future to save his life. 69,70-X-Men(w/Wolverine) x-over. 77-Cannonball (of X-Force) app. 87-Quesada-c/a(p) in monthly comic begins, ends #92. 88-1st app. Random 4.00
38,50,60-62,71,75: 38,50-(52 pgs.): 50-Liefeld/McFarlane-c. 60-X-Tinction Agenda x-over; New Mutants (w/Cable) x-over in #60-62; Wolverine in #62. 61,62-X-Tinction Agenda. 62-Jim Lee-c. 71-New team begins (Havok, Polaris, Strong Guy, Wolfsbane & Madrox); Stroman-c/a begins. 75-(52 pgs.) 5.00
40-Rob Liefield-c/a (4/89, 1st at Marvel?) 5.00
60,71-2nd printings. 60-Gold ink 2nd printing. 71-2nd printing ($1.25) 3.00
84-86 -Jae Lee a(p); 85,86-Jae Lee-c. Polybagged with trading card in each; X-Cutioner's Song x-overs. 4.00
87-Facsimile Edition (10/19, $3.99) Reprints #87 with original ads and letter column 4.00
92-($3.50, 68 pgs.)-Wraparound-c by Quesada w/Havok hologram on-c; begin X-Men 30th anniversary issues; Quesada-a. 6.00
92-2nd printing 4.00
100-($2.95, 52 pgs.)-Embossed foil-c; Multiple Man dies. 6.00
100-($1.75, 52 pgs.)-Regular edition 4.00
102-105,107: 102-bound-in card sheet 3.00
106-($2.00)-Newsstand edition 3.00
106-($2.95)-Collectors edition 4.00
108-124,126-148: 112-Return from Age of Apocalypse. 115-card insert. 119-123-Sabretooth app. 123-Hound app. 124-w/Onslaught Update. 126-Onslaught x-over; Beast vs. Dark Beast. 128-w/card insert; return of Multiple Man. 130-Assassination of Grayson Creed. 146,148-Moder-a 3.00
125-($2.95)-"Onslaught"; Post app.; return of Havok 4.00
149-Last issue 5.00
#(-1) Flashback (7/97) Matsuda-a 4.00
Annual 1-9: 1-(10/86-'94, 68 pgs.) 3-Evolutionary War x-over. 4-Atlantis Attacks; Byrne/Simonson-a;Byrne-c. 5-Fantastic Four, New Mutants x-over; Keown 2 pg. pin-up. 6-New Warriors app.; 5th app. X-Force cont'd from X-Men Annual #15. 7-1st Quesada-a(p) on X-Factor plus-c(p). 8-Bagged w/trading card. 9-Austin-a(i) 5.00
...Prisoner of Love (1990, $4.95, 52 pgs.)-Starlin scripts; Guice-a 5.00
... Visionaries: Peter David Vol. 1 TPB (2005, $15.99) r/#71-75 16.00
... Visionaries: Peter David Vol. 2 TPB (2007, $15.99) r/#76-78 & Incr. Hulk #390-392 16.00
... Visionaries: Peter David Vol. 3 TPB (2007, $15.99) r/#79-83 & Annual #7 16.00

NOTE: ***Art Adams** a-41p, 42p. **Buckler** a-50p. **Liefeld** a-40; c-40, 50i, 52p. **McFarlane** c-50i. **Mignola** c-70. **Brandon Peterson** a-78p(part). **Whilce Portacio** c/a(p)-63-69. **Quesada** a(p)-87-92, Annual 7. c(p)-78, 79, 82, Annual 7. **Simonson** c/a-10, 11, 13-15, 17-19, 21, 23-31, 33, 34, 36-39; c-12, 16. **Paul Smith** a-44-48; c-43. **Stroman** a(p)-71-75, 77, 78(part), 80, 81; c(p)-71-77, 80, 81, 84. **Zeck** c-2.*

X-FACTOR (Volume 2)
Marvel Comics: June, 2002 - No. 4, Oct, 2002 ($2.50)

1-4: Jensen-s/Ranson-a. 1-Phillips-c. 2,3-Edwards-c 3.00

X-FACTOR (Volume 3) (Also see All-New X-Factor)
Marvel Comics: Jan, 2006 - No. 262, Nov, 2013 ($2.99)

1-24: 1-Peter David-s/Ryan Sook-a. 8,9-Civil War. 21-24-Endangered Species back-up 3.00
25-49: 25-27-Messiah Complex x-over; Finch-c. 26-2nd printing with new Eaton-c 3.00
50-(12/09, $3.99) Madrox in the future; DeLandro-a/Yardin-c 4.00
200-(2/10, $4.99) Resumes original series numbering; 3 covers; Fantastic Four app. 5.00
201-224,224.1, 225-262 ($2.99) 201,202-Dr. Doom & Fant. Four app. 211,212-Thor app. 230-Wolverine app.; Havok & Polaris return 3.00
... Special: Layla Miller (10/08, $3.99) David-s/DeLandro-a 4.00
...: The Quick and the Dead (7/08, $2.99) Raimondi-a; Quicksilver regains powers 3.00
...: The Longest Night HC (2006, $19.99, dust jacket) r/#1-6; sketch pages by Sook 20.00
...: The Longest Night SC (2007, $14.99) r/#1-6; sketch pages by Sook 15.00
...: Life and Death Matters HC (2007, $19.99, dust jacket) r/#7-12 20.00
...: Life and Death Matters SC (2007, $14.99) r/#7-12 15.00
...: The Many Lives of Madrox SC (2007, $14.99) r/#13-17 15.00
...: Heart of Ice HC (2007, $19.99, dust jacket) r/#18-24 20.00
...: Heart of Ice SC (2008, $17.99, dust jacket) r/#18-24 18.00

X-FACTOR (4th series) (Leads into X-Men: The Trial of Magneto series)
Marvel Comics: Sept, 2020 - No. 10, Aug, 2021 ($4.99/$3.99)

1-($4.99) Leah Williams-s/David Baldeon-a; Northstar, Polaris, Daken app. 5.00
2,3,5-10-($3.99) 3-Shatterstar app. 10-Hellfire Gala tie-in; Scarlet Witch found dead 4.00
4-($4.99) "X of Swords" tie-in; Carlos Gomez-a 5.00

X-FACTOR FOREVER
Marvel Comics: May, 2010 - No. 5, Sept, 2010 ($3.99, limited series)

1-5-Louise Simonson-s/Dan Panosian-a; back-up origin of Apocalypse 4.00

X-51 (Machine Man)
Marvel Comics: Sept, 1999 - No. 12, Jul, 2000 ($1.99/$2.50)

1-7: 1-Joe Bennett-a. 2-Two covers 3.00
8-12: 8-Begin $2.50-c 3.00
Wizard #0 3.00

X-FILES, THE (TV)

GD 2.0 VG 4.0 FN 6.0 VF 8.0 VF/NM 9.0 NM- 9.2

Topps Comics: Jan, 1995 - No. 41, July, 1998 ($2.50)

-2(9/96)-Black-c; r/X-Files Magazine #1&2 5.00
-1(9/96)-Silver-c; r/Hero Illustrated Giveaway 5.00
0-($3.95)-Adapts pilot episode 4.00
0-"Mulder" variant-c 1 2 3 5 6 8
0-"Scully" variant-c 1 2 3 5 6 8
1/2-W/certificate 1 2 3 5 6 8
1-New stories based on the TV show; direct market & newsstand editions; Miran Kim-c on all 3 6 9 15 22 28
2 1 2 3 6 8 10
3,4 6.00
5-10: 6-Begin $2.95-c 5.00
11-41: 21-W/bound-in card. 40,41-Reg. & photo-c 4.00
Annual 1,2 ($3.95) 4.00
Afterflight TPB ($5.95) Art by Thompson, Saviuk, Kim 6.00
Classics #1: Hundred Penny Press Edition (12/13 $1.00) r/#1 3.00
Collection 1 TPB ($19.95)-r/#1-6. 20.00
Collection 2 TPB ($19.95)-r/#7-12, Annual #1. 20.00
...Fight the Future ('98, $5.95) Movie adaptation 6.00
Hero Illustrated Giveaway (3/95) 1 2 3 5 6 8
Special Edition 1-5 ($3.95/$4.95)-r/#1-3, 4-6, 7-9, 10-12, 13, Annual 1 5.00
Star Wars Galaxy Magazine Giveaway (B&W) 1 3 4 6 8 10
Trade paperback ($19.95) 20.00
Volume 1 TPB (Checker Books, 2005, $19.95) r/#13-17, #0, Season One: Squeeze 20.00
Volume 2 TPB (Checker Books, 2005, $19.95) r/#18-24, #1/2, Comics Digest #1 20.00
Volume 3 TPB (Checker Books, 2006, $19.95) r/#23-26, Fire, Ice, Hero Ill. Giveaway 20.00

X-FILES, THE (TV)
DC Comics (WildStorm): No. 0, Sept, 2008 - No. 6, Jun, 2009 ($3.99/$3.50)

0-($3.99) Spotnitz-s/Denham-a; photo-c 4.00
1-6-($3.50) 1-Spotnitz-s/Denham-a; 2 covers. 4-Wolfman-s 3.50
TPB (2009, $19.99) r/#0-6 20.00

X-FILES, THE (TV)
IDW Publishing: Apr, 2016 - Present ($3.99)

1-17: 1-Joe Harris-s/Matthew Dow Smith-a. 12,13-Flashback to Skinner in Viet Nam 4.00
... Annual 2014 (4/14, $7.99) Back-up story with Dave Sim-s/Currie-a; 2 covers 8.00
... Annual 2016 (7/16, $7.99) Greg Scott-a; Valenzuela & photo-c 8.00
...: Art Gallery (5/14, $3.99) Gallery of sketch card art by various incl. Kim & Staggs 4.00
...: Deviations (3/16, $4.99) What If... young Fox Mulder was abducted by aliens 5.00
...: Deviations 2017 (3/17, $4.99) Samantha Mulder and Scully team; Califano-a 5.00
... Funko Universe One Shot (5/17, $4.99) Short stories with Funko Pop-styled characters 5.00
... X-Mas Special (12/14, $7.99) Joe Harris-s/Matt Smith-a; Kesel-s/Southworth-a 8.00
... X-Mas Special 2016 (12/16, $7.99) Joe Harris-s/Wayne Nichols-a 8.00

X-FILES, THE: CASE FILES
IDW Publishing: 2018 ($3.99, limited series)

... - Florida Man 1,2 (4/18 - No. 2, 5/18) Dawson-s/Casagrande-a 4.00
... - Hoot Goes There? 1,2 (7/18 - No. 2, 8/18) Joe & Keith Lansdale-s/Califano-a 4.00

X-FILES COMICS DIGEST, THE
Topps Comics: Dec, 1995 - No. 3 ($3.50, quarterly, digest-size)

1-3: 1,2: New X-Files stories w/Ray Bradbury Comics-r. 1-Reg. & photo-c 4.00

NOTE: ***Adlard** a-1, 2. **Jack Davis** a-2r. **Russell** a-1r.*

X-FILES, THE: CONSPIRACY
IDW Publishing: Jan, 2014 - No. 2, Mar, 2014 ($3.99, limited series)

1,2-Bookends for 6-part Lone Gunmen series; Crilley-s/Stanisci-a; Kim & Corroney-c 4.00
X-Files/Ghostbusters: Conspiracy (1/14, $3.99) Part 2; Navarro-a 4.00
X-Files/Teenage Mutant Ninja Turtles: Conspiracy (2/14, $3.99) Part 3; Walsh-a 4.00
X-Files/Transformers: Conspiracy (2/14, $3.99) Part 4; Verma-a 4.00
X-Files/The Crow: Conspiracy (3/14, $3.99) Part 5; Malhotra-a 4.00

X-FILES, THE: GROUND ZERO (TV)
Topps Comics: Nov, 1997 - No. 4, March, 1998 ($2.95, limited series)

1-4-Adaptation of the Kevin J. Anderson novel 4.00

X-FILES, THE: JFK DISCLOSURE (TV)
IDW Publishing: Oct, 2017 - No. 2, Nov, 2017 ($4.99)

1,2-Tipton-s/Menton3-a 5.00

X-FILES, THE: ORIGINS (TV)
IDW Publishing: Aug, 2016 - No. 4, Nov, 2016 ($4.99)

1-4-Flipbooks with teenage Mulder and Scully 5.00

X-FILES, THE: ORIGINS – DOG DAYS OF SUMMER (TV)
IDW Publishing: Jun, 2017 - No. 4, Sept, 2017 ($3.99)

1-4-Flipbooks with teenage Mulder in 1974 and Scully in 1977 4.00

GD VG FN VF VF/NM NM-
2.0 4.0 6.0 8.0 9.0 9.2

X-FILES, THE: SEASON ONE (TV)
Topps Comics: July, 1997 - July, 1998 ($4.95, adaptations of TV episodes)
1-(Pilot Episode, r/X-Files #0), 2-(Deep Throat), Squeeze, Conduit, Ice, Space, Fire, Beyond the Sea, Shadows 1 2 3 5 6 8

X-FILES, THE: SEASON 10 (TV)
IDW Publishing: Jun, 2013 - No. 25, Jun, 2015 ($3.99)
1-25: 1-5-Co-written by Chris Carter; multiple covers on each. 6,7-Flukeman returns. 17-Frank Black app. 18-Doggett & Reyes app. 4.00
... #1: IDW's Greatest Hits (4/16, $1.00) r/#1 3.00

X-FILES, THE: SEASON 11 (TV)
IDW Publishing: Aug, 2015 - No. 8, Mar, 2016 ($3.99)
1-8: 1-Joe Harris-s/Matthew Smith-a 4.00

X-FILES, THE / 30 DAYS OF NIGHT
DC Comics (WildStorm)/IDW: Sept, 2010 - No. 6, Feb, 2011 ($3.99, limited series)
1-6-Steve Niles & Adam Jones-s/Tom Mandrake-a. 1-Three covers 4.00
TPB (2011, $17.99) r/#1-6; cover gallery 18.00

X-FILES, THE: YEAR ZERO (TV)
IDW Publishing: Jul, 2014 - No. 5, Nov, 2014 ($3.99)
1-5: 1-Karl Kesel-s; Greg Scott & Vic Malhotra-a; flashback to 1946 4.00

X-FORCE (Becomes X-Statix) (Also see The New Mutants #100)
Marvel Comics: Aug, 1991 - No. 129, Aug, 2002 ($1.00-$2.25)
1-($1.50, 52 pgs.)-Polybagged with 1 of 5 diff. Marvel Universe trading cards inside (1 each); 6th app. of X-Force; Liefeld-c/a begins 1 3 4 6 8 10
1-1st printing with Cable trading card inside 2 4 6 11 16 20
1-1st printing with Deadpool trading card inside 2 4 6 11 16 20
1-2nd printing; metallic ink-c (no bag or card) 6.00
2-Deadpool-c/story (2nd app.) 3 6 9 14 20 26
3,4: 3-New Brotherhood of Evil Mutants app. 4-Spider-Man x-over; cont'd from Spider-Man #16; reads sideways; 2-pg pin-up by Mignola 5.00
5-10: 6-Last $1.00-c. 7,9-Weapon X back-ups. 8-Intro The Wild Pack (Cable, Kane, Domino (not Copycat), Hammer, G.W. Bridge, & Grizzly); Liefeld-c/a (4); Mignola-a. 10-Weapon X full-length story (part 3). 5.00
11-2nd app. the real Domino (not Copycat); Deadpool-c/story (3rd app.) 3 6 9 16 24 32
12-14,20-22,24,26-33 3.00
15-Cable leaves X-Force; Deadpool-c/app. 2 4 6 10 14 18
16-18-Polybagged w/trading card in each; X-Cutioner's Song x-overs 4.00
19-1st Copycat 2 4 6 10 14 18
23-Deadpool-c/app. 6.00
25-($3.50, 52 pgs.)-Wraparound-c w/Cable hologram on-c; Cable returns 5.00
34-37,39-45: 34-bound-in card sheet 3.00
38,40-43: 38-($2.00)-Newsstand edition. 40-43 ($1.95)-Deluxe edition 3.00
38-($2.95)-Collectors edition (prismatic) 5.00
44-49,51-74: 44-Return from Age of Apocalypse. 45-Sabretooth app. 49-Sebastian Shaw app. 52-Blob app., Onslaught cameo. 55-Vs. S.H.I.E.L.D. 56-Deadpool app. 57-Mr. Sinister & X-Man-c/app. 57,58-Onslaught x-over. 59-W/card insert; return of Longshot. 60-Dr. Strange 68-Operation Zero Tolerance 3.00
50 ($3.95)-Gatefold wrap-around foil-c 4.00
50 ($3.95)-Liefeld variant-c 5.00
75,100-($2.99): 75-Cannonball-c/app. 4.00
76-99,101,102: 81-Pollina poster. 95-Magneto-c. 102-Ellis-s/Portacio-a 3.00
103-115: 103-Begin $2.25-c; Portacio-a thru #106. 115-Death of old team 3.00
116-New team debuts; Allred-c/a; Milligan-s; no Comics Code stamp on-c 4.00
117-129: 117-Intro. Mr. Sensitive. 120-Wolverine-c/app. 123-'Nuff Said issue. 124-Darwyn Cooke-a/c. 128-Death of U-Go Girl. 129-Fegredo-a 3.00
#(-1) Flashback (7/97) story of John Proudstar; Pollina-a 3.00
Annual 1-3 ('92-'94, 68 pgs.) 1-1st Greg Capullo-a(p) on X-Force. 2-Polybagged w/trading card; intro X-Treme & Neurtap 4.00
...And Cable '95 (12/95, $3.95)-Impossible Man app. 4.00
...And Cable '96, ...'97 ('96, 7/97) -'96-Wraparound-c 4.00
...And Spider-Man: Sabotage nn (11/92, $6.95)-Reprints X-Force #3,4 & Spider-Man #16 7.00
.../ Champions '98 ($3.50) 4.00
Annual 99 ($3.50) 4.00
...: Famous, Mutant & Mortal HC (2003, $29.99) oversized r/#116-129; foreward by Milligan; gallery of covers and pin-ups; script for #123 30.00
...New Beginnings TPB (10/01, $14.95) r/#116-120 15.00
...Rough Cut ($2.99) Pencil pages and script for #102 3.00
...Youngblood (8/96, $4.95)-Platt-c 5.00
NOTE: ***Capullo*** *a(p)-15-25, Annual 1; c(p)-14-27.* ***Rob Liefeld*** *a-1-7, 9p; c-1-9, 11p; plots-1-12.* ***Mignola*** *a-8p.*

X-FORCE
Marvel Comics: Oct, 2004 - No. 6, Mar, 2005 ($2.99, limited series)
1-6-Liefeld-c/a; Nicieza-s. 5,6-Wolverine & The Thing app. 3.00
X-Force & Cable Vol. 1: The Legend Returns (2005, $14.99) r/#1-6 15.00

X-FORCE (Also see Uncanny X-Force)
Marvel Comics: Apr, 2008 - No. 28, Sept, 2010 ($2.99)
1-Crain-a; Wolverine & X-23 app.; two covers (regular and bloody) by Crain on #1-5 4.00
2-21,23-28: 2,3-Bastion app. 4-6-Archangel app. 7-10-Choi-a. 9-11-Ghost Rider app. 26-28-Second Coming x-over; Granov-c. 26-Nightcrawler killed 3.00
22-($3.99) Necrosha x-over; Crain-a 4.00
...: Angels and Demons MGC #1 (5/11, $1.00) r/#1 with "Marvel's Greatest Comics" on-c 3.00
... Annual 1 (2/10, $3.99) Kirkman-s/Pearson-a/c; Deadpool back-up w/Barberi-a 4.00
... /Cable: Messiah War 1 (5/09, $3.99) Choi-a; covers by Andrews and Choi 4.00
... Special: Ain't No Dog (8/08, $3.99) Huston-s/Palo-a; Dell'Edera-a; Hitch-c 4.00

X-FORCE
Marvel Comics: Apr, 2014 - No. 15, Apr, 2015 ($3.99)
1-15: 1-Team of Cable, Fantomex, Psylocke & Marrow; Rock-He Kim-a. 4-6-Molina-a 4.00

X-FORCE
Marvel Comics: Feb, 2019 - No. 10, Sept, 2019 ($3.99)
1-10: 1-Team of Cable, Domino, Shatterstar, Warpath, Cannonball, Deathlok; Brisson-s 4.00

X-FORCE
Marvel Comics: Jan, 2020 - Present ($3.99)
1-($4.99) Team of Jean Grey, Wolverine, Domino, Beast, Colossus; Percy-s/Cassara-a 5.00
2-38-($3.99) 2-Kid Omega app. 6-Segovia-a. 7,8-Basaldua-a. 13,14-"X of Swords" tie-in 4.00
Annual 1 (6/22, $4.99) Shammas-s/Pimentel-a 5.00
...: Killshot Anniversary Special #1 (1/22, $4.99) Rob Liefeld-s/a; 7 covers 5.00

X-FORCE MEGAZINE
Marvel Comics: Nov, 1996 ($3.95, one-shot)
1-Reprints 4.00

X-FORCE: SEX AND VIOLENCE
Marvel Comics: Sept, 2010 - No. 3, Nov, 2010 ($3.99, limited series)
1-3-Dell'Otto-a/Kyle & Yost-s; Domino & Wolverine vs. The Hand & The Assassins Guild 5.00

X-FORCE: SHATTERSTAR
Marvel Comics: Apr, 2005 - No. 4, July, 2005 ($2.99, limited series)
1-4-Liefeld-c/s; Michaels-a 3.00
TPB (2005, $15.99) r/#1-4 & New Mutants #99,100 16.00

X-INFERNUS
Marvel Comics: Feb, 2009 - No. 4, May, 2009 ($3.99, limited series)
1-4-Illyana Rasputin in Limbo; Cebulski-s/Camuncoli-a/Finch-c 4.00

XIN: JOURNEY OF THE MONKEY KING
Anarchy Studios: May, 2003 - No. 3, July, 2003 ($2.99)
Preview Edition (Apr, 2003, $1.99) Flip book w/ Vampi Vicious Preview Edition 3.00
1-3-Kevin Lau-a. 1-Three covers by Lau, Park and Nauck. 2-Three covers 3.00

XIN: LEGEND OF THE MONKEY KING
Anarchy Studios: Nov, 2002 - No. 3, Jan, 2003 ($2.99)
Preview Edition (Summer 2002, Diamond Dateline supplement) 3.00
1-3-Kevin Lau-a. 1-Two covers by Lau & Madureira. 2-Two covers by Lau & Oeming 3.00
TPB (10/03, $12.95) r/#1-3; cover gallery and sketch pages 13.00

X LIVES OF WOLVERINE (Bi-weekly series alternating with X Deaths of Wolverine)
Marvel Comics: Mar, 2022 - No. 5, May, 2022 ($5.99/$4.99)
1-($5.99) Percy-s/Cassara-a; Omega Red & Logan at birth of Prof. X 6.00
2-5-($4.99) 2-Jean Grey app. 5-Omega Red app. 5.00

X-MAN (Also see X-Men Omega & X-Men Prime)
Marvel Comics: Mar, 1995 - No. 75, May, 2001 ($1.95/$1.99/$2.25)
1-Age of Apocalypse 1 2 3 5 6 8
1-2nd print 3.00
2-4,25: 25-($2.99)-Wraparound-c 4.00
5-24, 26-28: 5-Post Age of Apocalypse stories begin. 5-7-Madelyne Pryor app. 10-Professor X app. 12-vs. Excalibur. 13-Marauders, Cable app. 14-Vs. Cable; Onslaught app. 15-17-Vs. Holocaust. 17-w/Onslaught Update. 18-Onslaught x-over; X-Force-c/app; Marauders app. 19-Onslaught x-over. 20-Abomination-c/app.; w/card insert. 23-Bishop app. 24-Spider-Man, Morbius-c/app. 27-Re-appearance of Aurora (Alpha Flight) 3.00
29-49,51-62: 29-Operation Zero Tolerance. 37,38-Spider-Man-c/app. 56-Spider-Man app. 3.00
50-($2.99) Crossover with Generation X #50 4.00
63-74: 63-Ellis & Grant-s/Olivetti-a begins. 64-Begin $2.25-c 3.00
75 ($2.99) Final issue; Alcatena-a 4.00
#(-1) Flashback (7/97) 3.00
...'96, ...'97-($2.95)-Wraparound-c; '96-Age of Apocalypse 4.00
...: All Saints' Day ('97, $5.99) Dodson-a 6.00
.../Hulk '98 ($2.99) Wraparound-c; Thanos app. 4.00

XMAS COMICS
Fawcett Publications: 12?/1941 - No. 2, 12?/1942; (50¢, 324 pgs.)
No. 7, 12?/1947 (25¢, 132 pgs.)(#3-6 do not exist for this series, see 1949-1952 series)
1-Contains Whiz #21, Capt. Marvel #3, Bulletman #2, Wow #3, & Master #18; front & back-c by Raboy. Not rebound, remaindered comics; printed at same time as originals 503 1006 1509 3672 6486 9300
2-Capt. Marvel, Bulletman, Spy Smasher 232 464 696 1485 2543 3600
7-Funny animals (Hoppy, Billy the Kid & Oscar) 97 194 291 621 1061 1500

XMAS COMICS
Fawcett Publications: No. 4, Dec, 1949 - No. 7, Dec, 1952 (50¢, 196 pgs.)
4-Contains Whiz, Master, Tom Mix, Captain Marvel, Nyoka, Capt. Video, Bob Colt, Monte Hale, Hot Rod Comics, & Battle Stories. Not rebound, remaindered comics; printed at the same time as originals. Title logo and Santa's suit on cover are topped by red felt 135 270 405 864 1482 2100
5-7: 5-Green felt tree on-c. 6-Cover has red felt like #4. 7-Bill Boyd app.; stocking on cover is made of green felt (novelty cover) 106 212 318 673 1162 1650

X-MEN, THE (See Adventures of Cyclops and Phoenix, Amazing Adventures, Archangel, Brotherhood, Capt. America #172, Classic X-Men, Exiles, Further Adventures of Cyclops & Phoenix, Gambit, Giant-Size..., Heroes For Hope..., Kitty Pryde & Wolverine, Marvel & DC Present, Marvel Collector's Edition:..., Marvel Fanfare, Marvel Graphic Novel, Marvel Super Heroes, Marvel Team-Up, Marvel Triple Action, The Marvel X-Men Collection, New Mutants, Nightcrawler, Official Marvel Index To..., Rogue, Special Edition..., Ultimate..., Uncanny..., Wolverine, X-Factor, X-Force, X-Terminators)

X-MEN, THE (1st series)(Becomes Uncanny X-Men at #142)(The X-Men #1-93; X-Men #94-141) (The Uncanny X-Men on-c only #114-141)
Marvel Comics Group: Sept, 1963 - No. 66, Mar, 1970; No. 67, Dec, 1970 - No. 141, Jan, 1981; Uncanny X-Men No. 142, Feb, 1981 - No. 544, Dec, 2011
1-Origin/1st app. X-Men (Angel, Beast, Cyclops, Iceman & Marvel Girl); 1st app. Magneto & Professor X 5140 10,280 20,560 47,500 116,250 185,000
2-1st app. The Vanisher 241 482 723 1988 4494 7000
3-1st app. The Blob (1/64) 162 324 486 1337 3019 4700
4-1st Quicksilver & Scarlet Witch & Brotherhood of the Evil Mutants (3/64); 1st app. Toad; 2nd app. Magneto 1100 2200 3300 6600 8800 11,000
5-Magneto & Evil Mutants-c/story 115 230 345 920 2060 3200
6-Sub-Mariner app. 89 178 267 712 1606 2500
7-Magneto app. 71 142 213 568 1284 2000
8,9,11: 8-1st Unus the Untouchable. 9-Early Avengers app. (1/65); 1st Lucifer. 11-1st app. The Stranger. 57 114 171 456 1028 1600
10-1st S.A. app. Ka-Zar & Zabu the sabertooth (3/65) 75 150 225 600 1350 2100
12-Origin Prof. X; Origin/1st app. Juggernaut 279 558 837 2302 5201 8100
13-Juggernaut and Human Torch app. 52 104 156 411 931 1450
14-1st app. Sentinels 93 186 279 744 1672 2600
15-Origin Beast 46 92 138 340 770 1200
16-20: 19-1st app. The Mimic (4/66) 21 42 63 147 324 500

X-Force (2008) #1 © MAR

X-Men #50 © MAR

X-Men #268 © MAR

	GD 2.0	VG 4.0	FN 6.0	VF 8.0	VF/NM 9.0	NM- 9.2
21-27,29,30: 27-Re-enter The Mimic (r-in #75); Spider-Man cameo	15	30	45	100	220	340
28-1st app. The Banshee (1/67)(r-in #76)	40	80	120	296	673	1050
28-2nd printing (1994)	2	4	6	9	12	15
31-34,36,37,39: 34-Adkins-c/a. 39-New costumes	12	24	36	80	173	265
35-Spider-Man x-over (8/67)(r-in #83); 1st app. Changeling	40	80	120	296	673	1050
38,40: 38-Origins of the X-Men series begins, ends #57. 40-(1/68) 1st app. Frankenstein's monster at Marvel	12	24	36	84	185	285
41-48: 42-Death of Prof. X (Changeling disguised as). 44-1st S.A. app. G.A. Red Raven.	11	22	33	75	160	245
49-Steranko-c; 1st Polaris	46	92	138	340	770	1200
50-Steranko-c/a; Polaris cover	44	88	132	326	738	1150
51-Steranko-c/a	14	28	42	96	211	325
52	17	34	51	117	259	400
53-Barry Smith-c/a (his 1st comic book work)	12	24	36	79	170	260
54-1st app. Alex Summers who later becomes Havok; B. Smith-c	23	46	69	161	356	550
55-Summers discovers he has mutant powers	12	24	36	81	176	270
56,57,59-63,65-Neal Adams-a(p). 56-Intro Havok w/o costume. 60-1st Sauron. 65-Return of Professor X.	12	24	36	80	173	265
58-1st app. Havok in costume; N. Adams-a(p)	36	72	108	259	580	900
62,63-2nd printings (1994)	2	4	6	8	11	14
64-1st app. Sunfire	32	64	96	230	515	800
66-Last new story w/original X-Men; battles Hulk	14	28	42	94	207	320
67-70: 67-Reprints begin, end #93. 67-70: (52 pgs.)	9	18	27	63	129	195
71-93: 71-Last 15¢ issue. 72: (52 pgs.). 73-86-r/#25-38 w/new-c. 83-Spider-Man-c/story. 87-93-r/#39-45 with covers	9	18	27	57	111	165
94 (8/75)-New X-Men begin (see Giant-Size X-Men for 1st app.); Colossus, Nightcrawler, Thunderbird, Storm, Wolverine, & Banshee join; Angel, Marvel Girl & Iceman resign	140	280	420	980	1890	2800
95-Death of Thunderbird	17	34	51	117	259	400
96,97	12	24	36	79	170	260
98,99-(Regular 25¢ edition)(4,6/76)	12	24	36	82	179	275
98,99-(30¢-c variants, limited distribution)	29	58	87	209	467	725
100-Old vs. New X-Men; part origin Phoenix; last 25¢ issue (8/76)	16	32	48	111	246	380
100-(30¢-c variant, limited distribution)	36	72	108	259	580	900
101-Phoenix origin concludes	34	68	102	245	548	850
102-104: 102-Origin Storm. 104-1st brief app. Starjammers; Magneto-c/story	8	16	24	56	108	160
105-107-(Regular 30¢ editions). 106-(8/77)Old vs. New X-Men. 107-1st full app. Starjammers; last 30¢ issue	8	16	24	54	102	150
105-107-(35¢-c variants, limited distribution)	36	72	108	259	580	900
108-Byrne-a begins (see Marvel Team-Up #53)	8	16	24	56	108	160
109-1st app. Weapon Alpha (becomes Vindicator)	15	30	45	103	227	350
110-116: 110-Phoenix joins	6	12	18	42	79	115
117-119: 117-Origin Professor X	6	12	18	37	66	95
120-1st app. Alpha Flight, story line begins (4/79); 1st app. Vindicator (formerly Weapon Alpha); last 35¢ issue	12	24	36	79	170	260
121-1st full Alpha Flight story	11	22	33	73	157	240
122-128: 123-Spider-Man x-over. 124-Colossus becomes Proletarian	5	10	15	34	60	85
129-Intro Kitty Pryde (1/80); last Banshee; Dark Phoenix saga begins; intro. Emma Frost (White Queen)	17	34	51	117	259	400
130-1st app. The Dazzler by Byrne (2/80)	11	22	33	76	163	250
131-133: 131-Dazzler app.; 1st White Queen-c. 133-1st Wolverine solo-c	5	10	15	34	60	85
134-Phoenix becomes Dark Phoenix	8	16	24	54	102	150
135-1st Dark Phoenix-c	6	12	18	42	79	115
136,138: 138-History of the X-Men recounted; Dazzler app.; Cyclops leaves	5	10	15	31	53	75
137-Giant; death of Phoenix	6	12	18	42	79	115
139-Alpha Flight app.; Kitty Pryde joins; new costume for Wolverine	5	10	15	33	57	80
140-Alpha Flight app.	5	10	15	33	57	80
141-"Days of Future Past" part 1; intro Future X-Men & The New Brotherhood of Evil Mutants; 1st app. Rachel (Phoenix II); Death of alt. future Franklin Richards; classic cover	10	20	30	69	147	225

X-MEN: Titled THE UNCANNY X-MEN No. 142, Feb, 1981 - No. 544, Dec, 2011

	GD 2.0	VG 4.0	FN 6.0	VF 8.0	VF/NM 9.0	NM- 9.2
142-"Days of Future Past" part 2; Rachel app.; deaths of alt. future Wolverine, Storm & Colossus	7	14	21	46	86	125
143-Last Byrne issue	4	8	12	25	40	55
144-150: 144-Man-Thing app. 145-Old X-Men app. 148-1st app. Caliban; Spider-Woman, Dazzler app. 150-Double size	2	4	6	11	16	20
151-154,156,157,159-161,163,164: 161-Origin Magneto. 163-Origin Binary. 164-1st app. Binary as Carol Danvers	2	4	6	9	13	16
155-1st app of The Brood	4	8	12	27	44	60
158-1st app. Rogue in X-Men (6/82, see Avengers Annual #10)	4	8	12	25	40	55
162-Wolverine solo story	3	6	9	16	23	30
165-Paul Smith-c/a begins, ends #175	2	4	6	11	16	20
166-170: 166-Double size; Paul Smith-a. 167-New Mutants app. (3/83); same date as New Mutants #1; 1st meeting w/X-Men; ties into N.M. #3,4; Starjammers app.; contains skin "Tattooz" decals. 168-1st brief app. Madelyne Pryor (last page) in X-Men (see Avengers Annual #10)	2	4	6	8	11	14
171-Rogue joins X-Men; Simonson-c/a	3	6	9	21	33	45
172-174: 172,173-Two part Wolverine solo story. 173-Two cover variations, blue & black. 174-Phoenix cameo	2	4	6	8	11	14
175-(52 pgs.)-Anniversary issue; Phoenix returns	3	6	9	14	20	25
176-185,187-192,194-199: 181-Sunfire app. 182-Rogue solo story. 184-1st app. Forge (8/84). 190,191-Spider-Man & Avengers x-over. 195-Power Pack x-over	2	4	6	8	10	12
186,193: 186-Double-size; Barry Smith/Austin-a. 193-Double size; 100th app. New X-Men; 1st app. Warpath in costume (see New Mutants #16)	2	4	6	8	11	14
200-(12/85, $1.25, 52 pgs.)	3	6	9	16	23	30
201-(1/86)-1st app. Cable? (as baby Nathan; see X-Factor #1); 1st Whilce Portacio-c/a(i) on X-Men (guest artist)	3	6	9	21	33	45
202-204,206-209: 204-Nightcrawler solo story; 2nd Portacio-a(i) on X-Men. 207-Wolverine/Phoenix story	2	4	6	8	11	14
205-Wolverine solo story by Barry Smith	3	6	9	14	20	26
210,211-Mutant Massacre begins	3	6	9	16	23	30
212,213-Wolverine vs. Sabretooth (Mutant Mass.)	3	6	9	18	28	38
214-220,223,224: 219-Havok joins (7/87); brief app. Sabretooth.	2	4	6	8	10	12
221-1st app. Mr. Sinister	5	10	15	34	60	85
222-Wolverine battles Sabretooth-c/story	3	6	9	17	25	34
225-242: 225-227: Fall Of The Mutants. 226-Double size. 240-Sabretooth app. 242-Double size, X-Factor app., Inferno tie-in	2	4	6	8	10	12
243,245-247: 245-Rob Liefeld-a(p)	2	4	6	8	10	12
244-1st app. Jubilee	4	8	12	28	47	65
248-1st Jim Lee art on X-Men (1989)	3	6	9	17	25	34
248-2nd printing (1992, $1.25)	1	3	4	6	8	10
249-252: 252-Lee-c	1	3	4	6	8	10
253-255: 253-All new X-Men begin. 254-Lee-c	1	3	4	6	8	10
256-Betsy Braddock (Psylocke) 1st app. as purple-haired Asian in ninja costume; Jim Lee-c/a	3	6	9	19	30	40
257-Jim Lee-c/a; Psylocke as Lady Mandarin	2	4	6	9	13	16
258-Wolverine solo story; Lee-c/a	2	4	6	9	13	16
259-Silvestri-c/a; no Lee-a	1	3	4	6	8	10
260-265-No Lee-a. 260,261,264-Lee-c	1	3	4	6	8	10
266-(8/90) 1st full app. Gambit (see Annual #14)-No Lee-a	10	20	30	67	141	215
267-Jim Lee-c/a resumes; 2nd full Gambit app.	3	6	9	16	24	32
268-Capt. America, Black Widow & Wolverine team-up; Lee-c/a	3	6	9	21	33	45
268,270: 268-2nd printing. 270-Gold 2nd printing	2	4	6	8	11	14
269,273,274: 269-Lee-a. 273-New Mutants (Cable) & X-Factor x-over; Golden, Byrne & Lee part pencils	1	3	4	6	8	10
270-X-Tinction Agenda begins	2	4	6	8	10	12
271,272-X-Tinction Agenda	2	4	6	8	10	12
275-(52 pgs.)-Tri-fold-c by Jim Lee (p); Prof. X	2	4	6	8	10	12
275-Gold 2nd printing						6.00
276-280: 277-Last Lee-c/a. 280-X-Factor x-over	1	2	3	5	6	8
281-(10/91)-New team begins (Storm, Archangel, Colossus, Iceman & Marvel Girl); Whilce Portacio-c/a begins; Byrne scripts begin; wraparound-c (white logo)	2	4	6	9	12	15
281-2nd printing with red metallic ink logo w/o UPC box ($1.00-c); does not say 2nd printing inside						5.00
282-1st brief app. Bishop (cover & 1 page)	3	6	9	21	33	45
282-Gold ink 2nd printing ($1.00-c)	2	4	6	8	10	12
283-1st full app. Bishop (12/91)	2	4	6	11	16	20
284-299: 284-Last $1.00-c. 286,287-Lee plots. 287-Bishop joins team. 288-Lee/Portacio plots. 290-Last Portacio-c/a. 294-Peterson-a(p) begins (#292 is 1st Peterson-c). 294-296 ($1.50)-Bagged w/trading card in each; X-Cutioner's Song x-overs; Peterson/Austin-c/a on all						6.00
297-Gold Edition	13	26	39	86	188	290
300-($3.95, 68 pgs.)-Holo-grafx foil-c; Magneto app.	1	3	4	6	8	10
301-303,305-309,311						4.00
303,307-Gold Edition	6	12	18	38	69	100
304-($3.95, 68 pgs.)-Wraparound-c with Magneto hologram on-c; 30th anniversary issue;						

GD 2.0 | VG 4.0 | FN 6.0 | VF 8.0 | VF/NM 9.0 | NM- 9.2

Jae Lee-a (4 pgs.) 2 4 6 8 10 12
310-($1.95)-Bound-in trading card sheet 4.00
312-$1.50-c begins; bound-in card sheet; 1st Madureira 5.00
313-321: 318-1st app. Generation X 4.00
316,317-($2.95)-Foil enhanced editions 5.00
318-321-($1.95)-Deluxe editions 5.00
322-Onslaught 5.00
323,324,326-346: 323-Return from Age of Apocalypse. 328-Sabretooth-c. 329,330-Dr. Strange app. 331-White Queen-c/app. 334-Juggernaut app.; w/Onslaught Update. 335-Onslaught, Avengers, Apocalypse, & X-Man app. 336-Onslaught. 338-Archangel's wings return to normal. 339-Havok vs. Cyclops; Spider-Man app. 341-Gladiator-c/app. 342-Deathbird cameo; two covers. 343,344-Phalanx 4.00
325-($3.95)-Anniversary issue; gatefold-c 6.00
342-Variant-c 2 4 6 9 13 16
347-349:347-Begin $1.99-c. 349-"Operation Zero Tolerance" 4.00
350-Newsstand version 2 4 6 10 14 18
350-($3.99, 48 pgs.) Prismatic etched foil gatefold wraparound-c; Trial of Gambit; Seagle-s begin 2 4 6 11 16 20
351-359: 353-Bachalo-a begins. 354-Regular-c. 355-Alpha Flight-c/app. 356-Original X-Men-c 4.00
354-Dark Phoenix variant-c 2 4 6 8 10 12
360-($2.99) 35th Anniv. issue; Pacheco-c 5.00
360-($3.99) Etched Holo-foil enhanced-c 6.00
360-($6.95) DF Edition with Jae Lee variant-c 2 4 6 8 10 12
361-374,378,379: 361-Gambit returns; Skroce-a. 362-Hunt for Xavier pt. 1; Bachelo-a. 364-Yu-a. 366-Magneto-c. 369-Juggernaut-c 4.00
375-($2.99) Autopsy of Wolverine 6.00
376,377-Apocalypse: The Twelve 1 3 4 6 8 10
380-($2.99) Polybagged with X-Men Revolution Genesis Edition preview 5.00
381,382,384-389,391-393: 381-Begin $2.25-c; Claremont-s. 387-Maximum Security 4.00
383-($2.99) 5.00
390-Colossus dies to cure the Legacy Virus 2 4 6 8 11 14
394-New look X-Men begins; Casey-s/Churchill-c/a 5.00
395-399-Poptopia. 398-Phillips & Wood-a 4.00
400-($3.50) Art by Ashley Wood, Eddie Campbell, Hamner, Phillips, Pulido and Matt Smith; wraparound-c by Wood 6.00
401-421: 401-'Nuff Said issue; Garney-a. 404,405,407-409,413-415-Phillips-a. 416-Asamiya-a begins. 421-Garney-a 4.00
422-($3.50) Alpha Flight app.; Garney-a 5.00
423-(25¢-c) Holy War pt. 1; Garney-a/Philip Tan-c 4.00
424-449,452-454: 425,426,429,430-Tan-a. 428-Birth of Nightcrawler. 437-Larroca-a begins. 444-New team, new costumes; Claremont-s/Davis-a begins. 448,449-Coipel-a 4.00
450-X-23 app.; Davis-a 3 6 9 14 20 25
451-X-23 app.; Davis-a 3 6 9 14 20 25
455-459-X-23 app.; Davis-a 6.00
460-471: 460-Begin $2.50-c; Raney-a. 462-465-House of M. 464-468-Bachalo-a 4.00
472-499: 472-Begin $2.99-c; Bachalo-a. 475-Wraparound-c. 492-494-Messiah Complex 4.00
500-($3.99) X-Men new HQ in San Francisco; Magneto app.; Land & Dodson-a; wraparound covers by Alex Ross and Greg Land 6.00
500-Classic X-Men Dynamic Forces var.-c by Ross 2 4 6 10 14 18
500-X-Men variant-c by Michael Turner 4 8 12 22 32 40
500-X-Men sketch variant-c by Michael Turner 13 26 39 89 195 300
500-X-Women variant-c by Dodson 3 6 9 14 20 25
500-X-Women sketch variant-c by Dodson 11 22 33 76 163 250
501-511,515-521,523-525: 501-Brubaker & Fraction-s/Land-a. 523-525-Second Coming 4.00
512-514,522-($3.99). 513,514-Utopia x-over. 522-Kitty Pryde returns to Earth; Portacio-a 5.00
526-543-($3.99) 526-The Heroic Age; aftermath of Second Coming. 530-534-Land-a 540-543-Fear Itself tie-in, Juggernaut attacks; Land-a. 542-Colossus becomes the Juggernaut 5.00
534.1 (6/11, $2.99) Pacheco-a/c 4.00
544-(12/11, $3.99) Final issue; Land-a/c; Mr. Sinister app. 2 4 6 10 14 18
#(-1) Flashback (7/97) Ladronn-c/Hitch & Neary-a 4.00
... No. 1 Facsimile Edition (9/19, $3.99) Reprints #1 with original ads 4.00
... No. 4 Facsimile Edition (1/21, $3.99) Reprints #4 with original ads 4.00
... No. 137 Facsimile Edition (9/19, $3.99) Reprints #137 with original ads 4.00
... No. 266 Facsimile Edition (1/20, $3.99) Reprints #266 with original ads and letters 4.00
Special 1(12/70)-Kirby-c/a; origin The Stranger 12 24 36 79 170 260
Special 2(11/71, 52 pgs.) 8 16 24 54 102 150
Annual 3(1979, 52 pgs.)-New story; Miller/Austin-c; Wolverine still in old yellow costume 5 10 15 30 48 65
Annual 4(1980, 52 pgs.)-Dr. Strange guest stars 3 6 9 16 23 30
Annual 5(1981, 52 pgs.) 2 4 6 8 10 12
Annual 6-8('82-'84 52 pgs.)-6-Dracula app. 1 2 3 5 6 8
Annual 9,10('85, '86)-9-New Mutants x-over cont'd from New Mutants Special Ed. #1; Art Adams-a. 10-Art Adams-a 2 4 6 8 10 12
Annual 11-13:('87-'89, 68 pgs.): 12-Evolutionary War; A.Adams-a(p). 13-Atlantis Attacks 5.00
Annual 14(1990, $2.00, 68 pgs.)-1st app. Gambit (minor app., 5 pgs.); Fantastic Four, New Mutants (Cable) & X-Factor x-over; Art Adams-c/a(p) 4 8 12 28 47 65
Annual 15 (1991, $2.00, 68 pgs.)-4 pg. origin; New Mutants x-over; 4 pg. Wolverine solo back-up story; 4th app. X-Force cont'd from New Warriors Annual #1 5.00
Annual 16-18 ('92-'94, 68 pgs.)-16-Jae Lee-c/a(p). 17-Bagged w/card 5.00
Annual '95-(11/95, $3.95)-Wraparound-c 5.00
Annual '96,'97-Wraparound-c 5.00
.../Fantastic Four Annual '98 ($2.99) Casey-s 5.00
Annual '99 ($3.50) Jubilee app. 5.00
Annual 2000 ($3.50) Cable app.; Ribic-a 5.00
Annual 2001 ($3.50, printed wide-ways) Ashley Wood-c/a; Casey-s 5.00
Annual (Vol. 2) #1 (8/06, $3.99) Storm & Black Panther wedding prelude 5.00
Annual (Vol. 2) #2 (3/09, $3.99) Dark Reign; flashback to Sub-Mariner/Emma Frost 5.00
Annual (Vol. 2) #3 (5/11, $3.99) Escape From the Negative Zone; Bradshaw-a 4.00
....At The State Fair of Texas (1983, 36 pgs., one-shot); Supplement to the Dallas Times Herald 2 4 6 9 12 15
...: The Dark Phoenix Saga TPB 1st printing (1984, $12.95) 25.00
...: The Dark Phoenix Saga TPB 2nd-5th printings 20.00
...: The Dark Phoenix Saga TPB 6th-10th printings 20.00
... Days of Future Past TPB (2004, $19.99) r/#138-143 & Annual #4 20.00
... Eve of Destruction TPB (2005, $14.99) r/#391-393 & X-Men #111-113; Churchill-c 15.00
...:Dream's End (2004, $17.99)-r/Death of Colossus story arc from Uncanny X-Men #388-390, Cable #87, Bishop #16 and X-Men #108,110; debut pages from Giant-Size X-Men #1 18.00
... From The Ashes TPB (1990, $14.95) r/#168-176 15.00
... Future History - The Messiah War Sourcebook (2009, $3.99) Cable's files on X-Men 4.00
...: God Loves, Man Kills ($6.95)-r/Marvel Graphic Novel #5 7.00
...: God Loves, Man Kills Extended Cut (6/20 - No. 2 10/20, $4.99) 1-Reprint with 5 new opening pages by Claremont & Anderson; creator interviews. 2-New 5-page epilogue 5.00
...: God Loves, Man Kills - Special Edition (2003, $4.99)-reprint with new Hughes-c 5.00
...: God Loves, Man Kills HC (2007, $19.99) reprint with Claremont & Anderson interviews; original artist Neal Adams' six sketch pages and interview 20.00
...: Hope (5/10, $2.99) Collects Cable and Hope back-ups; Dillon-a 3.00
House of M: Uncanny X-Men TPB (2006, $13.99) r/#462-465 and selections from Secrets Of The House of M one-shot 14.00
...In The Days of Future Past TPB (1989, $3.95, 52 pgs.) 10.00
...: No More Humans HC (2014, $24.99) Carey-s/Larroca-a 25.00
...Old Soldiers TPB (2004, $19.99) r/#213,215 & Ann. #11; New Mutants Ann. #2&3 20.00
...Poptopia TPB (10/01, $15.95) r/#394-399 16.00
...: Rise & Fall of the Shi'Ar Empire HC (2007, $34.99, dustjacket) r/#475-486; bonus art 35.00
...: Rise & Fall of the Shi'Ar Empire SC (2008, $29.99) r/#475-486; bonus art 30.00
...: Season One HC (2012, $24.99) Origin re-told; Hopeless-s/McKelvie-a 25.00
...: Sword of the Braddocks (5/09, $3.99) Psylocke vs. Slaymaster; Claremont-s 4.00
...: The Complete Onslaught Epic Book 1 TPB (2007, $29.99) r/X-Men #53-54, Uncanny X-Men #334-335, Fantastic Four #414-415, Avengers #400-401, Onslaught: X-Men, Cable #34 and Incredible Hulk #444 30.00
...: The Complete Onslaught Epic Book 2 TPB ('08, $29.99) r/Excalibur #100, Wolverine #104, X-Factor #125-126, Amazing Spider-Man #415, Green Goblin #12, Spider-Man #72, Punisher #11, X-Man #18 & X-Force #57 30.00
...: The Extremists TPB (2007, $13.99) r/#487-491 14.00
...: The Heroic Age (9/10, $3.99) Beast, Steve Rogers and Princess Powerful app. 4.00
Uncanny X-Men Omnibus Vol. 1 HC (2006, $99.99, dust jacket) r/Giant-Size X-Men #1, (Uncanny) X-Men #94-131 & Annual #3; cover gallery, promo and sketch art 140.00
Uncanny X-Men 3D #1 (3/19, $7.99) Reprints #268 polybagged with 3-D glasses 8.00
Vignettes TPB (9/01, $17.95) r/Claremont & Bolton Classic X-Men #1-13 18.00
Vignettes Vol. 2 TPB (2005, $17.99) r/Claremont & Bolton Classic X-Men #14-25 18.00
... Vol. 1: Hope TPB (2003, $12.99) r/#410-415; Harris-c 13.00
... Vol. 2: Dominant Species TPB (2003, $11.99) r/#416-420; Asamiya-c 12.00
... Vol. 3: Holy War TPB (2003, $17.99) r/#421-427 18.00
... Vol. 4: The Draco TPB (2004, $15.99) r/#428-434 16.00
... Vol. 5: She Lies with Angels TPB (2004, $11.99) r/#437-441 12.00
... Vol. 6: Bright New Mourning TPB (2004, $14.99) r/#435,436,442,443 & (New) X-Men #155,156; Larroca sketch covers 15.00
...Vs. Apocalypse Vol. 1: The Twelve TPB (2008, $29.99) r/#376-377, Cable #73-76, X-Men #96,97 and Wolverine #145-147 30.00
... - The New Age Vol. 1: The End of History (2004, $12.99) r/#444-449 13.00
... - The New Age Vol. 2: The Cruelest Cut (2005, $11.99) r/#450-454 12.00
... - The New Age Vol. 3: On Ice (2006, $15.99) r/#455-461 16.00
... - The New Age Vol. 4: End of Greys (2006, $14.99) r/#466-471 15.00
... - The New Age Vol. 5: First Foursaken (2006, $11.99) r/#472-474 & Annual #1 12.00

NOTE: ***Art Adams*** *a-Annual 9, 10p, 12p, 14p; c-218p.* ***Neal Adams*** *a-56-63p, 65p; c-56-63.* ***Adkins*** *a-34, 35p; c-31, 34, 35.* ***Austin*** *a-108i, 109i, 111-117i, 119-143i, 186i, 204i, 228i, 294-297i, Annual 3i, 7i, 9i, 13; c-109-111i, 114-122i, 123, 124-141i, 142, 143, 196i, 204i, 228i, 294-297i, Annual 3i.* ***J. Buscema*** *c-42, 43, 45.* ***Buscema/Tuska*** *a-45.* ***Byrne*** *a(p)-108, 109, 111-143, 273; c(p)-113-116, 127, 129, 131-141.* ***Capullo*** *c-14.* ***Ditko*** *r-86, 89-91, 93.* ***Everett*** *c-73.* ***Golden*** *a-273, Annual 7p.* ***Guice*** *a-216p, 217p.* ***G. Kane*** *c(p)-33, 74-76, 79, 80, 94, 95.* ***Kirby*** *a(p)-1-17 (#12-17, 67r-layouts); c(p)-1-17, 25, 30 (18, 26-parts).* ***Layton*** *a-105i; c-112i, 113i.* ***Jim Lee*** *a(p)-248, 256-258, 267-277; c(p)-252, 254, 256-261, 264, 267, 268 ,270, 275-277, 286.* ***Perez*** *a-Annual 3p; c(p)-112, 128, Annual 3.* ***Peterson*** *a(p)-294-300, 304(part); c(p)-294-299.* ***Whilce Portacio*** *a(p)-281-286, 289, 290; a(i)-267; c-281-285p, 289p, 290; c(i)-267.* ***Romita, Jr.*** *a-300; c-300.* ***Roussos*** *a-84i.* ***Simonson*** *a-171p; c-171, 217.* ***B. Smith*** *a-53, 186p, 198p, 205, 214; c-53-55, 186p, 198, 205, 212, 214, 216.* ***Paul Smith*** *a(p)-165-170, 172-175, 278; c-165-170, 172-175, 278.* ***Sparling*** *a-78p.* ***Steranko*** *a-50p, 51p; c-49-51.* ***Sutton*** *a-106i.* ***Art Thibert*** *a(i)-281-286; c(i)-281, 282, 284, 285.* ***Toth*** *a-12p, 67p(r).* ***Tuska*** *a-40-42i, 43-46p, 88i(r); c-39-41, 77p, 78p.* ***Williamson*** *a-202i, 203i, 211i; c-202i, 203i, 206i.* ***Wood*** *c-14i.*

UNCANNY X-MEN AND THE NEW TEEN TITANS (See Marvel and DC Present...)

X-MEN (2nd Series)(Titled New X-Men with #114) (Titled X-Men Legacy with #210)
Marvel Comics: Oct, 1991 - No. 275, Dec, 2012 ($1.00-$2.99)

1 a-d (four different covers, $1.50, 52 pgs.)-Jim Lee-c/a begins, ends #11; new team begins (Cyclops, Beast, Wolverine, Gambit, Psylocke & Rogue); new Uncanny X-Men & Magneto app.; 3 6 9 16 23 30
1 e ($3.95)-Double gate-fold-c consisting of all four covers from 1a-d by Jim Lee; contains all pin-ups from #1a-d plus inside-c foldout poster; no ads; printed on coated stock 3 6 9 15 22 28
1-20th Anniversary Edition-(12/11, $3.99) r/#1 with double gatefold-c; Jim Lee pin-ups 5.00
2,3,5-7: 5-Byrne scripts. 6-Sabretooth-c/story 1 2 3 5 6 8
4-1st app. Omega Red; Wolverine back to old yellow costume (same date as Wolverine #50); last $1.00-c 4 8 12 25 40 55
8-10: 8-Gambit vs. Bishop-c/story; last Lee-a; Ghost Rider cameo cont'd in Ghost Rider #26. 9-Wolverine vs. Ghost Rider; cont'd/G.R. #26. 10-Return of Longshot 1 2 3 5 6 8
11-Regular edition; X-Men vs. Mojo 2 4 6 13 18 22
11-Silver ink 2nd printing; came with X-Men board game 5 10 15 31 53 75
12,13,17-24,26-29,31: 12,13-Art Thibert-c/a. 28,29-Sabretooth app. 6.00
14-16-($1.50)-Polybagged with trading card in each; X-Cutioner's Song x-overs; 14-Andy Kubert-c/a begins 1 2 3 5 6 8
25-($3.50, 52 pgs.)-Wraparound-c with Gambit hologram on-c; Professor X erases Magneto's mind 3 6 9 15 22 28
25-30th anniversary issue w/B&W-c with Magneto in color & Magneto hologram & no price on-c 5 10 15 31 53 75
25-Gold 5 10 15 30 50 70
30-($1.95)-Wedding issue w/bound-in trading card sheet 1 3 4 6 8 10
32-37: 32-Begin $1.50-c; bound-in card sheet. 33-Gambit & Sabretooth-c/story 5.00
36,37-($2.95)-Collectors editions (foil-c) 6.00
38-44,46-49,51-65: 42,43- Paul Smith-a. 46,49,53-56-Onslaught app. 51-Waid scripts begin, end #56. 54-(Reg. edition)-Onslaught revealed as Professor X. 55,56-Onslaught x-over; Avengers, FF & Sentinels app. 56-Dr. Doom app. 57-Xavier taken into custody; Byrne-c/swipe (X-Men,1st Series #138). 59-Hercules-c/app. 61-Juggernaut-c/app. 62-Re-intro. Shang Chi; two covers. 63-Kingpin cameo. 64- Kingpin app. 5.00

X-Men #505 © MAR

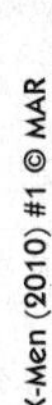

X-Men (2010) #1 © MAR

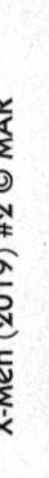

X-Men (2019) #2 © MAR

	GD 2.0	VG 4.0	FN 6.0	VF 8.0	VF/NM 9.0	NM- 9.2
45-($3.95)-Annual issue; gatefold-c						6.00
50-($2.95)-Vs. Onslaught, wraparound-c	1	2	3	5	6	8
50-($2.95)-Vs. Onslaught, wraparound foil-c	1	2	3	5	6	8
50-($2.95)-Variant gold-c.	4	8	12	25	40	55
50-($2.95)-Variant silver-c.	2	4	6	11	16	20
54-(Limited edition)-Embossed variant-c; Onslaught revealed as Professor X	4	8	12	23	37	50
66-69,71-74,76-79: 66-Operation Zero Tolerance. 76-Origin of Maggott						4.00
70-($2.99, 48 pgs.)-Joe Kelly-s begin, new members join						5.00
75-($2.99, 48 pgs.) vs. N'Garai; wraparound-c						5.00
80-($3.99) 35th Anniv. issue; holo-foil-c						6.00
80-($2.99) Regular-c						5.00
80-($6.95) Dynamic Forces Ed.; Quesada-c						7.00
81-93,95,98,99: 82-Hunt for Xavier pt. 2. 85-Davis-a. 86-Origin of Joseph. 87-Magneto War ends. 88-Juggernaut app.						4.00
94-($2.99) Contains preview of X-Men: Hidden Years						5.00
96,97-Apocalypse: The Twelve	1	2	3	5	6	8
100-($2.99) Art Adams-c; begin Claremont-s/Yu-a						5.00
100-DF alternate-c	2	4	6	8	11	14
101-105,107,108,110-114: 101-Begin $2.25-c. 107-Maximum Security x-over; Bishop-c/app. 108-Moira MacTaggart dies; Senator Kelly shot. 111-Magneto-c. 112,113-Eve of Destruction						4.00
106-($2.99) X-Men battle Domina						5.00
109-($3.50, 100 pgs.) new and reprinted Christmas-themed stories						5.00
114-(7/01) Title change to "New X-Men," Morrison-s/Quitely-c/a begins						4.00
114-(8/10, $1.00) "Marvel's Greatest Comics" reprint						3.00
115-Two covers (Quitely & BWS)						5.00
116-125,127,129-149: 116-Emma Frost joins. 117,118-Van Sciver-a. 121,122,135-Quitely-a. 127-Leon & Sienkiewicz-a. 132,139-141-Jimenez-a. 136-138-Quitely-a. 142-Sabretooth app.; Bachalo-c/a thru #145. 146-Magneto returns; Jimenez-a						3.00
126-($3.25) Quitely-a; defeat of Cassanova						4.00
128-1st app. Fantomex; Kordey-a	4	8	12	23	37	50
150-($3.50) Jean Grey dies again; last Jimenez-a						4.00
151-156: 151-154-Silvestri-c/a						3.00
157-169: 157-X-Men Reload begins						3.00
170-184: 171- Begin $2.50-c. 175,176-Crossover with Black Panther #8,9. 181-184-Apocalypse returns						3.00
185-199,201-229,231-249,251-261: 185-Begin $2.99-c. 188-190,192-194,197-199-Bachalo-a. 195,196,201-203-Ramos-a. 201-204-Endangered Species back-up. 205-207-Messiah Complex x-over. 208-Romita Jr.-a. 210-Starts X-Men: Legacy. 228,229-Acuña-a. 235-237-Second Coming x-over. 238-The Heroic Age. 245-Age of X begins						3.00
200-($3.99) Two wraparound covers by Bachalo & Finch; Bachalo & Ramos-a						4.00
230-($3.99) Acuña-a; Rogue vs. Emplate						4.00
250-($4.99) Suayan-c/Pham-a; back-up r/New Mutants #27						5.00
261.1-(3/12, $2.99) The N'Garai app.; Brooks-c						3.00
262-275-Brooks-c. 266-270-Avengers vs. X-Men tie-in						3.00
#(-1) Flashback (7/97); origin of Magneto						4.00
Annual 1-3 ('92-'94, $2.25-$2.95, 68 pgs.) 1-Lee-c & layouts; #2-Bagged w/card						5.00
Special '95 ($3.95)						5.00
... '96,...'97-Wraparound-c						5.00
.../ Dr. Doom '98 Annual ($2.99) Lopresti-a						5.00
... Annual '99 ($3.50) Adam Kubert-c						5.00
Annual 2000 ($3.50) Art Adams-c/Claremont-s/Eaton-a						4.00
...2001 Annual ($3.50) Morrison-s/Yu-a; issue printed sideways						4.00
...2007 Annual #1 (3/07, $3.99) Casey-s/Brooks-a; Cable and Mystique app.						4.00
...Legacy Annual 1 (11/09, $3.99) Acuña-a; Emplate returns						4.00
Animation Special Graphic Novel (12/90, $10.95) adapts animated series						12.00
Ashcan #1 (1994, 75¢) Introduces new team members						4.00
... Archives Sketchbook (12/00, $2.99) Early B&W character design sketches by various incl. Lee, Davis, Yu, Pacheco, BWS, Art Adams, Liefeld						4.00
...: Bizarre Love Triangle TPB (2005, $9.99)-r/X-Men #171-174						10.00
.../ Black Panther TPB (2006, $11.99)-r/X-Men #175,176 & Black Panther (2005) #8,9						12.00
...: Blinded By the Light (2007, $14.99)-r/X-Men #200-204						15.00
...: Blind Science (7/10, $3.99) Second Coming x-over; Parel-c						4.00
...: Blood of Apocalypse (2006, $17.99)-r/X-Men #182-187						18.00
...: Day of the Atom (2005, $19.99)-r/X-Men #157-165						20.00
Decimation: X-Men - The Day After TPB (2006, $15.99) r/#177-181 & Decimation: House of M - The Day After						16.00
...: Declassified (10/00, $3.50) Profile pin-ups by various; Jae Lee-c						4.00
...: Earth's Mutant Heroes (7/11, $4.99) Handbook-style profiles of mutants						5.00
...: Endangered Species (8/07, $3.99) prologue to 17-part back-up series in X-Men titles						4.00
...: Endangered Species HC (2008, $24.99, d.j.) over-sized r/prologue and 17-part series						25.00
...: Evolutions 1 (12/11, $3.99) Collection of variant covers from May 2011 Marvel titles						4.00
...: Fatal Attractions ('94, $17.95)-r/x-Factor #92, X-Force #25, Uncanny X-Men #304, X-Men #25, Wolverine #75, & Excalibur #71						18.00
...: Golgotha (2005, $12.99)-r/X-Men #166-170						13.00

	GD 2.0	VG 4.0	FN 6.0	VF 8.0	VF/NM 9.0	NM- 9.2
... Millennial Visions (8/00, $3.99) Various artists interpret future X-Men						4.00
... Millennial Visions 2 (1/02, $3.50) Various artists interpret future X-Men						4.00
...: Mutant Genesis (2006, $19.99)-r/X-Men #1-7; sketch pages and extra art						20.00
New X-Men: E is for Extinction TPB (11/01, $12.95) r/#114-117						13.00
New X-Men: Imperial TPB (7/02, $19.99) r/#118-126; Quitely-c						20.00
New X-Men: New Worlds TPB (2002, $14.99) r/#127-133; Quitely-c						15.00
New X-Men: Riot at Xavier's TPB (2003, $11.99) r/#134-138; Quitely-c						12.00
New X-Men: Vol. 5: Assault on Weapon Plus TPB (2003, $14.99) r/#139-145						15.00
New X-Men: Vol. 6: Planet X TPB (2004, $12.99) r/#146-150						13.00
New X-Men: Vol. 7: Here Comes Tomorrow TPB (2004, $10.99) r/#151-154						11.00
New X-Men: Volume 1 HC (2002, $29.99) oversized r/#114-126 & 2001 Annual						30.00
New X-Men: Volume 2 HC (2003, $29.99) oversized r/#127-141; sketch & script pages						30.00
New X-Men: Volume 3 HC (2004, $29.99) oversized r/#142-154; sketch & script pages						30.00
New X-Men Omnibus HC (2006, $99.99) oversized r/#114-154 & Annual 2001; Morrison's original pitch; sketch & script pages; variant covers & promo art; Carey intro.						140.00
...: Odd Men Out (2008, $3.99) Two unpublished stories with Dave Cockrum-a						4.00
... Original Sin 1 (12/08, $3.99) Wolverine and Daken; Deodato & Eaton-a						4.00
... Origin: Colossus (7/08, $3.99) Yost-s/Hairsine-a; Piotr Rasputin before joining X-Men						4.00
... Phoenix Force Handbook (9/10, $4.99) bios of those related to the Phoenix; Raney-c						5.00
...: Pixies and Demons Director's Cut (2008, $3.99) r/FCBD 2008 story with script						4.00
... Pizza Hut Mini-comics-(See Marvel Collector's Edition: X-Men in Promotional Comics section)						
... Premium Edition #1 (1993)-Cover says "Toys 'R' Us Limited Edition X-Men"						4.00
...: Rarities (1995, $5.95)-Reprints						6.00
...: Return of Magik Must Have (2008, $3.99) r/X-Men Unlimited #14, New X-Men #37 and X-Men: Divided We Stand #2; Coipel-c						4.00
...: Road Trippin' ('99, $24.95, TPB) r/X-Men road trips						25.00
...: Supernovas ('07, $34.99, oversized HC w/d.j.) r/X-Men 188-199 & Annual #1						35.00
...: Supernovas ('08, $29.99, SC) r/X-Men 188-199 & Annual #1						30.00
...: The Coming of Bishop ('95, $12.95)-r/Uncanny X-Men #282-285, 287,288						13.00
...: The Magneto War (3/99, $2.99) Davis-a						4.00
...: The Rise of Apocalypse ('98, $16.99)-r/Rise Of Apocalypse #1-4, X-Factor #5,6						17.00
... Visionaries: Chris Claremont ('98, $24.95)-r/Claremont-s; art by Byrne, BWS, Jim Lee						25.00
... Visionaries: Jim Lee ('02, $29.99)-r/Jim Lee-a from various issues between Uncanny X-Men #248 & 286; r/Classic X-Men #39 and X-Men Annual #1						30.00
... Visionaries: Joe Madureira (7/00, $17.95)-r/Uncanny X-Men #325,326,329,330,341-343; new Madureira-c						18.00
... Vs. Hulk (3/09, $3.99) Claremont-s/Raapack-a; r/X-Men #66						4.00
...: Zero Tolerance ('00, $24.95, TPB) r/crossover series						25.00

NOTE: ***Jim Lee** a-1-11p; c-1-6p, 7, 8, 9p, 10, 11p. **Art Thibert** a-6-9i, 12, 13; c-6i, 12, 13.*

X-MEN (3rd series)
Marvel Comics: Sept, 2010 - No. 41, Apr, 2013 ($3.99)

	GD 2.0	VG 4.0	FN 6.0	VF 8.0	VF/NM 9.0	NM- 9.2
1-41: 1-6-"Curse of the Mutants" x-over; Medina-a. 7-10-Spider-Man app.; Bachalo-a. 12-Continued from X-Men Giant-Size #1. 16-19-FF & Skull the Slayer app. 20-23-War Machine app. 16-Deadpool app. 28-FF & Spider-Man app. 38,39-Domino & Daredevil team-up						4.00
15.1 ($2.99) Pearson-c/Conrad-a; Ghost Rider app.						3.00
...: Curse of the Mutants - Blade 1 (10/10, $3.99) Tim Green-a						4.00
...: Curse of the Mutants - Smoke and Blood 1 (11/10, $3.99) Crain-c						4.00
...: Curse of the Mutants Spotlight 1 (1/11, $3.99) creator profiles and interviews						4.00
...: Curse of the Mutants - Storm and Gambit 1 (11/10, $3.99) Bachalo-a; 2 covers						4.00
...: Curse of the Mutants - X-Men vs. Vampires 1,2 (11/10 - No. 2, 12/10, $3.99) Bradshaw-c						4.00
... Giant-Size 1 (7/11, $4.99) Medina & Talajic-a; cover swipe of Giant-Size X-Men #1						5.00
...: Regenesis 1 (12/11, $3.99) Splits X-Men into 2 teams; Tan-a/Bachalo-c						4.00
... Spotlight 1 (7/11, $3.99) Character profiles and creator interviews						4.00
...: With Great Power 1 (2011, $4.99) r/#7-9						5.00

X-MEN (4th series)
Marvel Comics: Jul, 2013 - No. 26, Jun, 2015 ($3.99)

	GD 2.0	VG 4.0	FN 6.0	VF 8.0	VF/NM 9.0	NM- 9.2
1-26: 1-All-female team; Brian Wood-s/Olivier Coipel-a. 5,6-Battle of the Atom						4.00
100th Anniversary Special: X-Men (9/14, $3.99) Takes place in 2061; Furth-s/Masters-a						4.00

X-MEN (5th series)
Marvel Comics: Dec, 2019 - No. 21, Aug, 2021 ($4.99/$3.99)

	GD 2.0	VG 4.0	FN 6.0	VF 8.0	VF/NM 9.0	NM- 9.2
1-($4.99) Hickman-s/Yu-a; follows House of X and Powers of X series; intro Serafina						5.00
2-21-($3.99) 5-Serafina app.; Silva-a. 6-Mystique app.; Buffagni-a. 9-The Brood app. 10,11-Empyre tie-in. 13-15-"X of Swords" tie-in. 17-Booth-a. 21-Hellfire Gala tie-in						4.00
...: Marvels Snapshots 1 (11/20, $4.99) Flashback to Cyclops' childhood; Alex Ross-c						5.00

X-MEN (6th series)
Marvel Comics: Sept, 2021 - Present ($4.99/$3.99)

	GD 2.0	VG 4.0	FN 6.0	VF 8.0	VF/NM 9.0	NM- 9.2
1-($4.99) Duggan-s/Larraz-a; new team; debut of the Treehouse						5.00
2-19-($3.99) 4-Nightmare app. 6-Intro. Captain Krakoa. 8-M.O.D.O.K. app.						4.00
Annual 1 (2/23, $4.99) Foxe-s/Di Vito-a; spotlight on Firestar						5.00
...& Moon Girl 1 (11/22, $4.99) Wolverine and Havok app.						5.00
...: Curse of the Man-Thing 1 (7/21, $4.99) Orlando-s/Broccardo-a						5.00
...: Hellfire Gala 1 (9/22, $7.99) 2nd gala; Immortality is revealed; new team chosen						8.00

	GD 2.0	VG 4.0	FN 6.0	VF 8.0	VF/NM 9.0	NM- 9.2

...: The Onslaught Revelation 1 (11/21, $4.99) Spurrier-s/Quinn-a; Legion app. 5.00

X-MEN (Free Comic Book Day giveaways)
Marvel Comics: 2006; May, 2008

FCBD 2008 Edition #1-(5/08) Features Pixie; Carey-s/Land-a/c 3.00
.../Runaways: FCBD 2006 Edition; new x-over story; Mighty Avengers preview; Chen-c 3.00

X-MEN ADVENTURES (TV)
Marvel Comics: Nov, 1992 - No. 15, Jan, 1994 ($1.25)(Based on animated series)

1,15: 1-Wolverine, Cyclops, Jubilee, Rogue, Gambit. 15-($1.75, 52 pgs.) 2 4 6 9 12 15
2-14: 3-Magneto-c/story. 6-Sabretooth-c/story. 7-Cable-c/story. 10-Archangel guest star. 11-Cable-c/story. 4.00

X-MEN ADVENTURES II (TV)
Marvel Comics: Feb, 1994 - No. 13, Feb, 1995 ($1.25/$1.50)(Based on 2nd TV season)

1-13: 4-Bound-in trading card sheet. 5-Alpha Flight app. 4.00
...Captive Hearts/Slave Island (TPB, $4.95)-r/X-Men Adventures #5-8 5.00
...The Irresistible Force, The Muir Island Saga ($5.95, 10/94, TPB) r/X-Men Advs. #9-12 6.00

X-MEN ADVENTURES III (TV)(See Adventures of the X-Men)
Marvel Comics: Mar, 1995 - No. 13, Mar, 1996 ($1.50) (Based on 3rd TV season)

1-13 4.00

X-MEN: AGE OF APOCALYPSE
Marvel Comics: May, 2005 - No. 6, June, 2005 ($2.99, weekly limited series)

1-6-Bachalo-c/a; Yoshida-s; follows events in the "Age of Apocalypse" storyline 4.00
... One Shot (5/05, $3.99) prequel to series; Hitch wraparound-c; pin-ups by various 4.00
X-Men: The New Age of Apocalypse TPB (2005, $20.99) r/#1-6 & one-shot 21.00

X-MEN ALPHA
Marvel Comics: 1994 ($3.95, one-shot)

nn-Age of Apocalypse; wraparound chromium-c 2 4 6 10 14 18
nn ($49.95)-Gold logo 55.00

X-MEN/ALPHA FLIGHT
Marvel Comics Group: Dec, 1985 - No. 2, Dec, 1985 ($1.50, limited series)

1,2: 1-Intro The Berserkers; Paul Smith-a 5.00

X-MEN/ALPHA FLIGHT
Marvel Comics Group: May, 1998 - No. 2, June, 1998 ($2.99, limited series)

1,2-Flashback to early meeting; Raab-s/Cassaday-s/a 4.00

X-MEN AND POWER PACK
Marvel Comics: Dec, 2005 - No. 4, Mar, 2006 ($2.99, limited series)

1-4-Sumerak-s/Gurihiru-a. 1-Wolverine & Sabretooth app. 3.00
...: The Power of X (2006, $6.99, digest size) r/#1-4 7.00

X-MEN AND THE MICRONAUTS, THE
Marvel Comics Group: Jan, 1984 - No. 4, Apr, 1984 (Limited series)

1-4: Guice-c/a(p) in all 5.00

X-MEN: APOCALYPSE/DRACULA
Marvel Comics: Apr, 2006 - No. 4, July, 2006 ($2.99, limited series)

1-4-Tieri-s/Henry-a/Jae Lee-c 3.00
TPB (2006, $10.99) r/series; cover gallery 11.00

X-MEN ARCHIVES
Marvel Comics: Jan, 1995 - No. 4, Apr, 1995 ($2.25, limited series)

1-4: Reprints Legion stories from New Mutants. 4-Magneto app. 4.00

X-MEN ARCHIVES FEATURING CAPTAIN BRITAIN
Marvel Comics: July, 1995 - No. 7, 1996 ($2.95, limited series)

1-7: Reprints early Capt. Britain stories 5.00

X-MEN: BATTLE OF THE ATOM
Marvel Comics: Nov, 2013 - No. 2, Dec, 2013 ($3.99, bookends for X-Men title crossover)

1,2: 1-Bendis-s/Cho-a/Art Adams-c; bonus pin-ups of the various X-teams 4.00

X-MEN: BLACK
Marvel Comics: Dec, 2018 ($4.99, series of one-shots, back-up Apocalypse story in each)

...: Emma Frost 1 - Williams-s/Bachalo-a; Sebastian Shaw app.; Apocalypse part 5 5.00
...: Juggernaut 1 - Thompson-s/Crystal-a; Apocalypse part 4 5.00
...: Magneto 1 - Claremont-s/Talajic-a; Apocalypse part 1 5.00
...: Mojo 1 - Aukerman-s/Bradshaw-a; Apocalypse part 2 5.00
...: Mystique 1 - McGuire-s/Failla-a; Apocalypse part 3 5.00

X-MEN BLACK SUN (See Black Sun:...)

X-MEN: BLUE (Continued from All-New X-Men)
Marvel Comics: Jun, 2017 - No. 36, Nov, 2018 ($4.99/$3.99)

1-($4.99) Bunn-s/Molina-a; Juggernaut & Black Tom Cassidy app. 5.00
2-24,26-36-($3.99): 4-Jimmy Hudson joins. 7-9-Secret Empire tie-ins. 13-15-"Mojo Worldwide." 18-Generation X app. 21,22-Venom app. 4.00
25-($4.99) Bunn-s/Molina-a; Sebastian Shaw & Bastion app. 5.00
Annual 1 (3/18, $4.99) Poison-X part 1; Venom app.; Bunn-s/Salazar-a 5.00

X-MEN BOOKS OF ASKANI
Marvel Comics: 1995 ($2.95, one-shot)

1-Painted pin-ups w/text 4.00

X-MEN: CHILDREN OF THE ATOM
Marvel Comics: Nov, 1999 - No. 6 ($2.99, limited series)

1-6-Casey-s; X-Men before issue #1. 1-3-Rude-c/a. 4-Paul Smith-a/Rude-c. 5,6-Essad Ribic-c/a 4.00
TPB (11/01, $16.95) r/series; sketch pages; Casey intro. 17.00

X-MEN CHRONICLES
Marvel Comics: Mar, 1995 - No. 2, June, 1995 ($3.95, limited series)

1,2: Age of Apocalypse x-over. 1-wraparound-c 5.00

X-MEN: CLANDESTINE
Marvel Comics: Oct, 1996 - No. 2, Nov, 1996 ($2.95, limited series, 48 pgs.)

1,2: Alan Davis-c(p)/a(p)/scripts & Mark Farmer-c(i)/a(i) in all; wraparound-c 4.00

X-MEN CLASSIC (Formerly Classic X-Men)
Marvel Comics: No. 46, Apr, 1990 - No. 110, Aug, 1995 ($1.25/$1.50)

46-110: Reprints from X-Men. 54-(52 pgs.). 57,60-63,65-Russell-c(i); 62-r/X-Men #158 (Rogue). 66-r/#162 (Wolverine). 69-Begins-r of Paul Smith issues (#165 on). 70,79,90,97 (52 pgs.). 70-r/X-Men #166. 90-r/#186. 100-($1.50). 104-r/X-Men #200 4.00

X-MEN CLASSICS
Marvel Comics Group: Dec, 1983 - No. 3, Feb, 1984 ($2.00, Baxter paper)

1-3: X-Men-r by Neal Adams 6.00
NOTE: *Zeck c-1-3.*

X-MEN: COLOSSUS BLOODLIINE
Marvel Comics: Nov, 2005 - No. 5, Mar, 2006 ($2.99, limited series)

1-5-Colossus returns to Russia; David Hine-s/Jorge Lucas-a; Bachalo-c 3.00
TPB (2006, $13.99) r/#1-5 14.00

X-MEN: DEADLY GENESIS (See Uncanny X-Men #475)
Marvel Comics: Jan, 2006 - No. 6, July, 2006 ($3.99/$3.50, limited series)

1-($3.99) Silvestri-c swipe of Giant-Size X-Men #1; Hairsine-a/Brubaker-s 4.00
2-6-($3.50) 2-Silvestri-c; Banshee killed. 4-Intro Kid Vulcan 3.50
HC (2006, $24.99, dust jacket) r/#1-6 25.00
SC (2006, $19.99) r/#1-6 20.00

X-MEN: DIE BY THE SWORD
Marvel Comics: Dec, 2007 - No. 5, Feb, 2008 ($2.99, limited series)

1-5-Excalibur and The Exiles app.; Claremont-s/Santacruz-a 3.00
TPB (2008, $13.99) r/#1-5; handbook pages of Merlyn, Roma and Saturne 14.00

X-MEN: DIVIDED WE STAND
Marvel Comics: June, 2008 - No. 2, July, 2008 ($3.99, limited series)

1,2-Short stories by various; Peterson-c 4.00

X-MEN: EARTHFALL
Marvel Comics: Sept, 1996 ($2.95, one-shot)

1-r/Uncanny X-Men #232-234; wraparound-c 4.00

X-MEN: EMPEROR VULCAN
Marvel Comics: Nov, 2007 - No. 5, Mar, 2008 ($2.99, limited series)

1-5: 1-Starjammers app.; Yost-s/Diaz-a/Tan-c 3.00
TPB (2008, $13.99) r/#1-5 14.00

X-MEN: EVOLUTION (Based on the animated series)
Marvel Comics: Feb, 2002 - No. 9, Sept, 2002 ($2.25)

1-9: 1-8-Grayson-s/Udon-a. 9-Farber-s/J.J.Kirby-a 3.00
TPB (7/02, $8.99) r/#1-4 9.00
Vol. 2 TPB (2003, $11.99) r/#5-9; Asamiya-c 12.00

X-MEN FAIRY TALES
Marvel Comics: July, 2006 - No. 4, Oct, 2006 ($2.99, limited series)

1-4-Re-imagining of classic stories; Cebulski-s. 2-Baker-a. 3-Sienkiewicz-a. 4-Kobayashi-a 3.00
TPB (2006, $10.99) r/#1-4 11.00

X-MEN/ FANTASTIC FOUR
Marvel Comics: Feb, 2005 - No. 5, June, 2005 ($3.50, limited series)

1-5-Pat Lee-a/c; Yoshida-s; the Brood app. 3.50
HC (2005, $19.99, 7 1/2" x 11", dustjacket) oversized r/#1-5; cover gallery 20.00

X-MEN/ FANTASTIC FOUR
Marvel Comics: Apr, 2020 - No. 4, Sept, 2020 ($4.99, limited series)

1-4-Zdarsky-s/Dodson-a; Franklin recruited by X-Men; Doctor Doom app. 5.00

X-MEN FIRST CLASS
Marvel Comics: Nov, 2006 - No. 8, Jun, 2007 ($2.99, limited series)

1-8-Xavier's first class of X-Men; Cruz-a/Parker-s. 5-Thor app. 7-Scarlet Witch app. 3.00
... Special 1 (7/07, $3.99) Nowlan-c; Nowlan, Paul Smith, Coover, Dragotta & Allred-a 4.00
... - Tomorrow's Brightest HC (2007, $24.99, d.j) r/#1-8; cover & character design art 25.00
... - Tomorrow's Brightest SC (2007, $19.99) r/#1-8; cover & character design art 20.00

X-MEN FIRST CLASS (2nd series)
Marvel Comics: Aug, 2007 - No. 16, Nov, 2008 ($2.99)

1-16: 1-Cruz-a/Parker-s; Fantastic Four app. 8-Man-Thing app. 10-Romita Jr.-c 3.00
... Giant-Size Special 1 (12/08, $3.99) 5 new short stories; Haspiel-a; r/X-Men #40 4.00
... - Mutant Mayhem TPB (2008, $13.99) r/#1-5 & X-Men First Class Special 14.00

X-MEN FIRST CLASS FINALS
Marvel Comics: Apr, 2009 - No. 4, July, 2009 ($3.99, limited series)

1-4-Cruz-a/Parker-s. 1-3-Coover-a 4.00

X-MEN FIRSTS
Marvel Comics: Feb, 1996 ($4.95, one-shot)

1-r/Avengers Annual #10, Uncanny X-Men #266, #221; Incredible Hulk #181 5.00

X-MEN FOREVER
Marvel Comics: Jan, 2001 - No. 6, June, 2001 ($3.50, limited series)

1-6-Jean Grey, Iceman, Mystique, Toad, Juggernaut app.; Maguire-a 4.00

X-MEN FOREVER
Marvel Comics: Aug, 2009 - No. 24, July, 2010 ($3.99)

1-24: 1-Claremont-s/Grummett-a/c. 7-Nick Fury app. 4.00
... Alpha 1 (2009, $4.99) r/X-Men (1991) #1-3; 8 page preview of X-Men Forever #1 5.00
... Annual 1 (6/10, $4.99) Wolverine & Jean Grey romance; Sana Takeda-a/c 5.00
... Giant-Size 1 (7/10, $3.99) Grell-a/c; Lilandra & Gladiator app.; r/(Uncanny)X-Men #108 4.00

X-MEN FOREVER 2
Marvel Comics: Aug, 2010 - No. 16, Mar, 2011 ($3.99)

1-16: 1-Claremont-s/Grummett-a/c. 2,3-Spider-Man app. 9,10-Grell-a 4.00

X-MEN: GOLD
Marvel Comics: Jan, 2014 ($5.99, one-shot)

1-50th Anniversary anthology; short stories by various incl. Stan Lee, Simonson, Claremont, Thomas, Olliffe, Wein, Molina, McLeod, Larroca; Coipel-c 6.00

X-MEN: GOLD
Marvel Comics: Jun, 2017 - No. 36, Nov, 2018 ($4.99/$3.99)

X-Men: Fairy Tales #1 © MAR

X-Men Noir #1 © MAR

X-Men '92 #8 © MAR

	GD	VG	FN	VF	VF/NM	NM-
	2.0	4.0	6.0	8.0	9.0	9.2

1-($4.99) Syaf-a; Storm, Nightcrawler, Old Man Logan, Colossus, Kitty Pryde team 5.00
2-24-($3.99): 4-6-Silva-a. 7,8-Secret Empire tie-ins; Lashley-a. 13-15-"Mojo Worldwide" 4.00
25-($4.99) Guggenheim-s/Siqueira-a; Captain Britain app. 5.00
26-29,31-36: 26-29-Til Death Do Us Part; prelude to wedding of Kitty Pryde & Colossus 4.00
30-($4.99) Wedding of Rogue and Gambit; leads into Mr. & Mrs. X series; Marquez-a 5.00
Annual 1 (3/18, $4.99) Excalibur reunion; Capt. Britain app.; Martinez-a 5.00
Annual 2 (10/18, $4.99) McGuire-s/Failla-a; 14-year-old Kitty Pryde at summer camp 5.00

X-MEN: GRAND DESIGN
Marvel Comics: Feb, 2018 - No. 2, Mar, 2018 ($5.99, limited series)
1,2-Origins and early days of the X-Men re-told; Ed Piskor-s/a/c 6.00

X-MEN: GRAND DESIGN - SECOND GENESIS
Marvel Comics: Sept, 2018 - No. 2, Oct, 2018 ($5.99, limited series)
1,2-Days of the X-Men from #94 (1975) to #186 (1984) re-told; Ed Piskor-s/a/c 6.00

X-MEN: GRAND DESIGN - X-TINCTION
Marvel Comics: Jul, 2019 - No. 2, Aug, 2019 ($5.99, limited series)
1,2-Days of the X-Men from mid-'80s to early '90s re-told; Ed Piskor-s/a/c 6.00

X-MEN: HELLBOUND
Marvel Comics: July, 2010 - No. 3, Sept, 2010 ($3.99, limited series)
1-3-Second Coming x-over; Tolibao-a/Djurdjevic-c; Majik rescued from Limbo 4.00

X-MEN: HELLFIRE CLUB
Marvel Comics: Jan, 2000 - No. 4, Apr, 2000 ($2.50, limited series)
1-4-Origin of the Hellfire Club 3.00

X-MEN: HIDDEN YEARS
Marvel Comics: Dec, 1999 - No. 22, Sept. 2001 ($3.50/$2.50)
1-New adventures from pre-#94 era; Byrne-s/a(p) 5.00
2-4,6-11,13-22-($2.50): 2-Two covers. 3-Ka-Zar app. 8,9-FF-c/app. 4.00
5-($2.75) 4.00
12-($3.50) Magneto-c/app. 5.00

X-MEN: KING BREAKER
Marvel Comics: Feb, 2009 - No. 4, May, 2009 ($3.99, limited series)
1-4-Emperor Vulcan and a Shi'ar invasion; Havok, Rachel Grey and Polaris app. 4.00

X-MEN: KITTY PRYDE - SHADOW & FLAME
Marvel Comics: Aug, 2005 - No. 5, Dec, 2005 ($2.99, limited series)
1-5-Akira Yoshida-s/Paul Smith-a/c; Kitty & Lockheed go to Japan 3.00
TPB (2006, $14.99) r/#1-5 15.00

X-MEN LEGACY (See X-Men 2nd series)

X-MEN LEGACY (Marvel NOW!)
Marvel Comics: Jan, 2013 - No. 24, Apr, 2014; No. 300, May, 2014 ($2.99)
1-24: 1-Legion (Professor X's son); Spurrier-s/Huat-a. 2-X-Men app. 5,6-Molina-a 3.00
300-(5/14, $4.99) Spurrier, Carey & Gage-s/Huat, Kurth & Sandoval-a; Mann-c 5.00

X-MEN LEGENDS
Marvel Comics: Apr, 2021 - No. 12, May, 2022 ($4.99/$3.99)
1-($4.99) Nicieza-s/Booth-a; the 1990s version of the X-Men & Cable app. 5.00
2-12-($3.99) 3,4,11-X-Factor; Louise Simonson-s/Walt Simonson-a. 7-9-Hama-s/Tan-a 4.00

X-MEN LEGENDS
Marvel Comics: Jul, 2022 - No. 6, Apr, 2023 ($3.99)
1-6: 1,2-Follows events of Incredible Hulk #181; Roy Thomas-s/Dave Wachter-a 4.00

X-MEN: LIBERATORS
Marvel Comics: Nov, 1998 - No. 4, Feb, 1999 ($2.99, limited series)
1-4-Wolverine, Nightcrawler & Colossus; P. Jimenez 4.00

X-MEN LOST TALES
Marvel Comics: 1997 ($2.99)
1,2-r/Classic X-Men back-up stories 4.00

X-MEN: MAGNETO TESTAMENT
Marvel Comics: Nov, 2008 - No. 5, Mar, 2009 ($3.99, limited series)
1-5-Max Eisenhardt in 1930s Nazi-occupied Poland; Pak-s/DiGiandomenico-a. 5-Back-up story of artist Dina Babbitt with Neal Adams-a 4.00

X-MEN: MANIFEST DESTINY
Marvel Comics: Nov, 2008 - No. 5, Mar, 2009 ($3.99, limited series)
1-5-Short stories of X-Men re-location to San Francisco; s/a by various 4.00
... Nightcrawler 1 (5/09, $3.99) Molina & Syaf-a; Mephisto app. 4.00

X-MEN: MESSIAH COMPLEX
Marvel Comics: Dec, 2007 ($3.99)
1-Part 1 of x-over with X-Men, Uncanny X-Men, X-Factor and New X-Men; 2 covers 4.00
... - Mutant Files (2007, $3.99) Handbook pages of x-over participants; Kolins-c 4.00

HC (2008, $39.99, oversized) r/#1, Uncanny X-Men #492-494, X-Men #205-207, New X-Men #44-46 and X-Factor #25-27 40.00

X-MEN '92 (Secret Wars tie-in)
Marvel Comics: Aug, 2015 - No. 4, Nov, 2015 ($4.99, limited series)
1-4-Koblish-a; Cassandra Nova app. 2-4-X-Force app. 4-Apocalypse cameo 5.00

X-MEN '92 (Follows Secret Wars)
Marvel Comics: May, 2016 - No. 10, Feb, 2017 ($3.99)
1-10: 1-Firmansyah-a; Omega Red & Alpha Red app. 2-U-Go Girl joins. 3,4-Dracula app. 9,10-New Mutants app. 4.00

X-MEN '92: HOUSE OF XCII
Marvel Comics: Jun, 2022 - No. 5, Nov, 2022 ($3.99, limited series)
1-5: 1-Foxe-s/Espin-a 4.00

X-MEN NOIR
Marvel Comics: Nov, 2008 - No. 4, May, 2009 ($3.99, limited series)
1-4-Pulp-style story set in 1930s NY; Van Lente-s/Calero-a 4.00
...: Mark of Cain (2/10 - No. 4, 5/10, $3.99) Van Lente-s/Calero-a 4.00

X-MEN OMEGA
Marvel Comics: June, 1995 ($3.95, one-shot)
nn-Age of Apocalypse finale 2 4 6 9 13 16
nn-($49.95)-Gold edition 55.00

X-MEN: ORIGINS
Marvel Comics: Oct, 2008 - Sept, 2010 ($3.99, series of one-shots)
...: Beast (11/08) High school years; Carey-s; painted-a/c by Woodward 5.00
...: Cyclops (3/10) Magneto app.; Delperdang-a/Granov-c
2 4 6 9 12 15
...: Deadpool (9/10) Fernandez-a/Swierczynski-s 4 8 12 25 40 55
...: Emma Frost (7/10) Moline-a; r/excerpt from 1st app. in Uncanny X-Men #129
2 4 6 9 12 15
...: Gambit (8/09) Mr. Sinister, Sabretooth and the Marauders app.; Yardin-a
3 6 9 14 20 26
...: Iceman (1/10) Noto-a 5.00
...: Jean Grey (10/08) Childhood & early X-days; McKeever-s; Mayhew painted-a/c 5.00
...: Nightcrawler (5/10) Cary Nord-a; r/excerpt from 1st app. in Giant-Size X-Men #1 5.00
...: Sabretooth (4/09) Childhood and early meetings with Wolverine; Panosian-a/c
1 2 3 5 6 8
...: Wolverine (6/09) Pre-X-Men days and first meeting with Xavier; Texeira-a/c 5.00

X-MEN: PHOENIX
Marvel Comics: Dec, 1999 - No. 3, Mar, 2000 ($2.50, limited series)
1-3: 1-Apocalypse app. 4.00

X-MEN: PHOENIX - ENDSONG
Marvel Comics: Mar, 2005 - No. 5, June, 2005 ($2.99, limited series)
1-5-The Phoenix Force returns to Earth; Greg Land-c/a; Greg Pak-s 3.00
HC (2005, $19.99, dust jacket) r/#1-5; Land sketch pages 20.00
SC (2006, $14.99) 15.00

X-MEN: PHOENIX - LEGACY OF FIRE
Marvel Comics: July, 2003 - No. 3, Sep, 2003 ($2.99, limited series)
1-3-Manga-style; Ryan Kinnard-s/a/c; intro page art by Adam Warren 3.00

X-MEN: PHOENIX - WARSONG
Marvel Comics: Nov, 2006 - No. 5, Mar, 2007 ($2.99, limited series)
1-5-Tyler Kirkham-a/Greg Pak-s/Marc Silvestri-c 3.00
HC (2007, $19.99, dustjacket) r/#1-5; variant cover gallery and Handbook pages 20.00
SC (2007, $14.99) r/#1-5; variant cover gallery and Handbook pages 15.00

X-MEN: PIXIE STRIKES BACK
Marvel Comics: Apr, 2010 - No. 4, July, 2010 ($3.99, limited series)
1-4-Kathryn Immonen-s/Sara Pichelli-a/Stuart Immonen-c 4.00

X-MEN: PRELUDE TO SCHISM
Marvel Comics: Jul, 2011 - No. 4, Aug, 2011 ($2.99, limited series)
1-4-Jenkins-s/Camuncoli-c. 1-De La Torre-a. 2-Magneto childhood. 3-Conrad-a 3.00

X-MEN PRIME
Marvel Comics: July, 1995 ($4.95, one-shot)
nn-Post Age of Apocalypse begins 2 4 6 8 10 12

X-MEN PRIME
Marvel Comics: May, 2017 ($4.99, one-shot)
1-Preludes to X-Men: Blue #1, X-Men: Gold #1 and Weapon X #1 5.00

X-MEN RARITIES
Marvel Comics: 1995 ($5.95, one-shot)

GD 2.0 | VG 4.0 | FN 6.0 | VF 8.0 | VF/NM 9.0 | NM- 9.2

nn-Reprints hard-to-find stories 6.00

X-MEN: RED
Marvel Comics: Apr, 2018 - No. 11, Feb, 2019 ($4.99/$3.99)

1-($4.99) Asrar-a; Jean Grey, Nightcrawler, Namor, Wolverine (X-23) team 5.00
2-11-($3.99) 4-Black Panther app. 4.00
Annual 1 (7/18, $4.99) Taylor-s/Alixe-a; Black Bolt app. 5.00

X-MEN: RED
Marvel Comics: Jun, 2022 - No. 10, Mar, 2023 ($4.99/$3.99)

1-($4.99) Ewing-s/Caselli-a; new Brotherhood of Mutants is formed 5.00
2-10-($3.99) Cable app. 5-7-Judgment Day tie-ins 4.00

X-MEN ROAD TO ONSLAUGHT
Marvel Comics: Oct, 1996 ($2.50, one-shot)

nn-Retells Onslaught Saga 4.00

X-MEN: RONIN
Marvel Comics: May, 2003 - No. 5, July, 2003 ($2.99, limited series)

1-5-Manga-style X-Men; Torres-s/Nakatsuka-a 3.00

X-MEN: SCHISM
Marvel Comics: Sept, 2011 - No. 5, Dec, 2011 ($4.99/$3.99, limited series)

1-($4.99) Aaron-s/Pacheco-a/c 5.00
2-5-($3.99) 2-Cho-a/c. 3-Acuña-a/c. 4-Alan Davis-a/c. 5-Adam Kubert-a 4.00

X-MEN: SEARCH FOR CYCLOPS
Marvel Comics: Oct, 2000 - No. 4, Mar, 2001 ($2.99, limited series)

1-4-Two covers (Raney, Pollina); Raney-a 4.00

X-MEN: SECOND COMING
Marvel Comics: May, 2010 - No. 2, Sept, 2010 ($3.99)

1-Cable & Hope return to the present; Bastion app.; Finch-a; covers by Granov & Finch 4.00
2-Conclusion to x-over; covers by Granov & Finch 4.00
...: Prepare (4/10, free) previews x-over; short story w/Immonen-a; cover sketch art 3.00

X-MEN / SPIDER-MAN ("X-Men and Spider-Man" on cover)
Marvel Comics: Jan, 2009 - No. 4, Apr, 2009 ($3.99, limited series)

1-4: 1-Team-up from pre-blue Beast days; Kraven app.; Gage-s/Alberti-a 4.00

X-MEN SPOTLIGHT ON... STARJAMMERS (Also see X-Men #104)
Marvel Comics: 1990 - No. 2, 1990 ($4.50, 52 pgs.)

1,2: Features Starjammers 5.00

X-MEN SURVIVAL GUIDE TO THE MANSION
Marvel Comics: Aug, 1993 ($6.95, spiralbound)

1 7.00

X-MEN: THE COMPLETE AGE OF APOCALYPSE EPIC
Marvel Comics: 2005 - Vol. 4, 2006 ($29.99, TPB)

Book 1-4: Chronological reprintings of the crossover 30.00

X-MEN: THE EARLY YEARS
Marvel Comics: May, 1994 - No. 17, Sept, 1995 ($1.50/$2.50)

1-16: r/X-Men #1-8 w/new-c 4.00
17-$2.50-c; r/X-Men #17,18 5.00

X-MEN: THE END
Marvel Comics: Oct, 2004 - No. 6, Feb, 2005 ($2.99, limited series)

1-6-Claremont-s/Chen-a/Land-c 3.00
... Book One: Dreamers and Demons TPB (2005, $14.99) r/#1-6 15.00

X-MEN: THE END - HEROES AND MARTYRS (Volume 2)
Marvel Comics: May, 2005 - No. 6, Oct, 2005 ($2.99, limited series)

1-6-Claremont-s/Chen-a/Land-c; continued from X-Men: The End 3.00
... Vol. 2 TPB (2006, $14.99) r/#1-6 15.00

X-MEN: THE END (MEN & X-MEN) (Volume 3)
Marvel Comics: Mar, 2006 - No. 6, Aug, 2006 ($2.99, limited series)

1-6-Claremont-s/Chen-a. 1-Land-c. 2-6-Gene Ha-c 3.00
... Vol. 3 TPB (2006, $14.99) r/#1-6 15.00

X-MEN: THE EXTERMINATED
Marvel Comics: Feb, 2019 ($4.99, one-shot)

1-Prelude to Uncanny X-Men #1 (2019); Hope and Jean Grey story; Deadpool app. 5.00

X-MEN: THE MANGA
Marvel Comics: Mar, 1998 - No. 26, June, 1999 ($2.99, B&W)

1-26-English version of Japanese X-Men comics: 23,24-Randy Green-c 4.00

X-MEN: THE MOVIE
Marvel Comics: Aug, 2000; Sept, 2000

Adaptation (9/00, $5.95) Macchio-s/Williams & Lanning-a 6.00
Adaptation TPB (9/00, $14.95) Movie adaptation and key reprints of main characters; four photo covers (movie X, Magneto, Rogue, Wolverine) 15.00
Prequel: Magneto (8/00, $5.95) Texeira & Palmiotti-a; art & photo covers 6.00
Prequel: Rogue (8/00, $5.95) Evans & Nikolakakis-a; art & photo covers 6.00
Prequel: Wolverine (8/00, $5.95) Waller & McKenna-a; art & photo covers 6.00
TPB X-Men: Beginnings (8/00, $14.95) reprints 3 prequels w/photo-c 15.00

X-MEN 2: THE MOVIE
Marvel Comics: 2003

Adaptation (6/03, $3.50) Movie adaptation; photo-c; Austen-s/Zircher-a 4.00
Adaptation TPB (2003, $12.99) Movie adaptation & r/Prequels Nightcrawler & Wolverine 13.00
Prequel: Nightcrawler (5/03, $3.50) Kerschl-a; photo cover 4.00
Prequel: Wolverine (5/03, $3.50) Mandrake-a; photo cover; Sabretooth app. 4.00

X-MEN: THE 198 (See House of M)
Marvel Comics: Mar, 2006 - No. 5, July, 2006 ($2.99, limited series)

1-5-Hine-s/Muniz-a 3.00
... Files (2006, $3.99) profiles of the 198 mutants who kept their powers after House of M 4.00
Decimation: The 198 (2006, $15.99, TPB) r/#1-5 & X-Men: The 198 Files 16.00

X-MEN: THE TIMES AND LIFE OF LUCAS BISHOP
Marvel Comics: Apr, 2009 - No. 3, June, 2009 ($3.99, limited series)

1-3-Swierczynski-s/Stroman-a. 1-Bishop's birth and childhood 4.00

X-MEN: THE TRIAL OF MAGNETO
Marvel Comics: Oct, 2021 - No. 5, Feb, 2022 ($3.99, limited series)

1-5-Leah Williams-s/Lucas Werneck-a. 5-Thunderbird returns 4.00

X-MEN: THE ULTRA COLLECTION
Marvel Comics: Dec, 1994 - No. 5, Apr, 1995 ($2.95, limited series)

1-5: Pin-ups; no scripts 4.00

X-MEN: THE WEDDING ALBUM
Marvel Comics: 1994 ($2.95, magazine size, one-shot)

1-Wedding of Scott Summers & Jean Grey 4.00

X-MEN: THE WEDDING SPECIAL
Marvel Comics: Jul, 2018 ($4.99, one-shot)

1-Prelude to wedding of Kitty Pryde & Colossus; art by Nauck, Land & Cresta 5.00

X-MEN: TO SERVE AND PROTECT
Marvel Comics: Jan, 2011 - No. 4, Apr, 2011 ($3.99, limited series)

1-4-Short story anthology by various.1-Bradshaw-c. 2-Camuncoli-c 4.00

X-MEN TRUE FRIENDS
Marvel Comics: Sept, 1999 - No. 3, Nov, 1999 ($2.99, limited series)

1-3-Claremont-s/Leonardi-a 4.00

X-MEN 2099 (Also see 2099: World of Tomorrow)
Marvel Comics: Oct, 1993 - No. 35, Aug, 1996 ($1.25/$1.50/$1.95)

1-($1.75)-Foil-c; Ron Lim/Adam Kubert-a begins 1 2 3 5 6 8
1-2nd printing ($1.75) 3.00
1-Gold edition (15,000 made); sold thru Diamond for $19.40 20.00
2-24,26-35: 3-Death of Tina; Lim-c/a(p) in #1-8. 8-Bound-in trading card sheet. 35-Nostromo (from X-Nation) app; storyline cont'd in 2099: World of Tomorrow 4.00
25-($2.50)-Double sized 4.00
Special 1 ($3.95) 4.00
...: Oasis ($5.95, one-shot) -Hildebrandt Bros.-c/a 6.00

X-MEN ULTRA III PREVIEW
Marvel Comics: 1995 ($2.95)

nn-Kubert-a 4.00

X-MEN UNIVERSE
Marvel Comics: Dec, 1999 - No. 15, Feb, 2001 ($4.99/$3.99)

1-8-Reprints stories from recent X-Men titles 5.00
9-15-($3.99) 4.00

X-MEN UNIVERSE: PAST, PRESENT AND FUTURE
Marvel Comics: Feb, 1999 ($2.99, one-shot)

1-Previews 1999 X-Men events; background info 1 3 4 6 8 10

X-MEN UNLIMITED
Marvel Comics: 1993 - No. 50, Sept, 2003 ($3.95/$2.99, 68 pgs.)

1-Chris Bachalo-c/a; Quesada-a. 2 4 6 8 10 12
2-11: 2-Origin of Magneto script. 3-Sabretooth-c/story. 10-Dark Beast vs. Beast; Mark Waid script. 11-Magneto & Rogue 6.00
12-33: 12-Begin $2.99-c; Onslaught x-over; Juggernaut-c/app. 19-Caliafore-a. 20-Generation X app. 27-Origin Thunderbird. 29-Maximum Security x-over; Bishop-c/app. 30-Mahfood-a. 31-Stelfreeze-c/a. 32-Dazzler; Thompson-c/a 33-Kaluta-c 5.00
34-37,39,40-42-($3.50) 34-Von Eeden-a. 35-Finch, Conner, Maguire-a. 36-Chiodo-c/a; Larroca, Totleben-a. 39-Bachalo-c; Pearson-a. 41-Bachalo-c; X-Statix app. 5.00
38-($2.25) Kitty Pryde; Robertson-a 4.00
43-50-($2.50) 43-Sienkiewicz-c/a; Paul Smith-a. 45-Noto-c. 46-Bisley-a. 47-Warren-s/Mays-a. 48-Wolverine story w/Isanove painted-a 4.00
X-Men Legends Vol. 4: Hated and Feared TPB (2003, $19.99) r/stories by various 20.00
NOTE: *Bachalo c/a-1.* ***Quesada*** *a-1.* ***Waid*** *scripts-10*

X-MEN UNLIMITED
Marvel Comics: Apr, 2004 - No. 14, Jun, 2006 ($2.99)

1-14: 1-6-Pat Lee-c; short stories by various. 2-District X preview; Granov-a 3.00

X-MEN UNLIMITED...
Marvel Comics: May, 2022 - Present ($5.99)

...: Latitude 1 (5/22, $5.99) Hickman-s/Shalvey-a 6.00
...: X-Men Green 1,2 (7/22, 11/22, $5.99) Duggan-s/Laiso-a. 2-Sauron app. 6.00

X-MEN VS. AGENTS OF ATLAS
Marvel Comics: Dec, 2009 - No. 2, Jan, 2010 ($3.99, limited series)

1,2-Pagulayan-a. 1-McGuinness-c. 2-Granov-c 4.00

X-MEN VS. DRACULA
Marvel Comics: Dec, 1993 ($1.75)

1-r/X-Men Annual #6; Austin-c(i) 1 2 3 5 6 8

X-MEN VS. THE AVENGERS, THE
Marvel Comics Group: Apr, 1987 - No. 4, July, 1987 ($1.50, limited series, Baxter paper)

1-Silvestri-a/c 2 4 6 8 10 12
2-4: 2,3-Silvestri-a/c. 4-Pollard-a/c 5.00

X-MEN VS. THE BROOD, THE
Marvel Comics Group: Sept, 1996 - No. 2, Oct, 1996 ($2.95, limited series)

1,2-Wraparound-c; Ostrander-s/Hitch-a(p) 4.00
TPB('97, $16.99) reprints X-Men/Brood: Day of Wrath #1,2 & Uncanny X-Men #232-234 17.00

X-MEN VISIONARIES
Marvel Comics: 1995,1996,2000 (trade paperbacks)

nn-($8.95) Reprints X-Men stories; Adam & Andy Kubert-a 9.00
...2: The Neal Adams Collection (1996) r/X-Men #56-63,65 30.00
...2: The Neal Adams Col. (2nd printing, 2000, $24.95) new Adams-c 25.00

X-MEN/WILDC.A.T.S.: THE DARK AGE (See also WildC.A.T.S./X-Men...)
Marvel Comics: 1998 ($4.50, one-shot)

1-Two covers (Broome & Golden); Ellis-s 5.00

X-MEN: WORLDS APART
Marvel Comics: Dec, 2008 - No. 4, Mar, 2009 ($3.99, limited series)

X-Men: Schism #2 © MAR

X-Men: World's Apart #1 © MAR

X-O Manowar (2013) #18 © VAL

	GD	VG	FN	VF	VF/NM	NM-
	2.0	4.0	6.0	8.0	9.0	9.2

1-4-Storm and the Black Panther vs. the Shadow King. 1-Campbell-c 4.00

X-MEN: WORST X-MAN EVER
Marvel Comics: Apr, 2016 - No. 5, Aug, 2016 ($3.99, limited series)

1-5: 1-Intro. Bailey Hoskins; Max Bemis-s/Michael Walsh-a. 3,4-Magneto app. 4.00

X-NATION 2099
Marvel Comics: Mar, 1996 - No. 6, Aug, 1996 ($1.95)

1-($3.95)-Humberto Ramos-a(p); wraparound, foil-c 5.00
2-6: 2,3-Ramos-a. 4-Exodus-c/app. 6-Reed Richards app 3.00

X NECROSIA
Marvel Comics: Dec, 2009 ($3.99)

1-Beginning of X-Force/X-Men/New Mutants x-over; Crain-a; Selene returns 4.00
...: The Gathering (2/10, $3.99) Wither, Blink, Senyaka, Mortis & Eliphas short stories 4.00

X OF SWORDS (Marvel Event crossing over Wolverine, Cable, and the X-Men titles)
Marvel Comics: Nov, 2020 - Jan, 2021 ($6.99/$4.99)

...: Creation (11/20, $6.99) Part 1 of crossover; Hickman & Howard-s/Larraz-a 7.00
...: Destruction (1/21, $4.99) Part 22 conclusion; Hickman & Howard-s/Larraz & Gracia-a 5.00
...: Handbook (11/20, $4.99) Profile pages of the mutants of Krakoa 5.00
...: Stasis (12/20, $4.99) Part 11 of crossover; Hickman & Howard-s/Larraz & Asrar-a 5.00

X-O MANOWAR (1st Series)
Valiant/Acclaim Comics (Valiant) No. 43 on: Feb, 1992 - No. 68, Sept, 1996 ($1.95/$2.25/$2.50, high quality)

0-(8/93, $3.50)-Wraparound embossed chromium-c by Quesada; Solar app.; origin Aric (X-O Manowar) 1 3 4 6 8 10
0-Gold variant 3 6 9 21 33 45
1-Intro/1st app. & partial origin of Aric (X-O Manowar); Barry Smith/Layton-a; Shooter & Englehart-s 3 6 9 21 33 45
2,3: 2-B. Smith/Layton-c. 3-Layton-c(i) 2 4 6 8 10 12
4-1st app. Shadowman; Harbinger app. 4 8 12 23 37 50
5,6: 5-B. Smith-c. 6-Begin $2.25-c; Ditko-a(p) 1 2 3 5 6 8
7-15: 7,8-Unity x-overs. 7-Miller-c. 8-Simonson-c. 12-1st app. Randy Calder. 14,15-Turok-c/stories 4.00
15-Hot pink logo variant; came with Ultra Pro Rigid Comic Sleeves box; no price on-c 1 3 4 6 8 10
16-24,26-43: 20-Serial number contest insert. 27-29-Turok x-over. 28-Bound-in trading card. 30-1st app. new "good skin"; Solar app. 33-Chaos Effect Delta Pt. 3. 42-Shadowman app.; includes X-O Manowar Birthquake! Prequel 3.00
25-($3.50)-Has 16 pg. Armorines #0 bound-in w/origin 4.00
44-66: 44-Begin $2.50-c. 50-X, 50-O, 51, 52, 63-Bart Sears-c/a/scripts 3.00
67 1 2 3 5 6 8
68-Revealed that Aric's past stories were premonitions of his future 3 6 9 16 23 30
...: Birth HC (2008, $24.95) recolored reprints #0-6; script and breakdowns for #0; cover gallery; new "The Rise of Lydia" story by Layton and Leeke 25.00
Trade paperback nn (1993, $9.95)-Polybagged with copy of X-O Database #1 inside 15.00
Yearbook 1 (4/95, $2.95) 4.00
NOTE: ***Layton** a-1i, 2i(part); c-1, 2i, 3i, 6i, 21i. **Reese** a-4i(part); c-26i.*

X-O MANOWAR (2nd Series)(Also see Iron Man/X-O Manowar: Heavy Metal)
Acclaim Comics (Valiant Heroes): V2#1, Oct, 1996 - No. 21, Jun, 1998 ($2.50)

V2#1-21: 1-Mark Waid & Brian Augustyn scripts begin; 1st app. Donavon Wylie; Rand Banion dies; painted variant-c exists. 2-Donavon Wylie becomes new X-O Manowar. 7-9-Augustyn-s. 10-Copycat-c 3.00

X-O MANOWAR (3rd series)
Valiant Entertainment: May, 2012 - No. 50, Sept, 2016 ($3.99)

1-Robert Venditti-s/Cary Nord-a/Esad Ribic-c; origin re-told 4.00
1-Pullbox variant-c by Nord 5.00
1-Variant-c by David Aja 10.00
1-QR Voice variant-c by Jelena Kevic-Djurdjevic 25.00
2-24: 2-Origin continues. 2,3-Kevic-Djurdjevic-c. 5-8-Ninjak app.; Garbett-a. 9,10-Hairsine-a 11-14-Planet Death; Nord-a. 19-21-Unity tie-in 4.00
2-5,8-14-Pullbox variant covers. 2-Lozzi. 3-Suayan. 4-Kramer. 5-Tan. 14-Eight-bit art 5.00
25-($4.99) Hitch-a; Armor Hunters app., Owly & Wormy short story by Runton 5.00
26-37,39-49: 26-29-Armor Hunters tie-in. 30-32-Armorines app. 34-37-Dead Hand. 47-49-Polybagged with micro-print 4.00
38-(7/15, $4.99) Wedding of Aric and Saana; Doctor Mirage app.; flashbacks 5.00
50-(9/16, $4.99) Polybagged; wraparound-c by 50 artists; art by various 5.00
#0 (10/14, $3.99) Flashback to Aric before his kidnapping; Clay Mann-a 4.00
Annual 2016 #1 (5/16, $5.99) Art by JG Jones, Perez, McKone, Gorham, De La Torre 6.00
...: Commander Trill #0 (12/15, $3.99) Origin of Trill; Venditti-s/Portela-a 4.00
...: Valiant 25th Anniversary Special (6/15, $3.99) Origin of Shanhara; Venditti-s/Cafu-a 4.00

X-O MANOWAR (2017) (4th series)
Valiant Entertainment: Mar, 2017 - No. 26, Apr, 2019 ($3.99)

1-26: 1-Kindt-s/Giorello-a; Aric on planet Gorin. 4-6 Braithwaite-a. 7-9-Crain-a 4.00

X-O MANOWAR (5th series)
Valiant Entertainment: Mar, 2020 - No. 9, Dec, 2021 ($3.99)

1-9-Hallum-s/Laiso-a. 1-Bonus preview of Final Witness #1 4.00

X-O MANOWAR FAN EDITION
Acclaim Comics (Valiant Heroes): Feb, 1997 (Overstreet's FAN giveaway)

1-Reintro the Armorines & the Hard Corps; 1st app. Citadel; Augustyn scripts; McKone-c/a 5.00

X-O MANOWAR/IRON MAN: IN HEAVY METAL (See Iron Man/X-O Manowar: Heavy Metal)
Acclaim Comics (Valiant Heroes): Sept, 1996 ($2.50, one-shot)
(1st Marvel/Valiant x-over)

1-Pt 1 of X-O Manowar/Iron Man x-over; Arnim Zola app.; Nicieza scripts; Andy Smith-a 5.00

XOMBI
DC Comics (Milestone): Jan, 1994 - No. 21, Feb, 1996 ($1.75/$2.50)

0-($1.95)-Shadow War x-over; Simonson silver ink varnish-c 1 3 4 6 8 10
1-John Byrne-c 1 2 3 5 6 8
1-Platinum 2 4 6 9 12 15
2-21 5.00

XOMBI
DC Comics: May, 2011 - No. 6, Oct, 2011 ($2.99)

1-6-Rozum-s/Irving-a/c 3.00

X-PATROL
Marvel Comics (Amalgam): Apr, 1996 ($1.95, one-shot)

1-Cruz-a(p) 3.00

X-RAY ROBOT
Dark Horse Comics: Mar, 2020 - No. 4, Nov, 2020 ($3.99)

1-4-Mike Allred-s/a. 4-Madman app. 4.00

XSE
Marvel Comics: Nov, 1996 - No. 4, Feb, 1997 ($1.95, limited series)

1-4: 1-Bishop & Shard app. 3.00
1-Variant-c 4.00

X-STATIX
Marvel Comics: Sept, 2002 - No. 26, Oct, 2004 ($2.99/$2.25)

1-($2.99) Allred-a/c; intro. Venus Dee Milo; back-up w/Cooke-a 4.00
2-9-($2.25) 4-Quitely-c. 5-Pope-c/a 3.00
10-26: 10-Begin $2.99-c; Bond-a; U-Go Girl flashback. 13,14-Spider-Man app. 21-25-Avengers app. 26-Team dies 3.00
... Vol. 1: Good Omens TPB (2003, $11.99) r/#1-5 12.00
... Vol. 2: Good Guys & Bad Guys TPB (2003, $15.99) r/#6-10 & Wolverine/Doop #1&2 16.00
... Vol. 3: Back From the Dead TPB (2004, $19.99) r/#11-18 20.00
... Vol. 4: X-Statix Vs. the Avengers TPB (2004, $19.99) r/#19-26; pin-ups 20.00

X-STATIX PRESENTS: DEAD GIRL
Marvel Comics: Mar, 2006 - No. 5, July, 2006 ($2.99, limited series)

1-5-Dr. Strange, Dead Girl, Miss America, Tike app. Milligan-s/Dragotta & Allred-a 3.00
TPB (2006, $13.99) r/series 14.00

X-TERMINATION (Crossover with Astonishing X-Men and X-Treme X-Men)
Marvel Comics: May, 2013 - No. 2, Jun, 2013 ($3.99)

1,2-Lapham-s/David Lopez-a 4.00

X-TERMINATORS
Marvel Comics: Oct, 1988 - No. 4, Jan, 1989 ($1.00, limited series)

1-1st app.; X-Men/X-Factor tie-in; Williamson-i 5.00
2-4 4.00

X-TERMINATORS
Marvel Comics: Nov, 2022 - No. 5, Mar, 2023 ($4.99, limited series)

1-($4.99)-Leah Williams-s/Carlos Gomez-a; Dazzler, Boom-Boom, Jubilee, X-23 app. 5.00
2-5-($3.99) 4.00

X, THE MAN WITH THE X-RAY EYES (See Movie Comics)

X-TINCTION AGENDA (Secret Wars tie-in)
Marvel Comics: Aug, 2015 - No. 4, Nov, 2015 ($3.99, limited series)

1-4-Guggenheim-s/Di Giandomenico-a; Havok & Wolfsbane app. 4.00

X-TREME X-MEN (Also see Mekanix)
Marvel Comics: July, 2001 - No. 46, Jun, 2004 ($2.99/$3.50)

1-Claremont-s/Larroca-c/a 4.00
2-24: 2-Two covers (Larroca & Pacheco); Psylocke killed 3.00
25-35, 40-46: 25-30-God Loves, Man Kills II; Stryker app.; Kordey-a 3.00
36-39-($3.50) 3.50
Annual 2001 ($4.95) issue opens longways 5.00

	GD	VG	FN	VF	VF/NM	NM-
	2.0	4.0	6.0	8.0	9.0	9.2

... Vol. 1: Destiny TPB (2002, $19.95) r/#1-9 20.00
... Vol. 2: Invasion TPB (2003, $19.99) r/#10-18 20.00
... Vol. 3: Schism TPB (2003, $16.99) r/#19-23; X-Treme X-Posé #1&2 17.00
... Vol. 4: Mekanix TPB (2003, $16.99) r/Mekanix #1-6 17.00
... Vol. 5: God Loves Man Kills TPB (2003, $19.99) r/#25-30 20.00
... Vol. 6: Intifada TPB (2004, $16.99) r/#24,31-35 17.00
... Vol. 7: Storm the Arena TPB (2004, $16.99) r/#36-39 17.00
... Vol. 8: Prisoner of Fire TPB (2004, $19.99) r/#40-46 and Annual 2001 20.00

X-TREME X-MEN
Marvel Comics: Sept, 2012 - No. 13, Jun, 2013 ($2.99)
1-13: 1-Pak-s/Segovia-a; Dazzler with alternate reality Wolverine, Nightcrawler, Emma 3.00
7.1-(2/12) Cyclops & The Brood app. 3.00

X-TREME X-MEN
Marvel Comics: Jan, 2023 - Present ($3.99)
1-3-Claremont-s/Larroca-c/a 4.00

X-TREME X-MEN: SAVAGE LAND
Marvel Comics: Nov, 2001 - No. 4, Feb, 2002 ($2.99, limited series)
1-4-Claremont-s/Sharpe-c/a; Beast app. 3.00

X-TREME X-POSE
Marvel Comics: Jan, 2003 - No. 2, Feb, 2003 ($2.99, limited series)
1,2-Claremont-s/Ranson-a/Migliari-c 3.00

X-23 (See debut in NYX #3)(See NYX X-23 HC for reprint)
Marvel Comics: Mar, 2005 - No. 6, July, 2005 ($2.99, limited series)
1-Origin of the Wolverine clone girl; Tan-a 3 6 9 16 24 32
1-Variant Billy Tan-c with red background 3 6 9 17 25 34
2-6-Origin continues 1 3 4 6 8 10
2-Variant B&W sketch-c 2 4 6 9 12 15
One shot 1 (5/10, $3.99) Urasov-c/Liu-s; Wolverine & Jubilee app.
3 6 9 19 30 40
...: Innocence Lost MGC 1 (5/11, $1.00) r/#1 with "Marvel's Greatest Comics" cover logo 3.00
...: Innocence Lost TPB (2006, $15.99) r/#1-6 20.00

X-23
Marvel Comics: Nov, 2010 - No. 21, May, 2012 ($3.99/$2.99)
1-Marjorie Liu-s/Will Conrad-a; origin retold; Luo-c 3 6 9 17 26 35
1-Djurdjevic variant-c 3 6 9 19 30 40
1-Dell'Otto variant-c 26 52 78 180 404 625
2-Luo-c 2 4 6 8 11 14
2-Mayhew variant-c 7 14 21 46 86 125
3-21: 3,10-12,17-19-Takeda-a. 8,9-Daken app. 13-16-Spider-Man app.; Noto-a. 20-Jubilee app.; Noto-a. 21-Silent issue; Noto-a 4.00

X-23
Marvel Comics: Sept, 2018 - No. 12, Jul, 2019 ($4.99/$3.99)
1-($4.99) Tamaki-s/Cabal-a; Honey Badger and the Stepford Cuckoos app. 5.00
2-12-($3.99) 7-Intro X-Assassin 4.00

X-23: TARGET X
Marvel Comics: Feb, 2007 - No. 6, July, 2007 ($2.99, limited series)
1-Kyle & Yost-s/Choi & Oback-a 3 6 9 14 20 26
2-6: 6-Gallery of variant covers and sketches 6.00
TPB (2007, $15.99) r/#1-6; gallery of variant covers and sketches 16.00

X-UNIVERSE
Marvel Comics: May, 1995 - No. 2, June, 1995 ($3.50, limited series)
1,2: Age of Apocalypse 5.00

X-VENTURE (Super Heroes)
Victory Magazines Corp.: July, 1947 - No. 2, Nov, 1947
1-Atom Wizard, Mystery Shadow, Lester Trumble begin
161 322 483 1030 1765 2500
2 68 136 204 435 743 1050

X-WOMEN
Marvel Comics: 2010 ($4.99, one-shot)
1-Milo Manara-a/Chris Claremont-s; a female X-Men adventure; Quesada afterword 5.00

XYR (See Eclipse Graphic Album Series #21)

YAK YAK
Dell Publishing Co.: No. 1186, May-July, 1961 - No. 1348, Apr-June, 1962
Four Color 1186 (#1)- Jack Davis-c/a; 2 versions, one minus 3 pgs.
8 16 24 56 108 160
Four Color 1348 (#2)-Davis c/a 7 14 21 46 86 125

YAKKY DOODLE & CHOPPER (TV) (See Dell Giant #44)
Gold Key: Dec, 1962 (Hanna-Barbera)
1 8 16 24 51 96 140

YANG (See House of Yang)
Charlton Comics: Nov, 1973 - No. 13, May, 1976; V14#15, Sept, 1985 - No. 17, Jan, 1986 (No V14#14, series resumes with #15)
1-Origin; Sattler-a begins; slavery-s 2 4 6 13 18 22
2-13(1976) 1 2 3 6 9 10
15-17(1986): 15-Reprints #1 (Low print run) 6.00
3,10,11(Modern Comics-r, 1977) 6.00

YANKEE COMICS
Harry 'A' Chesler: Sept, 1941 - No. 7, 1942?
1-Origin The Echo, The Enchanted Dagger, Yankee Doodle Jones, The Firebrand, & The Scarlet Sentry; Black Satan app.; Yankee Doodle Jones app. on all covers
258 516 774 1651 2826 4000
2-Origin Johnny Rebel; Major Victory app.; Barry Kuda begins
116 232 348 742 1271 1800
3,4: 4-(3/42) 97 194 291 621 1061 1500
4 (nd, 1940s; 7-1/4x5", 68 pgs, distr. to the service)-Foxy Grandpa, Tom, Dick & Harry, Impy, Ace & Deuce, Dot & Dash, Ima Slooth by Jack Cole (Remington Morse publ.)
21 42 63 124 202 280
5-7 (nd; 10¢, 7-1/4x5", 68 pgs.)(Remington Morse publ.)-urges readers to send their copies to servicemen. 18 36 54 107 169 230

YANKEE DOODLE THE SPIRIT OF LIBERTY
Spire Publications: 1984 (no price, 36 pgs)
nn-Al Hartley-s/c/a 2 4 6 9 13 16

YANKS IN BATTLE
Quality Comics Group: Sept, 1956 - No. 4, Dec, 1956
1-Cuidera-c(i) 17 34 51 98 154 210
2-4: Cuidera-c(i) 11 22 33 62 86 110

YARDBIRDS, THE (G. I. Joe's Sidekicks)
Ziff-Davis Publishing Co.: Summer, 1952
1-By Bob Oskner 40 80 120 246 411 575

YARNS OF YELLOWSTONE
World Color Press: 1972 (50¢, 36 pgs.)
nn-Illustrated by Bill Chapman 2 4 6 9 12 15

YEAH!
DC Comics (Homage): Oct, 1999 - No. 9, Jun, 2000 ($2.95)
1-Bagge-s/Hernandez-a 3.00
2-9: 2-Editorial page contains adult language 3.00

YEAR OF MARVELS, A
Marvel Comics: ($4.99)
...: The Amazing (6/16) Spider-Man vs. The Vulture; Ant-Man 5.00
...: The Incredible (8/16) Spider-Man & D-Man story; Wolverine (X-23) & She-Hulk story 5.00
...: The Unbeatable (12/16) Nick Fury story; Rocket Raccoon & Tippy-Toe story 5.00
...: The Uncanny (2/17) Hawkeye (Kate Bishop) story; Punisher story 5.00
...: The Unstoppable (10/16) Nova & Iron Man story; Winter Soldier story 5.00

YEAR OF THE VILLAIN: HELL ARISEN
DC Comics: Feb, 2020 - No. 4, May, 2020 ($4.99, limited series)
1,2-Apex Lex vs. The Batman Who Laughs; Tynion IV-s/Epting-a. 1-Crime Syndicate app. 5.00
3-First full app. of Punchline; Joker app. 5 10 15 30 50 70
4-Perpertua app.; leads into the Death Metal series 5.00

YEAR ONE: BATMAN/RA'S AL GHUL
DC Comics: 2005 - No. 2, 2005 ($5.99, squarebound, limited series)
1-Devin Grayson-s/Paul Gulacy-a 6.00
TPB (2006, $9.99) r/#1,2 10.00

YEAR ONE: BATMAN SCARECROW
DC Comics: 2005 - No. 2, 2005 ($5.99, squarebound, limited series)
1-Scarecrow's origin; Bruce Jones-s/Sean Murphy-a 6.00

YEARS OF FUTURE PAST (Secret Wars Battleworld tie-in)
Marvel Comics: Aug, 2015 - No. 5, Nov, 2015 ($4.99/$3.99, limited series)
1-($4.99) Bennett-s/Norton-a; Art Adams-c; Kitty Pryde, Wolverine, Colossus app. 5.00
2-5-($3.99) Storm, Magneto, Mystique, Blob, Sentinels app. 4.00

YEAR ZERO
AWA Studios: Apr, 2020 - No. 5, Sept, 2020; Nov, 2020 - No. 5, Mar, 2021 ($3.99)
1-5-Benjamin Percy-s/Ramon Rosanas-a 4.00
Vol. 0 (10/22 - No. 5, 2/23) 1-5-Prequel to the series; Kraus-s/Sudzuka-a 4.00
Vol. 2 (11/20 - No. 5, 3/21) 1-5-Percy-s/Ryp-a 4.00

YELLOW CLAW (Also see Giant Size Master of Kung Fu)
Atlas Comics (MjMC): Oct, 1956 - No. 4, Apr, 1957
1-Origin by Joe Maneely 258 516 774 1651 2826 4000
2-Kirby-a 168 336 504 1075 1838 2600
3-Kirby-a 155 310 465 992 1696 2400
4-Kirby/Severin-a 161 322 483 1030 1765 2500
NOTE: *Everett c-3. Maneely c-1. Reinman a-2i, 3. Severin c-2, 4.*

YELLOWJACKET COMICS (Jack in the Box #11 on)(See TNT Comics)
E. Levy/Frank Comunale/Charlton: Sept, 1944 - No. 5. Jan, 1945; No. 6, Dec, 1945 - No. 10, June, 1946
1-Intro & origin Yellowjacket; Diana, the Huntress begins; "Famous Tales of Terror" begins with E.A. Poe's "The Black Cat" adaptation 97 194 291 621 1061 1500
2-Yellowjacket-c begin, end #10; no "Famous Tales of Terror"
61 122 183 390 670 950
3,5: 3-"Famous Tales of Terror" with Poe's "The Pit and the Pendulum" adaptation. 5-No "Famous Tales of Terror" 55 110 165 352 601 850
4-"Famous Tales of Terror" with Poe's "Fall of the House Of Usher" adaptation; Palais-a
58 116 174 371 636 900
6-Last "Famous Tales of Terror", with Poe's "The Tell Tale Heart" adaptation
55 110 165 352 601 850
7-Classic Skull-c; "Tales of Terror" begins by Alan Mandel-narrated by the Ancient Witch, wearing a red cloak, stirring her bubbling cauldron at beginning and end of story just like E.C.'s Old Witch 5 years later; tells story "The Avenging Hand!" similar to "The Maestro's Hand!" in Crypt of Terror #18. (1st horror series?) Toth-a (1 pg. gag feature)
74 148 222 470 810 1150
8-"Tales of Terror" narrated by the Old Witch; classic splash & end panel with skull & bones; early "return from the grave story" 45 90 135 284 480 675
9,10-"Tales of Terror" in each, narrated by the Old Witch in a red cloak, w/classic splash and end panels 45 90 135 284 480 675
NOTE: *The Old Witch in #7-10 above may have inspired creation of E.C.'s Old Witch. Her costume, dialogue, use of bubbling cauldron, skull and bones and even the title "Tales of Terror" were possibly used.*

YELLOWSTONE KELLY (Movie)
Dell Publishing Co.: No. 1056, Nov-Jan, 1959/60
Four Color 1056-Clint Walker photo-c 6 12 18 41 76 110

YELLOW SUBMARINE (See Movie Comics)

YOGA HOSERS: A SUNDANCE SUPER SPECIAL
Dynamite Entertainment: 2016 ($10.00, one-shot)
1-Prologue to the Kevin Smith movie; Smith-s/Jeff Quigley-a 10.00
1-Third printing (2017, $3.99) 4.00

YOGI BEAR (See Dell Giant #41, Golden Comics Digest, Kite Fun Book, March of Comics #253, 265, 279,

X-23 (2018) #1 © MAR

Year Zero #1 © AWA

Young Avengers (2013) #1 © MAR

	GD 2.0	VG 4.0	FN 6.0	VF 8.0	VF/NM 9.0	NM- 9.2

291, 309, 319, 337, 344, Movie Comics under "Hey There It's..." & Whitman Comic Books)

YOGI BEAR (TV) (Hanna-Barbera) (See Four Color #990)
Dell Publishing Co./Gold Key No. 10 on: No. 1067, 12-2/59-60 - No. 9, 7-9/62; No. 10, 10/62 - No. 42, 10/70

	GD	VG	FN	VF	VF/NM	NM-
Four Color 1067 (#1)-TV show debuted 1/30/61	13	26	39	89	195	300
Four Color 1104,1162 (5-7/61)	8	16	24	56	108	160
4(8-9/61) - 6(12-1/61-62)	5	10	15	34	60	85
Four Color 1271(11/61)	6	12	18	40	73	105
Four Color 1349(1/62)-Photo-c	8	16	24	54	102	150
7(2-3/62) - 9(7-9/62)-Last Dell	5	10	15	33	57	80
10(10/62-G.K.), 11(1/63)-titled "Yogi Bear Jellystone Jollies" (80 pgs.); 11-X-Mas-c	6	12	18	41	76	110
12(4/63), 14-20	4	8	12	28	47	65
13(7/63, 68 pgs.)-Surprise Party	6	12	18	40	73	105
21-30	3	6	9	19	30	40
31-42	3	6	9	16	24	32

YOGI BEAR (TV)
Charlton Comics: Nov, 1970 - No. 35, Jan, 1976 (Hanna-Barbera)

	GD	VG	FN	VF	VF/NM	NM-
1	5	10	15	31	53	75
2-6,8-10	3	6	9	16	24	32
7-Summer Fun (Giant, 52 pgs.)	4	8	12	27	44	60
11-20	3	6	9	15	22	28
21-35: 28-31-partial-r	2	4	6	11	16	20
Digest (nn, 1972, 75¢-c, B&W, 100 pgs.) (scarce)	3	6	9	18	28	38

YOGI BEAR (TV)(See The Flintstones, 3rd series & Spotlight #1)
Marvel Comics Group: Nov, 1977 - No. 9, Mar, 1979 (Hanna-Barbera)

	GD	VG	FN	VF	VF/NM	NM-
1,7-9: 1-Flintstones begin (Newsstand sales only)	3	6	9	16	23	30
2-6	2	4	6	11	16	20

YOGI BEAR (TV)
Harvey Comics: Sept, 1992 - No. 6, Mar, 1994 ($1.25/$1.50) (Hanna-Barbera)

V2#1-6 3.00
...Big Book V2#1,2 ($1.95, 52 pgs): 1-(11/92). 2-(3/93) 4.00
...Giant Size V2#1,2 ($2.25, 68 pgs.): 1-(10/92). 2-(4/93) 4.00

YOGI BEAR (TV)
Archie Publ.: May, 1997

1 3.00

YOGI BEAR'S EASTER PARADE (See The Funtastic World of Hanna-Barbera #2)

YOGI BERRA (Baseball hero)
Fawcett Publications: 1951 (Yankee catcher)

	GD	VG	FN	VF	VF/NM	NM-
nn-Photo-c (scarce)	81	162	243	518	884	1250

YONDU (Guardians of the Galaxy)
Marvel Comics: Jan, 2020 - No. 5, Apr, 2020 ($3.99, limited series)

1-5-Zac Thompson & Lonnie Nadler-s/John McCrea-a; future Yondu app. 4.00

YOSEMITE SAM (...& Bugs Bunny) (TV)
Gold Key/Whitman: Dec, 1970 - No. 81, Feb, 1984

	GD	VG	FN	VF	VF/NM	NM-
1	5	10	15	31	53	75
2-10	3	6	9	16	23	30
11-20	2	4	6	11	16	20
21-30	2	4	6	9	13	16
31-50	2	4	6	8	10	12
51-65 (Gold Key)	1	2	3	5	7	9
66,67 (Whitman)	2	4	6	8	10	12
68(9/80), 69(10/80), 70(12/80) 3-pack only	5	10	15	30	50	70
71-78: 76(2/82), 77(3/82), 78(4/82)	2	4	6	9	13	16
79-81 (All #90263 on-c, no date or date code; 3-pack): 79(7/83). 80(8/83). 81(2/84)-(1/3-r)	3	6	9	16	24	32

(See March of Comics #363, 380, 392)

YOSSEL
DC Comics: 2003/2011 ($14.99, B&W graphic novel)

SC-Joe Kubert-s/a/c; Nazi-occupied Poland during World War II 15.00

YOU ARE DEADPOOL
Marvel Comics: Jul, 2018 - No. 5, Jul, 2018 ($3.99, weekly limited series)

1-5-Ewing-s; interactive role-playing adventure. 3-Man-Thing app. 4-Bullseye app. 4.00

YOU ARE OBSOLETE
AfterShock Comics: Sept, 2019 - No. 5, Jan, 2020 ($3.99)

1-5-Matthew Klickstein-s/Evgeniy Bornyakov-a/Andy Clarke-c 4.00

YOU LOOK LIKE DEATH: TALES FROM THE UMBRELLA ACADEMY
Dark Horse Comics: Sept, 2020 - No. 6, Feb, 2021 ($3.99, limited series)

1-6-Gerald Way & Shaun Simon-s/I.N.J. Culbard-a; spotlight on Klaus 4.00

YOUNG ALLIES
Marvel Comics: Aug, 2010 - No. 6, Jan, 2011 ($3.99/$2.99)

1-($3.99) Wraparound-c; Nomad, Araña, Firestar, Gravity, Toro team-up; origin pages 5.00
2-6-($2.99) 2-Lafuente-c/McKeever-s/Baldeon-a. 6-Miyazawa-c; Emma Frost app. 4.00

YOUNG ALLIES COMICS (All-Winners #21; see Kid Komics #2)
Timely Comics (USA 1-7/NPI 8,9/YAI 10-20): Sum, 1941 - No. 20, Oct, 1946

	GD	VG	FN	VF	VF/NM	NM-
1-Origin/1st app. The Young Allies (Bucky, Toro, others); 1st meeting of Captain America & Human Torch; Red Skull-c & app.; S&K-c/splash; Hitler-c; Note: the cover was altered after its preview in Human Torch #5. Stalin was shown with Hitler but was removed due to Russia becoming an ally	1400	2800	4200	9800	19,400	29,000
2-(Winter, 1941)-Captain America & Human Torch app.; Simon & Kirby-c	459	918	1377	3350	5925	8500
3-Remember Pearl Harbor issue (Spring, 1942); Stan Lee scripts; Vs. Japanese-c/full-length story; Captain America & Human Torch app.; Father Time story by Alderman	432	864	1296	3154	5577	8000
4-The Vagabond & Red Skull, Capt. America, Human Torch app. Classic Red Skull-c	622	1244	1866	4541	8021	11,500
5-Captain America & Human Torch app.	309	618	927	2163	3782	5400
6,7: 6-Japanese/Nazi war-c	284	568	852	1818	3109	4400
8-Classic Schomburg WWII Japanese bondage-c	300	600	900	2010	3505	5000
9-Hitler, Tojo, Mussolini-c.	400	800	1200	2800	4900	7000
10-Classic Schomburg Hooded Villain bondage-c; origin Tommy Tyme & Clock of Ages; ends #19	239	478	717	1530	2615	3700
11-16: 12-Classic decapitation story; Japanese war-c. 16-Last Schomburg WWII-c	174	348	522	1114	1907	2700
17-20	135	270	405	864	1482	2100

NOTE: ***Brodsky** c-15. **Ferstadt** a-3. **Gabriele** a-3; c-3, 4. **S&K** c-1, 2. **Schomburg** c-5-13, 16-19. **Shores** c-20.*

YOUNG ALLIES 70TH ANNIVERSARY SPECIAL
Marvel Comics: Aug, 2009 ($3.99, one-shot)

1-Bucky & Young Allies app.; Stern-s/Rivera-a; Terry Vance rep. from Marvel Myst. #14 5.00

YOUNG ALL-STARS
DC Comics: June, 1987 - No. 31, Nov, 1989 ($1.00, deluxe format)

1-31: 1-1st app. Iron Munro & The Flying Fox. 8,9-Millennium tie-ins 4.00
Annual 1 (1988, $2.00) 4.00

YOUNG AVENGERS
Marvel Comics: Apr, 2005 - No. 12, Aug, 2006 ($2.99)

	GD	VG	FN	VF	VF/NM	NM-
1-1st app Kate Bishop; intro. Iron Lad, Patriot, Hulkling, Asgardian; Heinberg-s/Cheung-a	8	16	24	54	102	150
1-Director's Cut (2005, $3.99) r/#1 plus character sketches; original script	5	10	15	33	57	80
2-8,10,11: 3-6-Kang app. 7-DiVito-a. 9-Skrulls app.						4.00
9-1st Kate Bishop-c	3	6	9	14	19	24
12-1st Kate Bishop as Hawkeye	3	6	9	17	25	34

... Special 1 (2/06, $3.99) origins of the heroes; art by various incl. Neal Adams, Jae Lee, Bill Sienkiewicz, Gene Ha, Michael Gaydos and Pasqual Ferry 4.00
... Vol. 1: Sidekicks HC (2005, $19.99, dustjacket) r/#1-6; character design sketches 20.00
... Vol. 1: Sidekicks TPB (2006, $14.99) r/#1-6; character design sketches 15.00
... Vol. 2: Family Matters HC (2006, $22.99, dustjacket) r/#7-12 & YA Special #1 23.00
... Vol. 2: Family Matters SC (2007, $17.99) r/#7-12 & YA Special #1 18.00
HC (2008, $29.99, d.j.) oversized reprint of #1-12 and Special #1; script & sketch pages 30.00

YOUNG AVENGERS (Marvel NOW!)
Marvel Comics: Mar, 2013 - No. 15, Mar, 2014 ($2.99)

1-15: 1-Loki assembles team; Marvel Boy, Miss America app.; Gillen-s/McKelvie-a/c. 11-Loki ages back to adult. 14,15-Multiple artists 3.00
1-Variant-c by Bryan Lee O'Malley 6.00
1-Variant-c by Skottie Young 6.00

YOUNG AVENGERS PRESENTS
Marvel Comics: Mar, 2008 - No. 6, Aug, 2008 ($2.99, limited series)

1-6: 1-Patriot; Bucky app. 2-Hulkling; Captain Marvel app. 3-Wiccan & Speed. 4-Vision. 5-Stature. 6-Hawkeye; Clint Barton app.; Alan Davis-a 3.00

YOUNGBLOOD (See Brigade #4, Megaton Explosion & Team Youngblood)
Image Comics (Extreme Studios): Apr, 1992 - No. 4, Feb, 1993 ($2.50, lim. series); No. 5-(Flip book w/Brigade #4); No. 6, June, 1994 - No. 10, Dec, 1994 ($1.95/$2.50)

	GD	VG	FN	VF	VF/NM	NM-
1-Liefeld-c/a/scripts in all; flip book format with 2 trading cards; 1st Image/Extreme Studios title.	2	4	6	8	10	12
1,2-2nd printing						3.00
2-(JUN-c, July 1992 indicia)-1st app. Shadowhawk in solo back-up story; 2 trading cards inside; flip book format; 1st app. Prophet, Kirby, Berzerkers, Darkthorn	2	4	6	10	14	18

3,0,4,5: 3-(OCT-c, August 1992 indicia)-Contains 2 trading cards inside (flip book); 1st app. Supreme in back-up story; 1st app. Showdown. 0-(12/92, $1.95)-Contains 2 trading cards; 2 cover variations exist, green or beige logo; w/Image #0 coupon. 4-(2/93)-Glow-in-the-dark

GD VG FN VF VF/NM NM-
2.0 4.0 6.0 8.0 9.0 9.2

cover w/2 trading cards; 2nd app. Dale Keown's The Pitt; Bloodstrike app. 5-Flip book w/Brigade #4 3.00
6-($3.50, 52 pgs.)-Wraparound-c 4.00
7-9: 7, 8-Liefeld-c(p)/a(p)/story. 8,9-(9/94) 9-Valentino story & art 3.00
10-Spawn app.; death of Chapel 1 2 3 5 6 8
Battlezone 1 (May-c, 4/93 inside, $1.95)-Arsenal book; Liefeld-c(p) 3.00
Battlezone 2 (7/94, $2.95)-Wraparound-c 4.00
Image Firsts: Youngblood #1 (3/10, $1.00) reprints #1 3.00
...Super Special (Winter '97, $2.99) Sprouse -a 4.00
Yearbook 1 (7/93, $2.50)-Fold out panel; 1st app. Tyrax & Kanan 4.00
Vol. 1 HC (2008, $34.99) oversized r/#1-5, recolored and remastered; sketch art and cover gallery; Mark Millar intro. 35.00
TPB (1996, $16.95)-r/Team Youngblood #8-10 & Youngblood #6-8,10 17.00

YOUNGBLOOD
Image Comics (Extreme Studios)/Maximum Press No. 14: V2#1, Sept, 1995 - No. 14, Dec, 1996 ($2.50)

V2#1-10,14: Roger Cruz-a in all. 4-Extreme Destroyer Pt. 4 w/gaming card. 5-Variant-c exists. 6-Angela & Glory. 7-Shadowhunt Pt. 3; Shadowhawk app. 8,10-Thor (from Supreme) app. 10-(7/96). 14-(12/96)-1st Maximum Press issue 3.00

YOUNGBLOOD (Volume 3)
Awesome/ Awesome-Hyperwerks #2: Feb, 1998 - No. 2, Aug, 1998 ($2.50)

1-Alan Moore-s/Skroce & Stucker-a; 12 diff. covers 3.00
2-(8/98) Skroce & Liefeld covers 3.00
...Imperial 1 (Arcade Comics, 6/04, $2.99) Kirkman-sMychaels-a 3.00

YOUNGBLOOD (Volume 4)
Image Comics: Jan, 2008 - No. 9, Sept, 2009; No. 71, May, 2012 - No. 78, Jul, 2013 ($2.99/$3.99)

1-7-Casey-s/Donovan-a; two covers by Donovan & Liefeld on each 3.00
8-Obama flip cover by Liefeld; Obama app. in story 3.00
9-(9/09, $3.99) Obama flip cover by Liefeld; Free Agent rejoins; Obama app. in story 4.00
71-74: 71-(5/12, $2.99) Liefeld & Malin-a; three covers 3.00
75-(1/13, $4.99) Five covers; Malin-a 5.00
76-78-($3.99) Malin-a 4.00

YOUNGBLOOD (Volume 5)
Image Comics: May, 2017 - No. 11, May, 2018 ($3.99)

1-11-Bowers-s/Towe-a; multiple covers on each. 1-Back-up story w/Liefeld-s/a. 4,5-Bloodstrike flip book; Liefeld-s/a 4.00

YOUNGBLOOD: STRIKEFILE
Image Comics (Extreme Studios): Apr, 1993 - No. 11, Feb, 1995 ($1.95/$2.50/$2.95)

1-10: 1-($1.95)-Flip book w/Jae Lee-c/a & Liefeld-c/a in #1-3; 1st app. The Allies,Giger, & Glory. 3-Thibert-i asisst. 4-Liefeld-c(p); no Lee-a. 5-Liefeld-c(p). 8-Platt-c 3.00
NOTE: *Youngblood: Strikefile began as a four issue limited series.*

YOUNGBLOOD/X-FORCE
Image Comics (Extreme Studios): July, 1996 ($4.95, one-shot)

1-Cruz-a(p); two covers exist 5.00

YOUNG BRIDES (True Love Secrets)
Feature/Prize Publ.: Sept-Oct, 1952 - No. 30, Nov-Dec, 1956 (Photo-c: V1 #1-6, V2 #1,2)

V1#1-Simon & Kirby-a 53 106 159 334 567 800
2-S&K-a 32 64 96 188 307 425
3-6-S&K-a 27 54 81 162 266 370
V2#1-7,10-12 (#7-18)-S&K-a 24 48 72 140 230 320
8,9-No S&K-a 14 28 42 81 118 155
V3#1-3(#19-21)-Last precode (3-4/55) 14 28 42 76 108 140
4,6(#22,24), V4#1,3(#25,27) 13 26 39 72 101 130
V3#5(#23)-Meskin-c 13 26 39 74 105 135
V4#2(#26)-All S&K issue 22 44 66 130 213 295
V4#4(#28)-S&K-a 19 38 57 112 179 240
V4#5,6(#29,30) 14 28 42 76 108 140

YOUNG DR. MASTERS (See The Adventures of Young Dr. Masters)

YOUNG DOCTORS, THE
Charlton Comics: Jan, 1963 - No. 6, Nov, 1963

V1#1 4 8 12 27 44 60
2-6 3 6 9 16 23 30

YOUNG EAGLE
Fawcett Publications/Charlton: 12/50 - No. 10, 6/52; No. 3, 7/56 - No. 5, 4/57 (Photo-c: 1-10)

1-Intro Young Eagle 21 42 63 122 199 275
2-Complete picture novelette "The Mystery of Thunder Canyon"
12 24 36 67 94 120
3-9 9 18 27 52 69 85
10-Origin Thunder, Young Eagle's Horse 9 18 27 47 61 75
3-5(Charlton)-Formerly Sherlock Holmes? 7 14 21 37 46 55

YOUNG GUNS SKETCHBOOK
Marvel Comics: Feb, 2005 ($3.99, one-shot)

1-Sketch pages from 2005 Marvel projects by Coipel, Granov, McNiven, Land & others 4.00

YOUNG HEARTS
Marvel Comics (SPC): Nov, 1949 - No. 2, Feb, 1950

1-Photo-c 25 50 75 150 245 340
2-Colleen Townsend photo-c from movie 17 34 51 100 158 215

YOUNG HEARTS IN LOVE
Super Comics: 1964

17,18: 17-r/Young Love V5#6 (4-5/62) 2 4 6 9 13 16

YOUNG HELLBOY: ASSAULT ON CASTLE DEATH
Dark Horse Comics: Jul, 2022 - No. 4, Feb, 2023 ($3.99, limited series)

1-4-Mignola & Sniegoski-s/Rousseau-a; Lobster Johnson app. 4.00

YOUNG HELLBOY: THE HIDDEN LAND
Dark Horse Comics: Feb, 2021 - No. 4, Jun, 2021 ($3.99, limited series)

1-4-Mignola & Sniegoski-s/Rousseau-a; Prof. Bruttenholm app. 4.00

YOUNG HEROES (Formerly Forbidden Worlds #34)
American Comics Group (Titan): No. 35, Feb-Mar, 1955 - No. 37, Jun-Jul, 1955

35-37-Frontier Scout 12 24 36 67 94 120

YOUNG HEROES IN LOVE
DC Comics: June, 1997 - No. 17; #1,000,000, Nov, 1998 ($1.75/$1.95/$2.50)

1-1st app. Young Heroes; Madan-a 4.00
2-17: 3-Superman-c/app. 7-Begin $1.95-c 3.00
#1,000,000 (11/98, $2.50) 853 Century x-over 3.00

YOUNG INDIANA JONES CHRONICLES, THE
Dark Horse Comics: Feb, 1992 - No. 12, Feb, 1993 ($2.50)

1-12: Dan Barry scripts in all 3.00
NOTE: ***Dan Barry** a(p)-1, 2, 5, 6, 10; c-1-10. **Morrow** a-3, 4, 5p, 6p. **Springer** a-1i, 2i.*

YOUNG INDIANA JONES CHRONICLES, THE
Hollywood Comics (Disney): 1992 ($3.95, squarebound, 68 pgs.)

1-3: 1-r/YIJC #1,2 by D. Horse. 2-r/#3,4. 3-r/#5,6 4.00

YOUNG JUSTICE (Also see Teen Titans, Titans/Young Justice and DC Comics Presents: ...)
DC Comics: Sept, 1998 - No. 55, May, 2003 ($2.50/$2.75)

1-Robin, Superboy & Impulse team-up; David-s/Nauck-a 6.00
2,3: 3-Mxyzptlk app. 4.00
4-20: 4-Wonder Girl, Arrowette and the Secret join. 6-JLA app. 13-Supergirl x-over. 20-Sins of Youth aftermath 3.00
21-49: 25-Empress ID revealed. 28,29-Forever People app. 32-Empress origin. 35,36-Our Worlds at War x-over. 38-Joker: Last Laugh. 41-The Ray joins. 42-Spectre-c/app. 44,45-World Without YJ x-over pt. 1,5; Ramos-c. 48-Begin $2.75-c 3.00
50-($3.95) Wonder Twins, CM3 and other various DC teen heroes app. 4.00
51-55: 53,54-Darkseid app. 55-Last issue; leads into Titans/Young Justice mini-series 3.00
#1,000,000 (11/98) 853 Century x-over 3.00
...: A League of Their Own (2000, $14.95, TPB) r/#1-7, Secret Files #1 15.00
...: 80-Page Giant (5/99, $4.95) Ramos-c; stories and art by various 5.00
...: In No Man's Land (7/99, $3.95) McDaniel-c 4.00
...: Our Worlds at War (8/01, $2.95) Jae Lee-c; Linear Men app. 3.00
...: Secret Files (1/99, $4.95) Origin-s & pin-ups 5.00
...: The Secret (6/98, $1.95) Girlfrenzy; Nauck-a 3.00

YOUNG JUSTICE (Based on the 2011 Cartoon Network series)
DC Comics: No. 0, Mar, 2011 - No. 25, Apr, 2013 ($2.99)

0-19: 1-Miss Martian joins; Joker app. 2-Joker-c/app. 5-Kid Flash & Aqualad origins 3.00
20-25: 20-(11/12) Starts Invasion; 5 years later 3.00
FCBD 2011 Young Justice Batman BB Super Sampler (7/11) Flash app. 3.00

YOUNG JUSTICE
DC Comics (Wonder Comics): Mar, 2019 - No. 20, Jan, 2021 ($4.99/$3.99)

1-($4.99) Robin, Wonder Girl & Impulse team; intro Jinny Hex & Teen Lantern; Bendis-s 5.00
2-20-($3.99): 2-Gleason & Lupacchino-a. 3-Gleason & Bogdanovic-a. 7-Capt. Carrot and the Kingdom Come Justice League app. 8-10-Earth-3 counterparts app. 13-Warlord app.; art by Grell (5 pages). 20-Red Tornado app. 4.00

YOUNG JUSTICE: SINS OF YOUTH (Also see Sins of Youth x-over issues and Sins of Youth: Secret Files)
DC Comics: May, 2000 - No. 2, May, 2000 ($3.95, limited series)

1,2-Young Justice, JLA & JSA swap ages; David-s/Nauck-a 4.00
TPB (2000, $19.95) r/#1,2 & all x-over issues) 20.00

YOUNG JUSTICE: TARGETS (Based on the 2011 Cartoon Network series)
DC Comics: Sept, 2022 - No. 6, Feb, 2023 ($3.99, limited series)

1-6: 1-Greg Weisman-s/Christopher Jones-a 4.00

YOUNG KING COLE (...Detective Tales)(Becomes Criminals on the Run)
Premium Group/Novelty Press: Fall, 1945 - V3#12, July, 1948

V1#1-Toni Gayle begins 43 86 129 271 461 650
2 22 44 66 128 209 290
3-4 20 40 60 117 189 260
V2#1-7(8-9/46-7/47): 6,7-Certa-c 15 30 45 88 137 185
V3#1,3-6,8,9,12: 3-Certa-c. 5-McWilliams-c/a. 8,9-Harmon-c
15 30 45 85 130 175
2-L.B. Cole-a; Certa-c 21 42 63 122 199 275
7-L.B. Cole-c/a 27 54 81 158 259 360
10,11-L.B. Cole-c 31 62 93 182 296 410

YOUNG LAWYERS, THE (TV)
Dell Publishing Co.: Jan, 1971 - No. 2, Apr, 1971 (photo-c)

1 3 6 9 17 26 35
2 2 4 6 11 16 20

YOUNG LIARS (David Lapham's...)(See Vertigo Double Shot for reprint of #1)
DC Comics (Vertigo): May, 2008 - No. 18, Oct, 2009 ($2.99)

1-18: 1-Intro. Sadie Dawkins; David Lapham-s/a/c in all 3.00
...: Daydream Believer TPB (2008, $9.99) r/#1-6; Gerald Way intro. 10.00
...: Maestro TPB (2009, $14.99) r/#7-12; Peter Milligan intro. 15.00
...: Rock Life TPB (2010, $14.99) r/#13-18; Brian Azzarello intro. 15.00

YOUNG LIFE (Teen Life #3 on)
New Age Publ./Quality Comics Group: Summer, 1945 - No. 2, Fall, 1945

1-Skip Homeier, Louis Prima stories 24 48 72 142 234 325
2-Frank Sinatra photo on-c plus story 25 50 75 150 245 340

YOUNG LOVE (Sister title to Young Romance)
Prize(Feature)Publ.(Crestwood): 2-3/49 - No. 73, 12-1/56-57; V3#5, 2-3/60 - V7#1, 6-7/63

V1#1-S&K-c/a(2) 97 194 291 621 1061 1500
2-Photo-c begin; S&K-a 41 82 123 256 428 600
3-S&K-a 29 58 87 172 281 390
4-6-Minor S&K-a 20 40 60 117 189 260
V2#1(#7)-S&K-a(2) 27 54 81 158 259 360
2-5(#8-11)-Minor S&K-a 17 34 51 98 154 210
6,8(#12,14)-S&K-c only. 14-S&K 1 pg. art 20 40 60 114 182 250
7,9-12(#13,15-18)-S&K-c/a 25 50 75 150 245 340
V3#1-4(#19-22)-S&K-c/a 22 44 66 132 216 300
5-7,9-12(#23-25,27-30)-Photo-c resume; S&K-a 19 38 57 111 176 240
8(#26)-No S&K-a 13 26 39 72 101 130
V4#1,6(#31,36)-S&K-a 17 34 51 98 154 210

Youngblood #71 © Rob Liefeld

Young Justice (2012) #18 © DC

Your Pal Archie #4 © ACP

	GD 2.0	VG 4.0	FN 6.0	VF 8.0	VF/NM 9.0	NM- 9.2

2-5,7-12(#32-35,37-42)-Minor S&K-a 15 30 45 84 127 170
V5#1-12(#43-54), V6#3,7,9(#57,61,63)-Last precode 12 24 36 67 94 120
V6#1,2,4-6,8(#55,56,58-60,62) S&K-a 14 28 42 76 108 140
V6#10-12(#64-66) 10 20 30 56 76 95
V7#1-7(#67-73) 5 10 15 33 57 80
V3#5(2-3/60),6(4-5/60)(Formerly All For Love) 5 10 15 30 50 70
V4#1(6-7/60)-6(4-5/61) 4 8 12 28 47 65
V5#1(6-7/61)-6(4-5/62) 4 8 12 28 47 65
V6#1(6-7/62)-6(4-5/63), V7#1 4 8 12 27 44 60
NOTE: **Meskin** *a-14(2), 27, 42.* **Powell** *a-V4#6.* **Severin/Elder** *a-V1#3. S&K art not in #53, 57, 61, 63-65. Photo-c most V1 #1-6, V2 #3, V3#5-V5#11.*

YOUNG LOVE
National Periodical Publ.(Arleigh Publ. Corp #49-61)/DC Comics: #39, 9-10/63 - #120, Wint./75-76; #121, 10/76 - #126, 7/77

39 6 12 18 41 76 110
40-50 4 8 12 28 47 65
51-68,70 4 8 12 25 40 55
69-(68 pg. Giant)(8-9/68) 7 14 21 44 82 120
71,72,75-77,80 3 6 9 20 31 42
73,74,78,79-Toth-a 3 6 9 21 33 45
81-99: 88-96-(52 pg. Giants) 3 6 9 19 30 40
100 3 6 9 20 31 42
101-106,115-120 3 6 9 16 24 32
107 (100 pgs.) 8 16 24 52 99 145
108-114 (100 pgs.) 7 14 21 48 89 130
121-126 (52 pgs.) 4 8 12 27 44 60
NOTE: **Bolle** *a-117.* **Colan** *a-107r.* **Nasser** *a-123, 124.* **Orlando** *a-122.* **Simonson** *c-125.* **Toth** *a-73, 78, 79, 122-125r.* **Wood** *a-109r(4 pgs.).*

YOUNG LOVER ROMANCES (Formerly & becomes Great Lover...)
Toby Press: No. 4, June, 1952 - No. 5, Aug, 1952
4,5-Photo-c 15 30 45 88 137 185

YOUNG LOVERS (My Secret Life #19 on)(Formerly Brenda Starr?)
Charlton Comics: No. 16, July, 1956 - No. 18, May, 1957
16,17('56): 16-Marcus Swayze-a 16 32 48 94 147 200
18-Elvis Presley picture-c, text story (biography)(Scarce)
116 232 348 742 1271 1800

YOUNG MARRIAGE
Fawcett Publications: June, 1950
1-Powell-a; photo-c 18 36 54 105 165 225

YOUNG MEN (Formerly Cowboy Romances)(...on the Battlefield #12-20(4/53); ...In Action #21)
Marvel/Atlas Comics (IPC): No. 4, 6/50 - No. 11, 10/51; No. 12, 12/51 - No. 28, 6/54
4-(52 pgs.) 34 68 102 199 325 450
5-11 22 44 66 128 209 290
12-23: 12-20-War format. 21-23-Hot Rod issues starring Flash Foster
22 44 66 132 216 300
24-(12/53)-Origin Captain America, Human Torch, & Sub-Mariner which are revived thru #28; Red Skull app.
432 864 1296 3154 5577 8000
25-28: 25-Romita-c/a (see Men's Advs.). 27-Death of Golden Age Red Skull
194 388 582 1242 2121 3000
25-2nd printing (1994) 2 4 6 10 14 18
NOTE: **Berg** *a-7, 14, 17, 18, 20; c-17?* **Brodsky** *c-4-9, 13, 14, 16, 17, 21-25.* **Burgos** *c-26-28.* **Colan** *a-14, 15, 20.* **Everett** *a-18-20.* **Heath** *a-13, 14.* **Maneely** *c-10-12, 15.* **Pakula** *a-14, 15.* **Robinson** *c-18. Captain America by* **Romita**-*#24?, 25, 26?, 27, 28. Human Torch by* **Burgos**-*#25, 27, 28. Sub-Mariner by* **Everett**-*#24-28.*

YOUNG MONSTERS IN LOVE
DC Comics: Apr, 2018 ($9.99, 80 pages, one-shot)
1-Horror short stories by various; Swamp Thing, Raven, Deadman app.; Kelley Jones-c 10.00

YOUNG REBELS, THE (TV)
Dell Publishing Co.: Jan, 1971
1-Photo-c 3 6 9 14 19 24

YOUNG ROMANCE COMICS (The 1st romance comic)
Prize/Headline (Feature Publ.) (Crestwood): Sept-Oct, 1947 - V16#4, June-July, 1963 (#1-33: 52 pgs.)
V1#1-S&K-c/a(2) 161 322 483 1030 1765 2500
2-S&K-c/a(2-3) 53 106 159 334 567 800
3-6-S&K-c/a(2-3) each 40 80 120 246 411 575
V2#1-6(#7-12)-S&K-c/a(2-3) each 37 74 111 218 354 490
V3#1-3(#13-15): V3#1-Photo-c begin; S&K-a 24 48 72 142 234 325
4-12(#16-24)-Photo-c; S&K-a 24 48 72 142 234 325
V4#1-11(#25-35)-S&K-a 23 46 69 136 223 310
12(#36)-S&K, Toth-a 24 48 72 142 234 325
V5#1-12(#37-48), V6#4-12(#52-60)-S&K-a 23 46 69 138 227 315
V6#1-3(#49-51)-No S&K-a 14 28 42 80 115 150
V7#1-11(#61-71)-S&K-a in most 18 36 54 105 165 225
V7#12(#72), V8#1-3(#73-75)-Last precode (12-1/54-55)-No S&K-a
13 26 39 74 105 135
V8#4(#76, 4-5/55), 5(#77)-No S&K-a 12 24 36 69 94 120
V8#6-8(#78-80, 12-1/55-56)-S&K-a 15 30 45 83 124 185
V9#3,5,6(#81, 2-3/56, 83,84)-S&K-a 15 30 45 83 124 185
4, V10#1(#82,85)-All S&K-a 16 32 48 94 147 200
V10#2-6(#86-90, 10-11/57)-S&K-a 9 18 27 61 123 185
V11#1,2,5,6(#91,92,95,96)-S&K-a 9 18 27 61 123 185
3,4(#93,94), V12#2,4,5(#98,100,101)-No S&K 6 12 18 38 69 100
V12#1,3,6(#97,99,102)-S&K-a 9 18 27 61 123 185
V13#1(#103)-Powell-a; S&K's last-a for Crestwood 9 18 27 61 123 185
2,4-6(#104-108) 5 10 15 35 63 90
V13#3(#105, 4-5/60)-Elvis Presley-c app. only 9 18 27 62 126 190
V14#1-6, V15#1-6, V16#1-4(#109-124) 5 10 15 34 60 85
NOTE: **Meskin** *a-16, 24(2), 33, 47, 50.* **Robinson/Meskin** *a-6.* **Leonard Starr** *a-11. Photo c-13-32, 34-65. Issues 1-3 say "Designed for the More* **Adult** *Readers of* **Comics**" *on cover.*

YOUNG ROMANCE COMICS (Continued from Prize series)
National Periodical Publ.(Arleigh Publ. Corp. No. 127): No. 125, Aug-Sept, 1963 - No. 208, Nov-Dec, 1975
125 9 18 27 59 117 175
126-140 5 10 15 34 60 85
141-153,156-162,165-169 4 8 12 28 47 65
154-Neal Adams-c 5 10 15 34 60 85
155-1st publ. Aragonés-s (no art) 5 10 15 33 57 80
163,164-Toth-a 5 10 15 30 50 70
170-172 (68 pg. Giants): 170-Michell from Young Love ends; Lily Martin, the Swinger begins
5 10 15 33 57 80
173-183 (52 pgs.) 4 8 12 27 44 60
184-196 3 6 9 21 33 45
197-204-(100 pgs.) 8 16 24 55 105 155
205-208 3 6 9 19 30 40

YOUNG ROMANCE: THE NEW 52 VALENTINE'S DAY SPECIAL
DC Comics: Apr, 2013 ($7.99, one-shot)
1-Short stories by various; Superman/Wonder Woman-c by Rocafort; bonus valentines 8.00

YOUNG X-MEN
Marvel Comics: May, 2008 - No. 12, May, 2009 ($2.99)
1-12: 1-Cyclops forms new team; Guggenheim-s/Paquette-a/Dodson-c. 11,12-Acuña-a 3.00

YOUR DREAMS (See Strange World of...)

YOUR HIGHNESS
Dark Horse Comics: 2011 ($7.99, one-shot)
nn-Prequel to 2011 movie; Danny McBride & Jeff Fradley-s/Phillips-a/c 8.00

YOUR PAL ARCHIE
Archie Comic Publications: Sept, 2017 - No. 5, Feb, 2018 ($3.99)
1-5-New stories with classic-style Archie gang, plus back-up reprints in #1-4 4.00

YOUR UNITED STATES
Lloyd Jacquet Studios: 1946
nn-Used in **SOTI**, pg. 309,310; Sid Greene-a 32 64 96 188 307 425

YOUTHFUL HEARTS (Daring Confessions #4 on)
Youthful Magazines: May, 1952 - No. 3, Sept, 1952
1- "Monkey on Her Back" swipes E.C. drug story/Shock SuspenStories #12; Frankie Laine photo on-c; Doug Wildey-a in all 47 94 141 296 498 700
2,3: 2-Vic Damone photo on-c. 3-Johnny Raye photo on-c
29 58 87 172 281 390

YOUTHFUL LOVE (Truthful Love #2)
Youthful Magazines: May, 1950
1 40 80 120 246 411 575

YOUTHFUL ROMANCES
Pix-Parade #1-14/Ribage #15 on: 8-9/49 - No. 5, 4/50; No. 6, 2/51; No. 7, 5/51 - #14, 10/52; #15, 1/53 - #18, 7/53; No. 5, 9/53 - No. 9, 8/54
1-(1st series)-Titled Youthful Love-Romances 40 80 120 246 411 575
2-Walter Johnson c-1-4 25 50 75 150 245 340
3-5 22 44 66 128 209 290
6,7,9-14(10/52, Pix-Parade; becomes Daring Love #15). 10(1/52)-Mel Torme photo-c/story. 12-Tony Bennett photo-c, 8pg. story & text bio.13-Richard Hayes (singer) photo-c/story; Bob & Ray photo/text story. 14-Doris Day photo/text story
20 40 60 120 195 270
8-Frank Sinatra photo/text story; Wood-c/a 31 62 93 182 296 410
15-18 (Ribage)-All have photos on-c. 15-Spike Jones photo-c/story. 16-Tony Bavaar photo-c
20 40 60 117 189 260
5(9/53, Ribage)-Les Paul & Mary Ford photo-c/story; Charlton Heston photo/text story
19 38 57 111 176 240

	GD	VG	FN	VF	VF/NM	NM-
	2.0	4.0	6.0	8.0	9.0	9.2

6-9: 6-Bobby Wayne (singer) photo-c/story; Debbie Reynolds photo/text story. 7(2/54)-Tony Martin photo-c/story; Cyd Charise photo/text story. 8(5/54)-Gordon McCrae photo-c/story. (8/54)-Ralph Flanagan (band leader) photo-c/story; Audrey Hepburn photo/text story 19 38 57 109 172 235

YTHAQ: NO ESCAPE
Marvel Comics (Soleil): 2009 - No. 3, 2009 ($5.99, limited series)
1-3-English language version of French comic; Arleston-s/Floch-a 6.00

YTHAQ: THE FORSAKEN WORLD
Marvel Comics (Soleil): 2008 - No. 3, 2009 ($5.99, limited series)
1-3-English language version of French comic; Arleston-s/Floch-a 6.00

Y: THE LAST MAN
DC Comics (Vertigo): Sept, 2002 - No. 60, Mar, 2008 ($2.95/$2.99)
1-Intro. Yorick Brown; Brian K. Vaughan-s/Pia Guerra-a/J.G. Jones-c 6 12 18 41 76 110
2 2 4 6 11 16 20
3-5 1 2 3 5 6 8
6-10 5.00
11-59: 16,17-Chadwick-a. 21,22-Parlov-a. 32,39-41,48,53,54-Sudzuka-a. 3.00
60-($4.99) Final issue; sixty years in the future 6.00
... Double Feature Edition (2002, $5.95) r/#1,2 2 4 6 9 12 15
... Special Edition (2009, $1.00) r/#1, "After Watchmen" trade dress on cover 3.00
... - Cycles TPB (2003, $12.95) r/#6-10; sketch pages by Guerra 13.00
... - Girl on Girl TPB (2005, $12.99) r/#32-36 13.00
... - Kimono Dragons TPB (2006, $14.99) r/#43-48 15.00
... - Motherland TPB (2007, $14.99) r/#49-54 15.00
... - One Small Step TPB (2004, $12.95) r/#11-17 13.00
... - Paper Dolls TPB (2006, $14.99) r/#37-42 15.00
... - Ring of Truth TPB (2005, $14.99) r/#24-31 15.00
... - Safeword TPB (2004, $12.95) r/#18-23 13.00
... - Unmanned TPB (2002, $12.95) r/#1-5 15.00
... - Whys and Wherefores TPB (2008, $14.99) r/#55-60 15.00
... - The Deluxe Edition Book One HC (2008, $29.99, dustjacket) oversized r/#1-10; Guerra sketch pages 30.00
... - The Deluxe Edition Book Two HC (2009, $29.99, dustjacket) oversized r/#11-23; full script to #18 30.00
... - The Deluxe Edition Book Three HC (2010, $29.99, dustjacket) oversized r/#24-36; full script to #36 30.00
... - The Deluxe Edition Book Four HC (2010, $29.99, dustjacket) oversized r/#37-48; full script to #42 30.00
... - The Deluxe Edition Book Five HC (2011, $29.99, dustjacket) oversized r/#49-60; full script to #60 30.00

Y2K: THE COMIC
New England Comics Press: Oct, 1999 ($3.95, one-shot)
1-Y2K scenarios and survival tips 6.00

YUPPIES FROM HELL (Also see Son of...)
Marvel Comics: 1989 ($2.95, B&W, one-shot, direct sales, 52 pgs.)
1-Satire 4.00

ZAGO (..., Jungle Prince) (My Story #5 on)(See Unusual Comics)
Fox Feature Syndicate: Sept, 1948 - No. 4, Mar, 1949
1-Blue Beetle app.; partial-r/Atomic #4 (Toni Luck) 87 174 261 553 952 1350
2,3-Kamen-a 77 154 231 493 847 1200
4-Baker-c 103 206 309 659 1130 1600

ZANE GREY'S STORIES OF THE WEST
Dell Publishing Co./Gold Key 11/64: No. 197, 9/48 - No. 996, 5-7/59; 11/64 (All painted-c)
Four Color 197(#1)(9/48) 12 24 36 84 185 285
Four Color 222,230,236('49) 8 16 24 55 105 155
Four Color 246,255,270,301,314,333,346 6 12 18 37 66 95
Four Color 357,372,395,412,433,449,467,484 5 10 15 33 57 80
Four Color 511-Kinstler-a; Kubert-a 5 10 15 35 63 90
Four Color 532,555,583,604,616,632(5/55) 5 10 15 33 57 80
27(9-11/55) - 39(9-11/58) 4 8 12 28 47 65
Four Color 996(5-7/59) 5 10 15 33 57 80
10131-411-(11/64-G.K.)-Nevada; r/4-Color #996 3 6 9 21 33 45

ZANY (Magazine)(Satire)(See Frantic & Ratfink)
Candor Publ. Co.: Sept, 1958 - No. 4, May, 1959
1-Bill Everett-c 19 38 57 111 176 240
2-4: 4-Everett-c 14 28 42 76 108 140

ZATANNA (See Adv. Comics #413, JLA #161, Supergirl #1, World's Finest Comics #274)
DC Comics: July, 1993 - No. 4, Oct, 1993 ($1.95, limited series)
1 1 3 4 6 8 10
2-4 6.00
...: Everyday Magic (2003, $5.95, one-shot) Dini-s/Mays-a/Bolland-c; Constantine app. 4 8 12 23 37 50
Special 1(1987, $2.00)-Gray Morrow-c/a 2 4 6 10 14 18

ZATANNA
DC Comics: Jul, 2010 - No. 16, Oct, 2011 ($2.99)
1-Dini-s/Roux-a/c 2 4 6 11 16 20
1-Variant-c by Bolland 3 6 9 19 30 40
2-6-Variant-c by Bolland 2 4 6 10 14 18
2-10,12: 4,5,7-Hardin-a. 7-Beechen-s. 8-Chang-a 6.00
11,13,14-Hughes-c 2 4 6 11 16 20
15-Hughes-c 5 10 15 34 60 85
16-Hughes-c 7 14 21 44 82 120
...: Shades of the Past TPB (2011, $19.99) r/#7-16; cover gallery 32.00
...: The Mistress of Magic TPB (2011, $17.99) r/#1-6; variant cover gallery 24.00

ZAZA, THE MYSTIC (Formerly Charlie Chan; This Magazine Is Haunted V2#12 on)
Charlton Comics: No. 10, Apr, 1956 - No. 11, Sept, 1956
10,11 17 34 51 98 154 210

ZEALOT (Also see WildC.A.T.S: Covert Action Teams)
Image Comics: Aug, 1995 - No. 3, Nov, 1995 ($2.50, limited series)
1-3 3.00

ZEGRA (Jungle Empress) (Formerly Tegra)(My Love Life #6 on)
Fox Feature Syndicate: No. 2, Oct, 1948 - No. 5, April, 1949
2 90 180 270 576 988 1400
3-5 61 122 183 390 670 950

ZEN INTERGALACTIC NINJA
No Publisher: 1987 -1993 ($1.75/$2.00, B&W)
1 8 16 24 54 102 150
2-Copyright-Stern & Cote 3 6 9 21 33 45
3-6: Copyright-Stern & Cote 2 4 6 8 10 12
V2#1-4-($2.00) 4.00
V3#1-5-($2.95) 4.00
... :Christmas Special 1 (1992, $2.95) 4.00
... :Earth Day Special 1 (1993, $2.95) 4.00

ZEN (Intergalactic Ninja)
Zen Comics Publishing: No. 0, Apr, 2003 - No. 4, Aug, 2003 ($2.95)
0-4-Bill Maus-a/Steve Stern-s. 0-Wraparound-c 3.00

ZEN, INTERGALACTIC NINJA (mini-series)
Zen Comics/Archie Comics: Sept, 1992 - No. 3, 1992 ($1.25)(Formerly a B&W comic by Zen Comics)
1-3: 1-Origin Zen; contains mini-poster 4.00

ZEN INTERGALACTIC NINJA
Entity Comics: No. 0, June-July, 1993 - No. 3, 1994 ($2.95, B&W, limited series)
0-Gold foil stamped-c; photo-c of Zen model 5.00
1-3: Gold foil stamped-c; Bill Maus-c/a 5.00
0-(1993, $3.50, color)-Chromium-c by Jae Lee 4.00
...Sourcebook 1-(1993, $3.50) 4.00
...Sourcebook '94-(1994, $3.50) 4.00
... Spring Spectacular 1 (1994, $2.95, B&W) Gold foil logo 4.00

ZEN INTERGALACTIC NINJA: APRIL FOOL'S SPECIAL
Parody Press: 1994 ($2.50, B&W)
1-w/flip story of Renn Intergalactic Chihuahua 5.00

ZEN INTERGALACTIC NINJA COLOR
Entity Comics: 1994 - No. 7, 1995 ($2.25)
1-($3.95)-Chromium die cut-c 5.00
1, 0-($2.25)-Newsstand; Jae Lee-c; r/...All New Color Special #0 4.00
2-($2.50)-Flip book 4.00
2-($3.50)-Flip book, polybagged w/chromium trading card 5.00
3-7 4.00
Summer Special (1994, $2.95) 4.00
Yearbook: Hazardous Duty 1 (1995) 4.00
Zen-isms 1 (1995, 2.95) 4.00
Ashcan-Tour of the Universe-(no price) w/flip cover 4.00

ZEN INTERGALACTIC NINJA COMMEMORATIVE EDITION
Zen Comics Publishing: 1997 ($5.95, color)
1-Stern-s/Cote-a 6.00

ZEN INTERGALACTIC NINJA: HARD BOUNTY
1First Comics: 2015 - No. 6 ($3.99, limited series)
1-Stern-s/Mychaels-a 4.00

ZEN INTERGALACTIC NINJA MILESTONE
Entity Comics: 1994 - No. 3, 1994 ($2.95, limited series)
1-3: Gold foil logo; r/Defend the Earth 4.00

ZEN INTERGALACTIC NINJA STARQUEST
Entity Comics: 1994 - No. 6, 1995 ($2.95, B&W)
1-6: Gold foil logo 4.00

ZEN, INTERGALACTIC NINJA: THE HUNTED
Entity Comics: 1993 - No. 3, 1994 ($2.95, B&W, limited series)
1-3: Newsstand Edition; foil logo 4.00
1-($3.50)-Polybagged w/chromium card by Kieth; foil logo 5.00

ZERO GIRL
DC Comics (Homage): Feb, 2001 - No. 5, Jun, 2001 ($2.95, limited series)
1-5-Sam Kieth-s/a 3.00
TPB (2001, $14.95) r/#1-5; intro. by Alan Moore 15.00

ZERO GIRL: FULL CIRCLE
DC Comics (Homage): Jan, 2003 - No. 5, May, 2003 ($2.95, limited series)
1-5-Sam Kieth-s/a 3.00
TPB (2003, $17.95) r/#1-5 18.00

ZERO HOUR: CRISIS IN TIME (Also see Showcase '94 #8-10)
DC Comics: No. 4(#1), Sept, 1994 - No. 0(#5), Oct, 1994 ($1.50, limited series)
4(#1)-0(#5) 4.00
"Ashcan"-(1994, free, B&W, 8 pgs.) several versions exist 3.00
TPB ('94, $9.95) 10.00

ZERO KILLER
Dark Horse Comics: Jul, 2007 - No.6, Oct, 2009 ($2.99)
1-6-Arvid Nelson-s/Matt Camp-a 3.00

ZERO PATROL, THE
Continuity Comics: Nov, 1984 - No. 2 ($1.50); 1987 - No. 5, May, 1989 ($2.00)
1,2: Neal Adams-c/a; Megalith begins 5.00
1-5 (#1,2-reprints above, 1987) 4.00

06 PROTOCOL, THE
AfterShock Comics: Sept, 2022 - Present ($4.99, limited series)
1,2-Lee Turner-s/Cliff Richards-a 5.00

ZERO TOLERANCE
First Comics: Oct, 1990 - No. 4, Jan, 1991 ($2.25, limited series)
1-4: Tim Vigil-c/a(p) (his 1st color limited series) 3.00

Y: The Last Man #46 © Vaughan & Guerra

Zatanna (2010) #7 © DC

Zombies vs. Robots #1 © IDW

	GD 2.0	VG 4.0	FN 6.0	VF 8.0	VF/NM 9.0	NM- 9.2

ZIGGY PIG – SILLY SEAL COMICS (See Animal Fun, Animated Movie-Tunes, Comic Capers, Krazy Komics, Silly Tunes & Super Rabbit)
Timely Comics (CmPL): Fall, 1944 - No. 4, Summer, 1945; No. 5, Summer, 1946; No. 6, Sept, 1946

	GD	VG	FN	VF	VF/NM	NM-
1-Vs. the Japanese	43	86	129	271	461	650
2-(Spring, 1945)	28	56	84	165	270	375
3-5	22	44	66	128	209	290
6-Infinity-c	24	48	72	142	234	325
I.W. Reprint #1(1958)-r/Krazy Komics	5	10	14	20	24	28
I.W. Reprint #2,7,8	5	10	14	20	24	28

ZIGGY PIG – SILLY SEAL COMICS (Marvel 80th Anniversary salute)
Marvel Comics: May, 2019 ($3.99, one-shot)

1-Tieri & Cerilli-s/Chabot-a; Doctor Doom app.; Deadpool cameo 4.00

ZIP COMICS
MLJ Magazines: Feb, 1940 - No. 47, Summer, 1944 (#1-7?: 68 pgs.)

	GD	VG	FN	VF	VF/NM	NM-
1-Origin Kalathar the Giant Man, The Scarlet Avenger, & Steel Sterling; Mr. Satan (by Edd Ashe), Nevada Jones (masked hero) & Zambini, the Miracle Man, War Eagle, Captain Valor begins	476	952	1428	3475	6138	8800
2-Nevada Jones adds mask & horse Blaze	284	568	852	1818	3109	4400
3-Biro robot-c	300	600	900	2070	3635	5200
4,5-Biro WWII-c	226	452	678	1446	2473	3500
6,7-Biro-c	206	412	618	1318	2259	3200
8-Bondage/torture-c by Biro	258	516	774	1651	2826	4000
9-Last Kalathar & Mr. Satan; classic-c	300	600	900	2070	3635	5200
10-Inferno, the Flame Breather begins, ends #13	300	600	900	2010	3505	5000
11-Inferno without costume	187	374	561	1197	2049	2900
12-Biro bondage/torture-c with dwarf ghouls	219	438	657	1402	2401	3400
13-Electrocution-c	258	516	774	1651	2826	4000
14-Biro bondage/torture guillotine-c	226	452	678	1446	2473	3500
15-Classic spider-c	239	478	717	1530	2615	3700
16-Female hanging execution-c by Biro (Rare)	265	530	795	1694	2897	4100
17-Last Scarlet Avenger; women in bondage being cooked alive-c by Biro	443	886	1329	3234	5717	8200
18-Wilbur begins (9/41, 1st app.); headlights sci-fi-c	649	1298	1947	4738	8369	12,000
19-Horror-c	271	542	813	1734	2967	4200
20-Origin & 1st app. Black Jack (11/41); Hitler-c	383	766	1149	2681	4691	6700
21-Sinister Nazi using lethal chemical weapons on the General-c	232	464	696	1485	2543	3600
22-Classic Nazi Grim Reaper w/sickle, V for Victory-c	811	1622	2433	5920	10,460	15,000
23-Nazi WWII-c	181	362	543	1158	1979	2800
24,25: 25-Last Nevada Jones	155	310	465	992	1696	2400
26-Classic Nazi/Japanese "Remember Pearl Harbor!" WWII cover; Black Witch begins; last Captain Valor (scarce)	300	600	900	2010	3505	5000
27-Intro. Web (7/42) plus-c app.; Japanese WWII-c	343	686	1029	2400	4200	6000
28-Origin Web; classic Baron Gestapo Nazi WWII-c	309	618	927	2163	3782	5400
29-The Hyena app. (scarce); Nazi WWII-c	300	600	900	1950	3375	4800
30-WWII-c	290	580	870	1856	3178	4500
31,35-WWII-c. 35-Last Zambini, Black Jack	232	464	696	1485	2543	3600
32-Classic skeleton Nazi WWII-c	541	1082	1623	3950	6975	10,000
33-Japanese war-c showing nurses bound, blindfolded, lined up at a firing squad	649	1298	1947	4738	8369	12,000
34-Japanese WWII bondage & hanging-c; 1st Applejack app.	300	600	900	1980	3440	4900
36-38: 38-Last Web issue	116	232	348	742	1271	1800
39-Red Rube begins (origin, 8/43)	81	162	243	518	884	1250
40-43	65	130	195	416	708	1000
44-46: WWII covers. 45-Wilbur ends	74	148	222	470	810	1150
47-Last issue; scarce	81	162	243	518	884	1250

NOTE: ***Biro** a-5, 9, 17; c-3-17. **Meskin** a-1-3, 5-7, 9, 10, 12, 13, 15, 16 at least. **Montana** c-29, 30, 32-35. **Novick** c-18-28, 31. **Sahle** c-37, 38, 40-46. Bondage c-8, 9, 33, 34. Cover features: Steel Sterling-1-43, 47; (w/ Blackjack-20-27 & Web-27-35), 28-39; (w/Red Rube-40-43); Red Rube-44-47.*

ZIP-JET (Hero)
St. John Publishing Co.: Feb, 1953 - No. 2, Apr-May, 1953

	GD	VG	FN	VF	VF/NM	NM-
1-Rocketman-r from Punch Comics; #1-c from splash in Punch #10	132	264	396	838	1444	2050
2	63	126	189	403	689	975

ZIPPY THE CHIMP (CBS TV Presents...)
Pines (Literary Ent.): No. 50, March, 1957; No. 51, Aug, 1957

	GD	VG	FN	VF	VF/NM	NM-
50,51	9	18	27	50	65	80

Z NATION (Based on the 2014 TV series on Syfy)
Dynamite Entertainment: 2017 - No. 6, 2017 ($3.99)

1-6: 1-Engler & Van Lente-s/Menna-a; multiple covers 4.00

ZODIAC STARFORCE
Dark Horse Comics: Aug, 2015 - No. 4, Feb, 2016 ($3.99, limited series)

1-4-Kevin Panetta-s/Paulina Ganucheau-a. 2-Wada-c. 4-Babs Tarr-c 4.00

ZODIAC STARFORCE: CRIES OF THE FIRE PRINCE
Dark Horse Comics: Jul, 2017 - No. 4, May, 2018 ($3.99, limited series)

1-4-Kevin Panetta-s/Paulina Ganucheau-a 4.00

ZODY, THE MOD ROB
Gold Key: July, 1970

	GD	VG	FN	VF	VF/NM	NM-
1	3	6	9	16	23	30

ZOMBIE
Marvel Comics: Nov, 2006 - No. 4, Feb, 2007 ($3.99, limited series)

1-4-Kyle Hotz-a/c; Mike Raicht-s 4.00
...: Simon Garth (1/08 - No. 4, 4/08) Hotz-s/a/c 4.00

ZOMBIE BOY
Timbuktu Graphics/Antarctic Press: Mar, 1988 - Nov, 1996 ($1.50/$2.50/$2.95, B&W)

1-Mark Stokes-s/a 4.00
...'s Hoodoo Tales (11/89, $1.50) 4.00
... Rises Again (1/94, $2.50) r/#1 and Hoodoo Tales 4.00
1-(Antarctic Press, 11/96, $2.95) new story 4.00

ZOMBIE KING
Image Comics: No. 0, June, 2005 ($2.95, B&W, one-shot)

0-Frank Cho-s/a 5.00

ZOMBIE PROOF
Moonstone: 2007 - Present ($3.50)

1-3: 1-J.C. Vaughn-s/Vincent Spencer-a; two covers by Spencer and Neil Vokes 4.00
1-Baltimore Comic-Con 2007 variant-c by Vokes (ltd. ed. of 500) 6.00
2-Big Apple 2008 Convention Edition; Tucci-c (ltd. ed. of 250) 6.00
3-Convention Edition; Beck-c (ltd. ed. of 100) 6.00
...: Zombie Zoo #1 Virginia Comicon Exclusive Edition (2012, ed. of 150) 10.00
...: Zombie Zoo - WVPOP Exclusive Edition (2012) 10.00

ZOMBIES ASSEMBLE
Marvel Comics: Jul, 2017 - No. 3, Aug, 2017 ($4.99, B&W, manga style back to front)

1-3-English translation of Avengers Japanese manga; Komiyama-s/a 5.00
#0-(9/17) Follows Tony Stark after Avengers: Age of Ultron; Komiyama-s/a 5.00

ZOMBIES ASSEMBLE 2
Marvel Comics: Oct, 2017 - No. 4, Jan, 2018 ($4.99, B&W, manga style back to front)

1-4-Continuation of story from Zombies Assemble #1-3; Komiyama-s/a 5.00

ZOMBIES CHRISTMAS CAROL (See Marvel Zombies Christmas Carol)

ZOMBIES!: ECLIPSE OF THE UNDEAD
IDW Publ.: Nov, 2006 - No. 4, Feb, 2007 ($3.99, limited series)

1-4-Torres-s/Herrera-a; two covers 4.00

ZOMBIES!: FEAST
IDW Publ.: May, 2006 - No. 5, Oct, 2006 ($3.99, limited series)

1-5: 1-Chris Bolton-a/Shane McCarthy-s. 3-Lorenzana-a 4.00

ZOMBIES!: HUNTERS
IDW Publ.: May, 2008 ($3.99)

1-Don Figueroa-a/c; Dara Naraghi-s 4.00

ZOMBIES VS. ROBOTS
IDW Publ.: Oct, 2006 - No. 2, Dec, 2006 ($3.99, limited series)

1-Chris Ryall-s/Ashley Wood-a; two covers by Wood 18.00
2 12.00

ZOMBIES VS. ROBOTS
IDW Publ.: Jan, 2015 - No. 10, Oct, 2015 ($3.99/$4.99)

1-8-Short stories by Chris Ryall-s/Ashley Wood-a and others 5.00
9,10-($4.99) Two covers on each 6.00

ZOMBIES VS. ROBOTS AVENTURE
IDW Publ.: Feb, 2010 - No. 4, May, 2010 ($3.99, limited series)

1-4-Short stories; Ryall-s; art by Matthews III, McCaffrey, & Hernandez; Wood-c 5.00

ZOMBIES VS. ROBOTS: UNDERCITY
IDW Publ.: Apr, 2011 - No. 3, Jun, 2011 ($3.99, limited series)

1-3-Chris Ryall-s/Mark Torres; two covers on each by Torres and Garry Brown 5.00

ZOMBIES VS. ROBOTS VS. AMAZONS
IDW Publ.: Sept, 2007 - No. 3, Feb, 2008 ($3.99, limited series)

1-3-Chris Ryall-s/Ashley Wood-a; two covers by Wood on each 6.00

ZOMBIE TALES THE SERIES

BOOM! Studios: Apr, 2008 - No. 12, Mar, 2009 ($3.99)
1-Niles-s; Lansdale-s/Barreto-a; two covers on each 5.00

ZOMBIE WAR
IDW Publishing: Oct, 2013 - No. 2, Nov, 2013 ($3.99, limited series)
1,2-Kevin Eastman & Tom Skulan-s/Eastman & Eric Talbot-a; 2 covers on each 4.00

ZOMBIE WORLD (one-shots)
Dark Horse Comics
... :Eat Your Heart Out (4/98, $2.95) Kelley Jones-c/s/a 4.00
... :Home For The Holidays (12/97, $2.95) 4.00

ZOMBIE WORLD: CHAMPION OF THE WORMS
Dark Horse Comics: Sept, 1997 - No. 3, Nov, 1997 ($2.95, limited series)
1-3-Mignola & McEown-c/s/a 4.00

ZOMBIE WORLD: DEAD END
Dark Horse Comics: Jan, 1998 - No. 2, Feb, 1998 ($2.95, limited series)
1,2-Stephen Blue-c/s/a 4.00

ZOMBIE WORLD: TREE OF DEATH
Dark Horse Comics: Jun, 1999 - No. 4, Oct, 1999 ($2.95, limited series)
1-4-Mills-s/Deadstock-a 4.00

ZOMBIE WORLD: WINTER'S DREGS
Dark Horse Comics: May, 1998 - No. 4, Aug, 1998 ($2.95, limited series)
1-4-Fingerman-s/Edwards-a 4.00

ZOO ANIMALS
Star Publications: No. 8, 1954 (15¢, 36 pgs.)
8-(B&W for coloring) 10 20 30 56 76 95

ZOO FUNNIES (Tim McCoy #16 on)
Charlton Comics/Children Comics Publ.: Nov, 1945 - No. 15, 1947
101(#1)(11/45, 1st Charlton comic book)-Funny animal; Al Fago-c
25 50 75 150 245 340
2(12/45, 52 pgs.) Classic-c 15 30 45 86 133 180
3-5 12 24 36 69 97 125
6-15: 8-Diana the Huntress app. 10 20 30 56 76 95

ZOO FUNNIES (Becomes Nyoka, The Jungle Girl #14 on?)
Capitol Stories/Charlton Comics: July, 1953 - No. 13, Sept, 1955; Dec, 1984
1-1st app.? Timothy The Ghost; Fago-c/a 14 28 42 82 121 160
2 9 18 27 50 65 80
3-7 8 16 24 44 57 70
8-13-Nyoka app. 10 20 30 58 79 100
1(1984) (Low print run) 1 3 4 6 8 10

ZOOHUNTERS, THE
Aspen MLT: Nov, 2014 - No. 4 ($3.99, limited series)
1-4-Peter Stiegerwald-s/a; five covers on each 4.00

ZOONIVERSE
Eclipse Comics: 8/86 - No. 6, 6/87 ($1.25/$1.75, limited series, Mando paper)
1-6 3.00

ZOO PARADE (TV)
Dell Publishing Co.: #662, 1955 (Marlin Perkins)
Four Color 662 6 12 18 38 69 100

ZOOM COMICS
Carlton Publishing Co.: Dec, 1945 (one-shot)
nn-Dr. Mercy, Satannas, from Red Band Comics; Capt. Milksop origin retold
52 104 156 328 552 775

ZOOT (Rulah Jungle Goddess #17 on)
Fox Feature Syndicate: nd (1946) - No. 16, July, 1948 (Two #13s & 14s)
nn-Funny animal only 34 68 102 199 325 450
2-The Jaguar app. 25 50 75 150 245 340
3(Fall, 1946) - 6-Funny animals & teen-age 17 34 51 100 158 215
7-(6/47)-Rulah, Jungle Goddess (origin/1st app.) 155 310 465 992 1696 2400
8-10 90 180 270 576 988 1400
11-Kamen bondage-c 142 284 426 909 1555 2200
12-Injury-to-eye panels, torture scene 81 162 243 518 884 1250
13(2/48) 71 142 213 454 777 1100
14(3/48)-Used in **SOTI**, pg. 104, "One picture showing a girl nailed by her wrists to trees with blood flowing from the wounds, might be taken straight from an ill. ed. of the Marquis deSade" 206 412 618 1318 2259 3200
13(4/48),14(5/48)-Western True Crime #15 on? 90 180 270 576 988 1400
15,16 77 154 231 493 847 1200

ZORRO (Walt Disney with #882)(TV)(See Eclipse Graphic Album)
Dell Publishing Co.: May, 1949 - No. 15, Sept-Nov, 1961 (Photo-c 882 on)
(Zorro first appeared in a pulp story Aug 19, 1919)
Four Color 228 (#1) 27 54 81 189 420 650
Four Color 425,617,732 12 24 36 82 179 275
Four Color 497,538,574-Kinstler-a 12 24 36 82 179 275
Four Color 882-Photo-c begin;1st TV Disney; Toth-a 14 28 42 96 211 325
Four Color 920,933,960,976-Toth-a in all 10 20 30 66 138 210
Four Color 1003('59)-Toth-a 10 20 30 66 138 210
Four Color 1037-Annette Funicello photo-c 12 24 36 81 176 270
8(12-2/59-60) 7 14 21 48 89 130
9-Toth-a 8 16 24 51 96 140
10,11,13-15-Last photo-c 7 14 21 46 86 125
12-Toth-a; last 10¢ issue 8 16 24 51 96 140
NOTE: ***Warren Tufts** a-4-Color 1037, 8, 9, 10, 13.*

ZORRO (Walt Disney)(TV)
Gold Key: Jan, 1966 - No. 9, Mar, 1968 (All photo-c)
1-Toth-a 7 14 21 44 82 120
2,4,5,7-9-Toth-a. 5-r/F.C. #1003 by Toth 4 8 12 28 47 65
3,6-Tufts-a 4 8 12 27 44 60
NOTE: *#1-9 are reprinted from Dell issues. **Tufts** a-3, 4. #1-r/F.C. #882. #2-r/F.C. #960. #3-r/#12-c & #8 inside. #4-r/#9-c & insides. #6-r/#11(all); #7-r/#14-c. #8-r/F.C. #933 inside & back-c & #976-c. #9-r/F.C. #920.*

ZORRO (TV)
Marvel Comics: Dec, 1990 - No. 12, Nov, 1991 ($1.00)
1-12: Based on TV show. 12-Toth-c 4.00

ZORRO (Also see Mask of Zorro)
Topps Comics: Nov, 1993 - No. 11, Nov, 1994 ($2.50/$2.95)
0-(11/93, $1.00, 20 pgs.)-Painted-c; collector's ed. 3.00
1,4,6-9,11: 1-Miller-c. 4-Mike Grell-c. 6-Mignola-c. 7-Lady Rawhide-c by Gulacy. 8-Perez-c. 10-Julie Bell-c. 11-Lady Rawhide-c 4.00
2-Lady Rawhide-app. (not in costume) 5.00
3-1st app. Lady Rawhide in costume, 3-Lady Rawhide-c by Adam Hughes
2 4 6 9 12 15
5-Lady Rawhide app. 4.00
10-($2.95)-Lady Rawhide-c/app. 4.00
The Lady Wears Red (12/98, $12.95, TPB) r/#1-3 13.00
Zorro's Renegades (2/99, $14.95, TPB) r/#4-8 15.00

ZORRO
Dynamite Entertainment: 2008 - No. 20, 2010 ($3.50)
1-Origin retold; Wagner-s; three covers 3.50
2-20-Two covers on all 3.50

ZORRO BLACK & WHITE NOIR
American Mythology Prods.: 2022 ($3.99, limited series)
1-New stories in B&W plus reprint with Toth-s/a 4.00

ZORRO: FELIZ NAVIDAD
American Mythology Prods.: 2022 ($3.99, one-shot)
1-Christmas-themed short stories and reprints 4.00

ZORRO FLIGHTS
American Mythology Prods.: 2021 - Present ($3.99, limited series)
1-Don McGregor-s/Vincenzo Carratu-a; preview of Zorro: The Dailies 4.00

ZORRO: GALLEON OF THE DEAD
American Mythology Prods.: 2020 - No. 4, 2021 ($3.99, limited series)
1-4-Mike Wolfer-s/Alessandro Miracolo-a 4.00

ZORRO IN THE LAND THAT TIME FORGOT
American Mythology Prods.: 2020 - No. 4, 2021 ($3.99, limited series)
1-4-Mike Wolfer-s/Alessandro Ranaldi-a 4.00

ZORRO: LEGENDARY ADVENTURES
American Mythology Prods.: 2018 - Present ($3.99)
1-4-English reprints of French Zorro comics from 1975-1976; Robert Rigot-a 4.00
... Book 2 (2019 - No. 4, 2019, $3.99) 1-4-Art by Marcello & Rigot 4.00

ZORRO MASTERS
American Mythology Prods.: 2019; 2022 ($3.99)
1-Reprints Four Color #1003; art by Alex Toth 4.00
Vol. 2 1-Reprints Four Color #976 & Dell issue #12 (1960); art by Alex Toth 4.00

ZORRO MATANZAS
Dynamite Entertainment: 2010 - No. 4, 2010 ($3.99, limited series)
1-4-Mayhew-a/McGregor-s 4.00

ZORRO NEW WORLD
American Mythology Prods.: 2021 - No. 4, 2022 ($3.99, limited series)
1-4-Reprints of stories from the 1990 Marvel series; Mario Capaldi-a 4.00

ZORRO RIDES AGAIN
Dynamite Entertainment: 2011 - No. 12, 2012 ($3.99)
1-12: 1-6-Wagner-s/Polls-a. 7-12-Snyder III-a. 10-Lady Zorro on cover 4.00

ZORRO: RISE OF THE OLD GODS
American Mythology Prods.: 2019 - No. 4, 2019 ($3.99, limited series)
1-4-Jason Pell-s/Puis Calzada-a. 1-Main cover by Kaluta 4.00

ZORRO: SACRILEGE
American Mythology Prods.: 2019 - No. 4 ($3.99, limited series)
1-4: 1,2-Mike Wolfer-s/Mauricio Melo-a. 1-Main cover by Kaluta. 3,4-Miracolo-a 4.00

ZORRO: SWORDS OF HELL
American Mythology Prods.: 2018 - No. 4, 2019 ($3.99, limited series)
1-4-David Avallone-s/Roy Allan Martinez-a 4.00

ZORRO TIMELESS TALES
American Mythology Prods.: 2020 ($3.99, limited series)
1,2-Nadaud-s/Marcello-a; art in the style of the Toth stories 4.00

ZOT!
Eclipse Comics: 4/84 - No. 10, 7/85; No. 11, 1/87 - No. 36 7/91 ($1.50, Baxter-p)
1 5.00
2,3 4.00
4-10: 4-Origin. 10-Last color issue 3.00
10 1/2 (6/86, 25¢, Not Available Comics) Ashcan; art by Feazell & Scott McCloud 4.00
11-14,15-35-($2.00-c) B&W issues 3.00
14 1/2 (Adventures of Zot! in Dimension 10 1/2)(7/87) Antisocialman app. 3.00
36-($2.95-c) B&W 5.00
... The Complete Black and White Collection TPB (2008, $24.95) r/#11-36 with commentary, interviews and bonus artwork 25.00

Z-2 COMICS (Secret Agent...)(See Holyoke One-Shot #7)

ZULU (See Movie Classics)

ZVRC (Zombies vs Robots Classics)
Image Comics: Mar, 2022 - No. 4, Jun, 2022 ($3.99/$5.99/$6.99, limited series)
1-($3.99)-Chris Ryall-s/Ashley Wood-a 4.00
2,4-($5.99) 6.00
3-($6.99) 7.00

Terry's Comics

WHO IS TERRY'S OLD SCHOOL COMICS?

TERRY'S COMICS IS A COMIC BOOK DEALER WHO IS ALSO A COLLECTOR. TERRY'S COMICS IS ALWAYS LOOKING FOR QUALITY COMICS TO HELP COLLECTORS FILL IN THEIR COLLECTIONS.

CGC AUTHORIZED DEALER

WHY SELL YOUR COMICS TO TERRY?

TRAVEL: I WILL COME TO VIEW YOUR COLLECTION.
CASH OFFERS: I CAN PAY FOR YOUR ENTIRE COLLECTION IN CASH.
HIGH PRICES PAID: I ALWAYS NEED NEW MATERIAL.
LOCATION: ASSOCIATTES all across the United States.
NO COST APPRAISALS: I DO NOT CHARGE YOU TO APPRAISE YOUR COLLECTION.*
FINDERS FEE: I PAY A FINDERS THAT LEADS ME TO A COLLECTION PURCHASE.
CONSIGNMENT: CONSIGNMENTS ARE FULLY DOCUMENTED AND INSURED.
* THERE IS A CHARGE FOR WRITTEN PROFESSIONAL EVALUATION FOR INSURANCE

25¢

TERRY'S COMICS

WHY BUY YOUR COMICS FROM TERRY?

Experience: We have been buying and selling vintage comics since 1976.
Customer Service: We have thousands of satisfied, repeat customers.
Tight Grading: Grading is as strict as possible to keep all our customers happy.
Guarantee: We offer a full refund if you are not satisfied.
Selection: Large selection of vintage comics.
Credentials: Overstreet Price Guide adviser, CGC authorized dealer.
Fast Shipping: Most orders are shipped within two business days of payment.

percentage of guide I pay you:
TIMELY: 80-200%
ATLAS: 55-200%
COVERLESS: 10-100% OF GOOD
DC GOLDEN AGE: 50 - 150%
MISC. GOLDEN AGE: 60-100%
MARVEL SILVER AGE: 40-100%
DC SILVER AGE: 40-90%
ALL OTHERS: 20-200%

I WILL PAY YOU FOR POOR TO MINT GOLD & SILVER AGE COMICS, I WANT SUPERHERO, HORROR, CRIME, WAR, TEEN, ROMANCE, CLASSICS, ETC.

I CAN AND WILL BEAT ANY OFFER FOR TIMELY/ATLAS COLLECTIONS.

I WANT TO BUY YOUR JUNKY OLD COMICS.

PHONE: (360) 846-3714
(714) 288-8993
E-MAIL: Terry@terryscomics.com
info@terryscomics.com
WEBSITE: terryscomics.com

PayPal VERIFIED
MasterCard VISA AMERICAN EXPRESS DISCOVER NETWORK

TERRY'S COMICS
PO BOX 1186
KELSO, WA 98626

© Gilberton

FRANK MILLER PRESENTS
ANCIENT ENEMIES
ENTER: THE GEEK
DiDIO BEYRUTH
2 OF 6
MILLER KUBERT MARANVILLE SILVESTRI
FOUR
FRANK MILLER'S RONIN BOOK II
MILLER · TAN · HENRIQUES
DAN DIDIO CALAFIORE
FRANK MILLER PRESENTS
FRANK MILLER'S PANDORA
FIERCELY INDEPENDENT

FMP

Bill Hughes
Paid You How Much?

CALL NOW FOR IMMEDIATE PAYMENT!!

ALWAYS SEEKING THE FOLLOWING:

Pre-1965 Disney Comics & Posters
Vintage Tarzan Books, Comics & Posters
Pre-1960 Western Comics & Posters
Early Popeye, Betty Boop & Krazy Kat
Vintage Our Gang, Marx Bros., 3-Stooges
Vintage Lone Ranger, Dick Tracy, Green Hornet
Charlie Chaplin, Buster Keaton, Harold Lloyd
Horror & Sci-Fi Poster and Stills
High-Grade Warren & Skywald Magazines
Pre-1937 Pulps & Fantasy Books

William Hughes' Vintage Collectables

P.O. Box 270244
Flower Mound, TX 75027
Office: 972-539-9190
Mobile: 973-432-4070

www.VintageCollectables.net
Email: whughes199@yahoo.com
eBay User Name: comic-warehouse

Senior Advisor
Overstreet
Price Guide

SHIELDS UP

Everyone knows the days of keeping unbagged comic books lying around are long gone – bags and boards are a forgone conclusion in this modern world of collecting. But what about when a bag and board aren't enough? Do you want to lie awake all night worrying that your comic is developing irreversible stresses that will reduce its value a thousandfold? You need something a little tougher to keep that comic safe, and Ironguard Supplies has just the thing. In addition to a full range of bags and boards in all sizes, Ironguard now offers comic toploaders, rigid sleeves that will keep your comic protected from even the most unforgiving longbox. Sleep easy, my friend.

Get 20% off with code

OVERSTREET

See the full line at ironguardsupplies.com

/ironguardsupplies

© 2022 Ironguard Supplies. All rights Vreserved.

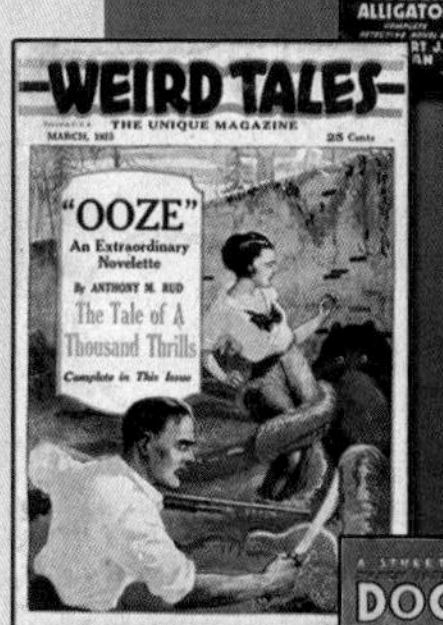

ACTIVELY BUYING

High prices paid. All genres wanted. One piece or lifetime collections. No collection too large or small.

ACTIVELY SELLING

Thousands of Pulps in stock.
We love servicing your want lists.
Items added to our website weekly.

www.FantasyIllustrated.net

DEALING SINCE 1969

Prompt professional service. Specializing in Pulp magazines and science fiction/fantasy/horror first editions. Vintage paperbacks and comic books.

Contact DAVE SMITH

(425) 750-4513 • (360) 652-0339
rocketbat@msn.com
P.O. Box 248 Silvana, WA 98287
www.FantasyIllustrated.net

SAVE THE DATE

FREE COMIC BOOK DAY

May 4, 2024

freecomicbookday.com

TM

SUBSCRIBE & FOLLOW

WE BUY OLD COMICS!

$ $ $ $ 1930's TO 1980's $ $ $ $

GOLDEN AGE * SILVER AGE * BRONZE AGE

COMIC INTERLUDE

Buying * Selling * Trading Comic Books Since 1987!

- Over 35 Years Experience -

- Overstreet Advisor -

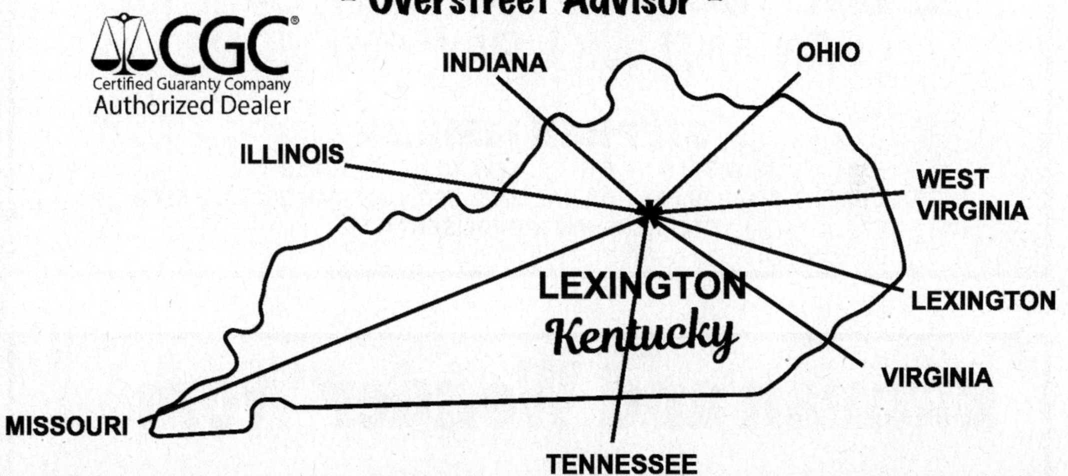

Why call us? Because We're confident we will pay you more!
We buy all Titles Any condition. Any collection big or small
Visit our retail store in Lexington for a free appraisal

WE ARE ALWAYS BUYING:

Comic Book Collections from 1930's to 1980's
Horror & Adventure Magazines from 1940's to 1980's
Pulp Magazines from 1900's to 1950's
Original Artwork Comic Book Covers, Pages, Sketches

Contact: Kevin Forbes / Owner 859-321-4325
Email: thecomicinterludeky@gmail.com
393 Waller Ave., Ste. 10, Lexington, KY 40502

WANTED

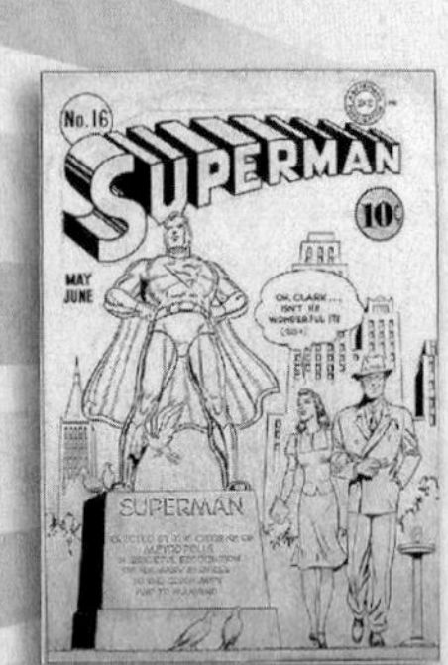

COMIC BOOK ART

COMIC STRIP ART

BEFORE YOU SELL YOUR ART, CALL ME.
I CAN AND WILL PAY YOU MORE.

STEPHEN FISHLER
36 W 37TH ST, 6TH FL, NEW YORK, NY 10018
TOLL-FREE 1.800.229.6387 OR CALL 212.260.4147 FAX 212.260.4304
STEPHENF@METROPOLISENT.COM

Batman and Wonder Woman Collectors

P.O. Box 604925
Flushing, NY
11360-4925

email: batt90@aol.com
wwali@aol.com

COMIC CAVE CANADA

CA-A-A-AVE MA-A-A-N!

MS. TAMARA

#1 DEALER IN CANADA

LARGEST PRIVATE COLLECTOR IN CANADA
NOW OFFERING HIS SERVICES TO THE PUBLIC.
INVESTMENT GRADE QUALITY HIGH END BOOKS ALWAYS FOR SALE.

OVER ONE MILLION COMICS SOLD/BOUGHT LAST YEAR! WATCH OUR DAILY AUCTIONS ONLINE! DOWNLOAD THE "WHATNOT" APP AND FOLLOW: COMICCAVECANADA FOR EXCITING REAL TIME SHOWS! WATCH OUR SHOW ON YOUTUBE 'CAVEMAN COLLECTIBLES' PRESTIGIOUS SHOWROOM IS BY APPOINTMENT ONLY FOR PREFERRED COLLECTORS-CALL FOR DETAILS.

WE BUY AND SELL ALL COMIC BOOKS!
TOP VALUE AND FAIR MARKET PRICES PAID!

LARGEST VINTAGE COMIC BOOK COLLECTION IN CANADA
WITH OVER 150,000 VINTAGE 10,12 & 15 CENT MARVEL AND DC COMICS
2000 LONG BOXES WITH BRAND NEW UNCIRCULATED
OLD STOCK FROM 1973-2016

Authorized CGC dealer: submissions, collector sales, appraisals.
CGC pre-screen advice/opinion before submissions are free at Comic Cave Canada.
Trust in the 'Caveman' Sean Prosje. Caveman is an Overstreet advisor
Professional clean and press services with 'no damage' guarantee.
Don't risk your precious books with amateurs.

CGC COMICCAVECANADA.COM whatnot

905-808-8185 1104 Hwy 5 West, Dundas, Ontario, L9H 5E2 Canada

FIRST
COMICS NEWS
FIRST COMICS NEWS
COLUMNISTS
Alex Wright
Barry Gregory
Ben Herman
Bill Black
Bob Almond
Christopher Watts
Dærick Gröss Sr.
Matthew Pulido
Miguel Ortiz
Tanya Tate
Tim Chizmar
CONTRIBUTORS
Al Nickerson
Buzz Dixon
Holly Golightly
Howard Chaykin
J. C. Vaughn
Joshua 1:9 Holley
Mike Bullock
Scott McDaniel
PODCASTERS
Jamie Coville
Mark Torres
Roland Mann
Steven Butler
REPORTERS
Chris Squires
Eric N. Bennett
Francis Sky
Grant Offenberger
Joeseph Simon
Mark Davis
Martin Boruta
Peter Breau
Phil Latter
REVIEWERS
Francis Garbut
Giovanni Aria
Joshua Pantalleresco
Ric Croxton
Wayne Hall
EDITORIAL STAFF
Matthew Szewczyk ♦ MANAGING EDITOR
Richard Vasseur ♦ BUREAU CHIEF CANADA
Rik Offenberger ♦ EDITOR-IN-CHIEF
CLASSIC HEROES
© DC Comics
INDIE HEROES
© G-Man Comics
MOVIE HEROES

COSMIC COMICS!
BUY SELL TRADE
Est. 1996
LAS VEGAS, NV
4,000 SQFT. OF COMIC GOODNESS
LOCATED MINUTES FROM THE STRIP!
BRIAN SAYS:
OVER 50.000 BACK ISSUES FROM THE 1950'S TO THE PRESENT!
10,000+ GRAPHICS NOVELS!
PLUS, T-SHIRTS, TOYS AND DO-DADS!
Mention this ad for 10% off Back Issues
3830 E Flamingo Las Vegas, NV 89121
702-451-6611 • info@cosmiccomicslv.com
WWW.COSMICCOMICSLV.COM

BUSINESS CARD ADS

To have your ads seen here
in future editions,
contact our Advertising Dept.
Gemstone Publishing, Inc.
10150 York Rd., Suite 300
Hunt Valley, MD 21030
or e-mail feedback@gemstonepub.com.

BUYINGOLDCOMICS.COM

PAYING CASH FOR YOUR COMIC BOOK COLLECTION!

ALWAYS BUYING COMICS .COM

10,000 Backissues & Counting!
10% off 1st order with code:
OVERSTREET23

simple tragic collectibles

Your 24/7 online comic store!
simpletragic.com

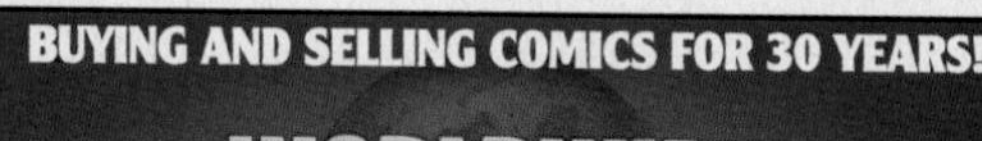

WORLDWIDE COMICS

ALWAYS BUYING! CALL US TODAY!

SENIOR OVERSTREET ADVISOR

wwcomics.com

STEPHEN RITTER • stephen@wwcomics.com

Tel: (830) 368-4103 • 29369 Raintree Ridge, Fair Oaks Ranch, TX 78015 (San Antonio Area)

COMICS GUARANTY, LLC Charter Member Dealer

BATMAN WONDER WOMAN COLLECTORS

E-mail: batt90@aol.com
wwali@aol.com

COLLECTORS
P.O. Box 604925
Flushing, NY 11360-4925

Richard A. Vincent

THE COLLECTION DRAWER CO.
1818 S. Quebec Way, Suite #12-12
Denver, Colorado 80231-5616
303-368-7873

Email: Rich@CollectionDrawer.com
www.collectiondrawer.com

The lowest prices in Kentucky and Tennessee on New & Back Issue Comic Books, Graphic Novels, Trade Paperbacks & more!

Since 1977

SPECIALIZING IN BUYING LARGE COLLECTIONS!
(At our place our yours; we travel for large acquisitions)

Largest selection of Back Issue Comic Books in Kentucky or Tennessee (100,000+)

ALL NEW COMICS, GRAPHIC NOVELS & TRADE PAPERBACKS DISCOUNTED

FREE SUBSCRIPTION SERVICE
(No minimum or advance deposit required.)

2 Store Locations in Kentucky: Louisville * Bowling Green
3 Stores in Middle Tennessee: Nashville * Madison * Murfreesboro

Call individual store locations or check online for our hours.
www.TheGreatEscapeOnLine.com

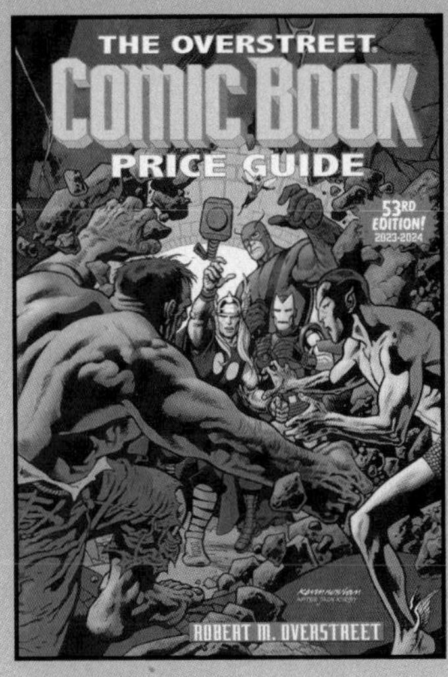

DEALERS • PUBLISHERS • COLLECTORS

ADVERTISE IN OVERSTREET®

53 YEARS OF REACHING SERIOUS COMIC BOOK FANS!

FOR MORE INFORMATION, EMAIL US AT

FEEDBACK@GEMSTONEPUB.COM

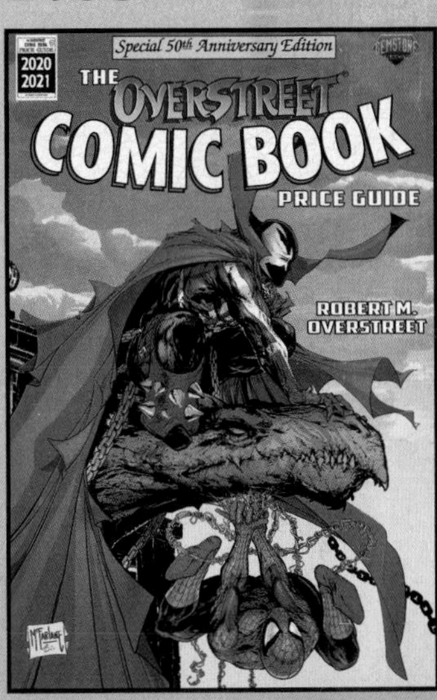

WWW.GEMSTONEPUB.COM

ll characters ©2023 respective Copyright holders. Overstreet® is a
egistered Trademark of Gemstone Publishing. All rights reserved.

DIRECTORY LISTINGS

(PAID ADVERTISING - STORE LISTINGS)

You can have your store listed here for very reasonable rates. Send for details for next year's Guide. The following list of stores have paid to be included in this list. We cannot assume any responsibility in your dealings with these shops. This list is provided for your information only. When planning trips, it would be advisable to make appointments in advance. Remember, to get your shop included in the next edition, contact us for rates.

Gemstone Publishing, Inc.
10150 York Rd., Suite 300
Hunt Valley, MD 21030
E-MAIL: feedback@gemstonepub.com

Items stocked by these shops are noted at the end of each listing and are coded as follows:

(1) Golden Age Comics
(2) Silver Age Comics
(3) Bronze Age Comics
(4) New Comics & Magazines
(5) Back Issue magazines
(6) Comic Supplies
(7) Collectible Card Games
(8) Role Playing Games
(9) Gaming Supplies
(10) Manga
(11) Anime
(12) Underground Comics
(13) Original Comic Art
(14) Pulps
(15) Big Little Books
(16) Books - Used
(17) Books - New
(18) Comic Related Posters
(19) Movie Posters
(20) Trading Cards
(21) Statues/Mini-busts, etc.
(22) Premiums (Rings, Decoders)
(23) Action Figures
(24) Other Toys
(25) Records/CDs
(26) Blu-rays/DVDs/VHS
(27) Doctor Who Items
(28) Simpsons Items
(29) Star Trek Items
(30) Star Wars Items
(31) POP! Vinyls/HeroClix

ALABAMA

Bob's Comics
979 Gadsden Highway
Birmingham, AL 35235
(205) 833-6914
comicbkbob@aol.com
(1-6)

Quality Comix
500 Eastern Blvd.
Suite 101
Montgomery, AL 36117
PH: (800) 548-3314
info@qualitycomix.com
www.qualitycomix.com
(a-c)

CALIFORNIA

The Comic Cellar
135 W. Main St.
Alhambra, CA 91801
(626) 570-8743
comiccellar@comiccellar.com
www.comiccellar.com
(1-6, 10, 12, 13, 18, 30, 31)

Legacy Comics and Cards Inc.
123 W Wilson Ave.
Glendale, CA 91203
(818) 247-8803
legacyhgc@gmail.com
legacycomics.com
(1-10, 12, 14, 18, 20, 21, 23, 24, 30, 31)

Comic Cult HD
9594 I Ave. Ste F
Hesperia, CA 92345
(760) 998-2730
comiccultHD@gmail.com
(1-7, 9, 12, 18, 21, 23, 30, 31)

Current Comics
400 Lighthouse Ave.
Monterey, CA 93940
(831) 333-1085
CurrentComics831@gmail.com
www.CurrentComics.net
(1-7, 9-11, 16-18, 20, 23, 27, 30, 31)

ArchAngels
4629 Cass Street #9
Pacific Beach, CA 92109
(310) 480-8105
rhughes@archangels.com
www.archangels.com

Funny Business
896 N. Garey Ave.
Pomona, CA 91768
(909) 868-1974
samanieg@verizon.net
(2, 4-6, 10, 12, 21, 24)

Paper Hero's Comics
26771 Bouquet Canyon Rd.
Santa Clarita, CA 91350
(661) 513-9700
staff@paperheroscomics.com
paperheroscomcis.com
(1-4, 6-9, 13, 15, 20, 22, 30, 31)

Geoffrey's Comics
4068 Redondo Beach Boulevard
Unit 1
Torrance, CA 90504
(310) 538-3198
geoffreyscomics@gmail.com
geoffreyscomics.com
(1-7, 9, 10, 17, 18, 20, 21, 23, 30, 31)

COLORADO

RTS Unlimited, Inc.
P. O. Box 150412
Lakewood, CO 80215-0412
PH: (303) 403-1840
FAX: (303) 403-1837
RTSUnlimitedinc@gmail.com
www.RTSUnlimited.com
(1-3, 5, 6, 12, 13, 18, 19)

JNJ Comic Books and Games LLC
3929-A E 120th Ave.
Thornton, CO 80233
(720) 297-0988
jnjscomicbooks@gmail.com
jnj-comic-books-and-games.business.site/?m=true
(1-4, 6-9, 13, 20, 23, 31)

Hero Headquarters
8757 Sheridan Blvd
Westminster, CO 80003
(303) 426-0768
herohq@msn.com
(1-12, 15-24, 27-31)

CONNECTICUT

Matt's Sportscards and Comics
348 Hazard Ave.
Enfield, CT 06082
(860) 741-2522
mattssportscardsandcomics@gmail.com
cardandcomicshop.com
(1-15, 18, 20, 21, 23, 24, 27, 29-31)

Sarge's Comics and Games
124 State St
New London, CT 06320
(860) 443-2004
sargescomics@gmail.com
(1-12, 14-18, 20-31)

DELAWARE

Ogre's Grove
129 Union St
Milton, DE 19968
(302) 643-2125
Ogresgrove@gmail.com
www.ogresgrove.com
(1-7, 9, 10, 12, 13, 18, 21, 23, 29, 30)

FLORIDA

Main Street Comics & Memorabilia
415 E. Main Street Suite C
Bartow, FL 33830
(863) 537-7703
mainstreetcomicsbartow@yahoo.com
www.facebook.com/ComicsBartow
(2, 4, 6, 7, 10, 11, 13, 18, 20, 21, 23, 24, 29, 30, 31)

The Comics Club, Inc.
714 West Lumsden Road
La Viva Plaza
Brandon, FL 33511
(813) 653-4111
mail@comicsclub.com
www.comicsclub.com
(2-4, 6-9, 18, 24)

Emerald City Comics
4902 113th Ave. N
Clearwater, FL 33760
(727) 398-2665
email@emeraldcitycomics.com
emeraldcitycomics.com
(1-10, 12, 13, 15, 17-24, 27-31)

Phil's Comic Shoppe
6512 W Atlantic Blvd
Margate, FL 33063
(954) 977-6947
philscomix@att.net
www.ebay.com/str/philscomicshoppe
(1-6, 10, 12, 13)

PCB Hobby
11939 Panama City Beach Pkwy
Panama City Beach, FL 32407
(850) 320-8388
sales@pcbcomics.com
http://pcbcomics.com
(1-4, 6-9, 12, 13, 20, 31)

Yancy Street Comics
9409 US HWY 19
381-A
Port Richey, FL 34668
(727) 817-0888
yancystreetcomicshop@gmail.com
www.yancystcomics.com
(1-6, 10, 13, 18, 19, 21, 23, 24, 29-31)

Cover Price Comics
4012 SW Alice St.
Port St. Lucie, FL 34953
(347) 2544073
coverpricecomicsonline@gmail.com
www.coverpricecomics.com
(4, 6, 9, 10, 13, 18, 21, 23, 24, 29-31)

All Books & Comics
1395 US Highway 1 South
St. Augustine, FL 32084
(904) 829-0944
jack.tolzmann@gmail.com
(1-4, 6, 10, 13, 16, 18, 21, 23, 24, 27-31)

Comic Central, Inc.
1425 WP Ball Blvd
Sanford, FL 32771
(407) 321-5111
www.comic-central.com
(2-4, 6, 8, 10, 18, 21, 23, 30, 31)

Classic Collectible Services
P.O. Box 4738
Sarasota, FL 34230
(855) CCS-1711
CCSpaper.com

CGC
P.O. Box 4738
Sarasota, FL 34230
PH: (877) NM-COMIC
FAX: (941) 360-2558
www.CGCcomics.com

World of Comics
2133 S. Ridgewood Ave.
South Daytona, FL 32119-3015
(386) 760-0555
worldofcomics1983@gmail.com
(1-6, 8, 10-12, 16, 18-30)

David T. Alexander Collectibles
P.O. Box 273086
Tampa, FL 33618
(813) 968-1805
davidt@cultureandthrills.com
www.dtacollectibles.com
(1-3, 5, 12-15, 18-20, 22, 24, 29,30)

Pedigree Comics, Inc.
12541 Equine Lane
Wellington, FL 33414
PH/FAX: (561) 422-1120
CELL: (561) 596-9111
E-Mail: DougSchmell@pedigreecomics.com
www.pedigreecomics.com

GEORGIA

Comicpresser.com
Atlanta, GA
(507) 400-0661
info@comicpresser.com
www.comicpresser.com

Dr. No's Comics & Games SuperStore
3372 Canton Road
Suite 104
Marietta, GA 30066
(770) 422-4642
manager@drnos.com
www.drnos.com
(1-7, 9, 10, 12, 17-19, 21-24, 27, 29-31)

Visions Comics and Games
214 Sycamore Grove Ct.
Rockmart, GA 30153
(678) 685-4696
logan@visionsgaming.com
visionsgaming.com

Neighborhood Comics
1205 Bull St.
Savannah, GA 31401
(912) 349-3095
team@neighborhoodcomics.com
neighborhoodcomics.com
(1-6, 10, 12, 13, 18, 21, 23-25, 28, 30)

Galactic Comics and Games
21 E Vine St.
Statesboro, GA 30458
(912) 489-3123
galacticcg@gmail.com
https://galacticcg.com/
(2,-11, 14, 16-24, 27, 29-31)

HAWAII

Other Realms Ltd.
1130 N Nimitz HWY
RM C140
Honolulu, HI 96817
(808) 596-8236
OtherRealms@hawaii.rr.com
https://other-realms.com
(1-4, 6-10, 12, 21, 23, 24, 29-31)

ILLINOIS

Alternate Reality Inc.
3149 West 111th Street
Chicago, IL 60655
(773) 881-4376
arcomics@msn.com
http://MYALTERNATEREALITY.COM
(2, 4-10, 12, 17-19, 23, 24, 27-31)

3 Keys Comics
595 W Exchange St.
Crete, IL 60417
(708) 279-7643
scott@3keyscomics.com
http://3keyscomics.com
(1-3, 5, 6, 10, 13, 14, 21, 23, 31)

Amazing Fantasy Comics and Games
20505 S. La Grange Rd.
Frankfort, IL 60423
(815) 469-5092
afbooks_frankfort@sbcglobal.net
www.afbooks.com
(2-10, 18, 21, 23, 24, 27-31)

One Stop Comics
111 South Ridgeland
Oak Park, IL 60302
(773) 910-9903
onestopcomics@sbcglobal.net
http://onestopcomics.net
(1-31)

Beyond Tomorrow Comics & Cards
327 N. Northwest Hwy.
Fleetwood Center
Palatine, IL 60067
(847) 705-6633
beyondtomorrowcomics@gmail.com
(2-6, 10, 12, 16-18, 21, 23, 24, 26-31)

Mellow Blue Planet
2212 5th Avenue
Rock Island, IL 61201
(309) 788-1653
comicman70@gmail.com
mellowblueplanet.com
(1-6, 8-12, 15, 17-21, 23, 24, 26-31)

Killens Games Comics Toys
2501 Wabash Ave
White Oaks Mall
Springfield, IL 62704
(217) 726-5801
killenx@gmail.com
http://killenenterprises.com
(1-13, 16, 18-31)

INDIANA

Comics Ina Flash
P.O. Box 3611
Evansville, IN 47735-3611
PH/FAX: (812) 401-6127
comicflash@aol.com
www.comicsinaflash.com

Comic Quest
8401 N Kentucky Ave. Suite B
Evansville, IN 47726
(812) 474-1133
sales@comicquest.com
www.comicquest.com
(1-10, 17-19, 21, 23, 24, 27-31)

BCT-Books Comics & Things
5808 W Jefferson Blvd.
Suite C
Fort Wayne, IN 46804
(260) 755-2425
judys@bctcomics.com
www.bctcomics.com
(1-10, 18, 20-24, 27, 29-31)

Book Comics & Things
2212 Maplecrest Rd.
Fort Wayne IN 46815
(260) 493-6116
bct@bctcomics.com
www.bctcomics.com
(1-10, 18, 20-22, 24, 27, 29-31)

Collectors Paradise
5618 E Washington St.
Indianapolis, IN 46219
(317) 357-2291
dianaduncan@msn.com
(2-6, 18, 20, 21, 23, 24, 29-31)

Mancave Comics & Collectables LLC
1310 South Miller Ave.
Shelbyville, IN 46176
(812) 614-8253
tmc304@tds.net
(1-9, 16, 18, 19, 21, 23, 24, 29-31)

IOWA

Alter Ego Comics
331 7th Avenue
Marion, IA 52302
(319) 373-8935
info@alteregoia.com
www.alteregoia.com
(1-4, 6, 23, 31)

Oak Leaf Comics & Collectibles
221 North Federal
Mason City, IA 50401
(641) 424-0333
miket@dustcatchers.com
www.dustcatchers.com
www.oakleafcomics.com
(1-13, 15, 16, 18-25, 27-31)

StarFighter Comics
4501 Southern Hills Drive #23
Sioux City, IA 51106
(712) 224-0070
starfightercomics@gmail.com
http://starfightercomics.com
(1-11, 16, 17, 20, 21, 23, 24, 27-31)

KANSAS

B-Bop Comics South
8709 Metcalf
Overland Park, KS 66212
(913) 383-1777
b-bopcomics@att.net
(1-8, 10-21, 23, 24, 27-31)

KENTUCKY

The Great Escape
2945 Scottsville Road
Suites B17 & B18
Bowling Green, KY 42104
PH: (270) 782-8092
FAX: (270) 843-3090
thegreatescapebg@gmail.com
www.TheGreatEscapeOnLine.com
(1-31)

Comic Interlude
393 Waller Ave.; Ste. 10
Lexington, KY 40502
PH: (859) 321-4325
thecomicinterludeky@gmail.com

The Great Escape
2433 Bardstown Road
Louisville, KY 40205
PH: (502) 456-2216
FAX: (502) 456-5964
thegreatescapelouisville
@gmail.com
www.TheGreatEscapeOnLine.com
(1-31)

LOUISIANA

Excalibur Comics, Cards & Games
937 E. 70th Street
Shreveport, LA 71106
PH: (318) 868-4389
FAX: (318) 868-4369
excaliburccg@gmail.com
excaliburcomicscardsandgames.com
(1-10, 20, 21, 23, 31)

MAINE

Top Shelf Coins & Comics
115 Maine St.
1st Floor
Bangor, ME 04401
(207) 947-4939
topshelf@tcomics.com
www.tcomics.com
(1-6, 15)

El Rey Comics
75 Bishop Street #1
Portland, ME 04103
(207) 405-9831
adrian@elreycomics.com
www.elreycomics.com
(4)

MARYLAND

Third Eye Comics
209 Chinquapin Round Rd.
Suite 200
Annapolis, MD 21401
(410) 897-0322
info@thirdeyecomics.com
http://thirdeyecomics.com
(2-12, 17-25, 27, 29, 31)

E. Gerber
1720 Belmont Ave.; Suite C
Baltimore, MD 21244

Esquire Comics.com
Mark S. Zaid, ESQ.
P.O. Box 3422492
Bethesda, MD 20827
PH: (202) 498-0011
esquirecomics@aol.com
www.esquirecomics.com
(2-11, 18, 21, 23, D, E)

KC's Comics
2807 Belair Road
Fallston, MD 21047
(410) 877-3152
kcscomicshop@gmail.com
(1-4, 6, 21, 23, 31)

Diamond Comic Distributors
10150 York Road, Suite 300
Hunt Valley, MD 21030
PH: (443) 318-8001

Diamond International Galleries
10720 Gilroy Rd., Suite 300
Hunt Valley, MD 21031
pokevin@DiamondGalleries.com
www.DiamondGalleries.com

Reece's Rare Comics
PO Box 399
Monrovia, MD 21770
PH: (240) 367-3662
alex@reececomics.com
www.reececomics.com
(1, 2, 3, 5, 6)

Cards Comics and Collectibles
51 Main St.
Reisterstown, MD 21136
PH: (410) 526-7410
FAX: (410) 526-4006
cardscomicscollectibles
@yahoo.com
www.cardscomicscollectibles.com
(1-4, 6, 7, 10, 20, 23, 5)

BLC Comics
3702 Old Crain Hwy
Upper Marlboro, MD 20772
(301) 861-9888
jamesmusgrovemedia
@gmail.com
(2-5, 10, 29, 30)

MASSACHUSETTS

Gary Dolgoff Comics
116 Pleasant St.
Easthampton, MA 01027
PH: (413) 529-0326
FAX: (413) 529-9824
gary@gdcomics.com
www.gdcomics.com
(1-3, 5, 7, 12-16, 20, 21, 23, 24)

Federation Comics
Fulfilling orders for
Bill Cole Enterprises Inc.
3065 Cranberry Highway
Suite B17
East Wareham, MA 02538
PH: (781) 986-2653
sales@bcemylar.com
www.bcemylar.com

That's Entertainment
56 John Fitch Highway
Fitchburg, MA 01420
(978) 342-8607
fitch@thatse.com
www.ThatsE.com
(1-11, 16-31)

His and Hers Comics
40 Bank Row Street
Greenfield, MA 01301
(413) 325-8133
hisandherscomicsgreenfield
@gmail.com
(1-6, 10-12, 20, 21, 23, 24, 29-31)

The Comic Book Palace
620 Primrose St.
Haverhill, MA 01830
(978) 372-1477
cbpalace@aol.com
(1-4, 6, 7, 9, 20)

SuperworldComics.com
456 Main St., Suite F
Holden, MA 01520
PH: (508) 829-2259
PH: (508) UB-WACKY
Ted@Superworldcomics.com
www.Superworldcomics.com
(1-3, 13)

Harrison's Comics
252 Essex St.
Salem, MA 01970
(978) 741-0786
harrisonscomics@hotmail.com
(1-31)

Silver Moon Comics
1 E India Square Mall #131
Witch City Mall
Salem, MA 01970
(978) 594-8641
silvermooncomics@yahoo.com
www.silvermooncomics.com
(1-8, 12-21, 23, 24, 28-31)

The Outer Limits
437 Moody Street
Waltham, MA 02453
PH: (781) 891-0444
askouterlimits@aol.com
www.eouterlimits.com
(1-30)

That's Entertainment
244 Park Avenue
At the corner of Lois Lane
Worcester, MA 01609
(508) 755-4207
webmaster@thatse.com
www.ThatsE.com
(1-31)

MICHIGAN

Collectible Assets, LLC
3277 12 Mile Rd
Berkley, MI 48072
(248) 548-7213
thetraveler
@timetravelersonline.com
www.timetravelersonline.com
(1-10, 12, 14, 15, 18, 20, 21, 23, 24, 27-31)

Comix Corner
32032 Utica
Fraser, MI 48026
(586) 219-3468
pazzaz88@yahoo.com
(4, 6, 10, 23, 31)

The Comic Signal, LLC
4318 Plainfield Ave NE,
Suiite H
Grand Rapids, MI 49525
(616) 259-8017
donnieboy67@gmail.com
(1-9, 21, 23, 31)

Harley Yee Comics
P.O. Box 51758
Livonia, MI 48151-5758
PH: (800) 731-1029
FAX: (734) 421-7928
HarleyComx@aol.com
www.HarleyYeeComics.com

Fanfare
4415 S Westnedge Ave.
Kalamazoo, MI 49008
(269) 349-8866
comics@fanfareland.com
http://fanfareland.com
(1-11, 14, 15, 18, 20, 21, 23, 24, 27, 29-31)

MINNESOTA

NerdinOut
1802 2nd St. SW
Rochester, MN 55902
(507) 322-0008
sales@nerdinout.com
www.nerdinout.com
(1-11, 15-21, 23, 24, 29-31)

MISSOURI

B-Bop Comics North A Division of Friendly Frank's Inc.
6320 NW Barry Road
Kansas City, MO 64154
(816) 746-4569
b-bopcomics@att.net
(1-14, 16-21, 23, 24, 27-31)

Massey's Comics
727 S. Jefferson Avenue
Lebanon, MO 65536
(417) 532-0652
masseyscomics@gmail.com
Facebook.com/MasseysComics
(1-4, 6-10, 12, 16, 18, 20, 21, 23, 24, 30, 31)

Not Just Comix!
339 W. Main St.
Park Hills, MO 63601
(573) 431-4587
(2-10, 18)

Comic Book Relief
2300 N 3rd St.
St. Charles, MO 63301
(636) 9401244
info@comicbookrelief.com
www.comicbookrelief.com
(1-6, 10, 11, 18, 19, 21, 23, 24, 30, 31)

NEBRASKA

Trade A Tape Comic Center
145 S 9th St.
Lincoln, NE 68508
(402) 435-6063
tradeatape@neb.rr.com
(1-6, 10)

NEVADA

Cosmic Comics!
3830 E. Flamingo Rd.; Ste F-2
Las Vegas, NV 89121
PH: (702) 451-6611
info@CosmicComicsLV.com
CosmicComics.vegas
(1-10, 17-19, 21, 23, 29-31)

Torpedo Comics
7300 Arroyo Crossing Pkwy
Unit 105
Las Vegas, NV 89113
PH: (702) 444-4432
BMarvelman@aol.com
(1-6, 10-15, 21, 23, 27-30)

NEW HAMPSHIRE

Rare Books & Comics
James F. Payette
P.O. Box 750
Bethlehem, NH 03574
PH: (603) 869-2097
FAX: (603) 869-3475
JimPayette@msn.com
www.JamesPayetteComics.com
(1-3, 5, 14-16)

Jetpack Comics & Games
37 North Main Street
Rochester, NH 03867
(603) 330-9636
JetpackComics@gmail.com
www.JetpackComics.com
(1-10, 12, 13, 16-18, 20, 21, 23, 24, 27-31)

NEW JERSEY

Manifest Comics and Cards
766 Broadway, Suite 3
Bayonne, NJ 07002
(201) 535-5330
manifestcomics@gmail.com
http://manifestcomics.com
(3, 4, 6-9, 18, 19, 31)

Nationwide Comics
Buying All 10¢ & 12¢ original priced comics
Derek Woywood
Clementon, NJ 08021
PH: (856) 217-5737
dwoywood@yahoo.com
www.philadelphiacomic-con.com
(1, 2, 4-8, 13, 14, 17)

Secret Origins Comics & More
888 Haddon Ave.
Collingswood, NJ 08108
(856) 448-5496
secretoriginscomics@gmail.com
http://secretoriginscomics.com
(2-4, 6-8, 10, 12, 23, 31)

The Joker's Child Inc.
12-23 River Road
Fair Lawn, NJ 07410
(201) 794-6830
info@jokerschild.com
http://jokerschild.com
(1-7, 10, 11, 17, 20, 23, 24, 28-31)

Pyramid Comics and Cards
24 Main Street
Sparta, NJ 07871
PH: (973) 729-5343
FAX: (973) 729-4307
sales@pyramidcomics.com
www.pyramidcomics.com
(4, 6)

JHV Associates
(By Appointment Only)
P. O. Box 317
Woodbury Heights, NJ 08097
PH: (856) 845-4010
FAX: (856) 845-3977
JHVassoc@hotmail.com
(1, 2, 14, 19)

NEW MEXICO

Astro-Zombies
3100 Central Ave. SE
Albuquerque, NM 87106
(505) 232-7800
info@astrozombies.com
www.astrozombies.com
(1-10, 12, 13, 18, 21, 23-31)

Comic Warehouse Albuquerque
9617 Menaul Blvd NE
Albuquerque, NM 87112
PH: (505) 293-3065
FAX: (505) 237-1000
comics@c-warehouse.com
facebook.com/comicwarehouse
(1-4, 6, 10)

NEW YORK

Excellent Adventures Comics
110 Milton Ave (Rt #50)
Ballston Spa, NY 12020
(518) 884-9498
Jbelskis37@aol.com
www.excellentadventurescomics.com
(1-6, 11-16, 18-24, 27-30)

Dork Forest Comics
14 East Main Street
Clifton Springs, NY 14432
(315) 462-6011
dorkforestcomics@yahoo.com
(1-10, 18, 23-31)

HighGradeComics.com
17 Bethany Drive
Commack, NY 11725
PH: (631) 543-1917
FAX: (631) 864-1921
BobStorms@HighGradeComics.com
www.HighGradeComics.com
(1-3, 5)

Superhero Comics Express
146 Jericho Tpke
Floral Park, NY 11001
(516) 328-9290
rbrindisi@nyc.rr.com
(1-7, 10, 18, 20, 21, 23, 24, 29, 30, 31)

The Comic Box
840B North Broadway
Massapequa, NY 11758
(516) 795-2528
thecomicboxny@gmail.com
www.instagram.com/thecomicboxny/
(1-6, 10, 12, 18, 23, 24, 27, 28, 30, 31)

Best Comics
1300 Jericho Turnpike
New Hyde Park, NY 11040
PH: (516) 328-1900
FAX: (516) 328-1909
TommyBest@aol.com
www.bestcomics.com
(1, 2, 4, 6, 13, 20, 21, 23, 29,30)

October Country Comics
246 Main St. Ste #5
New Paltz, NY 12561
(845) 255-1115
info@octobercountrycomics.com
www.octobercountrycomics.com
(2-10, 17, 20, 21, 23, 24, 30, 31)

ComicConnect.com
36 West 37th St.; 6th Floor
New York, NY 10018
PH: (212) 895-3999
FAX: (212) 260-4304
support@comicconnect.com
www.comicconnect.com
(1-3, 13, 14, 19, 22)

Metropolis Collectibles
36 West 37th St.; 6th Floor
New York, NY 10018
PH: (800) 229-6387
FAX: (212) 260-4304
E-Mail: buying@metropoliscomics.com
www.metropoliscomics.com

Dave and Adam's
55 Oriskany Dr.
Tonawanda, NY 14150
PH: (888) 440-9787
FAX: (716) 838-9896
service@dacardworld.com
www.dacardworld.com
(1-9, 13, 18, 20, 23, 24, 27-31)

Dave and Adam's
2217 Sheridan Dr.
Tonawanda, NY 14223
PH: (716) 837-4920
sheridan-store@dacardworld.com
www.dacwstore.com
(1-3, 6-9, 13, 20, 23, 24, 27-31)

Long Island Comics
276 Little East Neck Road
West Babylon, NY 11704
(631) 321-4822
frank@licomics.com
licomics.com
(2-6, 26)

Dave and Adam's
8075 Sheridan Dr.
Williamsville, NY 14221
PH: (716) 626-0000
Transit-store@dacardworld.com
www.dacwstore.com
(1-4, 6-9, 13, 18, 20, 23, 24, 27-31)

NORTH CAROLINA

Fan-Tastic Cards & Comics
100 District Dr. Unit 010
Asheville, NC 28803
(828) 505-0515
support@fan-tasticshop.com
http://fan-tasticshop.com
(4, 6, 7, 20)

Heroes Aren't Hard to Find
417 Pecan Avenue.
Charlotte, NC 28204
PH: (704) 375-7462
www.heroesonline.com

Nostalgia Newsstand
201 W 9th St.
Greenville, NC 27834
(252) 758-6909
nostalgianewsstand@gmail.com
www.facebook.com/NostalgiaNewsstandNC/
(1-6, 12, 18, 21, 23, 24, 28-31)

DreamDaze Comics Fun & Games
2801-1B Ward Blvd.
Wilson, NC 27893
(252) 281-5586
ddcfg@dreamdazecfg.com
www.dreamdazecfg.com
(2-4, 6-10, 17, 18, 20-24, 27-31)

OHIO

Queen City Comic and Card Company
6101 Montgomery Road
Cincinnati, OH 45213
(513) 351-5674
qccomics@aol.com
queencitycomics.com
(1-7, 9, 12, 18-20, 23, 29, 30)

Rockin' Rooster Comics & Games
5000 Glenway Ave.
Cincinnati, OH 45238
(513) 661-7625
rockinroostercomics@gmail.com
http://rockinroostercomics.com
(1-10, 18, 21-24, 27, 29, 31)

Up Up & Away!
4016 Harrison Avenue
Cincinnati, OH 45211
(513) 661-6300
cheviot@upupandawaycomics.com
www.uuacomics.com
(1-6, 10, 12, 21, 23, 24, 27-31)

Up Up & Away!
9687 Kenwood Road
Cincinnati, OH 45242
(513) 936-6300
blue_ash@upupandawaycomics.com
www.uuacomics.com
(1-6, 10, 12, 13, 18, 21, 23, 24, 27-31)

Cosmic Comics & Games
17 W National Rd.
Englewood, OH 45322
(937) 836-0083
cosmicomicsandgames@gmail.com
www.cosmic-comics-games.com
(1-4, 6-9, 13, 16, 18-21, 23, 24, 26-31)

Queen City Comic and Card Company
6600-V Dixie Highway
Fairfield, OH 45014
(513) 860-5805
qccomics@aol.com
queencitycomics.com
(2- 7, 18, 20, 23, 31)

Comics and Friends, LLC
7850 Mentor Ave.; Suite 1054
Mentor, OH 44096
PH: (440) 255-4242
comics.and.friends.store@gmail.com
www.comicsandfriends.com
(1-7, 9, 10, 12-14, 18, 20, 21, 23-31)

New Dimension Comics
Ohio Valley Mall
67800 Mall Ring Rd Unit 875
Saint Clairsville, OH 43950
PH: (740) 695-1020
ohiovalley@ndcomics.com
www.ndcomics.com

Wonder Comics and More
100 N. Miami St.
Trenton, OH 45067
(513) 468-4001
wondercomicsmore@gmail.com
(1-12, 14, 16-21, 23, 24, 26, 31)

Jim and Dan Comics LLC
1 East Dayton Street
West Alexandria, OH 45381
(937) 839-7068
jimdancomics@gmail.com
www.jimdancomics.com
(1-16, 18, 20-25, 27-31)

World's Greatest Comics
5974 Westerville Rd.
Westerville, OH 43081
(614) 891-3000
worldsgc@gmail.com
www.wgcomics.com
(1-6, 13, 18, 21, 23)

OKLAHOMA

Impulse Creations Comics & Collectibles
8228 E 61 St, Ste 121
Tulsa, OK 74133
staff@impulsecreations.com
http://ImpulseCreations.com
(2-10, 17, 21, 23, 24, 26, 27, 29-31)

Want List Comics
(Appointment Only)
P.O. Box 701932
Tulsa, OK 74170
PH: (918) 299-0440
E-Mail: wantlistcomics777@gmail.com
(1-3, 13-15, 19, 20, 24, 29)

OREGON

Future Dreams
1847 E Burnside St. Suite 116
Portland, OR 97214
(503) 231-8311
fdb@futuredreamsbooks.com
http://futuredreamsbooks.com
(1-12, 14-19, 21, 23, 24, 26, 27, 29, 30)

Tasteecat Comics
2621 SE Clinton St.
Portland, OR
(503) 236-8133
@tasteecatcomics
tasteecatcomics.com

PENNSYLVANIA

New Dimension Comics
108 South Main Street
Butler, PA 16001
PH: (724) 282-5283
butler@ndcomics.com
www.ndcomics.com
(1-12, 14, 15, 18, 20, 21, 23, 24, 27-31)

New Dimension Comics – Cranberry
20550 Route 19
#20 Piazza Plaza
Cranberry Township, PA 16066
(724) 776-0433
cranberry@ndcomics.com
www.ndcomics.com
(1-4, 6-10, 12, 14, 15, 17, 18, 20-24, 27-31)

Codex Comics & Collectibles
125 West High Street
Ebensburg, PA 15931
(814) 472-2233
codexcomics@yahoo.com
http://codexcomicshop.com
(1, 2, 4, 6-10, 15, 17, 18, 21, 23, 31)

ITEM CODES
(1) Golden Age Comics
(2) Silver Age Comics
(3) Bronze Age Comics
(4) New Comics & Magazines
(5) Back Issue magazines
(6) Comic Supplies
(7) Collectible Card Games
(8) Role Playing Games
(9) Gaming Supplies
(10) Manga
(11) Anime
(12) Underground Comics
(13) Original Comic Art
(14) Pulps
(15) Big Little Books
(16) Books - Used
(17) Books - New
(18) Comic Related Posters
(19) Movie Posters
(20) Trading Cards
(21) Statues/Mini-busts, etc.
(22) Premiums (Rings, Decoders)
(23) Action Figures
(24) Other Toys
(25) Records/CDs
(26) DVDs/VHS
(27) Doctor Who Items
(28) Simpsons Items
(29) Star Trek Items
(30) Star Wars Items
(31) HeroClix

New Dimension Comics
Megastore
516 Lawrence Ave.
Ellwood City, PA 16117
PH: (724) 758-2324
ec@ndcomics.com
www.ndcomics.com
(1-12, 14, 15, 18, 20, 21, 23, 24, 27-31)

New Dimension Comics
630B East Waterfront Dr.
Homestead, PA 15120
PH: (412) 655-8661
waterfront@ndcomics.com
www.ndcomics.com
(1-12, 14, 15, 18, 20, 21, 23, 24, 27-31)

Uncanny!
160 North Gulph Road
Suite 2361
King of Prussia, PA 19406
(610) 337-1555
uncannykop@gmail.com
http://Uncannyonline.com
(2-12, 18-21, 23, 24, 29-31)

Comic Zen
301-A W Main St
Lansdale, PA 19446
(267) 263-4219
comiczenpa@gmail.com
http://www.comiczenpa.com
(3, 4, 6-8, 10, 18, 21, 23, 31)

Uncanny!
272 Montgomery Mall
North Wales, PA 19454
(610) 828-5848
uncannypm@gmail.com
http://Uncannyonline.com
(2-12, 18-21, 23, 24, 29-31)

Ontario St. Comics
2235 E. Ontario St.
Philadelphia, PA 19134
PH: (215) 288-7338
(2-4, 6, 7, 10, 20, 21, 23, 31)

Eide's Entertainment, LLC
1121 Penn Ave.
Pittsburgh, PA 15222
PH: (412) 261-0900
eBay: Eides_Entertainment
eides@eides.com
www.eides.com
(1-31)

Isle Of Comics
56 West Southern Avenue
South Williamsport, PA 17702
(570) 322-4753
IsleOfComics@hotmail.com
www.IsleOfComics.com
(1-4, 6, 12, 21, 23, 24, 30, 31)

New Dimension Comics
Pittsburgh Mills
590 Pittsburgh Mill Circle
Tarentum, PA 15084
PH: (724) 758-1560
mills@ndcomics.com
www.ndcomics.com
(1-12, 14, 15, 18, 20, 21, 23, 24, 27-31)

Hake's Americana & Collectibles
P.O. Box 12001
York, PA 17402
PH: (866) 404-9800
www.hakes.com

SOUTH CAROLINA

Borderlands Comics and Games
410 S. Pleasantburg Dr.
Greenville, SC 29607
(864) 235-3488
BorderlandsComics@gmail.com
www.borderlands.us
(1-10, 14, 16, 18, 20, 21, 23, 24, 27-31)

TENNESSEE

Comics Universe
1869 Hwy 45 By-Pass
Jackson, TN 38305
PH/FAX: (731) 664-9131
rethelmiller@gmail.com
(1-4, 6, 18, 23)

BrickHouse Collectibles
163 West End Avenue
Knoxville, TN 37934
(865) 392-1019
BrickHouseCollectibles
@gmail.com
(4, 6-10, 20, 24)

The Great Escape
105 Gallatin Road North
Madison, TN 37115
PH: (615) 865-8052
FAX: (615) 865-8779
thegreatescapemadison
@gmail.com
www.TheGreatEscapeOnLine.com
(1-31)

Batcave Treasures LLC
7535 US Highway 64
Memphis, TN 38133
(815) 514-6104
batcavetreasures@sbcglobal.net
https://batcave-treasures.com/
(4, 6-13, 17, 19-21, 23, 24, 27-31)

The Great Escape
810 NW Broad St., Suite 202
Murfreesboro, TN 37129
PH: (615) 900-1937
FAX: (615) 962-9562
thegreatescapemurfreesboro
@gmail.com
www.TheGreatEscapeOnLine.com
(1-31)

The Great Escape
5400 Charlotte Avenue
Nashville, TN 37209
PH: (615) 385-2116
FAX: (615) 297-6588
contactus
@thegreatescapeonline.com
www.TheGreatEscapeOnLine.com
(1-31)

Cadets Toys and Comics
4910 Main Street
Suite 114
Spring Hill, TN 37174
(615) 302-8260
hello@cadetstoys.com
http://cadetstoys.com
(1-7, 10, 17-19, 21, 23, 24, 30, 31)

TEXAS

Comic Heaven
P.O. Box 900
Big Sandy, TX 75755
PH: (903) 539-8875
www.ComicHeaven.net

Comic Book Certification Service (CBCS)
2700 Summit Ave., Suite 100
Plano, TX 75074
www.CBCScomics.com

Heritage Auction Galleries
2801 W. Airport Freeway
Dallas, TX 75261-4127
PH: (877) 437-4827
www.HA.com

Worldwide Comics
29369 Raintree Ridge
Fair Oaks Ranch, TX 78015
PH: (830) 368-4103
stephen@wwcomics.com
wwcomics.com

William Hughes' Vintage Collectables
P.O. Box 270244
Flower Mound, TX 75027
PH: (972) 539-9190
PH: (973) 432-4070
Whughes199@yahoo.com
www.VintageCollectables.net

Lewisville Comics
2417 South Stemmons Fwy.
#106
Lewisville, TX 75067
(972) 315-3664
info@lewisvillecomics.com
www.lewisvillecomics.com

Monster's Lair Comics
2416 19th St
Lubbock, TX 79401
(806) 701-5800
monsterslair.shop@gmail.com
(1-6, 12-14, 20, 21, 23, 24, 30, 31)

VIRGINIA

Dave Anderson
5192 Dawes Avenue
Alexandria, VA 22311
(703) 578-1222
danderson8991@gmail.com
(1,2,13,14)

Victory Comics
586 So. Washington St.
Falls Church, VA 22046
(703) 241-9393
victorycomics.fc@gmail.com
http://victorycomics.com
(1-11, 18, 20, 21, 23, 24, 27-31)

Gateway Comics and Toys
2340 Plank Rd.
Fredericksburg, VA 22401
(540) 621-9274
sales@
gatewaycomicsandtoys.com
www.gatewaycomics.com
(1-10, 12, 14-31)

Jersey's Cards & Comics
1818 Todds Lane
Hampton, VA 23666
(757) 825-0097
jerseysHampton@aol.com
http://jerseycc.com
(4, 6-10, 18-20, 23, 24, 30, 31)

Jersey's Cards, Comics and Games
4852 George Washington
Memorial Highway
Hayes/Gloucester, VA 23072
(804) 824-9790
jerseysgloucestr@aol.com
http://jerseyscc.com
(1, 2, 4-11, 13, 16, 18-21, 23, 24, 30, 31)

Stories Comics
9040 West Broad Street
Henrico, VA 23294
(804) 874-1829
storiescomics@outlook.com
www.storiescomics.com
(1-6, 10, 12, 21, 23, 24, 27 29-31)

Four Color Fantasies
80 Weems Lane
Winchester, VA 22601
(540) 662-7377
fourcolorfantasies@gmail.com
(1-6, 8, 9, 12)

Nova Gateway Comics and Toys
3112 P.S. Business Center Dr.
Woodbridge, VA 22192
(540) 621-9274
sales@
gatewaycomicsandtoys.com
www.gatewaycomicsandtoys.com
(1-7, 9, 14, 16-24, 27-31)

Jersey's Cards, Comics and Games
5906A George Washington
Memorial Highway
Yorktown, VA 23692
(757) 890-2842
jerseysyorktown@aol.com
http://Jerseyscc.com
(1 2, 4, 6-11, 15, 17, 19-21, 23, 24, 30, 31)

WASHINGTON

Mill Geek Comics
17624 15th Ave SE
Suite #105a
Bothell, WA 98012
(425) 415-6666
millgeekcomics@gmail.com
www.millgeekcomics.com
(1-4, 13, 30)

Pristine Comics
2008 South 314th Street
Federal Way, WA 98003
PH: (253) 941-1986
www.PristineComics.com

Terry's Comics
Buying All 10¢ & 12¢
Original priced comics
P.O. Box 1186
Kelso, WA 98626
PH: (714) 288-8993
Cell: (360) 846-3714
info@TerrysComics.com
www.TerrysComics.com
(1, 2, 4-8, 13, 14, 17)

Golden Age Collectables
1501 Pike Place
Ste #401, Lower Level
Seattle, WA 98101
PH: (206) 622-9799
FAX: (206) 622-9595
gacollect@gmail.com
www.goldenagecollectables.com
(1-4, 6-10, 15, 18, 21, 23, 24, 29-31)

Fantasy Illustrated
P.O. Box 248
Silvana, WA 98287
PH: (425) 750-4513
rocketbat@msn.com
www.fantasyillustrated.net.com
(1, 2, 14, 16)

Comic World
1204 4th Avenue
Huntington, WV 25701
(304) 638-3591
(1-4, 6, 18, 23, 31)

WISCONSIN

Inner Child Collectibles and Comics
5921 Sixth Avenue "A"
Kenosha, WI 53140
PH: (262) 653-0400
StevenKahn@sbcglobal.net
innerchildcomics.com
(1-6, 12-16, 18, 19, 21-24, 27-30)

CANADA

ALBERTA

Beat Box Comics & Collectibles
5205 B Duncan Ave.; Box 720
Blackfalds, AB T0M 0J0
beatboxcomics@gmail.com
beatboxcomics.ca
(2, 3, 4, 6, 18, 21,24, 28, 30, 31)

Alpha Comics
#9 7005 - 18th Street S.E.
Calgary, AB T2C 1Y1
(403) 453-0187
admin@alphacomics.com
alphacomics.ca
(2-4, 6, 23, 24)

MANITOBA

Doug Sulipa's Comic World
Box 21986
Steinbach, MB., R5G 1B5
PH: (204) 346-3674
FAX: (204) 346-1632
dsulipa@gmail.com
www.dougcomicworld.com
(1-5, 8, 12, 14-20, 25, 26, 29,30)

Book Fair
340 Portage Ave.
Winnipeg, MB R3C 0C3
PH/FAX: (204) 957-0142
info@bookfaircomics.com
www.bookfaircomics.com
(1-10, 15-18, 20, 23)

204Comics
5-1549 St. Mary's Road
Winnipeg, MB R2M 5G9
(204) 306-2400
info@204comics.com
www.204comics.com
(1-4, 6, 10, 12, 13, 31)

ONTARIO

Aardvark Comics
516 Plains Rd.
Unit 4
Burlington, ON L7T 2E1
905-639-2161
jeffrfy@gmail.com
www.aardvarkcomics.com
(1-6, 13-15, 23, 30, 31)

Fantasy Realm
227 Pitt Street
Cornwall, ON K6J 3P8
(613) 933-7997
fantasyrealm@cogeco.ca
www.facebook.com/
fantasyrealmcornwall
(2-7, 9, 10, 18, 20, 21, 23, 29-31)

Comic Cave Canada
1104 Hwy 5 West
Dundas, ON L9H 5E2
(905) 808-8185
www.comiccavecanada.com

Big B Comics
1045 Upper James St.
Hamilton, ON L9C 3A6
(905) 318-9636
mailbox@bigbcomics.com
www.bigbcomics.com
(1-7, 9, 10, 12, 13, 21-24, 27-31)

Burdin's Comics
725 Barton Street East
Hamilton, ON L8L 3A7
(905) 312-6642
gburton34@hotmail.com
(4-10, 15, 18, 21, 23, 24, 27, 29-31)

Kingston Nexus
270 Bagot Street
Kingston Gaming Nexus
Kingston, ON K7L 3G5
(613) 546-2565
kingstonnexus@gmail.com
www.kingstonnexus.ca
(1-10, 12, 17, 20-24, 27, 29-31)

Knowhere
88 Cawthra Ave.
Toronto, ON M6N 3C2
(647) 406-7926
knowhere.canada@gmail.com
www.knowherecomics.com
(2-6, 10, 11, 20, 24, 29)

Pendragon Comics and Cards
Cloverdale Mall
181-250 The East Mall
Toronto, ON M9B 3Y8
(416) 253-6974
pendragoncomics@gmail.com
pendragoncomics.com
(1-7, 12, 14, 16, 20-24, 28-31)

Treehouse Collectibles
164 Donlands Ave.
Toronto, ON M4J 3P8
(647) 436-9553
treehousecollectibles@gmail.com
treehousecollectibles.ca
(1-8, 20, 21, 23-25, 27-30)

QUEBEC

Librairie Première Issue
27 A D'Auteuil
Québec, QC G1R 4B9
418-692-3985
lib.premiere.issue@gmail.com
www.bsidepremiereissue
@gmail.com
(2-4, 6, 8, 12)

Multinational Comics & Cards
Montreal, QC
PH: (514) 891-6666
Larry.mcd1985@gmail.com
www.multinationalcomics.com
(1-9, 16-24, 26, 29,30)

NETHERLANDS

Henk Comics and 10, Store
Zeedijk 101a
Amsterdam, Noord Holland
1012 AV
henk@comics.nl
www.comics.nl
(2-7, 10-12, 18, 19, 21,23, 24, 27-30)

PHILIPPINES

Comic Odyssey
Space 3909, Level 3,
Robinsons Galleria
Ortigas
Quezon City, Metro Manila
1100
(637) 914-0040
sandy@comic-odyssey.com
www.comic-odyssey.com
(3, 4, 6, 7, 10, 18, 23, 31)

INTERNET

ComicLink Auctions & Exchange
PH: (617) 517-0062
buysell@ComicLink.com
www.ComicLink.com

Get Cash For Comics
PH: (888) 440-9787; ext. 117
buying@getcashforcomics.com

Goldin
PH: (856) 767-8550
sell@goldin.co
goldin.co/comics

Multinational Comics & Cards
PH: (514) 891-6666
Larry.mcd1985@gmail.com
www.multinationalcomics.com
(1-9, 16-24, 26, 29,30)

MyComicShop.com
PH: (817) 860-7827
buytrade@mycomicshop.com
www.mycomicshop.com

The Evil Lair
PH: (845) 513-3845
Thom@Evillaircomic.com
TheEvilLair.com
(4, 5, 7, 10, 20, 21, 23, 31)

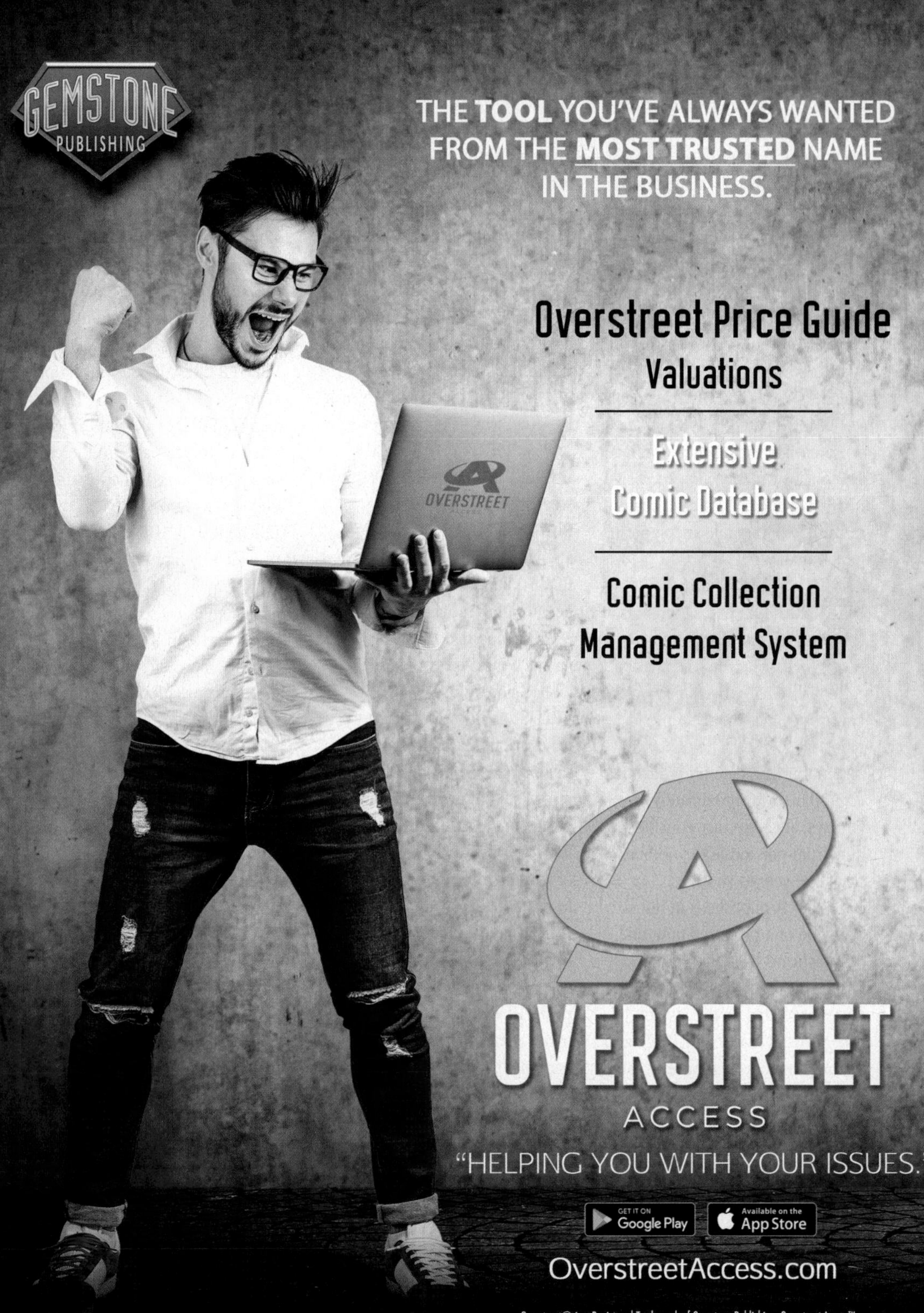
GEMSTONE
PUBLISHING
THE TOOL YOU'VE ALWAYS WANTED
FROM THE MOST TRUSTED NAME
IN THE BUSINESS.
Overstreet Price Guide
Valuations
Extensive
Comic Database
Comic Collection
Management System
OVERSTREET
OVERSTREET
ACCESS
"HELPING YOU WITH YOUR ISSUES."
GET IT ON Google Play
Available on the App Store
OverstreetAccess.com
Overstreet® is a Registered Trademark of Gemstone Publishing. Overstreet Access™ and the OA logo™ are trademarks of Gemstone Publishing. All rights reserved.

GLOSSARY

a - Story art; **a(i)** - Story art inks; **a(p)** - Story art pencils; **a(r)** - Story art reprint.

ADULT MATERIAL - Contains story and/or art for "mature" readers. Re: sex, violence, strong language.

ADZINE - A magazine primarily devoted to the advertising of comic books and collectibles as its first publishing priority as opposed to written articles.

ALLENTOWN COLLECTION - A collection discovered in 1987-88 just outside Allentown, Pennsylvania. The Allentown collection consisted of 135 Golden Age comics, characterized by high grade and superior paper quality.

ANNUAL - (1) A book that is published yearly; (2) Can also refer to some square bound comics.

ARRIVAL DATE - The date written (often in pencil) or stamped on the cover of comics by either the local wholesaler, newsstand owner, or distributor. The date precedes the cover date by approximately 15 to 75 days, and may vary considerably from one locale to another or from one year to another.

ASHCAN - A publisher's in-house facsimile of a proposed new title. Most ashcans have black and white covers stapled to an existing coverless comic on the inside; other ashcans are totally black and white. In modern parlance, it can also refer to promotional or sold comics, often smaller than standard comic size and usually in black and white, released by publishers to advertise the forthcoming arrival of a new title or story.

ATOM AGE - Comics published from 1946-1956.

B&W - Black and white art.

BACK-UP FEATURE - A story or character that usually appears after the main feature in a comic book; often not featured on the cover.

BAD GIRL ART - A term popularized in the early '90s to describe an attitude as well as a style of art that portrays women in a sexual and often action-oriented way.

BAXTER PAPER - A high quality, heavy, white paper used in the printing of some comics.

BC - Abbreviation for Back Cover.

BI-MONTHLY - Published every two months.

BI-WEEKLY - Published every two weeks.

BONDAGE COVER - Usually denotes a female in bondage.

BOUND COPY - A comic that has been bound into a book. The process requires that the spine be trimmed and sometimes sewn into a book-like binding.

BRITISH ISSUE - A comic printed for distribution in Great Britain; these copies sometimes have the price listed in pence or pounds instead of cents or dollars.

BRITTLENESS - A severe condition of paper deterioration where paper loses its flexibility and thus chips and/or flakes easily.

BRONZE AGE - Comics published from 1970 to 1984.

BROWNING - (1) The aging of paper characterized by the ever-increasing level of oxidation characterized by darkening; (2) The level of paper deterioration one step more severe than tanning and one step before brittleness.

c - Cover art; **c(i)** - Cover inks; **c(p)** - Cover pencils; **c(r)** - Cover reprint.

CAMEO - The brief appearance of one character in the strip of another.

CANADIAN ISSUE - A comic printed for distribution in Canada; these copies sometimes have no advertising.

CCA - Abbreviation for **Comics Code Authority**.

CCA SEAL - An emblem that was placed on the cover of all CCA approved comics beginning in April-May, 1955.

CENTER CREASE - See Subscription Copy.

CENTERFOLD or CENTER SPREAD - The two folded pages in the center of a comic book at the terminal end of the staples.

CERTIFIED GRADING - A process provided by a professional grading service that certifies a given grade for a comic and seals the book in a protective **Slab**.

CF - Abbreviation for Centerfold.

CFO - Abbreviation for Centerfold Out.

CGC - Abbreviation for the certified comic book grading company, Comics Guaranty, LLC.

CIRCULATION COPY - See Subscription Copy.

CIRCULATION FOLD - See Subscription Fold.

CLASSIC COVER - A cover considered by collectors to be highly desirable because of its subject matter, artwork, historical importance, etc.

CLEANING - A process in which dirt and dust is removed.

COLOR TOUCH - A restoration process by which colored ink is used to hide color flecks, color flakes, and larger areas of missing color. Short for Color Touch-Up.

COLORIST - An artist who paints the color guides for comics. Many modern colorists use computer technology.

COMIC BOOK DEALER - (1) A seller of comic books; (2) One who makes a living buying and selling comic books.
COMIC BOOK REPAIR - When a tear, loose staple or centerfold has been mended without changing or adding to the original finish of the book. Repair may involve tape, glue or nylon gossamer, and is easily detected; it is considered a defect.
COMICS CODE AUTHORITY - A voluntary organization comprised of comic book publishers formed in 1954 to review (and possibly censor) comic books before they were printed and distributed. The emblem of the CCA is a white stamp in the upper right hand corner of comics dated after February 1955. The term "post-Code" refers to the time after this practice started, or approximately 1955 to the present.
COMPLETE RUN - All issues of a given title.
CON - A convention or public gathering of fans.
CONDITION - The state of preservation of a comic book, often inaccurately used interchangeably with Grade.
CONSERVATION - The European Confederation of Conservator-Restorers' Organizations (ECCO) in its professional guidelines, defines conservation as follows: "Conservation consists mainly of direct action carried out on cultural heritage with the aim of stabilizing condition and retarding further deterioration."
COPPER AGE - Comics published from 1984 to 1992.
COSMIC AEROPLANE COLLECTION - A collection from Salt Lake City, Utah discovered by Cosmic Aeroplane Books, characterized by the moderate to high grade copies of 1930s-40s comics with pencil check marks in the margins of inside pages. It is thought that these comics were kept by a commercial illustration school and the check marks were placed beside panels that instructors wanted students to draw.
COSTUMED HERO - A costumed crime fighter with "developed" human powers instead of super powers.
COUPON CUT or COUPON MISSING - A coupon has been neatly removed with scissors or razor blade from the interior or exterior of the comic as opposed to having been ripped out.
COVER GLOSS - The reflective quality of the cover inks.
COVER TRIMMED - Cover has been reduced in size by neatly cutting away rough or damaged edges.
COVERLESS - A comic with no cover attached. There is a niche demand for coverless comics, particularly in the case of hard-to-find key books otherwise impossible to locate intact.
C/P - Abbreviation for **Cleaned and Pressed**. See **Cleaning**.
CREASE - A fold which causes ink removal, usually resulting in a white line. See **Reading Crease**.
CROSSOVER - A story where one character appears prominently in the story of another character. See **X-Over**.
CVR - Abbreviation for Cover.
DEALER - See **Comic Book Dealer**.
DEACIDIFICATION - Several different processes that reduce acidity in paper.
DEBUT - The first time that a character appears anywhere.
DEFECT - Any fault or flaw that detracts from perfection.
DENVER COLLECTION - A collection consisting primarily of early 1940s high grade number one issues bought at auction in Pennsylvania by a Denver, Colorado dealer.
DIE-CUT COVER - A comic book cover with areas or edges precut by a printer to a special shape or to create a desired effect.
DISTRIBUTOR STRIPES - Color brushed or sprayed on the edges of comic book stacks by the distributor/wholesaler to code them for expedient exchange at the sales racks. Typical colors are red, orange, yellow, green, blue, and purple. Distributor stripes are not a defect.
DOUBLE - A duplicate copy of the same comic book.
DOUBLE COVER - When two covers are stapled to the comic interior instead of the usual one; the exterior cover often protects the interior cover from wear and damage. This is considered a desirable situation by some collectors and may increase collector value; this is not considered a defect.
DRUG PROPAGANDA STORY - A comic that makes an editorial stand about drug use.
DRUG USE STORY - A comic that shows the actual use of drugs: needle use, tripping, harmful effects, etc.
DRY CLEANING - A process in which dirt and dust is removed.
DUOTONE - Printed with black and one other color of ink. This process was common in comics printed in the 1930s.
DUST SHADOW - Darker, usually linear area at the edge of some comics stored in stacks. Some portion of the cover was not covered by the comic immediately above it and it was exposed to settling dust particles. Also see **Oxidation Shadow** and **Sun Shadow**.
EDGAR CHURCH COLLECTION - See **Mile High Collection**.
EMBOSSED COVER - A comic book cover with a pattern, shape or

image pressed into the cover from the inside, creating a raised area.

ENCAPSULATION - Refers to the process of sealing certified comics in a protective plastic enclosure. Also see **Slabbing**.

EYE APPEAL - A term which refers to the overall look of a comic book when held at approximately arm's length. A comic may have nice eye appeal yet still possess defects which reduce grade.

FANZINE - An amateur fan publication.

FC - Abbreviation for Front Cover.

FILE COPY - A high grade comic originating from the publisher's file; contrary to what some might believe, not all file copies are in Gem Mint condition. An arrival date on the cover of a comic does not indicate that it is a file copy, though a copyright date may.

FIRST APPEARANCE - See **Debut**.

FLASHBACK - When a previous story is recalled.

FOIL COVER - A comic book cover that has had a thin metallic foil hot stamped on it. Many of these "gimmick" covers date from the early '90s, and might include chromium, prism and hologram covers as well.

FOUR COLOR - Series of comics produced by Dell, characterized by hundreds of different features; named after the four color process of printing. See **One Shot**.

FOUR COLOR PROCESS - The process of printing with the three primary colors (red, yellow, and blue) plus black.

FUMETTI - Illustration system in which individual frames of a film are colored and used for individual panels to make a comic book story. The most famous example is DC's *Movie Comics* #1-6 from 1939.

GATEFOLD COVER - A double-width fold-out cover.

GENRE - Categories of comic book subject matter; e.g. Science Fiction, Super-Hero, Romance, Funny Animal, Teenage Humor, Crime, War, Western, Mystery, Horror, etc.

GIVEAWAY - Type of comic book intended to be given away as a premium or promotional device instead of being sold.

GLASSES ATTACHED - In 3-D comics, the special blue and red cellophane and cardboard glasses are still attached to the comic.

GLASSES DETACHED - In 3-D comics, the special blue and red cellophane and cardboard glasses are not still attached to the comic; obviously less desirable than Glasses Attached.

GOLDEN AGE - Comics published from 1938 (*Action Comics* #1) to 1945.

GOOD GIRL ART - Refers to a style of art, usually from the 1930s-50s, that portrays women in a sexually implicit way.

GREY-TONE COVER - A cover art style in which pencil or charcoal underlies the normal line drawing, used to enhance the effects of light and shadow, thus producing a richer quality. These covers, prized by most collectors, are sometimes referred to as **Painted Covers** but are not actually painted.

HC - Abbreviation for Hardcover.

HEADLIGHTS - Forward illumation devices installed on all automobiles and many other vehicles... OK, OK, it's a euphemism for a comic book cover prominently featuring a woman's breasts in a provocative way. Also see **Bondage Cover** for another collecting euphemism that has long since outlived its appropriateness in these politically correct times.

HOT STAMPING - The process of pressing foil, prism paper and/or inks on cover stock.

HRN - Abbreviation for Highest Reorder Number. This refers to a method used by collectors of Gilberton's *Classic Comics* and *Classics Illustrated* series to distinguish first editions from later printings.

ILLO - Abbreviation for Illustration.

IMPAINT - Another term for **Color Touch**.

INDICIA - Publishing and title information usually located at the bottom of the first page or the bottom of the inside front cover. In some pre-1938 comics and many modern comics, it is located on internal pages.

INFINITY COVER - Shows a scene that repeats itself to infinity.

INKER - Artist that does the inking.

INTRO - Same as **Debut**.

INVESTMENT GRADE COPY - (1) Comic of sufficiently high grade and demand to be viewed by collectors as instantly liquid should the need arise to sell; (2) A comic in VF or better condition; (3) A comic purchased primarily to realize a profit.

ISSUE NUMBER - The actual edition number of a given title.

ISH - Short for Issue.

JLA - Abbreviation for Justice League of America.

JSA - Abbreviation for Justice Society of America.

KEY, KEY BOOK or KEY ISSUE - An issue that contains a first appearance, origin, or other historically or artistically important feature considered especially desirable by collectors.

LAMONT LARSON - Pedigreed collection of high grade 1940s comics with the initials or name of its original owner, Lamont Larson.

LENTICULAR COVERS or "FLICKER" COVERS - A comic book cover overlayed with a ridged plastic sheet such that the special artwork underneath appears to move when the cover is tilted at different angles perpendicular to the ridges.

LETTER COL or LETTER COLUMN

- A feature in a comic book that prints and sometimes responds to letters written by its readers.

LINE DRAWN COVER - A cover published in the traditional way where pencil sketches are overdrawn with india ink and then colored. See also **Grey-Tone Cover**, **Photo Cover**, and **Painted Cover**.

LOGO - The title of a strip or comic book as it appears on the cover or title page.

LSH - Abbreviation for Legion of Super-Heroes.

MAGIC LIGHTNING COLLECTION - A collection of high grade 1950s comics from the San Francisco area.

MARVEL CHIPPING - A bindery (trimming/cutting) defect that results in a series of chips and tears at the top, bottom, and right edges of the cover, caused when the cutting blade of an industrial paper trimmer becomes dull. It was dubbed Marvel Chipping because it can be found quite often on Marvel comics from the late '50s and early '60s but can also occur with any company's comic books from the late 1940s through the middle 1960s.

MILE HIGH COLLECTION - High grade collection of over 22,000 comics discovered in Denver, Colorado in 1977, originally owned by Mr. Edgar Church. Comics from this collection are now famous for extremely white pages, fresh smell, and beautiful cover ink reflectivity.

MODERN AGE - A catch-all term applied to comics published since 1992.

MYLAR™ - An inert, very hard, space-age plastic used to make high quality protective bags and sleeves for comic book storage. "Mylar" is a trademark of the DuPont Co.

ND - Abbreviation for **No Date**.

NN - Abbreviation for **No Number**.

NO DATE - When there is no date given on the cover or indicia page.

NO NUMBER - No issue number is given on the cover or indicia page; these are usually first issues or one-shots.

N.Y. LEGIS. COMM. - New York Legislative Committee to Study the Publication of Comics (1951).

ONE-SHOT - When only one issue is published of a title, or when a series is published where each issue is a different title (e.g. Dell's *Four Color Comics*).

ORIGIN - When the story of a character's creation is given.

over guide - When a comic book is priced at a value over *Guide* list.

OXIDATION SHADOW - Darker, usually linear area at the edge of some comics stored in stacks. Some portion of the cover was not covered by the comic immediately above it, and it was exposed to the air. Also see **Dust Shadow** and **Sun Shadow**.

p - Art pencils.

PAINTED COVER - (1) Cover taken from an actual painting instead of a line drawing; (2) Inaccurate name for a grey-toned cover.

PANELOLOGIST - One who researches comic books and/or comic strips.

PANNAPICTAGRAPHIST - One possible term for someone who collects comic books; can you figure out why it hasn't exactly taken off in common parlance?

PAPER COVER - Comic book cover made from the same newsprint as the interior pages. These books are extremely rare in high grade.

PARADE OF PLEASURE - A book about the censorship of comics.

PB - Abbreviation for Paperback.

PEDIGREE - A book from a famous and usually high grade collection - e.g. Allentown, Lamont Larson, Edgar Church/Mile High, Denver, San Francisco, Cosmic Aeroplane, etc. Beware of non-pedigree collections being promoted as pedigree books; only outstanding high grade collections similar to those listed qualify.

PENCILER - Artist that does the pencils...you're figuring out some of these definitions without us by now, aren't you?

PERFECT BINDING - Pages are glued to the cover as opposed to being stapled to the cover, resulting in a flat binded side. Also known as **Square Back or Square Bound**.

PG - Abbreviation for Page.

PHOTO COVER - Comic book cover featuring a photographic image instead of a line drawing or painting.

PIECE REPLACEMENT - A process by which pieces are added to replace areas of missing paper.

PIONEER AGE - Comics published from the 1500s to 1828.

PLATINUM AGE - Comics published from 1883 to 1938.

POLYPROPYLENE - A type of plastic used in the manufacture of comic book bags; now considered harmful to paper and not recommended for long term storage of comics.

POP - Abbreviation for the anti-comic book volume, *Parade of Pleasure*.

POST-CODE - Describes comics published after February 1955 and usually displaying the CCA stamp in the upper right-hand corner.

POUGHKEEPSIE - Refers to a large collection of Dell Comics file copies believed to have originated from the warehouse of Western Publishing in Poughkeepsie, NY.

PP - Abbreviation for Pages.

PRE-CODE - Describes comics published before the **Comics Code Authority** seal began appearing on covers in 1955.

PRE-HERO DC - A term used

to describe *More Fun* #1-51 (pre-Spectre), *Adventure* #1-39 (pre-Sandman), and *Detective* #1-26 (pre-Batman). The term is actually inaccurate because technically there were "heroes" in the above books.

PRE-HERO MARVEL - A term used to describe *Strange Tales* #1-100 (pre-Human Torch), *Journey Into Mystery* #1-82 (pre-Thor), *Tales To Astonish* #1-35 (pre-Ant-Man), and *Tales Of Suspense* #1-38 (pre-Iron Man).

PRESERVATION - Another term for **Conservation**.

PRESSING - A term used to describe a variety of processes or procedures, professional and amateur, under which an issue is pressed to eliminate wrinkles, bends, dimples and/or other perceived defects and thus improve its appearance. Some types of pressing involve disassembling the book and performing other work on it prior to its pressing and reassembly. Some methods are generally easily discerned by professionals and amateurs. Other types of pressing, however, can pose difficulty for even experienced professionals to detect. In all cases, readers are cautioned that unintended damage can occur in some instances. Related defects will diminish an issue's grade correspondingly rather than improve it.

PROVENANCE - When the owner of a book is known and is stated for the purpose of authenticating and documenting the history of the book. Example: A book from the Stan Lee or Forrest Ackerman collection would be an example of a value-adding provenance.

PULP - Cheaply produced magazine made from low grade newsprint. The term comes from the wood pulp that was used in the paper manufacturing process.

QUARTERLY - Published every three months (four times a year).

R - Abbreviation for Reprint.

RARE - 10-20 copies estimated to exist.

RAT CHEW - Damage caused by the gnawing of rats and mice.

RBCC - Abbreviation for Rockets Blast Comic Collector, one of the first and most prominent adzines instrumental in developing the early comic book market.

READING COPY - A comic that is in FAIR to GOOD condition and is often used for research; the condition has been sufficiently reduced to the point where general handling will not degrade it further.

READING CREASE - Book-length, vertical front cover crease at staples, caused by bending the cover over the staples. Square-bounds receive these creases just by opening the cover too far to the left.

REILLY, TOM - A large high grade collection of 1939-1945 comics with 5000+ books.

REINFORCEMENT - A process by which a weak or split page or cover is reinforced with adhesive and reinforcement paper.

REPRINT COMICS - In earlier decades, comic books that contained newspaper strip reprints; modern reprint comics usually contain stories originally featured in older comic books.

RESTORATION - Any attempt, whether professional or amateur, to enhance the appearance of an aging or damaged comic book using additive procedures. These procedures may include any or all of the following techniques: recoloring, adding missing paper, trimming, re-glossing, reinforcement, glue, etc. Amateur work can lower the value of a book, and even professional restoration has now gained a negative aura in the modern marketplace from some quarters. In all cases a restored book can never be worth the same as an unrestored book in the same condition. There is no consensus on the inclusion of pressing, non-aqueous cleaning, tape removal and in some cases staple replacement in this definition. Until such time as there is consensus, we encourage continued debate and interaction among all interested parties and reflection upon the standards in other hobbies and art forms.

REVIVAL - An issue that begins republishing a comic book character after a period of dormancy.

ROCKFORD - A high grade collection of 1940s comics with 2000+ books from Rockford, IL.

ROLLED SPINE - A condition where the left edge of a comic book curves toward the front or back; a defect caused by folding back each page as the comic was read.

ROUND BOUND - Standard saddle stitch binding typical of most comics.

RUN - A group of comics of one title where most or all of the issues are present. See **Complete Run**.

S&K - Abbreviation for the legendary creative team of Joe Simon and Jack Kirby, creators of Marvel Comics' Captain America.

SADDLE STITCH - The staple binding of magazines and comic books.

san francisco collection - (see **Reilly, Tom**)

SCARCE - 20-100 copies estimated to exist.

SEDUCTION OF THE INNOCENT - An inflammatory book written by Dr. Frederic Wertham and published in 1953; Wertham asserted that comics were responsible for rampant juvenile deliquency in American youth.

SET - (1) A complete run of a given title; (2) A grouping of comics for sale.

SEMI-MONTHLY - Published twice a month, but not necessarily **Bi-Weekly**.
SEWN SPINE - A comic with many spine perforations where binders' thread held it into a bound volume. This is considered a defect.
SF - Abbreviation for Science Fiction (the other commonly used term, "sci-fi," is often considered derogatory or indicative of more "lowbrow" rather than "literary" science fiction, i.e. "sci-fi television."
SILVER AGE - Comics published from 1956 to 1970.
SILVER PROOF - A black and white actual size print on thick glossy paper hand-painted by an artist to indicate colors to the engraver.
SLAB - Colloquial term for the plastic enclosure used by grading certification companies to seal in certified comics.
SLABBING - Colloquial term for the process of encapsulating certified comics in a plastic enclosure.
SOTI - Abbreviation for **Seduction of the Innocent**.
SPINE - The left-hand edge of the comic that has been folded and stapled.
SPINE ROLL - A condition where the left edge of the comic book curves toward the front or back, caused by folding back each page as the comic was read.
SPINE SPLIT SEALED - A process by which a spine split is sealed using an adhesive.
SPLASH PAGE - A **Splash Panel** that takes up the entire page.
SPLASH PANEL - (1) The first panel of a comic book story, usually larger than other panels and usually containing the title and credits of the story; (2) An oversized interior panel.
SQUARE BACK or SQUARE BOUND - See **Perfect Binding**.
STORE STAMP - Store name (and sometimes address and telephone number) stamped in ink via rubber stamp and stamp pad.
SUBSCRIPTION COPY - A comic sent through the mail directly from the publisher or publisher's agent. Most are folded in half, causing a subscription crease or fold running down the center of the comic from top to bottom; this is considered a defect.
SUBSCRIPTION CREASE - See **Subscription Copy**.
SUBSCRIPTION FOLD - See **Subscription Copy**. Differs from a **Subscription Crease** in that no ink is missing as a result of the fold.
SUN SHADOW - Darker, usually linear area at the edge of some comics stored in stacks. Some portion of the cover was not covered by the comic immediately above it, and it suffered prolonged exposure to light. A serious defect, unlike a **Dust Shadow**, which can sometimes be removed. Also see **Oxidation Shadow**.
SUPER-HERO - A costumed crime fighter with powers beyond those of mortal man.
SUPER-VILLAIN - A costumed criminal with powers beyond those of mortal man; the antithesis of **Super-Hero**.
SWIPE - A panel, sequence, or story obviously borrowed from previously published material.
TEAR SEALS - A process by which a tear is sealed using an adhesive.
TEXT ILLO. - A drawing or small panel in a text story that almost never has a dialogue balloon.
TEXT PAGE - A page with no panels or drawings.
TEXT STORY - A story with few if any illustrations commonly used as filler material during the first three decades of comics.
3-D COMIC - Comic art that is drawn and printed in two color layers, producing a 3-D effect when viewed through special glasses.
3-D EFFECT COMIC - Comic art that is drawn to appear as if in 3-D but isn't.
TITLE - The name of the comic book.
TITLE PAGE - First page of a story showing the title of the story and possibly the creative credits and indicia.
TRIMMED - (1) A bindery process which separates top, right, and bottom of pages and cuts comic books to the proper size; (2) A repair process in which defects along the edges of a comic book are removed with the use of scissors, razor blades, and/or paper cutters. Comic books which have been repaired in this fashion are considered defectives.
TTA - Abbreviation for *Tales to Astonish*.
UK - Abbreviation for British edition (United Kingdom).
UNDER GUIDE - When a comic book is priced at a value less than Guide list.
UPGRADE - To obtain another copy of the same comic book in a higher grade.
VARIANT COVER - A different cover image used on the same issue.
VERY RARE - 1 to 10 copies estimated to exist.
VICTORIAN AGE - Comics published from 1828 to 1883.
WANT LIST - A listing of comics needed by a collector, or a list of comics that a collector is interested in purchasing.
WAREHOUSE COPY - Originating from a publisher's warehouse; similar to file copy.
WHITE MOUNTAIN COLLECTION - A collection of high grade 1950s and 1960s comics which originated in New England.
X-OVER - Short for **Crossover**.
ZINE - Short for **Fanzine**.

CGC

How the Company Has Grown and How It Works

By the CGC Grading Team

The world of comic book collecting has grown and matured considerably since the introduction of CGC (Certified Guaranty Company) in 2000. Before CGC was founded, comic book transactions required sellers to grade their own comic books, a practice that often lacked consistency and impartiality. They also had to check their books for restoration, which was limited to each seller's skills at detection. During the first decades of fandom most sales took place through mail order, as well as local comic shops or the occasional convention. The advent of the internet changed all that, allowing global buying and selling, regardless of a person's location or experience. While this greatly expanded the comic book market, it also greatly increased the potential for inaccurate grading and restoration detection.

CGC was created to help bring order and stability to comic book sales, and to put an end to the risk and the chaos that accompanied online sales. CGC is the first and largest third-party comic book grading service, totally independent and impartial. A proven and respected commitment to integrity, accuracy and consistency has made CGC the leader in its field, becoming a tool to help people with their buying and selling decisions. The universally accepted CGC Grading Scale ensures consistency and gives both dealers and collectors a sense of dependability when making purchasing decisions. With CGC certification, a collector knows what he or she is getting based on an accurate and comprehensive description that can be found on the CGC certification label.

If you've ever wondered how it's done, here's a look at how CGC came together and how a book is certified.

The Formation of the Company

In January 2000, CGC was launched as part of the Certified Collectibles Group, which includes Numismatic Guaranty Corporation (NGC), the largest third-party coin grading company in the world; Numismatic Conservation Services (NCS), the leading authority in numismatic conservation; Paper Money Guaranty (PMG), the world's leading currency certification company; Classic Collectible Services (CCS), the world's premier comic book restoration, restoration removal and pressing company; Certified Sports Guaranty (CSG), a fast-growing grading service for sports cards; Authenticated Stamp Guaranty (ASG), an expanding stamp grading service; and Collectibles Authentication Guaranty (CAG), service for preserving the authenticity and provenance of collections.

The Certified Collectibles Group sought out talented and ethical individuals to grade comic books. Experts needed a history of working with comics as well as necessary skills to verify a comic book's authenticity and to detect restoration that can affect its value. To identify these individuals, many of the most respected individuals in the hobby were consulted, and based on their recommendations, a core grading team was selected.

The members of the CGC grading team come from diverse backgrounds, and many were comic book dealers at some time in their careers. Experience in the commercial sector can be an essential ingredient in becoming familiar with market standards.

When it was time to develop a uniform grading standard, the hobby's leaders were once again called upon. Everyone agreed that the *Overstreet Guide* was the foundation of this standard, but there were a number of subjective interpretations of its published definitions. It was critical to understand how these guidelines were being applied to the everyday buying and selling of comics. To accomplish this, approximately 50 of the hobby's top experts took part in an extensive grading test. Their grades were averaged and an accurate grading standard reflecting the collective experience of the hobby's most prominent individuals was thus developed. CGC now had the best standard and the best team to apply it.

With the graders in place and the grading scale established, the next step was to develop a tamper-evident holder for the long-term storage and display of certified comics. This proved to be a technical challenge. Exhaustive material tests were conducted to determine that the holders were archival safe. To create a true first line of defense, it was determined that the comic book should be sealed in a soft inner well, then sealed again inside a tamper evident hard plastic case with interlocking ridges to enable compact storage. The CGC-certified grade appears on a label sealed inside the holder for an additional level of security.

Submitting Books

Comic books may be submitted for certification in two ways: they can be submitted by authorized dealers or by Collectors Society members. The Collectors Society is an online community with direct access to certification service from CGC, and submissions can be prepared using the CGC online submission form. Both dealers and Collectors Society members typically send their comics to CGC's offices by registered mail or through an insured express company. Submissions are also accepted at many of the comic cons that occur around the country throughout the year. CGC will grade on-site at selected shows.

Receiving the Books

CGC's Receiving Department opens packages that have arrived and verifies that the number of books in each package matches the number shown on the submitted invoice and checks the submission for any damage sustained in shipping. Once this is done, a more detailed comparison is made to ensure that their invoice descriptions correspond to the actual comics. This information is entered into a computer, and from this time forth, the comics will be traceable at all stages of the grading process by their invoice number and their line number within that invoice. Each book is checked to see that it is properly prepared for grading in an appropriately sized comic bag with backing board and then is labeled with a numbered barcode containing the pertinent data of invoice number and line-item information for quick reading by the computer.

The Grading Begins

The book is then passed on to the graders. The grading process begins by having the book's pages counted and entering into the computer any peculiarities or flaws that may affect a book's grade. Some examples of this would be "Spine Stress Lines Break Color," "Right Top Front Cover Small Crease Breaks Color," "Top Back Cover Tear with Crease" and "Staple Rusted ." This information is entered into the "Graders Notes" field and a grade is assigned. The book is also examined for restoration; if any form of restoration work is detected, this information is entered into the computer, broken down by each form of restoration found.

When other graders examine the comic, they do not see any previous assigned grades, so as to not influence their evaluation. Graders are able to view previous Graders Notes while determining their own grade. The Grader may then add to the existing commentary if he or she believes more remarks are in order. The Grading Finalizer is the last person to examine the book. He or she makes a final restoration check before determining their own grade, at which time the grades and notes entered by the previous graders are reviewed. If all grades match or are very close, they will assign the book's final grade. The book is then forwarded to the Encapsulation Department for sealing. If there is disagreement among the graders, a discussion will ensue until a final determination is made and the book can be forwarded.

Each comic book receives a restoration check and the results appear on the label.

CGC RESTORED GRADE

X-Men #1

Marvel Comics, 9/63

Restoration includes: color touch, pieces added, tear seals, cover cleaned, interior lightened, reinforced.

OFF-WHITE Pages

Encapsulating the Comics

After each comic has been graded and the necessary numbers and text entered into their respective data fields, all the comics on a particular invoice are taken from the Grading Department into the Encapsulation Department. Here, appropriately color-coded labels are printed bearing the proper descriptive text, including each book's grade and identification number. This is critical, as it serves to make each certified comic unique and is also a significant deterrent to counterfeiting CGC's valued product. All of the above information is duplicated in a barcode, which also appears on the comic's label.

The newly printed labels are stacked in the same sequence as the comics to be encapsulated with them, ensuring that each book and its label match one another. The comic is now ready to be fitted inside an archival-quality interior well, which is then sealed within a transparent capsule, along with the book's color-coded label. This is accomplished through a combination of compression and ultrasonic vibration.

The Comics are Shipped

After encapsulation, all comics are sent to Quality Control for inspection. Here, they are examined to make certain that their labels are correct for both the grade and its accompanying descriptive information. Quality Control also inspects each book for any flaws in its holder, such as scuffs or nicks. CGC is careful to make certain that the comics it certifies are not only accurately graded, but attractively presented as well. When all the comics have been inspected, they are delivered to our Shipping Department for packaging. The comics are counted, and their labels checked against the original invoice to make certain that no mistakes have occurred. A Shipping Department employee then verifies the method of transport as selected by the submitter on the invoice and prepares the comics for delivery or they are held in CGC's vault for in-person pick-up by the submitter.

No matter whether the US Postal Service or a private carrier is used, the method of packaging is essentially the same. The encapsulated comics are placed inside sturdy cardboard boxes. CGC has developed a custom shipping box to enable the highest level of stability during shipping. A copy of the submitter's invoice is included before the box is sealed and heavy tape is used to prevent accidental or unauthorized opening of the box while it is in transit.

The barcode of every comic book is scanned before it is placed into its shipping box. The status of the book is changed to "shipped" in our tracking system, and we retain a record of what books were shipped in which box. This is the final crucial step of our detailed internal tracking system.

The CGC Label

Comic books certified by CGC bear color-coded labels that have different meanings. Whenever purchasing a CGC-certified comic, be certain to note not only the book's grade but also its label category. A Universal label is denoted by the color blue and indicates that a book was not found to have any qualifying defects or signs of restoration. There is one exception to this policy: At CGC's discretion, comics having a very minor amount of color touch or glue may still qualify for a Universal label provided such restoration is noted underneath the assigned grade.

As its name implies, the Restored label, identified by its purple color, is used for books found to have restoration work performed on them. The grade assigned is based on the book's appearance, with the restoration noted. The Restoration scale determines the quality (A, B, or C) and quantity (between 1 and 5) of any restoration present, and is as follows:

Quality (Aesthetic) Scale – (Determined by materials used and visual quality of work)

A (Excellent)

- Color touch using acrylic or watercolor. Color match near perfect, no bleed through
- Tear seals, reinforcement, split seals and reattachment applied with rice paper and wheat paste
- Piece fill applied with leafcasting or rice paper, seamless with correct thickness and flexibility
- Cleaning with no evidence of fading, dimensional change, excessive whiteness, ripples, cockling, or ink smudging
- Staples cleaned or replaced with vintage or rustproof staples
- Staples replaced exactly as they were
- Filled edges cut evenly
- Book feels and looks natural

B (Fine)

- Color touch using pencil, pen, crayon, or chalk. Apparent upon close inspection, but no bleed through
- Color touch using acrylic or watercolor with average color matching
- Piece fill applied with cadaver comic parts or poorly applied rice paper. Apparent upon close inspection and to the touch
- Cover cleaning exhibiting color fading, dimensional change, ink smudging, or excessive whiteness or cockling
- Interior cleaning exhibiting slight puffiness, cockling, or excessively white
- Crooked or repositioned staples
- Re-glossing agent used on cover

C (Poor)

- Color touch using pen, marker or white out. Poor color matching or bleed through evident
- Piece fill using regular paper, obvious at arm's length
- Tear seals, reinforcement, split seals and reattachment using household glue

Quality Scale – (Determined primarily by extent of piece fill and color touch)

1 (Slight)
Tear seals, spine split seals, reinforcement, piece reattachment, leafcasting, cleaning, replaced staples, re-glossing, glue. Piece fill can be no bigger than the size of two bindery chips. Color touch must be light, in small areas like spine stresses, creases or bindery chip fill.

2 (Slight/Moderate)
Piece fill can be up to ½" x ½" cumulative in size on the cover and up to 1" x 1" on the interior. Color touch can be up to 1" x 1" in area. An excessive amount of glue used on the cover or interior pages.

3 (Moderate)
Piece fill up to the size of 1" x 1" and/or color touch covering up to 2" x 2". Interior piece fill up to 2" x 2"

4 (Moderate/Extensive)
Piece fill up to the size of 2" x 2" on the cover and 4" x 4" on the interior. Color touch up to 4" x 4" in area.

5 (Extensive)
Piece fill over 2" x 2" on the cover and 4" x 4" on the interior. Color touch over 4"x 4".

The presence of trimming on a comic book will receive a CGC purple restored label. But if only trimming is present, it will not garner a quality or quantity rating, only displaying the word "apparent." If restoration is present in addition to trimming, the trimming will have no bearing on the quality or quantity assigned to the restoration.

The Conserved Label is similar to the blue Universal label but is differentiated by a silver bar across the top. Conservation is noted in a similar fashion on the label as on the purple CGC Restored Label. This label is applied to any comic book with specific, professional repairs done to improve the structural integrity and long-term preservation. These repairs include tear seals, support, staple replacement, piece reattachment, leafcasting, and certain kinds of cleaning:

Conservation Repairs

- Tear seals
- Spine split seals
- Reinforcement
- Piece reattachment
- Some cover or interior cleaning (water or solvent)
- Staples cleaned or replaced
- Leafcasting

Materials Used for Conservation Repairs:

- Rice paper
- Wheat glue
- Vintage staples
- Archival tape

The Qualified label is green, indicating one qualifying defect is present on a book, and includes detachments, missing parts, and unverified signatures. An example of such a qualifying feature would be a Marvel Value Stamp missing from an interior page that does not affect the story. If such a book appears 9.6 otherwise but would downgrade to 3.5 due to the missing stamp, assigning a grade of 3.5 does not fully represent the appearance of the comic to a collector. Through use of the green Qualified label, a comic buyer is able to make an informed decision as to what he is purchasing in terms of its overall desirability. Because of the complexity involved, green labels are seldomly assigned. In addition, high grade comic books that have an unwitnessed signature, and therefore are not eligible for the Signature Series label (see below), get the Qualified label. This is the most common use for the Qualified label and shows what the grade of the book would have been if the signature was not present. Qualified labels are always used for married parts; if no restoration is present, a comic book with a married cover, wrap or page will always receive a Qualified label.

The Qualified label is green, indicating one qualifying defect is present on a book, and includes detachments, missing parts, and unverified signatures. An example of such a qualifying feature would be a Marvel Value Stamp missing from an interior page that does not affect the story. If such a book appears 9.6 otherwise but would downgrade to 3.5 due to the missing stamp, assigning a grade of 3.5 does not fully represent the appearance of the comic to a collector. Through use of the green Qualified label, a comic buyer is able to make an informed decision as to what he is purchasing in terms of its overall desirability. Because of the complexity involved, green labels are seldomly assigned. In addition, high grade comic books that have an unwitnessed signature, and therefore are not eligible for the Signature Series label (see below), get the Qualified label. This is the most common use for the Qualified label and shows what the grade of the book would have been if the signature was not present. Qualified labels are always used for married parts; if no restoration is present, a comic book with a married cover, wrap or page will always receive a Qualified label.

The Evolution of CGC and CCG

In October of 2003, CGC began to certify comic book related magazines. The certification process and label system for magazines is the same as for comic books. Some examples of comic book-related magazines that CGC certifies are *MAD Magazine*, *Vampirella*, *Creepy*, *Eerie* and *Famous Monsters of Filmland*.

More recently CGC introduced grading and encapsulation for *Sports Illustrated* and *Playboy* magazines, Movie Lobby Cards, Photographs and Concert Posters. In 2016, CGC launched a redesign of its holder with enhanced strength, design, clarity and tamper-proof features. In 2020, CGC launched CGC Trading Cards, a division devoted to grading the most popular TCGs, such as *Pokémon* and *Magic: The Gathering*. CGC has graded nearly 10 million collectibles to date.

In a move intended to strengthen CGC's commitment to promoting the comic collecting hobby and enhance the collecting experience, the Certified Collectibles Group acquired Classics Incorporated, the world's premier comic book restoration, restoration removal and pressing company, in 2012. Previously located in Dallas, Texas, Classics Incorporated relocated to Sarasota, Florida, to become an independent member of the Certified Collectibles Group under the new name Classic Collectible Services (CCS). Customers who wish to send books in for pressing, restoration or restoration removal are able to send them to CCS and have them transfer directly to CGC for grading — creating a synergistic relationship that saves customers time, shipping and insurance expenses.

For more information on comic book certification, pressing, restoration, and CGC's many other services, please visit our website at www.CGCcomics.com

Grab yourself a refreshment!

• Marv Wolfman •
(Teen Titans)

• Larry Houston •
(X-Men animated)

• Rick Hoberg •
(Star Wars)

• Chris Ulm •
(Ultraverse/Rune)

• Shaun McLaughlin •
(Superman animated)

• Ed Catto •
(Captain Action)

• Kevin VanHook •
(Bloodshot)

Geekview Tavern
on YouTube

Host & bartender Dave Olbrich
(publisher Malibu Comics, Ultraverse, Bravura, Eternity)

All the geeky comic books, television, and movies you love!

www.youtube.com/@geekview

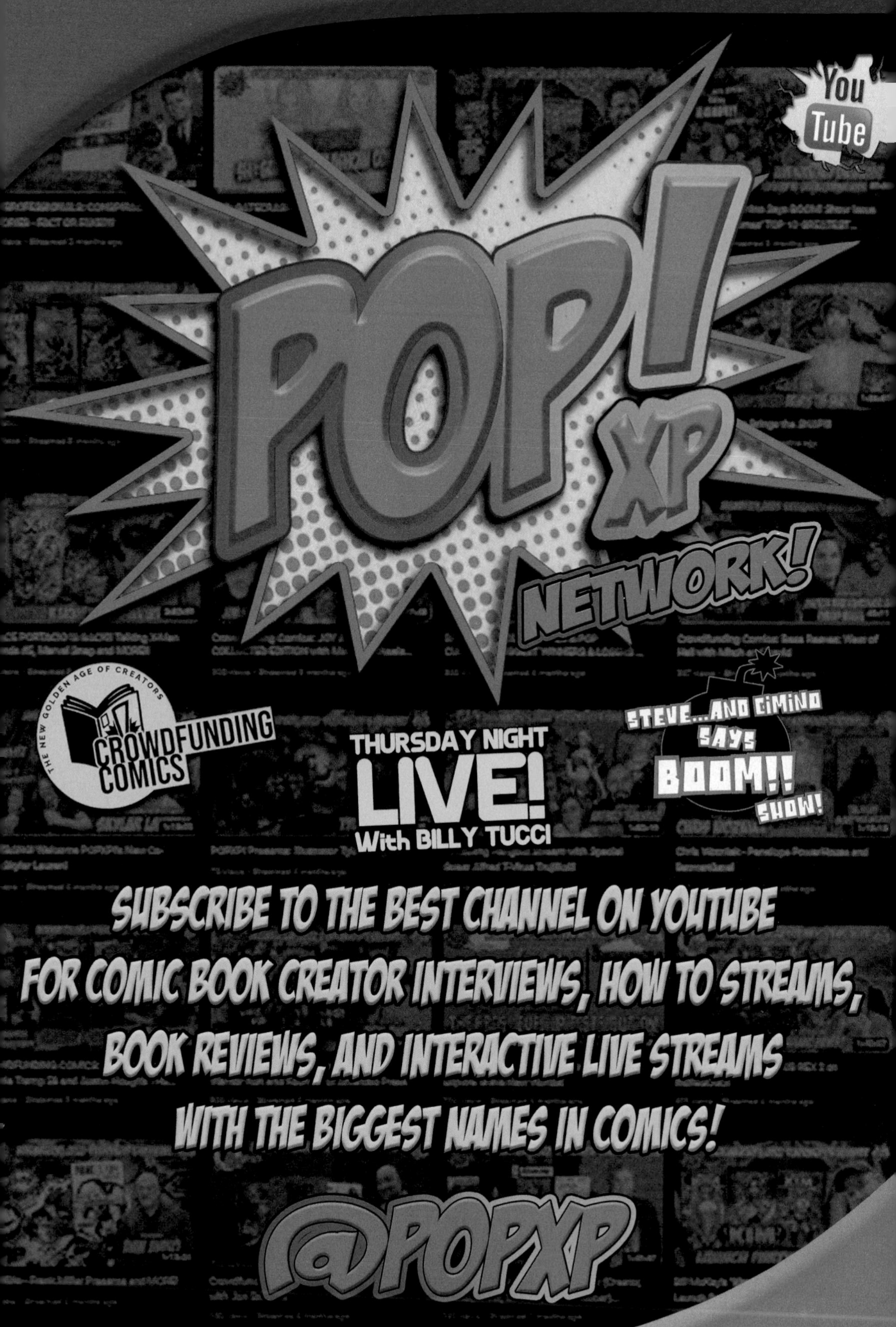

You Tube
POP! XP
NETWORK!
THE NEW GOLDEN AGE OF CREATORS
CROWDFUNDING COMICS
THURSDAY NIGHT LIVE! With BILLY TUCCI
STEVE...AND CIMINO SAYS BOOM!! SHOW!
SUBSCRIBE TO THE BEST CHANNEL ON YOUTUBE
FOR COMIC BOOK CREATOR INTERVIEWS, HOW TO STREAMS,
BOOK REVIEWS, AND INTERACTIVE LIVE STREAMS
WITH THE BIGGEST NAMES IN COMICS!
@POPXP

FRANK FRAZETTA'S

DEATH DEALER

IVERSON • MARTINO • DELGADO • BASCLE

FRANK FRAZETTA'S

DEATH DEALER

One acclaimed illustration spawned a still-growing industry

With his horned helmet and obscured facial features, the axe-carrying, armor-clad warrior sits atop a horse and permanently looks ready for battle, evoking whole stories from a single image: Frank Frazetta's Death Dealer.

The character of the Death Dealer first appeared in Frazetta's 1973 painting of the same name. The popularity of the piece spawned additional paintings of the character by the artist. In addition to the paintings, the Death Dealer's familiar image has appeared on comic books, novels, statues, action figures, D&D miniatures, and the cover to Molly Hatchet's debut album. The US Army's III Corps uses the character as its mascot, as does the US Marine Corps VNM-164 helicopter squadron.

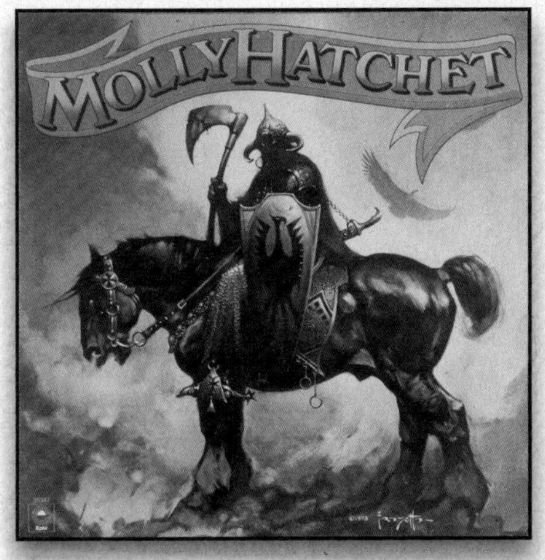

In other words, even with "Death" in the character's name, it took on a life of its own. Considering the emotions and story inspirations Frazetta's work has evoked over decades, perhaps it's not too surprising that this particular piece has been the catalyst for so much.

"Unlike most of his artistic contemporaries in the latter 20th century, Frank Frazetta didn't try to impress the cultural establishment with his profound insights or stylistic radicalism. His subjects were beautiful women, heroic men and fearsome monsters, usually captured in dramatic scenes of action and adventure. His style was classical Italian Renaissance, sometimes compared to Michelangelo or Rafael, with an edge of Brooklyn attitude," author Rob Salkowitz

wrote in *Forbes*. "The power of his imagination and his incomparable draftsmanship are credited with supercharging entire genres of literature and music, as the presence of one of his cover illustrations just about guaranteed commercial success for everything from fantasy paperbacks to heavy metal rock albums."

The Society of Illustrators gave Frazetta an Award of Excellence in their 15th Annual Exhibition of American Illustration. In the artist's biography on the organization's site, Nick Meglin wrote, "With only his imagination as reference, Frazetta paints with such persuasive accuracy that the viewer often accepts one of his landscapes as if it were the camera's vision. And it is executed with such craft that none can doubt the artist had painted that vista on-the-spot, regardless of its inter-planetary location."

In this universe-building era in which we presently reside, it's not too surprising that Opus Comics and parent Incendium saw tremendous potential in the master illustrator's legacy.

"There's a real power to Frazetta works, of course many of the pieces include idealized anatomy and heroic figures, but there is a weight and movement that really captures the imagination, the visual communication of the mood and the action is superb. Frank made mention of his process to keep foreground elements to a minimum and backgrounds somewhat abstract, it's his focus on the characters, and the entire illustration supporting the figure, that really reinforces his creations and gives the viewer enough room to conjure up the broader scenario for themselves, I've always found it a very captivating and engaging portfolio, the characters leap off the canvas and yet there's so much left to explore," said Opus Comics' Llexi Leon.

In March 2022 they launched *Frank Frazetta's Death Dealer*, written by Mitch Iverson (*DOTA:*

Dragon's Blood) and illustrated by Stefano Martino (*Stranger Things*) with colorist Luis Antonio Delgado (*Teenage Mutant Ninja Turtles: The Last Ronin*). Some of the top artists in the industry have taken the opportunity to walk in Frazetta's shoes and create variant covers for the project.

"We've been fortunate in that many wonderfully talented artists have reached out to us with regards to contributing to the Frazetta comic titles; it's evident that Frank's work has inspired a lot of the great established and up-and-coming artists, so we've seen some truly awesome interpretations come through from many fan-favorite creators," Leon said.

As we approached press time for *The Overstreet Comic Book Price Guide* #53, the company announced that *Frank Frazetta's Death Dealer* #1 would receive its fourth printing. Clearly, there's an audience for it. This isn't, though, the character's first time in comics.

Previously, *Death Dealer* was the title character in a four-issue series from Verotik in 1995. Former Misfits vocalist Glenn Danzig served as writer and publisher. The series featured art by Simon Bisley, Liam Sharp, and Arthur Suydam.

In 2007 and 2008, Image Comics published the series *Death Dealer: Shadows of Mirahan* written by Joshua Ortega and illustrated by Nat Jones with colorist Jay Fotos. The hardcover collecting the issues can command higher prices.

In addition to the success Opus has seen with *Frank Frazetta's Death Dealer,* they have added a five-issue mini-series, *Frank Frazetta's Dawn Attack*, and an anthology, *Frank Frazetta's Tales of Science-Fantasy*. They both follow the same formula as Death Dealer, drawing their inspiration from Frazetta's paintings and challenging today's top artists to live up to his legacy.

–J.C. Vaughn

THE AVENGERS

60 YEARS OF ASSEMBLING

By Amanda Sheriff

Comic books is a visual medium with much of the story told through the art. But if there's one phrase that can excite readers as much as a powerful punch delivered to the chin of a villain, it's the battle cry of Earth's Mightiest Heroes: "Avengers assemble!"

What began as a small group of heroes gathered to stop a charismatic and calculating villain (and an opportunity to introduce readers to more characters and their other books) has evolved into an all-star team that is recognized around the world. The Avengers consistently fight villains with insatiable quests for power in dramatic confrontations to save not just our world but all of existence across the multiverse. Comprised of Marvel's greatest superheroes, they handle massive threats that are far too challenging for a single warrior. Each individual's extraordinary superpowers, genius innovation, and magical talents combine to form a mighty front in facing the most dire situations.

The degree of difficulty in their missions creates fertile ground for storytelling that hits not just the ethos, but the pathos too. Underneath their suits, masks, and armor, the Avengers are real people who are strong-willed, opinionated, and don't always agree on how they should neutralize threats. Characters who are the singular stars of their own comics must set aside their hubris and personal priorities, however hard that might be, to work as a team. By compromising, relinquishing sole control of a fight, and trusting that they'll have each other's backs, the Avengers give readers deeper stories.

The Avengers assembled for the first time in *The Avengers* #1 (September 1963), created by writer Stan Lee and artist Jack Kirby. Originally a fivesome of Iron Man, Thor, the Hulk, Ant-Man (Hank Pym), and the Wasp, the team has seen a rotating roster of members with humans, Inhumans, mutants, androids, supernatural beings, aliens, and even former villains.

Many of the greatest minds in comics have written or drawn the Avengers over their 60-year history. They have dwelt in the hands of writers like Roy Thomas, Kurt Busiek, John Byrne, Mark Millar, Mark Gruenwald, Steve Englehart, Roger Stern, Brian Michael Bendis, Jim Starlin, Jonathan Hickman, and Rick Remender. Artists such as Don Heck, John Buscema, Sal Buscema, George Pérez, Neal Adams, John Romita Jr., Steve Epting, Adam Kubert, Mike Deodato Jr., and Leinil Yu have brought them to life. This list of comic luminaries is just a sampling of the talent that has worked on Avengers comics.

Their first team conflict was an Asgardian incident when Loki sought revenge against his brother Thor. After defeating Loki, Ant-Man noted how well they worked together and suggested forming a team (which was then named by the Wasp). The Hulk left soon after they became a team and was replaced by Captain America, in issue 4 (notably, Cap's first Silver Age

appearance). Together they fought big league villains like Baron Zemo, Masters of Evil, Kang the Conqueror, Wonder Man, and Count Nefaria.

Heroes need a place to hang their capes, which came in the headquarters in New York City. Courtesy of Tony Stark, Avengers Mansion was introduced in *The Avengers* #2 (November 1963). It has been overseen by their butler Edwin Jarvis, outfitted with state of the art technology, and is home to their indispensable Quinjet.

The Avengers started seeing members rotating in and out, with the departures of the founders, minus Cap, who were replaced by former villains Hawkeye, Scarlet Witch, and Quicksilver. Throughout the 1960s, Ant-Man (now as Goliath) and the Wasp returned, then Hercules joined, Black Panther was added after helping them defeat Grim Reaper and Klaw, and Vision was introduced to the team. An intrateam milestone occurred when Hank (now as Yellowjacket) and Janet got married.

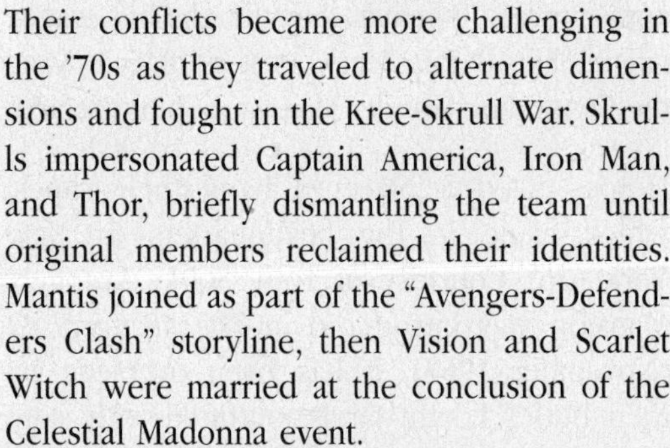

Their conflicts became more challenging in the '70s as they traveled to alternate dimensions and fought in the Kree-Skrull War. Skrulls impersonated Captain America, Iron Man, and Thor, briefly dismantling the team until original members reclaimed their identities. Mantis joined as part of the "Avengers-Defenders Clash" storyline, then Vision and Scarlet Witch were married at the conclusion of the Celestial Madonna event.

They faced a bureaucratic foe starting in *Avengers* #165 (November 1977) when Henry Peter Gyrich became their liaison to the U.S. National Security Council. Since he was not a fan of superhumans, Gyrich was adamant that the Avengers follow government rules or lose their status with the country. He demanded that the team be trimmed to seven members and that Falcon be added to comply with affirmative action laws. The last decree didn't sit well with Falcon, who didn't want to be the subject of tokenism, and Hawkeye, who would lose his spot on the team.

A big team conflict occurred in the early '80s, surrounding Hank Pym's erratic behavior. He became hostile toward Janet, which culminated in Hank hitting her during an argument. In another incident, he attacked an enemy after a fight had ended. Hank was suspended from the team for a period then made peace with Janet, though they decided not to remain as couple, and he retired from being a superhero.

Several major storylines followed, including when Vision took over the world's computer systems to create world peace, the West Coast Avengers were formed, the second Baron Zemo and the Masters of Evil infiltrated Avengers Mansion, and Zeus transported the Avengers to Olympus for a trial when he blamed them for Hercules' injuries.

Tigra, She-Hulk, Monica Rambeau as Captain Marvel, Starfox, Mockingbird, and Namor joined the team. Since there were now so many members whose abilities were needed in different situations, both the Avengers

and West Coast Avengers changed their team policies to allow members to be active when available and on reserve when not. Then they merged into one team with two bases.

Vision and Scarlet Witch had a rough time in the '80s. It was discovered that their children were illusions, Vision was disassembled by government agents, and the results drove Scarlet Witch insane. Though she recovered, some of her latent powers were discovered which became part of future conflicts.

The Avengers titles were featured in a 1989 crossover event when Loki gathered some of Marvel's greatest villains in "Acts of Vengeance," pitting Magneto, Doctor Doom, Kingpin, Red Skull, the Mandarin, and Wizard against the team.

Characters like Black Widow, Vision, Hercules, Black Knight, Sersi, and Crystal became primary features in the title as the Avengers started facing villains that were more homicidal, which made the team question their rule against killing villains. This was a focal point in the 1992 "Operation: Galactic Storm" event when the Avengers were involved in a situation between the Kree and the Shi-ar Empire. Iron Man and several others executed the Supreme Intelligence, which didn't sit well with Captain America, though it was revealed that Kang was manipulating Iron Man.

In the mid-'90s "Heroes Reborn," many of the Avengers and the Fantastic Four died trying to stop Onslaught, but were actually transported to a pocket universe. The continuity briefly changed – turning Tony Stark into a teenager, Hawkeye was deaf, and the Wasp was mutated into an insect state – but was returned to normal in *Avengers* Vol. 3 #1 (February 1998). Some of the new members included Wonder Man, Silverclaw, Firestar, Justice, and Triathlon.

Scott Lang as Ant-Man, Jack of Hearts, and a new Captain Britain were the next members to join the team around the time that the

Avengers were given international authority by the United Nations. In the 2004-2005 "Avengers Disassembled" event, some were killed, and the team lost a measure of their credibility. The villain of the story was revealed to be Scarlet Witch who had been driven insane by the loss of her children. When the Avengers disbanded after the event, the New Avengers was formed, comprised of Iron Man, Captain America, Spider-Man, Spider-Woman, Wolverine, Luke Cage, Ronin, and Sentry.

In 2006-2007 Marvel crafted the Civil War story arc that split its heroes over the new Superhuman Registration Act. Iron Man supported the act, along with Mister Fantastic, Ms. Marvel, and She-Hulk, while Captain America was opposed to it. Since Cap disagreed with some of his teammates, he started a Secret Avengers team with Hercules, Falcon, Iron Fist, and Luke Cage. It culminated in a major battle with Cap nearly killing Iron Man before realizing that the fight had hurt the people they always tried to protect.

The period saw a few different Avengers teams, featuring many heroes. Luke Cage led a team with some New Avengers members, who dealt with the Secret Wars event, Iron Man formed a Mighty Avengers team, and Hank Pym started a team of Avengers that operated on an international level.

The next iteration of the Avengers was formed in early 2010, with Thor, Hawkeye, Spider-Man, Wolverine, Captain America, Spider-Woman, and Iron Man, with Maria Hill as the team leader. Luke Cage maintained his team with Iron Fist, Power Woman, and the Thing joining his crew. In 2011, the "Shattered Heroes" story resulted in changes to the main team lineup with Wolverine and Spider-Man leaving to be involved in the New Avengers, and Quake, Storm, and Vision joining the main team.

TO BE CONTINUED...

PREVIEWS world
PULLBOX

THE CONTINUATION OF YOUR NEXT GREAT STORY IS ONLY A PAGE AWAY.

A **PICTURE** IS WORTH A THOUSAND WORDS.

BIDS **STARTING**
AS LOW AS **$1.00**

DIGAuction.com

*Come "**DIG**" through our collection.*

MULTIPLE COMIC AUCTIONS EVERY WEEK! | **NO** BUYER'S PREMIUM

An *Uncanny Avengers* series was created in 2012 with members of the Avengers and the X-Men working together. During the Axis event, several heroes and villains went through a moral inversion, prompting Steve Rogers to assemble a team with Magneto, Doctor Doom, Deadpool, Enchantress, Loki, Mystique, Carnage, and others who are temporarily heroic characters.

In the aftermath of 2015's "Secret Wars," Avengers Idea Mechanics was formed to take on threats beyond just fighting the villains, and Iron Man formed a team in *All-New All-Different Avengers* with Vision, Ms. Marvel, Miles Morales as Spider-Man, Sam Wilson as Cap, and Jane Foster as Thor. A Hydra version of the Avengers was formed in Secret Empire, with Hydra Cap, Odinson, Deadpool, a possessed Scarlet Witch, virus-infected Vision, Taskmaster, and Doctor Octopus. That team disbanded with Odinson rejecting Hydra Cap, Vision and Scarlet Witch being cleansed of their afflictions, and others helped free some of the Champions.

With "Secret Wars" safely behind, the eighth volume of *Avengers* was launched in May 2018, with the return of core members Captain America, Iron Man, and Thor, joined by Captain Marvel, She-Hulk, Black Panther, Robbie Reyes as Ghost Rider, Blade, and Doctor Strange. The new incarnation of the team has battled the Dark Celestials and been confronted by Namor and the new Winter Guard. They stood against the kingdom of vampires with Blade's help, discovered the new wielder of the Starbrand, were challenged by Khonshu, and fought each other for the power of the Phoenix.

The Avengers have long been a favorite among comic book readers, but in the late 2000s their comic book stories were brought out of their niche status and into the pop culture consciousness through the Marvel Cinematic Universe. From the start, the MCU has gotten award-winning actors and big name stars to play comic book characters with a variety of directors who have used their specific talents to capture the style and tone of different characters. They created highly detailed, rich cinematic experiences with dramatic stories about men and women of honor and lighthearted turns about the misadventures of loveable screwups.

The MCU has overseen the creation of a giant complicated web of stories weaved together to make each entry important. This larger tapestry was given life through Infinity Stone appearances, cameos and team-ups, well placed foreshadowing, and expositive stingers. They didn't rush things into mediocre movies or bombard viewers with too much content all at once, nor did they drag things out to the point of becoming irrelevant or irritating for viewers. From the storytelling standpoint, it's an unprecedented exercise in complexity and meticulously planned interconnectedness. It's also proven to be a highly lucrative venture.

Since *Iron Man* soared into theaters in 2008, the Avengers have become synonymous with box office gold, gaining legions of new fans who were previously unfamiliar with many of the team's roster of heroes and foes. They have continually broken box office records, become the most bankable movies for going on 15 years, and inspired many movie fans to become first time comic readers.

In their 60 years of existence, the Avengers have left an indelible mark on comics and pop culture. They have kept the storytelling fresh with members rotating in and out on a regular basis, new iterations on different coasts, even welcoming villains when the occasion called for it. Facing insurmountable odds, they have inspired readers time and again by proving that even world-ending events could be resolved with bravery, grit, and teamwork. Whatever the situation, they can always be counted on to, well, avenge.

MARVEL

1/7 SCALE BUSTS

AVAILABLE NOW:

SPIDER-MAN

Coming
Spring 2023

USE CODE OVERSTREET TO GET 20% OFF IN-STOCK AT DIAMONDSELECTTOYS.COM

DIAMONDSELECTTOYS.COM

© 2023 MARVEL

Diamond Select Toys and Collectibles is a trademark of Diamond Select Toys and Collectibles, LLC. © 2023 Diamond Select Toys and Collectibles. All Rights Reserved. Comic Shop Locator Service and CSLS logo © Diamond Comic Distributors Inc. All Rights Reserved. Final product may vary.

THE OVERSTREET HALL OF FAME

The Overstreet Hall of Fame was conceived to single out individuals who have made great contributions to the comic book arts.

This includes writers, artists, editors, publishers and others who have plied their craft in insightful and meaningful ways.

While such evaluations are inherently subjective, they also serve to aid in reflecting upon those who shaped the experience of reading comic books over the years.

This year's class of inductees begins on this next page.

THE PREVIOUS INDUCTEES

Class of 2006
Murphy Anderson
Jim Aparo
Jim Lee
Mac Raboy

Class of 2007
Dave Cockrum
Steve Ditko
Bruce Hamilton
Martin Nodell
George Pérez
Jim Shooter
Dave Stevens
Alex Toth
Michael Turner

Class of 2008
Carl Barks
Will Eisner
Al Feldstein
Harvey Kurtzman
Stan Lee
Marshall Rogers
John Romita, Sr.
John Romita, Jr.
Julius Schwartz
Mike Wieringo

Class of 2009
Neal Adams
Matt Baker
Chris Claremont
Palmer Cox
Bill Everett
Frank Frazetta
Neil Gaiman
William M. Gaines
Carmine Infantino
Jack Kirby
Joe Kubert
Paul Levitz
Russ Manning
Todd McFarlane
Don Rosa
John Severin
Joe Simon
Al Williamson

Class of 2010
Sergio Aragonés
M.C. Gaines
Archie Goodwin
Winsor McCay
Mike Mignola
Frank Miller
Robert M. Overstreet
Mike Richardson
Jerry Robinson
Joe Shuster
Jerry Siegel
Jim Steranko
Wally Wood

Class of 2011
Jack Davis
Martin Goodman
Dean Mullaney
Marie Severin
Walt Simonson
Major Malcolm Wheeler-Nicholson

Class of 2012
John Buscema
Dan DeCarlo
Jean Giraud (Moebius)
Larry Hama
Kurt Schaffenberger
Bill Sienkiewicz
Curt Swan
Roy Thomas

Class of 2013
Mark Chiarello
Mike Deodato, Jr.
Bill Finger
Jack Kamen
Bob Kane
Andy Kubert

Class of 2014
George Evans
Lou Fine
Gardner Fox
Terry Moore
Dave Sim
Jeff Smith

Class of 2015
Paul Gulacy
Don McGregor
Alex Schomburg
Mark Waid

Class of 2016
Darwyn Cooke
Russ Heath
Rob Liefeld
R.F. Outcault
Tim Truman

Class of 2017
Mike Grell
Osamu Tezuka
Jim Valentino
Mark Wheatley
Bernie Wrightson

Class of 2018
C.C. Beck
Howard Chaykin
Denny O'Neil
Katsuhiro Otomo
Marc Silvestri
Len Wein

Class of 2019
Sal Buscema
José Luis García-López
Michael Wm. Kaluta
Rumiko Takahashi

Class of 2020
Kevin Eastman
Louise Simonson
Dick Sprang

Class of 2021
Denys Cowan
David Mack
William Moulton Marston
June Tarpé Mills

Class of 2022
Ross Andru
Johnny Craig
J.G. Jones

Gene Colan was an artist easily recognized for crafting textured composition, fluid figures, and heavy shadows. He made significant contributions to Marvel on titles like *Daredevil*, and was the co-creator of Sam Wilson/The Falcon, Carol Danvers (later Ms. Marvel, then Captain Marvel), and Blade the vampire hunter. His career began in 1944 at Timely on crime comics and at National Comics on war books. He was a prominent Silver Age Marvel artist, illustrating *Captain America*, *Doctor Strange*, and an 82-issue run on *Daredevil*. By the '70s, he had prominent stints on the horror comic *Tomb of Dracula* and the cult classic *Howard the Duck*. Colan's next move was at DC on *Batman* and *Detective Comics*, which included the introduction of Killer Croc, and *Wonder Woman*, where he co-designed Wonder Woman's "WW" emblem. Later in his career, Colan returned to familiar territory, including vampire stories in *The Curse of Dracula* and the last issue of *Blade* Vol. 3, and his Marvel classics, *Daredevil* and *Captain America*. Colan died in June 2011.

- Amanda Sheriff

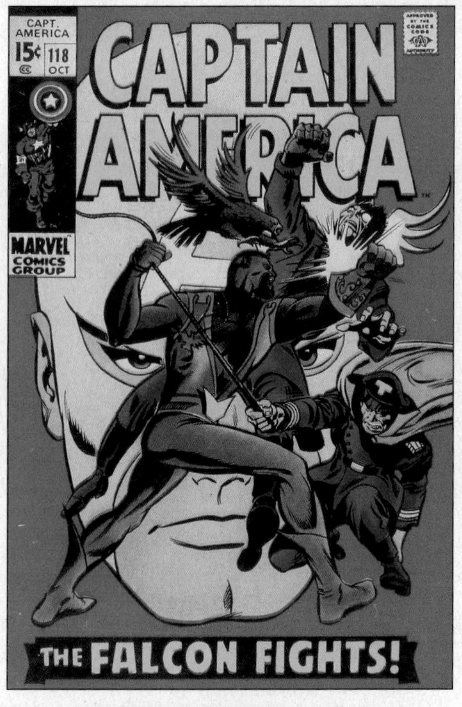

CAPTAIN AMERICA #118
October 1969. © MAR

DAREDEVIL #47
December 1968. © MAR

DETECTIVE COMICS #532
November 1983. © DC

DOCTOR STRANGE #180
May 1969. © MAR

IRON MAN #1
May 1968. © MAR

NATHANIEL DUSK #1
February 1984. © DC

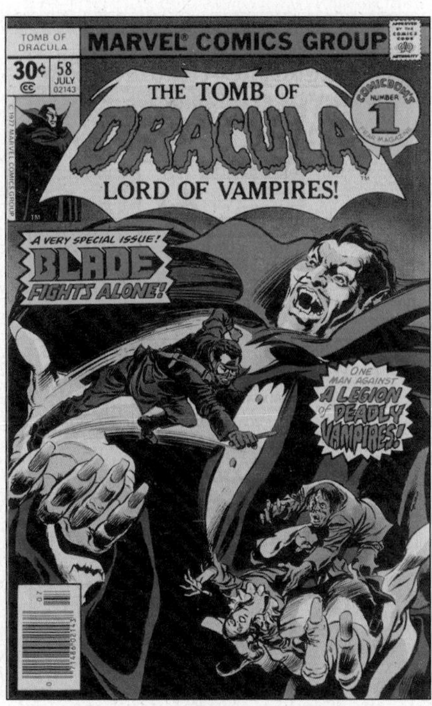

TOMB OF DRACULA #58
July 1977. © MAR

HALL OF FAME

In an influential 60-year career, Sheldon "Shelly" Moldoff's early work includes time as one of Bob Kane's ghost artists. He co-created Poison Ivy and Mr. Freeze. His first published art was a sports filler on the inside back cover of *Action Comics* #1. He was a prominent DC cover artist during the Golden Age, including Green Lantern's first appearance in *All-American Comics* #16. He drew the first image of Shiera Sanders in costume as Hawkgirl and was the primary Hawkman artist of the time, illustrating him in Justice Society of America adventures and other stories. Moldoff also worked on *Moon Girl* EC's and other titles. In the 1950s to '60s, he ghosted for Kane on Batman comics, co-creating characters like the original Bat-Girl and Batwoman, Bat-Mite, Ace the Bat-Hound, and he revived the Riddler. After leaving mainstream comics, Moldoff worked in animation and drew promotional comics for restaurant chains. In 2000, he returned to DC to illustrate a portion of *Superman and Batman: World's Funnest.* Moldoff died in February 2012.

\- *Amanda Sheriff*

ALL-AMERICAN COMICS #21
December 1940. © DC

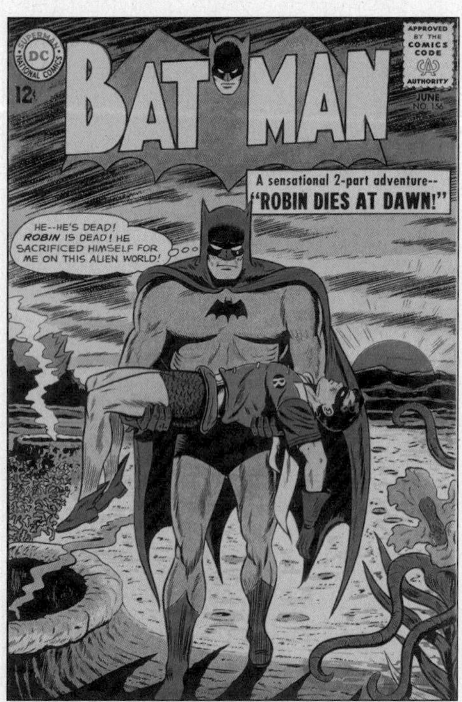

BATMAN #156
June 1963. © DC

DETECTIVE COMICS #233
July 1956. © DC

FLASH COMICS #1
January 1940. © DC

FLASH COMICS #37
January 1943. © DC

MOON GIRL #3
Spring 1948. © WMG

THIS MAGAZINE IS HAUNTED #4
April 1952. © FAW

HALL OF FAME

Christopher Priest (born James Christopher Owsley) is a writer-editor, who edited Spider-Man, wrote Green Lantern, and played a part in the formation of Milestone Media. His editing career began in the late 1970s on Marvel's *Crazy Magazine* and *Conan*. After his first writing gig on *The Falcon* mini-series, he became the editor of Spider-Man comics. He wrote *Power Man and Iron Fist*, which included Iron Fist's controversial death, and wrote *Conan the Barbarian* and *Amazing Spider-Man*. At DC he wrote Green Lantern stories in *Action Comics Weekly, The Ray*, *Justice League Task Force*, *Steel*, and multiple specials. He also edited titles for DC's Impact Comics line. He co-created and wrote Quantum and Woody for Valiant. Moving back to Marvel, he wrote an acclaimed run on *Black Panther* as well as *Deadpool*. After a break from comics, he wrote a *Quantum and Woody* mini-series for the revived Valiant. He also wrote significant runs on *Deathstroke* and *Justice League* as a part of DC Rebirth.

- *Amanda Sheriff*

AMAZING SPIDER-MAN #288
May 1987. © MAR

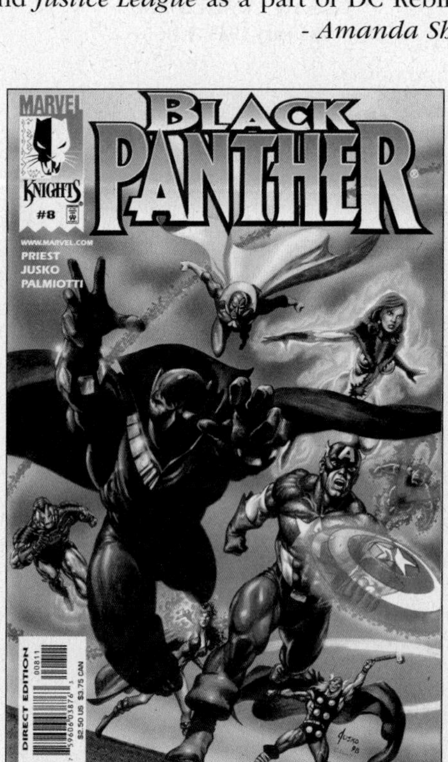

BLACK PANTHER #8
May 1999. © MAR

DEATHSTROKE #1
October 2016. © DC

CHRISTOPHER PRIEST

GREEN LANTERN: EMERALD DAWN #1
December 1989. © DC

POWER MAN AND IRON FIST #120
November 1985. © MAR

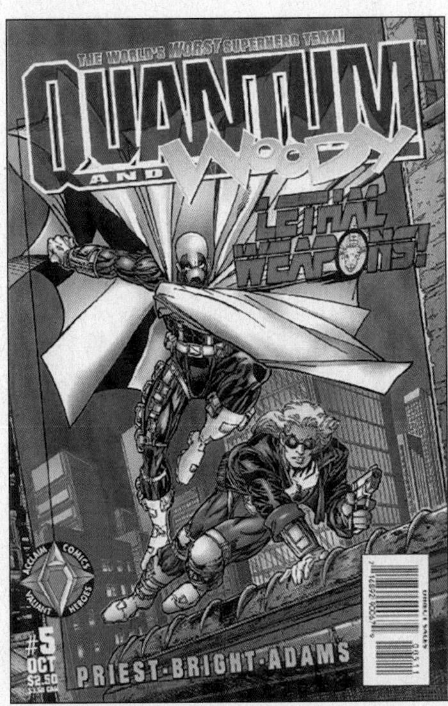

QUANTUM & WOODY #5
October 1997. © VAL

VAMPIRELLA VOL. 5 #2
2019. © DYN

FIND NEW WORLDS AND DISCOVER NEW STORYLINES AT YOUR LOCAL COMIC SHOP

OVERSTREET ADVISORS

DARREN ADAMS
Pristine Comics
Seattle, WA

WELDON ADAMS
Heritage Auctions
Dallas, TX

GRANT ADEY
Halo Certification
Brisbane, QLD, Australia

BILL ALEXANDER
Collector
Sacramento, CA

DAVID T. ALEXANDER
David Alexander Comics
Tampa, FL

TYLER ALEXANDER
David Alexander Comics
Tampa, FL

LON ALLEN
Heritage Auctions
Dallas, TX

DAVE ANDERSON
Want List Comics
Tulsa, OK

L.E. BECKER
Comic*Pop Collectibles
Wixom, MI

JIM BERRY
Collector
Portland, OR

PETER BILELIS, ESQ.
Collector
South Windsor, CT

MIKE BOLLINGER
Hake's Auctions
York, PA

STEVE BOROCK
Senior Consignment Director
ComicLink
Portland, ME

SCOTT BRADEN
Comics Historian
Red Lion, PA

RUSS BRIGHT
Mill Geek Comics
Marysville, WA

RICHARD BROWN
Collector
Detroit, MI

MICHAEL BROWNING
Graphic Novel Specialist

SHAWN CAFFREY
Finalizer/Modern Age Specialist
CGC

MICHAEL CARBONARO
Dave & Adam's
New York

BRETT CARRERAS
VA Comicon
Richmond, VA

GARY CARTER
Collector
Coronado, CA

CHARLES CERRITO
Hotflips
Farmingdale, NY

JEFF CERRITO
Hotflips
Farmingdale, NY

JOHN CHRUSCINSKI
Tropic Comics
Lyndora, PA

PAUL CLAIRMONT
PNJ Comics
Winnipeg, MB
Canada

ART CLOOS
Collector/Historian
Flushing, NY

GARY COLABUONO
Dealer/Collector
Arlington Heights, IL

BILL COLE
Bill Cole Enterprises, Inc.
South Dartmouth, MA

TIM COLLINS
RTS Unlimited, Inc.
Lakewood, CO

JON B. COOKE
Editor - Comic Book Artist Magazine
West Kingston, RI

JACK COPLEY
Coliseum of Comics
Florida

ASHLEY COTTER-CAIRNS
Goldin
Montreal, Canada

JESSE JAMES CRISCIONE
Jesse James Comics
Glendale, AZ

JAIME ADRIANO DAEZ
Collector/Dealer
Metro Manilla, Philippines

BROCK DICKINSON
Collector
St. Catharines, ONT
Canada

GARY DOLGOFF
Gary Dolgoff Comics
Easthampton, MA

JOHN DOLMAYAN
Torpedo Comics
Las Vegas, NV

SHELTON DRUM
Heroes Aren't Hard to Find
Charlotte, NC

WALTER DURAJLIJA
Big B Comics
Hamilton, ONT
Canada

KEN DYBER
Tasteecat Comics
Portland, OR

DANIEL ERTLE
Modern Age Specialist
CBCS
Dallas, TX

MICHAEL EURY
Author
Concord, NC

JAMES FAIR
Diamond Int. Galleries
Hunt Valley, MD

D'ARCY FARRELL
Pendragon Comics
Toronto, ONT Canada

BILL FIDYK
Collector
Annapolis, MD

PAUL FIGURA
Quality Control Specialist
CBCS
Dallas, TX

JOSEPH FIORE
ComicWiz.com
Toronto, ONT Canada

STEPHEN FISHLER
Metropolis Collectibles, Inc.
New York, NY

DAN FOGEL
Hippy Comix LLC
Cleveland, OH

KEVIN FORBES
Comic Interlude
Lexington, KY

ERIC FOURNIER
Guardian Comics
Pickering, ON,
Canada

KEIF A. FROMM
Collector/Historian
Hillsborough, NJ

DAN GALLO
Dealer/Comic Art Con
Westchester Co., NY

JAMES GALLO
Toy & Comic Heaven
Willow Grove, PA

STEPHEN H. GENTNER
Golden Age Specialist
Portland, OR

JOSH GEPPI
Diamond Int. Galleries
Sapphire Studios
Hunt Valley, MD

STEVE GEPPI
Diamond Int. Galleries
Hunt Valley, MD

DOUG GILLOCK
ComicLink
Portland, ME

SEAN GOODRICH
Goldin
Maine, USA

TOM GORDON III
Monumental Holdings LLC
Westminster, MD

JAMIE GRAHAM
Graham Crackers
Chicago, IL

ANDY GREENHAM
Forest City Coins
London, ON Canada

ERIC J. GROVES
Dealer/Collector
Oklahoma City, OK

GARY GUZZO
Atomic Studios
Boothbay Harbor, ME

JOHN HAINES
Dealer/Collector
Kirtland, OH

JIM HALPERIN
Heritage Auctions
Dallas, TX

JAY HALSTEAD
International Comic
Exchange
Hamilton, ON Canada

MARK HASPEL
Finalizer/
Pedigree Specialist
CGC

JEF HINDS
Jef Hinds Comics
Madison, WI

TERRY HOKNES
Hoknes Comics
Saskatoon, SK
Canada

GREG HOLLAND, Ph.D.
Collector
Alexander, AR

JOHN HONE
Collector
Silver Spring, MD

STEVEN HOUSTON
Torpedo Comics
Las Vegas, NV

BILL HUGHES
Dealer/Collector
Flower Mound, TX

ROB HUGHES
Arch Angels
Pacific Beach, CA

ROBERT ISAAC
Red Hood Comics
Las Vegas, NV

JEFF ITKIN
Elite Comic Source
Portland, OR

ED JASTER
Heritage Auctions
Dallas, TX

DR. STEVEN KAHN
Inner Child Comics
& Collectibles
Kenosha, WI

NICK KATRADIS
Collector
Tenafly, NJ

TERRENCE KEEGAN
Platinum Age Specialist
Phillipines

DENNIS KEUM
Fantasy Comics
Goldens Bridge, NY

IVAN KOCMAREK
Comics Historian
Hamilton, ON
Canada

ROBERT KRAUSE
CGC Vintage Comics Grader
Lakewood Ranch, FL

TIMOTHY KUPIN
Koops Comics
Lawton, OK

BENJAMIN LABONOG
Primetime Comics
Stockton, CA

BEN LICHTENSTEIN
Zapp Comics
Wayne, NJ

STEPHEN LIPSON
Comics Historian
Mississauga, ON

PAUL LITCH
Primary Grader
CGC

DOUG MABRY
The Great Escape
Madison, TN

JOE MANNARINO
Heritage Auctions
Ridgewood, NJ

NADIA MANNARINO
Heritage Auctions
Ridgewood, NJ

BRIAN MARCUS
Cavalier Comics
Wise, VA

WILL MASON
Dave & Adam's
New York

HARRY MATETSKY
Collector
Middletown, NJ

JIM McCALLUM
Guardian Comics
Pickering, ON Canada

KELLY McCLAIN
Hake's Auctions
York, PA

JON McCLURE
Comics Historian,
Writer
Astoria, OR

TODD McDEVITT
New Dimension Comics
Cranberry Township,
PA

PETER MEROLO
Collector
Sedona, AZ

JOHN JACKSON MILLER
Historian, Writer
Scandinavia, WI

BRENT MOESHLIN
Quality Comix
Montgomery, AL

STEVE MORTENSEN
Miracle Comics
Santa Clara, CA

MARC NATHAN
Cards, Comics &
Collectibles
Reisterstown, MD

JOSHUA NATHANSON
ComicLink
Portland, ME

MATT NELSON
President
CGC

TOM NELSON
Top Notch Comics
Yankton, SD

JAMIE NEWBOLD
Southern California
Comics
San Diego, CA

KAREN O'BRIEN
Comics Journalist
Dyer, IN

VINCE OLIVA
Grader
CGC

IN MEMORIAM

RICHARD OLSON
Collector/Academician
Poplarville, MS

TERRY O'NEILL
Terry's Comics
Orange, CA

MICHAEL PAVLIC
Purple Gorilla Comics
Calgary, AB, Canada

JIM PAYETTE
Golden Age Specialist
Bethlehem, NH

BILL PONSETI
Fantastic Worlds
Comics
Scottsdale, AZ

SEAN PROSJE
Comic Cave Canada
Dundas, ON, Canada

RON PUSSELL
Redbeard's Book Den
Crystal Bay, NV

ALEX REECE
Reece's Rare Comics
Monrovia, MD

AUSTIN REECE
Reece's Rare Comics
Monrovia, MD

ROB REYNOLDS
ComicConnect
New York, NY

STEVE RICKETTS
CBCS Pressing
Dallas, TX

STEPHEN RITTER
Worldwide Comics
Fair Oaks Ranch, TX

CHUCK ROZANSKI
Mile High Comics
Denver, CO

SEAN RUTAN
Hake's Auctions
York, PA

BARRY SANDOVAL
Heritage Auctions
Dallas, TX

BUDDY SAUNDERS
MyComicShop.com
Arlington, TX

CONAN SAUNDERS
MyComicShop.com
Arlington, TX

MATT SCHIFFMAN
Bronze Age Specialist
Bend, OR

DOUG SCHMELL
Pedigree Comics, Inc.
Wellington, FL

BRIAN SCHUTZER
Sparkle City Comics
Neat Stuff Collectibles
North Bergen, NJ

ALIKA SEKI
Maui Comics and Collectibles
Waiehu, HI

TODD SHEFFER
Hake's Auctions
York, PA

FRANK SIMMONS
Coast to Coast Comics
Rocklin, CA

CHRIS SIMONS
I Like Comics
Vancouver, WA

MARC SIMS
Big B Comics
Barrie, ON, Canada

LAUREN SISSELMAN
Comics Journalist
Baltimore, MD

MARK SQUIREK
Collector/Historian
Baltimore, MD

TONY STARKS
Silver Age Specialist
Evansville, IN

WEST STEPHAN
CBCS
Dallas, TX

AL STOLTZ
Basement Comics
Havre de Grace, MD

DOUG SULIPA
"Everything 1960-1996"
Manitoba, Canada

MAGGIE THOMPSON
Collector/Historian
Iola, WI

MICHAEL TIERNEY
The Comic Book Store
Little Rock, AR

TED VAN LIEW
Superworld Comics
Worcester, MA

JOE VERENEAULT
JHV Associates
Woodbury Heights, NJ

JASON VERSAGGI
Collector
Langhorne, PA

FRANK VERZYL
Long Island Comics
West Babylon, NY

BOB WAYNE
Collector
Fort Worth, TX

JEFF WEAVER
Victory Comics
Falls Church, VA

LON WEBB
Dark Adventure Comics
Norcross, GA

RICK WHITELOCK
New Force Comics
Lynn Haven, FL

MIKE WILBUR
Diamond Int. Galleries
Hunt Valley, MD

ALEX WINTER
Hake's Auctions
York, PA

HARLEY YEE
Dealer/Collector
Detroit, MI

ROBERT YOUNG
Borderlands Comics and Games
Greenville, SC

MARK ZAID
EsquireComics.com
Bethesda, MD

VINCENT ZURZOLO, JR.
Metropolis Collectibles, Inc.
New York, NY

COMING SEPTEMBER 2023

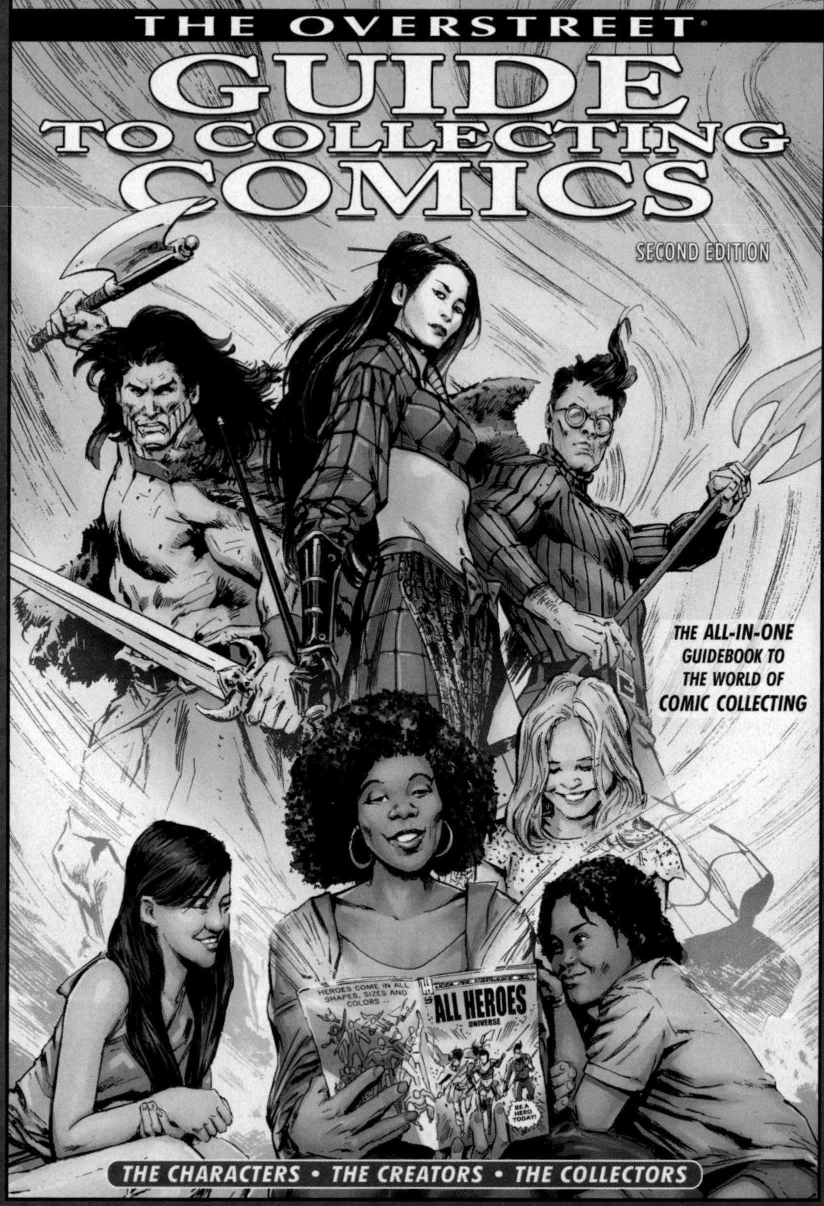

Ironjaw ©2023 Nemesis, Inc. Shi ©2023 William Tucci. Kent Menace ©2023 Scott Braden & Mike Malbrough. Overstreet® is a Registered Trademark of Gemstone Publishing. All rights reserved.

Whether you're picking up new comics off the shelves each week or bidding on the highest of the high-end back issues, there are things you need to know in order to collect effectively. This book introduces them.

- How do you collect comics?
- How do you care for them?
- How do you grade them?
- How do you sell them?
- Who have been the greatest comic creators?
- How do you turn your comics hobby into a job in the industry?

This brand new edition of *The Overstreet Guide To Collecting Comics* offers answers and insights into these questions and more facing new collectors and experienced enthusiasts alike.

GEMSTONE PUBLISHING

www.gemstonepub.com

OVERSTREET PRICE GUIDE BACK ISSUES

The Overstreet® Comic Book Price Guide has held the record for being the longest running annual comic book publication. We are now celebrating our 53rd anniversary, and the demand for the Overstreet® price guides is very strong. Collectors have created a legitimate market for them, and they continue to bring record prices each year. Collectors also have a record of comic book prices going back further than any other source in comic fandom. The prices listed below are for NM condition only, with GD-25% and FN-50% of the NM value. Canadian editions exist for a couple of the early issues. Abbreviations: SC-softcover, HC-hardcover, L-leather bound.

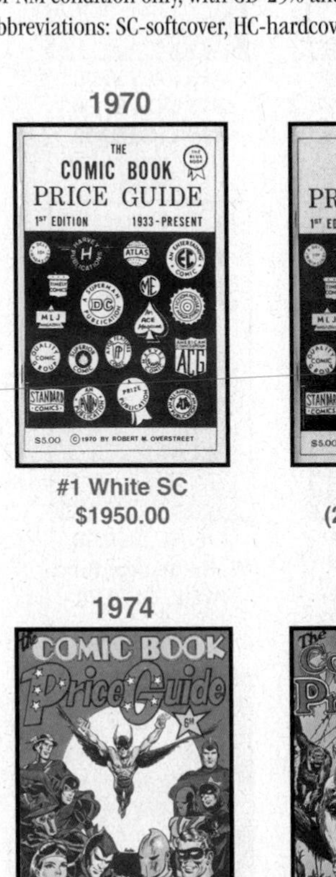

1970	1970	1972	1973
#1 White SC $1950.00	#1 Blue SC (2nd Printing) $1600.00	#2 SC $650.00 #2 HC $1100.00	#3 SC $325.00 #3 HC $950.00

1974	1975	1976	1977
#4 SC $165.00 #4 HC $475.00	#5 SC $155.00 #5 HC $260.00	#6 SC $105.00 #6 HC $155.00	#7 SC $155.00 #7 HC $230.00

1978	1979	1980	1981
#8 SC $130.00 #8 HC $180.00	#9 SC $130.00 #9 HC $180.00	#10 SC $140.00 #10 HC $190.00	#11 SC $85.00 #11 HC $115.00

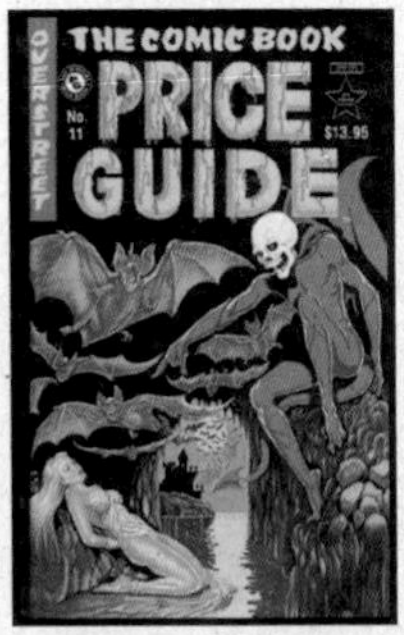

1982

#12 SC $85.00
#12 HC $115.00

1983

#13 SC $85.00
#13 HC $115.00

1984

#14 SC $55.00
#14 HC $110.00
#14 L $190.00

1985

#15 SC $55.00
#15 HC $80.00
#15 L $170.00

1986

#16 SC $60.00
#16 HC $85.00
#16 L $180.00

1987

#17 SC $55.00
#17 HC $110.00
#17 L $170.00

1988

#18 SC $45.00
Art with black background

1988

#18 HC $65.00
White background
#18 L $170.00

1989

#19 SC $50.00
#19 HC $60.00
#19 L $190.00

1990

#20 SC $32.00
#20 HC $50.00
#20 L $150.00

1991

#21 SC $40.00
#21 HC $60.00
#21 L $160.00

1992

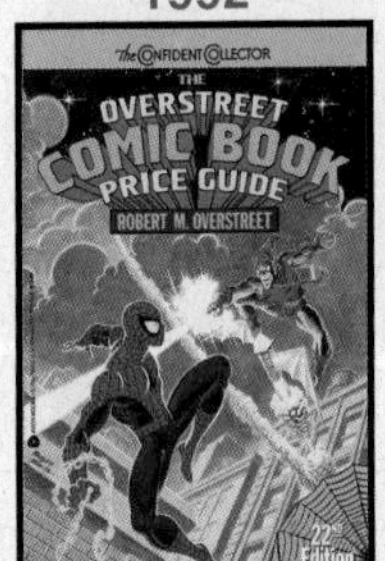

#22 SC $32.00
#22 HC $50.00

1993

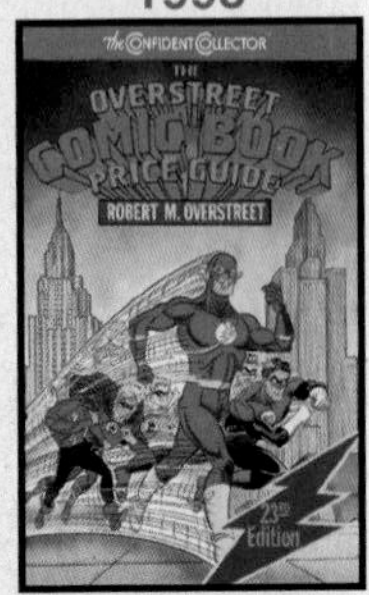

#23 SC $32.00
#23 HC $50.00

1994

#24 SC $26.00
#24 HC $36.00

1995

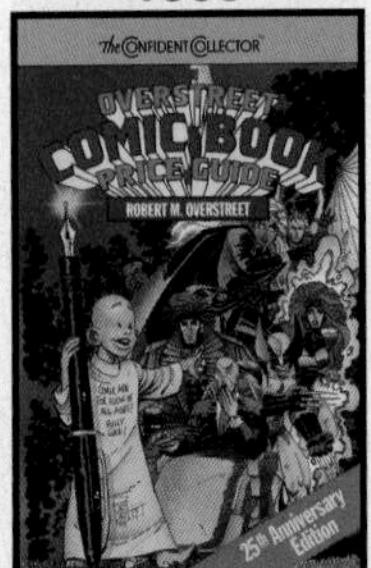

#25 SC $26.00
#25 HC $36.00
#25 L $110.00

1996

#26 SC $20.00
#26 HC $30.00
#26 L $100.00

1997	1997	1998	1998	1999	1999

#27 SC $22.00 #27 HC $38.00 #27 L $125.00	#27 SC $22.00 #27 HC $38.00 #27 L $125.00	#28 SC $20.00 #28 HC $35.00	#28 SC $20.00 #28 HC $35.00	#29 SC $25.00 #29 HC $40.00	#29 SC $20.00 #29 HC $37.00

2000	2000	2001	2001	2001	2002

#30 SC $22.00 #30 HC $32.00	#30 SC $22.00 #30 HC $32.00	#31 SC $22.00 #31 HC $32.00	#31 SC $22.00 #31 HC $32.00	#31 Bookstore Ed. SC only $22.00	#32 SC $22.00 #32 HC $32.00

2002	2002	2003	2003	2003	2004

#32 SC $22.00 #32 HC $32.00	#32 Bookstore Ed. SC only $22.00	#33 SC $25.00 #33 HC $32.00	#33 SC $25.00 #33 HC $32.00	#33 Bookstore Ed. SC only $25.00	#34 SC $25.00 #34 HC $32.00

2004	2004	2005	2005	2005	2006

#34 SC $25.00 #34 HC $32.00	#34 Bookstore Ed. SC only $25.00	#35 SC $25.00 #35 HC $32.00	#35 SC $25.00 #35 HC $32.00	#35 Bookstore Ed. SC only $25.00	#36 SC $25.00 #36 HC $32.00

2006

#36 SC $25.00
#36 HC $32.00

2006

#36 Bookstore Ed.
SC only $25.00

2007

#37 SC $25.00
#37 HC $32.00

2007

#37 SC $30.00
#37 HC $35.00

2007

#37 Bookstore Ed.
SC only $30.00

2008

#38 SC $30.00
#38 HC $35.00

2008

#38 SC $30.00
#38 HC $35.00

2008

#38 Bookstore Ed.
SC only $30.00

2009

#39 SC $30.00
#39 HC $35.00

2009

#39 SC $30.00
#39 HC $35.00

2009

#39 Bookstore Ed.
SC only $30.00

2010

#40 SC $30.00
#40 HC $35.00

2010

#40 SC $30.00
#40 HC $35.00

2010

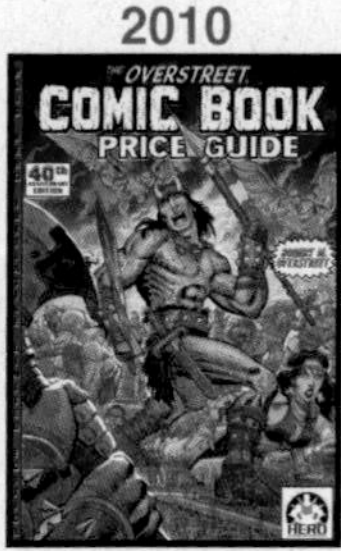

#40 HERO Ed.
HC only $35.00

2011

#41 SC $30.00
#41 HC $35.00

2011

#41 SC $30.00
#41 HC $35.00

2011

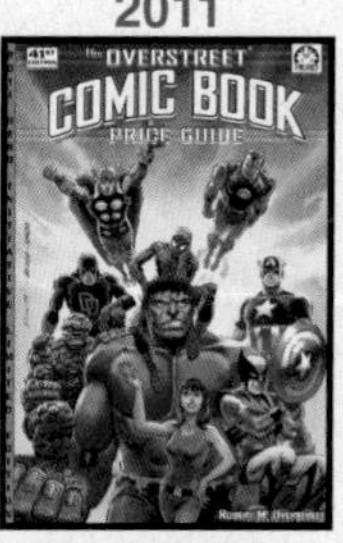

#41 HERO Ed.
HC only $35.00

2012

#42 SC $30.00
#42 HC $35.00

2012

#42 SC $30.00
#42 HC $35.00

2012

#42 HERO Ed.
HC only $35.00

2013

#43 SC $30.00
#43 HC $35.00

2013

#43 SC $30.00
#43 HC $35.00

2013

#43 HERO Ed.
HC only $35.00

2014

#44 SC $30.00
#44 HC $35.00

2014

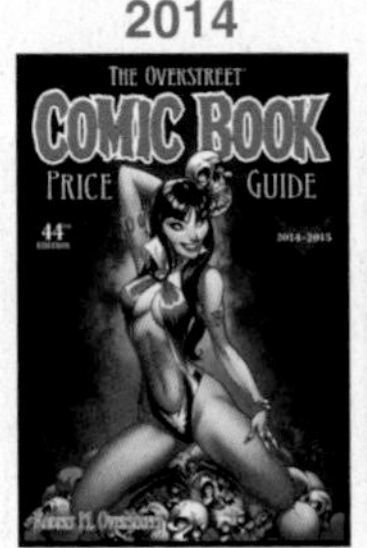

#44 SC $30.00
#44 HC $35.00

2014

#44 HERO Ed.
HC only $35.00

2015

#45 SC $30.00
#45 HC $35.00

2015

#45 SC $30.00
#45 HC $35.00

2015

#45 SC $30.00
#45 HC $35.00

2015

#45 SC $30.00
#45 HC $35.00

2015

#45 HERO Ed.
HC only $35.00

2016

#46 SC $30.00
#46 HC $35.00

2016

#46 SC $30.00
#46 HC $35.00

2016

#46 SC $30.00
#46 HC $35.00

2016

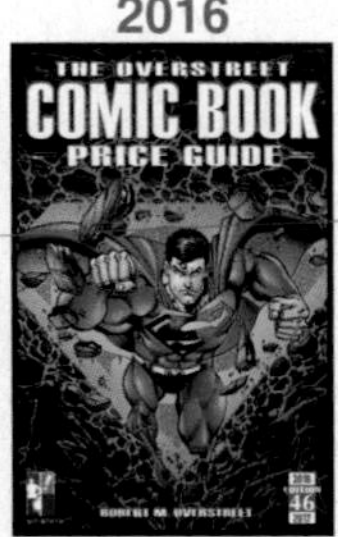

#46 HERO Ed.
HC only $35.00

2017

#47 SC $30.00
#47 HC $35.00

2017

#47 SC $30.00
#47 HC $35.00

2017

#47 SC $30.00
#47 HC $35.00

2017

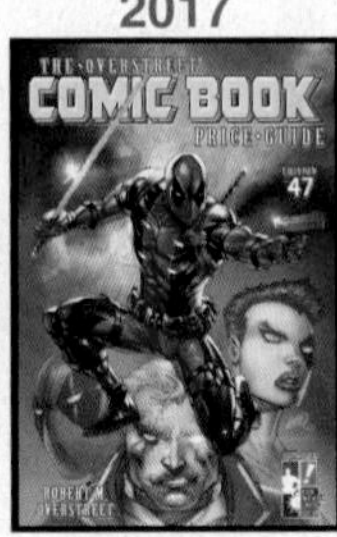

#47 HERO Ed.
HC only $35.00

2018

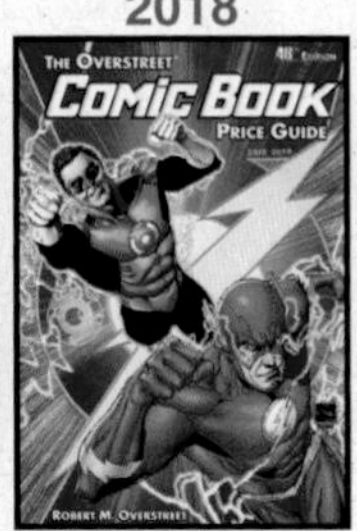

#48 SC $30.00
#48 HC $35.00

2018

#48 SC $30.00
#48 HC $35.00

2018

#48 SC $30.00
#48 HC $35.00

2018

#48 HERO Ed.
HC only $35.00

2019

#49 SC $30.00
#49 HC $35.00

2019

#49 SC $30.00
#49 HC $35.00

2019

#49 SC $30.00
#49 HC $35.00

2019

#49 HERO Ed.
HC only $35.00

2020

#50 SC $40.00
#50 HC $50.00

2020

#50 SC $30.00
#50 HC $37.50

2020

#50 SC $30.00
#50 HC $37.50

2020

#50 HERO Ed.
HC only $37.50

2021

#51 SC $30.00
#51 HC $37.50

2021

#51 SC $30.00
#51 HC $37.50

2021

#51 HERO Ed.
HC only $37.50

2022

#52 SC $35.00
#52 HC $45.00

2022

#52 SC $35.00
#52 HC $45.00

2022

#52 SC $35.00
#52 HC $45.00

2022

#52 HERO Ed.
HC only $45.00

2022

#52 Exclusive Overstreet Advisor Ed.
HC only, print run of 200 copies

BACK ISSUE GUIDES

Many (but not all!) backdate editions of *The Overstreet Comic Book Price Guide* are available for sale on the Gemstone Publishing website. All of the past editions we offer are as-new uncirculated copies (unless otherwise noted), and supplies on most are very limited.

www.gemstonepub.com

2001 | 2002 | 2003 | 2004 | 2005

#31 Big Big CBPG $35.00

#32 Big Big CBPG $35.00

#33 Big Big CBPG $37.00

#34 Big Big CBPG $37.00

#35 Big Big CBPG $37.00

2006 | 2007 | 2008 | 2012 | 2013

#36 Big Big CBPG $37.00

#37 Big Big CBPG $37.00

#38 Big Big CBPG $37.00

#42 Big Big CBPG $45.00

#43 Big Big CBPG $45.00

2014 | 2015 | 2016 | 2017 | 2018

#44 Big Big CBPG $45.00

#45 Big Big CBPG $47.50

#46 Big Big CBPG $47.50

#47 Big Big CBPG $47.50

#48 Big Big CBPG $47.50

2019 | 2020 | 2021 | 2022 | 2022

#49 Big Big CBPG $49.50

#50 Big Big CBPG $49.50

#51 Big Big CBPG $49.50

#52 Big Big CBPG $54.95

#52 Big Big CBPG $54.95

ADVERTISERS' INDEX

A

B

C

D

E

F

G

H

A **PICTURE** IS WORTH A THOUSAND WORDS.

BIDS **STARTING** AS LOW AS **$1.00**

DIGAuction.com

*Come "**DIG**" through our collection.*

MULTIPLE COMIC AUCTIONS EVERY WEEK! | **NO** BUYER'S PREMIUM

THE **TOOL** YOU'VE ALWAYS WANTED FROM THE **MOST TRUSTED** NAME IN THE BUSINESS.

Overstreet Price Guide
Valuations

Extensive
Comic Database

Comic Collection
Management System

OVERSTREET
ACCESS

"HELPING YOU WITH YOUR ISSUES."

OverstreetAccess.com

Overstreet® is a Registered Trademark of Gemstone Publishing. Overstreet Access™ and the OA logo™ are trademarks of Gemstone Publishing. All rights reserved.

COMING MARCH 2024!

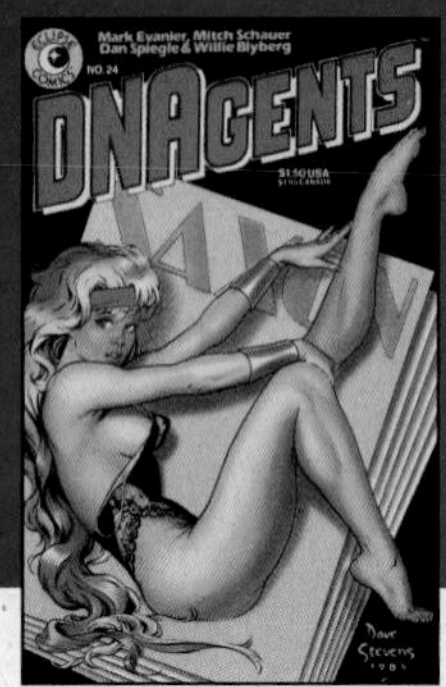

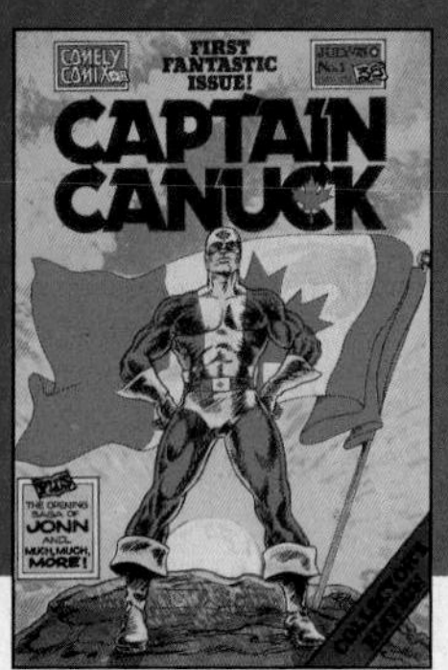

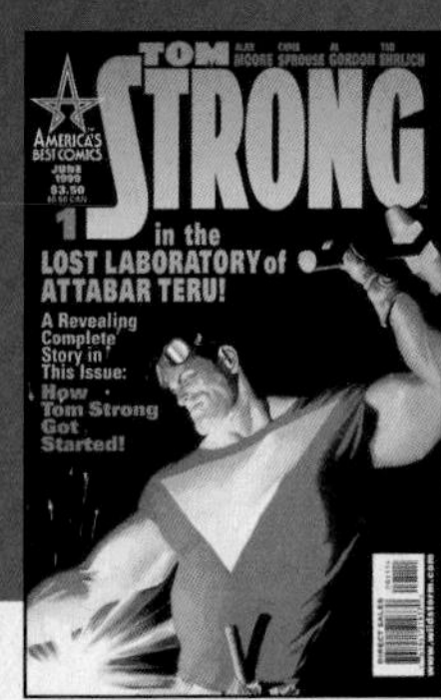

Featuring Fawcett's Marvel Family • Marvel 2099
America's Best Comics • BOOM!'s Stan Lee Universe • Captain Canuck
DNAgents • Scout • and MORE!

Timothy Truman's SCOUT

From the pages of *Starslayer*, Grimjack and his graphic novel *Time Beavers* onward through his career, writer-artist Timothy Truman has offered readers hard-boiled action and no small amount of grit. It was at Eclipse that Truman created what is perhaps his signature title, *Scout*. And while Eclipse as a whole was clearly a non-universe, *Scout* and its spin-offs describe a single coherent reality.

"I'd always been interested in Native American culture when I was growing up. My great-grandmother on my father's side was a full-blooded Cherokee, and I'm sure that played a part in it. In college, the interest intensified, and I started reading a lot of scholarly studies and histories about various Native American tribes. Finally, my wife Beth purchased a big, thick book by a historian named Arthur Haley called *Apaches: A Culture and History Portrait* and gave it to me for my birthday. That book really set the scene for coming up with *Scout*. I became intensely interested in Apache culture. It was the Reagan era, so, as an unrepentant leftist, I saw things going on around me that concerned me quite a bit. So, I speculated about what might happen if these things were allowed to progress and eventually pictured this bleak future where America had basically become an impoverished third-world nation. It seemed to me that the only person who might have any sort of hope of existing in such a future would be someone with these old school traditional Apache cultural ideals that I was reading about. So, before I knew it, the whole scenario for the *Scout* series appeared, Truman said.

FIRST PUBLICATION:
Scout #1
(September 1985)

LAST PUBLICATION:
Scout: War Shaman #16
(December 1989)

REVIVAL(S):
Scout: Marauder
graphic novel (TBD)

"The story takes place in the near future in a sort of ravaged, impoverished, dystopian United States. The country has split off into various smaller states or governments, the main one being centered in the American Southwest, called New America. The star of the series is an Apache named Emanuel Santana who is AWOL from a special Army training program. Scout learns, or at least thinks, that he is the reincarnation of the mythical Apache hero, Child of Water, and that it's his mission to destroy the Four Monsters of Apache legend. The monsters have taken the form of four businessmen and statesmen aligned with acting President, Jerry Grail – himself a former pro-wrestler. The reader never knows whether or not the Monsters are real or just a figment of Santana's imagination," he said.

Scout #1 (September 1985) kicked off the original series, which ran 24 issues and concluded in October 1987. *Swords of Texas* #1 kicked off a four-issue mini-series that same month, and *New America* #1 launched another four-issue mini-series the following month. 1987 also saw the release of the *Scout Handbook*. *Scout: War Shaman* #1 (March 1988) launched a 16-issue run that concluded in December 1989.

"The second series, *Scout: War Shaman*, takes place about a decade or so after the first series, chronologically, during which time Scout married and had two small children, Tahzey and Victorio. After his wife dies, he and the boys set out on a trek across the southwest. Most people were really taken with the second series, the fact that you have this outlaw who has been branded a terrorist by the government, who is on the run and must worry about the welfare and safety of his two small children. In what was a pretty dramatic step for the time, at the end of the series, Scout dies. One boy, Tahzey, is adopted by one of Santana's allies, a militant missionary named Rev. Sanddog Yuma. However, the fate of the youngest boy, Victorio, is uncertain. When we last see him, he's very much alone, hiding in some rocks. Keeping his fate uncertain was a deliberate move on my part, as readers will hopefully discover in Scout: Marauder," Truman said.

Timothy Truman's original art for Scout #8 Page 2 (1986).
Image courtesy of Heritage Auctions.

2 LOST UNIVERSES

LOST UNIVERSES 3

Full color! • Every comic listed is also pictured! • The latest prices!
Original art! • Interviews, feature articles and more!
Inside information on the birth, death, and revivals of Lost Universes!

THE OVERSTREET COMIC BOOK PRICE GUIDE TO

LOST UNIVERSES

2ND EDITION

ALL NEW!

Spider-Man 2099 cover by Butch Guice!

Plus a Scout cover by Timothy Truman!

BY ROBERT M. OVERSTREET & J.C. VAUGHN

Spider-Man 2099 ©2023 MARVEL. Captain Marvel (Shazam) ©2023 DC Comics. DNAgents ©2023 Mark Evanier & Will Meugniot. Scout ©2023 Timothy Truman. Overstreet® is a Registered Trademark of Gemstone Publishing. All rights reserved.

Interested in advertising?
Email feedback@gemstonepub.com!

GEMSTONE PUBLISHING

WWW.GEMSTONEPUB.COM

HERITAGE®

COMICS & COMIC ART AUCTIONS

WHEN IT'S TIME TO SELL, CONSIGN TO HERITAGE

THE WORLD'S LARGEST COLLECTIBLES AUCTIONEER

1.5 Million+ Online Bidder-Members

We have provided cash advances as high as $10 million against individual comic consignments

2.8 Million+ different people visit our website each month on average (source: SimilarWeb.com, October 2022), no other comic dealer even comes close.

SOLD FOR $840,000! June 2021

SOLD FOR $264,000! June 2021

SOLD FOR $3,600,000! September 2021

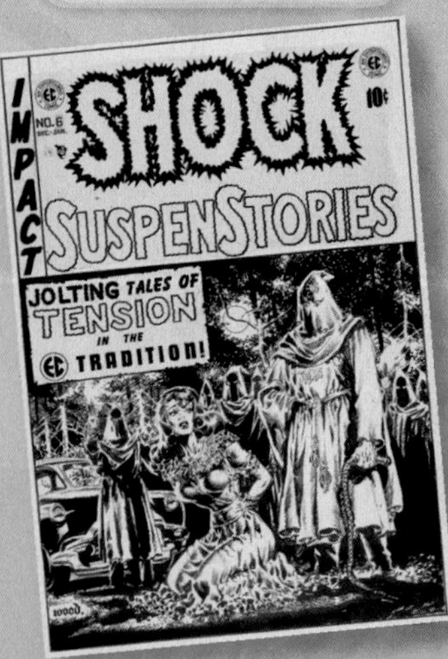

To discuss selling your comics or art at auction, call or email us today!

LEARN HOW HERITAGE GETS YOU MORE MONEY - SEE OUR ADS ON PAGES 6 AND 7!

DALLAS | NEW YORK | BEVERLY HILLS | CHICAGO | PALM BEACH
LONDON | PARIS | GENEVA | BRUSSELS | AMSTERDAM | HONG KONG

Always Accepting Quality Consignments in 50+ Categories
Immediate Cash Advances Available

HERITAGE AUCTIONS
THE WORLD'S LARGEST COLLECTIBLES AUCTIONEER

COLLECTOR BUYING PRE-1965 COMIC BOOKS AND RELATED COLLECTIBLES

COMIC BOOKS

CLUB KITS • PREMIUMS

OTHER CHARACTER COLLECTIBLES

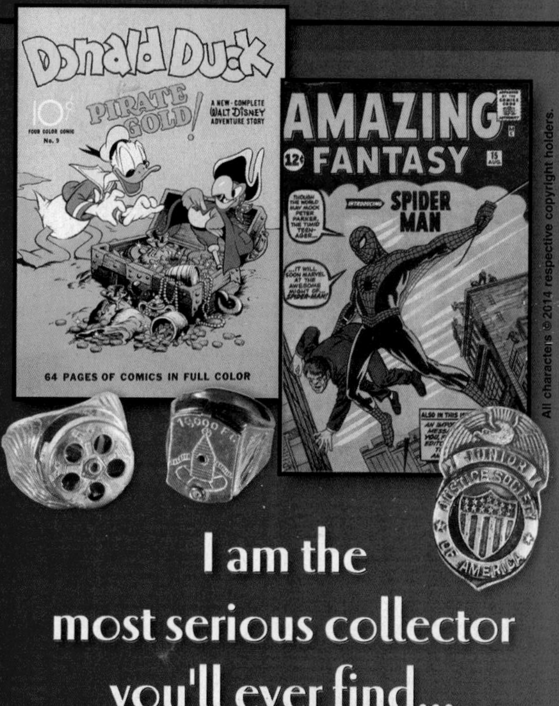

All characters © 2014 respective copyright holders.

I am the most serious collector you'll ever find...

I LOVE THIS STUFF!

SEND YOUR SALE LIST!

Stephen A. Geppi
10150 York Road, Suite 300
Hunt Valley, MD 21030
410-598-1773
gsteve@diamondcomics.com

COLLECTOR BUYING MOST PRE-1967 COMIC BOOKS

PARTICULARLY INTERESTED IN:
Superhero comic books
Anything related to Batman
Anything related to Superman
Original comic book art
Pulp magazines

Why Sell to Me?

THIS IS A HOBBY, NOT A BUSINESS. THEREFORE, I CAN & WILL PAY MORE. I WILL BUY ENTIRE COLLECTIONS OR INDIVIDUAL PIECES. IMMEDIATE CASH IS ALWAYS AVAILABLE FOR PURCHASES.

DR. DAVID J. ANDERSON, D.D.S. • 5192 DAWES AVENUE
SEMINARY PROFESSIONAL VILLAGE • ALEXANDRIA, VA 22311
(703) 578-1222
DANDERSON8991@GMAIL.COM